PEARS
CYCLOPAEDIA

1995–96

A BOOK OF REFERENCE AND BACKGROUND
INFORMATION FOR ALL THE FAMILY

EDITED BY

CHRISTOPHER COOK

M.A. Cantab., D.Phil. Oxon., F.R. Hist. S.

One Hundred and Fourth Edition

The Editor desires to express his gratitude to readers for their criticisms and suggestions and to all those who in one way or another have contributed to this latest edition. Correspondence on editorial matters should be addressed to Dr. Christopher Cook, "Pears Cyclopaedia", Pelham Books Ltd., 27 Wrights Lane, Kensington, London W8 5TZ.

PELHAM BOOKS

Published by the Penguin Group
Penguin Books Ltd, 27 Wrights Lane, London W8 5TZ, England
Penguin Books USA Inc., 375 Hudson Street, New York, New York 10014, USA
Penguin Books Australia Ltd, Ringwood, Victoria, Australia
Penguin Books Canada Ltd, 10 Alcorn Avenue, Toronto, Ontario, Canada M4V 3B2
Penguin Books (NZ) Ltd, 182–190 Wairau Road, Auckland 10, New Zealand

Penguin Books Ltd, Registered Offices: Harmondsworth, Middlesex, England

First published 1897
© Pelham Books Ltd. 1995

Printed in England by Clays Ltd., St Ives plc

A CIP catalogue record for this book is available from the British Library.

0 7207 2052 4

CONTENTS

Sections are arranged alphabetically, or chronologically, or have a detailed Table of Contents.

THE STORY OF PEARS

Success stories in publishing, even in the economic climate of the 1990s, still abound. Success stories which go from strength to strength for 100 editions are, by any standards, unique. In 1991 *Pears Cyclopaedia* passed that historic publishing landmark. In September 1991, the 100th edition of the world famous reference book took its familiar place on the shelves of bookshops across the world. This latest edition (the 104th) was published in Autumn 1995.

The origins of *Pears Cyclopaedia* are no less fascinating than its phenomenal success—a success which produced sales of 3 million copies by the 1930s and at least as many again since. That success dates to 1865, when a young man of 24 joined the business of A&F Pears Ltd, soap makers to Queen Victoria. At a well-known Academy of Dancing and Deportment in the West End, Thomas J Barratt made the acquaintance of the eldest daughter of Mr Francis Pears. Miss Pears became Mrs Barratt, and Mr Barratt became the London Manager of Pears!

Thomas Barratt was an advertising genius. He declared that he would advertise as no soapmaker had ever advertised before. In the then relatively new profession of advertising, he made Pears Soap a world-wide name. Such advertisements as "Bubbles" and "Two years ago I used your soap, since when I have used no other" achieved lasting fame.

But perhaps the most original advertisement of all for Pears Soap was the little red *Pears Shilling Cyclopaedia*, first printed for A&F Pears by David Bryce and Son of Glasgow. It was published in December 1897, the year of Queen Victoria's Diamond Jubilee. This first edition contained an English dictionary, a medical dictionary, a gazetteer and atlas, desk information and a compendium of general knowledge entitled "A Mass of Curious and Useful Information about Things that everyone Ought to know in Commerce, History, Science, Religion, Literature and other Topics of Ordinary Conversation".

The idea was to keep the general public informed on the issues of the day, to equip them for social discourse, satisfy their curiosity and widen their learning. Topics ranged from hard facts to questions of etiquette, from why the Russians needed a port on the Mediterranean to the longevity of the clergy!

Although *Pears Cyclopaedia* slipped its connections with soap back in 1960 when the publishing rights passed to Pelham Books, there has been astonishing editorial continuity (only two editors since 1946, only three in the first 50 years). Now the price is a little more than the original shilling, but *Pears* still represents remarkable value for over 1,000 pages packed with information.

Many of the popular features of the first edition have been retained. The medical section, the gazetteer and atlas, the sections on Economics, Science, Literature, Ideas and Beliefs, Historical Events and General Information are all still there. Also there are topics of current social and political interest, specially commissioned for each edition. There are newer, equally-popular favourites in the present edition, including Classical Mythology, Sporting Records, the Biblical Glossary, Music and the Environment. It is this blend of innovation and tradition—the tried and tested facts and figures alongside authoritative new articles in every edition that has made *Pears* so popular with generation after generation.

The single most important factor in the *Pears* success story, and the key to its truly unique publishing phenomenon, is that *it is the only book of its kind to be fully revised and updated by a team of experts every year*. Over thirty contributors, under the editorship of historian Dr Chris Cook, ensure that every section contains the most-up-to-date information available.

Schools and colleges, offices and libraries, students and researchers, newspapers, radio and TV stations—for all these, and many more, for whom readily accessible, reliable facts at their fingertips are needed, *Pears Cyclopaedia* remains an invaluable companion.

THE EDITOR

Dr Chris Cook was born in Leicester in 1945. He was educated at St Catharine's College, Cambridge (where he took 1st Class Honours in History) and at Nuffield College, Oxford (where he completed his doctorate under AJP Taylor). He has subsequently combined an academic career (he was recently appointed a Visiting Research Fellow at the London School of Economics) with a variety of writing and editorial work. He is a Fellow of the Royal Historical Society.

He first wrote for *Pears Cyclopaedia* in 1970, before becoming Assistant Editor (to Mary Barker) and eventually Editor in 1976. Among his best-known books on modern Britain are *The Slump* (co-authored with John Stevenson) and *A Short History of the Liberal Party, 1900–1992*. For Longman, he has co-authored the 3-volume series of Longman Handbooks to modern British, European and World History.

HISTORICAL EVENTS

Historical events from the earliest times to the present. For events in pre-history the reader may also like to consult the relevant sections on geology and our early ancestors in the Science section. This edition includes a detailed chronicle of the dramatic events of the early 1990s that have seen the fall of the Soviet Union, the redrawing of the map of Eastern Europe and fundamental changes in the Middle East and South Africa.

CHRONICLE OF EVENTS

Note.—For classical history and for the past millennium most dates are well established. For other periods there is sometimes considerable uncertainty. Many of the dates in ancient history are either dubious or approximate, sometimes both. For dates on evolution prior to 100 million years ago the reader is invited to consult the table on **F48.**

B.C.   **PREHISTORY**

70,000,000   Earliest known primate (*Plesiadapis*).

35,000,000   *Aegyptopithecus,* ancestral ape from the Fayum.

20,000,000   *Proconsul,* possible ancestor of hominids in East Africa.

3,700,000   First hominids in East Africa – *Australopithecus.*

2,100,000   First hominid stone toolmaker – *Homo habilis;* present in Africa until 1,800,000 years ago.

1,600,000   Earliest *Homo erectus* in East Africa, present there and in Europe and Far East until 200,000 years ago.

500,000   Archaic modern man, *Homo sapiens,* present in Africa until 30,000 years ago.

100,000   Neanderthal Man, present in Europe until 35,000 years ago: Anatomically modern man, *Homo sapiens sapiens* present in Africa, dispersed worldwide.

70,000   Neanderthalers (Europe, Asia, N. Africa). Rhodesian Man (S. Africa). Solo Man (Java). Flake tools.

40,000   First cold phase ends. Neanderthal race becoming extinct. Second cold phase. *Homo sapiens* (modern man). Implements show significant advances: small knife-blades, engraving tools. Paintings and sculpture; magic rites and ceremonies. Cro-Magnons with Aurignacian culture.

18,000   Final culmination of last ice age. Aurignacian culture dying out to be replaced by Solutrean and then by the Magdalenian cultures. Great flowering of Palaeolithic art.

15,000   First immigrants from Asia to cross Bering Straits?

15,000   Last glaciers in Britain disappeared. Proto-Neolithic in Middle East. Agricultural settlements (*e.g.,* Jericho). Settled way of life leading to such skills as weaving, metallurgy; inventions such as ox-drawn plough, wheeled cart.

5,000   Britain becomes an island (land connection with continent severed by melting ice-sheets).

B.C. **CIVILISATION IN THE MIDDLE EAST**

4300–3100   Formation of urban settlements in S. Mesopotamia during the Uruk Period. Cuneiform writing developed.

3150   First Egyptian Dynasty; capital at Memphis. Hieratic writing already perfected. Early Minoan Age (Crete). Pictorial writing, copper, silver, gold in use. Early Mycenaean civilisation begins.

2900–2334   Early Dynastic Mesopotamia (Sumer & Akkad). Sumerian dominance; Royal Cemetery of Ur.

2870   First settlements at Troy.

2850   Golden Age of China begins (legendary).

B.C.

2700–2200   Old Kingdom (Pyramid Age) in Egypt.

2400   Aryan migrations.

2334–2279   Sargon of Agade; his Akkadian empire collapses soon after the death of his grandson Naram-Sin in 2218.

2205   Hsia Dynasty begins in China (legendary).

2200   Middle Minoan Age: pottery, linear writing in pen and ink.

1800–1400   Stonehenge built and rebuilt.

1792–1750   Hammurabi king of Babylon; law code.

1766–1122   Shang Dynasty in China.

1720–1550   Hyksos in Egypt. War chariots introduced. Hebrews entered Egypt (Joseph) *c.* 1600.

1552–1069   Egyptian New Kingdom: at zenith under XVIIIth Dynasty. Chronology more certain: Late Minoan Age; Linear B script.

1500   Powerful Mitanni (Aryan) kingdom in Asia Minor. Phoenicia thriving—trade with Egypt and Babylonia. Vedic literature in India.

1450   Zenith of Minoan civilisation.

1400   Ugarit (N. Syria) culture at its zenith. Cretan civilisation ends: Knossos burnt. Temple at Luxor built.

1352–1338   Amenhotep IV (Akhenaten), the "heretic" Pharaoh. Diplomatic archive of Tell el-Amarna.

1350   Zenith of Hittite civilisation.

1275   Israelite oppression (Rameses II); Exodus from Egypt (Moses). Phoenician settlements—Hellas and Spain (Cadiz). Tyre flourishing.

1250   Israelites invade Palestine (Joshua).

1200   Attacks on Egypt by "Peoples of the Sea". Downfall of Hittite kingdom. Siege of Troy (Homeric). Beginning of sea-power of independent Phoenician cities.

1122–256   Chou Dynasty in China.

1115   Magnetic needle reputed in China.

1005–925   Kingdom of David and Solomon: Jerusalem as Sanctuary.

1000   *Rig Veda* (India).

925–722   Israel and Judah divided.

893   Assyrian chronological records begin.

850   Foundation of Carthage (traditional).

781   Chinese record of an eclipse.

776   First Olympiad to be used for chronological purposes.

753   Foundation of Rome (traditional).

750   Greek colonists settling in Southern Italy.

745   Accession of Tiglath-Pileser III; Assyrian Power at its height.

722   Capture of Samaria by Sargon II: Israel deported to Nineveh.

700   Homer's poems probably written before this date. Spread of the iron-using Celtic Hallstatt culture about this time.

625   Neo-Babylonian (Chaldean) Empire (Nineveh destroyed 612).

621   Publication of Athenian laws by Draco.

610   Spartan constitution, made rigid after Messenian Wars: later attributed to Lycurgus.

B.C.

594 Athenian constitution reformed by Solon.

586 Capture of Jerusalem: Judah deported to Babylon (partial return 538).

561 Pisistratus tyrant of Athens.

560 Accession of Croesus—prosperity of Lydia.

538 Babylon taken by Persians: Empire founded by Cyrus, soon covers almost all of civilised Middle East.

509 Roman Republic founded (traditional).

508 Democratic constitution in Athens.

500 Etruscans at height of their power in Northern Italy.

GREAT AGE OF GREECE

499 Revolt of Ionian Greek cities against Persian king Darius.

494 Secession of Plebeians from Rome. Tribunes established.

490 Battle of Marathon: Athenian repulse of Persian attack.

480 Death of Buddha. Battle of Thermopylae: Spartans under Leonidas wiped out by Persians. Battle of Salamis: Persian fleet defeated by Athenians under Themistocles; Persian invasion of Greece halted.

479 Battles of Plataea and Mycale: Greek victories by land and sea respectively destroy Persian invasion force. Death of Confucius.

477 League of Delos founded by Athens for defence against Persia; soon becomes Athenian Empire. (467 Naxos kept in by force.)

461 Pericles comes to power in Athens.

458 Cincinnatus saves Rome (traditional).

456 Death of Aeschylus.

447 Building of Parthenon begun.

431 Death of Phidias. Outbreak of Great Peloponnesian War between Athens and Sparta. Pericles "Funeral Oration" (according to Thucydides).

425 Death of Herodotus.

416 Massacre of Melos by Athenians.

415 Sicilian Expedition: flight of Alcibiades from Athens to Sparta.

413 Loss of entire Athenian expeditionary force at Syracuse.

406 Death of Euripides and Sophocles.

405 Battle of Aegospotami: Athenian navy destroyed by Sparta.

404 Athenian surrender to Sparta: beginning of Spartan hegemony in Greece.

403 Beginning of epoch of Warring States in China.

400 Death of Thucydides, Greek historian (?).

399 Execution of Socrates.

390 Occupation of Rome by Gauls under Brennus.

371 Battle of Leuctra: Spartans defeated by Thebans: beginning of Theban hegemony in Greece.

370 Death of Hippocrates of Cos (?).

347 Death of Plato.

343 Last native Egyptian Dynasty ends; Persians reconquer Egypt.

338 Battle of Chaeronea: Greek city-states defeated by Philip II of Macedon, who becomes supreme in Greece.

336 Assassination of Philip of Macedon: accession of Alexander.

334 Alexander's invasion of Persian Empire. Battle of Granicus, first victory.

333 Battle of Issus: Alexander defeats Darius of Persia.

332 Alexander's siege and capture of Tyre, occupation of Egypt.

B.C

331 Battle of Arbela (Gaugamela)—final defeat of Darius.

330 Death of Darius and end of Persian Empire. Alexander heir to civilisations of Middle East.

326 Battle of Hydaspes: Alexander conquers the Punjab.

323 Death of Alexander at Babylon. Beginning of Hellenistic Age in Middle East and Eastern Mediterranean. Ptolemy I founds dynasty in Egypt. Alexandria becomes intellectual centre of Hellenic world.

322 Death of Demosthenes.

321 Death of Aristotle. Maurya dynasty unites N. India.

312 Seleucus I founds dynasty in Asia.

300 Zeno the Stoic, Epicurus and Euclid flourishing.

ROME: CONQUESTS AND DECAY OF REPUBLICAN INSTITUTIONS

290 End of Third Samnite War. Rome dominates Central Italy.

280 Translation of Pentateuch into Greek.

275 Battle of Beneventum: Rome finally defeats Pyrrhus and the Greek cities of Southern Italy. Rome dominates all Italy.

274 Asoka becomes ruler of two-thirds of Indian sub-continent.

264 Beginning of First Punic War (Rome *v.* Carthage).

260 Battle of Mylae: first great Roman naval victory.

255 Defeat and capture of Regulus by Carthaginians.

250 Incursion of "La Tène" Iron Age people into Britain.

241 End of First Punic War. Sicily becomes first Province of Rome.

221 Kingdom of Ch'in completes conquest of all Chinese states under Shih Huang-ti.

218 Outbreak of Second Punic War: Hannibal crosses Alps.

216 Battle of Cannae: Hannibal wipes out great Roman army.

214 Great Wall of China constructed (by linking existing walls).

213 Burning of Chinese classics.

212 Capture of Syracuse by Romans and death of Archimedes.

207 Battle of Metaurus: defeat and death of Hasdrubal. End of Hannibal's hopes of overcoming Rome.

205 Roman provinces organised in Spain.

202 Battle of Zama: Hannibal defeated by Scipio Africanus, 202–A.D. 220 Han Dynasty in China.

201 End of Second Punic War. Rome dominates Western Mediterranean.

196 After defeating Macedon, Rome proclaims independence of Greek city-states. Death of Eratosthenes the geographer (?).

160 Death in battle of Judas Maccabaeus: Jewish revolt against Seleucids continues successfully.

149 Outbreak of Third Punic War.

146 Carthage destroyed. Roman province of Africa formed. Roman provinces of Macedonia and Achaea formed, and most of remainder of Greece reduced to vassal status.

134 First Servile War; Revolt of slaves in Sicily under Eunus. Suppressed 132.

133 Siege and destruction of Numantia by Romans. Tiberius Gracchus Tribune. Attempted land reforms. Murdered 132.

129 Roman province of Asia formed from lands bequeathed by Attalus of Pergamum.

124 Chinese Grand College to train Civil Service officials.

123 Caius Gracchus Tribune. Attempted land reforms. Murdered 121.

110 Chinese expansion to include most of south-east of modern China, under Emperor Wu Ti. Commercial activity in Indian Ocean.

B.C.

106 Jugurtha captured by Marius and Sulla.

104 Second Servile War: revolt of slaves in Sicily under Tryphon and Athenion. Suppressed 101.

102 Chinese expedition to Ferghana and possible knowledge of West.

101 Battle of Vercellae: Marius ends threat of Cimbri to Rome.

91 Social War: revolt of Italian cities against Rome. Suppressed 88. Roman franchise granted to most Italians.

88 Civil Wars of Marius and Sulla begin.

87 Massacre in Rome by Marius.

82 Proscriptions in Rome by Sulla.

75 Belgic invasion of south-eastern Britain.

73 Third Servile War: revolt of slaves in southern Italy under Spartacus the gladiator. Suppressed 71.

63 Conspiracy of Catiline exposed by Cicero.

60 First Triumvirate: Pompey, Caesar, Crassus.

58 Beginning of Caesar's conquest of Gaul.

55 Caesar's first British expedition: second, 54.

53 Battle of Carrhae: destruction of Roman army under Crassus by Persians.

52 Revolt of Vercingetorix against Caesar.

50 Migration to Britain of Commius and his followers.

49 Caesar crosses the Rubicon. Beginning of war against Pompey and the Senate.

48 Battle of Pharsalus: defeat of Pompey by Caesar.

46 Caeser's calendar reforms.

44 Murder of Caesar.

43 Second Triumvirate: Antony, Octavian, Lepidus.

42 Battle of Philippi: defeat and death of Brutus and his associates.

31 Battle of Actium: naval victory of Octavian over Antony and Cleopatra. Octavian unchallenged master of the Roman world.

THE ROMAN EMPIRE

27 Octavian given the title of Augustus by the Senate.

19 Death of Virgil.

8 Death of Horace.

4 Birth of Jesus (date not certain).

A.D.

6 Civil Service Examination system in China.

9 Radical reforms by Wang Mang (short Hsin dynasty 9–23). Annihilation of Roman army under Varus by Teutonic tribesmen under Arminius.

10 Cunobelinus reigning over much of south-east Britain from Colchester.

14 Death of Augustus.

17 Death of Livy.

18 Death of Ovid.

30 Crucifixion of Jesus (date not certain).

43 Roman invasion of Britain under Aulus Plautius.

51 Caractacus taken to Rome as prisoner.

60 Revolt of Boudicca.

63 Great Fire of Rome.

64 Death of St. Paul (date not certain).

65 Death of Seneca.

66 Jews of Palestine rebelled against Roman rule.

68 Death of Nero—end of Julio-Claudian line of Roman Emperors.

70 Jerusalem taken and Jewish revolt supressed by Titus.

79 Destruction of Pompeii and Herculaneum by eruption of Vesuvius.

A.D

80 Completion of Colosseum (Flavian Amphitheatre).

83 Battle of Mons Graupius: Agricola crushes Caledonians.

96 Accession of Nerva: first of the "Five Good Emperors."

97 Chinese expedition under Kang Yin (lieutenant of Pan Ch'ao) penetrates to Persian Gulf.

117 Death of Trajan, accession of Hadrian. Roman Empire at its greatest extent.

122 Beginning of Hadrian's Wall (Tyne–Solway) by Aulus Platorius Nepos.

135 Suppression of Bar-Cochba's revolt and Dispersion of Jews.

142 Construction of Antonine Wall (Forth–Clyde) by Quintus Lollius Urbicus.

180 Death of Marcus Aurelius, last of the "Five Good Emperors." Beginning of the "Decline" of the Roman Empire (Gibbon).

193 Praetorian guards murder Emperor Pertinax, sell Empire to highest bidder (Didius Julianus).

196 Clodius Albinus, governor, withdraws forces from Britain to support his attempt to become Emperor. Northern Britain overrun by barbarians.

208 Septimius Severus visits Britain to punish Caledonians (death at York 211).

212 Edict of Caracalla. Roman citizenship conferred on all free inhabitants of Empire.

220 End of Han Dynasty: China divided and frequently invaded for next three centuries.

227 Sassanid Empire in Persia.

230 Emperor Sulin—Japanese history emerging from legendary stage.

251 Goths defeat and kill Emperor Decius.

259 Break-away "Gallic Empire" set up: suppressed 273.

273 Defeat of Zenobia and destruction of Palmyra by Emperor Aurelian.

284 Accession of Diocletian, who reorganises Roman Empire (293) with rigid social laws and heavy taxation.

287 Carausius attempts to found independent "Empire of Britain": suppressed 297.

306 Constantine proclaimed Emperor at York.

313 Edict of Milan. Christianity tolerated in Roman Empire.

320 Gupta dynasty reunites India.

325 Council of Nicaea: first general Council of the Church.

367 Successful attack on Britain by Picts, Scots, Saxons.

369 Restoration of Roman authority in Britain by Theodosius.

378 Battle of Adrianople: Goths defeat and kill Eastern Roman Emperor Valens.

383 Magnus Maximus withdraws forces from Britain to support his attempt to conquer north-western part of Empire.

388 Magnus Maximus defeated and killed in Italy.

395 Death of Emperor Theodosius the Great: the division of the Empire into East and West at his death proves eventually to be the final one.

406 Usurper Constantine III withdraws forces from Britain to support his claims: probable end of Roman military occupation of Britain.

410 Sack of Rome by Alaric the Goth. Emperor Honorius tells Britons to arrange for their own defence.

THE BARBARIAN INVASIONS

415 Visigoths begin conquest of Spain.

419 Visigothic kingdom of Toulouse recognised by Roman government.

429 Vandals begin conquest of North Africa.

432 St. Patrick begins mission in Ireland.

A.D.

446 "Groans of the Britons"—last appeal to Rome (traditional).

451 Châlons: Attila the Hun repelled from Gaul by mixed Roman–Barbarian forces.

452 Attila's raid into Italy: destruction of Aquilea and foundation of Venice by refugees.

455 Rome pillaged by Vandals.

476 Romulus Augustulus, last Western Roman Emperor, deposed by Odovacar: conventionally the end of the Western Roman Empire.

481 Clovis becomes King of the Franks, who eventually conquer Gaul (d. 511).

493 Theodoric founds Ostrogothic Kingdom in Italy (d. 526).

515 Battle of Mount Badon: West Saxon advance halted by Britons, perhaps led by Arthur (?).

BYZANTIUM AND ISLAM

527 Accession of Justinian I (d. 565).

529 Code of Civil Law published by Justinian. Rule of St. Benedict put into practice at Monte Cassino (traditional).

534 Byzantines under Belisarius reconquer North Africa from Vandals.

552 Byzantine reconquest of Italy complete.

563 St. Columba founds mission in Iona.

568 Lombard Kingdom founded in Italy.

570 Birth of Mohammed.

577 Battle of Deorham: West Saxon advance resumed.

581–618 Sui Dynasty in China.

590 Gregory the Great becomes Pope.

597 St. Augustine lands in Kent.

605 Grand Canal of China constructed.

618–907 T'ang Dynasty in China: their administrative system lasts in essentials for 1,300 years.

622 Hejira or flight from Mecca to Medina of Mohammed: beginning of Mohammedan era.

627 Battle of Nineveh: Persians crushed by Byzantines under Heraclius.

632 Death of Mohammed: all Arabia now Moslem. Accession of Abu Bakr, the first Caliph.

634 Battle of Heavenfield: Oswald becomes king of Northumbria, brings in Celtic Christianity.

638 Jerusalem captured by Moslems.

641 Battle of Mehawand: Persia conquered by Moslems.

643 Alexandria taken by Moslems.

645 Downfall of Soga clan in Japan, after establishing Buddhism: beginning of period of imitation of Chinese culture.

650 Slav occupation of Balkans now complete.

663 Synod of Whitby: Roman Christianity triumphs over Celtic Christianity in England.

685 Nectansmere: end of Northumbrian dominance in England.

698 Carthage taken by Moslems.

711 Tarik leads successful Moslem invasion of Spain.

718 Failure of second and greatest Moslem attack on Constantinople. Pelayo founds Christian kingdom of Asturias in Northern Spain.

726 Byzantine Emperor Leo III begins Iconoclast movement: opposed by Pope Gregory II, and an important cause of difference between Roman and Byzantine churches.

THE HOLY ROMAN EMPIRE AND THE TRIUMPH OF CHRISTIANITY IN EUROPE: NORSEMEN AND NORMANS

732 Poitiers: Moslem western advance halted by Charles Martel.

735 Death of Bede.

750 Beginning of Abbasid Caliphate (replacing Omayyads)

A.D

751 Pepin King of the Franks: founds Carolingian dynasty. Ravenna taken by Lombards: end of Byzantine power in the West.

754 Pepin promises central Italy to Pope: beginning of temporal power of the Papacy.

778 Roncesvalles: defeat and death of Roland.

786 Accession of Haroun-al-Rashid in Baghdad.

793 Sack of Lindisfarne: Viking attacks on Britain begin.

795 Death of Offa: end of Mercian dominance in England.

800 Coronation of Charlemagne as Emperor by Pope Leo III in Rome.

814 Death of Charlemagne: division of empire.

825 Ellandun: Egbert defeats Mercians and Wessex becomes leading kingdom in England.

827 Moslem invasion of Sicily.

840 Moslems capture Bari and occupy much of Southern Italy.

843 Treaty of Verdun: final division of Carolingian Empire, and beginning of France and Germany as separate states.

844 Kenneth MacAlpin becomes king of Picts as well as Scots: the kingdom of Alban.

862 Rurik founds Viking state in Russia: first at Novgorod, later at Kiev.

866 Fujiwara period begins in Japan. Viking "Great Army" in England: Northumbria, East Anglia and Mercia subsequently overwhelmed.

868 Earliest dated printed book in China.

872 Harold Fairhair King of Norway.

874 Iceland settled by Norsemen.

885–6 Viking attack on Paris.

893 Simeon founds first Bulgar Empire in Balkans.

896 Arpad and the Magyars in Hungary.

899 Death of Alfred the Great.

900 Ghana at the height of its power in North West Africa.

907–960 Five Dynasties in China: partition.

910 Abbey of Cluny founded: monastic reforms spread from here.

911 Rolf (or Rollo) becomes ruler of Normandy.

912 Accession of Abderrahman III: the most splendid period of the Omayyad Caliphate of Cordova (d. 961).

928 Brandenburg taken from the Slavs by Henry the Fowler, King of Germany.

929 Death of Wenceslas, Christian King of Bohemia.

937 Battle of Brunanburh: crowning victory of Athelstan. West Saxon kings now masters of England.

955 Battle of Lechfeld: Magyars finally defeated by Otto the Great and settle in Hungary.

960–1279 Sung Dynasty in China.

965 Harold Bluetooth king of Denmark, accepts Christianity.

966 Mieszko I king of Poland, accepts Christianity.

968 Fatimids begin their rule in Egypt.

982 Discovery of Greenland by Norsemen.

987 Hugh Capet king of France: founder of Capetian dynasty.

988 Vladimir of Kiev accepts Christianity.

991 Battle of Maldon: defeat of Byrhtnoth of Essex by Vikings—renewed Viking raids on England.

993 Olof Skutkonung, king of Sweden, accepts Christianity.

1000 Leif Ericsson discovers North America.

1001 Coronation of St. Stephen of Hungary with crown sent by the Pope.

1002 Massacre of St. Brice's Day: attempt by Ethelred to exterminate Danes in England.

A.D.

1014 Battle of Clontarf: victory of Irish under Brian Boru over Vikings.

1016 Canute becomes king of England; builds short-lived Danish "empire."

1018 Byzantines under Basil 11 complete subjection of Bulgars.

1040 Attempts to implement Truce of God from about this time.

1046 Normans under Robert Guiscard in southern Italy.

1054 Beginning of Almoravid (Moslem) conquests in West Africa.

1060 Normans invade Sicily.

1066 Norman conquest of England under William I.

1069 Reforms of Wang An-Shih in China.

THE CRUSADES

1071 Manzikert: Seljuk Turks destroy Byzantine army and overrun Anatolia.

1073 Hildebrand (Gregory VII) becomes Pope. Church discipline and Papal authority enforced.

1075 Seljuk Turks capture Jerusalem.

1076 Kumbi, capital of Ghana, sacked by Almoravids: subsequent break-up of Ghana Empire.

1084 Carthusians founded by St. Bruno at Chartreuse.

1086 Compilation of Domesday Book.

1094 El Cid takes Valencia.

1095 Council of Clermont: Urban II preaches First Crusade.

1098 Cistercians founded by St. Robert at Citeaux.

1099 First Crusade under Godfrey of Bouillon takes Jerusalem.

1100 Death of William Rufus in the New Forest. Baldwin I: Latin Kingdom of Jerusalem founded.

1106 Tinchebrai: Henry I of England acquires Normandy, captures his brother Robert.

1115 Abelard teaching at Paris. St. Bernard founds monastery at Clairvaux.

1119 Order of Knights Templars founded.

1120 Loss of the White Ship and heir to English throne.

1122 Concordat of Worms: Pope and Emperor compromise on the Investiture Controversy, but continue to quarrel over other matters (Guelfs and Ghibellines).

1135 Stephen takes English crown: civil wars with Matilda and anarchy ensue.

1143 Alfonso Henriques proclaimed first king of Portugal.

1144 Moslems take Christian stronghold of Edessa.

1148 Second Crusade fails to capture Damascus.

1150 Carmelites founded about this time by Berthold.

1152 Accession of Emperor Frederick Barbarossa.

1154 Henry of Anjou succeeds Stephen: first of Plantagenet kings of England.

1161 Explosives used in warfare in China.

1169 Strongbow invades Ireland: beginning of Anglo-Norman rule. Saladin ruling in Egypt.

1170 Murder of Thomas Becket in Canterbury cathedral.

1171 Spanish knightly Order of Santiago founded.

1176 Battle of Legnano: Frederick Barbarossa defeated by the Lombard League. Italian autonomy established.

1185 Kamakura Period in Japan: epoch of feudalism: until 1333.

1187 Hattin: destruction of Latin kingdom of Jerusalem by Saladin.

A.D

1189 Third Crusade launched: leaders—Frederick Barbarossa, Philip Augustus of France, Richard Lionheart of England.

1191 Capture of Acre by Crusaders.

1192 End of Third Crusade without regaining Jerusalem. Richard I seized and held to ransom in Austria on return journey.

1198 Innocent III becomes Pope.

1202 Fourth Crusade, diverted by Venetians takes Zara from Byzantines.

1204 Fourth Crusade captures Constantinople, founds Latin Empire. King John of England loses Normandy to France.

1206 Temujin proclaimed Genghiz Khan (Very Mighty King) of all the Mongols: soon controls all of Central Asia.

1208 Albigensian Crusade launched: the first against Christians.

1212 Battle of Las Navas de Tolosa: decisive victory of Spaniards over Moors. The Children's Crusade.

THE CULMINATION OF THE MIDDLE AGES

1215 Fourth Lateran Council: the authority of the mediaeval Church and Papacy at its zenith. Dominicans recognised by the Pope. Magna Carta extorted by barons from John.

1223 Franciscans recognised by the Pope.

1229 Emperor Frederick II, through diplomacy, recognised by Moslems as King of Jerusalem.

1230 Teutonic Knights established in Prussia.

1237 Golden Horde (Mongols) begin subjugation of Russia.

1241 Mongol incursions into Central Europe.

1250 St. Louis of France captured on his Crusade in Egypt. Mamelukes become rulers of Egypt. Mandingo king declares his independence of Ghana and embraces Islam.

1256 Conference of Baltic ports; the first form of the Hanseatic League.

1258 Provisions of Oxford: barons under Simon de Montfort force reforms on Henry III of England. Baghdad destroyed by Mongols.

1264 Battle of Lewes: Montfort's party become rulers of England.

1265 Simon de Montfort's Parliament, Battle of Evesham: defeat and death of de Montfort.

1274 Death of Thomas Aquinas.

1279–1368 Mongol Dynasty in China (Kublai Khan).

1231 Repulse of Mongol attack on Japan.

1282 Sicilian Vespers: rising of Sicilians against French ruler.

1284 Completion of Edward I of England's conquest of Wales.

1290 Expulsion of Jews from England. Death of Maid of Norway: Edward I begins attempts to rule Scotland.

1291 Fall of Acre: end of Crusading in Holy Land. Everlasting League of Uri: beginnings of Swiss Confederation.

1294 Death of Roger Bacon, the founder of experimental science.

1295 "Model Parliament" of Edward I (anticipated in 1275).

1308 Death of Duns Scotus.

THE DECLINE OF THE MIDDLE AGES

1309 Papacy moves to Avignon: beginning of the Babylonish Captivity.

1312 Suppression of Templars by king of France and Pope.

1314 Battle of Bannockburn: victory of Robert Bruce secures Scottish independence.

1321 Death of Dante.

1325 Zenith of Mandingo Empire of Mali (North West Africa) under Mansa Musa; superseded at end of 15th century by Songhai empire.

1327 Deposition of Edward II; subsequently murdered.

A.D.

1336 Ashikaga Period in Japan: great feudal lords semi-independent of authority of Shogun.

1337 Death of Giotto.

1338 Beginning of Hundred Years' War between England and France.

1340 Battle of Sluys: English capture French fleet.

1344 Swabian League: weakness of Imperial authority in Germany obliges towns to form leagues for mutual protection.

1346 Battles of Crecy and Neville's Cross: spectacular English victories over French and Scots.

1347 Calais taken by Edward III of England. Cola di Rienzi attempts to reform government of Rome: killed 1354.

1348 Black Death reaches Europe (England 1349, Scotland 1350).

1351 Statute of Labourers: attempt by English Parliament to freeze wages.

1353 Statute of Praemunire: restraints placed on Papal intervention in England.

1354 Ottoman Turks make first settlement in Europe, at Gallipoli.

1355 Death of Stephen Dushan: collapse of Serbian Empire which he had built.

1356 Battle of Poitiers: capture of King John of France by Black Prince. "Golden Bull" regulates Imperial elections in such a way as to place power in the hands of the German princes: valid until 1806.

1358 The Jacquerie: rising of French peasants.

1360 Peace of Bretigny: Edward III makes great territorial gains in France.

1362 English becomes the official language in Parliament and the Law Courts.

1363 Timur (Tamerlane) begins his career of conquest in Asia.

1368–1644 Ming Dynasty in China.

1370 Bertrand du Guesclin Constable of France: regains much territory from the English. Peace of Stralsund: Hansa in complete control of Baltic Sea.

1377 Pope returns to Rome: End of Babylonish Captivity.

1378 Disputed Papal Election: Beginning of Western Schism.

1380 Battle of Chioggia: decisive victory of Venice over Genoa. Battle of Kulikovo: Dmitri Donskoi of Moscow wins first major Russian victory over Golden Horde.

1381 Peasants' Revolt in England under Wat Tyler.

1384 Death of John Wyclif.

1385 Battle of Aljubarotta: Portugal safeguards independence from Castile.

1386 Battle of Sempach: Swiss safeguard independence from Habsburgs. Jagiello (Vladislav V) unites Lithuania and Poland.

1389 Battle of Kossovo: crushing defeat of Serbs and neighbouring nations by Turks.

1396 Battle of Nicopolis: "the last crusade" annihilated by Turks.

1397 Union of Kalmar: Denmark, Norway and Sweden united under one crown: dissolved 1448.

1398 Timur invades and pillages Northern India.

1399 Richard II deposed by Henry IV: first of the Lancastrian kings of England.

1400 Owen Glendower revolts in Wales. Death of Chaucer.

1401 De Haeretico Comburendo: the burning of heretics made legal in England.

1410 Battle of Tannenberg: Poles and Lithuanians break power of Teutonic Knights.

1415 Battle of Agincourt: great success of Henry V of England in France. Council of Constance ends Western Schism, burns John Hus.

1420 Treaty of Troyes: English claims to French throne recognised. Hussite Wars begin: Bohemian heretics defend themselves successfully.

A.D

1429 Relief of Orleans by Joan of Arc.

1431 Burning of Joan of Arc.

1433 Rounding of Cape Bojador: first great achievement in exploration ordered by Henry the Navigator.

1434 Cosimo die Medici begins his family's control of Florence.

1435 Congress of Arras: Burgundians withdraw support from England, in favour of France.

1438 Albert II became German king and began Hapsburg rule over Holy Roman Empire, 1438–1806.

1440 Death of Jan van Eyck.

1450 Rebellion of Jack Cade against government of Henry VI of England.

1453 Battle of Castillon: final English defeat and end of Hundred Years' War. Constantinople taken by Turks: end of Byzantine or Eastern Roman Empire.

RENAISSANCE, DISCOVERIES, "NEW MONARCHIES"

1454 First dated printing from movable types in Europe: Papal indulgence printed at Mainz.

1455 First battle of St. Albans: beginning of Wars of the Roses.

1458 Mathias Corvinus becomes king of Hungary. George of Podiebrad becomes king of Bohemia.

1461 Battle of Towton: Yorkist victory in a particularly bloody battle. Louis XI becomes king of France.

1467 Charles the Bold becomes Duke of Burgundy.

1469 Marriage of Ferdinand of Aragon with Isabella of Castile: union of the main kingdoms of Spain (1474). Lorenzo the Magnificent becomes ruler of Florence.

1470 Warwick ("The Kingmaker") turns Lancastrian, dethrones Edward IV.

1471 Return of Edward IV: Lancastrians crushed at Barnet and Tewkesbury. Ivan III of Moscow takes Novgorod: Muscovy rising to supremacy in Russia.

1476 Caxton sets up his press at Westminster.

1477 Battle of Nancy: defeat and death of Charles the Bold: end of the greatness of Burgundy.

1479 Pazzi conspiracy against the Medici in Florence.

1481 Inquisition becomes active in Castile (1484 in Aragon).

1485 Battle of Bosworth Field: beginning of Tudor period in England.

1487 Lambert Simnel's rising fails.

1488 Bartholomew Diaz rounds Cape of Good Hope.

1491 Brittany acquired by King of France (by marriage).

1492 Rodrigo Borgia becomes Pope Alexander VI. Granada, last Moorish foothold in Western Europe, conquered by Spain. Christopher Columbus discovers the West Indies.

1493 Sonni Ali brings Songhai Empire to height of its prestige: Timbuktu renowned centre of literary culture.

1494 Italy invaded by French led by Charles VIII: beginning of Italian Wars and "modern" European diplomacy and international relations. Treaty of Tordesillas: Spain and Portugal agree to divide unexplored part of world; subsequently approved by Pope.

1496 Hapsburg–Spanish marriages: foundation of later empires.

1497 Perkin Warbeck captured by Henry VII (hanged 1499). John Cabot discovers Newfoundland.

1498 Savonarola burned. Vasco da Gama at Calicut: the sea route to India found.

1499 Amerigo Vespucci charts part of the South American coast.

A.D.
1500 Brazil discovered by Pedro Cabral.

1503 Casa de Contratación established at Seville; beginnings of Spanish colonial government. Fall of Caesar Borgia.

1507 Alfonso de Albuquerque becomes Viceroy of Portuguese Empire in the East.

1513 Accession of Pope Leo X, zenith of Renaissance Papacy. Machiavelli writes *The Prince*. Balboa discovers the Pacific (South Sea). Battle of Flodden: James IV of Scotland defeated and killed by English.

1514 Battle of Chaldiran: Turkish victory begins long series of wars between Turkish and Persian Empires.

REFORMATION, HAPSBURG–VALOIS WARS

1515 Francis I becomes king of France: victory of Marignano ends legend of Swiss invincibility. Thomas Wolsey becomes Lord Chancellor of England and Cardinal.

1516 Algiers taken by Barbarossa; beginning of the Corsairs.

1517 Martin Luther nails up his Ninety-five Theses: beginning of the Reformation. Turks conquer Egypt.

1519 Charles V inherits Hapsburg lands and elected emperor. Magellan begins first circumnavigation of the world. Death of Leonardo da Vinci.

1520 Suleiman the Magnificent becomes Sultan; Turkish power at its height. Field of Cloth of Gold; celebrated diplomatic meeting, spectacular but with no results.

1521 Mexico conquered by Hernando Cortes. Belgrade taken by the Turks. Diet of Worms: Luther commits himself irrevocably. Charles V divides his dominions: Austrian and Spanish Hapsburgs.

1522 Rhodes taken by the Turks; Knights of St. John move to Malta. Election of Adrian VI, first non-Italian Pope since 1378.

1523 Swedes expel Danish overlords, elect Gustavus Vasa King.

1524 Peasants' War in Germany (suppressed 1525).

1525 Battle of Pavia: defeat and capture of Francis I by Imperialists.

1526 Battle of Mohács: Turkish victory ends Hungarian independence. Foundation of Danubian Hapsburg Monarchy (Hungarian and Bohemian crowns united with Austrian patrimony of Hapsburgs): Holy Roman Empire prolonged for 300 years. Battle of Panipat: Babar begins Moslem conquest of India, founds Mogul Empire.

1527 Sack of Rome by Imperialists. Italy under control of Charles V.

1529 Siege of Vienna by the Turks. Peace of Cambrai; pause in Hapsburg–Valois struggle, end of serious French intervention in Italy. Diet of Speyer: origin of the name Protestant.

1532 Peru conquered by Francisco Pizarro.

1533 Ivan IV (the Terrible) becomes Tsar. Marriage of Henry VIII and Catherine of Aragon declared null.

1534 Act of Supremacy: Henry VIII asserts control over English Church.

1535 Coverdale's English Bible printed. Execution of Thomas More and John Fisher.

1536 Execution of Anne Boleyn. Dissolution of smaller Monasteries by Henry VIII and Thomas Cromwell (remainder dissolved 1539). Pilgrimage of Grace: Northern rising because of religious grievances.

1538 Chibchas of Bogota conquered by Gonzalo de Quesada.

1540 Francisco de Coronado begins explorations in North America. Society of Jesus recognised by Pope.

1541 John Calvin regains authority in Geneva.

1542 First Portuguese reach Japan. New Laws of the Indies: first attempt to legislate for welfare of colonial natives, by Spanish government.

1543 Death of Copernicus.

1545 Opening of Council of Trent: the Counter-Reformation.

A.D
1547 Death of Henry VIII: Somerset Protector in the name of the boy king, Edward VI.

1549 First English Book of Common Prayer. Kett's Rebellion in Norfolk, because of economic grievances.

1550 Deposition of Protector Somerset: Northumberland rules England.

1553 Lady Jane Grey proclaimed Queen by Northumberland on death of Edward VI: Mary I succeeds. Servetus burned by Calvin.

1555 Latimer and Ridley burned by Mary. Religious Peace of Augsburg: policy of *cuius regio, eius religio* accepted in Germany.

1556 Charles V abdicated imperial powers in favour of brother Ferdinand. Cranmer burned. Akbar becomes Mogul Emperor (d. 1605).

1557 Macao becomes permanent Portuguese port in China.

1558 Calais lost by English to French. Elizabeth I becomes Queen of England.

1559 Peace of Cateau-Cambrésis: end of Hapsburg–Valois duel.

RELIGIOUS WARS

1561 Mary, Queen of Scots, returns to Scotland.

1562 First War of Religion in France: wars continue intermittently until 1598.

1563 Thirty-nine Articles define Elizabethan Church settlement.

1564 Birth of Shakespeare; death of Michelangelo.

1565 Malta beats off Turks.

1567 Deposition of Mary, Queen of Scots. Alva in the Netherlands: severe rule.

1568 Flight of Mary, Queen of Scots, to England: imprisonment. San Juan de Ulua: defeat of Hawkins, and end of his slave-trading voyages. Beginning of Anglo-Spanish maritime feud. Revolt of Moriscos of Granada (suppressed 1570).

1569 Rebellion of Northern Earls (Catholic) in England.

1570 Elizabeth I anathematised by Pope.

1571 Battle of Lepanto: spectacular defeat of Turkish sea-power by Don John of Austria. Bornu (or Kanem) in Central Sudan at its zenith under Idris III.

1572 Dutch "Sea Beggars" take Brill. Massacre of St. Bartholomew in France. Polish Crown elective again, on death of Sigismund II.

1576 Catholic League formed in France, led by Guise family.

1577 Drake begins voyage round world (returns 1580).

1578 Battle of Alcazar-Quivir: death of King Sebastian of Portugal. Parma re-establishes Spanish rule in Southern Netherlands.

1579 Union of Utrecht: seven northern provinces of Netherlands form what becomes Dutch Republic. Death of Grand Vizier Sokolli: decline of Turkish power begins.

1580 Philip II of Spain becomes king of Portugal.

1582 Gregorian Calendar (or New Style) introduced by Pope Gregory XIII.

1584 Assassination of William the Silent.

1585 Hidéyoshi Dictator of Japan: unification of the country. English intervention in Spanish–Dutch War.

1587 Execution of Mary, Queen of Scots. Drake "singes King of Spain's beard." Shah Abbas I (the Great) becomes ruler of Persia (d. 1629).

1588 Spanish Armada defeated.

1589 Death of Catherine de' Medici, Queen-Mother of France.

1592 Moorish conquest of African Songhai Empire.

1593 Henry IV of France becomes Catholic.

1598 Edict of Nantes: French Protestants guaranteed liberty of worship. End of French Wars of Religion.

1600 English East India Company founded. Tokugawa Period begins in Japan (Ieyasu takes title of Shogun, 1603): lasts until 1868.

A.D.
1601 Rebellion and execution of Earl of Essex, Elizabethan Poor Law.

1602 Dutch East India Company founded.

1603 Irish revolts finally suppressed by Mountjoy. Accession of James VI of Scotland as James I of England: Union of English and Scottish Crowns.

1604 Hampton Court Conference: James I disappoints Puritans.

1605 Gunpowder Plot.

1607 Virginia colonised by London company: Jamestown founded.

1608 Quebec founded by Champlain.

1609 Twelve Years' Truce between Spain and United Provinces: Dutch independence in fact secured. Expulsion of Moriscos from Spain.

1610 Assassination of Henry IV of France.

1611 Plantation of Ulster with English and Scottish colonists. Authorised Version of the Bible in England.

1613 Michael Romanov becomes Tsar: the first of the dynasty.

1614 Napier publishes his explanation of logarithms.

1616 Death of Shakespeare and Cervantes. Edict of Inquisition against Galileo's astronomy.

1618 "Defenestration of Prague": Bohemian assertion of independence begins Thirty Years' War.

1620 Pilgrim Fathers settle in New England.

1624 "Massacre of Amboina": English driven out of spice islands by Dutch. Richelieu becomes Chief Minister in France.

1628 Murder of Duke of Buckingham. Petition of Right by Commons to Charles I. Fall of La Rochelle: French Protestants lose political power. Harvey publishes his work on the circulation of blood.

1629 Charles I begins Personal Rule.

1630 Gustavus Adolphus of Sweden enters Thirty Years' War, turns tide against Imperialists.

1631 Sack of Magdeburg, one of the worst incidents of the Thirty Years' War.

1632 Battle of Lützen: death of Gustavus Adolphus.

1633 William Laud appointed Archbishop of Canterbury. Thomas Wentworth takes up his post as Lord Deputy of Ireland.

1634 Dismissal and murder of Imperialist general Wallenstein.

1635 John Hampden refuses to pay Ship Money.

1636 Japanese forbidden to go abroad.

1637 Russian pioneers reach shores of Pacific.

1638 Covenant widely signed in Scotland.

1639 First Bishops' War: Charles I comes to terms with Scots.

1640 Second Bishops' War: Charles I defeated by Scots. Long Parliament begins: abolition of Royal prerogatives. Great Elector (Frederick William) becomes ruler of Brandenburg. Revolt of Catalonia (finally suppressed 1659). Revolt of Portugal: Duke of Braganza proclaimed king.

1641 Japanese exclude all foreigners (except for small Dutch trading fleet). Massacre of Protestants in Ireland. Wentworth (Earl of Strafford) executed. Grand Remonstrance of Commons to Charles I.

1642 Charles I attempts to arrest the Five Members. Outbreak of English Civil War: first general engagement, Edgehill. Death of Richelieu.

1643 Mazarin becomes Chief Minister of France. Battle of Rocroi: French victory, end of Spanish reputation for invincibility. English Parliament agrees to Solemn League and Covenant, secures services of Scots army.

1644 Marston Moor: decisive battle of English Civil War. North lost to Charles I. Tippemuir: Montrose begins victorious Royalist

A.D
campaign in Scotland. 1644–1911 Manchu dynasty in China.

1645 Formation of New Model Army. Naseby: main Royalist army crushed. Battle of Philiphaugh: Montrose's army destroyed.

1646 Charles I surrenders to Scots.

1647 Charles I handed over to Parliament. Charles I seized by Army. Charles I flees to Carisbrooke Castle.

1648 Second Civil War: New Model Army defeats Scots and Royalists. "Pride's Purge": Parliament refashioned by Army. Peace of Westphalia ends Thirty Years' War.

ASCENDANCY OF FRANCE

1649 Charles I executed. England governed as Commonwealth. Cromwell in Ireland. New Code of Laws in Russia completes establishment of serfdom.

1651 Battle of Worcester: Cromwell's final victory, now master of all Britain. First English Navigation Act. Hobbes' *Leviathan* published.

1652 Foundation of Cape Colony by Dutch under Van Riebeek. First Anglo-Dutch War begins (ends 1654).

1653 Cromwell dissolves Rump, becomes Protector.

1655 Major-Generals appointed to supervise districts of England. Jamaica seized by English.

1656 Grand Vizier Kiuprili: revival of Turkish government.

1658 Death of Cromwell.

1659 Peace of the Pyrenees: France replaces Spain as greatest power in Western Europe.

1660 Restoration of monarch in Britain: Charles II. Royal Society founded.

1661 Death of Mazarin: Louis XIV now rules in person. "Clarendon Code"; beginning of persecution of Non-conformists in England.

1664 New York taken by English: Second Anglo-Dutch War ensues (ends 1667).

1665 Great Plague of London.

1666 Great Fire of London. Newton's discovery of law of gravitation.

1667 Dutch fleet in the Medway. War of Devolution begins: first of Louis XIV's aggressions.

1668 Portuguese Independence recognised by Spain.

1669 Death of Rembrandt.

1670 Secret Treaty of Dover between Charles II and Louis XIV. Revolt of peasants and Don Cossacks under Stenka Razin (suppressed 1671).

1672 Third Anglo-Dutch War begins (ends 1674). Murder of De Witt brothers: William of Orange becomes leader of Dutch against French invasion.

1673 Test Act deprives English Catholics and Non-conformists of public offices. Death of Molière.

1675 Battle of Fehrbellin: Swedes defeated by Great Elector; rise of Prussian military power. Greenwich Royal Observatory founded.

1678 "Popish Plot" of Titus Oates utilised by Shaftesbury and the Whigs to bring pressure on Charles II.

1679 Bothwell Brig: suppression of Scottish Covenanters. Habeas Corpus Act passed.

1680 Chambers of Reunion: Louis XIV uses legal arguments to complete annexation of Alsace.

1681 Oxford Parliament: Charles II overcomes his opponents, begins to rule without Parliament.

1683 Rye House Plot. Siege of Vienna by the Turks: last major Turkish attack on Europe.

1685 Sedgemoor: Monmouth's rebellion crushed by James II. Revocation of Edict of Nantes: persecution of French Protestants by Louis XIV.

A.D.

1688 Seven Bishops protest against James II's policy of toleration, and are acquitted. William of Orange lands in England: flight of James II. "The Glorious Revolution."

1689 Derry relieved: failure of James II to subdue Irish Protestants. Killiecrankie: death of Dundee and collapse of Highland rising. Bill of Rights defines liberties established by "Glorious Revolution."

1690 Locke's *Two Treatises on Government* published. Beachy Head: French victory over Anglo-Dutch fleet. Boyne: defeat of James II by William III.

1691 Capitulation of Limerick: surrender of Irish supporters of James II on conditions which are not fulfilled.

1692 Massacre of Glencoe. Government's "lesson" to Highlanders. La Hogue: Anglo-Dutch fleet regains command of the sea.

1693 National Debt of England begun.

1694 Bank of England founded.

1695 Press licensing abandoned: freedom of the press in England.

1696 Peter the Great sole Czar.

1697 Peace of Ryswyck between Louis XIV and William III. Peter journeys "incognito" to the West.

1699 Treaty of Karlowitz: great Turkish concessions to Austrians. Death of Racine.

1700 Great Northern War, involving all Baltic powers, begins (ends 1721). Battle of Narva: Russians defeated by Charles XII of Sweden. Death of Charles II of Spain: under French influence Louis XIV's grandson Philip of Anjou named successor.

1701 War of the Spanish Succession begins. Hungarian revolt led by Francis Rakoczi against Austrians. Elector of Brandenburg receives title of King of Prussia. Act of Settlement establishes Protestant Hanoverian Succession in England.

1703 Methuen Treaty between England and Portugal. St. Petersburg founded.

1704 Gibraltar taken by Rooke. Blenheim: Marlborough stops France from winning war.

1706 Ramillies: Marlborough's second great victory. Turin: Eugene defeats French in Italy.

1707 Almanza: Anglo-Austrian forces in Spain defeated by French under Berwick. Act of Union: English and Scottish Parliaments united. Death of Aurungzib, last powerful Mogul.

1708 Oudenarde: Marlborough's third great victory.

1709 Pultava: Charles XII's invasion of Russia smashed by Peter the Great. Malplaquet: Marlborough's fourth great victory—at great cost in lives.

1710 Tory government in England.

1711 Dismissal of Marlborough.

1713 Peace of Utrecht: England makes advantageous peace with Louis XIV. Bourbon king of Spain grants Asiento (monopoly of Spanish American slave trade) to England.

1714 Peace of Rastatt between France and Austria. Death of Queen Anne: accession of George I. Beginning of Hanoverian Dynasty in Britain. Whig oligarchy rules.

1715 Jacobite Rising defeated at Preston and Sheriffmuir. Death of Louis XIV. France under Regent Orleans.

ENLIGHTENED DESPOTS: FIRST BRITISH EMPIRE

1716 Septennial Act: English Parliament prolongs its life from three to seven years. Prince Eugène of Savoy defeated Turks at Petrovaradin (Yugoslavia).

1720 Collapse of Law's system of banking ("Mississippi Bubble") in France. "South Sea Bubble" in England.

A.D.

1721 Robert Walpole becomes first Prime Minister. Peace of Nystad: Sweden no longer a major power at end of Great Northern War. Russian gains.

1723 Death of Christopher Wren.

1727 First Indemnity Act for Non-conformists.

1729 Methodists begin at Oxford.

1730 Resignation from government of Townshend, who becomes agricultural pioneer.

1733 First Family Compact between Bourbon kings of France and Spain. Withdrawal of Walpole's Excise Bill. John Kay invents flying shuttle, first of the great textile inventions. Jethro Tull publishes *The Horse-Hoeing Husbandry*, advocating new agricultural methods.

1738 Lorraine ceded to France.

1739 Nadir Shah with Persian army sacks Delhi, ruins Mogul power. War of Jenkins' Ear begins between Spain and Britain.

1740 Frederick II (the Great) becomes king of Prussia. Maria Theresa succeeds to Austrian dominions. Frederick seizes Silesia, begins War of the Austrian Succession.

1742 Fall of Walpole.

1743 Dettingen: George II, last British king to command his army in the field, defeats French.

1745 Fontenoy: Duke of Cumberland defeated by Marshal Saxe. Jacobite Rebellion under Prince Charles Edward: initial success, victory of Prestonpans, march to Derby.

1746 Culloden: Jacobites destroyed by Cumberland.

1748 Treaty of Aix-la-Chapelle: Frederick retains Silesia, elsewhere status quo.

1750 Death of J. S. Bach.

1751 First volume of the *Encyclopédie* published in France. Clive takes and holds Arcot: checks plans of Dupleix in Southern India. Chinese conquest of Tibet.

1752 Britain adopts New Style calendar.

1753 British Museum begun by government purchase of Sloane's collection.

1755 Lisbon earthquake. Braddock's defeat and death at the hands of French and Indians.

1756 Diplomatic Revolution (alliance of Austria with France) achieved by Kaunitz; Britain and Prussia perforce became allies. Seven Years' War begins. Minorca taken from British by French (Byng executed 1757). Black Hole of Calcutta: suffocation of many British prisoners.

1757 Pitt Secretary of State, main influence in British government. Rossbach: one of Frederick II's numerous victories against heavy odds, Plassey: Clive conquers Bengal.

1759 "Year of Victories" for Britain: Quebec, Minden, Lagos, Quiberon Bay. James Brindley designs Worsley-Manchester Canal: the beginning of this form of transport in Britain. Voltaire publishes *Candide*. Death of Handel.

1760 Wandewash: decisive defeat of French in India, by Coote.

1761 Panipat: Mahrattas heavily defeated by Afghans. Fall of Pitt.

1762 Catherine II (the Great) becomes Czarina. Rousseau's *Social Contract* and *Emile* published.

1763 Peace of Paris: British colonial gains, First British Empire at its height. Peace of Hubertusburg: Frederick II retains his gains. Pontiac's Conspiracy: failure of Red Indian attempt to destroy British power.

1764 John Wilkes expelled from Commons. James Hargreaves invents spinning jenny.

1766 Henry Cavendish proves hydrogen to be an element.

1768 Royal Academy of Arts founded.

1769 Richard Arkwright erects spinning mill (invention of water frame).

1770 Struensee comes to power in Denmark (executed 1772). "Boston Massacre." James Cook discovers New South Wales.

1772 First Partition of Poland between Russia, Prussia and Austria.

A.D.
1773 Society of Jesus suppressed by Pope (restored 1814). Revolt led by Pugachov in Russia (suppressed 1775). "Boston Tea Party."

1774 Warren Hastings appointed first Governor-General of India. Treaty of Kutchuk Kainarji; great Turkish concessions to Russia. Karl Scheele discovers chlorine. Joseph Priestley's discovery of oxygen.

1775 Watt and Boulton in partnership at Soho Engineering Works, Birmingham. Lexington: first action in American War of Independence.

1776 American Declaration of Independence. Adam Smith's *Wealth of Nations* published.

1777 Saratoga: surrender of British army under Burgoyne to Americans.

1779 Beginning of great Franco-Spanish siege of Gibraltar (raised finally, 1783). Samuel Crompton invents spinning mule.

1780 Joseph II assumes sole power in Austria. Armed neutrality of maritime nations to restrain British interference with shipping.

1781 Joseph II introduces religious toleration, abolishes serfdom in Austria. Yorktown: surrender of British under Cornwallis.

1782 Battle of the Saints: Rodney's victory save British West Indies.

1783 Treaty of Versailles: American independence recognised. Pitt the Younger becomes Prime Minister of Britain. First flights in hot-air (Montgolfier) and hydrogen (Charles) balloons.

1784 Death of Dr. Samuel Johnson.

1785 Edmund Cartwright invents the power loom.

1787 American Constitution drafted.

1788 Impeachment of Warren Hastings begins (ends 1795): English fleet commanded by Captain Arthur Phillip landed in Australia.

FRENCH REVOLUTION AND NAPOLEON

1789 Washington first President of U.S.A. French Revolution begins. Storming of the Bastille (July 14).

1790 Civil constitution of the Clergy in France.

1791 Flight of Louis XVI and Marie Antoinette to Varennes.

1792 Battle of Valmy: French Revolution saved from intervention of European kings. Denmark becomes first country to prohibit slave trade. France becomes a Republic.

1793 Louis XVI beheaded. Second partition of Poland.

1794 "Glorious First of June." Fall of Robespierre and end of Jacobin Republic. Negro revolt in Haiti led by Toussaint L'Ouverture.

1795 The Directory established. "Whiff of Grapeshot": Napoleon Bonaparte disperses Paris mob, Oct. 5. Batavian Republic set up by France.

1796 First Italian campaign of Bonaparte: victories of Lodi, Arcola.

1797 Treaty of Campo Formio: Bonaparte compels Austria to make peace. Britain left to fight France alone.

1798 Bonaparte goes to Egypt. Battle of the Nile. Vinegar Hill rebellion in Ireland suppressed.

1799 New coalition against France: Suvorov and Russians victorious in Italy. Bonaparte returns to France. *Coup d'état* of Brumaire, Nov. 9. Consulate set up.

1800 Parliamentary Union of Great Britain and Ireland.

1801 Treaty of Lunéville: Austria makes peace; great French gains in Germany.

1802 Peace of Amiens between Britain and France. *Charlotte Dundas*, first practical steamship, on Clyde.

1803 Insurrection in Ireland under Robert Emmet. Britain again at war with France.

A.D
1804 Bonaparte becomes Emperor. Spain declares war against Great Britain. Serbian revolt against Turks under Kara George.

1805 Battle of Trafalgar, Nelson's great victory and death, Oct. 21. Battle of Austerlitz, Dec. 2.

1806 Death of Pitt, Jan. 23. Confederation of the Rhine: Napoleon's reorganisation of Germany, July 12. End of Holy Roman Empire, Aug. 6. Prussia overthrown at Jena. Napoleon declares Great Britain in a state of blockade—"Continental System."

1807 Slave trade abolished in British Empire. Treaty of Tilsit: with Alexander of Russia his friend, Napoleon controls all of Europe. Occupation of Portugal by French, to enforce Continental Blockade.

1808 Occupation of Spain by French. Spanish rising: guerilla warfare. Peninsular War begins. Battle of Vimeiro (defeat of French by Wellington), Aug. 21.

1809 Battle of Corunna and death of Sir John Moore, Jan. 16. Attempted risings in Germany against Napoleon: Austria renews war. Treaty of Schönbrunn, Oct. 14.

1810 Self-government established in Argentina: first South American state to become independent of Spain.

1811 Massacre of Mamelukes at Cairo. Luddite riots.

1812 Retreat from Moscow: destruction of Napoleon's Grand Army.

1813 War of Liberation starts in Germany. Defeat of French by Wellington at Vitoria, June 21

1814 Soult defeated by Wellington at Toulouse, April 10. Abdication of Napoleon, April 11; Louis XVIII king of France. Congress of Vienna (concluded June 1815) under guidance of Metternich. Resettlement of Europe, usually by restoration of kings. Germanic Confederation under Austrian supervision. Poland ruled by Czar. Kingdom of Netherlands to include Belgium.

THE OLD ORDER RESTORED

1815 Escape of Napoleon from Elba. Battle of Waterloo, June 18. Corn Law in Britain to safeguard agricultural interests by keeping up prices. Quadruple Alliance (Austria, Russia, Prussia, Britain) to maintain Vienna settlement and hold regular meetings ("Congress System") —frequently confused with Holy Alliance, which was simply a declaration of Christian principles. Napoleon sent to St. Helena, Oct. 16.

1818 Bernadotte made king of Sweden (Charles XIV), Feb. 6.

1819 Singapore founded by Stamford Raffles. Beginning of Zollverein (Customs Union) in Germany under Prussian influence. Parliamentary reform meeting at Manchester dispersed by military ("Peterloo"), Aug. 16.

1820 Death of George III, Jan. 29.

1821 Death of Napoleon at St. Helena, May 5.

1822 Congress of Verona: congress system breaks down with refusal of Britain (Canning) to intervene against revolutions.

1823 "Monroe Doctrine" announced by U.S.A. President. Dec. 2.

1824 Repeal of Combination Acts in Britain which had forbidden Trades Unions. Charles X king of France.

1825 Independence of all Spanish American mainland now achieved. Nicholas I Czar of Russia. First railway, Stockton to Darlington, opened.

1826 First crossing of Atlantic under steam by Dutch ship *Curaçao*. Menai suspension bridge opened.

1827 Battle of Navarino, Turkish and Egyptian fleet destroyed. Death of Beethoven.

1828 Death of Chaka, great Zulu conqueror.

1829 Greece independent. Catholic Emancipation Act in Britain. Metropolitan Police established.

A.D.

1830 Death of George IV, June 26. Louis Philippe ousts Charles X. Belgium breaks away from Holland. Russian Poland revolts.

1831 First Reform Bill introduced by Lord John Russell. Leopold of Saxe-Coburg becomes king of independent Belgium. British Association founded. Faraday discovers electromagnetic induction.

1832 Reform Bill passed, June 7. Walter Scott, Jeremy Bentham, and Goethe die. Electric telegraph invented by Morse.

1833 Beginning of "Oxford Movement" in English Church. First government grant made to English schools. First British Factory Act.

1834 Poor Law Amendment Act: tightening up of relief in Britain "Tolpuddle Martyrs" victimised to discourage British working-class movement. Carlist wars begin in Spain.

1835 Municipal Reform Act revises British local government. The word "socialism" first used. "Tamworth Manifesto" of Peel defines aims of Conservative Party.

1836 People's Charter states programme of Chartists. Great Trek of Boers from British South African territory. Texas achieves independence of Mexico.

1837 Queen Victoria succeeds to the throne.

1838 National Gallery opened.

1839 First Afghan war begins. Chartist riots at Birmingham and Newport. Anti-Corn Law League founded. Aden annexed by Britain.

1840 Penny postage instituted. Queen Victoria marries Prince Albert of Saxe-Coburg-Gotha. "Opium War" with China begins. Union Act gives Canada responsible government. Last convicts landed in New South Wales.

1841 Hong Kong acquired by Britain.

1842 Chartists present second national petition and put themselves at the head of strikes. Great potato famine in Ireland begins.

1846 Repeal of the Corn Laws. Peel resigns.

1847 British Museum opened.

REVOLUTIONS AND NEW NATIONS

1848 Monster meeting of Chartists on Kennington Common, procession abandoned, Apr. 10. General revolutionary movement throughout the Continent. Louis Philippe abdicates: French Republic proclaimed. Swiss Federal Constitution established after defeat of Sonderbund (Catholic succession movement). Rising in Vienna: flight of Metternich, accession of Francis Joseph. Nationalist risings in Bohemia and Hungary. Frankfurt Parliament: attempt to unite Germany on liberal principles. Communist Manifesto produced by Marx and Engels. U.S.A. makes great territorial gains from Mexico. Gold discovered in California.

1849 Collapse of revolutionary movements. Rome republic besieged by French (June 3), defended by Garibaldi, holds out until July 2. Austrians take Venice, Aug. 22. Repeal of old Navigation Laws. Punjab annexed by Britain.

1850 Cavour becomes Prime Minister of Sardinia. Don Pacifico affair: privileges of British citizenship at their highest defended by Palmerston.

1851 Great Exhibition in Hyde Park. First satisfactory submarine telegraph cable between Dover and Calais laid. Gold in Australia.

1852 Independence of Transvaal recognised by Britain. Napoleon III Emperor of the French.

1853 U.S. Commodore Perry lands in Japan: beginning of Western influence. Russia and Turkey at war.

1854 War declared against Russia by France and Britain. Allied armies land in Crimea, Sept. 14 (Alma, Siege of Sevastopol, Balaklava, Inkerman). Orange Free State set up.

1855 Sardinia joins Britain and France against Russia. Fall of Sevastopol and end of Crimean War. Alexander II Czar of Russia.

A.D

1856 Peace Treaty signed at Paris. Bessemer invents process for large-scale production of steel. Livingstone completes journey across Africa.

1857 Indian Mutiny. Relief of Lucknow. Canton captured by English and French.

1858 *Great Eastern* launched. Crown assumes government of India. Treaty of Aigun, by which China cedes Amur region to Russia.

1859 Darwin publishes *Origin of Species*. French support for Piedmont in war with Austria (Magenta, Solferino). Piedmont receives Lombardy. Harper's Ferry raid: John Brown hanged, Dec. 2.

1860 Garibaldi and the Thousand Redshirts in Sicily and Naples; most of Italy united to Piedmont. Vladivostok founded; Russia strongly established on N.W. Pacific.

1861 Abraham Lincoln takes office as Pres. of U.S. American Civil War commences with 11 states breaking away to form Southern Confederacy. Bull Run (July 21) Confederate success ends Federal hopes of easy victory. Victor Emmanuel proclaimed by first Italian Parliament as king of Italy. Emancipation of Serfs in Russia. Death of Prince Albert, Dec. 14.

1862 Bismarck becomes leading minister in Prussia. Garibaldi attempts to seize Rome but wounded at Aspromonte. Aug. 29. Cotton famine in Lancashire.

1863 Polish rising against Russia (suppressed 1864). French in Mexico. Battle of Gettysburg, July 1–3. Maximilian of Austria made emperor of Mexico.

1864 Cession of Schleswig-Holstein to Prussia and Austria. First Socialist International formed. Taiping rebellion in China ended. Federal army enters Atlanta, Sept. 2: General Sherman captures Savannah ("From Atlanta to the sea"). Dec. 22. Geneva Convention originated.

1865 Death of Cobden, Apr. 2. General Lee surrenders to Grant, Apr. 9. Lincoln assassinated, Apr. 14. Thirteenth Amendment to Constitution: slavery abolished in U.S. Death of Palmerston, Oct. 18. Lister introduces antiseptic surgery in Glasgow. Tashkent becomes centre of Russian expansion in Central Asia. Mendel experiments on heredity. William Booth founds Salvation Army.

1866 Austro-Prussian War over Schleswig-Holstein ("Seven Weeks War"). Prussian victory at Sadowa (July 3). Venice secured for Italy, who had, however, been defeated by Austrians at Custozza (June 24) and Lissa (July 20). Treaty of Prague, Aug. 23.

1867 North German Confederation founded. Emperor Maximilian of Mexico shot. Dominion of Canada established. Russia sells Alaska to America for $7 million. Garibaldi makes second attempt to seize Rome, but defeated by Pope with French support at Mentana, Nov. 3. Second Parliamentary Reform Bill passed (Disraeli "dished the Whigs").

1868 Shogunate abolished in Japan: Meiji period of rapid Westernisation under Imperial leadership begins. Ten Years' War (1868–78); struggle for Cuban independence from Spain. Disraeli succeeds Derby as Prime Minister but defeated in general election by Gladstone, Nov.

1869 General Grant, Pres. of U.S. Irish Church disestablished. Suez Canal formally opened.

1870 Napoleon III declares war against Prussia. French defeated at Woerth, Gravelotte, and Sedan. Paris besieged. Rome and Papal states annexed to kingdom of Italy. Irish Land Act passed. Forster's Education Act puts elementary education within reach of all British children. Papal Infallibility announced.

1871 William I of Prussia proclaimed German emperor at Versailles, Jan. 18. Paris capitulates, Jan. 28. Commune of Paris proclaimed, Mar. 28. Peace signed at Frankfurt-on-Main, May 10. Government troops enter Paris and

A.D.

crush Communards, May 28. Thiers President of the Republic, Aug. 31. Mont Cenis tunnel opened. Trade Unions in Britain legalised.

RIVAL IMPERIAL POWERS

1872 Secret ballot introduced in Britain. Death of Mazzini, Mar. 10.

1873 Death of Livingstone, May 4. Ashanti war.

1874 Disraeli succeeds Gladstone as Prime Minister.

1875 England purchases Khedive's shares in Suez Canal, Nov.

1876 Bulgarian massacres. Serbo-Turkish war. Bell invents the telephone. Custer defeated and killed in last large-scale Red Indian success. Porfirio Diaz in power in Mexico (until 1911). Victoria declared Empress of India.

1877 Transvaal annexed to British Empire. War between Russia and Turkey. Satsuma rebellion in Japan: final unsuccessful attempt to halt new ideas.

1878 Congress of Berlin: general Balkan settlement. Cyprus leased to Britain (annexed 1914). Second war with Afghanistan (ended 1880). Edison and Swan produce first successful incandescent electric light.

1879 Dual control (Britain and France) in Egypt. Zulu War. Gladstone's Midlothian Campaign. Tay Bridge destroyed, Dec. 28.

1880 Beaconsfield ministry succeeded by second Gladstone ministry. Transvaal declared a republic.

1881 British defeat at Majuba: independence of Transvaal recognised. France occupies Tunis. Gambetta becomes Prime Minister of France. Revolt of the Mahdi in the Sudan. Pasteur's famous immunisation experiment to show that inoculated animals can survive anthrax.

1882 Lord Frederick Cavendish, Irish Secretary, assassinated in Phoenix Park, Dublin, May 6. Triple Alliance (Germany, Austria, Italy) first formed. Alexandria bombarded, July 11. Cairo occupied by British troops, Sept. 14.

1883 National Insurance begun in Germany. Death of Wagner.

1884 Wolseley heads expedition to Khartoum to rescue Gordon. French establish complete protectorate in Indo-China. Evelyn Baring takes over administration of Egypt. Russians capture Merv. Berlin Conference defines rights of European Powers in Africa. Third Parliamentary Reform Bill. Parsons invents his turbine. Greenwich meridian internationally recognised as prime meridian. Fabian Society founded.

1885 Khartoum captured; Gordon slain, Jan. 26.

1886 Upper Burma annexed by Britain. Home Rule Bill defeated in Commons. All Indians in U.S.A. now in Reservations. Daimler produces his first motor car. Completion of Canadian Pacific Railway. Gold discovered in the Transvaal.

1887 Queen Victoria's Jubilee celebration, June 21.

1888 William II German Emperor. County Councils set up in Britain.

1889 Mayerling: tragic death of Prince Rudolf of Austria, Jan. 30. Flight of General Boulanger, after attempting to become master of France. Second Socialist International set up. Great London dock strike, Aug. 15–Sept. 16. Parnell Commission concludes sittings, Nov. 23 (129th day).

1890 Parnell ruined by divorce case: Irish politicians split. Sherman Anti-Trust Law: first attempt in U.S.A. to break cartels. Opening of Forth Bridge, Mar. 4. Bismarck resigns, Mar. 17. Caprivi succeeds. Heligoland ceded to Germany.

1891 The United States of Brazil formed.

1892 Panama Canal financial scandals in France.

1893 Home Rule Bill passes third reading in Commons, Sept. 1: Lords reject Bill, Sept. 8.

1894 Opening of Manchester Ship Canal, Jan. 1.

A.D

Gladstone resigns, Mar. 3, Lord Rosebery succeeds. Armenian massacres by Turks: repeated at intervals for next quarter of century. Japan declares war against China. Dreyfus convicted of treason.

1895 Opening of Kiel canal, June 21. Rosebery resigns, June 22; Salisbury Ministry succeeds. Treaty of Shimonoseki: Japan gets Formosa, free hand in Korea. New Cuban revolution breaks out against Spanish. Marconi sends message over a mile by wireless. Röntgen discovers X-rays. Freud publishes his first work on psycho-analysis. Jameson Raid, Dec. 29.

1896 Jameson raiders defeated by Boers, Jan. 1. Adowa: Italian disaster at hands of Abyssinians, the first major defeat of a white colonising power by "natives." Gold discovered in the Klondike.

1897 Cretan revolt leads to Greek–Turkish War. Hawaii annexed by U.S.A. Queen Victoria's Diamond Jubilee, June 22. Great Gold Rush began.

1898 Port Arthur ceded to Russia. Spanish–American War. *Maine*, U.S. warship blown up in Havana harbour. Treaty of Paris, Dec. 10: Cuba freed, Puerto Rico and Guam ceded to U.S.A., Phillippines surrendered for $20 million. Death of Gladstone, May 19. Battle of Omdurman, decisive defeat of Mahdists, Sept. 2. Empress of Austria assassinated, Sept. 10. The Curies discovered Radium.

1899 Boer War begins, Oct. 10.

1900 Boers attack Ladysmith, Jan. 6. Battle of Spion Kop, Buller repulsed with severe losses, Jan. 14. Relief of Kimberley, Feb. 15. Ladysmith relieved, Feb. 28. Mafeking relieved, May 17. Boxer outbreak in China, May. Annexation of Orange Free State, May 26. Roberts occupies Johannesburg, May 31. "Khaki Election." Annexation of the Transvaal, Oct. 25. Australian Commonwealth proclaimed, Dec. 30.

1901 Queen Victoria dies, Jan. 22. Trans-Siberian Railway opened for single-track traffic.

1902 Anglo-Japanese Alliance, Jan. 30. Death of Cecil Rhodes, Mar. 26. Treaty of Vereeniging ends Boer War, May 31.

1903 Congo scandal: celebrated case of misrule and exploitation. Royal family of Serbia assassinated, May 29. First controlled flight in heavier-than-air machine—Orville and Wilbur Wright at Kitty Hawk, U.S.A., Dec. 17.

1904 Russo-Japanese War begins, Feb. 8. Japanese victory at Yalu River, May 1. British forces under Younghusband reach Lhasa, Aug. 3. Treaty with Tibet signed at Lhasa, Sept. 7.

1905 Port Arthur falls to Japanese, Jan. 3. "Bloody Sunday" massacre at St. Petersburg, Jan. 22. Destruction of Russian fleet under Rozhdestvenski at Tsushima by Admiral Togo (May). Treaty of Portsmouth (U.S.A.) ends Russo-Japanese war. Separation of Church and State in France. Norway separates itself from Sweden.

1906 General strike in Russia. San Francisco destroyed by earthquake and fire, Apr. 18. Simplon tunnel opened for railway traffic, June 1. First Duma (Parliament with limited powers) in Russia. Liberal "landslide" majority in Britain: Labour M.P.s appear. Movement for Women's Suffrage becomes active in Britain. Algeciras Conference: Franco-German crises resolved in favour of France. Death of Ibsen. Vitamins discovered by F. G. Hopkins.

1907 New Zealand becomes a dominion.

1908 Annexation of Congo by Belgium. Young Turk revolution. Annexation of Bosnia and Herzegovina by Austria: severe rebuff for Russia. Asquith becomes Prime Minister of Britain.

1909 Old Age Pensions in Britain. Peary reaches North Pole. Blériot makes first cross-Channel flight. House of Lords rejects Lloyd George's budget. Union of South Africa formed. Henry Ford concentrates on producing Model T chassis: beginnings of cheap motors.

A.D.
1910 Accession of George V on death of Edward VII, May 6. Liberals win two General Elections. Labour Exchanges established in Britain. Death of Tolstoy and Florence Nightingale.

1911 Parliament Act: power of Lords decisively reduced. British M.P.s paid for first time. National Insurance in Britain. Great British rail strike. Tripoli taken from Turkey by Italy. Chinese Revolution. Amundsen reaches South Pole, Dec. 14.

1912 China becomes a Republic under Sun Yat Sen. *Titanic* disaster off Cape Race, Apr. 14–15. Great British coal strike. Scott's last expedition. Outbreak of Balkan Wars.

1913 Treaty of Bucharest: most of Turkey-in-Europe divided among Balkan states.

FIRST WORLD WAR

1914 Archduke Francis Ferdinand, heir to the Hapsburg thrones, assassinated at Sarajevo, June 28. Austria-Hungary declares war against Serbia, July 28. Germany declares war against Russia, Aug. 1. Germany declares war against France, Aug. 3. German invasion of Belgium: Great Britain declares war against Germany, Aug. 4. Great Britain declares war on Austria-Hungary, Aug. 12. British Expeditionary Force concentrated before Mauberge, Aug. 20. Battle of Mons; Japan declared war on Germany, Aug. 23. Battle of the Marne, Sept. 5–9. Trench warfare began on Aisne salient, Sept. 16. Three British cruisers (*Aboukir*, *Hogue*, and *Cressy*) sunk by one U-boat, Sept. 22. First Battle of Ypres, Oct. 12–Nov. 11. Raiding of German cruiser *Emden* until destroyed, Nov. 9. Battle of Coronel: German cruisers *Scharnhorst* and *Gneisenau* sink British cruisers *Good Hope* and *Monmouth*, Nov. 1. Great Britain declares war against Turkey, Nov. 5. Destruction of German squadron off Falkland Is., Dec. 8. British protectorate over Egypt proclaimed, Dec. 17. First Zeppelin appeared over British coast, Dec. 20.

1915 Turkish army defeated in Caucasus, Jan 5. Great Britain declared blockade of Germany, Mar. 1. Battle of Neuve Chapelle, Mar. 10–13. Naval attack on Dardanelles called off, Mar. 22. First landing of British, Australian, New Zealand troops on Gallipoli Peninsula, Apr. 25. Second Battle of Ypres, Apr. 22–May 25: Germans first used gas. Sinking of *Lusitania*, May 7. Battle of Aubers Ridge, May 9–25. Italy declares war on Austria, May 22. British Coalition Government formed, May 26. Italian army crosses Isonzo, June 2. Zeppelin destroyed by R. A. J. Warneford, June 7. Second landing of Allied troops at Suvla Bay. Italy declares war on Turkey, Aug. 20. Turks defeated at Kut-el-Amara, Sept 28. Serbia conquered by Austria and Bulgaria, Nov. 28. French and British troops occupy Salonika, Dec. 13. British troops withdraw from Anzac and Suvla, Dec. 20.

1916 Evacuation of Gallipoli completed, Jan 8. Opening of Battle of Verdun, Feb. 21. Republican rising in Ireland, Apr. 24. First Daylight Saving Bill passed. Fall of Kut, Apr. 29. Battle of Jutland, May 31. Brusilov's offensive in Galicia begins, June 4. Kitchener drowned when *Hampshire* struck mine, June 5. Battle of the Somme, July 1–Nov. 13: British losses: 420,000. Italians capture Gorizia, Aug. 10. Hindenburg and Ludendorff chiefs of German staff, Aug. 27. Rumania declares war against Austria and Germany. Aug. 27. Tanks first used by British, Sept. 15. Death of Francis Joseph of Austria, Nov. 21. Lloyd George forms War Cabinet, Dec. 6. Joffre replaced by Nivelle, early Dec.

1917 Unrestricted submarine warfare begins, Feb. 1. British troops occupy Baghdad, Mar. 11. Revolution in Russia, Mar. 12. U.S.A. declares war on Germany, April 6. Battle of Arras, Apr. 9–14: Vimy Ridge taken by Canadians, Apr. 10. Pétain replaced Nivelle, May 15. Messines Ridge taken by British, June 7. First American contingents arrive in France, June 26. Allenby assumes Palestine

A.D
command, June 29. Third Battle of Ypres opened, July 31. Russia proclaimed a Republic, Sept. 15. British victory on Passchendaele Ridge, Oct. 4. French victory on the Aisne, Oct. 23. Caporetto: Italians severely defeated by Austrians. Oct. 24. Bolshevik Revolution, Nov. 7 (Oct. 25 O.S.). Passchendaele captured by British, Nov. 6. Balfour declaration recognised Palestine as "a national home" for the Jews, Nov. 8. Hindenburg Lines smashed on 10-mile front, Nov. 20. Fall of Jerusalem, Dec. 9. Russo-German armistice signed, Dec. 15.

1918 Treaty of Brest-Litovsk, Mar. 3. German offensive against British opened on Somme, Mar. 21, Battle of Arras, Mar. 21–Apr. 4. Second German offensive against British, Apr. 9–25. British naval raid on Zeebrugge and Ostend, Apr. 23. Foch appointed C.-in-C. Allied armies, Apr. 14. Peace signed between Rumania and Central Powers, May 7. *Vindictive* sunk in Ostend harbour, May 9. Last German offensive against French, July 15. British, Canadians, and Australians attack in front of Amiens, Aug. 8. Allenby destroyed last Turkish army at Megiddo, Sept. 19. Bulgarians signed armistice, Sept. 29. General Allied offensive in West began, Sept. 26. Germans accepted Wilson's Fourteen Points, Oct. 23. Great Italian advance, Oct. 24. Turkey surrenders, Oct 30. Austria accepts imposed terms, Nov. 3. Popular government in Poland (Lublin), Nov. 7. Revolutionary movement begins in Germany, Nov. 8. Kaiser abdicates and escapes to Holland, Nov. 9. Armistice signed by Germans, Nov. 11. Proclamation of Kingdom of Serbs, Croats and Slovenes in Belgrade, Dec. 1.

THE TWENTIES AND THIRTIES

1919 Peace Conference in Paris, Jan. 18. Einstein's theory of Relativity confirmed experimentally during solar eclipse, March 29. First direct flight across Atlantic by Sir J. Alcock and Sir A. W. Brown, June 15. Interned German fleet scuttled at Scapa Flow, June 19. Treaty of Peace with Germany signed at Versailles, June 28. Treaty of St. Germain: break-up of Austrian Empire, Sept. 10.

1920 Peace Treaty ratified in Paris. First meeting of League of Nations, from which Germany, Austria, Russia, and Turkey are excluded, and at which the U.S.A. is not represented. Prohibition in U.S.A. Peace Treaty with Turkey signed at Sèvres: Ottoman Empire broken up Aug. 10. Degrees first open to women at Oxford Univ., Oct. 14.

1921 Riots in Egypt, May 23. In complete disregard of the League of Nations, Greece makes war on Turkey. Heligoland fortresses demolished, Oct. 14. Irish Free State set up by Peace Treaty with Britain, Dec. 6.

1922 Four-Power Pacific Treaty ratified by U.S. Senate, Mar. 24. Heavy fighting in Dublin, the Four Courts blown up, July 2. Defeat of Greek armies by the Turks, Aug.–Sept. Mussolini's Fascist "March on Rome," Oct. 28.

1923 French troops despatched to Ruhr, Jan. 11. Treaty of Lausanne, July 24. Earthquake in Japan, Tokyo and Yokohama in ruins, Sept. 1. Rhine Republic proclaimed, Bavaria defies the Reich, Oct. 20. Turkish Republic proclaimed; Kemal Pasha, first President, Oct. 29.

1924 Lenin dies, Jan. 21. First Labour Ministry in Britain under MacDonald, Jan. 22; lasts 9 months. George II of Greece deposed and a Republic declared, Mar. 25. Dawes Plan accepted by London conference; Ruhr evacuation agreed to, Aug. 16.

1925 Hindenburg elected German President, Mar. 26. Treaty of Locarno signed in London, Dec. 1. Summer Time Act made permanent.

1926 Ibn Saud proclaimed king of the Hedjaz in Jeddah, Jan. 11. Evacuation of Cologne by British forces, Jan. 31. General strike in Britain.

1927 Lindbergh flies Atlantic alone, May 21.

1928 Earthquake in Greece, Corinth destroyed. Apr. 23. Capt. Kingsford-Smith flies the

A.D.
Pacific, June 9. General Nobile rescued by aeroplane from Arctic one month after disaster, June 24. Kellogg Pact accepted by Gt. Britain, July 18. German airship with 60 persons crosses Atlantic, Oct. 15. Women in Britain enfranchised on same basis as men.

1929 Second Labour Ministry under MacDonald. Graf Zeppelin makes numerous successful inter-continental flights. Commander Byrd flies over South Pole, Nov. 30. American slump and Wall Street crash.

1930 *R.101* destroyed in France on first flight to India, 48 lives lost, Oct. 5—end of British interest in airships.

1931 Great floods in China. Resignation of Labour Government and formation of Coalition under MacDonald. Invergordon naval mutiny.

1932 Manchuria erected into Japanese puppet state of Manchukuo, Feb. 18. Sydney Harbour Bridge opened, Mar. 19. Ottawa Imperial Conference.

1933 Hitler appointed Chancellor by Hindenburg, Jan. 30, and step by step gains supreme control. German Reichstag set on fire, Feb. 27.

1934 Dollfuss, Austrian Chancellor, murdered by Austrian Nazis, July 25. Death of Hindenburg, Aug. 2. Hitler becomes Dictator. Alexander of Yugoslavia assassinated in Marseilles, Oct. 9.

1935 Saar plebiscite for return to Germany, Jan. 13. Baldwin succeeds MacDonald as Prime Minister, June 7. War begins between Italy and Abyssinia, Oct. 3. Ineffectual economic "sanctions" by League of Nations against Italy, Nov. 18.

1936 Accession of King Edward VIII, Jan. 20. Repudiation of Locarno Treaty by Germany, Mar. 7. Remilitarisation of Rhineland, Mar. 8. Italian troops occupy Addis Ababa, May 5. Civil War breaks out in Spain, July 18. Inauguration of BBC high definition TV, Nov. 2. King Edward VIII abdicates after a reign of 325 days, Dec. 10. The Duke of York succeeds his brother as King George VI, Dec. 12.

1937 Coalition Ministry under Chamberlain, May 28. Japanese begin attempted conquest of China—"China incident," July 7.

1938 Austria annexed by Germany, Mar. 13. British navy mobilised, Sept. 28. Munich Agreement between Chamberlain, Daladier, Hitler, and Mussolini, Sept. 29.

1939

February 27 Great Britain recognises General Franco's Government.

March 16 Bohemia and Moravia annexed by Hitler and proclaimed a German Protectorate. **22** Memel ceded to Germany by Lithuania. **28** Anti-Polish press campaign begun by Germany.

April 1 Spanish War ends. **7** Italy seizes Albania. **14** First British talks with Russia. **27** Conscription introduced in Great Britain. **28** Hitler denounces Anglo-German Naval agreement and the Polish Non-Aggression Treaty.

May 12 Great Britain signs defensive agreement with Turkey. **22** Italy and Germany sign pact. **23** France and Turkey sign defensive agreement. **25** Anglo-Polish treaty signed in London.

July 10 Chamberlain re-affirms British pledge to Poland.

August 23 German-Soviet Pact signed by von Ribbentrop. **25** Japan breaks away from the Anti-Comintern Pact. **28** Holland mobilises. **31** British fleet mobilised.

SECOND WORLD WAR

September 1 Poland invaded by German forces. Great Britain and France mobilise. **1–4** Evacuation schemes put in motion in England and Wales: 1,200,000 persons moved. **2** Compulsory military service for all men in Britain aged 18 to 41. **3** War declared (11 a.m.) between Britain and Germany as from 5 p.m. **4** British liner *Athenia* sunk by submarine. R.A.F. raid the Kiel Canal entrance and bomb German warships. **6** First enemy air raid on Britain. **8** Russia mobilises. Russian troops on Polish border. **11** British troops on French soil. **17**

A.D
Russian troops cross the Polish frontier along its entire length. Russian and German troops meet near Brest Litovsk: loss of *Courageous*. **27** Capitulation of Warsaw. **29** Nazi-Soviet pact signed in Moscow approving partition of Poland: Introduction of petrol rationing in Britain.

October 14 *Royal Oak* sunk in Scapa Flow with a loss of 810 lives.

November 8 Bomb explosion in the Bürgerbräukeller at Munich after Hitler's speech. Germans using magnetic mines. **29** Diplomatic relations between Russia and Finland severed. **30** Finland attacked by Russia.

December 11 Italy leaves the League of Nations. **13** Battle of the River Plate: engagement of German warship *Admiral Graf Spee* by H.M. cruisers *Exeter*, *Ajax*, and *Achilles*. **14** Rejection by Russia of the League of Nations' offer of mediation in the Russo-Finnish war. Russia expelled from the League of Nations. **17** *Admiral Graf Spee* scuttles herself in the entrance of Montevideo harbour.

1940

February 14 Finnish advanced posts captured by Russians. **16** 299 British prisoners taken off the German Naval Auxiliary *Altmark* in Norwegian waters. **26** Finns lose the island fortress of Kolvisto. Finns retreat from Petsamo.

March 12 British ships to be fitted with a protective device against magnetic mines. Finland concludes a peace treaty whereby she cedes to Russia the Karelian Isthmus, the town of Vipuri and a military base on Hango Peninsula.

April 9 Invasion of Denmark and Norway by Germany. **15** British troops arrive in Norway. **19** British soldiers land in the Faroes.

May 2 British troops withdrawn from Norway. **10** Holland, Belgium and Luxembourg invaded by German forces. Parachute troops landed near Rotterdam. British troops cross the Belgian border. British troops land in Iceland. Rotterdam bombed. **11** National Government formed under Churchill. **13** Queen Wilhelmina arrives in London. **14** Rotterdam captured. Holland ceases fighting. Allied troops land near Narvik. **17** Belgian Government moves to Ostend. **24** German forces enter Boulogne. **27** Belgian army capitulates on the order of King Leopold. British forces to be withdrawn from Flanders. Narvik captured by Allied forces. **29** Ostend, Ypres, Lille and other Belgian and French towns lost to the Germans.

June Evacuation of British army from Dunkirk (May 27–June 4): 299 British warships and 420 other vessels under constant attack evacuate 335,490 officers and men. **5** Hitler proclaims a war of total annihilation against his enemies. **8** German armoured forces penetrate French defences in the West near Rouen. **10** Italy declares war on Great Britain and France. **14** Paris captured by German forces. **15** Soviet troops occupy Lithuania, Latvia and Estonia. **22** French delegates accept terms for an Armistice. **25** Hostilities in France cease at 12.35 a.m.

July 1 Channel Islands occupied by Germany. **3** French naval squadron at Oran immobilised. **10** Battle of Britain began.

August 19 British withdrew from Somaliland. **25** British began night bombing of Germany.

September 6 King Carol of Rumania abdicates in favour of his son Michael. **7** London sustains severe damage in the largest aerial attack since war commenced. **15** Battle of Britain ends with British victory: German aeroplanes destroyed, 1,733; R.A.F. losses, 915. **23** Japanese troops enter Indo-China.

October 7 German troops enter Rumania. **28** Greece rejects an Italian ultimatum.

November 1 Greeks repel Italian attacks, **5** H.M.S. *Jervis Bay* lost defending Atlantic convoy from German warship *Admiral Scheer*. **11** Italian fleet at Taranto crippled by Fleet Air Arm. **14** Coventry heavily attacked, the Cathedral destroyed. **22** Albanian town of Koritza captured by the Greeks.

December 2 Bristol heavily bombed. **11** Sidi Barrani captured by British forces: beginning

A.D.

of Wavell's destruction of Italian forces in Cyrenaica. **29** City of London severely burned by incendiary bombs: Guildhall and eight Wren Churches destroyed.

1941

January 5 Bardia captured. **22** Tobruk captured by Australian troops.

February 7 Benghazi captured. **26** Mogadishu, capital of Italian Somaliland, occupied by Imperial troops. German mechanised troops in Libya.

March 4 British raid Lofoten Islands. **11** U.S. Lease and Lend Bill signed by Roosevelt. **27** Keren—main battle in British conquest of Abyssinia and Somaliland. **28** Cape Matapan: Italian fleet routed by British. **30** Rommel opens attack in N. Africa.

April 4 Addis Ababa entered by Imperial troops. **6** Greece and Yugoslavia invaded by German troops. **8** Massawa capitulates. **11** Belgrade occupied by German forces. **13** Bardia given up by British. Tobruk holds out. **24** Empire forces withdrawing from Greece. **27** Athens captured by the Germans.

May 2 Evacuation from Greece completed. **10** Rudolf Hess descends by parachute in Scotland. **20** Crete invaded by German air-borne troops. **24** H.M.S. *Hood* sunk. **27** German battleship. *Bismarck* sunk; British forces withdrawn from Crete.

June 2 Clothes rationing commences. **4** William II (ex-Kaiser of Germany) dies. **18** Treaty of friendship between Turkey and Germany signed. **22** Germany attacks Russia. **24** Russia loses Brest Litovsk.

July 3 Palmyra (Syria) surrenders to Allied forces. **7** U.S. forces arrive in Iceland. **9** General Dentz, the French High Commissioner in Syria, asks for Armistice terms. **25** Fighting round Smolensk.

August 25 British and Russian troops enter Persia. **27** The Dnepropetrovsk dam blown up by the Russians.

September 18 Crimea cut off from mainland. **19** Kiev entered by Germans.

October 6 German attack on Moscow. **16** Soviet Government leaves Moscow. Odessa occupied by German and Rumanian troops. **19** Taganrog on Sea of Azov captured by Germans. **26** Kharkov captured by the Germans.

November 14 *Ark Royal* sunk. **18** Libyan battle opens: Eighth Army's first offensive. **23** Bardia and Fort Capuzzo captured by British. **24** H.M.S. *Dunedin* torpedoed. **25** H.M.S. *Barham* sunk. **30** Russians re-take Rostov.

December 1 Points rationing scheme in force in Britain. **4** German attack on Moscow halted. **7** Japanese attack on Pearl Harbor. **8** Japanese forces land in Malaya. **9** British forces in Tobruk relieved. **10** H.M.S. *Repulse* and *Prince of Wales* sunk off Malaya by Japanese. Phillippines invaded by Japanese. **25** Hongkong surrenders to Japanese.

1942

January 2 Manila and Cavite taken by Japanese. **23** Japanese forces land in New Guinea and the Solomon Islands.

February 9 Soap rationed. **12** Escape through English Channel of German ships *Scharnhorst*, *Gneisenau*, and *Prinz Eugen*. **15** Singapore surrenders to Japanese. **27** Battle of Java Sea.

March 9 Surrender of Java to Japanese.

April 15 George Cross awarded to the island of Malta.

May 4–8 Battle of Coral Sea. **7** Madagascar invaded by British forces. **7** U.S. forces sink 11 Japanese warships off the Solomon islands. **30** Over 1,000 bombers raid Cologne. Canterbury bombed.

June 3–7 Midway Island. U.S. naval victory turns tide in Pacific. **20** Tobruk captured by the Germans.

July 16 R.A.F. make first daylight raid on the Ruhr.

August 6 Germans advancing towards the Caucasus. **10** American forces land in the Solomon

A.D

Islands. **11** Malta convoy action (loss of H.M.S. *Eagle*, *Manchester*, *Cairo*, and one destroyer). **19** Raid on Dieppe. **23–25** Battle of Solomons.

September 6 Germans halted at Stalingrad.

October 23 El Alamein: Allied offensive opens in Egypt.

November 4 Rommel's army in full retreat. **5** Red Army holding firm at Stalingrad. **7** Allied invasion of N. Africa. **27** German forces enter Toulon. French Fleet scuttled.

December 2 First self-sustained, controlled nuclear chain reaction in uranium achieved by group working under Enrico Fermi at Chicago. **24** Admiral Darlan assassinated.

1943

January 6 German armies in the Caucasus and the Don elbow in retreat. **18** Leningrad 16-month siege ended. **23** Tripoli occupied by the Eighth Army. **27** American bombers make their first attack on Germany. **31** Remnants of the German army outside Stalingrad surrender.

February 9 Guadalcanal Island cleared of Japanese troops. **16** Kharkov retaken by the Russians.

March 1–3 Battle of Bismarck Sea. **23** 8th Army penetrates the Mareth Line.

May 7 Tunis and Bizerta captured by Allies. **12** All organised German resistance in Tunisia ceases. **16** Dams in the Ruhr breached by the R.A.F. **22** Moscow dissolves the Comintern.

June 3 French Committee for National Liberation formed in Algiers.

July 10 Allied invasion of Sicily. **25** Mussolini overthrown. **28** Fascist Party in Italy dissolved.

August 17 Sicily in Allied hands.

September 3 Italian mainland invaded. **7** Italy surrenders. **9** British and American troops land near Naples. **10** Rome seized by the Germans. **14** Salamaua captured from the Japanese. **23** *Tirpitz* severely damaged (sunk Nov. 12, 1944). **25** Smolensk taken by the Russians.

October 1 Naples taken. **25** Russians capture Dnepropetrovsk and Dneprodzerzhinck.

November 6 Kiev taken by the Russians. **26** Second Battle of Solomons. **28** Churchill, Roosevelt, and Stalin meet in Teheran.

December 2 Men between 18 and 25 to be directed to the mining industry by ballot in Britain. **26** Sinking of German battleship *Scharnhorst*.

1944

January 22 Allied landings at Anzio. **28** Argentina breaks with the Axis Powers.

February 1 American forces land on the Marshall Islands. **2** Russians penetrate Estonia.

March 15 Cassino (Italy) destroyed by American bombers.

May 9 Sevastopol captured by Russians. **18** Capture of Cassino and Abbey by Allies. **19** 50 Allied officers shot after escaping from a German prison camp. **30** Battle for Rome commences.

June 4 Allied forces enter Rome. King of Italy signs decree transferring his powers to Prince Umberto, his son. **6** *D-Day*: invasion of Europe (over 4,000 ships in invasion fleet). **7** Defeat of Japanese thrust at India, outside Imphal. **9** Heavy fighting near Caen. **12** First V-1 falls on England. **18** Cherbourg peninsula cut by the Americans. Russians break through the Mannerheim Line.

July 3 Minsk captured by Russians. **9** Caen captured by Allies. **20** "Bomb plot" on Hitler's life. **21** Guam captured by Americans.

August 1 Uprising in Warsaw. **4** Myitkyina falls to Allied forces. **15** Allied forces land in southern France. Marseilles taken. Rumania surrenders. **25** Paris liberated. Rumania declares war on Germany.

September 3 Allies in Belgium. **4** Antwerp and Brussels taken by Allies. Holland entered. Finland "ceases fire." **6** Bulgaria asks for an armistice. **7** Boulogne entered by Allies. Bulgaria declares war on Germany. **8** First V-2 falls on England. **11** Allied forces fighting on

A.D.
Reich territory. **17** Allied airborne troops landed at Arnhem. **22** 1st Battle of Philippines.
October 3 Warsaw rising crushed by Germany. **14** Allies occupied Athens. **15** Hungary requested armistice. **20** US troops took Aachen. **25** Battle of Leyte Gulf: Japan's sea-power broken.
December 6 Civil war in Athens. **16** German counter-attack in Ardennes.

1945

January 5 Athens fighting ended. **9** US troops landed on Luzon. **13** Red Army occupied Budapest. **17** Red Army occupied Warsaw. **27** Red Army entered Auschwitz. **28** Burma Rd to China reopened.
February 4 Yalta Conference. **14** Dresden bombed. **19** US troops landed on Iwo Jima.
March 6 Allies took Cologne.
April 1 US invaded Okinawa. **11** Red Army entered Vienna. **12** Pres Roosevelt died. **27** Russian–US link-up in Germany. **28** Mussolini killed by Italian partisans. **29** German and Italian armies in Italy surrendered. **30** Suicide of Hitler.
May 2 Russians took Berlin. **3** British took Rangoon. **4** German forces in NW Germany, Holland and Denmark surrendered. **8** World War II ended. **13** VE Day. **28** Air attacks on Japan.
June 26 World Security Charter to establish UN signed in San Francisco.
July 5 Allies recognised Polish government. **26** Labour won General Election: new PM Clement Attlee. **31** Potsdam Conference.
August 6 Atomic bomb destroyed Hiroshima. **8** Nagasaki atom bomb. **14** Unconditional surrender of Japan. **15** VJ Day.
September 5 Allies reoccupied Singapore.

"COLD WAR": AFRO-ASIAN INDEPENDENCE

October 15 Laval executed. **24** Quisling executed.
November 16 Unesco founded in Paris. **20** Nuremberg trial opened.
December 27 IMF and World Bank established.

1946

February 1 Trygve Lie 1st UN Secretary-General.
March 5 Churchill's "Iron Curtain" speech.
April 18 League of Nations wound up.
May 25 Jordan independent.
June 30 US atom bomb test at Bikini.
July 13 £937m US loan to Britain. **22** King David Hotel, British HQ in Jerusalem, blown up.
August 1 Paris Peace Conference.
October 16 Nuremberg sentences carried out: Goering's suicide. **23** General Assembly of UN opened in New York.

1947

January 1 Coal nationalised. **14** Vincent Auriol 1st Pres of French IVth Republic.
February 20 Lord Mountbatten last Viceroy of India.
June 5 "Marshall Plan" inaugurated.
August 3 UN mediation ended Indonesia fighting. **15** India and Pakistan independent after partition.
October 6 International organisation of Communist Parties Cominform set up. **14** Sound barrier broken.
November 20 Princess Elizabeth married.
December 15 "Big 4" talks on Germany broke down.

1948

January 1 Railways nationalised. **4** Burma independent. **30** Gandhi assassinated.
February 1 Malayan federal constitution came into force. **27** Communists seized power in Czechoslovakia.
March 10 Czech Foreign Minister Jan Masaryk found dead.
April 1 Electricity nationalised. **16** OEEC set up.
May 14 British Mandate in Palestine ended: new State of Israel proclaimed.

A.D
June 28 Cominform expelled Yugoslavia.
July 1 Berlin airlift. **5** NHS inaugurated.
August 1 Economic union of French, US and British zones in Germany.
September 4 Queen Wilhelmina of Netherlands abdicated. **9** N Korea independent, following S Korea. **17** UN mediator in Palestine assassinated.
November 3 Harry Truman elected US Pres. **14** Prince Charles born.
December 10 UN adopted Declaration of Human Rights.

1949

January 22 Chinese Communists took Peking.
April 1 Newfoundland became province of Canada. **4** 12 nations signed N Atlantic Treaty. **18** Republic of Ireland proclaimed.
May 1 Gas nationalised. **12** Berlin blockade lifted. **23** Federal Republic of Germany proclaimed.
August 8 1st meeting of Council of Europe.
September 14 Dr Adenauer 1st Chancellor of FDR. **21** Soviet atom bomb test.
October 1 People's Republic of China proclaimed under Chairman Mao Tse-tung. **12** German Democratic Republic proclaimed in Soviet sector.
December 8 Chinese Nationalist government set up Formosa HQ. **27** Indonesia independent.

1950

January 26 Indian republic proclaimed under Pres Rajendra Prasad.
February 14 USSR–China alliance signed. **23** Labour won General Election.
June 25 N Korea invaded S Korea. **27** US air, naval, and later ground forces supported S Korea.
July 8 Gen MacArthur C-in-C of UN forces in Korea.
August 1 Chinese membership rejected by UN. **7** US offensive in Korea.
September 6 British troops in action in Korea.
October 19 UN forces took Pyongyang. **21** China invaded Tibet. **26** New Chamber of House of Commons opened.
November 26 Chinese offensive into N Korea.
December 4 Chinese took Pyongyang. **19** Gen Eisenhower appointed head of Nato forces.

1951

January 4 N Korean and Chinese troops captured Seoul. **17** French held back Viet Minh offensive in Tonkin.
March 19 Treaty of Paris signed to create European Coal & Steel Community.
April 11 Gen MacArthur replaced by Lt-Gen Ridgway.
May 2 Persian oil industry nationalised. **3** Festival of Britain opened.
June 7 British diplomats Burgess and Maclean vanished.
July 8 Korean ceasefire talks. **16** King Leopold of Belgians abdicated. **20** King Abdullah of Jordan assassinated.
September 1 Tripartite Security Treaty between US, Australia and New Zealand. **8** Japanese peace treaty.
October 16 Pakistan's PM Ali Khan assassinated. **19** British troops seized Suez Canal Zone. **25** Conservatives won General Election: Churchill PM.
December 24 Libya independent.

1952

February 6 George VI died: Accession of Queen Elizabeth II.
March 21 Kwame Nkrumah Gold Coast's 1st PM.
April 23 Japan regained sovereign and independent status.
May 27 European Defence Community Treaty signed.
June 23 US air attack on N Korea hydro-electric plants.
July 23 Military coup in Egypt: later King Faroukh abdicated. **30** Eva Peron died.

A.D.

August 1 Parliament ratified Bonn Agreement: W Germany again independent. **16** Lynmouth floods. **26** S African protests against racial laws.
September 8 Gen Neguib military Gov-Gen of Egypt.
October 3 Britain's 1st atomic bomb test in Monte Bello Is. **20** State of Emergency in Kenya over Mau Mau atrocities.
November 4 Republican Gen Eisenhower won US Presidental Election. **30** US hydrogen bomb test reported.

1953

February 3 E coast floods.
March 5 Stalin died. **14** Krushchev emerged as USSR leader. **24** Queen Mary died. **25** Polio vaccine announced. **31** New UN Sec-Gen Dag Hammarskjöld.
April 8 Mau Mau leader Jomo Kenyatta jailed.
May 29 Hillary and Tensing climbed Everest.
June 2 Elizabeth II crowned: ceremony televised. **17** E Berlin anti-Soviet riots. **18** Egyptian republic proclaimed.
July 27 Korean armistice signed.
August 14 Soviet hydrogen bomb test.
November 21 Piltdown skull exposed as hoax. **29** French took Dien Bien Phu.
December 23 Former KGB chief Beria executed.

1954

January 9 Sudan self-governing. **16** New French Pres René Coty.
February 3 1st Central African Federation parliament opened.
March 22 London gold market reopened.
April 18 Nasser took power as Egypt's PM. **21** USSR joined Unesco.
May 4 Roger Bannister's 4-min mile. **8** Dien Bien Phu fell to Viet Minh. **17** Racial segregation banned in US state schools.
June 2 New Irish PM John Costello. **17** New French PM Pierre Mendès-France.
July 3 Food rationing ended. **21** Sino-French pact to end Indo-China war.
August 5 Persian oil dispute settled.
October 19 Anglo-Egyptian Suez Canal Agreement.
November 1 Algerian nationalist riots.
December 2 Senator McCarthy censured by Congress. **18** Cyprus riots for union with Greece.

1955

February 8 Marshall Bulganin Soviet PM and 1st Sec of Communist Party. **23** New French PM Edgar Fauré. **25** 1st meeting of SEATO.
April 5 Sir Winston Churchill resigned: new PM Sir Anthony Eden. **18** Hungarian PM Imre Nagy dismissed. **24** Afro-Asian Conference of 29 non-aligned nations. **29** Vietnam civil war.
May 5 W Germany attained full sovereignty; Western European Union established. **26** Conservatives won General Election.
June 2 Soviet-Yugoslav relations normalised. **15** UK–US nuclear cooperation agreed.
July 18 "Big 4" Geneva conference.
August 20 Riots in Algeria and Morocco.
September 15 EOKA guerrillas outlawed: British troops in Cyprus. **19** Gen Peron ousted. **22** ITV 1st broadcast.
October 6 New Greek PM Constantine Karamanlis. **20** Syria–Egypt mutual defence treaty. **26** S Vietnam declared independent republic.
November 2 New Israeli PM David Ben-Gurion.
December 7 Clement Attlee resigned. **14** New Labour Party leader Hugh Gaitskell.

1956

January 1 Sudan proclaimed independent republic.
February 25 Krushchev denounced Stalin. **29** Alabama race riots.
March 2 King Hussein of Jordan dismissed Lt-Gen Glubb, Commander of Arab Legion. **9** Archbishop Makarios deported to Seychelles. **23** Pakistan Islamic Republic within Commonwealth.
April 18 Krushchev and Bulganin in London.
June 13 British troops left Canal Zone. **23** Nasser elected Pres of Egypt unopposed. **29** Polish anti-Soviet riots.
July 26 Egypt seized Canal Zone.

A.D

October 23 Hungarian uprising against Soviet domination. **25** Anti-Soviet Polish unrest. **29** Israel invaded Egypt seizing Sinai peninsula. **31** Anglo-French forces bombed Egyptian military targets.
November 1 Premium bonds launched. **4** Soviet tanks crushed Hungarian revolt. **5** Anglo-French troops seized Canal Zone. **6** Pres Eisenhower re-elected. **8** UN Canal Zone ceasefire. **16** Canal blocked. **21** UN troops controlled Canal Zone. **30** Flood of Hungarian refugees.
December 5 140 arrests in S Africa for alleged treason. **7** Anglo-French troops left Port Said.

1957

January 1 Egypt abrogated 1954 Anglo-Egyptian Treaty; Saarland returned to W Germany. **9** Sir Anthony Eden resigned: new PM Harold Macmillan.
February 15 New Soviet Foreign Minister Andrei Gromyko.
March 6 Ghana independent; De Valera won Eire General Election. **25** Treaty of Rome setting up EEC and EAEC (Euratom) signed by Benelux, France, Germany and Italy.
April 8 Suez Canal reopened. **17** Archbishop Makarios in Athens.
May 15 UK's 1st hydrogen bomb test.
June 11 Canada's new Convervative government under John Diefenbaker.
July 1 International Geophysical Year began. **8** Eire State of Emergency against IRA. **25** Tunisia became republic under Pres Bourguiba.
August 8 Myxomatosis rife. **30** Malaya independent.
September 4 Wolfenden Report published. **15** Chancellor Adenauer re-elected. **23** Asian flu epidemic. **25** National Guard sent in to enforce desegregation in Little Rock, Arkansas.
October 4 Soviet satellite launched. **11** Jodrell Bank radio telescope inaugurated.
November 3 Soviet satellite carrying dog in orbit.
December 19 Nato conference agreed US nuclear bases in Europe.

1958

January 1 Treaty of Rome came into force. **3** British W Indies Federation inaugurated. **28** Turkish Cypriot riots. **31** US satellite launched.
February 1 Syria and Egypt proclaimed United Arab Republic. **6** Munich plane crash: Manchester Utd lost 8 players. **14** Short-lived Jordan–Iraq union. **17** CND founded.
March 2 Dr Vivian Fuchs completed 1st crossing of Antarctica. **8** Yemen entered federation with UAR. **27** Bulganin ousted.
April 4 1st Aldermaston march. **17** Nationalists won S African General Election. **21** Maltese PM Dom Mintoff resigned.
May 13 Algerian French nationalists rebelled. **23** Hovercraft unveiled. **29** Gen de Gaulle returned to power.
June 9 Gatwick airport opened. **20** Greek Cypriots rejected British peace plan.
July 14 King Faisal of Iraq assassinated: republic established. **15** US marines in Lebanon. **17** British troops in Jordan. **24** 1st life peers announced. **26** Prince Charles named Prince of Wales.
August 5 US nuclear submarine passed under N Pole.
September 2 New S African PM Dr Verwoerd. **9** Notting Hill race riots. **28** French referendum approved Vth Republic.
October 2 EOKA campaign renewed. **9** Pope Pius XII died. **28** Angelo Roncalli elected Pope as John XXIII. **31** 1st heart pacemaker implanted.
December 8 Draft agreement at 3-power Geneva test ban talks. **21** De Gaulle 1st Pres of Vth Republic. **27** Soviet cooperation agreed with UAR on Aswan dam project. **31** Thalidomide implicated in birth defects.

1959

January 1 Cuba's Batista regime overthrown by Fidel Castro. **12** USSR *Lunik I* satellite 1st to escape Earth's gravity.
February 2 Indira Gandhi leader of India's Congress Party. **23** Archbishop Makarios returned to

A.D.

Cyprus. **26** State of Emergency in S Rhodesia: black nationalist parties dissolved.

March 4 Anti-British riots in Nyasaland: Hastings Banda arrested. **17** Lhasa uprising against Chinese rule: Dalai Lama fled.

May 6 "Cod war" with Iceland. **15** Jodrell Bank transmitted radio message to USA via moon.

June 17 Eamon de Valera voted Eire's Pres. **26** St Lawrence Seaway opened.

July 5 3 animals recovered safely after Soviet space flight. **18** Castro assumed Cuba's Presidency.

August 18 BMC launched Mini.

September 14 Soviet *Lunik II* landed on moon. **27** Ceylon's PM Bandaranaike assassinated.

October 8 Conservatives won General Election. **26** *Lunik III* sent back photos of dark side of moon.

November 1 Nationalist riots in Belgian Congo. **2** M1, 1st UK motorway, opened. **20** EFTA agreement signed.

December 1 12 nations signed Antarctic Treaty. **3** Fréjus dam disaster. **14** Archbishop Makarios 1st Pres of Cyprus.

1960

January 1 French "new franc" introduced. **29** French settlers' revolt in Algeria.

February 2 De Gaulle granted emergency powers. **3** Harold Macmillan's "Wind of change" speech in Cape Town. **13** French atomic test in Sahara. **29** Agadir earthquake.

March 21 Sharpeville massacre in S Africa: 67 dead.

April 1 Hastings Banda freed. **9** Murder attempt on Dr Verwoerd. **19** Flood of E German refugees. **27** S Korean Pres Synghman Rhee resigned.

May 1 US U-2 military reconnaissance aircraft shot down over USSR. **7** Leonid Brezhnev new Soviet PM. **17** Paris "Big 4" Summit failed; Kariba Dam inaugurated. **25** Turkish military coup.

June 22 Krushchev attacked Mao and Chinese policies. **30** Belgian Congo became independent republic of Congo under PM Patrice Lumumba.

July 1 Ghana and Somalia became republics. **6** Congolese army mutiny: whites fled Leopoldville. **11** Katanga declared independence from Congo under Moise Tshombe. **21** Mrs Bandaranaike world's 1st woman PM.

August 8 Coup in Laos: new PM Prince Souvanna Phouma. **16** Cyprus declared republic.

September 14 Congolese army took power under Col Mobutu.

October 2 Talks to end "Cod war". **12** Disruptive behaviour from Krushchev at UN General Assembly. **20** *Lady Chatterley's Lover* trial.

November 9 Democrat John Kennedy elected US Pres. **21** Fighting between Congolese army and UN troops.

December 2 Lumumba arrested; Archbishop of Canterbury met Pope. **31** National Service ended; Farthing abolished.

1961

January 8 Referendum in France and Algeria backed de Gaulle; Portland spy ring arrests.

February 13 Lumumba dead.

March 21 US military aid to Laos. **26** French army rising in Algiers collapsed after 4 days.

April 12 Yuri Gagarin in 1st manned space flight. **19** Cuban exiles in Bay of Pigs invasion. **20** Angolan revolt.

May 1 1st betting shops opened. **5** Alan Shepherd made 1st US manned space flight. **17** S Korean military coup. **31** S Africa independent and left Commonwealth.

June 3 Kennedy-Krushchev Vienna talks. **27** Michael Ramsay enthroned as 100th Archbishop of Canterbury.

August 10 Britain formally applied to join EEC. **13** E Berlin border sealed: later Berlin Wall erected. **14** Kenyatta freed.

September 18 Dag Hammarskjöld killed in Congo plane crash. **30** Syria seceded from UAR.

October 10 Volcanic eruption on Tristan da Cunha: entire population evacuated. **23** 30 megaton Soviet atomic test. **24** Malta independent. **30** Stalin's body moved from Red Sq.

November 7 Adenauer elected Chancellor for 4th term. **28** UN condemned S African apartheid policy.

A.D

December 15 Eichmann sentenced to death for crimes against Jewish people. **17** Indian troops invaded Goa and other Portuguese colonies.

1962

January 4 More US military aid for S Vietnam. **14** UK smallpox outbreak.

February 8 OAS bomb campaign in France and Algeria.

March 2 Nehru's Congress Party won Indian General Election. **14** Geneva disarmament talks reopened. **15** Liberals won Orpington by-election.

April 8 Algerian peace accord. **13** International agreement on marine pollution. **26** 1st UK satellite *Ariel* launched.

May 10 US troops in Laos. **13** New Indian Pres Dr Radhakrishnan. **25** Coventry cathedral consecrated.

July 1 Commonwealth Immigrants Act came into force. **3** Algeria independent. **10** 1st live tv US–Europe link-up via *Telstar*.

August 22 De Gaulle escaped 4th assassination attempt.

September 3 Trans-Canada highway opened. **27** Yemen proclaimed republic.

October 22 Cuban missile crisis. **28** Soviet missile sites in Cuba to be dismantled. **26** Fighting on China–India border.

November 7 Nelson Mandela jailed for incitement. **20** US Cuban blockade lifted. **21** Ceasefire in China–India border dispute. **26** US Turkish bases to be removed. **29** Anglo-French agreement on Concorde. **30** New UN Sec-Gen U Thant.

December 8 British troops clashed with Brunei rebels opposing Malaysian Federation. **9** Dr Julius Nyrere 1st Pres of Tanganyika. **15** Rightwing victory in S Rhodesian General Election.

1963

January 15 Moise Tshombe finally ended Katanga secession. **18** Hugh Gaitskell died. **22** Franco-German Treaty on political and military cooperation. **29** Britain refused EEC membership; "Kim" Philby disappeared from Beirut.

February 1 Nyasaland self-governing under PM Hastings Banda. **8** Military coup in Iraq: PM Kassim executed. **9** Joshua Nkomo jailed in S Rhodesia. **14** Harold Wilson new Labour leader; 1st successful kidney transplant.

March 8 Military coup in Syria. **27** Beeching Report axed railways. **29** Central African Federation collapsed.

April 6 US–UK Polaris agreement. **8** Liberals won Canadian General Election. **23** New German Chancellor Ludwig Erhart.

May 11 Greville Wynne in Moscow spy trial. **18** Federal troops sent to quell Alabama race riots. **20** Sukarno Life Pres of Indonesia. **25** OAU founded. **27** Kenyatta elected PM in Kenya's 1st General Election.

June 3 John XXIII died. **5** John Profumo, Secretary of State for War, resigned. **6** Martial law in Teheran after Ayatollah Khomeini arrested. **13** Buddhist riots in Saigon. **16** Valentina Tereshkova 1st woman in space. **21** Giovanni Battista Montini elected Pope as Paul VI. **26** Pres Kennedy in W Berlin.

July 22 Stephen Ward on trial in "Profumo affair" aftermath. **26** Skopje earthquake.

August 8 "Great Train Robbery": £2·6m. mailbags stolen. **5** US–UK–USSR test ban treaty. **28** Dr Martin Luther King's "Freedom March" on Washington. **30** Moscow–Washington "hot line" inaugurated.

September 16 Federation of Malaysia created: anti-British riots. **17** Fylingdales early warning missile system operational.

October 1 Nigeria declared republic within Commonwealth. **18** Harold Macmillan resigned: new PM Earl of Home, later Sir Alec Douglas-Home.

November 1 Military coup in S Vietnam. **22** Pres Kennedy assassinated: Vice-Pres Lyndon Johnson sworn in.

December 12 Kenya independent.

1964

January 4 Pope visited Holy Land. **29** Further S Vietnam military coup.

February 11 Turkish–Greek Cypriot fighting.

A.D.
March 19 UN peacekeeping troops in Cyprus.
April 9 Labour won 1st GLC elections. **13** New S Rhodesian PM Ian Smith. **21** BBC-2 on air. **22** Tanganyika and Zanzibar united as Tanzania.
May 27 Nehru died.
June 2 New Indian PM Lal Shastri; PLO founded. **4** Britain's *Blue Streak* rocket launched. **12** Life sentence on Nelson Mandela for treason. **14** Francois Duvallier Haitian Pres-for-Life.
July 2 US Civil Rights Act. **6** Nyasaland independent as Malawi. **10** Congo's new PM Moise Tshombe.
August 2 US destroyer attacked by N Vietnam in Gulf of Tonkin: US air raids in reprisal.
September 2 Indonesian troops landed in Malaysia. **21** Malta independent within Commonwealth.
October 15 Krushchev deposed: new Communist Party leader Leonid Brezhnev, new PM Kosygin; Labour won General Election: new PM Harold Wilson. **16** Chinese atomic test. **24** N Rhodesia independent as Zambia under Pres Kaunda.
November 1 Vietcong guerrillas attacked US S Vietnamese base. **2** King Saud of Saudi Arabia deposed by brother Faisal. **3** Pres Johnson won US Presidential Election. **17** Arms embargo on S Africa. **26** Belgian paratroopers rescued hostages from Congo rebels.
December 12 Kenya proclaimed republic under Pres Kenyatta.

1965

January 12 Indonesia left UN. **24** Churchill died.
February 7 US air raid on N Vietnam. **24** US bombed Vietcong in S Vietnam.
March 7 US marines in S Vietnam. **18** Soviet cosmonaut made 1st spacewalk. **25** Ceylon's new PM Senanayaka. **28** Alabama civil rights protest. **30** US Saigon embassy bombed.
April 30 US marines in Dominica after military coup.
May 7 Rhodesia Front won Rhodesian General Election. **11** E Pakistan cyclone: 16,000 dead.
June 19 Algerian Pres Ben Bella ousted by Col Boumedienne. **29** US offensive against Vietcong.
July 29 Edward Heath new Conservative leader.
August 9 Singapore seceded from Malaysia. **11** Riots in Watts, Los Angeles.
September 8 India invaded Pakistan after Kashmir fighting: Pakistan air raids on New Delhi and later Bombay. **12** 50,000 more US troops in S Vietnam. **30** UK's 1st woman High Court judge.
October 7 Post Office Tower opened. **17** US and UK anti-Vietnam war protests. **22** India and Pakistan accepted UN ceasefire. **29** Rhodesia conciliation talks failed.
November 11 Rhodesian UDI: Britain declared regime illegal: sanctions imposed. **25** Gen Mobutu deposed Congo's Pres Kasavubu.
December 8 Vatican Council II closed. **17** Rhodesian oil embargo. **19** Pres de Gaulle re-elected.

1966

January 11 Indian PM Shastri died: new PM Indira Gandhi. **15** Army coup in Nigeria. **31** US bombing of N Vietnam resumed: UK Rhodesia trade ban.
February 24 Army coup in Ghana while Pres Nkrumah abroad.
March 31 Labour won General Election.
April 19 Australian troops in Vietnam.
June 30 France left NATO; US bombed Hanoi.
July 20 6-month pay and prize freeze. **30** US bombed Vietnam demilitarised zone; England won World Cup. **31** US urban race riots.
Augst 11 Indonesia–Malaysia peace agreement. **13** Chinese cultural revolution began.
September 6 Dr Verwoerd assassinated: new S African PM John Vorster. **30** Bechuanaland became independent republic of Botswana; Ancient statues saved from waters of Aswan Dam.
October 3 Basutoland independent as Lesotho; Nigerian tribal fighting. **21** Aberfan coal tip disaster.
November 1 Vietcong shelled Saigon. **9** Florence floods; new Irish PM Jack Lynch.
December 1 Dr Kiesinger new W German Chancellor. **2** Harold Wilson and Ian Smith in inconclusive talks on HMS *Tiger*. **16** UN mandatory oil

A.D
sanctions against Rhodesia. **22** Rhodesia left Commonwealth.

1967

January 18 New Liberal leader Jeremy Thorpe. **27** Flash fire killed 3 US astronauts during ground test.
February 22 Gen Suharto in power in Indonesia. **26** Major US offensive against Vietcong.
March 9 Stalin's daughter defected to West. **18** *Torrey Canyon* wrecked off Land's End: major pollution. **24** Army coup in Sierra Leone.
April 1 UK's 1st Ombudsman. **14** Conservatives won GLC elections. **21** Greek colonels seized power.
May 11 Britain applied to join EEC. **30** Biafra seceded from Nigeria.
June 5 6 Day War: Israel seized territory from Egypt, Jordan and Syria. **17** 1st Chinese H-bomb test.
July 1 Moise Tshombe arrested when plane hijacked to Algiers; BBC-2 began colour broadcasts. **7** Nigerian troops invaded Biafra. **15** De Gaulle in Quebec. **27** US urban race riots.
August 9 Biafran troops in Nigeria.
September 1 Majority verdicts allowed in UK criminal courts. **3** Swedish traffic switched to right. **20** *QEII* launched.
October 9 Che Guevara killed; New drink-driving laws. **22** Anti-Vietnam war demonstrations in US, UK and W Europe. **25** Abortion Bill passed. **31** Foot-and-mouth disease epidemic.
November 19 £ devalued. **29** Aden independent republic as S Yemen.
December 3 1st successful human heart transplant. **17** Australian PM Harold Holt drowned.

1968

January 5 Alexander Dubcek new moderate Czechoslovak PM. **9** New Australian PM John Gorton. **23** Intelligence ship *USS Pueblo* seized by N Korea. **31** Vietcong Tet offensive against S Vietnam cities: raid on US Saigon embassy.
February 24 US and S Vietnam troops recaptured Hue.
March 6 Black Rhodesians hanged in defiance of Queen's reprieve. **15** Foreign Secretary George Brown resigned. **17** Grosvenor Sq anti-Vietnam war demonstration.
April 4 Martin Luther King assassinated: riots throughout USA. **6** New Canadian Liberal PM Pierre Trudeau. **12** Student riots throughout Europe after shooting of W German student leader Rudi Dutschke. **21** Enoch Powell's immigration speech.
May 5 Student riots in Paris began. **9** Soviet troops on Czech border. **16** Ronan Point tower block collapsed. **19** French General Strike. **30** De Gaulle dissolved National Assembly and called General Election.
June 5 Robert Kennedy assassinated. **30** De Gaulle won landslide victory in French General Election.
July 1 Last EEC customs barriers removed; 36 nations signed Nuclear Non-Proliferation Treaty. **10** Couve de Murville succeeded Pompidou as French PM. **29** Papal encyclical against artificial contraception.
August 22 Warsaw Pact troops invaded Czechoslovakia.
September 11 Soviet tanks left Prague. **16** UK 2-tier postal system. **26** Theatre censorship abolished. **27** France vetoed UK EEC membership.
October 4 Warsaw Pact troops to remain in Czechoslovakia. **6** Londonderry riots against sectarian discrimination. **9** *HMS Fearless* Rhodesia talks failed.
November 1 US halted bombing of N Vietnam. **5** Republican Richard Nixon won US Presidential Election. **7** Prague anti-Soviet demonstrations.
December 27 3 US astronauts completed 10 orbits of moon.

1969

January 3 N Ireland sectarian violence. **19** Student Jan Palach set himself on fire in Wenceslas Sq in anti-Soviet protest.
February 3 Yasser Arafat PLO leader.
March 2 Soviet–China border clashes. **17** New Israeli PM Golda Meir. **19** British troops in

A.D.

Anguilla. **25** Pres Ayub Khan ousted by army coup under Gen Yahya Khan.

April 17 More troops sent to N Ireland; Dubcek replaced as Czech Communist Party leader by Gustav Husak. **18** Bernadette Devlin, civil rights worker, elected in Mid-Ulster by-election, UK's youngest MP. **23** Nigerian troops took Umuahia. **28** De Gaulle resigned after referendum defeat. **29** N Ireland PM Terence O'Neill resigned.

May 1 New N Ireland PM Maj James Chichester-Clark.

June 8 Spain closed Gibraltar border. **15** New French Pres Georges Pompidou: PM Jacques Chaban-Delmas.

July 1 Prince of Wales invested at Caernarvon. **21** Neil Armstrong and "Buzz" Aldrin 1st men on moon; Sen Edward Kennedy in court over Chappaquiddick drowning. **22** Gen Franco named Prince Juan Carlos as future Spanish King.

August 12 3 days of riots in Londonderry after Apprentice Boys' March: 500 dead. **15** British troops took over N Ireland security.

September 1 King Idris of Libya deposed by army revolutionaries under Muammar Gaddafi: republic proclaimed. **3** Ho Chi Minh died. **10** 7,000 troops in N Ireland. **24** Ton Duc Thang new N Vietnamese Pres. **28** Army erected Belfast "peace line": barricades dismantled: traffic curfew.

October 1 Olaf Palme Swedish PM. **10** N Ireland "B Specials" disbanded. **12** Troops used tear gas in N Ireland. **14** 50p coin issued. **15** "Vietnam moratorium" in USA. **21** New W German Chancellor Willi Brandt.

November 2 Starvation in Biafran refugee camps: Nigeria banned Red Cross aid.

December 18 UK death penalty permanently abolished.

1970

January 1 UK age of majority 18. **12** Biafra capitulated. **16** New Libyan PM Gaddafi; UK Hong Kong flu epidemic.

February 9 Equal Pay Bill passed in Commons. **11** Decentralisation of NHS announced.

March 1 US planes bombed "Ho Chi Minh trail" in E Laos. **2** Rhodesia declared republic. **18** Cambodia's Prince Sihanouk ousted. **19** 1st meeting between E and W German leaders.

April 2 Battle between Israeli and Syrian troops. **8** Israeli air raid on Nile delta village. **16** Clifford Dupont 1st Pres of Rhodesia. **17** *Apollo 13* crew rescued. **30** US troops in Cambodia.

May 4 4 student anti-war protesters shot dead at Kent State University, Ohio.

June 7 Jordan troops attempted to expell Palestinian guerrillas. **19** Conservatives won General Election: new PM Edward Heath. **26** Dubcek expelled from Communist Party. **30** UK, Denmark, Ireland and Norway opened talks on EEC entry.

August 2 1st use of rubber bullets in N Ireland. **30** Malayan PM Tengku Abdul Rahman resigned.

September 4 New Chilean Pres Socialist Salvador Allende. **12** Palestinian terrorists blew up 3 hijacked airliners in Jordan desert: 56 hostages held. **14** Palestinian guerrillas in control of N Jordan and Jordan's 2nd city Irbid. **22** New Malayan PM Abdul Razak. **27** Jordan–PLO truce signed in Cairo: PLO expelled from Jordan. **28** Nasser died. **30** All Western hostages freed in exchange for terrorists held by UK, W Germany and Switzerland.

October 5 New Egyptian Pres Anwar Sadat; Quebec separatists kidnapped British diplomat. **10** Quebec Minister Pierre Laporte kidnapped. **16** Trudeau outlawed FLQ and invoked emergency powers. **18** Laporte found dead. **19** Major oil find in N Sea by BP.

November 9 De Gaulle died. **13** Defence Minister Gen Assad seized power in Syria. **20** E Pakistan tidal wave: 150,000 dead.

December 3 Kidnapped British diplomat freed. **8** Pakistan's 1st free elections: Zulfikar Ali Bhutto victorious in W, Sheikh Mujibur Rahman in E.

December 14 Anti-government riots in Poland's Baltic ports: Communist Party leader Gomulka replaced by Gierek.

1971

January 1 Divorce Reform Act in force. **2** Ibrox Park football disaster. **3** Open University inaugu-

A.D

rated. **8** British ambassador to Uruguay kidnapped by Tupamaros guerrillas. **15** Aswan High Dam inaugurated. **25** Ugandan Pres Obote ousted by army coup under Idi Amin.

February 4 Rolls-Royce bankrupt; Swiss women given vote in national elections. **9** 1st British soldier killed in N Ireland. **15** UK decimal day. **20** Idi Amin Uganda's self-appointed Pres.

March 23 New N Ireland PM Brian Faulkner. **26** Sheikh Mujibur Rahman declared E Pakistan independent as Bangladesh: civil war erupted: Rahman jailed. **29** Lt Calley found guilty of My Lai massacre.

April 5 Thousands dead in E Pakistan fighting. **10** Split between "official" and "provisional" IRA. **18** UAR, Syria and Libya formed Federation of Arab Republics. **22** Jean Claude Duvallier succeeded as Haitian Pres.

May 3 Erich Honeker Gen Sec of E German Communist Party. **13** Labour took over GLC. **14** 2m E Pakistan refugees in India. **28** Egypt–USSR friendship treaty.

June 6 Cholera epidemic in W Bengal: border with Bangladesh sealed. **15** Education Sec Mrs Thatcher announced end of free school milk. **30** 3 Soviet cosmonauts dead at end of space flight.

July 20 Anglo-Maltese defence talks collapsed.

August 10 Internment without trial in N Ireland: riots and firebomb attacks. **22** Right-wing coup in Bolivia.

September 9 British ambassador freed in Uruguay. **24** 90 Soviet diplomats expelled as spies. **27** Chequers talks on N Ireland between 3 PMs.

October 25 China admitted to UN. **27** Congo changed name to Zaire. **28** Parliament voted to join EEC. **31** IRA bomb at PO Tower.

November 23 India–Pakistan border fighting. **24** Rhodesia agreement signed.

December 3 Pakistan declared war on India. **6** India recognised Bangladesh. **7** Libya nationalised £80m BP assets. **17** Pakistan agreed ceasefire. **20** New Pakistan PM Zulfikar Ali Bhutto. **21** New UN Sec-Gen Kurt Waldheim. **26** US resumed N Vietnam bombing.

1972

January 9 Miners' strike. **12** Sheikh Mujibur Rhaman PM of Bangladesh. **13** Ghana coup led by Col Acheampong. **20** UK unemployment passed 1m. **22** Treaty of Brussels signed to admit UK, Denmark, Ireland and Norway to EEC. **30** "Bloody Sunday": army shot 13 Derry marchers dead; Pakistan left Commonwealth.

February 2 British embassy in Dublin burned down. **16** Widespread prolonged power cuts as miners' crisis deepened: State of Emergency declared. **22** IRA Aldershot bomb: 7 dead. **25** Miners ended strike.

March 4 2 killed, 146 injured by Belfast restaurant bomb. **21** 6 died in Belfast shops bombing. **30** Direct rule imposed in N Ireland; N Vietnamese offensive.

April 10 46 nations signed convention to ban biological warfare. **14** US retaliatory bombing of Hanoi and Haiphong. **18** Bangladesh joined Commonwealth.

May 3 Hue evacuated. **9** Israeli troops freed 92 hostages and killed Black September guerrillas at Lydda airport. **16** Segregationist Gov Wallace of Alabama crippled by gunman. **22** Ceylon became republic of Sri Lanka. **28** Duke of Windsor died. **29** Brezhnev–Nixon talks. **30** Tel Aviv airport massacre by PFLP; Official IRA agreed ceasefire.

June 16 5 burglars caught in Watergate building, Democrat campaign HQ; W German Red Army Faction guerrillas captured. **22** Provisional IRA ceasefire. **23** £ floated.

July 1 Pres Nixon's campaign manager resigned. **14** N Ireland ceasefire failed. **31** "Operation Motorman": army dismantled N Ireland barricades.

August 6 50,000 Ugandan Asians expelled to UK. **11** Last ground troops left Vietnam. **20** S Vietnamese troops retreated.

September 1 New Icelandic fishing limit 50 miles. **5** Black September guerrillas killed Israeli athletes at Munich Olympics, kidnapped others: hostages, 5 guerrillas and policeman killed in airport gun battle. **12** Icelandic gunboat sank 2 British trawlers.

October 5 United Reformed Church formed. **13** Bank rate abolished (new term MLR).

A.D.

November 6 Government froze prices, pay, rent and dividend increases for 90 days. **7** Pres Nixon re-elected. **19** Chancellor Brandt re-elected. **20** Silver Wedding of Queen and Prince Philip.

December 2 Gough Whitlam 1st Australian Labor PM since 1946. **18** US resumed bombing of N Vietnam. **21** Treaty between W and E Germany. **23** Nicaraguan earthquake devastated Managua.

1973

January 1 UK, Eire and Denmark joined EEC. **27** Vietnam ceasefire signed.

February 1 EEC Common Agricultural Policy came into effect. **5** 1st Loyalists detained without trial in N Ireland. **12** 1st US prisoners released by N Vietnam. **21** Israeli fighters brought down Libyan Boeing 727: 104 dead.

March 1 Fine Gael and Labour coalition won Irish General Election: new PM Liam Cosgrave. **8** 2 bombs in central London. **9** N Ireland referendum: 591,820 in favour of retaining UK links. **11** French General Election: Gaullists and allies won absolute majority.

April 1 VAT introduced in UK.

May 7 Pres Nixon denied all knowledge of Watergate. **10** Elections for 36 new metropolitan district councils. **18** Royal Navy frigates sent to protect British trawlers in disputed 50-mile limit off Iceland. **31** Erskine Childers succeeded Pres de Valera of Eire.

June 1 Greece declared republic. **7** Skylab astronauts freed solar panels saving mission. **21** Mr Brezhnev and Pres Nixon signed arms limitation agreement.

July 31 1st sitting of N Ireland Assembly ended in chaos.

August 2 Summerland fire at Douglas, IOM. **19** George Papadopoulos 1st Pres of Greece.

September 3 Dr Henry Kissinger new US Secretary of State. **7** Len Murray new TUC General Secretary. **11** Allende government overthrown in Chile. **14** King Gustav of Sweden died. **20** Chelsea barracks bombed.

October 6 Arab–Israeli war began. **8** UK's 1st commercial radio station opened. **10** US Vice Pres Spiro Agnew resigned. **12** Gen Peron new Pres of Argentina with his wife as Vice Pres **16** Government embargo on arms sales to Middle East. **17** Arab oil producers cut supplies until Israel withdrew from occupied territories. **22** UN ceasefire agreed by Israel, Egypt and Jordan. **31** 3 Provisional IRA leaders freed from Mountjoy prison by hijacked helicopter.

November 8 UK–Iceland "cod war" ended. **12** Miners began overtime ban and ambulance drivers selective strikes. **14** Wedding of Princess Anne and Capt Mark Phillips. **25** Army coup in Greece.

December 5 50 mph speed limit imposed to conserve fuel. **6** Gerald Ford new US Vice Pres. **12** Rail drivers union ASLEF began overtime ban. **20** Spain's PM Admiral Carrero Blanco assassinated. **31** 3-day week imposed.

1974

January 1 Direct rule in N Ireland ended: new N Ireland Executive took office; Golda Meir won Israeli General Elections. **8** Lord Carrington Energy Secretary at head of new department. **9** Commons debate on energy crisis. **18** Israel and Egypt agreed withdrawal of forces. **22** Loyalists expelled from N Ireland Assembly.

February 10 Miners strike began. **28** UK General Election: no clear majority.

March 4 Edward Heath resigned: new minority Labour government. **9** UK resumed 5-day week. **11** Miners returned to work.

A.D

April 10 Golda Meir and Cabinet resigned. **14** Fighting on Golan Heights and Mt Hermon. **24** S African General Election: Nationalist party won. **25** Army uprising in Portugal: regime in power since 1926 overthrown.

May 6 Chancellor Brandt resigned on discovery of E German spy in Chancellery. **15** Gen Spinola new Pres of Portugal; Israeli troops stormed village school in Ma'alot where children held hostage by Arab terrorists. **16** Herr Schmidt new W German Chancellor. **19** Giscard d'Estaing won French General Election. **28** N Ireland Executive collapsed: direct rule from Westminster resumed.

June 1 Flixborough chemical works explosion. **3** New Israeli PM Mr Rabin.

July 9 Pierre Trudeau won Canadian General Election. **13** Senate Watergate Committee Report. **15** Pres Makarios overthrown in Cyprus coup. **17** Bomb at Tower of London. **18** Statutory incomes policy ended. **20** Turkish invasion of Cyprus. **24** Supreme Court ordered surrender of 64 White House tape recordings. **26** Greek junta collapsed: Mr Karamanlis returned to power. **27** 3 articles of impeachment adopted by Judiciary Committee of House of Representatives against Pres Nixon.

August 6 Pres Nixon resigned. **9** Gerald Ford sworn in as US Pres.

September 8 Emperor Haile Selassie deposed. **30** New Portuguese Pres Gen da Costa Gomes.

October 5 Guildford pub bombings: 2 dead, 70 hurt. **10** Labour won UK General Election: overall majority of 3. **15** Riots at Maze prison.

November 2 Vladivostock Summit between Pres Ford and Mr Brezhnev. **7** Woolwich pub bombings: 2 dead. **17** Mr Karamanlis won 1st Greek General Election since 1967. **21** Birmingham pub bombings: 21 dead, 120 hurt. **29** Anti-Terrorism Act proscribing IRA.

December 3 Defence cuts announced. **7** Archbishop Makarios returned to Cyprus. **18** Wave of bombs in London. **25** Cyclone devastated Darwin, Australia.

1975

January 1 Watergate defendants found guilty. **24** Dr Coggan enthroned 101st Archbishop of Canterbury. **25** Shaikh Mujibur Rahman new Pres of single party state in Bangladesh.

February 11 Mrs Thatcher elected leader of Conservative Party. **13** Turkish Cypriots declared separate state.

March 13 Portugal's new Supreme Revolutionary Council took power. **25** King Faisal of Saudi Arabia assassinated. **26** S Vietnamese troops evacuated Hué and Da Nang.

April 17 Phnom Penh government surrendered to Khmer Rouge. **21** Pres Thieu resigned as N Vietnamese troops encircled Saigon. **25** 1st elections in Portugal for 50 years. **30** Vietnam War ended.

June 5 EEC referendum: UK in favour by 2:1 majority. **5** Suez Canal reopened. **12** Mrs Ghandi convicted of illegal use of government officials in 1971 campaign.

July 1 S S Ramphal new Commonwealth Secretary-General. **29** Military coup in Nigeria: new Head of State Brig Murtala Mohammed.

August 7 Hottest-ever August day in London. **15** Pres Rahman of Bangladesh assassinated. **27** Bombings in Caterham and London.

September 9 Prince Sihanouk returned to Cambodia. **24** Government steps to check unemployment.

October 3 Dutch industrialist kidnapped in Limerick. **15** Iceland extended fishing rights to 200

A.D.

miles. **21** UK unemployment over 1m. **26** Battles in Beirut between Christian Phalangists and left-wing Muslims.

November 3 Queen formally inaugurated North Sea oil. **11** Angolan independence; Australian Governor-General dismissed Labor government. **22** Prince Juan Carlos crowned King of Spain.

December 4 Detention without trial ended in N Ireland. **10** "Cod war" began. **11** IRA Balcombe St siege in London. **14** Liberal Country Party won Australian General Election. **18** Education Bill compelling comprehensive education published. **29** Sex Discrimination and Equal Pay Acts came into force.

1976

January 19 Commons Devolution debate.

February 11 MPLA recognised as Angola's legal government by OAU. **13** Nigerian Pres Murtala Mohammed assassinated. **March 1** Ulster Convention dissolved: direct rule continued. **16** Harold Wilson resigned. **24** Senora Peron of Argentina deposed. **25** Basil Hume enthroned as Archbishop of Westminster.

April 5 New PM James Callaghan.

May 10 Jeremy Thorpe resigned Liberal leadership. **28** Soviet–US treaty on underground nuclear explosions.

June 1 "Cod war" ended. **16** Riots in African township Soweto near Johannesburg. **24** Vietnam reunified.

July 2 Government emergency powers to control water shortage. **4** Israeli raid on Entebbe airport to free 100 hostages. **7** David Steel new Liberal leader. **10** Explosion at Hoffman-La Roche plant at Seveso: contamination over 7km radius. **14** Official handing-over to Tanzania and Zambia of Chinese-built Tanzam railway. **21** UK ambassador to Eire assassinated. **28** Earthquake destroyed Tangshan, China.

August 25 PM Chirac of France resigned.

September 2 European Commission on Human Rights found Britain guilty of torture in N Ireland. **10** Zagreb air collision. **20** Sweden's Social Democratic Party ousted after 20 years. **24** Ian Smith accepted UK and US proposals for Rhodesian majority rule.

October 3 Bishop Muzorewa returned to Rhodesia from exile. **4** British Rail high-speed train entered service. **6** Military coup in Thailand. **25** National Theatre officially opened. **28** Geneva conference on Rhodesia's future.

November 1 Jimmy Carter elected Pres of USA. **15** Formal end of Lebanon's civil war: Syrian peacekeeping troops in Beirut.

December 16 Michael Manley won Jamaican General Election. **17** Vladimir Bukovsky, Soviet dissident, and Senor Corvalán, Chilean Communist veteran, exchanged.

1977

January 1 EEC extended fishing limits to 200 miles. **24** Rhodesia talks collapsed.

February 15 1976 deaths exceeded live births for 1st time. **17** Uganda's archbishop and 2 Cabinet ministers killed in mysterious circumstances.

March 1 James Callaghan's government went into minority. **7** Zulfikar Ali Bhutto won Pakistan election. **22** Mrs Gandhi resigned after election defeat. **23** Lib-Lab pact: no-confidence vote defeated. **24** New Indian PM Moraji Desai and Janata Party government sworn in. **27** Tenerife airport disaster.

April 21 Martial law in Pakistan. **22** Ekofisk Bravo oilfield disaster.

A.D

May 13 N Ireland 11-day strike collapsed. **17** Menachem Begin's Likud Party won Israel election. **18** International Commission of Jurists reported Ugandan atrocities.

June 1 New UK road speed limits. **7** Silver Jubilee celebrations in London. **11** 11-day S Moluccan sieges ended in Holland. **15** 1st Spanish elections since 1936, won by PM Suarez's Union of Democratic Centre. **16** Fianna Fail won Eire General Election.

July 5 Pakistan army deposed PM Bhutto. **21** Mrs Bandaranaika's Sri Lanka Freedom Party defeated.

August 10 Panama Canal Agreement concluded. **13** Violence at Lewisham National Front march. **25** Scarman Report on Grunwick dispute.

October 31 Effective revaluation of £.

November 4 Mandatory UN arms embargo on S Africa. **14** Firemen's strike. **15** Son for Princess Anne. **19** Egyptian Pres Sadat and Israeli PM Begin met in Israel; Bay of Bengal cyclone killed 25,000. **30** National Party won S African General Election.

December 10 Malcolm Fraser's Conservative coalition won Australian General Election: Labor leader Gough Whitlam resigned. **21** OPEC froze oil prices.

1978

January 1 Air India plane crash off Bombay. **4** PLO London representative shot dead. **25** Government defeat on Scottish devolution. **29** Rhodesia talks in Malta with Joshua Nkomo and Robert Mugabe.

February 4 Ethiopian Ogaden offensive. **19** Egyptian commandos stormed hijacked plane at Larnaca.

March 3 Internal settlement agreed in Rhodesia between Ian Smith and 3 black Nationalist leaders. **8** New Italian PM Giulio Andreotti. **15** Israeli thrust into S Lebanon. **16** Aldo Moro, 5 times Italy's PM, kidnapped and murdered; *Amoco Cadiz* aground off Brittany: massive pollution.

April 3 1st regular radio broadcasts from Parliament. **10** Transkei, 1st tribal homeland to gain independence, cut diplomatic links with S Africa. **17.** No cases of smallpox anywhere during previous year. **26** Arab terrorist attack on bus on West Bank. **27** Afghanistan's Pres Daoud deposed in pro-Soviet coup.

May 1 1st UK May Day Bank Holiday. **24** Princess Margaret and Lord Snowdon divorced.

June 3 New Bangladeshi Pres Gen Zia ur-Rahman. **12** Provisional IRA leader Seamus Twomey sentenced in Dublin.

July 5 Ghanaian Pres Acheampong resigned. **9** Former Iraqi PM Gen Razzale al-Naif shot in London. **25** World's 1st "test tube" baby born. **31** Lib-Lab pact ended.

August 6 Pope Paul VI died. **13** Beirut PLO HQ bombed. **22** Gunmen held hundreds hostage in Nicaraguan parliament. **26** Cardinal Albino Luciani of Venice elected as Pope John Paul I.

September 8 Martial law in Tehran. **11** Martial law in Nicaragua. **16** Earthquake in Iran killed 11,000. **17** Camp David talks between Pres Sadat and PM Begin concluded framework for Middle East peace treaty. **28** Pope John Paul I died; New S African PM Pieter Botha.

October 10 New Kenyan Pres Daniel arap Moi. **15** Cardinal Karol Wojtyla of Cracow 1st non-Italian Pope for 450 years as John Paul II. **20** 4-week siege of Beirut lifted.

November 25 National Party won New Zealand

A.D.

General Election. **26** Clashes in Iran during 24-hour general strike. **27** Japanese PM Fukuda resigned. **30** Publication of *The Times* suspended until 13 Nov 1979.

December 7 New Japanese PM Masayoshi Ohira. **17** OPEC announced oil price rise. **20** Israeli attack on Lebanese terrorist bases.

1979

January 1 New Iranian PM Dr. Bakhtiar. **4** Guadeloupe Summit between UK, US, W Germany and France. **7** Phnom Penh captured by Vietnamese and rebel troops. **15** Road haulage strike. **16** Shah left Iran. **17** UK admitted Vietnamese refugees. **20** Rhodesian whites only referendum: 6:1 in favour of transfer to majority rule.

February 1 Ayatollah Khomeini returned to Iran from exile in Paris. **5** New Iranian PM Dr Bazargan. **14** "Concordat" between government and TUC. **15** Army take-over in Chad. **28** Final meeting of white Rhodesian House of Assembly.

March 1 Scots voting in favour of devolution failed to reach 40% requirement: Welsh voted overwhelmingly against devolution. **13** Government of Grenada overthrown. **26** Israel–Egypt peace treaty signed. **28** Radiation leak at Three Mile Island nuclear plant, Pennsylvania. **30** Shadow N Ireland Secretary Airey Neave assassinated. **31** Final withdrawal of British navy from Malta.

April 1 Islamic Republic in Iran. **2** 1st visit of Israeli PM to Egypt. **4** Former Pakistani PM Bhutto executed. **11** Kampala captured by Tanzanian troops and Ugandan exiles: new Ugandan leader Prof Yusofo Lule. **23** 1 died, 300 arrested in clashes at Southall National Front march.

May 3 UK General Election: Margaret Thatcher 1st woman PM: Conservative overall majority 43. **16** Government removed legal obligation towards comprehensive education. **22** Joe Clark's Progressive Conservatives formed minority Canadian government. **29** Bishop Muzorewa Zimbabwe Rhodesia's 1st black MP.

June 4 S African Pres Vorster resigned after "Muldergate" scandal; Ghanaian forces led by Flt-Lt Rawlings took power. **11** Conservatives won UK European elections. **18** Pres Carter and Pres Brezhnev signed SALT II treaty. **20** Ugandan Pres Lule deposed. **22** Jeremy Thorpe acquitted in Old Bailey conspiracy trial.

July 13 Abortion Law tightened. **17** Pres Somoza fled Nicaragua.

August 14 Gales wrought havoc in Fastnet yacht race. **18** Heart transplant carried out at Papworth Hospital near Cambridge. **19** Former Cambodian leader Pol Pot convicted in his absence of murder of 3m people. **27** Earl Mountbatten killed by bomb on boat in Sligo.

September 10 London talks on Zimbabwe Rhodesia constitution. **19** 3-party non-Socialist coalition won Swedish elections. **20** Emperor Bokassa of Central Africa Empire ousted. **26** UK compulsory metrication abandoned. **29** 1st-ever Papal visit to Eire.

October 1 Civilian rule restored in Nigeria. **17** El Salvador colonels imposed martial law. **19** ITV strike ended. **23** Foreign exchange controls removed.

November 1 Military coup in Bolivia. **4** Iranian students occupied US embassy in Tehran. **9** US computer fault led to full-scale nuclear alert. **14** Iranian assets in US frozen.

December 5 Dutch Parliament rejected Nato's Cruise missile plan. **11** New Irish PM Charles Haughey. **12** Nato approved stationing of US missiles in Europe. **21** Rhodesian treaty signed. **27** Afghanistan's Pres Amin ousted in Soviet-backed coup.

A.D

1980

January 7 Mrs Gandhi's Congress Party won Indian General Election. **22** Dr Andrei Sakharov, winner of 1975 Nobel peace prize, sent into USSR internal exile. **27** Israel–Egypt border reopened.

February 12 Publication of Brandt Report "North South". **18** Pierre Trudeau won Canadian General Election.

March 4 Robert Mugabe's ZANU(PF) party formed government with absolute majority in Zimbabwe Rhodesia. **24** Archbishop Romero shot dead at altar in San Salvador. **25** Robert Runcie enthroned as Archbishop of Canterbury. **27** Oil accommodation rig overturned in North Sea.

April 2 Riots in St Pauls area of Bristol. **3** 13-week steel strike ended. **9** Israeli troops moved into Lebanon. **13** US Olympic Committee voted to boycott Moscow Games. **18** Rhodesia became independent as Zimbabwe. **20** Clashes at Lewisham National Front march. **25** Unsuccessful attempt to free US hostages in Iran. **30** Queen Beatrix of the Netherlands invested.

May 5 SAS stormed besieged Iranian embassy in London. **18** Mount St Helens erupted.

June 22 Liberals won Japanese General Election. **23** Sanjay Ghandi, son of Indian PM, died in plane crash. **30** New Icelandic Head of State Ms Vigdis Finnbogadottir.

July 17 Military coup in Bolivia. **19** Moscow Olympics opened.

August 13 French fishermen blockaded Channel ports.

September 7 Hua Guofeng resigned as Chinese leader: replaced by Zhao Ziyang. **10** Libya and Syria to merge as unitary Arab state. **22** Outbreak of Iran–Iraq War.

October 5 Helmut Schmidt re-elected W German Chancellor. **10** Algerian earthquake: 4,000 dead. **15** James Callaghan resigned as Labour leader. **18** Liberal and Country coalition won Australian General Election. **23** Soviet PM Kosygin resigned. **24** Polish independent trade union Solidarity recognised by Polish authorities. **27** Hunger strike at Maze prison.

November 4 Ronald Reagan elected Pres of USA. **10** New Labour leader Michael Foot. **23** Earthquake in S Italy.

December 8 Dublin Summit between Mrs Thatcher and Charles Haughey; John Lennon shot dead in New York. **15** Dr Milton Obote sworn in as Ugandan Pres. **17** Prof Alan Walters appointed PM's personal economic adviser.

1981

January 1 Greece joined EEC. **10** New Portuguese PM Dr Francisco Pinto Balsemao. **20** US hostages left Iran. **21** Sir Norman Stronge and his son, former Stormont MPs, killed by IRA. **25** Roy Jenkins, Shirley Williams, William Rodgers and David Owen launched Council for Social Democracy; Mao's widow Jiang Qing convicted. **27** Joshua Nkomo appointed Minister without Portfolio in attempt to prevent Zimbabwe confrontation.

February 3 Norway's first woman PM Dr Gro Harlem Brundtland. **12** Rupert Murdoch bought *The Times*. **23** Failed military coup in Spain.

March 18 £1m EEC food aid to China. **26** Social Democratic Party launched. **30** Pres Reagan shot outside Hilton Hotel in Washington.

April 5 Pres Brezhnev in Czechoslovakia talks on Polish crisis. **11** Brixton riots.

May 9 Bomb exploded at Sullum Voe during Royal inauguration. **10** François Mitterrand won French Presidential Election. **13** Pope shot by Turkish gunman. **22** Peter Sutcliffe convicted of Yorkshire

A.D.
Ripper murders. **30** Bangladeshi Pres Zia ur-Rahman assassinated.

June 8 Israeli planes destroyed Iraqi nuclear reactor. **10** 8 IRA prisoners escaped from Crumlin Rd jail. **13** Blanks fired at Queen during Trooping of Colour. **16** Liberal-SDP alliance announced. **21** Socialists won French General Election. **22** Ayatollah Khomeini dismissed Iran's Pres Bani-Sadr. **30** PM Begin secured continuation of Israeli coalition government; New Irish PM Dr Garret FitzGerald.

July 3 Southall race riots. **4** Toxteth riots. **15** Red Cross to mediate at Maze prison. **29** Wedding of Prince Charles and Lady Diana Spencer.

August 20 MLR suspended. **25** S African troops crossed into Angola. **30** Iran's Pres and PM killed by bomb.

September 1 Army take-over in Central African Republic. **4** French ambassador assassinated in Beirut. **18** France abolished capital punishment.

October 4 Maze hunger strike ended. **6** Pres Sadat assassinated. **10** IRA bomb in Chelsea: 2 dead. **14** New Egyptian Pres Hosni Mubarak. **18** Left-wing victory in Greek General Election; Gen Jaruzelski new leader of Polish Communist Party. **26** Oxford St IRA bomb killed disposal expert.

November 6 Anglo-Irish Intergovernmental Council agreed. **14** Unionist MP Rev Robert Bradford shot dead.

December 8 Arthur Scargill new leader of National Union of Mineworkers. **11** Javier Perez de Cuellar new UN Secretary-General. **13** Martial law in Poland. **14** Israel annexed Golan Heights. **19** Penlee lifeboat lost during rescue attempt. **31** Military coup in Ghana.

1982

January 4 EEC rejected USSR and Poland sanctions. **13** Air crash in central Washington. **26** UK unemployment reached 3m.

February 4 Laker Airways collapsed. **15** Oil rig sank off Newfoundland. **19** De Lorean car company failed.

March 9 Charles Haughey new Irish PM. **16** Pres Brezhnev froze deployment of Soviet missiles in Europe. **18** Argentinians in S Georgia to dismantle whaling station raised Argentinian flag. **19** 3-year ban on England cricketers in unofficial S African tour. **23** Coup in Guatemala. **24** Martial law in Bangladesh after coup.

April 2 Argentina invaded Falkland Is. **5** Lord Carrington and 2 Foreign Office ministers resigned: new Foreign Secretary Francis Pym. **25** British troops recaptured S Georgia; Israel handed over Sinai to Egypt.

May 2 Argentine cruiser *General Belgrano* sunk in British attack. **4** British destroyer HMS *Sheffield* hit by Exocet missile. **7** Britain extended total exclusion zone to within 12 miles of Argentine coast. **15** British commando raid on Argentine airstrip at Pebble I. **21** British troops established bridgehead at San Carlos. **28** Paratroops captured Goose Green and Darwin; Papal visit to UK.

June 3 Israeli ambassador shot in London. **4** Israel bombed Beirut's Palestinian quarter. **6** British took Bluff Cove and Fitzroy. **7** Argentine raid on *Sir Tristram* and *Sir Galahad* off Bluff Cove. **14** Falklands ceasefire. **17** Argentinian Pres Gen Galtieri ousted. **21** Prince William of Wales born. **23** Labour National Executive acted against Militant Tendency. **25** New US Secretary of State George Shultz.

July 1 New Argentinian Pres Gen Bignone. **2** Roy Jenkins new SDP leader. **9** New Orleans air crash. **20** IRA bombs in Hyde Park and Regent's Park.

August 4 Israeli tanks invaded W Beirut. **12**

A.D
Ceasefire in Lebanon. **17** China and US agreed Taiwan policy. **21** PLO guerrillas left Beirut.

September 14 Princess Grace of Monaco died; Lebanese leader Bashire Gemayal killed by bomb. **17** Palestinian refugees killed in W Beirut camps. **19** Swedish Social Democrats won General Election.

October 1 New W German Chancellor Christian Democrat leader Helmut Kohl. **8** Polish government dissolved Solidarity. **11** Tudor warship *Mary Rose* raised. **21** SDLP and Sinn Fein refused to take seats won in Ulster Assembly election. **28** Socialists elected in Spain. **31** Thames barrier inaugurated.

November 1 Channel 4 tv opened. **10** Soviet leader Leonid Brezhnev died: new leader Yuri Andropov. **24** El Al went into liquidation. **25** Eire's new government formed by Fine Gael and Labour coalition.

December 6 Bomb at bar in Ballykelly killed 16. **12** 30,000 women ringed Greenham Common missile base in protest.

1983

January 25 EEC agreed common fishing policy. **31** New UK seat belt law.

February 9 Derby winner Shergar stolen in Co Kildare.

March 5 Labor Party won Australian General Election. **6** Christian Democrats won W German General Election. **22** New Israeli Pres Chaim Herzog.

April 4 White Senator and 2 others killed by Zimbabwe dissidents. **18** US embassy in W Beirut bombed: many dead. **21** New UK £1 coin. **24** Austrian Chancellor Dr Bruno Kreisky resigned. **26** 8 famine relief workers kidnapped in Ethiopia by Tigré People's Liberation Front.

May 1 Demonstrations in 20 Polish cities. **16** 1st use of wheel clamps by London police. **17** Israel-Lebanon agreement on troop withdrawal. **18** State of Emergency in Sri Lanka. **23** S African raids on Maputo. **30** Williamsburg Summit of 7 industrialised nations (G7).

June 9 Conservative majority of 144 in UK General Election. **13** New SDP leader David Owen. **14** All-party Commons defence committee endorsed "Fortress Falklands" policy. **15** New Speaker of Commons Bernard Weatherill. **16** Mr Andropov elected Soviet Pres. **24** Syria expelled PLO leader Yasser Arafat.

July 3 Home of former Ulster MP Gerry Fitt burnt out by IRA. **15** 6 killed by bomb at Orly airport. **16** 20 killed in helicopter crash near Scilly Is. **25** Anti-Tamil riots in Colombo.

August 4 Italy's 1st Socialist PM since 1946 Bettino Craxi. **5** Lebanese mosque explosion: 19 dead. **8** Military coup in Guatemala. **11** Chad town Faya-Largeau fell to Libyan troops. **14** French troops in NE Chad. **21** Philippine opposition leader shot dead at Manila airport. **31** S Korean airliner disappeared near Japan: USSR later admitted shooting it down.

September 4 Israeli army withdrew from Chouf mountains above Beirut. **15** Israeli PM Begin resigned. **23** Abu Dhabi air crash: 112 dead. **25** 38 IRA prisoners escaped from Maze prison: prison officer stabbed to death. **26** *Australia II* won America's Cup.

October 2 New Labour leader Neil Kinnock. **10** New Israeli government led by Yitzhak Shamir. **14** Cecil Parkinson resigned. **19** Grenada's PM Maurice Bishop shot by troops: Gen Hudson Austin in control. **23** Suicide bombers killed 229 US marines and 58 French paratroops in Beirut. **25** Troops from US and 6 Caribbean states invaded Grenada. **30** Earthquake in E Turkey. **30** Radical Party leader Raul Alfonsin won Argentine General Election.

A.D.
November 3 S African white minority voted to give limited representation to Asians and Coloureds. **12** New leader of Irish Republican movement Gerry Adams. **14** 1st Cruise missiles at Greenham Common. **15** Turkish Cypriot UDI under Rauf Denktash. **16** Yasser Arafat retreated to Tripoli. **21** Unionist Party withdrew from N Ireland Assembly in protest at Darkley Gospel Hall killings. **23** USSR quit Geneva disarmament talks. **26** £26m Heathrow bullion robbery. **27** Air crash near Madrid: 181 dead. **28** European space lab launched at Cape Canaveral.

December 6 1st UK heart–lung transplant. **7** Official Unionist Edgar Graham shot dead at Queen's University Belfast. **10** Bomb at Woolwich barracks. **15** NGA industrial action ended. **17** Harrods bomb: 6 dead, many injured. **31** Military coup in Nigeria: new leader Maj-Gen Mohammed Buhari.

1984

January 9 Share prices exceeded 800 on FT index. **20** £1m Christie's diamond robbery. **25** Government ban on union membership at GCHQ. **29** Basque terrorists murdered Spanish general.

February 3 Indian diplomat Ravindra Mhatre kidnapped and murdered in Birmingham. **5** Lebanese Cabinet resigned. **8** British peacekeeping troops left Lebanon followed by French, Italians and US. **9** Soviet Pres Andropov died: succeeded by Konstantin Chernenko. **15** Druze and Shi'ite militiamen drove Lebanese army from S Beirut. **29** Canadian PM Pierre Trudeau resigned.

March 6 Maze deputy prison officer shot dead. **12** Miners strike against pit closures. **15** £5m Woburn Abbey silver robbery. **20** UK blamed for collapse of EEC Summit. **23** Foreign Office clerk jailed for leaking documents to *The Guardian*.

April 3 Coup in Guinea after death of Pres Sekou Touré. **17** WPC Yvonne Fletcher shot dead outside Libyan embassy: 10-day siege.

May 7 Christian Democrat Napoleon Duarté won Salvadorean Presidential election. **8** USSR and Warsaw Pact countries boycotted Olympics. **13** Angolan rebels freed 16 hostages. **18** IRA killed 4 members of security forces. **23** Lancs underground pumping station explosion: 15 dead.

June 1 Pres Reagan visited Ireland; Mrs Thatcher and PM Botha in Chequers talks. **5** US increased military role in Gulf. **6** Sikh fanatics in Golden Temple of Amritsar surrendered to Indian army: leader died. **14** UK European elections: Conservatives kept majority. **16** New Canadian Liberal Party leader and PM John Turner. **20** Education Secretary announced new GCSE examinations.

July 5 Abducted Nigerian exile found in crate at Stansted. **9** York Minster fire. **12** Robert Maxwell acquired Mirror Group newspapers. **13** Labour Party won New Zealand General Election. **17** French government resigned. **25** Soviet cosmonaut 1st woman to walk in space. **29** Los Angeles Olympics opened. **31** Air France Boeing hijacked.

August 21 S African Coloured elections won by Labour Party: many arrests. **26** Wakefield salmonella outbreak. **31** TUC backed pit strike.

September 3 Riots in Transvaal townships. **4** Conservatives won Canadian General Election: new PM Brian Mulroney. **5** New Israeli government of national unity; TUC rejoined Neddy. **20** US Beirut embassy bombed. **26** Sino-British declaration on Hong Kong's future.

October 12 IRA bomb at Grand Hotel, Brighton. **23** Violence in S African townships. **30** Kidnapped Polish priest Fr Popieluszko found dead; Famine in Ethiopia. **31** Indian PM Mrs Gandhi assassinated by Sikh bodyguard: new PM her son Rajiv.

November 4 New Nicaraguan Pres Daniel Ortega. **6** Pres Reagan re-elected. **19** Mexico City gas explosion: 600 dead. **30** Taxi driver taking miner to work killed by concrete post dropped from bridge.

A.D
December 1 Labor Party won Australian General Election. **3** Leak of poison gas from pesticide factory in Bhopal, India: 2,500 dead, thousands blinded; Massive gains in 1st day's trading in British Telecom shares. **4** Kuwait airliner hijacked to Tehran. **18** Local authorities told to cut capital spending by £1bn in 1985. **28** Rajiv Gandhi won Indian General Election

THE END OF THE COLD WAR

1985

January 3 12,000 Ethiopian Jews airlifted to Israel. **15** Civilian Pres for Brazil. **20** Tamil bomb on Sri Lankan train: 36 dead. **22** 1st House of Lords debate televised. **29** Oxford University refused PM honorary degree.

February 4 Spain–Gibraltar border reopened. **18** Riots at Crossroads shanty town, S Africa. **19** S African anti-apartheid leaders arrested. **20** PM addressed joint session of US Congress. **25** £ at record low against $. **28** IRA bombed Newry police station.

March 3 Miners' strike ended. **4** New Zealand PM reaffirmed ban on nuclear weapons. **4** Beirut car bomb: 80 dead. **10** Pres Chernenko died: succeeded by Mikhail Gorbachev. **12** Geneva arms control talks. **15** Belgian government agreed to deploy Cruise missiles. **21** 19 blacks shot dead in Uitenhage on Sharpeville anniversary. **29** Greek political crisis.

April 6 Sudanese Pres Numeiri deposed by army. **11** Tamil bomb killed 24 in Colombo just prior to Mrs Thatcher's arrival.

May 1 US trade ban on Nicaragua; Ethiopia's largest famine relief camp cleared by troops. **10** Pres Reagan froze defence spending. **11** Bradford City FC fire: 55 dead. **15** Sri Lankan Tamil terrorists killed 146. **22** Fighting in Beirut. **24** Tidal wave swamped Bangladesh islands: thousands dead. **29** 38 killed when wall collapsed at Heysel stadium, Brussels, before Liverpool v Juventus match.

June 10 Israel completed withdrawal from Lebanon. **12** Shi'ite gunmen blew up Jordanian aircraft after releasing hijack hostages. **19** Frankfurt airport bomb; Tripoli car bomb: 60 dead. **23** Air India Boeing crashed in Irish Sea.

July 2 New USSR Pres Andrei Gromyko: Foreign Minister Eduard Schevardnadze. **7** Robert Mugabe won Zimbabwe General Election. **10** Greenpeace ship *Rainbow Warrior* sunk in Auckland, NZ. **13** Live Aid concert for African famine relief. **19** Dam collapse at Stava, Italy: 260 dead. **21** S African State of Emergency. **27** Ugandan Pres Obote ousted.

August 2 Tristar crash at Dallas-Fort Worth. **12** Japanese Boeing 747 crashed near Tokyo: 524 dead. **17** E Beirut car bomb killed 54. **22** Manchester airport disaster: 54 dead. **27** Nigerian government ousted.

September 9 Riots in Handsworth, Birmingham. **11** S African citizenship restored to 8m blacks in tribal homelands. **17** Chancellor Kohl's secretary defected to E Berlin. **28** Brixton riots.

October 1 Israeli air raid on PLO's Tunisian HQ. **6** Policeman killed in riots on Broadwater Farm estate, Tottenham. **7** Italian cruise ship *Achille Lauro* hijacked by PLO. **20** Commonwealth leaders agreed measures against S Africa.

November 2 S African government controls on media riot coverage. **14** W Colombian volcano erupted: 20,000 dead. **15** N Ireland agreement signed by Mrs Thatcher and Dr Garret FitzGerald. **21** Reagan–Gorbachev Summit. **24** Egyptian commandos stormed hijacked Boeing in Malta.

December 5 UK to withdraw from Unesco. **6** UK to participate in US Strategic Defence Initiative

A.D.

(SDI). **13** Westland helicopters in deal with US and Italian consortium. **27** Terrorist attacks on Israeli check-in desks at Rome and Vienna airports.

1986

January 7 Pres Reagan cut economic links with Libya. **9** Michael Heseltine and later Leon Brittan resigned over Westland affair: George Younger new Defence Secretary. **19** Rebel forces claimed victory in Aden. **20** Anglo-French twin tunnel Channel rail link agreed. **24** N Ireland by-elections due to mass resignation of MPs. **26** *Sunday Times* and *News of the World* printed at Wapping despite print union action. **28** *Challenger* shuttle crashed on take-off.

February 7 Jean-Claude Duvalier left Haiti. **16** Mario Suares won Portuguese Presidential Election. **25** Mrs Corazon Aquino took power in Philippines. **28** Swedish PM Olof Palme assassinated.

March 2 Legal independence for Australia. **12** New Swedish PM Ingvar Carlsson. **16** New French PM Jacques Chirac. **24** US navy destroyed missile battery on Gulf of Sidra. **31** GLC and 6 Metropolitan councils abolished.

April 5 Berlin disco bomb. **15** US bombed Benghazi and Tripoli in retaliation for Libyan terrorism. **17** 2 UK hostages killed in Lebanon. **26** Major accident at Chernobyl nuclear power plant, USSR: 19 deaths, radioactive cloud over Scandanavia. **30** Police invaded Golden Temple at Amritsar.

May 19 S African commando attacks on Zimbabwe, Zambia and Botswana.

June 6 Chief Constable of W Yorks to replace John Stalker in N Ireland "shoot-to-kill" inquiry. **8** New Austrian Pres Dr Kurt Waldheim. **12** Renewed State of Emergency in S Africa. **20** S Africa legalised 180-day detention without trial; Ban on sheep movement in Cumbria and N Wales due to radiation. **27** EEC Summit called for release of Mandela and recognition of ANC; International Court of Justice ruled US support for Nicaraguan Contras illegal.

July 6 Liberal Democratic Party won Japanese General Election. **22** Commons voted to ban corporal punishment in schools. **23** Prince Andrew named Duke of York on marriage to Sarah Ferguson. **25** Appeal Court banned publications by former MI5 officer Peter Wright.

August 5 Commonwealth sanctions against S Africa. **7** Ulster loyalist mob crossed border into Eire. **18** Mr Gorbachev announced unilateral freeze on nuclear testing. **25** Gas escape from volcanic crater in Cameroon: 1,500 dead.

September 1 Soviet cruise liner sank after collision: 400 dead. **5** Commandos stormed hijacked PanAm jet at Karachi. **16** Kinross goldmine fire in Transvaal: 177 dead.

October 2 US sanctions against S Africa. **7** *The Independent* newspaper launched; New statefunded city technology colleges announced. **12** Reagan–Gorbachev Summit collapsed over Star Wars programme; Queen visited China. **19** Pres Samora Michel of Mozambique killed in S Africa plane crash: new Pres Joaquim Chissano. **20** New Israeli PM Likud leader Yitzhak Shamir. **26** Conservative Party deputy chairman Jeffrey Archer resigned. **27** "Big Bang" in City: computer failed. **29** Final section of M25 opened.

November 10 EEC (except Greece) backed sanctions against Syria. **13** Pres Reagan admitted arms sales to Iran. **24** Barclays Bank pulled out of S Africa. **25** John Poindexter and Col Oliver North dismissed over sale of arms to Contras.

December 1 DTI investigation into Guinness affair. **11** Israel bombed Palestinian targets near Tripoli. **23** Dr Andrei Sakharov returned to Moscow.

A.D

1987

January 12 Rate Support Grant settlement: cuts of up to 30% imposed on 20 local authorities. **16** General Secretary of Chinese Communist Party Hu Yaobang resigned. **20** Archbishop of Canterbury's special envoy Terry Waite kidnapped in Beirut. **24** 3 US and one Indian professor kidnapped from Beirut University. **25** Chancellor Kohl's centre-right coalition won German election. **27** Mr Gorbachev offered Soviet people choice of election candidates: criticism of Brezhnev era.

February 10 140 political prisoners released in USSR. **12** Peaceful Moscow human rights demonstration dispersed violently. **22** 4,000 Syrian troops in W Beirut to enforce peace.

March 6 Zeebrugge ferry disaster: 292 dead. **10** Ireland's new PM Charles Haughey.

April 13 9 trains set alight in Soweto. **25** Lord Justice Gibson and Lady Gibson killed by N Ireland car bomb. **27** Egyptian government closed PLO offices.

May 1 Government abandoned plan to dump nuclear waste. **5** Congressional hearing into Irangate affair. **6** National Party won S African whites-only election: 1m blacks on protest strike. **12** New Nationalist PM of Malta. **14** Coup led by Lt-Col Sitiveni Rabuka in Fiji. **17** USS *Stark* hit by Iraqi Exocet: 37 dead. **26** US authorised Kuwaiti tankers in Gulf to fly US flag; Sri Lankan government offensive to recapture Jaffna Peninsula. **29** German Matthius Rust landed in Red Sq; S African commandos attacked Maputo targets.

June 1 Lebanese PM Rashid Karami murdered. **11** UK General Election: Conservatives won 3rd term with 101 majority. **12** Princess Anne created Princess Royal. **15** Christian Democrats won Italian General Election. **27** Controversy over Cleveland child abuse.

July 3 Former Gestapo chief Klaus Barbie found guilty of crimes against humanity. **13** Labor Party won Australian General Election. **17** France and Iran cut diplomatic relations. **20** Social Democrats won Portuguese General Election. **29** Indo-Sri Lankan peace accord signed: Colombo riots.

August 6 David Owen resigned as SDP leader after party voted to open merger talks with Liberals. **12** Pres Reagan accepted responsibility for Iran-Contra affair: no knowledge of diversion of funds. **17** Suicide of Rudolf Hess. **19** Hungerford massacre: 16 dead. **27** Pres Aquino crushed 5th coup in 18 months. **29** New SDP leader Robert Maclennan.

September 3 Bangladesh monsoon: 24m homeless. **4** UN Security Council endorsed Iran–Iraq peace plan. **5** Israeli air raid on Palestinian refugee camp: 40 dead. **7** Lebanese kidnappers released W German hostage. **9** Iraqi air raids on Iran. **12** New Caledonia voted to remain part of France. **23** Home Secretary ended sale of arms to Iran.

October 1 Los Angeles earthquake: 7 dead; 5 foreign tankers attacked in Gulf. **6** Fiji declared a republic. **15** Coup in Burkina Faso; US-protected supertanker hit by Iranian Silkworm missile. **16** Hurricane in S England: 19 dead. **17** Indian army crushed Jaffna rebels. **19** "Black Monday": London and NY shares crashed. **22** Iran attacked Kuwait oil loading terminal. **26** Lord Mackay succeeded Lord Havers as Lord Chancellor. **31** 150 tonnes of arms seized off Brittany.

November 1 Deng Xiaoping resigned from Chinese Poliburo: replaced by Zhao Ziyang. **5** Former ANC chairman Govan Mbeki released after 23 years. **7** Tunisian Pres Bourguiba ousted. **8** Enniskillen Remembrance Day bomb: 11 dead. **11** Moscow reformist leader Boris Yeltsin dismissed; Arab Summit declared support for Iraq. **18** King's Cross fire: 31 dead. **24** US and USSR agreed to scrap intermediate range nuclear weapons. **28** S African Boeing crashed in Indian Ocean: 160 dead.

A.D.

December 8 Pres Reagan and Mr Gorbachev signed INF agreement. **16** Roh Tae Woo won allegedly rigged S Korean Presidential Election. **17** Milos Jakes succeeded Czechoslovakian Pres Husak. **20** Manila ferry disaster: 2,000 drowned. **29** Space record of 11 months by Soviet cosmonaut. **31** Robert Mugabe executive Pres of Zimbabwe: Joshua Nkomo 1 of 2 Vice Pres.

1988

January 3 Mrs Thatcher longest-serving 20th century UK PM. **4** Purchases by W German and Japanese banks halted US $ slide. **8** Further Wall St crash. **11** Secret Belfast talks between SDLP and Sinn Fein. **17** Leslie Manigat won Haitian General Election amid protests.

February 2 3 women abseiled into Lords in Clause 28 protest. **5** 2 UN relief workers kidnapped in Lebanon. **7** W Bank and Gaza strip violence. **14** PLO officials killed by bomb in Limassol. **16** Prevention of Terrorism Act made permanent. **17** US Lt-Col William Higgins kidnapped in S Lebanon. **21** New Cyprus Pres George Vassiliou. **26** Panamanian National Assembly dismissed Pres Delvalle; Soviet paratroops in Armenian capital Yerevan.

March 1 31 dead in riots in Azerbaijan city Sumga'it: Soviet tanks moved in. **3** Liberals and SDP formed Social & Liberal Democrats. **6** 3 IRA members shot dead in Gibraltar after bomb plan uncovered. **10** Prince Charles' friend Hugh Lindsay killed by avalanche: Prince escaped. **14** Gulf War flared; Israel imposed curfew in Gaza and W Bank. **16** Loyalist gunman killed 3 at IRA funeral. **17** US troops in Honduras. **18** State of Emergency in Panama. **19** 2 British soldiers lynched in vicinity of Republican funeral. **25** Government review of justice in N Ireland. **28** S African commandos killed 4 in Botswana. **29** Head of ANC assassinated in Paris.

April 4 3,000 Indian troops moved to Pakistan border. **5** Kuwait Airways 747 hijacked to Mashad, Larnaca, then Algiers. **7** ANC lawyer Albie Sachs injured by car bomb in Mozambique. **10** 80 killed in Islamabad and Rawalpindi arsenal fire. **14** Geneva accord on withdrawal from Afghanistan. **15** PLO military commander Abu Jihad murdered. **17** Iraq recaptured Faw peninsula. **18** John Demjanjuk found guilty on Treblinka charges. **24** Kanak militants rioted in New Caledonia.

May 1 IRA killed 3 British servicemen in Holland. **2** Israeli troops in Lebanon rounded up Palestinian guerrillas. **8** Pres Mitterrand re-elected: new French PM Michel Rocard. **10** Coalition re-elected in Denmark. **17** Commandos stormed Golden Temple. **22** Hungarian Communist Party leader ousted. **27** Syrian troops moved into Shi'ite S Beirut. **29** Moscow Summit: Pres Reagan and Mr Gorbachev signed INF treaty.

June 2 Mine disaster in Borken, W Germany. **10** Millenium of Christianity celebrated in USSR; S Africa extended press curbs. **15** IRA bomb killed 6 soldiers at Lisburn fun-run. **19** Haitian coup: civilian leader fled. **21** Toronto Economic Summit. **23** IRA shot down army helicopter at Crossmaglen; EEC agreed farm price freeze. **26** A320 airbus crash at French air show. **27** 57 dead in Gare de Lyon train crash.

July 1 Communist Party conference approved Gorbachev's democratising proposals. **3** USS *Vincennes* shot down Iranian airbus "by mistake": 200 dead. **5** Former priest held in Brussels over IRA arms procurement. **6** Explosion on North Sea oil rig Piper Alpha: 170 dead. **12** Nagorno-Karabakh's Armenian majority voted to leave Azerbaijan. **19** Soviet team at Greenham Common for missile check. **22** New EEC Commissioner Leon Brittan. **23** 3 killed by IRA landmine intended for Justice Higgins. **25** Ne Win retired as leader of Burma's ruling Socialist Party after 26 years; UN Gulf peace talks. **28** New SLD leader Paddy Ashdown; Winnie Mandela's Soweto home burned down.

A.D

August 1 Bomb at N London barracks killed soldier. **6** Train crash at Gare de l'Est: SNCF Chairman resigned. **8** Iran-Iraq ceasefire; Soviet troops withdrew from Kabul. **11** 6,000 North Sea seals died from canine distemper. **12** British soldier shot dead in Ostend; Burmese leader Sein Lwin resigned after week of violence: 1,000 dead. **17** Pakistan's Pres Zia killed in plane explosion. **21** 24,000 massacred in Burundi. **22** All-day opening in English and Welsh pubs. **25** Heart of Lisbon gutted by fire. **28** Ramstein air disaster. **31** Nelson Mandela suffering from TB.

September 3 Lee Kuan Yew won Singapore's General Election. **4** 20m homeless in Bangladesh flooding. **6** Kurdish leader's appeal to UN to intervene against genocide. **7** 2 stranded cosmonauts landed successfully. **12** W German hostage freed in Beirut. **13** Devastating hurricane in Jamaica and Mexico. **14** Papal Mass pilgrims held hostage in Maseru: S African troops stormed bus. **17** Seoul Olympics opened. **18** Further coup in Burma. **19** Polish PM resigned. **20** New Pres of UN General Assembly Argentina's Dante Caputo. **22** Lebanon's Pres Gemayal appointed Christian PM. **31** Mr Gorbachev new Soviet Pres.

October 2 Estonian Popular Front founded. **3** Indian hostage released in Beirut. **6** State of Emergency in Algiers. **9** Serb protests in Yugoslavia. **10** Czechoslovakian PM resigned. **19** Ban on broadcast interviews with pro-violence groups in N Ireland. **20** Criminals' right to silence abolished in N Ireland. **28** Police crushed Prague rally.

November 3 Failed coup in Maldives. **8** George Bush won US Presidential Election. **10** Hungary legalised political opposition parties. **14** Agreement to end Sudan civil war. **21** Brian Mulroney won Canadian General Election. **22** State of Emergency in Azerbaijan. **23** "Sharpeville 6" reprieved. **24** Police clashed with students in Westminster student loans protest. **27** US banned PLO leader. **30** New Pakistani PM Benazir Bhutto.

December 4 Edwina Currie, junior Health Minister, in "salmonella in eggs" row. **7** Pres Gorbachev announced armed forces cuts; Yasser Arafat voiced Palestinian recognition of Israel's existence; Disastrous Armenian earthquake: Pres Gorbachev abandoned US trip. **12** Clapham rail crash. **21** PanAm jumbo jet crashed on Lockerbie: 281 killed: caused by terrorist bomb. **22** Namibian independence accord signed by S Africa, Cuba and Angola. **29** 2 French girls freed in Lebanon by Abu Nidal; Rajiv Gandhi on 1st working visit to Pakistan by Indian PM for 28 years. **20** Brezhnev's son-in-law jailed for bribery.

1989

January 4 US jets shot down 2 Libyan MiGs. **7** Emperor Hirohito of Japan died. **8** Boeing 737 crashed on M1 embankment near Kegworth, Leics. **10** Czechoslovakia to stop export of Semtex explosive. **18** 1st steps towards legalisation of Solidarity. **20** Nagorno-Karabakh under Moscow's direct control. **31** White Paper proposed market-orientated NHS.

February 3 Alfredo Stroessner ousted in Paraguay after 35 years: replaced by Gen Rodriguez; Michael Manley won Jamaican General Election. **14** Ayatollah Khomeini ordered execution for blasphemy of Salman Rushdie, author of *The Satanic Verses*. **21** Leading Czech playwright Vaclav Havel jailed; 2 of Winnie Mandela's bodyguards charged with murder of young activist.

March 2 EC agreed to ban CFCs by 2000. **7** China imposed martial law in Lhasa. **24** *Exxon Valdez* aground off Alaska: 12m gallons oil spilt. **26** Soviet General Election: many senior officials defeated: Moscow victory for Boris Yeltsin.

April 12 Hungarian re-shuffle: hardliners removed. **14** Georgia's Communist leader, Pres and PM resigned. **15** 95 Liverpool supporters crushed to death in Hillsborough disaster; Death of Hu Yaobang sparked Beijing student riots. **19** Explosion on USS *Iowa*.

A.D.

May 13 Briton Jackie Mann kidnapped in Beirut.
14 Peronist Carlos Menem won Argentine General
Election.
June 2 Tiananmen Sq massacre. **3** Ayatollah
Khomeini died. **4** Solidarity won Polish elections.
15 Labour won UK European elections. **30**
Military coup in Sudan.

July 5 Pres Botha met Nelson Mandela. **19** Gen
Jaruzelski executive Pres of Poland. **21** Burmese
opposition leader Aung San Suu Kyi under house
arrest. **24** Cabinet re-shuffle: Geoffrey Howe
deputy PM and Leader of Commons, John
Major Foreign Secretary. **28** Israelis kidnapped
Hizbollah sheikh Abdul Obeid. **31** Lebanese
terrorists killed US hostage Lt-Col William
Higgins.

August 1 1st Cruise missiles left Greenham
Common. **13** Inconclusive 4-day battle for Beirut.
14 Pres Botha resigned: acting S African Pres
F W de Klerk. **23** Independence demonstration
in Baltic states. **24** 1st non-communist Polish
PM for 45 years, Solidarity's Tadeusz
Mazowiecki.

September 6 Pres de Klerk's National Party won
S African General Election. **11** Hungary opened
border allowing E German refugees to escape. **13**
Huge peaceful anti-apartheid protest in Cape
Town. **14** Sam Nujoma, Swapo Pres, returned to
Namibia after 30 years. **18** Hungary announced
transition to democracy. **19** Vietnamese army left
Cambodia. **22** IRA bomb at Royal Marines School
of Music, Deal.

October 1 Thousands of E German refugees escaped
through Warsaw and Prague embassies. **2** E
Germany closed borders after demonstrations for
reform. **4** Soviet workers given right to strike. **13**
ANC's Walter Sisulu released after 25 years. **16**
CITES banned ivory trade to save African
elephant. **17** San Francisco earthquake. **18** E
German leader Erich Honecker resigned: succeeded by Egon Krenz. **19** "Guildford 4" released.
24 Soviet guarantee of Communist parliamentary
seats to end. **26** Chancellor of Exchequer Nigel
Lawson resigned: new Chancellor John Major,
Douglas Hurd Foreign Secretary.

November 8 E German cabinet and politburo
resigned. **9** E Germany opened borders to West:
demolition of Berlin Wall began. **10** Bulgarian
Communist leader Todor Zhivkov ousted. **12**
Swapo won Namibian General Election. **17** Violent anti-government demonstration in Prague.
22 Lebanese Pres Moawad killed by bomb. **23** S
African troops withdrew from Namibia after 74
years. **24** Communist leader Milos Jakes and
Czechoslovak politburo resigned. **28** Soviet parliament restored Azerbaijan's powers over Nagorno-
Karabakh. **29** Indian PM Rajiv Gandhi resigned;
Serbia and Slovenia cut relations.

December 1 Czechoslovakia began demolition of
Iron Curtain along Austrian border; E German
Communist Party voted away monopoly of
power. **3** Malta Summit: Pres Bush and Pres
Gorbachev declared end of Cold War. **6** Egon
Krenz resigned. **7** Lithuanian parliament abol-
ished guarantee of Communist supremacy. **10**
Czechoslovak Pres Husak resigned. **11** Leipzig
demonstration for German reunification. **14** E
German Stasi disbanded. **16** Huge violent demon-
stration against Romanian Pres Ceausescu in
Timisoara. **17** New Brazilian Pres Fernando
Collor de Mello. **20** US troops invaded Panama. **23**
Fighting in Romania. **25** Ceausescus executed. **26**
Ion Iliescu Pres of National Salvation Front
government and Romania's provisional leader. **28**
Alexander Dubcek Chairman of Czechoslovak
Federal Assembly; Vaclav Havel, playwright
and human rights activist, Pres until elections;
Bulgarian demonstration for democracy;
Lithuania launched USSR's 1st multiparty
system; Latvia abolished Communist power
monopoly.

A.D.

THE CHANGING WORLD ORDER

1990

January 3 Manuel Noriega surrendered to US
troops; KGB troop reinforcements in Azerbaijan.
11 Independence rally in Vilnius; Armenian
parliament voted itself the right to veto Soviet
laws. **14** Armenian nationalist leaders declared
mobilisation against Azerbaijan. **15** Bulgaria
abolished Communist monopoly rule. **20** Soviet
troops took control of Baku. **22** Yugoslavia's
Communist Party voted to abolish Party's monopoly of power. **25** Hurricane-force winds battered S of England: 46 died.

February 1 New coalition government in Bulgaria **2**
30-year ban on ANC lifted: Gen Aoun besieged E
Beirut. **5** Temporary Government of National
Responsibility in E Germany; Indian troops
opened fire on 4,000 Pakistanis who crossed into
Kashmir state to protest against Indian rule. **7**
Soviet Communist Party abolished monopoly
rule. **11** Nelson Mandela freed after 25 years. **13**
Conference of World War II allies and E and W
Germany ("4 + 2") agreed German reunification
formula. **23** 6-month ambulance dispute settled.
24 Pro-democracy demonstrations in Moscow,
Belorussia and Ukraine. **26** Nicaraguan General
Election won by Violeta Chamorro's coalition
National Opposition Union.

March 6 Soviet parliament passed law sanctioning
private property. **8** Farzad Bazoft, Iranian-born
journalist on *Observer* newspaper, sentenced to
death in Baghdad for espionage. **11** Lithuania's
Supreme Council proclaimed independence. **18**
Right-wing Alliance for Germany won E German
General Election. **21** Soviet military presence
increased in Lithuania; Namibian Independence
celebrated. **23** Mongolia abolished Communist
monopoly of power. **28** Heathrow customs officials
foiled smuggling of nuclear triggers to Iraq. **30**
Estonian parliament proclaimed start of transition to independence. **31** Violence at massive anti-
Community Charge demonstration in London.

April 1 Riot at Strangeways Prison, Manchester. **8**
King Birendra lifted ban on political parties in
Nepal. **11** Teesside Customs & Excise officers
detained steel cylinders ("supergun") bound for
Iraq. **15** Guerrilla revolt in NE Liberia; Right-
wing coalition formed Slovenian government. **19**
Pres de Klerk rescinded 2 laws central to
apartheid. **22** US hostage Robert Polhill released
by Islamic Jihad. **30** US hostage Frank Reed
freed in Beirut.

May 1 Moscow's May Day parade: Pres Gorbachev
jeered. **4** Latvia declared independence. **13** Baltic
States Summit requested independence talks
with Pres Gorbachev. **20** Romanian elections:
NSF won huge victory. **27** First free elections in
Poland for 50 years. **29** Boris Yeltsin elected Pres
of Russian republic; Opposition League for Democracy, led by Aung San Suu Kyi, won Burmese
elections.

June 1 Pres Bush and Pres Gorbachev signed
accord on reduction of nuclear missiles. **7** Warsaw
Pact Summit pledged radical transformation. **8**
First free Czechoslovakian elections for 44 years:
Russian parliament voted its laws to take prec-
edence over those of USSR. **9** New right-wing
Israeli government under Yitzhak Shamir. **11**
Alberto Fujimori new Peruvian Pres. **12** Russian
Federation formally proclaimed sovereignty. **13**
USSR eased Lithuanian blockade. **20** Chancellor
of Exchequer John Major proposed new currency
unit, the Ecu, backed by EMF; Ion Iliescu new
Romanian Pres. **22** Checkpoint Charlie in Berlin
Wall removed. **25** IRA bomb at Carlton Club. **26**
Pres Bush abandoned pledge not to raise
taxes.

July 6 Nato Summit agreed joint peace declaration
with Warsaw Pact countries. **10** Pres Gorbachev
re-elected Leader of Soviet Communist Party. **12**
Boris Yeltsin resigned from Soviet Communist
Party. **16** Ukraine issued declaration of sovereignty. **17** Solidarity split with formation of

A.D.

splinter groups. **20** IRA bomb at Stock Exchange. **23** Iraqi troops massed on Kuwaiti border. **27** Attempted coup in Trinidad; Belorussia declared itself a sovereign state within USSR. **30** Ian Gow MP killed by IRA bomb. **31** Estonia seceded from USSR.

August 2 Iraqi forces invaded Kuwait. **4** US Marines in Monrovia. **6** Pakistani PM Benazir Bhutto dismissed; Pretoria Minute: political prisoners freed, ANC hostilities suspended. **7** US ships, planes and troops in Gulf as part of multinational defence force. **8** Iraq annexed Kuwait; Leader of Winnie Mandela's bodyguard sentenced to death for murder of teenage activist. **15** Pres Saddam Hussein offered Iran peace treaty. **15** Yugoslav Republic of Croatia faced insurrection by rebel Serbs. **20** Western hostages in Kuwait held at military bases and potential targets. **24** Irish hostage Brian Keenan released by Islamic Dawn Organisation. **31** E and W Germany signed unification treaty.

September 1 Boris Yeltsin demanded resignation of Soviet government. **4** Thousands in Jordanian refugee camps in appalling conditions; Prime Ministers of N and S Korea met for the first time. **10** Pres Samuel Doe killed by rebels in Monrovia; All Cambodian factions accepted peace formula to end civil war. **12** 4 Allied Powers of World War II signed Treaty handing back full sovereignty to single united German state. **13** Sri Lankan commandos ended 96-day siege of Jaffna peninsula. **18** Former Governor of Gibraltar Air Chief Marshal Sir Peter Terry severely injured by IRA. **24** Soviet parliament granted Pres Gorbachev wide powers to rule by decree for 18 months. **26** Soviet parliament agreed bill on freedom of conscience and religious practice. **27** IRA bomb discovered shortly before London terrorism conference began; 50 dead in riots against Indian PM Singh's plans striking against caste system.

October 3 Germany celebrated reunification. **8** UK joined ERM; **19** Palestinians killed by Israeli troops when youths attacked worshippers at Wailing Wall. **13** Gen Michel Aoun surrendered after Syrian air attack on Beirut HQ. **24** Pakistan General Elections: Benazir Bhutto's PPP defeated. **25** Crash of Polly Peck International. **27** Rwanda asked OAU for peacekeeping force between government troops and rebels. **28** EC agreed 2nd stage of economic and monetary union: Britain alone in dissent. **30** Militant Hindus attacked mosque built over Hindu holy site in Ayodhya, Uttar Pradesh; Contact between French and British Channel Tunnel construction teams.

November 1 Sir Geoffrey Howe resigned from Cabinet; Communist Party swept from power in Soviet Georgia. **7** Rwandan rebel leaders killed. **8** British economy in recession. **9** Mary Robinson Eire's first woman and youngest-ever President. **10** New Indian PM Chandra Shekhar. **17** Pres Gorbachev presented constitutional reforms giving him increased powers and reinforcing Federal Council. **21** CSCE conference closed with signing of Charter of Paris for a New Europe. **22** Mrs Thatcher resigned. **25** Nationalist parties in Bosnia-Herzegovina won first free elections for 52 years. **27** John Major won Conservative leadership. **28** New Cabinet included Norman Lamont as Chancellor of Exchequer, Kenneth Baker Home Secretary, Michael Heseltine Environment Secretary. **29** UN resolution to use force against Iraq. **30** Zambian parliament passed Bill to allow opposition parties.

December 2 Chancellor Köhl won German elections. **6** Saddam Hussein announced immediate release of all foreign hostages. **7** Gatt talks collapsed. **9** Lech Walesa won Polish Presidential election. **13** Oliver Tambo, ANC President, in S Africa after 30-year exile. **15** Violent anti-Communist protests in Albania. **20** Soviet Foreign Minister Eduard

A.D.

Shevardnadze resigned. **24** Pres Gorbachev won greater powers from Soviet parliament: conservative politician Gennady Yanayev Vice-Pres. **27** Russia's parliament cut contribution to USSR budget by 80%.

1991

January 1 Fierce fighting in Mogadishu. **7** Soviet paratroopers in Baltic states. **8** Lithuanian PM Kasimiera Prunskiene resigned. **13** Soviet troops seized tv centre in Vilnius: 14 dead, thousands defended Parliament buildings: Boris Yeltsin and Baltic Presidents in UN appeal. **17** Huge air and missile attack on Iraq by US, British and Saudis, to liberate Kuwait in Operation Desert Storm. **18** Scud missile attacks on Israel. **19** Key Baghdad buildings damaged by missiles. **20** Scud missiles brought down by Patriot missiles: 5 dead when "Black Beret" pro-Communist troops opened fire in Riga. **25** Iraq released millions of gallons of Kuwait oil into Gulf. **26** Pres Siad Barre of Somalia fled. **29** Nelson Mandela and Chief Buthelezi made peace; New Somali Pres Ali Mahdi Mohamed. **31** Iraqi armoured columns broken up by Allied artillery and aircraft.

February 1 Repeal of remaining S African apartheid laws. **7** IRA attack on Downing St; Allied bombers destroyed Iraqi bridges. **8** 147 Iraqi aircraft now in Iran. **10** Lithuanian referendum in favour of independence. **13** US missiles destroyed Baghdad bunker: 300 civilians killed. **19** Boris Yeltsin demanded Pres Gorbachev's resignation. **20** Huge statue of Enver Hoxha toppled in Tirana: Pres Alia announced new government. **22** Iraqis set fire to Kuwait's oil installations. **23** Military junta seized power in Thailand. **24** Ground war for liberation of Kuwait began. **26** Kuwait City liberated. **27** Allied ceasefire in Gulf War.

March 1 Unrest in Iraq among Shi'ite Muslims. **3** Peace agreement between Allies and Iraq; Estonian and Latvian referendum in favour of independence. **4** S Iraq towns occupied by Shia Muslim resistance. **5** Kurdish guerrillas clashed with army in N Iraq. **7** Albanian refugees arrived in S Italian ports. **12** Political prisoners freed in Albania. **14** "Birmingham 6" released. **15** Kurdish guerrillas claimed control of Kurdistan. **17** Referendum on future of united USSR: minimal victory for Pres Gorbachev. **18** 16,000 Shia Muslims reported killed in S Iraq; 300,000 Soviet miners on strike. **28** 100,000 anti-Gorbachev radicals rallied in Moscow.

April 1 Kurdish revolt in N Iraq collapsed. **4** Refugee crisis on Turkish and Iranian borders; Russian parliament approved special powers for Boris Yeltsin to tackle economic crisis. **9** Soviet Georgia declared independence. **15** EC lifted remaining sanctions against S Africa; European Bank for Reconstruction & Development launched. **18** Iraq agreed to establishment of UN "humanitarian centres". **21** Sri Lankan ethnic violence. **23** New Council Tax unveiled to replace Poll Tax. **26** Rebels advanced on Addis Ababa.

May 5 Virtual civil war between Serbs and Croats. **6** Pres Gorbachev gave Boris Yeltsin control of Russian coalfields in exchange for cooperation in resolving USSR crisis. **9** S African government prohibited carrying of weapons in townships. **13** Winnie Mandela found guilty on kidnap and assault charges. **15** New French PM Edith Cresson. **19** Croatian referendum in favour of independence. **21** Rajiv Gandhi assassinated; Pres Mengistu of Ethiopia fled. **24** Clandestine Israeli airlift of Falasha Jews from Ethiopia. **26** First-ever Presidential elections in USSR held in Georgia: won by nationalist leader Zviad Gamsakhurdia. **29** Ethiopian People's Revolutionary Democratic Front in control in Addis Ababa.

June 5 Pres Bendjedid of Algeria postponed

A.D.
elections, and dismissed government. 9 Mt Pinatubo in Philippines erupted. 13 Boris Yeltsin elected Russian Pres. 16 Plan for Kurdish safe haven close to collapse as Allied troops pulled out. 17 Congress (I) Party won Indian General Election; S Africa formally abolished apartheid. 25 Slovenia and Croatia declared independence. 26 "Maguire 7" convictions overturned. 28 Iraqi soldiers opened fire on UN nuclear inspectors. 29 Yugoslav/Slovenian fighting.

July 1 Warsaw Pact disbanded, a few days after Comecon. 2 Fighting in Croatia. 4 UK–China agreement on new Hong Kong airport. 5 Bank of Commerce & Credit International (BCCI) collapsed. 6 ANC's first National Congress ended with Nelson Mandela as new Pres and democratically-elected National Executive. 19 S African government admitted funding Inkatha party to undermine ANC; 678 dead in fighting between Tamil rebels and Sri Lankan army. 20 Boris Yeltsin banned Communist Party in factories, offices and local government. 22 John Major launched Citizens' Charter. 25 Fighting continued in Croatia.

August 8 British hostage John McCarthy released by Islamic Jihad. 11 US hostage Edward Tracy freed by Revolutionary Justice Organisation. 19 Pres Gorbachev deposed in dawn coup: Emergency Committee of 8 hardliners in control: Yeltsin denounced coup. 21 Estonia and Latvia declared independence: 3 killed outside Russian parliament: coup collapsed. Yeltsin assumed control of Soviet troops: Pres Gorbachev reinstated: Soviet troops withdrew from Lithuania; statues of Lenin demolished. 23 Pres Gorbachev addressed Russian parliament with ill-received defence of Communist Party: Soviet Foreign Minister dismissed: Russia, Lithuania and Latvia banned Communist Party: Communist activity in workplaces banned in Moldavia and Tajikistan: Communism banned in KGB and among troops. 24 Pres Gorbachev resigned as Communist Party leader, and dissolved Party organisation: Ukraine declared independence. 25 Armenia, Georgia and Belorussia declared independence. 26 Vukovar in E Croatia besieged by Serbs and Yugoslav troops. 28 Central Committee of KGB dissolved. 29 Soviet Parliament voted to curtail Pres Gorbachev's power. 30 Azerbaijan, Kirghizia and Uzbekistan declared independence.

September 3 Nagorno-Karabakh declared independence from Armenia. 3 Russia in control of all former Soviet nuclear weapons. 5 Pres Gorbachev made sweeping constitutional changes. 6 Guatemala recognised Belize as independent nation after 100 years. 9 Leningrad formally reverted to former name, St Petersburg; Macedonian citizens voted for independence. 15 Pro-democracy party won Hong Kong's first election. 18 Yugoslav ceasefire collapsed. 24 British hostage Jackie Mann released; Iraqi troops surrounded UN inspectors in Baghdad; French and Belgian troops in Zaire. 26 Romanian government resigned. 30 Military coup in Haiti: Pres Aristide fled.

October 2 Dubrovnik besieged. 3 DPP Sir Allan Green resigned. 13 Communists ousted in Bulgarian multi-party elections. 20 Israel to attend Middle East peace conference. 21 Israel handed over 15 Arab prisoners: later US hostage Jesse Turner released. 22 EC and EFTA agreed to form world's largest common market. 30 Middle East peace conference in Madrid. 31 Pres Kaunda defeated in Zambia's 1st multi-party presidential election by Victor Chiluba.

November 5 Body of international media magnate Robert Maxwell found in sea off Canary Is. 8 EC sanctions on Yugoslavia; Forcible repatriation of Vietnamese boat people. 12 100 civilians massacred by Indonesian army in E Timor. 13 Brazil set aside 94,000 sq km of Amazon rainforest for Yanomami Indians. 18 Hostages Terry Waite (UK) and Tom Sutherland (US) released by Islamic Jihad; Gen Aideed took control in

A.D.
Mogadishu. 22 £ fell to lowest against Deutschmark since joining ERM. 24 Ian Richter released from Iraqi prison after 5 years. 25 "Tottenham 3" freed; Poland's 1st democratic Sejm for 50 years.

December 1 Ukrainian referendum in favour of independence. 2 US hostage Joseph Ciccippio freed by Revolutionary Justice Organisation. 3 US hostage Alan Steen freed by Islamic Jihad; Kenya to legalise opposition parties. 4 Terry Anderson released by Islamic Jihad; £600m missing from Mirror Group pension fund. 6 Siege of Dubrovnik renewed. 8 Leaders of Russia, Ukraine and Belorussia agreed new Commonwealth of Independent States, and declared USSR defunct. 10 Maastricht Summit agreed Treaty of European Union: Britain obtained exclusive opt-out clauses on single currency and social charter. 19 Australian Labor Party voted to replace PM Bob Hawke with Paul Keating, former Treasurer. 20 Opening of Convention for a Democratic S Africa (Codesa). 21 8 former Soviet republics joined CIS. 25 Pres Gorbachev resigned as Pres of USSR. 26 Soviet parliament met for last time. 27 1st Algerian multi-party General Elections: victory for Muslim Fundamentalists in 1st stage.

1992

January 1 New UN Secretary-General Boutros Boutros Ghali. 3 Fighting in Nagorno-Karabakh. 6 Pres Gamsakhurdia fled Tbilisi. 7 5 EC peace monitors killed near Varazdin; Military Council set up to rule Georgia. 12 Algerian Higher Security Council cancelled elections and introduced martial law. 13 Fighting in Mogadishu. 16 Mohammed Boudiaf returned to Algiers as Leader of Council of State. 27 Maxwell pension funds wound up with loss of millions of pounds. 30 Taoiseach Charles Haughey resigned.

February 1 Pres Bush and Pres Yeltsin agreed arms cuts and aid. 6 Croatian Pres Tudjman accepted plan for UN peacekeeping force. 7 Franco-Russian solidarity pact 1st treaty between the 2 for over 100 years. 11 IRA bomb in Whitehall as N Ireland talks opened at 10 Downing St; Albert Reynolds new Taoiseach. 14 Hizbollah leader killed by Israeli helicopter strike. 19 N and S Korea declared end to 40-year confrontation. 21 UN experts began destruction of Iraq's chemical weapons. 28 Iraq defied UN order to destroy missile equipment. 29 Bosnia-Herzegovina referendum in favour of independence.

March 4 Algeria banned Islamic Salvation Front. 5 Codesa agreed outline of power-sharing interim government. 10 Eduard Shevardnadze Pres of Interim State Council to rule Georgia. 11 Sudanese government offensive against Southern rebels. 17 S African referendum in favour of Pres de Klerk's moves to end apartheid; Car bomb attack on Israeli embassy in Buenos Aires; UN peacekeeping troops in Croatia. 26 Ethnic fighting in Bosnia-Herzegovina. 31 UN arms embargo on Libya.

April 2 France's new PM Pierre Bérégovoy. 3 Pres Alia of Albania resigned. 6 Fierce fighting in and around Sarajevo between Muslims and Serbs; EC recognised Bosnia. 9 General Election: Conservative majority of 21 and record-breaking 4th term of office; Gen Noriega guilty on drug charges. 10 IRA bombs in London: 3 dead. 11 Cabinet reshuffle: Kenneth Clarke Home Secretary, Michael Heseltine Trade & Industry Sec, Malcolm Rifkind Defence Sec, Sir Patrick Mayhew N Ireland Sec. 13 Neil Kinnock resigned Labour leadership. 16 Pres Banda dissolved Malawi's parliament. 22 Serbs fought Muslims in Sarajevo. 27 Betty Boothroyd 1st-ever woman Speaker of Commons. 29 Los Angeles riots: 44 dead.

May 4 13 Christians killed in S Egypt by Muslim extremists. 5 EC monitors withdrew from Sarajevo. 11 Azeris conceded last stronghold in Nagorno-Karabakh. 18 Ghana lifted ban on multi-party politics. 19 Serbian troops held 3,500

A.D.

women and children hostage in Bosnia. **20** Fighting in Bangkok between troops and pro-democracy demonstrators; Serbs fired on UN peacekeeping forces in Sarajevo attempting to rescue 5,000 Muslim refugees. **23** Italy's leading anti-Mafia judge assassinated by car bomb in Palermo. **24** Thailand's unelected PM Gen Suchinda resigned. **27** Mortar bombs in Sarajevo marketplace: 16 dead.

June 6 Czechoslovakian General Election: victory for populist Slovak Vladimir Meciar. **18** Kevin and Ian Maxwell charged with conspiracy to defraud. **20** UN Sarajevo peacekeeping activities suspended; Czech and Slovak political parties agreed to split Czechoslovakia into 2 separate states. **20** Yitzhak Rabin's Labour Party won Israeli General Election. **25** French confrontation with Cornish fishing boats. **29** Pres Mohammed Boudiaf of Algeria assassinated. **30** N Ireland Protestant leaders and Irish government met in 1st talks for 70 years.

July 3 Fighting in Sarajevo. **7** $ at lowest for 17 months. **9** Chris Patten sworn in as Governor of Hong Kong. **12** Leaders of Bosnia-Herzegovina appealed to UN to prevent massacre by Serbs. **18** John Smith new Labour Party Leader. **19** Muslim refugees forced from homes by Serbs in "ethnic cleansing"; Anti-Mafia judge Paolo Borsellino killed by car bomb. **20** Czechoslovak Pres Vaclav Havel resigned. **26** Iraq agreed nuclear inspection. **30** UN peacekeeping forces sent to Somalia; **31** Marsh Arabs of S Iraq bombarded by Iraqi troops.

August 2 Israel to permit Arab police in occupied territories. **3** Confirmation of Serbian detention camps where torture and killings had occurred. **10** Ban on Protestant Ulster Defence Association. **18** British troops in Iraq and Bosnia to protect UN aid convoys. **25** Serb bombardment destroyed National Library and historic treasures in Sarajevo: 90 dead. **27** Iraq accepted exclusion zone; Lord Owen new EC peace negotiator. **28** 3,000th sectarian death in N Ireland. **31** Shell attack on Sarajevo market.

September 2 Government troops accused of genocide in S Sudan. **3** New Slovak constitution signed in Bratislava. **6** Racial violence in Germany. **7 28** ANC supporters shot dead by Ciskei troops as protest march crossed border. **9** Georgian forces and Abkhazia rebels agreed ceasefire. **11** £ close to ERM floor. **12** Abimael Guzman, leader of Peru's Shining Path guerrillas, captured. **14** UN troops landed in Somalia. **15** 68 Bosnian wounded evacuated to UK for treatment. **16** "Black Wednesday": £ withdrawn from ERM in *de facto* devaluation. **17** Khmer Rouge rejoined UN Cambodia talks. **20** French referendum on Maastricht Treaty: narrow majority in favour. **21** EC Foreign Ministers agreed ratification of Maastricht Treaty. **24** National Heritage Minister David Mellor resigned. **27** Chief Buthelezi cut communication with S African government.

October 4 El Al cargo Boeing 747 crashed into flats in Amsterdam. **5** £ at record low; Unità alleged rigged Angolan elections. **7** Sweeping plans for Hong Kong democracy. **11** Serbian warplanes defied UN ban; Eduard Shevardnadze Georgian Parliamentary speaker. **12** IRA Covent Garden pub bomb. **13** Government and British Coal announced closure of 31 collieries. **15** 1st British troops in Croatia to support UN. **16** Pres Babangida declared Nigerian primary Presidential election void. **26** Last Russian troops left Poland. **30** IRA bomb in Whitehall; Angolan war erupted.

November 3 Democrat Bill Clinton Pres of USA; Gatt talks collapsed. **4** Government 3-vote majority in Commons Maastricht debate. **7** British patrol retaliated when under fire in central Bosnia. **9** 1st Anglo-Russian treaty for 226 years.

A.D.

11 Church of England General Synod voted narrowly in favour of ordination of women. **13** Attacks on UN troops and aid workers in Mogadishu. **14** Belfast betting shop attack. **16** Formal alliance between Iran and Islamic Resistance Movement (Hamas) in occupied territories. **20** Windsor Castle fire; Agreement in Gatt talks, later rejected by France: French farmers protested. **23** Turkish women died in fire started by neo-Nazis in Mölln near Hamburg. **26** Queen volunteered to pay income tax on private income. **27** UN aid convoy to Srebrenica halted by Serb women's road-block.

December 2 German parliament won veto on EMU in Maastricht debate. **4** US troops in Somalia on food aid mission. **6** 200,000 Hindu militants destroyed Ayodhya mosque; Swiss referendum against joining European Economic Area. **8** Serb troops controlled road linking Sarajevo and airport. **9** Prince and Princess of Wales separated. **12** EC Edinburgh Summit: deal saving Maastricht Treaty. **14** New Russian PM former Communist Viktor Chernomyrdin. **16** Israel expelled 418 suspected Hamas supporters. **28** US aircraft carrier deployed in Gulf to enforce air exclusion zone. **29** Brazil's Pres Collor resigned to avoid impeachment; Kenyan Presidential Election won by Pres arap Moi: allegations of vote-rigging. **31** Bosnian leader Radovan Karadzic grounded aircraft indefinitely.

1993

January 1 Inauguration of single European market; 2 new states, Czech Republic and Slovakia, came into being. **5** EC report confirmed rape of 20,000 Bosnian Muslim women by Serb forces. **7** US marines stormed weapons arsenal in Mogadishu. **8** Missile batteries in S Iraq moved in apparent compliance with ultimatum. **10** Iraq banned UN nuclear inspectors. **12** Iraq mounted 3rd raid on UN compound in Kuwait. **13** Allied aircraft bombed air defence centres in S Iraq. **15** Police captured Sicily's Mafia chief Salvatore "Toto" Riina. **19** Iraq declared unilateral ceasefire: UN nuclear inspectors given clearance. **24** Croat troops seized Maslenica bridge connecting N Croatia with Adriatic. **26** Vaclav Havel 1st President of new Czech state. **28** Croat troops recaptured Peruca dam, mined by retreating Serbs; Riots in Kinshasa: 1,000 dead including French ambassador.

February 10 Assassination attempt on Iranian Pres Rafsanjani. **12** S African government and ANC agreed plans for elected black and white interim government. **14** Lithuania's 1st genuinely democratic Presidential Election won by Algirdas Brazauskas. **15** Attorney-General ruled Social Chapter defeat would not prevent Maastricht ratification; Michal Kovak voted 1st Slovak President. **23** Communist anti-Yeltsin march in Moscow. **24** US troops in Somalia shot dead supporters of Gen Aideed. **25** 10,000 dead in Huambo Siege. **26** Terrorist bomb under World Trade Center, Manhattan.

March 1 US aid drops to Bosnian Muslim enclaves. **5** S African multi-party talks resumed after 9 months. **8** Government defeated in Commons Maastricht debate. **10** Russia's Congress attacked Pres Yeltsin. **11** Gen Morillon, UN commander in Bosnia, set up temporary HQ in Srebrenica to safeguard enclave. **13** Labor won record 5th term in Australian General Election. **16** VAT on domestic fuel in 2-stage plan announced in Budget. **20** IRA bombs in Warrington: 2 children dead: Pres Yeltsin declared his own "special powers", pending referendum; Gen Morillon escorted 684 refugees from Srebrenica. **23** Bosnian Serbs withdrew from UN peace talks. **25** Muslims and Croats signed full UN peace plan in New York. **26** UN Security Council voted to take over Somalia peacekeeping. **27** New Chinese Pres Jiang Zemin. **28** Conservative landslide in French General Election. **29** New French PM Edouard

A.D.

Balladur; Somali factions signed UN peace agreement. **30** Italian government crisis.

April 1 French conceded in fishing dispute. **2** State of Emergency in Azerbaijan. **4** Vancouver Summit: $1·6bn aid package to Russia. **8** UN admitted former Yugoslav republic Macedonia. **10** Chris Hani, Gen Sec of S African Communist Party and ANC leader, shot dead. **12** Nato enforced Bosnian "no fly" zone; Talks between Sinn Fein leader Gerry Adams and SDLP leader John Hume. **14** Waco siege ended: many dead. **21** Syria, Jordan and Lebanon to rejoin Middle East peace talks. **22** John Major claimed recession was over. **24** IRA bomb in Bishopsgate. **25** Russian referendum: 58% backed Pres Yeltsin.

May 1 Sri Lankan Pres Premadasa assassinated. **4** Asil Nadir, former Chairman of Polly Peck, fled to N Cyprus. **6** Conservatives lost control of 15 county councils in local elections. **7** Radovan Karadzic accepted 'safe havens'. **15** 96% against Vance-Owen peace plan in Bosnian Serb referendum. **18** Danish Maastricht Referendum: 56·8% in favour; Italian police captured top Mafia suspect. **24** Eritrean independence. **26** Pan-Africanist Congress boycotted S African constitutional negotiations. **27** Florence terrorist bomb: 6 dead, Uffizi museum damaged; Norman Lamont dismissed in Cabinet reshuffle: new Chancellor of Exchequer Kenneth Clarke. **29** Turkish women died in arson attack at Solingen, Germany. **30** Fighting intensified in Sarajevo and Gorazde.

June 1 11 killed by Serb shells at Sarajevo football match. **5** Pres Yeltsin's Russian constitutional congress; Gen Aideed's troops killed 23 Pakistani UN troops. **6** 1st democratic Latvian elections since 1931 won by centre-right alliance. **7** Bosnian government accepted "safe haven" plan: Croat/Muslim battle for Travnik. **8** IRA bombs at Gateshead and later N Shields. **10** In Vitez Muslim gunmen forced British UN troops to surrender weapons. **11** US air strike against HQ and arsenals of Gen Aideed. **13** 52 Bosnian Muslims killed in Serb rocket attack on Gorazde hospital. **15** Bosnia ceasefire agreed at Sarajevo airport. **22** Pres Banda and 2 opposition groups agreed to institute Malawi constitutional reform. **23** Bosnian ethnic division plan welcomed by Serbs and Croats, denounced by Muslims: Nigerian military government annulled Presidential Election. **24** N Ireland Minister Michael Mates resigned; Moshood Abiola, unofficial winner of Nigerian Election, declared himself Pres. **25** Head of European Bank for Reconstruction & Development resigned. **27** Joint Serb-Croat offensive against Maglaj. **30** Bosnian Muslims overran Croatian base in Mostar.

July 3 Pres Clinton announced 1-year suspension of nuclear testing. **4** Muslim forces attacked Serbs surrounding Sarajevo. **5** 65 S African township deaths. **10** Georgian government forces broke separatists' blockade of Sukhumi. **11** Iraq refused UN order to seal missile testing equipment. **12** 16 Somalis killed in US helicopter attack on Gen Aideed's control centre; Sarajevo mortar attack. **16** 8m acres flooded in US Mid-West. **17** Bosnian troops took Fojnica. **18** Maslenica bridge reopened. **19** Iraq allowed UN to inspect weapons development programme. **22** Government defeated in Commons Maastricht vote. **25** Israeli air raids against Hizbollah positions in S Lebanon. **29** ERM on verge of collapse; John Demjanjuk acquitted of Nazi death camp crimes. **30** Bosnian factions assented to ethnic division of country.

August 2 Emergency meeting of EC Finance Ministers: *de facto* suspension of ERM. **4** Serb troops captured Mt Igman overlooking Sarajevo. **7** Buckingham Palace opened to public. **9** 5-year-old Irma Hadzimuratovic, wounded by Serb mortar, flown to London for treatment after media exposure and John Major's intervention. **10** 100,000 dead in Angolan civil war. **12** Pres Yeltsin ordered Russian parliament to submit to

A.D.

elections or face dissolution. **14** Serbs withdrew from Mts Igman and Bjelanica. **16** Transitional State Council for Liberia. **18** Muslims, Serbs and Croats agreed to place Sarajevo under UN rule for 2 years, after 3-way division of Bosnia decided. **22** 55,000 Bosnian Muslims, including 30,000 refugees, trapped in E Mostar. **26** Gen Babangida stepped down: new hand-picked interim government. **27** Muslims held UN convoy "hostage" in Mostar as protection against Croats. **29** Yasser Arafat won PLO executive committee support for radical peace plan giving Palestinians control of Gaza strip and Jericho.

September 1 Geneva talks collapsed when Bosnian factions failed to agree peace plan. **6** UN helicopters attacked Gen Aideed's Mogadishu stronghold after 7 Nigerian peacekeepers killed. **9** PLO Chairman Yasser Arafat signed mutual recognition agreement with Israel. **13** Israel-PLO agreement signed at White House. **14** Jordan and Israel signed agreement. **21** Pres Yeltsin dissolved Russian parliament, and announced rule by decree: parliament swore in Speaker Alexander Rutskoi as Pres. **22** Pres Yeltsin supported by army, security forces, ministers, central bank and many world leaders. **23** S Africa's parliament passed Bill granting disenfranchised black majority a legal say in affairs of state. **24** US and Commonwealth lifted S African trade sanctions. **25** Russian Parliament (White House) telephones, power and hot water cut off. **27** Abkhazian rebels took Sukhumi: Pres Shevardnadze fled. **29** Labour Party Conference passed John Smith's "One man one vote" motion. **30** Earthquake in Maharashtra, central India: 22,000 dead.

October 4 Russian troops stormed White House: Alexander Rutskoi, Ruslan Khasbulatov and other leaders surrendered: 170 dead. **12** Germany's highest court approved Maastricht Treaty. **13** UN economic sanctions against Haiti re-imposed. **19** Benazir Bhutto Pakistan's new PM. **23** IRA bomb in Shankill Rd, Belfast: 10 dead. **25** Sinn Fein leader Gerry Adams banned from mainland Britain; Canadian General Election: landslide victory for Liberals. **28** Irish government's 6-point statement of principles for peace welcomed in Downing St. **30** 7 killed by Loyalist gunmen in Rising Sun pub, Greysteel, Co Londonderry.

November 1 European Union established as Maastricht Treaty came into force. **8** Pres Yeltsin approved final draft of new constitution. **9** Stari Most, Mostar's celebrated 16th century bridge, destroyed by Croats. **11** Russian marines deployed in Zugdidi to support Georgian government. **16** Iraqi intruders in Kuwaiti border incident. **17** Pres de Klerk and Nelson Mandela ratified S Africa's 1st democratic constitution; US Congress endorsed N American Free Trade Agreement (Nafta). **18** Bosnia factions agreed to suspend hostilities and guarantee UN aid deliveries; Gen Sani Abacha, Nigeria's new military ruler, banned political parties and all democratic institutions. **24** £300,000 arms and explosives from E Europe seized, bound for N Ireland loyalist paramilitaries. **27** UK government admitted 9 months of clandestine contact with IRA. **28** Hong Kong–China talks failed.

December 3 John Major and Albert Reynolds in N Ireland talks. **7** Transitional Executive Council (TEC) inaugurated in Cape Town. **12** Vladimir Zhirinovsky's ultra-nationalist Liberal Democratic Party won most seats in Russian Election: referendum in favour of wider powers for Pres Yeltsin. **15** Downing St Declaration by John Major and Taoiseach Albert Reynolds on future of N Ireland; Gatt talks agreement. **19** Ruling Socialist Party under Slobodan Milosevic won Serbian General Election. **21** Croats and Serbs agreed Muslim demand for one-third Bosnia-Herzegovina territory. **30** Sudan expelled British ambassador.

A.D.

1994

January 1 Armed guerrillas seized 6 S Mexican towns. **4** 23 dead in Sarajevo shelling. **5** Environment Minister Tim Yeo resigned; National Curriculum testing restricted. **7** Bushfires ringed Sydney; Inkatha boycott of S African General Election. **8** Parliamentary Private Secretary at Health Ministry resigned. **9** Earl of Caithness, Minister for Aviation & Shipping, resigned; Bosnia peace talks reopened with redrawn map. **11** Poland, Hungary, Slovakia and Czech Republic accepted Nato's Partnership for Peace plan. **13** District Auditor's inquiry charged Westminster City Council with gerrymandering. **17** State of Emergency after Los Angeles earthquake; John Major revealed to have approved £234m aid to Malaysia for Pergau dam, linked to arms deal. **19** Serb-Croat pact to normalise relations. **22** 6 children killed by mortar bombs while playing in Sarajevo. **23** Troop build-up in S Sudan. **28** British aid worker kidnapped and executed in Bosnia. **30** US granted Gerry Adams visa for 2-day visit to New York conference. **31** Breakthrough in PLO–Israel talks.

February 1 Westerners attacked by Algerian Muslim extremists. **4** Violent French fishermen's protests. **5** Mortar attack on Sarajevo market: 68 dead. **7** Parliamentary Private Secretary at Defence Ministry Stephen Milligan found dead. **10** Nato 10-day deadline to Bosnian Serbs to withdraw weapons from Sarajevo area or risk air strikes. **12** Parliamentary Private Secretary at Foreign Office Hartley Booth resigned. **15** N Korea to allow inspection of nuclear installations. **17** Russian Deputy Foreign Minister Vitaly Churkin persuaded Bosnian Serbs to withdraw Sarajevo artillery. **20** All Serb heavy weapons withdrawn from Sarajevo exclusion zone or under UN control. **22** S Iraq dykes opened to flood Shia Muslim resistance. **23** Russian parliament granted amnesty to hardline leaders of 1991 coup and 1993 rebellion. **25** Jewish extremist settler shot dead 40 Arabs in Hebron mosque; Malasia banned new UK trade deals. **28** US jets shot down 4 Bosnian Serb aircraft after attacks on muslim towns, Nato's first-ever aggresive intervention.

March 1 Bosnian Muslims and Croats signed US-brokered peace agreement. **4** Far-right white Afrikaner Volksfront, as well as Zulu Inkatha, registered for S African election; Islamic militants guilty of World Trade Center bombing. **9** IRA mortar attack on Heathrow airport. **10** Controversy over government use of PII certificates. **11** S Africa's white Freedom Front confirmed election participation; Slovak PM Meciar ousted. **12** S African government and TEC ended existence of Bophuthatswana. **13** Chief of Defence Staff Sir Peter Harding resigned. **19** Khmer Rouge Pailin HQ fell to government troops. **20** N–S Korea talks failed. **22** Ciskei government collapsed; PLO–Israel draft accord on armed presence to protect W Bank and Gaza Palestinians; Evidence of secret nuclear bomb programme in N Korea. **25** US troops left Somalia. **27** Italian General Election won by right-wing alliance led by Silvio Berlusconi. **28** ANC security guards attacked Inkatha marchers carrying Zulu weapons: 30 dead. **31** State of Emergency in Natal and KwaZulu.

April 1 Renewed Serb "ethnic cleansing" in N Bosnia. **2** 400 Algerian Muslim extremists killed in month-long army crackdown. **6** Presidents of Rwanda and Burundi died in rocket attack on plane bringing them from Addis Ababa Summit. **7** Civil war in Rwanda: hundreds dead, including PM. **8** Japanese PM Hosokawa resigned. **9** Thousands killed in Rwanda; 130 dead in Natal; Islamic extremists assassinated Egypt's police chief. **10** Nato air strike on Serbian troops advancing on Gorazde; Argentinian Elections supported constitutional reform. **11** 2nd Nato air

A.D.

strike on Bosnian Serb troops. **12** RPF (Rwandan Patriotic Front) Tutsi rebels captured Kigali: government fled; 450 recent S African ANC/Inkatha deaths; Pres Clinton paid $14,600 to rectify tax affairs; Tougher film and video censorship announced. **13** Hamas suicide bomber killed 5 on Tel Aviv bus. **15** Russia declined to join Nato PFP programme; Inflation at lowest for 26 years. **17** Bosnian army's defence of Gorazde failed: UN-Serb agreement to restore peace. **18** Controversy over form of D-Day commemoration. **19** Agreement brought Inkatha Freedom Party into S African Elections: Zulu monarchy upheld by constitution; Paul Touvier 1st Frenchman convicted of World War II crimes. **21** Giant tortoises rescued from Galapagos Is fires; New mammal species, Giant Muntjac, found in Vietnam rainforest. **22** New S Korean PM Lee Yung Dug. **23** Western allies' troops began Berlin withdrawal. **24** Bosnian Serbs withdrew from Gorazde after Nato ultimatum; S African car bomb attacks by white extremists; Armando Calderon Sol won El Salvador's 1st post-war Presidential Election. **25** New Japanese PM Tsutomi Hata. **26** New S African constitution came into force: long queues to vote in Elections; Rwanda ceasefire: 330,000 refugees in neighbouring countries. **28** Iranian chargé d'affaires reprimanded over IRA-Iran links. **29** Fighting between N and S Yemen: 400 dead; PLO-Israel economic agreement. **30** Spanish government corruption scandal.

May 2 Pres de Klerk conceded Election victory to Nelson Mandela: ANC won 7 of 9 provinces, 63% vote. **3** 200,000 dead as Rwanda genocide continued; Dutch Elections: centre left coalition government defeated; Gerry Adams, Sinn Fein leader, granted US visa. **4** Israel and PLO signed agreement to end 27-year occupation of Gaza and W Bank, initiating Palestinian self-rule. **5** Conservatives heavily defeated in local elections: Labour won 40% vote. **6** Total UN embargo on Haiti to restore democracy; Channel Tunnel officially opened. **7** TB epidemic in Siberia. **8** Conservative Whip Michael Brown MP resigned; Former Communists won Hungarian Elections. **9** Nelson Mandela elected Pres of S Africa; Yemen civil war stalemate. **10** New Italian PM Silvio Berlusconi announced right-wing government including neo-Fascists; 1st Gaza military base handed over to Palestinian police. **11** Minister for Disabled narrowly survived resignation demands. **12** Labour leader John Smith died suddenly. **13** Jericho under Palestinian control. **16** Universal dismay at latest Bosnian partition plan; Some London police to be armed. **17** UN African peacekeepers deployed as Rwanda fighting continued; 1st democratic Malawi Presidential Election: Pres-for-Life Dr Hastings Banda defeated by United Democratic Front's Baliki Muzuli. **18** Bosnia factions given peace agreement ultimatum. **19** Detailed government answers to Sinn Fein questions on Downing St Declaration; 1st Channel Tunnel freight service. **20** Islamic militants killed 2 Israeli soldiers in Gaza strip; Civil Rights (Disabled Persons) Bill stopped in Commons by Conservative manoeuvring; Former Albanian Pres Alia tried for embezzlement; Virtual declaration of independence by Crimean parliament. **21** UVA attacked Dublin bar. **22** 40,000 mutilated bodies, mostly minority Tutsi, washed down River Kagera into Lake Victoria: Uganda declared 3 disaster areas: mainly Tutsi RPF seized Kigali airport from mainly Hutu government army; Flood of Haitian refugees to US. **23** UK outbreak of necrotising fasciitis; N Yemeni troops advanced; S Yemen declared independence; Chancellor Kohl's candidate Roman Herzog elected Pres of Germany. **24** 270 pilgrims crushed to death in Mecca; Russia agreed to join Nato PFP; 4 Muslim fundamentalists jailed for World Trade Center bombing. **26** US renewed China's trading partner status despite human rights abuses. **27** John Major's remarks about beggars caused controversy; Alexander Solzhenitsyn returned to Russia. **28** Angolan government air raids on Huambo, Unità stronghold. **29** Saddam Hussein assumed Iraq premiership to tackle economic crisis.

A.D.

June 1 S Africa rejoined Commonwealth; Rail signalmen voted for strike action in pay claim. **2** Helicopter crash on Mull of Kintyre killed 29 anti-terrorism experts; Israeli attack on Hizbollah near Baalbek: 26 dead. **4** D-Day commemoration. **6** 2 Britons taken hostage by Kashmiri guerrillas; 160 dead in China's worst-ever air crash. **8** Bosnia's Serbs, Croats and Muslims agreed 1-month informal ceasefire; N Korea offered international inspection of nuclear sites as scientists disposed of final evidence; Political activity banned in Gaza mosques. **9** In by-elections, Liberal Democrats won Eastleigh from Conservatives; Labour held 4 other seats; 63 Rwandan civilians, 22 clergy dead in RPF advance; Conservative Iranian newspapers attacked Pres Rafsanjani's defence of US trade links. **10** Labour leadership contest opened between Margaret Beckett, John Prescott, Denzil Davies and Tony Blair. **11** Moshood Abiola, winner of annulled 1993 Nigerian election, declared himself head of rival government: later escaped house arrest. **12** European Election results showed ruling parties lost seats across Europe: In UK, Labour won 62 seats with 44% vote; Austrian referendum in favour of EU membership; Pakistan's former PM Sharif on embezzlement charges. **13** N Korean threat to quit International Atomic Energy Agency; 79 Islamic extremists killed by Algerian security forces. **14** Angola aid cut when Unita withdrew security clearance for UN and Red Cross planes; Kurdish factional fighting in N Iraq. **15** 24-hour national rail strike after reports that Cabinet ministers intervened to prevent settlement; US proposed mandatory N Korea arms embargo and sanctions. **16** Former US Pres Jimmy Carter met Pres Kim Il Sung in Pyongyang to resolve nuclear crisis; N Yemen shelled Aden: 47 killed. **17** Turkey banned pro-Kurdish political party. **18** N and S Korean leaders agreed nuclear summit; UVF attack on Loughinisland pub killed 6. **19** Spanish-French "tuna wars" over use of illegal drift nets. **20** Agriculture Minister Gillian Shepphard blocked inadequate proposed EC animal transport controls; Iran's holiest shrine in Mashbad bombed; 25 dead. **21** 3 terrorist bombs in Turkish Mediterranean resorts. **22** Pres Clinton announced N Korea's agreement not to reload nuclear reactor or reprocess fuel: inspection allowed; 2nd rail strike, followed by others throughout summer. **23** French troops entered Rwanda form Zaire on humanitarian mission; Kashmiri guerrillas freed British hostages. **24** EU Corfu Summit: Pres Yeltsin signed Partnership & Cooperation Agreement. **25** John Major vetoed appointment of Belgian PM Jean-Luc Dehaene as EC Pres: later emergency summit announced. **28** Germany announced UK beef ban; S African penguin rescue operation after oil spill on Robben and Dassen Is. **29** Hong Kong parliament backed Governor Chris Patten's democracy plan; New Japanese PM Socialist Tomiichi Murayama. **30** Monklands E by-election narrowly won by Labour; 60% rise in world-wide Aids cases in 1993.

July 1 PLO Chairman Yasser Arafat returned to Gaza; Baby girl 4 hours old abducted from Nottingham hospital. **4** RPF took Kigali. **5** Yasser Arafat in Jericho: Palestine National Authority (PNA) sworn in; US, Russian and EU Foreign Ministers unveiled Bosnian peace plan and map in Geneva; Government backed 10-year renewal of BBC Charter. **6** Detained Nigerian opposition leader Moshood Abiola accused of treason; Former Italian PM Giuliano Andreotti accused of Mafia membership. **7** Bosnian Pres Alija Izetbegovic approved peace plan and map assigning 51% Bosnia to Muslim-Croat federation: Bosnian Serbs promised to consider plan; N Yemeni troops took Aden: S Yemen leaders fled; Cambodian parliament voted to outlaw Khmer Rouge; Crew of 7 murdered on Italian ship in Algerian port. **8** Lord Archer investigated for insider share dealing: later cleared; Chinese PM Li Peng cut short German visit after demonstrations against human rights abuses; N Korea-US nuclear inspection talks; Turkish troops in Zenica. **9** N Korean Pres Kim Il Sung's death followed by hysterical mourning; G7 Naples Summit admitted Russia, effectively creating G8; Refugees fled RPF offensive in NW Rwanda. **10** 2 Conservative ministerial aides suspended after accusations of

A.D.

tabling Commons questions for cash; Ukraine's Presidential Election won by former Pres Leonid Kuchma. **11** Israel sealed Gaza border after clashes. **12** Commons inquiry into "cash for questions" and MPs' fees; Haiti expelled UN human rights monitors: opposition members massacred; Bosnia truce renewed; Kim Jong Il to succeed father as N Korean Pres; Record London air-pollution; 2 tons terrorist explosive seized at Heysham, Lancs. **13** Former W Australian PM Brian Burke jailed for fraud. **14** Defence Secretary Malcolm Rifkind announced £2bn defence cuts: 18,700 job losses, Rosyth naval shipyard downgraded; Trinidadian hanged after 5 years in death cell despite Privy Council order for stay of execution; 3 dead in E Timor clashes with troops. **15** Emergency EU Summit endorsed Luxembourg PM Jacques Santer as new EU Pres; New Hungarian PM Gyula Horn. **16** Nottingham baby Abbie Humphries restored to parents; 1st of 21 fragments of Comet Shoemaker-Levy 9 collided with Jupiter. **17** 3 mortar rounds fired at Goma airport by RPF caused refugee stampede: 35 dead. **18** RPF claimed control of all Rwanda outside French "safe haven" and declared civil war over; Hizbollah car bomb outside Jewish Centre in Buenos Aires: 100 dead; Israel-Jordan peace talks opened; Pro-democracy protests in Lagos as oil strike entered 3rd week: 20 dead; EU brokered UK beef compromise with Germany. **19** RPF swore in new Hutu Pres and Hutu PM, with Tutsi Vice Pres and Defence Minister; Bomb on Panamanian plane carrying Jewish passengers: 21 dead; New European Parliament Pres German Socialist Klaus Hänsch; Italian PM Berlusconi dropped emergency decree curbing magistrates' powers. **20** Cabinet reshuffle: Gillian Shephard new Education Sec, Brian Mawhinney Transport Sec, William Waldegrave Agriculture Sec, Michael Portillo Employment Sec, Jeremy Hanley Chairman of Conservative Party; 1st Belarus Pres Alexander Lukashenko sworn in. **21** Tony Blair new Labour leader with 57% vote: John Prescott deputy leader; European Parliament narrowly approved Jacques Santer as EC Pres; Thief unwittingly foiled IRA bombers when he stole bag containing Semtex. **22** Pres Clinton announced massive aid for Rwanda, later matched by UK, EU, Germany and France. **23** Military coup in Gambia. **25** King Hussein of Jordan and Israeli PM Rabin signed declaration ending 46-year conflict; Trinidad to seek capital punishment law reform; 14,000 dead in cholera epidemic in refugee camps in Goma, Zaire. **26** Car bomb outside Israel's London embassy: 13 injured; 2nd bomb outside Jewish charity HQ: Hamas claimed responsibility; Italian government corruption crisis deepened. **27** Bangladeshi feminist writer Taslima Nasrin under Muslim extremist death threats; Turkish air raid inside Iraq killed 70 Kurds; Panic as Russia's MMM investment fund collapsed. **28** Khmer Rouge kidnapped 3 Westerners: Water companies ordered to peg price increases. **29** Neil Kinnock new British EC Commissioner; 2 shot dead outside Florida clinic by anti-abortionists; 29 IRA bombs injured 47 in Newry attack. **31** Serb Pres Milosevic urged Bosnian Serbs to accept peace plan.

August 2 Indian opposition boycotted parliament in corruption protest. **3** Bosnian Serbs rejected peace plan; French embassy in Algiers attacked by Armed Islamic Group: suspected militants arrested in France; Riots in Qazvin, Iran. **4** 2 Havana police killed during attempted ferry hijacking to US; Israeli raids on S Lebanon Hizbollah bases. **5** US-N Korea nuclear talks resumed; Nato airstrike on Bosnian Serb positions near Sarajevo after exclusion zone violation. **7** New Colombian Pres Ernesto Samper; 8,000 in Muslim extremist rally at Wembley. **8** New Israel-Jordan border crossing near Eilat inaugurated: Yitzhak Rabin 1st Israeli PM to visit Jordan. **9** Typhus in Goma refugee camps. **12** "Cradle to grave" NHS ended with abandonment of guaranteed care of elderly; John Paul Getty II gave £1m to keep Canova's *Three Graces* in UK. **13** New Dutch Purple Coalition government under Wim Kok. **14** Guatemalan Republican Front of former ruler Gen Efraim Rios Montt won Congressional

A.D.
Election. **15** Venezuelan terrorist Carlos "the Jackal" arrested in Khartoum and taken to Paris; Michael Portillo, who signed 1992 European directive on disabled employment, as new Employment Sec embarrassed by consequences; Russian plutonium seized from smugglers in Germany; Palestinian security forces arrested 35 Hamas activists. **16** Republican Senators' delay tactics effectively killed US Health Bill; Sri Lanka Election won by Chandrika Kumaratunga. **17** King Letsie III of Lesotho dissolved parliament: 4 protesters killed. **21** Mexican Election won by ruling PRI party's Ernesto Zedillo; Riots in Tabriz, Iran's 3rd city. **22** 2,548 Cuban refugees picked up by US coastguards in one day: held at US naval base Guantanamo Bay; House of Representatives finally approved Pres Clinton's Crime Bill. **23** Former PM Sharif admitted Pakistan had nuclear weapons. **24** Lord Archer admitted "grave error" in share deal. **26** Irish US delegation met Sinn Fein in Belfast; 1st British patient received mechanical heart. **27** Bosnian Serb referendum rejected Bosnia-Herzegovina partition; RPF revenge killings against returning refugees. **28** Sunday Trading Act came into force. **29** Cholera, anthrax and diphtheria epidemics in former USSR. **30** Stock Exchange reopened Archer share inquiry. **31** IRA declared ceasefire: UK government demanded evidence of permanence; US ultimatum to Haiti's military government; China to dismantle Hong Kong's democratic structure after 1997; Russian army left Latvia and Estonia.

September 1 4 republican prisoners transferred to N Ireland jails. **2** Lesotho government reinstated. **4** Loyalist car bomb attack on Belfast Sinn Fein HQ. **5** UN Population Conference opened in Cairo. **6** Irish Taoiseach Albert Reynolds met Sinn Fein leader Gerry Adams. **7** N Ireland security relaxed. **9** Cuba-US agreement to end refugee exodus. **10** Pope visited Croatia. **11** Crimean Pres Meshkov disbanded parliament. **12** Suicide pilot crashed light aircraft on White House lawn; Separatist PQ won control of Quebec provincial government. **15** Pres Clinton's TV address on imminent Haiti operation; Last Marines left Somalia; Renewed fighting in Liberia. **16** Broadcasting ban on N Ireland extremists lifted; Former Pres Carter led mediating delegation to Haiti. **18** Conservative government defeated in Swedish General Election. **19** Gen Cedras given 28 days to quit Haiti: US troops began peaceful occupation; Plague epidemic in India. **20** Zulu King Goodwill Zwelithini banished Inkatha leader Chief Buthelezi from court; 800,000 Muslims and Croats expelled from Bosnian Serb territory since 1992; Burma's military leaders met Aung San Suu Kyi. **21** Fossilised remains of oldest humans (*Australopithecus ramidus*) found in E Africa. **22** Employment Sec Michael Portillo used UK's opt-out mechanism over paternity leave legislation; Nato aircraft attacked Bosnian Serb troops W of Sarajevo. **24** Gerry Adams in US. **25** Haitian police killed by US Marines in Cap Haitien in violent protest against military regime. **28** 910 drowned in Baltic ferry disaster; Signal workers' strike settled.

October 1 Slovakia Elections won by Vladimir Meciar's nationalist party. **2** US troops began arrest and disarming of Haitian paramilitaries. **3** Failed coup in Azerbaijan; Channel Tunnel car service began. **4** At Labour Party conference Tony Blair announced replacement of Clause IV: "common ownership of means of production"; UN eased Serbian blockade; Chief Abiola's treason trial postponed indefinitely; Antarctic ozone damage at record level. **5** 48 Solar Temple cult members found dead in Switzerland. **6** Labour Party conference narrowly reasserted backing for Clause IV. **7** Armoured Iraqi troops massed on Kuwait border. **9** Build-up of US Gulf troops against Iraqi threat; Violence at London anti-Criminal Justice Bill demonstration; Austrian General Election: far-right FPO gains; Inquiry demanded into Mrs Thatcher's 1985 arms deal from which her son allegedly profited. **10** Gen Cedras stepped down in Haiti. **11** Saddam

A.D.
Hussein withdrew troops. **13** N Ireland Loyalist paramilitary groups announced ceasefire. **14** Hamas-held Israeli hostage killed in rescue attempt; Egyptian Nobel laureate writer Naguib Mahfouz stabbed by Islamic militant. **15** Pres Aristide returned to Haiti. **16** Chancellor Kohl narrowly won 4th term; Finnish referendum in favour of EU membership. **17** Queen visited Russia; N Korea agreed to limit nuclear ability. **19** Tim Smith N Ireland Minister, and later Neil Hamilton Minister at DTI, resigned over "questions for cash" affair; Hamas suicide bomb in Tel Aviv: 22 dead. **20** Israel sealed off Gaza strip and West Bank. **21** John Major opened way to talks with Sinn Fein: bans on leaders lifted, border roads opened. **23** Cerebral malaria epidemic in India. **24** Opposition candidate in Sri Lanka Presidential Election killed by Tamil suicide bomber. **25** New body established under Lord Nolan to oversee standards in public life. **26** Israel-Jordan peace treaty signed; Major oil spill from Siberian pipeline; Royal Commission demanded drastic cuts in car use and pollution. **29** New EC Pres Jacques Santer stripped UK Commissioner Sir Leon Brittan of part of portfolio; Gun attack on White House.

November 1 3 UK hostages freed by Indian police from Kashmir militants; 3 Western Khmer Rouge hostages found dead. **2** Storms in S Egypt: 475 dead. **3** Government abandoned Post Office privatisation plans. **4** Serb-held Kupres fell to Bosnian Croats; Chief Abiola's release on bail approved by court but not implemented. **6** Muslims seized territory from Serbs near Bihac; NW Italy floods: 53 dead. **7** David Martin Parliamentary Private Sec at Foreign Office resigned over Post Office privatisation. **8** Republican landslide victory in US mid-term elections. **10** IRA murdered N Ireland postal worker: IRA prisoners' early release in Irish Republic cancelled; High Court ruled UK Pergau dam aid illegal; Saddam Hussein recognised Kuwait. **11** US abandoned Bosnia arms embargo; Angolan government troops took Huambo; Unità leader Jonas Savimbi fled. **13** Swedish referendum in favour of EU membership; E Timor riots. **14** World's 1st woman PM Mrs Bandaranaike returned to power in Sri Lanka under her daughter Pres Chandrika Kumaratunga; UK National Lottery inaugurated. **16** Queen's speech at State Opening of Parliament: increased contributions to EU budget: universal retirement age (65); improved disabled rights; John Major declared European Budget Bill a confidence issue. **17** Albert Reynolds resigned as Taoiseach; Ministers' controversial 4·7% pay rise. **18** Gaza's PLO police fired on Hamas militants: 11 dead; Serb jets attacked UN "safe area" Bihac with napalm and cluster bombs. **19** Bertie Aherne new Fianna Fail leader; 2nd Serb air attack on Bihac. **20** Writer Wole Soyinka, Nigeria's Nobel laureate, fled to Paris. **21** 39 Nato planes bombed Serb air base SW of Bihac; £205,000 pay rise for British Gas chief executive. **22** Serb advance into Bihac outskirts; Italian PM Berlusconi investigated for corruption. **23** 2 Nato airstrikes on Bosnian Serb air defences near Bihac; Unità troops broke ceasefire while leader Jonas Savimbi endorsed peace accord. **24** Nato refused to endorse Bihac rescue plan: pitched battle within safe haven area. **28** Government won Commons vote on European Finance Bill: Whip withdrawn from 8 Conservative abstainers; Serbs took Bihac; Norwegian referendum against EU membership. **29** Budget day: public spending cuts: VAT on fuel at 17·5% from April: petrol, car tax, cigarettes up. **30** Russian jets attacked Grozny: refugees fled; Italian liner *Achille Lauro* sank off Somalia after fire.

December 1 New Mexican Pres Ernesto Zedillo. **2** UN halted Nato air missions over Bosnia. **4** Serb Pres Milosevic backed negotiated Bosnian peace settlement. **5** US Treasury Sec Lloyd Bentsen resigned. **6** Government defeat on planned VAT increase on fuel; CSCE gathering failed to agree on Bosnia: retitled Organisation for Security and Cooperation in Europe. **7** Russian air raids on Grozny; EU £231m aid for N Ireland; Southern

A.D.
Ocean whale sanctuary came into effect. **8** Chancellor of Exchequer's mini-budget to recoup £1bn lost by "VAT on fuel" defeat: alcohol, cigarettes, petrol up. **9** Sinn Fein talks at Stormont; EU Essen Summit: E European leaders special guests; 300 Chinese children died in cinema fire. **11** Russia invaded Chechnya. **12** Bosnian Muslim attack on UN armoured vehicle in Bihac: further attack near Mt Igman; £30,000 bonus for Head of Prison Service. **13** Russian tanks blockaded Grozny: fierce fighting. **14** UK unemployment down to 2·4m. **15** 29% swing to Labour in Dudley W by-election; New Irish Taoiseach John Bruton. **16** Commander of Grozny-bound armoured column defied orders, refusing to attack civilians; 9,000 MoD job losses; Gibraltar finally complied with EU directives on banking procedure. **17** US helicopter shot down in N Korea: pilot died. **18** Russian troops attacked Grozny: day and night air raids; Former US Pres Carter on Bosnia peace mission; Bulgarian General Election: former Communist BSP won outright majority. **19** UK agreed EU directive on key part-time workers' rights. **21** Cargo plane crashed near Coventry: 5 dead. **22** Italian PM Berlusconi resigned as coalition crumbled; Compromise agreement allowed Spanish and Portuguese trawlers into UK and Irish waters; Sarajevo shelled. **23** Dublin released 9 IRA prisoners; Christmas ceasefire in Bosnia; Russian parliament demanded Chechnya ceasefire; Tutsi-Hutu fighting in Bujumbura. **26** Algerian Muslim extremist hijack of French airliner ended at Marseille airport: 4 guerrillas, 3 hostages dead. **27** 4 RC priests killed by Algerian Muslim fundamentalists in reprisal. **28** Grozny blitz; All 158 opposition MPs resigned after 40 days of strikes in Bangladesh. **29** Bihac ceasefire failed. **30** 2 murders at Boston abortion clinic. **31** Russian troops reached central Grozny: fierce fighting, many dead; Bosnian Muslims signed 4-month truce.

1995

January 1 Austria, Finland and Sweden joined EU; France assumed EU Presidency; New Brazilian Pres Henrique Cardoso. **3** 3 dangerous prisoners escaped from Parkhurst prison for 5 days: riots at Everthorpe prison, Humberside; Gaza unrest after 3 Palestinian police shot dead by Israeli troops; Live animal export protests at Shoreham, W Sussex. **4** Bosnian Serbs broke Bihac truce. **5** Former Malawi Pres Banda under house arrest for 1983 murders; Peking curtailed Tibetan religious worship. **6** S African politician Joe Slovo died. **8** Sri Lankan government truce with Tamil guerrillas. **9** Egon Krenz charged with killings on former E German border. **10** Chechnya defied Russian surrender ultimatum; Parkhurst Prison Governor dismissed. **11** Pres Yeltsin assumed direct control of Russian armed forces; 7 dead in peasant uprising in Chiapas state, Mexico. **12** Army to end Belfast daytime patrols; Saddam Hussein's brutal punishment by amputation of limbs of thieves, deserters, *etc.* revealed. **13** Animal welfare protesters blockaded Swansea airport. **14** Lamberto Dini nominated new Italian PM pending economic and electoral reforms. **16** Somali militiamen controlled Mogadishu streets. **17** Over 4,000 dead in Kobe earthquake. **18** Spanish Fishing Rights Bill narrowly passed after UK compensation doubled to £53m; Inflation up to 2·9%: unemployment fell to 2,414,000; 18,000-year-old Ice Age paintings found in Ardèche caves. **19** Grozny Presidential palace fell to Russians; 8 foreign workers taken hostage by Sierra Leone rebels; Shoreham live animal exports to end. **20** EU to review use of veal crates. **22** Islamic Jihad car bomb in central Israel: 21 dead, 62 injured. **23** Portuguese PM Silva resigned; CSA overhaul announced. **26** 50th anniversary of Auschwitz liberation commemorated. **30** Severe floods in Netherlands, Belgium, N France: thousands evacuated; Virtual civil war in Sierra Leone. **31** Cumbria rail crash: 1 dead.

A.D.
February 1 *Times* leaked draft London-Dublin plan for N Ireland's future; Woman protester against animal exports killed in Coventry airport accident; Russia issued arrest warrant against Chechen leader Dzhokhar Dudayev. **3** Irish Republic freed 3 IRA prisoners; Controversy over Lord Wakeham's merchant bank appointment soon after leaving Cabinet. **4** Ceasefire to end 11-day Peru-Ecuador border conflict. **6** Maoris disrupted New Zealand National Day celebrations; US space shuttle Discovery and Russia's Mir space station rendezvous. **7** Scottish Office Minister Allan Stewart resigned; IMF declined to make huge loan to Russia. **8** Pres Yeltsin claimed major victory in battle for Grozny; Palestinian police seized 90 Gaza Islamic militants. **9** Stormont bugging device find halted Sinn Fein talks; Greece rejected EU plan for customs union with Turkey. **10** Air Chief Marshal Sir Sandy Wilson resigned; £267m compensation agreement for Maxwell pension funds; Mexican government declared war on Zapatista guerrillas. **11** Junior Home Office Minister Charles Wardle resigned; 11 women resigned from ANC Women's League after controversy involving Winnie Mandela. **12** 50th anniversary of Dresden bombing commemorated; Allan Boesak, S Africa's UN ambassador-designate, resigned. **13** 2-day Chechnya ceasefire. **14** Inflation up to 3·3%. **15** England fans in Dublin football riot: far-right extremist links; Chechnya ceasefire extended. **16** Huge Labour win in Islwyn by-election; 100 computers vandalised in Dept of Transport burglary. **17** N Ireland Sec Sir Patrick Mayhew lifted 10 exclusion orders against terrorists. **18** UN Afghanistan peace plan under threat with emergence of Taliban Koranic students militia. **19** "Mass trespass" in Windsor Castle grounds against Criminal Justice Act. **21** Huge Russian attack on Chechen separatists; Phone-tapping scandal threatened Presidential campaign of French PM Balladur. **22** Joint Anglo-Irish document on N Ireland's future published; France expelled 5 alleged US spies. **23** French seamen's protest against employment of foreign ferry crews. **24** Plymouth animal exports halted; 20 dead in Karachi mosque massacre: 153 dead in recent Sunni/Shia factional violence. **26** 233-year-old Barings merchant bank collapsed. **27** 2 Pakistani Christians acquitted of blasphemy fled to Germany; Car bomb in Zakho, Kurdish N Iraq: 54 dead. **28** Last UN peacekeepers left Somalia; Polish PM Pawlak ousted.

March 1 Government defeated Labour motion on European policy by 5 votes. **2** Nick Leeson, Barings Bank financial trader involved in collapse, arrested in Frankfurt; Sir John Banham, Chairman of Local Government Commission, resigned. **5** Inkatha MPs ended S. African parliament boycott. **6** Spanish peseta and Portuguese escudo devalued after emergency meeting to realign ERM; Croat alliance with Bosnian Muslims and Bosnian Croats. **7** Dutch bank ING bought Barings in £1·6bn deal; Robert Hughes, Junior Minister for Citizens Charter, resigned. **8** Government agreed to direct meetings between ministers and Sinn Fein before surrender of arms or explosives; 2 US diplomats killed in Karachi by Muslim extremists. **9** Canada arrested Spanish trawler off Grand Banks fishing fields, Newfoundland; Queen in Belfast; Government approved Westland helicopter order; 100 senior army officers made compulsorily redundant. **12** John Major visited Israel. **13** Tony Blair secured overwhelming National Executive support for new Clause IV; Chief executive of Student Loans Company dismissed. **14** Maze Prison riot: 20 prison officers injured. **15** UK intervened in Spain/Canada fishing dispute. Italian PM Dini won confidence vote. **17** Pres Clinton urged IRA to relinquish arms. **19** 3 Belgians, 2 government soldiers killed in Bujumbura ambush; 2 Israelis killed in Palestinian bus ambush in Hebron. **20** Sarin nerve gas attack on Tokyo subway; Turkish troops shelled N Iraq Kurd targets; Queen in S. Africa: Nelson Mandela awarded OM. **21** 35,000 Turkish troops with armoured support captured mountainous area of Iraqi Kurdistan; Rupert Pennant-Rea, Deputy Governor of Bank of England, resigned. **22** Belgian Foreign Minister resigned. **24** Ethnic clashes in Burundi: many dead, thousands fled; Routine army patrols in Belfast to end. **25** Iraq jailed 2 US citizens

A.D.

who strayed over Kuwait border. **26** Conservative Party allegations of BBC bias. **27** Winnie Mandela dismissed from S. African government. **28** Leading Haitian opposition politician assassinated; High Court approved Leeds and Halifax Building Societies merger; Plan to widen M25 abandoned;

A.D.

UN Global Warming Summit opened in Berlin. **30** Arctic ozone layer suffered worst-ever damage during 1994–5 winter. **31** Israeli helicopter attack killed Hizbollah leader; Romanian airbus crash 60 dead; US peacekeepers handed over duties to UN in Haiti.

THE MAY 1995 LOCAL ELECTIONS
ENGLAND AND WALES

Seats at Stake

Voting took place in the following authorities:
■ 36 English metropolitan districts, for one third (827) of the seats;
■ 107 English districts for one third (1,617) of seats;
■ 167 English districts for all seats (7,580);
■ 14 English "shadow" all-purpose unitary councils (784) including the new Isle of Wight authority;
■ 22 Welsh "shadow" all-purpose councils (1,273) which replace the eight counties and 37 districts in 1996.

Gains and Losses

	Seats	Net Change
Conservative	2056	− 2027
Labour	5615	+ 1799
Lib. Dem.	2702	+ 495
Plaid Cymru	113	+ 11
Others/NOC	1582	− 299

Council Control

Labour	155
Others/NOC	138
Lib. Dem.	45
Conservative	8

Among the many councils won by Labour were:
Calderdale
Dartford
Dover
Exeter
Gloucester
High Peak
Hove
Kettering
Kirklees
Lancaster
Northampton
Oldham
Portsmouth
Southampton
Walsall

Among councils won by Liberal Democrats were:
East Dorset
Guildford
Horsham
Mid-Devon
Mid-Sussex
North Dorset
Pendle
Salisbury
South Norfolk
West Devon

THE APRIL 1995 LOCAL ELECTIONS
SCOTLAND

Voting took place on 6 April 1995 for the 29 unitary authorities due to take office in 1996. The outcome of the voting was:

Party	Seats	Votes	% Vote
Labour	613	742,557	43·6
SNP	181	444,918	26·1
Liberal Democrats	123	166,752	9·8
Conservative	82	196,109	11·5
Independents	155	130,642	7·7
Others	5	23,170	1·3

No less than 20 of the 29 new authorities were won by Labour. Neither the Conservatives nor Liberal Democrats won any. The SNP won control of 3 (Angus, Moray, Perthshire and Kinross), Independents won 3 (Argyll and Bute, Borders, Highland) and there was no overall control in Aberdeenshire, Dumfries and Galloway and East Renfrewshire.

PROMINENT
PEOPLE

Glimpses of some of the famous
people in the history of the world.
See also Section D for leading
British politicians; Section E for
composers; Section M for prominent English novelists; and Section
W for major figures in the history
of the cinema.

PROMINENT PEOPLE

A

Abel, Sir Frederick (1826–1902). English military chemist, an authority on explosives. He and his friend James Dewar patented the propellant cordite (*see* **Section L**).

Abelard, Peter (1079–1142), one of the founders of scholastic moral theology, b. at Pallet (Palais) near Nantes. He lectured in Paris, where he was sought by students, though persecuted for alleged heresy. His main achievement was to discuss where others asserted. His love for Héloïse, a woman of learning, ended in tragic separation and in a famous correspondence.

Abercrombie, Sir Patrick (1879–1957), architect and town-planner. He was consulted on the replanning of Plymouth, Hull, Bath and other cities and produced a plan for Greater London, 1943.

Acton, 1st Baron (John Emerich Edward Dalberg Acton) (1834–1902), English historian. He planned the *Cambridge Modern History*.

Adam, Robert (1728–92), architect, one of four Scottish brothers. He developed a characteristic style in planning and decoration and his achievements in interior design include Harewood House, Yorks.; Osterley Park, Middlesex; Syon House, Middlesex; Kedleston Hall, Derbyshire; Luton Hoo, Bedfordshire; and Kenwood. *See* **Neo-Classical Style, Section L.**

Adams, John (1735–1826), succeeded Washington as president of the U.S.A. He was the first of the republic's ambassadors to England.

Adams, John Couch (1819–92), English mathematician and astronomer. He shared credit for the discovery of the planet Neptune (1846) with the French astronomer Leverrier, working independently.

Adams, Samuel (1722–1803), American revolutionary statesman, b. Boston. He advocated "no taxation without representation" as early as 1765; promoted the "Boston tea-party"; and in 1776 signed the Declaration of Independence.

Adams, William (*c.* 1564–1620), navigator, b. Gillingham, Kent; the first Englishman to visit Japan. He found favour with the shogun Ieyasu, and an English and Dutch trading settlement was established till 1616.

Addams, Jane (1860–1935), American sociologist who founded Hull House, Chicago, in 1889.

Addison, Joseph (1672–1719), writer and Whig politician. He contributed to the *Tatler*, and was co-founder with Steele of the *Spectator*.

Adelard of Bath (*c.* 1090–*c.* 1150), English mathematician who translated into Latin the *Arithmetic* of Al-Kwarizmi and so introduced the Arabic numerals to the West (*see* **L8–9**).

Adenauer, Konrad (1876–1967), chancellor of the West German Federal Republic, 1949–63; founder and chairman of the Christian Democratic Party, 1945–66. To a defeated Germany he gave stable constitutional government and a place in the Western alliance. He promoted reconciliation with France but resisted accommodation with Russia.

Adler, Alfred (1870–1937), Austrian psychiatrist, founder of the school of individual psychology. An earlier pupil of Freud, he broke away in 1911, rejecting the emphasis on sex, regarding man's main problem as a struggle for power to compensate for feelings of inferiority. *See* **Adlerian psychology, Section J.**

Adrian, 1st Baron (Edgar Douglas Adrian) (1889–1977), English physiologist. He shared with Sherrington the 1932 Nobel Prize for medicine for work on the electrical nature of the nerve impulse. Pres. Royal Society 1950–5; Pres. British Association 1954; Chancellor Leicester Univ. 1958–71; Chancellor Cambridge Univ. 1967–75; O.M. 1942.

Adrian IV (Nicholas Breakspear) (d. 1159), pope 1154–50, the only English pope, b. near St. Albans. He crowned Frederick Barbarossa Holy Roman Emperor. Granted overlordship of Ireland to Henry II.

Aeschylus (524–456 B.C.), founder of Greek tragic drama. Of the many plays he wrote, only seven have come down to us, including *The Seven against Thebes*, *Prometheus Bound*, and a trilogy on Orestes.

Aesop (? 6th cent. B.C.), semi-legendary fabulist, originally a slave. The fables attributed to him probably have many origins.

Agassiz, Louis (1807–73), Swiss-American embryologist, author of *Lectures on Comparative Embryology*, intended for laymen, *Researches on Fossil Fishes*, and *Studies on Glaciers*. He was an opponent of Darwinian evolution.

Agricola, Gnaeus Julius (37–93), Roman governor of Britain, who subdued the country except for the Scottish highlands. His son-in-law Tacitus wrote his life.

Agrippa, Marcus Vipsanius (63–12 B.C.), Roman general.

Ahmad Khan, Sir Syed (1817–98), Indian educationist and social reformer who founded what is now the Aligarh Muslim University.

Airy, Sir George Biddell (1801–92), English mathematician who was astronomer royal for over 40 years, 1835–81. He set up a magnetic observatory at Greenwich.

Akbar, Jalal-ud-din Mohammed (1542–1605), Mogul emperor of India, son of Humayun. He extended the imperial power over much of India, stabilised the administration, promoted commerce and learning; and, though a Muslim, respected Hindu culture and tolerated Christian missions. His reign saw a flowering of Mogul culture.

Akhenaten, the name adopted by the heretic pharaoh **Amenhotep IV** (d. 1338 B.C.), who introduced a short-lived but influential religious and artistic reformation. He sought to convert his people from their polytheistic beliefs to a more compassionate religion based on the one supreme sun-god Aten (hence his name). His pacifism caused the temporary loss of most of Egypt's overseas territories. His wife was Nefertiti and he was succeeded by Tutankhamen, who gave in to the conservative forces of the priesthood.

Alanbrooke, 1st Viscount (Alan Francis Brooke) (1883–1963), British field-marshal; chief of the imperial general staff 1941–46. Sir Arthur Bryant's *The Turn of the Tide* and *Triumph in the West* are based on his war diaries.

Alarcón, Pedro Antonio de (1833–91), Spanish novelist. His short story, *El Sombrero de tres picos* (The Three-Cornered Hat) became the subject of Falla's ballet and of Hugo Wolf's opera *Der Corregidor*.

Alaric I (376–410), Visigothic chief who, as first auxiliary to the Roman emperor Theodosius, later attacked the empire and sacked Rome in 410.

Alban, St. (d. *c.* 303), proto-martyr of Britain, converted by a priest to whom he had given shelter. He suffered under Diocletian at Verulam (now St. Albans), where in the 8th cent. King Offa of Mercia founded the abbey of that name.

Albert, Prince Consort (1819–61), son of the Duke of Saxe-Coburg-Gotha, married Queen Victoria in 1840. He helped the queen with political duties, projected the international exhibition of 1851, and in 1861 in a dispute with the United States advised a conciliatory attitude which averted war. He died of typhoid fever and is commemorated by the Albert Memorial in Kensington Gardens.

Albertus Magnus (**Albert the Great**) (1206–80), Dominican scholastic philosopher, b. Swabia. His interest in nature as an independent observer marked the awakening of the scientific spirit. Among his pupils was Thomas Aquinas.

Alcibiades (*c.* 450–404 B.C.), Athenian general and statesman. Pupil and friend of Socrates, he was an egoist whose career brought Athens disaster. He was murdered in Phrygia.

Alcott, Louisa May (1832–88), American author of books for girls, notably *Little Women*.

Alcuin (735–804), English scholar, who settled on the Continent and helped Charlemagne with the promotion of education.

Aldred (d. 1069), Saxon archbishop of York who crowned William the Conqueror.

Aldrich, Henry (1647–1710), English composer of church music, theologian and architect. He designed Peckwater quadrangle at Christ Church, the chapel of Trinity College, and All Saints' Church, Oxford, and wrote the "Bonny Christ Church bells."

Alekhine, Alexander (1892–1946), world chess champion, 1927–35, 1937–46. He was born in Moscow but later became a French citizen.

Alembert, Jean le Rond d' (1717–83), French mathematician and philosopher, one of the encyclopaedists, a leading representative of the Enlightenment.

Alexander of Tunis, Earl (Harold Leofric George Alexander) (1891–1969), British field-marshal, b. Ireland. Directed retreat at Dunkirk 1940, and Burma 1942; C.-in-C. Allied Armies in Italy 1943–4; Supreme Allied Commander, Mediterranean 1944–5; Governor-general of Canada 1946–52.

Alexander II (1818–81), reforming Tsar of Russia, succeeded his father Nicholas in 1855. In 1861 he emancipated the serfs and in 1865 established provincial elective assemblies. Later his government became reactionary; he was assassinated by Nihilists; the pogroms followed.

Alexander the Great (356–323 B.C.), Greek conqueror. Educated by Aristotle, he succeeded his father Philip as king of Macedon in 336 B.C. He led the Greek states against Persia; and, crossing the Hellespont, he defeated Darius and sacked Persepolis. He captured Egypt and founded Alexandria. He penetrated to India. D. at Babylon.

Alexandra, Queen (1844–1925), daughter of Christian IX of Denmark, married the Prince of Wales (afterwards Edward VII) 1863.

Alfieri, Vittorio, Count (1749–1803), Italian poet and dramatist.

Alfonso the Wise (1221–84), king of León and Castile, known for his code of laws and his planetary tables. He caused the first general history of Spain to be written. Dethroned 1282.

Alfred the Great (849–99), king of Wessex who became a national figure. From the outset he had to repel Danish invaders. After years of effort he won the battle of Ethandun (Edington), and subsequently, probably in 886, made peace with Guthrum, leaving to the Danes the north and east. He built ships, was an able administrator, and promoted education, his own translations from the Latin being part of the earliest English literature.

Al-Kwarizimi (fl. c. 830), Persian mathematician said to have given algebra its name.

Allenby, 1st Viscount (Edmund Henry Hynman Allenby) (1861–1936), British general. He served on the Western front 1914–16, commanded in Palestine 1917–18, capturing Jerusalem on 9 December 1917.

Allende, Salvador (1908–73), Chilean radical leader, a Marxist democrat, who won the presidency 1970. He tried to bring social reform by democratic means but met his death resisting the military coup in which it is alleged the American CIA played a role.

Alleyne, Edward (1566–1626), actor and founder of Dulwich College.

Al-Mamun (813–33), caliph of Baghdad, son of Harun-al-Rashid. He built an observatory at Baghdad where observations were long recorded.

Ampère, André Marie (1775–1836), French physicist who propounded the theory that magnetism is the result of molecular electric currents. The unit of electric current is named after him.

Amundsen, Roald (1872–1928), Norwegian explorer, the first to navigate the north-west passage and to reach the south pole. Sailing in the fishing smack *Gjoa*, he made the north-west passage in 3 years, 1903–6, and in 1911 sailed to the Antarctic in the *Fram*, reaching the pole on 14 December 1911, a month before his English rival Scott. His attempt to rescue Nobile after

his crash in the airship *Italia* cost him his life.

Anacreon (c. 569–475 B.C.), Greek lyric poet.

Anaxagoras (488–428 B.C.), Ionian philosopher who came to Athens 464 B.C. and inspired Pericles and the poet Euripides with his love of science. His rational theories outraged religious opinion.

Anaximander (611–547 B.C.), Miletan philosopher, pupil of Thales, the first among the Greeks to make geographical maps, and to speculate on the origin of the heavenly bodies. He introduced the sundial from Babylon or Egypt.

Anaximenes (b. c. 570 B.C.), the last of the Miletan school founded by Thales. For him the primal substance was air. He was the first to see the differences between substances in quantitative terms.

Andersen, Hans Christian (1805–75), Danish writer, especially of fairy tales such as *The Little Mermaid* and *The Ugly Duckling*.

Anderson, Elizabeth Garrett (1836–1917), one of the first English women to enter the medical profession. She practised in London for many years and later became mayor of Aldeburgh, her native town, the first woman to hold the office of mayor. Sister of **Millicent Garrett Fawcett**.

Andrea del Sarto (1487–1531), Italian painter, b. Florence, the son of a tailor. Known as the "faultless painter," his chief works are the frescoes of the Annunziata at Florence and his Holy Families. He died of the plague.

Andrée, Salomon August (1854–97), Swedish explorer who attempted in 1897 to reach the north pole by balloon. In 1930 a Norwegian scientific expedition discovered the remains of the Andrée expedition on White Island.

Andrew, St., one of the apostles of Jesus, brother of Simon Peter, whose festival is observed on 30 November. He became the patron saint of Scotland in the 8th cent.

Andrewes, Sir Christopher (1896–1988), British medical researcher. Prominent virologist. Helped discover the common cold virus. Director, World Influenza Centre until 1961.

Andropov, Yuri Vladimirovich (1914–84), Russian statesman. Counsellor, subsequently Ambassador, to Hungary, 1953–7. Chairman, State Security Committee (K.G.B.), 1967–82. Succeeded Brezhnev as Secretary-General of C.P.S.U., 1982; State President, 1983–84.

Angelico, Fra (1387–1455), Italian painter. An exquisite colourist, Fra Giovanni (his Dominican name) painted especially religious frescoes, mainly at Florence and Rome.

Ångström, Anders Jöns (1814–74), Swedish physicist who studied heat, magnetism, and spectroscopy; hence the ångström unit used for measuring the wavelength of light.

Anne, Queen (1665–1714), Queen of Gt. Britain and Ireland. A daughter of James II, she succeeded William III in 1702. The act of union with Scotland was passed in 1707. A well-intentioned woman without marked ability, she was influenced by favourites, at first by the Duchess of Marlborough, but in the main she was guided by Tory and high church principles (she established Queen Anne's Bounty to improve church finances). Her reign was notable for literary output (Swift, Pope, Addison, Steele, Defoe), developments in science (Newton), architecture (Wren, Vanbrugh), and for the Duke of Marlborough's victories in war.

Anouilh, Jean (1910–87), French dramatist, whose plays with various settings—classical, historical and contemporary—include *Eurydice*, *Antigone*, *The Lark*, *Becket*, *The Fighting Cock*.

Anselm, St. (1033–1109), Italian scholar who succeeded Lanfranc as archbishop of Canterbury.

Anson, 1st Baron (George Anson) (1697–1762), English admiral who sailed round the world 1740–44, his squadron being reduced during the voyage from seven ships to one. An account was compiled by his chaplain.

Antoninus Pius (86–161), Roman emperor, successor of Hadrian. In his reign, which was peaceful, the Antonine wall between the Forth and the Clyde was built to protect Britain from northern attack.

Antonius Marcus (Mark Antony) (c. 83–30 B.C.), Roman triumvir. He supported Caesar, and after the latter's death was opposed by Brutus and Cassius, and defeated by Octavian; committed suicide. His association with the Egyptian queen Cleopatra is the subject of Shakespeare's play.

Antony, St. (c. 251–356), early promoter of the monastic life. B. in Upper Egypt, he retired into the desert, where he was tempted, but attracted disciples and founded a monastery. Took part in the Council of Nicaea 325. (From his supposed help against erysipelas derives its name of St. Antony's fire.)

Apelles, 4th cent. B.C., Greek painter whose chief paintings, which have not survived, were of Alexander the Great holding a thunderbolt and of Aphrodite rising from the sea.

Apollinaire, Guillaume (Wilhelm Apollinaris Kostrowitzi) (1880–1918), French poet representative of the restless and experimental period in the arts before the first world war. He invented the term *surrealism* (*see* **Section L**).

Apollonius of Perga (fl. 220 B.C.), Greek mathematician of the Alexandrian school, remembered for his conic sections; introduced the terms *ellipse, parabola,* and *hyperbola.*

Apollonius Rhodius (fl. 250 B.C.), scholar and poet of Alexandria and Rhodes, librarian at Alexandria. His epic *Argonautica* is about the Argonaut heroes.

Appert, Nicholas (1752–1841), sometimes known as François Appert, invented the method of preserving animal and vegetable foods by means of hermetically sealed cans or tins, and paved the way for the creation of a vast world industry.

Appleton, Sir Edward Victor (1892–1965), English physicist, best known as the discoverer of the ionised region of the upper atmosphere which became known as the Appleton layer. His researches led to the development of radar. Nobel prizewinner 1947.

Aquinas, Thomas, St. (*c.* 1225–74), scholastic philosopher and Dominican friar of Italian birth, whose philosophico-theological system (called Thomism) is still accepted by Catholic ecclesiastics. He understood Aristotle well and interpreted his thought in accord with Christian teaching. His most important works are *Summa contra Gentiles* and *Summa theologica.*

Arafat, Yasser (b. 1929), Palestinian leader. The acknowledged leader of the PLO (Palestine Liberation Organization). Shared Nobel Peace Prize for his efforts to secure agreement with Israel (*see* **Section C**).

Arago, Dominique François Jean (1786–1853), French astronomer and physicist, remembered for discoveries in electromagnetism and optics.

Archimedes (287–212 B.C.), Greek mathematician, b. Syracuse, son of an astronomer; remembered for his contributions to pure mathematics, mechanics, and hydrostatics, notably the Archimedean screw for raising water, the conception of specific gravity, the doctrine of levers, and the measurement of curved areas. Not less than his scientific knowledge was his practical skill. He was killed by the Romans in the siege of Syracuse.

Argand, Aimé (1755–1803), Swiss physician, inventor of the lamp bearing his name, which was the first to admit a current of air to increase the power of the flame, by use of a chimney glass and circular wick.

Ariosto, Ludovico (1474–1533), Italian poet, author of *Orlando Furioso.*

Aristides (d. *c.* 468 B.C.), Athenian general and statesman, called "the just"; fought at Marathon.

Aristippus (*c.* 435–356 B.C.), founder of the Cyrenaic school of philosophy. He taught that man should aim at pleasure, but held that the pleasant was identical with the good.

Aristophanes (*c.* 444–*c.* 385 B.C.), Greek dramatist and comic poet, who satirised Athenian life. Among his plays are *The Clouds* and *The Birds.*

Aristotle (384–322 B.C.), Greek philosopher, pupil of Plato, after whose death in 347 he left Athens to become tutor to the young prince Alexander of Macedon. Subsequently at Athens he established his famous school in the garden known as the *Lyceum,* where he lectured in the *peripatos* (cloister) which gave his school of philosophy its name *Peripatetic.* He took the whole field of knowledge as his subject, giving it unity, and providing a philosophy which long held its own.

Arkwright, Sir Richard (1732–92), English inventor. A native of Preston, and originally a barber, he experimented with cotton-spinning machines. His "water frame" (run by water power), patented in 1769, was an early step in the industrial revolution. In 1790 he made use of Boulton and Watt's steam-engine. Rioters sacked one of his mills in 1779.

Armstrong, Neil (b. 1930), US astronaut, the first man to set foot on the moon, 21 July 1969.

Arne, Thomas Augustine (1710–78), English composer, remembered for *Rule, Britannia!* (from a masque called *Alfred*), and for Shakespearean songs such as *Where the Bee Sucks.* He also wrote operas (women singers appeared in *Judith* in 1761) and oratorios.

Arnold, Thomas (1795–1842), English headmaster, whose influence at Rugby (1828–42) gave it a high position among public schools.

Arrhenius, Svante August (1859–1927), Swedish chemist, a founder of modern physical chemistry. Received 1903 Nobel prize for the theory of electrolytic dissociation (ionisation).

Artaxerxes, the name borne by several ancient Persian kings. The first Artaxerxes, son of Xerxes, reigned 464–424 B.C.; he was succeeded by Darius II 424–404 B.C., who was followed by Artaxerxes II, who reigned until 358 B.C. Artaxerxes III, the last to bear the name, was a treacherous man and was poisoned in 338 B.C.

Arthur (*c.* 500), fabled Celtic warrior, whose feats, although referred to in passing in early Celtic writings, were first narrated in Geoffrey of Monmouth's *Historia* (*c.* 1135). In mediaeval times his legend developed an extensive literature, woven together by Sir Thomas Malory in his *Morte d'Arthur,* printed in 1485.

Arundel, Thomas (1353–1414), archbishop of Canterbury 1396, and for a time lord chancellor. An enemy of heresy, he persecuted the Lollards.

Ashdown, Paddy (b. 1941), Leader of the Social and Liberal Democrats since 1988. M.P. Yeovil, 1983–

Asimov, Isaac (1920–92), Russian-born American scientist and author, who wrote almost five hundred works, including science fiction (*e.g., The Foundation* trilogy, 1952–53), and scientific, literary and religious textbooks, guides and reference books (*e.g., The Intelligent Man's Guide to Science,* 1960; *Asimov's Guide to the Bible,* 1969–70; *Asimov's Guide to Shakespeare,* 1970).

Aske, Robert, (*c.* 1500–37), leader of the Pilgrimage of Grace 1536, directed against the Henrician Reformation; executed 1537.

Asoka (*c.* 269–232 B.C.), Indian emperor and upholder of Buddhism. At first he expanded his empire by conquest, but on being converted to Buddhism rejected war and aimed at the good of his people. He sent Buddhist missionaries as far as Sri Lanka and Syria. Art flourished. Many rock inscriptions commemorate his doings.

Asquith, Herbert Henry, 1st Earl of Oxford and Asquith (1852–1928), Liberal prime minister 1908–16, having previously served under Gladstone. His government enacted social reforms including old-age pensions (1908) and unemployment insurance (1911), but as a war minister he had to give way to Lloyd George. He resigned leadership of his party in 1926. His daughter **Violet** (1887–1969) was an eloquent speaker.

Asser, a Welsh monk of the 9th cent., traditionally author of a life of King Alfred.

Astor, John Jacob (1763–1848), founder of the millionaire family, was a native of Heidelberg, emigrated to America, and made a fortune by trading in fur.

Astor, Viscountess (Nancy Witcher Astor, *née* Langhorne) (1879–1964), the first woman M.P. to take her seat in the Commons. An American by birth, wife of the 2nd Viscount Astor.

Atatürk, Kemal (1881–1938), builder of modern Turkey. A fine soldier, he defended the Dardanelles against the British in 1915 and drove the Greeks out of Turkey in 1922. President of the Turkish Republic, and virtually dictator, 1923–38.

Athanasius, St. (296–373), upholder of the doctrine of the Trinity against Arius, who denied the divinity of Christ. He was bishop of Alexandria. He is not now thought the author of the creed which bears his name.

Athelstan (895–940), grandson of Alfred the Great, was crowned king of England in 925, and was the first ruler of all England.

Attenborough, Sir David (b. 1926), British traveller and zoologist. Commentator in TV series *Life on Earth* (1979) and *The Living Planet* (1983). His latest TV series, *The Private Life of Plants* (1995) received great acclaim. His brother **Lord Attenborough** (b. 1923) is an actor, film producer and director (*e.g. Gandhi,* 1982).

Attila (406–53), invading king of the Huns from Asia. He defeated the Roman Emperor

Theodosius, and entered Gaul, but was defeated in 451 near Châlons-sur-Marne.

Attlee, 1st Earl (Clement Richard Attlee) (1883–1967), Labour prime minister 1945–51, having served as deputy to Churchill 1942–5. Called to the Bar in 1905, he lectured at the London School of Economics 1913–23, was mayor of Stepney 1919, and parliamentary leader of his party 1935–55. His government helped to create a welfare society and granted independence to India.

Auchinleck, Sir Claude John Eyre (1884–1981), British field-marshal; G.O.C. North Norway 1940; C.-in-C. India 1941, 1943–7; Middle East 1941–2.

Auden, Wystan Hugh (1907–73), poet, b. in England and naturalised an American. Succeeded C. Day Lewis as professor of poetry at Oxford 1956–61.

Auer, Leopold (1845–1930), Hungarian violinist and teacher; Mischa Elman and Jascha Heifetz were among his pupils.

Augustine of Canterbury, St. (d. c. 605), first archbishop of Canterbury. He was sent from Rome in 597 by Gregory the Great to convert the English peoples.

Augustus, Caius Octavianus (63 B.C.–A.D. 14), first Roman emperor. Great-nephew of Julius Caesar, he was for 12 years triumvir with Mark Antony and Lepidus; then reigned alone. His reign was notable for peace, and for writers like Horace and Virgil; hence Augustan age for a great period in literature (the title Augustus was given him by the Senate).

Aurelius, Marcus Antonius. *See* **Marcus Aurelius Antoninus.**

Auriol, Vincent (1884–1966), French politician. President of the Fourth Republic 1947–54.

Aurangzeb (1618–1707), Mogul emperor of India. Son of Shah Jehan, he obtained power by acting against his father and brothers. In his long reign the Mogul empire reached its fullest extent; but he estranged Hindus and Sikhs; and when he died his authority was in dispute and the Mogul empire broke up.

Austen, Jane (1775–1817), author of *Emma, Mansfield Park, Northanger Abbey, Persuasion, Pride and Prejudice,* and *Sense and Sensibility.* Though confining herself to the personal relations of the English middle classes, she combined artistry, accuracy, imaginative power, satiric humour, sense, and genuine feeling with the ability to create a range of living characters. She spent the first 25 years of her life at her father's Hampshire rectory. She was unmarried.

Austin, 1st Baron (Herbert Austin) (1886–1941), English motor manufacturer, pioneer of the small car—the 7-horsepower car—which he put on the market in 1921.

Avenzoar (Ibn Zuhr) (c. 1090–1162), Arab physician, b. Seville. His chief work was the *Tasir.*

Averroës (Ibn Rushd) (1126–98), Arab philosopher, b. Córdova. He believed in the eternity of the world (not as a single act of creation as demanded by the current theology of Islam, Christianity and Judaism, but as a continuous process) and in the eternity of a universal intelligence, indivisible but shared in by all. He expounded Aristotle to his countrymen, but his teaching was modified by Neoplatonism.

Avicenna (Ali ibn-Sina) (980–1037), Arab philosopher and physician, of Bukhara, whose influence on mediaeval Europe was chiefly through his *Canon of Medicine,* in which he attempted to systematise all the medical knowledge up to his time.

Avogadro, Amedeo (1776–1856), Italian physicist, remembered for his hypothesis, since known as Avogadro's Law, that equal volumes of gases under identical conditions of temperature and pressure contain the same number of molecules.

Avon, Earl of. *See* **Eden, Anthony.**

Ayrton, William Edward (1847–1908), English electrical engineer, inventor of a number of electrical measuring instruments. His first wife, **Matilda Chaplin Ayrton** (1846–83), was one of the first woman doctors, and his second wife, **Hertha Ayrton** (1854–1923), became known for her scientific work on the electric arc and sand ripples and for her work for woman suffrage.

Ayub Khan, Mohammed (1907–74), Pakistani military leader; president of Pakistan, 1958–69.

Azikiwe, Nnamdi (b. 1904), Nigerian statesman;

president of Nigeria, 1963–6.

B

Babbage, Charles (1801–71), British mathematician. He designed an analytical engine, the forerunner of the modern digital computer.

Baber, Babar or Babur (Zahir ud-din Mohammed) (1483–1530), founder of the Mogul dynasty which ruled northern India for nearly three centuries; a descendant of Tamerlane.

Bach, Johann Sebastian (1685–1750), composer. B. at Eisenach, Germany, he was successively violinist, church organist, and chief court musician. It was as organist at the Thomaskirche, Leipzig, that he composed the St. Matthew and the St. John Passion and the B minor Mass. His work was in the school of the contrapuntal style (especially the fugue and the chorale); after his day it lost favour, but this century it has gained ground continually.

Bach, Carl Philipp Emanuel (1714–88), 3rd son of the above, and one of the first experimenters in the symphonic and sonata forms.

Backhaus, Wilhelm (1884–1969), German pianist, gifted in interpreting classical and romantic concertos.

Bacon, Francis, Lord Verulam (1561–1626), English philosopher. He threw over Aristotelian deductive logic for the inductive method (*see* **Baconian method, Section J**); remembered for the impulse his writings gave to the foundation of the Royal Society (c. 1662). His chief work is the *Novum Organum.* His career as statesman under Elizabeth and James I was brought to an end by charges of corruption.

Bacon, Francis (1909–92), Dublin-born artist. A realist who depicted the complexity of human emotions (*e.g.* his *Study after Velazquez* of 1953).

Bacon, Roger (c. 1219/20–94), founder of English philosophy, advocate of the value of observation and experiment in science. He first studied arts at Oxford but when he returned from lecturing in Paris he devoted himself to experimental science, especially alchemy and optics. He became a Franciscan friar in 1257.

Baden-Powell, 1st Baron (Robert Stephenson Smyth Baden-Powell) (1857–1941), founder of Boy Scouts (1908) and Girl Guides (1910) to promote good citizenship in the rising generation; Chief Scout of the World 1921–41. As a young cavalry officer in the South African war he defended Mafeking.

Baer, Karl Ernst von (1792–1876), German naturalist, b. Estonia, founder of the science of embryology. He discovered the mammalian ovum (1827). An opponent of Darwin's theory.

Baffin, William (1584–1622), British navigator and explorer who in 1616 discovered the bay which separates the north-east coast of Canada from Greenland, which bears his name.

Bagehot, Walter (1826–77), English economist and journalist, editor of *The Economist.* Among his works are *The English Constitution, Physics and Politics,* and *Lombard Street.*

Baird, John Logie (1888–1946), Scottish television pioneer, inventor of the televisor and the noctovisor.

Baker, Sir Benjamin (1840–1907), English civil engineer. With Sir John Fowler he built the Forth bridge and the London Metropolitan railway. He designed the vessel which brought Cleopatra's Needle to London. In Egypt he was consulting engineer for the Aswan dam.

Baker, Sir Herbert (1862–1946), English architect who designed the Bank of England, Rhodes House, Oxford, and, with Sir E. Lutyens, New Delhi.

Bakst, Léon (1868–1924), Russian painter who designed scenery and costumes for Diaghilev's ballets.

Baldwin of Bewdley, 1st Earl (Stanley Baldwin) (1867–1947), Conservative prime minister, 1923–4, 1924–9, and 1935–7. His handling of the crisis over Edward VIII's proposed marriage ended with the king's abdication.

Balewa, Sir Abubakar Tafawa (1912–66), federal prime minister of Nigeria, 1960–6; murdered during the crisis of January 1966.

Balfour, 1st Earl (Arthur James Balfour) (1848–1930), statesman and writer. He was Conservative prime minister 1902–5. As foreign secretary under Lloyd George, he was responsible for a declaration on Palestine.

Ball, John (d. 1381), English priest and a leader of the Peasants' Revolt, after which he was executed. The couplet *When Adam delved, and Eve span, Who was then the gentleman?* is attributed to him.

Balladur, Edouard, (b 1929), French centre-right politician. Prime Minister, March 1993–. Unsuccessful candidate for President, 1995.

Balliol, John de (d. 1269), founder of Balliol College, Oxford; a regent for Scotland; sided with Henry III against his barons.

Balliol, John de (1249–1315), king of Scotland. Son of the above, he claimed the throne against Robert Bruce and was chosen by the arbitrator, Edward I of England, whose overlordship he acknowledged. Later, on renouncing homage, he was taken captive and d. in retirement. His son Edward Balliol (d. 1363) obtained the kingdom for a time, acknowledging Edward III of England and surrendering Lothian; but retired on an annuity, 1356.

Balzac, Honoré de (1799–1850), French novelist of wide influence, and author of over eighty novels to which he gave the covering title of *La Comédie Humaine,* depicting the appetites and passions of the new social class born of the revolution and Napoleon.

Bancroft, Sir Squire (1841–1926), Victorian actor-manager.

Bandaranaike, Solomon West Ridgway Dias (1899–1959), socialist prime minister of Ceylon from 1956 until his assassination. His widow, **Mrs Sirimavo Bandaranaike,** became the world's first woman premier, 1960–5, 1970–7 and again after 1994, while his daughter, **Chandrika Bandaranaike Kumaratunga,** (b. 1945) has been president of Sri Lanka since 1994.

Banks, Sir Joseph (1743–1820), an amateur scientist of wealth who accompanied Captain Cook on his expedition to the Pacific 1768–76.

Banting, Sir Frederick Grant (1891–1941), Canadian physician who with C. H. Best discovered insulin.

Bantock, Sir Granville (1868–1946), composer of songs, orchestral and choral music.

Barbarossa (Ital. = red beard), surname of two brothers who were Barbary pirates: **Uruz** (*c.* 1474–1518), was killed by Spaniards, and **Khaireddin** (*c.* 1483–1546) conquered Tunis for the Turks and died in Constantinople.

Barbirolli, Sir John (1899–1970), conductor of the Hallé Orchestra 1943–70; succeeded Toscanini as conductor of the New York Philharmonic Symphony Orchestra 1937–42.

Barbusse, Henri (1874–1935), French writer, author of the war novel *Le Feu,* which portrays in a starkly vivid way the experience of the common soldier.

Barham, Richard Harris (1788–1845), English humorist, author of *The Ingoldsby Legends,* written under his pen-name of Thomas Ingoldsby. His best-known poem is *The Jackdaw of Rheims.*

Barnardo, Thomas John (1845–1905), founder of homes for orphan-waifs; devoted himself to the protection, education, and advancement of destitute children.

Barrie, Sir James Matthew (1860–1937), Scottish author and dramatist. His novels include *A Window in Thrums.* Among his plays are *Dear Brutus, The Admirable Crichton,* and *Peter Pan* which gained great popularity with children.

Barrow, Isaac (1630–77), divine and mathematician, tutor of Sir Isaac Newton.

Barry, Sir Charles (1795–1860), architect of the houses of parliament at Westminster, the details of which were contributed by his assistant A. W. Pugin.

Barth, Karl (1886–1968), Swiss theologian, described by the late Pope John as a Protestant St. Thomas Aquinas.

Bartók, Bela (1881–1945), Hungarian composer. From an early age he was deeply interested in folk-song which inspired his researches into Hungarian and Rumanian peasant music. He left for America in 1940, where he lived precariously and apparently unhappily until the end of the war made a return possible, regrettably too late. *See Section E.*

Bartolommeo, Fra (di Paolo) (1475–1517), Italian painter. At first influenced by Savonarola, he later resumed painting. Some of his best work

is at Lucca.

Bartolozzi, Francesco (1725–1815), Italian engraver, who settled in England and became a founder-member of the Royal Academy; noted for his stipple engravings.

Bashkirtseva, Maria Konstantinovna (1859–84), a Russian girl, achieved eminence as a painter in Paris, author of a famous diary.

Bassi, Agostino (1773–1856), Italian amateur microscopist who first suggested that infectious diseases might be caused by the invasion of the body by micro-organisms.

Batten, Jean Gardiner (1909–82), New Zealand airwoman who flew solo from England to Australia in 1934.

Baudelaire, Charles Pierre (1821–67), French poet of originality and sensitivity, best known for his *Les Fleurs du Mal.* His life was darkened by poverty and ill-health. He was also a talented draughtsman.

Bax, Sir Arnold (1883–1953), composer and Master of the King's Musick 1942–52. One of his best-known works is the poem, *Tintagel* (1917).

Baxter, Richard (1615–91), noncomformist divine, b. Shropshire; author of many books on theology; imprisoned after the Restoration by Judge Jeffreys.

Bayard, Pierre de Terrail, Seigneur de (*c.* 1474–1524), French knight, known as the "chevalier sans peur et sans reproche." He fought in campaigns against Italy and fell at the battle of Romagnano.

Bayle, Pierre (1647–1706), French philosopher, author of the *Dictionnaire historique et critique* (1697). His sceptical views influenced Voltaire and the encyclopedists of the 18th cent.

Baylis, Lilian Mary (1874–1937), manager of the Old Vic theatre from 1898 and of Sadler's Wells from 1931.

Beardsley, Aubrey Vincent (1872–98), black-and-white artist, who published much work, some of it controversial (as in the *Yellow Book*).

Beatles, The (Paul McCartney (b. 1942), John Lennon (1940–80), George Harrison (b. 1943), Ringo Starr (b. 1940)), a Liverpool pop group whose highly original and melodic songs held the attention of youth all over the world, especially during the period 1963–5 when they were in their prime. They parted in 1971 and went their separate ways. Lennon was shot dead in New York in 1980.

Beatty, 1st Earl (David Beatty) (1871–1936), British admiral; succeeded Jellicoe as commander of the Grand Fleet 1916–19. Commanding the British battlecruisers, he fought the German fleet on 28 August 1914 in the Heligoland Bight, and on 31 May 1916 off Jutland.

Beaufort, Sir Francis (1774–1857), hydrographer of the navy, who introduced the wind scale (1805) which bears his name. *See Section Z.*

Beaumont, Francis (1584–1616), and **Fletcher, John** (1579–1625), joint authors of many plays, including *The Maid's Tragedy* and *Philaster.*

Beaverbrook, 1st Baron (William Maxwell Aitken) (1879–1964), British newspaper owner and politician, a Canadian by birth. He gave energetic service as minister of aircraft production 1940–1. He controlled the *Daily Express, Sunday Express,* and *Evening Standard.*

Becket, Thomas (1118?–70), saint and martyr. An able chancellor, 1155–62, on becoming archbishop of Canterbury he made the position of the church his first care; and, coming into conflict with Henry II, was murdered in Canterbury cathedral. His shrine became a place of pilgrimage.

Beckett, Samuel (1906–89), Anglo-Irish dramatist and novelist, b. Dublin. Plays include *Waiting for Godot, Endgame, Krapp's Last Tape, Happy Days, Not I*; novels include *The Nouvelles* (3 stories), the trilogy: *Molloy, Malone Dies, The Unnamable,* and *How It Is.* His work expresses man's isolation, bewilderment and suffering. Nobel Prize for Literature, 1969.

Becquerel, Antoine Henri (1852–1908), French physicist who in 1896 discovered radioactivity in uranium. Shared with the Curies the 1903 Nobel prize in physics.

Bede, the Venerable (673–735), English historian and scholar; lived at Jarrow. His chief work is his *Ecclesiastical History* to 731.

Beecham, Sir Thomas (1879–1961), English conductor and impresario. Founded the London Philharmonic Orchestra in 1931; introduced into England the operas of Richard Strauss, Russian operas, and the Diaghilev ballet;

championed the music of Delius.

Beecher, Henry Ward (1813–87), American preacher whose church was at Brooklyn.

Beerbohm, Sir Max (1872–1956), critic and caricaturist, master of irony and satire. His works include *Zuleika Dobson* and *A Christmas Garland*, and he contributed to the *Saturday Review*.

Beethoven, Ludwig van (1770–1827), composer. B. at Bonn (his father being a tenor singer at the Elector's court), at 17 he went to Vienna, was recognised by Mozart, and eventually settled there; he never married; gradually he became deaf. In the development from simplicity to complexity of musical treatment, he stands midway between Mozart and Wagner; but in him were uniquely combined the power to feel and the mastery of musical resources necessary to express his feelings. Between the years 1805 and 1808 he composed some of his greatest works: the oratorio *Mount of Olives*, the opera *Fidelio*, and the *Pastoral* and *Eroica* symphonies besides a number of concertos, sonatas, and songs. The symphonies, nine in number, rank as the greatest ever written. *See* Section E.

Begin, Menachem (1913–92), b. Poland; active in Zionist movement since youth; leader of Israeli *Likud* party; prime minister 1977–83. Made peace with Egypt (1979) but failed to solve Palestinian problem; took Israel into war in Lebanon (1982) which led to the end of his premiership and to renewed conflict in that country.

Behring, Emil von (1854–1917), German bacteriologist, founder of the science of immunology. Nobel prizewinner 1901.

Behring, Vitus (1680–1741), Danish navigator who entered the Russian service and in 1728 discovered the strait which bears his name.

Belisarius (505–65), Roman general under Justinian who fought against the Vandals.

Bell, Alexander Graham (1847–1922), inventor, b. Edinburgh, emigrated to Canada in 1870, later becoming an American citizen. In 1876 he exhibited an invention which was developed into the telephone. He devoted attention to the education of deaf-mutes.

Bell, Gertrude Margaret Lowthian (1868–1926), the "uncrowned queen of Arabia," was a traveller in the Middle East; her knowledge aided Britain in the first world war.

Bellini, family of Venetian painters: **Jacopo** (*c.* 1400–70) and his two sons, **Gentile** (1429–1507), whose works include the *Adoration of the Magi* (National Gallery); and **Giovanni** (*c.* 1429–1516), brother-in-law of Mantegna, and teacher of Giorgione and Titian.

Belloc, Hilaire (1870–1953), versatile writer whose works include *The Bad Child's Book of Beasts, The Path to Rome, Hills and the Sea, Cautionary Tales*, and historical studies of Danton, Robespierre, and Richelieu. B. in France, he became a British subject in 1902.

Bellow, Saul (b. 1915), American novelist and short-story writer, author of *Adventures of Augie March, Henderson the Rain King, Herzog, Mr. Sammler's Planet* and *Humboldt's Gift*. Nobel prize 1976.

Belzoni, Giovanni Battista (1778–1823), Egyptologist. B. at Padua, he settled in England in 1803. His first interest was in hydraulics, and for this purpose he went to Egypt to Mehemet Ali. There he explored Thebes, Abu Simbel, and one of the pyramids, sending some sculptures to the British Museum.

Benavente y Martinez, Jacinto (1866–1954), Spanish dramatist, whose plays include *Los Intereses Creados* (Bonds of Interest). Nobel prizewinner 1922.

Benedict, St. (*c.* 480–*c.* 550), patriarch of western monasticism. B. at Nursia, and at first a hermit at Subiaco, he attracted numerous followers and grouped them in twelve monasteries. Later he went to Monte Cassino, where he formulated the Benedictine rule, of wide application in Western Christendom.

Beneš, Eduard (1884–1948), Czechoslovak statesman; co-founder with Thomas Masaryk of the Czech Republic after the break-up of the Austro-Hungarian monarchy (1918).

Ben Gurion, David (1886–1973), Zionist leader. He helped organise the Jewish Legion in 1918, and was prominently connected with the Labour movement in Palestine in between the world wars. Prime minister of Israel 1948–63.

Bennett, (Enoch) Arnold (1867–1931), English author, who wrote of the pottery towns where he was brought up. His novels include *Clayhanger* and *Hilda Lessways*.

Bennett, James Gordon (1841–1918), proprietor of the *New York Herald*. He sent out Stanley on an expedition to find Livingstone.

Bennett, Sir William Sterndale (1816–75), English composer, pianist and teacher, best known for his oratorio *The Woman of Samaria*, songs and piano pieces. Founded the Bach Society.

Bentham, Jeremy (1748–1832), utilitarian philosopher and writer on jurisprudence. His main works are *Government* and *Principles of Morals and Legislation*.

Bentley, Richard (1662–1742), classical scholar who did pioneer work in textual criticism.

Benz, Karl (1844–1929), German engineer whose motor car produced in 1885 was one of the first to be driven by an internal combustion engine.

Beresford, 1st Viscount (William Carr Beresford) (1768–1854), British general. He fought under Wellington in the Peninsular War and reorganised the Portuguese army.

Berg, Alban (1885–1935), Austrian composer whose best-known work is the three-act opera *Wozzeck*, based upon a drama by Büchner, which has become a modern classic.

Bergson, Henri Louis (1859–1941). French philosopher, exponent of the theory of creative evolution and the life force. Nobel prizewinner 1927. *See* Vitalism, Section J.

Bériot, Charles Auguste de (1802–70), Belgian violinist, whose wife was the operatic contralto Malibran. His son, **Charles Wilfrid de Bériot** (1833–1914) was a pianist who taught Ravel.

Berkeley, George (1685–1753), idealist philosopher and critic of Locke. His spiritual outlook led him to believe that reality exists only in the eye of God, that it is undiscoverable by science, though it can be revealed by religion. His chief works are *A New Theory of Vision* (1709) and *Principles of Human Knowledge* (1710). Of Irish birth, he became bishop of Cloyne.

Berlin, Irving (1888–1989), American composer of popular songs, b. Russia; pioneer of both ragtime and jazz music.

Berlin, Sir Isaiah (b. 1909), British philosopher, b. Riga; Chichele Prof. of Social and Political Theory at Oxford 1957–67. His works include *Karl Marx, The Hedgehog and the Fox*, and *The Age of Enlightenment*. O.M. (1971). A biography by John Gray appeared in 1995.

Berlioz, Hector (1803–69), composer. B. near Grenoble, the son of a doctor, his romantic sensibility, taste for the grand (as in his *Requiem*), and response to literary influence made him a prime figure in the French romantic movement. His works include the symphony *Romeo and Juliet*, and the operas *Benvenuto Cellini* and *Beatrice and Benedict*. *See* Section E.

Bernadotte, Count Folke (1895–1948), nephew of the late King Gustav of Sweden. U.N. mediator for Palestine 1947. Assassinated by Jewish terrorists.

Bernadotte, Jean Baptiste (1764–1844), a French commander who served under Napoleon, and in 1810 was chosen heir to the throne of Sweden. In 1818 he succeeded as Charles XIV.

Bernal, John Desmond (1901–71), physicist, b. Ireland. Prof. of Physics, Birkbeck College, Univ. of London, 1937–63, Prof of Crystallography, 1963–8. Author of *The Social Functions of Science, Science in History, The Origin of Life*. Lenin peace prize 1953.

Bernard, Claude (1813–78), French physiologist whose discoveries eventually paved the way for the work of Pavlov and Hopkins.

Bernard of Menthon (923–1008), patron saint of mountaineers. He founded Alpine hospices in the passes that bear his name.

Bernard, St. (1090–1153), abbot of Clairvaux, which became a chief centre of the Cistercian order. This order aimed at seclusion and austerity, and practised manual work. His writings had wide influence in Europe.

Bernhardt, Sarah (1844–1923), French tragedienne, b. Paris, daughter of Dutch jewess. She became a member of the Comédie Française after the siege of Paris. Her first performance in London was in 1879. Her successes included *Phèdre, La Dame aux Camélias, Fédora, Théodora*, and *La Tosca*.

Bernini, Gian Lorenzo (1598–1680), Italian baroque sculptor. Born Naples. Did much work in Rome, designing the piazza for St. Peters.

Bernstein, Leonard (1918–90), Popular American composer, conductor and pianist. His scores for musicals included *Candide* (1956) and *West Side Story* (1957).

Berthelot, Marcellin Pierre Eugène (1827–1907), French chemist and politician. The first to produce organic compounds synthetically.

Berzelius, Jöns Jakob (1779–1848), Swedish chemist, founder of electrochemical theory. His work was mainly concerned with the exact determination of atomic and molecular weights and he devised the system of chemical symbols in use today.

Bessemer, Sir Henry (1813–98), inventor of the process of converting cast-iron direct into steel. This revolutionised steel manufacture, reducing the cost of production and extending its use.

Best, Charles Herbert (1899–1978), Canadian physiologist, who with F. G. Banting discovered the use of insulin in the treatment of diabetes.

Betjeman, Sir John (1906–84), English poet, author and broadcaster; Poet Laureate, 1972–84.

Bevan, Aneurin (1897–1960), British socialist politician, architect of the National Health Service which came into operation in 1948.

Beveridge, 1st Baron (William Henry Beveridge) (1879–1963), British economist who drew up the Beveridge Plan (1942), which formed the basis of the present social security services.

Bevin, Ernest (1881–1951), British trade union leader, who later became a forceful foreign secretary. He was assistant general secretary of the Dockers Union (his masterly advocacy of the London dockers' case in 1920 earned him the title of "the dockers' K.C."), later general secretary of the Transport and General Workers Union; Minister of Labour 1940–5, and Foreign Secretary 1945–51.

Beyle, Marie Henri. *See* Stendhal.

Bhave, Vinova (b. 1895), Indian reformer, leader of the Sarvodaya movement. A follower of Gandhi, in 1951 he began a walking mission to persuade landlords to help landless peasants.

Bichat, Marie François Xavier (1771–1802), French physiologist whose study of tissues founded modern histology. His theory was that life is "the sum of the forces that restrict death."

Biddle, John (1615–62), unitarian. He taught in Gloucester: was several times imprisoned for his controversial writings; and died of fever contracted in prison.

Binyon, Laurence (1869–1943), poet, art critic, and orientalist, who worked at the British Museum 1893–1933.

Birch, Samuel John Lamorna (1869–1955), English landscape painter in watercolour, known for his Cornish and Australian studies.

Birkbeck, George (1776–1841), founder of mechanics' institutes, first at Glasgow, later in London (the Birkbeck Institution developed into Birkbeck College, London University).

Birkenhead, 1st Earl of (Frederick Edwin Smith) (1872–1930), English lawyer and politician; lord chancellor 1919–22; secretary for India 1924–8.

Bishop, Sir Henry Rowley (1786–1855), English composer who wrote *Home, sweet Home*, glees, and operas.

Bismarck, Otto Eduard Leopold von, Prince Bismarck, Duke of Lauenburg (1815–98), Prusso-German diplomat and statesman, chief architect of the German empire. He was of Junker family. As Prussian ambassador at St. Petersburg (1859–62) and at Paris (1862), he learned to assess the European situation. He was recalled to Berlin by the king to become chief Prussian minister; and when the house of representatives would not pass a military bill he closed the house. He used a dispute over Schleswig-Holstein to bring about the defeat of Austria at Königgratz in 1866; and he provoked the Franco-Prussian war of 1870–1 when France was defeated at Sedan. Germany then became united under the military leadership of Prussia, with the king as emperor, instead of by the slower processes of democracy. He presided over the Berlin Congress of European powers in 1878. In 1884 he began a colonial policy. His authoritarian system, in spite of its inherent defects, was at least based on cautious and accurate assessment of power politics. This factor was not understood by

William II, who succeeded as emperor in 1888, and dismissed the "iron chancellor" in 1890.

Bizet, Georges (1838–75), properly **Alexandre César Léopold**, French composer, chiefly remembered for his opera *Carmen*.

Björnson, Björnstjerne (1832–1910), Norwegian poet, dramatist and novelist. His work provides an image of Norwegian life from the period of the sagas (*Kong Sverre*) to contemporary problems (*Over Aevne*).

Black, Sir James (b. 1924), Eminent British scientist. Discovered life-saving drug used to prevent heart attacks. Awarded Nobel Prize for Medicine, 1988.

Black, Joseph (1728–90), Scottish chemist. A professor first at Glasgow, later at Edinburgh, he was the first to undertake a detailed study of a chemical reaction. He laid the foundation of the quantitative science of heat and his discovery of latent heat was applied by Watt in improving his steam-engine.

Blackett of Chelsea, Baron (Patrick Maynard Stuart Blackett) (1897–1974), British physicist whose work on nuclear and cosmic ray physics gained him a Nobel prize in 1948; author of *Military and Political Consequences of Atomic Energy* (1948), *Lectures on Rock Magnetism* (1956), *Studies of War* (1962). Pres. British Assoc. 1956; Pres. Royal Society 1966–70; O.M. 1967.

Blackmore, Richard Doddridge (1825–1900), English novelist and author of *Lorna Doone*.

Blackstone, Sir William (1723–80), English judge. His *Commentaries on the Laws of England* is a classic.

Blackwood, Algernon (1869–1951), English novelist and writer of short stories.

Blackwood, William (1776–1834), originator of *Blackwood's Magazine*.

Blair, Robert (1699–1746), Scottish poet, author of *The Grave*.

Blair, Anthony Charles Lynton (b. 1953), Labour politician. Leader of the Labour Party since 1994 (following the death of John Smith). M.P. for Sedgefield, 1983–. Committed to a modernised Labour Party with a new constitution.

Blake, Robert (1599–1657), Parliamentary general and an admiral in the Cromwellian navy in the Dutch and Spanish wars.

Blake, William (1757–1827), English poet, mystic, and artist, son of a hosier in Carnaby market, Soho. A solitary and deeply religious man, he had a hatred of materialism. He produced his own books, engraving on copper plates both the text of his poems and the illustrations. His *Book of Job* is a masterpiece in line-engraving in metal, his poems range from the mystical and almost incomprehensible to the delightfully simple *Songs of Innocence*. He has been called "the great teacher of the modern western world." His art is in many ways reminiscent of that of the Spanish painter Goya.

Blanqui, Louis Auguste (1805–81), French revolutionary leader, master of insurrection. He invented the term "dictatorship of the proletariat," and his social theories, stressing the class struggle, influenced Marx. Active in 1830, 1848, and 1871, he spent 37 years in prison.

Blériot, Louis (1872–1936), French airman; the first to fly the English Channel from Calais to Dover, on 25 July 1909.

Bligh, William (1754–1817), sailor, b. Plymouth. He accompanied Cook 1772–4, and discovered bread-fruit; but was in 1789 cast adrift from *The Bounty* by his mutinous crew. As governor of New South Wales (1806) he fought to suppress the rum traffic.

Blind, Karl (1826–1907), German agitator, b. Mannheim. He was active in the German risings of 1848, and imprisoned; but escaped and settled in England, remaining in touch with men like Mazzini and Louis Blanc.

Bliss, Sir Arthur (1891–1975), English composer; succeeded Sir Arnold Bax as Master of the Queen's Musick 1953.

Bloch, Ernest (1880–1959), composer, whose music is characterised by Jewish and oriental themes. B. in Geneva, he became a naturalised American.

Blondin, Charles (1824–97), French rope performer, who crossed the Niagara Falls on a tight-rope.

Blücher, Gebhard Leberecht von (1742–1819), Prussian general. He fought against Napoleon, especially at Lützen and Leipzig; and he completed Wellington's victory at Waterloo by his timely arrival.

Blum, Léon (1872–1950), French statesman, leader of the French Socialist Party. His efforts strengthened the growth of the Popular Front and the campaign against appeasement of Hitler. He held office only briefly and was interned in Germany 1940–5.

Blumlein, Alan Dower (1903–42), British electronics engineer and inventor, chiefly remembered for his fundamental work on stereophony.

Blunden, Edmund Charles (1896–1974), English poet and critic; professor of poetry at Oxford 1966–8.

Blunt, Wilfrid Scawen (1840–1922), English poet and political writer who championed Egyptian, Indian, and Irish independence; imprisoned in 1888 for activities in the Irish Land League.

Blyton, Enid (1897–1968), enduringly popular writer of more than 700 children's books. A teacher in South London, she is perhaps best remembered for the 'Famous Five' books, the 'Secret Seven' adventures and, of course, Noddy.

Boadicea (Boudicca), queen of the Iceni in eastern Britain, who fought against the Roman invaders, but was defeated in A.D. 61 and killed herself. Archaeologists tentatively identified her palace at Gallows Hill, Thetford, Norfolk.

Boccaccio, Giovanni (1313–75), Italian author, father of the novel. He is chiefly known for his *Decameron* (set in the neighbourhood of Florence during the plague), and for his life of Dante.

Boccherini, Luigi (1743–1805), Italian cellist and composer of chamber music.

Bode, Johann Ehlert (1747–1826), German astronomer remembered for his theoretical calculation (known as Bode's law) of the proportionate distances of the planets from the sun.

Boethius (480–524), Roman scientific writer who translated the logical works of Aristotle and provided the dark ages with some elementary mathematical treatises.

Bohr, Niels Henrik David (1885–1962), Danish nuclear physicist whose researches into the structure of the atom gave him great authority in the world of theoretical physics. With Rutherford he applied the quantum theory to the study of atomic processes. Nobel prize 1922.

Boieldieu, François Adrien (1775–1834), French composer especially of operas, including *La Dame blanche*.

Boileau-Despréaux, Nicolas (1636–1711), French literary critic and poet, best known for his *Satires*.

Boito, Arrigo (1842–1918), Italian poet and composer; he wrote the libretti of *Otello* and *Falstaff* for Verdi.

Boleyn, Anne (1507–36), queen of Henry VIII and mother of Queen Elizabeth. She was maid-in-waiting to Catherine of Aragon and her successor when Catherine's marriage was annulled. She failed to produce a male heir and was beheaded on a charge of adultery.

Bolivar, Simón (1783–1830), South American revolutionary, called the Liberator, b. Carácas. He led independence movements in the north-west of South America against Spanish rule, aiming at a South American federation. He founded Grand Colombia (now Venezuela, Colombia, Panama, Ecuador). Revered as a Latin-American hero.

Bonaventura, St. (1221–74), Franciscan theologian, b. Orvieto. His mystical theory of knowledge was in the Augustinian tradition.

Bondfield, Margaret Grace (1873–1953), as minister of Labour, 1929–31, she was the first woman to enter the cabinet and become a privy councillor.

Bondi, Sir Hermann (b. 1919), British mathematician and astronomer, b. Vienna: chief scientist to Min. of Defence, 1971–7.

Bone, Sir Muirhead (1876–1953), architectural draughtsman and etcher, b. Glasgow; excelled in dry-point and drawings of intricate scaffolding; official war artist in both world wars.

Boniface, St. (680–754), apostle of Germany. B. at Crediton, Devon, his name being Wynfrith, he became a Benedictine monk, and went as missionary to Friesland, securing papal approval. He founded Fulda Abbey and became archbishop of Mainz, but was martyred.

Bonnard, Pierre (1867–1947), French painter of landscapes, still life, and nudes.

Booth, Edwin Thomas (1833–93), American Shakespearean actor, brother of John Wilkes Booth who assassinated President Lincoln.

Booth, William (1829–1912), founder and first general of the Salvation Army, b. Nottingham. In 1865, with the help of his wife, Catherine Booth, he began mission work in the East End of London, which led to the creation in 1878 of the Salvation Army on military lines. It developed branches in many parts of the world. His son Bramwell (d. 1929) and his daughter Evangeline were among his successors. *See also* **Salvation Army, Section J.**

Boothroyd, Betty, *see* **D16.**

Borges, Jorge Luis (1899–1986), Argentine poet, critic, and short story writer. Some of his work has been translated into English, including *A Personal Anthology* and *Labyrinths*.

Borgia, Caesar (1476–1507), Italian general. The son of Pope Alexander VI, at 17 he was suspected of murdering his brother. He became captain-general of the church, and made himself master of Romagna, the Marches, and Umbria. Banished by Pope Julius II he met his death fighting in Spain.

Borlaug, Norman Ernest (b. 1914), American wheat scientist, responsible for the "green revolution" which transformed agriculture in the less-developed countries of the world. Awarded Nobel prize for peace 1970.

Borodin, Alexander Porfyrievich (1833–87), Russian composer who taught chemistry and founded a school of medicine for women. In a busy professional life he wrote two symphonies, two string quartets, the symphonic sketch *In the Steppes of Central Asia* and the opera *Prince Igor*. *See* **Section E.**

Borrow, George Henry (1803–81), English author, for many years agent for the British and Foreign Bible Society; in the course of his wanderings he studied gypsy life and wrote of his experiences in *Lavengro*, *Romany Rye*, *Bible in Spain*.

Bose, Subhas Chandra (1897–1945), Indian nationalist leader; killed in a plane crash.

Boswell, James (1740–95), Scottish author of *The Life of Dr. Johnson*, with whom he spent some years in intimacy. His own journals and letters recently published form an extensive literary collection.

Botha, Louis (1862–1919), South African soldier and statesman. In command of Transvaal forces 1899–1902 in the Boer war, he became prime minister of the Transvaal in 1907, and first premier of the Union of South Africa in 1910.

Bottesini, Giovanni (1821–89), Italian double-bass player.

Botticelli, Sandro (c. 1445–1510), Italian painter. He worked under Fra Lippo Lippi, and was influenced by Savonarola. His art is delicate and poetic. His *Birth of Venus* is in the Uffizi Gallery, Florence, and his *Mars and Venus* in the National Gallery. He illustrated Dante's *Inferno*.

Bottomley, Horatio (1860–1933), English politician, journalist, and notorious financier, who died in poverty after serving a prison sentence for fraud.

Botvinnik, Mikhail (1911–95), Russian chess player: world champion 1948–57, 1958–60, 1961–3.

Boughton, Rutland (1878–1960), English composer of the opera *The Immortal Hour*, and writer on the history and philosophy of music.

Boult, Sir Adrian (1889–1983), conductor of the London Philharmonic Orchestra 1950–7, and of the B.B.C. Symphony Orchestra 1930–50. Musical Director B.B.C. 1930–42.

Boulton, Matthew (1728–1809), engineer who in partnership with James Watt manufactured steam-engines at his Soho works near Birmingham. He also minted a new copper coinage for Great Britain.

Bowdler, Thomas (1754–1825), issued for family reading expurgated editions of Shakespeare and Gibbon, hence the term "bowdlerise."

Boyce, William (1710–79), London organist and composer, who also collected the works of English church composers. He was master of the orchestra of George III.

Boyd Orr, 1st Baron (John Boyd Orr) (1880–1971), British physiologist and nutritional expert. Director-general World Food and Agriculture Organisation 1945–8. Nobel prize 1949.

Boyle, Robert (1627–91), English scientist who with Robert Hooke laid the foundations of the modern sciences of chemistry and physics. He established the law which states that the volume of a gas varies inversely as the pressure upon it, provided temperature is constant. His chief work is the *Sceptical Chymist* (1661).

Bradley, Omar Nelson (1893–1981), American general. In the second world war he commanded in Tunis, Sicily, and Normandy.

Bradman, Sir Donald George (b. 1908), Australian cricketer who captained Australia in test matches against England 1936–48.

Bragg, Sir William Henry (1862–1942), English physicist. He held the chair of physics at Adelaide, Leeds, and London, and was professor of chemistry at the Royal Institution 1923–42. Pres. Royal Society 1935–40.

Bragg, Sir William Lawrence (1890–1971), son of the above. He succeeded Rutherford at the Cavendish laboratory, Cambridge, 1938–53. Dir. Royal Institution 1954–66. Shared with his father the 1915 Nobel prize for their fundamental work on X-rays and crystal structure.

Brahe, Tycho (1546–1601), Danish astronomer. At his island observatory at Uraniborg, provided by his sovereign, he carried out systematic observations which enabled Kepler to work out his planetary laws.

Brahms, Johannes (1833–97), composer. B. in Hamburg (son of a double-bass player). He was a friend of the Schumanns. *See* **Section E.**

Braille, Louis (1809–52), French educationist, who, as teacher of the blind, perfected his system of reading and writing for the blind. As the result of an accident when he was three years old he was himself blind.

Bramah, Joseph (1749–1814), English inventor of the safety-lock and hydraulic press which bear his name. He also invented the modern water-closet (1778) and a machine for printing the serial numbers on bank-notes.

Brandes, Georg Morris Cohen (1842–1927), Danish literary critic who exerted a vitalising influence on literature and art.

Brandt, Willy (1913–92), first social democratic chancellor of the Federal Republic of Germany, 1969–74. His main achievements were the Moscow and Warsaw treaties (1972) the treaty between E. and W. Germany (1973) which recognised their sovereign existence and the Brandt Report setting out a world development programme. Resigned party leadership, 1987.

Brangwyn, Sir Frank (1867–1956), artist of Welsh extraction, b. Bruges; first worked for William Morris making cartoons for textiles; he excelled in murals and in etching.

Breakspear, Nicholas. *See* **Adrian IV.**

Brecht, Bertolt (1898–1956), German dramatist and poet, b. Augsburg, whose brilliant experimental theatre was characteristic of the period in Germany between the two world wars. A Marxist, he left Nazi Germany in 1933 and returned after the war to direct the Berliner Ensemble in E. Berlin and develop his influential techniques of production. His plays include *The Threepenny Opera* (with music by Kurt Weill), *Mother Courage* and *The Caucasian Chalk Circle*. He may be regarded as the most original and vigorous dramatist and producer of this century.

Brennan, Louis (1853–1932), inventor, b. Ireland. His inventions include a gyro-directed torpedo and a mono-rail locomotive.

Breton, André (1896–1966), French poet, founder of the surrealist literary movement in France and a close friend of Apollinaire.

Brewster, Sir David (1781–1868), Scottish physicist, noted for his research into the polarisation of light; invented the kaleidoscope. He helped to found the British Association for the Advancement of Science.

Brezhnev, Leonid Ilyich (1906–82), succeeded Khrushchev as First Secretary of the Soviet Communist Party in 1964. Under his leadership the Soviet Union achieved strategic parity with the United States, society became more stable, education and living standards steadily improved, though the economy was put under strain with expectations not matching performance.

Bridges, Robert (1844–1930), poet laureate 1913–30. His *Testament of Beauty* (1929) has been called "a compendium of the wisdom, learning and experience of an artistic spirit."

Bridgewater, 3rd Duke of (Francis Egerton) (1736–1803), founder of British inland navigation by

his canal, to the design of James Brindley (*q.v.*) from Manchester to his coal mines at Worsley, later extended to join the Mersey at Runcorn.

Bridie, James (pseudonym of Osborne Henry Mavor) (1888–1951), Scottish author and dramatist. The first of his many successful plays was *The Anatomist*, produced in 1931. Other plays include *Tobias and the Angel*, *Jonah and the Whale*, *Mr. Bolfrey*, *Dr. Angelus*.

Bright, Sir Charles Tilston (1832–88), English telegraph engineer who supervised the laying of the British telegraph network and the Atlantic cables (1856–8).

Bright, John (1811–89), radical Quaker statesman and orator, b. Rochdale; friend of Cobden, with whom he promoted the movement for free trade.

Brindley, James (1716–72), English canal builder, b. Derbyshire, of poor parents, apprenticed as a millwright. He was employed by the Duke of Bridgewater (*q.v.*) and designed and constructed the Bridgewater canal, carrying it over the R. Irwell by an aqueduct, the first of its kind. He also built the Grand Trunk canal linking the Mersey with the Trent.

Britten, Baron (Edward Benjamin Britten) (1913–76), English composer, closely associated with the Aldeburgh festival. O.M. 1965. *See* **Section E.**

Broca, Paul (1824–80), French pathologist, anthropologist and pioneer in neuro-surgery. He localised the seat of speech in the brain and originated methods for measuring brain and skull ratios.

Broch, Hermann (1886–1951), Austrian novelist, author of the trilogy *The Sleepwalkers*. Lived in U.S.A. after 1938.

Broglie, prominent family of Piedmontese origin; **Victor Maurice** (1647–1727), and **François Marie** (1671–1745) were marshals of France; **Louis Victor, Prince de Broglie** (b. 1892) received the Nobel prize for his work on quantum mechanics, and his brother **Maurice, Duc de Broglie** (1875–1960), also a physicist, is noted for his work on the ionisation of gases, radioactivity, and X-rays.

Brontë, Charlotte (1816–55), forceful novelist, daughter of an Anglican clergyman of Irish descent, incumbent of Haworth, Yorkshire. She published under a pseudonym *Jane Eyre*, which was at once successful and was followed by *Shirley* and *Villette*. Her sister **Emily** (1818–48) wrote poetry and also *Wuthering Heights*; and **Anne** (1820–49) wrote *Agnes Grey*.

Brooke, Rupert (1887–1915), English poet who died during the first world war, whose works, though few, showed promise and include the poems *Grantchester* and *The Soldier*.

Brougham and Vaux, 1st Baron (Henry Peter Brougham) (1778–1868), English legal reformer; advocate of Queen Caroline against George IV; helped to found London university.

Brown, Sir Arthur Whitten (1886–1948), together with Sir John Alcock (d. 1919) in 1919 made the first transatlantic flight, crossing from Newfoundland to Ireland in 16 hr. 12 min.

Brown, John (1800–59), American abolitionist. His action in inciting Negro slaves to rebel in 1859 led to the civil war. He was hanged after failing to hold the U.S. arsenal at Harper's Ferry which he had captured. Known as "Old Brown of Osawatomie" and regarded as a martyr.

Browne, Charles Farrer (1834–67), American humorist who wrote under the pseudonym of Artemus Ward.

Browne, Hablot Knight (1815–82), English artist, the "Phiz" of many book illustrations, including Dickens's *Pickwick Papers*.

Browne, Sir Thomas (1605–82), author of *Religio Medici* and *Urne-Buriall*, was born in London and practised in Norwich as a physician.

Browning, Elizabeth Barrett (1806–61), English poet. Owing to an injury in childhood, she spent her youth lying on her back, but her meeting with Robert Browning, whom she married, brought a remarkable recovery. In her lifetime her works were more read than those of her husband. They include *Cry of the Children*, *Sonnets from the Portuguese*, and *Aurora Leigh*.

Browning, Robert (1812–89), English poet. Because of his involved style his reputation grew only slowly. In *Strafford* and *The Blot on the 'Scutcheon* he attempted drama also. He married Elizabeth Barrett and lived mainly abroad. His works include *Dramatis Personae* and *The Ring and The Book*.

Bruce, Robert (1274–1329), Scottish national leader against Edward I and Edward II of England. Crowned king in 1306, after years of struggle he defeated Edward II at Bannockburn in 1314.

Bruce, William Spiers (1867–1921), Scottish polar explorer who led the Scottish national antarctic expedition in the *Scotia* 1902–4 and set up a meteorological station on the South Orkneys.

Bruch, Max (1838–1920), German composer and conductor, best known for his G minor violin concerto.

Bruckner, Anton (1824–96), Austrian composer and organist. *See* **Section E.**

Brummell, George Bryan (1778–1840), "Beau Brummell," fashion leader and friend of the Prince Regent (George IV).

Brunel, Isambard Kingdom (1806–59), English civil engineer, son of *Sir Marc Isambard Brunel* (1769–1849), whom he assisted in building the Thames (Rotherhithe) tunnel. He was engineer of the Great Western Railway and built the ocean liners, the *Great Western*, the *Great Britain* (brought back from the Falkland Is. to Bristol in 1970), and the *Great Eastern*. His other works include the Clifton suspension bridge over the R. Avon at Bristol and the Royal Albert bridge over the R. Tamar at Saltash.

Brunelleschi, Filippo (1377–1446), Italian architect, b. Florence; he adapted the ideals of the Roman period. His work in Florence includes the Pitti Palace, the churches of San Lorenzo and San Spirito, and the cathedral dome.

Bruno, Giordano (1548–1600), Italian philosopher. A Dominican friar, he came to favour the astronomical views of Copernicus and was burnt at the stake.

Bruno, St. (*c.* 1032–1101), German monk, founder in 1084 of the Carthusian order at La Grande Chartreuse in the French Alps.

Brutus, Marcus Junius (85–42 B.C.), conspirator against Julius Caesar; later committed suicide.

Buchanan, George (1506–82), Scottish humanist who spent most of his life in France lecturing and writing Latin poems, plays, and treatises.

Buchner, Eduard (1860–1917), German chemist, remembered for his work on the chemistry of fermentation. Nobel prizewinner 1907.

Büchner, Georg (1813–37), German dramatist. Dying at 24, his limited output (principally *Dantons Tod* and the fragment *Wozzeck*) is marked by power and maturity.

Buckle, Henry Thomas (1821–62), author of *The History of Civilisation in England.*

Buddha. *See* **Gautama, Siddhartha.**

Budge, Sir Ernest Alfred Wallis (1857–1934), archaeologist who conducted excavations in Mesopotamia and Egypt.

Buffon, Georges-Louis Leclerc, Comte de (1707–88), French naturalist, author of the *Histoire naturelle* (44 vols., 1749–1804).

Bulganin, Nikolai Alexandrovich (1895–1975), Soviet prime minister 1955–8; defence minister 1947–9, 1953–5. Retired 1960.

Bull, John (*c.* 1562–1628), English composer; possibly composer of *God save the Queen.*

Bülow, Hans Guido von (1830–94), German pianist and conductor. He married Liszt's daughter Cosima, who later left him to marry Wagner.

Bunsen, Robert Wilhelm (1811–99), German chemist, discoverer of the metals caesium and rubidium, and inventor of the Bunsen burner, battery, and pump. Made important observations in spectrum analysis.

Bunyan, John (1628–88), was originally a travelling tinker and is believed to have served in the Parliamentary army. He joined an Independent church in Bedford in 1655 and became a popular preacher. After the Restoration he was thrown into prison, and there wrote *The Pilgrim's Progress*. Of his 60 works, the best known after *Pilgrim's Progress* are *The Holy War, Grace Abounding*, and *Mr. Badman*.

Burckhardt, Jacob Christoph (1818–97), Swiss historian, author of *The Civilisation of the Renaissance in Italy.*

Burghley, 1st Baron (William Cecil) (1520–98), English statesman. After holding office under her two predecessors, he was Queen Elizabeth I's secretary of state, 1558–72, and lord high treasurer, 1572–98.

Burke, Edmund (1729–97), Whig writer and political philosopher. B. in Dublin, he became secretary to Lord Rockingham and entered parliament in 1765. He advocated the emancipation (though not the independence) of the American colonies; and better administration in India; but was against the French revolution.

Burnett, Gilbert (1643–1715) bishop of Salisbury, b. Edinburgh. He wrote a *History of his Own Times*, which deals with many events of which he had personal knowledge.

Burnet, Sir John James (1859–1938), architect, b. Glasgow. The north front of the British Museum (King Edward's galleries) is his most important work in London.

Burney, Fanny (Madame D'Arblay) (1752–1840), originator of the simple novel of home life. Daughter of the organist, Dr. Burney, she published *Evelina* in 1778, and this brought her into court and literary society. She also wrote *Cecilia* and *Camilla.*

Burns, Robert (1759–96), Scottish poet. The son of a cottar, his first poems published in 1786 were at once successful, and he bought a farm. The farm failed, but he had a post as exciseman, and continued to write simply with tenderness and humour. Among his best-known poems are *Auld Lang Syne, Scots wa hae, Comin' through the rye*, and *The Banks of Doon.*

Burton, Sir Richard Francis (1821–90), British explorer and orientalist, who made a pilgrimage to Mecca and Medina in 1853 disguised as a Moslem. He explored Central Africa and translated the *Arabian Nights* (16 vols.).

Burton, Robert (1577–1640), English cleric and scholar, author of *The Anatomy of Melancholy.*

Busby, Sir Matt (1909–94), legendary football manager who took Manchester United from tragedy to triumph.

Bush, George Herbert Walker (1924–), American politician. Vice-President of America, 1981–89. Elected 41st President, November 1988. Inaugurated, January 1989. First Vice-President to be elected President since Martin van Buren in 1836. His popularity soared in 1991 after the Gulf War, but quickly fell over domestic economic problems which contributed to his defeat in 1992.

Busoni, Ferruccio Benvenuto (1866–1920), pianist and composer of three operas (the last *Dr. Faust*, unfinished at his death), much orchestral and chamber music, and works for the piano. *See* **Section E.**

Butler, Joseph (1692–1752), English bishop, remembered for his *Analogy of Religion*, published in 1736 in reply to deistic attacks.

Butler, Nicholas Murray (1862–1947), American educationist who shared with the sociologist Jane Addams the 1931 Nobel peace prize.

Butler, Baron (Richard Austen Butler) (1902–82), Conservative M.P. for Saffron Walden 1929–65. Brought in Education Act 1944; helped secure Conservative acceptance of the welfare state; held high office 1951–64. "Butskellism" applied to Conservative social and economic policies of the '50s. Described as "the best prime minister we never had." Life peerage 1965.

Butler, Samuel (1612–80), English verse-satirist, author of the poem *Hudibras* against the Puritans.

Butler, Samuel (1835–1902), English novelist and satirist, author of *Erewhon* and its sequel *Erewhon Revisited*. Other works include *The Fair Haven, Life and Habit*, and *Evolution Old and New*, in which he attacked Darwinism. His autobiographical novel *The Way of All Flesh* and his *Notebooks* were published after his death.

Butt, Clara (1872–1936), English contralto; made her début in London in 1892.

Buxton, Sir Thomas Fowell (1786–1845), English social reformer; succeeded Wilberforce as leader of the anti-slavery group in parliament.

Buys Ballot, Christoph Henrich Diedrich (1817–90), Dutch meteorologist who formulated the law which bears his name (an observer with back to wind in northern hemisphere has lower pressure to left; in southern hemisphere to right).

Byrd, Richard Evelyn (1888–1957), American rear-admiral, explorer and aviator. He flew over the north pole, 1926; and in 1929 made the first flight over the south pole. He made other expeditions in 1925, 1933–5, 1939 and 1946.

Byrd, William (1543–1623), English composer of church music, sacred choral music, string music, vocal and instrumental music; and a founder of the school of English madrigalists. He was organist of Lincoln cathedral at 20 and later of Queen Elizabeth's chapel royal. *See* Section E.

Byron, 6th Baron (George Gordon Byron) (1788–1824), English romantic poet who influenced European literature and thought. At 20 he published *Hours of Idleness*, which was violently attacked by the *Edinburgh Review*. This provoked his retaliatory *English Bards and Scotch Reviewers*, which caused a sensation. His *Childe Harold's Pilgrimage* appeared in 1812. His married life was unhappy. He went to help the Greeks in their struggle for independence and died at Missolonghi.

C

Cable, George Washington (1844–1925), American author and social critic, b. New Orleans, whose writings reflect the colour problems of his day: *Ole Creol Days, The Silent South*.

Cabot, John (1425–*c.* 1500), Genoese explorer who settled in Bristol and sailed westwards under letters-patent from Henry VII of England in 1497. Discovered Newfoundland and Nova Scotia, believing them to be part of Asia, and may have reached the mainland of America before Columbus did. His son:

Cabot, Sebastian (1474–1557), was born in Venice, and in 1509 in search of a north-west passage to Asia sailed as far as Hudson Bay. Entered Spanish service in 1512, and spent several years exploring the Plate and Paraná rivers. Re-entered English service in 1548 and organised expedition to seek a north-east passage to India, which resulted in trade with Russia. English claim to North America is founded on the voyages of the Cabots.

Cabral, Pedro Alvarez (*c.* 1467–*c.* 1520), Portuguese navigator, friend of Vasco da Gama, discovered Brazil, which he named "Terra da Santa Cruz."

Cadbury, George (1839–1922), liberal Quaker philanthropist of Cadbury Bros., mainly responsible for the pioneer garden city of Bournville.

Cadogan, Sir Alexander (1884–1968), English diplomat. He helped to draft the charter of the United Nations organisation and became Gt. Britain's representative on the Security Council.

Caedmon, the first English Christian poet, lived in the 7th cent. and, according to Bede, was first a cowherd and later a monk at Whitby. His poetry was based on the scriptures.

Caesar, Caius Julius (*c.* 101–44 B.C.), Roman general and writer. Under the declining republic, he was assigned in 61 the province of Gaul; in the course of pacifying it he invaded Britain (55 B.C.). Opposition in Rome to his career, mainly from Pompey, provoked him in 49 to the defiance of crossing the Rubicon with his army. He defeated Pompey, whom he pursued to Egypt, where he established Cleopatra as queen. At Rome he became dictator, and his reforms include the Julian calendar. He was murdered in 44. His career paved the way for Rome becoming an empire under his nephew Octavian.

Calderón de la Barca, Pedro (1600–81), Spanish dramatist, representative of contemporary Spanish thought, who also wrote court spectacles for Philip IV. Among his best-known works are *La Vida es Sueño* and *El divino Orfeo*.

Callaghan, Lord (Sir James Callaghan) (b. 1912), Labour's fourth prime minister, 1976–9; parliamentary leader of the Labour Party, April 1976, following Sir Harold Wilson's resignation: elected for South Cardiff 1950–87; served as Chancellor of the Exchequer, Home Secretary, and Foreign Secretary in the Labour administrations, 1964–70, 1974–76. Succeeded by Foot as leader, 1980. Order of the Garter, 1987.

Calvin, John (1509–64), French Protestant reformer and theologian. B. in Picardy, he broke with the Roman Catholic church about 1533, and subsequently settled in Geneva, where from 1541 he established a theocratic regime of strict morality. His theology was published in his *Institutes*; while, like Luther, he accepted justification by faith without works, he also believed in predestination. His doctrines spread on the continent, in Scotland and to some extent in England. *See* Section J.

Camden, William (1551–1623), English antiquary and historian. His *Britannia* appeared in 1586.

Cameron, Sir David Young (1865–1945), Scottish etcher and landscape painter.

Cameron, Richard (1648–80), Scottish preacher who revolted in defence of the Solemn League and Covenant. Killed at Airds Moss (Ayrshire).

Cameron, Verney Lovett (1844–94), English explorer, the first to cross the African continent from east to west. He surveyed Lake Tanganyika and in 1872 went out to find Livingstone.

Camillus, Marcus Furius (4th cent. B.C.), Roman general. When the Gauls attacked in 387 B.C., he was made dictator and defeated them.

Camões, Luis Vaz de (1624–80), Portuguese poet, author of *Os Lusiadas*, an epic of Portuguese history and discovery.

Campbell, Colin, 1st Baron Clyde (1792–1863), Scottish general who was commander-in-chief in India during the Mutiny.

Campbell, Sir Malcolm (1885–1948), racing driver who held the land-speed record of 301 mile/h (1935) and water-speed record of 141·7 mile/h (1939). His son **Donald** held the water-speed record of 276·33 mile/h (1964); killed in 1967 at Coniston.

Campbell, Mrs. Patrick (Beatrice Stella Tanner) (1865–1940), English actress of beauty and wit, friend of G. B. Shaw.

Campbell, Thomas (1777–1844), Scottish poet, who at 22 published *The Pleasures of Hope*. His war poems include *Ye Mariners of England* and *The Battle of the Baltic*. He was one of the founders of University College, London.

Campbell-Bannerman, Sir Henry (1836–1908), Liberal statesman, prime minister 1905–8.

Camus, Albert (1913–60), French existentialist philosopher and writer, native of Algeria. Preoccupied with the themes of the Stranger and the Absurd, the works for which he is particularly remembered are the philosophical essay *Le Mythe de Sisyphe*, the plays *Caligula* and *The Price of Justice*, and the novel *L'Etranger*. Nobel prize 1957. Killed in car crash.

Canaletto (Antonio Canal) (1697–1768), Italian artist. B. at Venice, he painted views of his city. From 1746 to 1756 he worked mainly in London. Some of his work is in the National Gallery, and there is a collection at Windsor.

Canning, George (1770–1827), English statesman. He was an advocate of Catholic emancipation, and was the first to recognise the free states of South America.

Cannizzaro, Stanislao (1826–1910), Italian chemist who carried forward the work of Avogadro in distinguishing between molecular and atomic weights.

Canova, Antonio (1757–1822), Italian sculptor. B. at Venice, he infused grace into the classical style.

Canton, John (1718–72), English physicist and schoolmaster, the first to verify in England Franklin's experiments on the identity of lightning with electricity. He was the first to demonstrate that water is compressible and produced a new phosphorescent body (Canton's phosphorus) by calcining oyster shells with sulphur.

Canute (*c.* 994–1035), king of the English, Danes and Norwegians. The son of a Danish king, after some years of fighting he established himself as king of England and ruled with wisdom and firmness.

Capablanca, José Raoul (1888–1942), Cuban chess player, world champion from 1921 to 1927 when he was beaten by Alekhine.

Caractacus or **Caradoc**, a king in west Britain, who resisted the Romans in the first century. After capture he was freed by the emperor Claudius.

Carey, George Leonard (b. 1935), 103rd Archbishop of Canterbury. Enthroned April 1991. Born Barking, East London. Son of hospital porter. Bishop of Bath and Wells, 1987–91.

Carey, William (1761–1834), first Baptist missionary to India. Helped found Baptist Missionary Society (1792), whose bicentenary in 1992 celebrated the work of William Carey. An Oriental scholar, he published 24 translations of the scriptures as well as compiling Indian dictionaries.

Carissimi, Giacomo (1604–74), Italian composer, b. near Rome. He introduced more instrumental variety into the cantata and oratorio, and brought the recitative to perfection. His *Jephtha* is still in print, and there are collections of his works at Paris and Oxford. *See* Section E.

Carlyle, Thomas (1795–1881), Scottish author. Of peasant stock, he went to Edinburgh university, but later lived mainly in England where he lectured. He married Jane Welsh. His individual views pervade his historical writing. His best-known works include *Sartor Resartus, Heroes and Hero Worship, Cromwell's Letters and Speeches,* and the *French Revolution.*

Carnegie, Andrew (1835–1919), philanthropist b. Dunfermline; emigrated to America 1848; after early struggles established the Carnegie iron works. He made munificent gifts to Free Libraries and other educational work.

Carnot, Lazare Nicolas Marguerite (1753–1823), French military engineer, prominent in the French revolutionary wars, 1792–1802. His son, **Sadi Carnot** (1796–1832), was a physicist and engineer who worked on the motive power of heat, establishing the principle that heat and work are reversible conditions.

Caroline, Queen (1768–1821), was married to George IV when he was Prince of Wales. They soon separated, but when he became king in 1820, she tried to assert her position. The question came before parliament. In spite of some public sympathy she was unsuccessful.

Carrel, Alexis (1873–1944), American surgeon who won the Nobel prize in 1912 for his success in suturing blood vessels in transfusion and in transplantation of organs. A Frenchman by birth, he returned to France in 1939.

Carroll, Lewis. *See* Dodgson, Charles Lutwidge.

Carson, Baron (Edward Henry Carson) (1854–1935), Irish barrister, solicitor-general for Ireland 1892; attorney general 1915; first lord of the admiralty 1916–17; member of the war cabinet 1917–18. He led a semi-militant organisation against Home Rule.

Carson, Rachel (1907–64), American biologist, remembered for *The Silent Spring.*

Carter, Howard (1873–1939), Egyptologist who was associated with Lord Carnarvon in discovering in 1922 the Tomb of Tutankhamun.

Carter, James Earl (b. 1924), American Democratic President 1977–81; former Governor of Georgia. His main achievements were the treaty between Israel and Egypt, the Panama Canal treaty, Salt II (though not ratified) and the settling of the release of American hostages held captive in Iran. More recently he has achieved successes as a negotiator in Somalia, North Korea, Haiti and Bosnia.

Cartier, Jacques (1494–1557), French navigator, b. St. Malo, who explored Canada, especially the gulf and river of St. Lawrence.

Cartwright, Edmund (1743–1823), English inventor of the power-loom, and also of a wool-combing machine, important steps in the weaving side of the textile revolution.

Cartwright, John (1740–1824), brother of the above; reformer and agitator against slavery.

Caruso, Enrico (1873–1921), Italian tenor, b. Naples.

Carver, George Washington (1864–1943), American Negro agricultural chemist of world repute.

Casabianca, Louis de (c. 1752–98), captain of the French flagship *L'Orient* at the Battle of the Nile. He and his ten-year-old-son died together in the burning ship.

Casals, Pablo (1876–1973), Spanish cellist and conductor, son of an organist, b. Vendrell, Tarragona. He exiled himself from Spain in 1938.

Casanova de Seinfalt, Giacomo (1725–98), Italian adventurer, author of licentious memoirs.

Casement, Roger David (1864–1916), Irish nationalist. While in British consular service exposed abuses in Belgian Congo. Knighted 1911 (degraded 1916). Hanged after 1916 Easter Rising. His remains are in Glasnevin cemetary, Dublin.

Cassini, French family of Italian origin, distinguished for work in astronomy and geography. Through four generations (1671–1793) they were heads of the Paris Observatory.

Cassius, Caius Longinus, Roman general who opposed the dictatorship of Julius Caesar, and took part in his murder. He died in 42 B.C. after being defeated by Mark Antony.

Castle, Baroness (Barbara Anne Castle) (b. 1910), Socialist politician who held high Cabinet office

under Harold Wilson. As Transport Secretary (1965–68), she introduced the breath test. Later attempted to reform the trade unions with *In Place of Strife.* A tireless campaigner for social justice.

Castlereagh, Viscount (Robert Stewart Castlereagh) (1769–1822), British minister of war and foreign secretary, who took a leading part in the Napoleonic wars. Committed suicide.

Castro, Fidel (b. 1927), Cuban revolutionary. After two unsuccessful attempts he succeeded in 1959 in overthrowing a police-state. He has initiated reforms in agriculture, industry, and education. His acceptance of Russian support led to the "missiles crisis" of 1962. The fall of Soviet communism has left his regime isolated.

Catherine, St. (4th cent.). Traditionally a virgin martyr in Alexandria, though not mentioned before the 10th cent. Legend represents her as tied to a wheel.

Catherine de' Medici (1519–89), Italian-born wife of Henry II and mother of three French kings (she was regent for Charles IX). Her antagonism to the Protestants may have led to the massacre of St. Bartholomew's day. She was able, and appreciated art and literature, but was unscrupulous and cruel.

Catherine of Aragon (1485–1536), first wife of Henry VIII of England, was daughter of Ferdinand and Isabella of Spain, and mother of Mary Tudor. After the Pope had refused to release Henry VIII from the marriage an English declaration of nullity was obtained (thus precipitating a movement towards the Reformation).

Catherine the Great (1729–96), Empress Catherine II of Russia. Daughter of a German prince, she married in 1745 the future Peter III, a weakling, later deposed and murdered. Intelligent, cultivated, autocratic, she proved a capable ruler for a time but was opposed by the landed interests and, despite plans for reform, her reign was marked by imperialist expansion and extension of serfdom.

Cato, Marcus Porcius (234–149 B.C.), Roman statesman and writer. His tenure of office as censor was characterised by austerity and conservatism. Advocated opposition to Carthage.

Catullus, Caius Valerius (c. 84–54 B.C.), Roman poet who wrote lyrics to Lesbia. His poems show sincere feeling and also Greek influence.

Cavell, Edith Louisa (1865–1915), English nurse who cared for friend and foe in Brussels in 1914–15, but was executed by the Germans for helping Allied fugitives to escape.

Cavendish, Henry (1731–1810), English scientist, a contemporary of Black, Priestley, Scheele, and Lavoisier, remembered for his investigations into the nature of gases. He discovered hydrogen and the chemical composition of water. The Cavendish Laboratory is named after him.

Cavour, Camilio Benso di (1810–61), Italian statesman who, as premier of Sardinia, helped to bring about the unification of Italy.

Caxton, William (1422–91), the first English printer and publisher, a man of wide-ranging abilities. He probably learnt the art of printing at Cologne (1471–2), setting up his own printing press at Westminster (1476). He printed Chaucer's *Canterbury Tales,* Malory's *Le Morte d'Arthur* and Aesop's *Fables.*

Cecil of Chelwood, 1st Viscount (Robert Cecil) (1864–1958), English politician who helped draft the Charter of the League of Nations. Nobel prize for peace 1937.

Cecilia, St. (2nd or 3rd cent.), patron saint of music, often represented playing the organ.

Cellini, Benvenuto (1500–71), Italian sculptor and goldsmith. B. at Florence, he worked for some years in Rome. His bronze statue *Perseus with the head of Medusa* is at Florence. His life was adventurous and he wrote an *Autobiography* which is revealing of himself and his time.

Celsius, Anders (1701–44), Swedish physicist and astronomer who invented the centigrade thermometer.

Ceresole, Pierre (1879–1945), Swiss founder of International Voluntary Service. His pacifism led him to become a Quaker.

Cervantes, Saavedra Miguel de (1547–1616), Spanish novelist and dramatist, b. at Alcalá de Henares. He was injured at the battle of Lepanto, and thereafter struggled to earn a livelihood from literature. His *Don Quixote* describes the adventures of a poor gentleman, confused in mind, who on his horse Rosinante with his squire Sancho Panza seeks adventures; it satirised chivalry, but is also a permanent criticism of life. Of his plays only two survive.

Cézanne, Paul (1839–1906), French painter, b. in Aix-en-Provence, the son of a wealthy banker and tradesman. He developed a highly original style, using colour and tone in such a way as to increase the impression of depth. He said that he wanted "to make of Impressionism something solid and durable, like the art of the Museums." Like Giotto, six hundred years before, he more than any other artist determined the course European painting was to take. *La Veille au Chapelet* and *Les Grandes Baigneuses* are in the National Gallery. He was a friend of Zola.

Chadwick, Sir Edwin (1800 00), English social reformer whose most important work was as Secretary of the Poor Law Board.

Chadwick, Sir James (1891–1974), English physicist, one of Rutherford's collaborators in the field of atomic research. Discovered the neutron in 1932, one of the main steps in the discovery of the fission process which led to the production of the atom bomb.

Chagall, Marc (1889–1985), Russian painter, b. at Vitebsk; the forerunner of surrealism.

Chamberlain, Joseph (1836–1914), English statesman. He began with municipal work in Birmingham. At first a Liberal under Gladstone, he became Conservative. He opposed Home Rule for Ireland, and was the first advocate of a partial return to protection.

Chamberlain, Neville (1869–1940), son of Joseph. He was prime minister 1937–40, when he appeased Hitler by the Munich agreement, 1938.

Chambers, Sir William (1726–96), British architect, b. Stockholm. He rebuilt Somerset House and designed the pagoda in Kew Gardens.

Champlain, Samuel de (1567–1635), French navigator who founded Quebec (1608), and discovered the lake known by his name.

Champollion, Jean François (1790–1832), French egyptologist, who found the key to the decipherment of hieroglyphics in the Rosetta stone (**L106**).

Chantrey, Sir Francis Legatt (1781–1841), English sculptor who left a fortune to the Royal Academy for the purchase of works of British art.

Chaplin, Sir Charles Spencer (1889–1977), first international screen star, with more than 50 years' achievement. B. in London, his mother was a music-hall singer and he made his début at five. In 1910 he went to the United States; and with the Keystone Company in Los Angeles (1914–15) he made films in which his early hardships are reflected in humour and sadness. His films include *Shoulder Arms, The Kid, The Gold Rush, City Lights, The Great Dictator, Modern Times,* and *Limelight. Autobiography* (1964).

Chapman, George (1559–1634), Elizabethan poet, dramatist, and translator of the *Iliad* and *Odyssey*. His best-known play is *Bussy d'Ambois*.

Chapman, Sydney (1888–1970), English mathematician and geophysicist, noted for his work on the kinetic theory of gases, geomagnetism, and solar and ionospheric physics. An upper layer of the atmosphere and a crater on the moon are named after him.

Charcot, Jean Baptiste (1867–1936), French explorer, who in 1903–5 and 1908–10 commanded expeditions to the south polar regions. Charcot Island in the Antarctic is named after him.

Chardin, Jean Baptiste Siméon (1699–1779), French painter of still life and domestic scenes.

Chares (c. 300 B.C.), Greek worker in bronze from Rhodes, sculptor of the Colossus of Rhodes, one of the seven wonders of the world.

Charlemagne (742–814), Charles the Great. From being King of the Franks, he came to govern an empire comprising Gaul, Italy, and large parts of Spain and Germany, and was crowned Emperor by the Pope in Rome on Christmas Day, A.D. 800. His revival of the Western Empire was the foundation of the Holy Roman Empire (*q.v.*).

Charles, Jacques Alexandre César (1746–1823), French physicist, the first to use hydrogen gas in balloons and who anticipated Gay-Lussac's law on the expansion of gases.

Charles Edward (Stuart) (1720–88), the Young Pretender (*i.e.*, claimant of the English throne), grandson of James II, led an unsuccessful rising in 1745 and died in exile.

Charles (Philip Arthur George) (b. 1948), Prince of Wales, Duke of Cornwall and Rothesay, eldest son of Queen Elizabeth II; married Lady Diana Spencer, daughter of 8th Earl Spencer, 1981.

Charles I (1600–49), King of England, Scotland, and Ireland, succeeded his father James I in 1625. Personally sincere, and having an appreciation of art, he was yet ill-fitted to cope with the political problems of his time. His marriage with the French princess Henrietta Maria was unpopular. He supported Archbishop Laud's strict Anglicanism, and he also attempted to rule without parliament. Defeated in the Civil War which broke out in 1642, he spun out negotiations for a settlement till he was beheaded in 1649.

Charles II (1630 05), King of England, Scotland, and Ireland, son of Charles I; after the Civil War escaped to France, and returned in 1660 when the monarchy was restored. His religious sympathies were Roman Catholic and his personal life was amorous; but in political matters he was shrewd and realistic, and contrived not to "go on his travels" again. He promoted the development of the navy, but had to accept the laws enforcing religious conformity imposed by parliament.

Charles V (1500–58), Hapsburg ruler, succeeded his grandfather, Maximilian I, as emperor of the Holy Roman Empire, and as heir to Ferdinand and Isabella succeeded to the Spanish crown. His rivalry with Francis I of France led to prolonged war. He crushed a revolt of peasants in 1525. He presided in 1521 at the Diet before which Luther appeared, after which religious struggle continued in Germany till the Augsburg settlement of 1555. In that year he retired to a monastery in Spain.

Charles XII of Sweden (1682–1718), a brave but rash and ambitious general. He repelled Russian attacks at Narva in 1700, but subsequntly pursuing military adventure he was defeated by Peter the Great at Poltava in 1709; and on invading Norway was killed.

Chateaubriand, François René, Vicomte de (1768–1848), French writer and diplomat. In a varied career he was at first an emigré, and later served as diplomat under both Napoleon and Louis XVIII. He was a friend of Mme. Recamier. His writings include *Mémoires d'outre-tombe*.

Chatham, 1st Earl of (William Pitt) (1708–78), English statesman and orator. His energetic conduct of the Seven Years War was an important contribution to English victory and to acquisitions in Canada and India at the peace (1763), though by then he was out of office. In the dispute with the American colonies he upheld their right to resist imposed taxation, and collapsed while making a last speech on this dispute.

Chatterton, Thomas (1752–70), English poet who tried to pass off his writings as newly discovered ancient manuscripts. Killed himself at the age of 17.

Chaucer, Geoffrey (1340?–1400), English poet. His main work, *The Canterbury Tales*, gives a vivid picture of contemporary life.

Chekhov, Anton (1860–1904), Russian dramatist and short-story writer, whose plays include *The Cherry Orchard, Uncle Vanya,* and *The Three Sisters*. His stories include *The Steppe, The Sleepyhead, The Post, The Student,* and *The Bishop*. He was of humble origin and while a student at Moscow supported his family by writing humorous sketches and tales.

Chernenko, Konstantin Ustinovich (1911–85) Soviet politician. Succeeded Andropov (q.v.) as General Secretary of the Communist Party, February 1984, but his ineffectual rule lasted a mere 13 months.

Cherubini, Luigi (1760–1842), Italian-born musician, director of the Paris Conservatoire.

Cheshire, Lord (Group Captain Leonard Cheshire) (1917–92) War hero (most decorated World War II pilot) who founded the world-wide homes for the disabled.

Chesterfield, 4th Earl of (Philip Dormer Stanhope) (1694–1773), English statesman, whose *Letters* to his natural son, Philip Stanhope, are full of grace, wit, and worldly wisdom.

Chesterton, Gilbert Keith (1874–1936), English essayist, novelist and poet, who also wrote studies of Charles Dickens and Robert Browning. His works include *The Napoleon of Notting Hill* and *The Ballad of the White Horse*.

Chevalier, Albert (1861–1923), English music-hall comedian known for his coster sketches.

Chiang Kai-shek (1887–1975), Chinese general. He

at first fought for Sun Yat-sen. After the latter's death (1925), as commander of the Kuomintang army, he attempted to unite China; but he was more anxious to defeat the Communists than to repel the Japanese in Manchuria in 1931. In 1949 retired to Formosa after military defeat by the Communists.

Chichester, Sir Francis (1902–72), English seaman, who sailed his *Gipsy Moth IV* into Sydney harbour in 1966 after a 107-day voyage from Plymouth, and back again round the Horn.

Chippendale, Thomas (1718–79), designer of furniture, b. Otley, Yorks, son of a joiner. His designs are shown in *The Gentleman and Cabinet Maker's Director*, 1754.

Chirac, Jacques (b. 1932), French Gaullist politician, elected President of France, May 1995, Prime Minister, 1974–76 and 1986–88.

Chirico, Giorgio de (1888–1978), painter associated with the surrealist school, born in Greece of Italian parents.

Chomsky, Noam (b. 1928), American theoretical linguist, professor of Linguistics, Massachusetts Institute of Technology; inventor of transformational grammar.

Chopin, Frédéric François (1810–49), Polish pianist and composer, son of a French father and Polish mother. He has been called "the poet of the piano" because of the originality and delicacy of his playing. He enjoyed Paris intellectual and musical society, was a friend of George Sand, and played in numerous concerts all over Europe. He died of consumption. *See* Section E.

Chou En-lai (1898–1976), Chinese revolutionary statesman, administrator and diplomat. He organised revolt in Shanghai 1927, later formed close partnership with Mao Tse-tung, took part in the "long march" 1934–5, becoming prime minister of the new China in 1949.

Chrysostom, St. John (c. 347–407), preacher. Chrysostom means golden-mouthed. First at Antioch, and later as patriarch of Constantinople, he was an eloquent teacher; but by outspokenness he lost the Empress Eudoxia's favour and died from ill-treatment.

Churchill, Lord Randolph Henry Spencer (1849–95), Conservative politician, who held brief office only. He was father of Winston Churchill.

Churchill, Sir Winston Leonard Spencer (1874–1965), British statesman and author, son of the last-named. He entered parliament in 1900. He served as a junior officer with the British forces abroad; and during the Boer War he acted as war correspondent. He held the following ministerial posts; Under-Secretary for the Colonies 1905–8; President of the Board of Trade 1908–10; Home Secretary 1910–11; First Lord of the Admiralty 1911–15, 1939–40; Chancellor of the Duchy of Lancaster 1915; Minister of Munitions 1917; Minister of War 1918–21; Minister of Air 1919–21; Secretary of State for the Colonies 1921–2; Chancellor of the Exchequer 1924–9; Prime Minister and Minister of Defence 1940–5; Prime Minister 1951–5. He was rector or chancellor of three universities. Cast in the heroic mould, he lived a full life. His main achievement was as leader of the British people in the second world war. His writings include a biography of his ancestor, Marlborough, and histories of the first and second world wars. He exhibited at the Royal Academy. Hon. American citizenship conferred 1963.

Cibber, Colley (1671–1757), a London actor and dramatist. His best comedies are *The Careless Husband* and *Love's Last Shift*.

Cicero, Marcus Tullius (106–43 B.C.), Roman orator and philosopher, many of whose letters and speeches survive. He held political office but was killed by the troops of the triumvirate.

Cid (El Campeador) (c. 1035–99), name given to the Spanish knight Rodrigo Diaz, a soldier of fortune who fought against Moors and Christians alike. Myth made him a national hero of knightly and Christian virtue.

Cierva, Juan de la (1895–1936), Spanish engineer who invented the autogiro.

Cimabue, Giovanni (Cenni di Pepo) (1240–1302), early Florentine painter. His only certain work is the St. John in Pisa cathedral.

Cimarosa, Domenico (1749–1801), Italian composer. His best-known opera is *Il Matrimonio Segreto*. He held revolutionary views.

Cimon (c. 512–449 B.C.), Athenian statesman and

general, son of Miltiades. He defeated the Persian fleet at the mouth of the Eurymedon in 468. He worked for cooperation with other states, including Sparta.

Cipriani, Giambattista (1727–85), Italian painter of historical subjects who worked in London; a founder member of the Royal Academy.

Clare, John (1793–1864), Northamptonshire labourer who became a poet. *Poems Descriptive of Rural Life and Scenery*, and *The Village Minstrel* were among his publications. He died in the county lunatic asylum.

Clarendon, 1st Earl of (Edward Hyde) (1609–74), English statesman and historian. He was chancellor to Charles II, and his daughter married the future James II, but he fell and died in exile. He wrote a *History of the Rebellion*.

Clark, Baron (Kenneth McKenzie Clark) (1903–83), English art historian. He was director of the National Gallery 1934–45, Slade professor of fine arts at Oxford 1946–50, and chairman of the Arts Council 1953–60. Life peer 1969. O.M. 1976.

Clarke, Kenneth, *see* D16.

Clarkson, Thomas (1760–1846) devoted his life to the abolition of slavery and shares with Wilberforce credit for the passing of the Act of 1807 abolishing the British slave trade.

Claude Lorrain (Gelée) (1600–82), French landscape painter. B. near Nancy, he settled in Rome. A close student of nature, he excelled in depicting sunrise or sunset, and founded a "picturesque" tradition.

Claudius (10 B.C.–A.D. 54), Roman emperor. After the murder of Caligula, he was proclaimed emperor almost accidentally by the Praetorian Guard. He was a sensible administrator. In his time the empire was extended to include Britain, Thrace, and Mauretania. He was probably poisoned by his wife Agrippina.

Clausewitz, Karl von (1780–1831), German military expert whose *Vom Kriege*, expounding his theories on war, dominated Prussia in the 19th cent.

Cleisthenes (6th cent. B.C.), Athenian constitutional reformer. Charged with redrawing the constitution of Athens after her occupation by Sparta in 510 B.C., he extended the work of Solon (q.v.). Henceforth all Athenians had equality of rights in the election of officials, regardless of wealth.

Clemenceau, Georges (1841–1929), French statesman of radical views; twice premier, 1906–9, 1917–20. He was a defender of Dreyfus.

Cleon (c. 495–429 B.C.) Athenian politician and demagogue, infamous for his extreme anti-Spartan position during the Peloponnesian War and his opposition to Pericles (q.v.).

Cleopatra (69–30 B.C.), daughter of Ptolemy XII, the seventh queen of Egypt by that name, a brilliant, ambitious woman. In 51 she became joint sovereign with her younger brother Ptolemy XIII. She was banished to Syria, but, obtaining the help of Caesar, regained the kingdom. She and Caesar became lovers, and in 47 she bore him a son Caesarion (later Ptolemy XV). After Caesar's murder she returned to Egypt. She met the triumvir Mark Antony and bore him twins; he deserted his wife and broke with his brother-in-law Octavian (later Augustus). Antony and Cleopatra were, however, defeated in 31 B.C.; Antony fell upon his sword, and Cleopatra killed herself with an asp bite. Her life inspired Shakespeare's *Antony and Cleopatra* and Shaw's *Caesar and Cleopatra*.

Clinton, Bill (William Jefferson) (b. 1946), 42nd President of the United States, defeating George Bush in November 1992. Inaugurated, January 1993. Born in Hope, Arkansas. A Rhodes Scholar at Oxford. Former Democrat governor of Arkansas. For the problems facing his administration, *see* Section C.

Clive, 1st Baron (Robert Clive) (1725–74), English general who helped to lay the foundations of English power in India. B. near Market Drayton, he entered the service of the East India Company. He contemplated suicide, but Anglo-French rivalry, culminating in the Seven Years War, gave scope for his military powers in the siege of Arcot and the battle of Plassey. As a governor he showed administrative capacity. In his later life he was unpopular which led to his suicide.

Clovis (c. 465–511), Merovingian king of the Franks and a convert to Christianity. He defeated the Burgundians and West Goths, and fixed his court at Paris.

Clyde, Lord. See Campbell, Colin.

Cobbett, William (1763–1835), English controversialist. He is chiefly known for his *Rural Rides*, but also published a weekly *Political Register* from 1802.

Cobden, Richard (1804–65), English advocate of free trade. The son of a Sussex farmer, he led agitation against the laws restricting import of corn, and they were repealed in 1846. He was impoverished by his public work and was helped by subscription.

Cochrane, Thomas, 10th Earl of Dundonald (1775–1860), British seaman, who crippled a French fleet in Biscay (1809), aided the liberation of Chile and Peru from Spanish rule (1819–22), of Brazil from Portuguese rule (1823–5), and assisted the Greeks in their struggle to throw off the Turkish yoke (1827).

Cockcroft, Sir John Douglas (1897–1967), Cambridge nuclear physicist who shared with E. T. S. Walton the 1951 Nobel prize. They had worked together at Cambridge in the historic "atom-splitting" experiments beginning with the transmutation of lithium into boron. He was directly involved in Britain's first nuclear power programmes.

Cockerell, Christopher (b. 1910), English inventor of the hovercraft, which works on the aircushioning principle. See Hovercraft, Section L.

Cocteau, Jean (1891–1963), French writer and artist in widely varied forms of art.

Cody, Samuel Franklin (1861–1913), American aviator, the first man to fly in Britain (1,390 ft. on 16 Oct. 1908). He became a British subject in 1909. Killed while flying.

Cody, William Frederick (1846–1917), American showman, known as "Buffalo Bill," whose Wild West Show toured America and Europe.

Coggan, Donald (b. 1909), enthroned 101st archbishop of Canterbury, January 1975; archbishop of York 1961–74; Canterbury 1975–80.

Cohn, Ferdinand Julius (1828–98), German botanist, founder of the science of bacteriology.

Coke, Sir Edward (1552–1634), English legal author, judge, and rival of Francis Bacon. His legal works are his *Reports* and *Institutes*.

Colbert, Jean Baptiste (1619–83), French statesman under Louis XIV, who fostered new industries, encouraged commerce, reformed the finances and established the navy on a sound basis. A patron of literature, science, and art.

Cole, George Douglas Howard (1889–1959), English economist and political journalist, professor of social and political theory at Oxford, 1944–57. Among his writings are *The Intelligent Man's Guide through World Chaos*, and *A History of Socialist Thought* (5 vols.).

Coleridge, Samuel Taylor (1772–1834), English poet, critic, and friend of Wordsworth, with whom he published *Lyrical Ballads*. His poems include *The Ancient Mariner*, *Christabel*, and *Kubla Khan*.

Coleridge-Taylor, Samuel (1875–1912), English composer, the son of a West African doctor practising in London and an Englishwoman. He is best known for his Hiawatha trilogy.

Colet, John (c. 1467–1519), English humanist and divine, founded St. Paul's School (1512). As scholar and friend of Erasmus he helped to bring the new learning to England.

Colette (Sidonie Gabrielle Claudine Colette) (1873–1954), French author of the *Claudine* stories, *Chéri* and *La Fin de Chéri*.

Collier, John (1850–1934), English painter noted for his "problem" pictures.

Collingwood, 1st Baron (Cuthbert Collingwood) (1750–1810), British admiral whose ship, the *Royal Sovereign*, led the fleet to battle at Trafalgar, and who on Nelson's death assumed command.

Collingwood, Robin George (1889–1943), English philosopher, historian, and archaeologist, associated with Oxford from 1908 to 1941. His philosophical thought is best studied in *Speculum Mentis*, *Essay on Philosophical Method*, *Idea of Nature*, and *Idea of History*.

Collins, Michael (1890–1922), Irish politician and Sinn Fein leader. He successfully organised guerrilla warfare, and mainly negotiated the treaty with Britain in 1921, but was killed in a Republican ambush on his return.

Collins, William (1788–1847), English landscape and figure painter.

Collins, William Wilkie (1824–89), son of the above; one of the first English novelists to deal with the detection of crime. *The Woman in White* appeared in 1860.

Colt, Samuel (1814–62), of Hartford, Connecticut, invented the revolver in 1835. It was used in the war with Mexico.

Columba, St. (521–97), founder of the monastery of Iona, b. Ireland. From the island shrine he made missionary journeys to the Highlands of Scotland. The founder of Christianity in Scotland.

Columbanus, St. (c. 540–615), Irish abbot who founded a number of monasteries in continental Europe. See Monasticism, Section J.

Columbus, Christopher (c. 1451–1506), Italian navigator, b. Genoa, who, prevailing upon Ferdinand and Isabella of Spain to bear the expense of an expedition, in 1492 discovered the Bahamas, Cuba, and other West Indian islands. In 1498 he landed on the lowlands of S. America.

Comenius, John Amos (1592–1670), Czech educationist and pastor, advocate of the "direct" method of teaching languages, of the use of pictures in education, and of equality of educational opportunity for girls.

Compton, Arthur Holly (1892–1962), American physicist whose work on X-rays established what is known as the Compton effect (1923). While professor of physics at the university of Chicago (1923–45) he helped to develop the atomic bomb. Nobel prizewinner 1927.

Compton, Karl Taylor (1887–1954), scientist-administrator, brother of the above.

Compton-Burnett, Dame Ivy (1884–1969), English novelist whose books deal with family relationships and include *Pastors and Masters*, *Men and Wives*, *A House and Its Head*, *Manservant and Maidservant*.

Comte, August (1798–1857), French philosopher, founder of positivism. See Positivism, Section J.

Condé, Louis, Prince de (1621–86), French general who defeated Spain at Rocroi in 1643.

Confucius or K'ung Fu-tse (c. 551–478 B.C.), Chinese philosopher, founder of the system of cosmology, politics, and ethics known as Confucianism. See Confucianism, Section J.

Congreve, William (1670–1729). Restoration dramatist, whose witty plays include *The Way of the World* and *Love for Love*.

Conrad, Joseph (1857–1924), English novelist of Polish birth, whose parents were exiled to Russia for political reasons. He became master mariner in the British merchant service, and began to write novels after he left the sea in 1884. His novels include *Almayer's Folly*, *Lord Jim*, *Nostromo*.

Conscience, Hendrik Henri (1812–83), Flemish novelist who wrote *The Lion of Flanders*.

Constable, John (1776–1837), English landscape painter, b. East Bergholt, Suffolk. Unlike his contemporary Turner, who journeyed over the Continent with his sketchbook, he found his scenes within a few miles of his home. His work was more popular in France than in England at the time and affected the Barbizon school and Delacroix. Examples of his work are in the National Gallery (*The Hay Wain*, *Flatford Mill*, and *The Cornfield*), the Victoria and Albert, and the Tate (*The Valley Farm*).

Constant, Jean Joseph Benjamin (1845–1902), French painter of portraits and Oriental subjects.

Constantine (274–338), called "the Great," the first Christian Roman emperor. He was proclaimed at York by the army in 306. He stabilised the empire after a period of decline, and founded a new capital at Constantinople. A Christian council was held under his auspices at Nicaea in 325, and he was baptised on his death-bed.

Cook, James (1728–79), English navigator, son of an agricultural labourer. He entered the Royal Navy and gained a high reputation for his scientific skill. He made voyages of discovery to New Zealand and Australia in the ships under his command, *Endeavour*, *Resolution*, and *Adventure*. He anchored at Botany Bay in 1770 on his first voyage and gave it that name because of the interesting plants found on its shores. He also surveyed the Newfoundland coast. In an attempt to find the north-west passage he was murdered at Hawaii.

Cook, Thomas (1808–92), pioneer of railway excursions and tourism. His first organised trip was from Leicester to Loughborough in 1841.

Cooper, Sir Astley Paston (1768–1841), English surgeon and author of medical textbooks.

Cooper, James Fenimore (1789–1851), American novelist, who produced stirring stories of adventure, among them *The Spy, The Last of the Mohicans, The Pathfinder,* and *The Deerslayer.*

Cooper, Samuel (1609–72), English miniaturist, represented with his brother Alexander (d. 1660) in the Victoria and Albert Museum. Among his miniatures is a portrait of Cromwell.

Copernicus, Nicolas (1478–1543), founder of modern astronomy, b. at Torun in Poland. He studied at Cracow and at a number of Italian universities before settling at Frauenburg in 1512 where he became canon of the cathedral. More of a student than a practical astronomer, he spent most of his private life seeking a new theory of the heavenly bodies. In his *On the Revolution of the Celestial Orbs,* published after his death, he broke with the past and put forward the novel theory that the planets, including the earth, revolve round the sun.

Coppée, François Joachim (1842–1908), French poet, novelist and dramatist.

Coquelin, Benoit Constant (1841–1909), and Coquelin, **Ernest** (1848–1909), (Coquelin aîné et cadet), brothers, were leading lights of the French theatre.

Corelli, Arcangelo (1653–1713), Italian composer and violinist, who established the form of the concerto grosso. *See* **Section E.**

Corneille, Pierre (1606–84), French dramatist, who ranks with Racine as a master of classical tragedy. *Le Cid, Polyeucte,* and *Le Menteur* marked a new era in French dramatic production.

Cornwallis, 1st Marquess (Charles Cornwallis) (1738–1805), British general who commanded the British forces which surrendered to the Americans at Yorktown in 1781, thus ending the war of independence. He was twice governor-general of India.

Corot, Jean Baptiste (1796–1875), French landscape painter.

Correggio, Antonio Allegri da (1494–1534), Italian painter, b. Correggio. His style anticipates the baroque. His *Ecce Homo* is in the National Gallery.

Cortés, Hernando (1488–1547), Spanish adventurer, b. Medellin, Estremadura, who captured Mexico for Spain, crushing an ancient civilisation.

Coulton, George Gordon (1858–1947), scholar and historian of the Middle Ages. In his *Five Centuries of Religion* he sets forth his interpretation of monastic history in England from the Conquest to the Reformation.

Couperin, a family of French musicians who were organists at St. Gervais, Paris, from about 1650 till 1826. **François Couperin** (1668–1783), called "Couperin the Great," is the best known today for his harpsichord music.

Cousin, Victor (1792–1867), French educationist and philosopher, founder of the eclectic school.

Cousins, Samuel (1801–87), English mezzotint engraver of plates after Reynolds, Millais, Landseer, and Hogarth.

Cousteau, Jacques-Yves (b. 1910), French underwater explorer, pioneer of aqualung diving.

Couve de Murville, Maurice (b. 1907), French diplomat; de Gaulle's foreign minister 1958–68.

Coverdale, Miles (1488–1568), one of the early English reformers, b. Yorkshire, later to become bishop of Exeter. He assisted Tyndale in translating the Pentateuch and completed his own translation of the Bible in 1535. The Psalms still used in the Prayer Book and many of the phrases in the authorised version of 1611 are from his translation.

Coward, Sir Noel (1899–1973), British playwright, actor, director and composer. His first success (*The Young Idea,* 1923) was followed by a succession of witty and sophisticated plays and comedies. His many popular songs included 'Mad Dogs and Englishmen'.

Cowdrey, Sir Colin (b. 1932), English cricketer. Scored 42,719 runs in first-class cricket (and 107 centuries). First captained England, 1959. President of MCC, 1986–7.

Cowper, William (1731–1800), English religious poet. His work is characterised by simplicity and tenderness. His best-known poems are *John Gilpin* and *The Task.*

Cox, David (1783–1859), English landscape painter. A collection of his works is in the Birmingham Gallery and the Tate Gallery.

Crabbe, George (1754–1832), English poet of grim humour; author of *The Village* and *The Borough.*

Craig, Edward Gordon (1872–1966), son of Ellen Terry, producer and author of books on stagecraft.

Cranmer, Thomas (1489–1556), archbishop of Canterbury under Henry VIII, and Edward VI; an ardent promoter of the Reformation. On Mary's accession he at first consented to return to the old faith, but when called upon to make public avowal of his recantation, refused, and was burnt at the stake. His contributions were the English Bible and Book of Common Prayer.

Crichton, James (1560–82), Scottish adventurer who for his scholarly accomplishments was called "the admirable Crichton." Killed in a brawl.

Crick, Francis Harry Compton (b. 1916), English molecular biologist. With James D. Watson discovered the structure of DNA (1953). Jointly (with Watson and Maurice H. Wilkins) awarded 1962 Nobel Prize for Medicine and Physiology. Author of *The Astonishing Hypothesis: the Scientific Search for the Soul* (1994).

Cripps, Sir Stafford (1889–1952), British Labour statesman. As chancellor of the exchequer in post-war Britain, his programme was one of austerity.

Crispi, Francesco (1819–1901), Italian statesman, who aided Garibaldi and was later premier.

Crispin, St. (c. 285), martyr with his brother. By tradition they were Roman and became shoe-makers, hence patron saints of shoemaking.

Croce, Benedetto (1886–1952), Italian philosopher and critic. His philosophy is expounded in the four volumes of *Filosofia dello Spirito* (which has been translated into English). He founded and edited *La Critica* in 1908, a review of literature, history, and philosophy. He was strongly opposed to fascism.

Croesus (d. c. 546 B.C.), last king of Lydia, reputed to be of immense wealth. Conquered and condemned to death by Cyrus, he was reprieved when Cyrus heard him recall Solon's saying "Call no man happy till he is dead."

Crome, John (1769–1821), English landscape painter, b. Norwich.

Cromer, 1st Earl of (Evelyn Baring) (1841–1917), British diplomat who, as British comptroller-general in Egypt from 1883 to 1907, did much to maintain order, improve the finances and promote development.

Crompton, Samuel (1753–1827), English inventor of the spinning-mule (1779), which substituted machinery for hand work. He was b. near Bolton, a farmer's son, and benefited little by his invention.

Cromwell, Oliver (1599–1658), Protector of the commonwealth of England, Scotland, and Ireland. B. at Huntingdon, he represented Huntingdon in parliament. When civil war broke out, he served under the Earl of Essex; and then reorganised the parliamentary army, winning victories at Marston Moor and Naseby. Tortuous negotiations with Charles I could not be brought to an end, and he promoted the king's trial and execution in 1649. He defeated the Scots at Dunbar. When continued difficulties beset government he became Protector in 1653, but was soon obliged to govern by major-generals. His handling of Ireland enhanced the difficulties of that country. An able general and a strong character, he was personally tolerant (an Independent), sincere and devout; but he was in the revolutionary's dilemma—that there is no easy exit from a revolutionary situation.

Cromwell, Richard (1626–1712), son of the above, and his successor in the protectorate.

Cromwell, Thomas (1485–1540), English statesman, who succeeded Wolsey in the service of Henry VIII, and carried out the dissolution of the monasteries. Fell from favour and was executed.

Crookes, Sir William (1832–1919), English physicist who discovered the element thallium (1861) and invented the Crookes tube (1874) which was used by J. J. Thomson and others in their researches into the conduction of electricity in gases. He was also an authority on nutrition.

Cruikshank, George (1792–1878), caricaturist and book illustrator, whose work includes illustrations to *Grimm's Fairy Tales,* and *Oliver Twist.*

Cuéllar, Javier Pérez de (b. 1920), Peruvian diplomat. UN Secretary-General, 1982–end of

1991. Succeeded in negotiating Iran-Iraq ceasefire (1988) but failed to prevent Gulf War (1991).

Cummings, Bruce Frederick (1889–1919), English zoologist, better known however as the author of *Diary of a Disappointed Man* (1919) written under the pseudonym W. N. P. Barbellion.

Cunard, Sir Samuel (1787–1865), founder of the Cunard line of steam ships. He was born in Nova Scotia, of a Welsh family of Quakers.

Cunningham of Hyndhope, 1st Viscount (Andrew Browne Cunningham) (1883–1963). British admiral in two world wars, b. Edinburgh. He served as C.-in-C., Mediterranean, 1939–42 and Feb.–Oct. 1943; naval C.-in-C. for the assault on North Africa 1942; and first sea lord 1943–6.

Curie, Marie Sklodowska (1867–1934), first great woman scientist, b. Poland. Her father was a professor of physics at Warsaw. She came to Paris to study at the Sorbonne and married **Pierre Curie** (1859–1906), professor of physics. Thus began a fruitful collaborative career that led to the discovery of radium for which they shared the 1903 Nobel prize for physics. In 1911 Mme. Curie received the Nobel prize for chemistry. Pierre Curie was killed in an accident. *See also* **Joliot-Curie.**

Curzon of Kedleston, 1st Marquess (George Nathaniel Curzon) (1859–1925), statesman and administrator; viceroy of India 1898–1905; member of Lloyd George's war cabinet 1916–18; foreign secretary 1919–24.

Cuthbert, St. (*c.* 635–87), Celtic monk who became prior of Old Melrose (on the Tweed) and later of Lindisfarne. For a time he lived in seclusion on one of the Farne islands. The story of his life we owe to Bede.

Cuvier, Georges (1769–1832), French naturalist, noted for his system of classification of animals and his studies in comparative anatomy. His *La Règne Animal* (1819) became a standard work.

Cuyp, Albert (1620–91), Dutch landscape painter of sea and river views.

Cyprian, St. (d. 258), bishop of Carthage, and early Christian writer who was martyred.

Cyrus (559–529 B.C.), Persian emperor. He founded the Achaemenid line, having defeated the Medes. By conquering Lydia and Babylonia, he controlled Asia Minor. He was a wise ruler, allowing the Jews to rebuild their temple.

D

Daguerre, Louis Jacques Mandé (1789–1851), French photographic pioneer, who invented the daguerrotype process. *See* **Section L.**

Dahl, Roald (1916–90), British author of Norwegian parentage. He wrote macabre, ingenious stories, including those in *Kiss, Kiss* (1960), and highly popular books for children, such as *Charlie and the Chocolate Factory* (1964). Some of his stories were dramatised for the TV series, *Tales of the Unexpected.*

Daimler, Gottlieb (1834–1900), German inventor, with N. A. Otto of Cologne, of the Otto gas engine. The Mercédès car, exhibited at Paris in 1900, was named after the daughter of Emile Jellinek, Austrian banker and car enthusiast.

Dalai Lama, *see* **Section L.**

Dale, Sir Henry Hallett (1875–1968), English physiologist. He shared the 1936 Nobel prize for medicine for his work on the chemical transmission of nerve impulses.

Dalhousie, 1st Marquess of (James Andrew Broun Ramsay) (1812–60), governor-general of India. He annexed the Punjab and later other states; opened the civil service to Indians and acted against suttee.

Dalton, John (1766–1844), English chemist and mathematician, a Quaker teacher of Manchester. In 1808 in the first number of his *New System of Chemical Philosophy* (1808–27) the modern chemical atomic theory was first propounded by him. According to this the atoms of the chemical elements are qualitatively different from one another.

Damien, Father (1840–89), Belgian missionary priest, originally named Joseph de Veuster, who, witnessing the sufferings of the lepers confined on the Hawaiian island of Molokai, obtained permission to take charge, and remained there until he himself died of leprosy.

Damocles, 5th cent. B.C., Syracusan flatterer who

pronounced the tyrant Dionysius the happiest of men. To illustrate the uncertainty of life, Dionysius invited him to a banquet, where a naked sword hung over his head by a hair. Hence the expression "Sword of Damocles" to mean impending danger or threat.

Damrosch, Walter Johannes (1862–1950), American conductor and composer, b. Breslau, Prussia. He promoted musical development in the U.S., especially while conductor of the New York Symphony Society which his father, Leopold Damrosch (1832–1885) had founded in 1878.

D'Annunzio, Gabriele (1863–1938), Italian poet, dramatist and nationalist. In 1919 he led a raid on Fiume and seized it, but was eventually forced to surrender. His bodyguard wore the black shirt, later the uniform of the Fascists.

Dante Alighieri (1265–1321), Italian poet, a figure of world literature. He was b. at Florence in a troubled period. Though he saw her but once or twice, he loved a lady whom he called Beatrice, who is believed to have been Bice Portinari who married Simone di Bardi; she died in 1290, after which Dante wrote his *Vita Nuova*. His next work *Convivio* was philosophical. He joined the party of the Bianchi, attained municipal office, but was imprisoned and in 1301 fled. His *Divina Commedia* is a description of hell, purgatory, and heaven, a work of moral edification, replete with symbolism. He d. at Ravenna.

Danton, Georges Jacques (1759–94), French revolutionary. To his eloquent lead in 1792 was largely due the defeat of the foreign forces attempting to quell the revolution. He was a member of the committee of public safety, and sought to modify the extremists, but was displaced by Robespierre and was executed.

D'Arblay. *See* **Burney.**

Darby, Abraham (1677–1717), member of the Quaker family of ironmasters of Coalbrookdale, Shropshire, who paved the way for the industrial revolution by developing iron metallurgy. His grandson **Abraham** (1750–91) built the first cast-iron bridge (1779) over the Severn at Coalbrookdale.

Darius I (548–486 B.C.), Persian king and founder of Persepolis. He extended the borders of the Persian empire beyond the Indus, and reorganised it into satrapies. He declared "God's plan for the earth is not turmoil but peace, prosperity and good government." On clashing with the Greeks, however, he was defeated at Marathon. **Darius II** was a natural son of Artaxerxes I and d. 405 B.C. **Darius III** (d. 331 B.C.) was the last of the Persian kings, and was defeated by Alexander and assassinated.

Darling, Grace Horsley (1815–42), English heroine who by putting off in a small boat from the lighthouse on one of the Farne islands, of which her father was keeper, saved the shipwrecked crew of the *Forfarshire.*

Darnley, Henry Stewart, Lord (1545–67), second husband of Mary, Queen of Scots (1565). He plotted the murder of her secretary Rizzio, and was subsequently himself murdered.

Darwin, Charles Robert (1809–82), English naturalist, b. Shrewsbury, one of the pioneers of experimental biology. After returning from his formative voyage round the world as naturalist on the *Beagle* (1831–6), he spent nearly twenty years building up evidence for his theory of evolution before publishing it in *The Origin of Species* (1859). In it he argued that the evolution of present-day morphology had been built up by the gradual and opportunistic mechanism of natural selection.

Daudet, Alphonse (1840–97), French writer who covered a wide range and whose works include *Lettres de mon Moulin*, *Robert Helmont*, and *Tartarin de Tarascon.*

David I (1084–1153), King of Scotland. As uncle of Matilda, daughter of Henry I of England, he supported her claim to the English crown, but was defeated. In Scotland he promoted unity and development.

David II (1324–71), King of Scotland. He was son of Robert Bruce. In invading England he was captured at Neville's Cross, 1346.

David, Sir Edgeworth (1848–1934), Australian geologist who accompanied Shackleton's antarctic expedition, 1907–9, leading the party that reached the south magnetic pole.

David, Jacques Louis (1748–1825), French painter of classical subjects and an ardent republican.

David, St., patron saint of Wales who lived in south Wales in the 6th cent.

Davidson, 1st Baron (Randall Thomas Davidson) (1848–1930), archbishop of Canterbury, 1903–28.

Davies, Sir Walford (1869–1941), English organist, composer, and broadcaster on music.

Davies, William Henry (1871–1940), Welsh poet. He spent some years tramping in both England and America, and his work shows knowledge of and love for nature. He wrote *Autobiography of a Super-tramp*.

Da Vinci. *See* Leonardo.

Davis, Jefferson (1808–89), American civil war leader. B. in Kentucky, he was made president of the Confederate States when the civil war broke out. After the war he was tried for treason, but discharged. He wrote *The Rise and Fall of the Confederate Government*.

Davis, John (*c.* 1550–1605), Elizabethan explorer and discoverer of Davis's Strait, the channel between the Atlantic and Arctic oceans on the west of Greenland. Invented the backstaff, or Davis's quadrant.

Davitt, Michael (1846–1906), Irish nationalist. The son of a peasant who later came to England, he joined the Fenians, and in 1870 was sentenced to penal servitude. On his release he helped to found the Land League in 1879; was again imprisoned; and wrote *Leaves from a Prison Diary.* He was subsequently returned to parliament.

Davy, Sir Humphry (1778–1829), English chemist, b. Penzance. Much of his work found practical application, *e.g.*, the miner's safety lamp which still bears his name. His *Elements of Agricultural Chemistry* (1813) contains the first use in English of the word "element." He took Michael Faraday as his assistant at the Royal Institution.

Dawber, Sir Guy (1861–1938), English architect. As chairman of the Council for the Preservation of Rural England, he did much to bring about the restoration of buildings nationwide.

Day Lewis, Cecil (1904–72), poet and critic; professor of poetry at Oxford from 1951–6. He succeeded Masefield as poet laureate in 1968.

Debussy, Claude Achille (1862–1918), composer and leader of the French Impressionist school in music. Among his works are *Suite bergamasque*, containing the popular *Clair de lune*; *L'après-midi d'un Faune*, inspired by the poem of Mallarmé, and *La Mer*. He also wrote an opera *Pelléas et Mélisande*.

Defoe, Daniel (1660–1731), English political writer; also author of *Robinson Crusoe, Moll Flanders*, and a *Tour of Gt. Britain*. His *Shortest Way with Dissenters* brought him imprisonment.

De Forest, Lee (1873–1961), American inventor who was the first to use alternating-current transmission, and improved the thermionic valve detector by which wireless and sound films were made possible.

Degas, Edgar (1834–1917), French impressionist painter and sculptor, son of a banker. He painted subjects from everyday life—dancers, café life, the racecourse.

De Gasperi, Alcide (1881–1954), Italian politician who founded the Christian Democrat Party.

de Gaulle. *See* Gaulle, Charles de.

De Havilland, Sir Geoffrey (1882–1965), pioneer of civil and military aviation in Britain; designer of the famous Moth machines.

De Klerk, Frederik Willem (b. 1936), South African State President from 1989 to May 1994. Currently Vice-President. He launched a far-reaching reform process in South Africa. Shared Nobel Peace Prize, 1993, with Nelson Mandela.

Delacroix, Ferdinand Victor Eugène (1798–1863), French painter of the Romantic school.

De la Mare, Walter John (1873–1956), English poet and novelist whose work has a characteristic charm. Much of it was written for children.

Delane, John Thadeus (1817–79), editor of *The Times*, 1841–77, who did much to establish that paper's standing.

Delaroche, Paul (1797–1856), French historical painter.

Delibes, Clément Philibert Léo (1836–91), French composer of much graceful music, including operas, of which *Lakmé* is the best known, and ballets, among them *Coppélia.*

Delius, Frederick (1862–1934), English composer of German parentage. His music, highly idiosyncratic in idiom, was more readily received in Germany than in England until promoted by Sir Thomas Beecham. *See* **Section E.**

Delors, Jacques, (b. 1925), French socialist politician. Leading advocate of European federalism. President, European Commission, 1985–95.

Democritus (*c.* 470–*c.* 400 B.C.), one of the first scientific thinkers, pupil of Leucippus (fl. *c.* 440 B.C.). He took an atomic view of matter, denied the existence of mind as a separate entity, and counted happiness and inner tranquility as important moral principles. His attitude was not shared by his contemporary, Socrates, nor by Plato and Aristotle, but was accepted by Epicurus. The atomic theory thus passed into the background for many centuries.

Demosthenes (384–322 B.C.), Greek orator who, by his *Philippics*, roused the Athenians to resist the growing power of Philip of Macedon.

Deng Xiaoping (b. 1904), Chinese politician, b. Szechwan; rehabilitated at Eleventh Party Congress (1977); effective leader of China in 1980s, target of May 1989 student revolt. *See* **Section C.**

De Quincey, Thomas (1785–1859), English essayist and critic; friend of Wordsworth and Southey. He wrote *Confessions of an English Opium-eater*.

De Reszke, Jean (1853–1925) and **De Reszke, Edouard** (1856–1917), Polish operatic singers, the first a tenor, the second a baritone.

Derwentwater, 3rd Earl of (James Radcliffe) (1689–1716), leader of the English Jacobite movement. He was defeated at Preston in 1715 and beheaded.

Descartes, René (1596–1650), French mathematician, pioneer of modern philosophy. Unconvinced by scholastic tradition and theological dogma, he sought to get back to why anything can be said to be true, which turned out to be a fruitful line of thought. The basis of his Cartesian philosophy is summed up in his own words, *Cogito, ergo sum* (I think, therefore I am).

Desmoulins, Camille (1760–94), French revolutionary. He represented Paris in the National Convention, and wrote witty and sarcastic pamphlets and periodicals. An ally of Danton.

Deutscher, Isaac (1907–67), Marxist historian, biographer of Stalin and Trotsky. B. in Poland, he joined the outlawed Polish Communist Party but was expelled for his anti-Stalinist views. In 1939 he came to London.

De Valéra, Eamon (1882–1975), Irish statesman, b. New York, son of a Spanish father and an Irish mother. He was imprisoned for his part in the Easter rising of 1916. He opposed the treaty of 1921; and in 1926, when the republican Fianna Fáil was founded, he became its president. Fianna Fáil won the election of 1932, and he then became president of the Executive Council, 1932–7; prime minister, 1937–48, 1951–4, 1957–9; president of the republic, 1959–73. He promoted Irish neutrality in the second world war and encouraged the use of the Irish language, and in spite of early intransigence his leadership was moderate.

de Valois, Dame Ninette (b. 1898), Irish-born ballet dancer and choreographer. She toured Europe with Diaghilev, 1923–5, and in 1931 founded the Sadler's Wells Ballet School (now Royal Ballet School), of which she became director. *Autobiography* (1957).

Dewar, Sir James (1842–1923), chemist and physicist, a native of Kincardine. He succeeded in liquefying hydrogen, and invented the vacuum flask. The explosive cordite was the joint invention of himself and Sir Frederick Abel.

Dewey, John (1859–1952), American philosopher, psychologist, and educationist. A follower of William James and an exponent of pragmatism.

De Witt, Jan (1625–72), Dutch republican statesman, who carried on war with England and later negotiated the Triple Alliance, but was overthrown by the Orange Party and murdered.

Diaghilev, Sergei Pavlovich (1872–1929), Russian ballet impresario and founder of the Russian ballet. Among those associated with him are Anna Pavlova, Vaslav Nijinsky, Tamara Karsavina, Leonide Massine, Michel Fokine, the choreographer, L. N. Bakst, the painter, and Igor Stravinsky, the composer.

Dickens, Charles (1812–70), popular English

novelist of the 19th cent., with enormous output and capacity for vivid story-telling. Of humble origin, he was extremely successful. His best-known works are perhaps *Pickwick Papers*, *Oliver Twist*, *A Christmas Carol* (this influenced the observance of Christmas), *Dombey and Son*, *David Copperfield*, *Little Dorrit*, and *Great Expectations*. His great-granddaughter, **Monica Dickens** (1915–92), wrote popular novels and some light-hearted autobiographical books (*e.g.*, *One Pair of Hands*, 1939).

Dickinson, Emily (1830–86), American poet whose writing has a mystic quality. She lived a cloistered life and published almost nothing in her lifetime.

Dickinson, Goldsworthy Lowes (1863–1932), English author, an interpreter and upholder of the Greek view of life.

Diderot, Denis (1713–84), French man of letters, critic of art and literature, and editor of the *Encyclopédie* (1713–84) to which many writers of the Englightenment contributed.

Diemen, Anthony van (1593–1645), Dutch promoter of exploration. As governor-general in the Far East, he promoted Dutch trade and influence; and despatched Abel Tasman, who in 1642 discovered New Zealand and Van Diemen's Land (now Tasmania).

Diesel, Rudolf (1858–1913), German engineer, inventor of an internal combustion engine which he patented in 1893. *See also* L34.

Diocletian (245–313), Roman emperor and persecutor of Christianity. He divided the empire under a system of joint rule; later abdicated; and built a palace in Dalmatia.

Diogenes (412–322 B.C.), Greek cynic philosopher who lived in a tub and told Alexander to get out of his sunshine. He sought virtue and moral freedom in liberation from desire.

Dionysius the elder and younger, tyrants of Syracuse in the 4th cent. B.C.

Dirac, Paul Adrien Maurice (1902–84), English physicist who shared with Erwin Schrödinger the 1933 Nobel prize for their work on Heisenberg's theory of quantum mechanics. O.M. (1973).

Disney, Walter Elias (1901–66), American film cartoonist, creator of Mickey Mouse. He is known for his *Silly Symphonies*, *Snow White and the Seven Dwarfs*, and *Pinocchio*. Held strongly anti-semitic views.

Disraeli, Benjamin, Earl of Beaconsfield (1804–81), British statesman and novelist who helped to form modern Conservatism in England. The son of Isaac (*q.v.*), he published his first novel at 21, and later *Coningsby* and *Sibyl*, which helped to rouse the social conscience. He entered parliament in 1837 and was prime minister 1868 and 1874–80, when he arranged the purchase of shares in the Suez canal. He was rival of Gladstone and friend of Queen Victoria.

D'Israeli, Isaac (1766–1848), father of Benjamin (*q.v.*) and author of *Curiosities of Literature*.

Dobson, Austin (1840–1921), English writer of light verse and of 18th cent. biography.

Dodgson, Charles Lutwidge (1832–98), English writer. Under the pseudonym Lewis Carroll, he wrote poems and books for children, including *Alice's Adventures in Wonderland*. In private life he was a lecturer in mathematics at Oxford.

Dolci, Carlo (1616–86), one of the last Florentine painters.

Dolci, Danilo (b. 1924), Italian social reformer who dedicated himself to the rehabilitation of the people of Sicily in their desperate poverty.

Dominic, St. (1170–1221), founder of the Friars Preachers or Black Friars. B. in Castile, he and his followers sought to teach the ignorant. In 1216 they were formed into an order and vowed to poverty. The order spread widely.

Domitian (Titus Flavius Domitianus) (A.D. 51–96), Roman emperor, son of Vespasian. Emperor from A.D. 81. He ruled despotically, aroused the hatred of the senate, and was assassinated as a result of a palace conspiracy.

Donatello (Donato di Niccolò) (*c.* 1386–1466), Italian sculptor, b. Florence, son of Niccolò di Betto di Bardo. He was the founder of modern sculpture, producing statues independent of a background, designed to stand in the open to be viewed from all angles. Among his masterpieces are the statues of *St. George* and *David* (in the Bargello, Florence) and his equestrian *Gattamelata* in Padua, the first bronze

horse to be cast in the Renaissance.

Donizetti, Gaetano (1797–1848), Italian composer. The best known of his sixty operas are *Lucia di Lammermoor*, *La Fille du Régiment*, and *Don Pasquale*. *See* **Section E**.

Donne, John (1572–1631), English metaphysical poet and preacher (dean of St. Paul's). His poems and sermons marked by passion, wit, and profundity of thought have received full publicity only in the present century. His writings include *Elegies*, *Satires*, *Songs and Sonnets*, *Problems and Paradoxes* and the *Holy Sonnets*.

Doré, Gustave (1833–83), French artist who painted scriptural subjects and illustrated Dante, Milton, and Tennyson.

Dostoyevsky, Feodor Mikhailovich (1001–01), Russian novelist, b. Moscow. As a result of his revolutionary activity he was sent to hard labour in Siberia. In his books, which include *Crime and Punishment*, *The Brothers Karamazov*, *The Idiot*, and *The Possessed*, he explored the dark places of the human spirit to a degree not previously attempted.

Douglas of Kirtleside, 1st Baron (William Sholto Douglas) (1893–1969), British airman; commanded Fighter command, 1940–2, Coastal command, 1944–5. A Labour peer.

Douglas, Norman (1868–1952), novelist and travel writer. A Scot, born in Austria, he made his home on the Mediterranean. His works include *South Wind*.

Doulton, Sir Henry (1820–97), English potter and the inventor of Doulton ware.

Dowden, Edward (1843–1913), English literary critic and Shakespearean scholar.

Dowding, 1st Baron (Hugh Caswell Tremenheere Dowding) (1882–1970), British airman; commanded Fighter command during the Battle of Britain period (1940).

Dowland, John (*c.* 1563–1626), English composer of songs with lute accompaniment. His son Robert was later Court lutenist to Charles I.

Doyle, Sir Arthur Conan (1859–1930), British writer, b. Edinburgh, creator of the detective Sherlock Holmes and his friend and foil, Dr. Watson. He was trained as a doctor but gave up his medical practice in 1890 to devote himself to writing.

Doyle, Richard (1824–83), humorous artist on the staff of *Punch*.

D'Oyly Carte, Richard (1844–1901), English theatrical manager, who built the Savoy theatre and there produced Gilbert and Sullivan operas.

Draco (7th cent. B.C.), Athenian lawmaker who redrew the constitution of Athens in 621 B.C. and substantially increased the penalties for debt, thus giving his name to particularly severe laws.

Drake, Sir Francis (*c.* 1540–96), English seaman. In 1577–80 he sailed round the world in the *Golden Hind*. In 1587 he destroyed a number of Spanish ships in Cadiz harbour; and under Lord Howard he helped to defeat the Spanish Armada in 1588.

Draper, John William (1811–82), American chemist, b. near Liverpool. He was the first, using Daguerre's process, to take a successful photograph of the human face (1840), and the moon.

Dreiser, Theodore (1871–1935), American novelist of austere realism. Author of *An American Tragedy*.

Dreyfus, Alfred (1859–1935), French victim of injustice. Of Jewish parentage, in 1894 he was accused of divulging secrets to a foreign power, and was sentenced by a military secret tribunal to imprisonment for life on Devil's Island in French Guiana. At a new trial in 1899 he was again found guilty. Efforts continued to be made on his behalf, and in 1906 he was entirely exonerated, restored to his rank in the army, and made a Chevalier of the Legion of Honour.

Drinkwater, John (1882–1937), English poet and playwright. His plays include *Abraham Lincoln*, and *Oliver Cromwell*.

Drummond, William (1585–1649), Scottish poet and Royalist pamphleteer. He was laird of Hawthornden.

Drury, Alfred (1857–1944), English sculptor, especially of statues of Queen Victoria at Bradford and Portsmouth.

Dryden, John (1631–1700), prolific English poet and dramatist, who also wrote political satire (*Absalom and Achitophel*). He was hostile to the revolution of 1688, and thereafter mainly translated classical writers, including Virgil.

Du Barry, Marie Jean Bécu, Comtesse (1746–93), mistress of Louis XV of France and guillotined by the revolutionary tribunal.

Dubček, Alexander (1921–92), Czech political leader. First Secretary, Slovak Communist Party, 1968-69. His reform programme (the 'Prague Spring') prompted the Russian invasion of August 1968. Restored to public life, 1989.

Du Chaillu, Paul Belloni (1835–1903), traveller in Africa, who in 1861 and 1867 published accounts of his explorations. A French-American.

Dufferin and Ava, 1st Marquess of (Frederick Temple Hamilton-Temple Blackwood) (1826–1902), British diplomat, writer, and governor-general of Canada and viceroy of India.

Dulles, John Foster (1888–1959), U.S. Secretary of State in the Republican administration 1953–9. A staunch Cold War warrior.

Dumas, Alexandre (1802–70), French romantic novelist, among whose many works are *The Three Musketeers*, *The Count of Monte Cristo*, and *The Black Tulip*.

Dumas, Alexandre (1824–95), French dramatist, son of the above; author of *La Dame aux Camélias*.

Du Maurier, George (1834–96), contributor to *Punch* and author of *Trilby*.

Dummett, Professor Michael (b. 1925), English philosopher. Succeeded Ayer as Wykeham Professor of Logic at Oxford University. Author of *Logical Basis of Metaphysics* (1990). Anti-racist.

Dundee, 1st Viscount (John Graham of Claverhouse), (1648–89), Scottish soldier ("Bonnie Dundee"). Employed to suppress the conventers, he was defeated at Drumclog, but victorious at Bothwell Brig. At the revolution of 1688 he supported James II, and was killed in the (victorious) battle of Killiecrankie.

Dundonald, Earl of. *See* Cochrane, Thomas.

Duns Scotus, John (c. 1265–1308), Scottish scholastic philosopher, b. at Maxton near Roxburgh, opponent of Thomas Aquinas. He joined the Franciscans, studied and taught at Oxford and Paris, and probably d. at Cologne. He challenged the harmony of faith and reason.

Dunstable, John (c. 1380–1453), the earliest English composer known by name. He was a contemporary of the Netherlands composers Dufay and Binchois. *See* **Section E.**

Dunstan, St. (908–88), reforming archbishop of Canterbury. He lived through seven reigns from Athelstan to Ethelred, and was adviser especially to Edgar. Under him Glastonbury Abbey became a centre of religious teaching.

Dupleix, Joseph François (1697–1763), French governor in India. He extended French influence and power in the Carnatic, but his plans were frustrated by his English opponent, Clive. He was recalled in 1754 and died in poverty.

Dürer, Albrecht (1471–1528), German painter and engraver. B. at Nuremberg, he was (like his Italian contemporary, Leonardo) a man of intellectual curiosity and scientific insight. His best work is in his copper engravings, woodcuts, and drawings; the former include *The Knight, Melancholia*, and *St. Jerome in his Study*. He was the friend of Luther and Melanchthon.

Durham, Earl of (John George Lambton) (1792–1840), governor-general of Canada after the disturbances of 1837, and in 1839 presented to parliament the *Durham Report*, which laid down the principle of colonial self-government.

Durrell, Gerald (1925–95). Zoo pioneer, conservationist and writer on animals. Author of best-selling *My Family and Other Animals*. Founded Jersey Zoo, 1958. His story-telling ability reached a generation of conservationists.

Duse, Elenora (1861–1924), Italian tragedienne.

Duval, Claude (1643–70), notorious highwayman who came to England from Normandy and was eventually hanged at Tyburn.

Dvořák, Antonin (1841–1904), Czech composer whose music is rich in folk-song melodies of his native Bohemia. In 1884 he conducted his *Stabat Mater* in London. His *New World* symphony was composed in New York, where he was head of the National Conservatoire (1892–5). *See* **Section E.**

Dyson, Sir Frank Watson (1868–1939), English astronomer who was astronomer royal 1910–33, and astronomer royal for Scotland 1905–10.

Dyson, Sir George (1883–1964), English composer and writer. In *The New Music* he analysed the

technique of modern schools of composition. He composed several choral works such as *The Canterbury Pilgrims* and *Nebuchadnezzar*, which still remain popular.

E

Earhart, Amelia (1898–1937), American air pioneer. First woman to fly the Atlantic alone. Disappeared in 1937 during a Pacific flight.

Eastlake, Sir Charles Lock (1793–1865), English painter of historical and religious works.

Eastman, George (1854–1932), American inventor of the roll photographic film and Kodak camera.

Easton, Florence (Gertrude) (1882–1955), English operatic soprano of great versatility. Repertoire of 88 roles. Last woman to sing with Caruso in 1920.

Eck, Johann von (1486–1543), German Catholic theologian and opponent of Luther.

Eddington, Sir Arthur Stanley (1882–1944), English astronomer (Greenwich observatory 1906–13; Cambridge observatory 1914–44). His works include *The Nature of the Physical World*.

Eddy, Mrs Mary Baker (1821–1910), American founder of the Church of Christ Scientist. Her *Science and Health with Key to the Scriptures* was published in 1875. *See* **Christian Science, Section J.**

Edelinck, Gerard (1640–1707), Flemish engraver, b. Antwerp, the first to reproduce in print the colour, as well as the form, of a picture.

Eden, Robert Anthony, 1st Earl of Avon (1897–1977), British statesman. He entered parliament in 1923; became foreign secretary in 1935 (resigning in 1938 over Chamberlain's negotiation with Mussolini and rebuff to President Roosevelt); deputy prime minister in 1951; succeeded Sir Winston Churchill in 1955. His Suez policy divided the country. He resigned for health reasons in 1957. Earldom 1961.

Edgar (943–75), King of England 959–75. He was advised by Archbishop Dunstan.

Edgar Atheling (c. 1060–c. 1130), was the lawful heir of Edward the Confessor, but in the Norman invasion could not maintain his claim.

Edgeworth, Maria (1767–1849), Irish novelist, whose stories include *Castle Rackrent*, *The Absentee*, and *Belinda*.

Edinburgh, Duke of (Philip Mountbatten) (b. 1921), consort of Queen Elizabeth II. He relinquished his right of accession to the thrones of Greece and Denmark on his naturalisation in 1947 when he took the name of Mountbatten. He is the great-great-grandson of Queen Victoria, grandson of Admiral Prince Louis of Battenberg, and nephew of the late Earl Mountbatten of Burma.

Edison, Thomas Alva (1847–1931), American inventor of the transmitter and receiver for the automatic telegraph; the phonograph; the incandescent lamp (shared with the British inventor Swan); and many devices for the electrical distribution of light and power. From being a newsboy on the railway and later a telegraph clerk, he became a master at applying scientific principles to practical ends. He set up a laboratory at Menlo Park, New Jersey.

Edmund II (Ironside) (c. 990–1016), the son of Ethelred, king of the English, made a compact with Canute to divide England, but soon afterwards died.

Edward the Confessor (c. 1004–1066), English king who preceded the Norman Conquest and founded Westminster Abbey. He was canonised in 1161.

Edward the Elder (c. 870–c. 924), son of Alfred, succeeded him as king of the West Saxons in 899. He overcame the Danes and reoccupied the northern counties.

Edward I (1239–1307), King of England, succeeded his father Henry in 1272. Able and energetic, his legislation influenced the development of the land law, and he summoned parliamentary assemblies. A soldier, he conquered Wales, building castles, but could not maintain his hold on Scotland.

Edward II (1284–1327), succeeded his father Edward I as king of England in 1307 and was defeated by the Scots at Bannockburn. Weak and inept, he was murdered in 1327.

Edward III (1312–77), succeeded his father Edward II as king of England in 1327. Popular and ambitious he began the Hundred Years

War with France. He fostered the woollen industry. Latterly he became senile.

Edward IV (1442–83), able but dissolute Yorkist leader whose reign (1461–70, 1471–83) brought about a revival in the power of the monarchy, in English sea power, and in foreign trade (in which he himself took part). Spent 1470–71, in exile. Began rebuilding of St. George's chapel, Windsor. Patron of Caxton.

Edward V (1470–83), succeeded his father Edward IV at the age of 12 and was a pawn in the quarrels of baronial relatives. He and his brother were shut up in the Tower by his uncle, Richard, Duke of Gloucester, and there probably murdered, though proof has not been established.

Edward VI (1537–53), succeeded his father, Henry VIII, as king of England when in his tenth year. He was delicate and studious, and his government was carried on successively by the Dukes of Somerset and Northumberland; while under Archbishop Cranmer the prayer book was issued. He was induced to name Lady Jane Grey his successor.

Edward VII (1841–1910), King of Great Britain and Ireland. The son of Queen Victoria, he married Princess Alexandra of Denmark in 1863, and succeeded his mother in 1901. Interested mainly in social life and in international contacts. He visited India in 1875.

Edward VIII (1894–1972), King of Great Britain, succeeded his father George V 1936, and abdicated later that year because of disagreement over his proposed marriage. He was created Duke of Windsor, and was governor of the Bahamas 1940–45. The Duchess of Windsor died in 1986.

Ehrlich, Paul (1854–1915), German bacteriologist, who at Frankfurt-on-Main carried out work in immunology. He discovered salvarsan for the treatment of syphilis. Nobel prizewinner 1908.

Eiffel, Alexandre Gustave (1832–1923), French engineer, one of the first to employ compressed air caissons in bridge building. Among his works are the Eiffel Tower (1887–9) and the Panama Canal locks.

Einstein, Albert (1879–1955), mathematical physicist whose theory of relativity superseded Newton's theory of gravitation. He was born in Ulm of Jewish parents, lived for many years in Switzerland, and held a succession of professorial chairs at Zurich, Prague, and Berlin. In 1921 he was awarded the Nobel prize for his work in quantum theory. He was driven by the Nazis to seek asylum in America and became professor at the Institute of Advanced Study at Princeton 1933–45. In August 1939 at the request of a group of scientists he wrote to President Roosevelt warning of the danger of uranium research in Germany and stressing the urgency of investigating the possible use of atomic energy in bombs. *See* Relativity, Section F, Part II.

Eisenhower, Dwight David (1890–1969), American general and statesman. He was C.-in-C. Allied Forces, N. Africa, 1942–3; and in the European theatre of operations, 1943–5; and was Republican President, 1953–61.

Eisenstein, Sergei Mikhailovich. *See* W7.

Eleanor (1246–90), Queen of Edward I. After her death in 1290 the king had memorial crosses erected at the twelve places where her body rested on its way from Grantham to Westminster.

Elgar, Sir Edward (1857–1934), English composer, specially of choral-orchestral works for festivals. His oratorios include *The Kingdom, The Apostles,* and *The Dream of Gerontius*; he also wrote the *Enigma Variations,* and the tone-poem *Falstaff. See* Section E.

Elgin, 7th Earl of (Thomas Bruce) (1766–1841), British diplomat who, with the object of saving them, conveyed some sculptures from the Parthenon in Athens to the British Museum.

Eliot, George (1819–80), pen-name of Mary Anne (later Marion) Evans, b. Warwickshire. Her novels include *Adam Bede, The Mill on the Floss, Silas Marner, Middlemarch,* and *Daniel Deronda.* Her works show deep insight. She lived with the writer George Lewes from 1854 until his death 25 years later. (Although Lewes had been deserted by his wife it was not then possible to obtain a divorce.) She brought up his three children.

Eliot, Thomas Stearns (1888–1965), poet and critic. He was born in St. Louis, Missouri, and became a British subject in 1927. His poems include *Prufrock and Other Observations,*

The Waste Land, The Hollow Men, Ash Wednesday, Four Quartets; his verse dramas *Murder in the Cathedral* and *The Family Reunion.* He described himself as "classical in literature, royalist in politics, and Anglo-Catholic in religion". Nobel prizewinner 1948.

Elizabeth (b. 1900), Queen Consort of George VI, daughter of the 14th Earl of Strathmore. Before her marriage in 1923 she was Lady Elizabeth Angela Marguerite Bowes-Lyon.

Elizabeth I (1533–1603), Queen of England, daughter of Henry VIII, succeeded her sister Mary in 1558. Politically and intellectually able and firm, though personally vain and capricious, she chose to serve her able men such as William Cecil; and her long reign was one of stability, victory over the Spanish, and adventure in the New World; while the Church of England was established. It was however marred by the execution of Mary, Queen of Scots.

Elizabeth II (Elizabeth Alexandra Mary of Windsor) (b. 1926), Queen of Gt. Britain and N. Ireland, ascended the throne Feb. 1952 on the death of her father George VI. Her Consort, Prince Philip, Duke of Edinburgh, is the son of Prince Andrew of Greece and a descendant of the Danish royal family. They have four children: **Charles, Prince of Wales** (b. 1948), **Princess Anne** (b. 1950), **Prince Andrew** (b. 1960), and **Prince Edward** (b. 1964). Princess Anne was styled the Princess Royal in June 1987. She married Commander Tim Laurence in 1992, the first royal remarriage after a divorce since Henry VIII.

Ellis, Havelock (1859–1939), English writer whose *Studies in the Psychology of Sex* was influential in changing the public attitude towards sex. His books were first published in America.

Emerson, Ralph Waldo (1803–82), American poet and essayist, b. Boston, member of the transcendentalist group of thinkers. Among his best-known poems are *Woodnotes, Threnody, Terminus, Brahma, The Problem.*

Emin Pasha, the name adopted by **Eduard Schnitzer** (1840–92), a German explorer associated with Gen. Charles Gordon in the Sudan as a medical officer; and governor of the Equatorial Province 1878–89, when he was menaced by the Mahdi and rescued by Stanley. He had contributed greatly to African studies.

Emmet, Robert (1778–1803), Irish patriot, led the rising of 1803, was betrayed, and executed.

Empedocles (c. 500–c. 430 B.C.), Greek philosopher, b. Agrigentum in Sicily, founder of a school of medicine which regarded the heart as the seat of life, an idea which passed to Aristotle, as did his idea that all matter was composed of four elements: earth, air, fire, and water.

Engels, Friedrich (1820–95), German socialist, son of a wealthy textile manufacturer, lifelong friend of Karl Marx, with whom he collaborated in writing the *Communist Manifesto* of 1848. Through him Marx acquired his knowledge of English labour conditions.

Epaminondas (c. 418–362 B.C.), Theban general who led the Boeotian League against the attempt of Sparta to dominate Greece in the early 4th cent. B.C. and even defeated her army at the battle of Leuctra in 371 B.C.

Epicurus of Samos (342–270 B.C.), refounded the atomic view of matter put forward by Democritus, and held that peace of mind comes through freedom from fear, the two main sources of which he regarded as religion and fear of death. The Epicureans were a rival sect to the Peripatetics and Stoics.

Epstein, Sir Jacob (1880–1959), sculptor, b. New York of Russian–Polish parents. His work includes *Rima,* in Hyde Park; *Day* and *Night* on the building of London Underground headquarters; *Genesis,* exhibited in 1931; *Lazarus,* in New College, Oxford; the *Madonna and Child* group in Cavendish Square, London; the figure of *Christ in Majesty* in aluminium in Llandaff cathedral; a sculpture for the T.U.C. headquarters in London; and a bronze group for Coventry cathedral.

Erasmus, Desiderius (1466–1536), Dutch Renaissance humanist, who spent several years in England and was the friend of Dean Colet and Sir Thomas More. He aimed at ecclesiastical reform from within and scorned the old scholastic teaching. He thus prepared the way for Luther. His *Praise of Folly* is still widely read.

Erhard, Ludwig (1897–1977), German economist and politician; succeeded Adenauer as Chancellor of the West German Federal Republic, 1963–7.

Essex, 2nd Earl of (Robert Devereux) (1566–1601), favourite of Queen Elizabeth I in her old age. Unsuccessful as governor-general of Ireland, he returned to England against the Queen's wish; plotted; and was executed.

Ethelbert, King of Kent at the close of the 6th cent., accepted Christianity on the mission of St. Augustine.

Ethelred II (c. 968–1016), King of England. Unable to organise resistance against the Danish raids, he was called the Unready (from Old Eng. uraed = without counsel).

Etty, William (1787–1849), English artist of historical and classical subjects.

Eucken, Rudolf Christoph (1846–1926), German philosopher of activism, which puts personal ethical effort above intellectual idealism. Nobel prizewinner 1908.

Euclid, Greek mathematician of the 3rd cent. B.C. Famous for his *Elements*.

Euler, Leonhard (1707–83), Swiss mathematician, remembered especially for his work in optics and on the calculus of variations. He was called by Catherine I to St. Petersburg, where he was professor, 1730–41, and by Frederick the Great to Berlin, 1741–66. He became blind but continued his work.

Euripides (480–406 B.C.), Greek tragic dramatist, who is known to have written about 80 plays of which 18 are preserved, including *Alcestis*, *Medea*, *Iphigenia*, and *Orestes*. He displayed a sceptical attitude towards the myths.

Eusebius (264–340), ecclesiastical historian. His *Ecclesiastical History* gives the history of the Christian church to 324. He also wrote a general history, *Chronicon*.

Evans, Sir Arthur John (1851–1941), English archaeologist, known for his excavations at Knossos in Crete and his discovery of the pre-Phoenician script.

Evans, Dame Edith Mary (1888–1976), English actress, whose celebrated roles were Millamant in *The Way of the World*, the Nurse in *Romeo and Juliet*, and Lady Bracknell in *The Importance of Being Earnest*.

Evans, Sir Geraint Llewellyn (1922–92), much-loved Welsh opera singer. Principal Baritone, Royal Opera House, Covent Garden, 1948–84. Son of a Welsh miner.

Evelyn, John (1620–1706), cultured English diarist who gives brilliant portraits of contemporaries. A book collector and librarian who wrote *Sylva*, a manual of arboriculture. His magnificent library was sold by Christies in 1977.

Eyck, Jan van (c. 1389–1441), Flemish painter, whose best-known work is the altarpiece in Ghent cathedral. His brother **Hubert** (c. 1370–1426) is associated with him.

F

Fabius, the name of an ancient Roman family who over many generations played an important part in early Roman history. **Quintus Fabius Maximus Verrucosus** (d. 203 B.C.) saved Rome from Hannibal by strategic evasion of battle; hence his name *Cunctator* (delayer), and the term Fabian policy.

Fabre, Jean Henri Casimir (1823–1915), French naturalist, whose study of the habits of insects was recorded in his *Souvenirs entomologiques*.

Faed, name of two Scottish genre painters, **Thomas** (1826–1900), and **John** (1819–1902). A third brother, **James**, engraved their works.

Fahrenheit, Gabriel Daniel (1686–1736), German physicist, b. Danzig. He introduced c. 1715 the mercury thermometer and fixed thermometric standards.

Fairbairn, Sir William (1789–1874), Scottish engineer. In 1817 he took the lead in using iron in shipbuilding.

Fairfax, 3rd Baron (Thomas Fairfax) (1612–71), parliamentary general in the English civil war, and victor of Marston Moor. In 1650 he withdrew into private life.

Falconer, Hugh (1806–65), British botanist and palaeontologist, b. Forres, Scot.; physician to East India Co.; introduced tea into India.

Falla, Manuel (1876–1946), Spanish composer whose music is highly individual with a strong folk-song element. *See* **Section E.**

Faraday, Michael (1791–1867), English experimental physicist, founder of the science of electromagnetism. He was the son of a Yorkshire blacksmith and at 13 became apprenticed to a bookseller in London. In 1813 he became laboratory assistant to Sir Humphry Davy at the Royal Institution, succeeding him as professor of chemistry in 1833. He set himself the problem of finding the connections between the forces of light, heat, electricity, and magnetism and his discoveries, translated by Maxwell (*q.v.*) into a single mathematical theory of electromagnetism, led to the modern developments in physics and electronics. He inaugurated the Christmas lectures for juvenile audiences at the Royal Institution.

Farman, Henri (1874–1958), French aviator, one of the pioneers of aviation.

Farouk I (1920–65), King of Egypt, 1936–52. He was forced to abdicate after the 1952 coup.

Farrar, Frederick William (1831–1903), English clergyman, author of the schoolboy story *Eric*.

Faulkner, William (1897–1962), American novelist, whose series of novels, *The Sound and the Fury*, *As I Lay Dying*, *Light in August*, *Sanctuary*, depict the American South. Nobel prize 1949.

Fauré, Gabriel Urbain (1845–1924), French composer and teacher. His works include chamber music, nocturnes, and barcarolles for piano, an opera *Pénélope*, some exquisite songs, and *Requiem*. Ravel was among his pupils.

Fawcett, Millicent Garrett (1847–1929), educational reformer and leader of the movement for women's suffrage; one of the founders of Newnham College, Cambridge. Wife of the blind Liberal politician and economist, **Henry Fawcett** (1833–84) and sister of **Elizabeth Garrett Anderson**.

Fawkes, Guy (1570–1606), a Yorkshire catholic, who with Catesby and other conspirators planned the Gunpowder Plot. Though warned, he persisted and was captured and hanged.

Fénelon, François de Salignac de la Mothe (1651–1715), archbishop of Cambrai and author of *Telemachus*.

Ferdinand II of Aragon (1452–1516), who married Isabella of Castile, and with her reigned over Spain, saw the Moors expelled from Spain, equipped Columbus for the discoveries that led to Spain's vast colonial possessions, and instituted the Inquisition.

Ferguson, James (1710–76), Scottish astronomer who, from being a shepherd-boy, educated himself in astronomy, mathematics, and portrait painting.

Fermi, Enrico (1901–54), Italian nuclear physicist whose research contributed to the harnessing of atomic energy and the development of the atomic bomb. Nobel prizewinner 1938.

Feynman, Richard (Philips), (1918–88), American physicist, born of working-class Jewish parents. Helped develop the atomic bomb. Won Nobel Prize for Physics (1965) for work on quantum electrodynamics.

Fichte, Johann Gottlieb (1762–1814), German nationalistic and Romantic philosopher who paved the way for modern totalitarianism.

Field, John (1782–1837), Irish composer of nocturnes, pupil of Clementi and teacher of Glinka. His work served as a model for Chopin.

Fielding, Henry (1707–54), English novelist, author of *Tom Jones*, *Joseph Andrews*, and *Amelia*, as well as plays.

Fildes, Sir Luke (1844–1927), English painter and woodcut-designer.

Finsen, Niels Ryberg (1860–1904), Danish physician who established an institute for light therapy and invented the Finsen ultra-violet lamp. Nobel prizewinner 1903.

Firdausi, *pen-name of* **Abu'l Kasim Mansur** (940–1020), Persian poet, author of the epic *Shah-Nama* or Book of Kings.

Fisher of Lambeth, Baron (Geoffrey Francis Fisher) (1887–1972), archbishop of Canterbury, 1945–61; Headmaster, Repton School, 1914–32.

Fisher, Herbert Albert Laurens (1865–1940), English historian and educational reformer.

Fisher, Sir Ronald Aylmer (1890–1962), British scientist who revolutionised both genetics and the philosophy of experimentation by founding the modern corpus of mathematical statistics.

FitzGerald, Edward (1809–83), English poet who translated the *Rubaiyát* of Omar Khayyám (1859).

Fitzroy, Robert (1805–65), British meteorologist, who introduced the system of storm warnings which were the beginning of weather forecasts.

Flammarion, Camille (1842–1925), French astronomer, noted for his popular lectures and books which include *L'Astronomie Populaire*.

Flamsteed, John (1646–1719), the first English astronomer royal, for whom Charles II built an observatory at Greenwich (1675) where he worked for 44 years.

Flaubert, Gustave (1821–80), French novelist, and creator of *Madame Bovary*. Other works were *Salammbô, L'Education sentimentale*, and *Bouvard et Pécuchet*.

Flaxman, John (1755–1826), English sculptor, b. York, employed as modeller by Josiah Wedgwood. He then took to monumental sculpture.

Flecker, James Elroy (1884–1915), English poet whose works include *Golden Journey to Samarkand, Hassan* (staged in London, 1923), and *Don Juan*, as well as many lyrics.

Fleming, Sir Alexander (1881–1955), Scottish bacteriologist who discovered the antibacterial enzyme lysozyme in 1922 and penicillin in 1928. Full recognition came during the war when Florey separated the drug now used from the original penicillin. Awarded Nobel prize jointly with Florey and Chain, 1945.

Fleming, Sir Ambrose (1849–1945), British scientist whose invention of the radio valve in 1904 revolutionised radio telegraphy and solved problems of radio-telephony. This eventually made possible high quality sound transmission, and thus led to broadcasting and television.

Fletcher, John (1579–1625), English dramatist who collaborated with Francis Beaumont (*q.v.*) in writing many pieces for the stage.

Flinders, Matthew (1774–1814), English navigator and explorer who made discoveries in and around Australia. He sailed through Bass Strait, so called in honour of his surgeon.

Florey, Baron (Howard Walter Florey) (1898–1968), British pathologist, b. Australia. Shared 1945 Nobel prize with Fleming and Chain for work on penicillin.

Foch, Ferdinand (1851–1929), French general, b. Tarbes. In the first world war he halted the German advance at the Marne (1914), and was engaged in the battles of Ypres (1914 and 1915) and the Somme (1916). In 1918 he became supreme commander of the British, French, and American armies and dictated the terms of Allied victory.

Fokine, Michel (1880–1944), Russian dancer, choreographer to Diaghilev's company, and creator of *Les Sylphides, Prince Igor, Scheherazade, Firebird*, and *The Spectre of the Rose*.

Fokker, Anthony (1890–1939), Dutch aircraft engineer, b. Java. The Fokker factory in Germany made warplanes for the Germans in the first world war.

Fonteyn, Dame Margot (Mme. Roberto de Arias) (1919–91), prima ballerina of the Royal Ballet and acclaimed by many as the greatest ballerina of her age.

Foot, Michael (b. 1913), British journalist and politician; leader of the Labour Party 1980–83; pubs. inc. biography of Aneurin Bevan.

Ford, Gerald R. (b. 1913), American Republican President 1974–7; automatically succeeded Richard Nixon when he resigned.

Ford, Henry (1863–1947), founder of Ford Motor Company (1903), of which he was president until 1919, when he was succeeded by his son, Edsel B. Ford (1893–1943). He was the pioneer of the cheap motor car.

Forester, Cecil Scott (1899–1966), English novelist, author of the *Captain Hornblower* series.

Forster, Edward Morgan (1879–1970), English novelist, author of *The Longest Journey, A Room with a View, Howards End, A Passage to India*. O.M. 1969.

Foscari, Francesco (*c.* 1372–1457), Doge of Venice and victor over Milan.

Fourier, Charles (1772–1837), French socialist who propounded a system of associated enterprise which although utopian stimulated social reform.

Fourier, Jean Baptiste Joseph (1768–1830), French mathematical physicist. He played an active part in politics, holding administrative posts in Egypt and Isère, yet finding time for his own research, especially on the flow of heat.

Fowler, Sir John (1817–98), was the engineer of the first underground railway (the London Metro-

politan) and with his partner Sir Benjamin Baker, of the Forth bridge.

Fox, Charles James (1749–1806), English Whig statesman. Son of the 1st Lord Holland, he entered parliament at 19. He held office only for brief periods between 1770 and 1806, but he upheld the liberal causes of the day (American independence, the French revolution, and parliamentary reform), and was one of the impeachers of Warren Hastings.

Fox, George (1624–91), founder of the Society of Friends, son of a weaver of Fenny Drayton, Leicestershire.

Foxe, John (1516–87), English martyrologist, author of *History of the Acts and Monuments of the Church* (better known as *Fox's Book of Martyrs*).

Frampton, Sir George James (1860–1928), English sculptor of the Peter Pan statue in Kensington Gardens and the Edith Cavell memorial.

France, Anatole (1844–1924), French writer, especially of short stories. Nobel prize 1921.

Francis I (1494–1547), King of France. Brilliant but ambitious and adventurous, he fostered learning and art, and met Henry VIII at the Field of the Cloth of Gold. His rivalry with the Emperor Charles V involved France in prolonged war, especially in Italy (he was captured at Pavia, 1525). He persecuted the Protestants.

Francis of Assisi, St. (1181/2–1226), founder of the Franciscan Order. Son of a wealthy cloth merchant, in 1208 he turned from a life of pleasure to poverty and the complete observance of Christ's teaching. He and his friars went about preaching the gospel by word and example, and the brotherhood increased rapidly. He was canonised in 1228.

Francis, Sir Philip (1740–1818), English politician, reputed author of the *Letters of Junius*.

Franck, César Auguste (1822–90), composer and organist, b. at Liège in Belgium. *See* **Section E.**

Franco, Francisco (1892–1975), Spanish general and dictator. He led the Fascist rebellion against the Republican government (1936) and with German and Italian help ended the civil war (1939), after which he ruled Spain with utter ruthlessness.

Franklin, Benjamin (1706–90), American statesman. B. at Boston, he was at first a printer and journalist. He then took an interest in electricity, explained lightning as of electrical origin, and invented the lightning conductor. He was active in promoting the Declaration of Independence in 1773; he negotiated French support; and helped to frame the American constitution.

Franklin, Sir John (1786–1847), English Arctic explorer. His expedition in the *Erebus* and the *Terror* to find the north-west passage ended disastrously, and all attempts to find survivors failed.

Franks, Baron (Oliver Shewell Franks) (1905–92), British academic, diplomat and banker; British ambassador to U.S.A. 1948–52; provost of Worcester College, Oxford 1962–76; chosen to head Falklands inquiry 1982. O.M. 1977.

Fraunhofer, Joseph von (1787–1826), optical instrument-maker of Munich, the first to map the dark lines of the solar spectrum named after him.

Frazer, Sir James George (1854–1941), Scottish anthropologist, author of *The Golden Bough*.

Frederick I (*c.* 1123–90). Holy Roman Emperor, nicknamed Barbarossa. A strong personality, he sought to impose his will on the city-states of northern Italy and the papacy, and was defeated at Legnano in 1176 but was more successful with a conciliatory policy (1183). He had also to contend with opposition at home. He died on the third crusade.

Frederick II (1194–1250), Holy Roman Emperor, grandson of the above, and son of the heiress of Sicily. Brilliant and enlightened, he attracted to his court in Sicily Jewish, Mohammedan, and Christian scholars; founded the university of Naples; was a patron of the medical school of Salerno; wrote a treatise on falconry; and commissioned a code of laws. Politically he was less successful, having trouble with the Lombard cities, and being involved with the papacy especially as regards his delay in going on crusade; but after negotiations with the sultan of Egypt he actually was crowned king of Jerusalem.

Frederick II (the Great) (1712–86), King of Prussia. Having inherited from his father a well-drilled army, in 1740 he seized Silesia from Austria, and retained it through the resulting war and the Seven Years war. He also took part in the partition of Poland. An able administrator and and outstanding general he made Prussia powerful and strengthened its military tradition. He corresponded with Voltaire and he also played the flute.

French, Sir John, 1st Earl of Ypres (1852–1925), first British commander-in-chief in the first world war; replaced by Sir Douglas Haig in 1915.

Freud, Sigmund (1856–1939), psychiatrist and founder of psychoanalysis; b. Moravia, studied medicine in Vienna, where he lived until 1938 when the Nazi invasion of Austria sent him into exile in London where he died. His theories of the mind illumined the way we think about ourselves. His grandson, the artist **Lucien Freud** (b. 1911), was awarded the O.M. (1993).

Friedman, Milton (b. 1912), American economist. Leading proponent of monetarism. Professor of Economics, University of Chicago, 1948–82. Strongly influenced Thatcherite monetary policy.

Friese-Greene, William (1855–1921), English inventor of the cinematograph. His first film was shown in 1890. He died in poverty.

Frink, Elisabeth (1930–93), English sculptor whose figurative work made her one of the most-loved artists of her day.

Frobisher, Sir Martin (1535–94), first British navigator to seek the north-west passage from the Atlantic to the Pacific through the Arctic seas. He is commemorated in Frobisher's Strait. He also fought against the Spanish Armada.

Froebel, Friedrich Wilhelm August (1782–1852), German educational reformer, founder of the Kindergarten system.

Froissart, Jean (1337–1410), French author of *Chronicles* covering the history of Western Europe from 1307 to 1400.

Frost, Robert (1874–1963), American poet, author of *Stopping by Woods on a Snowy Evening, Birches, The Death of the Hired Man, After Apple-Picking*.

Froude, James Anthony (1818–94), English historian and biographer of Carlyle.

Fry, Christopher (b. 1907), English poet and dramatist of Quaker family; author of *The Lady's Not for Burning, Venus Observed, The Dark is Light Enough, Curtmantle, A Yard of Sun* and the religious play *A Sleep of Prisoners*.

Fry, Elizabeth (1780–1845), English prison reformer. She lived at Norwich and belonged to the Society of Friends.

Fry, Roger (1866–1934), English art critic and painter; introduced the work of Cézanne and the post-impressionists into England; author of *Vision and Design*.

Fuchs, Leonhard (1501–66), German naturalist whose compendium of medicinal plants was for long a standard work. He was professor of medicine at Tübingen and the genus *Fuchsia* is named after him.

Fuchs, Sir Vivian Ernest (b. 1908), British geologist and explorer; leader of the British Commonwealth Trans-Antarctic Expedition 1957–8, the first to cross the Antarctic continent.

Fuller, Thomas (1608–61), English antiquarian and divine, author of *Worthies of England* and a *Church History of Britain*.

Fulton, Robert (1765–1815), American engineer who experimented in the application of steam to navigation, and in 1807 launched the *Clermont* on the Hudson.

Furniss, Harry (1854–1925), caricaturist, b. Wexford. He came to London as a young man, served on the staff of *Punch* and illustrated the works of Dickens and Thackeray.

G

Gade, Niels Vilhelm (1817–90), Danish composer. While studying at Leipzig he met Mendelssohn, whom he succeeded as conductor of the Gewandhaus orchestra.

Gagarin, Yuri Alexeyevich (1934–68), Soviet cosmonaut, the first man to be launched into space

and brought safely back (12 April 1961). His flight was made in the front portion of a multistage rocket which made a single circuit of the earth in 108 min. Killed in an air crash.

Gainsborough, Thomas (1727–88), English landscape and portrait painter, b. at Sudbury in Suffolk. His portraits are marked by informality and grace.

Gaiseric or Genseric (c. 390–477), king of the Vandals, the ablest of the barbarian invaders of the Roman empire. He led his people from Spain into Africa, took Carthage, gained control of the Mediterranean and sacked Rome in 455.

Gaitskell, Hugh Todd Naylor (1906–63), Labour politician and economist. He represented Leeds South from 1945; was chancellor of the exchequer 1950–1; and leader of the Labour opposition 1955–63.

Galbraith, John Kenneth (b. 1908), American university professor of economics, b. Canada; author of *The Affluent Society* (1958), *The Liberal Hour* (1960), *The New Industrial State* (1967), *The Age of Uncertainty* (1977). He was ambassador to India 1961–3.

Galdós, Benito Pérez. See **Pérez Galdós.**

Galen, Claudius (131–201), physician, b. Pergamum (Asia Minor) of Greek parents. He systematised medical knowledge with his idea of purposive creation by the will of God; and thus discouraged original investigation. Many of his treatises survive, and his influence lasted for more than a thousand years.

Galileo (1564–1642), Italian scientist whose experimental-mathematical methods in the pursuit of scientific truth laid the foundations of modern science. He became professor of mathematics at Pisa university when he was 25 and lectured at Padua for 18 years. He made a number of fundamental discoveries, *e.g.*, in regard to the hydrostatic balance, thermometer, telescope, and foreshadowed Newton's laws of motion. He detected the four major satellites of Jupiter, the ring of Saturn, and the spots of the sun. He supported the superiority of the Copernican over the Ptolemaic theory, and was put under house arrest for so doing. He died the year Newton was born. Rehabilitated by Catholic Church, 1992.

Galsworthy, John (1867–1933), English novelist and playwright, author of *The Forsyte Saga*, a series of novels dealing with the history of an upper middle-class family. Nobel prize 1932.

Galton, Sir Francis (1822–1911), founder of eugenics, cousin of Darwin. His early work *Meteorographica* (1863), contains the basis of the modern weather chart. He was an early advocate of using finger-prints for rapid identification, and was one of the first to apply mathematics to biological problems.

Galvani, Luigi (1737–98), Italian physician and physiologist, whose experiments at Bologna demonstrated the principle of animal electricity.

Gama, Vasco da (c. 1460–1524), Portuguese navigator. Discovered the sea route to India in 1498 by rounding the Cape of Good Hope.

Gandhi, Indira (1917–84), daughter of Nehru, succeeded Shastri in 1966 to become India's first woman prime minister. She suffered a defeat at the polls in 1977 but was spectacularly successful in 1980. Assassinated 1984. Succeeded by her son, Rajiv Gandhi, who was assassinated in May 1991.

Gandhi, Mohandâs Karamchand (Mahatma) (1869–1948), Indian patriot, social reformer and moral teacher. From 1893 to 1914 he lived in South Africa opposing discrimination against Indians. In the movement for Indian independence after 1914 he dominated Congress, instituted civil disobedience, and advocated non-violence; and he sought to free India from caste. After independence he strove to promote the co-operation of all Indians but was assassinated on his way to a prayer meeting. His teaching of non-violence has had great influence.

Garbo, Greta (1905–90), Swedish film actress of poetical quality. Her films included *Queen Christina* and *Ninotchka*.

García, Manuel de Popolo Vincente (1775–1832), Spanish tenor, composer, and singing master. His son **Manuel Patricio Rodriguez** (1805–1906) was tutor to Jenny Lind. Both his daughters (Mme. Malibran and Mme. Viardot) were operatic singers, and his grandson and great-grandson baritones.

Garcia Lorca, Federico. *See* Lorca.

Gardiner, Samuel Rawson (1890–1902), English historian of the Stuart period.

Garibaldi, Giuseppe (1807–82), Italian soldier and patriot, who with Mazzini and Cavour created a united Italy. In 1834 he was condemned to death for helping in a republican plot to seize Genoa, but escaped to S. America. He returned in 1848 to fight for Mazzini but was again forced to flee. In 1851 he returned and gave his support to Cavour, taking part in the Austrian war of 1859. In 1860 with a thousand volunteers he freed Sicily, took Naples, and handed over the Two Sicilies to Victor Emmanuel who was proclaimed king.

Garrick, David (1717–79), English actor and theatrical manager. Brought up at Lichfield, he was taught by Samuel Johnson.

Garrison, William Lloyd (1805–79), American philanthropist who worked to end slavery.

Gaskell, Mrs. Elizabeth Cleghorn (1810–65), English novelist, author of *Mary Barton*, *Cranford*, and a *Life of Charlotte Brontë*. She was brought up by an aunt in the little Cheshire town of Knutsford.

Gaulle, Charles de (1890–1970), French general and statesman, son of a headmaster of a Jesuit school; first president of the Fifth Republic 1959–69. He fought in the first world war until his capture in 1916. In the second world war he refused to surrender (1940) and raised and led the Free French forces, with headquarters in England. He came to political power in 1958; allowed Algerian independence in 1962 in face of an army and civilian revolt, initiated closer ties with West Germany (Franco-German treaty 1963), recognised Communist China, withdrew from NATO, building his own nuclear force, vetoed Britain's entry into the Common Market (1963 and 1967); and based his government on personal prestige and use of the referendum in place of parliamentary approval. He was taken by surprise by the rising of students and workers in 1968 and resigned after losing the referendum in 1969.

Gauss, Karl Friedrich (1777–1855), German mathematician. He spent most of his life at the university of Göttingen where he set up the first special observatory for terrestrial magnetism. He made major contributions to astronomy, mathematics, and physics. The unit of magnetic induction is named after him.

Gautama, Siddhartha (Buddha, the enlightened) (*c.* 563–*c.*483 B.C.). B. near Benares, a rajah's son, he gave himself up to the religious life and attracted many disciples. Concerned with man's sorrow and suffering, he planned a movement which could be universally shared, in which kindness to others, including animals, took a leading part. His teaching is summarised in the "four noble truths" and the "eightfold path" (*see* **Buddhism, Section J**). After his death his teaching spread (with the help of the King Asoka) over much of India and through eastern Asia as far as Japan, and developed varying schools of thought.

Gautier, Théophile (1811–72), French poet and novelist, author of *Mademoiselle de Maupin.*

Gay, John (1685–1732), English poet, author of *The Beggar's Opera* (set to music by Pepusch) and *Polly.*

Gay-Lussac, Joseph Louis (1778–1850), French chemist, who showed that when gases combine their relative volumes bear a simple numerical relation to each other and to the volume of their product, if gaseous (1808), *e.g.*, one volume of oxygen combines with two volumes of hydrogen to form two volumes of water vapour.

Ged, William (1690–1749), Scottish printer who patented stereotyping.

Geddes, Sir Patrick (1854–1932), Scottish biologist and a pioneer in town and regional planning, who invented the term conurbation.

Geikie, Sir Archibald (1835–1924), Scottish geologist. His brother James specialised in glacial geology.

Genghis Khan (1162–1227), Mongol conqueror. After years of struggle to make good his succession to his father, he overran the greater part of Asia bringing devastation wherever he went.

Geoffrey of Monmouth (1100–54), chronicler, b. Monmouth, later bishop of St. Asaph. His chronicle drew on his creative imagination.

George I (1660–1727), became King of Great Britain in 1714 as descendant of James I. His chief minister was Sir Robert Walpole. Himself personally undistinguished, his reign saw political development; and in spite of the Jacobite threat (rising in 1715) it began a period of dynastic stability.

George II (1683–1760), son of the above, succeeded in 1727, and survived a more serious Jacobite rising in 1745. His long reign helped the development of constitutional government, for he kept within the limitations of his powers and capacity; and it saw the extension of English power in India and North America.

George III (1738–1820), grandson of George II reigned 1760–1820. Sincere and well intentioned, but not politically able, he suffered from mental illness due to intermittent porphyria. His reign saw a clash with John Wilkes, the rise of Methodism, and agrarian and industrial revolution; also the loss of the American colonies, the extension and the questioning of English power in India (Warren Hastings), and prolonged French wars.

George IV (1762–1830), eldest son of George III, reigned 1820–30, having become Prince Regent in 1812. Styled "the first gentleman of Europe," he is remembered for his interest in art and architecture. His married life was unfortunate, and the monarchy was at a low ebb; while his reign was a time of distress and of demand for reform.

George V (1865–1936), was the second son of Edward VII and Queen Alexandra. His elder brother died in 1892 and, in 1901, on his father's accession, he became heir to the throne. He joined the Navy as a cadet in 1877. In 1893 he married Princess Mary of Teck. He succeeded in 1910 and discharged his office conscientiously. In 1932 he began the royal broadcast on Christmas Day and in 1935 celebrated his silver jubilee.

George VI (1895–1952), second son of George V, was called to the throne in 1936 on the abdication of his elder brother, Edward VIII. His personal qualities gained wide respect.

George, Henry (1839–97), American political economist whose "single tax" on land values as a means of solving economic problems is expounded in his *Progress and Poverty* (1879).

George, St., patron saint of England, adopted by Edward III. He is believed to have been martyred by Diocletian at Nicomedia in 303 (and not, as believed by Gibbon, to be confused with George of Cappadocia). The story of his fight with the dragon is of late date.

Gershwin, George (1898–1937). American jazz pianist and song-writer, composer of *Rhapsody in Blue* and the Negro folk-opera *Porgy and Bess.*

Gesner, Conrad (1516–65), Swiss naturalist, b. Zurich. His magnificently illustrated volumes describe animal and vegetable kingdoms.

Ghali, Boutros Boutros (b. 1922), Egyptian politician and international civil servant. Secretary-General, United Nations, since January 1992.

Ghiberti, Lorenzo (1378–1455), Florentine sculptor whose bronze doors, beautifying the baptistry in Florence, were described by Michelangelo as fit for the gates of paradise.

Ghirlandaio, Domenico (1449–94), Florentine painter. Most of his frescoes are in Florence, including the cycle of the life of the Virgin and the Baptist in S. Maria Novella. Michelangelo began his apprenticeship in his workshop.

Giacometti, Alberto (1901–66), Swiss sculptor and painter, who worked mainly in Paris and produced abstract symbolic constructions.

Giap, Vo Nguyen (1912–86), Vietnamese general who defeated the French at Dien Bien Phu (1954) and withstood American intervention in the Vietnam war which followed. Replaced in 1980 as defence minister. Retired in 1982.

Gibbon, Edward (1737–94), English historian of the *Decline and Fall of the Roman Empire.*

Gibbons, Grinling (1648–1720), English woodcarver and sculptor, b. Rotterdam, was brought to the notice of Charles II by Evelyn, the diarist. The choir stalls of St. Paul's and the carving in the Wren library at Trinity College, Cambridge, are his work.

Gibbons, Orlando (1583–1625), English composer of church music. *See also* **Section E.**

Gibson, Sir Alexander Drummond (1926–95). Founder and music director of the Scottish Opera

Company. One of the foremost Scottish musicians of the century.

Gide, André (1869–1951), French writer of many short novels in which he gives expression to his struggle to escape from his protestant upbringing (*Strait is the Gate*, *The Counterfeiters*). In his memoir *Si le grain ne meurt* he tells the story of his life up to his marriage.

Gielgud, Sir John (b. 1904), English actor and producer, grand-nephew of Ellen Terry, to whom, the Hamlet of his generation, the present popularity of Shakespeare is largely due.

Gilbert, Sir Alfred (1854–1934). English sculptor and goldsmith. His sculptures include *Eros* in Piccadilly Circus.

Gilbert, Sir Humphrey (1537–83), English navigator. He was knighted by Queen Elizabeth for service in Ireland. In 1583 he discovered Newfoundland, but was drowned the same year.

Gilbert, William (1540–1603), English physician to Queen Elizabeth. His book *On the Magnet*, published in Latin in 1600, was the first major contribution to science published in England.

Gilbert, Sir William Schwenck (1836–1911), English humorist and librettist, of the Gilbert and Sullivan light operas. First known as author of the *Bab Ballads*, from 1871 he collaborated with Sir Arthur Sullivan, his wit and satire finding appropriate accompaniment in Sullivan's music. Their operas include *H.M.S. Pinafore*, *Patience*, *Iolanthe*, *The Mikado*, *The Gondoliers*, and *The Yeomen of the Guard*.

Gill, Eric (1882–1940), English sculptor and engraver, whose works include the *Stations of the Cross* (Westminster Cathedral), *Prospero and Ariel* (Broadcasting House), *Christ Driving the Money-changers from the Temple* (Leeds University). He designed the George VI stamps.

Gillray, James (1757–1815), English caricaturist who produced over a thousand political cartoons.

Giotto di Bondone (1267–1337), Florentine artist. A pupil of Cimabue, he continued the development away from Byzantine tradition towards greater naturalism. His frescoes survive in the churches of Assisi, Padua, and Florence. He designed the western front of the cathedral at Florence and the campanile.

Gissing, George Robert (1857–1903), English novelist whose works deal with the effect of poverty. The best known is *New Grub Street*.

Giulio Romano or **Giulio Pippi** (*c.* 1492–1546). Italian artist, was a pupil of Raphael. He was also an engineer and architect.

Gladstone, William Ewart (1809–98), English Liberal statesman. B. at Liverpool, he entered parliament in 1832 as a Tory and held office under Peel. From 1852 he served several terms as chancellor of the exchequer and was Liberal prime minister 1868–74, when his legislation included the education act of 1870, the ballot act, the disestablishment of the Church of Ireland and an Irish land act. In 1874 when Disraeli came to power, he temporarily withdrew, but made a come-back in 1879 with his Mid-Lothian campaign. He was again prime minister 1880–5, 1886 and 1892–4; he carried a parliamentary reform act, and advocated home rule for Ireland but was unable to carry it.

Glazunov, Alexander Constantinovich (1865–1936), Russian composer, pupil of Rimsky-Korsakov. The first of his eight symphonies was composed when he was 16.

Glendower, Owen (*c.* 1350–*c.* 1416), Welsh chief, who conducted guerrilla warfare on the English border. He figures in Shakespeare's *Henry IV*.

Glinka, Mikhail Ivanovich (1804–57), Russian composer, first of the national school, best known for his operas, *A Life for the Tsar*, and *Russlan and Ludmilla*, based on a poem by Pushkin. *See* **Section E.**

Gluck, Christoph Wilibald (1714–87), German composer, important in the development of opera. He studied in Prague, Vienna and Italy, and his first operas were in the Italian tradition; but with *Orfeo ed Euridice* (1762) his style became more dramatic. There followed *Alceste*, *Armide*, and *Iphigénie en Tauride*. *See* **Section E.**

Goddard, Robert Hutchings (1882–1945), American pioneer of rocket development. He achieved (1926) the first rocket flight with a liquid-fuelled engine. By 1937, bigger rockets were reaching altitudes of several thousand metres.

Gödel, Kurt (1906–78), American mathematician.

Devised Gödel's proof, the vitally important proof of modern mathematics which declares that there will always exist statements that can be neither proven nor disproven in any mathematical system which has a finite number of axioms.

Godfrey of Bouillon (*c.* 1061–1100), Crusader on the first crusade. On capturing Jerusalem declined title of "king", preferring that of protector of the Holy Sepulchre.

Godiva, Lady (1040–80), English benefactress. According to tradition, she obtained from her husband Leofric, Earl of Chester, concessions for the people of Coventry by riding naked through the town.

Godwin, Earl of the West Saxons (d. 1053), was the father of Edith, wife of King Edward the Confessor, and of Harold, last Saxon king.

Godwin William (1756–1836), English political writer and philosopher, author of *Political Justice* (which criticised many contemporary institutions) and a novel *Caleb Williams*. He married **Mary Wollstonecraft** (1759–97), author of *A Vindication of the Rights of Women*; and their daughter, **Mary Wollstonecraft Godwin** (1797–1851) wrote *Frankenstein* and married Shelley.

Goethe, Johann Wolfgang von (1749–1832), German poet and thinker. B. at Frankfurt-on-Main, his first notable work was a romantic play, *Götz von Berlichingen*, followed by a novel *Werthers Leiden*. In 1776 he became privy councillor to the Duke of Weimar, whom he served for many years. He had wide-ranging interests, and made discoveries in anatomy and in botany. Among his later writings are the play *Iphigenie* and the novel *Wilhelm Meister*. His best-known work however is *Faust*.

Gogol, Nikolai Vasilievich (1809–52), Russian novelist and dramatist. His comedy, *The Government Inspector*, satirised provincial bureaucracy; and his novel, *Dead Souls*, deals with malpractice in the purchase of dead serfs.

Golding, Sir William (1911–93), novelist, whose imaginative and experimental fiction includes *Lord of the Flies* (1954) and *The Spire* (1964). Awarded the Nobel Prize for Literature (1983).

Goldsmith, Oliver (1728–74), Irish poet, dramatist and novelist. The son of a poor curate, he came to London in 1756, and eventually joined the circle of Dr. Johnson. He is best known for his novel *The Vicar of Wakefield* and his play *She Stoops to Conquer*.

Goncourt, Edmond Louis Antoine Huot de (1822–96) and **Jules Alfred Huot de** (1830–70), French brothers, remembered for their *Journal des Goncourts*, an intimate account of Parisian society.

Góngora y Argote, Luis de (1561–1627), Spanish poet, b. Córdova. In *Polifemo* and *Soledades* he attempted to express the core of poetry in new experimental forms.

Goodyear, Charles (1800–60), American inventor who discovered the art of vulcanising rubber.

Goossens, Sir Eugene (1893–1962), English conductor and composer of Belgian descent. His compositions include *Judith* and *Don Juan de Mañara*; brother of **Léon**, oboe virtuoso, and of **Sidonie** and **Marie Goossens**, harpists.

Gorbachev, Mikhail (b. 1931). Soviet politician. Succeeded Chernenko (*q.v.*) as General Secretary of the Communist Party, 1985. His accession marked the end of the "old-guard" leadership. Identified with policies of *glasnost* (openness) and *perestroika* (restructuring). President of the USSR from 1988 until his resignation on 25 December 1991. He presided over revolutionary changes both in Eastern Europe and Russia, but faced a growing political crisis over economic reforms, the rise of his rival, Boris Yeltsin, as well as the forces of nationalism. The abortive coup in 1991 weakened his position, leading to the collapse of the USSR. Nobel Peace Prize, 1990. *See* **Section C.**

Gordon, Charles George (1833–85), Scottish soldier. After service in the Crimea and China, in 1873 he was made governor of the Equatorial provinces of Egypt; and he was a notable governor of the Sudan, 1877–80. When a rising was led by the Mahdi, he was sent out in 1884 to the garrisons in rebel territory. Killed at Khartoum.

Gordon, Lord George (1751–93), agitator, led No-Popery riots in London in 1780.

Gore, Albert (b. 1948), US Vice-President since 1993. Former Senator from Tennessee.

Gorky, Maxim (Alexey Maximovich Peshkov) 1868–1936), Russian writer. From the age of ten he worked at many trades from scullion on a Volga steamboat to railway guard, while learning to write: see *My Childhood*. His early work was romantic. He spent many years abroad, but returned in 1928, a supporter of the Soviet regime. His later work is marked by social realism.

Gosse, Sir Edmund (1849–1928), English poet and critic, known for his literary studies of the 17th and 18th centuries; and for his memoir *Father and Son*.

Gounod, Charles François (1818–93), French composer, known for his operas *Faust* and *Roméo et Juliette*, though his lyrical gifts are shown in earlier works, such as *Le Médicin malgré lui* and *Mireille*.

Gower, John (1325–1408), English poet of the time of Chaucer, author of *Confessio Amantis*.

Goya y Lucientes, Francisco José (1746–1828), Spanish painter and etcher b. nr. Saragossa. He became court painter to Charles III in 1786. His portraits are painted with ruthless realism; his series of satirical etchings (*Los Caprichos* and the *Disasters of War*) expose man's inhumanity and express his hatred of the cruelty and reaction of his day.

Gracchi, the brothers Tiberius (163–133 B.C.) and **Gaius** (153–121 B.C.) who, as Tribunes of the People, tried to reform the system of public landholding and liberalise the franchise at Rome, but were both killed when the Senate suppressed their followers.

Grace, William Gilbert (1848–1915). English cricketer who scored 54,896 runs, including 126 centuries, and took 2,876 wickets.

Grahame, Kenneth (1859–1932), Scottish writer of books for children, including *The Golden Age*, *Dream Days*, and *Wind in the Willows*.

Grahame-White, Claude (1879–1959), the first Englishman to gain an aviator's certificate, 1909.

Grant, Ulysses Simpson (1822–85), American general of the civil war, and president of the United States from 1869 to 1876.

Granville-Barker, Harley (1877–1946), English dramatist, actor, and producer, who promoted the plays of Ibsen, Shaw, *etc.* His own works include *The Voysey Inheritance*.

Grattan, Henry (1746–1820), Irish statesman, who struggled for Irish legislative independence and for Catholic emancipation (though himself a Protestant) and parliamentary reform; but unsuccessfully.

Graves, Robert Ranke (1895–1985), English writer, author of *Goodbye to All That*, written after the first world war; and of *I Claudius* and *Claudius the God*; besides poetry.

Gray, Thomas (1716–71), English poet, author of *Elegy written in a Country Churchyard* and *Ode on a Distant Prospect of Eton College*.

Greeley, Horace (1811–72), American newspaper editor, founder of the New York *Tribune* (1841).

Green, John Richard (1837–83), English historian, author of *Short History of the English People*.

Greenaway, Kate (1846–1901), English artist, who depicted children, especially in book illustrations.

Greene, Graham (1904–91), English novelist and journalist, whose novels (*The Power and the Glory*, *The Heart of the Matter*, *The End of the Affair*, *The Quiet American*, *Our Man in Havana*, *A Burnt-out Case*, *The Comedians*, *The Honorary Consul*), like his plays (*The Complaisant Lover*) and films (*Fallen Idol*, *The Third Man*) deal with moral problems in a modern setting. C.H. (1966), O.M. (1986). Widely regarded as the greatest English novelist of the second half of the century.

Greer, Germaine (b. 1939). Feminist and writer. Born in Melbourne, Australia. Her most famous work is *The Female Eunuch* (1970) which exposed the misrepresentation of female sexuality by a male-dominated society.

Gregory, St. (*c.* 240–332), converted King Tiridates of Armenia, so founding the Armenian church.

Gregory I (the Great), St. (*c.* 540–604), Pope 590–604, was the last great Latin Father and the forerunner of scholasticism. The main founder of the temporal power and the political influence of the papacy, he also maintained the spiritual claims of Rome, enforcing discipline, encouraging monasticism, defining doctrine *etc.* He sent Augustine on a mission to England.

Gregory VII (Hildebrand) (*c.* 1020–85), Pope 1073–85. He strove for papal omnipotence within the church and for a high standard in the priesthood (especially by stamping out simony and

clerical marriage). He also upheld the papacy against the Holy Roman Empire, and the emperor Henry IV did penance for three days in the snow at Canossa.

Gregory XIII (1502–85), Pope 1572–85; introduced the Gregorian calendar.

Gregory, James (1638–75), Scottish mathematician. He invented a reflecting telescope and was the first to show how the distance of the sun could be deduced by observations of the passage of Venus across the disc of the sun. Successive generations of the family reached distinction.

Grenville, Sir Richard (1541–91), English sea captain, who with his one ship engaged a fleet of Spanish war vessels off Flores in 1591, an exploit celebrated in Tennyson's ballad *The Revenge*.

Gresham, Sir Thomas (1519–79), English financier and founder of the Royal Exchange. Son of a Lord Mayor of London, he was an astute moneyfinder for four successive sovereigns, including Queen Elizabeth I. "Gresham's Law" is the statement that bad money drives out good.

Greuze, Jean Baptiste (1725–1805), French artist, known especially for his studies of girls. His *Girl with Doves* is in the Wallace Collection.

Grey, 2nd Earl (Charles Grey) (1764–1845), British Whig statesman under whose premiership were passed the Reform Bill of 1832, a bill abolishing slavery throughout the Empire (1833), and the Poor Law Amendment Act, 1834.

Grey, Lady Jane (1537–54), Queen of England for a few days. The daughter of the Duke of Suffolk, she was put forward as queen by protestant leaders on the death of her cousin, Edward VI; but overcome by the legal claimant, Mary Tudor, and executed.

Grieg, Edvard Hagerup (1843–1907), Norwegian composer, b. Bergen. He presented the characteristics of his country's music with strong accentuation. He is best known for his incidental music to *Peer Gynt*.

Griffin, Bernard William (1899–1956), Roman catholic archbishop of Westminster, 1944–56.

Griffith, Arthur (1872–1922), the first president of the Irish Free State, 1921; founder of the *Sinn Fein* movement.

Griffith, David Wark (1880–1948), American film producer, who introduced the close-up, and the flash-back, and developed leading actors.

Grimaldi, Joseph (1779–1837), British clown who won enormous acclaim at Covent Garden.

Grimm, the brothers Jakob Ludwig Karl (1785–1863), and **Wilhelm Karl** (1786–1859), German philologists and folk-lorists, best known for their *Fairy Tales*. Jakob published a notable philological dictionary, *Deutsche Grammatik*. The brothers also projected the vast *Deutsches Wörtebuch* which was completed by German scholars in 1961.

Grimond, Lord (Joseph) (1913–93), Leader of the Liberal Party, 1956–67. M.P. (Orkney and Shetland), 1950–83. A much-loved figure.

Grimthorpe, 1st Baron (Edmund Beckett Denison) (1816–1905), horologist who invented the double three-legged escapement for the clock at Westminster, familiarly known as "Big Ben" (the name of the bell). Known as Sir Edmund Beckett.

Gromyko, Andrei Andreevich (1909–89), Russian diplomat and statesman. President, USSR, July 1985–88, Foreign Minister, 1957–85.

Grossmith, George (1847–1912), English actor. With his brother, **Weedon Grossmith**, he wrote *Diary of a Nobody*. His son, **George Grossmith** (1874–1935) was a comedian and introduced revue and cabaret entertainment into England.

Grote, George (1794–1871), English historian, author of a *History of Greece*.

Grotius (Huig van Groot) (1583–1645), Dutch jurist, the founder of international law. He was condemned to life imprisonment for religious reasons, but escaped to Paris, where he wrote *De Jure Belli et Pacis*.

Grouchy, Emmanuel, Marquis de (1766–1847), French general, who served under Napoleon; after Waterloo led defeated army back to Paris.

Grove, Sir George (1820–1900), English musicologist, author of *Dictionary of Music and Musicians*. By profession he was a civil engineer.

Guedalla, Philip (1889–1944), English historian, author of *The Second Empire*, *Palmerston*, *etc.*

Guevara, Ernesto "Che" (1928–67), revolutionary hero, b. Argentina. He took part in the Cuban guerrilla war and became a minister in the Cuban government 1959–65. He was killed while leading a band of guerrillas against American-trained Bolivian troops.

Guido Reni (1575–1642), Italian painter of the Bolognese school whose works are characteristic of the Italian baroque of his period and include the *Aurora* fresco in the Rospigliosi palace at Rome, and *Crucifixion of St. Peter* (Vatican).

Guinness, Sir Alec (b. 1914), English actor of extraordinary versatility. Awarded an Oscar for *The Bridge on the River Kwai*. C.H. (1995).

Gustavus Adolphus (1594–1632), King of Sweden, the "Lion of the North." After a campaign in Poland he entered the Thirty Years' war in support of Swedish interests and Protestant distress, won the battle of Breitenfeld in 1631 and was killed in action the next year.

Gutenberg, Johann (*c.* 1400–68), German printer, b. Mainz, the first European to print with movable types cast in moulds. The earliest book printed by him was the Mazarin Bible (*see* **L76**).

Guy, Thomas (1644–1724), English philanthropist. A printer, he made money by speculation; and in 1722 founded Guy's Hospital in Southwark.

Gwyn, Nell (*c.* 1650–87), English actress and mistress of Charles II by whom she had two sons. Of Hereford origin, she sold oranges in London and became a comedienne at Drury Lane.

H

Habgood, John Stapylton (b. 1927), Archbishop of York, 1983–95. Formerly Bishop of Durham, 1973–83.

Hadley, George (1685–1768). He developed Halley's theory of the trade winds by taking into account the effect of the earth's rotation and the displacement of air by tropical heat (1735).

Hadrian (76–138), Roman emperor. An able general, he suppressed revolts, and he was also a lover of the arts. He visited Britain *c.* A.D. 121 and built a protective wall between Wallsend-on-Tyne and Bowness-on-Solway.

Hafiz, pseudonym of **Shams ad-Din Mohammed** (d. *c.* 1388), Persian lyrical poet. His principal work is the *Divan*, a collection of short sonnets called *ghazals*. The sobriquet *Hafiz*, meaning one who remembers, is applied to anyone who has learned the Koran by heart.

Hahn, Otto (1879–1968), German chemist and physicist, chief discoverer of uranium fission.

Hahnemann, Samuel Christian Friedrich (1755–1843), German physician who founded homoeopathy (treatment of disease by small doses of drugs that in health produce similar symptoms).

Haig, Douglas, 1st Earl of Bermersyde (1861–1928), British field-marshal, b. Edinburgh. He replaced French as commander-in-chief in France, 1915–19, leading the offensive in August 1918; and after the war presided over the British Legion.

Haile Selassie I (1891–1975), Emperor of Ethiopia 1930–74. He spent the years of the Italian occupation 1936–41 in England. Deposed 1974.

Hakluyt, Richard (1553–1616), English writer on maritime discovery. B. in Herefordshire, he spent some time in Paris. From 1582 (when *Divers Voyages* appeared), he devoted his life to collecting and publishing accounts of English navigators, thus giving further impetus to discovery.

Haldane, John Burdon Sanderson (1892–1964), biologist and geneticist, noted not only for his work in mathematical evolutionary theory but for explaining science to the layman. He emigrated to India in 1957. He was the son of **John Scott Haldane** (1860–1936), b. Edinburgh, who studied the effect of industrial occupations upon health.

Haldane, 1st Viscount (Richard Burdon Haldane) (1856–1928). British Liberal statesman. As war minister in 1905 he reorganised the army and founded the Territorials.

Hale, George Ellery (1868–1935), American astronomer, after whom is named the 200-inch reflecting telescope on Mount Palomar.

Halévy, Ludovic (1834–1903), French playwright, who collaborated with Henri Meilhac in writing libretti for Offenbach and Bizet.

Halifax, 1st Earl of (Edward Frederick Lindley Wood) (1881–1959), British Conservative politician; foreign secretary during the period of appeasement of Germany; as Lord Irwin, viceroy of India 1926–31.

Halifax, 1st Marquess of (George Savile) (1633–95), English politician of changeable views, who wrote *Character of a Trimmer*.

Hallam, Henry (1777–1859), English historian, best known for his *Constitutional History*. He was father of Arthur Hallam, friend of Tennyson.

Hallé, Sir Charles (1819–95), German-born pianist and conductor, who settled in Manchester and organised an orchestra of high-class talent. He married the violinist Wilhelmine Neruda.

Halley, Edmond (1656–1742), English astronomer royal 1720–42. He published observations on the planets and comets, being the first to predict the return of a comet (*see* **Section L**). He furthered Newton's work on gravitation, setting aside his own researches. He made the first magnetic survey of the oceans from the naval vessel *Paramour*, 1698–1700. His meteorological observations led to his publication of the first map of the winds of the globe (1686).

Hals, Frans (*c.* 1580–1666), Dutch portrait painter, b. at Mechlin. He is best known for his *Laughing Cavalier* in the Wallace Collection, and for portraits in the Louvre and at Amsterdam.

Hamilton, Alexander (1755–1804), American statesman and economist. With Madison and Jay he wrote the *Federalist* (1787). As secretary of the Treasury (1789–95) he put Washington's government on a firm financial footing and planned a national bank. He was the leader of the Federalists, a party hostile to Jefferson. He was killed in a duel.

Hamilton, Emma, Lady (*née* **Lyon**) (*c.* 1765–1815), a beauty of humble birth who, after several liaisons, was married in 1791 to Sir William Hamilton, British ambassador at Naples. There she met Nelson, and later bore him a child, Horatia.

Hammarskjöld, Dag (1905–61), Swedish Secretary-General of the United Nations, 1953–61. He was killed in an air crash while attempting to mediate in a dispute between Zaïre and the secessionist province of Katanga. Posthumous Nobel peace prize.

Hammond, John Lawrence (1872–1949), English historian of social and industrial history, whose works (with his wife Barbara) include *The Town Labourer* and *The Village Labourer*.

Hampden, John (1594–1643), English parliamentarian and civil war leader. He refused to pay Charles I's ship money in 1636. When civil war broke out, he raised a regiment and was killed on Chalgrove Field.

Hamsun, Knut, pen-name of Knut Pedersen (1859–1952), Norwegian author who in his youth struggled for existence, visited America twice and earned his living by casual labour. *The Growth of the Soil* won him the Nobel prize in 1920. Other great novels are *Hunger* and *Mysteries*.

Handel, George Frederick (1685–1759), German composer, son of a barber-surgeon to the Duke of Saxony; b. Halle, the same year as Bach; spent much of his life in England composing operas and oratorios. His operas, of which there are over 40, include *Atalanta, Berenice* and *Serse*, and his oratorios, of which there are 32, include *Saul, Israel in Egypt, Samson, Messiah, Judas Maccabaeus,* and *Jephtha*. Before he died he became blind and relied upon his old friend and copyist John Christopher Smith to commit his music to paper. *See* **Section E**.

Hannibal (247–182 B.C.), Carthaginian general. He fought two wars against Rome. In the first he conquered southern Spain. In the second he overran Gaul, crossed the Alps, and defeated the Romans in successive battles, especially at Cannae. Thereafter his forces were worn down by Roman delaying tactics; he was defeated by Scipio at Zama and later poisoned himself.

Harcourt, Sir William Vernon (1827–1904), Liberal politician who revised death duties.

Hardicanute (1019–42), son of Canute, and last Danish king of England.

Hardie, James Keir (1856–1915), Scottish Labour leader, one of the founders of the Labour party. He first worked in a coal-pit; in 1882 became a journalist; and in 1892 was the first socialist to be elected to the House of Commons (for West Ham – South). He edited the *Labour Leader* 1887–1904. He was the first chairman of the parliamentary Labour party, 1906. A

B30

pacifist, he opposed the Boer war.

Hardy, Thomas (1840–1928), English novelist and poet, was trained as an architect and practised for some time, but became known in 1871 with *Desperate Remedies*. In 1874 his *Far from the Madding Crowd* was published. Following that came a series of novels, including *The Trumpet-Major, The Mayor of Casterbridge, Tess of the D'Urbervilles*, and *Jude the Obscure*. In 1908 he completed a dramatic poem, *The Dynasts*, whose central figure is Napoleon. His underlying theme is man's struggle against neutral forces, and he depicts the Wessex countryside.

Hargreaves, James (1720–78), English inventor, b. Blackburn. His spinning-jenny was invented in 1764 and became widely used, though his own was broken by spinners in 1768 and his invention brought him no profit.

Harkness, Edward Stephen (1874–1940), American banker and philanthropist, who in 1930 founded the Pilgrim Trust in Gt. Britain.

Harley, Robert, 1st Earl of Oxford and Mortimer (1661–1724), English statesman and collector of MSS. He held office under Queen Anne, and brought a European war to an end with the treaty of Utrecht. After the Hanoverian succession he lived in retirement, and formed the MSS. collection, now in the British Museum, which bears his name.

Harold II (1022–66), last Saxon king of England, was son of Earl Godwin. He was chosen king in succession to Edward the Confessor. He had at once to meet a dual invasion. He defeated the Norwegian king at Stamford Bridge; but was himself defeated by William of Normandy at the battle of Hastings (fought at Battle 1066).

Harriman, William Averell (1891–1986), American public official. He was adviser to President Roosevelt and later presidents especially on Marshall Aid and foreign affairs.

Harris, Joel Chandler (1848–1908). American author, creator of Uncle Remus and Brer Rabbit in Negro folk-tales.

Harrison, Frederic (1831–1923), English philosopher and lawyer, author of *The Meaning of History* and *The Philosophy of Common Sense*. He was president of the Positivist committee.

Harrison, John (1693–1776), "Longitude Harrison," English inventor of the chronometer, b. near Pontefract, Yorkshire, the son of a carpenter.

Harty, Sir Hamilton (1880–1941), composer and for some years conductor of the Hallé orchestra.

Harun al-Rashid (Aaron the Upright) (763–809), 5th Abbasid caliph of Baghdad. His court was a centre for art and learning, but he governed mainly through his vizier until the latter lost favour and was executed in 803. The *Arabian Nights* associated with him are stories collected several centuries later.

Harvey, William (1578–1657), English physician and discoverer of the circulation of the blood. B. at Folkestone, he studied at Padua while Galileo was there, and was physician to James I and Charles I. His treatise on circulation was published in Latin in 1628.

Hastings, Warren (1732–1818), English administrator in India. As governor-general of Bengal for the East India Company he revised the finances and administration and put down disorder. On his return to England he was impeached for alleged corruption, and, though acquitted, lost his fortune in his own defence. Later however he received a grant from the company.

Hauptmann, Gerhart (1862–1946), German dramatist and novelist. B. in Silesia, he lived at first in Berlin and later abroad. His play *The Weavers* deals with a revolt of 1844 and has a collective hero. Other works include *Die versunkene Glocke, Der arme Heinrich*, and *Rose Bernd*. Nobel prizewinner 1912.

Havel, Vaclav (b. 1936) Czech playwright, dissident and statesman. Imprisoned, 1979–83. President of Czechoslovakia, December 1989–1992. President of new Czech Republic since January 1993.

Havelock, Sir Henry (1795–1857), British general who helped to put down the Indian mutiny.

Hawke, 1st Baron (Edward Hawke) (1705–81), English admiral, who in 1759 defeated the French at Quiberon in a tremendous storm.

Hawking, Stephen William (b. 1942), British theoretical physicist. Lucasian Professor of Mathematics, Cambridge University, since 1979. Author of *300 Years of Gravitation* (1987) and *A Brief*

History of Time (1988). Awarded C.B.E., 1982. Companion of Honour (1989). Sufferer from motor neurone disease. His latest book is *Black Holes and Baby Universes and other essays* (1993).

Hawkins, Sir John (1532–95), English sailor and slave-trader. Born at Plymouth. In 1562 he was the first Englishman to traffic in slaves. Treasurer of the Navy, 1585–88. He helped to defeat the Spanish Armada in 1588, commanding the *Victory*. Died at sea off Puerto Rico, 12 November 1595.

Hawthorne, Nathaniel (1804–64), American author. His works include *The Marble Faun, The Scarlet Letter* and *The House of the Seven Gables*.

Haydn, Franz Joseph (1732–1809), Austrian composer, belongs to the classical period of Bach, Handel, and Mozart. He has been given the title "father of the symphony." Much of his life was spent as musical director to the princely Hungarian house of Esterhazy. In 1791 and again in 1794 he visited London, where he conducted his Salomon symphonies. His two great oratorios, *The Creation* and *The Seasons*, were written in old age. *See* **Section E**.

Hayek, Friedrich August (von) (1899–1992), Austrian economist. The 'father of monetarism.' Director, Austrian Institute for Economic Research, 1927–31. Tooke Professor of Economic Science, London University, 1931–50. Strongly influenced development of Thatcherite monetary policies. Shared Nobel Prize for Economics, 1974. Awarded Companion of Honour, 1984.

Hazlitt, William (1778–1830), English essayist and critic. His writings include *The Characters of Shakespeare's Plays, Table Talk*, and *The Spirit of the Age*. His grandson **William Carew Hazlitt** (1834–1913) was a bibliographer and writer.

Heath, Sir Edward (b. 1916), British statesman, leader of the Conservative Party 1965–75; prime minister 1970–74; leader of the opposition 1965–70, 1974–75. In 1973 he took Britain into the EEC. Order of the Garter, 1992. 'Father of the House' since 1992.

Hedin, Sven Anders (1865–1952), Swedish explorer of Central Asia; wrote *My Life as Explorer*.

Heenan, John Carmel (1905–76). English Roman Catholic prelate, archbishop of Westminster 1963–76; member of Sacred College (1965–76).

Hegel, Georg Wilhelm Friedrich (1770–1831), German idealist philosopher, b. Stuttgart, whose name is associated with the dialectic method of reasoning with its sequence of thesis —antithesis—synthesis. He studied theology at Tübingen with his friend Schelling. He taught philosophy at Jena, Nuremberg, Heidelberg, and Berlin. He produced an abstract philosophical system which was influenced by his early interest in mysticism and his Prussian patriotism. His doctrines were very influential in the 19th cent. and led to modern totalitarianism. *See* **Dialectical Materialism, Section J**.

Heidenstam, Verner von (1859–1940), Swedish author and poet, leader of a new romantic movement. Nobel prizewinner 1916.

Heifetz, Jascha (b. 1901), Russian-born violinist, a U.S. citizen. He was the first musician to win a reputation in England by gramophone records before a personal appearance.

Heine, Heinrich (1797–1856), German lyric poet, b. Düsseldorf. He lived mostly in Paris.

Heisenberg, Werner (1901–76), German physicist, noted for his theory of quantum mechanics and the Uncertainty Principle. Nobel Prize, 1932.

Helmholtz, Herman von (1821–94), German physicist and physiologist. He published his *Erhaltung der Kraft* (Conservation of Energy) in 1847, the same year that Joule gave the first clear exposition of the principle of energy. His pupil Heinrich Hertz discovered electromagnetic radiation in accordance with Maxwell's theory.

Heloïse (c. 1101–64), beloved of Abelard (*q.v.*). Her letters to him are extant.

Hemingway, Ernest (1898–1961), American novelist of new technique and wide influence. His works include *A Farewell to Arms, Death in the Afternoon, For Whom the Bell Tolls, The Old Man and the Sea*. He committed suicide. Nobel prizewinner 1954.

Henderson, Arthur (1863–1935), British Labour politician, b. Glasgow. He worked mainly for disarmament. President, World Disarmament Conference, 1932–5. Nobel peace prize 1934.

B31

Henrietta Maria (1609–69), the daughter of Henry IV of France and wife of Charles I.

Henry, Joseph (1797–1878), American physicist and schoolteacher who independently of Faraday discovered the principle of the induced current. The weather-reporting system he set up at the Smithsonian Institution led to the creation of the U.S. Weather Bureau.

Henry I (1068–1135), King of England. The youngest son of William the Conqueror, he ascended the throne during the absence on crusade of his elder brother Robert of Normandy. His long reign brought order and progress, not entirely destroyed by the anarchy under his successor Stephen.

Henry II (1133–89), King of England. He was son of Matilda, daugher of Henry I, and Geoffrey Plantagenet, count of Anjou; and his lands stretched to the Pyrenees. He was a strong ruler to whom we largely owe the establishment of the common law system and permanent administrative reforms. His conflict with the Church led to the murder of archbishop Becket.

Henry III (1207–72), King of England, succeeded his father John in 1216. Himself devout and simple, his long reign was troubled by a partly factious baronial opposition.

Henry IV (1367–1413), grandson of Edward III and heir to the Duchy of Lancaster, became king of England in 1399. More solid and practical than his cousin Richard II, whom he had supplanted, he consolidated the government.

Henry V (1387–1422), son of Henry IV, succeeded his father as king of England in 1413. A successful commander, he renewed the French war and won the battle of Agincourt, but died young.

Henry VI (1421–71), son of Henry V, succeeded his father as king of England in 1422 as a baby. Gentle and retiring, he inherited a losing war with France. He founded Eton, and King's College, Cambridge. The Yorkist line claimed the crown from his (the Lancastrian) line, and the Wars of the Roses led to his deposition and death. Ruled 1422–61, 1470–71.

Henry VII (1457–1509) succeeded Richard III as king of England after defeating him in 1485. The first Tudor king, he was firm and shrewd, even avaricious; he built Henry VII's Chapel in Westminster Abbey, and encouraged John Cabot to sail to North America.

Henry VIII (1491–1547), King of England, succeeded his father Henry VII in 1509. A prince of the Renaissance, skilled in music and sports, he loved the sea and built up the navy. His minister Cardinal Wolsey fell when Henry, seeking divorce to obtain a legal heir, rejected papal supremacy and dissolved the monasteries. Ruthless and ostentatious, he executed Sir Thomas More and spent his father's wealth. The father of **Edward VI**, **Mary I** and **Elizabeth I**.

Henry IV of France (Henry of Navarre) (1553–1610). Prior to becoming king, he was the leader of the Huguenots; and although on being crowned he became a Catholic, he protected the Protestants by the Edict of Nantes. He then became a national king, but was later assassinated by Ravaillac, a religious fanatic.

Henry the Navigator (1394–1460), Portuguese promoter of discovery, son of John I. His sailors discovered Madeira and the Azores.

Henschel, Sir George (1850–1934), singer, composer, and conductor. B. in Breslau, he became a naturalised Englishman. Founder and conductor of the London Symphony Concerts (1886).

Hepplewhite, George (d. 1786), English cabinet-maker whose name is identified with the style which followed the Chippendale period.

Heraclitus of Ephesus (c. 540–475 B.C.), Greek philosopher. His discovery of a changing world (he lived in an age of social revolution when the ancient tribal aristocracy was beginning to give way to democracy) influenced the philosophies of Parmenides, Democritus, Plato, and Aristotle, and later, of Hegel.

Herbert, George (1593–1633), the most purely devotional of English poets.

Hereward the Wake, the last Saxon leader to hold out against the Normans. His base in the fens was captured in 1071 but he escaped. His exploits were written up by Kingsley.

Herod the Great (c. 73–4 B.C.). At first governor of Galilee under the Romans, he obtained the title of king of Judaea in 31 B.C. The massacre of the Innocents reported in St. Matthew (though not corroborated in any contemporary history) is in keeping with his historical character.

Herodotus (c. 485–425 B.C.), Greek historian, called by Cicero, the father of history. He travelled widely collecting historical evidence.

Herrick, Robert (1591–1674), English lyric poet. His poems include Gather ye Rose Buds, Cherry Ripe, and Oberon's Feast.

Herriot, Edouard (1872–1957), French Radical-Socialist statesman. A scholar, long-time mayor of Lyons. Three times prime minister. President of the National Assembly 1947–54.

Herschel, Sir John (1792–1871), British astronomer who continued his father's researches and also pioneered photography, a term introduced by him. One of his twelve children introduced fingerprints into criminology.

Herschel, Sir William (1738–1822), German-born astronomer who came to England from Hanover as a musician; father of the above. Unrivalled as an observer, and with telescopes of his own making he investigated the distribution of stars in the Milky Way and concluded that some of the nebulae he could see were separate star systems outside our own. He discovered the planet Uranus in 1781.

Hertz, Heinrich Rudolf (1857–95), German physicist, whose laboratory experiments confirmed Maxwell's electromagnetic theory of waves and yielded information about their behaviour.

Herzl, Theodor (1860–1904), founder of modern political Zionism, was b. Budapest. He convened a congress at Basle in 1897.

Heseltine, Michael. See **D17**.

Hesiod (fl. c. 735 B.C.), Greek poet, author of Work and Days, which tells of life in the country.

Hill, Octavia (1838–1912), English social reformer concerned with the housing conditions of the poor, a pioneer in slum clearance in London; founder (with Sir Robert Hunter and Canon Rawnsley) of the National Trust.

Hill, Sir Rowland (1795–1879), originator of the penny postal system. He was secretary to the Postmaster-General 1846–54, then chief secretary to the Post Office until 1864.

Hillary, Sir Edmund (b.1919), New Zealand mountaineer and explorer. Won world-wide fame when he and Sherpa Tenzing were the first to reach the summit of Mt. Everest in 1953. Order of the Garter (1995).

Hindemith, Paul (1895–1963), German composer and viola player. He is associated with the movement in Gebrauchsmusik, which regarded music as a social expression. He incurred Nazi hostility and his later life was spent abroad. His numerous works include chamber works, songs, operas, ballet music, symphonies, and the oratorio Das Umaufhörliche. See also **Section E**.

Hindenburg, Paul von (1847–1934), German field-marshal. In 1914 he defeated the Russians at Tannenberg. In his old age a national hero, President of the German Reich, 1925–34.

Hinshelwood, Sir Cyril Norman (1897–1967), English chemist. He shared with Prof. Semenov of Russia the 1956 Nobel prize for chemistry for researches into the mechanism of chemical reactions. Pres. Royal Society, 1955–60.

Hinton of Bankside, Baron (Christopher Hinton) (1901–83), as managing director of the industrial group of the U.K. Atomic Energy Authority he played an important part in the building of Calder Hall. O.M. 1976.

Hippocrates of Chios (fl. c. 430 B.C.), Greek mathematician, the first to compile a work on the elements of geometry.

Hippocrates of Cos (fl. c. 430 B.C.), Greek physician, whose writings are lost, but who is believed to have established medical schools in Athens and elsewhere, and to have contributed towards a scientific separation of medicine from superstition. Traditionally he is the embodiment of the ideal physician.

Hirohito, Emperor of Japan (1901–89), acceded to the throne in 1926. In 1946 he renounced his legendary divinity. Much controversy surrounds his role in Japanese aggression in the 1930s and his part in the Second World War. Succeeded by his son, **Akihito**, the 125th Emperor.

Hitler, Adolf (1889–1945), German dictator, founder of National Socialism, b. in Austria, son of a customs official. He was in Vienna for 5 years with no regular work before going to Munich in

1913; enlisted in Bavarian infantry at outbreak of the Kaiser's war. At the end of the war conditions in Germany favoured the growth of a fascist movement and under his leadership the National Socialist (Nazi) party climbed to power. He became Reich chancellor in 1933 and on the death of Hindenburg in 1934 Führer; and commander-in-chief Wehrmacht 1935. Under his regime working class movements were ruthlessly destroyed; all opponents—communists, socialists, Jews—were persecuted and murdered. By terrorism and propaganda the German state was welded into a powerful machine for aggression. There followed the occupation of the Rhineland (1936), the annexation of Austria and Czechoslovakia (1938–9) the invasion of Poland and declaration of war by Great Britain and France (1939), the invasion of Russia (1941). Final defeat came in 1945; on 30 April he committed suicide as the Russian troops closed in on Berlin.

Hobbes, Thomas (1588–1679), English philosopher who published *Leviathan* in 1651. He favoured strong government and supported the supremacy of the state, but his arguments aroused antagonism even among royalists. He was an enthusiast for scientific enquiry.

Hobhouse, Leonard Trelawney (1864–1929), English sociologist. His books include *The Theory of Knowledge, Morals in Evolution,* and *Development and Purpose.*

Ho Chi-minh (1892–1969), leader of the Vietnam revolutionary nationalist party of Indo-China, which struggled for independence from France during and after the second world war. His main purpose was to weld together the nationalistic and communistic elements in Vietnam. As president of North Vietnam he fought to extend his control over South Vietnam, defying the United States.

Hodgkin, Sir Alan (b. 1914), British biophysicist working in the field of nerve impulse conduction. During the second world war he worked on the development of radar. Pres. Royal Society, 1970–75. Nobel prizewinner, 1970; O.M. 1973.

Hodgkin, Dorothy Crowfoot (1919–94), the third woman to win the Nobel prize in chemistry, awarded in 1964 for her X-ray analysis to elucidate the structure of complex molecules, notably penicillin and vitamin B-12. She and her team at the Department of Molecular Biophysics at Oxford succeeded in 1969 in determining the crystalline structure of insulin. O.M. (1965).

Hofbauer, Imre (d. 1990), Hungarian-born artist, whose brilliance was portrayed in his compassionate studies of the down-trodden.

Hogarth, William (1697–1764), English engraver and painter, who satirised his time with character, humour, and power, especially in his *Harlot's Progress, Rake's Progress, Marriage à la Mode, Industry and Idleness,* and *The March to Finchley.*

Hogg, Quintin (1845–1903), educationist and philanthropist who purchased the old Polytechnic Institution in 1882 and turned it into a popular college providing education at moderate rates. His grandson, **Lord Hailsham,** was lord chancellor 1970–4, 1979–83, 1983–87.

Hokusai, Katsushika (1760–1849), Japanese landscape artist of the Ukiyo-e (popular school).

Holbein, Hans, the elder (c. 1465–1524), German painter, b. Augsburg, father of:

Holbein, Hans, the younger (1497–1543), German painter, b. Augsburg; settled in London 1532. He won the favour of Henry VIII, for whom he painted many portraits. He is also known for his series *The Dance of Death.*

Holden, Charles (1875–1960), British architect, designer of public buildings, including British Medical Asscn. Building, London; Underground Head Offices; Senate House *etc.*

Holden, Sir Isaac (1807–97), British inventor of woolcombing machinery.

Hölderlin, Johann Christian Friedrich (1770–1843), German poet, friend of Hegel. His works include the novel *Hyperion* and the elegy *Menon's Laments for Diotima.* In his middle years his mind became unhinged.

Holford, Baron (William Graham Holford) (1907–75), British architect and town-planner; planned post-war redevelopment of City of London, including precincts of St. Paul's.

Holmes, Oliver Wendell (1809–94), American author. His writings include *Autocrat of the Breakfast Table, The Professor of the Breakfast Table,* and *The Poet at the Breakfast Table.*

Holst, Gustave Theodore (1874–1934), British composer of Swedish descent whose compositions include *The Planets* suite, *The Hymn of Jesus,* an opera *The Perfect Fool,* and a choral symphony. An outstanding teacher. *See* **Section E.**

Holyoake, George Jacob (1817–1906), English social reformer and secularist. He wrote a history of the co-operative movement.

Holyoake, Keith Jacka (1904–83), New Zealand politician; prime minister 1960–72.

Home of the Hirsel, Lord (Alex Douglas-Home) (b. 1903), British Prime Minister, 1963–64 (after renouncing his peerage as 14th Earl of Home). Foreign Secretary, 1960–63, 1970–74. Created Life Peer, 1974. His younger brother was the playwright **William Douglas-Home** (1912–92).

Homer (c. 700 B.C.), epic poet. He is supposed to have been a Greek who lived at Chios or Smyrna, and has been regarded as the author of the *Iliad* and the *Odyssey,* though this is tradition rather than ascertained fact.

Hood, 1st Viscount (Samuel Hood) (1724–1816), British admiral who in 1793 was in command of the Mediterranean fleet and occupied Toulon.

Hood, Thomas (1799–1845), English poet. His poems include *The Song of the Shirt, The Dream of Eugene Aram* and *The Bridge of Sighs.* He was also a humorist and punster.

Hooke, Robert (1635–1703), English physicist. His inventions include the balance spring of watches. He was also an architect and drew up a plan for rebuilding London after the Great Fire. His *Diary* is published.

Hooker, Richard (1554–1600), English theologian, author of *Ecclesiastical Polity.* He was Master of the Temple, 1585–91. For his choice of words he was known as "Judicious Hooker".

Hopkins, Sir Frederick Gowland (1861–1947), English biochemist, pioneer in biochemical and nutritional research. He first drew attention to the substances later known as vitamins. Pres. Royal Society 1930–5. Nobel prize 1929.

Hopkins, Gerard Manley (1844–89), English poet of religious experience and of a novel style.

Hopkins, Harry (1890–1946), Franklin Roosevelt's personal assistant at foreign conferences, and in the New Deal and Lend-Lease.

Hopkinson, John (1849–98), English engineer. By developing the theory of alternating current and of the magnetic current in dynamos he paved the way to the common use of electricity.

Hoppner, John (1758–1810), English portrait painter, b. Whitechapel, of German parents.

Horace (Quintus Horatius Flaccus) (65–8 B.C.), Roman satirist and poet, son of a Greek freedman. He wrote *Satires, Epodes, Odes,* and *Epistles.* He fought on the republican side at Philippi, but became poet laureate to Augustus.

Horniman, Annie Elizabeth Fredericka (1860–1937), founder of the modern repertory system in England. Her father F. J. Horniman founded the Horniman Museum.

Hosking, Eric (1909–91), bird photographer. A highly skilled ornithologist and tireless champion of the grace and beauty of birds.

Hoskins, William George (1908–92), the great local historian of England and the English. Author of *The Making of the English Landscape* (1955) and numerous other stories.

Houdini, Harry (Erich Weiss) (1874–1926), American illusionist, son of a Hungarian rabbi. Famed for his escapes from handcuffs.

Housman, Alfred Edward (1859–1936), English poet, author of *A Shropshire Lad;* he was also a classical scholar. His brother Laurence (1865–1959) was a playwright and wrote *Little Plays of St. Francis* and *Victoria Regina.*

Howard, John (1726–90), English prison reformer. Imprisoned in France in wartime, he subsequently investigated English prisons, securing reforms; and later also continental prisons, dying in Russia of gaol fever.

Howard of Effingham, 2nd Baron (Charles Howard) (1536–1624), afterwards Earl of Nottingham; commanded the fleet which defeated the Spanish Armada (1588), and took part in the capture of Cadiz (1596).

Howe, Elias (1819–67), American inventor of the sewing machine.

Howe, Julia Ward (1819–1910), American suffragette, author of *Mine eyes have seen the glory.*

Howe, 1st Earl (Richard Howe) (1726–99), British admiral whose victories over the French in two wars included that off Ushant on 1 June 1794 ("the glorious first of June").

Hua-Guofeng (b. 1922), b. Hunan, succeeded Mao Tse-tung as Chairman of the Chinese Communist Party, 1976–81.

Hubble, Edwin Powell (1889–1953), American astronomer, noted for his work on extragalactic nebulae. With the 100-inch telescope on Mount Wilson he detected the Cepheid variables.

Hudson, Henry (d. 1611), English navigator credited with the discovery of the Hudson river and Hudson Bay, where mutineers turned him adrift to die. He was on a voyage to find a passage by the north pole to Japan and China.

Hudson, William Henry (1841–1922), naturalist, b. Buenos Aires of American parents, naturalised in England (1900). His books include *The Purple Land*, *Green Mansions*, and *Far Away and Long Ago*. Hyde Park bird sanctuary was established in his memory.

Huggins, Sir William (1824–1910), British astronomer who pioneered in spectroscopic photography.

Hughes, Ted (b. 1930), English poet. Succeeded Sir John Betjeman as Poet Laureate (*see* **L97**) in December 1984.

Hughes, Thomas (1822–96), English novelist, author of *Tom Brown's Schooldays*, which is based on Rugby school.

Hugo, Victor Marie (1802–85), French poet, dramatist, and novelist, who headed the Romantic movement in France in the early 19th cent. His dramas include *Hernani*, *Lucrèce Borgia*, *Ruy Blas*, and *Le Roi s'amuse*. Of his novels *Notre Dame* belongs to his early period, *Les Misérables*, *Les Travailleurs de la mer*, and *L'Homme qui rit* were written in Guernsey.

Humboldt, Friedrich Heinrich Alexander, Baron von (1769–1859), German naturalist and explorer whose researches are recorded in *Voyage de Humboldt et Bonpland* (23 vols., 1805–34), and *Kosmos* (5 vols., 1845–62).

Hume, Cardinal (George) Basil (b. 1923), Catholic Benedictine monk. Abbot of Ampleforth, 1963–76, when he became Archbishop of Westminster.

Hume, David (1711–76), Scottish philosopher who developed the empiricism of Locke into the scepticism inherent in it. His main works are *Treatise of Human Nature* and *Dialogues Concerning Natural Religion*.

Hunt, Holman (1827–1910), English artist, one of the founders of the Pre-Raphaelite movement. His pictures include *The Light of the World*.

Hunt, Baron (John Hunt) (b. 1910), leader of the 1953 British Everest Expedition when Tenzing and Hillary reached the summit.

Hunt, Leigh (1784–1859), English poet and essayist. In 1813 he was fined and imprisoned for libelling the Prince Regent in *The Examiner*. He was a friend of Keats and Shelley.

Hurd, Douglas, *see* **D17**.

Hus, Jan (1369–1415), Bohemian religious reformer. Strongly influenced by Wyclif, he urged reform both of abuses in the church and of doctrine. Sentenced to death or recantation, he suffered martyrdom on 6 July 1415. His death caused a civil war which lasted many years.

Hussein, Saddam (b. 1938), dictator of Iraq, 1979–. Launched the war with Iran in 1980 and the invasion of Kuwait, 1990. *See* **Section C**.

Hutton, James (1726–97), an Edinburgh doctor who founded modern geological theory.

Hutton, Sir Leonard (1916–90), foremost English cricketer. Captained England 23 times, scoring 364 in 1938 against Australia.

Huxley, Aldous (1894–1963), English novelist, author of *Brave New World*.

Huxley, Sir Julian (1887–1975), biologist and writer, grandson of T. H. Huxley and brother of Aldous; first director general of Unesco 1946–8; one of the founders of the International Union for the Conservation of Nature and of the World Wild Life Fund.

Huxley, Thomas Henry (1825–95), English biologist, b. Ealing. He started life as assistant-surgeon on H.M.S. *Rattlesnake* and during the voyage (1846–50) studied marine organisms. After the publication of Darwin's *Origin of Species* he became an ardent evolutionist and gave the first recognisably modern lecture on the origin of life to the British Association in 1870.

He coined the term "agnostic". By his lectures and writings, he popularised science.

Huygens, Christian (1629–95), Dutch mathematician, physicist, and astronomer, son of the poet **Constantijn Huygens** (1596–1687); discovered the rings of Saturn, invented the pendulum clock, and developed the wave theory of light in opposition to Newton's corpuscular theory.

Hyde, Douglas (1860–1949), Irish scholar, historian, poet, and folk-lorist; first president of Ireland in the 1937 constitution, 1938–45.

Hypatia of Alexandria, the only woman mathematician of antiquity. She excited the enmity of Christian fanatics. Murdered in A.D. 415.

I

Ibsen, Henrik Johan (1828–1906), Norwegian playwright and poet, who dealt with social and psychological problems and revolutionised the European theatre. His chief works are *Ghosts*, *The Wild Duck*, *The Master Builder*, *A Doll's House*, *Hedda Gabler* and the poetic drama, *Peer Gynt*.

Ingres, Jean Auguste Dominique (1780–1867), French historical and classical painter. His paintings include *La grande odalisque* in the Louvre.

Innocent III (*c.* 1160–1216), Pope 1198–1216. He asserted the power and moral force of the papacy over the Emperor Otto IV, Philip II of France, and John of England. He launched the fourth crusade, encouraged the crusade against the Albigensian heretics, and held the 4th Lateran council. His pontificate marks the zenith of the mediaeval papacy.

Inönü, Ismet (1884–1973), Turkish soldier and statesman; president 1938–50 and 1961–5.

Ionesco, Eugene (1912–94), French playwright of the Absurd, b. Romania, whose influential plays include *The Bald Prima Donna*, *The Chairs*, and *Rhinoceros*.

Iqbal, Sir Muhammad (1877–1938), poet-philosopher, b. Slalkot (Pakistan). He wrote both poetry and prose in Urdu, Persian, and English, and his work is marked by mystic nationalism.

Ireland, John (1879–1962), English composer, popularly known for his setting of Masefield's *Sea Fever*, but also a composer of chamber music and sonatas for pianoforte and violin.

Irving, Sir Henry (1838–1905), English actor. At the Lyceum theatre from 1871, later with Ellen Terry, he gave notable Shakespearean performances, especially as Shylock and Malvolio.

Irving, Washington (1783–1859), American essayist, whose works include *Tales of a Traveller* and *The Sketch Book*, also biographies.

Isabella of Castile (1451–1504), reigned jointly with her husband, Ferdinand II of Aragon, over a united Spain, from which the Moors and the Jews were expelled. During their reign the New World was discovered.

Ismail Pasha (1830–95), grandson of Mehemet Ali, was Khedive of Egypt, and became virtually independent of the Sultan. Under him the Suez canal was made, but his financial recklessness led to Anglo-French control and to his own abdication.

Ismay, 1st Baron (Hastings Lionel Ismay) (1887–1965), British general who was chief of staff to Sir Winston Churchill in the second world war.

Ito, Hirobumi, Prince (1841–1909). Japanese statesman, four times premier, who helped to modernise his country. He was assassinated.

Ivan the Great (1410–1505) brought the scattered provinces of Muscovy under one control and put an end to Tartar rule.

Ivan the Terrible (1530–84), crowned as first Tsar of Russia in 1547, was an autocratic ruler who consolidated and expanded Russia.

J

Jackson, Andrew (1767–1845), American general who was twice president of the United States.

Jackson, Reverend Jesse Louis (1941–). American clergyman and civil rights leader. Sought Democratic nomination, 1984 and 1988.

Jackson, Thomas Jonathan (1824–63), "Stonewall Jackson," was general on the Southern side in the American Civil War; killed at Chancellorsville.

Jacobs, William Wymark (1863–1943), English

novelist, b. London, author of humorous sea and other stories.

Jacquard, Joseph Marie (1752–1834), French inventor whose loom provided an effective method of weaving designs.

Jahangir (1569–1627), 3rd Mogul emperor and patron of art.

James I (1566–1625), King of England (1603–25) and, as James VI, King of Scotland (1567–1625). He was the son of Mary Stuart and succeeded to the English throne on the death of Elizabeth I. His reign saw the Gunpowder Plot of 1605 and the publication of the Authorised Version of the Bible, but it also marked an increasingly critical attitude of the Puritans towards the established church. Described as "the wisest fool in Christendom."

James II (1633–1701), King of England and, as James VII, King of Scotland (1685–8), was the younger son of Charles I. Personally honest, and an able admiral, he lacked political understanding; and when, having put down Monmouth's rebellion, he tried and failed to obtain better conditions for his fellow Roman Catholics, he was obliged in 1688 to flee the country.

James, Cyril Lionel Robert (1901–89), Trinidadian historian, literary critic, political theorist and activist. Also a cricket writer. Author of *Nkrumah and the Ghana Revolution* (1977) and *Spheres of Existence* (1980).

James, Henry (1843–1916), American novelist. He lived mainly in England. His work, noted for intellectual subtlety and characterisation, includes *The American, Daisy Miller, The Portrait of a Lady, What Maisie Knew*, and *The Spoils of Poynton*.

James, William (1842–1910), American psychologist and philosopher, brother of Henry. He was a protagonist of the theory of pragmatism developed by his friend C. S. Peirce, and invented the doctrine which he called "radical empiricism." His major works are *The Principles of Psychology, The Will to Believe*, and *The Meaning of Truth*.

Janáček, Leoš (1854–1928), Czech composer and conductor, and student of folk music, b. in Moravia, son of a village schoolmaster, creator of a national style. His best-known opera is *Jenufa*. *See Section E*.

Jefferies, Richard (1848–87), English naturalist of poetic perception, b. in Wiltshire, author of *Gamekeeper at Home* and *The Life of the Fields*.

Jefferson, Thomas (1743–1826), American president, 1801–9. He created the Republican Party, by which the federalists, led by Hamilton, were overthrown, and helped to draft the Declaration of Independence. He tried unsuccessfully to bring an end to slavery. He negotiated the Louisiana Purchase of 1803.

Jeffreys, 1st Baron (George Jeffreys) (1648–89), English judge who held the "bloody assize" after Monmouth's unsuccessful rebellion. In 1686 he was sent to the Tower and there died.

Jellicoe, 1st Earl (John Rushworth Jellicoe) (1859–1935), British admiral. He fought the uncertain battle of Jutland in 1916, after which the German fleet remained in harbour.

Jenkins, Lord (Roy Jenkins) (b. 1920), British politician, b. Wales; Pres. EEC Commission 1977–80; served as Labour's Home Sec. 1965–7; Chanc. of Exchequer 1967–70. Elected M.P. for Glasgow Hillhead for Social Democrats (1982). Leader, SDP 1982–June 1983. Elected Chanc., Oxford University, 1987–. Defeated in 1987 General Election. Awarded Order of Merit (1993).

Jenner, Edward (1749–1823), English physician, b. in Gloucs., pupil of John Hunter. His discovery of vaccination against smallpox (1798) helped to lay the foundations of modern immunology.

Jerne, Niels Kai (1911–94), Danish microbiologist and Nobel laureate. The "Grand Old Man of Immunology".

Jerome, Jerome Klapka (1859–1927), English humorous writer, author of *Three Men in a Boat*.

Jerome, St. (*c.* 331–420), scholar, whose translation of the Bible into Latin (the Vulgate) became for centuries the standard use.

Jesus Christ (c. 4 B.C.–A.D. 30), founder of Christianity, the son of Mary whose husband was Joseph, was born in a critical period of Jewish history. His home was at Nazareth in Galilee, but virtually nothing is known about his early life. When he was about 30 he began the mission which he believed to have been entrusted to him,

proclaiming the Kingdom of God was at hand. His teaching is summarised in the Sermon on the Mount, and its main theme is love, especially for the poor and downtrodden. He was later crucified. The main source of his life is the New Testament. The title "Christ" comes from the Greek word *christos* = anointed, which is the Greek translation of the Hebrew title *Messiah*. Modern dating has amended the probable year of his birth.

Jiang Zemin (b. 1926), Chinese politician. Currently State President of China.

Jiménez, Juan Ramón (1881–1958), Spanish lyric poet. Nobel prizewinner 1956.

Jinnah, Mohammed Ali (1876–1948), Pakistani statesman. B. at Karachi, he became president of the Muslim League and succeeded in 1947 in establishing the Dominion of Pakistan, becoming its first governor-general.

Joachim, Joseph (1831–1907), Hungarian violinist and composer.

Joan of Arc, St. (Jeanne d'Arc) (1412–31), French patriot, called the Maid of Orleans; of peasant parentage (she was b. at Domrémy), she believed herself called to save France from English domination; and by her efforts Charles VII was crowned at Rheims in 1429. Captured by the Burgundians and sold to the English; burned as a heretic; canonised in 1920.

Joffre, Joseph Jacques Césaire (1852–1931), French general. He was commander-in-chief of the French army in the 1914–18 war.

John, St., the Baptist (executed A.D. 28), the forerunner of Jesus Christ.

John, St., the Evangelist, one of the twelve apostles of Jesus Christ, a Galilean fisherman, son of Zebedee and brother of James; traditionally author of the fourth Gospel.

John (1167–1216), youngest son of Henry II, was King of England from 1199. Able but erratic and arbitrary, he lost Normandy. Baronial opposition to him, under the influence of Archbishop Stephen Langton, acquired a national character, and in 1215 he was obliged to seal Magna Carta (*see* **Section L**).

John of Gaunt (1340–99). Duke of Lancaster, son of Edward III and father of Henry IV.

John XXIII (1881–1963), elected Pope in 1958, succeeding Pius XII, was formerly Cardinal Angelo Giuseppe Roncalli, patriarch of Venice. He sought to bring the Church closer to modern needs and to promote Christian unity.

John Paul II, (b. 1920), succeeded Pope John Paul I after his sudden death in 1978; formerly Cardinal Karol Wojtyla, archbishop of Cracow; first Pope to come from Poland. Assassination attempt made 1981. Historic meeting with Gorbachev, 1989.

John, Augustus (1878–1961), British painter and etcher, b. in Wales: noted for his portraits.

Johnson, Amy (1904–41), was the first woman aviator to fly solo from England to Australia. She lost her life serving in the Air Transport Auxiliary in the second world war.

Johnson, Lyndon Baines (1908–73), President of the United States, 1963–9. He became president on Kennedy's assassination and followed a progressive policy at home, but his achievements were clouded by the war in Vietnam.

Johnson, Samuel (1709–84), English lexicographer and man of letters, b. at Lichfield. His *Dictionary* was published in 1755, and was followed by *Rasselas, The Idler* (a periodical), and *Lives of the Poets*. He was a focus of London literary life of his day, and his biographer, James Boswell, has vividly portrayed his circle.

Joliot-Curie, Jean Frédéric (1900–58), and his wife Irène (1896–1956), French scientists who discovered artificial radioactivity. Nobel prizewinners 1935. Joliot-Curie was one of the discoverers of nuclear fission. Irène was the daughter of Pierre and Marie Curie. Both were communists, and both died from cancer caused by their work.

Jones, Ernest Charles (1819–69), English Chartist leader and poet.

Jones, Sir Harold Spencer (1890–1960), British astronomer royal, 1935–55. His major research was to determine the mean distance of the earth from the sun, 93,004,000 miles.

Jones, Inigo (1573–1652), architect of the English renaissance who studied in Italy and inspired the use of Palladian forms in England. His buildings include the banqueting hall in Whitehall and the queen's house at Greenwich. He also designed furniture and introduced the proscenium arch and movable scenery on the English stage.

Jonson, Ben (1573–1637), English poet and dramatist. His plays include *Every Man in his Humour*, *Volpone*, and *The Alchemist*; and his poems *Drink to me only with thine Eyes*. He also produced court masques.

Josephine, Empress (1763–1814), wife of Napoleon I, *née* de la Pagerie, she was previously married to the Vicomte de Beauharnais. She was divorced from Napoleon in 1809.

Josephus, Flavius (38–*c*. 100), Jewish historian, author of *History of the Jewish War*.

Joule, James Prescott (1818–89), English physicist, pupil of Dalton, who researched on electromagnetism and determined the mechanical equivalent of heat. See **Section L**.

Jowett, Benjamin (1817–93), English scholar. He translated Plato's *Dialogues*, and he was an influential Master of Balliol College, Oxford.

Jowitt, Earl (William Allen Jowitt) (1885–1957), British Labour politician and Lord Chancellor. He wrote *The Strange Case of Alger Hiss*.

Joyce, James (1882–1941), Irish author, b. Dublin. His *Ulysses* gives a microscopic picture of a day in the life of two Irishmen, and flouted the conventions of his day. Other works include *Portrait of the Artist* and *Finnegans Wake*. He spent most of his life on the Continent.

Juin, Alphonse (1888–1967), French general who took part in the Allied invasion of Tunisia and the Italian campaign in the second world war.

Julian the Apostate (331–63), Roman emperor who tried to restore paganism in the empire. He was killed in war against Persia.

Jung, Carl Gustav (1875–1961), Swiss psychiatrist. A former pupil of Freud, he later formulated his own system of analytical psychology. See **Section J**.

Junot, Andoche (1771–1813), French general defeated by Wellington in the Peninsular War.

Jusserand, Jean Jules (1855–1932), French author and diplomat, who wrote on English literature and wayfaring life in the Middle Ages.

Justinian I (483–565), Roman emperor in the East. He and his wife Theodora beautified Constantinople, and his general Belisarius was successful in war. He codified Roman law.

Juvenal (60–140), Roman poet and Stoic, remembered for his *Satires*.

K

Kafka, Franz (1883–1924), German-speaking Jewish writer, b. Prague, whose introspective work, the bulk of which was not published till after his early death from tuberculosis, has had a notable influence on later schools, especially the surrealists. It includes the three novels *The Trial*, *The Castle*, and *America*.

Kālidāsa (*c*. A.D. 400), chief figure in classic Sanskrit literature. No facts are known about his life and date, but certain evidence places him in the 5th cent. Seven of his works survive: two lyrics, *Ritu-samhara* (The Seasons), and *Megha-dūta* (Cloud Messenger); two epics, *Raghu-vamsa* (Dynasty of Raghu) and *Kumara-sambhava* (Birth of the War-god); and three dramas, *Śakúntalá*, *Málavikágnimitra*, and *Vikramorvaśtya*.

Kant, Immanuel (1724–1804), German philosopher, author of *Critique of Pure Reason* (1781), *Critique of Practical Reason* (1788), and *Critique of Judgement* (1790). He came from a Pietist family of Königsberg, where he lectured, but the Prussian government forbade his lectures as anti-Lutheran. He was influenced by the writings of his neighbour Hamann (see **Romanticism, Section J**) and by Rousseau and Hume, and his own work was of immense influence in shaping future liberal thought. He believed in the freedom of man to make his own decisions and considered the exploitation of man as the worst evil. In *Perpetual Peace* he advocated a world federation of states.

Kapitza, Pyotr (1894–1984), Russian physicist who worked on atomic research with Rutherford at the Cavendish Laboratory, Cambridge, and returned to Russia in 1935. Member of the Soviet Academy of Sciences and Fellow of the Royal Society. Nobel Prize for Physics, 1978.

Kauffman, Angelica (1741–1807), Anglo-Swiss painter, a foundation member of the Royal Academy and the first woman R.A.

Kaulbach, Wilhelm von (1805–74), German painter who illustrated the works of Goethe and Schiller.

Kaunda, Kenneth (b. 1924), African leader of international standing, son of Christian missionaries. He was president of Zambia, 1964–91.

Kean, Charles John (1811–68), English actor-manager son of Edmund. He married Ellen Tree. In the 1850s played with her in spectacular revivals at the Princess's Theatre, London.

Kean, Edmund (1787–1833), English tragic actor. He made his name as Shylock.

Keats, John (1795–1821), English poet who in his short life produced poems notable for richness of imagination and beauty of thought. They include *Odes*, *Isabella*, and *The Eve of St. Agnes*.

Keble, John (1792–1866), English clergyman associated with the Tractarian movement (**J52**) and author of *The Christian Year*.

Keller, Helen Adams (1880–1968), American author and lecturer who overcame great physical handicaps (blind and deaf before the age of two) to live an active and useful life.

Kelvin of Largs, 1st Baron (William Thomson) (1824–1907), British mathematician and physicist, b. Belfast, known for his work on heat and thermodynamics, and contributions to electrical science and submarine telegraphy. In the domain of heat he stands to Joule as Maxwell stands to Faraday in the history of electrical science, both bringing pre-eminently mathematical minds to bear on the results of experimental discoveries. He introduced the Kelvin or Absolute scale of temperature and was one of the original members of the Order of Merit.

Kemble, Fanny (1809–93), English actress. She came of a noted theatrical family, her father and uncle respectively being the actors Charles Kemble and John Philip Kemble, and her aunt, Mrs. Siddons.

Kempenfelt, Richard (1718–82), English admiral, who sank with his ship the *Royal George* together with 600 of the ship's company off Spithead through a shifting of the guns which caused it to capsize.

Kempis, Thomas à (1380–1471), name by which the German mystic Thomas Hammerken was known, was a monk of the Augustinian order, whose life was mainly spent at a monastery near Zwolle. The author of *The Imitation of Christ*.

Kennedy, John Fitzgerald (1917–63), President of the U.S.A., 1961–3, the youngest and the first Roman Catholic to be elected; son of a financier. He had world-wide pre-eminence and gave the American people a sense of purpose to meet the challenges of a scientific age. He opposed racial discrimination and initiated a new era of East–West relations; but his foreign policy sowed the seeds of the Vietnam war. He and his brother Robert (1925–68) were assassinated, the latter while campaigning for the presidency in 1968. Robert Kennedy was Attorney General, 1961–64 and promoted the Civil Rights Act.

Kent, William (1684–1748), English painter, furniture designer, landscape gardener, and architect, protégé of Lord Burlington, whose buildings include the great hall at Holkham and the Horse Guards, Whitehall.

Kenyatta, Jomo (1893–1978), African leader who became president of Kenya in 1964.

Kepler, Johann (1571–1630), German astronomer and mystic, for a short time assistant to Tycho Brahe whose measurements he used in working out his laws of planetary motion, which are: 1. Planets move round the sun not in circles, but in ellipses, the sun being one of the foci. 2. A planet moves not uniformly but in such a way that a line drawn from it to the sun sweeps out equal areas of the ellipse in equal times. 3. The squares of the period of revolution round the sun are proportional to the cubes of the distances. The explanation of these laws was given by Newton.

Kerensky, Alexander (1881–1970), Russian politician. Prime Minister of Provisional Government, July–November 1917. Rest of life in exile.

Keyes, 1st Baron (Roger John Brownlow Keyes) (1872–1945), British admiral who led the raid on Zeebrugge in 1918.

Keynes, 1st Baron (John Maynard Keynes) (1883–1946), British economist, who was a Treasury representative at the Versailles peace conference, and published his views in *The Economic Consequences of the Peace*. His *Treatise on Money* (1930) and *The General Theory of Employment, Interest and Money* (1936) influenced economic thought all over the world.

Khachaturian, Aram Ilich (1903–78), Armenian-born composer who wrote the popular *Sabre Dance* and *Spartacus* (from which the Love Song was used in T.V.'s Onedin Line.)

Khomeini, Ayatollah (1900–89), Iranian religious leader. After 16 years in exile, returned to Iran in 1979 after the overthrow of the Shah. Architect of Islamic Republic of Iran. Virulently anti-Western. Waged costly, futile war with Iraq.

Khrushchev, Nikita Sergeyevich (1894–1971), Russian statesman who became leader of the Soviet Union soon after the death of Stalin; first secretary of the Soviet Communist Party, 1953–64; prime minister, 1958–64. After the harsh years of the Stalinist régime he pursued a policy of relaxation both in home and foreign affairs. Relations with America improved but those with China became strained.

Kierkegaard, Sören (1813–55), Danish philosopher and religious thinker, whose views have influenced existentialism. His main work is *Either–Or*.

King, Martin Luther (1929–68), American clergyman and Negro integration leader; awarded the 1964 Nobel peace prize for his consistent support of the principle of non-violence in the coloured people's struggle for civil rights. Assassinated at Memphis, Tennessee.

King, Mackenzie (1874–1950), prime minister of Canada, 1921–5, 1926–30, and 1935–48.

Kingsley, Charles (1819–75), English clergyman and novelist, author of *Hypatia*, *Westward Ho!*, *Hereward the Wake* and *The Water Babies*.

Kinnock, Neil, (b. 1942), Labour politician. Leader of the Labour Party 1983–92. Played a large part in reshaping the party for the 1992 election but resigned after Labour's fourth successive election defeat. EU Commissioner (with responsibility for Transport) since 1995.

Kipling, Rudyard (1865–1936), British writer, b. Bombay. His vivid work portrays contemporary British rule in India and includes *The Light that Failed*, *Stalky and Co.*, *Kim*, and the *Barrack Room Ballads*. Among his books for children are the *Just So Stories*, *Puck of Pook's Hill* and the *Jungle Books*. Nobel prize 1907.

Kirchhoff, Gustav Robert (1824–87), German mathematical physicist, who with R. W. Bunsen discovered that in the gaseous state each chemical substance emits its own characteristic spectrum (1859). He was able to explain Fraunhofer's map of the solar spectrum. Using the spectroscope, he and Bunsen discovered the elements caesium and rubidium.

Kissinger, Henry (b. 1923), American Secretary of State 1973–7 and special adviser on national security affairs to Richard Nixon; inventor of shuttle-service diplomacy. Shared Nobel peace prize for 1973 with Le Duc Tho.

Kitchener of Khartoum, 1st Earl (Horatio Herbert Kitchener) (1850–1916), English general. In 1898 he won back the Sudan for Egypt by his victory at Omdurman. He served in the South African war; and in the first world war he was secretary of war, 1914–16. He was drowned on his way to Russia.

Klee, Paul (1879–1940), Swiss artist, whose paintings, in a restless, experimental period, are small-scale, delicate dream-world fantasies of poetical content.

Klemperer, Otto (1885–1973), German-born conductor, renowned as interpreter of the Beethoven symphonies. Expelled by the Nazis he became an American citizen and returned to Europe in 1946. He had been principal conductor of the Philharmonic Orchestra since 1959.

Kneller, Sir Godfrey (1646–1723), portrait painter, b. at Lübeck, who settled in England and was patronised by successive English sovereigns.

Knox, John (1514–72), Scottish reformer, b. near Haddington. While in exile at Geneva he was influenced by Calvin. On return to Scotland he was a leader of the reforming party against Mary, Queen of Scots. He wrote a *History of the Reformation in Scotland*.

Koch, Robert (1843–1910), German bacteriologist who discovered the bacillus of tuberculosis, and worked on cholera and cattle diseases.

Kodály, Zoltán (1882–1967), Hungarian composer and teacher. He worked with Bartok in the collection of folk-tunes. See Section E.

Kohl, Helmut (b. 1930), Chancellor of the Federal Republic of Germany. First Chancellor of reunited Germany after 1990. One of the most powerful figures in contemporary European politics. Narrowly re-elected Chancellor, 1994. A Christian Democrat. See Section C.

Kokoschka, Oskar (1886–1980), Austrian portrait and landscape painter. Settled in England.

Korolyov, Sergei (1907–66), Russian space scientist, who designed the world's first earth satellite, the first manned spaceship and the first moon rocket.

Kosciusko, Tadeusz (1746–1817), Polish patriot. After experience gained in America in the War of Independence, he led his countrymen against Russia in 1792 and 1794 in opposition to the partition of Poland.

Kossuth, Louis (1802–94), Hungarian patriot, who in 1848 led a rising of his countrymen against the Hapsburg dynasty, but had to flee to Turkey and later to England.

Kosygin, Alexei Nikolayevich (1904–80), succeeded Nikita Khrushchev as chairman of the Council of Ministers of the U.S.S.R. (prime minister) in 1964; key technocrat and economic organiser; resigned on health grounds, 1980.

Krebs, Sir Hans (1900–81), British biochemist, b. Germany. Taught at Cambridge and Sheffield and became Professor of Biology at Oxford in 1954. Nobel prize 1953.

Kreisler, Fritz (1875–1962), Austrian violinist, who composed violin music and an operetta. He became an American citizen in 1943.

Krenek, Ernst (b. 1900), Austrian composer of partly Czech descent, whose compositions include the jazz opera *Jonny spielt auf*.

Kropotkin, Peter, Prince (1842–1921), Russian anarchist, geographer and explorer, who was imprisoned for favouring the political action of a working men's association, but escaped to England. He wrote on socialistic and geographical subjects. Returned to Russia, 1917.

Kruger, Stephanus Johannes Paulus (1825–1904), Boer leader, who in 1881 was appointed head of the provisional government against Britain, and later president. When the war of 1899–1902 turned against the Boers, he vainly sought help in Europe.

Krupp, Alfred (1812–87), founder of the German gun factories at Essen. He installed in a disused factory left him by his father a new steam-engine from England, began to make cast steel, and from 1844 specialised in armaments. The firm's factories made the Big Bertha guns which shelled Paris in 1918.

Krylov, Ivan Andreyevich (1768–1844), Russian writer of fables (the Russian La Fontaine.)

Kubelik, Jan (1880–1940), Czech violinist who at the age of 12 played in public.

Kublai Khan (1216–94), grandson of Genghis Khan, was the first Mongol emperor of China. He extended the Mongol empire by conquest, and lived in unparalleled splendour. His court was described by Marco Polo and is the subject of a poem by Coleridge.

L

La Fayette, Marie Joseph Paul Roch Yves Gilbert du Motier, Marquis de (1757–1834), French soldier and statesman. He fought for the colonists in the American War of Independence; and in the 1789 French revolution he proposed a declaration of rights and was commander of the National Guard till his moderation made him unpopular. When the monarchy was restored he was an opposition leader, and took part in the revolution of 1830.

La Fontaine, Jean de (1621–95), French poet and fabulist, b. in Champagne, a friend of Molière, Boileau, and Racine, all brilliant writers of the reign of Louis XIV.

Lagerlöf, Selma (1858–1940), Swedish novelist and first woman member of the Swedish Academy, Nobel prizewinner 1909.

Lagrange, Joseph Louis, Comte (1736–1813), French mathematician, of Turin and Paris, whose interest in astronomy led him to distinguish two types of disturbance of members of the solar system, the periodic and the secular.

He was called by Frederick the Great to Berlin to succeed Euler.

Lalande, Joseph Jerome LeFrançais de (1732–1807), French astronomer, author of *Traité d'astronomie.*

Lamarck, Jean Baptiste Pierre Antoine de Monet de (1744–1829), French biologist whose explanation of evolution was that new organs are brought into being by the needs of the organism in adapting to its environment and that the new characters acquired during its life-time can be passed on to the offspring through heredity, resulting in evolutionary change. *See* **F30.**

Lamb, Charles (1775–1834), English essayist, b. London. A clerk in the East India Office, he devoted his life to his sister Mary, who was of unstable mind. He is chiefly known for his *Essays of Elia,* and his letters, which have a blend of humour and tenderness.

Lambert, Constant (1905–51), English composer and critic, and conductor of Sadler's Wells ballet. His *Rio Grande* is in jazz idiom.

Landor, Walter Savage (1775–1864), English writer, b. Warwick, remembered for his *Imaginary Conversations* and poems.

Landseer, Sir Edwin (1802–73), English animal painter, b. London. He painted the *Monarch of the Glen* and designed the lions in Trafalgar Square.

Lane, Edward William (1801–76), English Arabic scholar, translator of the *Arabian Nights.*

Lanfranc (*c.* 1005–89), ecclesiastic. B. at Pavia, he became a prior in Normandy, and in 1070 an energetic archbishop of Canterbury.

Lang, Andrew (1844–1912), Scottish man of letters, whose output includes *Myth, Ritual and Religion,* poems, fairy-tales, and fiction.

Lang, 1st Baron (Cosmo Gordon Lang) (1864–1945), was archbishop of Canterbury, 1928–42.

Langland, William (1330?–1400?), English poet, probably educated at Malvern, author of *The Vision of Piers the Plowman.*

Langton, Stephen (1151–1228), archbishop of Canterbury, and adviser to the insurgent barons who induced King John to grant Magna Carta.

Lansbury, George (1859–1940), British Labour politician, founder of the *Daily Herald.* He improved London's amenities.

Lâo Tsze (old philosopher) (*c.* 600 B.C.), traditional founder of Taoism in China. *See* **Section J.**

Laplace, Pierre Simon, Marquis de (1749–1827), French mathematician and astronomer, author of *Celestial Mechanics* (1799–1825). He believed that the solar system had condensed out of a vast rotating gaseous nebula.

Lara, Brian Charles (b. 1969), West Indies cricketer. Born Trinidad. An accomplished batsman who made the highest-ever score in test cricket (375 against England at Antigua in April 1994). This was followed by 501 not out for Warwickshire against Durham at Edgbaston (also in 1994).

La Rochefoucauld, François, Duc de (1613–80), French writer, author of *Reflections and Moral Maxims.*

Lasker, Emanuel (1868–1941), German chess player, world champion, 1894–1921.

Lassalle, Ferdinand (1825–64), German socialist who took part in the revolutionary movement of 1848 and organised workers movements.

Lassus, Orlandus (Lasso, Orlando di) (*c.* 1532–94), Flemish composer and choirmaster, contemporary of Palestrina, writer of *chansons,* madrigals, and sacred music. *See* **Section E.**

Latimer, Hugh (*c.* 1485–1555), English Protestant martyr, became bishop of Worcester in 1535, and was executed under Queen Mary.

Laud, William (1573–1645), archbishop of Canterbury and adviser to Charles I. His attempt to get conformity for his high church policy made him unpopular and he was impeached and beheaded.

Lauder, Sir Harry (1870–1950), Scottish comic singer of wide popularity. He also wrote *Roamin' in the Gloamin'.*

Laval, Pierre (1883–1945), French politician who collaborated with the Germans, 1940–45.

Lavoisier, Antoine Laurent (1743–94), French chemist, b. Paris, was the first to establish the fact that combustion is a form of chemical action. We owe the word *oxygen* to him.

Law, Andrew Bonar (1858–1923), Conservative politician, prime minister 1922–3.

Lawrence, David Herbert (1885–1930), English poet and novelist, b. Notts., a miner's son. He tried to interpret emotion on a deeper level of consciousness. His works, which have had wide influence, include *The White Peacock, Sons and Lovers, The Rainbow, Women in Love,* and *Lady Chatterley's Lover;* his plays had to wait half a century before coming to the stage in the 1960s.

Lawrence, Sir Thomas (1769–1830), English portrait painter.

Lawrence, Thomas Edward (1888–1935) (Lawrence of Arabia), British soldier who led the Arabs against the Turks in the war of 1914–18, and wrote *The Seven Pillars of Wisdom.*

Leacock, Stephen (1869–1944), Canadian humorist.

Lean, Sir David (1908–91), British film director who won 28 Oscars. His films included *Dr Zhivago* (1965) and *A Passage to India* (1984). *See* **Section W.**

Leavis, Frank Raymond (1895–1978), British critic, who edited *Scrutiny,* 1932–63, and whose works include *The Great Tradition, D. H. Lawrence, Novelist,* and *"Anna Karenina" and Other Essays.*

Lecky, William Edward Hartpole (1838–1903), Irish historian, author of *England in the Eighteenth Century.*

Leclerc, Jacques Philippe (Philippe, Comte de Hautecloque) (1902–47), French general. He led a Free French force in Africa in the second world war and liberated Paris in 1944.

Le Corbusier (1887–1965), pseudonym of Charles Édouard Jeanneret, Swiss architect, whose books and work (especially his Unité d'Habitation at Marseilles and the Punjab capital at Chandigarh) have influenced town-planning.

Le Duc Tho (1911–90), member of the Politburo of the N. Vietnamese Workers' Party who was his country's chief negotiator at the Vietnam truce talks 1970–3. He would not accept the 1973 Nobel peace prize awarded jointly with Dr. Kissinger until peace had "really been restored in S. Vietnam."

Lee of Fareham, 1st Viscount (Arthur Hamilton Lee) (1868–1947), British politician who presented Chequers Court to the nation as prime minister's residence.

Lee Kuan Yew (b. 1923). First Prime Minister of Singapore, 1959–90. Helped establish prosperity of Singapore, but little opposition was tolerated.

Lee, Robert Edward (1807–70), American Confederate general in the Civil War, who made the surrender at Appomattox.

Lee, Sir Sidney (1859–1926), English critic. Joint editor of the *Dictionary of National Biography.*

Leech, John (1817–64), Humorous artist and political cartoonist who contributed numerous drawings to *Punch.* He illustrated Surtees' novels and Dickens's *A Christmas Carol.*

Lehár, Franz (1870–1948), Hungarian composer. Among his most popular operettas are *The Merry Widow* and *The Count of Luxembourg.*

Leibnitz, Gottfried Wilhelm (1646–1716), German philosopher and mathematician, who invented the differential and integral calculus (1684) independently of Newton whose previous work on the same subject was not published until 1687. It was Leibnitz's nomenclature that was universally adopted.

Leicester, Earl of (Robert Dudley) (1533–88), English soldier, commanded English troops in the Netherlands, 1585–7, without much success, and in 1588 commanded forces assembled against the Armada. He was husband of Amy Robsart.

Leif Ericsson (fl. 1000), discoverer of Vinland on the north-east coast of America; b. Iceland, son of the Norse explorer, Eric the Red, who colonised Greenland.

Leighton, 1st Baron (Robert Leighton) (1830–96), English painter whose works include *Paolo and Francesca.* He was also a sculptor.

Lely, Sir Peter (Pieter van der Faes) (1618–80), Dutch painter who settled in London and painted court portraits.

Lenin (Vladimir Ilyich Ulyanov) (1870–1924), Russian revolutionary leader and statesman. From 1893 to 1917 he worked underground in Russia and abroad for the revolutionary cause. During this time the Social-Democratic party was formed; within it developed an uncompromising revolutionary group, the Bolsheviks, and of this group Lenin was the leading spirit. In April 1917 he and his fellow exiles returned; after the November revolution he headed the new government having to face both war and

B38

anarchy. In 1921 his "new economic policy" somewhat modified the intensive drive towards planned industrial development. He was born in Simbirsk (now Ulyanovsk) on the middle Volga.

Leonardo da Vinci (1452–1519), Italian artist and man of science, son of a Florentine lawyer and a peasant. He described himself (when applying to Lodovico Sforza, Duke of Milan, for the post of city planner) as painter, architect, philosopher, poet, composer, sculptor, athlete, mathematician, inventor, and anatomist. His artistic output is small in quantity, and he is best known for his *Last Supper* in the refectory of Santa Maria delle Grazie in Milan and his *Mona Lisa* in the Louvre. He recorded his scientific work in unpublished notebooks written from right to left in mirror writing. The anatomy of the body (himself carrying out dissections), the growth of the child in the womb, the laws of waves and currents, and the laws of flight, all were studied by this astonishing man who believed nothing but had to see for himself.

Leoncavallo, Ruggiero (1858–1919), Italian composer of the opera *Pagliacci*.

Leonidas was king of Sparta at the time of the invasion of Greece by Xerxes (480 B.C.), and led the defence of the pass of Thermopylae, where he fell.

Lermontov, Mikhail Yurevich (1814–41), Russian poet and novelist, exiled to the Caucasus for a revolutionary poem addressed to Tsar Nicholas I on the death of Pushkin. He has been called the poet of the Caucasus. His novel *A Hero of Our Time* was written at St. Petersburg. He lost his life in a duel.

Le Sage, Alain René (1668–1747), French author, b. in Brittany, who wrote *Gil Blas* and *Le Diable Boiteux*. He was also a dramatist and his plays include *Turcaret*.

Lesseps, Ferdinand, Vicomte de (1805–94), French engineer who while serving as vice-consul at Alexandria conceived a scheme for a canal across the Suez isthmus; the work was completed in 1869. He also projected the original Panama canal scheme, which failed.

Lessing, Gotthold Ephraim (1729–81), German philosopher, dramatist, and critic, noted for his work *Laokoon* and his play *Minna von Barnhelm*.

Leucippus (fl. 440 B.C.), Greek philosopher, founder with Democritus of atomism, a theory of matter more nearly that of modern science than any put forward in ancient times. One of his sayings survives: "Naught occurs at random, but everything for a reason and of necessity."

Leverhulme, 1st Viscount (William Hesketh Lever) (1851–1925), British industrialist and philanthropist. He founded Lever Bros. which later became Unilever Ltd., and was a practical exponent of industrial partnership. He gave Lancaster House to the nation.

Leverrier, Urbain Jean Joseph (1811–77), French astronomer who, working independently of J. C. Adams of Cambridge, anticipated the existence of the planet Neptune which was later revealed by telescopic search.

Lévi-Strauss, Claude (b. 1908), French social anthropologist, b. Belgium, exponent of the theory of symbolic structures. He has written works on anthropology, religion, myths and language. The final vol. of his *Introduction to a Science of Mythology* about the myths and rituals of American Indians was published in 1981.

Lewis, Sinclair (1885–1951), American writer of novels satirising small-town life and philistinism. His works include *Main Street, Babbitt* and *Elmer Gantry*. Nobel prizewinner 1931.

Liaquat Ali Khan (1895–1951), leader of the Moslem League (1946) and first premier of Pakistan in 1947. He was assassinated.

Lie, Trygve (1896–1968), Norwegian politician. Secretary-General of the United Nations, 1946–52.

Lilburne, John (1614–57), English agitator and pamphleteer, leader of the Levellers in the Civil War period.

Linacre, Thomas (c. 1460–1524), English humanist and physician, who translated Galen's works and founded the College of Physicians.

Lincoln, Abraham (1809–65), American president. Born in Kentucky, he became a lawyer and was returned to Congress from Illinois in 1846. He was a leader of the Republican party which was formed in 1856 to oppose slavery. He became

president in 1861, in which year the Confederate States proposed to withdraw from the Union, and war broke out. The phrase "government of the people, by the people, for the people" comes from his Gettysburg speech of 1863. He was assassinated in 1865.

Lind, Jenny (1820–87), Swedish singer, popular in Europe, and known as the Swedish nightingale. She founded musical scholarships.

Linnaeus (1707–78), Swedish botanist, remembered for his system of defining living things by two Latin names, the first being its *genus*, and the second its *species*. His method is expounded in *Philosophia Botanica* (1751). In 1757 he was ennobled as Karl von Linné. He studied, taught and died at Uppsala.

Lippi, Fra Filippo (1406–69), Italian artist, b. Florence. Frescoes in Prato cathedral are his main work. His son **Filippino** (1457–1504) finished Masaccio's frescoes in the Carmine, Florence, and executed others, for instance in Santa Maria Novella.

Lippmann, Gabriel (1845–1921), French physicist who invented a capillary electrometer and was a pioneer in colour photography. Nobel prizewinner 1908.

Lippmann, Walter (1889–1974), American journalist of influence, writing for the New York *Herald Tribune*, 1931–62.

Lipton, Sir Thomas Johnstone (1850–1931), Scottish business man and philanthropist. B. Glasgow, he emigrated to America, but returned to Scotland and established extensive chainstores for groceries. He unsuccessfully competed in yachting for the America's Cup.

Lister, Baron (Joseph Lister) (1827–1912), English surgeon, son of **J. J. Lister** (1786–1869), an amateur microscopist. He founded antiseptic surgery (1865) which greatly reduced mortality in hospitals.

Liszt, Franz (1811–86), Hungarian pianist and composer. His daughter Cosima became the wife of Hans von Bülow and later of Wagner. *See* Section E.

Litvinov, Maxim (1876–1952), Russian diplomat, of revolutionary origin, who first as ambassador in London, then as commissar for foreign affairs, and 1941-3 ambassador to the U.S., gained respect and understanding for his country.

Livingstone, David (1813–73), Scottish explorer in Africa. He discovered the course of the Zambesi, the Victoria Falls and Lake Nyasa (now Lake Malawi), and roused opinion against the slave trade. At one time believed lost, he was found by Stanley (*q.v.*) on 10 Nov. 1871.

Lloyd-George of Dwyfor, 1st Earl (David Lloyd George) (1863–1945), Liberal statesman of Welsh origin. He was M.P. for Caernarvon, 1890–1944; and as chancellor of the exchequer he introduced social insurance, 1908–11. The war of 1914–18 obliged him to become a war premier (superseding Asquith), and he was subsequently one of the main figures at the peace conference. In 1921 he conceded the Irish Free State. His daughter, **Lady Megan Lloyd George**, was M.P. for many years, latterly for the Labour Party.

Lloyd Webber, Sir Andrew (b. 1948), British composer. His musicals include *Jesus Christ Superstar* (1970), *Evita* (1978), *Cats* (1981), *Starlight Express* (1983) and *Phantom of the Opera* (1986), and *Sunset Boulevard* (1993).

Locke, John (1632–1704), English liberal philosopher and founder of empiricism, the doctrine that all knowledge is derived from experience. His chief work in theoretical philosophy, *Essay Concerning Human Understanding*, was written just before the revolution of 1688 and published in 1690. Other writings include *Letters on Toleration, Treatises on Government*, and *Education*.

Lombroso, Cesare (1836–1909), Italian criminologist, whose *L'uomo delinquente* maintained the existence of a criminal type distinguishable from the normal.

Lomonosov, Mikhail Vasilievich (1711–65), Russian philologist and poet who systematised Russian grammar and orthography.

London, Jack (1876–1916), American author of adventure tales such as *Call of the Wild*.

Longfellow, Henry Wadsworth (1807–82), American poet, popular in his lifetime, author of *The Golden Legend* and *Hiawatha*.

Lope de Vega Carpio, Félix (1562–1635), Spanish

writer of immense output. First a ballad-writer, he took to play-writing and founded the Spanish drama. The number of his plays is said to have been 1,500, the earlier ones historical, the later ones dealing with everyday life; but most are lost.

Lorca, Federico Garcia (1899–1936), Spanish poet and dramatist of Andalusia. Among his works are *Llanto por Ignacio Sánchez Mejías*, an unforgettable lament on the death of a bullfighter, and *Canción de Jinete* with its haunting refrain, "Cordoba, far away and alone." He was brutally murdered by Franco sympathisers at the outbreak of the civil war.

Louis IX (1214–70), St. Louis, King of France. Of saintly character (as described in Joinville's *Memoirs*), he also carried out practical reforms. He died on crusade.

Louis XIV (1638–1715), King of France. A despotic ruler, builder of Versailles, he also dominated the Europe of his day; but he sowed the seeds of future trouble for France by his exhausting wars. He revoked the Edict of Nantes which had given religious freedom to the Huguenots since 1598. His reign, however, was a great period for literature.

Louis XV (1710–74), King of France. Extravagant and self-indulgent, his reign marked a declining period for the monarchy, but produced some fine art.

Louis XVI (1754–93), King of France. Well-meaning but incapable, he saw the outbreak of the French revolution of 1789, in which he and his queen Marie Antoinette were executed.

Louis, Joe (Joseph Louis Barrow) (1914–81), American Negro boxer, who became world heavyweight champion in 1937, successfully defending his title 26 times.

Low, Archibald Montgomery (1888–1956), British scientist who worked in varied fields, including wireless, television, and anti-aircraft and anti-tank apparatus.

Low, Sir David (1891–1963), British cartoonist, b. New Zealand, associated with the *Evening Standard* and later the *Guardian*; creator of Colonel Blimp.

Lowell, Robert (1917–77), American poet, author of the verse play *The Old Glory*, and *Life Studies*, an autobiographical volume in verse and prose.

Loyola, St. Ignatius (1491–1556), Spanish founder of the Jesuits, a missionary order working directly under the Pope.

Lucretius (99–55 B.C.), Roman poet, author of *De rerum natura*, a long philosophical poem advocating moral truth without religious belief.

Ludendorff, Erich (1865–1937), German general who directed German strategy in the first world war.

Lugard, 1st Baron (Frederick John Dealtry Lugard) (1858–1945), British colonial administrator in Africa, especially Nigeria, and exponent of the system of indirect rule through native chiefs.

Lukács, Georg (1885–1971), Hungarian writer, Marxist thinker and literary critic. His ideas are expounded in *History and Class Consciousness* (1923), *Studies in European Realism* (1946, Eng. tr. 1950), *The Historical Novel* (1955, Eng. tr. 1962).

Luther, Martin (1483–1546), German Protestant reformer. After spending time in a monastery, he was ordained priest (1507), and lectured at Wittenberg university. In 1517 he protested against the sale of indulgences; and when summoned before the Diet of Worms made a memorable defence. He was protected by the Elector of Saxony, and translated the Bible. German Protestantism culminated in the Augsburg confession (1530). *See also* **Lutheranism, Section J.**

Luthuli, Albert (1899–1967), African non-violent resistance leader, an ex-Zulu chief. Killed in train accident. Nobel prize for peace 1960.

Lutyens, Sir Edwin Landseer (1869–1944), English architect both of country houses and public buildings; designed the cenotaph, Whitehall; city plan and viceroy's house, New Delhi, British Embassy, Washington and Liverpool Roman catholic cathedral.

Lyell, Sir Charles (1797–1875), Scottish geologist, whose *Principles of Geology* (1830–33) postulated gradual geological change and helped to shape Darwin's ideas. His terminology—Pliocene (*Greek* = more recent), Miocene (less recent)

and Eocene (dawn)—is still in use.

Lynn, Dame Vera (b. 1917), immensely popular singer, the 'Forces' sweetheart' immortalised in such songs as *We'll Meet Again* and *White Cliffs of Dover.*

Lysenko, Trofim (1898–1976), Russian biologist who maintained that environmental experiences can change heredity somewhat in the manner suggested by Lamarck.

Lytton, 1st Baron (Edward George Earle Lytton Bulwer-Lytton) (1803–73), English novelist and playwright, author of *The Last Days of Pompeii.*

M

Macadam, John Loudon (1756–1836), Scottish inventor of the "macadamising" system of road repair.

MacArthur, Douglas (1880–1964), American general. He defended the Philippines against the Japanese in the second world war, and was relieved of his command in 1951 in the Korean war.

Macaulay of Rothley, 1st Baron (Thomas Babington Macaulay) (1800–59), English historian, poet and Indian civil servant. His poems include *Lays of Ancient Rome.* In India he reformed the education system.

Macaulay, Zachary (1768–1838), anti-slavery agitator, father of the above.

Macbeth (d. 1057), Scottish king, married Gruoch, granddaughter of Kenneth, king of Alban. He was mormaer of Moray, succeeding Duncan in 1040 after killing him in fair fight. His reign of seventeen years was prosperous, but he was killed by Duncan's son, Malcolm, in 1057. Shakespeare's play is based on the inaccurate *Chronicle* of Holinshed.

MacDiarmid, Hugh (1892–1978), pseudonym of Christopher Murray Grieve, Scottish poet, leader of the Scottish literary renaissance; author of *A Drunk Man Looks at the Thistle.*

Macdonald, Flora (1722–90), Scottish Jacobite heroine who saved the life of Prince Charles Edward after the defeat at Culloden Moor in 1746.

Macdonald, Sir John Alexander (1815–91), Canadian statesman, first prime minister of the Dominion of Canada.

MacDonald, James Ramsay (1866–1937), Labour politician of Scottish origin, premier 1924 and 1929–31; also of a coalition 1931–5. His action over the financial crisis of 1931 divided his party.

MacDonald, Malcolm (1901–81), son of above, held positions overseas in the Commonwealth, the last as special representative in Africa.

Machiavelli, Niccolò (1467–1527), Florentine Renaissance diplomat and theorist of the modern state. His book *The Prince* (1513), dedicated to Lorenzo, Duke of Urbino, is concerned with the reality of politics—what rulers must do to retain power. His *Discourses* is more republican and liberal.

Mackail, John William (1859–1945), British classical scholar, translator of the *Odyssey.*

Mackenzie, Sir Compton (1883–1972), British writer, whose works include *Carnival, Sinister Street,* and a monumental autobiography.

McLuhan, Herbert Marshall (1911–80), Canadian author of a number of books on contemporary communications, including *The Gutenberg Galaxy, The Mechanical Bride. See* **Section J.**

Macmillan, Harold (1894–1986), British Conservative statesman, prime minister 1957–63; During his premiership came the crises of the Berlin Wall and the Cuban missiles (in which his personal diplomacy played an influential role), de Gaulle's veto to our entry into Europe, the signing of the Partial Test-Ban Treaty and his "wind of change" speech which hailed African independence. Chancellor of Oxford University (1960–86), O.M. 1976. Created Earl of Stockton, 1984.

McMillan, Margaret (1860–1931), Scottish educational reformer, b. New York, and pioneer of open-air nursery schools.

Macneice, Louis (1907–63), British poet, playwright, and translator.

Macready, William Charles (1793–1873), British actor and manager, especially associated with Shakespearean roles.

Maeterlinck, Maurice (1862–1949), Belgian man of letters, whose plays include *La Princesse Maleine*, *Pelléas et Mélisande*, and *L'Oiseau Bleu*. Nobel prizewinner 1911.

Magellan, Ferdinand (*c.* 1480–1521), Portuguese navigator, and commander of the first expedition (1519) to sail round the world.

Mahler, Gustav (1860–1911), Austrian composer and conductor; a writer of symphonies and songs, a classical romantic, much influenced by Anton Bruckner and Wagner. *See* Section E.

Mahavira, Vardhamana Jnatiputra (6th cent. B.C.), Indian historical (as opposed to legendary) founder of Jainism, which teaches the sacredness of all life. *See* Jainism, Section J.

Maintenon, Françoise d'Aubigné, Marquise de (1635–1719), second wife of Louis XIV. Her first husband was the poet Scarron.

Major, John (b. 1943), Prime Minister since November 1990. Leader of the Conservative Party, 1990– . M.P. (Con.) Huntingdon since 1979. Foreign Secretary, 1989. Chancellor of the Exchequer, 1989–90. His early months in office were dominated by the Gulf War, economic problems and the reform of the poll tax. His victory in the 1992 election heralded grave problems for his government over Europe and great electoral unpopularity.

Makarios III (1913–77), Greek Orthodox archbishop and Cypriot national leader. Deported by the British to the Seychelles in 1956, he returned in 1957. First President of Cyprus.

Malibran, Marie Félicité (1808–36), Spanish mezzosoprano.

Malory, Sir Thomas (*c.* 1430–71), English writer. From earlier sources and legends of King Arthur and the Knights of the Round Table, he compiled the *Morte d'Arthur* printed by Caxton in 1485.

Malraux, André (1901–76), French novelist and politician. His works include *La Condition humaine*, *L'Espoir*, and *Psychologie de l'art* (tr. in 2 vols.), *Museum without Walls*, and *The Creative Act*). Served under de Gaulle.

Malthus, Thomas Robert (1766–1834), English clergyman and economist who in his gloomy essay *The Principle of Population* contended that population tends to increase faster than the means of subsistence and that its growth could only be checked by moral restraint or by disease and war. *See* Malthusianism, Section J.

Mandela, Nelson Rolihlahia (b. 1918), President of South Africa, May 1994– ; son of chief of Tembu tribe; imprisoned on political grounds 1964–90. His release from prison in February 1990 transformed the political scene in South Africa. Elected Deputy President, ANC, 1990. Historic agreement (1993) with President De Klerk to form Government of National Unity after multi-party elections. Shared Nobel Peace Prize with De Klerk, 1993. The ANC victory in April 1994 paved the way for him to become President. His autobiography, *Long Walk to Freedom*, was published in 1994. Honorary Order of Merit, 1995. *See* Section C.

Manet, Edouard (1832–83), French painter. His Impressionist pictures include *Olympia* and *Un bar aux Folies-Bergères* (the latter at the Courtauld).

Mann, Thomas (1875–1955), German writer who won world recognition at the age of 25 with his novel *Buddenbrooks*. His liberal humanistic outlook had developed sufficiently by 1930 for him to expose national socialism. He left Germany in 1933 to live in Switzerland, then settled in the U.S. Other works are *The Magic Mountain*, and the *Joseph* tetralogy. Nobel prizewinner 1929.

Mann, Tom (1856–1941), British Labour leader for more than fifty years.

Manning, Henry Edward (1808–92), English cardinal; archbishop of Westminster 1865–92. He was an Anglican churchman before he entered the church of Rome.

Mansfield, Katherine (Kathleen Beauchamp) (1890–1923), short-story writer, b. Wellington, New Zealand, whose work was influenced by the short stories of Chekhov. Her second husband was John Middleton Murry, literary critic.

Manson, Sir Patrick (1844–1922), Scottish physician, the first to propose that the malarial parasite was transmitted by the mosquito.

Manuzio, Aldo Pio (1450–1515), Italian printer, founder of the Aldine press in Venice which issued books famed for their beautiful type and bindings.

Manzoni, Alessandro (1785–1873), Italian novelist and poet, b. Milan, whose historical novel *I Promessi Sposi* (The Betrothed) won European reputation.

Mao Tse-tung (1893–1976), Chinese national and Communist leader. B. in Hunan, of rural origin. As a young man he worked as assistant librarian at Peking University. He understood how to win peasant support for a national and progressive movement. Attacked by Chiang Kai-shek, he led his followers to the "long march" to N.W. China, whence later they issued to defeat both Japanese and Chiang and proclaim a People's Republic in 1949, and later to promote the "great leap forward" of 1958–9 (the commune movement). He stood for an egalitarian democratic society, unbureaucratic, with revolutionary momentum. He promoted the "cultural revolution" from 1965 to 1969. *See* Maoism, Section J.

Marat, Jean Paul (1743–93), French revolution leader, largely responsible for the reign of terror, and assassinated by Charlotte Corday.

Marconi, Guglielmo Marchese (1874–1937), Italian inventor and electrical engineer who developed the use of radio waves. In 1895 he sent long-wave signals over a distance of a mile, and in 1901 received in Newfoundland the first transatlantic signals sent out by his station in Cornwall, thus making the discovery that radio waves can bend around the spherically-shaped earth. Nobel prizewinner 1909.

Marcus Aurelius Antoninus (121–180 A.D.), Roman emperor and Stoic philosopher of lofty character, whose *Meditations* are still read.

Marcuse, Herbert (1898–1979), political philosopher. B. Berlin, he emigrated to the U.S. during the Nazi regime. A critic of Western industrial society, he saw the international student protest movement as the catalyst of revolutionary change.

Maria Theresa (1717–80), Empress, daughter of the Hapsburg Charles VI. Able and of strong character, she fought unsuccessfully to save Silesia from Prussian annexation. She promoted reforms in her dominions. She married the Duke of Lorraine and had 16 children.

Marie Antoinette (1755–93), Queen of France, was daughter of the above and wife of Louis XVI; accused of treason, she and her husband were beheaded in the French revolution.

Marie Louise (1791–1847), daughter of Francis I of Austria, became the wife of Napoleon and bore him a son (Napoleon II).

Marius, Caius (157–86 B.C.), Roman general who defended Gaul from invasion; later civil war forced him to flee from Rome, and on his return he took terrible revenge.

Mark Antony. *See* Antonius, Marcus.

Marlborough, 1st Duke of (John Churchill) (1650–1722), English general, victor of Blenheim, Ramillies, Oudenarde and Malplaquet. His wife, Sarah Jennings, was a favourite of Queen Anne.

Marlowe, Christopher (1564–93), English dramatist and precursor of Shakespeare. His plays include *Dr. Faustus*, *Tamburlaine the Great*, *Edward II*, and *The Jew of Malta*. His early death was due to a tavern brawl.

Marryat, Frederick (1792–1848), English author of sea and adventure stories, including *Peter Simple*, *Mr. Midshipman Easy*, and *Masterman Ready*. A captain in the Royal Navy.

Marshall, George Catlett (1880–1959), American general. U.S. chief of staff 1939–45; originated the Marshall Aid plan. Nobel prize for peace 1953.

Martial, Marcus Valerius (*c.* 40–104), Roman poet, b. in Spain, remembered for his epigrams.

Marvell, Andrew (1620–78), English poet and political writer. He was Milton's assistant.

Marx, Karl (1818–83), German founder of modern international communism, b. Trier of Jewish parentage. He studied law, philosophy and history at the universities of Bonn and Berlin, and later took up the study of economics. In conjunction with his friend Engels he wrote the *Communist Manifesto* of 1848 for the Communist League of which he was the leader. Because of his revolutionary activities he was forced to leave the continent and in 1849 settled in London. Here, mainly while living at 28 Dean Street, Soho, he wrote *Das Kapital*, a deep analysis of the economic laws that govern modern society. In 1864 he helped to found the first International. He ranks as one of the most original and influential thinkers of modern times. He was buried in Highgate cemetery. *See* Marxism, Section J.

Mary I (1516–58), Queen of England, was daughter of Henry VIII and Catherine of Aragon. A Roman Catholic, she reversed the religious changes made by her father and brother, and about 300 Protestants were put to death. She married Philip of Spain.

Mary II (1662–94), Queen of England with her husband the Dutch William III. As daughter of James II, she was invited to succeed after the revolution of 1688 and expelled her father.

Mary Stuart, Queen of Scots (1542–87), daughter of James V of Scotland and Mary of Guise, she laid claim to the English succession. She was imprisoned in England by Elizabeth and beheaded. Her husbands were the dauphin of France (d. 1560), Lord Henry Stewart Darnley (murdered 1567) and Bothwell.

Masaryk, Jan Garrigue (1886–1948), Czech diplomat. The son of Thomas, he was Czech minister in London 1925–38, and foreign secretary while his government was in exile in London and after it returned to Prague, 1940–8.

Masaryk, Thomas Garrigue (1850–1937), Czech statesman and independence leader. He was the first president of Czechoslovakia, 1918–35.

Mascagni, Pietro (1863–1945), Italian composer of *Cavalleria Rusticana.*

Masefield, John (1878–1967), English poet. His best-known works are *Salt-Water Ballads* (as a boy he ran away to sea), and *Reynard the Fox.* He became poet laureate in 1930.

Maskelyne, John Nevil (1839–1917), English illusionist. He also exposed spiritualistic frauds.

Massenet, Jules Emile Frédéric (1842–1912), French composer of songs, orchestral suites, oratorios, and operas, among them *Manon* and *Thaïs.*

Massine, Léonide (1896–1979), Russian dancer, one of Diaghilev's choreographers.

Masters, Edgar Lee (1869–1950), American poet remembered for his *Spoon River Anthology.*

Matisse, Henri (1869–1954), French painter, member of a group known as *Les Fauves* (the wild beasts) for their use of violent colour and colour variation to express form and relief.

Matsys (Massys), Quentin (1466–1530), Flemish painter, b. Louvain, settled Antwerp; he worked at a time when Italian influence was gaining ground. His *Money-changer, and his Wife* is in the Louvre.

Matthews, Sir Stanley (b. 1915), first footballer to be knighted. He made 880 first-class appearances, 54 for England. Played in the legendary 1953 Cup Final (when Blackpool beat Bolton Wanderers 4–3).

Maugham, William Somerset (1874–1965), British writer, b. Paris. He practised as a doctor till the success of *Liza of Lambeth* (1897) followed by *Of Human Bondage.* He was a master of the short story and his work reflects his travels in the East. In both world wars he served as a British agent.

Maupassant, Guy de (1850–93), French writer whose novels and short stories show penetrating realism. His stories include *Boule de Suif, Le Maison Tellier,* and *La Parure.*

Mauriac, François (1885–1970), French writer whose novels deal with moral problems and include *Le Baiser au Lépreux* and the play *Asmodée.* Nobel prizewinner 1952.

Maurois, André (Emile Herzog) (1885–1967), French writer whose works include lives of Shelley and Disraeli.

Maxim, Sir Hiram Stevens (1840–1916), American inventor of the automatic quick-firing gun.

Maxton, James (1885–1946), Scottish Labour politician and pacifist; entered parliament 1922; chairman of I.L.P. 1926–31, 1934–9.

Maxwell, James Clerk (1831–79), Scottish physicist. He wrote his first scientific paper at 15, and after teaching in Aberdeen and London became first Cavendish professor of experimental physics at Cambridge. His mathematical mind, working on the discoveries of Faraday and others, gave physics a celebrated set of equations for

the basic laws of electricity and magnetism. His work revolutionised the understanding of fundamental physics.

May, Peter (Barker Howard) (1929–94). English cricketer. The finest post-war batsman produced in Britain. A long-serving and successful captain.

Mazarin, Jules (1602–61), cardinal and minister of France was b. in Italy. In spite of opposition from the nobles, he continued Richelieu's work of building up a strong monarchy.

Mazeppa, Ivan Stepanovich (1644–1709), Cossack nobleman, b. Ukraine (then part of Poland, before E. Ukraine passed to Russia, 1667). He fought unsuccessfully for independence allying himself with Charles XII of Sweden against Peter I of Russia (Poltava, 1709). Byron wrote a poem about him.

Mazzini, Giuseppe (1805–72), Italian patriot. B. Genoa, he advocated a free and united Italy, and from Marseilles he published a journal, *Young Italy.* Expelled from the Continent, he took refuge in London in 1837. In 1848 he returned to Italy, and became dictator of the short-lived Roman republic, which was put down by French forces. His contribution to Italian unity was that of preparing the way.

Mechnikov, Ilya (1845–1916), Russian biologist who discovered that by "phagocytosis" certain white blood cells are capable of ingesting harmful substances such as bacteria (*see* Diseases of the Blood, Section P). For his work on immunity he shared the 1908 Nobel prize for medicine.

Medawar, Sir Peter Brien (1915–87), British zoologist, author of *The Art of the Soluble* and *The Future of Man*; president of the British Association 1969. Nobel prizewinner 1960. O.M. 1981.

Medici, Florentine family of merchants and bankers who were politically powerful and who patronised the arts. Cosimo the Elder (1389–1464) was for over 30 years virtual ruler of Florence. His grandson, Lorenzo the Magnificent (1449–92), poet, friend of artists and scholars, governed with munificence. His grandson, Lorenzo, was father of Catherine de' Medici, Queen of France (*q.v.*). A later Cosimo (1519–74) was an able Duke of Florence and then Grand-Duke of Tuscany, which title the Medicis held until 1737.

Méhul, Etienne Nicolas (1763–1817), French operatic composer. *Joseph* is his masterpiece.

Meir, Golda (1898–1978), leading member of the Israeli Labour Party, her premiership included the Six Day and Yom Kippur wars.

Meitner, Lise (1878–1969), co-worker of Otto Hahn (*q.v.*) who interpreted his results (1939) as a fission process.

Melanchthon, Philip (1497–1560), German religious reformer, who assisted Luther, and wrote the first Protestant theological work, *Loci communes.* He drew up the Augsburg confession (1530).

Melba, Nellie (Helen Porter Mitchell) (1861–1931), Australian soprano of international repute.

Melbourne, 2nd Viscount (William Lamb) (1779–1848), English Whig statesman, was premier at the accession of Queen Victoria.

Mendel, Gregor Johann (1822–84), Austrian botanist. After entering the Augustinian monastery at Brünn he became abbot and taught natural history in the school. His main interest was the study of inheritance, and his elaborate observations of the common garden pea resulted in the law of heredity which bears his name. His hypothesis was published in 1866 but no attention was given to it until 1900. *See* Section F, Part IV.

Mendeleyev, Dmitri Ivanovich (1834–1907), Russian chemist, first to discover the critical temperatures. He formulated the periodic law of atomic weights (1869) and drew up the periodic table (*see* Section F), predicting the properties of elements which might fill the gaps. Element 101 is named after him.

Mendelssohn-Bartholdy, Felix (1809–47), German composer, grandson of Moses Mendelssohn, philosopher. He belongs with Chopin and Schumann to the early 19th cent. classic-romantic school, and his music has delicacy and melodic beauty. He was conductor of the Gewandhaus concerts at Leipzig for a time and often visited England. *See* Section E.

Menuhin, Lord (Yehudi Menuhin) (b. 1916), famous violinist, b. New York of Russian Jewish parentage.

He first appeared as soloist at the age of seven and has international repute. Founded a School for musically gifted children. Acquired British citizenship, 1985. Awarded Order of Merit, 1987.

Menzies, Sir Robert Gordon (1894–1978), Australian Liberal statesman, P.M. 1939–41, 1949–66.

Mercator, Gerhardus (Gerhard Kremer) (1512–94), Flemish geographer who pioneered the making of accurate navigational maps. He worked out the map which bears his name in which meridians and parallels of latitude cross each other at right angles, enabling compass bearings to be drawn as straight lines.

Meredith, George (1828–1909), English writer, b. Portsmouth. His novels include *The Ordeal of Richard Feverel*, *The Egoist*, *Evan Harrington*, *Diana of the Crossways*, and *The Amazing Marriage*. His poetry has had renewed attention; the main works are *Modern Love* and *Poems and Lyrics of the Joy of Earth*.

Mesmer, Friedrich Anton (1733–1815), Austrian founder of mesmerism (*see* **J32**).

Mestrovič, Ivan (1883–1962), Yugoslav sculptor of international repute. He designed the temple at Kossovo. He later lived in England, and examples of his work are in London museums.

Metastasio, Pietro (Pietro Bonaventura Trapassi) (1698–1782), Italian librettist who lived in Vienna and provided texts for Gluck, Handel, Haydn, and Mozart.

Michelangelo (Michelagniolo Buonarroti) (1475–1564), Italian painter, sculptor and poet. Of a poor but genteel Tuscan family, his first interest in sculpture came through his nurse, wife of a stone-cutter. He was apprenticed to Domenico Ghirlandaio. Like Leonardo, he studied anatomy, but instead of spreading his talents over a wide field, he became obsessed with the problem of how to represent the human body. In him, classical idealism, mediaeval religious belief, and renaissance energy met. Perhaps his most impressive work is the ceiling of the Sistine Chapel (a surface of about 6,000 square feet), the *Last Judgement* behind the chapel altar, his marble *Pieta* (St. Peter's) the statue of *David* (Academy, Florence), the great figure of *Moses* (San Pietro in Vincoli, Rome), and the four allegorical figures *Day, Night, Dawn, Twilight* (intended for the tombs of the Medici family at San Lorenzo, Florence).

Michelet, Jules (1798–1874), French historian who wrote a history of France in 24 vols. and of the revolution in 7 vols.

Michelson, Albert Abraham (1852–1931), American physicist, b. Poland. He collaborated with E. W. Morley in an experiment to determine ether drift, the negative result of which was important for Einstein. Nobel prizewinner 1907.

Mickiewicz, Adam (1798–1855), Polish revolutionary poet, author of *The Ancestors* and *Pan Tadeusz*.

Mill, John Stuart (1806–73), English philosopher. A member of Bentham's utilitarian school, he later modified some of its tenets. His main work is *On Liberty*, which advocates social as well as political freedom and warns against the tyranny of the majority. *The Subjection of Women* supported women's rights. He also wrote *Principles of Political Economy*. He was godfather to Bertrand Russell.

Millais, Sir John Everett (1829–96), English artist, b. Southampton; in his earlier years a pre-Raphaelite (*Ophelia*). Later works include *The Boyhood of Raleigh* and *Bubbles*. He married Mrs. Ruskin after the annulment of her marriage.

Millet, Jean François (1814–75), French painter of rural life, sometimes in sombre mood; his works include *The Angelus*.

Millikan, Robert Andrews (1868–1954), American physicist, who determined the charge on the electron and discovered cosmic rays. Nobel prizewinner 1923.

Milne, Alan Alexander (1882–1956), English humorist and poet whose work for children is still widely read.

Milner, 1st Viscount (Alfred Milner) (1854–1925), British administrator, especially in South Africa; author of *England in Egypt*.

Milstein, César (b. 1927) Argentinian-born molecular biologist. Joint Nobel Prize for Medicine, 1984. Created Companion of Honour, 1995.

Miltiades (d. 489 B.C.), one of the leaders of the Athenian army against the Persians at Marathon.

Milton, John (1608–74), English poet, author of

Paradise Lost. B. in London, he wrote while still at Cambridge *L'Allegro, Il Penseroso, Comus*, and *Lycidas*. The Civil War diverted his energies for years to the parliamentary and political struggle, but during this period he defended in *Aereopagitica* the freedom of the press. After he had become blind he wrote *Paradise Lost* and a sonnet *On His Blindness*.

Minot, George Richards (1885–1950), who with W. P. Murphy discovered the curative properties of liver in pernicious anaemia. Shared Nobel prize 1934.

Mirabeau, Gabriel, Honoré Victor Riquetti, Comte de (1749–91), French revolutionary leader. His writings and speeches contributed to the revolution of 1789.

Mistral, Frédéric (1830–1914), French poet, and founder of a Provençal renaissance. His works include *Lou Trésor dóu Félibrige* and a Provençal dictionary. Nobel prizewinner 1904.

Mitchell, Reginald Joseph (1895–1937), British aircraft designer. Famous for developing the *Spitfire*.

Mithridates (*c.* 132–63 B.C.), King of Pontus, in Asia Minor; after early successes against the Romans was defeated by Pompey.

Mitterrand, François Maurice Marie (b. 1916), French socialist politician, proclaimed fourth president of the Fifth Republic, 21 May 1981. Re-elected May 1988 for second 7-year term until 1995. The longest serving President of the Fifth Republic.

Modigliani, Amedeo (1884–1920), Italian painter and sculptor, b. Livorno. His portraits and figure studies tend to elongation and simplification. He lived mainly in Paris.

Moffatt, James (1870–1944), Scottish divine who translated the Bible into modern English.

Mohammed (570–632), the founder of Islam, the religion of the Moslems, received the revelation of the Koran (their sacred book), and the command to preach, at the age of 40. By his constant proclamation that there was only One God he gathered around him a loyal following, but aroused the hostility of other Meccans, who worshipped idols. The Moslems were forced to flee to Medina in 622, but grew in strength sufficiently to return to Mecca eight years later, and establish the Kaaba as the goal of the pilgrimage in Islam. Mohammed always described himself as only the messenger of God. *See* Islam, Section J.

Molière (Jean Baptiste Poquelin) (1622–73), French playwright. B. in Paris, he gained experience as a strolling player, and subsequently in Paris, partly in the king's service; he wrote an unsurpassed series of plays varying from farce as in *Les Précieuses ridicules* to high comedy. Among his plays are *Tartuffe, Le Misanthrope*, and *Le Bourgeois gentilhomme*.

Molotov, Vyacheslav Mikhailovich (1890–1986), Russian diplomat. He succeeded Litvinov as commissar for foreign affairs, 1939–49, and was chief representative of the Soviet Union at numerous post-war conferences.

Moltke, Helmuth, Count von (1800–91), Prussian general and chief of staff (1858–88) during the period when Prussia successfully united Germany.

Mond, Ludwig (1838–1909), German chemist who in 1867 settled in England as an alkali manufacturer and in partnership with John Brunner successfully manufactured soda by the Solvay process.

Monet, Claude (1840–1926), French painter, leader of the Impressionists, the term being derived in 1874 from his landscape *Impression soleil levant*. He liked painting a subject in the open air at different times of day to show variation in light.

Monier-Williams, Sir Monier (1819–99), English Sanskrit scholar whose works include grammars, dictionaries, and editions of the *Sákuntalá*.

Monk, George, 1st Duke of Albemarle (1608–69), English general and admiral, whose reputation and moderation were mainly responsible for the return of Charles II in 1660.

Monmouth, Duke of (James Scott) (1649–85), English pretender, natural son of Charles II; centre of anti-Catholic feeling against succession of Duke of York (later James II). His troops, mostly peasants, were routed at Sedgemoor (1685) by John Churchill (later Duke of Marlborough). Beheaded on Tower Hill.

Monnet, Jean (1888–1979), French political economist, "father of the Common Market." He drafted the Monnet plan for French economic recovery (1947) and the plan to establish the European Coal and Steel Community.

Monroe, James (1758–1831), president of the U.S. He propounded the doctrine that the American continent should not be colonised by a European power.

Montagu, Lady Mary Wortley (1689–1762), English writer. From Constantinople where her husband was ambassador she wrote *Letters* of which a complete edition was published 1965–7. She introduced England to the idea of inoculation against smallpox.

Montaigne, Michel de (1533–92), French essayist of enquiring, sceptical and tolerant mind.

Montcalm, Louis Joseph, Marquis de (1712–59), French general, who unsuccessfully commanded the French at Quebec against Wolfe.

Montesquieu, Charles-Louis de Secondat, Baron de la Brède et de (1689–1755), French philosopher. His works include *Lettres persanes*, a satire on contemporary life; and *De l'esprit des lois* giving his political philosophy. The latter was based largely, but to some extent mistakenly, on English practice, and its influence led the U.S. constitution to separate the executive (President) from the legislature (Congress).

Montessori, Maria (1870–1952), Italian educationist, who developed an educational system based on spontaneity.

Monteverdi, Claudio (1567–1643), Italian composer who pioneered in opera. His chief dramatic work is *Orfeo* (1607). See **Section E.**

Montezuma II (1466–1520), Aztec emperor of Mexico when the Spanish under Cortés invaded.

Montfort, Simon de, Earl of Leicester (c. 1208–65), English statesman. He led the barons in revolt against the ineffective rule of Henry III, but he differed from other rebels in that he summoned a parliamentary assembly to which for the first time representatives came from the towns. He was killed at Evesham.

Montgolfier, the name of two brothers, **Joseph Michel** (1740–1810) and **Jacques Etienne** (1745–99), French aeronauts who constructed the first practical balloon, which flew 6 miles.

Montgomery of Alamein, 1st Viscount (Bernard Law Montgomery) (1887–1976), British field-marshal; commanded 8th Army in North Africa, Sicily, and Italy, 1942–4; commander-in-chief, British Group of Armies and Allied Armies in Northern France, 1944. He served as Deputy Supreme Allied Commander Europe (NATO), 1951–8. Memoirs published in 1958.

Montrose, Marquess of (James Graham) (1612–50), Scottish general. In the Civil War he raised the Highland clansmen for Charles I and won the battles of Tippermuir, Inverlochy, and Kilsyth; but was finally defeated and executed. He was also a poet.

Moody, Dwight Lyman (1837–99), American revivalist preacher, associated with Ira D. Sankey, the "American singing pilgrim."

Moore, George (1852–1933), Irish novelist, author of *Confessions of a Young Man, Esther Waters,* and *Evelyn Innes.*

Moore, Henry (1898–1986), English sculptor in semi-abstract style, son of a Yorkshire coalminer. Examples of his work are to be seen all over the world, in the Tate Gallery, St. Matthew's Church, Northampton, the Unesco building in Paris, in Kensington Gardens, *etc.*

Moore, Sir John (1761–1809), British general, who trained the infantry for the Spanish Peninsular campaigns and conducted a brilliant retreat to Corunna, where he was mortally wounded after defeating the French under Soult.

Moore, Thomas (1779–1852), Irish poet, author of *Irish Melodies, Lalla Rookh,* and *The Epicurean* (novel). He also wrote a life of Byron.

More, Sir Thomas (1478–1535), English writer and statesman. In 1529 he succeeded Wolsey as lord chancellor, but on his refusal to recognise Henry VIII as head of the church he was executed. His *Utopia* describes an ideal state. He was canonised 1935.

Morgan, Sir Henry (c. 1635–88), Welsh buccaneer who operated in the Caribbean against the Spaniards, capturing and plundering Panama in 1671. Knighted by Charles II and made deputy-governor of Jamaica.

Morgan, John Pierpont (1837–1913), American financier who built the family fortunes into a vast industrial empire.

Morland, George (1763–1804), English painter of rural life.

Morley, 1st Viscount (John Morley) (1838–1923), English biographer and Liberal politician. He held political office, but is mainly remembered for his life of Gladstone. He also wrote on Voltaire, Rousseau, Burke, and Cobden.

Morley, Thomas (c. 1557–1603), English composer of madrigals, noted also for his settings of some of Shakespeare's songs. He was a pupil of Byrd, organist of St. Paul's cathedral, and wrote *Plaine and Easie Introduction to Practicall Music* (1597) which was used for 200 years.

Morris, William (1834–96), English poet and craftsman. His hatred of 19th-cent. ugliness, his belief in human equality, and in freedom and happiness for all, combined to make him a socialist, and he accomplished much for the improvement of domestic decoration. He was a popular lecturer, founded the Socialist League and the Kelmscott Press.

Morrison of Lambeth, Baron (Herbert Morrison) (1888–1965), British Labour statesman. From being an errand-boy, he rose to become leader of the London County Council. During the war he was Home Secretary, and he was deputy prime minister, 1945–51.

Morse, Samuel Finley Breeze (1791–1872), American pioneer in electromagnetic telegraphy and inventor of the dot-and-dash code that bears his name. He was originally an artist.

Mountbatten of Burma, 1st Earl (Louis Mountbatten) (1900–79), British admiral and statesman. In the second world war he became chief of combined operations in 1942. As last viceroy of India, he carried through the transfer of power to Indian hands in 1947 and was the first governor-general of the dominion. His assassination by Irish extremists evoked world-wide horror.

Mozart, Wolfgang Amadeus (1756–91), Austrian composer. B. Salzburg, he began his career at four and toured Europe at six. In 1781 he settled in Vienna, where he became a friend of Haydn and where his best music was written. His genius lies in the effortless outpouring of all forms of music, in the ever-flowing melodies, in the consistent beauty and symmetry of his compositions, and in the exactness of his method. Among the loveliest and grandest works in instrumental music are his three great symphonies in E. flat, G minor, and C (called the "Jupiter"), all written in six weeks in 1788. Three of the greatest operas in musical history are his *Marriage of Figaro* (1786), *Don Giovanni* (1787), and *The Magic Flute* (1791). His last composition, written under the shadow of death, was the *Requiem Mass,* a work of tragic beauty. See **Section E.**

Mugabe, Robert Gabriel (b. 1924), first prime minister of independent Zimbabwe after his election victory in March 1980.

Muggeridge, Malcolm (1903–90), broadcaster, journalist and writer who became an ardent Christian.

Müller, Sir Ferdinand (1825–96), German-born botanist who emigrated to Australia, where he was director of the Melbourne Botanical Gardens, 1857–73, and whence he introduced the eucalyptus into Europe.

Mulroney, (Martin) Brian (b. 1939), Prime Minister of Canada, 1984–93. Elected leader of the Progressive Conservative Party, 1983. First Conservative leader from Quebec in nearly 100 years.

Mumford, Lewis (1895–1990), American writer on town-planning and social problems. His works include a tetralogy: *Technics and Civilisation, The Culture of Cities, The Condition of Man,* and *The Conduct of Life; The Myth of the Machine,* and *The Urban Prospect.*

Munnings, Sir Alfred (1878–1959), English painter, especially of horses and sporting subjects.

Murdock, William (1754–1839), Scottish engineer and inventor, the first to make practical use of coal gas as an illuminating agent (introduced at the Soho works, Birmingham, 1800).

Murillo, Bartolomé Esteban (1617–82), Spanish painter, b. Seville, where he founded an Academy. His early works, such as *Two Peasant Boys* (Dulwich) show peasant and street life; his later paintings are religious, *e.g.,* the *Immaculate Conception* in the Prado.

Murray, Gilbert (1866–1957), classical scholar of

Australian birth who settled in England. A teacher of Greek at the universities of Glasgow and Oxford, he translated Greek drama so as to bring it within the reach of a wide public.

Mussolini, Benito (1883–1945), Fascist dictator of Italy 1922–43. From 1935 an aggressive foreign policy (Abyssinia and Spain) was at first successful, and in June 1940 he entered the war on the side of Hitler. Defeat in North Africa and the invasion of Sicily caused the collapse of his government. He was shot dead by partisans while trying to escape to Switzerland.

Mussorgsky, Modest Petrovich (1839–81), Russian composer whose masterpiece is the opera *Boris Godunov* after the play by Pushkin. His piano suite *Pictures at an Exhibition* was orchestrated by Ravel. *See* **Section E.**

N

Naipaul, Sir Vidiadhur Surajprasad (b. 1932), Trinidadian novelist and writer, whose novels include *A House for Mr Biswas* (1961). He was awarded the Booker Prize for *In a Free State* (1971) and was knighted in 1990.

Nanak (1469–1538), Indian guru or teacher, who tried to put an end to religious strife, teaching that "God is one, whether he be Allah or Rama." *See* **Sikhism, Section J.**

Nansen, Fridtjof (1861–1930), Norwegian explorer. In 1893 his north polar expedition reached the highest latitude till then attained—86° 14'. He published an account called *Farthest North*. He was active in Russian famine relief, 1921. Nobel peace prize 1922.

Napier, John (1550–1617), Scottish mathematician, b. Edinburgh, invented logarithms (published 1614) and the modern notation of fractions, improvements in the methods of mathematical expression which helped to advance cosmology and physics.

Napoleon I (**Bonaparte**) (1769–1821), French emperor and general, of Corsican birth (Ajaccio). Trained in French military schools, he became prominent in the early years of the revolution, with uncertainty at home and war abroad. In 1796 he became commander of the army in Italy and defeated the Austrians, so that France obtained control of Lombardy. He then led an expedition to Egypt but Nelson destroyed his fleet. After further Italian victories, he made a *coup d'état* in 1799, and in 1804 became emperor. Against continuing European opposition, he defeated the Austrians at Austerlitz, and his power in Europe was such that he made his brothers Joseph, Louis, and Jerome kings of Naples, Holland, and Westphalia; but in Spain he provoked the Peninsular War, and his armies were gradually driven back by the Spanish, helped by Wellington; while his invasion of Russia in 1812 ended in a disastrous retreat from Moscow; and in 1814 the Allies forced him to abdicate and retire to Elba. He emerged again in 1815 to be defeated at Waterloo and exiled to St. Helena. His government at home was firm and promoted some reforms (*e.g.*, legal codification), but the country was weakened by his wars. In Europe, in spite of the suffering caused by war, there was some spread of French revolutionary ideas, and equally a reaction against them on the part of authority. The imperial idea lingered in France, and Napoleon's remains were brought to Paris in 1840. He married first Josephine Beauharnais and second Marie Louise of Austria. Marie Louise was the mother of **Napoleon II** (1811–32).

Napoleon III (1808–73), son of Napoleon I's brother Louis. He returned to France in the revolution of 1848, and in 1851 came to power by a *coup d'état*. In his reign Paris was remodelled. His foreign policy was adventurous (the Crimean war, intervention in Mexico, war against Austria and Italy); but when he was manoeuvred by Bismarck into the Franco-Prussian war and defeated at Sedan he lost his throne and retired to England. His wife was Eugénie de Montijo.

Nash, John (1752–1835), English architect who planned Regent Street, laid out Regent's Park, enlarged Buckingham Palace, and designed Marble Arch and the Brighton Pavilion.

Nash, Paul (1889–1946), English painter and designer, official war artist in both world wars. Best-known pictures are *The Menin Road* of 1918 and *Totes Meer* of 1941.

Nash, Walter (1882–1968), New Zealand Labour politician; prime minister 1957–60.

Nasmyth, James (1808–90), Scottish inventor of the steam-hammer, which became indispensable in all large iron and engineering works.

Nasser, Gamal Abdel (1918–70), leader of modern Egypt and of the Arab world. He led the 1954 coup that deposed General Neguib. He became president of the Egyptian Republic in 1956 and of the United Arab Republic in 1958. His nationalisation of the Suez Canal in 1956 precipitated a short-lived attack by Britain and France. Israeli-Arab hostility led to the June war of 1967. He carried out reforms to bring his people out of near-feudalism, including the building (with Russian help) of the Aswan High Dam.

Needham, Joseph (1900–95), British biochemist, historian of science, orientalist. Author of the monumental multi-volume work of scholarship *Science and Civilisation in China.*

Nehru, Pandit Jawaharlal (1889–1964), Indian national leader and statesman, first prime minister and minister of foreign affairs when India became independent in 1947. A leading member of the Congress Party, during which time he was frequently imprisoned for political activity. He played a part in the final negotiations for independence. Under his leadership India made major advances. In world affairs his influence was for peace and non-alignment. His daughter **Indira Gandhi,** (*see* **B25**) became India's first woman prime minister in 1966.

Nelson, 1st Viscount (Horatio Nelson) (1758–1805), English admiral. Son of a Norfolk clergyman, he went to sea at 12 and became a captain in 1793. In the French revolutionary wars he lost his right eye in 1794 and his right arm in 1797. Rear-admiral in 1797, he defeated the French at Aboukir Bay in 1798. He was also at the bombardment of Copenhagen in 1801. In 1805 he destroyed the French fleet at Trafalgar, in which battle he was killed. His daring and decision made him a notable commander. He loved Emma Hamilton.

Nernst, Walther Hermann (1864–1941), German scientist who established the third law of thermodynamics that dealt with the behaviour of matter at temperatures approaching absolute zero. Nobel prizewinner 1920.

Nero, Claudius Caesar (A.D. 37–68), Roman emperor, the adopted son of Claudius. He was weak and licentious and persecuted Christians. In his reign occurred the fire of Rome.

Newcomen, Thomas (1663–1729), English inventor, one of the first to put a steam-engine into practical operation. In 1705 he patented his invention, the pumping-engine used in Cornish mines until the adoption of Watt's engine.

Newman, Ernest (1868–1959), English music critic, whose chief work is the *Life of Richard Wagner.*

Newman, John Henry (1801–90), English priest and writer, who became a cardinal of the Roman church in 1879, and was a founder of the Oxford Movement. (*See* **J52**) He is best remembered for his *Apologia pro Vita Sua* in which he described the development of his religious thought. He wrote *Lead, kindly Light,* set to music 30 years later by J. B. Dykes, and *The Dream of Gerontius,* set to music of Elgar.

Newton, Sir Isaac (1642–1727), English scientist, b. Woolsthorpe, Lincs. (the year Galileo died). He studied at Cambridge but was at home during the plague years 1665 and 1666 when he busied himself with problems concerned with optics and gravitation. Through his tutor Isaac Barrow he was appointed to the Lucasian chair of mathematics at Cambridge in 1669 and remained there until 1696 when he was appointed Warden, and later Master of the Mint. He was a secret Unitarian and did not marry. His three great discoveries were to show that white light could be separated into a sequence of coloured components forming the visible spectrum; to use the calculus (invented by him independently of Leibnitz) to investigate the forces of nature in a quantitative way; and to show by his theory of gravitation (for which Copernicus, Kepler and Galileo had prepared the way) that the universe was regulated by simple mathematical laws.

His vision was set forth in the *Philosophiae Naturalis Principia Mathematica* of 1687, usually called the *Principia*. It was not until 200 years later that Einstein showed there could be another theory of celestial mechanics.

Ney, Michel (1769–1815), French general who served under Napoleon, especially at Jena, Borodino, and Waterloo.

Nicholas II (1868–1918), last emperor and Tsar of Russia, son of Alexander III. His reign was marked by an unsuccessful war with Japan (1904–5), and by the 1914–18 war. Ineffective and lacking ability, he set up a Duma in 1906 too late for real reform. Revolution broke out in 1917 and he and his family were shot in July 1918.

Nicholson, Sir William (1872–1949), English artist known for his portraits and woodcuts. His son, **Ben Nicholson, O.M.**, (1894–1981) was a giant of English painting, with styles from Cornish landscapes to his controversial white minimalism.

Nicolson, Sir Harold (1886–1968), English diplomat, author, and critic. His works include *King George V*; and *Diaries and Letters*. His wife was **Victoria Sackville-West** (1892–1962).

Niemöller, Martin (1892–1984), German Lutheran pastor who opposed the Nazi regime and was confined in a concentration camp. He was president of the World Council of Churches in 1961.

Nietzsche, Friedrich Wilhelm (1844–1900), German philosopher, in his younger years influenced by Wagner and Schopenhauer. His teaching that only the strong ought to survive and his doctrine of the superman are expounded in *Thus spake Zarathustra, Beyond Good and Evil* and *The Will to Power*.

Nightingale, Florence (1820–1910), English nurse and pioneer of hospital reform, who during the Crimean war organised in face of considerable official opposition a nursing service to relieve the sufferings of the British soldiers, who called her "the lady with the lamp." Her system was adopted and developed in all parts of the world.

Nijinsky, Vaslav (1892–1950), Russian dancer, one of the company which included Pavlova, Karsavina and Fokine, brought by Diaghilev to Paris and London before the 1914–18 war. In *Les Sylphides, Spectre de la Rose* and *L'Après-midi d'un Faune* he won a supreme place among male dancers.

Nikisch, Arthur (1855–1922), Hungarian conductor of the Boston Symphony Orchestra, 1889–93. He was piano-accompanist to the Lieder singer, Elena Gerhardt.

Nimitz, Chester William (1885–1966), American admiral, commanded in the Pacific 1941–5.

Nixon, Richard Milhous (1913–94), Republican president (for two terms) of the U.S., 1969–74. In foreign affairs he negotiated the withdrawal of American troops from S. Vietnam and began a process of reconciliation with China and détente with the Soviet Union. But at home the Watergate conspiracies brought disgrace and an end to his presidency. His resignation in August 1974 rendered the impeachment process unnecessary; he accepted the pardon offered by his successor, President Ford.

Nkrumah, Kwame (1909–72), Ghanaian leader, first premier of Ghana when his country achieved independence in 1957. Promoted the Pan-African movement; but unsound finance and dictatorial methods led to his overthrow in 1966.

Nobel, Alfred Bernhard (1833–96), Swedish inventor and philanthropist. An engineer and chemist who discovered dynamite, he amassed a fortune from the manufacture of explosives; and bequeathed a fund for annual prizes to those who had contributed most to the benefit of mankind in the fields of physics, chemistry, medicine, literature and peace.

Nolan, Sir Sidney Robert (1917–92), foremost Australian artist and set designer. Best known for his works depicting 19th cent. outlaw Ned Kelly. He brought Australian painting to world attention. O.M. 1983.

North, Frederick (1732–92), favourite minister of George III who held the premiership from 1770 to 1782. (He held the courtesy title of Lord North from 1752.) The stubborn policies of George III led to the American war of independence.

Northcliffe, 1st Viscount (Alfred Charles Harmsworth) (1865–1922), British journalist and newspaper proprietor, b. near Dublin. He began

Answers in 1888 with his brother Harold, (later Lord Rothermere). In 1894 they bought the *Evening News*, and in 1896 the *Daily Mail*. In 1908 he took over *The Times*.

Northumberland, John Dudley, Duke of (1502–53), English politician who attempted to secure for his daughter-in-law Lady Jane Grey the succession to the throne after Edward VI.

Nostradamus or **Michel de Notre Dame** (1503–66), French astrologer and physician, known for his prophecies in *Centuries*.

Novalis, the pseudonym of Baron Friedrich von Hardenberg (1772–1801), German romantic poet and novelist, whose chief work is the unfinished *Heinrich von Ofterdingen*.

Nuffield, 1st Viscount (William Richard Morris) (1877–1963), British motor-car manufacturer and philanthropist, and until he retired in 1952 chairman of Morris Motors Ltd. He provided large sums for the advancement of medicine in the university of Oxford, for Nuffield College, and in 1943 established the Nuffield Foundation, endowing it with £10 million.

Nureyev, Rudolf Hametovich (1938–93), the most celebrated ballet dancer of modern times. Born nr. Lake Baikal. Soloist, Kirov Ballet, Leningrad, 1958–61. Naturalised Austrian citizen, 1982. Ballet Director, Paris Opéra, 1983–89. Principal Choreographer, 1989–92. He won extraordinary acclaim, enhancing the stature of dance as a form of art.

Nyerere, Julius (b. 1922), Tanzanian leader. He became first premier of Tanganyika when it became independent in 1961; and president. In 1964 he negotiated its union with Zanzibar. Resigned as President, 1985.

O

Oates, Lawrence Edward (1880–1912), English antarctic explorer. He joined Scott's expedition of 1910, and was one of the five to reach the south pole; but on the return journey, being crippled by frost-bite, he walked out into the blizzard to die.

Oates, Titus (1649–1705), English informer and agitator against Roman catholics.

O'Casey, Sean (1880–1964), Irish dramatist whose plays include *Juno and the Paycock*, *The Silver Tassie*, *Red Roses for Me*, and *Oak Leaves and Lavender*.

Occam (**Ockham**), **William of** (c. 1270–1349), English scholar and philosopher and one of the most original thinkers of all time. He belonged to the Order of Franciscans, violently opposed the temporal power of the Pope, espoused the cause of nominalism and laid the foundations of modern theories of government and theological scepticism. *See* **Occam's razor, Section J.**

O'Connell, Daniel (1775–1847), Irish national leader. A barrister, he formed the Catholic Association in 1823 to fight elections; his followers aimed at the repeal of the Act of Union with England, and formed a Repeal Association in 1840; but the formation of the Young Ireland party, the potato famine, and ill-health undermined his position and he died in exile.

O'Connor, Feargus (1794–1855), working-class leader in England, of Irish birth. He presented the Chartist petition in 1848.

O'Connor, Thomas Power (1848–1929), Irish nationalist and journalist, sat in parliament 1880–1929 and founded the *Star*.

Oersted, Hans Christian (1777–1851), Danish physicist who discovered the connection between electricity and magnetism.

Offa (d. 796), king of Mercia (mid-England), was the leading English king of his day, and built a defensive dyke (**L90**) from the Dee to the Wye.

Offenbach, Jacques (1819–80), German-Jewish composer, b. Cologne, settled at Paris, and is mainly known for his light operas, especially *Tales of Hoffmann*.

Ohm, Georg Simon (1787–1854), German physicist, professor at Munich, who in 1826 formulated the law of electric current–Ohm's law, (**L90**).

Olivier, Baron (Laurence Kerr Olivier) (1907–89), British actor and director, especially in Shakespearean roles. He also produced, directed, and played in films, including *Henry V*, *Hamlet*, and *Richard III*, and in television drama. In

1962 he was appointed director of the National Theatre (which opened in 1976) and in 1970 received a life peerage. O.M. 1981.

Oman, Sir Charles William (1860–1946), English historian, especially of mediaeval warfare and of the Peninsular War. He also wrote memoirs.

Omar ibn al Khattab (581–644), adviser to Mahomet, succeeded Abu Bakr as 2nd caliph. In his reign Islam became an imperial power. He died at the hands of a foreign slave.

Omar Khayyám (c. 1050–1123), Persian poet and mathematician, called Khayyám (tent-maker) because of his father's occupation. His fame as a scientist has been eclipsed by his *Rubaiyat*, made known to English readers by Edward FitzGerald in 1859.

O'Neill, Eugene Gladstone (1888–1953), American playwright who won success in 1914 with the one-act play, *Thirst*. His later plays include *Anna Christie*, *Strange Interlude*, *Mourning Becomes Electra*, *The Iceman Cometh*. Nobel prize, 1936.

Oppenheimer, J. Robert (1904–67), American physicist who was director of atomic-energy research at Los Alamos, New Mexico, 1942–5, when the atomic bomb was developed but in 1949 he opposed work on the hydrogen bomb on moral grounds.

Orchardson, Sir William Quiller (1835–1910), Scottish painter, b. Edinburgh, best known for his *Napoleon I on board H.M.S. Bellerophon* and *Ophelia*.

Origen (c. 185–254), Christian philosopher and Biblical scholar, who taught at Alexandria and Caesarea, and was imprisoned and tortured in the persecution of Decius, 250

Orpen, Sir William (1878–1931), British painter of portraits, conversation pieces, and pictures of the 1914–18 war.

Ortega y Gasset, José (1883–1955), Spanish philosopher and essayist, known for his *Tema de Nuestro Tiempo* and *La Rebelión de Las Masas*.

Orwell, George (Eric Arthur Blair) (1903–50), English satirist, b. India, author of *Animal Farm* and *Nineteen Eighty-Four*.

Osborne, John (1929–94), playwright, was one of the "Angry Young Men" of the 1950s. His play *Look Back In Anger* (1956) marked a revolution in English theatre. His other plays include *The Entertainer* (1957), *Luther* (1961) and *Inadmissible Evidence* (1965).

Osler, Sir William (1849–1919), Canadian physician and medical historian, authority on diseases of the blood and spleen.

Ossietzky, Carl von (1889–1938), German pacifist leader after the first world war; sent by Hitler to a concentration camp. Nobel peace prize 1935.

Oswald, St (c. 605–42), won the Northumbrian throne by battle in 633 and introduced Christianity there.

Otto I (the Great) (912–73), founder of the Holy Roman Empire (he was crowned king of the Germans in 936 and emperor at Rome in 962). The son of Henry I of Germany, he built up a strong position in Italy (as regards the papacy) and in Germany where he established the East Mark (Austria).

Otto, Nikolaus August (1832–91), German engineer who built a gas engine (1878) using the four-stroke cycle that bears his name.

Ouida (Maria Louise Ramée) (1839–1908), English novelist of French extraction, whose romantic stories include *Under Two Flags*.

Ovid (43 B.C.–A.D. 18), Latin poet (Publius Ovidius Naso), chiefly remembered for his *Art of Love* and *Metamorphoses*. He died in exile.

Owen, Lord (David Owen). *See* D17.

Owen, Robert (1771–1858), Welsh pioneer socialist, b. Montgomeryshire. As manager, and later owner, of New Lanark cotton mills he tried to put his philanthropic views into effect; other communities on co-operative lines were founded in Hampshire and in America (New Harmony, Indiana) but although unsuccessful they were influential in many directions. He inaugurated socialism and the co-operative movement.

Owens, Jesse (1913–80), American black athlete whose 1936 Olympic triumph infuriated Hitler.

P

Pachmann, Vladimir de (1848–1933), Russian pianist gifted in the playing of Chopin.

Paderewski, Ignace Jan (1860–1941), Polish pianist and nationalist. He represented his country at Versailles and was the first premier of a reconstituted Poland. He died in exile.

Paganini, Niccolo (1782–1840), Italian violinist and virtuoso who revolutionised violin technique.

Pahlevi, Mohammed Riza Shah (1919–80), last Shah of Iran. Pro-Western ruler of Iran whose ruthless suppression of opposition helped precipitate an Islamic revolution. Went into exile, January 1979.

Paine, Thomas (1737–1809), political writer, b. Norfolk, son of a Quaker. Spent 1774–87 in America supporting the revolutionary cause. On his return to England wrote *The Rights of Man* in reply to Burke's *Reflections* on the French revolution which led to his prosecution and flight to France where he entered French politics and wrote *The Age of Reason*, advocating deism. His last years were spent in America but this time in obscurity.

Palestrina, Giovanni Pierluigi da (c. 1525–94), Italian composer of unaccompanied church music and madrigals. *See* Section E.

Palgrave, Sir Francis (1788–1861), English historian and archivist, an early editor of record series. His son **Francis Turner Palgrave** (1824–97) was a poet and critic and edited *The Golden Treasury*; another son, **William Gifford Palgrave** (1826–88) was a traveller and diplomat.

Palissy, Bernard (c. 1510–89), French potter who discovered the art of producing white enamel, after which he set up a porcelain factory in Paris which was patronised by royalty.

Palladio, Andrea (1508–80), Italian architect, b. Padua, whose style was modelled on ancient Roman architecture (symmetrical planning and harmonic proportions) and had wide influence; author of *I Quattro Libri dell' Architettura*.

Palmer, Samuel (1805–81), English landscape painter and etcher, follower of Blake whom he met in 1824. *Bright Cloud* and *In a Shoreham Garden* are in the Victoria and Albert Museum.

Palmerston, 3rd Viscount (Henry John Temple) (1784–1865), English Whig statesman. At first a Tory, he was later Whig foreign secretary for many years, and prime minister 1855 and 1859–65. His vigorous foreign policy wherever possible took the lead and bluntly asserted English rights.

Pancras, St. (d. 304), patron saint of children, was (according to tradition) baptised in Rome where he was put to death at the age of fourteen in the persecution under Diocletian.

Panizzi, Sir Anthony (1797–1879), Italian bibliographer and nationalist. Taking refuge in England after 1821, he became in 1856 chief librarian of the British Museum, undertook a new catalogue and designed the reading room.

Pankhurst, Emmeline (1858–1928), English suffragette who, with her daughters Christabel and Sylvia, worked for women's suffrage, organising the Women's Social and Political Union.

Panufnik, Sir Andrzej (1914–91), Polish-born composer. His first major work, the *Graduation Concert* was performed in 1935. The first Pole to be knighted.

Papin, Denis (1647–1714), French physicist and inventor. He invented the condensing pump, and was a pioneer in the development of the steam-engine. Not being a mechanic, he made all his experiments by means of models.

Paracelsus (Theophrastus Bombastus von Hohenhelm) (1493–1541), Swiss physician whose speculations though muddled served to reform medical thought. He criticised the established authorities, Galen and Aristotle, and experimented and made new chemical compounds. His earliest printed work was *Practica* (1529).

Park, Mungo (1771–1806), Scottish explorer in west Africa, where he lost his life. He wrote *Travels in the Interior of Africa* (1799).

Parker of Waddington, Baron (Hubert Lister Parker) (1900–72) Lord Chief Justice, 1958–70.

Parker, Joseph (1830–1902), English Congregational preacher, especially at what later became the City Temple.

Parnell, Charles Stewart (1846–91), Irish national leader. To draw attention to Ireland's problems, he used obstruction in parliament. He was president of the Land League but was not implicated in crimes committed by some members. His party supported Gladstone, who became converted to Home Rule. His citation in divorce proceedings brought his political career to an end.

Parry, Sir William Edward (1790–1855), English explorer and naval commander in the Arctic, where he was sent to protect fisheries and also tried to reach the north pole.

Parsons, Sir Charles Algernon (1854–1931), English inventor of the steam-turbine, who built the first turbine-driven steamship in 1897.

Pascal, Blaise (1623–62), Frenchman of varied gifts, b. at Clermont-Ferrand. At first a mathematician, he patented a calculating machine. His *Lettres provinciales* influenced Voltaire. In 1654 he turned to religion, and his incomplete religious writings were published posthumously as *Pensées*. *See* Jansenism, J28(2).

Pasternak, Boris Leonidovich (1890–1960), Russian poet and writer. B. Moscow, he published his first poems in 1931. For some years his time was spent in translating foreign literature, but in 1958 his novel *Dr. Zhivago*, which describes the Russian revolution and is in the Russian narrative tradition, was published abroad, though banned in the Soviet Union. He was awarded a Nobel prize but obliged to decline it.

Pasteur, Louis (1822–95), French chemist, b. at Dôle in the Jura, whose work was inspired by an interest in the chemistry of life. His researches on fermentation led to the science of bacteriology and his investigations into infectious diseases and their prevention to the science of immunology. The pathological–bacteriological import of his researches came about mainly through his disciples (Lister, Roux, and others) and not directly, though all founded on his early non-medical investigations on organisms of fermentation, etc., which were of great importance in industry, and fundamentally. He spent most of his life as director of scientific studies at the Ecole Normale at Paris. The Institute Pasteur was founded in 1888.

Patmore, Coventry (1823–96), English poet. *The Angel in the House* deals with domesticity. Later became a Roman catholic, and *The Unknown Eros* is characterised by erotic mysticism.

Patrick, St. (c. 389–c. 461), apostle of Ireland, was born in Britain or Gaul, and after some time on the continent (taken thither after his capture by pirates) went as missionary to Ireland, where after years of teaching and a visit to Rome he fixed his see at Armagh. He wrote *Confessions*.

Patti, Adelina (1843–1919), coloratura soprano, b. in Madrid of Italian parents, and of international repute.

Paul, St. (c. A.D. 10–64), Jew to whom was mainly due the extension of Christianity in Europe. B. Tarsus (in Asia Minor), he was a Pharisee, and became converted about A.D. 37. His missionary journeys took him to the Roman provinces of Asia, Macedonia, and Greece (Rome had already had Christian teaching); and his epistles form nearly half the New Testament and were written before the gospels. He helped to develop both the organisation of the early church and its teaching. The date order of his epistles is to some extent conjectural. It is believed that he was executed in Rome. His Hebrew name was Saul.

Paul VI (Giovanni Battista Montini) (1897–1978), elected Pope in 1963 on the death of John XXIII. His encyclical *Humanae Vitae* (1968) condemned contraception.

Pauli, Wolfgang (1900–58), Austrian-born physicist who first predicted theoretically the existence of neutrinos. Nobel prize 1945.

Pauling, Linus Carl (1901–94), American scientist. Won 1954 Nobel Prize for Chemistry (for work on molecular structure). Won 1963 Nobel Prize for Peace (the only person to receive two Nobel Prizes outright).

Pavarotti, Luciano (b. 1935), Italian operatic tenor. Acclaimed for such roles as Rodolfo in *La Bohème*, the Duke of Mantua in *Rigoletto etc*.

Pavlov, Ivan Petrovich (1849–1936), Russian physiologist, known for his scientific experimental work on animal behaviour, particularly conditioned reflexes and the relation between psychological stress and brain function. Nobel prizewinner 1904.

Pavlova, Anna (1882–1931), Russian ballerina, b. St. Petersburg, excelling in the roles of *Giselle* and the *Dying Swan*.

Peabody, George (1795–1869), American philanthropist, a successful merchant who lived mainly in London. He gave large sums to promote education and slum clearance.

Peacock, Thomas Love (1785–1866), English novel-

ist, b. Weymouth. His works included *Headlong Hall* and *Nightmare Abbey*.

Pearson, Lester Bowles (1897–1972), Canadian politician who served as minister for external affairs 1948–57, and prime minister 1963–8. He supported the UN. Nobel peace prize 1957.

Peary, Robert Edwin (1856–1920), American arctic explorer, discoverer of the north pole (1909).

Peel, Sir Robert (1788–1850), English Conservative statesman, b. in Lancashire, son of a manufacturer. He first held office in 1811. With Wellington he enacted toleration for Roman catholics in 1829. As home secretary he reorganised London police. He developed a new policy of Conservatism, and in 1846, largely as a result of the Irish famine, he repealed the corn laws.

Peirce, Charles Sanders (1839–1914), American physicist and philosopher of original mind, founder of the theory of pragmatism later developed by his friend William James. *See* J49.

Penfield, Wilder Graves (1891–1976), Canadian brain surgeon, author of *The Cerebral Cortex of Man, Epilepsy and the Functional Anatomy of the Human Brain*. O.M.

Penn, William (1644–1718), English Quaker and founder of Pennsylvania. The son of Admiral William Penn, he persisted in becoming a Quaker, and on receiving for his father's services a crown grant in America he founded Pennsylvania. He wrote *No Cross, No Crown*.

Penney, Baron (William George Penney) (1909–91), British scientist. His nuclear research team at A.E.A. developed the advanced gas-cooled reactor (A.G.R.) chosen for the Dungeness "B" and Hinkley Point "B" power stations.

Pepys, Samuel (1633–1703), English diarist and naval administrator. His diary, 1660–69, was kept in cipher and not deciphered till 1825. It gives vivid personal details and covers the plague and fire of London. (The first complete version of the diary was issued in 1970.)

Pereda, José Maria de (1833–1906), Spanish regional novelist (around his native Santander).

Pérez Galdós, Benito (1843–1920), Spanish novelist and dramatist, who has been compared to Balzac for his close study and portrayal of all social classes, especially in the series of 46 short historical novels *Episodios nacionales*. His longer novels, *Novelas españolas contemporáneas*, some of which are translated, number 31.

Pergolesi, Giovanni Battista (1710–36), Italian composer, best known for his humorous opera *La Serva Padrona* and his *Stabat Mater*.

Pericles (c. 490–429 B.C.), Athenian statesman, general, and orator, who raised Athens to the point of its fullest prosperity, and greatest beauty, with the Parthenon, Erechtheum, and other buildings; but he died of plague following the outbreak of the Peloponnesian war.

Perkin, Sir William Henry (1838–1907), English chemist, b. London, who while seeking to make a substitute for quinine discovered in 1856 the first artificial aniline dye, mauve.

Perry, Frederick John (1909–95), the greatest player in the history of British lawn tennis. Last British player to win singles titles at Wimbledon (1934, 1935 and 1936).

Persius Flaccus Aulus (A.D. 34–62), Roman satirist and Stoic philosopher.

Perugino, Pietro (1446–1524), Italian artist. He worked in the Sistine Chapel at Rome and he taught Raphael.

Perutz, Max Ferdinand (b. 1914), British chemist. Nobel Prize, 1962 (with J. C. Kendrew). Founding father of the world-renowned Laboratory of Molecular Biology at Cambridge.

Pestalozzi, Johann Heinrich (1746–1827), Swiss educational reformer whose theories laid the foundation of modern primary education. His teaching methods were advanced for his time. He wrote *How Gertrude Educates Her Children*.

Pétain, Henri Philippe (1856–1951), French general and later collaborator. In the first world war he was in command at Verdun. Headed the pro-German Vichy regime in World War II.

Peter I, the Great (1672–1725), emperor of Russia. Son of Alexei, he succeeded his brother after some difficulty. He reorganised the army, and, after coming to Deptford to learn shipbuilding, he created a navy. To some extent he westernised Russian social life, and created a new capital at St. Petersburg (1703). In war with

Charles XII of Sweden he was at first defeated, but later victorious at Poltava (1709). He married a peasant, Catherine, who succeeded him.

Peter the Hermit (c. 1050–1115), French monk who preached the First Crusade, originated by pope Urban II at the council of Clermont. He went on the crusade himself, but gave up at Antioch.

Petrarch, Francesco (1304–78), Italian poet, son of a Florentine exile. He is chiefly remembered for his poems To Laura, but he was also a scholar who paved the way for the Renaissance.

Petrie, Sir Flinders (1853–1942), British egyptologist. He excavated in Britain (1875–90), Egypt (1880–1924), and Palestine (1927–38). See his Seventy Years of Archaeology.

Phidias (5th cent. B.C.), Greek sculptor especially in gold, ivory and bronze, worked at Athens for Pericles. No certain examples of his work are extant, but the Elgin marbles in the British Museum may be from his designs.

Philip II of France (1165–1223), son of Louis VII. He went on the Third Crusade with Richard I of England, but in France is mainly remembered for firm government, the recovery of Normandy from England, and the beautifying of Paris.

Philip II of Macedonia (382–336 B.C.), a successful commander, made his the leading military kingdom in Greece and was father of Alexander the Great.

Philip II of Spain (1527–98), succeeded his father Charles V in Spain and the Netherlands, also in Spanish interests overseas. In the Netherlands his strict Roman catholic policy provoked a revolt which ended in 1579 in the independence of the United Provinces. He married Mary Tudor of England; and after her death sent the ill-fated Armada against Elizabeth in 1588.

Philip V of Spain (1683–1746), first Bourbon king, succeeded his great-uncle Charles II and was grandson of Louis XIV. His accession provoked European war.

Phillip, Arthur (1738–1814), first governor of New South Wales. Under his command the first fleet of 717 convicts set sail from Britain to Australia, and with the founding of Sydney in 1788 colonisation of the whole country began.

Phillips, Stephen (1868–1915), English poet who wrote verse dramas, including Paolo and Francesca.

Piast, first Polish dynasty in Poland until the 14th cent. and until the 17th cent. in Silesia.

Piazzi, Giuseppe (1746–1826), Italian astronomer who discovered Ceres, the first of the asteroids to be seen by man.

Picasso, Pablo Ruiz (1881–1973) Spanish painter, b. Málaga; received his early training in Catalonia and settled in Paris in 1903. He and Braque were the originators of Cubism (c. 1909). His influence over contemporary art is comparable with that exercised by Cézanne (q.v.) over the artists of his time. Perhaps the best-known single work is his mural Guernica, painted at the time of the Spanish civil war, expressing the artist's loathing of fascism and the horrors of war. His genius also found scope in sculpture, ceramics, and the graphic arts, and he designed décor and costumes for the ballet.

Piccard, Auguste (1884–1962), Swiss physicist, noted for balloon ascents into the stratosphere and for submarine research. In 1960 his son Jacques made a descent of over 7 miles in the Marianas trench in the western Pacific in a bathyscaphe designed and built by his father.

Pilsudski, Joseph (1867–1935), Polish soldier and statesman who in 1919 attempted by force to restore Poland's 1772 frontiers but was driven back. From 1926 he was dictator.

Pindar (522–443 B.C.), Greek lyric poet.

Pinero, Sir Arthur Wing (1855–1934), English dramatist whose plays include Dandy Dick, The Second Mrs. Tanqueray and Mid-Channel.

Pirandello, Luigi (1867–1936), Italian dramatist and novelist whose plays include Six Characters in Search of an Author. Nobel prizewinner 1934.

Pissarro, Camille (1830–1903), French impressionist painter of landscapes; studied under Corot.

Pitman, Sir Isaac (1813–97), b. Trowbridge, English inventor of a system of phonographic shorthand.

Pitt, William (1759–1806), English statesman. Younger son of the Earl of Chatham, (q.v.) he entered parliament at 21 and became prime minister at 24 in 1783 when parties were divided and the American war had been lost. He rose to the position, and held office with scarcely a break till his death. An able finance minister, he introduced reforms, and would have gone further, but Napoleon's meteoric rise obliged him to lead European allies in a long struggle against France. He died worn out by his efforts.

Pius XII (1876–1958), elected pope 1939. As Eugenio Pacelli, he was papal nuncio in Germany and later papal secretary of state. It has been argued that, as pope in wartime, he could have taken a stronger line against Nazi war crimes.

Pizarro, Francisco (c. 1478–1541), Spanish adventurer, b. Trujillo. After Columbus's discoveries, he conquered Peru for Spain, overthrowing the Inca empire. He was murdered by his men.

Planck, Max (1857–1947), German mathematical physicist, b. Kiel, whose main work was on thermodynamics. In 1900 he invented a mathematical formula to account for some properties of the thermal radiation from a hot body which has since played an important role in physics. Nobel prizewinner 1918. See Quantum theory, Section I.

Plato (427–347 B.C.), Athenian philosopher, pupil of Socrates, teacher of Aristotle. He founded a school at Athens under the name of the Academy, where he taught philosophy and mathematics. His great work is his Dialogues, which includes the Republic, the longest and most celebrated. His known writings have come down to us and constitute one of the most influential bodies of work in history. See also Mind and Matter, Section J.

Playfair, 1st Baron (Lyon Playfair) (1818–98), a far-sighted Victorian who stood for the greater recognition of science in national life. He forsook his profession as professor of chemistry at Edinburgh to enter parliament. Pres. British Association 1885.

Plimsoll, Samuel (1824–98), English social reformer, b. Bristol. He realised the evil of overloading unseaworthy ships, and as M.P. for Derby he procured the passing of the Merchant Shipping Act, 1876 which imposed a line (the Plimsoll Mark) above which no ship must sink while loading.

Pliny the Elder (A.D. 23–79), Roman naturalist, author of a Natural History. He died of fumes and exhaustion while investigating the eruption of Vesuvius. His nephew, Pliny the Younger (A.D. 62–113), wrote Letters notable for their charm and the insight they give into Roman life.

Plotinus (c. 203–c. 262), Greek philosopher, was the founder of Neoplatonism, which had considerable influence on early Christian thought. See also God and Man, Section J.

Plutarch (c. 46–120), Greek biographer, whose Lives portray 46 leading historical figures (in pairs, a Greek and a Roman whose careers were similar). Although based on myth his Life of Lycurgus about life in Sparta had a profound influence on later writers, e.g., Rousseau and the romantic philosophers. He was educated at Athens but visited Rome.

Poe, Edgar Allan (1809–49), American poet and story-writer, b. Boston, Mass. His poems include The Raven, To Helen, and Annabel Lee, and his stories, often weird and fantastic, include Tales of the Grotesque and Arabesque.

Poincaré, Raymond Nicolas (1860–1934), French statesman. He was president 1913–20, and as prime minister occupied the Ruhr in 1923.

Pole, Reginald (1500–58), archbishop of Canterbury, cardinal of the Roman church and antagonist of the reformation. He opposed Henry VIII's divorce and went abroad in 1532, writing De Unitate Ecclesiastica; as a result of which his mother, Countess of Salisbury, and other relatives were executed. Under Queen Mary Tudor he became archbishop and died the year she did.

Pollard, Albert Frederick (1869–1948), English historian, especially of the Tudor period, and first director of the Institute of Historical Research.

Polo, Marco (1256–1323), Venetian traveller, who made journeys through China, India, and other eastern countries, visiting the court of Kubla

Khan, and leaving an account of his travels.

Pompadour, Jeanne Antoine Poisson, Marquise de (1721–64), mistress of Louis XV of France. She exercised disastrous political influence.

Pompey (106–48 B.C.), Roman commander, who cleared the Mediterranean of pirates, and became triumvir with Caesar and Crassus.

Pompidou, Georges Jean Raymond (1911–74), French administrator and politician who succeeded de Gaulle as president 1969.

Pope, Alexander (1688–1744), English poet, b. London, of a Roman catholic family, and largely self-educated. His brilliant satire was frequently directed against his contemporaries. He is especially remembered for *The Rape of the Lock*, *The Dunciad*, *Essay on Criticism*, and *Essay on Man*.

Popper, Sir Karl Raimund (1902–94), British philosopher of science, b. Vienna; author of *The Open Society and Its Enemies* (1945), *Conjectures and Refutations* (1963), *Objective Knowledge* (1972). He rejects the doctrine that all knowledge starts from perception or sensation and holds that it grows through conjecture and refutation. One of the most influential philosophers of the 20th century. C.H. (1982).

Potter, Dennis (1935–94), television dramatist, wrote many innovative and stimulating plays. These included three six-part serials: *Pennies from Heaven* (1978), *The Singing Detective* (1986) and *Lipstick on your Collar* (1993).

Pound, Ezra Loomis (1885–1972), American poet and writer on varied subjects, a controversial figure. Noted for his translations of Provençal, Latin, Chinese, French, and Italian poets.

Poussin, Nicolas (1593–1665), French painter. He lived in Rome 1624–40, 1642–65. His *Golden Calf* is in the National Gallery.

Powys, John Cowper (1872–1964), English writer, best known for his novel *Wolf Solent* and his essays *The Meaning of Culture* and *A Philosophy of Solitude*. His brothers, *Theodore Francis* (1875–1953) and *Llewelyn* (1884–1939) were also original writers.

Prasad, Rajendra (1884–1963), Indian statesman, first president of the Republic of India, 1950–62.

Praxiteles (4th cent. B.C.), Greek sculptor, whose main surviving work is *Hermes carrying Dionysus*.

Preece, Sir William Henry (1834–1913), Welsh electrical engineer, associated with the expansion of wireless telegraphy and telephony in the United Kingdom. He was connected with Marconi and introduced the block system.

Prichard, James Cowles (1786–1848), English ethnologist who perceived that people should be studied as a whole. His works include *Researches into the Physical History of Mankind* and *The Natural History of Man*. He practised medicine.

Priestley, John Boynton (1894–1984), English critic, novelist, and playwright, b. Bradford. His works include the novels *The Good Companions*, *Angel Pavement*, and the plays *Dangerous Corner*, *Time and the Conways*, *I Have Been Here Before*, and *The Linden Tree*, O.M. 1977.

Priestley, Joseph (1733–1804), English chemist who worked on gases, and shared with Scheele the discovery of oxygen. A presbyterian minister, he was for his time an advanced thinker. In 1794 he settled in America.

Prior, Matthew (1664–1721), English poet. In early life he was a diplomat. He was a neat epigrammatist and writer of occasional pieces. His works include *The City Mouse and Country Mouse* and *Four Dialogues of the Dead*.

Pritchett, Sir ' Victor Sawdon (b. 1900), novelist, short-story writer and critic. His *Complete Short Stories* were published in 1990 and his *Complete Essays* in 1992. Companion of Honour 1993.

Prokofiev, Serge Sergeyevich (1891–1953), Russian composer, whose music has a strong folk-song element, rich in melody and invention. He has written operas; *The Love of Three Oranges*, *The Betrothal in a Nunnery*, *War and Peace*; ballets: *Romeo and Juliet*, *Cinderella*; symphonies, chamber music, and the music for Eisenstein's films *Alexander Nevsky*, *Ivan the Terrible*.

Protagoras (c. 480–411 B.C.), Greek philosopher, chief of the Sophists, noted for his scepticism and disbelief in objective truth, and for his doctrine that "man is the measure of all things."

Proudhon, Pierre Joseph (1809–65), French socialist. In 1840 he propounded the view that property is theft. His main work is *Système des contradictions économiques* (1846).

Proust, Marcel (1871–1922), French psychological novelist, author of a series of novels known under the title of *A la recherche du temps perdu*. His works have been admirably translated into English by C. K. Scott Moncrieff and revised by T. Kilmartin and D. J. Enright.

Ptolemy of Alexandria (Claudius Ptolemaeus) (fl. A.D. 140), astronomer and founder of scientific cartography. In the *Almagest* he attempted a mathematical presentation of the paths along which the planets appear to move in the heavens. His other great work was his *Geographical Outline*.

Puccini, Giacomo (1858–1924), Italian composer, b. Lucca, whose operas include *Manon Lescaut*, *La Bohème*, *Tosca*, *Madam Butterfly*, and *Turandot* (completed by a friend).

Pupin, Michael Idvorsky (1858–1935), physicist and inventor (telephony and X-rays), b. Idvor, Hungary (now in Yugoslavia); went to America penniless 1874 to become professor of electro-mechanics at Columbia University.

Purcell, Henry (1659–95), English composer, b. Westminster, son of a court musician. He became organist of the chapel royal and composer to Charles II. His best works are vocal and choral. *See* **Section E.**

Pusey, Edward Bouverie (1800–82), English theologian, a leader of the Oxford or Tractarian movement with Keble and at first also with Newman, till the latter became Roman catholic. The movement aimed at revival.

Pushkin, Alexander (1799–1837), Russian writer, b. Moscow, whose place in Russian literature ranks with Shakespeare's in English. He wrote in many forms—lyrical poetry and narrative verse, drama, folk-tales and short stories. Musicians have used his works as plots for operas—the fairy romance *Russlan and Ludmilla* was dramatised by Glinka; the verse novel *Eugene Onegin* and the short story *The Queen of Spades* were adapted by Tchaikovsky, and the tragic drama *Boris Godunov* formed the subject of Mussorgsky's opera. Like Lermontov, who too was exiled, he was inspired by the wild beauty of the Caucasus. He was killed in a duel defending his wife's honour.

Pym, John (1584–1643), English parliamentary leader in opposition to Charles I. He promoted the impeachment of the king's advisers, Strafford and Laud. A collateral descendant is **Lord Pym**, Conservative Foreign Secretary, 1982–June 1983.

Pythagoras (c. 582–500 B.C.), Greek philosopher, b. on the island of Samos, off the Turkish mainland, which he left c. 530 to settle at Croton, a Greek city in southern Italy. He was a mystic and mathematician, and founded a brotherhood who saw in numbers the key to the understanding of the universe.

Q

Quasimodo, Salvatore (1901–68), Italian poet of humanity and liberal views whose works include *La vita non e sogno*. Nobel prizewinner 1959.

Quesnay, François (1694–1774), French economist, founder of the physiocratic school who believed in *laissez-faire* and influenced the thought of Adam Smith. *See* **Physiocrats, Section J.**

Quiller-Couch, Sir Arthur Thomas (1863–1944), English man of letters, b. Bodmin, known as "Q." He edited the *Oxford Book of English Verse*. King Edward VII Professor of English, Cambridge University, 1912–44.

R

Rabelais, François (c. 1495–1553), French satirist. At first in religious orders, he later studied medicine and practised at Lyons. His works, mainly published under a pseudonym, are full of riotous mirth, wit and wisdom. The main ones are *Gargantua* and *Pantagruel*.

Rachel, Elisa (Elisa Felix) (1821–58), Alsatian-Jewish tragic actress. Her chief triumph was in Racine's *Phèdre*.

Rachmaninov, Sergey Vasilyevich (1873–1943), Russian composer and pianist, b. Nijni-Novgorod (now Gorki), best known for his piano music, especially his *Prelude*. After 1917 he settled in America. *See* **Section E.**

Racine, Jean (1639–99), French tragic poet whose dramas include *Andromaque*, *Iphigénie* and *Phèdre*. An orphan, he was brought up by grandparents who sent him to Port Royal school where he acquired a love of the classics. In Paris he became a friend of Molière, whose company acted his first play, and of Boileau, with whom he became joint historiographer to Louis XIV. *Esther* and *Athalie* were written for Madame de Maintenon's schoolgirls.

Rackham, Arthur (1867–1939), English artist and book-illustrator, especially of fairy tales.

Radhakrishnan, Sir Sarvepalli (1888–1975), Indian philosopher and statesman, vice-president of India 1952–62, president 1962–7. He was at one time a professor at Oxford.

Raffles, Sir Thomas Stamford (1781–1826), English colonial administrator who founded a settlement at Singapore in 1819. He was also a naturalist, and founded the London Zoo.

Raikes, Robert (1735–1811), English educational pioneer, whose lead in the teaching of children at Gloucester on Sundays led to an extensive Sunday School movement.

Raleigh, Sir Walter (1552–1618), adventurer and writer. He found favour at the court of Elizabeth I, helped to put down the Irish rebellion of 1580, and in 1584 began the colonisation of Virginia, introducing potatoes and tobacco to the British Isles. At the accession of James I he lost favour and was sent to the Tower, where he wrote his *History of the World*. Released in 1615 to lead an expedition to the Orinoco, he was executed when it failed.

Raman, Sir Chandrasekhara Venkata (1888–1970), Indian physicist whose main work has been in spectroscopy. For his research on the diffusion of light and discovery of the "Raman effect" he was awarded the 1930 Nobel prize.

Rameau, Jean Philippe (1683–1764), French composer and church organist whose works on musical theory influenced musical development.

Ramón y Cajal, Santiago (1852–1934), Spanish histologist who made discoveries in the structure of the nervous system. Shared 1906 Nobel prize.

Ramphal, Sir Shridath 'Sonny' (b. 1928), Guyanese statesman. Secretary-General of the Commonwealth, 1975 to 1990. Foreign Minister, Guyana, 1972 to 1975. First black Chancellor of a British university.

Ramsay, Sir William (1852–1916), Scottish chemist, and discoverer with Lord Rayleigh of argon. Later he discovered helium and other inert gases, which he called neon, krypton, and xenon. Nobel prizewinner 1904.

Ramsey, Arthur Michael (1904–88), archbishop of Canterbury, 1961–74. He was professor of divinity at Cambridge 1950–2; bishop of Durham 1952–6; archbishop of York 1956–61. Widely travelled, he worked hard for church unity.

Ranke, Leopold von (1795–1886), German historian, one of the first to base his work on methodical research. His chief work is a *History of the Popes*.

Raphael (Raffaello Santi) (1483–1520) of Urbino was the youngest of the three great artists of the High Renaissance. He was taught at Perugia by Perugino, and then at Florence he came under the influence of Leonardo and Michelangelo. Raphael's Madonnas, remarkable for their simplicity and grace, include the *Madonna of the Grand Duke* (Palazzo Pitti), the *Sistine Madonna* (Dresden) the *Madonna with the Goldfinch* (Uffizi), the *Madonna of Foligno* (Vatican), and the *Ansidei Madonna* (National Gallery). He painted the frescoes on the walls of the Stanza della Segnatura in the Vatican, and designed 10 cartoons for tapestries for the Sistine Chapel. After the death of Bramante he was appointed architect for the rebuilding of St. Peter's.

Rasputin, Grigori Yefimovich (1869–1916), Russian peasant from Siberia, a cunning adventurer who at the court of Nicholas II exerted a malign influence over the Tsarina through his apparent ability to improve the health of the sickly Tsarevich Alexis. He was murdered by a group of nobles.

Rathbone, Eleanor (1872–1946), social reformer who championed women's pensions and in her book *The Disinherited Family* set out the case for family allowances.

Ravel, Maurice (1875–1937), French composer, pupil of Fauré, one of the leaders of the impressionist movement.

Rawlinson, Sir Henry Creswicke (1810–95), English diplomat and archaeologist. He made Assyrian collections now in the British Museum and translated the Behistun inscription of the Persian king Darius. He also wrote on cuneiform inscriptions and on Assyrian history.

Ray, John (1627–1705), English naturalist. A blacksmith's son, he went to Cambridge, travelled in Europe, and produced a classification of plants. He also wrote on zoology.

Rayleigh, 3rd Baron (John William Strutt) (184?–1919) English mathematician and physicist. He studied sound and the wave theory of light; and with Sir William Ramsay discovered argon. Nobel prizewinner 1904.

Read, Sir Herbert (1893–1968), English poet and art critic. His writings include *Collected Poems*, *The Meaning of Art*, and an autobiography, *Annals of Innocence and Experience*.

Reade, Charles (1814–84), English novelist. His chief work is *The Cloister and the Hearth*. He also wrote *Peg Woffington*, *It is Never too Late to Mend*, and *Griffith Gaunt*, aimed at social abuses.

Reagan, Ronald (b. 1911). U.S. President, 1981–89; former T.V. and film star, 1937–66. Governor of California, 1967–74. Won Republican victory, 1980. Re-elected in landslide victory, 1984. His popularity remained, helping ensure the election of George Bush (*q.v.*) as his successor. Awarded Order of the Bath, June 1989, by the Queen.

Réaumur, René Antoine Ferchault de (1683–1757), French naturalist who invented a thermometer of eighty degrees, using alcohol.

Récamier, Jeanne Françoise (*née* Bernard) (1777–1849), French beauty and holder of a noted salon. Her husband was a banker.

Regnault, Henry Victor (1810–78), French chemist and physicist, who worked on gases, latent heat, and steam-engines.

Reith, 1st Baron (John Charles Walsham Reith) (1889–1971), Scottish civil engineer, first director-general of the B.B.C. 1927–38

Rembrandt (Rembrandt Harmenszoon van Rijn) (1606–69), Dutch painter and etcher, b. Leiden, a miller's son, one of the most individual and prolific artists of any period. His output includes portraits, landscapes, large groups, etchings, and drawings. He settled in Amsterdam establishing his reputation with *The Anatomy Lesson*, painted in 1632. In 1634 he married Saskia, a burgomaster's daughter. *The Night Watch* was painted in 1642; it was not well received and Saskia died the same year, leaving the infant Titus. The path from relative wealth to lonely old age is depicted in his self-portraits. Caring little for convention or formal beauty, his work is characterised by bold realism and spiritual beauty, by vitality and simplicity. His understanding of the play of colour and the effects of light can give his pictures a mystical beauty, as in the atmospheric painting *The Mill*. His figures, even for religious pictures, were taken from real life, the Jews in the etching *Christ Healing* from the Jewish quarter where he lived. He met the misfortunes of later life by withdrawing from society, but it was then that he produced his greatest works.

Renan, Ernest (1823–92), French writer who, though not accepting the orthodox viewpoint, wrote on religious themes, especially a *Life of Jesus*.

Reni, Guido. *See* Guido Reni.

Rennie, John (1761–1821), Scottish civil engineer who built the old Waterloo and Southwark bridges and designed the granite London bridge which stood until recently. He also designed docks at London, Liverpool, Leith, Dublin, and Hull; constructed Plymouth breakwater; made canals and drained fens.

Renoir, Pierre Auguste (1841–1919), French impressionist painter, b. Limoges. His works include portraits, still-life, landscapes, and groups, including *La Loge*, *Les Parapluies*, *La première Sortie*, *La Place Pigalle*. He was later crippled with arthritis.

Reuter, Paul Julius, Freiherr von (1816–99), German pioneer of telegraphic press service, who in 1851 fixed his headquarters in London.

Reymont, Vladislav Stanislav (1868–1925), Polish novelist, author of *The Peasants*. Nobel prizewinner 1924.

Reynolds, Sir Joshua (1723–92), English portrait painter, b. Plympton, Devon. His portraits, which include *Mrs. Siddons*, are remarkable for expressiveness and colour and he was a sympathetic painter of children. He was first president of the R.A. from 1768 till his death.

Rhodes, Cecil John (1853–1902), English empire-builder. B. at Bishop's Stortford, he went to South Africa for health reasons and there prospered at the diamond mines. He became prime minister of what was then Cape Colony and secured British extension in what is now Zimbabwe and Zambia. He withdrew from politics after the failure of the Jameson Raid of 1895. He founded scholarships at Oxford for overseas students.

Ricardo, David (1772–1823), English political economist of Jewish descent. By occupation a London stockbroker, he wrote a useful work, *Principles of Political Economy*.

Richard I (1157–99), succeeded his father Henry II as king of England in 1189. A patron of troubadours and a soldier (Lion-heart), he went on the third Crusade and took Acre, but could not recover Jerusalem from Saladin. On his return journey across Europe he was imprisoned and ransomed. He was killed in war with France.

Richard II (1367–1400), son of the Black Prince, succeeded his grandfather Edward III as king of England in 1377. Artistic and able, but erratic and egocentric, he personally at the age of fourteen met the Peasants' Revolt in 1381, making untenable promises. Latterly his rule became increasingly arbitrary, and he was deposed and imprisoned in 1399.

Richard III (1452–85), King of England (1483–5), younger brother of the Yorkist, Edward IV, is believed to have murdered his two nephews in the Tower. He was defeated and killed at Bosworth by the invading Earl of Richmond, who as Henry VII brought to an end the Wars of the Roses, Richard's character is disputed, but he was able and might have been a successful ruler.

Richards, Sir Gordon (1904–86), foremost English jockey who rode 4,870 winners. Knighted in 1953 after he won the Epsom Derby on *Pinza*.

Richardson, Sir Albert Edward (1880–1964), British architect, author of *Georgian Architecture*.

Richardson, Sir Owen Willans (1879–1959), English physicist who worked on thermionics, or emission of electricity from hot bodies. Nobel prizewinner 1928.

Richardson, Sir Ralph David (1902–83), English actor who worked at the Old Vic, on the West End stage, and at Stratford-on-Avon, and appeared in films, including *South Riding*, *Anna Karenina*, and *The Fallen Idol*.

Richardson, Samuel (1689–1761), English author of *Pamela*, *Clarissa*, and *The History of Sir Charles Grandison*, exercised considerable influence on the development of the novel.

Richelieu, Armand Jean du Plessis, Duc de (1585–1642), French statesman, cardinal of the Roman church. As minister to Louis XIII from 1624 till his death, he built up the power of the French crown at home in central government, and by his military preparedness and active foreign policy gave France a lead in Europe.

Ridley, Nicholas (1500–55), English Protestant martyr, bishop of Rochester and later of London. He was burnt with Latimer.

Rienzi, Cola di (1313–54), Italian patriot, b. Rome, led a popular rising in 1347 and for seven months reigned as tribune, but had to flee, was imprisoned, and eventually murdered.

Rilke, Rainer Maria (1872–1926), German lyric poet, b. Prague. His work, marked by beauty of style, culminated in the *Duino Elegies* and *Sonnets to Orpheus*, both written in 1922, which gave a new musicality to German verse. His visits to Russia in 1899 and 1900 and his admiration for Rodin (who had been his wife's teacher) influenced his artistic career.

Rimbaud, Jean Nicolas Arthur (1854–91), French poet, b. Charleville, on the Meuse. In his brief poetic career (4 years from about the age of 16) he prepared the way for symbolism (*Bateau ivre*, *Les Illuminations*) and anticipated Freud (*Les déserts de l'amour*). He became in-

timate with Verlaine and at 18 had completed his memoirs. *Une saison en enfer*. He died at Marseilles.

Rimsky-Korsakov, Nikolai Andreyevich (1844–1908), Russian composer whose works include the operas *The Maid of Pskov*, *The Snow Maiden*, *Le Coq d'or*, and the symphonic suite *Scheherezade*. He was a brilliant orchestrator and re-scored many works, *e.g.* Borodin's *Prince Igor*.

Rizzio, David (1533?–66), Italian musician and secretary of Mary, Queen of Scots. He was murdered in her presence at Holyrood by her jealous husband, Darnley.

Robbia, Luca Della (1400–82), Florentine sculptor who introduced enamelled terra-cotta work.

Roberts of Kandahar, 1st Earl (Frederick Sleigh Roberts) (1832–1914), British general. He took part in the suppression of the Indian Mutiny, in the Afghan war (relieving Kandahar), and when in command in South Africa in the Boer War he relieved Kimberley and advanced to Pretoria.

Robertson, Sir William (1860–1933), the first British soldier to rise from private to fieldmarshal. His son, **Brian Hubert, 1st Baron** (1896–1974) was chairman of the British Transport Commission, 1953–61.

Robeson, Paul (1898–1976), American Negro singer, b. Princeton, especially remembered for his singing of Negro spirituals, and his appearance in works ranging from *Showboat* to *Othello*.

Robespierre, Maximilien Marie Isidoire de (1758–94), French revolutionary. A country advocate, b. Arras, he was in 1789 elected to the States General and in 1792 to the Convention. He became a leader of the Jacobins, the more extreme party which came to power under stress of war and after the king's execution in 1793. In this crisis, the Committee of Public Safety, of which he was a member and which used his reputation as a cloak, sent many to the guillotine. He opposed the cult of Reason and inaugurated the worship of the Supreme Being. In the reaction from the reign of terror he was denounced, tried to escape, but was guillotined.

Robinson, Mary (b. 1944), President of Republic of Ireland since 1990 (1st woman President). Labour politician, lawyer and prominent campaigner for women's rights.

Robinson, William Heath (1872–1944), English cartoonist and book-illustrator, especially known for his humorous drawings of machines.

Rob Roy (Robert McGregor) (1671–1734), Scottish freebooter who helped the poor at the expense of the rich, and played a lone hand in the troubled times of the Jacobite rising of 1715.

Robsart, Amy (1532–60), English victim (it is believed) of murder. The wife of Robert Dudley, Earl of Leicester, she was found dead at Cumnor Place. Her death was used by Scott in *Kenilworth*.

Rockefeller, John Davison (1839–1937), American philanthropist, b. Richford, N.Y. He settled in Cleveland, Ohio, and with his brother William founded the Standard Oil Company, making a fortune. His philanthropic enterprises are carried on by the Rockefeller Foundation. **Nelson Rockefeller** (1908–79), Gov. of New York 1958–73, Vice-Pres. of the United States 1974–7, was his grandson.

Rodin, Auguste (1841–1917), French sculptor, b. Paris. His best-known works include *Le Penseur*, *Les Bourgeois de Calais*, the statues of Balzac and Victor Hugo, and *La Porte d'Enfer*, a huge bronze door for the Musée des Arts Décoratifs, which was unfinished at his death.

Rodney, 1st Baron (George Rodney) (1719–92), English admiral, who served in the Seven Years War and the War of American Independence; in the latter war he defeated the French fleet under de Grasse.

Rogers, Sir Richard (George) (b. 1933), Architect of international repute. His creations include Lloyd's Building in London, the Pompidou Centre in Paris and the European Court of Human Rights building in Strasbourg. Reith Lecturer, 1995.

Roland de la Platière, Manon Jeanne (1754–93), a leading figure in the French revolution. Her husband **Jean Marie** (1734–93), belonged to the more moderate or Girondist party, and when threatened escaped; but she was imprisoned and executed. She wrote *Letters* and *Memoirs*.

Rolland, Romain (1866–1944), French author,

whose main work is a ten-volume novel, *Jean-Christophe*, the biography of a German musician, based on the life of Beethoven, and a study of contemporary French and German civilisation. Nobel prizewinner 1915.

Rolls, Charles Stewart (1877–1910), with **Henry Royce** (1863–1933) the co-founders of Rolls-Royce car manufacturers (at Derby in 1907).

Romilly, Sir Samuel (1757–1818), English lawyer and law-reformer, who aimed at mitigating the severity of the criminal law.

Rommel, Erwin (1891–1944), German Field-Marshal. He took part in the 1940 invasion of France, and was later successful in commanding the Afrika Korps till 1944. He committed suicide.

Romney, George (1734–1802), English artist, b. in Lancashire. He painted chiefly portraits, especially of Lady Hamilton, and lived mainly in London, but returned to Kendal to die.

Röntgen, Wilhelm Konrad von (1845–1923), German scientist who in 1895 discovered X-rays. Nobel prizewinner 1901.

Roosevelt, Franklin Delano (1882–1945), American statesman, a distant cousin of Theodore Roosevelt. During the first world war he held office under Wilson, and though stricken with poliomyelitis in 1921 continued his political career, becoming governor of New York in 1929 and U.S. president in 1933 (the first to hold office for more than two terms), till his death. A Democrat, he met the economic crisis of 1933 with a policy for a "New Deal" (*see* **Section L**). He strove in vain to ward off war. Towards other American countries his attitude was that of "good neighbour." After Pearl Harbor, he energetically prosecuted the war, holding meetings with Churchill and Stalin, and adopting a "lend-lease" policy for arms. He kept contact with his people by "fireside talks." His wife **Eleanor** (1884–1962) was a public figure in her own right.

Roosevelt, Theodore (1858–1919), American president. Popular because of his exploits in the Spanish-American war, he was appointed Republican vice-president in 1900, becoming president when McKinley was assassinated, and was re-elected 1905. He promoted the regulation of trusts; and his promotion of peace between Russia and Japan gained the Nobel prize, 1906.

Rops, Félicien (1833–98), Belgian artist, known for his often satirical lithographs and etchings.

Ross, Sir James Clark (1800–62), Scottish explorer of polar regions, who accompanied his uncle Sir John, and himself discovered the north magnetic pole in 1831. He commanded the *Erebus* and *Terror* to the antarctic (1839–43). His discoveries included the Ross ice barrier.

Ross, Sir John (1777–1856), Scottish explorer of polar regions, uncle of the above. He searched for the north-west passage and discovered Boothia peninsula.

Ross, Sir Ronald (1857–1932), British physician, b. India, who discovered the malaria parasite. Nobel prizewinner 1902.

Rossetti, Dante Gabriel (1828–82), English poet and painter, son of **Gabriele** (1783–1852), an exiled Italian author who settled in London in 1842. With Millais, Holman Hunt and others he formed the Pre-Raphaelite brotherhood which returned to pre-Renaissance art forms. His model was often his wife, Elizabeth Siddal. His poems include *The Blessed Damozel*. His sister **Christina Georgina** (1830–94) wrote poetry, including *Goblin Market*.

Rossini, Gioacchino Antonio (1792–1868), Italian operatic composer. *See* **Section E**.

Rostand, Edmond (1868–1918), French dramatist, whose *Cyrano de Bergerac* made a sensation in 1898.

Rothenstein, Sir William (1872–1945), English portrait painter. His son, **Sir John** (1901–92), was an art historian and until 1964 director of the Tate Gallery.

Rothschild, Meyer Amschel (1743–1812), German financier, founder of a banking family, b. Frankfurt. His five sons controlled branches at Frankfurt, Vienna, Naples, Paris and London (**Nathan Meyer**, 1777–1836). Nathan's son, **Lionel** (1808–79), was the first Jewish member of the House of Commons.

Roubiliac, Louis François (1695–1762), French sculptor who settled in London and carved a statue of Handel for Vauxhall gardens and one of Newton for Trinity College, Cambridge.

Rouget de Lisle, Claude Joseph (1760–1836), French poet, author of words and music of the *Marseillaise*, revolutionary and national anthem.

Rousseau, Henri (1844–1910), influential French "Sunday" painter, called "Le Douanier" because he was a customs official; self-taught, he was for long unrecognised as an artist of considerable talent and originality; he used the botanical gardens for his jungle scenes.

Rousseau, Jean-Jacques (1712–78), French political philosopher and educationist, b. Geneva, herald of the romantic movement. After a hard childhood he met Mme. de Warens who for some years befriended him. In 1741 he went to Paris where he met Diderot and contributed articles on music and political economy to the *Encyclopédie*. La *Nouvelle Héloïse* appeared in 1760, *Emile*, and *Le Contrat Social* in 1762. *Emile* is a treatise on education according to "natural" principles and *Le Contrat Social*, his main work, sets forth his political theory. It begins, "Man is born free and everywhere he is in chains." Both books offended the authorities and he had to flee, spending some time in England. Later he was able to return to France. His views on government did much to stimulate the movement which culminated in the French Revolution.

Royce, Henry, *see under* **Rolls, Charles Stewart.**

Rubens, Sir Peter Paul (1577–1640), Flemish painter. B. in exile, his family returned to Antwerp in 1587. He studied in Italy and visited Spain. His range was wide, his compositions vigorous, and he was a remarkable colourist. *Peace and War, The Rape of the Sabines,* and *The Felt Hat* are in the National Gallery.

Rubinstein, Anton Grigorovich (1829–94), Russian pianist and composer, who helped to found the conservatoire at St. Petersburg (Leningrad); as did his brother **Nicholas** (1835–81) at Moscow.

Rücker, Sir Arthur (1848–1915), English physicist, who made two magnetic surveys of the British Isles, 1886, and 1891.

Ruisdael, Jacob van (*c.* 1628–82), Dutch painter of landscapes, b. Haarlem. Several of his works are in the National Gallery, including *Coast of Scheveningen* and *Landscape with ruins*.

Runcie, Lord (b. 1921), 102nd Archbishop of Canterbury, 1980–91. Bishop of St. Albans, 1970–80; Historic first official visit to the Vatican, 1989.

Rupert, Prince (1619–82), general, son of Frederick of Bohemia and his wife Elizabeth, daughter of James I of England. He commanded the Royalist cavalry in the English civil war, but was too impetuous for lasting success.

Rushdie, (Ahmed) Salman (b. 1947), controversial author of *The Satanic Verses* (1988 Whitbread Novel Award). Under death sentence (*fatwa*) by Muslim ayatollahs. He has also published *The Moor's Last Sigh* and, in 1994, *East, West* (a book of short stories).

Ruskin, John (1819–1900), English author and art critic, b. London. His *Modern Painters* in 5 volumes was issued over a period of years, the first volume having a strong defence of Turner. He helped to establish the Pre-Raphaelites. Other notable works include *The Seven Lamps of Architecture, The Stones of Venice* and *Praeterita. Unto this Last* develops his views on social problems, and he tried to use his wealth for education and for non-profitmaking enterprises. Ruskin College at Oxford is named after him. In 1848 he married Euphemia Gray, but in 1854 she obtained a decree of nullity and later married Millais.

Russell, 3rd Earl (Bertrand Arthur William Russell) (1872–1970), English philosopher, mathematician, and essayist, celebrated for his work in the field of logic and the theory of knowledge, and remembered for his moral courage, belief in human reason and his championship of liberal ideas. He published more than 60 books, including *The Principles of Mathematics* (1903). *Principia Mathematica* (in collaboration with A. N. Whitehead; 3 vols., 1910–13), *The Problem of Philosophy* (1912), *Mysticism and Logic* (1918), *The Analysis of Mind* (1921), *An Inquiry into Meaning and Truth* (1940), *History of Western Philosophy* (1945), and a number on ethics and social questions. His *Autobiography* (3 vols.) appeared 1967–9. He was the grandson of Lord John Russell and John Stuart Mill was his godfather. Nobel prize for literature 1950; O.M. 1949.

Russell, 1st Earl (John Russell), (1792–1878), English statesman, third son of the 6th Duke of Bedford. He had a large share in carrying the parliamentary reform bill of 1832. He was Whig prime minister 1846–52 and 1865–6. He was also a historian and biographer.

Russell of Killowen, 1st Baron (Charles Russell), (1832–1900) British lawyer, b. Ireland; lord chief justice 1894–1900. He defended Parnell.

Rutherford, 1st Baron (Ernest Rutherford) (1871–1937), British physicist, b. New Zealand, eminent in the field of atomic research. His experiments were conducted at Manchester and Cambridge and attracted young scientists from all over the world. In 1911 he announced his nuclear theory of the atom and in 1918 succeeded in splitting the atom. His work prepared the way for future nuclear research.

Ruysdael, Jacob van. *See* **Ruisdael.**

Ruyter, Michiel Adrianszoon de (1607–76), Dutch admiral who ranks with Nelson. He fought against England and in 1667 caused alarm by sailing up the Medway as far as Rochester and up the Thames as far as Gravesend. He was mortally wounded at Messina.

S

Sachs, Hans (1494–1576), German poet, b. Nuremberg. A shoemaker, he wrote over 6,000 pieces, some dealing with everyday life, many (including *Die Wittenbergische Nachtigall*) inspired by the Reformation.

Sachs, Julius von (1832–97), German botanist, founder of experimental plant physiology. He demonstrated that chlorophyll is formed in chloroplasts only in light.

Sadat, Mohammed Anwar El (1919–81), Egyptian statesman, President of Egypt 1970–81. His visit to Israel in Nov. 1977 was a bold and courageous move which led to the Camp David peace treaty with Israel. Assassinated 1981.

Sádi or **Saadi** (Muslih Addin) (*c.* 1184–1292), Persian poet, b. Shiraz, best known for his *Gulistan* (Flower Garden).

Sainte-Beuve, Charles Augustin (1804–69), French critic, b. Boulogne. He studied medicine, abandoning it for journalism, and after attempting to write poetry, turned to literary criticism. His work reveals the wide range of his intellectual experience and includes *Causeries du lundi* and *Histoire de Port-Royal*.

Saint-Just, Antoine (1767–94), French revolutionary, a follower of Robespierre.

St. Laurent, Louis Stephen (1882–1973), Canadian politician, prime minister 1948–57.

Saint-Saëns, Charles Camille (1835–1921), French composer, for 20 years organist at the Madeleine. His compositions include symphonic and chamber music and the opera *Samson et Dalila*, which was produced by Liszt at Weimar in 1877. *See* Section E.

Saint-Simon, Claude, Comte de (1760–1825), French socialist, who in his *L'Industrie* and *Nouveau christianisme* prepared the way for much later thought.

Saintsbury, George Edward (1845–1933), English critic and literary historian.

Sakharov, Andrei Dimitrievich (1921–89), Soviet nuclear physicist and human rights campaigner. Nobel prizewinner 1975.

Sala, George Augustus (1828–95), English journalist who contributed to *Household Words* and was a notable foreign correspondent.

Saladin (el Melik an-Nasir Salah ed-Din) (1137–93), sultan of Egypt and Syria and founder of a dynasty, who in 1187 defeated the Christians near Tiberias and took Jerusalem. This gave rise to the unsuccessful Third Crusade, in which Richard I of England joined. His great qualities were admired by his opponents, and his administration left many tangible signs in such matters as roads and canals.

Salazar, Antonio d'Oliveira (1889–1970), Portuguese dictator, having first been premier in 1932, a new constitution being adopted in 1933. He gave Portugal stability, but refused to bow to nationalism in Portuguese Africa and India.

Salimbene de Adamo (1221–*c.* 1228), mediaeval chronicler, b. Parma, whose vivid description of life in the 13th cent. is embodied in his *Cronica*.

Salisbury, 3rd Marquess (Robert Arthur Talbot Gascoyne-Cecil (1830–1903), English Conservative statesman, prime minister 1885–6, 1886–92, 1895–1902, mainly remembered for his conduct of foreign affairs during a critical period, culminating in the Boer War.

Samuel, 1st Viscount (Herbert Samuel) (1870–1963), British Liberal statesman of Jewish parentage. He published philosophical works, including *Practical Ethics*.

Sand, George (1804–76), pseudonym of the French writer Aurore Dupin Dudevant. Her publications are extensive and varied, and include the novel *Mauprat*, rural studies, and an autobiography *Histoire de ma vie*. She was associated with Alfred de Musset and Chopin.

Sandow, Eugene (1867–1925), German "strong man" who opened an Institute of Health in London.

Sanger, Frederick (b. 1918), British scientist noted for his work on the chemical structure of the protein insulin. Nobel prizewinner 1958, and 1980. O.M. (1986).

Sankey, Ira David (1840–1908), American evangelist and composer, associated with Moody.

San Martin, José de (1778–1850), South American national leader in securing independence from Spanish rule to his native Argentina, Chile and Peru.

Santayana, George (1863–1952), American philosopher and poet, b. Madrid, of Spanish parentage. He was professor of philosophy at Harvard, 1907–12. His books include *The Sense of Beauty*, *The Life of Reason*, and *The Realms of Being*.

Santos-Dumont, Alberto (1873–1932), Brazilian aeronaut who in 1898 flew a cylindrical balloon with a gasoline engine. In 1909 he built a monoplane.

Sappho of Lesbos (fl. early 6th cent. B.C.), Greek poetess, of whose love poems few remain.

Sardou, Victorien (1831–1908), French dramatist popular in his day. Sarah Bernhardt created famous parts in *Fédora*, *Théodora* and *La Tosca*; *Robespierre* and *Dante* were written for Irving.

Sargent, John Singer (1856–1922), American painter, b. Florence, who worked mainly in England, especially on portraits.

Sargent, Sir Malcolm (1895–1967), popular British conductor, who conducted the Promenade Concerts from 1950 till his death, and succeeded Sir Adrian Boult as conductor of the B.B.C. Symphony Orchestra, 1950–7.

Sartre, Jean-Paul (1905–80), French existentialist philosopher, left-wing intellectual, dramatist, essayist and novelist. His major philosophical work is *L'Etre et le Néant* and his plays include *Les Mouches*, *Huis Clos*, *Crime passionel*, *La Putain respectueuse*, and *Les Séquestrés d'Altona*. He was awarded (though he declined it) the 1964 Nobel prize.

Sassoon, Siegfried (1886–1967), English poet and writer with a hatred of war. He is mainly known for *The Memoirs of a Foxhunting Man*, the first part of the *Memoirs of George Sherston*.

Savonarola, Girolamo (1452–98), Florentine preacher and reformer, a Dominican friar, who denounced vice and corruption not only in society but also in the Church itself, especially attacking Pope Alexander VI. He was excommunicated, imprisoned, and with two of his companions, hanged and burned. His passion for reform made him impatient of opposition and incapable of compromise, yet he was a notable figure and commands the respect of later ages. George Eliot's *Romola* portrays him.

Scarlatti, Alessandro (1659–1725), Italian musician who founded the Neapolitan school of opera. He composed over 100 operas, 200 masses, and over 700 cantatas and oratorios. His son **Domenico** (1685–1757) was a harpsichord virtuoso whose work influenced the evolution of the sonata. The chief years of his life were spent at the Spanish court in Madrid. *See* Section E.

Scheele, Carl Wilhelm (1742–86), Swedish chemist, discoverer of many chemical substances, including oxygen (*c.* 1773—but published in 1777 after the publication of Priestley's studies).

Schiaparelli, Giovanni Virginio (1835–1910), Italian astronomer, noted for having observed certain dark markings on the surface of the planet Mars which he called canals (recent close-range photographs show none).

Schiller, Johann Christoph Friedrich von (1759–1805), German dramatist and poet, b. Marbach in Württemberg, began life as a military surgeon. His play *The Robbers* with a revolutionary theme was successful in 1782 in Mannheim. After a stay at Dresden, where he wrote *Don Carlos*, and at Jena, where he wrote a history of the Thirty Years War, he became the friend of Goethe and removed to Weimar, where he wrote *Wallenstein*, *Mary Stuart*, *The Maid of Orleans* and *William Tell*. He is a leading figure in the European romantic movement.

Schirrmann, Richard (1874–1961), German originator of youth hostels. A schoolmaster, in 1907 he converted his schoolroom during holidays to a dormitory. The Verband für deutsche Jugendherbergen was founded in 1919, and the International Youth Hostels Federation in 1932, with Schirrmann as first president.

Schlegel, Friedrich von (1772–1829), German critic, b. Hanover, prominent among the founders of German ·omanticism, whose revolutionary and germinating ideas influenced early 19th-cent. thought. His brother, **August Wilhelm** (1767–1845), made remarkable translations of Shakespeare (which established Shakespeare in Germany), Dante, Calderón, and Camões.

Schliemann, Heinrich (1822–90), German archaeologist, who conducted excavations at Troy and Mycenae. He has been the subject of numerous biographies mostly based on his own writings which are now viewed with some scepticism.

Schmidt, Helmuth (b. 1918), German social democrat (SPD) statesman; succeeded Brandt as Chancellor of West Germany 1974–83.

Schnabel, Artur (1882–1951), American pianist of Austrian birth, regarded as a leading exponent of Beethoven's pianoforte sonatas.

Schoenberg, Arnold (1874–1951), Austrian composer of Jewish parentage who in 1933 was exiled by the Nazi regime and settled in America, teaching at Boston and Los Angeles. Among his works are the choral orchestral *Gurre-Lieder* and *Pierrot Lunaire*, a cycle of 21 poems for voice and chamber music. *See* Section E.

Schopenhauer, Arthur (1788–1860), German philosopher, b. Danzig, important historically for his pessimism, and his doctrine that will is superior to knowledge. His chief work is *The World as Will and Idea*. He regarded his contemporary Hegel as a charlatan.

Schubert, Franz Peter (1797–1828), Austrian composer, b. Vienna, the son of a schoolmaster, and a contemporary of Beethoven. He wrote not only symphonies, sonatas, string quartets, choral music and masses, but also over 600 songs of unsurpassed lyrical beauty. He might almost be called the creator of the German *Lied* as known today.

Schumann, Robert Alexander (1810–56), composer of the early 19th cent. German romantic school. He wrote much chamber music, four symphonies, a piano concerto, and choral music, but it is his early piano pieces and songs that give constant delight. His wife **Clara** (1819–96) was one of the outstanding pianists of her time.

Schweitzer, Albert (1875–1965), Alsatian medical missionary, theologian, musician and philosopher, b. at Kaysersberg. After publishing learned works, he resigned a promising European career to found at Lambaréné in French Equatorial Africa a hospital to fight leprosy and sleeping sickness and made it a centre of service to Africans. His funds were raised by periodic organ recitals in Europe. His motivation was not patronage but atonement. Nobel peace prize 1952. O.M. 1955.

Scipio, Publius Cornelius (237–183 B.C.), Roman general in the second Punic War, known as Scipio Africanus the elder. **Scipio Africanus the younger** (185–129 B.C.) was an adoptive relative and an implacable opponent of Carthage (destroyed 146).

Scott, Charles Prestwich (1846–1931), English newspaper editor. Under his editorship (1872–1929) the *Manchester Guardian* (now *The Guardian*) became a leading journal.

Scott, Sir George Gilbert (1811–78), English architect in the Gothic revival. He restored many churches and designed the Albert Memorial and the Martyrs' Memorial at Oxford.

Scott, Sir Giles Gilbert (1880–1960), English archi-

tect, grandson of above, designed the Anglican cathedral at Liverpool and planned the new Waterloo Bridge.

Scott, Robert Falcon (1868–1912), English antarctic explorer. He led two expeditions; one 1901–4 which discovered King Edward VII Land; and another 1910–12 which reached the south pole and found the Amundsen records; but while returning the party was overtaken by blizzards and perished 11 miles from their base. *See also* **Antarctic exploration, L7**. His son, **Sir Peter Scott** (1909–89), was an artist, ornithologist and pioneer conservationist.

Scott, Sir Walter (1771–1832), Scottish novelist and poet, b. Edinburgh. He was educated for the law, but came to know and love the Border country, and his interests were literary; and in 1802–3 he issued a collection of ballads, *Border Minstrelsy*. Poems such as *Marmion* and *The Lady of the Lake* followed. His novels appeared anonymously, beginning with *Waverley* in 1814; and continuing with *Guy Mannering*, *The Antiquary*, *Old Mortality*, *Rob Roy*, and *The Heart of Midlothian*. From 1819 he turned also to English history, with *Ivanhoe* and *Kenilworth*. In 1826 he became bankrupt, largely as the fault of his publishing partner.

Scott-Paine, Hubert (1891–1954), pioneer in the design and construction of aircraft and sea-craft.

Scriabin, Alexander (1872–1915), Russian composer and pianist, who relied to some extent on extra-musical factors such as religion, and in *Prometheus* tried to unite music and philosophy.

Seeley, Sir John Robert (1834–95), English historian, author of a life of Christ, *Ecce Homo*.

Segovia, Andrés (1894–1987), Spanish concert-guitarist. He adapted works by Bach, Haydn, Mozart etc. to the guitar.

Selfridge, Harry Gordon (1858–1947), American-born merchant who in 1909 opened a new style of department store in Oxford Street.

Semmelweis, Ignaz Philipp (1818–65), Hungarian obstetrician, a pioneer in the use of antiseptic methods, thus reducing the incidence of puerperal fever.

Seneca, Lucius Annaeus (*c.* 4 B.C.–A.D. 65), Roman stoic philosopher who was a tutor to Nero, but lost favour and was sentenced to take his own life.

Senefelder, Alois (1772–1834), Bavarian inventor of lithography about 1796.

Senna, Ayrton (1960–94), Brazilian motor racing champion. The leading driver of his generation, he won 41 Grands Prix victories and was Formula One World Champion in 1988, 1990 and 1991. He was killed in the 1994 San Marino Grand Prix at Imola.

Severus, Lucius Septimius (146–211), Roman emperor, and a successful general. On a visit to Britain he suppressed a revolt, repaired Hadrian's Wall, and died at York.

Sévigné, Marie de Rabutin-Chantai, Marquise de (1626–96), French woman of letters. Her letters to her daughter Françoise written in an unaffected elegance of style give a moving picture of fashionable French society.

Sgambati, Giovanni (1841–1914), Italian pianist (pupil of Liszt), composer and teacher, who revived interest in classical instrumental music.

Shackleton, Sir Ernest Henry (1874–1922), British explorer, who made four antarctic expeditions; that of 1909 reached within 100 miles of the south pole. He died on his last expedition.

Shaftesbury, 7th Earl of (Anthony Ashley Cooper) (1801–85), English philanthropist largely responsible for legislation reducing the misery of the industrial revolution. He was for 40 years chairman of the Ragged Schools Union.

Shakespeare, William (1564–1616), England's greatest poet and dramatist, b. Stratford-on-Avon. Little is known of his career up to his eighteenth year, when he married Anne Hathaway. He came to London at the height of the English renaissance and soon became connected with the Globe theatre as actor and playwright. Thirty-eight plays comprise the Shakespeare canon. Thirty-six were printed in the First Folio of 1623 (the first collected edition of his dramatic works), of which eighteen had been published during his lifetime in the so-called Quartos. *Henry VI* (3 parts), *The Two Gentlemen of Verona*, *The Comedy of Errors*, *The Taming of the Shrew*, *Richard III*, *Titus Andronicus* and *Love's Labour's Lost* seem to have been the earliest, followed by *Romeo and Juliet*, *A Midsum-*

mer Night's Dream, Richard II and *King John.* Then followed *The Merchant of Venice, Henry IV* (2 parts), *Henry V, Much Ado About Nothing, The Merry Wives of Windsor,* and *As You Like It.* Then came some of his greatest plays: *Julius Caesar, Troilus and Cressida, Hamlet, Twelfth Night, Measure for Measure, All's Well that Ends Well, Othello, King Lear, Macbeth, Timon of Athens, Antony and Cleopatra* and *Coriolanus.* Shakespeare's career ended with *Pericles, Cymbeline, The Winter's Tale, The Tempest, King Henry VIII* and *The Two Noble Kinsmen* (often ascribed to him). In mastery of language, in understanding of character, in dramatic perception, and in skill in the use of ritual he has never been surpassed.

Sharp, Granville (1735–1813), English abolitionist of slavery. Founder of colony of Sierra Leone.

Shastri, Shri Lal Bahadur (1904–66), Indian politician who became prime minister of India after the death of Nehru in 1964. He died of a heart attack at the end of the Soviet-sponsored Tashkent talks.

Shaw, George Bernard (1856–1950), Irish dramatist who conquered England by his wit and exposure of hypocrisy, cant, and national weaknesses, and whose individual opinions found expression in musical criticism, socialist pamphlets and plays. His plays include *Man and Superman, Heartbreak House, Back to Methuselah, Saint Joan, The Apple Cart,* and *Buoyant Billions,* and most have important prefaces. In 1884 he joined the newly-born Fabian Society. Nobel prizewinner 1925.

Shelley, Percy Bysshe (1792–1822), English poet, b. Horsham. He was a master of language and of literary form, and a passionate advocate of freedom and of new thought. Sent down from Oxford for his pamphlet *The Necessity of Atheism,* he came under the influence of William Godwin; and, after his first marriage came to an unhappy end, married the latter's daughter, Mary Wollstonecraft, herself a writer. In the same year began his friendship with Byron. His works include *The Revolt of Islam, The Masque of Anarchy* (an indictment of Castlereagh), *The Cenci* (a play on evil), and *Prometheus Unbound,* besides lyrics such as *To a Skylark* and *Ode to the West Wind.* He was accidentally drowned while sailing near Spezzia.

Sheppard, Hugh Richard (Dick) (1880–1937), Anglican divine and pacifist. He made St. Martin-in-the-Fields a centre of social service and also founded the Peace Pledge Union.

Sheraton, Thomas (1751–1806), English cabinetmaker, b. Stockton, whose *Cabinetmaker's Book* promoted neo-classical designs.

Sheridan, Richard Brinsley (1751–1816), British dramatist, b. Dublin. He was a brilliant writer of comedies, especially *The Rivals, The Duenna, The School for Scandal,* and *The Critic.* He acquired and rebuilt Drury Lane theatre, which reopened in 1794, but was burnt down in 1809; and this, with his lack of business sense, brought him to poverty, in spite of his friends' efforts to help him. He was also in parliament.

Sherman, William Tecumseh (1820–91), American general, who served especially in the Civil War. He took part in the battles of Bull Run and Shiloh, was appointed in 1864 to the command of the southwest, and with 65,000 men marched across Georgia to the sea. In 1865 he accepted Johnston's surrender.

Sherrington, Sir Charles Scott (1857–1952), English scientist, an authority on the physiology of the nervous system. His research led to advances in brain surgery. His principal work is *Integration Action of the Nervous System* (1906). Shared with E. D. Adrian the 1932 Nobel prize.

Shirley, James (1596–1666), English dramatist. His tragedies include *The Traitor,* and his comedies *Hyde Park.* His death was hastened by the Great Fire.

Sholokhov, Mikhail Aleksandrovich (1905–84), Russian novelist, author of *And Quiet Flows the Don.* Nobel prizewinner 1965.

Shostakovich, Dimitri (1906–75), Russian composer whose music is complex, profound, and deeply significant of the Soviet age in which he lived. His works include operas, ballets, symphonies, chamber music, and music for films. Hero of Soviet Labour 1966. *See* Section E.

Sibelius, Jean (1865–1957), Finnish composer imbued with national feeling. His works include seven symphonies, a violin concerto, and several tone poems, notably *Finlandia,* and some based on the Finnish poem *Kalevala.* *See* Section E.

Sickert, Walter Richard (1860–1942), British artist, b. Munich. He was influenced by Degas, and has himself influenced later painters. His *Ennui* is in the Tate Gallery.

Siddons, Sarah (1755–1831), English actress especially in tragic parts. She was daughter of the manager Roger Kemble and her reputation was almost unbounded.

Sidgwick, Henry (1838–1900), English philosopher who wrote *Methods of Ethics,* and who also promoted women's education, with the foundation of Newnham and Girton colleges at Cambridge.

Sidney, Sir Philip (1554–86), English poet and writer, best remembered for his *Arcadia, Apologie for Poetrie,* and *Astrophel and Stella,* all published after his death. He was killed at the battle of Zutphen, where he passed a cup of water to another, saying "Thy necessity is greater than mine."

Siemens, Sir William (1823–83), German-born electrical engineer who settled in England and constructed many overland and submarine telegraphs. He was brother of **Werner von Siemens,** founder of the firm of Siemens-Halske.

Sienkiewicz, Henryk (1846–1916), Polish novelist and short-story writer; best known of his historical novels is *Quo Vadis?* Nobel prize, 1905.

Sikorski, Vladislav (1881–1943), Polish general and statesman, prime minister of the Polish government in exile (1939) and commander-in-chief of the Polish forces. Killed in an aircraft accident at Gibraltar.

Simpson, Sir James Young (1811–70), Scottish obstetrician who initiated the use of chloroform in childbirth.

Sinclair, Upton (1878–1968), American novelist whose documentary novel *The Jungle* on the Chicago slaughter yards caused a sensation in 1906.

Singer, Isaac Merritt (1811–75), American mechanical engineer who improved early forms of the sewing-machine and patented a single-thread and chain-stitch machine.

Sisley, Alfred (1839–99), French impressionist painter of English origin, who painted some enchanting landscapes, such as *Meadows in Spring* in the Tate Gallery. He was influenced by Corot and Manet.

Sitwell, Edith (1887–1964), English poet, a great experimenter in verse forms. *Gold Coast Customs, Façade* (set to music by William Walton) and *Still Falls the Rain* are probably best known. She had two brothers, **Osbert** (1892–1969) and **Sacheverell** (1897–1988), both poets and critics.

Slim, 1st Viscount (William Slim) (1891–1970), British soldier who rose from private to field-marshal. He commanded the 14th Army in Burma, was chief of the Imperial General Staff 1948–52, and governor-general of Australia 1953–60.

Sloane, Sir Hans (1660–1753), British collector, b. Ireland. He practised in London as a physician. His library of 50,000 volumes and his collection of MSS. and botanical specimens were offered under his will to the nation and formed the beginning of the British Museum.

Slovo, Joe (1926–95), Lithuanian-born white champion of black nationalism in South Africa. Chairman of the South African Communist Party and former Chief of Staff of the armed wing of the African National Congress.

Slowacki, Julius (1809–49), Polish romantic poet, a revolutionary, he lived in exile in Paris. His work includes the poetic dramas *Kordian, Balladyna* and *Lilli Weneda,* written in the style of Shakespeare; and the unfinished poem *King Spirit* which reveals his later mystical tendencies.

Smeaton, John (1724–92), English engineer; he rebuilt Eddystone lighthouse (1756–59), improved Newcomen's steam-engine, and did important work on bridges, harbours, and canals. He also invented an improved blowing apparatus for iron-smelting.

Smetana, Bedřich (1824–84), Czech composer, creator of a national style. He was principal conductor of the Prague National Theatre, for which he wrote most of his operas, including *The Bartered Bride* and *The Kiss.* Best known of his other compositions are the cycle of symphonic poems *My Country* and the string quartets *From My Life.* He became totally deaf in 1874, suffered a mental breakdown, and died in an asylum. *See* **Section E.**

Smiles, Samuel (1812–1904), Scottish writer, b. Haddington, in early life a medical practitioner, remembered for *Self Help* (1859), and his biographies of engineers of the industrial revolution.

Smith, Adam (1723–90), Scottish economist, b. Kirkcaldy. In Edinburgh he published *Moral Sentiments*. Later he moved to London, and his *Wealth of Nations* (1776) is the first serious work in political economy.

Smith, Sir Grafton Eliot (1871–1937), Australian anatomist who did research on the structure of the mammalian brain. His works include *The Evolution of Man.*

Smith, John (1580–1631), English adventurer who in 1605 went on a colonising expedition to Virginia and was saved from death by the Red Indian Pocahontas.

Smith, John (1938–94), leader of the Labour Party, 1992–94. His much-respected, modernising leadership was ended by his untimely death. He is buried on the island of Iona. His widow, Elizabeth, was created a Life Peer in the 1995 New Year Honours.

Smith, Joseph (1805–44), American founder of the Mormons. He claimed that the *Book of Mormon* was revealed to him. In 1838 feeling against the Mormons culminated in a rising and Smith was murdered. He was succeeded by Brigham Young. *See* **Mormonism, Section J.**

Smith, Sydney (1771–1845), Anglican divine and journalist, who founded the *Edinburgh Review* and supported Catholic emancipation.

Smith, William (1760–1839), English surveyor and canal-maker, the first to map the rock strata of England and to identify the fossils peculiar to each layer.

Smith, Sir William Alexander (1854–1914), Scottish founder of the Boys' Brigade (1883), the oldest national organisation for boys in Britain.

Smith, William Robertson (1846–94), Scottish biblical scholar whose "Bible" contribution to the 9th edition of *The Encyclopaedia Britannica* resulted in an unsuccessful prosecution for heresy.

Smollett, Tobias George (1721–71), Scottish novelist whose work is characterised by satire and coarse humour. His main novels are *Roderick Random*, *Peregrine Pickle*, and *Humphrey Clinker*.

Smuts, Jan Christian (1870–1950), South African statesman and soldier. B. in Cape Colony, during the Boer War he fought on the Boer side. He was premier of the Union 1919–24, 1939–48, and worked for cooperation within the Commonwealth and in the world, but his party was defeated in 1948 by Malan's Nationalists.

Smyth, Ethel Mary (1858–1944), English composer and suffragette. Her main works are operas (*The Wreckers* and *The Boatswain's Mate*) and a *Mass in D.* She studied at the Leipzig Conservatory.

Snow, Baron (Charles Percy Snow) (1905–80), English physicist and novelist, author of the essay *The Two Cultures and the Scientific Revolution*, and a sequence of novels *Strangers and Brothers* (11 vols.).

Snyders, Frans (1597–1657), Flemish still-life and animal painter who studied under Breughel.

Soane, Sir John (1753–1837), English architect who designed the Bank of England. He left the nation his house and library in Lincoln's Inn Fields (Soane Museum).

Sobers, Sir Garfield (b. 1936), West Indies and Nottinghamshire cricketer who ranks as one of the greatest all-rounders. Knighted 1975.

Socinus or **Sozzini Laelius** (1525–62), Italian founder of the sect of Socinians, with his nephew **Faustus** (1539–1604). Their teachings resemble those of Unitarians.

Socrates (470–399 B.C.), Greek philosopher and intellectual leader, was the son of a sculptor of Athens. He distinguished himself in three campaigns (Potidaea, Delium, and Amphipolis). Returning to Athens, he devoted himself to study and intellectual enquiry, attracting many followers; through these, especially Xenophon and Plato, we know of his teachings, for he wrote nothing. In 399 B.C. he was charged with impiety and with corrupting the young, found guilty, and accordingly died by drinking hemlock; *see* Plato's *Apology*, *Crito*, and *Phaedo.*

Soddy, Frederick (1877–1956), English chemist, who in Glasgow about 1912 laid the foundation of the isotope theory. Nobel prizewinner 1921.

Solon (638–558 B.C.), Athenian lawgiver, who in a time of economic distress cancelled outstanding debts, and introduced some democratic changes.

Solzhenitsyn, Alexander Isayevich (b. 1918), Russian novelist, b. Rostov-on-Don; author of *One Day in the Life of Ivan Denisovich*, a documentary novel depicting life in one of Stalin's prison camps where he spent many years of his life. He was expelled from the Soviet Writers' Union in 1969, and from his country in 1974, returning in 1994. Nobel prize 1970.

Somerset, Duke of (Edward Seymour) (1506–52), lord protector of England in the time of the young Edward VI, but he fell from power and was executed.

Sophocles (495–406 B.C.), Athenian dramatist, who was awarded the prize over Aeschylus in 468. Of over a hundred plays of his, the only extant ones are *Oedipus the King*, *Oedipus at Colonus*, *Antigone*, *Electra*, *Trachiniae*, *Ajax*, *Philoctetes*.

Sopwith, Sir Thomas (1888–1989), British designer of 'Sopwith Camel' biplane. Chairman, Hawker Siddeley Group after 1935.

Sorel, Georges (1847–1922), French advocate of revolutionary syndicalism, author of *Reflections on Violence* (1905). The irrational aspects of his philosophy (derived from Bergson) appealed to Mussolini and the Fascists.

Soult, Nicolas Jean de Dieu (1769–1851), French general who fought under Napoleon in Switzerland and Italy, at Austerlitz, and in Spain.

Sousa, John Philip (1854–1932), American bandmaster and composer of some stirring marches.

Southey, Robert (1774–1843), English poet and historian. In 1803 he settled near Coleridge at Keswick, and in 1813 became poet laureate. His best work was in prose: histories of Brazil and of the Peninsular War; lives of Nelson, Wesley, *etc.*

Southwell, Robert (1561–95), English poet and Jesuit martyr, beatified 1920. His poems include *The Burning Babe.*

Spaak, Paul Henri (1899–1972), Belgian statesman, first president of the U.N. General Assembly in 1946. Secretary-general of NATO, 1957–61.

Spartacus (d. 71 B.C.), Thracian rebel. A Roman slave and gladiator in Capua, he escaped and headed a slave insurrection, routing several Roman armies, but was defeated and killed by Crassus.

Speke, John Hanning (1827–64), British explorer. In 1858 he discovered the Victoria Nyanza; and in 1860 with J. A. Grant traced the Nile flowing out of it.

Spence, Sir Basil Urwin (1907–76), Scottish architect, mainly known for the new Coventry cathedral, for Hampstead civic centre and for university architecture. O.M. 1962.

Spencer, Herbert (1820–1903), English philosopher. B. Derby, he was at first a civil engineer, then a journalist (sub-editor of the *Economist*), when he wrote *Social Statics.* He coined the phrase (1852) "the survival of the fittest" and his *Principles of Psychology* (1855), published four years before Darwin's *Origin of Species*, expounded doctrines of evolution. Author of the ten-volume *Synthetic Philosophy.*

Spencer, Sir Stanley (1891–1959), English artist of visionary power. His two pictures of the *Resurrection* are in the Tate Gallery. He also painted Cookham regatta.

Spengler, Oswald (1880–1936), German historicist who held that every culture is destined to a waxing and waning life cycle and that the West European culture was entering its period of decline. His principal work is *The Decline of the West.* His views prepared the way for national socialism.

Spenser, Edmund (1552–99), English poet, b. London and educated at Cambridge. His *Shepheards Calendar* appeared in 1579. In 1580 he went to Ireland as the lord deputy's secretary, and later acquired Kilcolman castle, where he wrote most of his main work, *The Faerie Queene.* His castle was burnt in an insurrection in 1598, when he returned to London. He is called "the poet's poet."

Spinoza, Baruch (1632–77), Dutch philosopher, b. Amsterdam, whose parents came to Holland from Portugal to escape the Inquisition. An independent thinker, his criticism of the Scriptures led to his being excommunicated from the synagogue. He supported himself by grinding and polishing lenses. He owed much to Descartes but was mainly concerned with religion and virtue. His philosophical theories are set out in the *Ethics* which was published posthumously. In the light of modern science his metaphysic cannot be accepted but his moral teaching has enduring validity.

Spofforth, Reginald (1770–1827), English writer of glees, including *Hail, Smiling Morn.*

Spurgeon, Charles Haddon (1834–92), English Baptist who preached at the vast Metropolitan Tabernacle, London, from 1861 (burnt down 1898).

Staël, Anne Louise, Baronne de Staël-Holstein (1766–1817), French writer. Daughter of the finance minister, Necker, she married the Swedish ambassador, and kept a salon. Her *Lettres sur Rousseau* appeared in 1788. After the revolution she lived partly abroad, partly in France, and after a visit to Italy wrote her novel *Corinne* (1807).

Stalin (Joseph Vissarionovich Djugashvili) (1879–1953), Soviet statesman who for nearly 30 years was leader of the Russian people. He originally studied at Tiflis for the priesthood, but became an active revolutionary and took part in the civil war after 1917. After Lenin's death, he ousted Trotsky and became the outstanding figure. He modernised agriculture on socialist lines by ruthless means, and his series of five-year plans from 1929 made Russia an industrial power. On the German invasion in 1941 he assumed military leadership; and later attended Allied war conferences. After his death some of his methods and the "personality cult" were denounced by Khrushchev, and this had far-reaching political consequences in other Communist countries.

Stanford, Sir Charles Villiers (1852–1924), Irish composer of instrumental, choral, operatic, and other music.

Stanley, Sir Henry Morton (1841–1904), British explorer, b. Denbigh. He fought for the Confederates in the American Civil War. He then became a correspondent for the *New York Herald*, was commissioned to find Livingstone, and did so in 1871 at Ujiji, and with him explored Lake Tanganyika. In 1879 he founded the Congo Free State under the Belgian king. His works include *Through the Dark Continent* and an *Autobiography.*

Stark, Freya Madeline (1893–1993), British writer and explorer of the Arab world.

Steel, Sir David (b. 1938), Liberal Democrat politician. Leader, Liberal Party, 1976–88. Acting Joint Leader, Social and Liberal Democrats, 1988.

Steele, Sir Richard (1672–1729), British essayist, b. Dublin. He founded the *Tatler* (1709–11), to which Addison also contributed, and later the *Spectator* (1711–12) and the *Guardian* (1713).

Steen, Jan (1626–79), Dutch genre painter, b. Leiden, son of a brewer. *The Music Lesson* and *Skittle Alley* are in the National Gallery, the *Lute Player* in the Wallace collection.

Steer, Philip Wilson (1860–1942), English painter, especially of landscapes and of portraits.

Stefansson, Vilhjalmur (1879–1962), Canadian arctic explorer of Icelandic parentage; his publications include *Unsolved Mysteries of the Arctic.*

Stein, Sir Aurel (1862–1943), British archaeologist, b. Budapest. He held archaeological posts under the Indian government and explored Chinese Turkestan.

Stendhal, pseudonym of Marie Henri Beyle (1783–1842), French novelist, b. Grenoble. He was with Napoleon's army in the Russian campaign of 1812, spent several years in Italy, and after the revolution of 1830 was appointed consul at Trieste, and afterwards at Civitavecchia. In his plots he recreates historical and social events with imaginative realism and delineates character with searching psychological insight. His main works are *Le Rouge et le Noir*, and *La Chartreuse de Parme.*

Stephen (1105–54), usurped the crown of England from Henry I's daughter in 1135; and, after anarchy, retained it till his death.

Stephen, Sir Leslie (1832–1904), English writer, critic, and biographer. He edited the *Cornhill Magazine* (1871–82), and the *Dictionary of National Biography* (1882–91), and was the father of Virginia Woolf.

Stephenson, George (1781–1848), English engineer; a locomotive designer, b. at Wylam near Newcastle, a colliery fireman's son. As engine-wright at Killingworth colliery he made his first locomotive in 1814 to haul coal from mines. He and his son Robert built the *Locomotion* for the Stockton and Darlington Railway (1825), the first locomotive for a public railway. His *Rocket* at 30 miles an hour won the prize of £500 in 1829 offered by the Liverpool and Manchester Railway. He also discovered the principle on which the miners' safety lamp was based. First president of the Institution of Mechanical Engineers.

Stephenson, Robert (1803–59), English engineer, son of the above, engineered railway lines in England and abroad, and built many bridges including the Menai and Conway tubular bridges.

Sterne, Laurence (1713–68), English novelist and humorist. His main works are *Tristram Shandy* and *A Sentimental Journey.* He led a wandering and unconventional life, dying in poverty. His work helped to develop the novel.

Stevenson, Adlai (1900–65), American politician, an efficient governor of Illinois, 1949–53; ambassador to the U.N., 1960–5, and unsuccessful presidential challenger to Eisenhower 1952 and 1956.

Stevenson, Robert (1772–1850), Scottish engineer and builder of lighthouses, who invented "intermittent" and "flashing" lights.

Stevenson, Robert Louis (1850–94), Scottish author, b. Edinburgh. He suffered from ill-health and eventually settled in Samoa. His main works are *Travels with a Donkey, Treasure Island, Kidnapped, Dr. Jekyll and Mr. Hyde,* and *The Master of Ballantrae.*

Stinnes, Hugo (1870–1924), German industrialist who built up a huge coalmining, iron and steel, and transport business, and later entered politics.

Stockton, Earl of. See Macmillan, Harold

Stoker, Bram (Abraham Stoker) (1847–1912), Irish author of the horror story *Dracula* and *Personal Reminiscences of Henry Irving.*

Stokes, Sir George Gabriel (1819–1903), Irish mathematician and physicist to whom is due the modern theory of viscous fluids and the discovery that rays beyond the violet end of the spectrum (the ultra-violet rays) produce fluorescence in certain substances.

Stopes, Marie Carmichael (1880–1958), English pioneer advocate of birth control. Her *Married Love* appeared in 1918, and she pioneered birth control clinics.

Stowe, Harriet Beecher (1811–96), American author of *Uncle Tom's Cabin* (1852), written to expose slavery.

Strachey, John St. Loe (1901–63), English Labour politician and writer. He held office under Attlee, 1945–51.

Stradivari, Antonio (1644–1737), Italian maker of violins, b. Cremona, first in his art.

Strafford, 1st Earl of (Thomas Wentworth) (1593–1641), English statesman. He supported Charles I with a "thorough" policy, both as president of the north and as lord deputy in Ireland, where he introduced flax. His efficiency made him a special target when parliament met, and he was impeached and executed.

Strauss, David Friedrich (1808–74), German theologian, whose *Life of Jesus* attempted to prove that the gospels are based on myths.

Strauss, family of Viennese musicians. **Johann Strauss** (1804–49), the elder, was a composer of dance music, who with Joseph Lanner established the Viennese waltz tradition. His son, **Johann Strauss** (1825–99), the younger, although not so good a violinist or conductor as his father, was the composer of over 400 waltzes, which include *The Blue Danube* and *Tales from the Vienna Woods.* Two of his brothers, **Josef Strauss** (1827–70) and **Eduard Strauss** (1835–1916) were also composers and conductors.

Strauss, Richard (1864–1949), German composer and conductor, the son of a horn player in the opera orchestra at Munich. He succeeded von Bülow as court musical director at Meiningen. His works include the operas *Salome, Elektra,* and *Der Rosenkavalier,* the symphonic poems *Don Juan, Till Eulenspiegel,* and *Don Quixote,* and many songs. See **Section E.**

Stravinsky, Igor (1882–1971), Russian composer and conductor, pupil of Rimsky-Korsakov. His ballets. *The Fire Bird* (1910). *Petrushka*

(1911), representative of his early romantic style, and the revolutionary *The Rite of Spring*, which caused a furore in 1913, were written for the ballet impresario Diaghilev. He adopted a neo-classical style in later works, for example, in the ballets *Pulcinella* and *Apollo Musagetes* and the opera-oratorio *Oedipus Rex*. He brought new vigour and freedom to rhythm and younger composers have been much influenced by his music. He became a French citizen in 1934 and a U.S. citizen in 1945. See **Section E**.

Strindberg, Johan August (1840–1912), Swedish writer of intense creative energy. His work is subjective and reflects his personal conflicts. He produced some 55 plays as well as novels, stories, poems, and critical essays. *Lucky Peter, Gustav Adolf, Till Damascus, The Father, Miss Julie* are some of his plays.

Suckling, Sir John (1609–42), English poet, author of *Why so pale and wan?* He invented cribbage.

Sudermann, Hermann (1857–1928), German writer of plays and novels, including *Frau Sorge* (translated as Dame Care).

Sulaiman the Magnificent (1494–1566), sultan of Turkey, conqueror, and patron of art and learning, who dominated the eastern Mediterranean but failed to capture Malta.

Sulla (138–78 B.C.) Roman general, he supported the oligarchy of the Senate against the demagogues Marius (Julius Caesar's uncle) and Cinna and established himself dictator in 82 B.C.

Sullivan, Sir Arthur Seymour (1842–1900), Irish composer, mainly known for the music he wrote for light operas with W. S. Gilbert as librettist, especially *The Pirates of Penzance, Patience, The Mikado, The Yeomen of the Guard* and *The Gondoliers*. He also wrote sacred music which was popular at the time. He and George Grove discovered Schubert's lost *Rosamunde* music.

Sully, Maximilien de Béthune, Duc de (1560–1641), French statesman, finance minister to Henry IV.

Summerson, Sir John (1904–92), the most distinguished British architectural historian of his generation. Recipient of Royal Gold Medal for Architecture (1976). Most often associated with John Nash and the Georgian period. Longest-serving Curator of Sir John Soane's Museum.

Sun Yat Sen (1867–1925), Chinese revolutionary, idealist and humanitarian. He graduated in medicine in Hong Kong, but after a rising failed in 1895 he lived abroad, planning further attempts, which succeeded in 1911 when the Manchus were ousted and he became president.

Sutherland, Graham Vivian (1903–80), British artist. He painted the 80th birthday portrait of Winston Churchill for parliament, and designed the tapestry for Coventry cathedral. O.M. 1960.

Suu Kyi, Aung San (b. *c.* 1945), Opposition leader in Myanmar (Burma). Nobel Peace Prize, 1991.

Swan, Sir Joseph Wilson (1829–1914), British scientist who shares with Edison the invention of the incandescent electric lamp.

Swedenborg, Emanuel (1689–1772), Swedish author of *Arcana Coelestia, The Apocalypse Revealed, Four Preliminary Doctrines*, and *The True Christian Religion*. He claimed that his soul had been permitted to travel into hell, purgatory, and heaven. His works became the scriptures of his followers, the Swedenborgians.

Sweelinck, Jan Pieterszoon (1562–1621), Dutch organist and composer of sacred music. In his fugues he made independent use of the pedals, and prepared the way for Bach. See **Section E**.

Swift, Jonathan (1667–1745), English satirist, b. Dublin of English parents. He crossed to England in 1688 to become secretary to Sir William Temple, and took Anglican orders, but did not obtain promotion. His *Tale of a Tub* and *The Battle of the Books* appeared in 1704. At first active in Whig politics, he became Tory in 1710, writing powerful tracts such as *Conduct of the Allies* (1711). In 1714 he retired to Ireland as Dean of St. Patrick's. His devoted women friends followed him—Hester Johnson (d. 1728), the Stella of his *Journal*, and Esther Vanhomrigh (d. 1723), the Vanessa of his poetry. Here he wrote his best work, including *Gulliver's Travels* (1726) and *The Drapier's Letters*.

Swinburne, Algernon Charles (1837–1909), English poet and critic. He first won attention with a play, *Atalanta in Calydon*, in 1865, followed by *Poems and Ballads*. Later followed *Songs before Sunrise, Bothwell*, and *Mary Stuart*.

Swithin, St. (d. 862), English saint, bishop of Winchester. Violent rain for 40 days fell in 971 when his body was to be removed to the new cathedral; hence the superstition as to rain on 15 July.

Symonds, John Addington (1840–93), English author who wrote on the Italian Renaissance.

Synge, John Millington (1871–1909), Irish poet and playwright, author of *Riders to the Sea* and *The Playboy of the Western World*.

T

Tacitus, Gaius Cornelius (*c.* 55–120), Roman historian. His chief works are a life of his father-in-law Agricola, and his *Histories* and *Annals*.

Tagore, Rabindranath (1861–1941), Indian poet and philosopher who tried to blend east and west. His works include the play *Chitra*. Nobel prize 1913 (first Asian recipient).

Talbot, William Henry Fox (1800–77), English pioneer of photography which he developed independently of Daguerre. He also deciphered the cuneiform inscriptions at Nineveh.

Talleyrand-Périgord, Charles Maurice de (1754–1838), French politician and diplomat, led a mission to England in 1792 and was foreign minister from 1797 until 1807. He represented France at the Congress of Vienna.

Tallis, Thomas (*c.* 1510–85), English musician, with Byrd joint organist to the chapel royal under Elizabeth. He composed some of the finest of our church music.

Tamerlane (Timur the Lame) (1336–1405), Mongol conqueror. Ruler of Samarkand, he conquered Iran, Transcaucasia, Iraq, Armenia, and Georgia, and invaded India and Syria. He defeated the Turks at Angora, but died marching towards China. A ruthless conqueror, he was also a patron of literature and the arts. The line of rulers descended from him are the Timurids. He is the subject of a play by Marlowe.

Tarquinius: two kings of Rome came from this Etruscan family; **Lucius the Elder** (d. 578 B.C.); and **Lucius Superbus**, or the proud, (d. 510 B.C.) whose tyranny provoked a successful rising and brought an end to the monarchy.

Tartini, Giuseppe (1692–1770), Italian violinist, who wrote *Trillo del Diavolo*. He discovered the "third sound" resulting from two notes sounded together, a scientific explanation of which was later given by Helmholtz.

Tasman, Abel Janszoon (1603–59), Dutch navigator despatched by Van Diemen. He discovered Tasmania or Van Diemen's Land, and New Zealand, in 1642.

Tasso, Torquato (1544–95), Italian epic poet, b. Sorrento, author of *Gerusalemme Liberata*. He also wrote plays, *Aminta* and *Torrismondo*.

Tawney, Richard Henry (1880–1962), British historian, b. Calcutta, pioneer of adult education, and leader of socialist thought—the first critic of the affluent society. His works include *The Acquisitive Society, Equality, Religion and the Rise of Capitalism*.

Taylor, Alan John Percivale (1906–90), Foremost English historian. Broadcaster, lecturer and radical. Author of such works as *English History, 1914–45*. The best-known (and by many the best-loved) historian of his generation.

Taylor, Sir Geoffrey Ingram (1886–1975), British scientist, noted for his work on aerodynamics, hydrodynamics, *etc.* O.M. 1969.

Taylor, Jeremy (1613–67), English divine, b. Cambridge, author of many religious works, of which the chief are *Holy Living* and *Holy Dying*.

Tchaikovsky, Peter Ilyich (1840–93), Russian composer. His music is melodious and emotional and he excelled in several branches of composition. Among his works are the operas *Eugene Onegin* and *The Queen of Spades* (both from stories by Pushkin), symphonies, including the *Little Russian* and the *Pathétique*, ballets, including *Swan Lake, The Sleeping Beauty*, and *The Nutcracker*, the fantasies *Romeo and Juliet*, and *Francesca da Rimini*, the piano concerto in B flat minor, the violin concerto in D, and numerous songs. See **Section E**.

Tedder, 1st Baron (Arthur William Tedder) (1890–1967), British air marshal. From 1940 he reorganised the Middle East Air Force and later became deputy supreme commander under Eisenhower for the invasion of Europe.

Teilhard de Chardin, Pierre (1881–1955), French palæontologist and religious philosopher. He went on palæontological expeditions in Asia, but his research did not conform to Jesuit orthodoxy, and his main works were published posthumously, *The Phenomenon of Man* and *Le Milieu Divin*.

Telemann, Georg Philipp (1681–1767), German composer, b. Magdeburg. His vitality and originality of form are appreciated today after a long period of neglect. His works include church music, 46 passions and over 40 operas, oratorios *etc*.

Telford, Thomas (1757–1834), Scottish engineer, originally a stonemason. He built bridges (two over the Severn and the Menai suspension bridge), canals (the Ellesmere and Caledonian canals), roads, and docks.

Tell, William, legendary Swiss patriot, reputedly required by the Austrian governor Gessler to shoot an apple from his son's head, and the subject of a play by Schiller. The story is late, but the Swiss confederation did first arise in the 14th cent. with Schwyz, Uri, and Unterwalden.

Temple, Frederick (1821–1902), English divine. He was headmaster of Rugby, 1857–69, and archbishop of Canterbury, 1897–1902.

Temple, William (1881–1944), English ecclesiastic, son of above, was a leading moral force in social matters and a worker for ecumenism. He was headmaster of Repton, 1910–14, and became archbishop of Canterbury in 1942.

Temple, Sir William (1628–99), English diplomat and writer, was instrumental in bringing about the marriage of Princess Mary with William of Orange. Swift was his secretary.

Templewood, 1st Viscount (Samuel John Gurney Hoare) (1880–1959), British Conservative politician. He piloted the India Act through the Commons while secretary for India, 1931–5; and as foreign secretary he negotiated an abortive pact with Laval.

Teniers, David, the elder (1582–1649), and the **younger** (1610–94), Flemish painters of rural life and landscape. The elder lived at Antwerp and the younger at Brussels.

Tenniel, Sir John (1820–1914), English artist, principal cartoonist for *Punch* 1864–1901 and illustrator of Lewis Carroll's *Alice* books.

Tennyson, 1st Baron (Alfred Tennyson) (1809–92), English poet-laureate, b. Somersby, Lincs. A master of language, his publications extended over 60 years, mirroring much of his age. *In Memoriam* reflects his grief for his friend Arthur Hallam. Apart from his lyrics, his longer works include *The Princess, Maud, Idylls of the King*, and *Enoch Arden*.

Terence, Publius Terentius Afer (*c.* 184–159 B.C.), a Latin poet and dramatist, an African (Berber), who rose from the position of a slave.

Teresa, St. (1515–82), influential Spanish religious reformer and writer, b. Avila, a woman of boundless energy and spiritual strength. She entered the Carmelite order about 1534, established a reformed order in 1562 (St. Joseph's, Avila), and also founded, with the help of St. John of the Cross, houses for friars. Her writings which rank high in mystical literature include *The Way of Perfection* and *The Interior Castle*.

Terry, Ellen Alice (Mrs. James Carew) (1848–1928), English actress, especially in Shakespearean parts with Sir Henry Irving, and in the plays of her friend Bernard Shaw.

Tertullian Quintus (*c.* 160–220), Carthaginian theologian whose works, especially *Apologeticum*, have profoundly influenced Christian thought.

Tesla, Nikolai (1856–1943), Yugoslav physicist and inventor; went to America 1883; pioneer in high-tension electricity.

Tettrazzini, Luisa (1871–1940), Italian soprano, especially successful in *Lucia di Lammermoor*.

Tetzel, John (*c.* 1465–1519), German Dominican preacher, whose sale of indulgences for St. Peter's building fund provoked Luther.

Thackeray, William Makepeace (1811–63), English novelist, b. Calcutta, author of *Vanity Fair, Pendennis, Esmond, The Newcomes, The Virginians, Philip*, and *Lovel the Widower*. He edited the *Cornhill Magazine* from the first number in 1860, his most notable contributions

being *Roundabout Papers*. He also wrote *Yellowplush Papers* and *The Book of Snobs* and lectured on *The English Humorists* and *The Four Georges*.

Thales of Miletus (*c.* 624–565 B.C.), earliest of the Greek scientists, he created a sensation by his prediction of an eclipse of the sun, which was visible at Miletus in 585 B.C. He looked upon water as the basis of all material things, and in his mathematical work was the first to enunciate natural laws. *See* **God and Man (Section J)**.

Thant, Sithu U (1909–74), Burmese diplomat; secretary-general of the U.N. 1962–1972.

Thatcher, Baroness (Margaret Hilda Thatcher) (b. 1925), leader of the Conservative Party 1975–90; prime minister, 1979–90; first woman to lead a western democracy; secured landslide victory, June 1983; M.P. (Finchley), 1959–92. Historic third successive election victory, June 1987. On 3 Jan 1988 became longest serving P.M. since Asquith. By 1990 she faced increasing unpopularity, reflected in a challenge to her leadership. Deserted by many in her party, she resigned on 28 November 1990. Created Baroness Thatcher of Kesteven, 1992. Order of the Garter (1995).

Themistocles (*c.* 523–458 B.C.), Athenian soldier and statesman. He fortified the harbour of Piraeus and created a navy, defeating the Persians at Salamis in 480 B.C. He prepared the way for later greatness, but fell from power and died in exile.

Theocritus (*c.* 310–250 B.C.), Greek poet, especially of pastoral subjects. His short poems came to be called *Idylls*.

Theodoric the Great (455–526), King of the East Goths, who conquered Italy. Himself an Arian, he practised toleration, and his long reign was peaceful and prosperous.

Theodosius the Great (346–95), Roman emperor of the East (the Empire being divided in 364). He was baptised as a Trinitarian, issuing edicts against the Arians, and after a judicial massacre at Thessalonica he did penance to (St.) Ambrose.

Theophrastus (*c.* 372–287 B.C.), Greek philosopher, who succeeded Aristotle as teacher at Athens and inherited his library. He is best known for his botanical works and his *Characters* (moral studies).

Thierry, Augustin (1795–1856), French historian, known for his *History of the Norman Conquest*.

Thiers, Louis Adolphe (1797–1877), French statesman and historian. After a varied political career, he became president in 1871, helping to revive France after defeat. He wrote a history of the Revolution.

Thomas, Dylan (1914–53), Welsh poet, whose highly individual *Eighteen Poems* (1934) brought him instant recognition. There followed *Twenty-five Poems* and *Deaths and Entrances*. *Under Milk Wood*, a play for voices, has more general appeal.

Thompson, Sir D'Arcy Wentworth (1860–1948), Scottish zoologist whose *On Growth and Form* (1917), written in lucid and elegant style, has influenced biological science.

Thomson, Sir George Paget (1892–1975), English physicist, son of Sir J. J. Thomson; author of *The Atom, Theory and Practice of Electron Diffraction, The Inspiration of Science*. Nobel prizewinner 1937.

Thomson, James (1700–48), Scottish poet who wrote *The Seasons* and *The Castle of Indolence*.

Thomson, James (1834–82), poet and essayist, b. near Glasgow. Wrote *The City Of Dreadful Night*.

Thomson, Sir Joseph John (1856–1940), English physicist and mathematician, leader of a group of researchers at the Cavendish laboratory, Cambridge. He established in 1897 that cathode-rays were moving particles whose speed and specific charge could be measured. He called them corpuscles but the name was changed to electrons. This work was followed up by the study of positive rays which led to the discovery of isotopes, the existence of which had earlier been suggested by Soddy. Nobel prizewinner 1906.

Thoreau, Henry David (1817–62), American essayist and nature-lover, who rebelled against society and lived for a time in a solitary hut. His chief work is *Walden*. He was a friend of Emerson.

Thorez, Maurice (1900–64), French communist leader from 1930 and after the second world war.

Thorndike, Dame Sybil (1882–1976), English actress. She made her début in 1904, and played in Greek tragedies, in the plays of Shakespeare and Shaw, and in Grand Guignol. Her husband was Sir Lewis Casson.

Thornycroft, Sir William Hamo (1850–1925), English sculptor, whose works include a statue of General Gordon in Trafalgar Square.

Thorpe, Sir Thomas Edward (1845–1925), English chemist who researched in inorganic chemistry and with his friend Arthur Rücker made a magnetic survey of the British Isles.

Thorwaldsen, Bertel (1770–1844), Danish sculptor whose works include the Cambridge statue of Byron.

Thucydides (c. 460–399 B.C.), Greek historian, especially of the Peloponnesian War in which he himself fought. He was not merely a chronicler, but saw the significance of events and tried to give an impartial account. The speeches attributed by him to leaders include the beautiful funeral oration of Pericles.

Tiberius, Claudius (42 B.C.–A.D. 37), Roman emperor who succeeded Augustus. His early reign was successful but his later years were marked by tragedy and perhaps insanity. He is the Tiberius of Luke 3.1.

Tillett, Benjamin (1860–1943), English trade-union leader, especially of a dockers' strike in 1889 and a transport-workers' strike in 1911.

Tillotson, John (1630–94), English divine, a noted preacher who became archbishop of Canterbury in 1691.

Tindal, Matthew (1655–1733), English deist, author of *Christianity as old as the Creation*.

Tintoretto (1518–94), Venetian painter whose aim it was to unite the colouring of Titian with the drawing of Michelangelo. His numerous paintings, mostly of religious subjects, were executed with great speed, some of them on enormous canvases. His *Origin of the Milky Way* is in the National Gallery. His name was Jacopo Robusti, and he was called Il Tintoretto (little dyer) after his father's trade.

Tippett, Sir Michael Kemp (b. 1905), English composer whose works include the operas *The Midsummer Marriage*, *King Priam*, and *Knot Garden*, and the song-cycles *Boyhood's End* and *The Heart's Assurance*. O.M. 1983. *See* **Section E**.

Titian (Tiziano Vecelli) (c. 1487–1576), Venetian painter. He studied under the Bellinis and was influenced by Giorgione, for example, in his frescoes at Padua. His mature style is one of dynamic composition and full colour, as in his *Bacchus and Ariadne* (National Gallery). Among his principal works are *Sacred and Profane Love* (Borghese Gallery, Rome), and some in the Prado, Madrid.

Tito (Josip Broz) (1892–1980), Yugoslav leader, b. Kumrovec. In 1941 he organised partisan forces against the Axis invaders, liberated his country, and carried through a communist revolution. In 1945 he became the first communist prime minister and in 1953 president. He successfully pursued an independent line for his country. Order of Lenin (1972).

Titus (A.D. 39–81), Roman emperor, son of Vespasian, brought the Jewish war to a close with the capture of Jerusalem. He completed the Colosseum.

Tizard, Sir Henry Thomas (1885–1959), English scientist and administrator. He was chairman of the Scientific Survey of Air Defence (later known as the Tizard Committee) that encouraged the birth of radar before the second world war and turned it into a successful defence weapon. He was chief scientific adviser to the government, 1947–52.

Tocqueville, Alexis, Comte de (1805–59), French liberal politician and historian, author of *Democracy in America*, still relevant reading.

Todd, 1st Baron (Alexander Robertus Todd) (b. 1907), Scottish biochemist, noted for his work on the structure of nucleic acids. Nobel prizewinner 1957; Pres. Royal Society 1975. Chancellor Univ. of Strathclyde. O.M. 1977.

Tolkien, John Ronald Reuel (1892–1973), Academic and writer. Professor of English language and literature at Oxford, 1945–59. Famous as creator of *The Hobbit* (1937), *The Lord of the Rings* (3 vols, 1954–5) and *The Silmarillion* (1977).

Tolstoy, Leo Nikolayevich, Count (1828–1910), Russian writer and philosopher, b. Yasnaya Polyana. Of noble family, he entered the army and fought in the Crimean War. Beginning

with simple, natural accounts of his early life (*Childhood* and *Boyhood*), he proceeded to articles on the war, and so eventually to perhaps his best work, the long novel *War and Peace*, followed by *Anna Karenina*. Increasingly preoccupied with social problems, he freed his serfs before this was done officially, and refused to take advantage of his wealth. His later works include *The Kreutzer Sonata* and *Resurrection*.

Tooke, John Horne (1736–1812), English politician and pamphleteer, was a supporter of Wilkes and later of Pitt. He was tried for high treason, but was acquitted.

Torquemada, Tomas de (1420–98), first inquisitor-general of Spain.

Torricelli, Evangelista (1608–47), Italian physicist, pupil of Galileo. He invented the barometer and improved both microscope and telescope.

Toscanini, Arturo (1867–1957), Italian conductor, b. Parma. He had a remarkable musical memory, and was at the same time exacting and self-effacing.

Toulouse-Lautrec, Henri de (1864–1901), French painter, whose pictures portray with stark realism certain aspects of Parisian life in the nineties, especially the *Moulin Rouge* series. Many are in the Musée Lautrec at Albi.

Tovey, Sir Donald Francis (1875–1940), English pianist and composer. His compositions include chamber music, a piano concerto, and an opera *The Bride of Dionysus*; and his writings *Essays in Musical Analysis*.

Toynbee, Arnold (1852–83), English historian and social reformer. The settlement Toynbee Hall was founded in his memory.

Toynbee, Arnold Joseph (1889–1975), nephew of above, English historian, known mainly for his 10-volume *A Study of History*, an analysis of many civilisations. He was for 30 years director of the Institute of International Affairs.

Traherne, Thomas (c. 1636–74), English religious poet, b. Hereford; author also of *Centuries of Meditations*.

Trajan (c. 53–117), Roman emperor, was a successful general and firm administrator. He was born in Spain.

Tree, Sir Herbert Beerbohm (1853–1917), English actor-manager of the Haymarket theatre until 1897 when he built His Majesty's theatre. Sir Max Beerbohm was his half-brother.

Trenchard, 1st Viscount (Hugh Montague Trenchard) (1873–1956), British air-marshal. He served with the Royal Flying Corps in the first world war and became the first air marshal of the R.A.F. He was largely responsible for the R.A.F. college at Cranwell and was also concerned in establishing Hendon police college.

Trent, 1st Baron (Jesse Boot) (1850–1931), British drug manufacturer, b. Nottingham. He built up the largest pharmaceutical retail trade in the world, and was a benefactor of Nottingham.

Trevelyan, George Macaulay (1876–1962), English historian, known for his *History of England* and *English Social History*.

Trevelyan, Sir George Otto (1838–1928), English liberal politician, father of above. He wrote a life of his uncle Lord Macaulay.

Trevithick, Richard (1771–1833), English mining engineer and inventor, b. near Redruth, Cornwall. His most important invention was a high-pressure steam-engine (1801) and he is commonly (and rightly) acknowledged as the inventor of the steam locomotive for railways.

Trollope, Anthony (1815–82), English novelist. His early life was a struggle, the family being supported by his mother's writings. His own career was in the post office, but by strict industry he produced many novels especially portraying clerical life (the *Barchester* series) and political life (the *Phineas Finn* series).

Trotsky, Leo (Lev Davidovich Bronstein) (1879–1940), Russian revolutionary, b. of Jewish parents in the Ukraine, one of the leaders of the Bolshevik revolution. As commissar of foreign affairs under Lenin he led the Russian delegation at the Brest-Litovsk conference. He differed from Stalin on policy, believing in "permanent revolution," according to which socialism could not be achieved in Russia without revolutions elsewhere, and was dismissed from office in 1925 and expelled from the Communist party in 1927. In 1929 he took up exile in Mexico where he was assassinated.

Trudeau, Pierre Eliott (b. 1919), Liberal prime minister of Canada 1968–79, 1980–84.

Truman, Harry S. (1884–1972), U.S. President, 1945–53. He inherited the presidency on Roosevelt's death in 1945 when he took the decision to drop the first atom bomb, and he won the election of 1948. He intervened in Korea and dismissed General MacArthur.

Tulsi Das (1532–1623), Indian poet whose master piece *Ram-Charit-Mānas* (popularly known as the *Ramayana* and based on the Sanskrit epic of Vālmiki) is venerated by all Hindus.

Turenne, Henri de la Tour d'Auvergne, Vicomte de (1611–75), French commander who was successful in the Thirty Years' War.

Turgenev, Ivan Sergeyvich (1818–83), Russian novelist, friend of Gogol and Tolstoy, who spent part of his life in exile. His works include *Fathers and Children, Smoke,* and *Virgin Soil.*

Turing, Alan Mathison (1912–54), computer genius. Developed concept (1936) of Turing machine. Deeply unhappy personal life.

Turner, Joseph Mallord William (1775–1851), English landscape painter, b. London, a barber's son. He entered the Royal Academy and was at first a topographical watercolourist. Later he turned to oil and became a master of light and colour, achieving magical effects, especially in depicting the reflection of light in water. His works include *Crossing the Brook, Dido building Carthage, The Fighting Temeraire, Rain, Steam and Speed.* He also made thousands of colour studies. He encountered violent criticism as his style became more abstract which led to Ruskin's passionate defence of him in *Modern Painters.* He bequeathed his work to the nation.

Tussaud, Marie (1761–1850), Swiss modeller in wax who learnt from her uncle in Paris, married a Frenchman, and later came to England where she set up a permanent exhibition.

Tutankhamen (d. c. 1327 B.C.), Egyptian pharaoh of the 18th dynasty, son-in-law of Akhenaten, whose tomb was discovered by Howard Carter in 1922, with the mummy and gold sarcophagus intact. He died when he was 18.

Tutu, Desmond Mpilo (b. 1931), South African churchman. Archbishop of Cape Town since 1986. Nobel Peace Prize, 1984. Outstanding opponent of apartheid.

Twain, Mark (Samuel Langhorne Clemens) (1835–1910), American humorist. His *Innocents Abroad* was the result of a trip to Europe. His works include *A Tramp Abroad, Tom Sawyer, Huckleberry Finn,* and *Pudd'nhead Wilson.*

Tweedsmuir, 1st Baron (John Buchan) (1875–1940), Scottish author of biographies, historical novels, and adventure stories, including *Montrose* and *Thirty-nine Steps.* He was governor-general of Canada 1935–40.

Tyler, Wat (d. 1381), English peasant leader. He was chosen leader of the Peasants' Revolt of 1381 (due to various causes), and parleyed at Smithfield with the young king Richard II, but was killed.

Tyndale, William (c. 1494–1536), English religious reformer, translator of the Bible. He had to go abroad, where he visited Luther and his New Testament was printed at Worms. When copies entered England they were suppressed by the bishops (1526). His Pentateuch was printed at Antwerp, but he did not complete the Old Testament. He was betrayed, arrested, and executed. Unlike Wyclif, who worked from Latin texts, he translated mainly from the original Hebrew and Greek and his work was later to become the basis of the Authorised Version of the Bible.

Tyndall, John (1829–93), Irish physicist whose wide interests led him to research on heat, light, and sound, and on bacteria-free air and sterilisation. He discovered why the sky is blue (Tyndall effect) and pioneered popular scientific writing, *e.g., Heat as a Mode of Motion.*

U

Unamuno, Miguel de (1864–1936), Spanish philosopher, poet, essayist, and novelist, author of *El Sentimiento Trágico de la Vida* (The Tragic Sense of Life).

Undset, Sigrid (1882–1949), Norwegian novelist, daughter of an antiquary, author of *Jenny, Kristin Lavransdatter,* and *Olav Audunsson.* Nobel prizewinner 1928.

Unwin, Sir Raymond (1863–1940), English architect of the first garden city at Letchworth.

Ursula, St., said in late legend to have been killed by Huns at Cologne with many companions while on pilgrimage. It took rise from a 4th cent. inscription which simply referred to virgin martyrs.

Usher or **Ussher, James** (1581–1656), Irish divine who in 1625 became archbishop of Armagh, and whose writings include a long-accepted chronology, placing the creation at 4004 B.C.

V

Valentine, St., was a christian martyr of the reign of the emperor Claudius II (d. A.D. 270). The custom of sending valentines may be connected with the pagan festival of Lupercalia.

Valéry, Paul (1871–1945), French poet and essayist, strongly influenced by the symbolist leader, Mallarmé. His poems include *La jeune Parque, Charmes,* and *Le cimetière marin.*

Vanbrugh, Sir John (1664–1726), English architect and playwright. His buildings include Blenheim Palace and his plays *The Provok'd Wife.*

Vancouver, George (1758–98), British navigator who served under Captain Cook, also doing survey work, and who sailed round Vancouver island.

Vanderbilt, Cornelius (1794–1877), American merchant and railway speculator who amassed a fortune and founded a university at Nashville. His son, **William Henry Vanderbilt** (1821–85), inherited and added to it.

Van Dyck, Sir Anthony (1599–1641), Flemish painter, b. Antwerp. He studied under Rubens, travelled in Italy, and then settled in England with an annuity from Charles I. He excelled in portraits, especially of Charles I and Henrietta Maria, and of their court.

Vane, Sir Henry (1613–62), English parliamentary leader during the civil war period, though not involved in the execution of Charles I. He was executed in 1662.

Van Gogh, Vincent (1853–90), Dutch painter of some of the most colourful pictures ever created. With passionate intensity of feeling he painted without pause whatever he found around him—landscapes, still life, portraits; his was a truly personal art. His life was one of pain, sorrow, and often despair, and in the end he committed suicide.

Vauban, Sebastien de Prestre de (1633–1707), French military engineer, whose skill in siege works (*e.g.,* at Maestricht 1673) was a factor in the expansive wars of Louis XIV. He protected France with fortresses and also invented the socket bayonet.

Vaughan Williams, Ralph (1872–1958), English composer, b. Gloucestershire. After Charterhouse and Cambridge he studied music in Berlin under Max Bruch and, later in Paris, under Ravel. He wrote nine symphonies besides a number of choral and orchestral works, operas (including *Hugh the Drover, Riders to the Sea*), ballets, chamber music, and songs. He showed great interest in folk tunes. *See* Section E.

Velasquez, Diego (c. 1460–1524), Spanish conquistador, first governor of Cuba.

Velasquez, Diego Rodriguez de Silva y (1599–1660), Spanish painter, b. Seville, especially of portraits at the court of Philip IV, and also of classical and historical subjects. He made two visits to Italy (1629–31, 1649–51), studying the Venetian painters, especially Titian, which hastened the development of his style. Among his masterpieces are *The Maids of Honour, The Tapestry Weavers* (both in the Prado), the Rokeby Venus and a portrait of Philip IV (both in the National Gallery), the landscape views from the Villa Medici (Prado) and *Juan de Pareja* (sold in London in 1970 for £2·25 million).

Venizelos, Eleutherios (1864–1936), Greek statesman, b. Crete. He became prime minister in 1910 and held this office intermittently. He promoted the Balkan League (1912), forced the king's abdication (1917), and brought Greece into the war on the Allied side, securing territorial concessions at the peace conference, but his expansionist policy in Turkish Asia failed.

Verdi, Giuseppe (1813–1901), Italian composer, b. near Busseto in the province of Parma. His early works include *Nabucco*, *Ernani*, *I Due Foscari*, and *Macbeth*; a middle period is represented by *Rigoletto*, *Il Trovatore*, *La Traviata*, *Un Ballo in Maschera*, and *Don Carlos*; to the last period of his life belong *Aïda*, *Otello*, and *Falstaff* (produced when he was 80). *See* **Section E.**

Verlaine, Paul (1844–96), French poet, one of the first of the symbolists, also known for his memoirs and confessions. His works include *Poèmes saturniens*, *Fêtes galantes*, *Sagesse*, and *Romances sans paroles*. He was imprisoned for two years in Belgium for shooting and wounding his friend Rimbaud. He died in poverty in Paris.

Vermeer, Jan (1632–75), Dutch painter, b. Delft. His main paintings are of domestic interiors, which he makes into works of art, as in *Lady at the Virginals* (National Gallery). His reputation has grown during the last century.

Verne, Jules (1828–1905), French writer of science fiction, including *Five Weeks in a Balloon*, *Twenty Thousand Leagues Under the Sea*, *Round the World in Eighty Days*.

Vernier, Pierre (1580–1637), French inventor of the small sliding scale which enables readings on a graduated scale to be taken to a fraction of a division.

Veronese, Paolo (1528–88), Italian painter of the Venetian school, whose works include *Marriage Feast at Cana in Galilee*, *The Feast in the House of Simon*, and *The Presentation of the Family of Darius to Alexander*, *His Adoration of the Magi* is in the National Gallery.

Veronica, St., legendary woman who was said to hand her kerchief to Christ on the way to Calvary, to wipe his brow, and his impression was left on the kerchief. In its present form her legend dates from the 14th cent.

Verwoerd, Hendrik Frensch (1901–66), South African politician, b. Amsterdam, exponent of the policy of apartheid; prime minister 1958–66. He was assassinated.

Vespasian, Titus Flavius (A.D. 9–79), Roman emperor. He was sent by Nero to put down the Jews and was proclaimed by the legions. He began the Colosseum.

Vespucci, Amerigo (1451–1512), Florentine explorer, naturalised in Spain, contractor at Seville for Columbus. He later explored Venezuela. The use of his name for the continent arose through a mistake.

Vico, Giambattista (1688–1744), Italian philosopher of history and of culture, b. Naples. His ideas were developed in his *Scienza nuova* (science of history) but it was not until our own day that its originality as a thinker was fully recognised.

Victor Emmanuel II (1820–78), first king of Italy. King of Sardinia, he was proclaimed king of Italy in 1861 after the Austrians had been defeated and Garibaldi had succeeded in the south. Rome was added in 1870.

Victoria (1819–1901), Queen of the United Kingdom of Gt. Britain and Ireland and Empress of India, was granddaughter of George III and succeeded her uncle, William IV, in 1837. In 1840 she married Prince Albert of Saxe-Coburg-Gotha, who died in 1861. Conscientious, hard-working, and of strict moral standards, she had by the end of a long life (jubilees 1887 and 1897) won the affection and respect of her subjects in a unique degree. Her reign saw industrial expansion, growing humanitarianism, literary output, and in the main prolonged peace; and by its close the British empire and British world power had reached their highest point.

Villeneuve, Pierre de (1763–1806), French admiral defeated by Nelson at Trafalgar and captured along with his ship, the *Bucentaure*.

Villon, François (1431–?1463), French poet, b. Paris, who lived at a turbulent time at the close of the Hundred Years War. After fatally stabbing a man in 1455 he joined the *Conquillards*, a criminal organisation. They had a secret language (the *jargon*) and it was for them that he composed his ballads. His extant works consist of the *Petit Testament* (1456),

originally called *Le Lais*, and the *Grand Testament* (1461), masterpieces of mediaeval verse.

Virgil (Publius Vergilius Maro) (70–19 B.C.), Roman epic poet, b. at Andes near Mantua, he went to Rome to obtain redress for the military confiscation of his farm. He was patronised by Maecenas, and wrote his pastoral *Eclogues*, followed by his *Georgics*. His best-known work, the *Aeneid*, deals with the wanderings of Aeneas after the fall of Troy till his establishment of a kingdom in Italy.

Vivaldi, Antonio (c. 1675–1743), Venetian composer, violin master at the Ospedale della Pieta. His output of orchestral works was prolific and Bach arranged some of his violin pieces for the harpsichord. *See* **Section E.**

Volta, Alessandro (1745–1827), Italian physicist of Pavia, who, working on the results of Galvani, invented the voltaic pile, the first instrument for producing an electric current. It provided a new means for the decomposition of certain substances. His name was given to the volt, the unit of electrical potential difference.

Voltaire (François Marie Arouet) (1694–1778), French philosopher and writer. His first essays offended the authorities, and he spent the years 1726–9 in England, where he wrote some of his dramas. Returning to France, he published his *Philosophical Letters*, which aroused the enmity of the priesthood. At this juncture, the Marquise du Châtelet offered him the asylum of her castle of Cirey, and for the next 15 years he made this his home, writing there his *Discourses of Man, Essay on the Morals and Spirit of Nations, Age of Louis XIV*, etc. His most celebrated book was *Candide*, in which he attacked the theory of Optimism. Its observations include *"pour encourager les autres"* (about Admiral Byng's execution) and its final message: *"il faut cultiver notre jardin."*

Vondel, Joost van don (1587–1679), Dutch poet who lived at Amsterdam. Most of his dramas are on biblical subjects, and the two most famous are *Jephtha* and *Lucifer*.

Voroshilov, Klimentiv Efremovich (1881–1969), Soviet general who commanded the Leningrad defences in 1941. U.S.S.R. president, 1953–60.

Vyshinsky, Andrei Yanuarievich (1883–1954), Soviet jurist and diplomat; conducted the prosecution of the Moscow treason trials, 1936–8.

W

Wade, George (1673–1748), English general and military engineer who, after the rising of 1715, pacified the Scottish highlands, constructing military roads and bridges. In the 1745 rising Prince Charles' forces evaded him.

Wagner, Richard (1813–83), German composer, b. Leipzig. He achieved a new type of musical expression in his operas by the complete union of music and drama. He made use of the *Leit-motif* and was his own librettist. His originality and modernism aroused a good deal of opposition, and he was exiled for some years. But he was supported by loyal friends, including Liszt, the young King Ludwig of Bavaria, and the philosopher Nietzsche. He began the music of the *Ring des Nibelungen* in 1853, but it was not until 1876 that the whole of the drama (Rheingold, Valkyrie, Siegfried, Götterdämmerung) was performed at Bayreuth under the conductor Hans Richter. Other operas are *The Flying Dutchman*, *Rienzi*, *Tannhäuser*, *Lohengrin*, *Tristan und Isolde*, *Die Meister-singer von Nürnberg*, and *Parsifal*, a religious drama. He married Liszt's daughter Cosima.

Walcott, Derek (b. 1930), West Indian poet and playwright, whose works include *Collected Poems 1948–1984* (1986) and *Omeros* (1990). He won the Queen's Gold Medal for Poetry (1988), the W. H. Smith Literary Award (1991), and the Nobel Prize for Literature (1992).

Waldheim, Kurt (b. 1918), Austrian diplomat; succeeded U Thant as secretary-general of the United Nations. Held office, 1972–81. President of Austria, 1986–92.

Walesa, Lech (b. 1943), Polish trade unionist. Shipyard worker in Gdansk. Leader of *Solidarity*. Awarded 1983 Nobel Peace Prize. President of Poland since 1990.

Waley, Arthur (1889–1966), English orientalist, known for his translations of Chinese and Japanese poetry and prose. The first to bring the literature of those countries to the western world.

Walker, George (1618–90), hero of the siege of Londonderry in 1688, who kept the besiegers at bay for 105 days.

Wallace, Alfred Russel (1823–1913), British naturalist, b. Usk, Monmouth, joint author with Darwin of the theory of natural selection. In 1858, while down with illness in the Moluccas, he sent a draft of his theory to Darwin in England who was amazed to find that it closely agreed with his own theory of evolution which he was on the point of publishing. The result was a reading of a joint paper to the Linnean Society.

Wallace, Edgar (1875–1932), English novelist and playwright, known for his detective thrillers.

Wallace, Sir Richard (1818–90), English art collector and philanthropist. His adopted son's wife bequeathed his collection to the nation (Wallace Collection, Manchester Square, London).

Wallace, Sir William (c. 1274–1305), Scottish patriot. He withstood Edward I, at first successfully, but was defeated at Falkirk, taken to London and brutally murdered.

Wallenstein, Albrecht von (1583–1634), German soldier and statesman during the Thirty Years War. An able administrator of his own estates, he sought the unity of Germany, but was distrusted and eventually assassinated.

Waller, Edmund (1606–87), English poet of polished simplicity, author of *Go, lovely rose.* He was able to agree with both parliamentarians and royalists.

Wallis, Sir Barnes Neville (1887–1979), British scientist and inventor whose many designs include the R100 airship, the Wellington bomber, the swing-wing aircraft, and the "bouncing bomb" that breached the Ruhr dams in 1943.

Walpole, Horace, 4th Earl of Orford (1717–97), younger son of Sir Robert Walpole, English writer, chiefly remembered for his *Letters,* his *Castle of Otranto,* and his "Gothic" house at Strawberry Hill.

Walpole, Sir Hugh Seymour (1884–1941), English novelist, b. New Zealand. His works include *Fortitude, The Dark Forest,* and *The Herries Chronicle.*

Walpole, Sir Robert, 1st Earl of Orford (1676–1745), English Whig statesman, who came to office soon after the Hanoverian succession and is considered the first prime minister—a good finance minister, a peace minister, and a "house of commons man."

Walter, Bruno (1876–1962), German-American conductor, especially of Haydn, Mozart, and Mahler.

Walter, John (1776–1847), English newspaper editor. Under him *The Times,* founded by his father John Walter (1739–1812), attained a leading position.

Walton, Izaak (1593–1683), English writer, especially remembered for *The Compleat Angler.* He also wrote biographies of Donne, Hooker, and George Herbert.

Walton, Sir William Turner (1902–83), English composer, whose works include concertos for string instruments, two symphonies, two coronation marches, *Façade* (setting to Edith Sitwell's poem), and an oratorio, *Belshazzar's Feast.* O.M. 1967.

Warbeck, Perkin (1474–99), Flemish impostor, b. Tournai, who claimed to be the younger son of Edward IV with French and Scottish backing, but failed and was executed.

Warwick, Earl of (Richard Neville) (c. 1428–71), "the kingmaker." At first on the Yorkist side in the Wars of the Roses, he proclaimed Edward IV king; but later changed sides and restored the Lancastrian Henry VI. He was killed at Barnet.

Washington, Booker Taliaferro (1858–1915), American Negro educationist, author of *Up from Slavery.*

Washington, George (1732–99), first U.S. president. B. in Virginia, of a family which originated from Sulgrave, Northants., he served against the French in the Seven Years War. When the dispute between the British government and the Americans over taxation came to a head, he proved a successful general, and Cornwallis's surrender to him at Yorktown in 1781 virtually

ended the war. In 1787 he presided over the Philadelphia convention which formulated the constitution, and was president 1789–97.

Watson, John Broadus (1878–1958), American psychologist, an exponent of behaviourism. *See* Behaviourism, Section J.

Watson-Watt, Sir Robert (1892–1973), Scottish physicist, who played a major part in the development of radar.

Watt, James (1736–1819), Scottish engineer and inventor, b. Greenock. He made important improvements to Newcomen's steam-engine by inventing a separate condenser (applying Black's discoveries (1761–4) on latent heat) and other devices based on scientific knowledge of the properties of steam. He was given support by Matthew Boulton, a capitalist, and settled down in Birmingham with him. He defined one horse-power as the rate at which work is done when 33,000 lb are raised one foot in one minute. He also constructed a press for copying manuscripts. The watt as a unit of power is named after him.

Watteau, Jean Antoine (1684–1721), French painter. He painted pastoral idylls in court dress. His works include *Embarquement pour Cythère* in the Louvre.

Watts, Isaac (1674–1748), English hymn-writer, author of *O God, our help in ages past.*

Watts-Dunton, Walter Theodore (1836–1914), English poet and critic, friend of Swinburne whom he looked after until his death in 1909.

Waugh, Evelyn (1902–66), English satirical writer, author of *Vile Bodies, The Loved One, Brideshead Revisited, Life of Edmund Campion, The Ordeal of Gilbert Pinfold,* and an autobiography, *A Little Learning.*

Wavell, 1st Earl (Archibald Percival Wavell) (1883–1950), British field marshal. He served in the first great war on Allenby's staff and in the second he commanded in the Middle East 1939–41, defeating the Italians; and in India 1941–3. He was viceroy of India 1943–7.

Webb, Matthew (1848–83), English swimmer, the first to swim the English Channel (1875).

Webb, Sidney James, Baron Passfield (1859–1947), and his wife **Beatrice,** *née* Potter (1858–1943), English social reformers and historians. They combined careful investigation of social problems (their books include *History of Trade Unionism* and *English Local Government*) with work for the future; they were members of the Fabian Society, launched the *New Statesman,* and helped to set up the London School of Economics. He held office under Labour.

Weber, Carl Maria Friedrich Ernst von (1786–1826), German composer, who laid the foundation of German romantic opera. His reputation rests principally on his three operas, *Der Freischütz, Euryanthe,* and *Oberon.* He was also an able pianist, conductor, and musical director. *See* Section E.

Webster, Daniel (1782–1852), American statesman and orator. He held office more than once and negotiated the Ashburton Treaty which settled the Maine–Canada boundary.

Webster, Noah (1758–1843), American lexicographer, who published an *American dictionary of the English language.*

Wedgwood, Dame Cicely Veronica (b. 1910) English historian, author of *William the Silent, Thomas Wentworth, The Thirty Years' War, The King's Peace, The Trial of Charles I*; a member of the Staffordshire pottery family. O.M. 1969.

Wedgwood, Josiah (1730–95), English potter, who at his Etruria works near Hanley produced from a new ware (patented 1763) pottery to classical designs by Flaxman, and gave pottery a new impetus.

Weill, Kurt (1900–50), German composer of satirical, surrealist operas, including *Die Dreigroschenoper* and *Mahagonny* (librettist Brecht). His wife, the Viennese actress **Lotte Lenya** (d. 1981) will be remembered for her singing of the Brecht songs and the interpretation of her husband's works. They left Europe for the United States in 1935.

Weingartner, Felix (1863–1942), Austrian conductor, also a composer and writer of a text book on conducting.

Weismann, August (1834–1914), German biologist. He worked on the question of individual variability in evolution, stressing the continuity of the germ plasm and rejecting the idea of inheritance of acquired characteristics.

Weizmann, Chaim (1874–1952), Israeli leader, b. Pinsk. He came to England in 1903 and taught biochemistry at Manchester. He helped to secure the Balfour Declaration (1917), promising a Jewish national home. In 1948 he became first president of Israel.

Wellesley, Marquess (Richard Colley Wellesley) (1760–1842), British administrator. He was a successful governor-general of India, and was brother of the Duke of Wellington.

Wellington, 1st Duke of (Arthur Wellesley) (1769–1852), British general. B. in Ireland, he joined the army and gained experience in India. In the Peninsular War he successfully wore down and drove out the invading French when Napoleon escaped from Elba, Wellington defeated him at Waterloo. Thereafter he took some part in politics as a Tory, but in the last resort was capable of accepting change.

Wells, Herbert George (1866–1946), English author. B. London, he was at first a teacher. He believed in progress through science, and became one of the most influential writers of his time. His long series of books includes romances of the Jules Verne variety (*The Time Machine, The Island of Dr. Moreau, The Invisible Man*), sociological autobiography (*Love and Mr. Lewisham, Kipps, Tono-Bungay, The History of Mr. Polly, Mr. Britling Sees it Through*), and popular education (*Outline of History, The Science of Life, The Work, Wealth and Happiness of Mankind, The Shape of Things to Come, The Fate of Homo Sapiens*). He was an early and successful educator of the common man. He was also a founder member of the Fabian Society.

Wenceslaus, St. (907–929), Patron saint of Czechoslovakia. A Christian ruler, murdered by his brother Boleslav on his way to Mass. The 'Good King' of the Christmas carol.

Wesley, Charles (1707–88), English hymnwriter. He was the companion of his brother John, and wrote over 5,500 hymns, including *Love divine* and *Jesu, lover of my soul*.

Wesley, John (1703–91), English evangelist and founder of Methodism (at first a nickname applied to friends of himself and his brother), b. at Epworth. After a trip to Georgia and after encountering Moravian influence, he began to teach on tour, covering in over 50 years more than 200,000 miles and preaching over 40,000 sermons. He made religion a live force to many ignorant folk of humble station who could only be reached by a new and direct challenge. He made a feature of the Sunday school and increased the use of music (the brothers' first hymnbook appeared in 1739). He did not plan separation from the Anglican church, though it was implicit in his ordination of a missionary, and it took place after his death. *See also* **Methodism, Section J.**

Westermarck, Edward Alexander (1862–1939), Finnish sociologist. His works include *History of Human Marriage, Origin and Development of the Moral Ideas*, and *The Oedipus Complex.*

Westinghouse, George (1846–1914), American engineer who invented an air-brake for railways (1868) called by his name, and pioneered the use of high tension alternating current for the transmission of electric power.

Westmacott, Sir Richard (1775–1856), English sculptor of Achilles in Hyde Park.

Wharton, Edith (1862–1937), American novelist and friend of Henry James. Her works include *House of Mirth* and *Custom of the Country.*

Whately, Richard (1787–1863), English archbishop of Dublin. He wrote treatises on *Rhetoric* and *Logic.*

Wheatstone, Sir Charles (1802–75), English physicist, one of the first to recognise Ohm's law. In 1837 he (with W. F. Cooke) patented an electric telegraph. He also introduced the microphone.

Wheeler, Sir Charles (1892–1974), English sculptor, especially on buildings. His autobiography is *High Relief.* P.R.A., 1956–66.

Whistler, James Abbott McNeill (1834–1903), American artist. B. at Lowell, he studied in Paris and settled in England. He reacted against the conventions of his day, and Ruskin's uncomprehending criticism of his work resulted in a lawsuit. Among his main works are

studies of the Thames, and a portrait of his mother, now in the Louvre.

White, Sir George Stuart (1835–1912), British general. Defended Ladysmith in the Boer War.

White, Gilbert (1720–93), a father of English ecology. His book *The Natural History and Antiquities of Selborne*, published in 1789, became the bible of the ecology movement.

White, Patrick (1912–90), Australian novelist whose books include *The Aunt's Story, Riders in the Chariot, The Solid Mandala* and *The Eye of the Storm.* Nobel prize 1973.

Whitefield, George (1714–70), English evangelist, b. Gloucester. He was at first associated with the Wesleys, but differed from them on predestination. His supporters built him a "Tabernacle" in London, and he had other chapels elsewhere, but founded no lasting sect.

Whitgift, John (1530–1604), archbishop of Canterbury in the time of Elizabeth I (from 1583). His policy helped to strengthen Anglicanism.

Whitman, Walt (1819–92), American poet, b. Long Island. He led a wandering life and did hospital work in the Civil War. He aimed at forming a new and free American outlook. His works include *Leaves of Grass, Drum Taps,* and *Democratic Vistas.*

Whittier, John Greenleaf (1807–92), American Quaker poet, b. Haverhill, Mass. He wrote against slavery (*Justice and Expediency*), turning to poetry after the Civil War, especially remembered for *Snow-bound.*

Whittington, Richard (c. 1358–1423), English merchant. Son of a Gloucestershire knight, he became a London mercer and was mayor of London 1398, 1406, 1419. The cat legend is part of European folklore.

Whittle, Sir Frank (b. 1907), pioneer in the field of jet propulsion. The first flights of Gloster jet propelled aeroplanes with Whittle engines took place in May 1941. O.M. (1986).

Whymper, Edward (1840–1911), English wood-engraver and mountaineer. He was the first to climb the Matterhorn.

Wilberforce, William (1759–1833), English philanthropist, b. Hull. He was the parliamentary leader of the campaign against the slave trade, abolished in 1807. He then worked against slavery itself, but that further step was only taken in the year of his death.

Wilcox, Ella Wheeler (1855–1919), American writer of romantic sentimental verse.

Wilde, Oscar Fingall (1854–1900), Irish author and dramatist, son of a Dublin surgeon and leader of the cult of art for art's sake. His works include poems, fairy-tales, short stories, and witty plays—*Lady Windermere's Fan, A Woman of No Importance, An Ideal Husband,* and *The Importance of Being Earnest.* In a libel action he was convicted of homosexual practices and imprisoned for two years, when he wrote *The Ballad of Reading Gaol.*

Wilder, Thornton Niven (1897–1975), American author and playwright. Among his books are *The Bridge of San Luis Rey* and *Ides of March.*

Wilkes, John (1727–97), English politician. A Whig, he violently attacked George III in his paper the *North Briton*, and as a result of unsuccessful proceedings against him, general warrants were determined illegal. He was again in trouble for obscene libel; his defiance of authority brought him popularity, and he was four times re-elected to parliament but refused his seat, until his opponents gave way. He helped to establish freedom of the press.

Willcocks, Sir William (1852–1932), British engineer, b. India, who carried out irrigation works in India, Egypt, South Africa, and Mesopotamia. He built the Aswan dam (1898–1902).

Willett, William (1856–1915), English advocate of "daylight savings," adopted after his death.

William I of England (1027–87), the "Conqueror," Duke of Normandy, claimed the English throne as successor to Edward the Confessor, and defeated Harold II at Hastings in 1066. An able commander and a firm ruler, he crushed Saxon resistance, especially in the north, transferred most of the land to his Norman followers, and drew England into closer relations with the continent, as did his archbishop Lanfranc. He ordered the Domesday survey.

William II of England (1056–1100), the Conqueror's son, surnamed Rufus, succeeded in

1087. Capricious and self-indulgent, his reign was troubled, and he was shot (by accident or design) while hunting in the New Forest.

William III of England (1650–1702), King of England, Scotland, and Ireland (1689–1702), son of William II of Orange and Mary, daughter of Charles I. He married Mary, daughter of the Duke of York (later James II) while stadtholder of Holland. In 1688, when James had fled the country, he was invited to succeed and he and Mary became joint king and queen. The revolution of 1688 brought to England tolerance of Protestant worship, but William was mainly concerned with war against France, ended in 1697.

William IV of England (1765–1837), third son of George III, succeeded his brother George IV in 1830; called the "sailor king." The reform bill of 1832 and other reform measures were carried without obstruction from him.

William I of Germany (1797–1888), King of Prussia and first German emperor. He succeeded to the throne in 1861 and continued resistance to reform, appointing Bismarck as chief minister, and supporting him through the Austro-Prussian and Franco-Prussian wars. His personal character was simple and unassuming.

William II of Germany, the Kaiser (1859–1941), King of Prussia and German emperor from 1888, was grandson of William I and of Queen Victoria. He was intelligent but impetuous, and believed in military power. He dismissed Bismarck. In 1914 his support of Austria helped to precipitate European war, and the resulting defeat brought his abdication, after which he lived in retirement at Doorn in Holland.

William the Silent (1533–1584), Dutch national leader. Prince of Orange, he led the revolt of the Protestant Netherlands against the rule of the Spanish Philip II. The union of the northern provinces was accomplished in 1579, and Spanish rule was renounced by 1584, in which year William was assassinated.

Williams, Sir George (1821–1905), founder of the Young Men's Christian Association.

Williamson, Malcolm (b. 1931), Australian composer, pianist and organist; succeeded Sir Arthur Bliss as Master of the Queen's Musick.

Willis, Ted (Lord Willis) (1914–92), socialist politician and playwright. His best-known play is *Woman in a Dressing Gown* (1962), and he created the TV series, *Dixon of Dock Green* (1953–75).

Wilson, Edmund (1895–1972), American critic, author of *Axel's Castle* (1931), *The Triple Thinkers* (1938), *The Wound and the Bow* (1941), *To the Finland Station* (1940), *The Shores of Light* (1952), *The Dead Sea Scrolls* (1955).

Wilson of Rievaulx, Lord (Sir Harold Wilson) (1916–95), British statesman, leader parl. Labour Party 1963–76; prime minister 1964–6, 1966–70, 1974–6. Entered parliament 1945 as member for Ormskirk; elected for Huyton 1950–83. Returned as Prime Minister on four occasions. Resigned March 1976. Founder of the Open University.

Wilson, Richard (1714–82), British landscape painter, b. Montgomeryshire. Admired by Turner and Constable.

Wilson, Thomas Woodrow (1856–1924), American statesman. He was U.S. president 1913–21, brought America into the first world war and advocated the League of Nations, but was not a successful negotiator at the peace conference and could not carry his country into the League. He introduced prohibition and women's suffrage.

Wingate, Orde Charles (1903–44), leader of the Chindit forces engaged behind the Japanese lines in Burma during the second world war.

Winifred, St., the 7th cent. patron saint of North Wales, said in late legend to have been killed by her rejected suitor, Prince Caradoc, but restored by her uncle.

Wiseman, Nicholas Patrick (1802–65), cardinal, b. in Spain of an Irish family. In 1850 on the restoration in England of the Roman Catholic hierarchy he became first archbishop of Westminster, and reorganised and developed his church in Great Britain.

Wittgenstein, Ludwig Josef Johann (1889–1951), Austrian linguistic philosopher whose main works were the *Tractatus Logico-Philosophicus* of his early period, much admired by Russell, and the *Philosophical Investigations*.

Wodehouse, Pelham Grenville (1881–1975), English humorist, creator of Jeeves in the Bertie Wooster stories. He became a U.S. citizen.

Wolf, Friedrich August (1759–1824), German classical scholar, a founder of scientific classical philology.

Wolf, Hugo (1860–1903), Austrian song-writer. In his settings of over 300 German lyrics, including many of Mörike and Goethe, he achieved union of poetry and music. *See* **Section E.**

Wolfe, James (1727–59), British general, b. Westerham. He showed early promise in the Seven Years' War, and was given command of the expedition against Quebec, which in spite of its strong position he captured, but lost his life.

Wolsey, Thomas (*c.* 1475–1530), English cardinal. A butcher's son at Ipswich, he entered the church, becoming archbishop of York and cardinal, while in the same year (1515) he became Henry VIII's lord chancellor. But in spite of his ability he was unable to secure papal sanction for the king's divorce from Catherine of Aragon, and fell from power and died.

Wood, Sir Henry Joseph (1869–1944), English conductor, founder of the Promenade Concerts which he conducted from 1895 till his death.

Woodcock, George (1904–79), English trade union leader. T.U.C. general secretary 1960–69; first chairman of the Commission on Industrial Relations, 1969–71.

Woodsworth, James Shaver (1874–1942), Canadian politician, parliamentary leader of the Co-operative Commonwealth Federation.

Woodville, Elizabeth (1437–91), wife of Edward IV. Her daughter Elizabeth married Henry VII.

Woolf, Virginia (1882–1941), English writer, daughter of Sir Leslie Stephen and wife of Leonard Woolf with whom she founded the Hogarth Press. Her works develop the stream-of-consciousness technique and include *To the Lighthouse, Mrs. Dalloway, The Waves, A Room of One's Own.*

Woolley, Sir Richard van der Riet (b. 1906), succeeded Sir Harold Spencer Jones as astronomer royal (England), 1956–72.

Wootton of Abinger, Baroness (Barbara Frances Wootton) (b. 1897), English social scientist. Her works include *Social Science and Social Pathology, Crime and the Criminal Law*, and an autobiography *In a world I never made.*

Wordsworth, William (1770–1850), English poet, b. Cockermouth. He went to Cambridge, and in 1798 with Coleridge issued *Lyrical Ballads*, a return to simplicity in English poetry. He settled at Grasmere with his sister Dorothy (1771–1855), to whose insight his poems owe much. Among his best works are his sonnets and his *Ode on the Intimations of Immortality*, besides his *Prelude.*

Wren, Sir Christopher (1632–1723), English architect, b. Wiltshire. After the great fire (1666) he prepared an abortive plan for rebuilding London, but did in fact rebuild St. Paul's and more than fifty other city churches, including St. Stephen, Walbrook, and St. Mary-le-Bow. Other works include Chelsea Hospital, portions of Greenwich Hospital, the Sheldonian theatre, Oxford, and Queen's College library, Oxford. He had wide scientific interests (he was professor of mathematics at Gresham College, London, and professor of astronomy at Oxford) and helped to found the Royal Society.

Wright, (William Ambrose) Billy (1924–94), the golden-boy of post-war English football. A former captain of Wolves and England, he won 105 caps for England, captaining his country 90 times.

Wright, Frank Lloyd (1869–1959), American architect, initiator of horizontal strip and all-glass design. Buildings include the Imperial Hotel, Tokyo, and the Guggenheim Museum, New York.

Wright, Orville (1871–1948), American airman who with his brother Wilbur (1867–1912) in 1903 was the first to make a controlled sustained flight in a powered heavier-than-air machine, flying a length of 852 ft. at Kitty Hawk, N.C.

Wyatt, James (1746–1813), English architect who built Fonthill Abbey.

Wyatt, Sir Thomas (1503–42), English poet (and diplomat) who introduced the sonnet from Italy.

Wyatt, Sir Thomas the younger (*c.* 1520–54), son of above, unsuccessfully led a revolt against Queen Mary on behalf of Lady Jane Grey.

Wycherley, William (1640–1715), English dramatist of the Restoration period. A master of satiric comedy, his plays include *Love in a*

Wood, The Plain Dealer and *The Country Wife.*

Wyclif, John (*c.* 1320–84), English religious reformer. He taught at Oxford, later becoming rector of Lutterworth. He insisted on inward religion and attacked those practices which he thought had become mechanical. His followers, called Lollards, were suppressed, partly for political reasons. The Wyclif Bible, the first translation of the Latin Vulgate into English, was mainly the work of his followers at Oxford.

Wykeham, William of (1324–1404), English churchman. He held office under Edward III and became bishop of Winchester in 1367. He founded New College, Oxford, and Winchester School, and improved Winchester cathedral.

Wyllie, William Lionel (1851–1931), English marine painter of *The Thames Below London Bridge.*

Wyspianski, Stanislav (1869–1907), Polish poet, dramatist and painter. His plays *The Wedding, Liberation,* and *November Night* treat of national themes.

X

Xavier, St. Francis (1506–52), "apostle of the Indies," b. at Xavero in the Basque country. He was associated with Loyola in founding the Jesuits, and undertook missionary journeys to Goa, Ceylon, and Japan.

Xenophon (444–359 B.C.), Athenian general and historian. He commanded Greek mercenaries under the Persian Cyrus, and on the latter's death safely marched the Ten Thousand home through hostile country. His chief works are the *Anabasis,* the *Hellenica,* and *Cyropaedia.*

Xerxes (*c.* 519–465 B.C.), King of Persia, was son of the first Darius. In 481 B.C. he started on an expedition against Greece when, according to Herodotus, he had a combined army and navy of over two and a half million men. He defeated the Spartans at Thermopylae, but his fleet was overcome at Salamis. He reigned from 485 to 465 B.C. and met his death by assassination.

Ximénes de Cisneros, Francisco (1436–1517), Spanish statesman and churchman. He became cardinal in 1507; carried out monastic reforms; and directed preparation of a polyglot bible, the *Complutensian;* but as inquisitor-general he was fanatical against heresy. He was adviser to Queen Isabella; in 1506 regent for Queen Juana; and himself directed an expedition to conquer Oran and extirpate piracy.

Y

Yeats, William Butler (1865–1939), Irish lyric poet and playwright, b. near Dublin, a leader of the Irish literary revival. His plays were performed in the Abbey Theatre (which with **Lady Gregory** (1852–1932) he helped to found), and include *Cathleen Ni Houlihan, The Hour Glass,* and *Deidre.* A complete edition of the *Collected Poems* appeared in 1950.

Yeltsin, Boris Nikolayevich (b. 1931), Russian politician. President, since May 1990, of the Russian Federation. At first an ally of Gorbachev (*q.v.*) then a rival. Yeltsin's role in opposing the August 1991 coup greatly strengthened his power and undermined the old Soviet Union. Architect of the Commonwealth of Independent States. He successfully overcame the 1993 communist rising in Moscow, but now (1995) faces grave economic problems, a resurgence of nationalism and fascism and severe criticism of his handling of the Chechenya war. *See* **Section C.**

Yonge, Charlotte Mary (1823–1901), English novelist. Influenced by Keble, she wrote novels which faithfully reflect some aspects of Victorian life; one such is *The Daisy Chain.* She also wrote historical fiction *e.g. The Dove in the Eagle's Nest.*

Young, Brigham (1801–77), American Mormon leader, and president in 1844 after the founder's death. He was a main founder of Salt Lake City. He practised polygamy. *See* **Section J.**

Young, Francis Brett (1884–1954), English novelist, author of *My Brother Jonathan* and *Dr. Bradley remembers.*

Young, James (1811–83), Scottish chemist, b. Glasgow, whose experiments led to the manufacture of paraffin oil and solid paraffin on a large scale.

Young, Thomas (1773–1829), English physicist, physician and Egyptologist, b. Somerset, of Quaker family. He established the wave theory of light and its essential principle of interference, put forward a theory of colour vision, and was the first to describe astigmatism of the eye. He was largely responsible for deciphering the inscriptions on the Rosetta stone.

Younghusband, Sir Francis Edward (1863–1942), English explorer and religious leader. He explored Manchuria and Tibet, and wrote on India and Central Asia. He founded the World Congress of Faiths in 1936 (*see* **Section J**).

Ypres, 1st Earl of. *See* **French.**

Ysaÿe, Eugène (1858–1929), Belgian violinist and conductor, noted chiefly for his playing of the works of Bach and César Franck.

Yukawa, Hideki (1907–81), Japanese physicist, who received the 1949 Nobel prize for predicting (1935) the existence of the meson.

Z

Zadkiel (angel in rabbinical lore), pseudonym of two astrologers: **William Lilly** (1602–81) and **Richard James Morrison** (1794–1874).

Zadkine, Ossip (1890–1967), Russian-born sculptor who made play with light on concave surfaces.

Zaharoff, Sir Basil (1849–1936), armaments magnate and financier, b. Anatolia of Greek parents. He was influential in the first world war.

Zamenhof, Ludwig Lazarus (1859–1917), Polish-Jew who invented Esperanto. He was by profession an oculist.

Zeno of Citium (?342–270 B.C.), philosopher, founder of the Stoic system. He left Cyprus to teach in Athens.

Zeppelin, Ferdinand, Count von (1838–1917), German inventor of the dirigible airship, 1897–1900. It was used in the first world war.

Zeromski, Stefan (1864–1925), Polish novelist, author of *The Homeless, The Ashes, The Fight with Satan.*

Zhukov, Georgi Konstantinovich (1896–1974), Soviet general, who led the defence of Moscow and Stalingrad and lifted the siege of Leningrad in the second world war, and accepted the German surrender in 1945.

Zhukovsky, Vasily Andreyevich (1783–1852), Russian poet and translator of German and English poets. For many years he was tutor to the future Tsar Alexander II.

Zola, Emile Edouard (1840–1902), French novelist, b. Paris, of Italian descent. His series, *Les Rougon-Macquart,* portrays in a score of volumes (the best known of which are perhaps *L'Assommoir, Nana* and *Germinal*) the fortunes of one family in many aspects and in realistic manner. He had the moral courage to champion Dreyfus.

Zorn, Anders Leonhard (1860–1920), Swedish sculptor, etcher, and painter.

Zoroaster (Zarathustra) (fl. 6th cent. B.C.), Persian founder of the Parsee religion. He was a monotheist, and saw the world as a struggle between good (Ahura Mazda) and evil (Ahriman). *See* **Zoroastrianism, Section J.**

Zoshchenko, Mikhail (1895–1958), Russian writer of humorous short stories, which include *The Woman who could not Read and other Tales* and *The Wonderful Dog and other Stories.*

Zosimus (fl. *c.* 300), the first known alchemist. He lived in Alexandria.

Zuccarelli, Francesco (1702–88), Italian artist of fanciful landscapes. He spent many years in London and was elected a founder member of the R.A. (1768).

Zuckermann, Baron (Solly Zuckermann) (1904–93), British biologist; chief scientific adviser to British governments; 1940–71. Author of *Scientists and War* and *The Frontiers of Public and Private Science.* O.M. 1968.

Zwingli, Ulrich (1484–1531), Swiss religious reformer. He taught mainly at Zurich, where he issued a list of reformed doctrines, less extreme than those of Calvin.

Zwirner, Ernst Friedrich (1802–61), German architect who restored Cologne cathedral.

BACKGROUND TO WORLD AFFAIRS

This section is in three parts. The first provides an up-to-date chronicle of political changes in Britain since 1979, including the record of the Conservative Government up to the 1995 local elections. The second part provides a wide-ranging guide to events and movements elsewhere in the world. The third section consists of a series of special topics. This edition includes articles on the political ferment in Russia, the crisis in Mexico, and the presidential elections in France. There is also an analysis of the contemporary Labour Party under Tony Blair.

TABLE OF CONTENTS

BACKGROUND TO WORLD AFFAIRS

This section is in three parts. The first outlines the political history of the United Kingdom since 1979. The second part provides a wide-ranging guide to events elsewhere in the world and takes stock of the changing patterns in international relations. The third section contains special topics on particular themes. The reader is invited to turn to **Section D** for further key facts and figures relating to the British political system.

I. SURVEY OF THE BRITISH POLITICAL SCENE

BRITISH POLITICAL EVENTS 1979–95

The 1979 General Election.

After the fall of the Labour Government on 28 March 1979, polling day was fixed for 3 May, coinciding with local government elections in most of England and Wales. The campaign was overshadowed by the murder on 30 March of Airey Neave, Opposition spokesman on Northern Ireland and one of Mrs. Thatcher's closest advisers, when a bomb planted in his car by Irish extremists exploded in the House of Commons car park. This led to a tightening of security with fewer meetings and other public appearances by leading politicians. Television thus played an even more dominant role than in recent elections with the main focus being on the party leaders. Generally it was a very quiet campaign disrupted only by various incidents involving supporters and opponents of the National Front, the most serious of which was at Southall where one person was killed and over 300 arrested. The Conservatives started the campaign with an overwhelming lead in the opinion polls, largely reflecting the winter's industrial troubles. During the campaign the gap between the parties narrowed but the Conservative lead was maintained and it was confirmed by the actual results. There was a swing of 5·2% to the Conservatives, sufficient to give them an overall majority of 44 in the House of Commons. There were, however, significant regional variations. The swing to the Conservatives was largest in southern England, it was smaller in the north, and in Scotland there was a very small swing to Labour. The most dramatic change in Scotland was the collapse of support for the Nationalists whose share of the vote was almost halved and they lost 9 of their 11 seats. The performance of the Liberals was patchy. Overall their vote fell by 1 million and they lost 3 seats but some of their MPs, including their leader David Steel, greatly increased their majorities. The National Front did very badly, all its candidates losing their deposits and securing only 0·6% of the poll. Among the casualties of the election were Shirley Williams, Labour's Education Minister, Teddy Taylor, the Conservative spokesman on Scotland, and Jeremy Thorpe, former leader of the Liberal Party.

Mrs. Thatcher's Government.

Mrs. Thatcher's arrival at 10 Downing Street attracted great interest, not only because she was the first woman Prime Minister of a Western state, but also because of the radical policies she had advocated in Opposition. Some of her closest associates were appointed to senior posts in the Cabinet, particularly on the economic side (for instance Sir Geoffrey Howe as Chancellor of the Exchequer and Sir Keith Joseph as Industry Secretary) but the Cabinet also included many who had been closely identified with the approach of her predecessor, Edward Heath. Among them were William Whitelaw (Home Secretary), Lord Carrington (Foreign Secretary), James Prior (Employment Secretary) and Peter Walker (Minister of Agriculture). However, even though he had campaigned energetically for the Conservatives during the election, no place was found in the Government for Edward Heath himself.

A Radical Programme.

The Queen's Speech for the first session of the new Parliament (lasting from May 1979 until October 1980) was an ambitious one both in its scale and in the magnitude of the changes it proposed. Among the most important measures were: the abolition of statutory price controls; changes in the law on picketing and the closed shop; repeal of the devolution legislation; granting council tenants a statutory right to purchase their homes; denationalisation of the nationalised airline and freight and aerospace industries and a reduction generally in the powers of state intervention in industry; and repeal of the requirement that local authorities introduce comprehensive education. Legislation giving effect to most of these changes was introduced in the autumn of 1979 and, although the congestion of the Parliamentary timetable led to some problems, the Government's comfortable majority ensured that it reached the statute-book by the end of the session.

Taxation and Public Spending.

During the election campaign the Conservatives attracted widespread support with their promises to cut direct taxation and eliminate wasteful public spending. Although many commentators thought that the economic situation would preclude fulfilment of public expectations immediately, the Chancellor confounded such scepticism by cutting the standard rate of income tax from 33% to 30%, with even greater reductions at higher levels, in his first Budget in June 1979. To finance these cuts he announced, as expected, reductions in public spending but he also had to increase VAT by 7% and petrol duty by 10p a gallon and to raise interest rates. These changes, however, added to the inflationary pressure already in the economy and in November the Chancellor had to raise interest rates to record levels and to make additional cuts in public spending affecting all sectors except for the armed forces and the police. These cuts were reflected in the withdrawal of some services, increased charges for others, reductions in staffing and in the winding-up of various government agencies.

The Labour Party Constitution.

As in the past, Labour's electoral defeat was followed by internal dissent, on this occasion centred upon those parts of the Party's constitution dealing with the powers of Party members to control their leaders. In October 1979, the Party Conference endorsed two changes in the constitution, requiring sitting MPs to be re-selected during the life of each Parliament and giving the final say on the election manifesto to the National Executive Committee. These decisions were referred to the committee of inquiry it also agreed to establish into the Party's organisation. Disagreement over the composition of this committee delayed the start of its work until January 1980. James Callaghan was re-elected Leader of the Party shortly after the General Election and most of the members of the outgoing Cabinet were elected to the Shadow Cabinet; one notable absentee was Tony Benn who chose to return to the backbenches in order to have greater freedom to speak on a wide range of issues.

Europe: A Fresh Start?

The campaign for the first direct elections to the European Parliament attracted little public interest, particularly as it came immediately after the General Election, and this was reflected in a very low turnout on polling day, 7 June. The result was a further victory for the Conservatives who won 60 of the 78 British seats. The new Government promised that it would be more positive than its predecessor in its attitude towards the EEC but it soon found itself in conflict with all its partners over its demand that Britain's net contribution to the EEC Budget be reduced by £1,000 million. Britain was also alone in calling for a tough response, including a boycott of the Moscow Olympics, to the Soviet invasion of Afghanistan in January 1980. Finally there were rows with particular countries, for example with France over the latter's refusal to permit imports of British lamb and with Germany over Britain's policy on North Sea oil.

Rhodesia: Return to Legality.

Elections, under the terms of the internal settlement, were held in Rhodesia in April 1979, leading to the formation in June of a coalition government led by Bishop Abel Muzorewa. Contrary to expectations, the Conservative Government did not recognise this government and continued to seek all-party agreement. The turning point occurred during the Commonwealth Conference at Lusaka in August 1979 where agreement was reached on the basic elements of a settlement. This led to three months of difficult negotiations in London, under the chairmanship of the Foreign Secretary, Lord Carrington, which culminated in the signing of a ceasefire and the lifting of sanctions in December 1979. Under its terms, a Cabinet Minister, Lord Soames, was appointed Governor for the period leading up to independence which was to be achieved following elections in February 1980. These elections, supervised by British and Commonwealth officials, resulted in a landslide victory for one of the Patriotic Front leaders, Robert Mugabe. Following the formation of a coalition government, including two whites, independence was officially achieved in April 1980, Zimbabwe becoming the 43rd member of the Commonwealth.

Trade Unions and the Law.

One consequence of the Government's tough economic policies was an increase in unemployment. In the public sector the Government's plans to cut jobs and its reluctance to support industries in financial difficulty caused widespread alarm among the trade unions. However, an early collision between the Government and the unions was not expected, partly because of the refusal of the Employment Secretary, James Prior, to be stampeded into tough action against the unions, and partly because of the reluctance of the unions to take on the Government so soon after it had received a mandate in an election in which public dislike of union power had played a major part. However, these predictions were confounded by a crisis at British Steel. The world recession and the strict limits placed by the Government on its financial support for the industry forced British Steel to announce major redundancies, with dramatic implications for the level of employment in places such as Corby and Port Talbot. British Steel was also unable to offer its employees wage increases corresponding to the rate of inflation. Tension on both issues culminated in January 1980 in the first national steel strike for over 50 years.

Growing World Tension.

The Government, and Mrs. Thatcher in particular, acquired a reputation for taking a tough stance on international issues. Its determination to resist Soviet aggression led it to allow American Cruise missiles to be stationed in Britain and to decide to replace Polaris with Trident missiles as Britain's strategic nuclear deterrent (decisions that were opposed by a revived Campaign for Nuclear Dis-armament). Its attempt to organise a boycott of the Moscow Olympics in protest at the Soviet invasion of Afghanistan had only limited success and its strong recommendation against participation was heeded by only a minority of British sportsmen. Relations with Europe, however, became

more cordial, assisted by the settlement, albeit on terms less favourable than the Prime Minister had hoped, of the dispute over Britain's contribution to the EEC budget. EEC governments acted in concert on various issues such as the Middle East and the American hostages in Iran. The problems of Iran spread dramatically to London at the end of April when seven gunmen seized the Iranian Embassy, taking 24 people hostage. Under the full view of TV cameras, the siege was successfully ended by the SAS a few days later.

Leadership of the Labour Party.

Constitutional questions dominated the Labour Party throughout 1980 and into 1981. At the 1980 Annual Conference the earlier decision to require reselection of sitting MPs was confirmed but the plan to give the National Executive Committee the final say on the election manifesto was reversed. The most controversial decision, however, was to take the election of the Party leader out of the hands of the Parliamentary Labour Party alone and to set up an electoral college consisting of Labour MPs, the constituency parties and the affiliated trade unions. No agreement could be reached in October on the precise composition of such a college and a special conference was convened for this purpose in January 1981. In the midst of all this uncertainty, James Callaghan announced his retirement. The election of his successor therefore took place under the old system and, on the second ballot, the PLP elected Michael Foot by a margin of ten votes over Denis Healey. Denis Healey was subsequently elected Deputy Leader.

Deepening Recession.

The Government's counter-inflation policies, implemented at a time of worldwide recession, had a severe effect upon levels of output and employment. Industry was especially hard hit by the record interest rates and by the strength of the pound. Although inflation did fall steadily, public attention switched increasingly to unemployment which early in 1981 reached 2½ million. The Government came under bitter attack from the trade unions, although the 13-week steel strike was ended without major concessions and the TUC's Day of Action in May 1980 met with only limited success, and more woundingly from the CBI and some prominent Conservative backbenchers. These problems led ministers to relax their policy of non-intervention in industry and large amounts of money were pumped into some of the major lossmakers such as British Leyland and British Steel. Despite accusations that it was making U-turns, the Government insisted that its overall economic strategy was unchanged. Confirmation of this was provided by the Chancellor of the Exchequer. Although interest rates were lowered in November 1980 and March 1981, offsetting action was taken to restrict monetary growth. In the Budget in March substantial increases in personal taxation were imposed and windfall taxes were applied to the profits of the banks and oil companies.

The Birth of the Social Democratic Party.

During 1980 various leading members of the Labour Party became increasingly critical of its decisions on its constitution and on policy (such as the support at the Annual Conference for unilateral nuclear disarmament and withdrawal from the EEC). Led by Shirley Williams, David Owen and William Rodgers (popularly known as the Gang of Three), their disillusionment was heightened by the Special Conference at Wembley in January 1981 which not only reaffirmed the decision to establish an electoral college but also decided that its composition should be: trade unions 40%, constituency parties 30% and Labour MPs 30%. A week later, the Gang of Four (having been joined by Roy Jenkins on his retirement as President of the EEC Commission) published the Limehouse Declaration announcing the formation of a Council for Social Democracy. Initially this was not a separate party but only a group to campaign for moderate leftwing policies, but in March 1981 12 Labour MPs (including David Owen and William Rodgers) resigned the Party Whip and announced that they would not be seeking re-election as Labour MPs.

On 26 March 1981, to a fanfare of publicity, the Social Democratic Party was formally launched. In the House of Commons the SDP consisted initially of 14 MPs (13 ex-Labour and 1 ex-Conservative). One of its first decisions was to negotiate an electoral alliance with the Liberals.

Healey versus Benn.

In April 1981 Tony Benn announced his intention of standing against Denis Healey for the Deputy Leadership of the Labour Party, thereby bringing into play for the first time the new procedures which had been agreed at the Wembley conference at the beginning of the year. In a bruising six months of campaigning, Benn and Healey were joined by a third candidate, John Silkin, who offered himself as a conciliator between the Party's left and right wings. At the electoral college, held the day before the Annual Conference in Brighton in October, Silkin was eliminated in the first ballot and in a photofinish, in which the abstention of a number of MPs who had supported Silkin was decisive, Healey defeated Benn by the narrowest of margins. The ensuing conference produced further victories for the parliamentary leadership, notably in the election of the National Executive Committee and on the control of the Party's election manifesto. Although there was growing pressure from within the Party for a truce, symbolised by a meeting of the NEC and trade union leaders at Bishops Stortford in January 1982, Michael Foot's problems were by no means solved. Tension persisted between Tony Benn, who failed to secure election to the Shadow Cabinet in November, and his parliamentary colleagues. Under pressure from MPs, the NEC instituted an inquiry into the influence in the constituency parties of a Trotskyite group, the Militant Tendency.

"Wets" versus "Dries".

The Chancellor's tough Budget in March 1981 brought to the surface the tensions that had existed for some time within the Government and the Conservative Party generally. In an attempt to reassert her authority, Mrs. Thatcher undertook a major ministerial reshuffle in September. Among those dismissed was one of her most outspoken critics (who became widely known as "wets"), Sir Ian Gilmour, and another, James Prior, was switched from the Department of Employment to the Northern Ireland Office. Most of those who were promoted were loyal colleagues of the Prime Minister. Particularly significant were the appointments of Norman Tebbit as Secretary of State for Employment, charged with the task of introducing new legal curbs upon the trade unions, and of Nigel Lawson as Secretary of State for Energy who lost no time in announcing the Government's intention of privatising important parts of the state-owned North Sea oil and gas industries. The reshuffle, however, failed to silence the Prime Minister's critics within the Cabinet. After a lengthy battle, they succeeded in forcing the Chancellor of the Exchequer to make some relaxations in his plans for public spending in 1982–3 although he insisted upon recouping part of the cost in increased employee national insurance contributions. Their determination to press for a more radical change in economic strategy was strengthened by the continuing rise in the level of unemployment, which in January 1982 passed the 3 million mark, and by the financial problems of many companies which resulted in a record number of bankruptcies.

Social Unrest.

The Government's economic policies were alleged to be one of the contributory factors behind the ugly street violence which broke out in Brixton in April 1981 and in various cities, notably Liverpool, Manchester and London, three months later. Following the Brixton riots, the Government appointed a distinguished judge, Lord Scarman, to inquire into their causes. His report, completed in November, concluded that there had been a breakdown of confidence between the coloured community and the police against a background of urban deprivation, racial disadvantage and a rising level of street crime. The Liverpool riots prompted the Prime Minister to send a top-level task force, led by a Cabinet minister, Michael Heseltine, to investigate the area's problems and to find ways of overcoming them. Unemployment continued to keep down the number of industrial disputes. The Government became

embroiled, however, in a major dispute with its own employees. Incensed by the Government's failure to honour its agreement that civil service pay should be fixed on the basis of fair comparison with equivalent work in the private sector, civil servants began a series of selective strikes in March which lasted for 21 weeks and had a major impact upon the work of the Government, for instance seriously disrupting the collection of tax revenue.

The Liberal/SDP Alliance.

Labour's continuing problems and the Government's economic record provided fertile ground for the launching of the Liberal/SDP Alliance. Its first real test (although it was formally endorsed by the Liberal Assembly only in September) occurred at a parliamentary by-election in Warrington in July 1981 where, in a safe Labour seat of a kind generally considered to be unpromising for the SDP, Roy Jenkins almost succeeded in overturning the Labour majority. Three months later, a Liberal, who had lost his deposit in the 1979 General Election, won the Conservative marginal seat of Croydon North West. Most dramatic of all, however, was Shirley Williams' victory in the safe Conservative seat of Crosby in late November. She thus became the first MP to be elected under the SDP's colours but the 24th member of its parliamentary group, nine further Labour MPs having transferred their allegiance since the inauguration of the Party in March. The SDP did not contest the county council elections in May but it won many local by-elections and, as a result of the defection of a majority of the Labour councillors in Islington, it took control of its first council. At the end of 1981 the opinion polls predicted a decisive victory for the Alliance were there to be an immediate general election. However, its popularity began to decline during the first few months of 1982 as the SDP (by then the third largest party in the House of Commons with 27 MPs) began to finalise its constitution and policy programme and as strains emerged in its alliance with the Liberals over the distribution of seats for the next general election. Nonetheless its momentum was maintained by Roy Jenkins' victory in the Glasgow, Hillhead by-election in March 1982, although in the May local elections it secured very few successes.

The Falkland Islands Crisis.

The Argentinian invasion of the Falkland Islands, British colonial territory in the South Atlantic, at the beginning of April 1982 provoked a major political crisis in Britain. At a special session of Parliament, the first to be held on a Saturday since the Suez crisis of 1956, there was almost universal condemnation of the Government's failure to take action to defend the Falklands against Argentinian aggression. Both the Foreign Secretary, Lord Carrington, and the Defence Secretary, John Nott, offered their resignations to the Prime Minister but only the former resigned (to be replaced by Francis Pym), along with two of his ministerial colleagues at the Foreign Office. Amidst great patriotic fervour, the Government despatched a major naval task force to re-take the islands. As it sailed on its long voyage to the South Atlantic, the United States Secretary of State, Alexander Haig, shuttled back and forth between London and Buenos Aires in an attempt to find a diplomatic solution to the crisis.

War in the South Atlantic.

A month after the task force had set out, military action commenced with British aircraft bombing Port Stanley airfield and clashes in the air and at sea. Following further unsuccessful efforts to reach a negotiated settlement, this time by the Secretary-General of the United Nations, British troops landed on East Falkland and, after 3½ weeks of bitter fighting, they encircled Port Stanley and secured the surrender of the Argentinian forces. During the conflict, over 1,000 lives were lost (255 British and 720 Argentinian). Fearing further Argentinian aggression, the Government had to make arrangements for a large permanent garrison on the islands. It also established a top-level committee of inquiry, under the chairmanship of Lord Franks, to investigate the events leading up to the crisis.

The Peace Movement.

The achievements of the task force resulted in strong public support for the armed forces and there were scenes of great jubilation on their return to this country. In other respects too defence attracted considerable public attention. The Campaign for Nuclear Disarmament organised a number of major demonstrations against the Government's nuclear weapons policy and peace camps were established at some of the bases where Cruise missiles were due to be sited in the autumn of 1983, such as Greenham Common near Newbury. Unilateral nuclear disarmament was adopted by the Labour Party as official policy at its 1982 Conference and it was recommended by a committee of the Church of England, although early in 1983 this recommendation was rejected by the Church's Synod in favour of multilateral disarmament, but with the proviso that Britain should never be the first to use nuclear weapons. To counter the arguments of the peace movement, Mrs. Thatcher appointed one of the Government's most effective orators, Michael Heseltine, to be Secretary of State for Defence in January 1983, replacing John Nott who some months earlier had announced his intention of retiring from politics at the next general election.

The Difficulties of the Opposition.

In some respects 1982 was an easier year for the leadership of the Labour Party. Michael Foot and Denis Healey were re-elected as Leader and Deputy Leader unopposed and they increased their control over the National Executive Committee. However, the Party's problems were by no means resolved. At a time of national crisis and patriotic fervour the task of Opposition leader is never easy and this was one factor contributing to a steady decline in the popularity of Mr. Foot among the electorate. His difficulties were exacerbated by continuing rows within the Party. Following receipt of the report into the activities of the Militant Tendency, it was decided to require all groups that wished to operate within the Party to register and to meet certain conditions laid down by the NEC. In the opinion of the NEC, Militant failed to satisfy these conditions but action to expel its leaders was delayed by legal complications. These and other problems were reflected in the Party's electoral popularity. In October 1982 it narrowly succeeded in winning the Conservative marginal seat of Birmingham, Northfield, but in February 1983 it suffered the crushing blow of losing Bermondsey, one of the safest Labour seats in the country. This setback was to some extent offset by the retention of the marginal seat of Darlington a month later.

The 1983 General Election.

Throughout most of 1982 the Government, and Mrs. Thatcher in particular, enjoyed a commanding lead in the opinion polls. This was a remarkable achievement for a government in the fourth year of its existence, particularly in view of the continuing upward trend in unemployment, and it largely reflected public approval of the Government's handling of the Falklands crisis (and it was exonerated by the Franks Committee for not having averted the Argentinian invasion). From early 1983 onwards the continuing Conservative lead in the opinion polls fuelled speculation about an early general election. The Prime Minister, who could easily have dampened such speculation, did not do so. Instead, having seen an analysis of the municipal election results in May, she decided on a snap poll on 9 June.

Potentially, the election could have been of exceptional interest. For the first time since the 1920s it was a three-horse race, with the Liberal/SDP Alliance contesting every seat in mainland Britain. The constituency map had also been extensively redrawn since 1979, with many well-known MPs having to fight new constituencies. In practice, however, it produced few excitements. The commanding lead of the Conservatives was never challenged during the campaign and interest therefore focused upon the contest between Labour and the Alliance for second place. Labour's difficulties were aggravated, in what was an increasingly presidential-style campaign, by unfavourable comparisons drawn by most voters between Mr. Foot and Mrs. Thatcher.

A Decisive Conservative Victory.

From the very first result there was no doubt about the outcome of the election. With the Labour vote in retreat everywhere and with the Alliance polling well but failing to secure a real breakthrough, the Conservatives coasted to a decisive victory, winning an overall majority of 144, only two short of the massive majority won by Labour in the landslide of 1945. (For the full results, *see* **D3–4**.) In terms of votes, however, the Conservative share of the vote (43%) had *fallen* since 1979. What had happened was that the Conservatives had won a large number of seats because the opposition was divided, with the Alliance eating seriously into the Labour vote. Labour's share of the vote (28%) was the lowest since the early 1920s and it held only two seats in southern England outside London. Elsewhere it managed to hold on to seats and, with 209 MPs, was easily the second largest party. The Alliance polled almost as many votes as Labour (26%) but because its vote was less concentrated it won many fewer seats (only 23), and had to be content with coming second in as many as 313 constituencies. The result was a particular disappointment for the SDP, most of whose leading members, apart from Roy Jenkins and David Owen, were defeated. Other prominent casualties in the election included Tony Benn, Albert Booth, Joan Lestor and David Ennals, all former Labour Ministers.

Mrs. Thatcher's Second Term.

Strengthened by her success at the polls, Mrs. Thatcher made various ministerial changes designed to increase her dominance over the Cabinet. She sacked Francis Pym, who had been Foreign Secretary since the start of the Falklands crisis but with whom she had never enjoyed an easy relationship, and replaced him with Sir Geoffrey Howe, who had been her loyal Chancellor of the Exchequer since 1979. In his place, she promoted Nigel Lawson, a keen supporter of her economic policies. As a reward for his work as Party Chairman, she appointed Cecil Parkinson to head a new department, combining Trade and Industry. William Whitelaw left the Home Office but remained Deputy Prime Minister and was elevated to the House of Lords as a Viscount. This was the first hereditary peerage to be conferred since 1964. (However, neither he nor the second such peer, the former Speaker, George Thomas, had male heirs; the hereditary principle was to be fully restored only in 1984 when an earldom was conferred upon Harold Macmillan on the occasion of his 90th birthday.) Victory at the polls, however, did not assure Mrs. Thatcher of an easy time. On various issues, including reductions in NHS manpower, control of local authorities, fuel prices and housing benefits, there was open criticism from Conservative backbenchers, sometimes about the substance of what the Government was doing, and often about its presentation. The most serious embarrassment concerned the personal life of Cecil Parkinson. The disclosure that his former secretary was expecting his child did not lead to his immediate resignation. However, further revelations during the Party Conference, which but for this would have been a victory celebration, made his departure from the Government inevitable and resulted in the appointment of Norman Tebbit to replace him (he had earlier handed over the Party Chairmanship to John Selwyn Gummer).

New Opposition Leaders.

Shortly after the General Election, both Michael Foot and Denis Healey announced their intention of standing down as Leader and Deputy Leader of the Labour Party at the Party Conference in October 1983. Four candidates stood for the leadership, but early in the campaign it soon emerged that left-winger, Neil Kinnock, would be the easy winner over Roy Hattersley, the leading "moderate" candidate. Interest therefore focused upon the contest for the deputy leadership where, although there were again four candidates, the race was between Hattersley (both he and Kinnock had agreed to stand for both offices and to serve under the other) and Michael Meacher, the standard bearer for the left in the absence of Tony Benn. Although there were close decisions in a number of trade unions, Hattersley emerged as a comfortable winner, thus giving the Party the so-called "dream ticket" of balanced leadership which many supporters believed was essential if it was to rebuild its electoral support. That this was going to be a lengthy process was acknowledged in the choice of a leader aged only 41. A similar development occurred also in the SDP where David Owen, aged 45, was elected unopposed to replace Roy Jenkins as leader.

The Cruise Missile Debate.

Failure to reach a negotiated arms control agreement on intermediate-range missiles led the Government to proceed with the deployment of US Cruise missiles in Britain. This decision was endorsed by the House of Commons in October 1983 which also rejected a proposal for a dual-key control system, designed to ensure that the missiles could be used only with the consent of the British Government. This decision, and that of the German Parliament to commence deployment of Pershing II missiles, resulted in a Soviet walkout from the arms control talks at Geneva. The first Cruise missiles arrived in Britain at Greenham Common, near Newbury, in November and were operational by Christmas. Demonstrations against these developments continued throughout the year and were fuelled by tensions in the Anglo-American alliance over the US invasion in October 1983 of the Caribbean island of Grenada, an independent member of the Commonwealth, despite the serious reservations of the British Government. Sir Geoffrey Howe's handling of this crisis and of the decision early in 1984 to ban trade unions from the Government Communications Centre (GCHQ) was widely criticised. At the same time, however, there were signs that Western leaders' attitudes towards the Warsaw Pact were softening, symbolised by Mrs. Thatcher's visit to Hungary in February 1984, her first visit to a Communist country, by her decision to travel to Moscow for the funerals of Presidents Andropov and Chernenko, and by her warmth towards the new Soviet leader, Mr. Gorbachev, on his accession to office in March 1985.

Implementing its Manifesto.

The Queen's Speech for the first session of the new Parliament contained few surprises. Various measures, such as the privatisation of British Telecom and bills on data protection and police powers, had been introduced in the last Parliament but had been lost as a result of the early dissolution; others, including the abolition of the Greater London Council and the metropolitan county councils, the creation of a quango to run London Transport, and new curbs on local authorities, had featured prominently in the Conservative Manifesto. The Government also proceeded with its plans further to regulate the activities of trade unions, introducing legislation requiring the periodic election of union officials, and the holding of secret ballots before strike action and to decide whether to maintain a fund for financing political objectives. The prospect of a further five years of Conservative rule injected a new realism in most union leaders and this, coupled with a less strident tone on the part of ministers following Tom King's appointment to replace Norman Tebbit as Secretary of State for Employment, led to concessions on the last of these proposals. Industrial relations problems, however, remained in the public eye, especially in the printing industry where there were a number of serious disputes, including a confrontation between the National Graphical Association and a Warrington newspaper publisher which led to protracted litigation and in the mining industry, where a bitter battle against pit closures developed.

Privatisation.

Privatisation—limiting the role of the state and extending the operation of market forces—was one of the hallmarks of the Government. It embarked upon the biggest change in the boundary between the public and private sectors since 1945. It encouraged the contracting out to private firms of work that previously was undertaken by public bodies (e.g. local authority cleansing and refuse collection services, NHS cleaning, laundry and catering); it relaxed statutory monopoly powers and licensing arrangements in various sectors (e.g. buses and telecommunications); and it sold all or part of a number of public enterprises. During its first term

these included selling a majority stake in British Aerospace, in the oil-producing side of the British National Oil Corporation—Britoil—and in Cable and Wireless. These were dwarfed by the sales of just over 50% of British Telecom in November 1984 and of almost all the shares in British Gas – the largest ever flotation of a company – two years later. Other sales during its second term included Jaguar, the Trustee Savings Bank and British Airways and, during 1987, the Government disposed of its remaining shareholding in BP and sold British Airports.

Miners' Strike.

In March 1984 the National Coal Board (NCB) announced plans to close various pits to eliminate excess capacity. This exacerbated tensions that already existed in the industry and rapidly escalated into a national strike. Given the history of relations since the early 1970s between the miners and the Conservatives, a major confrontation seemed inevitable. But few predicted its length or bitterness. The NCB, whose chairman Ian MacGregor had earlier established a reputation for toughness at British Steel, with the full backing of the Government, was determined not to surrender; its attitude was matched by that of the striking miners, led by Arthur Scargill, who were driven on by the feeling that they were defending the very existence of their communities. The NUM, however, failed to bring the economy to its knees as it had done in 1972–4. Not only was it unsuccessful in attracting effective support from the rest of the trade union movement, it also was itself divided, with about one third of its members, especially in the prosperous Nottinghamshire coalfield, refusing to join the strike. The Government too went to some lengths to ensure that alternative sources of fuel were available. The NUM's attempts to prevent working miners getting to work led to violent scenes between pickets and the large numbers of police who were deployed, often in riot gear, to restrain them. Eventually, after various abortive rounds of negotiation, striking miners, many of whom were suffering severe financial hardship, started to trickle back to work and, after almost exactly a year, the NUM decided to end the strike without reaching an agreement with the NCB. Quite apart from the damage that it did to the economy, the strike imposed major strains upon both the TUC and the Labour Party. The Labour leadership sought to distance itself from the more extreme statements and behaviour of Arthur Scargill and his followers while supporting the miners' case. It was criticised, however, for not giving more wholehearted support by the left wing of the Party, whose ranks in Parliament had been strengthened in March 1984 by the victory of Tony Benn in a by-election at Chesterfield.

Brighton Bombing.

The Conservative Party Conference in October 1984 at Brighton was overshadowed by a bomb explosion at the Grand Hotel where most of the Cabinet was staying. Mrs. Thatcher herself had a narrow escape and, among those seriously injured were Norman Tebbit and the Chief Whip. Responsibility was claimed by the IRA. A month earlier, Jim Prior had resigned as Secretary of State for Northern Ireland, choosing to return to the backbenches, thus removing from the Cabinet yet another critic of the Government's economic strategy. Ministers continued to be embarrassed by backbench revolts on various issues but the Government's majority in the Commons was never endangered. In the Lords, however, it was forced to amend its plans, for example over the cancellation of the GLC and metropolitan county elections in 1986. One Opposition backbencher, Tam Dalyell, had his persistence in probing the Government's account of the sinking of the Argentinian ship, the General Belgrano, during the Falklands crisis rewarded when a leak by a senior civil servant in the Ministry of Defence, Clive Ponting, revealed inconsistencies. Controversially, the Attorney-General decided to prosecute Mr. Ponting under the widely discredited Official Secrets Act and when, contrary to all expectations, he was acquitted a major political row erupted.

Close to Dollar Parity.

The damage inflicted on the economy by the

miners' strike (estimated by the Chancellor of the Exchequer to have cost £2¾ billion) was one of the factors behind a slide in the exchange rate. Miscalculations by the Government, however, also contributed to the rapid decline in the dollar value of sterling. Faced with the imminent possibility of parity between the pound and the dollar, the Chancellor was forced to re-introduce minimum lending rate and to force up interest rates. This eventually succeeded in calming the nerves of the money markets. But it had an adverse effect on the prospects of economic revival. The Government was widely attacked for its failure to take direct action to alleviate the problem of unemployment not only by the Opposition but also by some of the most senior members of its own Party and by prominent members of the Church of England. One such critic was the Earl of Stockton, formerly Harold Macmillan, who took advantage of the first televised debate from the House of Lords in January 1985 to reach a wide audience for his views.

Getting the Message Across.

By the summer of 1985, the Government's popularity was at a low ebb. Continuing record levels of unemployment, cuts in many public services, and long-running industrial disputes (the year-long miners' strike was followed by an equally protracted teachers' dispute), all contributed to the worst by-election defeat for the Conservatives for many years at Brecon and Radnor in July. In an attempt to improve the Government's standing, Mrs. Thatcher made a number of important changes in the Cabinet in September. As Party Chairman she appointed her close ally, Norman Tebbit (and to assist him in getting the Government's message across she recruited best-selling author, Jeffrey Archer, as his deputy). In the sensitive area of law and order she shifted Douglas Hurd from Northern Ireland to the Home Office. His predecessor, Leon Brittan, who was generally regarded as a poor performer on TV and who had been widely criticised for putting pressure on the BBC to cancel a programme on political extremism in Northern Ireland, replaced Norman Tebbit as Secretary of State for Trade and Industry. For a few months these changes seemed to have been successful, even though the new Home Secretary was immediately embroiled in controversy over the outbreak of rioting in Handsworth in Birmingham and in Brixton and Tottenham in London and over the tactics adopted by the police in attempting to restore order.

Stronger Labour Leadership.

Although Labour did well in the county council elections in May 1985, it continued to share the spoils of the Government's unpopularity with the Alliance which succeeded in breaking the two-party hold on most of the counties in England and in winning the Brecon and Radnor by-election. The strains within the Labour movement caused by the miners' strike persisted as a result of the creation of a breakaway union, the Union of Democratic Miners, which successfully challenged the National Union of Mineworkers in parts of the country. In addition, the Labour leadership was challenged to support various left-wing Labour controlled local authorities in their defiance of the new financial curbs that had been imposed by the Government. At the Party's Annual Conference, Neil Kinnock answered those who had criticised him for lack of leadership by making a vigorous attack both upon Arthur Scargill and upon hard left Labour councillors, particularly in Liverpool. His stand won him support among Labour M.P.s and in the opinion polls but it did not resolve the problems facing the Labour Party. The NEC launched an inquiry into the running of the Liverpool District Party which early in 1986 recommended action which could lead to the expulsion of various leading members. Labour councillors in Liverpool and Lambeth were also confronted with bankruptcy and disqualification following court action initiated by the District Auditor over their delay in setting a rate. They and other Labour councillors facing similar penalties pressed the Labour leadership to indemnify them on Labour's return to power.

The Westland Saga.

The Government's calmed nerves were soon disturbed by an extraordinary internal battle over the fate of a West Country helicopter manufacturer, Westland plc. Throughout the Christmas recess an unusually public row simmered between two Cabinet ministers over the merits of two alternative solutions to the financial problems of the company. The Defence Secretary, Michael Heseltine, campaigned hard for a European solution whereas the Trade and Industry Secretary, Leon Brittan, with the backing of the Prime Minister, favoured leaving the decision to the company's shareholders which in effect meant that the company would be bailed out by the American firm, Sikorsky. The first casualty was Michael Heseltine who walked dramatically out of a Cabinet meeting, refusing to accept the Prime Minister's attempt to shackle his campaign. The next fortnight saw intense political controversy, fuelled by allegations first over different versions of a meeting between Leon Brittan and the chief executive of Westland and then over the unprecedented leaking of a letter to Michael Heseltine from the Solicitor-General. Although he retained the support of the Prime Minister, Leon Brittan's position became untenable and he followed his adversary onto the backbenches. Westland continued to dominate the headlines for some weeks but the focus of attention switched to the company itself and its shareholders, who eventually backed the American option. The Government, however, was immediately involved in a new political row over the future of the state-owned car firm, British Leyland, when it was disclosed that discussions had reached an advanced stage over the sale of different parts of the company to General Motors and Ford. The Government was forced to break off its negotiations with Ford over Austin-Rover and this change of course further dented the Government's reputation.

Anglo-Irish Agreement.

Westland and British Leyland were not the only sources of trouble for the Government in the early months of 1986. In November 1985, Mrs. Thatcher and the Irish premier, Dr. Fitzgerald, signed an Anglo-Irish Agreement. Both Governments affirmed the status of Ulster as part of the UK so long as this was the wish of the majority of its people; and they set up an inter-governmental conference to enable the Irish Government to comment on certain aspects of Northern Irish affairs, and to foster improved cross-border cooperation, particularly on security, establishing an inter-governmental conference to discuss issues of common interest This provoked the resignation of all the Unionist M.P.s in protest at what they saw as the first step towards a united Ireland and their stand attracted the support of a number of senior Conservative M.P.s, one of whom, Ian Gow, who earlier had been one of Mrs. Thatcher's closest aides, resigned from the Government. All but one of the Unionists were re-elected in by-elections held in January 1986. The Government's refusal to abandon the Agreement, however, led to a one-day strike in the province in February and to further acts of defiance.

A World Leader.

After six years in office, Mrs. Thatcher had become one of the most experienced political leaders in the world. She enjoyed a very close relationship with President Reagan, demonstrating her support by allowing US aircraft based in Britain to be used in a reprisal attack on centres of terrorism in Libya in April 1986 and by refusing to join international criticism of Reagan over the sale of arms to Iran in exchange for hostages (the so-called Irangate Affair). On other issues too Mrs. Thatcher took an independent line. Although condemning apartheid in South Africa, she refused to support the call for economic sanctions. In an attempt to maintain unity, a Commonwealth Eminent Persons Group, which included the former Conservative Chancellor, Lord Barber, was sent on a mission to South Africa to investigate means of promoting peaceful political change. Despite its negative conclusions, published in 1986, Mrs. Thatcher persuaded her EEC colleagues to send Sir Geoffrey Howe on a further mission. Its failure resulted in a Commonwealth decision to take various economic measures against South Africa but the British Government agreed only to impose voluntary bans upon new investment and the promotion of tourism and, in conjunction with the EEC, to stop imports of iron and steel.

Big Bang in the City.

Westland was not the only cause of unusual public attention on the business world. A rash of company mergers and takeovers gave rise to extensive advertising campaigns as rival bidders sought to influence shareholders' votes. The battle over the future of the Distillers Company was particularly bitter. However, the eventual victor, Guinness, was widely criticised when a number of undertakings given at the time of the takeover were not honoured and, following disclosure of improprieties during the course of the bid, its chief executive, Ernest Saunders, and a number of his advisers were forced to resign. This affair, coupled with the radical changes that occurred in the City of London in October 1986, led to pressure on the Government to introduce tighter regulation of the financial markets. The so-called 'Big Bang' opened up membership of the Stock Exchange and extended competition in share dealing and in financial services generally. One consequence was a rapid growth in foreign involvement in the City with new firms offering extremely high salaries to attract key staff. Although the Government did introduce some new statutory controls, it stuck to its view that self-regulation was more likely to be effective.

Election Speculation.

The Government also benefited from the spectacularly successful publicity generated by Mrs. Thatcher's visit to the Soviet Union in April 1987. This confirmation of her stature as a world figure contrasted sharply with the reception accorded to Mr. Kinnock by President Reagan when he visited Washington to explain Labour's non-nuclear defence strategy.

The 1987 General Election.

A good performance by the Conservatives in the local elections in May 1987 led Mrs. Thatcher to seek an immediate dissolution of Parliament with polling day on 11 June. More than ever before, the style of the campaign was determined by the media. Every TV and radio station provided near-saturation coverage and the parties responded by seeking to exploit all the time and space offered to them. The result was an almost presidential campaign with a succession of 'photo-opportunities' of the party leaders. Unlike 1983, the Labour Party was in much better shape to mount this kind of campaign, making full use of the relative youth and informality of its leader, Neil Kinnock. However, the three weeks of the campaign were remarkably uneventful with no incident seriously disrupting the stage management of the party managers. Nor did all the money and effort expended by the parties appear to have much effect upon public opinion. With only one hiccough, the Conservatives' lead in the opinion polls remained secure. Labour's position improved by a few points but it was almost entirely at the expense of the Alliance.

Third Conservative Victory.

At the eve of the poll the only uncertainty concerned the size of the Conservative majority and the impact that tactical voting might have in some marginal constituencies. From the first declared result in Torbay, it was clear that the majority was going to be larger than most commentators had predicted and that the Alliance in particular was not going to benefit from tactical voting on a scale comparable with that seen in recent by-elections. The final outcome was an overall majority for the Conservatives of 101 over all other parties, a fall of only 43 from its landslide in 1983. They gained 12 seats, and lost 29; Labour gained 26, mainly in Scotland and the North of England, and lost 6; and the Alliance gained 3 and lost 8. Nationally, there had been a swing of 2.5% from Conservative to Labour since 1983 but this figure hides the extent of Labour's success in Scotland (where it won 50 out of the 72 seats) and Wales, and its poor showing in London (where it lost 3 seats) and the South East. As never before, the political map of Britain was divided

with the Conservatives overwhelmingly predominant south of a line from the Wash to the Severn, and Labour strengthening its hold on the urban areas in the North. For details of the election result, *see* D3–4.

Mrs. Thatcher's New Cabinet.

The election hattrick – Mrs. Thatcher was the first Prime Minister since Lord Liverpool in 1827 to win three successive election victories – was a personal triumph for the Prime Minister. Relatively few changes were made in the Cabinet but their effect was to strengthen still further her position. Out went John Biffen, who had criticised Mrs. Thatcher's style and some of her policies; following strains during the campaign between Downing Street and party headquarters, Norman Tebbit also left the Cabinet at his own request, but he retained the Chairmanship of the Party until the Autumn. Lord Young, who had played an increasingly influential role during the Election, was promoted, Cecil Parkinson was brought back after nearly four years on the backbenches following his personal difficulties, and most of the newcomers, such as John Moore and John Major, were close personal supporters of the Prime Minister.

Strains in the Alliance.

The Election result was especially disappointing for the Alliance. Far from breaking the mould of two-party politics, its overall vote fell, it suffered a net loss of 5 seats including some of its leading M.P.s, and it failed to win almost any of the marginal seats it had targeted. On the other hand it had still gained 23% of the votes cast. Reflecting on this performance over the weekend after polling day, David Steel called for the 'democratic fusion' of the two wings of the Alliance into a single united party. His initiative set in train many months of protracted and increasingly bitter negotiations. On the Liberal side, the overwhelming majority of the Party accepted the case for merger albeit tinged for many with regret at the passing of the party which traced its origins to the eighteenth century. The SDP however split in two. Its leader, David Owen, supported by two of his Parliamentary colleagues, mounted a powerful campaign against merger; the other two M.P.s, one of whom—Robert Maclennan—was elected leader after the SDP voted to open negotiations with the Liberals, and prominent members such as Shirley Williams and Roy Jenkins took the opposite view. During the first few months of 1988, the negotiations were concluded and the outcome ratified by both parties. The new party, the Social and Liberal Democrats (SLD), was launched in March 1988. Initially it had joint leadership—David Steel and Robert Maclennan—but in July 1988 Paddy Ashdown was elected leader, defeating Alan Beith.

The Next Moves Forward.

Far from running out of steam, the Government embarked upon a radical programme for its third term of office. Its initial agenda, following closely its election manifesto, included the abolition of domestic rates and their replacement by a flat-rate community charge, or poll tax as its critics preferred to claim; privatisation of the electricity supply, steel and water industries; far-reaching reform of education, including giving schools the right to opt out of local authority control and the abolition of the Inner London Education Authority; introduction of radical changes in the social security system; and further reforms of housing, immigration control and industrial relations. With its substantial majority, the Government's prospects were set fair. However, its standing and self-confidence suffered a severe blow from almost the only area of government in which radical changes had not been introduced since 1979: the National Health Service. Throughout the Autumn public attention focused relentlessly upon the financial difficulties being experienced by many health authorities, especially in large cities, which were leading to closed wards and postponement of operations. The Government's defence of its record, based largely on statistics which demonstrated substantial increases in overall spending on the NHS, failed to carry weight against a barrage of individual instances of breakdown in services. To make matters worse, the Secretary of State for Social Services, John Moore, was away on extended sick-leave. In an attempt to regain the initiative, the Prime Minister launched in January 1988 a fundamental review of the NHS.

Tax-cutting Budget.

The Government's difficulties with the NHS had a damaging effect upon Conservative morale and worked wonders for the Opposition. After many unrewarding years, Labour had found an issue on which the Government was vulnerable and its case attracted strong public support. In other areas however the Government continued to ride high. In his 1988 Budget the Chancellor was able to achieve his goal of reducing the standard rate of income tax by a further 2p to 25p, and of introducing various major tax reforms. His approach was criticised by his opponents on two grounds. It was argued first that priority should have been given to increasing public spending, particularly on the NHS, rather than to cutting taxes, and second that the principal beneficiaries of the Budget were the well-off. This charge was fuelled a month later when changes in social security benefits hit many low earners. One change in particular, relating to housing benefit, led to such pressure on Conservative backbenchers that the Government was compelled to revise its decision. Ministers also faced a difficult few months in securing the passage of controversial legislation on the community charge and educational reform through the House of Lords. Its task there was exacerbated by the retirement through ill-health early in 1988 of Viscount Whitelaw whose popularity and experience had proved invaluable in the past both in Cabinet discussions and in Parliamentary business. On the other hand, the Government still enjoyed the exceptional good fortune of a divided and ineffective Opposition. Despite its better showing in Parliament, the Labour leadership was distracted for much of 1988 by a challenge which under the protracted electoral college system took six months to resolve; and the Social and Liberal Democrats had the daunting task of rebuilding their support in competition with David Owen's Social Democratic Party.

Mid-term Difficulties.

By the end of 1988, Nigel Lawson's tax-cutting Budget was looking ill-advised. Booming consumer spending had led to the recurrence of two all too familiar problems: inflation and a trade deficit. Inflation, the Government's own touchstone of economic success, rose steadily, reaching almost 8% by March 1989. The balance of payments deficit at the turn of the year broke all previous records. Virtually alone, the Chancellor remained confident that these were merely temporary and minor hiccoughs in the country's economic recovery which could be overcome by the single weapon of increasing interest rates. In other respects too the Government was experiencing mid-term difficulties. It faced an uphill task in convincing the public of the merits of major measures such as the introduction of the community charge, or poll tax, and privatisation of water and electricity. Its reputation for competence also began to look tarnished. Increasing public concern about food safety was highlighted in angry exchanges between the Ministry of Agriculture and the Department of Health over salmonella in eggs which led to the resignation of the outspoken junior Health Minister, Edwina Currie; and a run of transport disasters turned an unusual and unflattering spotlight on the performance of the Secretary of State for Transport, Paul Channon. Most damaging of all, the Government's problems over the NHS persisted. In mid-1988, Mrs. Thatcher split the DHSS, appointing Kenneth Clarke to take a high profile in Health, and relegating the hapless John Moore to Social Security. The benefits of this change were soured by bitterness over the handling of nurse regrading and by continuing uncertainty over the outcome of the Prime Minister's Review. The eventual White Paper, published in January 1989, heralded far-reaching changes and was greeted by almost universal opposition, spearheaded by the doctors.

A Divided Opposition.

Despite all these problems, the Conservatives' lead in the opinion polls did not disappear im-

mediately. In part this reflected the electoral collapse of the Centre. The SLD and the SDP seemed intent upon destroying each other, not only splitting the former Alliance share of the vote—thereby enabling the Conservatives to scrape home in the Richmond by-election in February 1989—but also reducing their combined support as they no longer appeared a credible alternative. Labour benefited also from their disarray but, after three successive election defeats, it had its own problems of credibility. Following the 1987 Election, Neil Kinnock initiated a fundamental review of all aspects of Labour policy. Although he beat off easily the challenge to his position from Tony Benn at the 1988 Conference, his attempts to present a new image were dented by continuing difficulties over defence policy which highlighted the role of the trade unions in the Party's affairs. Labour's problems were compounded by the loss of the safe seat of Glasgow Govan to the Scottish National Party in November 1988.

A Decade in Office.

May 1989 marked the tenth anniversary of Mrs. Thatcher's accession to office. Throughout the decade she had dominated British politics to an extent unequalled in recent history. Within the Conservative Party her critics, with just one or two exceptions, had either retired or sat impotent on the backbenches. Radical changes had been implemented in almost every area of government, frequently against bitter opposition, and the Prime Minister often seemed to set the agenda and dictate the solution regardless of the issue—exchange rate policy, football hooliganism, and the environment to name just three recent examples. Abroad too she had outlasted most of her allies and adversaries. The former, led by President Reagan, feted her as a leading world statesman; and even those who disagreed accorded her considerable respect. However fate allowed little time for celebration. In June the Conservatives were defeated in the elections for the European Parliament, a result attributed to Mrs Thatcher's negative attitude towards Europe. In an attempt to restore her fortunes, the following month the Prime Minister undertook a more radical reshuffle than had been expected. In particular she moved a reluctant Sir Geoffrey Howe from the Foreign Office to the Leadership of the House of Commons with the courtesy title of Deputy Prime Minister. The handling of the negotiations with her most senior colleague, and her apparently cavalier treatment of a number of others tarnished her reputation. Nor did the promotion of John Major to Foreign Secretary inspire confidence. His inexperience in this field and his closeness to Mrs Thatcher signalled Downing Street's determination to control foreign policy. In the Autumn matters were no easier for the Prime Minister. Continuing tension between the Chancellor, Nigel Lawson, and her personal economic adviser, Sir Alan Walters, led to the Chancellor's abrupt resignation in October. To fill the gap, John Major was moved to the Treasury and Mrs Thatcher had to appoint a much more independently minded Douglas Hurd to the Foreign Office. Finally she had to face the indignity of a challenge to her position as Conservative leader from a backbench critic, Sir Anthony Meyer. Although not a credible challenger, he nonetheless attracted 33 votes and there were also about 25 abstentions.

Delors Plan and the Social Charter.

Always a determined defender of UK interests within the EEC, Mrs Thatcher took every opportunity of challenging the moves towards greater integration and a shift of power from national capitals to Brussels. She angered European opinion by refusing to reappoint Lord Cockfield as one of the British members of the European Commission and delivered a swingeing attack on the aspirations of many continental Europeans at a ceremony at the College of Europe in Bruges. During 1989 Britain became increasingly out of step with its partners. On monetary integration there were differences of view between the Prime Minister on the one hand and her Chancellor and Foreign Secretary on the other. At the Madrid Summit in June they obtained her reluctant acquiescence in the first stage of the Delors Plan (prepared by the

President of the Commission, Jacques Delors) including Britain's acceptance in principle to join the exchange rate mechanism (ERM) of the European Monetary System (EMS). However, Britain alone opposed stages 2 and 3 of the Plan, leading to monetary union and a single currency. Britain was also isolated in its opposition to the Social Charter, a wide-ranging statement of rights on employment, including pay, working hours, leave and free time, social benefits, vocational training, equal opportunities, worker consultation and participation, which Mrs Thatcher argued would impose excessive burdens on industry and introduce undesirable state control.

Out of Line or Ahead of Time?

On other overseas issues Britain was becoming increasingly isolated. The special relationship with the USA became weaker with the retirement in January 1989 of Mrs Thatcher's close personal friend Ronald Reagan, and his replacement as President by George Bush who appeared to be closer to a number of other European leaders. On the question of sanctions against South Africa, Mrs Thatcher was at odds with both the Commonwealth, producing her own communiqué at the Heads of Government conference in Kuala Lumpur in October 1989, and the EEC. Britain welcomed the reforms introduced by the new State President of South Africa, F. W. de Klerk, and the release of Nelson Mandela in February 1990 after 27 years in detention. In the Government's view, these steps called for a positive response through a progressive relaxation of sanctions lest they provoked a white backlash; its partners argued that pressure required to be maintained to ensure the dismantling of apartheid and the ending of the state of emergency.

Elsewhere, however, Mrs Thatcher claimed to be ahead of her colleagues. She had been one of the first world leaders to recognise the significance of Gorbachev's rise to power; and the changes that swept the Soviet Union and Eastern Europe during the second half of 1989 were heralded as part of the same process of freeing people from the shackles of state control and socialism that she had introduced in Britain. In contrast, the return to repression in China cast doubt on China's promises regarding Hong Kong and, faced with a "haemorrhage of talent", the Government had—despite criticism from its own supporters—to grant full British citizenship to about 50,000 leaders of the colony and their families. The Government also attracted international criticism over its decision to repatriate those Vietnamese boat people who did not qualify for refugee status. On a happier note, diplomatic relations were restored with Argentina, eight years after the Falklands War.

Return to Two-Party Politics.

The early months of 1989 saw an upturn in the Labour Party's fortunes. Neil Kinnock began to score some Parliamentary victories over the Prime Minister; there was a general view among commentators that Labour's frontbench team matched and probably outshone their counterparts; and the White Paper on the NHS provided an issue on which they were able to lead public opinion. This was reflected in two victories at the polls: the Vale of Glamorgan by-election in May and the Euro-elections in June. At the Party Conference in October, Mr Kinnock completed his transformation of the Party's image by winning overwhelming endorsement of the outcome of the policy reviews. Throughout the Autumn, Labour maintained a firm lead in the opinion polls and, in February 1990, this had stretched to around 15% and Neil Kinnock was rated above Mrs Thatcher. The Government's difficulties remained unabated. Despite unprecedently high interest rates, inflation showed little sign of falling; public doubts about its handling of the NHS were compounded by a six-month pay dispute with ambulancemen; and April 1990 heralded the introduction of the poll tax in England and Wales. British politics appeared to have returned to its familiar two-party character. Both the SLD—restyled as Liberal Democrats following a poll of members—and the SDP remained in the doldrums, suffering the discomfort of losing third place in the Euro-elections to the Greens. Their 15% share of the vote reflected a marked increase in environmental concern which affected all parties.

This prompted Mrs Thatcher to replace Nicholas Ridley as Environment Secretary with a more environmentally friendly Chris Patten and to introduce a "Green" Bill in the 1989–90 session. This was not the only move towards "softening" the Government's image, prompted in part by the introduction of TV cameras into the House of Commons in November 1989.

Conservatives in Disarray.

The unpopularity of the poll tax surpassed the worst fears of those Conservatives who had opposed its introduction. As local councils declared the initial level of tax, in almost every case—Tory and Labour controlled—well in excess of the Government's estimate, they were met by strong protest. Nor did the violence of some of the demonstrations, especially at a rally in London, rebound on the Government's critics. By April 1990 Labour's lead in the polls was over 20%, and the Prime Minister's personal popularity had plummetted. Better than expected local election results in May temporarily calmed Conservative nerves. Despite a difficult summer during which Labour's lead grew steadily, the autumn started well for the Government which appeared to be regaining the initiative, including the surprise announcement in October of Britain's entry into the exchange rate mechanism of the EMS. However, later the same month, any hopes of a revival in its electoral fortunes were dashed by the loss of one of the safest Conservative seats, Eastbourne, to the Liberal Democrats in a by-election following the murder by the IRA of Ian Gow. This reflected the impact of economic pressures, on this occasion hitting the previously prosperous South-East as much as other parts of the country, and a poor campaign. Against this background, the sudden resignation of Sir Geoffrey Howe after eleven years in the Cabinet and until his removal from the Foreign Office in 1989 one of Mrs Thatcher's closest advisers, would in any case have had a serious effect upon Conservative morale. But it was his resignation speech that proved devastating. His criticisms of her approach to key issues, particularly Europe, and of her style precipitated the end of her premiership.

The Departure of Mrs Thatcher.

Sir Geoffrey's attack and the response it evoked forced Michael Heseltine into declaring his candidature for the leadership of the Conservative Party. Since leaving the Cabinet in 1986 over Westland, he had in effect been preparing the ground for a bid for the leadership but he had stated repeatedly that he would not challenge Mrs Thatcher. Now, if he did not stand, there was the risk that others would step in to test the strength of the anti-Thatcher forces. Following a short campaign, in which Mr Heseltine skilfully made use of hostility towards the poll tax, he succeeded in attracting 152 votes, sufficient to force the contest to a second ballot under the Conservative Party's complex rules which require the winner to have a margin of at least 15% to win outright in the first round. In characteristic style, Mrs Thatcher declared within minutes of the announcement of the result that she would stand again. The following day, however, she was persuaded to consult her colleagues. After interviewing each of her Cabinet, she came reluctantly to the conclusion that her position was untenable, and announced her withdrawal. This opened the field to two further candidates: Douglas Hurd and John Major. A week later John Major topped the poll and, to avoid a third ballot, both his rivals stood down. On 28 November, Mrs Thatcher left Downing Street for the last time as Prime Minister, technically undefeated but having lost the confidence of her colleagues, and at the end of the longest premiership this century.

The Advent of John Major.

Although he was Mrs Thatcher's preferred choice as successor, John Major started to distance himself from her, immediately in the style of his Government and increasingly in policy as well. His Cabinet contained more changes than predicted. Norman Lamont, his campaign manager, was promoted to Chancellor of the Exchequer; Chris Patten succeeded Kenneth Baker as Party Chairman; and in a tactically astute move, Michael Heseltine was appointed to the Department of the Environment with the crucial task of finding a way out of the poll tax crisis. The new Prime Minister declared his intention of establishing a less presidential style. He sought to capitalise on his reputation as a "man in the street", and he began to talk of the social impact of policies and of the need for close collaboration with Europe in a manner little heard from his predecessor. However, before he had much opportunity to make his mark, he faced the exceptional challenge of war.

Gulf War.

In August 1990 Iraq invaded and annexed Kuwait. President Bush, with the active encouragement of Mrs Thatcher, pressed the UN Security Council first to impose economic sanctions and then to set a deadline for withdrawal. Meanwhile, a multinational coalition of forces was assembled in Saudi Arabia under American leadership and including a significant British contingent. Despite repeated efforts to find a diplomatic solution, the Iraqi President, Saddam Hussein, refused to withdraw. Shortly after the expiry of the UN deadline in January 1991, the coalition forces commenced an air attack, of unprecedented intensity and accuracy, on strategic targets in Iraq and Kuwait. This was followed by a land war in which heavy coalition casualties had been feared. However, Iraqi resistance had been worn down by weeks of air bombardment. The occupying troops surrendered or fled with only minimal force such that Kuwait was retaken and a ceasefire declared in a matter of days and with almost no coalition casualties. The war quickly established Mr Major on the international stage and – although British involvement was supported by Neil Kinnock and Paddy Ashdown – it gave the Prime Minister early opportunities to project himself as a national leader which, it was thought, would result in substantial political dividends for the Conservatives.

Conservative fortunes were indeed revived by the war and by the honeymoon enjoyed by any new leader. However, their impact was more short-lived than had been expected. British politics reverted very quickly to domestic issues, in particular the economic recession and the poll tax. Rather than riding on the crest of a victory wave of popularity, the Government was rebuffed in one of the biggest electoral upsets ever when it lost Ribble Valley in March 1991, again to the Liberal Democrats. Without question, the poll tax had been the cause of its defeat. Finding a solution was, however, proving more elusive than Ministers had hoped. In the Budget, the Chancellor sought to limit the damage caused by the tax by announcing a rebate of £140 per person, recouped by a 2½% increase in VAT. Two days later, Michael Heseltine announced that in 1993 the poll tax would be replaced by a new local tax based on property but also including a personal element. The details, which would establish whether this was to be the "son of poll tax" or a return to the rates, had still to be worked out, and proved to be difficult for a Government torn between loyalty towards the underlying principles of the poll tax – once described by Mrs Thatcher as her flagship – and recognition of its apparently fatal unpopularity in the minds of a majority of the electorate. To ease the burden of local government finance, Mr Heseltine also heralded a reform of local government to create a single-tier structure throughout the country.

A New Political Scene.

Perversely, after being attacked under Mrs Thatcher for being dictatorial, the Government was now accused of dithering. In the early Spring the opinion polls showed the Conservatives and Labour to be level-pegging, and a marked improvement in the fortunes of the Liberal Democrats, now unchallenged as the third party following the decision in June 1990 to wind up the SDP. Party politics were also transformed by the disappearance of one towering personality. The three major parties were led by individuals – John Major, Neil Kinnock and Paddy Ashdown – of similar age and standing. On policy too there was a convergence towards the centre. Labour had already moved in this direction as a result of its policy reviews and new image. Now the Conservatives were muting their radical stance and discarding the Thatcherite rhetoric. The pros-

pects for the General Election, due before June 1992, seemed therefore wide open. Following a poor Conservative showing in the May local elections (with widespread Labour and Liberal Democrat gains), speculation concerning an early election was dampened. The loss of the Monmouth by-election (on 16 May) to Labour dealt any lingering expectations of an early election a final blow. On a swing of over 12½%, in the second safest Conservative seat in Wales, Labour swept to victory with a 2,406 majority. Against this electoral background, with unemployment rising swiftly and interest rates still worryingly high, the country was set for a long and protracted battle in the run-up to the General Election.

Politics in the second half of 1991 and the first months of 1992 were shaped, firstly, by the knowledge that the General Election would have to take place by July of 1992, and secondly, that the economic setting within which the election would take place would be unpropitious for the government.

The Major Administration.

John Major devoted the first fifteen months before the election to establishing a distinctive image for himself and the government he led. He was constrained by some opinion within his own party from distancing himself too greatly from Margaret Thatcher in policy towards public spending, the economy in general, and European integration but spurred on by the knowledge that he had to set a course for the Conservative Party and the country different from that of his predecessor. In practice, Mr. Major's administration set a course for public policy sharply at variance with that which he had inherited. Willing as Mrs. Thatcher had been to modify principle for political advantage, Mr. Major effectively reinstated the politics of pragmatism as the first article of governing faith. This development was evident in five respects:

* The Government announced that the Poll Tax was to be abandoned and replaced by a "Council Tax" based on the value of property.
* Policy towards Europe was refashioned. Negotiations over European integration leading up to the Maastricht summit in December 1991 resulted in Britain securing a clause enabling it to opt out of Community agreements on social policy, and to stand back from monetary union. The Prime Minister took pains to commit himself rhetorically to the defence of Britain's national interests and sovereignty, and opposed any movement towards a federal European state in which sovereignty would be formally and legally divided between the Community and the member states. However, the agreement he secured was much closer in content to that which (for example) Douglas Hurd sought than that with which Margaret Thatcher would have been content. In practice, Major's diplomacy was almost as skilful as his marginalisation of right-wing dissenters within the Conservative Party. Mrs. Thatcher eventually supported him in a formal Commons vote on the outcome of Maastricht.
* The "Citizens' Charter" was launched in the summer of 1991 and relaunched six months later to underline the government's determination to promote the rights enjoyed by consumers of public services, including central and local government. Although its provisions did not extend to private industry and commerce, it showed Major's shrewdness in identifying widespread dissatisfaction at the quality of service received from public bodies with a belief that some public services could be held accountable without necessarily privatising them thoroughly. The programme assisted the government's aim to portray itself as mindful of the needs of consumers.
* Under Mr. Major, the government was on several occasions to show tactical flexibility and a willingness to spend money in order to defuse damaging issues. The compensation of haemophiliacs infected by the AIDS virus through being given contaminated blood was but one instance which marked a change of style at No. 10 Downing Street, and a shift towards the image of a caring government.
* Monetary policy, which since the entry into the Exchange Rate Mechanism had been effectively set in Germany rather than London, remained tight throughout the pre-election period. Al-

though nominal rates fell, real rates remained very high as the rate of inflation also dropped. Faced with a persisting recession, weak confidence among business people about commercial prospects, and the imminence of the General Election, fiscal policy was dramatically loosened. The Public Expenditure proposals in the autumn of 1991 heralded a fiscal loosening with a Public Sector Borrowing Requirement (PSBR) of £10·5 billion. This was furthered by the Budget of 10 March 1992 which saw a fiscal stimulus of some £5 billion in the form of lower taxes, and a surge in the expected Public Sector Borrowing Requirement to £27 billion.

The Election Background.

On 9 April 1992, Britain went to the polls in one of the most keenly-contested and closely fought contests of the post-war period. The election ended many months of "phoney" electioneering and was held against a background of claims and counter-claims concerning the state of the British economy. Repeated forecasts by Treasury ministers in the autumn and winter of 1991/2 of imminent recovery from recession reflected their genuine expectations that a Spring election would be called with interest rates drifting down, inflation under firm control, and the first stirrings of economic growth apparent. The election was actually called in less propitious circumstances when the Prime Minister had lost almost all room for tactical manoeuvre. The economy remained in deep and prolonged recession, public spending was rising rapidly (resulting in a Public Sector Borrowing Requirement of £28 billion), the politically-sensitive reforms of the National Health Service were in troubled mid-course, and the final Poll Tax bills were about to arrive. There remained the potentially damaging constitutional question of Scotland's increasingly uncertain relationship with the rest of the Kingdom.

The April 1992 Election.

Against the published indications of every major polling organisation and the large exit polls conducted on the day of the election, the Conservatives were returned with an overall majority. The results were as follows:

		Votes	
Con	Lab	Lib Dem	Nat/other
41·9	34·4	17·8	5·9
		Seats	
Con	Lab	Lib Dem	Nat/other
336	271	20	24

The new parliament has a different appearance from the old. Several senior members of the Labour and Conservative Parties retired: Denis Healey, Michael Foot, Norman Tebbit, David Owen, Cecil Parkinson, and most notably of all, Margaret Thatcher, did not seek re-election. Others were defeated: both Chris Patten (Chairman of the Conservative Party) and Lynda Chalker (the Overseas Development Minister) lost their seats in Bath and Wallasey respectively. Mr Major's new administration is also very different from the old: Kenneth Baker, the former Home Secretary, left the government as did Tom King, the former Defence Secretary, and (briefly) Peter Brooke, the former Northern Ireland Secretary. Two women joined the Cabinet: Gillian Shephard, at Employment, and Virginia Bottomley, at Health. John Wakeham, former Leader of the House of Commons, was appointed Leader of the House of Lords, whilst Michael Heseltine, who had a characteristically vigorous and energetic campaign, won the post he had long coveted: Secretary of State for Trade and Industry, whilst Kenneth Clarke became the new Home Secretary.

The remarkable achievement of a fourth successive term of office for the Conservatives brought a further round of internal dissension within the Labour Party, but only a brief respite for the Prime Minister, John Major, from the three, linked problems of ratification of the Maastricht Treaty, Britain's membership of the Exchange Rate Mechanism of the European Monetary System, and the country's continuing economic recession.

Advent of John Smith.

Neil Kinnock, under whom the Labour Party had largely shed its electorally lethal image of unfitness for government, announced shortly after his party's election defeat that he would resign the Leadership. John Smith, a conservative Scots advocate who had previously held the position of Shadow Chancellor, was overwhelmingly elected to succeed him over the challenge of Bryan Gould. Mr Smith was the sole member of the Shadow Cabinet elected by the Parliamentary Labour Party in 1993 himself to have been a member of a Labour Cabinet. Cautious by instinct, and forensic by legal training, Smith set in train a Commission under the Chairmanship of Sir Gordon Borrie to review the nature, purposes, and structure of the Welfare State as a prelude to establishing new policies for welfare and (by implication) for taxation. To the evident frustration of some colleagues, not all of them on the left of the party, the assumption which underlay Smith's approach in his first six months as leader was that the Conservative majority in the Commons would hold, whatever the outcome of the debate on Maastricht, for the full term of the Parliament.

During the autumn of 1992, Mr Smith's apparent assumption appeared open to doubt when, following consistent, vigorous, assertions of the centrality of ERM membership to the government's anti-inflation strategy, the markets' doubts about its credibility overwhelmed the Treasury's capacity to resist. Britain's withdrawal from the mechanism provoked a wider crisis within the mechanism (see the European Community, **C14**) and widened divisions between pro- and anti-Europeans within the Conservative Party. Freed of the need to maintain the value of sterling within its ERM bands, however, the government began to cut short-term interest rates aggressively and frequently in order to stem the fall in output and (which marked a significant shift in government rhetoric) to improve prospects for employment.

A Sea of Troubles.

The economy nonetheless continued to contract, albeit at a slower rate than for most of 1991, and unemployment grew rapidly, reaching a total of 3 million in January 1993. Confidence showed signs of fragile recovery in early 1993, but house prices continued to weaken, and the rate of business failures remained high. Under these circumstances, British Coal's proposal in the autumn of 1992 to close thirty of the remaining coal mines following the privatised electricity companies' decisions to buy much less coal from British suppliers in the future than they had done in the past, provoked a storm of protest from opposition and government benches which the government headed off only at the price of an expensive and humiliating retreat. Whilst inflation was brought down to levels comparable with major European competitors, the recession damaged not only the industrial base, but greatly harmed public sector finances. So rapidly did the Public Sector Borrowing Requirement (PSBR) grow, that many in the Conservative Party (who had campaigned in the April 1992 General Election on a platform of implacable opposition to tax increases) were by the spring of 1993 agreeing that increases in taxation and reductions in public spending were required in order to close the rapidly growing gap between income and expenditure.

Conservatives in Disarray.

A damaging by-election defeat at the previously safe Conservative seat of Newbury, Berkshire, precipitated the dismissal of the Chancellor of the Exchequer, Mr. Norman Lamont, from his post in the summer of 1993. The Chancellor was scarcely solely to blame for the deterioration in public finances, the sluggish recovery, or the Conservatives Government's deep unpopularity (not least among its core voters in the South of England). Nevertheless, his lack of empathy and finesse in dealing with a public bruised by a long recession and very high real interest rates, had long been a source of grumbling discontent for the government. Defeat at Newbury intensified it, and precipitated the Chancellor's departure from the government led by the man whose close political ally he had been.

For the remainder of 1993 and in the first months of 1994, morale on the Conservative backbenches and, more tellingly, in local Conservative Associations, remained low; exceptionally poor public opinion poll ratings, though of little moment in the middle of a parliament, added to the discomfiture of government and party. Disunity within the parliamentary party posed considerable difficulties for government whips and business managers, despite the removal of the single greatest focus of anti-EC discontent within the Party by the final ratification of the Maastricht Treaty. The rightwing faction which had caused such turmoil within the Parliamentary Party in the eighteen months following the 1992 election victory on the European Question, remained unreconciled to the weakening of the tone and substance of policy under Mrs. Thatcher's successor.

Some of the government's misfortunes were self-inflicted, reflecting a combination of poor staff work and (more especially) uncertainty and fitfulness in direction from the Prime Minister himself. The clearest example was that of a strange, misconceived, attempt at the Party Conference in the autumn of 1993 to launch a campaign of "Back to Basics", the content of which was differently defined by different politicians and groups in the party, but part of which was originally intended by some in the Party to have a morally cleansing effect upon politics. The campaign collapsed in the first weeks of 1993 amidst sundry scandalous revelations about the private lives of certain government ministers, further diminishing the Prime Minister's authority and the government's cohesion.

Crisis for the Prime Minister.

The prospects for the premiership of John Major deteriorated rapidly in the spring of 1994. Partly this was due to his position over British voting rights in an enlarged Europe (he suddenly adopted an unrealistic tough stance, only to abandon it with equal speed). But it was the electoral trough in which the party found itself which proved even more problematic. In the opinion polls, the party was at rock bottom. In the May local elections, the electoral day of reckoning arrived.

The outcome of the local elections was a disaster for the Conservatives. Across the length and breadth of the country, normally loyal towns deserted the Conservatives. The litany of losses included Kingston, Colchester and Winchester. The resurgent Liberal Democrats made a net gain of 388 seats, Labour a gain of 88 and the Conservatives a loss of 429. Not only did these results increase speculation on John Major's ability to survive, but they appeared to herald heavy losses in the European elections.

The Advent of Tony Blair.

The sudden death of Mr Smith on 12 May 1994 forced a labour leadership contest and threw the party's future direction into question. (For Labour under Tony Blair, see Special Topic, C78–80). Campaigning for the forthcoming European Parliamentary elections was suspended until after Mr Smith's funeral on 20 May. The delay gave an increasingly buffeted Mr Major a short breathing space. But failure in May's local elections was followed by disaster in the 9 June European elections. The Tories took 18 seats with 28% of the vote, their lowest share in any 20th century election. Labour won 62 seats with 44% of the vote, while the Liberal Democrats' 17% gained them only two seats. In the Eastleigh by-election on the same day, a Tory majority of almost 18,000 was turned into a Liberal lead of over 9,000 votes.

The July 1994 Cabinet Reshuffle.

Against this background of growing unpopularity, Mr Major reshuffled his Cabinet on 20 July, replacing four senior ministers. The changes coincided with the release of the Pergau Dam report which criticised linking aid funding with arms purchases and called the conduct of former defence minister Lord Younger "reprehensible". The following day Tony Blair was elected Labour leader. Even prolonged industrial action by railway signal staff through the summer gave the government no comfort, as public opinion appeared sympathetic to the strikers' case.

Although, as ministers argued, there were distinctly improving economic indicators, the govern-

ment could not translate this to a "feel good factor" in the public mind. Instead, its reputation was further threatened by the emergence of a "sleaze factor". In August Lord Archer, a political confidant of Mr Major, was exonerated following accusations that he had used insider knowledge in share dealings. At the end of October two junior ministers resigned after admitting they had asked Parliamentary questions for payment while they were backbenchers. Mr Major moved quickly to establish a standing committee under Lord Nolan, a senior judge, to investigate and make recommendations on office holders' conduct. The public mood was not improved by reports of directors of privatised utilities awarding themselves massive pay increases.

Widening Conservative Divisions.

Conservative divisions became more openly intense in the autumn. There was no reference to Post Office privatisation in the Queen's Speech on 16 November because backbench Tory resistance (echoing the policy's unpopularity in the country) made the Cabinet doubt the likelihood of passing the legislation proposed. Even more dangerous for the government's survival were fundamental disagreements within the party over Britain's future in Europe.

Mr Major announced on 16 November that he would treat the European Community (Finance) Bill as a vote of confidence. This was aimed at "Eurosceptic" backbenchers reluctant to see Britain's contribution to Europe increase from 1·2 to 1.7% as the Bill proposed. As the vote approached, a memorandum to Mr Major from party vice-chairman John Maples was leaked on 20 November. The memorandum set out the government's weakness in painful detail. "What we are saying on the economy," it reported, "is completely at odds with Conservative supporters' experience." Mr Maples also revealed party fears of Mr Blair's popularity. "If Blair turns out to be as good as he looks, we have a problem."

The "Eurosceptics".

On the European Bill's second reading on 27 November, the government won two crucial votes comfortably. But the Tory whip was withdrawn from eight backbench "Eurosceptics" who abstained on one or both. When a ninth voluntarily relinquished the party whip, Mr Major was theoretically at the head of a minority government. Further humiliation followed when, on 6 December, the government suffered defeat in its attempts to impose the full rate of VAT on household fuel and heating. The measure was rejected by 319 votes to 311 as 17 Tory backbenchers voted against the government. A week later at Dudley West the Tories suffered their worst by-election defeat at the hands of Labour for 50 years.

Mr Major attempted to unite his divided party, and to preserve his own position, by attacking Labour's proposals on home rule for Scotland and Wales. Playing the union card had worked effectively in the 1992 general election but the situation was now more problematic because, paradoxically, of the apparent success of his Northern Ireland policy.

The Northern Ireland Peace Process.

If there was one bright spot for the government – and one for which opposition parties gave Mr Major ungrudging praise – it was in the events following the December 1993 Downing Street Declaration. Sinn Fein delayed a formal response and asked for clarification on the Unionist community's veto. But on 31 August 1994, the IRA announced a ceasefire. In the previous 25 years 3,169 people had been killed, 38,680 injured, and there had been 10,001 bombings. Mr Major welcomed the ceasefire but, aware of Unionist fears, said there had been no "secret deals" with the IRA. On 13 October the loyalist para-militaries announced an end to violence.

As the ceasefire continued, Mr Major announced the possibility of talks involving Sinn Fein before Christmas. But the Ulster Unionists remained concerned about their long-term position in any agreement reached between London and Dublin.

On 18 January 1995 Unionist members at Westminster threatened withdrawal of support from what was now, in effect, a minority government. The threats became more pronounced with the leak on 1 February of a draft document on cross border bodies proposing a voice for Dublin in Northern Ireland affairs. The future of the peace process became unclear.

A further attempt by Mr Major to reunite his party came over Europe. Having taken the whip from the more determined Eurosceptics, he moved towards them in the New Year. There was an increasing emphasis on nationalism and British participation in a single European currency was rejected, at least until "the time was right". But divisions within the Cabinet (reportedly 17–5 pro-Europe) were thrust into the open when chancellor of the exchequer Mr Clarke derided Eurosceptic fears that monetary union implied political union on 9 February. He was contradicted the next day by employment secretary Michael Portillo. It appeared the two wings of the party were positioning themselves for a future leadership contest.

The Government suffered further humiliation when the Tory candidate lost his deposit at the Islwyn by-election on 17 February, pushed from second to fourth place with 3·9% of the vote. The atmosphere of collapse continued when Britain's oldest merchant bank, Barings, went into receivership on 26 February after making estimated losses of £750 million on the derivatives market and the failure of a last-minute Bank of England rescue attempt.

The one bright spot for the government was Northern Ireland, where the ceasefire held. But even here there was disappointment at slow progress towards a settlement, largely due to disagreement over the Provisional IRA giving up its weapons. A joint Anglo-Irish Framework Document unveiled on 22 February aroused much disapproval from Ulster Unionists. The document proposed an assembly for Northern Ireland, a charter of rights, an end to the Irish territorial claim, and a joint parliamentary forum of representatives from the south and the north. The right of the people of Northern Ireland to decide their own future would be given legislative backing. By mid-April preparations were under way for discussions on the proposals by the province's main political parties. Sinn Fein continued to be excluded because of the continuing impasse over paramilitary weapons.

The government's European policies brought it close to parliamentary defeat once again on 1 March as a number of Tory backbenchers abstained and former chancellor of the exchequer Norman Lamont voted with the opposition. Mr Major appeared increasingly unfortunate in his friends when his chancellor, Kenneth Clarke, admitted on 16 March that voters were not giving the government credit for economic recovery and suggested that the "feel bad factor" might last for much longer. Former party treasurer Lord McAlpine declared that a period in opposition could be healthy. The government's majority fell to 12 with the death on 20 March of the only Ulster Unionist backbencher to consistently support the prime minister.

The Scottish Local Elections.

Mr Major attempted to regain the political initiative from an increasingly confident Labour Party on 2 April by offering voters a package of future legislation which included more nursery places, a harder line on asylum seekers, a charter for victims of crime and a reduction in income tax to 20p. But four days later the Tories were humiliated at the hands of Labour and Nationalists in local authority elections in Scotland. They took only 11% of the vote and won in only 82 of the 1,161 seats contested, losing control of six councils.

Humiliation in England and Wales.

The municipal elections of 4 May 1995 were a disaster for the Conservatives and a triumph for both Labour and the Liberal Democrats. Voters were electing over 11,700 councillors in 324 English authorities and the entire councils in the 22 new unitary Welsh authorities. The Conservatives finished with a net loss of over 2,000 seats, Labour with some 1,800 net gains and the Liberal Democrats 495 net gains. Labour were estimated to have polled 48% of the vote, the Conservatives 25% and the Liberal Democrats 23%. Further details of council control are given on **A38**.

Coming on top of Tony Blair's easy victory in modernising Clause IV at the special Party Conference (*see* **C78–80**), the political landscape in Britain had now been greatly changed. The Conservatives (and not least the Prime Minister himself) were on the defensive. Labour were now looking to a general election (which had to be held by May 1997) with more confidence of victory than for many years.

II.   THE CHANGING WORLD SCENE

WESTERN EUROPE

FRANCE.

The presidential elections of May 1988 brought to an end two years of 'cohabitation' between the Socialist President, Francois Mitterrand and the neo-Gaullist Prime Minister, Jacques Chirac. Of the nine candidates who stood in the first round on 24 April only the two best-placed candidates, Mitterrand and Chirac, went through to the run-off ballot a fortnight later. In this second poll the outgoing Socialist President defeated his right-wing rival by 54·02 to 45·98 per cent of the votes cast thereby becoming the first French President to be re-elected for a second seven year term of office by popular vote. Mitterrand's re-election was not a decisive victory for socialism. His election programme contained few left-wing proposals; his success reflected his ability to attract centrist votes. This fact, together with the continued decline of the Communist Party vote and the impressive performance of the neo-fascist candidate, Jean-Marie Le Pen confirmed the extent to which French politics has shifted to the Right since 1981.

The voters were unimpressed; Mitterrand won a landslide victory on 8 May winning over 50% of the votes cast in all but 19 of the 96 metropolitan departments. His victory was Gaullien; national and personal in character. Elected with centrist support, Mitterrand confirmed his opening to the centre by appointing Michel Rocard, leader of the social-democratic wing of the PS as Prime Minister and asking him to form a centre-left coalition government. Despite long negotiations with leading UDF politicians including the former UDF President, Giscard d'Estaing, Rocard was unable to form a government which was acceptable to the right-wing Parliament. Just one week after his re-election President Mitterrand therefore dissolved the National Assembly in order to seek a Socialist parliamentary majority. The legislative elections were held on 5 and 12 June.

The June Legislative Elections.

These elections, called a week after President Mitterrand's re-election on 8 May 1988 were held under the double ballot, single member constituency electoral system. Re-elected with centrist support, Mitterrand continued his policy of *ouverture* towards the centre during the election campaign in an attempt to divide the "system" Right. However, the two principal right-wing parties, the neo-Gaullist RPR (*Rassemblement pour la République*) and the more centrist UDF (*Union pour le Démocratie Française*) which had supported rival candidates in the presidential election hurriedly formed a new electoral alliance, the URC and agreed to support a joint candidate in each constituency. Early polls forecast a large overall majority for the President's Socialist Party together with the marginalisation or even the elimination of both the PCF and FN (both of which had benefited from proportional representation in 1986).

The polls proved only partially correct. As predicted, the FN lost all but one of its 33 seats (including that belonging to the FN leader Jean-Marie Le Pen in Marseilles). The PCF's electoral fortunes meanwhile revived and (partly because of PS backing for PCF candidates on the second round) the Party retained 27 of its 33 seats. The biggest surprise was the failure of the PS to obtain an overall majority. Several factors help to explain this result. The PS was the party most affected by the record abstention level in the first round—complacency and election fatigue kept many voters away from the polls. Secondly, the PS election message to voters was ambiguous: appeals to voters to give the President a stable parliamentary majority (and electoral deals with the PCF) were combined with Mitterrand's public statements in favour of an opening to the centre. Finally, while many centrists and Communists had been willing to support Mitterrand in the presidential contest they refused to vote for a Socialist Party candidate in the parliamentary elections.

The Fight for the Succession.

French politics in the second half of 1989 and the early months of 1990 were marked to a striking degree by the contending for advantage on both the right and the left by candidates for the Presidency since it seemed improbable that Mitterrand would choose to seek a third term upon the expiry of his second in 1995.

On the left, no politician possessed Mitterrand's weight and popularity which enabled him to chart his own course with relative freedom on the foundation of strict party discipline. At the biennial congress of the French Socialist Party in March 1990 at Rennes, Laurent Fabius (Mitterrand's second Prime Minister) beat a group led jointly by Pierre Mauroy (Mitterrand's first Prime Minister, and currently the Party's first secretary) and Lionel Jospin (Education Minister, and formerly first secretary of the party), into second place and Michel Rocard, the leading social democratic figure on the right of the party (and Mitterrand's current Prime Minister), into third for the post of party secretary. The contest was superficially bound up with ideological dispute but in fact had more to do with personal politicking with a view to the presidential election in 1995 (or before in the event that Mitterrand chose to retire early), than with substantive differences over policy. Whilst Rocard's position continued to be somewhat distinctive, there was little ideological distance between Mauroy and Fabius but much animus.

On the right, the three major figures of the 1970s and 1980s, Giscard d'Estaing, Jacques Chirac, and Raymond Barre, came under increasing pressure from new contenders for power. All three senior figures were in any case handicapped by Mitterrand's crushing of Chirac in the 1988 presidential elections, and by his having pursued a converative economic policy with conspicuous success since 1983.

Political Developments in 1991.

Events in both the right and left party groupings were of absorbing interest, and possible longer-term significance, during 1990 and early 1991. On the left, Mitterrand saw his popularity slip in the autumn of 1990 in the wake of amnesties granted to politicians charged with campaign finance offences. France's participation in the Gulf War nonetheless caused almost as significant a recovery in Mitterrand's public opinion poll ratings as America's did in Bush's. His strengthened standing enabled him to accept the offer of resignation by the defence minister, Jean-Pierre Chevenement, who had more or less openly resisted France's embroilment in a war which in his view threatened her long-term interest in fostering closer links with Arab powers (including Iraq). Chevenement's replacement was Pierre Joxe, whose views on French foreign and defence policy were closer to Mitterrand's.

On the right, the RPR and UDF agreed to a collaborative federation of their two parties (the *Union pour France*) with the intention of agreeing upon candidates for the 1992 local and 1993 legislative elections, and of finding through a primary system a single candidate in the 1995 Presidential elections. This was the first factor tending to divide the RPR; the second (as in the British Conservative Party) was policy towards Europe. The RPR, heavily influenced by Charles Pasqua, adopted in December 1990 a hostile policy towards monetary union. In the fragile world of French party politics, these changes left many dissatisfied. Michel Noir, the Mayor of Lyons, and Michele Barzach, a former health minister, resigned their parliamentary seats and their membership of the RPR in order to stand for re-election as independents against official RPR candidates. Noir's victory raised the prospect that the right in France might fragment further, perhaps with a new party led by him.

A Woman Prime Minister.

The resignation of Michel Rocard in May 1991 and his replacement by Edith Cresson presaged a year of extreme difficulty for President Mitterrand and for the government. Between the time of her appointment and the regional elections of March 1992, politics were notable primarily for the weakness of the government, for the disruptive effects of the issue of immigration upon the public agenda and the extraordinary erosion in support for the Socialist Party. In times of economic prosperity, the impact of immigration as an issue would be slight but in circumstances of persistently high unemployment, its salience is higher and its significance altogether greater. Support for the National Front as measured by opinion polls was at 15% in early 1992, but support for the Front's policy on immigration is twice as great. The significance of this difference was not lost on politicians in other parties: Jacques Chirac and Giscard d'Estaing have both attempted to woo those who favour stricter limits on immigration with thinly disguised appeals to racial prejudice.

Background to Electoral Disaster.

A hint of the electoral disaster which awaited the Socialist Party in the Spring regional elections was apparent in a by-election near Lille on 26 January 1992: having polled 31% in the first round of voting there in the general election in 1988, the Socialist candidate took a mere 13% in 1992. Faced with parliamentary elections in 1993, the pressure upon Mitterrand to revive both his own and his party's prospects was great.

Regional elections held on 22 March, and cantonal polls on 29 March, resulted in heavy defeats for the ruling Socialist Party. Faced with a deepening of the government's unpopularity, President Mitterrand replaced Edith Cresson with Pierre Bérégovoy, who had held the post of Finance Minister since 1984.

Difficulties of Bérégovoy.

France's establishment of credibility for its policy of a strong Franc within the Exchange Rate Mechanism (ERM) came under fierce pressure in 1992 and early 1993. The primary cause of the difficulty was the policy of the Bundesbank to keep German interest rates high in order to choke off German inflation. Since the franc was linked to the Deutschmark within the ERM, the French government was obliged to maintain French interest rates at much higher levels than were consistent with the need to stimulate French domestic demand. President Mitterrand's popularity suffered as unemployment rose relentlessly, and the Socialist government of M. Bérégovoy slid towards defeat in the parliamentary elections of March 1993.

The right-wing RPR of Jacques Chirac, and the centre-right UDF of Giscard d'Estaing, fought the legislative elections under the allied banner of the Union for France (UPF). The alliance declared that a new government of the right would seek to reduce unemployment by stimulating economic growth, extend the privatisation programme begun under Chirac's Prime Ministership between 1986 and 1988 to the remainder of the large state-run enterprises, create an independent Bank of France, and persist with a broadly pro-European policy.

Landslide for the Right.

The elections resulted in a landslide victory for the right-wing coalition, the crushing of the Socialist Party and its allies, the resistance of the Communist Party to final elimination, and the failure of the two Ecologist parties and the National Front to gain any seats in the Assembly. The final results were as follows:

Party	Percentage of National Vote	Seats
RPR	28·27	247
UDF	25·84	213
FN (National Front)	5·66	—
Other right-wing parties	3·56	24
Radical Left		6
Other left-wing parties }	3·32	
Socialists	28·25	54
Communists	4·61	23

The result marks a complete transformation from the old party balance in the Assembly where the left had enjoyed a slender majority in coalition with their allies, and the Communists. Legislatively and politically devastated, the Socialists are now too marginal to pose any significant threat to the huge right-wing majority. The next Presidential elections will take place in 1995 (unless President Mitterrand resigns through ill-health before then). Until then, opposition to the new government, (in which Edouard Balladur, the senior RPR politician, is the new Prime Minister) will come from within the governing alliance of the RPR and the UDF.

Although it is organised as a single party, divisions on monetary and European policies within the RPR were apparent even in the flush of election victory, fuelled by the contending ambitions of senior figures within it. A federation of five parties, the UDF is even less cohesive: two of its constituent parts (the Republican Party, and the CDS) enjoyed considerable autonomy in the Assembly between 1988 and 1993 and may now be tempted to break away from the UDF entirely not least because it will take little for opposition within the UDF to Giscard's leadership to break through the surface. Imposing discipline upon such an unwieldy and unstable base as the RPR and UDF now present in the Assembly will be exceptionally difficult.

Balladur as Prime Minister.

Nevertheless, there is for Mitterrand little prospect that his systematic outmanoeuvring of the RPR Prime Minister Jacques Chirac under the earlier cohabitation between 1986 and 1988 will be repeated with Edouard Balladur in the remaining two years of his Presidency. Their internal fissures notwithstanding, the position of the two large right-wing parties is altogether stronger now than it was then, and Mitterrand himself will not be a candidate for re-election in 1995. Moreover, Michel Rocard, the politician regarded as the Socialists' likeliest candidate in 1995, was defeated in his attempt to retain his seat in the Assembly; his Presidential prospects are, accordingly, damaged and those of his rivals, Jacques Delors and Laurent Fabius, somewhat enhanced. Having chosen to stay out of the government and to remain as Mayor of Paris, Jacques Chirac presents a powerful obstacle to the ambitions of any and all candidates on the left. His party, created by Francois Mitterrand in 1971, is now demoralised and discredited, and the centre of French partisan gravity has shifted.

Recent Developments.

Persisting recession, manifested most starkly in an exceptionally high unemployment rate of 12% in December 1993, provided the backcloth against which French politics were played out in 1993 and against which French politicians manoeuvred in preparation for the Presidential elections in 1995. In such circumstances, it was remarkable that Prime Minister Edouard Balladur should not only have survived his first year in office, but positively thrived. Against all the odds, Balladur secured a remarkably advantageous deal for French farmers in the GATT round talks (which were concluded successfully in December 1993) by forcing other EU member states and the United States to accept terms which they had previously rejected outright.

Balladur also proved himself more adept at political manoeuvre than his political friends and enemies alike had anticipated. Partly because the President would not himself be a candidate for re-election in 1995, Balladur's relations with President Mitterrand have been much less problematic than Chirac's had been in the first cohabitation of a conservative Prime Minister with a Socialist President between 1986 and 1988. An untroubled relationship with Mitterrand aided Balladur's ambitions: a successful Premiership provided him with a strong platform for 1995.

The 1995 Presidential Elections.

For the background to the 1995 elections and an analysis of the results, *see* **Special Topic, C82**.

GERMANY.

The West German electorate went to the polls on 25 January 1987, and confirmed the coalition led by Helmut Kohl in office, albeit with a reduced share of the vote. Herr Kohl's partners in the coalition, the Free Democrats led by Hans-Dietrich Genscher, emerged strengthened from the elections; their share of the vote increased from 7·0% in 1983 to 9·1% in 1987.

	CDU/ CSU	FDP	SPD	Die Grünen	Others
% share of the vote	44·3	9·1	37·0	8·3	1·3
Seats in the Bundestag	223	46	186	42	—

The election campaign was dull, thereby emulating the tone of Chancellor Kohl's leadership. Kohl's approach to government posed few electoral problems in a setting of economic strength, but seemed less likely to suffice for the more difficult and challenging circumstances posed by the strength of the D-Mark and the resultant pressure on Germany's traditional export markets. His campaign slogan of *Weiter so, Deutschland* ('More of the same') reflected the Chancellor's innate caution and disinclination to translate Germany's economic strength into political leadership, either within Europe or in relations with the United States.

The FDP's new strength was reflected in the apportionment of Cabinet places following Herr Kohl's reelection as Chancellor by the Bundestag on 12 March 1987. In addition to its control of the Foreign, Economics and Justice ministries, the Party now took the education portfolio. The change was largely symbolic since West Germany's federal structure devolves most education responsibilities to the states. Herr Franz Josef Strauss opted not to accept a Cabinet portfolio but instead to remain Prime Minister of Bavaria, itself an indication that Strauss may privately have judged the new government to have a short life.

The INF Treaty.

The Intermediate Nuclear Force Treaty negotiated by the Soviet Union and the United States in December 1987 had considerable implications for West Germany. The modernisation of NATO's intermediate missiles had taken place in part as a result of the anxiety of Helmut Schmidt (then Chancellor) about the weakening of the linkage between conventional forces and the American strategic deterrent. The successful elimininatinn of the Soviet Union's SS20s, the United State's Cruise, and Pershing IIs, and Germany's own Pershing Is, nonetheless caused most German politicians to look either for cuts in short-range weapons (as Herr Genscher, the FDP Foreign Minister sought) or their complete withdrawal (as the SPD wished).

The Coalition under Pressure.

Pressure on the governing coalition grew in the early months of 1988. The CDU lost ground in the opinions polls, falling to just 40% (the same as the SPD) in early March, whilst the FDP (buoyed by Herr Genscher's popularity) moved ahead to 12%. Worse still for Chancellor Kohl, his CDU appeared likely to do badly in state elections in the Spring, just as it had done in 1987. Herr Strauss, frustrated by his powerlessness, criticised Herr Stoltenberg, the West German finance minister, for deciding to tax the incomes of churches and charities, and for raising taxes on petrol and tobacco in an attempt to cut the burgeoning West German budget deficit. The real objects of Herr Strauss's attack were Foreign Minister Genscher and Chancellor Kohl, both of whom held jobs which he had spent his life seeking; its probable consequence was the further weakening of the CDU. Chancellor Kohl's difficulty was that he was torn between on the one hand attempting to appeal to centrist voters who had been wooed by the SPD and *Die Grünen*, and on the other of trying to retain the coalitional support of Bavarian conservatives. Some of the latter, especially farmers disaffected by West German concessions in the EC, began to drift away from the CSU towards extreme right-wing parties.

Political Developments in 1988.

The intermediate-range nuclear question having been settled by the INF Treaty between the United States and the Soviet Union, short-range nuclear modernisation emerged in 1988 as a politically embarrassing question for the West German government. Whereas Britain and the United States were firmly committed to modernising American Lance missiles in West Germany, the German government sought to postpone a decision. In public, Herr Kohl and Herr Genscher argued that to modernise the missiles without delay would be an inappropriate move at a time when negotiations on conventional forces were proceeding well. Privately, both Kohl and Genscher were concerned at the impact a decision to modernise would have on German public opinion, and upon their respective parties' prospects at the Federal elections in 1990.

A left-led coalition formed of the SPD and *Die Grünen* was formed in early March 1989 to govern West Berlin. The move was significant for coming less than two years before national elections. If the coalition was successful, both parties within it could employ it to attempt to defeat Helmut Kohl's CDU-led government. If it failed, Kohl would himself have an opportunity to embarrass his opponents.

The Berlin elections were also notable for revealing the strength of the Republicans, an extreme right-wing party which derives its popularity from unremitting hostility to foreigners and which won 7·5% of the vote and eleven seats on the City Council. The Republicans' electoral prospects are rosier in the wake of the death in 1988 of Franz-Josef Strauss, the ebullient and powerful leader of the right-wing CSU. With Strauss gone, the Republicans offer a new vehicle for right-wing protest outside the political mainstream of the four major parties. Another outlet exists in the shape of the National Democrats, the much older neo-Nazi party, which secured 6·6% of the vote in local elections in Frankfurt in March.

Chancellor Kohl's position within the CDU and the CDU-FDP alliance which he led accordingly came under scrutiny in the months after the poor results in Berlin and in other local elections. Criticism focussed upon his seeming inability to respond to the challenges posed from the right, and to the implications that this had for the vulnerability of CDU's electoral base. As the national elections approached in December 1990, so Kohl's room for manoeuvre lessened, and the possibility of a new national coalition of the SPD, the FDP, and the Greens emerging after the poll, grew.

	December 1990
Alliance '90/Eastern Greens	8
PDS (ex-Communists)	17
SPD	239
FDP	79
CDU/CSU	319

Developments in East Germany.

Between 7 and 11 September 1987, Herr Honecker, the East German party leader, paid his first official visit to West Germany. The fact that the visit went ahead at all was a mark of the improved condition of relations between the United States and the Soviet Union; when the visit was first planned, three years before, the Russians vetoed the proposal. The visit was in itself remarkably unspectacular: the agreements signed during the visit were relatively insignificant and had in any case been well-flagged in advance. Nonetheless, the occasion marked an extraordinary shift since Chancellor Willy Brandt struggled against intense domestic opposition in the early 1970s to establish his policy of *Ostpolitik*. This was reflected in increased trade, a decrease in tensions generally, and a marked increase in visits among friends and families across the border. Early in 1988, it appeared likely that Chancellor Kohl would visit East Germany later in the year, and possibly include a visit to East Berlin – an especially sensitive matter in view of the two countries' wholly different views of the city's status.

Figures released by the West German government in January 1988 showed that many East Germans used the additional travel permits granted by the East German government to enter West Germany and stay. Some 1·29 million travel permits were issued to persons under pensionable age in 1987; of these, as many as 12,000 stayed in the West – double the number of escapees in the same year. The issue posed a dilemma for the East German authorities: if travel restrictions were increased, discontent in the East was likely to rise, and escape attempts might well become more common. On the other hand, a more liberal policy towards travel permits clearly carried the risk that many (especially the young, and professional persons who could earn more in the west) would not return.

Honecker Soldiers On.

As her Eastern European neighbours adapted to perestroika in the Soviet Union in different ways, the East German Communist Party showed no sign in 1988 and early 1989 of shifting from its self-assigned path of rigid adherence to the command economy which, in contrast to the experience elsewhere in Comecon countries, had brought about considerable economic success for East Germany. The waning of state repression in Hungary, Poland, and the Soviet Union similarly had little effect upon politics in East Germany. Yet the authorities in East Berlin had to contend with the continuing exposure of the population to currents of western opinion and news through West German television. The East German population were hence well aware of the primacy which western analysts and journalists accorded Soviet economic and political developments. Equally, they knew well that the reforms within several Comecon member states aroused at best cold indifference among Erich Honecker and his colleagues, and more commonly their ill-concealed scorn.

The Road to Reunification.

From 1990, discussion of German politics can no longer be easily divided into East and West. The East German Communist regime collapsed in late 1989, as waves of East Germans took advantage of the ending of travel restrictions between Hungary and Austria to leave their crumbling country. As the regime disappeared by Christmas 1989, the East German state had begun its own process of disappearance by Easter 1990. The official celebrations attending the 40th anniversary of the East German state were marked by the attendance of Mikhail Gorbachev whose policies had done so much to undermine Communist rule in eastern Europe, and by mass unrest in Leipzig, Dresden, and East Berlin. In the space of a few weeks, the remaining shreds of legitimacy attaching to Herr Honecker's administration fell away. His successor was Egon Krenz, who had the distinct political disadvantage of having had responsibility for internal security and of rigging the municipal elections in May 1989. He lasted but a few weeks until his replacement by Hans Modrow, the reformist Mayor of Dresden.

The End of the Berlin Wall.

On 9 November, the Berlin Wall was breached. In the ten months preceding that momentous event, 200,000 East Germans had left for the West; in the week that followed it, 3 million East Germans followed (most of them simply to visit and return). The regime fell away from beneath its leaders; on 3 December, the Politburo and Central Committee resigned. Politicians who had only weeks before exercised absolute power now found themselves under investigation for corruption and abuse of power.

Formation of New Parties.

New parties sprang up, and old ones which for forty years had been quiescent allies of the ruling Communist Party now broke free, finding independent voices. Elections were set for 18 March 1990. In the three months between the effective collapse of Communism and the elections, West and East German politics became inextricably linked. Two states, with two economic systems, remained. But the one nation now looked to a fusing of its nationhood with statehood, and the calculations of German voters on both sides of the disappearing border were made with unity in mind. As the elections approached, so the timetable for unity shortened. Foreign politicians gradually accommodated themselves to the prospect of unity. Where Mikhail Gorbachev and

Margaret Thatcher had as late as December 1989 been powerfully antipathetic to German unity, they were forced by the extraordinary speed of events to acquiesce in its inevitability. From early 1990 onwards, discussion proceeded not about whether unity would take place but about the circumstances under which it would occur, and with what speed.

The March 1990 Elections.

The election on 18 March took place between three main groupings: the Alliance for Germany which was a coalition of three conservative parties favouring rapid reunification, immediate introduction of the Deutschmark to the east on the basis of a one-for-one exchange rate, and a free-market economy; the Social Democratic Party which favoured a more gradual approach to unity and a social market economy; and the Democratic Socialist Party, the successor to the discredited Communist Party. The campaign was dominated by West German political parties and the leading West German politicians, and resulted in a landslide victory for the conservative Alliance for Germany. This result had not seemed remotely likely as recently as two weeks before polling day but the East German CDU's commitment to rapid reunification and a market economy swung the day. The new East German Prime Minister, Lothar de Maizière, was faced with the remarkable task of overseeing the process of the elimination of the East German state and its absorption into a new Federal Republic.

The rest of 1990 continued to be a year of breathless political development in Germany: on 1 July, the East German monetary system was merged with the West's, and the soft-currency Ostmark was replaced by Europe's most important currency, the Deutschmark. On 3 October, the two states became one country. Two months later, on 2 December, a united Germany voted in the first nation-wide elections since 1932.

The West German party system was reproduced in the eastern *lander*. There were nonetheless differences between parties in the west and those in the east: the PDS won almost no support in the west but retained some in the east, whilst the CDU nominally had merely an ally in the east in the shape of the German Social Union (DSU). In fact, the electoral rule which permitted the formation of joint lists in those cases where parties were not competitors enabled the CDU to run alongside the DSU. The PDS, with a regionally-skewed voter base, was disadvantaged for the same reason. For this election only, the east was treated as a separate voting area: if a party achieved 5% of the vote there, it would qualify for representation in the Bundestag.

Kohl Returns to Power.

The architect of the process of unification, Helmut Kohl, was returned to power at the head of CDU/ CSU/FDP coalition. The conservative part of that coalition, the CDU/CSU, won just 43·8% of the vote–its poorest performance since 1949. The FDP won 11·0%. This thoroughly creditable performance reflected the popularity of the Foreign Minister, Hans Dietrich-Genscher, in the eastern *lander*, and the success of the FDP's plea to voters that they receive sufficient support to enable them to act as a counterweight to Herr Kohl's conservatives. The SDP won 33·5%, giving them their worst result since the heavy defeat of 1957 when Chancellor Adenauer won an overall victory; the Greens won just 3·9% (which, because they fell below the 5% barrier, caused them to be excluded from the Bundestag). Green representation was not eliminated, however, because the coalition in the eastern *lander* between Alliance '90 and the Greens brought them 5·9% of the regional vote. Extreme right-wing Republicans, feeding off the discontent among some conservatives at Herr Kohl's decision to recognise the Oder-Neisse line as Poland's western border, won 2·1% of the vote (and hence no seats).

The Aftermath of Victory.

The task facing Herr Kohl in the aftermath of electoral victory was huge. At home, it amounted to nothing less than the complete reconstruction of what had once been East Germany. The former

Communist state's soft-currency markets in the Soviet Union had been lost; its goods were hopelessly outdated and hence uncompetitive in West European markets. The most obvious consequence was that the cost of unification would be enormous. The eastern *lander* would inevitably make huge demands for capital reconstruction on the west, and substantial rises in public spending for unemployment and social security.

These pressures were reflected in significant rises in German interest rates in the six months following monetary unification in July. The risk that private investment might as a result be "crowded out" was not insignificant. Tax rises, which Kohl resisted in the latter half of 1990 in order to preserve his political position ahead of the December elections, were eventually implemented (though nominally to finance Germany's financial contribution to the allied efforts in the Gulf crisis).

Abroad, Germany struggled with the problem encapsulated by the Gulf crisis – that of reconciling her post-war democratic, consensualist traditions at home with diplomatic and even military involvement abroad. It seemed more likely than not that Kohl would seek to entrench Germany ever more firmly in the European Community. In addressing these questions, Kohl found himself more heavily constrained politically than he would have wished by the new-found weight of the FDP, especially by Genscher. Having played so spectacular a part in the theatre of reunification, Kohl found himself with a more difficult role in the expensive task of reconstructing a nation whose two parts had, in thirty years of enforced division grown further apart than many Germans had believed. The dragging weight of the collapse of East German industry was also very much greater than had been generally anticipated and placed additional strains upon the coalition in Bonn.

Chancellor Kohl suffered a humiliating reverse in elections on 21 April 1991 in the south-western state of Rhineland-Palatinate. In the first test of Kohl's diminishing popularity since the national elections of December 1990, the conservative Christian Democrats lost office after 44 years on a swing of 7% to the Social Democrats. It was a reflection of disenchantment at the economic problems brought about by unification.

The Rebuilding of East Germany.

Chancellor Kohl's government continued in 1991 and early 1992 to struggle with the immense task of rebuilding the East German economy in the face of a gently rising inflation rate, tight monetary policy, an economy which hovered on the edge of recession, and increasing wage pressures. Taxes were increased in July 1991 in an attempt to finance some of the costs of unification, but government borrowing nonetheless grew sharply.

As her exposed position during the Gulf War indicated, the collapse of the Soviet Union and the associated political order in eastern Europe gave Germany a greatly enhanced importance in continental and world politics which the diplomacy surrounding preparations for the European summit at Maastricht confirmed. In the short-term, Maastricht did nothing to alter the dominance which the Bundesbank, the German central bank, exercised over European monetary policy. Both Britain and France found during 1991 that their sovereignty over monetary conditions was severely circumscribed by the need to maintain the positions of their currencies within the European Exchange Rate Mechanism, and that German interest rates set the bench-mark for all others. These are high in an attempt to force inflation down; they will be kept high even at the price of the economy drifting into recession. In fact, the economy is not experiencing recession in the way that the United States and Britain have for the past two years. It will grow during 1992—slowly in the west, but much more rapidly in the east. The strains of unification will persist for some time, both in the eastern and in the western *Länder*. In the east, unemployment and short-time working is now widespread but eastern workers are still massively subsidised by those in the west where productivity levels are far higher. If productivity in the east is to rise to internationally-competitive levels, unemployment will also rise as newly-privatised firms reduce their costs.

Strains on Kohl.

Under such extraordinary strains, Helmut Kohl's CDU performed remarkably strongly, drawing roughly equal support to the SPD as measured by opinion polls. However, the calculations of the FDP remain pivotal to politics in Bonn as they do in the *Länder*. The possibility exists that the FDP could seek to join the SPD in a coalition after the next elections in 1994. In early 1992, the SPD was still to address convincingly the question with which it had struggled during the 1980s: who should face Kohl for the Chancellorship. Two candidates suggest themselves: Björn Engholm, the Prime Minister of Schleswig-Holstein who was elected Party Chairman in the early summer of 1991, and Hans-Ulrich Klose who is the new SPD Floor Leader in the Bundestag.

In April 1992, the pressure on Kohl intensified with the resignation of the long-serving Foreign Minister, Genscher, and the outbreak of public sector strikes.

Gathering Economic Recession.

Germany slid rapidly into economic recession in the autumn of 1992, with industrial production falling by an annual rate of 20% in the final quarter. Some sectors, such as vehicles and machine tools, two vertebrae of the German economy, faced much more dramatic falls in demand and output. Demand at home fell as cyclical recession was intensified by the Bundesbank's action in sustaining exceptionally high real interest rates in order to choke off what its ruling Council rightly regarded as an unacceptably high rate of inflation of more than 4%. At the same time, export markets were weak because of recession elsewhere in western Europe, sluggish demand in Eastern Europe because of a shortage of foreign exchange, rising labour costs which made German products increasingly uncompetitive, and a Deutschmark which the chaos of September 1992 had left significantly overvalued. For eastern Germany, the problems were yet more serious, primarily because labour costs there began to close on those in west Germany, so rendering the east's lack of competitiveness yet more serious. The costs to western Germany of unification remained punishingly high, adding greatly to public spending and to the underlying fiscal imbalance.

Opposition Weakness.

The opposition SPD failed completely to exploit the economic disorder over which the CDU/FDP coalition presided, not least because there exists no obvious policy response to the combination of stubbornly high inflation, deepening recession, fiscal disorder, and (which is novel for Germany) a balance of payments deficit. One of the few polls to take place in the twelve months up to March 1993 was municipal elections in Hesse at the end of the period for which, significantly, turnout fell. The SPD's support fell by more than 8 percentage points, and the CDU's by 2·3 percentage points but the Greens recovered their share by nearly 2 percentage points leaving the FDP unchanged. The most remarkable aspect of the result, however, was the surge of extreme right-wing parties. The largest of them, the Republican Party (whose leader was a former SS officer) gained 8·3% of the total vote.

Rise of the Right.

The rise of the extreme right was fed in 1992 and early 1993 by the large influx of refugees from eastern Europe, especially those fleeing civil war in Bosnia: by the end of 1992, Germany's foreign-born population stood at approximately 5·5 million. The problem was further exacerbated by internal migration from the eastern *länder*. During the summer and autumn of 1992, attacks (some of them murderous) upon immigrants intensified debate within Germany about the country's condition and direction. The government's problems in dealing with levels of immigration more than 50% higher than in 1991 were compounded both by Germany's carrying a significantly higher share of the total refugee burden than her EC partners and by high rates of unemployment.

Economic Pressures.

Linked demographic and economic pressures arising from reunification continued to make life difficult for German politicians and people in 1993 and early 1994. The establishment of structures and values conducive to democratic stability was overwhelmingly the dominant consideration in German politics for the first forty years of its existence. Under the extraordinary strains of integrating an economic and ecological disaster zone of the eastern *länder* into the west, the structures and values which served Germany well between 1949 and 1989 are now being found wanting. Unemployment grew to more than 8% by the end of 1993;

Adjustment would be easier were German political leaders of greater stature. However, skilled as he had proved in keeping his own party reasonably united, and in maintaining a coalition with the FDP since 1982, Federal Chancellor Helmut Kohl had yet to convince the German population of the necessity for fiscal stringency if reunification was to succeed, and the German economy's competitiveness to be improved. The major opposition force, the Social Democratic Party (SPD) was in little better condition than the governing coalition. Although it was boosted by local elections in Brandenburg in December 1993, its new leader, Rudolf Scharping, was even less charismatic than the Chancellor himself.

The 1994 Elections.

Despite securing its second lowest vote since the establishment of the Federal Republic in 1949, the CDU emerged from the elections on 16 October 1994 as the largest party in the Bundestag. The results of the election, in which the turnout was 79%, were:

	Percentage share of the vote	Change	Seats	Change
CDU/CSU	41·5	−2·3%	294	−25
SPD	36·4	+2·9%	252	+13
FDP	6·9	−4·1%	47	−32
The Greens	7·3	+3·4%	49	+49
PDS	4·4	+2·0%	30	+13

The CDU/CSU's continuation in office in coalition with the FDP (which squeaked back into the Bundestag, thanks largely to CDU/CSU supporters voting tactically to boost the centrist party's vote as a means of increasing the prospects of the CDU/CSU forming the government) owed much to Chancellor Kohl. Exploiting the strong economic recovery evident throughout 1994, Kohl's dominating personality reassured a plurality of German voters as he had done (albeit with more conviction) following reunification in 1990. A month after the election, the Bundestag reelected Kohl, by the narrowest of margins, as Chancellor.

Although the election's outcome did not alter the Chancellor's formal position, it changed his political circumstances considerably. Not only was the CDU/CSU's position in the Bundestag weaker but his FDP partners emerged from the election damaged and in some disarray, and the SPD remained in control of the upper house (the Blundesrat). The medium-term significance of the elections was the heightened possibility that the FDP would be disabled by internal party wrangling, obliging the CDU/CSU to look to the SPD as a new partner in government.

ITALY.

The 1992 General Election.

The elections of April 1992 sent shockwaves through the political system. The Christian Democrats saw their share of the vote fall to 29·7%—its lowest since the war. Socialist support slipped from 14·3% to 13·6% (with heavy losses in Milan). The PDS (the re-named Communists) took 16·1%, the hard-line Communists 5·6%. The real victors were the Northern League, under the ebullient Sr. Bossi, who took 8·7% of the vote and 55 seats. The outcome effectively left Italian politics virtually deadlocked. The crisis intensified when President Cossiga announced he was resigning. However, the assassination of the leading anti-Mafia judge, Giovanni Falcone, galvanised the politicians into

electing the veteran Christian Democrat, Oscar Luigi Scalfaro, as President.

The Gathering Crisis.

Not until three months after the inconclusive General Election of April 1992 was a new government formed when Giuliano Amato, a Socialist and academic, became Prime Minister in a four-party coalition. His political prospects at the outset were poor: he exercised little sway over his own party (which was in any event entering a period of crisis following revelations of corruption), and none over the Christian Democrats who emerged from the elections damaged and divided among themselves. The hiatus and disarray focussed attention upon the burgeoning public sector deficit (which grew by a quarter in the first three months of 1992, partly in order to sweeten public opinion in advance of the election) and the currency instability to which it gave rise.

Contrary to general expectations, Amato exploited the instability around him, concentrated political and public attention upon the deficit, and succeeded in wringing support from Parliament in July 1992 for a package of spending cuts and tax increases designed to cut the deficit in the short-term, and of privatisation measures intended to reduce the scope of the public sector in the medium to long-term. Among the spending reductions were measures to control public sector pay more tightly, to restrain growth in public sector employment, to control public sector pensions, and to raise the retirement age. Buttressed by the considerable advantage of there being no credible alternative either to him or to his government, Amato pressed ahead with the policy of attacking the root causes of the structural deficit and survived two devaluations of the lira against the Deutschmark and, finally, Italy's withdrawal from the ERM.

Yet within a year of taking office, Amato was faced with a problem whose scale was so large as to threaten not only him and the government he led but the regime itself: endemic corruption in the public and private sectors was finally brought out into the open. Bribery has for so long been accepted practice at the meeting points of Italian politics and commerce that its exposure through relentless judicial investigations risks enmeshing a large part of the business and political classes. Some of Italy's most senior business leaders were by the early Spring of 1993 arrested on corruption charges, whilst Parliament voted in early March to lift immunity from prosecution of Bettino Craxi, the former Prime Minister. Similar requests by the judicial authorities for Parliamentary immunity to be lifted from other MPs suspected of corruption slowed legislative processes, and raised the possibility that thorough investigation would disable the Italian state.

In the referendum on the electoral system for the Italian Senate, voters turned out in large numbers to give overwhelming support for reform. However, it is far from certain that the introduction of a new voting system will result in a clear mandate for a coherent government because divisions within Italy are likely to persist along regional lines and to be reflected in a newly-elected Senate.

D'Amato's government finally collapsed in April 1993, its support having crumbled away in the chaos of the enlarged revelations of corruption. President Scalfaro appointed Carlo Ciampi, formerly Governor of the Bank of Italy, as Prime Minister.

The 1994 Election Background.

In 1993, Italy was convulsed by reform so rapid as might justify the term "revolutionary". In advance of parliamentary elections in March 1994, the entire party system changed. Mainstays of the old regime, especially the Christian Democrats and the Socialists, effectively imploded under the devastating impact of continuing revelations about the depth and breadth of the systematic corruption of public life. Coupled with deep regional divisions, electoral volatility, and public opinion polls which gave no party more than one-fifth of the vote, the risks to Italy's stability and coherence from elections fought under new rules by new parties were great. Proportional representation was not completely ended: one-quarter of the seats would continue to be allocated by proportional representation. Accordingly, many voters would continue to vote as they previously did: for the party they support rather than the tactically rational option of voting for the party best placed to defeat the party to which they were most intensely opposed. With three groupings in most constituencies, individual calculations about the party for which it was most rational to vote were rendered exceptionally difficult.

The new system, therefore, offered no guarantee that threats to the country's stability could be overcome: in the months leading up to the elections, parties congregated in three loose coalitions, none of which were internally stable and some of which were greatly weakened by serious fault lines (especially of region) running through them.

The New Electoral System.

The new electoral laws provided for the following:
* single-member, single-seat constituencies for 75% of the seats in parliament, with 25% of the seats allocated in proportion to the votes received.
* a threshold excludes from representation in the lower house (the Chamber) those parties which gain less than 4% nationally, and from the upper house (the Senate) those parties which gain less than 10% calculated regionally.
* opinion polls are prohibited in the fortnight prior to the election.

Such a combination of circumstances and rules made it improbable that any one of the eighteen parties contesting the elections could expect to gain more than one-fifth of the total vote. The three groupings within which the parties were organised were as follows:
* *The Centre* parties formed loose groupings around the "Pact for Italy", dominated by former Christian Democrats.
* *The Left* formed a broad alliance under the banner of the "Progressives"—the first occasion since 1948 that left-wing parties in Italy had overcome the differences between them for electoral purposes. The grouping included the Greens, the former Communist PDS, the remnants of the discredited Socialists, the Network movement, Liberals, Catholic radicals, the Marxist Communist Refoundation Party, and free-enterprise centrists.
* *The Right* was more deeply divided. Little common ground existed between the neo-fascist National Alliance and the Northern League on the one hand, and Silvio Berlusconi's *Forza Italia* on the other. The National Alliance, a remarketed version of the neo-fascist MSI, had its greatest strength in the south; the Northern League, a populist movement built around the charismatic leadership of Umberto Bossi on a programme of protest against the large state subsidies to the south, espoused a federalist programme which the National Alliance explicitly rejected. *Forza Italia* was unencumbered by principle, and fuelled by novelty. The three parties nevertheless found it expedient to campaign on the same platform.

The Outcome.

The electoral campaign of the political novitiate Berlusconi was powerfully assisted by his ownership of half of Italy's media outlets. By dint of the collapse of the centre parties, and his energetic campaigning exploitation of his electronic media ownership, Berlusconi's *Forza Italia* emerged from the elections as the single largest party. The election resulted in the right-wing alliance winning an absolute majority in the Chamber of Deputies, with 366 seats out of the total of 630, but just failing to win a majority of the 315 seats in the Senate. Given that neither Bossi nor Fini possessed the political stature necessary to make a plausible bid for the Premiership, Berlusconi was in a powerful position to assume the office, the delaying and bargaining tactics of his erstwhile colleagues in the other two right-wing parties notwithstanding. In the space of little more than two months, Berlusconi had propelled himself from magnate to Prime-Minister designate. On 28 April Berlusconi was finally invited to try to form a Cabinet.

The Berlusconi Administration.

The election of a new government led by media magnate Silvio Berlusconi following the elections of March 1994 heightened expectations of an end to the politics of stagnation and corruption. In fact, Berlusconi made little progress in gaining control of public finances. Moreover, in his tenacious grip upon his vast media interests, he represented in his own person and politics the ills which he had set out to right. Nor did the realigned political system which resulted in the formation of the centre-right grouping of the Northern League, the neo-fascist National Alliance, and Berlusconi's own party vehicle, *Forza Italia*, establish a firm basis for government.

Berlusconi's government fell in December 1994 following the Northern League's departure from the coalition in an attempt to force the creation of a new parliamentary commission to reform the franchising of television. The issue of media ownership concentration had weakened Berlusconi, and prompted the creation of an exceptionally weak new, technocratic, government under the leadership of Lamberto Dini, a former Director-General of the Bank of Italy. The government's durability will turn on the view taken by international markets of the credibility of its budget strategy, but an election is unlikely before new electoral laws can be implemented.

SPAIN.

As most observers anticipated, the General Election in Spain held on 22 June 1986 resulted in a clear victory for the party of the incumbent Prime Minister, Felipe Gonzalez, albeit with a smaller majority than in 1982. The outcome was in many ways remarkable for a Socialist leader who had practised monetarist economic policies and under whom unemployment had risen by 800,000 (the amount by which in 1982 he had pledged himself to reduce it). However, the improved standing of the regionalist parties and of the small groupings to the Socialist Party's left were reminders (if the Prime Minister needed them) of the persistence of the Catalan and, more seriously, the Basque questions, and of the unpopularity of his economic policies with the left.

The 1988 Party Congress.

At the Party Congress in January 1988, Mr. Gonzalez and his lieutenants such as the Deputy Prime Minister, Alfonso Guerra, easily overcame the dissent within the trade unions and from the few left-wingers prepared to state publicly their opposition to the Prime Minister's policies of high economic growth, the attraction of capital to Spain, and of a firm if not uncritical partnership with NATO and the EC. The policies won the overwhelming approval of Congress. The left had nowhere to turn: there was in early 1988 no more prospect of a credible challenge being mounted to Gonzalez's leadership from among their ranks, or from among assorted regional interests discontented with central control of policy and politics, than there was of a united centre or right-wing opposition emerging in the foreseeable future. Although the PSOE's public opinion poll rating fell to 40% at the beginning of the year, Mr. Gonzalez was his party's most powerful asset with voters and immune from serious challenge from within his own party or from another.

Relations between the Spanish Socialist government of Felipe Gonzalez and the socialist UGT trade union federation led by Nicolas Redondo worsened markedly during 1988 and early 1989. The main point of contention was social welfare policy which is very much less generous in Spain than in most other advanced Western European countries. Welfare policy is of particular importance in Spain because of the politically awkward combination of a nominally socialist government and the very high unemployment rate of 18·5%. Less than one-third of Spain's unemployed qualify for unemployment benefit; pledges made by the government in 1984 to raise the proportion to about half have not been met. The government's spending projections accord welfare spending no higher priority for the next four years. In these circumstances, the high expectations which the unions had of Mr. Gonzalez's administration following the increases in welfare benefits in his first year as Prime Minister have been dashed. The unions' response has been to overturn the corporatist arrangement between government, employers and unions to determine the level of national pay settlements.

The October 1989 Election.

The Prime Minister of Spain, Felipe Gonzalez, called an election for 20 October 1989, eight months before he was obliged to do so. High unemployment and a widening trade deficit apart, the economic achievements of the government he led were sufficiently impressive for him to seize the opportunity. Opportunism was precisely the charge levelled against the Prime Minister by his opponents in the conservative People's Party (led by a former member of Franco's government, Manuel Fraga) and the Social and Democratic Centre (led by the able former Prime Minister, Adolfo Suarez). There was much truth to it, The Socialist government had benefitted from a weak and divided opposition, and had paid little regard to the needs of the unemployed. The conservative and centrist opposition parties were tainted by reason of the association of their senior members with the old fascist regime; their support was accordingly limited.

The result of the election was to confirm the dominance of the Socialist Party. It remained by far the largest party with 176 seats, though with a majority of only one, and lost support on its left to the United Left with 17 seats, dominated by the Communist Party who tapped the discontent with the Socialists' parsimonious welfare policy, and its toleration of high unemployment. The People's Party benefitted from its running a new candidate for Prime Minister: Jose Maria Aznar who, unlike Fraga, was entirely untainted by links to Francoism. They won 106 seats but, as the People's Party gained, so the CDS under Suarez lost ground sharply with its total of seats falling to just 14.

The Socialists' circumstances deteriorated further during 1990. By the ruthlessness with which he dealt with those who opposed him, the deputy prime minister, Alfonso Guerra, deeply antagonised colleagues within the Cabinet and the Socialist Party. Guerra was an intimate political ally of Felipe Gonzalez who had increasingly ceded to him effective direction over the internal affairs of the Socialist Party whilst the Prime Minister concentrated upon foreign affairs. Precisely because he was a rough operator within the party, Guerra was immensely useful to Gonzalez: the party was kept in line, but not by the Prime Minister himself.

As Gonzalez gradually accepted more of the market-based economic prescriptions of right-wing colleagues within the government, he came under pressure from them to sack Guerra on account of his resistance to them. Guerra's resignation in January 1991 would not have occurred at the time it did had it not been for the involvement of his brother, Juan, in a scandal in Seville. If Juan's occupancy of an office in a government building there (whilst holding no government post) was not improper, it appeared so to many. Even so, Alfonso Guerra retained his post in the Socialist Party and is unlikely now to make the (decidedly free-market) government's job easier now that he is outside it than when he was within it. Gonzalez's delayed response was to use the opportunity of a reshuffle of his Cabinet to move the government further to the right. Two who gained were Narcis Serra, promoted to Guerra's old post as deputy prime minister, and Carlos Solchaga who had been powerfully opposed by Guerra when he was in office.

Socialist Electoral Success.

Guerra's departure from the government in 1991 was followed in 1992 by the resignation of the Health Minister, Julian Garcia Valverde after a land deal involving the state railway system of which he was then in charge came to public notice. However, the popularity of Prime Minister Gonzalez was relatively unaffected by the continuing problem of corruption in public life, and the Socialist Party continued to dominate Spanish electoral politics: in May 1991, the Socialists secured 38% of the vote in regional and local elections, two percentage points more than they had won in 1987. The overall gains masked their loss of control in the cities of Seville, Oviedo and Valencia which had previously been significant bases of power, and the continuing rise

of the People's Party as the main party of opposition. The vote of the Democratic and Social Centre again fell, prompting the resignation of the party's leader, Adolfo Suarez.

The Unemployment Spiral.

The Socialists' electoral success occurred with unemployment remaining stubbornly high. Some groups facing the prospect of unemployment (most notably miners facing pressures from the European Commission for a reduction in employment levels) reacted with violence. Employment and incomes policy continued to be the single greatest source of division within the Socialist Party, and its prominence will grow as the conditions set for European Monetary Union bear down upon Spanish wage inflation. Nevertheless, the government's position is not threatened: the economy continues to grow faster than most of her competitors, and the rate of inflation has fallen to approximately 5%. However, 1992 sees Spain thrust onto the international stage with the holding of Expo 92 in Seville, and the staging of the Olympics in Barcelona. The occasions offer parallel opportunities to Prime Minister Gonzalez to promote Spain's image as a dynamic European economy and society in preparation for elections either in 1993 or, if the Prime Minister senses the prospect of victory earlier, in the autumn of 1992.

Spain's International Role.

Spain's international prominence in 1992 was one of the few valuable cards in Prime Minister Gonzalez's hand in the Spring of 1993 after ten years of PSOE government: both the Barcelona Olympics and Expo 92 in Seville were undoubted successes (but both also proved heavy drains on the public purse). For 1993 and 1994, Spain will also have a seat on the United Nations Security Council. The governing PSOE's electoral fortunes were nonetheless shaped more by continuing economic difficulty, epitomised in tax increases and expenditure cuts in the summer of 1992, devaluations of the peseta in September and November by 5% and 6% respectively, and an accompanying reimposition of exchange controls.

In the wake of the first devaluation, Finance Minister Solchaga, leader of the liberal economic faction of the PSOE, announced new, severe, restraints upon public spending. As elsewhere in Europe, so in Spain: domestic politics were driven by domestic economic policy which was in turn heavily shaped by policy regarding European monetary union.

Electoral Problems.

The difficulty for the Spanish government was that the electoral timetable increased the political costs of tight fiscal and monetary policies: both the small United Left Party and the right of centre People's Party (PP) benefited from the government's discomfiture. By the time that the People's Party held its annual convention in early February 1993, it was barely four percentage points behind the PSOE in the opinion polls. Whilst Prime Minister Gonzalez was still an accomplished leader of a factious party (divided especially deeply over privatisation and labour market reforms), the fall in support during 1992 for his party and for his leadership of it gave heart both to the PP and to the smaller regional parties. Gonzalez's decision to call an election for 6 June 1993 resulted in a hotly-contested election, with the PSOE and PP competing to gain ascendancy. In the event, the Socialist Party clung on to power, losing its absolute parliamentary majority but seeing off the Popular Party challenge.

Of the 350 seats at issue in elections for the lower house, the Socialist Party (PSOE) won 159 on 38·6% of the vote. It thereby lost the overall majority which it had won at the 1989 General Election, but retained a plurality over the opposition conservative People's Party (PP) which won 141 seats (an increase of 34 over 1989) on 34·8% of the popular vote. The votes for other parties were squeezed by the two large blocs: the Basque Nationalist Party (PNV) and Catalan Convergence and Union (CiU) parties won five and seventeen seats respectively, whilst the United Left won nineteen seats—only two more than in 1989. Despite losing its overall majority, the PSOE performed well in both the Basque country and Catalonia. The centre party, CDS, a significant force in the 1980s, fell from fourteen seats to one. The minor parties also found themselves marginalised in the 208 Senate races: there, the PSOE won 96 seats, and the PP 93.

Freed of compelling pressures to reach accommodations with other parties, Gonzalez was able to continue with his liberal economic reforms in the knowledge that to do so would make it more difficult for conservative opponents in the PP and the CiU (which, though nationalist, is dominated by business interests) to attack him. To that extent, the failure of his attempt to secure a formal coalition with the nationalist parties of the centre-right was not crucial. In the first eight months of the new government's life, however, it did grant the nationalist parties unusual influence over macroeconomic policy, and enable them to extract concessions from the government with respect to a new package of devolution measures.

Labour Market Deregulation.

The PSOE's electoral weakness among younger voters prompted the Prime Minister to intensify his deregulation of Spanish labour markets whilst seeking to keep public sector wage rises beneath the prevailing rate of inflation. Gonzalez's objective of cutting the very high levels of unemployment, especially among the young, was clear. Given that the Europe-wide problem of joblessness was, at nearly a quarter of the working population, especially severe in Spain, the Prime Minister was not alone in regarding the matter as the highest political priority. Nevertheless, his chosen measures of cutting the real level of state pensions, and reducing unemployment benefits by yet larger amounts, risked open conflict with the deputy leader of the PSOE, Alfonso Guerra—although they attracted the support of the opposition PP.

Political Crisis in Spain.

As problems of public finance, falling business confidence, and rising inflation crowded in upon the government in 1994, Spanish politics were thrown into crisis by the alleged involvement of the government's Anti-Terrorist Liberation Groups (GAL) in the illegal killing of twenty-three suspected members of the Basque separatist ETA movement in the 1980s. The charges came after a rash of corruption allegations: one concerned the UGT trade union (whose links with the PSOE are close), and another the alleged preferential government treatment of the Prime Minister's brother-in-law. The GAL case was more damaging than either. It reached high into the Spanish government, entangling the former security chief and, possibly, both the Interior Minister and Gonzalez himself. Were the judicial investigation actually to inculpate the Prime Minister, the government's prospects of survival would be slender because the Catalan CiU party would be bound to withdraw its support. Even if Gonzalez were to escape embroilment in the scandal, the government was bound to be weakened by the revelations.

EASTERN MEDITERRANEAN

GREECE.

As elsewhere in Europe, politics in Greece are powerfully affected by the collapse of Communism in Eastern Europe and the resurgence of nationalist sentiments and ethnic loyalties. Greece is alarmed by the possibility of Macedonian claims on parts of northern Greece being launched in the wake of the collapse of Yugoslavia, and anxious at the fate of the Greek minority in Albania. More generally, Greece is wary of the opportunities for the extension of Turkish influence in Moslem regions of the Balkans. The Greek government faces more familiar problems deriving from the competitive pressures on EC members in the implementation of European Monetary Union. Inflation remains much higher than her EC competitors (22% in 1991), and the public sector borrowing requirement is growing.

The August 1992 Reshuffle.

Prime Minister Constantine Mitsotakis reshuffled his Cabinet on 7 August 1992 in an attempt to address the grave problem presented by the large budget deficit which, although it has fallen as a percentage of GDP since 1990, remains stubbornly high. The most significant appointment is that of Stefanos Manos as Minister of Finance in addition to his existing responsibilities as Minister for National Economy. For Greece even to approach the convergence condition set under the Maastricht agreement (government debt should not exceed 60% of GDP; the annual deficit should not exceed 3% of GDP), public finances will have to improve dramatically under his leadership of the Finance Ministry.

Mr. Manos's remedy for the uncomfortable combination of high inflation and comparatively high public debt was conventional, but politically risky: it involved an extension of the tax net (partly in order to cover the large black economy) and a reduction in some marginal rates of tax, coupled with increases in some indirect taxes, restraint in public sector pay, reductions in social security benefits, and cuts in public sector employment. This package met with intense resistance from public sector workers in the latter half of 1992.

The October 1993 Elections.

In the general election held on 10 October 1993, the Socialists were returned to power under the leadership of Andreas Papandreou with 47% of the vote and 170 seats in parliament. The New Democracy party, in government since 1989 under the leadership of Constantine Mitsotakis, fell well short by gaining slightly less than 40% of the vote and only 111 seats. Political Spring, the faction within New Democracy whose departure from the governing party brought about the general election, took less than 5% of the vote and only ten seats. The unreformed Communist Party also won less than 5%, taking nine seats.

Within PASOK's unpromising economic inheritance, the problem of public indebtedness posed the gravest problem for the new government. The government's first budget, presented six weeks after its victory at the polls, provided for modest budget reductions in those areas of government spending where the political costs of cuts could be sustained. Tax rises in the Spring of 1994 will contribute to the closing of the yawning gap in public finance which, in combination with an understanding on wages with employers and unions, should diminish inflationary pressures, and enable exceptionally high Greek interest rates to be cut slightly.

Greek politics in 1994 were shaped increasingly by politicians' focus upon the Presidential elections scheduled for May 1995. Elected by the 300-member Parliament, the President must secure the votes of 180 members to be elected. Since PASOK has only 170 Parliamentary seats, its success in promoting one of its own to the Presidency will hinge upon its capacity to win additional support from another party, or a faction from within the increasingly divided New Democracy opposition. Political manoeuvring is complicated by the difficult economic circumstances in which Papandreou's government finds itself, especially with regard to growing public sector wage pressures and the linked problem of a budget deficit resistant to attempts at control.

TURKEY.

The October 1991 Election.

The True Path Party, led by Suleyman Demirel, emerged from the elections of 20 October 1991 as the largest party in Parliament, but the largest gains were made by the Welfare Party, led by the conservative (and Islamic) Necmettin Erbakan.

The government which emerged was a coalition between Demirel's True Path and Erdal Inonu's Social Democratic Party. Demirel became Prime Minister, and Inonu Deputy Prime Minister. Surprisingly, the arrangement quickly came to appear settled. Inonu's hold over his party is firmer than many observers had expected, and such disturbance as there has been in the government's first six months has arisen mostly from awkward relations between Demirel and President Ozal. Although the party political base of the government is reasonably stable, the problems which it faces are great. At home, inflation remains very high (70% in 1991), and economic growth is sluggish.

The Kurdish Question.

Terrorist attacks by the Kurdistan Workers' Party (PKK) upon Turkey both from within the country and also from bases in Iraq, and the establishment of an Iraqi Kurdish administration in northern Iraq after the elections in Iraqi Kurdistan in May 1992, combined to present the Turkish government with an intensely difficult and persistent diplomatic problem. Opposed to the formation of a permanent Kurdish state in northern Iraq because of the implications for its own control over the mostly Kurdish part of south-eastern Turkey, aware that the PKK may have fallen under the protection of Saddam Hussein, but knowing also that the Iranian government supports the PKK, Turkey was caught between its need to defeat the terrorist threat and its wish to maintain good working relations with the major powers in the region, especially Iran.

The Death of Ozal.

Turgut Ozal, the dominant figure in Turkish politics during the 1980s, died suddenly on 17 April 1993. As President of Turkey since 1989, Ozal's formal powers were few but he continued to do much to enhance Turkey's international standing and influence abroad and to exercise great (though increasingly contested) influence over politics at home. Parliament elected Suleiman Demirel as President to succeed him.

Intensified violence in the Kurdish areas of south-eastern Turkey, coupled with an inflation rate in 1993 of 71%, presented Prime Minister Ciller with two problems of exceptional difficulty. Whilst the economy grew in 1993 by approximately 7%, the political repercussions of such a high inflation rate threatened the standing of Ciller's True Path Party (TPP) and the stability of its coalition with the Social Democratic Populist Party. Impending local elections due in March 1994 made addressing one of the primary causes of the inflation (a huge public sector spending deficit) even more difficult than it otherwise would have been, as parliament's weakening of the government's tax reforms in December 1993 showed. The March local elections revealed a huge rise in support for Islamic fundamentalists. Operations against the PKK reached new heights in 1993: the PKK's temporary ceasefire ended at the end of May, and Ciller's attempts to find an opening to a negotiated settlement ran up against the rock of opposition from the powerful Turkish Armed Forces to any arrangement providing for increased Kurdish autonomy. Despite intensified operations against the PKK, the insurgency went undefeated.

Turkey and the EU.

Implementation of a customs union between Turkey and the EU, delayed by Greece in an attempt to win concessions from Ankara on Cyprus, was not assisted by European displeasure with Turkey's brutal handling of her internal security problems. The economy's dire condition provided no relief for the beleaguered government, either. Production fell by one-fifth in the second half of 1994, international trade fell by one-tenth between January and September, and the value of the Turkish lira against the US dollar more than halved between January and December.

On 13 March Istanbul was placed under military curfew after 16 people had died in the worst street violence since 1980. Rioting began after Islamic fundamentalist gunmen fired on moderate Muslims in a working class district, killing two and wounding 25 people. Two groups—the Turkish Revenge Brigade and the Great Eastern Islamic Raiders—claimed responsibility. On the following day thousands clashed with police in Ankara during protests against the killings organised by human rights groups and trade unions. There were similar demonstrations in other towns and on 16 March four people were killed in further clashes with police in Istanbul.

But attention immediately shifted to Turkey's long-running campaign against Kurdish Workers' Party (PKK) separatist guerillas as on 19 March the PKK killed 18 soldiers in a mountain ambush in the east of the country. Turkey responded immediately. On 20 March 35,000 troops advanced 25 miles into northern Iraq in an assault against 20 alleged PKK camps. This incursion into the United Nations protection zone had an immediate detrimental effect on Turkey's relations with the EU.

THE FORMER SOVIET UNION

Note: For the events leading to the collapse of the Soviet Union, the fall of Gorbachev and the political and economic crisis engulfing Russia, *see* Special Topic, C71–3.

EASTERN EUROPE

POLAND.

Poland marked in 1989 a less complete break with the past than either Czechoslovakia or Hungary but one which was still a significant further shift away from totalitarianism. The elections of June 1989 marked a stunning rebuff to the Communist Party (PUWP) but the restrictive rules under which the elections took place ensured that the old order could not be completely and immediately swept away. The election resulted in 160 out of 161 Solidarity candidates being victorious, giving it almost all of the 35% of the seats in the Sejm for which it had been permitted to compete. It became apparent by August 1989 that the new Prime Minister, General Kiszczak, would be unable to form a government.

Tadeusz Mazowiecki emerged as the country's first non-Communist leader in forty years. Mazowiecki, a 63 year old lawyer, was a former editor of a Catholic monthly journal, and of Solidarity's weekly newspaper in 1981. He led a government where the defence and interior ministries are in Communist hands, the fellow-travelling Peasants and Democrat parties had four and two ministries respectively, and Solidarity took the remaining six. The Peasants Party is a misnomer since the party enjoys scarcely any support from peasants; Rural Solidarity is the main political force among Poland's farmers but it played little role in the formation of the government. Its composition reflected Mr. Lech Walesa's judgement of what was prudent under the circumstances. Walesa had taken charge of the task of forming a government only after Solidarity's negotiations with the two small parties collapsed.

In early 1990, the Polish Communist Party (the PUWP) dissolved itself, to be replaced by two parties: the Social Democratic Party of the Polish Republic (which inherited most of the PUWP's physical assets) and the Union of Social Democrats. The first is led by Alex Kwasniewski who disarmingly observed that only a "crazy" person would have wanted the post. The second is headed by Tadeusz Fiszbach, formerly the PUWP leader in Gdansk.

The Presidential Elections.

In the first round of voting for the Polish Presidency on 25 November 1990, the prime minister, Tadeusz Mazowiecki (with just 18% of the vote) was defeated by a Polish-Canadian businessman, Stanislaw Tyminski (with 23%) and Lech Walesa (with 40%). Tyminski was a bizarre candidate, much given to the making of irresponsible promises. In the course of the campaign, he declared that he would bring full employment and instant riches; he evoked old-fashioned Polish nationalist sentiments even to the ludicrous extent of declaring "economic war" upon the west. Tyminski owed his support more to discontent with Mazowiecki's repeated messages of economic gloom and what appeared to many Poles to be the sluggish response of the country's economy to the end of Communism. Mazowiecki resigned as Prime Minister, and Tyminski was duly defeated by Lech Walesa in the second round of the Presidential election.

Two prominent Solidarity politicians (Bronislaw Geremek and Jan Olszewski) declined Walesa's invitation to serve as Prime Minister in succession to Mazowiecki. Krzysztof Bielecki, who favoured a more vigorous free-market and privatisation programme, was eventually appointed. The combination of a lack of constitutional clarity and immense policy problems prompted Walesa to transform the Presidency into a powerful executive post with a council to advise him. The Sejm, whose legitimacy was weakened by its being only partly-democratic, was further marginalised by Walesa's creation of the Council (as he intended that it should be). As elsewhere in eastern Europe, the political vehicle for democratic revolution proved unwieldy for the task of democratic reconstruction: Solidarity split into several parts in preparation for national elections.

The 1991 Elections.

Poland's first free parliamentary elections for more than half a century were held in late October 1991 but most voters chose not to participate, and no clear result emerged from the confusion of 125 parties competing for seats. Of these, more than twenty parties won representation in the Sejm, with no single party exercising dominance. After the election, three unstable groupings of parties existed within the Sejm:
* three parties were loosely-organised around what had been Solidarity. Damaged by the unpopularity of the government's harsh economic reforms and marketisation policies, the grouping attracted only about one-fifth of the total votes;
* the second was a group of four Christian Democratic parties with about 27% of the votes, and a rather larger proportion of the seats in the Sejm. Although this group would appear to be reasonably cohesive, there are lines of fissure within it caused by increasingly bitter differences over the role of the Catholic Church in public life;
* the third centred around the successors to the Communist Party which, feeding off widespread discontent among both industrial and rural workers, received 21% of the total vote.

Growing Economic Crisis.

Formation of a stable government from such a multiply-divided Sejm proved exceptionally difficult. Divisions of opinion about how the Communist past should be confronted ran deep, while the social and political costs of compliance with western bankers' (and especially the IMF's) agendas for economic reform exacerbated discontents. Unemployment grew rapidly during 1991 to more than 11% of the workforce. The new government of Jan Olszewski shifted economic course somewhat in early 1992, placing a new emphasis on the need for greater exports and higher investment at the expense of consumption. Olszewski attempted to reassure the IMF that he remained determined to drive down the rate of inflation below 50% in 1992, but it is clear that the government's anti-inflationary credentials will be severely tested over the next three years.

The Fall of Olszewski.

Having persistently delayed taking difficult economic and financial decisions, especially those on privatisation and wage restraint, the populist Olszewski government fell on 5 June 1992 following the publication of a list of names of prominent figures who either had collaborated, or were alleged to have collaborated, with state security agencies during the years of Communist rule. Ironically, on the very day that it fell, the government succeeded in pushing its restrictive budget, providing for a budget deficit of less than 5% of GNP, through parliament—thereby meeting the condition set by the IMF for continued support.

The Brief Suchoka Administration.

The successor centre-left coalition government of seven parties was formed by Hanna Suchoka, a prominent member of the anti-Communist Democratic Alliance in the early 1980s. Facing a wave of major strikes in the coal mining, car, and tractor manufacturing industries in the months following her appointment, Ms. Suchoka faced down some of the most critical whilst seeking less conflictual,

participatory, means of settling with unions and business her industrial and labour market policy. Ms. Suchoka also steered the government firmly in a free-market direction, bearing down upon inflation by restraining wage settlements and achieving strong growth in exports. By the end of 1992, it was apparent that Poland was slowly emerging from recession.

In early 1993, the prospect of more rapid economic reform grew with the granting by Parliament to the government of the right to rule by decree in key areas such as privatisation and the development of closer relations with western economies. The IMF, evidently content with the progress made by Prime Minister Suchoka and her government of economically liberal ministers, gave its approval in March 1993 to a new US$660 million standby loan facility. The IMF's confidence was premature.

The Transition to a Market Economy.

Tight restraints on public spending, coupled with anxieties about the implications of continuing privatisation, implemented by the government as part of the IMF package, contributed to a worsening of relations in the spring of 1993 between Suchoka's Solidarity-headed Democratic Union (UD) government and the trade unions. Growing industrial unrest, and the difficulty of establishing and maintaining a majority for economic reform, eventually resulted in the calling of a general election for September 1993 which the government lost. That Suchoka lost was unsurprising, for the pain of transition to a market economy was considerable, though unevenly borne: the rate of inflation reached 35% in 1993 (but was expected to moderate in 1994 to approximately 28%), whilst unemployment rose to 16% in January 1994 with intense local pockets at rates substantially above the national average rate. The unemployed, public sector workers, farmers, and pensioners formed the backbone of the coalition which ousted Suchoka's government.

The Advent of Pawlak.

Reflecting the difficulty in distributing Cabinet posts, the new government of the Polish Peasant Party (PSL) and the Democratic Left Alliance (SLD) was some weeks in the making. Led by Prime Minister Waldemar Pawlak of the PSL, the government was beset by internal strains and tensions arising from the contradictory pressures of its supporters on the one hand and external creditors on the other. The government continued to seek to protect vulnerable groups within its coalition from the worst of the unemployment and depressed real incomes which were accompanying the transition from state socialism whilst pressing ahead with a wide-ranging programme of privatisation. The political judgment was apparent in the budget agreed in February 1994: the tax net was widened in order to pay for increases in state benefits, and overall spending increases were limited to about 8%.

The Crisis of February 1995.

Growing tensions between the two parties of the governing coalition, the Democratic Left Alliance (SLD) and the Polish Peasant Party (PSL) in 1994 led to Prime Minister Waldemar Pawlak, a member of the PSL, being replaced in February 1995 with Jozef Oleksy, a member of the SLD, Speaker of the Sejm, opponent of President Walesa, and a man with a reputation for being an astute bargainer and conciliator.

The crisis and its disposition was intimately connected to the contest for the Presidency in mid-1995, the prospect of which proved sufficient to stifle creative governance. Walesa constantly staked out positions in opposition to the government during 1994. As part of an attempt to remove his most powerful potential opponent for the Presidency, Walesa had sought to manoeuvre Alexander Kwasniewski, leader of the SLD, into the Premiership. The move having failed, Kwasniewski's long-term prospects were good – whether he opted to stand for the Presidency against Walesa, or to seek the Premiership under a reformed constitution in which the President's role was greatly reduced.

THE FORMER CZECHOSLOVAKIA.

In October 1989, Vaclav Havel was a prisoner of a Communist-run Czechoslovakia; on 29 December, he was sworn in as the newly-democratic Czechoslovakia's President. Alexander Dubcek, the country's leader during the "Prague Spring" of 1968 which was ended by the Soviet invasion in the August of that year and who lived in internal exile for most of the twenty-two years that followed, was elected chairman of the federal assembly in Prague on 27 December 1989.

Democratic Revolution.

Czechoslovakia's democratic revolution was slow to arrive. A large demonstration in Prague on 17 November 1989, brutally treated by police in baton-charges, spawned others on succeeding nights in other Czech and Slovak cities. Too late for their own good, the Prime Minister, Ladislav Adamec and the Communist Party secretary, Milos Jakes, made small concessions to those demonstrating for Czechoslovakian reforms as far-reaching as those in Poland and Hungary. Within a fortnight, Communist power in Czechoslovakia collapsed and Civic Forum, the opposition peacefully led by the inspirational Vaclav Havel, emerged as the dominant political force. On 10 December, what was left of the Communist leadership accepted the formation of a government in which they were a minority. The new foreign minister was Jiri Dienstbier, a founder of Charter 77, the human rights group and spokesman for Civic Forum. Other ministers were also drawn from the ranks of dissidents, until recently marginalised (many of them imprisoned) by the old communist regime.

Painful Economic Adjustment.

The process of economic adjustment grew more painful during 1991: industrial production fell to approximately three-quarters of 1990 levels, whilst GDP fell by a fifth and continued to fall further (albeit at a slower rate) in the early months of 1992. Under the austere policies of Finance Minister Vaclav Klaus, the prize of virtually zero inflation was achieved by the summer of 1991. The second phase of the government's privatisation plan attracted substantial public support.

Wide variations in economic activity were apparent within the Federation: Slovakia's economy was hampered by the Republic being mired in the old anxieties and fears of anti-semitism, the narrowest nationalism, and persisting public support for Communist officials and attachment to Communist norms. The Czech Republic, less dependent than Slovakia upon trade with former Comecon countries, stood to benefit disproportionately from the lowering of tariff barriers with the European Community (EC), embodied in the terms of a membership association agreed with the EC in November 1991. Slovakia already absorbed more than its fair share of public expenditure, and contributed less than one-fifth of Czechoslovakia's total exports.

THE CZECH REPUBLIC AND SLOVAKIA.

On 1 January 1993, Czechoslovakia split into its two constituent republics, the Czech Republic, and Slovakia. From the time of elections in June 1992 to the Federal Assembly and the two National Councils, the outcome had appeared likely because the two parties which had emerged the strongest from the polls were plainly unwilling to create a federal government. Czechoslovakia polarised by party along the boundary between the two republics, making a federal accommodation improbable.

Prospects for the New Nations.

From the time of the elections until formal separation, both Republics prepared for separation, but it was plain that the Czech Republic's economic and political future was brighter than that of Slovakia. Whereas the latter's unemployment rate at the time of separation was more than 10% and rising, the Czech Republic's rate was a mere 2·5%—exceptionally low by comparison with other European industrial democracies. The liberal, free-market policies of the thoroughly democratic

Czech Republic contrast sharply with the barely-reformed policies of Slovakia where the Communist political class continues to exercise power. The Slovakian government's appeal derives from its exploitation of crude nationalist sentiment in its disputes with Hungary, Poland, and the Ukraine which serve as a diversion from continuing economic failure. Having been integrated for so long, the economies of the two Republics will not be quickly separated but financial and commercial tensions between the two have nonetheless arisen with disturbing rapidity. Such tensions are likely to intensify as Slovakian frustration with the onset of economic decline grows.

The Economic Outlook.

The gap in economic performance between the Czech Republic and Slovakia increased further in 1993: the Czech economy grew at the very slow rate of 1%, whilst the Slovakian economy shrank by a further 6·4%. The gap between the two will probably grow further in 1994, albeit at a slower rate than in 1993; overall economic performance in the Czech Republic will depend heavily upon demand in Germany which now absorbs a high proportion of Czech exports (themselves fuelled by a deliberately undervalued Czech Crown). Slovakia's export industries are much less well-equipped to meet the rigours of international competition: a deterioration in Slovakian export performance in 1993 prompted the Slovakian government to devalue its currency—the Slovakian Crown—adding to domestic inflationary pressures.

The Czech Republic's economic prospects are good. Whilst those assessments of the Czech economy which identify it as having the vigour and dynamism of Singapore and South Korea are misplaced, its attraction to foreign investors and its early, proven, capacity to compete in West European markets bode well. It remains much the most dynamic and soundly-based large manufacturing economy in Eastern Europe.

Recent Developments.

The coalition government in Prague lost little of its stability or popularity in 1994 but potential sources of division within the ruling coalition seemed likely to grow in 1995 as manoeuvring took place in advance of the 1996 elections. Old Communists, enjoying renewed popularity elsewhere (not least in Slovakia) in Eastern Europe while dressed in new clothes, remained marginalised in the Czech Republic. The economy at last began once again to grow (albeit slowly) in 1994, sustained continuing high levels of employment, and exhibited remarkable fiscal discipline. At 11%, inflation was high, but half the rate of that in 1993.

Slovakia, too, enjoyed a measure of success: inflation was only a little higher than in the Czech Republic, whilst growth of output (fuelled by a vigorous export performance) was strong. Structural change proceeded more slowly in Slovakia than in its neighbour, however, reflecting the more divisive and unstable character of its domestic politics.

HUNGARY.

Dissolution of the Communist Party.

At its congress in October 1989, the Hungarian Communist Party dissolved itself, reforming as the Hungarian Socialist Party to be led by Tezso Nyers. The proclaimed programme of the new party was that of commitment to a multi-party system (an accommodation to a fast-developing reality) and a social market economy. The move was prompted by the Communist Party's poor performance in by-elections held during the summer and early autumn, and by fears within the party about its likely fate in the general election to be held in March 1990.

The elections took place in two stages, with an absolute majority of the vote required for election. Voters had the task of voting for individual constituency candidates and for nationwide party lists; of the 386 seats in the parliament, 176 came from constituencies and the remaining 110 from party lists. In the first round of voting, the Hungarian Socialist Party fared poorly, falling to fourth place by gaining just under 11% of the vote for the party lists. Just ahead of it was the rural conservative Independent Smallholders' Party.

The two major parties after the first round were the conservative Hungarian Democratic Forum, and the liberal Alliance of Free Democrats. It seemed improbable that the second round of voting would result in either of them having an overall majority. A coalition between them, or between one of them and one or more small parties, would therefore be necessary for the formation of a government. The Democratic Forum's most likely coalition partner would be the Christian Democratic People's Party whereas the Alliance's would be the slightly larger Federation of Young Democrats.

In the second round of voting, the Democratic Forum secured 165 of the 386 seats; the Smallholders Party 43, and the Christian Democratic People's Party 21. A coalition of these three would give a total of 228 seats, and an overall majority of 72. Opposition parties included 92 Free Democrats, and 33 Socialists. The President of the Hungarian Democratic Forum and the country's probable Prime Minister, Jozsef Antall, declared after his party's success that Hungary's first priority would be to seek membership of the European Union.

The 1990 Elections.

A series of elections in 1990 resulted in Jozsef Antall's coalition government becoming established in parliament but facing vigorous opposition from the Alliance of Free Democrats and the Alliance of Young Democrats, the two liberal parties, who won local elections in October. Unlike in Romania, the key institutions of state and society were not dominated by remnants of the old regime: the mass media was independent (although parts of it were owned by western media corporations) and the Courts were by late 1990 fully independent of the executive. Also in contrast to circumstances in Romania and some other parts of eastern Europe, privatisation proceeded apace and relatively smoothly, helped greatly by the preparation for entry into a market economy which had occurred during the two decades before the democratic revolution.

The transition was not, of course, costless. As in other former communist countries, many stood to lose by the ending of the command economy and did not hesitate to tell the takers of opinion polls of their gloom. There were harder indications of discontent, too: demonstrations by drivers of cabs and trucks followed the imposition of heavy increases in petrol and diesel fuel prices in October 1990.

Like other East European economies, Hungary suffered a fall in national output in 1991. The fall in GDP was relatively small, however—only about 6%, and the rate of decline slowed considerably towards the end of the year and the beginning of 1992. The lagging indicator of unemployment nonetheless rose remorselessly in 1991 and will continue to increase during 1992 as firms seek to cut costs and improve labour productivity by reducing workforces.

A Changing Economy.

Partly because of early market reforms under Communism, Hungary was less dependent than other former Comecon members on the Soviet Union; adjustment to the world (and especially the European) markets therefore came as less of a shock to Hungarians and was further cushioned by substantial investment in Hungary from abroad. Nonetheless, many of those newly unemployed in 1991 had worked for firms engaged in trade with the Republics of the former Soviet Union. Germany has now replaced the Soviet Union as Hungary's largest partner in foreign trade, and exports to the whole of western Europe grew rapidly in 1991. Progress is being made in the fight against inflation: the rate stood at 35% in 1991 but is unlikely to be much more than half this in 1992.

Hungarian Minorities Abroad.

Hungarian politics in 1992 was heavily marked by the savage war in neighbouring Croatia and Serbia, and by the hostility towards ethnic Hungarians in Romania and Slovakia. By the late summer of 1992, the government estimated that it had absorbed more than 320,000 refugees (Hungarians, Croatians and others) from Croatia and Vojvodina (still home to more than 400,000 ethnic Hungarians) which is under Serbian control. The Hungarian government finds itself in a position where governments of adjoining states find that an appeal to anti-Hungarian sentiment is one of the few popular causes amidst the chaos of economic collapse.

The Death of Antall.

Prime Minister Jozsef Antall died in mid-December 1993, and was succeeded by Peter Boross, Minister of the Interior in Antall's administration. With only six months before elections fell due, Boross conspicuously lacked the moderate Antall's appeal to those beyond the Hungarian Democratic Forum Party (MDF). Whereas Antall sought wide support, Boross's career suggested that his politics were more narrowly right-wing; moreover, Boross lacked a firm base in the party (which he had joined only in 1992). MDF's prospects were clouded by three further factors, all of which made the election's outcome exceptionally difficult to predict:

* the damaging effects of the split in the party in June 1993 when its nationalist and liberal factions broke away;
* the electoral pact concluded between FIDESZ and SZDSZ, the two main liberal parties;
* the resurgence of support in opinion polls for the Socialist Party (MSZP) to the point where, in early 1994, it ran neck-and-neck with FIDESZ.

Foreign Policy Developments.

In foreign policy, Hungary's relations with its neighbours in Slovakia, Serbia and (in particular) Romania continued to be made difficult by conflicting views about the status of Hungarian minorities in those countries. Hungary's anxieties were heightened by an agreement between Slovakia and Romania to adopt an agreed policy towards ethnic minorities within their two states. The problem presented by the Hungarian minority in the Romanian province of Transylvania was especially severe and not easily susceptible of solution, not least because nationalist parties in both Hungary and Romania were content to exploit the question for factional ends. The domestic political support lent to the Romanian government by extreme nationalist parties limited Bucharest's capacity to adopt a more enlightened policy towards the Hungarian minority within its borders. The visit to Bucharest of the Hungarian Foreign Minister in September 1993 drew no concessions from his hosts, an outcome which, in turn, enabled right-wing nationalist opinion in Hungary to use the issue to put pressure on the administration in Budapest.

The May 1994 Elections.

The Hungarian Socialist Party (MSZP), led by Gyula Horn, emerged from the elections of May 1994 with an overall majority in parliament. Seeking to broaden support within Hungary and reassure opinion among western governments and investors about his determination to marginalise the left-wing of his party and its trade union allies, Horn nonetheless chose to form a coalition with the Alliance of Free Democrats (SZDSZ). The new government's programme included policies to reform parliament (including election law), the media, education, and local government. Its first eight months in office revealed that the major strains within the government lay within the MSZP, not within the SZDSZ. However, to the extent that the Prime Minister was tempted to accommodate the political pressures to his left, he risked the coalition's stability. Given that the bulk of government debt in Hungary is short-term, and that foreign investors lacked confidence, Horn's freedom of manoeuvre was slight.

ROMANIA.

The Revolution in Romania.

Having watched the rapid progress of the democratic revolutions in Eastern Europe with as a great a horror as others experienced exhilaration, President Ceausescu's own brutal Stalinist regime collapsed within the space of a few days in December 1989. Within five weeks of the opening of the choreographed Communist Party Congress in Bucharest, Ceausescu was overthrown. After a 'trial' by a kangaroo court, he and his wife were shot on Christmas Day.

The revolution began with demonstrations in Timisoara which were ended bloodily by troops on 17 December. Attempting to bolster his support by a rally in Bucharest on 21 December, troops again opened fire—but this time on demonstrators who defied Ceausescu by openly denouncing him. The army's loyalty to Ceausescu quickly evaporated, and he was obliged to leave the headquarters of the Communist Party by helicopter in order to escape the wrath of the crowds at its doors.

The revolution was bloody. During the three days between the capture of Ceausescu and his wife Elena and their execution, the *Securitate* secret police fought a rearguard action against the army and the people. The number of persons killed is unknown, but probably not more than 2,000. Unsurprisingly, politics in Romania were unsettled afterwards.

The May 1990 Elections.

Assisted massively by its inheritance of the organisational structures and propaganda machine of the former Communist Party, and by the pervasively anti-democratic political culture, the National Salvation Front dominated the campaign for the elections held on 20 May 1990 for the Presidency, the Chamber of Deputies, and the Senate. The elections were effectively administered and adjudicated by officials sympathetic to the Front; even the counting of votes was often undertaken by openly partisan officials. The two major opposition parties were accordingly seriously handicapped. In some cases, opposition candidates and supporters were physically intimidated by Front supporters.

The Advent of Iliescu.

Ion Iliescu, the National Salvation Front candidate, was elected to the Presidency with 85·1% of the vote. His nearest opponent, Radu Campeanu of the National Liberal Party won just 10·6%, and Ion Ratiu of the National Christian Democratic Peasant Party won 4·3%. Iliescu did best in wholly Romanian provinces, less well in ethnically mixed areas, and poorly in the Hungarian provinces. In elections to the Chamber of Deputies, the Front gained two-thirds of the vote, and 263 of the 396 seats. As elsewhere in Eastern Europe, the umbrella party which dominated the course of revolutionary events came under strain as the responsibilities of government fell upon it. In contrast to the relatively smooth break-up of Civic Forum and the establishment of a stable party system in Czechoslovakia, however, the future of representative politics in Romania appeared unclear in early 1991: the government enjoyed little trust but the parliamentary opposition was weak, divided, and mostly incompetent. Lacking legitimacy, Mr. Petre Roman's government was seriously hampered in its attempts to implement the radical economic reform plan announced in November 1990.

The Fall of Roman.

Violent protest by miners at their poor pay and conditions of work in September 1991 led to Roman's resignation on 1 October and to a freeze on rents, the prices of coal, fuel-oil, and basic foodstuffs. In practice, severe shortages continue to drive up prices of energy and food, made worse by a poor harvest in the autumn of 1991. The dissatisfaction of the miners was shared by workers in other industries who had seen little or no economic benefit in the period of nearly two years since the overthrow of Ceausescu's regime.

The divisions within the NSF were explained more by jockeying for power than by doctrinal differences. As Prime Minister, Roman had introduced market reforms which were resisted by his conservative opponents within the divided National Salvation Front (NSF) but his departure from office did not mark a retreat from market reforms. Roman's successor, Teodor Stolojan, is as much an advocate of freemarket reforms as Roman himself, but is not himself a party politician. He had served as Finance Minister under Roman's Premiership and in his first month as Prime Minister announced plans for the convertibility of the Romanian currency, the leu, for the continuation of marketisation.

The 1992 Elections.

The Presidential elections resulted in a victory for Iliescu, whilst the Parliamentary elections saw his former communist allies in the Democratic National Salvation Front (DNSF) emerge as the largest party. Of the many other parties with representation in the legislature, only the Democratic Convention (DC) was a significant force.

Unlike the elections of May 1990, those of the autumn of 1992 were not (as several hundred international observers mostly confirmed) blatantly rigged. Yet nor were they entirely fair: the ruling party's election funds were supported from state sources, whilst the DC was granted no greater access to the electronic media than the weakest of the 90 parties registered as taking part in the elections. Iliescu's party was not subject to the same limitation because of the President's heavy exposure on state-run television and radio news programmes.

Continuing Problems.

The election results gave little cause for optimism about progress towards either full democracy or economic reform. Iliescu ran for re-election breathing hostility towards business people and foreign investors, and advocating a slow-down in economic reform. Moreover, Iliescu's dependence upon a coalition in parliament composed of his own supporters in the DNSF together with deeply conservative nationalist, and Communist, forces was likely to cause him to adopt policies more hostile to ethnic minorities (especially to the 1·8 million ethnic Hungarians living in Romania) and still less receptive to investment in Romania by foreign companies. There remained a serious risk of popular dissatisfaction boiling over into street protest.

Deepening Economic Crisis.

The economic crisis deepened in 1993 to the point where international institutions such as the IMF became alarmed at the lack of progress in implementing economic reforms. Key reforming personnel in Prime Minister Nicolae Vacaroiu's minority government were dismissed in the summer. Their departure resulted from conservative and nationalist pressures from parties within Vacaroiu's weak coalition: the ruling Party of Social Democracy of Romania (PSDR), formerly the Democratic National Salvation Front, was itself increasingly conservative on economic issues, whilst the extreme nationalist Romanian National Unity Party (RNUP) and the xenophobic Greater Romania Party (GRP) sought to exploit economic discontent for narrow ethnic advantage. Their fiercest opposition was directed against foreign ownership of former Romanian state assets (an inevitable product of the embryonic privatisation programme), and privatisation itself. Rural discontent was increasingly evident, too, in pressure from the National Peasant Party-Christian Democrats (NPP-CD) for faster land reform.

Recent Developments.

Meanwhile, economic indicators reflected the extent of the problem: by the end of 1993, the annual inflation rate exceeded 300%, unemployment was rising rapidly through the 10% barrier, and the national currency, the lei, had lost two-thirds of its January 1993 value against the dollar. Weakened further by corruption within his government, Vacaroiu sought to fend off pressure from the RNUP leader, Gheorghe Funar, by making concessions in an attempt to slake the latter's nationalist thirst. On 2 February 1994, an agreement was reached between the PSDR and RNUP with the agreement that they would seek to include the neocommunist Socialist Labour Party (SLP) and the GRP in the coalition. The prospects for a liberal society and a reformed economy were greatly lessened by the nature of the new coalition.

YUGOSLAVIA.

Yugoslavia after Tito.

In the years following Tito's death, successive Yugoslav leaders struggled with the consuming problems of economic crisis, corruption in public life, and the profound difficulty of governing a country composed of eight provinces each of which enjoyed substantial autonomy from the weak centre, Belgrade.

By the beginning of 1989, Yugoslavia's inflation rate had risen to 250%, its rate of unemployment to 15%, and its external debt to $22 billion. Its many factions had little in common with each other than their passports (of which many wished to divest themselves) and, as the old year ended, the government of Mr. Branko Mikulic resigned

Such a combination of circumstances would test the resolve of a country with a resilient political structure and organisation. Yugoslavia failed that examination. The country was throughout 1988 and early 1989 rent by strife centering upon the person and political ambitions of Slobodan Milosevic, the leader of the Communist Party in Serbia. Mr. Milosevic was concerned in particular to keep the mostly Albanian province of Kosovo in line by defending the rights of minority Serbs within it. Kosovo's Albanians are wholly opposed to an increase in Serbian influence over the affairs of their province which since 1974 has enjoyed almost as much autonomy from Serbia as the six federal republics of Yugoslavia. More than 1,000 Kosovo miners staged a hunger strike in February 1989 with the aim of forcing the removal of senior officials of the Communist Party in Kosovo whom most of the Albanians there regarded as Mr. Milosevic's placement. Whilst the Yugoslavian federation as a whole rejected the demands of the discontented Kosovo Albanians, the striking miners enjoyed support from the northern republics of Slovenia and Croatia whose own relations with Serbia became increasingly strained throughout 1988. The combination of extreme discontents among the peoples of the Republics, and economic failure in the federation as a whole, induced severe political weakness.

For long one of the most liberal Eastern European communist states, Yugoslavia's political progress towards a western-style democracy was decidedly less smooth in 1989 and early 1990 than processes elsewhere. The explanation for the difference lies with the peculiarly fractured character of Yugoslavia, and the intensity with which nationalist passions are fought out. There is no simple or single path from communist autocracy to capitalist democracy in Yugoslavia because so many political forces pull in different directions.

The Collapse of Communism.

The Communist Party had by the Spring of 1990 effectively crumbled away. At its congress in January 1990, the Slovenian delegation withdrew following attempts by Serbia to weaken plans for the introduction of multi-party democracy and the translation of the Yugoslav Communist party into a more thoroughly devolved federation. (The Slovenian and Croatian parties had already decided to move towards a multi-party system Slovenia's parliament declared the Republic independent in early March 1990. Prime Minister Markovic struggled to keep the country together, conscious always of the threat presented by Milosevic's assertion of nationalist values in general, and of Serbian nationalist power over Kosovo in particular. In Kosovo, under direct rule from Serbia, Milosevic sent in troops to quell demonstrations calling for an end to the state of emergency. At least 25 ethnic Albanians were killed in the unrest.

A Divided Nation.

Free elections in 1990 revealed again the extent of the divisions within the country. In Serbia, Milosevic led the Socialist Party to an overwhelming victory on a platform demanding that Yugoslavia remain a federal state; it was a policy with which the Montenegrins were agreed. In Croatia and Slovenia, centre-right governments were elected on confederal platforms of varying kinds. For Slovenia this meant a condition approaching independence: the Republic's parliament declared in February 1991 that its laws were to take precedence over federal ones, and took steps to prepare its own currency. In Croatia, President Tudjman was more cautious—mostly because he knew full well that Croatian secession would be regarded by Serbia as intolerable because of the substantial Serbian presence there; Slovenian independence would matter less to the dominant Serbia. The governments of Bosnia and Hercegovina and of Macedonia attempted to forge a complicated "asymmetric community" compromise arrangement between themselves, Montenegro, and Serbia as a group of inner Republics in confederal association with Croatia and Slovenia on the other.

In the event that attempts at compromise fail, and the federation collapses, the major danger is of attempts being made to alter boundaries between the republics to take account of minority aspirations. Under Milosevic, attempts might well be made to incorporate Serbian majority areas in other republics. Ominously, the Serbs in Croatia had already declared themselves sovereign, and there were bloody armed clashes between Croatian troops and local Serbs in the early Spring of 1991. Tension also grew between Milosevic and anti-communist demonstrators, two of whom were killed by riot police in mid-March.

The Fear of Serbia.

Anti-communism in Serbia added a further fault line to those many that already threatened Yugoslavia's continued existence. Milosevic, who as recently as December had appeared unassailable, was seriously weakened by his response to the upsurge of anti-communist sentiment. The repression of demonstrations, and the temporary imprisonment of Vuk Draskovic, the leader of the Serbian National Renewal Movement, confirmed the fears of many Croatians and Slovenians about Serbia's violent potential. Yet puncturing the myth of Serbian unity may in the longer-run have enhanced the possibility that Yugoslavia might, in a more confederalist form, survive. Anti-Milosevic forces in Serbia, many of them democratic, are often no less pro-Serbian than those against whose Communist rule they protest, but a constrained Milosevic may be easier for Democratic Serbs, and other Yugoslavs, to deal with. However, as in the Soviet Union, the possibility of military intervention remains: the (mostly Serbian) officer corps are unlikely to acquiesce in the fragmentation of Yugoslavia.

By early summer, Yugoslavia was on the verge of civil war. Violence, particularly in Croatia, threatened to tear the fragile unity of the nation apart. The army, whose presence in key areas was steadily increasing, was poised for a military takeover. Once again, the historic rivalries and mistrust of Serbs and Croats looked set to precipitate a bloodbath.

CROATIA AND SLOVENIA.

By the end of 1991, the old Yugoslavia no longer existed. Slovenia declared independence in the summer of 1991 without arousing a warlike response from Belgrade. Croatia's attempted declaration of independence provoked a bloody civil war which brought heavy loss of life and immense destruction of property throughout Croatia, but especially in and around ethnic Serbian enclaves. Under German pressure, the European Community (EC) recognised early in 1992 the independence of Croatia and Slovenia. Nevertheless, the EC proved unable to broker a peace between Serbia and Croatia, and German diplomatic (but not logistic or military) support for Croatia did little to quell the conflict. War subsided only under waning Serbian enthusiasm, exhaustion, and the proposed intervention of the United Nations and the eventual introduction of a UN peace-keeping force in the Spring of 1992.

The process of Yugoslavian disintegration spread beyond Croatia and Slovenia: both Bosnia-Hercegovina and Macedonia voted in early 1992 for independence but each case was full of ethnic and border complications. Bosnia-Hercegovina contained Croat, Serbian, and Muslim minorities, whilst Macedonia's unwillingness to renounce its claim to part of northern Greece caused the Greek government to oppose the republic's independence.

BOSNIA-HERCEGOVINA.

In 1992 and early 1993, conflict in Bosnia-Hercegovina exploded into vicious and deadly inter-ethnic strife and civil war. The United Nations was drawn more deeply into the war through its policy of attempted peace-keeping and protection of food convoys to beleaguered towns. European Community diplomacy failed to control the conflict whilst the United States, unsure how its military forces might be used, what political objectives should be set, or when and how its forces might be withdrawn, abstained from direct armed involvement. Neither for the European Community nor for the United States did the conflict in Bosnia-Hercegovina immediately and directly threaten vital strategic interests. Yet the risk that the war will spread to other parts of the Balkans through Kosovo (largely under the control of Serb militias, despite the fact that the province has an Albanian ethnic majority) and Macedonia remains high. If it were to do so, Greece and Bulgaria would almost certainly become involved, possibly with devastating consequences for regional and European security. More immediately, failure to contain or end the civil war has left civilians on all sides, but especially Muslims, to suffer from violence, hunger, and homelessness on scales unseen in European politics since the Second World War. The movement of refugees from the areas ravaged by war and famine was vast, affecting probably one-tenth of former Yugoslavia's population.

The Owen–Vance Proposals.

Having failed to control the conflict's escalation, the UN Security Council imposed an embargo on trade and oil with Serbia in July 1992. However, some trade in oil and other supplies continued from Greece, Romania, Russia, and the Ukraine; their fragile economic condition means that none of the latter three can in practice afford to cease completely all trading with Serbia, their traditional ally. The UN peace envoys, Cyrus Vance (the former US Secretary of State) and Lord Owen (the former British Foreign Secretary) produced a peace plan in early 1993 which sought to avoid the partition of Bosnia-Hercegovina by creating ten regions organised in a confederation which preserved the outline of the Bosnian state but gave few powers to the weak centre at Sarajevo. Opposition to the plan ranged wide, from Muslims within Bosnia (who remained resolutely opposed to rewarding the Serbs for their aggression) to the United States (whose politicians and people identified Serbia as the aggressor) and Muslim states outside the region (which interpreted western reluctance to respond to Serbian and Croatian aggression and atrocities as evidence of double standards).

For the western states, however, the cost of deploying ground troops to impose a peace through the restoration of the territorial *status quo ante* was likely to be exceedingly high. Hence by June 1993 the end of the conflict was no further forward. The United States had no wish to intervene militarily. The Owen-Vance proposals were increasingly unrealistic and the Bosnian Serbs equally increasingly intransigent. Within Serbia itself political conflict was growing.

Developments in 1993.

Although 1993 passed without the Bosnian conflict spilling over into adjacent zones of potential strife, events gave no good cause for optimism either that the underlying problems could be made the subject of a bargained settlement or that they could reliably be confined within Bosnia's borders. No semblance of international agreement about political objectives, or the diplomatic and military means to achieve them, were apparent in 1993 beyond the continued deployment of UN troops to safeguard convoys of relief supplies. Economic sanctions, pursued with new vigour through tighter patrolling of waterborne traffic along the River Danube, neither diminished Serbian nationalist resolve (although they contributed to the collapse of the Serbian economy, and harmed the economies of Greece and Romania) nor undermined the powerful political position of the Serbian President, Slobodan Milosevic. (The latter's circumstances were, in any event, greatly strengthened in 1993 by his election victory in Serbia.) Neither Serbian nor Croatian governments risk significant unpopularity with their domestic constituencies by pursuing expansionist policies in Bosnia. On the contrary, the domestic political risks for both the Serbian and the Croatian leaders lie with their being accused by yet more hard-line nationalist opponents to their right on the grounds of allegedly appeasing EC and UN opposition.

The HVO Setbacks.

Within Bosnia, circumstances are less clear-cut. The Croatian Defence Forces (HVO), despite having been lent substantial military support by the Croatian Army throughout 1993, lost 40% of its territory in Bosnia following the end of its working alliance with the Bosnian Army in the early summer of 1993. Rising western public discontent with the continuing slaughter throughout Bosnia in general, but with the barbarous Serbian shelling of Sarajevo in particular, led to a belated assertion of NATO resolve to take air action against Serbian artillery emplacements in the event that such guns were not ceded to UN control within a specified time period. That threat induced the Russian government to deploy troops in UN uniform to police the withdrawal of their Serbian allies' artillery from the zone drawn around Sarajevo by NATO.

The dangers of the UN (and American and European) policy towards Bosnia were glaringly exposed in April 1994. The brutal (and bloody) Serb onslaught on Goradze, a supposedly "safe haven", proved how futile UN policy was. The safe haven was not safe for its Muslim civilians (nor indeed anyone else) and it was hard to see who the UN protection force was protecting.

Recent Developments.

Shelling of Goradze continued despite a NATO ultimatum to Bosnian Serbs on 22 April 1994. But a one month ceasefire was agreed between Bosnian Serbs and the Bosnian Federation of Muslims and Croats on 9 June. It was, however, almost continuously violated. The Contact Group members (Britain, France, Germany, the United States and Russia) unveiled new peace proposals on 6 July. The Bosnian Serbs were to relinquish some of their military gains and the Federation of Bosnia-Hercegovina would be awarded 51% of Bosnian territory. The June ceasefire was further extended to 10 August. Serb President Milosevic added weight to the impetus for settlement by imposing sanctions on the Bosnian Serbs and closing the border on 5 August. But on 28 August Bosnian Serbs made their position clear by overwhelmingly rejecting the peace plan in a referendum.

A Bosnian government offensive which opened on 3 November met with early successes as its forces captured a number of Serb occupied towns. But by 14 November Bosnian Serbs had regained 80% of their losses. As the Contact Group attempted to formulate acceptable peace proposals in December, former US President Carter negotiated a four month ceasefire which came into effect on 1 January 1995. But clashes continued in the Bihac area and on 4 January the UN Security Council asked for 6,000 reinforcements to the 23,000 peacekeeping force. As spring approached, heavy fighting resumed and it appeared that all out civil war had begun again.

THE MIDDLE EAST

ISRAEL.

In December 1987 violence erupted amongst the 1·5 million Palestinians in the occupied West Bank and Gaza Strip areas. Anti-Israeli strikes, demonstrations and riots were met by mass arrests, beatings and expulsions. There was international condemnation of the Israeli policy of beating demonstrators graphically shown on television around the world, but the Israeli government also came under pressure to take even firmer action from Jewish settlers in the occupied areas.

In April 1988 an Israeli special service unit assassinated the PLO military commander, Abu Jihad, who was believed to be masterminding the Palestinian unrest, at his home in Tunis.

General elections for the 120-member Knesset

took place on 1 November 1988. The result was again inconclusive, with both Labour and Likud losing seats to the smaller parties. Likud won 39 seats to Labour's 38. The religious parties secured a record number of eighteen seats, compared with twelve in 1984. Mr. Shamir began negotiations for the support of the ultra-orthodox parties, but these became bogged down over their demands for the enforcement of religious laws and a narrowing of the definition of who was a Jew.

Mr. Shamir also had talks with the Labour Party, until at the end of November Labour's political bureau voted to break them off. But President Herzog called on Mr. Shamir to form a wide and stable government, and finally, on 19 December, Likud and Labour reached agreement on the formation of another national unity coalition. Mr Shamir was to continue as Prime Minister, while Mr. Peres took over the Finance Ministry, indicating Labour's intention of concentrating on the economy, rather than on the problems of foreign affairs and the Palestinian question.

The Continuing Intifada.

How Israel should respond to the continuing intifada in the occupied territories threatened the coalition's survival from the outset. Meetings in February 1989 between Labour MPs and West Bank Palestinian leaders were approved by Finance Minister Shimon Peres, Labour's leader, but attacked by the Prime Minister, Mr Shamir. Behind this disagreement lay the question of whether or not Israel should eventually talk with the PLO. In March the US government called on Israel and the PLO to reduce tensions in the occupied territories and acknowledged the PLO's growing political status. Mr Arens, the Israeli Foreign Minister, reiterated his determination not to talk with the PLO.

Visiting the United States in April, Mr Shamir offered elections to Palestinians in the occupied territories leading to eventual autonomy as part of a wider Arab-Israeli settlement. Despite opposition from some members of his own Likud party, Mr Shamir gained cabinet approval for the proposal on 14 May. US Secretary of State James Baker's advice on 22 May that Israel should begin dialogue with the Palestinians was condemned by Mr Shamir as "useless". By July continuing opposition from Likud forced Mr Shamir to modify his proposals. No elections would take place until the intifada ended; no East Jerusalem resident could stand in the elections (ruling out the candidacy of influential PLO figures); and Israel would not tolerate the creation of a Palestinian state. The PLO claimed these conditions "closed the door" to any agreement while Mr Peres said he refused to "accept the dictates of Mr Shamir". Labour now seemed prepared to abandon the coalition, its leaders recommending this on 20 July. Collapse was averted when Mr Shamir confirmed the elections proposal still stood without mentioning the new conditions.

On 18 September Egyptian President Mubarak presented a 10 point peace plan to Israeli Defence Minister Mr Rabin in Cairo. His suggestion that Israeli representatives should meet a Palestinian delegation in Cairo for preliminary talks on election arrangements provoked further division within the coalition. The proposal was increasingly pressed by US Secretary of State Baker. On 6 October the 12-strong inner cabinet divided evenly on discussions with Palestinians, the six Likud members voting against and Labour voting for.

The violence of the intifada had meanwhile intensified, with over 500 Palestinians and 22 Israelis reported killed by June. There was growing polarisation between Jewish and Arab communities, particularly on the West Bank where Jewish vigilantes were arming to attack Arab areas.

The March 1990 Crisis.

US pressure for talks to begin in Cairo brought Israel's political crisis to a head. The cabinet attempted to hold off collapse by postponing a decision on 7 March 1990. But on 13 March Mr Shamir dismissed Labour leader Mr Peres and the remaining Labour ministers resigned. Mr Shamir's government lost a Knesset confidence vote by 60–55 on 15 March and Israel faced the prospect of a Labour-led coalition or a general election.

Mr Peres's attempts to form a Labour-led coalition finally foundered in late April. Mr Shamir, after protracted negotiations with small religious and right-wing parties, formed a Likud-led coalition on 11 June, albeit with only a two seat majority. It was the most conservative government in Israel's history, with a hard-line position on peace talks with the Palestinians.

Mass Soviet Immigration.

Mr Shamir's government saw mass Soviet Jewish immigration as the main issue. By late August almost 100,000 immigrants had landed in Israel, compounding employment and housing problems. The immigration issue had a wider aspect, with Arab fears that Soviet Jews would displace Palestinians in the occupied West Bank and Gaza. The official government position remained that they would be neither encouraged nor discouraged from settling in the territories.

For much of 1990 the violence of the three-year intifada had been declining. But on 8 October police shot 19 stone-throwing Palestinian demonstrators in Jerusalem, the highest number of deaths in a single incident since clashes began. This aroused immediate world criticism, the United States condemning the excessive force used. As controversy failed to subside Mr Shamir appointed a commission to investigate the incident. Meanwhile, troops were deployed to enforce a strict curfew against Palestinians in the Gaza and much of the West Bank. In the following weeks eight Israelis were killed by Palestinians.

Israel and the Gulf Crisis.

In December Israel's treatment of Palestinians came under increasing UN criticism, supported by the United States. On 21 December the UN demanded international monitoring on conditions in the occupied territories. Israel rejected this and accused the United States of attempting to appease its Arab allies in the Gulf crisis. But Israel's stance in the Gulf crisis – and particularly its restraint in the face of Iraqi Scud missile attacks which began on 17 January 1991 – won international approval. Mr Shamir balanced this restraint with an increasingly hawkish approach to the Palestinians, one encouraged by the PLO's support for Iraq. On 2 February he appointed Mr Rehavam Ze'evi of the Moledet Party to the cabinet, against the opposition of some of his Likud colleagues. Mr Ze'evi believed that only the expulsion of the 1·5 million Palestinians in the occupied territories could ensure peace for Israel.

Israel and the Peace Talks.

Shamir's government had been consistent in its position once it came to office in June 1990. It refused to countenance ceding territory either in the West Bank or on the Golan. Some of its members argued that Israel had a historical right to this land which was the heartland of Judaism in biblical times, others argued that Israel would be overly vulnerable to military attack without it. In accord with traditional Israeli policy it refused to recognise the PLO or grant the Palestinians national rights. Instead it sought to cultivate an alternative leadership based in the occupied territories which would accept Israeli control in return for a limited devolution of administrative powers.

Israel was extremely reluctant to attend the Madrid peace conference, arguing that it would risk coming under international pressure to concede territory in return for a paper treaty which would not really end Arab hostility. Israelis have been disappointed by their peace treaty with Egypt which, although it has held, has not resulted in warm relations. Israeli suspicions were exacerbated during the Gulf War when Palestinians, despite their moderate pronouncements, supported Iraq's missile attacks on Israel. Shamir only consented to attend the conference after he had obtained guarantees from Baker that Israel's conditions would limit the scope of the talks. The main conditions were: Palestinians to be represented only as part of the Jordanian delegation; their delegates to have no official links with the PLO; no discussion of the status of Jerusalem—which Shamir regards as irrevocably Israeli; and no discussion of a

Palestinian state. In addition to these carrots, President Bush wielded a stick by postponing consideration of $10 billion in loan guarantees that Israel was requesting to help it settle immigrants.

The Washington Talks.

Israeli and Arab negotiators met for a second round of peace talks in Washington from 13–16 January 1992 but little emerged beyond procedural agreements. There were, however, repercussions for Mr. Shamir as two far-right parties left the coalition on 19 January after reports that he was considering offering Palestinian self-rule in the occupied territories. Pressure continued for Israel to end its settlements policy in the Gaza Strip and West Bank and on 24 February the US threatened to halt a $10 billion loan guarantee unless settlement was halted. As violence continued in the occupied territories, Israel was condemned by the UN for allowing "continued deterioration of the situation".

The June 1992 Elections.

Israel held elections on 23 June, with Labour under the leadership of Yitzhak Rabin who had ousted Shimon Peres on 19 February. Labour representation in the Knesset increased from 39 to 44, while Likud's fell from 41 to 32. Mr. Rabin was confirmed as prime minister on 13 July. Israel cancelled projected settlement plans in the occupied territories and, in a meeting between Mr. Rabin and President Bush on 11 August, the $10 billion loan guarantee was restored. Peace talks with Arab negotiators re-commenced on 21 October, though they were hampered by uncertainty over the forthcoming US presidential elections. But the talks were halted on 17 December when Israel seized over 400 alleged members of the outlawed fundamentalist Islamic Resistance Movement (Hamas) following the murder of a police officer and attempted to deport them to Lebanon. Lebanon refused to accept them and the deportees were stranded in the border area in harsh conditions, arousing international criticism and the threat of UN sanctions.

Easing of PLO Restrictions.

However, on 19 January 1993 the Israeli parliament lifted the ban on political contacts with the PLO. Mr. Rabin reduced the Hamas deportees' two-year term of exile in March, opening the way for the resumption of Arab-Israeli peace talks. On 24 March Ezer Weizman was elected president by parliament to replace Chaim Herzog. The following day Benjamin Netanyahu replaced Yitzhak Shamir as leader of the right-wing opposition Likud party. Increasing violence—15 Israelis and 25 Palestinians were killed in March alone—prompted the government to seal off Gaza and the West Bank at the end of March, preventing 120,000 Palestinians entering Israel to work.

The Gaza Strip/Jericho Proposals.

In secret talks with PLO representatives in May, Israeli negotiators suggested a possible withdrawal of troops from the Gaza Strip and Jericho. A meeting between a cabinet minister and PLO chairman Yasir Arafat on 5 August in effect ended the ban on official contacts. On 13 August foreign minister Shimon Peres said Israel would continue to negotiate with Palestinian representatives despite its awareness that some were PLO officials. The Israeli cabinet accepted a draft accord with the Palestinians—negotiated in parallel discussions with the official talks—on 31 August.

Recognition of the PLO.

As agreement neared, Israel recognised the PLO on 9 September. A peace accord was signed by Mr. Rabin and Mr. Arafat in Washington on 13 September by which Israeli troops would withdraw from the Gaza Strip and Jericho on the West Bank on 13 December. Parliament ratified the agreement on 23 September and detailed negotiations on the withdrawal opened on 11 October. However, on 14 November discussions stalled over Israel's demand to control border crossings and protect settlers. Meanwhile, violence continued and by mid-Decem-

ber 38 Palestinians and 18 Israelis had been killed since the September agreement. The detailed negotiations over the Washington settlement which continued into 1994 raised obstacles which prevented Israel's withdrawal from the agreed areas.

Recent Developments.

See **Special Topic C76–8** for the search for peace in the Middle East.

EGYPT.
Egypt and the Arab World.

During 1987 Egypt's isolation, caused by the peace with Israel, came to an end. The Arab summit at Amman in November 1987 agreed that relations with Egypt were a matter for individual states. A number of Arab countries, including Saudi Arabia, Morocco and Iraq, proceeded to restore full diplomatic relations with Egypt. Egypt's return to the Arab fold was confirmed by President Mubarrak's attendance at the Arab League conference in Casablanca in May, the first attended by Egypt since 1979.

Mubarrak's Moderate Course.

Mr Mubarrak continued to exercise a moderating influence as Middle Eastern tension heightened. Domestically, he dismissed his hard-line anti-Islamic fundamentalist Interior Minister Zaki Badr, who had been accused of sanctioning police brutality, on 12 January 1990. On 2 May Mr. Mubarrak visited Syrian President Assad in Damascus, the first such meeting since ties were broken in 1977. On 15 May Egypt ended over a decade of strained relations with the Soviet Union when Mr Mubarrak met President Gorbachev in Moscow.

Egypt and the Gulf Crisis.

Egypt condemned Iraq's invasion of Kuwait and Mr Mubarrak was prominent in orchestrating Arab opposition to President Saddam, calling on 8 August for the formation of a joint Arab peacekeeping force. The advance guard of what would eventually be a 40,000-strong Egyptian contingent landed in Saudi Arabia on 11 August. The US acknowledged Egypt's support in October by writing off $7 billion worth of debts. Mr Mubarrak faced some domestic opposition to his Gulf policy, notably from the Moslem Brotherhood which demanded the withdrawal of Egyptian troops when bombing of Iraq began in January 1991. Government officials stressed that Egypt's support for force went only as far as removing Iraq from Kuwait and not overthrowing President Saddam and destroying Iraq's armed forces.

Egypt after the Gulf War.

1991 was a triumphant year for Egyptian diplomacy. By supporting the US against Iraq, Egypt benefited from injections of large amounts of aid from the Gulf oil states as well as from the West. The advent of the Madrid peace process saw Egypt taking a leading role in cajoling the Arabs into accepting US conditions, although at the same time Cairo presented itself as the Arab interlocutor with Israel and the US by sharpening its rhetoric. Furthermore, Egyptian diplomats succeeded in being elected to two major international posts— Ismat Abd al-Magid as Secretary-General of the Arab League and Boutros Boutros Ghali as Secretary-General of the UN. However, Egyptian diplomats suffered one notable defeat. The Damascus Declaration, which had been signed on 6 March by Egypt, Syria and the six members of the Gulf Cooperation Council (Saudi Arabia, Kuwait, Bahrain, Qatar, United Arab Emirates, Oman), proved to be a dead letter. The Declaration had envisaged the use of Egyptian and Syrian troops to defend the GCC states in return for financial aid. However the GCC governments have preferred to rely on expanding their own armed forces and forging closer military ties with the US and Britain.

Economic Problems in Egypt.

Domestically, Mubarrak's government provoked popular worries when in April it agreed on a package of austerity and economic liberalisation measures with the IMF. With unemployment already between 15 and 20%, it was feared that reforming Egypt's inefficient state industries would, exacerbate social and economic tensions. Pressures on the labour market were eased somewhat when agreements were concluded in August between Egypt and Libya for the free movement of labour and goods across their common border.

Growing Fundamentalist Influence.

Cairo was struck by an earthquake on 12 October 1992 in which over 500 died and 5,000 badly constructed homes in the poorer districts were destroyed. Riot police were deployed on 17 October as demonstrators attacked the government's slow response to the disaster. Islamic fundamentalist groups were active in constructing shelters and providing food to the earthquake victims. Fundamentalists were also involved in attacks on foreign tourists in June and October intended to exert economic pressure on the government. There were a number of clashes between fundamentalist Moslems and Christians. On 8–9 December 10,000 para-military forces were deployed in a Cairo slum area popularly known as the "Islamic Republic of Imbaba" to arrest over 500 Islamic militants. Although President Mubarak declared that his government was "in full control", fundamentalist influence was growing in the face of rising unemployment whilst attacks on tourists continued.

Escalating Fundamentalist Violence.

Violence intensifed in 1993. The fundamentalist al-Gamaa al-Islamiya (Islamic Group) claimed responsibility for a bombing in Cairo on 26 February, the first of many to come. As the trial began on 9 March of 49 Islamic Group members for plotting to overthrow the state and killing foreign tourists, security forces attacked a mosque in the southern city of Aswan killing 14 alleged militants. President Mubarak accused Iran and Sudan of training and supporting the activists.

The Egyptian government continued to seek international investment to develop the economy. In February and March reforms were announced to speed privatisation and to ease exchange controls. Despite criticism of widespread corruption, economic stagnation and the erosion of political and civil liberties, President Mubarak was elected unopposed by parliament to a third six-year term on 21 July. In October President Mubarak visited Washington to press President Clinton to continue over $2 billion annually in aid, the bulk of which went to the military.

On 26 November Ates Sedki, the long-serving prime minister, narrowly escaped death from a car bomb in Cairo. The militant Islamic organisation Jihad claimed responsibility. A planned "National Dialogue" to discuss Egypt's political crisis was postponed until April 1994 and President Mubarak ruled out the participation of Islamic groupings. Following the shooting of seven militants in Cairo, the Islamic Group warned all foreigners to leave Egypt on 2 February 1994.

Recent Events.

During 1994 the government managed to make headway against the violent fundamentalist groups opposing it. An energetic programme of mass arrests, shoot to kill policies, extraditions from abroad and police infiltration of groups pushed the rebels on the defensive and forced them to largely limit their activities to their Upper Egyptian strongholds around Assiut. The opposition did however score successes. In April gunmen killed General Rauf Khayrat, the head of the anti-terror branch of the State Security Investigation Section and later in the year attacked the Red Sea tourist resort of Hurghada. Terrorists also stabbed and injured the Nobel-Prize Winning novelist Naguib Mahfouz, accusing him of supporting the secularisation of society. They did not however manage to disrupt the UN Population Conference held in Cairo amid tight security.

The government's main concern remained the implementation of the IMF reform programme. This made progress, with the country recording a growth rate of 4% and reduced budget deficits.

The burden of reforms however fell on the poor and floods and oil fires in the south of the country in November once again highlighted the inefficiency and corruption of the state.

On the diplomatic front, President Mubarak sought to raise Egypt's profile and take the lead in the Arab world by raising the issue of Israel's undeclared nuclear arsenal. In the run-up to the review conference of the Nuclear Non-Proliferation Treaty in April he aroused Israeli and American annoyance by leading a united Arab call for Israel to adhere to the Treaty and give up its nuclear arms.

JORDAN.

On 1 January 1991 premier Mudar Badran brought five members of the Moslem Brotherhood into his cabinet, giving them the ministries of health, education, social welfare, religious affairs, and justice. It was thought this move would moderate rather than intensify fundamentalist pressures on King Hussein. As the air war against Iraq began on 17 January Jordan declared the attack a "brutal act of aggression". King Hussein's opposition to the war was a result of fears that Jordan would be dragged into the conflict, especially if Israel became involved, and in response to popular opinion which saw Desert Storm as a Western-Zionist conspiracy against the Arabs. President Bush on 8 February accused King Hussein—following an emotional speech the latter delivered after further anti-US demonstrations—of supporting President Saddam and attempting to split the anti-Iraq coalition. On 20 February both houses of parliament passed pro-Iraqi resolutions.

Democratisation and Economic Crisis in Jordan.

In the wake of Iraq's defeat, Jordan faced a severe economic crisis as its trading links with Iraq, its largest trading partner, were disrupted by the sanctions imposed on Iraq; it was forced to support the hundreds of thousands of refugees who fled Iraq and Kuwait in the months leading up to the war; and aid from the Gulf States and the US was slashed in response to King Hussein's vocal opposition to the war. By April, however, Jordan was engaged in an intensive round of diplomacy and reestablished its ties with Syria, France, the US and the Gulf States. On 20 April US Secretary of State James Baker visited Amman and eventually the US released $55 million of aid it had been withholding. At the end of the year Jordan finally agreed to take part in the Madrid peace talks as part of a joint Jordanian-Palestinian delegation.

Domestically, King Hussein continued his attempts to democratise his regime in a controlled manner. On 9 June a National Charter was approved by a cross party commission. Under the Charter the King guaranteed the continuance of a pluralist system in return for pledges from all parties to accept the legitimacy of the monarchy. The adoption of the Charter ameliorated King Hussein's concerns that several of the country's parties were seeking to undermine the regime as they perceived it as an artificial British creation, and gave him the confidence to carry on the democratisation process. On 19 June a new government was installed under Tahir Masri. The appointment of the liberal Masri, prominent in Palestinian circles, indicated that Hussein wanted to lessen the influence of the Muslim Brotherhood—who were destabilising the situation by encouraging armed infiltration across the Israeli border—and proceed with the building of a more equitable Jordanian-Palestinian state. The lead up to the Madrid talks however overshadowed other issues in Jordanian politics. In October the Muslim Brotherhood and the Constitutional Bloc (a group of traditionalist notables) signed a no-confidence motion opposing both Masri's plans for Madrid and his distribution of cabinet seats in favour of the leftists. Unable to form a new cabinet, Masri resigned in favour of Sharif Zyid bin Shakir a month later. With strong personal backing from the King, bin Shakir mollified both the Brotherhood and the Bloc and narrowly won a vote of no-confidence in December.

Jordan and her Neighbours.

Although Jordan had backed Iraq during the

Gulf Crisis, on 6 July 1992 King Hussein had to deny that Jordan had been involved in a coup attempt against President Saddam of Iraq at the end of June. However, King Hussein attempted reconciliation with Egypt by visiting victims of the Cairo earthquake on 14 October. Relations had been strained by Jordan's pro-Iraqi stance. On 29 October Israel announced that Jordanian and Israeli negotiators had prepared a discussion document on a peace settlement.

The 1993 Elections and Peace.

Jordan held its first multi-party elections for the parliament's lower house for 37 years on 8 November 1993. No party won a clear majority but candidates close to King Hussein—described as "traditionalists"—took 59 of the 80 seats. Representation of the Islamic Action Front, a fundamentalist grouping opposed to peace talks with Israel, fell from 22 seats to 16.

During 1994 King Hussein faced the prospect of persuading the opposition that a peace treaty was in the country's interests (*see* **Special Topic C76–8**). After the signing of a treaty in October he faced the prospect of selling it to Jordanians. The Islamist opposition remained resolutely opposed but the King insisted on the necessity of approving the agreement. In an effort to ensure support in his core constituency, he raised pay for teachers, promised benefits to the military and cut import duties.

THE PALESTINIANS.

On 30 May 1990 Palestinian guerrillas attempted a seaborne attack on Israel. Yasser Arafat dissociated the PLO, which had renounced terrorism, from the attack but did not denounce it. In response the US suspended any dialogue with the PLO on 20 June. Iraq's invasion of Kuwait in August divided the PLO. The PLO did not support an Arab League resolution condemning Iraq on 3 August and on 10 August opposed sending Arab troops to Saudi Arabia. The PLO leadership was under pressure from militants in the Israeli-occupied territories to give outright support to Iraq but was aware that this would anger the organisation's financial backers, notably Saudi Arabia.

In the occupied territories themselves a PLO moderate declared on 17 October that the PLO might sanction the use of arms in self-defence by Palestinians if violence intensified. With the ending of the Gulf crisis dialogue appeared to have resumed with the US as Secretary of State James Baker met West Bank and Gaza Palestinians on 12 March. On 14 March a leading official offered concessions to Israel in return for recognition of a Palestinian state. The PLO would not demand a return to Israel's pre-1967 borders and the new state would be demilitarised for a transitional period. Israel rejected the suggestion and West Bank Palestinians dissociated themselves from it.

Palestinian Dilemmas.

As a result of its support for Iraq during the Gulf crisis, the PLO was ostracised by its erstwhile backers and cut off from its sources of finance in the Gulf States. Thus weakened, the organisation was wracked by debates over the best approach to the Madrid peace process. Although Yassir Arafat retained control over the movement and the moderate Palestinian negotiators based in the occupied territories were fêted for their performance at Madrid, the *intifada* became increasingly violent as frustrated youths increasingly used guns and bombs against Israeli targets.

The PLO chairman, Mr. Arafat, survived an air crash on 8 April 1992. Although there was some discontent among activists over his leadership, there appeared to be no obvious successor. In June the moderate Fatah faction attempted to end a longstanding feud with the fundamentalist Islamic Resistance Movement (Hamas) in the interest of common action in the occupied territories. Hamas opposed Fatah's support for Arab–Israeli peace talks. The agreement was temporary and by the end of 1992 Hamas, which called for the destruction of Israel and the creation of an Islamic Palestine, had significant influence among Arabs in the occupied territories. Israel offered Palestinians detailed plans for self-rule in the West Bank and Gaza Strip on 25 August, with elections proposed for May 1993. The offer was rejected for falling short of Palestinian demands for full self-government with a national parliament, a position that hardened as the moderate leadership faced increased pressure from activists. This came against the background of continuing clashes with Israeli forces in the occupied territories. The worst outbreak came between 7–18 October, when three Israelis were killed, 18 Palestinians, and hundreds wounded in demonstrations which followed Palestinian prisoners' hunger strikes.

On 10 March 1993 Palestinian negotiators, despite US and Russian urging, refused to rejoin the Arab–Israel peace process unless Israel ended its deportation policy. However, prompted by Syria, Egypt and Jordan, the delegation agreed on 21 April to resume talks without preconditions. Hamas condemned the decision and threatened "grave popular consequences". In May a secret meeting between PLO and Israeli representatives culminated in proposals for an Israeli withdrawal from Gaza and Jericho.

Progress Towards Peace.

The peace talks concluded on 1 July with no apparent progress. However, there was a secret meeting between PLO chairman Yasir Arafat and an Israeli cabinet minister on 5 August. But the PLO now faced divisions as criticism grew of Mr. Arafat's personal rather than collective leadership style, his willingness to accept a partial rather than complete Israeli withdrawal from the occupied territories, and allegations of financial mismanagement in the organisation. Nonetheless, on 26 August the Palestinian delegation announced agreement with Israel on a draft agreement reached in negotiations conducted parallel to the official discussions. On 31 August the PLO accepted Israel's right to exist.

The Peace Accord, 1993.

A peace accord signed by Mr. Arafat and Mr. Rabin in Washington on 13 September proposed an Israeli withdrawal from the Gaza Strip and Jericho on the West Bank beginning on 13 December. The areas would come under Palestinian self-government. The PLO central council, at a meeting boycotted by its most radical elements, ratified the agreement on 12 October by 63 votes to eight but criticisms of Mr. Arafat's autocratic style continued. Detailed negotiations with Israel over the withdrawal ran into obstacles when Israel demanded the right to protect Jewish settlers, to control border crossings and on the exact extent of Jericho. On 13 December the PLO and Israel agreed to postpone the deadline for implementation a further ten days.

See **Special Topic C76–8.**

LEBANON.

As a result of Syrian and Iranian moves towards the West, the Western hostages kidnapped by Lebanese groups in the mid-1980s were gradually released in the wake of the Gulf War. British journalist John McCarthy was released on 8 August and carried a letter from his kidnappers to the UN Secretary-General. UN mediation followed and in a complicated process of behind the scenes dealing Western hostages (Jackie Mann, Joseph Cicippio, Terry Waite, Tom Sutherland, Jesse Turner and Terry Anderson) were released in parallel with the return of the bodies of Israeli servicemen lost in Lebanon and Arab prisoners held in Israeli jails. In what it claimed was an unrelated move, in December the US released $178 million in compensation for sequestrated Iranian military equipment.

The Austerity Programme.

On 3 February 1992 the government announced an emergency austerity programme. A lack of foreign aid and investment was preventing the recovery of Lebanon's economy following the 16-year civil war. The General Federation of Labour Unions staged a general strike on 6 March in protest against soaring inflation. A further strike on 5 May, accompanied by rioting, precipitated the resignation of the prime minister, Omar Karami. He was replaced on 13 May by Rashid al-Solh, a Sunni Moslem. Lebanon's first parliamentary elections for 20 years were held in successive rounds on 23 August, 30 August and 6 September. The contest was for seats in a 128-seat parliament divided equally between Moslems and Christians, but the Phalangist Party and other leading Christian factions withdrew in protest against the continuing presence of 35,000 Syrian troops. Other Christian candidates took their places but this prevented the emergence of a cohesive Christian parliamentary bloc. Nabih Berri's Amal movement emerged as the largest single group with 18 seats. Mr. Berri was elected speaker on 20 October with the support of 105 of the 128 deputies. On 22 October Sunni Moslem Rafik al-Hariri was appointed premier. His cabinet, in which he also took the ministry of finance, contained 15 Christian and 15 Moslem members.

Reconstruction and War.

On 18 March 1993 the government announced a ten-year $10 billion dollar programme to rebuild the infrastructure devastated in the 1975–90 civil war. But tension with Israel was growing and on 27 March Lebanese and Israeli tanks exchanged fire in the south of the country. From 25–31 July Israel mounted air and artillery attacks on Hizbollah bases and villages in the area, pushing 300,000 Lebanese refugees north to Beirut. Premier al-Hariri called on the UN to force Israel to end the attacks and threatened to leave the Arab–Israeli peace talks. On 31 July a ceasefire was negotiated.

During 1994 the government proceeded with its ambitious plans for the rebuilding of Beirut and managed to attract foreign capital and business interest. A share issue in Solidere, the holding company set up to manage the reconstruction of an entirely new central business district of Beirut was heavily oversubscribed and a Eurodollar bond issue was also successful. Nonetheless, capital was slow to return as the country remained potentially unstable. The Christians felt themselves excluded from power and many emigrated. The Christian Lebanese Forces militia leader Samir Jaja became the first militia leader to be tried for murder after he was accused of bombing a Maronite church, leading to further accusations that the government was biased against the Christian community. The south meanwhile remained in a state of conflict as Hizbollah guerillas attacked the Israeli-backed occupation forces and Lebanon remained beholden to Syria in the peace talks.

IRAN.

Death of Ayatollah Khomeini.

On 4 June 1989, the ailing Ayatollah Khomeini died. By his creation of the Islamic Republic of Iran he had earned his place in history, but the nature and policy of the government that would follow were uncertain.

Ali Khamenei was immediately appointed supreme religious leader in succession to Ayatollah Khomeini. But the confidence of Majlis (parliament) speaker Ali Akbar Hashemi Rafsanjani of his own success in the forthcoming presidential elections suggested a possible future moderation in Iranian policies. On 28 July Rafsanjani took 94·5% of the vote.

The Advent of Rafsanjani.

Taking office on 3 August, President Rafsanjani offered help in the Lebanon hostage crisis, signifying a moderation of Iran's attitude towards the United States. Ayatollah Khameini's attack on the US and his rejection of the possibility of negotiations demonstrated continuing divisions within the government. But President Rafsanjani's nomination of a cabinet with a large sprinkling of economic pragmatists, and its acceptance by the Majlis on 29 August, implied a growing mood in favour of reform. On 6 November the US released $567 million Iranian assets frozen since 1979. Although President Rafsanjani had said only a few days earlier that it was too soon to begin discussions with

the United States, this did suggest an underlying easing of relations.

Moves Towards Moderation.

An inflow of aid and assistance following a serious earthquake in June 1990 appeared to strengthen President Rafsanjani's attempts to improve relations with the West. Despite denunciations from hard-liners, he declared, "Kindness affects relations." Iran's position was also strengthened by its role in the August 1990–February 1991 Gulf crisis. Iran denounced Iraq's invasion of Kuwait and supported the UN trade embargo against Iraq. Iran benefited from higher oil prices arising from the crisis, enabling a continuation of President Rafsanjani's attempts to reconstruct the economy. On 15 August Iran achieved most of its demands in a final settlement of the 1980–88 war with Iraq. Iran remained neutral in the crisis and took the opportunity to renew contacts with a range of Western and Arab states. Relations with Britain, broken off in March 1989, were restored on 27 September 1990. However, a new crisis gripped Iran in the wake of the mass influx of refugees from Iraq in April 1991. The crisis was ameliorated by an inflow of international aid, but it added to the refugee burden on Iran which already housed up to 1·5 million Afghan refugees.

The Internal Power Struggle Continues.

During the spring Rafsanjani continued his policy of improving relations with the West, paying visits to France and Germany in May. At the same time the regime sought to woo the millions of educated Iranians who had fled into exile. As the Iranian Ambassador in Bonn stated, "we are keeping the doors open to all of them". This represented a reversal of previous policy under which exiles had been condemned as enemies of the regime.

Although Iran received plaudits from the West in return for facilitating the release of hostages held in Lebanon, it experienced several setbacks on the international scene. Relations with Saudi Arabia improved but Tehran was pointedly excluded from discussions on a new Gulf security structure and Kuwait's signing of a defence pact with the US on 4 September worried Iran as it meant the stationing of US troops close to Iran's border. Franco-Iranian relations worsened when discussions over the resolution of a financial dispute stalled after France refused to resume supporting Iran's nuclear energy programme and by the killing of an Iranian exile, Shapour Bakhtiar, in Paris on 6 August by Iranian agents. Later in the year as the Arab states came on board the US programme for a peace process, Iran found itself isolated as the sole remaining rejectionist state. Iran was particularly annoyed at Syria's participation as the two states still enjoyed a fairly close relationship. During August these external reverses were overshadowed by a tide of domestic disturbances sparked by the faltering economy and struggles between conservative hardliners and more liberal forces.

As the US-sponsored peace process got under way, Iranian hardliners led by Ayatollah Khameini attempted to sabotage what they saw as Muslim capitulation to Western blandishments. On 19 October Iran convened a conference of Palestinians opposed to the peace process, and the leading hardline cleric Ali Akbar Mohtashemi called for the official Palestinian delegates to Madrid to be executed. Rafsanjani nonetheless continued his campaign to weaken his conservative opponents, and in December 100 MPs called for the removal of Khameini.

The 1992 Election.

The first elections to the 270 seat Majlis, Iran's parliament, since the death of Ayatollah Khomeini in 1989 were held on 10 April and 8 May 1992 and resulted in a setback for Islamic radicals who had previously held 60% of seats. Although there were no formal political parties, the results were seen as a victory for the moderate supporters of President Rafsanjani's Society of Combatant Clergymen. Mr Rafsanjani sought to attract foreign investment by moving towards a free market economy. The radicals, who were increasingly blamed for Iran's economic stagnation, favoured retaining a centralised economy. On 5 May the Supreme Council of Investment removed limits on the share foreign owners could have in Iranian businesses. But poverty in Iran had led to the growth of squatter communities in urban areas and in April and May there was serious rioting in five major cities. President Rafsanjani's attempts to rebuild relations with the west suffered a setback when, on 2 November, a government-backed religious charity announced an increase in the $2 million reward for the assassination of *Satanic Verses* author Salman Rushdie. President Rafsanjani survived an assassination attempt on 10 February 1993.

Recent Developments.

On 25 May 1993 Iranian aircraft bombed bases in Iraq sheltering opposition People's Mujahedeen guerrillas. The guerrillas had attacked oil pipelines in Iran and claimed to have killed hundreds of government troops. In elections on 11 June President Rafsanjani was elected to a second four-year term in a four man contest. His opponents were selected by the Council of Guardians, a body of conservative Islamic clerics. President Rafsanjani took 63% of the votes cast and his nearest opponent, former labour minister Ahmed Tavakoli, won 24%. The low turn-out, 56% as opposed to 70% four years earlier, was attributed to apathy caused by economic hardship and dissatisfaction with clerical rule.

During 1994 the radical-moderate struggle continued to swing back and forth. A fall in oil prices was a severe blow to the economy and to Rafsanjani's reform plans. Although he claimed that the five year development plan completed in 1994 was a success, it had built up foreign debts of $20–$30 billion. The reform programme provoked discontent as it involved cutting subsidies and grants to religious institutions and major riots took place in several cities, including Qazvin. Terrorist violence also swept the country with bombs in Shia shrines, including Mashhad, and the murder of several Christian clergymen. The government blamed these on opposition Mujahidin guerillas but it is likely that they were attempts by the regime to create a state of siege and make people rally round the regime. Attempts to attract foreign investors were set back by the government's inability to reform the exchange rate system and a resistance to allowing foreign investment. The exiled opposition claimed during the year that the end of the regime was nigh and elected a President in exile. The government responded by bombing Mujahidin bases in Iraq in November.

IRAQ.
The Invasion of Kuwait.

During the spring and summer of 1990 Iraq came under increasing Western criticism as a result of its burgeoning non-conventional weapons programme. On 15 March the execution of a British journalist raised a storm, and on 2 April Saddam threatened to devastate Israel if it attacked Iraq's weapons programme.

In July Saddam Hussein accused Kuwait of stealing £1·3 billion worth of oil from disputed border territory and claimed that Kuwait was conspiring to undermine Iraq's economy by excessive oil production. He demanded compensation and moved troops towards the frontier. Iraq agreed to a Kuwaiti proposal for discussions but these broke down on 1 August. The following day Iraq invaded Kuwait, claiming to have been invited to support a popular uprising. The Emir, Sheikh Jabir Ahmed al-Sabah, fled to Saudi Arabia. Iraq installed a puppet republican government but at the end of August annexed Kuwait as Iraq's 19th province.

UN Condemnation.

The UN Security Council condemned the invasion on 9 August and followed this by imposing mandatory economic sanctions. President Bush warned Iraq not to attack Saudi Arabia and King Fahd of Saudi Arabia invited friendly states to defend his country against a possible Iraqi attack. The US flew troops to the Gulf, while the Soviet Union sent two warships. Britain followed suit. A coalition was emerging which eventually included the US, Britain, Egypt, France, the Gulf States, Kuwait, Morocco, Pakistan, Saudi Arabia, Syria, Argentina, Australia, Belgium, Canada, Denmark, Greece, Italy, Holland, Norway, Portugal, the Soviet Union, Spain, Bangladesh, Senegal, Niger, and Czechoslovakia.

The West's immediate concern was the fate of thousands of American, British and other foreign nationals in Kuwait and Iraq. On 16 August Iraq ordered British and US citizens in Kuwait to report for internment. Iraq announced they would be used as human shields to protect military installations against attack. On 19 August President Saddam offered their return if the US withdrew from the Gulf. In December President Saddam authorised the release of all remaining hostages.

Iraq appeared isolated, even within the Arab world. On 10 August 12 of the 20 Arab League states agreed to send troops to defend Saudi Arabia. President Saddam attempted to drive a wedge between Arab leaders and their people by calling for a "holy war" against America and Israel. He demanded Israel's withdrawal from the West Bank and Gaza, linking the Palestinian issue with the Gulf crisis. Iraq also improved relations with Iran, conceding the disputed Shatt-al-Arab. But Iran's neutrality was to be a further significant feature of the crisis.

Operation Desert Shield.

The build-up of coalition forces—Operation Desert Shield—ran parallel with peace moves.

On 29 November the UN Security Council authorised the use of "all necessary means" to free Kuwait if Iraq had not withdrawn by 15 January 1991. The five permanent members guaranteed that Iraq would not be attacked if she withdrew immediately from Kuwait. This was linked with growing concerns about what precisely the objective of the West, and above all the United States, was: the liberation of Kuwait or the overthrow of President Saddam.

The UN deadline expired at 5.00 GMT on 16 January. Shortly before midnight the war between the coalition and Iraq—Operation Desert Storm—began. Over the next six weeks Iraq and Kuwait suffered almost continual air bombardment. The attacks were met with anti-aircraft fire but there was limited reaction from Iraq's 700-strong air force, 132 of its best aircraft fleeing to Iran for sanctuary.

Retaliation by Iraq.

Iraq's main military response was to launch Scud missiles against Israel and Saudi Arabia. Israel was hit by 39 missiles. The missile attacks' importance lay in their potential political effects rather than their military impact. If Israel retaliated, Arab support for the coalition might weaken. President Bush urged restraint on Israel, backing this with the deployment of anti-Scud Patriot missiles in Israel.

At the same time Iraq released a large oil slick from Kuwait, apparently in an attempt to pollute the Gulf. The firing of Kuwaiti oil wells followed with serious environmental consequences.

The impact of continual bombing on civilians raised international concern. On 13 February two bombs hit what the coalition claimed was a military command bunker in Baghdad. The bunker was sheltering 400 civilians, mainly women and children. Hundreds were killed.

On 15 February President Saddam announced Iraq's readiness to withdraw from Kuwait but, once again, insisted on a linkage with Israel's occupation of the West Bank and Gaza. President Bush denounced the statement as a "cruel hoax" and called for President Saddam's overthrow. A Soviet peace formula, including withdrawal from Kuwait and accepted by Iraq on 22 February, was rejected by President Bush and Iraq was warned to withdraw within 24 hours. On 24 February the allied land offensive opened.

The Allied Land Offensive.

Iraq fielded the world's fourth largest army, with 555,000 regular and 480,000 reserve troops. An estimated 545,000 were deployed in or near Kuwait with a further quarter of a million in northern Iraq.

The army included 2,595 tanks, 1,625 artillery pieces and 1,945 armoured personnel carriers. As the land battle began 1,300 tanks, 800 armoured vehicles and 1,100 artillery pieces had reportedly been destroyed by bombing. The largest allied force—commanded by General Norman Schwarzkopf—was the American, with 527,000 combat and support troops, 3,400 tanks and armoured vehicles, and almost a thousand aircraft. The British force, the second strongest, was led by Lt.-Gen. Sir Peter de la Billière.

The 100-Hour War.

The battle for Kuwait lasted 100 hours. The main allied attack was directed towards the Euphrates Valley, while a French Rapid Action Force went to the west, encircling an estimated 500,000 Iraqi troops. Iraqi forces—including the elite Republican Guard—offered minor resistance, and allied casualties were light. Iraq's casualties were estimated at between 50 and 150,000 and 175,000 troops were taken prisoner. On 25 February Baghdad Radio reported that the withdrawal from Kuwait had begun. Allied air forces bombed the retreating army on the road to Basra, turning it into what one press report described as a "slaughterhouse". On 26 February President Saddam conceded that Kuwait was no longer part of Iraq. As US marines and local resistance fighters took control of Kuwait City the exiled Emir declared martial law.

The Kurdish Rebellion.

Taking advantage of Iraq's preoccupation with Kuwait, Kurdish rebels launched a major offensive, taking a string of towns including Zakho, Dahuk, and Kirkuk. After the Gulf War ceasefire, however, Saddam Hussein turned his army loose on them. The flight of the Kurdish people to bleak mountain refuges awakened the conscience of the world. Allied forces moved into northern Iraq to establish 'safe havens' for the Kurds. In May, UN personnel also moved in.

These safe havens enabled the Kurds to return to their towns and Kurdish guerrillas replaced Iraqi security forces in much of northern Iraq. At the same time a major uprising broke out in the south of the country as disaffected soldiers and the Shia population followed President Bush's advice to rise up and remove Saddam. These rebels received aid from Iran but none from the West and were rapidly crushed by Saddam's forces. Kurdish leaders however, emboldened by Western support, began to negotiate an autonomy agreement with Saddam. The negotiations progressed slowly as Saddam waited for the West to lose interest and Kurdish leaders disagreed among themselves.

Having failed to support the Kurdish and Shia rebellions when they were strong enough to threaten Saddam, the US set out to keep him weak by arranging for the UN to supervise the dismantling of Iraq's arsenal of non-conventional weapons. UN investigations revealed that Iraq had a far more sophisticated and extensive nuclear programme than originally believed. Trade sanctions were also maintained as a way of encouraging Iraqis to remove their leader, but a succession of coup attempts took place in vain. Iraq also consistently refused to accept two UN resolutions that would allow her to sell a limited amount of oil to pay for vital food imports, as the money would have been controlled directly by the UN.

Continued Repression and Dictatorship.

Charges by the UN Security Council on 12 March 1992 that Iraq was failing to comply with the 1991 ceasefire—particularly on the inspection and dismantling of weapon-making facilities—were followed by British and US warnings of air-strikes. Iraq agreed to comply on 20 March. There were reports of an attempted coup against President Saddam on 29 June by members of the elite Republican Guard, followed by the purging of hundreds of officers. On 30 July President Saddam reshuffled his cabinet, dismissing two senior ministers. In August Iraq re-asserted its claim to Kuwait as Iraq's "19th province". As the repression of Shiites intensified, Britain, France and the US ordered Iraq to cease military and civil flights over Shiite areas, threatening to shoot down any aircraft that disobeyed. Allied air patrols in the area began

on 27 August and an Iraqi jet fighter was shot down on 27 December. Meanwhile, opposition to President Saddam solidified when delegates from over 30 groups—including Kurds, Turks, Shiites, socialists and dissident officers—met in Kurd-controlled north-east Iraq in September to unify their campaign against the President.

Punitive Air Strikes.

The UN Security Council repeated its charges on 11 January 1993 that Iraq was continuing to violate the cease fire terms by obstructing UN weapons investigators and making two incursions into Kuwait. US and British aircraft mounted punitive attacks on Iraq on 13, 17 and 18 January, destroying missile batteries and attacking an industrial complex north of Baghdad which had formerly been a nuclear plant. President Saddam ordered his forces to cease fire in what had been an undeclared war on 19 January and conceded entry to UN inspectors. Forty civilians were killed in the air attacks.

Recent Events.

The UN voted to extend economic sanctions on 29 March 1993 because of continuing repression of Kurds in the north and Shi'ite Moslems in the south, and refusal to co-operate with the commission setting the border with Kuwait. Sanctions imposed in the wake of the Gulf War had been intended to heighten dissatisfaction among the Iraqi people with President Saddam. But his position appeared as secure as ever, while the suffering caused to the most vulnerable sections of the people was intense.

From 7–14 July Iraq discussed with UN officials its appeal to allow the sale of $1·6 billion of oil to buy essential food and medicines. While no decision was made, Iraq announced on 19 July its willingness to allow long-term UN monitoring of its weapons production. But accusations in November that Iraq had recently used chemical weapons against Shi'ites in the south made the lifting of sanctions unlikely.

Throughout 1994 the US and Britain continued to insist on the continuation of sanctions even through Turkey, Russia and France, were keen to restore ties with Iraq in order to restore trade relations. The sanctions were crippling the economy and impoverishing Iraqis even further, leading Saddam himself to assume the prime-ministership and impose draconian anti-profiteering measures. In a desperate attempt to force the UN to reconsider he moved Republican Guard divisions towards Kuwait, leading the Western allies to deploy troops to the region. There was however no indication that he wanted to fight, especially since the army was plagued by desertion and lack of supplies. The UN weapons inspectors announced on 10 October that they had destroyed the bulk of Iraq's weapons of mass destruction and installed a monitoring regime. This was to remain in place for at least six months before the embargo on oil sales could begin to be lifted but it appeared likely that the US and Britain would seek to retain sanctions until Saddam fell. Even Iraq's acceptance of the existence of Kuwait and the UN-drawn border in November failed to convince Washington and London to soften their stance, despite signs that they were becoming increasingly isolated in the international community.

The opposition meanwhile showed little sign of being able to topple the regime. In the south the army continued to drain the marshes and evict villagers while in the north, Kurdish groups fought among themselves and the Iraqi National Congress took a lower profile. The intra-Kurdish clashes led to widespread human rights abuses and to a Turkish invasion aimed at the Kurdish Workers Party (PKK) on the grounds that the Turkish border was no longer secure.

Pressure meanwhile intensified on Saddam Hussein as his troops clashed with Shia fighters in the south and Kurds in the north even as reports emerged of a coup attempt in which his son Udai was wounded. The US continued to insist that sanctions be maintained but Iraq co-operated with UN weapons inspectors and tempted a range of countries with lucrative oil and commercial concessions.

SYRIA.

In 1963 Syria was taken over by conspirators belonging to the Ba'ath party and pro-Nasserites. The latter were ousted the same year and younger, more radical members of the Ba'ath soon removed the old guard. In 1966 these radicals took power and were instrumental in provoking the 1967 war with Israel. One of their number, Hafiz al-Assad, took power himself in 1970 and instituted a more pragmatic rule. Still fiercely anti-Israeli, he mended fences with the conservative Arab monarchies and liberalised the economy. After being isolated by Egypt's separate peace negotiations with Israel in the mid and late 1970s, Syria was left as the main Arab confrontation state. After Israel's invasion of Lebanon in 1982 Syria managed to bring about the withdrawal of both the Israeli army and multinational peacekeeping forces through the use of proxy guerrilla operations. In 1985 Syria asserted its influence over Jordan when it persuaded King Hussein to reject proposals for separate talks with Israel. At the same time Syrian-Iraqi hostility, which derives in part from a split in the Ba'ath party in the mid-1960s, led to the development of a close Syrian-Iranian alliance in the Iran-Iraq War.

Syria and the Gulf War.

Assad refused to attend an emergency Arab League summit meeting held in Baghdad on 28-30 May 1990 to discuss growing Middle East tension because of Syria's enmity to Iraqi President Saddam. He visited Egypt on 14-16 July and declared Syria's willingness to join the Arab-Israeli peace process. On 14-15 August Syrian troops began arriving in Saudi Arabia to counter the Iraqi threat. There were demonstrations in Syria against Syrian alignment with the US against Iraq. President Assad declared Syria's willingness to increase its military commitment when he met US Secretary of State James Baker on 14 September but requested greater financial aid from the Gulf States. On 23 November President Assad met US President Bush in Geneva, the first meeting with an American president since 1977.

On 6 March 1991 Syria signed the "Damascus Declaration" with Egypt, Saudi Arabia and five smaller Gulf States, calling for increased economic, military and political co-operation in the region. This declaration did not bring Syria the benefits it had hoped for as the Gulf States chose to rely on Western military guarantees instead.

Syria and Lebanon.

One of the benefits of its pro-Western stance in the war against Iraq was the acceptance by the US of Syrian hegemony over Lebanon. In 1976 Syria had invaded to prevent the state coming under the control of radical leftist and Palestinian groups who would have provoked a war with Israel, but its influence extended over only part of the country. In 1991 the US rewarded Syria by allowing it to formalise its hegemonic role in Lebanon, in spite of Israeli objections.

In addition, Syria received substantial financial aid from the Gulf States. This was used to buy armaments to bolster its position in the negotiations with Israel.

Assad's Fourth Term.

On 12 March 1992 President Assad inaugurated his fourth term by accusing the United States of mounting an arms blockade against the Arab states while allowing Israel to build up its arsenal. The US had attempted to intercept a ship allegedly transporting Scud missiles to Syria. However, President Assad told the US Secretary of State on 21 February 1993 that he was anxious to resume Arab-Israeli peace talks suspended on 17 December 1992.

The talks (which resumed on 27 April) were threatened when, on 25 July 1993, Syrian soldiers in Lebanon's Bekaa Valley were killed in Israeli air attacks on guerrilla villages. But Syrian forces refrained from retaliatory action and, while condemning Israel, did not withdraw from the peace negotiations. Syria was involved in negotiating a ceasefire with Israel, Lebanon and Hizbollah forces and appeared to take steps to prevent further Iranian weapons reaching the guerrillas. In talks on 16 January 1994 President Assad told US President

Clinton that Syria wanted "normal" relations with Israel.

On the domestic front, Assad's plans for a smooth succession were blown off course by the death of his son and anointed successor Basil in a car crash on 21 January. Although the President has since sought to build up another of his sons, Bashar, Basil's death opens the way for a power struggle between Assad's estranged brother Rifaat and the generals who run the country's intelligence services. Meanwhile, the economic reform programme made gradual progress as limited foreign investment began to enter the country.

For further developments in the peace process, *see* **Special Topic. C76-8**.

SAUDI ARABIA.

Saudi conservatives had feared that the massive influx of Western troops would undermine the strict traditional nature of Saudi society. Although contacts between troops and the population were kept to a minimum, Saudi liberals attempted to take advantage of the situation. A group of professional women made their claim for more liberalism by driving their cars, normally prohibited for women. The regime bowed to pressure from the conservative clergy and cracked down on such manifestations.

Although the war was very costly for Saudi Arabia, the halt in production of oil from Iraq and Kuwait proved beneficial and allowed Saudi Arabia to increase its market share. The major change resulting from the war however, has been the Saudi government's new-found self assertiveness in international affairs. Seeing that their previous policy of buying off potential threats, such as the Palestinians and Iraq, had failed, the government ruthlessly slashed its aid to Arab states who had not supported the war. Workers from these countries were expelled *en masse*. Although the signing of the Damascus Declaration in March 1991 appeared to herald the beginning of a policy of swapping Gulf oil wealth for Egyptian and Syrian military manpower, Saudi Arabia soon reneged on the commitment and chose to increase the size of its armed forces instead.

Demands for Liberalisation.

On 1 March 1992 King Fahd acknowledged growing demands from the business community for greater liberalisation of the country's social and economic system by issuing an 83-article "Basic System of Government", Saudi Arabia's first written constitution. A 61-member Consultative Council, chosen by the king, would have the right to propose and review laws and treaties and to question ministers but would not be permitted to overrule the king or his cabinet. In addition, the decrees devolved greater authority to provincial governments and took a step towards guaranteeing some human rights by weakening the authority of the religious police. Ultimate power, however, remained with the king.

The royal family felt its absolute rule challenged by the formation of a Committee for the Defence of Legitimate Rights (CDLR) by six Islamic conservatives on 3 May 1993. The committee's leader declared it was intended to "help eliminate injustice, support the oppressed and defend the rights prescribed by sharia (Islamic law)." On 12 May the committee was outlawed. But on 29 December King Fahd opened a new 61-man consultative council, the Shura, as part of his long-awaited political reforms. Sessions of the Shura were to be held in private and it was intended to act as a "partner" to King Fahd, who had the final say.

Rising Discontent.

The CDLR was forced into exile in London in April 1994 and launched a fax campaign to discredit the Royal Family, accusing them of corruption and un-Islamic behaviour. The regime responded by arresting the leaders, pressuring the British government to return the exiles and taking more of a say in religious affairs in order to control the agenda domestically. The fundamentalist opposition, although regarded as of little consequence by many Saudis, tapped a vein of discontent with King Fahd's rule as the country's post-Desert Storm debts forced it to cut spending and to give the private sector a greater role. The Kingdom was also embarrassed by its open support for the Yemeni secessionists who were defeated in that country's civil war. Relations between the Kingdom and Yemen remained poor. In the wake of a border clash in January the two sides opened talks on resolving their border dispute.

These talks led to the signing on 25 February of a Memorandum of Understanding under which the two countries pledged to hold further talks to settle their long-running border dispute.

YEMEN.

The Yemen Arab Republic and the People's Democratic Republic of Yemen merged into the Republic of Yemen on 22 May 1990. General Ali Abdullah Saleh was elected head of state by both parliaments and took charge of a five-man council which was to rule Yemen over a 2½-year transitional period before elections were held. Mr Ali Salem al-Badh, secretary-general of the South's ruling Yemeni Socialist Party became vice president and Mr Haydar Abu Bakr al-Attas prime minister.

Yemen and the Gulf Crisis.

During the Gulf Crisis Yemen followed Jordan in seeking to avoid condemnation of Iraq. There were rumours that Iraqi aircraft had been flown to Yemen for safekeeping. The Gulf States responded to this perceived pro-Iraqi stance by expelling over 800,000 Yemeni workers. This was a severe strain on the economy, but an upturn was in sight with the opening of the first oil well in a newly discovered oil field. Domestically, adjustment to unification proceeded apace. Tensions were inevitable as the more populous and wealthy but socially conservative northerners mingled with the more westernised southerners.

In the April 1993 elections, President Ali Abdullah Saleh's General People's Congress (GPC) emerged as the largest single party, followed by vice-president Ali al-Bahd's Yemeni Socialist Party (YSP).

Tensions between the GPC and YSP however escalated with the southerners claiming they were being excluded from power. In late 1993 Bahd withdrew from government and a series of clashes between the rival northern and southern armies led to the outbreak of full scale hostilities in February 1994. The north tried to crush the south but southern troops resisted for over two months. On 21 May the southern leadership declared their secession from the union but on 7 July Aden fell to northern forces and the YSP leadership fled into exile. Perhaps 7,000 people died in the war and Saleh afterwards moved to consolidate his control over the country. A new government was formed excluding the YSP. The two armed forces were united and demands made for the return of the exiled leadership.

KUWAIT.

The Iraqi Invasion.

Kuwait was occupied by Iraq for seven months from 2 August 1990, the emir going into exile in Saudi Arabia, (*see* **C37**). On the liberation in February 1991 the emir placed Kuwait under martial law for three months. There were clear divisions between the government which had been in exile and the opposition groups which had remained in occupied Kuwait. On 9 March 1991 the emir promised US Secretary of State James Baker that there would be an early return to democracy.

Recent Events.

However, Kuwait's rulers have made little effort to accede to democratic pressures. Instead they have sought to ensure Kuwait's future security by concluding a defence pact with the US and replacing "politically unreliable" Arab workers with more neutral Asians. In the process Kuwait was heavily criticised by the West for its often brutal treatment of its Palestinian population, most of whom have been forced to leave the country. The country's other main concern has been dealing with

the aftermath of the invasion, putting out the oil wells fired by Iraq and clearing the unexploded ordnance littering the countryside.

The National Assembly Elections.

On 16 April 1992 the United Nations awarded Kuwait a small portion of Iraqi territory in a border adjustment. On 5 October—under pressure internally and from its Gulf War allies—Kuwait held its first National Assembly elections since 1985. The election campaign was marked by criticism from opposition candidates of the Sabah family's monopoly of political power and on financial mismanagement. Political parties were illegal and the candidates represented loose opposition groupings. Under Kuwait's strict voting laws only 14% of the country's citizens were eligible to vote. Opposition candidates nonetheless won 31 of the 50 Assembly seats on an 85% turnout.

On 17 October the premier, Crown Prince Saad al-Abdallah Al Sabah announced a new 16 member cabinet which included six opposition deputies. Members of the royal family retained the defence, foreign and interior portfolios.

On 27 April 1993 Kuwait's defence minister announced the arrest of ten Iraqis for planning to assassinate US President Bush during a visit earlier in the month. In the face of continuing low-level Iraqi incursions and Iraq's refusal to accept a frontier delineated by the United Nations in 1992, the government revealed plans to build a security trench along the 120-mile border. Islamic fundamentalism appeared to be strengthening its position with 39 of parliament's 50 elected members signing a motion advocating a change in the constitution to make Islam the sole (rather than the "main") source of Kuwaiti law.

In the face of a vociferously critical National Assembly, the government's main concern was the country's soaring budget deficit and debts. Austerity plans were resisted by parliament though the Emir encouraged citizens and expatriates to give voluntarily to a fund to help pay the costs of supporting western troops rushed to defend Kuwait in October. In foreign affairs, Kuwait continued to urge the international community to maintain pressure on Iraq and sealed its border with a ditch and sensor system.

SOUTH ASIA

INDIA.

On 17 October 1989 a beleaguered Mr Gandhi, his position clearly undermined by the scandal, announced that parliamentary elections would be held in November, two months earlier than constitutionally necessary. Four days previously his government had lost two important votes in the upper house on local government changes. Congress failed to win the necessary two-thirds majority on both occasions, the first time an Indian government had suffered what amounted to humiliation since 1952. In addition, from September the government was faced with violent clashes between Hindus and Moslems in Kota, Badain and Indore. 170 were killed in two weeks of rioting in Bihar state.

Mr Gandhi faced a united opposition. Five regional organisations rallied in a National Front under Janata Dal, the People's Party. Its manifesto issued on 20 October denounced government corruption and promised increased autonomy for state governments. Congress in its manifesto proposed legislation to improve the position of women and, to encourage rural support, the creation of self-governing village councils.

The November campaign proved to be the bloodiest since independence, with 120 deaths. Turnout for the 525 lower house seats contested was a little under 60%. Congress took 192 seats, a dramatic decline from the 415 it had won in 1984. Much of its lost support was in the hitherto traditionally loyal north. An allied party in the south won a further 11 seats. For the opposition, Janata Dal and two smaller associated parties took a total of 144 seats; the right-wing Hindu BJP (the Indian People's Party), 88; and four left-wing parties, 51. Though Congress remained the largest single party it was well short of a majority.

A New Prime Minister.

National Front leader Vishwanath Pratap Singh became Prime Minister on 2 December, heading a minority government supported by the BJP and four left-wing parties. He promised an investigation into the Bofors scandal, a freedom of information act, and encouragement for agriculture and small-scale industry. In announcing his cabinet Mr Singh broke with tradition by appointing a Moslem, Mohammed Sayeed, as home affairs minister. Mr Gandhi's Congress party suffered further defeats in state elections held in March 1990, losing control of a number of traditionally Congress northern and central states. The most striking successes came for the right-wing BJP, suggesting that Mr Singh would face increasing demands from the BJP for its support.

Threats to the Government.

By July 1990 Janata Dal's hold on power was already weakening, confronted by separatist violence in Kashmir and from Sikhs in Punjab, together with coalition conflicts. Thirteen ministers resigned in protest against the appointment of the son of deputy prime minister Mr Devi Lal as chief minister in the state of Haryana. Mr Singh, declaring he had lost the support of his party, announced his own resignation. When this was rejected Mr Singh engineered the chief minister's dismissal and the 13 ministers withdrew their resignations. On 1 August Mr Singh dismissed Mr Lal, ending the cabinet crisis but risking further threats to his narrow majority.

In August Mr Singh announced that the quotas restricting civil service posts to members of the lower castes would be increased from 22% to 40%. This was an attempt to detach lower caste support from Congress (I). Middle and upper caste students, already facing unemployment, began protest riots in New Delhi on 23 August. These reached a peak in late September, by which time over 50 people had died. On 1 October the Supreme Court ordered a delay in implementation of the new quotas.

The Ayodhya Crisis.

A further crisis came in October over a Hindu fundamentalist campaign to build a temple on the site of a mosque in Ayodhya. Mr Singh resisted the proposal—which led to intense inter-communal violence—as a violation of Moslem rights. On 23 October a BJP leader of the campaign was arrested. BJP immediately withdrew from the coalition. In the ensuing upheaval Mr Singh was ousted in November in a Janata Dal revolt. Following Mr Gandhi's refusal of a presidential invitation to form a government Mr Singh was replaced as prime minister by Mr Chandra Shekhar, leader of the Janata Dal socialist faction. Mr Shekhar's position was even weaker than that of his predecessor.

The Advent of Chandra Shekhar.

On 11 January 1991 the lower house speaker ruled that eight MPs had disqualified themselves by defecting from Mr Singh's government, forcing the dropping of five key ministers and reducing Mr Shekhar's base in the 545-seat lower house to 54. He now depended on the goodwill of Mr Gandhi's Congress (I). But on 5 March Congress announced a boycott of parliamentary proceedings after Mr Gandhi alleged police were keeping his home under surveillance under government orders. Parliament was dissolved on 13 March and elections were called for May.

Assassination of Rajiv Gandhi.

The election campaign, against a backcloth of rising Hindu militancy, became increasingly violent. On 21 May, addressing an election rally 30 miles from Madras, Rajiv Gandhi was assassinated by a terrorist bomb. India (and the world) was stunned. The remaining elections were postponed. After unsuccessfully attempting to instal Rajiv's widow as his successor, the party chose veteran Congressman and former Foreign Secretary P. V. Narasimha Rao as party leader. The Gandhi dynasty was ended and India entered a new and uncertain political future.

India under Rao.

The next round of the delayed elections took place on 15–16 June. Congress (I) failed to win an independent parliamentary majority, taking 218 seats and having the support of a further 17 members. The BJP increased its representation from 88 to 120 seats. On 20 June Mr. Rao defeated an attempt to oust him from the party leadership and was sworn in as prime minister. Echoing Mr. Gandhi's pre-election speeches, Mr. Rao proposed a free market, austerity and the encouragement of foreign investment as the solution to the country's economic problems. In November his government shored up its precarious minority hold on power with a number of by-election successes. Mr. Rao's government also made a number of radical foreign policy moves, ending 30 years of diplomatic coldness with China on 13 December, and recognising Israel. Congress (I) was successful in state assembly and parliamentary elections held in Punjab on 19 February 1992, the first since 1985. But this was largely because the Sikh Akali Dal party boycotted the elections and separatist terrorists kept the turnout down to 28% by intimidation. Mr. Rao's government faced increasing united opposition criticism of the inflation and unemployment brought on by its economic policies.

Communal Violence and Hindu Extremism.

On 9 March 1992 the prime minister Narasimha Rao won an important vote on his economic programme which amounted to a vote of confidence forced by the opposition Bharatiya Janata Party (BJP). But on 31 March his foreign minister was forced to resign following allegations of involvement in the long-running Bofors corruption scandal. India was rocked by intense violence following the destruction of a mosque in the northern town of Ayodhya by Hindu extremists on 6 December. By 13 December over 1,200 people had been killed and an estimated 5,000 injured in clashes between Hindus, Moslems and the security forces throughout India. The government reacted by banning three Hindu and two Moslem extremist organisations. On 16 December three state governments run by the opposition BJP were dismissed on the orders of the cabinet because of alleged BJP involvement in the destruction of the mosque. The rioting intensified popular discontent with the government, and this was not defused by a cabinet reshuffle undertaken by Mr. Rao on 17 January 1993 in which 14 ministers were dismissed. Violence struck again when, on 12 March, the Bombay business quarter was hit by terrorist bombs which killed over 300 people and wounded more than 1,000.

Claims against Pakistan.

On 21 April the government announced it had evidence linking Pakistan's intelligence services to the bombings. Inter-communal clashes continued and on 3–4 May over 100 people were killed in the north-eastern state of Manipur. Premier Rao's alleged indecisiveness in the face of communal strife was at the centre of a no confidence motion in parliament on 28 July. A unified challenge by the normally fragmented opposition also accused his government of encouraging corruption. Earlier, on 16 June, a stockbroker involved in a securities scandal alleged he had paid Mr. Rao $300,000 in November 1991 for future political favours, an allegation Mr. Rao denied. Mr. Rao's government narrowly won the vote by 265 to 251.

Mr. Rao's Congress (I) did creditably in regional elections held in November while the BJP failed to build on what it hoped would be a "Hindu wave". The elections had been seen as a mid-term verdict on the central government. But Mr. Rao faced a further crisis when his finance minister Manmohan Singh, the driving force behind India's move to a market economy, was accused in a parliamentary report of "constructive responsibility" for a £860 million financial scandal. Mr. Rao's government finally secured an absolute majority in parliament when, on 30 December, ten members of a faction of Janata Dal joined Congress.

Strikes, Demonstrations and Electoral Defeats.

A strike called by the opposition BJP on 10 February 1994 against price rises in essential commodities won wide support. In his 1994–95 budget proposals on 28 February, finance minister Manmoham Singh remained committed to growth despite concern over the level of public borrowing.

But on 4 March the ruling Congress (I) suffered a serious setback at the hands of the BJP in elections for four upper house seats in Gujarat, taking two instead of the expected three.

Economic developments had further repercussions when there were violent demonstrations in New Delhi on 5–6 April against India's accession to the Uruguay Round of the General Agreement on Tariffs and Trade, which the opposition claimed weakened national sovereignty. Strikes brought large areas of the country to a halt on 15 April. Tension continued with Pakistan, with mutual expulsion of diplomats in August and renewed allegations of Pakistan's involvement in the March 1993 bombings.

Mr Rao's position was threatened by his party's disastrous results in state elections in December. Congress (I) lost three of the four crucial southern states, including Mr Rao's home state of Andhra Pradesh. He responded by threatening a party purge, blaming the losses on infighting. A leading rival, Arjun Singh, resigned from the cabinet, declaring his "disillusion with the leadership." Mr Singh was suspended from the party on 24 January 1995 for "indulging in anti-party activities." As Congress (I) faced another round of state elections in February, it appeared that Mr Rao might face serious revolt from within his party.

The position of Mr Rao's government was further undermined by defeat in state elections in March 1995. In the economically crucial state of Maharashtra, a right wing alliance of the BJP and Shiv Sena ejected Congress from power for the first time in 44 years. In neighbouring Gujarat the BJP succeeded in winning sole power. In both states poorer voters were protesting against the impact of the central government's economic liberalisation programme.

SRI LANKA.

In December 1988 UNP leader Mr Premadasa succeeded Mr Jayawardene as president in elections marked by intense JVP violence. President Premadasa ended a five-year state of emergency. In the February 1989 parliamentary elections, the first for 12 years, the ruling UNP took 125 of the 225 seats. In May India announced the withdrawal of its 45,000 strong peace-keeping force by the end of 1989 while President Premadasa began talks with the Tamil Tiger leaders which led to a ceasefire in June. But continuing JVP-inspired violence forced a renewed state of emergency on 20 June. President Premadasa called further peace talks in February 1990. The Tamil Tigers announced an end to armed action in favour of forming a political party and the government appeared to have ridden the worst of JVP violence. President Premadasa promised an early end to the state of emergency and reforms to promote communal harmony. But violence renewed on 11 June when Tamil Tigers launched attacks on police stations in the east, capturing and then killing hundreds of police.

Tamil Tiger Ceasefire.

On 1 January 1991 the Tigers declared a unilateral ceasefire. The government responded with a seven-day suspension of military operations, but abandoned the ceasefire at army insistence. Sustained air and sea raids were then mounted against Tiger strongholds on the Jaffna peninsula in what appeared to be a preliminary to a decisive ground attack. The Tigers ended their ceasefire on 25 January. The Tamil community accused the government of targetting its bombing attacks on civilians.

On 2 March the deputy defence minister Ranjan Wijeratne was assassinated in a bomb explosion. He had led the fight against the Tamil Tigers and had strongly opposed entering into negotiations with them. President Premadasa did, however, favour talks and on 3 August, the day after government troops broke a four-week siege by Tamils of an important military base, he renewed his invitation to the Tamils. But on 30 August, facing opposition party calls for his impeachment for corruption and abuse of power, President Premadasa suspended parliament for a month. In October he announced that he had succeeded in thwarting an attempt to force his resignation. At the end of October the army cut off the last access

route to the Tamil Tiger controlled Jaffna peninsula, effectively blocking food supplies to the one million population. On 23 February 1992 the leader of the Tigers, Vellupillai Prabhakaran, offered to moderate Tamil calls for independence and called for UN mediation to find a political settlement.

Sri Lanka suffered its worst violence of 1992 when Tamil separatist rebels killed 127 people in raids on four villages on 15 October.

The Assassination of Premadasa.

On 1 May 1993 President Premadasa was killed by a suicide bomber at a ruling United National Party rally in Colombo. The Tamil Tigers denied responsibility for the murder. Prime minister Dingiri Banda Wijetunge was appointed acting president.

President Wijetunge appointed Ranil Wickremasinghe prime minister on 7 May. The ruling UNP party took the majority of seats in provincial council elections held on 17 May, although the opposition Sri Lanka Freedom Party led a left-wing coalition to electoral success in Colombo. Elections were not held in the northern and eastern parts of the country, the scene of the most intense violence. On 18 August the Tamil Tigers announced their agreement to talks with the government. The Tigers had previously demanded a separate Tamil state but were now willing to accept limited autonomy within a federal structure. But on 11 November the Tigers attacked the Pooneryn base killing up to 500 government troops, the heaviest losses of the ten-year insurgency.

President Wijetunge announced on 2 February 1994 that he proposed to amend the constitution to abolish the direct national presidential poll and instead have parliament vote to choose the president. The intention was to further weaken the electoral influence of the minority Tamil community.

The ruling United National Party (UNP) suffered a serious setback in provincial council elections held on 24 March 1994. The rise in support for the opposition People's Alliance – led by the Sri Lanka Freedom Party (SLFP) – was seen as a vote of no confidence in President Wijetunge. The UNP did, however, put on a better performance in local council elections held in the eastern and northern provinces on 1 March. But there were bombings in Colombo on 8–9 April, responsibility being claimed by the previously unknown Tamil group Ellalan Force.

Following the government's loss of a confidence vote on 5 May, President Wijetunge dissolved parliament. In elections held on 16 August the UNP took 94 seats and the Alliance 105, although it failed to gain an absolute majority. Chandrika Bandaranaike Kumaratunga was appointed prime minister on 18 August. The Tamil Tiger leadership welcomed her election as opening the way for a possible end to ethnic violence. On 31 August Mrs Kumaratunga lifted the economic embargo on Tiger controlled areas. But clashes continued, a Tiger training camp being destroyed on 26 September while rebels killed 14 soldiers two days later.

The 1994 Presidential Elections.

On 24 October 56 people, including UNP leader and presidential candidate Gamini Dissanayake, were killed in a bomb blast. The Tamil Tigers denied responsibility. Mr Dissanayake was replaced by his widow. In the elections held on 9 November, Mrs Kumaratunga became president with 62% of the vote, the UNP candidate taking 35%. President Kumaratunga appointed her mother, Mrs Bandaranaike (prime minister from 1960–65, 1970–77), premier on 14 November. The Tamil Tigers announced a ceasefire immediately after Mrs Kumaratunga's election. However, on 1 January 1995 a leader of the People's Liberation Organisation of Tamil Eelam was assassinated, his organisation blaming rival Tamil Tigers.

PAKISTAN.

On 17 August 1988 President Zia was killed when his C-130 transport aircraft exploded a few minutes after taking off from Bahawalpur, seventy miles from the Indian border. All those on board were killed, including the US ambassador to Pakistan, Mr. Arnold Raphel. The subsequent enquiry ruled out an accident or a missile attack, leaving sabotage—perhaps by Afghan agents or disaffected elements in the army—as the most likely cause.

A state of emergency was declared, and the chairman of the Senate, Mr. Ghulam Ishaq Khan, became acting president, with a council of military and civilian leaders. He announced that elections would go ahead as planned in November, and supported a decision by the Supreme Court in October, setting aside President Zia's order that they could not be contested by political parties.

The Triumph of Miss Bhutto.

Voting in the national elections took place on 16 November 1988. Miss Bhutto's Pakistan People's Party (PPP) won 95 of the 207 elected Muslim seats in the National Assembly, plus a further twelve when indirect elections took place for the twenty seats reserved for women. Her main opponents, the Islamic Democratic Alliance, won 54 seats. The next largest party was the Mohajir Qaumi Movement (MQM), with thirteen seats, representing the Urdu-speaking population of Sind who had come as refugees after partition. Two weeks of uncertainty followed the elections. This came to an end when Miss Bhutto reached an understanding with the leader of the MQM, Mr. Altaf Hussein. When the National Assembly met, President Ishaq Khan named Miss Bhutto as prime minister.

In December 1988 Miss Bhutto won a vote of confidence in the National Assembly by 148 votes to 55. Miss Bhutto supported the election of President Ishaq Khan for a five-year term, and he received 348 votes compared with her nearest rival's 91. In appointing her cabinet Miss Bhutto kept personal control of the defence and finance ministries, so that she would be responsible for relations with the army and the country's economy, her two main potential problem areas in 1989.

Throughout 1989 Miss Bhutto's authority appeared increasingly vulnerable. Islamic fundamentalist leaders claimed her position as prime minister violated the teachings of the Koran and demanded her replacement by a man. Her Pakistan People's Party suffered a setback in national and provincial by-elections fought in January. Its main opponents, the Islamic Democratic Alliance, took seven of the 13 National Assembly places contested and three of the seven provincial legislature seats. Miss Bhutto's party won four and three respectively, with independents taking the remainder. The PPP did, however, retain its position as the National Assembly's largest party.

In March Miss Bhutto moved to strengthen her position by attempting to oust Nawaz Sharif, chief minister of the Punjab, Pakistan's largest and wealthiest state, and her leading political rival. He easily won a vote of no confidence and by early 1990 appeared, with some success, to be ruling Punjab as a virtually autonomous state. Miss Bhutto followed this by appointing her mother as, in effect, deputy prime minister and, in May, dismissing the chief of the Inter Services Intelligence Directorate in an effort to retain control over the military. There were, nonetheless, reports—unconfirmed by the government—of an attempted military coup in September.

Miss Bhutto's administration came under increasing criticism for inefficiency, corruption—with rumours touching her closest family—and a failure to fulfill any of its election promises. In November, shortly after Pakistan had rejoined the Commonwealth, the Islamic Democratic Alliance forced a confidence vote in the National Assembly. The ensuing 107 votes against Miss Bhutto were only 12 short of the 119 necessary to drive her from office. Miss Bhutto responded by reshuffling her cabinet. Ghulam Mustafa Jatoi, the IDA leader, proclaimed the result the "beginning of the end" for Miss Bhutto.

In early 1990 tension between Pakistan and India resumed over the disputed Kashmir region. In July 1989 Indian prime minister Mr Gandhi had visited Miss Bhutto to improve relations. But soon after his successor, Mr Singh, had taken office Indian troops were firing on Moslem demonstrators in Kashmir.

The Dismissal of Benazir Bhutto.

On 6 August 1990 President Ghulan Ishaq Khan dismissed Miss Bhutto, accusing her of corruption and nepotism. A state of emergency was declared

and Mr Jatoi was appointed interim prime minister pending elections in October. Miss Bhutto said the move was unconstitutional and that it had been dictated by the army. President Khan ordered the criminal code to conform with Islamic law on 15 August, reversing Miss Bhutto's previous attempts to secularise the judicial process. On 10 September Miss Bhutto was charged with corruption and abuse of power involving business contracts. Her husband, Asif Ali Zardari, was already in custody for corruption and was later charged with kidnapping and extortion. Miss Bhutto faced a hearing on 2 October but proceedings were abandoned when the court was stormed by thousands of her supporters.

On 24 October the Islamic Democratic Alliance won a decisive victory in the elections, taking 105 seats in the 217-seat National Assembly. This, with the support of smaller parties, guaranteed an IDA majority. The Pakistan People's Party saw its seats halved to 45. Miss Bhutto immediately alleged widespread electoral fraud intended to prevent her return to office. The PPP went on to further massive defeat in the provincial assembly elections three days later, most notably in Miss Bhutto's home province of Sindh.

Pakistan under Sharif.

On 10 April 1991 prime minister Nawaz Sharif placed legislation before parliament instituting *Sharia* (Islamic law) in place of the secular code. This had been one of the main promises of the four right-wing parties making up the IDA. His government also made rapid moves towards privatisation, as well as increasing police powers and making widespread arrests of opposition leaders. Mr. Sharif's first anniversary of office in November was marked by a series of public hangings, the first since President Zia. But there were growing divisions within the IDA. Senator Samiul Haq, a leading opponent of Mr. Sharif, criticised slowness in implementing the Islamic law bill. Attempts were made to discredit Mr. Haq in November when he, together with other critics, faced allegations of involvement in a sex scandal. Miss Bhutto's opposition PPP meanwhile accused Mr. Sharif and his interior minister Shujaat Hussein of involvement in corruption. Growing public dissatisfaction with Mr. Sharif led to reports of moves within the IDA to remove him from the leadership.

There were clashes in Islamabad on 18 November when the opposition leader Benazir Bhutto was prevented from leading a People's Democratic Alliance march on the national assembly demanding the resignation of the prime minister, Mr. Sharif. Ms. Bhutto was placed under house arrest and thousands of her supporters detained. Ms Bhutto threatened to defy a government ban on public appearances but, as unrest subsided, restrictions on demonstrations were lifted.

On 18 April 1993 President Ghulam Ishaq Khan dissolved parliament and dismissed premier Nawaz Sharif's 30-month old governing coalition, accusing Mr Sharif's government of 'maladministration, corruption and nepotism' and of using terrorism against opponents. Balakh Sher Mazari, a dissident member of the Pakistan Muslim League, was appointed caretaker prime minister. The new cabinet included four members of Ms Bhutto's Pakistan People's Party, among them her husband Asif Zardari. National elections for a new government were promised for 14 July. However, instability further increased when Nawaz Sharif was re-instated on 25 May by the High Court.

However, on 26 May the Supreme Court declared President Khan's dismissal of Mr. Sharif unconstitutional. Mr. Sharif returned to office, winning a vote of confidence on 27 May. But the power struggle between the two continued until, on 18 July, both resigned following a deal negotiated by the army, with the imposition of martial law posed as an alternative. Senate chairman Wasim Sajjad became acting president and Moeen Qureshi was appointed caretaker premier. National and provincial assemblies were dissolved and elections were set for early October.

The Return of Benazir Bhutto.

In the elections, Ms. Benazir Bhutto's Pakistan People's Party (PPP) emerged as the largest in the national assembly, though the rival Pakistan

Muslim League was stronger in the Punjab parliament, and her administration depended on the support of independents. On 14 November former PPP deputy leader Farooq Lehari was sworn in as president, strengthening Ms. Bhutto's position. However, a feud within the Bhutto family—with Ms. Bhutto's mother Nusrat backing Ms. Bhutto's estranged brother Murtaza's claim to PPP leadership—led to clashes in which police fired on Murtaza's supporters on 5 January 1994. Murtaza had been arrested on his return to Pakistan on 3 November for allegedly leading the Al-Zulfikar terrorist group.

On 19 February 1994 Ms Bhutto was acquitted on the corruption charge which had been a cause of her downfall in August 1990. A week later she moved against her main opponent, Nawaz Sharif, imposing direct rule in North West Frontier Province. The PPP and its allies took power in the province following a no confidence vote against their rivals on 24 April. Nationally, in biennial elections for 37 Senate seats held on 2 March, the PPP had taken 16 seats, making it the largest single party in the Senate. However, a wave of political violence erupted in Hyderabad and Karachi in late April in which 29 people were killed. The government blamed a group representing Urdu speaking Muslim migrants from India. Tension with India was heightened by a mutual expulsion of diplomats on 11–13 July.

Opposition Accusations.

The opposition parties announced their withdrawal from National Assembly committees on 16 August, alleging government corruption. Of 20 recently appointed judges, 13 were members of the ruling PPP. The government was further embarrassed by the claim of former premier Nawaz Sharif on 23 August that Pakistan had developed a nuclear weapon. Ms Bhutto denounced his claim as "highly irresponsible". Thousands were arrested and thirteen people were killed in a nation-wide strike called by the opposition on 12 October. On 17 November 17 died in gun battles between rival political factions in Karachi provoked by the murder of a leader of the Mohajir Qusami Movement.

AFGHANISTAN.

In March 1992 Mr. Najibullah offered to resign as president to pave the way for an interim government. But on 16 April he was overthrown by his ministers. The capital was encircled by rival mujahedin guerrilla groups. The leader of the largest group, Ahmed Shah Massoud, reached agreement with disaffected generals and became defence minister. His main rival was Gulbuddin Hekmatyar, head of the Islamic fundamentalist Hizbe Islami. But on 24 April the exiled mujahedin political leadership in Pakistan agreed on the formation of a 50-strong interim council under the presidency of Professor Sibghatullah Mojadidi. Professor Mojadidi arrived in the capital on 29 April and appealed for unity and for international aid to rebuild the country after 14 years of civil war. However, Hizbe Islami forces which had been driven from Kabul posed a continuing threat to the new government from outside the capital. In the months that followed, and throughout 1993, intermittent fighting continued.

Civil War in 1994.

Fighting between rival groups continued through early 1994. A truce negotiated on 14 February to allow food supplies into a beleaguered Kabul broke down the following day, as did an attempted ceasefire a week later. However, on 6 March prime minister Hekmatyar's forces responded to a UN appeal and allowed food convoys through.

The government claimed territorial gains in the north of the country against Mr Hekmatyar's main ally, the Uzbek militia leader General Abdul Rashid Dostam, on 10 March. But civilian casualties continued to mount in Kabul, with over 200 killed in rebel rocket attacks on 20 March. Despite UN-backed ceasefire negotiations, fighting continued into May. On 22 May Mr Hekmatyar rejected a proposal by President Rabbani that both should resign as a preliminary to fresh elections. Clashes

continued through the summer, with over 100 people killed in July and a further 400 in September. UN peacemaking efforts appeared to have borne fruit when, on 6 November, five factions loyal to President Rabbani announced acceptance in principle of proposals for a ceasefire and a transfer of power to a grand assembly. There was no word from rebel premier Hekmatyar.

The Forces of the Taliban.

A new element entered into the equation with the emergence in September of fundamentalist students, the "taliban", in the south east of the country. Through a combination of violence and bribery they succeeded in defeating and disbanding local warlords' armies. By early December the taliban controlled three provinces and threatened to move on Kabul. A Taliban rocket attack on Kabul in late March weakened much of the moral support the movement had gathered since October 1994 but it retained control over eight of the 30 provinces.

BANGLADESH.

In August 1986 General Ershad resigned as army chief of staff, accepted nomination as the Jatiya Party's presidential candidate, and announced presidential elections for October. A seven-party opposition alliance led by the Bangladesh Nationalist Party boycotted the elections and General Ershad was elected with 83·6% of the votes cast. He lifted martial law in November and sought popular support by enlarging the civilian cabinet. But a bill introduced in July 1987 allowing army representation in district councils provoked strikes and demonstrations. A state of emergency was declared and parliament dissolved. The opposition parties boycotted parliamentary elections held in March 1988. The state of emergency was lifted in April.

Through 1988 and 1989 Bangladesh suffered a wave of natural disasters. In February 1989 President Ershad returned from Britain with a promised £15 million in aid to be confronted by a devastating tornado, a cholera epidemic, and a drought which threatened to halve the summer harvest. In August he dismissed Vice-President Nurul Islam for incompetence, replacing him with Moudud Ahmed. Kazi Zafar Ahmed became prime minister.

On 4 December 1990 President Ershad was driven from office following seven weeks of violently anti-government demonstrations. Shahabuddin Ahmed was appointed acting president. General Ershad and three former ministers were charged with corruption on 26 January 1991. Rioting continued in the run-up to Bangladesh's first genuinely democratic elections on 27 February. The conservative Bangladesh Nationalist Party—led by Mrs Khaleda Zia, widow of the assassinated President Zia—emerged as the leading party with 138 seats but no overall majority. The Awami League trailed with 88 seats. Gen. Ershad's Jatiya Party took 35 seats, and the fundamentalist Jamaat-i-Islami 18. In 1991, Bangladesh was devastated again by a cyclone causing 130,000 deaths.

On 16 February former President Ershad failed to attend trial, on charges of illegally possessing firearms, because of illness. But on 12 June he was sentenced, despite his protests that the charges were politically motivated, to ten years' imprisonment. He had still to face corruption charges.

Continuing Political Violence.

Campus political violence—in which 80 had died in a year—prompted the prime minister Khaleda Zia to order the ruling Bangladesh Nationalist Party to dissolve its student association central committee on 7 September 1992. The opposition Awami League had suspended the activities of its student wing a day previously. But it appeared in October that an end might be near to insurgent activity by the Santi Bahini guerrilla group in south-eastern Bangladesh which had claimed over 2,000 lives in the past 18 years.

There were violent clashes between supporters of the ruling BNP and opposition Awami League members during local elections on 30–31 January 1994. On 20 March the Awami League led protests against alleged vote-rigging at a by-election won, to widespread surprise, by the BNP. Continuing demands for the resignation of the prime minister, Mrs Khaleda Zia, and an immediate general election, led to riots on 7 April in which three died. Eight opposition parties boycotted parliament's inaugural session on 5 May in support of their demand for a caretaker government and fresh elections.

Death Sentence on Taslima Nasreen.

On 28 May 1994 leaders of the Islamic opposition parties renewed their call for a death sentence to be imposed on the author Taslima Nasreen for blasphemy. Ms Nasreen had been under police protection since calling in October 1993 for a revision of the Koran to recognise women's rights. Her flight to Sweden on 10 August prompted Islamic extremist charges of government complicity.

Opposition to the government intensified with a wave of strikes and violence from 10–13 September led by the Awami League. Further strikes followed in November, with clashes between government and opposition supporters. On 11 December the High Court ruled a boycott of parliament conducted by opposition MPs since March illegal but on 29 December 153 MPs from the Awami League, the Jatiya Party, Jamat-e-Islami and a number of smaller parties resigned en masse. They rejected Mrs Zia's offer the following day to stand down as premier a month before elections due in February 1996.

THE FAR EAST

CHINA.

The 1989 Student Rising.

In the spring of 1989 the Communist government faced a serious challenge to its authority, triggered by the death on 15 April of Hu Yaobang, the disgraced former party general-secretary. Beijing University students demanding his rehabilitation staged a sit-in outside the Great Hall of the People. On the day of his funeral, 22 April, there were demonstrations in a dozen major cities. Deng Xiaoping warned of possible bloodshed. But on 27 April a march by 100,000 students in Beijing calling for democracy and attacking party corruption passed off peacefully. On 4 May 300,000 demonstrators filled Tiananmen Square, signifying growing popular support. Students began a hunger strike in the square on 13 May, demanding political reforms of the kind being enacted in the Soviet Union, their presence disrupting a visit by Mr Gorbachev on 15 May.

The hunger strikers called for a televised dialogue with the government as, on 17 May, a million people marched in Beijing, others demonstrated in 20 cities, and workers announced they would strike in support of the students. Divisions opened in the party hierarchy, with Zhao Ziyang apparently favouring dialogue while the Prime Minister, Li Peng, announced that martial law would come into force on 20 May. The people of Beijing massed in the square to prevent the troops entering.

Massacre in Tiananmen Square.

As the students in the square perceptibly tired hardliners within the party prevailed. On 4 June thousands of troops and scores of tanks moved in, staging a bloody massacre in which 2,500 were initially reported killed. With the world watching the carnage on television, China appeared on the brink of chaos. Sporadic clashes continued in Beijing and in cities throughout China over the next two days. There were reports that the 38th Army, which had refused to enforce the martial law decree, was facing the 27th Army and a clash seemed possible.

But on 8 June Li Peng appeared on television and praised the troops who had put down the protesters. The following day the party leadership, minus Zhao Ziyang, presented a united front on television. The official government media called on citizens to inform on "counter-revolutionary" dissidents. Arrests of activists now began alongside a government

propaganda campaign to minimise the extent of casualties in the Tiananmen Square massacre. By 21 June 1,500 activists had been arrested, including Guo Haifong, a prominent student leader. All independent student and workers organisations were ordered to disband. As the arrests continued protesters received heavy punishment and nine were executed publicly in Shanghai.

Purge of Student Sympathisers.

The party now began a purge of what it saw as its own unreliable elements. Several leading officials were ousted at a Central Committee meeting on 24 June, including Zhao Ziyang, who was dismissed for "counter-revolutionary rebellion" and replaced by Jiang Zemin. Many lower level party members were expelled for having supported the democracy movement. In a keynote speech on 28 June Deng Xiaoping denounced the protesters, praised the army, and warned of "evil influences from the West".

By July unofficial reports claimed 10,000 had been arrested and the government itself admitted 2,500. Through the summer arrests, prison sentences and executions continued. The party did, however, acknowledge the legitimacy of some of the protesters' complaints. The party Politburo announced a programme to combat government and party corruption on 28 July. On 6 September Li Peng pointed to inflation, party corruption and inequalities in wealth as justifiable grievances, though he rejected the wider demands raised in the summer demonstrations.

The 40th anniversary of Communist rule was celebrated in Tiananmen Square on 1 October with parades behind a heavy security cordon.

Background of Economic Discontent.

Although the dramatic events of the summer had passed and resistance crushed, the government faced economic problems that might provoke a renewal of discontent and unrest. An austerity programme introduced in September 1988 to combat inflation of over 30% had resulted in falling living standards and rising unemployment. Articles in the party and army press implied that troops would be used again if the party felt itself to be in danger. With unconfirmed reports that 1,500 officers and soldiers faced courts martial for mutiny in the protests, the party conducted a campaign of ideological indoctrination to guarantee the army's loyalty.

Rise of Jiang Zemin.

At the meeting of China's parliament, the National People's Congress, in March 1990, there was an easing of the austerity programme. Deng Xiaoping resigned on 22 March as chairman of the State Military Commission, handing its leadership to Jiang Zemin. Although the party leadership appeared to be attempting to distance itself from the Tiananmen Square massacre, Li Peng declared on 20 March that "socialist China will stand firm as a rock" and dissent would be punished. The party was determined that China would not follow the path of the Soviet Union and Eastern Europe.

On 24 April Li Peng met President Gorbachev in Moscow, the first such high-level visit for 26 years. The two leaders signed a 10-year economic and scientific co-operation treaty and agreed on troop cuts along the Sino–Soviet border.

On 3–4 June Beijing University students mounted demonstrations to commemorate the first anniversary of the crushing of the pro-democracy movement. Students were injured in clashes with police and the authorities sealed off Tiananmen Square to prevent demonstrators entering.

Economy in Recession.

China's economy remained in recession, largely as a result of the 1988 austerity measures. In March 1990 the Finance Minister had admitted that the economic situation was "grim". Reports in June put unemployment at its highest for ten years, with foreign investment slowing dramatically. A Party Central Committee meeting in December attempted to reconcile divisions between reformist and conservative factions and approve a new five-year economic plan. A vaguely worded compromise emerged, combining a recognition of the need to encourage Western investment with a determination to resist dramatic reform.

The Dissident Trials.

The need not to offend potential foreign investors—together with government hopes of minimising the significance of the 1989 pro-democracy demonstrations—appeared to influence the treatment of dissidents. The trials began in December 1990 of individuals involved in the 1989 Beijing protests including student leaders Guo Haifeng and Wang Dan, both of whom received—as did other students—relatively lenient sentences. But an unknown number of workers were more harshly dealt with.

Moves towards eventual unity with Nationalist Taiwan continued. Since 1983 mainland China had favoured a "one country, two systems" solution. In December 1990 Taiwan president Lee Teng-hui announced the ending of the 'state of war' with China that had existed for over 40 years and advocated a peaceful reunification. Economic ties had already been strengthened but Chinese proposals in December for talks between the Communist and Nationalist parties were rejected by Taiwan.

At the opening of China's parliament, the National People's Congress, on 23 March 1991, prime minister Li Peng acknowledged the role market forces could play in developing the economy. But he stressed that China would remain a socialist society. Despite a worsening budget deficit, increased military spending was announced. Conflicts between reformists and anti-reformists continued. The appointment of Deng Zhu, the mayor of Shanghai, as a vice premier with responsibility for developing the eastern coastal area and promoting links with the West, appeared to represent a victory for the reformist line of Deng Xiaoping.

Death of Mao's Widow.

On 14 May Jiang Qing, Mao's widow and a member of the 1970s "gang of four", committed suicide. The official announcement of her death was delayed until the second anniversary of the Tiananmen Square massacre on 4 June had passed. In Beijing there were limited student demonstrations to commemorate the 1989 events.

On 10 August China agreed in principle to sign the 1968 Nuclear Non-proliferation Treaty. But on 13 November, as Beijing prepared for what was seen as a diplomatically significant visit by US Secretary of State James Baker, an internal government document was leaked which alleged the United States was seeking the collapse of communism in China. The document appeared to represent the view of many senior government officials. Mr Baker left Beijing on 17 November declaring that a gulf in relations remained. There was, however, a distinct improvement in relations with offshore Taiwan, with proposals in February 1992 for China and Taiwan to open liaison offices in each other's capitals.

Economic Liberalisation in China.

China's parliament, the National People's Congress, met from 12 March to 3 April 1992. The meeting closed with some embarrassment for China's premier, Li Peng, as his final statement was strengthened by the Congress to emphasise the free market reforms advocated by Deng Xiaoping. Li was known to prefer a greater element of state planning. China's economic liberation bore fruit with the renewal of relations with South Korea on 24 August. In September China's central bank announced plans to create a stock exchange regulatory body modelled on the US Securities and Exchange Commission.

The 14th Party Congress.

The 14th Party Congress held from 12–18 October, the first since 1987, reaffirmed the policy of market-oriented economic reform combined with strict party control. This was underlined by general secretary Jiang Zemin who stressed the need for social and political stability if economic reform was to succeed. The Central Committee selected by

the Congress balanced reformers and more traditional hardliners. The Congress set an annual growth rate target of 9% for the 1991–95 five-year plan, another rebuff for premier Li who favoured a more moderate 6%.

The March 1993 Congress.

At the opening session of the National People's Congress on 15 March 1993 Mr. Li, despite his identification with conservative forces in the Communist Party, outlined a sweeping programme of economic change aimed at strengthening market reforms and re-structuring the state sector by reducing the number of government departments and cutting the bureaucracy by 25%.

The Congress continued with the election on 27 March of Jiang Zemin—the party general secretary and chairman of the central military commission—as state president to succeed Yang Shangkun. On 29 March a new constitution was approved, China's fifth since 1949. China's economic reforms were formally enshrined in the constitution as a move to a "socialist market economy". Closer relations with Taiwan appeared to be developing following meetings in Singapore between two organisations representing the respective governments. Agreement was reached on 29 April on educational, cultural and scientific co-operation.

Unrest in Sichuang and Tibet.

Resentment among China's 800 million peasants that their incomes were lagging behind those of factory workers and entrepreneurs expressed itself in riots in early June in Sichuan province. China's cabinet, the State Council, responded by ordering local officials to reduce taxes previously imposed. There were also clashes in Qinghai province on 7 October between thousands of Moslem demonstrators and Chinese troops. The demonstrations followed increasingly violent incidents over the previous five years.

The government also faced demonstrations in Tibet, which had been annexed by China in 1959. On 24 May Tibetans began protesting in the capital Lhasa against high prices in largely Chinese-owned shops. The clashes with Chinese troops lasted five days and spread beyond the capital. Already, on 27 April, Tibet's exiled political and spiritual leader, the Dalai Lama, had appealed to US President Clinton to urge China to stop moving ethnic Chinese into Lhasa, reducing the ethnic Tibetans to a minority. On 2 June Tibet's governor offered talks with the Dalai Lama, provided the claim for independence was abandoned. Discussions were reportedly held in August but no details emerged.

In the long-delayed Communist Party central committee plenary session which opened on 11 November, reformists attempted to push through tax reforms favouring central government. A final communiqué issued on 14 November announced sweeping reforms in state industries, banking, taxation, social security, foreign trade and investment, and officially abandoned communism. But on 21 December the government reimposed price controls on 27 basic commodities because of fears that rising prices might provoke popular unrest.

An Inflationary Economy.

Currency and taxation reforms announced in December 1993 increased inflationary pressures in the economy. By January 1994, inflation reached 30% in some urban areas. Premier Li Peng instituted price controls on 20 basic commodities in mid-March in recognition of widespread concerns about inflation. Economic development became entangled with human rights issues when US Secretary of State Warren Christopher visited China in March and suggested that concessions on "most favoured nation" trading status depended on China's human rights record. Mr Li said China would never accept American "human rights concepts".

Crackdown on Dissidents.

A crackdown on dissidents came in April – an open show of defiance to the United States. As the anniversary of the 1989 Tiananmen Square massacre approached, the government extended its powers to detain and restrict dissidents. Nevertheless, on 26 May President Clinton announced his decision to renew "most favoured nation" status and abandoned any linkage with human rights. China introduced further laws against dissidents on 4 June. However, on 5 July the National People's Congress approved a new labour law which included an eight-hour day, a minimum wage and improved conditions. The law, which came into effect on 1 January 1995, ended the guarantee of a job for life.

Nine dissidents who had called for trade union rights and political reforms were imprisoned on 16 December. Several were prominent members of the Free Labour Union of China, a group set up in 1991. China's growing emphasis on internal repression and an intensified nationalism in foreign affairs were seen in part as a result of the declining health of the 90–year old Deng Xiaoping.

China after Deng.

As Mr Deng's health was rumoured to be declining, Communist Party leader Jiang Zemin consolidated his authority and prepared the framework for an orderly transition. In March 1995, he succeeded in appointing two supporters as vice premiers, despite some opposition from delegates to the National People's Congress. Mr Jiang had also succeeded in creating a power base through a series of promotions. A former mayor of Shanghai, Mr Jiang took over running the party after the 1989 Tiananmen Square massacre. The resignation of Chen Xitong, Secretary of the Beijing Party Committee, was further evidence of the power struggle beginning in China in early summer 1995.

HONG KONG

Hong Kong was first occupied by the British as a trading post in January 1841 and China's cession of the island to Britain was confirmed by the Treaty of Nanking in 1842. South Kowloon and Stonecutters Island were ceded by China in the Treaty of Peking in 1860, and in 1898 the New Territories, which consist of the area north of Kowloon and other islands around Hong Kong, were leased to Britain for 99 years. Hong Kong was occupied by the Japanese from 1941 to 1945. The approaching expiry of the lease on the New Territories led to the initiation of diplomatic discussions between Britain and China on the future of Hong Kong in 1979 with a visit by Sir Murray MacLehose, governor of Hong Kong, to Beijing. Mrs. Thatcher herself visited Beijing in 1982. Britain had initially taken the line that the 19th century "unequal treaties", as the Chinese termed them, were not invalid, but it was forced to concede that sovereignty over Hong Kong would have to be surrendered.

The 1984 Agreement.

A new phase in the negotiations began in July 1983 and by December Britain had also given up its proposal for retaining an administrative role in Hong Kong after 1997. Deng Xiaoping insisted that an agreement should be reached by September 1984, and on 26 September the Sino-British declaration on the future of Hong Kong was initialled in Beijing. China will resume the exercise of sovereignty from 1 July 1997. Except in foreign and defence affairs, however, the Hong Kong Special Administrative Region will have a considerable degree of autonomy, and for at least fifty years the social and economic system and "life-style" of Hong Kong will remain unchanged.

In 1985 the British colonial administration began to give way to a form of representative government. In September indirect elections were held for 24 seats to represent professionals, local councils and special interest groups on the new 56-seat Legislative Council. The remaining seats were filled by government officials and appointees. The first session of the Council was held at the end of October.

The Chinese National People's Congress formally approved the 1984 agreement on the future of Hong Kong in April 1985, but the Chinese government was unhappy about the introduction of democracy into the colony. China stressed that in 1997 sovereignty passes to her and not to the people of Hong Kong, whose form of government would finally be decided by Beijing. In December 1985 a senior Chinese official, Mr Ji Pengfei, visited Hong Kong but pointedly did not formally meet the Legislative Council.

In October 1986 Queen Elizabeth II paid a successful visit to Hong Kong after her tour of China. Following the death of the governor, Sir Edward Youde, Sir David Wilson was appointed to be his successor in January 1987.

China's Attitude to Democratisation.

In January 1987 the important step was taken of promoting a group of Hong Kong citizens to senior civil service posts to emphasise the role of the local population in the last phase of British rule. At the same time the government was working on a Green Paper discussing the options for representative government. In March 1987 an independent body was established to sound out public opinion in Hong Kong on political reform.

Hong Kong had continued to enjoy an economic boom in 1986, but uncertainty about the future was evident in the increasing number of citizens emigrating (some 10,000 to Canada during the year) or applying for second passports. Anxiety increased after Hu Yaobang was brought down by conservative forces in China in January 1987. Although the Chinese government assured Hong Kong that nothing had changed, a more decidedly frosty reception was expected for the Green Paper's proposals on democratisation.

A Green Paper on representative institutions was published by the government of Hong Kong in May 1987. It emphasised that there were now divided opinions over the desirability of direct elections in the immediate future. After consultations the White Paper published in February 1988 ruled out direct elections, albeit for only 10 of the 56 seats on the Legislative Council, until 1991. Voting again took place in September 1988 for the 24 seats on the Legislative Council representing professionals, local councils and special interest groups.

The Basic Law.

Prospects for the development of truly democratic government in Hong Kong did not look particularly encouraging following a meeting in January 1989 of representatives drafting the Basic Law relating to the territory's administration after 1997. The draft was generally conservative. It proposed that the chief executive of the Hong Kong Special Administrative Region should be chosen by an electoral college for the first three five-year terms of office. Only after fifteen years would a referendum be held to decide whether the chief executive should be elected by universal suffrage.

The convulsions in China, led by mass student protests, once again cast major doubts on future stability in Hong Kong itself.

Repercussions of Tiananmen Square.

The 1989 upheavals in China had immediate repercussions in Hong Kong, which faced absorption by its Communist neighbour in 1997. Hong Kong stock market prices fell by 22% on 5 June as troops moved against protesters in Beijing. There were two days of protests by hundreds of thousands of demonstrators and a general strike on 7 June.

On 5 June Mrs Thatcher said events in Beijing could not alter Britain's obligation to cede Hong Kong. She refused to guarantee refuge to the 3·25 million of Hong Kong's 5·7 million citizens who had a right to British passports. On 2 July the Foreign Secretary, Sir Geoffrey Howe, faced angry crowds in the colony as he repeated that Britain could accommodate only a few who had been "of service" to the UK.

British Citizenship Scheme.

Early in 1990 Britain promised legislation to allow entry to 50,000 selected citizens and their families after 1997 should China threaten their liberties. Britain also promised a bill of rights and a Basic Law to establish democratic government. But as negotiations with China on the Basic Law continued, 1,000 people a day were leaving Hong Kong by February 1990. China refused to accept proposals that Hong Kong's 60 strong legislative council should have half its members directly elected by universal suffrage by 1997 and be fully elected by 2003, insisting initially on 18 and agreeing in March to 20. The attempt to draft a bill of rights appeared stalemated by the difficulty of reconciling local demands for legally guaranteed human rights after 1997 with China's suspicion of any such legislation.

When the deadline under the British citizenship scheme expired on 28 February 1991 only approximately 60,000 applications had been received rather than the expected 300,000. Residents who might have qualified apparently preferred to seek entry to Canada, Australia or the US.

The 1991 Elections.

In March 1991 Hong Kong held its first elections for 19 consultative district boards, the lowest tier of a limited democratic system. Pro-democratic liberal candidates won 80 out of 274 seats, the Federation of Trade Unions and the business-based Liberal Democratic Federation—both of which favoured closer links with China—took 50 each. Turnout was only 32·5%.

On 4 September visiting British prime minister John Major stressed his commitment to democracy but Martin Lee, leader of the United Democrats—Hong Kong's largest party—said Britain showed a "lack of concern for the rights and freedom" of the Hong Kong people. The United Democrats emerged as the strongest party in elections for 18 of the 60 seats on the Legislative Council on 15 September, the first direct elections in 150 years of British rule. They won 12 seats and other pro-democracy parties took the remaining six.

In November China appeared to be reneging on guarantees it had made in the 1984 Sino-British agreement on the transfer of power. On 21 November there were suggestions that China's parliament, the National People's Congress, would determine the power and functions of a post-handover court of final appeal. On 4 December the Hong Kong legislature overwhelmingly rejected a Sino-British agreement on the structure of the court. Opposition leader Mr. Lee said the Legislative Council refused to be a "rubber stamp".

The Appointment of Chris Patten.

On 9 July 1992 former Tory Party chairman Mr. Chris Patten took office as governor. Mr. Patten announced his plans on 7 October for the transition to China's takeover in 1997, including extended democracy, despite China's declared opposition. He proposed increasing the number of Legislative Council seats directly elected from 18 to 20, with 10 remaining indirectly elected and 20 selected from constituencies. This would expand the electorate from 110,000 to 2·7 million. Increased public spending on education, welfare and environmental protection was also promised.

China denounced the political proposals as "irresponsible and imprudent" while Hong Kong's pro-democracy leaders called for full democracy. Mr. Patten made no progress on the issue during a visit to Beijing from 20–23 October but the Legislative Council approved the proposals on 11 November. China responded by threatening to repudiate all commercial agreements made by the Hong Kong government. Nonetheless, on 1 December Mr. Patten announced that he would submit more detailed plans to the Legislative Council in February 1993 but the formal tabling of a bill was postponed until 12 March in a vain effort to secure China's agreement. China's premier Li Peng responded immediately at the opening session of the National People's Congress on 15 March, denouncing the bill.

Growing Chinese Hostility.

Chinese attacks on Mr. Patten continued through March and April, with charges that his proposals violated the 1990 Basic Law agreement. However, on 22 April talks were resumed. They made slow progress and Mr. Patten threatened to submit the reforms to the Legislative Council regardless of China's views. He offered a compromise proposal on 14 October that local and Legislative Council elections could be discussed separately. Argument now centred on 1995 elections for the 60-member Legislative Council, whose term of office would continue for two years after handover in 1997. China alleged that Mr. Patten's democracy plans were an attempt at undermining China's influence

and formally broke off negotiations on 2 December following Mr. Patten's announcement that he was launching the first stage of his reforms. China said it would reverse reforms that took place without its agreement.

The crisis intensified when, following Mr. Patten's tabling of reform legislation, China declared an end on 15 December to all co-operation and announced it would not recognise the results of either local or Legislative Council elections but would hold fresh elections on handover in 1997. While the pro-Beijing Liberal Party expressed dismay, the pro-democracy United Democrats insisted that Mr. Patten's proposals did not go far enough. Mr. Patten urged a resumption of negotiations on 24 January 1994 but insisted he would continue with reform whether China agreed or not.

Recent Events.

The first part of Mr Patten's political reform package was approved by the Legislative Council on 24 February. China said this ended any possibility of further negotiations, adding that bodies elected under the reforms would be "definitely terminated" in 1997. On 18 April the United Democrats and Meeting Point announced their merger into a Democratic Party. Two days later businessmen and members of the professional community concerned to promote harmonious relations with China formed the Hong Kong Progressive Alliance.

An official visit in May by the senior Chinese official with responsibility for Hong Kong affairs, Lu Ping, was marked by his refusal to meet Mr Patten on the grounds that he was "too busy". On 31 August China instituted laws confirming that the entire Hong Kong political structure would be removed in 1997. Nevertheless, elections were held on 18 September for 346 district board seats. On a 33% turnout, almost half the seats were won by Independents. The Democratic Party took 75 seats, the pro-China Democratic Alliance (DAB) 37 and the pro-business Liberal Party 18. Lu Ping declared that China would appoint an interim Legislative Council in 1997 and scrap Mr Patten's reforms.

JAPAN.

The February 1990 Elections.

At the general election on 18 February 1990 the Socialists failed to capitalise on a year of scandals. 73·27% of the 90 million eligible voters turned out. The LDP, with over 25 million votes, took almost 50% of the popular vote, while the Socialists gained a little under 25%. The Socialists had expanded at the expense of rival opposition parties rather than taking votes from the LDP. The LDP returned with 275 MPs but support from 15 of the 21 independents elected put their new parliamentary strength at 290, only five short of the pre-election position. The Socialists won 136 seats. Although Mr Kaifu's personal position in the LDP now seemed secure he faced an opposition majority in the Upper House.

The Kaifu Administration.

By June 1990 Mr Kaifu's personal popularity in an opinion poll stood at 63%, the highest figure for a prime minister since polls began in 1964. LDP leaders visited North Korea from 24–28 September and, after apologising for the "unhappy past which Japan had inflicted on Korea", signed an agreement to ease relations between the two states. But Mr Kaifu faced the continuing problem of an upper house controlled by the opposition, with Komeito ("clean government party") holding the casting vote. An attempt to build a centre-right LDP-Komeito coalition foundered in December 1990, partly because of continuing revelations of financial impropriety. The position of Mr Kaifu, faced by opponents in the faction-ridden LDP, appeared precarious. On 29 December he unexpectedly reshuffled his cabinet, taking the opportunity to strengthen his position in the wake of public indignation over a former minister's involvement in tax evasion. He replaced 17 members, many of whom had been linked with the Recruit scandal.

Mr Kaifu was thwarted in his attempt to deploy

troops in the Gulf by parliamentary and public opposition, the SDP declaring it would violate Japan's pacifist constitution. The proposal was also rejected by Komeito, to which Mr Kaifu still looked for possible support. Instead, Japan pledged a $9 billion aid package restricted largely to food and medical supplies. But LDP in-fighting continued as Mr Kaifu faced obstacles in his attempt to secure tax increases to fund the package.

Elections and Scandals.

Mr. Kaifu was strengthened by a creditable LDP performance in the April 1991 local elections. Support for the opposition Social Democrats fell and on 21 June the party's leader, Takako Doi, announced her resignation. But in July the government faced a financial scandal involving Japan's leading securities companies. Finance minister Ryutaro Hashimoto resigned in October, apologising for the scandals that had emerged during his period of office. On 4 October Mr. Kaifu, having lost support in bitter party faction conflicts, unexpectedly stood down as LDP leader. Kiichi Miyazawa, who had resigned as finance minister in 1988 in the Recruit scandal, emerged as his successor.

Japan under Miyazawa.

Mr. Miyazawa became prime minister on 5 November and formed a cabinet including ministers who had resigned following previous scandals. Mr. Miyazawa promised to clean up Japanese politics and ordered a 10% ministerial pay cut.

There had been growing international concern at Japan's failure to play a part in the world order commensurate with its economic strength. In response the Diet (lower house) passed a United Nations Peacekeeping Operations Co-operation Bill on 3 December allowing troops to be deployed abroad for the first time since World War Two in a peacekeeping role.

On 13 January 1992 a close aide of Mr. Miyazawa was arrested after admitting receiving payments from a steel company. Mr. Miyazawa was further weakened by an overwhelming LDP by-election defeat on 9 February. Allegations of financial scandal involving politicians, businessmen and criminal gangs emerged in February, prompting speculation that almost 40 years of LDP rule were coming to an end. The leading opposition parties made moves towards forming a united social democratic slate of candidates for the July elections to the upper house of the Diet.

The Nikkei Collapse.

Further bad news for Mr. Miyazawa's government came on 11 March 1992, when the Tokyo stock exchange Nikkei index fell to its lowest figure since the October 1990 crash. There was a slowing down of Japan's growth rate, with leading electronics companies hit particularly hard. But Mr. Miyazawa achieved a political success on 15 June when the Diet approved a bill authorising future deployment of troops abroad as members of UN peace-keeping forces. The Liberal Democratic Party's position was further strengthened on 26 July when it regained control of the Diet Upper House. The Nikkei index fell to its lowest level since 1986 on 29 July. The government's response was an $87 billion economic stimulus programme on 29 August to encourage growth by increased public expenditure on infrastructure, education and housing, together with loans to smaller businesses. Despite this, confidence within the business community was reported at its lowest for 15 years in September.

The Shin Kanemaru Scandal.

Mr. Miyazawa was touched by scandal on 27 August when Shin Kanemaru, head of the LDP's most influential faction, resigned as vice-chairman of the LDP after admitting receiving a $4 million political payment from a transport company. Mr. Kanemaru's support for Mr. Miyazawa had been crucial in the latter's successful leadership bid in 1991. A public outcry forced Mr. Kanemaru's resignation from the Diet on 14 October. Continuing revelations now became entangled with the government's plans to stimulate the economy as the opposition refused to discuss them unless leading

LDP members testified to a Diet committee investigating financial connections between the LDP, business and organised crime. Former premier Noboru Takeshita and Mr. Kanemaru testified at the end of November. On 1 December the Lower House of the Diet approved the government's economic proposals.

On 6 January 1993 the Socialists elected a new leader, Sadao Yamahana. Further pressure on premier Kiichi Miyazawa to initiate political reform came on 6 March with the arrest of Mr. Kanemaru for tax evasion. The ruling LDP's position was further weakened by continuing recession and on 2 April a public spending package of $118 billion was proposed to boost the faltering economy. The LDP's reluctance to confront its own corruption came to a head with the government's loss of a confidence motion on 18 June by 225–220 as 39 LDP members voted with the opposition. On 21 June ten LDP members left to form the New Initiative Party. Two days later a further 44 LDP members set up the Renewal Party under the leadership of Tsutumo Hata.

The 1993 Election Upheaval.

The LDP lost its majority in elections for the 511-seat Diet on 18 July. The LDP took 223 seats (as against 275 in 1990). Three new parties that had emerged from the LDP won a total of 103 seats, the Renewal Party taking 55, the Japan New Party 35 and the New Initiative Party 13. The Socialists, undergoing their own internal problems, failed to capitalise on the LDP misfortunes, taking only 70 seats. Yohei Kono replaced Mr. Miyazawa as LDP leader. On 6 August New Japan Party leader Morihiro Hosokawa became prime minister of a seven party coalition government.

The government placed reform bills before parliament proposing the introduction of single member constituencies and proportional representation, state subsidies to parties and tighter controls over political donations. But arguments within the coalition, together with resistance from the LDP, slowed their progress. Coalition confidence was shaken when Ichiro Ozawa, the influential secretary-general of the Renewal Party, admitted receiving money from a construction company at the centre of the corruption scandal. The four reform bills were passed by the lower house on 18 November.

The Changing Political Scene.

Defence minister Keisuke Nakanishi's resignation on 2 January 1994, following his suggestion that the clause in the constitution outlawing the use of force and a standing army should be reconsidered, further delayed already slow progress in the upper house. Socialists protested at his statement and the LDP used it as an opportunity to paralyse debate. On 21 January the reform package was defeated following the defection of 17 Socialists. Mr. Hosokawa threatened to resign and on 28 January the reforms were accepted following a last minute compromise with LDP leader Mr. Kono.

But the government's problems were not over. On 4 February Mr. Hosokawa was forced to abandon a £93 billion economic reflation programme involving a shift from direct to indirect taxation following its rejection by five of his coalition partners. A new storm began on 9 February when he was accused of having accepted bribes from a company at the heart of Japan's corruption scandal. There were, in addition, fears of a trade war when discussions between Mr. Hosokawa and US President Clinton on 11 February failed to resolve a £49 billion trade imbalance. As the coalition appeared increasingly fragmented, on 14 February the leaders of the Renewal Party and Komeito proposed the formation of a new centre-right party.

The Hata Administration.

Japanese politics was thrown into further confusion on 8 April when Mr. Hosokawa resigned as prime minister following corruption allegations against him that had paralysed all government activity. Mr. Hosokawa was accused of accepting large loans in the 1980s.

Eventually he was succeeded by Tsutomu Hata, the former foreign minister. However, the socialists refused to support him and a minority government ensued.

The survival of Mr Hata's administration seemed in doubt when the SDJP's 74 members withdrew from the coalition on 26 April, removing his overall majority. Mr Hata's cabinet, announced on 28 April, contained a majority of Shinseito members. But on 7 May his justice minister, Shigeto Nagano, was forced to resign following a storm of protest over his denial of the 1937 "Rape of Nanking" in which 300,000 Chinese had been murdered.

Mr Hata, in his address to the Diet on 10 May, appealed for opposition co-operation on political and tax reforms. The main parties agreed to allow his government to survive long enough to introduce a budget. But, following the approval of a budget on 7 June, the LDP threatened Mr Hata with a no confidence motion and he resigned on 25 June. The Diet appointed SDPJ leader Tomiichi Murayama Japan's first socialist premier by 261 votes to 214 on 29 June. The cabinet he announced the following day, while including SDPJ and Sakigake members, was dominated by the LDP.

Japan under Murayama.

An electoral reform package was passed by both houses of the Diet in November. The legislation, which was due to come into effect on 25 December, replaced the multi-member electoral system with single member constituencies elected by proportional representation and introduced state financing of political parties. Tax reductions were brought in to boost the economy and, by encouraging imports, to placate Japan's international trading partners.

Meanwhile, the opposition redeployed its forces into a single party. On 10 December Shinshinto (New Frontier Party) was formally inaugurated. It was an amalgamation of nine separate parties (including Shinseito, Komeito, the Japan New Party, and the Democratic Socialist Party) with 214 Diet members. Shinshinto was led by former premier Toshiki Kaifu, with Ichiro Ozawa as secretary-general.

The Kobe Earthquake.

The port city of Kobe was struck by Japan's worst earthquake for half a century on 17 January 1995. Over 5,000 were killed, 300,000 made homeless and almost 90,000 buildings destroyed. The government was criticised for its handling of the aftermath of the disaster.

Tokyo suffered a horrific terrorist attack when nerve gas was released into the capital's underground system on 20 March, killing ten people and injuring 5,000. There were early suspicions that the perpetrators were members of an extreme religious sect, the Aum Shinrikyo.

KOREA (NORTH AND SOUTH).

In May 1991 North Korea announced it would seek UN membership, abandoning its former opposition to the two states having separate seats. North and South Korea took their seats at the UN on 17 September. President Roh presented a proposal for Korean unification to the General Assembly on 24 September. The prime ministers of both states met in Pyongyang on 22–24 October and on 13 December North and South Korea signed a non-aggression treaty, pledging to respect each other's economic and social systems and to negotiate a peace treaty to replace the 1953 armistice. But fears that North Korea was close to producing a nuclear weapon remained an obstacle. On 18 December President Roh declared the South free of nuclear arms and on 31 January 1992 North Korea signed the International Atomic Energy Agency inspection accords.

Growing North-South Links.

In March 1992 the South Korean cabinet was reshuffled following the ruling Democratic Liberal Party's loss of its National Assembly majority. In April the two main opposition parties—the Democratic Party and the National Unification Party—began boycotting the Assembly in protest against the postponement of local elections until 1995. There were, however, further signs of co-operation between North and South Korea on 14 March when

they agreed to mutual inspection of suspected nuclear weapons sites. On 7 May southern premier Chung Won Shik and northern premier Yon Hyong Muk announced an agreement to reunite relatives in both parts of the country who had not met since the Korean War. Agreement in principle to re-establish air, land and sea links followed on 28 July, while South Korea established diplomatic relations with China on 24 August.

The Advent of Kim Young Sam.

The South Korean opposition parties ended their Assembly boycott on 18 September when President Roh announced his resignation as head of the Democratic Liberal Party. But on 9 October the party's chairman resigned after conflict with the DLP presidential candidate Kim Young Sam. Further resignations culminated in the creation of a New Korea Party by DLP dissidents on 25 October. In the presidential elections on 18 December Mr. Kim—following a bitterly fought campaign—won a comfortable victory, taking over 42% of the vote against six other candidates.

As South Korea's first civilian president since 1961, Mr. Kim attempted to re-assert political control over the armed forces by dismissing eight senior officers in March and April 1993. Kim Il Sung's son, Kim Jong Il, was appointed chairman of North Korea's National Defence Committee on 9 April, a sign that he was his father's most likely successor. On 12 December President Kim's younger brother, 71-year-old Kim Yong-ju was appointed vice-president following 18 years of political exile.

The Nuclear Confrontation.

On 11 June 1993 North Korea suspended withdrawal from the Nuclear Non-proliferation Treaty and agreed to resume contacts with the International Atomic Energy Agency (IAEA). But in November North Korea refused to allow inspectors into the country. President Clinton threatened the possible use of force. North Korea agreed to inspection at seven nuclear facilities on 5 January 1994, but refused access to two further sites, arousing suspicions of weapons production capability.

Tension intensified when North Korea denounced the IAEA and said any further pressure would be met with "a resolute measure". North Korea threatened war at talks with the south on 19 March, warning that Seoul would become a "sea of fire". In response, President Clinton agreed to deploy anti-missile batteries in the South, while South Korea's 650,000-strong army was placed on alert.

On 24 March Russia proposed an international conference to resolve the dispute and supported a planned UN resolution threatening economic sanctions. North Korea replied that sanctions would be construed as a declaration of war, At China's request sanctions were not referred to in the UN Security Council resolution asking North Korea to allow the IAEA inspectors to complete their work. North Korea nonetheless rejected the request and on 4 April declared that it would resume its "peaceful nuclear activities".

Meanwhile, in South Korea, President Kim Young Sam's anti-political corruption reforms came into effect on 16 March 1994. The government and opposition also reached agreement on revising the National Security Law, which was much criticised on human rights grounds. On 22 April premier Lee Yung Duk was replaced by Lee Hoi Chang. The National Assembly approved the change by 170 votes to 10, but proceedings were boycotted by the Democratic Party, the main opposition grouping, on the grounds that the move would weaken the anti-corruption campaign.

Death of Kim Il-Sung.

President Kim Il-Sung died on 8 July. The transition of power to his son, Kim Jong Il, appeared far from smooth, with hints of a power struggle. It was not until October that Kim's hold seemed secure. Improving relations with South Korea and the United States seemed in doubt as meetings agreed by the former president were abandoned. However, on 10 September North Korea allowed IAEA inspectors into two further nuclear sites. In October North Korea agreed to halt her nuclear programme in return for American technical aid and improved diplomatic relations. On 7 November the South Korean president lifted the ban on trade with and investment in the North.

North Korea formally ended its nuclear programme on 29 November. But the new accord with the United States was threatened when an American helicopter was shot down in December, killing one crew member. The pilot was released after two weeks of delicate negotiations. Doubts about Kim Jong Il's position resurfaced when he failed to make the traditional New Year Day address on 1 January 1995.

VIETNAM.

On 5 April 1989 Vietnam announced that 45,000 troops would withdraw unconditionally from Cambodia by 30 September, ending an occupation lasting over ten years in which over 25,000 had been killed and 55,000 seriously wounded. Vietnam proposed the formation of an international commission to monitor both the withdrawal and an end to foreign arming of anti-Cambodian government guerrillas. The last troops left on 26 September. But within a month several thousand had returned in the guise of "advisors", as Vietnam admitted in February 1990, to assist a Cambodian regime still vulnerable to guerrilla attack.

Vietnam made attempts in 1989 to improve relations with the United States. As a token of good will Vietnam returned the bodies in April and June of a number of US troops killed in the war, though the government denied claims that Vietnam continued to hold American prisoners. Vietnam also allowed 10,000 former political prisoners and their families to emigrate to the United States.

The Modernisation of the Economy.

Domestically, the communist party took steps to modernise the economy and to confront growing popular dissatisfaction symbolised by the thousands of "boat people" fleeing Vietnam. On 6 March 1989 party secretary-general Nguyen Van Linh appointed Pham Van Kai, a leading advocate of economic reform, to the post of state planning minister. In December 1989 the Politburo, recognising the fate of European communist governments, made moves to encourage internal party democracy, wider debate and a more pragmatic approach. Open attacks on party privileges and corruption appeared in the press. Party secretary Nguyen Van Linh was expected to resign at a central committee plenum to be held in March 1990.

The Central Committee session ended on 27 March 1990. Nguyen Van Linh retained his post to ensure party unity. The following day the expulsion was announced of Tran Xuan Bach, a prominent reformist, from both the ruling Politburo and the Central Committee. He had pressed for rapid reform and openly supported events in Eastern Europe. The Central Committee communique nevertheless reaffirmed its commitment to economic and political change.

On 29 September Foreign Minister Nguyen Co Thach met US Secretary of State James Baker, the highest level meeting between the two states since the ending of the Vietnam war and a sign of improved relations. Discussion centred on moves to end the conflict in Cambodia, where Mr Thach had earlier acknowledged that Vietnam military "advisers" remained.

The 1991 Party Congress.

At the opening session of the Communist Party congress on 24 June 1991 secretary-general Nguyen Van Linh reaffirmed the party's determination to retain power, but acknowledged the need for economic liberalisation. He also called for improved relations with the United States and China. During the congress he stood down on age and health grounds, to be succeeded by Do Muoi. Nguyen Co Thach resigned as foreign minister and Politburo member. Also leaving the Politburo were President Vo Chi Cong and interior minister Mai Chi Tho. There were further government changes when, on 9 August, Vo Van Kiet—an economic liberal—replaced Do Muoi as prime minister.

Relations with America and China.

The quest for improved relations with the United States and China bore fruit. On 23 October Vietnam foreign minister Nguyen Mah Cam and US Secretary of State James Baker agreed that the signing of the Cambodian peace treaty opened the way towards normalisation of relations. On 5 November, following a visit to Beijing by Do Muoi and Vo Van Kiet, diplomatic links were restored with China. Mr. Kiet also conducted a round of visits to other southeast Asian states, the first by a Vietnamese premier since 1978, seeking aid for development. A new draft constitution unveiled on 30 December reiterated the move towards free market reforms, proposed an increase in the powers of the elected National Assembly, but reaffirmed the determination to continue with one-party rule.

The 1992 Constitution.

In April 1992 the 395-member National Assembly adopted a new constitution reaffirming the Communist Party's determination to continue market-orientated economic development under strict party control. On 23 September the National Assembly elected the conservative General Le Duc Anh as state president. The following day the reformist Vo Van Kiet was re-elected as prime minister.

The End of Isolation.

French President Mitterrand visited Vietnam from 9–11 February 1993, the first Western leader to do so since unification in 1976. The visit signalled the end of Vietnam's international economic isolation. Free market reforms continued with new measures announced on 3 June to encourage the privatisation of over 10,000 state enterprises. The United States refused to end its economic embargo imposed in 1964, but on 2 July President Clinton withdrew opposition to multi-lateral loans and, as a result, donor countries promised Vietnam $1·86 billion in aid and credits in November. However, argument over the pace of economic reform caused rifts within the Communist Party and a special party congress due to be held in November was continually postponed. Opening the national assembly session in December, premier Vo Van Kiet said the economy was growing by 8% a year while inflation had been reduced to 4%. On 3 February 1994 the US trade embargo was finally lifted, though President Clinton stressed this did not mean diplomatic relations would be normalised.

Relations with America.

Improved relations with the United States were symbolised from 26 February to 20 March 1994 by a joint search for US servicemen still missing from the Vietnam War. This was accompanied by discussions on financial claims and on the opening of liaison offices in each other's capitals. In April Australian premier Paul Keating met Vietnamese leaders and promised a doubling of aid over the coming four years. Following agreement with the United States on financial claims, liaison offices were opened at the end of January 1995.

CAMBODIA (KAMPUCHEA).

The Peace Accord.

Thirteen years of war ended with the signing in Paris on 23 October 1991 of a peace treaty by the SNC members and 18 other states. Under the treaty, elections would be held in 1993 to a 120-seat assembly which would draw up a new constitution. In the interim the United Nations would share power with the SNC, with direct UN control over some ministries and the deployment of a monitoring force.

Leaders of the factions now began their return to the capital, Phnom Penh. Prince Sihanouk arrived on 14 November and was declared interim head of state on 20 November. KPNLF leader Son Sann returned to Cambodia on 21 November. On 27 November Khieu Samphan, the Khmer Rouge leader, returned to Phnom Penh but was attacked by angry crowds and fled to Bangkok. The first meeting of the SNC in Cambodia was delayed as Khieu Samphan refused to return in the face of demonstrations which were initially directed against the Khmer Rouge but which broadened into protests against government corruption and the privatisation of state assets. As the demonstrations continued and the SNC appeared to wield little real authority, the government closed schools and colleges in Phnom Penh on 23 December.

UNTAC Problems.

The head of the UN peace-keeping force which was to administer the transition to democracy arrived in Cambodia on 15 March 1992. But as he arrived, Khmer Rouge troops were attacking in Kompong Tom province in an attempt to consolidate their territory before the UN force was deployed. The UN negotiated a ceasefire on 1 April. Representatives of the four factions making up the Supreme National Council signed UN charters guaranteeing civil, political, economic and cultural rights on 20 April. But on 10 June the Khmer Rouge refused to comply with the 1991 agreement to place its forces in camps under UN supervision until it was convinced that all Vietnamese troops had left Cambodia. Fighting was reported between the Khmer Rouge and coalition forces.

A further obstacle was placed in the way of peace efforts when, on 4 January 1993, Prince Sihanouk announced that he would end co-operation with the UN Transitional Authority in Cambodia (UNTAC) and with the government.

The elections finally took place in May 1993 but seemed to solve nothing. Allegations of fraud and intimidation were made and, amidst all these, the only likely victor (as much by intrigue as the ballot box) appeared to be Prince Sihanouk.

The Return of Sihanouk.

Prince Sihanouk declared himself head of state on 5 June and proposed a transitional coalition government of the Cambodian People's Party (the CPP, which gained 38·2% of the vote in the May elections) and the United National Front for an Independent, Neutral, Peaceful and Co-operative Cambodia (Funinpec, led by Sihanouk's son Prince Norodom Ranariddh, which had won 45·5%). Both parties agreed to work together on 18 June, dividing cabinet seats equally, with Prince Sihanouk as "chief of state", and Prince Ranariddh and CPP leader Hun Sen as co-presidents. The 120-member constituent assembly was to draft a new constitution.

In August the newly unified Cambodian Armed Forces captured two Khmer Rouge strongholds on the Thai border. Khmer Rouge president Khieu Samphan called for discussions. Despite talks with the newly titled King Sihanouk in Beijing, and an offer from him of a place in the government, Khmer Rouge forces launched an offensive in the central provinces in December.

In early February 1994 government forces captured the Khmer Rouge northern headquarters at Anlong Ven, only to lose it on 2 March. On 19 March the government announced the capture of the Khmer Rouge national headquarters at Pailin, losing it again on 19 April. Following an appeal by King Norodom Sihanouk, both sides agreed to peace talks, but these were abandoned following disputes over the venue. However, government and Khmer Rouge leaders met in the North Korean capital on 27–28 May. The king's ceasefire proposals were accepted by the government but rejected by Khmer Rouge leader Khieu Samphan.

Meanwhile, fighting continued in the west of the country, as Khmer Rouge forces advanced following their recapture of Pailin. On 7 July the National Assembly outlawed the Khmer Rouge, who responded two days later by forming a "provisional government" of national union and national salvation" based in the northern province of Prey Vihear. The government alleged on 2 January 1995 that Khmer Rouge forces had seized thousands of civilians and killed hundreds over the previous three months.

BURMA (MYANMAR).

In September 1988 student-led protests brought down the 28-year regime of General Ne Win. But at least 5,000 pro-democracy activists were killed by the military junta—the State Law and Order Restoration Council (SLORC)—which succeeded him. SLORC promised free elections and an early return to civilian rule. However, in June 1989 Aung San Suu Kyi, leader of the National League for Democracy (NLD), the main opposition grouping, was placed under house arrest. In January 1990 she, and other leading opposition figures, were banned from standing in elections to be held in May, the first for 30 years.

The NLD won 397 of the 485 National Assembly seats in elections held on 27 May. The National League took 48 seats and the military-backed National Unity Party ten. Despite promises of an early transition to civilian government, the ruling SLORC appeared reluctant to relinquish control. Fifty NLD officials were arrested following the May elections and in November two opposition leaders were imprisoned for spying. On 18 December the opposition Democratic Front of Burma—made up of the NLD and a 21-party Democratic Alliance of Burma—formed a provisional government on the edge of civil war. On 21 December SLORC outlawed the National League for Democracy.

In October 1991 the government was embarrassed by an announcement of the award of the Nobel Peace Prize to the National League for Democracy (NLD) leader, Aung San Suu Kyi, who had been under house arrest since July 1989. On 10 December students defied the military government by demonstrating against its refusal to allow her to collect the prize. In response the government ordered the closing of all higher educational institutions the following day.

On 23 April General Than Shwe was appointed head of the ruling military council and named as prime minister the following day. The release of 12 political prisoners, including Burma's last democratically-elected leader U Nu, followed. The military council declared its willingness to begin talks with opposition leaders within two months and to call a national convention within six months.

Signs of Compromise.

A suggestion of the new leadership's comparative moderation came on 2 May 1992 when opposition leader Aung San Suu Kyi, under house arrest since 1989, was reunited with her family. In September the curfew and martial law provisions imposed in 1988 were lifted and attempts made to encourage foreign investment and tourism. In January 1993 SLORC called a four-day national convention to lay down guidelines for a new constitution. The convention chairman, Major-General Myo Nyunt, insisted that the armed forces would continue to play a leading role in a new democratic system.

On 20 May US President Clinton urged the SLORC to release Aung San Suu Kyi from house arrest and to recognise her party's victory in the May 1990 elections. But on 20 July her house arrest was extended into a fifth year. On 21 July, the 7,000 strong Kachin Independence Organization, one of the guerrilla forces at the heart of anti-SLORC resistance, announced a ceasefire with the government.

The possibility of opposition leader Aung San Suu Kyi's release faded when on 15 February SLORC extended her house arrest into 1995 on the grounds that she would use her freedom to "create unrest". On 9 April the national convention formed to co-ordinate drafting of a new constitution was adjourned until 2 September. Hopes rose that Ms Suu Kyi's release might be imminent when she had discussions with two leading SLORC members on 20 September.

THE PHILIPPINES.

The May 1992 Elections.

President Aquino did not seek a second term in the 1992 presidential elections. Her preferred candidate was the former Defence Minister, General Fidel Ramos. Early returns showed considerable strength (especially in Manila) for the "Iron Lady of the East" (Miriam Santiago) campaigning on an anti-corruption ticket. Imelda Marcos trailed far behind. Eventually, as votes from the rural areas were counted, Ramos took a convincing lead.

Fidel Ramos was declared victor in the presidential election on 16 June 1992 with 5·34 million votes, 24% of the total. Miriam Santiago was second with 20% and Eduardo Cojuango took 18%. Joseph Estrada was elected vice-president. Mrs. Aquino handed over to Mr. Ramos on 30 June. President Ramos called on left and right wing guerrillas to end their armed struggle. The Communist Party was legalised in September to dissuade it from further insurgency. President Ramos also indicated a wish to renew friendly relations with the United States, suggesting that the US could station troops in the Philippines after evacuating its final base in November. In an attempt to encourage foreign investment in the economy, the government lifted exchange controls on 1 September.

Political Developments.

On 17 February 1993 charges against opposition leader Juan Ponce Enrile and Col. Gregorio Honasan of involvement in the December 1989 rebellion were dropped when prosecution witnesses failed to testify. Vice-president Joseph Estrada escaped an assassination attempt on 20 March allegedly organised by the communist New People's Army. The Communist Party itself split in July, with 40% of its members rejecting central committee authority.

As part of a campaign against corruption and human rights abuses, President Ramos dismissed 62 high-ranking police officers on 24 April. On 2 August he launched a birth control programme intended to reduce population growth from 2·48% a year (among the highest in Asia) to 2% by 1998. President Ramos said this was necessary because of growing pressure on resources but the Roman Catholic hierarchy condemned the proposal.

The 1993 Ceasefire.

A ceasefire came into force between the government and the New People's Army (NPA) in mid-December 1993. Negotiations then opened between government representatives and the National Democratic Front, the NPA political wing. On 11 January the government announced that it would attempt to negotiate a ceasefire with the Moro Islamic Liberation Front (MILF), a Muslim secessionist group. Security forces captured a leading member of the Communist Party on 4 May 1994.

INDONESIA.

Indonesia's independence from the Netherlands—proclaimed in August 1945—was formally recognised on 27 December 1949. Dr Sukarno became president. In 1957 he introduced "guided democracy", replacing the elected parliament with an appointed legislature. Following an attempted coup in 1965, the Indonesian Communist Party was banned and thousands of its supporters killed. In March 1966 the army assumed emergency powers under General Suharto. He was elected president by the People's Consultative Assembly in March 1968 and went on to be re-elected in 1973, 1978 and 1983.

President Suharto's "New Order" gave the army a pivotal place in Indonesian politics, attempting a balance between the communists on the left and Islamic fundamentalists on the right. The army was also involved in counter-insurgency operations in East Timor—which was integrated into Indonesia in July 1976 following Portugal's withdrawal in 1975—and in Irian Jaya, which Indonesia had occupied in 1963. Politics was dominated by the official party, Golkar. In 1972 four Moslem parties—Indonesia's population is 90% non-orthodox Moslem—merged into the United Development Party (PPP). President Suharto's official ideology was "Pancasilia", the tenets of which are belief in God, humanitarianism, national unity, social justice and democracy. By the mid-1980s, despite PPP fears that Pancasilia implied a one-party state and limitations on religious freedom and despite violent outbreaks in 1984, Indonesia achieved a greater degree of stability than many developing countries.

The Golkar Victory.

In general elections held in April 1987 Golkar won a landslide victory, increasing its share of the vote from 64% to 74% against a divided PPP. In March

1988 President Suharto was appointed to a fifth five-year term. There was some relaxation during 1988 of the strict military control over East Timor. But in February 1989 Indonesia suffered its most serious religious violence since 1984 when 30 people were killed in clashes between troops and Moslem rebels in southern Sumatra. On 23 February Indonesia re-established diplomatic relations with China, China pledging not to interfere in Indonesian internal affairs.

East Timor Massacre.

On 12 November 1991 troops opened fire on demonstrators at the funeral of a separatist sympathiser in East Timor. Indonesia had occupied the area in 1976 and the number of troops deployed to counter Fretelin separatist guerrillas had reached 10,000. The army admitted 50 demonstrators were killed but unofficial estimates were 180. On 13 November the army apologised and army commander Gen. Try Sutrisno promised an investigation. In February 1992 the army reported that six senior officers had been punished for the massacre.

The June 1992 Elections.

In parliamentary elections held on 9 June 1992 the ruling Golkar party retained its majority, though with a lower percentage of the vote than in 1987. Golkar took 67%, the Moslem United Development Party (PPP) 17·5%, and the Indonesian Democratic Party (PDI) 15%. During the campaign opposition candidates criticised nepotism and the lack of a free press. Golkar had pointed to the economic prosperity achieved over the past 20 years with, according to the World Bank, an annual growth rate of 6% and a reduction in those living below the poverty line from 60% in 1970 to 15% in 1990.

Security forces captured the leader of the Revolutionary Front for the Independence of East Timor (Fretilin), Jose Alexandre Gusmao, in November 1992. Over 1,000 members surrendered following his capture. His successor, Antonio Gomes da Costa, was arrested in April 1993. Gusmao was sentenced to life imprisonment on 21 May but this was reduced to 20 years by the President in August in response to world-wide protests.

President Suharto was unanimously elected for a sixth consecutive five-year term on 10 March 1993 by the appointed People's Consultative Assembly. General Try Sutrisno was elected vice-president. Both nominations had been accepted by the opposition Indonesian Democratic Party. President Suharto made sweeping cabinet changes on 17 March, dismissing 20 of the 36 ministers from their posts.

Industrial Unrest.

In his 1994 New Year message President Suharto promised greater political openness. Two weeks later the government repealed the 1986 Labour Law which had allowed military intervention in industrial disputes – a move intended to influence the United States' stance on trade concessions. Through January and February thousands of workers struck against their employers' refusal to pay a newly introduced minimum wage. The government responded by threatening to prosecute the employers. The newly formed Indonesian Prosperous Labour Union (SBSI) called a successful one-hour national strike on 11 February. But an SBSI organised strike in the Sumatran city of Medan degenerated into anti-Chinese rioting and looting on 14 April, with the Chinese accused of being the only beneficiaries of economic reform. SBSI general secretary Muchtar Pakpahan was given a three year gaol sentence on 7 November for incitement.

The End of an Era?

The promise of an end of an era came on 12 March when President Suharto announced his unwillingness to stand for a seventh consecutive term in the 1998 elections. But tension continued in East Timor, with serious clashes on 14 July 1994. The government was embarrassed by renewed riots on

12–13 November timed to coincide with the arrival of world leaders for the Asia-Pacific Economic Co-operation summit. There were further ethnic clashes in East Timor, when at least one person was killed in rioting in Dili on 2 January 1995.

AFRICA

ETHIOPIA.

The Fall of Mengistu.

On 5 March 1990 President Mengistu said Ethiopia should shift from a centralised to a more liberal mixed economy. He was also reported to favour a multi-party political system. But he clearly feared for his own survival and made a pessimistic speech at a 1 May rally. The army had suffered 30,000 casualties in three unsuccessful attempts to recapture Massawa. The EPLF was tightening its siege of Asmara where 100,000 government troops were surrounded. The USSR was increasingly distancing itself from President Mengistu. On 21 May he angered his own army commanders by announcing the execution of 12 senior officers for their involvement in a May 1989 coup attempt.

On 5 June the government announced it would cease bombing the EPLF-held port of Massawa to enable UN food aid to reach Eritrea and Tigre where 4·5 million faced starvation. But by December 1990, when 6 million were threatened by an almost total crop failure in Eritrea and parts of Tigre, Massawa had still not opened, though negotiations continued between the government, the UN and the EPLF. In February 1991 the Ethiopian People's Revolutionary Democratic Front, a coalition headed by the Tigray People's Liberation Front, mounted an offensive that succeeded in severing three strategic roads to Addis Ababa. In May 1991 the revolt came to a climax. Mengistu fled the country and, shortly afterwards, triumphant rebel forces entered Addis Ababa.

The Abandonment of Marxism.

Peace talks between representatives of the government and its three main opponents were held in London from 26–28 May. The EPRDF leader, Mr. Meles Zenawi, returned to Ethiopia on 1 June and announced his organisation's abandonment of Marxism in favour of a free market economy and the ending of state controls over agriculture. In July representatives of 24 of Ethiopia's political and ethnic groups agreed a charter which guaranteed human rights, proposed elections in two years, and recognised the right of regional and ethnic groups to self-rule. The EPLF formed a separate provisional government in Eritrea pending a referendum on independence to be held in 1993. On 5 July the conference elected an 87-seat legislature, the Council of Representatives. The EPRDF emerged as the largest group on the Council, followed by the Oromo Liberation Front. The Council was to administer the country for two years and draft a new constitution. But with the removal of the former government's repression, there was an upsurge in ethnic conflict and banditry. By January 1992 relief operations in the east of the country were threatened by continued clashes between the EPRDF, the Oromo Liberation Front and other smaller groups.

A New Constitution.

On 13 April 1994 the council of representatives discussed the text of a draft constitution and agreed to rename the country the Federal Democratic Republic of Ethiopia. Amharic was to be the official national language but federation members would have their own official languages. Despite this apparent political success, Premier Tamirat Layne announced on 7 May that almost seven million of the country's population were suffering the effects of famine and drought and that the situation could be worse than that of 1984–85. Elections held to the 547-seat Constituent Assembly on 5 June were boycotted by several opposition parties. The ruling Ethiopian People's Revolutionary Democratic Front took 484 seats.

ERITREA.

In a three-day referendum that ended on 25 April 1993, Eritreans voted almost unanimously in favour of independence from Ethiopia. Eritrea, formerly an Italian colony and then a British protectorate, was federated to Ethiopia in 1952 and annexed ten years later. The Eritrean People's Liberation Front (EPLF) armed struggle began in 1961. The EPLF occupied the Eritrean capital Asmara in May 1991, ending 30 years of war.

Recent Developments.

In February 1994 the EPLF transformed itself into a political party named the People's Front for Democracy and Justice (PFDJ) under the continuing chairmanship of President Issaias Afewerki. It was agreed in March that the National Assembly would consist of 75 PFDJ central council members and a further 75 popularly elected members.

SOMALIA.

Mohammed Siad Barre became president after seizing power in a military coup in 1969. In May 1988 the predominantly Issaq-clan Somali National Movement (SNM) began operations against his forces in the north. In 1989 the Somali Patriotic Front (SPF)—largely made up of the Ogadeni clan—opened an offensive in the south. A third insurgent group, the mainly Hawiye clan United Somali Congress (USC), was also formed in 1989. Government forces were accused of indiscriminate bombing and shelling of civilians as they sought to subdue the rebel movements. By February 1990 an estimated 50,000 civilians had been killed and 500,000 refugees had fled the country.

Bitter Civil War.

In December 1990 a beleaguered President Barre legalised opposition parties and offered multi-party democracy. His offer was rejected by the three groups which had agreed on military and political co-operation to overthrow the president. USC forces claimed to be in control of most of the capital, Mogadishu. On 2 January 1991 President Barre appealed for a ceasefire in Mogadishu but this, and his invitation to hold talks with all opposition groups, was rejected. President Barre fled on 27 January as the insurgents took complete control of the capital. The USC announced the formation of an interim government in co-operation with the southern SPM and the northern SNM on 29 January, Ali Mahdi Mohammed taking the office of president and Umar Arteh Ghalib that of premier. Somali faced a breakdown in food supplies and public services. In addition, despite the apparent agreement between the insurgent groups, bitter fighting continued unabated outside the capital.

The Republic of Somaliland.

In May, northern Somalia established an independent republic of Somaliland led by President Abdirahman Ahmed Ali. This area remained relatively peaceful. Fighting broke out in the capital Mogadishu on 17 November between forces loyal to the interim president, Ali Mahdi Mohamed, and those of his rival in the ruling United Somali Congress (USC), Gen. Mohamed Farah Aidid. Both belonged to competing factions within the Hawiye clan and Somalia faced renewed civil war. By the end of December 4,000 had died in a ruined Mogadishu. Talks between representatives of the combatants held under UN auspices in February 1992 appeared to bring peace no nearer.

The UN Ceasefire.

The two main antagonists agreed to a UN negotiated ceasefire on 14 February. But individual factions and bandits continued fighting in the capital Mogadishu. In April the UN agreed to send observers to monitor the ceasefire and on 30 April the first relief supplies of food arrived since December 1991. As a quarter of Somalia's six million population faced starvation, the UN agreed on the deployment of troops to protect the food shipments. On 17 September a fleet of US warships carrying over 2,000 marines began patrolling the coastal waters. But as attacks on supply convoys continued, the United States proposed more aggressive action, offering 30,000 troops on 26 November. General Aidid, weakened by the loss of an important rural stronghold, welcomed the offer. On 3 December the UN agreed to send a US-led force to ensure food reached the population. The first of a projected 30,000 strong force, headed by US Marines, landed in Somalia on 9 December. Intermittent clashes with bandits and demonstrators followed.

However, by 7 January 1993 it appeared, following the visit of the UN secretary-general, that the 14 main political factions in Somalia had reached agreement on the formation of a government of national reconciliation. Militia groups were called upon to cease fire. Meanwhile, US Marines launched a series of attacks on weapons markets in the capital Mogadishu to seize arms caches. In February a reported 1·5 million Somalis faced starvation in the war-shattered economy.

UN Peace-keeping Force.

The Security Council agreed on 26 March to replace the bulk of the US troops in Somalia with a 28,000 strong UN force, initially for six months from May. The following day the Somali war lords and clan chiefs agreed to form a transitional council to rule until the formation of a national government. However, no date was set for its creation and the Somaliland Republic, an independent state in the north of the country since 1991, was not party to the agreement.

On 5 June 23 Pakistani troops in the UN force were killed in Mogadishu. General Aidid denied responsibility but from 12–16 June UN forces mounted attacks in Mogadishu vainly seeking out his hiding place. Resentment against the UN force heightened when Pakistani troops killed 20 civilians protesting against the attacks. Aidid remained in hiding, denying on 9 August that his forces were responsible for killing four US soldiers the previous day. A UN-negotiated ceasefire between the clans broke after two weeks when fighting resumed in Mogadishu between supporters of General Aidid and Ali Mahdi Mohammed on 25 October. As the two held peace talks in early December, it was announced that the UN force would withdraw on 31 March 1994 (together with the last of the US contingent) because of growing unwillingness to provide troops.

Attempts at Reconciliation.

Rival militia clashes which began on 11 February 1994 took 60 lives in two days and continued through the month. But on 24 March a peace agreement was signed by General Aidid and his main rival interim president Ali Mahdi Mohammed. The last United States troops left the following day. But optimism faded as the first meeting scheduled under the agreement failed to take place on 15 April, both sides accusing the other of undermining the pact. A further meeting of the main factions to prepare for a national reconciliation conference was postponed for the fourth time in two months on 27 May.

A reconciliation conference organised by General Aidid on 1 November was boycotted by President Mohammed's Somali Salvation Alliance. The continuing inability of the factions to resolve their differences prompted the UN Security Council to announce on 4 November that the 15,000 strong peace force would be withdrawn by 31 March 1995.

ALGERIA.

Rise of Fundamentalism.

The dominant feature of recent Algerian politics has been the fall from power of the FLN and the rise of the growing fundamentalist Islamic movement, the Islamic Salvation Front (FIS). In local and regional elections held during 1990 the FIS won unprecedented victories against the FLN. During the Gulf Crisis the FIS, led by Dr. Abbasi Madani, capitalised on popular support for Iraq by organising large demonstrations and called for President Chadli Benjedid's resignation. In response the FLN-controlled parliament introduced changed electoral reforms designed to debilitate the FIS in the run-up to the country's first ever general election scheduled for 27 June 1991. The FIS reacted by organising strikes and demonstrations calling for the removal of the laws. As these escalated clashes broke out with the army in which hundreds were injured. The climax came on 4 June when President Chadli Benjedid declared a state of siege, accepted the resignation of Mouloud Hamrouche's government and postponed the election.

The new Prime Minister, Sid-Ahmed Ghozali, assembled a non-partisan government which promised to hold the elections by the end of the year and to amend the electoral laws. Notwithstanding this, clashes between the army and the FIS continued and the security forces accused the FIS deputy leader Ali Belhaj of involvement in a plot to train paramilitary subversives. At the end of June renewed clashes left over 30 dead. The government reacted by arresting Madani, Belhaj and other FIS leaders. At the same time President Benjedid announced his resignation from the FLN, thus leaving the FLN virtually unrepresented in government and opening the way for him to serve out his term as a non-partisan Head of State.

Ghozali's attempts to formulate electoral laws agreeable to all parties proceeded slowly and were overshadowed by FIS demands for the release of their leaders. Internal disagreements within FIS, between hardliners who opposed elections in principle and the pragmatists who wanted to take part, were only resolved a week before the elections in favour of the latter. The first round of elections, in which only eight million of the 13 million electorate turned out, took place on 26 December and the FIS swept the board, winning 188 seats to the FLN's 15. The second round of elections were scheduled for 16 January 1992. On 11 January, however, President Benjedid suddenly resigned and an army-dominated "Higher Security Council" took over. The Council cancelled the scheduled vote and imposed martial law.

The State of Emergency.

On 9 February 1992 the five-man Higher Security Council imposed a one-year state of emergency following a week of clashes with FIS supporters in which at least 40 died. Although there were over 5,000 FIS supporters in detention, the cabinet was reshuffled on 22 February to include two ministers with former FIS connections to appease fundamentalist opinion. On 4 March FIS was outlawed. In apparent response, Mr. Boudiaf was assassinated on 29 June while delivering a speech. He was succeeded on 2 July by Ali Kafi, like Boudiaf a veteran of the liberation war against the French. On 8 July President Ghozali resigned and was replaced by Belaid Abdesalam. An anti-terrorism law introduced on 1 October offered underground FIS members an amnesty if they surrendered and withdrew from activity. When the amnesty expired on 3 December the government imposed an indefinite night curfew. However, presidential elections were promised by the end of 1993. On 6 January 1993 press censorship was imposed and special courts set up to deal with Islamic fundamentalists.

The Crisis Intensifies.

The year-long state of emergency was extended indefinitely on 8 February 1993. Violence continued with the attempted assassination of the defence minister on 13 February. The High State Council alleged foreign involvement in terrorism, breaking off relations with Iran and withdrawing its ambassador from Sudan on 27 March, allegedly by fundamentalists. The High State Council proposed a three-year transition to democracy on 21 June. In the council's place a broader body would draft a constitution and expedite free market reforms.

On 21 August Belaid Abdesalam was replaced as prime minister by foreign minister Redha Malek. The dismissal of the defence minister and the armed forces chief suggested the government was dissatisfied with the effectiveness of anti-fundamentalist measures. Islamic militants now began to mount attacks on foreigners. By the end of the year Algeria was in a state of virtual civil war.

A two-day conference on the transition to democracy, opened on 25 January 1994, was boycotted by all significant political groupings, with only 60 minor parties attending, despite conciliatory gestures by the government. In its draft programme the High State Council proposed a new ruling body and a state-nominated national assembly of transition. In the wake of the failure of the conference, the appointment of defence minister General Lamin Zeroual as president on 30 January underlined the position of the military in the government.

Bitter Civil War.

The situation continued to spiral out of control in the months that followed. The extremist fundamentalist group, the Armed Islamic Group (GIA) struck heavy blows against the oil industry by beginning to target expatriate and Algerian workers. On 5 August the GIA also struck at the regime's French backers, killing five French officials in Algiers. France responded by cracking down on Islamist suspects in France. President Zeroual sought to split the Islamists by allowing FIS leaders Madani and Belhaj out of prison to attend talks in October. The two leaders however refused to condemn violence and were returned to their cells. Zeroual continued to seek a political solution, announcing that Presidential elections would be held in 1995 but at the same time he allowed military hard-liners to escalate their operations. The government rejected a multiparty proposal to hold a dialogue including the FIS in early 1995 and France was dragged into the conflict with the hijacking of an Algerian airliner to Marseilles. By early 1995 up to 30,000 people had been killed in the conflict.

LIBYA.

In the late 1980s, there were signs that Col. Gaddafi was attempting to moderate both his domestic and foreign stance. A lessening of state controls and a shift to a more market oriented economy encouraged definite improvements in Libyan citizens' lives. Col. Gaddafi acknowledged the legitimacy of complaints against his internal security forces. But it was in the international arena that Libya appeared to be taking decisive, if occasionally erratic, steps to end its isolation.

Relations with Chad and Egypt.

Gaddafi suggested in January 1989 that he and President-elect Bush—whom he later described as "wise and mature"—should discuss the issues dividing Libya and the US. There were reports that Libya had reduced funding of terrorist movements. On 17 February Libya became a founder member with Algeria, Mauritania, Morocco and Tunisia of the Arab Mahgreb Union, a North African common market. Commemoration the 20th anniversary of Col. Gaddafi's rule opened on 31 August with a treaty ending Libya's war with Chad. Having re-opened the border with Egypt and restored air links, Col. Gaddafi drove to meet Egyptian President Mubarrak on 16 October, a visit the President returned the following day. They agreed to co-operate on a range of agricultural and transport matters and announced that Egypt and Libya had no differences over Arab issues.

Libya and the Gulf Crisis.

Libya's attitude towards the Gulf crisis appeared ambiguous. At an Arab League summit on 9–10 August 1990 Libya voted with Iraq and the PLO against sending an Arab peace-keeping force to Saudi Arabia in response to the invasion of Kuwait. But on 20 August Col. Gaddafi criticised Iraq for holding civilian hostages and declared Libya's willingness to participate in a UN naval blockade of Iraq. However, Libya voted against an Arab League resolution which called for Iraq to withdraw from Kuwait and to pay reparations.

Gains and Losses.

In December 1990 the US withdrew its support for Chadian President Hissène Habré, whom it had previously supported against Libya. This allowed Idriss Deby, backed by France and Libya to take power. Libya gained as guerrilla forces of the US-backed anti-Gaddafi National Front for the Salvation of Libya were expelled from the country. Libya also continued its policy of improving ties with its

neighbours, focusing on economic integration. Libyan–Egyptian border controls were removed in August 1991 and President Mubarrak presided over the opening of the "Great Man-Made River", a major scheme to provide irrigation for Libyan agriculture.

These diplomatic gains were put at risk in November when British and American investigators charged Libyan intelligence agents with responsibility for the bombing of an American airliner that crashed over Lockerbie, Scotland in December 1988 and France accused Libya of masterminding the bombing of a French airliner over Niger in September 1989. The US and Britain demanded the extradition of the Libyan personnel, but Gaddafi denied responsibility. He announced an internal investigation into the affair and launched an intense diplomatic campaign to resist US and British pressure. He promised to halt his support for terrorist groups such as the Provisional Irish Republican Army.

UN Sanctions.

As allegations of Libyan involvement in international terrorism continued, the UN Security Council agreed to impose limited sanctions—a ban on air travel and arms sales to Libya—unless two agents suspected of responsibility were handed over for trial by 15 April. President Gaddafi suggested he would hand over the agents to an Arab government.

A visit by Libyan pilgrims to Islamic holy places in Israel on 31 May was interpreted as an attempted diplomatic overture by President Gaddafi and bitterly criticised by the PLO. The pilgrimage ended abruptly on 2 June when the group's spokesman called for the overthrow of Israel's "Zionist occupation". On 11 November the UN security council voted to impose tighter economic sanctions against Libya from 1 December unless two men suspected of involvement in the December 1988 Lockerbie aircraft bombing were handed over for trial.

A Continuing Stand-Off.

The stand-off continued throughout 1994 with Col. Gaddafi declaring his willingness to have the two suspects tried by the International Court of Justice (ICJ) but the UK and France rejected this proposal. Gaddafi is unlikely to hand over the two men since to do so would damage his credibility among his domestic supporters. On 8 April the UN voted to once again renew sanctions. This decision is reviewed every 120 days but so far European countries with economic interests in Libya have resisted US pressures to extend the sanctions to cover Libyan oil sales. Gaddafi suffered another blow in March when he had to accept a ruling by the ICJ rejecting Libya's claims to the Aouzou strip in Chad. Egypt however continued to improve its relations with Libya, announcing its intention to join the Arab Maghreb Union in November.

NIGERIA.

Continuing Austerity.

At the beginning of 1989 the Nigerian government launched a new austerity budget, designed to channel investment and scarce resources into agriculture and small-scale industry, in order to continue the process of reducing Nigerian dependence on oil revenues.

President Babaniga continued his economic reforms by easing restrictions on foreign investment in January 1989. A 40% limit on foreign ownership of enterprises imposed in the 1970s was raised to 100%, except in banking and insurance, mining and oil prospecting. The intention was to encourage investment and assist in the government's privatisation programme. Within days the IMF approved $620 million credit to aid Nigerian development. Economic and political liberalisation appeared to be running parallel when in May Mr Babaniga lifted a five year ban on political activity.

Anti-Government Demonstrations.

But there was clearly intense discontent with the austerity programme's effects. On 24 May—shortly after he had returned from Britain with the promise of £60 million in aid—students mounted demonstrations against the alleged corruption of Mr Babaniga and his government. These spread across nine states, were joined by non-students protesting against the government's economic policies, and became increasingly violent. The official death toll was 22 but unofficial figures suggested over 100 were killed. The government closed all universities, renewed its ban on political activity and arrested hundreds. As the unrest waned Mr Babaniga announced an easing of his economic reforms, but a failed coup attempt by junior officers early in 1990 demonstrated his political problems. The rising had been in protest against the domination of the Christian south of the country by the Moslem north. Mr Babaniga survived but there were signs that the continuation of his harsh austerity programme was encouraging a widespread unpopularity.

In April 1991 there was serious rioting in the north of Nigeria between Christians and fundamentalist Shi'ite Moslems demanding the implementation of *Sharia* (Islamic law). Over 200 were killed. There were further clashes with more deaths in October.

Transition to Civilian Rule.

The beginning of the promised transition from military to civilian rule began in December with gubernatorial and state assembly elections. The elections were contested by two parties created by the military government in 1989, the right-wing National Republican Convention and the left-wing Social Democratic Party. On 19 December the NRC leader, Mr. Tom Ikimi, whose party won a majority of the state governorships, alleged that ballot-rigging had taken place and called for fresh polls in four states.

Currency Devaluation.

On 9 March 1992 the Nigerian government floated the country's currency, in effect devaluing by 20%. This led in May to riots over rising prices. On 10 May the Campaign for Democracy demanded the government's resignation, backed by a National Association of Nigerian Students' call for a general strike on 13–14 May. There were clashes in Lagos in which seven died. Against this background, elections on 4 July to the new National Assembly went off peacefully. Only two parties were allowed to compete, the Social Democratic Party (SDP) and the National Republican Convention (NRP). The SDP took 47 Senate seats to the NRP's 37. The SDP won 310 House of Representatives seats, the NRP 267.

The Presidential Election Saga.

Presidential elections were due to be held on 5 December but on 6 October the Armed Forces Ruling Council overturned party primaries for alleged irregularities and dismissed leading SDP and NRP officials. On 17 November the presidential elections were put back to 12 June 1993, with the handover to civilian rule now rescheduled to 27 August. President Babangida swore in a 29-member transitional council on 4 January 1993, headed by businessman Mr. Ernest Shonekan, to govern Nigeria until the handover to an elected president.

On 28 March two Islamic candidates were selected for the state-sponsored parties, Bashir Tofa for the NRC and Moshood Abiola for the SDP and the elections were held on 12 June. But when the Association for a Better Nigeria (a group which wanted President Babangida to retain power) alleged fraud, President Babangida refused to allow the result to be released. (A Nigerian human rights group said that the SDP candidate had won 58·4% of the vote and the NRC 41·6%).

On 26 June President Babangida promised once again to hand over to civilian rule on 27 August after fresh elections. But the following day the SDP called for resistance to military rule and 30 senior army officers were reported to have resigned. A general strike was held in Lagos on 5 July and 25 people were killed in demonstrations the following day. On 16 July President Babangida announced new elections for 14 August. The SDP said it would not participate.

President Babangida stood down on 26 August, installing a replacement interim government led by Mr. Shonekan which was declared illegal by the

Lagos high court on 10 November. Demonstrations in support of the victor in the 12 June elections, Mr. Abiola, merged on 12 November with riots over a seven-fold rise in fuel prices. The Nigeria Labour Congress threatened a general strike if the rises were not rescinded.

The Advent of Abacha.

As the strike went ahead, Mr. Shonekan resigned on 17 November. He was replaced by the defence minister, General Sani Abacha, who declared himself chairman of a new Provisional Ruling Council, scrapped the national legislature and banned Nigeria's two political parties. There were clashes as pro-democracy demonstrators took to the streets. However, on 21 November the Labour Congress called off the strike, weakening the pro-democracy activists. On 23 November General Abacha appointed Baba Gana Kingibe, Moshood Abiola's running mate in the June elections, to the ruling council. He also dismissed 17 high-ranking officers close to former President Babangida from the army.

The government announced the first phase of the promised transition to civilian rule on 22 April 1994. A Constructional Conference was to be convened on 28 May, with candidates approved by the Provisional Ruling Council (PRC). However, the first round of elections for delegates to the Constitutional Conference held on 23 May was boycotted by the newly established National Democratic Coalition (Nadeco) – an alliance of politicians, former military officers and civil rights groups.The boycott was welcomed by Mr Abiola, who declared himself president in Lagos on 11 June, the anniversary of the 1993 elections. Two weeks later he was arrested for treason, a charge he denied when he appeared in court on 6 July.

The Oil Strike.

The powerful oil workers struck against his arrest and the annulment of the 1993 elections on 5 July. Transport was soon paralysed and Nigeria's export earnings were threatened. As the 250,000 strikers rejected a government appeal for talks, there were clashes in Lagos and in Abuja. Mr Abiola's trial was persistently adjourned because of his poor health. On 3 August the Nigerian Labour Congress (NLC) called an indefinite general strike. The government responded by dissolving the NLC executive and the strike was called off.

Widespread Opposition Arrests.

Sensing the opposition's weakness as the oil workers' stike collapsed on 4 September, the government announced decrees giving itself "absolute power" to legislate to maintain order. Mass arrests of opposition figures followed immediately and the PRC's four civilian members were dismissed on 27 September. Mr Abiola remained in detention – despite the granting of bail by the Court of Appeal on 4 November – and his trial was set for January 1995. Nobel prize winning writer Wole Soyinka fled the country on 3 November, denouncing its "despotic and corrupt military regime". The panel appointed by General Abacha to write a new constitution appeared to confirm charges that its role was to legitimise his dictatorship when, on 6 December, it voted in favour of another year of military rule.

GHANA.

Ghana became independent from Britain on 6 March 1957. The country was led by Dr. Kwame Nkrumah, who became president when Ghana was declared a republic in 1960. Ghana became a one-party state in 1964. Nkrumah's government became increasingly autocratic and extravagant, and this led to his overthrow in a military coup while he was on a state visit to China in February 1966. Military rule continued until elections were held in August 1969, which were won by the Progress Party led by Dr. Kofi Busia. In turn he was deposed by the army under General Acheampong in January 1972.

Plans were made for a return to civilian rule, but shortly before the elections in 1979 General Acheampong and the Supreme Military Council were overthrown in a coup staged by junior officers led by Flight-Lieutenant Jerry Rawlings. An Armed Forces Revolutionary Council took power, and in an anti-corruption drive, executed senior officers, including General Acheampong. The scheduled elections took place and resulted in a victory for Dr. Hilla Limann and the People's National Party. In December 1981, however, Rawlings staged a second coup, which dismissed parliament, suspended the constitution and banned political parties. A defence council chaired by Flight-Lieutenant Rawlings ruled by decree.

In 1987 Jerry Rawlings was still a popular and respected figure, but his regime had critics from both the left and the right. A National Commission for Democracy, set up in June 1984, had been consulting groups throughout Ghana, but its progress was slow. Ghanaians were reported to be frustrated that they had no say in the running of the country, whilst Jerry Rawlings seemed to have no clear plans for Ghana's long-term future.

In August 1990 troops from Ghana landed in Liberia as part of an Economic Community of West African States peace-keeping force attempting to end the civil war in that country.

The 1992 Referendum.

A referendum on 28 April 1992 approved a new multi-party constitution, ending an 11-year ban on political activity. Presidential elections were held on 4 November 1992. Flight-Lieutenant Jerry Rawlings won 58·5% of the four million votes cast. His nearest opponent, New Patriotic Party candidate Albert Adu Boahen, took 30·2%. President Rawlings's victory was seen as a vindication of his economic reform programme, and his anti-corruption campaign. But opponents criticised his human rights record and persistent repression of dissent. President Rawlings's National Democratic Party went on to sweeping victory in parliamentary elections held in December, taking 189 of the 200 seats following an opposition boycott of the elections.

Ghana placed its army on alert on 1 February 1993 following anti-government unrest in neighbouring Togo. The government denied any aggressive intent and, despite its sympathy with the opposition, denied involvement in an assassination attempt on the Togolese president on 25 March.

Ethnic Violence.

Ghana faced serious violence when, on 3 February 1994, there were clashes between members of the Konkomba and Namumba ethnic groups. By 10 February disorder had spread across seven districts in the north of the country. Over a thousand people were killed and a further 150,000 fled to escape the fighting. As clashes continued in May, parliament extended a state of emergency throughout the area.

KENYA.

Demands for Democracy.

During 1990 Kenya saw growing demands for multi-party democracy. A coalition of churchmen, human rights activists, lawyers and politicians accused President Moi's KANU government of corruption and repression. On 3 May the American ambassador told Kenyan businessmen that the US preferred to aid countries with democratic institutions. Kenya was one of the largest recipients of US aid in Africa. Though Mr Moi criticised the ambassador he announced he would allow discussion of democracy.

However, on 16 June he announced the debate was over and said the Kenyan people supported KANU as the sole party. Roman Catholic church leaders issued a pastoral letter condemning his attitude. Arrests of unofficial opposition leaders on 4–5 July provoked demonstrations and rioting which spread from Nairobi to other towns. On 11 July the government announced 20 people had been killed and 1,000 arrested. Mr Moi countered US criticism with accusations of "gross interference".

On 13 February 1991 former vice-president Oginga Odinga, a prominent critic of President Moi, announced the formation of the National Democratic Party (NDP). Its main objective was to repeal the 1982 constitution by which Kenya had become a one-party state.

The Launch of FORD.

In August the Forum for the Restoration of Democracy (FORD), a coalition of lawyers, trade unionists, clergy and politicians, was launched under Mr. Odinga's leadership. But in September 1991 Mr. Moi reportedly said that since Kenya was "at least 200 years behind" the West in economic development, democratisation could not be expected for at least two centuries. Nonetheless, FORD called a mass rally in Nairobi on 16 November to demand the drafting of a new constitution. Dissident leaders, including Mr. Odinga, were arrested under the Public Order Act before the rally, and Mr. Moi denounced the organisers as "anarchists and tribalists".

The murder of Mr. Ouko in February 1990 continued to reverberate politically, with allegations that Mr. Ouko had been about to prepare a report on corruption within KANU and that senior government figures were involved in his death. Two, including the internal security head, were arrested but released for lack of evidence.

Moves to Democracy.

Mr. Moi's apparent reluctance to undertake economic and political reform was influencing the attitude of Western aid donors. A meeting of donors organised by the World Bank in Paris on 21 November deferred a decision on future aid to Kenya for six months pending progress on reforms. Mr. Moi announced that a multi-party system would be introduced in the near future and on 3 December KANU's governing council recommended restoration of the constitutional right to form opposition parties. On 23 December Mr. Moi called for a purging of corrupt KANU members before multi-party elections were held in 1992. But there were increasing defections of current and former ministers from the weakened ruling party to FORD, which registered as a legal opposition party in January 1992.

Tribal Unrest in West Kenya.

Following the registration of the Forum for the Restoration of Democracy (FORD) as a legal party, a second opposition party, the Democratic Party was formed on 18 January 1992. At the first legal demonstration in Kenya for 22 years 100,000 people protested against the government. But on 20 March President Moi banned all political gatherings, blaming tribal fighting in the rural western provinces. The fighting, which had claimed 2,000 lives, was between the combined Kikuyu, Luo and Luyha tribes and members of the smaller Kalenjin tribe, President Moi's tribe which had come to dominate political life since his rise to power. There were counter-accusations from FORD and the government that each had provoked the violence.

The Split in FORD.

On 13 October FORD split into two parties, FORD-Asili and FORD-Kenya. As the first elections for 26 years approached, opposition divisions increased Mr. Moi's chance of retaining power. The elections on 29 December were marked by widespread irregularities and President Moi took 1·9 million votes against the opposition parties' total 3·3 million. In the parliamentary elections his Kenya African National Union (KANU) took 112 of the 200 seats. On 4 January 1993 the main opposition parties—FORD-Asili, FORD-Kenya, and the Democratic Party—formed a united front to oppose President Moi and called for the elections to be re-run. Mr. Moi responded by suspending the first session of the new parliament on 27 January.

Parliament was reconvened on 23 March 1993. President Moi criticised economic measures imposed by the World Bank and IMF as "unrealistic" and announced the reintroduction of export and currency controls. Nevertheless, the World Bank promised on 21 April to resume aid, saying that President Moi's government had demonstrated a commitment to economic reform. There were, however, allegations that KANU leaders were diverting state funds to enrich themselves. In June Mr. Odinga alleged in parliament that President Moi and Vice-president George Saitoti had misappropriated huge sums, an allegation they both denied.

On 23 November the Paris Club of government aid donors agreed to make $850 million aid available over the next 12 months. This was in spite of continuing tribal clashes which had left 1,500 dead and 300,000 displaced and which the opposition accused the government of encouraging.

The Death of Odinga.

Mr. Odinga, the leader of the parliamentary opposition, died aged 82 on 21 January 1994. Mr. Odinga was one of the last survivors of the generation that had led the struggle for independence from Britain. His death opened up the possibility of a struggle for the leadership of the forces opposing President Moi.

Economic Reforms.

However, Michael Wamalwa Kijana was appointed acting chair of FORD-Kenya on 3 February 1994. In February, and again in May, finance minister Musalia Mudavadi announced further economic reforms intended to encourage foreign investment and economic growth. On 3 January 1995 the stock exchange was opened to foreigners and the finance minister declared his intention to repeal currency controls imposed thirty years earlier.

SOUTH AFRICA.

In January 1989 73-year old President Botha suffered a mild stroke. During his recovery the Minister of Constitutional Affairs, Mr. Heunis, was sworn in as acting president. In February Mr. Botha stood down as leader of the National Party and the Transvaal leader, Mr. F. W. de Klerk was elected in his place. Although Mr. Botha at first insisted that he had no plans for early retirement, in early May he announced a general election to be held on 6 September. The Botha era was effectively over.

Mr Botha played a final surprising card by inviting imprisoned African National Congress leader Mr Nelson Mandela to discussions on 5 July. Then, following a bitter cabinet argument, he resigned on 14 August. His replacement as acting president, Mr F. W. de Klerk, declared that South Africa stood "on the threshold of a new era".

The 1989 Elections.

As the September elections approached the anti-apartheid movement mounted a civil disobedience campaign against the state of emergency, culminating in a widely supported general strike. The elections tested the white electorate's reaction to the National Party's reforms. In June the NP had promised South Africa's 23 million blacks limited "democratic participation". NP representation fell from 123 seats to 93, the party failing for the first time to win over 50% of white votes. The right-wing Conservative Party's seats increased from 22 to 39 while the reformist Democratic Party's support rose from 21 to 33. Though the NP lost ground to the right and to the left, President de Klerk claimed a "clear mandate" for change.

Towards A New Era.

South Africa now entered a decisive period. On 10 October eight leading political prisoners, all of whom had been jailed for life with Mr Mandela, were released. The following day Mr de Klerk met three black clergy, including Archbishop Desmond Tutu, for "talks about talks". In November Mr de Klerk announced an end to segregated beaches and a moderation of the Group Areas Act, a cornerstone of apartheid. On 13 December he followed in the steps of his predecessor by meeting Mr Mandela.

Events now moved rapidly. On 2 February 1990 Mr de Klerk declared at the opening of parliament, "The time for talking has arrived" and delivered five concessions. Over 60 banned organisations were legalised, including the ANC, the Pan-Africanist Congress, the Communist Party, the multiracial United Democratic Front, and the Azanian People's Organisation. There was to be a moratorium on hangings. The Separate Amenities Act would be repealed. Detention without trial would be limited to six months. Finally, Mr Mandela would be unconditionally released. The response of anti-apartheid organisations was mixed. White extremists denounced the concessions as a surrender.

The Release of Nelson Mandela.

Mr Mandela was freed on 11 February. His 25 years in prison had become a symbol to the world of white repression; now his release symbolised the hope of change. At a welcoming rally Mr Mandela described President de Klerk as a "man of principle" but said the armed struggle would continue as long as apartheid remained. But Mr Mandela was faced immediately with the need to seek reconciliation with the Zulu national Inkatha movement led by Chief Mangosuthu Buthelezi, chief minister of the Kwazulu homeland. Since 1988 Natal province had been undergoing virtual civil war between Inkatha and the ANC/UDF in which over 2,500 had died. Mr Mandela agreed to discussions between the three organisations on 2 April, but when Natal ANC activists complained they had not been consulted he had to cancel the meeting, revealing divisions within the ANC.

Divisions Amongst Nationalists.

A further demonstration of divisions within the anti-apartheid movement had come earlier in March when the ANC announced plans to create a broad black coalition to negotiate with the government. The Pan-Africanist Congress leadership in exile rejected negotiations. Mr Joe Modise—commander of the ANC's military wing—expressed fears that the ANC was being rushed into premature negotiations. Nevertheless, it was announced on 16 March that "talks about talks" between Mr de Klerk and the ANC would begin on 11 April. But on 26 March police fired on a black march in Sebokeng, killing 11 and wounding 250. Mr Mandela was initially reluctant to allow this to prevent the talks but widespread anger in the black community forced their abandonment. Mr Mandela, admitting that differences existed within the ANC but unwilling to go into detail, met Mr de Klerk for personal discussions on 5 April.

Formal ANC-government talks on 2-4 May concluded with a joint agreement on the need for a peaceful solution. The government would consider ending the state of emergency while the ANC would review its commitment to armed struggle. On 7 June Mr de Klerk announced the end of the state of emergency in all but Natal province, the scene of continuing factional fighting. The far-right then responded with a wave of terrorist bombings in June and July. On 7 August, following ANC-government discussions, the ANC ended its 30-year armed struggle. In return Mr de Klerk promised a phased release of political prisoners and a gradual return of exiled dissidents. Arguments about what precisely was an end to the armed struggle was continued, delaying the promised releases.

ANC–Inkatha Violence.

Violence between Inkatha and ANC supporters continued, spreading for the first time in July from Natal into the black townships near Johannesburg. By mid-September over 700 had died. On 21 August Mr de Klerk and Chief Buthelezi called jointly for an end to the violence. The ANC accused white security forces of supporting Inkatha in an attempt to sabotage ANC-government negotiations. On 11 September Mr Mandela told Mr de Klerk that, although the ANC had renounced the armed struggle, his movement was finding it difficult to resist supporters' calls for defence against Inkatha. Within 24 hours of a joint call for an end to the violence from Mr Mandela and Chief Buthelezi on 29 January 1991 there were further killings. On 8 February the ANC, Inkatha, the Azanian People's Organisation and the Pan-Africanist Congress appealed for an end to the internecine violence. The clashes and the deaths continued.

In September 1990 Mr de Klerk visited the United States and for the first time used the expression "one man, one vote" in the context of South Africa's future constitutional settlement. But he qualified this by saying there would be a need to safeguard the interests of the minority, implying a white veto.

ANC National Conference, 1990.

The ANC held its first national conference in December 1990. The organisation's president, Mr Oliver Tambo, newly returned from 30 years exile, questioned the ANC's insistence on sanctions. But the conference demanded their continuation and went on to call for an immediate interim government and constituent assembly, both of which Mr de Klerk had previously rejected. The conference revealed the ANC's political weakness and lack of organisation, with divisions between the older leaders and younger more radical activists.

The End of Apartheid.

On 1 February 1991 Mr de Klerk declared the end of the apartheid era. He announced that legislation was being prepared to abolish the three pillars of apartheid, the Group Areas Act, the Land Act and—perhaps most significant of all—the Population Registration Act, which divided all South Africans into rigid racial categories. The ANC welcomed the announcement but pointed to the necessity for fundamental economic reform to enable the black majority to benefit from these changes. Three days later the ANC, and Mr Mandela in particular, faced a potentially embarrassing period when Mrs Winnie Mandela came to trial on kidnapping and assault charges. She was subsequently convicted and sentenced, but released on bail pending an appeal.

The legislative framework of apartheid was dismantled when, on 5 June 1991, the Land and Group Areas Acts were repealed. The repeal of the Population Registration Act followed on 17 June. But violence in the townships continued, and a meeting between Mr. Mandela and Chief Buthelezi on 30 March failed to find a solution. On 18 May—as deaths reached 15 a day—the ANC broke off power-sharing talks with the government because of its failure to respond to ANC suggestions on ending the clashes. On 14 September the government, the ANC and Inkatha agreed on a peace plan, following a week in which 125 had died.

The ANC held its annual conference from 2–7 July. Mr. Mandela was elected president to replace the ailing Mr. Tambo. Cyril Ramaphosa, the leader of the National Union of Mineworkers, was elected general secretary and was to head the ANC team negotiating on a new state constitution. The ANC eased its stance on international trade sanctions, with Mr. Mandela calling for "flexibility".

The Inkatha Scandal.

On 19 July the government was shaken by political scandal when it admitted making secret payments to Inkatha in 1989–90. The revelations threatened to undermine Mr. de Klerk's reforming credentials. The National Party was also in conflict with its ultra-right opponents. On 9 August two Afrikaner Resistance Movement (AWB) members were killed in clashes with the police. The paramilitary AWB, hitherto predominantly Afrikaner, appeared to be attracting support among traditionally liberal English-speaking whites.

Both the ANC and the government issued outlines of a post-apartheid constitution as part of the negotiating process. In April the ANC called for a unitary rather than a federal state; a two-chamber parliament; a president elected either directly or by parliament; an independent judiciary and a bill of rights; and affirmative action for those "who in the past have been disadvantaged by discrimination". President de Klerk issued the National Party's proposals in September. These included a collective presidency made up of the leaders of the three largest parties; a two-chamber parliament, with one house elected by proportional representation and the other—which had veto powers—with membership apportioned among nine regions. Although there were significant points of agreement, the ANC rejected the government's draft on the grounds that whites would "retain the accumulated privileges of apartheid".

The CODESA Gathering.

The preliminary meeting of the long awaited multi-party constitutional conference—the Convention for a Democratic South Africa (CODESA)—opened on 20 December. The 19 delegations included representatives from the National Party, the ANC, Inkatha, the Democratic Party, the coloured and Indian minority parties, and from the ten black "homelands". The Conservative Party and white right-wing groups were absent, as was the Pan Africanist Congress, a leading rival to the ANC for black support. Despite an early clash between Mr. Mandela and President de Klerk on the continued existence of the ANC's armed wing, there was agreement on common principles. Mr. de Klerk repeated an earlier offer to include black leaders in an interim cabinet. On 29 December Mr. Mandela said the ANC would guarantee whites a block of seats in a new parliament for a limited period.

Reaction from the Right.

President de Klerk was, however, facing increased resistance from his right. His support among whites was called into question by a Conservative Party by-election victory at Potchefstroom on 19 February 1992. Mr. de Klerk announced that he would call a referendum among white voters on 17 March to test his mandate to negotiate constitutional change. This initially appeared to be an impulsive gamble. But Mr. de Klerk had outmanoeuvred his ultra-right opponents by the speed of his action. The question the whites would have to decide upon was announced on 24 February: "Do you support the continuation of the reform process which the state president began on 2 February 1990 and which is aimed at a new constitution through negotiation?" Both the Conservative Party and the AWB initially called for whites to boycott the referendum and a right-wing united front seemed likely. But younger moderates in the Conservative Party forced the CP leader, Mr. Treurnicht, to reverse his decision and to campaign instead for a No vote. On 5 March the government and the ANC agreed, should Mr. de Klerk win the referendum, on the establishment of a multi-racial Interim Government Council to oversee the transition to democracy. This would comprise all parties who were members of CODESA.

The Referendum Triumph.

Mr. de Klerk's victory in the referendum appeared overwhelming. Only one out of the country's 15 regions returned a No vote. On an 85·08% turnout, 1,924,186 (68·6%) voted Yes against 875.619 who voted No. It was estimated that 62% of Afrikaners had supported Mr. de Klerk and 79% of English-speakers. Mr. de Klerk declared that South Africa had "closed the book on apartheid", though he added that "nothing is going to be easy". Mr. Mandela welcomed the result, calling it a mandate to speed negotiations for the interim government. The result intensified divisions within the Conservative Party, with suggestions that the moderates might break away and enter into negotiations. South Africa's underlying economic problems, however, remained. The economy was suffering a three-year recession, with inflation in double figures, and 55% of blacks unemployed. Mr. de Klerk had promised that a Yes vote would encourage essential investment. But foreign investors remained afraid of the ANC's socialist policies.

The ANC faced deep political embarrassment as Mrs. Mandela faced further allegations of involvement in criminal violence. On 13 April Mr. Mandela announced that he and his wife were to separate. The ANC was, however, strengthened when, on 21 April, five white Democratic Party MPs announced they would sit as independents and support the ANC in the 178-seat parliament. The future of the deeply-divided liberal Democratic Party seemed uncertain. In May revelations emerged of state involvement in the assassination of four black activists in the late 1980s which threatened progress being made in the continuing CODESA negotiations.

The Second CODESA Session.

The second CODESA session on 15–16 May broke down after disagreement on the form a multi-racial transitional government should take. It was agreed, however, that five working parties should continue discussions. The ANC, impatient with slow progress towards the end of white domination and under pressure from its own rank and file, announced on 31 May a "mass action" campaign to remove the "de Klerk regime from power". Township violence between ANC and Inkatha supporters continued— 1,400 had died since the beginning of 1992—and a commission of enquiry blamed both sides. Mr. Mandela accused the government of manipulating the rivalry in its own interests.

The Boipatong Massacre.

The ANC "mass action" demonstrations began on 16 June. Inkatha, the Pan-Africanist Congress (PAC) and the Azanian People's Organisation (APO) refused their support. On 17 June 40 people were killed in Boipatong township by 200 Zulus, allegedly with police logistical support. The ANC withdrew from CODESA on 23 June, refusing to return until the government took "practical steps" to end township violence. Tension between the government and the ANC worsened when on 1 July the Congress of South African Trade Unions (COSATU) called for a general strike. Mr. de Klerk accused COSATU and the ANC of attempting to seize power but offered concessions on the future interim government. ANC-government talks on the release of political prisoners were resumed on 28 July. The general strike, opposed by Inkatha, the PAC and the APO, was supported by four out of seven million black workers on 3–4 August.

On 10 September, following a further massacre in which 28 ANC supporters were killed, the ANC accepted Mr. de Klerk's proposal for talks on ways of ending the violence. Mr. de Klerk and Mr. Mandela met on 26 September and agreed to resume negotiations on a non-racial constitution. The ANC would end its "mass action" tactics. Chief Buthelezi withdrew from CODESA the following day, angry at government pledges to ban the carrying of weapons by Inkatha supporters. A constitutional amendment on 21 October cleared the way for the appointment of black ministers in a future interim government.

A Government of National Unity?

The government announced agreement with the ANC on 12 February 1993 on a proposed government of national unity for the five years following a final constitutional settlement. Mr. Mandela, however, said there remained problems over the government's insistence on a white minority veto. He favoured majority rule with the majority party inviting other parties to join a government. Threats of rebellion in ANC ranks against power-sharing were defused. The resumption of constitutional talks in March appeared likely when, on 19 February, Chief Buthelezi agreed that Inkatha would join them. A reshuffle on 21 February which introduced one Indian and two coloured MPs into the Cabinet was a clear preparation for future multi-racial elections.

The Assassination of Chris Hani.

However, progress seemed threatened when on 10 April prominent ANC activist and Communist Party leader Chris Hani was assassinated. A member of the ultra-right Afrikaner Weerstandsbeweging (AWB) was charged with the murder. Five other whites, including a leading member of the pro-apartheid Conservative Party and his wife were arrested in the weeks folowing. At least 47 people were killed in the build-up to Mr Hani's funeral, including 19 in a massacre in Sebokeng township. President de Klerk warned of the danger of civil war as the ANC called a widely supported general strike to mark Mr Hani's funeral. On 24 April Oliver Tambo, the respected national chairman of the ANC, died. As the ANC leadership appeared it might lose control of its township supporters disappointed at the slow progress in negotiations, the ANC, COSATU and the Communist Party appealed for calm.

The assassination of Chris Hani on 10 April had the effect of strengthening rather than undermining the determination of the ANC itself and the government to accelerate power-sharing negotia-

tions. But the ANC leadership could not ignore the growing frustration of young radicals in the townships. Three years of negotiations had, in their view, yielded no real improvement in their lives. As an obvious safety valve, the ANC called on 16 April for six weeks of "mass action", ostensibly to speed President de Klerk into agreeing the election date for a new transitional government. Mr. de Klerk replied that he would not be "blackmailed".

Right-Wing Activism.

On 3 June 1993, the multi-party constitutional forum proposed 27 April 1994 as the date for the election of a National Assembly to serve as an interim legislature and draw up a new constitution. This was opposed by the Concerned South Africans Group (soon to be renamed the Freedom Alliance), which united the far right Conservative Party, the splinter Afrikaner People's Union, Inkatha, and two "homeland" governments. They argued that the majority were ill-prepared for the complexities of an election.

Right-wing activism intensified when, on 25 June, hundreds of white militants stormed the conference centre where negotiations were continuing on the future government. Meanwhile, violence between ANC and Inkatha followers was now costing 20 lives a day. On 23 June Mr Mandela and Chief Buthelezi met for the first time in two years and urged their followers to end the clashes. But a further 800 died in the following two months.

The Draft Constitution.

On 2 August a draft transitional constitution which attempted to satisfy objections to an over strong central state was unveiled. It did not, however, meet Inkatha's demand for an autonomous Zulu region or that of the white right for a separate Afrikaner homeland. Nevertheless, the constitution was ratified on 18 November. Voting for a 400 member National Assembly and a 90 member Senate was to be by proportional representation. The Freedom Alliance continued to withhold agreement, but on 22 December the predominantly white parliament formally approved the transitional constitution by 237 votes to 45.

The Pan Africanist Congress suspended its anti-white terror campaign on 16 January 1994 and agreed to participate in elections. The following day, over 10,000 Zulus demonstrated in Pretoria demanding autonomy. The situation remained tense. White extremists mounted bombing campaigns in the western Transvaal and Orange Free State. The massacre of 15 ANC election workers in Natal on 19 February gave a bitter foretaste of an increasingly feared civil war. The ANC and the government's joint offer to the Freedom Alliance of constitutional compromise on 21 February was immediately rejected.

By March, however, the Freedom Alliance was splintering. On 10 March President Mangope was forced to resign in Bophuthatswana. The "homeland" came under South African administration as anti-Mangope demonstrators had demanded. But there were fears that the elections might be postponed as violence mounted. On 28 March ANC-Inkatha clashes in central Johannesburg left 10 dead and 250 wounded. Over 50 people had died in Natal over the previous two days. The Independent Electoral Commission, which was to administer the elections, announced on 5 April that without a political settlement, polling in KwaZulu would be virtually impossible. President de Klerk, Chief Buthelezi and Mr Mandela could not reach agreement at a meeting on 8 April and international mediators failed to make a breakthrough. At the eleventh hour, however, Chief Buthelezi, having won concessions on the Zulu monarchy's role, agreed to participate in the elections.

The April 1994 Elections.

Despite right-wing bomb outrages, there was a heavy turnout in the elections. The ANC won a sweeping victory with 63% of the vote, the National Party retained a considerable following, and Inkatha (with 10% of the vote) won in its KwaZulu homeland. On 2 May Mr de Klerk conceded defeat. The way was clear for Mr Mandela to be formally inaugurated as president on 10 May. ANC deputy chair Thabo Mbeki became first deputy president, with Mr de Klerk as second deputy president.

A multi-racial cabinet was appointed on 11 May. Among the leading appointments were Chief Buthelezi as Home Affairs Minister and Joe Modise (formerly commander of the ANC armed wing) as Defence Minister. Joe Slovo, the Communist Party leader, became Housing Minister, while Derek Keys remained Finance Minister. In a statement welcomed by the white business community, President Mandela promised on 24 May that he would limit government spending, reduce the budget deficit and avoid tax increases. But on 5 July Mr Keys resigned as Finance Minister, although he agreed to remain in office until October for the sake of continuity.

Problems of the Government.

Of even more concern to the government was evidence of growing frustration and disappointment at slow progress in reform. It faced a wave of industrial unrest and demonstrations for increased wages and to an end to racial discrimination in employment. By the end of July, 48 separate strikes were taking place and the union federation COSATU warned the government to balance its concern with the interest of employers with those of its supporters. Police fired rubber bullets at demonstrators protesting in Johannesburg against a 500% increase in water and electricity prices. Clashes continued between ANC and Inkatha supporters but, despite almost 50 deaths in the last week of August in KwaZulu, the state of emergency imposed in March was lifted. Inkatha itself was riven by a power struggle between Chief Buthelezi and King Goodwill Zwelithini, forcing Chief Buthelezi to concede on 25 September that an independant Zulu kingdom was unlikely.

President Mandela's government's introduction of the Land Rights Act on 11 November represented the first legislation aimed at reversing the effects of apartheid since the election. The Act – which created a land claims court and an arbitration commission – was intended to redress the grievances of people dispossessed by white land confiscation.

The popular housing minister, Joe Slovo, died in the New Year and was given a full state funeral on 15 January 1995.

NAMIBIA.

Namibia finally became independent on 21 March 1990. At a celebratory rally President Nujoma said Namibia would have a mixed economy and called for foreign investment to end his country's dependence on South Africa. In February Namibia had adopted a Western-style constitution, guaranteeing the most liberal multi-party democracy of any African state.

Relations with South Africa remained strained. On 14 March 1991 delegates from Namibia and South Africa met in Cape Town to discuss the future ownership of Walvis Bay, an important port on Namibia's Atlantic coast which South Africa had retained when Namibia gained independence. The meeting ended with no agreement.

In Namibia's first post-independence elections in December 1994, Swapo won an easy victory against the opposition Democratic Turnhalle Alliance (DTA) and the smaller United Democratic Front. Although assured of a two-thirds parliamentary majority, President Nujoma said no move would be made to revise the constitution without popular consultation.

ZIMBABWE.

In June 1987 the government announced that it planned to abolish separate white representation in parliament. Seven years after the Lancaster House settlement it was possible to enact this with seventy votes in favour rather than one hundred as was previously the case. The departing whites were replaced by the nominees of all races chosen by the eighty black MPs.

Despite events earlier in the year Mr. Mugabe and Mr. Nkomo finally reached agreement on the merger of the two parties in December 1987. Mr. Mugabe became the party's first secretary and president, while Mr. Nkomo became one of the two vice-presidents. On the last day of 1987 President

Banana retired and Mr. Mugabe became Zimbabwe's first executive President. In January 1988 an expanded cabinet was sworn in, with Mr. Nkomo nominated to oversee several ministries concerned with rural development. Two other ZAPU members and a white MP were also given cabinet posts. In April 1988 special meetings of ZAPU and ZANU endorsed the merger of the two parties. Mr. Nkomo was appointed the party's interim second vice-president.

The road to a one party state did not run as smoothly as Mr Mugabe might have hoped. In March and April 1989 his government was shaken by a scandal involving senior members. In November 1988 Mr Mugabe had appointed an investigative commission under Justice Sandura to examine press allegations of ministerial involvement in corrupt dealing in state manufactured automobiles. Before the results of the inquiry were made public six of Mr Mugabe's associates resigned, including his defence minister. The most senior of them, Mr Maurice Nyagumbo, committed suicide on 20 April. Sandura, reporting on 13 April, called for the prosecution of former and present ministers and of two MPs. A junior minister was later given nine months for perjury, a sentence personally quashed by Mr Mugabe.

The affair added little to the popularity of a government held responsible for the unemployment of a million of Zimbabwe's nine million citizens.

Economic Problems in Zimbabwe.

Mr Mugabe concentrated on Zimbabwe's pressing economic problems in a speech on 18 April, the ninth anniversary of the country's independence. Growth since 1980, he said, had been inadequate and he proposed to remedy this by creating a more market oriented economy, encouraging foreign investment, and reducing administrative interference in business. Mr Mugabe insisted, however, that his ambition for Zimbabwe remained socialism.

But Edgar Tekere, a former close ally in the independence struggle expelled from ZANU-PF in 1988 for alleging government corruption and for his opposition to a one-party state, favoured a more thorough-going capitalist economy combined with multi-party democracy. He announced on 30 April the formation of a new party, the Zimbabwe Unity Movement (ZUM).

The Zimbabwe Unity Movement.

Mr Mugabe described the new party as "the joke of the year" but his government nevertheless banned ZUM demonstrations and public meetings and there were rumours of assassination attempts on Mr Tekere. The move to a one-party state continued. At a ZANU-PF "Victory Congress" early in 1990 Mr Mugabe shook hands with the leaders of PF-ZAPU, the largest opposition party, and said the two tribal based parties had pledged to work closely together. At the same time he renewed the state of emergency first introduced by the Smith regime in 1965, to protests from the churches and human rights groups. Mr Mugabe's position appeared strengthened by the results of the March 1990 elections. He was returned as President with 78% of the votes cast, Mr Tekere winning 16%. In the contest for the new single chamber parliament ZANU-PF took 116 of the 120 seats and ZUM only two. But only 54% of Zimbabwe's 4·8 million eligible voters turned out (the figure had been 95% in previous elections) and apathy was deepest among the urban working-class. There were also charges of ballot rigging. Nevertheless, Zimbabwe was expected to become a one party state in 1990.

Land Redistribution.

An important issue in the elections had been land redistribution. In December 1990 constitutional obstacles to the state purchase of white-owned land for redistribution to black peasants expired. Mr Mugabe's government had already bought three million hectares and in January 1991 the Minister of Lands & Agriculture announced proposals to buy a further six million hectares, half the country's commercial land, for redistribution. White commercial farmers feared they would be inadequately compensated and appealed to the government to moderate its approach.

The Abandonment of Marxism.

The radical land bill would allow the government to set its own purchase price. This appeared to threaten the interests of the 4,500 white farmers who owned 30% of the country's most fertile land. The proposals were criticised by Zimbabwe's chief justice and a Catholic human rights group. But events in Eastern Europe were having an impact on the ideological stance of Zimbabwe's ruling ZANU-PF. In June 1991 the party formally abandoned Marxism–Leninism. President Mugabe said that party members argued that as socialism was being abandoned by other countries "there was no reason why we should continue to stick to it". The central committee voted to remove all references to "Marxism–Leninism" and "scientific socialism" from the party constitution. However, the government tabled a bill in February 1992 to purchase half the white-owned land for redistribution.

On 6 March President Mugabe declared that the drought affecting southern Africa was having a disastrous effect on Zimbabwe and appealed for foreign aid. His government was criticised for ignoring earlier warnings from white farmers of the potential crisis. On 1 April ministers met their South African counterparts to discuss South African assistance in transporting food to Zimbabwe, ending a previous refusal to have such contacts.

The government continued to attempt to encourage private enterprise following the abandonment of socialism in 1991. In April 1993 the long-standing ban on foreign investment in the Zimbabwe stock market was lifted and investors allowed to remit profits. But industrialists called for greater economic liberalisation, the development of tourism and a reduction in public spending.

The Regrouping of the Opposition.

An attempt was made to form an effective opposition to Mr Mugabe when, on 27 January 1994, Bishop Abel Muzorewa announced the merger of the United African National Council (UANC) with Edgar Tekere's Zimbabwe Unity Movement (ZUM). Revelations in March and April that much of the white-owned land compulsorily purchased under the 1992 Land Acquisition Act had been leased to officials and civil servants embarrassed the government. Mr Mugabe instituted an official enquiry and on 3 May many of the leases were cancelled.

The 1995 Elections.

In elections to the 150 seat parliament held on 8/9 April 1995, Mr Mugabe's ruling Zanu-PF emerged with 118 seats against two for the opposition, due largely to an apathetic 50% turnout and a lack of opposition candidates. Zanu-PF was unopposed in 55 seats. A further 20 seats were filled by presidential appointees and ten allocated to traditional chiefs.

MOZAMBIQUE.

The 16 year civil war—in which 600,000 had died and four million had become refugees—ended with the signing of a truce by President Chissano and Alfonso Dhlakam of Renamo in Rome on 7 August 1992. To have continued the conflict in the midst of the drought affecting much of southern Africa would have guaranteed mass starvation among Mozambique's population. In addition, arms supplies to Renamo had been diminishing as its principal backer South Africa moved towards democracy. A formal peace treaty was signed on 4 October. Both sides agreed to disband their forces under UN supervision and to create a new 30,000 strong army equally representing the government and Renamo. Multi-party elections were planned for September 1993. But there were fears that, however genuine the hopes of both leaders, they might not exert sufficient control over their followers to guarantee a long-term cessation of violence. By late November it was clear that the plan had fallen behind schedule. Zimbabwe announced that it would halt the planned withdrawal of its 5,000 troops protecting the road and rail corridor to Beira.

Elections were now scheduled for October 1994 but in November 1993 the opposition movement Renamo objected to the government's proposals on votes for Mozambicans overseas and on the composition of the body responsible for implementing decisions taken by the multiparty national electoral commission. UN peacekeeping officials warned that unless agreement was reached the elections might be delayed.

The government faced increasing criticism from both Renamo and the UN in January 1994 for the slowness of withdrawal of its forces to confinement areas. Following President Chissano's announcement on 11 April that multi-party elections would be held in October, government and Renamo representatives agreed on the formation of a new Mozambique Defence Armed Forces (FADM). The new force was set up on 16 August. In elections for the 250 seat legislature held on 27–28 October, Frelimo candidates took 129 seats with 44% of the vote, Renamo winning 112 seats with 38%. Mr Chissano was re-elected president with 53% of the vote, the Renamo candidate Afonso Dhlakama taking 34%. Renamo, however, boycotted the inaugural session of parliament, finally agreeing to take its seats on 30 December.

ANGOLA.

After 16 years of war, peace at last came nearer to reality in Angola with the formal signing on 31 May 1991 of the Estoril Accord in Lisbon between the warring factions.

Following the signing, President dos Santos and UNITA leader Jonas Savimbi met Portuguese businessmen to discuss the rebuilding of Angola's devastated economy. In April 1991 the MPLA had formally abandoned its Marxist ideology and declared itself to be a social democratic party. UNITA had meanwhile announced its transformation from a guerrilla army to a political party. On 16 June UNITA representatives arrived in the capital Luanda for the first time since 1975 to set up a political office. On 19 July President dos Santos appointed Fernando Franca van Dunem as prime minister, restoring the office abolished in 1977. On 29 September Mr. Savimbi returned to Luanda to open his campaign for presidential elections due to be held in 1992.

Presidential and parliamentary elections planned for September 1992 were threatened by clashes in August between government and UNITA supporters. However, voting on 29–30 September was relatively peaceful. But as the initial results came in Mr. Savimbi declared the elections had been rigged and—ignoring offers of a post in a national unity government—threatened to renew fighting. On 6 October UNITA withdrew from the newly-formed joint Armed Forces of Angola (FAA) and, after unsuccessful mediation attempts, several thousand UNITA members began to take up position in their former rural strongholds. On 11 October there were clashes in the capital Luanda.

The Election Outcome.

The final election results were announced on 17 October. President dos Santos took 49·6% of the vote and Mr. Savimbi 40·1%, with the remainder divided between nine other candidates. In elections for the 223 seat parliament, the MPLA took 54% of the vote and UNITA 30·1%. Mr. Savimbi rejected the results. There was heavy fighting in Luanda on 30 October in which 1,000 were killed before a truce was agreed. But, as parliament was due to open, clashes were renewed. Mr. Savimbi said on 29 November that he was willing to join a national unity government, but only if UNITA was given major ministries. However, by early January 1993 full-scale civil war had returned. On 23 January the government put forward a peace proposal as the tide had turned and UNITA forces appeared to be meeting with success. There were three days of talks which began between the two sides in Addis Ababa on 27 January but, as 2·5 million people faced starvation, the talks faltered and UNITA advances continued.

Continuing Civil War.

The peace talks were suspended on 1 March 1993 following UNITA's repeated failure to attend. On 8 March the government admitted the loss to UNITA of Huambo, Angola's second largest city, following a 56-day battle in which 10,000 people—mainly civilians—had died. UNITA, which now controlled over half the country, immediately offered to re-open discussions. Pressure was placed on UNITA to end the fighting when, on 19 May, the US government (formerly a staunch supporter of UNITA) finally recognised the MPLA government 17 years after Angola had gained independence.

Peace talks in Zambia were halted in November by government demands that UNITA should disarm its civilian supporters and there was confusion on 5 December when a government spokesman denied earlier reports that agreement on a ceasefire had been reached.

Despite continued clashes between government and UNITA forces, negotiators were able to agree on 30 January 1994 on the need for "national reconciliation". By the end of April the two sides agreed on a second round of presidential elections. However, as UNITA forces attacked the government-held towns of Cuito and Cabinda, the UN Security Council demanded an end to the fighting. On 30 May UNITA was offered four ministerial portfolios but its representatives abandoned negotiations following an upsurge of fighting in Cuito in which over 300 people were killed.

The Formal Peace Accord.

Negotiations remained deadlocked through the summer, with argument centred on UNITA's demand that it be given governorship of Huambo province. A general agreement was reached on 31 October as government military pressure on UNITA forces intensified. UNITA's main stronghold of Huambo fell on 10 November. Mr Savimbi threatened to refuse to sign a peace agreement unless the government withdrew. Following the government's announcement of a ceasefire on 16 November, the peace accord was formally signed in Lusaka on 20 November by President dos Santos and General Eugenio Manuvakola, UNITA's secretary general.

ZAMBIA.

Multi-Party Elections, 1991.

In November 1991 Zambia held its first multi-party elections for 23 years. President Kaunda's United National Independence Party (UNIP) had ruled Zambia (formerly Northern Rhodesia) since independence in 1964. Following elections in 1968 President Kaunda intensified a programme of nationalisation and moved towards a one-party state, which was imposed in 1972. But the nationalisation of copper mining, and the attempt to provide extensive social services, proved expensive. Zambia had been among Africa's richest countries in 1964 but by the 1980s living standards had fallen dramatically as copper reserves declined and agriculture failed. UNIP's rule became more oppressive.

Formation of the MMP.

Against this background of economic failure, President Kaunda was forced in July to recognise the formation of an opposition Movement for Multi-Party Democracy (MMP). The MMP leader, Frederick Chiluba, had been chairman of the 300,000 strong Zambia Congress of Trade Unions since 1974 and was a longstanding opponent of one-party rule. The MMP, which advocated a market economy, an end to agricultural subsidies, and the encouragement of foreign investment through the privatisation of mining, had broad support among unions, business, and students.

The combined presidential and National Assembly elections saw an overwhelming defeat for the UNIP. The MMD won 135 assembly seats and UNIP the remaining 15. In the presidential election Mr. Chiluba took 62% of the vote. President Chiluba called for respect to be shown to Dr. Kaunda, whom he called "the father of the nation". Mr. Levy Mwanawasa was appointed vice-president and Zambia began a programme of economic reform which included devaluation and the ending of food subsidies. President Chiluba appealed for patience with his government's austerity policies.

Despite an apparently smooth transition to parliamentary democracy with elections in November 1991 President Chiluba declared a state of emergency on 4 March 1993. Ten people were detained, including the son of former President Kaunda. The foreign minister, Vernon Mwaanga, accused the opposition UNIP of receiving funds from Iran and Iraq to seize power through an insurrection, an accusation UNIP officials denied.

The Cabinet Restructuring.

On 11 February 1994 President Chiluba was forced to restructure his cabinet following allegations that two ministers were involved in corruption and drug trafficking. The Zambia Congress of Trade Unions (ZCTU), President Chiluba's former power base, had called on him to carry out a drastic purge of the cabinet. ZCTU remained unsatisfied, accusing seven of the remaining ministers of involvement in the scandal. Western aid donors forced the resignation of the foreign minister, community affairs minister and deputy speaker of parliament. In July President Chiluba dismissed his legal affairs minister and in the same month vice-president Levy Mwanawasa resigned, accusing the government of condoning greed. He was replaced by Brigadier-General Godfrey Miyanda. The former president, Mr Kaunda, announced that it might be necessary for him to return to politics.

THE UNITED STATES

America under Bush.

In the election of 8 November 1988, George Bush was elected the 41st President of the United States. His percentage of the popular vote was 54%, but in the electoral college (where the outcome is actually decided) he won with a lopsided majority. This is explained by the effect of the rule by which a small victory in a state gives the winner all of that state's electoral college vote. This transformed tiny popular margins in California, Illinois, and Pennsylvania into complete victories. Mr. Bush won all of the largest states except for New York, and secured a total of 426 electoral college votes to Governor Dukakis's 112.

The ten states which Mr. Dukakis won were all in the north: Massachusetts, New York, Rhode Island, and West Virginia in the north-east; Iowa, Minnesota (the only state won by Walter Mondale in 1984) and Wisconsin in the mid-west; and Oregon and Washington in the Pacific north-west. Dukakis also won the District of Columbia, which has been safely and overwhelmingly Democratic since the District's voters were first enfranchised at Presidential elections in 1964. Bush won everywhere else. In some major states, such as California and Illinois, he did so with the tiniest pluralities; in the south, and the mountain states, he won with the greatest of ease. However, Bush's margins in the farming belt were noticeably smaller than Reagan's had been in 1980 and 1984—the crisis in American farming harmed the Republican ticket. Two of the nation's fastest-growing states, Florida and Texas, went solidly for Bush; the south was in general his strongest region.

Early Period in Office.

The President's first fifteen months in office were quiescent, and major problems of public policy lay effectively unaddressed. In his single major economic initiative, the proposal to reduce capital gains tax, the President failed when the Senate rejected the move. His greatest opportunity for dealing with them passed with the close of the first session of his first Congress in December 1989. Unlike President Reagan, Mr. Bush did not exploit the window of opportunity in his first year to establish clear priorities for his administration, and to urge Congressional action upon them. By the comparable point in his first term, Reagan had signed all of his major legislation on the economy and defence into law.

The President's weak legislative record was nonetheless combined in the early months of 1990 with widespread democratic revolution abroad from Nicaragua to South Africa and to Eastern Europe, and with extraordinarily high public approval ratings for the President from the American public. Not since President Kennedy's first year has an American President enjoyed such great approval from the American public. Bush has set out deliberately to redefine the nature of the Presidency, to keep public expectations low, and to ensure that his few foreign initiatives (such as the invasion of Panama in December 1989) were marked with quick and overwhelming success.

America and the Gulf.

American politics in the second half of 1990 and the first half of 1991 were dominated by the Gulf War. The victory over Iraq was nominally one achieved by the coalition forces; in practice, it was won by the United States. The utility of the broad coalition for the United States was political and diplomatic; the huge and complicated military operation was made easier by the addition of British, French, and forces from several Arab nations but it was not essential for the outcome. Had it been required to do so, the United States alone could have achieved the same military result.

A Military Triumph.

The outcome was a spectacular military and political triumph for the United States, and for President Bush in particular. Bush's decided preference for foreign and defence policy over domestic policy was vindicated in the most emphatic and clear-cut fashion. Iraq was not only ejected from Kuwait but the United States emerged from the military engagement as the overwhelmingly dominant world power once more. The corrosive doubts about the nation's conventional military capability which had been fostered in Korea and seemingly confirmed in Vietnam were here laid to rest. The thesis of American decline which had shortly before appeared so compelling to many commentators in the United States and abroad seemed less so in the wake of complete victory. Using the United Nations as a vehicle for its policy, the United States fought the Gulf War on its own terms; the Soviet Union had the means to play a marginal diplomatic role only. Whilst the festering domestic problems of the fiscal deficit, education, a weakening infrastructure, and poverty lay unaddressed, the President showed by the steadiness of his judgment abroad that the application of American military power abroad could achieve results which much foreign opinion, most of his political opponents and many of his nominal party colleagues in Congress thought beyond not only his capacity but that of the United States.

The Ascendancy of Bush.

The single most important short-run implication for the United States of President Bush's successful leadership in the Gulf was the immense bolstering of his political position. With the Presidential Primary elections just ten months away at the conclusion of the war, the President was beyond challenge in his own party and (barring a dramatic and wholly unforeseen chain of damaging events) probably beyond defeat by a Democratic contender. Except for Senator Albert Gore of Tennessee, all of Bush's potential Democratic opponents in Congress voted against the President in the Congressional votes sanctioning the initiation of hostilities. Bush's campaign strategists for 1992 would certainly ensure that those votes were hung around the necks of Democratic opponents.

In the Spring of 1991, it seemed improbable that a powerful Democratic candidate could be induced to run against Bush in 1992. Only Gore had an unblemished foreign policy record (he not only supported Bush in the vote on the Gulf War but had himself served in Vietnam) and that was unlikely to be sufficient to stop a President with the highest opinion poll ratings in American history.

The Budget Imbroglio.

In November 1990, the President's circumstances had been very different. His poll ratings had then been driven sharply lower by the annual imbroglio over the Federal budget in the course of which he abandoned his 1988 election pledge not to agree to a rise in taxation. That move brought down upon his head the wrath of the right-wing of his own party in Congress, and caused many of his 1988 supporters to be deeply disillusioned (once again) with the fickleness of political leaders. The President's complete failure to address systematically the root causes of the disastrous structural fiscal deficit and the crises in public education and in health care mattered greatly before victory in war squeezed them all from the news headlines and changed completely the political agenda. Nonetheless, the domestic problems will rise up the agenda once more as memories of war begin to fade.

The 1990 Elections.

Elections took place to state legislatures, Governorships, the whole of the US House of Representatives, and to 34 seats in the US Senate in elections held on Tuesday, 6 November 1990. The results of the contests were important for public policy both in the states and in Washington, DC. All Presidents view these mid-term elections with trepidation since they invariably result in his party sustaining losses in Congress, the legislature whose support he needs for his policies to be made effective but which the separation of powers prevents him from controlling. In the event, Bush suffered the reverses familiar to all modern Presidents in the mid-terms of his own first year where the Democrats extended slightly their majorities in both the House and the Senate. The new party balances give the Democrats leads of 267 to 167 in the House, and 56 to 44 in the Senate. In the races for state Governorships, the Democrats maintained their advantage, but the Republicans made a net gain of two. The President's failure to advance a coherent domestic programme coupled with the political bonus deriving from his leadership in war, diminished the significance of the results in the short-term but made impossible the implementation of an alternative and much more radical privatisation agenda favoured by some of his staff.

The Gulf War Aftermath.

The political benefits of American triumph in the Gulf War ebbed away as the primary season of 1992 approached. Whilst the American victory called the political judgment of his would-be Democratic opponents into question, President Bush found his own judgment a political issue because of the failure of the Allied operation against Iraq to bring about Saddam Hussein's downfall. Moreover, the desperate plight of the Kurds in the north of Iraq and the Shi'ites in the south of the country meant that public attention in the United States focused upon the respects in which the war had failed as much as upon those in which it had succeeded.

If the President found the aftermath of the Gulf War politically uncomfortable, domestic economic policy presented altogether greater difficulties for him. In retrospect, as he acknowledged at the beginning of the primary contests in 1992, he had weakened himself by agreeing to the budget package of November 1990 by which income taxes were raised. The terms of that settlement had divided the President's Republican colleagues in Congress. Many within the Party who had identified closely with President Reagan's fiscal radicalism opposed the deal; others whose fear of the consequences of the federal deficit being allowed to grow out of control outweighed their preference for lower taxes supported it.

The Buchanan Challenge.

The dispute within the Republican Party opened wider with the announcement by Mr. Pat Buchanan, a former speech-writer to Presidents Nixon and Reagan, that he would oppose President Bush's bid for renomination by the Republican Party. The fissures within the Republican Party became plain as the campaign for the first primary of the season began in New Hampshire. It quickly became apparent that although Buchanan could not win the nomination against the President he could inflict significant damage upon him.

The Democrats Divided.

The Democrats, however, were scarcely free of difficulties of their own. The early primaries produced a clear leader in Governor Bill Clinton of Arkansas with former Senator Paul Tsongas of Massachusetts some way behind. Clinton, however, had been weakened by charges of marital infidelity and of sharp business practice. Whilst he was able to repair his campaign in the primaries, refurbishing it for the Presidential election itself is an altogether more demanding proposition. One of the consequences of the peculiar American practice of conferring the procedure of nomination upon primary and caucus electorates rather than upon party elites is that the coalition required for nomination may differ sharply from that required for election.

The Los Angeles Riots.

The tensions in American society were vividly brought to world attention by the devastating race riots in Los Angeles at the end of April. They resulted in 58 deaths, the worst civil disorder in America this century.

America since 1992.

For the election of 1992, the Clinton victory and the record of the Clinton administration, see **Special Topic C73–5.**

CANADA
The November 1988 Elections.

In a campaign which turned on the parties' contrasting policies toward one issue, the free-trade agreement between Canada and the United States, Brian Mulroney's Progressive Conservatives won 43% of the vote in the Canadian General Election of 21 November 1988, and an overall majority in the House of Commons. The immediate consequence was that the Prime Minister pressed the free-trade legislation (which had been delayed by the election) on the legislature and the agreement quickly became accomplished fact.

The Progressive Conservatives won 170 seats, the Liberals 82, and the New Democrats 43. As so often in Canadian elections, the parties' share of the vote varied widely across the country. In contrast to previous elections, however, the Liberals' stronghold of Quebec Province fell to Mr. Mulroney's colleagues who won 58 of its 75 seats (in 1980, the year of the Quebec Party's huge advance, they had won must one).

Although Mr. Mulroney's defence of the Free-Trade agreement, and the Liberal leader Mr. John Turner's attacks upon it, served to give a sharp focus to the campaign, public opinion of it shifted considerably in the weeks before the election. That the Agreement involves some risk for Canada is clear: as it opens up the markets of her huge neighbour to the south, so it carries the implicit threat that capital and job opportunities will move south, imperilling Canada's economic security. The voters, on balance, saw greater attraction in the possibility of the former than in the risk of the latter.

The Meech Lake Accord.

By early 1990, the terms of the Meech Lake Accord had become the focus of intense political disagreement which threatened the stability of the federation. The Accord had been negotiated in 1987 by Prime Minister Mulroney and the premiers of the ten provinces in an attempt to make the constitution acceptable to the people of Quebec. Among the concessions made to Quebec in the Accord were the recognition of French in Quebec and English elsewhere as the dominant languages; a requirement that amendments to the constitution win the support of the federal government and all ten provinces; greater influence for the provinces in the appointment of Supreme Court justices and members of the Senate; the granting of authority to Quebec to control foreign immigration into the province; and restrictions on federal programmes and spending authority.

In order to become law, the Accord had to win the approval of all provincial legislatures by 23 June 1990. The 23 June deadline for ratification of the Meech Lake Accord passed without either Newfoundland or Manitoba agreeing to ratify the amendments. Indeed, neither province actually voted on the amendments: Manitoba's procedures were derailed by a dispute over aboriginal rights, whilst the premier of Newfoundland adjourned the

legislature in protest at what he claimed (with some justice) was the intense pressure exerted upon the province by Ottawa. The atmosphere of constitutional crisis grew, though slowly. The political uncertainty harmed Canada's commercial prospects, and did great damage to Prime Minister Mulroney's standing. It also caused major difficulties for the Liberal Party since Quebec's premier, Robert Bourassa, had to meet the nationalist aspirations of much of his electorate, whilst remaining alert to the attempts of the *Parti Quebecois* to outflank him; his relations with some other Liberal premiers were accordingly poor.

The 1991 Liberal Conference.

At a conference in March 1991, Quebec's Liberal Party accepted a party report which demanded that a referendum be held by 1992 on the question of independence for the province unless, in effect, autonomy was not conceded before then. Under the Quebec Liberals' proposals, the federal government would be left with defence, monetary policy, and customs duties collection as its main remaining functions. Were Quebec to achieve this degree of autonomy, the central government would be dramatically weakened, the maritime provinces physically isolated from the rest of Canada, and the country's very existence imperilled.

Canada in Recession.

Canada's heavy dependence upon exports was painfully evident in 1991. Recession in the United States reduced demand there for Canadian exports in 1991 which in turn depressed economic activity. Gross Domestic Product fell by slightly more than 1% during the year, company profits fell, unemployment rose, and government finances deteriorated sharply. Downward pressure on federal spending intensified during the year and in early 1992, but could not overcome the additional spending arising from increased unemployment benefits. Growth in the Canadian economy, politically essential for a recovery in the fortunes of Mulroney's administration, is now dependent upon an end to the recession in the United States. The main benefit of a high exchange rate policy for the Canadian dollar and of reduced economic activity is now apparent in a low rate of inflation (approximately 4%). Dependent as Canada is upon her trade with the United States, frictions in the trading relationship are becoming ever more apparent. For Mulroney's purposes, it is essential to quieten the discontent which many Canadians feel with the implementation of the 1986 free trade agreement with the United States.

Politically weakened by the poor condition of the economy, Mulroney and his colleagues continued to struggle with the constitutional crisis engendered by the failure of the Meech Lake Accord.

New Constitutional Proposals.

Following two years of often acrimonious discussion, a new set of constitutional proposals was unanimously agreed by the ten provincial premiers and the Prime Minister at a meeting in August 1992. The plan provided for:
*a special status for the province of Quebec which was to be recognised as a "distinct society" with new powers which included the right to 25% of the seats in the House of Commons, irrespective of whether its population fell in relation to that of the rest of the country;
*a new Senate with a revised allocation of seats designed to favour the western provinces;
*recognition of the right of native peoples to self-government.

In the referendum of 26 October 1992, six of the provinces voted to reject the referendum as, by a margin of 54–46, did Canada as a whole. Quebec's voters rejected it, mostly because they held that the proposals conceded too little to francophone Canada, whilst all four western provinces rejected it because they deemed it to concede too much. Accordingly, there was no majority for a reform which would accommodate Quebec's aspirations, but nor was there a majority for Canda to fragment. The only remaining majority was for the *status quo*, but only by default.

The Resignation of Mulroney.

In the aftermath of the referendum, Canadian politics continued much as before: the government's popularity remained at an extremely low ebb, weakened by sluggish recovery from economic recession, high real interest rates and large government debt. Canada's weak economic condition had short-run political implications because a federal election had to take place before September 1993. The Conservatives were not to be led into that election by Brian Mulroney. After ten years in post, Mulroney resigned in February 1993, to be replaced by Kim Campbell.

Kim Campbell's replacement of Brian Mulroney as Prime Minister was followed by a shrewdly-judged set of Cabinet changes in late June 1993 by which she attempted to conciliate factions in the Conservative Party and sundry regional and provincial interests which had felt themselves marginalised under her predecessor's administration.

The Election Disaster.

Despite the freshness which Campbell's Premiership lent it, the Progressive Conservative Party slid in the elections of October 1993 to the heaviest defeat ever suffered by a governing party in Canada. It was left with 17% of the vote, and only two seats; among those to lose was Prime Minister Campbell herself. The Liberal Party, under the leadership of Jean Chretien, won more than 42% of the popular vote, and a Parliamentary majority of 177.

Votes were skewed by province: the Liberals won heavily in the Atlantic Provinces and in Ontario; Mr. Preston Manning's populist Reform Party's 52 seats were won mostly in the provinces of British Columbia and Alberta; the moderately left-wing New Democratic Party's representation fell to just nine seats, all of them from western provinces; the Bloc Quebeçois's (BQ) 54 seats were won entirely from within Quebec. Such regional partisan concentration carried both an opportunity and a risk also for Chretien as the new Prime Minister.

* The opportunity lay in no other party having any claim to be able to address the persisting problem presented by the BQ's strength in Quebec. Of the three significant parties, the Liberals alone stood for a federal solution to the Quebec question.

* The risks sprang both from the growing discontent within Quebec and from particular opposition dislike within the province towards the new Prime Minister: Chretien had led the opposition to the Meech Lake Accord by which Quebec would have enjoyed enhanced powers both over federal policy-making and its own. The Liberals' election platform was consistent with Chretien's opposition, thereby making the concessions to Quebec, necessary to accommodate secessionist opinion, all the more difficult to make.

The Chretien Agenda.

Mr. Chretien's political inheritance is exceptionally difficult. In addition to the Quebec question, economic problems loom large. His Liberal government has, in particular, to address the persisting problem of the large federal budget deficit. It was apparent at the end of 1993 that the deficit for 1994 would, in the absence of large public expenditure reductions, considerably exceed the deficit forecast at the time of the Conservative Government's last budget in the Spring of 1993. (Provincial governments, especially Quebec and Ontario, also faced large deficits in their own budgets.) Given the Liberals' spending commitments to stimulate job creation and to maintain old age pensions and welfare payments, the Federal deficit will not be cut without considerable political difficulty.

The Reduction of the Deficit.

Intensifying budgetary pressures in 1994 galvanised the government into setting a target for the reduction of the deficit to 3% of GDP by the 1996/7 financial year. The difficulty of reaching the target was enhanced by rising interest rates, thereby increasing the government's borrowing costs further. Political opposition to public spending reductions came not only from those groups whose

federal subsidies were threatened, but from provincial governments which depended heavily upon federal financial support. Difficulties of public finance apart, the Canadian economy enjoyed a strong year in 1994: economic growth was running at slightly more than 4·0% per annum, price inflation was a mere 0·4%, production was rising, and real incomes were growing. Even unemployment, although still significantly higher than the levels in the United States, was falling.

The prospect of cuts in Federal support for Provincial government programmes complicated the handling of Quebec's possible secession, a major question which the Parti Quebecois government pressed in 1994 to the point of introducing legislation claiming unfettered jurisdiction for the province over fiscal, foreign, and defence policy. A referendum will be held during 1995 on the question of whether Quebec voters support the bill, a move which, whilst it may not result in support for effective independence, is likely to mark a further weakening in the evolution of Canada towards a looser federation.

LATIN AMERICA

EL SALVADOR.

Following the ceasefire, the Farabundo Marti Liberation Front (FLMN) participated in the 1994 elections as a legitimate political party in coalition with Democratic Convergence (CD). In the first round of presidential elections on 20 March 1994, the strength of support for FMLN–CD candidate Rubin Zamora in the rural areas prevented ruling ARENA candidate Armando Calderón Sol from winning an absolute majority. Coalition complaints of voting irregularities were supported by UN observers who insisted they be put right before the second round.

In the second round on 24 April Calderón was the clear winner, taking 818,264 votes (68·2%) to Zamora's 368,980 (31·6%). In simultaneous elections to the 84-seat Legislative Assembly ARENA took 39 seats to the FMLN-CD's 21. ARENA also captured 200 of the 262 municipal councils. Talks began immediately to resolve issues identified during the 1992 peace talks, particularly the need for electoral, judicial and land reforms and the reduction of the army. By September continued delays in implementing the peace accords were a source of tension.

Split in the FMLN.

The FMLN's difficulties in moving from revolutionary to constitutional politics were revealed at its national council meeting on 9 May. A damaging split emerged between Marxist and moderate factions. Eight leading members of the National Resistance Armed Forces (FARN) and the People's Revolutionary Army (ERP) ignored an FMLN decision not to participate in the election of the president of the Legislative Assembly's directorate, supported the ARENA candidate, and went on to accept seats on the directorate. Divisions continued to the extent that in December 1994 moderate leader Joaquín Villalobos withdrew from the FMLN umbrella because of what he alleged was its continuing Marxist-Leninist ideological stance. Meanwhile, a privatisation programme instituted by the government aroused increasing opposition from the trade unions as 1995 opened.

GUATEMALA.

The Advent of Ramiro de León.

Ramiro de León became president in June 1993. A peace proposal in July was rejected by the Guatemalan National Revolutionary Union (UNRG) in October. However, on 10 January 1994 agreement was reached between the two. An Assembly was formed to negotiate a peace treaty by the end of the year, headed by the Bishop of Zacapa.

But the country entered a new phase of violence when, on 1 April, the President of the Constitutional Court was assassinated, allegedly because of his role in ruling that President Serrano's attempted coup of May 1993 had been unconstitutional. The murder of a prominent congressional deputy was followed by that of an influential businessman. A wave of kidnappings, some involving foreigners, threatened to have a drastic effect on the country's economy. There were suggestions of military involvement, aimed at creating an atmosphere of tension which would hinder the development of the peace process with URNG.

Security and the Army.

Against this background, President León transferred responsibility for internal security to the army. He denied that this represented a step back from democratisation and congressional elections were set for 14 August, although the number of deputies was reduced from 116 to 80. The Guatemalan Republican Front (FRG) — with 32 seats — emerged as the largest single party. However, an alliance of the National Advancement Party (PAN), the National Liberation Movement (FLN) and the Democratic Union (UD) took control of the congressional directorate, naming PAN's Arabella Castro de Comparini as its leader. But the fact that only 20% of the electorate participated in the elections showed a general cynicism towards politicians.

Further peace talks with the URGN collapsed on 29 November after failure to reach agreement on human rights issues.

MEXICO.

For the political and financial crisis in Mexico, *see* **Special Topic C75–6.**

NICARAGUA.

Relations with the Sandanistas.

As Violeta Chamorro tried to maintain control, right-wing elements in her coalition became increasingly critical of continued dialogue with the Sandanistas. With three years remaining before the next elections, the Sandanistas called for a national unity government. But in an atmosphere of almost perpetual electoral campaigning, all parties adopted increasingly polarised positions. A demobilisation agreement with the 3–80 Northern Front (FN 3–80) was threatened in February 1994 by continuing disagreement over allocation of land to the former rebels. Demobilisation went ahead in March.

In late July and early August 1994 there were bomb explosions in Managua and León. There were no casualties and the bombings were regarded more as political protests than terrorist acts. The Sandanistas denied involvement and there were suggestions that they were the responsibility of the Front for Popular Struggle (FLP), a radical breakaway from the FSLN.

Ortega Re-asserts Control.

Divisions sharpened within the Sandanista movement. Former president Daniel Ortega was re-elected FSLN secretary general on 22 May 1994 and, with the election of eight hardline supporters to the 15-member national directorate, won complete control of the party. The newly elected Sandanista assembly determined on firmer opposition to the Chamorro government. On 18 May President Chamorro had announced—under pressure from right-wing critics—that Ortega's brother would retire as army commander in chief on 21 February 1995. There was further evidence of Sandanista divisions in September. The moderate leader of the 39-strong National Assembly FSLN group, Sergio Ramirez Mercado, was dismissed for disobeying party directives. He was replaced, however, by another moderate, Dona María Téllez. A party split became almost inevitable with the resignation in October of former culture minister Ernesto Cardenal, followed by further resignations in November. The conflict culminated on 10 January 1995 with the resignation of Dr Ramírez, following Dona María Téllez's announcement that she was leaving the Sandanista national directorate.

SOUTH AMERICA

ARGENTINA.

President Menem used legislative elections in

October 1993 as a test of the acceptability of his aim to stand as a candidate for a second term in 1995. In a December 1993 pact, the two main parties—the Peronist Judicialist Party (PJ) and the Radical Civic Union (UCR) – agreed that Constituent Assembly members to be elected in April 1994 would have 90 days to endorse or reject constitutional reforms. These reforms included a reduction of the presidential term of office from six to four years; direct elections of the president and vice-president; and stronger legislative control over the executive.

The April 1994 Elections.

President Menem was disappointed by the results of the Constituent Assembly elections held on 10 April 1994. The PJ maintained its position as the leading party with 136 of the 305 seats, but did not gain an outright majority. The UCR, which had endorsed his reform proposals, took 75 seats. A striking result was the 37·5% of the vote in the capital for the newly formed centre-left Big Front coalition. With an eye to his hopes of re-election, President Menem announced a $7 billion anti-poverty plan at the 1 May inauguration of the assembly.

Prices and Free Market Economics.

The government's free market policies provoked the largest demonstration since President Menem took office. On 6 July over 50,000 demonstrators marched on Buenos Aires. Despite being banned the previous day, a general strike took place on 2 August. Opposition to government policies came from trade unionists and parties across the political spectrum. The new constitution was enacted on 22 August. This was followed by a freeze on public sector recruitment and the privatisation of all state enterprises, including the nuclear power industry, on 31 August in an attempt to balance the budget. These measures had reduced Argentina's inflation level from 5,000% to 5% in 1994 and there was a significant increase in economic growth.

Despite a 1·2% increase in prices in January 1995 President Menem began campaigning for re-election on 5 May, apparently with strong support among the electorate.

BRAZIL.

As 1994 opened the public sector approached breakdown and the new government was faced with corruption scandals. It was estimated that Brazil was losing $150 billion through tax evasion. Finance minister Cardoso attempted to rescue the government's anti-inflation programme with a Social Emergency Fund in February 1994. Having introduced this, Mr Cardoso announced his resignation on 20 March, timed to enable him to stand as the Social Democratic Party candidate in the October presidential election.

As monthly inflation of 45% provoked a series of nationwide pay strikes by the police and other state employees, the Federal Supreme Court ordered public sector strikes on 19 May. The armed forces' leadership were also restive about cuts in their budget and recommended that President Franco dissolve Congress. Public opinion appeared sympathetic to military intervention. As part of the economic stabilization programme, a new currency—the *real* — was introduced on 1 July and strict limits were set on the money supply. Inflation fell sharply.

The Advent of Cardoso.

Constitutional reforms enacted in May reduced the presidential term from five to four years. In presidential elections on 3 October, Mr Cardoso took 45% of the vote in an eight candidate race. His closest challenger, Luis Inacio Lula da Silva of the Workers' Party, polled 25%.

President Cardoso, whose term began in January 1995, had promised to concentrate on the fight against poverty. But as the effects of the Mexican crisis spread through Latin America, he abandoned promises to spend up to $20 billion on Brazil's infrastructure, putting stabilization and economic growth before immediate measures to help the poor. On 3 February presidential plans for constitutional reform were hampered by his decision to veto a 42% rise in the minimum wage. At the same time he announced that he and his ministers would take a 25% cut in salary. Opinion polls showed a slip in his popularity among the electorate from 70% at the start of his term to 36%.

CHILE.

Chile remained the most buoyant economy in South America. The October 1993 elections produced a landslide victory for Christian Democrat leader Eduardo Frei, the candidate of the ruling centrist coalition. Mr Frei took office in the first democratic transfer of power since 1970 on 11 March 1994. He promised that constitutional reforms would continue, but there seemed little possibility that the provision in the 1980 Constitution that the government could have no say in the appointment and dismissal of military commanders would be removed.

Trade Union Activism.

Despite the apparent success of the economy, trade unionists organised by the Chilean Unitary Labour Centre (CUT) marched on the capital Santiago on 11 July protesting against both the government and employers and demanding direct negotiations on wages and social conditions. Criticisms that the government lacked political initiative led to a cabinet reshuffle on 20 September. President Frei promised that the government was now entering a second phase and would concentrate on education, the infrastructure and increased production to raise the living standards of the poor.

PERU.

Continued failures of economic policy and President Fujimori's authoritarian style eroded his popularity in 1993. President Fujimori was disappointed by the narrow majority in an October 1993 referendum on a new constitution granting the president extra powers and allowing him to stand for a second term. He had staked his personal reputation on the outcome.

The president's problems were compounded by his relationship with his wife. Mrs Higuchi, as she called herself, accused the government of corruption and broken promises. She also objected to a new electoral law preventing relatives of the president from standing for political office. On 24 August 1994 President Fujimori announced that she would no longer perform her official functions as First Lady. On 12 September, Mrs Higuchi, now officially separated from her husband, announced her intention to stand as president for a newly formed political party, Harmony 21st Century. Polls suggested she had the support of 6% of voters. Former UN Secretary General Javier Perez de Cuellar, who announced his candidacy on 22 September, had 24% support. However, on 20 October Harmony 21st Century was disqualified from congressional elections when the National Electoral Board ruled that the party failed to qualify as a valid political party.

War with Ecuador.

Electoral campaigning was overshadowed when a longstanding boundary dispute with Ecuador in an area said to be rich in gold and oil erupted into serious clashes on 29 January. The date marked the 53rd anniversary of the signing of the Rio Treaty in 1942 which ended a war over the disputed territory. On 6 February ceasefire proposals were rejected by Ecuador. Talks were resumed in Brasilia on 10 February but both countries seemed on the edge of all-out war and there was growing concern throughout Latin America about the implications for economic investment in the region.

The war, however, did not dent Fujimori's election hopes. He won the presidency with over 60% of the vote.

AUSTRALASIA

AUSTRALIA.

The Second World War had a profound psychological and political impact on the Australian national identity. The fall of Singapore and the bombing of Darwin had revealed Britain's inability to defend

Australia, exposing her vulnerability to attack. Reliance on American power for protection initiated a radical shift in defence policy culminating in the 1951 Pacific Security treaty for mutual defence or ANZUS pact. Although emotional ties with Britain and Europe remained strong, Asia became of increasing economic and strategic importance. Britain's entry into the EEC in 1973 emphasised the need for new markets, with Japan rapidly becoming Australia's largest trading partner. By 1993 East Asia accounted for 58% of Australian exports compared to only 21% in 1957. Domestically, post-war electoral domination by the Liberal-Country coalition ended with the 1972 victory of Labour under Gough Whitlam. Many progressive social and economic reforms quickly followed, whilst conscription ended and Australia withdrew from Vietnam. Whitlam was dramatically dismissed in 1975 by the Governor-General, precipitating a constitutional crisis and ushering in eight years of Liberal-Country government. Labour was swept back into power in 1983 under Bob Hawke, who went on to lead the party to three more election victories in 1984, 1987 and 1990.

The Keating Administration.

Paul Keating became Labour leader and Prime Minister in December 1991 at his second attempt, continuing his predecessor's economic reforms with further privatisation and deregulation. The recession deepened as unemployment rose to 11% in 1993 and the current account deficit deteriorated to A $16bn. Whilst manufacturing was badly affected, the agricultural sector continued to decline, accounting for only 4% of GDP and 29% of exports in 1993 compared to 25% and 80% respectively in 1950. The fragile economic recovery was threatened by prolonged drought and widespread bushfires in Eastern Australia destroying livestock, crops and native fauna. Despite the recession and a series of State election setbacks, Labour scored a surprise victory in the March 1993 General Election, capitalising on popular opposition to the Liberal-National coalition plan for a goods and services tax. Labour won 45% of the vote and 80 seats to the coalition's 44% and 65 seats, with Independents gaining 2 seats. Although all the State governments, with the exception of Queensland, were controlled by the coalition, recent national polls still placed Labour ahead of a divided Opposition. Keating has promoted regional economic co-operation, following the removal of trade barriers with New Zealand in 1990. The success of the 1993 GATT world trade talks was crucial for an Australian economy competing with European and American subsidies and is fundamental to the planned creation of an Asia-Pacific free trade area by 2020.

The Changing Population.

Until 1946 when mass immigration from war-torn Europe began, the population was predominantly of Anglo-Celtic origin. By 1993, 23% of the population were born outside Australia, and non-Europeans, largely excluded until the White Australia policy was abandoned in 1973, now constitute the majority of immigrants. "Multiculturalism" has replaced "assimilation" as official policy towards immigrant communities, achieving a fairly harmonious accommodation of ethnic diversity. However, concern over jobs during the recession led to the government halving the annual intake quota to 65,000, and increasing antipathy towards Asian communities has become more apparent. Comprising only 1·5% of the population, Aborigines remain a disadvantaged minority with higher infant mortality, lower life expectancy and living standards below average. Promotion of Aboriginal rights has progressed with the historic High Court decision to recognise land rights existing before European settlement in 1788 (the Mabo ruling). A Government enquiry into treatment of Aborigines has prompted a $A500m programme of reconciliation to improve their lives over the next ten years.

A New Cultural Identity.

The choice of Sydney for the 2000 Olympics reflects the Australian influence on world sport and its importance domestically. Cricket, rugby and the Melbourne Cup horse race remain national pastimes. In the arts, the era of 'cultural cringe' typified by Dame Edna Everage and Sir Les Patterson has been replaced by a new self-confidence. Growing international recognition of Australian cinema has recently been matched by increasing popular success at the box office of films such as *Strictly Ballroom*, giving audiences a glimpse of Australian life distinct from the ever-popular television soap operas.

Time For A Republic?

The most debated topic in Australia today remains the future of the monarchy. Tentative moves in the 1970s towards a republic, with a new national anthem and the scrapping of royal patronage, were given fresh impetus by the Whitlam crisis. By 1986 the Australia Act had established the independence of Australian Law, abolishing Westminster's residual legislative and judicial controls. Keating, a confirmed republican, placed the issue back at the top of the national agenda by announcing in September 1993 that, subject to a referendum, Australia would become a republic by 2001, the centenary of the Commonwealth. Recent opinion polls have shown the country to be fairly evenly divided, with republicanism particularly strong among new immigrants and younger Australians, where allegiance to the Crown is weakest. During a recent visit, Prince Charles gained the respect of many not only by being unfazed at having blanks fired at him, but also by declaring that Australia's future was a matter for Australia alone. It seems inevitable that as emotional ties to Britain weaken and Australia develops a stronger national identity based on changing trade patterns, an increasingly diverse population and a new self-confidence, a republic will not be far away. Die-hard monarchists may be outraged when Keating accuses Britain of abandoning Australia during World War Two, but the 'clever country' with its huge natural resources and access to Asian markets is set to assert its independence. The Sydney Olympics may yet be opened by an Australian president under a new Australian flag.

NEW ZEALAND.

The Bolger Ascendancy.

Across the Tasman Sea, recent political and economic troubles have overshadowed an emerging republican debate. The National Party under Jim Bolger, having won the 1990 election as voters introduced an austerity package to reduce the budget deficit. Pensions, benefits, the health and education services were all deeply affected, as was National's popularity, but inflation and unemployment did finally start to fall and Bolger narrowly won again in November 1993 with a majority of 1.

The next election will be fought under the new mixed-member proportional system (MMP), which combines proportional representation and first-past-the-post, and has already precipitated new coalitions and internal party squabbling. Labour's 1985 declaration of a nuclear-free zone, enforced by legislation in 1987, put the future of the ANZUS pact in doubt, although relations with the USA have improved since US warships no longer carry tactical nuclear weapons. Relations with the Maori population, 10% of the total, slowly continue to improve with the creation of a Ministry of Maori Development in 1991. Bolger is pushing for a republic by 2000, but opinion polls consistently put support at below 30% though the fact that a republic is finally being discussed is significant. New Zealand, with a smaller, more homogenous population, may take longer than her neighbour in choosing to become a republic but will probably take that course eventually.

III. SPECIAL TOPICS

RUSSIA IN REVOLUTION

The August 1991 Coup.

In August 1991, on the eve of the new Union Treaty being signed, a motley and incompetent group of conservatives attempted to seize power in the Soviet Union by force and halt the process of disintegration for which the new Treaty was a flimsy cover. The coup lasted for less than a week by the end of which the dynamics of politics had changed completely. Gorbachev, who had been kept under house arrest in the Crimea during the attempted coup, returned to Moscow to find his power base collapsing beneath him, the Communist Party totally discredited, and his arch-rival, Boris Yeltsin, positioned to assume the reins of power. As Gorbachev's attempt to maintain a federal Soviet Union had failed, so his attempt to reform the Communist Party from within had come to naught. By the end of 1991, the Soviet Union ceased to exist, Gorbachev was no longer President, Yeltsin had abandoned the new Union Treaty and become President of Russia, and the successor Commonwealth of Independent States (CIS) had emerged. *Perestroika* had failed to save Communism from itself but had set in motion forces which its authors could not control and which ultimately caused the state to collapse.

The Commonwealth of Independent States.

The CIS was however little more than a loose and unstable confederation of eleven of the former fifteen Republics of the Soviet Union; the three Baltic states remain entirely outside its ambit. Each of the eleven CIS states appears determined to pursue its own governance and policies in its own way. The single greatest indictment of the CIS is that it has proved impossible to establish unified armed forces: Russia and the central Asian states are the only member states to have agreed to the establishment of a common force structure.

Russia is the dominant member of the CIS, but desperately weakened by economic collapse and internal divisions. The former central Asian Republics of the USSR are effectively dependent upon her, incapable of seeking wider influence or alliances of their own. In external policy, only Russia is a state of international significance, and then only as a supplicant; almost all of its foreign currency reserves in 1992 are being spent upon food. Armenia and Belarus will remain within the Russian sphere of influence, not least as protection against their neighbouring states of Azerbaijan and the Ukraine. Even the Baltic states, in the vanguard of the movement towards national self-determination, must maintain close relations with Russia both because of important trading relations and to placate substantial Russian minorities within their borders. Of other CIS members, only the Ukraine has an agricultural and economic base sufficiently strong to grant it a significant degree of independence from Moscow. Azerbaijan continues to be locked in a viciously debilitating war with Armenia over the disputed region of Nagorno-Karabakh, and Georgia was rent by virtual civil war resulting in the overthrow of President Zviad Gamsakhurdia early in 1992.

The Problems Yeltsin Faced.

Within Russia, Yeltsin's political honeymoon quickly ended. His role during the attempted coup was genuinely heroic: he bravely defied the plotters in public even as others privately sought accommodation, temporised, or gave different indications of support to different participants. Suddenly thrust into power, Yeltsin has had to abandon the luxuries of opposition and to learn rapidly the art of government. He is however scarcely a democrat. He rules by decree and takes little account of parliament but the weakness of the Russian state and the collapse of its economy results in him having little authority or influence. Many of his decrees smack more of aspiration than of clear-minded policy, and are without effect; the democratic revolution in Russia has destroyed not only a regime but ways of

thought, and modes of administration. Those administrative agencies which exist are often poorly-adapted to the demands of a market economy and the disordered growth of civil society.

The fragmentation of policy formation and the disintegration of policy implementation spring not only from the inadequacy of public administration but from divisions within Russia itself. Both the Russian government and people are themselves divided between different varieties of nationalists and democrats, represented by a plethora of parties and movements. Even under Communism, Russia's ethnic divisions were recognised by the establishment of twenty so-called autonomous Republics. Many of these, under the leadership of former Communists striving to remain in power by playing the nationalist card, were now pressing for nominal autonomy to be more fully realised. However, most of the republics physically within Russia were actually dominated by ethnic Russians which encouraged "Russia first" adherents to work for the retention of all borders between the former Republics of the Soviet Union, and to maintain Russia's own territorial integrity. Vice-President Alexander Rutskoi led the group. He was prepared to sacrifice economic and financial reform for the sake of achieving narrowly nationalist objectives.

The Economic Reform Process.

Time was short if economic reform was to become entrenched in Russia. Price liberalisation on almost all consumer goods had been accomplished with remarkable speed and had aroused less resistance than many had feared. Under the pressure of increased prices for most foodstuffs, the rate of inflation was high, but falling. The inflation rate at the end of 1992 was likely to be about 240%, about a quarter of that at the end of 1991. The fiscal deficit was to be cut—indeed, it is officially forecast (though probably optimistically) to be eliminated by the end of 1992 through further heavy cuts in defence spending from 20% to 10% of the total budget, reductions in public employment, a wide-ranging programme of privatisation, and revenue from the Value Added Tax (VAT) which was introduced in the first week of 1992.

Economic relations between Russia and the other CIS Republics were weak and chaotic—a testimony to the failure of the CIS to aggregate the diverse interests of its members on behalf of common objectives. The rouble would in the short to medium term remain the currency of CIS member states but as the introduction of coupons by the governments of the Ukraine and Belarus suggest, pressures from within individual states for an end to Russia's domination of economic relations was strong. Moreover, many Republics evinced less enthusiasm for market reforms than Yeltsin and his more liberal advisers. Much of the early impetus behind coordination of economic policy had been dissipated.

Continuing Power Struggle.

Russian politics in 1992 and early 1993 were dominated by the continuing struggle between President Yeltsin and his conservative opponents in the Congress of People's Deputies. At the December 1992 Congress, Yeltsin's appointee as Prime Minister, the leading reformist Yegor Geidar, was ejected from office following intense pressure from conservatives, moderates and industrialists. The most active group opposing Geidar was Civic Union whose members favoured investment in and regulation of key areas of the economy including energy, transport, food production, and the defence sector.

On 14 December, Viktor Chernomyrdin, a former Minister of Energy and a key figure in Civic Union, was appointed Prime Minister. His appointments to the Cabinet reflected the influence within Congress of nationalists, former Communists, and (especially) industrialists. The influence of the latter in particular was in turn reflected in an extension of subsidies to the energy sector, a strengthening of price controls, and a budget deficit moving back up to 10% of GNP.

The March 1993 Congress.

The dispute between Yeltsin and Congress, and hence over economic and industrial policy, grew in intensity during the four-day session of Congress in March 1993. Yeltsin's authority weakened rapidly during the four days. His belligerent responses to criticism and lightly-coded references to the possibility that he might take "extreme measures" aggravated his already weak position: the Chairman of the Congress, Khasbulatov, openly accused Yeltsin of seeking to bring the armed forces into politics. The outcome was that Yeltsin appeared to have concluded that no further compromise with the Congress was possible, and that it was therefore expeditious to hold a referendum on two questions:

*the distribution of power between Congress and the President;

*the private ownership of land.

It remained unclear whether a referendum could in practice be held without the parliamentary sanction required by the constitution. Congress actually voted overwhelmingly against the holding of a referendum but the stakes were so high that Yeltsin had little option but to attempt a circumvention of Congress by seeking popular backing.

The Referendum.

The crisis in relations between Yeltsin and parliament came to a head in the referendum held on 25 April. 64·6% of eligible voters turned out to vote. Of these, 58% responded in the affirmative to the question of whether they trusted Boris Yeltsin, and 52·9% supported his economic reforms. However, less than 33% supported the calling of early Presidential elections, and only 44% backed his request for early parliamentary elections.

The outcome greatly assisted Yeltsin, but denied him that which he had most prized: the effective capitulation of his opponents in parliament. New draft constitutional proposals from Yelsin would, if implemented, further strengthen his hand but were certain to be fought bitterly by those in parliament who would have most to lose by them.

1993 witnessed an intensification of Russia's political crisis, issuing in an attempted coup in the first week of October. Elections which followed in December confirmed the widespread dissatisfaction with the government and the electorate's desperate search for new and less painful remedies. Under conditions of disorder, fluidity, a stifling and cross-cutting patch-work of regulatory agencies, and a grave lack both of coherent authority and legitimacy, Western companies declined to supply the investment capital without which Russia had no prospect of significant economic recovery.

The October Rising.

Having publicly mused on the possibility of doing so as early as the late winter of 1993, President Yeltsin dissolved the Supreme Soviet and the Congress of People's Deputies by decree issued on 21 September 1993. The action drew sympathetic murmurings from Western political leaders abroad (who had firmly identified their interests with Yeltsin's), rather less whole-hearted backing from Russian public opinion, and (understandably) intense opposition from members of the parliament. It marked, nevertheless, an astonishing transformation for a politician who had himself in 1991 defended Parliament against anti-democratic forces but who had shown in the interim that he lacked the political judgment and skill to build coalitions with the Parliamentary majority. Western political leaders continued to support Yeltsin in the violent confrontation between the Parliamentary forces and Yeltsin's heavily-armed troops which besieged them in the White House (the Parliament Building in Moscow) between the 3rd and 4th of October, 1993. Electricity and water supplies to the White House and the Constitutional Court Building were cut off by Yeltsin's forces which on 4 October overwhelmed the Parliament's defenders.

Contrary to most reports in the western media, the Parliamentary majority was not composed of a majority of communist and fascist forces; only a minority (albeit a significant one) fell into either or both categories. Nevertheless, in the six to eight months prior to the coup attempt in October, political relations between the President and Parliament were strife-ridden and wholly unproductive. Politics polarized in frozen unproductivity.

The Fundamental Problems.

Part of the difficulty was, fundamentally, constitutional: the order by which Russia was governed in the early 1990s was wholly inadequate to cope with the strains imposed upon it by transition to a amarket economy and democracy. The jurisdictions of government's several parts were uncertain and the subject of vitriolic dispute. Boundaries between decrees issued by the President, and laws written by the Parliament, were unclear. Government's ineffectiveness was such that both laws and decrees were often simply disregarded (to the extent that they were known at all beyond the major cities). Politics in Russia was also marked by a striking lack of democratic culture and understanding, made worse by poor judgment: the arts of coalition-building were foreign to many senior politicians. The President himself was scarcely exempt from the charge, as his extraordinarily risky running battles with the Speaker of the Parliament, Ruslan Khasbulatov, and his Vice-President Alexsandr Rutskoy, graphically showed.

Yeltsin's crushing of the opposition was altogether more decisive than his fitful governing in the year preceding the crisis, but equally undiscriminating: by no means all who opposed him between 1991 and 1993 or during the coup were anti-democratic, but Yeltsin treated them similarly. Once he had overcome the immediate challenge, Yeltsin moved quickly to proscribe seventeen political parties and organisations accused of complicity in the uprising, including Communist organisations, and some nationalist groups. He also moved to abolish the Constitutional Court (thereby overturning the old constitution), and decided that parliamentary elections should be held in mid-December.

The Rise of Zhirinovsky.

Yeltsin's gamble on a favourable election outcome did not entirely succeed, not least because he had himself failed to organise a pro-reform Presidential party. Results of the elections to the 450 member State Duma (the lower house) held on 12 December gave 24% of the vote held on the party lists to the ill-named Liberal Democratic Party, an extreme nationalist party led by Vladimir Zhirinovsky; the other three major parties, taking between 12 and 14% of the vote, were Russia's Choice (a pro-reform party), the Communist Party and the Agrarian Party. However, Russia's Choice performed very much more strongly in the one half of the Duma's seats allocated by first-past-the-post rules in territorial constituencies. With seventy-eight deputies overall, Russia's Choice emerged as the largest grouping in the Duma but found itself opposed by all other major parties on the key questions of budgetary control and economic reform. Whilst a new constitution, approved by referendum on the day of the elections, gave the President much greater powers to set the agenda for government, the widespread discontent reflected in Zhirinovsky's support indicated that Yeltsin would have to tread warily.

The Resignation of Gaidar.

The political constraints under which Yeltsin laboured quickly became apparent in the resignation on 17 January 1994 of his Deputy Prime Minister Yegor Gaidar (and the Parliamentary leader of Russia's Choice) following the latter's failure to persuade colleagues of the need for strict budgetary controls in pursuit of a coherent anti-inflation strategy. Whilst Gaidar's departure harmed the cause of reform in the short-term and was unwelcome to Yeltsin, it strengthened the position of Prime Minister Chernomyrdin whose adoption of a more restrained reformist stance proved politically productive in the early months of 1994. Advocates of radical economic reform were marginalised, or offered terms for their continuance in office which were intentionally unacceptable to them and so left government. (Among the latter, Finance Minister Boris Fedorov was the most notable example.) Yeltsin was also mindful of the influence of Zhirinovsky, whose nationalism was expressed in language so violent that voters who sought a powerful vehicle for expressing their anger with economic decline found one in him and his party. The alarm of foreign governments at Zhirinovsky's rise notwithstanding, his support had more to do with domestic decline than with enthusiasm for foreign adventures.

Economic Dislocation.

Russia's stability and democratic prospects came under pressure from two sources in 1994 and early 1995. One, that of continuing economic dislocation, was familiar; the other, that of the Russian military action against Chechnya, rapidly became so. In neither case, however, were the wider apocalyptic forecasts about the significance for Russia justified.

The total output of the Russian economy at the end of 1994 was about half what it had been in 1989 and continued to fall: the government's forecast that the rate of decline would ease was cold comfort. In the face of the collapse in output, employment levels also fell. Whilst reliable data are difficult to generate, estimates of unemployment for mid-1995 range between one-quarter and one-third of the population; no credible estimate of the budget deficit for 1995 places it at much less than 10% of Gross Domestic Product. Anti-inflation policy did meet with some success in 1994, however: the rate continued to fall, but still stood at about 300% by the end of the year.

The Chechnya Crisis.

Within and without Russia, intervention in Chechnya to crush a local separatist rebellion stirred memories of imperialism which sanguine observers had thought the Soviet Union's collapse to have stopped. In fact, the brutal intervention was a better indication of the divisions within the Russian hierarchy than of a new policy towards the periphery. Whilst it is unlikely that Russian military action against Chechnya will have great significance for policy towards other Russian regions, the startling military incompetence which the intervention revealed posed economic and political questions.

Economically, the Chechnya operation placed the budget under further strain: one well-informed Russian journalist estimated the costs of intervention to be in the region of $2·0 billion. The wider risk lay in the exploitation of the Chechnyen operation by ministries attempting to bolster their own budgets.

Politically, the intervention prompted sundry anxieties—that control over policy was slipping towards hard-line nationalists, that Yeltsin was losing control over the military and security apparatus, and that parliamentary elections (due in 1995) and presidential elections (due in 1996) might be postponed. In fact, the Chechnya operation is more likely to weaken extreme nationalists (such as Zhirinovsky and his Liberal Democratic Party) than to strengthen them. Postponement of the parliamentary elections remains possible, but is not without risk. Yeltsin's political unpopularity makes him a probable loser in the presidential election, but there is little good reason to think that the broad movement towards a liberal polity, and market-based economy, is imperilled.

THE CLINTON PRESIDENCY

Introduction.

The election in November 1992 of Governor William J. (Bill) Clinton of Arkansas as the 42nd President of the United States was unsurprising given the prominent lead that the Democrats had in the opinion polls throughout the campaign. However the manner of his election was unusual in that the general election of 1992 (in which the whole of the House of Representatives and one-third of the Senate was also up for election) was dominated by the participation of an independent candidate, Ross Perot of Texas. Clinton handsomely beat the incumbent Republican President George Bush by 370 votes to 168 in the electoral college, but his share of the popular vote (43%) was actually less than that achieved by the losing Democratic challenger in 1988, Michael Dukakis. The difference between the election of 1992 and the previous contest was the dramatic fall in the national

Republican vote; George Bush's share fell an unprecedented 16%, the worst performance by an incumbent president since the Great Depression. Ross Perot claimed the vote of very nearly one American in five—the best result for a third party candidate since 1912; had he not been in the race the final result would have been much closer. Nonetheless Clinton's success should not be underestimated—even in circumstances in which the total vote was divided among three candidates, he nearly succeeded in achieving the average Democratic share of the past 20 years.

A Disappointing Start.

As he completed his first year in office in January 1994, the only thing about Bill Clinton's presidency which the majority of his fellow Americans could agree upon was that he had failed to fulfil the mandate for "change" for which he had campaigned so effectively before the presidential election four-teen months earlier. If most voters have remained ambivalent and confused about President Clinton's intentions, allegiances and political competence, so has official Washington; his first year in office was marked both by signal legislative triumphs and by a series of mistakes which, if none amounted to a full-blown crisis, at least together suggested an Administration prone to lurching from one avoid-able issue to another. The president seemed fated to be unable to maintain public confidence in his direction for more than a few weeks at a time and as a result was subject to violent swings in the public estimation of his ability.

The Legislative Record.

These misfortunes stood in stark contrast to President Clinton's actual record of achievement, particularly in his relationship with Congress, which public opinion somehow contrived to overlook or at least discount. With Congress Clinton managed a better first year record even than the popular Eisenhower, being supported by the legislature in nine out of ten votes; neither was he obliged to resort to the power of presidential veto to block legislation with which he disagreed, in stark contrast to his predecessor who used the veto 21 times during his last year in office. Clinton proved particularly adept at persuading Congress to enact his legislative agenda—during his first year he was able to pass bills which had been languishing for years (such as the Brady bill on gun-control), though a number of these were partisan measures which had been blocked by President Bush and which were simply awaiting the election of a Democratic president.

Clinton's most important achievements were to secure the passage of his budget in August and then three months later to win congressional ratification of the North American Free Trade Agreement (NAFTA) with Canada and Mexico. Failure to win either could have undermined his presidency in its first year. The budget was the closer of the two, passing the Senate only on the casting vote of Vice President Al Gore. Although at the time this was seen as indicative of Clinton's difficulties in main-taining support for his programme within his own party, in retrospect the tortured passage of the budget was part of a wider institutional and sectorial conflict in American politics. Seeking the largest reduction in the federal budget deficit in history—$500 billion over five years—the president was dependent upon legislators of both parties who wished to hold out for a deeper cut and yet who refused to accept the abolition of specific pro-grammes or services which benefited their own constituents. This problem was not unique to the Clinton presidency and undoubtedly it will resurface in the future, but the consequences were likely to be diminished in the medium term by the robust growth (c. 3%) which the United States enjoyed during 1993 as the economy finally moved out of the longest recession since the war. The spectre of unemployment which so damaged President Bush during the 1992 election and upon which Clinton campaigned so effectively seemed to be diminish-ing.

Securing the ratification of NAFTA was arguably the more important congressional victory. In origin this was a Republican measure and in supporting it the president was obliged to build a coalition with the minority Republicans and to disappoint both the bulk of his own party in Congress, which remained ambivalent about free trade, and particularly the trades unions (a bold move given that these supply most of the party's campaign funds). In the end Clinton's margin of victory in the November vote was more comfortable than for the budget, despite the fact that he had come to support NAFTA rather late in the day. The political consequences of this episode were particularly important because it marked a signal victory over the anti-free trade platform of the maverick 1992 presidential candidate Ross Perot, who had led the opposition to NAFTA but whose star was seen to wane during the year. However success was achieved partly at the expense of the most vigorous round of political horse-trading seen in Washington for years, as the president struck individual deals with numerous members of Congress.

Problems of Political Management.

Unfortunately for Clinton the benefits of such achievements were undermined by his political management of the Administration, which during the first year seemed unfocused or on occasion inept. Charges of a failure of presidential leadership were given weight by the successes of the Republican party, which won six of the year's most important state and mayoral elections (including New York City); however it could fairly be maintained that this was simply a continuation of the anti-incumbent feeling which had brought Clinton himself to the White House and was likely to hurt the Democrats more because they held the majority of federal and state offices. More importantly the transition from the Bush Administration was accomplished with agonising slowness, such that by the end of the first year only half of the one thousand presidential appointments requiring Senate confirmation had actually been made. This problem was compounded by the nature and fate of individual candidates for office. Critics claimed that initial cabinet appointments were an attempt to placate as many interests as possible, in pursuit of a campaign pledge to name a cabinet which reflected America's ethnic and social diversity. Many nominations were bungled—most seriously Clinton required three attempts to appoint an Attorney-General—perhaps reflecting a new Administration's lack of understanding both of Washington politics and of its candidates' credentials. However a concerted attempt to counter the impression of inexperienced management was made in the early summer with the appointment as White House director of communications of the veteran David Gergen, who had served under President Reagan; the extent to which Clinton has subsequently appeared more 'presidential' indicates that this has been at least partly successful.

The Personality of the President.

The origin of Clinton's woes partly lies in the personality of the president himself. To a greater extent than his two predecessors he is distinguished by an intellectual vigour and natural curiosity that have led him towards hyperactivity in office and, more seriously, produced a certain inability to establish priorities among issues.

Foreign Policy Failures.

The sphere in which Clinton's weaknesses have been most seriously apparent has been foreign policy. The record is not distinguished. Even before his election Clinton was calling for bolder action by the United States on a host of international issues—Bosnia, Somalia, Russia, or nuclear weapons proliferation—but in office he has proved singularly unable either to carry his foreign allies with him on most occasions or to provide a concrete statement of what US policy should be in a post-Cold War world. The new concept of the "enlargement" of democratic market relations and institutions has remained quite vague. Clinton's Secretary of State Warren Christopher, who served under President Carter, has proved pragmatic but often discreet to the point of invisibility; and opposition from established interests at home or abroad has frequently resulted in the Administration quickly backing down. This was most clearly visible during the first year in Clinton's relationship with the US military. The first weeks of his presidency were occupied by an avoidable confrontation over the issue of privacy of homosexuals serving in the armed forces and the year ended with the enforced resignation of the Secretary of Defense Les Aspin, who never in fact fully established his own team at the Pentagon. The primary responsibility for this must lie with the president, who persistently gave the impression that he considered foreign policy to be largely an intrusion onto his domestic agenda.

The Failure of Health Care Reform.

The problems of political management which had bedevilled the Administration since its inception were made cruelly obvious during the course of 1994 by the fate of health care reform. This had been only a minor theme in Clinton's campaign in 1992, but once elected he had identified health care in particular as an issue which would distinguish him as a "New Democrat"—one who consciously rejected "big government" solutions to social and welfare questions. In the realm of health care action would be needed in some form or other to control the spiralling costs of the two main government programmes for the unemployed poor and the elderly, Medicaid and Medicare.

In September 1993 the President proposed to Congress a bill to achieve universal national health insurance coverage within five years, by requiring compulsory employer-funded insurance for the working population with limited subsidy from the state. The Clinton plan explicitly rejected the so-called "single payer" model operated by neighbouring Canada (in which the government would arrange insurance), in favour of amending the existing system. To that extent it was an incremental and rational proposal. However it quickly attracted considerable political opposition. This was partly motivated by the fact that the plan had been produced by a White House task force chaired by Mrs. Hillary Clinton, who was seen by cultural conservatives as a symbol of the very interventionist, 1960s-style liberalism which President Clinton claimed to have rejected. More importantly, the plan had been devised independently of the Democratic leadership in Congress and with little attempt to seek the bipartisan support of the Republican opposition. In retrospect this was seen to be a serious oversight.

The fate of the health care bill in Congress became a testament to how reform measures may become the victim of electoral politics. President Clinton received a significant boost in the opinion polls when he unveiled his plan—declaring dramatically that he would veto any final version which did not provide universal coverage—and the Senate minority leader Robert Dole was moved to agree that there was a "crisis" in the American health system. However as the bill passed through numerous congressional committees it emerged that there was little support for many of its features, which were understood to oblige employers and employees to purchase health care cover from only a limited number of providers or to restrict one's choice of doctor. The already insured middle class (not yet affected significantly by runaway costs) criticised the plan as too bureaucratic. The Democratic and Republican leaderships in Congress both proposed their own versions, promising more limited coverage by a later date; but even these could not gain sufficient support, and the House and the Senate recessed in the summer of 1994 without having taken any final vote on the reform bill. In September the retiring Democratic Senate majority leader George Mitchell was obliged to tell the President that the issue was effectively dead.

The Mid-Term Elections.

The loss of health care reform was perhaps made inevitable by the imminence of the mid-term congressional elections in November, when all of the House and one-third of the Senate would be re-elected. The Republican leadership—having agreed that health care was in crisis when that interpretation was popular—quickly recognised that the majority of Americans would not yet welcome fundamental change, particularly if it raised taxes or led to job losses by increasing employers' costs. Clinton's reform proposals allowed them to characterise him as a traditional "big government" Democrat, now out of touch with the concerns of ordinary Americans. The election campaign was remarkable for the extent to which he was personally vilified. Great efforts were made by the Republicans nationally to associate moderate or liberal congressional Democrats with the President's style and philosophy. In part this strategy was an attempt to build upon increasing public dissatisfaction with "politics as usual" and in particular with the image of the federal government and of Congress itself, which opinion polls showed a majority of voters now regarded as representative of private rather than public interests. Indeed the campaign was marked in several states by popular movements to amend the state constitutions by referendums limiting the number of terms which an individual might serve in Congress.

The Republican Landslide.

The outcome of the elections themselves on 9 November was truly extraordinary. The Republican strategy succeeded beyond all expectation, as congressional Democrats suffered devastating losses across the country. Many liberal and moderate grandees of the party were swept from office, such as the Speaker of the House of Representatives, Thomas Foley (the first incumbent Speaker to fall since 1860), or Governors Mario Cuomo of New York and Ann Richards of Texas in state races. The Democrats lost 53 seats in the House and the Republicans none, which gave the latter control of the House for the first time since 1954 and ultimately control of Congress. Much of the credit for the victory must go to the vigorous national campaign waged by the Republican whip in the House, Newt Gingrich, who was to assume the Speakership when Congress reconvened in January 1995.

The Contract with America.

Gingrich was able to unite Republican candidates behind a ten-point manifesto which he dubbed a "Contract with America"—many of whose provisions such as welfare reform, increased defence spending and tax cuts for the middle class harked back to the Reagan era. These proved extremely popular among voters, especially in the more conservative South which in this election now completed its transition from being the bedrock of the Democratic Party to being an almost exclusively Republican region.

The Capture of Congress.

The Republican seizure of Congress opened up the prospect of two very difficult years for President Clinton before the next presidential election in November 1996. He recognised the extent of the damage in his State of the Union address in January 1995 when he explicitly tried to align himself with middle class concerns, promising action on welfare and crime and seeking limited tax cuts. However, the Republican honeymoon may prove as short as any president's, especially as the congressional leadership struggles to find ways to meet its campaign pledges both to reduce taxes and balance the federal budget by the end of the century. These are likely to require cuts in public expenditure which would decimate many social programmes favoured by the middle class, such as aid to education. Moreover the Republicans cannot assume that the rejection of Clintonism marks any acceptance of their own programme—a typically low turnout of some 40 percent of voters means that the "Contract with America" has in fact been endorsed by little more than one-fifth of the potential electorate.

Popular Alienation from Politics.

The popular disillusion with politics is now marked by widespread alienation from the existing electoral system, as great swathes of the population (in particular minority groups and the poor) do not participate by voting. If the Republicans fail to implement their own agenda, the Democratic losses of 1994 may well be reversed within two years and President Clinton (the so-called "Comeback Kid") may yet be able to mobilise the widespread discontent with Washington to his own advantage, as he did in 1992. Such an achievement would, however, be almost without parallel in American history.

The Oklahoma Bombing.

The worst urban terrorism ever to be experienced in the United States devastated the FBI building in April 1995 in Oklahoma City, the very heart of middle America. As the death toll mounted to 167, it appeared that the perpetrators might have links with far-right militia groups, adding a new dimension to those trying to counter extremism.

CRISIS IN MEXICO

The Background: The Zapatistas.

As the North American Free Trade Agreement (NAFTA) with the US and Canada was to come into force, there was an uprising on 1 January 1994 in the southern Chiapas region by the previously unknown Zapatista National Liberation Army (EZLN). Armed Indians—who named themselves after the early 20th century revolutionary Emiliano Zapata—seized four towns, including the tourist resort San Cristobal de Las Casas, holding it for 24 hours. They protested against the effects on the indigenous population of the economic integration with the US and Canada which NAFTA proposed and demanded major social reforms.

Federal forces moved rapidly against the Zapatistas and by 6 January the rebels had retreated to the mountains, where they continued guerrilla action, backed by the local peasants, until a ceasefire was agreed on 12 January. Over 120 people were killed in the fighting. Talks were held with the government from 22–24 February which, while addressing Chiapas regional problems, failed to consider the EZLN demands for local self-rule, national democratic reform and land redistribution.

The Murder of Colosio.

Tension rose when, on 23 March, PRI presidential candidate Luis Colosio was murdered. There were allegations that his party was involved in the killing. He was replaced as candidate by Ernesto Zedillo. Unrest continued as the EZLN feared the effects of Colosio's death. There were reports of land seizures by Indians and other peasants in Chiapas. On 12 June the Zapatistas rejected the government's peace terms, claiming that 97·9% of EZLN supporters were against it. The ceasefire, however, held.

Zedillo was elected president with 49% of the vote on 21 August, the centre-right National Action Party (PAN) candidate taking 26%. In elections to the Chamber of Deputies, the PRI took 277 of the 500 seats, PAN 18 and the centre-left Party of Democratic Revolution (PRD) 5. In Chiapas, Amado Avendano, running for the governorship with the backing of the PRD and Zapatista support, claimed he had been denied victory by electoral fraud. He formed a "rebel transitional government" and demanded fresh elections. Outside Chiapas, violence continued and on 28 September the PRI general secretary was assassinated. There were gains for the opposition parties in municipal elections held on 13 November, PAN gaining control of 5 towns and the PRD of 20.

The Financial Crisis.

Formally taking office on 1 December, President Zedillo was faced with EZLN remobilisation on 20 December. This triggered a financial crisis, forcing a devaluation of the peso on 24 December and a floating of the currency the following day. As the anniversary of the Chiapas uprising approached, the EZLN called for a mass protest against the government. Meanwhile, as the peso fell 40% against the dollar, President Zedillo announced an emergency austerity programme on 2 January 1995 in an effort to reduce Mexico's $28 billion dollar current account deficit and so restore international financial confidence. The programme of spending cuts, tax increases, privatisation and wage curbs threatened to increase unemployment but was backed by business leaders and the state-controlled trade unions.

President Zedillo had been attempting to resolve the country's crisis without resort to the International Monetary Fund but on 5 January finance minister Guillermo Ortiz was forced to apply to the IMF for a stand-by loan. A week later the PRD led a widely supported protest at the president's residence against the government's measures.

The first face-to-face talks held on 16 January under the auspices of a national Mediation Commission between government and Zapatista representatives served only to demonstrate the gulf dividing the two parties.

US Aid for Mexico.

The financial crisis continued and at the end of the month US President Clinton failed to persuade his Congress to approve a $40 billion loan guarantee to Mexico. However, the terms of the proposed loan—which called on Mexico to offer its oil reserves to the United States until 2005 as a guarantee—roused intense opposition. Populist opposition leader Cuauhtemoc Cardenas supported by dissidents from the ruling PRI, demanded a plebiscite on the issue. Despite President Clinton's failure, Mexico was pledged a total of $15 billion by the western countries, together with a further $7·8 billion approved by the IMF. This, however, did little to reassure financial markets or shore up the position of the peso.

The Four-Party Reform Pact.

President Zedillo attempted to strengthen his political position on 8 February by signing a sweeping reform pact between the four main parties. He declared that Mexico was taking "a step towards a full democracy without a stain". But an opposition leader said it was Mexico's "last chance. Either we go to democratic stability or we go to chaos." Now apparently secured in his own position, President Zedillo switched to a harder line against the Zapatistas. On 9 February he revealed that the movement's leader, the mysterious "Subcomandante Marcos" was a middle class left-winger, attempting to undermine Zapatista claims to be the voice of the rural poor. Troops were deployed to occupy towns and villages as a preliminary to attacking rebel-held territory. President Zedillo was gambling on shedding the weak image he had earned since becoming president, on winning over hardliners within his increasingly divided party, and on reassuring international investors and lenders. But, as "Marcos" taunted the government with its inability to capture him, the ruling Institutional Revolutionary Party lost the governorship of Jalisco state to the opposition National Action Party, only the fourth such loss in over 60 years.

However, on 14 February President Zedillo suddenly changed course over the Zapatistas and ordered the army to halt its search for Marcos. On the same day the governor of Chiapas—the validity of whose election was disputed by a wide-ranging opposition—stood down and was replaced by an interim governor. President Zedillo proposed an amnesty for EZLN guerrillas and appealed to the movement to join efforts to seek a political solution.

The government reached agreement with the United States on 21 February on the terms of the $20 billion loan to rescue Mexico's stricken economy. These included interest rates of 50% and US control of Mexico's annual $7 billion oil production as collateral. Politicians of all three leading parties predicted that the country would suffer its worst economic recession of the century.

Economic breakdown was accompanied by increasing fragmentation of the political system. On 26 February the attorney general reported that the murder of the PRI presidential candidate in March 1994 had been carried out by individuals in his own party and that there had been an official cover up. A week later the brother of the former President Salinas was arrested for involvement in the murder of the PRI secretary general in September 1994.

The Collapse of the Peso.

The 66th anniversary of the PRI's accession to power on 4 March was marked by the peso falling to an all time low and the announcement by former President Salinas that he was beginning a hunger strike. He was protesting against accusations that he was responsible for the country's economic plight and attempting to detach himself from the charge levelled against his brother. Mr Salinas went into self-imposed exile in the United States on 12 March.

As the peso continued to fall – and as accusations surfaced of high level involvement in drug running – the finance minister finally announced the government's programme to restore international confidence in the economy on 10 March. He proposed a 35% increase in fuel prices, raising VAT on consumer goods and a 10% reduction in government spending. Although this was to be balanced by an increase in the minimum wage and subsidies on basic foods, many workers' and employers' organisations denounced the proposals. Within a few days the package was on the brink of collapse as opposition within the PRI mounted.

MIDDLE EAST PEACE PROCESS

Progress in 1994.

During 1994 the US-sponsored peace talks between Israel and her Arab neighbours made significant progress but at the same time led to outbreaks of violence which bode ill for the future stability of the region. In the course of the year Israel made peace with Jordan, advanced on the implementation of the 1993 accords with the Palestinians and saw a slight thaw in relations with Syria. The prospects for economic integration throughout the region also looked rosier at the end of the year than at the start. The year however also saw the first violent clashes between Yasser Arafat's security forces and the Islamist opposition groups and a rise in disillusionment among Palestinians as to the benefits of the peace process. Hardline Israeli settlers also intensified their often violent activities against the talks.

An Inauspicious Start.

The year opened with mixed, but largely negative, portents. On 9 January Yasser Arafat concluded talks in Cairo with Israeli Foreign Minister Shimon Peres, agreeing on a framework for implementation of the September Declaration of Principles (DoP) signed in Washington. Although an agreement was necessary to keep the process going, critics soon charged that Arafat had given too much away and had in fact largely accepted Israel's conditions for the interim period, which will last until talks begin on the final status of the occupied territories. In particular, Arafat accepted Israel's insistence on de facto control over the border crossings into Gaza and Jericho, the territories to be initially transferred to Palestinian control according to the DoP; he also agreed to postpone discussion of the fate of Israeli settlements on Palestinian territory, and agreed to allow Israeli troops to continue to be responsible for the security of these enclaves.

The Hebron Massacre.

Implementation of these measures was brought to an abrupt halt on 25 February when an Israeli settler and army officer, Baruch Goldstein, perpetrated a massacre at the Ibrahmi mosque in Hebron, gunning down 48 Palestinian worshippers. The massacre brought to the fore the question of Israeli settlements and the vulnerability of Palestinians under occupation to acts of Jewish terrorism as well as repression by the army. In the weeks following the massacre it was revealed that Israeli soldiers had no orders to fire on settlers attacking Palestinians and the occupation forces clamped a curfew on the Palestinian residents of Hebron, allowing settlers to move freely and, in some cases, applaud Goldstein. In the course of riots that erupted throughout Israel and the occupied territories after the attack, the Israeli Defence Forces (IDF) killed at least another 27 Palestinians.

Revenge by Hamas.

The massacre was "avenged" on 6 April by Hamas, the main Palestinian Islamist movement, when it killed seven Israeli civilians with a car-bomb in Afula. The peace process nonetheless resumed as both Rabin and Arafat had invested too much to be able to retreat from their positions. Face was saved with the stationing in Hebron of 160 lightly armed European observers, the Temporary International Presence in Hebron (TIPH). In the event the IDF did not permit TIPH to perform any useful role in protecting the human rights of Palestinians in Hebron, but the measure permitted Arafat to resume talks. At the same time, Israel once again closed the occupied territories in the wake of the Afula bombing, dealing a further blow to the desperate economy of Gaza whose workforce depends on labouring jobs inside Israel.

The talks resulted in the 4 May signing between Arafat and Rabin of what became known as the Cairo Agreement. This settled the details left hanging in February and paved the way for the redeployment of the IDF and their replacement by a newly-constituted Palestinian police force. This police force gradually deployed in the liberated areas of Gaza and Jericho and was welcomed by the population. Arafat himself set up his headquarters in Gaza on 1 July where he was greeted with some joy and hopes that he would soon improve the economic and political lot of the Strip's residents.

Economic Worries.

The incoming Palestinian National Authority (PNA) faced a host of problems. Not only did it have to continue negotiations with Israel in the face of Rabin's insistence on maintaining the upper hand, it also had to cope with rejection both of the concept of the peace process, by *Hamas* and Islamic *Jihad*, and of the concessions that had been made in Cairo, by most factions within the Palestine Liberation Organisation (PLO) other than Arafat's *Fatah*. The PNA also faced a chronic credibility problem as Arafat failed to force Rabin to make good on promises to release the estimated 4,000 Palestinian prisoners still held in Israeli jails.

Most pressing, though, was the economic and financial crisis faced by the PNA. On 29 April Israel and the PLO had signed an economic agreement in Paris laying down the rights of the PNA to open banks, collect taxes and supervise trade. Israel agreed to hand over a portion of the taxes paid by Palestinian workers in Israel. International donors such as the European Union and the World Bank had pledged billions of dollars in aid in recognition that, in view of the 50% unemployment in Gaza, political support for the process would wane without rapid economic regeneration.

The majority of the pledged aid has, however, not been forthcoming as a result of disputes over control of the funds, with the result that even the PNA's policemen were not fed or properly housed when they first took up their posts. International donors have been reluctant to release funds to Arafat, as head of the PNA, as they complain at lack of proper accounting procedures and are concerned he will use the money to disburse as patronage and not put it into economically viable projects. Arafat has, however, resisted international pressures to allow the Palestinian Economic Council for Development and Reconstruction (Pecdar) to utilise the funds under international supervision. He has argued that it is a limitation on Palestinian sovereignty not to give the head of state control over the funds and points out that the international lending agencies are, to a large degree, operating at the behest of the United States to retain control over the Palestinian entity. The upshot of the dispute is that aid has been very slow to reach the PNA and little has been done to resolve Gaza's economic crisis. On 14 September Rabin and Arafat signed an agreement in Oslo which it was hoped would unblock some $2·5 billion of funds and reached an agreement on temporary funding of the Palestinian police forces but the sudden resignation of Ahmad Quray, head of Pecdar, did not bode well for the PNA's financial stability.

Potential for Civil War.

The more dramatic sign of crisis within the Palestinian body politic has been the cycle of escalating clashes between the PNA, *Hamas* and Islamic *Jihad*. Islamic *Jihad* has only limited support among Palestinians but has vowed to continue to fight Israel and has attacked military and civilian targets. Many of these attacks have been designed to embarrass the PNA since they are carried out within the self-rule areas where the PNA is responsible for security. In November the ongoing Israeli–Islamic *Jihad* covert war erupted into a series of events which threatened to derail the peace process. On 2 November suspected Israeli agents killed an Islamic *Jihad* leader, Hani Abed, with a car bomb in Gaza, leading *Jihad* to respond by using a suicide bicycle bomb to kill

three IDF officers near the Netzarim settlement in the Gaza Strip. Under pressure from Israel, the PNA cracked down and arrested numerous Islamists and attempted to restrict Islamist protest demonstrations. On 18 November this policy led to tragedy with, for the first time, PNA police firing on Gaza demonstrators and killing 16 people. Arafat and his aides have been happy to crack down on Islamic *Jihad*, regarding it as an Iranian-inspired minor faction, but the resulting bloodshed has reduced popular support for the peace process.

Relations between Arafat and *Hamas* have been even more delicate. *Hamas* has continued to attack Israelis in Israel and outside the self-rule areas in an attempt to disrupt the peace talks. In October a major crisis erupted when *Hamas* kidnapped an IDF officer. He was held in the West Bank and three kidnappers, an IDF officer and the hostage were all killed in a botched rescue attempt by Israeli commandos on the 15th. Four days later a *Hamas* suicide bomber blew himself up in Tel Aviv along with 22 bus passengers. Arafat responded to *Hamas* attacks by rounding up members of the movement but he has been reluctant to launch an all-out campaign. *Hamas* has the support of up to a quarter of the population of the Gaza Strip and neither side wants civil war. Instead, Arafat has sought to encourage those elements in *Hamas* who urge that the movement should open a dialogue and take part in the preparation for elections for the PNA, the date for which has constantly been postponed, so as to better influence the direction of Palestinian society and politics. On 25 November *Hamas* staged a major rally to protest at the previous week's massacre which passed off peacefully since PNA policemen took a low profile.

Dissension within the PLO.

Arafat has been further undermined by dissension in his own ranks. The major factions within the PLO, the Popular Front and the Democratic Front, oppose his conduct of the peace talks, arguing that he has made too many concessions to the Israelis. More disturbingly, Arafat has been deserted by more and more of his followers from within *Fatah*, his core constituency. Farouq Qaddumi, previously the PLO's *de facto* foreign minister, has been working to co-ordinate opposition to the peace agreement. In elections to professional associations as well as in meetings of the PLO executive committee, dissatisfaction with Arafat's leadership has become more evident. This dissatisfaction is motivated both by the perception that Arafat has been giving away too much to the Israelis and by his autocratic leadership and failure to consult his colleagues. Between 21 and 23 November *Fatah* staged big rallies in Palestinian population centres intended to demonstrate Arafat's continuing grip on power. Within days Arafat asserted his position even more forcefully, ordering an attack on forces loyal to a rebel *Fatah* commander, Munir Maqdah, who had split off from Fatah in 1993. In the fighting, in Ain al-Hilwe refugee camp in Lebanon, eight militiamen were killed.

Has the Palestinian Track a Future?

By the end of the year, the future of the Palestinian track of the peace talks looked rocky indeed. The Israeli government had a security-led view of the process in which it expected Arafat and the PNA to act as a proxy police force in protecting Israel from Islamist terrorism, something the IDF had been unable to do. Israel consistently refused to take steps which would give Arafat any credit among his people—humiliating his security forces, refusing to remove even the most provocatively-located settlements, replacing Palestinian labour with imported cheap labour, and giving Jordan's King Hussein a greater say in the affairs of Jerusalem than Arafat who claimed the city as his capital. Rabin, operating with a wafer thin majority and under attack from the right wing of his party as well as from Likud, had little room to manoeuvre between an Israeli public opinion enraged by Islamist attacks on the one hand, and the necessity of shoring up Arafat as a "moderate" bulwark on the other.

At the same time, however, there were indications that the negotiators were engaged in a process with its own momentum. Palestinian public support for the process, though diminished, remained. Civil powers were being gradually transferred to the PNA and the PNA security forces were, if covertly, extending their presence across the West Bank. Although most observers at year end found the scene depressing, it was likely that the process would stumble along, although to an uncertain fate. It remained unclear whether Arafat would in the end get anything more than limited autonomy over scattered centres of Palestinian population surrounded and isolated by Israeli settlements and military installations.

Jordan's Leap.

In contrast with the chaotic Palestinian scene, Jordan's King Hussein moved swiftly and relatively easily to achieve his goal of peace with Israel. At the beginning of the year it had been unclear how willing he would be to move out ahead of either the PLO or of Syria, both of which were unenthusiastic to a rapid Jordanian deal with Israel. King Hussein nonetheless concluded that the benefits of rapid establishment of relations were worth the risks. On 25 July Hussein and Rabin signed a declaration in Washington, vowing to end their state of war. Despite hiccups, this was followed on 26 October by a formal peace treaty signed on the Israeli–Jordanian border.

An Israeli–Jordanian peace had never been predicted to pose too many problems since the ostensible issues of contention, Jordanian claims over territory and water rights, were never regarded by either country as of great strategic moment. The two countries had been "best of enemies" for many years and had long covertly co-operated. Israel nonetheless regarded the treaty as of historic significance as, from November onwards, Israelis could now cross another of their land borders and the two countries could work together openly on development, trade and tourism projects. In addition, Israel proved adept at using Jordan to apply pressure on Arafat. Israeli negotiators agreed on a "special role" for Hussein in relation to the Jerusalem holy places, a move which infuriated the Palestinian leadership. A low-key struggle for control of the West Bank subsequently resumed with the PNA banning a pro-Jordanian newspaper.

For King Hussein the treaty was more of a gamble. His signature provoked opposition in parliament, especially from Islamist deputies who opposed the peace and claimed that Jordan had sold out the Palestinians due to US pressure. The extent of pressure became evident over the summer and autumn as Washington took a series of steps which encouraged Hussein to go along. These included easing the UN-mandated inspection regime for ships entering Aqaba port, forgiving much of Jordan's debt to the US and offering military aid to the country.

Syrian Deadlock.

Throughout the year the Syrian–Israeli track of negotiations moved with glacial slowness, if at all. President Hafiz al-Asad seemed ready to make a deal with Israel, in exchange for the return of all of the Golan Heights. He was, however, wary of being pressured by Israel and the US into accepting a deal which would not give him what he wanted. He was intensely annoyed by King Hussein's separate agreement and watched cautiously as Arafat's deal teetered on the brink of disaster. During frequent meetings with US Secretary of State Warren Christopher, who shuttled between Middle Eastern capitals throughout the year, he followed a two track strategy. On the one hand, he made clear his willingness to talk. Foreign Minister Farouq al-Sharaa, in a conciliatory gesture, addressed the Israeli public on Israeli TV. On the other hand, he continued to support the Islamist movement *Hizbollah* which mounted attacks on the IDF in South Lebanon.

Although Damascus was cautious in its pronouncements and careful not to give too much away before obtaining an Israeli commitment to withdraw, the main blockage seemed to come from Israel. Rabin had to face intense opposition to withdrawal from the Golan lobby, which argued against the withdrawal of settlements from the Golan. This lobby, which included several Labour parliamentarians, mounted strong and effective protests against the talks with Syria. Needing to sell the PLO and Jordanian deals, Rabin was in a weak position to confront this movement as well and consequently went slowly on the Syrian track. Unlike Arafat or Hussein, Asad has

not felt that he is under pressure to come to a quick agreement and so Rabin has been unable to bend Syria to Israel's will in the same way that he did with Jordan and the PLO.

The Emergence of "Middle Easternism".

Despite the traumas on the Palestinian front and the coldness on the Syrian front, it did appear at the end of the year that progress towards a new Middle Eastern order was unstoppable. The US, and Israel which enjoys closer relations with Washington from which it has for many a year, has been pushing hard for the development of regional economic ties which would bring together the region from the Maghreb, through the Middle East, to the Gulf. This wish was given expression at the 31 October–1 November Casablanca economic summit which brought together Western businessmen with potential regional customers. Plans that are afoot include joint development of the Red Sea region as a tourist centre and international sharing of electricity.

Arab countries with close ties to the US have spearheaded the drive to incorporate Israel into the region. Morocco established an interests section as a preliminary to setting up diplomatic relations while Oman and Qatar have expressed their intentions to follow suit. The Gulf Co-operation Council ended the secondary boycott of Israel and Kuwait called for the total lifting of the boycott.

In sum, recent developments have fulfilled the expectations of many observers of the region. The overwhelming strength of the US and the economic crises facing many Arab states have led to great strides in plans for a new Middle East incorporated into the international economic and political system and linking Israel with its neighbours. Violence and instability have however spread at the same time as goodwill. It remains to be seen whether this instability is purely part of the transition process or whether it will escalate to the extent where it may derail the peace process.

THE NEW LABOUR PARTY

The Death of John Smith.

The sudden death of Mr. Smith on 12 May 1994 caused an outpouring of grief for a figure who was now seen, like Mr. Gaitskell in 1963, as Labour's (and Britain's) "lost leader". His deputy, Mrs Beckett, took over as acting leader and proved effective in the role. However, on 21 July, Labour turned to its centrist 41-year-old home affairs spokesman, Tony Blair, electing him leader with 57% of the vote. The more traditionalist John Prescott, who had also stood for the leadership, was elected as his deputy.

Although described by one commentator as a politician apparently "almost wholly lacking in ideological ballast", Mr. Blair had, as a shadow minister, effectively destroyed the Tory party monopoly on law and order with the slogan that Labour would be "tough on crime, tough on the causes of crime".

The Leadership Campaign.

In his leadership campaign Mr. Blair accepted the principle of a minimum wage, but would give no figure; he favoured full employment, but was unwilling to provide a target or a timetable. He advocated changes to Labour's commitment to public ownership and would make no promises about taking the privatised utilities back into public ownership. Like Mr. Smith before him, Mr. Blair would increasingly face criticism for the imprecision of Labour's intentions. However, Labour maintained, and improved upon, its lead in the opinion polls. Mr. Blair was also subject to remarkably flattering media coverage.

Mr. Blair faced his first test as leader when, despite pressure from union leaders, he refused to back the rail signallers' industrial action on the eve of the annual TUC congress. Denying he was sitting on the fence, Mr. Blair said it was "not the function of politicians to start barging into industrial disputes".

At the Labour Party conference there were calls, particularly during the economic debate on 3 October, for what GMB leader John Edmonds described as some "concrete" to be mixed with the rhetoric, particularly on full employment and the minimum wage. But on television Mr. Blair, though he pledged a future Labour government to introduce a minimum wage "sensibly and effectively", would not be drawn on a figure.

In his conference speech on 4 October, Mr. Blair promised full employment as a goal, that Britain would sign the European Social Chapter on workers' rights, a Bill of Rights and Freedom of Information Bill, a Scottish Parliament and a Welsh Assembly, and a reduction in the powers of the House of Lords. But his call for a revision of the party constitution's Clause Four, Part IV—the section setting out Labour's objective of public ownership—caused inner party turmoil. Since Mr. Gaitskell's thwarted attempt to abandon Clause Four in 1960, no Labour leader (whatever his private feelings) had attempted such a move.

The NEC Elections.

In elections to the 29-strong National Executive Committee on 2 October there had been a small, but nonetheless remarkable, resurgence of the left. The previous year's conference had seen an eradication of the left on the NEC. With one member one vote being used for the first time in 1994, two Campaign Group members—Dennis Skinner and Diane Abbott—were surprisingly elected to the NEC by the party's constituency section. Their election demonstrated suspicions about the direction in which Mr. Blair hoped to take what he called "New Labour". A potentially humiliating defeat for Mr. Blair on Clause Four seemed imminent. In the event, on 5 October the conference voted to retain the clause only by the narrowest of margins—50·9 to 49·1%.

The Social Justice Commission Report.

Since Mr. Smith's appointment of a Social Justice Commission under Sir Gordon Borrie in December 1992, Labour had been able to deflect questions on many of its policies. The Commission's report, *Strategies for National Renewal*, was published on 24 October. It covered welfare reforms, employment and wages, taxation and educational opportunity and recommended the most fundamental shake-up of the welfare state in its 50-year history. Echoing US President Bill Clinton, Mr. Blair said in supporting the report, "I want to give people a hand up, not a handout." Although it was not a party document, the report was taken as a framework for Labour's longer term policies.

A New General Secretary.

Mr. Blair now moved to confirm his hold on the party. On 17 October Larry Whitty, Labour general secretary for the past nine years, was replaced by Tom Sawyer, a leading trade union ally of Mr. Blair. It was thought his appointment would help influence union leaders in Mr. Blair's Clause Four campaign. A week later Mr. Blair completed a sweeping reshuffle of his front bench and the whips' office. There were, however, some surprises, including the appointment of Campaign Group member "Red Dawn" Primarolo to the Treasury team.

As the budget approached, shadow chancellor Gordon Brown unveiled Labour's recommendations. These concentrated on benefit reforms and tax changes to help the unemployed, including a proposed £600m in tax relief for employers to encourage them to take 300,000 people back into work. During the budget debate Mr. Blair accused the government of having "only one aim in mind—large tax cuts in the budget before the next election". Mr. Brown, meanwhile, continued with a cautious strategy, refusing to allow any large spending commitments and denying plans to increase taxation for all but the very rich.

Opinion Poll Popularity.

Mr. Blair was clearly proving an asset, consolidating the popularity for the party achieved by Mr. Smith. The party's position in the opinion polls remained strong and party membership was increasing. A leaked report to the prime minister from Tory vice-chairman John Maples revealed in November how much the new leader's attractiveness to the public was feared. "If Blair turns out

to be as good as he looks," Mr. Maples reported, "we have a problem." He suggested setting backbench "yobbos" on the opposition leader in the Commons, a threat Mr. Blair turned to his advantage. But it was Mr. Blair's turn to be embarrassed when it was revealed early in December that he intended to send his son to a grant maintained secondary school when party policy was to discontinue them on taking office.

The Clause Four Campaign.

The Clause Four campaign cleared its first hurdle when the NEC agreed by 20–4 on 30 November that a revision of the party's constitution was necessary. There were, however, criticisms—and not only from the left of the party—that this was an unnecessary diversion when Labour should be concentrating its energies on attacking an increasingly vulnerable government.

On 14 December the NEC accepted Mr. Blair's proposal to put a new version of the party's aims to a special conference on 29 April. His intention was clearly to ensure the question was resolved before Clause Four supporters could rally support at the summer trades union conferences and the party conference in October. When 32 Labour European Parliament members challenged Mr. Blair by placing an advertisement in *The Guardian* on 9 January 1995 supporting Clause Four, he accused them of "not learning from our history, but merely living in it."

Mr. Blair faced two sets of problems in his campaign. The first was the resistance to the proposed change from some trade union leaders. There were reports early in the New Year that some were offering a trade-off: they would support him in return for pledges to renationalise the privatised public utilities, particularly the railways. The second problem was that many constituency party members were staunch supporters of Clause Four as it stood. A *Tribune* survey found that of 60 constituency parties, 58 had voted to retain Clause Four. In the era of one person one vote, it would be embarrassing for Mr. Blair if he were to depend on the union block vote to further modernise the party.

Mr. Blair insisted on 25 January that it was essential that the majority of constituency parties supported the change. To win this support, he and deputy leader Mr. Prescott planned a programme of rallies in ten towns and cities from 26 January to 2 March. Early reports suggested opinion was moving Mr. Blair's way and on 4 February Labour's youth conference voted 68% for change to 17% against.

Further support for change came at the party's Scottish conference on 10 March when trade unions and constituency activists backed Mr. Blair's proposals by 58·3% to 41·6%

Mr. Blair and his deputy formally introduced their revised Clause 4 to the party's National Executive Committee (NEC) on 13 March. In 350 words, they pledged Labour to a "dynamic" mixed economy in a society where "power, wealth and opportunity are in the hands of the many, not the few." Labour, to the approval of traditionalists, was described as a "democratic socialist party". The NEC overwhelmingly endorsed the new wording by 23 to 3 (with five trade union abstentions). As Labour's lead in the opinion polls over the Conservatives continued—by mid-March it stood at over 30%—Mr. Blair took his party deeper into Tory ideological territory in a speech on 22 March in which he attacked truancy, anti-social council tenants and reminded voters that they had duties as well as rights.

The Unison Vote.

But on 13 April Mr. Blair was unexpectedly halted in his triumphal progress when Britain's largest union, Unison, voted 55 to 47 against abandoning Clause 4 at a national delegate conference. It became clear that the party's reformers were meeting more resistance from the trade unions than they expected as the influential Transport and General Workers' Union appeared ready to line up against change.

Blair Triumphant.

In the event, the April party conference gave overwhelming support to the reform of Clause IV. The final votes were 65·23% in favour of change,

34·77% against. The constituencies (with 30% of the total vote) voted 90% for change. The unions, with 70% of the vote, voted only 54·6% for change, with such unions as the TGWU, Unison, RMT and the NUM voting against.

DEVELOPMENTS IN
THE EUROPEAN UNION

At the beginning of 1995 the European Union moved into a new phase of its development. With this fresh start came the end of an era when, on January 19, the outgoing head of the European Commission, Frenchman Jacques Delors, left office after an eventful 10 years. Another tour de force in Europe, his seriously ill compatriot President François Mitterrand, was also close to the end of his term. Delors handed over leadership to the former Luxembourg prime minister, Jacques Santer, who took over an enlarged executive of 20 members, more than half of them newly appointed. Also in January, three new members, Austria, Sweden and Finland joined the Union, expanding it to 15 states, with a total population of some 370 million people and a budget of almost US$100 billion.

The Norwegian Referendum.

The refusal of Norwegians to vote to join the EU in a November 1994 referendum, against the wishes of their government, was a disappointment but few dwelt upon the setback. More pressing was consideration of the four main challenges facing the Union: the increasing likelihood of a "multi-speed" Europe, in which a "hard core" of states disposed towards more rapid economic and social integration would split from those otherwise inclined or unable; European Monetary Union (EMU); further enlargement to incorporate the newly-democratic countries of Eastern Europe; and the creation of a joint defence and common foreign policy after failing to stop the war in Bosnia. Against a background of strong economic growth across western Europe, the forthcoming inter-governmental conference (IGC), in 1996, to review the Maastricht treaty and overhaul EU institutions is expected to be the key forum for debating these issues.

The "Maastricht 2" Treaty.

Any "Maastricht 2" treaty will reflect the victory of either those countries, such as Germany, who want a politically and economically integrated federal Europe or those, such as Britain, who favour a looser approach. The question of a two- or multi-speed Europe has long been taboo within the EU. At its root is the problem of keeping the Union's integrated structure while at the same time expanding its membership. The issue surfaced on 1 September 1994, when the German Christian Democrats (CDU), leader of the country's coalition government, and its CSU partner broke ranks. In a paper they proposed a Franco-German-led "inner circle" of five states who were committed to faster integration. They also called for a more powerful European Parliament at the expense of the Council of Ministers, on which the national governments are represented. Italy, one of the six original founding members of the European Community (in 1957) would be excluded from the hard core, initially consisting of France, Germany, Belgium, Luxembourg and the Netherlands, as would Britain and Spain. Earlier, the French prime minister, Edouard Balladur had suggested the EU could organise on the model of three concentric circles, with a core of countries—which he did not name—surrounded by a second circle of present members unable or unwilling to integrate rapidly. An outer ring would embrace economically weak east European states which had little chance of meeting the criteria for full EU membership in the short term.

At the end of September the European Parliament overwhelmingly denounced the multi-speed option, but warned that ways would have to be found to allow countries wishing to integrate further to do so if a minority of states—notably the UK and Denmark—continued to undermine EU unity. One possible way would be to end the 36-year-old principle that treaty changes can be vetoed by a single country. Hans van den Broek, EU commissioner for external affairs, has suggested that changes in the Rome, Maastricht or other treaties should come into effect if ratified by 80 per cent of EU citizens and member states. John Major has threatened to exercise Britain's national

veto if any "significant constitutional change" is agreed at the IGC.

The British "Opt-Out".

The European Parliament's resolution decried British and Danish opt-outs from the Maastricht treaty as the cause of "dangerous speculation about an *à la carte* Europe"—the freedom to accept or reject core EU obligations. In this respect, of course, a form of variable geometry already exists in practice. For instance, alone among the then 12 member states, Britain opted out of the social chapter of the Maastricht Treaty on European Union, negotiated in 1991. The protocol provides for legislation on such issues as social security, employment rights and working conditions. In effect, in the interests of winning agreement, Britain was allowed to escape the social costs of the single market. Critics among the majority complained that the greater attractiveness to foreign investment this manoeuvre achieved was precisely the sort of competitive advantage the social chapter aimed to eliminate. There are other examples of variable geometry. Denmark bans foreigners from buying second homes on its soil; Sweden has kept its state monopoly on alcohol sales and Swedes can legally sell snuff banned elsewhere in the EU; Ireland is not a member of the Western European Union, the EU's defence arm; and France is not a member of Nato's integrated command.

The Schengen Accord.

From 26 March 1995, nine EU members finally implemented the so-called Schengen Accord, progressively removing border controls between themselves. The convention, an integral part of the "harmonisation" envisaged in the Single Market Act of 1986, guarantees the free movement of people along with goods, services and capital in the Community. All of the original 12 EU countries except Britain, Ireland and Denmark are taking part. Of the new members, Austria has observer status and the Nordic countries are expected to join eventually. Schengen will alleviate some of the obstacles in the way of the single market, but many others remain. In September 1994 the EU's Economic and Social Committee identified 59 such obstacles, including the failure of members to recognise each other's commercial, and financial standards and professional qualifications.

Perhaps the most likely outcome of the multi-speed Europe debate—possibly to be agreed at the IGC—is the eventual adoption of a Euro-constitution or something similar, incorporating an agreed set of minimum obligations to the EU and distinguishing between legal Union-wide responsibilities or "competences" and those which are reserved for the national governments.

Much of the discussion of political union and of variable geometry has been stimulated by the difficulties the then 12 EU members had in approving the Maastricht Treaty, whose main purpose was to timetable the three phases of European Monetary Union (EMU). Drafted in 1991, it came into effect only in November 1993. The ratification process showed up an alarming lack of enthusiasm among EU citizens. In the countries where the treaty was put to a referendum, the French voted only narrowly for it and the Danes voted "yes" only after once rejecting it. Political considerations led Denmark and Britain to ratify only after negotiating opt-outs, inter alia, from EMU. Adding to the painful realisation of the political dimension to a process essentially rooted in economics was the effective collapse of the Exchange Rate Mechanism (ERM), which semi-fixes exchange rates within the community (*see* **Section G**).

EMU Target Dates.

Although few believe 1997 is a realistic target for EMU, in 1994 community-wide economic recovery brought renewed speculation that it was once again possible by 1999, at least for a privileged majority led by the German D-Mark. By the end of the year only Luxembourg and Ireland had actually met the criteria. The European Commission was even more upbeat, arguing in its 1995 Annual Economic Report that the earlier target was still valid. Its figures suggested that eight countries, Austria, Britain, Denmark, Germany, France, Ireland, Luxembourg, and the Netherlands could be in a position to join. Even if this were the case, there appears to be little enthusiasm for EMU among the populations of Europe. In a 1994 Commission opinion poll of citizens of the 12 states before Austria, Finland and Sweden joined, only 53 per cent of those asked supported a single currency. Significantly, there were majorities against in Denmark—which would require a referendum before joining—Britain and Germany. The British results could enhance the likelihood of a referendum, already hinted at by John Major, with the expectation that a "no" vote would help heal internecine divisions by silencing pro-EU voices within his party.

The Economic Prospects.

If EU economies grow at expected rates, the European Commission's zeal could prove justified. The export and investment-led revival has brought predictions of a comfortable average of 3·0 to 3·5 per cent growth until the end of the century. By the end of 1994 economic policy co-ordination within the community was at an unprecedented level and annual inflation was low, although it had crept up fractionally to 3·1 per cent[a]in December—the first rise in five years. All EU countries, including the new members, saw prices increase by less than 3 per cent, except for Portugal, Italy and Spain, which were on 4·0 per cent or just above. Only Greece lagged far behind, on 10·8 per cent. However, unemployment remains an intractable problem. As 1995 began, to Jacques Delors' great frustration, more than 17 million people were seeking work. Best estimates were that there would be some 11 million still jobless by the end of the century notwithstanding the economic recovery.

The Expansion of the EU.

Already the world's largest trading bloc, the EU could almost double in size within the next 20 years. Within a decade there might be more than 20 members. Enthusiasm for expansion appears undimmed. Yet several questions remain unanswered. Should the Union keep expanding until the entire continent of Europe is on board? If so, should eligibility to the status of being "European" be judged on the basis of religion, territory or simply economic compatibility? The institutions of Europe, currently more inter-governmental than supra-national, would have to be given greater powers to administer such a vast, diverse bloc of member states. Could paralysis result from sovereignty being ceded by member governments to the point of national policy-making impotence, while the supranational institutions remain too weak and lacking in democratic legitimacy to implement policy in their place? Might popular alienation from the remote centre of this huge edifice encourage nationalism and even war?

In the meantime, perhaps more for reasons of fear and self-interest than of kinship or altruism, there is broad consensus that the former communist east European states should be admitted to the union as soon as they are able to fulfil the necessary conditions. At the December 1994 heads of state summit at Essen, Germany, the host, Chancellor Helmut Kohl, carried the debate on the EU's enlargement to the east, paving the way for six former communist countries to join the union, together with Cyprus and Malta. Leaders of the six, Poland, Hungary, the Czech Republic, Slovakia, Romania and Bulgaria were present at Essen. The summit agreed to grant them an infrastructure package designed to build transport links across the continent and assist economic growth. Their gross domestic products currently average less than one third the EU average and the economies tend to reflect the distortions of their communist past. A US$6·65 billion plan to prepare for the six's membership, including trade concessions and the promise of regular meetings with Brussels, was also announced although no timetable was offered.

Reform of CAP.

At the summit, Jacques Delors warned that the EU could not afford to continue the controversial and costly Common Agricultural Policy after the eastern expansion. The prospect of competing on equal terms with East European producers strikes terror into the hearts of the subsidised western farmers, although in recent years exports to the east have risen faster than imports, despite EU farm trade concessions. The Commission has played down the likely cost to agriculture of enlargement, arguing that it could be 15 years before the former communist farmers are competitive and that during the transition eastern farm prices would gradually converge.

Chancellor Kohl won the support of the southern states, generally less enamoured of enlargement than the north, with a commitment to a US$3·3 billion five year Mediterranean development package. The member states with Mediterranean coastlines, France, Spain and Italy, who will each in turn hold the 6-month rotating EU presidency from January 1995, have complained that the post-1989 tilt to the east has led to neglect of serious problems beyond the union's southern flank. Crises in North Africa—such as that in Algeria—and the Middle East have left the southern state nervous of a northward push by economic migrants or political refugees. They have called loudly for greater EU financial assistance as a preventative measure. Northern states favour granting market access over financial aid. Their southern neighbours prefer aid not markets: they stand to lose most from competition from north African producers and yet do not bear the brunt of increases in EU spending.

A Common Foreign Policy?

Although the Maastricht treaty declared that "a common foreign and defence policy is hereby established", no infrastructure was provided for the purpose. It allowed only for inter-governmental joint action on the basis of unanimity—from which Britain negotiated an opt-out in order to be free, when necessary, to pursue its supreme national interest. Hitherto joint foreign actions have been confined to such matters as election monitoring, although the EU was involved in the administration of the Bosnian town of Mostar. The Western European Union (WEU), the EU's defence arm, has been built up slowly in the shadow of Nato. Recently Nato has been trying to change its structure to allow the WEU to play a greater role in independent European action. France has called for the establishment of a foreign policy-making system and joint body to represent the EU internationally, as the European Commission does in domestic policy. It also demanded joint military forces in order to avoid in future the powerlessness experienced during the Bosnian war. So far, progress towards this end amounts only to the Franco-German Eurocorps—an embryonic European army—and a Mediterranean aero-naval force set up by France, Spain and Italy under WEU auspices.

The Task for Santer.

Clearly high hopes are riding on the IGC in 1996 to solve a multitude of problems. For Jacques Santer, on whom much of the responsibility lies for shaping the debate in the run-up to the conference, his predecessor, the energetic Jacques Delors, is a hard act to follow. Though a socialist, Delors takes much of the credit for masterminding the reforms which shook the EC out of what he termed "Eurosclerosis" and steering it towards the Single European Act and then the Maastricht treaty, which created the EU.

Santer, who was chosen as compromise candidate after Britain vetoed the appointment of Belgian prime minister Jean-Luc Dehaene, got off to an impressive start. He successfully defused threats by the expanded European Parliament to exercise its new powers, granted under Maastricht, to veto Commission appointments. After a series of US Senate-like hearings, during which several commissioners came in for biting criticism, the new President's appointees were approved by a four to one majority. Both sides were quick to claim the vote had enhanced the democratic legitimacy of the two institutions, although few seriously believed the Parliament, the EU's only directly elected body, would step over the brink so soon. However, long dismissed as ineffectual and parodied as passengers on a rich gravy train, MEP's pointedly reminded the new commissioners that they could be removed from office later if their performance was wanting.

A mild-mannered pragmatist, Santer cleverly pressed all the right buttons when before the vote he pledged to MEPs his strong commitment to integration, strengthened a committee on women's rights and agreed to review the accord governing relations between the Commission and the Parliament. Having passed through this first official test of his diplomatic acumen with flying colours, he was free to walk the minefield of consensus building among the EU's fractious membership. On all the available evidence this is an impossibly difficult task. But the same could have been said of that which faced Delors a decade earlier. If he does manage to achieve the impossible, Santer might even receive the greatest accolade of all: his own image stamped on the bills of Europe's first unified currency.

THE FRENCH PRESIDENTIAL ELECTIONS

The Background.

High unemployment, pervasive political corruption, and Mitterrand's distinctive variant upon General de Gaulle's theme of *grandeur*, realised in the building of hugely expensive public monuments in Paris, dominated the campaign for the 1995 election.

Having begun 1995 trailing Prime Minister Edouard Balladur by a significant margin in the opinion polls, Jacques Chirac recovered, partly by reason of the Prime Minister's errors of judgement, to a point where, by mid-April, he enjoyed a clear lead. Not only did his victory in the first round over Balladur, and the Socialist candidate, Lionel Jospin, seem assured, but all polls also gave Chirac a majority in the second round. Chirac's strength derived from his authority over the Gaullist RPR, and his success in establishing a distinctive image. In contrast to Balladur, whose chilly aloofness made political recovery yet more difficult, Chirac gave every indication of relishing the campaign. Balladur gave the appearance of accepting the inevitability of high unemployment; Chirac, reviving old Gaullist memories of the activist and interventionist state, did not.

Chirac versus Balladur.

In fact, neither Chirac nor Balladur nor even Jospin provided any clear policy for reducing unemployment, restoring some measure of social cohesion to a divided France or of public faith in the democratic legitimacy of political institutions. Nor would a President Chirac or Balladur, both quintessential members of the Fifth Republic's governing elite, be likely fundamentally to wish to occupy an office whose grandeur was conspicuously diminished. The reason for the weakness of political debate lay partly in the substantive difficulty of the questions involved, but partly also in the lines of fracture which lay just beneath the surface both of Chirac's and of Balladur's support: Chirac's coalition among the political elite extended to free-market neo-liberals, old-style Gaullists of a newly-hostile anti-European kind, and social conservatives. His own platform, notably that on Europe, reflected the tensions which this variegated coalition

implied: on the one hand, he committed himself to implementation of European Monetary Union whilst on the other declining to give a date by which such union might be achieved. His insistence upon the primacy of the Franco-German axis in foreign and monetary policy was, similarly, in tension not only with his quasi-Gaullist insistence upon the nation-state as the building-block of an expanded European Union, but also with laxer fiscal and more generous welfare policies than Balladur's.

Outcome of the First Round.

The first round of voting surprised observers, and confounded all pollsters, by giving Lionel Jospin a plurality victory over Chirac and pushing Balladur to third place, as the table shows.

Candidate	Party	Votes (mill.)	%
Jospin	Socialist	7·10	23·3
Chirac	RPR	6·35	20·8
Balladur	RPR	5·66	18·6
Le Pen	National Front	4·57	15·0
Hue	Communist	2·63	8·6
Laguiller	Trotskyist	1·62	5·3
de Villiers	Movement for France	1·44	4·7
Voynet	Greens	1·01	3·3
Cheminade	New Solidarity	0·09	0·3

Jospin and Chirac each entered the second round with the customary task of expanding their small plurality coalitions into winning majority ones, and faced unusual difficulties in doing so. The pattern of the vote revealed unusually complicated political divisions: indeed, the proportion of the first-round vote won by the two leading candidates was the smallest in the history of the Fifth Republic. Whilst the combined right-wing vote of 60% presented Jospin with a more difficult task than Chirac of coalition-building, Le Pen's heavy support gave the extreme right leverage over Chirac which gave him little freedom of manoeuvre in making his political calculations.

Narrow Chirac Victory.

In the event, after a lacklustre campaign in which Jospin emerged as a strong challenger, Chirac won a narrow victory by 52% to 48%, becoming the fifth president of the Fifth Republic. On his third attempt, he had secured the presidency. However, his numerous electoral pledges, during the campaign, on unemployment and social affairs, together with his somewhat Byzantine policy statements on Europe, all suggested his presidency might be a difficult one.

POLITICAL COMPENDIUM

This compendium provides a compact reference work of key facts and figures for an understanding of modern British politics. It is fully revised each year to take account of the latest political events. Readers will also find that the preceding section, *Background to World Affairs*, complements this part of the book.

TABLE OF CONTENTS

POLITICAL COMPENDIUM

A. THE MONARCHY

The Queen is a constitutional monarch. In law she is the head of the executive, an integral part of the legislature, head of the judiciary, commander-in-chief of the armed forces and temporal head of the Church of England. In practice, the Queen's role is purely formal; she reigns, but she does not rule. In all important respects she acts only on the advice of her ministers. However, she still plays an important role symbolically as Head of State and Head of the Commonwealth.

Monarchs since 1900

1837–1901	Victoria
1901–1910	Edward VII
1910–1936	George V
1936	Edward VIII
1936–1952	George VI
1952	Elizabeth II

B. GENERAL ELECTIONS

For electoral purposes the United Kingdom is divided into 651 constituencies (650 before the 1992 General Election) each returning one MP to the House of Commons. All British subjects and citizens of the Irish Republic are entitled to vote provided they are 18 years old and over and are included on the electoral register which is compiled annually. The only exceptions are members of the House of Lords and those incapacitated through insanity or imprisonment. Anyone who is entitled to vote and aged at least 21 may stand as a candidate, the only exceptions being undischarged bankrupts, clergymen in the established church and the holders of certain other public offices. All candidates have to pay a deposit of £500, which is forfeited unless they receive 5% of the votes cast. In each constituency the winning candidate has only to obtain a simple majority.

General elections must be held every five years,

General Elections, 1918–92

VOTES CAST (thousands)

	Conservative	Labour	Liberal*	Communist	Plaid Cymru	SNP	Others
1918	4,166	2,546	2,753	—	—	—	1,296
1922	5,500	4,241	4,189	34	—	—	462
1923	5,538	4,438	4,311	39	—	—	260
1924	8,039	5,489	2,928	55	—	—	126
1929	8,656	8,390	5,309	51	1	—	243
1931	12,320	6,991	1,509	75	2	21	293
1935	11,810	8,465	1,422	27	3	30	273
1945	9,988	11,995	2,248	103	16	31	752
1950	12,503	13,267	2,622	92	18	10	290
1951	13,745	13,949	731	22	11	7	177
1955	13,312	12,405	722	33	45	12	313
1959	13,750	12,216	1,639	31	78	22	125
1964	12,023	12,206	3,093	46	70	64	168
1966	11,418	13,095	2,328	62	61	128	171
1970	13,145	12,198	2,117	38	175	307	384
1974 (Feb.)	11,910	11,646	6,059	33	171	632	958
1974 (Oct.)	10,501	11,457	5,347	17	166	840	897
1979	13,698	11,532	4,314	17	133	504	1,024
1983	12,991	8,437	7,775	12	125	331	952
1987	13,761	10,030	7,340	6	124	417	859
1992	14,092	11,563	6,003	–	154	630	1,178

* 1983 and 1987 figures for Liberals include the SDP total.

The Speaker has been regarded as a candidate of the party he represented before appointment.

SEATS WON

	Conservative	Labour	Liberal*	Communist	Plaid Cymru	SNP	Others (GB)	Others (NI)	Total
1918	383	73	161	0	0	0	9	81	707
1922	344	142	115	1	0	0	10	3	615
1923	258	191	158	0	0	0	5	3	615
1924	412	151	40	1	0	0	10	1	615
1929	260	287	59	0	0	0	6	3	615
1931	521	52	37	0	0	0	3	2	615
1935	429	154	21	1	0	0	8	2	615
1945	213	393	12	2	0	0	16	4	640
1950	299	315	9	0	0	0	0	2	625
1951	321	295	6	0	0	0	0	3	625
1955	345	277	6	0	0	0	0	2	630
1959	365	258	6	0	0	0	1	0	630
1964	304	317	9	0	0	0	0	0	630
1966	253	364	12	0	0	0	0	1	630
1970	330	288	6	0	0	1	1	4	630
1974 (Feb.)	297	301	14	0	2	7	2	12	635
1974 (Oct.)	277	319	13	0	3	11	0	12	635
1979	339	269	11	0	2	2	0	12	635
1983	397	209	23	0	2	2	0	17	650
1987	376	229	22	0	3	3	0	17	650
1992	336	271	20	0	4	3	0	17	651

Others (NI): Ireland in 1918, Northern Ireland only 1922–79. Ulster Unionists regarded as Conservatives 1922–70.

The Speaker has been regarded as an MP of the party he represented before appointment.

* 1983 and 1987 figures for Liberals include SDP MPs. The 1992 figures are for the Liberal Democrats.

By-Elections 1945– May 1995 **

Parliament	Government	No. of By-elections	Changes	Con. + −		Lab. + −		Lib./All.* + −		Others + −	
1945–50	Lab.	52	3	3	—	—	—	—	—	—	3
1950–51	Lab.	16	0	—	—	—	—	—	—	—	—
1951–55	Con.	48	1	1	—	—	1	—	—	—	—
1955–59	Con.	52	6	1	4	4	—	1	1	—	1
1959–64	Con.	62	9	2	7	6	2	1	—	—	—
1964–66	Lab.	13	2	1	1	—	1	1	—	—	—
1966–70	Lab.	38	16	12	1	—	15	1	—	3	—
1970–74	Con.	30	8	—	5	1	3	5	—	2	—
1974	Lab.	1	0	—	—	—	—	—	—	—	—
1974–79	Lab.	30	7	6	—	—	1	1	—	—	—
1979–83	Con.	20	6	1	4	1	1	4	1	—	—
1983–87	Con.	31†	6	—	4	1	1	4	—	1	1
1987–92	Con.	24	8	—	7	4	1	3	—	1	—
1992–	Con.	12	4	—	4	1	—	3	—	—	—

* Liberal 1945–79; Alliance (Liberal and SDP) 1979–89, Liberal Democrat after 1990.
† Includes 15 by-elections held in Northern Ireland in January 1986 following Unionist resignations in protest at Anglo-Irish Agreement.
** Since 1992 the following seats have changed hands at by-elections: Newbury, Christchurch and Eastleigh (all from Conservative to Liberal Democrat) and Dudley West (from Conservative to Labour).

Composition of House of Commons, May 1995

Conservatives	331
Labour	271
Liberal Democrats	23
Ulster Unionists	9
Scottish Nationalists	3
Plaid Cymru	4
SDLP (NI)	4
Democratic Unionists	3
Speaker	1
Vacant	2
	651

but may occur more frequently either because no government can command a majority in the House of Commons or at the request of the Prime Minister. If a seat falls vacant between general elections a by-election is held on a date usually chosen by the party which previously held the seat. Elections are generally held on Thursdays.

TURNOUT AND PARTY SHARE OF VOTES CAST

Turnout (%)		Share of Poll (%)		
		Conservative	Labour	Liberal
1918	59	39	24	26
1922	71	38	30	29
1923	71	38	31	30
1924	77	48	33	18
1929	76	38	37	23
1931	76	59	32	7
1935	71	54	39	6
1945	73	40	48	9
1950	84	44	46	9
1951	83	48	49	3
1955	77	50	46	3
1959	79	49	44	6
1964	77	43	44	11
1966	76	42	48	9
1970	72	46	43	8
1974 (Feb.)	78	38	37	19
1974 (Oct.)	73	36	39	18
1979	76	44	37	14
1983	73	42	28	26*
1987	75	42	31	23*
1992	78	42	34	18**

* includes SDP figures.
** Liberal Democrats

C. POLITICAL PARTIES

To understand the operation of the British system of government it is essential to appreciate the importance of the party system. Since the seventeenth century two parties have usually been predominant, at different times Tories and Whigs, Conservatives and Liberals, and since the 1930s Conservatives and Labour. Parties exist to form governments, and the path to this goal lies in the House of Commons, for the party which obtains a majority of seats has the right to have its leaders form the government. The other party forms Her Majesty's Opposition.

To this end parties in this country have been highly disciplined organisations. The opposition accepts that, unless the government's majority is very small, it is unlikely to defeat it in the Commons, and it thus sees its role as one of criticising government policy and setting forth an alternative programme.

Party Leaders

The Conservative Party leader is elected by the members of its parliamentary party. In 1993, Labour adopted a new democratic system for electing future leaders. This system was used to elect Tony Blair in 1994 after the death of John Smith. The Social and Liberal Democrat leader is elected by party members nationally.

Leaders (at May 1995)

Conservative	Mr John Major
Labour	Mr Tony Blair
Social and Liberal Democrat	Mr Paddy Ashdown
Plaid Cymru	Mr Ieuann Wyn Jones
Scottish National	Mrs Margaret Ewing
Ulster Unionist	Mr James Molyneaux

Past Leaders

Conservative Party Leaders

1900–2	Marquis of Salisbury
1902–11	A Balfour
1911–21	A Bonar Law
1921–22	A Chamberlain
1922–23	A Bonar Law
1923–37	S Baldwin
1937–40	N Chamberlain
1940–55	(Sir) W Churchill
1955–57	Sir A Eden
1957–63	H Macmillan
1963–65	Sir A Douglas-Home
1965–75	(Sir) E Heath
1975–90	Mrs M Thatcher
1990–	J Major

Labour Party Leaders

1906–8	J K Hardie
1908–10	A Henderson
1910–11	G Barnes
1911–14	J R MacDonald
1914–17	A Henderson
1917–21	W Adamson
1921–22	J Clynes
1922–31	J R MacDonald
1931–32	A Henderson
1932–35	G Lansbury
1935–55	C Attlee
1955–63	H Gaitskell
1963–76	H Wilson
1976–80	J Callaghan
1980–83	M Foot
1983–92	N Kinnock
1992–94	J Smith
1994–	T Blair

Liberal Party Leaders

1900–8	Sir H Campbell-Bannerman
1908–26	H Asquith
1926–31	D Lloyd George
1931–35	Sir H Samuel
1935–45	Sir A Sinclair
1945–56	C Davies
1956–67	J Grimond
1967–76	J Thorpe
1976–88	(Sir) D Steel

Social and Liberal Democratic Party Leader

1988–	P Ashdown

Party Officers

Conservative Party

Chairman of the Party Organisation
(appointed by the Leader of the Party)

1959–61	R Butler
1961–63	I Macleod
1963	I Macleod ⎫
	Lord Poole ⎭
1963–65	Viscount Blakenham
1965–67	E du Cann
1967–70	A Barber
1970–72	P Thomas
1972–74	Lord Carrington
1974–75	W Whitelaw
1975–81	Lord Thorneycroft
1981–83	C Parkinson
1983–85	J Selwyn Gummer
1985–87	N Tebbit
1987–89	P Brooke
1989–90	K Baker
1990–92	C Patten
1992–94	Sir N Fowler
1994–	J Hanley

Chairman of Conservative (Private) Members'
Committee (or the 1922 Committee)

1955–64	J Morrison
1964–66	Sir W Anstruther-Gray
1966–70	Sir A Harvey
1970–72	Sir H Legge-Bourke
1972–84	E du Cann
1984–92	Sir C Onslow
1992–	Sir M Fox

Labour Party

General Secretary

1944–62	M Phillips
1962–68	A Williams
1968–72	Sir H Nicholas
1972–82	R Hayward
1982–85	J Mortimer
1985–94	L Whitty
1994–	T Sawyer

Chairman of the Parliamentary Labour Party

1970–74	D Houghton
1974	I Mikardo
1974–79	C Hughes
1979–81	F Willey
1981–87	J Dormand
1988–92	S Orme
1992–	D Hoyle

Social and Liberal Democratic Party

President
(election by Party members)

1988–90	I Wrigglesworth
1990–94	C Kennedy
1994–	R Maclennan

Chief Executive

1988–89	A Ellis
1989–	G Elson

Scottish National Party—National Secretary:
A Morgan

Plaid Cymru—General Secretary: K Davies

D. PARLIAMENT

Parliament consists of the Queen, the House of Lords and the House of Commons. Over the centuries the balance between the three parts of the legislature has changed such that the Queen's role is now only formal and the House of Commons has established paramountcy over the House of Lords. Because of the party system the initiative in government lies not in Parliament but in the Cabinet. But Parliament, and especially the Commons, has important functions to play not only as the assembly to which the government is ultimately responsible but also in legitimising legislation, voting money and in acting as a body in which complaints may be raised.

House of Lords

Composition. The House of Lords comprises about 1,200 peers, made up in 1995 as follows:

Hereditary Peers	764
Life Peers	400
Lords of Appeal	10
Archbishops and bishops	26

No new hereditary peers were created between 1964 and 1983. Since then, there have been 3: Viscounts Tonypandy (George Thomas) and Whitelaw, and the Earl of Stockton (Harold Macmillan who died in December 1986). Less than 300 peers attend more than one-third of the Lords' proceedings, although 621 peers voted in the debate over Maastricht. Figures of party strengths in the Lords are not easy to obtain, but one source identified 472 Conservatives, 113 Labour and 54 Social and Liberal Democrats in early 1995.

Functions.

(1) Legislation. Some bills on subjects which are not matters of partisan controversy are initiated in the Lords. It also examines in detail many bills which originated in the Commons, but its part is limited by the Parliament Acts, under which it cannot require the Commons to agree to amendments nor delay a bill indefinitely.

(2) Debate. The Lords provides a forum for men and women, distinguished in most fields of national life, to discuss issues of importance free from the reins of party discipline.

(3) Court of appeal. The Lords is the highest court of appeal. Only the law lords take part in its legal proceedings.

House of Commons

Composition. The House of Commons comprises 651 MPs (650 before the 1992 General Election) elected to represent single-member constituencies (524 in England, 72 in Scotland, 38 in Wales and 17 in Northern Ireland). Its proceedings are presided over by the Speaker, who is elected by MPs, at the beginning of each session. The present Speaker, Miss Betty Boothroyd (the first woman Speaker) was elected to the office in 1992.

MPs sit on parallel rows of seats, known as benches, with those who support the government on one side of the chamber and the rest on the other side. Members of the government and the spokesmen of the Opposition are known as "frontbenchers"; other MPs are "backbenchers".

Functions.

(1) Legislation. There are two types of legislation—*public acts*, most of which are introduced by the government, but which can also be introduced

by individual MPs, and *private acts*, which confer special powers on bodies such as local authorities in excess of the general law and which are subject to special procedures.

All public legislation must pass through the following stages before becoming law:

First Reading. The bill is formally introduced.

Second Reading. The general principles of the bill are debated and voted.

Committee Stage. Each clause of the bill is debated and voted.

Report Stage. The bill is considered as it was reported by the committee, and it is decided whether to make further changes in individual clauses.

Third Reading. The bill, as amended, is debated and a final vote taken.

The Other House. The bill has to pass through the same stages in the other House of Parliament.

Royal Assent. The Queen gives her assent to the bill which becomes law as an Act of Parliament.

(2) Scrutiny of government activities. There are a number of opportunities for the opposition and the government's own back-benchers to criticise government policy. They can question ministers on the floor of the House; they can table motions for debate and speak in debates initiated by the government; and they can take part in one of the select committees set up to scrutinise government activity.

Committees. The House of Commons uses committees to assist it in its work in various ways. They are of two types:

Standing Committees. A standing committee is a miniature of the House itself, reflecting its party composition, and consists of between 20 and 50 MPs. Its function is to examine the Committee Stage of legislation. Usually seven or eight such committees are needed.

Select Committees. A select committee is a body with special powers and privileges to which the House has delegated its authority for the purpose of discovering information, examining witnesses, sifting evidence and drawing up conclusions which are then reported to the House. A few select committees are established *ad hoc*, but the majority are semi-permanent, although the House can always wind them up at any time.

Since 1979, there have been 13 or 14 select com-

E. HER MAJESTY'S GOVERNMENT
The Cabinet (as at 4 May 1995)

Prime Minister, First Lord of the Treasury and Minister for the Civil Service	Mr John Major
Lord Chancellor	Lord Mackay
Secretary of State for Foreign and Commonwealth Affairs	Mr Douglas Hurd
Chancellor of the Exchequer	Mr Kenneth Clarke
Secretary of State for the Home Department	Mr Michael Howard
Secretary of State for Trade and Industry and President of the Board of Trade	Mr Michael Heseltine
Secretary of State for Transport	Dr Brian Mawhinney
Secretary of State for Defence	Mr Malcolm Rifkind
Lord Privy Seal and Leader of the House of Lords	Viscount Cranborne
Lord President of the Council and Leader of the House of Commons	Mr Antony Newton
Secretary of State for the Environment	Mr John Gummer
Secretary of State for National Heritage	Mr Stephen Dorrell
Secretary of State for Employment	Mr Michael Portillo
Secretary of State for Social Security	Mr Peter Lilley
Chancellor of the Duchy of Lancaster and Minister for the Citizen's Charter	Mr David Hunt
Secretary of State for Scotland	Mr Ian Lang
Secretary of State for Northern Ireland	Sir Patrick Mayhew
Secretary of State for Education and Science	Mrs Gillian Shephard
Secretary of State for Health	Mrs Virginia Bottomley
Minister of Agriculture, Fisheries and Food	Mr William Waldegrave
Chief Secretary to the Treasury	Mr Jonathan Aitken
Secretary of State for Wales	Mr John Redwood
Minister without Portfolio and party chairman	Mr Jeremy Hanley

Ministers not in the Cabinet

Agriculture, Fisheries and Food, Minister of State	Mr Michael Jack
Defence, Ministers of State	Mr Roger Freeman
	Mr Nicholas Soames
Education and Science, Minister of State	Mr Eric Forth
Employment, Minister of State	Miss Ann Widdecombe
Environment, Ministers of State	Mr David Curry
	Mr Robert Atkins
	Viscount Ullswater
Foreign and Commonwealth Office, Ministers of State	Mr Douglas Hogg
	Mr David Davis
	Mr Alastair Goodlad
Minister for Overseas Development	Baroness Chalker
Health, Minister of State	Mr Gerry Malone
Home Office, Ministers of State	Baroness Blatch
	Mr David Maclean
	Mr Michael Forsyth
Northern Ireland Office, Ministers of State	Sir John Wheeler
	Mr Michael Ancram
Scottish Office, Minister of State	Lord Fraser of Carmyllie
Social Security, Ministers of State	Lord Mackay of Ardbrecknish
	Mr William Hague
Trade and Industry, Ministers of State	Mr Tim Eggar
	Mr Richard Needham
	Earl Ferrers
Transport, Minister of State	Mr John Watts
Treasury, Financial Secretary	Sir George Young
Paymaster General	Mr David Heathcoat-Amory
Economic Secretary	Mr Anthony Nelson
Parliamentary Secretary, Treasury	Mr Richard Ryder
Attorney General	Sir Nicholas Lyell
Lord Advocate	Lord Rodger of Earlsferry
Solicitor General	Sir Derek Spencer
Solicitor General for Scotland	Mr Thomas Dawson

Principal Ministers 1900–1945

	Prime Minister	Chancellor of the Exchequer	Foreign Secretary	Home Secretary	Leader of the House of Commons
1900–2	Marquis of Salisbury	Sir M Hicks-Beach	Marquis of Salisbury Marquis of Lansdowne	Sir M White-Ridley C Ritchie	A Balfour
1902–5	A Balfour	C Ritchie A Chamberlain	Marquis of Lansdowne	A Akers-Douglas	A Balfour
1905–8	Sir H Campbell-Bannerman	H Asquith	Sir E Grey	H Gladstone	Sir H Campbell-Bannerman
1908–16	H Asquith	D Lloyd George R McKenna	Sir E Grey	H Gladstone W Churchill R McKenna Sir J Simon Sir H Samuel	H Asquith
1916–22	D Lloyd George	A Bonar Law A Chamberlain Sir R Horne	A Balfour Earl Curzon	Sir G Cave E Shortt	A Bonar Law A Chamberlain
1922–23	A Bonar Law	S Baldwin	Earl Curzon	W Bridgeman	A Bonar Law
1923–24	S Baldwin	S Baldwin N Chamberlain	Earl Curzon	W Bridgeman	S Baldwin
1924	J R MacDonald	P Snowden	J R MacDonald	A Henderson	J R MacDonald
1924–29	S Baldwin	W Churchill	(Sir) A Chamberlain	Sir W Joynson-Hicks	S Baldwin
1929–35	J R MacDonald	P Snowden N Chamberlain	A Henderson Marquis of Reading Sir J Simon	J Clynes Sir H Samuel Sir J Gilmour	J R MacDonald
1935–37	S Baldwin	N Chamberlain	Sir S Hoare A Eden	Sir J Simon	S Baldwin
1937–40	N Chamberlain	Sir J Simon	A Eden Viscount Halifax	Sir S Hoare Sir J Anderson	N Chamberlain
1940–45	W Churchill	Sir K Wood Sir J Anderson	Viscount Halifax A Eden	H Morrison Sir D Somervell	C Attlee* Sir S Cripps A Eden

* Churchill deputed day to day business to Attlee.

Principal Ministers 1945– May 1995

Prime Minister		Chancellor of the Exchequer	Foreign Secretary	Home Secretary	Leader of the House of Commons
1945-51	C Attlee	H Dalton Sir S Cripps H Gaitskell	E Bevin H Morrison	C Ede	H Morrison C Ede
1951-55	Sir W Churchill	R Butler	Sir A Eden	Sir D Maxwell-Fyfe G Lloyd George	H Crookshank
1955-57	Sir A Eden	R Butler H Macmillan	H Macmillan S Lloyd	G Lloyd George	R Butler
1957-63	H Macmillan	P Thorneycroft D Heathcoat Amory S Lloyd R Maudling	S Lloyd Earl of Home	R Butler H Brooke	R Butler I Macleod
1963-64	Sir A Douglas-Home	R Maudling	R Butler	H Brooke	S Lloyd
1964-70	H Wilson	J Callaghan R Jenkins	P Gordon Walker M Stewart G Brown M Stewart	Sir F Soskice R Jenkins J Callaghan	H Bowden R Crossman F Peart
1970-74	E Heath	I Macleod A Barber	Sir A Douglas-Home	R Maudling R Carr	W Whitelaw R Carr J Prior
1974-76	H Wilson	D Healey	J Callaghan	R Jenkins	E Short
1976-79	J Callaghan	D Healey	A Crosland D Owen	R Jenkins M Rees	M Foot
1979-90	Mrs M Thatcher	Sir G Howe N Lawson J Major	Lord Carrington F Pym Sir G Howe J Major D Hurd	W Whitelaw L Brittan D Hurd D Waddington	N St John-Stevas F Pym J Biffen J Wakeham Sir G Howe J MacGregor
1990-	J Major	N Lamont K Clarke	D Hurd	K Baker K Clarke M Howard	J MacGregor A Newton

mittees, each one scrutinising the work of one or two government departments (e.g. Agriculture, Foreign Affairs, Treasury and Civil Service); and various others including the following: European Legislation, Members' Interests, Parliamentary Commissioner for Administration, Privileges, Public Accounts, and Statutory Instruments.

Central Government

The executive work of central government is performed by the Prime Minister and the other ministers of the Crown. The power of executive action is not given to a government department as a corporate body but to the minister individually, who is responsible for the exercise of his duties legally to the Queen and politically to Parliament. For this reason, all ministers must be members of either the Commons or the Lords.

At the head of the government structure is the Cabinet, which consists of the leading members of the majority party in the Commons, selected by the Prime Minister. Most Cabinet ministers are the heads of government departments, which are staffed by civil servants, but there are usually some without departmental responsibilities. Although legally ministers are individually responsible for the exercise of government powers, politically it is accepted that the Cabinet is collectively responsible for government policy. It thus acts as one man, and a minister who disagrees with the Cabinet must either resign or remain silent.

Size of the Government 1945–93

	Cabinet Ministers	Non-Cabinet Ministers	Junior Ministers	Total
1945	20	20	49	89
1950	18	22	44	84
1960	20	23	45	88
1965	23	33	55	111
1970	17	26	41	84
1975	24	31	54	109
1993	22	28	46	96

F. HER MAJESTY'S OPPOSITION

The leader of the largest party opposed to the government is designated Leader of Her Majesty's Opposition and receives an official salary. The leading spokesmen of the Opposition meet together as a committee and are generally known as the Shadow Cabinet. A Conservative Shadow Cabinet, officially known as the Leader's Consultative Committee, is selected by the leader of the party. Labour Shadow Cabinets, officially known as the Parliamentary Committee, are elected by the Parliamentary Labour Party, but the leader retains the right to invite members to take charge of particular subjects.

G. OTHER EXECUTIVE BODIES

A large number of semi-autonomous agencies have been established to carry out functions on behalf of the government, usually because a particular function is considered to be unsuitable for a normal government department. In this category are bodies such as the British Broadcasting Corporation and the Commission for Racial Equality which need to be insulated from the political process, and the nationalised industries, most of which are managed by public corporations so as to secure managerial flexibility. Some public control over these bodies is maintained by means of various powers which ministers possess.

H. THE CIVIL SERVICE

The civil service is the body of permanent officials who, working in the various departments, administer the policy of central government. It consists of some 567,000 people (2·5% of the working population), of whom 499,000 are non-industrial civil servants and the rest industrial workers in places such as the ordnance factories and naval dockyards. Over 80% of the civil service work outside Greater London, mainly in the regional and local offices of departments such as Health, Social Security, Employment and the Inland Revenue.

The political head of each department is a minister, but, as he often has no previous experience of the field to which he is appointed and his tenure of office may be fairly short-lived, great

Labour's Shadow Cabinet (as at May 1995)

The Shadow Cabinet in full

Leader of the Opposition	Mr Tony Blair
Deputy Leader	Mr John Prescott
Foreign Affairs	Mr Robin Cook
Health	Ms Margaret Beckett
Treasury and Economic Affairs	Mr Gordon Brown
Social Security	Mr Donald Dewar
Employment	Ms Harriet Harman
Chief Secretary to Treasury	Mr Andrew Smith
Environment and London	Mr Frank Dobson
Scotland	Mr George Robertson
Northern Ireland	Ms Mo Mowlam
National Heritage	Mr Chris Smith
Trade and Industry	Mr Jack Cunningham
Transport	Mr Michael Meacher
Wales	Mr Ron Davies
Defence	Mr David Clark
Home Affairs	Mr Jack Straw
Education	Mr David Blunkett
Overseas Development	Ms Joan Lestor
Agriculture	Mr Gavin Strang
Shadow Commons Leader, Citizen's Charter	Ms Ann Taylor

Chief Whip	Mr Derek Foster
Chair of the Parliamentary Labour Party	Mr Doug Hoyle
Leader in the House of Lords	Lord Richard
Chief Whip in the Lords	Lord Graham of Edmonton

Major Public Bodies

	Chairman
Arts Council	Lord Gowrie
Bank of England	Mr Eddie George
British Broadcasting Corporation	Mr Marmaduke Hussey
British Coal	Sir David White
British Rail	Mr John Welsby
Civil Aviation Authority	Mr Christopher Chataway
Commission for Racial Equality	Mr Herman Ouseley
Equal Opportunities Commission	Ms Kamlesh Bahl
Higher Education Funding Council for England	Sir Ron Dearing
Independent Television Commission	Sir George Russell
London Regional Transport	Mr Peter Ford
Monopolies and Mergers Commission	Mr Graeme Odgers
National Consumer Council	Lady Wilcox
Post Office	Mr Michael Heron
Radio Authority	Sir Peter Gibbings
Railtrack	Mr Robert Horton

responsibility falls on the shoulders of the permanent civil servants in his department. Civil servants remain largely anonymous and their relationship with their minister is a confidential one. They are non-political in the sense that they serve all political parties impartially.

Civil Service Numbers

	Total		*Total*
1914	779,000	1970	702,000
1938	581,000	1979	732,000
1950	972,000	1994	533,000
1960	996,000		

Note: The drop in numbers between 1960 and 1970 is the result of the exclusion of Post Office staff, who ceased to be civil servants in 1969. Otherwise the size of the civil service grew by more than 50,000 between 1960 and 1970.

Senior Civil Servants

Head of the Home Civil Service

1945–56	Sir E Bridges
1956–63	Sir N Brook
1963–68	Sir L Helsby
1968–74	Sir W Armstrong
1974–78	Sir D Allen
1978–81	Sir I Bancroft
1981–83	{ Sir R Armstrong / Sir D Wass
1983–88	Sir R Armstrong
1988–	Sir R Butler

Head of the Diplomatic Service

1945–46	Sir A Cadogan
1946–49	Sir O Sargent
1949–53	Sir W Strang
1953–57	Sir I Kirkpatrick
1957–62	Sir F Hoyer Millar
1962–65	Sir H Caccia
1965–68	Sir S Garner
1968–69	Sir P Gore-Booth
1969–73	Sir D Greenhill
1973–75	Sir T Brimelow
1975–82	Sir M Palliser
1982–86	Sir A Acland
1986–94	Sir P Wright
1994–	Sir J Coles

Permanent Secretary to the Treasury

1945–56	Sir E Bridges
1956–60	{ Sir N Brook / Sir R Makins
1960–62	{ Sir N Brook / Sir F Lee
1962–63	{ Sir N Brook / Sir W Armstrong
1963–68	{ Sir L Helsby / (Sir) W Armstrong
1968	{ Sir W Armstrong / Sir D Allen
1968–74	Sir D Allen
1974–83	Sir D Wass
1983–91	Sir P Middleton
1991–	Sir T Burns

Secretary to the Cabinet

1938–47	Sir E Bridges
1947–63	Sir N Brook
1963–73	Sir B Trend
1973–79	Sir J Hunt
1979–88	Sir R Armstrong
1988–	Sir R Butler

I. LOCAL GOVERNMENT

Local government in the United Kingdom is the creation of Parliament. Its structure is laid down by Parliament, and local authorities may only exercise those powers which Parliament either commands or permits them to exercise. Their functions include responsibility for all education services, except further and higher education, most personal welfare services, housing, public health, environmental planning, traffic management and transport, in each case subject to some central government control.

The structure of local government varies in different parts of the country. In non-metropolitan England (often known as the shire counties), there is a two-tier system.

In London and the six metropolitan areas there has been, since April 1986 (when the Greater London Council and the metropolitan county councils were abolished), a single-tier system with a few special bodies undertaking county-wide functions. In March 1991, the Government proposed a major review of the structure of local government.

Currently (May 1995) the final future shape of local government in England remains unclear. However, elections for 14 English "shadow" all-purpose unitary councils (including the new Isle of Wight authority) took place in May 1995. Among authorities to be reorganised will be Avon, Humberside and Cleveland, all created in 1974. Berkshire has become the only old shire authority to be abolished under the review.

In Wales, 22 all-purpose councils are to replace the 8 counties and 37 district councils in 1996. Elections to these "shadow" councils took place in May 1995.

In Scotland, 29 single-tier authorities replace the existing 2-tier structure from 1 April 1996. These new authorities were elected in April 1995. There are single-tier island councils in Orkney, Shetland and the Western Isles.

For a summary of seats gained and lost in the local elections of May 1995, *see* **A38**. *See also* **D12** for current control of metropolitan councils.

First-tier Authorities (as at May 1995)

Name	Population in 1989	Political control in 1995 *	Number of districts	Administrative capital
ENGLAND				
Non-Metropolitan Counties				
Avon	953,000	NOM.	6	Bristol
Bedfordshire	531,000	NOM.	4	Bedford
Berkshire	749,000	NOM.	6	Reading
Buckinghamshire	634,000	Con.	5	Aylesbury
Cambridgeshire	655,000	NOM.	6	Cambridge
Cheshire	959,000	NOM.	8	Chester
Cleveland	553,000	Lab.	4	Middlesbrough
Cornwall	464,000	SLD.	6	Truro
Cumbria	492,000	NOM.	6	Carlisle
Derbyshire	929,000	Lab.	9	Matlock
Devon	1,030,000	NOM.	10	Exeter
Dorset	657,000	NOM.	8	Dorchester
Durham	597,000	Lab.	8	Durham
East Sussex	712,000	NOM.	7	Lewes
Essex	1,532,000	NOM.	14	Chelmsford
Gloucestershire	530,000	NOM.	6	Gloucester
Hampshire	1,546,000	NOM.	13	Winchester
Hereford and Worcester	675,000	NOM.	9	Worcester
Hertfordshire	987,000	NOM.	10	Hertford
Humberside	856,000	Lab.	9	Beverley
Isle of Wight	131,000	SLD.	2	Newport
Kent	1,524,000	NOM.	14	Maidstone
Lancashire	1,391,000	Lab.	14	Preston
Leicestershire	892,000	NOM.	9	Leicester
Lincolnshire	587,000	NOM.	7	Lincoln
Norfolk	749,000	NOM.	7	Norwich
Northamptonshire	576,000	Lab.	7	Northampton
Northumberland	304,000	Lab.	6	Newcastle-upon-Tyne
North Yorkshire	722,000	NOM.	8	Northallerton
Nottinghamshire	1,015,000	Lab.	8	Nottingham
Oxfordshire	578,000	NOM.	5	Oxford
Shropshire	403,000	NOM.	6	Shrewsbury
Somerset	461,000	SLD.	5	Taunton
Staffordshire	1,039,000	Lab.	9	Stafford
Suffolk	641,000	NOM.	7	Ipswich
Surrey	1,000,000	NOM.	11	Kingston-upon-Thames
Warwickshire	483,000	NOM.	5	Warwick
West Sussex	705,000	NOM.	7	Chichester
Wiltshire	558,000	NOM.	5	Trowbridge
WALES				
Counties				
Clwyd	411,000	Lab.	6	Mold
Dyfed	353,000	NOM.	6	Carmarthen
Gwent	447,000	Lab.	5	Cwmbran
Gwynedd	241,000	NOM.	5	Caernarfon
Mid Glamorgan	538,000	Lab.	6	Cardiff
Powys	117,000	Ind.	3	Llandrindod Wells
South Glamorgan	404,000	Lab.	2	Cardiff
West Glamorgan	363,000	Lab.	4	Swansea
SCOTLAND				
Regions				
Borders	103,000	NOM.	4	Newtown St. Boswells
Central	271,000	Lab.	3	Stirling
Dumfries and Galloway	147,000	NOM.	4	Dumfries
Fife	345,000	Lab.	3	Glenrothes
Grampian	501,000	NOM.	5	Aberdeen
Highland	202,000	Ind.	8	Inverness
Lothian	741,000	Lab.	4	Edinburgh
Strathclyde	2,333,000	Lab.	19	Glasgow
Tayside	393,000	NOM.	3	Dundee
Islands Councils				
Orkney	19,000	NP.	—	Kirkwall
Shetland	23,000	NP.	—	Lerwick
Western Isles	32,000	NP.	—	Stornoway

NOM.—No overall majority.   NP.—Non-party
* The May 1993 elections left 28 county councils with NOM, 14 Labour, 3 Lib. Dem., 1 Con. and 1 Ind. in England and Wales.

Second-tier Authorities (as at May 1995)

	Number	Range of population
England Non-Metropolitan District Councils	296	24,000—416,000
Wales District Councils	37	20,000—282,000
Scotland District Councils	53	9,000—856,000

Metropolitan Councils in England

	Name	Population in 1990	Political control (May 1995)
London	Barking & Dagenham	148,000	Lab.
	Barnet	310,000	NOM.
	Bexley	220,000	NOM.
	Brent	255,000	Con.
	Bromley	299,000	Con.
	Camden	184,000	Lab.
	Croydon	317,000	Lab.
	Ealing	294,000	Lab.
	Enfield	262,000	Lab.
	Greenwich	213,000	Lab.
	Hackney	192,000	Lab.
	Hammersmith and Fulham	149,000	Lab.
	Haringey	190,000	Lab.
	Harrow	194,000	NOM.
	Havering	233,000	NOM.
	Hillingdon	235,000	Lab.
	Hounslow	196,000	Lab.
	Islington	170,000	Lab.
	Kensington and Chelsea	131,000	Con.
	Kingston-on-Thames	136,000	SLD.
	Lambeth	238,000	NOM.
	Lewisham	227,000	Lab.
	Merton	164,000	Lab.
	Newham	207,000	Lab.
	Redbridge	232,000	NOM.
	Richmond-on-Thames	164,000	SLD.
	Southwark	220,000	Lab.
	Sutton	169,000	SLD.
	Tower Hamlets	164,000	Lab.
	Waltham Forest	212,000	NOM.
	Wandsworth	256,000	Con.
	Westminster	173,000	Con.
Greater Manchester	Bolton	265,000	Lab.
	Bury	176,000	Lab.
	Manchester	444,000	Lab.
	Oldham	221,000	Lab.
	Rochdale	208,000	NOM.
	Salford	235,000	Lab.
	Stockport	291,000	NOM.
	Tameside	218,000	Lab.
	Trafford	215,000	NOM.
	Wigan	310,000	Lab.
Merseyside	Knowsley	158,000	Lab.
	Liverpool	466,000	NOM.
	St. Helens	189,000	Lab.
	Sefton	300,000	NOM.
	Wirral	336,000	Lab.
South Yorkshire	Barnsley	222,000	Lab.
	Doncaster	293,000	Lab.
	Rotherham	254,000	Lab.
	Sheffield	527,000	Lab.
Tyne & Wear	Gateshead	206,000	Lab.
	Newcastle-upon-Tyne	278,000	Lab.
	North Tyneside	193,000	Lab.
	South Tyneside	156,000	Lab.
	Sunderland	296,000	Lab.
West Midlands	Birmingham	993,000	Lab.
	Coventry	304,000	Lab.
	Dudley	305,000	Lab.
	Sandwell	296,000	Lab.
	Solihull	204,000	NOM.
	Walsall	263,000	Lab.
	Wolverhampton	250,000	Lab.
West Yorkshire	Bradford	468,000	Lab.
	Calderdale	197,000	Lab.
	Kirklees	376,000	Lab.
	Leeds	712,000	Lab.
	Wakefield	314,000	Lab.

Local Government Structure (showing numbers of authorities of each type) (1995)

	England			Wales	Scotland	
1st Tier	Metropolitan District Councils 36	Non-Metropolitan County Councils 39	London Borough Councils * 32	County Councils 8	Regional Councils 9	Islands Councils 3
2nd Tier		Non-Metropolitan District Councils 296		District Councils 37	District Councils 53	
3rd Tier	Parish Councils 221	Parish Councils 8,919		Community Councils	Community Councils	Community Councils

* Excluding the City of London.

Table derived from J Stanyer and B C Smith, *Administering Britain* (Martin Robertson, 1980), p. 119.

Local Government—Division of Functions (1995)

Service	England and Wales			Scotland
	Metropolitan areas	Non-Metropolitan areas	Greater London	
Education	District	County	Borough[1]	Region
Personal social services	District	County	Borough	Region
Police and fire services	Joint boards[2]	County	Home Secretary/Joint Board[3]	Region
Planning	District	Shared	Borough	Shared
Highways	District[3]	Shared	Borough[3]	Shared
Environmental Health	District	District	Borough	District
Housing	District	District	Borough	District

Notes:

1. In Inner London a special body, the Inner London Education Authority (ILEA), ran the education service until its abolition in 1990.

2. Joint boards are composed of borough and district councillors, appointed by the councils within the metropolitan area or Greater London.

3. In the metropolitan areas except London, passenger transport services are run by joint boards; London Regional Transport has, since 1984, been appointed by central government.

J. REDRESS OF GRIEVANCES

In the first instance most citizens who are aggrieved by the decision of a public body take up their complaint with the body concerned, either personally or in writing. If this does not satisfy them they have a number of options which vary according to the type of body and the nature of their complaint.

Central Government

1. *MPs.* MPs may be contacted by letter, and many of them hold regular surgeries in their constituencies. On receipt of a complaint they can write to the minister in charge of the department concerned or ask a question in Parliament. If the complainant alleges maladministration (*e.g.*, arbitrary action, undue delay) this can be referred to the *Parliamentary Commissioner for Administration* (usually known as the Ombudsman) who is empowered to investigate complaints and report his findings to Parliament.

2. *Tribunals and inquiries.* In certain areas of government (*e.g.*, social security), special tribunals exist to adjudicate on disputes between citizens and government. In others (*e.g.*, planning) an inquiry can be set up. In both cases the machinery is less formal and more flexible than the ordinary courts.

3. *Courts of law.* On certain restricted matters (*e.g.*, that a public body has acted outside its lawful powers), citizens have recourse to the ordinary courts.

Local Government

1. *Councillors.* Local councillors can be contacted in the same way as MPs. They can also refer complaints of maladministration to a *Commissioner for Local Administration* (or local Ombudsman). There are five commissioners, three in England and one each in Scotland and Wales, each investigating complaints in a particular part of the country.

2. *Tribunals and inquiries* (as above).

3. *Courts of law* (as above).

Other Public Bodies

1. *National Health Service.* Each health authority has its own complaints procedure subject to a national code of practice. Complaints, other than those involving the exercise of clinical judgement, may be taken to the *Health Service Commissioner*. Special procedures exist for complaints against doctors.

2. *Nationalised Industries.* Each industry has a consumer council which exists both to take up individual complaints and to represent the views of consumers to the board of management for the industry (*e.g.*, The Post Office Users National Council, the Transport Users Consultative Committees). In four former nationalised industries, privatised during the 1980s – telecommunications, gas, water and electricity – independent regulatory bodies have been created to ensure the companies do not abuse monopoly power and to deal with consumers' complaints.

Parliamentary Commissioner for Administration
(and Health Service Commissioner since 1973)

1967–71	Sir Edmund Compton
1971–76	Sir Alan Marre
1976–78	Sir Idwal Pugh
1979–85	Sir Cecil Clothier
1985–90	Sir Anthony Barrowclough
1990–	Mr William Reid

Office of Gas Supply (OFGAS)
Ms Clare Spottiswoode

Office for Standards in Education (OFSTED)
Professor S Sutherland

Office of Telecommunications (OFTEL)
Mr D Cruickshank (Director-General)

Office of Water Services
Mr I C R Byatt (Director-General)

Office of Electricity Regulation
Professor S Littlechild (Director-General)

K. PRESSURE GROUPS

Large numbers of groups exist to exert pressure on government by direct consultation with ministers and civil servants, lobbying Parliament and general publicity campaigns. Some exist to defend interests such as labour, business or consumers; others promote particular causes such as the prevention of cruelty to children or the banning of blood sports. Of great importance in contemporary politics are the groups representing labour and business.

Trade Unions

About 38% of the working population belong to a trade union. Among the largest unions are:

UNISON *
Transport and General Workers' Union
Amalgamated Electrical and Engineering Union
General, Municipal, Boilermakers' and Allied Trades Union
Manufacturing, Science, Finance Union
Union of Shop, Distributive and Allied Workers

* Formed by the merger of NALGO, NUPE and COHSE.

Union	Principal Officer
UNISON	A Jinkinson
AEEU	W Jordan
TGWU	W Morris
GMBATU	J Edmonds
MSF	R Lyons
USDAW	S Tierney

69 trade unions, representing over 80% of total union membership, are affiliated to the *Trades Union Congress*, which is the federal body of the trade union movement, representing its views to government and others, and giving assistance on questions relating to particular trades and industries.

TUC General Secretaries since 1946

1946–60	(Sir) V Tewson
1960–70	G Woodcock
1970–74	V Feather
1974–84	L Murray
1984–93	N Willis
1993–	J Monks

Business

The peak organisation representing British business is the *Confederation of British Industry*, formed in 1965. Its members now comprise over 11,000 individual enterprises (mainly in the private sector but also including most nationalised industries) and over 200 representative organisations (employers' organisations, trade associations *etc.*).

Director-Generals of the CBI

1965–69	J Davies
1969–76	(Sir) C Adamson
1976–80	(Sir) J Methven
1980–87	(Sir) T Beckett
1987–92	(Sir) J Banham
1992–95	H Davies

Business is also represented by large numbers of associations which promote the interests of individual industries and sectors (*e.g.*, the Society of Motor Manufacturers and Traders, the Retail Consortium, the Association of Independent Businesses).

Other major groups

Campaign for Nuclear Disarmament
Consumers Association
European Movement
Friends of the Earth
National Society for the Prevention of Cruelty to Children
Royal Society for the Prevention of Accidents
Royal Society for the Prevention of Cruelty to Animals
Royal Society for the Protection of Birds
Shelter (National Campaign for the Homeless)

L. THE MEDIA

1. Principal Newspapers

The principal national dailies, with their proprietors and circulation, are set out on **D15**.

There are also a number of provincial morning daily newspapers in England (*e.g.*, *The Birmingham Post and Gazette*, *The Liverpool Daily Post*, *The Yorkshire Post*). Scotland has five morning dailies, of which the most important are *The Scotsman*, *The Glasgow Herald* and *The Daily Record*. Wales has one, *The Western Mail*, and Northern Ireland two, *The News-Letter* and *Irish News*.

A Press Complaints Commission has replaced the voluntary Press Council to consider complaints against the Press and to promote standards.

Chairman, 1995– Lord Wakeham

2. Broadcasting

British Broadcasting Corporation

Established in 1926 as a public service body and financed by licence fees paid by all owners of TV sets. It is directed by a board of governors appointed by the government.

Services: Radio—5 national networks; 36 local radio stations. TV—2 channels.

Chairman of the Board of Governors, 1986– Mr Marmaduke Hussey

Director-General, 1993– John Birt

Independent Television Commission

Established in 1991, as successor to Independent Broadcasting Authority to license programme contracting companies and to regulate their output. Independent broadcasting is financed by advertising revenue.

Services:—One channel, operated by 15 regional companies, and a second (Channel 4) run by two organisations (one for England and Scotland, the other for Wales). A common news service is provided for all the companies by Independent Television News Ltd.

Chairman, 1991– Sir George Russell

Radio Authority

In 1991 it inherited the Independent Broadcasting Authority's responsibilities in relation to radio.
Services: 50 local radio stations.
Chairman, 1995– Sir Peter Gibbings

Editorially all broadcasting authorities are expected to show political balance. Two bodies exist to deal with complaints and standards:

Broadcasting Complaints Commission – to adjudicate on complaints of unjust or unfair treatment in sound or TV programmes. The Commission is to merge with the Broadcasting Standards Council (*see below*) in 1996.
Chairman, 1995– Canon Peter Pilkington

Broadcasting Standards Council – to establish a code on the portrayal of sex and violence and standards of taste and decency, to monitor programmes and consider complaints.
Chairman, 1993– Lady Howe

Paper	Proprietors	Circulation Mar 1995 (millions)	General political stance
National Dailies			
Daily Express	United Newspapers	1·3	Right
Daily Mail	Associated Newspapers	1·8	Right
Daily Mirror	Mirror Group Newspapers	2·5	Left
Daily Star	United Newspapers	0·7	Right
Daily Telegraph	Telegraph Newspaper Trust	1·1	Right
Financial Times	Pearson Longman	0·3	Right
Guardian	Guardian and Manchester Evening News	0·4	Centre
Independent	MGN-led Consortium	0·3	Ind.
Sun	News International	4·1	Right
The Times	News International	0·6	Right
Today	Lonrho International	0·6	Right
National Sundays			
Independent on Sunday	MGN-led Consortium	0·3	Ind.
Mail on Sunday	Associated Newspapers	1·9	Right
News of the World	News International	4·8	Right
Observer	Guardian and Manchester Evening News	0·5	Centre
Sunday Express	United Newspapers	1·4	Right
Sunday Mirror	Mirror Group Newspapers	2·5	Left
Sunday People	Mirror Group Newspapers	2·1	Left
Sunday Telegraph	Telegraph Newspaper Trust	0·7	Right
Sunday Times	News International	1·3	Right

M. SCOTLAND, WALES AND NORTHERN IRELAND

The structure of government in Scotland, Wales and Northern Ireland differs from that in England.

Scotland

Most central government functions in Scotland are the responsibility of a single department, the Scottish Office, based in Edinburgh and represented in the Cabinet by the Secretary of State for Scotland. On many matters special Scottish legislation is enacted by Parliament and administrative structure (*e.g.* the local government system—see **D13**) and practice (*e.g.* the educational system) differ from that in England.

Wales

The Welsh Office, based in Cardiff and represented in the Cabinet by the Secretary of State for Wales, performs many central government functions in Wales but its responsibilities are narrower than its Scottish counterpart. In other respects too government in Wales resembles more closely that in England.

Northern Ireland

From 1921 until 1972 Northern Ireland was governed under the scheme of devolution embodied in the Government of Northern Ireland Act 1920. This created the Northern Ireland Parliament, generally known as Stormont after its eventual location. Executive powers were formally vested in the Governor of Northern Ireland, but were in effect performed by a Prime Minister and small cabinet, responsible to Stormont.

The recent troubles in the province led the UK Government in 1972 to suspend the Government of Northern Ireland Act. Since then, apart from a period of four months in 1974, Northern Ireland has been ruled direct from Westminster, the powers of government being vested in the Secretary of State for Northern Ireland. Most local government functions in the province are performed either by the Secretary of State or by special boards. There are, however, 26 elected district councils with limited functions, mainly in the environmental field. Under the terms of the Anglo-Irish agreement, signed in November 1985, the Republic of Ireland has been granted consultative status on certain issues. Following the Downing Street Declaration, extensive consultations took place on a framework document for the future government structure in Northern Ireland. See **C15**.

N. BRITAIN IN EUROPE

Since joining the European Economic Community (now the European Union) in 1973, the United Kingdom has participated in the principal institutions of the European Union as follows:

Council of Ministers and Commission

The Council of Ministers is the main decision-making body within the Union, consisting of representatives of the 15 member states (12 before 1995), each government delegating one of its ministers according to the business under discussion. The principal UK delegate is the Secretary of State for Foreign and Commonwealth Affairs.

The Commission heads a large bureaucracy in Brussels which submits proposals to the Council of Ministers, implements its decisions, and has powers of its own to promote the Community's interests. Its members are appointed by agreement among the member states for 4-year renewable terms. Members are pledged to independence of national interests.

President of the Commission: Mr Jacques Santer (Luxemburg)

UK Commissioners:
Sir Leon Brittan
Mr Neil Kinnock

European Parliament

Apart from general powers of supervision and consultation, the Parliament, which meets in Luxembourg and Strasbourg, can dismiss the Commission and has some control over the Community Budget. Until 1979 it consisted of members nominated by the national parliaments of the member states. The first direct elections were held in June 1979, the second in June 1984, and the third in June 1989. The fourth elections were held in June 1994, when Britain elected 87 MEPs, 6 more than in 1989. Five extra seats were given to England and one to Wales.

UK Seats Won, 1979–94

	1979	1984	1989	1994
Conservative	60	45	32	18
Labour	17	32	45	62
Liberals (Lib Dems)	0	0	0	2
Scottish Nationalist	1	1	1	2
Democratic Unionist	1	1	1	1
Official Unionist	1	1	1	1
Social Democratic and Labour	1	1	1	1

UK Party Leaders:
Conservative　Lord Plumb
Labour　　　　Mr Wayne David

European Court of Justice

The European Court is responsible for interpreting and applying the Community treaties. Its decisions are binding in the member countries. It consists of thirteen judges and six advocates-general, appointed by the member governments for 6-year renewable terms.

O. BRITAIN AND THE UN

Britain was one of the founding members of the United Nations Organization which was created in 1945. The UN (May 1995) has 104 member states. Its principal organs, with headquarters in New York, are:

the General Assembly in which each member state has one vote and which normally meets once a year in September;

the Security Council which has five permanent members (China, France, Russia, UK, USA) and ten non-permanent members elected for a two-year term.

Also linked with the UN are various international organizations, including the International Court of Justice (based in the Hague), the International Labour Organization (based in Geneva), the Food and Agriculture Organization (based in Rome), the UN Educational, Scientific and Cultural Organization (based in Paris) and the World Health Organization (based in Geneva).

UN Secretary-General: Mr Boutros Boutros Ghali (Egypt).

UK Permanent Representative to the UN and Representative on the Security Council: Sir John Weston.

P. WHO'S WHO IN BRITISH POLITICS 1979–95
(for MPs, present constituency only is indicated)

Aitken, Jonathan, b. 1942; MP (Con) Thanet South, 1983–. Chief Secretary to the Treasury, 1994–.

Ashdown, Paddy, b. 1941; MP (Lib) 1983–8, (SLD) since 1988 (Yeovil); Leader, Social and Liberal Democratic Party since 1988.

Baker, Kenneth, b. 1934; MP (Con) since 1968 (Mole Valley); Secretary of State for the Environment 1985–6, for Education and Science 1986–9, Chancellor of Duchy of Lancaster and Chairman of the Conservative Party 1989–90; Home Secretary 1990–92.

Beckett, Margaret, b. 1943; MP (Lab) 1974–9 and since 1983 (Derby South); joined Treasury frontbench team, 1989; close ally of John Smith; Deputy Leader 1992–94. Shadow Health Secretary, 1994–.

Beith, Alan, b. 1943; MP (Lib) 1973–88, (SLD) since 1988 (Berwick); Deputy Leader, Liberal Party 1985–8; contender for leadership of SLD, 1988.

Benn, Anthony Wedgwood, b. 1925; MP (Lab) 1950–83 (except for short period between father's death and renunciation of the family peerage) and since 1984 (Chesterfield); Minister of Technology 1966–70, Secretary of State for Industry 1974–5 and for Energy 1975–9; Member Labour Party NEC 1959–60 and 1962-93.

Blair, Tony, see **B8**.

Boothroyd, Betty, b. 1929; MP (Lab) since 1973 (West Bromwich until 1974, then West Bromwich West). Speaker of the House of Commons since May 1992 (the first woman to be elected to the Speakership).

Bottomley, Virginia, b. 1948; MP (Con) Surrey South-West, May 1984–. Secretary of State for Health, 1992–.

Brittan, Sir Leon, b. 1939; MP (Con) 1974–89; Chief Secretary to the Treasury 1981–3, Secretary of State for Home Department 1983–5, and for Trade and Industry 1985–6; EEC Commissioner since 1989; Vice-President, 1995–.

Brown, Gordon, b. 1951; MP (Lab) since 1983 (Dunfermline East); Shadow spokesman on trade 1989–92; Shadow Chancellor, 1992–.

Butler, Sir Robin, b. 1938; entered civil service in 1961, Treasury 1961–9, 1975–82 and 1985–7, Principal Private Secretary to Prime Minister 1982–5, Secretary to the Cabinet and Head of the Home Civil Service since 1988.

Callaghan, Lord, b. 1912; MP (Lab) 1945–87 (Cardiff South and Penarth); Chancellor of the Exchequer 1964–7, Home Secretary 1967–70, Foreign Secretary 1974–6, Prime Minister 1976 01 Leader of Labour Party 1976 80.

Carrington, Lord, b. 1919; Member of House of Lords since 1938; Leader of Opposition in the Lords 1964–70 and 1974–9; Secretary of State for Defence 1970–4, for Energy 1974, and for Foreign and Commonwealth Affairs, 1979-82; Secretary-General of NATO 1984–8; Chairman Conservative Party Organisation 1972–4.

Clarke, Kenneth, b. 1940; MP (Con) since 1970 (Rushcliffe); Paymaster General 1985–7, Chancellor of the Duchy of Lancaster 1987–8, Secretary of State for Health 1988–90, for Education 1990–92. Home Secretary 1992–3, Chancellor of the Exchequer since 1993.

Cook, Robin, b. 1946; MP (Lab) since 1974 (Livingston); Shadow spokesman on health 1987–92; Shadow Trade and Industry spokesman, 1992–4. Shadow Foreign Secretary, 1994–.

Cunningham, Jack, b. 1939; MP (Lab) since 1970 (Copeland); Shadow Leader of the House of Commons 1989–92; Shadow Foreign Secretary, 1992–4. Shadow Trade and Industry Secretary, 1994–.

Dobson, Frank, b. 1940; MP (Lab) since 1979 (Holborn and St. Pancras); Shadow spokesman on Transport and London, 1993–4. Shadow Environment spokesman, 1994–.

Donaldson, Lord, b. 1920; Barrister since 1946, QC 1961; High Court Judge 1966–79, President, National Industrial Relations Court 1971–4; Lord Justice of Appeal 1979–82; Master of the Rolls, 1982–92.

Dorrell, Stephen, b. 1952; MP (Con) Loughborough, 1979–. Secretary of State for National Heritage, 1994–.

Edmonds, John, b. 1944; National Industrial Officer, General and Municipal Workers Union (later General, Municipal, Boilermakers and Allied Trades Union) 1972–85, General Secretary since 1985.

Foot, Michael, b. 1913; MP (Lab) 1945–55 and 1960–92 (Blaenau Gwent); Secretary of State for Employment 1974–6, Lord President of the Council and Leader of the Commons 1976–9; Member Labour Party NEC 1971–83, Deputy Leader 1976–80, Leader, 1980–3.

Fowler, Sir Norman, b. 1938; MP (Con) since 1970 (Sutton Coldfield); Secretary of State for Transport 1979–81, for Social Services 1981–7 and for Employment 1987–90. Chairman of the Conservative Party, 1992–94.

Gould, Bryan, b. 1939; MP (Lab) 1974–9 and 1983–94 (Dagenham); Shadow spokesman on the environment 1989–92; Member, Labour Party NEC 1988–92. Unsuccessfully contested leadership, 1992. Returned to New Zealand, 1994.

Green, Pauline, b. 1948; MEP (Lab) London North, 1989–. Leader, Socialist Group, European Parliament since 1994.

Hanley, Jeremy, b. 1945; MP (Con) Richmond and Barnes, 1983–. Chairman of the Conservative Party (and Minister without Portfolio) since 1994.

Hattersley, Roy, b. 1932; MP (Lab) since 1964 (Birmingham Sparkbrook); Secretary of State for Prices and Consumer Protection 1976–9; Shadow Home Secretary 1987–92; Deputy Leader 1983–92. Announced (Feb 1994) retirement from Commons at next election.

Healey, Lord, b. 1917; MP (Lab) 1952–92 (Leeds East); Secretary of State for Defence 1964–70, Chancellor of the Exchequer 1974–9; Member Labour Party NEC 1970–5 and 1980–3, Deputy Leader 1980–3.

Heath, Sir Edward, see **B30**.

Heseltine, Michael, b. 1933; MP (Con) since 1966 (Henley); Secretary of State for the Environment 1979–83; for Defence 1983–6; for the Environment 1990–92. Secretary of State for Trade and Industry since 1992.

Howard, Michael, b. 1941; MP (Con) since 1983 (Folkestone and Hythe); Secretary of State for Employment 1990–92, for the Enviroment, 1992–3. Home Secretary since 1993.

Howe, Lord, b. 1926; MP (Con) 1964–6 and 1970–92 (Surrey East); Solicitor-General 1970–2, Minister for Trade and Consumer Affairs 1972–4, Chancellor of the Exchequer 1979–83, Secretary of State for Foreign and Commonwealth Affairs 1983–9, and Leader of the House of Commons (and Deputy Prime Minister) 1989–90.

Hume, John, b. 1937; MP (SDLP) Foyle, 1983–. Leader, Social Democratic and Labour Party, since 1979. MEP (SDLP) Northern Ireland, 1979–.

Hunt, David, b. 1942; MP (Con) Wirral West, 1983–. Secretary of State for Wales, 1990–3; for Employment, 1993–4. Chancellor of the Duchy of Lancaster and Minister for the Citizen's Charter since 1994.

Hurd, Douglas, b. 1930; MP (Con) since 1974 (Witney); Minister of State, Foreign Office 1979–83, Home Office 1983–4, Secretary of State for Northern Ireland 1984–5, for Home Department 1985–9, and for Foreign and Commonwealth Affairs since 1989.

Jenkins, Lord, b. 1920; MP (Lab) 1948–76, (SDP) 1982–7 (Glasgow Hillhead); Home Secretary 1965–7 and 1974–6, Chancellor of the Exchequer 1967–70; Deputy Leader of Labour Party 1970–2; President, EEC Commission 1977–80; co-founder of Social Democratic Party 1981 and Leader, 1982–3.

Kaufman, Gerald, b. 1930; MP (Lab) since 1970 (Manchester Gorton); Minister of State, Department of Industry 1975–9; Shadow Foreign Secretary, 1987–92.

King, Tom, b. 1933; MP (Con) since 1970 (Bridgwater); Minister for Local Government 1979–83, Secretary of State for the Environment Jan.–June 1983, for Transport June–Oct. 1983, for Employment 1983–5, for Northern Ireland 1985–9, and for Defence, 1989–92.

Kinnock, Neil, see **B36**.

Lamont, Norman, b. 1942; MP (Con) since 1972 (Kingston-upon-Thames); Financial Secretary, Treasury 1986–9, Chief Secretary 1989–90, Chancellor of the Exchequer, 1990–3.

Lawson, Lord, b. 1932; MP (Con) (Feb.) 1974–92 (Blaby); Editor, *The Spectator*, 1966–70; Financial Secretary to the Treasury 1979–81, Secretary of State for Energy 1981–3, Chancellor of the Exchequer 1983–9.

Mackay, Lord, b. 1927; Member of House of Lords since 1979; Advocate since 1955, QC 1965; Lord Advocate 1979–84; Lord of Appeal 1985–7; Lord Chancellor since 1987.

Major, John, b. 1943; MP (Con) since 1979 (Huntingdon); Chief Secretary to the Treasury 1987–9, Secretary of State for Foreign and Commonwealth Affairs 1989, Chancellor of the Exchequer 1989–90, Prime Minister since 1990; Leader, Conservative Party since 1990.

Meacher, Michael, b. 1939; MP (Lab) since 1970 (Oldham West); Shadow spokesman on social security 1989–92; on Development and Cooperation, 1992–3, Citizen's Charter, 1993–4. Member, Labour Party NEC 1983–8. Shadow Transport spokesman, 1994–.

Monks, John, b. 1945; official of Trades Union Congress. Deputy General Secretary, 1987–93, General Secretary since 1993.

Owen, Lord, b. 1938; MP (Lab) 1966–81, (SDP, Ind. Soc. Dem. after 1990) 1981–92 (Plymouth Devonport); Secretary of State for Foreign and Commonwealth Affairs 1977–9; co-founder of Social Democratic Party 1981 and Leader 1983–7 and from 1988 until its dissolution in 1990. Co-Chairman, Peace Conference on ex-Yugoslavia, 1992–. Created Companion of Honour, 1995.

Paisley, Rev. Ian, b. 1926; MP (Protestant Unionist 1970–4, Democratic Unionist since 1974) since 1970 (Antrim North); M.E.P. since 1979; member of Stormont 1970–2, NI Assembly 1973–5, NI Constitutional Convention 1975–6, NI Assembly since 1982.

Patten, Christopher, b. 1944; MP (Con) 1979–92 (Bath); Secretary of State for the Environment 1989–90; Chancellor of the Duchy of Lancaster, 1990–92; Chairman of the Conservative Party, 1990–92. Governor of Hong Kong since 1992.

Portillo, Michael Denzil Xavier b. 1953; MP (Con) Southgate, Dec. 1984–. Chief Secretary to the Treasury since 1992.

Prescott, John, b. 1938; MP (Lab) since 1970 (Hull East); Shadow spokesman on Transport, 1988–93; on Employment, 1993–4. Deputy Leader of the Labour Party, 1994–.

Prout, Lord, b. 1942; MEP (Con) 1979–94 (Shropshire and Stafford); Chief Whip, European Democratic Group 1983–7, Leader, 1987–94.

Ridley, Lord, 1929–93; MP (Con) 1959–92 (Cirencester and Tewkesbury); Secretary of State for Transport 1983–6, for the Environment 1986–9, and for Trade and Industry 1989–90.

Rifkind, Malcolm, b. 1946; MP (Con) Edinburgh Pentlands, Feb 1974–. Secretary of State for Scotland, 1986–90; for Transport, 1990–92; for Defence, 1992–.

Shephard, Gillian, b. 1940; MP (Con) Norfolk South-West, 1987–. Secretary of State for Employment, 1992–3; Minister of Agriculture, Fisheries and Food, 1993–4. Secretary of State for Education since 1994.

Smith, John, see **B56**.

Steel, Sir David, see **B57**.

Tebbit, Lord, b. 1931; MP (Con) 1970–92 (Chingford); Secretary of State for Employment 1981–3, for Trade and Industry 1983–5, Chancellor of the Duchy of Lancaster 1985–7; Chairman, Conservative Party Organisation 1985–7.

Thatcher, Baroness, see **B59**.

Waddington, Lord, b. 1929; MP (Con) 1979–90 (Ribble Valley); Government Chief Whip 1987–9, Home Secretary 1989–90; Leader, House of Lords 1990–92. Governor of Bermuda, 1992–.

Walker, Lord, b. 1932; MP (Con) 1961–92 (Worcester); Secretary of State for the Environment 1970–2 and for Trade and Industry 1972–4, Minister of Agriculture 1979–83, Secretary of State for Energy 1983–7 and for Wales 1987–90.

Weatherill, Lord, b. 1920; MP (Con) 1964–92 (Croydon North East); Conservative Whip 1970–9; Deputy Speaker 1979–83, Speaker, 1983–92.

Whitelaw, Viscount, b. 1918; MP (Con) 1955–83; Lord President of the Council and Leader of the Commons 1970–2, Secretary of State for Northern Ireland 1972–3, for Employment 1973–4 and Home Secretary 1979–83, Lord President of the Council and Leader of the House of Lords 1983–8; Chairman Conservative Party Organisation 1974–5.

Williams, Baroness, b. 1930; MP (Lab) 1964–79, (SDP) 1981–3; Secretary of State for Prices and Consumer Protection 1974–6 and for Education and Science 1976–9; Member Labour Party NEC 1970–

81; co-founder of Social Democratic Party 1981 and President 1982–8; joined SLDP, 1988.

Willis, Norman, b. 1933; official of Trades Union Congress since 1959. Deputy General Secretary 1977–84, General Secretary, 1984–93.

Wright, Lord, b. 1931; entered Diplomatic Service in 1955, Deputy Under Secretary, Foreign and Commonwealth Office 1982–4, Ambassador to Saudi Arabia 1984–6, Permanent Under Secretary 1986–94.

Younger, Lord, b. 1931; MP (Con) 1964–92 (Ayr); Secretary of State for Scotland 1979–86 and for Defence 1986–9.

Q. GLOSSARY OF POLITICAL PLACES AND TERMS

Political Places

Cathays Park	Location of Welsh Office in Cardiff
Chequers	Country house of Prime Ministers in Buckinghamshire
Congress House	Headquarters of TUC in London
Downing Street	The heart of government: No. 10 is the Prime Minister's official residence; No. 11, that of the Chancellor of the Exchequer; and No. 12, the offices of the Government Chief Whip
Fleet Street	Traditional home of the main national newspapers (most of which have now moved elsewhere)
St. Andrew's House	Location of the Scottish Office in Edinburgh
Smith Square	Location of Conservative Party headquarters (formerly Labour Party also)
Stormont	Location of Northern Ireland Parliament until 1972; now NI Assembly and Northern Ireland Office
Transport House	Former headquarters of Labour Party (shared with Transport and General Workers' Union) in Smith Square
Walworth Road	Current headquarters of Labour Party. Named John Smith House in 1994

Political Terms

Backbencher	An MP who is neither a member of the Government nor an official Opposition spokesman
Chiltern Hundreds	A fictional office of profit under the Crown, acceptance of which requires an MP to vacate his seat (*i.e.* the means by which an MP can resign)
Crossbencher	A member of the House of Lords who does not take a Party whip (see below)
Father of the House	MP with the longest *continuous* service in the Commons.
Frontbencher	An MP who is a member of the Government or an official Opposition spokesman
Guillotine	A means of curtailing debate on parliamentary legislation
Hansard	The official report of debates in both houses of Parliament
Hung Parliament	A Parliament in which no party has an overall majority (also known as a balanced Parliament)
PLP	Parliamentary Labour Party
PR	Proportional representation (an alternative electoral system favoured by the Liberal Democrats)
Shadow Cabinet	The official Opposition's counterpart to the Cabinet (hence Shadow Chancellor *etc*)
Tactical voting	Voting behaviour determined by calculation of which party has the best chance of winning in a particular constituency
Tories	Abbreviation for Conservatives
Whips	Name given to the party managers in Parliament and to the written instructions they issue to MPs, the urgency of which is denoted by the number of times they are underlined (*e.g.* three-lined whip = extremely important)
1922 Committee	Conservative backbenchers' committee

THE
WORLD OF
MUSIC

The art of music as it has developed in the Western world, with an outline historical narrative, a glossary of musical terms and an index to composers. A Special Topic provides an introduction to recent developments in new music technology.

TABLE OF CONTENTS

THE WORLD OF MUSIC

In writing this section no special knowledge on the part of the reader is assumed; it is for those who want to know about the history of music, how different styles evolved, and how one composer influenced another. It is a background to music as the science section is a background to science, and just as the latter cannot show the reader the colours of the spectrum but only tell of Newton's experiments and of the relationship between colour and wavelength, so in this section we can only describe man's achievements in the world of sound. But knowing something about a composer, his work, and when he lived can help to bring fuller understanding and enjoyment when listening to his music.

The section is in four parts:

I. Historical Narrative and Discussion
II. Glossary of Musical Terms
III. Index to Composers
IV. Special Topic: New Music Technology

I. HISTORICAL NARRATIVE AND DISCUSSION

The history of music, like that of any people or art, is not one of uninterrupted progress towards some ideal perfection. For five centuries or more music in the West has achieved peaks of accomplishment in one style or another before society has dictated or composers have felt the need for something new and different. Thus Wagner's music-drama *Parsifal*, lasting five hours, is not necessarily a more rewarding work than what Monteverdi achieved in *Orfeo* 250 years earlier. More complex yes, more rewarding—well, that is for the listener to judge.

We must keep this in mind when considering the development of music from a starting point of, say, Gregorian chant down to the complicated structures of a Schoenberg in our own day. In this development there is no true dividing line between one period and another, nor must simplifying terms such as "classical" or "romantic" be taken too literally.

The earliest history of Western music as we know it today is closely bound up with the Church, for music had to be provided for services. The earliest Christian music was influenced by Greek songs, few of which unfortunately have survived, and by the music of synagogues, where the art of chanting originated. The modal system of the ancient Greeks was highly organised. The earliest Greek scale was from A to A and the four descending notes A,G,F,E became the basis of their musical theory, and it is from them that Western music learned to call notes after the letters of the alphabet. A scale can begin on any note and always includes two semitones upon which much of the character of a melody depends.

The Greek modes were based on the white notes only; the Dorian, Phrygian, Lydian, and Mixolydian began respectively on E,D,C, and B. Their character was thus decided by the position of the semitones, and they formed the basis, often corrupted, of the mediaeval modes. This system was transmitted through Latin writers such as Boethius and Cassiodorus, and through Arabic writers. The eight Church modes were not established until the 8th or 9th cent. Their four plagal modes, as they are called, started in each case, for technical reasons, a fourth below the authentic modes.

By the end of the 6th cent. Gregorian chant had developed so far that some sort of permanent record was required. *Neumes*, signs placed over the Latin text, were the earliest attempt at musical notation. Gradually lines came into use until a four-line stave was established, probably in the 11th and 12th cent., and with them clef signs, although the treble clef as we know it today did not appear until the 13th cent.

And what is this music—plainchant—like? It is an unaccompanied, single line of melody, which, when we have become used to its "antique" flavour is heard to have a wide range of spiritual and emotional expression, not excluding word painting. The texts used came from the Liturgy. These beautiful, extended lines of flowing, flexible melody can still be heard on Sundays in Roman Catholic cathedrals and churches.

Polyphony is Born.

The 10th cent. saw the appearance of a book called *Musica Enchiriadis* (whose authorship is disputed) which introduced theories about unison singing in which the melody is doubled at the fourth or fifth. Organum, or diaphony, is used to describe this method of writing, a term which confusingly could also be used for a kind of singing where melismatic melody was heard over a drone note on the organ. Rules came into fashion defining which intervals were allowed and which parts of the church services could be sung in more than one part. By the time of Guido d'Arezzo (*c.* 990–1050), a Benedictine monk who helped advance notation, contrary motion was permitted as the cadence was approached, another technical advance. Gradually the voices became more and more independent, and the third, so long considered a discord, came into use. Pérotin, of Notre Dame, was the first composer to write for three and four voices, and he and his great predecessor Léonin were the great masters of early polyphony. The proximity and spikiness of Pérotin's harmony is almost modern-sounding, and as with Gregorian chant, once we have adjusted ourselves to the sound, this music can be a rewarding experience.

Early Secular Music.

In mediaeval France, towards the end of the 11th cent., there developed what has become known as the age of the troubadours, poet-musicians. They were the successors to the *jongleurs*, or jugglers, and minstrels about whom we know little as practically none of their music has survived. The troubadours hymned the beauty of spring and of ladies. Contemporary with them in Germany were the Minnesingers. Their songs were mostly set in three modes. Adam de la Halle (d. 1287), because so much of his music survives, is perhaps the best known of the troubadours. He was a notable composer of *rondels*, an early form of round, of which the English *Sumer is icumen in*, written by a monk of Reading *c.* 1226, is a fine example. In that modes were used, the troubadours' music remained definitely akin to that of ecclesiastical hymns, although there is an undoubted feeling of our modern major scale in some of the songs.

Ars Nova and Early Renaissance.

The term *ars nova* derives partly from writings of Philippe de Vitry (1291–1361) who codified the rules of the old and the new music in a valuable treatise. This *new art* represented a freeing of music from organum and rhythmic modes, and an increase in the shape and form of melodic line. France was the centre of music during the 14th cent. and apart from Philippe de Vitry the leading composer was Guillaume de Machaut (1300–77), who wrote many secular works as well as a polyphonic setting of the Mass. His music is notable for its vigour and tenderness as well as for its technical expertise. Meanwhile in 14th-cent. Italy a quite separate branch of *ars nova* was developing. Imitation and canon were to be noted in the music of Italian composers, and vocal forms such as the Ballata, Madrigal (which often included instrumental accompaniment) and Caccia (a two-voice hunting song in canon) were common. The greatest Italian composer of this period was the blind organist and lutenist Francesco di Landini (c. 1325–97). Italian pieces of the time, as compared with their French counterparts, are notable for their sensual rather than their intellectual qualities, a difference—it has been noted—between The Southern and The Northern New Art.

England was less affected by *ars nova*, but surviving music shows the influence of the Continent. Not until the 15th cent. did she begin to make a significant contribution to the history of music. Both John Dunstable (c. 1380–1453), who was no less eminent as a mathematician and an astronomer than as a musician, and his contemporary Lional Power advanced the technique of music by their method of composition (use of the triad, for instance) and mellifluous style. Their musicianship was much appreciated on the Continent. Dunstable depended less upon the use of *cantus firmus*—a fixed melody—and increased the use of free composition.

After Dunstable the next great figure in European music was Guillaume Dufay (c. 1400–74), the most celebrated composer of the Burgundian school. His music is distinguished for its blend of flowing melody, cleverly wrought counterpoint and tender expressiveness. Much travelled, Dufay was a man of catholic outlook. Together with Dunstable and the Burgundian Gilles Binchois he bridged the gap between 14th cent. *ars nova* and the fully developed polyphony of the 15th cent.

Composers of the 14th and 15th cents. also showed an interest in secular music, and many of their songs (those of Binchois particularly) have been preserved.

The results of Dufay's good work can be heard in the flowering of the Franco-Netherland school later in the 15th cent. Its two most notable representatives are Ockeghem (c. 1420–95) and his pupil Josquin des Prés (c. 1450–1521), who carried musical expressiveness even further than Dufay; their work can also be grand and majestic. Indeed Josquin's wide range, from the humorous to the dignified, partially accounts for his justly deserved high reputation. He was a master of counterpoint but tempered his mechanical ingenuity with imaginative insight.

Throughout the Renaissance choral music was breaking away, as we have seen, from its earlier bonds. The mediaeval tradition of having the *cantus firmus* in the tenor went by the board; the use of dissonance, when only two voices were used in mediaeval times, was abandoned in favour of euphony; and all the voices, democratically, came to share the musical lines. Composers also began to respect their texts; where words were previously fitted to the music, the reverse was now the case. In Josquin's music, indeed, we have the first attempts at symbolism: matching verbal ideas with musical ones. The importance of this musical renaissance has been realised only over the past thirty years. At last the Renaissance composers are coming to be seen not merely as historical figures relevant only in so far as their work culminated in the great classical composers,

but as masters in their own right, whose music should be nearly as familiar to us as is that of a Mozart or a Beethoven.

With the exception of Dufay, little is known of the lives of the musicians so far mentioned. Most of them were in the service of royal or ducal households where they were in charge of the chapel choir, or else they worked in or around the great cathedrals, teaching at choir-schools. They were well rewarded for their services and their social position was probably high.

During recent years there has been an appreciable revival of interest in mediaeval music. Numerous ensembles have emerged with their own ideas about how it should be performed—an indication that it is alive and not just part of the history of music. It can communicate just as well as the music of later eras.

The Sixteenth Century.

By the 16th cent. music in England was a steadily expanding art and much encouraged. Music-making in the home was becoming quite the fashion in social circles. The Chapels Royal remained the chief musical centres but the music was changing with the development of new secular forms so that it was not so much religious as a part of life. Composers began their lives as choirboys and received a thoroughgoing education, both theoretical and practical.

Carrying on from where Josquin and his contemporaries left off, Palestrina in Italy, Victoria in Spain, Lassus in the Netherlands, and Byrd in England brought the polyphonic style to its zenith. At the same time came the rise of the madrigalists, first in Italy, then in the Netherlands; and then the beginnings of instrumental music as it came to be known in the succeeding centuries.

The vocal composers began to use chordal (homophonic) as well as contrapuntal (polyphonic) methods of writing—examples are Victoria's *Ave Verum Corpus* and Palestrina's *Stabat Mater*—but polyphony was still the fullest most magnificent instrument of composition, as for instance in Byrd's *O Quam Gloriosum* which shows an eager response to the mood and to the inflection of the words in a kind of vocal orchestration. A feature of all these composers' music, but more especially that of Victoria (c. 1535–1611) and Palestrina (1525–94), is its serene simplicity and fervour of utterance. Palestrina was perhaps more spacious in his effects, Victoria the more passionate. How well we can imagine—and sometimes hear—their music resounding down the naves of the great cathedrals of Europe.

The music of Lassus (c. 1532–94) is distinguished both in sheer amount and in vitality. His mastery in the field of motets was unrivalled, encompassing a wide range of subject and mood. He and his fellow Flemish composers, Willaert, de Monte and Arcadelt, were also expert in the Madrigal, a form popular in Italy and England as well. The Madrigal was a contrapuntal setting of a poem, usually not longer than twelve lines, in five or six parts. The subject (of the poetry) was usually amorous or pastoral. It was a short-lived, but highly prolific vogue. Orlando Gibbons (1583–1625), Thomas Weelkes (c. 1573–1623), and John Wilbye (1574–1638) were the most prominent English exponents.

Instrumental Music.

By the end of the 14th cent. instrumental music began to become something more than mere anonymous dance tunes or primitive organ music. Instruments often accompanied voices, or even replaced them, so that the recorder, lute, viol, and spinet indoors, and sackbuts and shawms outdoors, had already been developed by the time instrumental music came to be written down. Gradually a distinction grew up between what was appropriate to the voice and what was suitable for instruments, Byrd, Gibbons, and Giles Farnaby in England, the great blind keyboard player, Cabezón (1510–66) in Spain, and Frescobaldi (1583–1643) in Italy produced valuable instrumental works. Perhaps the *Parthenia* and the *Fitzwilliam Virginal Book*, collections of Early English Keyboard music, give as fair a representative idea as any of the development of instrumental form at this time.

In chamber music musicians often played collections of dance tunes strung together to make a whole; or they chose fantasies (or "fancies"), where a composer altered a tune as he wished. Then there were sets of variations on a ground, that is a simple tune played over and over again on a bass viol.

As far as brass instruments are concerned, they were often used on festive occasions in spacious halls or in cathedrals. The Venetian composer Andrea Gabrieli (c. 1510–86) was the first to combine voice and instruments and his nephew Giovanni Gabrieli (1557–1612) carried the process further to produce sacred symphonies, often using antiphonal effects.

Drama in Music.

Not until the end of the 16th cent. did anyone begin to think about combining drama and music, and so "invent" the new art we know today as opera. A group of artistic intelligentsia met together in Florence and conceived the idea of reviving the ancient declamation of Greek tragedy. They took Greek mythological subjects, cast them in dramatic form, and set them to music, not in the choral polyphonic style of the Madrigal, but with single voices declaiming dialogue in music. The earliest examples of what was called *Dramma per Musica* were Peri's *Dafne* in 1597 (now lost) and his *Euridice*, in which he co-operated with Caccini. The new style came to its full flowering with the appearance of Monteverdi (1567–1643), whose genius would surely have shone in any age.

Monteverdi's first opera, *Orfeo*, produced in 1607, is a landmark of dramatic expression, and it is nothing less than a catastrophe that so many of his later operas have been lost. His *Orfeo* provides the basic ground work for the operas of the next two centuries: recitative, accompanied recitative, and aria. His last opera *L'Incoronazione di Poppea*, written when he was at the great age (for those days) of 75, succeeds in its aim of creating a free, fluid form, slipping easily from recitative to arioso and even aria without the strict, closed forms that were to be used in the 17th and 18th cent. He focuses attention to an almost unbelievable extent on character rather than situation. He creates real people with all their faults and foibles—the kittenish, sexually attractive Poppaea, the power-drunk, infatuated Nero, the noble Seneca, and the dignified, rejected empress Octavia. As recent productions have shown these characters leap from the musical page as if they had just been created, each unerringly delineated in musical terms. Only the vocal line, the continuo, and the very incomplete instrumental ritornelli parts have been preserved, but in sensitive, knowledgeable hands tonal variety in the shape of wind and string parts can be added, as we know certain instruments were available to the composer.

Monteverdi's successors were Cavalli (1602–76), Cesti (1623–69) and Stradella (1642–82), who gave the solo voice more and more prominence encouraged by the advent of the castrati's brilliant voices. These artificially created singers had a vogue and popularity similar to "pop" singers of today, fêted wherever they appeared. The aria became more extended and ornate, and dramatic verisimilitude gradually but inexorably took second place to vocal display. An aria was nearly always in *da capo* form, the first section being repeated after a contrasting middle one.

Sixteenth- and Seventeenth-century Church Music.

Of course, the invention of a new dramatic style affected church music too. The concentration on the vertical aspect of music (homophony) as opposed to the horizontal (polyphony) led to the increasing importance of the voice in religious music. In Italy, it is true, there was the late-flowering, great madrigalist Carlo Gesualdo (1560–1614), whose harmonic daring still astonishes us today, but by 1600 the cantata was coming to replace older forms in church music. In its simplest form this was a story told in accompanied recitative, Giacomo Carissimi (c. 1604–74) was one of the first significant composers of this new form. He too was in on the birth of the oratorio, whose forerunner was the *sacra rappresentazione* (mystery or miracle play) of early 16th-cent. Florence. Then in the mid-16th cent. St. Philip Neri brought in elements from popular plays on sacred subjects in his services in Rome, designed to hold the attention of youth—rather as certain parsons have tried with "pop" services today. Emilio del Cavalieri (c. 1550–1602) and Carissimi developed the form adding arias and choral movements, omitting actual representation. Alessandro Scarlatti (1660–1725), whose oratorios bear a close resemblance to his operas, brought oratorio to its zenith in Italy.

Heinrich Schütz (1585–1672), Bach's great predecessor, was the founder of German church music. His historical place has never been called into question but only in recent times have the intrinsic merits of his own music come to be recognised. He studied with Giovanni Gabrieli in his youth and later came under the influence of Monteverdi, so it was not surprising that he brought Italian ideas across the Alps to Germany and wrote the first German opera *Daphne*, now sadly lost. He also introduced his country to the Italian declamatory style and to the new kind of concertato instrumental writing. But his dramatic religious works were his greatest contribution to musical development. He wrote with a devout intensity, bringing to life the scriptural texts by closely allying his urgent music to the words. His three settings of the Passions—Matthew, Luke, and John—paved the way for Bach's even more remarkable works in this genre. Two contemporaries of Schütz, Johann Herman Schein (1586–1630) and Samuel Scheidt (1587–1654), were both important figures in German Reformation music.

Lully, Purcell, and Seventeenth-century Opera.

France resisted the tide of Italian opera, although paradoxically it was an Italian, Jean-Baptiste Lully (c. 1632–87), who charted the different course of French opera which was from the beginning associated with the court ballet. His musical monopoly during the reign of Louis XIV was put to good use. In his thirteen operas the libretto, usually on classical, allegorical themes, plays a vital part in the composition, which is therefore less clearly divided between recitative and aria than in Italian opera. The orchestration and the ballets assume greater importance than in the traditional Italian form. It was, in short, a more realistic, less stylised art.

In England, opera developed out of the entertainment known as the Masque, a succession of dances, accompanied by voices and instruments and often incorporated in a drama or spectacle. Henry Lawes's (1596–1662) setting of Milton's *Comus* is probably the most famous of these entertainments. The *Venus and Adonis* of John Blow (1649–1708) can be called the first English opera because here the music is gradually gaining the ascendancy over the spoken word. However, it was Purcell (c. 1659–95), Blow's pupil, with *Dido and Aeneas*, who really gave dramatic life to the new medium by giving his characters a true musical personality that was subtler than anything the mere spoken word could achieve. The grief-laden lament of the dying Dido "When I am laid in earth" has an expressive power, achieved by extraordinarily bold harmonic effects, never before and seldom since achieved. The opera was in fact written for a young ladies' boarding school. Purcell followed it with several outstanding semi-operas—such as *The Fairy Queen* (to Dryden's text). His untimely death at the age of 36 probably robbed us of several full-length operas—and perhaps a consequence of this was that English music after him did not develop as it should have done.

His verse anthems and much of his instrumental music, especially the Fantasias, are also rich in imaginative mastery through his original use of harmony and counterpoint. However, a large number of his pieces were written for a specific occasion and many of the odes are set to impossibly trite texts. At least his genius was partly acknowledged in his own day, and he was appointed organist in Westminster Abbey where he was buried with due pomp. He is said to have died through catching cold when locked out of his own house at night.

Vivaldi and the Rise of Instrumental Music.

Out of the dance suites popular in the 16th cent. and the beginning of the 17th (known in Italy as the *Sonata da Camera*) developed the concerto. This began as two groups of instrumentalists compared and contrasted with each other as in Giovanni Gabrieli's *Sonata piano e forte*. With Arcangelo Corelli (1653–1713) the concerto grosso took a more definite shape, alternating a solo group of instruments with the main body of strings in three or more contrasting movements. Giuseppe Torelli (1658–1709), Francesco Geminiani (1687–1762) and Tommaso Albinoni (1671–1750) were other notable contributors to the form, but none of the composers so far mentioned has today achieved the popularity of the priest Antonio Vivaldi (c. 1678–1741), himself a violinist, who had at his disposal the orchestra at the Ospedale della Pieta in Venice. The young women at this music school also contributed the vocal side of the concerts there of which there are many descriptions. One says: "They sing like angels, play the violin, flute, organ, oboe, cello, bassoon—in short no instrument is large enough to frighten them ... I swear nothing is so charming than to see a young and pretty nun, dressed in white, a sprig of pomegranate blossom behind one ear, leading the orchestra, and beating time with all the grace and precision imaginable." For this body, Vivaldi wrote about 500 concertos which maintain a remarkably even quality, but "The Four Seasons" are perhaps the most felicitous.

Meanwhile organ music was advancing rapidly in technique. Girolamo Frescobaldi (1583–1643) and Jan Pieterszoon Sweelinck (1562–1621) wrote works that provided the foundation of the Italian and Northern German schools of organ music. Their ricercares gradually developed into the fugue, a vein so richly mined by Bach. Among their successors the most notable figure before Bach was Johann Pachelbel (1653–1706).

Other keyboard music, especially for the harpsichord, was the particular province of France; and Jean-Philippe Rameau (1683–1764) and François Couperin (1668–1733) were both masters of keyboard style and harmonic invention. They wrote many pieces of subtle charm and exquisite craftsmanship.

Bach (1685–1750).

The two giant figures of Bach and Handel bestride the first half of the 18th cent. Their differences are perhaps greater than their similarities. Bach wrote essentially for himself (although of course, he had to satisfy his employers at Cöthen and Leipzig) while Handel was composing to please his wide public. Bach was a provincial, always remaining in central Germany; Handel was widely travelled. Bach was devoutly religious, almost ascetic; Handel was more a man of the world. They never met.

To summarise Bach's vast output in a short space is virtually impossible. One can only try to distil the flavour of his music. He brought the art of polyphony to the highest pitch of mastery that has ever been achieved or is ever likely to be achieved. In his famous "Forty-Eight" and "the Art of the Fugue" he explored all the fugal permutations of the major and minor keys. At the same time his music rose above technical brilliance to achieve, especially in his organ music,

the two Passions, many of the church cantatas, and the B minor Mass, intense emotional and expressive power. The cantatas, from his Leipzig appointment (1723) onwards, were integrated into the services. They consisted usually of a chorus based on a Lutheran hymn tune, recitatives, several extended arias, and a concluding chorus usually a straightforward version of the hymn tune in which the congregation joined. There are some two hundred of these works and they contain a wealth of comparatively unknown and sometimes even unrecognised beauties. The St. John and the St. Matthew Passion extend these procedures to a grand scale, an Evangelist telling the New Testament story in vivid recitative, the chorus taking the part of the crowd, soloists pondering in arias on the meaning of the Gospel, and Jesus's words being sung by a bass. Anyone who has heard either of these works well performed cannot help but dismiss from his mind any idea of Bach as a mere dry-as-dust musical mathematician. In the St. Matthew Passion, every suggestion in the text that can possibly be illustrated by a musical equivalent is so illustrated. The Old Testament Pharasaic law is represented by strict musical forms such as the canon; Christ's sayings are given noble arioso life; and the arias reflect truly the New Testament's compassionate message. Technically the work is a marvel; expressively it is eloquent. The B minor Mass, although it contains borrowings from many of his own works, still stands as a satisfying monumental whole in which Bach's choral writing achieved a new richness, the adaptations being in accord with their new setting.

Bach's instrumental music, especially the violin concertos and the unaccompanied works for violin and cello, not only show the immense range of his powers but also contain many of his deeper thoughts, whereas the orchestral suites and the Brandenburg concertos are more extrovert, particularly the rhythmically exuberant fast movements.

Bach closes an era—that of the later contrapuntalists—by achieving the *ne plus ultra* in fugal composition; his last, incomplete work, The Art of the Fugue, is evidence of that. In recent years there has been a trend towards playing Bach's music on original instruments of his time (or replicas) and singing it with appropriately sized, sometimes all-male choirs.

Handel (1685–1759).

During his lifetime Handel was far more widely recognised as a great composer than Bach, and his music, unlike Bach's, maintained its place in popular esteem until the re-discovery of Bach and the dominance of the symphony placed Handel somewhat in the background.

During the latter part of the 19th cent. Handel's name was mainly associated with mammoth, anachronistic performances of a small sample of his oratorios at the Crystal Palace and elsewhere in England. In his lifetime these works, and all his other pieces in the genre, were sung by a small choir who were outnumbered by the instrumental players. Over the past few years authentic-sized performances of his oratorios and a revival of interest in his operas have revealed the real Handel, unknown to our grandparents.

The operas were neglected partly because the vocal prowess they required—and which the castrati so brilliantly supplied—was no longer available and because their dramatic life, at least according to 19th- and early 20th-cent. tenets, hardly existed. Now it is realised that this neglect has deprived us of an unending stream of glorious melody and of much daring harmony. But perhaps it is in the hitherto disregarded oratorios, such as *Semele*, that Handel's innate dramatic sense and musical range are to be heard gloriously fulfilled, and the pastoral serenade *Acis and Galatea* is surely one of the most delightful scores ever composed.

Handel was a colourful, imaginative orchestrator, and this can be heard both in his accompaniment to vocal music and in his concerti grossi, op. 3 and 6, the earlier set exploiting a diversity of interesting string and wind combination. In his writing he was at home in a polyphonic or homophonic style as his superb choruses show. His organ concertos, of which he was the "inventor" (to quote a contemporary source), were often played between the acts of his oratorios. They are alternately expressive and exuberant pieces calling for some virtuosity from the player. His occasional works, such as the Water Music and Fireworks Music show his ingenuity in extending the range of the typical 17th cent. suite to serve a particular occasion.

Handel's working life was mostly spent in England where his Italian operas were acclaimed. In the years between his arrival here in 1711 and 1729 he wrote nearly thirty operas. It was only when the public tired of these and his reputation slumped that he turned to oratorio with equal success.

Bach and Handel between them crowned the age of polyphony that had lasted for two hundred years or more. After them, it is hardly surprising that composers began looking for a new style, already anticipated in the music of Rameau and particularly Dominico Scarlatti (1685–1737), whose harpsichord sonatas foreshadowed the classical sonata form that was to dominate music for the next two hundred years. The change in musical style about 1750 was partly the result of a change in musical patronage. Bach was the last great composer to earn his living through being employed by the church. The new patrons were the nobility who liked to have a composer on hand to write for the various evening entertainments of the time. For this purpose the princes and dukes had their own orchestras and their own small opera houses. The music required had to be elegant, formal, galant. Haydn was exceptionally fortunate in having an employer, Prince Nicholas of Esterhazy, who allowed him to write more or less as he wished so that he was able to develop symphonic form into something more than a pleasing way of passing an evening.

The early symphonists, culminating in Haydn, broke away from Bach's contrapuntal treatment of the orchestra. Instruments now came to be treated in a more colourful manner according to their particular timbre. The court of Mannheim had an orchestra of a standard unheard hitherto, and Johann Stamitz (1717–57) and his son Karl (1745–1801) influenced the great composers who were to follow in their footsteps. The composition of their orchestra was flexible, oboes, flutes, and horns often being added to the standard string section. Bach's son Carl Philipp Emanuel (1714–88) added to and developed symphonic and sonata form, especially as regards keys and subjects.

Haydn and Mozart.

These two figures dominate the second half of the 18th cent. as Bach and Handel do the first. In a brief space only a general picture can be presented of their huge output and influence. Of Haydn's 104 symphonies (there may even be others) nearly all are worthy of study and hearing. The craftsmanship is always remarkable, the invention ever new. Indeed without Haydn's harmonic daring or his melodic ingenuity, the even greater symphonic thought of Beethoven would have been impossible: Haydn laid the groundwork on which his successor built towering edifices. A work such as the 93rd symphony in D is typical of his mature style with its searching introduction, powerfully wrought, earnestly argued first movement, beautiful Largo and resourceful bustling finale. Haydn did not fight shy of contrapuntal writing: the development section of this symphony's first movement and the finale are evidence of that, but it was only as an integral part of a predominantly homophonic technique.

Mozart's symphonies are not so different in form from Haydn's but—and this must be a subjective judgment—he put more emotional feeling into his. Nobody could listen to the heart-

searching first movement of his 40th symphony without being deeply moved. It was in his final three works in the medium that Mozart brought his symphonic art to perfection, and these obviously had an effect on Haydn's later symphonies written after them. For passion and tenderness contained within a classical form these late symphonies, and many other of Mozart's works, have yet to be surpassed.

Haydn, who has been rightly termed "the Father of the Symphony", was also the founder of the string quartet—perhaps the most perfect, because the most exactly balanced, form of musical expression. The four instruments—two violins, viola, and cello—discuss, argue, commune with each other over the whole gamut of feeling. In his quartets Haydn's mastery of structure is even more amazing than in his symphonies. Mozart's quartets (especially the six devoted to Haydn) and even more his quintets achieve miracles of beauty in sound, nowhere more so than in the first movement of the G minor (his most personal key) quintet. The two late piano quartets show how the piano *can* be ideally combined with strings. His clarinet quintet is also a masterly work.

Haydn did not leave any concertos of consequence. Mozart's, especially those for piano, are among his greatest works. As a brilliant clavier player himself, he showed a consummate skill in writing for the keyboard. Although the instrument he knew was slightly less advanced than the piano today, his concertos call for virtuosity in execution, yet they are as searching in emotional content as the late symphonies and quartets. Indeed the C major concerto (K. 467) and the C minor (K. 491) may be said to hold the quintessential Mozart. As well as twenty (mature) piano concertos, Mozart wrote six for the violin, four for the horn, and eighteen others, but none of these, delightful as they are, can be placed in quite the same class.

Of their church music, Haydn's sixteen masses and his oratorios—*The Creation* and *The Seasons* (both late works)—are perhaps more worthy of attention than Mozart's various masses, but we must not forget Mozart's final work—the Requiem or the serene late Motet *Ave Verum Corpus*.

Eighteenth-century Opera.

Mozart—for many the first great opera composer—did not, of course, create his masterpieces out of nothing. In France, Lully was followed by Rameau (1683–1764), who carried on his tradition of using classical themes but developed a more flexible style of recitative and greatly increased vividness of expression. But it was Gluck (1714–87) who more than anyone broke out of the straitjacket of the now ossified Italian form of opera—dominated by the singer—and showed just what could be achieved in moving human terms. Drama in music really came of age with his *Orfeo e Euridice* (1762), *Alceste* (1767) and *Iphigénie en Tauride* (1779). His simplicity and poignancy of expression were not lost on Mozart.

Meanwhile in Germany a kind of opera called *Singspiel* appeared during the 18th cent. Breaking away from classical themes, mundane stories were told in dialogue and music.

Until quite recently Haydn's operas were dismissed as unworthy representations of his genius but, chiefly through the enlightening efforts of the Haydn scholar, H. C. Robbins Landon, some of his fifteen surviving works in the medium have been successfully revived. They have proved to be perfectly viable for the stage and, especially in the ensembles, full of that delightful invention to be found in the rest of his opus, if on a less fully developed scale. Still as musical drama they inevitably fall far short of Mozart's achievements, for the younger composer seems to have had an instinctive feeling for the stage. Into his operas he poured his most intense, personal music. He vividly portrays the foibles, desires, loves, and aspirations of mankind.

The earlier, immature stage pieces of his youth led to such works as *Lucio Silla* (1772) and *La*

Finta Giardiniera (1775) with their first glimpses of the glories to come. His first indubitably great opera is *Idomeneo* (1781). Despite its unpromisingly static plot, *Idomeneo* reveals Mozart's stature through its ability to breathe new life into a conventional *opera seria* form. Though influenced by Gluck it is yet more human and touching in its musical expression. To succeed this Mozart wrote a much more frivolous piece *Die Entführung aus dem Serail*. Stemming from the *Singspiel* tradition, it none the less creates real-life characters who have much charming music to sing.

After three lesser pieces Mozart embarked on his four masterpieces—*Le Nozze di Figaro* (1786), *Don Giovanni* (1787), *Cosi fan tutte* (1790), and *Die Zauberflöte* (1791).

Figaro, as well as being a delightful comedy, explores more fully than any previous opera situation and character, which find expression in beautiful arias and in two finales of symphonic proportion. In *Don Giovanni*, less satisfactory as a dramatic structure, the range of musical characterisation and insight into human motives is widened still further. *Cosi* lyrically but humorously expresses the follies of love. Mozart could not help but love his characters and his music for them is at one and the same time amusing and heartfelt, *Die Zauberflöte*—The Magic Flute—displays Mozart's deep-felt concern for his fellow men and for truth in an opera of great spiritual strength. Nor has opera any more loveable personality than the birdcatcher Papageno. Mozart's final opera *La Clemenza di Tito*, extolling imperial magnanimity, has never achieved the success or popularity of his other maturer stage works, though it contains much excellent music, and has recently been revived with honour in several opera houses.

Beethoven.

Mozart was the last major composer to depend, to any large extent, on private patronage for his living, and even he left the service of the Archbishop of Salzburg because he could not stand the restrictions imposed on his freedom. Henceforth composers would have to stand on their own two feet with all the advantages (liberty) and disadvantages (lack of security) that implied. Beethoven (1770–1827) was the first such composer of importance.

Although his work is usually divided into three periods, that division is somewhat too arbitrary, for no other composer in history, with the possible exception of Wagner, has shown such a continual development of his genius. Coming at just the right moment in musical history, he crowned the achievements of Haydn and Mozart with music of the utmost profundity of thought and feeling that looks back to its classical heritage and forward to the romantic movement of the 19th cent. His influence on musical thinking and writing is incalculable.

His first period shows his strong melodic gifts and the beginning of his individuality in developing form and structure to suit his own ends and match his particular genius. Unusual keys are explored, unusual harmonic procedures employed. With the "Eroica" (his third symphony) he established his position as a great composer. The unity of purpose he here achieved within a long and diverse structure is truly staggering, even today. In the first movement alone the formal invention and cogency went far beyond what even Mozart had achieved in his "Jupiter" symphony, and the second movement—a vast funeral March—has an overwhelmingly tragic emotional content. But the "Eroica" was followed by six equally great symphonies, each one as varied, as inventive, as unified as the others. The ninth symphony is significant both for its length and its finale. Here Beethoven crowns three superb instrumental movements with a choral movement that, as well as summing up all that has gone before, expresses in music the joy in existence more ecstatically than any other work.

The burning intensity of Beethoven's genius is just as evident in his chamber music. His quartets are the product of a revolutionary age in which the social graces and formal restraint of the 18th cent. were thrown off in a search for a more personal mode of expression. The early op. 18 set, and the Razoumovsky quartets, op. 59, go even beyond the range of Haydn's and Mozart's works in the medium but it was in his late quartets, his final musical testament, that Beethoven refined and distilled his art for posterity. No words can possibly describe their unique quality, but any and every chance should be taken to make their acquaintance; the effort required will be more than amply rewarded.

The early piano concertos do not reach quite that level of attainment, but the last three, together with the violin concerto, are on a par with the finest of the symphonies and quartets, as well as being considerable tests of the performers' technique. The Triple Concerto for piano, violin, and cello is an unusual and rewarding work.

Beethoven's grandest choral work—and one of the most noble in existence—is the Mass in D (*Missa Solemnis*). Its vast scale and sublime utterance often defeat performers, but when it is successfully done there is no more spiritually uplifting experience for the listener, except perhaps Beethoven's only opera, *Fidelio*. This simple escape story was transformed by Beethoven's creative fire into a universal symbol of liberty, the composer identifying himself with the struggle for freedom from tyranny and release from darkness.

Beethoven lived in a period of war and revolution. A passionate believer in the brotherhood of man and in liberty, he was shocked to find his ideals thrown over by revolutionaries-turned-dictators. His own tragedy of deafness, which came upon him at the moment of his triumph, nearly submerged him, but in the end he won through and produced the string of masterpieces from the "Eroica" onwards. Hope springing from despair, love from hatred, victory over defeat, these are the unquenchable legacies left by Beethoven.

The Romantic Movement.

Inevitably, the Romantic movement in literature that burst forth about 1800 was bound to have its counterpart in music. And so it was. Breaking the classical bonds, composers such as Schubert, Schumann, Liszt, and Berlioz sought a new freedom in musical expression. Form became of less importance than content; and that content often had literary connections. For their purposes a larger orchestra was needed and supplied, but the miniature, the song especially, because of its very personal connotation, was also a favourite form.

Schubert (1797–1828)—described by Liszt as "the most poetic of musicians"—is perhaps the greatest lyrical genius in musical history. In him the Viennese tradition and influence of Haydn, Mozart, and Beethoven reached its zenith. The song was always Schubert's starting point, so it is hardly surprising that his reputation as a song writer has never been impaired but in his symphonic and instrumental works too it is always his inexhaustible fund of melody that first calls for attention. Nobody could listen to his "Trout" quintet, for piano and strings, his octet, his fifth symphony, or his song cycle *Die Schöne Müllerin* without being enchanted and invigorated by the sheer tunefulness of the music. But there is much more to Schubert than this: his understanding of the possibilities of harmonic change, his grasp of orchestral coloration (in the great C major symphony, for instance), his free use of sonata structure.

Although Mozart, Haydn, and Beethoven had all contributed to the song as an art form, it was with Schubert that it achieved its first full flowering. If he had written nothing but his songs, his place in the musical firmament would be assured. With his *Erlkönig* in 1815 the German *Lied* came of age and from then until the end of his life he wrote more than six hundred songs, hardly a dud among them. Whether it is the charm of *Heidenröslein*, the drama of *Der Doppelgänger* or the numbed intensity of the *Winterreise* cycle, Schubert unerringly went to the heart of a poet's meaning; indeed he often raised poor verses to an inspired level by his settings. And for the first time the pianist shares a place of equal importance with the singer.

There is only room to mention one or two other composers, some of them wrongly neglected, who were roughly contemporaries of Beethoven and Schubert: the Czech Dussek (1760–1812), who like Beethoven bridges the classical–romantic gulf, Boccherini (1743–1805), the two Italian opera composers Cimarosa (1749–1801) and Paisiello (1740–1816), the Frenchman Méhul (1763–1817) and the German Hummel (1778–1837).

Weber (1786–1826) lacked Beethoven's energy and constructive powers and Schubert's sheer lyrical profundity, but he is an important figure, especially in the field of opera, where his *Der Freischütz* and *Oberon* led the way to a more flexible, dramatically realistic form of opera. His vivid imagination exactly fitted the new romantic mood abroad. The sheer beauty in the melodic shape of his music is also not to be denied. His instrumental works are attractive but insubstantial.

Mendelssohn and Schumann.

Mendelssohn (1809–47) was the civilised craftsman among the Romantic composers. A boy genius—many of his finest works were written before he was twenty—he maintained the importance of classical form while imbuing it with his own affectionate brand of poetic sensibility. His third and fourth symphonies—the "Scottish" and "The Italian"—(and possibly the fifth "The Reformation"), his string quartets (some of which go deeper than the rest of his music), octet, violin concerto, first piano concerto, and of course, the incidental music to "A Midsummer Night's Dream" represent his tidy yet effervescent style at its most winning.

Schumann (1810–56) is less easy to categorise. His early romantic flame was burnt out by some flaw in his intellectual and/or emotional make-up, and his inspiration seems to have declined in later years. No matter, by then he had given us the marvellous song cycles of 1840, an ever fresh piano concerto, many fine piano solos, including the mercurial, popular *Carnaval* and four symphonies, which, if not structurally perfect, contain much lovely music. The joys and sorrows of love and the feeling for natural beauty are all perfectly mirrored in these charming, lyrical works, and in the genial piano quintet.

Romantic Giants.

Berlioz (1803–69) and Liszt (1811–86) are the two most typical representative composers of the Romantic era. Both have always been controversial figures, with ardent advocates and opponents either unduly enthusiastic or unfairly derogatory. Berlioz might be termed the perfect painter in music. With an uncanny mastery of orchestral sound he could conjure up the countryside, the supernatural and the historical with the utmost ease. He based his music on the "direct reaction to feeling" and a desire to illustrate literature by musical means. That his technical expertise was not always the equal of his undoubted genius, can be heard in many of his larger works such as the dramatic cantata *The Damnation of Faust* and the dramatic symphony *Romeo and Juliet*, yet most people are willing to overlook the occasional vulgarity for the ineffable beauty of his many fine pages, but brutal cuts in his music, such as are often made in, for instance, his epic opera *The Trojans* only have the effect of reducing the stature of his works. We must accept him, warts and all. Anyone who has seen the two parts of *The Trojans*, presented complete in one evening at Covent Garden, will realise that Berlioz knew what he was about.

His output is not quantitatively large but includes several monumental works, as well as The

Trojans, The *Requiem* ("Grand Messe des Morts") requires a tenor solo, huge chorus and orchestra, and brass bands, although Berlioz uses these forces fastidiously. The *Symphonie funèbre et triomphale* calls in its original form, for choir brass, and strings. But Berlioz was just as happy writing on a smaller scale as his exquisite song cycle, to words of Théophile Gautier, *Nuits d'Eté*, shows. Gautier perhaps summed up better than anyone Berlioz's singular talent: "In that renaissance of the 1830s Berlioz represents the romantic musical idea, the breaking up of old moulds, the substitution of new forms for unvaried square rhythms, a complex and competent richness of orchestration, truth of local colour, unexpected effects in sound, tumultuous and Shakespearian depth of passion, amorous or melancholy dreaminess, longings and questionings of the soul, infinite and mysterious sentiments not to be rendered in words, and that something more than all which escapes language but may be divined in music."

During his lifetime Liszt was fêted and honoured not only by his musical colleagues but by the world at large, which idolised him and his piano. Then his reputation took a plunge from which it has only recently recovered. To be sure much of his early music is glitter and gloss, but his symphonies and tone poems—especially the Faust Symphony, the Dante Symphony (both, of course, inspired by literature), and *Orpheus* and *Prometheus*—and his late piano works show that he was an extraordinary harmonic innovator. The piano sonata in B minor brings his romantic, wilful temperament within a reasonably stable, pianistic form, and as such is a landmark in the repertory of the instrument. Liszt's output was prodigious, but the inquiring listener should explore the more original of his compositions already mentioned to form a true picture of his fertile genius.

Chopin.

Chopin (1810–49) was the master of the keyboard, par excellence. His development of the technical and expressive capabilities of the piano is unique in musical history. His inventive powers were poured out with nervous passionate energy and in a highly individual style through twenty astonishing, possibly agonised years of creative activity before his early death. A Chopin melody, limpid, transparent, singing, can be recognised easily by anyone, but his style gradually developed into something more subtle, more satisfying than pure melody. He took the greatest care of every detail so that any alteration, however small, upsets the perfect balance of his work. His poetic sensibility can be found in any of his works; for his constructive ability we must turn to the Ballades, the B minor Sonata, and the Barcarolle, while the Preludes and Studies blend technical powers and emotional expressiveness in ideal proportions.

Nineteenth-century Opera.

After Mozart's operas and Beethoven's *Fidelio* the medium might have been expected to decline. Instead it took on a new, if different, lease of life that culminated in Verdi's extraordinary output.

Rossini (1792–1868) created a world of exuberant high spirits in his operatic works that are as cheerful and heart-warming today as they were a hundred or more years ago.

He always worked in and around the lyric theatres of Italy and between 1810 and 1830 poured out a stream of works, not all of which can be expected to be masterpieces. However, *Il Barbiere di Siviglia*, *L'Italiana in Algieri*, *La Cenerentola* and *Le Comte Ory* will always delight audiences as long as opera houses exist. Although these works are difficult to sing really well, their vitality and charm can never be submerged even by poor voices or indifferent staging.

His German contemporaries were critical of his confidence and frivolity, but his works show a consistency of invention and an irresistible tunefulness that anyone might envy. In recent years, there has been a renewed interest in his more serious operas—*Otello* (1816), *La Gazza Ladra* (1817), *Semiramide* (1823), *La Siège de Corinthe* (1820), and *Guillaume Tell* (1829)—which were certainly surpassed in dramatic power by his successors but which nevertheless are not to be despised or neglected.

William Tell, to give it its most popular title, was his last work for the stage although he lived on for nearly forty years in retirement in Paris, scene of many of his greatest successes. There he enjoyed good living, dispensing *bons mots*, and occasionally composing trifles. An exception is the unpretentious *Petite Messe Solennelle*, written originally for soloists, chorus, a harmonium, and two pianos. Rossini later orchestrated it, but he would not allow it to be performed during his lifetime. The first public performance was on 28 February 1869, as near as possible to the 78th anniversary of the composer's birth on Leap Year Day 1792.

In contrast to the mercurial Rossini, Vincenzo Bellini (1801–85) was an exquisite, romantic figure dealing with exquisite, romantic stories, an operatic equivalent to Chopin, who much admired him. His delicate, sinuous vocal line (in the arias) and brilliant acrobatics in the final sections (cabalettas) require singers of the utmost accomplishment to do them justice, although his music is never as florid as Rossini's. His most typical and popular works are probably *La Sonnambula* (1831), *Norma* (1831) and *I Puritani* (1835). The first is a tender, homely country story, the second an almost heroic lyrical drama of sacrifice, and the third a rather unsatisfactory historical story redeemed by its appealing music. In our own day singers of the calibre of Maria Callas, Joan Sutherland, Guiletta Simionato, and Marilyn Horne have brought Bellini's operas a popularity almost equal to that they enjoyed at the time they were written.

Gaetano Donizetti (1797–1848) was an even more prolific operatic composer than Rossini. He wrote at least 75 works, mostly for the Italian stage, several of which, such as *Alfredo il Grande* or *Emilia di Liverpool*, are never likely to be revived, but during the past few years, with the renewed interest in what are called the *Ottocento* operas, many of his serious operas have been resuscitated and found as enjoyable in performance as his more frequently heard comedies.

He was a well-grounded musician and although his invention is often criticised for being too tied to the conventions of his day performances often belie this reputation, his dramatic instinct proving sure. *Lucia di Lammermoor*, because of the chances it offers to a coloratura soprano with tragic pretensions, has always held the stage and of late, *Lucrezia Borgia*, *Anna Bolena*, *La Favorita*, and *Poliuto* have all been successfully revived. Of his lighter works, the comedies *L'Elixir d'Amore* and *Don Pasquale* have never declined in popularity. One of his last works was *Linda di Chamounix* (1842) which he wrote for Vienna where it aroused such enthusiasm that the Emperor appointed him Court Composer and Master of the Imperial Chapel.

French Opera.

The taste in Paris was for more and more lavish productions. Following Spontini (1774–1851), whose works were comparatively austere, came Halévy (1799–1862) and Giacomo Meyerbeer (1791–1864) whose operas contain all the ingredients that came to be expected of "Grand Opera"—spectacle, huge ensembles, showpieces for the soloists, and extended, if superfluous ballet. Drawing from Italian, German, and French traditions Meyerbeer's works contained everything the public wanted, yet today they are seldom revived, perhaps because his creative powers were essentially derivative, yet when they *are* given, operas like *Les Huguenots*, *Le Prophète*, and *L'Africaine* still have the power to fascinate and his influence on his successors, notably Wagner, was considerable.

Verdi.

Italian opera in the 19th cent. culminated in the works of Giuseppe Verdi (1813–1901), who rose from a peasant background to become his country's most noted composer, as well as something of a natural hero during the period of the Risorgimento. His earliest works, indeed, often roused his hearers to patriotic fervour. For instance, *Nabucco* (1841), with its theme of an oppressed people seeking deliverance, was treated as a symbol of the Italians' fight for freedom.

Musically, Verdi developed out of all recognition during the course of his long career. The continuously flowing structure of his last two operas *Otello* and *Falstaff* is very far removed from the start-stop formulas, inherited from his predecessors, of his first works, yet even they are touched, in harmonic subtleties, orchestral felicities, and a sense of drama, by a spark of genius, a burning inspiration that sets him apart from all other operatic composers. *Ernani* (1844), *I due Foscari* (1844), and *Luisa Miller* (1849) all have foretastes of glories to come even if as a whole they are flawed dramas, and these "galley years", as Verdi himself later described them, gave him the essential know-how to produce his later, greater operas, as well as establishing him incontrovertibly as the most popular Italian composer of the time.

However, it was with *Rigoletto* (1851), *Il Trovatore* (1853), and *La Traviata* (1853) that Verdi first really staked his claim to immortality. In these pieces his increasing dramatic mastery is married to a wonderful flow of lyrical melody, at the same time controlled by a fine musical sensibility. They were followed by four operas—*Simon Boccanegra* (1857), *Un Ballo in Maschera* (1858), *La Forza del Destino* (1862), and *Macbeth* (revised version, 1865)—in which Verdi overcame complexities of story line by his continually developing musical powers. This period is crowned by *Don Carlos* (written for the Paris Opéra, 1867) a masterly exercise in combining private and public situations in a single, grand, and characterful work. In some respects Verdi never surpassed the subtlety of his writing in this opera. *Aïda* (1871) carried on the process but the characterisation in this ever-popular piece is less refined than in *Don Carlos*, if the grandeur of the design is more spectacular.

The success of *Otello* (1887) owes nearly as much to the skill of Boito whose literary ability combined with musical knowledge (he was himself a composer) presented Verdi with an ideal libretto for his seamless music in which the drama moves inevitably to its tragic end. Recitative, aria, ensemble are fused in a single, swiftly moving music-drama, which in its very different way equals that of Wagner. *Falstaff* (1893) achieves the same success in the field of comic opera, a brilliant, mercurial ending to a distinguished career. If Verdi had written only these two final masterpieces his place in musical history would have been assured.

Brahms.

Brahms (1833–97) has justly been described as "a romantic spirit controlled by a classical intellect," for while complying with most of the formal regulations of sonata form he imbued them with an emotional content that accorded with his time. Indeed Schumann declared that he was the "one man who would be singled out to make articulate in an ideal way the highest expression of our time."

Perhaps in his chamber music will be found the quintessence of his art. The piano and clarinet quintets, the two string sextets, the horn trio, and the violin sonatas all are designed on a large scale yet the expression remains intimate, the design and structure clear.

The symphonies and concertos, though, remain his most popular works; they are part of the solid repertory of every orchestra and most piano and violin players in the world. Their high seriousness, constant lyrical beauty, and control of form are deeply satisfying. They do not provide the extremes of passion and excitement provided by his contemporaries, but their study provides continuous absorption and delight. The double concerto for violin and cello deserves a mention as a unique work in music.

Brahms wrote more than two hundred songs in which the desire for melodic beauty takes precedence over the words and meaning. Many are set to poor poetry, but hidden away are still some unexplored treasures, and the Four Serious Songs, at least, are tragic masterpieces. In a lighter vein the two sets of *Liebeslieder Walzer* for four voices are irresistible. The choral Requiem, too, is a fine work.

Bruckner.

In recent years Bruckner's reputation *vis-à-vis* his great contemporary Brahms has been enhanced in England. The old conception of him as a naïve Austrian unable to grasp the fundamentals of symphonic architecture has died hard, and the prevailing popularity of his grandest works is at last gaining him his rightful place in the 19th cent. firmament. The nine symphonies and the masses are his chief claim to immortality. They contain melodies of unforgettable beauty, symphonic paragraphs of unparalleled grandeur, and an appreciation of formal development that, though different, is equally as valid as that of Brahms. The movements of his symphonies are long and he often pauses, as if for breath and to admire the scenery, before he reaches the climactic peak of his musical journey. His idiom is best approached by a newcomer to his work through the fourth and seventh symphonies as they are perhaps the easiest to understand, but the fifth, sixth, eighth, and ninth (unfinished) are just as beautiful—and cogently argued—once one has acquired the knack, so to speak, of listening to his music. Most of these works are now to be heard in their original form, stripped of the veneer of "improvements" suggested to the diffident composer by his friends.

The masses, which translate Bruckner's symphonic ideas to the choral plain, and Bruckner's delightful string quintet are worth investigating.

Wagner.

Praised only this side of idolatry by his admirers, unmercifully criticised by his detractors, Richard Wagner (1813–83) is perhaps the most controversial composer in musical history. And so it was bound to be with such a revolutionary figure, whose writings, other than his music, contain, to say the least, dubious theories and whose operas, composed to his own libretti, broke the bonds of the form as known until his time. He regarded music-drama as a fusion of all the arts—music, literature, painting—in one unity. With *The Ring of the Nibelungs* he achieved his purpose; no other work of art has ever tried to encompass the whole of existence. Today, and surely forever, musicians, philosophers, and writers will argue over its meaning, and each age will reinterpret it according to its own lights.

But before he reached this pinnacle of achievement, Wagner gradually transformed opera—through *Rienzi*, *The Flying Dutchman*, *Tannhäuser*, and *Lohengrin*—so that a new mould was fashioned to take what he wanted to pour into it. He introduced the *Leitmotiv*, a musical theme that could be associated with a particular person, situation, or idea, each time it occurred. Slowly he developed the musical form so that the drama could unfold continuously without breaks for arias. By the time he began to write *Tristan and Isolde* and *Die Meistersinger*, he had perfected his methods and had he never undertaken *The Ring* that tragedy and that comedy would have assured him his place in the musical firmament. Indeed, *Die Meistersinger* is considered a masterpiece even by those who are not willing or prepared to accept the rest of the Wagnerian ethos.

The length and complexity of these operas, and of *Parsifal*, a work of unique beauty in spite of

certain *longueurs*, means that it is almost essential to prepare oneself by homework, with libretti and records, before attempting to assimilate them in the opera house. The added effort is well worth while for the ultimate musical satisfaction they bring because Wagner was more than an operatic reformer; he opened up a new harmonic language (especially in the use of chromaticism) that was logically to develop into the atonality of the 20th cent.

Wolf.

As Wagner was the culmination of the 19th cent. symphonic and operatic tradition, so Hugo Wolf (1860–1903) summed up, if he did not surpass, the achievements in song-writing of Schubert, Schumann, and Loewe (1796–1869).

Wolf was a lonely, pathetic man. He lived much of his life in poverty, and eventually lost his reason and died of an incurable disease. These circumstances account perhaps for his almost feverish bursts of creative activity, which were also the outward sign of his burning genius. His greatest contributions to the art of *Lieder* were his extraordinary insight into the poet's meaning and the harmonic means by which he heightened the expression of the words. He raised the importance of the piano part even higher than had Schumann, and in some of his songs the vocal part takes the form of a free declamation over a repeated idea in the piano. However, in the main the vocal and piano parts are interweaved with great subtlety, and he unerringly matched the very varied moods of the poems he chose to set. His greatest creative period was between early 1888 and early 1890 when songs poured from his pen daily—more than 50 settings of the German poet Mörike, 20 of Eichendorff, more than 50 of Goethe, and more than 40 of Heyse and Geibel (the Spanish Song-book). Later he composed songs from Heyse's Italian Song-book and the three Michelangelo sonnets. And the range of his creative understanding was wide, taking in the almost wild passion of the Spanish songs, the humanity and humour of the Italian love-songs, the titanic power of *Prometheus* (Goethe), the varying moods of the Mörike book, and the intangible power of the Michelangelo sonnets. There are almost inexhaustible riches here for the inquiring mind to discover. Outside *Lieder*, Wolf's output is small, but it includes a sadly neglected opera, *Der Corregidor*, the Italian Serenade for string quartet (alternatively for small orchestra) and a tone poem *Penthesilea*.

Ernest Newman, his greatest champion, summed up his work most aptly: "Wolf practically never repeats himself in the songs; every character is drawn from the living model. It is a positively Shakespearian imagination that is at work—Protean in its creativeness, inexhaustibly fecund and always functioning from the inside of the character or the scene, not merely making an inventory from the outside."

National Movements.

During the course of the 19th cent., alongside the emergence of national political identity, came the rise of nationalism in music, fertilising traditional Western—that is basically German—musical forms with folk material. Of these groups the Russian is certainly the most important, if not the most vital.

Glinka (1804–57) was the first important Russian composer of the national school and, although his two operas *A Life for the Tsar* (sometimes called *Ivan Susanin*) and *Russlan and Ludmilla* are strongly influenced by Italian models, they do introduce Russian song and harmony into the texture. He undoubtedly influenced Borodin (1833–87), Cui (1835–1918), Balakireff (1837–1910), Mussorgsky (1839–81) and Rimsky-Korsakov (1844–1908)—the so-called "Five" of 19th-cent. Russian music. However, each was very much of an individualist too. Borodin was a lecturer in chemistry who wrote in his spare time. His two symphonies, two string quartets led up to his most notable work, the opera *Prince Igor*, left incomplete at his death. Balakireff, friend and adviser to the rest of the group, wrote little himself, but his orchestral works and the piano fantasia, *Islamey*, are worthy of investigation.

Modest Mussorgsky (1839–81) is today seen as the most important and inspired of "The Five." More than the others he used Russian song and Russian speech as the basis of his operas in which he portrayed the lives and destinies of his own people. Although his capacities were seriously impaired by an uncongenial job, poverty, and drinking, he produced two great operas, *Boris Godunov* and *Khovanshchina*, and another *Sorochintsy Fair* that is immensely enjoyable. *Boris* should be given in its original, with spare orchestration, but more often than not it is heard in Rimsky-Korsakov's more elaborate revision. In any case the opera exists in various versions, none of them necessarily the right one; what is important is to hear it in one or the other because of its great portrayal of Boris's personality set against the background of the Russian people, unforgettably presented in choral outbursts. *Khovanshchina* was completed by Rimsky-Korsakov, *Sorochintsy Fair* by Tcherepnin (although other versions also exist). Mussorgsky's songs explore a new vein of naturalistic vocal declamation. Each of the four *Songs and Dances of Death* is a miniature drama worthy of Wolf, although of course in a quite other idiom. The *Nursery* songs miraculously conjure up a child's world as seen from a child's point of view. Many of the individual songs, the *Sunless* cycle too, should be investigated.

Rimsky-Korsakov (1844–1908) is perhaps a less attractive figure because so much of his music seems heartless or merely decorative, but this judgment is probably made on the strength of hearing *Shéhérazade* and the *Capriccio Espagnol* a few too many times. Such of his 15 operas as are played evince a (literally) fantastic mind and lyrical vein, and it is a pity that *Sadko*, *The Snow Maiden*, and *The Tsar's Bride*, at least, are not heard more often.

Tchaikovsky.

Peter Ilyich Tchaikovsky (1840–93) is a more universally admired figure than any of "The Five" and his music is indubitably closer to the mainstream than theirs in that it adheres more nearly to Western European forms. His popularity is due to his unhesitating appeal to the emotions and to his tender, often pathetic melodic expression. His lyrical gift is stronger than his sense of architecture, as he himself admitted. Yet his later symphonies—the fourth, fifth, and sixth (the *Pathétique*)—are all cogently enough argued and invigorating, as can be heard in the hands of a conductor willing to emphasise their formal power rather than their tendency towards sentimentality; the orchestral craftsmanship is also superb. The three piano concertos and the violin concerto offer rare opportunities for virtuoso display within a reasonably dramatic structure and his various overtures are always exciting to hear.

The three ballets—*The Sleeping Beauty*, *Swan Lake*, and *Nutcracker* show Tchaikovsky's skill on a smaller and perhaps more congenial scale, but only two of his operas—*Eugene Onegin* and *The Queen of Spades*—survive in regular performance. They demonstrate his ability to delineate character and his always eloquent melodic invention. His songs often felicitously capture a passing mood or emotion.

Bohemia (Czechoslovakia).

The Czech national school is dominated by two composers—Smetana (1824–84) and Dvořák (1841–1904). In his own country Smetana holds a unique position as the father of his country's music—which is remarkable when you consider that he lived in a country that was then under Austrian rule and never spoke the Czech language perfectly. Yet his music is filled with the spirit of Czech history and national life, and many of his operas, his most important contribution, deal purely with national subjects. The reawakening of interest in things national, after Austria's defeat by Italy in 1859, led to the establishment of a Provisional Theatre in 1862 and Smetana's first opera *The Brandenburgers in Bohemia* was produced there in 1866, but its success was eclipsed by the enormous popularity of *The Bartered Bride*, which appeared the same year. Its melodic charm, lively characterisation and cosy humour have carried it round the world and it is the one Smetana opera to be in the repertory of most opera houses. However, his next opera *Dalibor* (1868) is considered by some authorities as his masterpiece. It is conceived on a heroic scale, and frequently rises to great dramatic heights. His later operas include *Libuše* (1872) a solemn festival tableau, *The Two Widows* (1874), a delightful comedy, *The Kiss* (1876), *The Secret* (1878), and *The Devil's Wall* (1882).

His main orchestral work *Má Vlast* (My Country), written between 1874 and 1879, is a cycle of six symphonic poems nobly depicting the life and legends of his country. He composed only three mature chamber works—an elegiac piano trio, written in 1855 in memory of the death of his eldest daughter, and two string quartets, both autobiographical. The first in E minor (1876)—"From My Life"—tells of his youth and aspirations until a terrible, screeching E in *altissimo* describes the onset of deafness; the second in D minor, sadly neglected, was described by the composer as an attempt to explain the "whirlwind of music in the head of one, who has lost his hearing," and was probably influenced by Beethoven's later music.

Dvořák combined a fecund melodic gift with an intelligent grasp of structure. His symphonies and chamber music are mostly written in classical form, yet the works are imbued with a spontaneity and freshness that have not lost one whit of their charm over the years.

He wrote nine symphonies and, although only the last three or four are regularly performed, they are mostly mature works, several of which, for instance No. 7 in D minor (formerly known as No. 2) reach a tragic grandeur at times. They are all orchestrated in a masterly way and are full of delightful detail. Dvořák wanted to show that a Brahms could come out of Bohemia—and he succeeded in doing so while maintaining a definitely individual flavour, strongly influenced by natural rhythms.

He wrote three concertos, one each for piano, violin, and cello. The earlier ones are interesting without being quite in the first flight of the composer's output, but the cello concerto of 1895 is perhaps the composer's crowning achievement—warm, mellifluous, romantic.

He wrote chamber music throughout his long creative life. Some of the early works are weak and derivative, but the later string quartets, the "Dumky" trio, and the piano quartet and quintet are expressive and full of unforced invention. Dvořák felt himself somewhat hampered when setting words, nevertheless his *Stabat Mater* and *Te Deum* are both deeply felt choral works and he wrote songs throughout his career, many of them very fine indeed. He wrote ten operas, but only *Rusalka* (1901) has gained a foothold outside Czechoslovakia.

Janáček.

The Moravian composer Leoš Janáček (1858–1928) spent most of his life in Brno as a working musician. His music has recently come to be recognised as some of the most original written in the past hundred years. His operas, in which he closely followed the inflection of the speech of his native land, are his finest works. Over the score of his last opera, *From the House of the Dead*, he wrote the words "In every human being there is a divine spark", and it is this deep love of humanity that permeates all his works. Of his operas *Kátya Kabanová* (1921) and *The Cunning Little Vixen*

(1924), the *Makropoulos Affair* (1926), and *From the House of the Dead* (adapted from a Dostoyevsky novel, 1928) are the most important and they have all been produced in Britain in recent years. His original genius is self-evident in all of them.

Among his orchestral works *Taras Bulba* and *Sinfonietta* should be noted, and his two string quartets, very difficult to play, should be better known. The song cycle, *Diary of one who has disappeared*, for tenor, contralto, and three female voices with piano, and the Glagolithic Mass contain music of much expressive beauty.

Hungary.

The Hungarian musical outburst came somewhat later than that of other countries. Its great figure is Bela Bartók (1881–1945) who, as well as being a national figure, has proved an influential composer in the whole of 20th-cent. music. His mind was full of folk music, but it was transmuted by his strongly personal style and powerful intellect into something highly original. His music is tense and volatile but this restlessness is sometimes relieved by a kind of other-wordly, ethereal lyricism, as in the lovely slow movements of his quartets.

Bartók was affected as much by the musical innovations of Debussy and Stravinsky (see below) as by East European, notably Magyar, folk music and many of his works are an attempt to meld the two.

The most important part of his output is undoubtedly his string quartets which cover most of his creative life. To this intimate form he confided his personal innermost thoughts and in it conducted his most far-reaching musical experiments, thereby extending its boundaries beyond anything previously known. As with Beethoven's late quartets many of Bartok's rely on organic or cyclic development while remaining just within the laws of classical form. As Mosco Carner puts it, "For profundity of thought, imaginative power, logic of structure, diversity of formal details, and enlargement of the technical scope, they stand unrivalled in the field of modern chamber music."

The most important of his orchestral works are the three piano concertos, of which the first two are harsh and uncompromising, and fiendishly difficult to play, while the third, written in 1945, is mellower and more diatonic. The second violin concerto (1937–8) shows the various elements of Bartók's style in full flower, by turns exuberant, passionate, and brilliant. The *Music for Strings, Percussion and Celesta* (1937) is remarkable for its strange sonorities and its fascinating texture. The *Concerto for Orchestra* (1944) is more immediately appealing and again shows the composer in complete command of a large canvas. Of the piano works *Mikrokosmos* (1935) and the sonata for two pianos and percussion (1937) are worth investigating.

His chief stage pieces are *The Miraculous Mandarin* (1919), a harsh, cruel ballet which drew appropriately dramatic music from the composer, and the opera *Duke Bluebeard's Castle* (1911), a luscious, original score that makes one regret that he wrote no more operas later in his career.

Kodály (1882–1967) was from early years closely associated with Bartók and with him collected Hungarian folk melodies using many of them in his music. He worked in many forms and the more important of his works are the *Peacock Variations* for orchestra, the choral *Psalmus Hungaricus* and *Te Deum*, The *Dances of Galánta*, and the opera *Háry János*, and the sonatas for cello and for unaccompanied cello.

Sibelius, Nielsen and Grieg.

Among Scandinavian composers the Finn Jean Sibelius (1865–1957) and the Dane Carl Nielsen (1865–1931) are outstanding. Sibelius is a lone northern figure ploughing his own furrow

oblivious or, at any rate, ignoring the unusual developments that were taking place in Central Europe, yet his seven symphonies are strong as granite, honest, rugged works that will undoubtedly stand the test of time. They are not by any means all similar in mood, or even form. The first is very much influenced by Tchaikovsky and Borodin, the second and third show a more personal style developing, the fourth is terse and tragic, the fifth lyrical, bright, and lucid; the sixth is perhaps most typically Sibelian in its evocation of primeval nature, and the seventh—in one continuous movement—is a more purely abstract piece, notable for its structural logic and the grandness of its themes. The violin concerto is the most easily understood of the composer's main works and has a grateful part for the soloist.

The tone poems *The Swan of Tuonela*, *Pohjola's Daughter*, *En Saga*, *Night Ride and Sunrise*, *The Bard*, and *Tapiola* uncannily evoke the icy words of the legends of the far north, and the primeval forces of nature. Sibelius's one string quartet *Voces Intimae* and many of his songs are worth hearing too. His music, reviled in some quarters during the 1950s, has since been restored to favour, and seems to be enjoyed again by critics and the general public alike.

Carl Nielsen (1965–1931) is another individualist. His six symphonies, like Sibelius's seven, are the most important part of his output, but whereas Sibelius was dealing with a huge, uninhabited northern landscape, Nielsen is more friendly and serene in his music, which is seldom forbidding, always inventive, throwing a new light, through unusual ideas about harmony, structure and tonality, on traditional forms. He also wrote highly individual concertos for the flute and clarinet, four string quartets and two operas—the dramatic, rather Brahmsian *Saul and David* (1902) and a delightful comedy, *Maskarade* (1906), full of lyrical music.

The Norwegian composer Edvard Grieg (1843–1907) was essentially a miniaturist whose range of feeling was not wide but whose music is always gentle and appealing. His most notable works are the romantic piano concerto, the atmospheric incidental music to Ibsen's play *Peer Gynt*, the charming Lyric Suite, and the small piano pieces. Not an important composer, then, but always an attractive one.

Elgar and the English Revival.

After the death of Purcell there is hardly a name in English music worth speaking of until the 19th cent. when Hubert Parry (1848–1918) and Charles Villiers Stanford (1852–1924), actually an Irishman, led a revival. Their music is seldom heard today, but their pioneer work paved the way for Edward Elgar (1857–1934). Although all were influenced by Brahms they nevertheless managed to establish a new English tradition that has been carried on in our own day. Elgar's symphonies are laid out on a grand, leisurely scale and they are both eloquent and exhilarating. His violin concerto has an elegiac slow movement as has the glorious cello concerto and both contain many fine opportunities for the soloist. The cello concerto is as appealing a work as any by Elgar expressing his innermost thoughts. His *Enigma Variations* are a series of portraits in sound of his friends, but there is another overall theme to go with them that has never been identified. This has not prevented the work from becoming Elgar's most popular, not surprisingly when one considers its charm and melodiousness. Three other orchestral pieces that should not be neglected are his symphonic study *Falstaff*, a many-sided musical picture of the Fat Knight, and the overtures *Cockaigne*, a happy evocation of London, and *In the South*, inspired by a visit to Italy. His three late chamber works, written when he was 61, are reticent, economic pieces that remove any misconception of Elgar as a bombastic composer. His songs are mostly feeble, but the oratorios, notably *The Dream of Gerontius*, show the composer's ability to control a large canvas. The composer himself wrote over the score of *Gerontius*,

"This is the best of me"—a verdict with which we can readily agree.

French Music.

César Franck (1822-90) was the main figure in mid-19th-cent. musical France and his influence spread even wider than his music of which only the D minor Symphony, the Symphonic Variations for piano and orchestra, the piano quintet, and the violin sonata are likely to be encountered today. The leading French opera composers of that time were Gounod (1818-93), Bizet (1838-75) and Massenet (1842-1912). Gounod's *Faust*, Bizet's *Carmen* (composed just before his untimely death when he caught cold after a swim) and Massenet's *Manon* all retain a deserved place in the repertory; each is a well-judged mini-drama unafraid of romantic ardour and forceful, histrionic strokes. Some of Massenet's other numerous operas, such as *Werther* and *Don Quichotte*, have enjoyed a revival in recent years.

Concurrently with similar movements in French painting and poetry came the French Impressionist composers at the end of the 19th cent. Their leader—and one of the great seminal forces of modern music—was Claude Debussy (1862-1918). His aim was to capture a mood or sensation, and he did that by more or less inventing a fresh system of harmony using a whole-tone scale, unusual chords, and by creating in the orchestra new, highly personal textures—there is no mistaking the Debussy idiom once you have heard at least one piece by him. His impressionistic style did not lead him, however, to abandon form as some have suggested, and his main works are just as closely organised as those by classical German composers. His music is sensuous and poetic yet nearly always structurally satisfying as well.

His reputation, at least with the general musical public, rests largely on his orchestral music, a few piano pieces and his only opera *Pelléas et Mélisande*. *La Mer* is a scintillating evocation of the sea in all its moods; *Nocturnes*, *Images*, and *Prélude à l'Après-midi d'un Faune* exactly suggest different places, times, moods—the "Iberia" and "Gigues" sections of *Images*, calling to mind respectively the spirit of Spain and the flickering light of a rainy English night. *Pelléas*, based on a Symbolist drama by Maeterlinck, tells a story of love, jealousy, and murder in predominantly restrained yet emotionally loaded terms. It is an elusive original work that has no predecessor or successor. Intensely atmospheric, rivetingly beautiful, it weaves an irresistible spell over the listener.

Debussy's chamber music is unjustly neglected. His string quartet (1893) was one of the first works in which he displayed his new and strange world of sound, and the three late sonatas, one for violin, one for cello, and the third for flute, viola, and harp are elliptical, compressed pieces which seem to be questing disjointedly into new regions of sound. His songs too, are worthy of investigation, and his piano music, especially the twenty-four Preludes and some of the shorter pieces, contain some of his most imaginative and original ideas and thoughts.

Gabriel Fauré (1845-1924) is a difficult figure to place. He lived through all kinds of musical revolutions yet they seemed to affect the character of his work very little. He has never been, and is never likely to be, a widely known or popular composer, yet his music has a reticence and delicacy that is very appealing. Despite his dreamy, retiring art he was not a recluse, but a very sociable man.

He was content with forms as he found them, but he imbued them with a very personal, human style. Perhaps his art is best heard in his songs. They are not overtly passionate or dramatic but the long, sinuous melodies and subtle harmonies are exquisitely wrought. Of the song-cycles, *La Bonne Chanson*, *Cinq Mélodies* (Verlaine), *Le Chanson d'Eve*, and *L'Horizon Chimérique* are best known. The last written in 1922, when the composer was seventy-seven, is a beautiful setting

of words by a soldier killed in the first World War. There are also many remarkable single songs, many of them settings of poems by Verlaine. His opera *Pénélope*, based on the classical heroine, is unjustly neglected.

He wrote few orchestral pieces, but the *Ballade* for piano and orchestra and the *Pavane* are among his most typical, and delicate compositions, and his outstanding piano music, modelled on Chopin's, includes Nocturnes, Impromptus, and Barcarolles. His chamber music covers more than half a century from the violin sonata of 1876 to the string quartet written the year he died. In that period he composed two piano quartets, two piano quintets, another violin sonata and two cello sonatas, the later works failing to allow quite the unforced lyrical grace of the earlier ones. Perhaps Fauré is best approached with the first piano quartet, a charming, easily assimilated work, and the beautiful choral *Requiem*.

Saint-Saëns (1835-1921), an accomplished, cultivated musician, has had a "bad press" but his craftsmanship, as displayed in his symphonies, concertos, and *Samson et Dalila* (one among his 12 operas) is not to be despised.

Henri Duparc (1844-1933), despite a very long life, is known today only for a group of songs he wrote before he was forty. They are among the most emotionally direct yet tasteful melodies ever written. Paul Dukas (1865-1935) is another figure off the beaten track, as it were. He, too, is known only for a handful of compositions. He was strongly influenced by Vincent d'Indy (1851-1931) and the school who strongly opposed Debussy's new ideas, yet he could not help but come under Debussy's spell. Dukas's one great work is his opera *Ariane et Barbe-Bleue*, the text adapted from a Maeterlinck play written with the composer in mind.

Maurice Ravel (1875-1937), a pupil of Fauré, followed in Debussy's footsteps, although his later pieces were more ascetic. Indeed, he was one of the most fastidious of composers, always seeking, and often finding, artistic perfection. The works he wrote before 1918 are definitely of the Impressionist School and it would be difficult to imagine more beautiful sounds than are to be found in the ballet *Daphnis el Chloé*, in the song-cycle *Shéhérazade*, and the piano fantasy *Gaspard de la Nuit*. His first style was summed up in the A minor piano trio (1915). In his later music Ravel was struggling, not always successfully, to keep up with new developments such as jazz and atonality. The piano concerto, for instance, shows very strongly the influence of jazz.

Outstanding orchestral works of his, other than *Daphnis* are *Rapsodie espagnole* (1907), *La Valse* (1920), a sumptuous evocation of the Vienna waltz, and the ever-popular *Boléro*. Two chamber works, besides the trio, are masterpieces—the string quartet (1902-3) and the Introduction and Allegro for Harp, String Quartet, Flute, and Clarinet. This Septet composed in 1906, ravishes the senses with magical sound.

Ravel's piano pieces are perhaps his most notable contribution to music, combining an extraordinary feeling for the instrument's technical possibilities with the sensibility of a Chopin, and in this field *Jeux d'eau*, *Miroirs*, and *Ma Mère l'Oye*, all written just after the turn of the century, come very close to the perfection of *Gaspard de la Nuit*. His songs show his unusual appreciation of the need to fuse poetic and musical values, and he set exotic poems for preference. His output in this field includes the cycle *Histoires naturelles* (1906), acutely observed settings of five poems about birds and animals; *Cinq Mélodies populaires grecques* (1907), charming settings of Greek folk songs; *Trois Poèmes de Mallarmé* (1913); and *Chansons madécasses* (1926), suitably exotic settings of three poems by an 18th-cent. Creole poet called Parny. Finally in 1932 came *Don Quichotte à Dulcinée*, three poems by Paul Morand, Ravel's last composition.

Ravel wrote two operas—the slight but moderately amusing *L'Heure espagnole* (1907), nicely orchestrated in a faintly and appropriately Spanish style and *L'Enfant et les Sortilèges* (1925) to a story by Colette, a delicious fantasy about a naughty child who gets his due punishment for tormenting animals and destroying furniture.

French music after Debussy and Ravel was dominated by the slighter composers known as *Les Six*, the most important of whom were Arthur Honegger (1892–1955, Swiss born), Darius Milhaud (1892–1974) and Francis Poulenc (1890–1963). Each has contributed music of some wit and charm to the repertory. They were influenced by Erik Satie (1866–1925), an eccentric but interesting figure who wrote works with odd titles such as *Three Pear Shaped Pieces*. His music is entirely unsentimental, often ironic.

Spain.

Felipe Pedrell (1841–1922) has been aptly described as the midwife of Spanish nationalist music. As a musicologist and teacher he strongly influenced the two main composers of the school, Manuel de Falla (1876–1946) and Enrique Granados (1867–1916). Falla's output was not large and most of it was written around the years of the first world war. The pre-war years were spent in Paris where Falla came under the influence of Debussy. However his style is individual and evokes all the passion and gaiety of his native land. Perhaps his most typical works are in two ballets *Love the Magician* (1915) and *The Three-Cornered Hat* (1919). The opera *La Vida Breve* (1905) despite its weak libretto also has much appeal. The vivacity and smouldering passion at the heart of the country's character is conjured up by the *Seven Popular Songs* (1914) and the *Nights in the Gardens of Spain* (1916) for piano and orchestra. His later works, especially the harpsichord concerto of 1926, show Falla tending towards a less ebullient, more restrained style. The second opera, *Master Peter's Puppet Show* (1923) is a miniaturist work, refined and intense. His third opera *Atlantida*, left unfinished at his death, was completed by his pupil Ernesto Halffter and first staged in 1962.

Granados was perhaps a more restrictedly Spanish composer than Falla, but his music is unfailingly attractive and deserves to be better known. The opera *Goyescas* (1916) is most famous for the second interlude and opening of Act III—*La Maja y el Ruiseñor* (The Lover and the Nightingale), a haunting, sinuous melody for soprano, generally heard in its original form as a piano solo.

The chief claim to fame of Albéniz (1860–1909) is *Ibéria*, masterly descriptive pieces for piano. Many of his other piano works are now more well known in the form of very effective guitar arrangements. Turina (1882–1949), attempted a more cosmopolitan style, but his most often heard music is typically Spanish.

The Late German Romantics.

While composers such as Debussy, Sibelius, Stravinsky and Schoenberg (see below for the latter pair) were striking out along new paths, Richard Strauss (1864–1949) continued in the trend of 19th-cent. German composers; he was the tradition's last great figure. At least two of his operas—*Salome* and *Elektra*—were considered shocking at the time, but today we can hear that they are essentially big-scale, romantic works—natural successors to Wagner's—however startling the harmonies may once have seemed.

If Strauss did not achieve the granite intellectual greatness of Beethoven or Wagner, there is no denying his melodic genius and powers of fertile invention which overlaid the streak of vulgarity and inflation in his musical make-up. His first outstanding achievement was in the field of the symphonic poem, where he carried the work of composers such as Liszt and Berlioz to its logical conclusion. Starting with *Don Juan* in 1888 and ending with *Sinfonia Domestica* in 1903 he wrote a series of kaleidoscopic works, full of enormous vitality, endless melody, and fascinating orchestration. The most easily assimilated—and the most popular—are *Don Juan* and *Till Eulenspiegel* but some of the longer works, notably *Also Sprach Zarathustra* (based on Nietzsche's

prose poem) and *Don Quixote* (based, of course, on Cervantes's great work) will reward the persistent, inquiring mind with long hours of enthralled listening. Other works sound somewhat dated in their bombastic over-confidence, though Strauss's skill in composition seldom flagged at this stage of his long creative career. The symphonic poems all tell something of a story usually based on a literary source, but it is not essential to the enjoyment of the music to know what this is, although it may be helpful.

Strauss's reputation is even more solidly based on his fifteen operas, the earliest of which *Guntram* was first performed in 1894, the last, *Capriccio*, in 1942. During these years the essentials of Strauss's style changed little, though it became very much more refined as the years passed. His first operatic period ended with the violent, sensual tragedies *Salome* (1905) and *Elektra* (1909), the latter being his first collaboration with his chief librettist, Hugo von Hofmannsthal. Then came their unique *Der Rosenkavalier* (1911), which filters the charm and the decadence of 18th-cent. Vienna through early 20th-cent. eyes. This was followed by *Ariadne auf Naxos* (1912). Originally intended to be given after Molière's *Le Bourgeois Gentilhomme*, it was later presented (1916) without the play but with an amusing Prologue, written by von Hofmannsthal. *Die Frau ohne Schatten* is the most grandiose result of the Strauss–Hofmannsthal partnership. It is a complex psychological allegory, but Strauss's contribution is not on as consistently lofty a level as is his librettist's. *Intermezzo* (1924), which has a libretto by Strauss himself, is a largely autobiographical domestic comedy, which has lately gained in reputation as a compact, charming piece. With *Die Aegyptische Helena* (1928), an opera on a mythical theme, and *Arabella* (1933), another sensuous Viennese comedy, the Strauss–Hofmannsthal collaboration ended on account of the librettist's death. Strauss then wrote *Die Schweigsame Frau* (1935) to a libretto by Stefan Zweig, based on a play by Ben Jonson, and *Friedenslag* (1938), *Daphne* (1938)—a beautiful opera—and *Die Liebe der Danae* (written 1938–40) with Josef Gregor as librettist. His swan-song was *Capriccio*, a dramatisation of the old argument about the relative importance of words and music in opera. The libretto is by the conductor Clemens Krauss and the opera, a serene, melodious work, was a fit end to a great operatic career.

However, Strauss went on composing till nearly the end of his life, adding a group of late orchestral pieces to his already large catalogue of works. The *Metamorphosen* for 23 solo string instruments, is probably the best of these. During his long creative career he wrote numerous songs, many of them, such as *Morgen*, *Wiegenlied* and *Ruhe*, *meine Seele* of surpassing beauty.

Other notable figures in German music at this time were Max Reger (1873–1916), a somewhat ponderous but highly accomplished composer who, in a quarter of a century of creative life, wrote more than 150 works, of which his sets of variations, his piano concerto, and chamber music are probably the most impressive. Hans Pfitzner (1869–1949), another German traditionalist, is chiefly remembered today for his opera *Palestrina*, about events, now known to be spurious, in the life of the 16th-cent. Italian composer.

Twentieth-century Music.

Gustav Mahler (1860–1911), the Austrian Jewish composer, is one of the most important figures in 20th-cent. music. In a sense he bridges the gulf between the late Romantics, who were tending more and more towards chromaticism and away from established key relationships, and the atonalists, who abandoned the key system entirely. His detractors maintain that his inflation of allegedly banal Viennese beer-house music to unheard-of lengths rules him out of court as a serious writer. His admirers would claim that his music encompasses the whole of life in enormous, valid structures. The truth, if truth there be, perhaps lies somewhere in between: if his material does not always justify the length of his symphonies, and if there are occasional imperfections and *longueurs*, these shortcomings are worth enduring for the sake of the depth of utterance, the humanity and the poetry of the great pages. He admitted himself that "I cannot do without trivialities," but it is out of these impurities that he forged his titanic victories.

His music is undoubtedly best approached through his songs, where the words force him to discipline his wide-ranging vision. *Lieder eines fahrenden Gesellen* (1884), to his own words, *Kindertotenlieder* (1901–4), to poems by Rückert, and some individual songs perfectly relate words to music, and are all of a poignant loveliness. Similarly *Das Lied von der Erde* (1908), especially the last of the six songs, is a touching farewell to the world, nobly expressed.

The ten symphonies, however, are Mahler's most impressive legacy to posterity. They are almost impossible to characterise briefly so vast are they in terms of both length and variety. The first, fourth and ninth are probably the easiest to grasp but the fifth, sixth and seventh, despite flaws, contain some of his most awe-inspiring conceptions. The second and third, both of which use soloists and chorus, are revolutionary in orchestration and structure; they both try, inevitably without complete success, to carry out the composer's dictum, "a symphony should be like the world—it must contain everything." The eighth is even more gargantuan, but as in all Mahler's work size does not mean loss of clarity or an overloading of the structure. Part one—a mighty choral invocation—is a visionary setting of the mediaeval hymn *Veni Creator Spiritus*. Part two, which incorporates adagio, scherzo, and finale in one, is a setting of the final scene of Goethe's *Faust*. Until recently all of Mahler's unfinished tenth symphony that was ever performed was the Adagio, but the musicologist and Mahler scholar, the late Deryck Cooke, provided a performing version of the symphony to critical and popular acclaim during the 1960s and thus added a noble, and also optimistic epilogue to the Mahler opus. The debate over the quality of Mahler's music is likely to continue; one fact, however, that cannot be gain-said is his popularity with an ever-increasing audience, largely made up of young people. There must be something in his uncertainty and intense self-inquiry that accords with the mood of the youthful mind.

Schoenberg and the Second Viennese School.

Arnold Schoenberg (1874–1951) revolutionised Western music by his twelve-note method—a system which uses all the notes of the chromatic scale "and denies the supremacy of a tonal centre," as Schoenberg himself puts it. This serial technique of composition, as it is commonly called, naturally sounds strange to an ear acclimatised to music written, as it were, with a home base, but Schoenberg and his disciples Berg and Webern showed that the system could produce works that were something more than mere intellectual exercises. None of the more recent advances in music would have been possible, even thinkable, without Schoenberg's pioneer work.

Schoenberg always considered himself as much as a composer as a theorist or teacher, and his works are supposed to appeal as much to the emotions as to the intellect, although to be understood they do, of course, require the listener's concentrated attention. To appreciate how his ideas developed it is necessary to hear first his pre-atonal music, such as the *Gurrelieder* (1900–1) and *Verklärte Nacht* (1899), in which he carried Wagnerian chromaticism to extreme lengths. The *Gurrelieder*, in particular, is a luxuriant, overblown work that shows the Wagnerian idiom in an advanced stage of decay, in spite of many beautiful pages of music. In his succeeding works the feeling of tonality began to disappear until in the Three Piano Pieces (opus 11), of 1909, he finally rejected tonality, although the new 12-note scheme is not yet evident; traces of the old order can still be heard. The succeeding works were mostly short, highly compressed, and very expressive. Schoenberg was reaching out for a new system,

which would "justify the dissonant character of these harmonies and determine their successions." By 1923 he had formulated his 12-note system and the Five Piano Pieces (opus 23), and the Serenade (opus 24) of that year, can thus be considered the first works that used a note-row as the fundamental basis of their composition. Between 1910 and 1915, however, the Russian composer Alexander Skryabin (1872–1915) had attempted to define a new method of composition of his own employing the "mystic chord" of ascending fourths, but his scheme proved comparatively abortive when compared with Schoenberg's. Josef Hauer (1883–1959) also developed a 12-note system which he propounded in 1919 and he always considered himself, rather than Schoenberg, as the true founder of the system. He later worked out a system of tropes (*i.e.*, half-series of six notes).

To return to Schoenberg, in later works he shows much more freedom and assurance in the use of his system. The wind quintet (1924), the Variations for Orchestra, opus 31 (1927–8), the third (1926), and fourth (1936) string quartets, and the string trio (1946) are modern classics of their kind; they require concentrated listening and a degree of understanding of the unfamiliar style of composition. The set of songs with piano *Das Buch der hängenden Gärten* (opus 15), written in 1908, *Pierrot Lunaire*, opus 21 (1912) and the Four Songs, opus 22 (1913–14) provide a kind of bridge between tonality and atonality that the adventurous mind should cross. The monodrama *Erwartung* (1909) is another fascinating work, but perhaps the unfinished *Moses and Aaron* (1932) is Schoenberg's masterpiece as its production at Covent Garden in 1965 showed. Here, for certain, the composer matched his obvious intellectual capacities with an evident emotional content and managed to combine *Sprechgesang* (speech-song) and singing with a real degree of success.

It is only in recent years that Schoenberg's music has had a real chance to make its mark through the essential prerequisite of frequent performance. If his idiom now seems approachable, and a reasonably natural outcome of late 19th-cent. developments, it is perhaps because other, more recent composers have extended the boundaries of sound much further.

Schoenberg's two most respected disciples were Anton Webern (1883–1945) and Alban Berg (1885–1935). Webern's output is small, reaching only to opus 31, and many of his works are very brief. They are exquisitely precise, and delicate almost to a fault. He was trying to distil the essence of each note and in so doing carried the 12-note system to its most extreme and cerebral limit. His music has often been described as pointillist in the sense that one note is entirely separated from the next, there being little discernible melody. Beyond Webern's music, there is indeed the sound of nothingness, and he was rightly described during his lifetime as the "composer of the *pianissimo espressivo*". In his later works, Webern tended towards a strict, and often ingenious use of form and the Variations for Orchestra of 1940 are a good example of this and of his delicacy of orchestration. Webern's influence has perhaps been greater than the impact of his own music, even though he has had no direct successor.

Berg's music is much more accessible. Like Webern his total output was not large, but nearly all his works are substantial additions to the repertory. He is also the directest link between Mahler and the second Viennese School, as Mahler's music influenced him strongly. He studied with Schoenberg from 1904 to 1910. His music is more intense, more lyrical, and less attenuated in sound than Schoenberg's or Webern's. His humanity and abiding compassion can be heard most strongly in his finest opera *Wozzeck* (1925) and his violin concerto (1935), written as an elegy on the death of Manon Gropius, a beautiful 18-year-old girl. Both works are very carefully designed yet formal considerations are never allowed to submerge feeling, and the note-row is fully integrated into the structure.

Both *Wozzeck* and the unfinished but rewarding

Lulu are concerned with society's outcasts who are treated with great tenderness in both operas. The later work is entirely dodecaphonic, all the opera's episodes being based on a theme associated with Lulu. Between these operas Berg wrote the highly complex Chamber Concerto for piano, violin, and thirteen wind instruments (1925) and the expressive *Lyric Suite* (1926). Among his other works the Seven Early Songs (1908–9) and the concert aria *Der Wein* (1929) are notable.

Stravinsky.

Igor Stravinsky (1882–1971) was another vital figure in 20th-cent. music. If his influence has been in quite another and perhaps less drastic direction than Schoenberg's it is hardly less important. Indeed, future musical historians may consider his achievement the more significant. He has been compared with the painter Picasso in his almost hectic desire to keep up with the times, yet, although he wrote in a number of very different styles over a period of fifty years, every work of his is stamped with his own definitive musical personality. His most revolutionary and seminal work is undoubtedly *The Rite of Spring* (written for the ballet impresario Diaghilev), which caused a furore when it first appeared in 1913, and although it no longer shocks, the rhythmical energy, the fierce angular thematic material, and the sheer virtuosity of the orchestration will always have the power to excite new audiences. Before *The Rite* Stravinsky had written two ballets for Diaghilev—*The Firebird* and *Petrushka*—that are no less filled with vitality and new, albeit not so violent, sounds. During the next thirty years Stravinsky wrote a series of ballet works, gradually becoming more austere and refined in composition. *Apollo* (1928) and *Orpheus* (1947) belong among his most attractive scores.

Stravinsky did not confine himself in stage works to the ballet. *The Nightingale* (1914) is a charming, early opera; *The Soldiers Tale* (1918) is a witty combination of narration, mime, and dance; *Les Noces* (1923) is a concise, original choreographic cantata for soloists and chorus; *Oedipus Rex* (1927) is a dignified version of the Sophocles play, which can be staged or given on the concert platform; either way it is a moving experience. *Perséphone* (1934), a melodrama for reciter, tenor, chorus, and orchestra is an appealling, lucid score. After the war his most important stage work by far was *The Rake's Progress* (1951), with a libretto by W. H. Auden and Chester Kallman. This fascinating opera is deliberately based on 18th-cent. forms and the music itself is neo-classical, always attractive, sometimes haunting.

Stravinsky was no laggard in writing for the concert-platform either. The finest of his orchestral pieces are probably the fervent choral *Symphony of Psalms* (1930), the violin concerto (1931) and the aggressive compact Symphony in Three Movements (1945). Of his chamber music the octet (1923), a duo concertant (1932), and septet (1952) are probably the most important, but no piece, even the dryest and most pedantic, is without redeeming features.

Stravinsky is often thought of as an aloof, detached figure. He has been castigated for his lack of lyrical warmth. But in spite of his own professed desire to drain his music of specific emotion, craftsmanship and originality, often with a strange other-worldly beauty added, are unmistakably there throughout his many scores. Quirky and annoying he may be, dull never.

Busoni and Puccini.

Italian music in the early part of the century was dominated by two very different composers—Ferruccio Busoni (1866–1924) and Giacomo Puccini (1858–1924). Busoni is a difficult figure to place. His austere, intellectual power is never called in question, but he seldom, if ever, succeeded in translating his technical prowess into altogether successful compositions. We can admire the strength, honesty, and often beauty of such works as his huge piano concerto (1903–4), *Fantasia Contrappuntistica* (1912)—for piano solo—and his unfinished opera *Doktor Faust* without ever capitulating to them entirely. None the less, it has to be admitted that those who have studied his music closely have always fallen completely under his spell. In style his music is anti-Romantic and often neo-Classical yet he was an ardent admirer of Liszt and more especially of Liszt's realisation of the possibilities of the pianoforte. Busoni, himself a great pianist, carried on where Liszt had left off in his own piano music, in which form and expression often find their perfect balance. *Doktor Faust* is undoubtedly his most important opera but *Die Brautwahl* (1908–10) and *Turandot* (1917) have many points of interest too.

Puccini's *Turandot*—his last opera—is a much grander version of the same Gozzi fable and the culmination of this great opera composer's work. His achievement is at an almost directly opposite pole to Busoni's. Not for him the severity or intellectuality of his contemporary. He sought and found an almost ideal fusion of straight-forward lyricism and dramatic truth. His music unerringly follows the pathos and passion of the stories he sets and all his characters "live" as human beings. That, and his abundant flow of easy, soaring melody, are the reasons for his immense popular success, unequalled by any other 20th-cent. composer. Whether it is the pathetic Mimi (*La Bohème*—1896) and Cio-Cio-San, (*Madam Butterfly*—1904), the evil Scarpia (*Tosca* —1900), the cunning Schicchi (*Gianni Schicchi*—1918), the ardent Rodolfo (*La Bohème*) and Cavaradossi (*Tosca*), or the ice-cold Turandot (*Turandot*—1926). Puccini's musical characterisation is unfailing. And he backs his *verismo* vocal writing with an orchestral tissue that faithfully reflects the milieu of each opera, for instance, Japanese for *Butterfly*, Chinese for *Turandot*, while never losing his particular brand of Italian warmth. His orchestration is always subtle and luminous.

Other Italian composers who wrote operas in the *versimo* style of Puccini were Leoncavallo (1858–1919), Mascagni (1865–1945), and Giordano (1867–1948). Mascagni's *Cavalleria Rusticana* and Leoncavallo's *Pagliacci* have formed an inseparable bill and a regular part of the repertory in most opera houses.

Prokofiev, Shostakovich, and Rachmaninov.

Sergey Prokofiev (1891–1953) spent part of his creative life in his native Russia, part of it (1918–34) abroad, mostly in Paris. His early music, apart from the popular Classical Symphony (1916–17) tended to be acid and harsh, but on his return to Russia his style, though still frequently satirical, became warmer, more Romantic. The third piano concerto (1917) and the second symphony (1924) are good examples of the former period, the ballets *Romeo and Juliet* (1935) and *Cinderella* (1941–4) and the fifth (1944) and sixth (1946) symphonies of the latter. His music gives the impression of immense rhythmical energy, as in the outer movements of several of his nine piano sonatas, but this fierce drive is often leavened by the soft, wistful lights of his slow movements. His second string quartet (1941), perhaps, presents all the elements of his music in the kindest light.

His strong leaning towards fantasy and mordant parody is felt in his earlier operas *The Love of the Three Oranges* (1921) and *The Fiery Angel* (1922–5). Towards the end of his life much of Prokofiev's music fell into official disfavour.

Dmitri Shostakovich (1906–75) also suffered from attacks on his style. He had to conform to Stalin's requirements for writing music, but he survived and continued to produce music of universal appeal, as, for example, his later string quartets. Like Prokofiev, his music falls into two very distinct styles: one humorous and spiky, the other intense, very personal and often large-scale in its implications. Not all his symphonies reach the expressive depths of numbers one, five, six, eight, ten and fourteen, but they all have rewarding passages, and his violin and cello concertos are of high quality. He also wrote fifteen string quartets, a piano quintet (an attractive piece) and two operas: the satirical *The Nose* (1930) and *Katrina Ismailova* (1934, revised 1959), originally known as "Lady Macbeth of Mtsensk."

Although Sergey Rachmaninov (1873–1943) was born in Russia, he left his home country in 1918, disliking the Soviet régime, and lived mostly in Switzerland and the United States. His music is chiefly notable for its Romanticism, nostalgic melody, nervous energy and, in the piano works, its opportunities for displays of virtuosity. The first three piano concertos, the third symphony, the piano preludes, and the Rhapsody on a theme of Paganini, are his most typical and attractive works, and many of his songs are touching and beautiful. He wrote three operas.

Weill and Hindemith.

Kurt Weill (1900–50) is chiefly known for his sociopolitically pointed operas, such as *Die Dreigroschenoper* (1929), *Mahagonny* (1929), *Der Jasager* (1930) and *Happy End* (1929), all effective works on the stage, and for his particular brand of brittle, yet fundamentally romantic music. His influence on later composers has been considerable.

Paul Hindemith (1895–1963) in his later years wrote in a strictly tonal, often neo-classical idiom, after being one of the most advanced intellectuals of his time. As well as many chamber and orchestral works, he wrote three formidable operas: *Die Harmonie der Welt*, *Cardillac* and *Mathis der Maler*.

Ives and Copland.

Charles Ives (1874–1954) is generally recognised as the first American composer of major stature. Most of his works were composed before about 1920, while he was pursuing a successful career in insurance. Ives' music is noted for its thorough-going electicism and his refusal to be bound by rules and conventions. His work anticipates many 20th century techniques, such as polytonality and polyrhythm, which he seems to have arrived at independently of others. Folk songs, hymn tunes, dance music and the sound of the brass band all appear in his compositions, many of which are evocative of his New England background (*e.g. Three Places in New England*, the *Holidays Symphony*, the *Concord* Sonata). It was not until the 1930s that Ives began to achieve recognition, but his influence on later American composers can hardly be exaggerated.

Aaron Copland (1900–90) was a composer who had absorbed a variety of influences—from his Jewish background, contemporary Europe, American folk music and jazz, Latin American music—while writing music which is instantly recognisable as his own in its clean textures and taut rhythms. Early works such as the Piano Concerto (1927) show the use of jazz styles, while the Piano Variations (1930) combine inventiveness and technical discipline in a tough, concentrated and highly dissonant piece. A move towards a simpler, more immediately appealing idiom is evident in pieces like *El Salón México* (1936), and the ballets *Billy the Kid* (1938), *Rodeo* (1938) and *Appalachian Spring* (1944) and the Third Symphony (1946). These works remain Copland's most popular and frequently performed pieces. A number of works from the 1950s and 1960s experiment with serial techniques, while retaining his individual voice.

Vaughan Williams, Holst and Delius.

The twentieth century revival of music in England owes much to Ralph Vaughan Williams (1872–1958) and Gustav Holst (1874–1934). The English folk song revival, associated with Cecil Sharp, was in full swing during their formative years, and both composers produced arrangements of folk songs as well as assimilating the folk idiom into their own styles. The influence of 16th century polyphony is also strong in Vaughan Williams' music, the most obvious example being the *Fantasia on a Theme by Thomas Tallis* (1909). Vaughan Williams' strongest works (*e.g.* the first, fourth, fifth and sixth sym-

phonies, the ballet *Job*, the choral *Dona Nobis Pacem*) show his characteristic alternation of the forceful and the contemplative.

Holst was a more enigmatic figure. Only his suite *The Planets* and the choral work *The Hymn of Jesus* have established themselves in the regular repertory, but his bold harmonic experiments and the austerity, even mysticism, of his style as heard in the opera *Savitri* and the orchestral piece *Egdon Heath* are perhaps more typical of this meditative, original composer.

Frederick Delius (1862–1934) was the major English composer to fall under the sway of French impressionism, though his English (north country) background, his friendship with Grieg, and the time he spent in America all contributed to the formation of his musical style. He lived in France from 1888 onwards. His most important works are the atmospheric tone-poems for orchestra, such as *Brigg Fair*, the vocal and orchestral *A Mass of Life*, *Sea Drift* and *Appalachia*, and the opera *A Village Romeo and Juliet*.

Walton, Britten and Tippett.

Sir William Walton (1902–83) became known as an *enfant terrible* with the witty and irreverent *Facade* (1923) for speaker and chamber orchestra (with words by Edith Sitwell). The poetic Viola Concerto (1929) shows another side of his musical character. His First Symphony (1934–5) is an arresting, dramatic score and the colourful oratorio *Belshazzar's Feast* (1931) is a landmark in choral music. Walton's rhythms show the influence of jazz and of Stravinsky but he is generally felt to be a quintessentially English composer. An Elgarian element is clear in such occasional pieces as the coronation marches *Crown Imperial* (1937) and *Orb and Sceptre* (1953).

Benjamin Britten (1913–76) did as much as anyone to establish English music on the forefront of the international stage. Much of his music seems to have an immediate appeal to large audiences and certainly his many stage works earned him quite exceptional prestige both at home and abroad. *Peter Grimes* (1945), *Billy Budd* (1951), *Gloriana* (1953), *A Midsummer Night's Dream* (1960) all show his mastery of stage technique and the first two are also moving human documents. On a smaller scale he has achieved as much with his chamber operas—*The Rape of Lucretia* (1946), *Albert Herring* (1947), *The Turn of the Screw* (1954)—and the three Parables for Church Performance—*Curlew River* (1964), *The Burning Fiery Furnace* (1966) and *The Prodigal Son* (1968). His operatic output was crowned by *Death in Venice* (1973). If he had written nothing else, these dramatic works would have marked him out as a composer of outstanding imaginative gifts. In addition to these, however, the choral works culminating in the *War Requiem* (1962), the various song cycles written, like so much else, for his friend Peter Pears, the *Serenade* for tenor, horn and strings, *Nocturne* for tenor and orchestra, the three *Canticles*, and the *Spring Symphony* are further evidence of both his intense emotional commitment and his technical skill. Despite the strong influence of such composers as Purcell, Schubert, Verdi, Mahler and Berg, his style is entirely his own; his musical personality combines, it has been said, "a deep nostalgia for the innocence of childhood, a mercurial sense of humour and a passionate sympathy with the victims of prejudice and misunderstanding."

This last quality is also evident in the emotional make up of Sir Michael Tippett (b. 1905), as expressed in such works as the oratorio *A Child of our Time* (1941) one of his earliest successes, which shows both his compassion and his ability to write on a large scale. This and the Concerto for Double String Orchestra (1939) remain his most popular works. Tippett has been open to a wide range of influences, both musical (from English Madrigals, Monteverdi and Beethoven to Negro spirituals and jazz) and non-musical (*e.g.* the ideas of Jung). His early style—often richly lyrical and affirmative of the continued power of tonality—reached its culmination in his allegorical opera *The Midsummer Marriage* (1952), the Piano Concerto (1955) and the Second Symphony (1957). A new style, spare and incisive, with structure arising from the juxtaposition of contrasting ideas rather than from a process of development, is evident in his second opera, *King Priam* (1961) and its offshoots, the Second Piano Sonata (1962) and the Concerto for Orchestra (1963). The mystical, ecstatic *The Vision of St. Augustine* (1965), a complex, difficult but rewarding work, is one of his finest from this period. The opera *The Knot Garden* (1970) exemplifies again Tippett's concern with human relationships and the need for self-knowledge. Tippett has never ceased to explore and experiment; his inspiration now seems as fresh as ever. His most recent works, *The Mask of Time*— a huge choral piece—and the Fourth Piano Sonata (1984) have something of the quality of summarising statements about the musical and non-musical concerns of a lifetime.

Olivier Messiaen and Elliott Carter.

Amongst the many schools and groups of composers in the twentieth century, two major figures stand apart, Olivier Messiaen and Elliott Carter. Both born in 1908, each is an individualist of great influence and stature who has pursued his own path to a personal style of composition.

A devout Catholic, Messiaen viewed himself as a theological composer and music as a medium for a profound communication, celebration and contemplation of the love and mystery of God. Few of his works are liturgical but most have religious and doctrinal themes, for example *La Nativité du Seigneur* (1935) for organ and *Vingt Regards sur l'Enfant-Jésus* (1944) for piano. Messiaen was inspired to compose by hearing the music of Debussy. This influence can be particularly seen in Messiaen's flexible rhythms, sensitive scoring and use of timbre. Indeed, he identifies sounds with colours and views composition as painting. The other major early influence was that of the East, particularly Indian music. Messiaen often uses Hindu rhythmic patterns alongside Greek poetic metres, plainsong and other medieval techniques and Stravinskian devices. The sum of these can be seen in *Quatuor pour la fin du temps* for violin, clarinet, cello and piano which he composed in a prisoner of war camp in 1940. A very complex work, it reflects the primacy Messiaen gives to rhythmic control. Its overwhelming impression however is of lush and exotic sounds and textures. Similarly, the vibrant colours and rhythms of the massive *Turangalila-symphonie* (1946–8) for orchestra effectively realise the ideas of life and vitality embodied in the Sanskrit title.

After *Turangalila*, Messiaen adopted a less luxurious style. It was works such as the *Livre d'orgue* (1951) which profoundly influenced many young composers of post-war years in the use of systematic transformations of rhythm and dynamics using a system of modes in a quasi-serial fashion. For Messiaen it is the seven harmonic modes, inspired by Debussy, Liszt and the Russian "Five", which are perhaps more important because they give his music its unique sound quality.

The 1950s saw the integration of the final element crucial to Messiaen's music; birdsong. A keen ornithologist, he collected and accurately notated the songs of many birds for incorporation into compositions. *Catalogue d'oiseaux* (1951–8) is a collection of thirteen piano pieces featuring French bird songs. For Messiaen birdsong represented, "the true lost face of music", and it provided a source of inspiration for many of his major post-war works. Since 1960, his style has become simpler and less complex to the ear. To encounter the many elements of his music one can do little better than to listen to *La Transfiguration de Notre Seigneur Jésus-Christ* (1963–9) for one hundred voices, seven instrumental soloists and a large orchestra. Its subject is the mystery of God, his relationship with man and nature as a revelation of God. Messiaen draws upon all his compositional techniques in a spellbinding and overwhelming work that is a profound affirmation of faith. It is fitting that his most recent work is a vast opera (1973–83), *St François d'Assise* about the saint who is best known for his great spirituality and for gaining inspiration and insight from nature.

Carter's reputation is based on a small number of works. He has concentrated on problems of language and structure in a dramatic context unlike Messiaen's preoccupations with colour and the communication of religious truths. Carter's early works reflect a variety of influences: Stravinsky, Hindemith and the English Virginalists. He con-

sciously aimed at a simple, lyrical, accessible style, for example, in the ballet, *Pocahontas* (1938–9) and *Holiday Overture* (1944). During those war years however there occurred a change of direction. The Piano Sonata (1945–6) saw the start of a compositional style where instruments were endowed with personalities who act as protagonists in a drama. His ideas crystallised in the *String Quartet No. 1* (1950–1) after an absorbing study of the music of Ives, Cowell and African and Oriental music. It led to the use of very complex rhythmic relationships and a very tightly-knit pitch structure that could be traced back to a simple and small source, in this case a four-note chord. After this Carter refined his portrayal of his dramatis personae such that in *String Quartet No. 2* (1959) his players each have a separate personality defined by melodic material, gestures and rhythms. They converse, argue and enact that work's dramatic programme. *String Quartet No. 3* (1971) marked a shift in approach. Although the players were still "personalities", the work relied heavily on the use of contrast between strict and flexible writing between members of two duos. The *Symphony of Three Orchestras* (1975–7) and *Triple Duo* (1983) continue to explore the possibilities of simultaneous presentation of independent and sometimes unrelated processes. Carter's music makes rewarding, though not always easy, listening.

MUSIC SINCE 1945—THE AVANT GARDE

Serialism.

The early post-war years saw a renewed interest in "twelve-note techniques" otherwise known as "serialism". Composers like Stravinsky and Dallapiccola (1904–75), who had shunned serialism in earlier years, began to experiment and absorb serial techniques into their musical style. Stravinsky, for example, in works such as *Threni* (1957–8) explored ideas of varied repetition both of small ideas and large sections, in a serial context. A clear example to listen to is the fifteen-minute *Requiem Canticles* (1964–6). During the progression from its Prelude to Postlude, one can hear the piece subtly develop. The succeeding movements, and phrases within movements, slightly alter that which has gone before, evolving into something fresh.

This period also saw the emergence of a new generation of composers, keen to jettison the past and begin anew. Serialism was a favoured tool, its revival stemming from Paris, where Webern's pupil René Leibowitz was teaching, and the USA where Schoenberg had fled from Nazi Germany. The American Milton Babbitt (b. 1916) was much concerned with codifying serial techniques. His younger European contemporaries Pierre Boulez (b. 1925) and Karlheinz Stockhausen (b. 1928) sought to increase the number of musical elements that could be controlled by a predetermined method. They sought to emulate the rigorous methods of Webern, hoping to control not only pitch, but also rhythm, timbre and intensity of attack. In doing so they hoped to create an impersonal, emotionally restrained music.

Attention went first to controlling rhythm. Forerunners of this control can be seen in movement three of Berg's *Lyric Suite* and in Webern's Op.30 Variations. However, the catalyst came from Messiaen. He inspired his pupil Boulez to explore the possibilities of rhythmic and dynamic serialism in his Second Piano Sonata (1951). The performance of Messiaen's *Modes de valeurs et d'intensités* (1949) at the Darmstadt Summer School proved decisive for Stockhausen. Although not serial, the piece established scales of pitch, length of note (duration), loudness and attack. The 1950s were to see this potential for serialism taken to extremes. Boulez reached "total serialism" in *Structures 1a* for piano. However, having attained it he soon became frustrated with its restrictions. Some of the more fantastic and exotic elements of earlier works were allowed to reappear. *Le Marteau sans Maître* (1952–4) for mezzo-soprano and six instruments is a masterly setting of three surreal poems by René Char, with instrumental interludes. For the listener it is the contrasts of timbres, of flexible and regular pulsing rhythms, of sound and silence that are spellbinding. The virtuosic serial workings are hidden.

Stockhausen reached total serialism in *Kreuzspiel*

(1951) for oboe, bass clarinet, piano and percussion. Each note's pitch, length, dynamic and timbre are part of a predetermined plan. All are concerned with "Kreuzspiel" or "crossplay". Its various processes reverse or change over throughout so that at the end we have returned full circle. The effect is of clear-cut lines where each note is weighted. However, despite the intention of the composer, the effect is not unemotional, especially with the insistent throbbing of the percussion, and the piece builds to a series of climaxes before dying away. *Punkte* (points) (1952) for orchestra finds each note being treated as an isolated point of sound. It illustrates some of the problems of total serialism; often very difficult to play, it can be monotonous or lack focal points, appearing to be random rather than rigorously controlled. Stockhausen therefore transferred his attention to using not points but bursts of sound and moved towards possibly his most significant contribution to music, "moment form". There, different aspects of a note, chord or sound are suspended in eternity for contemplation and re-examination. Works became longer, slower and had a greater emphasis on colour and the effects of spatial separation, both between sounds and between their sources. *Carré* (1959–60) uses four orchestras between which chords move and evolve. Stockhausen wrote "you can confidently stop listening for a moment . . . each moment can stand on its own and at the same time is related to all the other moments". Although unifying principles in pitch content *etc.* might be present, "strict" serialism had been gently left behind, until *Mantra* (1970). This work for two pianos, percussion and two electronic ring modulators is totally based on a thirteen-note row, the mantra, with a different duration, mode of attack and dynamic for each note. These permeate the whole piece. For example, each of the thirteen sections is dominated by one of the thirteen types of attack. The work's climax is the coda where the 156 versions of the mantra used are rushed through in a few minutes. The work is important, not only as marking a return to serialism and notated music, but also in its rediscovery of melody—something unthinkable twenty years earlier.

Mathematics and Music.

The younger generation of composers have often used mathematical systems for composing which are not necessarily serial. A good example is Sir Peter Maxwell Davies (b. 1934). The use of durational ratios, ciphers and magic squares features prominently in his work, partly reflecting his interest in medieval music. A magic square is a number square where the sum of any line is the same. This becomes the basis for a composition by assigning notes to the numbers—a technique that Davies has often used since the mid-1970s. For example, in *Ave Maris Stella* (1975), each of the nine movements uses a different transformation of the square and follows a characteristic route through the square. The work is governed by the square at all levels: it even determines the precise length of each movement. Far from being a mathematical exercise however the piece shows masterly control which is particularly revealed in its drama and the beauty of its colours.

Mathematical processes of a different type have been taken up by the Greek, Xenakis (b. 1922), possibly because of his original training as an engineer and architect in France. His rejection of serialism led to the use of "stochastic" principles, derived from the mathematical laws governing probability. He also applied mathematical set theory to composition. The use of these ideas however is not audible. In *Nomos Alpha* (1965) for solo cello, for example, it is the use of contrasts, of texture, dynamic, register and timbre which give shape and form for the listener.

Chance.

Although for many serialism represented the way of reviving music after the excesses of romanticism, some looked beyond Europe to the East. John Cage (b. 1912) found inspiration there, studying Zen Buddhism in the early 1950s. By using the "chance operations" of the Chinese *I Ching* (Book of Changes) Cage brought a new radical approach to Western music. *Music of Changes* (1951) for piano is fully notated but its content is the result of operations where chance has a role. The use of "indeterminacy" or "chance" gave the performer an active role in determining the course of a piece. This might come about by providing "graphic notation"—an artist's impression of what the piece might sound like. Thus Earle Brown's *December 1952* is a visual design to be realised on any instrument as the performer sees fit. Alternatively the composer could give the performer control over the order of sections or their content. *Twenty-five pages* (1953) by Brown is for one to twenty-five pianos. Each person has twenty-five pages and may arrange them in any order before commencing. Thus music was no longer to be necessarily a progression of fixed and immutable steps to an endpoint. This and other traditional assumptions about music were challenged in Cage's most well-known outrage, *4′ 33″*.The performer does not play any notes at all. The music consists of the sounds in the environment that occur during a period of four minutes and thirty-three seconds.

In 1957, both Stockhausen and Boulez took to chance having realised that total control was an impossibility. The more rigorous the control of musical elements, the more impossible it became to realise it accurately. Stockhausen's first experiment with chance techniques was Piano Piece XI which is a single page with nineteen fragments of music. They may be played in any order but the tempo, dynamic and attack must be that shown at the end of the previous fragment. After one fragment has been played three times the work ends. Boulez's Third Piano Sonata was less free. There the choices are in the nature of varying routes through the piece. Boulez saw his music as using a form of control that is not random but akin to throwing a dice. Limited choices in the combination of instruments and their choice of lines form the basis of *Pli selon pli* (1957–65) for soprano and orchestra, offering Boulez a way "to fix the infinite".

For Stockhausen, chance has been a way to encourage performer participation and the development of "intuitive music-making". In *Prozession* (1967) for example, performers react to what is going on guided by plus or minus signs in the score which denote whether the response should be positive or negative. It has worked well in combination with the ideas behind moment form. *Stimmung* (1968) is a 45 minute meditation on one chord whose parts and overtones emerge and merge into the whole, punctuated by erotic poems, magic numbers and words which are delivered in response to chance operations. The culmination of these ideas may be seen in *Aus den Sieben Tagen* (1968) where the score for each of the seven movements is a short poem.

Use of indeterminacy does not necessarily have to be so extreme. For György Ligeti (b. 1923) and Witold Lutoslawski (1913–93) use of controlled chance techniques has provided a way for composing atonal music without embracing serialism. During 1955–60 Lutoslawski evolved a harmonic language which used twelve-note chords for expression and colour. In 1960 he heard a performance of Cage's Piano Concerto and realised that he could use chance techniques to add a rhythmic freedom and new types of texture to his music. The exact combination of sounds at any given moment is often a matter of chance but the overall effect is planned. Textures are created by the constant repetition of small melodic ideas and simple rhythms in different parts, creating a kaleidoscope of sound, and by lines of counterpoint set off against each other, often sliding from one note to another blurring the transition between chords. The music of Lutoslawski is a fine example of the use of chance as a tool in compositions which still have strong links to tradition. The direction and drama of works such as *Mi-Parti* (1976) and his Third Symphony (1983) are firmly in the composer's hands, relying heavily on his skilful sense of harmonic movement, use of colour and proportion. Only small rhythmic details are left to chance.

Ligeti has also made use of textures created by chance operations. The contrast of such sections with fixed areas has been a way of creating large structures as in his *Requiem* (1963–5). The idea of clocks and clouds underlies several of his works of the late 1960s and 1970s: in the Double Concerto for flute, harp and orchestra (1972) we hear the transition from dense clusters or clouds of notes to regular clock-like single notes. Chance techniques have been an important element in creating these.

Electronic Music.

An important part of the post-war struggle with musical language has been the development of electronic means to generate, manipulate and record sounds. Its pioneer was the Frenchman Edgard Varèse (1883–1965). Before the war he had been an independent and radical composer much concerned with the exploration of new sounds. This had led to an emphasis on the exploitation of percussion effects in works such as *Intégrales* (1924–5) and *Ionisation* (1933). The following work *Ecuatorial* (1934) explored further, using primitive electrically generated sounds produced by two Ondes Martenot. However the catalyst for further development was the invention of the tape recorder which provided an easy means to store sounds that could then be rearranged by cutting and rejoining the tape in different ways. Varèse explored these possibilities in *Déserts* (1949–54) which alternated recorded and instrumental sounds in an atmospheric work which really seems to conjure up the aridity and emptiness of the desert. Recorded sound offered the possibility of creating illusions of aural space by technical manipulation and by judicious positioning and control of loudspeakers. This is a fundamental part of Varèse's great masterpiece, *Poème Electronique* (1958) which used soprano, chorus, bells, organs and artificial sounds. Its spatial effects were achieved by using many loudspeakers positioned around a specially designed pavilion at the 1958 Brussels Exhibition.

Generally, electronic music-making required a studio and the 1950s saw the setting up of important studios in Paris and Cologne. In Paris Pierre Schaeffer (b. 1910) pioneered "musique concrète" which used altered and rearranged natural sounds, for example, the sound of a steam train, to create a musical piece. At Cologne where Stockhausen worked, the emphasis was on creating new synthetic sounds.

Electronic music had the potential to generate complex, accurate serial structures through precise electronic operations. Boulez's studies in this however did not satisfy him and he neglected the medium until 1970 when he became Director of IRCAM (*Institut de Recherche et de Coordination Acoustique/Musique*). Stockhausen however found electronic music an ideal medium to create a musical unity far beyond that of serialism; pitch, timbre, rhythm and form could be seen as different aspects of the same thing—vibration. He did not restrict himself to pure synthetic sounds and in 1955–6 created perhaps his most well-known electronic work, *Gesang der Jünglinge*. This combines synthetic sounds with a recorded boy's voice to portray the three boys in the fiery furnace from the Book of Daniel.

With *Kontakte* (1958–60) for piano, percussion and tape, Stockhausen began an exploration of the interplay between live performers and electronic sound which still preoccupies him today. The work explores "contact" between real and artificial sounds and between the elements of music. Compared to pure electronic music, the presence of the live performers made it easier to listen to, providing a visual focus and making each performance unique. The next step was to create "live" electronic music where performers created their electronic sounds on stage. Cage had already begun this in 1960 with *Cartridge Music*. Unlike Stockhausen's first attempt, *Mikrophonie I* (1964–5), *Cartridge Music* gives much freedom to the performer in creating the electronic effects. A desire to create a world music led to one of the most vast electronic works to date, *Hymnen* (1966–7), a two-hour work for quadraphonic tape or tapes, soloists and optional symphony orchestra. Stockhausen constructed it out of national anthems from all over the world. Inspired by the occult *Urantian Book*, he became more ambitious still, seeking a galactic music. *Sirius* (1977) for four soloists and electronic music deals with the arrival on earth of four visitors from the star Sirius.

In America, developments have followed a different course. There, the use of computer synthesised sounds has been the main interest because of the computer's superior control and accuracy. It has allowed the continuation of abstract composition where complicated operations are achieved simply and effectively. Computer synthesis can also be applied to existing material. For example, *Chronometer* (1971) by Harrison Birtwistle (b. 1934) (an English composer working at that time in New York) is based on clock sounds.

Minimalism.

The transformation of existing material on tape has been a crucial part of an American movement dating from the 1960s known as 'Minimalism'. Its chief exponents are Steve Reich (b. 1936), Philip Glass (b. 1937), Terry Riley (b. 1935) and La Monte Young (b. 1935). Minimal music uses material which is limited in pitch, rhythm and timbres; the elements are subjected to simple transformations relying heavily on repetition. Of great importance are the subtle evolution from one idea to another as repetitions are modified, and the use of "phasing" techniques. Phasing is the effect of altering the rate of repetition between parts repeating the same material so that it is no longer synchronised. The effect of works such as *Drumming* (1971) by Reich may appear long and non-dramatic. However, the listener is not expected to concentrate all the time but to become aware of a piece's various elements and processes. The music's patterns will change as the listener's attention shifts from one aspect to another. As in moment form, minimalist works owe much to Indian concepts of time as a circular rather than linear phenomenon. In recent years, the minimalists have developed their style and there are greater differences between the four. Philip Glass has written four operas, *Einstein on the Beach* (1975), *Satyagraha* (1980), *Akhnaten* (1983) and *The Making of the Representative for Planet 8* (1986) while recent works by Reich such as *Desert Music* (1983) are less monochrome, exploiting bright sound colours and far from minimal forces.

Music Theatre.

During the early post-war years many composers were grappling with the tools of composition. Only more "traditional" writers such as Britten, Tippett and Hans Werner Henze (b. 1926) were engaged in writing opera. By 1970 however, most composers were including elements of theatre in their work even if they were not necessarily engaged in writing full-scale operas.

One of the major composers of "traditional" opera has been Henze. His first three operas draw heavily on the past. For example, *Boulevard Solitude* (1952) updates the story of Manon, a nineteenth-century favourite. After moving to Italy in 1953, Henze's stance appeared more traditional still as lyrical elements became more dominant in contrast to the abstract athematic style of contemporaries such as Stockhausen. Increasingly Henze's operas began to reflect his preoccupation with socialism. The *Bassarids* (1966), for example, examines through a mythological guise the precipitation of social upheaval and disruption. The oratorio *Das Floss der "Medusa"* (1968) is dedicated to Che Guevara and provoked such struggles between police and left-wing students at its premiere that Henze went to Cuba for a year. There he was inspired to write *El Cimarrón* (1969–70), a vocal monologue portraying a Cuban runaway slave accompanied by flute, guitar and percussion. For a while, Henze continued to reject the traditional opera format because of its bourgeois overtones, preferring a more intimate, chamber style. But in 1976 Henze returned to opera with *We come to the River*. It reflected a renewal of Italianate lyricism, the exploitation of opera's full potential and a less overt political message.

Luigi Nono (b. 1924) also exploited theatre for political ends, beginning with *Intolleranza* (1960). However he found greater resource than Henze in contemporary developments, taking full advantage of the opportunities offered by electronics. *Contrappunto dialettico della mente* (1967–8) includes the sounds of political demonstrations. Like Henze, Nono also returned to the opera house after a long break from large-scale opera with *Al gran sole carico d'amore* (1972–4), which consolidated the techniques he had developed in the previous decade.

"Theatre" became a dominant characteristic in the works of Luciano Berio (b. 1925). One of his most famous works is *Circles* (1960) for female voice, harp and percussion. The virtuosic technique used there and in other works was inspired by the phenomenal vocal elasticity of his then wife, Cathy Berberian. 'Circles' are depicted at many different levels in the work's structure and content. More importantly, these are underlined by the singer moving about the stage during the performance. Berio's next few works became overtly political, culminating in *Laborintus II* (1965) which was intended as an attack on capitalism via a musical collage and extracts from Dante's *Inferno*. Many of Berio's larger scale works since *Laborintus II* have been theatrical in their virtuosity and instrumental technique. For example, *Sequenza IV* (1965) demands a pianist with very agile feet. This type of dramatic gesture is much seen in Stockhausen's work, particularly those written for his own music ensemble, for example, *Solo* (1966). Since *Alphabet für Liege* (1972) his work has become increasingly theatrical and from 1978, Stockhausen has been working on an opera project *Licht*. Twenty years earlier, such a project would have been unthinkable.

The small-scale synthesis of text, music and gesture characteristic of Berio has greatly influenced British work in music theatre, notably the work of Sir Peter Maxwell Davies and Sir Harrison Birtwistle. Davies' work is very powerful particularly through its use of parody and wild use of outrageous gesture. *Vesalii Icones* (1969) uses a naked male dancer portraying parts of the Stations of the Cross and scenes from the anatomy text by Vesalius. It is a good example of parody, particularly of what Davies views as nineteenth-century grossness—it includes a vile distortion of a Victorian hymn tune which turns into a foxtrot, both played on a honky-tonk piano. Many of his works feature a single vocal soloist, with instrumental back up, who plays the part of a crazed, obsessive individual. For example, *Eight Songs for a Mad King* (1969) features the instrumentalists in giant bird cages who must suffer the mad ravings of George III played by the singer.

Davies has written two full-scale operas to date, *Taverner* (1962–8) and *The Martyrdom of St. Magnus* (1976) and is currently working on a third, *Resurrection*. Taverner deals with two fundamental preoccupations of Davies—the nature of faith and betrayal—and uses both musical and dramatic parody to convey its message. *St. Magnus* was written after Davies moved to Orkney. It reflects a change in style, uses only a small orchestra and is for production "in the round".

Birtwistle's first major dramatic work was a chamber opera, *Punch and Judy* (1966) which uses grotesque and violent gestures. However, while Davies' roots may lie with early Schoenberg, Birtwistle has found inspiration in the clear-cut lines and ritualism of Stravinsky. Possibly his most significant work to date is *The Mask of Orpheus* (1973–5 and 1981–3). This deals with Birtwistle's central dramatic concern, the conflicts between the individual ego and the collective unconscious. An important aspect of the work is the use of electronics, developed at IRCAM to create atmospheric "auras", for example, "cloud" music, and six mime interludes. Crucially, Apollo gives utterance to his commands through electronic fragments which vary in length from a second to almost a minute.

The Contemporary Music Scene.

While earlier sections have already covered part of the 1980s, little mention has been made of some younger composers. It is difficult to stand back from the music of the present, but here is a brief survey of some British composers working now who deserve attention.

Brian Ferneyhough (b. 1940) is continuing to expand the chamber music repertoire using traditional structures as a framework for music in which micro-tones play an increasingly important part. He is currently working on a seven-part cycle of chamber works of which three are complete; *Superscripto* for solo piccolo (1981), *Carceri d'Invenzione I* (1982) and *Carceri d'Invenzione II* (1985) for chamber orchestra (II with solo flute). Robin Holloway (b. 1943) has also been active in composing smaller scale works, often lyrical, of which recent examples are his *Viola Concerto* (1985) and the bleak *Ballad* for harp and chamber orchestra (1985). Nigel Osborne (b. 1948) has used electronic and non-Western music in his work, gravitating recently towards vocal works. 1986 saw the premiere of his theatre piece, *Hells Angels*. Other recent operas are *Where the Wild Things Are* (1984) and *Higglety, Pigglety Pop!* (1985) by Oliver Knussen (b. 1952) which attracted acclaim for a young composer already noted for his symphonies, vocal and chamber work. Tim Souster (b. 1943) has been active in composing and promoting electronic music of all types, some influenced by rock music. A recent example is his *Quartet with Tape* (1985). Meanwhile choral music is flourishing with new works by Paul Patterson (b. 1947) which often involve new types of notation and vocal technique, and several ritualistic works by John Tavener (b. 1948), inspired by his Eastern Orthodox faith. For example *Doxa* (1982) sets a single word from the Eastern liturgy. A meteoric rise to fame has been achieved by George Benjamin (b. 1960) starting with *Ringed by the Flat Horizon* (1980) written while still at Cambridge.

The contemporary scene is varied, exciting and constantly changing. It is well worth exploring both for itself and because it speaks to us as the music of our time.

II. GLOSSARY OF MUSICAL TERMS

A. Note of scale, commonly used for tuning instruments.

Absolute Music. Music without any literary descriptive or other kind of reference.

A Capella. Literally "in the church style." Unaccompanied.

Accelerando. Quickening of the pace.

Accidental. The sign which alters the pitch of a note; ♯ (sharp) raises and a ♭ (flat) lowers note by one semitone, ✕ (double sharp) and ♭♭ (double flat) alter by two semitones.

Accompaniment. Instrumental or piano part forming background to a solo voice or instrument that has the melody.

Ad lib. (L. *ad libitum*). Direction on music that strict time need not be observed.

Adagio. A slow movement or piece.

Aeolian mode. One of the scales in mediaeval music, represented by the white keys of the piano from A to A.

Air. A simple tune for voice or instrument.

Alberti Bass. Characteristic 18th century keyboard figuration derived by splitting chord(s) of an accompanying part. Tradition credits Alberti as its inventor.

Allegretto. Not quite so fast as *Allegro.*

Allegro. Fast, but not too fast.

Alto. An unusually high type of male voice; also the vocal part sung by women and boys with a low range.

Ambrosian Chant. Plainsong introduced into church music by St. Ambrose, bishop of Milan (d. 397), and differing from Gregorian chant.

Andante. At a walking pace, not so slow as *Adagio* nor as fast as *Allegretto.*

Animato. Lively.

Answer. Entry in a fugue or invention which imitates or "answers" the theme at a different pitch.

Anthem. Composition for use in church during a service by a choir with or without soloists.

Antiphonal. Using groups of instruments or singers placed apart.

Appoggiatura. An ornament consisting of a short note just above or below a note forming part of a chord.

Arabesque. Usually a short piece, highly decorated.

Arco. Direction for string instruments to play with bow.

Aria. Vocal solo, usually in opera or oratorio, often in three sections with the third part being a repeat of the first. An *Arietta* is a shorter, lighter kind of aria.

Arioso. In the style of an aria; halfway between aria and recitative.

Arpeggio. Notes of a chord played in a broken, spread-out manner, as on a harp.

Ars antiqua. The old mediaeval music, based on organum and plainsong, before the introduction of *Ars nova* in 14th cent.

Ars Nova. New style of composition in 14th century France and Italy. It has greater variety in rhythm and independence in part-writing.

Atonal. Not in any key; hence *Atonality.*

Aubade. Morning song.

Augmentation. The enlargement of a melody by lengthening the musical value of its notes.

Ayre. Old spelling of *air.*

B. Note of scale, represented in Germany by *H.*

Bagatelle. A short, generally light piece of music. Beethoven wrote 26 Bagatelles.

Ballad. Either a narrative song or an 18th-cent. drawing-room song.

Ballade. A substantial and dramatic work, often for piano. Notable examples are by Chopin and Brahms.

Ballet. Stage entertainment requiring intrumental accompaniment; originated at French court in 16th and 17th cent.

Bar. A metrical division of music; the perpendicular line in musical notation to indicate this.

Barcarolle. A boating-song, in particular one associated with Venetian gondoliers.

Baritone. A male voice, between tenor and bass.

Baroque. A term applied, loosely, to music written in the 17th and 18th cent., roughly corresponding to baroque in architecture.

Bass. The lowest male voice; lowest part of a composition.

Bass Drum. Largest of the drum family, placed upright and struck on the side.

Bassoon. The lowest of the woodwind instruments, uses double reed.

Beat. Music's rhythmic pulse.

Bel canto. Literally "beautiful singing"—in the old Italian style with pure tone and exact phrasing.

Berceuse. Cradle song.

Binary. A piece in two sections is said to be binary in form. The balance is obtained by a second phrase (or section) answering the first.

Bitonality. Use of two keys at once.

Bow. Stick with horsehair stretched across it for playing string instruments.

Brass. Used as a collective noun for all brass or metal instruments.

Breve. Note, rarely used nowadays, with time value of two semibreves.

Bridge. Wood support over which strings are stretched on a violin, cello, guitar, etc.

Buffo(a). Comic, as in *buffo bass* or *opera buffa.*

C. Note of scale.

Cabaletta. Final, quick section of an aria or duet.

Cadence. A closing phrase of a composition or a passage, coming to rest on tonic (key note).

Cadenza. Solo vocal or instrumental passage, either written or improvised, giving soloist chance to display technical skill to audience.

Calando. Becoming quieter and slower.

Canon. A piece or section of music resulting from one line of music being repeated imitatively in the other parts which enter in succession.

Cantabile. Song-like, therefore flowing and expressive.

Cantata. Vocal work for chorus and/or choir.

Cantilena. Sustained, smooth melodic line.

Cantus firmus. Literally "fixed song." Basic melody from 14th to 17th cent., around which other voices wove contrapuntal parts.

Canzonet. Light songs written in England *c.* 1600.

Carillon. A set of bells in tower of church, played from a keyboard below.

Carol. Christmas song.

Castrato. Artificially-created male soprano and alto, fashionable in 17th and 18th cent. (The castration of vocally gifted boys prevailed in Italy until the 19th cent.)

Catch. A part-song like a round, in vogue in England from 16th to 19th cent.

Cavatina. An operatic song in one section, or a slow song-like instrumental movement.

Celesta. Keyboard instrument with metal bars struck by hammers.

Cello. Four-stringed instrument, played with bow, with a bass range. Comes between viola and double bass in string family.

Cembalo. Originally the Italian name for the dulcimer, but sometimes applied to the harpsichord.

Chaconne. Vocal or instrumental piece with unvaried bass.

Chamber Music. Music originally intended to be played in a room for three or more players.

Chanson. Type of part-song current in France from 14th to 16th cent.

Chant. Singing of psalms, masses, etc., in plainsong to Latin words in church.

Choir. Body of singers, used either in church or at concerts.

Chorales. German hymn tunes, often made use of by Bach.

Chord. Any combination of notes heard together. *See also* Triad.

Chording. Spacing of intervals in a chord.

Chorus. Substantial body of singers, usually singing in four parts.

Chromatic. Using a scale of nothing but semitones.

Clarinet. Woodwind instrument with single reed in use since mid-18th cent.

Clavichord. Keyboard instrument having strings struck by metal tangents, much in use during 17th and 18th cent. as solo instrument.

Clavier. Used in German (*Klavier*) for piano, in England for any stringed keyboard instrument.

Clef. Sign in stave that fixes place of each note.

Coda. Closing section of movement in Sonata form.

Coloratura. Term to denote florid singing.

Common chord. See Triad.

Common Time. Four crotchets to the bar, 4/4 time.

Compass. Range of notes covered by voice or instruments.

Composition. Piece of music, originated by a composer's own imagination; act of writing such a piece.

Compound Time. Metre where beats are subdivided into threes rather than twos.

Con Brio. With dash.

Concert. Public performance of any music.

Concertato. Writing for several solo instruments to be played together.

Concerto. Work for one or more solo instruments and orchestra.

Concerto grosso. Orchestral work common in 17th and 18th cent. with prominent parts for small groups of instruments.

Concord. Opposite of discord, *i.e.*, notes that when sounded together satisfy the ear. (Conventional term in that its application varies according to the age in which one lives.)

Conduct. To direct a concert with a baton.

Consecutive. Progression of harmonic intervals of like kind.

Consonance. Like Concord.

Continuo. Bass line in 17th and 18th century music. Played by a bass instrument and keyboard, the latter improvising on the indicated harmonies.

Contralto. A woman's voice with a low range.

Counterpoint. Simultaneous combination of two or more melodies to create a satisfying musical texture. Where one melody is added to another, one is called the other's counterpoint. The adjective of counterpoint is contrapuntal.

Counter-tenor. Another name for male alto.

Courante. A dance in triple time.

Crescendo. Getting louder.

Crook. Detachable section of tubing on brass instruments that change the tuning.

Crotchet. Note that equals two quavers in time value.

Cycle. Set of works, especially songs, intended to be sung as group.

Cyclic form. Form of work in two or more movements in which the same musical themes recur.

Cymbal. Percussion instrument; two plates struck against each other.

D. Note of scale.

Da Capo (abbr. D.C.). A *Da Capo* aria is one in which the whole first section is repeated after a contrasting middle section.

Descant. Additional part (sometimes improvised) sung against a melody.

Development. Working-out section of movement in sonata form. *See* Sonata.

Diatonic. Opposite of chromatic; using proper notes of a major or minor scale.

Diminished. Lessened version of perfect interval, e.g., semitone less than a perfect fifth is a diminished fifth.

Diminuendo. Lessening.

Diminution. Reducing a phrase of melody by shortening time value of notes.

Discord. Opposite of concord, *i.e.*, notes that sounded together produce a clash of harmonies.

Dissonance. Like discord.

Divertimento. A piece, usually orchestral, in several movements; like a suite.

Dodecaphonic. Pertaining to 12-note method of composition.

Dominant. Fifth note of major or minor scale above tonic (key) note.

Dorian Mode. One of the scales in mediaeval music, represented by the white keys on the piano from D to D.

Dot. Placed over note indicates staccato; placed after note indicates time value to be increased by half.

Double bar. Two upright lines marking the end of a composition or a section of it.

Double bass. Largest and lowest instrument of violin family; played with bow.

Drone bass. Unvarying sustained bass, similar to the permanent bass note of a bagpipe.

Drum. Variety of percussion instruments on which sound is produced by hitting a skin stretched tightly over a hollow cylinder or hemisphere.

Duet. Combination of two performers; composition for such a combination.

Duple Time. Metre in which there are two beats to a bar.

Dynamics. Gradations of loudness or softness in music.

E. Note of scale.

Electronic. Term used to describe use of electronic sounds in music.

Encore. Request from audience for repeat of work, or extra item in a programme.

English horn (*Cor anglais*). Woodwind instrument with double reed of oboe family.

Enharmonic. Refers to use of different letter names for the same note, *e.g.* F and E♯. Often exploited to achieve modulation between distantly related keys.

Ensemble. Teamwork in performance; item in opera for several singers with or without chorus; a group of performers of no fixed number.

Episode. Section in composition usually divorced from main argument.

Exposition. Setting out of thematic material in a sonata-form composition.

Expression marks. Indication by composer of how he wants his music performed.

F. Note of scale.

False relation. A clash of harmony produced when two notes, such as A natural and A flat, are played simultaneously or immediately following one another.

Falsetto. The kind of singing by male voices above normal register and sounding like an unbroken voice.

Fanfare. Flourish of trumpets.

Fantasy. A piece suggesting free play of composer's imagination, or a piece based on known tunes (folk, operatic, etc.).

Fermata. Pause indicated by sign ⌒ prolonging note beyond its normal length.

Fifth. Interval taking five steps in the scale. A perfect fifth (say, C to G) includes three whole tones and a semitone; a diminished fifth is a semitone less, an augmented fifth a semitone more.

Figure. A short phrase, especially one that is repeated.

Fingering. Use of fingers to play instrument, or the indication above notes to show what fingers should be used.

Flat. Term indicating a lowering of pitch by a semitone, or to describe a performer playing under the note.

Florid. Term used to describe decorative passages.

Flute. Woodwind instrument, blown sideways. It is played through a hole, not a reed. Nowadays, sometimes made of metal.

Folksong. Traditional tune, often in different versions, handed down aurally from generation to generation.

Form. Course or layout of a composition, especially when in various sections.

Fourth. Interval taking four steps in scale. A perfect fourth (say, C to F) includes two whole tones and a semitone. If either note is sharpened or flattened the result is an augmented or a diminished fourth.

Fugato. In the manner of a fugue.

Fugue. Contrapuntal composition for various parts based on one or more subjects treated imitatively but not strictly.

G. Note of scale.

Galant. Used to designate elegant style of 18th-cent. music.

Galliard. Lively dance dating back to 15th cent. or before.

Gavotte. Dance in 4/4 time, beginning on third beat in bar.

Giusto. Strict, proper.

Glee. Short part-song.

Glissando. Rapid sliding scales up and down piano or other instruments.

Glockenspiel. Percussion instrument consisting of tuned steel bars and played with two hammers or keyboard.

Grace note. See Ornament.

Grave. In slow tempo.

Grazioso. Gracefully.

Gregorian Chant. Plainsong collected and supervised mainly by Pope Gregory (d. 604).

Ground Bass. A bass part that is repeated throughout a piece with varying material on top.

Guitar. Plucked string instrument of Spanish origin, having six strings of three-octave compass.

H. German note-symbol for *B.*

Harmony. Simultaneous sounding of notes so as to make musical sense.

Harp. Plucked string instrument of ancient origin, the strings stretched parallel across its frame. The basic scale of C flat major is altered by a set of pedals.

Harpsichord. Keyboard stringed instrument played by means of keyboard similar to a piano but producing its notes by a plucking, rather than a striking action.

Homophonic. Opposite of polyphonic, *i.e.,* indicated parts move together in a composition, a single melody being accompanied by block chords, as distinct from the contrapuntal movement of different melodies.

Horn. Brass instrument with coiled tubes. Valves introduced in 19th cent. made full chromatic use of instrument possible.

Hymn. Song of praise, especially in church.

Imitation. Repetition, exactly, or at least recognisably, of a previously heard figure.

Impromptu. A short, seemingly improvised piece of music, especially by Schubert or Chopin.

Improvise. To perform according to fancy or imagination, sometimes on a given theme.

In alt. The octave above the treble clef; *in altissimo,* octave above that.

Instrumentation. Writing music for particular instruments, using the composer's knowledge of what sounds well on different instruments.

Interlude. Piece played between two sections of a composition.

Intermezzo. Formerly meant interlude, now often used for pieces played between acts of operas.

Interval. Distance in pitch between notes.

Ionian mode. One of the scales in mediaeval music, represented on piano by white keys between C and C, identical therefore to modern C major scale.

Isorhythmic. Medieval technique using repetitions of a rhythm but with different notes. Much used in 15th century motets.

Jig. Old dance usually in 6/8 or 12/8 time.

Kettledrum (It. pl. *Timpani*). Drum with skin drawn over a cauldron-shaped receptacle, can be tuned to definite pitch by turning handles on rim, thus tightening or relaxing skin.

Key. Lever by means of which piano, organ, etc., produces note; classification, in relatively modern times, of notes of a scale. Any piece of music in major or minor is in the *key* of its tonic or keynote.

Keyboard. Term used to describe instruments with a continuous row of keys.

Key-signature. Indication on written music, usually at the beginning of each line, of the number of flats or sharps in the key of a composition.

Kitchen Department. Humorous term for percussion section of an orchestra.

Lament. Musical piece of sad or deathly significance.

Largamente. Spaciously.

Largo. Slow.

Leading-motive (Ger. *Leitmotiv*). Short theme, suggesting person, idea, or image, quoted throughout composition to indicate that person, etc.

Legato. In a smooth style (of performance, etc.).

Lento. Slow.

Libretto. Text of an opera.

Lied (pl. *Lieder*). Song, with special reference to songs by Schubert, Schumann, Brahms, and Wolf.

Lute. String instrument plucked with fingers, used in 15th- and 16th-cent. music especially.

Lydian mode. One of the scales in mediaeval music, represented by white keys of piano between F and F.

Lyre. Ancient Greek plucked string instrument.

Madrigal. Contrapuntal composition for several voices, especially prominent from 15th to 17th cent.

Maestoso. Stately.

Major. One of the two main scales of the tonal system with semitones between the third and fourth, and the seventh and eighth notes. Identical with 16th-cent. Ionian mode.

Mandolin(e). Plucked string instrument of Italian origin.

Manual. A keyboard for the hands, used mostly in connection with the organ.

Master of the King's (or Queen's) Musick. Title of British court appointment, with no precise duties.

Melisma. Group of notes sung to a single syllable.

Mélodie. Literally a melody or tune; has come to mean a French song (cf. German *Lied*).

Metronome. Small machine in use since the beginning of the 18th cent., to determine the pace of any composition by the beats of the music, *e.g.*, = 60 at the head of the music indicates sixty crotchets to the minute.

Mezzo, Mezza. (It. = "half") *Mezza voce* means using the half voice (a tone between normal singing and whispering). *Mezzo-soprano*, voice between soprano and contralto.

Minim. Note that equals two crotchets in time value.

Minor. One of the two main scales of the tonal system (cf. major), identical with 16th-cent. Aeolian mode. It has two forms—the harmonic and melodic, the former having a sharpened seventh note, the latter having the sixth and seventh note sharpened.

Minuet. Originally French 18th-cent. dance in triple time, then the usual third movement in symphonic form (with a contrasting trio section) until succeeded by scherzo.

Mixolydian mode. One of the mediaeval scales represented by the white keys on the piano from G to G.

Modes. Scales prevalent in the Middle Ages. *See* Aeolian, Dorian, Ionian, Lydian, Mixolydian, Phrygian.

Modulate. Changing from key to key in a composition, not directly but according to musical "grammar".

Molto. Much, very; thus *allegro molto*.

Motet. Sacred, polyphonic vocal composition. More loosely, any choral composition for use in church but not set to words of the liturgy.

Motive, motif. Short, easily recognised melodic figure.

Motto. Short, well-defined theme recurring throughout a composition, cf. *Idée fixe* in Berlioz's *Symphonie Fantastique*.

Movement. Separate sections of a large-scale composition, each in its own form.

Music drama. Term used to describe Wagner's, and sometimes other large-scale operas.

Mutes. Devices used to damp the sound of various instruments.

Natural (of a note or key). Not sharp or flat.

Neoclassical. Clear-cut style, originating during 1920s, that uses 17th and 18th century forms and styles. It constituted a reaction to the excesses of romanticism.

Ninth. Interval taking nine steps, *e.g.*, from C upwards an octave and a whole tone to D.

Nocturne. Literally a "night-piece" hence usually of lyrical character.

Nonet. Composition for nine instruments.

Notation. Act of writing down music.

Note. Single sound of specified pitch and duration; symbol to represent this.

Obbligato. Instrumental part having a special or essential rôle in a piece.

Oboe. Woodwind instrument with double reed, descended from hautboy; as such, in use since 16th cent., in modern form since 18th cent.

Octave. Interval taking eight steps of scale, with top and bottom notes having same "name"; C to C is an octave.

Octet. Composition for eight instruments or voices.

Ondes Martenol. Belongs to a class of melodic instruments in which the tone is produced by electrical vibrations controlled by the movement of the hands not touching the instrument.

Opera. Musical work for the stage with singing characters, originated *c.* 1600 in Italy.

Opera buffa (It.), *Opéra bouffe* (Fr.). Comic opera (in the English sense), *not* to be confused with *Opéra comique* (Fr.) which is opera with spoken dialogue and need not be humorous.

Opera seria. Chief operatic form of 17th and 18th cent., usually set to very formal librettos, concerning gods or heroes of ancient history.

Operetta. Lighter type of opera.

Opus (abbr. *Op.*). With number following *opus* indicates order of a composer's composition.

Oratorio. Vocal work, usually for soloists and choir with instrumental accompaniment, generally with setting of a religious text.

Orchestra. Term to designate large, or largish, body of instrumentalists originated in 17th cent.

Orchestration. Art of setting out work for instruments of an orchestra. To be distinguished from *Instrumentation (q.v.).*

Organ. Elaborate keyboard instrument in which air is blown through pipes by bellows to sound notes. Tone is altered by selection of various stops, and, since the 16th cent., a pedal keyboard has also been incorporated.

Organum. In mediaeval music a part sung as an accompaniment below or above the melody of plainsong, usually at the interval of a fourth or fifth; also, loosely, this method of singing in parts.

Ornament. Notes that are added to a given melody by composer or performer as an embellishment.

Overture. Instrumental introduction or prelude to larger work, usually opera. Concert overtures are simply that: *i.e.*, work to be played at start of a concert.

Part. Music of one performer in an ensemble; single strand in a composition.

Part-song. Vocal composition in several parts.

Passacaglia. Composition in which a tune is constantly repeated, usually in the bass.

Passage. Section of a composition.

Passion. Musical setting of the New Testament story of Christ's trial and crucifixion.

Pastiche. Piece deliberately written in another composer's style.

Pavan(e). Moderately paced dance dating from 16th cent. or earlier.

Pedal. Held note in bass of composition.

Pentatonic. Scale of five consecutive notes, *e.g.*, the black keys of the piano.

Percussion. Collective title for instruments of the orchestra that are sounded by being struck by hand or stick.

Phrygian Mode. One of the scales of mediaeval music, represented by the white keys on piano from E to E.

Piano. Soft, abbr. *p*; *pp* = *pianissimo*, very soft; instrument, invented in 18th cent., having strings struck by hammer, as opposed to the earlier harpsichord where they are plucked. The modern piano has 88 keys and can be either "upright" (vertical) or "grand" (horizontal).

Pianoforte. Almost obsolete full Italian name for the piano.

Pitch. Exact height or depth of a particular musical sound or note.

Pizzicato. Direction for stringed instruments, that the strings should be plucked instead of bowed.

Plainchant, Plainsong. Mediaeval church music

consisting of single line of melody without harmony or definite rhythm.

Polka. Dance in 2/4 time originating in 19th cent. Bohemia.

Polonaise. Polish dance generally in 3/4 time.

Polyphony. Combination of two or more musical lines as in *counterpoint*.

Polytonality. Simultaneous use of several keys.

Postlude. Closing piece, opposite of Prelude.

Prelude. Introductory piece.

Presto. Very fast. *Prestissimo.* Still faster.

Progression. Movement from one chord to next to make musical sense.

Quartet. Work written for four instruments or voices; group to play or sing such a work.

Quaver. Note that equals two semiquavers or half a crotchet.

Quintet. Work written for five instruments or voices; group to play or sing such a work.

Rallentando. Slowing down.

Recapitulation. Section of composition that repeats original material in something like its original form.

Recitative. Term used for declamation in singing written in ordinary notation but allowing rhythmical licence.

Recorder. Woodwind instrument, forerunner of flute.

Reed. Vibrating tongue of woodwind instruments.

Register. Set of organ pipes controlled by a particular stop; used in reference to different ranges of instrument or voice (*e.g.*, chest register).

Relative. Term used to indicate common key signature of a major and minor key.

Répétiteur. Member of opera house's musical staff who coaches singers in their parts.

Rest. Notation of pauses for instrument in composition, having a definite length like a note.

Retrograde. Term used to describe a melody played backwards.

Rhapsody. Work of no definite kind with a degree of romantic content.

Rhythm. Everything concerned with the time of music (*i.e.*, beats, accent, metre, etc.) as opposed to the pitch side.

Ritornello. Passage, usually instrumental, that recurs in a piece.

Romance, Romanza. Title for piece of vague song-like character.

Romantic. Term used vaguely to describe music of 19th cent. that has other than purely musical source of inspiration.

Rondo. Form in which one section keeps on recurring.

Rubato. Manner of performing a piece without keeping strictly to time.

Sackbut. Early English name for trombone.

Saxophone. Classified as wind instrument, although made of brass, because it uses a reed.

Scale. Progression of adjoining notes upwards or downwards.

Scherzo. Literally "a joke". Often used as a light movement in the middle of a sonata type work.

Score. Copy of any music written in several parts.

Second. Interval taking two steps in scale, *e.g.*, C to D flat, or to D.

Semibreve. Note that equals two minims or half a breve.

Semiquaver. Note that equals half a quaver.

Semitone. Smallest interval commonly used in Western music.

Septet. Composition for seven instruments or voices.

Sequence. Repetition of phrase at a higher or lower pitch.

Serenade. Usually an evening song or instrumental work.

Seventh. Interval taking seven steps in the scale.

Sextet. Composition for six instruments or voices.

Sharp. Term indicating a raising of pitch by a semitone.

Shawm. Primitive woodwind instrument, forerunner of oboe.

Simple time. Division of music into two or four beats.

Sinfonietta. Small symphony.

Sixth. Interval taking six steps in the scale.

Solo. Piece or part of a piece for one performer playing or singing alone.

Sonata. Term to denote a musical form and a type of composition. In *sonata form* a composition is divided into exposition, development and recapitulation. A *sonata* is a piece, usually for one or more players following that form.

Song. Any short vocal composition.

Soprano. Highest female voice.

Sostenuto. Sustained, broadly.

Sotto voce. Whispered, scarcely audible, applied to vocal as well as instrumental music.

Spinet. A small keyboard instrument belonging to the harpsichord (*q.v.*) family.

Sprechgesang. (Ger. Speech-song.) Vocal utterance somewhere between speech and song.

Staccato. Perform music in short, detached manner.

Staff. Horizontal lines on which music is usually written.

Stop. Lever by which organ registration can be altered.

String(s). Strands of gut or metal set in vibration to produce musical sounds on string or keyboard instruments. Plural refers to violins, violas, cellos, and basses of orchestra.

Study. Instrumental piece, usually one used for technical exercise or to display technical skills, but often having artistic merits as well (*e.g.*, Chopin's).

Subject(s). Theme or group of notes that forms principal idea or ideas in composition.

Suite. Common name for piece in several movements.

Symphony. Orchestral work of serious purpose usually in four movements, occasionally given name (*e.g.*, Beethoven's "Choral" symphony).

Syncopation. Displacement of musical accent.

Tempo. Pace, speed of music.

Tenor. Highest normal male voice.

Ternary. A piece in three sections is said to be in ternary form. The balance is obtained by repeating the first phrase or section (though it need not be exact or complete) after a second of equal importance.

Tessitura. Compass into which voice or instrument comfortably falls.

Theme. Same as *subject* but can also be used for a whole musical statement as in "theme and variations."

Third. Interval taking three steps in scale.

Time. Rhythmical division of music.

Timpani. See Kettledrum.

Toccata. Instrumental piece usually needing rapid, brilliant execution.

Tonality. Key, or feeling for a definite key.

Tone. Quality of musical sound; interval of two semitones.

Tonic Sol-fa. System of musical notation to simplify sight-reading.

Transcribe. Arrange piece for different medium, instrument, or voice than that originally intended.

Transition. Passage that joins two themes of sections of a composition.

Transpose. To move a musical idea, theme or piece to a different key from its original.

Treble. Highest part in vocal composition; high boy's voice.

Triad. Three note chord. Usually consists of a note and those a third and fifth above.

Trio. Work written for three instruments or voices; group to play or sing such a work.

Trombone. Brass instrument with slide adjusting length of tube.

Trumpet. Metal instrument of considerable antiquity; modern version has three valves to make it into a chromatic instrument.

Tuba. Deepest-toned brass instrument with three or four valves.

Twelve-note. Technique of composition using full chromatic scale with each note having equal importance. Notes are placed in particular order as the thematic basis of works.

Unison. Two notes sung or played together at same pitch.

Valve. Mechanism, invented in early 19th cent. to add to brass instruments allowing them to play full chromatic scale.

Variation. Varied passage of original theme. Such variations may be closely allied to or depart widely from the theme.

Verismo. Term to describe Italian operas written in "realist" style at the turn of this century.

Vibrato. Rapid fluctuation in pitch of voice or instrument. Exaggerated it is referred to as a "wobble" (of singers) or tremolo.

Viol. String instrument of various sizes in vogue until end of 17th cent.

Viola. Tenor instrument of violin family.

Violin. Musical four-string instrument, played with bow, of violin family, which superseded viol at beginning of 18th cent.

Virginals. English keyboard instrument, similar to harpsichord of 17th and 18th cent.

Vivace. Lively.

Voluntary. Organ piece for church use, but not during service.

Waltz. Dance in triple time, fashionable in 19th cent.

Whole-tone scale. Scale progressing by whole tones. Only two are possible, one beginning on C, the other on C sharp.

Xylophone. Percussion instrument with series of wood bars tuned in a chromatic scale and played with sticks.

Zither. String instrument laid on knees and plucked. Common in Central-European folk music.

III. INDEX TO COMPOSERS

IV. SPECIAL TOPIC

Note: This new section has been written for *Pears* by Godric Wilkie.

NEW MUSIC TECHNOLOGY

Introduction.

Music Technology is a generic term which describes that wide range of electronic equipment which has specific application in music making. Music technology includes reproduction systems such as CD; recording systems such as tape recorders; sound processing systems such as mixing consoles, equalisation, echo or reverberation devices; sound generating systems such as synthesisers, samplers and drum machines; and devices for controlling any of these. Music technology is extremely pervasive throughout all activities in music making. It allows composers to produce their own publisher-ready scores of engraver quality. It allows musical performances to be recorded, processed and reproduced. It allows completely new sounds and timbres to be synthesised and played like those of any acoustic instrument. It allows the creation of different ambient environments for sound and music, from small room, to large hall, to cave. It allows recordings to be edited in such a way as to exclude mistakes from a performance. It can also facilitate the music ambitions of those who have no formal training in music, allowing them to produce convincing musical works. This pervasiveness has increased as the technology has developed, in particular with the introduction of digital electronics.

Early History.

From the 1930s until the early 1980s music technology was largely based on analogue electronics, systems of discrete components such as amplifiers and filters which process voltage in various ways, where the voltage represents or is an "analogue" of sound or music. For much of this time music technology was essentially studio technology used by recording engineers, many of whom had an electronics background. Their emphasis was to use this equipment to ensure the best possible signal was recorded to tape. This approach is exemplified by the introduction of "equalisation" or EQ. Early microphones were not efficient at all audio frequencies particularly above about 10 kHz. This inefficiency was exacerbated by the long cable runs which were sometimes necessary (any length of cable will reduce the strength of high frequencies—the longer the cable the more noticeable this effect is). In order to compensate for these problems, engineers developed special types of amplifier called filters which would increase (or decrease) the amount of signal at a given frequency. The intention was to make the recorded signal "equal" to the heard signal by increasing the level of those frequencies which had been reduced by the electrical equipment from microphone to tape. A similar system was used to compensate for comparable inefficiencies in tape recorders. Although some would describe such filters as a "tone control" they tended to be used for technical rather than creative reasons, and consequently the use of this equipment was seen as a technical rather than musical activity.

It was not until the late 1950s that the electronic equipment used in studios began to be designed to enhance a signal creatively rather than to compensate for technical deficiencies. Spring and plate reverberators are examples of this. These electromechanical devices were used to superimpose a sense of acoustic space on a signal comparable to the effect of a room or hall. The principal effect is to make a sound of short duration take a longer time to decay, a feature of large acoustic spaces. The longer the springs or the larger the plates, the longer the decay and the bigger the acoustic space that could be simulated. Reverberators were used if it was considered that the signal sounded too "dry" or close.

Some French composers who became interested in using recording technology creatively were responsible for a style of composition called *Musique Concrète*. The style exploited the possibilities for transforming everyday, real or "concrete" sounds using tape recorders and other pieces of studio equipment such as equalisers and reverberators. Recorded sounds could be replayed at different speeds on a tape player, thus simultaneously altering their pitch and duration (slowing the tape lowered the pitch and increased duration while speeding the tape had the opposite effects). Taped sounds could also be replayed backwards, thus reversing them in time. Another possibility was that a sequence of sounds could be recorded or edited onto a length of tape whose ends had been joined together in a loop. This could then be played for as long as desired, causing the sequence to be repeated (as it sometimes was) ad nauseam. Any of these techniques could be combined together and with other studio techniques.

Other Experiments.

The American composer Steve Reich experimented with the effect of two or more duplicate loops containing the same sound sequence replayed on machines running at slightly different speeds. The sounds all start together but gradually start to drift apart causing a "phasing" effect which Reich used as the name for this type of work *c.f.* "it's ronna rain". Later Reich adapted a machine-less version of this basic notion, by requiring instrumental performers to play the same musical phrase at slightly different tempi *c.f.* Piano Phase, Violin Phase – an example of the crossover of a technique from music technology to composition and performance.

Other than the Theremin, an electronic device which sounded not unlike a musical saw and the Ondes Martenôt, there were few purely electronic musical instruments. In the mid 1960s the synthesiser was developed separately by the Americans Buchla and Moog. These instruments looked more like pieces of test equipment (to which they were in fact closely related electronically) than musical instruments, with large arrays of control knobs, switches and cables. However their development encouraged a new group of musicians with complimentary musical and technical ability.

Early Synthesisers.

Early synthesisers consisted of a collection of modules each with a specific electronic function, such as oscillators, filters and amplifiers. While modules like this had been around for some time, the particular innovation for which Buchla and Moog are to be remembered was to provide each type of module with an input to which a voltage could be applied in order to control the behaviour of that module. For example increasing the "control voltage" applied to an oscillator caused its pitch to increase proportionally. Applying the same change in control voltage to an amplifier module would increase the volume of an audio signal passing through it.

Oscillators, electronic devices which create a continuous tone, produced the basic pitch and timbral content of the sound being synthesised. The timbre could be further modified by filter and amplifier modules. Modules such as envelope generators could produce time-varying voltages which when applied to filters and or amplifiers were useful to break the continuous tone into the various "attack" and "decay" dynamics of normal sounds. Other modules such as noise generators, sample and hold or ring modulators could be used for more esoteric effects. Arranging a keyboard that could produce a change in voltage according to which key was pressed, made what would otherwise have been an odd assortment of test-gear into a musical instrument. Many of these synthesisers were entirely modular to the extent that the user could buy an empty frame to fill with modules of his or her choice. The modules also had to be connected together, usually by patch cords like those in a primitive telephone exchange, in order to form a useful configuration. This allowed considerable flexibility, but was complex, expensive and occasionally unreliable. It became apparent that there was a very commonly used configuration for the modules, and it was not long before compact synthesisers with this sort of prewired configuration became available. An instrument of this type was the popular "Minimoog". In passing it is worth noting that most early synthesisers were monophonic (capable of playing only one note at a time) or at best duophonic.

The new sounds possible with this sort of equipment captured the imagination of performers (mostly keyboard players) from both the classical and rock worlds. This increased demand led to a number of manufacturers in America, Europe and Japan competing to produce ever more complex and extensive (e.g. polyphonic) synthesisers for both professional and domestic use.

It was not long before some of these technically-minded musicians wanted to achieve, while they performed on stage, the same sort of effects that recording engineers could produce in the studio, so synthesiser manufacturers obligingly added effects units such as echo and reverb machines to their catalogue.

Multitrack Tape Recorders.

Multitrack tape recorders which allowed the gradual building up of a musical texture, layer by layer on up to 16 or 24 tape tracks had become available to recording studios in the mid-1970s. By the early 1980s it became possible to offer compact 8 and 16 track versions which were sufficiently cheap to be purchased by musicians for their own use. Soon records were released which had been recorded on equipment owned and operated by musicians in what were often referred to (especially by commercial studio owners in a pejorative sense) as "bedroom studios". It is a tribute to the abilities of many such musicians and the designers of budget or domestic recording equipment that these recordings were of a sufficiently high quality as to be immediately releasable. By this time the previously obvious division between recording technician and musician had become quite blurred.

The Advent of Computers.

Manufacturers of music technology products had to be competitive by offering innovative and more versatile products, while keeping these affordable. This was becoming difficult to achieve with analogue systems and they sought an alternative solution by adopting digital technologies, in other words computers.

Initially the computer content of these devices was not great or obvious as the manufacturers tended to make their new digital versions have the same appearance and controls as the existing analogue devices, despite the fact that their new products had many of the components of a personal computer. Also in this early stage the rôle of digital technology was often restricted merely to the control of analogue circuits which processed sound. For example, one innovation in sound synthesisers was the use of computer memory to store and recall the settings of the front-panel controls which determined the timbre produced. This allowed instantaneous change from one timbre to another from a single switch, compared with the laborious manual adjustment of each and every control on the panel of previous models. In this situation the computer inside the synthesiser is only required to monitor and memorise the adjustments to the controls made by the user. The sound was often still generated by analogue circuits as it had been in the past.

A number of universities had been using mainframe computers for sound generation, but these were extremely expensive general purpose machines. In 1983, Yamaha produced a system of sound synthesis called Frequency Modulation or FM, which was entirely digital, using just such an academic approach developed by Dr. Chowning of Stanford University, but aimed at a mass-market. This achievement was made possible by the conversion of the original mainframe-based system to a set of purpose-built integrated circuits which could be cheaply mass-produced.

While Chowning's original system looked like a large computer installation which almost incidentally had a musical keyboard attached to it, Yamaha's DX synthesisers were no less computers than Chowning's mainframe had been, but in order to maximise the interest generated in their new product Yamaha had realised the need to make it look familiar to musicians.

Features of Digital Synthesisers.

Unlike analogue synthesisers which had circuitry dedicated to the functions of oscillator, filter, amplifier etc., digital synthesisers only contain circuitry dedicated to the task of being a computer. It is the use of appropriate software which gives the "effect" of oscillators, etc. From an electronic point of view the oscillators do not exist but are instead "modelled" by the software. The user can view parameters relating to the oscillator, such as pitch or output level, on a screen and make adjustments. These are interpreted by the computer which performs a mathematical calculation. The result of this calculation is converted from a numerical or digital state to an audio signal which can be heard by the user (the component in a digital synthesiser which performs this latter function is not surprisingly called a Digital to Analogue Convertor or DAC).

One consequence of the "virtual" nature of the models in a digital synthesiser is that the operator's panel need not be covered with control knobs each with a dedicated function. Yamaha chose to have only one control for altering over 100 different synthesiser parameters one at a time. This made the machine cheaper to build and buy, and certainly made it look extremely novel when compared to contemporary analogue equipment. However for some it did complicate the process of setting up sounds.

Another consequence of digital technology was that it allows additive rather than subtractive synthesis. Analogue synthesisers which have filters are called subtractive because a harmonically rich waveform generated by an oscillator has harmonics selectively removed by the action of one or more filters in order to arrive at the desired timbre. It is a process rather like taking a large block of marble and chiselling away most of the material to leave a final shape. In practice this meant that novel or obviously electronic sounds were easy to generate while most attempts to reproduce synthetic versions of natural or acoustic sounds were less satisfactory. To stretch the sculpting analogy to breaking point, it was as if analogue synthesisers were a strange type of marble that allowed any number of abstract "modern art" forms to be produced, but somehow could not produce the classical figurative forms.

The Basis of Additive Synthesis.

It had been known since the 18th century that any sound was a complex of many pure tones called sine waves, more commonly referred to as "harmonics", "overtones" or "partials". In principle, and given enough sine wave oscillators and amplifiers, any sound could be synthesised by adding sine waves together. This is the basis of additive synthesis. Depending on how purist your point of view an additive synthesiser needs at least 16 to 32 oscillators (one per harmonic) to generate complex timbres convincingly, numbers too great to be practical to any but the most profligate analogue synthesiser owners. Given that a piece of software does not care how many oscillators it pretends to be (as long as the computer is fast enough to emulate them all) there is no such limitation for a digital synthesiser.

As a point of accuracy it should be noted that the Chowning/Yamaha system, while additive, only requires the modelling of two sine wave oscillators to produce a complex tone. But that does not affect the verity of the above description and indeed another Japanese manufacturer, Kawai, produced a range of more conventionally additive products which modelled 32 to 64 sine wave oscillators.

A major selling point of digital synthesisers when they first appeared was their ability to produce reasonably convincing impersonations of existing acoustic instruments (perhaps more convincing when compared with analogue attempts than with the real instrument). They were not merely limited to this however and the novel timbres they could produce were often markedly more satisfying and organic in nature than those available on analogue systems. This wider palette of sounds, coupled to the economy of mass produced computer components further enhanced the attractiveness of synthesisers to a broad range of musicians, including many less technical ones who might even have been horrified to discover they were using a computer.

The beauty of digital systems is their flexibility. In principle, once a manufacturer has a system of hardware and software which can manipulate sound (an ability which is part of what is known as digital signal processing (DSP) and which comes down to mathematical calculations), the behaviour of the system can be radically altered simply by installing different software. The same hardware can be used both to generate sound and to process sound, for example by adding reverberation. All that is required is for the software to perform its calculations in a different way. By the mid 80s it was possible to produce quite cheaply a synthesiser that was not only polyphonic (more than one note at a time) but multitimbral (able to play more than one sound at a time). Now a single unit could replace eight or even sixteen separate monotimbral synthesisers, allowing it to replay an entire musical arrangement.

In summary, these versatile digital synthesisers were essentially personal computers connected to digital to analogue converters running software which produced sound and even reverb and echo by performing mathematical calculations.

Advent of the "Sampler".

By the early 1980s, a variant of the digital synthesiser known as a "sampler" began to appear. The main difference was the addition of hardware in the form of an Analogue to Digital Converter (ADC). As one might imagine the ability of this component is to turn a sound into numbers which the computer and its software can manipulate. A sampler is thus a digital synthesiser which can record sound of short duration (typically up to a couple of minutes) and replay it in a very similar manner to the more familiar tape recorder. In fact a sampler is essentially a digital sound recorder. However this is a musician's sound recorder and any sound recorded can be played from a keyboard.

The existence of samplers led to something of a rediscovery of the techniques of *Musique Concrète* by musicians quite isolated, both by history and culture, from the earlier French school. Some of the results of the usage of samplers by musicians and DJs from the African-American and Hispanic-American dance-music genres "House" and "Hip-Hop" can be compared favourably with music by Pierre Schaefer *et al.* Part of the reason for this is that the principal techniques of replaying sounds at different pitches, playing sounds backwards and looping sounds which were central to *Musique Concrète* are very easy to achieve on a sampler, primarily because the user no longer has to manipulate small pieces of magnetic tape.

The Use of Samplers.

The use of samplers by musicians and indeed non-musicians has not been uncontroversial. One possibility is for a sampler user to record (or sample as it is more commonly called) a couple of bars of backing rhythm from an existing piece of music, for example the instrumental part of a chorus or introduction of a pop song. This small section of rhythm can be looped, to make it repeat for several minutes. On top of this, new and original music may be recorded, using the looped bars as a backing. Some may think this a perfectly legitimate practice, thinking, probably erroneously, that the rhythmic backing of a piece of music does not "belong" to anyone. In fact it is highly likely that the original is copyright material and the use of it in this way an infringement of the copyright holder's rights. Unfortunately the situation is not clear-cut. How much material needs to be recorded before a breach of copyright occurs? If one samples the loud tutti chord from Stravinsky's "Rite of Spring" and uses it as part of another otherwise original composition,

would this be sufficient to constitute such a breach? If something as identifiable as Stravinsky's Rite of Spring chord is clearly copyright, how about a single snare drum beat? Without a musical context how can snare drum beat be said to be unique or original? There is ample scope for lucrative employment for barristers.

When samplers first appeared and were used in this manner there was an initial flurry of breach of copyright actions including one which centred around the ownership of a single snare drum beat sampled from one record and used on another. It became clear to the record companies that it was not in their best interests to resort to this kind of litigation in an attempt to control samplers and their users and most of them arrived at schemes to settle disputes arising from this practice amicably (*i.e.* without paying lawyers). Such schemes include globally applied standard fees per unit time for samples or "knock-for-knock" arrangements where record companies allowed mutual sampling of one another's artists.

The principal limitation to the duration of sound which a sampler can record is the amount of memory available to it. In order to achieve on a sampler a reproduction quality comparable to that of Compact Disc, approximately 5 MB (megabytes) of memory are required for each minute of mono signal. If the sound is to be recorded as stereo then 10 MB are required per minute. The normal memory in a sampler is Random Access Memory (RAM) in the form of semiconductor "chips". This is relatively cost effective for amounts up to about 32 MB, which equates to approximately six minutes of mono recording or three in stereo. However for longer durations RAM becomes prohibitively expensive. It is possible for a sampler to record audio onto "hard disc" storage devices which currently are available in sizes of up to 4,000 MB and which would allow approximately six hours of continuous stereo.

Such a system can become a direct replacement for the analogue tape recorders found in recording studios. To draw a distinction in use between the musical applications of a sampler and the recording of tens of minutes of audio, systems with the latter ability are often referred to as "hard disc recorders" or "direct-to-disk systems", although from a hardware point of view these only differ from samplers in the type of memory they use to store sound. Hard disk recording systems began to appear during the late 1980s. There is a nice symmetry in the way recording technology has become available to musicians, while the sampling technology developed specifically for use by musicians has found its way into the recording studio in the form of hard disk recorders.

Hard Disk Recorders.

Hard disk recorders are often used quite differently from samplers and in many cases the reason for using them is the ease with which the material they record can be edited.

Owners of CDs of classical music may be surprised to know that, concert recordings excepted, few of the performances they contain are continuous. In fact most are actually a jigsaw of the best of a large number of "takes" which an editor has assembled according to instructions from the producer of the recording. This allows the performer to have many attempts at the music, confident that only the mistake-free or most musical efforts will finally be heard. It also allows the performer to play the music out of sequence, perhaps playing a particularly difficult section early on in the recording session before tiredness sets in. In some cases the performer may not actually play the entire piece from beginning to end during the recording, preferring to tackle a few bars at a time. The final recording session tapes may amount to several hours of material in order to guarantee a one hour flawless performance on CD. A few years ago recordings were literally cut with razor blades and joined with sticky tape. This was problematic for a number of reasons. It was fiddly; the razor had a tendency to become magnetic in use which could impart an audible "thump" at the edit point; and sections which needed to appear twice (in movements which have repeat sections and where it is desirable to use only one of the performed repeats both times) have to be copied, which can lead to degradation of the sound. Perhaps the biggest problem was that the original master recording effectively has to be destroyed in order to carry out the editing process. Although a safety copy could be made, this as always would be of a lesser quality.

Hard-disk systems allow editing which is "non-destructive". Because the system is digital the music is represented on the hard disk as numbers. In order to hear the music the numbers are "read" sequentially off the disk and converted to sound by the DAC. The reading process has no effect on the numbers. The system can access the numbers more or less instantly from any point (there is no equivalent of having to wind tape backwards or forwards) which means that any section of the music can be played instantaneously after any other section. There is also no limit to the number of times a section can be played before proceeding to the next. These capabilities make the job of editing very easy. The exact process differs from system to system but goes something like this. The hard-disk system is put in record and the master tape is played into it. If the master tape is a digital format like RDAT, then the copy on the system is a digital "clone" of the master tape which gives no loss of quality. If the master is an analogue tape then the copy on the system is still arguably without noticeable loss of quality. The operator or the producer then replays the music from the hard-disk system noting the good "takes". The required sections are selected by the operator and are usually named in some way. In fact all the operator has done is select two points in the music which represent the start and end points of this section, the computer knows to play everything between these two points. When all the required sections have been identified they can be assembled in the required order in what is known as a playlist. The operator simply places the names of the sections in the list in the order he or she wishes to hear them, even repeating them if desired. The computer then replays the music from the hard disk jumping immediately from the end point of one section to the start point of the next.

These jumps can generally not be heard. There is no pause as such but occasionally there may be a mismatch in the volume or tone of the music from one section to another and this can be noticeable. In fact because the sections to be joined may have been recorded at quite different times a common problem is that there may be a change in tempo between them. However in the hands of a skilful operator the computing power of the hard-disk system can be used to reduce or even remove problems like this. The system can be set to fade gradually from the end of one section into the start of the next. This is known as a crossfade. It is an effect which is not possible on analogue tape without making copies and the loss of quality that entails. Crossfades can often successfully mask many of the problems described above.

The hard disk system can also carry out a number of useful DSP functions. For example it may be desirable to reduce the volume of a section to match it with the adjacent ones. It is even possible to increase or reduce the tempo of a section by a small amount without affecting its pitch, a feat not possible on a conventional tape player. The ease with which such a system can edit music has encouraged producers to specify large numbers of edits which a few years ago would not have been practical. The existence of such perfected recorded versions of music raises interesting problems for the recording artist when the time comes for its performance in live concerts. In fact the whole editing process has been called into question by some purists who claim the results are not "musical". They consider that the emotional context of the music has been lost in the pursuit of a note-perfect performance. This may happen in some situations but in general producers are more interested in selecting the most musical renditions and are quite happy to allow the odd missed note. The proof of the pudding is perhaps that thousands of CDs featuring edited performances are sold every day, and their purchasers are usually unaware that they are listening to a musical jigsaw.

Mix Automation.

Many recording studios now feature mixing consoles whose "state" (the settings of all or many of the knobs, faders and switches etc.) can be stored by an internal computer. These states or "snapshots" as they are sometimes known can be recalled instantly, and in many cases it is possible to fade or move from one snapshot to another automatically. For obvious reasons this facility is called mix automation. If the mixing desk is entirely digital then it is a simple matter to automate every single function including EQ and effects levels etc.

Musical Instrument Digital Interface (MIDI).

Perhaps the most significant development in the history of music technology has been that of MIDI. In its original form the Musical Instrument Digital Interface was conceived as a standard means of describing many of the features of a musical performance in terms of numbers. The development of MIDI dates from about 1981 when initially American (and subsequently Japanese) synthesiser manufacturers were seeking a versatile means of connecting synthesisers together. Originally all that was intended was that a performer could connect some synthesisers together with a cable, such that when one of them was played one or more of the others would respond as if they had been played directly by the performer. This would allow the layering of sounds or simply make available sounds from one synthesiser on the keyboard of another.

Some systems of this kind had existed previously including the CV & Gate system, which had become notorious because few manufacturers configured their Control Voltage (CV) or Gate signals in quite the same manner, making the different systems often incompatible. Another problem with these earlier systems was that they had been developed with monophonic synthesisers in mind and were becoming cumbersome in the light of the newer polyphonic instruments. What is remarkable is that manufacturers agreed (eventually and not without a few hiccoughs) both to standardise the system before any machines using it were manufactured and to leave some parts of it "open-ended" in order to allow for evolution of the standard. The basic standard specifies a low-cost DIN connector cable for connecting the hardware and a "language" of commands which allows the essential features of a performance on an electronic instrument to be described. The first synthesisers featuring MIDI capability appeared in 1983 (the Yamaha DX synthesiser described above was one of these). Most samplers that appeared around this time also had MIDI.

The Consequences of MIDI.

It is not an exaggeration to state that this modest development revolutionised contemporary music making. The obvious consequence of the MIDI standard is that if a musical performance on one instrument can be described in terms of numbers, then those numbers can be stored on a computer and replayed at another time. For historical reasons this capability is called "sequencing". It is important to realise that what is stored is not the sound of the music but simply a description of its performance—the notes and chords that were used and their "velocity" (the speed at which the key was pressed) which is used to give the effect of loudness or brightness of timbre for each note, as well as articulations such as volume, sustain, pitch bend or vibrato etc. The performance can be replayed by different synthesisers or even the same synthesiser set to a different "patch" and as a consequence sound completely different. This situation is analogous to the various 19th century player-pianos and organs which were "played" by rolls of paper with holes punched in them. It is possible to transfer a roll (the sequence) made on a piano to another instrument which would sound different.

Computer based sequencers, samplers and synthesisers allow a musician to build up complex pieces of music, including sampled "real" instruments such as drums or vocals, a part at a time without using a tape recorder. The whole performance can then be stored permanently on a computer disk. All that is then required is to mix the sounds from the synthesisers and samplers to produce a stereo master, the only stage in which tape is involved. This was the start of the so called "Tapeless Studio".

Integrating the functionality of a sequencer with synthesised or sampled drum sounds in a single package created the "Drum Machine". This device allows the user to construct a rhythmic backing either for live performance or during the recording process.

The Evolution of MIDI Time Code (MTC).

Gradually the promised evolution of MIDI began to happen. One early development was the MIDI Sample Dump Standard which allows the numbers representing sound in one sampler to be transferred through the MIDI cable either to another sampler for replay, or to a computer for editing purposes. Standard MIDI Files allow sequences stored on one computer to be transferred to another. MIDI Time Code (MTC) allows a computer sequencer and a conventional tape recorder to be run in synchronisation, such that if the tape was wound to some point say near the end of a song, the computer would jump to the equivalent time in the sequence. In this way the synthesised or sampled parts of a piece of music could be kept in time with recorded tracks of vocals, guitar, sax etc. of the same piece of music. This was useful as it meant that valuable tape tracks need not be occupied by those parts of the music generated by the synthesisers, leaving them free for other things and allowing for more complex arrangements than the 16 or 24 tracks would normally allow.

MTC also allows a sequencer to be synchronised to video or film, thus ensuring that synthesised or sampled music, sound effects and even dialogue will match the picture to frame-exact accuracy. For the sake of accuracy it is worth pointing out that the ability to synchronise to tape, video and film was present in the original MIDI specification, however for various technical reasons this could be problematic. MTC is actually the absorption into the MIDI standard of the SMPTE time code standard which was already in use in the video, film and recording industries. MIDI can now be used to control all manner of devices involved in a musical show including the automation of the mixing desk and the lighting.

The Multimedia Dimension.

In recent years MIDI has been used as the key to multimedia—audiovisual presentations generated by computers—and has thus continued to expand beyond the musical horizons originally perceived for it. For some time computer games have been able to generate their own sound effects and music on the computer's internal loudspeaker. Now many of them are programmed to generate music via the computer's MIDI cable on external synthesisers and samplers, with much better quality sound. This will only work well if the composer of the music can ensure that the piano part will always be replayed using a piano sound and the electric bass part on an electric bass sound etc. Unfortunately most synthesisers have their sounds arranged quite arbitrarily and indeed two synthesisers of the same make might have entirely different sounds stored in them. In order to ensure that such games always replay their music on appropriate sounds, General MIDI (GM) has been developed. This essentially specifies a list of conventional and not so conventional sounds from pianos to drums in a particular layout. This means that any music that is GM compatible will be replayed correctly on a GM synthesiser.

Non-Keyboard MIDI Instruments.

Initially MIDI was developed with keyboard instruments in mind. It was not long before musicians playing other instruments got access to the advantages of a MIDI equipped instrument. The earliest non-keyboard MIDI instrument appeared in the form of pads which emulated the surface dynamics of a real drum kit. This allowed drummers to play sampled or synthesised sounds of drums or even non-drum sounds. One advantage was that a drummer could switch instantly from the sound of a jazz kit to a heavy rock kit, or even mix jazz, Latin percussion and heavy rock sounds on the same kit. A drummer might assemble a collection of vocal sounds and use these percussively. For a listener this is a quite different experience from hearing the same vocal sounds played from a keyboard.

The next development was the addition of MIDI to string instruments, primarily guitar but also members of the violin family. This was slightly more difficult to arrange from an engineering point of view. A keyboard or set of drum pads is simply a collection of switches which can produce an output which says which switch is "on" and how quickly it was switched on.

A conventional guitar cannot be viewed in this way, and the electronics of the MIDI guitar have to "listen" to the string to know what pitch it is vibrating at. They can then produce the appropriate MIDI output. The problem is that the analysis of the string's pitch takes at least half a cycle of its vibration. On the lowest pitched strings this delay can amount to several milliseconds. In other words the guitarist plucks a string, hears the guitar string, and then several milliseconds later hears whatever synthesiser etc. is connected by MIDI. In everyday activities a few milliseconds delay is neither here nor there, but in a musical context this phenomenon can be quite distracting.

Some solutions to this problem have been quite novel. One is to mount the string on an electromechanical transducer which injects a supersonic pulse into the core of the string. The pulse is then timed as it makes its journey from the transducer up to the point where the string is "stopped" by the performer and back. The time taken can be used to calculate the length of the string and hence the pitch required. Because this system works at very high frequencies the analytical delay is barely noticeable. Another solution is to do away with the conventional guitar altogether and make a purely electronic playing surface which resembles, but cannot itself sound like a guitar.

For the violin family of instruments the problem of analytical delay is not so great as these are more commonly bowed than plucked, giving a soft or delayed start to the note. However these instruments are, unlike a conventional guitar, fretless and this gives rise to a much greater problem. A fretless instrument can play any pitch including those "in between" the pitches of the piano keys or guitar frets. MIDI was not designed with this possibility in mind and only describes 127 discrete semitone pitches over a ten octave range. It is possible to get round this problem with varying degrees of success using standard MIDI commands. In practice most MIDI fiddle players simply accept that the electronic sound will come in semitone steps while the acoustic sound of the violin etc. need not.

The next non-keyboard MIDI controller type were the unfortunately named "Wind-controllers". These allow saxophonists, clarinettists and other keyed-instrument players as well as some valve-instrument or brass players to control MIDI devices. In general the MIDI wind controller is an electronic device, essentially a keyboard adapted into the required shape with the addition of detectors for lip pressure, breath strength etc. It is now possible for vocalists to control MIDI devices using a suitably equipped microphone, although this can suffer from some of the analytical delays and semitonal nature of the MIDI specification.

The visual impact of an instrumentalist producing sounds quite alien to those you might expect, for example a sax player performing a drum solo, can be quite stunning and adds another dimension to their performance, not to mention the immense broadening of the player's timbral repertoire which MIDI equipped technology brings with it.

MIDI also allows high quality printed scores to be produced by people with relatively little knowledge of transcription and engraving. Once a piece of music is assembled part by part into a sequence or a Standard MIDI File it is a relatively simple matter for it to be displayed in musical notion by the computer for editing or printing. The ability to perform a piece of music and have it instantly transcribed into notation is a long held dream of many composers, which to a greater or lesser extent is now realised by modern music technology. To be fair some types of music such as those which are highly variable in tempo or which use irregular beat relationships can fox the software into producing an unmusical result. Like any other technology the results are much better when controlled by an experienced user, but for most commonplace music these computer notation systems can produce quite publishable results without too much knowledge or effort.

The Impact of Artificial Intelligence.

The field of Artificial Intelligence has also had some impact on the work of composers with the creation of "expert systems" for composition which can compose authentically in a particular style. Examples include systems for generating chorales, fugues and inventions which are convincing enough to sound like "new" compositions by Bach; renaissance counterpoint in the manner of Palestrina, "cool jazz" and "swing" *etc. etc.* Some systems in development are able to do this interactively, that is a performer can play a melody which is automatically accompanied by a full arrangement in the appropriate style. Some high-level programming languages such as LISP and FORTH have been adapted to produce composition systems which produce music as an output from a program written in the language.

It is not intended that these systems replace traditional skills in composition. In fact they are usually created in an attempt to uncover what it is that composers do when they write music. The Bach and Palestrina expert systems were written in part as an analytical classification of the melodic, harmonic and contrapuntal techniques of those composers. However they can become fascinating tools for composers of almost any skill, and it is perhaps this single example which best typifies the power of music technology—the power to give control over musical materials to people who in an earlier generation might not have had this experience.

The Music Technology "A" Level.

Many young people have been attracted to music as a subject choice in their education primarily in response to their own experience with music technology. This year (1995) marks the first series of an "A" Level Music Technology paper, which directly tests students' knowledge of the field in an applied manner through both course work and a theory paper examination.

The most recent development in music technology is the combination of many of the facilities described above into a single system based on a personal computer. The computer on which this article was written includes some additional hardware in the form of analogue to digital and digital to analogue converters, digital signal processors as well as some software for sound synthesis, sampling, recording and editing, sequencing, notation and composition. It can assist in the composition of the music and produce notated parts for real musicians to play. It can function as an entirely computerised recording studio complete with multitrack recording of live performers onto hard disk, while replaying a sequence of synthesised and sampled sounds in perfect synchronisation. It can automate the mixing of the tracks and effects and provide many other musically useful functions. All this is in one package which can comfortably sit on a desktop.

Technology of any sort is a great democratiser: disabled people can have increased mobility by virtue of technology; the technology of air travel provides opportunities for travel undreamed of 100 years ago! Medical technology can enhance people's duration and quality of life. These examples are things which in less recent times were only open to the very wealthy. Technology has extended their availability to the averagely well off.

New Technology: Hopes, Fears and Opportunities.

In the late 1970s and early 1980s, some musicians as well as the unions to which they belong began to express fears that technology would deny them opportunities for work. Some players were concerned by the close imitations of their instruments now available on digital synthesisers, while some drummers openly stated that they might be "replaced" by drum machines. This is a historically common response of labourers to the changes brought about by technology. In fact no such replacement happened, simply a change in the rôle of drummers. Drum backings on recordings are now very often hybrids of sequenced and live performance. The basic beat, which is less challenging to play, is very often sequenced while other more interesting parts of the rhythm are performed by a drummer or percussionist, as it is thought the human "feel" would be missing from an entirely technology based performance.

Although music technology improves and develops all the time, and developments such as expert systems model the way humans interact with instruments, reproducing some of what makes a performance more human and less mechanical, it is unlikely that musicians will be replaced in the near future. What might happen is that there will be changes in the way musicians and composers are trained. This is because, as has been pointed out, music technology allows some people without formal musical training to produce results that are as compelling as those who have devoted many years to such training. The addition of music technology to the A level syllabus may be the first evidence of this change.

Some may claim that music technology is responsible for much music that is bland and unoriginal, and there may be some truth in the statement. The point is that the overall number of players and composers of music and the variety of styles is increasing because of the opportunities made available by music technology and the author is of the opinion that this can only be a beneficial development for human musical culture.

THE WORLD OF SCIENCE

A contemporary picture of scientific discovery, designed to explain some of the most important ideas in astronomy, physics, chemistry, biology, physical and social anthropology, and to give some account of recent research in various fields, including in this edition new special topics on modern molecular biology and the exploration of the planet Venus. Also included is a variety of useful scientific tables. Readers will also find many definitions of scientific terms in the General Information section.

TABLE OF CONTENTS

THE WORLD OF SCIENCE

In Parts I, II, and III the inanimate universe is described. This is the domain of cosmology, astronomy, geology, physics, and chemistry. There are already many interesting links which join this realm to that of the living and make it difficult to say where the boundary lies. Nevertheless it is still convenient to accord to the biological and social sciences two separate chapters, IV and V. Part VI provides some useful scientific tables. Part VII consists of specialist articles on topics of current scientific interest, including in this edition a study of the genetic revolution.

I. ASTRONOMY AND COSMOLOGY—THE NATURE OF THE UNIVERSE

The universe includes everything from the smallest sub-atomic particle to the mightiest supercluster of galaxies. The scientific view of the universe (not the only view but the one we are concerned with here) is a remarkable achievement of the human mind, and it is worth considering at the outset what a "scientific view" is, and what is remarkable about it.

A scientific view of something is always an intimate mixture of theories and observed facts, and not an inert mixture but a seething and growing one. The theories are broad general ideas together with arguments based on them. The arguments are designed to show that, if the general ideas are accepted, then this, or the other thing ought to be observed. If this, that, or the other actually are observed, then the theory is a good one; if not, then the theoreticians have to think again. Thus theoretical ideas and arguments are continually subjected to the severe test of comparison with the facts, and scientists are proud of the rigour with which this is done. On the other hand, theories often suggest new things to look for, *i.e.*, theories lead to predictions. These predictions are frequently successful, and scientists are entitled to be proud of that too. But it follows that no theory is immutable; any scientific view of any subject may, in principle, be invalidated at any time by the discovery of new facts, though some theories are so soundly based that overthrow does not seem imminent.

A remarkable aspect of the scientific view of the universe is that the same principles are supposed to operate throughout the whole vastness of space. Thus the matter and radiation in stars are not different from the matter and radiation on earth, and their laws of behaviour are the same. Therefore theories hard won by studies in terrestrial physics and chemistry laboratories are applied at once to the whole cosmos. Astronomy and cosmology are spectacular extensions of ordinary mechanics and physics.

LOOKING AT THE UNIVERSE

The universe is observable because signals from it reach us and some manage to penetrate our atmosphere.

First, there are waves of visible light together with invisible rays of somewhat longer (infra-red) and somewhat shorter (ultra-violet) wavelengths. These waves show us the bright astronomical objects and, to make use of them, astronomers have constructed telescopes of great power and precision backed up with cameras, spectroscopes, and numerous auxiliaries. The biggest telescope in the world is the 6 m reflector at Mt. Pastukhov in the northern Caucasus (USSR). The earth's atmosphere acts as a distorting and only partially transparent curtain and the erection of telescopes on satellites is beginning to extend optical telescope performance significantly. Indeed, the Hubble Space Telescope, launched in 1990, promises to dramatically expand our knowledge of the universe.

Secondly, there are radio waves of much longer wavelength than light. Radiotelescopes are sensitive radio receivers with specialised aerial systems. The scientific stature of modern radioastronomy was emphasised by the award in 1974 of the Nobel Physics Prize to two Cambridge radio astronomers, Ryle and Hewish.

Other types of radiation reach the earth from outer space. Cosmic radiation consists of fundamental particles, including protons (**F16**) of extremely high energy, moving at velocities very close to that of light. These particles can be detected by Geiger counters and by their tracks on photographic plates. X-rays and neutrinos (**F5**) are also generated by certain interesting classes of astronomical objects (**F5**). With the recent advent of satellite-borne detectors and apparatus buried in deep mines, new facets of cosmic-ray astronomy, X-ray astronomy, and neutrino astronomy are now rapidly deepening our knowledge of the nature of the universe and of the violent processes by which galaxies as well as individual stars and planetary systems evolve (**F6, F7**).

Great Distances and Large Numbers

To visualise the immense scale of the universe is almost as much a problem for the scientist as for the layman. The conventional shorthand is to express 1,000 as 10^3; 1,000,000 as 10^6. On this scale the earth is $1 \cdot 496 \times 10^8$ km away from the sun. Concorde, for example, the world's fastest airliner, took about $3\frac{1}{2}$ hours to travel 5,000 km from London to New York. The "Viking" spacecraft in 1976 took just over a year to travel the 200 million km to Mars. These distances, however, are minute by comparison with the distance even to the nearest star, Proxima Centauri, some 4×10^{13} km away. This distance is more conveniently expressed in terms of the travel time of light itself. With a velocity of nearly 300,000 km per second, in a year light travels about $9 \cdot 46 \times 10^{12}$ km. The distance to Proxima Centauri is therefore $4 \cdot 2$ light years. Even this distance, enormous on our terrestrial scale, is a small cosmic distance. The diameter of our Galaxy is about 10^5 light years, while the most distant objects yet observed lie over $1 \cdot 3 \times 10^{10}$ light years away.

PLANETS, STARS AND GALAXIES
The Solar System

The earth is the third, counting outward of nine planets revolving in nearly circular orbits round the sun. Some of their particulars are given in the Table (**F8**). The sun and its planets are the main bodies of the solar system. Mainly between the orbits of Mars and Jupiter revolve numerous small bodies—the minor planets or asteroids, the largest of which, Ceres, is only 1,000 km in diameter. Apart from these, the solar system is tenuously populated with particles varying in size from about a micron (10^{-6} m) to hundreds of metres in diameter. Some of these objects collide with the earth's atmosphere. The smaller particles (micro-meteoroids) are too small to be visible. Larger particles (meteoroids) cause the phenomenon known as meteors (commonly referred to as 'shooting stars') when they burn up at around 100 km altitude. The particle collides with air molecules. This causes frictional heating which usually results in complete vapourization of the particle. Even larger chunks, of rocky or iron composition, cause the rare and brilliant fireballs, some of which survive their high-speed flight through the earth's atmosphere and may later be recovered. Such objects (meteorites) are very important, providing examples of extraterrestrial rocks, and thus giving the composition of some of the most primitive material left in the solar system. Collisions with very large meteorites (or small asteroids) are now, fortunately, very rare. However, the large meteorite crater in Arizona is one recent reminder that such collisions still occur, although much less frequently now than earlier in the history of the planetary system. The surfaces of Mercury, the Moon, Mars, and Venus together with those of many other planetary satellites still show the scars from collisions with a multitude of objects of up to tens of km in diameter.

Comets are fascinating objects which, from time to time, provide a spectacular sight. More than 700 comets have been observed so far, and about six new ones are discovered each year. At the heart of every comet is a small nucleus. In 1986 the Giotto space probe revealed that Halley's comet has a potato-shaped nucleus measuring 15 km by 10 km. This nucleus consists of ices of various gases, chiefly water, interspersed with dust particles. In their highly elliptical orbits comets spend most of their life at great distances from the sun, where the temperature is very low because of the feeble solar radiation, so that all the "icy" materials are solid. Periodically, when each comet returns to the inner parts of the solar system, the increasing solar radiation heats the surface layers, evaporating the volatile ices, which carry the surface dust away from the comet nucleus. After this heating and evaporation process, the ultra-violet component of sunlight further breaks down the parent "icy" molecules, a process known as photo-dissociation, and many molecules become ionised. Solar-radiation pressure, acting on the dust constituents, and the solar wind acting on the ionised constituents, form the gigantic cometary tails which may reach 2×10^8 km in length—larger than the radius of the earth's orbit. *See also* L28.

The sun itself is a dense, roughly spherical mass of glowing matter, 1,392,000 km across. Its heat is so intense that the atoms are split into separated electrons and nuclei (**F11**) and matter in such a state is called plasma. At the sun's centre the temperature has the unimaginable value of about 15 million degrees Centigrade (a coal fire is about 800°C). Under such conditions the atomic nuclei frequently collide with one another at great speeds and reactions occur between them. The sun consists largely of hydrogen and, in the very hot plasma, the nuclei of hydrogen atoms interact by a series of reactions whose net result is to turn hydrogen into helium. This is a process which releases energy just as burning does, only these nuclear processes are incomparably more energetic than ordinary burning. In fact, the energy released is great enough to be the source of all the light and heat which the sun has been pouring into space for thousands of millions of years.

Emerging from the sun and streaming past the earth is a "solar wind" of fast-moving electrons and protons (**F11**) whose motion is closely linked with the behaviour of an extensive magnetic field based on the sun. In fact, the region round the sun and extending far into space past the earth is full of complex, fluctuating particle streams and magnetic fields which interact with planetary atmospheres causing, among other things, auroras and magnetic storms.

Stars

In colour, brightness, age, and size the sun is typical of vast numbers of other stars. Only from the human point of view is there anything special about the sun—it is near enough to give us life.

Even the possession of a system of revolving planets is not, according to some modern views, very unusual.

No star can radiate energy at the rate the sun does without undergoing internal changes in the course of time. Consequently stars evolve and old processes in them give rise to new. The exact nature of stellar evolution—so far as it is at present understood—would be too complex to describe here in any detail. It involves expansion and contraction, changes of temperature, changes of colour, and changes in chemical compositon as the nuclear processes gradually generate new chemical elements by reactions such as the conversion of hydrogen to helium, helium to neon, neon to magnesium, and so on. The speed of evolution changes from time to time, but is in any case very slow compared with the pace of terrestrial life; nothing very dramatic may occur for hundreds of millions of years. Evidence for the various phases of evolution is therefore obtained by studying many stars, each at a different stage of its life. Thus astronomers recognise many types with charmingly descriptive names, such as supergiants, blue giants, sub-giants, red, white and brown dwarfs.

The path of stellar evolution may be marked by various explosive events. One of these, which occurs in sufficiently large stars, is an enormous explosion in which a substantial amount of the star is blown away into space in the form of high-speed streams of gas. For about a fortnight, such an exploding star will radiate energy 200 million times as fast as the sun. Japanese and Chinese (but not Western) astronomers recorded such an occurrence in A.D. 1054, and the exploding gases, now called the Crab nebula, can still be seen in powerful telescopes and form a cloud six or seven light-years across. While it lasts, the explosion shows up as an abnormally bright star and is called a *supernova*. In late February 1987 a spectacular supernova occurred in our nearby galaxy the Large Magellanic Cloud. At a distance of only $1 \cdot 6 \times 10^5$ light years this supernova was the closest to the Earth for over 400 years. Many exciting findings are expected.

Groups of Stars

It is not surprising that ancient peoples saw pictures in the sky. The constellations, however, are not physically connected groups of stars but just happen to be patterns visible from earth. A conspicuous exception to this is the Milky Way, which a telescope resolves into many millions of separate stars. If we could view the Milky Way from a vast distance and see it as a whole we should observe a rather flat wheel of stars with spiral arms something like the sparks of a rotating Catherine wheel. This system of stars is physically connected by gravitational forces and moves through space as a whole; it is called a *galaxy*.

The Galaxy is about 10^5 light-years across and contains roughly 10^{11} stars. An inconspicuous one of these stars near the edge of the wheel is our sun; the prominent stars in our night sky are members of the galaxy that happen to be rather near us. Sirius, the brightest, is only $8 \cdot 6$ light-years away, a trivial distance, astronomically speaking.

The galaxy does not contain stars only, there are also clouds of gas and dust, particularly in the plane of the galaxy. Much of the gas is hydrogen, and its detection is difficult. However, gaseous hydrogen gives out radio waves with a wavelength of 21 cm. Radio telescopes are just the instruments to receive these, and workers in Holland, America, and Australia detected the gas clouds by this means. In 1952 they found that the hydrogen clouds lie in the spiral arms of the galaxy, and this is some of the strongest evidence for the spiral form.

Another important feature of the galactic scene is the weak but enormously extensive magnetic field. This is believed to have an intimate connection with the spiral structure.

Around the spiral arms, and forming part of the galaxy, are numerous globular clusters of stars. These are roughly spherical, abnormally densely packed, collections of stars with many thousands of members. Because of its form and density, a globular cluster may be assumed to have been formed in one process, not star by star. Thus all its stars are the same age. This is of great interest to astronomers, because they can study differences between stars of similar age but different sizes.

Galaxies

One might be forgiven for assuming that such a vast system as the galaxy is in fact the universe; but this is not so. In the constellation of Andromeda is a famous object which, on close examination, turns out to be another galaxy of size and structure similar to our own. Its distance is given in the table (**F8**). The Andromeda galaxy is the same basic structure as our own, but roughly half as big again. The Milky Way, the Andromeda nebula, and a few other smaller galaxies form a cluster of galaxies called the Local Group. It is indeed a fact that the universe is populated with *groups*, *clusters* and *superclusters*, of *galaxies*. A cluster may contain two or three galaxies, but some contain thousands.

By about 1920 it was known that there were at least half a million galaxies, and with the advent of the 2·54 m. Mt. Wilson telescope this number rose to 10^8 and has now been increased further by larger telescopes which can see out to distances greater than 10^{10} light years. Through the powerful telescopes the nearer galaxies reveal their inner structures. Photographs of galaxies are among the most beautiful and fascinating photographs ever taken, and readers who have never seen one should hasten to the nearest illustrated astronomy book. Most galaxies have a spiral or elliptical structure but about 2 per cent have peculiar wisps and appendages. Some galaxies are strong emitters of radio waves. A recently discovered type of galaxy is the starburst galaxy. This is an otherwise normal galaxy in which huge numbers of stars are forming in a small volume at its centre.

The Expanding Universe

Two discoveries about galaxies are of the utmost importance. One is that, by and large, clusters of galaxies are uniformly distributed through the universe. The other is that the distant galaxies are receding from us.

How is this known? Many readers may be familiar with the Doppler effect first discovered in 1842. Suppose a stationary body emits waves of any kind and we measure their wavelength, finding it to be L cm. Now suppose the body approaches us; the waves are thereby crowded together in the intervening space and the wavelength appears less than L; if the body recedes the wavelength appears greater than L. The Austrian physicist, J. Doppler (1803–53), discovered the well-known change of pitch of a train whistle as it approaches and passes us. The same principle applies to the light. Every atom emits light of definite wavelengths which appear in a spectroscope as a series of coloured lines—a different series for each atom. If the atom is in a receding body all the lines have slightly longer wavelengths than usual, and the amount of the change depends uniquely on the speed. Longer wavelengths mean that the light is redder than usual, so that a light from a receding body shows what is called a "red shift." The speed of recession can be calculated from the amount of red shift.

It was the American astronomer, V. M. Slipher, who first showed (in 1914) that some galaxies emitted light with a red shift. In the 1920s and 1930s the famous astronomer E. Hubble (1889–1953) measured both the distances and red shift of many galaxies and proved what is now known as Hubble's Law about which there is now some controversy. This states that the speed of recession of galaxies is proportional to their distance from us. This does not apply to our neighbours in the Local Group, we and they are keeping together. Hubble's Law has been tested and found to hold for the farthest detectable galaxies; they are about 7×10^9 light-years away and are receding with a speed approaching that of light.

The expansion of the universe does not imply that the Local Group is the centre of the universe —from any other viewpoint in the universe Hubble's Law would also be valid, and the distant galaxies would, similarly, all appear to be rapidly receding.

One possible implication of this most exciting scientific discovery is that, if the galaxies have always been receding, at an early time they must have been closer together. We can calculate that about 10^{10} years ago all the matter of the universe could have been densely packed. The truth or otherwise of this hypothesis is the most fundamental question of cosmology, and its testing still drives the quest to explore the universe, by larger and more sensitive telescopes, to the greatest possible distances.

Quasars, Pulsars and Black Holes

In November 1962 Australian radio astronomers located a strong radio emitter with sufficient precision for the Mt. Palomar optical astronomers to identify it on photographs and examine the nature of its light. The red shift was so great that the object must be exceedingly distant; on the other hand it looked star-like, much smaller than a galaxy. By the beginning of 1967 over a hundred of these objects had been discovered and other characteristics established, such as strong ultra-violet radiation and inconstancy, in some cases, of the rate at which radiation is emitted. Not all of these so-called quasars are strong radio emitters; some show all the other characteristics except radio emission. It has been estimated that the "quiet" kind are about a hundred times more numerous than the radio kind. One great problem here is: how can such relatively small objects generate such inconceivably great amounts of energy that they appear bright at such huge distances? Recent observations suggest that quasars are only the central visible part of an otherwise undetected galaxy. There may also be a massive black hole near the quasar centre.

Late in 1967, while investigating quasars, Cambridge radio astronomers discovered pulsars, a new type of heavenly body. Their characteristic is the emission of regular pulses of radio waves every second or so. A pulsar in the Crab nebula has a repetition rate even faster—about 1/30 sec— and it follows that pulsars must be very small bodies little if at all bigger than the Earth.

The existence of such small bodies raises again the problem of the ultimate fate of evolving stars. Much depends on their mass because this determines how strong the inward pull of gravity is. For a star to be at least temporarily stable the inward pull must be balanced by an outward pressure. In the sun this is the pressure of the burning hydrogen (**F6**) and the resulting average density is about 1·4 times that of water (**Table, F8**). In some stars the inward pressure is so great that collapse proceeds until it is balanced by a different type of outward pressure that sets in when electrons and atomic nuclei are forced into proximity. Stars so formed are called the "white dwarfs". They are millions of times denser than the sun—"a matchbox of their matter would weigh a ton"— and they are very small though not small enough to be pulsars. The latter are now generally thought to be a million times denser even than white dwarfs and to consist largely of tightly packed neutrons (*see* **F11**). Such bodies are called neutron stars.

Could the tendency of a massive star to fall inwards ever be so great that no outward pressure known to physics would suffice to balance it? Apparently it could! Many astrophysicists now hold on theoretical grounds that such a gravitational collapse could create a high density object whose gravitational field would be too strong to allow anything—including light waves—ever to leave the body. Such hypothetical objects are called "black holes" because, light and other signals being unable to emerge from them, their matter has literally disappeared from view. Black holes could be detected by the disturbance their gravitational attraction causes to neighbouring visible stars and also because atoms attracted by the black hole should emit intense X-rays before falling so far in that they too disappear into the black hole. Both of these detection methods have led some astronomers to conjecture (by 1973) that there is a black hole in the constellation Cygnus. There is another promising candidate for a black hole in the Large Magellanic Cloud. The theory of gravitational collapse raises profound and unresolved problems about our physical concepts.

Very recently, it has been conjectured that black holes, formed by the "death" of individual stars, and perhaps even on a massive scale at the centre of large and dense galaxies, have been responsible for "devouring" a very significant proportion of the total mass of the universe. Since this "devoured" mass is invisible by direct observation, we may have considerably underestimated the average density, and thus the total gravitational field of the universe.

THE ORIGIN AND DEVELOPMENT OF THE UNIVERSE

Scientists can only attempt to explain the universe by relating its observable structure to the features predicted by alternative theories of its origin and development. The time span of all our observations of the Cosmos is so small by comparison with the lifetime of the universe (more than 10^{10} years). Also, contrary to many other scientific disciplines, it is impossible to repeat the "experiment", under controlled conditions. We must, therefore, explore the evolution of the universe by using the fact that light from the most distant galaxies has taken about 10^{10} years to reach us, thus providing us with a crucial, if tantalisingly remote and thus indistinct, view of the universe at a much earlier epoch.

Several models of the universe have been based on Einstein's theory of General Relativity (F17). Einstein's equations may be solved to predict the evolution of the universe. However, there is a spectrum of solutions which vary from a continuous and indefinite expansion at the present rate to an eventual slowing and subsequent contraction to a dense state, again in the distant future, which hints at a "pulsating" universe.

The Steady-State Theory

As an alternative to the Evolutionary theory, Bondi, Gold, and Hoyle (1948) suggested the so-called "Steady-State" theory. This theory has no initial dense state or "origin" and, on a large scale, the density of galaxies and stars is always as at present. To permit this possibility, they proposed that matter—hydrogen atoms—is continuously created throughout space at a rate sufficient to compensate for the present observed expansion of the universe. Thus the average density of matter would always remain constant.

The Formation of Galaxies and Stars

On any theory of the universe, some explanation has to be found for the existence of clusters of galaxies. In all theories galaxies condense out from dispersed masses of gas, principally hydrogen.

It is believed on theoretical grounds each galaxy could not condense into one enormous star but must form many fragments which shrink separately into clusters of stars. In these clusters many stars, perhaps hundreds or thousands or even millions, are born. A small cluster, visible to the naked eye, is the Pleiades. The Orion nebula, visible as a hazy blob of glowing gas in the sword of Orion, is the scene of much star-forming activity at present. However, the best evidence yet for witnessing the birth of a star comes from observations by the Infrared Astronomical Satellite (IRAS). Deep within a gas and dust cloud called the Ophiuchus dark nebula, matter is falling inward in a manner predicted by contemporary theories of star formation. At the centre of this collapsing cloud there seems to be an embryonic star perhaps only 30,000 years old.

According to the Evolutionary theory the "initial dense state" consisted of very hot plasma in a state of overall expansion. The expanding plasma was both cooling and swirling about. The random swirling produces irregularities in the distribution of the hot gas—here it would be rather denser, there rather less dense. If a sufficiently large mass of denser gas happened to occur, then the gravitational attraction between its own particles would hold it together and

maintain its permanent identity, even though the rest of the gas continued to swirl and expand. Such a large mass would gradually condense into fragments to become a cluster of galaxies.

The Changing Scene

The 1960s witnessed revolutionary developments in both observational and theoretical astronomy. For example, it now seems agreed that remote sources of radio waves are more abundant the weaker their intensity. This strongly suggests that they are more abundant at greater distances. Thus the universe is not *uniform* as the original steady-state theory prescribed. Since greater distances correspond to earlier times, any extra abundance of objects observed at the greater distance means that the universe was denser in its younger days than now. This favours an evolutionary theory of the universe.

The same theory requires that the initial dense state of the universe—aptly christened "the primaeval fireball"—should contain intense electromagnetic radiation with a distribution of wavelengths characteristic of the high temperature. As the fireball, *i.e.*, the universe, expanded over a period of about 10^{10} years it cooled, and one feature of this process is that the wavelengths of the radiation increase and their distribution becomes characteristic of a much lower temperature. In fact, the wavelengths should now be concentrated round about 1 mm to 1 cm (corresponding to about $-270°$ C) and the radiation should approach the earth uniformly from all directions. Radiation just like this was detected in the 1960s by extremely sensitive instruments both at ground-based observatories and flown from balloon payloads high in the earth's atmosphere—above most of the water vapour and other constituents which interfere with such delicate observations. This "microwave background" radiation appears to be "cosmological", and thus supports strongly the evolutionary or "Big Bang" theory as opposed to the "Steady-State" theory, which cannot rationally explain the radiation.

The Formation of the Chemical Elements

A stable nucleus is one that lasts indefinitely because it is not radioactive. There are 274 known kinds of stable atomic nuclei and little likelihood of any more being found. These nuclei are the isotopes (F12) of 81 different chemical elements; the other elements, including, for example, uranium and radium are always radioactive. Some elements are rare, others abundant. The most common ones on earth are oxygen, silicon, aluminium, and iron. However, the earth is rather atypical. It is especially deficient in hydrogen, because the gravitational attraction of our small planet was not strong enough to prevent this very light gas from escaping into space.

It is possible to examine the chemical constituents of meteorites and to infer the composition of the sun and other stars from the spectrum of the light they emit. By such means, the conclusion has been reached that 93% of the atoms in our galaxy are hydrogen, 7% are helium; all the other elements together account for about one in a thousand atoms. A glance at the Table of Elements (*see* end of Sec.) will show that hydrogen and helium are two of the lightest elements: they are in fact the two simplest. The problem is to explain how the heavier chemical elements appear in the universe at all. It is here that a fascinating combination of astronomy and nuclear physics is required.

We have already referred to the fact that the energy radiated from the sun originates in nuclear reactions which turn hydrogen into helium. Why is energy given out? To answer this question we note that nuclei are made up of protons and neutrons (F11). These particles attract one another strongly—that is why a nucleus holds together. To separate the particles, energy would have to be supplied to overcome the attractive forces. This amount of energy is called *binding energy* and is a definite quantity for every kind of nucleus. Conversely, when the particles are brought together to form a nucleus the binding energy is *released* in the form of radiations and heat. Different nuclei consist of different numbers of particles, therefore the relevant quantity to consider is the *binding energy per particle*. Let us call this B. Then if elements of *high* B are formed out of those of *low* B there is a *release* of energy. *See also* **Nuclear Energy, L88.**

Now B is small (relatively) for light elements like lithium, helium, and carbon; it rises to a maximum for elements of middling atomic weight like iron; it falls again for really heavy elements like lead, bismuth, and uranium. Consequently, energy is released by forming middleweight elements either by splitting up heavy nuclei ("nuclear fission") or by joining up light ones ("nuclear fusion"). *See also* **L88.**

It is the latter process, fusion, that is going on in stars. The fusion processes can be studied in physics laboratories by using large accelerating machines to hurl nuclei at one another to make them coalesce. In stars the necessary high velocity of impact occurs because the plasma is so hot. Gradually the hydrogen is turned into helium, and helium into heavier and heavier elements. This supplies the energy that the stars radiate and simultaneously generates the chemical elements.

The Heaviest Elements

The very heavy elements present a problem. To form them from middleweight elements, energy has to be *supplied*. Since there is plenty of energy inside a star, a certain small number of heavy nuclei will indeed form, but they will continually undergo fission again under the prevailing intense conditions. How do they ever get away to form cool ordinary elements, like lead and bismuth, in the earth? One view links them with the highly explosive supernovae, to which we have already referred (**F4**(2)). If the heavy elements occur in these stars the force of the explosion disperses them into cool outer space before they have time to undergo the fission that would otherwise have been their fate. The heavy elements are thus seen as the dust and debris of stellar catastrophes. The view is in line with the steady-state theory, because supernovae are always occurring and keeping up the supply of heavy elements. In the evolutionary theory some of the generation of elements is supposed to go on in the very early stages of the initial dense state and to continue in the stars that evolve in the fullness of time. It cannot be claimed that the origin of the chemical elements is completely known, but we have said enough to show that there are plausible theories. Time and more facts will choose between them.

The Formation of the Planets

Precisely how the planetary system was formed is still not understood in detail. From extremely precise observations of the movements of some nearby stars, it seems certain that other planetary systems occur among our stellar neighbours. By inference, it is thus probable that among certain classes of stars, planetary systems are very common throughout the universe.

Two other facts are crucial for any theory of planetary system formation. First, all the planetary orbits lie nearly in the plane perpendicular to the axis of rotation of the sun. The planets' rotations about the sun are all in the same direction and their axes of rotation, with two exceptions (Venus and Uranus), are close to the polar axis of their orbit planes, and in the same sense as their orbital rotation about the sun. Secondly, there is a very strong inverse correlation between planetary distance from the sun and the planet's mean density, particularly if the correct allowance is made for the effects of gravitational compression in the deep interiors of planets (greater in large than in small planets).

Rather than theories which would place planetary formation as either the random collection of pre-formed planets by the sun in its path through the galaxy or as the consequence of a very near encounter between our sun and another star, it is now generally believed that the origin of the planetary system (and most of the satellites, etc.) was a direct consequence of the process which originally formed the sun.

As the primaeval solar nebula contracted, to conserve angular momentum, its rotation rate increased, and a diffuse equatorial disk of dust and gas formed. In the cold outer region ($10-20°$ K) of this disk, all materials except helium and possibly hydrogen could readily condense on dust particles. Near the centre the temperature was higher, increasingly so as the proto-sun heated up, initially by the energy released by its gravitational contraction and, later, by the thermonuclear processes (**F4**(1)).

The Process of Accretion

Within this rotating and swirling disk of gas and dust, the process of accretion proceeded. Low-velocity collision between dust particles from time to time allowed larger particles to be created, composed of a mixture of the heavier elements and also the "icy" materials, particularly so in the colder outer regions where more of the "ices" were in a frozen state. Virtually our only information on the composition of such particles comes from detailed study of meteorites and from spectroscopic observation of comets. Eventually rocks of the size of centimetres, metres, and even kilometres were built up in this way. The build-up, controlled by low-velocity collisions, particularly of "sticky" materials, and also by electrostatic charges, was, at all times, however, moderated by occasional destructive high-velocity collisions. The relatively high viscosity of the dust and gas mixture throughout the disk must have been very important in producing a relatively uniform, rotational motion throughout the disk.

When "rocks" a few kilometres in size had been created new factors became important. Gravitational forces firstly increased the capacity of the larger "rocks" to accrete additional dust and smaller particles and, secondly, allowed some retention of material after even high-velocity collisions which would have destroyed smaller pieces.

The next stage is possibly the most difficult to model. Within a relatively uniform disk containing large numbers of rocks up to a few kilometres in diameter mixed within the residual dust and a large amount of gas, and extending to well outside Pluto's orbit, a small number of massive planets were formed. Some debris now remains as the comets and asteroids; however this debris and all the major planets, including the massive Jupiter, represent in total only a very small percentage of the original material of the solar nebula which was not condensed to form the sun.

It would appear that relatively quickly, during a period of 10^7 or 10^8 years, the large numbers of kilometre-sized objects, by collision and mutual gravitational attraction, formed the nuclei of the present planets and probably, in most cases, their major satellites also, in orbits relatively similar to their present ones. The planet-building process was most efficient at distances from the sun corresponding to the present orbits of Jupiter or Saturn, a compromise between temperature decreasing with distance from the sun, allowing a greater percentage of the total material to be solid and thus available for accretion, and density of material being greater closer to the sun.

The Jovian Planets

The outer or "Jovian" planets must have grown quickly, sweeping up hydrogen and helium gas as well as solid particles. Closer to the sun, the "icy" materials, still mainly in gaseous form, could not contribute very significantly to the initial accretion process, so that only smaller planets could form. Owing to their smaller mass, gravitational field and thus lower "escape velocity," they were only able to accrete a small proportion of the heavier gas present within the inner part of the solar system. Thus, at present, these

THE SOLAR SYSTEM

	Mean distance from Sun (millions of km)	Diameter km	Period of Revolution	Average density (water = 1)	Number of Satellites
Sun	—	1,392,000			—
Mercury	57·9	4,880	88 days	5·4	0
Venus	108·2	12,104	224·7 days	5·2	0
Earth	149·6	12,756	365·26 days	5·5	1
Mars	227·9	6,787	687 days	3·9	2
Jupiter	778·3	142,800	11·86 years	1·3	16
Saturn	1,427	120,000	29·46 years	0·7	18
Uranus	2,869·6	51,118	84·01 years	1·2	15
Neptune	4,496·6	49,528	164·8 years	1·7	8
Pluto	5,900	c 3,050	247·7 years	0·6	1

Note: Chiron, an object recently discovered orbiting the sun between Saturn and Uranus has not been given "planet" status due to its small size.

"terrestrial" planets are much denser than the outer "Jovian" planets, much smaller in size, and contain very little hydrogen or helium. The planet-building process was probably ended by two factors: the gravitational disruptive effect of the planets already formed and the enhanced "solar wind" of the young sun, which swept much of the residual dust and gas out of the solar system.

Before the process was complete, however, the gravitational energy released by the material falling onto the proto-planets plus the radioactive heating of short-lived isotopes present at the time of planetary formation were responsible for melting most of the bodies of the planets and probably all the larger satellites and asteroids. This process allowed gravitational segregation of denser and lighter materials within the planets, and the production of the core, mantle and crustal regions of each of the terrestrial planets. Long after the dust and gas were driven from the solar system and the planet surfaces cooled and solidified, the residual larger rocks and asteroids, of which enormous numbers were originally still present, continued to be swept up by each of the planets. The record of this violent stage of the solar system's development can still be seen in the saturation cratering observed on the Moon, Mercury, and Mars.

In the past two decades, direct space exploration, using automated space probes (and manned spacecraft in the case of the Moon) has enormously increased our knowledge of the solar system. Notable have been the Mars "Viking" project, the Venus probes, the later Pioneer probes with Pioneer 11 flying on from Jupiter to Saturn, and the Voyagers 1 and 2, the latter visiting no less than four planets, ending with Neptune in 1989. The five space probes to Halley's comet in 1986 were also a huge success. Important discoveries have continued to be made by ground-based telescopes such as a new ring system of Uranus, the object Chiron, and the radar investigation of the terrain of Venus. Current and future space missions, such as the Galileo probe to Jupiter, the Cassini mission to Saturn, the Ulysses probe over the poles of the Sun, and the Hubble Space Telescope promise exciting new results.

THE EARTH

Structure

The earth has the shape of a slightly flattened sphere, with an equatorial radius of 6,378 km and a polar radius 21 km less. Its mass can be calculated from Newton's Law of Gravitation and from measurements of the acceleration due to gravity, and is $5·97 \times 10^{24}$ kg. The average density follows from these two figures and is about 5·5 grams per cubic centimetre. This is nearly twice the density of typical rocks at the surface, so there must be very much denser material somewhere inside, and the earth must have a definite internal structure.

This structure can be investigated using shock waves from earthquakes or large explosions. These are received at recording stations at different distances from their source, having penetrated to varying depths within the earth, and their relative times of arrival and characteristic forms enable the deep structure to be worked out. This consists of three main units, a core at the centre with a radius about half that of the earth, the mantle outside this, and the thin crust, about 35 km thick under the continents and 5 km thick under the oceans, forming a skin surrounding the mantle.

The composition of these three units can be deduced by observation and inference. For example, meteorites which arrive at the earth's surface from other parts of the solar system consist of three main types, composed of iron–nickel alloy, stony silicates, and a mixture of iron and silicates. Could these have originated from the break-up of some planet like the earth? If so, then perhaps the core of the earth is made up of iron–nickel alloy and the mantle of magnesium-rich silicates. Experiments on the physical properties of these materials at high pressures show strong similarities with the measured properties of the earth's interior. In addition, rocks composed of magnesium-rich silicates are found at the earth's surface in places where material seems to have come from great depth, such as in the debris from volcanic explosions. These may be direct samples of the earth's mantle.

Core, Mantle and Crust

By these arguments, and by many others, a picture can be built up of the internal structure of the earth. The core is composed of iron–nickel

SOME ASTRONOMICAL DISTANCES

(1 light-year = $9·46 \times 10^{12}$ km).

Object	Distance from Earth (light-years)	Velocity of recession (km per second)	Object	Distance from Earth (light-years)	Velocity of recession (km per second)
Sun	$1·6 \times 10^{-5}$	—	Andromeda Galaxy	$2·2 \times 10^{6}$	—
Nearest star (Proxima Centauri)	4·2	—	Galaxy in Virgo	$7·5 \times 10^{7}$	1,200
Brightest star (Sirius)	8·6	—	Galaxy in Gt. Bear	10^{9}	14,900
Pleiades	410	—	Galaxy in Corona Borealis	$1·3 \times 10^{9}$	21,600
Centre of Milky Way	$3·0 \times 10^{4}$	—	Galaxy in Bootes	$4·5 \times 10^{9}$	39,300
Magellanic clouds (the nearest galaxies)	$1·6 \times 10^{5}$	—	Very remote quasi-stellar object	$\sim 1·2 \times 10^{10}$	~280,000

alloy. It is liquid at the outside, but contains a solid inner core of radius about one-fifth of that of the earth.

Outside this the mantle is solid, and is made up mainly of magnesium–iron silicates of various kinds. By studying its physical properties through earthquake wave observations, the mantle may be divided into several zones, of which the most important is the asthenosphere. This is the part of the mantle between 70 and 300 km depth in which volcanic lavas are formed. In this region the mantle is everywhere quite near to the temperature at which it begins to melt, and is thus rather soft compared with the rest of the mantle. The presence of a soft asthenosphere accounts for many of the surface features of the earth, mountain belts and ocean basins, that make it so very different from cratered planets such as the Moon and Mars.

The sharp boundary between mantle and crust is called the Mohorovicic Discontinuity. Above it, the crust is different under continents and oceans. The thick continental crust has a composition that can broadly be called granitic, while the thin oceanic crust is poorer in silicon, sodium, and potassium and richer in calcium, iron, and magnesium. The continental crust has been built up over thousands of millions of years by welding together mountain belts of different ages, while the oceanic crust is made up of basalt lavas and is nowhere older than 250 million years.

Rocks

Rocks are naturally occurring pieces of the solid earth. If you take a rock and break it up into grains, then separate the grains into different heaps of like grains, each heap will consist of grains of the same *mineral*. For example, the kind of rock called granite can be divided into glassy grains of the mineral quartz, milky white or pink grains of the mineral feldspar, shiny black flakes of the mineral biotite, and shiny colourless flakes of the mineral muscovite. Both biotite and muscovite belong to the mica group of minerals. Each different mineral has a well-defined composition or range of composition, and a definite and characteristic arrangement of the atoms that compose it. There are several thousand known kinds of minerals, but only fifty or so are at all common.

There are three main kinds of rock; igneous rocks, formed by the solidification of molten lava; sedimentary rocks, formed from material laid down under gravity on the earth's surface; and metamorphic rocks, formed by heating or reheating of either of the other kind of rock. Each of these broad groups may be further subdivided. When *igneous rocks* solidify deep inside the earth, they cool slowly and large crystals have time to form. Coarse-grained igneous rocks such as granites are known as plutonic igneous rocks. Conversely the rapidly cooled fine-grained igneous rocks that form the volcanic lavas, such as basalts and rhyolites, are called volcanic igneous rocks. *Sedimentary rocks* can be divided into three kinds: Clastic sediments are those formed from mechanically abraded and transported fragments of pre-existing rocks and include sandstone, mudstone, and clay. Organic sediments are those composed, as are most limestones, of fragments of organically produced material such as shells, wood, and bone. Chemical sediments are formed by direct chemical action and include, most typically, salt deposits formed by evaporation of sea water. *Metamorphic rocks* are more difficult to subdivide. They are usually classified on the basis of their original composition and/or the maximum pressure and temperature to which they have been subjected. Chemical reactions in metamorphic rocks give rise to successions of minerals as the pressure and temperature change, so that examination of a metamorphic rock will often allow one to say how deeply it was buried and how hot it was.

Age of Rocks

There are two distinct ways of estimating the age of rocks. The first gives the *relative age*. It is based on the principle that in a sequence of sediments, older rocks lie underneath and younger ones above, that igneous rocks are younger than the rocks they intrude, and that folded rocks are formed earlier than the earth movements that fold them. Correlation of a sequence of rocks in one place with those in another is made by fossil faunas and floras. Thus a complete scale of relative ages can be built up, stretching back to the first rocks containing fossils (see the table in Part IV). The *age in years* can, on the other hand, be measured by using radioactive elements (Part II) contained in rocks. If the amount of a radioactive element present is measured, and the amount of the product of radioactive decay can also be found, then, using the known rates of decay, the time since the product started to accumulate (defined for this purpose as the age in years) can be measured. This method is particularly useful for studying rocks that do not contain fossils (igneous and metamorphic rocks, or those too old to contain fossils). By similar methods, the *age of the earth* can be obtained. This turns out to be about $4 \cdot 6 \times 10^9$ years. The rocks containing the first fossils are $2 \cdot 5$–3×10^9 years old, while organised life in abundance first appeared about $0 \cdot 6 \times 10^9$ years ago.

The Continents and the Ocean Floor

The outer part of the earth, namely, the asthenosphere and the solid mantle and crust overlying it, the lithosphere, is in a state of restless movement, and it is this movement that gives rise to the formation of oceans, continents, and mountain belts. The surface of the earth can be divided into a number of rigid plates of lithosphere, which move apart, or together, or slide past one another. Some of these plates are very large, such as the one which contains all of North America, all of South America, and about half of the Atlantic Ocean. Others are no more than a few thousand square kilometres in size. But they are all moving about relative to one another like ice floes in pack-ice. Where two plates move apart, hot material rises from the asthenosphere to fill the gap, partly melts, and gives rise to a chain of volcanoes and a thin volcanic crust. This is how ocean basins form and grow larger. In the Atlantic, the Mid-Atlantic Ridge marks the line along which plates are moving apart, and where new ocean is being formed. Long narrow pieces of ocean such as the Red Sea and the Gulf of California mark where a continent has just begun to split apart, and a new ocean is forming. Where two plates slide past one another, a great tear fault results. Such a fault is the San Andreas fault which runs from the Gulf of California to San Francisco. Jerky movement on this fault gave rise to the great San Francisco earthquake of 1906 and could give rise to another earthquake there at any time.

Where two plates move together, the result depends on the nature of the crust forming the plates. If at least one of the plates is oceanic, the oceanic crust dips down into the mantle and slides away to great depths until it eventually merges with the asthenosphere. Along this dipping sheet of crust, strong earthquakes occur and frictional heating of the sheet leads to melting and the production of quantities of lava. Examples of such boundaries are the Andes, where the Pacific Ocean bed dips beneath South America, and Indonesia, where the Indian Ocean bed dips below Asia. When both plates are continental, on the other hand, the crust is too thick and buoyant to slide into the mantle, and a collision results, giving rise to a fold mountain chain. Eventually the movement grinds to a halt, the plates weld together, and the fold mountains become dormant. The Himalayas were formed in this way from the recent collision of India and Asia. The evidence that has led to these conclusions is too complex to summarise here. It comes from a study of rock magnetism, earthquakes, the flow of heat from inside the earth and even from the shapes of the continents, that must match across the oceans by which they have been split apart. Confirmation has come from a series of holes drilled in the ocean which has shown how the crust becomes younger towards the centres of the oceans.

Rates of movement of plates have been calculated, ranging from a few millimetres a year to ten centimetres a year. The faster movements can be measured directly on the ground by such simple techniques as looking at the displacement of railway lines, walls, and roads, but the slower ones, and those beneath the oceans must be measured by more indirect geophysical methods. The mechanism by which this movement takes place is still unknown. Are the plates pulled by their sinking edges, or pushed by their rising edges, or moved by some other means? But it cannot be doubted that the movement does happen, and that it holds the key to the development of the earth's crust since the time it was first formed.

The Rest

There is a lot more to the study of the earth than has been possible to set down here. The oceans, the atmosphere, and the rocks of the crust all interact with one another in their development in a complex way. The surface of the earth has gradually changed as life has evolved over thousands of millions of years and ice ages have come and gone, changing the surface again and again. Just as important is the economic potential of the earth, on which we depend for all of our energy and all raw materials. This section has given the basic framework within which such further investigations are carried out, to help the reader understand as he reads more widely.

II. PHYSICS—THE FUNDAMENTAL SCIENCE OF MATTER

WHAT PHYSICS IS ABOUT

Anyone compelled by curiosity or professional interest to look into contemporary journals of pure physics research is soon struck by the fact that the old test-book division of physics into "heat, light, sound, electricity, and magnetism" has become very blurred.

Two different, though complementary, sections can be distinguished. First, there is the physics concerned with the properties of matter in bulk, with solids, liquids, and gases, and with those odd but very important substances, such as paints, plastic solutions, and jelly-like material, which are neither properly solid nor liquid. In this vast domain of physics questions like this are asked: Why is iron magnetic, copper not? What happens when solids melt? Why do some liquids flow more easily than others? Why do some things conduct electricity well, others badly, some not at all? During the last century, particularly the last few decades, it has become clear that such questions can be answered only by raising and solving others first. In particular, we must ask: (i) Of what nature are the invisible particles of which matter is composed? and (ii) How are those particles arranged in bulk matter?

The first of these two questions has generated the second major category of modern physics: this is the physics of particles and of the forces that particles exert on each other. In this field which represents science at its most fundamental questions like this are asked: If matter is composed of small units or particles, what are they like? How many kinds of particle are there? Do the particles possess mass? electric charge? magnetism? How do the particles influence each other? How can their motion be described and predicted?

The discussion which follows has been divided into two main parts (1) Particles and Forces, and (2) The Properties of Matter in Bulk, with part (1) describing the microscopic structure of matter and part (2) its macroscopic properties.

PARTICLES AND FORCES

Aristotle to Newton

The inference that matter should be composed of small particles or atoms originated, it is true, in classical times. The atomic idea was an attempt to solve the age-old problem of matter and its peculiar properties. The ancients had provided themselves with two solutions to the problem of matter:

(i) The theory of the four elements (earth, water, fire, air), from which all different forms of matter were composed by selecting different ratios of the four ingredients. This approach had been used by traditional philosophy and was adopted by Aristotle.

(ii) The theory of atomism which postulated the existence of atoms and empty space.

Atomism remained very much in the background in the development of Western Science and persisted even longer in the Arab world. The idea that matter is composed of "small units" was in reality forced into the mental development of mankind by the repeated application of the process of dimension halving. By the time of Newton atomism had come to the fore and Newton considered that God had made the Universe from "small indivisible grains" of matter. Nevertheless, the search for the "philosopher's stone" was still, in the seventeenth century, the main pursuit of many scientists, but the new chemistry of the seventeenth century made use of atomistic concepts. Newton's physics was a mechanics concerning particles in a vacuum and when Boyle described his gas law (i.e., Pressure × Volume is constant at a fixed temperature) he visualised matter as composed of particles with specific qualitative properties. It was, of course, the advance of experimental techniques which enabled scientists to test ideas and theories on the nature of matter.

Dalton and Atomic Theory

The modern view of atomism need be traced no farther than the beginning of the nineteenth century when Dalton and his contemporaries were studying the laws of chemical combination using precise weighing techniques. By that time the distinctions between elements, compounds, and mixtures were already made. Compounds and mixtures are substances which can be separated into smaller amounts of chemically distinguishable constituents. Elements (see end of Sec.) cannot be so divided. In a mixture the components may be mixed in any proportion and sorted out again by non-chemical means. In a compound the elements are combined in fixed proportions by weight. This last fact gives the clue to atomic theory.

Dalton pointed out that the fixed combining weights of elements could easily be explained if the elements consisted of atoms which combined in simple numerical ratios, e.g., 1 atom of element A with one of B, or one of B with two of C, and so on. For instance, 35·5 g of chlorine combine with 23·0 g of sodium to make 58·5 g of ordinary salt. If we assume one atom of chlorine links with one of sodium, then the atoms themselves must have weights in the ratio 35·5 to 23·0. This turns out to be consistent with the combining weights of chlorine and sodium in all other compounds in which they both take part. Sometimes two elements combine in several different proportions by weight. But this is easily explained by assuming that the atoms link up in a variety of ways e.g., one iron atom with one oxygen, or two irons with three oxygens, or three irons with four oxygens. Then the three different combining numbers of atoms arise from the three different numbers of atoms, using in each case the same ratio of oxygen atom weight to iron atom weight.

Atomic Weight

Over the century and a half since Dalton, these ideas have been repeatedly tested by chemical experiments No. one now doubts that every chemical element has atoms of characteristic weight. The atomic weight or more properly the relative atomic mass, of an element is by international agreement expressed relative to one isotope (*see* below) of carbon, namely carbon-12 which is given the relative mass of twelve. These numbers are only ratios; the real weight of one single oxygen atom is $2 \cdot 7 \times 10^{-23}$ g.

Valency

That the combinations of atoms in definite proportions was necessary to produce compounds, or more correctly molecules, was known from 1808. The reason why only one atom of sodium and one of chlorine was required to produce one molecule of salt was unknown. Further the seemingly odd combinations of two atoms of hydrogen (H) with one of oxygen (O) to give water (H_2O), while only one atom of hydrogen could combine with chlorine to give hydrogen chloride (HCl) could not be explained. This situation was not resolved until around 1860, when the chemical formulae of many molecules were known. It was then discovered that homologies existed in the elements, for example the series Na, K, Rb, Cs, or Fl, Cl, Br, I, and this culminated in the Periodic Table of the elements (see end Sec.). The valency of an atom was determined by its position in the periodic table and determined by the number of electrons (see below) which the atom has orbiting its nucleus. Atoms combined to form molecules in a manner which maintained the number of "valence" electrons in a stable grouping of 2, 8, or 18 (*see* **F24**). For example, sodium has one valence electron and chlorine seven, therefore the combination NaCl gives the stable grouping of eight; hydrogen has one and oxygen six, hence it requires two atoms of hydrogen and one of oxygen to give one stable molecule, H_2O. Other more complicated molecular structures and types of bonding between atoms are dealt with in the chemistry section. This discovery of particles smaller than the atom itself was necessary to fully comprehend the nature of valency in atomic combinations.

J. J. Thomson and the Electron

Matter is electrically uncharged in its normal state, but there exist many well-known ways of producing electric charges and currents—rubbing amber, or rotating dynamos, for example. It is therefore necessary to have some theory of electricity linked to the theory of matter. The fundamental experiment in this field was made by J. J. Thomson when, in 1897, he discovered the electron.

If you take two metal electrodes sealed inside a glass vessel and if the pressure of the air is reduced from atmospheric pressure, 76 cm of mercury, to 1 mm of mercury by mechanical pumping and then a high voltage, several kilo-volts, is applied to the electrodes, the negative electrode emits a "radiation" which causes the walls of the tube to glow. The rays are called *cathode rays*. The discovery of the electron was essentially a clarification of the nature of cathode rays. Thomson showed that they were streams of particles with mass and negative electric charge and a general behaviour unlike any other atomic particle known at that time. The importance of this discovery for the world of science cannot be overestimated, and its technical progeny are in every home and factory in X-ray machines, television tubes, and all electronic devices.

Rutherford–Bohr Atom

Since the electrons emerge from matter, they are presumably parts of atoms. The relation between the negative electrons and the positively charged constituents of matter was elucidated by the great experimenter Rutherford and the great theoretician Bohr. Their work, just before the First World War, showed that the positive charge, together with almost all the mass, is concentrated in the central core or nucleus of the atom about which the very light-weight electrons revolve. The diameter of an atom is about 10^{-8} cm, roughly one three-hundred-millionth part of an inch. The central nucleus has a diameter about 10,000 times smaller still. The nucleus and the electrons hold together because of the electric attraction between them.

The positive charge of the nucleus is responsible for holding the electron in the region of space around the nucleus. The electrostatic Coulomb force, if left on its own would quickly attract the electrons into the nucleus but since the electrons move in orbits, circular and elliptical, they experience an outward centrifugal force which balances the inward electrostatic force. The mechanism is similar to that which holds the earth in orbit around the sun, only here a gravitational force replaces the effect of the Coulomb force. Modern theories of the electronic structure of atoms are quantum mechanical (*see* below).

At this stage work could, and did, go on separately along several different lines:

(i) Electrons could be studied on their own. Nowadays the handling of beams of electrons of all sizes and intensities has become a major branch of technology.

(ii) The nucleus could be treated as a special problem, and this led to the mid-century flowering of nuclear physics, to the atomic bomb, and to nuclear power.

(iii) The behaviour of electrons in the atom could be analysed; this is the great domain of atomic physics which spreads into many other sciences as well.

Volumes have been written about each of these three fields, but we can spare only a few lines for each.

The Electron

Electrons are expelled from solids by light, heat, electric fields, and other influences. It has therefore been possible to study beams of electrons on their own *in vacuo*. Electrons inside matter, either as constituents, or temporarily in transit, can also be observed by their innumerable effects. These observations all show the particles to be indistinguishable one from another; all electrons are the same wherever they come from. They have a definite mass ($9 \cdot 11 \times 10^{-28}$ g), a negative electric charge, a magnetic moment, and a "spin" (intrinsic rotatory motion). No one has ever subdivided an electron or obtained an electric charge smaller than that on one electron. The electronic charge is therefore used as a basic unit of charge in atomic physics. The electron has come to be the best known of all the "fundamental particles." It is now used in research as probe for studying the structure of matter, for which it is ideally suited, since it is very much smaller than an atom. A whole field of electron-scattering research which studies the nature and structure of solids, liquids, and gases is being actively conducted in many laboratories.

The Nucleus

The early research programmes in nuclear physics were greatly facilitated by the occurrence in nature of certain unstable (radioactive) nuclei which emit fast-moving fragments. The latter can be used as projectiles to aim at other nuclei as targets; the resulting impacts yield much valuable information. This technique still dominates nuclear physics, though nowadays the projectiles are artificially accelerated by one or other of the large costly machines designed for the purpose.

The most important early discovery was that the nucleus consists of two types of fundamental particle—the positively charged *proton* and the electrically neutral *neutron*. These two are of nearly equal mass (about 1,800 times that of the electron), and like electrons, have a magnetic moment and spin. The proton charge is equal to the electron charge, though opposite in sign. Consider a moderately complex nucleus like that of iron. This usually has 30 neutrons and 26 protons. Its atomic weight therefore depends on the total number of neutrons plus protons, but the total charge depends only on the number of protons—called the *atomic number*. The latter is denoted by Z while the total number of neutrons plus protons is called the *mass number* and denoted by M. A species of nucleus with given values of Z and M is called a *nuclide*. Z is also the number of electrons in the atom, since the atom as a whole is electrically neutral. The atomic number determines the chemical nature of the atom (see below), so that by altering the number of *neutrons* in a nucleus we do not change the chemical species. It is therefore possible to find—and nowadays to make—nuclei of the same element which nevertheless differ slightly in weight because they have different numbers of neutrons. These are called *isotopes*. Iron isotopes are known with 26, 27, 28, 29, 30, 31, 32, and 33 neutrons, but all have 26 protons. Thus a set of isotopes consists of the various nuclides that have the same Z but different M's.

When the atomic properties of isotopes are measured it is found that small, hyperfine differences in the motions of the electrons around the respective nuclei exist. These result from the different total spin of the isotopes and its effect on the orbiting electrons. This influence of atomic properties by nuclear effects is important in that it provides a link between different fields of research

Stable Nuclides

The protons and neutrons in a nucleus are bound together by strong forces called *nuclear forces*. In many cases, the forces are so strong that no particles ever escape and the nucleus preserves its identity. There are two hundred and seventy-four different combinations of neutrons and protons of this kind, and they are called the *stable nuclides*. The earth is largely composed of such stable nuclides, because any unstable ones have, in the course of time, spontaneously broken up into stable residues.

Nevertheless, there are some unstable nuclei left on earth. They give rise to the phenomenon of radioactivity which was discovered by Becquerel in 1893.

Unstable Nuclides: Radioactivity

Becquerel found that certain chemicals containing uranium gave off rays capable of blackening a photographic plate, and shortly afterwards Marie and Pierre Curie discovered more substances, including radium, which produce similar but stronger effects. By now, about fifty chemical elements having radioactive properties are known to exist on earth, some, like radium, being strongly radioactive, others, like potassium, being so weak that the radiations are difficult to detect. These are called the *natural radioactive nuclides*.

The main facts about radioactivity are as follows: it is a *nuclear* phenomenon and (with minor exceptions) proceeds quite independently of whatever the electrons in the atom may be doing. Thus, the radioactivity of an atom is not affected by the chemical combination of the atom with other atoms, nor by ordinary physical influences like temperature and pressure. The radioactivity consists of the emission by the substance of certain kinds of rays. The early workers, Rutherford being the giant among them, distinguished three kinds of rays labelled a, β, and γ. These are described below. Whatever kind of ray is examined, it is found that the radiation from a given sample decreases gradually with time according to a definite law which states that the intensity of radiation decreases by half every T seconds. The number T, called the half-life, is constant for each radioactive material, but varies enormously from substance to substance. For instance, radium decreases its activity by a half every 1,622 years, whereas the half-life of one of the polonium isotopes is about 0.3×10^{-6} sec.

a-, β-, and γ-rays

The three most well-known types of radioactive emission are quite distinct from one another.

(i) a-rays or a-particles consist of two protons and two neutrons bound together. They are ejected from the radioactive nucleus with one of several well-defined speeds. These speeds are high, often of the order 10^9 cm per sec. Two protons and two neutrons are the constituents of the nucleus of helium, and a-particles are thus fast-moving helium nuclei.

(ii) β-rays are moving electrons. They may emerge from their parent nucleus with any speed from zero to a definite maximum. The maximum speed often approaches that of light, and is different for each isotope. The electron has a

positively charged counterpart, the positron (see below), and β-rays are sometimes positrons. To distinguish the two cases, the symbols β^- and β^+ are used. The naturally occurring β-radiations are almost all β^-.

(iii) γ-rays travel with the speed of light because they are in fact electromagnetic waves differing from light only in the extreme shortness of their wavelength. They have no electric charge.

It is unusual, though not unheard of, for the same radioactive substance to emit both a- and β-rays. On the other hand, γ-rays frequently accompany either a- or β-rays.

γ-rays pass through matter easily; in fact, they are extra penetrating X-rays. a-rays can be stopped by thin sheets of tissue paper. a-rays brought to rest pick up a pair of electrons from the surrounding matter and become neutral helium atoms, and helium gas from this source is consequently found imprisoned in certain radioactive rocks. β-rays are intermediate in penetrating power between a- and γ-rays.

We must now try to interpret these observations.

Radioactive Disintegration

A nucleus is a collection of neutrons and protons interacting with each other and possessing collectively a certain amount of energy. Just as some human organisations lose their coherence if they accept too many members, so nuclei can remain stable only if (i) the total number of particles is not too great, and (ii) neutrons and protons are there in suitable proportions. Radioactive nuclei are the ones for which either or both these conditions do not hold. Sooner or later such nuclei eject a fragment, thus getting rid of some energy they cannot contain. This is called a *radioactive disintegration*, and the fragments are the a-, β-, and γ-rays. a-emission relieves a nucleus of two neutrons and two protons and some energy; γ-emission simply carries off excess energy without altering the number or kind of particles left behind. β-emission is more complicated. There are no electrons normally present in a nucleus, but they are suddenly created and explosively emitted if a neutron changes into a proton; positive electrons are similarly generated if a proton changes into a neutron. β-emission is therefore a mechanism for changing the ratio of protons to neutrons without altering the total number of particles.

Both a- and β-emission change the Z of a nucleus, and the product, or daughter nucleus, is a different chemical element. a-emission also changes the M. It might happen that the daughter nucleus is unstable, in which case it too will disintegrate. Successive generations are produced until a stable one is reached. Part of such a family tree is shown below. The symbols above the arrows show the kind of rays emitted at each stage, the figures are the mass numbers, M, and the names and symbols of chemical elements can be found at the end of the Section.

$$\text{U}^{238} \xrightarrow{a} \text{Th}^{234} \xrightarrow{\beta} \text{Pa}^{234} \xrightarrow{\beta} \text{U}^{234} \xrightarrow{a} \text{Th}^{230} \xrightarrow{a}$$
$$\text{Ra}^{226} \xrightarrow{a} \text{Rn}^{222} \xrightarrow{a} \text{Po}^{218} \xrightarrow{a} \text{Pb}^{214} \xrightarrow{\beta} \text{Bi}^{214} \xrightarrow{\beta}$$
$$\text{Po}^{214} \xrightarrow{a} \text{Pb}^{210} \xrightarrow{\beta} \text{Bi}^{210} \xrightarrow{\beta} \text{Po}^{210} \xrightarrow{a} \text{Pb}^{206}$$
$$(\text{Pb}^{206} \text{ is stable lead}).$$

This family exists naturally on earth, because the head of the family, U^{238}, has so long a half-life (4.5×10^9 years) that there has not yet been time enough since its formation for it to have disappeared.

Artificial Radioactivity

Nowadays many new radioactive isotopes can be man-made. All that is required is to alter the M or Z (or both) of a stable isotope to a value which is incompatible with stability. The means for doing this is *bombardment, i.e.*, stable nuclei are exposed to the impacts of atomic particles such as streams of protons from an accelerator, the neutrons in an atomic reactor, or simply the a-particles from another radioactive substance.

The new material is called an *artificially radio-active isotope*. Artificial radioactivity is not different in kind from that of the naturally radio-active substances, but the half-lives are usually on the short side. Indeed, the isotopes in question would exist in nature but for the fact that their short half-lives ensured their disappearance from the earth long ago.

Suppose a piece of copper is exposed to the intense neutron radiation in an atomic reactor at Harwell.

The more abundant of the two stable isotopes of ordinary copper has thirty-four neutrons and twenty-nine protons (*i.e.*, $Z = 29$, $M = 63$). In the reactor many (not all) of these nuclei absorb a neutron, giving an unstable copper nucleus with $Z = 29$, $M = 64$. When removed from the reactor the specimen is observed to be radioactive with a half-life of 12·8 hours. It is somewhat unusual in that it gives out both β^- and β^+ rays. Some nuclei emit electrons, leaving a daughter nucleus with one more positive charge than copper, *i.e.*, a zinc nucleus ($Z = 30$, $M = 64$). One neutron has become a proton, and the re-sulting zinc nucleus is stable. The others emit positrons, leaving behind a nucleus in which a proton has been turned into a neutron ($Z = 28$, $M = 64$); this is a stable nickel nucleus. The overall process is one example of the artificial transmutation of the chemical elements which is now a commonplace of nuclear physics. It was first discovered by Irene and Frederick Joliot-Curie in 1934.

Lack of a Complete Theory

Consider now a collection of, say, one million radioactive nuclei of the same kind. It is im-possible to tell exactly when any one of them will disintegrate; it is a matter of chance which ones break up first. All we know is that, after a time equal to the half-life, only a half a million will survive unchanged. In general, the more excess energy a nucleus has, the more likely it is to break up, and therefore the shorter the half-life of that particular nuclear species. In principle, to cal-culate the half-life theoretically, one would have to have a reliable theory of nuclear forces and energies. This is still being sought after, so it is probably fair to say that while the laws of behaviour of radioactive isotopes are well and accurately known, the *explanation* of this behaviour in terms of the properties of protons and neutrons is by no means complete.

Nuclear Fission—Chain Reaction

A discovery important not just for nuclear physics but for the whole of mankind was made by Hahn and Strassman in 1939. This was the dis-covery of nuclear fission in uranium. One of the natural isotopes of uranium is an unstable one, U^{235}, with 143 neutrons and 92 protons. It norm-ally shows its instability by emitting a- and γ-rays. If uranium is bombarded with neutrons, some U^{235} nuclei temporarily gain an extra neutron, which makes them even less stable. This they show by splitting into two roughly equal parts, called fission fragments, together with two or three neutrons. There are two highly important things about this disintegration. One is that the two or three neutrons can promote further disintegrations in other uranium nuclei, and the process can therefore be self-propagating: it is then called a *chain re-action*. The other is that the total mass of the fission products is less than that of the original nucleus. This mass difference does not disappear without trace; it turns into energy according to a formula referred to in a paragraph below (**F18**(1)).

Nuclear Fusion

The ability of two light nuclei to combine and form a heavier nucleus is called fusion. A reac-tion of this nature does not form a chain process but proceeds in singly induced reactions. A typical fusion reaction is the formation of a helium nucleus (mass 3) from two deuterium nuclei which are made to collide at an energy of 60 keV (speed of 2·410⁶ m/s)

i.e., $^2D_1 + {}^2D_1 \rightarrow {}^3He_2$ (0·82 meV) + n(2·45 meV)

where the $^3He_2$ particle has kinetic energy of 0·82 meV and the free neutron has free kinetic energy of 2·45 meV. This type of reaction is exo-energetic, the additional kinetic energy coming from the tighter binding of the nucleus in ^3He than in the two separate deuterium nuclei. The energy released in this form of nuclear reaction is much more than that in a fission process and is respon-sible for the emitted energy of the sun which burns hydrogen to form helium.

Applications of Nuclear Reactions

The world has two uses for the energy released in nuclear reactions:

(1) nuclear weapons;
(2) nuclear power plants.

The only nuclear bombs to be used in anger employed the fission chain reaction proceeding at a rapid rate which quickly becomes uncontrollable and produces a tremendous explosion. The second generation of nuclear warhead uses the fusion reaction, which is initiated by a fission-reacting detonator to produce an even more des-tructive blast. The third generation of nuclear warhead uses the large flux of very energetic neutrons to kill biological material, but the blast effect is essentially zero, hence attacks with neutron bombs leave most non-biological material and structures intact.

In the second application the nuclear fission process is controlled to provide a constant source of energy to drive turbines which produce elec-tricity.

Both uses represent epoch-making technical achievements, but mankind has yet to show itself capable of bearing sanely the burden of respon-sibility which nuclear physicists have laid upon it. One thing is certain: the discoveries will not cease. Already, other fissionable elements have been made and used; new chemical elements have been created; nuclear plants ("atomic piles") have stimulated great demands for new materials that will stand the heat and radiation inside the reactor, and this promotes research in other fields of science; irradiation inside an atomic pile gives new, and potentially useful properties to old materials; nuclear power drives ships and submarines. It is difficult to write even briefly about contemporary nuclear physics without feel-ing keenly the ambiguity of its powerful promises.

Atoms

A nucleus surrounded by its full complement of electrons is an electrically neutral system called an atom. Neither the atom as a whole, nor its nucleus, counts as a "fundamental particle" because either can be subdivided into more elementary parts, thus:

atom $\longrightarrow$ electrons + nucleus $\longrightarrow$ electrons + neutrons + protons

The chemical identity of the atoms of a given element, which was Dalton's key idea, depends entirely on the number and motion of the elec-trons. For example, the simplest element, hydrogen, has one proton for a nucleus, and one electron. The latter is comparatively easily detached or disturbed by the electric forces exerted by neighbouring atoms, consequently hydrogen is reactive chemically, *i.e.*, it readily lends its electron to build chemical structures with other equally co-operative elements. The second element, helium, has a nucleus of two protons and two neutrons; outside are two electrons in a particularly stable arrangement. Both electrons orbit the nucleus in the same spacial orbit, but with their spin directions oppo-site and at 90° to the plane through the nucleus and the electrons. This pair of electrons is so difficult to disarrange that the special name of closed shells has been coined to cover such cases. The fact that two electrons can be present in the same orbit is only possible if their spins are anti-parallel (Pauli Exclusion Principle). In the case of a stable group of eight electrons they arrange themselves in groups of two and their spins antiparallel. Helium with its closed shell will not react chemically, whereas hydrogen, which has an open shell of only one electron, will react very quickly with other atoms.

As the nuclear charge increases, different electron arrangements of greater or lesser stability succeed one another, with every so often a closed shell corresponding to one of the chemically inert gases neon, argon, xenon, krypton.

Such considerations, pursued in sufficient detail, enable atomic physics to account for all the differences and similarities among the chemical elements and, in principle at least, for all other facts of chemistry as well.

Ions

Changes in the atomic properties of an atom are accomplished by altering the position of any electron from one orbit to another. In the limit when an electron is completely removed from the atom, leaving it positively charged, the atom is said to be ionised and is called a positive ion. An atom can be singly or multiply ionised up to a level equal to the number of electrons existing in the neutral atom. In addition, atoms can, through distortion of the existing electrons, accept an additional electron and become negative ions. These can be formed in a resonance scattering process and exist only for life-times of only 10^{-14}s or be formed by chemical reactions. The roles played by negative and positive ions in the upper atmosphere of the earth and stellar atmospheres have been of special interest to atomic physicists since the 1930s.

Maxwell and Electromagnetic Waves

Atoms are held together by the electric attraction of the nucleus for the electrons. Finer details of atomic behaviour depend on the magnetic moments of the particles. Any moving charged particle gives rise to magnetic effects, and in the dynamo a coil moving in a magnet produces an electric current. It can be seen therefore that electric and magnetic phenomena are intimately linked. Any region of space subject to electric and magnetic influences is called an *electromagnetic field*.

In 1862, before the discovery of the electron, Maxwell, while still in his twenties, had perfected a general theory of the electro-magnetic field. This theory today still describes correctly almost all electro-magnetic phenomena. The elegance of this theory is difficult to appreciate, but it alone was the only theory of pre-twentieth century physics which satisfied the prerequisites of Einstein's relativity theory (1905), *i.e.*, inherent in its structure was the concept of relativistic invariance. *Inter alia*, he proved that disturbances in the electric and magnetic conditions at one place could be propagated to another place through empty space, with a definite velocity, just as sound waves are propagated through air. Such electromagnetic disturbances in transit are called *electromagnetic waves*, and their velocity turned out experimentally to be the same as that of light and radio waves—which was a decisive argument to show that both of these phenomena are themselves electro-magnetic waves.

Einstein and Photons

In the years between about 1900 and 1920 this view was upset by Planck, Einstein, Millikan, and others, who focused attention on phenomena (radiant heat, photoelectricity) in which light behaves like a stream of particles and not at all like waves. A wave and a particle are two quite different things, as anyone will admit after a moment's contemplation of, say, the ripples on a pond and a floating tennis ball. The acute question was: is light like waves or particles?

Theoretical physicists have devised means of having it both ways. To say that light behaves as particles means that the waves of the electromagnetic field cannot have their energy subdivided indefinitely. For waves of a given frequency, there is a certain irreducible quantity of energy that must be involved whenever light interacts with anything. This quantity is the product hv where v is the frequency and h is a constant named after Planck. Each such unit is called a *quantum of the electromagnetic field* or a *photon* and is counted as one of the fundamental particles. Frequencies and wavelengths vary widely. Typical wavelengths are: radio—hundreds or thousands of metres; radar—a few centimetres; visible light—5×10^{-5} cm; X-rays—10^{-8} cm.

De Broglie and Particles

Since it seemed possible to attribute particle properties to electro-magnetic waves, then why not associate wave properties with particles. If an electron (mass m) is travelling with a velocity of v cm/s, then De Broglie (1923) suggested that its characteristic wavelength would be given by the relation $mv\ \lambda = h$; for example if $v = 10^5$ cm/s, $m = 9 \times 10^{-28}$ g, $h = 6 \cdot 610^{-27}$ erg-seconds, then $\lambda = 7,500$ Å, which is the same wavelength as red light. This proposal was confirmed in 1927 by Davisson and Germer when they showed that electrons could produce diffraction, a property until then only associated with light. These wave-like properties are now known to exist for all particles, and we now consider a particle with momentum mv to behave like a wave of wavelength $\lambda = h/mv$.

De Broglie made his revolutionary assertion in his doctoral thesis, and his examiners were so uneasy about the validity of the hypothesis that they were prepared to fail the young man in his examination. Happily for De Broglie, Einstein was visiting that particular university and he was asked his opinion of the idea; his reply ensured success for De Broglie and saved the examiners from future embarrassment.

Molecules

Electrical attractions and interactions of various kinds can cause atoms to combine with each other or themselves to form molecules. Two similar atoms, say hydrogen, combining to form the homonuclear diatomic molecule H_2, while two different atoms, hydrogen and chlorine, will form a heteronuclear diatomic molecule HCl. Molecules have a wide range of complexity, from simple pairs of atoms to highly intricate spirals and chains composed of thousands of atoms. The biological basis of all life is, of course, molecular in both origin and function.

Excited Atoms

Like nuclei, atoms, when given excess energy (insufficient to ionise them), will absorb the energy in one of the electrons, which is then displaced from its equilibrium state to a state (or orbit) of higher energy. It will remain there for typically 10^{-8} seconds before returning to its equilibrium position with the excess energy being emitted as light. The time an atom remains in its excited state can exceed 10^{-8} seconds; lifetimes of $0 \cdot 1$ second are known, and these metastable states are prevented by the atomic properties of the atom from decaying quickly to their equilibrium states. The colour of the light emitted is characteristic of the atom involved, with the more energetic transitions giving blue light while the less energetic transitions give red light. Hence the emitted colour (or wavelength) of the light can be used as a tool for chemical identification and study of the various transition probabilities in atoms.

Herein lies the explanation of innumerable natural and technical phenomena, such as the colours of glowing gases whether they exist in the sun and stars, in aurora, or in street-lamps and neon signs. Herein also lies the reason for the importance of spectroscopy, which is the study of the characteristic radiation from excited states for spectroscopy is not only a useful tool for the chemical identification of substances ("spectroscopic analysis") but was one of the main routes along which twentieth-century physicists broke through to a knowledge of the inner nature of the atom.

Forces in Nature

Nature uses four, possibly five, apparently different forces to make one particle interact with another. The weakest force is **gravity** which although present at all particle interactions, is insignificant in atomic and nuclear interactions. Gravity controls the mass distribution in the universe and the force has an infinite range of interaction.

The **electric force** which also has an infinite range of interaction is much stronger than the gravitational force and is responsible for the binding forces inside atoms by the attraction of nuclei for electrons.

Inside the nucleus two types of interaction take place which require different forces for their existence:

(1) the forces which hold neutrons and protons together in the nucleus and this is the **strong force,** and
(2) the **weak force** which controls the changes in charge state of nucleons, *e.g.*, the β-decay process when a neutron in a nucleus changes into a proton with the ejection of an electron is controlled by the weak force.

Both these nuclear forces are short-range with their radius of influence approximately 10^{-13} cm, with the weak force acting on all matter and the strong force acting on nucleons only. In today's parlance the strong force will act only on particles which are single multiples of quarks (see later). Since quarks exist (or more precisely, since their existence has been deduced), then it is necessary to have a force through which they can interact.

The fifth force of the universe is postulated to be the **colour force** which operates only on quark particles and has a mode of interaction which prevents a normal range restriction being placed on it. The proton, *i.e.*, the nucleus of atomic hydrogen, is composed of three quarks which move about freely within the shell of the proton; only when one quark tries to escape across the boundary of the proton does it experience the colour force which rebinds into the proton. Before we discuss further the interactions of these forces we must describe the range of particles which exist in physics.

Elementary Particles

When considering the word elementary in this context the reader should be wary of thinking that it implies some degree of absoluteness. The elementary mass of any particular particle is always highly qualified and subject to change. When a particle is discovered physicists measure its properties, *i.e.*, mass, electric charge, and spin, and determine which of the five forces to which it is subject. In addition, its life-time must be determined to see if the particle is stable or only a transient particle which will break up into other particles. The life-times of unstable particles are extremely short, ranging from 10^{-17}s to 10^{-21}s, and it is debatable if a particle which lasts only for 10^{-21}s should be called a particle. Generally now such short-lived particles are called resonances which are produced in an interaction which is only a step to the final product.

The rudimentary classification of particles is into four groups:

(1) photons
(2) leptons
(3) mesons
(4) baryons

All particles have an anti-particle which has the same mass but opposite charge as the real particle, the only exception being the photon, which is its own anti-particle and forms a group on its own. The leptons (electron, muon, and neutrino) form a stable group of particles and do not react to the strong or colour forces. This group of particles, and the photon, are perhaps the most fundamental of all particles. The mesons are unstable particles and (as will be seen later) exist only to act as a means which enables nucleons to interact with each other. They are subjected to the strong nuclear force. All particles heavier than the proton are called baryons, every one of them, except the proton, is unstable in some degree, and a vast number of them are known. Only a few are listed in the Table on page **F16.**

Mesons and baryons are collectively called hadrons. All of these unstable particles have been detected either in the cosmic flux falling on the earth or produced in the very high energy accelerating machines in Europe, the USA, and the USSR.

Strangeness

Some particles have long life-times $\sim 10^{-9}$ s, which is much larger than that encountered normally. Particles which possessed these long life-times were called "strange". Strangeness describes not a new property of matter but a different quality of matter which persists long enough to enable that particle to engage in strong nuclear-force interactions. Hence strangeness does not persist indefinitely. The decay of a strange particle into other particles with the abolition of strangeness proceeds via the weak nuclear force. The strange (and doubly strange) particles form highly symmetrised shapes when combined with non-strange particles. The pattern itself does not explain anything, but the underlying theory, known as Group Theory, does indicate by symmetry arguments which particle should be necessary to form a complete group. This mathematical procedure had a resounding success in 1964 when it predicted the existence of a triply strange particle known as "omega minus". The organisation of particles according to their properties of mass, spin, and strangeness in groups is now only an organisation exercise, and it will not tell us anything about the composition of nucleons.

Interactions of Particles

The method by which atomic, nuclear, and sub-nuclear particles interact is via the exchange of energy which can be considered as a particle exchange. The interaction between electric charges proceeds by the exchange of photons. For example, two charges feel each other by one charge emitting a photon which interacts with the second charge. Since the electric force has infinite range, its force-carrying particle has zero mass. The same criteria apply in the gravitational force, where the graviton is the particle which carries the force effect between particles of matter. Since the weak, strong, and colour forces are short-range, then their force-carrying particles have finite masses. The weak force is transmitted by W and Z particles and the strong force can be considered as transmitted by mesons. The quarks interact via the colour force, which is carried by gluons (mass at present unknown), which also feel the force themselves. The colour force does not distinguish between or acknowledge the existence of strangeness and charm.

A theory which combines the electric and weak forces into a single interaction has predicted the masses of the W and Z particles to be around 80 and 90 Gev respectively. In early 1983 experimental evidence was found by international groups at *CERN* for the existence of the W particle with the predicted mass thereby giving considerable support to this theory. A long term aim is to unify all the known forces of nature into a single interaction.

Quarks

The stability of the leptons contrasts sharply with the instability of the hadrons (excepting the proton), and this as well as other things had led physicists to consider that all hadrons were composed from different combinations of yet undiscovered particles. Gellmann has postulated the existence of three particles from which the nucleons, mesons, and hence all hadrons are composed. These "new" particles are attributed with fractional electric charges of $+\frac{2}{3}$, $-\frac{1}{3}$, and $-\frac{1}{3}$ of the electron charge. The particles were called quarks. The name quark was taken from the novel *Finnegans Wake* by James Joyce, the meaning of which is obscure, which is perhaps appropriate, but as students of Joyce will know, quark means "non sense", and other interpretations as to its meaning, such as the "sound of seagulls" or "quarts" are wrong. The three

SOME MEMBERS OF THE ATOMIC FAMILY

The numbers in brackets after the name denote first the electric charge and second, the mass. The charge on an electron is counted as -1 unit and the electron mass as $+1$ unit. Thus $(+1,207)$ means the particle has a positive charge of 1 unit and a mass 207 times that of the electron.

The mass energy of an electron is 0.51 MeV, hence conversion to mass energies can be made by multiplying the given mass by 0.51. Thus the muon has a mass energy of 106 MeV. Note: the letter M is used to denote quantities of millions and the letter G to denote quantities of thousand of millions.

Photon $(0, 0)$	A quantum of electromagnetic radiation, *e.g.*, light, X-rays, γ-rays. The concept was introduced by M. Planck in 1900 when he described the emission of light as taking place in "packets" rather than in a steady stream. The energy of a photon is proportional to the frequency of the radiation and inversely proportional to the wavelength.
	Leptons
Electron $(-1, 1)$	Discovered by J. J. Thomson in 1897. The number of orbital electrons in an atom determines its chemical properties. Actual rest mass $= 9.1 \times 10^{-28}$ g. Emitted as β-rays by some radioactive nuclei. A stable particle.
Positron $(+1, 1)$	Positive counterpart or, "anti-particle", to the electron. Predicted theoretically by P. A. M. Dirac in 1928 and first discovered in cosmic rays by C. D. Anderson in 1932. Emitted as β-rays by some radioactive nuclei. When positrons and electrons collide they usually annihilate each other and turn into γ-rays; consequently, positrons only last about 10^{-10} sec. within ordinary matter, but are stable in isolation.
Neutrino $(0, 0)$ and Anti-neutrino $(0, 0)$	These particles travel with the speed of light and are distinguished from one another by the relation of their spin to their direction of motion. A neutrino is emitted with the positron during positive β-decay; and an anti-neutrino with the electron during negative β-decay. Their interaction with matter is extremely slight. First postulated by Pauli in 1933 and detected in 1956. π-meson decay also produces neutrinos and anti-neutrinos but in 1962 it was proved experimentally that these are a different species. Thus there are two kinds of neutrino each with an anti-neutrino. All these particles are distinguished from photons by having different spin.
Muon $(\pm 1, 207)$	Similar to, but heavier than, the electron and positron; disintegrates into electron (or positron if positive) + neutrino + anti-neutrino.
	Mesons
Pion $(\pm 1, 273)$ or $(0, 264)$	The π-meson. Charged pions decay either into muons and neutrinos or into electrons and neutrinos. Neutral pions decay into γ-rays, into "positron-electron pairs", or both. Pions are intimately connected with nuclear forces, *i.e.*, with the "strong" interaction.
Kaon $(\pm 1, 966)$ or $(0, 974)$	The K-mesons. These decay in many different ways producing other mesons, electrons, and neutrinos.
	Baryons
Proton $(+1, 1836.1)$	The positively-charged constituent of nuclei; the hydrogen nucleus is one proton. Fast-moving protons occur in cosmic rays. Does not spontaneously disintegrate.
Anti-proton $(-1, 1836.1)$	Negative anti-particle of the proton. Its existence was long suspected. Artificially produced and detected for the first time in 1955. Will react with the proton to produce pions or kaons.
Neutron $(0, 1838.6)$	Discovered by J. Chadwick in 1932. The neutral constituent of nuclei. When free it spontaneously disintegrates into a proton, an electron, and an anti-neutrino, after an average lifetime of about 18 minutes. Passes through matter much more easily than charged particles.
Anti-neutron $(0, 1838.6)$	The anti-particle of the neutron from which it is distinguished by properties connected with its magnetic moment and spin. Will react with neutron to produce pions or kaons.
Lambda Particle $(0, 2183)$	Discovered in 1947. Decays into proton plus pion.
Sigma Particle $(0$ or ± 1; about $2330)$	Various modes of disintegration, producing neutrons, protons, mesons and lambda particles.
Omega Particle $(\pm 1, 3272)$	Predicted by recent theory and discovered at Brookhaven, New York, in 1964.
Psi Particle $(0,$ about $6100)$	Discovered independently by two laboratories in the USA 1974. Still under intensive study.

quarks were called up, down, and strange and have the properties given in the Table below:

Name	charge	spin	mass-energy (MeV)
up	$+\frac{2}{3}$	$\frac{1}{2}$	336
down	$-\frac{1}{3}$	$\frac{1}{2}$	338
strange	$-\frac{1}{3}$	$\frac{1}{2}$	540

These particles interact with each other via the colour force. Hence it can be seen that by taking different combinations of quarks, different hadrons can be built up. For example, the proton is two up quarks and one down, the neutron is two down and one up. The simplicity of this system can be appreciated, but the only experimental evidence to support the existence of quarks is indirect. No one has yet isolated a single quark! Many scientists are seeking ways to produce and detect them, but as yet (1982) no claims have stood the test of scrutiny. Of course as well as the three quarks up, down, and strange, there are the corresponding anti-quarks.

The K-mesons, for example, are composed of a quark and an anti-quark either with the spins of the two quarks aligned parallel to give a net spin of one, or aligned antiparallel to give a net spin of zero. The charges $+1$, -1, and 0 are simply determined by selecting the correct combination of up and down quarks.

Charm

In the quest to unite the weak and electric forces, theoreticians were forced to introduce yet another new particle into the quark family. This was a charmed quark with charge $+\frac{2}{3}$. The four members of the quark family seemed now to be symmetrical with the four members of the lepton group (electron, muon, and two neutrinos). Since the charmed quark had charge $+\frac{2}{3}$ and mass of 1,500 MeV, it could simply replace the up quark as a building brick in nucleons to produce charmed matter. For example, by replacing the up quark in a proton and a meson by a charmed quark we get a charmed proton and a charmed meson. The first experimental evidence of the existence of charm was obtained by the high-energy physics group at University College, London, working at CERN laboratory, when they established the existence of "a neutral current interaction" in neutrino scattering experiments. Although "naked" charm has never been detected, charmed mesons (masses of 1,865 and 2,020) have been detected by the SPEAR laboratory in USA and charmed anti-protons have also been detected with masses of 2,260 MeV. The experimentally determined masses are in sufficient agreement with theory to confirm the existence of the charmed quark. If a charmed quark combined with an anti-charmed quark it would form a particle of mass 3,000 MeV (3 GeV) and this has been given the name of the Gipsy particle. Several laboratories in 1976 reported the possible existence of a particle of this mass energy, and called it either a J particle or psi particle. The uncertainty has now been resolved and the existence of the Gipsy has been confirmed. It can exist in an excited state of 3·7 GeV, from which it decays by gamma-ray emission to a value of 3·1 GeV, the predicted value. It can further change its spin state and decay to a mass energy value of 2·8 GeV. The building bricks of matter now seemed complete!

The Top Quark: Recent Evidence

In 1995 scientists at Chicago claimed to have discovered the "top quark". The top quark exists for only a hundredth of a billionth of a billionth of a second before decaying into subatomic particles that leave their trails in a bubble chamber. If this proves to be the case, it will end one of the fiercest arguments in physics and complete the theory of matter.

QUANTUM THEORY AND RELATIVITY

Quantum Theory

In our discussion of the nature of the various particles in physics we have alluded to them as being classified with well-defined sizes and weights. Of course, once we consider the physics of matter on a scale which is smaller than that of our everyday comprehension, then the classical physics of Newton is insufficient and we must use quantum physics. In the atomic region of reality we are again faced with the problem of indivisibility where the Greeks stopped their thinking and called the smallest particles of the universe atoms. Today we know that each separate particle is composed of a definite amount of energy, and the larger the particle, i.e., the more energy it is composed of, the easier it is to detect. We also know that the exchange of force between nucleons is carried by particles and that this inchangeability between mass and energy is a reality of quantum theory. To see this more fully we must realise that quantum theory rests on the theory of measurement! If a particle, of any type or structure, is composed of an amount of energy ΔE, then it is necessary to make measurements on it for a certain minimum time before it is detected. This minimum time Δt is given by the equation $\Delta E \times \Delta t \geqslant \hbar$, where $\hbar$ is Planck's constant divided by 2π; hence it can be seen that the smaller ΔE, then the longer a measurement must be made to detect the particle. Correspondingly, the time of measurement itself introduces an uncertainty, ΔE, in the energy of the particle. As well as the parameters ΔE and Δt, a particular physical event can be expressed in terms of its momentum p and position q, and these can also be expressed in a relationship as $\Delta p \times \Delta q \geqslant \hbar$. Hence one can ask at what position in space, q, is a particular particle with momentum p? Or what exactly is the wavelength of a wave? It may be thought that the first question cannot reasonably be asked of a wave nor the second of a particle, but bearing in mind the dual roles of particles and waves discussed earlier, then these questions can be interchanged. We know that electrons behave both as particles and waves. Since electrons have something in common with both, one question cannot be answered precisely for electrons without ignoring the other; alternatively, both questions can be given an imprecise answer. As the wavelength of electrons is intimately connected with their speed, one has to accept an accurate knowledge of the speed (wavelength) and ignorance of position, or the converse, or inaccurate knowledge of both. This is the famous Heisenberg Uncertainty Principle. Quantum theory is a set of mathematical rules for calculating the behaviour of fundamental particles in accordance with the Uncertainty Principle. In spite of its equivocal sounding name, the principle has led to an enormous increase in the accuracy with which physical phenomena can be described and predicted. Quantum theory includes all that previous theories did and more.

Quantum theory grew up in the same epoch as the Theory of Relativity. Heroic attempts have been made to combine the two, but with only partial success so far. Relativity is concerned with all motion and all physical laws, but its characteristic manifestations occur only when something is moving with nearly the velocity of light. Quantum theory is likewise all-embracing, but its typical phenomena almost always occur when something on the minute atomic scale is in question. Co. Consequently, the vast majority of everyday mechanics needs no more than the classical theory laid down by Newton, which is neither relativistic nor quantum.

Relativity

Historically, relativity grew out of attempts to measure the speed with which the earth moved through that hypothetical medium called the ether, which was supposed at that time to be the bearer of light waves. To take a simple analogy: sound waves travel through still air with a certain definite speed, v. If you move through the air with speed v' towards oncoming sound waves, they will pass you at the speed $v + v'$. Michelson and Morley, in their celebrated experiment of 1887, failed to find the corresponding behaviour on the part of light. This is so important an experiment that it has been repeated, and repeatedly discussed ever since. In Octobe58 the latest and most accurate confirmation of the Michelson-Morley result was announced. It seems as if light always travels with the same speed relative to an observer, however fast he moves relative to anything else. Einstein put it this way: two observers moving with any constant velocity relative to each other will always agree that light travels past them at the same speed; this speed is denoted by c, and is approximately 186,000 miles per second.

It should be remembered that the limiting value of the velocity of light in relativity is a postulate introduced by Einstein not a conclusion which the theory provides. There may exist forms of matter which can travel faster than light!

Nevertheless, the postulate that the maximum velocity encountered in the universe is c, logically developed, leads to remarkable conclusions. For instance: if you walk from tail to nose of an aircraft at 4 m.p.h. and the plane is receding from me at 300 m.p.h., then you recede from me at 304 m.p.h. "Common sense", Newton, and Einstein would all agree on this. But if you could walk at $0.25c$ and the plane moved at $0.5c$, the Newtonian mechanics would give your recession speed as $0.75c$, whereas Einsteinian relativity would give about $0.67c$. Although at the everyday speed of 300 m.p.h., the disagreement, though present in principle, is absolutely negligible, at speeds near that of light it becomes very pronounced. Many experiments show that the relativity answer is right.

Equivalence of Mass and Energy

The most famous consequence of relativity theory from which we derive benefit is the knowledge that mass can be converted into energy. The amount of energy, E, which can be derived from a given mass, m, of any type of material is given by the celebrated equation $E = mc^2$. If we take one gram of ash and convert it into the free energy of which it is composed we would get 10^8 kilowatts of power, sufficient to heat 15 houses for a year. The heat provided by the material which produced the ash is equivalent to that obtained from burning a single match. The massive energy released by $E = mc^2$ has been demonstrated in the power of nuclear weapons, but this energy has also been put to peaceful uses in nuclear-powered electricity generating stations.

In fundamental particle physics the masses of particles were always expressed in units of mass energy using $E = mc^2$ as the conversion equation. This is a matter of convenience from the realisation that mass is simply a condensed form of energy. The mesons which are the force-exchanging particles in the strong interaction have a mass energy of approximately 130 MeV, which is equivalent to a real mass of only 210^{-26} grams. The energy of the sun is provided by the conversion of real mass into light energy through thermonuclear fusion processes.

Mass and Rest Mass

The concept of mass is not a simple idea to grasp, for as we have seen, the mass of a body which is at rest is equivalent to its inherent latent energy. Further complications and interpretations arise when the body starts moving and its mass is no longer necessarily a constant quantity.

A stationary body can be observed to have a mass called its *rest mass*. If the body moves, it has energy of motion and therefore, according to Einstein's mass-energy equation, it increases its mass. Mass thus depends on speed, but in such a way that there is very little change unless the speed approaches that of light. Many experiments on atomic particles demonstrate this. The interesting question now arises: do all fundamental particles have rest mass? or do some have mass derived solely from their energy? The answer appears to be that photons and neutrinos have no rest mass; all other particles have. The Table on **F16** gives their rest masses.

Special Theory of Relativity

The mathematical development of Einstein's ideas, leading to the conclusions just referred to, constitutes the Special Theory of Relativity.

Stated more generally, the theory raises the question whether two observers in uniform relative motion could ever detect, as a result of their relative speed, any difference in the physical laws governing matter, motion, and light. To this, Special Relativity answers: No. The detailed theory involves special consideration of the results the two observers would obtain when measuring (i) the spatial distance, and (ii) the time interval, between the same two events. It turns out that they would not agree on these two points. They would agree, however, on the value of a certain quantity made up jointly of the spatial distance and the time interval in a same what complex combination. The intimate mixture of space and time in this quantity has led to the treatment of the three space dimensions and time on an equivalent footing. Hence the frequent references to time as the "fourth dimension". Minkowski devised an extremely elegant presentation of relativity theory by using an extension of ordinary geometry to four dimensions. A line drawn in his four-dimensional space represents the path of a particle in space and time, i.e., the whole history of the particle. Thus the movement of particles in the ordinary world is turned into the geometry of lines in Minkowski's four-dimensional world of "space-time".

General Relativity and Gravitation

In 1915, 10 years after the publication of the Special Theory of Relativity, Einstein published his theory of General Relativity. This apparently innocuous extension of the ideas of special relativity to include accelerated relative motion opened up new and difficult fields of mathematical complexity which, when solved, enabled Einstein to include gravitation in the theory. In discussing the physics of atomic, nuclear, and subnuclear particles, we did not include the effect of the gravitational force, since in relation to the Electric, Weak, Strong, and Colour forces it is extremely small and can be neglected in the discussion of the structure of matter but not in the discussion of astronomical problems and the movements of large-scale electrically uncharged bodies.

It has been usual, ever since Newton, to say that two bodies of mass m_1 and m_2, separated by a distance r attract one another with a force proportional to $m_1 m_2/r^2$. This is Newton's inverse square law of gravitation which explains the movements of planets and comets and the falling to earth of an apple from a tree.

The apple's fall is accelerated, and we observe this by noting its position relative to certain marks fixed with respect to us, and by timing it with some sort of clock. This system of location in space and time may be called our "frame of reference". We therefore assert that, in our frame of reference, the apple falls down with an acceleration which Newton saw no alternative but to attribute to a thing called gravitational attraction. Galileo had shown that *all* bodies fall with the same acceleration at all points, and we can now rephrase this by saying that in our frame of reference there is a constant gravitational attraction or *uniform gravitational field*. (This last statement and Galileo's demonstration only refer strictly to points fairly near the earth's surface; at greater distances the gravitational field decreases and is therefore not uniform.)

Now suppose a collection of falling bodies is observed by us and an intelligent creature, designated C, inhabits one of them. C has his own frame of reference fixed relative to him and we have ours fixed relative to us. In C's frame neither his own body, nor any of the others, is accelerated, and therefore he has no reason to suppose a gravitational force is acting on them. We have, therefore, the following situation:

(i) in our frame, fixed relative to us, we find all the bodies falling subject to a gravitational pull;

(ii) in C's frame, undergoing accelerated fall relative to us, no gravitational field is apparent to C.

It looks, therefore, as if one has only to choose the correct frame of reference for the measurements in order to remove the need for any assumptions about the existence of gravitational fields. This is a simple illustration of the connection between gravitation and frames of reference for the measurement of space and time. Einstein's General Theory of Relativity extends this to cover non-uniform gravitational fields and shows that what Newton taught us to call the gravitational field of material bodies is better thought of as a peculiarity of the space and time in the neighbourhood of such bodies. Since space–time, as we mentioned above, can be expressed in geometrical terms, Einstein has transformed the theory of gravitation into an exercise (a difficult one) in the geometry of space–time. Other physicists, in Einstein's tradition, are trying to turn *all* physics into geometry, but no one knows whether this is really feasible.

All this abstruse work is much more than a demonstration of mathematical power and elegance. Observable phenomena which fall outside the scope of Newton's theory of gravitation are accounted for by relativity. One is the small but definite discrepancy between the actual orbit of the planet Mercury and the predictions of Newton's theory. Another is the effect of a gravitational field on the wavelength of light emitted by atoms. Similar atoms in different places in a gravitational field emit radiations with slightly different wavelengths. For example, the light from an atom in the intense field of a star should have slightly longer wavelength than the corresponding light from an atom on earth. This effect has always proved very difficult to detect with certainty. However, Einstein's prediction was verified with moderate accuracy in 1960 by a very subtle method which was purely terrestrial in its operation. The atoms being compared were placed at the top and bottom of a water tower and the difference in their emission was detected by means that belong rather to nuclear physics than to astronomy.

Quantum Theory and Relativity Combined

The atomic family table refers to "antiparticles". The theory which first introduced such things in 1934 is due to the Cambridge physicist Dirac and was epoch-making. Dirac conceived an equation to describe the motion of electrons subject to the laws of both quantum theory and relativity. His achievement was thus to synthesise these two great ideas. The spin of the electron was originally a supposition that helped to make sense of spectroscopic observations of light emitted from atoms. Dirac's equation made spin a logical consequence of the union of relativity and quantum theory. Perhaps even more important was the brilliant inference that the equation for the electron implied the existence of another particle having the same mass and spin but with a positive instead of a negative electric charge. This object is called the electron's antiparticle and is now well known as a positron.

Every particle is now believed to imply an antiparticle, so it is conceivable that the universe could have been (but isn't) an anti-universe, *i.e.*, all the electrons and protons might have been positrons and antiprotons and so on. The laws of physics would still have been applicable, however.

The gravitational force has an infinite range and therefore its force-carrying particles must travel at the speed of light. The graviton is the name of the particle which transmits the gravitational force between bodies with mass. To date (1983) no experiment has detected the existence of gravitons which are the postulated quanta of gravitational waves. There is an exact analogy between photons, the quanta of electro-magnetic radiation, and gravitons.

Conservation Laws

If charged particles interact, then it is found that the amount of electric charge existing after the reaction is the same as that which existed before the event. This is called the law of the conservation of charge. Many other conservation laws exist in physics, *e.g.*, conservation of mass

energy, angular momentum, linear momentum, and other more abstruse conservation laws exist in particle physics, *e.g.*, conservation of baryons, leptons, strangeness, isotopic spin, and parity. The last three conservation laws listed have been found to have a limited jurisdiction, and the violation of parity in the weak interaction was a great surprise to physicists.

Any reader who looks in a mirror knows that the left- and right-hand sides of his face are interchanged in the image. Fortunately mirrors do not also turn the image upside down, but, if they did, the face would then have undergone what is called "a parity transformation". A screwdriver driving a right-handed screw downwards becomes, on parity transformation, a screwdriver driving a left-handed screw upwards. The law of conservation of parity is a way of asserting that any physical process that goes on in the world could equally well go on—obeying the same laws—in a parity transformed world. There is nothing left-handed that does not in principle have a right-handed counterpart.

For many years this belief was strongly held. It came as something of a shock when, in 1957, after theoretical proposals by Lee and Yang in America, Wu and co-workers proved that parity was not always conserved. To understand Wu's experiment, we must recall that nuclei can have intrinsic spin. Suppose the axis of spin were downwards into the page and the rotation were suitable for driving an ordinary screw into the page. Then Wu showed that beta-rays from such a nucleus are emitted *preferentially upwards, i.e.*, against the direction of travel of the screw. The parity transformed version of this would have the beta-rays preferentially emitted in the same direction as the travel of the screw and, if parity is conserved, this process would happen too. But it does not. If the beta-rays in the experiment had been emitted in equal numbers up and down, then the parity transformed version would have had this feature too, and thus parity would have been conserved.

Modern research on elementary particles is greatly concerned to find out which types of process obey which conservation laws. The parity surprise is only one of the stimulating shocks that this type of work is heir to.

Conclusion

Over a century's development of the atomic ideas has brought a progressive, if jerky, increase in the mathematical precision of the theories. In some fields of particle physics, observations to one part in a million, or even better, can be explained, to that level of accuracy, by the existing theories. At the same time, however, the theories have lost visual definition. An atom as an invisible but none the less solid billiard ball was easy enough; so was a light wave conceived like a sound wave in air. Even after Rutherford, an atom consisting of a miniature solar system merely exchanged the solid billiard ball for a system of revolving billiard balls and was no great obstacle to visualisation. But since quantum theory and the Uncertainty Principle, every unambiguous visualisation of fundamental wave-particles leaves out half the picture, and although the electrons are in the atom, we can no longer represent them in definite orbits. The moral seems to be that visualisation is unnecessary, or at best a partial aid to thought.

THE PROPERTIES OF MATTER IN BULK

One of the most obvious and at the same time most wonderful things about the properties of matter is their great variety. Think of air, diamond, mercury, rubber, snow, gold, pitch, asbestos.... Even the differences of state of the same chemical substance are remarkable enough, ice, water, and steam, for example. One of the aims of physics is to reach an understanding of all these different properties by explaining them in terms of the behaviour of the particles discussed in the previous section (**F10–19**). The widespread success with which this imposing programme has been carried out indicates the maturity of physics. It is difficult to think of any major property of matter in bulk for which there is not some attempted theoretical explanation, though future physicists will no doubt regard some present-day theories as rudimentary or incorrect.

Physics, Statistics, and Thermodynamics

Take a number equal to the population of London, multiply it by itself, and multiply the product by another million. The answer is about the number of molecules in 1 cubic centimetre of ordinary air. They are constantly moving about and colliding with one another. Even if the nature of the molecules and their laws of motion were perfectly understood, it would clearly be impracticable to calculate the exact paths described by each particle of so vast an assembly. This difficulty brought into being a whole branch of physics concerned with calculating the overall or average properties of large numbers of particles. Just as statisticians will provide the average height, income, expectation of life, and so on, of the population of London, without knowing everything about every individual, so statistical physicists can work out average properties of molecules or atoms in large groups. This important branch of physics is called *Statistical Mechanics*. It was founded in the nineteenth century by Maxwell, Boltzmann, and Gibbs and is still being actively developed.

Consider now all the molecules in 1 cubic centimetre of air contained in a small box. They are continually bombarding the walls of the box and bouncing off. This hail of impacts (it is actually about 10^{23} impacts per square centimetre per second) is the cause of the pressure which the gas exerts against the walls of the box. Now suppose we pump air in until there is twice as much as before, though the box is still the same size and at the same temperature. This means that the density of the gas (*i.e.*, the mass of 1 unit of volume) has doubled. We should now expect twice as many impacts per second on the walls as before, and consequently twice the pressure. We therefore arrive at a conclusion that, if the volume and temperature of a gas are constant, the pressure of a gas is proportional to its density. This is one of the simplest statistical arguments that can be checked against observation; in fact, it stands the test very well.

Heat, Temperature, and Energy

The proviso about the temperature remaining the same is an important one for the following reason. In the nineteenth century there was much discussion about the nature of heat. To Joule we owe the now well-established view that heat is equivalent to mechanical work. In one of his experiments, in the 1840s, the work necessary to rotate paddle wheels against the resistance of water in a tank generated heat that caused a slight rise in the temperature of the water. Joule found out exactly how much work was equivalent to a given quantity of heat. However, one can do other things with work besides generate heat; in particular, work creates motion, as when one pushes a car. Bodies in motion possess a special form of energy, called kinetic energy, which is equal to the work done in accelerating them from a state of rest. We have, then, three closely connected ideas: work, heat, and kinetic energy. Now according to the views of the nineteenth century, which are still accepted, any heat given to a gas simply increases the kinetic energy of its molecules; the hotter the gas, the faster its molecules are moving. If, therefore, the gas in our box is allowed to get hotter, there is an increase in molecular speed, and the impacts on the walls become correspondingly more violent. But this means the pressure increases, so we have another law: if the density remains the same, the pressure increases if the temperature does.

Laws of Thermodynamics

Such considerations as these have been pursued with great elaboration and subtlety. The notions of heat, temperature, energy, and work—familiar but vague in everyday life—have been given precise definitions, and the relations between them have been enshrined in the Laws of Thermodynamics. Enshrined is perhaps a suitable word, because these laws are so soundly and widely based on experimental results that they have greater prestige than any others in physics. If any proposed physical law comes in conflict with thermodynamics then so much the worse for that law—it has to be revised. It is sometimes asserted that no one is properly educated who does not understand the Second Law of thermodynamics. We cannot, therefore, leave this section without at least stating the two best known thermodynamic laws:

First Law: *If any physical system is given a quantity of heat, and if the system performs some work, then the energy of the system increases by an amount equal to the excess of heat given over work done.* This law asserts that heat, energy, and work are convertible one into the other, and that all such transactions balance exactly. This is one form of a principle accepted as fundamental in all science, *viz.*, the Principle of the Conservation of Energy, according to which energy can never be created or destroyed, but only changed from one form to another.

Second Law: *It is impossible to make an engine which will continuously take heat from a heat source and, by itself, turn it all into an equivalent amount of mechanical work.* In fact, all engines which produce work from heat—steam engines for example—always use only a fraction of the heat they take in and give up the rest to some relatively cool part of the machine. The Second Law makes this obligatory on all work-from-heat devices. This statement of the Second Law has an engineering ring about and, indeed, it arose from the work of the nineteenth-century French engineer Carnot. Nevertheless, it can be rephrased in terms of the concept of entropy, and has been applied with unbroken success to all fields of science involving the transfer of heat and allied matters. It sets a definite limit to the kinds of physical and chemical process that can be conceived to take place. Nothing has been known to contravene it.

The States of Matter

The molecular motion in gases has been referred to in the previous section. Tacitly it was assumed that each molecule acted independently of all others, except that collisions occurred between them. In reality, molecules exert attractive forces on one another and, if a gas is cooled so that molecular movements become relatively sluggish, a time comes when the attractive forces succeed in drawing the molecules close together to form a liquid. This process is called condensation.

The molecules in a liquid are packed tightly together and they impede each other's movements. On the other hand, movement still persists, and the molecules struggle about like people in a milling crowd. Besides wandering about, the molecules vibrate. These motions represent the energy contained in the liquid.

The fact that the molecules, though irregularly packed, can still slip past one another and move from place to place, explains the essential property of liquids that distinguishes them from solids—ability to flow. As a matter of fact, although the rather vague assertion that in a liquid molecules are irregularly packed would be generally accepted, there is no agreed opinion on what the irregularity is actually like. Indeed, not only the precise structure of liquids, but the theory of liquids in general, is fraught with such considerable mathematical difficulties that the liquid state is much less well understood than the solid or gaseous.

Most solids are crystals. The popular idea of a crystal is of something which has a more or less regular geometrical form with faces that shut in the light—like snowflakes or gems. However, crystallinity really depends on a regular inner pattern of the atoms, and may or may not show itself on the visible surface. A lump of lead, for example, is crystalline, despite its appearance.

The actual arrangement of the atoms in a crystal can be extremely complex. Some are quite simple, however. The largest model of a crystal structure must surely be the 400-ft. "Atomium" building in the 1958 Brussels Exhibition. This consisted of eight balls, representing atoms, situated at the corners of a cube, and one more ball exactly in the middle. Imagine this repeated in all directions so that every ball is the centre of a cube whose corners are the eight neighbouring balls. This is known to crystallographers and physicists as the "body-centred cubic structure"; it is the actual arrangement of atoms in iron, sodium, chromium, and some other metals. If every ball, instead of being the centre of a cube, were the centre of a regular tetrahedron (a solid figure with four equal triangular faces), and had its four neighbours at the corners of the tetrahedron, then we should have the "diamond structure". This is how the carbon atoms are arranged in diamonds.

In crystals the atoms are locked into a regular ordered structure by attractive forces which give the solid its rigidity and prevent it from flowing. The atoms are so close together that any attempt to press them closer involves crushing or distorting the atoms—a process they resist strongly. This explains why solids (and liquids too) are so difficult to compress. Gases can easily be compressed because there is so much space between the molecules.

The distinction between solid and liquid is not so sharp as is commonly supposed. A lump of dough will not bounce, but is plastic; a steel ball-bearing is very elastic and bounces excellently, but one cannot mould it in the fingers. Neither dough nor steel qualifies for description as a liquid. There are, however, substances which can be moulded like plasticine into a ball that will then bounce very well on the floor like an elastic solid, and finally, if left on a flat table, will spread into a pool and drip off the edge like a liquid. There is no point in trying to force such things into rigid categories. One may say instead that for short, sharp impacts the material behaves like an elastic solid, but under long-sustained forces it flows like a liquid. The properties of these, and many other anomalous materials, are increasingly engaging the attention of those who study the science of flow—*rheology*. It is interesting to see how many familiar and important materials exhibit peculiar rheological behaviour—paint, dough, ball-pen ink, cheese, unset cement, and solutions of nylon and other plastics are only a few examples.

Inside a Crystalline Solid

We now return to our wallpaper analogy of crystal structure and give some free play to our visual imagination.

Suppose we have walls papered with a regular pattern of, say, roses, fuchsias, and green leaves. These represent the different kinds of atoms in the solid. Careful observation shows that the whole pattern is shimmering. The flowers and leaves are not stationary, but are undergoing slight random oscillations about their proper positions. In a crystal these movements are called thermal vibrations, and are never absent. The hotter the crystal, the more the vibration, and at a high enough temperature the vibrations become so great that the atoms get right out of position and the pattern disappears altogether, *i.e.*, the crystal melts. Thermal vibrations are essential to the theory of solids, and are responsible for numerous physical properties.

Next we note something extraordinary about some of the papered walls. On these the paper has been hung in irregular patches fitted together like a not very well-made jig-saw puzzle. Lines of roses which should be vertical are horizontal in some patches, oblique in others. This represents the situation in most ordinary solids, for they consist of many small pieces of crystal irregularly packed together. Such material is called *poly-crystalline*, and the small pieces are *crystal grains*. Crystal grains may be almost any size, sometimes visible to the naked eye, as often on galvanised iron.

However, on one wall, we see excellent regularity and no obvious patches at all. The physicist would call this a *single crystal*, and several techniques exist for preparing them. Natural single

crystals can be found, and there are some beautiful large single crystals of rock salt. But on examining the single crystal wall closely, we find a number of places where the paperhanger has failed to make adjacent pieces register perfectly—there is a slight disjointedness. This occurs in real single crystals, and the line along which the structure fails to register is called a *dislocation*. These are much studied by physicists because of their bearing on the mechanical properties of solids, on the yielding of metals under strong stress, for instance.

This by no means exhausts the possibilities of the wallpaper analogy; several other phenomena can be found. For example, in a place where there should be a fuchsia there is actually a daffodil—something completely foreign to the pattern. Or perhaps a small wrongly shaped leaf is jammed between the proper leaves in a place that should really be blank. These represent chemical impurity atoms. The first is called *substitutional*, because it occupies the position of an atom that should be there, the second is called *interstitial*, because it does not. Substitutional impurities of indium metal, deliberately added to the semi-conductor silicon, make possible the manufacture of transistors (*see* **Section L**). Some steels derive their valuable properties from inter-stitial carbon atoms within the iron pattern.

What physicists call a vacancy would occur if a flower or leaf were simply missing. Remembering that all the atoms are vibrating, we should not be surprised if occasionally an atom jumps into a neighbouring vacancy if there happens to be one, *i.e.*, the atom and the vacancy change places. Later this may occur again. In the course of time, a rose which was near the ceiling may make its way to the floor by jumping into vacant rose positions when they occur near enough. This process, which the physicist calls *diffusion*, is also analogous to the game in which numbers or letters can be moved about in a flat box because there is one vacant space to permit adjustment. The more vacancies there are in a crystal, the faster diffusion occurs. It is, in fact, very slow in solids, but is nevertheless evidence that apparently quiescent materials are really internally active.

Metals, Electricity, and Heat

There is ample evidence that inside metals there are large numbers of free electrons. To illuminate this statement let us take sodium metal as an example. One single sodium atom has a nucleus with eleven protons; there are therefore eleven electrons in the atom. The outermost one is easily detached, leaving a positively charged sodium ion behind. We may think of these ions arranged in the three-dimensional pattern characteristic of sodium crystals. It is the same as the iron structure previously described. The detached electrons, one per atom, occupy the spaces in between. The usual metaphor is that the structure of ions is permeated by a "gas" of electrons. Like all visualisations of fundamental particles, this must be taken as a rough approximation. The important point is that the electrons in the gas are not bound to individual atoms but may wander freely about the crystal, hindered only by the collisions they make with the vibrating ions.

This is the picture as it appeared to physicists of the first decade of this century, and we can explain many properties of metals with it. Naturally the theory has developed greatly since then, thanks to the great work of Lorentz, Sommerfeld, and Bloch; it now relies heavily on quantum theory, but it is surprising how little violence is done to modern ideas by the simple picture we are using.

The free electrons move randomly in all directions at thousands of miles per hour. If the metal is connected across a battery it experiences an electric field. Electrons are negatively charged particles, and are therefore attracted to the electrically positive end of the metal. They can move through the metal because they are free; this flow is not possible to those electrons which remain bound to the ions. The function of the battery is to keep the flow going and, for as long as it is going, it is the electric current.

The flow of electrons is not unimpeded. They

constantly collide with the ions and are deflected from the path of flow. This hindrance is what the electrician calls *electrical resistance*. The electric force, due to the battery or a dynamo, accelerates the electrons, thus giving them extra energy; but they lose this to the ions at collisions because the ions recoil and vibrate more than before. The net effect of innumerable collisions is to increase the thermal vibrations of the ions, *i.e.*, to make the metal hotter. This is the explanation of the fact well known to every user of electric irons; that electric current heats the conductor. If a strong current is passed through a wire, the heating is so great the wire glows, as in electric-light bulbs, or melts and breaks, as in blown fuses.

If one end of a metal rod is heated we soon feel the heat at the other end; metals are excellent thermal conductors. This is because the mobile free electrons carry the heat energy down the rod, passing it on to the ions by colliding with them. Substances without free electrons cannot do this, nor can they conduct electricity well; we have, in the free electrons, an explanation of the fact that the good electrical conductors are the good heat conductors. For technical purposes, it would be useful to have electrical insulators that would conduct heat well, and *vice versa*; but this is almost a contradiction in terms, and one can only compromise.

Non-conductors and Semi-conductors

There are some elements, and numerous compounds in which all the electrons are so tightly bound to their parent atoms that free electron flow is impossible. These materials are electrical and thermal insulators.

Let us return to our sodium atom. It readily loses its outer electron, forming a positive ion. The ion is very stable; indeed, its electron arrangement resembles the "closed shell" belonging to the inert gas neon. The chlorine atom, on the other hand, would have a very stable structure, resembling the inert gas argon, if only it could be given one extra electron to complete the closed shell. If the outer sodium electron were given to a chlorine atom we should have two stable ions, one positive and one negative. These would then attract each other and form a compound. This is just how common salt, sodium chloride, is formed, and its crystals consist of a regular network of alternate sodium and chlorine ions. As all the electrons are bound to ions, it is not surprising that salt will not conduct electricity or heat to any appreciable extent. Not all insulating compounds are built on this pattern, but all have structures which bind the electrons tightly.

We have seen (**F20**) that Nature does not permit a hard-and-fast distinction between solids and liquids; nor does she between conductors and insulators. Over a hundred years ago, Faraday knew of substances which would conduct electricity, but rather badly. A common one is the graphite in pencils. Others are the elements selenium, germanium, and silicon, and a considerable number of compounds. Such substances are called semiconductors.

Semi-conductors conduct badly because they have so few free electrons, many thousands of times fewer than metals. In very cold germanium—say, 200 degrees below freezing—all the electrons are tightly bound to atoms and the substance is an insulator. It differs from normal insulators in that, on warming it, the gradually increasing thermal vibration of the crystal detaches some of the electrons, for they are only moderately tightly bound. The warmer the crystal becomes, the more of its electrons become detached and the better it conducts electricity, By about the temperature of boiling water, there are so many freed electrons that conduction is moderately good, though less good than in metals. This is basic semi-conductor behaviour. Because transistors were made of germanium, and because they are of such great technical importance, more knowledge has accumulated about germanium than about any other material. *See also* **Transistor, Section L.**

Magnetism

The most important thing about magnetism is that it is inseparably connected with electricity. Oersted showed this in July 1820, when he deflected a magnetic compass needle by passing an electric current through a wire near it. Since then, many experiments have shown that wherever a current flows there will certainly be a magnetic field in the surrounding space. The laws of this are very well known now—they are the Maxwell equations previously referred to (**F14**). However, most people first meet magnetism when, as children, they pick up pins with a magnet. Where is the electricity here? and what is a magnet?

The explanation of magnetism exemplifies beautifully the technique of explaining the bulk properties of matter in terms of fundamental particles. In the atoms the electrons are moving, and a moving electric charge constitutes an electric current. Therefore each moving electron is a tiny source of magnetism. It does not immediately follow that every atom is a source of magnetism because it might—and often does—happen that the magnetic effect of different electrons in the atom cancel out. In helium atoms, for example, the two electrons have equal but opposed magnetic effects. Nevertheless, some atoms and ions have a net effect called their *magnetic moment*. This simply means they behave like tiny magnets. Crystals containing such atoms will be magnetic, though the magnetism is much weaker than in ordinary magnets because the different atoms largely annul one another's effects. In a very limited number of crystals, however, the magnetic ions act on one another in a special way which forces all the atomic magnets to point in the same direction. The total effect of many co-operating atoms is very strong and the crystal becomes what we normally call a magnet. Iron acts like this, so do cobalt and nickel, the rarer elements gadolinium and dysprosium, and a fair number of alloys. On the whole, this behaviour, which is called *ferromagnetism*, is very rare. The reason for the co-operation of all the atomic magnets is not explained to everyone's satisfaction yet, though the key idea was given by Heisenberg in 1928.

In the section dealing with the electron it was pointed out that every electron has an *intrinsic* magnetic moment. This is in addition to any effect simply due to the electron's motion round a nucleus. The net effects of ions are therefore partly due to the intrinsic magnetism of electrons. In the ferromagnetic metals the latter is by far the most important contribution. Thus we pick up pins, and benefit from magnets in other ways, because innumerable fundamental particles act in co-operation for reasons that are still somewhat obscure. It is interesting to ask whether the electrons responsible for magnetism are the same free electrons that allow the metals to conduct electricity. It is thought not.

We are accustomed to think of magnets as metallic. Actually the magnet originally discovered by the Chinese was the mineral lodestone, which is a non-metallic oxide of iron. Nowadays a number of non-metallic magnets are made. They are called *ferrites*, and some are insulators and some are semi-conductors. The combination of magnetism and insulation is technically very valuable in radio, radar, and other applications. The explanation of ferrite behaviour is related to that of metallic ferromagnetism, but is not the same.

Conclusion

The aim of the second part of this account of physics is to show how our conception of fundamental particles allows us to build theories of the properties of matter. This very aim shows that the two "major divisions" of physics referred to at the beginning (**F10**) are divided only in the way that labour is divided by co-operating workers to lighten the task. For the task of physics is a very great one—no less than to explain the behaviour of matter; and since the universe, living and inanimate, is made of matter, physics must necessarily underlie all the other sciences.

III. THE WORLD OF THE CHEMISTS

WHAT CHEMISTRY IS ABOUT

Chemistry is the scientific study of the preparation, composition and architecture of chemical compounds, and of the modes and mechanisms of their transformations or reactions. Natural (and other) processes can be classified as *physical*, in which no chemical reactions occur, for example water running down a hill, and *chemical* if changes occur in the chemical compounds involved. Common examples are the burning of fuel, whether in a biological cell, an internal combustion engine, or a lowly domestic grate. Biological changes at the molecular level in plants and animals generally consist of many chemical reactions, as do some geological changes in rocks and deposits. Chemistry therefore is rooted in physics and interpenetrates biology (biochemistry) and geology (geochemistry). Some of the main sub-divisions of chemistry are delineated in the Table. Chemists not only aim to discover new reactions by trial and error, but by seeking to understand chemical change aspire to design new compounds and reactions. New reactions can be used to produce useful physical *effects* in new ways—like light from the cold chemical candle (chemiluminescence) as the firefly does, and electricity from more efficient batteries and from fuel cells—or to produce new *synthetic products*. These can be faithful copies of compounds like penicillin which have been discovered first in nature, or completely new, invented, compounds like the sulphonamide drugs.

This research activity, which is mainly centred in the Universities, is the basis of a large chemical industry, one of the major manufacturing industries. Other branches which deal with more restrictive topics or use combinations of the above for specific goals have names which are self-explanatory, for example:—analytical chemistry, colloid chemistry, pharmaceutical chemistry, chemistry of dyes, petroleum chemistry, polymer chemistry, environmental chemistry, medicinal chemistry.

Main Divisions of Chemistry

	Elements, Compounds and reactions involved	Examples
Organic Chemistry	Carbon in combination mainly with H, O, N.	Natural products Carbohydrates Steroids Proteins
Inorganic Chemistry	All elements and compounds not covered in organic chemistry. Minerals and salts.	Inorganic polymers (*e.g.*, silicones) Transition metal complexes Organometallic compounds
Physical Chemistry	Mathematical and physical descriptions of organic and inorganic compounds and reactions.	Electrochemistry Chemical thermodynamics Molecular spectroscopy Photochemistry
Biochemistry	The chemistry of biological systems	Enzymes Biosynthesis.

ELEMENTS AND COMPOUNDS

Elements

The reader will find a description of the formation of chemical elements in Part I (**F6**). They are listed alphabetically in the Table of Elements (with their chemical symbols) and in order of atomic number (*see* **F11**) in the Periodic Table. Other details may be found in Section L. They vary widely in natural abundance terrestrially. In the earth's crust the most abundant elements are oxygen (O), silicon (Si), aluminium (Al), and iron (Fe). Our familiarity with them varies too, not only because of the rarity of some (thulium, Tm, and radium, Ra) and the artificiality of a few (plutonium, Pu) but because we meet some only in combination with other elements and not in their elemental state, for example, fluorine (F) in fluorides. The most familiar non-metallic elements besides oxygen and nitrogen in their gaseous molecular states (O_2 and N_2) are probably carbon (C), as graphite (or diamond!) and sulphur (S). Among the metallic elements most people know aluminium (Al), tin (Sn) and lead (Pb) from the main groups of the Periodic Table, and the transition metals: iron (Fe), chromium (Cr), nickel (Ni) as well as copper (Cu) and the precious metals silver (Ag), gold (Au) and platinum (Pt). Increasingly familiar because of their use in semi-conductors are the metalloids silicon (Si) and germanium (Ge).

Compounds

Most terrestrial matter as we know it can be classified in terms of the chemical compounds it contains, *i.e.*, is a mixture of compounds. Each compound consists of chemical elements in combination, the relative amount of each being characteristic and definite (Law of Constant Composition). Compounds vary not only in the number of elements combined but also in their proportions: carbon dioxide has twice as much oxygen per carbon as carbon monoxide (*see* atoms and molecules).

The properties of a compound can be, and normally are, very different from the properties of the elements it contains, a fact not commonly recognised in the popular imagination. When phrases like—"it's good for you, it's got iron in it". This does not mean that elemental metallic iron is present but rather that some seemingly beneficial compound of iron is present. The ambiguity is that although iron is essential to human life in the form of haemoglobin in the blood, it also can form highly poisonous compounds. Similarly arsenic (As), although notoriously poisonous as the element and in some of its compounds, was nevertheless contained in one of the first chemotherapeutic drugs ever produced, salvarsan. The point can be further illustrated with sodium chloride, a water-soluble white crystalline solid, which is a compound of the very reactive metal sodium (capable of reacting violently with water), and of chlorine (known as a poisonous green gas). Similarly diamond (a particular elemental form, or allotrope, of carbon) is one of the hardest known substances but may be combined with hydrogen (the highly inflammable gas which can combine with oxygen gas to give water), to give thousands of different derivatives which include benzene (a liquid), methane (a gas) and various hydrocarbon waxes and polishes.

ATOMS AND MOLECULES

Atoms vary in weight, structure and size from one element to the next (*see* **Part II, F10**). Molecules are made from whole numbers of atoms in combination. A particular molecule is characterised by the number of atoms of each of its constituent elements. It has a characteristic weight called its *molecular weight* (the sum of the weights of the atoms in it), and a characteristic three dimensional structure (*see below*).

An aggregate of molecules of the same type is a chemical compound, so that the molecule is to a compound as the atom is to an element.

The Mole

It is frequently very useful to know when the amounts of two compounds are the same, not in terms of their masses but in terms of the number of molecules each contains, since chemical reactions occur at the molecular level and involve small relative numbers of molecules of the reacting species at each step. Avogadro (*see* **B5**) suggested that equal volumes of gases under identical conditions contained equal molecular numbers (*see* **L12**) and it followed that it the weights of two substances were in the ratio of their relative molecular masses (molecular weights) then they too contained equal numbers of molecules. The approximate molecular weights of water (H_2O) and ethanol or ethylalcohol (C_2H_5OH) are 18 and 46 respectively and so 18 g of water for example contain the same number of molecules as 46 g of ethanol.

The amount of substance referred to in each case is called 1 mole. For any compound the weight of 1 mole is equal to the gramme molecular weight. Molecular weights (or relative molecular masses) are now referred to the carbon-12 atomic scale (*see* **F10**). The modern definition of the mole therefore is that it is the amount of substance which contains the same number of elementary particles as there are atoms in twelve grammes of carbon-12. This number, called Avogadro's number, is $6.022\,169 \times 10^{23}$.

Molecular Structure and Isomers

Modern spectroscopic and diffraction methods have enabled the details of molecular structures to be accurately determined not only with respect to the distances between atoms (normally in the range 1–5 Å, *i.e.*, 100–150 pm for adjacent atoms) and the angles which define the structure, but also with respect to the various internal motions (vibrations and rotations).

Sometimes two (or more) different compounds have the same molecular weight (and are called, therefore, *isomers*) but have different molecular structures in which the same atoms are arranged in different relative positions, and hence have different properties. If two isomeric structures are related as left and right hands are related, the isomers are stereoisomers of a particular class called enantiomers. An example is glucose. Even such subtle variation as this produces differences in properties which can be crucial in biological function or drug metabolism.

A familiar simple example of *structural* isomers are ethylalcohol (or ethanol) and dimethyl ether of formula C_2H_6O. They each can be represented by the structural formulae

$$CH_3 - CH_2 - OH \quad \text{and} \quad \begin{matrix} CH_3 \\ \diagdown \\ O \\ \diagup \\ CH_3 \end{matrix}$$

in which the lines represent some of the *covalent chemical bonds* (*see below*). It is these interatomic forces which hold the atoms in specific spatial arrangements. Some examples are shown in Fig. 1.

CHEMICAL BONDING

The number of possible arrangements of a given set of atoms is limited since each type of atom (each element) is capable of forming only a limited number of bonds, equal to its *valency*. The valency varies from element to element; hydrogen has a valency of one (exceptionally two); oxygen, two; nitrogen, three; and carbon four (hence the molecular formulae H_2, H_2O, NH_3 and CH_4 for hydrogen, water, ammonia and methane respectively).

In some compounds two atoms may be joined by a *multiple bond* so that the valency number may be reached. Examples are the double and triple bonds in ethylene (ethene) and acetylene (ethyne) respectively:

$$CH_2 = CH_2 \text{ and } CH \equiv CH$$

The modern theory of chemical bonding is electronic. Bonds are formed:

    (i) by the sharing of electrons in pairs between two bonded atoms (*covalent* bonding); or

    (ii) by the transfer of an electron from one atom to another to form oppositely charged ions (*ionic* bonding).

The ionic situation is electrically *polar* whereas pure covalent bonds have no polarity. If, however, the shared electrons are not shared equally between the bound atoms some effective electron transfer occurs and the bond has some polar character. Covalent bonds between *dissimilar* atoms are generally polar. If one of the two atoms provides *both* the shared electrons, the polarity is particularly high and the bond is called *dative covalent*.

VALENCIES OF THE ELEMENTS

Electronic Theory of Valency

These ideas of the chemical bond lead to a ready explanation of the valencies of the elements (which are periodic if the elements are arranged in order of atomic number) when combined with knowledge of the electronic structure of atoms.

In the original Bohr theory the electrons of atoms move in well defined orbits arranged in shells. The known elements use seven shells, and each element has its unique number of electrons equal to the atomic number, Z ranging from 1 in hydrogen to 103 in lawrencium. Each element also has its unique arrangement of its electrons in these shells. The build-up of electrons in the above sequence follows well-defined rules. The resulting electron configuration of the elements is an important starting point for a discussion of valency. The shells each have a limited capacity and the numbers of electrons that can be accommodated in the first four labelled 1, 2, 3, 4 (or sometimes K, L, M, N) are 2, 8, 18, 32 respectively. Each of these shells has sub-shells of which there are four main types designated s, p, d and f which can contain 2, 6, 10 and 14 electrons respectively. If all the orbits in a shell have electrons actually present in them the shell is filled or closed and this confers on the shell an unusual stability or inertness. Conversely, unfilled shells lead to activity and the electrons in the incompletely filled shells largely determine the chemical and physical properties of the element and are responsible for the combination of atoms to form molecules. These electrons are referred to as *valence electrons*. The inner shell, *i.e.*, the one nearest the nucleus, can accommodate only two electrons (the element helium has just that number) and the next two shells can hold eight each. Large atoms, *e.g.*, lead, radium, have many filled shells and, subject to special exceptions, the general rule is that the inner shells are the filled ones and the outer shell may be incomplete. Elements which have equal numbers of electrons in their outer shell resemble each other and come in the same Group of the Periodic Table. Thus the elements with complete electronic shells are chemically unreactive gases, *e.g.*, argon and neon (minor constituents of the atmosphere). Elements with just one electron in the outer shell are highly reactive metals, *e.g.*, sodium and potassium which lose this electron readily to give monopositive ions, *e.g.*, Na^+. These elements are called electropositive. Contrariwise elements with just one electron too few are electronegative and readily gain one electron either by sharing, or by capture (to form anions, *e.g.*, Cl^-).

More generally, at least for the light elements of Periods 2 and 3 of the Periodic Table, the valence of an element is given by the Group Number, N, *i.e.*, the number of valence electrons which must be lost by the electropositive metals, or by 8-N, the number of electrons which electronegative elements need to gain.

The covalence of an electronegative element is increased by one if it loses one electron to form a positive ion, and decreased by one if it gains an electron. Thus nitrogen with a covalence 3 can give either N^+ which can form 4 covalent bonds (in the ammonium ion, NH_4^+) or the N^- ion with

Valence Electrons (N) and Valency (V)

N = 1	2	3	4	5	6	7	8
V = 1	2	3	4	3	2	1	0
Hydrogen							Helium
Sodium	Magnesium	Aluminium	Carbon	Nitrogen	Oxygen	Flourine	Neon
Potassium	Calcium	Gallium	Silicon	Phosphorus	Sulphur	Chlorine	Argon
			Germanium	Arsenic		Bromine	
			Tin			Iodine	
	Barium		Lead				

←————————Metals————————→←——————————————→←————Non-metals:—————→
Positive ions   Covalent   Negative ions
                                 compounds   or covalent compounds

a covalency of 2 (*e.g.*, NH_2^-). Similarly oxygen can give H_3O^+, the hydroxonium ion (the acid principle in water), H_2O (water itself), and OH^- (the hydroxyl ion).

IONIC BONDS, SALTS AND ACIDS

These bonds are normally formed between electropositive elements (at the left of the Periodic Table, *e.g.*, sodium and potassium) and electronegative elements (at the right of the Periodic Table, *e.g.*, oxygen, fluorine, chlorine). The ionic charge may be determined from the valency: Na^+, Mg^{++}, Al^{+++}; $O^=$, Cl^-.

Ions may contain a number of atoms, as shown by many of the common anions: hydroxyl, OH^-; nitrate, NO_3^-; sulphate, $SO_4^=$; carbonate $CO_3^=$. Ionic solids formed from a metal ion and one of these anions are called *salts* and are derived from the parent *acid* in which the anion is bound to a *hydrogen ion* (or ions): HNO_3, nitric acid; H_2SO_4, sulphuric acid. Sulphuric acid can form two series of salts, one called *normal* based upon the $SO_4^=$ ion and a second (called acid salts since they contain a hydrogen) based upon the HSO_4^- ion. Phosphoric acid, H_3PO_4, has three series of salts. A substance which reacts with an acid to form a salt and water as the only products is called a *base*. An example is sodium hydroxide, NaOH (caustic soda). The Lewis definitions of acid and base are given below.

The ionic forces are less directional in character than covalent bonds are, but in solids the ions are in regular fixed arrangements (*see* **Part II**). Each anion is surrounded by cations and is attracted to them by electrostatic Coulomb forces. These are of long range and so the anion is attracted not only to the closest cations. Additionally each cation is surrounded by anions so that the bonding is not localised. The whole solid therefore is like a giant molecule and is not easily broken down by melting. This contrasts with covalent compounds in which the forces between molecules are small, the main attractions being within the molecule.

The structures adopted depend upon the relative numbers of the anions and cations (which are determined by ionic charges) and by the relative ionic sizes, which have been deduced from X-ray diffraction measurements.

COVALENT BONDS

In the simple theory the shared electron pairs are localised between two atoms. Multiple bonds result when there are more pairs shared. The multiplicity (or *bond order*) is integral. The theory may be extended by admitting that an electron pair may be shared between more than two atoms in *delocalised bonding* which can then give rise to fractional bond orders. The best example is benzene (and graphite) where nine pairs of electrons are shared between six carbon-carbon bonds giving a bond order of 1·5.

Modern Theories

Modern theories of valency make use of the concepts of quantum mechanics (*see* **F17**) in which each of the well-defined electron orbits of the s, p, d and f electrons in the Bohr theory is replaced by the idea of the electron cloud with a spatial electron density and distribution. Each of these electron clouds (now called an orbital) has a definite shape depending upon the type of electrons. The orbitals of s electrons are of spherical shape with a density that falls off with the distance from the nucleus. The peak density occurs at the old Bohr radius. Electrons of the p type have orbitals with double lobes giving the figure of eight or dumbell shape. There are three such orbitals in every shell except the first and they are arranged mutually at right angles. Each one can contain two electrons giving a total of six. The d orbitals are five in number. Each again can contain two electrons giving a total of ten. Four of these d orbitals have shapes like four-leaf clovers, whereas the fifth has two lobes, rather like the p orbitals but with the addition of a torus or doughnut. The shapes of the f orbitals are even more complicated. It is the shape of these orbitals and their relative spatial arrangement which gives the covalent bond its directional character. The idea of electron sharing between two atoms becomes the notion of overlap of an orbital on one atom with an orbital on another to give a bonding *molecular orbital* which can contain the pair of shared electrons. The bond energy is a maximum when this overlap is optimum and this occurs when the atoms are in certain definite positions thus giving the molecule its own characteristic shape.

Molecular shape

For elements from the second row of the Periodic Table the number of electrons in the valence shell can be eight arranged in four pairs of orbitals (one 2s and three 2p orbitals). These orbitals can be combined or *hybridised* to give the basic tetrahedral shape (*see* Fig. 1). Each of these can overlap with say an orbital of a hydrogen atom (the 1s) to give a bonding orbital which can accommodate two electrons. Alternatively each orbital can, if the atom has enough electrons, contain two non-bonding electrons called a *lone pair*. The basic molecular shapes of methane (CH_4), ammonia (NH_3), and water (H_2O) may then be rationalised as in Fig. 1.

The bond angle in methane is the tetrahedral angle (109° 28′). The angles in ammonia (107° 18′) and water (104° 30′) are smaller probably because the lone pair orbital is slightly more repulsive than the bonding orbital is. This closes down the angles between the bonds.

The lone pairs may be used to bind the hydrogen ions from acids to give tetrahedral NH_4^+ and pyramidal H_3O^+. It is the lone pairs therefore which give ammonia and water their basicity. In the modern concept of acids and bases due to Lewis, a base is an electron donor and an acid becomes an electron acceptor. This definition of an acid includes the older idea of it as a hydrogen ion producer in that the hydrogen ion is an electron acceptor but it is more general—a Lewis acid need not be a protic acid.

Bond Lengths

Many covalent bond distances have been measured

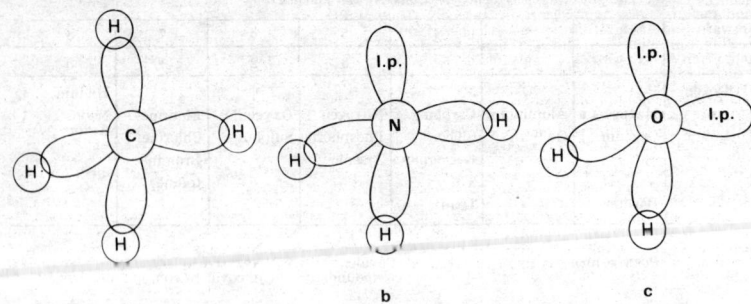

Fig. 1. The spatial arrangements of the atoms and orbitals in (a) methane (CH$_4$), (b) ammonia (NH$_3$) and (c) water (H$_2$O). The basic shape is tetrahedral and the hybridised orbitals are lone pair orbitals (l.p.) and bonding orbitals.

and each may be apportioned between the bound atoms to give a self-consistent set of covalent bond-radii for each element which can be used in predictions of molecular structures. These radii vary inversely with the bond order involved. Thus the carbon-carbon bond length varies from 154 pm (*i.e.*, 10^{12}m) for C−C to 135 pm for C=C.

Bond Energies

Bonds differ in their strength depending upon the atoms and the bond order. A double bond between two given atoms is stronger than a single bond but generally not as strong as two single bonds. Thus "unsaturated" compounds, which contain multiple bonds, will tend to form "saturated" compounds containing only single bonds since the energetics are favourable.

Functional Groups

Compounds may be further classified according to certain persistent groups of atoms which have a residual valency and can combine with other groups. Thus the methyl group (CH$_3$) related to methane (CH$_4$) by the removal of a hydrogen atom can combine with other atoms or groups of valency one: methyl chloride (chloromathane), CH$_3$Cl; methyl alcohol (methanol), CH$_3$OH; dimethyl ether, CH$_3$OCH$_3$. Common functional groups are shown in the table.

CHEMICAL ENERGETICS

Chemical reactions are accompanied by energy changes which can be utilised as heat (in fires) or mechanical work (in explosions or rockets), or to produce electric current in batteries. Chemical compounds can therefore be said to store energy and to possess "internal energy". The energy can be thought of as being stored in the chemical bonds. The energy change (at constant volume) in a reaction is then a result of changes (denoted ΔU) in the nett internal energy of the reactants and products by the law of the conservation of energy. If the conditions are those of constant pressure, the energy change is due to overall changes in a closely related properly called enthalpy (ΔH).

It was at one time thought that reactions would proceed only if energy was given out (*exothermic* processes). Although this is now known to be true at the lowest temperature, in other cases a second consideration, the entropy term, needs to be considered, as the existence of *endothermic* changes confirms. A new "energy" term defined to contain the entropy consideration and called the Gibbs Free Energy, G, may then be used. Natural or "spontaneous" processes are accompanied by a decrease in the nett value of G, and systems tend to assume whichever state has the lowest value of G.

Chemical Equilibrium

Certain chemical changes, like physical changes

Some Classes of Simple Organic Compounds

Name	General Description and Formula	Examples
Alkanes (or paraffins)	"Saturated" hydrocarbons of the general formula C_nH_{2n+2} Contain single bonds only	methane (CH$_4$) butane (C$_4$H$_{10}$)
Alkenes (olefins)	"Unsaturated" hydrocarbons of general formula C_nH_{2n} Contain double bonds	ethylene (C$_2$H$_4$) styrene (C$_6$H$_5$.C$_2$H$_3$)
Alkynes (acetylenes)	"Unsaturated" hydrocarbon of general formula C_nH_{2n-2} Contain triple bonds	acetylene (C$_2$H$_2$)
Enols (alcohols)	Contain the OH group, bound for example to an alkyl group $C_nH_{2n+1}OH$	methylalcohol (CH$_3$OH) ethylalcohol (C$_2$H$_5$OH)
Ketones	Contain the C=O group $C_nH_{2n+1}C=O$	acetone (CH$_3$)$_2$CO
Aldehydes	Contain the CHO group	formaldehyde (HCHO) acetaldehyde (CH$_3$CHO)
Aromatic hydrocarbons	Ring compounds with reactions similiar to the proto type, benzene (C$_6$H$_6$)	napthalene (C$_{10}$H$_8$) anthracene (C$_{14}$H$_{10}$)
Phenyl compounds	Derivatives of the phenyl group, C$_6$H$_5$	phenol (C$_6$H$_5$OH) aniline (C$_6$H$_5$NH$_2$)
Heterocyclic compounds	Ring compounds containing mainly carbon atoms and one or more other atoms, *e.g.*, nitrogen	pyridine (C$_5$H$_5$N) thiophene (C$_4$H$_4$S)

such as raising and lowering weights, or freezing and melting water, may be easily reversed. The forward and backward reactions which are proceeding continuously can then be made to balance out, given enough time, and the system is said to be in equilibrium.

Suppose that X and Y when mixed are partially converted to Z and an equilibrium mixture is obtained under certain defined conditions. The relative amounts $[X]$, $[Y]$, etc., are then definite and governed by the equilibrium constant defined as

$$K = \frac{[Z]}{[X][Y]}$$

Putting it in another way, if we know K we can predict the relative amounts of products and reactants, i.e., the extent to which the reaction proceeds. K in turn depends upon the change in Gibbs Free Energy for the reaction:

$$\Delta G = - RT \ln K$$

where R is the gas constant, and T the absolute temperature, and ln denotes the natural logarithm.

The efficiency of a reaction therefore can be predicted theoretically since values for ΔG can frequently be calculated from tabulated values of ΔH and ΔS. Such studies constitute *chemical thermodynamics*, the branch of thermodynamics (see **F20**) applied to chemical reactions. It is an essential consideration in industrial processes.

Bond Enthalpies

The enthalpy (**L40**) of a molecule can be thought of as the sum of the enthalpies associated with each covalent bond, for each of which there is a characteristic value. Determination and tabulation of these bond energies helps in the prediction of enthalpy changes in new reactions involving covalent molecules. Similarly for ionic solids.

THE SPEED OF REACTIONS—CATALYSIS

A good analogy to illustrate the difference between chemical thermodynamics and kinetics is the downhill flow of water. The water will seek the lowest point where it has the lowest potential energy, and in an analogous way a reaction will try to proceed to the state with the lowest Gibbs Free Energy. However, the speed of both water flow and reaction will depend upon a large number of factors, particularly the available *pathway* (or reaction mechanism). Indeed water at the top or a mountain or in a domestic bath may not flow down at all if a suitable path is blocked say by a hillock (or bath plug). The unblocking may involve the expenditure of energy, for example to lift the water over the dam (or pull out the plug). In reactions this type of energy is called the *activation energy*. It can be supplied in a number of ways (see below) such as heating. Sometimes it is small and (thankfully) at other times it is large enough that thermodynamically feasible reactions do not occur at all quickly. Each of us is, in fact, *thermodynamically* unstable with respect to our combustion products, mainly CO_2 and H_2O, i.e., we should burn (!), but fortunately we are *kinetically* stable.

A *catalyst* is a substance which will provide an alternative reaction pathway of low activation energy, i.e., it can speed up a reaction, without itself being consumed in the process. The analogy for the water flow would be a tunnel through the hillock. Catalysts are very important industrially, for example, in the manufacture of sulphuric acid (using platinised asbestos or vanadium pentoxide), in the Haber process for ammonia used for fertilisers (iron derivatives), and in the "cracking" of crude oil to give lighter oils (aluminium oxide). Natural catalysts are called *enzymes* (see **F31(2)**).

CLASSIFICATION OF REACTIONS

Chemical change can be brought about by a variety of techniques used separately or together:

mixing of single substances
heating single substances or mixtures
electrolysing solutions
exposure to light or radiation
addition of catalysts.

The changes can be classified according to the results produced:

Dissociation—breakdown into simpler substances or ions
Addition—in which one type of molecule or ion is added to another
Polymerisation—reaction of a substance (monomer) with itself to produce larger molecules of the same composition (polymer)
Substitution—in which one particular group in a molecule is replaced by another
Elimination—in which one particular group in a molecule is lost
Exchange—in which two groups are mutually substituted one by the other
Oxidation—removal of electrons (increase of oxidation number), e.g., Fe^{++} ferrous ion is oxidised to ferric, Fe^{+++}
Reduction—the converse of oxidation

More significantly modern classifications are based upon the precise *molecular mechanism* employed. Examples are

Nucleophilic attack—where an electron-rich reagent attacks a position of low electron density in a molecule
Electrophilic attack—where an electron-depleted reagent—an electrophile (for example, a positive ion)—attacks a position of high electron density
Bimolecular reaction—one which involves two molecules unlike a monomolecular reaction which involves only one in each step

Precise descriptions can be built up: substitution, nucleophilic, bimolecular.

ELECTROLYTES, ELECTROLYSIS AND ELECTROCHEMICAL CELLS

Electrolytic Solutions

Ionic solids can dissolve in some solvents especially if each has a high dielectric constant to cut down the force of attraction between oppositely charged ions. The process can be assisted by solvation of the ions and also by the entropy changes which favour the less ordered state of affairs—the liquid rather than the ordered solid.

Electrolysis

The oppositely charged ions are capable of independent movement and the application of an electric potential from an external battery or source of direct current to electrodes in the solution will cause the ions to move. The positive ions (cations) will move to the negatively charged electrode (the cathode) and the negatively charged ions (anions) to the positively charged anode. At the electrodes chemical changes occur and ions may be converted to uncharged species and deposited: for example, sodium ions (Na^+) to sodium metal, Na. This process is referred to as electrolysis. Faraday discovered two laws of electrolysis: (i) the amount of any substance deposited (or dissolved) is proportional to the amount of electricity used; (ii) the relative amounts of substances deposited by the same quantity of electricity are in the ratio of their *equivalent weights*.

For any ion discharged below a certain value of the applied voltage the *discharge voltage* is small. In an electrolyte containing many different ionic species therefore, each ionic discharge will occur only as the appropriate potential is reached. For solutions of acids, hydrogen (formed from H^+ ions) is discharged at the cathode, and oxygen (formed from OH^- ions) at the anode. Electrolysis is important commercially for the refining of metals, electroplating, and in the production of many basic chemicals.

Electrochemical Cells

Ever since 1800 when Volta produced an electric battery consisting of alternate plates of silver and zinc separated by cloth impregnated with salt, the search for new batteries has been continuous. In each new battery a different chemical process is harnessed to produce electrical energy. The battery must not only be feasible according to the laws of thermodynamics, but must be practicable and cheap for widespread consumer use.

The voltages developed in any battery can be predicted from a knowledge of the two processes occurring: one at the cathode and the other at the anode. Voltages can be ascribed to each of these "half cells" according to the chemical reaction which occurs and the condition used, for example concentrations of the reactants (the so-called "standard electrode potentials"). The voltage of any combination of two half cells is the sum of the half-cell voltages. Furthermore each of these voltages is related to the change in the Gibbs Free Energy for its reaction and can, in theory, therefore be predicted thermodynamically.

CHEMISTRY IN MODERN LIFE

Chemistry plays a crucial role in modern life, not least in the third world, as well as in the more developed nations. In the U.K. chemistry has been studied, developed and put to practical use as well as anywhere in the world in modern times. It is no accident that the largest specialised scientific society in the U.K. is the Royal Society of Chemistry (R.S.C.) and that its forerunner, The Chemical Society, lays claim to being the oldest in the world. The high quality of chemical science at the crucial level of basic research is indicated by the remarkable frequency with which the Nobel Prize in Chemistry has come to the U.K. The success is not confined to academic activity but, surely as a consequence, it extends to the economic life of the nation.

The U.K. chemical industry is among the largest in the world and one of the most successful. In national statistics it is included in the manufacturing sector alongside other sectors which have a high chemical component such as petroleum and petroleum products. Its output covers a very wide range. Firstly there are the so called "basic chemicals", such as sulphuric acid, which are utilised in the manufacturing processes of other sectors.

In agriculture chemicals are not only important in the form of bulk products such as fertilizer, without which modern agriculture could not operate efficiently, but also for the 'finer' chemicals such as herbicides and insecticides. Manufactured synthetic polymers and plastics are omnipresent in modern life, for example in architecture and building as well as in many familiar household products and uses. The list here is long and includes moulded casings for televisions and other electronic and electrical products, kitchen utensils, all forms of coverings from paints and varnishes to fabrics. Then there are the "fine" chemicals: cosmetics and pharmaceuticals, ranging from vanity products to the birth control pill and life-saving synthetic drugs. Petroleum products from oil cover an extremely wide range. Petroleum is a most valuable "feed stock" for other products and in this use it is arguably more unique and precious than as a fuel or energy source.

Nevertheless, chemistry has had as bad a press recently as other basic physical sciences have had, with the consequence that young people turned away at the turn of the decade from studying the sciences. In the popular mind, chemistry has become associated with pollution resulting from the manufacturing, use and misuse of synthetic chemicals, as well as industrial accidents. Indeed, the word "chemical" has been used increasingly in a pejorative way, even in informed broadcasting and reportage. Thus chemical fertilizers (meaning synthetic fertilizers) are distinguished falsely from organic fertilizers. This sort of practice ignores the fact that we ourselves consist of, use, rely on, are surrounded by naturally occurring chemicals, organic and inorganic, as well as the useful man-made synthetics.

The word *chemist* fares no better. Whereas the terms physicist, biologist, mathematician and scientist are generally used unambiguously, the word chemist is commonly used for the pharmacist or apothecary, at least in the U.K. if not generally in the rest of the world.

IV. BIOLOGY—THE SCIENCE OF LIFE

WHAT BIOLOGY IS ABOUT

Biology embraces the study of all living things which exist on earth at the present time and also the recognisable remains of those that are extinct. Living things or organisms range from the apparently simple micro-organisms such as viruses and bacteria to the largest animals and plants.

Living Processes

The enormous variation and complexity of living processes make the task of understanding and defining life a very difficult one. Every living organism undergoes continual physical and chemical changes which, in spite of their diversity, are referred to as the metabolism of the organism. Metabolism involves the processing of food materials, the production of waste products, and all the intermediate stages between these whereby energy and matter are provided for the operation, maintenance, and growth of the organism. These reactions are under very exact chemical or nervous control at every stage and can be slowed down or speeded up as the need arises. Thus the organism can react to changes in the environment in which it lives, adjusting its activities in relation to the external changes. Finally, organisms can reproduce either in an identical or very slightly modified form. In this process new individuals are produced and the species continues to survive. Differences between offspring and parents can, under certain circumstances, act cumulatively over many generations and so form the basis of evolutionary change in which new species of organism are ultimately formed.

Molecular Biology

It has been evident for many years that the most fundamental aspects of these living processes occur in basic structural units known as cells. The study of living processes at the molecular and cell level has been given a tremendous impetus in recent years by the advent of new techniques which enable microscopic and submicroscopic parts of cell to be examined. Physicists, chemists, and mathematicians have found themselves working alongside biologists in this field and several of the very notable advances have been made by physical scientists. Molecular biology is a term frequently used in describing this rapidly expanding and fascinating field of research.

EVOLUTION

Introduction.—The idea that species of living organisms could change over long periods of time was considered by some Greek writers and, much later, by the Frenchmen Buffon and Lamarck at the end of the 18th cent. Further, the work of the 18th cent. geologists such as James Hutton and William Smith provided a basis without which the major contribution of Darwin, the great 19th cent. naturalist, would have been impossible. Hutton showed that the earth's surface had undergone prolonged upheavals and volcanic eruptions with consequent changes in sea level. This implied that the earth was much older than had previously been supposed. Smith developed a method of dating the geological strata by means of the fossils found in them and demonstrated that widely different types of animals and plants existed at different periods of the earth's history. Later in this section (**F47–8**) a general picture is presented of the evolution of organisms from the simple to the complex and from the aquatic to the terrestrial environment.

These discoveries were in conflict with the Biblical account in the book of Genesis and, although various attempts were made to explain them away or discredit them, it became abundantly clear that through milllions of years life has been continually changing, with new species constantly arising and many dying out.

The Evidence for Evolution

1. *The Geological Record.*—It has already been pointed out that successively younger rocks contain fossil remains of different and relatively more complex organisms. The spore-bearing plants preceded the gymnosperms and the angiosperms arose much later. Similarly in the vertebrate series the fish appeared before the amphibia which were followed by the reptiles and later by the air breathing, warm-blooded birds and mammals. On a more restricted level the evolution of the horse has been worked out in great detail from the small Eohippus which was about a foot high and had four digits on the forefeet and three on the hind-feet to the large one-toed animal living today. However, such complete series are rare and the geological record is very incomplete. There are a number of gaps, particularly between the major groups of organisms. No satisfactory fossil evidence is known of the ancestors of the angiosperms (**F43**) so perhaps they did not grow in conditions which favoured their preservation as fossils. On the other hand, Archæopteryx provides an indisputable link between the reptiles and the birds.

Although we talk about the age of fishes, the age of reptiles and so on it must be emphasised that these are the periods during which particular groups were abundant or even dominant. Each group probably originated many millions of years before it became widespread. Further, some groups, such as the giant reptiles and the seed-ferns, died out completely whereas others, the fishes and true ferns for example, are still common today although many fishes and ferns that exist today are very different from those of the Devonian and Carboniferous periods (**F48**). On the other hand some species, for example the Maidenhair tree, have remained unaltered for many millions of years.

2. *Geographical Distribution.*—Nearly all the marsupials or pouched mammals are found in the Australian continent which was cut off from the mainland about 60 million years ago. All the fossil evidence indicates that at that time the eutherian or placental mammals did not yet exist. The marsupials are the only naturally occurring mammals in Australia (**F37(1)**) but since the isolation of the continent the group has given rise to a large number of species very similar in appearance to those which evolved elsewhere in the world among the eutherian mammals. There are marsupials which look like wolves, dogs, cats and squirrels; yet they have no close biological relationships to these animals. Further, some marsupials such as the kangaroos have evolved which are unlike any other creatures in the rest of the world. Quite clearly the isolation of Australia so long ago has resulted in the evolution of these distinct types, just as Darwin found in the Galapagos islands where each has its own distinct flora and fauna which differ also from those of the S. American mainland.

3. *Anatomy.*—The comparative study of the development and mature structure of the mammalian body provides much evidence that all the species have evolved from a single ancestral stock.

Although the arm of an ape, the leg of a dog, the flipper of a whale and the wing of a a bat appear very different externally they are all built on the same skeletal plan. It would be difficult to explain such similarities unless they had all evolved from a common type. There is also evidence that the early development of an animal recapitulates its biological history to a certain extent. For example, the gill slits found in fish are formed during the early stages in the development of a mammal although later they disappear. Finally, apparently useless vestigial structures sometimes occur which would be inexplicable unless regarded in the light of an evolutionary history. In man a small appendix and vestiges of a third eyelid occur but these are functionless although in other animals such structures are well developed and functional, *e.g.*, the appendix in the rabbit

4. *Human Selection.*—During his brief history on earth modern man has continually selected and bred animals and plants for his own use. We have only to look at the various breeds of dogs which have been developed from a single wild type to see that under certain circumstances great structural divergence can occur in a species even in a relatively short time.

The Darwinian Theory of Evolution.—Darwin amassed a great deal of information such as that outlined above which convinced him that evolution of life had taken place over millions of years. His was the first real attempt to collect all the evidence scientifically and no other satisfactory alternative explanation of all the facts he presented has been proposed. Perhaps even more important was his attempt to explain *how* evolution had actually occurred. He published his theory after many years of work in his book *The Origin of Species by Means of Natural Selection* in 1859. Some of his ideas have since been modified owing to our increased knowledge of genetics but they are so important that it is worth-while recounting the main points of his theory.

1. *The Struggle for Existence.*—It is clear that in nature there is a severe struggle for existence in all animals and plants. Over a period of time the number of individuals of a species in a given community does not vary greatly. This implies that the number of progeny which survive to become mature breeding individuals more or less replaces the number of mature ones that die. Generally speaking the reproductive output of a species is much greater than this. For example, a single large foxglove plant may produce half a million seeds each one of which is potentially capable of giving rise to a new individual. Obviously nearly all the progeny die before reaching maturity and the chance of any single one surviving is very remote.

2. *Variation.*—The individuals of any generation of human beings obviously differ from one another and such differences are found in other organisms. It is clear that they vary considerably in structure, colour, activity and so on. Darwin also pointed out that generally these variations were passed on from one generation to the next, for example, the children of tall parents tend to grow tall.

3. *Survival of the Fittest.*—If there is an intense struggle for existence in their natural environment among individuals of a species having different characteristics, those which are best "fitted" to a given set of conditions are most likely to survive to maturity. These will reproduce and the features which enabled them to survive will be passed on to their offspring. This

process is liable to continue and a species will become better adapted to its environment.

4. *Natural Selection.*—Over a long period of time the environment of a given species is never stable but will change in various ways. As it does so the characters which best fit the individuals to the changed environment will be selected (not consciously of course) and the species will change. The environment may change only in part of the range of the species and thus lead to divergence and the production of a new species alongside the old one.

Darwin and Lamarck.—Darwin pictured evolution as a slow continuous process with natural selection operating on the small inheritable variations found between the individuals of a species which were undergoing intense competition. This neglects the important effect of the environment on the growth and structure of the individual. It is obvious that external conditions will affect the development of an organism, for example the effect of various soil conditions on the growth of a plant or the amount of food material available to an animal. Lamarck maintained that the characters acquired by an individual owing to the effect of its environment could be passed on to its offspring. Undoubtedly characters are acquired by the individual during its growth but in spite of many attempts to prove otherwise no experiments have been done which prove conclusively that these are inherited by the offspring. Thus Lamarck's theory that evolution has occurred by the inheritance of acquired characters is not generally acceptable today.

Neodarwinism

Darwinism received something of a setback during the early years of modern genetics. There did not seem to be much in common between the large mutations studied by geneticists and the small continuous variations which Darwin thought were the basic material upon which selection acted. With time, it became evident that not all mutations are large in their effects and that much of the continuous variation which occurs does indeed have a genetic basis. Mathematicians such as J. B. S. Haldane and Sewall Wright showed that even very small selective advantages would cause genes to spread throughout populations as the generations passed by. Experiments and observations on natural populations showed that evolution—seen as progressive, adaptive genetic change —does indeed occur today. For example, the proportion of dark-coloured moths has greatly increased in many areas where smoke pollution occurs, as a result of predation by birds on the now more obvious light forms. Again, many pest insects have evolved genetic resistance to the insecticides used to attack them.

GENETICS

Mendelism

Genetics is the study of the mechanisms of the hereditary process. Modern genetics began with the experiments of Gregor Mendel, an Austrian monk in 1865. He studied the inheritance of different factors in peas by crossing different strains and counting the numbers of plants with different characters in the succeeding generations.

In one experiment Mendel crossed peas with round seeds with peas having wrinkled seeds. All of the offspring (known as the "first filial" or F1 generation) had round seeds. Mendel allowed these plants to pollinate themselves, and then measured the characteristics of their offspring (the F2 generation). There were 5,474 round-seeded plants and 1,850 wrinkled-seeded plants in the F2 generation, a ratio of very nearly three to one. The character of roundness can be described as being "dominant" over the "recessive" character of wrinkledness.

In order to explain his results Mendel suggested that the characters of roundness and wrinkledness were determined by particulate factors (now called *genes*), and that each plant possessed two genes for each feature. Suppose the gene for roundness is A and that for wrinkledness is a. Then the parental plants in Mendel's experiment will be represented by AA (round seeds) and aa (wrinkled seeds). The gametes (the ovules and the sperm nuclei of the pollen grains) will be A and a respectively. When these combine to form the F1 generation they will produce plants with the genetic constitution Aa. Both male and female gametes of the F1 generation are then of the two types A and a, and these can combine, on self-pollination, in four different ways:

F1	male gamete	female gamete	F2
	A	A	AA
Aa	A	a	Aa
	a	A	Aa
	a	a	aa

The individuals of the F2 generation will thus have genetic constitutions of AA, Aa and aa in the approximate proportions $1 : 2 : 1$. Since both AA and Aa individuals have round seeds, the ratio of round-seeded plants to wrinkled-seeded plants will be about three to one, which indeed it is.

Mendel's results were ignored for many years until their rediscovery at the beginning of this century. Mendelian ratios were then found to govern inheritance in a large number of other cases, such as coat colour in rabbits and cattle, and white eyes and other characteristics in the fruit fly *Drosophila*. In other cases characteristics are governed by more than one set of genes so the simple mathematical relationships are obscured. This occurs in quantitative features, such as yield in crop plants and weight in animals.

Chromosome Theory

The chromosomes are dark-staining filaments which, as we shall see later, can be observed in the nucleus at cell division. Their behaviour was described in the nineteenth century, but it was not clear what their function was. After the rediscovery of Mendel's work, Sutton suggested that the genes are carried on chromosomes, since the observed behaviour of the chromosomes corresponded very well with the theoretical behaviour of Mendel's factors.

Further evidence for the chromosome theory of inheritance came from study of the phenomenon known as sex-linkage, in which the expression of a gene depends upon the sex of the individual in which it is found. Haemophilia in man, for example, is a hereditary disease which is normally found only in males, although it is clear that females can act as carriers (Queen Victoria was one, since one of her sons, three of her grandsons and seven of her greatgrandsons were haemophiliacs). Cytological study shows that there is one pair of chromosomes which differ in the two sexes. In the female (in man and most animals) the two chromosomes of this pair are similar and are known as the X chromosomes. In the male one of these is replaced by a much smaller Y chromosome. Hence recessive genes which are found on only one X chromosome are expressed in the male, since there is no other dominant gene present. A female haemophiliac would have haemophilia genes on both X chromosomes; this could only arise from a carrier mother and a haemophiliac father, a very rare occurrence.

In recent years it has become clear that chromosomes are composed largely of the DNA molecules of the cell nucleus, to be discussed later (**F33-4**) and since it has become evident that genes are DNA molecules, we now have a firm chemical basis for the assumption that genes are carried on chromosomes. Genetics has thus to some extent become a branch of molecular biology.

Mutations

Sometimes a DNA molecule may not replicate itself exactly during the process of cell division. When this happens the gene which it constitutes has changed its character so as to produce a difference effect when expressed in the individual organism. Such a change is known as a gene mutation. It seems likely, for example, that Queen Victoria's haemophilia gene arose as a mutation in herself or in her mother. Mutations, as we shall see, are of vital importance in providing the genetic variation upon which evolutionary selection can act.

The frequency with which mutations occur is increased by certain chemicals and by ionising radiation. Hence the need for caution in exposing the body to X-rays and to radioactive materials, and the concern over the possible genetic effects of radioactive waste from power stations and from military testing programmes.

THE CELL

Cells were first seen in 1665 by Robert Hooke when he looked at a piece of cork under his primitive microscope. It was not until 1839, however, that Schlieden and Schwann produced the cell doctrine which visualised the cell as both the structural and functional unit of living organisation. Exceptions may be found to the cell doctrine. For example, some protozoa, algae, and fungi show very complex internal organisation but are not divided into cells; they are usually called acellular organisms. The viruses also constitute a difficulty since in many ways they are intermediate between living and dead matter. They are absolutely dependent on cells of other organisms for their continued existence. Outside living cells they are inert molecules which may take a crystalline form. Inside a host cell, however, they become disease-producing parasites which multiply and show many of the other properties of living organisms. They are minute and lack the complex organisation usually associated with cells. Notwithstanding their somewhat ambiguous position, the viruses are often treated as though they were single cells or parts of cells and their extreme simplicity has made them ideal material for many types of research at this level. The bacteria also lack some of the properties of cells but the differences are not so clearly defined as they are in the case of viruses.

Structure and Function of Cells

Though the constituent cells of a multicellular organism are usually specialised to perform particular functions, they have a great many features in common. The cell is often said to be made up of a substance called protoplasm, a term for the fundamental material of life which dates from the 19th cent. Protoplasm has two main constituents, the cytoplasm and the nucleus, and is bounded on the outside by a cell or plasma membrane. Plant cells generally have an additional wall composed primarily of cellulose and used for support. The nucleus is the controlling centre of the cell and has rather limited metabolic capabilities. The cytoplasm contains various subunits which operate to produce energy and new cell structure during the normal metabolism of the cell.

Cells take up the raw materials for metabolism through the cell membrane from extracellular fluid which surrounds them. The nutrients include carbohydrates, fats, proteins, minerals, vitamins, and water. Fats and carbohydrates are important principally as sources of energy, though both types of compound are found in permanent cell structure. Proteins are complex substances of high molecular weight which contain nitrogen in addition to the carbon, hydrogen, and oxygen found in the other compounds. They are of fundamental importance in the structure and function of the cell and are built up of a number of simple nitrogen-containing organic molecules called amino acids. There are twenty amino acids occurring commonly in nature so that the number of possible combinations in large protein molecules is quite clearly enormous. A group of proteins whose significance is well established are the enzymes which are the catalysts of chemical reactions in living cells. Each enzyme will control and speed up a specific reaction even though it is present in very small amounts and is usually unchanged at the end of the process. A large number of inorganic mineral salts are essential for cells to function normally. Some, such as sodium, potassium, and calcium salts, are needed in considerate quantity; others are required only in trace amounts and these include iron, copper, and manganese. The trace elements are usually important constituents of enzyme systems. Vitamins are also necessary in very small amounts and it seems reasonable to conclude that their function is also a catalytic one in parts of some enzyme systems.

I. CYTOPLASM

For a long time cytoplasm was thought to be a homogeneous and structureless substrate in which enzymes occurred as part of a general colloidal system. With the refinement of techniques such as electron microscopy and ultracentrifugation, more and more identifiable components have been found within the cytoplasm. It now seems certain that the material other than these recognisable particles is not a structureless matrix but a highly organised and variable complex.

Mitochondria and Oxidation

Mitochondria vary in shape from cylindrical rods to spheres and in size from 0·2 to 3·0 microns. When seen in the living cell they are in constant motion. The whole structure is enclosed within a thin double membrane, the inner layer of which is thrown into folds extending across the central cavity of the mitochondrion and dividing it into small chambers. The function of mitochondria is to provide energy for the reactions of the rest of the cell. Almost the whole machinery for the oxidation of foodstuffs is to be found in the mitochondria. Slight damage to the mitochondrion will render it unable to carry out a complete cycle of oxidative processes. Destruction of parts of the double membrane system prevents the production of energy-rich phosphate bonds in adenosine triphosphate (ATP) in which energy is stored and transported about the cell.

Chloroplasts and Photosynthesis

Chloroplasts are particles found in cells in the green parts of plants, in fact they contain the green pigment which is called chlorophyll. They are involved in the process known as photosynthesis in which energy absorbed from light is used to synthesise carbohydrates from carbon dioxide and water, oxygen being formed as a by-product.

Chloroplasts are disc-shaped or flat ellipsoids from 2 to 20 microns across, possessing a complex structure which in many ways is reminiscent of that found in mitochondria. A typical double membrane surrounds the structure and the inside is made up very largely of a stack of discs consisting of paired membranes connected at their ends to form closed systems. This seems to be a further development of the type of lamellated structure seen dividing the central cavity of a mitochondrion. The chlorophylls and other pigments, such as the orange yellow carotenoids, seem to be arranged in layers a single molecule thick in the chloroplast discs so that they are maximally exposed to light.

The importance of this process whereby plants can make use of the energy in sunlight to fix carbon dioxide and produce carbohydrates is quite clear. The whole animal population of the world, including man, is dependent on plants for food since even the meat-eating carnivores prey upon herbivores. Although scientists continue to make efforts to produce adequate food materials from simple compounds, there is still no better machinery known for doing this than the plant cell. Man is dependent on photosynthesis not only for his supplies of food but also for much of

his fuel, since much of the combustible material removed from the earth is of plant origin.

Endoplasmic Reticulum, Ribosomes, and Protein Synthesis.

A network of elaborate and oriented double membranes existing within parts of the cytoplasm can be seen in the electron microscope. In the space between the pairs of double membranes small granules are visible, either free in the space or attached to a membrane. The whole system is called the endoplasmic reticulum. When the cell is homogenised and centrifuged the endoplasmic reticulum appears as the microsomal fraction. Biochemical analysis after separation of the membranous from the granular components reveals that the former is composed largely of phospholipids and cholesterol, which are compounds closely related to fats, and the latter of ribonucleic acid (RNA).

Nucleic Acids

The term nucleic acid covers a class of substances, usually of great complexity, built up from smaller units called nucleotides. Each nucleotide consists of a base, united to a sugar, in turn united to phosphoric acid. Nucleotides are joined together in a linear fashion by means of the phosphoric acid residues to form a chain from which the bases project at right angles. Two types of sugar are found in naturally occurring nucleic acids and these are the ribose of RNA and the deoxyribose of desoxyribonucleic acids (DNA). We shall return to the latter when the nucleus is considered. Four nitrogen-containing bases occur in nucleic acids and in RNA—adenine, cytosine, guanine, and uracil. In DNA the uracil is replaced by thymine.

Protein Synthesis

There is good evidence that RNA is manufactured exclusively within the nucleus and subsequently moves out into the cytoplasm. Some of it, called ribosomal RNA, unites with protein to form the granules, or ribosomes, of the endoplasmic reticulum. Another form, called messenger RNA, also migrates from the nucleus to be associated with ribosomes but does not become incorporated into their permanent structure. It is also well established that the ribosomes are closely linked with protein synthesis in the cell because radioactive amino acids, when fed to an animal, are always found first in the ribosomes before any other cell structure. The specificiation for a particular protein is not carried on the ribosome which is merely the factory for making these complex molecules. It is thought that messenger RNA carries instructions from the nucleus which specify exactly the protein to be synthesised at a ribosome. This is done by means of a code in which a "triplet" of three nucleotide bases codes one amino acid (Fig. 1). Thus on a long molecule of RNA, three adjacent uracil bases would specify an amino acid called phenylalanine. If these were followed on the RNA molecule by one uracil and two guanines then the amino acid tryptophan would be specified and this would be joined to the phenylalanine. In this way complex protein molecules can be built up according to instructions emanating from the nucleus for each of the 20 different amino acids.

This system is responsible for building and maintaining much of the organisation of the cytoplasm. All the enzymes, for example catalysing every reaction within the cell will be specified and built up on the appropriate RNA template. The understanding of protein synthesis is of fundamental importance to the whole of biology and has particular significance in studies on cancer where cell growth becomes abnormal.

The Golgi Apparatus

The characteristic features of the Golgi apparatus are numbers of large vacuoles or spaces bordered by closely packed layers of double membranes. The latter look very much like the

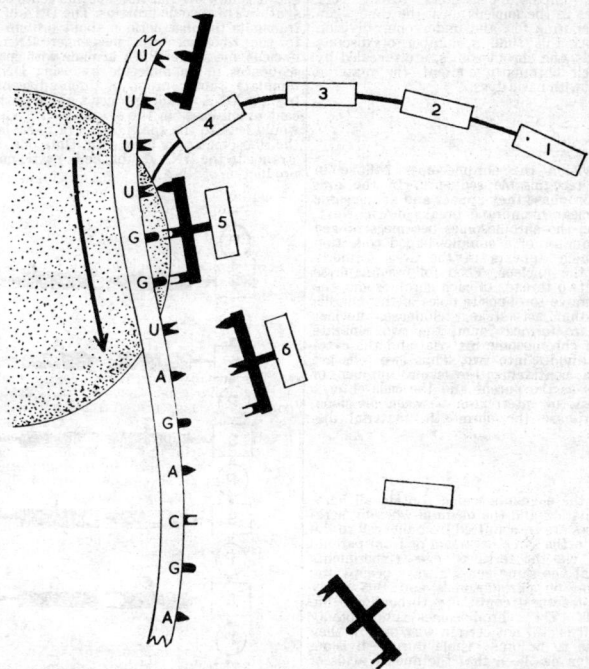

FIG. 1. This shows a portion of a molecule of messenger RNA, associated with a ribosome and synthesising a protein. Adenine specifies Uracil (U), Cytosine specifies Guanine (G), Thymine specifies Adenine (A), and Guanine specifies Cytosine (C). The ribosome is moving down the messenger RNA strand "reading" the triplet code. Amino acid 4, which is phenylalanine specified by UUU, has just been joined to three other amino acids and its carrier RNA released to the cytoplasm. Amino acid 5, tryptophan specified by UGG, is attached to its carrier RNA and in position ready to be joined to the protein chain by the ribosome. Amino acid 6, methionine specified by UAG is attached to its carrier RNA but has not been brought into position on the messenger RNA strand.Other amino acids and carrier RNA molecules exist free in the cytoplasm and have not yet associated.

membranes of the endoplasmic reticulum but do not have the ribosome particles along their edge. They are therefore known as "smooth" membranes in contrast to the "rough" membranes of endoplasmic reticulum. The function of the Golgi apparatus may be associated with secretory activity of the cell.

Cell Membrane

Though the cell membrane plays a most vital part in regulating what can enter and leave the cell, it remains rather poorly understood. It is thought to consist of a double layer of lipid molecules with a layer of protein probably outside the lipid. Fairly large molecules seem to be able to penetrate the membrane in relation to their fat solubility, which would support the hypothesis of its lipid framework. Small molecules and ions appear to penetrate in relation to their size, the smaller ones getting through more readily than the larger. This suggests that pores of a certain size exist in the membrane.

The cell membrane has mechanisms which can move ions and other substances against concentration differences either into or out of the cell. A fine microelectrode can be pushed into a cell and the electrical potential of the inside determined with respect to the outside. In all the cells studied so far there is a potential difference across the membrane which is produced by the non-uniform distribution on either side of ions, particularly those of sodium, potassium, and chloride.

Though these potentials have been studied in animal and plant cells generally, they are best known from the work on nerve cells where sudden changes in the membrane potential are the basis of nerve impulses. The basic process which produces the nerve impulse in any region of the nerve fibre has been shown to be a sudden increase in permeability of the membrane to sodium ions in that region. Transmission from one nerve cell to the next takes place at a special region called a synapse and when an impulse reaches this region it causes the release of a small amount of chemical transmitter substance which diffuses to the membrane of the adjacent cell. There it combines with the membrane in such a way as to change its permeability to ions and so produce a response in the second cell. A number of transmitter substances have now been identified and many of them are related chemically to tranquillisers and other drugs affecting the nervous system.

II. NUCLEUS

The main regions of the nucleus are the surrounding nuclear membrane, a mass of material known as chromatin, and a small sphere called the nucleolus. The nuclear membrane is a double structure very much like the membranes of the cell surface and endoplasmic reticulum. Suggestions have been made that these membranes are continuous at some regions within the cell. The status of chromatin was in doubt for many years. Light microscope studies reveal very little structure in the nucleus until the time when the cell is preparing for, and undergoing, division or mitosis. At this time a number of discrete double strands, the chromosomes, are revealed by virtue of their chromatin content—the material stains heavily with basic dyes.

Cell Division

During division the chromosomes behave in regular and recognisable sequence. In the first stage called prophase they appear and at the same time the nuclear membrane breaks down. Next, in metaphase, the chromosomes become arranged across the equator of a spindle shaped collection of fibrils which appears in the area formerly outlined by the nucleus. Then follows anaphase in which the two threads of each chromosome, the chromatids, move to opposite poles of the spindle. Finally in the last stage, telophase, nuclear membranes are formed round the two separate collections of chromosome material and the cytoplasm itself divides into two. Thus two cells are formed each containing the same number of chromosomes as the parent and the cells enter a period of rest, or interphase, between divisions. During interphase the chromatin material disappears.

Genes

These are the elements which contain all hereditary information and the medium whereby hereditary features are transmitted from one cell to the next, either in the same organism or from parents to offspring via the fertilised egg. Experiments indicated that the same genes always occupy the same position on chromosomes and this really demands a structural continuity through the life of the cell. The chromosomes undoubtedly persist, but it is still not certain why or how they change so as to become visible during division. One suggestion has been that the nucleic acids of which they are very largely made up condense during the period of prophase. In the resting nucleus the chromosomes may be much more swollen and occupy much of the nucleus.

The problem that has attracted the most attention and is possibly the most fundamental that biology has to offer is that of the nature of the genes. The important material of the genes is known to be deoxyribonucleic acid (DNA), made up of nucleotides as is RNA, though in this case the bases are adenine, cytosine, guanine, and thymine. The DNA molecule is large and complex. Two long chains of nucleotides are known to coil round in a double helix with the pairs of bases on each helix directed towards one another and linked by means of hydrogen bonds (Fig. 2). Furthermore, if adenine is the base on one chain, thymine must be its partner on the other and similarly guanine can link only with cytosine. Because of this pairing off of bases there is sufficient information in a single chain of nucleotides to resynthesise the double helix once more. Thus if we examine a section of a single strand of the helix and find bases in the order adenine, thymine, guanine, adenine, cytosine, we can predict that in similar positions on the other strand we shall find thymine, adenine, cytosine, thymine, guanine. The capacity of one half of a DNA molecule to specify the other half exactly, enables the system to be self-replicating in a way that is essential in a hereditary transmitter and fits in well with what is known of chromosome behaviour during cell division.

Transmission of Genetic Information

Long before the structure and significance of the DNA molecules was known, geneticists were finding that alterations in a gene, known as a mutation, usually affected a particular chemical reaction and this in turn caused the changes seen in the organism as a whole. The effect was due to the failure to synthesise a necessary enzyme and so the hypothesis "one gene = one enzyme" gathered currency. This view has now been extended to include proteins other than enzymes

and it is now certain that specific genes control the synthesis of specific proteins. The DNA of the genes transmits the instructions about protein synthesis to the ribosomes via messenger RNA. In the nucleus, messenger RNA is made with specific base sequences in its molecule by using DNA as the template; thus a group of three adjacent adenine bases in DNA would produce a group of three adjacent uracil bases in the synthesised RNA and this would lead to the specification of phenylalanine at the ribosome as we have seen. Only one of the two strands in the DNA double helix participates in the production of RNA.

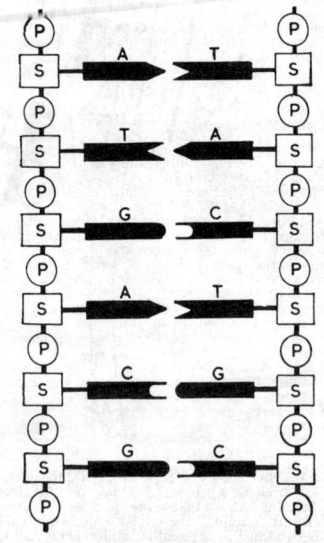

FIG. 2. A portion of a DNA molecule showing how it is made up of two strands of nucleotides. Each nucleotide consists of a base, which may be Adenine (A), Thymine (T), Guanine (G), or Cytosine (C), united to the Pentose Sugar, Desoxyribose (S), in turn joined to Phosphoric Acid (P). The nucleotides are linked through the phosphoric acid groups. The two strands are held together by hydrogen bonds between bases, adenine linking only with thymine, and guanine only with cyto-sine. They are twisted round each other so that the molecule is in the form of a double helix.

The processes involved in nuclear control and the transmission of information from cell to cell is summarised in the aphorism "DNA makes RNA and RNA makes protein." The system of carrying that information in the base sequences of DNA molecules has become known as the "genetic code." A remarkable landmark in the study of DNA occurred when, towards the end of 1967, Kornberg and his colleagues managed to synthesise a virus DNA in a test tube. The synthesised molecules proved to be capable of infecting bacteria in the same way that the naturally occurring virus would. The DNA was synthesised using an extracted virus DNA molecule as template and attaching nucleotides by means of appropriate enzymes. The newly made molecules were then separated from the template. It can hardly be claimed that this is the creation of life in a test tube since the template was extracted from a living virus. The experiment suggests many possibilities in experimental modification of the genetic constitution of an organism with all the far-reaching ethical consequences.

See **Special Topic, F70–76.**

MULTICELLULAR ORGANISATION

It is axiomatic, if evolutionary theory is accepted, that in the course of very long periods of time there has been a general change in multicellular organisation from the simple aggregation of cells with little individual differentiation, to the highly specialised and differentiated cells and tissues seen in complex animals and plants.

Furthermore the complex organisation must be built up in the lifetime of each animal or plant from the single-celled stage of the fertilised egg. The essential problems in development are: (1) how is the smooth succession of shape changes produced during cell division so that an appropriate and recognisable end product is reached?; (2) how do the cells *differentiate* during this temporal sequence so that those which form part of the eye, say, are different from those of liver and blood?

Method of Development

There are some important differences in the method of development in animals and plants. In animals there tends to be a relatively short period during which the basic structure is produced and after which growth, repair, and replacement may cause adjustment rather than major change. In higher plants, on the other hand, the apical regions of both roots and shoots remain in a permanently embryonic state and add material, which then differentiates, in a continuous process throughout the life of the plant. In spite of these differences—and in any case there are many exceptions—the two main problems in development are essentially similar in both animals and plants.

A great deal of work has been done on animal development since this takes place in a fairly stereotyped way during a short period of time. The fertilised egg of an animal divides in such a way as to form a hollow ball of cells, the blastula, which folds in on itself to produce a two-layered sac, the gastrula. A third layer, the mesoderm, is now added between the two layers, known as ectoderm on the outside, and endoderm on the inside. At this stage much of the animal's basic structure is established. Many aspects of this orderly sequence can be explained in terms of specific adhesive properties of cells, so that a cell will stick to others of the same type but not to unrelated types. Other mechanical properties such as elasticity, particularly in surface layers, are important in maintaining shape and producing appropriate changes during processes when one layer is folded in on another. Why cells should have the different physical properties necessary to produce an integrated whole embryo is not known, but certainly it cannot be thought that every cell has an absolutely fixed constitution and therefore a predetermined role in development. Large parts of developing embryos can be removed in early stages and their places taken by remaining cells so that intact organisms are still produced.

Formation of Specialised Tissues

This is essentially a problem in the regulation of gene activity since we know that each cell division produces daughter cells which are genetically identical. It seems likely therefore that instructions are carried on the chromosomes to cope with all requirements of the organism, but that in specialised cells only a small fraction of this full potential is realised. For a long time embryologists have known that egg cytoplasm shows regional differences which make identical nuclei behave differently, and it is thought that regional cytoplasm can in some way control gene activity. Techniques for the transplantation of nuclei in developing frog embryos have been perfected and it has been possible to put a nucleus from an intestinal cell of a tadpole into an enucleate egg. The egg will go on to develop normally even though its nucleus came from a fully specialised cell derived from endoderm. The embryo will form blood and muscle from the mesodermal layer and all the other components of an organism, under the influence of a nucleus which normally would have produced none of these things. One can conclude that all the genes are present, even in the nuclei of specialised cells, but that they have to be placed in a suitable cytoplasmic environment in order to be activated. Similar nuclear transplantation experiments indicate that genes can be "turned off" as well as "turned on" by an appropriate cytoplasmic environment, even though the nuclei come from cells which are so specialised as to stop dividing. The components of cytoplasm which control gene activity are still quite unknown.

A study of cell differentiation and the development of multicellular organisation leads us to the view that, important though the nucleus and its genes are in controlling cell activity, an integrated organism is the result of complex interactions between its constituent cells and between the cytoplasm of those cells and their nuclei.

THE CLASSIFICATION OF ORGANISMS

It was clear to the biologists of the 17th cent. that animals and plants could be fitted into different groups or species. John Ray, a leading biologist of the day, defined a species as a group of individuals capable of interbreeding within the group. This criterion, with its corollary that a species is reproductively isolated from organisms outside the group, has survived more or less unchanged to the present day. The early workers also saw that some species were very similar to one another while others were obviously dissimilar. Systems of classification based on the similarities and differences were drawn up so that all organisms could be fitted into an orderly scheme and species could be given names in accordance with the scheme. The most famous collector and classifier was the Swede, Linnaeus, who established his reputation in the 1730s. A very large number of animals and plants are known by the names given to them by Linnaeus.

Systematics, as this type of study is called, acquired a new significance after Darwin and the Theory of Evolution. The most satisfactory classification became one which reflected the evolution of the organisms classified, a so-called natural classification. It is not always easy to produce because ancestral types tend to become extinct and the problem then becomes one of reconstructing a whole branching system when only the ends of the branches are known. A great deal of the work on systematics has, of necessity, to be done on museum specimens which may be fossils or material preserved in some way by the collectors. The biological criterion of reproductive isolation cannot be used to define a species when the only available representatives are in a preserved state. In this case the scientist must resort to an assessment of structural differences in an attempt to decide whether two organisms are of different species. In recent years computer techniques have been used to compare large numbers of structural differences between groups of animals or plants, as well as physiological and biochemical characteristics. All these techniques have led to the realisation that even the species cannot be regarded as a static point in an evolutionary pattern. Some species die out and others arise as conditions in the environment slowly change.

When the systematist shifts his attention to the higher levels of classification the problems are just as great as at the species level. Different species having features in common can be grouped together into genera, genera into families, families into orders, orders into classes, and classes into phyla. The dividing lines between different groups at all levels is always difficult and in the final analysis somewhat arbitrary since at these levels we do not have any biological criterion such as exists for the species. The evolutionary status of the larger groups is also poorly defined. Many are now recognised to be polyphyletic, which is to say that there are several main evolutionary lines running right through the group.

THE ANIMAL KINGDOM

The animal kingdom is divided into about 24 large groups or phyla though the number varies between different classifications. Ten of the more important phyla are listed below.

1. Protozoa.—Microscopic, unicellular forms of great variety. Some may have more than one nucleus and others form colonies. Many are able to swim by waving hair-like flagella or cilia. Others move by putting out extensions of the body or pseudopodia into which the rest of the body then flows. Protozoa are found in the sea, in fresh water and in the soil. Some are parasitic and cause important diseases in animals and man such as sleeping sickness and malaria.

2. Porifera.—Sponges. Very primitive, multicellular animals whose cells display considerable independence of one another. Largely marine. The body which may become branched and plant-like is supported by a framework of spicules and fibres. The bath sponge is the fibrous skeleton of certain species.

3. Coelenterates.—Hydra, jellyfish, sea anemones, corals. Simple animals which have a body only two cells thick surrounding a gut cavity with a single opening to the outside. Largely marine. Many are colonial. Coral reefs are formed from the calcareous skeletons of these animals.

4. Platyhelminths.—Flatworms, which are free living in water, and liver flukes and tapeworms, which are parasitic. A third, solid block of cells, the mesoderm, has been developed between the two layers of cells seen in the coelenterates. A simple gut may be developed and the reproductive system is complex especially in the parasitic forms.

5. Nematodes.—Roundworms. The body is smooth and pointed at each end. Some of the most numerous and widespread of all animals. Free living in all environments and parasitic in practically all groups of plants and animals. At the same level of complexity as the Platyhelminths.

6. Annelids.—Segmented worms such as earthworms, marine worms and leeches. A system of spaces, the body cavity, is developed in the mesoderm so that movements of the main body of the animal and movements of the gut become more or less independent. Digestive, excretory, circulatory, nervous and reproductive systems are all well developed.

7. Arthropods.—A very large, diverse and important group of animals which includes crustaceans such as crabs, shrimps and water fleas; myriapods, such as centipedes and millepedes; insects; and arachnids, such as spiders and scorpions. The arthropods show many of the developments seen in annelids and in addition they possess a jointed, hard exoskeleton. Paired appendages grow out from the segments of the body and form antennae, mouth parts, walking legs, etc. The muscles within the skeleton are able to exert a fine control over the movement of the appendage. In order to grow these animals have to shed the exoskeleton periodically.

8. Molluscs.—Mussels, clams, oysters, squids, octopods and snails. Complex body form but somewhat different from annelid-arthropod type. Unsegmented body protected by shell which is variously developed in different types. It forms two valves in mussels and oysters, a spiral structure in snails, is reduced and internal in squids and completely lost in octopods.

9. Echinoderms.—Starfish, brittle stars, sea cucumbers, sea urchins, and sea lilies. All marine and all radially symmetrical, usually with five radii. Completely unlike the other advanced, major groups. Circulatory, excretory and nervous systems differently developed. Locomotion and feeding by means of hundreds of tube feet projecting from under surface.

10. Chordates.—Sea squirts, Amphioxus, fish, amphibia, reptiles, birds and mammals. Segmented animals which at some stage in their life have gill slits leading from pharynx to the outside and a supporting notochord from which, in all chordates except sea squirts and Amphioxus, is developed a vertebral column or backbone. Those animals with a backbone are commonly referred to as vertebrates, *all* those without as invertebrates. These are obviously names of convenience having no phylogenetic significance since they lump together totally unrelated phyla in one case and align these with a part of a single phylum in the other. The vertebrates have been investigated more completely than any other animals because of their direct structural and functional relationship with man himself. There are five well defined classes which are listed below. The first vertebrates were the fish and from them came the amphibia. The amphibia gave rise to the reptiles and both birds and mammals evolved from different reptilian stock.

(a) Fish

Cold blooded, aquatic animals breathing by means of gills. Sharks, rays and dogfish belong to a group known as the elasmobranchs characterised by a skeleton made of cartilage. Bony fish, most of them in a group called the teleosts, include almost all the fresh water fish and the common marine fish such as cod, mackerel, plaice, herring, etc.

(b) Amphibia

Cold blooded, more or less terrestrial animals which have to return to water to breed. Five fingered limbs are developed in place of the fins of fish. The egg hatches into a tadpole larva which is aquatic and breathes by gills. At metamorphosis the larva changes into the terrestrial adult which possesses lungs. Some amphibia such as the axolotl may become sexually mature as a larva and so never metamorphose into the adult. The class includes newts, salamanders, frogs and toads.

(c) Reptiles

Cold blooded and terrestrial. These animals do not return to water to breed because they have an egg with a relatively impermeable shell containing the food and water requirements of the developing embryo. There is no larval stage. Present day reptiles such as lizards, snakes and crocodiles are all that remains of a tremendous radiation of dinosaur-like creatures which occurred in the Mesozoic (**F48**).

(d) Birds

Warm blooded and adapted for aerial life. The characteristic feathers are both to insulate the body against heat loss and to provide the airfoil surfaces necessary for flight. The birds are an astonishingly uniform group and show less diversity of structure than much lower classification categories (*e.g.*, the teleosts) in other classes. The relationships of the 8,000 or more species of bird are difficult to establish because of this uniformity. It is clear that the flightless forms such as the ostrich are primitive and that the penguins are also in a separate category but the typical modern birds are classified in a large number of rather arbitrary orders. About half of all the known species are placed in one enormous order called the Passeriformes or perching birds.

(e) Mammals

Warm blooded animals which have been successful in a tremendous variety of habitats. Mammals are insulated from the environment by the characteristically hairy and waterproofed skin. They are, with two exceptions, viviparous which means that their young are born alive and in typical mammals at an advanced stage of development. In the marsupials of Australia the young are born at an early stage and transferred to a pouch where they develop further. The two exceptions referred to are primitive monotreme mammals known as the duck-billed platypus and spiny ant-eater and these animals lay eggs. The young of mammals are suckled by means of the milk producing mammary glands. The mammals include aquatic whales and dolphins, hoofed ungulates, flesh eating carnivores, rodents and insectivores, the aerial bats, and the tree climbing primates to which man himself belongs.

THE PHYSIOLOGY OF ANIMALS

In multicellular animals cells are of various types, constituting distinct tissues and organs which perform special functions in the body. Although each cell has its own complex metabolism there must be coordination between cells forming special tissues and between the tissues which form the whole organism in order for the body to function efficiently. The study of these functional interrelationships at the tissue and organism level of organisation is the province of the physiologist.

1. Movement, Fibrils and Skeletons

(a) **Muscles.**—The prime movers in almost all animal movement are large protein molecules in the form of microscopic fibrillar threads. In some way not yet fully understood these fibrils can convert the chemical energy stored in the high energy phosphate bonds of ATP into mechanical energy. In the long, thin cells forming the muscles of animals, it has been discovered that there are two sets of fibrils, one formed of a protein called myosin, the other of actin, arranged in a regular, interdigitating fashion. When the muscle contracts the fibrils slide past one another so that, although the fibrils themselves do not change in length, the muscle as a whole develops tension and shortens. Fine bridges extend from the myosin fibrils to attach on to the actin and it is here that the conversion of chemical to mechanical energy goes on.

(b) **Skeletons.**—In order for muscles to work effectively it is necessary for them to operate in some sort of skeletal system. Contraction but not relaxation is an active process; muscles must be arranged in antagonistic pairs so that one muscle can extend the other. A skeleton also provides a system of levers so that the muscles can do work against the environment in an efficient manner. A simple type of skeleton found in fairly primitive animals is the hydrostatic system of coelenterates and worms. Here the animal can be thought of as a fluid-filled bag or tube which can change shape but whose volume remains constant. By contraction of circular muscles the tube will become long and thin and conversely contraction of longitudinal muscles makes the tube short and fat. Examination of an earthworm will demonstrate how alternating waves of activity of this type passing from head to tail can move the animal over the ground. The earthworm shows an advance over

the simplest systems because the hydrostatic tube is broken up into small units by the segmentation of the body. This makes local responses possible. The next advance to be seen is the development in animals such as arthropods and vertebrates of a firm skeleton to which muscles are directly attached. The skeleton can then be used to support the body and to engage the environment. It seems to matter little whether an endoskeleton (vertebrates) or exoskeleton (arthropods) is developed since in both cases a tremendous radiation of fins for swimming, legs for walking and wings for flying can be seen. However in other respects these two types of skeleton show significant differences. The exoskeleton for example offers more protection than the endoskeleton while apparently setting an upper size limit. All the really big animals have endoskeletons.

(c) **Cilia.**—Fibrillar systems are also seen in the hair-like cilia which project from the surface of some cells. Cilia are important in a number of ways. They are the organelles of movement in many Protozoa, they are used to produce water currents past the bodies of some aquatic animals, and they are of great importance in moving fluid within the body of almost all animals. They beat in a regular fashion, the effective stroke being accomplished with the cilium held straight out from the surface and the recovery stroke with the cilium flexed at the base.

2. Feeding

All animals require complex organic substances, proteins, fats and carbohydrates, together with small amounts of salts and vitamins. These materials are obtained by eating the dead bodies of plants and other animals. They are taken into the alimentary canal and there broken down or digested by enzymes into simpler, soluble amino acids, sugars and fatty acids. These substances are absorbed and distributed to various parts of the body where they are used in cell metabolism (**F31–2**) or stored for future use.

Many animals, called macrophagous feeders, take in relatively large masses of food. Some such as frogs and snakes swallow their food whole, but many break it up first. Arthropods have modified appendages arranged round the mouth for cutting, some molluscs have a rasp-like radula with which to scrape off particles, and many mammals break up their food with jaws and teeth. The teeth are usually well adapted to the type of food. Carnivores have large, sharp canines, premolars and molars with which to tear the flesh of the prey, fish-eating seals have small peg-like teeth to grip the fish and herbivorous ungulates have flat grinding teeth with which they break up hard plant material.

In contrast, microphagous feeders collect small particles of food material from the environment by continuous filtration. In bivalve molluscs and many marine worms water currents are produced by beating cilia. Food is trapped within the confined space through which the water flows by means of a plentiful supply of sticky mucus in the filtering region. Some crustacea use fine hairs to sieve off food material, often from water currents created by the swimming movements. The most startling of filter feeders is the whalebone whale. As the whale swims forward a stream of water flows in at the front of the mouth and out at the sides via sheets of whalebone which filter off the organisms on which the animal feeds. Though macrophagy seems to favour the attainment of larger size there are exceptions! Another type of particulate feeding is seen in those animals which eat deposits of detritus as do many worms. Finally some animals take in only soluble food materials. These fluid feeders include internal parasites like the tapeworm which absorb substances over the surface of the body, and insects such as the aphid with sucking mouth parts.

3. Respiration. Gills, Lungs and Tracheae

All living cells respire and remain alive only if supplied with oxygen. In a multicellular body, however, many cells are remote from the oxygen of the environment and the need arises for an efficient respiratory system by which oxygen can be taken up and carbon dioxide released. In addition a circulatory system is necessary to transport the oxygen to and from the respiring cells.

(a) Simple Gas Exchange Systems

Animals such as protozoa do not need special structure for gas exchange. Diffusion over the whole body surface ensures an adequate supply of oxygen. Much larger animals such as earthworms also find it possible to rely on diffusion alone, partly because their consumption of oxygen is fairly low, and partly because their bodies are permeable all over. For various reasons most animals restrict the permeability of the outer layers of the body and under these conditions special respiratory areas have to be developed.

(b) Gas Exchange in Water

Aquatic animals, except those such as whales breathing at the surface, have to obtain their oxygen from the supplies which are dissolved in the water. This presents several problems because water is a dense medium, there is not a lot of oxygen in solution, and its diffusion rate is low. For these reasons there is a surprisingly functional uniformity in gill systems and they are very different from lungs. Gills are fine, finger-like processes with a good blood supply which are held out in a water stream. The water current is brought very close to the gill filaments so that the length of diffusion pathway for oxygen is minimal. There is a "counter current" flow of water and blood so that the water containing most oxygen comes into contact with the blood just leaving the gill. This ensures that most of the oxygen can be transferred from water to blood through the thin gill cells. The efficiency of "counter current" systems is well known to the engineer but they were invented by aquatic animals long before they were by man. These features can be seen in the gills of molluscs, crustacea and fish. The pumping devices which maintain the water currents also operate economically. Flow is maintained in crustacea by appendages modified to form beating paddles, in many molluscs by ciliary movement, and in fish by the operation of a double pump in mouth and opercular cavities. In almost all cases there is a continuous current over the gills, the water coming in one way and going out another. Thus the animal avoids reversing the flow with the consequent waste of energy in accelerating and decelerating a large mass of water. Fish, for example, take water in at the mouth and force it out through the gill slits (sharks) or operculum (teleosts).

(c) Gas Exchange in Air

Air breathing animals do not encounter these problems since the medium is less dense, contains a great deal (20%) of oxygen and diffusion rates are high. Lungs are therefore in the form of sacs whose walls are well supplied with blood. The area of the walls may be increased by folding so that the lung becomes spongy and full of minute air spaces called alveoli where the gas exchange goes on. Only the main airways receive fresh air as the lung expands; oxygen is renewed in the alveoli by diffusion. Ventilation of the lung is accomplished by a tidal flow of air in and out of the same tubular opening known as the trachea. The actual ventilating mechanism varies in different animals. In the amphibia for example air is forced into the lungs when the floor of the mouth is raised with the mouth and nostrils shut. The lungs are emptied by elastic recoil and by lowering the floor of the mouth. Higher vertebrates use a costal pump which changes the volume of chest and lungs by movements of the ribs. This change in volume is further assisted in mammals by the diaphragm, a sheet of muscle which lies beneath the lungs and separates thorax and abdomen. In many animals sound producing organs are associated with the lungs and trachea. The larynx is a vocal organ in frogs, some lizards, and most notably mammals. In birds voice production takes place in the syrinx situated further down at the base of the trachea.

A completely different gas exchanging system is seen in insects. Branching tubes, known as tracheae, run throughout the body and carry oxygen directly to the cells without the intervention of a blood system. The tracheae communicate with the outside world via a series of holes called spiracles. Although the main tubes may be actively ventilated, diffusion in the system accounts for a large part of the movement of oxygen between the outside world and cells.

4. Circulation

In the larger animals a transport system is necessary to convey materials about the body and in many, but not all, it is in the form of a blood system. Blood systems are of two types, closed and open.

(a) Open Systems

In an open circulatory system blood is pumped from the heart into a few major arteries but these very quickly give way to large tissue spaces or sinuses so that the tissues and organs of the body are directly bathed in blood. Blood flows slowly from the sinuses back to the heart. Both mollusc and arthropods possess an open system.

(b) Closed Systems

In a closed system blood is pumped round the body in a branching network of arteries and comes into contact with tissues and cells via very thin walled vessels called capillaries. Substances diffuse into and out of the blood through capillary walls. From capillaries, blood enters the veins and so returns to the heart. Blood flow in the tubes of a closed system is much more brisk and blood pressures tend to be higher than in an open system. In annelids the closed system is fairly simple with a vessel above the gut in which blood moves forward connecting to one below in which blood moves backwards. The blood is pumped by peristaltic contraction of the vessels and this system must be regarded as the precursor of a localised pump. Simple hearts are in fact seen in some annelids.

In vertebrates a well defined heart is always present, situated ventrally at the level of the forelimbs. In fish there is a single auricle and ventricle and the latter pumps blood directly to the gills. From the gills the blood is collected into a dorsal aorta which then branches to serve the rest of the body. Associated with the development of lungs and loss of gills in the tetrapods, we see a progressive modification of this simple pattern. The most posterior gill vessel is taken over as the lung or pulmonary artery and slowly a completely separate circuit evolves. This involves the division of the single heart into right and left sides, the former pumping blood to the lungs and the latter to the body. In the birds and mammals where the division is complete the system can be seen to be functionally satisfactory. Blood flows along the following route: left auricle to left ventricle, to body, to right auricle, to right ventricle, to lungs, to left auricle, and so on. Thus blood charged with oxygen in the lungs returns to the heart before being pumped to the body.

(c) Function of the Blood

Most of the materials transported by the blood such as nutrients, waste materials and hormones are carried in solution in the plasma. The respiratory gases, oxygen and carbon dioxide, are present in greater quantity than would be possible if they were in simple solution. Carbon dioxide is carried in the form of bicarbonate and oxygen combines with blood pigment. The best known blood pigment is haemoglobin which is found in a variety of animals and gives the red colour to blood. When oxygen is present in high concentration, as it is in the lungs, combination occurs to give oxyhaemoglobin. If the concentration of oxygen is low, as it is in the tissues, dissociation occurs and oxygen is given off leaving reduced haemoglobin. Carbon monoxide will combine more readily than oxygen with haemoglobin so that in carbon monoxide poisoning the blood cannot transport oxygen. The haemoglobin of vertebrates is contained in high concentration in red blood corpuscles. The amount of haemoglobin and, hence, oxygen carried is greater than if the pigment is not in corpuscles. In mammals the oxygen carrying capacity of blood is thirty times that of a similar quantity of water. Other blood pigments are the blue haemocyanin found in crustacea and molluscs, and the violet haemerythrin found in some worms. Also present in the blood are various types of white corpuscle which are part of the defence mechanism of the body and ingest invading bacteria. Special blood proteins such as fibrinogen, causing clot formation, and antibodies effective against foreign substances occur in the plasma.

5. Excretion, Ionic Regulation and Kidney Tubules

As the chemical reactions included under the term metabolism proceed, so numerous waste products accumulate. The most important of these are compounds containing nitrogen, such as ammonia, urea and uric acid, arising from the use of protein as an energy source. In terrestrial animals they are removed from the blood by the kidney. The basic unit of a kidney is the tubule; in worms these tubules are not concentrated into a solid kidney but occur, a pair in every segment, right down the body. The kidney tubule begins with an end sac, corpuscle or funnel which is closely associated with the body cavity or the blood system. Fluid is filtered from the body cavity or blood into the corpuscle whence it passes to the tubule proper. During passage down the tubule, useful materials are reabsorbed through the tubule cells into the blood whereas unwanted materials remain and pass to the outside world.

Although it is usual to think of kidney function being primarily one of nitrogenous excretion, it is quite common to find that in aquatic animals the kidneys are hardly used for this purpose. In these animals the tubules are primarily concerned in regulating the salt and water levels in the body, nitrogenous wastes being eliminated by diffusion through any permeable surface. In fresh water for example all animals have osmotic problems since the body fluids have a much greater osmotic pressure than the environment. Water tends to enter the body and salts tend to leave. Fresh water animals produce large quantities of very dilute urine, filtering off a lot of blood plasma into the tubules but reabsorbing all wanted materials including the invaluable salts. Fresh water crustacea, molluscs and fish all possess tubules of different morphology which show very similar functional properties.

Different environmental conditions impose different demands on the osmotic and ionic regulating machinery. In very dry conditions, such as in deserts, it is obviously of advantage to reabsorb as much water from the tubule as possible. All animals do this but it is interesting that only birds and mammals have discovered the secret of so concentrating the urine that its salt concentration is higher than that in the blood. This is done by means of a hairpin-like loop in the tubule called the Loop of Henle, another example of a counter current device.

6. Co-ordinating Systems

Overall co-ordination of the animal's body, so that it functions as a whole and reacts appropriately to environmental changes, is largely the province of two systems, one chemical or hormonal, the other nervous. In one respect these are systems for homeostasis, that is for preserving the *status quo*, in spite of considerable environmental fluctuation. Paradoxically they can also initiate change as, for example, one can see in the daily repertoire of complicated behaviour patterns produced by almost any animal.

(a) Nervous Systems

(i) *Sensory Information*

Before appropriate reactions can be produced to any stimulus it is necessary to measure its intensity, position, duration and, most important, character. This is done by sense organs which are usually specialised to receive stimuli of a single modality or character. Thus photoreceptors detect light, mechanoreceptors detect mechanical disturbance and chemoreceptors detect specific chemicals. In all cases the sense organs produce a message about the stimulus in the form of nerve impulses (*see* **F33**—Cell Membrane) which travel up the nerve from the sense organ to the rest of the nervous system. Change of stimulus intensity is usually signalled as a change in frequency of nerve impulses. The position of the sense organ which is active indicates the position of the stimulus within or without the body. The duration of the repeated discharge of nerve impulses indicates the duration of the stimulus.

(ii) *Simple Networks*

The simplest type of nervous system is the network of interconnected nerve cells (neurones) found in the coelenterates. Branching processes of the nerve cells communicate with neighbouring processes at special regions called synapses (**F33**). Quite complicated behaviour is possible even with this relatively simple system. If a sea anemone is prodded violently it will close up equally violently, showing that activity has spread throughout the network. If it is tickled gently it will respond with local contractions around the site of stimulation. The movements of feeding and locomotion are very delicately performed at appropriate times.

(iii) *Central Nervous Systems*

In the majority of animals all the nerve cells tend to become collected into a solid mass of tissue referred to as a central nervous system (C.N.S.). Within the mass the nerve cells are interconnected via synapses in the same way as in a nerve net. The connexions with sense organs and muscles are made via long processes called axons. Numbers of axons are usually bound together with connective tissue to form a nerve trunk. In annelids and arthropods the C.N.S. is seen as a ventral cord lying beneath the gut with a swelling or ganglion in each segment of the body. In molluscs, the ganglia are usually more closely grouped around the oesophagus, with the possible provision of a pair of ganglia further back in the viscera. Vertebrates possess a dorsal nerve cord which is uniform in diameter and not ganglionated, though nerves emerge from it in a segmental fashion. The segmental nerves arise in two separate bundles or roots. The dorsal root is made up entirely of sensory nerves conveying information to the C.N.S. The ventral root consists of motor nerves which convey nerve impulses to the muscles of limbs and alimentary canal together with other effector organs such as glands.

(iv) *Reflexes*

A reflex, in which stimulation of a sense organ or sensory nerve results in the almost immediate contraction of a muscle, is the simplest type of C.N.S. activity. Reflexes have been studied in all animals but the best known ones can be seen in frogs, cats, dogs, and sometimes humans. The very simplest is the stretch reflex, in which a stretched muscle is made to contract by activity coming into the C.N.S. from stretch receptors in the muscle. The activity is relayed directly to the motor neurones of the muscle concerned, making them active and thus causing the muscle to contract. This reflex is monosynaptic, *i.e.* there is only the single synaptic connexion between sensory nerve and motor neurone. The knee jerk in humans is a stretch reflex, the stretch being caused by hitting the muscle tendon as it passes over the knee. Much of the recent work on reflexes has been done on this simple system, notably by Eccles. The flexor reflex, which is seen as the sudden withdrawal of a limb from any painful stimulus, is more complicated. Although the stimuli may vary, the withdrawal response is always accomplished by contraction of flexor muscles which bring the limb in towards the body. The reflex is polysynaptic, *i.e.* several intermediate neurones connect the sensory nerves through to the motor neurones. More complicated still is the scratch reflex in which an animal is made to scratch its flank in response to an irritation or tickling in that region. This reflex demonstrates some of the more involved properties of the C.N.S. For example a dog will continue to scratch for a time after the tickling has stopped, so that the C.N.S. must continue to be active in the absence of sensory stimulation. This has been called after-discharge.

(v) *The Brain*

The C.N.S. functions in a more complicated way than is suggested by study of the reflexes and most of these higher activities are co-ordinated by the brain. A greater condensation of neurones is seen at the front end of the C.N.S. of all animals because of the larger numbers of sense organs in that region. Brains, which become the dominant part of the C.N.S., can be seen in arthropods, molluscs and vertebrates. The close association with sense organs is illustrated by the vertebrate brain which is divided into three regions: (a) forebrain (nose), (b) midbrain (eye) and (c) hindbrain (ear and taste). However, the brain is much more than a relay station for these stimulus modalities and it receives information from other parts of the body via the spinal cord. All this information is correlated and activity patterns initiated and transmitted to appropriate regions. In lower vertebrates, the roof of the midbrain (the optic tectum) is the important correlation centre and its effectiveness has been well established in studies on instinct and learning in fish. Another region of the brain of importance in all vertebrates is a dorsal upgrowth of the hindbrain called the cerebellum. This is a motor co-ordinating centre which ensures that all activities are performed in a smooth and well balanced way by the muscles and limbs of the body. In reptiles, the forebrain begins to take over the correlation role and in mammals this development reaches its peak in the cerebral cortex. In man the cortex overshadows the rest of the brain and contains some 1,000,000,000 neurones. It is easy to see the magnitude of the problem of understanding a system of this complexity. The bee's brain with far, far fewer cells can initiate complicated behaviour such as the hive dances. The possibilities offered by the human cortex seem vastly greater, though they are often realised in ways which give cause for concern. At the moment it would be quite impossible to build a computer with the properties of the human brain. To do this in the future would depend on major advances in computer technology and even greater advances in the knowledge of central nervous systems.

(b) Hormonal Regulation

Many aspects of an animal's metabolism are regulated, not by the nervous system, but by specific chemical signals known as hormones which are circulated in the blood stream. Growth, carbohydrate metabolism, salt balance, activity of ovaries and testes and their associated structures, and colour change are all regulated in some way by hormones. The substances are secreted by endocrine glands or ductless glands as they are often called. The important endocrine glands in vertebrates are the thyroid, parathyroid, adrenal, pancreas, the sex glands, and the pituitary.

In the past the endocrine and nervous systems were regarded as exerting an independent control in slightly different functional areas of the body. It is clear now that the integration of the two systems is much greater than was formerly envisaged and in vertebrates is accomplished through the pituitary gland. Secretions of this gland regulate almost all other endocrine glands and the secretions of the pituitary are either produced in the C.N.S. with which it is directly connected or are controlled by C.N.S. secretions. An astonishing, parallel development of other neurosecretory systems, such as those of the pituitary, has been found in a variety of animals and in all types the neurosecretory organ complex is the dominant endocrine gland of the body. In crustacea the so-

called X organ complex found within the eyestalk, and in insects neurosecretory cells connecting to the corpora cardiaca glands, occupy the functional position of the vertebrate pituitary. They all regulate growth, metabolism and reproductive physiology, either directly or through the medication of other endocrine glands.

7. Animal Behaviour

In discussing the nervous system we have already dealt with simple mechanisms such as the reflex. Very much more complicated are the instinctive and learned patterns of behaviour which are studied by animal psychologists and ethologists such as Lorenz and Tinbergen.

(a) Instinct

Instinct is inborn behaviour which does not have to be learnt and is usually performed in a stereotyped way. For example a gull will retrieve an egg taken out of its nest by shovelling it back with the underside of its beak. The gull will never replace an egg in its nest in any other way, for example by using a wing or leg, and once it has begun a retrieval it will usually continue the movements back to the nest even though the egg is taken away. An instinctive behaviour pattern is triggered off by a particular stimulus or "releaser" which may be a very small part of the total environment. A male stickleback will attack a very crude model with a red belly but will not attack an exact model without it. The red underside appears to be a much more important stimulus than general shape. A particular instinctive pattern cannot always be elicited and the reaction of an animal very largely depends on when the behaviour was last produced. The longer the time that elapses, the easier it is to trigger off the instinctive pattern until eventually it may appear in the absence of an appropriate set of environmental circumstances.

(b) Learning

Learning is that behaviour acquired during the organism's lifetime as a result of experience. Evidence of learning has been seen in many animals from worms upwards though, as might be expected, the more complicated types of learning are found only in those animals with elaborate nervous systems. A simple type of learning is seen when an animal, upon repeated exposure to a stimulus, gradually decreases the normal response which is usually one of flight, until eventually the response may disappear completely. This process is called habituation. More complex are the conditioned reflexes, which were first discovered by Pavlov. In these an animal can in some way connect a conditioned stimulus such as a bell, with an unconditioned stimulus such as meat, so that eventually it salivates when the bell is rung. Trial and error learning of the type needed to be successful in running a maze is more complicated still. In this there is a retrospective element because the reward at the end of the maze comes after all the responses. Many animals can run mazes but the white rat has been extensively used in experiments of this nature and there is a huge literature on this one animal. A final category of learning can be called insight learning; in this an animal shows evidence of resolving a new problem without trial and error. This type of learning involves the perception of relations between different parts of the environment and though there may be examples in arthropods and molluscs the clearest evidence of it is seen in the behaviour of birds and mammals.

8. Reproduction

A single animal may live for a short or long time, but eventually it dies, and the continuance of the species is dependent upon reproduction. Some protozoa, such as *Amoeba*, reproduce asexually by the simple division of the cell to produce two new individuals. Asexual reproduction also occurs in some coelenterates, such as jelly-fish, in which there is an alternation of sexual and asexual generations. However, the vast majority of animals only reproduce sexually.

This involves the fusion of two cells, the gametes, produced by adult individuals, and each zygote thus formed develops into an individual of the next generation. The gametes are of two kinds, the large, spherical, immobile ova produced by the female gonad or ovary and the much smaller motile sperms produced by the male gonad or testis. The motility of the sperms helps them to reach the passive ovum, which contains food reserves to support the early development of the embryo.

Worms.—The flat worms, particularly parasitic forms, have complicated life cycles, and many are hermaphrodite, *i.e.*, each individual has both male and female organs. Cross-fertilisation usually occurs, the sperms from one worm being introduced into the female duct of another. The round worms are unisexual, and internal fertilisation also occurs. Of the annelids the polychaete worms are unisexual, but the ova and sperms are shed into the sea, where fertilisation takes place. However, *Lumbricus* and the leeches are hermaphrodite, cross-fertilisation takes place and the eggs are laid in cocoons.

Arthropods.—Many crustacea are unisexual, though the sedentary barnacles are hermaphrodite. Internal fertilisation may occur, but in the crabs and crayfish pairing takes place and the sperms are deposited on the tail of the female. When the eggs are shed they become fertilised and remain attached to the abdominal appendages. Most crustacea have motile larval stages into which the eggs first develop. In *Daphnia*, the water-flea, parthenogenesis sometimes occurs, *i.e.*, the eggs develop without being fertilised. The sexes are separate in the arachnida and there are usually no larval stages except in the primitive king-crabs. The insects are also unisexual, and the fertilised eggs are laid after copulation. In some, *e.g.*, dragon-flies, an immature nymph similar to the adult is formed, but in flies, beetles, moths, and many others the egg hatches into a larval form. This then develops into a pupa, from which the final adult or imago is produced. In the social ant's nest the workers are sterile females with large heads, reduced eyes, and no wings. The males and queens are winged, and insemination of the latter occurs during the "nuptial" flight.

Molluscs and Echinoderms.—Most lamellibranchs are unisexual, although some species of scallops and oysters are hermaphrodite. There are motile larval forms, and in the swan mussel, *Anodonta*, the larvae develop in the mantle cavity of the parent and when liberated become attached to the gills or fins of fish, where they remain parasitic for some time. Some gastropods are unisexual, but the slugs and snails are hermaphrodite. In the latter cross-fertilisation occurs, the two approaching snails being stimulated to copulate by firing small sharp darts of calcium carbonate into each other. The echinoderms are unisexual, and fertilisation takes place in the sea. The egg first develops into a ciliated larval form.

Vertebrates.—The sexes are always separate in the vertebrates. In some cartilaginous fish, *e.g.*, dogfish, internal fertilisation occurs and the eggs are laid in protective sacs. In contrast, the bony fish shed ova and sperms into the water, where fertilisation takes place. Although pairing may take place in amphibia, fertilisation occurs in water, and there is usually an aquatic larval stage. The reptiles, birds, and mammals are independent of water for fertilisation, as copulation takes place and the sperms from the male are introduced directly into the female. Most reptiles and all birds lay eggs with hard shells. Development of the embryo in marsupial mammals begins in the female uterus, but is continued in a ventral pouch which surrounds the teat of the mammary gland. In the two living species of monotreme mammals the eggs are incubated in a similar pouch. Finally, in the eutherian mammals the embryo develops in the female uterus and is born at an advanced stage.

Diversity of Sexual Reproduction.—This brief survey will give some idea of the diversity of sexual reproduction in animals. External fertilisation is very much a matter of chance, and large numbers of gametes are produced which offset the great losses of gametes and embryos that this method involves. Internal fertilisation is more certain, and is also independent of external water—an important factor in land animals. In vertebrates particularly there is increase in the care of the young by the parents, involving the development of characters of behaviour as well as those of structure. Some fish lay their eggs in holes or nests which are protected by the male. Similarly, a few frogs build nests, while others carry the eggs about. The eggs of birds require a constant high temperature for their development, and they are usually incubated by the parents. After hatching the young are fed and guarded by the parents until they can leave the nest and fend for themselves. In the eutherian mammals the embryos are attached to the uterus wall by the placenta, *via* which food materials pass from the mother. The period of gestation is long, and after birth the young are supplied with milk from the mother until they are weaned and can feed themselves. Another feature in mammals is the period of "childhood" during which they play and learn and are protected and fed by their parents. The internal fertilisation, internal development, and care and protection of the young after birth which is so conspicuous in the higher vertebrates results in the reduction of losses during the vulnerable embryonic and young stages, and in consequence relatively few progeny are produced by a pair of individuals.

THE PLANT KINGDOM

There are various ways in which the main classes of the plant kingdom can be grouped, but a simple, up-to-date arrangement is given in the chart. Vascular plants are often known as the *Tracheophyta* because they all possess woody conducting elements. These are absent in nonvascular plants, and the bacteria, fungi, and algæ are often called *Thallophyta*, *i.e.*, they have a relatively simple plant body or thallus. Many of the bryophytes also possess a thallus, but in some there is a stem bearing leaves, although a true vascular system is absent. Many thallophytes are aquatic, whereas the tracheophytes are mostly land plants in which the development of woody tissues can be related to the attainment of the land habit as the plant kingdom evolved. However, the chart should not be taken as indicating the evolutionary relationships of the various groups. It is more a convenient arrangement which reflects the relative complexity of the plant body.

1. Bacteria.—This is a vast group of minute organisms of very simple structure. They are spherical or rod shaped and may exist as separate cells, some species being motile, or as long chains or irregular masses. Their minute size makes the elucidation of their structure very difficult. There is a wall of complex composition, and cytoplasm which contains glycogen and fat. Electron-microscope studies have revealed the presence of structures which appear to consist of nuclear material. Multiplication is by simple division, which may take place very rapidly. For example, *Bacillus subtilis* can divide every 20 minutes, so that in 8 hours a single cell may give rise to 16 millions. Recent research indicates that a sexual process may also occur. Bacteria can survive unfavourable conditions by producing a resistant spore within the cell. They do not possess chlorophyll, though a few are pigmented. Most obtain their food already formed, and are thus either saprophytes or parasites. The saprophytic bacteria occupy a vital position in the living world. They are responsible for most of the decay of dead organic matter, and it has been truly said that without them the surface of the earth would soon become completely covered with the dead bodies of animals and plants. Bacteria also play a vital part in the circulation of nitrogen in nature. By breaking down organic material, ammonia is released and ammonium carbonate is formed in the soil. This is oxidised by other bacteria to form nitrates, which can be absorbed

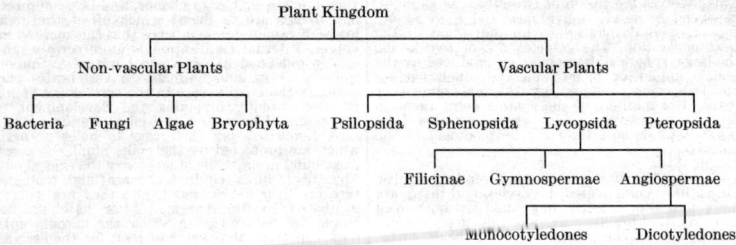

Plant Kingdom

Non-vascular Plants — Vascular Plants

Bacteria Fungi Algae Bryophyta Psilopsida Sphenopsida Lycopsida Pteropsida

Filicinae Gymnospermae Angiospermae

Monocotyledones Dicotyledones

by plants again. Yet other bacteria can "fix" atmospheric nitrogen, and one species, *Rhizobium leguminosum*, occurs in the root nodules of the pea plant. Such plants are often grown on poor soils and ploughed in, thus improving the fertility of the soil. The parasitic bacteria are also of great importance, as they are responsible for many diseases of plants, animals, and man.

2. Fungi.—This is a large group of plants, none of which contain chlorophyll. Hence, like the bacteria, they are either parasites on other living plants and animals or saprophytes which live on dead organic matter. Some are unicellular aquatic plants, but many have a body called a mycelium composed of many branched threads or hyphæ. In the higher fungi (*e.g.*, toadstools, bracket fungi, and puff-balls) complex reproductive structures are formed. All fungi produce spores. In the aquatic species these may be motile, but the majority form minute, airborne spores. The spore output is often very great, and a single mushroom may produce, 1,800 million spores. Some fungi are serious diseases of crop plants, such as potato blight and wheat rust.

3. Algae.—These are essentially aquatic plants which contain chlorophyll. They range from microscopic forms to the large seaweeds. The green algae (Chlorophyceae) live mostly in fresh water and may be unicellular, motile or non-motile, or filamentous, though a few found in tropical seas are more complex. The brown algae (Phaeophyceae) are mostly seaweeds which possess a brown pigment, fucoxanthin, which masks the green chlorophyll. They include the bladder-wracks (*Fucus*) and kelps (*Laminaria*) of our coasts and the seaweeds which form dense floating masses over hundreds of square miles of the Sargasso Sea. Other groups are the red algae (Rhodophyceae), mostly seaweeds of delicate form, the unicellular motile diatoms (Bacillariophyceae), and the blue-green algae (Cyanophyceae). All algae possess unicellular reproductive organs. Various types of life cycle occur, the most complex being found in the red algae.

4. Bryophyta.—These are the liverworts (Hepaticae) and the mosses (*Muscineae*). They are all small plants characterised by a sharply defined life-cycle. This consists of an alternation of generations, the "plant" being a gametophyte bearing sex organs. The latter are multicellular, the female archegonium containing a single stationary ovum and the male antheridium producing many motile sperms. The latter are released and swim in water to the archegonium, where fertilisation takes place. After this a sporophyte is formed which is always dependent on the gametophyte and never becomes free living. The sporophyte usually consists of an absorbing foot buried in the tissue of the gametophyte and a stalk or seta bearing at the top a single sporangium. In many mosses this is a complex structure with hygroscopic teeth which move apart only when dry, thus releasing the minute spores only when conditions are suitable for their dissemination in the air. The bryophytes are of little economic importance, and may be looked upon as an evolutionary side-line. However, they occupy suitable "niches" in many plant communities, and species of the bog-moss *Sphagnum* cover large areas where rainfall is high.

5. Psilopsida.—This is a small group of primitive, vascular, spore-bearing plants. Its only living representatives are two rare genera of the Southern Hemisphere. However, a number of fossil forms are known from the Devonian period. The best known are those found in the chert at Rhynie in Scotland. The plants are excellently preserved, and their internal structure can be easily seen. They were probably marsh plants with prostrate and erect leafless stems, although *Asteroxylon* had simple leaves.

6. Sphenopsida.—The only living members of this group are about twenty-five species of horse-tails (*Equisetum*). In the Carboniferous period many tree forms existed (*e.g.*, *Calamites*), the remains of which are very common in coal deposits.

7. Lycopsida.—In the Carboniferous period the tree clubmosses were also prominent members of the forests (*e.g.*, *Lepidodendron*). They often reached 30m in height, were branched or unbranched, and had large simple leaves. They also had extensive root systems. The only living members belong to a few genera of small herbaceous clubmosses, such as *Lycopodium* and *Selaginella*. Like the true mosses, they have an alternation of generations, but the elaborate plant with stem, leaves, and roots is the sporophyte, and the gametophyte is very small. In *Lycopodium* only one kind of spore is produced, and the resultant gametophyte is bisexual. *Selaginella* produces numerous small microspores which give rise to the very reduced male gametophytes and motile sperms and the few large megaspores which produce the female gametophytes. The latter are formed within the megaspore wall, which splits to allow the sperms to reach the small archegonia.

8. Filicinae.—These are the true ferns, which in some classifications are put with the horsetails and clubmosses in the Pteridophyta or vascular cryptogams (*i.e.*, vascular plants without seeds). The ferns have a long fossil history, and remains very similar to the living Royal ferns (*Osmunda*) are known from the Carboniferous. The ferns are widespread and particularly abundant in tropical forests. The majority are herbaceous perennial plants, but a few are aquatic, and there are some tree ferns, which may reach 6 m in height. Most ferns possess a stem bearing roots and large leaves or fronds. The plant is the sporophyte and produces numerous spores in sporangia borne on the fronds. Each spore gives rise to a minute green free-living gametophyte known as the prothallus, which bears the archegonia and antheridia. After fertilisation a young sporophyte develops, which at first draws nourishment from the prothallus. Thus, as in the Bryophyta, external water is essential for the motile sperms to swim in, and there is a clearly defined alternation of generations, but the sporophyte is a complex independent plant, and the gametophyte is reduced though free-living.

9. Gymnospermae.—These were the dominant land plants in the Mesozoic era, although fossil remains are found as far back as the Devonian. The living members still form large forests in the North Temperate regions. They are mostly tall evergreen trees with roots, stems, and small leaves. The conifers include the pines (*Pinus*), larches (*Larix*), and yews (*Taxus*). The cycads are a relic group of tropical plants with thick, unbranched trunks and large fern-like leaves. The maiden-hair tree of Japan (*Ginkgo biloba*) has also had a long geological history. Another interesting Gymnosperm is *Metasequoia*, a genus well known to palaeobotanists. In 1948 a few living specimens were found in a remote area of China. Seeds were collected and plants are now being grown in botanical gardens all over the world. The Gymnosperms are characterised by the production of "naked" seeds, which are usually born on cones. The male pollen grains, which are equivalent to the microspores of *Selaginella*, are carried by wind to the ovule of the female cone. The pollen germinates and the pollen tube carries the male gametes to the reduced archegonia borne on the female prothallus, which, unlike those of the ferns, is retained within the ovule on the parent plant. After fertilisation an embryo is formed, the prothallus becomes the food store or endosperm, and the outer part of the ovule becomes the seed coat. The cycads and *Ginkgo* retain a primitive feature in that the male gametes are motile and they swim to the archegonia from the pollen tube.

10. Angiospermae.—The apparent sudden rise of the Angiosperms in the Cretaceous period is still the "abominable mystery" it was to Darwin. Various suggestions have been put forward, but nothing definite is known about the origin of the group. The Angiosperms or flowering plants are now the dominant group over most of the land surface of the earth, and at least 250,000 species are known. Apart from the natural vegetation, the majority of our crop and garden plants are Angiosperms. They occur in every type of habitat and range in form from gigantic trees to minute plants, such as the duck-weeds. Some are climbers, others succulents, and a number have reverted to the aquatic habit. Although most possess chlorophyll, a few are partial (*e.g.*, Mistletoe) or complete parasites (*e.g.*, Dodder).

Flower, Fruit and Seeds.—The diagnostic feature of the group is the production of seeds, which are completely enclosed within the female part of the flower, the ovary. Basically a flower is a short reproductive shoot which bears several whorls of lateral organs. At the base are several, often green, protective sepals forming the calyx, and above this are the often brightly coloured petals of the corolla. Within this are the stamens of the androecium or male part of the flower. Centrally is the female gynoecium of one or more carpels containing the ovules. The parts of the flower may be free, as in the buttercup, or fused together. In many species the petals are fused (sympetalous), the stamens are borne on the corolla (epipetalous), and the carpels are fused to form a compound gynoecium (syncarpous). The stamens possess anthers, which produce pollen grains. These are shed and carried by insects or wind to the receptive stigmas of the carpels. Each produces a tube which grows down the style to the ovary and enters an ovule. The ovule is a complex structure containing an ovum and a primary endosperm nucleus. Two male nuclei are discharged from the pollen tube, one fuses with the ovum and the other fuses with the primary endosperm nucleus. After this "double fertilisation" an embryo is formed which is embedded in the nutritive endosperm and the outer tissues of the ovule form the seed coat or testa. The ovary of the carpel develops into the fruit containing the seeds. Fruits are of various kinds, being either dehiscent and opening when mature to release the seeds or indehiscent, with a succulent or dry wall. The indehiscent fruits are shed as a whole, and often contain only a single seed. Seeds and fruits show great variation in structure, and often have adaptations assisting dispersal. Some have hairs or wings which aid wind dispersal, whereas others have hooks or are sticky and are transported by animals. Some have flotation devices and may be carried a great distance from the parent plant by water. Seeds vary in size from the microscopic seeds of orchids to those of the double coconut, which may weigh 18 kg. Only about 10% of the weight of a seed is water, and the embryo, although alive, is dormant. The bulk of a seed consists of stored food material, commonly fats or starch and proteins, which may be contained in the endosperm surrounding the embryo, although in some species the endosperm is absorbed during seed development and the food is stored in the one or two swollen seed leaves or cotyledons of the embryo.

Classification of Flowering Plants.—John Ray (1627–1705) was the first botanist to recognise the two great divisions of the Angiosperms—the dicotyledons with two seed leaves and the monocotyledons with only one. This primary division of the flowering plants has stood the test of time and is still recognised. Other differences are also found between the two groups. The dicotyledons usually have net-veined leaves and the floral parts are in fours or fives, whereas the monocotyledons usually have leaves with parallel veins and the floral parts are in threes.

THE PHYSIOLOGY OF PLANTS

Some of the fundamental differences between animals and plants can be ascribed to the ways in which the two groups of living organisms satisfy their requirements for food material. In a simple way at least, an animal can be thought of as a mobile gastro-intestinal tract which is highly specialised to search out and receive food in convenient, concentrated packets. In typical land plants, however, a quite different organisation exists because the organic nutrition is based on the process of photosynthesis in which carbon dioxide from the air is combined with water from the soil to form simple carbohydrates. An expanded foliage system is necessary to absorb carbon dioxide and to expose the photosynthetic pigment, chlorophyll, to sunlight. Similarly, an expanded root system is needed to absorb the other ingredients of nutrition, water and mineral salts, from the soil.

The work of the plant physiologist is devoted to understanding the functional relationships between these two expanded systems of root and shoot. The production of carbohydrates by photosynthesis has already been discussed (**F32**).

The Spread of Roots

In addition, the physiologist is concerned with the progressive elaboration of root and shoot as the plant grows. Plants show much less specialisation of their cells into discrete tissues and organs than do animals and they also retain special areas, at root and shoot tips for example, where new cells are added to the structure throughout the life of the plant. In some cases whole plants can be regenerated from very few cells taken almost anywhere from a growing plant body. The orderly regulation of growth and differentiation is thus a basic property of much plant tissue.

1. Movement of Solutes and Water

The movement of water and inorganic solutes in a plant is primarily upwards from the roots where they are absorbed, to the leaves or growing regions where evaporation of water or the use of both water and salts occurs. Water and inorganic ions permeate freely through the cell walls and air spaces of the more peripheral cells of the roots. Equilibrium is established between the insides of cells in this region and the water and salts outside, water tending to enter by osmosis and the salts by diffusion or active transport. Increase in cell volume which would be caused by continual influx of materials is, of course, restricted by the inextensible cell wall. In the centre of the root is a region packed with the specialised conducting tissues called xylem and phloem. These form continuous channels through the root and into the shoot and clearly serve for the conduction of water and substances in solution. In the root this central region is separated from the more peripheral tissue by a single layer of cells, the endodermis. The endodermal layer can actively pump water and salts from the outer regions through into the longitudinal conducting strands of, in this case, the xylem. Evidence for this pumping activity can be seen in the exudation of liquid from the base of a plant stem cut close to ground level. In some cases pressures of 8 to 10 atmospheres have been generated in roots as a result of the pumping action of the endodermal cells.

Water is also moved up a plant by forces generated in the leaves. Constant evaporation from the walls of leaf cells, both on the surface and within the substance of the leaf, causes loss of water from the plant. The process is called transpiration and, within limits, the plant can control transpiration rate by regulating the ease with which water-saturated air passes to the exterior through perforations in the leaf surface called stomata. The diameter of these apertures can be regulated by movements of guard cells surrounding the stomatal openings. Loss of water from the leaf cells is made good by with-drawing more water from the xylem elements within the leaves and stem of the plant. Cohesive forces between water molecules prevent the continuous water columns within the xylem from breaking. The net result is that water is drawn up the stem as transpiration occurs in the leaves. Considerable suction pressures have been measured by suitable manometer systems at-tached to the cut stems of actively transpiring plants. In addition materials such as dyes or radioactive isotopes have been followed as they move up the conducting xylem vessels at rates which can usually be related to the rate of trans-piration.

2. Movement of Organic Substances

The organic substances, whose site of manu-facture is primarily in the leaves, have to be distributed to the rest of the plant body. It is thought that a second conducting tissue, the phloem, is mainly responsible for the distribution of these materials in solution. Ploem is found as a layer of tissue to the outside of the xylem vessels in a plant stem. It consists of conducting cells which are rather different from those of the xylem, which serve, as we have seen, mainly in the transport of water and salts. Whereas xylem tissues are composed of dead cells whose cell walls form effective longitudinal conducting channels, phloem is made up mainly of living cells. Elements called sieve tubes are the most important conducting cells in phloem and, during the initial stages of differentiation, a sieve tube has a full complement of cytoplasm and cell organelles. Later differentiation sees the pro-toplasmic structures break down, but even in mature sieve tubes protoplasmic strands join through the perforated ends of adjacent cells and may extend longitudinally through the conducting elements.

Ringing experiments in which a complete ring of phloem is cut from the outside of a plant, provide evidence of the tissue's function in longitudinal conduction of carbohydrates. Sugars accumulate above such a ring but not below it. Samples of fluid taken from sieve tubes have also revealed high concentrations of carbo-hydrates in the sap. The method used to obtain such samples is very ingenious. Several aphids (insects such as green fly) are known which parasitise the phloem translocation chan-nels of plants. The aphid is allowed to insert its stylet tip into the phloem vessels and is then anaesthetised and cut off the inserted stylet. Sap exudes from the stylet stump and can be col-lected and analysed.

3. Growth

Growth is usually, but not always, thought of as involving increase of size as measured by length, volume, or weight. In these terms any unit in a plant, whether root, shoot or fruit would follow a sigmoid growth curve with growth starting slowly, then speeding up, before finally slowing down at maturity leading on to death. Growth may also be considered as an increase in the number of cells, an increase in substances such as water, protein or DNA in the growing system, or an increase in complexity of organisa-tion.

The organisation of growth, no matter how it is measured, presents a number of interesting problems. In the first divisions of a fertilised egg, all cells divide. Very soon this property becomes localised, polarity is established, and the young embryo develops a shoot tip and a root tip. These have then become discrete regions of cell division. The cells behind them cease active division, enlarge by developing large vacuoles and form mature plant tissue. A circular strand of dividing tissue, called the cambium, is left in the stem between differen-tiated xylem and phloem. The cambium is responsible for growth in girth. The acquisition of polarity has far-reaching consequences, for the behaviour of a shoot tip is very different from that of a root. The shoot tip, for example, gives rise to leaf cells with photosynthesising chloroplasts and it grows upwards away from gravity and towards light. The root tip gives rise to cells which absorb salt and water, and it grows towards gravity and away from light.

Quite a lot is known about the mechanisms which regulate growth by cell enlargement in the regions behind the actively dividing tips. Cell enlargement is achieved by the secretion of water and solutes to form a substantial vacuole within the cell, thus causing an overall increase of volume and expansion of the cell wall. The degree of enlargement is affected by external stimuli such as light and gravity, producing the differential growth patterns seen when plants orientate to these stimuli. Substances, called plant hormones or auxins, are now known to be produced at the growing apex and to move back causing vacuole formation in the actively elongating region. The distribution of auxin is affected by light or gravity so that the plant will turn towards or away from the stimulus. Indoleacetic acid is the active growth substance occurring naturally in many plants. Several man-made substances are also effective and are widely used as weedkillers. Evidence is also accumulating to show that a group of substances exists in plants to control cell division, just as auxins regulate cell enlargement.

ECOLOGY—THE STUDY OF LIVING ORGANISMS IN THEIR ENVIRONMENT

The important branch of biology which deals with the relationship between living organisms and their environment must now be considered. Living organisms and the physical environment in which they exist form what is termed an eco-system. Obviously it would be possible to regard the whole world as a giant ecosystem, though for purposes of study it would be extremely un-rewarding and impractical. A pond, a rocky or sandy shore, a forest, and a peat bog are examples of ecosystems on a somewhat smaller scale, possessing different properties and containing populations of animals and plants that are dif-ferent both in number of individuals and in species represented. The ecologist seeks to understand why a particular species is present in certain numbers in an ecosystem in terms of that species' interaction with all other living organisms (biotic factors) and with the physical (abiotic) factors of the ecosystem.

1. Abiotic Factors

All living organisms will show ranges of toler-ance for abiotic factors such as temperature, humidity, salinity, oxygen levels, amount of light, etc. Clearly, if any factor in the environment moves outside the range of tolerance of a species, it becomes limiting for that particular species which is then excluded from the environment. Within the range of tolerance there will be an optimum value for each abiotic factor at which a species will survive best.

There is not a firm line separating suitable and unsuitable environments, but rather a steady shift from optimum values into conditions in which an organism finds it more and more difficult to survive.

One of the most important abiotic factors in an environment is the nature of the substrate upon or within which an organism moves and settles.

(a) **The Terrestrial Environment.**—Soil is the commonest substrate for terrestrial organisms. Particle sizes, ranging from the coarsest gravel soils, through sands and silts to the finely textured clays, have extensive effects on the flora and fauna of any area. Coarsely textured soils are obviously penetrated most easily both by roots and by soil animals. Soils of this type also allow the rapid movement of water and soil gases, but they have the serious disadvantage of poor water retention. The level at which water saturation occurs is known as the water table and is an important abiotic factor. The terrestrial environment tends on the whole to dehydrate organisms and there is always a marked dependence on water supplies.

Soil characteristics also vary with depth. A vertical section through any soil is referred to as its profile and has considerable bearing on the ecosystems in which the soil is involved. The layers, or horizons, of a soil profile vary enormously from one soil to another. Below a surface layer of organic debris one can, in general terms, distinguish a layer of soil from which substances have been leached (A horizon), soil containing the leached-out substances from the layer above (B horizon), the weathered parent material (C horizon), and finally the parent rock or some other stratum beneath the soil (D horizon).

Humus

Humus, which is formed from animal and plant remains and is located in the lower parts of the A profile, is of great importance in providing food for soil organisms and chemical elements such as nitrogen, phosphorus, and calcium for plant growth. It is also important in maintaining good soil structure and, though inorganic fertilisers can supply chemical elements, they have little or no effect on structure. Soil requires careful cultivation, and structure is easily disturbed by such things as heavy farm machinery, which can lead to the creation of impermeable layers with the disastrous exclusion of oxygen and oxygen-consuming organisms.

(b) **The Aquatic Environments.**—Marine and freshwater environments together cover more than 75 per cent of the earth's surface and, since they can be occupied throughout their entire depth, offer a much greater volume of living space than does the land. There is only a slight difference between the density of water and of living tissues, so that the bodies of aquatic organisms are very largely supported by the environment and do not need strong woody stems or powerfully muscled limbs to hold them up. Water has a high specific heat, which means that large amounts of heat are needed to raise its temperature. The result is that aquatic environments tend to show much smaller fluctuations in temperature than the terrestrial ones. In general, the larger the volume of water the smaller are the fluctuations in temperature, and so the fauna and flora of the oceans will not show wide temperature tolerance, whereas that of small pools will, but in neither case will the tolerance be so great as that shown by many terrestrial forms. Oxygen and carbon dioxide concentrations are very different in water and in air and are also variable from one aquatic environment to another, making them suitable for the support of different fauna and flora.

An important difference between the sea and freshwater is seen when their salt concentrations are determined.

Osmotic and ionic regulation

Organisms living in fresh or in sea water face quite dissimilar problems in osmotic and ionic regulation. Life evolved originally in the sea and the salt concentration in the blood of marine molluscs, crustaceans, and echinoderms, for example, is about the same as in sea water itself. Marine organisms have, on several occasions in the course of their evolution, moved into freshwater. Representatives of the worms, crustaceans, molluscs, and vertebrates have all independently invaded this very dilute habitat. What is more, all these animals show approximately the same types of modification to cope with the change. Their outer layers, in the main, become impermeable and the salt concentration of their blood is reduced considerably and to a spectacularly low level in the freshwater mussel. The kidneys become enlarged and produce a large volume of dilute urine. By these means freshwater animals can cut down loss of their salts (*see* **F39**). It is interesting that all terrestrial vertebrates, including the mammals have retained a salt concentration in their blood of about half the seawater level and this is partly attributable to their freshwater ancestry. The ultimate development of salinity tolerance is seen in such animals as the salmon and eel which move from fresh to salt water and back again during their life cycle.

2. Biotic Factors

(a) **Associations between Organisms.**—No organism can be considered to be independent of any other organism in an ecosystem but in some cases close associations of various types can be developed between different species or different members of the same species.

Commensalism is an association which benefits one member but has little effect on the other. Small organisms can live within the protective covering offered by a larger individual, as, for example, commensal crabs living within the shell of some species of oyster.

Symbiosis is a somewhat closer association in which both members benefit, as do certain species of green algae and the coelenterates in whose body tissues they live. The algae are protected and the coelenterates benefit from the food produced by the photosynthetic plant. Some symbiotic organisms are unable to survive outside the association. The lichens which are associations of algae and fungi, are examples of this type of symbiosis, as are some of the food-processing micro-organisms together with the animals in whose intestinal tracts they live.

Social animals. In some cases animals of the same species form social groups in which co-operative effort and division of labour makes them more successful in exploiting a particular environment. Social development is most obvious among certain insects such as termites, ants, wasps, and bees, and among the vertebrates. Social organisation in these groups may lead to the development of different behaviour patterns and ultimately, as in ants and bees, for example, to the evolution of a variety of structural modifications so that different castes are recognisable.

Parasitism. Not all associations are of mutual benefit and when one organism becomes sufficiently specialised so that it can live successfully on materials extracted from another, the latter is always adversely affected. Parasites, by causing disease in, and sometimes the death of, the host, can influence population growth and size. Important groups are bacteria, protozoa, fungi, nematodes (roundworms), and platyhelminths (tapeworms and liver flukes). Viruses are also important disease-producing agents which are incapable of an independent existence outside the cells of the host and utilise the host cell's metabolic pathways directly to synthesise new virus material.

Control of Parasites

Many parasites (and other pests which may disturb the comfort and health of man) can now be controlled to some extent, and, for a variety of reasons, such control procedures have extensive effects on the ecosystems involved. The regulation of some bacterial parasites by means of antibiotics, and control of the insect vectors of organisms such as the malaria parasite by means of insecticides, have both been important factors in the increase in human population. Though the beneficial effects of pest control of all types are clear, the process is not without its difficulties and dangers. Indiscriminate use of many chemical agents has led to the development of resistant strains. In any group of organisms, some will naturally be more resistant to a pesticide or antibiotic than others and these will be the survivors of any treatment that is less than totally effective. They will form the breeding stock for subsequent generations and so progressively more and more resistant types will evolve. Thus, there are now many strains of bacteria resistant to penicillin and other antibiotics. Even more alarming is the recent discovery that this resistance can be transferred in an infective way between bacteria of different species. Another complication associated with chemical control is that the agent concerned frequently affects a wide spectrum of organisms, including those that are in no sense injurious to man or his crops. Thus DDT kills bees and other pollinating insects unless its application to a crop is very precisely timed. In addition, the accumulation of quantities of chlorinated hydrocarbons such as DDT in the environment is known to have an injurious effect on organisms other than insects. Because these chemicals are broken down very slowly they now form a serious problem in environmental pollution.

Predation. A less direct association than that between parasite and host is the one which exists between predators and the prey which they capture and kill. However, interactions in both parasitism and predation have features in common particularly those affecting population numbers.

(b) **The Food Factor.**—Plants are the ultimate source of organic food for all animals. The most important food plants are those capable of photosynthesis (**F32**) in which organic material is synthesised from carbon dioxide and water, using radiant energy from the sun to drive the reaction.

Food Chains. Plants are eaten by herbivores which in turn are eaten by carnivores. It is possible to see many such sequences, called food chains, in all ecosystems. For example, in the open sea, green algae are the important photosynthetic organisms; these are eaten by a small crustacean, *Calanus*, which in turn forms a large part of the diet of the herring. Feeding relationships are usually of much greater complexity than is suggested by a simple food chain. Thus, *Calanus* represents about 20 per cent of the herring's diet but it is also eaten by many other marine animals as well. For example, it forms about 70 per cent of the total diet of larval sand eels. The larval eels are eaten in turn by the herring and may form 40 per cent of its diet. Because an animal's diet is usually quite varied and one species of animal or plant may be part of the food of a wide range of different animals, interactions are set up which are referred to as food webs. However, for general comparative purposes it is possible to disregard the detail of species and to group together all organisms with similar food habits. When this is done a relationship known as pyramid of numbers often appears in which organisms at the base of a food chain (the primary producers) are extremely abundant, while those at the apex (the final consumers) are relatively few in number.

Productivity. The validity of using numbers of individuals in such an analysis is often open to

question, especially when ecosystems are to be compared. For example, a comparison between numbers of herring and numbers of whales as final consumers in two pyramidal systems is not very informative. This difficulty is partially overcome by using estimates of the total weight (biomass) of organisms at each level rather than their number. Even this has disadvantages because determinations of biomass give a measure of the amount of material present at any one time (the standing crop) but give no indication of the amount of material being produced or the rate of its production (the productivity). In some parts of the sea, for example, the biomass of small animals forming the zooplankton is greater than that of the plant life or phytoplankton on which it depends for food. This seems to contravene the pyramid concept. However, the rate of production of new material by the phytoplankton is very much greater than by the zooplankton so that, if taken over a year, the total amount of plant material produced would far exceed the total production of animal material. Productivity is a concept of great practical and theoretical importance. It may be determined in terms of the actual organic material produced in an area over a set period of time or, more usefully, in terms of the amounts of energy transferred and stored at each food level, again over a set period of time.

Photosynthetic efficiency

Under natural conditions only 1 to 5 per cent of the light falling on a plant is converted by its photosynthetic system into chemical energy contained in the material of its tissues. Similarly herbivores which consume plants will pass on to their predators only some 10 per cent of the energy contained in the plant material they eat. These low values for photosynthetic efficiency and ecological efficiency respectively are due to the fact that most of the energy appears as heat during the metabolic reactions needed to sustain life and only a small amount is incorporated into new tissue. It is easy to see that the form of a pyramid of numbers can be explained in terms of low ecological efficiency, as can the observation that a food chain rarely has more than five links. The loss of energy at each stage must mean that each succeeding stage becomes smaller and smaller in number and that the number of stages is severely limited.

Human Population and Food. The present very large increase in human population and the predicted rise from 4,124 million in 1977 to 6,000 million in the year 2000 has led to a pressing need for the controlled exploitation of food resources in the world. Consideration of the processes of energy transfer suggests that man should be mainly herbivorous. They also suggest that present agricultural crops, with the possible exception of sugar cane, do not achieve as high a primary productivity as that encountered in some natural ecosystems. Crops rarely achieve complete plant cover of the land throughout the growing season so as to trap the maximum amount of sunlight. It would be necessary to mix crops to do this effectively and there would then be complicated harvesting problems.

If man remains an omnivore, as he almost certainly will, then his domestic food animals will continue to be herbivorous as they are at present, though whether they will be the same herbivores is less easy to predict. Beef cattle raised on grassland convert only 4 per cent of the energy in the plants of their environment into similar chemical energy in their tissues. At the present time intensive farming practices are being employed to improve conversion, usually by harvesting plant material, processing it, and bringing it to the animals which are housed in special buildings. This cuts down on the wastage of plant food because it can be grown under better conditions and less of it is consumed by animals other than the cattle. Careful breeding and the limitation of the period over which livestock is raised to that of maximum growth efficiency have also contributed to conversions of some 35 per cent, achieved in the case of broiler chickens and calves. The moral problems raised by these methods and the circumstances which make them necessary give rise to widespread concern.

Fish are also an important part of man's diet. Many populations have been overfished so that returns have gone down in spite of intensified fishing effort. The fisheries scientist is concerned to discover the limit at which the maximum number of fish can be taken without depleting the population year by year. Research is also going on into possible methods of enclosing and farming areas of the sea or estuaries.

Population Dynamics

Study of the numbers of organisms in a population, together with their change and regulation, forms a branch of the subject of considerable practical importance known as population dynamics.

Numbers of animals and plants tend to increase up to the capacity of the environment. The rate of increase will be determined by the balance between reproduction rate and mortality. As Malthus appreciated, adults of any organism tend to replace themselves by a greater number of progeny and, in the absence of losses by mortality and other factors, there is a vast potential for increase in all populations. If an organism doubles its number in a year, there will be a 1,000-fold increase in 10 years, and a 10 million-fold increase in 20 years. Increase of this type soon leads to shortages and overcrowding so that mortality goes up, the net rate of increase diminishes, and finally an equilibrium is reached with no further increase in number. The change with the passage of time follows and S-shaped curve. At equilibrium, the numbers are kept at a steady level by factors such as competition for food, refuge, or space.

Human population is increasing rapidly at the present time, mainly because of the fall in deathrate. Food production is also increasing, but in some areas the world supply and requirement are so evenly matched that drought or war are inevitably followed by a famine. Though the human population has not yet reached the stage of equilibrium, it is clear that ultimately it must be subject to forces of regulation similar to those that control populations of other organisms. Birthrate cannot exceed death-rate indefinitely in any living organism. By limiting the size of families it is possible for man to achieve a population equilibrium at levels lower than those at which regulative factors such as famine or aggression must begin to operate. Rational control of birth-rate seems to offer the best chance of averting a global population disaster.

THE GEOLOGICAL RECORD

The various stages in the history of the earth can be read by the geologists in the strata or layers of rock laid down since the planet began to solidify, and it is in these rocks, too, that the record of life upon earth may be traced.

No Life Rocks.—The earliest rocks in the record are known as the Azoic (no life) rocks, because they show no trace of living things, and these layers are of such thickness that they occupy more than half of the whole record. That is to say, for more than half the earth's history nothing living existed upon any part of the globe. For millions of years the surface of our planet was nothing but bare rock without soil or sand, swept by hot winds exceeding in violence the wildest tornadoes of today, and drenched by torrential downpours of tropical rain which, as we have seen elsewhere, gradually tore away the surface to form sandy sediments at the bottom of the seas. In such ancient rocks pushed above the surface by later upheavals we can still trace the marks of primeval oceans as they rippled upon the barren shores or of raindrops which left their imprint perhaps 1,500 million years ago.

Primitive Sea-life.—As we move upwards through the strata, however, traces of life begin to appear and steadily increase as we come to the more recent levels. The earliest signs appear in what is known as the Early Palaeozoic Age (or by some writers as the Proterozoic Age), when we find the fossilised remains of small shellfish, seaweeds, and trilobites—the latter were creatures somewhat like the plant-lice of modern times. All these primitive animals and plants lived in the shallow tidal waters of ancient seas; for as yet life had not invaded either the dry land or the deep oceans. It is, of course, clear that these creatures of Early Palaeozoic times were not the first living things; they were merely the first creatures capable of leaving fossilised remains, and without doubt must have had more primitive ancestors—amoebic-like forms, jellyfish, bacteria, and so on whose bodies were too soft to leave any traces in the record of the rocks.

The Age of Fishes.—Towards the end of the Early Palaeozoic Era, in what we now know as the Silurian period, there arose a new form of life: the first backboned animals, primitive fishes somewhat similar to the sharks of today; and in the division of the Upper Palaeozoic Era known as the Devonian, they had come to multiply so greatly that this is frequently described as the Age of Fishes.

First Land Animals and Plants.—It is from this time, too, that we find traces of animal and plant life upon the dry land. Both animals and plants had acute problems to solve before it became possible for them to live out of water; for both animals and plants had hitherto been supported by the surrounding water and respired by removing oxygen dissolved in the water. In land animals this problem was solved by a long series of adaptations from gills to lungs. Plants were able to invade the land because of the evolution of an impermeable outer cuticle which prevented water loss and also the development of woody tissues which provided support and a water-conducting system for the whole plant body.

Amphibia and Spore-bearing Trees.—The first type of vertebrates (backboned animals) to live upon dry land was the group of amphibia in the Carboniferous Age, which is today represented by the newts, frogs, toads, and salamanders. In all these forms the eggs give rise to a tadpole stage with gills which lives for some time entirely in water. Later the gills give place to a primitive form of lung which enables the animal to live upon land. Even so, amphibia are restricted more or less to swampy or marshy land, and without a damp environment they would dry up and shrivel to death. The most abundant forms of plant life in the Carboniferous period were the tree-like horsetails, clubmosses, and ferns, the fossilised tissues of which are found in the coal measures and are burned as household coal. But these plants also, as in the case of the amphibia, could exist only amongst the swamps and marshes, and life, although it had freed itself from the necessity of existence in the waters of the earth, still had to return to the water in order to reproduce itself. The highlands and the deeper waters of the planet were still empty of living things. Although the Carboniferous period had been a period of warmth and abundance, the Palaeozoic Era came to an end with a long cycle of dry and bitterly cold ages. Such long-term climatic changes were due, it is now supposed, to such factors as changes in the earth's orbit, the shifting of its axis of rotation, changes in the shape of the land masses, and so on. Long before the Ice Ages of more recent times, there are records in the rocks of alternating periods of warmth and cold as far back as the Azoic and Early Palaeozoic Eras. This long cold spell at the close of the Palaeozoic era came to an end about 220 million years ago, and was succeeded by a long era of widely spread warm conditions—the Mesozoic Era, the so-called Age of Reptiles.

The Mesozoic Era.—The reptiles first appeared in the Permian, but it was during the Mesozoic era that they became the dominant group of animals. The giant reptiles included the stegosaurus, the gigantosaurus, the diplodocus, and many other kinds which were far larger than any land animals living today. Some, for example the diplodocus, were 100 ft. long, although they were vegetarian in habit and were preyed upon by other almost equally huge flesh-eating reptiles. Some species, such as the plesiosaurs and ichthyosaurs, became secondarily aquatic, while the pterodactyl possessed wings with which it could glide and perhaps fly short distances. However, they all differed from the amphibia in that they had hard, dry skins, their lungs were more efficient, fertilisation was internal due to the development of copulatory organs, and they laid eggs with hard, protective shells.

It was also during the Mesozoic era that the warm-blooded birds arose. The birds, like the reptiles, lay eggs with hard shells, and they have several internal features found in the reptiles. The fossil bird Archaeopteryx, three specimens of which have been found in Germany, lived in the Jurassic period. Although it was obviously a bird, it retained many reptilian features. Earliest mammals are recognised in rocks of the late Palaeozoic but in the Mesozoic considerable evolution of the group took place. The fossil Trituberculata which are also found in the Jurassic, are believed to be related to forms from which both the marsupial and placental mammals arose. Although insects were present as far back as the Carboniferous, it was in the Mesozoic that many of the groups we know today first appeared.

Great changes also took place in the plant cover of the land during this era. The spore-bearing giant horsetails and tree clubmosses declined and were replaced by gymnosperms—trees bearing naked seeds. One large group of these, the cycadeoids, has become extinct, but the conifers and a few of the once abundant cycads still remain. The flowering plants or angiosperms also made their appearance, and towards the end of the Cretaceous their evolution was extremely rapid. In fact, many of the fossil leaves found in rocks of Cretaceous age are indistinguishable from those of some present-day flowering plants.

A New Era.—But, perhaps 150 million years later, all this seemingly everlasting warmth and sunshine, the lush tropical life, the giant reptiles who had ruled the world, were wiped out by a new period of bitter cold which only the hardy species could survive. A new Era known as the Caenozoic was beginning, ushered in by a period of upheaval and volcanic activity, following which the map of the world came to resemble more closely the picture we know today. The old period may have lasted several million years, and the main species to survive it were those which had come into existence towards the end of the Mesozoic Era, the seed-bearing flowering plants, the birds, and the mammals. The once all-powerful reptiles from this time onwards are represented only by the comparatively few and relatively small reptilian species of today: the snakes, lizards, crocodiles, and alligators. It was at this time, too, that, long after the creation of the mountains of Scotland and Norway (the so-called Caledonian revolution), or even of the Appalachian mountains (the Appalachian revolution), there arose the great masses of the Alps, the Himalayas, the Rocky Mountains, and the Andes. These are the mountain chains of the most recent, the Caenozoic revolution. Initially, as we have seen, the climate of the Caenozoic Era was cold, but the weather grew generally warmer until a new period of abundance was reached, only to be followed at the end of the Pliocene by a period of glacial ages generally known as the First, Second, Third, and Fourth Ice Ages.

CHRONICLE OF EVENTS

4,500,000,000	Formation of Earth's crust.
4,000,000,000	Australian fossil dated in 1993 at this age.
600,000,000	Earliest fossil evidence of invertebrates.
450,000,000	First jawless fishes appear in fossil record. First land plants.
400,000,000	First bony fishes appear. Early seed plants. First amphibians. First insects.
350,000,000	Earliest reptiles in fossil record.
270,000,000	First conifers; coal seams laid down.
220,000,000	Dinosaurs appear in fossil record; First fossil evidence of mammals (*Megazostrodon*).
135,000,000	Evolution of flowering plants; First bird in fossil record (*Archaeopteryx*). Dinosaur extinction begins (ends 65,000,000 years ago).

V. SCIENCES OF MAN

PHYSICAL ANTHROPOLOGY

MAN'S PLACE IN NATURE

In the broadest terms of scientific classification, humans are part of the *animal kingdom*—that is to say they are multicellular organisms which feed by ingesting complex organic substances and are capable of independent movement. More than one million animal species have been described (and the actual number may be nearer 10 million). Each belongs to one of the many phyla (singular *phylum*, meaning tribe or stock) into which the animal kingdom is divided. Humans belong to the phylum chordata, *subphylum* vertebrata, which includes all animals with a spinal cord enclosed within a vertebral column, and with a skull enclosing the brain.

Each phylum is divided into a number of *classes*, among which humans are classified as four-limbed vertebrates of the class mammalia: warmblooded animals with mammary glands which secrete milk for the nourishment of young, skin with hair or fur, a body cavity divided by a muscular diaphragm which assists respiration, three ear bones and seven neck vertebrae.

There are about 4,500 species of mammal, classified in three *subclasses*: the *prototheria*, which is a group of oviparous (egg-laying) mammals consisting solely of the duckbill platypus and spiny anteaters of Australia and New Guinea; the *metatheria*, represented by about 260 species of viviparous (live-bearing) marsupials whose young are born in a very immature state and carried by their mother in an external pouch for some time after birth; and the *eutheria*, which are mammals with a placenta permitting substantial development of the young before birth.

The great majority of mammals belong to the eutheria—including humans. The subclass itself is divided into *orders*, numbering 16 in all, which range from the insectivora (shrews, moles, hedgehogs *etc*) and pholidota (pangolins), to the proboscidea (elephants) and cetacea (whales). Lemurs, monkeys, apes and humans are grouped together in the primate order; all are tree-dwellers (or descendants thereof) whose distinctive similarities are their fingers, flat nails, and reduced sense of smell.

The primate order is split into three *suborders*: the prosimii, represented by the living lemurs, lorises and galagos; the tarsoidea (the living tarsiers); and the anthropoidea (monkeys, apes and humans). The anthropoidea order is divided into two *infraorders*: the platyrrhini, meaning flat-nosed and comprising the New World monkeys of central and south America; and the catarrhini (thin-nosed), which are the Old World monkeys, the gibbons, the apes, and humans.

The catarrhini infraorder divides into two *superfamilies*: the cercopithecoidea (Old World monkeys), and the hominoidea (gibbons, apes and humans); and the hominoid superfamily splits into three *families*: the hylobatiae (gibbons); the pongidae (apes), and the hominidae (humans). The hylobatids and pongids are distinguished by long arms and short legs, reflecting a predominantly arboreal way of life, while the principal distinguishing features of the hominid family are an habitual upright posture and bipedal gait, and a large brain.

Each zoological family is a group of related genera (sing. *genus*, meaning race, origin); a genus is a collection of closely related *species* (meaning kind, or sort), and a species is a group of individuals who are capable of breeding among themselves. There are several genera and numerous species of the hylobatid and pongid primate families alive today, but only one living species of hominid: modern humans – *Homo sapiens*.

It will be seen from the above that the relationships which form the basic structure of zoological classification set every species in the context of a greater whole—genus, family, order, and so on. *Homo sapiens* is no exception. Man is not the end-product of the entire evolutionary process, as is

commonly supposed. On the contrary, man's place in nature is at the end of a relatively short line radiating from among the millions which have evolved since life on Earth began more than 3·5 billion years ago.

The origin of the primates

The primates are essentially tropical animals. With the exception of humans, virtually all living species are arboreal, and 80 per cent of them are found in the tropical rain forests. Their most distinctive characteristic is the very general and unspecialised nature of their anatomical structure, and the highly specialised and adaptable nature of their behaviour. While other mammals evolved specialised physical characteristics (the giraffe's long neck, for example), the primates have retained the basic structure of the ancestral mammalian form and have instead adapted their behaviour to suit prevailing circumstances. The human hand is a case in point—it has the same number of bones operated by the same arrangement of muscles as the arboreal primates possessed 45 million years ago, yet the human hand serves a much greater variety of uses.

The fossil evidence indicates that primates have existed for at least 70 million years. They were one of the groups of placental mammals which survived the mass-extinction event which closed the Cretaceous period of geological time, about 65 million years ago. The dinosaurs were among those which disappeared with that event, and their passing marks the end of the epoch known as the Age of the Reptiles. Some reptiles survived, of course, but with the declining prominence of the dinosaurs the mammals flourished, heralding the Age of the Mammals with a burst of adaptive radiation which eventually took them into every ecological niche which the dinosaurs had previously occupied.

The early mammals had lived in the shadow of the dinosaurs for more than 100 million years before the Age of the Reptiles came to a close. They were small (typically about 10 cm long), and occupied parts of the environment that the large reptiles could not reach—the nocturnal world, for instance, (a temporal dimension in which the cold-blooded reptiles could not function), and rocky crags, holes and forest undergrowth. Here they evolved a high degree of sensory perception. Sight, sound, touch and smell assisted their capture of the invertebrate prey upon which they largely subsisted; integration of cerebral and physical equipment was crucial, and while the later evolution of the dinosaurs was concerned primarily with physical structure, that of the early mammals was concerned with the development of brain and behaviour. This equipped them well for the radiation which followed.

Of the various habitats available to the mammals as the Age of the Reptiles drew to a close, the ancestors of the primates took to the trees. Here they found a rich and varied diet—leaves, buds, fruit, insects, birds' eggs and nestlings—but also a suite of new demands. Life in the trees called for a shift in the emphasis of the mammals' environmental awareness. While the nose had probably been the most important organ of ground-dwelling mammals, the eyes were more crucial in the trees.

Because a tree is a spatially restricted environment, an arboreal animal needs to be particularly aware of its whereabouts. It must know if a potential predator is in the same tree, and if a fruit is at the end of a safe branch. It must be able to see clearly and judge distances accurately as it moves through the branches. These requirements favoured the evolution of stereoscopic vision, which was further enhanced by the advent of colour vision.

Life in the branches also called for greater agility. An ability to flex the paws and grasp things was advantageous; digits evolved into fingers, claws into fingernails. Front limbs became principally a means of holding on, while the rear limbs served as a means of propulsion and also of static support.

Thus the animals could leap safely about the trees, and also could sit with the spine erect, the head turning with a perceptive eye, the ears twitching.

It can be supposed that the attributes favouring an arboreal existence also promoted yet more cerebral development. A large brain relative to body size evolved; accommodating a larger brain required some restructuring of the skull, which in turn was affected by the masticatory demands of the foods which the animals ate—fruit, leaves, insects, meat. Such an omnivorous diet calls for neither the specialised canines and slicing teeth of the carnivores, nor the grinding molars of the herbivores. The ancestral set of general all-purpose teeth was retained. The jaws broadened and shortened, the face flattened, the eyes looked forward and the expanding brain took up more and more room at the back of the skull. These interactive and interdependent features evolved over millions of years, a mosaic of cause and effect from which evolved the order of mammals known as the primates.

In basic zoological terms, the primates which evolved from the early arboreal mammals are distinguished from all other placental mammals by the fact that they have retained the four kinds of teeth found in ancestral mammals (incisors, canines, premolars and molars); they can hold things between finger and thumb, they have frontally directed eyes and have a large brain, relative to body size. They are represented today by 193 living species, all but one of which are covered with hair.

Hominid ancestry

The broadest categories of the primate order were also the earliest to have existed in evolutionary time, and the divisions were created principally by the geographic isolation resulting from the breakup of Gondwanaland, the supercontinent on which the primates had originated. Thus, the tarsier suborder became confined to the islands of Indonesia and the Philippines, and the prosimian suborder is best represented today by the lemurs of Madagascar, where the infraorder has been isolated for close on 60 million years. Another infraorder of prosimian, represented by the pottos, lorises and bushbabies, remained on continental Africa and Asia, and has found isolation in a nocturnal way of life as other primates adopted a diurnal lifestyle.

Isolation similarly split the anthropoid suborder when the landmass of South America broke away from Gondwanaland about 40 million years ago, carrying with it the primate stock which evolved into the platyrrhines—the New World monkeys. Subsequently, the catarrhine stock left on Gondwanaland split into its two main groups, probably along the lines of diverging dietary preferences. One group adopted a mainly herbivorous diet and gave rise to the Old World monkeys or cercopithecoids (represented today by the baboons and the colobines), while the other retained a more omnivorous diet and produced the hominoids (gibbons, apes and humans).

The precise dates at which these splits occurred are uncertain, but the fossil evidence suggests that the hominoid line is at least 30 million years old. A putative ancestor from that time has been found in the Fayum, south west of Cairo. The land is arid desert now, but 30 million years ago it was tropical rain forest and swampland, laced with broad meandering rivers. Scientists excavating fossil beds in the region have recovered the remains of a creature which is described formally as *Aegyptopithecus zeuxis*, though it is more colloquially known as the "dawn ape". Jaws and teeth, a skull and the skeletal parts of several individuals suggest that *Aegyptopithecus* was diverse and very generalised in its physical form. Experts have reconstructed from the fossil evidence a picture of a small arboreal primate, about the size of a domestic cat, with a sinuous back, long limbs, and all four feet capable of both grasping branches and conveying food to the mouth. The eyes looked forward, indicating stereoscopic vision, and the brain was larger in proportion to bodyweight than that of any other mammal then alive.

The descendants of *Aegyptopithecus* and its kind appear to have been very successful in evolutionary terms. More than 50 species are known from the fossil record, and hence palaeoanthropologists are inclined to refer to the Miocene (the geological period extending from 26 million to 8 million years ago) as the Age of the Ape. One of these species, *Proconsul africanus*, is believed to represent the evolutionary line which led to the modern apes and humans.

First described from a nearly complete face and partial skull discovered by Mary Leakey on Kenya's Rusinga Island, Lake Victoria, in 1948, *Proconsul* was a tree-dwelling animal about the size of a baboon which roamed East Africa about 18 million years ago, sometime after the monkey and ape lines had diverged. More remains were recovered during the 1970s, enabling scientists to reconstruct a skeleton that was essentially 75 percent complete. The result showed an unexpected mixture of characteristics. *Proconsul* had a back-bone resembling that of the gibbon, shoulder and elbow joints like those of the chimpanzee, and the wrists of a monkey. Overall, *Proconsul* is quite unlike any living ape, but could be ancestral.

Around 17 million years ago, the African continental plate butted up against Europe, raising high mountains and creating a landbridge across which many African animals migrated into Eurasia for the first time. Among them were apes whose fossil remains have also been proposed as candidates for the ancestry of the ape and human lines. *Dryopithecus* was found in Greece, *Ramapithecus* and *Sivapithecus* in the Siwalik Hills of northern Pakistan. The fossil evidence was fragmentary, but for many years *Ramapithecus*, dating from 14 million to 7 million years ago, was almost universally accepted as the earliest known ancestor of the human line. During the early 1980s, however, the discovery of more complete ramapithecine remains showed that it and the sivapithecines are more likely to represent ancestors of the orang-utan on their evolutionary and migratory journey to the south-east Asian islands where they are found today. Consensus opinion now rates the dryopithecines as close cousins headed for extinction, and regards Africa as the cradle of mankind.

The emergence of mankind

The question of human origins has intrigued every generation. The biblical story of creation provided a longstanding and widely-accepted explanation, to which Charles Darwin (see **B18**) added a biological dimension with the publication of *The origin of species* in 1859. The controversy aroused by Darwin centred very largely around the mistaken idea that the theory of evolution implied that humans were descendants of the apes. This mistake is still encountered with surprising frequency, even though Darwin's original work and the many studies conducted since then all make the evolutionary proposition quite clear: humans are not descended from the apes, the two branches evolved simultaneously from a common ancestor which existed sometime in the past.

Among evolutionists, the question of human origins is basically a question of when the divergence of the ape and human lines occurred, and what the common ancestor looked like. For the greater part of the time since Darwin's day it has been assumed that the answers to these questions would be supplied by the fossil remains of the ancestral forms which might be recovered from geological deposits of ever-greater antiquity—if only those fossils could be found. Thus began the search for the missing link, as it became popularly known. By the 1960s the results of these fossil hunts had provided the basis for a widely-accepted scenario in which humans had evolved from *Ramapithecus* on a line which had split from the apes some 30 million years ago. Since the 1960s, however, this fossil-based scenario has been displaced by one based on biochemistry which puts the human/ape split at just 5 million years ago.

Instead of studying fossil bones, biochemists have used the genetic material (DNA—deoxyribonucleic acid) of related living species to measure the amount of time which has passed since they diverged from a common ancestor. This work is based on three findings: first, DNA accumulates random mutations and changes over time which are evident in the protein structure of all individuals of a species. Second, as two lineages diverge from a common ancestor, each lineage accumulates changes in its DNA which are different from those of the other. Third, the accumulation of changes tends to occur at a regular, almost clocklike rate through time. Clearly, the greater the differences, the longer the divergence, and biochemists have thus been able to put a timescale on the divergence of the apes and humans. The orang-utan split away from the African hominoid stock about 12 million years ago, and the gorilla lineage diverged from the common ancestor of apes and humans about 8 million years ago. The chimpanzee and human lineages were the most recent to diverge from the common ancestor, their split having occurred about 5 million years ago.

Origin of the hominid lineage

In one sense the facts of human origins can be reduced to a series of dates at which humans and related species diverged from their common ancestors. But an intriguing question remains even then: what caused the splits; why did the species diverge from their common ancestor?

A species is the result of reproductive isolation. If the individual members of a viable breeding population reproduce only among themselves for any length of time, the genetic changes which accumulate with each generation will eventually produce a closely-related population which is significantly different from both its ancestral stock and the other descendants of that stock. If the process continues long enough a discrete species will have evolved, one which can only produce fertile offspring among its own kind. It can be supposed with some certainty that the reasons for the isolation which provoked speciation lay in the prevailing ecological circumstances of the time. Food supply would have been a primary factor, and this would have been susceptible to other factors such as climatic variation, the incursion of competing animals, climatic changes, or simply the pressures of a growing population.

Any one or a combination of these ecological factors could have moved a viable breeding population of individuals into reproduction isolation where they might evolve into a discrete species. Migration is the most obvious course by which such isolation could have been achieved—but not the only one. Exploiting an alternative food resource, or adopting different social strategies could have achieved a similar degree of isolation even in close proximity with the ancestral population.

Precisely why the gorilla, chimpanzee and human lineages diverged between 8 million and 5 million years ago is not known. It may have been a consequence of the major climatic fluctuations which occurred during that time, when the overall pattern ranged from hot and dry to wet and very cold. The tropical forests retreated to the equatorial region, woodlands became dominant and grasslands proliferated. And with the changes in vegetation the composition of resident animal populations changed too. Many species became extinct, particularly among the browsers, while the grazers became more numerous. Doubtless the common ancestor of apes and humans was also affected by these developments, but the only certainties are that divergence and speciation occurred during that time, and that the distinctive characteristics of the living species can be considered as adaptations which proved advantageous to a reproductively isolated population.

The distinctive characteristics of humans are the adaptation to a terrestrial way of life and bipedal locomotion; the much reduced face and jaws, and the greatly enlarged brain. In evolutionary terms, bipedalism was the crucial development, and it has been suggested that this was a consequence of the climatic changes which reduced the forest area and thereby increased competition for its resources. Under pressure from other arboreal primates, the human ancestor found a niche on the savannah. Whatever the case, bipedalism offered extensive evolutionary advantages. This was not because bipedalism itself is a particularly effective means of locomotion but rather because it freed forelimbs from locomotor functions and made them available for other purposes. One of the most important of these was the use of tools, and subsequently toolmaking. When the ancestral hominids first colonised the terrestrial habitat they had few inbuilt defence mechanisms and the ability to use stones, sticks and bones to ward off predators must have been of considerable survival value (as has been observed among present-day chimpanzees when they take to the ground). Initially used for defence, tools eventually were used in attack, heralding the adoption of a hunting mode of life. Toolmaking is also thought to have been one of the practices which favoured the development of language, and, since toolmaking called for fine manipulative skills, hand and brain evolved together; particularly those parts of the brain concerned with precise motor control and tactile sensation.

Another consequence of freeing the forelimbs through bipedalism was that carrying became so much easier. Thus food and other items could be carried over considerable distances and this facilitated the establishment of a home base. Perhaps even more important, the human infant could be carried in its mother's arms and held close to her body, allowing a much closer and more intimate relationship between mother and child than is possible in other animals. In terms of its physical development, the human infant is born in a very immature state; in part because of the limitations to the size of the birth canal imposed by the demands of bipedalism. It is therefore long dependent on parental care. This raises problems in a society where pregnant women and nursing mothers become dependent upon the group for food. Social bonds were forged in response, and it has been argued that the evolution of the particular form of reproductive cycle found in humans, in which the female is receptive to the male throughout most of her menstrual cycle should be seen as a means of ensuring that a male will be willing to assume responsibility for females and offspring.

THE FOSSIL EVIDENCE OF HUMAN EVOLUTION

A fundamental premise of palaeoanthropology (the study of man in times past) rests on the contention that unequivocal evidence of human evolution would be found in fossils of known antiquity linking modern man to extinct ancestor. Ideally, the fossils should comprise a series of complete skeletons from a precisely dated sequence of time: this would enable scientists to trace the evolutionary development of humans with complete certainty. But the arbitrary nature of the fossilization process virtually eliminates all chance that such an ideal could ever be achieved or even approached. Far from ideal, palaeoanthropology has had to work with a slowly accumulating collection of diverse and often very fragmentary specimens ever since it became an established discipline in the mid-19th century. In the first fifty years only five specimens were discovered; another twenty-five years passed before a dozen were known, and even today the significant specimens could all be accommodated on a billiard table. The fossils have come from Europe, the Far East and Africa; they span over 3 million years, but as clues to the process of human evolution during that time they represent a minute fraction of mankind's potential ancestry. It has been calculated that ten skulls from East Turkana in Kenya (an exceptional collection covering 1 million years), for example, represent only one individual in every 100 million.

The shortage of evidence is compounded by other problems. Uncertainties concerning age, for instance, mean that differing features which may represent evolutionary change over time cannot be placed in chronological order. And many fossils are so broken, distorted or incomplete that unequivocal interpretation of their significance is rarely possible. In such cases, different authorities may emphasize the importance of different features with equal validity, and the points distinguishing their interpretations may be so slight that each depends as much upon the proponent's beliefs about the course of human evolution as upon the evidence being presented.

Beliefs have always been an important component of palaeoanthropological debate, and for many years they centred around the question of the order in which humans had acquired the characteristics which distinguish them from other primates. Which came first—the restructuring of the jaw and speech? The erect posture and bipedal gait? The enlargement of the brain? Two broad groupings developed in the science—one believing that enlargement of the brain had been the prime mover; the other contending that bipedalism had led the way—and as each new fossil was discovered it was immediately assessed according to those propositions. Neanderthal Man (1857) was initially dismissed as non-human on the basis of the shape and proportions of its brain; Java Man (1891) was promoted as small-brained but bipedal and dubbed *Homo erectus* because a thighbone was found in the same deposit as the skull; Piltdown Man (1912) was a forgery which found widespread acceptance because its large brain and apelike jaw confirmed the beliefs of prominent authorities; *Australopithecus* (1925) was rejected as a candidate for human ancestry because its small brain did not match the expectations of the day.

Subsequent discoveries, including fossils and a trail of fossilized footprints, have shown that hominids were fully bipedal more than 3.6 million years ago, though the configuration of skull and jaw remained distinctly apelike for some time thereafter, while brainsize did not begin to approach modern proportions until 1.5 million years ago.

Finding the fossils

Fossils (from the latin *fossilis*, meaning dug up) are the end products of a process in which organisms are buried and infiltrated by minerals which replace them, molecule by molecule, until, where organic material existed before, stone remains, exactly preserving the form of the original. Fossils have been the source of virtually all that is known about the evolution of life—from the oldest known forms (microscopic fossil algae dating back to 3.5 billion years) to modern times.

For an organism to become fossilized it must first of all be entrapped in a suitable material, away from the attention of scavengers and decomposers. Aquatic organisms comprise by far the greatest number of fossils, not only because they have been more numerous throughout the history of life, but also because the seabed or lake bottom favours fossilization. Terrestrial organisms are less commonly found as fossils (most are consumed or decomposed by other creatures soon after death), and hominid fossils are among the rarest of all.

Palaeoanthropologists wishing to find the fossil remains of early humans are limited by two major factors. First, humans evolved in the comparatively recent past and were not numerous until recent times—which means that the total number available for fossilization must always have been relatively small. Second, their way of life and the terrain they occupied were unlikely to favour the fossilization of their remains, and there are few places in the world where fossil beds of a suitable age and composition are exposed.

In scouring the world for potential fossil deposits, palaeoanthropologists have found ancient caves to be a most productive source of fossils (and not only of hominids). Whether originally used as shelters, or as dens to which predators such as leopards or hyenas may have retreated with their victims, bones left in the cave did not decay, but were fossilized as debris and rockfalls filled the caves. The first hominid fossils ever known to science were discovered at cave sites in Europe—Cannstadt in Germany (c.1700); Koestritz, Upper Saxony (1820); Kent's Cavern, Devon (1829); Engis in Belgium (1833), Gibraltar (before 1848), Neanderthal in Germany (1857). Several of the discoveries made before Darwin published his theory of evolution in 1859 received little notice at the time of discovery; some were lost. Investigations moved to the Far East at the end of the 19th century, where *Homo erectus* was recovered from riverbed deposits in Java (1891), and again in cave deposits near Peking during the 1920s.

Cave sites in South Africa have also proved to be a good source of hominid fossils. Alerted in the 1920s by quarrymen exploiting the lime-rich infills of ancient cave systems in the dolomitic hills, palaeoanthropologists have since recovered a number of important fossils from these sites.

The famed fossil sites of East Africa are predominantly volcanic in origin; the ash settling from eruptions associated with the formation of the Rift Valley having created conditions that were particularly suitable for the fossilization of bone. At Olduvai Gorge in Tanzania, where an ancient lake basin was inundated by successive eruptions of ash

and subsequently drained by geological faulting, a river has sliced through the deposits to reveal much evidence of the hominids who frequented the area from at least 2 million years ago. Volcanic eruptions similarly preserved the 3.6 million year old footprint trail at Laetoli, near Olduvai.

As at Olduvai, volcanic activity and a lakeside environment were also responsible for the preservation of hominid fossils dating from 3.1 million years ago which have been found in the Afar depression of Ethiopia, and those dating from 1.8 million years ago found in the Koobi Fora region of the Lake Turkana basin, northern Kenya.

Hominid fossil sites may be discovered by chance or by a geological survey which deliberately sets out to locate cave sites or sedimentary beds of an age and situation which renders them likely to contain hominid remains. In cave sites the fossils are nearly always embedded in a hard calcrete matrix from which they are removed by careful preparation after the rock has been removed from the cave. Open sedimentary beds often extend over many hundreds of square kilometres and specific sites worthy of excavation are usually identified by foot surveys leading to the discovery of fossil bone eroding from the side of a watercourse, or a steep slope cutting into the fossil deposits.

If fossil material is lying exposed on the surface, the site will be marked out with pegs and line in a grid of one-metre squares and the exact position of each fossil fragment will be recorded before it is removed. Each square is then excavated to a precise depth and the soil sieved as it is removed; the precise location of every fossil (or artifact, such as stone tools) is recorded as the excavations proceed. Meanwhile, geochronologists take samples from specific levels of the excavation for laboratory analysis which will give a sequence of dates for the deposit. Thus the final result of the excavation will be a collection of fossils and artifacts accompanied by precise information on their location and age. Such meticulous attention to detail enables palaeoanthropologists to assess the use of a site through time, and the developments (if any) which its users underwent during that period.

Assessing the age of hominid fossils

The age of a fossil is of paramount importance to the palaeoanthropologist in the assessment of its evolutionary significance. Until the late 1950s scientists could do no more than assess the age of their finds in *relative* terms, that is according to the kinds of other fossil animals found in the same deposit or sequence of deposits. The fossil record as a whole gives a broad picture of the order in which various animal forms have evolved and become extinct through the course of geological time. Hominid fossils are not found among the remains of dinosaurs, for instance, so must be younger; on the other hand, they must be older than any extinct animals (such as hyenas and pigs) which may be found in deposits overlaying the hominid beds.

Relative dating was always of limited use to palaeoanthropologists since human evolution occurred in a recent and extremely brief period of geological time (if the whole of Earth history was condensed into 24 hours, man would have existed for little more than one minute). The sequence of arrivals and extinctions identified in the fossil record is on a broad scale and therefore unable to give the resolution needed for meaningful assessment of hominid evolution through time. Estimates of the fossils' age in years were made from time to time, but they were rough estimates based on guesses of how fast evolution proceeds, and of the rate at which sedimentary deposits accumulate. Most underestimated the actual ages which were given when developments during the 1950s enabled geochronologists to give an *absolute* date for hominid fossil deposits.

Several methods of absolute dating have been applied to the study of fossil man:

Radiometric dating is based on the principle that a radioactive "parent" element decays into a stable "daughter" element at a constant rate. Once the rate of decay is known, the age of a sample can be calculated from the ratio of parent to daughter elements which it contains. It should be noted that it is not the fossils themselves that are dated, but the deposits in which they are found. The cave sites of South Africa and elsewhere are devoid of materials suitable for radiometric dating, but the volcanic beds of East Africa have proved especially informative in this respect because they contain the minerals necessary for the *potassium-argon* dating method, which measures the ratio of the radioactive isotope of potassium, K-40, to its decay product, the gas argon 40. Potassium-argon is used for the absolute dating of deposits between 230,000 and 26 million years old, which makes it particularly suited to the needs of palaeoanthropologists.

Fission-track dating is a method in which the age of a specimen is assessed from the tracks made by the fission of uranium atoms within them. The density and number of tracks already present in the specimen are compared with those produced when the specimen is exposed to neutron radiation in the laboratory. This comparison provides the basis for an estimate of age.

Radiocarbon dating: the radioisotope carbon-14 accumulates in living tissue, but begins to decay after death. The rate of decay is known, and so the proportion of carbon-14 remaining in a specimen is a measure of the time which has passed since the organism ceased to live. After about 50,000 years, however, so little carbon-14 remains that dating becomes impossible. This limited timespan makes the methods of little use to palaeoanthropologists, but it has proved immensely useful to archaeologists in the dating of wood and other organic materials.

Thermoluminescence: with the passage of time, certain substances accumulate energy in the form of electrons trapped at defects in the crystal lattice of their constituent minerals. When the materials are heated this energy is given off as a "puff" of light (thermoluminescence, or TL); the intensity of that light is a measure of how long the energy had been accumulating in the material, and this can be set against a known timescale to give an estimate of the material's age. The method has been particularly useful in dating archaeological finds such as pottery, where it is certain that the firing process reset the material's TL clock to zero when the pot was made, but it has also been used to date flints that were dropped in early man's campfires. These go back to 100,000 years ago.

Geomagnetic dating (also known as *palaeomagnetic dating*): makes use of the fact that the Earth's magnetic field has changed direction many times in its history. When metals are deposited in sediments they align with the prevailing magnetic field, which is then effectively "fossilized" as the sediments harden. The record of these directional changes through geological time establishes a sequence of broad time-segments which can be used for dating deposits directly, or as a check of other methods.

THE FOSSIL LINEAGE

From the earliest days of palaeoanthropological research, investigators have tended to consider the fossils in chronological order (on either the relative or the absolute timescale), from oldest to youngest, and to describe the differences between them as progressive evolutionary changes which have led, ultimately, to modern man. So long as the number of hominid fossils remained small, and the temporal distance between them large, this attractively simple scheme remained valid, inculcating a general readiness to believe that human evolution had been a straightforward single-line affair, unwaveringly directed towards its ultimate expression: *Homo sapiens sapiens* and contentious only in the matter of which human attributes were acquired first—restructuring of the jaw, the bipedal gait, or the large brain?

Straightforward and attractive, yes, but contradicting the evidence of evolution in many other mammalian lineages. The fossil remains of pigs, horses, and antelopes, for example, display a tremendous amount of variation, not only through the geological sequence, but also at any given point on it, indicating that their evolution had been more of a radiation than a single line, with extinctions and proliferations of species occurring at many points in their evolutionary histories. Indeed, the frequency of extinction and speciation found in the fossil record of most organisms whose remains have been found in large quantities suggests that such patterns are the rule. Why should humans be the exception?

The answer emerging from the tremendous advances made in palaeoanthropological research over the past twenty years is that they are not. Though the total number of fossil hominids is small (as was the total number of hominids available to be fossilized, especially when compared with the size of living pig, antelope and horse populations), it shows that there have been extinctions and speciations during the course of human evolution too.

The fossil hominids discovered so far date from over 3.5 million years ago to less than 30,000. This survey presents them in a series of broad groupings which represents both a chronological sequence and a presumed evolutionary progression, but it should be noted that the relationship of one fossil to another is not always a matter of universal agreement. A brief account of the discovery and initial description of each is given, together with some discussion of evolutionary status and affinities.

The australopithecines

The oldest known group of hominids, dating from 3.7 to 1.6 million years ago. Most authorities now accept four species—*Australopithecus afarensis*, *A. africanus*, *A. boisei* and *A. robustus*. The taxon was created in 1925 by Raymond Dart (1893–1988), professor of anatomy at the Witwatersrand University in South Africa, to accommodate a fossil skull which had been sent to him following its discovery during blasting activities at a lime quarry near Taung, in the northern Cape Province. The specimen comprised the greater part of a juvenile skull, together with an endocast of the right half of the brain (formed by the petrification of sediments which had filled the cranium after death). The face was complete and undistorted, with large rounded orbits, flattened nasal bones and a forward jutting jaw. Though the overall configuration of the specimen was essentially apelike, Dart noted several features which in his view made it more likely to represent the hominid lineage. The dental arcade was parabolic (it is more U-shaped in the apes); the erupting permanent teeth had a hominid cusp pattern; the braincast displayed certain hominid characteristics, and the foramen magnum (the hole in the base of the skull through which the spinal cord joins the brain) was set well forward beneath the skull, indicating that the head had been held erect at the top of the spine as in humans, and implying that the creature had been bipedal. In apes the foramen magnum is more to the rear of the skull and the head is slung forward, as befits their quadrupedal gait.

When Dart published his conclusions he claimed that his *Australopithecus africanus* (the southern ape of Africa) represented an early stage of human evolution. The claim was rejected, principally because it contradicted prevailing views. No evidence of early man had been found in Africa until then, and consensus opinion held that man had evolved in Asia or Europe, where the known fossils had been found. Furthermore, *A. africanus* had a small brain and a jaw of hominid configuration, which directly contradicted the faked Piltdown skull then still reinforcing the contention that a large brain and ape-like jaw would have characterised the earliest human ancestors. The leading authorities of the day dismissed *Australopithecus* as an ape, and therefore nothing to do with human evolution.

More than a decade later, in 1936, a retired Scots medical doctor and palaeontologist, Robert Broom (1866–1951), decided to look for more specimens of *Australopithecus* and re-investigate the matter of its relationship to human evolution. Broom was then 69. By the time he died in 1951 at the age of 84, he and his associates had recovered numerous australopithecine fossils from cave sites at Sterkfontein, Swartkrans and Kromdraai near Pretoria, in the Transvaal. Broom's findings confirmed Dart's assertion that the australopithecines were good candidates for the ancestry of man. Though Broom tended to create a new taxon for each of his finds, it soon emerged that two species were represented: the lightly-built *A. africanus*, which includes the Taung specimen and is often referred to as the *gracile* australopithecine; and the heavily-built *A. robustus*, the *robust* australopithecines. Mean brain size is estimated to have been 450 cc for *A. africanus*; 500 cc for *A. robustus*.

Dating the South African fossils has always been a problem, due to the confused geology of the infills and a lack of materials suitable for dating. The current consensus view suggests a date of about one million years ago, though some authorities claim that two million could be nearer the mark.

In 1959 Louis Leakey (1903–72) and his wife, Mary (1913–), recovered an almost complete skull, lacking the mandible, from deposits at Olduvai Gorge in Tanzania subsequently dated at 1.7 million years by the potassium-argon method. Though the skull showed definite affinities with the robust australopithecines from South Africa, it was thought to differ sufficiently to merit the creation of a new genus: *Zinjanthropus* (East African man), with the species name *boisei* honouring a benefactor. Subsequently the generic distinction has been dismissed and the specimen is now known as *Australopitheus boisei*.

Since 1969 teams under the direction of National Museums of Kenya Director, Richard Leakey (1944–), have recovered numerous australopithecine fossils with both gracile and robust affinities from 1.4 to 1.8 million year old deposits at East Turkana, northern Kenya. In 1985, the same team recovered a robust australopithecine skull from 2.5 million year old deposits on the west shore of Lake Turkana.

Between 1973 and 1977 joint French and American expeditions recovered large numbers of gracile australopithecine fossils from deposits dated at 2.6 to 3.3 million years ago in the Afar depression region of north-eastern Ethiopia. The fossils proved to be remarkably similar to others found at Laetoli, near Olduvai Gorge, by Mary Leakey in 1974–5 which were dated at 3.6 million years. In publishing the Afar findings, Donald Johanson, (1943–) and his co-authors concluded that the Afar and Laetoli material represented a single species which was sufficiently distinct from existing species to merit the creation of a new taxon: *Australopithecus afarensis*. Mary Leakey objected to this conclusion.

The fossil hominids discovered at Laetoli came from the same age deposit as a trail of fossilised footprints, and this circumstantial evidence invites the inference that the trail was made by those same hominids—*A. afarensis*. Evidence has been adduced for and against, but the issue remains contentious.

The affinities of the australopithecines

The South African discoveries established the australopithecines as viable candidates for the early ancestry of man, while fossils from East Africa and Ethiopia have shown that the species were widely dispersed through Africa between 3.7 and 1.6 million years ago. The distinction between the robust and gracile species is considered to represent differences in diet, the heavier teeth and facial build of the robust australopithecines reflecting the masticatory demands of an herbivorous diet while the lightly-built gracile australopithecines were adapted to a less demanding omnivorous diet. This distinction is presumed to represent a dietary specialization which led the robust australopithecines away from the ancestral australopithecine stock and ultimately to extinction, while the gracile line continued and thus represents the earliest known stage of hominid evolution.

Several schemes of australopithecine phylogeny (the evolutionary history of the group) have been proposed, their suggestions as to the manner by which the australopithecines evolved among themselves and ultimately into *Homo* differing principally on the questions of whether or not *A. afarensis* is accepted as a valid species, and whether the Afar and Laetoli fossils represent a single species or two distinct species. But despite their differences, no scheme denies that the australopithecines represent a pre-human phase of hominid evolution during which considerable advances were made in the development of the upright stance and bipedalism, and in the modification of the dentition, while expansion of the brain proceeded slowly; and all agree that the next stage of human evolution is presently understood to be represented by *Homo habilis*.

HOMO HABILIS

The taxon was created by Louis Leakey and his co-authors in a 1964 *Nature* paper describing hominid remains excavated at Olduvai Gorge in 1961 from deposits dated at 1.7 million years by the potassium-argon method. The fossils comprised a lower mandible, skull fragments, and a group of handbones. They were found in association with stone tools, and this was a persuasive factor in the authors' decision to assign the fossils to the genus *Homo*, since no tools had ever been found incontrovertibly associated with the australopithecines and it was generally considered that man by definition was a toolmaker. Hence the name, *Homo habilis*, colloquially translated as "handy man".

Further remains of *Homo habilis* were found at Olduvai in succeeding years, including teeth, limb bones and a badly crushed and distorted skull. Richard Leakey's team at East Turkana discovered the skull known as 1470 (from its museum accession number KNM ER 1470), which is informally described as *Homo habilis*, as are sundry other finds from East Turkana. Remains assigned to *Homo habilis* have also been recovered from excavations at the Swartkrans and Sterkfontein cave sites in South Africa, and at deposits in the Omo river basin in southern Ethiopia. In 1986, a new survey of the Olduvai Gorge deposits (led by Donald Johanson), recovered numerous fragments of skull, jaw and limb representing a single individual, which was subsequently assigned to *Homo habilis*.

The fossil evidence of *Homo habilis* recovered to date gives the species wide distribution through Africa, and a timespan dating from 2.1 to 1.8 million years ago. The species' mean brainsize is estimated to have been 750 cc.

The affinities of *Homo habilis*

Though the significance of the fossils was widely acknowledged, and the association of stone tools as a definition of man not questioned, *Homo habilis* did not find universal acceptance when the species was first proposed in 1964. All agreed that stone tools and an enlarged brain represented a significant step in the human direction, but some critics felt that the Olduvai material was insufficient evidence upon which to found a new species; others felt that if the material were to be assigned to a new species it should be within the genus *Australopithecus*, not *Homo*. The specimen certainly possessed a blend of gracile australopithecine and *Homo* characteristics which might be supposed to present an intermediatory stage between the two, but critics observed that in the then prevailing state of knowledge there was insufficient temporal and morphological space for a new species between *Australopithecus* and *Homo erectus* (the latter is generally accepted as the immediate antecedent of modern humans, *see below*). Louis Leakey, however, firmly believed that both *Australopithecus* and *Homo erectus* were aberrant offshoots from the hominid line which became extinct, and his promotion of *Homo habilis* as the oldest representative of the human line must be seen in the light of this belief.

The status of *Homo habilis* itself has not been much clarified in the quarter century since it was first described. Two main issues have arisen: First, the discovery of *Homo erectus* fossils from 1.6 million year deposits at East Turkana indicates that *Homo habilis* was one of at least three hominid species alive at that time (the other was *A. robustus*), which questions its status as an ancestor of *H. erectus*. Second, the *Homo habilis* fossils discovered at Olduvai in 1986 by Johanson and his team show a considerable degree of affinity with the *Australopithecus afarensis* material dating from more than 3.5 million years ago, which suggests that the ancestral form remained unchanged for a very long time, and that the *Homo* characteristics evident in later specimens of *H. habilis* must have evolved very quickly.

The evidence suggests that *Homo habilis* is still more of an idea in an evolutionary scheme than a well-defined example of anatomical fact linking one species to another. Only more evidence and rigorous analysis of early hominid variation will resolve the question of its status.

HOMO ERECTUS

The most widespread and longest-surviving of the fossil hominids. Remains have been found in north and east Africa, Europe, Indonesia and China. The fossils date from 1.6 million years ago (West

Turkana) to less than 300,000 years (China). Mean brain size ranges from 900 cc in early specimens to 1100 cc in late specimens.

The first known specimens were described by Eugene Dubois (1858–1940) in 1894 and included a calotte (the cranial vault) and a complete femur (thighbone) excavated from sedimentary deposits comprising freshwater sandstones, conglomerates and volcanic material at a bend of the Solo river in Central Java, Indonesia. The cranial capacity was relatively small (900 cc) while the femur was entirely human, and this combination led Dubois to assign the fossils to a new species: *Pithecanthropus erectus*, meaning erect ape-man, while the specimen became popularly known as Java Man. When fossils of similar configuration were found in China (Peking Man) both the Java and Peking material was assigned to the taxon *Homo* with sub-specific distinctions made for the Java (*Homo erectus javensis*) and Peking material (*Homo erectus pekinensis*). Subsequently, sub-specific distinctions were dropped and the taxon became known as *Homo erectus*.

Remains displaying *Homo erectus* characteristics have been recovered in Europe from sites in Germany (both East and West), Hungary, Greece, and France, and in 1960 a skull found at Olduvai Gorge extended the range of the species to Africa. Subsequently, further remains were found in Morocco and Algeria, in the Omo river basin of Ethiopia, and the Lake Turkana basin, northern Kenya.

In 1985 a virtually complete *Homo erectus* skeleton was found in deposits on the western side of Lake Turkana dated at 1.6 million years old. The remarkable preservation of the specimen is thought to be the result of the body having sunk quickly into lake silts after death. The skeleton is immature, its development matching that of a modern 12 year old. Estimates based on its limb size and modern growth rates suggest that the individual would have stood 1.68 m tall as an adult. Cranial capacity is as yet undetermined, but clearly relatively low. The forehead is low and recedes, as does the chin.

The affinities of *Homo erectus*

Though *Homo erectus* is well positioned in time to be both a descendent of earlier hominid forms and an ancestor of modern humans, several questions arise from its distribution and physical characteristics. Some authorities argue that the Asian and African forms are so distinct that the latter should not be assigned to *Homo erectus*. Others have suggested that the species represents a side branch of human evolution which became extinct, and its co-existence with *Homo habilis* at East Turkana indeed could be seen as reason for dismissing it from the human line.

There is also continuing debate on whether the relatively incomplete material from Europe represents the "true" *Homo erectus* or a group that should be more closely aligned to modern humans. This in turn raises the question of the *Homo erectus/Homo sapiens* transition: was this a gradual change, as some authorities see demonstrated in the Omo material? Or was there a long period of stasis followed by abrupt change, as the differences between the African and Asian fossils seem to indicate?

ARCHAIC HOMO SAPIENS

A term applied to specimens which might be said to exemplify the *Homo erectus/Homo sapiens* transition mentioned above, and also integral to the proposition that modern man evolved in Africa in the relatively recent past (*see* **F52**). The definitive specimen (Rhodesia Man) was found in the course of mining operations at Kabwe, Zambia in 1921, and comprises a complete cranium, teeth and skeletal fragments. Recent appraisal of the site and associated finds has suggested that the remains date from at least 125,000 years ago. Cranial capacity is 1280 cc, indicating an enlarged brain. Numerous other specimens assigned to the group have come from more than 30 sites spanning Africa from north to south and covering a timespan ranging from 500,000 to 30,000 years ago. Some display features characteristic of the ancestral hominids, others are entirely modern. An age of about 100,000 years has been given to comparable forms known from Qafzeh in Israel, but all other

evidence of anatomically modern man known from outside Africa is significantly younger. This is seen as indicating that modern man originated in Africa and migrated from the continent to populate the rest of the world not more than 200,000 years ago.

NEANDERTHAL MAN

The first specimen was discovered by quarrymen clearing a cave in the Neander valley, near Dusseldorf in 1857. Following its classification as a distinct species in 1864, *Homo neanderthalensis* soon became symbolic of the popular view of early man as an inferior and degenerate version of modern man. Based at first on a shortage of evidence and a determination to believe in the purity of the human line, this misconception was later reinforced by the distinguished palaeontologist Marcellin Boule (1861–1942) in a series of reports on Neanderthal remains found in cave sites at La Chapelle-aux-Saints and La Ferrassie between 1908–1912. Boule interpreted skeletal deformities as indicative of an habitual slouching gait and concluded that Neanderthal Man was every bit as degenerate as had been popularly supposed. Subsequent studies have shown that the deformities were the result of arthritis and that the Neanderthals were a sturdy and successful race, well-adapted to the environmental conditions of their time.

Discoveries of Neanderthal fossils at Engis in Belgium (1832), and Gibraltar (before 1848) predated the original find, and further remains have been found in Europe, Iraq and Israel. Bone structure and stout muscular attachments indicate that the Neanderthals were generally short and thick-set, with large feet and hands and a body form similar to that of modern cold-adapted people. Average brain size was over 1400 cc (some 10 percent larger than modern human, relative to body size) and exceeded 1700 cc in some large males. Dating of the fossil sites indicates that the Neanderthals lived from about 130,000 to 35,000 years ago. Thus they appear to have been a well-adapted and successful group of hunters and gatherers who ranged across Europe with the advance and retreat of the Ice Age.

The affinities of *Homo neanderthalensis*

Anatomical characteristics evident in both the Neanderthals and *Homo erectus* indicate that the two shared a common ancestry and possibly even a direct line of descent, but their relationship to modern man is far less clear. There are common characteristics, but much more that is different between the two forms. Moreover, it is generally felt that the proximity of the dates at which the Neanderthals disappeared and the modern humans became prevalent leave too little time for evolution to have effected the change from one to the other. After 100,000 years of unchallenged existence, the Neanderthals disappeared between 35,000 and 30,000 years ago. Only the remains of people anatomically indistinguishable from modern humans have been recovered from more recent sites.

This transition from Neanderthal to anatomically modern man poses what has become known as the "Neanderthal Problem": what happened to the Neanderthals in Europe? Only one of three explanations could apply: either the Neanderthals themselves were transformed into modern humans by a very rapid process of evolution, or they were overrun and replaced by modern humans who moved into Europe from some other point of origination, or they interbred with modern human immigrants and their distinctive characteristics were lost in the process. All three explanations have had their advocates. Argument and counter-argument have been pursued at length since the turn of the century, but genetic research (see below) indicating that modern humans originated in Africa and left the continent relatively recently strongly suggests that replacement was probably responsible for the disappearance of the Neanderthals. This need not have been a violent process. Some interbreeding also could have been involved, and the principal factor could have been better adaptation, perhaps of a behavioural or social nature. It has been suggested, for instance, that speech and enhanced social communication could have given the modern humans adaptive advantages in the changing, post-Ice Age climate of Europe which increased their reproductive rate and population growth while

Neanderthal numbers declined to the point of extinction.

HOMO SAPIENS SAPIENS

Fossil remains of anatomically modern humans are known from sites in Europe, Africa, the Near East, Asia and Australia. The first and most famous to be found was Cro-Magnon Man, unearthed in the Dordogne region of France in 1868 and dating from about 40,000 years ago. Fragmentary fossils of a wholly modern form recovered from a cave at the Klasie's river mouth in South Africa date back to more than 100,000 years ago, while those from the Mungo site in Australia are from 32,000 years ago. On present knowledge, these two finds represent the greatest time-depth and geographic dispersal of early modern humans

The dispersal of modern humans appears to have been rapid between 30,000 and 20,000 and became especially so with the domestication of animals and crop plants from about 10,000 years ago. Migration into the Americas was delayed until a landbridge across the Bering Straits opened through glacial ice about 18,000 years ago, but excavations have shown that modern humans were well-established as far south as the Chilean Andes by 12,000 years ago.

The spread and proliferation of anatomically modern humans is inextricably linked with the development of technological skills, art, and circumstantial evidence of social interaction. While the Neanderthals employed a stone tool technology little improved from earlier forms, the anatomically modern humans introduced the flint-flaking techniques by which a greater variety of tools were made. Personal adornment and careful burial of the dead were features of their lifestyle not evident among the Neanderthals, and cave paintings speak eloquently of their perceptive talents.

THE STUDY OF SOCIAL ANTHROPOLOGY

Social anthropology is concerned with the way men live as members of ordered societies. It has been described as a branch of sociology, or as the sociology of the simpler peoples. Neither description is wholly correct. A social anthropologist seeks to identify the *structure* of the society he studies and the *processes* of social interaction within it. His method is direct contact—what has been called "participant observation." Therefore he must deal with a unit small enough to be manageable with this technique. Nation-states, such as sociologists commonly work among, are too large. Most social anthropologists have done their work in what we call "small-scale" societies; that is, peoples who lacked such media of communication as writing or money, set alone mechanical means of transport, until these were brought to them from Europe. A social anthropologist may choose to work in some section of a society that possesses those techniques—in the ancient countries of the East or in Europe or America. In that case he confines himself to a microcosm such as a village or a factory. When he is writing of societies alien to his own and that of most of his readers he is obliged to describe their *culture* as well as their social relationships, since without such a description his readers would not be able to picture, or even understand, the social rules that are his main subject of study; this would be superfluous for a sociologist taking modern machine society for granted. Culture has been called the raw material out of which the anthropologist makes his analysis of social structure. It is the sum total of standardised ways of behaving, of lore and technique, of belief and symbolism, characteristic of any given society. The founders of social anthropology in Britain were B. Malinowski and A. R. Radcliffe-Brown.

The Notion of Roles

All the world, as Shakespeare said, is a stage, and this is a key metaphor for social anthropologists. Every individual does indeed play many parts, not consecutively but all together; for every social relationship carries with it the expectation of society that the parties to it will behave in approved ways. Father and children, ruler and subject, buyer and seller, husband and wife; every one of these words is the name of a *role* to be played by the person it describes. The playing of roles involves the recognition of claims and obligations as well as appropriate modes of behaviour in personal contacts. All these rules are called *norms*; when they are concerned with rights and obligations they are *jural norms*. A social norm is what people think ought to happen; unlike a statistical norm, it may or may not be what happens in the majority of cases.

Kinship and Marriage

In societies of simple technology most roles are ascribed, that is, the parts people will play in life are given them at birth by the fact of their parentage and of the group of which this makes them members. In other words, the most important principle of organisation is *kinship*. W. H. R. Rivers called this "the social recognition of biological ties." The ties in question can be called genealogical; they all derive from the recognition of common ancestry. Such ties may be fictitious, as when a child is adopted. But in the vast majority of cases the relationships that are recognised are actually biological.

No man can recognise for social purposes all the individuals with whom he has a common ancestor somewhere in the past, or even know of their existence; their number increases with every generation. In every society a selection is made, from the whole universe of genealogically related persons, of certain categories towards which an individual recognises specific obligations and on whom he can make specific claims. Such *corporate groups* of kin have a permanent existence; they recruit new members in each generation in accordance with recognised rules. Kin groups are concerned largely with the transmission of property, and for this and other purposes they recognise the common authority of a senior man; they are also religious groups, performing together rituals directed to their common ancestors.

The common patrimony of a kin group normally consists in land and livestock; in societies of more advanced technology it may be a boat, as in Hong Kong, or even, as in Japan, a family business. It may have non-material resources too, such as the right to supply chiefs or priests for the society as a whole; this may be put conversely as the right to hold political or religious office. Those who share a common patrimony have a common interest in preserving and increasing it. Wrongs done by their members to outsiders are compensated from their collective resources, and they have joint responsibility for seeking compensation if one of their own members is injured, particularly in the case of homicide.

Descent

Kin groups may be recruited according to a number of principles. A principle widely followed in small-scale societies is that of *unilineal descent*; that is, group membership is derived from one parent only, either the father (*patrilineal* or *agnatic*) or the mother (*matrilineal*). Property is *administered* by men in either system, but in the matrilineal system it is *inherited* from the mother; hence its control passes from a man to the sons of his sisters. In a unilineal system every individual recognises kin linked to him through the parent from whom he does not trace his descent; this is the principle of *complementary filiation*. The complementary kin are *matrilateral* where the descent rule is patrilineal, *patrilateral* where it is matrilineal. A unilineal descent group is called a *lineage*.

Descent can also be traced *cognatically*; that is, all descendants of a common ancestral pair may be recognised as forming one *kindred*. In such a system there is no permanent group patrimony; people inherit a share of the property of both their parents, and this is often conferred upon them when they marry, while their parents are still living. Or all the inhabitants of a village may share rights in its rice-fields or fishing ponds; a man chooses among what kin he will live, but he can have rights in one village only. In such a system there are no continuing groups defined by descent; the permanent group is territorial, consisting of the inhabitants of the village.

Marriage

Kinship status is defined by legitimate birth, and this in its turn by legal marriage. There are always rules against marriage with specified categories of kin, though these are not necessarily near kin. Some societies consider that the ideal marriage is that between the children of a brother and a sister; if such marriages are repeated through the generations they create a permanent link between two lineages. Marriage between members of the same lineage is nearly always forbidden; this is expressed in the term *lineage exogamy*. The general effect of the prohibitions is to spread widely through a society the links created by marriage, links that impose an obligation of friendship on groups that without them would be mutually hostile.

In a matrilineal system women bear children for their own lineage; it is expected that they should be fathered by a man who has married their mother according to the approval procedure, but a child's lineage membership is not affected by the marriage of its mother. But in a patrilineal society wives must be brought from outside to bear children for the group. Associated with this fact is the payment of *bridewealth*, which used to be mistakenly interpreted as the purchase of wives. This payment is what fixes the status of a woman's children; all those she bears while the bridewealth is with her lineage are reckoned as the children of the man on whose behalf it was paid, even if he is dead and she is living with another partner. In a matrilineal society the making of gifts is part of the marriage procedure, but they are of slight economic value in comparison with bridewealth. The difference is correlated with the difference in what the husband acquires by the marriage; in both cases he gains the right to his wife's domestic services and sexual fidelity, but where bridewealth is paid he can also count her children as his descendants and call on their labour when he needs it.

In societies where most roles are ascribed by the fact of birth, marriage is the most important field in which there is freedom of choice. But the choice is commonly exercised not by the couple but by their lineage seniors, who are more concerned with alliances between lineages than with the personal feelings of the pair. *Polygamy*, or the simultaneous marriage of a man to more than one woman, is permitted in lineage-based societies; indeed it is the ideal, though only a minority of men attain it. One reason why it is valued is that it enables a man who has the resources necessary for successive bridewealth payments to build up a network of alliances.

Authority Systems

Every society has some arrangements for the maintenance of order, in the sense that force may be used against those who infringe legitimate rights. In every society theft, adultery, and homicide are treated as offences. Where no individual has authority to punish these on behalf of the community, *self-help* is the approved course. Lineage membership is significant here; a man who is wronged will go with his kin to seek redress (for a theft or adultery) or vengeance (for the homicide of a kinsman). Vengeance can be bought off by the payment of compensation; but because the taking of life is a serious matter in the most turbulent of societies, there must also be a solemn reconciliation, with a sacrifice to the ancestral spirits, between the lineages of killer and victim. The recognition of an appropriate method of dealing with injuries has been described as "the rule of law" in its simplest form.

Within a lineage the senior man is expected to settle quarrels, and the ancestral spirits are believed to punish with sickness juniors who do not listen to him. When quarrels break out between members of different lineages, their elders may meet and seek a solution. Where there is no hereditary authority individuals may attain positions of leadership in virtue of their powers of mediation by persuasion.

In addition to the maintenance of rights, most societies require at some time arrangements for the organisation of collective activities. It is possible for there to be no ascribed role of organ-iser; in such a case leadership is a matter of competition. Competitive leadership in economic activities is characteristic particularly of the very small societies of New Guinea. What is needed here is not only powers of persuasion but resources to reward the participants. The very important principle, to be discussed later, that every gift ought at some time to be returned, is the basis of their position. A man who can put others in his debt can call upon their labour. It may take a long time to build up the necessary resources for acknowledged leadership, and leadership may be lost to a rival and is not necessarily passed to an heir.

Responsibility both for law and order and for collective activities may be shared on recognised principles among the whole adult male population. This is done where society is organised on the basis of *age*, a system widely found in east and west Africa. In such a system all adult men pass through a series of stages at each of which appropriate tasks are allotted to them. In its simplest form the division is made into "warriors" and "elders". This principle may be complicated in various ways, but the essence of it is that men in their prime are responsible for activities requiring physical strength, impetuosity, and courage, while their elders have the task of mediating in disputes, discussing public affairs, and performing sacrifices to the ancestors. Men in the warrior grade are the fighting force, and may also have the police functions of summoning disputants and witnesses before the elders, and seizing property from a man who has been adjudged to pay compensation and does not do so voluntarily. Sometimes specific public works are allotted to them, such as rounding up stray cattle or clearing weeds from paths or springs. It is also possible for community responsibilities to be shared in more complicated ways, as for example among the Yakö of Nigeria, where the adherents of particular religious cults are believed to call on the spirit which they worship to punish persons guilty of particular offences.

Where there are hereditary chiefs, both public works and the maintenance of law and order are the responsibility of the chief and his subordinate officials. Resources are accumulated for public purposes by the collection of tribute, and labour is obtained for public works by the recognition of the principle that persons in authority can claim the labour of those subject to them. Expectations are attached to the role of chief as to any other. Chiefs are expected to dispense justice fairly, to be generous to the poor, to reward loyalty, and to be successful in war, and they are reminded of these expectations in the course of the elaborate rituals performed at their accession. The prosperity of the whole land is commonly held to be bound up with the health of the chief and the favourable attitude towards him of supernatural beings. He may be obliged to obey all kinds of ritual restrictions to this end; for example it was believed of the ruler of Ruanda, in east Africa, that he must not bend his knee lest the country be conquered. Chiefs are either themselves responsible for the performance of ritual on behalf of the whole populace or must maintain priests to do this.

Social anthropologists have recently turned their attention to the process of competition for the commanding roles which any society offers. Some would claim to have discarded the idea of structure altogether in favour of that of process; yet the structure must be taken into account as the set of rules in accordance with which the game is played. There are societies where it is the rule that on the death of a chief his sons must fight for the succession, to test who is the strongest and has the largest following. There are others where the rule of succession may seem to be clear, and yet there can always be dispute as to who fits it best. Sometimes people pursue the struggle for power by accusing their rivals of witchcraft; sometimes by massing their followers behind them in a show of strength before which their adversaries retire; the first is the method of the Ndembu in western Zambia, the second that of the Pathans in the Swat Valley in Pakistan. Such confrontations occur at moments of crisis, but the process of building up support is going on all the time. The study of these processes is among the most interesting new developments in social anthropology.

Economic Systems

The typical methods of subsistence in societies of simple technology are food-gathering (hunting and collecting roots and berries), herding, and agriculture. The domestication of animals and plants came relatively late in man's history; without it there could have been no permanent settlement, no cities, no civilisation. But the life of those food-gatherers who still exist is not a hard one; they can get an adequate diet in a very short working week. The three modes of subsistence should not be thought of as forming a historical series; moreover, there are many varieties of each, depending on the nature of the environment and the techniques used.

We shall never know what brought about the "agricultural revolution" or why the greater number of our ancestors chose the harder, but more productive, life of cultivators. This may have been somehow made necessary by the pressure of population in certain areas. Nor shall we know when and how trade and exchange began. We can reject the argument of Adam Smith that people first provided themselves with enough to eat and then began to exchange the products of specialists for surplus food. Exchanges are made among and between peoples who suffer from periodic famines, and the objects which are most valued are not exchanged for food.

These exchanges are not conducted, however, through the medium of a currency which enables people to calculate the relative value of goods of different kinds, as does money in a commercial society. Certain goods can be exchanged only for certain others—in the highlands of New Guinea, for example, shells and the plumes of rare birds. This has led to much controversy on the question whether primitive peoples can be said to have money. Of course, if money is defined as a universal medium of exchange, they do not. But some modern anthropologists find that too strict a definition, and prefer to say that, whereas modern currencies are "general-purpose money," societies of simple technology have different kinds of "special-purpose money"—strings of shells, hoe-blades, iron bars and the like, which are used only in a limited range of transactions.

It is certainly true, however, that money of this kind cannot be made the means of very exact calculations of profit and loss. It is often assumed that where there is no such common medium of exchange people do not make any economic calculations, and dispose of their property in ways that are the reverse of business-like. The principal reason why this assumption is made is the great importance attached to the making of gifts. The essential difference between a gift and a commercial exchange is that no return is stipulated. In the commercial world goods are sold, services hired, at a price, and anyone who fails to pay has broken a contract and is liable to be punished. The obligation to return a gift is a moral one. Moreover, to compete in the giving of gifts seems at first sight the very opposite of competition in the acquisition of wealth. But in most societies people who have a surplus of wealth like to have a reputation for generosity; only in the affluent world of machine production people feel the need to have many more material possessions before they begin to think in terms of surplus.

The exchange of gifts plays a particularly large part in the societies of Melanesia, where men form partnerships for the express purpose of giving and receiving valuable objects, and earn prestige at least as much by giving as by receiving. This exchange of valuables, mostly shell ornaments, is so important that it has a name in the language of each society. The first such exchange system to be described by an anthropologist was the *kula* of the Trobriand Islands, observed by Malinowski. An important man had a partner in an island on either side of his own home; from one he received armbands and returned necklaces, from the other he received necklaces and returned armbands. These objects did not become part of a store of wealth for any man; nobody could hold one long before it was time to pass it on to his partner. To receive his gift a man sailed by canoe to his partner's home; he was there welcomed peaceably, and while he was making his formal visit the crew were bartering their goods on the shore with the local populace. Thus the *kula* partnership had the nature of a political alliance; it was a means of maintaining peaceful relations between populations which would otherwise have been hostile.

In the highland area of New Guinea identical objects are exchanged, so that the relative value of amounts given and received can be calculated. In some parts the ideal is that a return gift should be twice the original one. Naturally it is no small achievement to carry on a prolonged series of exchanges at such a rate. Very few men manage it, and those who do are the acknowledged leaders of their community. For each large gift he has made a man wears a little bamboo stick hung round his neck; thus his munificence is publicly proclaimed. A new partnership is initiated by making the minimum gift. Men make these partnerships with others not bound to them by kinship, notably with their relatives by marriage. Each partnership extends the range within which a man can count on friendly treatment. So widespread is the idea that gifts should be repaid, and services rewarded, after some delay, and at the discretion of the man making the return, that where the highland people have taken to growing coffee for sale, the large-scale planters do not pay wages but employ young men for planting who get their return by coming to them later for help in difficulties. Of course the young men would stop giving their work if they judged that the return was not adequate.

Gift-giving, then, is an investment, but not one that produces a direct material return. One anthropologist, R. F. Salisbury, has called it an investment in power. The second classic example of the uneconomic use of goods is the *potlatch* practised by the Kwakiutl and kindred tribes of the northwest coast of America. This was a public distribution of goods at which the recipients had to be given their gifts in strict order of rank. The giver earned prestige and power by the scale of his gifts, by his knowledge of the correct rank order, and by the famous deeds (*potlatches* and others) which he was able to claim as feats of himself and his ancestors. Rivals for precedence would assert their claim by vying with each other in the amounts they distributed. The Kwakiutl way of avenging an insult was what has been called the "rivalry gesture." The man who thought he had been insulted actually destroyed valuable property by throwing it on a fire, or into the sea, and his enemy had to match him in destruction or be humiliated.

Certainly this is not turning resources to material advantage. No more is the giving of a very expensive dinner-party in London or New York. But equally certainly, it is not done without calculation. In the affluent society people display their superior affluence because this demonstrates their prestige rating, just as in the *potlatch*; and they keep on good terms, through the hospitality they offer, with people from whom they may later seek a return in professional dealings, rather as in the Melanesian gift-exchanges. In fact a substantial proportion of the incomes of people in European societies who are by no means affluent goes into the making of gifts—to parents, to kin, to friends, to persons who have helped one or given one hospitality; gifts which are given as a matter of moral obligation. The difference between the uses to which resources are put in societies of simple and of complex technology is one only of degree. The proportion that is devoted to securing non-material advantages is higher in the small-scale societies, and so is the proportion of gift-giving to commercial exchange. In gift-giving there is no bargaining, but there is a clear expectation of return. The initiation of new social relationships by the making of gifts is not by any means confined to New Guinea. Bride-wealth which legitimises children is the most widespread example. Pastoral peoples in East Africa also make gifts of stock to selected friends in distant parts. The friend on his home ground is a sponsor for his partner, and he is expected to make return gifts from time to time, and may be asked for a beast if his partner is in difficulties. One could think of such an arrangement as a type of insurance.

A small number of social anthropologists have

specialised in the study of the economic systems of small-scale societies, and have asked whether the concepts devised for the analysis of monetary economies—such notions, for example, as capital and credit—can be applied to people who gain their livelihood directly from the resources of their immediate environment. Starting from the assumption that there is always some choice in the allocation of resources, they have observed how these choices are actually made in the societies where they have worked. They have asked how the value of such goods as are obtained by barter is measured; how labour is obtained, how directed and how rewarded for such enterprises as the building of a canoe or a temple, which call for the co-operation of large numbers. They have examined the use of media of exchange, asking how far any of these fulfil the functions that we associate with money.

The general conclusion of these studies is that peoples of simple technology are perfectly capable of rational calculation in the allocation of their resources, even though their calculations are rough by comparison with those of the entrepreneur in an industrial society. They know what to regard as an adequate return when they are bartering goods. They withhold goods from consumption when they are planning an enterprise; that is to say, a man who proposes to initiate such an activity as canoe-building, arranges to be able to feed his labour force.

Religion

At a time when people questioned whether "primitive" societies could be said to have religion, E. B. Tylor offered as a "minimum" definition of religion "the belief in spiritual beings." All societies of simple technology have such beliefs, and think that unseen personalised beings influence the course of nature by direct intervention, causing rain to fall if they are pleased with the actions of men and withholding it if they are angry, sending sickness as a punishment and so forth. In the great majority of such societies the most important spirits to be worshipped are those of dead ancestors. But there may also be a belief in gods responsible for particular aspects of the world, to whom offerings are made for protection or success in their special fields. Many preliterate peoples believe in a "high god" from whom all other spirits derive their power, and one school of anthropology sees this as evidence of an original state of higher religious consciousness from which man has declined; but this view is not widely held.

Rituals involving groups of people are commonly performed on occasions when changes of status are to be signalised. A child becomes a member of society not by being born, but at a naming or showing ceremony. A youth or girl becomes adult at initiation. Marriage, which makes a couple into potential parents and links their kin groups, is another such ritual.

In funerary rites the dead person is made into an ancestor, and his heir adopts his social personality and his responsibilities. The accession of a man to political office is surrounded by ritual, and chiefs frequently observe annual rites at the time of harvest, when it is the season, not the person, that is changing. These are *confirmatory* rituals, designed to keep society and the world on an even course. When something goes wrong, a drought or epidemic or an individual sickness, *piacular* rituals are performed to make peace with the spirits responsible for the disaster.

An essential aspect of many of these religions is the belief in witchcraft—that is that it is possible for humans to harm others merely by hating them. Witchcraft supplies an explanation of an undeserved misfortune. Diviners employ a multitude of techniques (which anthropologists rather inaccurately call oracles) to detect whether a disaster is a merited punishment or is due to witchcraft.

Every small-scale society has its myths—stories which tell how the word as people know it came to be. Sometimes their ritual re-enacts the myth; often the myth tells how the ritual was first performed and thereby gives a reason for its continuance. Then there are myths telling how death and evil came into the world. Some myths lend authority to the existing social order, and

particularly to the claims of ruling groups, by telling how the social structure was divinely ordained. Under the influence of the French anthropologist Lévi-Strauss, many anthropologists are beginning to see both myths and the symbolism of ritual as man's earliest attempt to order intellectually the world of his experience.

The existence of ultra-human beings on whom the affairs of men depended was universally taken for granted until a very short time ago. As long as this belief was held, the established order in any society was supported by the tenets of religion. But there are also revolutionary religions. In recent years anthropologists have been inspired by the many new religions that have arisen in developing territories to give more attention to this side of the subject. Notably in Melanesia, a succession of prophets have appeared with a message announcing the imminent coming of an ideal world from which all hardships would be banished, including the subjection of the indigenous peoples to colonial rulers. These events turned the attention of anthropologists, along with sociologists and historians, to the study of similar movements in the past, and we now have a considerable body of literature on such subjects as "the religions of the oppressed."

Closer study of traditional religions from this point of view has shown that they also often include symbolic reversals as part of their regular ritual. The high are brought low and the humble exalted. In his ritual installation a chief may be beaten and abused by his subjects, or a rite that confirms his authority may include a simulated rebellion. Women may assume for a day the garb and authority of men. There is a temporary suspension of the rules and cultural forms which differentiate the members of the ritual congregation. This may go as far as "ritual licence", in which actions that at other times are offences liable to punishment, notably sexual promiscuity, are permitted and must not be made a reason for quarrels. Or it may be simply that the participants are masked, stripped naked, or dressed identically. Such rituals affirm their common membership, or communitas, as it has been called, and where they express not merely unity and equality, but the reversal of high and low, they remind the powerful that they must not abuse their power. Rites of this kind form a phase in complex rituals. They are followed by a re-affirmation of the accepted order in its ideal form, where hierarchical relations maintain order without promoting injustice. This theory would interpret the new "subversive" religions as the response to situations in which the injustices of the powerful have gone too far for the re-assertion of communitas to be possible.

Social Change

No doubt all the societies that anthropologists have studied have been gradually changing throughout the centuries when their history was not recorded. But they experienced nothing like the rapidity of the changes that came to them when they were brought under the rule of European nations and introduced to mass production and a money economy. The effect of this has been in essence to widen the range of choice in the relationships that people can form. A man may choose to be dependent on an employer rather than on work in co-operation with his kin or village mates. He is more likely to rise in the world by going to school and getting a city job than by earning the respect of the villagers or the approval of a chief. Small-scale societies are now becoming merged in larger ones and the close ties of the isolated village are loosened. In the newly created industrial areas new specialised associations are formed to pursue professional and other interests. The social insurance that kinship provided is lacking, and it has not as yet been replaced by what the state offers in the highly industrialised societies. The minority that has whole-heartedly adopted the values of the industrialised world now produces the political rulers of new states. They are impatient to carry the majority along the same road, but there are profound conflicts of value between them and the still largely illiterate masses.

The first studies of this type of social change

were mainly interested in the effects of intrusive influence on traditional institutions in rural areas. Later, attention was turned to social relationships in the cities which have come into being, or greatly increased in size and population, as a result of the development of commerce and industry. Recent work is largely concerned with the extent to which immigrants to the cities preserve their sense of a distinctive home origin. Immigrant populations which have abandoned all their traditional customs often preserve a strong sense of a common identity which differentiates them from their neighbours, and sometimes they even create a myth of the possession of "special customs" that has no foundation in fact. This sense of a particularly close relationship between people from the same place of origin is called *ethnicity*. It has been argued that when the members of an *ethnic group* are in a privileged position they appeal to the sense of ethnicity to close the ranks against outsiders. The less fortunate might be more likely to unite on a non-ethnic basis to improve their position. Divisions based on ethnicity cut across those based on social class. This is a field in which the interests of social anthropologists and sociologists overlap. The conclusions drawn from studies in African cities could be, and no doubt will be, tested against work among immigrant populations in Europe and America.

Recent Trends in Social Anthropology

Structural Anthropology, as it has been developed in France by Lévi-Strauss, has the aim of establishing the universal characteristics of cultural, that is rule-governed, human behaviour, as opposed to the natural, instinctive behaviour of non-human species. Lévi-Strauss finds the distinguishing feature of man in communication by symbols, and holds that the way in which symbols are constructed reflects the structure of the human brain. As he uses the term social structure, it means the system of symbols by which a given society comprehends the world of its experience.

According to Lévi-Strauss communication is an exchange, and for him all exchange is communication. The prohibition of incest, which represents to him man's first move from natural to cultural life, obliges men to exchange their sisters, giving them to other men as wives. Then they exchange goods for goods or services. But for Lévi-Strauss the most important exchange is that of messages, and his central interest is in the codes in which the messages are embodied. Every code is an arbitrary set of symbols, the meaning of which depends on the way in which they are related. A code is based on a logical structure, so that social structure is the structure of a socially accepted code. It should be noted that the existence of the structure is not demonstrated independently of the code, but deduced from it, while the nature of the code is deduced from the supposed nature of the structure.

For the principles of structure Lévi-Strauss turns to the linguists, notably Roman Jakobson, according to whom all speech-sounds can be analysed into pairs of opposites; it is by recognising these opposites that children learn to speak and to distinguish meaning. Lévi-Strauss argues that the structure of the human brain leads men to classify the objects of their experience into opposites, then finding mediating terms to link the opposites. The recognition of differences is in his view the basis of classification, more important than the recognition of similarities. In totemism, a phenomenon which many anthropologists have tried to explain, awareness of differences between social groups is expressed by associating them with different animals. Exogamous descent groups, the groups which exchange sisters, are commonly called by the names of animal species. Each group has its totem animal, and they often believe that they must not eat this animal. The rules attached to these animal names form a code which can be decoded as: "We, Elephants, are different from them, Lions", not because either group is *like* elephants or lions, but because the groups differ as species differ. Any contrasting species would do; there is no intrinsic relation between Elephants and elephants just as there is none between the sounds of a word and its

meaning. Totemism, then, is an arbitrary code to express the principles on which a society is organised.

Lévi-Strauss' most massive work is devoted to the interpretation of myth. In his view the material of myth comes from the unconscious. He has made an extensive study of the myths of Amerindian peoples, and has found that stories in which the incidents are superficially dissimilar lead to the same conclusion (convey the same message), and on the way deal with oppositions (or contradictions) between rules or necessary facts of life and human wishes. The episodes of myths are the symbols of the code, and they can be combined in many different ways, but always according to an underlying, unconscious logic (structure). To explain this logic he draws comparisons with music and with mathematics. A musical note has no meaning in itself, only as an element in a melody or a chord. A musical composition plays with modifications or transformations of themes or harmonies, and just as a theme can be transposed into a different key, so a message can be conveyed in images that may refer to the objects of all the different senses; sight (light and darkness), taste (cooking—the first volume of his great book on myths is called *The Raw and the Cooked*), hearing (noise and silence) and so on. Note that all these codes are concerned with contrasts. From mathematics Lévi-Strauss takes the idea of a system of algebraic signs which can be combined in many permutations. Ultimately the theory of myth tells us that the important socially prescribed relations between persons of different status can be represented as relations between animal species, between kinds of food, between kinds of sound and silence, smells and tastes, aspects of landscape or any of these in combination.

According to Lévi-Strauss, although the deep structure of thought is unconscious, the classification of observed phenomena is conscious, and is the first activity of the human mind. Hence he rejects the view that peoples of simple technology are interested in natural phenomena only in so far as these have practical uses.

Cognitive Anthropology was first taken up as a special field in America, where its pioneers were Ward Goodenough, Charles E. Frake and Harold Conklin. It has much in common with the structuralism of Lévi-Strauss, but its practitioners are not interested in myths, and the majority make less extensive claims than he does. Some of them do believe that studies of the way in which different peoples classify the objects of their experience should lead to the discovery of universal cognitive principles, but they do not seek to reduce all categories to binary oppositions; rather they talk of *contrast sets*.

Studies in cognitive anthropology began with the examination of kinship terms by the method known as *componential analysis*. Instead of asking what relatives were grouped together under a designation found in English kinship, such as "father" or "brother", cognitive anthropologists looked for the essential *components* of any kin term, and found these to be sex, generation, and lineal or non-lineal relationship to the speaker or the person referred to by the term. This method was considered to give a truer picture of the principles according to which people group their relatives.

Cognitive anthropology has also been directed to other *domains* of experience, that is fields to which a distinguishable vocabulary is observed to apply; for example, to the classification of colours or of disease, but most of all to that of flora and fauna, or folk taxonomy, as this is called. These studies elucidate not only the principles according to which people group and distinguish the objects of their environment but also the factual knowledge they have of them.

Marxist anthropology has developed along with a general revival of interest in Marxist theory largely inspired by the new interpretation of Marxism introduced by the French writer Louis Althusser, not himself an anthropologist. The leading anthropological theorist in this field is Maurice Godelier, also in France. Like Lévi-Strauss, Marxists look for the unperceived structural laws on which all society rests, but they look in another direction. They find their answer in the *relations of production*, that is in the manner in which production is organised, and in particular the distribution of the resources which make production possible. They apply to the study of pre-capitalist societies the analysis which Marx himself made of capitalism, and seek to place the primitive and peasant societies of today, and also some vanished societies of which there are records, in their place in a line of developing social formations, each a transformation of its predecessor. Thus Marxist anthropology is in a sense an historical study, and can be contrasted with functional analysis in which societies are taken as they are when the observer sees them and treated, as Malinowski put it, as "going concerns". A functionalist study asks what keeps a society going; hence Marxists regard such studies as essentially conservative.

For Marxists a *social formation* is a combination of the forces of production and the relations of production. The forces of production consist in labour power and technical knowledge, and in the way production is organised. The relations of production are the relations between those who control the means of production—land or machines —and those who supply their labour power. Those who control the means of production are able to determine what share of the product shall go to the workers, and invariably they take more than a fair share. The state exists to practise this *extraction of surplus value*, as it is technically called. Accepted religious beliefs and other systems of ideas are not, as Lévi-Strauss and the cognitive anthropologists would have it, attempts to organise experience; they are delusions which conceal from the workers the way in which they are exploited. One social formation gives way to another when its *internal contradictions*—conflicts, incompatibilities—become too acute to be contained within the existing system. All aspects of a society are linked to the relations of production. Hence Marxist anthropologists do not admit the validity of cross-cultural comparisons between different institutions, such as kinship, economics, politics or religion, and argue that only social formations can be compared.

Thus they have given much more attention than earlier anthropologists to societies of hunters and gatherers, where nobody is dependent on others for the weapons that are the sole means of production. As soon as the means of production are appropriated by one section of society, the opposition of classes is observed. This change took place in the Neolithic period, when the invention of agriculture led to the recognition of rights in land. Even in those systems in which land is regarded as the common property of a group, the senior man or men who control its use are in a position to exploit their juniors, so that there are class divisions among kinsmen. It is also sometimes argued that where people believe that specialists in magic can influence the weather, or promote the growth of crops as the Trobriand magicians observed by Malinowski do, their knowledge is indispensable to production, and so they, too, make the workers dependent on them and can exploit them.

Marxist anthropologists make use of the ethnographic work of Malinowski and his pupils, who looked, as Malinowski had taught them, for the importance of reciprocity in exchange. Lévi-Strauss also discusses this in his theory of the exchange of women as the basis of kinship systems. But Marxists are concerned with inequalities rather than reciprocities in exchange, inequalities that those who own the means of production can impose. Thus they would not agree with Malinowski's followers, that there is any reciprocity in a state between rulers and ruled, that subjects pay tribute and rulers make their return both by maintaining order and in direct economic terms by the redistribution of wealth.

The study of ecology combines the work of anthropologists with that of human geographers and many natural scientists. It is associated with the name of the American anthropologist Julian Steward. Ecologists study the relations between society, technology and environment. They differ from the biologists who invented the term "ecology" in that they examine man's modification of his environment as well as his adaptation to it. Early ecological work concentrated on food-gathering populations who modify their environment very little, but it was soon extended to societies of pastoralists and cultivators.

Ecological studies have practical implications in various directions. They throw light on the success or failure of policies that are intended to raise standards of living, for example by persuading or compelling nomad pastoralists to become settled cultivators. A type of enforced change which has become widespread is the resettlement of populations whose homes have been flooded by the damming of rivers for hydro-electric projects; here the alteration in the environment is sudden and dramatic, quite unlike the effects of the unplanned changes of the past. It is usually accompanied by attempts to create a new environment that will make higher standards of living available, through housing schemes, new educational facilities, the introduction of new crops or farming methods, and so on. The proliferation of such schemes has been said to provide the anthropologist with a "laboratory situation" in which both policies and reactions can be compared. By combining ecological with medical studies it is possible to consider the prevalence of malnutrition or parasitic diseases in relation not only to the non-human environment but also to social groupings and norms which render certain populations, and particular categories within such populations, more vulnerable than others to these health hazards.

Another meeting-ground between anthropology and the natural sciences is in the new interest of sociologists in **ethology**, the study of the evolution of social behaviour. The classical exponents of this study have been Tinbergen in Holland and Lorenz in Austria. Close observation of the interaction between individuals and groups among non-human species has led many ethologists to conclude that animal populations may appropriately be regarded as societies. They hope to learn what tendencies among humans are genetically determined and so may not be amenable to deliberate attempts at social change. A subdivision of this study, human ethology, concentrates on minute details of behaviour with the aim of identifying gestures, facial expressions and the like that are found in all cultures, and so may be supposed to spring from affective systems common to all humanity. Yet a narrower subdivision is child ethology. Some anthropologists believe that these studies offer the key to the question What is Man? What are the characteristics that distinguish him from other animals, and how in fact did natural selection enable him to develop them?

These studies are still in their infancy, and in their present state they are vulnerable to some dangers. It is difficult, perhaps impossible, to use in the description of behaviour language which does not assume that what is described is social, the very question that the ethologists are asking. The assumption may be made unconsciously, but if it is consciously recognised it is possible to guard against it. The language used may also lead to the attribution to non-human animals of reactions that are specifically human (*anthropomorphism*). Zoologists may too readily assume that all human behaviour can be reduced to those reactions which are transmitted in our evolutionary heredity, forgetting that the processes of social conditioning are much more elaborate in man than in other animals. Anthropologists on their side may be too ready to seek the kind of interpretation of non-human behaviour that supports their *a priori* idea of the nature of man, *e.g.*, whether he is essentially aggressive or pacific, competitive or co-operative.

DEVELOPMENT ANTHROPOLOGY

Introduction

The word development became a technical term in colonial administration with the implementation in the British territories of the Colonial

Development and Welfare Act of 1940. With the passing of this measure Britain abandoned the principle that colonial territories should be self-supporting, and made available from British revenues grants for projects expected to improve the standard of living of the local populations. "Welfare" implied the expansion of social services: "development" was investment calculated to increase productivity. After the Second World War a similar policy was introduced in France, and as former colonial territories became independent the United States and the United Nations also contributed funds for their development; the United Nations proclaimed a "development decade" in 1960. The motives behind these policies were various: governments sought to extend their political influence, their trading relations and opportunities for their nationals, but a humanitarian element was also present. The development of resources had always been the aim of colonial powers, but now the emphasis was on the development of peoples.

The Problems of Development

In a sense anthropologists have been interested in problems of development from the time when, under the influence of Malinowski, British anthropologists turned from the reconstruction of the past to what he called "the anthropology of the changing African". African was taken as the type because it was the International African Institute, supported by large American grants, which supplied the bulk of the funds made available for research in anthropology in the period between the two world wars. Malinowski's pupils observed the effects that European penetration had had on African and other populations, and tended to concentrate on those which had been adverse. For a time they deplored economic development altogether, but they came to realise that the changes introduced by colonial rule were irreversible. They also had to recognise the fact that Western science and technology could and should be used for the benefit of non-Western peoples, particularly to raise standards of health and nutrition. Their attention was now focused on small-scale innovations with these aims, such as had of course always been attempted under colonial rule. The "community development" projects which had some vogue in West Africa in the period just before independence aimed at making much improvements through the efforts of the people expected to benefit from them, with some assistance from governments. Independent India adopted a community development policy which involved the division of the whole country into development areas under officials of the central government. Since the improvements sought were of a kind that any anthropologist would approve, it now became our task to explain the indifference or resistance which they so often encountered. Some also looked critically at the explanations in terms of "peasant conservatism" that were offered by people who were interested in development but not versed in anthropological theory.

The Awareness of Poverty

The interest in development which was manifested after the Second World War arose from a new awareness of the poverty of many millions of people in those newly independent countries that began to be called "under-developed", and later from the recognition that population was increasing faster than natural resources. These poorer countries were contrasted with the highly industrialised ones, which were assumed to be "developed", and it was further assumed that their problem was simply that too little capital had been invested in industry. Hence external finance was offered for development programmes which aimed at rapid industrialisation, and the next assumption made was that this would increase national productivity, as it often did, and thus would automatically raise standards of living. It proved, however, to do little to alleviate the poverty of the peasant majorities of the populations concerned.

Food Production

Attention then turned to the possibility of increasing food production and peasant incomes along with it, by introducing more efficient methods of farming. Since most anthropologists have worked among rural populations, it is here that they might be expected to have something to contribute, and that their advice has in fact sometimes been sought. An anthropologist may, for example, be appointed as a member of a UN development team; or a private company may engage one as consultant, as was done when copper was discovered on the island of Bougainville and the inhabitants were not satisfied with the compensation they were offered for the expropriation of their land. Sometimes one has been asked to comment on an elaborate multiple project such as the damming of a river for a hydro-electric scheme and the resettlement of the people whose homes would be flooded, and has been able to indicate situations that would have to be taken into account and persuade the planners to work to a slower timetable.

But more often anthropologists have come to the scene after a plan has been carried through, and have been able to see the various ways in which the results have differed from what was expected, and sometimes reasons why it has failed altogether—if, for example, a farm project does not attract or hold settlers.

The Colson–Scudder Survey

A well-known example of a study which was begun before the change that was planned and continued after it, is that made by Elizabeth Colson and the ecologist Thayer Scudder of the 56,000 Gwembe Tonga who were moved from their homes when the Kariba Dam was built on the Zambezi River. They made a detailed study of the Gwembe social organisation and adaptation to the environment in their traditional homes, and returned when the move was still a recent drama in most people's lives, and at intervals in later years. Their final study contrasted the adaptation to the move made by two village communities whose home environments had been very different and who had been moved to new sites only a few miles apart.

In their study of the resettlement process they called attention to the hardships that had been caused by requirements of technicians which were allowed to override consideration for human values. The height of the dam was raised after the preparations for resettlement had begun, so that the area to which many people had agreed to move was flooded and they had to be sent elsewhere. Those who had furthest to go had to be moved en bloc in a single day because the Public Works Department could only release the number of lorries needed for one day. New sites were not provided with water in time for the move, as had been promised.

This list of grievances illustrates both a failure to co-ordinate the activities of different technical departments of government and a lack of imaginative sympathy. But it also indicates that the agents of change must work within the limits of their technical resources. It would have been quite impracticable in this case, for example, for Public Works to transport several thousand people over 100 miles by a shuttle service, picking up families or even whole villages as and when they were ready to move. After all, the Kariba Dam had not been conceived as an operation to benefit the Gwembe Tonga. Anyone who is convinced that a project must go through can argue that the people who are affected will settle down after a temporary upset; and in a sense they do, as they come to take their new circumstances for granted.

Nevertheless, if those in authority think it important not to impose unnecessary hardships on those who are subject to their decisions, this detailed account of an exercise which is likely to be repeated in some form where dams are built, populations moved from disaster areas, refugees settled and so on, is a record to which they can look to see what mistakes they might avoid.

The Weinrich Study

A comparable study is that made by Dr. A. H. K. Weinrich (Sister Mary Aquina) of the African response to the various policies pursued by the government of Rhodesia (before independence) with the aim of improving African farming. Certain areas of land were earmarked for purchase by Africans who were required to show that they were efficient farmers. Others were irrigated and offered on lease to farmers who had to follow a closely controlled programme of work. The largest proportion of the area of land allotted to African occupation was "tribal trust land", where, after an attempt to enforce fixed standards of cultivation, the authorities fell back on the educational work of missionaries and extension officers. Dr. Weinrich investigated communities holding land in each of these three ways, and concluded that no great improvement in cultivation could be observed in any, except in the case of a minority of men and women who had followed courses of training to qualify as "master farmers". Her own conclusions were drastic: that *all* rights to agricultural land, including those of Europeans, should be conditional on efficient cultivation, and that every African cultivator should be held individually responsible for a specified area of land. Much more attention should be given to the education of peasant farmers in place of attempts at coercion, and farming communities should be given a say in the management of their own affairs. At the time when her findings were published, Zimbabwe had not achieved independence but whatever the type of government, it will have to deal with the problems that she has analysed.

These two examples are of action taken in territories where policy was dominated by European settler interests. Few such territories remain today, and it is the professed aim of the rulers of all the new states to seek the welfare of the indigenous populations. In such a context an anthropologist could be in a stronger position. If his views were asked in advance, he might be able to say that an apparently beneficial scheme would not really be so; or that it would need to overcome specific difficulties arising from existing power structures or modes of co-operation; or that the benefits would be lost if they were not accompanied by technical instruction (for instance, in the control of irrigated water supplies or the maintenance of pumps).

A difficulty in organising co-operation between anthropologists and development agents lies in the different time-scales with which they work. An anthropologist does not expect to speak with confidence about the people he studies until he has worked with them for at least a year. No doubt a development plan takes a year to complete, but once it has been adopted it is expected to be put into operation as soon as possible. Time-tables are drawn up, and even if deadlines are seldom met, there must be an attempt to meet them. In any event, decisions have to be taken at the moment when problems arise. Occasionally an anthropologist has actually been put in charge of a small-scale project and has had to face this dilemma.

Some would say, then, that the studies made after the event to explain failure or disappointment form the most valuable contribution of social anthropology; they are there as warnings or lessons for future planners, provided the planners will read them—but this is a risky assumption. Others would say that development agents should learn the elements of social anthropology as part of their training, and if they did, "village level" or "rural development" workers would certainly be more sensitive to the reception of their activities by villagers.

Intermediate Technology

Where there are the best prospects for fruitful co-operation is in the introduction of small-scale improvements such as are sometimes called "intermediate technology". Such improvements can sometimes be made by people who have made no academic study of anthropology at all, if they have enough local knowledge. It was an anthropologist working with a WHO team who pointed out that apparently simple additions to children's diet were far beyond the means of urban workers in Jakarta, but it was a doctor in India who discovered how to make existing food sources far more nutritious.

A field that anthropologists are only now beginning to enter is that of the traditional contribution of women to the farm and household economy. The exhortations and demonstrations of agronomists have commonly been directed to men, and men have been persuaded—sometimes—that methods involving harder work will bring in higher returns; it is not often noticed that the women may be doing the harder work while the men get the price of the crop. A move is now being made to train women for anthropological fieldwork among their own compatriots. They will have the general knowledge of social structure that must be the basis of any research, but they will concentrate their attention on women and on those aspects of co-operation in the household that have generally been taken for granted in the past. What are the chores that occupy a woman's day and how could they be lightened by the adoption of simple labour-saving devices? What are their ideas on the health and feeding of children and on the treatment, or recourse for aid, in sickness? How much independence of decision do they have, and in what contexts? One outcome of these studies is expected to be a fuller understanding of women's attitudes towards child-bearing and their receptiveness or resistance to the idea of family planning which is now beginning to be considered so urgently important in heavily populated countries.

The Anthropology of Development

A distinction has been drawn between "development anthropology", that is anthropology in the service of development and "the anthropology of development", or the study of interactions between all persons concerned in development, those who intend to bring benefits as well as the supposed beneficiaries. Studies of the latter type would depart from that focus on the reaction of intended beneficiaries which has been the main interest of anthropologists up to now, and would examine not only the motives of development planners but the interactions between the representatives of different interests engaged in planning. In the two African examples cited here, the benefit of the peasant cultivators was not the primary aim; the Kariba Dam was intended to provide electric power for industry, the various Rhodesian land policies, as Dr. Weinrich repeatedly emphasises, to enable an African population to subsist within limits set by the interests of a European one. Other plans are forced on governments by one crisis or another. But in addition, closer analysis would show how the competing interests of different technical agencies may influence the content of any development scheme and will certainly influence the allocation of resources within it. Governments are not the only empire-builders; divisions within them also seek to extend their power, and every expert thinks the most important benefits are those that depend on his own expertise (anthropologists are no exception). The most effective study of this kind that has been made is the work not of an anthropologist but of a political scientist, Robert Chambers, who followed in detail the history of the Mwea land settlement that was initiated in Kenya just before independence. He, however, was not solely interested in description as opposed to prescription; he travelled through Africa looking at settlement schemes, and concluded that the most important prerequisite for success was to keep government provision to the minimum and rely on self-help. But, brilliant as his analysis of the planning process is, it does not tell anyone how to plan better. It just throws light on human weakness and suggests the impossibility of making a perfect plan. A good many anthropologists would hope to offer more, even if they had to confine themselves to limited aspects of a plan.

VI. SCIENTIFIC TABLES
TABLE OF ELEMENTS

Element (Symbol)	Atomic Number	Atomic Weight	Valency	Element (Symbol)	Atomic Number	Atomic Weight	Valency
actinium (Ac)* . .	89	227		molybdenum			
aluminium (Al) .	13	26·9815	3	(Mo)	42	95·94	3, 4, 6
americium (Am)* .	95	243	3, 4, 5, 6				
antimony (Sb). . .	51	121·75	3, 5	neodymium (Nd)	60	144·24	3
argon (Ar)	18	39·944	0	neon (Ne).	10	20·17	0
arsenic (As) . . .	33	74·9216	3, 5	neptunium (Np)*	93	237	4, 5, 6
astatine (At)* . . .	85	210	1, 3, 5, 7	nickel (Ni)	28	58·71	2, 3
				niobium (Nb) . .	41	92·906	3, 5
barium (Ba)	56	137·34	2	nitrogen (N) . . .	7	14·0067	3, 5
berkelium (Bk)* .	97	247	3, 4	nobelium (No)*	102	254	
beryllium (Be). . .	4	9·0122	2				
bismuth (Bi)	83	208·980	3, 5	osmium (Os) . . .	76	190·2	2, 3, 4, 8
boron (B).	5	10·811	3	oxygen (O)	8	15·9994	2
bromine (Br). . . .	35	79·904	1, 3, 5, 7				
				palladium (Pd) .	46	106·4	2, 4, 6
cadmium (Cd) . . .	48	112·40	2	phosphorus (P) . .	15	30·9378	3, 5
calcium (Ca)	20	40·08	2	platinum (Pt) . .	78	195·09	2, 4
californium (Cf)* .	98	251		plutonium (Pu)*	94	244	3, 4, 5, 6
carbon (C)	6	12·0111	2, 4	polonium (Po)* . .	84	210	
cerium (Ce).	58	140·12	3, 4	potassium (K) . .	19	39·102	1
caesium (Cs)	55	132·905	1	praseodymium			
chlorine (Cl)	17	35·453	1, 3, 5, 7	(Pr)	59	140·907	3
chromium (Cr). . .	24	51·996	2, 3, 6	promethium			
cobalt (Co)	27	58·9332	2, 3	(Pm)*.	61	145	3
copper (Cu)	29	63·546	1, 2	protactinium			
curium (Cm)* . . .	96	247	3	(Pa)*	91	231	
				radium (Ra)* . .	88	226	2
dysprosium (Dy)	66	162·50	3	radon (Rn)* . . .	86	222	0
				rhenium (Re) . .	75	186·2	
einsteinium (Es)* .	99	254		rhodium (Rh) . .	45	102·905	3
erbium (Er)	68	167·26	3	rubidium (Rb) . .	37	85·47	1
europium (Eu). . .	63	151·96	2, 3	ruthenium (Ru) .	44	101·07	3, 4, 6, 8
				samarium (Sm) .	62	150·35	2, 3
fermium (Fm)* . .	100	253		scandium (Sc) . .	21	44·956	3
fluorine (F).	9	18·9984	1	selenium (Se) . .	34	78·96	2, 4, 6
francium (Fr)*. . .	87	223	1	silicon (Si)	14	28·086	4
				silver (Ag)	47	107·870	1
gadolinium (Gd) .	64	157·25	3	sodium (Na) . . .	11	22·9898	1
gallium (Ga)	31	69·72	2, 3	strontium (Sr) . .	38	87·62	2
germanium (Ge). .	32	72·59	4	sulphur (S)	16	32·064	2, 4, 6
gold (Au)	79	196·967	1, 3				
				tantalum (Ta) . .	73	180·947	5
hafnium (Hf) . . .	72	178·49	4	technetium (Tc)*	43	99	6, 7
helium (He)	2	4·0026	0	tellurium (Te) . .	52	127·60	2, 4, 6
holmium (Ho) . . .	67	164·930	3	terbium (Tb). . .	65	158·925	3
hydrogen (H) . . .	1	1·00797	1	thallium (Tl). . .	81	204·37	1, 3
				thorium (Th). . .	90	232·038	4
indium (In)	49	114·82	3	thulium (Tm) . .	69	168·934	3
iodine (I)	53	126·904	1, 3, 5, 7	tin (Sn)	50	118·69	2, 4
iridium (Ir).	77	192·2	3, 4	titanium (Ti). . .	22	47·90	3, 4
iron (Fe)	26	55·847	2, 3	tungsten (see wolfram)			
krypton (Kr) . . .	36	83·8	0	uranium (U) . . .	92	238·03	4, 6
lanthanum (La) . .	57	138·01	3	vanadium (V) . .	23	50·942	3, 5
lawrencium (Lr)*	103	257					
lead (Pb)	82	207·19	2, 4	wolfram (W) . . .	74	183·85	6
lithium (Li)	3	6·941	1				
lutetium (Lu) . . .	71	174·97	3	xenon (Xe)	54	131·30	0
magnesium (Mg)	12	24·305	2	ytterbium (Yb) .	70	173·04	2, 3
manganese (Mn)	25	54·9380	2, 3, 4, 6, 7	yttrium (Y) . . .	39	88·905	3
mendeleevium							
(Md)*.	101	256		zinc (Zn)	30	65·37	2
mercury (Hg) . . .	80	200·59	1, 2	zirconium (Zr). .	40	91·22	4

* In the cases of these elements, which are very rare or not found in nature, but have been artificially prepared, atomic weight in the chemical sense is meaningless; the integral mass of the most stable isotope known is given.

Note: In 1961 the isotope of carbon-12 replaced oxygen as a standard, the weight of its atom being taken as 12. This change of standard has meant a slight adjustment in atomic weights from the old chemical scale.
The new elements with an atomic number higher than that of uranium 238 (element 92) are termed Transuranics.

GAS LAWS

The Perfect or Ideal Gas Law: $pV = nRT$
where n is the number of moles in volume V at pressure p and absolute temperature T, and R is a universal constant.

Van der Waals' equation: $\left(p + \dfrac{a}{V^2}\right)(V - b) = nRT$

where a and b are constants, different for each gas.

PERIODIC TABLE

PERIODIC TABLE OF THE ELEMENTS

Key to Chart

Atomic Number → 5
Symbol → B
Atomic Weight → 10.811

GROUP / Period →	1A Alkali metals	2A Alkaline earth metals	3B	4B	5B	6B	7B	8	8	8	1B Noble metals	2B	3A	4A	5A	6A	7A	0 Inert gases
1	1 **H** 1·00797																	2 **He** 4·0026
2	3 **Li** 6·941	4 **Be** 9·0122											5 **B** 10·811	6 **C** 12·0111	7 **N** 14·0067	8 **O** 15·9994	9 **F** 18·9984	10 **Ne** 20·179
3	11 **Na** 22·9898	12 **Mg** 24·305											13 Al 26·9815	14 *Si* 28·086	15 **P** 30·9738	16 **S** 32·064	17 **Cl** 35·453	18 **Ar** 39·948
4	19 **K** 39·103	20 **Ca** 40·08	21 Sc 44·9559	22 Ti 47·90	23 V 50·942	24 Cr 51·996	25 Mn 54·938	26 Fe 55·847	27 Co 58·933	28 Ni 58·71	29 Cu 63·546	30 Zn 65·37	31 Ga 69·72	32 *Ge* 72·59	33 *As* 74·9216	34 *Se* 78·96	35 **Br** 79·904	36 **Kr** 83·80
5	37 **Rb** 85·4678	38 **Sr** 87·62	39 Y 88·9059	40 Zr 91·22	41 Nb 92·9064	42 Mo 95·94	43 Tc 99	44 Ru 101·07	45 Rh 102·905	46 Pd 106·4	47 Ag 107·870	48 Cd 112·40	49 In 114·82	50 Sn 118·69	51 *Sb* 121·75	52 *Te* 127·60	53 **I** 126·904	54 **Xe** 131·30
6	55 **Cs** 132·905	56 **Ba** 137·34	57 La* 138·91	72 Hf 178·49	73 Ta 180·947	74 W 183·85	75 Re 186·2	76 Os 190·2	77 Ir 192·2	78 Pt 195·09	79 Au 196·967	80 Hg 200·59	81 Tl 204·37	82 Pb 207·19	83 Bi 208·980	84 Po 210	85 **At** 210	86 **Rn** 222
7	87 **Fr** 223	88 **Ra** 226	89 Act 227															

Transition metals

* Lanthanides (see **L72**)

58 Ce 140·12	59 Pr 140·907	60 *Nd* 144·24	61 Pm 145	62 Sm 150·35	63 Eu 151·96	64 Gd 157·25	65 Tb 158·925	66 Dy 162·50	67 Ho 164·930	68 Er 167·26	69 Tm 168·934	70 Yb 173·04	71 Lu 174·97

† Actinides (see **L3**)

90 Th 232·038	91 *Pa* 231	92 U 238·03	93 Np 237	94 Pu 244	95 Am 243	96 Cm 247	97 Bk 247	98 Cf 251	99 Es 254	100 Fm 253	101 Md 256	102 No 254	103 Lr 257

Roman type—metals
Italic type—semiconductors
Bold type—non-metals

These designations refer to the normal materials usually at room temperature. Processes like heating or compressing can turn metals into insulators and vice versa.

Note: It may be possible by artificial methods such as bombardment by other nuclei to produce elements with atomic numbers greater than 103. However all the very heavy elements are unstable and decay spontaneously into lighter elements. Because the lifetime of such elements is short no element with an atomic number greater than Uranium (92) occurs naturally on earth.

MEASURES, UNITS AND METROLOGY

Before any quantity can be measured one must decide on the *units* used for measurement. For example, a 2 lb loaf of bread when weighed in ounces will give 32, *i.e.* 2 × 16. This is because there are 16 oz in a pound. It would be incorrect to say the weight of the loaf is 2 or 32. We say it is 2 lb or 32 oz and we can convert from one unit to another by knowing the ratio of their sizes.

If a standard pound is kept somewhere this can be used to calibrate other standard weights using accurate scales. These in turn can be used to calibrate other weights which in turn can be compared with the loaf with scales in order to weigh the bread. Nowadays, for scientific purposes, weights are compared with that of the *international prototype kilogram* (**L70**), kept at Sèvres in France. For a long time the length of an object was obtained by making a comparison, direct or indirect, with the standard metre if using the metric system or the standard yard if using the Imperial system. The standard metre was the length between two notches on a metal rod, kept at a controlled temperature, at Sèvres. Time is measured in seconds, which at one time was defined as a certain fraction of the tropical year.

Definitions of this kind are unsatisfactory for two reasons. First, the tropical year is not constant and even the most carefully kept metal rods are liable to change their dimensions over a long period of time. Secondly, it is not always convenient to do a comparison with an object kept in France. Nowadays every effort is made to define units in terms of some fundamental property of matter which is reproducible everywhere and does not require comparison with one particular object. The second is now defined using an atomic clock and can be measured to an accuracy of 1 part in 10^{12}. Variations in the rotation of the earth are far greater than this. The metre is nowadays defined in terms of the distance light travels in one second (**L82**). Although the kilogram could likewise be defined in terms of some fundamental quantity of matter, such as insisting the mass of an electron is $9.1083 × 10^{-31}$ kilogram, this quantity is only known to about 2 parts in 10^5. Comparisons with the standard kilogram can lead to an accuracy of the order 10^{-9}, so at present this definition of the kilogram stands.

The scientist nowadays mainly uses the S.I. system of units. SI is short for "Système International d'Unités" and it is a system of metric units now coming into international use through the agency of such bodies as the General Conference of the International Bureau of Weights and Measures and the International Organisation for Standardisation (ISO) in whose work Britain participates. Information about SI units is available in booklets published by the British Standards Institution, Sales Branch, 101–113 Pentonville Road, London, N.1.

Definitions of the Base Units

The system uses the seven *base quantities* listed below:

Quantity	Name of unit	Symbol of unit
Length	metre	m
Mass	kilogram	kg
Time	second	s
Electric current	ampere	A
Thermodynamic temperature	kelvin	K
Luminous intensity	candela	cd
Amount of substance	mole	mol

The seven S.I. base units are defined as follows:

The *metre* is the length travelled by light in a vacuum in 1/299 792 458 sec (**L82**).

The *kilogram* is the mass of the international prototype of the kilogram (**L70**). Scientists use the word "mass" where the layman would say "weight". Strictly speaking, weight is not a base quantity and is a measure of *force*.

The *second* is the duration of 9 192 631 770 periods of the radiation corresponding to the transition between the two hyperfine levels of the ground state of the caesium-133 atom (*see* **Clock L26**).

The *ampère* is that constant current which, if maintained in two straight parallel conductors of infinite length, of negligible circular cross-section, and placed 1 metre apart in vacuum, would produce between these conductors a force equal to $2 × 10^{-7}$ newton per metre of length.

The *Kelvin*, unit of thermodynamic temperature, is 1/273·16 of the thermodynamic temperature of the triple point of water (*see* **Absolute Temperature L3**).

The *Candela* is the luminous intensity, in the perpendicular direction, of a surface of 1/600 000 square metre of a black body at the temperature of freezing plantinum under a pressure of 101 325 newtons per square metre. Luminous intensity is a property of a *source* and is the amount of luminous flux (light) it throws out per steradian.

TABLE I

Quantity	Name of SI unit	Symbol	SI unit in terms of base units or derived units
frequency	hertz	Hz	$1\,\text{Hz} = 1\,\text{s}^{-1}$
volume	stere	st	$1\,\text{st} = 1\,\text{m}^3$
density	kilogram per cubic metre		$\text{kg}\,\text{m}^{-3}$
velocity	metre per second		$\text{m}\,\text{s}^{-1}$
force	newton	N	$1\ \text{N} = 1\,\text{kg}\,\text{m}\,\text{s}^{-2}$
pressure, stress	pascal	Pa	$1\,\text{Pa} = 1\,\text{N}\,\text{m}^{-2}$
viscosity (dynamic)	pascal second		$\text{Pa}\,\text{s}$
work, energy, quantity of heat	joule	J	$1\,\text{J} = 1\,\text{N}\,\text{m}$
power	watt	W	$1\,\text{W} = 1\,\text{J}\,\text{s}^{-1}$
quantity of electricity	coulomb	C	$1\,\text{C} = 1\,\text{A}\,\text{s}$
electric potential, EMF	volt	V	$1\,\text{V} = 1\,\text{W}\,\text{A}^{-1}$
electric field	volt per metre		$\text{V}\,\text{m}^{-1}$
electric capacitance	farad	F	$1\,\text{F} = 1\,\text{C}\,\text{V}^{-1}$
electric resistance	ohm	Ω	$1\,\Omega = 1\,\text{V}\,\text{A}^{-1}$
electric conductance	siemens	S	$1\,\text{S} = 1\,\Omega^{-1}$
magnetic flux	weber	Wb	$1\,\text{Wb} = 1\,\text{V}\,\text{s}$
magnetic flux density	tesla	T	$1\,\text{T} = 1\,\text{Wb}\,\text{m}^{-2}$
inductance	henry	H	$1\,\text{H} = 1\,\text{V}\,\text{s}\,\text{A}^{-1}$
magnetic field	ampère per metre		$\text{A}\,\text{m}^{-1}$
luminous flux	lumen	lm	$1\,\text{lm} = 1\,\text{cd}\,\text{sr}$
luminance	candela per square metre		$\text{cd}\,\text{m}^{-2}$
illuminance	lux	lx	$1\,\text{lx} = 1\,\text{lm}\,\text{m}^{-2}$
heat flux density, irradiance	watt per square metre		$\text{W}\,\text{m}^{-2}$
heat capacity	joule per kelvin		$\text{J}\,\text{K}^{-1}$
specific heat capacity	joule per kelvin per kilogram		$\text{J}\,\text{kg}^{-1}\,\text{K}^{-1}$
thermal conductivity	watt per metre per kelvin		$\text{W}\,\text{m}^{-1}\,\text{K}^{-1}$

The *mole* is the amount of substance of a system which contains as many elementary entities as there are atoms in 0·012 kilogram of carbon 12. Since this number is approximately $6·022\ 17 \times 10^{23}$ a mole of hydrogen molecules, for example, is approximately this number of hydrogen molecules.

In addition to the base units, two SI *supplementary units* are listed below:

Quantity	Name of unit	Symbol of unit
Plane angle	radian	rad
Solid angle	steradian	sr

They are defined as follows:

The *radian* is the plane angle between two radii of a circle which cut off on the circumference an arc equal in length to the radius.

The *steradian* is the solid angle which, having its vertex in the centre of a sphere, cuts off an area of the surface of the sphere equal to that of a square with sides of length equal to the radius of the sphere.

Derived Units

Most quantities that occur in nature are *derived quantities* and are measured in *derived units*. Speed is a derived quantity which can be measured in metres/sec, so that the units of speed involve the definition of two base units, *i.e.* metres and seconds. It is said that speed has the dimensions of [length]/[time], also written $[L][T]^{-1}$, since the metre is a measure of length and the second is a measure of time. In any equation in science the dimensions of both sides must always be the same and this is often a useful check of whether the equation is correct. If a mile = 1609·3 metre and an hour = 3600 sec, one mile/hr = 1609·3/3600 m s^{-1}. Conversions between any unit and any other unit which measures the same quantity can be similarly obtained.

Table I gives a list of some important derived quantities that occur in nature and in the fourth column the SI unit that is used to measure it. Some of these derived units have a name (usually that of a famous scientist) and a symbol which are given in the second and third columns. Thus for example, the SI unit of force is a kilogram metre sec^{-2}, but this unit is also given the name of a newton. A force of 5 kg m s^{-2} is 5 newton, which is sometimes written "5N".

Multiples and Fractions of Units

Within the SI system there are special prefixes for forming multiples and sub-multiples of its units.

Factor by which the unit is multiplied	Prefix	Symbol
10^{12}	tera	T
10^{9}	giga	G
10^{6}	mega	M
10^{3}	kilo	k
10^{2}	hecto	h
10	deca	da
10^{-1}	deci	d
10^{-2}	centi	c
10^{-3}	milli	m
10^{-6}	micro	μ
10^{-9}	nano	n
10^{-12}	pico	p
10^{-15}	femto	f
10^{-18}	atto	a

Examples: one thousandth of a metre is one millimetre (1 mm); one million volts is one megavolt (1 MV). These prefixes are *recommended* but other multiples and sub-multiples will be used when convenient, *e.g.*, the centimetre (cm), the cubic decimetre (dm^3).

The following is a selection of special points to note:

(i) The name litre now means 1 cubic decimetre or 10^{-3}m^3 and is a measure of volume.

(ii) Days, hours, and minutes are still used to measure time, though some scientists may prefer to use kiloseconds, etc.

(iii) The SI unit of plane angle is the radian (rad), but degrees, minutes and seconds are still used as well. $1° = \dfrac{\pi}{180}$ rad.; 1 rad = 57·295 78° = 57° 7′ 44·81″

(iv) A Celsius temperature, say 15 degrees, is written 15°C; note that 15C would mean 15 coulombs.

The Imperial System of Units

The SI system is not the only system of units in use today, although it is the one most favoured by scientists. The Imperial system is widely used in the U.K. and other English speaking countries and some Imperial weights and measures are given below:

Length.

1 nail	= 2¼ in
1 link	= 7·92 in
12 in	= 1 ft
3 ft	= 1 yd
22 yd	= 1 chain
10 chains	= 1 furlong
8 furlongs	= 1 mile = 1760 yd = 5280 ft

Area.

1210 yd²	= 1 rood
4 roods	= 1 acre = 4840 yd²
640 acres	= 1 mile²

Volume.

$$1728\ \text{in}^3 = 1\ \text{ft}^3$$
$$27\ \text{ft}^3 = 1\ \text{yd}^3$$

Capacity.

4 gills	= 1 pint
2 pints	= 1 quart
4 quarts	= 1 gallon
2 gallons	= 1 peck
4 pecks	= 1 bushel
8 bushels	= 1 quarter
36 bushels	= 1 chaldron
1 gal	= 277·274 in³

Weight (Avoirdupois).
(System used in commerce)

1 dram	= 27·343 75 grains
16 drams	= 1 oz = 437·5 grains
16 oz	= 1 lb = 7000 grains
14 lb	= 1 stone
28 lb	= 1 quarter
4 quarters	= 1 cwt = 112 lb
20 cwt	= ton = 2240 lb

Troy Weight.

1 pennyweight	= 24 grains
480 grains	= 1 ounce

The only unit of troy weight which is legal for use in trade in Britain is the ounce Troy, and weighings of precious metal are made in multiples and decimals of this unit.

The term *carat* is not a unit of weight for precious metals, but is used to denote the quality of gold plate, etc., and is a figure indicating the number of 24ths of pure gold in the alloy, *e.g.*, a 9 carat gold ring consists of nine parts of pure gold and fifteen parts of base metals.

Nautical Measures.

1 nautical mile = 6080 ft = 1853·18 m
1 knot = 1 nautical mile per hour = 1·151 mile/h

Note.—In future the international nautical mile of 1852 m will be used.

Note.—The British Pharmaceutical Code and the

British National Formulary—the official works of medicinal reference—no longer contain the apothecaries' units of measurement since medicine is now measured in metric units. Prescriptions are in 5 millilitre (*ml*) units; medicine bottles are in six sizes from 50 to 500 *ml*.

Selected Conversions between Units

Length

1 inch	= 2·54 cm
1 foot	= 30·48 cm
1 yard	= 0·9144 m
1 mile	= 1609·344 m
1 fathom	= 6 feet
1 nautical mile	= 1852 m
1 fermi	= 1 fm (femtometre)
1 Y unit	= 0·1002 pm (pico-metre)
1 angstrom	= 100 pm
1 micron	= 1 μ m
1 astronomical unit	= 149·6 Gm
1 light year	= 9460·70 Tm
1 parsec	= 30,857 Tm
	= 3·26 light years

For Angstrom, Light year, Parsec, Astronomical Unit *see* **Section L.**

Area.

1 hectare (ha)	= 10^4 m2 = 2·471 acre
1 acre	= 0·404686 ha
1 acre	= 4840 yd^2 which is approximately 70 yards square
1 mile^2	= 258·999 ha = 2·58999 km^2
1 barn	= $10\Omega^{28}$ m^2 (measure of nuclear cross-section)

Volume.

1 litre (l)	= 0.001 m^3
1 gallon UK	= 4.546 092 1
1 gallon UK is the volume of 10 lb water at 62 F
1 pint	= 0.568 l which is approximately 4/7 l
1 gallon US	= 0.8327 gallon UK

Mass and Weight

1 oz	= 0·02835 kg
1 lb	= 0·453 592 37 kg
1 cwt	= 50·80 kg
1 ton	= 2240 lb = 1016 kg = 1·016 tonne
1 tonne	= 1000 kg

Angle

		degree	minute	second	radian	revolution
1 degree	=	1	60	3600	$1·745 \times 10^{-2}$	$2·778 \times 10^{-3}$
1 minute	=	$1·667 \times 10^{-2}$	1	60	$2·909 \times 10^{-4}$	$4·630 \times 10^{-5}$
1 second	=	$2·778 \times 10^{-4}$	$1·667 \times 10^{-2}$	1	$4·848 \times 10^{-6}$	$7·716 \times 10^{-7}$
1 radian	=	57·30	3438	$2·063 \times 10^5$	1	0·1592
1 revolution	=	360	$2·16 \times 10^4$	$1·296 \times 10^6$	6·283	1

1 rt angle = 90°   1 grade = 0·01 rt angle

Time

		second	minute	hour	solar day	year
1 second	=	1	$1·667 \times 10^{-2}$	$2·778 \times 10^{-4}$	$1·157 \times 10^{-5}$	$3·169 \times 10^{-8}$
1 minute	=	60	1	$1·667 \times 10^{-2}$	$6·944 \times 10^{-4}$	$1·901 \times 10^{-6}$
1 hour	=	3600	60	1	$4·167 \times 10^{-2}$	$1·141 \times 10^{-4}$
1 solar day	=	86400	1440	24	1	$2·738 \times 10^{-3}$
1 year	=	$3·156 \times 10^7$	525,900	8766	365·24	1

Force

		newton	dyne	poundal	kg force	pound force
1 newton	=	1	10^5	7·233	0·1020	0·2248
1 dyne	=	10^{-5}	1	$7·233 \times 10^{-5}$	$1·020 \times 10^{-6}$	$2·248 \times 10^{-6}$
1 poundal	=	0·1383	13830	1	0·01410	0·03108
1 kg force	=	9·807	980700	70·93	1	2·205
1 lb force	=	4·448	$4·448 \times 10^5$	32·17	0·4536	1

Energy, Work, Heat

		joule	kW. hr	ft lb	calory	B.t.u
1 joule	=	1	$2·778 \times 10^{-7}$	0·7376	0·2389	$9·478 \times 10^{-4}$
1 kW. hr	=	$3·600 \times 10^6$	1	$2·655 \times 10^6$	$8·598 \times 10^5$	3412
1 ft lb	=	1·356	$3·766 \times 10^{-7}$	1	0·3238	$1·285 \times 10^{-3}$
1 calory	=	4·187	$1·163 \times 10^{-6}$	3·088	1	$3·968 \times 10^{-3}$
1 B.t.u.	=	1055	$2·931 \times 10^{-4}$	778·2	252	1

1 kW. hr (kilowatt hour) is 1 unit (Board of Trade unit) as measured by the electricity meter.
1 B.t.u. is a British thermal unit and is the amount of heat required to raise the temperature of 1 lb of water by 1° Fahrenheit.
1 Therm is 100 000 B.t.u. and is equivalent to the heat generated by 29·3 units of electricity.
1 calorie is the heat required to raise the temperature of 1 gm of water by 1° C. The calorie as used by weightwatchers is actually 1000 calories as defined above.
1 erg is 10^{-7} joule.
1 electron volt (eV) is $1·6 \times 10^{-19}$ joule.

Pressure

		pascal	millibar	atmosphere	torr	lb/sq in
1 pascal	= 1		0·01	$9·869 \times 10^{-6}$	$7·501 \times 10^{-3}$	$1·450 \times 10^{-4}$
1 millibar	= 100		1	$9·869 \times 10^{-4}$	0·7501	0·01450
1 atmosphere	= 101 300		1013	1	760	14·7
1 torr	= 133·3		1·333	$1·316 \times 10^{-3}$	1	0·01934
1 lb/sq in	= 6895		68·95	0·06805	51·72	1

1 pascal = 1 newton/sq metre = 10 dyne/sq cm
1 torr is the pressure due to 1 mm of mercury.
By atmosphere is meant "standard atmosphere" which is 760 mm or 29·92 inches of mercury.

Temperature

The Celsius scale is the same as the Centigrade scale. To convert from degrees Fahrenheit (°F) to degrees Celsius (°C), subtract 32 from the temperature in Fahrenheit and multiply by 5/9. To convert from Celsius to Fahrenheit multiply the temperature in Celsius by 9/5 and add 32. Applying this rule we obtain:

0° C = 32° F	20° C = 68° F
5° C = 41° F	25° C = 77° F
10° C = 50° F	30° C = 86° F
15° C = 59° F	35° C = 95° F

37° C (normal body temperature) is 98·6 ° F, −40° C = −40° F.

The absolute zero temperature (lowest possible temperature) is −273·15° C.
To convert from ° C to degrees Kelvin (° K) add 273·15 to the temperature in Celsius so that the absolute zero is 0° K.
To obtain the temperature according to the Rankine scale add 459·69 to the temperature in Fahrenheit. 0° Rankine is the absolute zero.

The c.g.s System in Electromagnetism

The centimetre gram second (c.g.s.) system of units is favoured by some scientists (notably theoretical physicists). There are in fact two sets of c.g.s. units: electrostatic units (e.s.u.) and electromagnetic units (e.m.u.). Electrostatic units are sometimes given the prefix *stat* and electromagnetic units sometimes given the prefix *ab*. Thus voltage can be measured in statvolts (e.s.u.) or abvolts (e.m.u.) as well as in volts (S.I.).

These two systems do not normally treat charge or current as base quantities as the S.I. system does but as derived quantities. In the electrostatic system the unit of electric charge, the statcoulomb is defined so that one statcoulomb of charge placed at a distance of 1 cm from another statcoulomb of electric charge in a vacuum repels it with a force of 1 dyne. In the electromagnetic system the abampere is such that if two parallel wires in a vacuum 1 cm apart both carry a current of 1 abampere the force between them is 2 dynes per cm length of wire. Also the force between two magnetic poles of unit strength one centimetre apart in a vacuum is one dyne. These two systems usually treat permittivity and permeability as dimensionless quantities, unlike the S.I. system.

In the table below $c = 2·997\ 925 \times 10^{10}$ and is the speed of light in cm s^{-1}.
The symbol "≃" means "is approximately equal to".
Thus $c \simeq 3 \times 10^{10}$ cm s^{-1}.

Quantity	S.I. Unit		e.m.u.	e.s.u.
Current	ampere	A	1 abampere = 10A	1 statampere = 1 abamp/c
				1 amp ≃ 3×10^9 statamp
Charge	coulomb	C	1 abcoulomb = 10 C	1 statcoulomb = 1 abcoulomb/c
EMF	volt	V	1 abvolt = 10^{-8} V	1 statvolt = c abvolt ≃ 300 V
Capacitance	farad	F	1 abfarad = 10^9 F	1 statfarad = 1 abfarad $\times c^{-2}$
				1 F ≃ 9×10^{11} statfarad
Permittivity	F m^{-1}			1 e.s.u./1 S.I.U. = $10^{11}/(4\pi c^2)$. Since the permittivity of a vacuum in e.s.u. is 1 this is equivalent to saying the permittivity of a vacuum in S.I. units = $10^{11}/(4\pi c^2) \simeq 1/(36\pi \times 10^9)$.
Magnetic field	A m^{-1}		1 oersted (e.m.u.) = $10^3/(4\pi)$ Am^{-1}	
Magnetic flux density	tesla	T	1 gauss (e.m.u.) = 10^{-4} tesla. 1 gauss is equivalent to a magnetic field of 1 oersted in a vacuum	
Magnetic flux	weber	Wb	1 maxwell (e.m.u.) = 10^{-8} Wb	
Inductance (self or mutual)	henry	H	1 abhenry = 10^{-9}H	
Permeability	H m^{-1}		1 e.m.u./1 S.I.U. = $4\pi \times 10^{-7}$. Since the permeability of a vacuum in e.m.u. is 1, this equivalent to saying the permeability of a vacuum in SI units = $4\pi \times 10^{-7}$.	

Units Related To Radioactivity

Radioactivity is the spontaneous disintegration of atomic nuclei to form lighter nuclei and to simultaneously emit fast moving particles. These particles are usually either a particles, electrons, neutrons, X rays or γ rays, the latter two being photons. These particles constitute radiation and can have a profound effect on the materials through which they pass, *e.g.* causing cancer in humans. Units are required to define the amount of radioactivity, exposure to radiation, absorbed dose of radiation and effective absorbed dose of radiation by human tissue.

The SI unit of radioactivity is the *bequerel* (Bq), which is the number of disintegrations per second. It is a measure of the amount of radioactive material present.

The emitted particles cause ionisation in a substance through which they pass. If this substance is a gas an electric field can be used to collect the ionised particles at electrodes before they recombine and enable the amount of ionisation produced to be measured. The number of SI units of exposure to radiation is the number of coulombs of electricity that would be produced in a kilogram of dry air by the radiation. The SI unit of exposure to radiation is the *coulomb* per kilogram.

Since the particles are fast moving they have energy. If they are absorbed by the medium through which they pass this energy is transmitted to the medium. The number of SI units of absorbed dose of radiation is the number of joules produced in a kilogram of this medium. The SI unit of absorbed dose of radiation is called the *gray* (Gy).

Some of the absorbed particles have more effect on human tissue than others. Each type of particle has a factor and the effective absorbed dose of radiation is the absorbed dose times the quality factor (g.v.) which is a weighted sum of the quality factors for each of the component particles. For a particles q.v. = 20, for neutrons q.v. = 10, for electrons, X rays and γ rays q.v. = 1. The SI unit of effective absorbed radiation dose is called the *Sievert* (Sv).

Number of Sv = Number of Gy × q.v.

Non SI units are also used to measure these quantities. The conversions are as follows:

1 Curie (Ci) = 3.7×10^{10} Bq,
1 Roentgen (R) = 2.58×10^{-4} C kg^{-1}
1 rad = 10^{-2} Gy
1 Roentgen Equivalent Man (REM) = 10^{-2} Sv

Quantity units	Name of SI unit	Symbol	SI unit in terms of base or derived
Radioactivity, disintegrations per second	becquerel	Bq	s^{-1}
Exposure to radiation	coulomb/kilogram		C kg^{-1}
Absorbed dose of radiation, joule/kilogram	gray	Gy	J kg^{-1}
Effective radiation dose absorbed by tissue	sievert	Sv	J kg^{-1}

VII. SPECIAL TOPICS

MODERN MOLECULAR BIOLOGY

Editor's Note.

This new article, written by Dr. James Howard Pringle of Leicester University, summarises the landmark steps in the history of molecular biology, from the discovery of nucleic acids in the nineteenth century to the first successful treatment of a human disease by means of recombinant DNA technology. For those not familiar with the terms used in molecular biology, a concise glossary of the main terms is given. A knowledge of the current revolution in genetics is fundamental to an understanding of modern biology.

All the structures and functions of living organisms are determined by their genes. Changes in genes lead to changes in structure and/or function, which can result directly in a variety of diseases, including inherited diseases and cancer. Genes are also important in infectious disease, because the properties of the bacteria and viruses that cause disease are determined by their genes. The new science of molecular biology, which has arisen in the last few years, allows scientists to study individual genes and the effects of changes within them. Studies of genes have given us a greater understanding of many diseases, as well as new methods for their diagnosis and treatment, and have also allowed us to start manipulating organisms ranging from viruses to animals to improve our ability to exploit them in biotechnology. Other areas in which molecular biology is important include the understanding of body development and of the evolutionary relationships between different organisms.

The Historical Background.

The technology to investigate our genes has been developed over the last 50 years to the extent that we can now manipulate human genes in vitro and use them to treat genetic disease. This achievement is a result of advances in molecular biology which allows complicated biological systems to be investigated by studying their genes. The spin off will enable mankind to understand the genetic basis of disease, to synthesise gene products commercially using biotechnology, to investigate the genetic diversity of living systems and to determine the evolutionary links between organisms. What follows is a historic account of the events leading to the establishment of modern molecular biology and the subsequent use of this technology to diagnose and eventually treat human genetic disease. The table highlights the milestones in the development of recombinant DNA technology, the "tools of the trade".

Although nucleic acids were discovered in the 19th century by Miescher, the development of modern molecular biology starts in 1944 when Avery and co-workers at the Rockefeller Institute in New York demonstrated for the first time that genetic information is held in nucleic acid not protein as previously believed. Nucleic acids, deoxyribonucleic acid (DNA) and ribonucleic acid (RNA) are information molecules allowing the genetic identity of an organism to be stored, retrieved and copied. DNA is the gene store found mainly in the chromosomes within the nucleus and is duplicated during cell division. RNA occurs mainly in the nucleolus, a structure within the nucleus as well as in the cytoplasm. Its main role in the cell is to aid the transfer of genetic information from genomic DNA to the synthesis of functional proteins, a process called gene expression.

The Work of Watson and Crick.

In 1953 Watson and Crick, working in Cambridge,

MILESTONES IN THE DEVELOPMENT OF RECOMBINANT TECHNOLOGY	
1869	Miescher isolated DNA for the first time.
1944	Avery proved that genetic information is carried by DNA rather than protein.
1953	Watson and Crick demonstrated the double-helical structure of DNA based on X-ray results of Franklin and Wilkins.
1957	Kornberg discovered DNA polymerase, the enzyme that copies strands of DNA (DNA replication).
1961	Marmur and Doty discovered that DNA single strands can reform the double-helical structure, establishing that nucleic acids can be specifically identified by renaturation reactions.
1966	Nirenberg, Ochoa, and Khorana elucidated the genetic code.
1967	Gellert discovered DNA ligase, the enzyme used to join DNA fragments together.
1970	Khorana synthesis of the first gene.
1970	Temin and Baltimore reverse transcriptase discovered RNA to DNA.
1970	Nathans and Hamilton Smith characterisation of DNA restriction nucleases, leading to their later purification and use of DNA sequence.
1972	Jackson first recombinant DNA molecules generated.
1972–1973	DNA cloning techniques were developed by the laboratories of Boyer, Cohen, Berg and their colleagues at Stanford University and the University of California at San Francisco.
1975	Southern developed gel-transfer hybridisation for the detection of specific DNA sequences.
1976	Kan, Golbus and Dozy first prenatal diagnosis using a gene specific probe.
1975–1977	Sanger and Barrell and Maxam and Gilbert developed rapid DNA-sequencing methods.
1977	Jeffries and Flavell discovery of gene splicing.
1977	Itakura somatostatin synthesised using recombinant DNA.
1978	Maniatis and colleagues construct human gene libraries.
1979	Burrell first recombinant vaccines.
1981–1982	Palmiter and Brinster produced transgenic mice.
1985	Mullis and co-workers invented the polymerase chain reaction (PCR).
1986	Start of the genome project.
1990	Gene therapy for the adenine deaminase gene.

proposed the double helical structure of DNA based on their interpretation of X-ray diffraction studies of Wilkins and Rosalind Franklin. The attraction of the proposed structure was that it accounted for the ability of the molecule to reproduce itself in such a manner that an identical replica of itself would be formed at each cell division.

DNA is composed of long chains of molecules called nucleotides which form each strand. The nucleotides are composed of a base (adenine, thymine, guanine and cytosine), a sugar (deoxyribose) and a phosphate molecule. The arrangement of bases in the DNA is not random: guanine in one strand pairs with the cytosine in the other strand and adenine always pairs with thymine. At nuclear division the two strands of DNA molecules separate and each chain is then copied using specific base pairing to generate a complementary strand. In 1957 Kornberg discovered DNA polymerase, the enzyme that copies strands of DNA during DNA replication.

The Composition of the Human Genome.

The human genome is made up of 23 pairs of chromosomes. Each chromosome contains a single molecule of DNA between 50–250 million nucleotide base pairs long. Therefore the human haploid genome is 3 thousand million base pairs long. What is the link between nucleotide and amino acid sequence and how many genes can such a large genome code for? The first successful attempt to break the genetic code was made by Nirenberg and Matthaei in 1961 while working in the National Institute of Health in the United States. Later it was shown that the genetic information in DNA molecules was stored in the form of triplet codes; a sequence of three nucleotide bases determines the identity of one amino acid; by 1966 a complete genetic code for all twenty amino acids had been established. In 1970 Khorana and his colleagues succeeded in synthesising a gene in vitro for the first time by assembling its constituent base pairs or sequence using DNA polymerase. Another important discovery by Marmur and Doty (1961) was the denaturation and renaturation properties of nucleic acids. High temperature can be used to separate DNA strands and when allowed to cool the DNA helix reforms by complementary base pair alignment. Therefore the information retained in the order of the nucleotide bases controls the specific identity of genes. Analysis of human DNA using renaturation experiments showed that a large proportion of the DNA is made up of repetitive sequences that do not code for genes. Thus although the genome is very large and could code for millions of genes the actual number is likely to be nearer thousands.

Recombinant DNA Techniques.

During the 1970s recombinant DNA techniques emerged as further analysis of nucleic acids and associated enzymes expanded. In 1970 Nathans and Hamilton Smith discovered a group of enzymes which occur in micro-organisms and they are now referred to as Class II restriction endonucleases. These enzymes were found to cleave the DNA molecule at sequence specific sites. It meant that DNA fragments of reproducible size could be produced and that DNA fragments containing a particular gene, for example, could be cut out from the rest of the DNA molecule.

The discovery of another enzyme which was subsequently proved to be of immense value in cloning genes was made by Temin and independently by Baltimore (1970). Genetic information is usually transferred from DNA to RNA by a process referred to as transcription and then the messenger RNA(mRNA) migrates into the cytoplasm where this genetic information is translated into protein. However, Temin and Baltimore and their colleagues showed that in retroviruses genetic information could flow in the reverse direction from RNA to DNA. This is referred to as RNA-directed DNA synthesis and the enzyme responsible is called reverse transcriptase. This enzyme provides a method of making a complementary copy of a gene referred to as complementary DNA(cDNA) and mRNA is converted to cDNA by the enzyme. For example, red blood cells contain only globin mRNA and therefore if this mRNA is reverse transcribed it is possible to make a globin cDNA copy. Other examples include using mRNA from the pancreas to clone the insulin gene. Globin cDNA is now used extensively to diagnose various haemoglobin abnormalities in the foetus and recombinant insulin is now used to treat insulin-dependent diabetes. Many other cDNAs have since been synthesised and sequenced and these find wide applications in the biotechnology industry.

Cloning Human Genes.

Cloning of the cDNA for genes was developed

from the experiments joining recombinant DNA fragments using the "sticky" or cohesive ends produced by some of the restriction enzymes to produce biologically functional hybrid DNA molecules. The two molecules are joined together by DNA ligase, an enzyme discovered by Gellert in 1967 which bonds the sugar phosphate molecules together. The first successful recombinant experiments were achieved in Edinburgh by Jackson in 1972. They were followed by the introduction of plasmid vectors to carry fragments of foreign DNA. Plasmids are naturally occurring small circular pieces of DNA found in the cytoplasm of bacteria. They are extrachromosomal and replicate independently of the host bacterial genomic DNA. By using a restriction endonuclease that cuts the plasmid DNA at a single site, the plasmid can be opened up and a foreign piece of DNA with the same restriction endonuclease sites inserted. Once ligated together the new recombinant plasmid can be introduced into a bacterial host and cloned. This is in fact the actual recombinant part of the process. In 1973 Boyer, Cohen and Berg constructed the first plasmid using a recombinant DNA technique, this plasmid is referred to as pSC101; p for plasmid, SC after its originator Stanley Cohen. Later, other plasmids were developed, perhaps the most important being pBR322, BR after the originators Bolivar and Rodriguez. If cDNA sequences are inserted into a plasmid designed or engineered to express the cDNA then recombinant protein can be produced and purified. To date a large variety of vectors have been constructed to clone and express genes in different organisms including bacteria, yeast, mammalian cells and plant cells. In order to clone large fragments of DNA, vectors have been designed from viruses and chromosomes. For example, yeast artificial chromosomes (YACs) have been used to clone large pieces of human DNA millions of nucleotides long.

The Work of Southern.

In 1975 Southern in Edinburgh pioneered a technique which proved essential for the subsequent developments in this field. If DNA is extracted from human tissues or cells, this DNA contains thousands of genes of the host organism. These genes must be selected or identified from the millions of fragments of DNA digested by restriction enzymes. How can a particular gene or nucleic acid sequence be identified among all this DNA? The first step is to separate the restricted fragments of DNA on an agarose gel, which results in the fragments separating under an electric current according to their size, smaller fragments migrating further than larger fragments. Among these fragments will be the ones containing the genes of interest. Southern's technique was to transfer the DNA fragments from the gel with an alkali buffer onto a nitrocellulose filter. This allows the fragments to be permanently fixed to the filter. The specific fragments can then be identified by hybridising a radiolabelled probe of nucleic acid fragments to the filter, where they will form double stranded molecules with their complementary strands. These hybrids are then displayed by autoradiography by exposing the filter to an X-ray film in the dark, radiolabelled bands on the X-ray film demonstrate the presence of DNA homologous to the probe. Modifications of this method can be used to identify mRNAs from total RNA extracted from cells or tissues using solvents. Hybridisation of probes to RNA filters is called Northern blotting and is used to assess which genes are expressed in different cells or tissues.

The methods developed for identifying genetic change using Southern blotting were the forerunner for prenatal diagnosis of genetic disease whereby certain genetic disorders in the foetus can be detected early in pregnancy. If the foetus proves to be affected with the genetic defect the parents may opt to have the pregnancy terminated. On the other hand, if the foetus proves to be unaffected the pregnancy is allowed to continue. In this way the parents can be sure that the child they will have will not be affected with an inherited genetic disorder. The usual procedure is to remove a small amount of amniotic fluid which surrounds the foetus by transabdominal amniocentesis or alternatively a small sample of the placenta called chorionic villi. Both procedures are safe in competent hands and

carry very little risk to the foetus. By looking for chromosomal changes in the foetal DNA it is possible to diagnose a variety of genetic diseases. Also, by making DNA from the foetal or placental sample it is possible to detect genetic change. This was first described in 1976 by Kan, Golbus and Dozy. They were able to show if the foetus was affected by a thalassaemia, a disorder in which the a-globin genes are deleted. This was observed by reduced hybridisation with the appropriate a-globin cDNA probe prepared from reticulocyte mRNA using reverse transcriptase.

This represented a major step forward in the field of prenatal diagnosis. It is now possible not only to identify a variety of genetic defects but also to give prenatal counselling giving parents the risk of having a genetically abnormal child and with the choices that incurs. In 1977, a year after Kan's report, there appeared two new and relatively simple methods for rapidly sequencing the bases in a DNA molecule. One of the methods was developed in the MRC Laboratory of Molecular Biology at Cambridge by Sanger and Barrell and the other at Harvard University by Maxam and Gilbert. The DNA sequencing methods evolved by these workers meant that given a piece of DNA it was now possible to analyse its nucleotide base sequence. This was to have far-reaching consequences.

Gene Structure Discoveries.

It was also at this time that recombinant DNA technology led to major discoveries concerning gene structure. It had always been assumed that genes were discrete and contiguous structures of DNA which coded for particular enzymes or peptides. However, in 1977 Jeffries and Flavell published the first report on the structure of a gene from a higher organism, i.e. the rabbit globin gene. It was found that the genes were in fact rarely contiguous stretches of DNA. It turned out that at least in higher organisms, almost all the genes are interrupted by so-called intervening sequences or introns, the remaining parts of the genes separated by introns being called exons. This led to the concept of gene splicing, subsequently it has been shown that during transcription the precursor RNA derived from introns is excised and the precursor RNA from non contiguous exons are spliced together to form functional mRNA. Thus exons and not introns specify the primary structure of the gene product. This finding was to have far reaching consequences particularly with regard for the use of DNA technology in biosynthesis.

Biosynthesis of Human Protein.

At the same time as the fine details of gene structure were beginning to be revealed the first biosynthesis of a human protein using DNA technology was reported by Itakura in 1977 and the first genetic engineering firm Genentech Incorporated in the United States was founded specifically to develop recombinant DNA methods for making medically important drugs. Itakura and his colleagues successfully obtained the bacterial expression of a cloned gene for somatostatin, a peptide hormone which among other things inhibits growth hormone and is used for the treatment of children with excessive growth. From knowing the amino acid structure of somatostatin they were able to infer the nucleotide base composition of its gene. This was relatively easy because somatostatin contains only 14 amino acids. The assembled synthetic gene, along with various regulators, was then inserted into the plasmid pBR322 and cloned in bacterium *Escherichia coli*. Since the first step many other valuable hormones and proteins have been synthesised using DNA technology. For example, Goeddel and his colleagues at Genentech published details of their successful synthesis of human insulin in 1979. Subsequently marketing approval for the genetically engineered insulin was obtained by the Eli Lilly Corporation in 1982 and is now available for the treatment of diabetes.

Factor VIII is another medically important gene essential for the treatment of haemophilia. This gene has also been cloned and expressed as a recombinant protein. The gene presented major cloning difficulties because the full length cDNA could not be synthesised so the gene had to be assembled from genomic DNA by cloning the many exon fragments into the vector in the correct order, a feat which took 8 man years.

Further Advances: The DNA Library.

As more experience was gained in cloning DNA sequences and confidence in the techniques grew the feasibility of possibly cloning DNA sequences from the entire human genome began to be entertained. The fragments produced by restriction enzymes and cloned into appropriate vectors could be stored and in this way a so-called library of individual genome could be produced. The pioneers in this regard were Maniatis and his colleagues in California, who reported the first successful construction of a gene library in 1978 and this was to prove extremely valuable for subsequent research. Currently DNA libraries are available for many organisms. In humans DNA libraries for each chromosome and cDNA libraries representing mRNA from different tissues and cells are available. The human genome project has the aim of identifying and sequencing all DNA libraries. This project became feasible with the development of automated DNA sequencing and computer analysis of the very large sequence database.

The Identification of Genetic Disorders.

Recombinant DNA technology had been so far used to detect defined genetic disorders in the foetus by demonstrating an abnormality in amniotic fluid cell DNA using gene specific probes. However, in many genetic disorders the identity of the basic biochemical defect is unknown and therefore a specific gene probe cannot be produced. Kan and Dozy in 1978 showed that an entirely different approach was feasible. The new approach depended on demonstrating that the disease producing gene is very closely linked to a particular restriction enzyme recognition site. It is known that variations in DNA sequence occur randomly throughout the entire genome and are apparently without any ill effects. These variations result in a loss of existing restriction sites or acquisition of new restriction sites. Such changes in DNA sequence mean that fragments produced by a particular restriction enzyme will be of different lengths in different people and they can be recognised by different mobilities on electrophoresis. They are referred to as restriction fragment length polymorphisms and are inherited as simple genetic traits obeying Mendelian laws of inheritance. If a disease producing gene could be shown from family studies to be closely linked to a restriction fragment length polymorphism then it would provide a method of detecting the disease without actually knowing anything about the gene itself. Kan and Dozy found that restriction enzyme DNA fragments incorporating the β globin gene were of different sizes depending on whether the chromosome carried the normal gene or the gene for sickle cell anaemia. Much work is currently directed towards finding such linkages using a variety of genetic markers. The repetitive DNA found throughout the genome has proven useful in this respect as micro-satellite DNA repeats show extensive variation and can be used to map most genetic traits.

By the late 1970s reports of successful gene cloning were becoming almost an everyday occurrence. One of particular importance was a report in early spring of 1979 by Burrell and his colleagues, then working in Edinburgh, of a successful cloning of the hepatitis B viral antigen. This was followed shortly afterwards by similar reports in the Pasteur Institute in Paris and Stanford Medical School in California. The importance of this work was that it opened up the possibility of producing an effective and safe vaccine against a relatively common disease which on occasions can lead to chronic ill health and even death. Following these reports DNA technology also began to be used to produce other viral antigens for use in developing vaccines as well as important biologically active proteins such as interferon. The production of vaccines and cellular proteins is a major commercial use for recombinant DNA technology. Though the emphasis has been so far largely on DNA in relation to medicine, at the same time significant developments were also taking place in relation to agriculture and

animal husbandry, for example the successful cloning of viral antigens of the foot and mouth disease by Clyde and his colleagues.

Advances with Cancer Genes.

The year 1982 saw the publication of the first attempts to isolate, clone and characterise human cancer genes, in this case a gene associated with bladder cancer. DNA was extracted from cancer cells, fragmented with restriction enzymes and then applied to a special line of cultured mouse fibroblasts referred to as NIH3T3. In tissue culture these cells became transformed and formed clumps rather than a flat single layer of cells when exposed to the whole tumour cell DNA from the cancer tissues. When the specific fragments of DNA capable of transforming NIH3T3 cells were identified the genes they contained were termed cancer genes or oncogenes. We all carry such genes and there is much speculation and interest at present in trying to find out how they may become activated. Another type of gene associated with cancer has been identified recently from cancers which show a hereditary form. These genes are called tumour suppressor genes as they normally prevent the development of cancer. Studies of hereditary cancers (such as retinoblastoma, Wilm's tumour and familial adenomatous polyposis) have identified the genes by linkage analysis providing a screening method to detect individuals at risk of developing these forms of cancer. Many problems still remain to be answered, in particular how oncogenes and tumour suppressor genes can lead to the development of cancer.

Transgenes.

One way of investigating an abnormal gene or cancer associated gene is to test its function by reinserting it into an organism and see what effect it has. By replacing the normal gene with the altered gene the function of the mutant protein can be tested. Palmiter and Brinster in 1982 injected linear DNA containing the gene of interest into fertilised mouse eggs which developed into mice with the foreign gene in many of their cells. Animals with the foreign gene in the germ line cells were then used to pass the foreign gene on to their progeny, creating permanently altered animals called transgenic organisms. The foreign genes are called transgenes. This approach can also be used to target and inactivate genes of interest producing "knockout" experiments which answer questions about the importance of a specific gene to normal growth and development.

Advances in DNA Technology.

By 1985 the availability of purified DNA polymerases and chemically synthesised DNA oligonucleotides has made it possible to amplify and clone specific DNA sequences rapidly without the need for living cells. The technique, called polymerase chain reaction (PCR) was invented by Mullis and co-workers in 1985 and allows the DNA from a selected gene or region of the genome to be amplified a thousand million fold provided that part of the nucleotide sequence is known. The principle of the technique is to double the amount of DNA in reaction cycles. Each cycle heat denatures the DNA producing single strands, followed by the oligonucleotide primers hybridising with the target complementary sequences as the DNA solution cools, followed by the synthesis of complementary DNA from the primer using the single strand as a template. By repeating the cycle 20–30 times and by using an enzyme which is able to withstand the high denaturation temperatures the DNA is amplified exponentially. Therefore the PCR is very sensitive so even DNA from single cells can be amplified and visualised using this method. The method has replaced many of the original DNA techniques for cloning specific genes and detecting genetic mutations, and it can be used to amplify RNA by first transcribing them into DNA with reverse transcriptase. It can be applied to the diagnosis of genetic diseases and to the detection of low levels of microbial infection. It can also be used to amplify genes from single cells taken at the first stages in the development of the embryo, improving early detection of genetic abnormalities. It has great promise in forensic medicine as a means of analysing minute traces of blood or other tissues and identifying the person from whom they came by their genetic "DNA fingerprint" using mini and micro satellite sequences.

The Future.

The most important medical application for this technology is its eventual use to treat genetic and other disease directly by gene therapy. Human genetic engineering raises unique safety, social, and ethical concerns. The first successful therapy was carried out in the National Institute of Health in the United States in 1990 on a 4-year-old girl suffering from adenosine deaminase (ADA) deficiency. Patients with ADA deficiency have a defect in DNA metabolism which affects growth of their immune system. By infecting the patients cultured lymphocytes with a retrovirus containing the normal recombinant ADA gene the defect was treated and the healthy cells were returned to the patient's blood. In future gene therapy will be used to treat cancer and acquired immune deficiency syndrome as well as a variety of genetically inherited diseases.

This brief history of the developments which have led to the establishment of modern molecular biology has only outlined some of the principal techniques and applications. The ability to manipulate our own genes will have far reaching consequences which we are only just realising. Although the human genome is genetically complicated the tools are now available to clone, sequence and investigate the function of every gene. The genetic revolution has arrived.

GLOSSARY OF TERMS

Biotechnology A set of methods for using living organisms to make a variety of products, including alcoholic drinks, bread, enzymes used in washing powders, and medical drugs.

Blotting A method of detecting specific nucleic acid sequences. A mixture of molecules is separated by size on a gel made of agarose, and a filter made of nylon or nitrocellulose is then placed on the gel, so that the nucleic acid molecules bind irreversibly to the filter. A nucleic acid of known sequence, which has been radioactively labelled, is then incubated with the filter so that the labelled nucleic acid sticks ("hybridises") with molecules of complementary sequence attached to the filter, so that the latter can be detected and the size can be measured. When DNA is attached to the filter, the procedure is called Southern blotting after its inventor; when RNA is attached to the filter, it is called Northern blotting. A similar method exists for proteins, using antibodies to detect specific proteins, which is called Western blotting.

cDNA An abbreviation for complementary DNA, which is a DNA "copy" of an mRNA molecule extracted from a cell; this is often the first step in cloning a gene, and is carried out using reverse transcriptase.

Chromosomes Chromosomes are structures found in the nuclei of plant and animal cells and consist of the cell's DNA, along with a number of specialised proteins. The functions of the chromosome are to minimise the space occupied by the DNA—in mammalian cells, up to 2 m of DNA has to be packed into a nucleus only 4–10 μm in diameter—and to distribute newly synthesised DNA to the daughter cells after cell division. Somatic cells (*i.e.* cells not specialising in reproduction) of different species contain different numbers of chromosomes, *e.g.* man (46), cat (38), mouse (40), honey bee (16),

Drosophila fruit fly (8), and potato (8). The chromosomes in each case consist of 2 sets of paired chromosomes; reproductive cells contain only 1 set of chromosomes, and are thus described as haploid. Bacteria contain a single chromosome, which is much simpler than the chromosomes of higher organisms, and is circular.

Cloning The production of genetically identical copies of a biological material, for example starting from a single cell. In recombinant DNA technology, cloning consists of joining a DNA molecule to a vector (*q.v.*) and putting the resulting recombinant molecule into a bacterium, where the vector then allows large quantities of the DNA molecule of interest to be made.

Cytoplasm The contents of a cell apart from its nucleus and other intracellular organelles (mitochondria, *etc.*).

Denaturation In general, the breakup of the higher structure of a biological polymer. For example, egg white becomes opaque on cooking because of denaturation of the protein albumin, caused by heat. In nucleic acids, denaturation refers to the breakage of the hydrogen bonds between the nucleotide bases that hold the two strands of a double-stranded DNA molecule together: heating a double-stranded molecule causes the two strands to separate (this is also called "melting"). If a solution of denatured DNA molecules is allowed to cool slowly enough for the separated strands to bump into each other, the double helix re-forms; this is called renaturation, and only occurs when the base sequences of two DNA molecules are complementary to each other (*see* Nucleic acids). Double-stranded molecules consisting of one DNA strand and one RNA strand ("heteroduplexes") can also be formed by this method.

Deoxyribonucleic acid (DNA) *See* Nucleic acid.

DNA Fingerprinting DNA fingerprinting consists of examining repetitive DNA in the genome for variations in the lengths of restriction fragments. The DNA from the genome is cut with a restriction enzyme known to cut repetitive sequences into short pieces and is then used in blotting experiments using probes that hybridise to the repetitive sequences. Every individual has his own pattern, so that fingerprinting can match blood to a particular person, and patterns are inherited from parent to child, allowing the method to identify relationships between individuals.

Exon *See* Intron.

Gene A unit of genetic information, *i.e.* the DNA sequence encoding one protein or RNA gene product.

Gene expression The process of making a product (protein or RNA) from a gene. Regardless of the gene product, the first step consists of transcribing the DNA to make an RNA copy; this can be the final product, or it can be translated to make a protein molecule.

Gene product When the information in a gene is copied, the final product is either a protein or an RNA molecule. The term gene product includes both of these. It does not usually include messenger RNA (mRNA), which is an intermediate between the DNA of the gene and the final protein.

Genetic code Sequence information in genes is used to specify amino acid sequences in proteins. There are four bases in nucleic acids and 20 amino acids in proteins, so a direct one-to-one correspondence is not possible. Groups of two bases could only store information about eight amino acids. Three bases (a "codon") can store information about 64 amino acids; this is the code that is used. Since there are only 20 amino acids in proteins, the code is quite redundant, most amino acids being represented by 2, 3 or 4 different codons, though these codons are generally related, e.g. GGA, GGT, GGC, and GGG all encode the amino acid glycine. Three of the 64 codons have the special function of telling ribosomes that the protein it is making has come to an end; these are called "stop codons".

Genetic disease A disease caused by a defect in a gene (*i.e.* a mutation) or in a chromosome. A well known example of a genetic disease caused by a point mutation is cystic fibrosis. Some types of leukaemia are associated with a chromosomal defect, where the long arms of chromosome 21 are shorter than normal (this is called the Philadelphia chromosome).

Genetic diversity The number of different *alleles* in a population. An *allele* is an individual's version of a particular gene, so the larger and more varied a population, the more different versions of a given gene it will contain, and the greater will be its genetic diversity. The importance of genetic diversity is that a larger allele pool makes a species better able to adapt to changing conditions.

Genome The total set of genetic information in an organism. Physically, the genome corresponds to the sum of all the chromosomes in a cell, *i.e.* all the DNA that the cell contains. The genome thus consists of all the genes encoding proteins and RNA molecules, as well as large amounts of non-coding or silent DNA. Much of this is made of repeated DNA sequences, which can be classified into a number of families.

Haploid Most animal cells contain two pairs of chromosomes—one from the father and one from the mother, and are called *diploid*. Reproductive cells (spermatozoa and oocytes) contain only one set of chromosomes and are called *haploid*. When a spermatozoon and an oocyte fuse, the resulting cell becomes diploid and develops into a new animal. A similar process occurs in plants.

Human genome project A large international collaborative project whose aim is to determine the nucleotide sequence of the entire human genome.

In vitro Used of an experiment that is not carried out in a living body.

In vivo Used of an experiment carried out in a living body.

Intron The nucleic acid sequence of a gene is often much longer than needed to encode the protein or RNA product of that gene. The part of the gene containing protein-encoding information is found to be split up into sometimes numerous small pieces called introns, which are separated by non-coding pieces called exons. Transcription produces an RNA copy (a pre-mRNA) containing both intron and exon sequences. Before the mRNA migrates out of the nucleus, the parts of the pre-mRNA corresponding to the exons are removed, a process called splicing.

Ligase An enzyme that is used in recombinant DNA technology for joining the ends of two DNA molecules together, usually after renaturation of sticky ends. Ligase is involved in the replication and repair of DNA.

mRNA An RNA molecule that is a copy of the base sequence of a gene, and carries that sequence from the nucleus to the cytoplasm to instruct the ribosomes to make a protein of the correct amino acid sequence.

Mutation A change in the sequence of bases in a gene. This can be a change from one base to another (point mutation), or loss or addition of one or more bases from or to a gene sequence (deletions and insertions respectively). Changes which do not alter the structure of the gene product, *e.g.* mutations in exons and mutations in codons that do not alter the amino acid encoded by those codons, are called silent mutations.

Nucleic acids Biological polymers consisting of a chain of sugars joined by phosphate groups, where each sugar carries a nucleotide base. There are two important nucleic acids, deoxyribonucleic acid (DNA), which is the chemical of which genes are made in most organisms, and ribonucleic acid (RNA), of which three types (mRNA, rRNA and tRNA) are involved in protein synthesis; some viruses carry their genes in the form of RNA. Nucleic acids store information in the sequence of chemical bases attached to the sugars; the bases in DNA are adenine (A), thymine (T), cytosine (C) and guanine (G), while those in RNA are the same except that uracil (U) replaces thymine. The two

ends of a nucleic acid molecule are different; one is called the 5′-end and the other is called the 3′-end. DNA is usually double-stranded; that is, two DNA molecules are linked together side by side and pointing in opposite directions as a double helix, joined by hydrogen bonds between the bases, which point towards the centre of the helix. Because of the chemical structures of the bases, C can only form hydrogen bonds with G and vice versa, T and U can only form bonds with A, while A forms hydrogen bonds with T in DNA and with U in RNA. Thus, if the sequence of bases in one of the two strands in a double-stranded DNA molecule is 5′-CATTG-3′, the "complementary" sequence in the other strand will be 3′-GTAAC-5′. The RNA sequence complementary to this DNA sequence will be 3′-GUAAC-5′. Two molecules that have similar sequences are said to be homologous.

Nucleolus A structure within the nucleus, consisting of copies of the cell's ribosomal RNA genes, which are sometimes needed in larger numbers than can be provided within the chromosomes, *i.e.* when cells have to synthesise large quantities of protein and thus need large numbers of ribosomes.

Nucleotides Nitrogen-containing bases attached to a sugar phosphate. See **Nucleic acids.**

Oligonucleotides Very short nucleic acid molecules. Oligonucleotides are often used as the probes in blotting studies and other recombinant DNA techniques because oligonucleotides of known sequences can easily be made in the laboratory.

Oncogenes A number of cancers have been found to be caused by viruses. The ability of a virus to cause cancer is conferred upon it by special genes, which are called oncogenes. Oncogenes are usually related to normal cellular genes involved in regulation of cell growth, and cancer due to oncogenes can be thought of as resulting from the abnormal expression of a normal gene.

Peptides Very short proteins.

Plasmid A small circular DNA molecule containing a replication origin (it is thus a replicon) commonly found in bacteria. Plasmids are widely used in recombinant DNA technology as vectors for cloning DNA fragments because of their small size. In nature, plasmids are responsible for a considerable proportion of bacterial antibiotic resistance—moving from cell to cell, they carry antibiotic resistance genes with them.

Polymerase chain reaction (PCR) A method for synthesizing relatively large amounts of a nucleic acid of known sequence, using polymerase enzymes and oligonucleotides.

Proteins Biological polymers made of amino acids, of which 20 are used in living organisms. The properties of a particular protein depend on the sequence of amino acids of which it is made, and this sequence is determined by the sequence of the nucleotide bases in the gene corresponding to the protein. Proteins can be structural (*e.g.* collagen) or they can be enzymes, which catalyse chemical reactions. Some proteins, such as haemoglobin, have the special function of transporting other chemicals around the body.

Recombinant DNA technology A more precise term for genetic engineering.

Repetitive sequences Much of the DNA in the genome of a higher organism does not contain genes, but consists of apparently functionless sequences, some of which are repeated head-to-tail. Genomes contain a number of families of related repeats, and up to 20% of the genome can consist of sequences present at up to 1,000,000 repeated copies.

Replicon A DNA molecule that is able to replicate in a cell. In order to do this, the molecule needs to carry a special sequence called a replication origin, which is the point at which synthesis of new copies of the DNA begins.

Restriction endonucleases Enzymes found in bacteria that cut DNA molecules; their function is to protect bacteria against infection from viruses. Class II restriction enzymes, the group which is important in recombinant DNA techniques, bind to a short (usually 4 or 6 bases) sequence and cut the DNA in or close to the recognition sequence.

Bacteria protect themselves against their own restriction enzymes by chemically modifying their DNA. Restriction enzymes allow DNA molecules whose sequences are known to be cut at predetermined positions. Many enzymes cut the two strands of a DNA molecule in slightly different places, to leave single-stranded overhangs ("sticky ends"); these can be renatured to join pieces of DNA together in a specific way.

Retrovirus A virus which stores its genetic information in the form of RNA instead of DNA; several are tumour-inducing viruses, and the viruses associated with AIDS are retroviruses. Replication of these viruses starts with making a DNA copy of the RNA genome, using the enzyme reverse transcriptase.

Reverse transcriptase A viral enzyme found in some viruses that use RNA instead of DNA for their genomes. This enzyme is an RNA-dependent DNA polymerase, and makes a DNA copy of the viral RNA, which is the first step in the replication of such viruses.

Ribonucleic acid (RNA) *See* Nucleic acids.

Splicing *See* Intron.

Transcription The process of copying a DNA molecule to make a complementary RNA copy of a gene. Transcription occurs in the nucleus of higher organism cells, and is carried out by enzymes called DNA-dependent RNA polymerases.

Transgene A foreign gene inserted into a higher organism (animal or plant). This is done by inserting the gene into the organism at an early stage of embryonic development; since all the cells of the adult come from these early embryo cells, all adult cells will contain the inserted gene. Such organisms are called transgenic animals or plants.

Translation The process of converting a gene sequence in the form of mRNA into a protein sequence. Translation is carried out by ribosomes.

Vector In recombinant DNA technology, a replicon that is used for cloning DNA sequences. Vectors are usually small and simple replicons, *i.e.* plasmids and bacteriophages.

NEW LIGHT ON VENUS

Introduction.

Venus is one of the most studied objects in the Solar System. Over the past few centuries astronomers have peered intently at the planet, striving to wrest what information they could from gazing at the Venusian cloud tops. Attempts to study Venus have been made considerably easier through modern technology, and over the past couple of decades or so over thirty spacecraft have been despatched to the planet.

The long-held fascination astronomers and scientists have with Venus is that in many respects it is a twin of our own Earth. Both planets lie close to each other in the Solar System and both have similar masses and compositions. However, space technology has shown us that there are major differences. The surface atmospheric pressure on Venus is a staggering 90 times that of the Earth while a runaway greenhouse effect has produced a mean Venusian surface temperature in excess of 500 °C. The Venusian atmosphere is comprised mainly of carbon dioxide, in similar amounts to that

on the Earth. Terrestrial carbon dioxide, however, is mostly contained inside reefs and limestone rocks.

Yet although inhospitable by terrestrial standards, Venus is fascinating geologically. Its surface plays host to many different types of feature including lofty mountain ranges, sweeping highland areas, impact craters, valleys and many spectacular volcanoes. In fact, volcanism has played a significant role in modelling the Venusian surface we see today.

The Magellan Probe.

Of all the space probes sent to explore Venus, by far the most successful is the American Magellan. Launched from the cargo bay of the Space Shuttle Atlantis in May 1989, Magellan was despatched towards Venus, arriving at the planet in August 1990. The probe was placed into a 3·3-hour elliptical orbit around the planet and, using the technique of radar-imaging, mapped 98 per cent of the Venusian surface over a period of 24 months.

The Volcanoes of Venus.

The first batch of data from Magellan showed clearly that Venus displayed evidence of volcanic activity (volcanism) practically everywhere on its surface. A whole range of features, ranging from huge shield volcanoes comparable in size to the largest terrestrial volcanoes down to small volcanic domes, were imaged by Magellan. In one region, that of the southern flanks of a highland area known as Tethus Regio, scores of domes pepper the surface. Volcanic domes appear everywhere on the Venusian surface and it is thought that Venus may play host to hundreds of thousands of these features. Many are seen to occur in swarms such as those near Tethus Regio.

Mylitta Fluctus is typical of the many large areas of lava flows recorded by Magellan. Measuring some 800 km by 400 km, the lava flows of Mylitta Fluctus flowed northwards from a 700-metre high volcano. Running down the volcano's flanks, the flows descended around a kilometre to the level plains where they widened out to form pools.

The lava flows imaged by Magellan appear to have been very fluid, similar to those thought to have formed the Venusian features known as "canali". These channels seem to have been formed from lava which was so liquefied that it was able to create riverlike formations similar in many ways to terrestrial rivers.

The Plains.

Most of the Venusian surface consists of flat rolling plains which, according to examination of data from earlier American Pioneer Venus missions, may have been covered by a planet-wide ocean some 25 metres deep. Although this water disappeared some 3 billion years or so ago, scientists cannot rule out the possibility that primitive life forms may have evolved in the Venusian oceans. Examination of Venus today reveals an almost total absence of water. The Venusian atmosphere contains around 1/100,000 the amount of water vapour present in that of the Earth while the high temperatures on Venus have ensured a completely dry and arid surface. The action of sunlight broke up the water into its constituent hydrogen and oxygen atoms, following which the hydrogen atoms slowly escaped into space.

The Highland Regions.

Rising up from the Venusian plains are a number of highland regions, including Aphrodite Terra and Ishtar Terra. Aphrodite Terra is comparable in size to Africa and straddles the Venusian equator. It contains a number of complex troughs including Diana Chasma, by far the deepest fracture on Venus with a depth of around 2 km and a width of some 300 km. Lying further to the north, Ishtar Terra is roughly the size of Australia and is one of the major Venusian highland blocks. It is comparable in elevation to the Tibetan Plateau on Earth but somewhat larger in area.

The Mountain Ranges.

As well as volcanoes, the Venusian surface contains a number of impressive mountain ranges, most notable of which is Maxwell Montes, named in honour of the Scottish physicist James Clerk Maxwell. Towering over 11 km above the Venusian surface, Maxwell Montes lies on the Ishtar Terra highland region and resembles terrestrial mountain ranges in that it appears to have been formed through compression of the upper layers of the Venusian crust.

Maxwell Montes contains faults and folds characteristic of terrestrial mountain ranges and, as with other Venusian features, these have suffered no erosion due to the absence of winds and lack of water on Venus. This lack of erosion carries the benefit of the preservation of geological features.

The Tesserae.

The western flanks of Maxwell Montes dip steeply to the surface while the eastern slopes are less steep, descending gradually towards Fortuna Tessera, a highland terrain adjoining the Maxwell range. As with mountain ranges, tesserae are characterized by folds and faults. Many of these rugged regions have been imaged by visiting spacecraft, including the Soviet Veneras 15 and 16 probes.

Some tessera regions are quite small, while others extend for thousands of kilometres across the Venusian surface. The main region of this type is Alpha Regio, a complex plateau measuring some 1,300 km across situated some 30° to the south of the Venusian equator. Standing a couple of kilometres above the surrounding plains and the first Venusian feature to be discovered by Earth-based radar, Alpha Regio is the result of prolonged periods of surface extension and compression and contains a mixture of troughs, fault valleys and ridges.

Another of the notable Venusian highland regions is Beta Regio, discovered by the Pioneer Venus orbiter probe. Beta Regio lies 30° or so north of the Venusian equator and plays host to Rhea Mons and Theia Mons, two possibly-active shield volcanoes which rise to around 4 km above the surrounding terrain. As was the case with Alpha Regio, Beta Regio was discovered back in the 1960s through Earth-based radar observations of Venus.

The highland regions of Venus are subject to a process known as gravitational relaxation, whereby Venusian gravity pulls on the rock, causing it to spread out over millions of years. This effect is made possible by the very high Venusian surface temperatures which exceed 500 °C. Gravitational relaxation is believed to be the main cause of the cracking and fracturing observed on the tesserae, produced as the surface is slowly deformed.

The Craters of Venus.

Impact craters are common features of the Venusian surface and there are many remarkable examples. A spectacular double-ring impact basin is located in eastern Maxwell Montes. Known as Cleopatra, this 100 km diameter, 2·5 km deep feature is pristine and well preserved. This could be indicative of its recent formation, or may be simply due to the lack of erosional processes on the Venusian surface.

Another impressive crater is Franklin. Measuring over 70 km in diameter Franklin is accompanied by extensive flows of material which were released following the impact that formed the crater. This matter could be either volcanic in origin, being released from the Venusian interior at the time of impact, or be formed from the melted rock.

The Cause of Impact Craters.

Venusian impact craters are caused by the bombardment of its surface by asteroids and cometary objects, and is a phenomenon found on the surfaces of all the terrestrial planets and many planetary satellites. However, the craters that populate the Venusian surface are found to range in diameter from several kilometres upwards, while on other planets, including the Earth, many smaller examples are found. The lack of small craters on Venus is due to the thick Venusian atmosphere which effectively protects the surface from impacts of small objects. Only the largest impacting bodies are able to penetrate the atmosphere, many smaller objects being broken up or destroyed before they reach the surface.

The craters of Venus are distributed across its surface fairly uniformly yet, based on observation of other planets, we would expect a more varied distribution. For example, geologically young areas, such as the lunar maria, contain few craters, while the much older highland areas contain a much denser crater population. This is due simply to the fact that younger areas have been exposed to meteorite impacts for a shorter period of time, most of the meteoritic bombardment of planetary surfaces having taken place during the early history of the Solar System.

Just why the craters of Venus should be so uniformly distributed has yet to be determined. One theory is that the Venusian surface was somehow 'cleared' some 500 million years ago, perhaps by a period of intense volcanic activity. The meteorite activity that has occurred from that time has taken place on a surface that has since undergone little further geological change. The pristine condition of the craters we see now also backs up their theory. Only around 2 per cent of the Venusian craters imaged by Magellan have been subject to covering by volcanic lava. Yet this could be regarded as being somewhat surprising in view of the fact that the Venusian surface contains so many volcanoes and fractures.

Another idea is that Venus undergoes regular periods of geological activity. Every 500 million years or so internal activity resulted in the surface being coated with lava, resulting in the obscuration of many of the craters. An extension of this idea suggests that these periods of activity ceased around 500 million years ago due to the surface of Venus having cooled down.

As we have seen on the lunar surface, the older highland regions are characterized by heavy cratering. The younger maria, produced as material welled up from the lunar interior to flood the low-lying areas, contain fewer craters. The observed amount of cratering therefore clearly determines the difference between older and younger regions.

However, the even distribution of craters on Venus has the effect of disguising any differences between ancient and relatively-recently formed regions of the Venusian surface. Just which theory explains the distribution of the Venusian craters may only be determined after the detailed mapping programme which will take place over the next few years and which will draw on the data obtained by Magellan.

Venus and Earth: Fundamental Differences.

Although often classed as a twin of Earth, Venus displays many fundamental geological differences from our planet. Perhaps the biggest of these is the absence of plate tectonics (see L97). On Earth, the major land masses move around the planet on huge plates which literally float across the surface.

It is at the plate boundaries that geological activity is most pronounced. New crust is formed at mid-ocean ridges, such as the Mid-Atlantic Ridge, where plates are moving apart and lava emerges from the Earth's interior. Ocean trenches occur where one plate slides beneath another, while huge mountain chains form at points where plates collide.

Venus displays a number of features seemingly typical of those arising from tectonic activity. For example, Diana Chasma (see above) and Dali Chasma, two huge canyons on Aphrodite Terra, each have a rim that is much higher than the other and from which the canyon wall descends steeply to the canyon floor. This suggests that each marks the location of part of the Venusian crust sliding under another.

Scientists believe that processes other than plate tectonics have modelled the Venusian surface. The reason why this should be so may be due to the high temperatures on the surface. As we have seen, the surface rocks are subject to gravitational relaxation. The crust is unable to form rigid plates and is only changed through the effects of the Venusian gravity. Stresses set up across wide areas create cracking and fracturing as the surface is deformed.

It was not until Magellan carried out its highly successful mission that we realized how limited our knowledge of Venus was. Earlier probes had given us a glimpse of the wonders that Earth's twin had to offer. Now Magellan has laid the Venusian secrets bare to the scientific community.

Future Probes.

Future missions to the planet will build on this. Atmospheric probes will provide us with more information on the dynamics of the Venusian atmosphere, as well as its composition and structure. Seismic measurements carried out by a series of landers, distributed at selected sites across the Venusian surface, could tell us a great deal about the internal structure of Venus. As is often the case, the Magellan mission has provided us with more questions than before it underwent its mission. It is expected that future exploration will help us to answer these questions.

BACKGROUND TO ECONOMIC EVENTS

The aim of this section is to help the ordinary reader (as well as the student) to follow economic events as they happen, and to understand the controversies that accompany them. The section looks not only at central problems of economic policy but at recent developments in Britain. It also examines the problems of the less-developed economies of the world.

TABLE OF CONTENTS

BACKGROUND TO
ECONOMIC EVENTS

This section is divided into four parts. Part I gives a brief description of the most important problems of economic policy. Part II is concerned with a more detailed survey of the British economy and the way in which it operates. In the course of this survey, the specialised terms used by economists are explained, and the attempt is made to present an intelligible summary of the information, facts and figures relevant to an understanding of economic events. There are five main sub-sections: International Trade and Payments; Employment; Production, and Industry; Incomes, Wages, and Prices; Money, Banking, and Finance; and Economic Aspects of the Public Services. Part III outlines the main economic problems faced by the less developed countries, and the economic policies of Britain and other developed countries towards the less developed world. Some suggestions for further reading are given at the end of Parts II and III. Part IV is written as shortly before publication as possible, and contains a survey of recent developments in the British economy.

I. CENTRAL PROBLEMS OF ECONOMIC POLICY

Why Economists Disagree.

On many of the most important issues Economics is in a state of disarray. Economic problems are in general as serious as they have ever been, yet the economics profession is more divided now than ever on the diagnosis of the problems and on the prescriptions for economic policy. Why is this the case?

It is important to distinguish between *positive* and *normative* economics, *i.e.*, between consideration of how the economy actually works and of how it ought to be made to work. Even if economists were unanimous in their understanding of the economy, different economists might nevertheless prescribe conflicting policies because they made different moral or political judgements. For instance, macroeconomic policy prescriptions might depend crucially on the relative strength of one's dislike for the two evils, inflation and unemployment. But disagreement among economists is not only about goals and objectives. In macroeconomics, the "Keynesian consensus" which held sway in the 1950s and 1960s gave way in the 1970s and 1980s to a variety of different schools of thought. This development reflected changes in the economy and the emergence of new and more pressing economic problems: a rise in the rates of inflation and unemployment and a fall in the rate of economic growth. The accepted analysis and prescriptions were found wanting. At the simplest level, the disputing schools divide into the *New Keynesians*, on the one hand, and the *Monetarists*, or *New Classical* school, on the other.

The two major political parties in Britain were, in the 1980s, committed to extreme and radically different approaches to the solution of Britain's economic problems. The Conservative Government, in office since 1979, placed its faith in *laissez faire* economics, in the efficient operation of market forces, and in Monetarist policies. The Labour Party did not accept that the uncontrolled play of market forces would be beneficial, and it favoured Keynesian reflation and an expansion of state activity and state control. In part, these different approaches were based on differences in economic analysis. For instance, the parties might disagree on what would be the consequences of import controls, or of incomes policy, or of running a budget deficit, or of reducing unemployment benefits. However, much of the disagreement is really based on differences in objectives, or on ideological considerations. Policies based on ideology or slogans can be dangerous. A great disservice is done by those who claim to have simple answers to what in reality are complex problems.

Economic relationships are complicated and changeable, and normally difficult to measure. Economists cannot conduct rigorous experiments in the way that natural scientists do. Everything is happening at once in an economy, and the influence of any one variable is not easy to isolate, even with

the use of sophisticated statistical techniques. This is another reason why economists disagree, and why they should always bear in mind the limitations of their knowledge.

Are Economists Useful?

Given their disagreements and the limitations of their knowledge, can economists perform a useful function? In the 1985 Reith Lectures, concerned with the influence of economic ideas on economic policy, David Henderson complained about the influence of what he called *do-it-yourself economics*. Over wide areas of policy the judgements of politicians and their officials, as also public opinion in general, are guided by beliefs and perceptions about the workings of the economy which owe little or nothing to the economics profession. The amateurs have not been driven from the field, and they are often in control of policy.

According to Henderson, do-it-yourself economics is based on peoples' intuitions and tends to be interventionist: politicians like to be active and to be seen to be active. These intuitions rarely extend beyond the immediate effects of the intervention, whereas professional economists analyse the less obvious, indirect and often unintended effects of interventions, which take place through the response of market forces. To give a simple example, rent controls appear to tackle the ill-effects of housing shortage but, by deterring investment in housing, they may exacerbate the shortage. Or mortgage interest tax relief may be electorally popular, but the economist's approach is to trace its consequences through to the end of the chain—higher house prices, losers as well as gainers, and less resources for non-housing. The professional approach is generally more quantitative than that of the amateur. Economists *can* often be useful, but their advice is ignored more frequently by policy-makers than that of, say, lawyers or engineers.

The Objectives of Economic Policy.

The central issues of economic policy concern certain desirable objectives. One important objective is the avoidance of unemployment. Between the wars, mass unemployment was Britain's most urgent problem: unemployment caused waste, hardship and poverty. After 1945, the maintenance of full employment was accepted as a primary objective of economic policy by all political parties. Until the late 1960s less than 2 per cent of the labour force was unemployed.

Unemployment can be either *cyclical* or *structural*. Cyclical unemployment, arising from a lack of demand in the economy, can be tackled by Government measures to increase total spending in the economy. Structural unemployment arises from a misallocation of resources. In the 1970s and 1980s structural unemployment grew as redundancies

rocketed in the increasingly uncompetitive manufacturing sector, *e.g.*, motor and engineering industries, and in declining industries such as steel and
coal. Moreover, cyclical unemployment grew as
world economic recession set in and deflationary
policies were introduced at home.

With the emergence during the last two decades
of new and greater problems of inflation, the
commitment to full employment first faltered and
then was withdrawn. The concern that has daunted
Governments in recent years is that expansionary
policies to eliminate cyclical unemployment might
fuel a spiral of inflation. Between 1985 and 1987,
and again in 1993, unemployment reached the
figure of 3 million, or 10 per cent of the labour force.

A second objective of economic policy has been
the cure of inflation. Between 1960 and 1970 retail
prices increased on average by 4·4 per cent per
annum; between 1970 and 1980 the inflation rate
averaged no less than 14 per cent per annum; and
between 1980 and 1990 by 6·5 per cent per annum.
Inflation can be harmful in various ways. It is associated with an arbitrary redistribution of purchasing power. Prices rise for everyone but some groups
in society are better able to protect themselves
against inflation. The feeling that particular groups
are falling behind is a source of much unrest and
discontent. Moreover, the general economic uncertainty that inflation brings can become a threat to
economic prosperity.

Two main explanations have been advanced to
account for inflation. The first stresses the role of
excess demand or spending power in the economy—
of too much money chasing too few goods. Such
demand-pull theories are put forward by Monetarists, who point to increases in the money supply in
generating demand, and by Keynesians who recommend restrictive monetary and fiscal policies
to curb excess demand, when it arises. The second
explanation stresses the role of excessive increases in costs, *e.g.*, wage costs or imported
raw material costs, in raising prices. Such *cost-push*
theories imply, for instance, that policies are
needed to restrain the power of trade unions to
raise wages. Neither explanation precludes the
other: both demand-pull and cost-push factors are
likely   to   have   contributed—with   different
strengths at different times—to inflation. Moreover, adherents of both views recognise that, once
expectations of continued inflation become entrenched, these expectations themselves sustain and
fuel the inflation.

A third objective of economic policy is the fostering of economic growth. Successive British Governments in the post-war period have tried to raise the
growth rate—the most important long run determinant of the standard of living. Britain's living
standards have until recently been rising: output per
head of population increased annually by 2 per cent
between 1960 and 1970, by 1·5 per cent between
1970 and 1980 and by 2·3 per cent per annum between 1980 and 1990. Nevertheless, the British
growth rate compares unfavourably with that
achieved by most other industrial countries.

The determinants of economic growth are not well
understood, but most economists would agree that
in order to raise the growth rate it is necessary to
encourage the community to save, and businessmen
to invest, a higher proportion of the national
income. In a fully employed economy the source of
increased output is higher productivity, *i.e.*, output
per worker. There is a danger, however, that higher
productivity growth will be achieved at the
expense of employment, as has largely been the case
in Britain since 1980.

A constraint on the achievement of the above
objectives has been the need to maintain balance
in international payments. The British balance of
payments position has been precarious, so that unfavourable turns of events have precipitated economic crises. Indeed, concern about the balance of
payments so dominated economic policy-making at
times during the post-war period that improvement
in the balance of payments was a major objective of policy. The expansion in the late 1970s of
North Sea oil production, and the resulting confidence of foreign investors, transformed the British
balance of payments. But this created new problems, particularly the adverse effect of the ensuing
high exchange rate on manufacturing, our traditional export sector and an important employer of
labour. The emergence of vast flows of funds in the
1980s meant that the balance of payments could be
increasingly regulated by means of interest rate
policy. But this in turn subordinated domestic
monetary policy to the foreign balances.

The Inter-relationship of Economic Problems.

The achievement of each of the objectives briefly
described above is extremely complex. The difficulties are further aggravated by the fact that
the problems are inter-related in such a way that
measures which are helpful for one objective can
make others more difficult to achieve. For example, a reduction of purchasing power might be
considered helpful in the control of inflation,
and might ease balance of payments problems by
reducing—or slowing down the increase of—imports. But it could also lead to an increase in unemployment, and to a slowing down in the rate of
growth of the economy. Many economic commentators now hold that it is no longer possible to
keep unemployment down to the levels of the
1950s and 1960s without unleashing cumulative
inflation, and that the control of inflation must
now have the highest priority. This must be the
rationale for the economic policies of the Conservative Government in office since 1979, as it
has paid little heed to the short run effects of its
policies on unemployment and economic growth. In
1980 the Government faced an inflation rate of 18
per cent and an unemployment rate of 6 per cent.
By 1987 it had got inflation down, to below 4 per
cent, but unemployment had risen to 10 per cent.

There are other examples of a conflict in policy
objectives. For instance, while the advent in the
1970s of a floating exchange rate can help to correct
the balance of payments, a depreciating pound can
in turn fuel inflation. The defence of a fixed
exchange rate can force interest rates higher and
higher, with unhelpful deflationary effects on the
economy – as happened in the early 1990s.

The Worsened Economic Climate.

In the mid-1970s, after 30 years of rapid
growth and unprecedented prosperity for the
major Western economies, the prospects for continued growth became much less favourable.
This resulted partly from the acceleration of
inflation in many countries, bringing with it
insecurity and militancy in industrial relations.
However, the main cause was the remarkable
increase in the price of oil in 1973 and again in
1979, a fuel on which the Western economies had
become heavily dependent. This produced a strong
burst of inflation; and, because much of the oil
revenue accruing to producers could not be spent,
gave rise to an unprecedented balance of payments
problem and severe world recession. There was a
danger that, through a lack of international co-
ordination and of business confidence and through
misplaced attempts by countries to cure their
immediate economic problems, mass unemployment
on the scale of the 1930s would again appear. The
international infectiousness of high interest rates,
economic recession and rapid inflation made it hard
for any one country to avoid these ills. The 1980s
and 1990s were a period of relatively slow world
economic growth.

II.   SURVEY OF THE BRITISH ECONOMY

1. INTERNATIONAL TRADE AND PAYMENTS

International Trade.
(i) Imports and Exports.

In 1992 the United Kingdom bought from abroad goods to the value of £126 billion (thousand million), or about £2,200 per head. Food accounted for 11 per cent of this total, raw materials and fuels another 10 per cent, and semi-manufactured goods bought for further processing 26 per cent. The biggest item was finished manufactures, which accounted for just over half of the total. This category of imports had increased sharply over a couple of decades. In 1968 finished manufactures were only a fifth and non-manufactures were over half of total imports. All this can be seen in the table, which compares 1968 with a recent year, 1992.

There are three main determinants of the level of British imports. One is the competitiveness of British with foreign producers. Britain imports those commodities which—at the ruling exchange rate between the pound and foreign currencies—can be bought more cheaply from foreign than from home producers. Secondly, the level of imports depends on the extent to which free trade is prevented by tariffs on imported goods or by other devices. Thirdly, as total incomes in the economy expand, there is a general increase in the demand for goods and services including imports. There-fore imports can be expected to vary with the total incomes in the country, known as the *national income*.

UNITED KINGDOM IMPORTS AND EXPORTS

Imports of goods (c.i.f.)	£ million		Percentage of total	
	1968	1992	1968	1992
Food, drink, and tobacco	1,900	13,426	24	11
Basic materials	1,207	4,668	15	4
Fuels and lubricants	902	7,014	11	6
Semi-manufactures	2,119	32,288	27	26
Finished manufactures	1,653	66,424	21	53
TOTAL*	7,900	125,867	100	100

Exports of goods (f.o.b.)				
Food, drink, and tobacco	430	8,706	7	8
Basic materials	232	1,879	4	2
Fuels and lubricants	168	6,967	3	6
Engineering products	2,657	44,420	41	41
Other manufactured goods	2,756	44,422	43	41
TOTAL*	6,442	108,508	100	100

*The column figures do not add up exactly to the totals because the latter include unclassified inputs.

Whereas in 1968 imports amounted to 23 per cent of national income, in 1992 the proportion was 28 per cent. One reason for this rise is the liberalisation of trade among the industrialised countries during the post-war period, and the tendency for trade in manufactures among these countries to increase. An example is the formation of the *European Economic Community* in 1956 and Britain's entry to it in January 1973. Another reason is the great

increase in the price of oil which occurred in the 1970s. Britain's oil import bill rose from £880 million in 1968 to £5·6 billion in 1976. Since then, however, North Sea oil has transformed the oil picture. Imports have fallen in volume, although they still amounted to £7·0 billion in 1992, and exports have risen, to a peak of £16·7 billion in 1985 and to £7·0 billion in 1992. For most of the 1980s Britain was a net exporter of oil.

Since the exports of one country must be the imports of another, the same factors in reverse, foreign competitiveness, access to foreign markets, and the level of foreign incomes determine the level of British exports. In 1992 these amounted to over £108 billion of which no less than 82 per cent were manufactures. In 1968 it was true to say that Britain gained from trade by exporting manufactures, in which she had a *comparative advantage*, in return for food and raw materials, which she was not suited to produce. This is still partly true; but increasingly—with the growth of trade and specialisation among the major economies—Britain gains from trade by exporting those manufactures in which her producers specialise and importing other manufactures. Among the main manufacturing exports are cars and commercial vehicles, tractors, aircraft and aircraft engines, finished steel, various forms of machinery, woollen fabrics, man-made fibres, and chemicals; among the main manufactured imports are wood products, aluminium, newsprint, cars, and aircraft. With the expansion of British oil production, the pattern of trade continued to show rapid change.

(ii) The Terms of Trade.

The value of trade increased more than twenty-fold between 1968 and 1992. This increase can be separated into two components, price and volume, of which price has been the more important. The ratio of the average price of exports to that of imports is known as the *terms of trade*; and a rise in the price of exports relative to imports indicates an improvement in the terms of trade. Thus, when we note in the table that the terms of trade deteriorated by some 11 per cent between 1968 and 1978 we mean that 11 per cent more exports by volume would have been needed in 1978 to buy the same amount of imports as in 1968. This deterioration reflected the commodity boom and the oil price increase which occurred in the 1970s.

VISIBLE TRADE: VOLUME AND PRICES

	1978 = 100	
	1968	1992
Value		
Imports	19	330
Exports	18	328
Volume		
Imports	68	192
Exports	57	163
Price		
Imports	27	188
Exports	30	196
Terms of trade	111	104

(iii) The Volume of Trade.

Superficially it would appear that any improvement in the terms of trade raises the value of British exports relative to imports. However, this is not always true: faster inflation in Britain, leading to a more rapid increase in export prices, would harm rather than help the balance of payments. If the prices of our export goods rise faster than the prices of our competitors in overseas markets it becomes progressively more difficult to sell our exports. Conversely, inflation in Britain makes it progressively more difficult to compete with imports. Growth in the volume of imports exceeded that in exports during the period 1978–92, and this may have been partly due to the faster increase in export prices. The trade balance may well be harmed by a rise in the price of imported primary products (as it was in the first decade); but the balance of trade in manufactures is worsened by an improvement in their terms of trade.

In the post-war period there was a considerable fall in Britain's share of world exports; from 20 per cent of exports of manufactures in 1954 to 12 per cent in 1967, the year of sterling devaluation, and to the figure of 6 per cent in 1991. Britain's main competitors in export markets—and particularly Germany and Japan, with 14 and 12 per cent respectively in 1991—were more successful in expanding their exports. Britain's competitive position in manufacturing has been persistently eroded over the years.

The Balance of Payments.

A detailed examination of recent movements in the British *balance of payments* is made in **Part IV.**

(i) The Balance of Visible Trade.

The *balance of (visible) trade* is the difference between exports and imports of goods. It is said to be in *surplus* if exports exceed imports and in *deficit* if imports exceed exports. In estimating the balance of trade it is important that imports and exports be valued on the same basis. The normal method in the trade returns is to measure imports *c.i.f.* (cost, insurance, and freight) and exports *f.o.b.* (free on board). In other words import prices are shown to include the cost of transporting them to Britain, and exports are valued at the prices when loaded in British ports.

(ii) Patterns of British Trade.

Germany and the United States are now Britain's largest trading partners, each with over 10 per cent of total British trade (exports plus imports) in 1992, followed by France, the Netherlands, Italy and Belgium. Britain's EC partners as a group accounted for no less than 54 per cent of her trade, and the rest of Western Europe for 10 per cent. The oil exporting countries as a group accounted for 4 per cent, and other less developed countries for 12 per cent of British trade in that year.

(iii) The Balance on Current Account.

The chronic deficit in the balance of visible trade has in normal years been offset by a surplus in the *balance of invisible trade*. This relates to international transactions in services as opposed to goods. The main components are: receipts from non-residents *less* payments to non-residents for services such as shipping, civil aviation, tourism, insurance, and financial services; receipts from foreign governments in respect of military bases in the country *less* payments by this country in respect of military bases abroad; receipts of gifts and grants made to this country, *less* gifts and grants made by this country; all receipts of interest, dividends, and profits earned on overseas investment *less* interest dividends, and profits paid out of foreign investment in this country.

(iv) Capital Flow.

The capital account of the balance of payments contains net private investment abroad (being the difference between investment abroad by United Kingdom residents and investment by foreigners in the United Kingdom). There are also large, short-term capital flows, sometimes referred to as *monetary movements*. These include bank lending and borrowing—trade credits, changes in sterling reserves held by foreign governments, and Euro-dollar transactions. Such funds can be highly volatile, moving out of a currency if there is a risk of its depreciation and into it if there is a chance of appreciation or if other currencies are suspect.

PATTERNS OF BRITISH TRADE, 1992

	British exports to: (£ billion)	British imports from: (£ billion)	Exports plus imports (as a percentage of the total)
European Community	60·5	65·6	53·9
of which:			
France	11·5	12·2	10·1
Belgium	5·7	5·7	4·9
Netherlands	8·5	9·9	7·9
Germany	15·1	19·0	14·6
Italy	6·1	6·8	5·5
Ireland	5·7	5·1	4·6
Spain	4·4	2·9	2·3
Rest of Western Europe	8·5	14·5	9·8
of which:			
Sweden	2·4	3·3	2·4
Switzerland	1·8	3·9	2·4
Eastern Europe	1·7	1·6	1·4
of which:			
former USSR	0·5	0·7	0·5
United States	12·2	13·7	11·1
Canada	1·6	1·9	1·5
Japan	2·2	7·4	4·1
Australia	1·4	1·0	1·0
Oil exporting countries	6·0	3·1	3·9
of which:			
Saudi Arabia	2·0	1·0	1·3
Other developing countries	12·7	15·6	12·1
of which:			
South Africa	1·1	0·9	0·9
India	1·0	0·9	0·8
Hong Kong	1·6	2·4	1·7
TOTAL	108·3	125·8	100·0

Therefore, monetary movements often accentuate a surplus or deficit in the other items of the balance of payments. They are also dependent on relative rates of interest at home and abroad, being attracted to financial centres which offer high interest rates.

(v) Foreign Exchange Reserves.

A deficit on current plus capital account can be financed through an increase in liabilities, *i.e.* by government borrowing from abroad, or by a reduction in assets, *e.g.*, a depletion of the official gold and foreign-exchange reserves. The official reserves are used to finance payments abroad which cannot be financed in any other way: they are a last line of defence in international trade.

The book-keeping identity of international payments and receipts requires that the flow of goods and services on current account should be precisely offset by the total *net transactions in assets and liabilities.* However, not all such transactions can be accurately recorded. There is generally an unrecorded capital flow, known as the *balancing item.* In some years the balancing item is so large that it actually exceeds the current account balance.

Correcting a Deficit.

If an imbalance in international payments persists, the deficit cannot be met indefinitely from official financing. At some stage the Government must take action to remove the deficit. What action can it take? There are a number of alternatives available, each with its advantages and disadvantages, and economic opinion is by no means unanimous on the choice of policy. Let us consider each of these alternatives in turn.

(i) Variation of the Exchange Rate.

The *exchange rate* is the ruling rate of exchange of

pounds for dollars or other currencies. It determines the value of British goods in relation to foreign goods. Under the post-war Bretton Woods arrangements (see G9), Britain and other countries maintained a constant value of their currencies in terms of gold, permitting only very minor fluctuations of the exchange rate about its par value. However, persistent balance of payments deficits or surpluses caused occasional adjustments of the official exchange rate, the response to persistent deficit being *devaluation* and to persistent surplus *upvaluation*. In 1972 the major countries adopted a system of fluctuating exchange rates. However, exchange rates are not permitted to fluctuate entirely freely, *i.e.*, so that the market supply and demand for foreign exchange are continuously equated. While the monetary authorities permit the foreign-exchange market to influence the exchange rate, they are prepared in the national interest to intervene in the market (by buying or selling their currency) and so to keep the exchange rate within bounds. Given some flexibility in the exchange rate, a tendency for a deficit to arise is thus met by a *depreciation* of sterling, and an incipient surplus by *appreciation*.

If the pound depreciates in terms of other currencies, British exports (which are paid for in pounds) become cheaper to foreigners and British imports (paid for by purchasing foreign currency) become more expensive to holders of pounds. In this way a fall in the value of the pound can improve the British balance of payments position by encouraging exports and discouraging imports.

But there are certain disadvantages attached to depreciation. The prospect of depreciation results in a speculative outflow of capital funds: and one fall may be taken as a sign that there will be a further fall in the future. Moreover, the rise in the price of imports of raw materials and consumption goods results in higher costs and prices and then in wage demands to maintain the British standard of living. It is possible that inflation will in this way neutralise the beneficial effects of depreciation.

The probable effect of a depreciation in Britain is initially to *worsen* the balance of trade, because the sterling price of imports is likely to be raised by more than that of exports. After about six months the effect of the depreciation on quantities —curbing imports and expanding the volume of exports—dominates, and the balance of trade improves. However, the improvement is maintained only if fiscal and monetary or incomes policies can prevent the fall in sterling from feeding through to domestic prices and costs and so both neutralising the gain in competitiveness and exacerbating inflation.

The pound was devalued in 1949, when an official exchange rate of £1 = $2·8 was established, and again in 1967, to a rate of £1 = $2·4. In 1972 the value of sterling in relation to other currencies was allowed to *float*. With widespread floating, an *effective exchange rate* is now calculated, which shows the value of sterling in relation to a bundle of other currencies, with each currency receiving a weight according to the extent of trade with Britain. This rate fluctuated from month to month, but with a strong downward tendency until 1977, followed by a recovery until 1980 due mainly to the advent of North Sea oil, and a subsequent fall. With the exchange rate equal to 100 in 1975, the weighted average value of sterling moved as follows:

1972	1975	1977	1980	1984	1987
123·5	100·0	81·2	96·1	78·8	70·6

1989	1990	1991	1992	1993	1994
72·6	71·6	71·9	69·3	62·8	62·7

Britain became a member of the *Exchange Rate Mechanism* (ERM) from October 1990 until sterling was forced out by speculation in September 1992. Membership of the ERM requires effectively fixing sterling (within narrow bands) to the *European Currency Unit* (ECU), so relinquishing the exchange rate as a policy variable. Whether exchange rates within the European Union should be fixed irrevers-

ibly will be an important issue in the coming years.

(ii) Exchange Controls and Convertibility.

A currency is fully *convertible* if it can be freely exchanged for any other currency at the ruling rates of exchange. Exchange controls impose restrictions on convertibility. In the early post-war period there was a world-wide shortage of dollars: if sterling had been convertible, there would have been a rush to obtain dollars, with the consequence that Britain's reserves would soon have been exhausted.

Exchange controls on residents can be enforced by requiring that earnings of foreign currencies (*e.g.* the proceeds from the sale of exports) be handed over to the exchange control authority in return for domestic currency; and by permitting the exchange of domestic for foreign currency (*e.g.*, to enable the purchase of imports) only for transactions approved by the exchange control authority. By restricting convertibility the Government can make it more difficult for funds to move into or out of the country.

Foreign exchange control has become a less feasible policy as a result of the revolution in information technology. The explosion in the way in which funds can be transferred and intermediation of all kinds can take place makes such controls increasingly impractical for any reasonably sophisticated economy (see Part IV).

(iii) Import Controls and Tariffs.

Import controls impose limitations on the quantity or value of goods which are permitted to enter a country; tariffs are duties levied on imported goods so that the price of those goods to consumers in a country is higher than the price received by the foreigners supplying the goods. In the early post-war years. Britain maintained strict import controls over a wide range of goods.

All countries impose tariffs. Some tariffs are primarily intended to raise revenue for the Government, and others are primarily intended to protect home industries by raising the price of competing goods from abroad. The rights of countries to raise tariffs, or to operate tariffs in a discriminatory way (*i.e.*, to offer lower tariffs on goods from some sources than on similar goods from other sources), are closely circumscribed by the rules of the *General Agreement on Tariffs and Trade* (GATT). The object of the GATT, now called the *World Trade Organisation*, is to work towards free trade, especially through a reduction in tariffs. The disadvantage of introducing import controls or tariffs to correct a deficit in the balance of payments is that the benefits of free trade are lost. Moreover, there is always the possibility of retaliation by trading partners.

Britain's powers to impose tariffs and quotas on imports were greatly circumscribed in 1973 by her accession to the European Economic Community, since this requires free trade within the Community and a common external tariff.

(iv) Deflation.

Until the late 1970s the U.K. balance of payments was far from secure. As a result, domestic economic policies were much influenced by balance of payments considerations. By ruling out devaluation and trade restrictions, the authorities had to fall back on *deflation* of the economy to correct periodic deficits. In other words, the Government took measures to discourage demand and so cut back incomes and employment. By reducing demand in general, the authorities secured a fall in demand for imports. Deflation is a painful method of correcting a deficit: not only does it have a direct effect on the level of incomes and employment, but it is also liable to slow down the rate of growth of the economy. This can happen because deflation can weaken the incentive to expand productive capacity by investing.

Deflation need not be the conscious policy. When inflation is high and the balance of payments weak, deflation may result from policies to raise domestic interest rates in order to protect sterling against speculative outflows of capital. This is a good description of British economic policy in the early 1990s.

(v) International Trade Flows.

We can divide the world into four trading groups: the industrial countries (mainly OECD), the oil-producing developing countries (OPEC), the other developing countries, and the (previously) communist countries. In 1992 the industrial countries accounted for 72 per cent of total world exports, 54 per cent being exports to countries within that group, 3 per cent to oil producers, 13 per cent to developing countries, and 2 per cent to communist countries. 80 per cent of the industrial countries' exports were manufactured products. The oil exports of the oil producers amounted to 5 per cent of world exports, 3 per cent going to the industrial countries. 55 per cent of the exports of the other developing countries were primary products. Their exports amounted to 20 per cent of the world total, most going to the industrial countries. Only 8 per cent of world trade occurred among the developing countries. The communist group exported 2 per cent of the world total, a fifth of which was traded within the group. Of the total world exports, 70 per cent were manufactures, 10 per cent fuels and 15 per cent primary products.

The International Monetary System.

(i) International Liquidity.

Imbalance in payments between countries is financed by transfers of gold or foreign-exchange reserves. These reserves are known as *international liquidity*. Their basic characteristic is general acceptability: they can perform their function only if they retain the confidence of those engaged in international transactions. In addition, countries in difficulty can finance international payments by means of their drawing rights on the International Monetary Fund. Each of these will be described below.

The amount of international liquidity required depends on various factors. One is the proneness of the international economy to sharp changes in the balance of payments among countries: high and variable rates of inflation and fluctuations in the oil price since the early 1970s have strengthened the need for liquidity. A second factor, having the same effect, is the remarkable increase that has occurred in international flows of short-term funds. Offsetting these, however, is the greater flexibility of exchange rates in recent years: the need for international liquidity would in principle be eliminated in a world of completely freely fluctuating exchange rates.

(ii) The International Monetary Fund.

The *International Monetary Fund* (IMF) was set up at Bretton Woods in 1944 with the object of working towards free trade at stable exchange rates. Under the original agreement establishing the Fund, members agreed to make their currencies convertible into other currencies and gold at fixed rates of exchange, and agreed not to impose exchange or import controls without the permission of the Fund.

The function of the Fund is to make foreign-exchange resources available to members which run into balance of payments difficulties. Each member country has a deposit (called its quota), paid partly in gold and partly in its own currency, with the Fund. The size of the deposit is fixed in relation to the country's share in world trade. In return, it is granted certain automatic drawing rights, which entitle it to borrow foreign currencies from the Fund. The Fund has power to make larger loans, and to grant standby credits to be drawn on if required. Before the Fund will make such loans and credits available it has to be satisfied that the borrowing country is taking appropriate action to correct the balance-of-payments disequilibrium. The relations between the IMF and the developing countries are examined on G50.

(iii) Gold.

Gold played a central role in the international monetary system during the 1950s and 1960s. Central banks were prepared to buy and sell gold at a fixed price in terms of their currencies, and gold was exchanged among them in settlement of imbalances. The price of gold was held for many years at $35 per fine ounce. However, this fixed price in the face of rising costs of gold production meant that gold supply could not increase rapidly enough to provide the international liquidity needed to finance expanding world trade. The *demonetisation* of gold is described in Part IV.

(iv) An International Currency?

The domestic currency of the United Kingdom is not backed by gold: on a ten-pound note the Governor of the Bank of England promises to pay the bearer on demand the sum of ten pounds—merely another note! Yet, within Britain, there is complete confidence in the currency, because it is generally acceptable and so convertible into goods and services. Just as gold no longer backs the domestic currency, there is no need for gold in settlement of international payments. All we need is a generally acceptable international currency, *i.e.*, one in which all countries have confidence.

Such a currency could be created by an international authority constituted for this purpose. However, it would involve loss of national autonomy and the vesting of considerable power in the international authority issuing the paper currency. And there is a fear that it will enable reckless governments to pursue inflationary policies without the discipline imposed by shortage of reserves, and that their inflation will be infectious. The very limited steps towards the creation of an international currency—the issue by the IMF of small quantities of *special drawing rights* —are described in Part IV.

(v) Foreign Exchange Reserves.

Surplus countries are prepared to hold short-term debt in foreign currencies—so earning a rate of interest—confident that their future trading deficits can be financed by payment of these currencies. They can perform their function only if there is confidence that they can be converted into other currencies and hence into goods and services at current exchange rates.

After World War Two the dollar replaced the pound as the main reserve currency, used in settlement of international payments. The United States ran a large and persistent payments deficit during the 1950s and 1960s, made possible by the willingness of the creditor countries to build up their dollar balances. Indeed, this increase in dollar balances was the main source of new international liquidity during that period. But there is necessarily a limit to such a process. The weakness in the U.S. balance of payments in fact added to the problem of international liquidity. The deficits produced periodic fears that the dollar would be devalued; and this resulted in speculation against the dollar, and contributed to the breakdown of the Bretton Woods system. The problems which have beset the dollar in recent years are explained in Part IV.

(vi) The Sterling Balances.

Foreign governments and individuals may hold balances in sterling (*e.g.*, Treasury bills, Government stocks, and bank accounts) to finance trading transactions or if the rate of interest paid on balances in London is higher than that paid in other financial centres. In late 1994 the sterling balances totalled £113 billion—more than the official reserves, which stood at £44 billion. However, by then the pound had largely given way to the yen and the deutschemark, which had joined the dollar as the major trading and reserve currencies.

(vii) The Eurocurrency Market.

The *Eurocurrency* (or *Eurodollar*) market is a market for bank deposits which are denominated in foreign currencies. It derives its name from the fact that most of the banks which accept these foreign currency deposits are in Europe (including Britain) and most of the deposits are denominated in U.S. dollars. The market has grown at remarkable speed since the 1960s. The reason for that growth was the profitability of Eurodollar transactions. Banks found that, particularly if only large units of money were handled, they could profitably borrow funds in country A and lend in country B, while paying interest rates higher than those paid in country A and charging rates lower than those charged in country B. Its growth was helped by the continuous deficit in the United States balance of payments, since this meant that banks and institutions received dollars which they were willing to hold and lend. OPEC funds obtained from their trade surpluses have tended to make their way into the market (as *petro-dollars*).

London and Tokyo are the largest international banking centres in the world, each accounting for nearly a quarter of the lending market. The external liabilities of UK banks can create problems for the regulation of economic activity. Movements in the market affect interest rates, credit and exchange rates in different countries, and they can thwart domestic monetary policies.

2. EMPLOYMENT, PRODUCTION, AND INDUSTRY

Population.

In 1993 the population of the United Kingdom was estimated to be 58·2 million—51·4 m. in England and Wales, 5·1 m. in Scotland, and 1·6 m. in Northern Ireland. Since 1971 the population has increased by only 4 per cent. This slow increase is accounted for by the birth rate (the number of live births per 100 people) of 1·4 exceeding the crude death rate of 1·1. In the period 1981–91 about 100,000 more people migrated to the United Kingdom than migrated from this country. In 1993 the balance was negative. An inflow of 215,900 people was more than offset by an outflow of 227,000.

The official estimate of the population of the United Kingdom in the year 2031 is 62·2 million. But prediction of future trends is difficult. For instance, it depends on immigration and emigration policies, the effect of improving medical services on the average length of life, trends in the age at which people marry, advances in techniques of birth control, and attitudes towards desirable family size. This projection is based on the belief that the birth rate will slightly exceed the death rate. It is also projected that the birth rate will gradually fall as the large generation born in the 1960s pass their peak child-bearing age.

The Labour Force.

Of the total population only some are of *working age*, *i.e.*, between the minimum school leaving age of 16 (15 before 1973) and retiring age—65 years for men and 60 for women. Of course, not all those of working age do work and not all those above working age have retired. In 1994 the labour force was 27·9 million. Of males aged 16 and over, 73 per cent were in the labour force compared with 50 per cent of females. The labour force is defined to include not only those who are gainfully employed (as employees or self-employed) but also the unemployed who are looking for work and those on work related government training programmes. Students and housewives are excluded unless they do some work for cash. One feature of the past decade or so has been a fall in the proportion of adult males going out to work, a fall which is expected to continue. It is caused by an increasing number of students and others undergoing full-time training and by more people retiring early. Those factors also affected the proportion of women going out to work, but they have been more than offset by a rising participation of married women, particularly in part-time work. This trend is again expected to continue.

Most of the labour force work for wages and salaries as employees. Of the total for the United Kingdom in 1994 of 27·9 million, 3·3 m. were employers or self-employed. 0·3 m. were in the Forces, 21·4 m. were employees, 0·3 m. were on work-related government training programmes, and 2·4 m. were recorded as unemployed. There has been an increase in the porportion of the workforce who are self-employed. So less than half the population who are at work have to produce not only for themselves but also for the rest of the

population who are either not in the labour force or who are unemployed.

The table shows the industries in which people work. As an economy develops there is a tendency for employment in the primary sector to decline as the production industries expand. As an economy gets richer still, the proportion of income spent on services increases, and employment in the service sector consequently rises whilst the proportion of the workforce in production industries declines. Thus, in 1955 services accounted for only 36 per cent of total employment; whereas by 1994 the proportion had risen to 73·4 per cent.

Employment and Unemployment.

In 1994 an average of 2,636,283 persons—9·4 per cent of the working population—were unemployed in the U.K. This figure excludes school-leavers. In most post-war years until the late 1960's the average was lower than 1·5 per cent. Even in January 1959, the worst month of the 1950s, the rate rose to less than 3 per cent, and in February 1963—an exceptional month owing to weather—to less than 4 per cent. These contrast with an average figure in 1937, the best year of the 1930s, of 11 per cent, and with a figure of 22 per cent at the bottom of the slump in 1932. The low unemployment of the post-war years was not maintained from the late 1960s. Unemployment grew to reach almost one million in early 1972. It then started to fall back with the general economic recovery, only to start rising again from late 1974 as the economy moved back into recession. Unemployment peaked in 1986 but fell sharply between then and the first half of 1990. The figures then began to rise sharply once again as the economy entered recession, topping 2 million by March 1991 and continuing to rise until early 1993.

Until the late 1960s 1–1·5 per cent unemployment was somewhere near the practicable minimum. Some unemployment is more or less inevitable. A seasonal rise in unemployment in the winter must be expected, *e.g.*, in seaside towns, and for this reason unemployment in January is higher than in June. Moreover, some unemployment is bound to be involved in job-changing and as the demands of industries change. Finally there is a core of people who are simply unemployable. "Full employment" means that there should be about as many jobs vacant as there are workers looking for jobs. A large excess of vacancies is evidence of inflationary pressure in the labour market, for it means that the employers needing workers to meet the demands for their products will have to compete with each other by bidding up wages.

Most commentators feel that the practicable minimum level of unemployment has increased since the late 1960s. By minimum they mean that any attempt to reduce unemployment below it, by injecting monetary demand, would be likely to cause increasing inflation or a deteriorating balance of trade. Many possible reasons have been advanced for the increase in this "equilibrium rate of un-employment"—that rate of unemployment consistent with stable inflation and balanced trade. One explanation is that as the fixed costs (like National Insurance) of employing workers went up, so employers were more careful to economise on labour. Another possible explanation was that the level of social security benefits as a whole was too high, causing people to demand an unrealistically high wage before accepting a job. Whilst the above factors, particularly the burden of National Insurance contributions, may well have played a role at times, it is unlikely that they have been persistently important. Many of the unemployed have skills which are redundant in an economy where the structure of industry is changing. Hence there may be an excess demand for some skills even when many people are without work—indeed this is the case at present. As well as skill mismatch of this sort, there may be geographical mismatch—that is the distribution of the population may not coincide with the distribution of job vacancies. This is one interpretation of Mr. Tebbit's famous exhortation: "Get on your bike!" However, there is grave disagreement amongst observers about the impor-tance of such mismatch explanations. No-one denies that there is a severe degree of mismatch in the British economy; the doubt concerns whether it has increased. Similar disagreement attends the claim that technological advance, reducing the need for labour, is a major factor. Interestingly many industrialists would put this as a prime explanation. Most economists would be inclined to disagree with them. They would put greater stress on a too rapid growth of real wages (that is wages compared to prices), causing employers to try to produce a given amount of output with smaller quantities of labour. Many used to put a large share of the blame for this on the shoulders of trade unions. If trade unions push up wages, employers may respond by putting up prices; unions then push up wages again in an attempt to obtain an increase in their living standards. Thus a wage-price spiral may cause increasing inflation. Governments concerned about inflation may therefore be forced to run the economy at lower levels of demand. The experience of the late 1980s when a surge in output growth and a sharp drop in unemployment contributed to a renewed increase in inflation and to a dramatic worsening of the balance of trade suggests that the equilibrium rate of unemployment has not fallen despite the supply-side reforms of the 1980s. Though unions are weaker, competition between employers for a limited stock of suitable workers, as well as a pervasive belief that rising real wages are important for motivating staff, may be amongst the more important. explanations of why the real wage and the equilibrium rate of unemployment remain high. Also of importance is the UK's failure to much improve its relatively inadequate performance (by international standards) in vocational education and training. Recently some commentators have laid stress on two other structural characteristics: the lack of coordinated wage bargaining and the lack of a time limit on social security benefit for the unemployed. Also prominent in contemporary debate is the contention that demand for unskilled labour is threatened by cheap labour in the Third World competing effectively in the production of standardised products.

Whatever the relative importance of these explanations, there is little doubt that the major cause of the rise in unemployment in the early 1980s was deficiency of aggregate demand for British goods. This in turn is was partly the consequence of restrictive government policies, and partly of our loss of international competitiveness. There is, however, dispute as to how much of this reduction in demand was necessary to stabilise inflation. Indeed there were some who thought that much of the fall in inflation rates in the early 1980s was the consequence of a massive slowdown in the rate of increase in world commodity prices and the consequentially slower growth of import prices. Equally there are those who believe that even if it was necessary in the above sense, it contributed to increasing the rate of equilibrium unemployment—because some of the workers who lost their jobs became hard to re-employ. Partly this was because of the effect of joblessness on their own attitudes and skills, and partly because of the perceptions of employers as to their worth. It may also have been difficult for the unemployed to "compete" with the employed by "bidding down" wages, since the latter may have great bargaining power vis a vis their employers for whom their departure would represent a major waste of training expenditure.

To some extent official unemployment figures are misleading, in that certain individuals may not record themselves as being out of work and will thus appear to drop out of the working population. Until 1982 the official unemployment figure was calculated on the number registered as available for work. Registration was a prerequisite for claiming unemployment benefit. Individuals not eligible for such benefits—particularly married women—often did not register as unemployed even if they still wished to work. Their only incentive for doing so was if they felt that the authorities would help them find a job. Further, the count did not include those who were temporarily stopped or working short time. Since late 1982 the official unemployment figures have been calculated according to the number actually claiming benefit, for which registering as available for work is no longer essential. Those under 18 are now not included in the unemployment figures, as they are assumed to be on a training scheme, to have a job, or to have remained in full-time

DISTRIBUTION OF EMPLOYEES IN EMPLOYMENT, GREAT BRITAIN, SEPTEMBER 1994
(Thousands)

Agriculture, forestry, and fishing	267
Coal, oil and natural gas extraction and processing	76
Electricity, gas, other energy and water supply	230
Manufacturing industries	4,227
Construction	766
Wholesale distribution and repairs	1,034
Retail distribution	2,280
Hotels and catering	1,231
Transport	852
Postal services and telecommunications	357
Banking, finance and insurance	2,726
Public administration	1,606
Education	1,752
Medical and other health services	1,575
Other services	965
GRAND TOTAL	20,999

education. The above are not the only changes that have been introduced in the last few years in the way that unemployment is measured. For example, older workers tend not to get included in the count, whilst many believe that the special employment and training measures (see **G16–17**) artificially deflate the unemployment figure. A combination of the changes in the way unemployment has been calculated, and the rapid expansion of demand in the second half of the decade, meant that recorded unemployment fell steadily between the middle of 1986 and early 1990, from a peak of over 3·36 million to 1·6 million. Thereafter, the emerging recession in the UK economy pushed unemployment back up, and at an accelerating rate. By the first quarter of 1991, seasonally adjusted unemployment was increasing by about 80,000 per month. Much to the surprise of many, unemployment started to fall slowly from early 1993. This came much earlier than had happened in the aftermath of earlier recessions. Though much of the increase in employment came in the form of part-time work, it is probably the case that the labour market was also witnessing the counterpart of a more thorough shedding of labour during the recession. Nevertheless in early 1995 about 2·4 million people remained unemployed.

Regional Unemployment.

Extreme variations in regional unemployment were not a general feature of the post-war period: only in Northern Ireland was unemployment persistently very high. Between 1965 and 1993 unemployment there ranged between 4·1 and 17·6 per cent. Nevertheless, regional inequalities existed and were magnified in absolute terms during most of the 1980s.

In 1994 the proportion of all workers unemployed in the UK was 9·4 per cent. Even within the more fortunate regions there are pockets of high unemployment. These are concentrated particularly in the inner areas of large cities, but also elsewhere. For example, in the South-East, Clacton had an unemployment rate of 17·2 per cent in 1994, whilst in the South West, Redruth had 17·3 per cent. This does not compare, however, with the 23·1 per cent rate in Strabane, Northern Ireland.

One of the main reasons for the traditional regional pattern of unemployment used to be that certain industries and services, in which big changes had been taking place, tended to be grouped in specific regions. Most of our early industrial centres had to be established close to coal, iron ore, and adequate water supplies. But employment in many long-established industries has been declining. Such industries include textiles, mining and quarrying, shipbuilding, and agriculture. On the other hand new and growing industries, and their related head offices, were concentrated in Greater London, the South East, and the Midlands. The growth of services, too, centred on the areas where industry was booming and population is increasing. In the absence of government

UNEMPLOYMENT AND VACANCIES
(United Kingdom, thousands)

	Unemploy-ment.† (Annual Average)	Vacancies. (Annual Average)	Unemploy-ment as a percentage of total labour force
1972	837	147	2·9
1974	600	298	2·0
1976	1,302	122	4·1
1978	1,383	210	4·4
1980	1,665	134	4·8
1982	2,917	114	0·5
1984	3,160	150	10·7
1986	3,292	189	11·2
1988	2,370	249	8·2
1990	1,665	174	5·8
1992	2,780	116	9·7
1994	2,636	157	9·4

† Prior to October 1982 the unemployment count consisted of those people registered at Jobcentres who were unemployed (the registrant count). From October 1982 the unemployment count consisted of those claiming unemployment-related benefits.

PERCENTAGE OF WORKERS
UNEMPLOYED, BY REGIONS

	Annual average* 1965	Annual average* 1994
North	2·4	11·7
Yorkshire and Humberside	1·0	9·8
East Midlands	0·8	8·3
East Anglia	1·2	7·4
South East	0·8	9·6
South West	1·5	7·5
Wales	2·5	9·4
West Midlands	0·0	9·9
North West	1·5	10·2
Scotland	2·8	9·9
Northern Ireland	5·9	11·5

* Excluding school-leavers.

intervention, it was thought that the process would tend to become cumulative, and regional inequalities would grow rather than diminish. The 1970s saw an interesting change. The West Midlands, traditionally after the South-East, the most prosperous area of the country, was severely hit by the particular impact of the recession on engineering, and appeared as one of the regions with higher than average unemployment. This is still the case today despite the fact that in the mid 1980's the West Midlands began to benefit from the ripple effect of the boom in the South East and as firms began to relocate some of their activities from the crowded South-East to areas where the labour market was less tight. Other areas of high unemployment saw little or no improvement in their relative position during the period of strong economic growth 1986–1988, the worst affected regions remaining Northern Ireland, Scotland, the North and North-West. This may have been linked to an additional factor—the relative concentration of unemployment in inner city areas in particular regions. Unemployment in the inner cities has grown more rapidly than elsewhere since the 1960s, and seems to be the result of limited growth of firms there together with only a slow emergence of new enterprise. When the economy slowed down in 1989 and entered recession in 1990 and 1991, a different pattern of regional unemployment started to emerge. In contrast to the recession of the early 1980s, the downturn affected service industries before manufacturing, so the initial rise in unemployment was heavily concentrated in the South East and in other regions where service industries predominate, such as East Anglia. Some commentators christened this the "yuppie recession". This had the effect of substantially narrowing regional variations in unemployment. A noteworthy aspect of these recent developments concerns Scotland and Wales. Traditionally both countries exhibited higher unemployment than the UK average. However the latest recession hit them less badly than many other areas of the UK.

As the Table shows, by 1994 they both had unemployment rates which were little different from the UK average. Perhaps even more remarkable was the experience of Northern Ireland where unemployment was actually lower than in 1988. It will be interesting to see what happens to the distribution of unemployment rates as we continue to emerge from recession. Some commentators expect the traditional pattern to reassert itself. The Table shows 1994 averages. By the end of that year the West Midlands, Yorkshire and Humberside, the North West, the North and Northern Ireland were experiencing above average unemployment. Unemployment in the South East and Scotland was also still a little above the national average, whilst in Wales it was exactly

equal to the national average. What the future holds for regional unemployment is uncertain. What is clear is that there are presently still discrepancies between regions in personal disposable income per head. For example in 1992, it was 31 per cent higher in the South East (the richest area) than in Wales (the poorest).

Regional Planning.

There are essentially two ways of tackling the problem of regional imbalances; taking jobs to the people or bringing people to the jobs. In so far as the latter alternative is chosen, the Government should encourage the mobility of labour, e.g., through retraining schemes or rehousing subsidies. However, the migration of population may damage community life in the denuded areas, and cause congestion, housing shortages, and over-crowding in the booming regions. The Government can create employment opportunities in the relatively depressed regions in various ways. It can try to induce expanding industries to set up new plants in these regions by offering tax incentives or grants; it can authorise additional expenditure on public works—e.g., by accelerating road-building programmes—to provide additional employment; it can place orders for the goods it needs—e.g., defence contracts—where work is required. It can also use physical controls on expansion in the better-off areas; between 1947 and 1981 factory building over a particular size, which was changed from time to time, required the granting of an *Industrial Development Certificate*.

(i) Labour's Policy in the 1960s.

On taking office in October 1964, the Labour Government made regional planning the responsibility of its Department of Economic Affairs. Britain was divided into eight regions, with the intention of producing a plan for each region.

Fiscal incentives to locate industry in the depressed regions were given, e.g., the cash grants provided in 1966 for new plants and machinery in manufacturing were at twice the national rate in the Development Areas. Buildings also received cash grants in Development Areas, in Intermediate Areas (where regional depression existed but in not such an acute form), and in Special Development Areas (where depression was most acute). By contrast, office building in London and some other cities was strictly limited. To encourage the mobility of labour, the Government introduced redundancy compensation and achieved some expansion in both public and private training facilities. In 1967 regional differentials in the selective employment tax were also introduced. This was known as the Regional Employment Premium (REP).

(ii) Policy in the 1970s.

In 1970 the incentive to invest in the Development Areas was affected by the Conservative Government's replacement of cash grants (except on buildings) by a system of initial allowances against tax. Whereas cash grants had been 40 per cent of investment in plant and machinery in Development

Areas and 20 per cent in other areas, there was now a 100 per cent initial allowance in Development Areas and 60 per cent initial allowances in other areas. The system of initial allowances is explained on **G15**.

Early in 1972 unemployment rates in Northern Ireland, Scotland, Wales and Northern England had reached high levels. The Government introduced 100 per cent allowances throughout the country on all investment in plant and machinery; the preferential treatment of investment in Development Areas was therefore ended. Instead *regional development grants*, in the form of cash payments towards investment in plant, machinery and buildings, were introduced. The Government also proposed in four years to triple expenditure on retraining facilities, and to pay a worker who had undergone retraining a housing grant if he moved house to take a new job; and also a grant to any worker in an assisted area who moved house to take a new job. It should be remembered, however, that strong measures were necessary merely to replace the Labour Government's system of cash grants, and the REP which it was planned to phase out in 1974. Though, in the event, REP was retained by the incoming Labour Government, it was finally replaced by more selective measures in 1977.

(iii) Conservative Policy in the 1980s.

In July 1979, the new Conservative Government announced some changes to be introduced over the 1979–83 period. The extent of the assisted areas would be gradually reduced, so as to cover 25 per cent instead of 40 per cent of the employed population and some areas were "down-graded". Industrial Development Certificate procedures were abolished in 1981.

In 1983 the Government introduced a Green Paper on regional policy. The suggestion was for a tighter and more selective approach, with aid being directed more at job creation, at small firms and at the services. But even this non-interventionist Government concluded that "wage adjustments and labour mobility cannot be relied upon to correct regional imbalance in employment opportunities". By the end of 1984 there were only two types of assisted areas in Britain—development and intermediate. In 1993 the development and intermediate areas were re-defined—they now cover about 34 per cent of the working population. Throughout the assisted areas help is available under the DTI's Enterprise Initiative for investment projects so long as they satisfy specified criteria. Regional Investment and Innovation Grants are available to help investment and innovation in firms with less than 25 employees. Small firms can also qualify for Innovation Grants. In addition, some help is forthcoming from the European Regional Development Fund and other European funds. The former is estimated to have contributed about £570 million to the UK in 1993. In Scotland industrial development is assisted by Scottish Enterprise and Highlands and Islands Enterprise through a network of Local Enterprise Companies. Similar roles are filled by the Welsh Development Agency and the Northern Ireland Department of Economic Development.

The Conservative Government's distrust of general regional assistance was confirmed by its decision in 1988 to abolish automatic regional grants. All assistance for the regions is now selective. The new philosophy is that the "market" will eventually erode the disparity in regional performance, as regional variations in pay encourage a redistribution in regional employment. It was generally thought that UDCs and enterprise zones were unlikely to have more than a marginal impact in reducing regional inequality.

The real value of expenditure on all regional incentives is currently less than half the levels of the early 1970s, although spending on both employment schemes and urban aid has increased.

Though regional problems remain, studies have shown that IDC's, financial incentives and REP, but particularly cash grants, have to a limited extent mitigated them. However, it was felt by many that the instruments were too blunt and insufficiently selective. It was also felt that in a slack labour market, regional policy was more likely to re-allocate a given number of jobs rather than

increase them in net terms. Alongside regional policy, therefore, were introduced measures on inner city decay (a problem even in non-assisted areas such as the South East), rural development and derelict land. In his March 1980 Budget the Chancellor announced proposals to establish about half a dozen "Enterprise Zones". These were small sites (of no more than 500 acres) with problems of economic and physical decay. The Zones were an experiment to test how far industrial and commercial activity could be encouraged by the removal of certain fiscal burdens, and by the removal or streamlined administration of statutory or administrative controls. In January 1995 there were 5 such zones. Although the government does not envisage extending the scheme massively, enterprise zones are seen to be an effective way of tackling particular local problems. Simplified Planning Zones are also designed to assist urban development. Currently the Government is placing renewed stress on the reclamation of derelict land. An additional measure, announced in the 1983 Budget, was the establishment of a number of 'freeports' which would enjoy similar relief from fiscal burdens, in particular local authority rates. By early 1985 there were 6 of these. However, the experiment with freeports proved to be unsuccessful. Of the six established only Southampton and Liverpool ever lived up to their initial expectations. The planned abolition of fiscal barriers within the EC after 1992 in any case removed much of the rationale for freeports.

In 1981 the Government set up two Urban Development Corporations (UDCs), one in London's Docklands and the other in Merseyside. The aim of the UDCs was to reclaim and develop derelict land for housing, commercial and recreational purposes. By early 1992 the London Docklands UDC had received over £1,300 million in Government aid and had obtained over £9 billion in private sector funding commitments. The London Docklands is the site for one of the largest single office developments in Europe, although progress was affected by the downturn in the UK commercial property market in the period 1989–92. From 1987 ten more UDCs were established in Birmingham, the West Midlands, Bristol, Leeds, Central Manchester, Greater Manchester, Sheffield, Teesside, Tyne and Wear, and Plymouth. In 1988 the Government also announced an Action For Cities programme to improve co-operation between Government departments, private enterprise and local authorities in order to rejuvenate derelict inner city areas. City Action Teams and Task Forces operate under this regeneration banner. City Grant (introduced in 1981) encourages private sector initiatives in the inner cities. The Urban Programme supported over 788 new firms in 1992–93. In 1991 the Government launched a further scheme—"City Challenge". This provides Government funding for particularly imaginative local authority schemes. Eleven local authorities had been awarded funds under this initiative and had started work by April 1992. Another twenty authorities were selected for the following year. There have been two recent developments. In the Autumn of 1992 a scheme called Capital Partnership was announced. This tops up local authority project investments with central funds. In 1993 a new Urban Regeneration Agency was established. The agency will be responsible for the Government's Derelict Land Programme and for the payment of City Grant.

National Income.

Gross domestic income (GDI) is the sum total of incomes received for the services of labour, land, or capital in a country. Gross domestic product (GDP) is the money value of all the goods and services produced in the country. So as to avoid double-counting, only the *value added* at each stage of production is included: firms' purchases of goods and services from other firms are excluded. The revenue from selling the GDP is either paid out to the hired factors of production—labour, land, and capital—or retained in the form of profits. Therefore, provided it is calculated net of taxes on goods produced, GDP must equal GDI. To estimate gross national income (GNI) from GDI it is necessary to add the net income—such as profits and interest—received from abroad. If an allowance is made for wear and tear of the nation's capital equipment, *i.e.*, for *capi-*

AN INTERNATIONAL GROWTH LEAGUE TABLE

| | Percentage change per annum, 1960 to 1980 | | | | |
	Output	Employ-ment	Output per head	Fixed investment as percentage of GDP, average, 1960-80	GNP per head, 1980 $
Japan	7·7	1·1	6·5	32·5	9,890
France	4·6	0·5	4·1	22·7	11,730
W. Germany	3·7	0·1	3·8	23·9	13,590
Italy	4·4	0·2	4·3	20·8	6,480
U.S.A.	3·5	2·0	1·5	18·2	11,360
U.K.	2·3	0·1	2·2	18·3	7,920

tal consumption, we arrive at net national income, better known as the *national income*.

In 1993 the gross national income of the United Kingdom was £632,263 million, implying a national income per head of £10,859. In 1955 the corresponding figure had been about £330 per head. However, only part of the increase in value was due to an increase in the quantity of goods and services produced; some of the increase simply reflected a rise in prices. It is important to calculate changes in the volume of output—known as *real output*—as well as changes in its value. Real output is calculated by the statistical device of constructing an index number. This is done by calculating the volume of goods and services provided in each year and then valuing these goods and services at the prices found in one particular year. Thus between 1955 and 1993 the money value of gross national product per head rose by nearly 3,200 per cent, whereas real per capita incomes little more than doubled, and the difference represented a rise in prices.'

The Quality of Life.

In real terms national income per head doubled between 1955 and 1993, an increase of almost 2·3 per cent per annum. National income per head is an indicator of the standard of living. However, this measure is necessarily a crude one. For instance, it cannot take into account new and better products, *e.g.*, television, man-made fibres, faster flight, long-playing records, or the lowly plastic bucket; nor does it indicate changes in the distribution of income between rich and poor; nor in the length of the working week.

Data of national income per head may also conceal important changes in the "quality of life", *e.g.*, in our physical environment. This is affected by such things as traffic congestion, noise, water-and air-pollution. Between 1961 and 1993 the number of private cars on British roads tripled, from 6·3 million to 23·3 million; the number of motor vehicles of all types more than doubled over the same period. Movement of civil aircraft over Britain quadrupled, although numbers fell after the outbreak of hostilities in the Gulf in 1990. The air in our cities became less polluted by smoke, sulphur dioxide, carbon monoxide and lead. Lead emissions from petrol engined vehicles have been more than halved since 1980. However, the number of our rivers, canals and estuaries which were grossly polluted remained significant, whilst complaints about noise were noticeably higher in the 1980s than before. In recent years environmental concerns have moved increasingly from the national to the international level. In particular the issue of global warming has become important. This is in part the consequence of emissions of carbon dioxide and carbon monoxide destroying the ozone layer. Noteworthy is that consumption—cars and aerosols, for example—as well as production contributes to this problem. Government anti-pollution policy is set out in the 1990 Environment Protection Act. There has been growing public concern with environmental issues, and an awareness that the Conservative government's "laissez faire" approach to industrial policy might prevent progress being made on issues such as carbon dioxide emissions from power stations. In answer to its critics, the government pointed to co-operation with international bodies such as the EC and the OECD in developing laws on pollution control. It also published a White Paper in September 1990 entitled "This Common Inheritance" which set out a policy framework for the 1990s. The paper was widely criticised by environmentalists as lacking substance, since it failed to support measures such as a carbon tax. Meanwhile the Environmental Protection Act of 1990 announced the phasing in of a so-called integrated system of pollution control. Important agencies in this process are the National Rivers Authority and Her Majesty's Inspectorate of Pollution. The new Environmental Action Fund, worth about £850,000 in 1994–95, supports projects with either direct or indirect environmental gains. At the beginning of 1994, BS7750 was published. This is described by the Government as 'the world's first standard for environmental management systems'.

Industrial Production.

It is fairly easy to measure output in the main manufacturing industries, and in many of the other industries producing goods. It is much more difficult to do so for the service industries: the output of a doctor or a teacher is not easily measured. So each month the Central Statistical Office calculates the *index of industrial production* covering the main production industries. Industrial production is thus an early indicator of economic trends (*see* Part IV), but historically it is prone to fluctuate more than the other components of GDP.

Manufacturing industry accounts for over 80 per cent of industrial production. Within manufacturing the following industries have expanded rapidly since World War II—chemicals, including drugs, plastics, cosmetics and detergents, coal and petroleum products, including oil refining, and instrument and electrical engineering. The slowest growing manufacturing industries are textiles, clothing, leather and shipbuilding, which are losing their markets to cheaper competitors. Those industries in which demand has stagnated tend to be the industries in which output per employee, *i.e.*, productivity, has stagnated. In 1994 manufacturing output was 16 per cent higher than in 1985, but 1 per cent lower than in 1990. At the same time employment in manufacturing fell from 5·9 million in 1982 to 4·5 million in 1992 to 4·3 million in 1994.

International Comparisons.

In the 1960s and 1970s Britain's GDP grew less rapidly than that of almost any other major Western country. The British economy was also characterised by a relatively slow growth of output per head, *i.e.*, productivity. Britain fell behind many of the European countries in terms of income per head. Some comparisons with other countries are made in the table above. However, these may be misleading because incomes are converted into pounds at official exchange rates, and these need not reflect relative costs of living.

Many explanations of Britain's poor performance were suggested, and there is by no means agreement on this matter among economists.

However, until recently there was general agreement that relatively slow productivity growth was the main culprit rather than an inadequate growth of capital and labour. The factors most often blamed were poor management, an inadequate and inefficient industrial relations system and low investment in training and research. Commentators differed in the relative importance they assigned to these different explanations, but agreed that low investment in physical plant and machinery was likely to have been the consequence rather than the primary cause of low growth. However in the last few years some economists have started to put renewed stress on the importance of capital and labour inputs. They argue that traditional analysis has under-estimated the effect of investment in either capital or labour. This is because there are knock-on effects on the rest of the economy which are hard to measure but nevertheless very real. For example, if a business spends money on developing a new product, the very existence of this new product creates opportunities for others. Think of the peripheral products and services which have relied on the development of cheap home computers.

A good deal of attention has been paid to the proportion of output which different countries devoted to physical *investment*, i.e., expenditure on plant, machinery and buildings—for use in future production. These investment ratios are shown in the table. With the exception of the U.S.A., all countries had investment ratios considerably higher than in the U.K. Since investment in dwellings contributes very little to growth, it may be appropriate to exclude this: however, similar results are obtained.

Recently economic theorists have stressed an important role for investment. Developing so-called endogenous growth theories, they have argued that, when a business invests in physical equipment or in training or in research and development, it creates potential opportunities not just for itself but for others. By this mechanism investment can have a substantial impact on productivity.

The performance of the British economy in the mid- to late 1980s was much better relative to other countries than was the case in the 1970s. Growth in total output averaged more than 2·1 per cent per annum in the period 1980–88, compared to a European average of 1·9 per cent in the same period. Productivity grew by an average 2·4 per cent per year from 1980 to 1989. **Part IV** includes a discussion of possible reasons for the UK's relatively better economic performance in the mid to late 1980s. Sceptics who believed that there had been no real underlying improvement have now been proved at least partly correct. The period of rapid growth 1986–88 finally ended because it met the UK's traditional constraints of high inflation and balance of payments weakness. The policy tightening invoked to cope with these depressed the UK economy and kept growth well below the European average in the period 1989–93.

Investment.

In 1993 gross investment in capital assets amounted to £96,611 million in the United Kingdom. This was 15·3 per cent of GNP. The net addition to the nation's stock of capital assets was only 30 per cent of total investment, the rest being needed to offset the wastage of assets already in use, i.e., to make good the *capital consumption*.

There are four main kinds of investment: plant and machinery, vehicles, dwellings, and other new buildings and works. In 1993 the four categories accounted for 34, 8·9, 19·9 and 37·1 per cent respectively. Investment may also be analysed by the purpose for which it is used. Social services such as education and health take a surprisingly small proportion of total investment. Distribution and other service industries take a large proportion: investment in electricity, gas and water alone accounts for 6·4 per cent of total non-dwelling investment. It is clear that some sectors of the economy are more capital-intensive than others. Manufacturing investment accounts for 12·8 per cent of the total. This is small in relation to the contribution of manufacturing to output, and has declined in recent years. Manufacturing investment fell more than any other form of investment in the recession at the beginning of the 1980s although it recovered markedly from 1983 onwards. Many of the fast-growing manufacturing industries—e.g.,

chemicals and electronics—use machinery and equipment per unit of output produced. However, these capital-intensive plants cannot pay unless they are worked at near full capacity. There is, however, evidence that the quality of investment undertaken has shown a marked improvement in recent years. The net real return on capital employed by all non-oil industrial and commercial companies stood at 7 per cent in 1993.

Increasing Investment.

Historically, the proportion of total output invested—the *investment ratio*—has been lower in Britain than in other countries with faster growth rates of output and productivity; and there is reason to believe that a higher proportion would have improved the growth rate to a certain extent. This was seen in the mid 1980s when a sharp acceleration in productivity growth was associated with a recovery of investment (particularly in manufacturing) from the very depressed levels of the early 1980s. But in a fully employed economy it is not possible to increase investment expenditures without curtailing other forms of expenditure, notably private and public consumption. This curtailment would have to be brought about by increasing taxation or encouraging people to save or by pruning public services. Yet the very act of restricting private consumption may induce private firms to *reduce* their investment expenditures. For society as a whole, increasing investment involves a choice between the loss in current consumption and the ensuing gain in future consumption. Of course not all consumption expenditure is equally important to the standard of living: some would agree that if British defence expenditure was pruned to permit more investment, there would be no loss to set against the future gain. This underlies the belief that the end of the Cold War will generate a substantial peace "dividend" in years to come.

In 1993 83·0 per cent of total investment in the United Kingdom was carried out in the private sector, 11·7 per cent by public authorities and 5·3 per cent by the public corporations. The Government has more control over investment in the public sector than in the private sector. Governments do possess various policy measures by which to influence private investment (*see also* **Part IV**) but private investment is volatile and highly dependent on businessmen's expectations, es-pecially their expectations about the future growth of their markets. It is no easy matter to raise the British investment ratio. Even in the sustained growth of the mid and late 1980s, investment rates were particularly high only for two or three years.

The Finance of Investment.

Any business is allowed to charge as a cost the depreciation of its assets. Normal depreciation allowances used to be based on the original cost of the asset and on its expected useful life. In a time of price inflation depreciation allowances calculated in this way will not provide sufficient finance to permit the replacement of assets at higher prices, and accountants have been slowly moving towards the concept of depreciation allowances being based on replacement costs.

Governments have, however, adopted certain fiscal devices to encourage replacement and net investment. Soon after the war initial allowances were introduced. Under this system firms were permitted to charge against profits in the first year of its life 20, or at times 40, per cent of the cost of any new equipment, and the system amounted to a loan of the tax saved in the first year, repaid over the life of the asset. In 1954 initial allowances for machinery were replaced by a system of investment allowances, under which a firm could charge against profits 20 per cent of the cost of any new machine, with the difference that all ordinary depreciation allowances were still chargeable. So the investment allowance was a grant, not a loan, of the saved tax. In 1966, initial and investment allowances on new plant and machinery in three sectors—manufacturing, mining, and shipping—were replaced by cash grants. Other plant and machinery and industrial building received higher initial allowances. In 1970 the Conservative Government reintroduced initial allowances in place of investment grants but in 1972 tried to encourage investment by granting free depreciation; *i.e.* 100 per cent allowance in the first year. The details of capital allowances changed from time to time over the following decade, but in the 1984 Budget a more radical change was announced. By 1986 first year allowances were scrapped, to be replaced by an annual allowance of 25 per cent and lower rates of Corporation Tax. In 1988–9 the Corporation Tax rate was reduced to 35 per cent, with a lower rate for small companies.

In response to the serious recession, the March 1991 Budget made a retrospective reduction in the Corporation Tax rate of 1% for the financial year 1990–91, and cut Corporation Tax by a further 1% to 33% for 1991–92 and beyond. The main rate is 33 per cent, with a reduced rate of 25 per cent for smaller companies (profits below £250,000 in a year). This leaves British rates of company taxation well below the European norm.

Apart from Government help, companies rely mainly on retained profits, which are often larger, taking companies as a whole, than their net investment. Other sources of company finance are borrowing in financial markets and the issue of company shares. As compared to many other countries, in Britain a relatively high proportion of external investment funds are raised by equity issue rather than by direct borrowing. Much public investment must be financed by the Treasury, except for relatively small amounts raised by public corporations on the financial markets. The 1979 Conservative Government announced its intention to seek private capital for some public investment projects, *e.g.* roadbuilding. The Government also maintained a new stress on helping small firms. This had been given particular impetus by the report of the Wilson Committee and by differentially favourable tax treatment in recent Budgets. The 1989 Enterprise Initiative continued this theme of assistance to small firms—by, for example, state-funded consultancy help. Some 10,400 consultancy projects were completed in 1993–94. Traditionally, investment measures are concerned with reducing the cost of capital. Many people believe that investment could be increased more effectively if more steps were taken to encourage a high and stable demand for output.

Labour Subsidies.

Initially Government subsidies were employed primarily as incentives for investment, particularly in a regional context. A 1972 Act, however, gave wide powers to the Government to offer financial assistance in almost any form to almost any enterprise, provided the assistance was "in the public interest". The Labour Government in 1974 greatly increased subsidisation, aimed chiefly at maintaining employment. These subsidies consisted chiefly of direct assistance to industries both within and outside the assisted areas and labour subsidies in the form of temporary employment and job creation schemes, aimed particularly at young people. Thus there was a new emphasis on subsidies which cheapened the cost of labour. Some of the schemes, like the Temporary Employment Subsidy, were pure subsidies in this sense. Others combined the subsidy element with measures to increase either the mobility or training of workers, the Youth Opportunities Programme, for instance. The new Conservative Government cut back on such schemes soon after its election in 1979, but did continue an emphasis on training, particularly with the Youth Training Scheme (later, Youth Training), which was significantly extended in 1986.

Two other major subsidies were introduced. The Community Programme encouraged sponsoring agencies or individuals to set up projects of community value to utilise unemployed labour. The Government provided a cash grant for each person employed, and paid their wage which was supposed to be equivalent to the going rate for the job in the area. A second subsidy was the Enterprise Allowance Scheme, which provided a small weekly payment to help the unemployed set up their own business. Subsequently, this was effectively replaced by the Business Start-Up Scheme. Until 1985 the Government had a fourth scheme called the Young Workers' Scheme, which paid employers

to take on youths, in order to help them gain work experience.

In 1986 and 1987 the Government shifted to more overt job subsidies, including the Job Start Scheme whereby a worker taking a job paying less than a specified minimum was paid the balance by the State. Other schemes were however phased out, including the New Workers Scheme (designed to encourage the young to accept low-paid employment) and the Job Release Scheme (which subsidised early retirement). Job-Sharing schemes however remained in place for longer.

By 1989 all training schemes for unemployed adults had been amalgamated under an umbrella Employment Training Scheme (later, Employment Training) which offered full-time training with an employer for all those who have been unemployed for at least six months. Job Restart interviews were provided for the long term unemployed, whilst help continued to be given via Employment Action.

Training.

An emphasis on training is an important part of the Government's supply strategy for the labour market. There had long been criticism of the British training effort. It was said that the school system was ill attuned to the needs of industry, that not enough young people continued with education or full-time training after the minimum school-leaving age. The old apprenticeship system was justly accused of being too rigid and of forming skills often inappropriate to changing technology. Financing of industrial training was thought to be insufficient. There was inadequate provision for the retraining of adults—so necessary if sufficient occupational flexibility was to be assured in a changing world.

In some respects matters had been getting worse. The recession of the early 1980s, for example, decimated training recruitment. Most of the old Industrial Training Boards were disappearing, without adequate substitutes being found. Yet at the same time, official thinking on training became more sophisticated after the mid 1970s. The present Government has issued many documents on the subject, perhaps the most significant being *The New Training Initiative* (1981), *Training for Employment* (1987), *Employment for the 1990s* (1988), and *People, Jobs and Opportunities* (1992).

Although training has been the focus of much attention, the main outcomes—Youth Training and Employment Training—were regarded by many as merely cosmetic devices to hide unemployment. The main criticisms of recent training programmes include lack of finance and a failure to address the key problem that arises under private sector provision of training, namely that unless an employer can guarantee that an employee stays in the firm for a considerable period of time, then the employer's return from the training investment is less than society's. The consequence is that if left to their own devices private employers will "underinvest". Rather than endorsing greater Government involvement to overcome this problem, a 1992 White Paper outlined a scheme whereby employers who lose workers whom they have trained might receive compensation either from the departing workers themselves or from their new employers. It is unlikely that this idea will be implemented. Meanwhile there has been some progress in the area of youth training and vocational education, with developments such as the Technical and Vocational Education Initiative. The school curriculum has been made more vocationally directed. The 1988 Education Act introduces a National Curriculum which, along with the recent switch from "O" Levels to GCSE, is intended to improve the vocational orientation of secondary education. More generally, the National Council for Vocational Qualifications is introducing a standard set of national qualifications to replace the myriad presently available. Some YT schemes were excellent whilst some industries were developing better alternatives to the old apprenticeship system, the Construction Industry Training Board, for instance.

The 1988 Employment Act incorporated all the Employment Training Schemes under the Employment Training Initiative. The scheme was workplace-based and was supported by a significant number of large employers. The scheme was designed to provide job-specific training over twelve months, and cost the government around £1·4 billion in 1989. Despite support from many employers, the scheme was criticised widely in the Trade Union movement where it was regarded as another means of attracting cheap labour and artificially reducing the official unemployment register. More generally there was some doubt about the quality of training being offered by some of the firms participating in the scheme.

As well as introducing the Employment Training Scheme, the 1988 Employment Act also brought substantial changes in structure of responsibility for training. At the local level, training is overseen by a network of Training and Enterprise Councils (TECs). These each cover a local labour market with a working population of approximately 250,000. Each TEC is an independent company, with two-thirds of its board being comprised of local employers. The reason for majority representation for businesses in TECs is that local industry should have the best insight into local skills needs. One difficulty is that the government has laid down fairly rigid rules about the seniority of the businessmen serving on TECs and this has caused recruitment difficulties in some areas. It is doubtful whether increased employer involvement in TECs will, in itself, make any difference to Britain's poor record in the area of skills training compared to other countries (particularly Japan and Germany). A deficiency in education and training is now widely blamed for the UK's bad industrial record and for the emergence of skills shortages at relatively high levels of unemployment. Meanwhile tentative steps have been taken to encourage individuals to take more responsibility for their own training decisions. A pilot scheme of Training Credits was introduced which is meant to give people the power to shop around for good training, whilst the 1991 Budget introduced tax relief for personal training expenditures. It is intended that a general Training Credits scheme will eventually replace YT in 1995. These credits will provide access to a new Modern Apprenticeship scheme. Meanwhile in 1993 Employment Training and Employment Action were replaced by two new schemes—Training for Work and Jobplan Workshops. Much progress has been made. More people are undergoing training and achieving qualifications, but the general view is that the UK still lags behind. Much of the training that is taking place is at a relatively low level.

Monopoly and Competition.

A trend to increasing size and increasing capitalisation has been going on now for many decades, and in the process it has changed the face of British industry. In the early 19th century the typical firm was the owner-managed textile mill. Then in the 1860s and 1870s came the discovery of cheap methods of making steel, with the consequential immense growth in the engineering industries. Most of the chemical industry is still newer, and there are many relatively 20th century industries such as aircraft, electronics and bio-technology.

In the capital-intensive industries the big firm predominates. In some it has become almost a monopoly; in others the pattern is of a few firms, all large. In 1995 the top British companies included oil firms (British Petroleum and Shell), tobacco firms (British American Tobacco and Imperial Tobacco), chemical firms (Imperial Chemical Industries and Unilever) and defence conglomerates such as British Aerospace (which included the Rover Group) and GEC. There is evidence that the extent of *concentration* of British industry—according to measures such as the proportion of the output of an industry produced by the largest three firms—has increased since 1945. For example, in 1993 only 516 of 131,122 businesses in manufacturing had more than 1,000 employees. Concentration increased particularly rapidly in the 1960s. There are two possible reasons for such an increase. The first is the natural growth of already large firms; the second is because of merger activity. This latter factor has been the more important in Britain. Although evidence is scanty, there is some suggestion that for a while in the mid 1970s, concentration stopped increasing, and it may even have fallen a little. In the late 1980s there was a massive increase in merger activity.

Competition goes on, but it has changed its form. Competition used to be largely by price. Now it is also by advertising and by variations in the quality and other features of the product—detergents and motor cars being good examples. In many industries, groups of firms producing similar products entered into agreements which had the effect of restricting competition, for example through schemes for price-fixing. The effect was to increase the price to the consumer and to reduce the amount of output available. Some authorities have estimated that the total "welfare" loss because of this was relatively small, and have argued that our major concern should be over the dangers of large corporations having substantial political power because of their size, and over their using this power to force the Government into unwise decisions about, for example, subsidising inefficient management.

Domestic monopolies are also limited by foreign competition, and by the discipline of "potential cross entry"—that is, the possibility that a powerful firm may be attracted into a new sector by the sight of very high profits. The British industrial scene has nevertheless changed substantially, not only with the emergence of very large and powerful domestic firms, but also with the extensive presence of foreign-owned multinationals. Finally, however, it is worth remembering the words of the Nobel Prize winning economist, Sir John Hicks, that the greatest return to a monopolistic existence is a quiet life. In other words, firms will try not to make "too large" profits for fear of attracting new competition. An interesting question, however, is how far the stock market "disciplines" firms into maximising their profits. If they do not, the argument goes, dividends will be low, investors will sell their shares whose price will be driven down, thus rendering the firm liable to be taken over.

Regulation of Competition and Monopoly.

(i) Restrictive Practices Court.

The Restrictive Trade Practices Acts of 1956 and 1968 outlawed many of the main forms of restrictive agreements preventing competition. Collective price-fixing was declared to be illegal unless an industry could show that the practice brought substantial benefit to the public. Collective price-fixing was the system under which a central association for the industry laid down minimum prices at which members might sell. Usually such a system was backed by arrangements for collective boycotts, under which members of the association would refuse to sell goods to wholesalers or retailers who broke the rules. Collective boycotts were also found in industries without collective price-fixing, one common purpose being to make sure that retailers did not sell a manufacturer's products below his recommended price. This form of collective resale price maintenance was also outlawed by the Acts.

Under the Acts any restrictive agreements of several specified kinds had to be registered with the Registrar of Restrictive Practices. He then had to decide whether there was a *prima facie* case for the discontinuation of the agreement, and, if he thought there was, the case was referred to a Restrictive Practices Court, containing both judicial and lay members. For an agreement to be upheld, the agreeing parties had to prove to the Court that the agreement conferred some substantial benefit on the public which out-weighed any injury it did to the public. A 1976 Act extended this legislation to cover service agreements.

In 1989 the government announced its intention to amend the existing legislation on Restrictive Trade Practices. It was intended that this would prohibit agreements which have the effect of preventing, restricting or distorting competition unless exemptions were given on the grounds of offsetting economic benefits. Many professional groups have voluntarily relaxed restrictive practices—for example, accountants, solicitors, stockbrokers, dentists and doctors. There has also been some legislation covering, for instance, the provision of legal services.

(ii) Resale Prices Act.

The Act of 1956 permitted individual manufacturers to enforce *resale price maintenance* (r.p.m.) for their own products. Few suppliers would want the publicity of enforcing r.p.m. through the courts, but they could still put some commercial pressure on price-cutters, *e.g.*, by offering less favourable terms or by refusing them supplies. The Resale Prices Act of 1964 prohibited all methods of enforcing minimum resale prices. However, goods which had been registered in due time with the Registrar of Restrictive Practices or had been approved by the Restrictive Practices Court, were exempted, temporarily in the former case and permanently in the latter. For r.p.m. to be approved by the Court, it had to be shown that some ensuing benefit to customers (*e.g.*, of increased quality or more retail outlets) outweighed any detriment. With the exception of books and some pharmaceuticals, where r.p.m. is still not unlawful, r.p.m. has largely been replaced by "recommended" retail prices, which are in effect maximum prices. This practice has been investigated by the Monopolies Commission, which found that it was not always against the public interest.

(iii) The Monopolies Commission.

The Restrictive Practices Acts left untouched those industries in which one firm is dominant: these remained the responsibility of the Monopolies Commission. This is an independent administrative tribunal, established in 1948, with powers to investigate and decide whether a monopoly (defined in terms of market share) is contrary to the "public interest."

The Monopolies and Mergers Act of 1965 strengthened control over monopolies and mergers. With regard to monopolies, the Government wished to provide itself with legal powers of enforcement: previously monopolies had been expected to comply voluntarily with the findings of the Monopolies Commission. The Act also permitted the Government to refer a merger or a proposed merger to the Monopolies Commission in cases where the merger would lead to monopoly (defined as control of at least one third of the market) or would increase the power of an existing monopoly, or where the value of the assets taken over exceeded £5 million (now £70 million). The 1965 Act was repealed in 1973 and replaced by the Fair Trading Act. The rules governing referral to the Monopolies Commission were changed in this later Act. Since 1989, the decision to refer a merger to the Monopolies Commission, and the criteria by which the commission examines the public interest, have become less rigidly defined. Considerations of formal market share are probably less important than for example, the existence of barriers to entry. The Companies Act of 1989 also introduced a number of changes aimed at improving procedures for merger control: a voluntary procedure for pre-notification of proposed mergers which would allow rapid approval; provision for the companies involved to accept statutory undertakings which might obviate the need for a full investigation by the Commission; and the temporary prohibition on dealing in one another's shares in the case of a merger referred to the Commission. The Act also strengthened powers given to the Secretary of State for Industry under the 1980 Competition Act to refer questions concerning the efficiency, cost or monopoly position of public sector bodies to the Commission.

In interpreting the public interest, the Monopolies Commission has to weigh up the negative aspects (of large size, high prices, reduced product choice and restricted entry for new firms into the market) against the benefits of greater resources for product innovation and lower costs due to synergy. More recently, emphasis has been placed upon the importance of international competition and it is argued that British firms need to be large to compete effectively. In 1993 the Monopolies Commission reported on ten "monopoly situations", three of them unfavourably.

(iv) The Fair Trading Act.

The 1973 Fair Trading Act placed the previously dispersed responsibilities for overseeing competition policies in the hands of a civil servant—the Director General of Fair Trading. The Monopolies

Acts of 1948 and 1965 were repealed and replaced by rather more comprehensive rules. Monopoly was now defined as control of one quarter of the market instead of one third. For the first time local monopolies were made subject to control. Also "complex monopolies" were made subject to investigation—that is situations where no one firm had 25 per cent of the market, but where several of them collaborated to restrict competition. The Director General of Fair Trading—as well as the Department of Trade and Industry—was enabled to refer monopoly situations to the Monopolies Commission; though it was still only the Department which could make references on mergers. Additionally the Director General took over the functions of the Registrar of Restrictive Practices and responsibility for general consumer protection, and set up a new body to assist in that aim—the Consumer Protection Advisory Committee.

In 1978 the Labour Government published a review of its general policy which recommended a more neutral policy towards mergers and that greater stress should be put on the importance of competition.

In 1980 the new Conservative Government introduced a Competition Act which strengthened the powers of the authorities to deal with practices which limited competition in both the public and private sectors. Procedures were also speeded up considerably. There was a new power to refer nationalised industries and other public bodies for investigation of their efficiency, costs, services to consumers, and possible abuse of monopoly position. Perhaps the most celebrated case of applying the authorities' new legislation involves the UK Stock Exchange. In return for a pledge from the Government not to prosecute, the Stock Exchange abolished the restrictive practices which governed entry into the stockbroking profession, and separate the broking from the market-making functions in the stock market—the so-called "Big Bang" in the City of London. Self-regulation for the City was enshrined in the Financial Services Act of 1986. Of increasing importance are EC provisions, Articles 85 and 86, which relate to anti-competitive practices which affect trade between member states.

(v) The Enterprise Initiative and Companies Act 1989.

A 1988 Enterprise White Paper proposed changes to competition policy, some of which were enacted in the course of 1989. Henceforth the main reason for referring mergers would be their likely effect on competition (see (iii) above). Though "public interest" referrals remain, the Government will intervene only rarely. Generally, it was claimed, the "market" would look after the public interest. When judging the impact of a merger on competition, due regard will be given to foreign competition and also to potential entrants. The latter represents a particular fashion among modern industrial economists, who argue that many apparently monopolistic or oligopolistic industries may in fact be constrained to behave in a relatively competitive manner by the possibility that other firms might be attracted into their sector by high profits. Accordingly Monopolies Commission hearings are increasingly concerned with the existence or otherwise of "barriers to entry". Mergers policy is not, however, without its critics, many of whom believe that the criteria for referral are now too lax, particularly compared to general practice in Europe. In 1993 the Government announced that it intended to take tougher measures against anti-competitive practices. In 1992 the Cadbury Committee, on the management of companies, provided a code of best practice for company boards.

(vi) Industrial Structure.

Mergers may lead to monopoly and to the abuse of monopoly power. But it would be wrong to presume that mergers are always bad: mergers—by facilitating research and other economies of large-scale production—may increase industrial efficiency. For this reason the *Industrial Reorganisation Corporation* (IRC) was set up in 1966 under Government auspices. Its functions were to promote industrial reorganisation in the interests of industrial efficiency, *e.g.*, by enabling industries to achieve economies of scale or by reorganising inefficiently managed firms. It assisted firms in agreed regroupings and could intervene to encourage a particular takeover which, in its estimation, was in the public interest. However its objective in making loans was to "prod" and not to "prop" inefficient firms. It supported mergers in electronics, trawling, nuclear power, mechanical engineering, and other industries. In 1970 the Conservative Government decided to wind up the IRC. However, some of the proposed functions of the National Enterprise Board, set up in 1975, were similar to those performed by the IRC (see **Part IV**). The 1979 Conservative Government initially streamlined the NEB, and subsequently amalgamated it with the National Research and Development Corporation to form the British Technology Group.

Nationalised Industries.

After the extensive privatisation of industries and utilities undertaken during the last decade, the Nationalised Industries now account for only about 1 per cent of GDP. In many cases—e.g., the railways and postal services—these remaining state industries are natural monopolies, in which the provision of competing services could be wasteful, although the present government seems determined to privatise even those industries where there appears to be a natural monopoly.

With the exception of steel—denationalised 1951-53 and re-nationalised in 1967—nationalisation was for a long time not extended into manufacturing industry. The post-1974 Labour Government nationalised the shipbuilding and aerospace industries, and established the British national Oil Corporation and the National Enterprise Board with wide powers to take holdings in private industry. Under the 1979 Conservative Government the post-war trend towards greater public ownership of industry was reversed (see **Part IV**).

A 1967 White Paper, amended in 1978, dictated that as well as achieving specified financial targets, nationalised industries should earn a target rate of return on their investments and price according to the marginal cost of a service.

With respect to pricing, it is government policy that subsidies can be made for some services which are justified on social grounds, e.g., grants to British Rail to continue unremunerative rail services, although these are due to be phased out over the next few years and have been halved in real terms since 1982. Cross-subsidisation of non-commercial services by commercial services within a nationalised industry is discouraged.

The present Government has challenged the whole concept of running publicly-owned industries even where a natural monopoly quite clearly exists. Industries remaining under state control have also been unable to raise sufficient outside investment capital because of the imposition of strict External Financing Limits. Public sector monopolies such as British Telecom and British Gas have been returned to the private sector and have remained largely monopolies. Prices are regulated to ensure that they reflect general inflation adjusted for changes in the industry's underlying cost structure. One difficulty is that prices may nevertheless be set too high because the regulator (for example, OFTEL for British Telecom) relies heavily on information which is provided by the monopolist. Restructuring of the industry may help overcome this difficulty, since this makes available several sources of information from the component firms and thus allows sensible comparisons to be made. This was one of the motives behind privatising electricity and water as area boards. The Government is also seeking to introduce competition in the provision of public services. For example, local authorities are now obliged to put services such as refuse collection out to public tender. Many traditional civil service functions have been put out to Agencies. Following the 1988 Education Act schools can effectively compete for pupils and as of April 1991 hospitals are essentially competing for patients referred through general practitioners.

3. INCOMES, WAGES, AND PRICES

Personal Income.

National income is a measure of the total income accruing to the residents in a country in return for services rendered (see **G13**). It therefore consists of the sum of wages, salaries, profits, and rents having allowed for depreciation. But not all this income accrues to persons, e.g., companies do not distribute all their profits to shareholders and some nationalised industries earn profits. This is part of national income but not of *personal income*. On the other hand, some personal incomes are not payments for services rendered. Such incomes are called *transfer incomes* to emphasise that their payment does not add to the national income, but only transfers income from one agent to another. Included in this category are retirement pensions, child benefit and student grants. In the United Kingdom in 1993 central and local government made transfer payments to the personal sector of £88·5 billion.

Personal Disposable Income.

Not all personal income is available for spending. In 1993 the State took 12 per cent of household income in *direct taxation*, and 3 per cent went as Social Security contributions, which being compulsory are in effect a form of tax. Another 2 per cent went in contributions to pension schemes. The remaining 83 per cent of income—called *personal disposable income*—was available for spending. However, not all disposable income need be spent on consumer goods and services; income can instead be saved. There are many possible motives for saving, e.g., to meet future contingencies, for a future purchase such as a house or car, for retirement, or for the income to be derived from saving. Saving as a fraction of personal disposable income fluctuated from 7 to 10 per cent between 1960 and 1971. By 1975 it had reached about 13 per cent. It remained high thereafter, and peaked at about 15 per cent in 1980. It then fell and was only 5·6 per cent in 1988 although it recovered rapidly to a level of 12·5 per cent in 1992. By the end of 1993 it was 11·8 per cent. Many explanations of this varying savings ratio have been advanced – it seems to be higher, the higher is the rate of inflation. In the mid-1980s the fall in savings was related to rapid growth in the value of personal sector wealth, particularly in housing.

The recent recovery of the ratio seems to be closely linked to the high level of uncertainty generated by the recession, and also with the fall in the real value of the personal sector's assets relative to its debt. This latter phenomenon is intimately linked to the decline in house prices.

Types of Personal Income.

The table shows the sources of household income. In 1993, the share of income from employment was 56 per cent. This rose considerably in the post Second World War period. The share of salaries grew relative to that of wages, not because average salaries rose faster than average wages but because the number of salaried workers expanded rapidly. With the development of the Welfare State there was an increase in the percentage of incomes derived from public grants—pensions, social security payments, student grants, etc.

SOURCES OF HOUSEHOLD INCOME,
1982 AND 1992

(As percentage of total)

	1983	1993
Wages and salaries	62	56
Self employment	8	10
Investments and rents	6	7
Annuities and pensions (other than social security benefits)	7	11
Social security benefits	14	13
Other sources	3	3

Over the post-war period as a whole, the share of self-employment income and incomes from property

DISTRIBUTION OF ORIGINAL, DISPOSABLE AND FINAL HOUSEHOLD INCOME, 1993

	Quintile groups of households				
	Bottom Fifth	Next Fifth	Middle Fifth	Next Fifth	Top Fifth
Original Income	2·3	6	15	25	52
Disposable Income	7·6	12	16	23	42
Final Income	6·6	11	16	22	44

fell while that from wages and salaries and from social security benefits tended to rise. Over the past ten years, however, income from self-employment has begun to increase a little, in line with a larger share of the self-employed in the labour force. The share of income from annuities and pensions is also tending to grow along with the expansion of privately-funded occupational pension schemes. This will be encouraged further by incentives to transfer out of the state pension scheme into private pension plans.

Inequality of Income.

In 1993, the top 20 per cent of income receivers (defined as households rather than individuals), received 52 per cent of total original income, whilst the bottom 20 per cent obtained only 2·3 per cent. Thus Britain is far from being an egalitarian society, but discrepancies have narrowed since before the war, though with a subsequent widening in the last decade or so.

Taxes on income are of course progressive, rising as income increases. This progressivity was reduced through the 1980s as higher rates of income tax were lowered. By the beginning of 1992 there was a standard rate of 25 per cent and just one higher rate of 40 per cent. The Budget of that year introduced an additional lower band of 20 per cent. The table shows the shares of disposable income. This is original income minus direct taxes and plus cash benefits. We can see that the effect is redistributive. In 1993 the share of the top 20 per cent fell to 42 per cent after allowing for these two items, whilst the share of the bottom 20 per cent rose to 7·6 per cent. Allowing for the effects of indirect taxation and benefits in kind produces final income. As the table shows, these two latter effects tend to be offsetting.

DISTRIBUTION OF
HOUSEHOLD INCOME (%)

	Bottom fifth	Net Income Next fifth	Middle fifth	Next fifth	Top fifth
1979	9·5	14·2	18·2	23·2	35·0
1981	8·9	13·5	17·5	22·8	37·3
1983	8·8	13·4	17·6	22·9	37·3
1985	8·6	13·1	17·5	23·2	37·6
1987	7·6	12·1	16·8	22·5	41·0
1988	8·0	11·0	16·0	23·0	42·0
1991/92	6·0	11·0	17·0	23·0	43·0

Thus the direct tax burden somewhat squeezes the distribution of incomes. But until the mid 1970s the narrowing dispersion of incomes before tax was of greater importance in making Britain rather more egalitarian than taxation policy. Since the late 1970s, however, inequality of pre-tax incomes has increased, whilst the tax system has become less redistributive. As the table about demonstrates, the distribution of income as defined by the share of net income has become less equal over the period since 1979. On this definition, the share of the bottom fifth has fallen from 9·5 per cent to 6 per cent, while that of the top quintile has risen from 35 per cent to 43 per cent.

Income and Spending Power.

In various ways figures for incomes alone underestimate the degree of inequality in British society. First, incomes are incomes as defined for income tax purposes. Any allowed expenses are excluded; and

for the self-employed and the higher ranks of management the expense allowance now adds substantially to spending power. Second, if one buys an asset which then rises in value one gains extra spending power. Such capital gains can be very important to the wealthy in periods of boom in ordinary share prices, land prices and house prices. Yet only in 1965 did capital gains become taxable and even then the rate of tax on capital gains was low in relation to the rate on additional income. Since 1988, capital gains have been taxed at the individual's or corporation's higher rate of tax, although there is a larger tax allowance.

Inequality of Wealth.

Spending power depends not only on income and capital gains but also on the sheer amount of capital owned. Data on the ownership of capital in Britain have to be estimated indirectly from information arising in connection with the payment of death duties, supplemented by information from capital transfer tax (from 1986 inheritance tax) returns and therefore cannot always be relied upon. An alternative method is to estimate the stock of wealth by working back from information on investment income, but this approach is also prone to error. It appears from the table that the most wealthy 1 per cent of the population own 18 per cent of all wealth, whilst 49 per cent of all wealth is owned by the richest 10 per cent. Even more strikingly, the poorer half of the population own only 8 per cent of total wealth. It should be emphasised, however, that the data refer to *individuals* rather than to *households*: this can give a misleading impression if, for example, the assets of married couples are generally registered in the name of one of the marriage partners rather than as jointly-owned assets. Nevertheless, it is fair to conclude from the data that the disparity of wealth is considerably greater than that of income. Moreover, there is a natural tendency for the inequality of wealth to grow because the higher income groups tend to save a higher proportion of their income and so to accumulate capital more readily. The Government by capital transfer tax tried but largely failed to neutralise this tendency.

Capital transfer tax (CTT) was introduced in 1974. Until then only transfers of wealth on death or shortly before death were taxable. The CTT had

WEALTH OF INDIVIDUALS IN BRITAIN,
1992

Percentage of wealth owned by:	
Most wealthy 1 percent of population	18
„ „ 5 „ „ „ „	37
„ „ 10 „ „ „ „	49
„ „ 25 „ „ „ „	72
„ „ 50 „ „ „ „	92

GROSS WEEKLY EARNINGS,
GREAT BRITAIN

(Average earnings, adults, April 1994)

	Manual	Non-Manual
Men	£280·7	£428·2
Women	£181·9	£278·4

AVERAGE GROSS WEEKLY EARNINGS
OF FULL-TIME ADULT MALE
EMPLOYEES, BY SELECTED
OCCUPATIONS, APRIL 1994

	£ per week
Medical practitioner . . .	788·3
General manager and administrator	667·2
Solicitor	624·7
University teacher . . .	564·8
Engineer, civil or structural . .	485·3
Production manager . . .	484·6
Accountant	482·6
Scientist	472·6
Primary teacher . . .	446·1
Policeman (sergeant and below) .	433·9
Telephone fitter	369·5
Electrician	346·2
Tool maker and fitter . . .	341·8
Coach and vehicle body builder .	289·3
Postal worker & mail sorter . .	274·0
Heavy goods driver . . .	263·7
General clerk	261·8
Bricklayer	252·4
Painter, decorator . . .	249·0
Unskilled building worker . .	241·2
Dustman	235·6
General farm worker . . .	217·7
Butcher	214·0
Hospital porter	202·6
Total workers . . .	362·1
of which: Manual . . .	280·7
Non-manual . . .	428·2

AVERAGE WEEKLY EARNINGS OF
MANUAL WORKERS IN CERTAIN
INDUSTRIES (£)
(April 1994)

	Men	Women
Mineral oil refining . .	464·8	—†
Printing and publishing . .	339·4	209·2
Motor vehicles . . .	334·2	228·5
Chemicals	330·0	297·1
Textiles	255·5	164·3
All manufacturing . .	*296·9*	*186·4*
Transport and		
communication . .	297·5	271·8
Public administration .	255·6	199·0
Retail distribution . .	233·4	166·4
All industries . . .	*280·7*	*181·9*

*Including industries not listed.

†Too small a number of women in this category to
be recorded.

differences within each industry between men and
women. There are two possible reasons why
women are paid less than men. One is that they
are crowded into lower-paying occupations. The
second is that they may have lower pay than men
within the same occupation. Either form of disadvantage could be the result of discrimination or
of women possessing inferior productive characteristics. In practice it is a very difficult distinction to
make. Equal opportunities and equal pay legislation
attempts to reduce discrimination. The Equal Pay
Act (1970) obliged a firm to pay men and women,
who are doing the same job, the same wage by the
end of 1975. In 1972 women in manual occupations
had median earnings which were about half those of
men. By 1978 this figure had risen to over 60 per
cent, though by the early 1980s this improvement
had slowed down, and by 1994 was only 64·8 per
cent. Women in non-manual occupations had
median earnings which were 65 per cent of their
male counterparts. These changes are explained by
the impact of the Act, by flat rate general increases
agreed under incomes policies, and by trade union
bargaining policy under inflation. There have been
renewed initiatives against sexual discrimination.
In particular, in 1984 an amendment to the Equal
Pay Act insisted that as well as paying men and
women doing the same job the same rate of pay,
parity of pay should also apply to jobs of equal
value. The Equal Opportunities Commission has
issued a Code of Practice which suggests positive
actions which employers might take to improve the
lot of women in employment. Recently this has
contributed to a catch-up for women in areas of the
retail trade. A number of "equal pay for work of
equal value" claims have been made under the 1984
Act and taken to the European Court of Human
Rights. Recent examples of such claims include
those filed by women upholsterers in the car
industry and by clerks in the banking industry. As
yet, such claims have been quite rare and have had
at most a marginal impact on pay differentials.

Overtime and short-time.

The earnings of any individual worker depend
on many factors, and are usually well above the
basic wage rate payable for a *standard working
week*. They include overtime earnings; and overtime working is common for men. In most weeks in
the 1970s 1–2 million operatives in manufacturing—about a third of the total—worked overtime to the extent of 8 to 9 hours. In 1994 32·7 per
cent of operatives worked an average of 9·7 hours of
overtime each. Nor is overtime confined to male
manual employment; it is found, for example, in
office work and even in some of the professions like
medicine and accountancy. The working week is
composed of standard hours and overtime hours.
Its length has diminished since before the war,
although the standard week has been more significantly reduced.

In most industries, for manual workers it was cut
from 48 to 44 hours soon after the war. A 42-hour
week was introduced between 1960 and 1962, and
there was a movement towards a 40-hour standard

---

many loopholes, but did something to redistribute
wealth. The 1986 Budget effectively abolished CTT
for gifts *inter vivos*, the tax (renamed inheritance
tax) applying on death or transfers made in the 7
years preceding death.

Wages and Salaries.

In 1993 56 per cent of personal income was
paid in the form of wages and salaries.

Earnings by Occupation.

Different occupations command different pay,
as the table shows. The figures are of average
earnings. The structure of pay reflects in part
the amount of responsibility which the different
jobs entail. The differentials reflect also the ease of
entry into various occupations. This in turn depends on the degree of specialised knowledge, skill
or talent required, and in a few cases it depends on
the extent to which artificial barriers to entry have
created scarcity. The structure of pay is also influenced, of course, by the degree of organisation and
bargaining strength of workers in different occupations. Finally, the relative strengths of demand
for different types of worker is important, as is the
force of custom.

Within the manual occupations the difference
between skilled, semi-skilled and unskilled pay
narrowed over the post-war years. This was most
marked during the war, in the years immediately
after the war and between 1970 and 1976 when
skilled workers were often granted the same flat rate
advances as unskilled. The last few years have seen
a reversal of such narrowing and indeed
further widening. Recent years have also seen a
widening of the gap between manual and non-
manual pay.

Earnings by Industry.

Even within the manual occupations there are
significant differences in earnings among industries. These are associated with the bargaining
strength of different groups of workers, with the
prosperity of the industry, and with the average
skill levels required in production. Manufacturing
industries as a whole pay relatively well. Public
administration (including local government, road-
men and the like) is a low-wage sector.

Earnings by Sex.

The table also shows very significant earnings

working-week in the late 1960s. More recently there have been pressures from unions, notably in engineering industries, to reduce the standard week below 40 hours, and indeed this has happened in many sectors. In much of the chemical industry, for example, it is often as low as 35 hours. The standard working week tends to be slightly less for white collar workers than for manual workers. Notwithstanding these developments total hours worked have increased for many people since the early 1980s.

Short-time, the working of less than the standard week, has not been common since the war. It has been important in particular industries at particular times: during 1994 it was far smaller than overtime. In 1994 31,000 operatives in manufacturing were on an average short time of 12·2 hours a week—a total 0·58 million hours lost as against 9·1 million hours of overtime in the same year. When the economy was growing very rapidly in the period 1986–88 it was disappointing that higher output was in many instances met through increased overtime rather than higher employment. This may have reflected natural caution on the part of employers about the durability of Britain's economic recovery at that time—a caution which appears justified in the light of the subsequent recession.

Earnings and Rates.

Overtime is not, however, the main reason why earnings exceed minimum wage-rates; for most workers earn more than the minimum in the standard working-week. One reason is payment by results, the system of payment under which the worker's wage depends partly on output or performance. A common form is still the piecework system, under which pieceworkers are paid a fixed low rate per hour for each hour worked plus a fixed piecework price for each operation performed; but increasingly employers tend to prefer, as a more effective incentive, some scheme under which the bonus payment is related to the output or some other measure of the performance of a larger group or to that of a whole factory. With such incentive schemes, earnings rise as productivity rises, and, as usually such workers also participate in advances in general wage-rates, the gap between earnings and wage-rates tends to widen for them. Merit-related pay is becoming increasingly fashionable, particularly in white-collar work. An example of such a scheme would be that each employee is given a cost of living increase each year plus an additional amount based on merit, as judged by an annual assessment. This principle has been extended further in some large firms, where employees receive performance-related bonuses according to whether or not they have met pre-determined objectives or targets. Some trade unionists regard this as a potentially severe threat to collective negotiations about pay.

Wage Determination.

In Britain there were 9 million trade union members in 268 unions at the end of 1993. Most of these unions are very small, 163 of them having less than 2,500 members. But 20 have memberships over 100,000. Union membership has fallen from its peak level of 13·3 million in 1979, and today is at its lowest level since 1946. The main job of unions is collective bargaining with employers. The structure and scope of collective bargaining changed significantly in the 1980s. Until the beginning of that decade in most industries most employers belonged to associations which bargained collectively on their behalf. Some big firms, however, preferred to remain outside the associations, and strike their own bargain with the unions. Before the war many firms tried to encourage the formation of Company Unions, i.e., of unions confined to employees of a single firm; but this became very uncommon. In some lowly paid trades minimum wages were fixed by Wages Councils set up by the Department of Employment: and representatives of the workers and employers, and independent members, met together to reach agreement on the settlement to be recommended to the Minister. But over most of industry the aim of collective bargaining was to reach voluntary agreement, and the Department of Employment intervened only when no agreement is reached. In 1974 the Labour Government set up the *Advisory Conciliation and Arbitration Service* (A.C.A.S.) to provide independent mediation and arbitration services.

The usual pattern of negotiation was like this. First, the union put in a claim for an all-round increase, usually much larger than it expected to get. Then after a time the employers replied, often offering a much smaller increase, and sometimes none at all. They then argued round a table until either they reached agreement or they definitely failed to reach agreement. If the latter happened the next step varied considerably from industry to industry. Many industries had their own "conciliation" machinery, in which outsiders tried to help the two sides to reach agreement. Some, though not many, also had their own "arbitration" machinery, in which outsiders could recommend a solution of the dispute, which was sometimes binding and sometimes not. It depended on what the two sides had agreed on in advance. Many industries had no machinery of their own and until 1974 depended on the general facilities the Minister responsible could offer. Thereafter they relied on the services of A.C.A.S. Just as neither unions nor employers were obliged to call in the Minister, so they were under no obligation to call in A.C.A.S.; the unions might opt to put pressure on the employers immediately either by strike action, or by banning overtime or piecework, or by other action.

After the Second World War plant bargaining developed as an increasingly important supplement to industry-wide bargaining in many sectors of the economy. Initially this was largely informal bargaining, with shop-stewards (unpaid lay trade union officials at the plant level) negotiating with management about, for example, special rates for working new machines. It is this which to a large degree was responsible for the growing gap between wage rates and earnings. The Donovan Commission, which was set up to inquire into the state of industrial relations and which reported in 1968, also saw it as a major cause of many of Britain's industrial relations problems, such as a high level of strike activity. Realising that it was impossible to put the clock back, the Commission recommended that plant bargaining procedures should be formalised, giving, for instance, proper channels for the resolution of wage disputes. In the 1970s there was indeed an increase in *formal* plant negotiations, with many plants setting their own wage rates and using national agreements purely as a minimum benchmark. This development probably improved the climate of industrial relations. In the mid 1970s some companies, especially in manufacturing, which had been concerned about the administrative cost as well as about the leapfrogging effects of plant agreements, had moved to single company bargains.

Thus in the years up to the 1980s there had been increasing decentralisation of bargaining. This continued apace during the 1980s with active Government encouragement. The multi-employer bargain declined considerably in significance and in many cases disappeared altogether. Thus the proportion of the workforce covered by such agreements fell from 60 per cent in 1978 to 35 per cent in 1989. At the same time pay setting in many companies was becoming more decentralised to profit and cost centres. Simultaneously the range of issues over which bargaining took place diminished, whilst even pay setting became more individualised.

It has always been the case, and still is, that more people are covered by collective bargaining than are union members. Nevertheless such has been the decline of unionism that increasingly large numbers of workers find that a collective bargain has little, if any, role to play in the determination of their pay. This is particularly true in the growing service sector and in small firms. The traditional heartlands of union influence are the public sector and the declining manufacturing industries. Although instances of formal de-recognition have been relatively few, even in these areas the influence of collective bargaining has waned. There has been a deliberate move to "individualise" the determining of pay; and here new fashions in payments systems, like performance pay, have played a large role.

WAGES AND PRICES
(1955 = 100)

	Weekly earnings	Index of retail prices	Real earnings
1955 . . .	100	100	100
1960 . . .	130	114	114
1965 . . .	175	136	129
1970 . . .	250	169	148
1975 . . .	540	313	173
1980 . . .	997	611	163
1985 . . .	1,537	865	178
1990 . . .	2,321	1,154	201
1994 . . .	2,847	1,310	222

INDEX OF RETAIL PRICES
(January 1987 = 100)

	1987 Weight*.	1993 Weight*.	Monthly average index.						
			1987	1988	1989	1990	1991	1992	1993
Food . . .	167	142	101	105	111	119	126	128	131
Catering . .	46	45	103	110	116	126	139	147	156
Alcoholic drink	76	76	102	107	113	124	139	148	155
Tobacco . .	38	35	100	103	106	114	130	144	156
Housing . .	157	158	103	113	135	164	161	160	151
Fuel and light	61	45	99	102	107	116	125	128	126
Household goods	73	76	102	106	110	115	123	127	128
Household services	44	47	102	107	113	120	130	137	142
Clothing and footwear	70	58	101	104	110	115	119	119	120
Personal goods and services .	38	37	102	107	114	123	133	142	148
Motoring expenditure	127	142	103	108	114	121	130	139	145
Fares and other travel	22	20	102	108	115	123	136	144	151
Leisure goods .	47	48	102	104	107	112	118	121	123
Leisure services .	30	71	102	108	115	125	139	150	157
Total . . .	*1,000*	*1,000*	*102*	*107*	*115*	*126*	*134*	*139*	*141*

* *i.e.*, proportionate importance of items in total expenditure in 1956 and in 1991.

Strikes.

The strike is the unions' weapon of last resort. Most unions maintain strike funds in order to support their members when they call them out on strike; but these funds are small, and strike pay is usually very much below normal wages. So unions cannot afford to call strikes irresponsibly, and major official strikes are relatively uncommon. Nevertheless, the big strikes are important; for the success or failure of one big strike can affect the results of all the other collective bargaining under way at the time.

Before the 1980s most strikes were neither large nor official. An official strike is one called by a union, usually by decision of the national executive, and is typically the result of collective bargaining about wages. But unofficial strikes called by local leaders were often about other matters. Few of the big unofficial strikes which plagued the docks were about wages; rather they reflected job insecurity and the poor state of labour relations in that industry. Much the same may be said about the continual strikes in shipbuilding, many of them caused by demarcation disputes concerning which jobs should be done by which type of skilled worker. Other strike-prone industries were mining and vehicles. In most industries there have always been very few strikes, and they have tended to be concentrated in the larger plants.

From the mid-1950s the number of strikes in Britain increased, except in coal mining. In 1969 and 1970 there was a huge jump in both the number of stoppages and working days lost. After that industrial disputes fell to a more normal level, and indeed by the early 1980s were at an historically very low level. Partly this reflected the impact of high unemployment, but may also have represented a more permanent improvement in Britain's strike record. When unemployment fell sharply in 1988 and 1989, the number of strikes did not increase disturbingly. In spite of a succession of transport strikes in the summer of 1989, and an ambulance dispute later in the year, working days lost in 1989 numbered just over 4 million, only a little above the average of the previous four years. Since then there has been a drop in the number of working days lost. The figure for 1993 was only 649,000.

In its Industrial Relations Act of 1971 the Conservative Government laid down new laws for the regulation of industrial relations and for the curbing of strikes. However, the Act was repealed by the incoming Labour Government in 1974, which itself brought in several new pieces of legislation, including the Trade Unions and Labour Relations Act, the Employment Protection Act, and the Trade Unions and Labour Relations (Amendment) Act. As well as increasing legal protection for the individual employee and extending trade union immunities and rights, this legislation was concerned to improve industrial relations practice. The belief behind the legislation was that this could be done by machinery which ensured, for example, that employers formally recognised unions for collective bargaining purposes and that unions had greater access to information to enable them to negotiate about issues (such as a firm's investment plans) which previously ignorance had precluded them from doing.

With the election of a Conservative Government in 1979, the direction of legislation altered again. The 1980 Employment Act introduced measures to moderate the closed shop, provide funds for secret union ballots about important issues such as industrial action, and to limit picketing to only the establishments at which strikes were taking place. A further Act in 1982 intensified pressure on the unions. In particular it introduced further measures against existing closed shops and increased the liability of unions for the actions of their members. In 1984 came the Trade Union Act concerned with union democracy. In this unions were denied immunity if strikes took place without ballots, voting members of union executives had to be elected, and periodic ballots on the political use of union funds were required. In 1988 a further piece of legislation was passed by Parliament, which, inter alia, made it illegal for unions to discipline members who refused to obey a strike call, even a legal one. Such legislative developments are likely to reduce unions' ability to call and prosecute strikes, and possibly also will diminish the scope for local union leaders to have a decisive impact on strike decisions. The process continues. A new Employment Act, passed in the final months of 1990, made further reforms to the closed shop and to the rules governing both secondary and unofficial industrial action. It removed Trade Union immunity for acts in contemplation or furtherance of trade disputes when there had been secondary action (redefined to include those working or performing services under contract) other than in the course of peaceful picketing. The Act also amended the Employment Act of 1980, making unions liable for the actions of all their officials, including their workplace representatives, during an industrial dispute. The 1990 Act also effectively outlawed the pre-entry closed shop by making it unlawful to refuse to employ someone on the grounds of union membership or lack of it. Much of the Conservative legislation was consolidated in the Trade Union and Labour Relations (Consolidation) Act of 1992.

In 1993 the Trade Union Reform and Employment Rights Act was enacted. It finally abolished Wages Councils, whose scope had been much reduced by legislation in 1986. Strike ballots had to be postal, and industrial action was only legal after a period of notice had been given. Two other provisions were of greater significance. First, henceforth workers would be able to decide for themselves which union to join. This provision could massively diminish the ability of the TUC to regulate competition amongst its member unions, and weaken its power still further. Second, workers would have to periodically re-affirm their willingness to have their subscriptions automatically deducted from their pay. This would eliminate any tendency for people to remain members of a union through inertia.

Prices and Real Incomes.

Prices rose very rapidly (by over 30 per cent) between 1949 and 1953, and earnings only just kept ahead in this period. But after that *real earnings* (*i.e.*, the command which money earnings have over goods and services) rose quite steadily until the early 1970s. Since then real earnings have increased more spasmodically (*see* Part IV).

Price Changes.

In the calculation of real wages it is usual to make use of the *index of retail prices*, commonly called the cost-of-living index. The index is calculated monthly by the Department of Employment, and it naturally has an influence on the course of wage negotiations.

Over the last forty years or so the allocation of consumers' expenditure amongst different items has altered substantially. Of growing importance in household budgets were housing and transport and vehicles, whilst of diminishing importance was food. As people grow richer they spend a smaller proportion of their income on food. Nor have price changes been the same for all types of goods and services. For example, during the same long period, prices of fuel and light went up by more than the average whilst those for clothing, drink and durable household goods rose by less.

The table (**G23**) shows how the allocation of expenditure has varied since 1987. Even over this brief period of time there have been some striking changes, whilst price rises have been very different from item to item.

The general retail price index is calculated by weighting each of the commodity price indexes by the proportionate importance of that commodity in total expenditure in a particular year, and then summing all the indexes, *i.e.*, the general index is a *weighted average* of its constituent indexes. A different pattern of expenditure would mean a different set of weights, and hence a different cost-of-living index. For instance, the poor—and particularly pensioners—spend a higher proportion on the basic necessities; food, fuel and light, and housing. It is possible that

the cost-of-living rose more for the poor than for the rich over these years.

The cost-of-living index has not risen evenly in Britain. There were spurts of rapid inflation in the periods 1950–52 and 1954–56, followed by a decade of relatively little inflation (averaging under 3 per cent per annum). After 1967, however, the rate of inflation accelerated, rising progressively from 2·5 per cent per annum between 1966 and 1967 to 7·0 per cent between 1971 and 1972. For more recent developments *see* Part IV.

The Causes of Inflation,

(i) Import Prices.

Prices charged in the shops are determined by a great many factors, over many of which the Government has little or no control. First among these is the price of imports. Prices of imported food and raw materials are determined in the world markets, in which Britain is only one of many purchasers. Prices in raw material and food markets can fluctuate wildly. Big increases in commodity prices occurred during the Korean war, in the early 1970's and in 1979 (*see* Part IV). The sharp increases in the prices of primary commodities contributed to British inflation at these and other times, but for most of the post-war period the rise in import prices has been less rapid than domestic inflation even allowing for unfavourable exchange rate movements which push up the price of imports in sterling terms.

The source of domestic inflation has to be looked for in the tendency of wages and salaries, or profits, or other incomes to rise faster than real output; and this one or other of them has done in almost every year since the war.

(ii) The Influence of Demand.

An explanation of domestically generated inflation is that it arises not so much from increased costs as from demand pressures increasing prices and profits. If there is an increase in aggregate demand for goods and services in the economy, how does the economy respond? If it is operating at less than full employment, producers are able to expand their production to meet the additional demand. But if full employment has already been achieved, it is the price level and not production which rises. Given an excess demand for goods and services, there is competitive bidding for the limited supplies and producers are able to sell at higher prices. A more sophisticated version of this argument recognises that full employment cannot be precisely defined: rather, there are degrees of less or more unemployment. Bottlenecks appear in different firms and industries at different stages; so that any increase in demand is met by an increase in both prices and production. But the lower the rate of unemployment, the more does the response take the form of price increases.

A variant of this approach is the so-called *quantity theory of money*, in which inflation is seen as a response to an increase in the supply of money; there is too much money chasing too few goods. The theory dates back at least to David Hume, but it was generally discredited as a result of the writings of Maynard Keynes in the 1930s. However, it was revived by Milton Friedman and has received some measure of acceptance among economists, especially in the United States.

The great shortages during and immediately after the war would no doubt have generated rapid demand inflation had it not been for rationing and price controls; and the spurt of inflation between 1954 and 1956 was associated with a very high pressure of demand. On the other hand, inflation has occurred even in periods of relatively high unemployment. Moreover, the method by which most firms price their products is on the basis of their costs; so that most prices are not directly sensitive to the pressure of demand. A more plausible mechanism by which demand might influence prices indirectly is through its effect on wages. In fact, there has been a lively debate as to the extent to which wages are influenced by the pressure of demand as opposed to being relatively independent of it. There is, however, general agreement that wages are the main driving force behind prices.

(iii) Wages and Inflation.

When employers grant a wage increase, they will immediately consider whether they should increase their prices to cover their increased wage-costs. As it is common practice for firms to fix the selling prices of their products by first calculating the direct cost of labour and of materials, and then adding on a percentage to cover overhead costs and profits, they will tend to want to raise their prices not only to cover the cost of the wage advance, but also to cover their percentage addition. Moreover, in deciding whether or not their customers will stand for such increases, firms will be influenced by the knowledge that their competitors have to pay the increased wages too, and will probably therefore be raising their prices. So industry-wide wage advances—and changes in costs of materials—are particularly likely to be passed on to the consumer; and, as wage-earners are also consumers, to generate further demands for wage advances to cover the increased prices.

Once this spiral gets going, it is very hard to stop it. In general, the requirement is that wage earnings should not rise faster than productivity (output per man). But as in some industries productivity is very slow to rise, and as it would be unfair and impracticable to exclude their workers from participating in any general rise in the standard of living, this requirement means that in industries with a rapid growth of productivity wage advances should be kept well below the rate of rise of productivity. For two reasons this is rather difficult. First, rising productivity often raises the wages of some workers in these industries automatically, because they are paid by results or through some incentive scheme. The rise of wages from this source takes the form of a tendency on the part of earnings in these industries to rise faster than wage-rates. Second, employers in the rapidly-growing industries have far less reason to resist demands for wage increases than those in slowly-growing industries. Indeed, they are quite likely to bid up wages in order to obtain and motivate labour rather than to try to hold down wages.

There are therefore major problems in preventing a faster rise in wages than in productivity, with its consequence of rising prices. And once a wage-price spiral has started, the problems become more acute because workers and employers become accustomed to substantial annual advances in money wages. A main source of continuing price inflation has been the tendency of money wages to continue to advance at a rate that was appropriate when the cost-of-living was going up sharply, but ceased to be appropriate in later years.

(iv) The Phillips Curve.

Even if wage behaviour is primarily responsible for inflation, the pressure of demand may still be important. If unemployment is low or falling rapidly, and unfilled vacancies high, there is competitive bidding among employers to obtain or retain their workers. Moreover, with the economy booming the bargaining strength of trade unions increases: employers are more willing to concede wage demands. These possibilities have led economists to postulate—and indeed to measure—the so-called *Phillips Curve* relationship: the lower the level of unemployment, the faster the rate of increase in money wages. Such a relationship has been found to exist in the British economy over some periods. But it is dangerous to postulate "general laws" in economics: in the 1970s inflation increased despite high and growing unemployment and governments in most Western countries were confronted with a phenomenon known as stagflation. Clearly, changes in the cost-of-living, expectations for the future, Government policies and the degree of militancy of trade unionists can all have a significant influence on wage behaviour; and the level of demand may at times be relatively unimportant.

There are many schools of thought attempting to explain developments from the late 1960s, but it is possible to discern two general approaches. The first is that trade unions behaved reactively. In other words, they responded in their wage demands to their expectations about prices and Government policies. A restrictive monetary policy might help moderate inflation, in that it might directly reduce prices and it might affect expectations. The second school of thought was that unions, as well as

responding to their perception of the events they faced, acted in a more initiatory way—to fulfil, for example, aspirations (developed perhaps over a long period of time) about what their real earnings, and therefore their share of the national cake, should be. In striving to realise these aspirations, they might be relatively unaffected by concern over rising unemployment. A likely explanation was that unions felt unconcerned about relatively minor variations in the unemployment rate, safe in the knowledge that Government was committed to the maintenance of full employment. In the mid-1970s such a commitment was quite explicitly abandoned. That, together with the experience of very high unemployment in the 1980s might, it was argued, tighten the demand constraint in more prosperous future times. No longer, it was argued, would unions or workers be able to count on being "protected from the consequences of their own actions". Many economists, therefore, were surprised at the persistence of quite high wage inflation during the very high unemployment of the mid-1980s. Their attempts to explain this are described in **Part IV.**

Modern approaches to inflation suggest that workers (or unions) have a "target" real wage and at the same time there is a "feasible" real wage which the economy can afford. Only when the two are equal will inflation be stable. At any given time there is a unique level of unemployment (or economic activity) at which the two will be consistent. If the Government attempts to run the economy at lower levels of unemployment, there will be a wage-price spiral of the sort already described, and as a consequence increasing inflation. Both the target wage and the feasible wage are determined by the underlying structures of the labour and product markets (*e.g.* the power of the unions, or the effectiveness of training, or basic productivity performance) as well as by the attitudes of workers and employers. Thus it is the supply-side which determines the level of unemployment at which it is safe to run the economy. The more unhealthy the supply-side, the higher this level of unemployment will be. Hence the modern stress on supply-side reform.

The Effects of Inflation.

British Governments have been concerned about inflation mainly because of its effects on British competitiveness, and hence on the balance of payments. If our costs rise relative to competitors' costs, British exporters find it more difficult to compete in foreign markets if they raise their prices; and if they keep prices down in order to compete, this implies their having to accept lower profit margins on exports than on sales in the home market, and so discourages exporting. Alternatively, this lack of competitiveness might be reflected in falling exchange rates, although membership of the ERM from the autumn of 1990 until the autumn of 1992 limited the scope for currency changes. Depreciation by itself is not necessarily a bad thing, but the danger is that it can start a spiral. An initial depreciation causes price inflation to increase at home, which causes further wage increases, which leads to further depreciation, and so on. The result could be hyper-inflation. This clearly has a major efficiency cost, since it will cause people to economise on the use of money in conducting their transactions.

Inflation can have other harmful consequences. It often produces a redistribution of income, with the strong gaining at the expense of the weak, *i.e.*, the poorly organised workers and the pensioners. In inflationary conditions income gains can appear to result not so much from work or sacrifice as from ingenuity and speculation and the exercise of economic and political power. Inflation can breed insecurity and industrial unrest. Among businessmen it increases uncertainty, reduces investment and hence growth. Finally, it causes a redistribution of income away from lenders to borrowers unless interest rates remain positive in real terms, as they are at present. What is clear is that the costs of inflation are significantly greater the more unanticipated it is.

Government Policy against Inflation.

There are several possible methods of attack on the inflationary spiral of wages and prices. Their usefulness will depend on the causes of the inflation.

One policy appropriate to most inflations, and also helpful to other objectives of economic policy, is to achieve a faster rate of productivity growth. The faster the growth of average productivity the faster can average incomes rise without an increase in average prices. Comprehensive and detailed government control of wages except as an emergency policy was thought for a long time to be impractical for political and institutional reasons, as was comprehensive and detailed control of prices. Experience suggested that such detailed policy, except as a temporary general "freeze", would be very difficult to operate and, if successful, would involve a major loss of flexibility in the economy. At the other extreme, general exhortations to unions to exercise restraint on wages, and to manufacturers to exercise restraint on prices, were thought to have little effect. After 1974 more people began to think that a semi-permanent incomes policy might in fact be a viable policy tool. This is discussed in **Part IV**.

The Government can attempt to regulate inflation by controlling purchasing power through its monetary and fiscal policies, the nature of which will be examined below. There is a danger that curbing demand also curbs the growth of output and productivity in the economy; so conflicting with other objectives of economic policy. Moreover, there is no certainty that inflation is sensitive to the rate of unemployment over the politically acceptable range of unemployment.

A final option is to try to impose an external inflationary discipline by linking the exchange rate to that of a low-inflation currency, removing the option of devaluation and thereby imposing a constraint upon employers' ability to pass on cost increases without loss of external competitiveness. By entering the ERM in October 1990 the Government effectively chose this option. Since leaving the ERM in the autumn of 1992, the Government has had to search for an alternative strategy.

4. MONEY, BANKING AND FINANCE

Economic Objectives and Demand Management.

The various economic objectives—full employment, balance of payments equilibrium, the control of inflation, *etc.*—which, as mentioned in **Part I**, have been shared by all post-war British Governments, are all to a greater or a lesser extent dependent for their attainment upon the type of *demand management* policy pursued by the government. By this is meant the policy, or set of policies, with which the government seeks to regulate the total level of expenditure on goods and services. The latter is the sum of consumption and investment expenditure by both the private sector (firms and consumers) and the public sector (the government and the nationalised industries). If the resulting level of aggregate demand for output is greater than the amount which can be produced with the economy's resources the result will be shortages leading to inflation and/or an increased demand for imports. If the level of demand is not high enough, on the other hand, the result will be a waste of resources, *i.e.*, workers will be unemployed and capital equipment will be underutilised. Hence it is crucial for the government to keep the pressure of demand at an appropriate level by regulating the various types of expenditure making up the total.

Fiscal and Monetary Policy.

One way in which the government can attempt to regulate demand is by fiscal policy, *i.e.*, the regulation of taxes and public expenditure (*see* **Part IV**). If the government believes, for example, that the level of demand is too high, it may seek to reduce it by raising taxes whilst leaving public expenditure unchanged, thereby reducing its *budget deficit* (*i.e.*, the excess of public spending over tax revenue). Since the private sector's expenditure plans are financed partly out of its after-tax income and partly out of borrowing, an increase in taxes will generally reduce private sector expenditure, so that total expenditure then falls if public expenditure is held constant. Conversely, the government can cut taxes or increase

public spending if it wants to expand the economy by increasing total expenditure.

However, fiscal policy of this type is not independent of *monetary policy, i.e.*, the regulation of interest rates or the stock of money in the economy. For example, if the government increases public spending it has to pay for the various resources which this involves. The finance may come from additional taxes, but if the government does not raise taxes the extra expenditure then has to be paid for in one of two ways: either the government increases its borrowing from the private sector by issuing government stock in return for money to pay for public expenditure; or the government prints new money for this purpose. In the latter case the supply of money is increased; in the former case interest rates will generally be increased, since the private sector will probably require higher interest rates if it is to be induced to lend extra funds to the government.

Economic Controversies.

The operation of monetary and fiscal policies has been a long-standing area of controversy among economists, although the nature of the disagreements has tended to alter somewhat over time. One traditional controversy has been between "Keynesian" and "monetarist" economists. The former take their lead from the English economist J. M. Keynes, whose most well-known work was published in the 1930s, whilst the pioneer of monetarism, in a series of books and articles in the 1950s and 1960s, was Milton Friedman of Chicago University. Keynesian ideas dominated economic policy making in Britain and elsewhere from the end of the second world war up to the late 1960s. Since the mid-1970s policy making has been predominantly monetarist, though by the mid-1980s some Keynesian elements appeared to be resurfacing. These various phases of policy making are described in more detail later, after the main principles of monetary and fiscal policies, and the sources of economic controversy, have been considered.

The Keynesian approach had a clear view about both the aims and the methods of macroeconomic policy making. The main aim was to achieve and maintain high levels of output and employment—Keynes's ideas were developed primarily in reaction to the mass unemployment of the inter-war period—and the main policy instrument for this purpose was fiscal policy. Keynesians argued that suitable choices of tax rates and of levels of public spending could maintain demand at a level high enough to secure continuous full employment. They also advocated that fiscal policy should be *fine tuned*, i.e. that tax and spending decisions should be frequently reviewed and amended in the light of short term changes in economic conditions.

From the mid-1950s onwards, Milton Friedman and others began to dispute both the aims and the methods of Keynesian policy makers. They had several important criticisms. First, they argued that on the basis of evidence from America, Britain, and elsewhere, the money supply was the main determinant of the level of economic activity, contrary to Keynesian ideas. Secondly, they were suspicious of fine tuning, arguing that frequent policy changes could destabilise rather than stabilise the economy. Thirdly, they questioned the policy aim of giving over-riding priority to the level of employment, arguing that this potentially conflicted with other aims such as the balance of payments and the control of inflation. Monetarists therefore urged governments to pay much more attention to controlling the money supply, and to a wider range of policy objectives.

From the mid-1970s to the mid-1980s monetarist prescriptions were broadly followed. The experience led to modifications in the traditional attitudes of both groups of economists.

Not many economists would now advocate an unqualified return to the sort of Keynesian policy-making practised in the 1950s and 1960s, and to this extent "Keynesianism" could be said to be discredited. However, experience of monetarism has suggested that some of its ideas are misleading or over-simplified as guides to policy-making, and some of its early advocates have modified or extended their policy prescriptions as a result. Equally, however, some of its ideas have won a measure of acceptance from former sceptics. In addition, new economic issues emerged in the 1980s, whose policy implications defy straightforward classification in either "Keynesian" or "monetarist" terms. As a result, many professional economists would now find it difficult to classify themselves as either "Keynesian" or "monetarist", even though these labels continue to be widely used in popular discussions of policy-making.

The Ricardian Approach.

Both monetarists and Keynesians agree that changes in the size of the government's budget deficit have significant effects on the economy—their disagreements concern the nature of the effects. A third school of thought, often called "Ricardian", argues in contrast that budget deficit changes may have little impact—in some circumstances no impact at all—upon economic activity. This approach gained many adherents in the 1970s and 1980s. It concentrates on the future effects, as well as the immediate impact, of a change in the budget deficit. If the government reduces taxes while holding its spending level constant, and increases its borrowing in order to replace the lost tax revenue, this new borrowing will have to be repaid, with interest, some time in the future. For example, new borrowing in 1993 using government bonds with a 5-year redemption period will have to be repaid in 1998. The Ricardian approach argues that when the repayment falls due this will require taxes to be raised. The Ricardian approach goes on to argue that the prospect of future tax increases is forseen by consumers at the time when the cut in taxes takes effect, and that consumers save the resulting increase in their current disposable incomes in order to be able to meet the anticipated extra tax bill in the future. Consequently, Ricardians argue, tax cuts do not stimulate economic activity because they do not generate increases in demand. The same argument applies in reverse.

The Ricardian approach thus argues that changes in budget deficits have little or no impact on economic activity, because they induce offsetting changes in savings, whereas both Keynesian and monetarist theories predict that the main impact is on current spending. The difference reflects the Ricardian assumption that consumers are willing, and able, to work out the future implications of current policy changes and to take account of both present and future effects in deciding on their current behaviour. Some economists argue that, in practice, most people are not sufficiently well informed nor sophisticated to pay much attention to the future implications of current tax changes. Other economists argue that, even if people are able to make sophisticated calculations, there is so much uncertainty about the future course of events that people are likely to discount them very heavily. Yet another complication is that if the repayment of current borrowing is sufficiently delayed, the burden may fall on future generations rather than on current tax payers.

Whilst all these arguments suggest reasons why changes in the size of the budget deficit are likely to lead at least to some change in the pressure of demand, and not simply to changes in savings, the Ricardian view has nonetheless become quite influential. This is partly because studies in many countries, but especially America, suggest that the impact of budgetary changes on demand pressure is often less strong than would be predicted by simple Keynesian ideas. In addition, Ricardian ideas have become quite influential in financial markets, which now routinely assess the longer term prospects of fiscal policy, as well as its immediate impact.

The Definition of "Money".

Money plays a central role in any modern economy: without it, all but the simplest buying and selling transactions would become difficult or impossible, since people would then have to use barter. In a barter economy goods are traded directly, so that anyone wishing to obtain, say, food has to pay for it by providing the food producer with some good or service which he requires. The obvious difficulty is that this relies on a "double coincidence" of wants: if the prospective food purchaser cannot supply anything which the food producer wants, the transaction cannot take place. Hence

barter only works well in very simple economies with a limited range of goods and with a high degree of self sufficiency. It cannot operate in an economy with a significant range of goods and services, and with specialisation of production. In these circumstances money is the essential oil which lubricates the economic process: an individual can buy a range of goods with the money earned from his job, instead of having to trade products directly.

Although most people probably have a clear idea of what they understand by "money", it is in fact an extremely difficult concept to define with precision. Economists tend to define it as anything which is readily acceptable as a means of payment. Evidently "money" in this sense constitutes "cash"—banknotes and coins—and also current account bank deposits, since possession of the latter allows the drawing of cheques which, normally, are a universally acceptable means of payment.

The total of cash and current account deposits at any given time is one possible definition of the supply of money existing at that time: in Britain it is known as "M1". However, it is by no means the only possible measure. The problem is that there are many other financial assets which are nearly as good as money in the sense that, although not themselves a means of payment, they can be converted quickly into money. These assets are often called "near money". An example of "near money" is *time deposits* at banks. These are accounts which pay interest and for which (as the name suggests) notice may have to be given if funds are to be withdrawn. They cannot automatically be used to draw cheques, and for this reason do not quite satisfy the economist's definition of "money", since they are not, in principle, a means of payment. In practice, however, funds can be transferred from them into current accounts—and then used for payment—with virtually no effort or delay. Indeed, banks will often honour cheques which are drawn on the strength of a time deposit account. For these reasons, such accounts are "nearly" as good as money, and might legitimately be included in a working definition. This sort of argument led to the development of a wider operational definition of money, known as "M3". M3 was defined as M1, plus time deposits, and also foreign currency accounts and public sector accounts. A variant on this, called *sterling M3* (i.e. excluding the foreign currency components of M3) was used as the main indicator of monetary policy in Britain for several years in the early 1980s, and indeed in 1984 M1 was abandoned as a formal policy target. It was replaced by MO, the so-called "monetary base", defined as notes and coins in circulation plus banks' deposits held at the Bank of England. The argument in favour of MO was that a growing proportion of M1 was made up of interest-bearing deposits and that it therefore increasingly represented peoples' savings decisions; hence it no longer provided a good guide to the amount of money available to finance current demands for goods and services. In contrast, because notes and coins constituted about 90 per cent of MO, the latter was a reliable indicator of current demand pressure.

Whatever the merits of MO as an indicator of demand pressure, it should be noted that it does not correspond to the definition of "money" as a means of payment because it excludes all current and deposit bank accounts, essentially on the grounds that holders of such accounts might choose to regard them as vehicles for savings rather than for financing current spending. It therefore narrows the definition of money beyond M1 by including only those elements for which there is no plausible demand other than as a means of payment.

Liquidity.

In contrast, many people criticised even the "wide" definition of money, M3, on the grounds that it exclude accounts at institutions other than banks. This is potentially important since total deposits with the banks are less than total deposits with non-bank institutions. If the government controls M1 (or M3) as a means of controlling aggregate demand, its policy may be circumvented if, say, people run down building society accounts in order to increase their current expenditure. Another way of putting this is to say that the range of "near money" assets extends beyond time deposits to include building society accounts, and perhaps even wider collections of assets. This has been recognised by the development of correspondingly wider working definitions of money, "M4" and "M5". M4 equals M3 plus building society accounts, and M5 equals M4 plus money market instruments such as Treasury Bills.

The traditional argument for concentrating on measures like M1 or M3 rather than on wider measures of liquidity was that building society accounts, and similar assets, could not be used directly as means of payment: it was necessary first to withdraw cash from a building society account before making a purchase. However, during the 1980s this changed rapidly, as the banks and the building societies began to compete much more closely. On the one hand the banks moved increasingly into the home loans business in an attempt to capture some of the traditional business of the building societies. Conversely, the building societies sought to take some of the banks' traditional business by offering accounts providing facilities close to those of current accounts at the banks. Towards the end of the 1980s most of the main building societies were issuing cheque books to account holders, and such cheques had become widely acceptable as a means of payment.

The building societies altered in other ways, widening their range of financial and housing services to the point at which the larger societies were more appropriately viewed as financial conglomerates—firms offering a full range of financial services—than in terms of their traditional role as lenders for house purchase. This trend was accentuated in 1989 when the second largest society, the Abbey National, took steps to convert itself from a mutual society—the traditional arrangement for building societies, whereby they are owned by their members—to a public company, quoted on the Stock Market, and so owned by shareholders. Members voted in favour of the proposal, making the Abbey National much more like a bank and much less like a traditional building society.

This brought to a head the question of whether or not building society accounts should be included in official definitions of "money". The Abbey National's deposits were included in M4 but not in M3, reflecting its previous role but not its new status. Faced with such confusion, and with the prospect that other building societies might make the same change, the monetary authorities decided to abandon M3 as a measure of "money", let alone as an active target of policy. Since then, therefore, M0 and M4 have been used as the main monetary indicators.

An "intermediate" measure, M2, has also been given more emphasis. Whereas M4 includes all private sector deposits in all banks and building societies, M2 includes only "retail" deposits, which mainly comprise deposits which pay no interest, together with cheque-bearing sight and time deposits. Hence, whilst M4 continues to provide a measure of "broad" money, M2 attempts to measure those parts of the total money stock which are likely to be used mainly for regular transactions rather than as a way of saving for the future. Hence M2 corresponds rather more closely than does M4 to the notion of money as a "means of payment", whilst M4 attempts to take account of the fact that many other financial assets can easily be turned into means of payment.

The Choice of Targets.

The fact that "money" can be defined in so many different ways, each having some plausible justification, poses an obvious problem: if it is important to control the money supply, which measure is the one to be controlled? This is of some practical importance since the various monetary aggregates often grow at very different rates. Over the longer term M1 has been steadily falling in size relative to M3: the ratio of M1 to M3 was about 2/3 in 1963 but less than 1/2 in the early 1980s. Similar variations also occur as between the various other possible measures of money supply and liquidity. Such variations in the growth of different monetary aggregates were one reason why monetary targets lost favour with the British government in the mid-1980s (*see* **Part IV**).

The Liquidity Spectrum.

By definition "money" is completely liquid. Building society accounts are clearly highly liquid assets. Other types of financial assets—*e.g.*, long-dated government stock, known as *gilt-edged securities*—are less liquid, since although the owner of such assets can easily exchange them for money, he cannot confidently predict the *price* at which he can do so. For example, he may have to sell at a time when the market price of government stock is unusually low, so that he realises relatively little money from the sale. Thus "liquidity" refers not only to the speed with which assets can be sold, but also to the predictability of the amount of money which the sale will realise. In practice, there is a *liquidity spectrum, i.e.*, a whole range of different types of asset, each possessing a different degree of liquidity. The spectrum includes not only financial assets but also real assets—houses, capital equipment, etc.—the latter being highly illiquid, *e.g.*, selling a house takes a long time, involves high transactions costs, and the sale price is unpredictable.

Liquidity and Expenditure.

Assets towards the illiquid end of the spectrum are obviously not "near money" and could never plausibly become so. However, the precise point at which the boundary should be drawn between "near money" assets and other, less liquid ones, is not clear. Indeed, many economists would argue that it is not sensible to try to define such a boundary. This is partly because its position is not objectively defined at any particular time, but more fundamentally because it cannot be regarded as fixed and immutable over time. The gradual change in the status of the building societies and their deposits illustrates the tendency for the boundary to shift.

The existence of a large spectrum of financial assets, and the tendency for the "near money" boundary to shift over time, emphasises the practical difficulty of controlling the money supply. If "money" and various forms of "near money" are in practice very close substitutes for one another, attempts by the government to control the money supply may be self defeating, because whatever the precise definition of "money" which is used, some liquid assets will be excluded, and the financial sector may then negate the effects of the controls by shifting towards greater use of other assets, not included in the definition and therefore not subject to control. This problem is often known as "Goodhart's Law", named after Charles Goodhart, formerly an economic adviser at the Bank of England. Goodhart's Law states that as soon as the government attempts to regulate any particular set of financial assets, these become unreliable as indicators of economic trends. The basic reason is that financial institutions can relatively easily devise new types of financial assets, and this allows them to negate the effects of controls on particular types of assets, based on particular definitions of the money supply. There is very little which the government can do to prevent it. The persistent failure by the government to achieve its monetary targets during the 1980s, and the wide divergences in different monetary series, led many economists, including those sympathetic in principle to the idea of monetary control, to question its practical usefulness.

One response by policy-makers during the 1980s was to try to control the money supply indirectly, by fixing interest rates, instead of attempting to control it directly. The principle behind this idea is that the demand for money varies inversely with interest rates. Higher interest rates tend to reduce the demand for money because they increase the *opportunity cost* of holding money, i.e. the amount of interest income which is sacrificed by keeping funds in money (which traditionally does not pay interest) instead of in some other financial asset on which interest is paid. If the monetary authorities reduce the money supply, the resulting shortage of money will tend to drive interest rates upwards as people try to sell other financial assets (so driving the price of these assets down, and driving up the interest rates payable on them) in order to build up their money balances. Faced with difficulties in controlling the money supply, however, the monetary authorities in the UK tended during the 1980s

THE NATIONAL DEBT IN SELECTED YEARS

	The National Debt (£bn.)	The National Debt as a percentage of national income
1900	0·6	31·9
1914	0·7	25·6
1921	7·6	147·7
1938	7·8	150·6
1946	23·0	259·6
1975	46·4	49·0
1988	171·0	38·0
1990	160·0	29·6
1991	163·7	28·8
1992	179·2	30·4

to reverse this procedure, pushing interest rates up in the expectation that this would reduce the demand for money and that the supply of money would then fall in line. The difficulty with this approach was similar to that with direct control of the money supply. Rapid changes in the financial sector have tended to make the relationship between interest rates and money demand difficult to predict. For example, most banks in the UK started to offer interest payments on current accounts during the 1980s. By thus reducing the opportunity cost of holding money, this had the effect of increasing the demand for money at each level of interest rates.

More generally, attempting to control the money supply by using interest rates is an indirect procedure which relies to a considerable extent upon factors beyond the government's control. The largest component of the money supply is deposits at the main banks. If interest rates are to be used to control the money supply, changes in interest rates have to be able to induce changes in the level of bank deposits. The mechanism involved is as follows. If interest rates rise, this will tend to reduce the demand for bank loans and overdrafts, since the cost of servicing these debts is increased. The resulting fall in bank borrowing reduces the pressure of demand for goods and services—since some of this is financed by borrowing—and this in turn reduces sales and sales receipts. This fall in receipts means that less money is deposited with banks; at this point the objective of reducing money supply by reducing bank deposits is achieved. However, whilst this mechanism is clear in principle, in practice its weak link is the relationship between interest rates and the demand for bank loans. In the early 1980s, for example, when interest rates were raised to what were then record levels, the demand for bank loans proved surprisingly resilient. One reason for this may have been the problems experienced by many individual companies, which found their cash flow positions squeezed between depressed sales revenue and relatively buoyant labour costs. For many firms, bank loans represented a possible way of easing these cash flow problems. In some cases the likely alternative was bankruptcy. In such circumstances it is not surprising that the demand for loans remained relatively strong, even in the face of high interest rates.

In practice, if interest rates are kept sufficiently high for a sufficiently long period of time, the demand for loans is likely to fall eventually, with consequent downward pressure on the money supply and on aggregate demand. The problem for policy-makers is in judging the appropriate level of interest rates in the context of such delayed reactions. If initial increases in rates have little or no immediate effect, there is a strong temptation to raise rates further—indeed, to continue raising them until the money markets respond. However, the danger is that rates will be raised much too far, so that the market response, when it comes, will be far stronger than planned or desired. Economists sometimes illustrate this by the analogy of someone pulling one end of a piece of elastic, in order to pull towards them a heavy weight which is attached to the other end. Initial gentle tugging does not move the weight, and there is a temptation to pull harder and harder. The end-result is that the person doing the pulling is likely to be hit in the face when the pressure reaches the point at which the weight is catapulted forwards.

Consider the British government's policy in 1989, when it raised interest rates to very high levels to reduce demand pressure. During 1989 the effect was very limited, but the subsequent recession proved to be far deeper and more prolonged than expected. The same problem can occur in reverse. In 1992 the government made a series of reductions in interest rates to stimulate economic activity. When these failed to have any immediate significant impact, the government came under pressure to make still further cuts, despite the danger that these would eventually produce an excessive response. Such pressures provide another illustration of the potential dfficulties caused by politicians' desires to be seen to respond actively to current problems—even if, sometimes, it would be better in the longer run not to respond.

These very considerable practical difficulties may have been one reason why the British government largely abandoned the idea of monetary targets in the second half of the 1980s, after a decade during which they had been central to policy-making. This and other policy developments are considered below.

The National Debt and Government Borrowing.

The *National Debt* is a measure of the total indebtedness of the government, excluding local authorities. The accompanying table shows how it has varied over time. Although the absolute size of the National Debt has risen steadily, this simply reflects inflation: as a proportion of national income the National Debt has fluctuated, rising sharply after each of the two World Wars—both of which saw borrowing on a massive scale by the government to finance the war effort—but falling slowly but steadily for 20 years up to 1975. From 1975 to the mid-1980s the proportion altered little; in the second half of the 1980s, it fell sharply.

The government borrows in several different ways. First, the issue of new bank-notes is a form of borrowing: as seen above it can be used to finance a budget deficit. Second, it borrows from foreign governments (see **G9**). Third, it borrows from companies through tax reserve certificates, whereby company taxes are paid at the later date when the taxes become legally due. Fourth, it borrows from private individuals through the various forms of national savings, e.g., Post Office accounts.

These four types of borrowing result in *non-marketable debt*, i.e., an individual who has a Post Office account cannot sell it in the market to another individual. Two other types of borrowing—gilt-edged securities and Treasury Bills—result in *marketable debt*, i.e., an individual who owns gilt-edged securities can sell them in the market to someone else. In practice, most gilt-edged and all Treasury Bills are held by institutions—banks, discount houses, etc.—rather than by private individuals. However, whereas Treasury Bills, representing short-term (usually three months) loans to the government are liquid assets (i.e., they can quickly be cashed at a predictable price), gilt-edged are illiquid. They represent promises to repay a certain sum of money at a specified date, e.g., government stock outstanding in 1985 had an average remaining life of 10·4 years, with significant redemptions due in each of the next five years. Occasionally stock is issued without a repayment date. Owners of such stock are in effect promised a fixed annual interest payment for ever. At any time prior to repayment gilt-edged can be traded, and there is a large market for such trading in which the market price (as opposed to the fixed repayment price) varies widely.

Interest Rates and Debt Financing.

As already seen, such variations in gilt-edged market prices cause changes in interest rates on all financial assets. Aside from the effects on aggregate demand, interest rate changes themselves have a large impact upon the financing of the National Debt, and hence upon overall public expenditure. For example, if restrictions on the growth of the money supply cause interest rates to rise, this increases the interest charges which the government has to pay on its existing debts. Furthermore, the accompanying fall in the market price of government stock may cause potential buyers of new issues of stock to anticipate further falls (*i.e.*, further increases in interest rates), in which case they will be reluctant to purchase the stock—and the government will be unable to finance its budget deficit—unless and until these further changes occur. When they do, the interest charges on the National Debt are further in-creased; and the market may still be unsettled, expecting yet further changes.

It is problems of this sort which at one time led many Keynesians to advocate a policy of promoting stable (or at least slowly changing) interest rates—an "orderly market" for financial assets—rather than a predetermined growth rate of the money supply. Monetarists object on the grounds that the government cannot in practice stabilise interest rates in this manner. They argue that although the government may be able to stabilise or even reduce interest rates in the short run by a rapid expansion of the money supply, this expansion will itself *increase* interest rates in the longer run. This is because, on the monetarist approach, the monetary expansion increases demand for real output, which in turn generally increases the rate of inflation. If this causes people to expect a higher future rate of inflation, gilt-edged stock then becomes less attractive to investors because of the associated decline in the anticipated real value of its fixed interest payments. The demand for gilt-edged stock there-fore falls, which pushes its price down and thus its effective interest rate up. This continues until the effective interest rate has risen sufficiently to offset the higher expected inflation. Interest rates else-where tend to get bid up at the same time, since banks, building societies, etc., have to protect their own reserves.

Monetarists therefore distinguish between the *nominal* interest rate, *i.e.*, the current money value of the interest rate, and the *real* interest rate, *i.e.*, the nominal rate minus the expected rate of price inflation on real output. They argue that firms and consumers are concerned about the real, not the nominal, interest rate; in this case nominal rates must inevitably rise if inflation increases—which it will do, on the monetarist argument, if the government, in pursuing a Keynesian policy of stabilising interest rates, over-expands the money supply. Hence the monetarists produce a paradox; a monetary policy which seeks to hold interest rates down may instead cause them to rise.

The Trend of Interest Rates in Britain.

It is difficult to deny that some element of the monetarist view of interest rates has operated in the post-war period, especially in more recent years. The accompanying table shows the course of (nominal) interest rates and yields on certain types of financial assets since the war. It can be seen that with the exception of the yield on Ordin-ary Shares—which is considered later—all rates showed a trend increase until the early 1980s. Since inflation and therefore, in all probability, inflation-ary expectations showed a similar trend, the rise in nominal interest rates was broadly consistent with the monetarist position. Furthermore, there was a tendency for all rates to rise in 1975–6, decline in 1977–8, and rise again in 1979–80. Inflation and therefore, presumably, inflation expectations fol-lowed a similar pattern.

For much of the 1980s the trends of the 1970s were reversed, with nominal interest rates gradually declining from their peak levels of 1979–81, albeit with some flunctuations. This is again broadly consistent with the monetarist viewpoint. Inflation in the UK fell quite sharply after 1981, stabilising at 3–5 per cent in the mid-1980s. Inflation expectations almost certainly fell in a similar fashion, as the Thatcher government's determina-tion to eliminate high inflation gradually gained credibility in financial markets and among the wider public, so helping to break the "inflation psychology" which had built up during the 1970s. Hence nominal interest rates would be expected to fall. However, in 1988 and 1989 inflation started to rise once again. Partly for this reason, nominal interest rates also began rising again after the middle of 1988. By early 1990 they had returned to even higher levels than at the beginning of the 1980s.

One point to note from the table is that *nominal* interest rates can be very misleading as a guide to *real* interest rates which, as explained above, are equal to nominal rates minus the expected rate of inflation. In the 1970s nominal rates were very high but for most of the time the rate of inflation was even higher, so that real interest rates were nega-tive. This was particularly marked in 1975–76, when nominal rates reached a then record high level of around 16 per cent. At the time, however, inflation was running at around 25 per cent, implying real interest rates of around minus 9 per cent—a record *low* level. The same has applied in reverse in the 1980s. Nominal interest rates fell to lower levels than in the 1970s, but inflation fell faster, so that by 1986 nominal interest rates of around 12 per cent coexisted with inflation of around 5 per cent, imply-ing real interest rates of plus 7 per cent—a record *high* level. Thus changes in nominal interest rates cannot be taken as a good guide to changes in the real cost of borrowing.

Inflation and National Debt Financing.

The distinction between real and nominal interest rates also substantially qualifies the earlier point about the effect of inflation on the financing of the National Debt. The latter consists mainly of debts which are fixed in money value. Hence, persistent inflation erodes their real value in terms of purchasing power. This substantially offsets the increased burden of interest payments when higher inflation raises nominal interest rates. In effect, the government loses through higher inflation in terms of interest payments, but gains in terms of the erosion of the real burden of its debts. Another way of making this point is that the burden of the National Debt really depends on real rather than nominal interest rates, and the latter are by no means a reliable guide to the former. For example, in the mid-1970s the official measure of the budget deficit was equivalent to over 6 per cent of national income, but after adjusting for inflation this was actually equivalent to a small surplus. The public sector's debt was being eroded by inflation by more than enough to offset its interest payments.

International Influences on Interest Rates.

Another substantial complication in considering interest rates concerns the relationship between in-terest rates in Britain and in other countries. The removal of exchange controls in 1979, and the much greater degree of competition and openness in foreign exchange markets which emerged in the 1980s, mean that changes in interest rates in other countries, especially Germany, have come to play a major role in determining British rates. Institutions such as pension funds, insurance companies, and large industrial companies which have substantial amounts of money to invest are now easily able to move money between alternative assets in different currencies. Consequently, if interest rates in Ger-many rise above those in Britain there will normally be a large movement of funds out of assets such as British government bonds, denominated in sterling, and into German marks in order to take advantage of the higher rates of return. The same applies if interest rates rise in other important financial centres such as Tokyo. Since selling of sterling assets implies a reduced demand for sterling and increased demand for other currencies, this tends to push down the exchange rate of sterling against other currencies. If the British government is reluctant to see a fall in the exchange rate it will then be forced to allow a rise in British interest rates in order to prevent it.

This problem played an important part in British economic policy at several times in the 1980s. The government wished to prevent rapid falls in the exchange rate because of the importance which it attached to reducing inflation: if the exchange rate falls this pushes inflation up because of the resulting rise in the sterling price of imported goods. Hence British interest rates in the 1980s were to a signifi-cant extent outside the control of the British government, depending instead on events in the world economy. The very large budget deficit of the United States tended to keep its interest rates at high levels, and this went a long way towards ex-plaining why British interest rates remained high even when inflation fell substantially. Of course, the government could have chosen to allow interest rates to fall, but only at the cost of abandoning a key part of its economic policy, namely the commit-ment to low inflation.

These international linkages became even more

PERCENTAGE YIELD ON FINANCIAL ASSETS
(Range during period)

	Treasury Bill rate	Long-dated government stock	Industrial ordinary shares dividend yield
1945–50	½	2–3	3½–5½
1951–60	1–6¼	3½–6	4½–7
1961–70	3¼–8	5–10	4–6
1971–78	5½–14½	7½–17½	3–12
1979–81	11–17	11–16	4½–8
1982–85	8½–14	10–13½	5–7½
1986–87	8–12	8½–11	3–4½
1988–90	7–14½	9–13½	4–5½
1991–92	7½–14	9–10	4½–5½
1993	5½–6½	7–8½	4½–5
1994	5½	8	5

important when, in October 1990, the government finally decided that the UK should join the Exchange Rate Mechanism (the ERM) of the European Monetary System (*see* **G61**). This involved a commitment to hold the pound within an agreed band of values against all other ERM currencies. This meant that all other policies became subordinate to the exchange rate. If, for example, the sterling exchange rate moved close to the bottom of its band, the UK government would be required to take offsetting action, the most likely such action being an increase in interest rates.

The German mark is normally the strongest currency in the ERM, so that Britain's entry was interpreted by many commentators as effectively fixing the pound's value to that of the mark. This still further emphasised the importance of international influences on domestic UK interest rates. Indeed, some people opposed Britain's entry to the ERM on precisely these grounds.

This argument was put increasingly strongly as the UK plunged into a very severe recession in 1991 and 1992. Critics argued that it was illogical to keep real interest rates at record high levels—as was the case for almost the whole of 1991—during a deep recession. In effect, they argued, Britain's interest rates were being decided according to the needs of the German rather than the British economy. Many of the critics felt vindicated when, after Britain left the ERM in September 1992, rates were rapidly reduced by 3 percentage points. On the other side of the argument, however, it was pointed out that, whether inside or outside the ERM, Britain was inescapably part of a highly integrated world economy, and that cuts in British interest rates would depress the exchange rate and so generate inflationary pressures.

The Commercial Banks.

If the government does adopt monetary targets, its main need is to find ways of influencing the behaviour of the commercial banks, known in England as the clearing banks. For as seen above, the main component of the money supply is the deposits of the clearing banks.

In Britain there are four main banks with one or more branches in every town. Each of them earns profits by borrowing at low or zero rates of interest—anyone holding a bank account is in effect making a loan to his bank—and lending out part of the resulting funds at higher interest rates. In normal circumstances—*i.e.*, unless there is a run on the banks—not all deposits will be withdrawn at once; therefore the banks need keep only a small proportion of their deposits in the form of cash. This proportion is known as the *cash ratio* and until 1971 the Bank of England required it to be at least 8 per cent. Also, between 1951 and 1971 the Bank of England requested that the banks held liquid assets—Treasury Bills, commercial bills, and money at call and short notice as well as cash—equal to at least 30 per cent of deposits. This was known as the *liquidity ratio*.

The commercial banks can "create" money because of their ability to accept deposits far in excess of their cash and liquid asset holdings; as economists would say, because they operate under a *fractional reserve system*. If a bank provides an overdraft facility to a customer who then draws cheques on the facility, the recipients of these cheques pay the proceeds into their bank accounts which are thereby enlarged; and this represents an increase in the money supply, since the enlarged accounts can be used to finance additional transactions. Thus any increase in the banks' cash and liquid asset holdings allows them to expand loans, overdrafts, etc.—and thereby the money supply—by a multiple amount.

The government can control the money supply by controlling the components of banks' cash and liquid asset holdings. A reduction in the latter can be engineered by *open market operations*, which involve the Bank of England's selling more gilt-edged than it otherwise would; this reduces the banks' liquidity, since, as already seen, gilt-edged are not regarded as liquid assets, so that their purchase involves a drain of liquidity from the banks. At the same time, as already seen, it will generally involve a rise in interest rates.

Financial Deregulation.

When the Thatcher government took office in 1979 it embarked on a series of measures to reduce the degree of government control over and regulation of the financial sector of the economy. Its general philosophy here, as in other economic contexts, was to increase the importance of market forces and reduce the role of the government. The first, and in some ways the most dramatic change was the removal, in October 1979, of all remaining foreign exchange controls (*see* **G52**). Further deregulation followed in stages. In June 1980 the government ended the Supplementary Special Deposits Scheme, which had required the banks to place zero interest deposits at the Bank of England to prevent the assets concerned from being used instead as a base for monetary expansion. In 1981 further changes in monetary control techniques were made. The reserve assets ratio was abolished. Instead, the banks undertook to keep an average of 6 per cent, and never normally less than 4 per cent, of their eligible liabilities as secured money with members of the London Discount Market Association and/or with money brokers and gilt-edged jobbers. They were also required to keep cash balances equal to ½ per cent of eligible liabilities in non-interest bearing accounts at the Bank of England. At the same time the Government abolished *Minimum Lending Rate*. It intended instead to set short term interest rates within an undisclosed band, thus abandoning its previous ability to influence the general level of interest rates by announcing a change in MLR. The main idea behind these changes was to attempt to introduce a greater role for market forces in the determination of interest rates.

Two further changes proved to have very important effects. In October 1983 the Building Societies Association ended its previous practice of recommending a common mortgage rate for all mortgage lenders. In future each lending institution was left free to choose its own rate. The main effect was to encourage new institutions to enter the housing finance market. The latter was also significantly affected when, in December 1986, the Bank of England withdrew its "guidance" on mortgage lending by financial institutions, thus leaving the market entirely unregulated. The main consequence was that the supply of credit, especially for housing finance, was sharply increased during the mid-1980s. This in turn contributed to an excessively rapid growth of demand, and the resurgence of inflation and balance of payments problems, during 1988 and 1989 (*see* **Part IV**).

The Stock Exchange.

Whilst short-term credit is mostly provided by banks and Finance Houses, long-term borrowing by companies is undertaken through the Stock Exchange. Firms in the private sector of the economy issue three main types of security on the Stock Exchange. *Debenture Stock* is simply a fixed-interest loan. *Preference Stock* is a fixed-interest loan with provisions for waiving the interest if no profits are earned. The most important type, representing the great majority of holdings, are *Ordinary Shares*. The owner of an Ordinary Share is, legally, a part-owner of the company concerned, with a right to participate in any net profits which it makes (though he has no legal right to any particular level of dividend or interest payment).

In contrast to government stock, a significant proportion of Ordinary Shares is owned by private individuals. However, an increasing proportion is owned by insurance companies and pension funds, which have grown in importance as private superannuation schemes have become more widespread. It is likely that the market for Ordinary Shares, like that for government stock, will eventually be completely dominated by such large institutional investors.

The attraction of Ordinary Shares to the investor wanting an outlet for his savings is that because they represent a part ownership of the firm concerned, their prices and dividends are likely to rise as the value of the firm increases. This is so whether the firm's value increases in real terms, because it is expanding, or simply in money terms, because of general inflation. Thus Ordinary Shares generally represent a reasonable "hedge" against inflation—unlike fixed-interest securities such as gilt-edged. It is for this reason that, as seen in the earlier table, the dividend yield on Ordinary Shares does not tend to rise with inflation: the demand for Ordinary Shares does not necessarily fall if inflation increases, so that their prices and yields are not affected in the same way as those of gilt-edged and other fixed-interest securities by changes in inflation rates.

The Big Bang.

In October 1986 several major changes occurred in the organisation of the Stock Exchange. These had been under active discussion and planning for several years, but because they were all formally introduced simultaneously, they became known as the *Big Bang*. The main changes consisted of alterations in the structure and ownership of firms operating in the stock market, removal of restrictions on charging for financial services, and new forms of regulation of activity.

Traditionally, stock market firms had been divided into "jobbers" and "brokers". The former were responsible for the trading of shares on the floor of the stock market, whilst the latter dealt with clients and provided business for the jobbing firms—clients wishing to buy or sell shares were not allowed to deal directly with jobbers. The market imposed what was known as the "single capacity" restriction: no firm was allowed to be both a jobber and a broker. It also imposed strict limits on the ownership of all member firms: they were required either to be partnerships, or to be limited companies with a maximum limit on the amount of capital which could be owned by non-member firms (*i.e.* firms not actually operating in the market). In addition, the market operated fixed minimum commission rates on share deals.

Although this structure had worked well in earlier years, during the 1970s and 1980s it started to become increasingly inappropriate. The main catalyst for change was the growing *internationalisation of financial markets* (*see* **G**58). This was the result of several forces. Technological developments were making it very easy for financial firms to obtain virtually instant information, at very low cost, about assets in any currency and any country. Simultaneously, firms needing finance, especially the large multinationals operating throughout the world, were becoming increasingly willing to consider finance from any source. In addition, the abolition of UK exchange controls in 1979 meant that UK financial institutions rapidly acquired a much more diversified range of assets and interests, and needed to deal regularly in markets throughout the world, and also to compete within the UK against foreign based financial firms. Their ability to do so was heavily constrained by the traditional arrangements: minimum commission requirements restricted competition, the single capacity arrangement was unwieldy, and the limits on outside capital ownership meant that most of the firms were undercapitalised in terms of the scale of risks which they needed to run in global operations.

The Big Bang swept away most of the old restrictions. It allowed "single capacity" firms to operate, ended minimum commission rates, and removed restrictions on the entry and the ownership of firms. The main result was a series of mergers between and takeovers of old-established stock market firms. After Big Bang, most of the firms operating in the market were merely parts of, or subsidiaries of, much larger financial conglomerates, many of them foreign owned. These large firms felt that they could raise their overall profitability by operating in the UK stock market, though for many of them this was only one part of a large range of financial activities. Big Bang effectively recognised that the London stock market, like other stock exchanges around the world, could no longer be organised so as to supply finance for solely UK-based firms. Instead, it was now a part of a global market for finance.

It was recognised that these new arrangements would need *regulation*, to protect the interests, and retain the confidence, of clients. The 1986 Financial Services Act provided the framework. This gave the Trade and Industry Minister the power to authorise firms as "fit and proper" to operate in the stock market, and in other financial contexts such as insurance services. In practice this power was largely delegated, in the first instance to the *Securities and Investments Board* (SIB), whose members were appointed by the Bank of England and the government.

The growing complexity, and volatility, of international financial markets led to growing fears that regulatory regimes, both in Britain and elsewhere, were inadequate. In Britain these fears were brought sharply into focus by the collapse of a merchant bank, Baring Brothers, in February 1995. Barings was forced into liquidation when one of its dealers in Singapore amassed trading losses beyond its ability to cover. These losses were mainly in what had become known as 'derivatives', a form of financial asset in which a contract is agreed to buy, or sell, assets at a fixed price at some specified future date (*see* **G**58).

This caused great concern in Britain. Although Barings was only a small bank in international terms, it was Britain's oldest merchant bank, and for much of the nineteenth century had been one of the world's leading financial institutions. There was considerable shock that such a long-established bank could be forced into bankruptcy in this way; some commentators speculated that the same problem could potentially affect other, much larger, banks. A particular point of concern was the increasingly international nature of financial institutions, by comparison with nationally-based regulatory regimes. To foresee the difficulties in Barings, for example, regulators in Britain would have needed to work closely with those in Singapore, but such cross-country co-operation remained extremely limited in scope.

Monetary Policy in Britain.

Until 1968 British monetary policy was in practice strongly Keynesian in the sense described earlier. Keynesian ideas began to come under increasingly strong intellectual challenge from monetarists in the 1960s, and by the second half of the 1970s monetarist ideas had become the dominant influence upon policy making. This happened in two stages. The first occurred in the autumn of 1976 when Britain applied to the I.M.F. for large credit facilities. One of the requirements which the I.M.F. imposed as a condition of granting these facilities was that the Government should lay down, and stick to annual *monetary targets, i.e.,* target annual growth rates in sterling M3. Successive governments adopted this approach for the next ten years.

The adoption of monetary targets in turn meant that the *public sector borrowing requirement* (p.s.b.r.) became a target, rather than a consequence, of policy. The p.s.b.r. is the combined deficit of the central government, local authorities and public corporations. It has to be financed by a combination of borrowing (from the private sector or from abroad) and increasing the money supply. Since domestic borrowing will push up interest rates, any government which has a monetary target and which is also unwilling to tolerate rises beyond a certain point in interest rates, will be compelled to limit the size of the p.s.b.r. This has to be done by a combination of tax rises and cuts in public spending. Thus targets for monetary growth carry implications for the government's tax and expenditure policies.

The second, and decisive, stage in the growth of monetarist influence was the election of a Conservative government in May 1979. The new government came into office committed to a monetarist approach to economic policy; several of its leading members declared themselves converts, to a greater or lesser extent, to the teachings of Professor Friedman, and rejected the Keynesianism of earlier post-war years.

Early in its term of office, therefore, the new government published its medium-term financial strategy, designed to operate over the period 1980-84. It aimed to secure steady cuts from year to year over this period in both the monetary growth rate, and the p.s.b.r. as a proportion of national income. The government took the view that the scale of past government borrowing had contributed a great deal to the rapid inflation rates of the 1970s.

Doubts about Monetarism.

By the end of 1981 the experience since 1976, and more especially since 1979, had begun to erode support for monetarist ideas, at least in their simple form. One area of doubt concerned the actual ability of the government to control money supply, however defined; this led to the 1981 changes in monetary control techniques mentioned above. A second argument revived the traditional Keynesian emphasis upon wider measures of liquidity: some economists, led by Nobel prize winner Professor James Meade, argued that the government should abandon monetary targets and instead set targets for the growth of *money national income*—the volume of output multiplied by its average price level—and should use a variety of fiscal instruments for this purpose, with monetary policy being used mainly to influence interest rates and the exchange rate. A third criticism of monetarism, also associated with Professor Meade and consistently advanced by another Nobel prize-winner, James Tobin of Yale University, and also many politicians, was that deflation had mainly reduced output and employment rather than inflation, and that this would always be the case unless the government returned to some form of *incomes policy*.

The Demise of Monetary Targeting.

In the course of the 1980s these criticisms gathered force. Despite its clear commitment to steady reductions in the growth rate of the money supply as a central part of its anti-inflation policy, Mrs. Thatcher's government persistently failed to achieve its monetary targets. Moreover its main target—£M3—became very volatile and, apparently, increasingly unreliable as a guide to underlying economic trends. In 1985-86, for example, £M3 grew very rapidly, suggesting that monetary policy was becoming lax, at just the time when real interest rates reached a record high level (which has traditionally been seen as an indication of tight monetary policy). By the middle of the 1980s it was clear that the government was attaching steadily less weight to formal monetary targets, and the 1987 Budget announced the end of £M3 as a target. This was certainly a substantial change from the period 1979-83, when £M3 was overwhelmingly the main policy instrument of macroeconomic policy.

New Controversies.

This modification of the Government's views was matched by changes in the views of many Keynesian economists. The traditional Keynesian view that money does not matter, which as discussed above dominated policy making for some twenty years after 1945, had been discarded by almost all the government's critics (some of whom pointed out Keynes himself had never argued that money was unimportant). Most economists accepted that there was sufficient evidence from the experience of the British economy in recent years to indicate that excessive expansion of the money supply was bound to lead to rises in inflation and nominal interest rates and was therefore harmful. In a sense, therefore, some of the traditional disputes between monetarists and Keynesians, which had persisted to the end of the 1970s, seemed to be coming to an end. Many monetarists accepted that simple monetary targeting was not sufficient; nearly all Keynesians accepted the need to prevent excessive monetary expansion.

New areas of controversy had partly replaced some of these traditional disagreements. For example, as the public sector borrowing requirement was reduced and eventually eliminated, giving way to a budget surplus during the 1987-8 financial year, there was much discussion on how this surplus should be used. Options included cutting tax rates, raising public spending, or repaying some of the accumulated National Debt. The Government, and many erstwhile monetarists, tended to favour the tax cutting option; many erstwhile Keynesians favoured increased public spending. However, this disagreement had little to do with traditional disputes about fiscal and monetary policies, and much more to do with alternative views about how best to stimulate the supply side of the economy. The Government argued that lower taxes would stimulate enterprise; those favouring higher spending argued that the rate of return on, for example, investment in education and training, would be very high. Hence traditional arguments about how best to regulate the *demand* side of the economy were increasingly being replaced by disputes about how to regulate the *supply* side—though many of the protagonists remained the same.

Another emerging argument concerned the appropriate degree of political control over monetary policy. Some economists, and some politicians, began to advocate an *independent Bank of England*, in the sense that the Bank's officials would be given the constitutional power to determine monetary policy themselves, rather than following the instructions of the elected politicians. Those advocating such a change believed that this would enhance the *credibility* of anti-inflation policies. They argued that politicians, facing electoral pressures, are always tempted to over-expand the economy, and consequently to adopt inflationary policies. Removing their power to control monetary policy would severely limit their ability to give in to such pressures. This in turn, so the argument went, would give a signal to other decision-makers in the economy that they should expect less inflationary pressure, which in turn would act, in a self-reinforcing way, to lower such pressures still further. For example, trade unions pressing for wage increases, and firms considering raising their selling prices, would think more carefully if they expected lower inflation generally in the economy. Advocates of such arguments pointed to the example of Germany, whose central bank, the Bundesbank, has long had considerable independence in the conduct of monetary policy.

Although this argument had some strong supporters, there were also many sceptics. Some economists argued that comparisons of a wider range of countries—as opposed to a focus only on the German example—gave little support to the idea that an independent central bank was certain to reduce inflationary pressures. Some politicians argued that it would be wrong in principle to hand control of monetary policy to people who were unelected and therefore in a sense unaccountable for their actions.

Whilst there was no consensus on the issue, it provided another good illustration of the extent to which the nature of economic controversies had altered. Few people questioned the inherent importance of monetary policy. Instead, the argument concerned the most effective way of implementing it, in the face of considerable consensus on its underlying objectives.

Confusion in Policy-Making.

The abandonment of monetary targetting in the second half of the 1980s coincided with what, in retrospect, appears to have been a considerable loss of cohesion in economic policy-making. Up to the mid-1980s the Thatcher governments, despite the various criticisms mentioned, had maintained a consistent approach to policy, with the defeat of inflation always the main priority and the use of monetary targets within the Medium Term Financial Strategy the main policy instrument. In the second half of the decade neither of these features was so clear cut. Whilst the Government continued to maintain that control of inflation was still the main priority, its actions suggested some modification. Similarly, whilst it continued to argue that

THE COST OF PUBLIC SERVICES
(£ million)

Expenditure.	1983	1993	Percentage increase 1983–93	Percentage of total 1993
Defence	16,592	24,279	46	8·9
Education	17,928	33,827	89	12·4
Health	19,900	36,828	85	13·5
Social Security benefits	38,634	93,298	142	34·2
Housing and community amenities	7,430	10,912	47	4·0
Agriculture, forestry and fishing	2,483	3,819	54	1·4
Transport and communication	6,058	6,820	13	2·5
Public order and safety	5,710	15,004	163	5·5
General public services	4,362	12,549	100	4·6
Other expenditure	22,032	35,464	61	8·8
Total expenditure	131,057	272,800	108	100

monetary control was vital, in practice it seemed relatively unconcerned at evidence that various monetary indicators suggested a danger of rapidly rising inflation.

Two episodes of policy making in particular illustrated these apparent changes. In 1986, £M3 exceeded its target by a large amount. The Government's response, as already mentioned, was to abandon £M3 as a target in the following year, thus ignoring the potential inflationary implications. This policy was justified by the Chancellor at the time on the grounds that £M3 had become too volatile to be a useful policy indicator. In effect Mr. Lawson was invoking Goodhart's Law. Whilst this had some intellectual justification, it is difficult to believe that the Government would have responded in the same way in the early 1980s. A second, similar policy episode occurred in 1988. By this time the Government was using M0 as its only formal monetary indicator. However, at the same time the Government had become increasingly preoccupied with exchange rate targets, and at the time the Chancellor was seeking to prevent the exchange rate of the pound from rising above three D-marks. To achieve this aim he was prepared to accept increases in M0 above the target range. Hence the Government in effect abandoned its monetary target in favour of an exchange rate target.

This emphasis on exchange rate targetting had emerged partly in response to pressure from companies engaged in large amounts of international trade, for whom volatile and unpredictable exchange rates had become an increasingly important problem. These firms argued in favour of policies aimed at stabilising exchange rates so as to make trading conditions more predictable. Many economists and policy makers were sympathetic to this view. However, economists emphasised that a policy of fixing or controlling the exchange rate was incompatible with one of monetary targetting. If the Government fixes the exchange rate it then has to allow the money supply to vary by whatever amounts are required to maintain the exchange rate target. However, it seemed that this point was not clearly grasped by the British Government, with the result that the clarity which had characterised policy making in the early 1980s was lost. After 1987 it became increasingly difficult to be sure about either the aims or the methods of policy making. This perception of confusion caused a gradual erosion of confidence in the Government by the financial markets.

When the Government took the decision to enter the Exchange Rate Mechanism of the European Monetary System in October 1990, it seemed that the confusion in policy-making had been resolved. Once again the Government had a clear strategy: all other policies were now subordinate to the requirement to maintain the sterling exchange rate within its agreed ERM bands, and this in turn was designed to re-emphasise the central importance of controlling inflation. However, the financial markets gradually lost confidence in the willingness or ability of the government to maintain the agreed exchange rate, and the resulting speculative pressure forced the pound out of the ERM again in September 1992. For the next few months, confusion about policy re-emerged in an even sharper form. The Government appeared to have no clear view about either the ultimate objectives of policy-making, or the appropriate policy tools. Gradually, however, a new view emerged which gave greater weight to encouraging growth in economic activity, whilst still stressing the importance of the inflation objective. The new emphasis on growth reflected the seriousness of the recession in which the economy had been trapped for the previous two years. The Government committed itself to adjusting taxes, public spending and interest rates in ways designed to give the economy the best possible chance of recovery. This marked a considerable shift of emphasis from policy-making in the 1980s.

5. ECONOMIC ASPECTS OF THE PUBLIC SERVICES

The Cost of Public Services.

In 1993, total public expenditure was £272,800 million, about £4,500 per head. Of this the bulk (over 80 per cent) was spent by central government, and the remainder by local authorities and public corporations. Total public expenditure has increased more than twentyfold since 1960, and rose as a proportion of GNP from 34 per cent to a peak of more than 50 per cent in 1983, before declining to 44 per cent in the period 1983–88. From 1988, the government's target of steady reductions in the share of public expenditure in GDP was prejudiced. In 1991, public spending's share in national income rose quite sharply as the recession and higher levels of unemployment pushed up expenditure on social security. Since Mr. Major became Prime Minister there had also been greater emphasis on public spending programmes such as health, and in its Spring 1993 Budget the Government intimated that the share of public spending in GDP would decline only marginally in the period to the mid-1990s.

Central Government collects in revenue considerably more than it spends itself, but transfers funds to the local authorities, to the National Insurance Fund, and to the public corporations. The expenditure of the public sector as a whole has generally exceeded its revenue, the difference being met by net borrowing. However, the buoyancy of privatisation receipts and the process of "real fiscal drag"—where tax allowances keep pace with inflation but not the rise in earnings so that tax payments as a percentage of earned incomes go up—provided some offset. There was a financial deficit in each year of the 1980s until 1988 when there was a surplus of £4·8 billion. There was a similar surplus in the following year, but then the Government started to move back into deficit as the recession pushed up spending, depressed tax revenues and curbed the Government's scope for further privatisations. The public sector deficit was forecast officially to stand at £35 billion in the financial year 1992–93 and at over £50 billion in 1993–94. Net public sector debt was forecast to be 39 per cent of GDP in 1993–94, compared to 50 per cent in 1979. Even on the Government's own rather optimistic forecasts, the public sector was envisaged to remain in deficit until late in the 1990s. In early 1995 it was estimated that the PSBR would decline from about 5 per cent of GDP in 1994–95 to about 1·5 per cent of GDP in 1997–98.

A breakdown of public expenditure is shown in the table (**G34**). Not all categories of public expenditure have expanded at the same rate. Over the period from 1983, for example, expenditure on public order and safety, social security, health and education increased faster than the total; expenditure on agriculture and on housing and community amenities fell behind the total.

Council Housing.

Expenditure on council housing (net of sales) amounted to 0·7 per cent of public expenditure in 1993. Housing expenditure consists of two quite different items. There is the capital cost of building new council houses or of improvement grants and the like. This is financed out of borrowing by local authorities from the Public Works Loan Board on the open market and through the proceeds of sales of existing council houses to tenants. There is also a recurrent cost, in the form of subsidies on council housing. April 1990 saw new financial arrangements for public sector housing, and a number of Government subsidies to council housing were consolidated into a Housing Revenue Account Subsidy of more than £4·4 billion in 1994–5. Direct subsidies to rents have fallen sharply in the past few years; and the new system, by "ring-fencing" local authorities housing revenue accounts, is intended to put councils' housing services on a more 'business-like footing". As a general rule, the Government's aim is to divert subsidies from the property to the person, via the housing benefit system.

For most of the post-war period governments provided a substantial subsidy to public sector housing, either in the form of help for new building, or as a direct subsidy to rents. The mix depended very much on the priorities of the day. From 1972 to 1975 there was a "fair rent" system, which then gave way to a system designed to subsidise the construction of new dwellings and improvements to the existing housing stock. The whole direction of policy for public sector housing was altered by the Housing Act of 1980. Since then, council house subsidies have been substantially reduced. Central government now calculates the amount by which it will finance housing subsidies on the assumption that local authorities charge council house tenants a "fair" or "market" rent. The result is that council rents have risen substantially in real terms. At the same time, private ownership has been encouraged *e.g.* through the sale of council houses. Between 1979 and 1993, just over 1·5 million council houses are estimated to have been sold. The Housing Act of 1988 further eroded the role of local authorities in the provision of housing by allowing public sector tenants to change their landlord if the authority in question was deemed to be unsatisfactory, and housing associations are becoming the main providers of new housing in the subsidised rented sector. Such associations now own and manage over 750,000 houses in England. Housing Action Trusts have been set up to take over responsibility for local authority housing in designated areas, although in many instances public sector tenants have been unwilling to risk a change of landlord even if dissatisfied with the standard of service provided by local authorities. An Act of 1993 was designed to add further impetus to tenant purchases.

The Housing Market.

Government housing policy must be seen in terms of the housing market as a whole. In 1992 there were about 23 million dwellings in the United Kingdom, 67 per cent being owner-occupied, 23 per cent council houses, and the other 11 per cent privately rented. The importance of owner-occupation has grown and that of private renting has declined: in 1960 they had accounted for 42 per cent and 32 per cent of the total respectively. Of the privately rented accommodation today, just under one third is military and company owned property let free to employees. One of the main aims of the 1988 Housing Act was to stimulate the private rented sector by deregulating rents on new private sector lettings. On an international comparison, the private rented sector in the early 1980s, as a percentage of total housing stock, was about 60 per cent in Switzerland, 50 per cent in Holland, 40 per cent in the USA, and 18 per cent in France. It should also be noted that the pattern of tenure

varies quite significantly across different parts of the U.K.—owner occupation ranges from 46 per cent in Scotland to 73 per cent in South-West England.

The switch to owner-occupation in the U.K. is largely the result of Government policy. Rent controls meant that there was little incentive to build houses for renting, nor even to maintain existing rented houses, although the 1988 Housing Act was intended to remove some of the disincentives to private rental. On the other hand, Government has given considerable tax advantages to owner-occupiers. Owner-occupied houses are exempt from the capital gains tax introduced in 1964, and owner-occupiers can also obtain tax relief on mortgage-interest payments on a principal of up to £30,000. In 1990, mortgage interest relief represented a direct subsidy to owner-occupiers worth some £6·2bn, a more than ten-fold increase since the early 1960s. The real cost of mortgage interest relief more than doubled during the 1980s alone. It is therefore unsurprising that steps have been taken to reduce this subsidy, even though mortgage interest relief is something of a political "sacred cow". The £30,000 limit for relief has been unchanged since March 1983, in spite of very rapid house price inflation since that date. Until August 1988 unmarried owner-occupiers could claim tax relief on multiples of £30,000, depending on the number sharing. Relief is now restricted to £30,000 per property. In the March 1991 Budget mortgage interest relief was restricted to the basic rate of income tax; previously higher rate tax payers could claim relief on interest payments at their highest marginal rate of income tax. Since the abolition of the Schedule A tax in 1961—whereby owner-occupiers paid tax on the rental income imputed to their houses—this tax relief on interest payments must be justified as an inducement to home-ownership; but it is also a considerable subsidy to owner-occupiers, who tend to be the relatively well-off. From 1994 mortgage interest relief was limited to 20 per cent and from April 1995 it was further limited to 15 per cent.

The year 1953 was a peak for public sector housebuilding in the United Kingdom when 256,000 council dwellings were completed. There was a trough in 1961 (119,000), a peak in 1967 (204,000) and a subsequent fall to 108,000 in 1973. Since the mid 1970s there has been a steady decline in the construction of public dwellings. In 1993 only 36,000 new houses were completed. By contrast, the number of private dwellings completed rose steadily from 63,000 in 1953 to a peak of 222,000 in 1968. Thereafter the number fell back to an annual average of slightly less than 200,000 in the early 1970s, and still further to an average of about 130,000 in the early 1980s, rising again in 1983 to about 148,000, and to a peak of 200,000 in 1988 before falling to 180,000 in 1989, 161,000 in 1990 and 154,000 in 1991. The total number of dwellings completed reached a peak of 414,000 in 1968, and fell to 270,000 in 1974. Since then, the best year has been 1976 (315,000), the worst 1992 (171,000), while 175,000 dwellings were completed in 1993.

Over the 15 years 1955–70 the rate of inflation in the price of modern existing houses averaged 5 per cent per annum: somewhat faster than the rise in the cost of living. After 1970 there was a great surge in house prices: between December 1970 and December 1972 the average rise was no less than 30 per cent per annum. There are various reasons for this remarkable inflation. Partly it reflected the rapid acceleration of general inflation; in such times it is sensible to hold one's wealth in the form of assets which will appreciate in value. It also reflected the decline in house-building after 1968, and a slowing-down in the rate at which building land became available. The precise timing of the inflation resulted from the sudden and large increase in the availability of building society mortgages. And as the inflation grew, so optimistic expectations helped to raise house prices still further. By 1974 the rate of increase had slowed down considerably. It slowed even further in 1975 and 1976. In 1978 and 1979 prices started to accelerate again, slackening off in 1980, only to start accelerating again at the end of 1982. This rise was sustained through to 1988, but 1989 through to early 1991 saw sharp falls in house prices, particularly in areas such as the South East and East Anglia where house price inflation had accelerated rapidly in the previous two years. By 1990 the housing market slowdown was evident in all regions, and nationally house prices fell by 5 per cent. Further declines were registered in 1991 and 1992, but the pattern varied from region to region. In particular there were signs of a recovery of the market in Northern England, Wales, Scotland and Northern Ireland. But there has been no real general recovery in prices.

In 1989 the number of dwellings exceeded the number of households by just under one million. Yet the picture is not as rosy as this implies. The regional distribution of supply and demand was not equally spread. The measured number of households understates the number of "units" needing accommodation—a married couple, for example, living in someone else's house. Such concealed units are thought to number 800,000. Much accommodation is substandard in some way or other—a 1986 survey of dwellings in England and Wales indicated that about 2·9 million homes or more than 12 per cent of the housing stock was unfit for habitation. In 1990 housing renewal areas were established in England and Wales to cover, inter alia, renovation and redevelopment of substandard housing. These complement housing action areas in Scotland and Northern Ireland, which have authority to channel funds for redevelopment where at least half the housing stock does not meet "statutory tolerable" standards. In spite of such initiatives, the above factors, together with personal financial and social problems, mean that a worrying number of people are homeless. Thus by 1993 134,100 households were accepted as homeless by the local authorities. The problem was particularly acute in London.

Education.

Educational expenditure accounted for 12 per cent of public expenditure in 1993. It had increased over the previous 25 years for two reasons. First the number of full-time pupils had grown. Second the more expensive sectors—secondary schools and universities—expanded most rapidly. For example, in 1993 there were 3·6 million students in state secondary schools as opposed to 3·2 million in 1961, although the 1993 figure was well below the comparable total for 1981 of 4·6 million. This reflects changing demographics. Falling birth rates meant that the secondary school population reached a peak in the mid-to-late 1970s, since when it has fallen. Higher education has also started to see the impact of these declining birth rates. Even so, there were 956,000 full-time students in higher education in 1992–93, compared with a total of 456,800 in 1970–71. The proportion of young people entering higher education rose from one in eight to one in five by 1990. The Government's target is for the proportion to rise to one in three by 2000. The autumn of 1993 saw a record entry which effectively met that target.

In December 1972 the Conservative Government published a White Paper setting out plans for the expansion of education over the following decade. More emphasis was to be placed on nursery schooling for the 3- and 4-year-olds: within 10 years it would be available to all children whose parents wanted them to attend. There would be a school building programme to replace old school buildings. Teacher training would be expanded to reduce pupil-teacher ratios further. Higher education would be expanded less rapidly than in the previous decade, and the emphasis would be placed on polytechnics and other non-university colleges. Unfortunately many of these plans were thwarted, largely as a result of cut-backs in total public expenditure. It is, however, generally recognised that education can be an economic investment for the future just as much as capital formation in, say, machinery or roads. There is a "private return" on "investment in education", which takes the form of higher earnings over the lifetime of the person educated; and there is a "social return" on public resources devoted to education being the greater contribution to the national product which trained and educated people can make. Although many of the 1972 White Paper plans were not implemented, both the 1974 Labour and 1979 Conservative Governments considered longer term policies for education. The key theme of a consultative White Paper in 1977 was the need to attune school curricula to the employment needs of school-leavers, and to encourage stronger ties between schools and industry. This has been a recurrent theme. Questions about longer term

educational requirements were initially subsumed under the present Conservative Government by debate on the relative merits of private and public sector education. There was also a renewed emphasis on making the later years of school education more directly related to labour market requirements, represented, for example, by the increased involvement in the mid 1980s of the Manpower Services Commission, and later the Training Commission, in school programmes, such as the Technical and Vocational Education Initiative.

In 1985 in a White Paper entitled "The Development of Higher Education into the 1990s", the Government also considered ways of improving the contribution of higher education to economic performance. Thus the links between full-time education and job training are being intensified. The system of National Vocational Qualifications is intended to unify academic and vocational credentials.

Such themes were continued in the Education Reform Act, passed in the 1988 Parliamentary session. It proposed the introduction of a National Curriculum, the establishment of City Technical Colleges and giving business greater representation on the new University Funding Council than it had had on the University Grants Committee. Many of the provisions of the 1988 Education Reform Act remain highly controversial, particularly those which relate to the National Curriculum and what is perceived to be over-rigid prescription of its content. Despite modifications to the original proposals, there is still widespread opposition to the formal testing of 7 and 14 year-olds, particularly the former. Many commentators see the Act as increasing central government's control over education—for example, LEAs have lost control of the Colleges of Further Education and of the former Polytechnics, while schools can choose to opt out of Local Authority control in favour of administration by central government if a majority of parents and governors so desire. At the same time the Act emphasises the theme of intensified competition in the provision of education. Schools now have to compete for pupils and universities for funding. In schools this is known as the policy of "open enrolment". The theme of greater competition was also evident in the higher education sector, where the "binary divide" between universities and polytechnics has been ended. All such establishments are now funded by the Higher Education Funding Council.

Social Security.

In 1988 the Social Security system underwent considerable change. In what follows we first describe the old system, before turning to the new.

There were two forms of social security: *National Insurance* and *Supplementary Benefits*. The former was non-means tested. They were designed to be exactly what the name indicated—insurance for when an individual met circumstances implying a loss of income, be that circumstance old age, unemployment or sickness. By contrast the latter were means tested, and were designed to keep people out of poverty. As such under the original Beveridge scheme, they were meant to be a safety net for the unfortunate few. The majority were to be covered by the insurance element. Formidable financing difficulties meant that this ideal was never achieved, and supplementary benefits attained an unwanted prominence in the British social security system.

(i) National Insurance.

Under this scheme employees receive rights to unemployment benefit, sickness benefit, retirement pensions, widows' benefits, injury and disablement benefits, *etc*. In 1993–94, 10 million pensioners received National Insurance pensions. For those below pensionable age, the major national insurance benefit available (under both the old social security system and the new one described in part (v) **G38**) is unemployment benefit. This was paid to 0·6 million recipients in 1993–94. Weekly rates are laid down for each benefit, *e.g.*, in April 1995 a rate of £46·45 was paid to a single person receiving unemployment benefit. The basic rate is increased according to the number of dependants. In 1966 an earnings-related supplement was introduced for benefits paid to persons between 18 and 65 (men) or

60 (women): the supplement being related to earnings in the previous tax year. The maximum total benefit, including increases for dependants, amounted to 85 per cent of earnings. This, together with tax rebates, meant a higher income out of work for a very few people. In 1982 the earnings-related unemployment supplement was withdrawn, whilst unemployment benefit became taxable.

By far the most important benefit is the retirement pension, paid as of right to contributors on retirement. Individuals may increase their rate of pension by staying on at work after the minimum retiring age of 65 for men and 60 for women. In April 1995 basic retirement pensions were £59·15 per week for single persons and £94·45 for a married couple. In its Autumn 1993 Budget the Government announced its intention to equalise retirement ages for men and women, but not until after the year 2010.

Social Security benefits used to be up-dated in November each year, to account for inflation in the year to the previous May. Under the Government's social security reforms (*see* **G38**), in 1986 the uprating took place in July, and in subsequent years in April.

(ii) The Financing of National Insurance.

The main source of finance for National Insurance payments is the National Insurance Fund. These funds are built up largely from the compulsory weekly National Insurance contributions which most of the adult population have to pay. For employees, both employer and employee pay a contribution. The self-employed also pay contributions of smaller size than the sum of the employer's and employee's contribution, but they are not entitled to unemployment benefit. Weekly contributions include a contribution to the cost of the National Health Service. As a result of the 1985 and 1989 Budgets, employers' and employees' national insurance contributions were cut for the lowest paid workers, in order to increase the incentives to work and to hire more labour. At the same time, while a maximum earnings limit for employees' contributions remains, the upper-earnings limit on employer's contributions has been abolished. In the 1989 Budget the structure of National Insurance payments was altered. Previously, the rate went from zero to more than 9 per cent once an individual hit the lower earnings limit. This meant that someone moving just above the lower limit for National Insurance contributions could face a marginal tax rate in excess of more than 100 per cent which was clearly a major disincentive. Although such traps have by no means been eradicated, National Insurance contributions are now charged at 2 per cent on earnings below the lower earnings limit once that limit has been reached, and thereafter at 10 per cent until the upper earnings limit.

The National Insurance Scheme is an odd mixture of insurance and tax. The levels of contributions, when the scheme started in 1948, were fixed on the actuarial principle that contributions by or on behalf of an individual plus a specified State contribution should on average suffice to pay for the benefits to which he was entitled. But the scheme did not allow for inflation and a rising standard of living. In particular a succession of increases granted in the rate of pensions has put an end to this actuarial probity. Instead the principle became established that the rate of contributions in each year, together with a transfer from the Government, should equal the total benefits paid out in that year. Expenditure on non-contributory benefits is covered by general revenues.

(iii) Reform of Pensions.

There are about ten million pensioners in Britain. Up to a quarter of these are kept out of poverty only by receiving income support. Many of the remainder find their living standards considerably reduced from when they were working. This is because the existing state retirement pension is inadequate. There are some occupational pension schemes which offer a better income, but these are still rather restricted in their coverage—of those currently of pensionable age, being available to many more non-manual than manual workers. Like personal savings, many of them also tend to have

only limited safeguards against inflation unless they are index-linked. In an era of rapidly rising prices, the pensioner is at a particular disadvantage. Widows form the poorest groups among them, with over half of them needing to draw a supplementary pension.

A scheme for graduated pensions was introduced for employees in 1961. Under the scheme there were two kinds of employees—*ordinary* and *contracted-out*. In the case of contracted-out workers, their employer (on whom the decision whether to contract out rested) had to institute a private superannuation scheme that gave at least as favourable terms as the new State scheme, including the provision that rights under the scheme should be transferable up to the limits of the State scheme. Transferability was the guarantee that the individual did not lose his pension rights when he changed his job. In practise transferability was never really achieved.

In 1969 the Labour Government made proposals in a White Paper to replace the National Insurance Scheme by a new scheme of superannuation and social insurance, in which both contributions and benefits would be related to the earnings of the individual. It argued that the existing scheme failed to provide security in old age. The new earnings-related contributions would be mostly higher than contributions under the existing scheme, especially among higher earners; and in return higher pensions and other benefits would be paid.

An important feature of the proposed scheme was that benefits were to take into account both changes in prices and in general living standards. Thus, for instance, a contributor who received earnings equal to the national average throughout his working life would receive a pension calculated on the national average earnings at the time he reached pension age, not on the money he received over his working life. Some two-thirds of employed men were contracted-out, *i.e.*, in occupational pensions schemes, in 1970. The Government intended that these schemes should continue to exist together with the State scheme, and it proposed to allow for partial contracting out of the State scheme.

These plans lapsed with the change of Government in 1970. The Conservative Government announced its proposals for reform in a White Paper published in 1971. It considered that the costs of earnings-related benefits would be too great; instead it favoured earnings-related contributions for basically flat-rate pensions. In addition it wished to encourage contracting out, so that almost all employees would also be members of a private occupational pension scheme, in which pensions would be related to past contributions. The Government recognised that it would have to ensure that occupational pension rights were transferable between jobs. Like the previous Government, it envisaged a legal guarantee that State pensions would be revised every two years. It also envisaged that the share which the State provides from taxation for National Insurance—about 18 per cent of contributions in 1970—would be maintained. Again the plan lapsed.

Meanwhile the Government had become aware of the need for a frequent adjustment of pension rates in an era of high inflation. In early 1975 the full pension entitlement was £10 for a single person and £16 for a married couple. In April 1995 the rates stood at £59·15 for a single person and £94·45 for a married couple. The difficulty of funding an adequate state pension when the number of pensioners is rising relative to the size of the workforce has led to a withdrawal from the goals for pensions laid down in the 1970s. These goals were for a two-tier pension. The bottom tier was a common flat-rate for everyone. The top tier was earnings-related—that is, a fixed proportion of the pensioner's previous earnings. Because of the flat-rate element, a low earner would be able to expect a pension which was a higher percentage of his working income than that obtained by a higher earner. Contributions to the scheme would be earnings related. The pensions would be fully protected against inflation, and women would enter the scheme on the same footing as men. There was an obvious emphasis on the need to protect women from poverty in retirement, after the death of the husband. There would be a maximum pension entitlement and a maximum contribution. For this reason among others, the Government planned to encourage new and improved occupational schemes, to exist alongside the state scheme. It was hoped that the scheme would come to full maturity by 1998, this long delay reflecting the formidable difficulties in financing the plan. In the meantime fully earnings-related contributions started in 1975, and minor earnings-related benefit in 1979. These replaced flat-rate National Insurance payments and graduated pension contributions.

A renewed concern in the early 1980s was with a particular aspect of occupational pensions—their transferability from job to job. Someone who left an occupational scheme had the choice of either leaving his pension rights at his old employer, and receiving a deferred pension at retirement age, usually unadjusted for inflation between his departure and retirement; or, if his old and new employers both agreed transferring the fund, from which effectively the pension is paid, to his new employer, usually at great loss to himself. The Government is attempting to introduce the full transferability of pension rights from job to job—at least for those who have been with an employer for more than two years. In changes introduced in 1988, employees were given the right to opt out of SERPS or of an employer's own scheme, and set up their own private pension plan. At the same time, a worker who left for another job after 2 years (instead as previously after 5 years) would be able to preserve his pension rights (with some protection for inflation) or have them transferred to a new scheme if the scheme was willing to accept them. The extent of take-up of personal pension schemes can be gauged by the cost to the Government in foregone National Insurance contributions as individuals contract out of the state pension scheme. National Insurance rebates to those taking out personal pensions amounted to £1·75 billion in 1989–90 and well over £2 billion in 1990–91, although this cost fell in 1991–92 as the take-up of personal pensions fell past its peak. Some 7·8 million people have now taken out personal pensions. The Social Security Act of 1990 contained provisions specifically designed to improve protection for occupational and personal pension schemes, including the appointment of a Pensions Ombudsman. The Social Security Act of 1993 introduced a 1 per cent additional rebate for personal pension holders aged 30 and over, and provided for a Treasury grant to be paid into the National Insurance Fund.

The advantage to the government of a shift into private pension schemes is that it will reduce the impact of demographic change, namely the cost of supporting a larger retired population relative to that of working age. Both private and state schemes are now operating on a fully funded basis *i.e.* the individual pays for his or her future pension entitlement, which contrasts with the "pay as you go" system in operation in many countries where pension payments are funded by current contributions.

Intense concern has started to be expressed about whether the State can continue to maintain the present pension system. The essential problem increasingly was seen to be the non-means tested component. Many commentators were starting to argue that eventually the bulk of pension payments would have to be means-tested.

(iv) Poverty in Britain.

Despite the existence of National Insurance there are many people in Britain whose income falls below that which the Government regarded as adequate. These people are supported from Government revenues by means of *income support*, formerly *supplementary benefits*, and before 1966 known as *National Assistance*. It was a fault of the National Insurance Scheme that so many have required this assistance. In 1993 1·6 million pensioners received income support, with many more getting extra help with rent. Of families whose head was in work, 447,000 received additional Family Credit, whilst well over half of the male unemployed were wholly dependent on additional state support. Anyone who is out of work for more than a year loses entitlement to unemployment benefit and becomes reliant on supplementary payments through what was the supplementary benefit system and is now income support (*see* (v) *below*). From 1996 all unemployed benefit recipients will be on a single benefit (the Jobseeker's Allowance), regardless of duration of unemployment. A major fault with the

earlier supplementary benefits scheme was that they could not be paid to those in employment whose earnings were below the benefit level, and if such persons became unemployed they could claim benefits only up to their normal earnings level. The *Family Income Supplement* was introduced in 1971 to alleviate hardship amongst low earners, but it has been estimated that only half of those eligible claimed F.I.S. The take-up of the new Family Credit payment, has been even lower.

In 1994–95 there were 6·1 million people receiving income support or family credit. The equivalent number in 1978–79 was 3 million. Apart from this increase in poverty, there are many households (at least 1·4 million) with income below the official poverty line.

(v) The Reform of Social Security.

In 1985 the Government issued a White Paper detailing reforms of the whole social security system. The basis of dissatisfaction was three-fold. First, the system was a complex and costly one to run. Second, it worked in such a way as to help some who, on official definitions of poverty, did not need assistance; whilst, conversely, it failed to provide it for some who did. Third, it created unemployment benefit traps, supplementary benefit traps and poverty traps. These imply that people who are unemployed or employed on low pay might be deterred from taking employment or taking jobs with higher pay, because the combined effects of the tax and benefit system mean that the consequential increase in their net income is negligible. Behind their proposed reforms was the concern about future financing difficulties, and a wish to make the system simpler. The main elements of the new system were introduced in April 1988.

On pensions, it was originally proposed to retain basic pensions, but to abolish earnings related pensions (SERPS). Instead, greater stress was to be placed on occupational pension schemes. Substantial political pressures caused a change of mind, and SERPS was retained, albeit in a modified form (see (iii) on **G**37). Universal child benefit was retained. But for low earnings families, FIS was replaced by *Family Credit*, paid through the pay packet. As compared to FIS it allows a smoother tapering of payments as original income increases. For those not in work, supplementary benefits were replaced by "*income support*", which is intended to be simpler and to involve a smaller range of payments. Benefits are at a lower rate for the under-25s and at a higher rate for pensioners. An additional sum is paid for each dependent child, as it is for single parents and the long-term sick and disabled. Beyond these, there are no additional payments. There is, however, a new *Social Fund* "to provide for exceptional circumstances and emergencies", payments from which are rationed through a system of strict budget limits for each Social Security Office. Recipients of income support are still entitled to free school meals and free welfare foods, unlike those getting family credit. There is also a new simplified scheme for housing benefits. Unemployment benefit, the maternity allowance (in revised form) and sickness benefit survived the 1988 review, but maternity and death grants were abolished. Substantial changes have been made in provisions for widowhood.

The Government's catchphrase for these reforms was "the twin pillars": state help combined with encouragement for private provision. Returning to the three major complaints about the previous system, certainly the revised one is cheaper to administer. It probably targets the benefits more accurately. It may also have alleviated the worst traps, but in substantially improving the lot of some in this respect, it has worsened it for more. Indeed, the present scheme is not a major departure, and falls far short of more radical proposals for a combined tax and benefit credit system.

Recently the Government has announced that in 1996 it will replace benefits for the unemployed with the Job Seekers' Allowance. It has also announced that Invalidity Benefit and Sickness Benefit will be replaced by the much more strictly tested Incapacity Benefit.

Public Revenue.

In the table on **G**39 we show the sources of revenue. No less than 53·6 per cent of the total

SOURCES OF PUBLIC REVENUE

Revenue.	1983 £m	1993 £m	Percentage increase 1983–93	Percentage of total revenue 1993
Taxes on income	*65,961*	*121,065*	*84*	*53·6*
of which paid by:				
personal sector	31,591	57,677	83	25·6
companies	5,616	15,010	167	6·6
national insurance contributions	18,449	33,781	83	15·0
Taxes on capital	*1,616*	*2,386*	*48*	*1·1*
of which:				
capital gains tax	974	1,118	15	0·5
Taxes on expenditure	*37,281*	*91,237*	*145*	*40·4*
of which levied on:				
alcohol	3,646	5,410	48	2·4
tobacco	3,759	6,359	69	2·8
Other revenues	*21,052*	*11,050*	*−48*	*4·9*
Total revenue	*125,910*	*225,738*	*79*	*100*
Net borrowing	12,611	34,141		
Total expenditure	*138,521*	*259,879*		

public revenue in 1993 came from taxes on income; almost half of this being personal income tax. Taxation of profits amounted to only 6·6 per cent of total public revenue. Taxes on expenditure accounted for 40 per cent of the total. Two commodities in particular were heavily taxed: alcoholic drink and tobacco. Together they accounted for 5·2 per cent of public revenue. These commodities are singled out partly for social reasons and partly because—in economists' jargon—the demand for them is *inelastic*; *i.e.*, the public reduces its consumption of drink and tobacco only slightly in response to a rise in their price. Indirect taxation—taking the form of excise duties and purchase taxes (value added tax after 1973)—used to be spread very unevenly over different sorts of expenditure. The introduction of Value Added Tax in 1973 tended to even out the incidence of indirect taxes on different goods and services, though tobacco, drink and motoring continued to be hit heavily.

Until 1989 in Scotland, and 1990 in England and Wales, the major method of collecting local taxes was through rates. A rateable value was assessed for each commercial or domestic property, corresponding roughly to its size, imputed rental value, and amenities. Each year, the appropriate local authority decided at what rate in the pound to tax this rateable value. On the dates mentioned above, the government substantially altered the local tax system in an ostensible effort to broaden the tax base for the domestic element. Instead of local taxes being paid on the basis of property ownership, each adult paid a flat rate charge or poll tax. Although some minor adjustment was made for personal circumstances, the tax was highly regressive and its introduction was very controversial. Part but not all of the objections related to the government's under-estimate of the burden of local government revenue which could fall on the personal sector. Local authorities were no longer levy rates on the business sector—these were charged uniformly by central government and the proceeds were then distributed to local authorities on some notional calculation of need. The large burden of local authority taxation falling on persons, particularly in previously low-rated areas, was tackled by an increasingly bureaucratic system of rebates. The first year of the poll tax in England and Wales merely served to demonstrate its unpopularity and its inefficiency in high collection costs. In order to defray the political consequences of the poll tax, the March 1991 Budget included a provision to reduce poll tax bills by £140 in 1991–92 and beyond, financed by a rise in the VAT rate from 15% to 17.5%. Even this failed to overcome objections to a tax which created far more losers than gainers, and in April 1991 the government announced plans to revert to a property-based system of local taxation, retaining only vestigial elements of the poll tax principle that all should contribute something to the cost of local services. The Government proposed that the new "Council Tax" would be a property tax banded according to the size of dwelling, thus reintroducing an element of progressivity. The Council Tax came into existence in 1993–4.

The Budget.

Each year in the Spring the Chancellor of the Exchequer used to announce his Budget for the coming fiscal year. In November 1993 the first unified Budget was presented, combining the Autumn expenditure exercise with the Spring taxation announcements. The most important and most difficult task in drawing up the Budget is to decide on the size of deficit to aim for. The deficit is the excess of public expenditure over public revenue; and it has to be financed by borrowing or by printing money. A large deficit is normally reflationary; sometimes that may be required to get the economy out of recession. A small deficit—and even more, a surplus—is deflationary, and is a means of holding a demand-pull inflation in check.

In 1970 there was a small surplus, and thus the net borrowing requirement was negative. After that the borrowing requirement became large and positive, peaking in the recessionary years 1979–82. In the 1980s more favourable economic circumstances and the one-off receipts from major privatisations enabled the public sector accounts to swing into surplus. In 1988 this surplus or Public Sector Debt Repayment (PSDR) was £12·4 billion (about 3 per cent of GDP) but it then fell to £9·6 billion in 1989 and only £1·9 billion in 1990. By 1991 the public finances had once again deteriorated markedly and were in deficit by some £8·8 billion. The reason for the elimination of the PSDR was a combination of much slower economic growth, difficulties with the privatisation programme, and a significant increase in government expenditure. The last of these was largely due to much higher public sector pay awards. A surplus is not itself indicative of a very tight fiscal policy, any more than a deficit automatically implies an expansionary stance. To assess the true fiscal stance, one must adjust the surplus/deficit for the effects of inflation, privatisation receipts, and the stage of the economic cycle, *i.e.* the level of unemployment.

The calculation of the precise deficit or surplus needed is a chancy business; for the level that is required depends on the amount of saving and on the amount of spending out of credit that people intend to do—and this is not easily predictable. It also depends on the change in the foreign balance. Nor can the Chancellor be sure his figures are right: estimating next year's revenue, and even next year's expenditure by the Government is difficult enough, but he needs to estimate also the likely trends of private income and expenditure, without really reliable information as to what they were in the past year. This has been particularly evident in recent years, when official economic statistics have been subject to massive error and subsequent revision, and the Chancellor's Budget forecasts for the year ahead have proved wildly inaccurate. One good example is provided by his 1988 Budget forecast for the balance of payments. In March 1988 the official forecast for the current account deficit in the year ahead was £4 billion—in the event the deficit was almost four times larger.

The introduction of advance *cash limits* on a large proportion of expenditure in 1976 was meant to give the Government greater control over projected spending. Prior to that the general rule had been to estimate public expenditure for the following year on the basis of its volume. If inflation was higher than predicted, then the tendency was to preserve volume by increasing the value of expenditure. Cash limits altered this, and in 1982 cash planning institutionalised this change. A large proportion of government spending was fixed in value terms, and if inflation exceeded the predicted rate, then volume suffered. From 1993 there was a major change in budgetary arrangements. For many years spending plans had been announced in the Autumn, and full budget proposals and tax changes the following Spring. From the autumn of 1000 there was a unified Budget.

In spite of such problems, fiscal policy—running large deficits when economic activity is low, and small ones or surpluses when it seems to be excessively high—is the most important action through which the economy can be kept on an even keel. Monetary policy may help; but the Budget decision of the Chancellor on changes in taxation and public expenditure is the key one. Indeed, it can be argued that the role of fiscal policy was enhanced by membership of the EMS Exchange Rate Mechanism (ERM). Even after withdrawal from ERM, the level of interest rates is now largely determined by the need to preserve sterling's value on the foreign exchanges, meaning that the only domestic policy tool over which the government has any direct control is the fiscal stance.

6. SOURCES OF STATISTICS: SOME SUGGESTIONS FOR FURTHER READING

The non-specialist will find that most of the statistics he needs are given in the *Annual Abstract of Statistics*, published every year by Her Majesty's Stationery Office. This comprehensive document includes figures on population, social conditions, education, labour, production, trade and balance of payments, national income and expenditure, wages and prices, and many other topics. For more up-to-date information, reference should be made to the *Monthly Digest of Statistics* which has a similar coverage and gives month-by-month figures. A selection of the more important series, presented in a manner which can more easily be understood by the layman, is given in another Stationery Office publication, *Economic Trends*, also issued monthly.

Fuller information on labour problems is given in the *Department of Employment Gazette*, and on financial matters in the *Bank of England Quarterly Bulletin*. These two periodicals include discussions on the statistics presented. *Social Trends* contains articles and detailed statistics on social, cultural and economic conditions in Britain.

For an analysis of developments in the economy see the *National Institute Economic Review*, a private publication issued by the National Institute for Economic and Social Research. The quarterly *Oxford Review of Economic Policy* (Oxford University Press) contains up-to-date articles on aspects of the economy.

For a comprehensive and systematic introduction to the British economy the reader is referred to A. R. Prest and D. J. Coppock, *The U.K. Economy: a Survey of Applied Economics* (Weidenfeld and Nicolson). Other introductory texts include N.F.R. Crafts and N. Woodward, *The British Economy since 1945* (Oxford), Tony Buxton et al., *Britain's Economic Performance*, (Routledge), J. Black, *The Economics of Modern Britain* (Martin Robertson), R. Dornbusch and R. Layard, *The Performance of the British Economy*, and D. Morris (ed), *The Economic System in the UK* (Oxford).

Interesting books on particular topics include J. Vickers et al., *Regulatory Reform* (MIT) and A. B. Atkinson, *The Economics of Inequality* (Oxford). A sourcebook on the EC is *The Economy of the European Community* (Office for Official Publications of the European Communities). An interesting survey of EC matters is E. Davies et. al. (eds), *1992: Myths and Realities*.

III.   THE LESS DEVELOPED ECONOMIES

Income Levels.

Two-thirds of the world's population live in dire poverty—a poverty which can scarcely be imagined by those accustomed to the standards of living attained in the relatively few developed countries of the world. The orders of world inequality may be seen from the table comparing annual gross national products per capita by region, converted into pounds sterling at official exchange rates. These figures are only very approximate because exchange rates are misleading indicators of purchasing power and because the averages conceal considerable income inequalities within some regions and countries. Nevertheless, it is clear that poverty is widespread in the world. The alleviation of this poverty is widely recognised as the most important economic—and indeed political—task of the remainder of the twentieth century. The 40 low-income developing countries referred to in the table have an average income per capita of £200 per annum, and contain 3,130 million people; over 2,400 million in 9 Asian countries and 440 million in 27 African countries.

According to a World Bank estimate, a third of the population of all developing countries in 1980 had a calorie intake below 90 per cent of the requirement laid down by the Food and Agricultural Organisation and the World Health Organisation; this meant that they did not get enough calories for an active working life. A sixth (340 million) had a calorie intake below 80 per cent: they did not get enough calories to prevent stunted growth and serious health risks. The areas particularly affected were South Asia and sub-Saharan Africa.

What is a Less Developed Country?

There are no less than 140 countries comprising the so-called "Third World," known variously as "less developed" or "developing" or "underdeveloped" or "poor" countries. There is a great diversity among them, and yet they have a number of features in common. Foremost is their poverty, but even poverty is not universal: some of the oil-producing countries such as Saudi Arabia, Kuwait and Libya have achieved very high levels of income per capita while retaining many of the other characteristics of less developed countries.

Most of the developing countries are primarily agricultural economies, with the bulk of the population engaged in *subsistence agriculture*. For many millions of peasant farmers the primary objective is to produce enough food for their family to subsist. India is a classic example, with no less than 70 per cent of its 870 million people dependent on agriculture for a living. Most less developed countries have only a small industrial sector as yet: it is rare for the output of the manufacturing sector to exceed 20 per cent of the gross domestic product. The main exceptions to this rule are the successful exporters of labour-intensive manufacturing goods, such as Hong Kong, Singapore, Taiwan and South Korea. Many of the less developed countries lack the necessary ingredients for successful industrialisation—capital, skills and entrepreneurship.

The developing countries vary enormously in size—from the teeming masses of India and China to scores of countries with less than a million people, including Bahrain, Botswana, Fiji, Gabon, Mauritius and many West Indian islands. The development problems and possibilities facing large and small countries are very different. The small size of most developing economies forces them to concentrate on the production of one or two primary products for world markets. Their high degree of specialisation and heavy dependence on exports and imports makes these econo-

GROSS NATIONAL PRODUCT PER CAPITA
BY GROUPS OF COUNTRY AND SELECTED
COUNTRIES, 1991

	(£ p.a.)
40 low-income developing countries	198
of which: Bangladesh	124
India	187
Sri Lanka	283
Tanzania	57
China	209
65 middle-income developing countries	1,402
of which: Turkey	1,006
Thailand	888
Brazil	1,662
Mexico	1,713
21 industrialised countries	12,174
of which: Spain	7,040
U.K.	9,358
Germany	13,373
U.S.A	12,576
Japan	15,228

POPULATION SIZE, GROWTH AND
DENSITY BY REGION

	Popula-tion 1990 (m).	Growth rate 1985–90 (% p.a.).	Density 1990 (per sq km).
North America	276	0·8	13
Europe	498	0·2	101
Former U.S.S.R.	289	0·8	13
Oceania	26	1·5	3
Africa	642	3·0	21
Latin America	448	2·1	21
Asia	3,113	1·9	113
of which:			
India	827	2·0	252
China	1,139	1·4	119
World Total	5,292	1·7	39

mies dangerously vulnerable to the vagaries of world trade and the world economy.

Enough has been said to show that, apart from their poverty, the less developed countries have other economic characteristics and problems in common. However, it is dangerous to generalise because there are also important differences. In particular, they vary in their degree of development and in their potential for development. A semi-industrialised, urbanised country such as Argentina has little in common with an utterly backward country such as Chad, and the economic prospects for an oil-rich country such as Indonesia are far brighter than for a country with few natural resources such as Tanzania.

Population Growth.

Many underdeveloped countries are experiencing an unprecedented population explosion: annual rates of increase of between 2 and 3 per cent—which double population in as little as 35 and 24 years respectively—are common. This is a phenomenon of the last four decades. Death rates have fallen sharply in response to improved health services and modern methods of control, *e.g.*, immunisation programmes and the eradication of malaria through DDT spraying. On the other hand, birth rates have been kept up by such factors as tradition, social prestige, religion, the need for security in old age and a lack of facilities for family planning.

The table indicates that over half the world's population lives in Asia, and that the developed regions account for under a quarter of the total. Apart from Australasia (into which immigration is high) the developed countries show slower rates of population growth than Africa, Latin America and Asia. The figures of population density may easily be misleading, since they take no account of the nature of the area, *e.g.*, deserts are included. But it is clear that Asia is more densely populated than Africa or Latin America.

Life Expectancy.

Although death rates have fallen in the developing countries, especially infant mortality, life expectancy is generally low in the poorest countries. Thus, for instance, the expectation of life at birth in 1992 was below 50 years in many countries of Africa, including Malawi, Ethiopia, Niger and Sierra Leone, and some in Asia, including Laos and Bhutan. Life in these countries is all too short.

Life expectancy is related to income per head. In most of the developed countries life expectancy at birth is about 77 years, being 76 in the United Kingdom, Germany and the United States and 79 in Japan in 1992. However, the average length of life depends also on the quantity and quality of medical provision and the degree of income inequal-

ity about the mean: life expectancy reached 70 years in some of the poorest countries, including China and Sri Lanka. Life expectancy is an important but neglected indicator of the "quality of life".

The Population Problem.

In many developing countries there is population pressure on the land, and many people want more land for farming. Population density is a hindrance in agricultural economies, but not necessarily in industrial economies: because it is industrialised and has accumulated much capital, Europe can support at a high standard of living a population more concentrated even than that of Asia.

As a result of rapid population growth the pressure of population on the land has increased. The consequences have been far more serious in countries such as Bangladesh (with a population density of 800 people per square kilometre in 1990) or India (252 per sq km) than in Zambia (11 per sq km) or Brazil (18 per sq km). In those countries with abundant land the expanding population can spread into unused areas; but as land becomes increasingly scarce, less and less productive land must be brought into cultivation and soil erosion and loss of fertility become major problems. A substantial increase in output is required to prevent a fall in per capita income as population grows, and an even greater increase is required if living standards are to be improved. Between 1979–81 and 1991 food production in the developing countries as a group increased by 43 per cent and per capita food production rose by only 13 per cent.

Even in those countries with plenty of land a rapid increase in population can have harmful effects. For instance, it diverts scarce investment resources away from directly productive investments such as factories and irrigation projects so as to meet the needs of the expanding population for more schools, hospitals, housing, cities and other public services.

Family Planning Programmes.

In many African and the poorer Latin American countries the rate of population growth appears to be constant or even rising, but in the more developed parts of Latin America and much of Asia there are signs that the growth rate has peaked and is now declining. The different experiences may reflect differences in government policies: in 1980 a quarter of less developed countries had no official family planning programme. The success stories include India, where in 1989, 45 per cent of married women used contraceptives and the birth rate fell from 4·1 to 3·0 per cent per annum between 1970 and 1991, China (72 per cent contraceptive use and a fall from 3·3 to 2·2 per cent) Colombia (66 per cent contraceptive use and a fall from 3·6 to 2·4 per cent) and South Korea (77 per cent contraceptive use and a fall from 3·0 to 1·6 per cent).

The successful cases show what can be done, but private incentives and attitudes still favour large families in many poor societies: simply providing facilities for family planning may not be enough. In Pakistan, for instance, contraceptive use only 14 per cent and the birth rate, which had barely fallen over the 21 years, was still over 4·0 per cent.

Problems of Agriculture.

There are many millions of peasant farmers throughout the Third World eking out a subsistence from the soil. The margin between what can be produced and what is required to support life is narrow: the failure of crops because of drought, floods or pests can lead to famine unless food is quickly supplied from outside the area affected. For instance, relief action by the international community was too slow to prevent the drought which struck the Sahel area of Africa in 1973 and 1974 from claiming some 100,000 lives, endangering future income by destroying seeds and livestock, and breaking up rural communities. Relief was again slow and patchy in response to the more widespread and severe African famines of 1984 and 1985.

Agricultural production may be held back by a shortage of land, or by the use of primitive tools and methods of cultivation (which may in turn be due to a lack of farming knowledge and skills or to a lack of funds for investment in land improvement or equipment), or by an unjust system of land tenure which deprives the farmer of incentive to raise his production. Perhaps all these problems must be tackled simultaneously.

The Green Revolution.

A technology is being introduced which can increase the yields from foodgrains by 50 per cent or more in tropical areas. This new technology is commonly thought to have caused a *green revolution*. It consists of new high-yielding seeds, largely for wheat and rice. Not only are the yields per acre higher but also shorter cropping cycles permit multiple cropping. The new technology economises on land and, being labour-intensive, provides more farm employment. The introduction of high-yielding cereals is probably the most decisive single factor in the emergence of India and Pakistan into the ranks of solid economic achievers.

However, we cannot assume that it is going to solve the problem of foodgrain shortage in the underdeveloped countries. As yet, the new seeds are less resistant to drought, floods and disease. To be effective, they require substantial inputs of fertiliser and of water; in many areas expensive irrigation will be essential to their success. Moreover, the fact that fertiliser and water are complementary inputs has meant that the green revolution has caught on—and been encouraged by governments—among the larger, more prosperous farmers in the better-watered, more prosperous regions. This is true of, *e.g.*, Mexico, Pakistan and the Philippines. Unless governments ensure that the benefits of the green revolution are widely spread, the effect might even be to harm small peasant farmers by increasing the competition from large farmers.

Land Reform.

There are many forms of land tenure in less developed countries. In black Africa communal or tribal ownership of land is common, with members of the community or tribe receiving rights to use the land individually. In parts of Asia and Latin America, there is private ownership of land, which—particularly where the land is densely populated—has often led to great inequality of land ownership. In some cases land tenure is characterised by absentee landlords and share-cropping tenants. The development of large estates produces a class of landless labourers.

The need for land reform varies according to the circumstances. In most cases the main argument is for greater social justice. In some cases it may be possible also to expand production by redistributing land more evenly or by giving land to share-cropping tenants and so improving their incentives. On the other hand, large farmers may have access to technology, skills and capital which small farmers lack: there is a danger that greater equity will be achieved only at the expense of efficiency. Hence the need to ensure that land reform is accompanied by a package of measures, *e.g.*, education, training and advice, and credit for fertiliser, tools

and land improvements. Few governments have succeeded in implementing serious land reform programmes. The main reason is that the system of land tenure in a country often reflects the balance of political power: land reform invariably faces political opposition from entrenched interests. By the same token, a successful land reform may alter the balance of political power so as to facilitate broad-based development.

Exports of Primary Products.

Almost all developing countries export primary products (foodstuffs, industrial raw materials or minerals) and import manufactured goods, especially the capital goods (plant, machinery and vehicles) required for development. This international division of labour has recently operated to the disadvantage of the developing countries. The world demand for their primary products has increased only very slowly. This is because people spend just a small part of their additional income on food (*e.g.*, tea, coffee, cocoa), because synthetic substitutes have been developed for many raw materials (*e.g.*, rubber, cotton, jute), because developed countries protect their own agriculture (*e.g.*, sugar) and because demand in the developed countries has moved towards commodities with low raw material content (*e.g.*, from heavy industries to services).

In consequence, the general trend has been for the prices of primary products to fall in relation to those of manufactured goods. There was a deterioration in the terms of trade of many developing countries, *i.e.*, they could now buy fewer imports for a given quantity of exports. Oil is a special case (*see* **G55**). When fuels are excluded, the terms of trade of the developing countries fell by 6 per cent between 1970 and 1980 and by 17 per cent between 1980 and 1993.

Unsatisfactory prices of primary commodities have contributed to the shortage of foreign exchange which restricts investment expenditure in many less developed countries. This was particularly marked in the 1980s. World recession and tardy growth depressed primary product prices and sales. The purchasing power of exports from the developing countries rose by 31 per cent between 1980 and 1993. However, this average reflected great diversity of experience. The major exporters of manufacturers gained 232 per cent, whereas the African countries and the major oil exporters lost 40 and 48 per cent of their purchasing power respectively.

Economic Instability.

The prices of various primary products tend to fluctuate violently from one year to another. Many developing economies depend heavily on the exports of one or two commodities. For instance, coffee is the most important product in Brazil, cotton in Egypt, copper in Zambia, sugar in Cuba, cocoa in Ghana and rice in Burma. Fluctuations in the world price of its main export cause instability in the export revenues of a country, and this in turn can produce fluctuations in income throughout its domestic economy.

Even the oil-producing developing countries, whose problems are in many ways quite different, have faced problems of economic instability. The governments of these countries have had to decide how best to use their vastly increased oil revenues so as to promote economic and social development without overturning their societies. The political events in Iran during the 1980s were closely related to the economic boom which oil produced. It may have been the prospect of lifting its heavy burden of indebtedness by means of additional oil revenues that caused Iraq to invade oil-rich Kuwait, and to threaten Saudi Arabia, in 1990.

Problems of Industrialisation.

In those underdeveloped countries where there is population pressure on the land, alternative employment has to be created in industry or services. Even in countries with a surplus of land, if there is heavy dependence on one or two primary products, industrialisation provides a means of diversifying the economy.

But industrialisation is not an easy course. Because the margin between agricultural production and food consumption is narrow, the surplus from the agricultural sector exchangeable for the products of other sectors *e.g.*, industry and services—is small; *i.e.*, the demand for the goods and services produced by other sectors is low. A second constraint on industrialisation is imposed by competition from abroad; new industries in an underdeveloped country have to compete with established industries in developed countries, which have the advantage of experience, a trained labour force and markets big enough for them to reap all the potential economies of large-scale production.

Industrialisation Strategies.

One means of overcoming the small size of market is to export manufactures to the developed countries. Developing countries with cheap labour are likely to have a comparative advantage in the manufacture of relatively labour-intensive commodities. A number of less developed countries have had remarkable success in following this strategy. Among their successful activities are textiles, clothing and labour-intensive components of electronic equipment. However, the developed countries often impose protective tariffs or quotas. Another form of manufacturing is the processing of primary products before exporting them. Here developing countries sometimes face the problem that tariffs are higher on the processed than on the unprocessed products.

A means of overcoming competition from the industries of the developed countries is by nurturing an infant industrial sector behind tariff walls—which is how the United States and Germany developed their industries in the face of British competition in the nineteenth century. A number of developing countries have adopted this strategy. However, it has its drawbacks. Sometimes the "infants" never grow up, and vested interests press for continued protection. Import-substituted industrialisation often means that raw materials or semi-processed goods are imported for local processing. There is a danger that fluctuations in export proceeds will periodically curtail imports of necessary intermediate goods. The under-utilisation of capital in the manufacturing sector because of foreign exchange shortages has frequently occurred in countries such as India, Pakistan, Tanzania and Ghana.

The Newly Industrialising Countries.

The remarkable success of a handful of developing countries—the *newly industrialising countries* (NICs)—in exporting manufactured goods raises the questions: why were they successful, and can others do the same?

South Korea is perhaps the most successful of the NICs. After a period in which government pursued a policy of industrialisation through import substitution, the policy was changed in the 1960s to one of promoting exports of labour intensive manufactures. This was achieved by devaluing the currency in order to encourage export industries in which the country would have a competitive advantage, and liberalising imports to discourage inefficient industrial production. In 1962 South Korea exported manufactures worth $10 million; in 1990 their value was $64,000 million. Between 1962 and 1990 the proportion of the labour force employed in industry rose from 10 to 30 per cent, manufacturing production rose by 17 per cent per annum, and GNP per capita rose by 7 per cent per annum. The labour-intensive nature of industrialisation, as well as its speed, helped to alleviate poverty through the market: first employment and later, as labour became less abundant, also real wages rose rapidly.

South Korea benefited from its trading relationships with Japan and its close ties with the United States in finding markets for its products. It has a well educated labour force: 87 per cent of the relevant age group in 1990 were enrolled in secondary school, which is higher than any other developing country. Industrialisation may also have benefited from stable autocratic government and a beleaguered sense of national purpose. In part the Korean success represents the harnessing of cheap labour in almost free trade conditions for exporters. However, the government also played an active role, *e.g.* it both generated high savings and successfully directed savings into the favoured sectors.

It will take much more than policies of *laissez faire* for other developing countries to be able to emulate South Korea. Moreover, since the world market for labour-intensive products is limited, only a minority of developing countries can take the Korean path.

The most successful NICs—known as the "Gang of Four"—are Hong Kong, South Korea, Taiwan and Singapore. As a group they exported manufactures equal to 8 per cent of world exports of manufactures in 1990.

Outward-Oriented Industrialisation Policies.

The success of the NICs has led many policy advisers to press for more outward-oriented industrialisation policies. The policy advice is gradually to dismantle the system of protection of import-substituting industries and to devalue the currency in order to provide incentives to export manufactures. It is argued that competition in world markets will act as a spur to domestic efficiency and help to divorce economic activities from domestic political processes.

The traditional view has been that few developing countries could succeed in breaking into world markets for manufactures. However, despite the growing resurgence of protectionism in the 1980s potential access to the markets of industrialised countries is better than it used to be, and broadly-based progress has been made. In 1970 manufactures accounted for 27 per cent of the exports of the developing countries, but in 1992 for 52 per cent. If the NICs constitute the "first division", a "second division" of countries has expanded manufacturing exports rapidly, including India, China, Pakistan, the Philippines, Thailand, Turkey, Malaysia, Brazil and Mexico. In 1992 manufacturing accounted for 39 per cent of the exports of low-income developing countries (excluding China and India), for over two-thirds in the case of China and India, and for 49 per cent of the total in the case of the middle-income developing countries.

Unemployment and Underemployment.

Unemployment and underemployment occur on a very considerable scale in both the rural and the urban areas of developing countries. Consider first the rural case. Because farm work is normally shared, underemployment—disguised unemployment—is more common than open unemployment. People work for only a part of the day or year. Where land is scarce, underemployment is chronic: people would like to work more if only they had more land. Unless the yield from the land can be raised, growth in population causes greater underemployment and reduces income per head on the land. Where land is abundant, underemployment is a seasonal phenomenon. People are fully employed in the busy season—harvesting and planting—but underemployed at other times of the year.

In the towns open unemployment is common with people queueing for *modern sector* jobs at the labour exchanges and at the factory gates. Rates of urban open unemployment in excess of 10 per cent are frequently recorded, *e.g.*, in Ghana, Colombia, Puerto Rico, Trinidad, Sri Lanka and the Philippines. Few developing countries can afford unemployment benefits, so that job-seekers remain openly unemployed only until their savings are used up or support by their relations is withdrawn. Then they have to scrape out a subsistence in the urban *traditional sector* while waiting and hoping for something better. Underemployment is rife in the easily entered traditional sector activities such as petty trading, hawking, beer brewing, fetching and carrying. A shoe-shiner may be on the streets for ten hours a day but have only a couple of customers. The more people enter these activities, the further average income per worker is depressed. In many less developed countries this self-employment in the traditional sector accounts for the majority of urban workers.

Migration to the Cities.

Urbanisation is proceeding at an unprecedented pace in much of the Third World. Over the decade 1970–80 the total urban population of the develop-

URBAN POPULATION AS A PERCENTAGE
OF TOTAL POPULATION IN SELECTED
DEVELOPING COUNTRIES, 1965 AND 1990

	1965	1990
41 low-income developing countries	17	38
of which: Ethiopia	8	13
India	19	27
Tanzania	5	33
Ghana	26	30
58 middle-income developing countries	42	60
of which: Egypt	41	47
Peru	52	70
Brazil	50	75
Iran	37	57
Jamaica	38	52
Oil exporters	30	50
of which: Libya	26	70

ing countries as a whole grew by 50 per cent and
over the period 1980–90 by 50 per cent again. The
table illustrates the pace of urbanisation in a
number of developing countries.

Rural people are being drawn to the cities at a rate
well in excess of the capacity of the cities to absorb
them productively. The reason for this migration
might be economic or social. The economic explanation runs in terms of an income differential between
the urban and the rural areas. Relatively unskilled
wages in the modern sector of the economy—often
governed by minimum wage legislation or trade
union bargaining—can be well above the incomes
to be derived from peasant agriculture. People
go to the town in search of modern sector wage
jobs, although they may actually end up underemployed in the low-income traditional sector.
Rural–urban migration may be a social phenomenon: rural people are attracted by the facilities and
"bright lights" of the cities. The recent expansion
of education in many countries may also play a
part, since a high proportion of the migrants are
school leavers.

Whatever the reasons, the consequences are
socially harmful and politically explosive.
Shanty towns and slums proliferate in the cities
and their outskirts; poverty, disease and crime
flourish.

In 1950 there were only two urban agglomerations in the world with more than 10 million inhabitants, New York and London. On present
trends, there will by the year 2000 be 25 such
cities, of which 20 will be in the third world and
the largest will be Mexico City with a forecast
population of 31 million.

Employment Creation.

As recognition has grown that unemployment,
in its open and disguised forms, is both high and
rising in many of the developing countries, so the
objective of creating productive employment has
received higher priority. For various reasons
the growth of modern sector employment has been
tardy and has lagged behind the growth of
output. One reason is that the modern sector
normally uses capital equipment and technology
which is imported from the developed countries.
This means that, even in countries with cheap and
abundant labour, the most profitable techniques of
production are often highly capital-intensive, so
that the amount of scarce investment funds required to equip a worker is high. Hence the case
for developing an *intermediate technology* which is
both profitable and suited to the needs of the
underdeveloped countries.

There is some danger that the establishment of
capital-intensive factories may actually harm
existing labour-intensive production. For instance, sandals can be made by small cobblers
using local leather (or old car tyres) or by a
large plant using imported plastic materials: a
new factory employing a few machine operators
might displace many more traditional craftsmen who have no alternative employment opportunities.

Governments, by encouraging or discouraging
particular forms and areas of investment, have the
power to influence the growth of employment.
In the rural areas the encouragment and organisation of labour-intensive developmental or community projects can assist in harnessing the one
abundant resource which almost all developing
countries possess: unskilled labour.

Educated Manpower.

Many underdeveloped countries are faced with
the dual problem of unskilled labour surpluses
and scarcities of skilled and educated manpower.
The problem is particularly acute in some of the
recently independent countries of Africa. To give
an extreme example: at the time of its independence in 1964, Zambia had only 100 Zambian university graduates and 1,200 secondary school
graduates in a population of 3·5 million. In such
countries the great shortage of educated and
skilled people enabled them to earn high incomes—
with the result that there was a very unequal
distribution of income. And even in countries where
surpluses have developed, the existence of an
international market for professional people such as
doctors and engineers helps to keep up their
earnings: these countries suffer from a "brain
drain" to the developed world.

In sub-Saharan Africa in 1991, 66 per cent of
children of the relevant age were at primary
school, 18 per cent at secondary school and only
two per cent in higher education; no more than a
half of adults were literate. The provision of
education on this meagre scale nevertheless took up
a sixth of government budgets. A reason for the
expensiveness of education is the cost of scarce
teachers: a primary school teacher's salary averaged
7 times the GNP per capita in Africa. In such
circumstances it is not easy to meet the demand for
universal primary education; especially if the sort
of education provided does not enable those who
receive it to become better farmers. The demand for
education is generally strong and unsatisfied in
Africa; often it is perceived as the passport to a
good urban job.

Educational Policies.

Economic development is not just a matter of
physical capital accumulation: it requires also an
increase in "human capital", *i.e.* in skilled and
educated manpower. Not only more knowledge but
also new habits and attitudes—*e.g.*, attitudes towards risk-taking, hard work and thrift.
Education—of the right sort and with suitable
content—is generally acknowledged to be important
for development, although the benefits of education
cannot be quantified at all satisfactorily.

EDUCATIONAL ENROLMENT RATIOS IN
DEVELOPING COUNTRIES, 1965 AND 1991

	Primary		Secondary		Tertiary	
	1965	1991	1965	1991	1965	1991
China	89	123	24	51	0	2
India	74	98	27	44	5	9
37 low-income developing countries	44	79	9	28	1	5
of which:						
Ethiopia	11	25	2	12	0	1
Tanzania	32	69	2	5	0	0
Sri Lanka	93	108	35	74	2	5
Pakistan	40	46	12	21	2	3
58 middle-income developing countries	85	104	22	55	5	18
of which:						
Egypt	75	101	26	80	7	19
Brazil	108	106	16	39	2	12
South Korea	101	107	35	88	6	40
Philippines	113	110	41	74	19	28

Note: A figure of zero indicates that it is closer to 0
than to 1 per cent, and a figure greater than 100 is
possible because of the difficulties of choosing the
appropriate age-group.

The table shows enrolment ratios (the percentage of children in the relevant age-group who are enrolled in education) at the primary, secondary and higher educational levels for selected developing countries in 1989. There is a strong tendency for enrolment ratios to increase with the income per head of a country. Educational provision remains extremely low in most of the low-income developing countries, particularly beyond the primary level. On the other hand, there are developing countries whose problem is now surplus rather than shortage of educated manpower. Such cases are common in Asia, e.g. India and the Philippines.

The table also shows that enrolment ratios increased rapidly in many countries between 1965 and 1991. The high financial returns accruing to the educated have generated powerful pressures for the expansion of state education, to which governments have often acceded. Rapid expansion in quantity has frequently been accompanied by a decline in quality of education. In the Philippines, for instance, where the same proportion are in tertiary education as in Britain (28 per cent), most are in institutions of poor quality.

Some governments have found that it is easier to expand an educational system than it is to expand an economy, and shortages have given way to surpluses. The response to surplus may take various forms: unemployment of the educated, or displacement of the less educated from their jobs, so pushing the unemployment down the educational ladder, or pressures on government to create unnecessary jobs for the educated in the public service. In this last case—true of Egypt, for example—scarce resources are doubly wasted.

Economic Aid.

The gap between living standards in the developing areas of the world and in the areas already developed has tended to widen in recent years. In the 1960s real income per capita rose in the developed countries by 3·8 per cent per annum on average, and in the less developed countries by 3·0 per cent per annum. A World Bank estimate for the 1970s has the annual average per capita growth of developing countries (2·8 per cent) exceeding that of developed countries (2·4 per cent). However, over the period of world economic recession and subsequent tardy recovery, 1980–90, GNP per capita in the developing countries grew by 1·2 and in the industrialised countries by 2·5 per cent per annum.

This masked wide variation in performance over the 1980s: GNP per capita in sub-Saharan Africa fell annually by 1·0 per cent and in Latin America by 0·5 per cent, whereas it rose by 3·0 per cent in South Asia and by no less than 5·2 per cent in East Asia. East Asia benefited from the rapid increase in agricultural production in China after the disbanding of the communes, and from the success of the NICS.

The main industrial countries—organised as a 21-member *Development Assistance Committee* (DAC)—have provided economic aid to the developing countries. The total net flow of economic assistance to the developing countries was $167 billion in 1993. Roughly $94 billion of this was net private investment and $69 billion official aid from governments. A fifth of the net *official development assistance* (ODA) was contributed by Japan ; the other principal donors were the United States, France, Germany, Italy and Britain in that order. Net private investment is volatile and cannot be relied upon.

The DAC nations have accepted three aid targets. One is that the net flow of private and official resources combined should exceed 1 per cent of each country's gross national product. In 1993, 4 out of 21 countries achieved this percentage. The second target is that net ODA should exceed 0·7 per cent of GNP; 4 countries managed this in 1993. The third target, more generally achieved, concerns the "grant element"—the extent to which ODA contains an element of grant as opposed to commercial loans.

The flow of resources from the DAC countries to the developing countries grew over the 1980s but, expressed as a proportion of GNP, it fell from 0·99 to 0·70 per cent between 1982 and 1993. Net ODA was the same proportion of GNP (about 0·33 per cent) in the two years. In real terms the flow of ODA rose by one per cent per annum over the period.

Forms of Aid.

Aid to the developing countries takes many forms, it serves many purposes and it is given for many reasons. Less developed countries need aid to provide finance for development projects; to provide foreign exchange with which imports for development purposes can be bought; and to provide the trained manpower and technical knowledge they lack. The motives of the donor are not always humanitarian. "Aid" can take a military form; it can be used to prop up an incompetent or unjust government, or to buy political support. Nor is aid always beneficial to the recipient country. It may be wasted on ill-conceived or prestige projects, or cause the government simply to relax its own efforts. Sometimes schools or hospitals are built with aid but there is a lack of local revenues with which to staff and run these institutions. Concern over donor's motives and instances of waste have led some people to react against aid-giving. However, the correct remedy is not to cut off aid but rather to prevent its misuse.

Donor governments may finance specific projects, or they may contribute to the general pool of funds available for expenditure by the governments of underdeveloped countries. But financial aid is not always enough. Many developing countries need technical assistance in planning their development, to ensure that development possibilities are exploited and that scarce resources are used to best advantage. Hence the many schemes for providing experts by individual countries and by the technical agencies of the United Nations, such as the Food and Agriculture Organisation (FAO), the World Health Organisation (WHO), the International Labour Organisation (ILO), the United Nations Educational, Scientific and Cultural Organisation (UNESCO), and so on. Hence also the schemes for educating and training people from the developing countries.

Foreign Private Investment.

One possible form of aid is private investment by firms from developed countries. These investments—setting up branch factories, for example—are concentrated in those projects which appear profitable to the investor. However, it is a characteristic of underdevelopment that there are few openings for profitable investment. Most of the U.K. private investment overseas, for example, has been concentrated in relatively highly developed countries of the world. Private investment cannot be relied upon to provide an adequate flow of resources.

Indeed, it has been questioned whether private investment constitutes aid to less developed countries at all. Its opponents argue that the benefits are often small or even negative: foreign-owned firms repatriate high profits and avoid tax by means of royalty payments to the parent company or unrealistic pricing of their transactions with the parent company; and these firms deter local enterprise. Supporters of foreign investment point to the high political risks which necessitate high profits in order to attract investors to developing countries, and question whether resources are available for any alternative path to development. A form of compromise which has become common in the Third World is a partnership arrangement between multinational companies and government or private firms in the host country.

Investment in Emergent Markets.

There was a substantial increase in private capital flows to developing countries in the 1990s, reflecting the policy reforms and welcoming stance in many developing countries and recession in many developed countries. Net capital flows averaged $92 billion per annum in the period 1990–93, of which more than a third ($34 billion) was net foreign direct investment. The major recipients were Asia (net capital inflow being $47 billion) and Latin America ($24 billion); Africa experienced a small net outflow. This development probably reflects a long term trend towards globalisation and diversification of investment and production away from the developed countries. It augurs well for the *emergent stock markets* of the world, such as in Argentina, Thailand, China and Malaysia.

FINANCIAL FLOWS FROM BRITAIN TO DEVELOPING COUNTRIES, 1970–1992

	Net total flows, official and private.		Net official development assistance.		
	£m.	% of GNP.	£m.	% of GNP.	Constant prices 1970 = 100
1970	520	1·02	186	0·36	100
1975	2,920	2·82	404	0·39	106
1980	5,253	2·29	797	0·35	119
1985	1,871	0·53	1,180	0·33	117
1992	2,675	0·45	1,833	0·30	101

British Aid

The table above shows how British assistance to developing countries has grown over the years, and how it has measured up to the international aid targets now accepted by the British Government. The first target is that the total net financial flow to developing countries should exceed 1 per cent of GNP. The large but fluctuating flows of private capital meant that this target was achieved in some of the years. The second target is for a net official development assistance (ODA) in excess of 0·7 per cent of GNP. We see that British ODA as a percentage of GNP was only half of the officially accepted target in each of the selected years. The table also shows that ODA has grown in value; in 1992 it equalled £32 per head of British population. However, if we allow for inflation by expressing official aid in real terms, we see that the volume of aid has risen little.

Government aid may be divided into multilateral aid and bilateral aid. Multilateral aid is given through the medium of the international development institutions: bilateral aid is given directly to the developing countries. Multilateral aid constituted 45 per cent of total British aid in 1992–93. Some 99 per cent of British ODA in 1991 took the form of grants, and the rest was loans. Two thirds of bilateral financial aid is formally tied to the purchase of British goods and services. Other aid is not tied formally, and may be used directly to finance local expenditure; but when it is used to finance imports directly, it has to be spent on British goods if these are available on competitive terms. Most multilateral aid is untied. The tying of aid tends to raise the costs to developing countries; but it also encourages countries to be more generous.

Aid takes the form not only of financial but also of technical assistance. Government expenditure on technical assistance amounted to 50 per cent of bilateral aid in 1992–93.

All British official aid is channelled and co-ordinated by the Overseas Development Administration. In addition there are various private associations concerned with promoting development, such as Oxfam, War on Want and World Development Movement.

Who Receives Most Aid?

In 1992–93 the countries which received the largest shares of British ODA were India (5·1 per cent), Bangladesh (2·7 per cent), and Zambia and Tanzania (2·3 per cent each). This contrasts with the pattern for the DAC countries' ODA as a whole: Egypt (5·5 per cent), Indonesia (3·9 per cent), China (3·5 per cent) and Israel (2·7 per cent). Generally, it helps to be a small country. British aid per head of recipient population in 1992–93 was greatest to the small micro-states such as Belize, Vanuatu, Anguilla and Grenada. Because of India's size, British aid per capita to that country was actually below average. The importance of Egypt and Israel as aid-recipients reflects United States foreign policy towards the Middle East.

The World Bank.

The International Bank for Reconstruction and Development (IBRD) known as the *International Bank* or as the *World Bank*, is an agency of the United Nations established in 1945. It has the primary function of making funds available to assist developing countries. Member nations agreed to subscribe quotas—fixed in much the same way as the quotas for the IMF—to the Bank. In fact, only a small proportion of the quotas has been called up by the Bank; the major part of the Bank's resources are borrowed—on the security of the remainder of the quotas—in financial centres.

Loans are made to finance specific projects and the Bank will normally make a loan only if it is satisfied that the investment will yield a revenue sufficient to enable the payment of interest on the loan, and the repayment of the sum lent. In 1994 the Bank made loans to the value of $21 billion. It is clear that some projects of great benefit cannot be financed in this way, because they would not yield returns quickly or large enough to meet the Bank's requirements for interest and repayment. Accordingly, the *International Development Association* has the power to make loans at low rates of interest and with more generous repayment conditions. The IDA contributes towards the development of education and agriculture ($7 billion in 1990).

UNCTAD.

In 1964 the first United Nations Conference on Trade and Development (UNCTAD) was held. For the first time the poorer nations of the world—77 were represented—came together to act as a pressure group on trading matters. The Conference made the following recommendations. Developing countries should be given free access to world markets for their manufactures and semi-manufactures by the elimination of quotas and tariffs. International *commodity agreements* should be made for each major primary commodity in world trade, to stabilise commodity prices.

Subsequent sessions of the Conference have been held at four-year intervals. UNCTAD has helped to modify international thinking. The developed countries have accepted more firmly the principle of discrimination in favour of developing countries.

Stabilising Export Earnings.

Two international facilities exist to help stabilise the export earnings of developing countries. One is the IMF's *Compensatory Financing Facility* (CFF). A country in balance of payments difficulty is eligible to draw up to 100 per cent of its quota with the IMF if exports fall below a defined trend for reasons generally beyond its control. In 1988 the scheme was extended to become the *Compensatory and Contingence Financing Facility* (CCFF), by providing also for contingency funding to help developing countries deal with external shocks to their economies.

The other facility is the EEC's *Stabex scheme*. It covers the 58 African, Caribbean and Pacific countries that are members of the Lomé agreement. Under the second Lomé agreement 44 primary products are eligible for support. These countries receive grants (if one of the 35 *least* developed countries) or interest-free loans if export earnings from a qualifying product fall below average earnings over the four preceding years by a certain percentage.

Thirdly, there is the UNCTAD *Common Fund*—agreed on in principle but still to be set up. The idea is that a central fund will finance buffer stocks under separate international commodity agreements, and will thereby stabilise commodity prices. Many countries ratified the agreement for establishing a Common Fund although their pledged contribution fell short of the capital required for its launching.

The Tokyo Round.

A round of multilateral trade negotiations was completed in Tokyo in 1979. It provided a legal basis within GATT for preferential treatment for developing countries, and offered them some trade liberalisation. The industrialised countries agreed to reduce tariffs generally, and by an average of 25 per cent for industrial and 7 per cent for agricultural products conventionally exported by developing countries. The extent to which developing countries actually gain, however, depends on whether developed countries make use of the *safeguard clause* which permits emergency protection on the grounds of serious injury to domestic industry: safeguard measures have frequently been invoked against imports from developing countries. Nevertheless, the prospects for success of export-based industrialisation in developing countries (*see* **G43**) were improved.

The Uruguay Round.

The *Uruguay Round* was a long drawn-out series of trade negotiations within the GATT (*see* **G9**), originally begun in Uruguay in 1986. After seven years a far-reaching trade agreement was finally concluded in December 1993. All 117 participant countries agreed to a text of over 500 pages containing 40 separate agreements. There was agreement to cut tariffs, on average, by 40 per cent—more than the original target of one-third. There was also agreement to extend the GATT disciplines to many services and to agriculture. The agreement committed the European Union to substantial liberation of its farm policies. The *World Trade Organisation* was set up to oversee and administer the outcome of the Uruguay Round.

It was important to tackle not only tariffs but also *non-tariff barriers* (NTBs) in the shape of voluntary export restraints, which had escalated in the 1980s. Although it was decided to phase out the *multifibre agreement*, a managed trade system for textiles and clothing, the most serious omission of the Uruguay Round was its failure to tighten discipline over *anti-dumping* laws, the favourite instrument for NTBs.

It was inevitable that progress on trade policies would be difficult because of perceived conflicts of interest. Even though the world as a whole might gain from freer world trade, any individual country might suffer. Many developing countries fear that greater competition from imports will threaten their protected industries, often born behind tariff barriers; and some developed countries fear that greater competition from low-wage countries will threaten their own production and employment in manufacturing. In that context, the Uruguay Round appeared to have reached a successful conclusion.

Food Policies.

In the last couple of decades food production in the developing countries has done little more than keep pace with the growth of population. Many developing countries have become net food importers, and this trend is likely to continue. In 1992 food imports represented no less than 9 per cent of the total merchandise imports of the 40 low-income developing countries and 11 per cent in the case of the 67 middle-income developing countries.

After poor harvests and famines in the early 1970s, most of the DAC donor countries decided to increase very substantially their aid to agriculture. An International Emergency Food Reserve was built up, and an IMF Food Facility was set up to provide financial assistance to offset fluctuations in countries' food import bills.

The Causes of Famine.

Famine is by no means always simply the result of a fall in food production which affects all people in the area uniformly. In the 1974 Bangladesh famine and the recent Ethiopian famines, those who suffered most were respectively the landless, who normally exchange labour for food, and pastoralists, who normally exchange cattle for food grains. The landless, losing their source of earnings because farmers no longer hired labourers, and pastoralists, seeing the prices of their emaciated beasts fall as more and more were marketed, could no longer buy food: these were the people who starved.

Inequality Within Countries.

The growth performance of the less developed countries over the last 30 years is good by the standards of the past. However, in some less developed countries these growth rates have been achieved without any apparent improvement in the lot of the masses.

The majority of the people are engaged in agriculture in the rural areas, whereas much of the development has taken place in industry and services in the urban areas. A minority of people have benefited—industrialists, bureaucrats, educated and skilled workers, organised labour in the modern sector of the economy—but the poor living in the urban slums, often in open or disguised unemployment, and the enormous numbers in the rural areas have been little affected by development. In many countries the fruits of development have not been widely spread. It is a widespread criticism that development policies have been biased towards industry and towards the cities, and that rural people in agriculture have been neglected. This outcome may be a reflection of the uneven distribution of political power within a developing country.

The growth of GNP per capita as a goal of development has been questioned, both within the less developed countries and among national and international aid agencies. Governments have shown a greater concern for poverty, employment creation and social equity. Many donors have modified their aid policies to try to reach the poor. For instance, in 1992–93 no less than 80 per cent of British bilateral aid went to low income (as opposed to middle income) developing countries, including 46 per cent to Sub-Saharan Africa. Of course, this redirection coincides to a considerable extent with the increased concern for agricultural development.

Basic Needs.

A direction in which international thinking has moved is towards the acceptance of a *Basic Needs* strategy of development. Essentially the aim is to alleviate absolute poverty, *i.e.*, to meet minimum standards of food, shelter, clothing and safe drinking water, and to satisfy certain other basic human needs. It is proposed that these standards be reached not so much by means of welfare transfers as by enabling the poor to help themselves through productive employment. The minimum standards are inevitably subjective, there are economic and political obstacles to the fulfilment of basic needs, and the approach does not translate easily into specific policies. Nevertheless, the basic needs strategy may have an impact on the priorities both of aid agencies and of recipient governments.

Inequality Among Countries.

Not all less developed countries have fared equally well in recent years. In particular there appears to be a tendency for disparities among less developed countries to widen. The countries which have performed well tend to be semi-industrialised and able to respond to opportunities for exporting manufactures to the developed countries, or to be well endowed with mineral or oil resources. Growth success stories include Turkey, China, Botswana, Thailand, South Korea, Taiwan, Malaysia and Singapore. Some of these are on the way to becoming self-reliant economically: they are known as the *newly industrialising countries* (NICs). The poorest countries—42 of which were designated the *least developed countries* (LLDCs)—are experiencing the greatest difficulty in escaping from the vicious circle of poverty. Between 1980 and 1990 their income per capita fell by 0·5 per cent per annun in real terms. A growing recognition of their problem has led the DAC countries to reallocate aid in favour of the least developed countries, and to offer aid on more concessionary terms to these countries.

We see in the table (**G48**) that it is the poorest areas of Sub-Saharan Africa and South Asia that have fared least well. East Asia is the area that has fared best.

LEVEL OF INCOME PER HEAD 1990 AND GROWTH OF INCOME PER HEAD 1965–90,
GROUPED BY REGION AND BY INCOME LEVEL

	Group	Income per head ($)	Growth of income per head (% p.a.)
By region	Sub-Saharan Africa	340	0·2
	South Asia	330	1·8
	East Asia	600	5·3
	Latin America	2,180	1·8
By income level	India	350	1·9
	China	370	9·8
	Other low income countries	320	1·7
	Lower middle income countries	1,530	1·5
	Upper middle income countries	3,410	2·8
All developing countries		840	2·5

The East Asian Economic Miracle?

East Asia has a remarkable record of high and sustained economic growth over the last quarter-century. Between 1965 and 1990 the 23 economies of East Asia averaged a growth in real income per capita of over 5 per cent per annum. Much of this seemingly miraculous growth is due to the performance of Japan, the "Gang of Four" (Hong Kong, Korea, Singapore and Taiwan) and three other successful economies, Indonesia, Malaysia and Thailand. What are the reasons for their success? What can other countries learn from their experience?

Most of them share a number of characteristics which point to the explanation. First, most have extremely high ratios of investment in physical capital to GDP, assisted by high saving rates. Rapid capital accumulation, then, is a necessary condition for rapid economic growth, but it may not be a sufficient condition. It, too, needs to be explained. A second common feature was rapid accumulation of human capital: educational participation rates were high even in the 1960s, and subsequently rose. Economic growth was probably also assisted by a sharp decline in population growth rates. Fourth, these countries have created a business-friendly environment, and have generally sought foreign technology and investment.

A fifth general feature was good economic management, which tended to be in the hands of bureaucrats, insulated from political influence and interest groups. It would be wrong to claim that these are free market economies: in several, government interventions to accelerate the pace of development have been pervasive. In particular, they have promoted exports in various ways: they have all adopted outward-orientated industrialisation policies (*see* **G43**). What distinguishes these countries from others is the quality rather than the quantity of government interventions.

Successful Economic Reform in China.

China is another country in East Asia that has performed remarkably well in recent years. The average annual growth rate of real income per capita in China over the period 1980–1991 was no less than 7·8 per cent. The reasons for its success are rather different from those for other East Asian countries. In 1976, when Mao died, it was a communist country with central planning and in which politics, rather than economics, was in command. Today it is in many respects a market economy in which the role of the state, previously all-pervasive, is rapidly diminishing. The economic reforms in China proceeded steadily in a way which brought greater prosperity to almost everyone. The successful reforms in China are to be contrasted with the current policy problems in Eastern Europe and the former USSR. The Chinese experience is worth examining.

Reforming Chinese Agriculture.

China contains no fewer than 1,150 million people, of whom 850 million (74 per cent) live in rural areas. The economic reforms began in the rural areas. Under Mao agriculture was collectivised and the peasants lacked incentives: farm production stagnated. The new leadership permitted the peasants to disband their communes and restore household production on family farms. Farm production grew by 8 per cent per annum between 1978 and 1984, as peasants responded to new opportunities and higher prices for their products.

There was a second transformation of the Chinese countryside: the growth of rural industry, owned collectively by villages or privately. By 1990 rural industry employed nearly 100 million people. It contributed greatly to the absorption of surplus labour on the land.

Reforming Urban China.

The urban reforms began in 1984. Although it had grown rapidly, industry—mainly state-owned—in urban China was inefficient. Enterprises had no autonomy within the centralised planning system. Prices and production were determined by the state, all output was sold to the state and all profits handed over to the state. The reforms took the form of decentralising decisions and introducing market sales and market prices alongside the state plan: gradually the market came to dominate the plan, and far more consumer goods were produced as the market for them expanded. By 1990, 42 per cent of urban households had a refrigerator, 59 per cent a colour television set, and 78 per cent a washing machine. Assisted by foreign investment and technology and by low labour costs, both rural and urban industry were increasingly able to export manufactures to the developed economies.

Prospects for the Chinese Economy.

If recent trends were to continue, China would become the largest economy in the world by 2015. However, various obstacles may slow down future economic growth. One is a shortage of highly educated workers, the result of giving priority to basic rather than higher education. Second, land is currently leased to households: without property rights, long term investments in agriculture could be deterred. Third, there is a problem of inefficient, loss-making enterprises which, together with fiscal decentralisation, has contributed to a growing budgetary problem for the state. Fourth, some people have got rich very quickly, and some regions—in particular, the coastal provinces—have prospered more than others. The rise in these income inequalities could contribute to social and political unrest, and so threaten economic progress. There is little sign as yet of political change to match the economic transformation.

Aid to Africa.

Of all the less developed regions, Africa has done least well in recent years. For instance, food production per capita in the developing countries of Africa was 10 per cent lower in 1980 than it had been 10 years before. In 1981 the World Bank undertook a study of the problem at the request of African governments. The ensuing report argued for a near doubling of external aid for these countries, and for policy changes by their governments, if a further fall in living standards was to be averted. These policy changes generally involved less state intervention in the economy and more rein to individual incentives and to the market. The report also

EXTERNAL DEBT OF
DEVELOPING COUNTRIES, 1980–93

	1980	1983	1988	1993
Total debt				
($ billion)	633	894	1,175	1,476
(per cent of exports)	82	133	146	116
Debt service				
($ billion)	103	119	153	174
(per cent of exports)	13	18	19	14

recognised the constraint on development imposed by a lack of trained manpower and of good management.

One problem will not be easy to deal with: the lack of political stability widely found in Africa, and in other parts of the Third World, is inimical to economic development. Violent changes of government are common, and there were in 1988 some 4 million African refugees who had fled from their own to neighbouring countries. The main "culprits" were Ethiopia, Angola, Rwanda, Burundi, Mozambique, Somalia and Chad.

Crisis and Response in Africa.

In 1983 and 1984 drought drove millions of Africans deeper into poverty. With the recurring drought and dismal statistics came vivid photographs of human suffering, conveying to the world an image of continent-wide disaster. The drought particularly affected countries in south eastern Africa, such as Mozambique, and the Sahel belt below the Sahara, e.g., Ethiopia, Sudan, and Chad. In 1983 cereal imports amounted to over a third of cereal production in two dozen affected African countries

A number of African governments accepted the need for measures to stimulate agricultural production, such as the raising of prices paid to producers for their crops and a transfer of investment priorities towards agriculture. Aid donors also responded to the crisis, giving short term assistance in the form of food aid and longer term assistance in the form of increased development aid.

The Prospects for African Development.

Africa has become the area that presents the greatest economic problem. Income per head in Sub-Saharan Africa fell sharply in the 1980s, by 9 per cent between 1980 and 1992. There are various reasons not associated with natural phenomena. First, population growth has continued to rise and now stands at 3·1 per cent per annum. Second, the terms of trade of the region deteriorated by 40 per cent between 1980 and 1993. Third, Africa's long term debt is now in excess of its GNP, making the region the most heavily indebted of all. Debt service obligations were 20 per cent of export revenues in 1992, but not all were actually paid, so that arrears accumulated. Both the level and the efficiency of investment have fallen.

With the World Bank forecasting a further fall in living standards, Africa is the focus of aid donors' attention. Some of Africa's problems are within the control of their governments, and aid agencies have increasingly made their aid to African countries conditional on the reform of economic policies. This is likely to involve a strategy requiring less government intervention, less top-down planning and more grass-roots development, and emphasising the development of institutional and human capacities to provide the enabling environment for economic growth.

Growing Indebtedness.

The external indebtedness of the developing countries grew rapidly in the 1970s and 1980s. Many developing countries failed to adjust fully to the worsened economic and trading conditions after the oil crisis of 1973, preferring instead to borrow heavily. After the second oil crisis in 1979–80, the world economy went into prolonged recession. Many developing countries were squeezed between stagnating foreign exchange earnings and heavy foreign exchange commitments. This precipitated

two problems: a *debt crisis* for certain heavily indebted developing countries and the need for *stabilization policies* among a broader group of developing countries.

The Debt Crisis.

Most developing countries had to go further into debt in response to the 1979 increase in the oil price. With nominal interest rates now very high and real rates positive, the burden of debt servicing become more onerous. The table shows how the external debts of developing countries increased between 1980 and 1983. In 1983 private bank claims on developing countries amounted to $417 billion. It was the more successful developing countries which had attracted private funds: Brazil and Mexico together accounted for some 40 per cent of this total.

A measure of the strain on developing countries is given by the ratio of debt and of debt servicing (annual interest and amortization payments) to annual foreign exchange earnings from exports. The table shows that these rose between 1980 and 1983. Countries with particularly high percentages included some newly industrialising countries with large oil imports whose export markets had contracted (e.g. Brazil and Korea), some low-income countries whose export prices fell in the world recession (e.g. Bolivia and Zaire) and some oil exporting countries whose export earnings collapsed (e.g. Mexico and Nigeria). The danger of default posed by the debt crisis was widely feared.

Of greatest benefit to the indebted nations would be a strong and sustained recovery of the world economy. In the event, world economic recovery—averaging 3·3 per cent per annum between 1983 and 1990—proved too tardy to solve the debt crisis. Part of the problem was the persistently high level of world interest rates and a deterioration in primary commodity markets.

Indebtedness increased every year between 1983 and 1993. The table shows that in 1993 the total external debt of developing countries was almost $1,500 billion, half of it owed to private banks, and that the ratio of debt servicing to exports was 14 per cent.

At the end of 1992 Mexico had external debt of $113 billion, Brazil $121 billion, Argentina $68 billion and Poland and Turkey each about $50 billion. In 1992 debt service represented no less than 23 per cent of exports in Brazil, 44 per cent in Mexico and 34 per cent in Argentina. Even greater relative burdens were borne by Guinea (93 per cent) and Algeria (71 per cent); some countries simply did not pay the interest that was due.

Solutions to the Debt Crisis.

Countries became increasingly dependent on new loans to service the old, and private banks were reluctant to provide these. In all the major cases a rescheduling of debt repayments was arranged, usually in conjunction with IMF programmes. However, in 1987 the formal procedures for managing debt problems were overtaken by informal actions. Brazil suspended debt service payments to private creditors, and a number of other Latin American and several smaller African countries accumulated arrears of interest to private creditors. The mounting arrears caused Western banks to raise their balance sheet provisions against loans to the problem debtors, writing the cost off against profits. In line with the *Brady Plan*, creditors negotiated reductions in debt and debt servicing with some of the major debtors.

Various proposals have been made for debt relief. One ambitious proposal, with the potential to solve the debt crisis, would be the creation of an international agency to take over claims from private banks, buying the debt at a discount. The debt could then be restructured to pass on the benefit of the discount to the debtors. The credit risk would thus pass from the private banks to the agency and its official shareholders.

Meanwhile, the problem continues although in relation to GDP and exports, the peak year was 1986. For creditors it represents a threat to the international financial system, albeit a receding one. For debtors, it represents economic hardship, a collapse of investment expenditures and increasing social and political problems. Between 1980 and

1992 real per capita income in the two groups most distressed by debt—the heavily indebted middle-income countries and the low-income sub-Saharan countries—fell by 11 per cent and by 9 per cent respectively.

Accelerating Inflation.

The serious macroeconomic strains which most developing countries experienced in the 1980s gave rise to accelerating inflation in many cases. Whereas the annual rate of inflation over the period 1983–1992 in OECD countries averaged 4·3 per cent, in developing countries it averaged 76 per cent. This average was of course much influenced by the hyperinflations in a few countries (Bolivia 221 per cent per annum, Brazil 370 per cent, Argentina 402 per cent, Israel 79 per cent and Nicaragua 656 per cent) but high inflation was a pervasive phenomenon. It was a response—sometimes acting as a safety valve—to such problems as foreign exchange shortage, loss of government revenue, food shortage, debt servicing, and tardy growth of or fall in real incomes. Once established, inflation could feed on itself by changing expectations and behaviour, and it became very difficult to eliminate.

The IMF and Stabilization Policies.

Many developing countries ran into serious balance of payments problems in the 1980s. The current account deficit of the developing countries taken as a whole, at $48 billion in 1986 – the worst year of the 1980s – was equivalent to 8 per cent of exports. Many sought temporary financial assistance from the International Monetary Fund (*see* G9).

As a condition of its larger loans the IMF generally requires a country to accept a series of *stabilization* measures. The typical stabilization package contains the following policies: a devaluation to assist the balance of payments, monetary and credit restrictions and reduced government budget deficits to reduce demand and curb inflation, and, more generally, the elimination of restrictions such as import controls and interest rate regulations in order to harness market forces.

The wisdom of such a package in a developing country is much disputed among economists. It is most obviously the correct remedy when the problem is one of general excess demand in the economy. However, when the problem arises from an extraneous shock, such as a fall in the world price of a major export or a rise in the price of imported oil, the IMF's remedies may prove to be inappropriate. Credit restrictions and cuts in government spending may depress the economy, reducing output and employment. This may temporarily alleviate the immediate problems of inflation and balance of payments deficit, but the effect on long run economic growth may be negative.

It is for these reasons that critics accuse the IMF of doctrinairely and narrowly focussing on monetary variables and ignoring structural problems and developmental objectives. The IMF, on the other hand, often sees itself as a handy scapegoat for unpopular measures made inescapable by domestic economic mismanagement.

The State versus the Market.

The role that the state should play in economic development has become a major issue. In past decades the governments of most developing countries have been extremely interventionist. The presumption was that markets do not work well in underdeveloped economies and that the state can improve on the market outcome by directly allocating resources. However, many countries lacked the skilled manpower required to make the economic bureaucracy efficient, and the economic powers taken by the state were often an invitation to corruption. By the end of the 1980s there was a widespread feeling that the pendulum had swung too far in favour of the state.

The 1990s have seen a move towards greater reliance on the market in many developing countries. In the words of John Maynard Keynes, "the important thing for government is not to do things which individuals are doing already, and to do them a little better or a little worse; but to do those things which at present are not done at all." In many developing countries there is a case for privatising state-owned enterprises and for doing away with price controls, import quotas, high tariffs, heavy subsidies and the like. At the same time, governments need to do more in those areas where markets alone cannot be relied upon, such as investing in health, nutrition, education, family planning and poverty alleviation, and building an efficient infrastructure within which private enterprises can flourish.

Structural Adjustment Policies.

The process whereby developing economies are redirected towards improved balance of payments, debt reduction, more openness to the world economy, less government intervention and greater use of markets, has come to be known as *structural adjustment*. It is being promoted by international donors and resisted by domestic vested interests. Many governments have accepted the need for structural adjustment; time will tell whether rhetoric becomes reality.

Much of the World Bank's lending now takes the form of *Structural Adjustment Loans*, providing funds to the government of a developing country on condition that it implements agreed structural adjustment policies. Supporters seek to justify such lending in terms of its results; opponents see it as an infringement of national sovereignty.

Environmental Issues.

To be economically sustainable development must also be environmentally sustainable. Much of the population increase in the 1990s will occur in environmentally fragile regions of the world. Desertification, deforestation, soil depletion through over-use of fragile land, and pollution are issues of growing concern.

Environmental degradation can contribute to famine (as in Ethiopia) and to devastating flooding (as in Bangladesh). Population pressures, poverty, inadequate systems of land tenure and the growing need for fuelwood lead to the cutting or burning of forests and the clearing of new land. This can be a problem of global as well as national dimensions on account of its effects on the global climate. Problems of pollution have become critical in many of the large urban agglomerations of the Third World. Sanitation, clean water and clean air are important aspects of the quality of life, and these require that government plays an active role.

Environmental Policies.

Environmental dangers are greater in poor countries which can little afford to invest in environmental protection and resource management. Their governments often find it difficult to monitor, regulate and control environmental pollution. Rather than attempt to regulate, it may be better to levy taxes on polluting equipment (*e.g.* combustion machinery) or fuels (*e.g.* petrol) according to the expected level of pollution. If, as in large cities, household use of energy is a major contributor to pollution, the types of fuel and equipment which reduce pollution might be subsidised and those that increase it might be taxed.

In 1989 the OECD nations agreed to give greater emphasis to environmental improvements in their aid policies. A *Global Environmental Facility* was established by donors to assist developing countries to undertake investment projects which would protect the global environment. These would include protection of the ozone layer, affected by *chlorofluorocarbon* [CFC] and other gas emissions, limiting "greenhouse" gas emissions (such as carbon dioxide and methane) that contribute to global warming, protecting biological species against extinction and protecting international waters against pollution (*e.g.* waste pollution and oil spills). Recognising the global advantages of such projects, the international donors are willing to offer this aid on concessional terms.

The United Nations Conference on Environment and Development, otherwise known as the *Earth Summit*, was held in Rio de Janeiro in June 1992. It failed to produce specific commitments concerning the environment, but it helped to change attitudes and emphasis. For instance, principles were agreed on forest conservation and the control of greenhouse gases. *See* **Section Y**.

Some Suggestions for Further Reading.

For an introduction to the subject the reader is referred to Jagdish Bhagwati, *The Economics of Underdeveloped Countries* (World University Library). Ian Little, in *Economic Development* (Basic Books) assesses the development record and the way in which ideas and policies have evolved. The Overseas Development Administration has compiled a handbook of *British Aid Statistics* (H.M.S.O.), The World Bank produces an annual *World Development Report*; each edition has a theme, the theme in the 1993 edition being *Investing in Health* and in the 1995 edition *Workers in an Integrated World*. The Organisation for Economic Co-operation and Development, comprising all the major developed countries, publishes an annual review of aid and development entitled *Development Cooperation* (O.E.C.D.).

An interesting quarterly publication of the I.M.F. and the World Bank, *Finance and Development*, is available free of charge: applications should be sent to *Finance and Development*, I.M.F. Building, Washington, D.C. 20431, U.S.A.

IV. RECENT DEVELOPMENTS IN THE BRITISH ECONOMY

1. INTERNATIONAL DEVELOPMENTS

The Balance of Payments.

The balance of payments problem has dominated events in the British economy until recent years and may do so again. It is therefore important to analyse the balance of payments in some detail; to understand why the balance of payments has been a problem; and to see its effects on economic policy. The balance of payments and its components are explained in detail on **G6–8**. The balance of payments in each year from 1986 to 1994 is shown in the table below.

The 1970s.

The competitive position of the United Kingdom was weakened in the early 1970s by rapid monetary expansion and an inflation more rapid than in other countries. There were sharp increases in demand for many consumer durables and the inability of domestic producers to expand their production correspondingly both constrained exports and accelerated imports. The trade balance deteriorated and there was a large outflow of short-term funds in mid-1972, which culminated in a sterling crisis and a floating of the pound. That was the first time that sterling had been allowed to float since a period in the 1930s, and it represented a contravention of the increasingly criticised Bretton Woods system (*see* **G9**). The pound then floated downwards, from about $2·60 = £1, and in March 1976 the pound fell below $2·00 for the first time.

The falling value of the pound was of no immediate assistance to the balance of payments: experience suggests that the improvement occurs only after a lag of a year or two. In the meantime

the depreciation pushed up the domestic price of imports of raw materials and foodstuffs, so raising both the costs of production and the cost of living. The downward floating of the pound made a counter-inflation policy both more difficult and more important.

Inflation in Commodity Markets.

The current account of the balance of payments deteriorated sharply in 1973. The most important reason was the higher price of imports: this period witnessed a remarkable inflation in the prices of various primary products in world markets. To give some examples, between the first quarter of 1972 and the last quarter of 1973 average price increases

in major world markets were as follows: cocoa 173 per cent, copper 115 per cent, cotton 127 per cent, rubber 123 per cent, wool 138 per cent and zinc 308 per cent. This unprecedented jump in primary commodity prices stemmed from the sharp and well-synchronised expansion of the major industrial economies during 1972 and 1973, and it was assisted by some speculative buying as a hedge against inflation.

The Oil Crisis, 1973.

An event of great importance to Britain and to other industrial countries was the decision of the Arab oil-producing states, taken in October 1973, to restrict oil supplies and to raise oil prices. The restriction of supplies was initiated as a short-run political weapon in the Arab–Israeli conflict; but it revealed a potential for obtaining higher prices which had not previously been exploited by the *Organisation of Petroleum Exporting Countries* (OPEC). In the past the world demand for oil had grown very rapidly—by about 8 per cent per annum between 1960 and 1973—but it had been successfully met by expansion of production. A slower growth of oil supply in relation to demand produced scarcity and a rocketing of price. Alternative sources of energy could not be developed—and thus the demand for oil could not be curtailed or even its growth retarded—for some years. However, maintenance of high prices depended on the ability of the

THE UK BALANCE OF TRADE IN OIL, 1974–93 (£ BILLION)
(Annual average)

1974–6	1977–9	1980–2	1983–5
− 3·9	− 2·5	+ 1·5	+ 5·5

1986–8	1989–91	1992	1993
+ 2·6	+ 1·0	+ 1·3	+ 2·0

THE UK BALANCE OF PAYMENTS 1986–94 (£ BILLION)

	1986	1987	1988	1989	1990	1991	1992	1993	1994
Exports (f.o.b.)	72·6	79·2	80·3	92·2	101·7	103·4	106·8	121·4	135·0
Imports (f.o.b.)	82·2	90·7	101·8	116·8	120·5	113·7	120·5	134·6	145·7
Visible balance	− 9·6	− 11·6	− 21·5	− 24·5	− 18·8	− 10·3	− 13·8	− 13·2	− 10·7
Invisible balance	9·6	7·1	5·3	3·0	1·8	4·0	1·9	2·9	7·2
Current balance	0·1	− 4·5	− 16·2	− 21·5	− 17·0	− 6·3	− 11·9	− 10·3	− 3·5
UK investment overseas	− 34·0	− 14·1	− 32·2	− 57·0	− 25·4	− 41·2	− 36·5	− 102·9	n.a.
Overseas investment in UK	18·0	29·0	27·6	33·2	23·9	28·7	28.0	49·5	n.a.
Other capital transactions	21·9	2·7	7·4	18·3	1·5	15·2	9·7	62·4	n.a.
Official reserves *	− 2·9	− 12·0	− 12·8	5·4	− 0·0	− 0·0	1·2	− 0·7	n.a.
Net capital transactions	− 3·1	4·3	9·4	19·3	11·1	11·1	2·4	8·3	n.a.
Balancing item	3·1	0·1	6·8	2·5	5·9	5·9	9·5	2·0	n.a.

* A positive sign denotes drawings on and a negative sign additions to the reserves. n.a. = not available

OPEC group to restrict oil supplies to the market despite the incentive of each individual country to take advantage of the high prices by expanding its sales. Comparing 1974 with 1973, the price of oil imported into Britain almost trebled.

Oil and the Balance-of-Payments.

Largely because of higher import prices Britain's current balance deteriorated sharply in 1974, when Britain recorded her worst ever current account deficit. In the wake of the oil crisis the world economy duly moved into severe recession. To this the British economy was no exception: real GDP stagnated in 1974 and fell in 1975. In 1976 the world economy began to emerge from its severe recession. This helped the British current account, but the deficit in total currency flow rose to a record level.

During 1975 the rate of inflation in Britain was some 15 per cent above the average for the OECD countries: it became clear that sterling would have to be depreciated further. Speculative outflows of funds forced the authorities to intervene strongly in the foreign exchange market by selling foreign exchange.

The exchange rate slid to a low point of $1·57 in October 1976, and the Bank of England's minimum lending rate was hurriedly raised to the unprecedented level of 15 per cent. The Government applied to the IMF to draw on the United Kingdom's credit tranche of $3·9 billion. The successful conclusion of these negotiations in January 1977, and the borrowing of more than £1 billion from the IMF, helped to restore confidence. However, the terms of the agreement involved some loss of control over domestic affairs: in his Letter of Intent to the IMF, the Chancellor agreed to restrictions on the rate of *domestic credit expansion* (DCE) and on the *public sector borrowing requirement* (PSBR).

North Sea Oil.

The table shows how the "oil deficit" in the balance of payments, huge in the mid-70s, gradually declined as North Sea oil production expanded, disappeared in the course of 1980, and was transformed into an "oil surplus", becoming as large as £5·5 billion in the mid-1980s, and then declining.

The future course of the British balance of payments depends considerably on the value of British oil production. The sharp build-up in production from almost nil in 1975 had arrived at about 100 million tonnes in 1980, roughly equal to U.K. net consumption of oil. Oil continues to be both exported and imported because of differences in quality: the United Kingdom exports a higher quality than it imports. British production of petroleum and natural gas amounted to 7 per cent of GDP in the peak year, 1984. The value of North Sea oil to Britain in the future depends on many imponderables, including the price of oil itself. This depends on the ability of the OPEC cartel to survive and on the growth of the world economy in relation to the supply (influenced by the development of new fields and by the political stability of major producers).

The exploitation of North Sea oil has been a mixed blessing. Through its strengthening of the balance of payments and consequent raising of the exchange rate, it has harmed the manufacturing sector. The problems of structural adjustment, of which rising unemployment was a symptom, brought a social cost. The precise extent to which manufacturing suffered as a result of North Sea oil has been debated among economists. Some economists attribute much of the slump in manufacturing—by 10 per cent between early 1979 and early 1982—to the 25 per cent rise in the exchange rate over the same period; others put most of the blame on the Government's deflationary monetary and fiscal policies. It is generally agreed, however, that if it had not been for North Sea oil, Britain in the post-1973 era would have had to devote additional resources to the production of manufactures for export simply to pay for more expensive oil.

Recovery in the late 1970s.

Pressure on sterling beginning in 1977 was met in part by the willingness of the monetary authorities

to let the exchange rate rise. From its lowest level of £1 = $1·58 in October 1976, it rose steadily to reach a peak of $2·44 in October 1980. The heavy balance of payments deficit of the United States and speculation against the dollar was partly responsible. However, sterling rose steeply against other currencies as well. This was partly due to North Sea oil production, its direct effect on the balance of payments and its indirect effect on foreign confidence in the British economy. Also important were the high interest rates engendered by the government's restrictive monetary policy and the low level of demand for imports caused by the recession in the domestic economy.

The End of Exchange Controls.

In October 1979 the new Conservative Government announced the immediate lifting of all remaining exchange control restrictions. Exchange controls had been in force in the United Kingdom for more than 40 years. The announcement meant that it was now possible for residents to obtain foreign exchange for outward portfolio investment or the purchase of holiday homes abroad without the payment of a premium, and to acquire unrestricted access to foreign exchange for direct investment abroad.

The effect was to induce a capital outflow which helped to keep the exchange rate from rising further. There was a strong outflow of portfolio investment in the early 1980s. However, this was probably in the national interest: the alternative methods of financing the current account surpluses—a buildup of foreign exchange reserves or a further appreciation of the exchange rate—were less attractive.

Balance of Payments Surplus, 1980–85.

With the economy slumping in 1980, the trade balance moved into surplus for the first time in many years. In 1981 and 1982 the trade balance was in even greater surplus, reflecting the growth of North Sea oil revenues and the deeper recession in the UK than abroad.

The appreciation of sterling helped to curb domestic inflation by keeping down the sterling price of imports (an imported good selling for $1 could now be bought for fewer pence). However, it also had a harmful effect on the manufacturing sector and on competitiveness (an exported good costing £1 would now have to be sold at a higher dollar price to cover costs). The current account surplus fell after 1982, reflecting a lagged adjustment to the unfavourable competitiveness of British products.

The effective weighted exchange rate of sterling against the currencies of Britain's trading partners peaked in late 1980. The subsequent fall was mainly due to a depreciation against the dollar, in turn attributable to the tight monetary policy and high interest rates prevailing in the United States.

Sterling fell sharply in 1984, mainly as a result of the appreciation of the dollar against all currencies. From an average of £1 = $1·46 in March 1984, the pound collapsed to $1·22 in October and to a low of $1·05 in March 1985. However, sterling depreciated against other currencies as well. The reason for the particular weakness of sterling appeared to be market fears about oil. There may also have been concern in the foreign exchange markets about the coal miners' strike and its possible repercussions on the balance of payments and the economy.

Is a Lower Oil Price Good for Britain?

The market price of oil collapsed early in 1986 (*see* **G**56). Was this a matter for concern, Britain being a net oil exporter? There were advantages as well as disadvantages, and Britain may on balance have been a beneficiary.

The obvious ill-effects are on the balance of payments and on North Sea oil tax revenues. The Government estimated that, if the price were $15 a barrel, oil would yield it £6 billion in 1986–7 instead of the £11·5 billion of 1985–6; and that each fall of one dollar in the price per barrel would reduce its revenue by £400 million. Moreover, if the pound came under speculative pressure it might be necessary to maintain high domestic interest rates, with adverse effects on investment and spending. Some fall in sterling would be beneficial. The depreciation required by the worsened balance of payments on current account would improve competitiveness, expand manufacturing and reduce unemployment. The loss of tax revenue from a fall of one dollar in the price per barrel could be offset by a six per cent depreciation of the pound against the dollar. The expansion of the economy would also increase tax revenue, and should not cause inflation because the lower oil price would tend to neutralise any inflationary pressures. Most important, the boost to economic growth in oil-importing countries and to world trade would be good for Britain.

Deteriorating Balance of Payments, 1986–90.

The British trade balance deteriorated sharply in 1986, the deficit increasing to £9·6 billion; and the current account surplus disappeared. This reflected the sharp fall in oil prices in 1986 as well as an increased deficit on trade in manufactures. The overall balance of payments was protected by relatively high interest rates in London. In 1987 the short term rate of interest (9·2 per cent) exceeded the average for the U.S., Japan, Germany and France by 3·5 percentage points. This interest rate differential and the movement of international funds out of the depreciating dollar explain why the UK official reserves increased rapidly—despite the deterioration in the current account—from $15·5 billion at the start of 1986 to a peak of $51·7 billion at the start of 1989.

Although the current account was cause for concern, the problem which the authorities faced was one of a short-term capital inflow—out of New York and into London with its high interest rates. The inflow threatened to appreciate sterling at a time when the current account justified a depreciation.

The policy dilemma which this posed led to a remarkable public conflict between the Prime Minister and the Chancellor of the Exchequer at the time of the 1988 budget: the former favoured a free market outcome and the latter stabilisation of the pound through official intervention. The Prime Minister was right in the sense that the authorities now have limited power to control the exchange rate in the face of huge capital flows. The Chancellor was right in the sense that the market, left to itself, is unlikely to produce the outcome that the balance of trade and the economy require. Both could be accused of exacerbating the problem through the Government's reliance on monetary policy and therefore on high interest rate policy.

The balance of payments deteriorated very sharply in 1988. The trade deficit rose to £21·5 billion and the current account to £16·2 billion (compared with a forecast of some £4 billion). What went wrong? The deterioration was in the visible rather than the invisible balance. The oil surplus fell to £2·1 billion, because of the fall in both the price and production of oil, but the main culprit was an increased volume of manufactured imports—up by no less than 19 per cent on 1987. This reflected the growth of demand in the British economy—GDP was up by 4·7 per cent. Despite this increase in production, demand outpaced available domestic capacity (see **G64**) and the excess demand was diverted to imports. The exchange rate also played a part. Sterling appreciated against a basket of currencies by 13 per cent between December 1986 and March 1988, reflecting the relatively high interest rates in London. This loss of competitiveness contributed to the rise in the trade deficit in 1988.

In 1989 the trade deficit was £24·5 billion and the current account deficit a record £21·7 billion. Most of the £5 billion deterioration over 1988 took place in the oil balance (due to temporary production problems) and the invisible balance (associated with high British interest rates). With the high cost of credit causing a fall in expenditure on investment and consumer durables and in stockholding by firms, output in the economy grew slowly, by only one per cent, in 1990. The economic recession improved the trade balance by no less than £6 billion in 1990. In particular, imports of capital goods were reduced and, reflecting the depressed market for cars in Britain, imports of cars were down and exports of cars were up.

A Policy Contradiction.

In 1988 British interest rates were raised in order to curb demand and reduce inflation. For instance, over the course of the year the Treasury bill rate rose from 8·5 to 13·0 per cent. Again, in 1989 and 1990, the Treasury bill rate averaged about 15 per cent, and it began to fall significantly only in 1991 when inflation began to fall. Yet this policy would exacerbate the balance of payments problem. High interest rates would attract funds from abroad and appreciate the pound at a time when an improvement in manufacturing competitiveness was needed. The heavy reliance placed by the Government on the manipulation of interest rates thus posed a policy contradiction. On the one hand, a higher interest rate was needed to curb inflation; on the other hand, it had the effect of curbing trade competitiveness.

A danger inherent in the policies pursued by the Conservative Government is that they would fail to solve, and would indeed contribute to, a serious structural problem. Between 1975 and 1992 employment in manufacturing fell by 3 million jobs, from 7·5 to 4·5 million. Monetary and interest rate policies and concern about inflation could keep the exchange rate at a level too high for the manufacturing sector to be competitive: they would thus contribute to the *de-industrialization* of Britain.

As an economy moves into economic recession the trade balance normally improves because the demand for imports is reduced. Correspondingly, an upswing in the economy is normally accompanied by a deterioration in the trade balance. Yet, despite the severe recession, the current account of the balance of payments was in significant deficit in both 1991 (£6 billion) and 1992 (£12 billion). During 1992 the volume of imports rose by 6·5 per cent whereas export volume rose by only 3 per cent. Moreover, import penetration in the manufacturing sector was higher in 1992, the recession year, than in 1988, the boom year: 47 per cent of demand for manufactured goods was met by imports in 1988, and 49 per cent in 1992.

The Effects of Entry to the EMS.

In October 1990 the decision was finally taken to make Britain a fuller member of the *European Monetary System* (EMS) by entering the *Exchange Rate Mechanism* (ERM) (see **G61**). This had important implications for the conduct of economic policy. Greater co-ordination of monetary policy with the rest of Europe would be required. The Bank of England would have to be given more independent responsibility and the setting of interest rates would be less subject to political control. There would be less scope for exchange rate realignment. With interest rates and exchange rates no longer so readily available as instruments to control the domestic economy, fiscal policy would become more important. The prospects for the UK economy would be more closely linked to the rest of Europe.

In the long run the wage and price inflation rate and the interest rate in Britain would have to be brought into line with those of Europe. However, the tendency for the British economy to generate excessive wage pressure remained firmly-rooted. There was a danger that the process of economic alignment would be a painful one, in which inflation was curbed by holding back demand in the economy. The difficulties facing the economy were compounded by the relatively high level of the exchange rate at which sterling entered the ERM. Maintaining the entry exchange rate might require a long and deep economic recession.

The current account deficit fell from £17·0 billion in 1990 to £6·3 billion in 1991. This improvement reflected the depth of the British recession which reduced demand for imports. Interest rates in Britain fell during 1991—by over 3 percentage points—but the need to maintain sterling within the permitted ERM band required the authorities to keep interest rates above German levels. German rates were rising and this prevented the government from reducing interest rates by as much as the recession warranted.

Black Wednesday.

German interest rates rose further in 1992, reflecting Bundesbank concern about inflation. Despite the severity of the economic recession in Britain (GDP fell by 3 per cent between 1990 and 1992), the current account remained in deficit (over

UK IMPORT PENETRATION AND
EXPORT SALES RATIOS IN
MANUFACTURING, 1975 AND 1989

	Imports as a percentage of home demand	
	1975	1989
Chemicals	23	42
Mechanical engineering	26	40
Electrical and electronic engineering	25	52
Office machinery and data processing equipment	71	95
Motor vehicles	26	51
Instrument engineering	47	60
Food, drink and tobacco	18	18
Textiles	22	48
Clothing and footwear	21	40
Paper, printing and publishing	20	22
Total manufacturing *	23	37

	Exports as a percentage of manufacturers' sales	
	1975	1989
Chemicals	32	47
Mechanical engineering	43	39
Electrical and electronic engineering	33	46
Office machinery and data processing equipment	69	93
Motor vehicles	43	33
Instrument engineering	48	54
Food, drink and tobacco	8	12
Textiles	22	32
Clothing and footwear	11	19
Paper, printing and publishing	9	10
Total manufacturing *	24	30

* Includes some industries not listed.

£6 billion in 1992). The markets lost confidence in the ability and commitment of the British Government, faced with weak international competitiveness and a depressed economy, to defend the pound within the EMS. Speculation fed on itself and, despite heavy (and costly) financial support by the Bank of England and the Bundesbank, the Government was defeated by the markets on *Black Wednesday*, 16 September. The pound dropped sharply, depreciating by some 16 per cent.

The old policy had failed, mainly because the government had joined the EMS at an over-valued rate for sterling. The government hastened to invent a new policy regime. Unemployment had reached 10 per cent and was still rising: it was decided to place greater emphasis on overcoming the recession. Indeed, some commentators regarded Black Wednesday as heaven-sent: the markets had saved the government from its self-imposed straightjacket.

Response to Devaluation.

The pound was worth 2·82 deutschmarks in August 1992 and 2·36 deutschmarks in February 1993. The treasury bill rate fell from 9·9 to 5·5 per cent over the same period, and other interest rates came down as well. The improved competitiveness provided a boost for producers, and lower interest rates eased the burden on mortgage-holders and encouraged investors. At last there was the prospect of an end to economic contraction.

In the four quarters after the devaluation there was an 11 per cent improvement in British competitiveness: the inflationary impact of the devaluation was very limited because of the extremely depressed state of the economy. With a lag, exports began to rise rapidly: by 3 per cent in 1993 and by no less than 11 per cent in 1994. The economy also began to recover, growing by 2 per cent in 1993 and by 4 per cent in 1994. This growth in aggregate demand stimulated imports, which increased in volume terms by 4 per cent in 1993 and by 5 per cent in

1994. The result was an improvement in the current account, the deficit falling to £2·4 billion in 1994. Britain was benefitting from export-led growth in the wake of the enforced devaluation of sterling.

The Competitiveness of Manufactured Products.

In which products has British manufacturing been losing competitiveness and in which has it been gaining? This question can be answered by examining the degree of import penetration (imports expressed as a percentage of home demand) and the export sales ratio (manufacturers' exports as a percentage of their sales), and their movements over time. These are shown in the table for selected industries for the years 1975 and 1989. The first thing to note is that the import share and the export share were very similar in 1975, and that both rose, the former more rapidly than the latter. This trend reflects the general increase in trade among nations, associated with the decline in trade barriers, the growth in importance of multinational companies and the United Kingdom's entry to the European Economic Community. In most of the industries listed both the import share and the export share increased. Nevertheless, the high exchange rate in the wake of North Sea oil and high interest rates weakened the competitive position of British manufactures: import share has increased more than export share in most industries, and especially in motor vehicles, textiles, clothing and footwear.

Britain's traditional manufacturing strengths were in all forms of engineering, chemicals and vehicles. Some of these sectors came under pressure. In the case of vehicles, for instance, the export share fell from 43 to 33 per cent, but the import share rose sharply, from 26 to 51 per cent. There are more foreign cars on the roads in every country, but the international competitiveness of British car and truck production has nevertheless declined. The demise of the British motor cycle industry is an example of this trend. Britain improved or maintained her competitive position in food and drink, office machinery and paper, printing and publishing.

The growing industries in a manufacturing sector which otherwise stagnated in recent years were pharmaceuticals, plastic products, scientific instruments, electronics and computers. It is high-technology, growth industries such as these that offer the best prospects for exporting in the 1990s. Using as the classifying criterion expenditure on *R and D* by different industries, it is found that high-technology industries increased production at 2·8 per cent per annum, compared with an overall manufacturing decline of 1·1 per cent per annum, during the period 1975–85. In 1985, when there was a trade deficit of £2·1 billion, this category of industries achieved a trade surplus of £1·1 billion.

International Investment.

One of the more successful items in the UK balance of payments has been net interest, profit, and dividends from private sources. After the freeing of controls on direct investment abroad in 1979, UK investment overseas rose sharply, from £5·9 billion in 1979 to £102·9 billion in 1993. This was accompanied by corresponding increases in interest, dividends and profit from abroad, which contributed to the net surplus on invisibles in the current account.

The remarkable expansion since 1960 of international investment, both by foreign companies in the United Kingdom and by British companies abroad, reflects the growing importance of *multinational companies* in the world economy. Some 165 multinationals account for 80 per cent of British private investment abroad. The multinationals tend to dominate the world markets for technologically advanced products. They account for no less than 60 per cent of trade in manufactures in the developed world. Their financial and market power, their global investment strategies, and their ability to avoid national taxation pose a challenge to the economic sovereignty of national governments.

Multinationals in Britain.

Just as many British companies operate abroad, so many foreign companies have subsidiaries and affiliates in Britain. Some household names—including the oil companies Esso, Mobil and Texaco, the motor companies Ford, Vauxhall and Nissan, the electrical companies Phillips and Hoover, and new technology companies like I.B.M., Kodak and Rank Xerox—are foreign-based. Events such as the takeover of Westland helicopters in 1986, Nestlés' takeover of Rowntree in 1988, and the purchase of Rover by BMW in 1994, brought the issue of foreign ownership into public debate.

Opponents of foreign takeovers may be motivated by crude nationalism or by a concern that production would become internationally more footloose. Although particular cases may require scrutiny, the liberal policies which British Governments have adopted towards both inward and outward foreign investment make sense. Countries which cut themselves off from the technological and other skills of multinational companies would find it difficult to compete internationally in the long run.

The International Economic System.

The international monetary system is explained on **G9–10**. The main problem facing the international economic system during the 1960s was an increasing shortage of international liquidity in the face of expanding world trade. This threatened the continuation of free trade. In the 1970s the focus moved to the problems of world inflation and to the international imbalance caused by the increased price of oil, and the resultant threat to economic growth. In the 1980s and 1990s the main problems were international debt, world recession and tardy economic growth. We trace the issues and events as they unfolded.

The Gold and Dollar Crises.

The United States ran a large and persistent payments deficit in the 1950s and 1960s. This was initially financed through the willingness of foreigners to run up dollar balances. However, distrust of the dollar grew, and since many speculators expected the devaluation of the dollar in terms of gold to be followed by a corresponding devaluation of other currencies, there was a growing demand for gold. To meet the crisis, two markets for gold were introduced in 1968, with private transactions taking place in the free market at a price determined by supply and demand, and transactions among central banks taking place in the official market at the official gold price.

In 1970 the deficit in the United States balance of payments rose to a record level. This was financed by creditor countries increasing their dollar balances. In 1971, massive speculation against the dollar forced the United States Government to suspend the convertibility of dollars into gold. Currencies of the major trading countries were then allowed to float upwards against the dollar by varying amounts.

Introduction of Flexible Exchange Rates.

The U.S. balance of payments on current account deteriorated and speculation against the dollar broke out again early in 1973. The dollar was devalued by 10 per cent and the EC countries agreed that their currencies would float against the dollar.

The international monetary system had entered a new era of flexible exchange rates. The Bretton Woods system, which had operated throughout the post-war period, had come to an end. No longer would countries be required to maintain fixed exchange rates subject only to periodic realignment in response to fundamental disequilibrium in their balance of payments. Although governments might wish to intervene to stop their currencies changing too rapidly and too far, most chose to unpeg their currencies.

The system had broken down because it could no longer perform its function. The imbalance between the United States and the other major countries was the immediate cause of the breakdown. Perhaps the more basic reasons, however, were the growing shortage of international reserves, the growing volume of internationally mobile short-term funds, and the more rapid and divergent national rates of inflation.

The First Oil Crisis.

The oil-producing countries ran a current account surplus in 1974 of no less than $59 billion, it having been $13 billion in 1973. This surplus involved a corresponding deficit for the oil-importing countries as a group. Such a transformation in the international balance of payments was unprecedented in its scale and speed. It involved a massive transfer of purchasing power from consumers to producers of oil. Since only a small part of the additional oil revenue was spent, this had a severe deflationary effect on the world economy.

The oil-producing countries had to invest their surplus funds abroad. These funds were highly mobile between recipient countries, thus introducing considerable instability in the currency flows of the western oil consumers. Many governments took restrictive measures to combat both domestic inflation and their balance of payments deficits. In 1974 and 1975 the industrial countries experienced the worst economic recession of the post-war period. For instance, the level of industrial production in the OECD group of countries was 10 per cent lower at the end of 1975 than it had been at the end of 1973.

The less developed countries sustained large deficits in the wake of the oil price increase. Their needs were met in part through lending by the IMF. The deposits made by oil-producers in western banks gave these banks an opportunity to lend on a much enlarged scale. Private lending to developing countries increased greatly; this sowed the seeds of the debt crisis of the 1980s (*see* **G49**).

The Second Oil Crisis.

The price of oil doubled over the course of 1979, rising from $13 to $25 a barrel. This was due to the halving of Iranian oil production after the revolution in Iran, and to a scramble for oil stocks by the consuming countries. In 1980, assisted by the outbreak of war between Iran and Iraq, the OPEC oil price averaged $32 a barrel.

These factors combined to cause economic stagnation in the OECD countries during 1980. The higher oil price led again to higher inflation (13 per cent in 1980) and an increased balance of payments deficit ($58 billion) in the industrial countries. The high inflation rates ensured that nominal interest rates would be high in the major countries, but one of the consequences of the restrictive monetary policies generally being pursued was to raise interest rates in real terms as well. For instance, the Eurodollar rate in London—over 17 per cent in late 1980 and early 1981—was well above inflation rates at that time. Both the restrictive policies and the high interest rates which they generated had a depressing effect on the major economies.

The Oil Market.

The table shows how average world prices of oil have moved since 1973, both in nominal terms and in real terms (nominal prices being deflated by the

WORLD PRICE AND PRODUCTION OF OIL, 1973–94

	Price (OPEC average)		Production (billion barrels)	
	Nominal ($ per barrel)	Real (1973 = 100)	OPEC	World
1973	3·5	100	11·3	21·2
1974	9·6	228	11·2	21·2
1978	13·1	222	10·9	23·1
1979	19·0	283	11·3	24·0
1980	31·9	428	9·8	23·1
1981	35·9	512	8·2	21·6
1985	28·0	442	5·8	20·8
1986	15·6	220	6·7	21·9
1987	17·1	218	6·5	21·8
1988	13·5	159	7·3	22·6
1989	16·9	200	8·1	23·3
1990	21·0	230	8·7	23·7
1991	17·9	189	8·8	23·6
1992	18·2	187	9·2	23·7
1993	15·2	166	9·4	23·7
1994	14·9	n.a.	9·5	24·0

CURRENT ACCOUNT OF MAJOR ECONOMIES,
1986–94 ($ billion)

	1986	1987	1988	1989	1990	1991	1992	1993	1994
United States	− 150	− 167	− 127	− 102	− 92	− 8	− 68	− 104	− 149
Japan	86	87	80	57	36	73	118	131	136
Europe	48	30	13	1	− 15	− 68	− 62	8	38
of which:									
Germany	40	46	51	57	47	− 20	− 22	− 20	− 16
United Kingdom	− 1	− 8	− 29	− 37	− 33	− 19	− 17	− 16	− 13

price of world exports of manufactures). The two great increases occurred in 1973–4 and 1979–80: both involved a more than doubling of the purchasing power of oil. Even with the collapse of OPEC in 1986, the oil price in real terms remained on a par with the 1974–5 level.

The table shows that world production of crude oil in 1985 was at the same level (21 billion barrels) as it had been in 1974. However, OPEC production was down to below 6 billion barrels. In particular, Saudi Arabia, which alone had produced over 3 billion barrels in 1974, was producing only half that amount a decade later. In 1974 OPEC had produced more than half of world production; now it produced only a third.

In 1985 Saudi Arabia was unwilling to continue withholding production so that other members— such as expansionist Libya, war-torn Iran and Iraq and heavily indebted Nigeria—could exceed their quotas: Saudi production expanded rapidly. Market forces took over. The spot price of oil collapsed, from just under $30 a barrel at the beginning of December 1985 to $10 a barrel at the beginning of April 1986. The cartel had fallen apart.

The OPEC members agreed to new quotas which, if adhered to, would reduce non-communist world production, then running at 17 billion barrels per annum. However, the strains within the organization proved to be too great and in October 1988 the OPEC price fell short of $12 a barrel.

The oil price was given a boost by Iraq's invasion of Kuwait in August 1990, and the uncertainty that this created. The free market price was $29 a barrel in January, just before the 100-hour battle, but it fell sharply after the defeat of the Iraqi forces. The fall reflected high world stocks and excess production of crude oil. The oil market could now be best characterised as a free-for-all. Early in 1994 the average OPEC price was down to $13 a barrel, reflecting depressed world demand, but it rose during the year, to $16, in response to the growth of the world economy.

Trade Fears.

The serious world recession after the second oil crisis raised unemployment. In 1982 30 million workers were unemployed in the 24 OECD countries. This led to intensified protectionist measures in many countries, aimed at preserving jobs by keeping out imports, whether from other industrial countries or from developing countries.

Western Europe and America have found increasing difficulty in competing in two areas: labour-intensive manufactures, such as textiles and clothing, and certain engineering products, such as cars and consumer electronics. The competiton has come from low-wage countries, in the former case, and from Japan, in the latter.

Not all developments were in the direction of protectionism, however. In 1986 representatives of 92 nations agreed to stage a new round of multilateral trade negotiations, to be called the Uruguay Round in succession to the Tokyo Round. The negotiations were intended to halt and reverse protectionism. The successful outcome of the negotiations in 1993 is described on G47.

Crisis in the Banking System.

During the second oil crisis the non-oil developing countries were in general not prepared to take the harsh measures needed to control their deficits, so long as they could obtain finance from somewhere. Although this response of the poor countries was understandable, it contributed to the growing problem of international indebtedness (*see* G49).

The difficulties experienced by the international banks were partly beyond their control, being due, for instance, to the rise in interest rates produced by restrictive monetary policies, and partly to their own lack of caution. Perhaps they were too much swayed by the competitive pressures to make loans from the additional deposits coming from the OPEC surplus, and complacently confident that "the authorities" would rescue banks which got into difficulties.

The Mexican debt crisis of late 1982 brought out the precariousness of the international banking system. After that, one substantial debtor country after another sought debt rescheduling or a standstill on repayments of principal. Stop-gap credits had to be cobbled together, and in addition the IMF emergency lending facility was enlarged, and agreement was reached to expand the IMF quota resources by about half.

World Recovery, 1983–89.

The world economy began to recover in 1983. In 1984 the increase in GDP of the industrial countries averaged no less than 5·0 per cent, the United States leading with a remarkable 6·8 per cent. Reflecting the considerable slack in the international economy, inflation did not accelerate in response to the recovery. The promising start to world recovery gave way to slower growth. The industrial countries managed an annual average growth rate of 3·5 per cent between 1984 and 1989. One consolation was that OECD inflation also fell, averaging 3·4 per cent per annum over the period 1984–89.

The Rise of the Dollar.

The United States recovery occurred despite a rising dollar. The effective exchange rate of the dollar against other currencies rose by 20 per cent in the 15 months up to March 1985. The reason for this appreciation is rather a puzzle. It was certainly not due to the strength of the current account. On the contrary, with rapid economic recovery the record American current account deficit of $35 billion in 1983 gave way to one of $80 billion in 1984. Rather, the relentless rise of the dollar has to be explained mainly in terms of developments in financial markets. Interest rates in the United States were high, and well above those in other countries. This was due to the strength of economic expansion and the consequent demand for funds, and to the vast Federal Government budget deficit which, on account of the restrictive monetary policy, was financed by debt issue. These high rates of interest, together with the anticipated profitability of the booming economy and the widespread sentiment that the dollar would continue to rise, attracted funds from abroad. By 1985 the loss of funds to the United States was putting authorities in other countries under pressure to raise interest rates in a way not required by domestic considerations.

The Falling Dollar.

With investment harmed by the high interest rate and export industries harmed by the high exchange rate, the United States economy slowed down sharply after 1984. This was an important reason why world economic growth fell back in those years. However, the long-expected depreciation of the dollar eventually came in March 1985: it had fallen 20 per cent against other currencies by the end of the year. It continued to fall: by late 1994 the dollar was only 53 per cent of its 1985 peak value. In 1995, it continued its fall.

The international imbalance in current accounts was huge. The large U.S. deficit, offset by the growing Japanese and West German surpluses, did not respond to the depreciation of the dollar, both because of the time-lags involved and because of the continuing Federal budget deficit. The latter deficit declined from a peak in 1983 of 5·2 per cent of GNP but remained huge, rising to 4·3 per cent in 1993.

World Financial Crisis, 1987.

The structural imbalances in the world economy came home to roost in the global financial crisis of October 1987. The most fundamental cause was a loss of confidence in the economic policies of the U.S. Government. No significant action had been taken to reduce the Federal budget deficit—action which would be needed to eliminate the trade deficit. Nor was there willingness on the part of the surplus countries, in particular Germany, to stimulate their economies sufficiently to help the United States out of its predicament.

The budget deficit and tight monetary policy increased U.S. interest rates in 1987. This posed a threat to equity prices, which had risen during the year on a speculative wave. Both in February—the *Louvre Accord*—and again in September, the governments of the Group of Seven agreed to co-operate in stabilising exchange rates and protecting the dollar against speculative depreciation. However, market operators became increasingly sceptical that the dollar could be supported in the face of the US trade deficit. In October the markets panicked, share prices plummeted and, as funds left the US, the dollar depreciated sharply. Stock exchanges around the world followed the New York lead.

The financial crisis led to fears that it would cause world-wide economic recession if business confidence was shaken and investment dried up. As a precaution, governments in various countries responded to the deflationary impetus by adopting more expansionary fiscal and monetary policies, hoping thereby to lower interest rates. In other respects, conditions in 1988 were favourable for faster world economic growth: world inflation was lower than it had been for many years, and oil and primary commodity prices were low. These propitious factors prevailed: the world economy grew more rapidly (by 4·3 per cent) in 1988 than it had done since 1984. Moreover, this was achieved without an acceleration of inflation.

World Recession, 1989–93.

It was the prospect of inflation accelerating which caused most governments—including those of the United States and the United Kingdom—to raise interest rates during 1988. As inflationary pressure built up (rising from 3·3 to 4·1 per cent in the industrial countries between 1988 and 1989) economic growth was reined in, as the table shows. The United States, Canada, Britain, France and Italy all moved into recession, and the economies of Eastern Europe contracted as planning and direction were dismantled without being replaced by markets and incentives. 1991 was a year of serious recession in the industrial economies, with the output of that group stagnating. 1992 and 1993 were years of continued poor growth performance and recession in the industrial countries. However, the industrialized countries managed to grow by 2·7 per cent in 1994, led by the United States, and the prospects for continued economic recovery in 1995 were good.

ANNUAL GROWTH RATES OF REAL GDP,
INDUSTRIAL COUNTRIES AND WORLD
ECONOMY, 1988–94

	1988	1989	1990	1991	1992	1993	1994
Industrial countries	4·3	3·2	2·3	0·5	1·5	1·3	2·7
World	4·6	3·4	2·2	0·6	1·7	2·3	3·1

The Economic Performance of Japan.

Japan's economy has outpaced all the major industrial economies in recent years. Over the period 1965–1989 annual growth of real income per head was no less than 4·3 per cent. Even in the 1980s it was 3·2 per cent, whereas inflation was only 1·4 per cent per annum. After the recession of the early 1980s the current account surplus was consistently above 2 per cent of GNP, partly offset by an outflow of long term capital, and the yen continued to appreciate in value. The Tokyo stock market rose inexorably—by over fourfold between 1982 and 1989.

By 1990 Japan's national income per capita (expressed in purchasing power parity) was 10 per cent higher than Britain's, and its total GNP was 55 per cent that of the United States. Japan, with its population of 124 million, had become an economic superpower. Its success is bound up with the hard work and thriftiness of its people.

In 1990 signs emerged that Japanese economic confidence and expectations were faltering. Despite a continuing current account surplus, the yen depreciated. The Nikkei share index fell sharply and interest rates were raised. It is not clear why confidence was lost. Commentators attributed the crisis to rising inflation and a deteriorating trade balance, but inflation was only 2 per cent per annum and the current account still in huge surplus. Speculative buying of shares and land is probably the culprit. The high level of share prices in relation to company profits strengthened the incentive to move capital abroad, and this realisation triggered the fall in the yen and in shares and the rise in interest rates.

While the yen recovered, asset prices did not. Between the end of 1989 and the end of 1992 share prices were halved. The fall in the prices of their assets placed the Japanese banks in financial jeopardy. The economy slowed down from a growth rate of 4·8 per cent in 1990 to 1·1 per cent in 1992 to −0·2 per cent in 1993, rising to only 0·8 per cent in 1994. The fear of a financial crisis sapped the economy, and in 1992 and again in 1993 the Japanese Government resorted to fiscal expansion as a means of stimulating the economy. Recorded unemployment remained low but this was because excess labour was retained by firms. The inexorable rise of the yen – by a quarter in real terms in the years 1993 and 1994 – was a brake on economic recovery.

Gold.

The rapid inflation and great uncertainty in the world economy in the 1970s contributed to the speculative demand for gold; this raised its price many times over in the free market. For instance, the instability after the Soviet invasion of Afghanistan catapulted the gold price to $700 in September 1980. Gold flourishes in times of uncertainty and expected inflation. The price of gold subsequently declined as inflation rates began to diminish and as real rates of interest rose.

LONDON GOLD PRICE, 1976–94
(U.S. $ per fine ounce, end-year)

1976	135	1988	411
1978	226	1990	386
1980	590	1991	362
1982	444	1992	344
1984	308	1993	384
1986	391	1994	383

Exchange Rate Arrangements.

At the start of 1995 the following exchange rate arrangements were in operation. 57 currencies, including the pound, the dollar and the yen, were independently floating. Another 33 currencies had "managed floats", *i.e.*, floating subject to a policy of periodic government intervention. Nine members of the EU, but not including Britain, maintained a co-operative arrangement to float together under the European Monetary System. Most developing countries pegged their currencies to those of major trading partners, 23 to the dollar, 14 to the French franc, 4 to the SDR, and 33 to some currency composite of their own choice.

Experience of Exchange-rate Flexibility.

One of the advantages claimed for greater flexi-

EXCHANGE RATES, 1995†

	Exchange rate against sterling, 1995 (£1 =)	Index of effective exchange rate, 1995 (1985 = 100)
Sterling	1·00	62·5
U.S. dollars	1·59	54·4
Deutschmark	2·40	130·0
Japanese yen	157·75	187·8

† January.

bility in exchange rates is that it diminishes the need for international liquidity. Variations in exchange rates should reduce the size of im-balances and therefore the resources required to tide over deficits.

However, it is not clear from recent experience that greater exchange-rate flexibility can produce equilibrium in international payments. It seems that the balance of payments takes a long time—perhaps two or three years—to adjust to a depreciation of the exchange rate. In the meantime there might be wage increases to compensate for the increase in the cost of living brought about by the depreciation. which in turn tend to neutralise the depreciation. For instance, the table indicates that, between 1985 and January 1995 the pound had depreciated against a basket of other currencies by 37 per cent and the dollar by 45 per cent, the mark had appreciated by 30 per cent and the yen by 88 per cent. Yet because of their different rates of inflation, the signs were that the competitiveness of British goods was no stronger than it had been in 1985. A worrying feature of the flexible exchange rate system is that it not only permits but also generates a far wider spread of inflation rates among the major countries.

The Integration of Financial Markets.

There is a growing worldwide integration of financial markets. Financial intermediation has become a footloose industry with only limited ties to particular national markets or stock exchanges. Borrowers and lenders in different countries are brought together often by intermediaries based in a third country. The major currencies are traded in most financial centres and dealing continues around the clock. There are now over 250 companies whose equity is traded around the world.

Much of this change is due to technological innovations in communications. The declining cost of communication has meant that arbitrage is now possible at only very small price differentials, and companies throughout the world are alive to the advantages of scanning money and currency markets on a worldwide basis to meet their requirements at least cost. The consequent competitive pressures have meant that those markets have become more integrated.

Markets for Risk.

Economic life is full of uncertainties and risks. Some individuals or companies dislike taking risks and are willing to pay to avoid them; others are willing to take risks in search of gain. Markets therefore develop in which risk is bought and sold like any other commodity. The most well-known are insurance markets. For instance, by pooling the risks of many customers, insurance companies can offer house insurance on terms that are attractive to most house-owners.

If the insurers are not as well informed as their customers, insurance markets may not work. For instance, if companies selling private health insurance cannot know about the health of individual customers and they therefore charge everyone the average premium, this can drive the healthy out of the market and push up the premiums. The healthiest of the remaining customers always have an incentive to withdraw, and so the market can collapse. This is an argument for having a national health service without permitting anyone to opt out of paying contributions.

Markets for Derivatives.

The explosive growth of *derivatives* since the 1980s has been one of the most profound innova-

tions in financial markets since the introduction of limited liability equity markets early in the nineteenth century. For a price, the amount and type of market risk associated with almost any combination of assets and liabilities can now be tailored to suit the needs of market participants.

A *derivative* market is a particular form of market for risk. A derivative is a tradable contract based on (or derived from) something which is actually marketed, such as a commodity (*e.g.* wheat, oil) or a financial asset (*e.g.* a currency, a share, or a share index). Instead of buying or selling the commodity or financial asset itself, the derivative is traded.

The most common derivatives are *futures* and *options*. A future obliges each party to the contract to fulfil it in the future. It is an obligation to buy, or to sell, (say) cocoa at some future date. An option is a similar contract to trade in the future, but it allows the choice of fulfilling the contract or letting the option to do so lapse.

Both futures and options provide ways of avoiding risk. If an exporter will need to sell its dollar proceeds in three months' time, it can sell dollars forward at a fixed price, so transferring the risk of a fall in the dollar to the market. Alternatively, it can, for a premium, take out an option to sell dollars forward. If the dollar falls, the option is used; if it rises, the producer can take advantage of the price rise by selling the dollars in the *spot* (*i.e.* actual) market.

Derivative markets have expanded greatly in recent years. Trading takes place by computer link, or on a trading floor at exchanges such as the London International Financial Futures Exchange (Liffe), or over-the-counter (*e.g.* at a bank).

The Dangers of Derivatives.

Professional investment managers use derivatives to hedge against risk, *i.e.* to sell risk in the sense of buying risk protection. A derivative can offer the same exposure to a market as the underlying commodity or share, but more quickly and at much lower initial outlay and cost. There is no need to own the commodity or asset. Herein lies a danger: derivatives can also be used to buy risk, *i.e.* to speculate in pursuit of big but risky profits.

It was precisely speculation of this sort that caused the collapse of Barings, Britain's oldest bank, in February 1995. An employee of Barings – a trader in the Singapore derivatives market – speculated on a future rise in the Japanese share market (the Nikkei share price index). Partly because of the Kobe earthquake, the index fell, and Barings incurred overwhelming losses of over £850 million.

Volatility of the Foreign Exchanges.

The movements in the 1970s towards greater flexibility of exchange rates and increased international liquidity helped to correct international imbalances. But there were various reasons for believing that they would not provide a permanent solution. Reasons have been given above for questioning whether exchange-rate flexibility can cope with the international imbalances of the 1980s. Moreover, the amount of short-term funds and the scope for speculation with them is greater than ever. The surpluses of the OPEC countries present a considerable problem. In September 1990 the OPEC countries had a stock of external financial assets of $190 billion, of which $65 billion was held in the United Kingdom, mainly in Eurocurrency bank deposits. International companies, with structures that span the remaining exchange control barriers, have accumulated vast sums which they move about in search of security and profit.

The burgeoning and integration of financial markets epitomised by the growth of the Eurocurrency market (*see* **G9**(2)), make control of short term capital flows very difficult and give rise to the possibility of exaggerated and destabilising movements in international exchange rates. For instance, the large differences in interest rates between financial centres in recent years, arising because of different inflation rates and monetary policies, stimulated huge and destabilising capital flows across the exchanges. The ensuing exchange rate fluctuations were detrimental to both private and public decision-taking. Exchange rates have become more responsive to expectations about currency revaluation and to interest rate arbitrage than to underlying current account imbalances.

Towards Greater Stability of Exchange Rates?

The early 1980s was a period in which governments made a virtue out of their reduced control over financial markets, and appeared to throw themselves on the mercies of the market. It also coincided with a world-wide shift in the political climate away from a belief in the efficiency of central control towards a greater reliance on the allocative forces of competition. Fairly "clean" floating of currencies (with little central bank intervention) was adopted, and exchange rate policies were not pursued. By the late 1980s, the inadequacies of this system—the volatility and economic irrationality of the behaviour of currencies—were more apparent, and the portents were that governments would attempt to intervene more vigorously in order to achieve greater exchange rate stability.

In 1987 the governments of the major economies moved towards a policy of stabilising exchange rates. In the *Louvre Accord* it was agreed to aim for particular exchange rates, which would be maintained within bands. In part this was because the major surplus countries were anxious to protect their export sectors from the consequences of further exchange rate appreciation, while the US wished to avoid the inflationary consequences of further depreciation. When confidence in the dollar was lost in 1987, however, and again when confidence in the pound was lost in 1992, the markets demonstrated the impotence of politicians in the face of powerful economic forces.

The European Union.

The *European Community* (EC), now called the *European Union* (EU), was set up by the Treaty of Rome, ratified in 1958. It consisted of six full members—Belgium, France, Holland, Italy, Luxembourg, and Western Germany. Britain had participated in the negotiations which led up to its formation, and had argued in favour of a looser "free trade area" without a common external tariff, and excluding trade in agricultural products. No compromise acceptable to the Six was found, and Britain joined with six other European countries—Austria, Denmark, Norway, Portugal, Sweden, and Switzerland—in forming the *European Free Trade Area* (EFTA).

Economic Arrangements of the EU.

The EU forms a common market with no tariffs or trade controls within it and a Common External Tariff (CET). There is a Common Agricultural Policy (CAP), which is maintained by a system of variable import levies setting *threshold prices* on imports of agricultural products from outside the Union, and by means of *intervention prices* at which agricultural products of the EU are purchased. The EU has a large Budget required mainly for supporting the CAP, *i.e.*, for subsidising farmers. There is free movement of both goods and labour within the Union, and a certain degree of fiscal harmonisation.

POPULATION (MILLIONS) AND GDP PER
HEAD (AVERAGE = 100) OF EC MEMBER
COUNTRIES, 1990

	Population	GDP per head*
Belgium	9·9	103
Denmark	5·1	104
Germany	62·7	113
Greece	10·0	53
France	56·3	109
Ireland	3·5	69
Italy	57·6	104
Luxembourg	0·4	125
Netherlands	14·9	104
Portugal	10·3	57
Spain	38·9	77
United Kingdom	57·3	104
Total	327·1	100

* Comparisons are based on purchasing power parities.

Accession to the Community 1973.

The United Kingdom acceded as a full member of the EC on 1 January 1973. Two of Britain's EFTA partners—Ireland and Denmark—joined on the same date, so forming an expanded Community of nine countries. Economic ties with the Community strengthened. In 1972 trade with the original six members of the EC accounted for about 23 per cent of total British trade, trade with the EFTA partners about 13 per cent, and with the Commonwealth 19 per cent. After accession, trade with the EC expanded sharply and the proportion of trade with the former EFTA countries and the Commonwealth fell. Excluding trade with the oil-exporting countries, British trade with the original EC countries rose from 25 per cent of the total in 1972 to 30 per cent in 1974. In 1992 no less than 54 per cent of British trade was with the EC.

The EU Budget.

It is in the British interest that the CAP—with its heavy support of farmers—be reformed. EU funds are available to protect farmers by buying excess food and building up stocks of food if the free market price falls below the intervention price. As a result "food mountains" have developed.

The British contribution to the EC Budget was initially small. Britain gained from "monetary compensation amounts," *i.e.*, refunds associated with the difference between the values of the pound in the foreign exchange markets and the *green pound*. The green pound is the agreed exchange rate between the pound and the other EU currencies which is used in calculating contributions to the Budget.

Britain's Budget Contribution.

Britain's net contribution to the EC budget rose to about £1 billion in 1980, *i.e.* about 60 per cent of the total net contributions to the Community budget. Yet Britain's GNP per head was then the third lowest of the Nine. The high level of Britain's net contribution reflected her heavy dependence on imported food: she has only a small agricultural sector whereas most of the Community budget is used for farm support. The British Government negotiated refunds on its contribution in the period 1980–3 but a more satisfactory deal was struck at Fountainebleau in 1984. The agreement made automatic arrangements for the future. The United Kingdom would receive a refund each year equal to two-thirds of the difference between its share of VAT payments to the Community (each country paid VAT to the Community at the rate of 1·4 per cent of value added) and its share in expenditure from the Community budget.

Reforming the Budget.

In 1984 EC farm ministers agreed to cut subsidies and freeze prices. The system of open-ended guarantees was to be largely discontinued in an effort to halt the growth of agricultural surpluses. Another aspect of the agricultural agreement was the decision to phase out the monetary compensation amounts, *i.e.*, the border taxes which iron out the effects of national currency fluctuations. Despite this talk, by July 1986 the surplus food stocks had reached new levels in almost all cases. In 1987 the President of the Commission declared that the objective should be to bring farm price intervention back to its original role of short term market stabilization.

In 1988 it was agreed that CAP expenditure should be limited to 74 per cent of GNP growth, *i.e.* if Community output grows annually by 4 per cent, CAP expenditure can grow by 3 per cent. In 1991 the Commission proposed to move from linking agricultural support to quantities produced (with its incentive to expand production) towards direct aid measures (*e.g.* depending on the size of farm). Reform of the CAP runs up against vested interests: progress is slow.

Agricultural Protectionism.

There is good cause for the reform of agricultural

policies not just in the EC but in the OECD countries generally. Agriculture is heavily supported in all the major economies—probably more so in Japan and the US than in the EC. A study of 7 major countries found that government assistance to agriculture exceeded one third of the value of their agricultural output. Half of this assistance came from tax-payers' pockets (subsidies) and half from consumers' pockets (higher prices).

This inefficient use of the world's resources is expensive to non-farming people in the rich countries and harmful to the people of the poor countries. Some progress in reducing agricultural protection in the OECD countries was made in the Uruguay Round negotiations of the GATT (see **G47**).

Towards Economic Integration

In 1970 the Commission of the EC published the *Werner Plan*, a report on the establishment of economic and monetary union. The plan aimed at transferring the principal economic decisions from the national to the Community level, and at establishing within the Community complete freedom of movement of goods, services, persons and capital, with fixed and constant rates of exchange between national currencies or, preferably, a common currency.

These ideas have far-reaching economic and political implications, since they involve a considerable reduction of national sovereignty. For instance, the loss of power to correct balance of payments deficits by means of trade controls or variation in the exchange rate implies either that the deficit country's currency should be generally acceptable to its creditors (so that the country within the Union—like a region within a country—simply cannot have a balance of payments problem), or the country must resort to deflation. And even if there is a common currency, it is very likely that resources will concentrate in some regions of the Union to the neglect of the other regions, possibly those far from the main centres of production and consumption. Complete mobility of resources is likely to produce a regional problem within the Union just as it can produce a regional problem within a country. But the Union may not, to the same extent as a country, possess the political power and determination required to remedy the problem.

Regional differences within the Community increased with the joining of Greece in 1981, of Spain and Portugal in 1986, and the incorporation of East Germany in 1990. The Community now united 330 million Europeans, but there were large differences in their incomes. Its population was almost as large as that of the US and Japan combined, and its output was similar to that of the US.

The Single European Act.

The Single European Act was introduced in 1986 to amend the Treaty of Rome. Its intention was to establish a free internal market in the Community by the end of 1992. This was defined as an area without frontiers in which the free movement of goods, persons, services and capital is ensured. The single market will involve the end of exchange controls, common financial services and technical standards, and mutual recognition of professional qualifications. The legislation was concerned to remove barriers—barriers that increase costs, impede entry to markets, or distort markets. Thus, for instance, it outlaws delays at customs posts, form-filling, the need to conform to different national rules and regulations, and national restrictions on purchases by governments and on professional practice.

The Act circumscribed the powers of member countries to impose a veto in all but sensitive issues. It also made provision for what is called "cohesion", which means reducing the gap between rich and poor regions of the Community. The Act should be seen as a very small step in the direction of a federal Europe.

Towards Monetary Union.

It was on the issue of monetary union that the first major economic problem for Britain arose after entry. The Community agreed in March 1973 to fix the exchange rates between member currencies and to float them together against the dollar. This

arrangement was known as the *snake in the tunnel*. Britain and Italy—then in balance of payments difficulties—decided to float independently.

There is a danger that the right to vary exchange rates be withdrawn from member countries without there being uniformity in other policies. If there is to be a monetary union, there should also be uniformity in other economic policies, even industrial relations and incomes policies! For if inflation is more rapid in Britain than in her partner countries, and if Britain is prevented from adjusting the exchange rates or imposing import restrictions against her partners to correct the ensuing balance of payments deficit, the Government might see no alternative but to deflate the economy: stagnation could ensue.

In 1987 the European Commission adopted proposals for the complete liberalisation of capital movements in the Community. Controls were removed in 1990 for most member countries. The liberalization should lead to the development of Community-wide financial and banking services, and the increased competition should make them cheaper.

The European Monetary System.

A modification of the snake, the *European Monetary System* (EMS) was introduced in 1979. A currency is permitted to float within a 2¼ per cent band on either side of the par rate between the currency and any other member's currency. Central bank intervention is required to keep the currency within the band. The participating currencies are defined in *European Currency Units* (ECUs), issued against the deposit of 20 per cent of national gold and foreign exchange reserves and used to settle intervention debts. There is a system of central bank "swaps" and short- and medium-term credit.

For some, the EMS is the response to a growing disillusionment with the operation of floating exchange rates and a strong desire to move towards greater exchange rate stability among close trading partners. For others, the EMS represents an early step on the path to European monetary union. The restriction on national sovereignty under the EMS is not large: it need only mean that exchange rate adjustments will be in discrete steps rather than by continuous and perhaps erratic floating.

The difference in inflation rates among countries in the EMS necessitated periodic currency realignments, in October 1981, June 1982, March 1983, April 1986 and January 1987. In each case the deutschmark was upvalued relative to the French franc: the combined result of these realignments was that the franc fell by 38 per cent against the mark. In early 1995 one ECU (representing a weighted bundle of EU currencies) was worth 79 pence.

The Debate Over the EMS.

Early in 1988 four EC countries had not entered the EMS: Britain, Greece, Spain and Portugal. Britain had resisted the blandishments of EMS members to join them. This was partly because of the large and unpredictable flows of funds in and out of sterling on account of London's role as a financial centre. However, the main reason was that, Britain being a net oil exporter, the British balance of payments is likely to move inversely to that of other EC countries as the world price of oil fluctuates. With the oil price falling sharply in 1986, Britain needed the power to permit a depreciation of sterling in order to maintain balance in payments.

Nevertheless, events were pushing Britain towards full membership of the EMS, involving entry to the *Exchange Rate Mechanism* (ERM). The ERM requires member countries to keep their exchange rates fixed within narrow bands and to adopt domestic monetary policies to achieve this target. Entry to the ERM was supported by most industrialists because exchange rate stability would reduce the uncertainty they faced in exporting and importing. In April 1989 a cabinet division emerged over entry to the ERM. The Chancellor of the Exchequer was in favour, mainly because it would impose an external constraint on Britain's inflation rate. However, the Prime Minister was against, mainly because it would involve loss of control over monetary policy. This disagreement was one of the factors that led to Nigel Lawson's resignation as Chancellor in October.

The Delors Plan.

The President of the European Community, Jacques Delors, was firmly in favour of economic and monetary union (EMU) of the Community. The *Delors Plan* on EMU was presented to the European Council's meeting in Madrid in June 1989. Its conclusions were in many ways similar to those of the Werner report. They envisaged a three-stage process of movement towards EMU. Stage one would consolidate the single market. Stage two would see the setting up of a European System of Central Banks (ESCB), but responsibility for policy would remain with national authorities. Stage three would involve an irrevocable locking of exchange rates, the creation of a single Community currency, binding constraints on national budgets, and a transfer of responsibility for monetary policy to the ESCB. The ESCB would also decide on exchange rate policy and manage all official reserves.

The British Response to Delors.

The British Government was unhappy both about the pace and ultimate form of EMU. Addressing the EC summit in Madrid in June 1989, the Prime Minister set terms for British entry to the ERM: there should first be liberalisation of financial markets, agreement on competition policy, an end to exchange controls, and completion of a single market. These conditions represented the first of Delors' three stages. In addition, the Prime Minister wanted British inflation to be closer to the European average between 1988 and 1989 British inflation was 7·8 per cent whereas the Community average was 5·1 per cent).

In November the Treasury published proposals for an evolutionary approach to EMU, as an alternative to the Delors plan. It proposed that, when stage one was complete, there should be a number of piecemeal measures to strengthen market competition and encourage integration, *e.g.* encouragement of private ECUs and the removal of restrictions on the use of Community currencies. The British Government was against binding rules on the size of budget deficits: budgetary policies should be left to national authorities. It proposed a multi-currency system which, through competition among monetary authorities, it expected to lead to convergence of inflation rates. It was concerned that Delors would take the control of monetary policy away from national governments while leaving those governments answerable to their electorates for policies over which they would have no control.

British Entry to the ERM.

In October 1990 John Major, then Chancellor of the Exchequer, announced that Britain would join the ERM. The exchange rate was set at a rate of £1 = 2·95 deutschmarks. However, the rate could be varied within a band of 6 per cent—considerably wider than the 2·25 per cent band applying to other EMS currencies.

It is interesting to note that the disagreement between the Prime Minister, Margaret Thatcher, her Chancellor of the Exchequer, Nigel Lawson, and her Deputy Prime Minister, Sir Geoffrey Howe, which led eventually to the resignation of all three of them, was related to the dispute over entry to the EMS. To many members of the public this seemed an obscure technical issue, but underlying the technicalities were important points of substance, relating to the most effective policies to control inflation and to maintain national sovereignty.

The subsequent emergence of John Major as the new Prime Minister, and his early statements adopting a more enthusiastic tone than his predecessor about the EMS, suggested that some of the uncertainty might have disappeared with Mrs Thatcher's removal. However, considerable doubt remained, focused particularly on the *Delors Plan* for the eventual development of the EMS towards permanently fixed exchange rates and, ultimately, a single European currency. The Prime Minister was opposed to this. However, the issue cut across party lines with all the major parties containing both supporters and opponents. The arguments involved the basic question: how much control over

economic policy should be surrendered by national governments? This issue seemed increasingly likely to be a dominant one in the 1990s.

The Treaty of European Union.

At a summit meeting held in Maastricht in December 1991, leaders of the Community member states—the *European Council*—agreed on a draft Treaty of European Union (the *Maastricht Treaty*). European economic and monetary union was now a gradual but irreversible commitment. It was agreed to establish a single currency by 1999, administered by a single independent central bank.

John Major signed the Treaty but secured important concessions: Britain was permitted to reserve its decision on moving to stage three; and Britain would not be required to participate in a social policy agreement, intended to provide a charter of social rights for workers. Federal goals were dropped from the draft Treaty, allegedly in return for concessions on other matters made by the British government. Britain's opposition to the Social Charter was based on grounds of cost and of ideology, *e.g.* it would "restore trade union practices that the government had spent much of the last twelve years eliminating".

Ratification of the Treaty.

Difficulties arose over the Maastricht Treaty as it required ratification by each one of the member countries. Some countries held a referendum. Only in Denmark was there a "no" vote, but this and the French referendum (narrowly in favour) cast doubt on the extent of popular support for closer union within the Community. At the meeting of Heads of State in Edinburgh in December 1992, it was agreed to make concessions to Denmark in the hope that these would pave the way to a successful referendum; and this proved to be the case. The British Government eschewed a referendum but managed to secure ratification of the Treaty in Parliament. The Community became the European Union on 1 November 1993.

Crisis in the Community, 1992.

Another reason for disquiet about the achievement of economic and monetary union according to the Maastricht timetable was the upheaval in the EMS in 1992. High interest rates in Germany posed problems for the countries with weak currencies and depressed economies. In particular, there was speculation against the lira and the pound. On 13 September, the lira was devalued 7 per cent by agreement, and on 17 September the pound was forced out of the EMS by speculation, despite massive supportive intervention (*see* **G54**). The lira was also then floated. The French franc came under speculative pressure but survived owing to Bundesbank support. The credibility of commitments to EMU was damaged by these shocks to the system.

A possible solution to the impasse would be the creation of a *two-speed* Community, with different countries approaching economic convergence at different speeds. An inner circle of countries, including Germany and France, would progress towards EMU according to the Maastricht timetable, whereas another group of countries within the Community, including Britain and Italy, would converge more slowly.

In the light of the 1992 crisis and subsequent strains on the system, the problems of restricting exchange rate fluctuations within the EMS were more widely acknowledged. In August 1993 it was agreed that all ERM currencies except the guilder and the mark would have wider bands of 15 per cent. However, Britain chose not to rejoin the ERM.

Expansion of the Community.

The Treaty on Economic Union provides that any European state whose system of government is democratic may apply to become a member of the Union. Turkey, Cyprus and Malta had submitted applications, as had the EFTA countries Austria, Sweden, Norway and Finland. The countries of Central and Eastern Europe could be expected to apply in the future. This outward-looking stance would have political benefits but, insofar as the

POSTWAR BRITISH ECONOMIC
EXPERIENCE

	Average annual rates of:		
	Unemploy-ment	Inflation	Growth of Gross National Product
1945–64	1·9	3·4	2·4
1965–69	2·1	4·3	2·5
1970–74	3·0	11·0	1·6
1975–79	5·5	14·1	1·7
1980–84	10·6	9·7	1·4
1985–89	9·0	5·1	3·5
1990	6·9	9·5	1·6
1991	8·8	5·9	−2·3
1992	9·9	3·8	−1·8
1993	10·3	1·8	2·0
1994	9·5	2·5	3·6

expansion widened economic inequality within the
EC, it might hold back EMU.

In 1994 the electorates of Austria, Finland
and Sweden voted to join the European Union,
and the Norwegians voted narrowly against. The
three countries entered the Union on 1 January,
1995.

The North American Free Trade Area.

The *North American Free Trade Area* (NAFTA)
was established in 1994. It is a free trade area of the
United States, Canada and Mexico, creating a
common market with roughly the same population
and income as the European Union.

The moves towards NAFTA began in the mid-
1980s, partly as a response to the success of the
European Community. The goals of NAFTA are to
eliminate barriers to trade and investment and to
improve regional co-operation. The United States
favours the expansion of NAFTA to include other
countries in the Americas; a likely contender being
Chile.

Economic Reform in Eastern Europe.

Over 40 years of centrally planned economic
systems have left a legacy of stagnating economies
with major structural and macroeconomic problems. Output per head remains well below that of
the EC countries. The remarkable political revolution that took place in almost all of Eastern Europe
in 1989 and 1990 provided the opportunity and the
challenge to introduce an economic revolution, with
the dismantling of central planning and the
introduction of market economies.

The problems of transition are considerable, as
the new governments have inherited large fiscal
deficits, rapid inflation, polluted environments and
heavy external indebtedness. For instance, in 1989
debt exceeded $1,000 per capita in Bulgaria, the
GDR, Hungary and Poland. The new electorates
have high expectations of rapid economic improvement, but the move to market prices involves large
price changes and associated changes in incomes
and vast transfers of resources, including the
closing down of unprofitable activities.

The European Bank for Reconstruction and Development.

The European Community took the initiative in
setting up a new international financial institution,
the European Bank for Reconstruction and Development (EBRD) to help the emerging democracies of
Eastern Europe in their transition to market
economies. The Bank, founded in 1991, has 42
member countries, headquarters in London, and a
capital base of 10 billion ECU, about £7 billion. It
can make equity investments in private enterprises,
loans to individual projects and provide technical
assistance for projects to these countries provided
that they are committed to democracy and a
market economy. An important element in the
Bank's work is investment designed to improve the
environment in Eastern Europe.

THE PUBLIC SECTOR
BORROWING REQUIREMENT
Annual averages

	£billion	as a percentage of gross domestic product
1979–82	10·3	4·3
1983–86	7·1	2·2
1987–88	−3·0	−0·7
1988–89	−14·0	−3·0
1989–90	−7·6	−1·7
1990–91	−0·5	−0·1
1991–92	13·8	2·4
1992–93	35·0	5·8
1993–94	45·9	7·2
1994–95	34·3	5·0

A negative sign indicates a public sector surplus.

2. INTERNAL DEVELOPMENTS

The Keynesian Era.

For some 25 years after the end of the Second
World War in 1945, successive British Governments
pursued broadly "Keynesian" policies, in the sense
that they gave top priority to the policy objective of
full employment, using fiscal policies—the manipulation of taxes and public spending—as their main
policy instrument. As the following table (**G62**)
shows, the policy was strikingly successful in its
own terms: unemployment was kept at a persistently low level throughout the period, most of the
time being well under half a million. However, there
were at least two important qualifications: the rate
of inflation showed a tendency to rise, albeit very
gradually, over the period; and the balance of
payments showed persistent weakness, which
became more pronounced whenever the economy
expanded too rapidly.

Problems of the 1970s.

In the early 1970s the inflation and balance of
payments problems became much more severe, and
the economy also experienced the simultaneous
problems of both high inflation and high unemployment. In the 1950s and 1960s, in contrast, these had
generally been inversely related. The Keynesian
policies of the 1950s and 1960s no longer seemed so
appropriate in these new circumstances. Indeed,
many economists, especially those persuaded by the
monetarist doctrines of Milton Friedman, argued
that expansionary Keynesian policies were part of
the problem rather than the solution.

In retrospect it is clear that many of the problems which emerged in the early and mid-1970s were
not only the product of over-expansionary Keynesian
policies but also reflected several adverse changes in
the world economy, all dating from the beginning of
the 1970s, which were outside the control of the
British government. These included a significant
slowdown in the growth of world trade; a sharp rise in
world-wide inflation; the emergence of negative real
interest rates in most countries; and—perhaps the
most dramatic—a vast rise in the international price
of oil. Over the decade as a whole real unit energy costs
rose drastically (*see* **G55**).

In such an unfavourable world economic climate
the British economy was bound to experience problems. The 1970s became the decade of *stagflation*—
a combination of both inflation and stagnation
(and thus unemployment). Britain was by no means
the only country to experience such problems.
However, Britain fared worse than most, and
mistakes by successive British governments were
partly to blame.

The Monetarist Era.

In the autumn of 1976 a loss of international
confidence in the government's economic policy led
to speculation against the pound and to a sharp
fall in its international value. The government had
to apply to the International Monetary Fund for a
loan. The latter was granted, but only on condition
that the government introduced *monetary targets*,
i.e. specified annual growth rates of the money
supply. The emergence of monetarism in Britain
really dates from this time.

The introduction of monetary targets meant that government spending could no longer be financed by unlimited monetary expansion, and thus forced the government to choose between cutting public spending, raising taxes, or increasing its borrowing (and therefore rising interest rates). The Labour government found all these options unpalatable, but at the 1979 General Election it lost power, and was replaced with a Conservative Government led by Margaret Thatcher, with Sir Geoffrey Howe as Chancellor.

Monetarism in Action, 1979–83.

In some respects the new Government's economic policy was little more than a continuation of the Labour Government's policy since 1976. The centrepiece of economic policy was the *Medium Term Financial Strategy*, which involved laying down targets for monetary growth and the p.s.b.r. for 3 to 4 years ahead. This policy was not substantially different in principle from that followed between 1976 and 1979.

The main change brought about by Mrs. Thatcher's Government was a change of attitudes towards economic policy, with the Keynesian priority of low unemployment finally giving way to the monetarist priority of low inflation. The two years 1980 and 1981 saw the sharpest recession for 50 years, with substantial falls in output and huge rises in unemployment. The gains, in terms of lower inflation, appeared from 1982 onwards, by which time it was clear that the "inflation psychology" of the 1970s—in which people had come to regard high and rising inflation rates as the normal state of affairs—had been broken: by 1982 few people anticipated a return to high inflation.

Another important policy change was the Government's long term commitment to securing reductions in public spending, in taxes, and in the p.s.b.r. These objectives—like the opposition to formal incomes policy—reflected its conviction that Government intervention was in general harmful to the economy, and that long term economic gains would follow if the extent of such intervention could be reduced. The table shows that the aim of a reduced p.s.b.r. was indeed achieved by 1982–83.

One of the main effects of the government's economic policy was a very sharp rise in the exchange rate between 1979 and 1981. This reflected two things. The first was North Sea oil (*see* **G52(1)**) and the second was the government's tough monetary policies, which pushed up interest rates in Britain and therefore attracted investment funds into Britain, increasing the demand for sterling and so raising its exchange value. The rise in the exchange rate was the principal cause of the fall in output and rise in unemployment between 1979 and 1982.

In 1983 the Prime Minister called a General Election. The economic policies pursued since 1979 were a principal issue in the campaign. The Government lost some support compared with the 1979 election but nevertheless secured a vastly increased Parliamentary majority: this contradictory result reflected the split in the opposition vote between Labour and the Alliance.

The Second Conservative Government.

After the election Mr Lawson, the new Chancellor, confirmed that the basis of the Government's macroeconomic policies was unchanged: it remained committed to controlling the public sector borrowing requirement, to securing further reductions in inflation, and if possible to cutting both taxes and public expenditure. However, an important new aspect of government policy soon appeared: the *privatisation* of large parts of the public sector. Indeed, this emerged as the most distinctive feature of the second Conservative Government.

The Privatisation Policy.

The Government committed itself to selling shares in existing public enterprises to the private sector. The Government had two motives for this policy. First, it anticipated raising some £2 billion per year through such sales, and this was intended to help finance the p.s.b.r. Secondly, it argued that most economic activity was more efficiently carried out by the private sector, and that privatisation would therefore ultimately raise the economy's overall level of efficiency and productivity.

Both these arguments were strongly attacked. Critics pointed out that there was no evidence from international comparisons of different countries to support the view that the size of the public sector had any appreciable effect upon economic performance.

Economic Policy in the mid-1980s.

The rapid rise in unemployment which had characterised Mrs. Thatcher's first term of office was not repeated in her second. The unemployment total reached 3 million and thereafter showed little trend in either direction until 1986, when it began to fall.

Inflation did not continue the sharp fall of 1980–83 but after 1983 stabilised in the region of 3 to 5 per cent, and the government could not succeed in lowering it further. Indeed there seemed to be little indication that it attached a high priority to doing so, though it continued to attach a very high priority to preventing any increase. One reason why it proved impossible to lower inflation further was that the growth of wages and salaries also stabilised at around 7 to 8 per cent per annum. With labour costs thus continuing to rise relatively rapidly, it was impossible to reduce price inflation. Indeed, throughout the second Conservative government, the growth of earnings considerably outstripped the growth of prices, so that people in work experienced significant improvements in their real living standards despite continued high unemployment.

Changes in Taxation.

The Chancellor introduced several types of tax change over the course of the Parliament. One was a reform of company taxation in which most tax reliefs and allowances on investment were phased out, and simultaneously the rate of Corporation Tax was sharply reduced. The aim was to increase post-tax company profits, whilst leaving individual firms free to decide on the best and most efficient way of using these profits, free from tax incentives which tended to make some types of investment more profitable than others. This fitted into the government's general philosophy of leaving decisions to private markets, with a minimum of direct government intervention.

Another major change was in personal taxation. When Mrs. Thatcher had first been elected in 1979, reductions in income tax had been one of her main aims. However, apart from the reduction of tax rates in Sir Geoffrey Howe's first Budget in 1979, little had been done by 1983. In her second government this objective was given a fresh priority, and over the course of the Parliament the Chancellor succeeded in cutting the standard rate of income tax from 30 to 27 per cent, and also in raising the tax thresholds by more than the rate of inflation. Hence the government succeeded in reducing the burden of income tax. At the same time other tax burdens—indirect taxes, and National Insurance contributions—were still substantially higher than in 1979. Hence it remained true for most people that their total tax burden was higher by the end of Mrs. Thatcher's second government than it had been when she was first elected. Only those earning more than around four times the national average had obtained a reduction in their overall tax burdens.

Economic Boom, 1987–89.

In June 1987 a General Election returned the government to power with only a small reduction in its Parliamentary majority, and with little change in its degree of popular support. Whilst the government had a number of proposals for radical changes, these were mostly in the field of social policy: in economic policy the emphasis was on continuity. This was reflected in the 1988 Budget, in which the basic rate of tax was cut from 27 per cent to 25 per cent, and the higher rates on relatively high incomes were slashed from a range of from 40 to 60 per cent to a new single rate of 40 per cent.

In the periods both before and after the 1987 election the economy experienced very rapid economic growth, at around 4·5 per cent per year. With hindsight it is clear that such growth rates were unsustainable, but at the time there was widespread optimism that the economy could continue along such a path, even though the growth rate was

AVERAGE ANNUAL GROWTH RATES OF
NATIONAL INCOME

	1973–8	1979–82	1983–6	1987–90	1991–3
Britain	1·4	0·3	3·4	3·0	−0·1
France	3·0	1·6	1·9	3·3	0·4
Germany	2·1	1·1	2·4	3·6	1·6
Italy	2·1	2·1	2·7	3·0	0·4
Canada	3·2	0·7	4·7	2·8	0·3
USA	2·7	0·8	4·0	2·7	1·6
Japan	3·3	4·1	3·8	4·9	1·7
OECD average	2·6	1·4	3·5	3·3	1·2

AVERAGE UNEMPLOYMENT RATES

	1973–8	1979–82	1983–6	1987–90	1991–3
Britain	5·0	9·2	11·7	8·1	10·3
France	4·0	6·9	9·6	9·7	10·5
Germany	2·8	4·2	7·2	5·7	4·6
Italy	6·3	8·0	10·2	10·7	9·9
Canada	6·9	8·3	10·7	8·0	10·9
USA	6·5	7·4	7·7	5·5	6·9
Japan	1·8	2·2	2·7	2·4	2·2
OECD average	4·6	6·5	7·9	6·6	7·3

AVERAGE ANNUAL INFLATION RATES

	1973–8	1979–82	1983–6	1987–90	1991–3
Britain	14·9	9·7	4·7	5·7	4·9
France	10·2	11·7	5·0	3·0	2·8
Germany	4·7	5·1	1·5	1·7	3·8
Italy	15·4	16·5	8·2	5·5	5·2
Canada	8·8	10·1	4·1	4·5	2·9
USA	7·7	9·8	3·2	4·4	3·4
Japan	10·7	4·7	1·6	1·5	2·1
OECD average	9·6	9·7	3·8	3·8	3·5

double the long term average. The Chancellor's tax cuts in his 1988 Budget helped to fuel such optimism. However, by mid-1988 there were unmistakeable signs of "overheating" in the economy, and the Chancellor was forced to alter course.

In retrospect it seems clear that some policy misjudgments occurred during 1987 and 1988, leading to too rapid an upswing. In part this probably represented a pessimistic view about the effects of the stock market crash of October 1987. At the time many commentators had predicted that this would lead to a large fall in demand, reflecting the fall in the value of share holdings. However, the crash did little more than correct the very large rise in share prices over the previous year, thus restoring share prices towards a longer run trend level. Hence in attempting to correct for the feared effects of the crash, especially with interest rate cuts, the Government probably over-reacted.

During 1989, the economic situation deteriorated sharply. Inflation continued to edge inexorably upwards, reaching approximately 7 per cent by the year-end. The current account deficit also mounted alarmingly. In response to these trends the Government increased interest rates in a series of steps. By the year-end interest rates were at record levels, being in the range 15 to 20 per cent, depending on the type of borrowing. The large gap between this level of interest rates and the inflation rate meant that real interest rates were also at a record high level.

Evaluating the 1980s.

These immediate difficulties obviously detracted from the Government's overall economic record. However, at the end of a decade throughout which Conservative governments under Mrs. Thatcher had been in power, it was possible to form some longer term judgements about the performance of the economy over the decade, and by inference about the policies pursued by the Government. At one extreme, leading members of the Government repeatedly asserted that they had achieved an "economic miracle". At the other extreme, one of their critics in the Labour party described the

1980s in Britain as "the decade which the locusts ate".

(i) Macroeconomic Indicators.

The accompanying tables summarise the performance of the British economy in relation to the other G7 countries (the world's seven major industrial economies) and also in relation to the average of all OECD countries (the 22 leading industrial economies). The figures provide little support for claims of an economic miracle. Britain's inflation rate improved (*i.e.* fell) a little compared with other countries in the early 1980s, but then rose again. Overall, Britain remained as a relatively high inflation economy. Britain also remained a relatively high unemployment economy, and indeed in this respect things worsened in the 1980s compared with the 1970s. In terms of economic growth, Britain's relative performance improved in the mid-1980s. However, as described later, this was partly because economic policy at this time generated an unsustainably rapid boom, the consequence of which was a subsequent deep recession in which, as the table shows, national income actually fell.

(ii) Economic Inequality.

A feature of the 1980s which many saw as unsatisfactory was a large increase in economic inequality. This had several causes. One was a widening in the dispersal of pre-tax earnings. Another was disproportionate cuts in the rates of tax levied on high incomes, particularly as a result of the tax changes made in the 1988 Budget. The combined effect of these two trends was that those in the top 10 per cent of income earners saw their real after tax earnings rise, on average, by 73 per cent from 1979 to 1988, whilst for those in the bottom 10 per cent the average rise was only 13 per cent. A third source of rising inequality was the growth in people unable to earn at all, including the long term unemployed and single parents unable to work because of family responsibilities. People in these categories, and some others including those retired people who were without occupational pensions or other income sources, and who were therefore dependent on the state pension, saw their incomes fall compared with those in regular employment.

(iii) Industrial Relations and Working Practices.

An area in which the Government claimed great success during the 1980s was improved labour relations. Compared with the 1960s and 1970s, the 1980s saw a large reduction in the amount of industrial conflict, measured either in terms of the total numbers of strikes or in terms of days lost through strikes. The Government argued that this was mainly the result of its various pieces of legislation during the 1980s, aimed at imposing clearer legal restraints on unions' ability to take strike action.

The Government also argued that a new, more constructive, spirit in management-employee relationships had fostered productivity gains. The figures for productivity growth in the table above are averages for the whole economy, and conceal a significantly better performance in some parts of the manufacturing sector. It was this improvement in industrial efficiency which Government supporters often claimed as its most significant achievement. The sources of this improvement were not wholly clear, but it certainly did not reflect investment in either productive equipment or research and development—the record on both of these was poor throughout the decade. Many commentators argued that the main source was changes in working practices, themselves the result partly of greater determination by management to overcome union resistance to change, and partly a forced response to the very deep recession of the early 1980s—when many companies were faced with a stark choice between improved efficiency or bankruptcy. Some research seemed to support this view: the biggest gains in productivity were often found in companies which had faced the greatest pressure for change, and which were also heavily unionised.

At the same time, it was not clear to what extent the Government's legislation on union activity and strike behaviour had established a *permanent* change in industrial relations. For one thing, the reduction in strike activity during the 1980s was matched in nearly all other countries. Indeed, Britain's record in relation to other countries was not discernibly better in the 1980s than in the 1970s. Another reason for doubt was the upsurge in strikes during 1988 and 1989 as the level of unemployment fell sharply, and many labour markets experienced significant labour shortages.

(iv) The Supply Side.

Another important feature of the economy during the decade was the emphasis put on the *supply side*. This contrasted with earlier decades during which the influence of Keynesian ideas had led to emphasis on policies to manipulate aggregate demand in order to regulate economic activity. In the 1980s demand management was mainly seen instead as subordinate to the aim of controlling inflation, and the Thatcher Governments argued that the key to improved economic performance lay in policies to improve the supply side. Their main methods were cuts in direct taxes, reform of the trade unions, and privatisation and deregulation.

It was a measure of the extent to which economic and political thinking changed during the course of the decade that most of the Government's critics increasingly came to accept the new emphasis on the supply side. Discussion instead began to focus upon the appropriate supply side policies. Many critics argued that the Government's policies were at best only marginally relevant to the most important supply side weaknesses in the British economy, which had to do with low levels of educational and training attainments. A series of detailed studies showed that, in a variety of industrial and service sectors, British labour productivity levels were very low in comparison with those in other countries, especially West Germany, France, and Japan. These large differences in productivity levels continued to show up even where employees were using similar types of productive equipment in both countries. The implication seemed to be that British employees' education and training were inferior, so preventing them from operating as effectively as their foreign counterparts—in the language of economics, Britain's *human capital* was inadequate. Related studies suggested reasons, by showing persistently lower educational achievements by British schoolchildren compared with children in other countries, persistently lower participation rates in higher education, and persistently lower investment in training and retraining.

In response to these findings, the Government could argue that it was taking a variety of actions. Its 1988 Education Act had introduced a national curriculum, with attainment targets designed to ensure that all children reached and were assessed on clearly identified educational target levels. It was aiming for a large increase in the number of students in higher education by the end of the century. In the training field, it had introduced the Youth Training Scheme and similar initiatives.

(v) The Shifting Debate.

The area of debate about economic policy had thus shifted drastically over the decade. What was certain, however, was that the British economy still had some deep-seated problems, especially relating to the quality of its human capital resources. There were doubts among some of the critics that these problems could be solved by the Thatcher Government, since their solution seemed to require significant increases in public spending, something to which the Government remained ideologically opposed. Similar problems were becoming evident in parts of Britain's transport system. For example, increasing congestion in London, and to a lesser extent in other major cities, threatened to become a significant obstacle to continued economic growth in these centres. Similarly, British business began to perceive the need for much improved transport links, especially high speed rail links, with continental Europe in the approach to the Single European Market of 1992. Again, however, alleviating congestion and improving rail networks seemed to require additional public spending. Some critics pointed out that Britain provided less public investment in transport infrastructure than its major trading partners in the European Community.

Hence, after a decade during which Mrs. Thatcher's Governments had consistently given priority to attempting to reduce levels of public spending in the economy, there remained serious arguments about the balance of public and private spending, and about the extent to which the country's supply side problems could be met without significant public sector intervention.

Economic Recession, 1990–92.

The unsustainably rapid expansion of 1987–88 had come to a halt by the beginning of 1989, but for a period of some 18 months the economy continued to grow slowly. In the middle of 1990, however, the trend altered abruptly, and the economy plunged into a deep recession which lasted for nearly two years, until the middle of 1992. The recession was the second deepest since the end of the second world war, behind the recession of 1979–81. The immediate cause was a drastic collapse in business confidence, which in turn reflected the cumulative effect of the tight monetary policy and high interest rates pursued by the government since mid-1988.

The steep fall in economic activity produced the intended fall in inflation, but also reversed the decline in unemployment. After falling for five years, unemployment started to rise again at the end of 1990. Unusually, the severest effects were felt in London and the south east, traditionally the most prosperous part of the economy: the biggest job losses occurred there. Another unusual feature of the recession was the extent to which employees in professional and managerial jobs were affected: traditionally, manual workers had always been the group most affected by economic downturns.

1991 proved to be one of the most economically difficult years since the Great Depression of the early 1930s, matched in severity only by the recession of 1979–81. During the year there was a sharp fall of nearly 2·5 per cent in GNP. Manufacturing output experienced a particularly severe fall, of over 5 per cent. Unemployment rose very sharply, passing the 2·5 million mark. There were two offsetting factors. First, inflation fell sharply, to a little over 4 per cent by the end of the year. Second, the trade balance also improved (*see* **G52**). However, improvement in both inflation and the trade balance would be expected at a time of deep recession.

The recession reflected a very sharp reduction in spending by both companies and individuals. Companies reduced their investment expenditure, which fell by over 10 per cent across the economy as a whole and by 19 per cent in manufacturing. In addition, companies engaged in heavy destocking, to the tune of some £3 billion. This meant that some sales were met out of accumulated stock, instead of from current production, so contributing to the fall in output. However, the fall in consumer spending was the single biggest source of reduced economic activity. Whilst all major consumption activities shared in the fall, consumer durables were the hardest hit, with car sales being especially depressed.

The sharp fall in spending could be attributed to three main factors. First, growing unemployment was directly reducing the spending power of the people affected. Second, it was also having a more widespread indirect effect, by reducing confidence in the future. Many people who still had jobs nonetheless felt insecure, fearing that their own firms' positions might weaken. In these circumstances consumers were less willing to spend a high proportion of their incomes. Firms similarly lacked confidence in the future.

The third source of reduced spending was as a reaction to what, in retrospect, seemed to have been excessive borrowing during the later part of the 1980s. The accompanying table gives some details. The unprecedentedly large level of borrowing seemed to have two causes. First, financial liberalisation and deregulation (*see* **Part II**) had made it easier for companies and individuals to borrow large amounts of money relative to their profit or income levels. Second, many people were overoptimistic about economic prospects at the time. The government's repeated claims of an "economic miracle" contributed to a perception that rapid growth in incomes, and cuts in taxes, could be sustained indefinitely. Consequently, many companies and individuals felt able to borrow heavily, expecting to be able to repay out of anticipated future profits or earnings. When the economy began to turn down, there was a sharp reaction. Both companies and individuals attempted to reduce their levels of indebtedness quickly and substantially. As the table indicates, borrowing fell sharply in 1990, and in 1991 the trend intensified. Such "boom and bust" behaviour helped to intensify the scale of the recession.

There was a wave of company bankruptcies during 1991. Some people who had obtained large mortgages for house purchases found that they could no longer afford the repayments, and had their houses repossessed by the banks or building societies who had made the loans. The housing market generally was very depressed, with average house prices falling by 8 per cent in real terms during 1991.

It was against the background of these very unfavourable circumstances that the general election took place in April 1992. The Conservatives proposed to keep the basic income tax rate constant at 25 per cent, and also proposed to keep a single higher rate of 40 per cent. However, they proposed a new lower rate of 20 per cent on the first £2,000 of taxable income, and suggested that in future years they would aim to increase the size of the income band to which this lower rate applied, with the eventual aim that it would entirely cover the income range over which income was taxed at 25 per cent—so effectively cutting the standard rate from 25 to 20 per cent.

Whilst there were differences among the parties, all of them were faced with some common problems. Chief among these was the weak state of the public finances. In his budget statement, Mr. Lamont predicted a p.s.b.r. of £28 billion for the fiscal year 1992–93, equal to around 4·5 per cent of national income. During the election, a leading accountancy firm published a report which argued that both the Conservative and the Labour parties were proposing tax and spending plans for the next five years which could not be achieved. On the Conservative side, their proposal to reduce the p.s.b.r. to zero would require substantial tax increases, the report argued, whereas the Conservatives were promising further tax cuts. On the Labour side, the report similarly argued that tax rises would be needed to fund many of Labour's spending plans; if taxes were not raised, most of the plans would have to be abandoned. This "fiscal reality gap" in the parties' plans mainly reflected what the report saw as their unrealistic assumptions about economic growth. High rates of growth and resulting extra tax revenue would make the parties' promises easier to achieve. However, whilst each party argued that its policies would generate higher growth, past experience gave good grounds for scepticism.

Following the Conservatives' narrow victory in the election, Mr. Lamont was reappointed as Chancellor, and implemented his budget measures. In the immediate aftermath of the election there was an improvement in both consumer and business confidence, but in both cases this proved to be short-lived, and the second half of 1992 was a period of almost unrelieved economic gloom. By the end of the year it was apparent that the "fiscal reality gap" had if anything been understated.

The government had fought the election on the basis that membership of the Exchange Rate Mechanism was the centrepiece of its economic policies. During the summer, however, market sentiment grew increasingly sceptical over the government's resolve to defend the fixed exchange rate of the pound against the other ERM currencies. Faced with increasingly strong market pressure, the government had to choose between leaving the ERM and letting the pound float downwards, or raising interest rates to even higher levels, in the middle of a recession, to protect the pound. In September the decision to leave the ERM was taken. In reality there was no choice. Immediately before leaving the government had raised interest rates by 5 percentage points, to 15 per cent, in a final attempt to stem market speculation of a devaluation; but market sentiment was not affected. Since such a rise in interest rates would have been totally devastating in the context of an already deeply depressed economy, the exit from the ERM was in effect forced.

With the constraint of a fixed exchange rate

NET BORROWING

	Industrial and commercial companies *	Personal sector **
1979–84 (annual average)	11·4	−0·8
1985	15·1	2·2
1986	20·7	3·4
1987	36·8	5·0
1988	61·7	4·4
1989	73·0	2·4
1990	32·1	1·3

* As a percentage of trading profits.
** As a percentage of disposable income.

removed, the 5 point rise in interest rates was reversed, and rates were quickly reduced by a further 3 points. The whole emphasis of policy making was altered: the Government quickly abandoned its emphasis on using the fixed exchange rate as a discipline, and began to focus on the need for economic expansion. Such an abrupt change of policy produced much confusion and cynicism, but with hindsight many people argued that the commitment to maintaining a fixed value of the pound, and the accompanying high interest rate policy, had been inappropriate in the context of what, by mid-1992, had become the longest recession since the end of the Second World War.

Slow Recovery 1993–94.

1993 saw an important innovation in the management of fiscal policy. Previously the annual budget statement, usually in March, had specified the government's tax plans for the year, whilst its annual statement of public expenditure plans was made in the autumn, usually in November. It had long been recognised that this did not make much sense, since the balance of taxes and spending is a crucial object of policy-making: tax and expenditure plans should be considered together rather than separately. Accordingly, the government decided that from 1993 onwards there would be a single Unified Budget, in November of each year, which would present both tax and spending plans. The transition to this new system meant that, exceptionally, 1993 saw two full-scale budgets, the first at the traditional time in March, and the second—the first unified budget—in November.

The most urgent priority of both budgets was to find ways of reducing the scale of the public sector borrowing requirement. For the fiscal year which ended at the time of the Chancellor's March budget, the p.s.b.r. was approximately £35bn., and the projected figures for the next three fiscal years were £51bn., £45bn. and £40bn. The 1992–93 figure was approximately 5·5 per cent of national income; the 1993–94 projected figure was around 8 per cent. Such figures represented a remarkable turnabout, since as recently as 1989–90 there had been a public sector surplus. The surpluses at the end of the 1980s had been unplanned, as had the scale of the deficits since then. Such large swings in the public sector finances mainly reflected the similarly large swings in economic activity, from the unsustainably rapid expansion of 1987 and 1988 to the deep recession of 1991 and 1992. The p.s.b.r. inevitably rises in recessions and falls during booms: as economic activity declines, unemployment increases, and this both increases total public spending (because of increased spending on unemployment benefits and family support) and reduces tax revenue (because the people who become unemployed are no longer receiving income on which they pay tax). This part of the p.s.b.r. is sometimes called the "cyclical deficit", and accounted for much of the increase in the p.s.b.r. since 1990. However, most observers believed that there was also a "structural deficit"— one which would remain even if the economy were restored to more normal levels of economic activity—and it was this part of the deficit which the government was under pressure to reduce.

The March 1993 Budget.

In his March Budget the Chancellor adopted an

unexpected, and previously largely untried, strategy for trying to reduce the p.s.b.r. without doing anything to harm the prospects of recovery. He announced significant increases in taxation, but postponed many of the measures until later tax years. His idea was that the prospect of future tax increases would demonstrate the government's commitment to reducing the p.s.b.r., while doing nothing to discourage any immediate rise in spending. The Chancellor's measures involved only a small net tax increase for 1993–94, of around £0·5bn., but the planned future tax increases were forecast to add £6·7bn. of extra revenue in 1994–95 and £10·3bn. in 1995–96.

The main immediate revenue-raising measure was the decision to freeze the main income tax allowances, rather than raising them in line with inflation. This was partially offset by a modest widening of the size of the 20 per cent tax band, with further widening planned for future years, thus continuing, albeit slowly, towards the longer term objective of making 20 rather than 25 per cent the basic rate of tax.

For future tax years there were several sources of significant extra tax revenue. The most contentious was the decision to levy Value Added Tax (VAT) on household fuel and power bills. These had previously been zero rated for VAT, but the Chancellor announced that VAT would be levied at 8 per cent in 1994–95, rising to the standard 17·5 per cent from 1995–96 onwards.

During the course of 1993 the economy showed signs of recovery from the long recession. Unexpectedly, unemployment began to fall quite sharply in the early months. Although the fall tailed off during the summer, it resumed in the atutumn, so that the year as a whole saw a fall in unemployment. This had not been generally predicted. Output grew by about 2 per cent during 1993, and this growth appeared to be fairly broadly based, affecting all major sectors of the economy except construction. The company sector as a whole found its position somewhat improved during the year. Profit margins rose, and the sector reported an overall financial surplus in the first half, for the first time since 1987. The balance of payments continued to show a sizeable deficit on current account.

An encouraging feature for the government was that the inflation rate continued to fall during 1993, reaching its lowest levels for nearly 30 years. Indeed, by the year-end the prices of some goods and services were actually falling—negative inflation—and, whilst there was no prospect of falling prices generally, projections for 1994 suggested a continuation of very low inflation. This encouraged the government to continue to reduce interest rates. By the end of the year nominal interest rates were lower than at any time during the 1980s.

It was hoped that low interest rates would help to revive the housing market, which had suffered an unprecedentedly severe depression since the end of 1988. This was partly a reaction to the unsustainable boom in property markets in the mid-1980s, when prices rose at an exceptionally rapid rate. In the housing market there had been elements of a "speculative bubble" in 1987–88, with people buying in anticipation of further price increases, which itself helped to sustain continuing price rises. This bubble burst in late 1988, and prices then fell substantially. As a result many house-owners found themselves holding "negative equity", meaning that the value of their house had fallen below the size of their mortgage debt. This had caused severe problems, and some recovery in the housing market was urgently needed to alleviate the problem. In this respect, however, low inflation was if anything a disadvantage, since it prevented any significant rise in house prices, so prolonging the negative equity problem.

Despite some signs of economic recovery, Mr. Lamont's position as Chancellor was difficult. He was widely felt to have lost credibility when the pound had to leave the ERM in 1992, after he had persistently denied that this would happen and had argued that ERM membership was at the centre of the government's economic policy. His credibility was further undermined when, after the pound had left the ERM, he revealed that he had all along been doubtful about the decision to enter in the first place. For these and other reasons his political position became very weak, and in the summer he was sacked from the government. His replacement as Chancellor was Kenneth Clarke.

The November 1993 Budget.

The November budget continued the strategy of the March budget. Mr. Clarke introduced significant further increases in taxes, over and above those announced in March. Mr. Clarke's measures were partly planned for introduction in April 1994, simultaneously with many of Mr. Lamont's delayed measures.

The Chancellor repeated the March decision to freeze the main personal tax allowances. Keeping these frozen for a second successive year raised around £550m. of extra revenue. A similar approach was taken to some other tax allowances. For example, tax relief on mortgage interest payments, previously allowed at the standard rate of 25 per cent, was reduced to 20 per cent from April 1994, with the intention of a further cut to 15 per cent in 1995. This appeared to signal the intention eventually to phase out mortgage interest tax relief altogether. Similarly, tax relief on the allowance for married couples was reduced to 20 per cent from April 1994 and then 15 per cent from April 1995.

These measures effectively increased the amounts which most people would pay in income tax, but the Chancellor left the income tax rates unchanged at the standard rate of 25 per cent and the lower and higher rates of 20 per cent and 40 per cent. He also decided not to add further to the one per cent increase in employee National Insurance contributions announced in the March budget. In addition, Mr. Clarke left VAT unchanged, neither increasing the rate nor widening the base to include previously zero-rated items. With the government still facing strong criticism over the March decision to impose VAT on domestic heating bills, it was perhaps reluctant to face any additional controversy.

On the spending side, the November budget announced some unexpectedly tough decisions. The aim was to reduce public spending as a proportion of national income from 45 per cent in 1993–4 to 42·5 per cent in 1996–7. Most major areas of public spending were affected, with cuts in previously planned programmes being announced in, for example, defence, social security, and road-building, and tight grant settlements being imposed on local authorities. Significant reductions in planned future spending were also intended to be achieved by reducing the size of the "contingency reserve", the sum set aside to meet unexpected events. Within the overall squeeze on spending, the budgets for health and education both fared relatively well, though this was potentially misleading in view of the probable sharp increases in demand for both health and education services, for example because of the growth in numbers of frail elderly people and of applicants for university places.

An important source of the projected savings in public spending was the intention to impose a freeze on public sector pay bills for the next three years. The Chancellor explained that this did not mean that individual wages and salaries were to be frozen, but rather that the total pay bill was to remain fixed. Individuals could still obtain increases in pay by raising their productivity. Critics argued that in much of the public sector a "rise in productivity" really implied a fall in the quality of service—for example, through increased class sizes in schools, or fewer nurses in hospital wards. There was thus the danger of a deterioration in the quality of public services.

On a longer term basis, the budget announced a significant change in future retirement pensions. From the year 2010 onwards, there would be phased increases in the age at which women qualified for the state retirement pension, until by 2020 it had risen from the current age of 60 to 65, the age at which men become eligible. This equalisation of state retirement ages was forced on the government by the European Court, which required equality of treatment between men and women. The government chose to raise the age for women, rather than lowering the age for men, because of its fears about the future cost of financing state pensions. There had been speculation that the government might consider phasing out the state pension altogether, but the budget decisions signalled that, at least for the moment, it had decided against this idea, though it continued to argue that people should make provisions for occupational or personal pensions rather than relying mainly on the state pension.

1994.

During 1994 many of the underlying trends in the economy were favourable. National income grew rapidly, by nearly 4 per cent over the year. Since the strongest growth was in exporting sectors, the balance of payments improved. At the same time inflation fell to its lowest level for a generation, and the public sector borrowing requirement began to fall sharply, helped both by the tax increases and by the fast growth rate. Many economists argued that the economic recovery was more soundly based than at comparable stages of previous economic cycles, and the government persistently argued that its policies had laid the foundation for steady, sustainable growth in the coming years.

However, the perceptions of many ordinary people appeared to be very different. The government remained deeply unpopular throughout the year, and a large part of the reason for this was undoubtedly that many voters did not feel that their own individual prospects were improving. This was partly reflected in the overall economic position. Although the economy as a whole grew fast during the year, consumer spending grew more sluggishly. This was desirable for the general health of the economy – since it allowed more goods to be exported, and prevented a large growth in imports – but it helped to explain consumers' scepticism about claims of economic recovery. The government's unpopularity was also a reflection of the considerable uncertainty and insecurity which afflicted many individuals and families. This left many people reluctant to contemplate extra spending. The uncertainty was primarily the result of the steep recession experienced during 1990–92. Many people had lost what they had previously considered to be secure jobs during that period, and had found it difficult or impossible to obtain new jobs. This partly reflected a trend, among both private and public sector employers, towards reducing the size of their 'core' labour forces, and contracting out some activities which had previously been done in-house. People looking for new jobs consequently found increased difficulty in obtaining the sort of employment they had previously regarded as normal; many instead found themselves taking temporary jobs, or working on a self-employed basis. The consequent insecurity and uncertainty helped to dampen consumer spending. A third dampening influence was the effect of the tax increases stemming from the decisions in the 1993 Budgets. These meant that after-tax incomes grew much less rapidly than pre-tax incomes.

Some economists argued that the continued depressed state of the housing market was a further contributory factor to sluggish consumer spending. This meant that the problem of 'negative equity' which had emerged at the start of the recession was still significant four years later.

The 1994 Budget.

All these influences combined to produce a conflict for the Chancellor between economic and political considerations in deciding on his Budget strategy. Politically, he was under pressure to help consumers, perhaps by cutting taxes, or, more realistically, by cancelling some of the tax increases planned for 1995 and announced in his 1993 Budget. However, economic considerations if anything pointed in the opposite direction, since national income was growing at an unsustainably rapid rate, and further increases in the growth rate triggered by consumer spending would risk a resurgence of inflation.

Faced with these conflicting pressures, the Chancellor chose to emphasise economic rather than political considerations, though cynics pointed out that he would be less likely to do this in the following year, when the next general election would be approaching. His main decision was to confirm virtually all the previously announced tax increases planned for April 1995, including reductions in tax relief on mortgage interest payments and in the size of the married person's allowance, and – more controversially – the second stage of the imposition of VAT on fuel. The total tax increases already planned for 1995 amounted to around £6·5 bn, and the overall effect of the Chancellor's

measures was to reduce this planned increase by approximately £1 bn, to £5·5 bn. This small reduction in the planned increases was mainly the result of increased tax allowances to people over retiring age, and of the decision to raise the band of income taxed at the lower, 20%, rate by more than enough to compensate for inflation. The latter decision was designed to help people on low incomes.

Other detailed tax changes included uprating of duties on tobacco and petrol, but not on alcohol. Higher petrol duties reflected a continuation of policy in previous Budgets of raising duty by more than the inflation rate in order to raise the real cost of private motoring. The freeze on alcohol duty reflected the increased difficulties of domestic producers and traders in the face of imports from the European Union, with most other member states having lower rates of duty. So far as income tax was concerned, the Chancellor left all the tax rates unchanged, but raised the main allowances in line with inflation, following two years in which the allowances had been frozen.

The Chancellor raised the main welfare benefits, including the state retirement pension, unemployment benefit and child benefit, in line with inflation. Additional welfare spending was announced in an attempt to offset the effect on low income groups of the second stage VAT increase on fuel. Measures included extra help with home insulation for people reliant on state benefits, and higher cold-weather payments. Conversely, the government tightened and restricted welfare spending on housing-related issues. Housing benefit payments were restricted for people living in unduly expensive properties. More controversially, the government also announced proposals to remove or restrict the payment of mortgage interest for people becoming ill, or unemployed. In future, people taking out new mortgages would be expected to insure themselves privately against such risks. This proposal was widely criticised. The main objection was that it would be difficult to obtain such insurance, and indeed that for some groups who were relatively prone to unemployment, it would be impossible, or at least prohibitively expensive. Critics argued that this would further damage confidence in an already very weak housing market.

Calculations of the overall effect of the tax and benefit proposals suggested that about 85 per cent of all households would be made worse off in 1995 by the Budget measures. On average they would reduce disposable income by about 1 per cent. The losses would be bigger for the poorest households, and smaller for the richest.

The most controversial proposal in the Budget was the decision to continue with the previously announced plan to raise VAT on fuel from the 8½ per cent rate introduced in April 1994 to the full 17 per cent in April 1995. The plan to tax fuel had been widely criticised when first proposed, on the grounds that it hurt that poorest section of the community disproportionately. These arguments all resurfaced after the Chancellor's Budget speech, and in a subsequent debate, Parliament voted against the second stage increase. In the face of this, Mr. Clarke withdrew the proposal, and recouped the lost tax revenue with higher excise duties.

As well as tax and welfare measures, the Budget also laid out the government's public spending plans. Compared with previous plans, the Budget announced a cut of £28 bn in total public spending over the next three years. This was partly because lower than predicted inflation meant that public sector costs had risen more slowly than expected. It also resulted from unexpected rapid economic growth, which had reduced unemployment by more than expected, with a consequent fall in the amount of public spending on unemployment and related welfare benefits. Within overall public spending, transport spending was reduced particularly sharply. This reflected two things. First, the government had partially reversed its previous emphasis on road-building, and a number of planned new roads were either postponed or cancelled altogether. Second, the government planned that a bigger proportion of capital spending projects would be financed privately rather than publicly.

Both of these points represented policy shifts by the government. The cut-back in road building partly reflected a simple desire to reduce spending, but it also resulted from what seemed to be a change of policy, in the light of research findings which suggested that road building did little or nothing to ease traffic congestion (because new roads tended to increase car usage). Also influencing the government's change of emphasis was the effect of research on the effects of traffic congestion on public health, especially through air pollution in city centres. Critics argued that the government had only partly accepted the implications of such research findings: it was cutting the roads programme, but not doing enough to encourage better quality public transport as a viable alternative to private cars.

The emphasis on private funding for publicly planned capital projects represented an increased priority for a policy first launched two years ago. Though the main emphasis was expected to be on transport projects, the Chancellor mentioned other areas, including the National Health Service, prisons, and universities. However, some critics argued that it was not clear whether policy was intended to improve public services by attracting additional finance, or whether instead it was simply a means of reducing the government's share of an unchanged total.

The effects of the continued policy of tax increases combined with the squeeze on public spending was a significant strengthening of the public sector finances. The public sector borrowing requirement, which had been £45 bn in the fiscal year 1993–4, was expected to have fallen to around £34 bn by the end of the 1994–5 tax year. This represented around 5 per cent of national income, as against 7 per cent in 1993–4. The Chancellor's announced tax and spending plans for the following three years implied further sharp falls, with the borrowing requirement being entirely eliminated by the end of the 1997–8 tax year, followed by surpluses thereafter. This in turn implied sharp falls in the ratio of accumulated public debt to national income. This ratio had fallen almost continuously during the 1970s and 1980s – from nearly 75 per cent in 1970 to under 30 per cent by 1990 – but had risen sharply, to over 45 per cent, during the recession. The Chancellor's projections envisaged a renewed fall over the coming years. In practice, however, there was room for doubt as to whether this would actually occur. The projections assumed unchanged policies, but most people anticipated that in his next Budget the Chancellor would be under irresistible political pressure to reduce taxes, whether or not the underlying economic situation justified such cuts.

Apart from taxes, spending, and borrowing, the Budget also included a package of measures designed to provide incentives to unemployed individuals to take jobs, and to employers to take them on. For example, employers taking on individuals who had previously been unemployed for two years or more were to receive a subsidy, and also a year's exemption from national insurance payments with respect to the new employees. The Budget also extended the range of welfare benefits available, on either a temporary or permanent basis, to people moving from unemployment into low-income jobs. The aim here was to make such moves worthwhile, by raising the overall income from being in work relative to being employed, while simultaneously helping public sector finances (since welfare benefits to people in work generally cost less than unemployment benefits).

Swings in Public Sector Finances.

By the time the 1994 Budget measures came fully into effect, in April 1995, the government would have completed a two-year phase of policy, starting with the April 1993 Budget, in which it had introduced the largest ever set of tax rises, apart from war-time emergencies. This had severely damaged the government's political standing, in the light of promise in the 1992 general election that it would not raise taxes. It was economically necessary in the light of the very large budget deficit which had emerged by 1992–3. This in turn had resulted partly from the recession, but in addition it had been exacerbated by the tax-cutting policies of the late 1980s. Over an eight-year period from 1987, the government had first lowered, and then raised, taxes by substantial amounts. Simultaneously the balance between tax revenue and spending had swung from a surplus to a huge deficit, before starting to strengthen again.

Such large swings severely dented the credibility of the government's claim that it was committed to 'sound finance'. There was also the question of whether or not the country would see a repeat of the process in future years. The fear was that the government would be tempted to cut taxes by unsustainably large amounts later in 1995, or in 1996, in the hope of winning the next general election. At the same time there was the apparent paradox that after a two-year period of unprecedented tax rises – the overall effect of which was that typical individuals and families were paying a higher share of their incomes in overall taxes than at nearly any time over the previous 20 years – it was simultaneously necessary to make deep cuts in public spending, which many people feared would severely damage essential public services. For example, there were projections that the cut in real spending on schools would cause sharp increases in class sizes, which in turn might damage the educational prospects of a generation of school children. The coexistence of deep cuts in public spending and large tax increases was mainly explained by continued high levels of unemployment, which structurally weakened public finances through lost tax revenue and increase welfare benefits. In the face of such continuing problems of unemployment, taxes, and spending, it was perhaps not surprising that the government's repeated claims of strong, and rapidly improving, economic situation were apparently unconvincing to most of the voters.

Prospects for Economic Growth.

The post-war economy has seen boom-periods and recessions, but generally speaking, the UK has tended to lag behind most other industrial countries in terms of economic growth (see **G14**). During this period various governments have adopted policies aimed at stimulating economic growth. Prior to Mrs Thatcher's Conservative government, which came to power in 1979, most of these measures were based on demand management policies. An early example of such policies was the National Plan introduced by the Labour government in 1965. The plan aimed for a growth rate of 4 per cent per annum but was abandoned after only a year when the economy was faced with a balance of payments crisis. Most policies aimed at expanding growth through stimulating demand have failed because of supply-side bottlenecks. The Conservative government under Mrs. Thatcher exhibited a major reversal in political judgement by persuading voters to reward government for long-term supply-side economic policies, although, given the problems encountered in the period 1989–92, the evidence that the UK has undergone a "supply-side" revolution under Mrs. Thatcher's stewardship is mixed.

(i) Pressures on the Industrial Sector.

In common with other industrialised economies, the UK has seen a major shift in the structure or composition of the economy. This has involved a significant reduction in its productive base, specifically the manufacturing sector, and a greater dependence on the service sector. This process is known as de-industrialisation. To illustrate the shift it is useful to look at the structure of the labour force. Between 1960 and 1994 the total number of employees in employment in the UK fell by about 2 per cent. Within this total, employment in manufacturing halved. This larger non-industrial sector imposes extra demands on industrial production. Capital goods for investment in services have to be provided from the output of the industrial sector, whilst industrial production is also needed for consumers employed in the services and elsewhere. Thus less is left over for investment in industry itself and for industrial exports. This has meant an inadequate growth of industrial capacity. Consequently when governments have attempted to stimulate the economy, bottlenecks quickly develop and imports of consumer goods increase rapidly. The result is balance of payments difficulties, which are only partially alleviated by increasing exports of services like insurance, and force the government into taking deflationary action. This vicious circle could only be broken by an upsurge in industrial investment, which until the last few years was prevented by declining profitability, or by a healthy growth of net exports of services which would both alleviate the balance of payments constraint and provide the funds for investment.

Some commentators have argued that the problem was a direct result of the growth in public sector employment in the 1960s and 1970s. This had to be paid for either by workers or private employers, and trade unions made sure that it was the employers; if, for example, income tax was raised, this was passed on in successful wage demands. The result was declining profitability. This analysis is at best speculative. It is not, for example, at all evident that public sector employment grew nearly as rapidly as implied. In certain activities such as local government there was a very rapid growth, but overall the ratio of general government to total employment increased only modestly—from 15 per cent in 1961 to 19·6 per cent in 1974. The ratio was 17 per cent in 1993. There was a rather more significant increase in public sector current spending on goods and services as a percentage of GDP; from 16·4 per cent in 1960 to 21·8 per cent by 1975 In 1989 it was 19·2, but because of the recession had risen to 21·2 by 1991 and was still high in 1993 at 23·6 per cent. It was argued that such figures understated the true change. They exclude transfers from people who produce to those who do not, such as pensioners, though this may be justifiable since such *transfer payments* do not represent final claims on resources by the public sector. It was argued that the claim of the public sector on output which could be sold increased by almost 50 per cent between 1961 and 1974 thus reducing the resources available for industrial investment. The present Conservative government, subscribing to this view, has been committed to reducing the share of public expenditure in GDP, believing that this is necessary to reduce taxes on both persons and companies. This, they believe, would restore work and profit incentives, although there is scant evidence in support of this view. Between 1979 and 1986 the share of public expenditure fell only slightly, mainly because of much greater demands on the social security system; thereafter some progress was made largely due to rapid economic growth only for this progress to be halted by the recession at the end of the decade. If the arguments mentioned above regain popularity then it is possible that the whole method of providing health care, education *etc.* will be called into question. This would be particularly sad if, as some of the points made above suggest, it is based on fallacious economic reasoning.

This is only one school of thought among those economists who are concerned that Britain is becoming *de-industrialised*. Another group of economists, also concerned with de-industrialisation, rejects the argument that it is the consequence of the expansion of the public sector. They stress the inability of British industry to maintain its share of world trade in manufactures, a share which fell in volume terms from almost 9 per cent in the early 1970s to less than 6 per cent by the mid-1980s, though there was subsequently a slight recovery to around 6 per cent. The forces causing this failure cannot be arrested by a once-and-for-all devaluation. On the demand side the conditions for an expansion of British exports are unfavourable; an important reason for this being that Britain tends to specialise in products for which demand tends to rise relatively slowly in response to increases in the standard of living. On the supply side, it is argued, there is a vicious circle of declining market share, declining profits and investment and declining competitive power. Some members of this group then point to the need for demand expansion, in order to stimulate output growth, and ultimately, higher productivity growth, which is the key to international competitiveness. The problem in Britain, though, appears to be in stimulating supply in an effective manner.

Yet other economists have argued that Britain's industrial structure, similar as it is to that of Germany, cannot account for our problems. Rather it is that Britain has narrowed the technological gap between herself and the US—for a long time the technical leader—more slowly than have her major competitors, thus failing to exploit the opportunities for unusually rapid growth. Recently particular stress has been put on Britain's supply-side faults leading to non-price competitiveness. Particularly emphasised are flaws in education and training at all levels—often dubbed as low quality-low skill equilibrium. By low quality is meant low specification. Too many British firms, it is argued, have got used to operating with relatively unskilled labour, and as a consequence tend to operate at the low specification end of product ranges. Therefore they can compete only on cost, and as is shown elsewhere Britain's record in this respect is not impressive. Even more worrying is that it is not countries like Germany and France with whom in the medium term we shall have to compete on cost, it is low wage emergent economies like Korea and Thailand. Countries which can move to the high end of a product range will find that their sales are much less dependent on price.

Whatever disagreement exists about causes, there is basic agreement that Britain does have an industrial problem. Not least is the question of which new activities—be they in industry and services—will replace those activities in which we were once strong but no longer are. A 1985 House of Lords Select Committee documented the decline of manufacturing, accelerated as it was by the general recession after 1979. To many it was too messianic in tone, both in regard to its view of the inevitability of manufacturing's demise and the lack of new activities to take its place. Be that as it may, it is worrying that Britain still lags in fundamental international competitiveness.

(ii) The National Enterprise Board.

In 1975 the Labour Government introduced an *Industry Act*. Underlying this Act was the feeling that private enterprise, on its own, had not done enough to stimulate a high rate of growth. The Act aimed to remedy this by setting up the *National Enterprise Board*. Its functions were: to assist the establishment, development or maintenance of any industrial enterprise or industry, to extend public ownership into profitable areas of manufacturing, to promote industrial democracy in undertakings controlled by it, and to hold and manage the securities of any other property in public ownership. The Board's borrowing capability was very modest in relation to the market value of the share capital of major British firms. Funds for aid could also be dispensed by the Board. Both the Minister for Industry and the Treasury had a responsibility to ensure that the Board earned an "adequate" return on capital employed.

Critics argued both that the Act was doctrinaire socialism and that it was not proved that such state intervention would have more favourable effects than the workings of free private enterprise.

Even before the NEB was effectively operational, state acquisitions in the private sector had proceeded apace. Normally the Government had provided help to ailing companies on condition of taking a shareholding, under the provisions of the Conservatives' 1972 Industry Act. State holdings in eight companies were handed over to the NEB at its inception. These companies were British Leyland, Rolls-Royce, Cambridge Instruments, Ferranti, Herbert, Brown-Boveri-Kent, Dunford and Elliott, and ICL. The NEB acquired shareholdings in another twenty-eight companies by early 1978.

When the Conservatives won the 1979 General Election there was some expectation that the National Enterprise Board would be abolished. Though this did not happen immediately, it soon became plain that the new Government did not intend to allow the Board any role other than that of overseeing a limited number of companies in need of temporary assistance. Subsequently the NEB was merged with the National Research and Development Corporation to form the British Technology Group. BTG's aims are noticeably different from those of the NEB. The aim of BTG, which has been privatized, is primarily to promote the development of new technology, often from the universities, into important commercial products. In order to assist the transfer of technology BTG can also provide finance, either through equity or project finance. BTG administers 10,000 patents covering about 1,500 technologies. Most of BTG's income is provided by its own licensing activities. In 1993–94 the Group's total revenue exceeded £29m.

(iii) Privatisation.

Soon after taking office, the Conservative Government announced its intention to sell off a portion of official holdings in several sectors—British Airways, British Aerospace, shipbuilding, freight and British Petroleum. The Government believed that reform of the nationalised industries was a key element in providing the framework for economic recovery, arguing that exposure to market forces through privatisation and competition was the best way to improve industrial performance. Since 1979, 50 major state-owned companies have been privatised, yielding the Government about £55 billion in extra revenue. Companies that have been privatised include British Gas, British Telecom, British Steel Corporation, Cable and Wireless, the National Freight Consortium, Amersham International, The Rover Group, Jaguar, Enterprise Oil, Britoil, Associated British Ports, Rolls-Royce, Royal Ordnance, BAA, nearly all the National Bus Company subsidiaries, the British Shipbuilders' warship-building yards, the regional water and sewage companies in England and Wales, and, most recently, the electricity distribution and generating industries, as well as British Coal. Plans for future privatisations include British Rail. The future of the Post Office is under review. Clearly those industries most easily sold have already been returned to private ownership (albeit often at a heavily discounted price); the remaining public sector industries are those where the case for privatisation is least valid, and which will be most difficult to sell.

One major effect of the privatisation program has been an increase in share ownership. In 1979 only 7 per cent of the population were shareholders; by 1993 this had increased to 24 per cent, although many individuals hold shares in only one or two companies. There has also been a fashion for privatisation abroad, but the process has been more intense in Britain than in any other country. Going alongside this programme, were programmes of "liberalisation" and of "franchising". By the former is meant the policy of allowing and encouraging competition in previously uncompetitive or regulated markets—for example, telecommunications and road passenger transport. By the latter is meant the process by which state establishments (*e.g.* hospitals) "put out" certain functions, which had previously been performed "in-house", to private companies (*e.g.* catering). This spread of sub-contracting, however, extends far beyond publicly provided activities.

(iv) An Approach to Industrial Strategy.

In 1975 a White Paper, entitled *An Approach to Industrial Strategy*, set out the Government's general views on planning for growth. The strategy was based on the fact that despite Britain's overall poor performance, some sectors had done very well. There was therefore a need to identify specific problems which had held back particular industries as well as a need to identify general problems. Some 40 sectoral working parties were established under the auspices of the National Economic Development Council, and were composed of representatives of management, workers and the Government. Their task was to analyse their own industry in detail and to agree a programme of action designed to improve competitive performance, and to make Britain a high-output, high-wage economy. Specifically they were asked to consider the following: how to get more out of existing investment and manpower in order to improve productivity; how to increase the level and quality of investment; how to improve non-price competitiveness; how to ensure that their sectors concentrate on the "correct" export markets; how to provide a sufficient supply of skilled workers. In 1978 the working parties presented their first reports. The planning provisions of the 1975 Industry Act were abandoned by the Conservative Government, but the NEDC Sector Working Parties continue to operate, albeit under a series of different titles. It is difficult to quantify their precise effects upon sectoral performance.

One area where the 1975 Industry Act had practical consequences was in the introduction of schemes of financial assistance to industry. The assistance was directed towards increases in productivity (*e.g.* by re-equipment), or to increases in product relevance to export markets, to improving non-price competitiveness and to improving marketing. In addition there was an export market entry guarantee scheme to cover the risks of entering new markets. Nevertheless, the crucial question re-

mained not just whether the performance of particular sectors could be improved, but whether it could be ensured that Britain produced the right mix of products to meet the threats to employment and to our trading balance of both technological change and foreign competition. On these issues, the present Government believes firmly that if Britain is to succeed, the impetus is most likely to come from risk-taking individual entrepreneurs and companies. In January 1988 the Department of Trade and Industry launched its Enterprise Initiative specifically to help small and medium-sized businesses. A total of £50 million was allocated in 1993–94 to help small independent businesses with consultancy costs for advice on design, quality, manufacturing systems, business planning, and financial and information systems. In Scotland and Wales the Enterprise Initiative is operated by the respective development agencies, and assistance is offered to firms with fewer than 500 employees. In the English assisted areas and Urban Programme Areas, two-thirds of project costs are provided; elsewhere 50 per cent. A 1994 White Paper on Competitiveness announced a series of measures to help small firms.

(v) British Oil Production.

The discovery of oil and gas in the UK Continental Shelf in the 1960s had major implications for the UK's long-term growth prospects. Arguably the main benefit has been to "cushion" our trade deficit as revenues from oil exports and a reduced dependence on imported oil have helped to offset a gradual deterioration in the balance on non-oil goods. The other side of the coin, however, is that after the first oil price shock in 1973 many oil producers' exchange rates became overvalued as the price of oil rose and also more volatile as exchange rates were influenced by expectations of future oil price movements. The UK, along with other oil producing nations suffered as a higher exchange rate eroded competitiveness and exacerbated the deterioration in the trade balance. Linked to this is the idea of Dutch disease which suggests that the loss of competitiveness resulting from petrocurrency status accelerates the process of de-industrialisation. Problems such as these were specific to the oil producing countries, but the repercussions of two oil price hikes, in 1973 and 1979, were felt world-wide.

The UK became self-sufficient in oil in 1981 and production of both gas and oil reached a peak in 1985 and 1986. In 1993 Britain was the world's tenth largest producer of crude oil and natural gas liquids, with an output of nearly 275,000 tonnes a day. The UK will remain self-sufficient for much of this decade. However, the viability of producing oil from offshore reserves depends on many economic factors, not least of which is the price of oil itself. Following the oil price collapse in 1986, the prospects for future production weakened, since the incentive for further exploration and development diminished. The subsequent recovery of prices in 1987 diminished but did not fully allay the concern, although the upturn in the world oil market following Iraq's invasion of Kuwait in August 1990 produced the first conclusive evidence of a recovery in Britain's oil exploration industry.

Meanwhile the Government tried to ensure that the state got a substantial share of the returns from offshore oil extraction. A major worry was the large degree of foreign ownership of the oil companies involved in the operations. A specific oil tax was initially proposed in the 1974 Oil Taxation Bill and implemented, in a modified form, in the 1975 Oil Taxation Act. Petroleum Revenue Tax (PRT) was introduced at 45 per cent and royalties at 12·5 per cent. Corporation tax was to be deducted from the residue at the standard rate. It was envisaged that this would allow the oil companies an adequate return on capital. A ring fence around a company's oil extraction activities prohibited losses made outside the North Sea being used to offset North Sea profits for corporation tax purposes. Concern had been expressed that such a tax system would discourage exploitation of the "marginal fields", that is the smaller oil-fields which might not justify the huge initial expenditure needed to make them productive. Several safeguards were, therefore, proposed. No petroleum revenue tax would be levied until a field had earned back 135 per cent of its capital outlay. Fields returning less than 30 per cent on investment after paying p.r.t. would have the tax refunded. There was also to be discretionary provision to return all or part of the 12½ per cent royalties. The Government reiterated its intention to press for 51 per cent state participation in the oil-fields, which it proceeded to do through the agency of the British National Oil Corporation.

Since its inception in 1975 the UK offshore taxation system has undergone many modifications. In August 1978 the rate of PRT was increased to 30 per cent while the PRT capital uplift was raised to 175 per cent from 135 per cent. In 1980 the PRT rate was once again increased, this time to 70 per cent. In March 1981, a fourth tax—Supplementary Petroleum Duty (SPD)—was introduced and was charged at 20 per cent of the landed value of gross revenues less an allowance equivalent to 0·5 million tonnes of oil per six-month period. In March 1982 SPD was replaced by Advance Petroleum Revenue Tax, identical to SPD save for the time of charges. The taxation system was becoming increasingly onerous for the oil companies and, as concern grew about the viability of developing marginal North Sea fields, modifications to the tax regime had to be made to ease the fiscal burden on oil. The main change was that a distinction was made between the tax treatment of the established Southern Basin fields and newer higher cost fields granted development approval after April 1982. For the latter group the PRT allowance was doubled to 1 million tonnes and royalty payments were abolished. In addition, Advance PRT was abolished from January 1987. In March 1988 the PRT allowance for the more profitable Southern Basin fields was reduced to 100,000 tonnes. In the Spring 1993 Budget the Chancellor announced his intention to reduce PRT from 75 per cent to 50 per cent for existing oilfields, and to eliminate it altogether for new fields. At the same time costs of new exploration and development would cease to be capable of being offset against tax.

In March 1978 the Government published a White Paper, *The Challenge of North Sea Oil*. In this it was estimated that by the mid-1980s North Sea Oil would increase national income by £6 billion per year and improve the balance of payments to the tune of £8 billion per year. Perhaps a more crucial aspect of the White Paper was that the annual benefit to government revenue was expected to be £4 billion. This estimate has, however, on occasions proved wide of the mark, largely because of fluctuations in the exchange rate and in the dollar price of oil. Revenues tailed off at the end of the decade, in part because of the disruption to North Sea activity caused by the Piper Alpha disaster in 1989. They were £2·0 billion in 1990–91 and turned negative in 1992.

The most crucial issue was how the extra revenue was to be used. The 1978 White Paper designated four priorities: more resources for industrial investment; funds for energy conservation and new energy investment; the reduction of the level of personal taxation; the improvement of certain essential services. It was clear that the Government believed that North Sea oil provided it with an opportunity to stimulate sustained growth, and the first two of the four priorities were obviously designed with this in mind. However, the election of a Conservative Government in 1979 signalled a change of emphasis.

In the 1980 Budget it was implied that henceforth the oil tax revenue would be used almost exclusively to reduce the size of the public sector borrowing requirement and the scale of personal and corporate taxation. In the previous year proposals were published to reduce BNOC's role. Its preferential position in future licensing was ended, as were special access to official finance through the National Oil Account and its statutory role as adviser to the Government. Effectively its role in exploration and production activities was abandoned. In early 1985, the Conservative government announced that BNOC was to be abolished, and that oil prices would be much more closely related to market developments. The authorities' other main energy worry was the fast rate of extraction of North Sea gas.

(vi) A Productivity Breakthrough?

The main cause of our poor relative growth rates in this post-war period was lower productivity increases than achieved in other countries: and as in other countries this growth slowed down in the 1970s. Between 1963 and 1973, the average annual growth of output per person employed was 2·9 per cent in the whole economy and 4·2 per cent in manufacturing. Productivity fell between 1973 and 1975, in the wake of the first oil-price shock. Between then and 1979, it grew at an average of 2·5 per cent per annum in the economy as a whole and at 2·1 per cent in manufacturing. Indeed but for North Sea oil, this performance would have looked even worse. Capital scrapping appears to have been an important contributory factor. With the second oil crisis and recession productivity declined in 1980. Between 1980 and 1989 productivity growth averaged 5·2 per cent in manufacturing and 2·3 per cent in the economy as a whole. In the recession after 1989 productivity growth slowed. However in 1992 it resumed a healthy growth, particularly in manufacturing. In 1992 productivity growth in manufacturing was 4·5 per cent and in 1993 was 4·2 per cent. The corresponding figures for the whole economy were 2·3 per cent and 3·1 per cent.

Many commentators have described the experience of the mid-1980s as a "productivity breakthrough". Certainly the U.K.'s performance improved significantly relative to that of its major competitors, at least in manufacturing. A number of possible explanations have been advanced for this. An initial boost was undoubtedly given by a very rapid shedding of labour. Some argue that much of the improvement was a statistical illusion caused by the "batting average effect". By this they mean the following. In the early 1980s there were what were then record levels of company liquidations and bankruptcies. If it was generally the least efficient companies which went to the wall, then their departure from the scene would have increased average measured productivity, without the performance of the surviving companies necessarily having improved one jot. However this explanation is probably a minor one, since it was by no means only weak firms which were driven out of business. The impact of new technology is cited by some writers as significant. Again it is probably only a minor factor, since other countries should have been affected in the same way, and yet the majority of them showed little improvement in productivity performance as compared to the 1970s. Almost certainly the major explanations lie in the changed attitudes and practices of management, unions and individual workers. People were frightened as they had never been before by the recession of the early 1980s. What is more the Government's anti-inflationary stance appeared credible—after all who had believed that any government would allow unemployment to rise so rapidly to 3 million? As a consequence management became more determined than ever before to achieve cost-cutting, flexible use of labour and efficiency. Workers and unions were more compliant, not least in the case of the unions because of massively reduced bargaining power.

Which mixture of explanations is correct is important for deciding whether the productivity breakthrough of the mid-1980s was a once-and-for-all phenomenon or whether it presaged a longer run improvement in our productivity performance. Despite evidence that working practices and management techniques continue to improve, an abrupt deterioration in productivity performance as the economy entered the difficult period 1989–91 has made many commentators more sceptical about the durability of the improved productivity performance earlier in the decade. Clearly, some of the deterioration in 1989–91 was cyclical; a more conclusive test will be the UK's productivity performance as the economy emerges from recession.

On balance, it seems reasonable to hope for a return to the productivity performance of the late 1960s. Changed management and worker attitudes should be a continuing source of productivity gain if these more realistic attitudes enable them to meet and react more effectively than formerly to the rapid pace of change in the modern industrial world.

Inflation.

(i) Wages and Prices.

Between 1971 and 1994 inflation averaged about 10 per cent a year. By 1994 prices were almost 600 per cent higher than they had been in 1971. Only a

RETAIL PRICES, AVERAGE EARNINGS,
REAL AVERAGE EARNINGS AND REAL
DISPOSABLE INCOMES
1971 = 100

	Retail prices	Average earnings	Real average earnings	Real disposable incomes
1971	100·0	100·0	100·0	100·0
1972	107·5	111·7	103·9	108·4
1973	117·3	127·2	108·4	115·4
1974	136·0	150·0	110·3	114·4
1975	168·7	189·7	112·4	114·9
1976	196·7	220·5	112·1	114·5
1977	228·0	240·3	105·4	112·0
1978	246·7	271·2	109·9	120·6
1979	279·9	313·1	111·9	127·6
1980	330·4	378·2	114·5	129·6
1981	369·6	426·5	115·4	128·7
1982	401·4	466·7	116·3	128·0
1983	419·6	506·2	120·6	131·4
1984	440·7	536·5	121·7	134·8
1985	467·3	581·9	124·5	138·5
1986	483·2	627·9	129·9	144·9
1987	503·3	676·7	134·5	150·0
1988	528·0	735·5	139·3	158·6
1989	569·2	802·4	141·0	167·2
1990	622·9	880·4	141·3	172·0
1991	659·5	950·8	144·2	171·9
1992	684·2	1,008·9	147·5	176·6
1993	695·1	1,042·4	150·0	176·2
1994	718·7	1,098·7	153·1	176·8

part of this increase can be attributed to an increase in import prices. During the same period average earnings rose by 12 per cent a year whilst, due to a poor productivity performance, unit labour costs (wages and salaries per unit of output) rose by over 10 per cent per annum. These increased costs were passed on to the consumer in the form of higher prices. Thus real earnings only increased by just under 2 per cent a year. The table shows annual average prices, earnings, real earnings and also real disposable income (*i.e.* the purchasing power of total personal incomes after income tax), all as indices based on 1971 = 100.

(ii) The Attack on Inflation.

Between the late 1960s and the mid 1970s there was growing price and earnings inflation. The reasons for this were complex, but significant were the growing aspirations for higher living standards expressed by workers in high pay claims. Employers were able to absorb only a fraction of their higher labour costs in their profit margins and passed the remainder on in higher prices, which caused the workers to make even greater pay demands. This behaviour was to a degree "validated" by relatively slack demand management policies. There were signs that governments in a number of Western countries were becoming increasingly concerned by such developments, a concern which became critical as they faced the inflationary implications of the oil crisis of 1973. The table shows a major spurt in inflation in 1974.

1975 saw an even higher rate of inflation. Average weekly earnings rose by over 26 per cent. Productivity fell and prices rose by about 24 per cent. Import prices made a smaller contribution to inflation than in the previous two years. Real earnings rose by 2 per cent, implying a further drop in the share of profits in domestic income. But through 1975 inflation moderated. Average earnings increases

started to slow down in the second quarter, and wholesale and retail prices followed with a lag. By the third quarter they were all increasing at about 15 per cent. The slowdown of average earnings in fact started before the imposition of the £6 incomes policy limit, and it has been suggested that this was caused by growing unemployment. Such an effect was, however, small compared with the direct impact of the £6 rule.

Domestic inflation moderated still further in 1976, retail prices being 16½ per cent higher than in 1975. The main contributor to this was the de-celeration in the rate of increase in labour costs. Average weekly earnings were 16 per cent higher than in 1975. Real earnings were therefore slightly lower than in the previous year, implying some recovery in the share of profits in domestic income. By far the largest influence on the de-celeration of wage inflation was the voluntary incomes policy, first the £6 limit and from August its successor, which aimed at a 4½ per cent increase in basic wage rates. However, in the last few months of the year price inflation showed a small increase. This upturn is explained by the sharp fall in the value of the pound during the year putting up the cost of raw materials and fuel purchased by British industry.

Retail prices were nearly 16 per cent higher in 1977 than in 1976, whilst earnings were less than 10 per cent higher. Real earnings, therefore, fell by nearly 6 per cent, and this meant some further recovery in the share of profits in national income. Real disposable income fell by the smaller amount of 2½ per cent, because of the reduction of taxes in the April and October budgets. Productivity improved hardly at all during the year, and so the earnings increases meant a similar increase in labour costs per unit of output, these costs feeding through to prices.

There was a considerable contrast between the two halves of 1977. In the year to July 1977 prices rose at the rate of about 17 per cent, inflation being exacerbated by the depreciation of sterling in 1976, and further fed by the delayed impact of earnings increases of 14 per cent during Stage I of incomes policy, which ended in July 1976. Since by early 1977 Stage II of the incomes policy was holding earnings increases down to 10 per cent, real personal income was badly squeezed in the first half of the year. These lower increases in earnings together with the appreciation of sterling had their effect on retail prices in the second half of the year. By early 1978 price inflation had fallen below 10 per cent. At the same time earnings had begun to increase at the rate of about 15 per cent per annum. This, together with the 1977 tax cuts, meant an appreciable recovery in real personal income.

Thus by early 1978 price inflation had fallen back into single figures, and it continued to fall steadily until the middle of the year. From then inflation started to increase again, so that by the spring of 1979 was going back into double figures.

Stage III of the incomes policy, which ran for the year ending July 1978, was looser than Stage II, and was accompanied by earnings increases of nearly 15 per cent. This was beginning to feed through to prices by the middle of 1978, and was the cause of the acceleration of inflation. By early 1979 earnings were rising at an annual rate of 14 per cent, and this despite continued low rates of increase of import prices and a renewed squeeze on profits, implied a likely further increase in price inflation. Real personal disposable income continued its recovery of late 1977. With earnings rising faster than prices and with only a modest increase in direct tax payments, r.p.d.i. improved substantially during 1978.

In early 1979, then, price inflation was starting to increase slowly but was still within single figures (at annual rates). Two important wage

RISE IN CONSUMER PRICES, PER CENT PER ANNUM

	1959–89	1989–90	1990–91	1991–92	1992–93	1993–94
U.S.	4·9	5·4	4·3	3·1	2·9	2·6
Japan . . .	5·6	3·0	3·3	1·7	1·3	0·6
France . . .	6·4	3·0	3·2	2·7	2·7	1·6
W. Germany .	3·5	2·7	3·5	4·0	4·1	3·0
Italy	9·1	6·4	6·3	5·1	4·4	4·1
U.K.	7·6	9·5	7·1	4·5	3·3	2·9

* Annual average.

settlements following strikes—the lorry drivers and local authority manual workers—set the pace for a higher rate of increase of earnings. By the end of 1979 they were rising at nearly 20 per cent per annum compared to about 14 per cent a year earlier. In December 1979 retail prices were going up at a rate of 17 per cent per annum. An increase in indirect taxation contributed 3 per cent to price inflation. But pay remained the main force driving prices. The Conservative Government was elected in May 1979 with the defeat of inflation a central plank of its economic policy. Despite a deflationary fiscal and monetary policy, retail prices continued to rise, reaching a year on year increase of over 20 per cent in the second quarter of 1980. Much of this was due to the effects of higher indirect taxes and continued wage pressure, and was despite an appreciation in the value of sterling. Towards the end of 1980 the rate of inflation began to fall. This was partly a consequence of the recession, both at home and abroad, making it difficult for firms to mark up over costs. Real wages rose, albeit slowly, implying a further squeeze on profits.

Inflation continued to fall in 1981, as pressure on wages eased and the recession became deeper. The year on year increase in retail prices was 12 per cent. Real personal disposable income fell by 1 per cent mainly because of the Chancellor's failure to index income tax allowances and bands in the 1981 Budget. The squeeze on disposable incomes continued into 1982 as the real burden of taxation rose further.

The fall in inflation continued in 1982 and into 1983, when the annual rates were 8¼ per cent and 4½ per cent respectively. This was despite a declining effective exchange rate. The recession and international competition were important influences making British industrialists very wary of putting up prices. At the same time earnings inflation was falling, being 9·4 per cent in 1982 and 8·5 per cent in 1983, whilst productivity was still increasing strongly.

After 1983 price inflation remained low, successive year-on-year figures until 1987 being 5·0 per cent, 6·0 per cent, 3·4 per cent and 4·2 per cent. The main cause of these slight variations was the course of oil prices. During 1987 inflation altered little. A strong pound, low world inflation and a resurgence of strong productivity growth all played their part. Inflation reached a low point of 3·3 per cent at the beginning of 1988, helped by a strong exchange rate. However, it soon became clear that inflationary pressures were emerging in the economy, largely as a result of excessive demand, but the trend was exacerbated by rising interest rates and sustained earnings growth. In early 1989, inflation averaged nearly 8 per cent and concerns over accelerating growth in labour costs forced the Government to maintain a tight monetary stance.

Ironically, higher interest rates feed through into higher retail prices via their effect on mortgage rates. This effect was seen clearly in 1989, when interest rates rose early in the year pushed inflation to a peak of 8·3 per cent in the spring. A period of unchanged interest rate levels allowed retail price inflation to fall back to 7·1 per cent in the early autumn, before another interest rate rise in October (this time to defend a weak pound) pushed inflation back to above 8 per cent in early 1990. Wage bargainers base their assessment of changed living costs on movements in retail prices, so an anti-inflationary policy based solely on the use of high interest rates may, perversely, create just the right conditions for a wage-price spiral.

More seriously, 1989 also saw a steady rise in underlying inflation. If one strips out the effect of mortgage interest rate changes, retail price inflation accelerated from under 5 per cent in early 1989 to nearly 6½ per cent in March 1990. This shows that inflationary pressures were building up quite independently of interest rate rises. One source of pressure was higher unit labour costs as earnings growth increased and productivity performance deteriorated. A second source was the exchange rate; between February 1989 and the end of the year the pound fell by around 15 per cent against the deutschemark and by 10 per cent against the US dollar. This clearly put up import prices.

The introduction of the poll tax was to raise retail price inflation (both 'headline' and underlying) still further. Combined with excise duty changes announced in the March 1990 Budget, the poll tax forced inflation up above 10% in the autumn of 1990. At its peak in September and October 1990, retail price inflation reached around 11 per cent. Excluding mortgage interest payments, underlying inflation rose well above 9 per cent in the final months of the year. Although underlying inflation remained stubbornly high, a succession of interest rate cuts in late 1990 and early 1991, combined with the unwinding of the effect of the poll tax on the index, brought headline inflation down to 6½ per cent in April 1991, to around 4 per cent by the end of 1991 and down still further by early 1993. But the fall in underlying inflation was smaller, though the deep recession has greatly constrained the ability of domestic producers to raise their prices. As the economy emerges from the recession it is thought that inflation will start to increase again. Inflation reached 1·2 per cent in June 1993. This was the lowest rate since February 1964. By February 1995 it had crept up to 3·3 per cent.

The growth in earnings had been a particular cause for concern: between 1980 and the end of the decade, our earnings were rising faster than those of most other OECD countries. Thus, despite improved productivity performance, wage costs per unit of output increased faster than those of our major competitors. In other words, they did even better on these critical variables than we did.

In this context, a remarkable fact is that throughout the early 1980s, when unemployment was rising, the real earnings of those in work continued to increase, as did real personal disposable income, which also incorporates the income of those not working. As the economy went into boom in 1987 and 1988 earnings inflation picked up. As late as 1990 earnings inflation showed little sign of slowing down, running at 9·5 per cent. By early 1991 it was still as high as 9·25 per cent. The unemployed did little to bid down pay. Rather it was forced up by high company profits, skill shortages, and the needs of employers—to attract good workers and to motivate their existing employees. During the course of 1991 earnings inflation moderated, though by early 1992 it was still in excess of 6 per cent per annum. By 1994 it was down to about 3·8 per cent per annum.

As a result of the above developments, inflation in Britain fell more into line with the rates prevailing in major competitor countries than had been the case in earlier years. However some commentators doubt whether this represents a permanent improvement in our relative inflation performance. Only time will tell; but it is slightly worrying that in 1993–94 Britain was exhibiting slightly higher inflation than the other countries (with the exception of Italy) listed in the table on **G73**.

Inflation Policy.

Britain's cost competitive position in world trade has deteriorated over the medium term in relation to that of her main rivals; this is one major reason for her recurrent balance of payments difficulties. The British share in total world exports of manufactures fell from the late 1950s until the mid-1970s. Thereafter there was some recovery. Nevertheless the recovery was small in relation to the losses of earlier years. There are essentially two methods of remedying this situation. There could be a depreciation of the pound in terms of other currencies, although this option was severely circumscribed by membership of the ERM. Alternatively, we must have a policy to limit the increase in British costs; either by increasing productivity growth or by limiting pay rises. Up to 1967 the Government concentrated on the latter alternative, either by restrictive budgetary policies or by *incomes policy*. In 1967 the pound was devalued, and from 1972 to October 1990 it was allowed to float, though the Government from time to time stepped in to prevent it floating freely. However, for many years it was generally believed that an incomes policy was still needed if any depreciation was to be successful, and if harshly restrictive monetary and fiscal policies were to be avoided. Other harmful effects of inflation are discussed in **Part II**.

(i) Incomes Policy under Labour.

In October 1964 the Labour Government's new Department of Economic Affairs was made responsible for achieving an incomes policy.

Its first objective was to achieve a "Joint Statement of Intent on Productivity, Prices and Incomes"; this was signed in December 1964. In this document the T.U.C. and the employers' organisations undertook to co-operate with the Government in producing an effective machinery for the implementing of an incomes policy.

It was Government policy that growth in earnings per employee should equal the planned growth in national output per employee of 3–3½ per cent per annum. Thus, in those industries (e.g., engineering) in which productivity growth exceeded this "norm", earnings should rise less rapidly than productivity, and in those industries in which productivity growth fell short of the norm, earnings could rise more rapidly than productivity. Growth in earnings per employee should exceed the norm only in exceptional cases; i.e., as a reward for increasing productivity by eliminating restrictive working practices; if necessary to transfer labour from one industry to another; if earnings were too low to maintain a reasonable standard of living; or if a group of workers had fallen seriously out of line with earnings for similar work.

To make specific recommendations on the basis of this policy, the Government set up a *National Board for Prices and Incomes*. The Board produced over 150 reports. There was no statutory authority to enforce its recommendations: reliance was placed on voluntary methods and the power of persuasion and public opinion. However, in late 1965 the Government introduced a compulsory "Early Warning" system, whereby it was notified in advance of any intended increase in incomes or in certain prices. As a result, the Government and the Board had time to consider increases before they were put into effect.

(ii) The Prices and Incomes Standstill.

A voluntary incomes policy is very difficult to implement, since it depends on co-operation among Government, workers, and employers; moreover, co-operation among representatives at the top may be undermined by "wage-drift" at the factory level. Thus the annual average of weekly wage-rates rose by 5 percentage points between 1965 and 1966. In fact all of this increase took place in the period before July 1966. Clearly the voluntary incomes policy was meeting with little success.

Therefore, as part of the July measures taken to deal with the balance of payments problem, the Government introduced a "prices and incomes standstill." Increases in prices and incomes were as far as possible to be avoided altogether until the end of 1966. Increases already negotiated but not yet implemented were deferred for 6 months. The first half of 1967 was a period of "severe restraint." Any price increases were carefully examined, and the norm for income increases was zero. Any increase in earnings had to be justified by one of the four conditions for exception, referred to above. To enforce its "freeze" the Government took the unprecedented step of asking Parliament for reserve powers (including penalties for offenders), which were to be used only if the need should arise. For the most part, there was a voluntary observation of the standstill; but from October 1966 the Government found it necessary to exercise its powers of compulsion in a few cases. These powers lapsed in August 1967.

There then followed a year in which there was to be a "nil norm" except where increases in incomes could be justified by one of the four exceptional criteria. The Government could no longer legally enforce its policy, but it did retain the power to delay price and pay increases. Whereas the Government succeeded in slowing down the rise in wages and prices during the year in which it took compulsory powers, in the second half of 1967 weekly wage rates rose at an annual rate of 6 per cent. The advantage gained from the previous restraint was diminished but not entirely lost.

(iii) Incomes Policy after Devaluation.

Incomes policy was made both more difficult and more important by the devaluation of the pound: more difficult in that devaluation involved a cut in the standard of living, and more important

in that it was important that the trading benefit from devaluation should not be neutralised by inflation.

In April 1968 the Government published a White Paper outlining its policy for the period until the end of 1969. Wage increases had still to be justified by the four criteria, and there was a "ceiling" of 3½ per cent per annum except for "productivity agreements" and low-paid workers. Price increases were permitted only as a result of unavoidable increases in costs per unit of output, and price reductions were required when these fell. The Government intended to rely on the voluntary cooperation of unions and employers over pay; but it decided to lengthen its delaying powers for pay and price increases up to 12 months, and take powers to enforce price reductions recommended by the Board.

Between November 1967 and November 1968 the retail price index rose by over 5 per cent, mainly due to the effect of devaluation on import prices. In the face of this rise in the cost of living the incomes policy met with firm resistance. In practice the ceiling of 3½ per cent per annum rapidly became the normal increase. In the first year after devaluation average earnings rose by 7·5 per cent. Workers were thus able to protect themselves against price inflation and to increase slightly their real incomes.

During 1969 wage and price inflation accelerated. In December the Government published a White Paper on its incomes policy for the period after 1969. It laid down a norm for wage increases of 2·5 to 4·5 per cent per annum: increases were to exceed the upper limit only in exceptional circumstances. Comparisons with other workers were not to be used, except in the case of public servants (e.g., teachers and nurses) whose productivity could not easily be measured. The Government's powers to delay the implementation of proposed wage and price increases were reduced. However, the incomes policy laid down in the White Paper was tempered by the imminence of a General Election and the recent cost of living increases; and it did not prevent a "wage explosion" occurring in 1970.

(iv) Conservative Policy.

On taking office in June 1970 the Conservative Government eschewed its predecessor's approach to incomes policy and disbanded the National Board for Prices and Incomes. To curb the inflation it maintained the economy in recession and squeezed company liquidity, hoping in this way to weaken wage pressures and strengthen the resistances of employers. In addition it attempted to resist demands for wage increases in the public sector, at the cost of prolonged strikes, e.g., in electricity supply, postal services and coal mining. In the former two cases it met with some success; in the case of the coal miners' strike early in 1972 the Government was unable to enforce its policy. In any event this form of incomes policy—like the "pay pause" of 1961—was both partial and discriminatory. The Government also intervened to curb price rises in the nationalised industries, e.g., postal charges and steel prices. The main initiative on prices came from the Confederation of British Industry (CBI): in July 1971, it asked its members to avoid price increases over the next twelve months or to limit them to 5 per cent or less in unavoidable cases. Over 170 leading British companies agreed to comply.

The Government measures were by no means a sure remedy for the inflation spiral. Moreover, even its apparent strategy of deterring wage demands by maintaining high unemployment was dropped in the reflationary budget of 1972. The Government appeared to place its faith in its Industrial Relations Act to solve wage inflation in the long run, by, as it saw matters, redressing the balance of power between unions and employers.

(v) The Pay and Price Standstill.

In 1972 wage demands became more difficult to contain because of the increase in the cost-of-living resulting from the effective devaluation of the pound in June and the rise in world food prices during the year. There was a marked increase in the number and seriousness of strikes (see G22). The principal cause was a sharp rise in disagreements over pay claims. In the six months between the first and third quarters of 1972 average weekly earnings rose by no less than 7 per cent. It was inevitable that the Government would intervene. The expectation of an impending freeze encouraged further wage and price increases, especially after the CBI's period of voluntary restraint had elapsed.

The Government first tried to achieve a tri-partite voluntary agreement with the CBI and the TUC. After this attempt had failed, in November the Conservative Government reversed its previous policy and introduced a statutory Prices and Pay standstill. In effect there was a standstill on all prices of goods and services other than imports and fresh foods, a standstill on rents, on dividends, and on all wages and salaries including those previously negotiated but not yet in operation. Offenders were liable to be fined.

(vi) The Price Commission and the Pay Board.

In early 1973 the Government formulated its policy for after the standstill in a series of documents, culminating in a Price and Pay Code. Two new agencies—a *Price Commission* and a *Pay Board*—were established to regulate prices, dividends, rent, and pay in accordance with the Price and Pay Code.

In Stage Two of the policy—lasting from the end of the pay standstill on 31 March until the autumn—the following criteria on pay applied. The total annual pay increase for any group of employees should not exceed £1 a week plus 4 per cent of the current pay bill excluding overtime. There was flexibility for negotiation of increases within a group: emphasis was to be on the lower paid and the maximum allowable increase was £250 a year. Exceptions to the limit were made for, *e.g.*, movement towards equal pay between the sexes, personal increments and promotion, and some improved pension benefits. The Pay Board had to be notified of all settlements involving less than 1,000 employees but settlements involving more than 1,000 employees required its prior approval. It became an offence to strike or threaten to strike to force an employer to contravene an order of the Pay Board.

Prices in Stage Two could be increased only to take account of *allowable* cost increases, and were to reflect only the percentage increases in these costs per unit of output since 1 October 1972. Moreover to allow for productivity growth, firms were permitted to pass on as price increases only a fraction of the increase in the wage costs allowed by the Code. Prices were also limited by the requirement that net profit margins should not exceed the average percentage level of the best two of the last five years. Exceptions were made for companies which could show that without higher profits their investment would be held back. Large firms had to give prior notice of price increases to the Price Commission, medium sized firms had to report regularly on prices, and small firms had to keep price records. Imports, fresh foods, auctioned goods, secondhand goods and interest charges were among the exemptions from the controls. Dividends could not be raised by more than 5 per cent over the previous year.

One of the problems facing the policy was the continued sharp rise in world food prices after the standstill was declared. This made public acceptance of the Government policy more difficult to achieve.

(vii) Stage Three.

Stage Three of the counter-inflation policy was introduced in October 1973. Price controls were similar to those under Stage Two. Wage increases negotiated for any group of workers were statutorily limited to an average of either £2·25 a week per head, or if preferred, 7 per cent per head, with a limit of £350 a year on the amount to be received by any one individual. However, further increases were permitted beyond these limits, to deal with certain specific matters: changes in pay structures, better use of manpower, efficiency schemes, "unsocial" hours, and progress towards equal pay for women. A novel aspect of the pay policy was the *threshold agreement* to safeguard against increases in the cost of living. It was possible for wage negotiators to bargain for a pay increase of up to 40p a week, payable if the retail price index reached 7 per cent above its level at the beginning of Stage Three, with up to another 40p a week for each percentage point it rose thereafter until the end of Stage Three in November 1974. It was claimed that these agreements were responsible for a large part of the wage and price inflation of 1974. Indeed in a purely statistical sense this was correct. The threshold was triggered eleven times, which meant an extra £4.40 per week for anyone under the scheme. It was estimated that 10 million workers were covered by such arrangements by October 1974. The idea behind thresholds was that unions, when negotiating wage increases, might have unduly pessimistic expectations about inflation. By introducing automatic compensation, such expectations would be taken out of the bargaining situation. Without this compensation, it might be argued, many groups would have refused to settle under Stage Three terms, and their pay increases would have been just as large or even larger than the ones which they actually obtained.

(viii) The Miners' Strike.

Over 6 million workers had settled under the Stage Three provisions by the end of February 1974. The National Union of Mine-workers, however, feeling strongly that their relative pay had fallen and recognising their new bargaining powers resulting from the oil crisis, refused to settle under Stage Three. A national overtime ban was begun in November which in January 1974 became a national strike. In November the Government declared a State of Emergency and in January introduced a three-day week for industry in order to conserve coal and electricity (which depended on coal). It was unwilling to waive the Stage Three legislation in the miners' case, despite a declaration by the Trade Union Congress that its member unions would not invoke a settlement of the miners' dispute in support of their own claims. The Government referred the NUM claim to the Pay Board, for the Board to determine whether the miners constituted a special case which justified a further increase in their relative pay. The Government then called a General Election. The Pay Board reported just after the election, and recommended that an additional increase be paid, on the grounds that the long-run contraction of the industry would in future be reversed and that higher relative pay would be necessary to recruit and retain sufficient mineworkers. The incoming Labour Government settled with the miners on terms very similar to those recommended by the Pay Board.

(ix) The Social Contract.

The Labour Party came to power pledged to deal firmly with prices but to abandon statutory wage controls. It took early action on house rents and food prices, by means of controls and subsidies. The Pay Board was abolished and the policy of compulsory wage restraint thus finally ended in July 1974. The Price Code and the Price Commission were, however, retained.

During the February 1974 general election campaign an agreement between the TUC and the Labour Party was announced. This became known as the *social contract*, and formed the backbone of the Labour Government's attempts to stem wage inflation. The idea was that, in return for the repeal of the Industrial Relations Act, the introduction of a measure of industrial democracy and various other concessions, the TUC would be able to persuade its members to co-operate in a programme of voluntary wage restraint. In this way it was hoped to avoid the strains caused by formal incomes policies, which have always appeared to trade unionists to leave them without any role to play. Under a voluntary system they could still do their job—that is bargain about wage rates. The terms of the contract were that there should be a twelve-month interval between wage settlements; and that negotiated increases should be confined either to compensating for price increases since the last settlement, or for anticipated future price increases before the next settlement. It is hardly surprising that most negotiators took the latter option. An attempt by the TUC to exclude this had failed.

(x) Voluntary Restraint.

By early 1975 it was evident that this policy had failed. Some wage settlements were of the order of 30 per cent. In July 1975 the Government announced that there would be a limit of £6 per week on pay increases, £6 representing 10% of average earnings. There were to be no exceptions to this, and those earning more than £8,500 a year were to get nothing at all. The Government had the prior agreement of the TUC, which agreed to try to persuade its members to comply. The policy was voluntary to the extent that there were no legal sanctions against individual unions, but in another sense there were very powerful sanctions. These operated through the Price Code. No firms could pass on in prices any part of a pay settlement above the limit.

The £6 limit was due to lapse in July 1976, and the April 1976 Budget gave the first indications of a possible successor. The Chancellor announced that he would make cuts in the effective amount of tax paid by private individuals, if he could secure trade union agreement to a second year of pay restraint. This would allow an increase in take-home pay with the employers bearing less than half the cost. Therefore prices would rise more slowly and our competitive position deteriorate more slowly than if the whole increase had been achieved by putting up money wages. There were, however, those who felt that the integrity of Parliament was threatened by making taxation decisions conditional on trade union agreement. Be that as it may, agreement was reached with the TUC. From August 1976 more severe limits on pay operated than under the £6 limit. For those earning less than £50 a week, wage increases were limited to £2.50; for those earning between £50 and £80 the limit was 5 per cent, whilst those earning more than £80 could get no more than a £4 per week increase. Average earnings at that time were about £75 per week, and the implied overall limit was about 4½ per cent.

There is no doubt that this pay policy was successful in holding down earnings. During the £6 policy, earnings rose by 14 per cent—a dramatic fall from the near- 30 per cent rise in the previous year. An all-round increase of £6 would have meant a 10 per cent rise. Another 2 per cent can be explained by the implementation of agreements made before August 1975, by moves towards equal pay, and by increased overtime earnings. This leaves only 2 per cent unaccounted for. Some of this "slippage" was no doubt evasion of the limits. There is no reason to think that there was any greater slippage from the 4½ per cent policy, and during the year of its operation (until August 1977) earnings rose by only 9 per cent. It is unclear whether the success of the policy was due as much to the threat of Price Code sanctions and to the recession in the economy as to the voluntary co-operation of the trade unions.

The 4½ per cent policy was due to lapse at the end of July 1977, and in the March 1977 Budget the Chancellor again offered the prospect of tax cuts if trade union agreement to a new stage could be reached. In the event the TUC agreed to continue its support for the 12-month rule, whereby no union should attempt more than one settlement in a year. It could not, however, agree to a limit of a specific amount. In return the Government gave a modest reduction in income tax, and introduced a "voluntary" policy of its own. This new Stage III policy was to last until the end of July 1978 and aimed for a national earnings increase of no more than 10 per cent during this time. No specific limit was to be put on individual negotiations, but the Government reserved the right to impose sanctions on firms whose settlements appeared inconsistent with the national target. These sanctions might be exercised through the Price Commission's controls on profit margins (though it was expected that these would lapse in July 1978), through public purchasing policy and the placing of contracts, and through consideration of industrial assistance. The Government did stress, however, the possibility that larger increases could be obtained by self-financing productivity deals.

By the spring of 1978 it seemed that earnings increases during this stage of policy would turn out to be as high as 14 per cent. The Government was reasonably successful in holding the public sector down to near 10 per cent, though there were some costly productivity deals, particularly in coal mining. But the main problem was in the private sector. Though the majority of wage-rate increases were at about 10 per cent, earnings drift together with consolidation of the previous two years' increases in rates worked out for overtime, piece rates or shiftwork were pushing earnings increases way above 10 per cent. In addition, productivity deals were incorporated in about 30 per cent of agreements, in each case adding between 6 per cent and 10 per cent to pay. It is unclear how many of these deals involved genuine cost saving, or how sanctions discouraged false deals of this sort.

In the early summer the Government announced its plans for the 1978–79 pay round. Its objective was to limit the growth in national earnings to around 5 per cent, and it was soon clear that its tactics were very similar to those it had employed in support of its 10 per cent target during the 1977–78 pay round: seeking to keep as many groups of workers as possible to settlements at or very near to the target figure by direct negotiations in the public sector and by the renewed threat of sanctions in the private sector; allowing additional increases for self-financing productivity deals; and using promises of additional increases in subsequent pay rounds in order to induce groups regarding themselves as "special cases" to settle for 5 per cent in the current round.

(xi) Conflict with the Unions.

A serious problem, however, was the TUC's hostility to the policy. Although the TUC had not supported the Government's 10 per cent target of the previous year, it had in practice helped the Government by putting pressure on unions to settle for increases which were not too obviously out of line with its policy. This time the TUC was not prepared to do this. Its reluctance stemmed partly from the opposition of some union leaders to continued pay controls but much more from the view that even if official union policy was to observe the 5 per cent guide-lines, the frustration apparently felt by many workers after three years of pay controls would lead to widespread unofficial strikes which would undermine union leaders' authority.

The Government therefore had to enforce its policy without TUC help. In the early autumn of 1978 it seemed to be having some success as several groups settled for not much more than the limit, but the policy was severely undermined by a two-month strike at Ford's which ended with a settlement of around 17 per cent. Subsequently Parliament refused to support the Government's proposed use of sanctions against Ford and other firms breaching the guidelines, so that the Government was left without any effective incomes policy in the private sector. As a result other groups of workers felt free to ignore the guidelines: the most spectacular breach of the policy being an increase of over 20 per cent for road haulage drivers after a disruptive strike in January 1979.

Such settlements in the private sector naturally made public sector workers unwilling to accept 5 per cent increases. The Government therefore offered 9 per cent more to most groups. However, this did not satisfy some of the lower-paid, public sector employees, particularly ambulance drivers and manual workers in hospitals and local authorities. They mounted a series of strikes, some of which—withdrawal of emergency ambulance services and disruption of hospitals—caused widespread concern and led to a growing public debate about the extent and the use of trade union power.

To deal with these problems the Government set up a new body, the Comparability Commission, to review the pay of those public sector workers who claimed that they had fallen behind comparable groups in the private sector: health and local authority workers were among the first to have their pay referred to the Commission.

(xii) Reluctant Union Acquiescence.

The new Conservative Government, which took office in May 1979, allowed the work of the Comparability Commission to continue until the end of 1980. Otherwise it eschewed a formal incomes policy. Its strategy to control earnings inflation consisted of two strands. The first was to use cash limits in the public sector and a tight monetary policy in the private. This might moderate settlements. If it did not, it was argued, it would at least make unions aware that high settlements had an unemployment cost. The second strand of policy was to reform the structure of bargaining, so as to redistribute the balance of power between union and employer. By the early autumn of 1980, the Government had moved in the direction of declaring specific limits in the public sector. Whilst they were managing to keep their settlements low in public services, they were less successful in nationalised industries. It was certainly hard to argue that pay inflation in the public sector as a whole was noticeably less than in the recession-hit private sector.

There was a muted union reaction to this policy. Though 1979 saw the largest number of working days lost through strikes in any year since 1926, by early 1981 working days lost, like the number of stoppages, were at a very low level, and thereafter on both measures, industrial strife remained very low. By early 1982 the Government's policies were having some measure of success. In the nationalised industries even the miners were held to just over 9 per cent. In the civil service, the government launched a sustained attack on automatic comparability-based pay determination, arguing that market forces should play a role. Thus grades—like computer staff—for whom demand was high were offered greater pay increases than others, whilst new entrants—of whom there was excess supply—were offered no pay increases at all. The Megaw Committee, the Government hoped, would permanently revise methods of pay determination in the Civil Service. In the weaker tax-dependent sections of the public sector—e.g. teachers—the Government was ruthless in enforcing very low pay settlements.

Meanwhile the recession kept settlements in the private sector at low levels. Through 1982 and into 1983 there was a further gradual reduction in pay inflation. In 1984 the policy was under some—albeit not serious—threat. There was evidence that the Government was finding it more difficult to hold the line in the public sector—a number of comparability deals were threatening. In the private sector, better economic fortunes were starting to result in some pay pressures. 1985 saw a continuation of these tensions in the public sector. Apart from the miners' strike, the Government faced severe difficulties from the civil servants and teachers. Yet, though it failed to hold public sector pay down to the 3 per cent cash limit, it was still managing to impose significantly lower settlements than in the private sector. In 1986 and 1987, however, pay in the public sector rose as rapidly as in private employment—by about 7 and 8 per cent respectively. In the period 1988–late 1990 earnings inflation started to edge up again as strong corporate profits and expectations of higher price inflation encouraged high pay demands. The Government was very eager to limit the extent of earnings increases and tried through high interest rates and a strong exchange rate to dissuade employers from conceding to what it considered to be excessive pay awards. In the public sector the Government faced severe opposition from several sectors. During the summer of 1989, British Rail and London Underground workers staged a series of one day strikes causing considerable disruption to businesses in central London, whose employees needed to commute. This was followed by a prolonged strike by the Ambulance service, who withdrew all but emergency services. The Government's policy throughout these disputes was to keep its distance from the negotiations and leave the discussions to the management and unions, presumably in an attempt to deflect criticism away from the Government at a time of increasing dissatisfaction with the Conservative Government and Mrs. Thatcher.

As earnings inflation threatened to take off during the boom, and was slow to come down at least in the early stages of the recession, many commentators began to doubt just how fundamentally the labour market had been reformed.

(xiii) **Membership of the ERM.**

After many years of debate the UK finally acceded to the Exchange Rate Mechanism of the EMS in October 1990. By accepting the discipline of linking the pound to a low-inflation currency (the deutschmark) the government effectively decided to make the exchange rate the main instrument of anti-inflation policy. Domestic interest rates were now largely determined by the need to keep sterling within its prescribed band; they could not therefore be used to target growth in the domestic money supply. Although the pound's value could still change if other members of the ERM agreed, it was largely the case that loss of competitiveness occasioned by higher-than-average wage inflation could not be accommodated by exchange rate depreciation. This was particularly serious given that most commentators believed that the pound joined at an overvalued level—sterling's purchasing power parity is generally estimated to be closer to DM2·40 than the DM2·95 central rate at which the UK entered. The hope was that wage bargainers in the UK reacted to the exchange rate discipline by accepting smaller pay rises and bringing competitiveness more into line with European competitors. If this did not happen, the UK would suffer much slower growth and higher levels of unemployment than would otherwise have been the case. When France and Italy joined the ERM it took many years for wage inflation to drop to German levels. Adjusting to the ERM would have been much easier if the government either had accepted the need for some form of incomes policy, or made genuine attempts to improve the supply side of the labour market e.g. through better education and training. ERM membership was only likely to be a relatively painless anti-inflation policy if accompanied by domestic measures designed to make the labour market work. The UK's withdrawal from the ERM in 1992 may only be temporary. But, in any event, the need for fundamental supply side reform remains.

(xiv) **Making the Labour Market Work.**

Incomes policies are often criticised on two grounds. The first is that, at best, they work for only a short time. The second is that they cause distortions in relative pay and prices. Hindsight might tell us that their success is no more short-run than is the impact of savage budgetary policies. It might also tell us that whatever allocative inefficiencies are involved, such inefficiencies are minor when compared with the vast waste of resources and personal anguish caused by very high levels of unemployment.

The Conservative Government seemed to believe that structural reform of the labour market was the only real alternative to incomes policies of the conventional kind. If there were features of the labour market which tended to produce inflationary pressures, better, it was argued, to root these out at source rather than tinker with them as an incomes policy would do. Thus the emphasis on trade union reform and on the recession producing permanent changes in attitudes. This concern also explains the emphasis on reducing the real value of social security benefits as a percentage of income in work. Thereby people would have a greater incentive to work and to accept reasonable wage settlements. This approach was confirmed in the 1985 White Paper, *The Challenge to the Nation*. Three desiderata were mentioned: individuals pricing themselves into jobs; flexibility in the face of change; freedom from regulation. In this spirit, the Government reformed Wages Councils in 1986, in particular totally removing juveniles from their orbit. It also further weakened employment protection legislation. The Government also encouraged employers to engage in more decentralised pay setting, in particular to break away from multi-employer industry wide agreements, and to concentrate more on paying according to their own specific needs. Whether this "strategy" will work or not is a vital, but undecided, question. Certainly the UK's failure to improve more significantly its relative unit labour cost performance casts some shadows of doubt. Yet many who are sceptical, now accept that our labour market problems are so deep-seated as to require structural action. They do not regard conventional incomes policies as sufficient. Rather they are seeking more permanent policies of this kind.

MONEY MATTERS

This popular section provides a concise yet authoritative introduction to the complex problems of money, investment and taxation. There is help and guidance on house-buying, income tax, VAT and the Council Tax. The section is updated annually to include the most recent budget changes.

TABLE OF CONTENTS

MONEY MATTERS

I. MONEY

1. SPENDING

Planning a Budget.

Most of us need some form of financial planning. Wages and salaries are usually paid in regular weekly or monthly instalments. The flow of expenditure, on the other hand, is normally much less even. Bills often seem to get lonely and like to arrive in batches. The way to deal with this problem is to work out an annual budget consisting of your major expenditures. An example is given in Table 1 though, of course, the actual figures will depend on your circumstances.

TABLE 1. *An Example of an Annual Budget*

	£
Council Tax	700
Mortgage or rent	2,000
House and contents insurance	200
Gas	200
Electricity	200
Telephone	200
Road tax	135
Car insurance	200
Television rental and licence	200
Life assurance	100
Holidays	1,000
Christmas expenses	500
Annual subscriptions	65
Clothing	400
Season ticket	—
	6,100
Allowance for price increases (say 5% of 6,100)	305
Estimated total bills	6,405
Monthly average	533·75

List the amounts you spent last year under each of the headings. As prices are likely to continue to rise, it is worth adding on a little extra to be on the safe side. In the example, average price increases of 5 per cent are allowed for. It is also sensible to add a small amount for unforeseen expenditure. Having calculated your estimated total bills for the forthcoming year, you can then calculate how much money has to be reserved each month or each week for these items. In the example, this works out at £533·75 per month, or £123·17 per week on average.

Preparing a budget like this has a number of advantages. First of all, by planning in this way you can save money. For example, it is cheaper to pay car tax once a year rather than every six months. Annual season tickets are cheaper than monthly or quarterly ones. Also, it is usually cheaper to pay your insurance premiums in one go, rather than by instalments. A second advantage is that you have a clear idea of your major expenses, so you know how much money there is left over for day-to-day expenses. Thirdly, because the money can be put aside when you are paid, the cash is usually ready when the bills come in.

It is also possible to arrange this through a bank with a budget account. What happens is that you calculate your monthly expenses as above. The bank then transfers that amount each month from your current account (more on this below) to a separate budget account. A separate cheque book is provided for this account. When the bills come in, you simply write out a cheque for them. Using a bank in this way does have an advantage in that you can overdraw on the budget account if a lot of bills come in early in the year. The bank will, however, expect the account to run mainly in credit. There is also a charge for this service.

2. SPENDING ECONOMICALLY

Many forms of expenditure are almost unavoidable. The new council tax and rent or mortgage payments cannot usually be altered unless you move home. Nevertheless, in many other areas savings can be made.

As a general guide, the Consumers' Association publishes a monthly magazine *Which?* This provides a great deal of information about the price and quality of different products. Information about subscriptions to this magazine can be obtained from *Which?*, Subscription Department, PO Box 44, Hertford SG14 1SH. Alternatively, it is available at libraries.

Food.

There are several points to remember when buying food. First of all, larger shops often sell goods at lower prices than smaller shops. As most people know, supermarkets often sell their own brands of many products. "Own brands" are, on average, cheaper than the brands of leading manufacturers. For example, on items such as peas, baked beans, soup and soap powder, own brands can be up to 15 per cent cheaper. On some lines, such as washing-up liquid, the savings can be even greater. There is no reason to suppose that own brands are inferior. They are commonly produced in the same place as the branded products. Often, the only difference is the packaging—and the price.

Other savings can be made with stores' special offers. Things like washing powder and toothpaste will be needed sooner or later; so it can make sense to buy these items when an offer is on, rather than waiting until you have run out.

When comparing prices, it is worth bearing in mind that the quantity varies as well. It is, therefore, better to compare the *unit cost* of products. This is the cost per ounce or pound. Packaging can easily make something look larger than it actually is.

Domestic Appliances.

Like food, the price of domestic appliances varies. Much of the variation depends on the number of extras. For example, a basic gas or electric cooker costs something in the region of £300. Such a cooker would serve a family quite adequately. If, however, you want a model with extras, then the cost can be £800 or more. A second important factor is where the appliance is sold. The price of the same model can vary considerably from place to place, so it is very worthwhile shopping around. There may also be a delivery charge. Discount warehouses are usually the cheapest place to buy appliances. The sales can also make a substantial difference to the price. Most appliances are likely to be cheaper in both winter and summer sales. Fridges are often particularly good bargains in winter sales, for obvious reasons. There is nothing inferior about domestic appliances sold in sales. Traders usually want to clear their premises for new lines. They also realise that January and the summer would otherwise be very lean times for them.

A particular question often arises as to whether to rent or to buy a television set. The advantages of renting are that repairs and service calls are included in the rent. If the set breaks down it is also likely to be repaired more quickly than if you owned a set. And if it cannot be fixed straight-away the rental company will provide a substitute until the original is repaired. On the other hand, it is generally true that it is cheaper to buy in the long run. This is true even if you buy the set on hire purchase. And if you decide to dispose of the set, you can always sell it. (Provided, of course, that any HP payments have been completed.)

Cars.

Cars are very expensive to buy and to run. It is quite common for the annual cost of running a car (including the drop in its secondhand value) to exceed £3,000. So it is worth thinking carefully about whether or not to buy a car. It may be cheaper to use taxis. They also have the advantage of removing any worries about parking, maintenance and drunken driving.

If you do decide to buy a car, the initial investment can be greatly reduced by buying a second-hand car. The value of most cars drops considerably in their first year. There are other advantages in buying second hand. A used car will have been run in and the teething troubles ironed out. However, if the car is more than three years old it must have an MOT (Ministry of Transport) test every year. The test is now very tough, so cars should be checked carefully before purchase.

If you do not get a guarantee from a reputable dealer you should consider having it examined by the A.A. or the R.A.C. They charge a fee for the service, but it may avoid a purchase you later regret. Alternatively, if faults are discovered it may enable you to negotiate a lower price.

Before setting out to buy a secondhand car it is sensible to study the market. Car price guides are widely available. They provide useful information on cars of different ages and condition. The two major sources of secondhand cars are professional dealers and private sellers. You are unlikely to get a bargain if you buy from a dealer, since they are very familiar with the value of used cars. If you buy privately you avoid the mark-up of the dealer, and so can expect to pay less. Even if you buy a new car, it can pay to ask for a discount, especially if you are paying cash. Dealers receive a sizeable discount on new cars. You may be able to persuade one to pass some of it on to you. Whatever sort of car you buy, new or old, you should give it a test drive. Even new cars are not immune from faults.

3. BORROWING

Under certain circumstances, it can be advantageous to borrow money. The biggest example in many peoples' lives is buying a house with the aid of a mortgage (see **H11**). On a much smaller scale most goods can be bought with the aid of credit. This does enable you to enjoy something without having to wait while you accumulate the cash to buy it outright. As prices rise, you may also be able to buy goods more cheaply through buying straightaway. And you save money buying things like season tickets annually. But there are some disadvantages with borrowing. Some people might find easy credit too much of a temptation and spend more than they can afford.

In addition, borrowing usually costs money. How much it costs depends on where the loan comes from. At the cheapest end of the scale are first mortgages. At the beginning of 1995 mortgage interest rates varied around 8 per cent and overdraft rates varied from 18 to around 22 per cent. The interest rate on personal loans was usually around 18 per cent. At the other end of the scale are second mortgages, some hire-purchase arrangements and check trading. The rates of interest at the top end can be 30 per cent per year or even more. There are many sources of credit, so only the main ones will be discussed here.

Banks.

A flexible way of borrowing from a bank is to arrange an overdraft. This allows you to overdraw your current account up to a limit agreed with the bank manager. Overdrafts are a relatively cheap way of borrowing since interest is charged only on the outstanding balance, but by being overdrawn you might incur higher bank charges. If you wish to overdraw regularly it may be worth comparing different banks' charges for overdrawn accounts. Unauthorised overdrafts should be avoided as they usually lead to higher interest and other charges.

With a personal loan you receive a lump sum and pay it back in regular instalments. This can make it easier to manage the repayments. Often the rate of interest will be fixed for the period of the loan. This is advantageous if interest rates rise during this time but not, of course, if interest rates fall. As with overdrafts, it may be worth shopping around to find the most favourable terms, and some building societies now offer personal loans as well.

Credit Cards.

Credit cards can be a convenient way of spreading the cost of purchases over a short period. They are also easy to use. When you buy something on credit the retailer makes out a sales voucher which you check and sign. The retailer then gives you a copy. You can also draw cash from a bank displaying the appropriate sign. Every month you are sent a statement showing how much you owe. You then have to repay a certain minimum amount. If you wish to pay more, or clear all the debt, you can.

Credit cards can be cheap if you only need the borrowing facility for a short time, or if you normally pay all your bills in one go. For longer term loans it is usually cheaper to borrow the money in a different way, such as with a bank loan. It is also now possible for sellers to charge a higher price for credit card transactions. At the time of writing (May 1992) few retailers actually imposed higher charges, but if this becomes common practice it might be worth considering another form of payment.

Credit cards are now issued by a wide range of financial institutions. Originally cards were issued free of charge but many now have an annual fee and others may follow. The rates of interest vary between cards and have fluctuated in recent years between 1.5 and 2.25 per cent per month. Some of the equivalent annual rates are as follows:

Rate per month %	Equivalent rate per year %
1.50	19.5
1.75	23.1
2.00	25.8
2.25	30.6

Normally no interest is charged if the statement is paid off in full. If only part payment is made, some cards still allow an interest-free period up to the date of the statement. After that, interest is charged on the outstanding balance. On this basis if you make a purchase just before the statement you may get about 20 to 35 days free credit. If, however, the purchase was made, say, three weeks before the statement, you could get up to 56 days free credit. If the retailer is slow in sending details of the purchase to the credit card centre the interest-free period may be even longer. For this reason, it can be useful to have two credit cards. If your statement dates differ, you can then use the card with the statement date furthest away. Credit cards can also be used overseas.

Other Cards.

There are several other cards. Store cards are operated in the same way as credit cards and sometimes offer special concessions. However the rate of interest charged is often higher than for credit cards and, of course, you can only use them in the issuer's shops. Charge cards, such as *American Express*, normally have no spending limits, but they do not offer extended credit and there is a charge for the card itself.

Hire Purchase.

The rates of interest on hire-purchase agreements are generally higher than those charged on bank or credit-card loans. To see this clearly, we should describe two ways of quoting interest rates. Salesmen sometimes quote "flat" rates of interest. This refers to the difference between the cash price and the cost if bought on credit. For example, suppose you could buy a cooker for £500 cash, or £625 payable in monthly instalments for one year. The extra cost of buying on credit is £125. This gives an annual flat rate of interest of 25 per cent on the £500 borrowed. But this is not the real rate of interest. The reason is that from the first month some of the capital has been repaid. In fact, the average amount borrowed throughout the year is just over £250. The true rate of interest on the balance outstanding (rather than the original loan) is over 40 per cent in this example. This calculation is known as the APR or annual percentage rate.

Insurance Companies.

If you have an insurance policy you may be able to borrow money from the insurance company on the strength of it. The policy would have to have a cash-in, or surrender value. The interest charged on such loans is often lower than other rates.

4. SAVING

There are several reasons why people save. They include the need to meet unforeseen expenditures, to provide for retirement or simply to buy large items such as a car. It is normally cheaper to pay cash rather than to buy on hire purchase. Although many people save only when they have money left over from their various outgoings, it is better to plan savings. That is, budget your income and expenditure and to regard savings as part of your regular outgoings. This allows capital to be built up on a regular basis.

Before deciding where to invest these savings there are factors that you should consider. The first is whether to invest for short or long periods of time. It is generally true that long-term savings attract a higher rate of interest. However, there are usually financial penalties or constraints that will restrict your ability to draw on the money when required. This loss of *liquidity* is important, since you may require money immediately to meet unforeseen expenditures.

Another consideration is the rate at which prices are increasing; that is the rate of inflation. The saver is particularly concerned with what goods or services money will buy in the future. The important rate of return of an investment is not the nominal or money rate of interest but the real rate of interest. If, for example, an investment offers a return of 7 per cent per annum and the rate of inflation is 5 per cent per annum, the real rate of interest is 2 per cent per annum. The individual requires 5 per cent per annum merely to maintain the purchasing power of his capital.

The real rate of interest is very important during periods of inflation because it may well be negative. For example, if the nominal rate of interest is 7 per cent per annum and the rate of inflation rises again, to say, 10 per cent per annum the real rate of interest is minus 3 per cent per annum. This means that when the saver withdraws money in the future, it will not buy the same quantity of goods or services it would have when the investments were made.

Having considered these general points, we can now look at the specific forms of investment open to the saver.

National Savings.

These are schemes provided by the Government. They include The National Savings Bank, Savings Certificates, Premium Bonds and the Save-As-You-Earn Scheme.

The National Savings Bank.

This was formerly known as the Post Office Savings Bank. There are over 20,000 post offices in the U.K. where you can deposit or withdraw money. There are two types of account available:

Ordinary accounts can be opened with as little as £10. They can also be opened for young children, but withdrawals are not normally allowed until the child reaches seven years of age.

Interest is calculated on each complete £1 deposited for a full calendar month. The money begins to earn interest from the first day of the month after it is deposited. It does not earn interest on the month in which it is withdrawn. You should therefore try to deposit money towards the end of the month and withdraw at the beginning of the month. There are two rates of interest. In 1994 these were 2·0 per cent and 3·25 per cent. The higher rate applies to balances of £500 or more, provided the account has been kept open for the whole calendar year. The lower rate applies to other balances. The interest is added on 31 December of each year, and the first £70 is tax free. The maximum amount normally allowed in an account is £10,000.

Up to £100 a day can be drawn on demand from your account. The bank book will be retained for checking if the withdrawal exceeds £50. If you require more than £100 you will have to allow a few days before you get your money. This is because you must apply in writing. Greater flexibility in withdrawing money can be achieved by having more than one account. For example, if you have two accounts you can draw up to £200 on demand. If you have a 'Regular Customer Account', you can withdraw up to £250 a day at your chosen post office and still retain your bank book. A person qualifies for a Regular Customer Account if he or she has used the chosen post office for at least six months.

The advantage of the system is its accessibility, since there are post offices in almost every town and village, and they are open six days a week. It is cheap, since there are no bank charges and money earns interest. Also, money is available on demand.

So, National Savings ordinary accounts are a good place to keep small amounts of money to meet unforeseen expenditures. On the other hand, the services offered are still limited, when compared with banks for example, and the rates of interest are relatively low.

Investment Accounts.

Like ordinary accounts, anyone over the age of seven can open an account. Children under seven can have one opened on their behalf. The minimum sum required to open an account is £20 and the maximum holding is £100,000. The rate of interest is higher than an ordinary account and is liable to tax, but tax is not withheld at source. Interest is calculated on a daily basis. This means that interest is earned on each whole pound for every day it is in the account. The interest is automatically credited on 31 December each year. The current rate of interest is displayed at post offices.

There is no limit on the amount of money that can be withdrawn. However, notice of one month is required. Investment accounts are better than ordinary accounts for long-term savers, although higher rates of interest can be obtained elsewhere.

Savings Certificates.

There have now (1995) been 42 issues of fixed interest Savings Certificates, but only one is on sale at any particular time. At the time of writing, the 42nd Issue was on sale. The minimum investment is £100, and an individual can invest up to £10,000. However there are special facilities for people cashing in earlier Issues of Certificates, which they have held for at least five years, and are reinvesting in the 42nd Issue. If they do this, they may hold up to £20,000 of 'Reinvestment Certificates' of the 42nd Issue in addition to any purchases made within the general £10,000 limit. This £10,000 (or £30,000) may be held in addition to any holdings of other National Savings Certificates. Instead of earning interest in the usual way, the value of the Certificates rises at an accelerating rate. As shown in Table 2, the increase in value of the 42nd Issue over five years is equivalent to a compound interest rate of 5·85 per cent per annum.

TABLE 2.   *The rates of return on £1,000 invested in the 42nd Issue of Savings Certificates*

Minimum Period held	Rate of interest (per annum from date of purchase)	
1 year	4·0%	£40·00
2 years	4·6%	£47·84
3 years	5·5%	£59·83
4 years	6·75%	£77·47
5 years	8·46%	£103·65
Total Return		£1,328·79

This is free of both income tax and capital gains tax. If allowance is made for the basic rate of income tax, 5·85 per cent is attractive to higher-rate tax payers. So, for example, Certificates to the value of £1,000 would become worth £1,328·79. Interest is earned for each completed period of three years. No interest is earned on Certificates cashed in the first year except for the 42nd Issue Reinvestment Certificates mentioned above.

You need not cash in Certificates when they reach maturity. In most cases, however, it will pay to do so. The General Extension Rate, the rate of interest currently paid on matured Certificates, is now well below most interest rates. Again anyone can hold certificates, including children under seven.

Index-linked Savings Certificates.

These were originally known as 'granny bonds' because when index-linked certificates were first issued they were only available to people over a certain age. This restriction no longer applies and the version currently available is the Eighth Issue. Provided the certificates are held for at least a year, their value is linked to increases in prices. Interest is also paid and the rate increases every year, from 1·25 per cent after the first year up to a maximum of 6·07 per cent after five years. If the certificates are held for five years the overall return is 3·0 per cent. (This is in addition to the increase in their value to match inflation and, once the interest is added to the capital, it is index-linked as well.) The repayments are also tax free.

The certificates are available in units of £100. You may buy up to £10,000 of the Seventh Issue in addition to any holdings you may have from previous issues. You may also reinvest from mature Savings Certificates and mature Yearly Plan Certificates up to a further £20,000 over the £10,000 limit.

The Yearly Plan.

This scheme was designed for regular investment but was withdrawn for new savers from 30 January 1995.

Premium Savings Bonds.

Premium Bonds are one of the most popular forms of national savings. No interest is earned as such on the bonds. Instead, you have a regular chance to win a cash prize each week and month.

All the prizes are tax free. However, before a bond is included in the draw it has to be held for three calendar months following the month in which it was bought. The winning numbers are generated by ERNIE (Electronic Random Number Indicator Equipment). The winning numbers are drawn entirely at random so that each bond has an equal chance of winning.

The size of the prizes varies from £50 to £100,000 and, from April 1994, there has been a monthly prize of £1,000,000. Prizewinners are notified by post, so it is important to notify the Bonds and Stock Office of any change of address. The numbers of prize-winning bonds and a complete list of unclaimed prizes can be consulted at major post offices. In addition most daily newspapers publish the numbers of bonds which have won the larger prizes. If you fail to claim a prize at the time of the draw, this can be done later.

Premium Bonds can be bought at post offices, and banks. Any person over the age of 16 can buy bonds. A parent, grandparent or guardian can buy bonds on behalf of their children. For individuals aged 16 or over the mimimum initial purchase is now £100 and the maximum holding is £20,000.

Capital Bonds.

Capital bonds are for people who wish to put some money away for a period of five years. They are available in multiples of £100 and the maximum amount held for all issues of capital bonds (except Series A) is £250,000. On each anniversary of the purchase interest is added and the rate of interest increases each year. The amount of interest is guaranteed over the period. At current rates (March 1995), the return is equal to 7·75 per cent compound. The bonds are repayable in full at the end of this period with all the interest due.

Although the interest is paid at the end of the five years, for income tax payers the interest is taxable each year. No further interest is earned after five years. Early repayment can be made after three months' notice is given but no interest is payable for repayments made in the first year.

FIRST Option Bonds.

FIRST stands for Fixed Interest Rate Savings Tax-Paid. This bond is for savings of at least £1,000 which are to be invested for at least a year or more. It is called an option bond because each year the investor has the option of either cashing in the bond without penalty or leaving it invested at a fixed rate of interest. No interest is payable if the bond is repaid before the first anniversary of purchase. If the bond is repaid between anniversary dates a lower rate of interest applies to the period between the most recent anniversary and the date of repayment. Investors may hold any amount between £1,000 and £250,000. Income tax is deducted at the basic rate. Non-taxpayers are able to reclaim the tax from the Inland Revenue but higher rate taxpayers have some further tax to pay.

Income Bonds.

These bonds provide a regular income from capital. The minimum investment is £2,000. Extra amounts can be invested in multiples of £1,000. The maximum holding is £250,000. The interest is paid on the fifth of each month and is taxable but tax is not withheld at source. In January 1995 the rate of interest was 6·5 per cent for holdings under £25,000 and 6·75 per cent for holdings of £25,000 or more. Repayments may be obtained by giving three months' notice, but if repayment is made in the first year the bond will earn only half the published rate of interest. The interest rate is adjusted from time to time and full details are available at post offices.

Pensioners' Guaranteed Income Bonds.

The Pensioners' Guaranteed Income Bonds are designed for people of 65 and over who want a monthly income from their capital. The minimum investment is £500 and the maximum £20,000. The interest rate is fixed and guaranteed for the first five years the bond is held. For the second series the rate of interest is 7·5 per cent. The interest is paid on the 19th of each month directly into the investor's bank or building society account.

Children's Bonus Bonds.

These are designed to be suitable gifts for children. They can be bought in units of £25 up to a maximum of £1,000 per child. Before making such a gift, therefore, it is worth checking that it would not take the child's holding over the maximum. The bonds can be bought for any child under 16 and will continue earning interest until the child is 21. A bonus is added every five years. As nothing further is earned after the 21st birthday they should then be cashed in. All interest and bonuses are tax-free.

Building Societies.

There are many building societies in the United Kingdom. Some of these are national, others local. All building societies are 'mutual' organisations set up for the benefit of their investing and borrowing members. However, the former Abbey National Building Society has converted itself into a public limited company and other societies may follow. There is no difference in the security of your money as between the small and large societies. If you want to be absolutely sure, you should choose one that has Trustee Status and is a member of the Building Societies Association.

For many years the interest rates quoted by building societies have been tax paid at the basic rate but non-taxpayers have not been allowed to claim the tax back. However the system was changed so that from 6 April 1991 non-taxpayers no longer have to suffer tax on the interest. Interest rates tend to be higher for regular savings and the longer you are prepared to commit your money.

Banks.

Banks offer two main types of account, current and deposit. Current accounts are for everyday transactions and are discussed later (**H8**). Deposit accounts are more suitable for savings.

The rates of interest offered on deposit accounts do tend to change more quickly than those offered by other schemes. This is because the deposit rate is based on each bank's base rate which change as interest rates generally change. The deposit rate is usually between 4¼ and 3 per cent below the base rate. The current rate offered by the various banks is usually on display at the bank branches. Interest is calculated on a daily basis. The interest is taxable, but in the past tax has not been deducted at source. However, from 6 April 1985, bank interest has been paid in the same way as building society interest. There is no minimum or maximum amount that can be deposited. You can only withdraw money at the branch at which you have an account. If you want ready access to your savings, deposit accounts can be attractive for small amounts of money. But you should look at the rates offered by National Savings and Building Societies before choosing a deposit account with a bank.

Tax Exempt Special Savings Schemes (TESSAs).

Tax Exempt Special Savings Schemes (TESSAs) were introduced in January 1991. They are operated by banks and building societies and the interest from them is free of income tax. Anyone over 18 can open a TESSA but can only have one at a time. A maximum of £3,000 can be invested in a TESSA in the first year and then up to £1,800 a year up to a total limit of of £9,000 over five years. Interest may be withdrawn during this period but only up to the "net of tax" level.

At the end of the five years the saver will receive a bonus consisting of the money which would otherwise have gone in tax, provided that the capital has remained untouched. Capital can be withdrawn at any time but this would lead to the loss of all tax advantages. After five years all or part of the capital built up (but not the accumulated interest) can be reinvested in a new TESSA. However, the overall investment limit of £9,000 remains, as does the rule that a TESSA has to last five years to qualify for relief.

Although the tax arrangements are the same for all TESSAs, different banks and building societies offer different conditions in terms of the minimum investment required, rates of interest etc. so it can be worth shopping around to find the most suitable one for you.

Personal Equity Plans.

Personal equity plans (PEPs) were introduced on 1 January 1987 to provide a tax incentive for investing in shares. Individuals over 18 can invest up to £6,000 a year in a PEP. (The £3,000 limit on investment in unit trusts and investment trusts was abolished from April 1992.) In addition to investing up to £6,000 in a general PEP in any one tax year a person may invest up to £3,000 in a single company PEP. All income and capital gains on investments in a PEP are free of tax. Originally, to qualify for tax relief, investments had to be retained for at least one full calendar year but this requirement was abolished in 1989.

PEPs are available from banks and investment companies. The plans have the advantage of permitting tax-free investment in shares, which is particularly beneficial for taxpayers subject to the higher rate of income tax and also to those paying capital gains tax. Obviously this benefit does not extend to non-taxpayers. As with any investment in shares there is the risk that share prices might fall. For this reason, it is sensible to view PEPs as a long term investment. Finally, in considering the tax benefits, you should take account of the charges made by the plan managers.

Gilt Edged Securities.

As well as raising taxes to finance its expenditure, the Government borrows from the general public. It does this by issuing gilt-edged stock. There are basically two types of stock, redeemable and irredeemable. Redeemable or dated stocks are those that the Government has agreed to repurchase on a certain date. Usually, two dates are given. This means that the Government cannot redeem them before the first date, but it must redeem them on or before the last date. Each stock has a *par* or face value of £100. This is the amount that will be repaid on redemption. An example of a redeemable stock is the 8¼ per cent Treasury Stock 1987–1990. Stocks that the Government is not committed to redeem are called irredeemable or undated stocks. The 2½ per cent consol introduced after the Second World War is an example.

The cost of buying or selling securities will depend on whether you go through a stockbroker or through the Department for National Savings, Bonds and Stock Office. It is cheaper to use the National Savings Stock Office, although you can only deal in stocks that are on the National Stock Register. There is no limit to the total amount you may hold. Application forms may be obtained from Post Offices.

The interest or *coupon rate* on a stock is normally paid half-yearly. Some pay quarterly, which is particularly useful for old-age pensioners, for example. This is based on the nominal or par value. For example, the 8¼ per cent Treasury Stocks pays £8·25 per year. However, the price that you pay for the stock will probably be less than par. The effective rate of interest or *running yield* will therefore be greater than 8¼ per cent.

Prices of stocks fluctuate so that their yield keeps in line with interest rates generally. This presents the possibility of a capital gain or loss. However, it is generally true that as the stock approaches redemption, the closer the price will be to par, and the smaller the capital gain. The further away redemption is, the lower the price of the stock, and hence the greater will be the capital gain if the stock is held to redemption. Government securities are a very marketable investment. They can be sold quickly if need be. Also, stocks are free of capital-gains tax if in your possession for more than one year.

Shares.

For the more adventurous, there is the possibility of investing in shares on the stock market. Since share prices can fall as well as rise, it is advisable to "spread your risk." This means that you must have a varied and balanced collection of shares in your portfolio. To do this will require a lot of capital and knowledge of the market. So it is best to seek professional advice from a stockbroker or your bank manager. People with more limited means will be better advised to participate indirectly in the stock market by holding units in a unit trust.

Unit Trusts and Investment Trusts.

Unit trusts sell 'units' to investors and use the proceeds to buy shares. This allows the investor to spread the risk of his or her investment over all the shares the trust owns. Unit trusts are run by professional managers who can be expected to know more than many investors about the merits of different securities. The value of the units of a trust are worked out each day in line with the value of the fund's stock market investments. Two prices are quoted. The 'offer' price is the price at which investors can buy units. The 'bid' price is the price at which the managers will repurchase units. The offer price is higher than the bid price and the difference contributes towards the cost of running the trust. In addition, there is usually a small half-yearly or yearly charge. Units can be bought and sold directly from the managers.

Investment trusts are companies which invest in securities. Like unit trusts they enable investors to spread their investment risk. However, unlike unit trusts they have a fixed share capital. The shares in investment trusts are bought and sold in the same way as those of other companies, but some investment trusts also have savings schemes which can be taken out directly with the managers.

Life Assurance as Saving.

Life assurance policies provide an alternative method of saving regular amounts for long periods of time. The various policies are considered in the section on insurance. However one version which should be considered under the heading of saving is the tax-exempt life insurance policies sold by Friendly Societies.

Friendly Societies: Tax-Exempt Policies.

Friendly Societies are allowed limited tax relief on life insurance and endowment business and can therefore offer tax-free savings plans. In 1995 the general limit on a person's premiums was increased from £200 to £270 a year.

5. BANKS

Most people are familiar with the high street banks. These are the clearing banks and are known as the Big Four. They are the National Westminster, Midland, Barclays and Lloyds. In addition, there are a number of smaller banks, such as the Royal Bank of Scotland and the Co-operative Bank. There are also the Girobank and the Trustee Savings Bank. Banks offer a variety of services, and we begin by considering current accounts.

Current Accounts.

A current account is a safe and easy way of making and receiving payments and is now offered by some building societies as well as banks. Many current accounts are operated free of charge if you stay in credit. If you go overdrawn or require additional services the charges vary considerably so it can be worth shopping around. To open an account you will have to supply samples of your signature, proof of identity and probably the names of two referees. These could be your employer and a friend with a bank account. To pay further amounts into your account, you simply fill in a paying-in slip provided by the bank. Some current accounts now attract interest but the rates are often very low indeed.

Making Payments.

With a current account you will receive a cheque book. This is used in making cash withdrawals from the bank or in making payments without using cash. A cheque is not money. It is merely a written instruction to the bank to pay an amount out of your account, to the person(s) named on the cheque. Cash can be obtained from your local branch. If you require cash from another you must make special arrangements or use a cheque card.

Cheque Cards.

Most retailers are reluctant to accept an unsupported cheque. This is because they do not know if you have sufficient money in your account for the bank to honour the cheque. And, of course, the cheque book may have been stolen. This problem is overcome by a cheque card. The card

guarantees that the bank will honour cheques up to £50 or sometimes more regardless of the state of the customer's account. You have to be a reliable and well-established customer before your bank will give you a cheque card. A cheque drawn on a cheque card cannot be stopped or cancelled.

Cash Cards.

Increasingly these cards can be used for more than just simply withdrawing cash from cash machines, for example checking the balance of the account or ordering statements. They are operated using your Personal Identification Number (PIN). This should be kept secret at all times and never written down where a thief could see it.

Debit Cards.

These are sometimes known as switch or connect cards and are the electronic version of cheques. Your card is swiped through a machine, you are asked to sign a voucher and the amount is then debited from your current account.

Standing Orders.

There are other ways of making payments apart from cheques. If asked, the bank will automatically make regular payments from your account. These "standing orders" are useful for paying such things as insurance premiums, subscriptions and mortgage repayments.

Direct Debiting.

Direct debits are slightly different from standing orders. In both cases you give your bank a written instruction to meet payments as they fall due. However, with direct debiting the recipient approaches your bank which then deducts the payment from your account. This can be convenient where the amount varies. The recipient has to tell you beforehand of the date and amount of payment. If you wish to cancel a direct debit instruction you should write to both your bank and the recipient.

Other Services.

In addition to the services mentioned, banks provide a whole range of other services. These include lending (considered in the section on Borrowing), deposit accounts (considered in the section on Saving), travel facilities, advice on investment, insurance and taxation, safe custody of items and many more. For further information on the additional services banks offer, contact your nearest branch.

Girobank.

The National Giro was set up by the Government to provide a low-cost current-account bank service. When Giro started it was considerably cheaper to run compared with a current account at a bank. However, the difference is now small. Giro can be opened via the post or through the 20,000 Post Offices in the U.K. These are generally open six days a week. You therefore have access to your account for more days and for longer hours than you do with the commercial banks.

6. INSURANCE

Insurance is a contract to pay a premium in return for which the insurer will pay compensation in certain eventualities, for example, fire or theft. In effect, insurance is a means of sharing certain risks. The traditional forms of insurance are general insurance and life assurance. The latter is usually called "assurance" because the cover is given against the occurrence of an event which is inevitable.

Life Assurance.

Life assurance provides a capital sum to your estate in the event of your death. Some policies also combine a savings element so that you receive a lump sum if you survive the period. These are called endowment policies. As a general point, it is just as important that you do not overburden yourself with life assurance as it is to have some form of cover. If you have to give up or surrender your policy before it matures there are usually severe financial penalties. There are three basic types of life assurance: term assurance, whole-life assurance and endowment assurance. All forms of life assurance used to attract tax relief. However, this was changed in the Budget of 13 March 1984 so that the tax relief does not apply to policies taken out after that date.

Term Assurance.

This type of policy provides life assurance for a fixed period of time. Should you die during the term of the policy your estate will receive the sum assured. However, if you survive the period you receive nothing. There are variations on the basic type of term policy. A *decreasing term* policy, for example, is often necessary if you have a mortgage. The sum assured decreases as you pay off the mortgage.

Other types of policies include level and convertible term policies. With *level term* policies the sum assured remains fixed throughout the term of the policy. A *convertible term* policy has the additional option of being able to convert it to another kind of policy later on, if you so desire. Term policies provide the cheapest form of life cover.

Whole-Life Assurance.

With this type of policy you are normally required to pay the premiums for the whole of your life-time. Like term assurance, the sum assured is paid out to your estate only on your death. Whole-life policies can either be with or without profits. A with-profits policy will be more expensive, since the sum received on your death will be the sum assured plus a share in the profits made by the company. Having to keep up the premiums after your retirement can be a problem, so *limited payment* policies are available. Premiums are paid until you reach a specific age, although life cover continues until your death. The premiums will be higher than for a straight whole-life policy.

Endowment Assurance.

Both whole-life and term policies normally provide benefit only on your death. With an endowment policy, benefit is still provided should you die before the maturity date of the policy. But if you survive this period you will receive the sum assured. Like whole-life policies, these policies can be with or without profits. Although the more expensive, with-profits endowment policies are the most popular form of life assurance in this country. However, the proportion of the premium used to provide death cover is small. This is because the chances of dying before the maturity date are usually low. Thus, the bulk of the premiums is used by the company to build up the capital sum on maturity.

Endowment policies are often used in conjunction with loans for house purchase, school fees and for providing for retirement. As well as with-profits investment policies, life assurance companies offer other investment policies. These include equity linked contracts, property bonds and policies linked to building societies. With unit-linked contracts the bulk of the premium is used to purchase units in a unit trust. Property bonds are very similar, except the investment is in property.

General Insurance.

As mentioned earlier, this provides cover for an eventuality that may never happen. The types of general insurance considered here are for house and possessions, motor vehicles, sickness and medical insurance.

Insuring your House.

If you are buying a house on a mortgage the building society will insist that it is insured. The sum that you will have to insure your house for may be more than what you paid for it. This is because the insurance value will be related to the cost of rebuilding the house. It is therefore important to adjust the amount for which the house is insured periodically to keep pace with inflation. Alternatively, you can take out policies which are "index-linked." Although most policies give the same kind of cover, there is no standard house insurance. So you should check to see if your policy covers all eventualities. This is particularly important if your area is prone to such events as flooding or subsidence.

Insuring your Possessions.

Unless you have a combined policy, the contents of your home and other possessions will not be covered by your house insurance. In the past insurance companies have reimbursed the purchase cost of articles, less a charge for wear-and-tear. However, you can get policies that do not make this deduction.

House and Possessions.

If you are a tenant living in rented accommodation you should only buy policies that cover the contents of the house and leave the landlord to buy insurance for the buildings. For owner-occupiers, it is best to buy a combined policy of house and possessions. This has the advantage that it will be generally cheaper than buying two separate policies.

Motor Insurance.

Motor insurance is compulsory by law. However, only a basic minimum is compulsory, and many people prefer to take out more comprehensive policies. Insurance companies offer two main types of policy; third party and comprehensive insurance.

Third-Party Motor Insurance.

The additional cover provided by this type of policy is the cost of repairing the other driver's car. Also, if you incur legal costs in dealing with a claim, these will be reimbursed if your insurer approves your actions. Since third-party insurance does not cover damage to your car, it is only suitable if your car is fairly old. "Third party, fire and theft" will cover you if your car is burnt out or stolen, but not if it is damaged in an accident.

Comprehensive Motor Insurance.

If your car is relatively new and hence more valuable, then you should consider a comprehensive policy. The most important additional benefit of such a policy is cover for loss or accidental damage to your car.

Sickness and Medical Insurance.

If you consider the benefits provided by the National Insurance schemes and the National Health Service to be inadequate, you can take out insurance that provides for you when ill. There are several schemes. *Hospital risk insurance* provides a sum only for the period you are in hospital. You may consider it best to have a *permanent health insurance*. This provides cover for the total period you are ill. In addition to providing an income for yourself when ill, there are schemes that provide for private medical treatment. The most well-known is the British United Provident Association (B.U.P.A.).

Buying Insurance.

Because of the bewildering variety of policies available it is often best to seek professional advice when buying insurance. This can be obtained from an insurance broker or your bank manager.

7. BUYING A HOUSE

Buying a house is very often preferable to renting a home. Your own house provides you and your family with a secure home. A house is also one of the soundest investments available to most people. In addition, a house can be a useful asset. For example, if you wish to move elsewhere the house can always be sold and the proceeds used to buy a home elsewhere. A house can be particularly valuable on retirement. With the mortgage paid off the retired owner can choose from a number of possible courses of action. He or she could continue living in it rent free. If the house proved too large for retirement part of it could always be let out to provide some additional income. Alternatively, the owner could move to a smaller home and the difference in the value of the two houses would provide a useful capital sum.

For many people there is no satisfactory alternative to buying a home. Most people are unlikely to be offered council accommodation. Furthermore, a home owner is likely to find it much easier to move than a council tenant. Councils are often reluctant or unable to offer new accommodation when their tenants wish to move; whereas an owner occupier can always sell his house and buy another elsewhere.

Accommodation rented privately also has its disadvantages. Reasonably priced rented accommodation is often difficult to find. Tenants sometimes pay nearly as much, or even more, in rent than they would have to pay for a mortgage on similar property. And mortgage interest normally attracts tax relief whereas rent does not. Finally, rents are likely to rise as inflation continues. Mortgage repayments on the other hand, although they fluctuate from time to time, are related to the original loan and not to the current value of the property.

The basic drawback of buying a house is the cost of buying and selling. The costs can include solicitor's and surveyor's fees and (in the case of selling) an estate agent's fee. Normally there will be the costs of fitting out a new home—the cost of curtains is one example. These costs clearly mean that it is not advantageous to buy a home if you expect to move in the near future.

An obstacle for many people is cash. One hundred per cent mortgages are uncommon, and the buyer has to find the difference between the mortgage offered and the price of the house. There are also the other fees mentioned above. The position may be illustrated with an example. Mr. and Mrs. Smith agree to buy a house for £50,000. The Smiths' building society is prepared to lend them 95 per cent of the value of the property. In this case, the loan would be £47,500 which leaves the Smiths £2,500 to find. On top of the £2,500, the Smiths have to pay a valuation fee to the building society of, say, £100. The valuation fee is related to the value of the property so that the higher the value, the higher the fee. If the price of the house exceeds £30,000 stamp duty also has to be paid. The rate of the stamp duty is currently 1 per cent of the value of the house. Note that duty is levied on the total price of the house, and not just the excess over £30,000. So, for example, the stamp duty on a £50,000 house would be £500. The Smiths also decide to have a professional survey of the house done in order to see if there are any defects in the property. The surveyor's fee depends on how detailed the buyer wishes the survey to be. In this example the fee is £200. Finally, the Smiths receive a solicitor's bill for £350. The solicitor's charge will depend partly on the value of the house, and partly on how much work the solicitor has to do to transfer the house from the seller to the buyer.

In this example, therefore, the Smiths need at least £3,650 of their own money. Frequently the amount of money needed will be greater than this.

For example, if the Smiths' mortgage were limited to 90 per cent of the value of the house they may have had to find at least £6,150.

Cost of the house	£50,000
Mortgage	£47,500
	2,500
Valuation fee	100
Survey fee	200
Solicitor's fee	350
Stamp duty	500
	£3,650

It should also be borne in mind that more money is needed to furnish the house. A first-time buyer needs almost everything from curtains to a cooker, and from doormats to a dinner service. Not all of these things need to be bought straight away of course. Nevertheless, some items, such as something to sleep on, and to eat off, will be needed almost immediately.

So it can be seen that, unless one is likely to move in the near future, buying a house can be a sensible decision. The key thing is to save up a reasonable sum of money towards the various costs. The next step is choosing a home.

Choosing a House.

Given the price of houses, selecting your future home is clearly not a decision to be rushed. Possibly the first thing to do is to work out how much you can afford to pay. If you need a mortgage, building societies and other lenders will give you a rough indication of the maximum amount they will lend. They cannot give a precise figure, however, because the amount a society will lend depends not only on your income but also the house itself. There is more on this below. The next stage is to decide where you would like to live. If you are not familiar with the area it pays to spend time studying a map in detail. That way you soon get an idea of the proximity of each area to your work, to the nearest shopping centre and so on. It is also worth thinking carefully about the type of house you want. You may, of course, be influenced by what is available. Nevertheless, if you have a fairly clear idea of what you want a lot of time can be saved by eliminating houses that are obviously unsuitable. Features to think about include whether you want a house, bungalow or flat; the number of bedrooms you require and whether you want a large, medium or small garden.

The next move is to find out as much as possible about the current state of the home market. Estate agents are always delighted to deluge prospective home buyers with details of many properties. Many of them might be unsuitable for you, but they will begin to give you an idea of the value of different houses. You may also change your mind about the sort of house you want. Estate agents are not the only source of information about houses for sale. Houses are often advertised privately, usually in the local newspaper. And because the seller will be saving hundreds of pounds in estate agent's fees, you might be able to buy a house advertised privately for a bit less than it were handled by an agent.

There are several other considerations that should be borne in mind. For example, if you are likely to have to move within a few years you may wish to buy a house which is relatively easy to resell. Such a house might be a fairly modern three-bedroomed semi-detached house which is close to shops and schools: rather than a "character" property in a remote area.

Buying a House.

The process of buying a house should not be rushed either. In fact, at this stage it is well to have two or three properties in mind. This reduces the disappointment should you fail to get your first choice. It also puts you in a better bargaining position over the price of the house. There is nothing sacred about the asking price. Sellers will often ask for a bit more than they think they will probably get. So, depending on the state of the market, it can often pay to offer less than the advertised price.

When a price is agreed, make it "subject to contract." Neither party is formally bound to the agreement until the contracts are actually signed. Before that happens there are a number of things to be done. First of all you will probably want a solicitor. It is not absolutely necessary to use a solicitor, but unless you are familiar with the procedure it is usually advisable to do so. If you need a mortgage the next thing to do is to give full details of the house you intend to buy to your building society or bank manager. He will then arrange to have the property surveyed and valued. The purpose of this is to safeguard the building society's money by making sure that the house is a good investment. When the building society is ready it will inform you how much it is prepared to lend on the house. Your solicitor should then be instructed to complete the remaining formalities.

As soon as the solicitors are satisfied about the technicalities of the purchase the next stage is the signing and exchange of contracts. The contract is usually prepared in duplicate with one copy to be signed by the buyer and one by the seller. The buyer is normally expected to pay a deposit of 10 per cent of the purchase price when contracts are exchanged. The exchange of contracts legally commits both parties to the purchase. This commitment stands regardless of what happens thereafter. This is why it is important for you or your solicitor or both to find out as much as possible about the property before the contract is signed. The contract will contain a number of details, including the date on which the deal will be completed. The date is usually a few weeks ahead and allows both parties to make final arrangements before the house is actually handed over. On the completion date the balance of the purchase money is paid, and the purchaser can take possession of the house.

The length of time between finding a house of your choice and taking possession can vary considerably. It depends on the number of complications involved. If everything goes well it would probably take between eight and ten weeks to buy the house. Such is the process of buying a home. However for many people the major consideration is the mortgage. It is therefore worth describing mortgages in greater detail.

Mortgages.

A "mortgage" is a technical term meaning that certain rights over one's property are given to someone else as security for a loan. In other words, if you buy a house with a loan you give a mortgage as security. In everyday usage, however, a mortgage refers just to the loan, even though the property is still used as security. Even if you can afford to pay cash, it is often worthwhile buying a house with the aid of a mortgage. There are several reasons for this. First of all, if the house is to be your main residence the mortgage interest on the first £30,000 borrowed qualifies for tax relief though this was reduced to 20 per cent from April 1994 and it is to be further reduced to 15 per cent from April 1995. Secondly, as inflation continues the value of money declines, and so the real value of the mortgage also declines. As a result, the mortgage repayments will not tend to rise in line with inflation.

It is true that interest rates fluctuate and that when they rise your mortgage repayments will rise as well. But sooner or later the rate of interest will fall again. In the meantime, higher interest payments are mitigated by higher tax relief. In addition, when interest rates rise it is sometimes possible to extend the repayment period, rather than increase the monthly repayments. The most common types of mortgage are repayment mortgages and endowment mortgages.

Repayment Mortgages.

Repayment mortgages are usually the most straightforward. They are repaid in equal monthly instalments. Each payment consists partly of interest and partly of a repayment of capital. In the early years the repayments consist almost entirely of interest. As the loan is paid off, the interest element declines.

There is some tax relief on mortgage interest. It is normally given directly by the Inland Revenue to the lender through a scheme called MIRAS (Mortgage Interest Relief At Source). However, the tax relief has been reduced in recent years and from 1995/96 is allowed only at a rate of 15 per cent on the first £30,000 of a mortgage loan.

Endowment Mortgages.

An "endowment mortgage" is a mortgage linked to an insurance policy. When the policy matures there should be sufficient funds to pay off the mortgage but this is not guaranteed. In the meantime you only pay interest on the loan. If you die before the end of the agreement the insurance policy would pay off the mortgage. Endowment mortgages usually cost more than repayment mortgages because of the premium for the insurance policy. However, there is the advantage that as with other insurance policies, it is possible to have a "with-profits" element in an endowment policy. This costs more, but it means that the insurance company not only guarantees to provide a minimum sum but also adds "bonuses" each year. The size of the bonus depends on the investment position of the company. When the policy matures the pay-out (including bonuses) should cover the mortgage and leave you with a substantial sum as well. It should be noted however, that there has been a recent trend towards reduced bonus rates and repayment mortgages might be more suitable for many people. Endowment policies should be regarded as a long-term arrangement.

If you surrender an endowment policy early you may receive little or nothing back.

Where to Get a Mortgage.

The majority of mortgages are supplied by building societies and in recent years banks have become an important source of mortgages. Some insurance companies also provide mortgages, but this is only a minor source of loans. Some employers, such as banks and building societies, will provide their employees with loans at favourable rates.

Getting a Mortgage.

The first thing to do is to plan ahead. As we have seen, you will probably need to put up a substantial sum of money of your own, so you should start saving as soon as possible. It can be advantageous to save by investing in a building society. When mortgage funds are in short supply societies are likely to consider their own investors before casual applicants. Building societies have fairly strong preferences about the sort of property they are prepared to lend on. For example, they are often very reluctant to lend on older property. Many building societies are also reluctant to lend on flats. Nevertheless, the lending policies of building societies differ, so if you are turned down by one society, try another. It can also help to ask people who are likely to have close contacts with building societies. Estate agents, your solicitor or bank manager may each be able to suggest a possible source.

How Much Can Be Borrowed?

The final question to be dealt with in this section is how much an individual will be allowed to borrow. As stated above, this partly depends on the value of the house concerned. But it also depends on the financial status of the borrower. Building societies have to safeguard their investors' money. Societies are careful not to lend more to anyone than they are likely to be able to repay. A person with a secure career may therefore be treated more favourably than a person whose future earnings are uncertain. Again, different societies have different policies. None the less, it is very rare for building societies to lend more than two and a half or three times your annual income. Most building societies will also take a spouse's income into account, but for a smaller proportion.

For example, suppose you went to a building society which was prepared to lend up to two and a half times your annual earnings plus an amount equal to your spouse's annual income. If you earn £20,000 and your spouse £10,000, the society would then be prepared to lend you up to £60,000:

Your income	£20,000	Maximum loan	£50,000
Spouse's income	£10,000	Maximum loan	£10,000
		Combined Limit	£60,000

The extent to which your spouse's income is taken into account depends on the lender.

II. TAXES

Taxation permeates almost every aspect of financial life. In addition, the entire subject is exceedingly complex, and the tax system is altered or amended at least once a year. All that will be attempted here, therefore, is a description of some of the most common situations faced by taxpayers. If your circumstances are more complicated you should consult your tax office, or take professional advice, or both.

For reasons which are largely historical, taxes are often divided into *direct* and *indirect* taxes. Direct taxes are paid to the Inland Revenue. There are four main types of direct taxation:

1. Income tax
2. Capital gains tax
3. Inheritance tax (formerly Capital transfer tax)
4. Corporation tax

It could also be argued that National Insurance Contributions are a form of tax and they are also described below.

Indirect taxes are collected mainly by the Customs and Excise. They include:

1. Value added tax
2. Customs and excise duties
3. Car tax
4. Stamp duties

Stamp duties are, however, the responsibility of the Inland Revenue.

In terms of the amount of revenue raised, income tax is by far the most important tax. It is also the tax most likely to affect the average taxpayer directly.

8. INCOME TAX

If you are resident in the United Kingdom tax is levied on your income whether it originates in the UK or from overseas. Even if you are not resident, tax is still levied on any income you have which originates in the UK. Tax is charged for each year of assessment; that is the year from 6 April to the following 5 April.

Income Subject to Tax.

Most types of income are taxable, including the following:

Income from employment. This includes wages, bonuses, commission. tips and benefits in kind, such as the private use of the company's car.

Income from self-employment, business, professions and vocations.

Interest, dividends and annuities.

Rent.

Pensions.

Income not Subject to Tax.

A few types of income are not subject to tax. The main groups are:

The first £70 of interest per person received from ordinary deposit accounts in the National Savings Bank.

Interest on National Savings Certificates and increases in the value of Index-Linked National Insurance Certificates. Also, interest from the Save-As-You-Earn scheme is exempt.

Sickness benefit (but not statutory sick pay), family credit, attendance allowance, maternity benefit, child benefit, housing benefit, invalidity benefit and non-contributory invalidity pension.

Educational grants and awards.

Compensation for loss of employment—up to £30,000.

War widows' pensions.

Wound and disability pensions.

Any wins from gambling, including Premium Bond prizes.

The capital element of annuity payments.

Profit-related pay, within certain limits.

Personal Allowances and Rates of Tax.

Almost everyone is entitled to at least one personal allowance which may be deducted before tax is levied on the remainder of a person's income. The allowances for 1994/95 and 1995/96 are shown in Table 3.

The basic personal allowance is available to individuals generally and there are two levels of higher personal allowances for those aged 65 and over and 75 and over. These higher personal allowances are reduced if total income exceeds a certain limit (£14,200 in 1994/95 and £14,600 in 1995/96). The allowance is reduced by £1 for every £2 that limit is exceeded until it reaches the normal single or married allowance. The married couple's allowance is normally given to the husband though since April 1993 it is possible to choose to split the allowance between spouses. Also, the wife may claim the whole of the married couple's allowance if the husband agrees. Although the married couple's allowance used to be granted at the full 25 per cent basic rate of tax, it has been restricted to 20 per cent from April 1994 and will be restricted to 15 per cent from April 1995.

The additional personal allowance may be claimed by a person who is single, separated, divorced or widowed and has a child living with

TABLE 3. *Personal Allowances Against Gross Income in 1994/95 and 1995/96*

	1994/95	1995/96
	£	£
Personal allowance	3,445	3,525
Personal allowance age 65–74	4,200	4,630
Personal allowance age 75 and over	4,370	4,800
Married couple's allowance	1,720	1,720
Married couple's allowance age 65–74	2,665	2,995
Married couple's allowance age 75 and over	2,705	3,035
Additional personal allowance	1,720	1,720
Widow's bereavement allowance	1,720	1,720
Blind person's allowance	1,200	1,200

him or her for at least part of the year. This allowance may also be claimed by a married man whose wife is incapacitated by illness or disability provided they are living with a child. The widow's bereavement allowance is granted only for the tax year in which the husband died, and the tax year following the bereavement unless the widow remarries. Like the married couple's allowance, the additional personal allowance and the widow's bereavement allowance have been restricted to 20 per cent from 1994 and 15 per cent for 1995. After these personal allowances (and any allowable expenses) have been deducted from gross income, the remaining taxable income is subject to the rates shown in Table 4. The new lower rate of tax was introduced for 1992/93, increased by £500 for both 1993/94 and 1994/95 and a further £200 for 1995/96.

TABLE 4.   *The Rates of Income Tax in 1994/95 and 1995/96*

	Taxable Income	
	1994/95	*1995/96*
	£	£
Lower rate– 20 per cent	1–3,000	1–3,200
Basic rate– 25 per cent	3,001–23,700	3,201–24,300
Higher rate– 40 per cent	over 23,700	over 24,300

9. ASSESSMENT AND COLLECTION

The administration of income tax is the responsibility of the Inland Revenue. In practice, the job is divided into two parts: assessment and collection. The "assessments" for tax are the responsibility of inspectors of taxes in over 700 tax offices spread throughout the country. When an individual's tax has been assessed the information is then passed to a collector of taxes who actually sends out the bill. If you receive a tax bill which you think is wrong you should contact the inspector. The collector has no power to amend the bill, his job is simply to collect the amounts decided between you and the inspector.

For historical reasons, income is divided into six groups known as "schedules." These are:

1. *Schedule A:* Income from property.

2. *Schedule B:* Income from commercial woodlands. Schedule B was finally abolished in 1988.

3. *Schedule C:* Certain interest and annuities paid out of public revenue.

4. *Schedule D:* Income from trades, businesses and professions. Also included are interest, rents and income not covered by other schedules.

5. *Schedule E:* This is the schedule that affects most people as it covers wages and salaries. It also deals with pensions.

6. *Schedule F:* Dividends and other distributions made by companies.

Pay-As-You-Earn.

By far the largest schedule is Schedule E. Nearly all Schedule E income is taxed through the Pay-As-You-Earn (PAYE) system. PAYE is the method used to deduct tax from wages, salaries and some pensions. In order to keep the deductions as accurate as possible, PAYE is operated on a cumulative basis. This means that your earnings, tax paid and so on are accumulated throughout the tax year. This is how it works. At the beginning, or before the start of the tax year, your tax-free allowances are added up. The total is then converted into a code number. For example, if your allowances came to £4,000 and you are married, then your code number would be 400H. The H suffix denotes that you are entitled to the married couple's allowance. If you are single or a working wife the suffix would be L (representing the "lower" single person's allow-

ance). If there are special circumstances, for example if you had a second job, the suffix would probably be T. There are also special suffixes for pensioners. The main ones are P for single people, and V for married pensioners. The new code K is used where the value of the perks from your job are greater than your personal allowances. This enables the excess to be collected through the PAYE system. If your current code number is different from the previous one the tax office will send you a "Notice of Coding." This will show the allowances the tax office has taken into account and how your code number has been calculated. If you do not receive a notice of coding you may request one. You should always check to see that you have received your full entitlement to allowances. Your code number is also sent to your employer so he knows how much tax to deduct from your earnings. It is worth noting that the higher your code, the lower the tax deducted from your pay.

It may be of interest to work through a simple example of PAYE operating. Suppose that a person's allowances for the year amount to £5,200, and the appropriate code is issued to his employer. The principle is that the annual allowances are divided by the number of pay periods in the year. If an individual is paid weekly, therefore, his allowances are divided by 52. In our example the individual would be granted £100 worth of allowances each week. This weekly allowance is then accumulated as the tax year progresses. Hence in, say, week 26 of the tax year the individual would be entitled to £2,600 worth of allowances. At the same time, the PAYE system accumulates the amount of earnings received. This enables the amount of tax to be deducted to be calculated accurately. Suppose the individual in our example earned £140 in Week 1 of the tax year. The employer knows from the code number that the person's allowances for that week amount to £100. The employer then deducts this £100 from the £140 gross pay, which leaves £40 of "taxable pay". The next stage is to calculate the tax due on the £40.

To assist him or her in this process, the employer has two sets of tax tables. The first table converts code numbers into weekly or monthly allowances. After these allowances have been deducted from gross pay the second set of tables is used to calculate the tax due on the remaining pay. In the example, there is £40 of taxable pay, so with a tax rate of, say, 30 per cent, £12 would be deducted in tax. Suppose that the wage in the second week was also £140. Because of the cumulative feature, the value of the allowances would now be £200. (£100 for the second week, plus £100 for the first week). Cumulative pay would now be £280. After deducting the allowances, taxable pay is now £80. The second set of tables would now show a total of £24 due in tax. However, £12 ("cumulative tax paid") was deducted in week 1. The amount of tax due in week 2, therefore, is a further £12 (£24 minus £12 deducted in week 1). This process then continues for the rest of the tax year.

PAYE has a number of advantages. These include accurate deductions of tax. The system can also repay tax during the year if the employee's pay falls substantially. Repayments occur when the value of the allowances accumulates faster than gross pay. The system does not always work in this way. For example, suppose you fail to send your tax return back to the tax office. You may find that you are then put on the Emergency Code (E). This code only gives you allowances equal to the single person's allowance, so if you are entitled to more you will have too much tax deducted. This, of course, provides you with an incentive to sort out your tax affairs with the Inland Revenue. In addition, a taxpayer who becomes unemployed will not normally receive any rebate due until after either he or she ceases to claim unemployment or supplementary benefit, or the end of the tax year. Also, rebates cannot usually be paid while a person is on strike.

Sometimes you may find that you have been put on what is known as a "week 1" basis. This means that tax is being deducted from your pay on a *non-cumulative* basis. In other words, every week is treated as though it were the first week of the tax year. One of the main results of the "week 1" basis is that it prevents tax repayments being made automatically if, say, your income falls through unemployment.

How to Check your Code Number.

As you can see from the above explanation, your code number is the factor that determines the amount of tax that is deducted from your pay. You can check your code number by examining your Notice of Coding. You should compare the allowances and expenses you claimed on your tax return with the ones listed on the Notice. One item which might appear on the Notice of Coding is "Tax unpaid for earlier years." This is to enable the tax office to collect outstanding tax by lowering the value of your code. The tax will then be collected slowly over the tax year rather than in one lump sum.

Appeals.

When your tax for the year is assessed you will be sent a Notice of Assessment. This is often not considered necessary if you are taxed under PAYE and your tax situation is straightforward, though you can still ask for one.

If you receive a Notice of Assessment which you think is wrong you must appeal within 30 days of the date appearing on the Notice. Appeals made after 30 days are normally allowed only if you can provide a satisfactory explanation such as being in hospital or abroad, and can show that the appeal was made without unreasonable delay. Most appeals are settled directly with the inspector. If you and the inspector cannot agree, then the case goes before the Commissioners of Income Tax. There are two types of Commissioners: the General Commissioners and the Special Commissioners. The General Commissioners are unpaid and recruited from members of the public. They sit with a clerk who provides advice on tax law. The Special Commissioners are professional civil servants who are experts in tax matters. It is often said that if your appeal is based on common sense, rather than the intricacies of tax law, you may do better to go to the General Commissioners. Each party pays its own costs for hearings before the Commissioners. If, however, the case is taken on to the High Court, or further, the loser usually pays the costs.

10. HOW TO COMPLETE A TAX RETURN

There are several types of tax return including:

1. *Form P1.* This form is mainly for people who earn a salary or a wage and do not have complicated tax problems. For example, if your main source of income is your job, and you have small amounts of interest from your savings but no other income you will probably receive form P1. (The "P" prefix, incidentally, stands for "Pay-As-You-Earn.")

The form P1 is simpler than some of the other forms. Most people who receive form P1 do not get one every year. When this happens, the reason is that the tax office is pretty sure that it has enough information to ensure you pay the right amount of tax without having to fill in a return every year. But, remember, it is your responsibility to tell the tax office if your tax liability changes as a result of a change in your circumstances.

For example, if you become entitled to a new allowance because, say, you get married, you should tell the inspector. Nobody else will. Alternatively, if you begin to receive a new source of income you should also tell the inspector. He may well find out anyway. For instance, banks must inform the Inland Revenue of the interest they pay to depositors. Concealing income can lead to demands for back tax plus interest. You may also be liable to penalties.

2. *Form 11P.* This form is designed for people with more complicated circumstances. For example, if you have a job and some other outside earnings you will probably be sent form 11P.

3. *Form 11.* This form is mainly for the self-employed.

General Points.

It is very worthwhile keeping a tax file containing all the information relevant to your tax affairs. The whole process of completing a tax return is much simpler if you keep all the relevant documents close together. These documents include items such as: P60 (from your employer); dividend advice slips; receipts for expenses. You may also be asked by the inspector to submit detailed records supporting expense claims. A second point is to keep a copy of your return. A photocopy is perhaps the best method of doing this. Alternatively, you can keep a separate record of what you put in the return as you go along.

Keeping a copy of your return has two advantages. First of all it will help you deal with any questions the inspector may have about your return. Secondly, it will enable you to complete your next return more easily. The tax office usually compares your latest tax return with your previous one to see if you have forgotten something. So it is better if you spot any omissions first. If you get into difficulties with your return, you can always telephone or write to the tax office whose address appears on the front of the form. If you wish to call personally, most tax offices are open for public enquiries between 10 am and 4 pm. But remember to take your tax file with you. It does not matter if you wish to make a personal call and your tax office is hundreds of miles away. This is often the case with Londoners and people who work for large nationwide companies. You can always call at a local office and in London there are special PAYE enquiry offices. (Their addresses are in the telephone directory.) Most enquiries can be handled without recourse to your official file. If the file is needed, the Inland Revenue can arrange to have it sent to a local office.

If you are sent a tax return you should complete and return it to the Inland Revenue within 30 days. If it is not returned by 31 October after the end of the tax year interest may be payable on tax payments delayed as a result.

The Return Itself.

As stated above, there are three main types of return, and there are some other variations. Most returns cover two years. They ask for details of your income and capital gains in the previous tax year, and have room for claims for allowances in the current year. Whichever return you receive you should always read the accompanying notes. The different returns sometimes ask different questions and are set out in a different way, but most include the following areas:

INCOME.

Income from Employment etc.

If you are an employee, you will receive a form P60 from your employer after 5 April each year. The P60 will show your total earnings and tax deducted under PAYE. It should do this even if you changed your job during the year. You should enter the total figure on the return, plus any bonuses, tips and so on. You should also enter any earnings from spare-time jobs. The same information should be entered for your wife.

The tax treatment of overseas earnings is unusually complicated—even by income-tax standards! If you are going to work abroad you should enquire about the tax implications. One place to start is with the Inland Revenue's explanatory leaflets.

Expenses in Employment.

The basic rule covering claims for employment expenses is that they must be incurred wholly, exclusively and necessarily in the performance of the duties of that employment. The rule is usually applied quite strictly. Thus, for example, travel expenses to and from work are not normally allowable because they are not incurred *in the performance* of the duties of the employment. Travelling expenses may be allowed, but only if incurred in the course of the employment.

Nevertheless, there are several types of expenditure which may be claimed. They include subscriptions to professional bodies, tools and some types of industrial clothing. Trade Unions often agree a fixed allowance with the tax office, but you can still claim for actual expenses if they exceed the agreed figure.

Income from Self-employment.

Any profits you make from self-employment should be entered here. This section covers both partnerships and sole traders. The figure required is your net profit for your accounting year which ended in the twelve months to 5 April 1991. If your total receipts are over £15,000, your profit figure should be supported by a set of accounts. If your total receipts are less than £15,000 a year you can complete the three line statement on Forms 11 and 11P. This requires total receipts, allowable expenses and the profit figure. If you do not know what your profits are when you complete the return you should write "per accounts to be submitted." Your accounts should then be sent to the Inspector as soon as possible.

Social Security Pensions and Benefits.

Certain pensions and social security benefits are tax-free and do not have to be entered on the tax return. Further details of these are given in the notes accompanying the return. All other pensions and social security benefits must be entered. "Retirement pension or old person's pension" refers to the state retirement pension. If you are approaching retirement you should inform the tax office. This will help the Revenue make sure that your tax affairs are kept up to date when you retire. Otherwise, it is possible that you many pay too much (or too little) tax until your affairs are sorted out.

Other Pensions.

If a pension is paid by a former employer it will usually be taxed through the PAYE system. At the end of the tax year, therefore, you should receive a form P60 showing the gross pension paid during the year. This section also covers pensions from abroad.

Income from Property.

Rent can be treated in one of two ways. If the accommodation is furnished *and* the rent covers services such as meals and cleaning the income will be treated as *earned* income. If the accommodation is unfurnished *or* it is furnished and the rent does not cover services the rent will be treated as *investment* income. The figures required are those for total income, expenses and net income. It is only the last of these, the net income, that is taxable, and included in the taxpayer's total income. The details of property income should be presented in a separate statement.

The expenses that may be claimed include:

Repairs and maintenance.

Insurance for the structure and its contents (but not insurance against loss of rent).

Costs of providing services to tenants.

Wear and tear for furniture and fittings. The allowance is usually 10 per cent of the rent receivable.

Management expenses. This includes items such as agents' commission for letting the property or collecting the rent.

Under the rent-a-room scheme, if you let a spare room in your home you can receive up to £3,250 rent a year tax-free. If you take advantage of this scheme you cannot also claim expenses in respect of the rent.

Dividends from United Kingdom Companies, etc.

Because dividends from UK companies and distributions from unit trusts are accompanied by a "tax credit," you do not have to pay basic-rate tax on them. However, you still have to enter the dividends and tax credits from each company or unit trust, in case you are liable to higher-rate tax or are entitled to a rebate. The necessary information will be shown on your dividend slips. If you do not have enough room, make out a separate list and submit it with the return. The totals should be entered on the return itself. One point should be made about unit trusts. Part of the first distribution you receive will be called *equalisation*. This is part of your capital, and *so should not* be entered on the return.

Other Dividends, etc.

This section requires you to enter the gross (before tax) amount of income from each source. Where tax has already been deducted from foreign income you should give the details.

Interest not Taxed before Receipt.

The first £70 of interest received from ordinary (but *not* investment) accounts with the National Savings Banks is exempt from tax. Your husband or wife is also entitled to a £70 exemption. You should still enter the total amounts of interest from both ordinary and investment accounts. Also enter interest from National Savings Income and Deposit bonds, British Government stocks bought on the National Savings Stock Register and any other taxable interest which you recieve without tax being deducted at source.

Interest from UK Banks and Building Societies.

Bank and Building society interest is "tax paid"—but this only saves you from tax at the basic rate. If you are liable to higher rates of tax you will have to pay more tax on the interest. The Inland Revenue will calculate the additional amount of tax payable. For this purpose, the interest payment will be *grossed up* to include tax at the basic rate.

All Other Income or Profit.

As you can guess, this section is for any source of income not covered elsewhere.

Capital Gains.

You should give details of the assets you have bought and sold during the tax year. Capital gains tax and how to calculate your gain or loss are discussed in greater detail below.

Personal Tax Allowances.

Unlike the income part of the return, which refers to income received in the previous year, the allowances section refers to your entitlement in the current year. Compared to some aspects of income tax, the allowances are relatively straightforward. The basic personal tax allowance is normally given automatically. This section of the return can be used to claim any of the other personal or higher allowances you are entitled to.

11. CAPITAL GAINS TAX

When you dispose of an asset or possession you may make a capital gains or a capital loss. An asset is property of any kind. It includes both property in the United Kingdom and property overseas. You are considered to have disposed of an asset if you sell it, lose it, exchange it or give it away. However, the transfer of a possession between a husband and wife who are not separated is not considered to be a disposal.

Tax-free Gains.

The following assets are exempt from capital gains tax:

Your home (but see below).

Personal possessions, household goods and other chattels, provided that each item is worth £6,000 or less at the time of its disposal. A set of goods, for example a pair of vases, is counted as one item. (*Chattels* means tangible, movable property.)

Animals, private cars, caravans and boats. Also other chattels which are wasting assets; that is assets expected to last 50 years or less.

Life assurance policies.

National Savings Certificates, British Savings Bonds and Save-As-You-Earn.

British government stocks if owned for more than one year or inherited. This exemption has been extended to corporate bonds (*e.g.* debentures) which are issued after 13 March 1984 and which are held for at least twelve months.

British money.

Foreign currency obtained for personal or family expenditure.

Winnings from betting or from Premium Bonds.

Gifts to charities.

Gifts to certain institutions such as the National Trust and the British Museum.

Your Own Home.

When you sell your house any capital gains you make will normally be exempt from tax. From 1980/81 onwards this exemption has applied (within certain limits) if you let part of your home. However, there are a number of circumstances in which you may get only partial exemption. For example, if you use part of your home for business you may not be allowed full exemption from capital gains tax. These circumstances are described in more detail in the Inland Revenue leaflet CGT4, *Capital Gains Tax—Owner-occupied houses.* You should enter any gains from the disposal of your house on your tax return in case they are not wholly exempt.

Capital Losses.

Your capital gains can be reduced by deducting allowable losses. An allowable capital loss is usually one which would have been taxable if it had been a gain. For example, a loss on an item which is exempt, such as your car, would *not* be considered an allowable loss. If your losses exceed your gains in the tax year you can carry the balance forward to set against gains in future years. You can also deduct allowable expenditure from your capital gains (or add them to your capital losses). Allowable expenditure includes the costs of acquiring or disposing of an asset; for example, commission, conveyancing costs and advertising. It also includes expenditure which increases the value of the asset, such as improvements to property.

Working Out Your Gain.

Normally your capital gain (or loss) is the amount you receive when disposing of the asset *minus* the original amount you paid for it. If you give the asset away, the market value at the time of disposal is used instead. The same method is used if you were originally given the asset, or if you inherited it.

Shares.

If you buy batches of the same share at different prices the cost of each share is considered to be the average cost. For example, suppose you purchase 100 shares in a company for £200. Three months later you buy a further 100 of the same shares for £300. You would then have a total of 200 shares which cost you £500. The average cost is, therefore, £2·50 per share. When you come to sell all or some of these shares the calculation of your gain or loss will be based on this average cost.

The Rates of Capital Gains Tax.

From its introduction in 1965 to 1988, capital gains tax was levied at a flat rate of 30 per cent. From 6

April 1988 capital gains have been charged at an individual's highest income tax rate. However the tax is only applied to an individual's gains over £5,800 (in the tax year 1992/93 onwards) during the year and £6,000 from 1995/96. Gains accruing prior to April 1982 are exempt.

12. INHERITANCE TAX
(Formerly **CAPITAL TRANSFER TAX**)

Inheritance tax emerged from the remains of the previous capital transfer tax in March 1986. Capital transfer tax applied to transfers of capital made both during life and on a person's death.

Capital transfer tax had replaced the old estate duty which was imposed on property passing at death, and gifts made within 7 years before death. The position has now turned full circle because, essentially, inheritance tax, like the old estate duty, is levied on transfers between individuals made on the death of the donor, or up to 7 years before his or her death.

The Tax.

Inheritance tax is payable on transfers made on or after 18 March 1986 on transfers made at death or in the years preceding death. Certain gifts, most of which are listed below, are exempt from tax. All other gifts which are not exempt and which are made within 7 years of death are taxable as soon as the total amount of taxable transfers exceeds the threshold for tax. For 1992/93 to 1994/95 the threshhold for tax was £150,000 and for 1995/96 the threshhold is £154,000.

Furthermore, there are rules, similar to those operated under estate duty, which apply where the donor continues to enjoy some benefit from a gift even after it has been 'given away'. For example, this might apply where a person gives his or her home to the children, but continues to live in it. If this happens, for the purpose of inheritance tax, the gift will normally be treated as if it had been given on the date such enjoyment finally ceases.

The method of valuing assets largely continues on from the previous capital transfer tax and estate duty. Assets are usually valued at the price they would fetch on the open market at the time of transfer.

The value of the estate on death will be taxed as the top slice of cumulative transfers in the 7 years before death. (For capital transfer tax the cumulation period was 10 years.)

From 1995/96 the tax is levied at a single rate of 40 per cent on transfers over the £154,000 threshold. However, where gifts are made between individuals more than 3 years before the death of the donor the rate of tax is reduced by the relevant percentage given in Table 5. Different rules apply to gifts into and out of trust, discretionary trust charges and gifts involving companies.

TABLE 5. *Relief for Lifetime Transfers*

Years between gift and death	Percentage of full charge
0–3	100
3–4	80
4–5	60
5–6	40
6–7	20
Over 7	0

Exempt Transfers.

Certain transfers are eligible for exemption in much the same way as they were under capital transfer tax, including the following:

Transfers up to £3,000 in any one year (unused relief may be carried forward for one year only).

Small gifts of up to £250 to any one recipient in any tax year.

Gifts made as part of normal expenditure.

Marriage gifts as follows:

Parents	£5,000 each
Grandparents	£2,500 each
Bride and groom	£2,500 to each other
Other people	£1,000 each

Transfers between husband and wife if the recipient is domiciled in the United Kingdom.

Gifts to charities and political parties. A 'political party' is defined for this purpose as one with two M.P.s, or one M.P. and not less than 150,000 votes for its candidates at the last general election.

Gifts for national purposes, *etc.* For example, gifts to the National Trust, National Gallery, universities and museums are exempt.

Other Relief.

There is also some relief for business assets, agricultural land and shares which represent a controlling interest in a company. In addition, a certain amount of relief is available for minority shareholdings in unquoted companies.

Administration and Collection.

The responsibility for the administration of inheritance tax lies with the Inland Revenue, and the procedures for assessment, appeals and penalties are similar to those for income tax. As with the previous capital transfer tax, the responsibility for dealing with Inland Revenue enquiries about transfers made before death lies with the personal representatives of the deceased. Where a person's death creates tax liability on gifts previously made, the main responsibility for the tax falls on the recipient, but with recourse to the donor's estate if necessary.

13. VALUE ADDED TAX

Value Added Tax (VAT) was introduced in the United Kingdom on 1 April 1973, and replaced the old Purchase Tax and Selective Employment Tax. One of the main reasons for changing the system was to harmonise the UK's indirect tax system with those of the other members of the Common Market, each of which now has some kind of value added tax.

As its name suggests, VAT is levied on the goods and services you buy. In the budget of June 1979, the standard and higher rates of VAT were amalgamated into a single rate of 15 per cent and this was increased to 17.5 per cent in April 1991. The government, however, has the power to vary the rates of VAT by up to a quarter during the year in the interests of economic management. Some goods and services are "zero-rated" and others are "exempted" from VAT, a distinction which is explained shortly.

Anyone who has a business with a turnover of £46,000 per year or more must register with the Customs and Excise. In some circumstances it can be advantageous to register even if you have a business with a turnover below this (*see* "Registration" on **H18**).

How VAT Works.

VAT is payable at every stage of production when goods and services are supplied either to another business or to the final consumer. VAT is also payable on imported goods (and some imported services). The tax is charged by the supplier, who then pays it over to the Customs and Excise. For example, a simple VAT invoice for a good would show:

	£
Goods supplied	100·00
VAT at 17·5%	17·50
Total payable	£117·50

When a business calculates how much VAT is payable to the Customs and Excise it can deduct any VAT it has been *charged* on the goods and services it has purchased itself. For instance, suppose a firm buys some wood for £100 (plus £17·50 VAT) which it turns into furniture and sells for £200 (plus £35 VAT). The tax position would

then be as follows:

	£	£
Receipts for furniture	200	
VAT charged to customer		35·00
Cost of wood	100	
VAT charged by supplier		17·50
VAT payable to Customs & Excise		£17·50

The final customer is charged £35 VAT and the Customs and Excise receives £35 in VAT (£17·50 from the furniture maker and £17·50 from the wood supplier).

In principle, each business pays tax on only the *value* it has *added* to its output. In our example above, the firm took £100 worth of wood and turned it into £200 worth of furniture. It could be said, therefore, that the firm has increased the value of the wood by £100. Accordingly, £17.50 VAT is payable to the Customs and Excise. Since each firm is taxed on its "value added," and charges the tax to its customer, the eventual VAT bill is related to the final value of the product and is paid by the final customer.

The way VAT is operated can be further illustrated by tracing the production of a good from the raw material stage through to the sale to the final customer. *See* Table on **H18**.

Zero-rated Supplies.

Goods and services that are "zero-rated" are in principle subject to VAT, but the rate applying to them is zero. This means that while VAT is not charged on these goods, businesses can still recover VAT paid on their own purchases. The effect of this arrangement is that zero-rated goods and services should be entirely free of VAT. For example, exports are relieved of VAT in this way.

Goods and services which are zero-rated may be summarised as follows:

Food—but not items such as pet foods, ice cream, soft drinks, alcoholic drinks, "meals out," and hot takeaway food and drink.

Water—except distilled water and bottled water.

Books—including newspapers, periodicals, music and maps (stationery is taxable).

Talking books and wireless sets for the blind.

News services. News services supplied to newspapers.

Fuel and Power—but not petrol and petrol substitutes. However VAT has been charged on domestic fuel and power from 1 April 1994 at a rate of 8 per cent.

Construction—of buildings.

Transport—except taxis, hired cars and boats and aircraft used for recreation.

Caravans—provided they are too large to be used as trailers on the roads. Houseboats are also zero-rated.

Gold and banknotes—but not gold coins or jewellery.

Drugs, medicines, medical and surgical appliances—provided they are purchased on a prescription.

Exports.

Charities.

Clothing and Footwear—for young children, industrial protective clothing and crash helmets.

Exempt Supplies.

Exempt goods and services are not subject to VAT, even in principle. A business cannot take any credit for VAT paid on the supplies used to produce exempt goods. Exemption is therefore less advantageous than zero-rating, but if a good falls into both categories it is zero-rated. Exempt items include:

Land.

Insurance including brokers' services.

Postal services, but not telephones and telex.

Betting, gaming and lotteries.

Finance such as banking.

Education—including incidental services.

Health.

Burial and cremation services.

Trade Unions and Professional Bodies

Sports Competitions.

	Basic Price £	VAT £	Amount Received by Customs and Excise (C & E) £
Manufacturer imports raw materials	1,000	175	
Manufacturer pays VAT to C & E			+175
Manufacturer sells goods to wholesaler	2,000	350	
Manufacturer pays VAT to C & E			+350 (£350 minus £175)
Wholesaler sells goods to retailers	3,000	525	
Wholesaler pays VAT to C & E			+175 (£525 minus £350)
Retailers sell goods to customers	5,000	875	
Retailers pay VAT to C & E			+350 (£875 minus £525)
Customers pay	5,000 plus 875 VAT		
Customs and Excise receive total			£875

The Tax Point.

The tax point is the date on which liability to VAT arises. There are rigid rules for fixing the tax point. This is to prevent businesses from gaining an unfair advantage from manipulating the date of transactions, either to delay the payment of VAT, or to take advantage of changes in the rates of tax.

Basically the tax point is the date when goods are despatched or made available to the customer. There are, however, two main exceptions to this. First, if an invoice is issued within 14 days of this time, the date of the invoice becomes the tax point. Secondly, if payment is made in advance, the date of payment becomes the tax point. It is also possible for particular businesses to make special arrangements with the Customs and Excise regarding the tax point.

Registration.

As already stated, anyone who has a business which has a taxable turnover of £46,000 or more a year must register with the Customs and Excise. For this purpose a "business" means any trade, profession or vocation. This includes partnerships, one-man businesses and free-lance work. It also includes clubs and associations such as sports clubs, but it does not include trade unions.

Businesses with a turnover of less than £46,000 a year are not liable to register, but it might be in their interests to do so. Where a trader pays more VAT for his supplies than he receives from his customers, he may be entitled to a rebate. This is most likely to happen where a business makes or supplies mainly items that are zero-rated or exported, but it may also happen with a new business. Rebates can be claimed only by registered traders.

To register for VAT, you simply contact the local VAT office (the address will be in the local telephone directory under "Customs and Excise"). You will then be sent form VAT 1, which you will have to complete and return. If a person wishes to de-register he may do so if he can satisfy the Customs and Excise that his taxable turnover (including the VAT) of all his business activities in the next 12 months will have fallen sufficiently. You can also, of course, deregister if you sell, cease trading or retire from your business.

VAT Records.

Businesses which are not exempt from VAT are required to keep certain records of their purchases and sales and the VAT relating to them. Furthermore, a *tax account* must be kept. This should contain a summary of the VAT totals from the main records and also VAT payments made to the Customs, or any repayments received.

Most businesses also have to issue *tax invoices* when making sales. Exceptions are retail businesses and sales of zero-rated goods and services. A tax invoice has to include the business's VAT registration number, the invoice number, the tax point and the tax charged.

Returns and Payment.

Traders registered for VAT have to make a return every three months whilst large VAT payers are required to make monthly payments on account.

Some traders who are likely to receive rebates may also be allowed to submit returns every month. The return must be made within 30 days of the end of the period to which it relates, and any VAT due should normally be paid at the same time.

Essentially, the return requires the trader to calculate the value of his sales and the VAT charged thereon. He must also add up all the purchases of his business and the VAT paid on these inputs. The basic calculation will then look something like this:

Total sales for the period	£10,000	
VAT received		£1,750
Total inputs (purchases) for the period	£8,000	
VAT paid		£1,400
Balance payable to the Customs & Excise		£350

Appeals.

There are independent VAT tribunals to deal with appeals over a wide range of issues. This includes whether or not a trader should be registered and, if so, what the effective date of registration is; the amount of VAT payable; the amount of credit that can be taken for VAT paid on a business's purchases; and the value of goods and services supplied. From the tribunal there is an appeal to the High Court and from there to the Court of Appeal on a point of law (but not questions of fact). In Scotland such appeals go to the Court of Session. There are time limits for submitting appeals, and the procedure for appealing to the VAT Tribunals is described in a booklet available from the local VAT office.

Retailers.

Retailers are in a special position because they are usually unable to record each sale separately. Retailers are not required to issue tax invoices unless asked by customers, and there are several special schemes for calculating the amount of VAT payable. Retailers usually charge a price which is inclusive of VAT, and the amount of VAT can be calculated by using the appropriate fractions. With the rate of 17·5 per cent the relevant fraction is 7/47ths of the gross price. For example, the amount of VAT payable on an article with a gross price of £117·50 would be £117·50 × 7/47 = £17·50.

Further Information.

The Customs and Excise provide a series of detailed leaflets which cover all aspects of VAT, and which are available free of charge from any VAT office.

14. NATIONAL INSURANCE CONTRIBUTIONS

There are four classes of National Insurance. Class 1 relates to employees, Classes 2 and 4 to the self-employed and Class 3 is voluntary.

The Class 1 contribution is paid partly by the employee and partly by the employer. Employees pay contributions of 2 per cent of their earnings up to the 'lower earnings limit' (£59 a week in 1995/96) and 10 per cent of earnings between the lower earnings limit and the 'upper earnings limit' (£440 a week in 1995/96). Employees contracted out of the state earnings related pension scheme pay a lower rate of contribution on earnings between the lower and upper earnings limits. No further contributions are required on earnings over the upper earnings limit and employees with earnings below the lower earnings do not pay any Class 1 contributions at all. A similar contribution is required from employers except that there is no upper earnings limit on the employer's contributions.

Class 2 contributions are payable by the self-employed and are levied at a flat rate of £5·85 in 1995/96. This contribution is payable if earnings from self-employment exceed a minimum amount which is £3,310 for 1995/96. The self-employed are also liable to Class 4 contributions which are related to the level of their profits. For the year 1995/96 the rate of contribution was 7·3 per cent of profits between £6,640 and £22,880. However from 1985/86, 50 per cent of this contribution receives relief from income tax. Finally Class 3 contributions are payable at a flat rate of £5·75 in 1995/96.

III. MISCELLANY

THE COUNCIL TAX

The new council tax was introduced in April 1993. The new tax is based on property but there is also a personal element. The property element is assessed using a new system of banding which is constructed around average property values. Every home in Britain is allocated to one of eight bands according to its value. Properties in the same band in a local authority area are assessed to tax on the same basis. The tax levied on homes in the highest band is limited to two and a half times the amount levied on homes in the lowest band.

The assessment to tax begins with the assumption that each home contains two adults, but households of three or more adults are not charged extra. However a personal element remains in that single adult households receive a discount of 25 per cent of the basic charge. Discounts are also extended to students. If the first or second adult in a household is a student, a student nurse or Youth Training trainee, he or she is entitled to a personal discount. So, for example, in a household of students and no other adults, two 25 per cent discounts are available.

For individuals with a second home, the tax should be reduced by two personal discounts so that only half the usual charge would apply.

People on low incomes may be entitled to Council Tax Benefit. The claim form for Income Support also includes a claim form for Council Tax Benefit. For those not claiming Income Support a claim form should be available from the Council, or Regional Council in Scotland.

Valuations for Council Tax.

The value of each home for the purposes of council tax is the value on 1 April 1991. This is worked out on the basis of the amount the home could have been sold for on the open market if it had been sold on 1 April 1991. Each home is put in one of the eight bands shown in Table A. The amount of council tax payable is then calculated on the basis of the band in which your home is placed.

TABLE A
COUNCIL TAX VALUATION BANDS

Band	£
A	Up to 40,000
B	40,001–52,000
C	52,001–68,000
D	68,001–88,000
E	88,001–120,000
F	120,001–160,000
G	160,001–320,000
H	Over 320,000

Appeals.

It is not possible, of course, to appeal against the amount of council tax your council decides to raise.

However, there are some grounds for appeal. One of these is where there has been a *material change* in the value of the home. This may arise, for example, because part of the dwelling has been demolished. There is no appeal on the grounds that there has been a general movement in house prices. A leaflet entitled "Council Tax—How to Appeal" should be available from your local council.

CHILD SUPPORT AGENCY

The 1991 Child Support Act came into effect on 5 April 1993 when the Child Support Agency (CSA), an arm of the Department of Social Security, began operating. The principle underlying the Act was that "absent parents" should pay maintenance for their children living with former partners ("people with care"), the majority of whom depended on social security benefits. Fewer than a third of the 1,300,000 lone parents caring for two million children in 1993 received child maintenance.

The CSA concentrated initially on lone parents making new claims for Income Support, Family Credit or Disability Working Allowance. They were asked to authorise the CSA to pursue absent parents for child maintenance. Parents already on these benefits were to be approached by the CSA between 1993–96. If a lone parent "unreasonably refused to co-operate" with the CSA her benefit would be reduced for 18 months. Refusal to co-operate was only accepted where there was a risk that pursuing the absent parent would cause the lone parent or a child living with her to suffer "harm or undue distress".

Child support maintenance was calculated by the CSA according to a rigid formula. It was argued that the amounts would be more consistent than those previously imposed in court settlements. Critics of the Act, though often agreeing with its principle, objected to the punitive nature of the "reduced benefit direction". They also complained that since whatever child maintenance a parent received was deducted from her benefit she would end up no better off. Indeed, it was claimed that the purpose of the CSA was primarily to reduce benefits expenditure, with estimated annual savings of £530 million. Making the services of CSA available to lone parents not on benefits are to be phased in up to 1997 and these parents will have to pay a fee.

By 1994, however, the operations of the Child Support Agency were increasingly attracting criticism – not just from fathers but from the women and children whom the Act had been designed to help.

The difficulties facing the Child Support Agency were highlighted in December 1994 when it was decided, because of a backlog of 350,000 cases, to suspend pursuing one-third of the absent fathers on its books.

In January 1995, after continuing criticism over the working of the Agency, the Social Services Secretary, Peter Lilley, announced several important changes. These included a new limit on how much an absent parent should pay (30% maximum of his or her net income) and greater discretionary powers for the CSA. Clean-break settlements, where both partners had agreed to a division of their capital, would now be taken into account by the agency, as would the housing costs of second families.

A limited right of appeal on assessments is conceded. The deadline of 1996 for separated parents not on benefit to begin using the CSA to overturn settlements agreed in court has been deferred indefinitely.

Payments by better-off absent parents will be cut substantially.

THE TAXPAYERS CHARTER

Under the new provisions and guidelines of this charter, the taxpayer is entitled to expect the Inland Revenue:

To be fair
- by settling your tax affairs impartially
- by expecting you to pay only what is due under the law
- by treating everyone with equal fairness

To help you
- to get your tax affairs right
- to understand your rights and obligations
- by providing clear leaflets and forms
- by giving you information and assistance at the enquiry offices
- by being courteous at all times

To provide an efficient service
- by settling your tax affairs promptly and accurately
- by keeping your tax affairs strictly confidential
- by using the information you give only as allowed by the law
- by keeping to a minimum your costs of complying with the law
- by keeping your costs down

To be accountable for what they do
- by setting standards for themselves and publishing how well they live up to them

If you are not satisfied
- they will tell you exactly how to complain
- you can ask for your tax affairs to be looked at again
- you can appeal to an independent tribunal
- your MP can refer your complaint to the Ombudsman

In return, they need you
- to be honest
- to give us accurate information
- to pay your tax on time.

THE PENSIONS BILL

In December 1994, the Government introduced a new pensions bill. Among its provisions, the bill aims to improve safeguards for those in company pension schemes and it will also equalise retirement ages for men and women. The main changes proposed in the bill are as follows:

A new Occupational Pensions Regulator will have powers to investigate and impose sanctions

State pension ages for men and women to be equalised at 65 by 2020

Company pension rights after 1997 will have to rise in line with inflation, up to a maximum of 5pc per annum

Older people will be encouraged to opt out of the State Earnings Related Pensions Scheme by age related rebates of up to 9pc of NI contributions

Members of company pension schemes will have the right to nominate one third of trustees

There will be statutory minimum solvency requirements for company pensions to hold sufficient assets to match liabilities

Where a pension scheme cannot meet its liabilities and the company becomes insolvent, a new statutory compensation scheme will make good 90pc of the deficit

Company pension schemes will be prohibited from investing more than 5pc of assets in the employer's company

Personal pension planholders may wait until they are 75 before buying an annuity.

MYTHS AND LEGENDS

This popular section gives a brief introduction to the myths and legends of Greece and Rome in an easily referable form. Great artists and writers throughout the ages have enriched their work by reference to these ancient tales of the classical world and some knowledge of them is indispensable to the full appreciation of our art and literature.

I. CLASSICAL MYTHOLOGY

A

Abas. In Greek mythology either (1) the son of Celeus and Metanira. His mockery of Demeter (q.v.) as she drank resulted in his being turned into a lizard, or
(2) the twelfth king of Argolis who owned a magic shield from which he derived authority. He was the father of Acrisius (q.v.) and Proetus (q.v.).

Abderus. The friend of Heracles (q.v.) in whose care Heracles left the mares of Diomedes (q.v.). The horses ate him and Heracles founded Abdera, a coastal town in Thrace, in his honour.

Absyrtus (or Apsyrtus). Half brother of the sorceress Medea (q.v.). When Aëtes pursued Jason (q.v.) and Medea, in order to recover the golden fleece, Medea slew the boy, cut his corpse into pieces and tossed the pieces into the sea. Because Aëtes stopped his ship to collect the pieces of his son for burial Jason and Medea were able to escape.

Abyla. See "Pillars of Hercules".

Acamas. Son of Theseus (q.v.) and Phaedra (q.v.), brother of Demophon (q.v.). He went to Troy (q.v.) with Diomedes (q.v.) to demand the return of Helen (q.v.). He and his brother also rescued their grandmother Aethra, who had been Helen's slave, when Troy fell.

Acastus. Son of Pelias King of Iolcos and one of the Argonauts (q.v.). When Medea (q.v.) caused his father's death he banished her and Jason (q.v.). Showed hospitality to Peleus (q.v.) but suspecting him of advances towards his wife he left Peleus to die at the hands of the Centaurs (q.v.). Later Peleus returned to slay the couple. Acastus was the father of Laodamia (q.v.).

Acestes. In Roman mythology a chieftain of Trojan descent who had settled in Sicily prior to the arrival of Aeneas (q.v.).

Achelous. A great river god, the son of Oceanus (q.v.) and Tethys (q.v.). By defeating Achelous Heracles (q.v.) won the hand of Deianeira (q.v.) daughter of Oeneus (q.v.).

Acheron. A real river of Epirus flowing into the Ionian Sea. Part of it runs underground which may account for its position in Greek mythology. Here it is the "river of grief" which flows in the underworld of the dead.

Achilles. A Greek warrior who is the principal character of the *Iliad*. The son of Peleus (q.v.) King of the Myrmidones at Phthia in Thessaly and Thetis (q.v.) one of the Nereids (q.v.). As a baby his mother dipped him in the Styx (q.v.) making him invulnerable save for his heel, by which she held him. He was educated in the arts of war and hunting, and in morality, by Cheiron (q.v.). His mother, knowing that he would die at Troy (q.v.) tried to prevent him joining the Greek expedition there by disguising him as a girl and sending him to the court of Lycomedes, king of Scyros. Here Lycomedes' daughter Deidamia, bore him a son, Neoptolemus (q.v.). Odysseus (q.v.) learned of this subterfuge and visited Lycomedes' court disguised as a merchant. While the king's daughters and the disguised Achilles were surveying his wares he suddenly produced swords which Achilles eagerly clasped, thus revealing himself. Achilles proved himself the most formidable warrior at Troy. At Tenedos on the way to Troy he killed King Tenes and his father Cyncus and by raiding Aeneas' (q.v.) cattle prompted him to join the Trojan forces. In the tenth year of the war Achilles quarrelled with Agamemnon (q.v.) over the captive girl Briseis and withdrew from the fighting. However he loaned his armour to Patroclus, his cousin and friend who was slain by Hector (q.v.). His death prompted Achilles to cease sulking in his tent and to return to the fray. Thetis gave him new armour made by Hephaestus (q.v.) and wearing this he slew Hector. He also killed Penthesilea (q.v.) and the

Greek Thersites (q.v.). After killing Memnon (q.v.) Achilles was shot in his vulnerable ankle at a battle near the Scaean gate (q.v.) Odysseus and Ajax (q.v.) recovered his body and argued over his armour.

Acis. In later Greek legend the young son of Faunus (q.v.) and a river nymph. He loved the sea-nymph Galatea (q.v.) and was killed by his jealous rival Polyphemus (q.v.). According to Sicilian tradition he was then turned into the river of the same name which runs at the foot of Mount Etna. This tradition first appears in the writing of Theocritus (q.v.) and later in Ovid's (q.v.) "Metamorphoses". It inspired paintings by Poussin and Claude and the opera *Acis and Galatea* by Handel.

Acrisius. Son of Abas (q.v.), twin brother of Proetus (q.v.) and King of Argos. Warned by an oracle that the son of his daughter Danaë (q.v.) would kill him he had her locked up in a brazen tower. But this was to no avail because Zeus (q.v.) visited her and fathered Perseus (q.v.), Acrisius then cast mother and son adrift on the sea, locked in a chest. Years later Perseus returned to Argos causing Acrisius to flee to Larissa. However Perseus, visiting Larissa to take part in the games, accidentally killed him with a discus.

Acropolis. In general terms a high citadel found in all Greek cities. The best known acropolis is that at Athens which was first inhabited around 2000 B.C. From time immemorial it was dedicated to Athene (q.v.).

Actaeon. Mythical huntsman and grandson of Cadmus (q.v.) of Thebes. Artemis (q.v.) turned him into a stag, torn to pieces by his own hounds because he inadvertently sight her bathing. The story is recounted in Ovid's (q.v.) "Metamorphoses" and recalled in the works of Titian, Veronese, Poussin, Rembrandt, Gainsborough and Parmigiano.

Admetus. King of Pherae in Thessaly and husband of the beautiful Alcestis (q.v.). Apollo (q.v.) offered to allow Admetus to avoid death if one of his family would die in his place. Alcestis offered herself but according to legend either Persephone (q.v.) refused the self-sacrifice or Heracles (q.v.) rescued Alcestis from Hades (q.v.). This forms the theme of one of Euripedes' best known plays and Gluck's opera *Alceste* (in which Apollo not Heracles saves her).

Adonis. A Syrian deity associated with the mystery of vegetation. He was a beautiful Cypriot youth, the son of Myrrha and her father. For this incest Myrrha was turned into a tree. Nine months later Adonis was born from the bark of the tree, taken up by Aphrodite (q.v.) and placed in the care of Persephone (q.v.). He spent alternate parts of the year with Persephone and Aphrodite who loved him. He was killed by a boar sent by Artemis (q.v.). Shakespeare's *Venus and Adonis* is based on Ovid's (q.v.) version of the tale while Shelley's elegy on the death of Keats, *Adonais*, derives its title from Bion's *Lament for Adonis*. Adonis was painted by Titian, Veronese and Poussin.

Adrastus. Son of Talaus and King of Argos. An oracle told him that his offspring would be a lion and a boar and in accordance with this he gave his daughter Argia to Polynices (q.v.) and her sister to Tydeus (q.v.) who bore images of these animals on their shields. He attempted to restore Polynices to his throne at Thebes (see **Seven against Thebes**). He survived this adventure—some say due to his magic horse Arion (q.v.)—and led a second expedition (of the Epigoni, q.v.) against Thebes, dying of grief when he heard that his son Aegialeus had fallen in the attack.

Aeacides. The descendants of Aeacus (q.v.).

Aeacus. Son of Zeus and Aegina and King of the Myrmidones. The Myrmidones were originally ants, transformed into men by Zeus at the request of Aeacus. He aided Poseidon (q.v.) and Apollo (q.v.) in the construction of the walls of Troy. He had two sons, Peleus (q.v.) and Telamon (q.v.) by his wife Endeis. He was also the father of Phocus (q.v.) by a Nereid. Aeacus later exiled Peleus (future father of Achilles) for the murder of Phocus. A model of virtue and piety, Aeacus was made one of the three judges of the Underworld.

Aeaea. In the Odyssey the island home of Circe (q.v.).

Aedon. In Greek mythology the wife of Zethus, king of Thebes. She was jealous of Niobe, wife of Zethus' brother Amphion (q.v.). In trying to murder Niobe's son she killed her own son Itylus by mistake. In pity Zeus (q.v.) turned her into a nightingale whose song still mourns Itylus.

Aegaeon. Alternative name for Briareus (q.v.).

Aegeus. King of Athens and father of Theseus (q.v.) by Aethra (q.v.) daughter of Pittheus king of Troezen. She brought Theseus up secretly at her father's court, during which time Aegeus married Medea (q.v.). When Theseus finally returned to his father's court Medea fled. Before Theseus went to slay the Minotaur (q.v.) he and Aegeus agreed that he would hoist a white sail when returning to Athens to signal his success. On returning Theseus forgot to do this and Aegeus seeing a black sail on his son's ship supposed him dead and, in grief threw himself into the sea, henceforth called the Aegean.

Aegisthus. The son of Thyestes (q.v.) by his daughter Pelopia. Pelopia exposed the baby but it was rescued by her husband Atreus (q.v.) who believed it to be his own son. Atreus was king of Mycenae and when Thyestes, an enemy, returned in later years he ordered Aegisthus to kill him. But father and son recognised each other and Aegisthus killed Atreus. Thyestes became king of Mycenae but Atreus had had two sons by Aerope, Menelaus (q.v.) and Agamemnon (q.v.). Agamemnon expelled Thyestes and reclaimed his father's throne. While Agamemnon was at Troy (q.v.) Aegisthus seduced his wife Clytemnestra (q.v.) and helped her murder him on his return. These two murderers of Agamemnon now ruled Mycenae. But at the urging of his sister Electra (q.v.) (whom Aegisthus would have liked to kill and whom he forced to marry a peasant) Agamemnon's son Orestes (q.v.) and his friend Pylades (q.v.) returned from exile in Phocis and with Electra's help avenged their father, slaying Aegisthus and Clytemnestra.

Aeneas. The Trojan hero regarded by the Romans as their ancestor. The son of Anchises (q.v.) and Aphrodite (q.v.). Led the survivors of the Trojan War to Italy. The lover of Dido. See under **Aeneid.**

Aeneid. Virgil's (q.v.) unfinished epic poem. In 12 volumes, it is written to honour Rome, to increase the prestige of Augustus (by recalling the deeds of his supposed ancestor) and to foretell prosperity to come. It describes Aeneas' (q.v.) wanderings after Troy fell, recounting his stay in Carthage and love for Dido (q.v.) the funeral games of his father Anchises (q.v.) in Sicily, a journey to the Underworld to visit his dead father's spirit and his arrival at the mouth of the Tiber where he landed on the Latin shore. Here he fought wars with the Latins and their allies before finally defeating Turnus the Rutulian prince and uniting the races by marrying Lavinia the Latin princess. He founded Lavinium, named in her honour.

Aeolian Isles. The present Aeolian Isles are off the North East of Sicily, forming part of the Liparia group. They are mentioned in the Odyssey.

Aeolus. In Greek mythology (1) the son of Helen and ruler of Thessaly, believed to be the brother of Dorus and Xuthus (q.v.) and the ancestor of the Aeolians or Aeolic Greeks, i.e. those inhabiting Aeolis.

(2) The son of Poseidon (q.v.) and ruler of the Aeolian isles (q.v.). Zeus (q.v.) made him guardian of the winds. He gave Odysseus (q.v.) a bag of winds which his men let loose and which blew the ship off course.

Aeschylus. See **B2.**

Aetolus. Legendary conqueror of Aetolia. The son of Endymion (q.v.) king of Elis, he was banished across the Corinthian Gulf after accidentally killing Apis in a chariot race.

Agamemnon. Son of Atreus (q.v.) and Aerope, brother of Menelaus (q.v.) and king of Mycenae. He married Helen's (q.v.) half-sister Clytemnestra (q.v.) and commanded the Greek forces at Troy (q.v.). Before the Greek fleet could leave Aulis to sail for Troy he had to sacrifice his daughter Iphigenia (q.v.). At Troy he quarrelled with Achilles (q.v.) when he seized Briseis from Achilles. He did this because Apollo (q.v.) had forced him to return Chryseis to her father, the Trojan Chryses (q.v.).

On his return to Mycenae he was murdered by Aegisthus (q.v.) and Clytemnestra. Clytemnestra attacked him with an axe while he was bathing. This occurred despite the warning given to Agamemnon by Cassandra (q.v.) whom he had brought back from Troy as his mistress. He was avenged by his children Orestes (q.v.) and Electra (q.v.). The story inspired Aeschylus' (q.v.) trilogy Orestia.

Aganippe. A fountain at the foot of Mt. Helicon, sacred to the Muses (q.v.) who are sometimes called Aganippides. It inspired those who drank from it. The fountain of Hippocrene, also sacred to the Muses, was known as Aganippis.

Agathyrsans. In the Aeneid (q.v.) a tribe in Thrace.

Aglaia. "The bright one": one of the Graces (q.v.).

Aides or **Aidoneus.** Hades (q.v.).

Ajax. (Greek Aias) In Greek legend two Ajaxes appear. The first was the son of King Telamon of Salamis. He killed Teuthras King of Teuthrania, an ally of Troy (q.v.) and took his daughter Tecmessa. At Troy he fought all day with Hector (q.v.) and at the end of the duel they exchanged gifts, Hector giving him a sword. With Menelaus (q.v.) he rescued the body of Patroclus (q.v.) and with Odysseus (q.v.) killed Glaucus and rescued the body of Achilles. Homer (q.v.) says the pair quarrelled over the armour and that Odysseus killed him. Later, when Odysseus summoned the spirits of the dead Ajax held aloof. But Sophocles (q.v.) in his Ajax calls on another tradition in which Ajax, disappointed at not being given the Palladium (q.v.) of Troy when the city fell, went mad, killing the Greek sheep under the delusion they were his rivals before impaling himself on the sword Hector had given him. The other Ajax was the son of Oileus, king of the Locrians. He was courageous but blasphemous. When Troy was sacked he dragged Cassandra (q.v.) from the altar of Athene (q.v.) where she sought refuge and gave her to Agamemnon (q.v.). On his return to Greece Poseidon (q.v.) saved him from shipwreck in a storm sent by Athene. Taking shelter on a rock he boasted himself more powerful than the goddess. She commanded Poseidon to crack the reef with his trident and Ajax drowned.

Alba Longa. The Latin city founded by Ascanius (q.v.) in the Alban Hills. In fact, as well as legend, Alba was the mother city of Rome which was probably founded as one of her western outposts. Alba was capital of the Latin League, a confederation of Latin states, but was eventually supplanted by Rome.

Alcaeus. See **Alcmene.**

Alcestis. Daughter of Pelias (q.v.) and the only one of his daughters not to follow Medea's (q.v.) advice and boil him alive. Married Admetus (q.v.) and was devoted to him.

Alcides. Another name for Heracles (q.v.) whose grandfather was reputed to be Alcaeus.

Alcinous. King of the mythical Phaeacians of the isle of Scheria. A grandson of Poseidon (q.v.), he married Arete his own sister. Father of the beautiful Nausicaa (q.v.). He entertained Odysseus and gave him a ship. He was also said to have entertained the Argonauts and refused to return Medea to her father. Scheria has been identified with Corfu.

Alcmaeon. In myth the son of Amphiaraus (q.v.) and Eriphyle (q.v.). One of the Epigoni (q.v.).

Alcmene. The wife of Amphitrion (q.v.) son of Alcaeus. Her brothers had been slain by the Taphians and she would not consummate her marriage until Amphitrion avenged them. While he was away warring with the Taphians Zeus (q.v.) appeared in his likeness and fathered Heracles (q.v.) upon her. Hermes (q.v.) was ordered to delay the dawn in order that Zeus might take his time—an amusing situation which has appealed to Plautus, Molière and Dryden. Later that night the real Amphitrion returned and fathered Iphicles (q.v.). In his Amphitryon 38 Jean Giraudoux claims 37 versions of the tale have preceded him. On the death of Amphitrion Alcmene married Rhadamanthus (q.v.).

Alcyone or **Halcyone.** (1) Leader of the Pleiades (q.v.), daughter of Atlas (q.v.) and Pleione.

(2) The daughter of Aeolus (q.v.) and wife of Ceyx. When Ceyx was lost at sea she drowned herself in sorrow. The sympathetic gods turned the pair to kingfishers which supposedly bred during the winter solstice. Then Aeolus forbids the wind to blow leaving the Aegean calm while they build and sit on their nest. This is the time of year

called the "Halcyon days". The story is told in Ovid's (q.v.) "Metamorphoses" and Chaucer's "Book of the Duchess".

Alecto. One of the Erinnyes (q.v.).

Alexander the Great. See **B3**

Amalthea. The she-goat which nursed the infant Zeus in the Dictaean cave in Crete. As a reward she was placed among the stars as Capricorn while one of her horns which had broken off became the Cornucopia, or horn of plenty.

Amazons. Mythical race of female warriors at one time believed by the Greeks to live in Thrace or Asia Minor. As the Greeks' knowledge of the world grew, so the homeland of the Amazons was held to be more distant. In the *Iliad* (q.v.) Priam (q.v.) is said to have warred with them, though they came to the aid of Troy (q.v.). Achilles (q.v.) slew their queen Penthesilea (q.v.). Heracles (q.v.) fought with them and seized the girdle of the queen Hippolyte (q.v.) while Theseus (q.v.) carried off either Hippolyte or Antiope (q.v.). Theseus' act caused the Amazons to invade Attica but Theseus defeated them in the streets of Athens. In antiquity it was thought they amputated their right breast (Greek *mazos*) in order to hold a bow better.

Ambrosia. The food of the Olympians which gave immortality.

Ammon. The Egyptian god Amun was known to the Greeks from the 7th century B.C. when they came into contact with his cult at the Siwa oasis. They identified him with Zeus. Alexander the Great consulted the oracle of Zeus and Ammon was recognised as the son of Zeus by the priests of the oracle. A legend grew up that Alexander was begotten by Ammon in the form of a snake.

Amphiaraus. See **Seven Against Thebes.**

Amphion. Twin brother of Zethus, sons of Zeus (q.v.) and Antiope (q.v.). Antiope was married to Lycus King of Thebes who divorced her. She was cruelly treated by his second wife Dirce. The twins were raised by herdsmen on Mt. Cithaeron. When they reached manhood they avenged their mother by killing Zethus and tying Dirce to the horns of a wild bull. The fountain into which her body was thrown henceforth bore her name. The twins now took possession of Thebes and built the fortifications below the Cadmea. Amphion, who had been given a lyre by Hermes (q.v.) played so skilfully that the stones moved into place of their own accord. They ruled jointly, Zethus marrying Thebe who gave her name to the city, and Amphion marrying Niobe (q.v.).

Amphitrion. Son of Alcaeus, husband of Alcmene (q.v.) and father of Iphicles (q.v.). Foster father of Heracles (q.v.). When Heracles killed his teacher Linus with Linus' own lyre, Amphitrion sent him away to keep cattle. Later Amphitrion was killed helping Heracles defeat the Minyans.

Amphitrite. The daughter of Nereus (q.v.) leader of the Nereids (q.v.). Persuaded by Delphinos to accept Poseidon (q.v.) (Delphinos was rewarded by having her image placed amongst the stars as the Dolphin). By Poseidon she was mother of Triton (q.v.). Her hatred of Scylla (q.v.), Poseidon's daughter by another, led her to turn Scylla into a monster with six barking heads and twelve feet.

Amphitroniades. Another name for Heracles (q.v.) whose putative father was Amphitrion (q.v.).

Amyclae. One of the most sacred sites in the Peloponnese, a sanctuary a few miles from Sparta consecrated to Hyacinthus (q.v.).

Anchises. A cousin of Priam (q.v.). For his piety he was allowed to sleep with Aphrodite (q.v.) who bore him Aeneas. When Troy (q.v.) fell Aeneas carried his father (now blind) to safety through the Dardanian gate of the city. He died in Sicily and was buried at Eryx. In the *Aeneid* (q.v.) he appears among the blessed spirits of the dead to foretell Rome's greatness. *Aeneas carrying his Father* is an early work of Bernini.

Ancus Martius. The legendary fourth king of Rome who succeeded Tullus Hostilius. A grandson of Numa Pompilius (q.v.) he ruled from 640 to 616 B.C. He was very religious but also succeeded in defeating the Latins. He was succeeded by Tarquin the Elder.

Andromache. A Trojan princess, wife of Hector (q.v.) and by him mother of Astyanax. When Troy fell her son was thrown from the city walls, despite her spirited defence of him with a pestle. She was carried off to Epirus by Neoptolemus (q.v.) and here married his brother in law Hellenus and

became joint ruler. She also had a son by Neoptolemus and was threatened by his jealous wife Hermione (see Racine's *Andromaque*). Her days were ended at Pergamum, the city founded by her and Neoptolemus' son, Molossus. In historic times the Molossi claimed descent from Molossus and Neoptolemus.

Andromeda. See **Cassiopeia.**

Antaeus. A Libyan giant, son of Poseidon (q.v.) and Ge (q.v.). An invincible wrestler until Heracles (q.v.), realising he drew his strength from his mother, held him in the air and squeezed him to death. He is featured in a painting by Pollaiuolo in Florence.

Antenor. The wisest of the Trojans. Priam (q.v.) sent him to reclaim Hesione from Telamon after Heracles (q.v.) sacked Troy (q.v.). He advised the Trojans to return Helen (q.v.) to Menelaus (q.v.) but they refused. His hatred for Deiphobus (q.v.) led him to help the Greeks steal the Palladium (q.v.). The husband of Theano and father of Laocoön (q.v.). After Troy fell he and his wife went to Italy and founded either Venice or Padua.

Antigone. Daughter of Oedipus (q.v.) and Jocasta (q.v.) she accompanied her father into exile (recalled in Sophocles' *Oedipus at Colonus*). After his death she returned to Thebes where her brother Eteocles (q.v.) and Polynices (q.v.) were warring on each other. Both perished in battle and her uncle Creon (q.v.) seized power. Because Polynices had fought against his own country Creon refused him burial. Antigone defied Creon and buried her brother with full rites and was imprisoned in a cave for doing so. Here she hung herself, and her betrothed, Creon's son Haemon, committed suicide in despair. The story and the ethical principles it raises are the basis of Sophocles' *Antigone*. In his work of the same name Anouilh reconsiders the arguments involved.

Antilochus. Son of Nestor (q.v.) a valiant Greek warrior at Troy (q.v.). Too young to sail from Aulis when the expedition began he arrived later. Slain by Memnon (q.v.) while defending his father.

Antinous. See **Odysseus.**

Antiope. (1) An Amazon, sister of Hippolyte (q.v.). According to some legends she was carried off by Theseus (q.v.), perhaps with the aid of Heracles (q.v.) and bore him Hippolytus (q.v.).

(2) A Theban princess who bore Amphion (q.v.) and Zethus to Zeus (q.v.) who visited her in the form of a satyr (q.v.). Her father exposed the children on Mt. Cithaeron. She was badly treated and imprisoned by Lycus and his wife Dirce (Lycus was either her husband, who divorced her to marry Dirce, or her uncle). She was later freed and avenged by her twin sons. Titian, Correggio and Watteau have all painted Zeus visiting Antiope as a satyr.

Aphaia. A goddess worshipped in Aegina and identified with the Cretan Britomartis.

Aphrodite. The goddess of love, desire and procreation, known to the Romans as Venus. She sprang from the seed of Uranus (q.v.), rising naked from the sea at Paphos in Cyprus. However, Homer (q.v.) holds her to be the daughter of Zeus (q.v.) and Dione, and makes her the wife of Hephaestus (q.v.). She was not faithful to Hephaestus, but bore children by Ares (q.v.), Poseidon (q.v.), Dionysus (q.v.), and Hermes (q.v.), She loved the mortals Adonis (q.v.) and Anchises (q.v.) by whom she bore Aeneas (q.v.), and tempted Paris (q.v.) to desert Oenone. It was to her that Paris gave the golden apple of discord, she being the "fairest" goddess. In return she promised him the most beautiful woman in the world. Around her waist she wore a magic girdle which made her beautiful and irresistibly desirable.

Apis. The sacred bull of Memphis which the Egyptians worshipped as a god.

Apollo. Son of Zeus (q.v.) and the mortal Leto; twin brother of Artemis (q.v.). As a child he killed the she-dragon Python on Mt. Parnassus and took over her role as the oracle at Delphi. Hence he was sometimes known as the Pythian or as Loxias "the Ambiguous". He was also a symbol of light and was known as Phoebus or "shining". Apart from being god of prophecy he was a god of song and music, having been given the lyre by Hermes (q.v.). He was the leader of the Muses (q.v.) and was sometimes called Musagetes. He could be a destroyer (he is always portrayed with bow and arrows) and sent plagues amongst the Greeks at Troy, but was also protective against evil and was father of Asclepius (q.v.). When Zeus slew Asclepius he retaliated by slaying the Cyclopes (q.v.)

and was punished by being sent as a servant to Admetus (q.v.) of Pherae in Thessaly. Prior to this Zeus had sent him as a bondsman to King Laomedan whom he helped to build the walls of Troy. This was punishment for his part in a conspiracy (led by Hera, Poseidon and himself) against Zeus. He loved Hestia (q.v.) but also seduced the nymph Dryope and attempted to seduce Daphne. When Daphne protested she was turned into a laurel tree. Amongst mortal women he at one time loved Cassandra (q.v.). With his sister Artemis he shot the giant Tityus, whom the jealous Hera sent to violate Leto; it was he who shot the vulture which tormented Prometheus and he also helped Paris (q.v.) shoot Achilles (q.v.). He was identified with the sun-god by later writers but in Homer (q.v.) he and Helios (q.v.) are quite distinct.

Arachne. A Lydian maiden who competed with Athene (q.v.) at a weaving contest. When she won the angry goddess forced her to hang herself before turning her into a spider and her weaving into a cobweb.

Arcadia. Green but mountainous region, isolated in the centre of the Peloponnese. Its inhabitants were primitive shepherds and peasants.

Arcas. The son of Zeus (q.v.) and Callisto (q.v.) who gave his name to Arcadia (q.v.).

Ares. The son of Zeus (q.v.) and Hera (q.v.) and the god of war. Associated with Mars, by the Romans. He was disliked by all the gods save Hades (q.v.) and Eris (q.v.) because of his love of battle for its own sake. He loved Aphrodite (q.v.), and Hephaestus (q.v.) once caught the pair in an invisible net exposing them to the ridicule of the other gods. The father of Penthesilea (q.v.) by Otrere. He was once defeated by Heracles (q.v.), was wounded by Diomedes (q.v.) and imprisoned for 13 months (till Hermes (q.v.) released him) in a brazen vessel by the Aloeidae (q.v.). Athene (q.v.) got the better of him on several occasions. He once stood trial on the site of the Areopagus.

Arethusa. A river and a river goddess of southern Greece. She was pursued under the sea to Sicily by the river god Alpheus. In Sicily she was identified with Artemis and a cult of Artemis Arethusa flourished at Syracuse.

Argo. A fifty-oared ship built for Jason (q.v.) by Argus. In its prow Athene (q.v.) fitted an oracular beam.

Argonauts. The heroes who sailed with Jason (q.v.) in the Argo (q.v.) to fetch the golden fleece from Colchis. Their ranks included Heracles (q.v.), Orpheus (q.v.) Castor and Polydeuces (q.v.) Echion, Idas (q.v.) and Lynceus (q.v.). The voyage was an adventurous one and after dallying at Lemnos they passed through the Hellespont and reached Mysia. Here Hylas (q.v.) was lost and Heracles stayed to look for him. At some point the Sirens (q.v.) were passed with the help of Orpheus (q.v.) and at Bebryces Polydeuces (see Castor) slew Amycus. In Thrace they rid Phineus (q.v.) of the Harpies (q.v.) and in return were told how to navigate the Symplegades (q.v.).

Argus. (1) The builder of the Argo (q.v.).
(2) A hundred-eyed giant set by Hera (q.v.) to watch Io (q.v.).
(3) The faithful hound of Odysseus (q.v.).

Ariadne. The daughter of Minos (q.v.) and Pasiphae (q.v.). She helped Theseus (q.v.) but he abandoned her at Naxos when Dionysus (q.v.) fell in love with her. He married her and gave her a crown of seven stars which became a constellation after her death.

Arimaspi. A mythical people of the Scythian steppes said to be neighbours of the Hyperboreans. They had one eye and constantly fought a group of griffins for the gold they guarded. Herodotus (q.v.) tells of a poem by Aristeas, a priest of Hyperborean Apollo, about them. Aristeas is clearly a *shaman*, able to separate body and soul and to be in two places at once. Aeschylus (q.v.) refers to them when describing Io's (q.v.) wanderings.

Arion. A fabulous horse, the offspring of Demeter (q.v.) and Zeus (q.v.). Demeter had taken the form of a mare and Zeus raped her in the form of a horse. She also gave birth to the nymph Despoena and possibly Persephone (q.v.) at the same time as Arion. It saved Adrastus (q.v.) at the siege of Thebes.

Aristaeus. The son of Apollo (q.v.) and a Lapith (see Lapithae) girl Cyrene. A minor deity, the protector of cattle, fruit trees and bee-keepers. Virgil (q.v.) makes Cyrene a nymph and says that Aristaeus fell in love with Eurydice who died of a snake bite she received while fleeing from him. In

punishment all his bees were killed. Cyrene sought the advice of Proteus (q.v.) and Aristaeus made sacrifices of cattle to placate the nymphs. Nine days later he found fresh swarms in the carcasses.

Aristophanes. See B4.

Artemis. The daughter of Zeus (q.v.) and Leto (q.v.) twin sister of Apollo (q.v.). Her Roman counterpart was Diana. She was often conflated with Hecate (q.v.) and Selene (q.v.), the moon goddess. A goddess of the chase and protectoress of children and young animals. She was also treated as a mother or earth goddess in the Asian tradition and was worshipped orgiastically at Ephesus. She was generally portrayed with a bow and arrow, made by Hephaestus (q.v.) and like Apollo could spread the plague and death. With her arrows she punished impiety (e.g. Niobe). A virgin who sternly protected her own chastity, she was known to punish unchastity in others e.g. Callisto (q.v.).

Ascanius. The son of Aeneas (q.v.) and Creusa, who escaped from Troy (q.v.) with his father. Another tradition makes his mother the Latin princess Lavinia. He succeeded his father as king and made Alba Longa (q.v.) his capital.

Asclepius or **Aesculapius.** The son of Apollo (q.v.) and Coronis, a god of healing whose worship spread to Rome after a plague in 293 B.C. He was taught healing by Cheiron the centaur (q.v.). Once he brought a dead man back to life and Zeus (q.v.) punished him, killing him with a thunderbolt. At Apollo's request he was placed among the stars.

Asopus. A river god, the son of Oceanus (q.v.) and Tethys (q.v.). The father of Evadne, Euboea and Aegina.

Astraeus. A Titan (q.v.) and by Eos the father of the beneficent winds. According to other traditions he also fathered the stars.

Astyanax. The son of Hector (q.v.) and Andromache (q.v.). He was a sensitive child frightened by the plume of his father's helmet. When Troy (q.v.) fell Andromache struggled to protect him but Neoptolemus (q.v.) threw him from the city walls. Another tradition says she took him to Neoptolemus' court in Epirus.

Atalanta. The Boeotian Atalanta was the daughter of Schoeneus and wife of Hippomenes, the Arcadian Atalanta, the daughter of Iasus and Clymene and wife of Milanion. Similar tales were told of her in both traditions. She was exposed by her father and suckled by a bear sent by Artemis (q.v.) with whom she was sometimes identified. She became a famous huntress and hunted the Calydonian Boar (q.v.). Though vowed to virginity she bore Meleager (q.v.) a son. She refused to marry any suitor except he who beat her in a foot race. Hippomenes (or Milanion) did this by placing three golden apples, gifts from Aphrodite (q.v.) in her path, causing her to stop and collect them.

Athamas. The son of Aeolus and king of Orchomenus in Boeotia. He loved Ino (q.v.) who bore him Learchus and Melicertes, but Hera (q.v.) forced him to marry Nephele who bore him Phrixus and Helle (q.v.). Hera drove him mad because he sheltered Dionysus (q.v.) and he killed Learchus. Ino flung herself into the sea with Melicertes and both became sea deities. Ino became Leucothea and Melicertes became Palaemon. Athamas fled to Thessaly.

Athene or **Athena.** Identified with Minerva by the Romans. The daughter of Zeus (q.v.) and Metis (q.v.). Though it was foretold she would be a girl, an oracle said that if Metis bore another child it would be a son who would depose Zeus. He then swallowed Metis and later suffered a terrible headache near Lake Triton. Hermes (q.v.) knew the cause and persuaded Hephaestus (q.v.) to cleave Zeus' skull. Out sprang Athene fully armed. She was the goddess of wisdom and patron of arts and crafts, a protectress of agriculture and also a warrior. Moreover, she was a virgin (see Pallas). She disputed possession of Athens with Poseidon (q.v.): he offered the city the horse, Athene the olive which was judged to be the better gift. Henceforth she was patron of the city which was a centre of her cult. Her epithet "glaucopis" meant "bright-eyed" or "owl-faced" and in the *Odyssey* (q.v.) she assumed the form of a bird. Athenian coins bore an owl and the saying "Owls to Athens" meant the same as "Coals to Newcastle". She was worshipped on the Acropolis. A defender of all heroes who worked for the good of mankind, e.g. Heracles (q.v.).

Atlantiades. Another name for Hermes (q.v.) whose mother Maia was the daughter of Atlas (q.v.).

Atlantis. A legendary island said to be to the west of the Pillars of Hercules (q.v.). Its inhabitants, once powerful and virtuous, became wealthy and degenerate and were conquered by the Athenians. Later the island sank beneath the ocean in a day and a night. It may be that the island Plato speaks of in *Timaeus* was part of Crete or some other island which suffered when a volcano on Suntorini (ancient Thera) erupted.

Atlas. A Titan (q.v.) the son of Iapetus and Clymene and brother of Prometheus (q.v.) and Epimetheus. For his part in the Titanomachia (q.v.) he was condemned to carry the sky on his shoulders and stood holding it far to the west of the Pillars of Hercules (q.v.). For a brief time Heracles (q.v.) shouldered his burden. It is said Perseus (q.v.) turned him to stone with Medusa's (q.v.) head and he was identified with Mt. Atlas in North-West Africa. The father of Calypso (q.v.) and the Pleiades (q.v.).

Atreus. *See* Thyestes.

Attis. A god of vegetation whose cult originated in Phrygia and involved a festival of death and resurrection in the Spring. A consort of Cybele (q.v.) according to one tradition he castrated himself in a religious frenzy and became head of her college of eunuch priests.

Augias. A king of Elis with more sheep and cattle than any other man. Heracles (q.v.) was given the task of cleansing his filthy stables which had not been cleared for many years. Heracles promised to cleanse them in a day in return for one tenth of the cattle. He did so by diverting the rivers Peneius and Alphaeus through them but Augias refused to pay him. Heracles later invaded Elis, killed Augias, his sons and their allies the Moliones and destroyed the city of Pylus which had also helped Augias. One tradition says he spared Augias.

Aurora. The Roman goddess of the dawn, associated with the Greek Eos (q.v.).

Autolycus. The son of Hermes (q.v.) and Chione, father of Anticleia and thus grandfather of Odysseus (q.v.). Also grandfather of Sinon (q.v.). He was renowned for trickery, cunning and theft.

Aventine. One of the hills of Rome and the southernmost. It was close to the Tiber, was outside the pomerium and was associated with the "plebians".

Avernus, Lake. The modern Lago di Averno near Naples, thought to be an entrance to the Underworld. This is how Aeneas (q.v.) was told to enter Hades (q.v.). Agrippa linked it with the Lucrine Lake while building the harbour of Portus Julius.

B

Bacchae. The female followers of the cult of Bacchus or Dionysus whose worship was characterised by wine-induced frenzies of a mystic nature. At the height of such frenzies they believed themselves to be at one with the god. Also known as Bacchantes, Maenads and Thyiads.

Bacchoi. Male equivalent of the Bacchae.

Bacchus. Latin name for Dionysus (q.v.).

Bassaris. A Bacchante (*See* Bacchae).

Baucis. *See* Philemon.

Bellerophon. Son of Glaucus (q.v.) King of Corinth. He killed one Bellerus and fled to Tiryns where Anteia, wife of the King Proetus falsely accused him of trying to seduce her. Proetus sent him to his father-in-law Iobates with a letter requesting Iobates to kill the bearer of it. Reluctant to kill a guest Iobates sent him to kill the Chimaera (q.v.). Capturing Pegasus (q.v.) with a golden bridle given to him by Athene (q.v.) he was able to accomplish the task. He was then sent to fight the Amazons (q.v.) and again triumphed. On his return to Tiryus he survived an ambush set by Iobates and finally persuaded the king of his innocence. Iobates made him his heir. One tradition says Bellerophon presumed to rise to Olympus on Pegasus but Zeus sent a gadfly which stung the horse. Pegasus threw Bellerophon to earth but itself entered Olympus.

Belus. One of Poseidon's (q.v.) sons and father of Danaus (q.v.), Cepheus (q.v.) and Aegyptus.

Biton and Cleobis. Sons of a priestess of Hera (q.v.) in Argos who drew their mother's chariot several miles to the goddess's temple when no oxen could be found. Their mother asked Hera to bestow on them the best of gifts for mortals, and they died in their sleep in the temple.

Boeotia. Region of northern Greece; the capital city was Thebes.

Bona Dea. A Roman fertility goddess. Only women worshipped her. Cicero (q.v.) recounts an occasion when his opponent Clodius (q.v.), disguised as a woman, entered an annual nocturnal ceremony of her worshippers over which the chief magistrate's wife presided.

Boreas. The Roman Aquilo; the north wind in Greek mythology. Son of Astraeus (q.v.) and Eos (q.v.) and brother of the other beneficent winds Zephyrus (q.v.), Notus (q.v.) and Eurus (q.v.). A friend of Athens who destroyed Xerxes' (q.v.) fleet. He carried off Oreithyia, daughter of Erechtheus king of Athens who bore him two sons Zetes (q.v.) and Calais (q.v.) and two daughters, Chione and Cleopatra, wife of Phineus.

Brauron. Site on the east coast of Attica. Centre of a cult of Artemis (q.v.). It was believed the locals had killed a she-bear, an animal sacred to the goddess, and that she demanded they worship her on the site, and that girls between the ages of 7 and 11 serve her and live in her temple. Also believed to be the burial place of Iphigenia (q.v.) after her sacrifice at Aulis.

Briareus or **Aegaeon.** One of the Hecatoncheires (q.v.).

Briseis. *See* Achilles.

Brontes. One of the Cyclopes (q.v.).

Brutus, Lucius Junius. According to a Roman tradition accepted by Livy (q.v.) the liberator of Rome from the Etruscan kings following the rape of Lucretia (q.v.). Also the first Roman consul in 509 B.C. He ordered the execution of his own sons when they became involved in a conspiracy to restore the monarchy.

C

Cacus. In Roman tradition this fire-breathing giant and his sister Caca were children of Vulcan (q.v.) who lived on the Palatine hill (q.v.), although Virgil in book 8 of the *Aeneid* (q.v.) makes it the Aventine (q.v.). Virgil tells how Cacus stole the cattle of Geryon (q.v.) from Hercules (q.v.) who pursued Cacus back to his cave, tracking him by the cattle's mooing. There he slew Cacus. This event has been portrayed in a painting by Poussin and a statue by Bandinelli in the Signoria, Florence.

Cadmus. Son of Agenor, king of Phoenicia and grandson of Poseidon (q.v.). When Zeus (q.v.) carried off his sister Europa (q.v.) he went to look for her but was told by the Delphic oracle (*see* Apollo) to relinquish the search and to follow a magical cow. Where the cow lay down he was to found a city. The place where it sank became the site of the Cadmea, the citadel of Thebes. Here Cadmus slew the dragon guarding the spring of Ares and on her advice sowed its teeth. The Sparti (q.v.) sprang up. Cadmus married Harmonia (q.v.) and their wedding was attended by the gods. Their children included Autonoe, Ino, Semele (q.v.) Agave Polydoros (q.v.) and Illyrius. In old age Cadmus, who had introduced the use of letters to Greece from Phoenicia, gave up his throne to his grandson Pentheus and went to reign in Illyria. Later he and Harmonia were received into Elysium (q.v.) in the form of serpents.

Caeneus. Originally the nymph Caenis turned into a man at her own request by Poseidon (q.v.). Accompanied the Argonauts (q.v.) and hunted the Calydonian Boar (q.v.). Invulnerable to normal blows he was killed by the Centaurs (q.v.) in their battle with the Lapithae (q.v.) when they buried him beneath a pile of trees. His soul left the body as a bird and in the Underworld again became female.

Calais. Twin brother of Zetes. Winged sons of Boreas (q.v.) and Oreithyia, they accompanied the Argonauts (q.v.) and drove off the Harpies (q.v.), tormenting Phineus (q.v.) husband of their sister Cleopatra.

Calchas. A renegade Trojan seer who helped the Greeks at Troy (q.v.). He foretold that Troy would not fall without Achilles' (q.v.) presence and that the sacrifice of Iphigenia (q.v.) was necessary to secure a favourable wind. It was he who advised Agamemnon to return the girl Chryseis to her father the Trojan priest Chryses. This caused Agamemnon to seize Briseis and sparked the quarrel with Achilles. Calchas later died of grief when surpassed in prophecy by Mopsus, a mysterious mythical figure who was also said to have sailed with the Argonauts (q.v.).

Calipe. See **Pillars of Hercules.**

Calliope. See **Muses.**

Callirhoë. Daughter of the river god Achelous (q.v.) and wife of Alcmaeon (q.v.). Alcmaeon gave her the necklace and robe of Harmonia (q.v.).

Callisto. Daughter of Lycaon (q.v.). One of Artemis' (q.v.) huntresses. She bore Arcas (q.v.) to Zeus (q.v.) who sought to conceal their affair from Hera (q.v.) by turning Callisto into a bear. Realising the ruse Hera had the bear hunted down but Zeus saved her and placed her amongst the stars as Arctos. Others say that Artemis turned her into a bear and Arcas hunted her. In this version Callisto became the Great Bear constellation and Arcas the Little Bear.

Calydonian Boar. A savage boar which Artemis (q.v.) sent to ravage Calydon because its king, Oeneus (q.v.) had not offered her proper sacrifice (see also Atalanta and Meleager). Pausanias (q.v.) tells of a story of long tusks found at Tegea, seen by Augustus and taken to Rome.

Calypso. A nymph of Ogygia who tended Odysseus (q.v.) there for eight years until Zeus (q.v.) ordered her to send him home to Ithaca. The name means "hidden" and she may have been a death goddess. At one point she offers the hero eternal youth, but he refuses, preferring real life. She bore him two sons.

Camilla. The Roman equivalent of an Amazon (q.v.) —a female warrior.

Capaneus. See **"Seven Against Thebes".**

Capricorn. See **Amalthea.**

Cassandra. Daughter of Priam (q.v.) and Hecuba and twin of Helenus. She was given the gift of prophecy by Apollo (q.v.) but when she disappointed him he decreed that no one would ever believe her prophecies. Several times her important warnings went unheeded, e.g. against Paris (q.v.) going to Sparta, and against the wooden horse (q.v.). She was taken as a slave by Agamemnon (q.v.) when Troy (q.v.) fell and became his mistress. She was murdered with him by Clytemnestra (q.v.).

Cassiopeia. The wife of Cepheus and mother of Andromeda. Her boast that Andromeda was more beautiful than the Nereids (q.v.) caused Poseidon (q.v.) to send a monster to ravage the kingdom. Only the sacrifice of Andromeda could prevent this. Perseus (q.v.), who found her chained naked to a rock by the sea, offered to save her if she would become his wife. Cepheus and Cassiopeia agreed to this and Perseus slew the beast. Her parents then attempted to renege on their promise, claiming Andromeda was promised to another. At her wedding to Perseus the other suitor and his followers attempted to seize the bride but Perseus turned them all to stone with the head of Medusa (q.v.). The images of Cepheus and Cassiopeia were set amongst the stars by Poseidon.

Castalian Spring. Sacred spring on Mt. Parnassus, near the site of the Delphic oracle. Here the young girl Castalia drowned herself to avoid Apollo's (q.v.) advances.

Castalides. A name for the Muses (q.v.).

Castor and Polydeuces. (Latin "Pollux") The "Dioscuri". The twin "Sons of Zeus", brothers of Helen (q.v.) and the sons of Leda (q.v.) the wife of Tyndareus of Sparta. One tradition says that they were born from an egg, like Helen, after Zeus had visited Leda in the form of a swan. Others say only Polydeuces was Zeus' son and that Castor being the son of Tyndareus was a mere mortal. Castor was a famous horse tamer and Polydeuces a great boxer. Sailing with the Argonauts (q.v.) Polydeuces slew Amycus son of Poseidon (q.v.) who lived on the isle of Bebrycos. Amycus was a renowned boxer who killed travellers by challenging them to a boxing match. They also hunted the Calydonian boar (q.v.). The Dioscuri fought a mortal battle with their cousins the twins Idas and Lynceus Zeus then killed Idas but Polydeuces begged to die with his brother. However Zeus decided they should live alternate days with the gods and under the earth. Their image was placed amongst the stars as Gemini. Poseidon gave them power over the wind and waves and they became protectors of seafarers. They were said to have appeared on horseback to help the Romans against the Latins in the battle of Lake Regillus in 484 B.C., after which their cult was adopted at Rome.

Centaurs. A race of savage creatures, half-man, half-horse which inhabited the woodlands and mountains, particularly those of Thessaly. They were the offspring of Ixion and a cloud. In Homer (q.v.) the centaurs appear as representatives of primitive desires, fighting, drinking and womanising, but later they are only portrayed as turning to violence when drunk. When they tried to abduct Deidamia (q.v.) from her wedding, they became involved in a famous battle with their neighbours the Lapithae (q.v.).

Centimani. See **Hecatoncheires.**

Cephalus. Husband of Procris who was carried off by Eos (q.v.). Eos released him but Procris, suspicious of the time he spent hunting, followed him into the woods. Hearing him praying for a breeze she supposed it to be his mistress (the Roman equivalent of Eos was Aurora, the Latin for breeze aura). Moving closer she was struck by his spear, which never missed, and killed. The story is told by Hesiod and Ovid and inspired paintings by Poussin and Claude.

Cepheus. King of Tegea and one of the Argonauts (q.v.). He and most of his 20 sons were killed helping Heracles (q.v.) fight Hippocoon.

Cerberus. A huge and savage dog, the offspring of Echidne (q.v.) and Typhon (q.v.) which guarded the entrance to Hades (q.v.). He is usually said to have had three heads, but Hesiod gives him fifty. His back was covered with serpents' heads and he had a snake for a tail. Heracles (q.v.) dragged him from the Underworld; Orpheus (q.v.) charmed him with music when seeking Eurydice while Aeneas (q.v.) drugged him with a cake of honey and narcotics, hence "a sop to Cerberus".

Cercyon. A son of Hephaestus (q.v.) reigning near Eleusis. Here he challenged all travellers to a wrestling match and killed them, until he challenged Theseus (q.v.) and was killed himself.

Ceres. Ancient Italian corn-goddess worshipped in a temple on the Aventine. Games and a spring festival, the Ceriala, were held in her honour. She was associated with Demeter (q.v.) from an early date and her daughter Proserpina with Persephone (q.v.).

Ceryneian Hind. A creature with brazen feet and golden antlers. One of Heracles' (q.v.) tasks was to catch it alive. He pursued it for a year and caught it without shedding blood by pinning its forelegs together with an arrow.

Chalybes. Mythical inhabitants of north Asia Minor said by some traditions to have invented iron working.

Chaos. In Greek creation myth Chaos was the infinite space existing before creation. From Chaos sprang Ge (q.v.), the Earth.

Charities. Also called the Gratiae or Graces by the Romans. They were originally divinities of nature. In the Iliad (q.v.) only one Charity is personified, Charis, wife of Hephaestus (q.v.). Later the three Graces appear, Aglaia, Thalia and Euphrosyne, friends of the Muses (q.v.) with whom they inhabited Mt. Olympus.

Charon. The surly ferryman who transported the dead across the Styx (q.v.) to Hades (q.v.). He only transported them if they had received the correct funeral rite and if their relatives had placed a small coin, his fare, under the tongues. However Heracles (q.v.) forced his passage and Orpheus (q.v.) charmed his with his lyre. Amongst the Etruscans (q.v.), as in modern Greek folklore, he was regarded as a synonym or figure of death. Virgil (q.v.) portrays him with unkempt white hair and eyes of fire in the 6th book of the Aeneid.

Charybdis and Scylla. Two monsters guarding the Straits of Messina. Charybdis swallowed the sea and vessels on it, three times a day, regurgitating what she swallowed each time. Opposite was Scylla, the daughter of Poseidon (q.v.) by a mortal, whom the jealous Amphitrite (q.v.) turned into a monster with six barking heads and twelve feet. Odysseus (q.v.) was forced to pass between the two evils and the equally undesirable choice between the pair has become proverbial.

Cheiron. Also called Chiron. A centaur (q.v.). A son of Cronus (q.v.) and Philyra, hence he is sometimes referred to as Philyrides. Unlike his fellow centaurs a wise and kindly being who learnt music, medicine, hunting and prophecy from Apollo (q.v.) and Artemis (q.v.). This learning he imparted to numerous heroes including Achilles (q.v.), the Dioscuri (q.v.), Jason (q.v.) and Peleus (q.v.). An immortal, he was accidentally wounded by the poisoned arrow of his friend Heracles (q.v.). In pain he longed for death. By surrendering his immortality he was relieved of life and suffering and placed among the stars as Sagittarius.

Chimeira. A monster with a lion's head, goat's body and a serpent for a tail. It could breathe fire. The offspring of Echidne (q.v.) and Typhon (q.v.), though some say it was begot by the Sphinx (q.v.) and Orthrus (q.v.). It was killed by Bellerophon (q.v.) while ravaging Lycia. The beast gave us the word "chimera" or fanciful notion.

Chryseis. (Cressida) Daughter of the Trojan seer and priest of Apollo (q.v.). Chryseis was captured by Agamemnon (q.v.) who refused to ransom her. Apollo then sent a plague on the Greek camp and when Calchas (q.v.) explained the cause Agamemnon released her. He then seized Briseis thus causing the quarrel with Achilles (q.v.). The medieval *Roman de Troie* tells how Troilus loved her, but she left him for Diomedes (q.v.). This is the basis of Chaucer's *Troilus and Criseyde* and Shakespeare's *Troilus and Cressida*.

Chrysippus. The son of Pelops (q.v.), murdered by his half-brother Atreus (q.v.) and Thyestes (q.v.) at the instigation of his step-mother Hippodameia (q.v.).

Chthonius. *See* **Spartii.**

Circe The daughter of Helios (q.v.) and Perse. A sorceress living on the island of Aeaea (Virgil (q.v.) identifies it with Circeii in Campania (q.v.)). She turned Odysseus' (q.v.) men into swine but he resisted by use of the herb "moly" given to him by Hermes (q.v.). Having forced her to restore his men he stayed a year with her and she advised him on his trip to the Underworld and return to Ithaca. She had a son, Telegonus by him and later married his son by Penelope (q.v.), Telemachus (q.v.). In the *Argonautica* of Apollonius of Rhodes she purifies Jason (q.v.) and Medea (q.v.) of murder on their return from Colchis. She was worshipped in Campania in the form of Feronia.

Cisseus. Father of Hecabe (q.v.).

Claros. Site of a shrine and oracle of Apollo (q.v.) to the south of Smyrna.

Cleobis. *See* **Biton.**

Clio. *See* **Muses.**

Cloacina. Ancient Roman divinity of "purification", later identified with Venus.

Cloelia. A Roman girl, legendary for having escaped from Porsenna (q.v.) when taken hostage and swimming back to Rome across the Tiber.

Clotho. One of the Fates (q.v.). She pulled the limbs of Pelops (q.v.) from the cauldron in which they were to be boiled, thus enabling his restoration to life.

Clytemnestra. Daughter of Tyndareus (q.v.) and a half-sister of Helen (q.v.) and Castor and Polydeuces (q.v.). Wife of Agamemnon (q.v.) by whom she bore Orestes (q.v.), Iphigenia (q.v.) and Electra (q.v.). While Agamemnon was at Troy (q.v.) she began an affair with Aegisthus (q.v.) and on his return the pair murdered him. She was killed by Orestes. Her murder of Agamemnon should be seen in the context of his infidelity with Cassandra (q.v.) and others and his sacrifice of Iphigenia. This is how Strauss views the matter in his opera *Elektra*.

Cocles. The "one-eyed", a nickname of Horatius (q.v.) who kept the bridge across the Tiber.

Cocytus. The river of wailing in Hades (q.v.).

Coeus. One of the Titans (q.v.).

Cornelia. Mother of the "Gracchi", daughter of Scipio Africanus and a model of what Romans of the Republic thought a matron should be. On the deaths of her sons she withdrew to Misenum and her home became a centre of culture. She appears in Plutarch's (q.v.) *Lives* of her sons and he tells us that when a visitor asked to see her jewels she presented her sons saying "These are my jewels".

Coronis. Thessalian princess made pregnant by Apollo (q.v.) but who fell in love with an Arcadian youth. Learning of this from a crow, Apollo sent Artemis (q.v.) to kill her. The unborn child was snatched from her and given to Cheiron (q.v.) to rear. The child was Asclepius (q.v.).

Corybantes. Priests of Rhea (q.v.) or Cybele (q.v.) in Phrygia and Asia Minor. Known for their dancing and performance of wild rites to the sound of drums and cymbals.

Corydon. Common Arcadian shepherd's name but in Virgil's (q.v.) second *Eclogue* the shepherd

Corydon laments his "faithless Alexis". From this Corydon has become a symbol of homosexual love.

Creon. A "ruler" or "prince" and the name often given to subsidiary characters in Greek legend, e.g. the brother of Jocasta (q.v.) who succeeds Oedipus (q.v.). *See also* **Jason.**

Cretan Bull. A magnificent white bull sent by Poseidon (q.v.) to Minos (q.v.) for sacrifice. Minos' wife Pasiphaë (q.v.) so admired the bull she had Daedalus (q.v.) construct a hollow cow for her to get inside. She then mated with the bull and later bore the Minotaur (q.v.). Minos also admired the bull and rather than sacrifice it, substituted another bull. The original bull escaped to ravage Crete until captured by Heracles (q.v.) and taken to Eurystheus (q.v.). Eurystheus freed it and it ravaged Greece until captured by Theseus (q.v.) at Marathon (q.v.) and sacrificed to Athene (q.v.).

Creusa. Feminine equivalent of Creon. The most famous is the daughter of Priam (q.v.), first wife of Aeneas (q.v.) and mother of Ascanius. She was lost in the escape from Troy (q.v.) when the city fell. When Aeneas looked for her he met only her ghost who bid him go forward to meet his destiny.

Croesus. Last king of Lydia who in the mid-6th century B.C. amassed a great fortune. His wealth is proverbial. Regarded as a model of piety for his gold offerings to Apollo (q.v.) at Delphi (q.v.). He met Solon and tried to persuade him to admit that Croesus was the happiest of men. Solon refused, saying that no man could be considered happy till his life had ended. The Delphic oracle told him that a great empire would fall if he invaded Persia. His own did. The Persian king Cyrus ordered him to be burnt alive but he called on Solon's name and told Cyrus of Solon's sayings. Cyrus pardoned him and made him an adviser. A later tradition says Apollo saved him and carried him to the land of the Hyperboreans.

Crommyum, Sow of. Wild sow slain by Theseus (q.v.).

Cronus. The son of Uranus (q.v.) and Ge (q.v.). The youngest of the twelve Titans (q.v.). When Ge stirred the Titans to revolt against Uranus she gave Cronus a flint sickle with which he castrated his father. Having deposed Uranus, Cronus reigned supreme and consigned the Cyclopes (q.v.) and the Hecatoncheires (q.v.) to Tartarus (q.v.). He married his sister Rhea (q.v.) and by her was father of Hestia (q.v.), Demeter (q.v.), Hera (q.v.), Poseidon (q.v.), Hades (q.v.) and Zeus (q.v.). Mindful of a curse by Uranus and Ge that he too be deposed by his own son, he swallowed each child at birth. But Rhea gave him a stone to swallow instead of Zeus and later gave him an emetic forcing him to regurgitate his other children. They now joined Zeus in a war on Cronus and the Titans. The Cyclopes aided them and gave Zeus the thunderbolt, Poseidon the trident and Hades a helmet of darkness or invisibility. Cronus was defeated and the Titans were consigned to Tartarus.

Cupid or **Amor.** Roman god of love, identified with the Greek Eros (q.v.).

Curetes. Priests of Rhea (q.v.) who drowned the cries of the infant Zeus (q.v.) as he lay in the Dictaean Cave by the clashing of their weapons. This prevented Cronus (q.v.) finding and devouring him. They were half-divine and in later times were conflated with the Corybantes (q.v.) who were also believed to be half-divine. All became part of Dionysus' ritual.

Cybele. The mother goddess of Phrygia where she and her lover Attis (q.v.) were worshipped in orgiastic rites and purification ceremonies including bathing in the blood of a sacrificed bull. Her symbol was a black stone and this was brought to Rome from Pessinus in 204 B.C. However it was only during the reign of Claudius that Roman citizens were allowed to serve as her priests and the oriental eunuchs serving her cult were always frowned upon. Her worship is described by Lucretius (q.v.) in book 2 and Catullus in his *Attis*. The artists of the classical world portray her with a crown of towers, a libation dish and tambourine, flanked by lions to show her control of wild nature.

Cyclops. Generally known to the Greeks as one-eyed giants living in a distant country, perhaps Sicily. In Homer (q.v.) the Cyclops Polyphemus is a man-eating son of Poseidon (q.v.), made drunk and blinded by Odysseus (q.v.) and his men whom he had captured and meant to eat. Hesiod (q.v.) refers to three Cyclops but describes them as Titans (q.v.). The three (Brontes, Steropes and Arges) were sons of Ge (q.v.) and Uranus (q.v.) who made weapons for Zeus (q.v.), Poseidon and Hades (q.v.) (see Cronus). Other traditions make them skilled craftsmen helping Hephaestus (q.v.) at his Sicilian forge. They were also builders of cities including Athens and the walls of Tiryns.

Cyllenius. Another name for Hermes (q.v.) who was said to have been born on Mt. Cyllene in southern Greece.

Cyncus. "The Swan", a mythical king of Liguria who loved Phaeton (q.v.) and was turned into a swan.

Cynthia. A name given to Artemis (q.v.). She and Apollo (q.v.) were thought to have been born on Mt. Cynthus in Delos and were thus referred to as Cynthia and Cynthus.

Cyrene. In myth the mother of Aristaeus (q.v.) by Apollo (q.v.) who carried her to Libya where she gave her name to the city of Cyrene.

Cythera. An island off the south-east coast of Greece noted for its sanctuary of Aphrodite (q.v.). She was thus referred to as "the Cytherean".

D

Dactyli. Greek equivalent of the Roman Chalybes (q.v.) the mythical beings who lived on Mt. Ida in northern Asia Minor and invented iron-working.

Daedalus. Mythical Athenian craftsman. His jealousy of his nephew Perdix of Talos, who was said to have invented the saw, caused him to throw Perdix from Athene's (q.v.) temple on the Acropolis (q.v.). Having thus committed murder he fled to Crete. Here he arranged the liaison between Pasiphaë (q.v.) and the Cretan Bull (q.v.) which produced the Minotaur (q.v.). Then, to conceal what had transpired from Minos (q.v.) he built the famous labyrinth to hide the Minotaur. When Minos discovered the truth he imprisoned Daedalus and his son Icarus in the labyrinth. Pasiphaë released them and Daedalus invented wings which, when attached to their shoulders by wax, enabled him and his son to fly. However Icarus flew too near to the sun, the wax melted, and he fell to his doom in the Icarian sea. Daedalus reached Cumae and then went to Sicily. Here King Cocalus welcomed him and when Minos arrived in pursuit Cocalus' daughters helped Daedalus kill him. In Sicily Daedalus was credited with many wonderful buildings including a honeycomb of gold for Aphrodite's (q.v.) temple on Mt. Eryx. His name has become synonymous with ingenuity and skill, hence "Daedal" and "daedalian" in the English language.

Damocles. Member of the court of Dionysius I, tyrant of Syracuse. Cicero tells how the tyrant had him eat a sumptuous dinner while a sword was suspended by a hair over his head. This illustrated the luxurious but precarious life style of the tyrant and "the sword of Damocles" has become proverbial.

Danaë. A princess of Argos, daughter of King Acrisius (q.v.). An oracle told the king that Danaë's son would kill him so he imprisoned her in a brazen tower. Zeus (q.v.) visited her in a shower of gold and fathered Perseus (q.v.). Acrisius cast them adrift in a box and they came to Seriphos. They were found by the fisherman Dictys and taken to the king Polydectes. He wished to marry Danaë and so, to get Perseus out of the way, sent him to fetch the head of Medusa (q.v.). Danaë was saved from Polydectes' advances when Perseus returned and, showing the head, turned him to stone.

Danai. A general name used by Homer for the Greeks assembled at Troy. It was meant to perpetuate the memory of a common ancestor, Danaus (q.v.).

Danaus. A king of Libya and the father of 50 daughters, the "Danaïdes". His brother Aegyptus, who had 50 sons, wanted a mass marriage, but Danaus fled with his daughters to Argos where he became king. Eventually Aegyptus' sons followed and demanded the "Danaïdes". Danaus agreed but gave each daughter a weapon with which they slew their husbands on the wedding night. All, that is, save Hypermestra who spared Lynceus. Lynceus killed Danaus and became king of Argos. In the Underworld the Danaïdes were condemned to carry water in sieves for ever. The story is told

by Pindar (q.v.) and the Danaïdes form the chorus in Aeschylos' (q.v.) Suppliants.

Daphne. The daughter of the river god Peneus or Ladon. A nymph pursued by Apollo (q.v.). To escape him she prayed either to her father or to the Earth to be turned into a laurel tree, which she was. Apollo made himself a laurel wreath as consolation and it became the prize at the Pythian Games held in his honour.

Daphnis. The son of Hermes (q.v.) and a nymph. She abandoned the infant but he was raised by Sicilian shepherds. Pan (q.v.) taught him the pipes and he was the originator of pastoral poetry. Later he was unfaithful to a nymph who loved him and in revenge she blinded him. His father ordered forth the fountain of Daphnis near Syracuse in his honour.

Dardanus. The son of Zeus (q.v.) and the Pleiad (q.v.) Electra. He founded Dardania on land given to him by Teucer. He was grandfather of Tros, great grandfather of Ilus (q.v.) and Ganymede (q.v.). Hence an ancestor of the Trojans who were sometimes called Dardanids, Dardans or Dardonians. Roman legend sometimes envisages him migrating to Dardania from Italy.

Deianeira. The daughter of Oeneus, king of Calydon and the wife of Heracles (q.v.) who won her hand by defeating the river god Achelous (q.v.). She bore him a son Hyllus. After accidentally killing Eunomus, Heracles took her and Hyllus into voluntary exile. When they came to cross the River Evenus the centaur (q.v.) Nessus offered to transport her on his back. However he tried to rape her and was killed by Heracles. As he lay dying he told her to take his blood as it was a charm which would keep Heracles in love with her. Later Heracles won Iole, daughter of Eurytus King of Oechalia, in an archery contest. When Eurytus refused to surrender Iole Heracles invaded Oechalia and defeated him. He then ordered Deianeira to send him a white shirt which he was to wear at a thanksgiving sacrifice to Zeus (q.v.). Deianeira, jealous of Iole, dipped the shirt in the blood of Nessus. But the blood was poisonous and when Heracles donned the shirt it burned his body and attempts to pull it off tore pieces of flesh from the hero. In agony he ordered Hyllus to build a funeral pyre on which he would find quick death and release from the pain. He also had Hyllus marry Iola. Deianeira, horrified at the result of her action, hanged herself. The story forms the plot of Sophocles' Women of Trachis.

Deidamia. The maiden who fell in love with Achilles (q.v.) and bore him Neoptolemus (q.v.).

Deiphobus. See Helen and Helenus.

Delis, Delius. Epithets of Artemis (q.v.) and Apollo (q.v.) who were born on Delos (q.v.).

Delos. Site of the important Ionian shrine of Apollo (q.v.). Here he was known as Phoebus ("the shining") or Lycius. When the jealous Hera (q.v.) pursued Leto (q.v.) she sought asylum where she could give birth to Apollo, her son by Zeus (q.v.). Delos, which was so poor it could lose nothing to Hera's wrath, accepted her.

Delphi. Site of Apollo's (q.v.) Dorian shrine and the most famous centre of his worship. Here he took his prophetic role having replaced Python. The oracle, located near the Castalian spring, was supposed to contain the omphalos or navel store of the Earth. A priestess, the Pythia, sat on a tripod chewing the intoxicating laurel leaf and voicing his utterances. Intoxicating vapours also issued from a chasm in the shrine. In this role Apollo was known as Loxias "the Ambiguous". (See Croesus). The priests of the shrine were not incorruptible and were known to take sides, e.g. with Sparta against Athens and with Philip of Macedon against Greece. The oracle had greatest influence during the period of overseas colonisation when its advice on location of colonies was always sought. The oracle encouraged Rome to defy Hannibal but was looted by Sulla. Nero visited it and Hadrian tried in vain to revive its prestige. Its decline came with the advance of Christianity and the growing interest in astrology as a means of prophecy. The temples at Delphi were sacked by Alaric in A.D. 396. Apollo's temple with its inscribed maxims "Know thyself" and "Nothing in excess" had stood on the highest point of Mt. Parnassus and had housed the sepulchre of Bacchus (q.v.) who was also worshipped at Delphi.

Demeter. The counterpart of the Roman Ceres, a

Greek corn-goddess responsible for the fertility of the earth. The daughter of Cronus (q.v.) and Rhea (q.v.) she became mother of Persephone (q.v.) or Kore ("the maiden") by her brother Zeus (q.v.). A 7th century B.C. Homeric *Hymn to Demeter* tells how Hades (q.v.) carried off Persephone from Eleusis twelve miles from Athens (Ovid says she was taken while gathering poppies in Sicily). Demeter scoured the earth for her until Helios (q.v.) told her what had occurred. She then shunned Olympus (q.v.) and wandered the earth, forbidding it to bring forth fruit and therefore threatening famine. Zeus finally agreed that Persephone could leave Hades provided she had not eaten in the Underworld. Hades agreed to let her go but tempted her into eating a pomegranate. She thus had to spend half a year with him in the Underworld and half with Demeter. Demeter again made the earth fertile but turned Ascalaphus, who had seen and reported Persephone eating the pomegranate, into an owl. She punished those who had been unkind to her during her wandering (see **Abas**) but rewarded those who had treated her hospitably. She taught Triptolemus, another son of Celeus (q.v.) the art of agriculture and gave him an ear of corn whose virtues he revealed to his fellow men. The Eleusian Festival was held in Demeter's honour from the 6th century B.C. and there was an annual procession from Eleusis to Athens. Those who spoke Greek were initiated into the mysteries of her cult. The Thesmophoria, a celebration of the foundation of laws, was held in her honour in many cities.

Demophon (1) The son of Theseus (q.v.) and Phaedra (q.v.) brother of Acamas (q.v.). He helped rescue his grandmother Aethra who had been Helen's (q.v.) slave, when Troy (q.v.) fell. Phyllis, a Thracian princess, loved him and committed suicide when he left her to visit Athens. She was then transformed into a tree.

(2) The son of Celeus and Metaneira. Demeter (q.v.) tried to reward the pair for their kindness to her by making Demophon immortal. To achieve this he had to be suspended above a fire, but Metaneira cried out thus breaking the spell and he perished.

Deucalion. The son of Prometheus (q.v.), husband of Pyrrha and father of Hellen. He was thus the ancestor of the Greeks. When Zeus (q.v.) decided to flood the earth in order to destroy mankind they escaped in an ark which finally made land on Mt. Parnassus. The couple prayed to Themis (q.v.) that mankind be restored and were told to scatter their mother's bones behind them. They took this to mean stones, the skeleton of Mother Earth. The rocks Deucalion scattered became men; those Pyrrha scattered became women.

Diana. Italian goddess of woods, women, childbirth and later, by association with the Greek Artemis (q.v.), the moon. Her cult was originally centred on the volcanic Lake Nemi at Aricia. The lake was known as Diana's mirror. The priest here, known as the rex, was always a runaway slave who had murdered his predecessor. A temple of Diana, said to have been founded by Servius Tullius also stood on the Aventine.

Dictaean Cave. A cave on Mt. Dicte, in Crete, the reputed childhood home of Zeus (q.v.). Hence he was known as Dictaeus.

Dictys. (1) The sailor who found Perseus (q.v.) and his mother Danaë (q.v.) adrift at sea in a chest.

(2) A Cretan said to have accompanied Idomeneus (q.v.) to the Trojan war. His diary of the war was supposedly buried near Cnossos and found in the reign of Nero.

Dido. A daughter of the king of Tyre originally called Elissa. Her husband Sychaeus was murdered but with a few followers she escaped to Libya and founded Carthage (**K31**). Local legend said she burnt herself on a funeral pyre to avoid marrying Iarbas, a native king. The Roman version, given in the *Aeneid* takes Aeneas (q.v.) to Carthage where Dido's unrequited love for him results in her death. Aeneas abandons her to fulfil his destiny as ancestor of Rome.

Didyma. A great sanctuary of Apollo (q.v.) at Miletus.

Dindyma. Mountain in Asia Minor and a centre of the Cybele's (q.v.) cult.

Diomedes. (1) A king of the Bistones in Thrace who possessed man-eating mares. A labour of Heracles (q.v.) was to bring them to Eurystheus (q.v.). This he did by stealing them and beating off

his pursuers. But while he was busy fighting, the mares devoured his friend Abderus. Heracles founded the city of Abdera in his honour. Eurystheus freed the horses on Mt. Olympus (q.v.) where wild beasts devoured them.

(2) The son of Tydeus, king of Argos. One of the Epigoni (q.v.). He also went to Troy (q.v.) and was a companion of Odysseus (q.v.). With Odysseus he sailed to fetch Achilles (q.v.) and later Neoptolemus (q.v.). He encouraged Agamemnon (q.v.) to sacrifice Iphigenia (q.v.) and helped Odysseus capture the Trojan spy Dolon. He wounded Aeneas (q.v.) and Aphrodite (q.v.) as she saved the Trojan. He also wounded Ares. He returned from Troy to find his wife had been unfaithful and went to settle in Daunia in Italy. Here he married Euippe, daughter of king Daunus. He was buried on one of the Diomedan islands.

Dionysus. The Roman Bacchus. Also called Bromius "the Boisterous". The son of Zeus (q.v.) and Semele, a mortal. Zeus visited her in the guise of a mortal but when she was six months pregnant the jealous Hera (q.v.) came to her as an old woman. She advised Semele to demand her lover appear in his true form. Zeus unwillingly agreed to do so and Semele was consumed by fire. The unborn child was sewn up in Zeus' thigh to be born as Dionysus. The child was given into the care of Athamas and Ino. He was disguised as a girl but Hera learned the truth and drove Athamas mad, causing him to kill his own son. Hermes (q.v.) then took Dionysus to Mt. Nysa in India where he was raised by nymphs. Zeus placed their images in the stars as the Hyades. Here he was taught the use of the vine by his tutor Silenus and his satyrs and here he invented wine. As an adult he journeyed through India, Egypt, Syria and Asia accompanied by a wild following of Maenads or Bacchae and Satyrs. As he went he founded cities and taught cultivation of the vine. When he reached Thrace, Lycurgus, king of the Edones, opposed him but was driven mad by Rhea (q.v.) and slew his own son. His people then had him torn apart by horses. King Pentheus of Thebes also opposed Dionysus and was torn apart by crazed Bacchae whose ranks included his mother and sisters. Entranced they took him for a wild animal. Sailing to Naxos Dionysus was captured by pirates for sale as a slave. He became a lion and turned the oars to serpents. Ivy grew on the mast. The terrified pirates jumped overboard and became dolphins. At Naxos he married Ariadne (q.v.) whom Theseus (q.v.) had deserted. He was eventually received into Olympus as a god, replacing Hestia (q.v.). He fetched his mother to Olympus from the Underworld and she was henceforth known as Thyone. Dionysus was the god of wine and intoxicating herbs like ivy and laurel. He was also the god of tillage and law giving. He was worshipped at Delphi (q.v.) and in the spring festival, the Great Dionysia. In Rome the mysteries of his cult were a closely guarded secret. His followers worshipped him in communal wine-induced frenzies and the ritual involved sacrifice of animals, flagellation and a mystical marriage of novices with the god.

Dioscuri. See **Castor and Polydeuces.**

Dirce. See **Antiope.**

Dis or Orcus. Hades (q.v.).

Dodona. Site of an oracle of Zeus (q.v.) in north west Greece near modern Janina. It was associated with the union of Zeus and Dione, a minor goddess. The oracle centred on an oak and messages were transmitted by the rustling branches and cooing of pigeons nesting in it. The priests were "Selloi" who slept on the ground and walked barefoot. It was visited by Croesus (q.v.) and Alexander the Great offered the sanctuary a large sum of money.

Dryope. The daughter of King Dryops. Apollo (q.v.) seduced her and she was carried off by the Hamadryads (nymphs of trees).

E

Echidne. A mythical creature, half-woman, half-serpent. Mother by Typhon (q.v.) of the Chimaera (q.v.), Sphinx (q.v.), Cerberus (q.v.), Hydra (q.v.), Nemean Lion, Orthrus (q.v.), and Ladon. Slain by Argus.

Echion. A son of Hermes (*q.v.*). An Argonaut (*q.v.*) who took part in the hunt of the Calydonian boar (*q.v.*).

Echo. A nymph who occupied Hera's (*q.v.*) attention by incessant talk while Zeus (*q.v.*) enjoyed himself with the other nymphs. In punishment Hera deprived her of the power of speech except to repeat the words of others. Echo loved Narcissus who refused her. Heart-broken she pined away to nothing, only her voice remaining. Artemis (*q.v.*) punished Narcissus for his heartlessness by making him fall in love with his own reflection. Despairingly he committed suicide and was turned into a flower.

Egeria. An Italian goddess or nymph whose worship was connected with that of Diana (*q.v.*). She was associated with water. It was believed she advised Numa Pompilius (*q.v.*) especially on religious matters and Livy tells us they met in a sacred grove near Rome.

Eileithyia. A goddess of childbirth whom the Greeks associated with Artemis (*q.v.*) and the Romans with Juno (*q.v.*).

Elatus. The father of Caeneus and one of the Lapithae (*q.v.*).

Electra. (1) A Pleiad (*q.v.*).

(2) The daughter of Agamemnon (*q.v.*) and Clytemnestra (*q.v.*). Treated as a slave by her mother and Aegisthus (*q.v.*) she later helped her brother Orestes (*q.v.*) and his friend Pylades (*q.v.*) avenge their father and married Pylades. This is the basis of Euripides' *Electra* and Strauss's *Elektra*. Freud gave the name "Electra complex" to female fixation on the father, the opposite of the "Oedipus complex".

Electryon. The son of Perseus (*q.v.*) and Andromeda (*q.v.*). King of Mycenae and father of Alcmene (*q.v.*) wife of Amphitrion (*q.v.*).

Eleusis. A sacred site twelve miles west of Athens facing Salamis. Here Celeus received Demeter (*q.v.*). Games and an oracle were found there. A cult involving "Mysteries" was centred there and administered by two families, the Eumolpidae and Kerykes. Ceremonies were held twice a year in Spring and Autumn and initiation to the mysteries, of which we know little, was open to all men, Greek or not, free or slave, who had not committed murder.

Elissa. *See* Dido.

Elpenor. One of Odysseus' (*q.v.*) crew who fell off the roof of Circe's (*q.v.*) palace while sleep-walking and broke his neck. When Odysseus visited the Underworld his shade begged for cremation and a burial mound in which his ear was to be planted.

Elysium. A blessed abode of the dead, placed by Homer near the Underworld but not in Hades (*q.v.*). The virtuous went here after death. It was a land of warmth never knowing cold or snow. Later it was associated with "Fortunate Isles" holding "Elysian Fields" which were believed to be far to the west, beyond the Pillars of Hercules (*q.v.*).

Empusae. Daughters of Hecate (*q.v.*). They were demons with the haunches of an ass who wore brazen slippers. Able to turn themselves into cows, bitches or young maidens, as the latter they lay with young men and sucked their blood as they slept.

Enceladus. A son of Ge (*q.v.*). One of 24 giants (*q.v.*) with serpents' tails whom Alcyoneus led in an assault on Olympus (*q.v.*). Buried under Mt. Etna in Sicily as a punishment.

Endymion. Either a shepherd of Caria or an Aeolian youth who became king of Elis. As he slept in a cave Selene (*q.v.*) the moon saw him and descended to kiss him. Captivated by his looks she made him fall into a dreamless everlasting sleep so that she could always gaze upon him. His son Aetolus conquered Aetolia.

Enipeus. A river god, beloved of Tyro (*q.v.*).

Eos. The goddess of the dawn, the Romans identified her with Aurora (*q.v.*). The daughter of Hyperion (*q.v.*) and Theira and sister of Helios (*q.v.*). She drove the chariot of Helios each morning to announce his arrival and traversed the sky with him as Hemera before landing in the west as Hespera. The wife of Astraeus and by him mother of the stars and all the winds save the east. She carried off several handsome youths including Orion (*q.v.*) Cephalus (*q.v.*), and Tithonus to whom she bore Memnon (*q.v.*). She requested Zeus (*q.v.*) to make Tithonus immortal but forgot to ask for eternal youth and as he aged he shrank to a cicada.

Epaphus. The son of Zeus (*q.v.*) and Io who ruled

Egypt and was said by some to be the sacred bull of Egypt, Apis (*q.v.*).

Epeus. A cowardly son of Panopeus who built the Trojan Horse.

Ephialtes. One of the 24 giants (*q.v.*) led by Alcyoneus. (*See also* Otus).

Epidaurus. Site of a famous sanctuary of Asclepius (*q.v.*) built in the 6th century B.C. Here pilgrims could see the tomb of the god.

Epigoni. Descendants of the "Seven against Thebes" (*q.v.*) who also attacked the city ten years after their fathers had done so. They were assembled by Adrastus (*q.v.*) and their ranks included his own son Aegialeus, Diomedes son of Tydeus, Sthenelus son of Capaneus and Eradne and Therseander. Like his father Polynices (*q.v.*) Therseander bribed Eriphyle (*q.v.*) into persuading Alcmaeon into joining the assault on Thebes. Aegialeus died at the walls of the city but the Theban prophet Teiresias advised the citizens to leave the city at night as he had foreseen the Argives (*i.e.* the Epigoni), capturing an empty city. He died next morning drinking from the well of Tilphussa. Adrastus died of grief hearing of his son's death while the remaining Epigoni were left holding an empty city. Alcmaeon went home to take revenge on Eriphyle (*q.v.*).

Erebos. A deep chasm in the Underworld.

Erebus. "Darkness", the son of Chaos (*q.v.*) and father of Aether and Hemera by "Night", his sister. Some traditions hold that the Fates (*q.v.*) were daughters of Erebus and Night and that they held sway even over Zeus (*q.v.*).

Erechtheus. Son of Pandion and grandson of Erichthonius (*q.v.*) with whom he is sometimes confused or identified. Both were reared by Athene (*q.v.*) and were associated with serpents. Both were mythical kings of Athens. When the Eleusians led by Eumolpus, a son of Poseidon (*q.v.*), invaded Athens, Erechtheus was told by an oracle to sacrifice his daughter Otonia. He did so and her sisters Protogonia and Panora also sacrificed themselves. He slew Eumolpus and was slain by lightning from either Poseidon or Zeus (*q.v.*).

Erichthonius. A son of Hephaestus (*q.v.*) by Athene (*q.v.*). The child was concealed in a chest by the normally chaste Athene and entrusted to the daughters of Cecrops of Athens who were forbidden to open it. However they did so and finding a serpent inside went mad and leaped to their death from the Acropolis (*q.v.*). Erichthonius eventually succeeded Cecrops as King of Athens and was grandfather of Erechtheus. It was said Erichthonius was the founder of the Panathenaean games in honour of Athene and that he was the first man to harness a team of four horses to a single chariot.

Eridanus. An Italian river god, later thought to be the River Po.

Erigone. The daughter of Icarius. Led to her father's grave by his faithful pet hound Maera, she hanged herself from the tree beneath which he lay.

Erinnyes. Three daughters of Mother Earth whom she conceived by the blood of Uranus (*q.v.*) when Cronus (*q.v.*) castrated him. They personified the conscience and were powerful divinities who punished crimes of sacrilege, especially matricide. They pursued Alcmaeon (*q.v.*) and drove Orestes (*q.v.*) mad and into exile. These winged creatures had serpent hair and lived in the Underworld. Their names were Alecto, Magaera and Tisiphone. Orestes was acquitted by Athene (*q.v.*) of matricide following his defence by Apollo (*q.v.*). To pacify the Erinnyes Athene gave them a grotto at Athens where they received libations and sacrifices. Henceforth they were euphemistically referred to as the Eumenides or "kindly ones".

Eriphyle. The sister of Adrastus (*q.v.*) and wife of the seer Amphiarus. Mother of Alcmaeon (*q.v.*). Polynices (*q.v.*) bribed her into persuading Amphiarus into joining the Seven Against Thebes (*q.v.*) despite the seer's prophecy that only Adrastus would survive their expedition. She received the necklace of Harmonia (*q.v.*) for this. Later Thersander bribed her with the magic robe of Harmonia into persuading Alcmaeon to join the Epigoni (*q.v.*). On returning from Thebes Alcmaeon slew her for her selfish deceit.

Eris. A female divinity personifying Quarrels and Strife for the Greeks.

Eros. The Greek god of love, identified with the Roman Cupid (*q.v.*) or Amor. A son of Aphrodite (*q.v.*), whom he often accompanied, by either her father Zeus (q.v.) or Hermes (q.v.). His half-brother was Anteros, son of Aphrodite and Ares (q.v.) who personified mutual love. It was only from the 4th century B.C. onwards that he came to be represented as a winged boy firing arrows of love which could wound both men and gods. (See **Psyche**).

Erymanthian Boar. A giant wild boar from Mt. Erymanthus which was ravaging the region of Psophis until captured by Heracles (q.v.). Whilst performing this task he was given wine made by Dionysus (q.v.) by the centaur Pholus. A dispute broke out with other centaurs, eager as ever for their share of the drink, and in the resulting battle Heracles accidentally wounded his friend Cheiron (q.v.). He caught and chained the boar in a snow drift and delivered it to Eurystheus (q.v.) before going to join the Argonauts (q.v.).

Erysichthon, Son of Triopas. He was punished with an insatiable hunger by the goddess Demeter (q.v.) for felling trees in one of her sacred groves.

Eryx. Mythical Sicilian hero. A son of Venus (q.v.) and a renowned boxer. The mountain near modern Trapani is named after him.

Eteocles. See **Seven Against Thebes**.

Etruscans. See **L41**.

Eumneus. Born of royal birth but given to Phoenician slave traders, Eumneus' story is told in Book 15 of the *Odyssey*. He became Odysseus' (q.v.) faithful swineherd.

Eumolpus. "The good singer", son of Poseidon (q.v.) and Chione. Chione threw him into the sea at birth but Poseidon saved him and he was raised at the court of King Tegyrius of Thrace before becoming a priest of Demeter (q.v.) and Persephone (q.v.) at Eleusis. Here he initiated Heracles (q.v.) into the mysteries and taught the hero the lyre. He later made war on Athens and was slain by Erechtheus (q.v.). His descendants became hereditary priests of the Eleusian mysteries.

Euphorbus. Son of Panthous, a Trojan who wounded Patroclus (q.v.) before he was slain by Hector (q.v.).

Euphrosyne. One of the Charities or Graces (q.v.).

Euripides. See **B23**.

Europa. Daughter of Agenor and Telephassa and a grand-daughter of Poseidon (q.v.). While she was on the sea-shore Zeus (q.v.) appeared in the form of a white bull and when she jumped on his back carried her off to Crete where he fathered three sons on her, Minos (q.v.), Rhadamanthus (q.v.) and Sarpedon (q.v.). The Cretan king married her and adopted the children. Zeus gave her a necklace fashioned by Hephaestus (q.v.) which rendered the wearer irresistibly beautiful.

Eurystheus. A grandson of Perseus (q.v.). He was conceived shortly after Heracles (q.v.) but when Zeus (q.v.) boasted that Heracles would rule the House of Perseus, Hera (q.v.) in her jealousy extracted a promise from Zeus that the next son born to the House of Perseus would be its ruler. She then delayed the birth of Heracles until after that of Eurystheus. Later, after Heracles had slain his children in a fit of madness he was told by the oracle to serve Eurystheus in order to be cleansed of guilt. Eurystheus, a cowardly and contemptible creature, set him twelve labours. After Heracles' death he decided to expel the Heracleidae (q.v.) or descendants of Heracles from Greece but they sheltered at Athens. Eurystheus attacked the city but was resisted by Theseus (q.v.), Iolaus (q.v.) and Hyllus (q.v.). An oracle demanded the sacrifice of one of Heracles' children and Macaria slew herself. Eurystheus was then defeated and slain by Alcmene.

Eurus. The South-East wind, son of Astraeus (q.v.) and Eos.

Euryale. One of the Gorgons (q.v.).

Eurydice. The wife of Orpheus (q.v.). She died from a snake bite and Orpheus followed her to the Underworld. Hades (q.v.) delighted by Orpheus' lyre playing allowed him to take her back to life provided he did not look back. Unfortunately at the gates of the Underworld the anxious Orpheus could no longer resist the temptation to gaze on her beauty nor acquiesce in her accusations of indifference. He turned round to see her and she was lost to him.

Eurytus. See **Deianeira**.

Euterpe. Muse of music and lyric poetry.

Evadne. The daughter of Iphis and wife of Capaneus

who killed herself on the funeral pyre of the Seven against Thebes (q.v.).

Evander. A mythical king of Arcadia who settled in Italy on the future site of Rome.

Evenus. The father of Marpessa. When Idas carried her off he drowned himself in the river which henceforth bore his name.

F

Fates. The personifications of impersonal destiny who sometimes seem to control even Zeus (q.v.), at others merely to perform his will. The concept developed of three Moirae (*Latin* Parcae) daughters of Zeus and Themis (q.v.), or of Erebus (q.v.) and Night. The first, Clotho, spans the thread of life, Lachesis who measured it, and Atropus who cut it. With Hermes (q.v.) they composed the Alphabet.

Faunus. An Italian god of the flocks, herds and wild countryside, later identified with Pan (q.v.). In this context he was half-human, half-goat and lived in Arcadia (q.v.). He had a shrine on the Palatine Hill. He is sometimes regarded not as one god but as numerous spirits of the woods or "fauns".

Faustulus. A kindly shepherd who, with his wife Acca Larentia, raised Romulus (q.v.) and Remus (q.v.). His name relates to Faunus (q.v.) and his wife's to Lares (q.v.) respectively the pastoral god of Latium and the tutelary deities of the Roman home. Up to Cicero's time Romans proudly pointed to a hut on the Palatine which was said to be that where Faustulus raised Romulus but, embarrassingly, a hut with similar claims also stood on the Capitol.

Fidius. Dius Fidius was a name for Jupiter (q.v.) as guarantor of Good Faith.

Flora. Italian goddess of flowers and the spring, worshipped at Rome from the mid 3rd century B.C. Ovid tells us the April festival in her honour, "Ludi Florales" was one of drunken boisterousness. As an earth nymph called Chloris she was pursued by Zephyr (q.v.) and changed into Flora whose breath spread flowers across the fields. The scene has been a subject for Botticelli, Titian and Poussin.

Fortuna. Roman goddess identified with Tyche (q.v.).

Fortunate Isles. See **Elysium**.

G

Gaea or Ge. The "Earth" who sprang from Chaos (q.v.). She was mother of Uranus (q.v.), the heavens, and Pontus the sea. By Uranus she was mother of the Hecatoncheires (q.v.), the Cyclopes (q.v.), the Titans (q.v.) and Themis (q.v.). When Uranus condemned the Cyclopes to Tartarus (q.v.) she instigated rebellion by the Titans and gave Cronus (q.v.) the flint sickle with which he castrated Uranus. From the blood which fell on her she bore Erinnyes (q.v.) and from the blood which fell into the sea came Aphrodite (q.v.). By Tartarus she was mother of Typhon (q.v.). She gave Hera (q.v.) a tree of golden apples which was guarded by the Hesperides (q.v.). The Romans identified her with their own earth goddess Tellus.

Gaetulians. A mythical savage tribe which the Romans placed in North Africa.

Galatea. (1) A sea nymph who loved the Sicilian shepherd Acis (q.v.). She was pursued by the Cyclops Polyphemus and to escape him threw herself into the sea off Sicily. She turned Acis into a river.

(2) See **Pygmalion**.

Ganymede. The most handsome of youths, the son of Tros (q.v.) and Callirhoë. Zeus (q.v.) loved the youth and taking the form of an eagle carried him off to become cup-bearer of the gods, leaving Tros two white horses in compensation. A subject for Correggio, Rubens, and Rembrandt.

Garamantians. Mythical North African tribe appearing in the *Aenead* (q.v.).

Ge. See **Gaea**.

Geryon. A three-bodied monster living on the island of Erythia far to the west of the known world.

Here he kept cattle guarded by Euryrion, son of Ares (q.v.) and Orthrus (q.v.). Heracles (q.v.) was sent to steal the cattle by Eurystheus (q.v.) and on his way to Erythia erected the "Pillars of Hercules" (q.v.), before sailing, on a boat provided by Helios (q.v.), to the island. He overcame Euryrion, Orthrus and Geryon and fetched the cattle to Eurystheus.

Giants (Gigantes). (1) The sons of Ge (q.v.) and Uranus (q.v.), twenty-four giants with serpents' tails who, to avenge the imprisonment of their brothers the Titans (q.v.), attacked the gods on Mt. Olympus (q.v.). Their leader was Alcyoneus and their ranks included Porphyrion, Ephialtes, Pallas, Minas, Enceladus and Polybotes. The gods finally triumphed due to the help of Heracles (q.v.) and the giants were buried under various volcanoes in punishment.

(2) In another version two giants, Ephialtes and Otus, the sons of Iphimedeia and Poseidon (q.v.), but called the Aloeidae after the name of Iphimedeia's husband Aloeus, attacked Olympus. At an early age the two imprisoned Ares (q.v.), then swearing to rape Hera (q.v.) and Artemis (q.v.) they stacked Mt. Pelion on top of Mt. Ossa in order to climb to the heavens. But Artemis lured them to Naxos and disguised as a doe leapt between them and they slew each other by accident. In Hades (q.v.) they were tied by vipers to a pillar back to back.

Glauce. Or Creusa, daughter of Creon. For her Jason (q.v.) forsook Medea (q.v.) and in revenge the sorceress sent Glauce a garment which enveloped her in flames and also killed Creon.

Glaucus. (1) King of Corinth, son of Sisyphus and Merope and father of Bellerophon (q.v.). He fed his horses on human flesh but Aphrodite (q.v.) caused them to devour Glaucus himself because he mocked her.

(2) His great-grandson, the grandson of Bellerophon who fought for the Trojans and was slain by Ajax (q.v.).

(3) The son of Minos (q.v.) and Pasiphaë (q.v.) who was drowned in a barrel of honey. The seer Polyides found the corpse and was entombed with the boy for failing to restore him. Both were saved when a serpent revealed a magic herb which resurrected Glaucus.

(4) A Boeotian fisherman who pursued Scylla (q.v.) and was turned into a sea god on eating a magic herb.

Golden Age. A concept of Hesiod's who lists four ages of man in his *Works and Days*: golden, silver, bronze and iron. Horace, Virgil, and Ovid also refer to it. A tranquil time when Cronus (q.v.) ruled as the ideal king.

Golden Bough. A gift Aeneas (q.v.) had to take to Proserpina (q.v.) before he could enter the Underworld. Also associated with the cult of Diana (q.v.) at Aricia where a runaway slave had to break the bough from a sacred tree before killing the priest and taking his place. Subject of a painting by J. W. M. Turner.

Gordian Knot. Gordius was a peasant who was acclaimed king of Phrygia by the inhabitants when he appeared in a wagon. An oracle had prophesied that the new king would appear thus. In thanksgiving he dedicated the cart to Zeus (q.v.) in the acropolis of Gordium. An oracle prophesied that he who untied the complex knot joining the yoke and pole would rule all Asia. It was eventually severed by Alexander the Great.

Gorgons or **Gorgones.** Three beautiful sisters, Medusa (q.v.), Stheno and Euryale, daughters of Phorcys and Ceto. Medusa slept with Poseidon (q.v.) in a temple of Athene (q.v.) and was transformed into a winged monster with serpent hair and brazen claws by the goddess as punishment. She could turn those who looked on her to stone. The Gorgons were sisters of the Graeae (q.v.). *See also* Perseus.

Graces (also **Gratiae**). *See* Charities.

Graeae. Sisters of the Gorgons (q.v.) who lived on Mt. Atlas. The three old women possessed only one eye and one tooth which they shared, passing them from one to the other. Perseus (q.v.) stole the eye and thus forced them to reveal the whereabouts of Medusa (q.v.) and also of the Stygian nymphs who gave him the winged sandals, magic wallet and helmet of Hades which Hermes (q.v.) said he needed in order to slay Medusa.

Gyes or **Gyges.** One of the Hecatoncheires (q.v.).

H

Hades. (1) The son of Cronus (q.v.) and Rhea (q.v.), brother of Zeus (q.v.) and Poseidon (q.v.). The Cyclopes (q.v.) gave him a helmet of darkness which made him invisible. When he and his brothers threw lots for their kingdoms Hades won the Underworld, home of the dead. His name was later extended to his realm itself. He was one of the few gods to like Ares (q.v.) and Hermes (q.v.) was his herald, conducting the shades of the dead to the Underworld. Because his name was too dread to mention he was often called "Pluto" (q.v.). No favours were expected of him so no temples were dedicated to him. He abducted Persephone (q.v.) and also chased the nymph Minthe (whom the jealous Persephone turned into a mint plant) and Leuce, who was turned into the white poplar.

(2) His realm, the Underworld, land of the dead. Its deepest reaches were called Tartarus (q.v.). Hades and Persephone ruled over it. Persephone was accompanied by Hecate (q.v.). There were five rivers in Hades, the Styx, Acheron, river of woe, Phlegethon, river of flame, Lethe, river of forgetfulness and Cocytus river of wailing. Three judges Minos (q.v.), Aeacus (q.v.) and Rhadamanthus (q.v.) decided on what would happen to souls, sending the evil for punishment, the virtuous to Elysium (q.v.) and those who had led indifferent lives to the drab asphodel fields.

Harmonia. The daughter of Ares (q.v.) and Aphrodite (q.v.) and the wife of Cadmus (q.v.). The gods attended their wedding and Aphrodite gave her the necklace which Zeus (q.v.) had given to Europa (q.v.). It had been made by Hephaestus (q.v.) and conferred irresistible beauty on the wearer. Athene (q.v.) gave her a robe which conferred divine dignity on its possessor. The couple had three children, Autonoe, Ino and Semele (q.v.). After Cadmus had resigned his throne to Pentheus (q.v.) the couple left Thebes and were eventually, in the form of serpents, received in Elysia (q.v.). The necklace and robe were later used to bribe Eriphyle.

Harpalyce. A mythical princess of Thrace, a fierce warrior and huntress.

Harpies (Greek "snatchers"). Originally spirits of the wind, in Homer they appear to carry people off to their death. Later they are portrayed as winged monsters with women's heads and claws, sent by the gods to torment mortals. They snatched and carried off people for their food.

Hebe. A personification of the Greek word for youth, the daughter of Zeus (q.v.) and Hera (q.v.). She was cupbearer to the gods until replaced by Ganymede (q.v.). Her Roman counterpart was Juventas. She married Heracles (q.v.) after his apotheosis.

Hecabe or **Hecuba.** The second wife of Priam (q.v.) who bore him 19 sons including Hector (q.v.) and Paris (q.v.). By Apollo (q.v.) the mother of Troilus (q.v.). Taken as a slave by Odysseus (q.v.) when Troy (q.v.) fell. Priam had entrusted their youngest son Polydorus, plus much gold, to Polymester, king of the Thracian Chersonese. He had murdered Polydorus and thrown his body into the sea. When Odysseus took her to the Thracian Chersonese she found the body, killed Polymester and his two sons, and escaped in the form of a bitch, Maera.

Hecate. An ancient goddess, later closely associated with Artemis (q.v.). Originally she was venerated by women, she was powerful in Heaven, Earth and the Underworld. But primarily she was seen as a goddess of the Underworld and companion of Persephone (q.v.). She was represented holding torches and accompanied by wolves. She was most formidable at the full moon with which she was associated. A practitioner of sorcery her image was worshipped at crossroads where she was portrayed with three heads or three bodies.

Hecatoncheires. The sons of Ge (q.v.) and Uranus (q.v.), three 100-handed giants called Cottus, Gyes or Gyges and Briareus or Aegaeon.

Hector. The eldest son of Priam (q.v.), Trojan hero of the Trojan War. Husband of Andromache (q.v.) and father of Astynax. He fought the great Ajax (q.v.) until nightfall when the two exchanged gifts. He slew Patroclus and in turn was slain by Achilles (q.v.) who dragged his body round the walls of Troy (q.v.). Priam begged for the corpse and his funeral is the closing scene of Homer's *Iliad*. A chivalrous warrior.

Helen. The daughter of Leda (*q.v.*) by Zeus (*q.v.*), hatched from an egg, and the sister of Clytemnestra (*q.v.*), Castor and Polydeuces (*q.v.*) (known as the Dioscuri). She was raised at the court of Leda's husband, Tyndareus of Sparta. As a child she was abducted by Theseus (*q.v.*) and Pirithous (*q.v.*) but being too young to marry, was left with Theseus' mother Aethra. The Dioscuri rescued her and Aethra became her slave. The most beautiful of women she had many suitors who swore to defend her chosen husband, Menelaus (*q.v.*). She was taken by Paris (*q.v.*) to Troy (*q.v.*) thus causing the Trojan war (*q.v.*) and "launching a thousand ships" (of the Greeks who went to reclaim her). When Paris died Helenus (*q.v.*) and Deiphobus quarrelled for her the latter forcibly marrying her. D, then she was homesick for Sparta and when Odysseus (*q.v.*) entered Troy in disguise told him so and gave him information useful to the Greek cause. When Troy fell Deiphobus was killed and mangled by Odysseus and Menelaus, but when Menelaus chased her, sword drawn, to punish her, she calmed him by baring her breast. In the *Odyssey* she was reconciled to Menelaus and became a domesticated and faithful wife. She bore him a daughter, Hermione. It appears that Helen may have been a pre-Greek goddess associated with birds and trees. Various tales are told of her. Stesichorus says that only her phantom went to Troy: the real Helen went to Egypt. Another legend says that at her death she was carried off to live eternally with Achilles (*q.v.*) on a "white isle". Others suggest that her mother was not Leda but Nemesis (*q.v.*).

Helenus. The son of Priam (*q.v.*) and Hecabe (*q.v.*), twin of Cassandra (*q.v.*) and a prophet. He quarrelled with his brother Deiphobus over Helen (*q.v.*) and when the latter forcibly married her fled Troy (*q.v.*) and was captured by Odysseus (*q.v.*). Calchas (*q.v.*) had said that only Helenus knew the secret oracles of how Troy would fall. He told Odysseus that the city would be taken in the summer if a bone of Pelops (*q.v.*) were brought to the Greeks, if Neoptolemus (*q.v.*) joined them, and if the Palladium (*q.v.*) were stolen. These things were done. After the war he was taken by Neoptolemus and prophesied a safe route home for him. When Neoptolemus settled in Epirus he gave part of the kingdom to Helenus who married Andromache (*q.v.*).

Helicon. A mountain in Boeotia (*q.v.*) sacred to Apollo (*q.v.*) and inhabited by the Muses (*q.v.*) who were thus called respectively Heliconiades and Heliconides.

Helios. The Roman "Sol". A Titan (*q.v.*) later identified with Hyperion and Apollo (*q.v.*), though some traditions make him the son of Hyperion and Theia. A sun-god, his chariot was drawn across the sky each day by four horses and at night he returned to the east floating on the stream of Ocean, which surrounded the earth, in a large cup. The husband of Rhode by whom he had seven sons and a daughter, Pasiphaë. He was father of Phaeton (*q.v.*) by Clymene and of Circe (*q.v.*) by Perse. He reputedly saw all, but missed Odysseus' (*q.v.*) men stealing his cattle. When he shone too brightly Odysseus (*q.v.*) fired an arrow at him. Admiring the hero's boldness he lent him his cup or boat with which to travel to Erythia. It was he who told Demeter (*q.v.*) that Hades (*q.v.*) had abducted Persephone (*q.v.*).

Hellas, Hellenes, Hellenism. The Greeks of the classical period termed themselves Hellenes and their country Hellas (in contrast to Homer's "Achaeans"). They traced their common descent from Hellen (*q.v.*) an eponymous hero. In modern times Hellenism refers to the culture flourishing in Greece, the Aegean isles, the Ionian coast of Asia Minor and Magna Graecia between the first Olympiad in 776 B.C. and the death of Alexander the Great in 323 B.C.

Hellen. Eponymous ancestor of the Greeks or Hellenes (*q.v.*), the son of Pyrrha and Deucalion (*q.v.*). His sons were Aeolus, Dorus and Xuthus.

Hephaestus. One of the Olympian gods, the son of Zeus (*q.v.*) and Hera (*q.v.*). The god of fire and metal work, known to the Romans as Vulcan (*q.v.*). He was hated by Hera because he was lame and she threw him down from Olympus and he landed in the sea where Thetis (*q.v.*) and Eurynome cared for him. Nine years later Hera

accepted him back but Zeus, angry with him for taking Hera's side in a quarrel, again cast him down. He was a day falling and landed on Lemnos. On returning to Olympus he sought to keep the peace between Zeus and Hera. The other gods always laughed at his lameness. His workshop was said to be on Olympus or else in Sicily, where the Cyclopes (*q.v.*) helped him in his labours. He made palaces for all the gods, the necklace of Harmonia (*q.v.*), the armour of Achilles (*q.v.*) and a wide variety of other wonderful articles. He was married either to Charis or to Aphrodite (*q.v.*) who deceived him with Ares (*q.v.*).

Hera. The Roman Juno, daughter of Cronus (*q.v.*) and Rhea (*q.v.*), sister and wife of Zeus (*q.v.*). A pre-Hellenic goddess, originally having power over all living things and vegetable life, she gradually lost these functions and eventually was only the goddess of marriage and childbirth. She was the mother of Ares (*q.v.*), Hephaestus (*q.v.*), Hebe (*q.v.*) and Ilythia (*q.v.*) by Zeus. Her virginity was renewed annually by bathing in a magical spring near Argos. Though she was the goddess of marital fidelity she had difficulty controlling the amorous adventures of her own husband (who had wooed her in the form of a cuckoo) and was violently jealous of his many affairs and cruel to her rivals and their offspring, *e.g.* Semele, Leto, Alcmene and Heracles. She once led a conspiracy against Zeus in which Poseidon (*q.v.*) and Apollo (*q.v.*) participated. Zeus was enchained and when he was freed he punished her by suspending her from the sky by the wrists with an anvil on each ankle. She helped Jason (*q.v.*) but was opposed to the Trojans because Paris (*q.v.*) did not give her the apple of discord. Her name means simply "lady".

Heracleidae. The children of Heracles (*q.v.*). Eurystheus (*q.v.*) attempted to expel them from Greece but failed.

Heracles. A hero who later became a god, a figure popular all over Greece and in Italy where the Romans knew him as Hercules. The son of Alcmene (*q.v.*) and Zeus (*q.v.*) and half-brother of Iphicles (*q.v.*). Alcmene fearing Hera's (*q.v.*) jealousy exposed him but by mistake Hera nursed him. After he had been returned to his mother Hera sent two snakes to kill him in his cradle, but he strangled them. He was taught to fight by Castor (*q.v.*), to play the lyre by Eumalpus, to wrestle by Autolycus (*q.v.*) and the art of archery by Eurytus. Linus also tried to teach him to play the lyre but, when he censured his awkward pupil, Heracles killed him with his own instrument. Amphitrion (*q.v.*) then sent him to keep cattle. At the age of 18, after a 50-day chase, he killed a huge lion on Mt. Cithaeron because it had been ravaging the herds of Amphitrion and Thespius. He did this with a wild olive club and later wore the pelt everywhere, though some other sources say he wore the pelt of the Nemean lion. In reward Thespius gave him his 50 daughters. At Thebes he defeated the Minyan heralds of Orchomenus who had come to demand tribute. Creon, king of Thebes, rewarded him by giving him his daughter Megara or Megera who bore him several children. His half-brother Iphicles married Creon's youngest daughter. Hera now made him mad and he killed his own children and two of Iphicles'. At Delphi the Pythia (*q.v.*), calling him Heracles for the first time, sent him to serve, for 12 years, his wretched cousin Eurystheus (*q.v.*) in order to purify himself of the murder. At the end of that time he would become immortal. With his nephew Iolaus (*q.v.*) as companion he embarked on 12 labours set by Eurystheus. These were to fetch the pelt of the Nemean lion, to kill the Hydra of Lerna (*q.v.*), to capture alive the Ceryneian Hind (*q.v.*), to capture alive the Erymanthian Boar (*q.v.*), to cleanse the stables of Augias (*q.v.*), to drive off the Stymphalian Birds (*q.v.*), to capture the Cretan Bull (*q.v.*), to fetch the horses of Diomedes (*q.v.*), to fetch the girdle of Hippolyte (*q.v.*), to steal the cattle of Geryon (*q.v.*), to fetch the golden apples of the Hesperides (*q.v.*) and to bring back Cerberus (*q.v.*). After capturing the Erymanthian Boar he had joined the Argonauts (*q.v.*) but his squire Hylas was spirited off by the Naiads (*q.v.*) while fetching water at Cios in Mysia and Heracles left the expedition to search for him. Having completed his service for Eurystheus he returned to Thebes and here gave Megara to Iolaus. But Hera again drove him mad and he killed Megara and her children. Some traditions say he also killed himself and his family. He now desired to marry Iole daughter of his friend Eurytus of Oechalia and won her in an archery contest. But Eurytus refused to surrender her because Heracles had slain his own children. The incident ended in Heracles killing Iphitus (q.v.) but he later seized Iole. To purify himself of this murder he went to serve Omphale (q.v.). After serving her he and Telamon saved Hesione, daughter of Laomedon (q.v.) and sacked Troy (q.v.). Heracles gave Hesione to Telamon and ransomed Priam (q.v.). Next he made war on Augias and Neleus (q.v.) and then on Hippocoon who had helped Neleus. In this he was assisted by Cepheus (q.v.) and he restored Tyndareus (q.v.). At this time he seduced the priestess Auge, daughter of Aleus king of Tegea, who bore him a son, Telephus. Now he married Deianeira (q.v.) who inadvertently caused his death. As Heracles ascended his funeral pyre, to be burned alive he gave his bow and quiver to Philoctetes (q.v.) who kindled the flame but thunderbolts demolished the pyre and he was carried on a cloud to Olympus. Here he was reconciled to Hera and married Hebe (q.v.), himself becoming an immortal. Numerous other legends concerning Heracles exist. We are told he rescued Alcestis (q.v.), helped the gods defeat the Giants (q.v.), defeated Antaeus (q.v.) and, when the Delphic Oracle would not give him an answer seized the sacred tripod and struggled with Apollo (q.v.) for it. Xenophon tells us that before beginning his adventures Heracles was confronted by two beautiful women, one offering a life of ease, the other of service to mankind and he had to choose between the two. Other writers tell of him having to choose between two roads offering similar alternatives to the women. From a mighty and boisterous hero the picture of Heracles gradually developed into a morality tale of selfless service and fortitude eventually rewarded and for this reason the Stoic philosophers of Rome idealised him.

Hercules. See **Heracles.**

Hermaphroditus. The son of Hermes (q.v.) and Aphrodite (q.v.) who refused the advances of the nymph Salmacis. Her request that their bodies be joined in one was then granted by the gods. The name gives us the word "hermaphrodite", a being with the characteristics of both sexes.

Hermes. The Roman Mercury. Originally a god of fertility. The son of Zeus (q.v.) and Maia, (daughter of Atlas (q.v.). He was born on Mt. Cyllene (hence he was sometimes referred to as Cyllenius). While still hours old he left the cradle and stole Apollo's (q.v.) cattle. He invented the lyre by stringing a tortoise shell with cow-gut and gave it to Apollo. This calmed Apollo's wrath and the two became friends. Zeus made him messenger of the gods and gave him his winged sandals (the Alipes), broadbrimmed hat (the Petasus) and herald's staff (caduceus) originally entwined with two white ribbons, later represented as entwined snakes. He conducted the souls of the dead to Hades (q.v.) and in this role was known as Psychopompus. The patron of travellers, traders and thieves and the father of Autolycus the thief, by Chione, and of Echion herald of the Argonauts (q.v.). He was the father of Pan (q.v.) by Penelope (q.v.) and a companion of the Muses (q.v.). He helped the Fates compose the alphabet, invented the musical scale, weights and measures and olive cultivation. A god of dice games. As herald he was eloquent and in Acts ch. XIV St. Paul, who spoke in tongues more than any man, is mistaken for him.

Hermione. The daughter of Helen (q.v.) and Menelaus (q.v.). Betrothed by Tyndareus (q.v.) to Orestes (q.v.) but given to Neoptolemus (q.v.) by Menelaus.

Hero. A priestess of Aphrodite (q.v.) at Sestos. Her lover Leander (q.v.) used to swim the Hellespont each night to see her but drowned when a storm extinguished the light she used to guide him. She then drowned herself. The subject of a play by Marlowe and paintings by Rubens and Turner.

Herodotus. See **B31.**

Heroes. To the Greeks a hero was the son of a mortal or divinity who was essentially superior to other men. They were venerated and received sacrifices because they were believed to help the living. Thus Theseus (q.v.) was supposed to have helped the Athenians at Marathon. "Heroic poetry" was epic poetry, telling of their deeds.

Hesiod. See **B31.**

Hesperides. "The daughters of evening" who lived in a land at the end of the world, far to the west. These maidens guarded a tree belonging to Hera (q.v.) which bore golden apples. They were assisted by a dragon, Ladon. Ge (q.v.) had given the tree to Hera on her wedding day. On the advice of Prometheus (q.v.) Heracles (q.v.) (who had been sent to get the apples by Eurystheus (q.v.)) persuaded Atlas (q.v.) to fetch three apples while he shouldered Atlas' burden. Atlas then refused to take the sky back on his shoulders but Heracles tricked him into doing so. On his return journey Heracles slew Antaeus (q.v.). Eurystheus gave the apples back to Heracles and he passed them to Athene to return to the Hesperides.

Hesperus. The evening star, the Greek form of the Latin vesper or evening.

Hestia. The sister of Zeus (q.v.) and Hera (q.v.), the goddess of the hearth worshipped by every family. Though Poseidon (q.v.) and Apollo (q.v.) tried to seduce her she swore to Zeus always to remain a virgin. The Romans worshipped her counterpart, the goddess Vesta (q.v.).

Hippodamia. (1) The daughter of Oenomaus, king of Elis. An oracle said he would die at the hands of his son-in-law so he challenged all her suitors to a chariot race. Victory meant they could marry Hippodamia, defeat meant death. His horses were the gifts of his father Ares (q.v.). However Pelops (q.v.) engineered his death and married Hippodamia.
(2) The wife of Pirithous (q.v.). When a drunken centaur (q.v.) abducted her on her wedding day the battle between the Lapithae (q.v.) and Centaurs occurred.

Hippolyte. A queen of the Amazons (q.v.) and sister of Antiope. Heracles (q.v.) had to fetch her golden girdle for Eurystheus. At first he was well received but Hera (q.v.) stirred the Amazons against him and in the fight he slew Hippolyte and took the girdle. Returning home he saved Laomedon's (q.v.) daughter Hesione. Another legend says Theseus (q.v.) abducted Hippolyte who bore him the son Hippolytus (q.v.).

Hippolytus. The son of Theseus (q.v.) and the Amazon Hippolyte (q.v.) or her sister Antiope (q.v.). When Theseus married again to Phaedra (q.v.), sister of Ariadne (q.v.), Phaedra fell in love with her stepson and committed suicide when he refused her. She left a note falsely accusing Hippolytus. Theseus prayed to Poseidon (q.v.) who was under an obligation to him, that Hippolytus would die the same day. Poseidon then sent a sea-monster which scared the youth's horses and he was dragged to death behind his chariot.

Homer. See **B32.**

Horae. The "hours", three daughters of Zeus (q.v.) and Themis (q.v.) and tutelary goddesses of nature and the seasons. They were bound to the soil and promoted fertility. Thus they were important and are involved in solemn oaths. However they rarely appear except in attendance on other gods and have no "adventures".

Horatii. Three Roman brothers whose tale is told by Livy. In the mid 7th century B.C. while Rome was ruled by Tullus Hostilius the city of Alba Longa (q.v.) was destroyed and its population transferred to Rome. According to legend the Horatii challenged the three Alban champions, the Curatii, to a sword battle. Two Horatii were killed but the third slew all the Curatii. On returning to Rome he met his sister, who had been engaged to one of the Curatii, weeping. He stabbed her to death. After ceremonies of expiation Tullus acquitted him of murder.

Horatius Cocles. Another of the Horatii family, the "one-eyed" (Cocles). In the 6th century B.C. he held the Etruscans at bay on the wooden Sublican bridge into Rome until it was pulled down beneath him. He then swam the Tiber to safety. The subject of a Lay by Macaulay.

Hyacinthus. A Peloponnesian youth loved by Apollo (q.v.) who was killed when the jealous Zephyrus (q.v.) diverted a discus to hit him. From his blood sprang the "hyacinth" flower. He had a shrine at Amyclae in Laconia and a three-day festival, the Hyacinthia, was held in his honour at Sparta.

Hyades. Nymphs who cared for Dionysus (q.v.) as a child on Mt. Nysa. Zeus (q.v.) placed their images in the sky as the "rain stars", part of the constellation of Taurus which rises at midnight in the rainy season.

Hydra of Lerna. The "water snake", offspring of Echidne (q.v.) and Typhon (q.v.) and raised by

Hera (q.v.). It was a monster with the body of a dog and 9 serpent heads. Heracles (q.v.) was sent to kill it by Eurystheus (q.v.). It lived at the source of the River Amymone in the swamp of Lerna. As Heracles lopped off a head two more grew. He also had to crush a giant crab which Hera placed among the signs of the zodiac. Finally he crushed the Hydra's heads with his club and Iolaus (q.v.) burned them to stop them regrowing. He dipped his arrows in the beast's blood thereby making them poisonous.

Hygeia. The wife or daughter of Asclepius (q.v.), a goddess of health.

Hylas. See **Heracles**.

Hyllus. The son of Heracles (q.v.) and Deianeira (q.v.). He conducted Heracles to his funeral pyre. Either he or Iolaus (q.v.) defeated Eurystheus (q.v.). Eventually he was slain by Echemus, king of Tegea.

Hymen. God of weddings.

Hyperboreans. A mythical race living far to the north, behind Boreas (q.v.) i.e. at the place where the north wind originates. Apollo (q.v.) spent time with them before going to Delphi and spent the winter months with them. A Hyperborean soothsayer, Olen, installed Apollo's oracle at Delphi. Their land was supposed to have perpetual sunshine and was a land of plenty, an earthly paradise where men lived in peace and ease on the fruits of the earth. Herodotus (**B31**) tells us that one of their priests, Aburis, travelled the world on a golden arrow and never needed to eat. He places their land in Southern Russia.

Hypenor. One of the Spartii (q.v.).

Hyperion. A Titan (q.v.) and sun-god, father of Helios (q.v.), Selene (q.v.) and Eos (q.v.), the sun, moon and dawn. In Keats' poem he is the last of the old gods to be deposed, the young Apollo (q.v.) taking his place.

Hypermestra. See **Danaus**.

Hypnus. The god of sleep.

I

Iacchus. Alternative name for Dionysus (q.v.) used in the Eleusian mysteries where he was regarded as the son of Zeus (q.v.) and Demeter (q.v.), not Semele (q.v.).

Iapetus. A Titan (q.v.), father of Prometheus (q.v.), Atlas (q.v.) and Epimetheus.

Iasion. Or Iasius or Iasus, the son of Zeus (q.v.) and Electra (q.v.), lover of Demeter (q.v.) who bore him a son Pluton. Zeus in his jealousy slew him with a thunderbolt.

Icarius. Father of Erigone. An Athenian to whom Dionysus (q.v.) taught cultivation of the vine and who gave wine to a band of shepherds. Mistaking drunkenness for witchcraft they slew him.

Icarus. See **Daedalus**.

Idaea. A nymph, mother of Teucer (q.v.) by Scamander (q.v.) of Crete.

Idas. The twin of Lynceus and a son of Poseidon (q.v.). He abducted Marpessa in a chariot given to him by Poseidon and fought Apollo (q.v.) for possession of her. Given the choice by Zeus (q.v.) she chose Idas. He and Lynceus took part in the voyage of the Argonauts (q.v.) and the hunt of the Calydonian boar (q.v.) and were killed in battle with their cousins the Dioscuri (q.v.).

Idomeneus. King of Crete who contributed 100 ships to the expedition against Troy (q.v.). Virgil adds that on his return from Troy he was caught in a storm and vowed to sacrifice the first person he met to Poseidon (q.v.) in return for safe passage. This proved to be his son and the sacrifice brought a pestilence on Crete. Idomeneus was banished to Calabria in Italy.

Ilia. A priestess of Vesta (q.v.) also called Rhea Silvia. The mother of Romulus (q.v.) and Remus.

Iliad. Homer's epic poem on the siege of Troy (q.v.). Although it hints at earlier and later events it covers only a period of weeks in the tenth year of the war, recounting Achilles' (q.v.) quarrel with Agamemnon (q.v.), the death of Patroclus (q.v.) and the death of Hector (q.v.). It ends with Achilles returning Hector's (q.v.) body to Priam (q.v.). Although many gods and heroes appear, Achilles and Hector are the main protagonists.

Ilioneus. An old and venerated Trojan who accompanied Aeneas (q.v.).

Ilithyiae. Daughters of Hera (q.v.) who helped women

in childbirth. Later only one goddess, Ilithyia, is mentioned in this connection.

Ilus. (1) The son of Tros (q.v.) and father of Laomedon (q.v.). An ancestor of the Trojans.

(2) Original name of Ascanius (q.v.) son of Aeneas (q.v.) and Creusa.

Inachus. The first king of Argos, son of Oceanus (q.v.) and Tethys. A river was named after him.

Ino. The daughter of Cadmus (q.v.) and Harmonia (q.v.), sister of Autonoe, Agave, Polydoras, Illyrus and Semele. She helped to rear Dionysus (q.v.) and her husband Athamas (q.v.) was punished for it by Hera (q.v.) who drove him into madness and the murder of his own children. Ino, Autonoe and Agave were Bacchae (q.v.) and they slew Pentheus, the son of Agave and heir to Cadmus, for opposing the worship of Dionysus. Ino committed suicide (see **Athamas**) and became a sea deity.

Io. The daughter of Inachus. Zeus (q.v.) loved her and turned her into a white heifer to deceive the jealous Hera (q.v.). He did not succeed in this and Hera set the hundred-eyed Argus to watch the heifer. But Hermes (q.v.) at Zeus' command cut off his head and placed his eyes in the tail of the peacock. He also sent a gadfly whose sting caused Io to wander the earth till she reached Egypt. On her wanderings she gave her name to the Ionian sea and to the Bosphorus ("ford of the cow"). In Egypt Zeus restored her to human form and she bore him a son, Epaphus, an ancestor of Danaus (q.v.).

Iobates. See **Bellerophon**.

Iolaus. Son of Iphicles (q.v.) and nephew of Heracles (q.v.) to whom he was charioteer and constant companion. He helped Heracles kill the Hydra (q.v.) and perform his other labours and in return Heracles gave him his wife Megara. He also sent Iolaus as the leader of his sons by the daughters of Thespius to settle in Sardinia.

Iolcus. The kingdom of Jason's (q.v.) father Aeson, usurped by his half brothers Pelias and Neleus.

Iole. See **Deianeira**.

Ion. The son of Xuthus and Creusa, brother of Achaeus. In Euripides' play *Ion* he is the son of Creusa and Apollo (q.v.) who is carried off to Delphi (q.v.), as a baby but is eventually restored to Creusa and adopted by Xuthus. The eponymous ancestor of the Ionian Greeks.

Iphicles. (1) One of the Argonauts (q.v.).

(2) The son of Amphitrion (q.v.) and Alcmene (q.v.) a night younger than Heracles (q.v.). The father of Iolaus (q.v.). He married the youngest daughter of Creon of Thebes when Heracles married Megara.

Iphigenia. The daughter of Agamemnon (q.v.) and Clytemnestra (q.v.), sacrificed by her father at Aulis to get a favourable wind for the Greek fleet sailing to Troy (q.v.). Euripides cites another tradition in which Artemis (q.v.) substituted a doe for Iphigenia at the last moment and carried her off to Tauris. Later Orestes (q.v.) found Iphigenia on the Tauric Chersonese and brought her home to Greece.

Iphitus. A son of Eurytus who argued that his father should deliver Iole (see **Deianeira**) to Heracles (q.v.). But in a rage Heracles slew him and though purified of the murder was told by an oracle to sell himself into slavery and give the proceeds to Iphitus' family.

Irene. The daughter of Zeus (q.v.) and Themis (q.v.), goddess of peace and one of the Horae (q.v.). The Romans identified her with Pax.

Iris. The personification of the rainbow and, in later myth, a messenger of the gods, particularly Hera (q.v.).

Isis. An Egyptian goddess, wife of Osiris and mother of Horus. In Hellenistic times she became one of the most important deities of the Mediterranean world, her cult arriving in Rome by the time of Augustus. Here the features of her worship, Egyptian priests, processions, initiation ceremonies etc. were described by Apuleius in his *Golden Ass*. One of her temples is preserved at Pompeii.

Ismene. The daughter of Oedipus (q.v.) and Jocasta (q.v.). She followed her father and her sister Antigone (q.v.) into exile.

Issa. The daughter of Macareus and his sister Canace, beloved by Apollo (q.v.).

Isthmian Games. Quadrennial games held at Corinth in honour of Poseidon (q.v.).

Ithaca. The island home of Odysseus (q.v.), one of the Ionian islands.

Itys, Itylus. *See* **Procne**.

Iulus. A name used for Ascanius (*q.v.*) by Virgil to indicate the descent of the Julian clan from Aeneas (*q.v.*).

J

Janus. A god of beginnings or new ventures, worshipped at Rome. He had a flamen (sacred priest) and was very important but the origin and nature of his worship is obscure. He had two faces and may represent the assimilation of an eastern god and an Etruscan (*see* **I41**) deity. Also associated with doorways and thresholds.

Jason. Son of Aeson, rightful king of Iolcus who was usurped by his half-brothers, Pelias and Neleus. The infant Jason was smuggled out of Iolcus and reared by Cheiron (*q.v.*) while Pelias expelled Neleus and ruled alone. When Jason returned to claim his birthright Pelias sent him to fetch the Golden Fleece from Colchis. This was the fleece of the ram on which Phrixus (*q.v.*) had escaped and which he had given to Aëtes, king of Colchis. Its presence was the cause of Colchis' prosperity and it hung from an oak tree in the grove of Ares (*q.v.*) where a dragon guarded it. After numerous adventures Jason and his Argonauts (*q.v.*) arrived at Colchis and Aëtes promised Jason the fleece if he could yoke two fire-breathing bulls with brazen feet made by Hephaestus (*q.v.*), and sow the grove of Ares with dragons' teeth left by Cadmus of Thebes (*q.v.*). Medea (*q.v.*) the sorceress gave him a fire-proof lotion which allowed him to complete the task and when her father Aëtes refused to give up the fleece, charmed the dragon to sleep while Jason stole it. Pursued by Aëtes the couple escaped when Medea murdered her half-brother Absyrtus and dropped pieces of his corpse into the sea, causing Aëtes to stop and collect them. They were purified of the murder by Circe (*q.v.*). At Iolchus Pelias had forced Aeson to commit suicide and in revenge Medea persuaded Pelias' daughters to boil their father alive pretending it would restore his youth. The couple were banished because of this and went to Corinth. Here Jason abandoned Medea for Glauce (*q.v.*) whom Medea killed. Jason took his own life though one tradition holds he was killed by the falling prow of the Argo (*q.v.*).

Jocasta. Daughter of Menoeceus, wife of Laius king of Thebes and mother of Oedipus (*q.v.*). When her unwitting incest with Oedipus brought a plague on Thebes Menoeceus sacrificed himself in answer to an oracle demanding the life of one of the Sparti (*q.v.*) *i.e.* a descendant of the "sown men". Jocasta hanged herself when she learned the truth of her marriage to Oedipus.

Jove. Alternative name for Jupiter (*q.v.*).

Juno. Italian goddess of womanhood and childbirth, associated by the Romans with the Greek Hera (*q.v.*) and regarded as the consort of Jupiter (*q.v.*).

Jupiter. Originally an Italian sky-god, later regarded by the Romans as *Dies Pater*—"Father Day", god of the day. Later still identified with Zeus (*q.v.*). His cult was introduced to Rome by the Etruscans and the temple to Jupiter Optimus Maximus (Best and Most High) stood on the Capitol. His *flamen*, the *flamen* Dialis was the most important of the college. He was guarantor of the *imperium* and city of Rome and triumphs were an act of Jupiter worship. Worshipped in various capacities as *Stator* (he who founds or maintains), *Teretrius* (he who strikes), *Ultor* ("Avenger") and *Tonans* ("Thunderer").

Juturna. (1) An Italian goddess of springs and streams.

(2) The sister of Turnus (*q.v.*).

Juventas. Italian goddess identified with Hebe (*q.v.*).

L

Labdacus. Mythical king of Thebes; a descendant of Cadmus (*q.v.*) and an ancestor of Oedipus (*q.v.*).

Lachesis. One of the Fates (*q.v.*).

Laelaps. A fleet-footed hound given to Procris by Cephalus (*q.v.*).

Laertes. The king of Ithaca, father of Odysseus (*q.v.*)

by Anticleia, daughter of the thief Autolycus. While Odysseus was at Troy (*q.v.*) Penelope's (*q.v.*) suitors forced him to retire to the country.

Laestrygones. A race of giant cannibals ruled by Lamus. At Telepylos, their capital city, Odysseus (*q.v.*) lost all but one of his twelve ships to them. Homer says their summer nights were so short that shepherds going out with their flocks in the morning met those returning at sunset. Traditionally located in eastern Sicily or at Formiae in central Italy.

Laius. *See* **Oedipus**.

Lamia. One of the Empusae (*q.v.*), daughter of Belus.

Lamus. *See* **Laestrygones**.

Laocoön. A Trojan prophet, son of Antenor and a priest of Apollo (*q.v.*) and Poseidon (*q.v.*). He warned the Trojans against the Wooden Horse (*q.v.*) and flung a spear at it. However he had angered Apollo by breaking his vows of celibacy and the god now sent two sea serpents which crushed him and his two sons. A famous group of statues depicting the scene, carved in Rhodes *c.* 25 B.C., now stands in the Vatican museum. The Trojans disastrously drew the wrong conclusion *viz.* that his death was punishment for striking the horse.

Laodamia. The daughter of Acastus and wife of Protesilaus of Thessaly, the first Greek ashore at Troy (*q.v.*) though he knew from an oracle the first Greek to land would die. Homer says he left his wife mourning and his house unfinished but Catullus, Virgil and Ovid follow another tradition in which she begged the gods that Protesilaus might return to life for three hours. When he died a second time she committed suicide. Wordsworth's poem *Laodamia* takes the tale as its subject.

Laodice. (1) A daughter of Priam (*q.v.*), sister of Cassandra (*q.v.*) and wife of Helicaon. When Troy (*q.v.*) fell the earth swallowed her.

(2) Alternative name for Electra (*q.v.*), Agamemnon's (*q.v.*) daughter.

Laomedon. The son of Ilus (*q.v.*), king of Troy (*q.v.*) and father of Hesione and Priam (*q.v.*). Apollo (*q.v.*) and Poseidon (*q.v.*) helped him build the walls of Troy and he refused to pay them. Poseidon then sent a sea monster to devour Hesione but Heracles (*q.v.*) saved her. Laomedon then refused to pay Heracles the agreed white horses left by Zeus (*q.v.*) in exchange for Ganymede (*q.v.*). Heracles and Telamon then sacked Troy and slew Laomedon and all his sons save Priam (*q.v.*).

Lapis Niger. Black marble paving in the Roman Forum said to cover the tomb of Romulus (*q.v.*).

Lapithae or **Lapiths.** Mythical tribe of Thessaly, governed by Pirithous, son of Ixion (*q.v.*) and thus half-brothers to the Centaurs (*q.v.*). At the wedding of Pirithous and Hippodamia, attended by Theseus (*q.v.*) a centaur tried to abduct the bride and a famous battle between the Lapithae and Centaurs ensued. It is described by Ovid and is depicted in the Parthenon and the frieze of Apollo's (*q.v.*) temple at Bassae. It is also the subject of a sculptured frieze by Michelangelo.

Lares. Originally fertility gods, worshipped by the Romans privately in the home and semi-publicly at crossroads. They were represented as youths with handfuls of fruit who wandered the farmstead incessantly whirling round and round. They kept away maleficent demons and ensured the prosperity of the family home. Each month they received offerings of oat cakes, milk, honey and flowers. Generally associated with the Penates, the spirits who guarded the household stores. Together the guardians of the hearth and home.

Larissa. A city in Thessaly near modern Volos. Reputed birthplace of Achilles (*q.v.*) hence his nickname "the Larissaen".

Lars Porsenna. Legendary Etruscan chief whom Livy tells us besieged Rome on behalf of the exiled Tarquinius Superbus. Lars means "overlord" and he is probably a symbol of Etruscan suzerainty over Rome. (*See* **Horatius Cocles**).

Latinus. Eponymous king of the Latini or Latins in Italy. Hesiod makes him the son of Odysseus (*q.v.*) and Circe (*q.v.*). Virgil makes him the son of Faunus (*q.v.*). Livy and Virgil portray him as opposing the settlement of Aeneas (*q.v.*) and the Trojans in Italy but then agreeing Aeneas should marry his daughter Lavinia. He next helps Aeneas fight Turnus king of the Rutuli, to whom Lavinia had been promised. Livy says he died in battle and Aeneas became king of the Latins; Virgil that he survived to celebrate the marriage and uniting of Latins and Trojans.

Leander. Mythical youth who drowned while swimming to meet Hero (*q.v.*).

Leda. Daughter of Thestius and wife of Tyndareus king of Sparta. Seduced by Zeus (*q.v.*) in the form of a swan she gave birth to two eggs, from one of which hatched Helen (*q.v.*) and Polydeuces (*q.v.*) from the other, Castor (*q.v.*) and Clytemnestra (*q.v.*). One tradition says that Helen was the daughter of Nemesis (*q.v.*) who left the egg for Leda to incubate.

Lemnos. A small island at the mouth of the Hellespont, home at one time of a primitive people known to the Greeks as the Pelasgi. Hephaestus (*q.v.*) was said to have landed on the island when Zeus (*q.v.*) hurled him out of heaven and supposedly had a forge here.

Lethe. "Forgetfulness" one of the rivers of the Underworld whose waters induced amnesia in those who drank of them. Virgil holds that here souls forgot their past prior to reincarnation and Ovid says that it flowed round the "cave of sleep".

Leto. Known to the Romans as Latona. The daughter of the Titans (*q.v.*) Coeus and Phoebe and the mother of Apollo (*q.v.*) and Artemis (*q.v.*) by Zeus (*q.v.*). While she carried the unborn gods the jealous Hera (*q.v.*) forced her to wander the earth until she finally gave birth to them at Ortygia, henceforth called Delos (*q.v.*). Hera sent the giant Tityus (*q.v.*) to rape her but her children slew him with their arrows. *See also* Niobe.

Leuce. A nymph loved by Hades (*q.v.*) who turned her into a white poplar tree.

Leucippus. (1) King of Messenia whose daughters Hilaera and Phoebe were abducted by the Dioscuri (*q.v.*) and whose brothers Idas (*q.v.*) and Lynceus (*q.v.*) fought to save them.

(2) The son of Oenomaus who loved Artemis (*q.v.*) To be near her he disguised himself as a nymph but when Apollo (*q.v.*) advised the nymphs to bathe naked he was discovered and torn to pieces by them.

Leucothea. Originally Ino, daughter of Cadmus (*q.v.*) and wife of Athamas who helped Zeus (*q.v.*) save Dionysus (*q.v.*) at the death of Semele (*q.v.*). In revenge Hera (*q.v.*) drove her mad and she leapt into the foaming sea to become the sea deity Leucothea—"the white goddess". In this role she helped Odysseus (*q.v.*) land on Scheria. Her son was Palaemon, a minor sea god.

Liber Pater. An ancient Italian god of the vine, early identified with Bacchus (*q.v.*) by the Romans.

Lichas. The herald of Heracles (*q.v.*) who took the shirt of Deineira (*q.v.*) to him. In his agony Heracles took him by the ankle, swung him round three times and threw him into the Euboean Sea where he became a rock of human shape which henceforth bore his name.

Linus. (1) The son of Psamathe of Argos and Apollo (*q.v.*). Fearful lest her father learn of her liaison with the god she exposed the baby who was reared by shepherds but later killed by her father's hounds. When her distress revealed her secret her father condemned her to death but Apollo sent a plague to the city which only abated when the Argives propitiated mother and son with dirges called *linoi*.

(2) The son of a Muse who was so gifted musically that the jealous Apollo killed him.

(3) Heracles' (*q.v.*) music tutor whom Heracles slew in a rage with his own lyre.

Lotophagi. ("The Lotus eaters"). A mythical people living on lotus fruit which induced trances and forgetfulness and made the eater lose any desire to return home. They gave the fruit to Odysseus' (*q.v.*) men. Herodotus placed them in western Libya, possibly the island of Jerba.

Luceres. One of the original three tribes into which Rome was divided and which were believed to date back to Romulus (*q.v.*). The other tribes were the Ramnes and Tities.

Lucifer. The "light bringer", the name given to the planet Venus which can be seen before dawn. In the evening sky the Greeks called it Hesperus.

Lucretia. Wife of Tarquinius Collatinus whose rape by Sextus, son of Tarquinius Superbus led her to stab herself in shame. Junius Brutus then swore by her spirit to expel the Tarquins which he did. The story is told by Livy and Ovid and inspired Shakespeare's poem *The Rape of Lucrece* and Brit-

ten's opera *The Rape of Lucretia*. A subject also for Titian, Botticelli, Tintoretto and Veronese.

Lucretius. *See* B39.

Lycaon. A mythical character who tricked Zeus (*q.v.*) by feeding him human flesh. Zeus killed him and all his sons save Nyctinus by lightning or turned them into wolves, hence Lycanthropy.

Lycomedes. The king of Scyros who murdered Theseus (*q.v.*). It was to his court that Thetis (*q.v.*) sent Achilles (*q.v.*), and Lycomedes' daughter Deidamia bore Achilles his son Neoptolemus (*q.v.*).

Lycurgus (1) Mythical king of Thrace who was made blind and mad for opposing the worship of Dionysus (*q.v.*).

(2) Mythical founder of the Spartan constitution and military regime, first mentioned by Herodotus and subject of a *Life* by Plutarch. Some traditions say the Pythia at Delphi gave him the constitution, others that he devised it while in Crete. In Sparta he was worshipped as a god.

Lynceus. (1) *See* Danaus.

(2) Twin of Idas (*q.v.*) noted for his keen eyesight.

Lyrnessus. City near Troy (*q.v.*) sacked by Achilles (*q.v.*).

M

Macareus. *See* Issa.

Macaria. *See* Eurystheus.

Machaon. The son of Asclepius the physician (*q.v.*).

Maenads. *See* Bacchae.

Maia. The daughter of Atlas (*q.v.*) and Pleione, eldest of the Pleiades (*q.v.*) and the most beautiful. By Zeus (*q.v.*) the mother of Hermes (*q.v.*). The Romans identified her with spring and as a nature goddess gave her name to the month of May.

Manes. "The good ones", the Roman name for the spirits of the dead, regarded as a collective divinity, *Di Manes*. On certain days they could leave the Underworld and were capable of great mischief. Thus they demanded propitiatory ceremonies at funerals and on set days when the head of the house, the *paterfamilias*, would go into the night and cast boiled beans to them. The Roman poets applied the term also to the gods of the Underworld and to the Underworld itself.

Marpessa. *See* Idas. The daughter of the river god Evenus.

Mars. Roman god of war, at one time also associated with agriculture. Later completely identified with Ares (*q.v.*).

Marsyas. A Phrygian, in some traditions a silenus (*q.v.*), who found the flute invented and discarded by Athene (*q.v.*). He challenged Apollo (*q.v.*) to a music contest, judged by the Muses (*q.v.*). Apollo won and had him flayed alive. The tears of the woodland spirits and animals which wept for him formed the river Meander.

Medea. The niece of Circe (*q.v.*) and daughter of Aëtes of Colchis some say by Hecate (*q.v.*). She loved Jason (*q.v.*) and helped him steal the Golden Fleece, murdering her half-brother in their escape. Having cut a goat in pieces, boiled them and pulled forth a lamb she persuaded the daughters of Pelias to boil him, causing his death. When Jason left her for Glauce (*q.v.*) she caused her death and slew her sons by Jason. She then escaped in a chariot drawn by winged serpents to Athens. Here she married Aegeus (*q.v.*). When Theseus (*q.v.*) returned she tried to poison him to secure the succession of her own son Medus (*q.v.*) but Aegeus recognised Theseus and saved him. She fled to wander the earth: some say she returned to Colchis and was reconciled to her father, others that she went to Asia Minor where her son gave his name to the Medes. She became an immortal.

Medus. Son of Medea (*q.v.*) and Aegeus (*q.v.*) eponymous ancestor of the Medes.

Medusa. *See* Gorgons. Slain and beheaded by Perseus (*q.v.*) as she slept. From her corpse sprang forth the fully grown Pegasus (*q.v.*) and the warrior Chrysaor.

Megaeia. One of the Erinnyes (*q.v.*).

Megara or **Megaera.** The eldest daughter of Creon of Thebes. Wife of Heracles (*q.v.*) and bore him several children. Later married Iolaus (*q.v.*) though one tradition says Eurystheus tried to kill her and Heracles instead killed Eurystheus. In revenge Hera (*q.v.*) drove Heracles mad and he killed Megara and his children.

Melampus. Son of Amythaon, a seer who introduced the worship of Dionysus (*q.v.*) to Greece. He and his brother Bias cured the women of Argos (including the daughter of the king, Proctus) of madness and received two thirds of his kingdom in reward.

Meleager. The son of Oeneus and Althaea. The Fates (*q.v.*) told his mother he would only die when a certain brand, which was on the fire, was burned. She extinguished and hid it. Meleager was one of the Argonauts (*q.v.*) and organised the hunt of the Calydonian Boar (*q.v.*). He fell in love with Atalanta who joined the hunt and having killed the boar himself gave her the hide on the pretext she had touched it first. This set the hunters quarrelling and in the dispute he killed his uncles, brothers of Althaea. She cursed their murderer, not realising the truth, and when she learned the Erinnyes (*q.v.*) were persecuting him because of the curse burned the brand and committed suicide. Her daughters (save Gorge and Deianeira) were turned into guinea-hens by Artemis. The son of Meleager and Atalanta was Parthenopaeus.

Melpomene. The Muse of Tragedy.

Memnon. The son of Eos (*q.v.*) and Tithonus, half-brother of Priam (*q.v.*). The king of Ethiopia who helped the Trojans and killed many Greeks. Achilles (*q.v.*) met him in single combat while Zeus (*q.v.*) weighed their fates in the balance. Achilles slew him but Zeus answered his mother's request that he be honoured by having the birds called *Memnonides* rise above his funeral pyre, then fall as a sacrifice. They annually visited his tomb on the Hellespont though one tradition says he survived the war and ruled five generations in Ethiopia before becoming an immortal. The Greeks assumed many monuments, which they called *Memnonia*, were dedicated to him including a huge statue in Egyptian Thebes.

Menelaus. Son of Atreus, younger brother of Agamemnon (*q.v.*) and husband of Helen (*q.v.*). When her father chose him from amongst many suitors he made the others swear to help him in any misfortune. He was thus able to summon the Greek forces for the war on Troy (*q.v.*). At one stage in the war he fought a duel with Paris (*q.v.*) to decide the war and was winning until Aphrodite (*q.v.*) carried Paris off. Because he failed to sacrifice to Athene (*q.v.*) he took eight years to return from Troy to Sparta.

Menoeceus. (1) *See* **Jocasta.**
(2) *See* **Seven against Thebes.**

Mentor. Friend and adviser of Odysseus (*q.v.*) who was too old to go to Troy (*q.v.*) and remained at Ithaca to watch over Odysseus' interests. Athene (*q.v.*) took his form to guide Telemachus' (*q.v.*) search for his father. The name is now synonymous with a trusted counsellor.

Mercury. The Roman equivalent of Hermes (*q.v.*).

Merope. A Pleiad. Wife of Sisyphus.

Metis. Counsellor of the young Zeus (*q.v.*) and his first wife. Mother of Athene (*q.v.*). Herself the daughter of Oceanus (*q.v.*) and Tethys.

Midas. Son of Gordius. *See* **Gordian Knot.** His hospitality to Silenus (*q.v.*) led Dionysus (*q.v.*) to grant him any wish: he wished that all he touched would turn to gold. When even his food became gold he begged to be relieved of his gift—and was—by bathing in the River Pactolus which was henceforth rich in gold. When he judged Pan (*q.v.*) a better musician than Apollo (*q.v.*) the latter gave him asses' ears which he hid under his hat. Only his barber knew, but when his barber told a hole in the ground, reeds grew from it which, via the wind, revealed his secret to the world.

Milanion. Husband of Atalanta (*q.v.*).

Miletus of Crete. The son of Aria and Apollo (*q.v.*), a beautiful youth over whom Minos (*q.v.*) and his brothers Rhadamanthus (*q.v.*) and Sarpedon quarrelled. Miletus chose Sarpedon and to escape Minos' jealousy they fled to Asia Minor where Miletus founded the city Miletus which bore his name.

Minerva. Etruscan goddess of wisdom, the arts and crafts. The Romans identified her with Athene (*q.v.*).

Minos. The son of Zeus (*q.v.*) and Europa (*q.v.*), brother of Rhadamanthus (*q.v.*) and Sarpedon (*q.v.*). Ruler of Crete and supported in this by Poseidon (*q.v.*) who gave him a magnificent white bull. *See* **Cretan Bull.** He gave Crete her laws and defended the island with the aid of Talos, a brazen

giant with a bull's head. He pursued the nymph Britomartis for nine months but she leapt into the sea. Artemis (*q.v.*) deified her and the two shared the epithet Dictynna. While besieging Nisa, the port of Megara, Scylla, the daughter of the king Nisus fell in love with Minos and cropped her hair on which Nisus' life depended. She let Minos into the city but he was repulsed by her parricide and deserted the girl who swam after his ship. According to one tradition her father's spirit in the form of an eagle seized her and she was transformed into the Ciris bird; according to another tradition Minos drowned her and she became a fish. Minos married Pasiphaë (*q.v.*) who bore him Ariadne (*q.v.*), Androgeos and Phaedra. When Androgeos won all the events at the Panathenaic games Aegeus (*q.v.*) had him murdered and in revenge Minos extracted a tribute of seven Athenian youths and maidens who were devoured by the Minotaur (*q.v.*). He was killed by the daughters of Cocalus of Sicily while pursuing Daedalus (*q.v.*) and became one of the three judges of the Underworld.

Minotaur. Offspring of Pasiphaë (*q.v.*) and the Cretan Bull (*q.v.*) which had the head of a bull and body of a man. It lived in a labyrinth devised by Daedalus (*q.v.*) where it devoured the maidens and youths of Athens delivered in tribute to Minos (*q.v.*). It was slain by Theseus (*q.v.*).

Minyans or **Minyae.** Prehistoric inhabitants of Boeotia (*q.v.*) and Thessaly whose reputed ancestor was Minyas.

Misenus. Trumpeter of Aeneas (*q.v.*) who was drowned by a Triton (*q.v.*) and buried in the Bay of Naples at the port which then bore the name Misenum (the modern Capo Miseno). From the time of Agrippa Misenum was a major Roman naval station.

Mithras. An Iranian deity whose worship was developed in Persia and spread throughout the Middle East. Known to the Greeks from the time of Herodotus his worship spread to Rome under the Republic and from the 2nd century A.D. spread throughout the empire. Mithras was linked with astrology and appears to have been linked with the sun following a fight with the sun-god. But the core of his cult was that man or the soul had fallen from grace and that Mithras could bring redemption and thus eternal life. Very popular with the Roman legions. Mithras was the one serious contender with Christianity for religious supremacy. His ritual involved seven stages of initiation and secret ceremonies conducted in underground caves or artificial subterranean chambers such as that found in London. These temples were called mithraea. *See also* **J35.**

Mnemosyne. "Memory", the daughter of Uranus (*q.v.*) and by Zeus (*q.v.*) the mother of the Muses (*q.v.*).

Moirae or **Moerae.** *See* **Fates.**

Monoecus. "The lone dweller", Latin name for Heracles (*q.v.*) who was said to have dwelt alone for a time in the region of modern Monte Carlo.

Mopsus. The son of Apollo (*q.v.*) and Manto, daughter of Teiresias. When he beat Calchas (*q.v.*) in prophecy Calchas died of grief.

Morpheus. The Greek *Hypnos.* The son of the god of "Sleep". A god who sends dreams and visions of human form. In Ovid's *Metamorphoses,* Sleep sends him to Alcyone (*q.v.*) in the form of her dead husband.

Musaeus. A mythical poet who succeeded Orpheus (*q.v.*), the first poet.

Muses or **Musae.** The daughters of Zeus (*q.v.*) and Mnemosyne (*q.v.*) who presided over the arts and sciences. Originally three in number, Hesiod later names nine. Clio was muse of history, Euterpe of lyric poetry and music, Thalia of comedy, Melpomene of tragedy, Terpsichore of song and dance, Erato of mime, Polyhymnia or Polymnia of the hymn, Calliope of epic poetry and Urania of astronomy, though the attributions vary.

Myrmidons or **Myrmidones.** Tribe of southern Thessaly which provided Achilles' (*q.v.*) contingent at Troy.

Myrtilus. The son of Hermes (*q.v.*). The charioteer of Oenomaus whose death he caused by removing the lynch pin of his chariot and substituting a wax replica. He did this because Pelops (*q.v.*) had bribed him with the promise of half his kingdom, but instead Pelops flung him into the sea. He cursed the House of Pelops as he died and his father placed him amongst the stars.

N

Naiads or **Naiades.** Fresh-water nymphs in Greek mythology. They carried off Hylas (q.v.).

Narcissus. See Echo.

Nauplius. A king of Euboea who lured ships returning from Troy (q.v.) to their doom on the promontory of Caphareus by lighting misleading fires.

Nausicaa. Daughter of Alcinous, king of the Phaeacians who found Odysseus (q.v.) after a shipwreck while playing ball with her friends on the beach. She looked after him and her father gave him a ship.

Nectar. The drink of the Greek gods which conferred immortality.

Neleus. Twin of Pelias (q.v.), sons of Poseidon (q.v.) and the nymph Tyro. The twins were exposed by their mother but reared by a horse breeder. When Tyro married Cretheus, king of Iolcus, he adopted the boys who were thus half-brothers of Aeson. Pelias then later seized the kingdom, imprisoned Aeson and expelled Neleus who went to Pylus with Bias and Melampus and became its king. He and all twelve of his sons bar Nestor (q.v.) were killed by Heracles (q.v.) for aiding Augias (q.v.) in his war against Heracles.

Nemesis. Greek goddess, daughter of Oceanus. Originally she was envisaged as allotting to men their share of happiness and unhappiness, thereby chastening the over-fortunate. Later she was portrayed as the punisher of crime, the goddess of retribution. Some say she laid the egg from which Helen (q.v.), Clytemnestra (q.v.) and the Dioscuri (q.v.) were born. She had a sanctuary at Rhamnus from around 430 B.C.

Nemi. A lake in the Alban mountains, site of a sanctuary and sacred wood of Diana (q.v.).

Neoptolemus. Also called Pyrrhus, a son of Achilles (q.v.) and Deidamia. Odysseus (q.v.) and Diomedes (q.v.) persuaded his grandfather Lycomedes to let him go to Troy (q.v.) after his father's death. He was one of the Greeks inside the Wooden Horse. He slew Polites, the son of Priam (q.v.) and Hecuba (q.v.) before their eyes. He killed Priam at the altar of Zeus, smashed the skull of Astyanax (q.v.), Hector's (q.v.) child, and sacrificed Polyxena, Priam's daughter, on his father's tomb. He was given Andromache (q.v.) but back in Greece married Hermione (q.v.) with the blessing of Menelaus (q.v.) despite her prior betrothal to Orestes (q.v.). When their marriage proved barren he went to Delphi (q.v.) to consult the oracle and was slain either by Orestes or the priests of Apollo (q.v.).

Nephele. A phantom conjured up by Zeus (q.v.) to deceive Ixion. She later married Athamas.

Neptune. Italian sea-god whom the Romans identified with Poseidon (q.v.).

Nereids or **Nereides.** Fifty beautiful sea nymphs, the daughters of Nereus (q.v.) and Doris, of whom the most famous were Amphitrite (q.v.) and Thetis (q.v.).

Nereus. An ancient and benevolent sea god, the son of Pontus (the sea) and Ge (q.v.). Husband of Doris, the daughter of Oceanus (q.v.) by whom he was father of the Nereids (q.v.).

Nero. See B44.

Nessus. See Deianeira.

Nestor. King of Pylos, only one of Neleus' (q.v.) twelve sons spared by Heracles. He participated in the Calydonian Boar (q.v.) hunt and the battle of Lapithae (q.v.) and Centaurs (q.v.). The oldest of the Greeks at Troy (q.v.) he was famous for his eloquence and wisdom. The father of Antilochus, a friend of Achilles (q.v.) and one of the bravest Greeks at Troy. Nestor was the only Greek to return home without mishap.

Nike. Goddess of Victory, not only in war but in musical and athletic competitions in Hesiod's *Theogony,* the daughter of the Titan Pallas and Styx. A minor deity, later envisaged not as one goddess but as several spirits, represented as young girls with wings who flew across the heavens to carry the crown to the victor. Zeus honoured Nike for helping the Olympian gods in the Titanomachia (q.v.). She was sometimes identified with Athene (q.v.).

Niobe. Daughter of Tantalus, sister of Pelops (q.v.) and wife of Amphion (q.v.) by whom she had seven sons and seven daughters (according to Ovid, Homer makes it six of each). She boasted of being superior to Leto (q.v.) who only had two children and in revenge Apollo (q.v.) slew her sons and Artemis (q.v.) her daughters. She wept for nine days and nights and Zeus (q.v.) then turned her into a stone on Mt. Sipylus.

Nisus. See Minos.

Nomius. "The pasturer", a name given to Pan (q.v.), Apollo (q.v.) and Hermes (q.v.) in their roles as protectors of flocks and pastures.

Notus. The south-west wind, known to the Romans as Auster. The son of Astraeus (q.v.) and Eos (q.v.).

Numa. The name of two Italian warriors in the *Aeneid.*

Numa Pompilius. Legendary king of Rome. The second king, successor of Romulus (q.v.) he was said to have ruled between 717 and 673 B.C. Said to be of Sabine (q.v.) origin he reorganised Roman religion under the guidance of Egeria (q.v.). He was said to have been initiated into the mysteries of Pythagoras, an obvious anachronism as he predates Pythagoras' 6th century visit to Italy, but his reputed religious reforms signify a new strand in Roman religion, a disinterested search for knowledge as opposed to inspired action. He founded the cult of Janus (q.v.), organised the priests in *collegia* and established the flamens, and reorganised the Salii whose war dances in honour of Mars (q.v.) reflected a very ancient Italic rite. He also appointed the Pontifex Maximus, a high priest with responsibility for ensuring religious rites were properly performed and for preventing the growth of undesirable foreign cults. He also reformed the Roman calendar to achieve the maximum coincidence of lunar and solar cycles.

Numicius. A sacred river in Latium between Ardea and Lavinium.

Numitor. The grandfather of Romulus (q.v.) and Remus (q.v.).

Nymphae or **Nymphs.** Minor deities, the spirits of nature. These daughters of Zeus (q.v.) were semi-mortal and were generally benevolent, though they could be malevolent particularly to unresponsive lovers. Each was the tutelary deity of a rock, tree, cave or fountain and was better known to the local peasants than the great gods of Olympus (q.v.). Lavishly decorated monumental fountains (a "*nymphaeum*") were dedicated to the nymphs by both Greeks and Romans.

Nysa, Mt. Mountain in Libya where, according to tradition, Dionysus (q.v.) was raised.

O

Oceanides. Sea nymphs (q.v.) of the ocean, daughters of Oceanus (q.v.). Hesiod says they were 40 in number.

Oceanus. One of the Titans (q.v.), the son of Ge (q.v.) and Uranus (q.v.). The only Titan not to revolt against Uranus (q.v.). In Aeschylus' *Prometheus Bound* he preaches submission to the authority of Zeus (q.v.). He was seen originally as the river encircling the world from which all rivers and seas sprang. He is thus depicted as the rim on Achilles' (q.v.) shield. The husband of Tethys and by her father of, among others, Metis.

Odysseus. The hero of Homer's *Odyssey,* itself the model for James Joyce's *Ulysses,* Ulysses being the Roman name for him. The son of Laertes, king of Ithaca, and Anticleia, daughter of the wily thief Autolycus. However, one tradition makes him the son of Sisyphus (q.v.). He married Penelope (q.v.). Warned by an oracle not to go to Troy (q.v.) he feigned madness when the heralds arrived by sowing salt, but when Palamedes placed his son Telemachus (q.v.) before the plough he was forced to disclose his sanity and join the expedition. Later, at Troy, he avenged himself by having a letter signed in Priam's (q.v.) hand placed in Palamedes' tent. The letter was found and Palamedes was stoned to death. But Odysseus himself tricked Achilles (q.v.) into revealing his true identity and joining the expedition. At Troy Odysseus and Diomedes (q.v.) entered the city at night to kill Rhesus the Thracian and steal his white horses, because it was prophesied that if they drank of the Scamander (q.v.) Troy would not fall. He quarrelled with Ajax (q.v.) over the armour of Achilles and some say he killed him. He captured Helenus and from him learned the secret oracles which told how Troy would fall. In accordance with these he stole the Palladium of Athene (*q.v.*). It was also Odysseus who devised the stratagem of the Wooden Horse. When Troy fell he took Hecuba (*q.v.*) as a slave. His journey home lasted ten years and involved many adventures. He first went to Cicones to procure jars of sweet wine and then visited the Lotophagi (*q.v.*). After leaving them he landed in Sicily where he blinded Polyphemus the Cyclops (*q.v.*). Next he visited Aeolus (*q.v.*) and as a result was blown off course and lost all his ships save one at Telepylos. In this he reached Aeaea, land of Circe (*q.v.*) and on her advice sought the aid of Teiresias, a dead seer in the Underworld. In the land of the Cimmerians he summoned Teiresias' shade, and also those of his mother and former comrades, though Ajax (*q.v.*) held aloof. Then, with Circe's counsel he navigated the Scylla and Charybdis (*q.v.*) and neutralised the spell of the Sirens (*q.v.*) by blocking his crew's ears with wax but having himself tied to the mast that he might hear their song. At Thrinacia his men slaughtered the cattle of Helios (*q.v.*) and were punished by Zeus (*q.v.*), all but Odysseus dying in a subsequent shipwreck. He drifted to Ogygia on flotsam, where he spent eight years with the nymph Calypso (*q.v.*). On a raft he made land at Scheria, was found by Nausicaa (*q.v.*) and given a ship to Ithaca (*q.v.*). Here he was recognised by Eumaeus (*q.v.*) despite his disguise as a beggar. He found Laertes (*q.v.*) in the country and Penelope (*q.v.*) besieged by suitors. This drunken and unruly crew were headed by one Alcinous, their most persistent member. Penelope had kept them at bay by promising to marry one of them when she had finished weaving a robe for Laertes: a robe she unpicked each night. But betrayed by her servants she was now being forced to choose a husband. Meanwhile Telemachus (*q.v.*) who had sailed away to find Odysseus returned to find him with Laertes and they plotted revenge. Still dressed as a beggar Odysseus entered the palace and was recognised only by his nurse Eurycleia and his faithful hound Argus who died on seeing his long lost master. Penelope now announced she would marry the suitor who could fire Odysseus' bow. Only he was able to bend and string it. The suitors having failed Odysseus strung the bow and with Telemachus slew the suitors. The *Odyssey* ends when Athene (*q.v.*) reconciles the hero and the kinsmen of the suitors who were seeking revenge. Teiresias had prophesied that Odysseus had to set out on another journey to appease Poseidon (*q.v.*) for the blinding of his son Polyphemus and would then live to an old age until death came from the sea. One tradition tells how Telegonus, Odysseus' son by Circe came looking for his father, landed and began plundering for supplies. Odysseus and Telemachus gave battle and Telegonus killed Odysseus, not recognising his father. He also took Telemachus and Penelope to Aeaca where Circe married Telemachus and he himself married Penelope.

Odyssey. *See under* **Odysseus.**

Oedipus ("Swollen-foot"). The son of Laius, king of Thebes, and Jocasta (*q.v.*). The Delphic oracle said Laius would be killed by his son so he had the baby exposed on Mt. Cithaeron with a nail driven through its feet—hence "Oedipus". But he was found by a shepherd and raised by Polybus, king of Corinth, as his own son. As an adult Oedipus learned from the oracle that he would kill his own father and marry his own mother and believing himself the son of Polybus, left Corinth. He met Laius on the road and killed him in a quarrel. Laius had been on his way to Delphi to seek advice on ridding Thebes of the Sphinx (*q.v.*). This Oedipus did and was made king by the Thebans. He married Jocasta and they had four children, Eteocles (*q.v.*), Polynices (*q.v.*), Antigone (*q.v.*) and Ismene (*q.v.*). When Thebes suffered a plague because of their incest Oedipus contacted the seer Teiresias and learned whose son he was. When she heard the truth Jocasta hanged herself and Oedipus blinded himself with the pins from her dress. With Antigone and later Ismene he went into exile at the grove of the Eumenides (*see* **Erinnyes**) at Colonos in Attica. Here he was received by the gods, having first cursed the sons who had neglected him, saying they would divide their kingdom by the sword.

Oeneus. King of Pleuron and Calydon, husband of Althaea and father of Tydeus (*q.v.*), Meleager (*q.v.*), Gorge and Deineira (*q.v.*). His realm was seized by his nephews but his grandson Diomedes (*q.v.*) avenged him and put Andraemon, husband of Gorge, on the throne. He accompanied Diomedes to the Peloponnesus where he was killed by two nephews who had escaped Diomedes. Deineira (*q.v.*) married Heracles (*q.v.*).

Oenomaus. A son of Ares (*q.v.*), king of Elis. An oracle said he would be killed by his son-in-law. Therefore he challenged all his daughter's suitors to a chariot race and if they won they would marry his daughter Hippodameia: if they lost they were put to death. His own chariot was drawn by wind-born horses, a gift from Ares. But he was murdered by Myrtilus at the instigation of Pelops (*q.v.*).

Oenone. A nymph who loved Paris (*q.v.*). He deserted her for Helen (*q.v.*) and when he was wounded by Philoctetes (*q.v.*) she refused to help him. Then, in remorse at his death, she committed suicide.

Oileus. One of the Argonauts (*q.v.*), and father of Ajax (*q.v.*).

Olympia. A small province in the western Peloponnesus, isolated from the centre and east of the Peloponnesus by high mountains. The site of a major sanctuary of Zeus (*q.v.*) whose worship replaced that of an early female divinity in the 9th century B.C. However, it was not till about 470 B.C. that a magnificent temple was built to Zeus. From 776 B.C. though, the Olympic games had been celebrated at Olympia in honour of Zeus. These quadrennial contests were international in character and an international truce accompanied their celebration. The prestige of the games was great and from 776 Greek chronology was based on the games, an "Olympiad" being a four-year cycle. Hence Olympiad 12, 1 denoted the 1st year in a four-year period after 11 previous Olympiads. If the number of Olympiads is multiplied by 4 and deducted from 776 we have our date *e.g.* $11 \times 4 = 44$, subtracted from 776 is 732 B.C.

Olympics. A term for any deity or muse inhabiting Olympus and not the Underworld.

Olympus Mt. The highest peak in Greece on the borders of Thessaly and Macedonia. Its 2975 m are almost inaccessible and it was not climbed until 1913. It was believed to be the home of the twelve Olympian gods.

Omphale. Queen of Lydia and widow of Tmolus who purchased Heracles (*q.v.*) as a slave. He served her for three years and one tradition says he dressed as a woman and swapped clothes with Omphale during this period.

Ops. Roman goddess of plenty, a consort of Saturn (*q.v.*) and the personification of abundance.

Orcus. The Roman name for Hades (*q.v.*) and for his realm.

Orestes. The son of Clytemnestra (*q.v.*) and Agamemnon (*q.v.*). As a child he was smuggled out of Mycenae by his sister Electra (*q.v.*) when Clytemnestra and Aegisthus (*q.v.*) seized power. He took refuge at the court of king Strophius in Phocis, becoming a close friend of Pylades (*q.v.*), the king's son. When of age he, Pylades and Electra killed Aegisthus and Clytemnestra, and Orestes was punished for his matricide by the Erinnyes (*q.v.*). He fled to the Acropolis of Athens and embraced the image of the goddess. Athene (*q.v.*) then summoned the Areopagus to judge his case. Apollo (*q.v.*), whose oracle had encouraged his crime, defended him on the grounds that fatherhood was more important than motherhood. Athene's casting vote found him innocent. Another tradition says Apollo told him he could be free of the Erinnyes by fetching the statue of Artemis (*q.v.*) from the Tauric Chersonese. Orestes and Pylades went to Tauris and were seized by the natives for sacrifice to Artemis. But it transpired that his sister Iphigenia (*q.v.*) was the priestess and she helped them steal the statue and return to Greece. They met Electra and went on to Mycenae where Orestes killed Aegisthus' son and became king. Later he slew his rival Neoptolemus (*q.v.*) and married his cousin Hermione.

Oreithyia. *See* **Boreas.** He turned her into a wind.

Orion. A giant, son of Poseidon (*q.v.*) who was a renowned hunter and very handsome. He loved Merope, daughter of Oenopion of Chios and was promised her hand in return for ridding Chios of wild animals. This he did but Oenopion would not give up Merope which led Orion to seduce her. Oenopion, with the help of his father Dionysus, blinded Orion who was told by the oracle he could only recover his sight by going to the east and gazing on the sun as it rose. This he did with the help of Hephaestus (*q.v.*) and once there Eos (*q.v.*) fell in love with him and Helios (*q.v.*) restored his sight. Later he joined Artemis (*q.v.*) in a hunt. Apollo (*q.v.*) angry at his boasting that he would kill all the wild beasts and afraid he would seduce Artemis contrived his death at the unwitting hands of Artemis. She placed his image in the stars, his constellation rising with the sun at the autumnal equinox.

Orpheus. The son of king Oeagrus of Thrace and Calliope (*q.v.*). The Greeks regarded him as the first great poet. He could enchant the beasts and trees with his lyre, a gift from Apollo (*q.v.*). After returning from the voyage of the Argonauts (*q.v.*) he married Eurydice (*q.v.*). His grief at losing her after redeeming her from Hades (*q.v.*) led to a failure to honour Dionysus (*q.v.*) at a Bacchanalia and he was torn to pieces by Bacchae (*q.v.*). The muses buried the pieces at the foot of Mt. Olympus (*q.v.*) save his head which was thrown into the River Hebrus still singing. The head and his lyre eventually floated to Lesbos (*q.v.*) and were finally placed amongst the stars at the request of Apollo and the Muses. *See also* **Orphism J38.**

Orthrus. A giant two-headed dog, the offspring of Typhon (*q.v.*) and Echidne (*q.v.*) and, some say, the father of the Sphinx (*q.v.*) and Chimaera (*q.v.*). It was set to watch the oxen of Geryon (*q.v.*) and was slain by Heracles (*q.v.*).

Ortygia (1) Port of Syracuse in Sicily.
(2) Port of Delos (*q.v.*), birthplace of Artemis (*q.v.*).

Otus and **Ephialtes.** Twin sons of Iphimedeia and Poseidon (*q.v.*), named Aloeidae after their mother's later husband Aloeus. At an early age they imprisoned Ares (*q.v.*) and later swore to rape Hera (*q.v.*) and Artemis (*q.v.*). In a vain effort to achieve this they placed Mt. Pelion on top of Mt. Ossa and attacked Heaven. But Artemis induced them to seek her at Naxos. Here she leapt between them in the form of a doe and they accidentally slew each other. In Tartarus (*q.v.*) their shades were tied back to back by bonds of vipers.

Ovid. *See* **B46.**

P

Palaemon. A sea god, the son of Athamas and Ino who was originally named Melicertes.

Palamedes. *See* **Odysseus.**

Pales. Italic deity of flocks and herds, worshipped on the Palatine.

Palicus. An obscure god or hero worshipped in Sicily and mentioned in the *Aeneid* (*q.v.*).

Palinurus. "Wind Astern", the helmsman of Aeneas. He managed the ship between the Scylla and Charybdis (*q.v.*) and in the storm off the coast of Carthage but later fell asleep and into the sea. He was cast ashore but murdered by local tribesmen. His shade begged Aeneas for carriage across the Styx (*q.v.*) so it could be at rest, but the Sybil refused as he had not been properly buried. However she promised him a shrine, Capo Pulinuro in Lucania near modern Salerno.

Palladium. A mythical statue of Athene given to Dardanus (*q.v.*) by Zeus (*q.v.*) to ensure the protection of Troy. By one tradition it was stolen by Odysseus (*q.v.*) and Diomedes (*q.v.*). By another Aeneas (*q.v.*) saved it and brought it to Rome where it saved the city several times in its early years.

Pallas. (1) A title of Athene (*q.v.*) given to her by the Achaens. Pallas, Kore and Parthenos signify a virgin, maiden or girl.
(2) One of the 24 Giants (*q.v.*) who rebelled against Zeus (*q.v.*).
(3) A brother of Aegeus (*q.v.*). *See also* **Theseus.**
(4) An ancestor of Evander (*q.v.*).
(5) Evander's son who went to follow Aeneas (*q.v.*).

Pan. A god, half-man, half-goat, said by some to be a son of Zeus (*q.v.*) by others to be the son of Hermes (*q.v.*) and Penelope with whom he inhabited Arcadia. He was a patron of shepherds and herdsmen and a lover of mischief. When not frolicking with the nymphs he liked to startle peasants and flocks inspiring "panic". He loved and

pursued Syrinx whose flight from him resulted in her being transformed into a reed from which he made a seven-piped flute, the syrinx. He also seduced Selene (*q.v.*). Sometimes identified with the Roman Faunus (*q.v.*).

Pandarus. A Trojan archer who broke a truce by shooting at the Greeks. In Chaucer's *Troilus and Criseyde* and Shakespeare's *Troilus and Cressida* he is Cressida's uncle and the lovers' go-between. The word "pandar" is derived from his name for this reason.

Pandora. "All gifts", the first woman fashioned and given life by Hephaestus (*q.v.*) and Athene (*q.v.*). Zeus (*q.v.*) sent her to punish man after Prometheus (*q.v.*) had given him fire. She married the brother of Prometheus, Epimetheus. Her curiosity led her to open a box which it was forbidden to touch, and from it sprang all the evils and diseases which beset mankind. Only hope was left at the bottom of the box.

Parcae. The Roman equivalent of the "Fates" or Horae.

Paris. Son of Priam (*q.v.*) and Hecuba (*q.v.*) who dreamed during her pregnancy that she would bring forth a blazing firebrand. As a child he was exposed on Mt. Ida. Raised by shepherds he was named Paris or sometimes Alexander ("defender of men") because of his courage. He loved and deserted Oenone (*q.v.*) which eventually caused his death. Promised the fairest of women by Aphrodite (*q.v.*) if he gave her the apple of discord, he did as she bade. Reunited with his parents he then left for Sparta whence he seduced Helen (*q.v.*) thus starting the Trojan War. At one point in the war Aphrodite saved him from death in a duel with Menelaus. He shot the arrow which slew Achilles (*q.v.*) at the Scaean Gate but was himself mortally wounded by Philoctetes (*q.v.*).

Parnassus, Mt. 2461 m peak in the Pindus range, north-east of Delphi (*q.v.*). Home of Apollo (*q.v.*) and the Muses (*q.v.*) hence the name "Montparnasse" for the hill in Paris on which centred the university and cultural life of that city. On the original's slopes was also the Corycian Cave, a centre of the Bacchae (*q.v.*).

Parthenon. *See* **L94.**

Parthenope. A nymph whose body was said to have washed up at Neapolis (Naples) around 600 B.C. She gave her name to the short-lived Parthenopean Republic of Naples established by Napoleon in 1799.

Parthenopeus. *See* **Seven Against Thebes.**

Parthenos. *See* **Pallas.**

Pasiphaë. Daughter of Helios (*q.v.*) and Persë, and wife of Minos (*q.v.*). Mother of the Minotaur (*q.v.*) by the Cretan Bull (*q.v.*) and of many children, including Ariadne (*q.v.*), Glaucus and Phaedra, by Minos.

Patroclus. Cousin and bosom companion of Achilles (*q.v.*) whom he met at the court of Peleus (*q.v.*) while in exile for an accidental murder. Slain by Hector (*q.v.*) while wearing Achilles' armour, his death persuaded Achilles to re-enter the Trojan War.

Pausanias. Spartan king who intervened to moderate Lysander's arrogant attitude towards Athens and other Greek cities after the Peloponnesian War.

Pegasus. Winged horse, offspring of Poseidon (*q.v.*) and Medusa (*q.v.*). It was captured by Bellerophon (*q.v.*) at the fountain of Pirene and helped him slay the Chimaera (*q.v.*). It struck Mt. Helicon with its hoof and brought forth the spring of Hippocrene, sacred to the Muses.

Peleus. The son of Aeacus, king of Aegina. With his brother Telamon he killed their half-brother Phocus and the two were expelled to Phthia in Thessaly by Aeacus. Here Eurytion purified them of murder. They took part in the Calydonian Hunt when they accidentally killed Eurytion. They then fled to the court of Acastus (*q.v.*) of Iolcis. Zeus (*q.v.*) married him to Thetis (*q.v.*) though he himself loved Thetis. This was because the oracle foretold that her son would be greater than his father. Their son was Achilles (*q.v.*). All the gods save Eris (*q.v.*) were invited to the wedding and in revenge she cast the Apple of Discord. Peleus later ruled the Myrmidones at Phthia.

Pelias. *See* **Jason.**

Pelicles. Son of Peleus *i.e.* Achilles (*q.v.*).

Peloponnesus. The "island of Pelops" (*q.v.*), the large southern peninsula of mainland Greece, attached to northern Greece by the Corinth isthmus.

Pelops. Son of Tantalus (*q.v.*) king of Lydia. Tantalus cut him in pieces and served him to the gods at a meal. Only Demeter (*q.v.*) grieving for Persephone (*q.v.*) did not realise and she ate Pelops' shoulder. Zeus (*q.v.*) restored him to life by having Hermes (*q.v.*) boil him in a pot. Demeter gave him an ivory shoulder, said to be the birthmark of his descendants. His shoulder blade was later taken to Troy (*q.v.*) by the Greeks as the oracle said this was necessary if the city were to fall. He married Hippodamia.

Pelorus. One of the Sparti (*q.v.*).

Penates. Roman deities of the home, confused from early times with the *genius* and the Lares. Eventually a wide variety of deities, *e.g.* Mars, Mercury, Venus, were regarded as *"di Penates"* that is, "guardians of the hearth".

Penelope. The wife of Odysseus (*q.v.*), usually seen as a symbol of fidelity. One tradition in the Peleponnesus made her adulterous and the mother of Pan (*q.v.*) by Hermes (*q.v.*) or by all of her many suitors.

Peneus. The son of Oceanus (*q.v.*) and Tethys. A river god and father of Daphne (*q.v.*) and Cyrene (*q.v.*). Identified with the River Peneus in Thessaly.

Penthesilea. Daughter of Otrere and Ares (*q.v.*), queen of the Amazons (*q.v.*) who helped the Trojans. Slain by Achilles (*q.v.*) they fell in love as she died and he later mourned her. When the wretched Thersites mocked his grief Achilles slew him which caused his kinsman Diomedes (*q.v.*) to throw her corpse into the Scamander. It was retrieved and honourably buried.

Pentheus. Grandson of Cadmus (*q.v.*) and king of Thebes. The subject of Euripedes' *Bacchae*. He refused to allow Dionysus (*q.v.*) into the city but the god, in disguise, persuaded him to dress as one of the Bacchae (*q.v.*) and watch their orgies. He was then torn to pieces by the Bacchae, led by his own mother who was in a trance.

Perdix (or **Talos**) *See* **Daedalus**.

Periclymenus. The son of Neleus (*q.v.*) and brother of Nestor (*q.v.*). An Argonaut (*q.v.*) he could assume any form he chose. Slain by Heracles (*q.v.*).

Periphetes. A giant residing at Epidaurus who murdered travellers with an iron club. Slain by Theseus (*q.v.*) who henceforth carried his club.

Perse. The daughter of Oceanus (*q.v.*). Wife of Helios (*q.v.*) to whom she bore Circe (*q.v.*), Pasiphaë (*q.v.*), Aeetes and Perses (*q.v.*).

Persephone. Daughter of Zeus (*q.v.*) and Demeter (*q.v.*). She spent the winter months with Hades (*q.v.*) when nothing grew and with Demeter she spent the fertile months. Thus she was a goddess of vegetation. She was also queen of the Underworld and was a symbol of death. Known to the Romans as Proserpina. Her companion in the Underworld was Hecate (*q.v.*).

Perses. The son of Helios (*q.v.*) and Perse (*q.v.*) father of Hecate (*q.v.*).

Perseus. Grandson of Acrisius (*q.v.*) king of Argos and the son of Zeus (*q.v.*) and Danae (*q.v.*). Raised at the court of Polydectes who sent him to fetch the head of Medusa (*q.v.*). Hermes (*q.v.*) gave him a sickle with which to do this and told him how, via the Graeae (*q.v.*) he could procure Hades' (*q.v.*) helmet of invisibility, winged sandals and a magic wallet to help him in the task. Once he had the head he petrified the Titan Atlas (*q.v.*) with it. He then flew to Aethiopia where he found Andromeda (*see* **Cassiopeia**). Returning to Seriphos he slew Polydectes, made Dictys (*q.v.*) king and returned to Argos. He went on later to exchange the kingdom of Argos for that of his cousin Megaperthes of Tiryns.

Phaebus ("Shining"). A name used for Apollo (*q.v.*) at Delos (*q.v.*) where he was associated with Artemis (*q.v.*).

Phaedra. The daughter of Minos (*q.v.*) and wife of Theseus (*q.v.*) to whom she bore Acamas and Demophon. *See also* **Hippolytus**.

Phaeton. The son of Helios (*q.v.*) and Clymene. Helios let him drive the chariot of the sun across the sky but he lost control of it and was killed by a thunderbolt from Zeus (*q.v.*) for almost setting the world on fire. He fell into the River Po and his sisters who mourned him were turned into poplar or alder trees and their tears into amber.

Phalanthus. Mythical founder of Tarentum in Italy.

Philemon. The husband of Baucis. This old Phrygian couple once received Zeus (*q.v.*) and Hermes (*q.v.*) with great hospitality.

Philoctetes. The son of Poecas, nephew of Protesilaus, and companion of Heracles (*q.v.*). He lit Heracles funeral pyre and received his bow and arrows. On the way to Troy (*q.v.*) one of the poisoned arrows wounded him, or he was bitten

by a snake on the island of Tenedos. The smell of the wound became so offensive that on the advice of Odysseus (*q.v.*) he was left on Lemnos. Later an oracle revealed that Troy would not fall till the bow and arrows of Heracles were brought to the Greeks and Odysseus and Diomedes (*q.v.*) fetched him to Troy. Here either Machaon or Podalirius, the sons of Asclepius (*q.v.*) cured him of his wound. He slew Paris (*q.v.*) and later settled in Italy.

Philomela. *See* **Procne**.

Phineus. King of Salmydessus in Thrace and the son of Agenor. He first married Cleopatra, then Idaca who falsely accused her stepsons of improper advances. Phineus imprisoned them and was made blind and pursued by the Harpies (*q.v.*). Eventually the Argonauts (*q.v.*) whose ranks included Zetes and Calais, Cleopatra's brothers, slew the Harpies. Phineus freed the stepsons and told Jason (*q.v.*) what course to set.

Phlegethon ("Blazing"). A river of the Underworld called the "river of flames" by Plato. The shades of those who had committed crimes of violence against their kin were roasted in it until they received forgiveness. ·

Phlegyas. A king of the Lapithae (*q.v.*) who burnt Apollo's (*q.v.*) shrine at Delphi and was punished for it in the Underworld by having to sit beneath a huge rock which was liable to fall at any time.

Phocis. Small mountainous province of northern Greece which held the oracle of Delphi.

Phocus. *See* **Peleus**.

Phoebe ("Bright"). In early myth the daughter of Heaven and Earth and mother of Leto (*q.v.*). Later identified with Artemis (*q.v.*). the moon-goddess.

Phoenix ("Red"). (1) Companion and tutor of Achilles (*q.v.*) who tried to reconcile him with Agamemnon (*q.v.*).
(2) The brother of Cadmus (*q.v.*) and Europa (*q.v.*), eponymous ancestor of the Phoenicians.
(3) A mythological Egyptian bird which died on a funeral pyre every 500 years before rising again from the ashes.

Phorcys. A sea-god, the father of Echidne (*q.v.*), Ladon, the Gorgons (*q.v.*) and the Graeae (*q.v.*).

Phrixus and **Helle**. Brother and sister, the children of Athamas king of Aeolia. Their stepmother, Ino (*q.v.*), had engineered their sacrifice by Athamas out of jealousy but they escaped on a flying ram with a golden fleece sent by Zeus (*q.v.*). Helle fell off into what was henceforth the Hellespont, but Phrixus reached Colchis and sacrificed the ram to Zeus (*see* **Jason**). The ram's image was placed amongst the stars as Aries.

Phyllis. *See* **Demophon**.

Picus. An ancient Italian god represented as a woodpecker *i.e.* '*picus*'.

Pierides. A name applied to the Muses (*q.v.*). It was derived from the inhabitants of Pieria, on the south coast of Macedonia, who were noted for their worship of the Muses.
Also a name for nine daughters of Pierus king of Macedonia who were defeated in a contest by the Muses and turned into birds.

Pillars of Hercules. Two pillars, Calpe and Abyla, erected on either side of the straits of Gibraltar by Heracles (*q.v.*).

Pilumnus. An ancient minor Italian god, "the spearman".

Pindar. *See* **B48**.

Pirithous. Son of Ixion (*q.v.*) and Dia, companion of Theseus (*q.v.*) and king of the Lapithae (*q.v.*). He led the fight on the Centaurs (*q.v.*). On the death of his wife Hippodamia he and Theseus abducted the young Helen (*q.v.*) of Troy. She fell by lot to Theseus who, in return and despite misgivings, promised to help Pirithous abduct a daughter of Zeus (*q.v.*) for himself. They attempted to abduct Persephone (*q.v.*) from the Underworld but Hades (*q.v.*) chained them to a rock. Heracles (*q.v.*) later freed Theseus but Pirithous was left to suffer torment for his sins.

Pleiades. The seven daughters of Atlas (*q.v.*) and Pleione and companions of Artemis (*q.v.*). Zeus (*q.v.*) turned them into doves and placed their image in the stars to save them from the attentions of Orion (*q.v.*) who pursued them for five years. A group of seven poets in 3rd century B.C. Alexandria also called themselves the Pleiad.

Plutarch. *See* **B48**.

Pluto. (1) A Roman name for Hades (*q.v.*), "the rich one" who owns the riches of the earth itself.

(2) A nymph who was mother of Tantalus (q.v.) by Zeus (q.v.).

Podarces. (1) See **Priam.**

(2) Son of Iphiclus, leader of the Thessalians who fought at Troy (q.v.).

Polites. A son of Priam (q.v.) and Hecabe (q.v.), slain before their eyes by Neoptolemus (q.v.).

Pollux. The Roman name for Polydeuces. See **Castor.**

Polydeuces. See **Castor.**

Polydorus. (1) The son of Cadmus (q.v.) and Harmonia and ancestor of Oedipus (q.v.) and other great Theban kings.

(2) The youngest son of Priam (q.v.) and Hecabe (q.v.).

Polymnia. See **Muses.**

Polynices. The son of Jocasta and Oedipus (q.v.), brother of Eteocles (q.v.), Antigone (q.v.) and Ismene (q.v.). See also **Seven Against Thebes.** When Creon refused to allow his burial Antigone (q.v.) disregarded the order and buried the corpse.

Polypemon. Also known as Procrustes, 'the stretcher'. A robber who tied travellers to a bed and if they were too tall he cut off their legs; if too short he put them on a rack. Theseus (q.v.) did the same to him.

Polyphemus. See **Cyclopes and Galatea.**

Polyxena. The daughter of Priam (q.v.) and Hecuba (q.v.) beloved by Achilles (q.v.) whose shade requested her sacrifice by Neoptolemus (q.v.) after Troy's (q.v.) fall. This is the theme of Euripedes' *Hecabe.*

Pomona. An Italian goddess of tree-fruits (*poma* e.g. apples. She was a minor deity but had her own priest and sanctuary near Rome. Ovid links her with Vertumnus, an Etruscan god with the power to change his shape. He was god of the changing seasons and the ripening fruits of autumn, and also of money changing. *Vertere* means "change" in Latin. He loved Pomona and pursued her disguised as a harvester, vine-dresser, herdsman and old woman, but only won her when he appeared as himself. His statue stood in the Vicus Tuscus, a busy street of brothels and shops named after him as an Etruscan.

Pontus. The sea, offspring of Ge (q.v.) the earth.

Pontus Euxinus. The "Hospitable Sea", the Greek name for the Black Sea. The name was an attempt to flatter and placate a hostile sea which was much feared by sailors.

Porphyrion. See **Giants.**

Porsenna. See **Lars Porsenna.**

Portunus. A Roman sea-deity associated with harbours.

Poseidon. The Roman N Ntune, a god of earthquakes, and later of the sea. The eldest son of Cronus (q.v.) and Rhea. When he and Zeus (q.v.) and Hades (q.v.) cast lots for their realms he won the sea and had an underwater palace near Aegae in Euboea. Here he kept horses with brazen hoofs and gold manes who drew his chariot across the sea. Its passage calmed the sea. Poseidon created the horse and invented the bridle. As a horse he raped Demeter (q.v.) who was disguised as a mare. Their offspring was the horse Arion and the nymph Despoena and, some say, Persephone (q.v.). He resented Zeus (q.v.) and helped Hera (q.v.) and Apollo (q.v.) enchain him. In punishment Zeus made him a servant of Laomedon (q.v.) and he built the Neptunilia Pergama, the walls of Troy. He helped the Greeks at Troy but hated Odysseus (q.v.) who blinded Polyphemus (q.v.). He disputed the possession of Athens with Athene (q.v.) and lost, but Zeus gave him the Isthmus of Corinth instead. Here the Isthmian games were held in his honour. He married Amphitrite (q.v.). By mortal women he had many children including Pegasus (q.v.) and the Aloeidae (q.v.). He is usually portrayed with a trident which he used to shake the earth.

Priam. The son of Laomedon (q.v.) and husband of Hecuba (q.v.). Originally called Podarces his name was changed to Priam i.e. "ransomed" because Heracles (q.v.) spared him and sold him to Hesione (q.v.) his sister. He had fifty sons and fifty daughters, nineteen of whom were by Hecuba and included Hector (q.v.), Paris (q.v.), Helenus (q.v.) and Cassandra (q.v.). He begged Achilles (q.v.) to return Hector's body. Eventually slain at the altar of Zeus (q.v.) by Neoptolemus (q.v.).

Priapus. The son of Dionysus (q.v.) and Aphrodite (q.v.). A fertility god whose worship spread from the Hellespont to Greece and later Rome, though he was never taken seriously. He was often por-

trayed in the form of a red-faced scarecrow with a large detachable phallus and in this role was used to scare birds. The phallus became a truncheon to ward off other intruders. He was also a protector of cultivated gardens and a god of sailors. In Petronius' *Satyricon* he pursues the hero Encolpius and makes him impotent. Horace and Martial write of him lightheartedly and 85 obscene poems about him – '*priapeia*' – exist of unknown authorship. His sacrificial animal was the donkey, a symbol of lust.

Procne. The daughter of Pandion, king of Athens. Pandion gave her to Tereus in return for his assistance and they had a son Itys. But Tereus wanted her sister Philomela. He made Procne a slave and tore out her tongue, then seduced Philomela saying Procne was dead. Procne could only alert her sister and be free by stitching a message to her robe. Once free she slew Itys, cooked pieces of the corpse and fed it to Tereus. When Tereus learnt what had happened he chased the sisters with an axe but the gods turned him into a hawk, Procne into a swallow and Philomela a nightingale though some traditions say it was Philomela who lost her tongue and became a swallow.

Procris. Daughter of Erectheus of Athens and the wife of Cephalus. Eos (q.v.) who also loved Cephalus showed him that Procris was easily seduced in return for gold. Procris then fled to Crete and lived for a time with Minos (q.v.). On returning to Athens disguised as a youth she brought with her a hound and spear, gifts from Artemis (q.v.), which never missed their quarry. Cephalus so wanted the gifts that the couple were reconciled. But Procris suspected Cephalus of having an affair with Eos and followed him on a hunt where he accidentally killed her with the spear.

Procrustes. See **Polypemon.**

Proetus. The son of Abas (q.v.) king of Argolis. His twin brother Acrisius (q.v.) expelled him and he fled to Lydia where he married Anteia (also called Stheneboea) daughter of king Iobates (see **Bellerophon**). He later returned to Argolis and forced Acrisius to give him half the kingdom. He ruled from Tiryns whose huge walls he built with the aid of the Cyclopes (q.v.). Eventually gave two thirds of his kingdom to Melampus (q.v.) and Bias.

Prometheus. A Titan (q.v.) and the brother of Epimetheus (q.v.) or "afterthought" and Atlas (q.v.). Sometimes said to be the maker of mankind. He supported Zeus (q.v.) against his brother Titans but stole fire from Olympus and gave it to men. This angered Zeus who took revenge on man through Pandora (q.v.) and punished Prometheus by chaining him to a rock in the Caucasus. Here an eagle tore at his liver each day. The liver was renewed daily and Prometheus suffered this torment until Heracles (q.v.) rescued him.

Proserpina. Roman counterpart of Persephone (q.v.).

Proteus. A sea god and a subject of Poseidon (q.v.). He had the power of prophecy and could change his form. He would avoid prophecy by changing form until tightly gripped; then he appeared in his true shape and spoke the truth. Said to live on the isle of Pharos in the Nile Delta. Menelaus (q.v.) mastered him while returning from Troy (q.v.) and forced him to reveal the way to Sparta.

Psyche. In Greek literature, the "soul" personified, often portrayed as a butterfly. As the centre of emotion she was tormented by "*eros*". Her beauty made Aphrodite (q.v.) jealous and she sent Eros (q.v.) to torment her. Instead he fell in love with her though he would not let her see him or disclose his identity. But at the bidding of her two sisters she sought to discover who he was. For the first time she saw him, holding a candle above him as he slept, but hot wax fell on him. He woke and left her to seek him. After many trials she found him, became immortal and was united with Eros for ever.

Pygmalion. (1) The king of Tyre and brother of Dido (q.v.).

(2) The king of Cyprus who made and fell in love with a maiden's statue. Aphrodite (q.v.) answered his prayers and gave the statue life as the girl Galatea. They married and had two sons, Paphus and Metharme. In some versions the tale he is a sculptor. The basis of Shaw's *Pygmalion* and the musical *My Fair Lady.*

Pylades. Husband of Electra (q.v.). See also **Orestes.**

Pyramus and Thisbe. The lovers in a tale by Ovid which he heard in the East. Living in Babylon they are forbidden to meet but converse through a chink in a wall. They arrange a meeting at the tomb of Ninus but Thisbe, arriving first, was chased away by a lion and dropped her veil. Finding this, Pyramus thought her dead and committed suicide. She returned and slew herself on his sword. Since that time the nearby mulberry has borne fruit the colour of blood. This is the basis of Bottom's tale in Shakespeare's *A Midsummer Night's Dream*.

Pyrrhus. Another name for Neoptolemus.

Pythia. The priestess of Apollo (*q.v.*) at Delphi (*q.v.*).

Python. A she-dragon of Mt. Parnassus who controlled the oracle at Delphi (*q.v.*). The boy Apollo (*q.v.*) slew her and the Pythia (*q.v.*) took over her task of giving voice to oracles.

Q

Quirinus. A very ancient Roman deity whose cult was centred on the Quirinal. The Romans eventually forgot his original character and he was identified with Mars (*q.v.*), though Romulus (*q.v.*) was also supposed to have adopted the name after his deification.

R

Rape of the Sabine Women. An episode recounted by Livy and Ovid to explain the intermarriage of the Roman settlers and natives. Romulus (*q.v.*) and his followers invited the surrounding tribes to celebrate a festival in the Circus Maximus then carried off the native girls. War broke out but the Sabine women, who had been well treated, intervened to restore peace. The event has been the subject of paintings by Poussin and Rubens and of a group of statues by Giovanni da Bologna.

Remus. *See* **Romulus.**

Rhadamanthus. The son of Zeus (*q.v.*) and Europa (*q.v.*), brother of Minos (*q.v.*) and Sarpedon (*q.v.*). Once the ruler of part of Crete but Minos forced him to flee to Boeotia (*q.v.*). Famed for his wisdom and justice he was made one of the judges of the Underworld after his death. He married Alcmene (*q.v.*) on the death of Amphitrion (*q.v.*).

Rhea. (1) A Titaness, daughter of Ge (*q.v.*) and Uranus (*q.v.*). *See* **Cronus.**
(2) *See* **Romulus.**

Rhesus. A Thracian king who helped the Trojans. An oracle said that if his magnificent snow-white horses ate the grass of the Trojan plain and drank of the River Scamander Troy would not fall. Diomedes (*q.v.*) and Odysseus (*q.v.*) raided his camp, slew him, and stole the horses.

Rhodos/Rhode. The daughter of Poseidon (*q.v.*), wife of Helios (*q.v.*).

Rome. The "eternal city" sited on the banks of the Tiber. Traditionally founded in 753 B.C. (year 1 of the Roman calendar) by Romulus (*q.v.*). It only really became a city in the 6th century under the Tarquins. Under the Republic it had a population of two or three hundred thousand, of 450,000 by the time of Augustus and 1,000,000 under the Antonines, though the population was occasionally reduced by wars, fires and plagues.

Romulus. The legendary founder of Rome (*q.v.*), twin brother of Remus and together the sons of Rhea or Rhea Silvia. She was the daughter of Numitor, king of Alba Longa (*q.v.*) who was deposed by his brother. Her uncle compelled her to become a Vestal Virgin (*q.v.*) but she bore Romulus and Remus, according to her, by Mars (*q.v.*). Her uncle then imprisoned her and threw the babies into the Tiber. The shepherd Faustulus (*q.v.*) found a wolf suckling them and reared them. When they reached manhood they returned to Alba Longa, restored Numitor to the throne and set off to found a city of their own. They went to the site of Rome and decided to consult the gods. Romulus chose the Palatine Hill, his childhood home, as the centre of the city, Remus the Aventine (*q.v.*). The gods favoured Romulus, sending him an extraordinary omen of twelve vultures, Remus only six. Thus Romulus was given the honour of founding Rome which he did by ploughing a furrow around the Palatine. As he commenced building the city wall Remus derisively jumped

over it, a quarrel ensued and Romulus slew him. Romulus took in fugitives in order to populate the city, found them wives by the "Rape of the Sabine women" (*q.v.*) and reigned for forty years before disappearing in a whirlwind on the Campus Martius. He was deified and identified with the Sabine god Quirinus (*q.v.*).

Rubicon. *See* **L107.**

S

Sabines. A branch of the Samnite race and one of the Sabellian peoples who occupied the Etruscanised area on the middle valley of the Tiber around Falerii. To the south of Rome they held the mountainous land between Rome and Campania. They were a constant threat to early Rome and the tradition that one Titus Tatius, a Sabine prince, was offered joint rule by Romulus (*q.v.*) may indicate a period of Sabine occupation or domination of Rome.

Sabinus. A mythical Sabine king.

Salmoneus. The son of Aeolus (*q.v.*) and brother of Sisyphus (*q.v.*). The founder of Salmone. His pride led him to emulate the thunder and lightning of Zeus (*q.v.*) who slew him and crushed his city with a thunderbolt.

Sarpedon. The son of Zeus (*q.v.*) and Europa (*q.v.*), brother of Minos (*q.v.*) and Rhadamanthus (*q.v.*). The three brothers quarrelled over the love of the youth Miletus (*q.v.*). Sarpedon went to Asia Minor and became king of the Lycians after helping king Cilix of Cilicia defeat them. Zeus allowed him to live three generations and he helped Troy (*q.v.*) in the Trojan war. Patroclus (*q.v.*) slew him.

Saturn. From *Satus i.e.* "sown". Ancient Mediterranean god of agriculture, possibly of Ligurian origin and particularly revered in Sardinia (*q.v.*) and Africa (*q.v.*). Later identified with Cronus (*q.v.*) who supposedly emigrated to Italy after being deposed by Zeus (*q.v.*). Here he presided over a mythical "Golden Age". His temple in Rome was consecrated in 497 B.C. and housed the state treasury. His festival, the Saturnalia, was celebrated near the winter solstice, originally on 17 December but from the 4th century A.D. on New Year's Day. During the celebrations complete licence was given, slaves took the place of their masters, presents were given, a "Lord of Misrule" appointed and merrymaking and disorder of every kind was rife. It may be that in primitive times his worship involved the sacrifice of humans because in classical times rush dummies in human shape (*argei*) were flung into the Tiber each year on 15 May in his honour.

Satyrs. Young spirits of wildlife, the woods and hillsides. Sons of Hermes (*q.v.*) closely associated with Dionysus (*q.v.*). They were possessed by lechery and a love of wine and embodied the fertile force of nature. Usually they were personified with pointed ears, horns and a tail like Pan's (*q.v.*).

Scaean Gate. The "left hand", the gate in the walls of Troy (*q.v.*) where Achilles (*q.v.*) fell.

Scamander, River. River in Asia Minor near Troy (*q.v.*), originally called the Xanthus. Its name was changed when the mythical Scamander (*q.v.*) of Crete founded a colony in Phrygia and jumped into the river.

Scamander. One-time king of Crete, father of Teucer (*q.v.*) by the nymph Idaea and therefore an ancestor of the Trojans.

Sciron. A robber who dwelt on the border of Attica and Megara. He preyed on travellers and forced them to wash his feet on the Scironian rock. He then kicked them off the rock into the sea to be eaten by a giant turtle. Theseus (*q.v.*) slew him.

Scylla. (1) *See* **Minos.**
(2) *See* **Charybdis.**

Scyrus. Aegean isle, half-way between Lesbos and Euboea and off the major trade routes. It was of no importance save in legend: here Achilles (*q.v.*) was hidden by Lycomedes. It was also here that Lycomedes threw Theseus (*q.v.*) from a rock while the hero was in voluntary exile from Athens after giving the city its first constitution. In 470 B.C. Cimon expelled the local populace in order to install Athenian colonists. At the same time he found the reputed body of Theseus and took it back to Athens amidst great pomp.

Selene. Eastern goddess whom the Greeks identified with Artemis (q.v.) and the Romans with Diana (q.v.) or the older moon goddess Luna. Both also identified her with Hecate (q.v.) and thus the two became associated with sorcery.

Semele. See **Dionysus.**

Semiramis. The wife of Ninus. These two were the mythical founders of Ninus or Nineveh.

Seven Against Thebes. Oedipus (q.v.) cursed his sons for neglecting him, saying they would divide their kingdom by the sword. To avoid this Eteocles and Polynices agreed to rule in turn but Eteocles then refused to give up the throne when his term expired. Polynices sought the help of Adrastus (q.v.) king of Argos and married his daughter Argia while her sister married Tydeus son of Oeneus of Calydon who was in exile because of a murder he had committed. Amphiaraus the seer (brother-in-law of Adrastus) prophesied death for all who marched on Thebes save Adrastus. But on the advice of Tydeus, Polynices bribed Eriphyle into persuading Amphiaraus to join them. These four were joined by Capaneus, Hippomedon and Parthenopaeus. The seven were initially successful but Teiresias (q.v.) prophesied that a Theban royal prince must sacrifice himself to save the city and Menoeceus did so. The fortunes of the seven now waned. Zeus (q.v.) killed Capaneus with a thunderbolt as he stormed the city walls. Tydeus was wounded by Melanippus but Athene (q.v.) intended to save him with an elixir from Zeus. But Amphiaraus, who had a grudge against him, persuaded him to drink the brains of Melanippus which so disgusted Athene she let him die. Hippomedon and Parthenopaeus were also slain. Polynices now fought a duel with Eteocles to settle the matter and both were mortally wounded. Amphiaraus was swallowed up by the earth and only Adrastus survived. See also **Antigone** and **Epigoni.**

Seven Hills of Rome. The Quirinal, Viminal, Esquiline, Caelian, Capitoline, Palatine and Aventine.

Seven Kings of Rome. Traditionally said to be Romulus, Numa Pompilius, Tullus Hostilius, Ancus Martius, Tarquinius Priscus, Servius Tullius and Tarquinius Superbus.

Seven Sages of Greece. Usually held to be Thales of Miletus, Bias of Priene, Solon, Chilo of Sparta who brought the bones of Orestes (q.v.) to Sparta, Periander of Corinth, Pittacus of Mytilene, a democrat, contemporary of Solon and opponent of Alcaeus, and Cleobulus of Rhodes.

Sibyl (Sibylla). A priestess and prophetess who uttered oracles. Localised in several places the term came to be used generically of many sibyls and Varro lists ten. The most famous was at Cumae in Campania and she told Aeneas (q.v.) how to enter the Underworld. Ovid says she was seven generations old when Aeneas met her and that Apollo (q.v.) had granted her request to live as many years as there were grains in a handful of sand. But she had forgotten to seek eternal youth and was now withered with age. In Petronius' *Satyricon* she hangs in a bottle and when asked what she wants replies "I want to die".

Sibylline Books. A Roman tradition tells how a sibyl (q.v.) offered Tarquinius Priscus nine prophetic books which he refused to buy at the price. She destroyed three and he still refused them; she burnt three more and he took the remaining three at the price demanded for the nine. Special priests kept them and they were consulted only when the Senate authorised it in time of need. In 83 B.C. the originals were destroyed by fire but replaced by new ones. Many later additions were made including Jewish and Christian forgeries and fourteen still exist. They were last consulted in the 4th century A.D. and shortly afterwards Stilicho had them burnt. The original books instructed the Romans to convey the sacred stone of Cybele to Rome.

Sigeum. Part of Troy (q.v.). Hence the Dardanelles were known as the "straits of Sigeum".

Sileni, Silenus. Scholars distinguish between *sileni* and satyrs (q.v.) but the two are very similar and the Greeks themselves seem to have made no distinction. They are regarded as companions of Dionysus (q.v.) and have pointed ears, flat noses and the tail of a horse or goat. By the 6th century B.C. one of their number, Silenus, stands out from his fellows for his wisdom and is sometimes said to have been the tutor of Dionysus. His special

knowledge comes from wine drinking and like his fellows he is usually drunk. An old man with horse-ears and tail he proves a good raconteur when captured, though something of a comic drunkard.

Silvanus. Ancient Italian god, a protector of uncultivated land.

Sinis or **Sinnis.** A robber of the Corinthian Isthmus who killed travellers by tying them to the tops of fir trees tied to the ground and then releasing the trees. Theseus (q.v.) slew him in the same fashion.

Sinon. A cousin of Odysseus (q.v.) and grandson of Autolycus the thief. When the Greeks pretended to leave Troy (q.v.) he remained in camp and persuaded the Trojans that the wooden horse was a gift in atonement for the theft of Athene's Palladium (q.v.). Once the horse was inside Troy he signalled the Greek fleet to return.

Sirens. In Homer two sisters who lure sailors to their death by their singing. Odysseus (q.v.) and the Argonauts (q.v.) withstood their fatal charms, the latter because Orpheus (q.v.) outsang them. They have been associated with the modern Galli islands. In non-Homeric tradition their number varies and they are portrayed as having the bodies of birds and heads of either sex. Some say they were daughters of Ge (q.v.) and companions of Persephone (q.v.) who escorted the dead to the Underworld. They were said to feed on the dead. Later they are given the heads of beautiful women and sing to console the dead they escort. Finally they lose their funerary and evil nature and develop fishes' tails like mermaids.

Sisyphus. The son of Aeolus and husband of the Pleiad Merope who bore him Glaucus. He was an ancestor of Bellerophon (q.v.) and also seduced Anticleia, mother of Odysseus (q.v.) and may have been his father. The founder of Ephyra (later Corinth) and an infamous rogue and knave he was condemned in the Underworld perpetually to push a large stone, uphill, only to see it always roll down, hence the term 'labour of Sisyphus' to denote a futile task.

Sophocles. See **B56.**

Spartii. "The sown men" who sprang up when Cadmus (q.v.) sewed the dragon's teeth. They were fully armed and fought amongst themselves until only five remained, Echion, Udaeus, Chthonius, Hyperenor and Pelorus. These helped Cadmus build the Cadmea, citadel of Thebes, and were ancestors of the Thebans. The title was also given to their descendants. Cadmus saved some of the teeth and Jason (q.v.) had to sow these to get the Golden Fleece.

Sphinx. A fabulous monster with a human head and the body of a lion. In Egyptian mythology where it originates it could be of either sex but in Greek myth is a female and lives north of Thebes. It was the offspring of Echidne (q.v.) and Typhon (q.v.) or possibly Orthrus (q.v.) and the Chimaera (q.v.) and plagued Thebes by strangling and devouring all who could not answer her riddle: what walks on four legs at dawn, two at noon and three in the evening? Oedipus (q.v.) answered correctly that it was man who first crawls, then walks upright and finally uses a stick in old age. The sphinx then leapt from her rock and was dashed to pieces.

Stentor. Greek herald in the Trojan war who supposedly had a voice equal to that of fifty men. He died after Hermes (q.v.) beat him in a shouting match. His name gives us the word 'stentorian' meaning extremely loud.

Steropes. One of the Cyclopes (q.v.).

Stheneboea. Another name for Anteia. See **Bellerophon.**

Sthenelus. (1) A king of Mycenae, the son of Perseus (q.v.) and Andromeda (q.v.). The husband of Nicippe by whom he was the father of Alcinoe, Medusa (q.v.) and Eurystheus (q.v.).
(2) The son of Capaneus and Evadne, a companion of Diomedes (q.v.) and one of the Epigoni (q.v.). One of the Greeks in the Wooden Horse (q.v.).
(3) A Trojan and companion of Aeneas (q.v.).

Stheno. One of the Gorgones (q.v.).

Strymon. River in Thrace, believed by the Greeks to be the home of the crane.

Stymphalian Birds. Monsters inhabiting Lake Stymphalus, a marshy area in northern Arcadia. They were huge birds with bronze beaks and claws that ate human flesh. They used their feathers as arrows. The birds were sacred to Ares (q.v.) but Heracles (q.v.) startled them with bronze castanets provided by Athene (q.v.) and shot them. Some say they flew to the Black Sea and were found there by the Argonauts (q.v.).

Styx. The river of "hate" in the Underworld and flowing several times around its perimeter. When dipped in it Achilles (q.v.) was made invulnerable. Ghosts could only cross it if they paid Charon (q.v.) to ferry them across and for this purpose a coin was placed beneath the tongue of corpses. On its far bank was Cerberus (q.v.). Aristophanes (q.v.) and others describe it as a marsh rather than a river though Herodotus (q.v.) identifies it with a trickle from the rock near Pheneus. Generally it was associated with the cascade on Mt. Chelmos further west whose cold waters stain the rock black. Plutarch and Arrian say Alexander the Great was poisoned by water from here brought to him in a mule's hoof.

Sul or Sulis. A Celtic deity identified with Minerva (q.v.) by the Romans. The patron of Aquae Sulis.

Symplegades. Floating islands, like icebergs, at the entrance to the Bosphorus. They clashed together and crushed ships. Jason (q.v.), on the advice of Phineus, let loose a dove which made them recoil and as they did so the Argo (q.v.) slipped between them. Henceforth they remained stationary.

Syrinx. An Arcadian nymph. See **Pan.**

T

Talaus. The father of Adrastus (q.v.).

Talos. (1) A mythical brazen giant with a bull's head said to protect Crete.
(2) See **Daedalus.** Another name for Perdix.

Tantalus. A wealthy king, the son of Zeus (q.v.) and the nymph Pluto. The father of Pelops, Broteas and Niobe. He was favoured by Zeus and was invited to Olympian banquets but stole nectar (q.v.) and ambrosia (q.v.) and revealed Zeus' secrets. He received the golden dog made by Hephaestus (q.v.) for Rhea (q.v.) (which had watched Zeus' cradle) from Pandareus. This incensed the gods but Tantalus denied having seen it. Pandareus was then put to a miserable death and his daughters were abducted by the Harpies (q.v.). His numerous other crimes included serving Pelops (q.v.) as a meal to the gods. For this he was punished in the Underworld, either by being placed beneath a huge rock which constantly threatened to fall and crush him or by being placed in a lake the waters of which receded whenever he tried to drink, while above his head were boughs of fruit "tantalisingly" behind his reach.

Tarchon. Legendary ancestor of the Etruscan "Tarquins" who lead a group of emigrants from Lydia to Italy and there founded Tarquinii and other Etruscan cities. He became an ally of Aeneas (q.v.).

Tarpeia. The daughter of Tarpeius, commander of the Roman garrison on the Capitol during the Sabine (q.v.) wars shortly after Rome's foundation. Her story is told by Livy. She treacherously offered to show the way into the citadel if the Sabine chief Tatius would give her that which his men "wore on their shield arms". By this she meant gold torques but instead the Sabines crushed her to death with their shields. The tale is an attempt to account for the name of the Tarpeian Rock (q.v.).

Tarpeian Rock. A precipice on the south-west corner of the Capitol from which traitors and other condemned criminals were thrown to their death. The last victim was an equestrian implicated in a conspiracy against Claudius in 43 A.D.

Tartarus. (1) Another name for Hades (q.v.) though in Homer it refers to the deepest reaches of the Underworld, a place of punishment to which the Titans (q.v.) and Centimani (q.v.) were consigned by Cronus (q.v.).
(2) Also the name of a son of Ge (q.v.) who was father, by his mother, of the monster Typhon (q.v.).

Teiresias or Tiresias. A blind Theban prophet, who, while young, had come upon Athene (q.v.) bathing in the nude. She had therefore blinded him but in compensation gave him the gift of prophecy. He revealed to Oedipus (q.v.) the truth of his incest. He helped Thebes against the Seven (q.v.) then died after drinking from the well of Tilphussa.

Odysseus (q.v.) consulted his shade in the land of the Cimmerians.

Telamon. The son of Aeacus and brother of Peleus (q.v.). After the two murdered their half-brother Phocus, his father expelled him to Salamis where he married Glauce and later succeeded her father as king. Next he married Periboea of Athens and she bore him Ajax (q.v.). A friend of Heracles (q.v.) and with him sacked Troy (q.v.). He carried off Hesione who bore him Teucer and his refusal to return her to her brother Priam (q.v.) was one cause of the Trojan war.

Telchines. Mythical beings, artists in metal work who made a sickle for Cronus (q.v.) and the trident for Poseidon (q.v.). They raised the infant Poseidon. At times they were destructive and interfered with the weather. They annoyed Zeus (q.v.) who drowned a number of them in a flood, and Apollo (q.v.) who took the form of a wolf to savage them.

Telemachus. See **Odysseus.**

Telephassa. The mother of Europa (q.v.) and Cadmus (q.v.) by Agenor.

Telephus. The son of Heracles (q.v.) and Auge (a priestess and daughter of Aleus, king of Tegea). Abandoned as a child, the Delphic oracle later directed him to the court of king Teuthras in Mysia where he found his mother married to Teuthras. He later succeeded Teuthras and married Laodice, daughter of Priam (q.v.). When the Greeks on their way to Troy (q.v.) landed in Mysia he repulsed them, but Dionysus (q.v.) caused him to trip on a vine and Achilles (q.v.) wounded him. An oracle told him he could only be cured by the one who wounded him while the Greeks were told they could not take Troy without his help. He therefore went to Achilles who cured the wound with rust from his spear and in return Telephus showed the Greeks the route to Troy.

Tempe. A vale in Thessaly where Apollo (q.v.) pursued Daphne (q.v.) and was purified of the killing of Python.

Tenedos. Small island off the coast of Asia Minor, south west of Troy (q.v.). Here Achilles (q.v.) slew king Tenes (q.v.) and his father Cyncus and here Philoctetes (q.v.) was wounded.

Tenes. The son of Apollo (q.v.) though reputed to be son of Cycnus, king of Colonae in Troas. His stepmother attempted to seduce him and, when he refused her, made false accusations against him. Cycnus then put Tenes and his sister Hemithea into a chest and cast it adrift at sea. It washed up on the isle of Leucophrys where Tenes became king and gave his name to the island, Tenedos (q.v.).

Tereus. See **Procne.**

Terpsichore. The muse of song and choral dance, portrayed with a lyre and plectrum.

Teucer. (1) The son of Scamander (q.v.) and the nymph Idaca. He gave the land to Dardanus (q.v.) on which Dardanus built Dardania. An ancestor of the Trojans.
(2) The son of Hesione and Telamon, half brother of Ajax (q.v.) behind whose shield he fought at Troy (q.v.).

Teucri. Name for the Trojans derived from that of their ancestor Teucer (q.v.).

Teuthras. See **Telephus.** The father of the girl Tecmessa. Ajax (q.v.) raided the Thracian Chersonese, slew him and abducted Tecmessa.

Tethys. A Titaness, mother of Oceanus (q.v.) of Metis.

Thalia. (1) Muse of comedy.
(2) One of the Charites (q.v.).

Thebe. The wife of Zethus, who gave her name to Thebes.

Themis. A Titaness, the daughter of Ge (q.v.) and Uranus (q.v.) and sister of Cronus (q.v.). The wife of Zeus (q.v.) before Hera (q.v.), she bore him the Horae (q.v.) and Moerae (q.v.). She determined religious rites, instituted laws and was the first to distinguish between that which was permitted and that which offended the divine order. Hence she became the personification of justice and represented the incarnation of divine law.

Therseander. See **Epigoni.**

Theocritus. See **B59.**

Thersites. A low-minded, ugly and mean spirited wretch amongst the Greek forces at Troy (q.v.). He accused Agamemnon (q.v.) of prolonging the war to serve his own interest until Odysseus (q.v.) beat him into silence.

Theseus. The son of Aethra, a princess of Troezen, by Aegeus (q.v.) though one tradition says Poseidon (q.v.) fathered him in the form of a bull.

Aegeus left her after seducing her but showed her a rock under which he had hidden his sword and sandals. Theseus was raised secretly by his mother at her father's court, and when he reached adolescence lifted the rock to claim Aegeus' sword and sandals. With these he set off for Athens and on the way had many adventures, slaying the wild sow of Crommyum, Sciron (q.v.), Periphetes (q.v.), Cercyon and Procrustes (q.v.). Arriving at Athens Aegeus recognised the sword and sandals and accepted him as his son despite the plots of Medea (q.v.). Theseus then scattered the Pallantides, fifty nephews of Aegeus and the sons of Pallas who hoped to claim the throne themselves. Next he captured the Cretan Bull (q.v.). But his greatest task was to go voluntarily to Crete to slay the Minotaur (q.v.). As one of the tribute demanded by Minos (q.v.) he was to be sacrificed to the monster but Minos' daughter Ariadne fell in love with him and gave him a sword with which to slay the beast and a thread by which he could retrace his steps through the massive labyrinth in which it lived. The couple then fled to Naxos where he left Ariadne and where she was loved by Dionysus (q.v.) whose sacred island it was. Aegeus tragically killed himself on Theseus' return and the hero then became king of Athens. Either alone or with Heracles (q.v.) he invaded the land of the Amazons and carried off either Antiope or Hippolyte. The Amazons attacked Athens but Theseus defeated them in the middle of Athens. By the Amazon queen he became father of Hippolytus (q.v.). Later he married Phaedra and was father by her of Acamas and Demophon (q.v.). A close friend of Pirithous (q.v.), the two shared many adventures. Eventually he returned again to Athens but was ousted by Menestheus and retired to Scyros where, for some reason he was murdered by Lycomedes. Unlike Heracles, Theseus was not worshipped throughout the Hellenistic world but was very much an Athenian hero and his reputed bones were brought to the city from Scyros in historical times. He is said to have gathered the villages of Attica into one state by the process of synoecismus.

Thetis. A Nereid (q.v.) who was raised by Hera (q.v.) and remained attached to her. Zeus (q.v.) and Poseidon (q.v.) desired her but it was foretold that her son would be greater than his father. She was thus forced to marry a mortal, Peleus (q.v.), but only after she had tried to avoid him by changing her shape, becoming various animals including a lion. Their wedding on Mt. Pelion was attended by all the gods save Eris (q.v.). They had a number of children who were killed when Thetis tried to make them immortal by throwing them into the fire. Peleus snatched their seventh child, Achilles (q.v.), from her as she tried yet again. Instead she dipped him in the Styx (q.v.). Angry at not giving birth to an immortal she left Peleus to live with her sister Neireids. She cared for Hephaestus (q.v.) when Zeus threw him into the sea, and for Dionysus (q.v.) though she and Briareus (q.v.) freed Zeus when the other gods enchained him.

Thoas. The son of Andraemon king of Calydon who took forty ships to Troy (q.v.) and was one of the Greeks in the Wooden Horse (q.v.).

Thyades. See **Thyia.**

Thyestes. The son of Pelops (q.v.) and Hippodamia and brother of Atreus, ancestor of the illustrious Atridae family. He and Atreus murdered their half-brother Chrysippus and fled to Mycenae. Here Atreus seized the kingdom and banished Thyestes. Thyestes had seduced Atreus' second wife Aerope and he now tricked Atreus into killing Pleisthenes, his son by his first wife. In revenge Atreus lured Thyestes to Mycenae, slew his three sons and served them to him. Thyestes unknowingly ate them. Not surprisingly he cursed the house of Atreus on learning the truth. The Delphic oracle told Thyestes he could get revenge by fathering a son on his own daughter Pelopia, a priestess at the court of Thesprotus of Sicyon. He raped her and Atreus later married her, believing her to be the daughter of Thesprotus. He raised Thyestes' son Aegisthus (q.v.) as his own.

Thyia. The first woman to worship and sacrifice to Dionysus (q.v.). She gave her name to the Attic women who participated in the orgies of Dionysus at Parnassus, the Thyiades. These women were also called Thyades, "raging women", a similar name but of different origin.

Thyone. See **Semele.**

Thyrsus. A wand carried by the Maenads, covered with ivy wreaths and surmounted by a fir cone.

Tiryns. City reputedly founded by Proetus (q.v.) and built with the help of the Cyclopes (q.v.). The actual site is a mound 300 yd long on the Gulf of Argolis. It was first inhabited in the 3rd millennium B.C. and held a chief's residence and town. Around 1600 B.C. a larger palace was built and ramparts constructed. In the 14th and 13th centuries the rampart was rebuilt and enlarged. Its impressive ruins remain.

Tisiphone. One of the Eumenides (q.v.).

Titanesses. Sisters of the Titans (q.v.), daughters of Ge (q.v.) and Uranus (q.v.). Their numbers included Rhea (q.v.), Themis (q.v.), Tethys and Mnemosyne.

Titanomachia. The ten-year war waged in Thessaly by Zeus (q.v.) and the Olympian gods against Cronos (q.v.) and the Titans (q.v.) led by Atlas (q.v.). Ge (q.v.) promised Zeus (who had usurped his Titan father Cronos) victory if he would free the Cyclopes (q.v.) and Hecatoncheires (q.v.) from Tartarus (q.v.). He did and the Cyclopes gave him the thunderbolt, Hades (q.v.) a helmet which conferred invisibility and Poseidon a trident. The three overcame Cronos and the Hecatoncheires stoned the other Titans who were defeated and consigned either to Tartarus or an island far to the west. Here the Hecatoncheires guarded them. Atlas was made to carry the sky as punishment but the Titanesses (q.v.) were spared. The war is the basis of Keats' Hyperion.

Titans. The sons of Ge (q.v.) and Uranus (q.v.). There were twelve of them though the lists given of their names are inconsistent. The most often named are Cronus (q.v.), Oceanus (q.v.), Hyperion, Iapetus and Atlas (q.v.). Brothers of the Titanesses (q.v.). When Uranus consigned the Cyclopes (q.v.) to Tartarus (q.v.) Ge persuaded Cronos and his brother Titans to depose Uranus. The Titans were in turn deposed in the Titanomachia (q.v.).

Tithonus. The son of Laomedon and Strymor and a half-brother of Priam (q.v.). By Eos (q.v.) the father of Memnon (q.v.). Eos begged Zeus (q.v.) to make him immortal, which he did, but forgot to ask for perpetual youth. Tithonus grew older and older until Eos tired of looking on him, turned him into a cicada and locked him in a cage.

Ties. One of the three primitive tribes of Rome.

Tityus. A giant son of Ge (q.v.) sent by Hera (q.v.) to violate Leto (q.v.) but Artemis (q.v.) and Apollo (q.v.) slew him with their arrows. In Hades (q.v.) he was pegged to the ground (he covered nine acres) while two vultures picked at his liver.

Tleopolemus. A son of Heracles (q.v.) who settled in Argos and later Rhodes.

Triptolemus. See **Demeter.**

Triton. The son of Poseidon (q.v.) and Amphitrite (q.v.) though sometimes several tritons are spoken of. He was a merman, his upper body being human, the lower fish. He blew a shell-trumpet, the concha, to calm the waves and Ovid tells us that he blew the concha to order the waters to recede after the Flood. (See **Deucalion**).

Troilus. A young son of Priam (q.v.) slain by Achilles (q.v.). His romance with Cressida is a medieval invention.

Trojan War. The ten-year siege of Troy (q.v.) and its eventual sack by Greek forces under Agamemnon (q.v.). The combined forces sought to restore Helen (q.v.) to Menelaus (q.v.). The story of the war is told in Homer's Iliad where Achilles (q.v.) is the major hero of the Greeks and Hector (q.v.) of the Trojans. According to Homer the war was ended by the Wooden Horse (q.v.) concocted by Odysseus (q.v.). The war is usually placed by tradition as occurring in the 12th century B.C. The war is not a purely mythical episode. Archaeological evidence from the site of Troy shows that the city occupying the seventh stratigraphical layer was destroyed by fire, though probably in the 14th century B.C. Archaeology also confirms the Iliad's description of the main towns in Trojan civilisation together with its picture of the Greek people and army.

Trophonius and Agamedes. Sons of Erginus who built a temple for Apollo (q.v.) at Delphi. They were rewarded by living merrily for six days and dying in their sleep on the seventh. Trophonius later had an oracle of his own at Lebadeia in Boeotia. Here, according to Pausanias, the questioner underwent a complex initiation, was dressed as a sacrificial victim and (carrying a honey-cake to placate the Underworld divinities) descended into a pot-hole. An underground stream swept him along some distance before he was returned to the light having heard invisible speakers in the cavern. Not surprisingly the questioner would look dazed and dejected and it became common to speak of a gloomy person as one who had been consulting Trophonius.

Tros. (1) The grandson of Dardanus (q.v.) and father of Ilus (q.v.) and Ganymede (q.v.). An ancestor of the Trojans, he gave his name to Troy (q.v.).
(2) A small town absorbed by the city of Troy (q.v.).

Troy. Also called Ilium, a city of Asia Minor near the sea not far from the straits of the Dardanelles. From its position the inhabitants could watch the sea traffic between the Aegean and Sea of Marmara. Many traders off-loaded cargo and used the land route to bypass the dangerous straits. Hence in the late 3rd millennium B.C. Troy became very prosperous from trade, a prosperity which returned at various periods in the 2nd millennium. In 1870 the German Heinrich Schliemann, an amateur archaeologist, sought the site near modern Hissarlik in Turkey. He found it and later excavations have distinguished nine strata of occupations, the richest dating from 2200 B.C. and the 7th showing signs of destruction by fire (See **Trojan War**). From the 14th century B.C. the site was of little importance until the Roman occupation when, as Ilium Nevum, it played a large part in provincial life. Homer's Troy had probably absorbed three neighbouring towns, Tros (q.v.), Dardania and Ilium and the names of three tribes, Ilians, Trojans and Dardanians are represented in the myths of its foundation.

Tyche or **Tuche.** The Roman "Fortuna", always more popular in Rome. A daughter of Zeus (q.v.) and the goddess of luck who bestowed or denied gifts to men according to her whims. She often accompanied Pluto (q.v.). She is portrayed juggling a ball, symbolising the instability of fate, or with a rudder to guide men's affairs.

Tydeus. Son of Oeneus and Calydon, husband of Deipyle. After committing a murder in his youth he fled to the court of Adrastus (q.v.). See **Seven Against Thebes.**

Tyndareus. The brother of Hippocoon who deposed him as king of Sparta, but Heracles (q.v.) reinstated him. Helen (q.v.) was brought up at his court (she was his wife Leda's (q.v.) child by Zeus (q.v.)). Helen married Menelaus (q.v.) who succeeded Tyndareus. Tyndareus had had all the Greek nobles who sought Helen's hand swear an oath to defend her chosen husband. This was the reason why the Greeks allied in support of Menelaus in the Trojan War (q.v.). Tyndareus also helped Agamemnon (q.v.) expel Thyestes (q.v.) and regain his throne.

Typhon. The monstrous offspring of Ge (q.v.) and Tartarus (q.v.), whose eyes could expel fire and whose limbs ended in snakes' heads. He attacked Olympus and the gods fled to Egypt disguised as animals, Zeus (q.v.) as a ram, Apollo (q.v.) as a cow, Dionysus (q.v.) as a goat, Hera (q.v.) as a white cow, Artemis (q.v.) as a cat, Aphrodite (q.v.) as a fish, Ares (q.v.) as a boar and Hermes (q.v.) as an ibis. Athene (q.v.) did not flee and persuaded Zeus to fight. In a great struggle Zeus was saved by Hermes and Pan (q.v.) and then defeated Typhon with his thunderbolts. He was then buried under Mt. Etna. By Echidne (q.v.) Typhon was father of a variety of monsters.

Tyro. A nymph, the mother of Pelias (q.v.) and Neleus (q.v.) by Zeus (q.v.) and of Aeson by Cretheus. The grandmother of Jason (q.v.).

U

Udaeus. One of the Spartii (q.v.).
Ulysses. The Roman name for Odysseus (q.v.).
Urania. The Muse of Astronomy.
Uranus. The Sky, offspring of Ge (q.v.) the earth and brother of Pontus, the sea. The father by Ge of the Hecatoncheires (q.v.), the Cyclopes (q.v.) and the Titans (q.v.). He threw the rebellious Cyclopes into Tartarus (q.v.). Ge then persuaded the Titans to rise against their father and avenge their brothers. She gave Cronos (q.v.) a flint sickle with which he castrated Uranus. The blood of Uranus which fell to earth produced the Erinyes and the blood which fell into the sea produced Aphrodite (q.v.). Uranus was deposed but cursed Cronos that his own children depose him.

V

Venus. Originally an Italian deity whose name meant "beauty" or "charm", she was a goddess of vegetable rather than animal fertility. She became identified with Aphrodite (q.v.) by way of Aphrodite's cult at Mt. Eryx in Sicily, said to have been founded by Aeneas (q.v.) on the death of Anchises (q.v.). In 217 B.C. Venus Erycina was given a temple at Rome and became completely associated with Aphrodite taking on her functions and attributes. She was patron goddess of Sulla and Pompey. In the imperial cult she played a very important role as the Julian family claimed descent from Aeneas and therefore Aphrodite. In this context she was Venus Genetrix, creator of all thing:, the universal mother and life giver.

Vesta. A primitive Roman goddess of the hearth, the counterpart of Hestia (q.v.). She was worshipped in each Roman house and officially in a circular temple in the Forum. The temple held a fire, said to have come from Troy (q.v.) which could never be allowed to go out. It was tended by the Vestal Virgins (q.v.). Her cult was purely Italian and never spread to the provinces.

Vestal Virgins. A college of priestesses of the cult of Vesta (q.v.). There were originally four of them, later six and finally seven. Candidates for the college were chosen at between six and ten years of age; both their parents had to be alive and they underwent a prolonged special training. They served for thirty years under the control of the Pontifex Maximus and during all this period had to remain virgins. The punishment for unchastity was burial alive. However they were highly honoured and had great privileges. For instance they could save from execution any criminal they met on the way to their death. They lived in a large residence near the temple of Vesta. The sacred fire of Vesta was tended by Vestal Virgins up to the 4th century A.D.

Virgil. See **B62.**
Victoria. The Roman goddess of victory, corresponding to the Greek *Nike* (q.v.).
Vulcan. The Roman god of fire, identified with Hephaestus (q.v.) and sometimes called Mulciber, "the smelter". His name gives us the word "volcano".

W

Wooden Horse of Troy. The "Trojan Horse", a stratagem devised by Odysseus (q.v.) which ended the Trojan War (q.v.). The Greeks had Epeius, son of Panopeus, build a large wooden horse. Athene (q.v.) helped him and it bore an inscription dedicated to her. Then twenty-three or more Greeks including Odysseus, Neoptolemus (q.v.), Sthenelus and Thoas hid inside it. The rest of the Greek force then burnt their camp and put to sea leaving only the wily Sinon (q.v.) to trick the Trojans into dragging the horse into Troy. (*See also* **Laocöon**). Inside the city Helen (q.v.) patted the horse and called out the names of those she suspected were inside it, but she was accompanied by the Trojan prince Deiphobus and Odysseus stopped the Greeks answering. At night the Greek fleet returned, Sinon let the men out of the horse, the gates of Troy were opened and the city was sacked.

X

Xenophon. See **B66.**
Xuthus. The son of Hellen and husband of Creusa, the daughter of Erectheus, king of Athens. By her the father of Achaeus and Ion. On the death of

Erectheus Xuthus was asked to determine which of the king's sons should succeed him. He chose Cecrops and was expelled to Achaia by the other heirs. Euripedes (*q.v.*) makes Ion the son of Apollo (*q.v.*) and Creusa.

Z

Zagreus. A son of Zeus (*q.v.*). He was torn apart and eaten by Titans (*q.v.*) except for his heart which Athene (*q.v.*) saved. He is sometimes identified with Dionysus (*q.v.*).

Zephyrus. The son of Astraeus and Eus. He was the west wind, originally imagined, like all winds, in the form of a horse. The father of Xanthus and Balius, the talking horses of Achilles (*q.v.*) which Poseidon (*q.v.*) had given to Peleus (*q.v.*) as a wedding gift. The husband of Iris (*q.v.*). He deflected the discus which killed Hyacinthus (*q.v.*). His Roman counterpart was Favonius.

Zetes. *See* **Calais.**

Zethus. *See* **Amphion.**

Zeus. The son of Cronos (*q.v.*) and Rhea (*q.v.*). He deposed his father and defeated the Titans (*q.v.*). Then he and his brothers Hades (*q.v.*) and Poseidon (*q.v.*) cast lots for their kingdoms and Zeus won the sky. The earth was common to all. Zeus was the king of the gods and was identified with Jupiter by the Romans. He was the father of men. In early legend his consort is Dione, but his consort on Mt. Olympus (*q.v.*) is the jealous Hera (*q.v.*). He first married Hetis who bore him Athene (*q.v.*) and his second wife was Themis (*q.v.*) who bore him the Horae and Maerae. Hera bore him Ares (*q.v.*), Hebe (*q.v.*) and Hephaestus (*q.v.*). His sister Demeter (*q.v.*) bore him Persephone (*q.v.*) and Eurynome bore him the Charities (*q.v.*) while by Mnemosyne he was father of the Muses (*q.v.*). By mortal women he was father of Hermes (*q.v.*), Apollo (*q.v.*) and Artemis (*q.v.*) and Dionysus (*q.v.*). Given the thunderbolt by the Cyclopes (*q.v.*) he was known as the thunderer.

IDEAS &
BELIEFS

This section explains many of the
ideas and beliefs that have dominated our history during the centuries. The arrangement is alphabetical and the subjects range from a
world-wide spectrum of religious
and philosophical terms to the
major political ideologies which
have shaped modern history.

IDEAS AND BELIEFS

THIS section explains many of the ideas and beliefs which people have held at different periods in history. Beliefs may be true or false, meaningful or totally meaningless, regardless of the degree of conviction with which they are held. Since man has been moved to action so often by his beliefs they are worth serious study. The section throws a vivid light on human history.

Man has always felt a deep need for emotional security, a sense of "belonging" This need has found expression in the framing of innumerable religious systems, nearly all of which have been concerned with man's relation to a divine ruling power. In the past, people have been accustomed to think of their own religion as true and of all others as false. Latterly we have come to realise that in man's religious strivings there is common ground, for our need in the world today is a morality whereby human beings may live together in harmony.

There is also to be found in man an irresistible curiosity which demands an explanation of the world in which he finds himself. This urge to make the world intelligible takes him into the realm of science where the unknown is the constant challenge. Science is a creative process, always in the making, since the scientist's conjectures are constantly being submitted to severe critical tests. Basic scientific ideas are discussed in **Section F**, while some of the major economic theories are to be found in **Section G**.

A

Activists, those in a political movement who insist on taking active steps towards their objectives rather than merely putting forward a programme. Lately activism has become an increasingly common facet of political life. This is probably because the undeniably rapid social changes which are taking place across the world at the moment are not generally being followed by appropriate shifts in political structures and ideals.

Acupuncture, a unique medical system originating in China and based on the established therapeutic effects of implanting fine gold needles in specific parts of the body. The site of needle implantation is decided according to traditional texts. The apparent lack of any logical relationship between the implantation sites and any known physiological or anatomical systems within the body has caused acupuncture to be held in low regard by Western medicine. Indeed it was certainly true that acupuncture and other similar practices tended to flourish in parts of the world where orthodox medicine has made little progress or where doctors and trained staff are scarce. Recent years however have seen a curious and unexpected revival of interest in acupuncture in Europe and America.

Adlerian Psychology. In 1911 the Viennese psychoanalyst Alfred Adler (1870–1937) together with his colleague Carl Gustav Jung broke with their friend Sigmund Freud over disputes concerning the latter's theoretic approach to psychoanalysis. Jung and Adler were themselves shortly also to part company, each to set up and develop his own "school" of psychoanalysis. Adler's system of psychotherapy is based on the idea, not of sex as a driving force as in the case of Freud, but on the concept of "compensation" or a drive for power in an attempt to overcome the "inferiority complex" which he held to be universal in human beings. The child naturally feels inferior to adults, but bullying, making him feel insignificant or guilty or contemptible, even spoiling, which makes him feel important within the family but relatively unimportant outside, increases this feeling. Or the child may have physical defects: he may be small or underweight, have to wear glasses, become lame, be constantly ill, or stupid at school. In these ways he develops a sense of inferiority which for the rest of his life he develops a technique to overcome.

This may be done in several ways: he may try to become capable in the very respects in which he feels incompetent—hence many great orators have originally had speech defects; many painters poor eyesight; many musicians have been partially deaf; like Nietzsche, the weakling, he may write about the superman, or like Sandow, the strong man, be born with poor health.

On the other hand he may overdo his attempt and overcompensate. Hence we have the bully who is really a coward, the small man who is self-assertive to an objectionable degree (Hitler, Napoleon, Stalin, and Mussolini were all small men) or the foreigner who like three of these men wanted to be the hero of his adopted country—Hitler the Austrian, Napoleon the Italian, Stalin the Georgian.

But what about the man who can do none of these things, who continues to fail to compensate? He, says Adler, becomes a neurotic because neurosis is an excuse which means "I could have done so-and-so but ..." It is the unconscious flight into illness—the desire to be ill. Adler's treatment involves disclosing these subterfuges we play on ourselves so that we can deal with the real situation in a more realistic way. Adlerian psychoanalysis still attracts supporters, but its golden days were when the founder was at the head of the movement in the U.S.A., when his views were considered to provide a more "acceptable" theory of the mind than the enormously controversial theories of Freud with their strong sexual orientation.

Adventists, a group of American religious sects, the most familiar being the Seventh-Day Adventist Church, which observes Saturday as the true Sabbath. With (1992) more than 5 million members throughout the world, it shares with other Adventists a belief in the imminent second coming of Christ (a doctrine fairly widespread in the U.S.A. during the early decades of the 19th cent. when the end of the world was predicted by William Miller for 1843, then for 1844). Modern Adventists content themselves with the conviction that the "signs" of the Advent are multiplying, the "blessed event" which will solve the world's ills. Believers will be saved, but the sects differ as to whether the unjust will be tortured in hell, annihilated, or merely remain asleep eternally.

Aestheticism. See **Section M, Part III.**

Agnosticism. See **God and Man.**

Albigenses, also known as Cathari. French heretical sect (named after the town of Albi in Provence) which appeared in the 11th cent. to challenge the Catholic Church on the way true Christians should lead their lives. They followed a life of extreme asceticism in contrast to the local clergy and their faith was adopted by the mass of the population, especially in Toulouse. Condemned as heretics by Pope Innocent III, the sect was exterminated in the savage Albigensian Crusade (1208–29), initially led by Simon de Montfort. (In his thoroughness, de Montfort also succeeded in destroying the high culture of the Troubadours.)

Alchemy, ancient art associated with magic and astrology in which modern chemistry has its roots. The earliest mention of alchemy comes from ancient Egypt but its later practitioners attributed its origins to such varied sources as the fallen angels of the Bible, to Moses and Aaron, but most commonly to Hermes Trismegistus, often identified with the Egyptian god Thoth, whose knowledge of the divine art was handed down only to the sons of kings (cf. the phrase "hermetically sealed"). Its main object was the transmutation of metals. Egyptian speculation concerning this reached its height during the 6th cent. in the Alexandrian period. Brought to Western Europe by the Moslems, one of its most famous Arab exponents was Jabir (c. 760–c. 815), known to the Latins as Geber, who had a laboratory at Kufa on the Tigris. One school of early Greek philosophy held that there was ultimately only one elemental matter of which everything was composed. Such men as Albertus Magnus (1206–80) and Roger Bacon (1214–94) assumed that, by removing impurities, this *materia prima* could be obtained. Although Bacon's ideas were in many ways ahead of his time, he firmly believed in the philosopher's stone, which could turn base metals into gold, and in an elixir of life which would give eternal youth. Modern science has, of course, shown in its researches into radioactivity, the possibility of transmutation of certain elements, but this phenomenon has little bearing on either the methods of the alchemist or the mysteries with which he surrounded them.

Anabaptists. See **Baptists.**

Analytical Psychology, the name given by Carl Gustav Jung (1875–1961) of Zürich to his system of psychology, which, like Adler's (*see* **Adlerian Psychology**), took its origin from Freud's psychoanalysis from which both diverged in 1911. Briefly, Jung differed from Freud: (1) in believing that the latter had laid too much emphasis on the sexual drive as the basic one in man and replacing it with the concept of *libido* or life energy of which sex forms a part; (2) in his theory of types: men are either extrovert or introvert (*i.e.* their interest is turned primarily outwards to the world or inwards to the self), and they apprehend experience in four main ways, one or other of which is predominant in any given individual—sensing, feeling, thinking, or intuiting; (3) in his belief that the individual's unconscious mind contains not only repressed materials which, as Freud maintained, were too unpleasant to be allowed into awareness, but also faculties which had not been allowed to develop—*e.g.*, the emotional side of the too rational man, the feminine side of the too masculine one; (4) in the importance he attaches to the existence of a collective unconscious at a still deeper level which contains traces of ancient ways of thought which mankind has inherited over the centuries. These are the *archetypes* and include primitive notions of magic, spirits and witches, birth and death, gods, virgin mothers, resurrection, etc. In the treatment of the neuroses Jung believed in the importance of (*a*) the present situation which the patient refuses to face; (*b*) the bringing together of conscious and unconscious and integrating them.

In the 1940s and 50s interest in Jung's ideas waned, at least in academic circles, as the emphasis among experimental psychologists shifted closer and closer to the "hard" scientific line. This was also true in the field of psychoanalysis where the Jungian as opposed to the Freudian point of view became progressively less popular. At the present time this trend is beginning to reverse, and while Jung's offbeat views on astrology, telepathy, etc., are still unfashionable, a reappraisal of the significance of his views on the nature of the unconscious is taking place and many psychologists feel that his contribution to our understanding of the nature of human mental processes has been greatly underrated. *See also* **Psychoanalysis.**

Anarchism, a political philosophy which holds, in the words of the American anarchist Josiah Warren (1798–1874), an early follower of Robert Owen, that "every man should be his own government, his own law, his own church." The idea that governmental interference or even the mere existence of authority is inherently bad is as old as Zeno, the Greek Stoic philosopher, who believed that compulsion perverts the normal nature of man. William Godwin's *Enquiry Concerning Political Justice* (1793) was the first systematic exposition of the doctrine. Godwin (father-in-law of Shelley) claimed that man is by nature sociable, co-operative, rational, and good when given the choice to act freely; that under such conditions men will form voluntary groups to work in complete social harmony. Such groups or communities would be based on equality of income, no state control, and no property: this state of affairs would be brought about by rational discussion and persuasion rather than by revolution.

The French economist Proudhon (1809–65) was the first to bring anarchism to the status of a mass movement. In his book *What is Property?* he stated bluntly that "property is theft" and "governments are the scourge of God". He urged the formation of co-operative credit banks where money could be had without interest and goods would be exchanged at cost value at a rate representing the hours of work needed to produce each commodity. Like Godwin, he disapproved of violence but, unlike Marx, disapproved of trade unions as representing organised groups.

In communistic anarchism these ideas were combined with a revolutionary philosophy, primarily by the Russians Michael Bakunin (1814–76) and Peter Kropotkin (1842–1921) who favoured training workers in the technique of "direct action" to overthrow the state by all possible means, including political assassination. In 1868 anarchists joined the First International which broke up a few years later after a bitter struggle between Bakuninists and Marxists. Subsequently small anarchist groups murdered such political figures as Tsar Alexander II of Russia, King Humbert of Italy, Presidents Carnot of France and MacKinley of America, and the Empress Elizabeth of Austria.

Anarchism and communism differ in three main ways: (1) anarchism forms no political party, rejects all relationship with established authority, and regards democratic reform as a setback; (2) communism is against capitalism, anarchism against the state as such; (3) both have the final goal of a classless society, but anarchism rejects the idea of an intermediate period of socialist state control accepted by communism. Philosophical anarchists, such as the American writer Henry David Thoreau (1817–62), were primarily individualists who believed in a return to nature, the non-payment of taxes, and passive resistance to state control; in these respects Thoreau strongly influenced Gandhi as did the Christian anarchist Tolstoy.

Anarchism has traditionally been criticised as being impractical—*e.g.*, in a non-authoritarian society, who is going to look after the sewers or clean the streets?—and there is a good deal of force to this argument. In fact anarchistic ideas became progressively less fashionable in the first half of this century. A curious and probably significant revival of interest has taken place in the past decade, however, probably because of a growing sense of disillusion, particularly on the part of young people, with the progress of orthodox political systems. *See also* **Syndicalism.**

Anglicanism, adherence to the doctrine and discipline of the Anglican Church, as the genuine representative of the Catholic Church. *See* **Church of England.**

Anglo-Catholicism. To Queen Elizabeth I the Church of England was that of the "middle way" in which human reason and commonsense took their place beside Scripture and Church authority. The extent to which these various factors are stressed creates the distinctions between "high" and "low" church. Anglo-Catholics tend to reject the term "Protestant" and stress the term "Catholic" and, although few accept the infallibility of the Pope some Anglo-Catholic churches have introduced much or all of the Roman ritual and teach Roman dogmas. The ordination in March 1994 of the first women priests to the Anglican ministry has caused a crisis in Anglo-Catholicism. *See* **Catholicism, Tractarianism**.

Animism. To early man and in primitive societies the distinction between animate and inanimate objects was not always obvious—it is not enough to say that living things move and non-living things do not, for leaves blow about in the wind and streams flow down a hillside. In the religions of early societies, therefore, we find a tendency to believe that life exists in all objects from rocks and pools to seas and mountains. This belief is technically known as *animatism*, which differs from *animism*, a somewhat more sophisticated view which holds that natural objects have no life in themselves but may be the abode of dead people, spirits, or gods who occasionally give them the appearance of life. The classic example of this, of course, is the assumption that an erupting volcano is an expression of anger on the part of the god who resides in it. Such beliefs may seem absurd today. but it is worth realising that we are not entirely free of them ourselves when we ascribe "personalities" of a limited kind to motor cars, boats, dolls, *etc*.

Anthropomorphism, the attribution of human form, thoughts or motives to non-human entities or life forms from gods to animals. At one end this can be summed up in the once widespread image of God as a "white-bearded old gentleman sitting on a cloud." At the other end is the very common tendency to invest domestic animals and pets with man-like wishes and personalities. At both extremes the belief could be seriously misleading. Firstly, it could be very unwise to assume that God, if he exists, necessarily thinks as humans do and has human interests at heart. Secondly, we shall learn very little about animal behaviour if we look upon them as mere extensions of our own personality, and we do them less than justice if we see them simply as human beings of diminutive intelligence.

Anthroposophy, a school of religious and philosophical thought based on the work of the German educationist and mystic Rudolf Steiner (1861–1925). Steiner was originally an adherent of Madame Blavatsky's theosophical movement (*cf* Theosophy) but in 1913 broke away to form his own splinter group, the Anthroposophical Society, following ideological disputes over the alleged "divinity" of the Indian boy Krishnamurti. Steiner was much influenced by the German poet and scientist, Goethe, and believed that an appreciation and love for art was one of the keys to spiritual development. One of the first tasks of his new movement was the construction of a vast temple of arts and sciences. known as the Goetheanum, to act as the headquarters of the society. This structure, which was of striking and revolutionary architectural style, was unfortunately burnt down in 1922 to be replaced by an even more imaginative one which today is one of the most interesting buildings of its kind in the world. Anthroposophy, which ceased to expand greatly following its founder's death, is nevertheless well-established in various parts of the world with specialised, and often very well equipped, schools and clinics which propagate the educational and therapeutic theories of the movement. These, which include the allegedly beneficial powers of music, coloured lights, etc., have made an increasing impact on modern educational ideas, but the schools have acquired a reputation for success in the training of mentally handicapped children. Today (1990) there are over 400 Steiner schools worldwide, many clinics and homes for the handicapped, adult education centres, an international management consultancy, and several hundred thousand acres under bio-dynamic cultivation without the use of chemical pesticides, herbicides, or fertilizers. Interesting work continues to be done, in pharmacology, botany, mathematics and physics, and architecture.

Anticlericalism, resentment of priestly powers and privileges, traceable in England to Wyclif's insistence in the 14th cent. on the right of all men to have access to the Scriptures. The translation of the Bible into the common tongue was a great landmark in the history of the Bible and the English language. Wyclif's principles were condemned by the Roman Church of his time but were readily accepted during the Reformation. Tudor anticlericalism arose from motives ranging from a greedy desire to plunder the riches of the Church to a genuine dislike of the powers of the priesthood whose spiritual courts still had the right to decide on points of doctrine or morals in an age when the layman felt he was well able to decide for himself. In innumerable ways the Church was permitted to extort money from the laity. It is generally agreed, says Trevelyan, that the final submission of church to state in England was motivated quite as much by anticlericalism as by Protestantism. The rise of the Reformed churches in England satisfied the people generally and anticlericalism never became the fixed principle of permanent parties as happened in France and Italy from the time of Voltaire onwards.

Antisemitism, a term first applied about the middle of the last century to those who were anti-Jewish in their outlook. Although this attitude was prevalent for religious reasons throughout the Middle Ages, modern antisemitism differed (*a*) in being largely motivated by economic or political conditions, and (*b*) in being doctrinaire with a pseudo-scientific rationale presented by such men as Gobineau (1816–82) and Houston Stewart Chamberlain (1855–1927), and later by the Nazi and Fascist "philosophers". Beginning in Russia and Hungary with the pogroms of 1882 it gradually spread south and westwards where, in France, the Dreyfus case provided an unsavoury example in 1894. Thousands of Jews from Eastern Europe fled to Britain and America during this period; for in these countries anti-semitism has rarely been more than a personal eccentricity. During the last war the murder of six million Jews by the Nazis and their accomplices led to a further exodus to various parts of the world and finally to the creation of the state of Israel.

The individual Jew-hater makes unconscious use of the psychological processes of projection and displacement: his greed or sexual guilt is projected on to the Jew (or Negro or Catholic) because he cannot bear to accept them as his own emotions, and his sense of failure in life is blamed on his chosen scapegoat rather than on his own inadequacy.

But there are social causes too and politicians in some lands are well versed in the technique of blaming unsatisfactory conditions (which they themselves may have in part produced) upon minority groups and persuading others to do the same. Historically, the Jew is ideally suited for this role of scapegoat; (1) in the Middle Ages when usury was forbidden to Christians but not to Jews, the latter often became moneylenders incurring the opprobrium generally associated with this trade (*e.g.*, to the simple-minded Russian peasant the Jew often represented, not only the "Christ-killer", but also the moneylender or small shopkeeper to whom he owed money); (2) many trades being closed to Jews, it was natural that they concentrated in others, thus arousing suspicions of "influence" (*i.e.* Jews are felt to occupy a place in certain trades and professions which far exceeds their numerical proportion to the population as a whole); (3) even with the ending of ghetto life, Jews often occupy *en masse* some parts of cities rather than others and this may lead to resentment on the part of the original inhabitants who begin to feel themselves dispossessed; (4) Jews tend to form a closed society and incur the suspicions attached to all closed societies within which social contacts are largely limited to members; marriage outside the group is forbidden or strongly disapproved of, and the preservation, among the orthodox, of cultural and religious barriers tends to isolate them from their fellow citizens. Since 1990, with the political changes in Russia and Eastern Europe, neo-fascist extremists have begun a resurgence of anti-semitism. *See* **Racism, Zionism, Judaism**.

Anti-vivisection, opposition to scientific experimentation upon live animals based, according to its supporters, both on the moral grounds of the suffering imposed, and also on the grounds that many doctors and scientists of repute have rejected the value of information gained in this way. It is true that the protagonists of the movement during its early days in the mid-19th cent. included a number of eminent physicians and surgeons. Many people today remain deeply concerned about the moral problems of vivisection, even though without animal experiments we would be unable to test out new drugs for safety before using them on human beings. There are in Britain two or three large national anti-vivisection societies and several smaller ones. Much of their work is co-ordinated through the British Council of Anti-Vivisection Societies. Animal experimentation is controlled by Act of Parliament which makes obligatory the possession of licences by experimenters, inspection of laboratories by the Home Office, and the issue of annual returns of experiments. Many people would like the number of experiments on animals reduced and the law changed to prohibit any experiments in which there is any risk of inflicting suffering. A recent opinion survey showed that while the public approves of medical experiment it strongly disapproves of animals being used for the testing of cosmetics and other chemicals which have nothing to do with medical research. Reform of the Cruelty to Animals Act 1876 has been called for in view of the enormous increase in the number of live animal experiments.

Apartheid. An Afrikaans word meaning "apartness", which refers to the policy of total racial discrimination between black and white South Africans as enforced by successive governments of that country from 1948 until the early 1990s when the system was dismantled. *See also* **Section C.**

Arianism, formed the subject of the first great controversy within the Christian Church over the doctrine of Arius of Alexandria (d. 336) who denied the divinity of Christ. The doctrine, although at first influential, was condemned at the Council of Nicaea (325), called by the Emperor Constantine, at which Arius was opposed by Athanasius, also of Alexandria, who maintained the now orthodox view that the Son is of one substance with the Father. Arius was banished but the heresy persisted until the 7th cent., especially among the barbarians, the Goths, Vandals and Lombards. Disbelief in the divinity of Christ has formed part of the doctrine of many sects since (*e.g.*) **Unitarianism** (*q.v.*).

Arminianism. A theological movement in Christianity, based on the teachings of the Dutch theologian Jacob Harmensen (or Hermansz) (1560–1609), whose name was Latinised as Jacobus Arminius. He reacted against the Calvinist doctrine of predestination. His followers formulated his three main beliefs as: divine sovereignty was compatible with real freewill in man; Christ died for all men (and not only the elect); and all who believe in him can be saved. Arminianism had an important influence on John Wesley and through him on Methodism.

Asceticism. The practice of self-discipline of both mind and body in order to achieve a spiritual ideal or goal. From the Greek *askein*, to practise or exercise. The term originally referred to the training carried out by athletes. The concept was then transformed into the idea of training for wisdom. This view is clearly articulated in Plato, who argued that one must free oneself from the desires of the body in order to achieve full spiritual insight. Since all religions exalt the soul over the body, the spiritual over the material, and eternal life over this world, they all have traces of asceticism. In many of them, there are adherents who have gone beyond self-denial to self-punishment. Important features of ascetic movements are celibacy, abdication of worldly possessions, abstinence and fasting. Some ascetics have dispensed with washing, or have isolated themselves in deserts or mountains. Extreme ascetics have resorted to self-laceration, wearing iron devices under their clothes, flagellation, even castration.

Ascetism has been very important in Christianity, most notably in the monastic movement (*see* **Monasticism**), though practices varied widely among monks, from the extravagant austerity of Egyptian hermits to the work-oriented community life of the Benedictines. Since the rise of Protestantism, however, extreme austerity has been less favoured. Hinduism also has a strong tradition of asceticism, and there are elements in Buddhism and Islam.

Assassins, a sect of Moslem Shi'ites, founded by the Persian Hasan i Sabbah (*c.* 1090), which for more than two centuries established a rule of terror all over Persia and Syria. The coming of the Mongols in 1256 destroyed them in Persia and the Syrian branch suffered a similar fate at the hands of the then Mamluk sultan of Egypt, *c.* 1270. It was a secret order, ruled over by a grand master, under whom the members were strictly organised into classes, according to the degree of initiation into the secrets of the order. The devotees, belonging to one of the lower groups, carried out the actual assassinations under strict laws of obedience, and total ignorance of the objects and ritual of the society. It is believed that the latter were given ecstatic visions under the influence of hashish, whence the term *hashshashin,* which became corrupted to "assassin".

Associationism. In psychology, the Associationist school of the 19th cent. accepted the association of ideas as the fundamental principle in mental life. It was represented in Britain by the two Mills and Herbert Spencer, in Germany by J. F. Herbart (1776–1841). To these, mental activity was nothing but the association of "ideas" conceived of as units of both thought and feeling—the emotion of anger or the perception of a chair were both "ideas"—and apart from them the self did not exist. Personality was simply a series of these units coming and going, adding to or cancelling each other out, in accordance with rigid and mechanistic scientific laws.

Astrology was once the best available theory for explaining the course of human life and bears much the same historical relationship to astronomy as alchemy does to chemistry. Originally it was divided into the two branches of Natural Astrology which dealt with the movements of the heavenly bodies and their calculations, and Judicial Astrology which studied the alleged influence of the stars and the planets on human life and fate. It was the former that developed into modern astronomy; the latter was, and remains, a primitive myth.

Astrology owes most to the early Babylonians (or Chaldeans) who, being largely nomadic in an environment which permitted an unobstructed view of the sky, readily accepted the idea that divine energy is manifested in the movements of the sun and planets. Gradually this concept became enlarged and the relative positions of the planets both in relation to each other and to the fixed stars became important together with the idea of omens—that, if a particular event occurred whilst the planets were in a particular position, the recurrence of that position heralded a recurrence of the same sort of event. Soon the planets became associated with almost every aspect of human life. They were bound up with the emotions, with parts of the body, so that astrology played quite a large part in medicine up to late mediaeval times. Not only was the position of the planet to be considered but also the particular sign of the zodiac (or house of heaven) it was occupying, and it was believed possible to foretell the destiny of an individual by calculating which star was in the ascendant (*i.e.* the sign of the zodiac nearest the eastern horizon and the star which arose at that precise moment) at the time of his birth. Astrology was popular among the Egyptians, the Romans (whose authorities found the Chaldean astrologers a nuisance and expelled them from time to time), and during the Middle Ages when astrologers were often highly respected.

Despite the apparent absurdity of astrological beliefs—for example, how could the pattern of light from stars billions of miles away possibly influence the temperament of single individuals on earth—a substantial number of intelligent and well-educated people take its study in all seriousness. The most interesting "convert" was the psychologist and philosopher, Carl Jung, who conducted a complex experiment in which he compared the "birth signs" of happily married and divorced couples and claimed to find that those most favourably matched in astrological terms were also those more likely to have permanent wedded bliss. Jung's findings were subsequently shown to have been based on a simple statistical fallacy, which did not prevent the brilliant but eccentric psychologist from offering them up as evidence in support of his own theory of "synchronicity" **(J50)**, an involved and vaguely metaphysical notion which suggests that events in the universe may be significantly related in a "non-causal" fashion. To add fuel to the controversy however, the French mathematician, Michel Gauquelin, has recently offered up fresh data which apparently supports the general astrological view. In a carefully controlled study he noticed statistically significant correspondences between certain astrological signs and the professions of a large number of Frenchmen whose birth time and date were accurately recorded. Gauquelin claims to have repeated his study on a second large sample of his fellow countrymen, though he has been unable to use English people as the exact times of birth are not recorded on their birth certificates! This apparent shot in the arm for astrology is still a matter of great scientific controversy, though Gauquelin's work has been given support from the distinguished British psychologist. H. J. Eysenck, who has pronounced his statistical data to to be incontrovertible. Both scientists, however, carefully refrain from discussing the implications of these curious findings, and the controversy will no doubt increase rather than decrease in the near future.

Atheism. *See* **God and Man.**

Atlantis, a mythical continent supposed to have lain somewhere between Europe and America and a centre of advanced civilisation before it was inundated by some great natural catastrophe in pre-Christian times.

Atomism. In philosophy, the atomists were a group of early Greek thinkers, the most important of whom were Leucippus (fl. *c.* 440 B.C.) and his younger contemporary Democritus (*c.* 460–370 B.C.). Prior to these men, although it had been agreed that matter must be composed of tiny ultimate particles and that change must be due to the manner in which these mingled or separated from each other, it was supposed that there existed different types of particle for each material—*e.g.* for flesh, wood, hair, bone. The atomists taught that atoms were all made of a single substance and differed only in the connections (pictured as hooks, grooves, points, etc.) which enabled them to join each other in characteristic ways. Theirs was the first move towards modern atomic theory and a predecessor of the modern concept of chemical linkages.

Authoritarianism, a dictatorial form of government as contrasted with a democratic one based on popular sovereignty. Its alleged advantages are the avoidance of the delays and inefficiency said to be characteristic of the latter.

Automatism, the production of material, written or spoken in "automatic" fashion—*i.e.,* apparently not under the conscious or volitional control of the individual. This psychologically perplexing phenomenon has occurred from time to time throughout the history of literature and art, and while it has occasionally produced work of great merit (much of William Blake's poetry, Coleridge's "Kubla Khan", etc.) the bulk of it is indifferent and often simply rubbish. Spiritualists claim that the work is produced under the direct guidances of the spirit world, and their argument has attracted considerable attention through the compositions of the pianist Rosemary Brown who, with little or no academic background in musical theory, has produced a number of "original" piano pieces allegedly composed by Beethoven, Mozart, etc., from the astral plane. While few music critics doubt Mrs. Brown's honesty and integrity, most consider her work to be clever pastiche and barely comparable in quality to the masterworks of the dead composers. Nevertheless automatism wants some explaining, and most psychologists today defer judgement, taking the view that it serves to remind us of the fund of material which lies in the unconscious mind, and which is prone to pop up from time to time without warning. Rather similar is the case of Matthew Manning, a young English student who produced clever and artistically intriguing drawings and

sketches, allegedly guided by the hands of famous dead artists.

B

Baconian Method, the use of the inductive (as opposed to the deductive or Aristotelian) method of reasoning as proposed by Francis Bacon in the 17th cent. and J. S. Mill in the 19th cent. Deduction argues from supposedly certain first principles (such as the existence of God or Descartes's "I think, therefore I am") what the nature of the universe and its laws *must* be, whereas the only means of obtaining true knowledge of the universe, in Bacon's view, was by the amassing of facts and observations so that when enough were obtained the certain truth would be known in the same way that a child's numbered dots in a playbook joined together by a pencilled line create a picture. However, this is not the way science progresses in practice (*see* **F3(1)**). Bacon underrated the importance of hypothesis and theory and overrated the reliability of the senses. In discussing the scientific tradition, Sir Karl Popper in his book, *Conjecture and Refutations*, says: "The most important function of observation and reasoning, and even of intuition and imagination, is to help us in the critical examination of those bold conjectures which are the means by which we probe into the unknown." Two of the greatest men who clearly saw that there was no such thing as an inductive procedure were Galileo and Einstein.

Bahá'i Faith, a faith which teaches the unity of all religions and the unity of mankind. It arose in Iran from the teachings of the Bab (Mirza Ali Mohammed, 1820–50) and the Bahá'u'lláh (Mirza Husain Ali, 1817–92), thought to be manifestations of God, who in his essence is unknowable. Emphasis is laid on service to others. It has communities in many states and is surprisingly strong in England with a substantial following among university students. Its aims—universal peace, love, fellowship, sexual equality, etc.—are so laudable that it is hard to disagree with anything in the movement. Since the ruling fundamentalist Islamic regime of the Ayatollahs came to power in Iran in 1979 members of the faith have been persecuted. The movement is now guided and administered by an elected order, "The Universal House of Justice". Today (1995) the movement has some 5–6 million followers, with some 8,000 in Britain.

Baptists, a Christian denomination whose distinctive doctrines are that members can only be received by baptism "upon the confession of their faith and sins" and that "baptism is no wise appertaineth to infants." Baptism is therefore by total immersion of adults. Modern Baptists base their doctrines upon the teaching of the Apostles and some hold that the Albigenses (*q.v.*) maintained the true belief through what they regarded as the corruption of the Roman Church in mediaeval times. On the other hand any connection with the Anabaptist movement during the Reformation is rejected and the beginning of the modern Church is traced to John Smyth, a minister of the Church of England who in Amsterdam came under the influence of the Arminians (*q.v.*) and Mennonites. Smyth died in 1612 when the first Baptist church in England was built at Newgate. This, the "General" Baptist Church, rejected Calvinistic beliefs and held the Arminian doctrine of redemption open to all, but some years later a split occurred with the formation of the "Particular" Baptist Church which was Calvinist in doctrine. In 1891 the two bodies were united in the Baptist Union and today the sect is spread throughout the world, notably in the United States. There are (1995) *c.* 150,000 Baptists in Great Britain.

The Anabaptist movement began in Zurich, Switzerland, in 1525, when Conrad Grebel, Felix Manz and Jörg Blaurock, their hearts moved by their failure to live according to the Gospel, decided to give their lives to following Christ's teaching, whatever the cost. The movement spread widely in Switzerland, Germany and Holland in the

16th century, and its followers suffered martyrdom by fire, water and the sword for the sake of their faith. They met with further condemnation and persecution because of the excesses of a violent and licentious group, known as the Münster Anabaptists, whom they disowned.

The wider movement was non-violent and stood for baptism on confession of faith, love to one's enemies and obedience to the Spirit of Christ's Sermon on the Mount. This movement is the spiritual precursor of several of the Peace Churches of today: the Hutterians (named after their founder, Jakob Hutter), the Mennonites (after Menno Simons), and, later, the Amish.

The most radical of these groups is that of the Hutterian Brethren, who live, work, and hold their goods in common like the first Christians.

Beat Generation, a term first used by the American writer Jack Kerouac (d. 1969), author of *The Town and the City* and *On the Road*, to define various groups spread across the face of the country, but notably in New York and San Francisco, who, belonging to the post-war generation, represented a complex of attitudes, mainly rebellious.

Behaviourism, a school of psychology founded in 1914 by J. B. Watson (1878–1958), an animal psychologist at Johns Hopkins University, Baltimore. Its main tenet was that the method of introspection and the study of mental states were unscientific and should be replaced by the study of behaviour. When animals or human beings were exposed to specific stimuli and their responses objectively recorded, or when the development of a child, as seen in its changing behaviour, was noted, these alone were methods which were truly scientific. Watson contributed an important idea to psychology and did a great deal towards ridding it of the largely philosophical speculations of the past. But he also went to absurd extremes, as in his view that thought is nothing but subvocal speech, consisting of almost imperceptible movements of the tongue, throat, and larynx (*i.e.*, when we think, we are really talking to ourselves), and his further opinion that heredity is, except in grossly abnormal cases, of no importance. He claimed that by "conditioning", the ordinary individual could be made into any desired type, regardless of his or her inheritance.

The work of Ivan Pavlov had begun about 1901, but was unknown in America until about ten years later, and it was through another Russian, Vladimir Bekhterev, that the concept of "conditioning" was introduced into the country. Bekhterev's book *Objective Psychology*, describing his new science of "reflexology", was translated in 1913 and played a great part in the development of Behaviourist ideas. The conditioned reflex became central to Watson's theory of learning and habit, formation (*e.g.*, he showed that a year-old child, at first unafraid of white rats, became afraid of them when they came to be associated with a loud noise behind the head). Finally all behaviour, including abnormal behaviour, came to be explained in terms of conditioned responses; these were built up by association on the infant's three innate emotions of fear, rage, and love, of which the original stimuli were, for the first, loud noises and the fear of falling; for the second, interference with freedom of movement; and for the third, patting and stroking.

Because of its considerable theoretical simplicity and its implicit suggestion that human behaviour could be easily described (and even modified or controlled), Pavlovian psychology appeared very attractive to the Communist regime in Russia, and before long it became the "official" dogma in universities and research laboratories. Whereas in America and Western Europe its severe limitations became gradually apparent, in Russia these were ignored or disguised for ideological reasons with the inevitable outcome that Soviet psychology failed to evolve and, at one stage, seemed to be no more than a pallid offshoot of physiology. The recent liberalisation which has been taking place throughout Soviet society has led to a considerable broadening of scientific horizons and Pavlovian ideas are no longer looked upon with such unquestioning reverence. In non-Communist countries simple Watsonian be-

haviourism has evolved into more sophisticated studies of animal learning, largely pioneered by the Harvard psychologist, Skinner. These techniques, which have shown that animals, from monkeys to rats, may be taught to solve a remarkable range of physical problems (such as pressing complex sequences of buttons or levers to escape from a cage) have themselves turned out to be rather disappointing in terms of advancing our general understanding of the workings of the human and animal brain. There is a growing feeling among psychologists that the real keys to the understanding of mankind will only be found through the study of man himself, and not his simpler animal cousins. *See also under entry* **Gestalt Psychology.**

Benthamism. *See* **Utilitarianism.**

Bermuda Triangle, an area of sea, bounded by Bermuda, Florida and Puerto Rico where unexplained disappearances of aircraft and ships have led to many fanciful theories. Natural phenomenon are the most likely explanation.

Bolshevism, an alternative name for **Communism** (*q.v.*), usually used in the West in a derogatory sense. When the Russian Social Democratic Party at a conference held in London in 1903 split over the issue of radicalism or moderation, it was the radical faction headed by Lenin (who subsequently led the 1917 Revolution and became first Head of State of the Soviet Union) which polled the majority of votes. The Russian for majority is *bolshinstvo* and for minority *menshinstvo*; hence the radicals became known as Bolsheviki and the moderates as Mensheviki, anglicised as Bolsheviks and Mensheviks. *See* **Communism, Marxism.**

Brahmanism. A religion of ancient India which evolved out of the Vedas about 1000–800 B.C. and is still powerful today. It provides the orthodox core of traditional Hinduism. Characteristics of the faith were elaborate ceremonies, material offerings, animal sacrifice, a dominant priestly caste (the Brahmins), and a development of the idea of Brahman as the eternal, impersonal Absolute Principle. *See also* **Hinduism.**

Buchmanism. *See* **Moral Re-Armament.**

Buddhism, one of the great Oriental religions. It arose against the background of Hinduism in north India in the 6th cent. B.C., its founder (real or legendary) being the Hindu prince Siddhartha Gautama, known as the Buddha or "Enlightened One". Distressed by the problem of human suffering from which even death allowed no escape—since Buddha accepted the Hindu doctrine of a cycle of lives—he left his palace and his beloved family to become a religious mendicant and ascetic, studying with limited success for six years the beliefs of Brahmin hermits and self-torturing recluses. After this long search he sat down under a tree (the Bo-tree) and finally came to understand the cause and release from suffering. The result of his meditations are enshrined in the "four noble truths" which are: (1) that all that lives experiences suffering; (2) suffering is caused by desire; (3) suffering ceases when desire is eradicated; (4) that it can be destroyed by following the "noble eightfold path" whose steps are: right views; right thought; right speech, plain and truthful; right conduct, including abstinence not only from immorality but also from taking life, whether human or animal; right livelihood, harming no one; right effort, always pressing on; right awareness of the past, the present, and the future; and lastly, right contemplation or meditation. The more man acquires merit by following these rules in his chain of lives, the sooner is *Nirvana* attained; he loses his individuality, not by annihilation, but "as the dewdrop slips into the shining sea," by merging with the universal life.

Buddhism teaches a way of liberation through ethics and meditation; A universal God plays no part in this religion, and in many Buddhist nations no word exists for the concept which was neither affirmed nor denied by Buddha himself but simply ignored. Nor did Buddha claim to be other than a man, although much superstition entered the religion at a later date; prayers were made to Buddha, ritual developed, sacred relics preserved under stupas, and the belief in a succession of Buddhas introduced; the sacred writings (*Tripitaka*) are divided into three parts;

for the layman, the monks, the philosophers. They were produced by devotees at three councils—the first held immediately after the death of Buddha at the age of 80, the last at the order of King Asoka in 244 B.C. The founder himself wrote nothing.

Buddhism spread to Sri Lanka, Nepal, Tibet, Mongolia, Indo-China, Myanmar (Burma), Thailand, China, and Japan, although on the whole losing influence in India. In Tibet, Buddhism developed into Lamaism (q.v.). In Sri Lanka and Burma it persisted in its pure form (the Theravada), while in China and Japan it developed into the Mahayana with its bodhisattvas and avatars. Today (1995) there are over 315 million Buddhists world-wide.

Bushido, the traditional code of honour of the Samurai or Japanese military caste corresponding to the European concept of knighthood and chivalry from which it took its separate origin in the 12th cent. Even today it is a potent influence among the upper classes, being based on the principles of simplicity, honesty, courage, and justice which together form a man's idea of personal honour.

C

Cabala, originally a collection of Jewish doctrines about the nature of the Universe, supposedly handed down by Moses to the Rabbis, which evolved into a kind of mystical interpretation of the Old Testament. Students of the history of religious belief have found its origins to be in fact extremely obscure, and some aspects appear to have been lifted from ancient Egyptian sources. Skilled Cabalists hold that the system contains a key to biblical interpretation based on the numerical values of the words and letters of the Scriptures which reveal hidden depths of meaning behind the allegorical Old Testament stories.

Calvinism, the branch of Protestantism founded basically (although preceded by Zwingli and others) by Jean Chauvin (1509–64), who was born in Noyon in Picardy. John Calvin, as he is usually called, from the Latin form of his name, Calvinius, provided in his *Institutions of the Christian Religion* the first logical definition and justification of Protestantism, thus becoming the intellectual leader of the Reformation as the older Martin Luther was its emotional instigator. The distinctive doctrine of Calvinism is its dogma of predestination which states that God has unalterably destined some souls to salvation to whom "efficacious grace and the gift of perseverance" is granted and others to eternal damnation. Calvinism, as defined in the Westminster Confession, is established in the Reformed or Presbyterian churches of France, Holland, Scotland, etc., as contrasted with the Lutheran churches, and its harsh but logical beliefs inspired the French Huguenots, the Dutch in their fight against Spanish Catholic domination, and the English Puritans. The rule set up under Calvin's influence in Geneva was marred by the burning at the stake of the anatomist Servetus for the heresy of "pantheism", or, as we should say, Unitarianism.

Perhaps its greatest single influence outside the Church was the result of Calvinist belief that to labour industriously was one of God's commands. This changed the mediaeval notions of the blessedness of poverty and the wickedness of usury, proclaimed that men should shun luxury and be thrifty, yet implied that financial success was a mark of God's favour. In this way it was related to the rise of capitalism either as cause or effect. Max Weber, the German sociologist, believed that Calvinism was a powerful incentive to, or even cause of, the rise of **capitalism** (q.v.): Marx, Sombart, and in England, Tawney, have asserted the reverse view—that Calvinism was a result of developing capitalism, being its ideological justification.

Capitalism is an economic system under which the means of production and distribution are owned by a relatively small section of society which runs them at its own discretion for private profit. There exists, on the other hand, a propertyless class of those who exist by the sale of their labour power. Capitalism arose towards the end of the 18th cent. in England where the early factory owners working with small-scale units naturally approved of free enterprise and free trade. But free enterprise has no necessary connection with capitalism; by the beginning of this century monopolies were developing and state protection against foreign competition was demanded. Capitalism is opposed by those who believe in socialism (q.v.), first, for the moral reasons that it leads to economic inequality and the exploitation of labour and the consuming public, and that public welfare rather than private profit should motivate the economic system; secondly, for the practical reason that capitalism leads to recurrent economic crises. Any major world economic crisis led to great hopes on the part of Marxists and Communists that capitalism was involved in its final death throes. It is worth commenting however, that the European war of the 1940s, the great depression of the 30s, the first world war and the Russian Revolution were also, in their turn, confidently held up by Communists as heralding capitalism's imminent collapse.

Cartomancy, the art of fortunes or predicting the future by playing cards or by the Tarot pack.

Catholicism. For those who are not Roman Catholics the term "Catholic" has two separate meanings. The more general refers to the whole body of Christians throughout the world, the more specific refers to a particular view of Christianity. In this latter sense the Church of England, the Orthodox Eastern Churches, and others consider themselves "Catholic" meaning that (a) they belong to Christ's Church as organised on an accepted basis of faith and order; (b) they insist on the necessity of "liturgical" worship through established forms (e.g., baptism, holy communion); (c) they emphasise the continuity of Christian tradition by the use of ancient creeds (e.g., the Apostles' Creed, the Nicene Creed) and regard the ministry as a succession (Apostolic succession) deriving from early practice. In this sense there is thought to be no necessary contradiction between Catholicism and Protestantism regarded as a renewal of the Church in the 16th cent. by an appeal to the Scriptures as interpreted by the early Fathers of the Church. This definition obviously excludes Quakers, Christian Scientists, and many Nonconformist sects. *See also* **Roman Catholic Church, J46.**

Characterology, the attempt made over many centuries to classify people into personality types on the basis of physical or psychological characteristics. The first attempt was made by Hippocrates in the 5th cent. B.C. who classified temperaments into the *sanguine* (or optimistic), the *melancholic*, the *choleric* (or aggressive), and the *phlegmatic* (or placid); these were supposed to result from the predominance of the following "humours" in the body: red blood, black bile, yellow bile, or phlegm respectively. Theophrastus, a pupil of Aristotle, described, with examples, thirty extreme types of personality (e.g. the talkative, the boorish, the miserly, etc.); these were basically literary and imaginative but about the same time "physiognomy" arose which attempted to interpret character from the face. Physiognomy became of importance again during the Renaissance and there are still those today who believe in it in spite of the fact that, broadly speaking, there is no connection whatever between facial features and personality (i.e. although it may be possible to tell from the features that a man is an idiot or some extreme abnormal type and some idea of character may be obtained from an individual's characteristic facial expressions, it is not possible to tell (as Johann Lavater, the best-known physiognomist of the late 18th cent. believed) from the shape of the nose, height of the brow, or dominance of the lower jaw, whether anyone is weak, intellectual or determined). The contention of the 19th cent. Italian criminologist Cesare Lombroso that criminals show typical facial characteristics— prominent cheekbones and jaw, slanting eyes, receding brow, large ears of a particular shape—was disproved by Karl Pearson early this century when he found that 3,000 criminals showed no major differences of features, carefully measured from a similar number of students at Oxford and Cambridge.

It has, however, been noted that people in general tend to be intellectual or emotional, inward- or outward-looking, and this observation is reflected in the classification of the Scottish psychologist, Alexander Bain (d. 1903), into intellectual, artistic, and practical; Nietzsche's Apollonian and Dionysian types; William James's "tender" and "toughminded"; and C. G. Jung's introvert and extrovert.

Some connection has been found between temperament and body-build. The German psychiatrist Ernst Kretschmer (1888–1964) showed that manic-depressive patients and normal people who are extroverted and tend to alternate in mood (as do manic-depressives to an exaggerated degree) were usually short and stout or thick-set in build; schizophrenics and normal people, who both show shyness, serious or introverted reactions, were usually tall and slender. The former of "pyknic" body-build are "cyclothyme" in temperament, the latter with "schizothyme" temperament are of two bodily types—the tall and thin or "asthenic" and the muscularly well-proportioned or "athletic". The American Sheldon has confirmed these observations on the whole and gone into further details. According to him the basic body types are: (1) *endomorphic* (rounded build), corresponding to Kretschmer's pyknic, normally associated with the *viscerotonic* temperament (relaxed, sociable); (2) *mesomorphic* (squarish, athletic build), normally associated with the *somatotonic* temperament (energetic, assertive); and (3) *ectomorphic* (linear build) normally associated with the *cerebrotonic* temperament (anxious, submissive, restless). Glandular and metabolic factors have considerable effect on human personality and also, to some extent, on physique. It is not too surprising, therefore, to find an association between body build (or "somatotype" as Sheldon termed it) and general mood. However, Sheldon's original clear-cut categories of body-type are no longer looked upon as reliable indicators of personality.

Chartism, a socialist movement in England (1837–55) which attempted to better the conditions of the working classes. Named after "The People's Charter" of Francis Place (1838), its programme demanded: (1) universal manhood suffrage; (2) vote by ballot; (3) equal electoral districts; (4) annual parliament; (5) payment of members; (6) abolition of their property qualifications. Chartism was supported by the Christian socialists (*q.v.*), J. F. D. Maurice (1805–72), and Charles Kingsley (1819–75) with certain qualifications. The movement, the first mass organisation of the industrial working class, had considerable influence on the evolution of socialist ideas in England. It is worth noting that its demands—with the exception of the unworkable "annual parliament"—have largely been met today, though at the time they were thought by many to be both outrageous and impossible. The movement failed at the time from internal divisions.

Chauvinism, a term applied to any excessive devotion to cause, particularly a patriotic or military one. The word is derived from Nicholas Chauvin whose excessive devotion to Napoleon made him a laughing-stock.

Chirognomy, the study of the shape of the hands and fingernails.

Chirology, the subject concerned with the hand as an indicator of psychological and medical significance. Chirology derives from an Oriental tradition concerning mental and physical healing and spirituality and as such encompasses many associated arts and studies of direct relevance to modern day living. Palmistry in the main is a crude folk art and does not attempt to understand or clarify its own teachings. The Cheirological Society was founded in 1889 by Katherine St. Hill to promote the systematic study of the hand as a serious subject worthy of scientific attention bereft of superstition and fakery. It still exists today and has members throughout the world.

Chiromancy, the study of lineal formations of the hand.

Chiropractic, the art of manipulation of the joints, in particular the spine, as a means of curing disease. Some qualified doctors employ its principles and, as with its near-neighbour osteopathy, it seems on occasions to be a useful complement to medical treatment.

Christadelphians, a religious denomination formed in the U.S.A. in the late 1840s by John Thomas, an Englishman. They strive to represent the simple apostolic faith of the 1st century and hold that the Scriptures are the wholly inspired, infallible Word of God. They believe in the mortality of mankind—the teaching of the immortality of the soul is not of Bible origin and that salvation is dependent of belief followed by a baptism of total immersion in water. They believe in the imminent, personal return of Jesus Christ to the earth to judge the living and dead and reward the righteous with Eternal life.

Christianity, the religion founded by Jesus Christ whose teaching is found in the New Testament's four Gospels. Simple as His creed may seem it soon became complicated by the various ways in which Christians interpreted it, and the differences within the early Church are reflected in the numerous Councils held to define truth from heresy. The Eastern Church of the Byzantine Empire from the 5th cent. onwards had differed in various ways from the See of Rome and by 1054 the breach became permanent. The 16th cent. Reformation was the other great break in the unity of the Church and, once Protestantism had given in effect the right to each man to interpret the Scriptures in his own way, the tendency to fragmentation increased so that, by 1650, there were no fewer than 180 sects, mostly dogmatic and intolerant towards each other. Today there are many more, some of which are mentioned in this section under the appropriate headings. Nevertheless there are signs today that the trend of disunity is being reversed. The modern ecumenical movement, which has its roots in the great missionary movement of the 19th cent., aims to bring about a reunion of Christendom by uniting Christians throughout the world on the simple basis of the acceptance of Jesus Christ as God and Saviour, *i.e.*, on the basis of Christian fellowship. The movement finds expression in the World Council of Churches (*q.v.*). The Christian life is expressed in the words of Christ: "Thou shalt love the Lord thy God with all thy heart and thy neighbour as thyself." For many it is the humanitarian side of Christianity that has meaning today; to accept responsibility for others, as well as for oneself. There are now (1995) an estimated 1,760,000,000 Christians world-wide.

Christian Science claims that it is a religion based on the words and works of Christ Jesus. It draws its authority from the Bible, and its teachings are set forth in *Science and Health with Key to the Scriptures* by Mary Baker Eddy (1821–1910) the discoverer and founder of Christian Science. A distinctive part of Christian Science is its healing of physical disease as well as sin by spiritual means.

The Church of Christ, Scientist, was founded in 1879 when 15 students of Mrs Eddy met with their teacher and voted to organize a church designed to commemorate the words and works of the Master, which should reinstate primitive Christianity and its lost element of healing.

A few years later the church took its present and permanent form as The Mother Church, The First Church of Christ, Scientist, in Boston, Massachusetts, which together with its branch churches and societies throughout the world, constitutes the Christian Science denomination. Now (1995) more than 100 years after its founding there are over 2,700 branches in 60 countries, as well as numerous groups not yet organized and about 300 organizations at universities and colleges.

Christian Socialism, a movement launched in 1848, a year of revolutions throughout the continent, by a group in England designed to commit the church to a programme of social reform. The leaders, notably J. F. D. Maurice, Charles Kingsley (both Anglican clergymen), and John Ludlow were deeply moved by the wretched conditions of the British working class and the two priests had, indeed, given active support to the

Chartist movement (q.v.). However, all insisted that socialism in its existing forms ignored the spiritual needs of mankind and must be tempered with Christianity. Tracts were written to expose the sweated industries, the consequences of unrestrained competition and the evils following the enclosure system; but, more concretely, Christian socialism fostered co-operative workshops and distributive societies based on those of the Rochdale pioneers, organised a working-man's college, and set up elementary classes for education. It also supported the emerging trade-union movement.

The traditions of Christian socialism have been carried on by the Fabian Society, by adherents of Guild Socialism, and by individuals who reject Marx's teaching of revolutionary change, and seek to bring it about by the methods of action through political parties, education, and encouragement of the unions. They believe that Christ's teachings can only be fully realised in a new society since Christianity implies social responsibility, and material factors are admitted to have an important bearing on the ability to lead a truly religious life.

Church of England. There is some evidence of possible continuity with the Christianity of Roman Britain, but in the main the Church derives from the fusion of the ancient Celtic church with the missionary church of St. Augustine, who founded the See of Canterbury in A.D. 597. To archbishop Theodore in 673 is ascribed its organisation in dioceses with settled boundaries, and in parishes. St. Augustine's church was in communion with Rome from the first, but the Church of England was not brought within papal jurisdiction until after the Norman conquest, and was at no time under the complete domination of Rome. It remains the Catholic Church of England without break of continuity, but during the Reformation the royal supremacy was accepted and that of the pope repudiated. It is the Established Church (i.e., the official church of the realm), crowns the sovereign, and its archbishops and bishops in the House of Lords can act as a kind of "conscience of the state" at every stage of legislation. The Church is organised in two ecclesiastical provinces (Canterbury and York) and 43 dioceses. Its traditional forms of worship are embodied in the Book of Common Prayer, but the Alternative Service Book of 1980 is now widely used. In 1992, the proportion of the public attending Sunday services dropped to 23 per thousand.

In November 1992, the General Synod finally accepted the ordination of women priests, despite bitter opposition from traditionalists. The first 32 women priests were ordained on 12 March 1994 in Bristol Cathedral. The first 42 Anglican women priests in Scotland were ordained in the Scottish Episcopal Church in December 1994. Meanwhile the Anglican Church faces a financial crisis, with its assets having been severely eroded in the 1980s. The Anglican Church is currently (1995) reviewing its wedding ban on divorcees.

The **Anglican Communion** comprises the churches in all parts of the world which are in communion with the Church of England. All the bishops of the Anglican Communion meet every ten years in the Lambeth Conference (first held in 1867), over which the Archbishop of Canterbury by custom presides as *primus inter pares*. At the 1968 Conference observers and laymen were admitted for the first time. The 1988 Conference paved the way for the eventual consecration of women bishops. The next Conference will meet in 1998.

Church of Scotland, the established national church of Scotland, presbyterian in constitution, and governed by a hierarchy of courts—the kirk-sessions, the presbyteries, the synods, and the General Assembly. *See* **Presbyterianism.**

Clairvoyance. *See* **Telepathy.**

Collectivism. The theory of the collective ownership or control of all the means of production, and especially of the land, by the whole community or state, i.e. the people collectively, for the benefit of the people as a whole. The term has also acquired a broader sense, to denote the view that the individual is subordinate to the social collectivity. An influential expression of collectivist ideas can be found in Rousseau's *Du contrat social* (1762). It is an important theme in Hegel and Marx, and has

been expressed in such movements as socialism, communism and fascism. Collectivism is to be contrasted with individualism (q.v.).

Colonialism. Colonialism refers to the kind of imperialism practised by European countries in for example Africa and S.E. Asia, where the colonised country was allowed to have partially autonomous legal and social institutions, while the mother country retained supreme power, and the colonial community had social and political rights denied to the natives. "Neo-colonialism" means the cultural and economic infiltration of developing countries by manipulation of market forces. *See also* **Imperialism.**

Communism, ideally refers to the type of society in which all property belongs to the community and social life is based on the principle "from each according to his ability, to each according to his needs." There would be public ownership of all enterprises and all goods would be free. Since no such society as yet exists, the word in practice refers to the attempt to achieve such a society by initially overthrowing the capitalist system and establishing a dictatorship of the proletariat (Marx identified the dictatorship with a democratic constitution). Communists believe that their first task is the establishment of socialism under which there remain class distinctions, private property to some extent, and differences between manual and brain workers. The state is regulated on the basis "from each according to his ability, to each according to his work". Lenin applied Marx's analysis to the new conditions which had arisen in 20th-cent. capitalist society. Marxism–Leninism develops continuously with practice since failure to apply its basic principles to changed circumstances and times would result in errors of dogmatism. Mao Tse-tung worked out the techniques of revolutionary action appropriate to China; Che Guevara the guerrilla tactics appropriate to the peasants of Latin America. His counsel "It is not necessary to wait until conditions for making revolution exist; the insurrection can create them", was the opposite of Mao Tse-tung's "Engage in no battle you are not sure of winning", and Lenin's "Never play with insurrection". Two fundamental principles of communism are (1) peaceful co-existence between countries of different social systems, and (2) the class struggle between oppressed and oppressing classes and between oppressed and oppressor nations. Maoism, for example, holds that it is a mistake to lay one-sided stress on peaceful transition towards socialism otherwise the revolutionary will of the proletariat becomes passive and unprepared politically and organisationally for the tasks ahead.

In Russia the civil war developed *after* the revolution; in China the communists fought their civil war *before* they seized power: the Yugoslav partisans won their own guerrilla war *during* their stand against the fascist powers—differences which had important political consequences. Russia suffered three decades of isolationism and totalitarian suppression ("an isolated and besieged fortress") before the advent of Gorbachev heralded a new openness (*glasnost*) in Soviet politics. Mao Tse-tung held to the orthodox Leninist view about capitalism and communism, regarded détente as a dangerous illusion, and compromise and "revisionism" as a fatal error. The ideological dispute between these two great communist powers which lasted from the '60s to the '80s ended with an improvement in inter-party relations, and a movement towards détente took place. The dramatic collapse of Communism in Eastern Europe during 1989 and the collapse of the Soviet Union itself in 1991 left only China, Cuba, Vietnam and North Korea as communist states (at least in theory) in the 1990s. *See also* **Maoism, Marxism, Trotskyism** and **Section C.**

Confucianism. Confucius (Latinised form of K'ung-Fo-tzu) was born in 551 B.C. in the feudal state of Lu in modern Shantung province. He was thus a contemporary of Buddha, although nobody could have been more dissimilar. Where Buddha was metaphysical in his thought, Confucius was practical; Buddha was original, Confucius had hardly an original idea in his head; Buddha wanted to convert individuals to an other-worldly philosophy,

Confucius wanted to reform the feudal governments of his time, believing that in this way their subjects would be made happier. Other religions have in their time, been revolutionary; Confucius was a conservative who wanted to bring back a golden age from the past. The only respect in which Confucius agreed with the Buddha was that neither was particularly interested in the supernatural.

Much of his time was spent in going from the court of one feudal lord to another trying to impress them by his example. For he suffered from the curious belief that the example set by the ruler influences his subjects. He made much of etiquette, trembling and speaking in low tones and behaving with "lofty courtesy" to his inferiors. Promoting the idea of "the golden mean", he was not impressed by heroic deeds or unusual people, and was greatly displeased when he heard that a truthful son had reported that his father had stolen a sheep: "Those who are upright", he said, "are different from this; the father conceals the misconduct of the son, and the son conceals the misconduct of the father." One feels that Confucius would have felt not at all out of place in an English public school. Virtue brings its own reward in this world, ceremonial is important, politeness when universal would reduce jealousy and quarrels; "reverence the spirits but keep them far off." Destiny decides to what class a man shall belong, and as destiny is but another name for Nature prayer is unnecessary, for once having received his destiny, a man can demand and obtain from Nature what he chooses, his own will decides.

Congregationalists, the oldest sect of Nonconformists who hold that each church should be independent of external ecclesiastical authority. They took their origin from the Brownists of Elizabeth's days. Robert Browne (c. 1550–c. 1633), an Anglican clergyman, who had come to reject bishops, was forced with his followers to seek refuge, first in Holland and then in Scotland where he was imprisoned by the Kirk. In later life he changed his views and is disowned by Congregationalists because of his reversion to Anglicanism. His former views were spread by Henry Barrow and John Greenwood who, under an Act passed in 1592 "for the punishment of persons obstinately refusing to come to church" (and largely designed for the suppression of this sect), were hanged at Tyburn. They had preached (a) that the only head of the church is Jesus Christ; (b) that, contrary to Elizabethan doctrine, the church had no relationship to the state; (c) that the

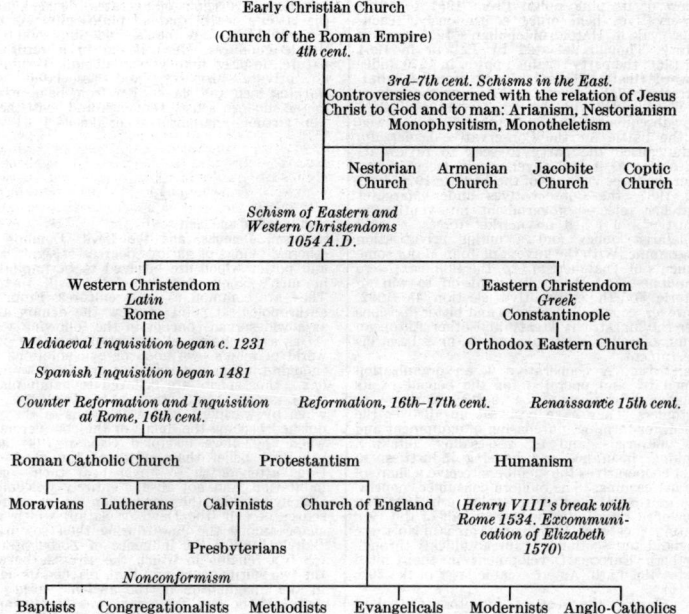

Early Christian Church

(Church of the Roman Empire)
4th cent.

3rd–7th cent. Schisms in the East.
Controversies concerned with the relation of Jesus
Christ to God and to man: Arianism, Nestorianism
Monophysitism, Monotheletism

| Nestorian Church | Armenian Church | Jacobite Church | Coptic Church |

*Schism of Eastern and
Western Christendoms
1054 A.D.*

Western Christendom
Latin
Rome

Eastern Christendom
Greek
Constantinople

Mediaeval Inquisition began c. 1231

Orthodox Eastern Church

Spanish Inquisition began 1481

*Counter Reformation and Inquisition
at Rome, 16th cent.*   *Reformation, 16th–17th cent.*   *Renaissance 15th cent.*

Roman Catholic Church   Protestantism   Humanism

Moravians   Lutherans   Calvinists   Church of England   (*Henry VIII's break with
Rome 1534. Excommunication of Elizabeth
1570*)

Presbyterians

Nonconformism

Baptists   Congregationalists   Methodists   Evangelicals   Modernists   Anglo-Catholics only statute-book was the Bible whereas the Articles of Religion and Book of Common Prayer were mere Acts of Parliament; (d) that each congregation of believers was independent and had the power of choosing its own ministers. The body fled once more to Holland and were among the Pilgrims who set sail in the *Mayflower* for America in 1620 whilst those who remained were joined by Puritans fleeing from Charles I. They became free once more to live in England under the Commonwealth only to be repressed again under Charles II. Finally full liberty of worship was granted under William III. In 1833 the Congregational Union of England and Wales was formed which had no legislative power. It had issued a Declaration of Faith by which no minister was bound· he was responsible to his own church and to nobody else. The sect is widespread both in Britain and the U.S.A. where it is held in special honour because of its connection with the Pilgrim Fathers. In 1972 the Congregational Church in England and Wales and the Presbyterian Church of England united to form the United Reformed Church. Those who did not join comprise the Congregational Federation.

Conservatism. The term "Conservative" came into general use after 1834 in place of the older name of "Tory". The modern Conservative Party has its origins in the period of "Tory Democracy" introduced by Disraeli between 1874 and 1880. Originally the party of church, aristocracy and landed gentry, Conservatism has been increasingly supported since the turn of the century by large business interests. Under Baldwin, Conservative-dominated administration held office for much of the inter-war period. The 1945 Labour victory caused the Conservative Party to undertake a basic review of its philosophy. From 1951 to 1964, Conservatives held office continuously, reaching a peak in Harold Macmillan's 1959 election victory. Though defeated by Labour in 1964 and 1966, the party regained power in 1970 under Edward Heath. The subsequent troubled administration, plagued with problems on the industrial front, ended with the February 1974 election. The subsequent defeat in October 1974, followed by the battle for the Conservative leadership, again caused the party to seek to review its philosophy as it had developed in recent years. After the three victories of the party in 1979, 1983 and 1987, the Conservatives under Margaret Thatcher rejected government intervention in industry and relied on market forces, a rigid monetarist policy and a major privatisation programme. With the advent of John Major some elements of Thatcherism (*e.g.* the Poll Tax) were abandoned and the party went on to win an historic fourth consecutive election in 1992. However, economic problems and bitter divisions over the Maastricht Treaty and other European issues, as well as electoral reverses, have beset his government.

Cooperativism. A cooperative is an organization owned by and operated for the benefit of its members, who may be either workers or customers. They have been set up all over the world, for farming, purchasing of equipment and raw materials, and in wholesaling, retailing, banking, insurance and housing industries. In most cooperatives the members receive a share of the net earnings. The modern consumer cooperative movement started in Rochdale in 1844 and developed rapidly in the second half of the 19th century, mostly in the industrial areas of Northern England and Scotland. It spread quickly through northern Europe. Development in the United States and Latin America came later in the 20th century.

Coptic Church, the sect of Egyptian Christians who, holding "Monophysite" opinions (*i.e.,* refusing to grant the two natures, God and Man, of Christ), were declared heretical by the Council of Chalcedon in 451. They practise circumcision and have dietary laws. Their language is a direct descendant of ancient Egyptian. Like the Armenians, they are regarded as an heretical branch of Eastern Christianity. Their religious head is the patriarch of Alexandria. The rise of Islamic fundamentalism threatens Egypt's 6 million Copts.

Counter-reformation. A movement in the 16th and 17th centuries in Europe, by which the Roman Catholic church reformed itself, defined its doctrines, strengthened its discipline and halted the advance of Protestantism. The Council of Trent (1545–1563) aimed at removing abuses within the church and defining Catholic thought in the debate with Protestantism. New, more active religious orders were founded, in particular the Jesuits (1534). The greater control exercised over church doctrine is also seen in the setting up of the Inquisition and an Index of Prohibited Books.

Creationism. The theory which attributes the origin of matter, the different species of plants and animals, *etc.,* to "special creation" out of nothing by a divinity. It is this doctrine which fundamentalist Christians have opposed to the evolutionary theories of Darwin, which have come to be accepted by most scientists since the publication of *The Origin of Species* in 1859. An attempt was made in the 1980s in the United States to have creationism taught alongside evolution, but failed in the U.S. Supreme Court. Creationism has no respectability as a scientific theory.

A second slightly older meaning of the term is in reference to the theory that God creates a soul for every being born. Aquinas believed that the soul was created out of nothing. This is to be contrasted with Traducianism, the doctrine that souls are generated from souls when and as bodies are generated from bodies.

Cynics, a school of philosophy founded in the time of Alexander the Great by Diogenes. Choosing to live like a dog by rejecting all conventions of religion, manners, or decency, and allegedly living in a tub. Diogenes unwittingly brought on his school the title "Cynic", meaning not "cynical", as the word is understood today, but "canine". His teacher, Antisthenes, who had been a disciple of Socrates, decided, after the latter's death, that all philosophy was useless quibbling and man's sole aim should be simple goodness. He believed in a return to nature, despised luxury, wanted no government, no private property, and associated with working men and slaves. Far from being cynics in the modern sense, Diogenes and Antisthenes were virtuous anarchists rather like old Tolstoy.

D

Deism. *See* **God and Man**.

Demonism, Demons, and the Devil. Demons are ethereal beings of various degrees of significance and power which are believed to be implicated in men's good, but especially evil, fortune. They are common to most cultures. From the anthropological point of view the demon arose as a widespread concept in the following ways: (1) as a psychological projection into the outer world of man's own good or evil emotions and thoughts; (2) as a survival of primitive animism (*q.v.*), thus spirits are believed to haunt places, trees, stones, and other natural objects; (3) when by warlike invasion the gods of the vanquished become the devils of the conquerors (as when the Jews occupied Canaan); (4) as a primitive belief that spirits of the dead continue after death to hover near their former habitation, and not always entirely welcome to the living; (5) the conception of a supreme source of evil (the Devil or Satan) which took shape among the Jews during their sojourn in Babylon under the influence of Zoroastrianism (*q.v.*), a religion in which the struggle between the two spirits, Good and Evil, reached its height in the imagination of the ancient world. The Satan of the Old Testament was first regarded as one of God's servants (in the Book of Job he goes up and down the earth to see whether God's commands are obeyed), but when the Jews returned from their captivity he had become identified with Ahriman, the spirit of evil, who was in continual conflict with Ahursa Mazda, the spirit of good. The primitive mind ascribed both good and evil to one power alone; the division into God and the Devil, priest and witch, belongs to a higher stage of civilisation. The worship of evil itself, or of its personification in Satan, is a curious practice which seems to have developed hand-in-hand with Christianity and to have received steady support from a small but measurable minority. Many of the ceremonies involved in Satanism or in the so-called Black Mass appear to have been no more than opportunities for sexual excesses of one kind or another—such indulgences being traditionally barred to devout Christians. The alleged power of sex as a form of magic was propagated by the talented but rather mad poet, Aleister Crowley (1875–1947). The self-styled "wickedest man in the world", Crowley was a pathetic rather than shocking figure and died a drug addict.

Determinism and Free-will. The question of whether man is, or is not, free to mould his own destiny is one which has exercised the minds of philosophers since Greek mythology conceived of the Fates as weaving a web of destiny from which no man can free himself. Socrates emphasised that man could through knowledge influence his destiny whilst ignorance made him the plaything of fate; Plato went further in pointing out that man can, and does, defeat the purposes of the universe and its divine Creator. It is our duty to live a good life, but we can live a foolish and wicked one if we chose. Aristotle wrote "Virtue is a disposition or habit involving deliberate purpose or choice". If this were not so morality would be a sham.

The Problem for Theology. The last of the great philosophers of Antiquity and one of the great influences in moulding Catholic theology was Plotinus (c. 204–70). Soul, he taught, is free, but once enmeshed in the body loses its freedom in the life of sense. Nevertheless, man is free to turn away from sensuality and towards God who is perfect freedom; for even when incarnated in matter the soul does not entirely lose the ability to rescue itself. This conception was carried over into the beliefs of the early Christian Apologists because it appeared to be in line with the teaching of Jesus that He had come to save man from sin. Sin implies guilt, and guilt implies the freedom to act otherwise; furthermore an all-good God cannot be responsible for the sin in the world which must be man's responsiblity and this again implies freedom. Pelagius (c. 355–c. 425), a Welsh priest, not only believed in free-will but questioning the doctrine of original sin, said that when men act righteously it is through their own moral effort, and God rewards them for their virtues in heaven. This belief became fairly widespread and was declared a heresy by the Church, being attacked notably by St. Augustine (354–430), a contemporary of Pelagius, who believed in predestination—that, since the sin of Adam, God had chosen who in all future history would be saved and who damned. This represents one tradition in Christianity: the determinism which leads to Calvinism (q.v.). St. Thomas Aquinas (1227–74), the greatest figure of scholasticism and one of the principal saints in the Roman Catholic Church, compromised between the two positions in the sense that, believing man to be free, he yet held that Adam's sin was transmitted to all mankind and only divine grace can bring salvation. But even when God wishes to bestow this salvation, the human will must co-operate. God foresees that some will not accept the offer of grace and predestines them to eternal punishment.

The Problem for Philosophy. With the Renaissance, thinkers began to free themselves from the domination of the Church and so study the world objectively and freely without preconceptions. But the more man turned to science, the more he discovered that the world was ruled by apparently inexorable laws and, since the scientist must believe that every event has a cause, he was led back to determinism. Man as part of the universe was subject to law too and all that existed was a vast machine. Francis Bacon (1561–1626) separated the fields of religion and science but left man subject completely to the will of God. Thomas Hobbes (1588–1679) was a rigid determinist and materialist although, having had trouble with the church in France whence, as a royalist, he had fled, he took care to announce that the Christian God is the Prime Mover.

Modern philosophy begins with René Descartes (1596–1650), a Frenchman who tried to reconcile the mechanical scientific universe of his time with the spiritual need for freedom. He did this by separating completely mind and body; the former, he said, is free, the latter completely determined. But, by admitting that the will can produce states of body, he was left with the problem of how this could happen—a problem which the so-called Occasionists solved to their own satisfaction by stating that the will is free and God so arranges the universe that what a person wills happens. Baruch Spinoza (1632–77), a Dutch Jew whose independence of thought had led to his excommunication from the Amsterdam Synagogue in 1656, was a complete determinist. He asserted that God and Nature are one, everything that happens is a manifestation of God's inscrutable nature, and it is logically impossible that things could be other than they are. Thus both Hobbes and Spinoza were determinists for entirely opposed reasons. The former as a materialist, the latter because he believed in the absolute perfection and universality of God. Yet the great religious mystic and mathematician Blaise Pascal (1623–62) held that, no matter what reason and cold logic may indicate we *know* from direct religious experience that we are free. John Calvin (1509–64) and Martin Luther (1483–1546) were both determinists. *See* **Calvinism, Lutheranism**.

To the more practical British philosophers, John Locke (1632–1704) and David Hume (1711–76), free-will was related to personality. Locke believed that God had implanted in each individual certain desires and these determine the will; the desires are already there, but we use our will to satisfy them. Hume argued that a man's behaviour is the necessary result of his character and if he had a different character he would act otherwise. Accordingly, when a man's actions arise from his own nature and desires he is free. He is not free when external events compel him to act otherwise (e.g., if he strikes another because his own nature is such he is free as he is not if he is compelled to do so against his desire). Leibnitz (1646–1716), although as a German metaphysical philosopher holding very different general views, said much the same thing—that choice is simply selecting the desire that is strongest. But most of the 18th cent. thinkers after Voltaire, with the great exceptions of Rousseau and the later German philosophers Kant, Fichte, Schopenhauer, and Hegel, who were initially influenced by him, accepted determinism. Rousseau (1712–78) began to stem the tide by his declaration that man is a free soul striving to remain free and only prevented from being so by society and the cold science which stifles his feeling heart. Once again the will became important as Kant (1724–1804) asserted that belief in freedom is a moral necessity although it cannot be proved by reason; the moral nature of man shows that there is a "transcendental" world beyond the senses where freedom applies. Fichte and Schelling found freedom in the Absolute ego or God, of whom each individual was part and thus also free. Hegel (1770–1831) saw the whole universe as evolving towards self-awareness and freedom in man although this could only be fully realised in a society that makes for freedom. Even God himself only attains full consciousness and self-realisation through the minds of such individuals as are free. This is the goal of the dialectical process. (*See* **Dialectical Materialism**.)

The Scientist's View. For the scientist the law of cause and effect is a useful hypothesis since, by and large, it is necessary for him to assume that all events are caused. Nevertheless the modern tendency is to think in terms of statistical probability rather than relentless mechanistic causality, and, although the free-will problem does not concern the scientist as such, it is clear that freedom and determinism (assuming the terms to have any meaning at all) are not necessarily opposed. In sociology, for example, we *know* that certain actions will produce certain results upon the behaviour of people in general, e.g., that raising the bank rate will discourage business expansion. But this does not mean that Mr. Brown who decides in the circumstances not to add a new wing to his factory is not using his free-will. Even in the case of atoms, as Dr. Bronowski has pointed out, the observed results of allowing gas under pressure in a cylinder to rush out occur because most of the atoms are "obeying" the scientific "law" relating to such situations. But this does not mean that some atoms are not busy rushing across the stream or even against it—they are, but the general tendency is outwards and that is what we note. Lastly, the modern philosophical school of Logical Analysis would probably ask, not whether Free-will or Determinism is the true belief, but whether the question has any meaning. For what scientific experiment could we set up to prove one or the other true? The reader will note that some of the philosophers mentioned above are using the words to mean quite different concepts.

Dialectical Materialism, the combination of Hegel's dialectic method with a materialist philosophy produced by Karl Marx (1818–83) and his friend Friedrich Engels (1820–95). It is the philosophical basis of **Marxism** (q.v.) and **Communism** (q.v.) "Dialectic" to the ancient Greek philosophers meant a kind of dialogue or conversation, as used particularly by Socrates, in which philosophical disputes were resolved by a series of successive contradictions: a thesis is put forward and the opposing side holds its contradiction or antithesis until in the course of argument a synthesis is reached in which the conflicting ideas are resolved.

From Thesis through Antithesis to Synthesis. Hegel in the 19th cent. put forward the view that this process applies to the course of nature and history as they strive towards the perfect state. But to him, as to the Greeks, the conflict was in the field of ideas. The "universal reason" behind events works through the ideas held by a particular society until they are challenged by those of another which supersedes them and in turn, usually by war, becomes the agent of universal reason until the arrival of a new challenger. Hegel therefore regarded war as an instrument of progress and his Prussian compatriots found no difficulty in identifying their own state as the new agent of progress by universal conquest. Feuerbach, Lassalle, and other early socialists were impressed by some of Hegel's ideas: *e.g.*, that societies evolved (with the assumption that finally their own ideal society would be achieved) and that truth, morals, and concepts were relative so that a type of society that was "good" at one time was not necessarily so at another. But Marx and Engels in effect turned Hegel upside-down, accepted his dialectic but rejected his belief that ideas were the motive force. On the contrary, they said, ideas are determined by social and economic change as a result of materialistic forces. (*See* **Calvinism**, where it is pointed out that the Marxist view is not that Calvin changed men's economic ideas but rather that a developing capitalism unconsciously changed his.) The historical materialism of Marxism purports to show that the inexorable dialectic determines that feudalism is displaced by capitalism and capitalism by creating a proletariat (its antithesis) inevitably leads to socialism and a classless society. The state, as a tool of the dominant class, withers away. Dialectical materialism is applied in all spheres. As a philosophy there is little to be said for it save that it has shown us the close dependence of man's thoughts upon current material and social conditions. But as a battle-cry or a rationalisation of Marxism it wields immense power over the minds of men. *See* **Marxism.**

Dianetics. *See* **Scientology.**

Diggers, one of the many sects which flourished under the Commonwealth (others were the Muggletonians, the Levellers, the Millennarians, and the Fifth Monarchy Men), so-called because they attempted to dig (*i.e.* cultivate) untilled land. Gerrard Winstanley, a profoundly religious man, and leader of the Diggers, believed in the economic and social equality of man and castigated the clergy for upholding the class structure of society. In his book *The True Leveller's Standard Advanced* (1649) he wrote: "Every day poor people are forced to work for fourpence a day, though corn is dear. And yet the tithing priest stops their mouth and tells them that 'inward satisfaction of mind' was meant by the declaration 'the poor shall inherit the earth.' I tell you, the Scripture is to be really and materially fulfilled. You jeer at the name 'Leveller'; I tell you Jesus Christ is the Head Leveller".

Doukhobors, a religious sect of Russian origin, founded by a Prussian sergeant at Kharkov in the middle of the 18th cent., and now mainly settled in Canada. Like many other sects they belong to that type of Christianity which seeks direct communication with God and such bodies tend to have certain traits in common, such as belief in the "inner light", opposition to war and authority in general, and often ecstasies which show themselves in physical ways such as shaking, speaking in strange tongues (glossolalia), and other forms of what to the unbeliever seem mass hysteria. Liturgy, ritual, or ceremony is non-existent. The Doukhobors were persecuted in Tsarist Russia, but in 1898 Tolstoy used his influence to have them removed to Canada where the government granted them uninhabited land in what is now Saskatchewan.

Dowsing. *See* **Radiesthesia.**

Druidism, the religion of Celtic Britain and Gaul of which Druids were the priesthood. They were finally wiped out by the Roman general Suetonius Paulinus about A.D. 58 in their last stronghold, the island of Anglesey. There are two sources of our present beliefs in Druidism: (1) the brief and factual records of the Romans, notably Pliny and Julius Caesar, which tell us that they worshipped in sacred oak groves and presumably practised a religion doing reverence to the powers of nature which must have had its roots in early stone age times and had many cruel rites, *e.g.*, human sacrifice; (2) the beliefs put forward by William Stukeley, an amateur antiquarian who from 1718 did valuable work by his studies of the stone circles at Stonehenge and Avebury. However, influenced by the Romantic movement, he later put forward the most extravagant theories which unfortunately are those popularly accepted by those without archaeological knowledge today. Stonehenge and Avebury were depicted as the temples of the "white-haired Druid bard sublime" and an attempt was made to tie up Druidism with early Christianity, above all with the concept of the Trinity. In fact, these circles have no connection with the Druids. They may have made ceremonial use of them but recent evidence suggests that the megalithic stones at Stonehenge belong to a Bronze Age culture (2100–1600 B.C.). Nor have Druidism and Christianity any relationship. Almost nothing is known of the religion.

Dualism, any philosophical or theological theory which implies that the universe has a double nature, notably Plato's distinction between appearance and reality, soul and body, ideas and material objects, reason and the evidence of the senses, which infers that behind the world as we perceive it there lies an "ideal" world which is more "real" than that of mere appearance. In religions such as Zoroastrianism or the Gnostic and Manichaeism heresies, it was believed that the universe was ruled by good and evil "principles"—in effect that there was a good God and a bad one. In psychology, dualism refers to the philosophical theories which believe mind and body to be separate entities. The opposite of dualism is monism which asserts the essential unity of the substance of the universe.

An essential problem in the dualistic view lies in the question as to how and where the two separate and distinct properties of the universe interact. Where, for example, does the "mind" actually mesh with the physical mechanics of the brain and body—where does the ghost sit in his machine? Descartes decided that mind and body must interact somewhere and he selected the pineal gland (an apparently functionless part of the brain) as the spot. But this did nothing to explain how two *totally different* aspects of nature can possibly influence each other, and today most philosophers and psychologists reject dualistic views of life and personality as posing more problems than they solve. *See also* **Psychology, Occam's Razor.**

E

Ecomovement. In the early 1970s widespread publicity was for the first time given to the urgent warnings of ecologists that the current exponential increase in (a) world population, (b) depletion of natural resources, and (c) pollution of the environment could not continue without global catastrophe. The most significant single event in the evolution of what is now being known as the "ecomovement" was probably the publication of the Club of Rome's paper on *The Limits to Growth*. From this sprang a movement, unfortunately initially drawn only from the middle class and better educated, which aimed to reduce environmental pollution, the extravagances of advertising and needless waste of natural resources. Its first campaigns were directed against such obvious targets as disposable glass bottles and unnecessary packaging and wrapping in shops and supermarkets. The ecomovement also protests against industrial firms which pollute rivers and seas and against aircraft noise and waste in general. Its early campaigns were greeted with some derision but have achieved dramatic point with the world pollution and economic crises which developed towards the end of the 1980s.

Ecumenism, a world movement which springs from the Christian belief that all men are brothers and that the Christian Church should be re-structured to give reality to the belief. Christ's church exists not to serve its own members, but for the service of the whole world. Some see the answer in a united church of a federal type (unity in diversity), others in an organic structure with one set of rules. The period since the convening of the Second Vatican Council by Pope John has been one of fervent discussion among Christian theologians with the aim of promoting Christian unity. *See* **World Council of Churches.**

Education. Education was no great problem to primitive man, but as societies became more complex people began to ask themselves such questions as: *What* should young people be taught? *How* should they be taught? Should the aim of their education be to bring out their individual qualities or rather to make them good servants of the state?

The first teachers were priests who knew most about the traditions, customs, and lore of their societies and thus the first schools were in religious meeting places. This was notably true of the Jews who learned from the rabbis in the synagogue.

The Greeks. We begin, as always, with the Greeks whose city-states, based on slavery, educated men (not women) for the sort of life described in Plato's *Dialogues*—the leisured life of gentlemen arguing the problems of the universe at their banquets or in the market-place. This made it necessary to learn debate and oratory (or rhetoric) especially for those who proposed to take up politics. The Sophist philosophy taught the need to build up convincing arguments in a persuasive manner, to learn the rules of logic and master the laws and customs of the Athenians, and to know the literature of the past so that illustrations might be drawn from it. These strolling philosophers who taught for a fee were individualists showing the student how to advance himself at all costs within his community.

Socrates had a more ethical approach, believing that education was good in itself, made a man happier and a better citizen, and emphasised his position as a member of a group. His method of teaching, the dialectic or "Socratic" method, involved argument and discussion rather than overwhelming others by rhetoric and is briefly mentioned under **Dialectical Materialism** (*q.v.*). Today this method is increasingly used in adult education where a lecture is followed by a period of discussion in which both lecturer and audience participate; for psychologists have shown that people accept ideas more readily when conviction arises through their own arguments than when they are passively thrust down their throats.

Socrates' pupil Plato produced in his book *The Republic* one of the first comprehensive systems of education and vocational selection. Believing that essentially men have very different and unequal abilities he considered that in an idealistic or utopian society they should be put into social classes corresponding to these differences, and suggested the following method: (1) For the first 18 years of a boy's life he should be taught gymnastics and sports, playing and singing music, reading and writing, a knowledge of literature, and if he passed this course sent on to the next stage; those who failed were to become tradesmen and merchants. (2) From 18–20 those successful in the first course were to be given two years of cadet training, the ones thought incapable of further education being placed in the military class as soldiers. (3) The remainder, who were to become the leaders of society, proceeded with advanced studies in philosophy, mathematics, science, and art. Such education was to be a state concern, state supported and controlled, selecting men and training them for service in the state according to their abilities.

Plato's pupil Aristotle even suggested that the state should determine shortly after birth which children should be allowed to live and destroy the physically or mentally handicapped; that marriage should be state-controlled to ensure desirable offspring. However, in their time the leisured and individualistic Sophists held the field and few accepted the educational views of Plato or his pupil.

Rome. The Romans were not philosophers and most of their culture came from Greece. Administration was their chief aptitude and Quintilian (A.D. *c.* 35–*c.* 95) based his higher education on the earlier classical tuition in public speaking, but he is important for emphasising the training of character and for his humanistic approach to the method of teaching that caused his *Institutio oratoria* to be influential for centuries later—indeed one might almost say up to the time of the great Dr. Arnold of Rugby. Education, he believed, should begin early but one must "take care that the child not old enough to love his studies does not come to hate them" by premature forcing; studies must be made pleasant and interesting and students encouraged by praise rather than discouraged when they sometimes fail; play is to be approved of as a sign of a lively disposition and because gloomy, depressed children are not likely to be good students; corporal punishment should never be used because "it is an insult as you will realise if you imagine it yourself". The world became interested not in *what* he taught but *how* he taught it; he was the pioneer of humanistic education and character-training from Vittorino d. Feltre (1378–1446) of Mantua, through Milton and Pope who commended his works to the modern educationists who have studied their pupils as well as their books.

The Middle Ages: The Religious View. With the development of Christianity education once more became a religious problem. The earliest converts had to be taught Christian doctrine and were given instruction in "catechumenal" schools before admission to the group, but as the religion came increasingly into contact with other religions or heresies a more serious training was necessary, and from these newer "catechetical" schools, where the method used was the catechism (*i.e.*, question and answer as known to all Presbyterian children today), the Apologists arose among whom were Clement of Alexandria and the great Origen. From this time education became an instrument of the church and in 529 the Emperor Justinian ordered all pagan schools to be closed.

As typical of the best in mediaeval education whilst the lamp of civilisation burned low during the Dark Ages, after the fall of Roman power, and survived only in the monasteries, we may mention St. Benedict (*c.* 480–*c.* 547) of Monte Cassino. There, in southern Italy, a rule was established which became a part of monastic life in general. Monastic schools were originally intended for the training of would-be monks, but later others were admitted who simply wanted some education; thus two types of school developed one for the *interni* and the other for *externi* or external pupils. Originally studies were merely reading in order to study the Bible, writing to copy the sacred books, and sufficient calculation to be able to work out the advent of holy days or festivals. But by the end of the 6th cent. the "seven liberal arts" (grammar, rhetoric, dialectic, arithmetic, geometry, music, and astronomy) were added.

The Renaissance. The close of the Middle Ages saw the development of two types of secular school. One came with the rise of the new merchant class and the skilled trader whose "guilds" or early trade unions established schools to train young men for their trades but ultimately gave rise to burgher or town schools; the other was the court school founded and supported by the wealthy rulers of the Italian cities—Vittorio da Feltre (mentioned above) presided over the most famous at Mantua.

These Renaissance developments are parallelled in northern Europe by the Protestant reformers who, having with Martin Luther held that everyone should know how to read his Bible in order to interpret it in his own way, were logically committed to popular education, compulsory and universal. In theory this was intended for biblical study, but writing, arithmetic, and other elementary subjects were taught and Luther said that, even if heaven and hell did not exist, education was important. Universal education is a Protestant conception.

Views of Philosophers. From this period onwards people were free to put forward any ideas about education, foolish or otherwise, and to create their own types of school. Of English philosophers who theorised about, but did not practise, education we may mention the rationalist Francis Bacon (1561–1626) who saw learning as the dissipation of all prejudices and the collection of concrete facts; the materialist and totalitarian Hobbes (1588–1679) who, as a royalist, believed that the right to determine the kind of education fit for his subjects is one of the absolute rights of the sovereign power or ruler; the gentlemanly Locke (1632–1704) whose ideal was a sound mind in a sound body to be attained by hard physical exercise, wide experience of the world, and enough knowledge to meet the requirements of the pupil's environment. The end result would be one able to get on with his fellows, pious but wise in the ways of the world, independent and able to look after himself, informed but reticent about his knowledge. Classics and religious study were not to be carried to excess, since Locke held that these subjects had been overrated in the past. Locke's pupil was the well-to-do, civilised young man of the 17th cent. who knew how to behave in society.

Jean-Jacques Rousseau (1712–78), a forerunner of the Romantic movement (*q.v.*), which despised society and its institutions, put emotion at a higher level than reason. His book *Emile* describes the education of a boy which is natural and spontaneous. Society, he holds, warps the growing mind and therefore the child should be protected from its influences until his development in accordance with his own nature is so complete that he cannot be harmed by it. During the first 4 years the body should be developed by physical training; from 5 to 12 the child would live in a state of nature such that he could develop his powers of observation and his senses; from 13 books would be used and intellectual training introduced, although only in line with the child's own interests, and he would be given instruction only as he came to ask for it. Moral training and contact with his fellows to learn the principles of sympathy, kindness, and helpfulness to mankind would be given between 15 and 20. Girls, however, should be educated to serve men in a spirit of modesty and restraint. His own five children he deposited in a foundling hospital.

Summary. Broadly speaking, then, there have been four main attitudes to education: (1) religious, with a view to a life beyond death; (2) state-controlled education, with a view to uniform subservience to authority; (3) "gentlemanly" education, with a view to social graces and easy congress in company; (4) the "child-centred" education, which attempts to follow the pupil's inner nature. It is unnecessary to mention the ordinary method of attempting to instil facts without any considerable degree of co-operation between pupil and teacher in order that the former may, with or without interest, follow some occupation in adult life; for this the philosophers did not consider. Today there remain the two fundamental principles: education for the advantage of the state and its ideology or education for individual development and freedom.

Four educationists of the modern period who have influenced us in the direction of freedom were Johann Pestalozzi of Switzerland (1746–1827) who, by trying to understand children, taught the "natural, progressive, and harmonious development of all the powers and capacities of the human being", Friedrich Froebel (1782–1852) of Germany, the founder of the Kindergarten who, like Pestalozzi, was influenced by Rousseau but realised the need to combine complete personal development with social adjustment; Maria Montessori (1869–1952) whose free methods have revolutionised infant teaching; John Dewey (1859–1952) who held that the best interests of the group are served when the individual develops his own particular talents and nature.

Egalitarianism. The doctrine that human beings are, in an important sense, equal and that it is desirable to remove inequalities by social and political means. It was part of the famous slogan of the French Revolution: "Liberty, Equality, Fraternity". There has been much debate, however, as to what extent human beings are, in fact, equal. Critics of equality as a political ideal argue that it conflicts with other more valuable ideals or social values, and that the different kinds of equality are not compatible.

Eleatics, the philosophers of Elea in ancient Greece who, at the time when Heraclitus (*c.* 535–475 B.C.) was teaching that change is all that exists and nothing is permanent, were asserting that change is an illusion. Of the three leaders of this school, Xenophanes asserted that the universe was a solid immovable mass forever the same; Parmenides explained away change as an inconceivable process, its appearance being due to the fact that what we see is unreal; and Zeno (the best-known today) illustrated the same thesis with his famous argument of the arrow which, at any given moment of its flight, must be where it is since it cannot be where it is not. But if it is where it is, it cannot move, this is based, of course, on the delusion that motion is discontinuous. The Eleatics were contemporaries of Socrates.

Elitism. A political theory, largely drawn from the writings of V. Pareto (1848–1923). Power in a society will always be exercised by a minority (the elite) which takes the major decisions. An elite gains its dominant position through possessing certain resources or qualities valued in that particular society, *e.g.* priests or soldiers or senior state officials. Elites normally aim to continue their domination, but are not always capable of doing so and become displaced by another elite. If elite rule is inevitable then there can be no hope of an egalitarian, socialist society. This analysis of the importance of elites has been very influential. Some sociologists have extended the theory in recent years to argue that in all developed countries there is a plurality of competing elites within different systems of control. Such systems are politics, trade union organisations, cultural and educational institutions.

Elitism is now sometimes used as a term of abuse, indicating the view that elites are desirable, and that the status and privileges of existing elites should be preserved.

Empiricism. While not a single school of philosophy, empiricism is an approach to knowledge which holds that if a man wants to know what the universe is like the only correct way to do so is to go and look for himself, to collect facts which come to him through his senses. It is, in essence, the method of science as contrasted with rationalism (*q.v.*) which in philosophy implies that thinking or reasoning without necessarily referring to external observations can arrive at truth. Empiricism is typically an English attitude, for among the greatest empirical philosophers were John Locke, George Berkeley, and David Hume. *See* Rationalism.

Encyclopedists. The writers (all men) who contributed to the *Encyclopedie* published in France from 1751 to 1772. The work's full title was *Encyclopedie, ou dictionnaire raisonne des sciences, des arts et des metiers*. It was designed as a synoptic description of all branches of human knowledge, and is perhaps the most characteristic work of the Enlightenment (*q.v.*). The *Encyclopedie* was inspired by Chambers' *Cyclopedia, or a universal dictionary of arts and sciences* published in London in 1728. The project began in 1745, with Denis Diderot and Jean d'Alembert as editors. The latter resigned in 1758, leaving Diderot to shoulder most of the work. In 1772 the project reached 28 volumes; between 1776 and 1780 7 supplementary volumes were published.

Besides Diderot and d'Alembert and many obscure writers, Voltaire, Rousseau and d'Holbach contributed. The work was a showcase for representatives of new schools of thought in all branches of intellectual activity. The work was tolerant, liberal, and also innovative in giving attention to trades and mechanical arts. In its scepticism, its emphasis on being scientific, and its criticism of superstition and contemporary social institutions, the *Encyclopedie* had immense influence.

Enlightenment. A European intellectual movement of the 18th century. Enlightenment thinkers aimed to bring clarity, order and reason, in a word, *light* to regions where formerly there had been mystery, superstition and blind authority, that is, darkness. Man would become enlightened by knowledge and progress to greater happiness and freedom. The movement affected the arts, the sciences, political and social life.

The Enlightenment was prepared by the rise of science from the 16th century on. In particular, the success of Newton (1642–1727) in encapsulating the laws that govern the motion of the planets gave great hopes in man's capacity to attain extensive understanding. According to the German philosopher Kant (1724–1804) the motto of the Enlightenment was "Have courage to use your own understanding". Scientific knowledge was the ideal. If something was held to be true, it had to be based on dispassionate rational investigation. This overrode any claim to knowledge based on authority. One great source of authority was the Christian church, which was widely criticised by Enlightenment thinkers (*e.g.* in Voltaire's *Candide*); another was the despotism and arbitrary power of many states at the time. Although there is now a tendency to be sceptical about the Enlightenment and the power of reason, the belief in human progress through increased knowledge has been one of the most powerful ideas of the last 200 years.

Epicureanism. The two great schools of the Hellenistic period (*i.e.* the late Greek period beginning with the empire of Alexander the Great) were the Stoics and Epicureans, the former founded by Zeno of Citium (not to be confused with Zeno the Eleatic) (*q.v.*), the latter by Epicurus, born in Samos in 342 B.C. Both schools settled in Athens, where Epicurus taught that "pleasure is the beginning and end of a happy life." However, he was no sensualist and emphasised the importance of moderation in all things because excesses would lead to pain instead of pleasure and the best of all pleasures were mental ones. Pleasures could be active or passive but the former contain an element of pain since they are the process of satisfying desire not yet satiated. The latter involving the absence of desire are the more pleasant. In fact, Epicurus in his personal life was more stoical than many Stoics and wrote "when I live on bread and water I spit on luxurious pleasures." He disapproved of sexual enjoyment and thought friendship one of the highest of all joys. A materialist who accepted the atomic theory of Democritus, he was not a determinist, and if he did not disbelieve in the gods he regarded religion and the fear of death as the two primary sources of unhappiness.

Epiphenomenalism. *See* **Mind and Body.**

Erastianism, the theory that the state has the right to decide the religion of its members, wrongly attributed to Erastus of Switzerland (1524–83) who was believed to have held this doctrine. The term has usually been made use of in a derogatory sense—*e.g.*, by the Scottish churches which held that the "call" of the congregation was the only way to elect ministers at a time when, about the turn of the 17th and 18th cent., they felt that Episcopalianism was being foisted on them. "Episcopalianism" (*i.e.* Anglicanism) with its state church, ecclesiastical hierarchy, and system of livings presented by patrons was to them "Erastian" in addition to its other "unscriptural practices."

Essenes, a Jewish sect which, during the oppressive rule of Herod (d. 4 B.C.), set up monastic communities in the region of the Dead Sea. They refused to be bound by the scriptural interpretations of the Pharisees and adhered rigorously to the letter of Holy Writ, although with additions of their own which cause them by orthodox Jews today to be regarded as a break-away from Judaism. Among their practices and beliefs were purification through baptism, renunciation of sexual pleasures, scrupulous cleanliness, strict observance of the Mosaic law, communal possession, asceticism. Akin in spirit, although not necessarily identical with them, were the writers of Apocalyptic literature preaching that the evils of the present would shortly be terminated by a new supernatural order heralded by a Messiah who would reign over a restored Israel. The casting out of demons and spiritual healing formed part of these general beliefs which were in the air at that time. The sect has an importance far beyond its size or what has been known about it in the past since the discovery from 1947 onwards of the Dead Sea Scrolls (*see* **Section L**) of the Qumran community occupying a monastery in the same area as the Essenes and holding the same type of belief. These scrolls with their references to a "Teacher of Righteousness" preceding the Messiah have obvious relevance to the sources of early Christianity and have given rise to speculations as to whether Jesus might have been influenced by views which, like His own, were unacceptable to orthodox Jews but in line with those of the Dead Sea communities. Scholars now think that early Christianity was not a sudden development but a gradual one which had its predecessors.

Ethical Church, a movement typical of 19th cent. rationalism which attempted to combine atheism (or at any rate the absence of any belief in a God which was inconsistent with reason or based on revelation) with the inculcation of moral principles. Prayers were not used and ordinarily the service consisted in the singing of edifying compositions interspersed with readings from poems or prose of a similar nature by great writers holding appropriate views. It terminated in a talk on an ethical or scientific theme. Conway Hall (built 1929) in Red Lion Square, London, belongs to the South Place Ethical Society, founded by Moncure Conway who preached at their Unitarian chapel in South Place, Finsbury, 1864–97.

Ethnocentrism, the exaggerated tendency to think the characteristics of one's own group or race superior to those of any others.

Eugenics, a 19th-cent. movement largely instigated by the British scientist and mathematician, Sir Francis Galton. Galton argued that many of the most satisfactory attributes of mankind—intelligence, physical strength, resistance to disease, etc.—were genetically determined and thus handed down in the normal process of inheritance. From this he reasoned that selective mating of physical "superior" individuals, and its converse, the controlled limitation on the breeding of criminals or the insane, would lead inevitably to a progressive improvement in the overall standards of the human race. In their simplest form these proposals are incontestable, though they do of course introduce marked restrictions on the choice of the individual for marriage and procreation. Worse yet is the way in which the argument can be misapplied or elaborated—as it was in Nazi Germany—to include the sterilisation of alcoholics, confirmed criminals and even epileptics. Nevertheless there remains the feeling that there are some aspects of eugenics which intuitively at any rate make good sense and of course the widespread application of birth control is itself an enactment of eugenic principles.

Euthanasia (mercy killing), the term applied to the painless killing of those (especially the old) suffering from unbearable pain and an illness for which there is no cure. In Britain, attempts in Parliament to introduce its legalisation have failed but in 1993 Holland voted to adopt routine legal procedures for euthanasia on the patient's request. Under these procedures, euthanasia is tolerated when the patient is conscious, suffers an incurable disease paired with intolerable pain and clearly requests a 'soft death'.

Evangelicalism, the belief of those Protestant sects which hold that the essence of the Gospel consists in the doctrine of salvation by faith in the atoning death of Christ and not by good works or the sacraments; that worship should be "free" rather than liturgical through established forms; that ritual is unacceptable and superstitious. Evangelicals are Low Churchmen.

Evangelism, the preaching of the Gospel, emphasising the necessity for a new birth or conversion. The evangelistic fervour of John Wesley and George Whitefield (*see* Methodism) aroused the great missionary spirit of the late 18th and 19th cent. George Fox, founder of the Society of Friends (*q.v.*), was also an evangelist. Evangelists can be Low, High, or Middle Churchmen.

Existentialism, a highly subjective philosophy which many people connect with such names as Jean-Paul Sartre (1905–80) or Albert Camus (1913–60) and assume to be a post-war movement associated with disillusion and a sordid view of life. However, existentialism stems from Sören Kierkegaard (1813–55), the Danish "religious writer"—his own description of himself—in such works as *Either/Or, Fear and Trembling,* and *Concluding Unscientific Postscript.* Between the two wars translations of Kierkegaard into German influenced Martin Heidegger's great work *Being and Time* and the other great existentialist Karl Jaspers; it has strongly influenced modern Protestant theology notably in Karl Barth, Reinhold Niebuhr, and Paul Tillich and beyond that field the French philosopher Gabriel Marcel, the Spanish writer Unamuno in his well-known *The Tragic Sense of Life,* and Martin Buber of Israel in his *I and Thou.* We have it on Heidegger's authority that "Sartre is no philosopher" even if it is to his works that modern existentialists often turn.

Existentialism is extremely difficult for the non-metaphysically-minded to understand, it deals, not with the nature of the universe or what are ordinarily thought of as philosophical problems but describes an attitude to life or God held by the individual. Briefly, its main essentials are: (1) it distinguishes between *essence, i.e.,* that aspect of an entity which can be observed and known—and its *existence*—the fact of its having a place in a changing and dangerous world which is what really matters; (2) existence being basic, each self-aware individual can grasp his own existence on reflection in his own immediate experience of himself and his situation as a free being in the world; what he finds is not merely a knowing self but a self that fears, hopes, believes, wills, and is aware of its need to find a purpose, plan, and destiny in life; (3) but we cannot grasp our existence by thought alone; thus the fact "all men must die" relates to the essence of man but it is necessary to be involved, to draw the conclusion as a person that "I too must die" and experience its impact on our own individual existence; (4) because of the preceding, it is necessary to abandon our attitude of objectivity and theoretical detachment when faced by the problems relating to the ultimate purpose of our own life and the basis of our own conduct; life remains closed to those who take no part in it because it can have no significance; (5) it follows that the existentialist cannot be rationalist in his outlook for this is merely an escape into thought from the serious problems of existence; none of the important aspects of life—failure, evil, sin, folly—nor (in the view of Kierkegaard) even the existence of God or the truth of Christianity—can be proved by reason. "God does not exist; He is eternal," was how he expressed it; (6) life is short and limited in space and time, therefore it is foolish to discuss in a leisurely fashion matters of life and death as if there were all eternity to argue them in. It is necessary to make a leap into the unknown, *e.g.,* accepting Christ (in the case of the Christian existentialist) by faith in the sense of giving and risking the self utterly. This means complete commitment, not a dependence on arguments as to whether certain historical events did, or did not, happen.

To summarise: existentialism of whatever type seems to the outsider to be an attitude to life concerning itself with the individual's ultimate problems (mine, not yours); to be anti-rationalist and anti-idealist (in the sense of being, as it seems to the believer, practical)—in effect it seems to say "life is too short to fool about with argument, you must dive in and become committed" to something. Sartre who called himself an "atheist existentialist" was apparently committed to the belief that "hell is other people," but for most critics the main argument against existentialist philosophy is that it often rests on a highly specialised personal experience and, as such, is incommunicable.

Existential Psychology, a new if rather diffuse movement in modern psychology with no specific founder but with a number of figures who have, perhaps against their will, acquired leader status. One of the key figures is the British psychiatrist, R. D. Laing, whose radical views on psychotherapy are counted as being heretical by the vast majority of his medical colleagues. Laing holds that many so-called neurotic and psychotic conditions are essentially not "abnormal" and merely represent extreme strategies by which an individual may adjust to environmental and personal stress. Instead of attempting to suppress or eliminate the psychosis in the traditional manner, one should lead the patient through it thus allowing the individual's "unconscious plan" for his own adjustment to be fulfilled.

Exorcism, the removal or ejection of an evil spirit by a ritual or prayer. It is easy to forget that the concept of insanity as representing a disorder of the brain, analogous to physical sickness of the body, is fairly recent in origin. Barely two centuries ago it was considered to be appropriate treatment to put lunatics into chains and beat them daily in the hope that the malevolent beings inhabiting them might be persuaded to depart. Tragically, many of the symptoms of severe forms of mental disorder induce such an apparent change in the personality of the individual as to suggest that an alien individual has indeed taken over their body, and this belief is still common in many parts of the world. Most religious systems have developed some ritual or set of rituals for expelling these demons, and while, not surprisingly, the practice of exorcism by the clergy has declined dramatically in the past century, it is still brought into play now and again in such circumstances as alleged hauntings, poltergeist phenomena, etc. From a scientific point of view, exorcism must be counted as a superstitious rite.

F

Fabian Society. In 1848 (the year of *The Communist Manifesto* by Marx and Engels) Europe was in revolt. In most countries the workers and intellectuals started bloody revolutions against the feudal ruling classes which were no less violently suppressed; hence on the continent socialism took on a Marxist tinge which to some extent it still retains. But at the same time England was undergoing a slow but non-violent transition in her political and industrial life which led the workers in general to look forward to progress through evolution. Marxism never became an important movement in England even though it took its origin here. There were many reasons for this: the agitation of the Chartists (*q.v.*); the writings of Mill, Ruskin, and Carlyle; the reforms of Robert Owen; the religious movement led by the Wesleys; the Co-operative societies; the Christian socialists. Furthermore legislation stimulated by these bodies had led to an extension of the franchise to include a considerable number of wage-earners, remedial measures to correct some of the worst abuses of the factory system, recognition of the trade unions, etc.

This was the background against which the Fabian Society was founded in 1884 with the conviction that social change could be brought about by gradual parliamentary means. (The name is derived from Quintus Fabius Maximus, the Roman general nicknamed "Cunctator," the delayer, who achieved his successes in defending Rome against Hannibal by refusing to give direct battle.) It was a movement of brilliant intellectuals, chief among whom were Sidney and Beatrice Webb, H. G. Wells, G. B. Shaw, Graham Wallas, Sidney Olivier, and Edward Pease. The Society itself was basically a re-search institution which furnished the intel-lectual information for social reform and sup-ported all contributing to the gradual attain-ment by parliamentary means of socialism.

The Webbs's analysis of society emphasised that individualist enterprise in capitalism was a hang-over from early days and was bound to defeat itself since socialism is the inevitable accompaniment of modern industrialism; the necessary result of popular government is con-trol of their economic system by the people themselves. Utopian schemes had been doomed to failure because they were based on the fallacy that society is static and that islands of utopias could be formed in the midst of an unchanging and antagonistic environment. On the con-trary, it was pointed out, society develops: "The new becomes old, often before it is con-sciously regarded as new." Social reorganisa-tion cannot usefully be hastened by violent means but only through methods consonant with this natural historical progression—gradual, peaceful, and democratic. The Fabians were convinced that men are rational enough to accept in their common interest developments which can be demonstrated as necessary; thus public opinion will come to see that socialisation of the land and industries is essential in the same way that they came to accept the already-existing acts in respect of housing, insurance, medical care, and conditions of work.

The Society collaborated first in the formation of the Independent Labour Party and then with the more moderate Labour Party and the trade unions and Co-operative movement. But in general it disapproved of independent trade union action since change should come from the government and take political form. The class-war of Marx was rejected and so too was the idea of the exclusive role of the working class —reform must come from the enlightened co-operation of all classes.

Faith Healing, the belief and practice of curing physical and mental ills by faith in some super-natural power, either allegedly latent in the individual (as with Christian Science) or drawn in some way from God. It is a characteristic of faith healing that it is supposed to be publicly demonstrable—*i.e.*, a "healer" will hold public meetings and invite sick people to come up to be cured on the platform. In the emotionally charged atmosphere which the healer generates, it is not unusual for people to show immediate and striking improvement in their illness, but the almost invariable rule is for relapses to occur within days or hours after the event. When remission is more permanent, the illness is generally hysterical in origin and will often return to the individual in some other form. Spiritualists claim that the healing in such cases is done not by "faith" but by direct interven-tion of the spirits of doctors, etc., who have died and passed on to another world. Per-haps the world's most famous faith healer in recent years was Harry Edwards (d. 1976), who had literally millions of letters from all parts of the world asking for the healing atten-tion of his spirit guides. Many doctors, while remaining immensely sceptical about the origins and extent of this kind of therapy, are inclined to admit that it might have benefits when the sickness is mildly hysterical in origin. The real danger, of course, comes when patients seek unorthodox therapy before consulting their doctor.

Falangists. The Fascist Party of Spain founded in 1933 by José Antonio Primo de Rivera, son of the man who was dictator of the country from 1923 to 1930. The Falange was the only political party allowed in Spain during the Franco era. *See* **Fascism.**

Fascism. From the end of mediaeval times with the opening up of the world, the liberation of the mind and the release of business enterprise, a new spirit arose in Europe exemplified in such movements as the Renaissance, the Reforma-tion, the struggle for democracy, the rise of capitalism, and the Industrial Revolution. With these movements there developed a certain tradition, which, in spite of hindrances and dis-agreement or failures, was universally held by both right- and left-wing parties however strongly they might fail to agree on the best means of attaining what was felt to be a universal ideal. The hard core of this tradition involved: belief in reason and the possibility of human progress; the essential sanctity and dignity of human life; tolerance of widely different religious and political views; reliance on popular government and the responsibility of the rulers to the ruled; freedom of thought and criticism; the necessity of universal education; impartial justice and the rule of law; the desirability of universal peace. Fascism was the negation of every aspect of this tradition and took pride in being so. Emotion took the place of reason, the "immutable, beneficial, and fruitful inequality of classes" and the right of a self-constituted élite to rule them replaced universal suffrage because absolute authority "quick, sure, unanimous" led to action rather than talk. Contrary opinions are not allowed and justice is in the service of the state; war is desirable to advance the power of the state; and racial in-equality made a dogma. Those who belong to the "wrong" religion, political party, or race are outside the law.

The attacks on liberalism and exaltation of the state derive largely from Hegel and his German followers; the mystical irrationalism from such 19th cent. philosophers as Schopenhauer Nietzsche, and Bergson; from Sorel (*see* **Syndicalism**) came the idea of the "myth", and an image which would have the power to arouse the emotions of the masses and from Sorel also the rationale of violence and justification of force. But these philosophical justifications of fascism do not explain why it arose at all and why it arose where it did—in Italy, Germany, and Spain. These countries had one thing in com-mon—disillusionment. Germany had lost the 1914–18 war, Italy had been on the winning side but was resentful about her small gains. Spain had sunk to the level of a third-rate power, and people were becoming increasingly restive under the reactionary powers of the Catholic Church, the landed aristocracy, and the army. In Marxist theory, fascism is the last fling of the ruling class and the bourgeoisie in their attempt to hold down the workers.

Italian Fascism. The corporate state set up by Benito Mussolini in Italy claimed to be neither capitalist nor socialist, and after its inception in 1922 the Fascist Party became the only recognised one. Its members wore black shirts, were organised in military formations, used the Roman greeting of the outstretched arm, and adopted as their slogan "Mussolini is always right". Membership of the Party was not allowed to exceed a number thought to be suited to the optimum size of a governing class and new candidates were drawn, after strict examinations, from the youth organisations. The Blackshirts, a fascist militia, existed sepa-rately from the army and were ruled by Fascist Headquarters.

At the head of government was Mussolini, "Il Duce" himself, a cabinet of fourteen ministers selected by him and approved by the King to supervise the various functions of government, and the Grand Council or direc-torate of the Fascist Party, all the members of which were chosen by the Duce. Parliament, which was not allowed to initiate legislation but only to approve decrees from above, consisted of a Senate with life-membership and a Chamber of Fasci and Corporations composed of nomi-nated members of the Party, the National

Council of Corporations, and selected representatives of the employers' and employees' confederations. Private enterprise was encouraged and protected but rigidly controlled; strikes were forbidden, but a Charter of Labour enforced the collaboration of workers and employers whose disputes were settled in labour courts presided over by the Party. All decisions relating to industry were government-controlled (*e.g.*, wages, prices, conditions of employment and dismissal, the expansion or limitation of production), and some industries such as mining, shipping, and armaments were state-owned.

Italian fascism served as a model in other countries, notably for the German National Socialist Party, in Spain and Japan, and most European nations between the wars had their small Fascist parties, the British version led by Sir Oswald Mosley being known as the British Union which relied on "strong-arm tactics", marches and violence. The Public Order Act of 1936 was passed to deal with it. Although fascism in all countries has certain recognisable characteristics, it would be wrong to think of it as an international movement taking fixed forms and with a clearly thought-out rationale as in the case of communism. There were minor revivals of interest in Fascism in Italy after 1945 and more recently in France with the emergence of the National Front led by M. Le Pen. Since 1989, elections in a variety of countries have showed increasing support for extreme right-wing or anti-immigrant parties. There is increasing support for neo-Fascism again in Italy and parts of Germany, the former communist states of eastern Europe, and (under Zhirinovsky) in Russia itself. *See* **Falangists, Nazism**.

Fatalism. *See* **Determinism**.

Feminism. Feminism is an expression which emerged in the mid-19th century. It is an international movement (there was, for example, a feminist congress in Paris in 1890), which aimed at ending female inequality in male-dominated societies. In early 20th century Britain feminism sought political advance through a militant campaign for women's suffrage. This, and the part played by women in World War One, made it impossible for a male elite to deny women the right to vote. But in each country it became increasingly clear to women that the political process alone left many of their needs unsatisfied, if not unrecognised. However, in post-World War Two Britain, legislation made a gesture towards outlawing discrimination against women at work with the 1970 Equal Pay Act and the 1975 Sex Discrimination Act.

Activist feminism, the "Women's Liberation Movement" of the 1960s and 1970s (primarily in America and Europe as well as Britain), centred on questions of sexuality and the right of women to make choices, for example, over when (and whether) to become pregnant. The contraceptive pill appeared to open up sexual choice for women and to liberate them from traditional responsibilities for home, family and the welfare of children. In practice, it appeared to many women that the pill (as well as having physical side-effects) merely relieved men from a recognition of their own responsibility. The 1967 Abortion Act in Britain implied an acceptance of a woman's right to control her own reproduction, a right which has been systematically but unsuccessfully challenged since. Many men—and much of the media—attempted to dismiss the movement as middle-class "bra-burners".

As western economies faltered in the late 1970s a recurring problem for the movement was consolidating the small gains that had been made. But the women's movement achievements cannot be measured by tangible results alone. A central aspect of the movement was "consciousness-raising", helping women recognise the social roots of their individual oppression. In their analysis of sexual stereotyping, late 20th century feminist writings—for example, Betty Friedan's *The Feminine Mystique* (1963) and Germaine Greer's *The Female Eunuch* (1970)—encouraged a change in some women's expectations. These writers, and many like them, enabled a new generation of women to challenge the dominant decision-making role of men and to demand acceptance of the principle of equality between the sexes. Dale Spender's *Man Made Language* (1980) pointed to

the ways in which the "sexist" structure of language internalised the perpetuation of male dominance. A simple, but not superficial, result of this is the acceptance of the abbreviation "Ms" rather than "Mrs" or "Miss" on the grounds that the latter presupposed that a woman's identity depended on her marital status.

Although feminism as a movement was loosely structured—there were, for example, early on, differing emphases between socialists, black women, working class women, and lesbians, based on their own experiences—the movement became increasingly fragmented during the 1980s. Some women, who were now building individual careers, distanced themselves from agitation and thought little more could be achieved by collective action. Single-issue pressure groups evolved, focusing on campaigns for change in areas of particular concern to women—for example, rape, pornography and health.

The Greenham Common Women's Peace Camp which began in the mid-1980s as a protest against the deployment of Cruise missiles in Britain, was able to develop from this into an exemplary feminist action which reverberated internationally. Self-organisation among miners' wives in the 1984–85 strike proved similarly effective.

The irony of "classical" feminism is that it became a concern of the generation that came to maturity in the late 1960s. Their children—and their younger sisters—had absorbed the earlier failures and successes and moved on. By the 1990s, for what became the older generation, there was a view that the earlier movement had implanted unrealistic expectations in women (particularly those with domestic responsibilities), the "double burden" of maintaining a career and home. This led at a time of growing recession and unemployment to an anti-feminist campaign or "backlash", not only among men (which was to be expected) but also among some women who described themselves as post-feminists. Susan Faludi, speaking for a younger generation in *Backlash: The Undeclared War Against Women* (1991) documents a process which has as a common thread the attempt to force women back into the home and a return to "traditional" family life. However, a significant recognition of the altered balance between the sexes came with the October 1991 House of Lords decision that rape within marriage was an offence. On the other hand, the ideological thrust behind the Child Support Agency which was set up in 1993 represented to many feminists an attempt by the British state—following Australia and the United States—to restore some lone parent women's economic dependence on men by threatening to reduce their benefits.

Fetichism, originally a practice of the natives of West Africa and elsewhere of attributing magical properties to an object which was used as an amulet, for putting spells on others, or regarded as possessing dangerous powers. In psychology the term refers to a sexual perversion in which objects such as shoes, brassières, hair, *etc.*, arouse sexual excitement.

Feudalism. The feudal system took its origins from Saxon times and broadly speaking lasted until the end of the 13th cent. It was a military and political organisation based on land tenure, for, of course, society throughout this period was based almost entirely on agriculture. The activities of men divided them into three classes or estates. The First Estate was the clergy, responsible for man's spiritual needs; the Second was the nobility, including kings and emperor as well as the lesser nobles; the Third was composed of all those who had to do with the economic and mainly agricultural life of Europe. The praying men, the fighting men and administrators, and the toilers were all held to be dependent on each other in a web of mutual responsibilities.

The theory of feudalism, although it by no means always worked out in practice, was as follows: the earth was God's and therefore no man owned land in the modern sense of the word. God had given the pope spiritual charge of men, and secular power over them to the emperor from whom kings held their kingdoms, and in turn the dukes and counts received the land over which they held sway from the king. Members of the Second Estate held their lands on the condition of fulfilling certain obligations to their overlord and to the people living under them, so when a noble received a fief or piece of land he became the vassal of the man who bestowed it. To him he owed military service for a specified period of the year, attendance at court, and giving his lord counsel. He undertook to ransom his lord when he fell into enemy hands and to contribute to his daughter's dowry and at the knighting of his son. In return the lord offered his vassal protection and justice, received the vassal's sons into his household and educated them for knighthood.

The system was complicated by the fact that large fiefs might be subdivided and abbots often governed church lands held in fief from nobles. The serf or toiling man dwelt on the land of a feudal noble or churchman where he rendered service by tilling the soil or carrying out his craft for his manorial lord in return for protection, justice, and the security of his life and land. He was given a share in the common lands or pastures from which he provided for his own needs. In the modern sense he was not free (although at a later stage he could buy his freedom) since he was attached to the soil and could not leave without the lord's permission. On the other hand he could neither be deprived of his land nor lose his livelihood. Feudal tenures were abolished in England by statute in 1660, although they had for long been inoperative. In Japan a feudal system existed up to 1871, in Russia until 1917.

Fideism. A term applied to religious doctrines which hold that the intellect or reason of man is incapable of attaining knowledge of divine matters and that religious faith is the way to truth. The word came into use in the late 19th century, although it is a doctrine that has a long history. The most notable modern thinker in this tradition is Soren Kierkegaard (1813–55).

Flying Saucers. In June 1947 an American private pilot, Kenneth Arnold, saw a series of wingless objects flying through the air at a speed which he estimated at thousands of miles an hour. He later told the press that the objects "flew as a saucer would if you skipped it across the water," and the phrase "flying saucers" was erroneously born. What Arnold actually saw has never been satisfactorily explained—it was probably a flight of jet fighters reflecting the sun's rays in a way that made them appear as discs—but since that date literally hundreds of thousands of people all over the world have reported the sighting of strange objects in the sky, coming in a bewildering range of shapes and sizes. Initially the American Air Force launched an official enquiry—Project Bluebook —to attempt to solve the mystery of these "unidentified flying objects" or "U.F.O.s," which folded in 1969 after hesitantly concluding that the sightings were probably misinterpretations of natural phenomena and that there was no evidence for the commonly held view that earth was being visited by spacecraft from some other planetary system. The University of Colorado's Condon Report supported this view, but its findings are now attacked as a 'debunking' exercise. So, despite this official attitude, belief in the existence of flying saucers and their origin as alien space vehicles is exceedingly widespread and is held very strongly by people in all walks of life. In 1959 this striking social phenomenon attracted the attention of the psychologist C. G. Jung. He noticed that the press were inclined to report statements that saucers existed when made by prominent people and not publish contrary statements made by equally prominent people. He concluded that flying saucers were in some way welcome phenomena and in his brilliant little book, *Flying Saucers—a modern myth*, he hypothesised that the U.F.O.s were the modern equivalent of "signs in the skies." It was Jung's contention that the saucers were looked upon as the harbingers of advanced alien civilisations who had come to save the world from its descent into nuclear catastrophe—archangels in modern dress in fact.

Whatever the validity of this imaginative view of U.F.O.s, it is undeniably true that they continue to exercise a great fascination for millions of people, some of whom invest them with definite religious significance.

Fourierism See **Utopianism**.

Freemasonry, a widespread, influential secret organisation of English origin. Although it can be traced back to the Middle Ages when itinerant working masons in England and Scotland were organised in lodges with secret signs for the recognition of fellow-members, modern freemasonry first arose in England in the early decades of the 18th cent. The first Grand Lodge was founded in London in 1716 and Freemasons' Hall was opened in 1776. With its clubs for discussion and social enjoyment (women were excluded) it met a need and became a well-known feature of English life. The movement quickly spread abroad to places which had direct trade links with England. The graded lodge structure, the social prestige conferred by membership, the symbolism, ritual and ceremony, and the emphasis on mutual help have had a lasting appeal. Interest in the occult had more appeal on the Continent than in England. Until a decade or so ago, membership conferred definite business and social advantages, particularly in small communities where the leading middle-class figures were generally members. Recently this advantage has markedly declined and freemason lodges nowadays tend to be little more than worthy charitable organisations. Fear of secret societies has given freemasonry many opponents; it was condemned by the Roman Catholic Church, banned by Fascist dictators, and denounced by the Comintern. A statement from the Congregation for the Doctrine of the Faith in 1981 reminded Catholics that under Article 2335 of the Code of Canon Law they are forbidden under pain of excommunication from joining masonic or similar associations.

Freudian theory. See **Psychoanalysis**.

Friends, The Society of. See **Quakers**.

Fundamentalism is a term covering a number of religious movements which adhere with the utmost rigidity to orthodox tenets; for example the Old Testament statement that the earth was created by God in six days and six nights would be held to be factual rather than allegorical or symbolic. Although the holding of rigid beliefs in the literal truth of the Bible might seem to be frequently contrary to modern scientific findings, the fundamentalists at least do not have the problems of compromise and interpretation to face, and to some people this is no doubt a great attraction. Since the coming to power of Khomeini in Iran, Islamic fundamentalism has become a potent force in much of the Middle East.

Futurism. See **Section L**.

G

Game Theory, an approach to understanding human and animal behaviour which takes the view that psychological insight is best gained by studying the decisions which all living things make constantly and which govern the course of their lives. It proposes that life is basically a strategic game following complex rules which can probably only be understood by a study of the "decision units" as and when they occur. Because one is dealing with highly variable animals controlled by highly complex brains, and not with simple clockwork or electro-mechanical systems, the study of the rules which operate in the game of life is enormously complicated and thus game theory has quickly taken off into advanced mathematics. Game theory, incidentally, can be used to apply to individual action or to the behaviour of groups. Little of any predictive value has been put forward by the protagonists of this approach, but the use of computers to tackle the complex mathematics involved may well lead to some interesting advances.

Gestalt Psychology. In the latter half of the 19th cent. it became evident to psychologists that in principle there was no good reason why "mental" events should not be just as measurable and manageable as "physical" ones. Intensive studies of learning, memory, perception, and so on were therefore undertaken and the beginnings of an empirical science of psychology were underway. In the early part of the 20th cent. the experiments of Pavlov (see **Behaviourism**) and his co-workers suggested that the behaviour of an animal, or even men, might ultimately be reduced to a descriptive account of the activities of nervous reflex loops—the so-called conditioned reflexes. With the publication of Watson's important book on Behaviourism in 1914 it looked as though the transfer of psychological studies from the field of philosophy to that of science could now take place. Actually the over-simplified picture of cerebral and mental pictures which Behaviourism offered was rather comparable to the billiard ball view of the universe so fashionable in Victorian science. Just as Behaviourism implied that there was a fundamental building block (the conditioned reflex) from which all mental events could be constructed, so Victorian physics assumed that the entire universe could be described in terms of a vast collection of atoms pushing each other around like billiard balls. The development of nuclear physics was to shatter the latter dream and at the same time a challenge to the naïve "reflex psychology" came from the Gestalt experimental school.

The founders of this school were Max Wertheimer, Kurt Koffka and Wolfgang Köhler, three young psychologists who in 1912 were conducting experiments—notably in vision—which seemed to expose the inadequacies of the behaviourist position. The Pavlov–Watson view, as we have said, implied that complex sensory events were no more than a numerical sum of individual nervous impulses. Wertheimer's group proposed that certain facts of perceptual experiences (ruled out of court as subjective and therefore unreliable by Watson) implied that the whole (Gestalt) was something more than simply the sum of its parts. For example, the presentation of a number of photographs, each slightly different, in rapid series gives rise to cinematographic motion. In basic terms, the eye has received a number of discrete, "still" photographs, and yet "motion" is perceived. What, they asked, was the sensory input corresponding to this motion? Some processes within the brain clearly added something to the total input as defined in behaviourist terms. An obvious alternative—in a different sense modality—is that of the arrangement of musical notes. A cluster of notes played one way might be called a tune; played backwards they may form another tune, or may be meaningless. Yet in all cases the constituent parts are the same, and yet their relationship to one another is evidently vital. Once again the whole is something more than the simple sum of the parts.

The implications of all this appeared to be that the brain was equipped with the capacity to organise sensory input in certain well-defined ways, and that far from being misleading and scientifically unjustifiable, human subjective studies of visual experience might reveal the very principles of organisation which the brain employs. Take a field of dots, more or less randomly distributed; inspection of the field will soon reveal certain patterns or clusters standing out—the constellations in the night sky are a good illustration. There are many other examples, and Wertheimer and his colleagues in a famous series of experiments made some effort to catalogue them and reduce them to a finite number of "Laws of Perceptual Organisation" which are still much quoted today.

Ghosts, belief in ghosts is one of the most common features of supernatural and mystical philosophy. At its roots it is based on the assumption that Man is essentially an individual created of two separate and distinct substances, mind and body. Most religious systems hold to this dualistic view (see **Dualism**), arguing that whereas the body is transient and destructible, the mind or spirit is permanent and survives the death of its physical host. The discarnate spirit is normally assumed to progress to some other realm ("Heaven," "Nirvana," "The Spirit World," etc.) whereupon it loses contact

with the mortal world. Occasionally, however, for one reason or another, the spirits may not progress and may become trapped and unable to escape the material world. Traditionally this is supposed to occur when the death of the individual is precipitated by some great tragedy —murder, suicide, etc.—when the site of the tragedy is supposed to be haunted by the earthbound spirit. Although the library of the Society for Psychical Research is crammed with supposedly authentic accounts of hauntings of this kind, scientific interest in ghosts has been waning rapidly in recent years. At one time, in particular in the latter part of the 19th cent., with the upsurge of scientific interest in Spiritualism (q.v.), there were even attempts to call up ghosts in the laboratory. These led to spectacular opportunities for fraud on the part of Spiritualist mediums and the like, but in the long run added little to the cause of science. As we have said, belief in ghosts is largely dependent upon a parallel belief that the mind or soul of man is something essentially separate from the body. With the decline in belief of this notion has come an inevitable decline in belief in ghosts. For a recent, different view, see Percy Seymour, The Paranormal: Beyond Sensory Science (Penguin, 1992). The debate continues!

Gnosticism. Among the many heresies of early Christianity, especially during its first two centuries, was a group which came under the heading of Gnosticism. This was a system or set of systems which attempted to combine Christian beliefs with others derived from Oriental and Greek sources, especially those which were of a mystical and metaphysical nature, such as the doctrines of Plato and Pythagoras. There were many Gnostic sects, the most celebrated being the Alexandrian school of Valentius (fl. c. 136–c. 160). "Gnosis" was understood not as meaning "knowledge" or "understanding" as we understand these words, but "revelation." As in other mystical religions, the ultimate object was individual salvation; sacraments took the most varied forms. Many who professed themselves Christians accepted Gnostic doctrines and even orthodox Christianity contains some elements of Gnostic mysticism. It was left to the bishops and theologians to decide at what point Gnosticism ceased to be orthodox and a difficult task this proved to be. Two of the greatest, Clement of Alexandria and his pupil Origen, unwittingly slipped into heresy when they tried to show that such men as Socrates and Plato, who were in quest of truth, were Christian in intention, and by their lives and works had prepared the way for Christ. Thus they contradicted Church doctrine which specifically said Extra ecclesiam nulla salus—outside the Church there is no salvation.

God and Man. The idea of gods came before the idea of God and even earlier in the evolution of religious thought there existed belief in spirits (see **Animism**). It was only as a result of a long period of development that the notion of a universal "God" arose, a development particularly well documented in the Old Testament. Here we are concerned only with the views of philosophers, the views of specific religious bodies being given under the appropriate headings. First, however, some definitions.

Atheism is the positive disbelief in the existence of a God. **Agnosticism** (a term coined by T. H. Huxley, the 19th cent. biologist and contemporary of Darwin) signifies that one cannot know whether God exists or not. **Deism** is the acceptance of the existence of God, not through revelation, but as a hypothesis required by reason. **Theism** also accepts the existence of God, but, unlike Deism, does not reject the evidence of revelation (e.g., in the Bible or in the lives of the saints). **Pantheism** is the identification of God with all that exists (i.e., with the whole universe). **Monotheism** is the belief in one God, **Polytheism** the belief in many (see also **Dualism**).

Early Greek Views. Among the early Greek philosophers, Thales (c. 624–565 B.C.) of Miletus, in Asia Minor, Anaximander (611–547 B.C.), his pupil, and Anaximenes (b. c. 570 B.C.), another Miletan, were men of scientific curiosity and their speculations about the origin of the universe were untouched by religious thought. They founded the scientific tradition of critical discussion. Heraclitus of Ephesus (c. 540–475 B.C.), was concerned with the problem of change. How does a thing change and yet remain itself? For him all things are flames—processes. "Everything is in flux, and nothing is at rest." Empedocles of Agrigentum in Sicily (c. 500–c. 430 B.C.) introduced the idea of opposition and affinity. All matter is composed of the so-called four elements—*earth, water, air*, and *fire*—which are in opposition or alliance with each other. All these were materialist philosophers who sought to explain the working of the universe without recourse to the gods.

Socrates, Plato, and Aristotle. Socrates (470–399 B.C.) was primarily concerned with ethical matters and conduct rather than the nature of the universe. For him goodness and virtue come from knowledge. He obeyed an "inner voice" and suffered death rather than give up his philosophy. He believed in the persistence of life after death and was essentially a monotheist. Plato (427–347 B.C.) was chiefly concerned with the nature of reality and thought in terms of absolute truths which were unchanging, logical, and mathematical. (*See* **Mind and Matter.**) Aristotle (384–322 B.C.) took his views of matter not from Democritus (atomic view) but from Empedocles (doctrine of four elements), a view which came to fit in well with orthodox mediaeval theology. Matter is conceived of as potentially alive and striving to attain its particular form, being moved by divine spirit or mind (*nous*). (An acorn, for example, is matter which contains the form "oak-tree" towards which it strives.) Thus there is a whole series from the simplest level of matter to the perfect living individual. But there must be a supreme source of all movement upon which the whole of Nature depends, a Being that Aristotle describes as the "Unmoved Mover", the ultimate cause of all becoming in the universe. This Being is pure intelligence, a philosopher's God, not a personal one. Unlike Plato, Aristotle did not believe in survival after death, holding that the divine, that is the immortal element in man, is mind.

Among the later Greek thinkers the Epicureans were polytheists whose gods, however, were denied supernatural powers. The Stoics built up a materialist theory of the universe, based on the Aristotelian model. To them God was an all-pervading force, related to the world as the soul is related to the body, but they conceived of it as material. They developed the mystical side of Plato's idealism and were much attracted by the astrology coming from Babylonia. They were pantheists. The Sceptics were agnostics.

From *Pagan to Christian Thought.* Philo, "the Jew of Alexandria," who was about 20 years older than Jesus, tried to show that the Jewish scriptures were in line with the best in Greek thought. He introduced the *Logos* as a bridge between the two systems. Philo's God is remote from the world, above and beyond all thought and being, and as His perfection does not permit direct contact with matter the divine *Logos* acts as intermediary between God and man. Plotinus (204–70), a Roman, and the founder of Neoplatonism, was the last of the great pagan philosophers. Like Philo, he believed that God had created the world indirectly through emanations—beings coming from Him but not of Him. The world needs God but God does not need the world. Creation is a fall from God, especially the human soul when enmeshed in the body and the world of the senses, yet (*see* **Determinism**) man has the ability to free himself from sense domination and turn towards God. Neoplatonism was the final stage of Greek thought drawing inspiration from the mystical side of Plato's idealism and its ethics from Stoicism.

Christianity: The Fathers and the Schoolmen. It was mainly through St. Augustine (354–430), Bishop of Hippo in North Africa, that certain of the doctrines of Neoplatonism found their way into Christianity. Augustine also emphasised the concept of God as all good, all wise, all knowing, transcendent, the Creator of

the universe out of nothing. But, he added, since God knows everything, everything is determined by Him forever. This is the doctrine of predestination and its subsequent history is discussed under **Determinism**.

In the early centuries of Christianity, as we have seen, some found it difficult to reconcile God's perfection with His creation of the universe and introduced the concept of the *Logos* which many identified with Christ. Further, it came to be held that a power of divine origin permeated the universe, namely the Holy Spirit or Holy Ghost. Some theory had to be worked out to explain the relationships of these three entities whence arose the conception of the Trinity. God is One; but He is also Three: Father, Son (the *Logos* or Christ), and Holy Ghost.

This doctrine was argued by the Apologists and the Modalists. The former maintained that the *Logos* and the Holy Spirit were emanations from God and that Jesus was the *Logos* in the form of a man. The Modalists held that all three Persons of the Trinity were God in three forms or modes: the *Logos* is God creating, the Holy Spirit God reasoning, and God is God being. This led to a long discussion as to whether the *Logos* was an emanation from God or God in another form; was the *Logos* of like *nature* with God or of the same *substance*? This was resolved at the Council of Nicaea (325) when Athanasius formulated the orthodox doctrine against Arius (*q.v.*): that the one God is a Trinity of the same substance, three Persons of the same nature—Father, Son, and Holy Ghost.

St. Thomas Aquinas (1227–74), influenced greatly by Aristotle's doctrines, set the pattern for all subsequent Catholic belief even to the present time. He produced rational arguments for God's existence: *e.g.*, Aristotle's argument that, since movement exists, there must be a prime mover, the Unmoved Mover or God; further, we can see that things in the universe are related in a scale from the less to the more complex, from the less to the more perfect, and this leads us to suppose that at the peak there must be a Being with absolute perfection. God is the first and final cause of the universe, absolutely perfect, the Creator of everything out of nothing. He reveals Himself in his Creation and rules the universe through His perfect will. How Aquinas dealt with the problem of predestination is told under **Determinism**.

Break with Mediaeval Thought. Renaissance thinkers, free to think for themselves, doubted the validity of the arguments of the Schoolmen but most were unwilling to give up the idea of God (nor would it have been safe to do so). Mystics (*see* **Mysticism**) or near-mystics such as Nicholas of Cusa (c. 1401–64) and Jacob Boehme (1575–1624) taught that God was not to be found by reason but was a fact of the immediate intuition of the mystical experience, Giordano Bruno held that God was immanent in the infinite universe. He is the unity of all opposites, a unity without opposites, which the human mind cannot grasp. Bruno was burned at the stake in 1600 at the instigation of the Inquisition (a body which, so we are told, never caused pain to anyone since it was the civil power, not the Inquisition, that carried out the unpleasant sentences) for his heresy.

Francis Bacon, who died in 1626, separated, as was the tendency of that time, science from religion. The latter he divided into the two categories of natural and revealed theology. The former, through the study of nature, may give convincing proof of the existence of a God but nothing more. Of revealed theology he said: "we must quit the small vessel of human reason ... as we are obliged to obey the divine law, though our will murmurs against it, so we are obliged to believe in the word of God, though our reason is shocked at it." Hobbes (d. 1679) was a complete materialist and one feels that his obeisance to the notion was politic rather than from conviction. However, he does mention God as starting the universe in motion; infers that God is corporeal but denies that His nature can be known.

From Descartes Onwards. Descartes (1596–1650) separated mind and body as different entities but believed that the existence of God could be deduced by the fact that the idea of him existed in the mind. Whatever God puts into man, including his ideas, must be real. God is self-caused, omniscient, omnipotent, eternal, all goodness and truth. But Descartes neglected to explain how mind separate from body can influence body, or God separate from the world can influence matter.

Spinoza (1632-77) declared that all existence is embraced in one substance—God, the all-in-all. He was a pantheist and as such was rejected by his Jewish brethren. But Spinoza's God has neither personality nor consciousness, intelligence nor purpose, although all things follow in strict law from His nature. All the thoughts of everyone in the world, make up God's thoughts.

Bishop Berkeley (1685 1750) took the view that things exist only when they are perceived, and this naturally implies that a tree, for example, ceases to exist when nobody is looking at it. This problem was solved to his own satisfaction by assuming that God, seeing everything, prevented objects from disappearing when we were not present. The world is a creation of God but it is a spiritual or mental world, not a material one.

Hume (1711-76), who was a sceptic, held that human reason cannot demonstrate the existence of God and all past arguments to show that it could were fallacious. Yet we must believe in God since the basis of all hope, morality, and society is based upon the belief. Kant (1724-1804) held a theory similar to that of Hume. We cannot know by reason that God exists, nor can we prove on the basis of argument anything about God. But we can form an idea of the whole of the universe, the one Absolute Whole, and personify it. We need the idea of God on which to base our moral life, although this idea of God is transcendent, *i.e.*, goes beyond experience.

William James (1842-1910), the American philosopher (*see* **Pragmatism**), held much the same view: God cannot be proved to exist, but we have a will to believe which must be satisfied, and the idea works in practice. Hegel (1770-1831) thought of God as a developing process, beginning with "the Absolute" or First Cause and finding its highest expression in man's mind, or reason. It is in man that God most clearly becomes aware of Himself. Finally Comte (1798-1857), the positivist, held that religion belongs to a more primitive state of society and, like many modern philosophers, turned the problem over to believers as being none of the business of science.

Good and Evil.

Early Philosophers' Views. The early Greek philosophers were chiefly concerned with the laws of the universe, consequently it was common belief that knowledge of these laws, and living according to them, constituted the supreme good. Heraclitus, for example, who taught that all things carried with them their opposites, held that good and evil were like two notes in a harmony, necessary to each other. "It is the opposite which is good for us". Democritus, like Epicurus (*q.v.*), held that the main goal of life is happiness, but happiness in moderation. The good man is not merely the one who *does* good but who always *wants* to do so: "You can tell the good man not by his deeds alone but by his desires." Such goodness brings happiness, the ultimate goal. On the other hand, many of the wandering Sophist teachers taught that good was merely social convention, that there are no absolute principles of right and wrong, that each man should live according to his desires and make his own moral code. To Socrates knowledge was the highest good because doing wrong is the result of ignorance: "no man is voluntarily bad." Plato and Aristotle, differing in many other respects, drew attention to the fact that man is composed of three parts: his desires and appetites, his will, and his reason. A man whose reason rules his will and appetites is not only a good but a happy man; for happiness is not an aim in itself but a by-product of the good life. Aristotle, however, emphasised the goal of self-realisation, and thought that if the goal

of life is (as Plato had said) a rational attitude towards the feelings and desires, it needs to be further defined. Aristotle defined it as the "Golden Mean"—the good man is one who does not go to extremes but balances one extreme against another. Thus courage is a mean between cowardice and foolhardiness. The later philosophers Philo and Plotinus held that evil was in the very nature of the body and its senses. Goodness could only be achieved by giving up the life of the senses and, freed from the domination of the body, turning to God, the source of goodness.

Christian Views. St. Augustine taught that everything in the universe is good. Even those things which appear evil are good in that they fit with the harmony of the universe like shadows in a painting. Man should turn his back on the pleasures of the world and turn to the love of God. Peter Abelard (1079-1142) made the more sophisticated distinction when he suggested that the wrongness of an act lies not in the act itself, but in the intention of the doer: "God considers not what is done but in what spirit it is done; and the merit or praise of the agent lies not in the deed but in the intention." If we do what we believe to be right, we may err, but we do not sin. The only sinful man is he who deliberately sets out to do what he knows to be wrong. St. Thomas Aquinas agreed with Aristotle in that he believed the highest good to be realisation of self as God has ordained, and he also agreed with Abelard that intention is important. Even a good act is not good unless the doer intended it to have good consequences. Intention will not make a bad act good, but it is the only thing that will make a good act genuinely good.

In general, Christianity has had difficulties in solving the problem of the existence of evil; for even when one accepts that the evil men do is somehow tied up with the body, it is still difficult to answer the question: how could an all-good God create evil? This is answered in one of two ways: (*a*) that Adam was given free-will and chose to sin (an answer which still does not explain how sin could exist anywhere in the universe of a God who created everything); (*b*) by denying the reality of evil as some Christians have chosen to do (*e.g.*, Christian Science *q.v.*). The Eastern religions, on the other hand (*see* **Zoroastrianism**), solved the problem in a more realistic way by a dualism which denied that their gods were the creators of the whole universe and allowed the existence of at least two gods, one good and one evil. In Christianity there is, of course, a Devil, but it is not explained whence his evil nature came.

Later Philosophic Views. Hobbes equated good with pleasure, evil with pain. They are relative to the individual man in the sense that "one man's meat is another man's poison." Descartes believed that the power to distinguish between good and evil given by God to man is not complete, so that man does evil through ignorance. We act with insufficient knowledge and on inadequate evidence. Locke, believing that at birth the mind is a blank slate, held that men get their opinions of right and wrong from their parents. By and large, happiness is good and pain is evil. But men do not always agree over what is pleasurable and what not. Hence laws exist and these fall into three categories: (1) the divine law; (2) civil laws; (3) matters of opinion or reputation which are enforced by the fact that men do not like to incur the disapproval of their friends. We learn by experience that evil brings pain and good acts bring pleasure and, basically, one is good because not to be so would bring discomfort.

Kant (*see* **God and Man**) found moral beliefs to be inherent in man whether or not they can be proved by reason. There is a categorical imperative which makes us realise the validity of two universal laws: (1) "always act in such a way that the maxim determining your conduct might well become a universal law; act so that you can will that everybody shall follow the principle of your action; (2) "always act so as to treat humanity, whether in thine own person or in that of another, in every case as an end and never as a means."

Schopenhauer (1788–1860) was influenced by Buddhism and saw the will as a blind impelling striving, and desire as the cause of all suffering. The remedy is to regard sympathy and pity as the basis of all morality and to deny one's individual will. This is made easier if we realise that everyone is part of the Universal Will and therefore the one against whom we are struggling is part of the same whole as ourselves.

John Stuart Mill and Jeremy Bentham were both representatives of the Utilitarian school, believing that good is the greatest good (happiness) of the greatest number (see **Utilitarianism**). Lastly, there is the view held mostly by political thinkers that good is what is good for the state or society in general (see **State and Man**).

Guild Socialism, a British form of syndicalism (q.v.) created in 1906 by an architect, A. J. Penty, who was soon joined by A. R. Orage, S. G. Hobson, and G. D. H. Cole. The guild socialists advocated a restoration of the mediaeval guild system as was being recommended by the French syndicalists whose programme involved a return to direct economic action, a functional industrial structure, return of craftsmanship, and distrust of the state. Guild socialists believed that value was created by society as a whole rather than by individuals singly, and that capitalist economists had recommended the acquisition of wealth without emphasising the social responsibilities which wealth should bring. The trade unions were to be organised to take over and run their own industries after nationalisation. Thus guild socialists were not only against capitalism but also against state socialism in which the state took over the control of industry. Political authority was held to be uncongenial to human freedom and therefore nothing was to be gained by the substitution of state bureaucracy for capitalist control. The National Guilds League, formed in 1915, advocated abolition of the wages system, self-government in industry and control by a system of national guilds acting in conjunction with other functional democratic organisations in the community. This body was dissolved in 1925, but the theories of guild socialism have undoubtedly influenced British socialism.

Gurdjieff, Russian–Greek mystic who set up an occult commune at La Prieure in France, to which were attracted a host of the intellectual and literary avant-garde of the 1920s. His teachings, which are immensely obscure, are presented in allegorical form in a lengthy philosophical novel, *All and Everything*, which has the peculiar sub-title "Beelzebub's Tales to his Grandson."

H

Hasidism (Chasidism). From the Hebrew *hasid*, pious or faithful one. A Jewish mystical movement which began in Poland in the 18th century, and which spread widely, first through Eastern Europe and then into Western Europe and America. The movement was founded by Israel ben Eliezer (1700–60), who came to be known as the Ba'al Shem Tov ("Master of the Good Name"). It was originally opposed to the authority of the rabbis and traditional Jewish practices. According to Hasidism, true religion comes not from study of the sacred texts but from purity of heart, prayer and observance of the commandments. The movement was also characterized by ecstatic forms of worship. Its present day followers are ultra-conservative orthodox Jews.

Hedonism. From Greek *hedone*, pleasure. The theory of ethics in which pleasure is regarded as the chief good, or proper end, of action. This is sometimes called ethical hedonism and is then distinguished from psychological hedonism, which is the theory that behaviour is primarily motivated by the pursuit of pleasure and the avoidance of pain. Psychological hedonism can of course be employed to support ethical hedonism.

This view, that only pleasure is ultimately good, has been held by many distinguished philosophers, including Epicurus, Locke, Hobbes, Hume, Bentham and Mill. In the case of the last two, it is closely associated with utilitarianism (q.v.). Although the term "pleasure" suggests physical enjoyments, hedonists have taken it to include intellectual pleasures also. They also argue that many things beside pleasure, such as virtue and knowledge, are desirable in that they produce pleasure.

Heresy, originally meant a sect or school of thought holding views different from others (e.g., Pharisees and Sadducees within Judaism). Later it came to mean beliefs contrary to orthodox teaching (e.g., Arianism, Jansenism, Pelagianism).

Hermeneutics. Originally, the study of the general principles of biblical interpretation. The term was imported into philosophy in the late 19th century to refer to a more general study of interpretation, namely the interpretation of the significance of human actions, utterances, products and institutions.

Hermeticism (or Hermetism). Philosophies based on the Hermetic writings, also called the Hermetica, works on occult, theological and philosophical subjects ascribed to the Egyptian God Thoth (referred to in Greek as Hermes Trismegistos, Hermes the thrice-greatest). This collection, written in Latin and Greek, dates from 2nd–3rd centuries A.D. It reached Europe, from the Arabs, in the late 15th century, and had some influence during the Renaissance. It continues to fascinate modern devotees of magic and astrology.

The term also has a literary sense. It refers to an Italian poetic movement of the 20th century, characterized by brevity and obscurity.

Hinduism, the religion and social institutions of the great majority of the people of India. Hinduism has no fixed scriptural canon but its doctrines are to be found in certain ancient works, notably the *Veda*, the *Brahmanas*, the *Upanishads*, and the *Bhagavad-gita*. The dark-skinned Dravidians invaded India between about 3250 and 2750 B.C. and established a civilisation in the Indus valley. They were polytheists who worshipped a number of nature-gods; some elements of their beliefs persisted into Hinduism. They were subdued by a light-skinned Nordic people who invaded from Asia Minor and Iran about 1500 B.C. The language of these Aryan people was Vedic, parent of Sanskrit in which their religious literature (the Vedas) came to be written after many centuries of oral transmission.

The *Veda* or Sacred Lore has come down to us in the form of mantras or hymns of which there are four great collections, the best-known being the *Rig-Veda*. These Vedic Aryans worshipped nature-deities, their favourites being Indra (rain), Agni (fire), and Surya (the sun). Their religion contained no idolatry but became influenced by the beliefs of the Dravidians, Sacrifice and ritual became predominant in a ceremonial religion.

As a reaction a more philosophic form arose (c. 500 B.C.) with its scriptures in the *Upanishads*. At its highest level known as Brahmanism belief is in a subtle and sophisticated form of monotheism (Brahman is an impersonal, all-embracing spirit), but there is a tolerant acceptance of more primitive beliefs. Thus Vishnu (a conservative principle) and Siva (a destructive principle) grew out of Vedic conceptions. The two great doctrines of Hinduism are *karma* and transmigration. The universal desire to be reunited with the absolute (*atman* or Brahman) can be satisfied by following the path of knowledge. Life is a cycle of lives (*samsara*) in which man's destiny is determined by his deeds (*karma*) from which he may seek release (*moksa*) through ascetic practices or the discipline of Yoga (q.v.). Failure to achieve release means reincarnation—migration to a higher or lower form of life after death—until the ultimate goal of absorption in the absolute is reached.

In the great Sanskrit epic poems *Ramayana* and *Mahabharata* the deity takes three forms, represented by the divine personalities of Brahma, Vishnu, and Siva. There are also lower gods, demi-gods, supernatural beings, and members of the trinity may even become incarnate, as Vishnu became identified with Krishna, one of the heroes of the *Mahabharata* and the well-known *Bhagavad-gita*.

The ritual and legalistic side of Brahmanism is the caste system based on the elaborate codes of the *Law of Manu*, according to which God created distinct orders of men as He created distinct species of animals and plants. Men are born to be Brahmans, soldiers, agriculturists, or servants, but since a Brahman may marry a woman from any of these castes, an endless number of sub-castes arise.

Hinduism has historically shown great tolerance for varieties of belief and practice. Ideas pleasant and unpleasant have been assimilated: fetichism, demon-cults, animal-worship, sexual cults (such as the rites of *Kali* in Calcutta). Today, as would be expected in a country which is in the throes of vast social change, Hinduism itself is changing. Under the impact of modern conditions new ideas are destroying old beliefs and customs. A militant political Hinduism is now threatening the cohesion of India. There are (1995) over 705,000,000 Hindus worldwide. *See also* **Jainism, Sikhism.**

Homoeopathy, an alternative branch of medicine whose motto *Similia Similibus Curantur* (like cures like) sums up its particular approach to therapy. In essence the homoeopathists claim that a disease can be treated by administering quite minute doses of a substance which produce symptoms (in the healthy person) similar to those induced by the disease itself. The founder and populariser of this unusual approach to medicine was the German Samuel Hahnemann who was born in 1775, a friend of the physician Mesmer who propagated hypnotherapy. Hahnemann lived to see his ideas spread across the civilised world (despite the grave theoretical difficulties implicit in the question of how the very minute dosages actually achieve any result at all). Recent years have seen a major growth in public demand for homoeopathy. This has been testified to by general practitioners and hospital staff. The increased interest in homoeopathy, furthermore, is worldwide. France and Germany have a very large number of homoeopathic doctors, and medical students are taught homoeopathy. Other countries, such as India and Australia are also experiencing this increased interest.

The amount of research being carried out in homoeopathy by medical doctors, physicists, molecular biologists, *etc.*, is phenomenal; furthermore, two real breakthroughs occurred in the UK when papers on homoeopathy were published in *The Lancet* in 1988 and in the *British Medical Journal* in 1989.

Humanism, the term applied to (1) a system of education based on the Greek and Latin classics; and (2) the vigorous attitudes that accompanied the end of the Middle Ages and were represented at different periods by the Renaissance, the Reformation, the Industrial Revolution, and the struggle for democracy. These include: release from ecclesiastical authority, the liberation of the intellect, faith in progress, the belief that man himself can improve his own conditions without supernatural help and, indeed has a duty to do so. "Man is the measure of all things" is the keynote of humanism. The humanist has faith in man's intellectual and spiritual resources not only to bring knowledge and understanding of the world but to solve the moral problems of how to use that knowledge. That man should show respect to man irrespective of class, race or creed is fundamental to the humanist attitude to life. Among the fundamental moral principles he would count those of freedom, justice, tolerance and happiness.

Today the idea that people can live an honest, meaningful life without following a formal religious creed of some kind does not seem particularly shocking. Persons seeking to find out more about humanism can apply for information to the British Humanist Association, 47, Theobald's Road, London WC1X 8SP.

Hussites, the followers of John Hus, the most famous pupil of John Wyclif. He was the rector of Prague University and, although it is now by no means certain that his beliefs were heretical, he was condemned to death for heresy and burnt at the stake in 1415 at Constance whence he had come with a safe conduct issued by the Emperor Sigismund of Hungary. The latter based his action on the doctrine that no faith need be kept with heretics, but it is obvious that the main objection to Hus was his contempt for authority of any kind. After their leader's death, the Hussites became a formidable body in Bohemia and Moravia. They took up

arms on behalf of their faith, their religion being strongly imbued with political feeling (hostility to Germanism and to the supremacy of the Roman Church). Their religious struggles for reform led to the Hussite Wars during which the movement splintered into several groups.

Hutterites. *See* **Mennonites, J31.**

I

I Ching, the Chinese "Book of Changes" which is supposed to provide a practical demonstration of the truths of ancient Chinese philosophy. The method consists of casting forty-nine sticks into two random heaps, or more simply, or tossing three coins to see if there is a preponderance of heads or tails. The coins are cast six times whereupon the head-tail sequence achieved is referred to a coded series of phrases in the book, which are supposed to relate in some way to the question held in the mind when the sticks or coins are being cast. The phrases are without exception vague, and platitudinous remarks such as "Evil people do not further the perseverance of the superior man," etc., abound. Consequently it is not difficult to read into such amorphous stuff a suitable "interpretation" or answer to one's unspoken question. The I Ching might well be looked upon as an entertaining parlour game, but it is currently a great fad in Europe and America and is taken with great seriousness by an astonishing number of people.

Idealism, in a philosophical sense, the belief that there is no matter in the universe, that all that exists is mind or spirit. *See* **Mind and Matter** and **Realism.**

Illuminati, a secret society founded in 1776 by Adam Weishaupt, a Bavarian professor of canon law at Ingolstadt, in an attempt to combat superstition and ignorance by founding an association for rational enlightenment and the regeneration of the world. "He tried to give the social ideals of the Enlightenment realisation by conspiratorial means" (J. M. Roberts, *The Mythology of the Secret Societies,* 1972). Under conditions of secrecy it sought to penetrate and control the masonic lodges for subversive purposes. Among its members were Goethe and Schiller. The Order spread to Austria, Italy and Hungary but was condemned by the Roman Catholic Church and dissolved in 1785 by the Bavarian government.

Immortality. The belief in a life after death has been widely held since the earliest times. It has certainly not been universal, nor has it always taken a form which everyone would find satisfying. In the early stages of human history or prehistory everything contained a spirit (*see* Animism) and it is obvious from the objects left in early graves that the dead were expected to exist in some form after death. The experience of dreams, too, seemed to suggest to the unsophisticated that there was a part of man which could leave his body and wander elsewhere during sleep. In order to save space, it will be helpful to classify the various types of belief which have existed in philosophical thought regarding this problem: (1) There is the idea that, although *something* survives bodily death, it is not necessarily eternal. Thus most primitive peoples were prepared to believe that man's spirit haunted the place around his grave and that food and drink should be set out for it, but that this spirit did not go on forever and gradually faded away. (2) The ancient Greeks and Hebrews believed for the most part that the souls of the dead went to a place of shades there to pine for the world of men. Their whining ghosts spent eternity in a dark, uninviting region in misery and remorse. (3) Other people, and there were many more of these, believed in the transmigration of souls with the former life of the individual determining whether his next life would be at a higher or lower level. Sometimes this process seems to have been thought of as simply going on and on, by others (*e.g.*, in Hinduism and Buddhism) as terminating in either non-sentience or union with God but in any case in annihilation of the self as self. Believers in this theory were the Greek philosophers Pythagoras, Empedocles, Plato (who believed that soul comes from God and strives to return to God, according to his own rather confused notions of the deity. If it fails to free itself completely from the body it will sink lower and lower from one body to another.) Plotinus held similar views to Plato, and many other religious sects in addition to those mentioned have believed in transmigration. (4) The belief of Plato and Aristotle that if souls continue to exist after death there is no reason why they should not have existed before birth (this in part is covered by (3)), but some have pointed out that eternity does not mean "from now on," but the whole of the time before and after "now"—nobody, however, so far as one knows, held that *individual* souls so exist. (5) The theory that the soul does not exist at all and therefore immortality is meaningless: this was held by Anaximenes in early Greek times; by Leucippus, Democritus, and the other Greek atomists; by the Epicureans from the Greek Epicurus to the Roman Lucretius; by the British Hobbes and Hume; by Comte of France; and William James and John Dewey of America. (6) The thesis, held notably by Locke and Kant, that although we cannot prove the reality of soul and immortality by pure reason, belief in them should be held for moral ends. (For the orthodox Christian view *see* **God and Man, Determinism and Free-will.**) From this summary we can see that many philosophies and religions (with the important exceptions of Islam and Christianity) without denying a future life do deny the permanence of the individual soul in anything resembling its earthly form (*see* **Spiritualism, Psychic Research**).

Imperialism, the practice by a country, which has become a nation and embarked upon commercial and industrial expansion, of acquiring and administering territories, inhabited by peoples usually at a lower stage of development, as colonies or dependencies. Thus the "typical" imperialist powers of the mid-19th cent. and earlier were Britain, France, Belgium, Holland, Spain and Portugal, whilst Germany, Italy, and Japan, which either did not have unity during this period or adequate industrial expansion, tried to make good their weakness in this direction by war in the late 19th cent. The term "imperialism" is not easy to define today (although often enough used as a term of abuse). There is economic imperialism exerted, not through armies, but through economic penetration. There is what may be described as ideological imperialism, *e.g.*, the anti-communist crusade that led America (in the name of freedom) into a disastrous and widely-condemned war in Vietnam; the dogmatism that led the former Soviet Union into the invasion of Czechoslovakia and Israel into occupying neighbouring lands.

Individualism. The doctrine that the single person is the basic unit of political analysis. The term covers all political and social philosophies that place a high value on the freedom of the individual. It is believed that the interests of the individual are best served by allowing him maximum freedom and responsibility. Society is seen as a collection of individuals. So individualism opposes controls over the individual, especially when they are exercised by the state. The most extreme form is anarchism, but all individualists believe that government interference should be kept to a minimum, and is hence associated with right-wing policies. It is opposed to collectivism (*q.v.*). The term was originally used critically, to refer to self-centred conduct or egoism as a matter of principle.

Irrationalism. An attitude that puts emotion and passion before reason, and which can be exploited for dubious ends.

Islam, the religion of the Arabic and Iranian world of which Mohammed (570–632) was the prophet, the word signifying submission to the will of God. It is one of the most widespread of religions. Its adherents are called Moslems or Muslims. Islam came later than the other great monotheistic religions (Judaism and Christianity) and drew its inspiration mainly from Judaism and Nestorianism. Mohammed accepted the inspiration of the Old Testament and claimed to be a successor to Moses, but recognised Jesus only as a prophet.

The sacred book of Islam is the Koran. Its revelations are contained in 114 *suras* or chapters: all but one begin with the words: "In the name of Allah, the Merciful, the Compassionate." It is written in classical Arabic, and Moslems memorise much or all of it. Its ethical teachings are high. Like orthodox Judaism Islam is a literal-minded religion lived in everyday life. No Moslem is in any doubt as to exactly how he should carry on in the events of his day. He has five duties: (1) Once in his life he must say with absolute conviction: "There is no God but Allah, and Mohammed is His Prophet". (2) Prayer preceded by ablution must be five times daily—on rising, at noon, in mid-afternoon, after sunset, and before retiring. The face of the worshipper is turned in the direction of Mecca. (3) The giving of alms generously, including provisions for the poor. (4) The keeping of the fast of Ramadan, the holy month, during which believers in good health may neither eat nor drink nor indulge in wordly pleasures between sunrise and sunset. (5) Once in his life a Moslem, if he can, must make the pilgrimage to Mecca. In addition, drinking, gambling, and the eating of pork are forbidden and circumcision is practised. Polygamy is permitted, although decreasing; sexual relations outside marriage are disapproved of; marriage is only with the wife's consent; and divorce may be initiated by either husband or wife. A great advantage in the spread of Islam has been its lack of race prejudice.

Mohammed's main achievements were the destruction of idolatry, the welding of warring tribes into one community, the progress of a conquest which led after his death to the great and cultured empire which spread throughout the Middle East into north Africa, north India, and ultimately to Spain. That it did not spread all over Europe was due to the Muslim defeat by Charles Martel at Poitiers in 732.

During the 1980s, militant Islam became a major political force in Iran (under Ayatollah Khomeini). Islamic fundamentalism is now, in the 1990s, a growing political force in, for example, Egypt and Algeria. There are (1995) over 970 m. Moslems in the world.

Britain's Moslem population (1995) numbers c 1·5 million. There are some 450 mosques and numerous prayer centres thoughout Britain. The first was established at Woking in Surrey in 1890. The Central Mosque in London has the largest congregation in Britain while other important centres include Liverpool, Manchester, Leicester and Glasgow.

J

Jainism. The Jains are an Indian sect, largely in commerce and finance. Their movement founded by Vardhamana, called Mahavira (the great hero), in the 6th cent. B.C. arose rather earlier than Buddhism in revolt against the ritualism and impersonality of **Hinduism** (*q.v.*). It rejects the authority of the early Hindu Vedas and does away with many of the Hindu deities whose place is largely taken by Jainism's twenty-four immortal saints; it despises caste distinctions and modifies the two great Hindu doctrines of *karma* and transmigration. Jain philosophy is based on *ahimsa*, the sacredness of all life, regarding even plants as the brethren of mankind, and refusing to kill even the smallest insect. The first Jain temple in the Western world opened in 1988 in Leicester. About one-tenth of India's population is Jain. Jainism claims 30,000 devotees in Britain (1995).

Jansenism, the name given by the Roman Catholic Church to the heresy of Cornelius Jansen (1585–1638), a Dutch-born professor of theology at Louvain, derived from his work *Augustinus*, published after his death. He proposed that without special grace from God, the performance of his commandments is impossible, that man has no free will, and that most human beings are condemned to damnation. The movement based on these ideas was very influential in France in the 17th century.

Jehovah's Witnesses, a religious body who consider themselves to be the present-day representatives of a religious movement which has existed since Abel "offered unto God a more excellent sacrifice than Cain, by which he obtained witness that he was righteous." Abel was the first "witness," and amongst others were Enoch, Noah, Abraham, Moses, Jeremiah, and John the Baptist. Pre-eminent among witnesses, of course, was Jesus Christ who is described in the Book of Revelation as "the faithful and true witness."

Most people are aware that the original movement was founded by Charles Taze Russell (Pastor Russell) of Allegany, Pittsburgh, Pennsylvania, U.S.A. in 1881 under the name, adopted in 1896, of the Watch Tower Bible and Tract Society. Following Pastor Russell's death in 1916 J F. Rutherford seized control of the Watch Tower Bible & Tract Society, dismissed the majority of the Board of Directors, began a revisionist change in doctrine and established dictatorial authority. In 1931 the present name (Jehovah's Witnesses) was adopted.

Their teaching centres upon the early establishment of God's new world on earth, preceded by the second coming of Christ. Witnesses believe this has already happened and that Armageddon "will come as soon as the Witness is completed." The millennial period will give sinners a second chance of salvation and "millions now living will never die" (the title of one of their pamphlets). The dead will progressively be raised to the new earth until all the vacant places left after Armageddon are filled.

Every belief held by the movement, it is asserted, can be upheld, chapter and verse, by reference to the Scriptures. Witnesses regard the doctrine of the Trinity as devised by Satan. In both wars Witnesses have been in trouble for their refusal to take part in war and six thousand suffered for the same reason in German concentration camps.

Jesus People, naive and exhibitionist revival of interest in the teaching and personality of Jesus Christ which featured from the 1960s as part of the American "Hippy" scene. The Jesus people or Jesus Freaks, as they are sometimes called, are generally white but not necessarily of an orthodox Christian background. The cult, like so many others of its kind seems to have developed in California and its adherents adopt the regimental attire (colourful costumes, long hair, beards, etc.) of the modern American Hippy, who is himself a descendant of the Beatnik.

Judaism, the relgion of the Jews, the oldest of the great monotheist religions, parent of Christianity and Islam, the development of which is presented in the Old Testament. The creed of Judaism is based on the concept of a transcendent and omnipotent One True God, the revelation of His will in the *Torah*, and the special relation between God and His "Chosen People." The idea of Incarnation is rejected, Jesus is not recognised as the Messiah. The *Torah* is the Hebrew name for the Law of Moses (the Pentateuch) which, Judaism holds, was divinely revealed to Moses on Mount Sinai soon after the exodus of the Israelites from Egypt (1230 B.C.). Many critics deny the Mosaic authorship of the first five books of the Bible and believe them to be a compilation from four main sources known as J(Jahvist), E (Elohist), D (Deuteronomist) and P (Priestly Code), distinguished from each other by the name used for God, language, style, and internal evidence. From the historical point of view an important influence on Judaism may have been the monotheism of Akhenaten, the "heretic" Pharaoh (note, for example, the striking resemblance between Psalm 104 and Akhenaten's "Hymn to the Sun").

The Talmud is a book containing the civil and canonical laws of the Jews and includes the Mishna, a compilation from oral tradition written in Hebrew, and the Gemara, a collection of comments and criticisms by the Jewish rabbis, written in Aramaic. There are in fact two Talmuds: the one made in Palestine (the Jerusalem Talmud), finished at the beginning of the 5th cent., and the other made in Babylon, completed at the end of the 6th cent.

Judaism at the beginning of the Christian era

had a number of sects: (1) the Pharisees (whose views include the first clear statement of the resurrection of the just to eternal life and the future punishment of the wicked) who held to the *Torah* and the universality of God; (2) the Sadducees, the upper class of priests and wealthy landowners, to whom God was essentially a national God and who placed the interests of the state before the *Torah*; they rejected ideas of resurrection and eternal life; (3) the Essenes (*q.v.*) who were regarded as a puritanical break-away movement by both parties. The views of the Pharisees prevailed.

Jewish writing continued through the years and some books were added to the *Torah*, among them the Three Major Prophets and certain books of the Twelve Minor Prophets. There were also the Apocalyptic writers who were unorthodox in their preaching of a divinely planned catastrophic end to the world with a "new Heaven and a new earth," preceded by a divine Messiah, and a future life—all of which beliefs influenced early Christianity. Judah Halevi of Toledo (c. 1085–c. 1140) and Moses Maimonides of Cordova (1135–1204) were the great Jewish philosophers.

Modern movements in Judaism stem from the Enlightenment, notably with Moses Mendelssohn in the 18th cent. who accepted, as was the tendency of the period, only that which could be proved by reason. He translated the Pentateuch into German thus encouraging German Jews to give up Yiddish and Hebrew for the language of the land and thereby preparing them for their vast contribution to Western civilisation. One of his disciples, David Friedländer (d. 1834) instituted "reform" Judaism. He wanted to eliminate anything that would hamper the relationships of Jews with their neighbours or tend to call in doubt their loyalty to their adopted state. A similar movement in America (1885) called for the rejection of dietary laws, the inauguration of Sunday services, and the repudiation of Jewish nationalism. Between "reform" and orthodoxy there arose the conservative movement which, in England, includes prayers in English in the service, does not segregate men and woman in the synagogue, and translates the Law in a more liberal way.

Judaism is essentially a social and family religion which, more than almost any other concerns itself with the observances of every aspect of daily life. As in Islam (*q.v.*) details are laid down in the most minute way for the behaviour of the orthodox.

The home is the main Jewish institution and Jews, like Catholics, cannot surrender their religion. Circumcision takes place eight days after birth, and a boy becomes a man for religious purposes at his Bar Mitzvah at the age of thirteen. Women are spared most of this because their place in the home is considered sufficiently sacred. Among festivals are Passover, recalling the Exodus; Rosh Hashanah (the Jewish New Year), the anniversary of the Creation and the beginning of ten days of penitence ending with Yom Kippur (the Day of Atonement), a day of fasting spent in the synagogue; Purim, celebrating the deliverance of the Jews from Haman; and Chanukah, celebrating their victory against the Syrians under their leader Judas Maccabeus. A new and semi-religious festival is the Yom Haatzmaut, the anniversary of the birth of the new Jewish state of Israel. The total numbers of world Jewry are estimated to be 17·8 million (1995).

K

Kabbala. *See* Cabala.

Ku Klux Klan. After the American Civil War (1861–65) southern conservatives and ex-Confederate leaders began to fear (as they had every reason to do) both Negro and poor White rule. Taxes were rising owing to radical legislation and the tax-burdened and disenfranchised planters finally took to illegal means to achieve their ends by trying to effect an alliance with the poor White and small farmer through appealing to his anti-Negro prejudice.

Hence the Ku Klux Klan was formed in 1866

as a secret society by a small group of Confederate veterans in Tennessee with the intention of frightening Negroes by dressing in ghostly white robes in the guise of the spirits of dead soldiers. But the movement spread like wild-fire throughout the South encouraged by small farmers and planters alike. General Nathan Bedford Forrest was appointed "Grand Wizard" of the Klan "empire" and in every community armed Klansmen riding at night horsewhipped "uppity" Negroes, beat Union soldiers, and threatened carpet-bag politicians (*i.e.*, fortune-hunters from the North). Soon several similar organisations arose, many of which did not stop at torture, burning property, and murder. In fact, although claiming to be a "holy crusade" the Klan was a vicious and contemptible organisation in which former Southern leaders trying to regain control deliberately set poor and middle-class Whites against the Negroes by appeal to race prejudice. Congress struck back with laws and intervention of Federal troops, and after a large number of convictions in South Carolina much of the violence stopped.

After the 1914–18 war the movement, dormant since 1900, revived as a sadistic anti-Negro, anti-Jewish, anti-Catholic society, spreading to the north as well as the south. By 1926, with its white-gowned hooligans and fiery crosses, the Klan began to subside once more. While it revived again in the mid-60s, the Klan has recently suffered a loss of support. Membership in 1993 was estimated at a mere 6,000. However, fuelled by unemployment and events such as the 1992 Los Angeles race riots, another 20,000 Americans belong to no fewer than 346 'white supremacy' groups.

L

Lamaism, the religion of Tibet. Its beliefs and worship derive from the Mahayana form of Buddhism which was introduced into Tibet in 749. The emphasis laid by its founder on the necessity for self-discipline and conversion through meditation and the study of philosophy deteriorated into formal monasticism and ritualism. The Dalai Lama, as the reincarnated Buddha, was both king and high priest, a sort of pope and emperor rolled into one. Under him was a hierarchy of officials in which the lowest order was that of the monks who became as numerous as one man in every six or seven of the population. The main work carried out by this vast church-state was the collection of taxes to maintain the monasteries and other religious offices. Second in power to the Dalai Lama was the Panchen or Tashi Lama believed to be a reincarnation of Amitabha, another Buddha. The last Dalai Lama fled to India in 1959 when the Chinese entered his country. For a brief period following his departure, the Panchen Lama surprised the Western world by publicly welcoming the Communist invasion, but he later renounced the regime and the suppression of Lamaism in Tibet continued unchecked.

Latter-day Saints. *See* **Mormons (J35).**

Levellers, an English military-politico-religious party prominent in the Parliamentary Army about 1647 which stood for the rights of the people. *See* **Diggers.**

Liberalism. The Liberal Party is the successor to the Whigs (a nickname derived from *Whiggamore*, used in the 17th cent. for Scottish dissenters) of the 18th and 19th cents. Under Gladstone's two great ministries (1868–74; and 1880–85), and again under Campbell-Bannerman and Asquith (1906–14) much reforming legislation was enacted. The Asquith–Lloyd George split of 1916, and the advent of Labour as a major party after 1918, have caused the Liberals to be relegated as a smaller, third party. In the decade after 1945, there were times when the Liberal Party barely survived. But revivals have since occurred under the leadership of Jo Grimond (1962), Jeremy Thorpe (1974), David Steel (1979) and Paddy Ashdown (since 1988).

Liberal philosophy is moderately radical and progressive in terms of social reform. But the party strongly disapproves of state control or any form of monopoly, private or public. The main proposals favoured by the party are co-ownership in industry, proportional representation, greater protection of individual liberties, and separate Parliaments for Wales and Scotland. Many younger members of the party hold views to the left of official party policy. The phenomenon of "community politics" has owed much to these younger, radical Liberals. The 1987 election setback heralded a merger ("democratic fusion") between the Liberals and their SDP Alliance partners. The new Social and Liberal Democratic Party (SLD) was formed in 1988. The first leader of the new party is Paddy Ashdown, MP for Yeovil. The new party (known as the Liberal Democrats) has been faced with the twin problems of putting forward a clear political ideology and also dealing with the revived Labour Party. In the 1992 election, it failed to make significant inroads, returning 20 MPs, having gained 4 seats but lost 6. Since 1992, it has won spectacular by-election victories (at Newbury and Christchurch in 1993, at Eastleigh in 1994) and sweeping local council successes. It also elected its first 2 MEPs in the June 1994 European elections.

Libertarianism, a political belief in free trade, individual liberty and respect for the lives and property of others. Essentially it is the modern day form of classical liberalism. Today the tradition is carried on by, among others: Frederick Hayek, Murray Rothbard, Ayn Rand and Robert Nozick.

Logical Positivism, a school of philosophy founded in Vienna in the 1920s by a group known as "the Vienna circle": their work was based on that of Ernst Mach, but dates in essentials as far back as Hume. Of the leaders of the group, Schlick was murdered by a student, Wittgenstein came to Britain, and Carnap went to America following the entry of the Nazis. Briefly the philosophy differs from all others in that, while most people have believed that a statement might be (a) true, or (b) false, logical positivists consider there to be a third category; a statement may be meaningless. There are only two types of statement which can be said to have meaning: (1) those which are tautological, *i.e.*, those in which the statement is merely a definition of the subject, such as "a triangle is a three-sided plane figure" ("triangle" and "three-sided plane figure" are the same thing); and (2) those which can be tested by sense experience. This definition of meaningfulness excludes a great deal of what has previously been thought to be the field of philosophy; in particular it excludes the possibility of metaphysics. Thus the question as to whether there is a God or whether free-will exists is strictly meaningless for it is neither a tautological statement nor can it be tested by sense experience.

Lollards, a body of religious reformers and followers of Wyclif who were reviled and persecuted in the reign of Richard II. The name "Lollard" comes from a Flemish word meaning "mutterer"—a term of contempt used to describe the sect. Under Henry V, determined efforts were made to crush the Lollards. Their leader, Sir John Oldcastle, was burnt at the stake (December 1417).

Luddites, a group of peasants and working men who deliberately destroyed spinning and farm machinery in England in the early part of the 19th cent., fearing that such devices would destroy their livelihood. Their name was taken from the eccentric Ned Lud who had done the same in a less organised way two or three decades earlier. The Luddites' worst fears were of course not realised, for far from putting human beings out of work the industrial revolution created jobs for a vastly increased population. Luddism, dormant for over a century, is beginning to appear again, if in muted form.

Lutheranism. The Reformation had a long history before it became, under Luther and Calvin, an accepted fact. The mediaeval Church had held (as the Catholic Church holds today) that the sacraments were the indispensable means of salvation. Since these were exclusively administered by the clergy, any movement which attacked clerical abuses was forced by sheer necessity to deny the Church's exclusive control of the means of salvation, before it could become free from dependence on a corrupt priesthood. Hence the Albigenses and the Waldenses (qq.v.), the followers of John Hus and Wycliff (see **Anticlericalism**), were bound to deny the authority of the Church and emphasise that of the Bible. Luther began his movement primarily in order to reform the Church from its gross abuses and the famous ninety-five theses nailed to the door of the Church at Wittenberg in 1517 were not primarily theological but moral complaints dealing with the actual behaviour of the clergy rather than Church beliefs. But, unlike the earlier reformers, Luther had arrived at the right moment in history when economic individualism and the force of nationalism were bound, sooner or later, to cause the authorities in Germany to line up on his side. Thus he began with the support of the peasants who were genuinely shocked at the abuse of indulgences and other matters, but ended up by being supported by the noblemen who wanted to destroy the power of the pope over the German states and looked forward to confiscating the lands and property of the Church. When the peasants wanted the reform of actual economic abuses relating to the feudal system, Luther took the side of the nobles against them. The contemporary movement in Switzerland led by Ulrich Zwingli had no such secular support, and Zwingli was killed in 1531.

Martin Luther (1483–1546) was the son of a miner in Eisleben in Saxony, entered the order of Austin Friars in 1505, and later taught at the newly founded university of Wittenberg. After the publication of the theses the real issue so far as the Church was concerned was whether he was willing or not to submit to the authority of his superiors; Luther refused to compromise with his conscience in the famous words: "Here I stand; I can do no other." In a further statement Luther recommended the formation of a German national church, the abolition of indulgences and other means whereby Rome obtained money from Germany, and an end to the celibacy of the clergy. For this he was naturally excommunicated. His teaching was based on the German translation of the Bible, but he was by no means a fundamentalist: e.g., he denied that the Book of Hebrews was written by Paul, would have nothing to do with the Apocrypha, and regarded the letter of James as "an epistle of straw." The Scriptures were open to all and could be interpreted by private judgment enlightened by the Spirit of God. Like Calvin, Luther was a predestinarian and determinist, but he was also a conservative and soon became alarmed about the position taken by many extremists once the Reformation was under way. He had really wanted the Church to reform itself, but when he alienated Rome he had perforce to rely more and more on the secular powers which finally resulted in the state-church form which became pronounced in Prussia and later elsewhere. Whereas Calvin wished the Church to be at least the equal of the State and in some respects its superior, Luther's rebellion resulted in the reverse, a state-controlled episcopalianism. See **Calvinism, Presbyterianism**.

Lycanthropy, the belief that men may, by the exercise of magical powers or because of some inherited affliction, occasionally transform into wolves. The so-called werewolf is an important feature of mid-European folklore and much the same can be said of the were-tigers and were-bears of Africa and the Far East. There is, needless to say, no such thing as a genuine werewolf known to biology, but it is not hard to see how legends of their existence could arise. There are a number of mental illnesses in which men may deliberately or unconsciously mimic the actions of animals and there are a number of endocrinological disorders which may cause gross changes in the features of the individuals, including the excessive growth of hair. In times when the physiological bases of such afflictions were not properly understood, sufferers from such complaints could easily be persuaded, either by themselves or others, that they were in fact wolfmen. Once the mythology of lycanthropy is established in a society, then of course it will be used

by unscrupulous individuals for their own ends —for example revenge killings by people dressed as animals—thus helping to perpetuate the legend.

M

McLuhanism. According to Marshall McLuhan (1911–80), a Canadian, and former professor of English at Toronto, the way people communicate is more important than what they communicate: hence his famous slogan, "the medium is the message." There have been two great landmarks in human understanding since we learnt to speak and write: the invention of the printed book and the present electronic revolution. The printed word took us step by step along the linear, logical path to understanding; television comes at us from all directions at once. "Electronic circuitry has overthrown the regime of 'time' and 'space' . . . Its message is Total Change."

McLuhan's importance lies in alerting us to the present clash between two great technologies, the literate and the electromagnetic, and in his vision, beyond the present chaos, of a world drawn tighter together in a "global village" where identity will merge in collectivity and we shall all be able to co-operate for the common good instead of being split up into warring nations.

Magic, a form of belief originating in very early days and based on the primitive's inability to distinguish between similarity and identity. The simplest example would perhaps be the fertility rites in which it is believed that a ceremony involving sexual relations between men and women will bring about fertility in the harvest. Or the idea that sticking pins in an image of an individual will bring about harm or even death to the real person. Magic is regarded by some as a form of early science in that man in his efforts to control Nature had recourse to magical practices when the only methods he knew had failed to bring the desired results. It filled a gap. By others magic is regarded as an elementary stage in the evolution of religion. It can be said to have served a purpose there too. Yet magic differs from religion, however closely at times it may come to be related with it in this important respect: religion depends upon a power outside and beyond human beings, whereas magic depends upon nothing but the casting of a spell or the performance of a ceremony—the result follows automatically.

The idea that "like produces like" is at the roots of imitative magic. It follows that an event can be compelled by imitating it. One engages in swinging, not for pleasure, but to produce a wind as the swing does; ball games are played to get rainy weather because the black ball represents dark rainclouds; other ball games, in which one attempts to catch the ball in a cup or hit it with a stick, represent the sexual act (as some gentlemen at Lords may be distressed to hear) and bring about fertility; in medicine until a few centuries ago herbs were chosen to cure a disease because in some respects their leaves or other parts looked like the part of the body affected (e.g., the common wildflower still known as "eye-bright" was used in bathing the eyes because the flower looks like a tiny eye). See **Witchcraft, Demonism**.

Malthusianism, the theory about population growth put forward by the Rev. Thomas Malthus (1766–1834) in An Essay on Population (1798). His three main propositions were (1) "Population is necessarily limited by means of subsistence." (2) "Population invariably increases where means of subsistence increase unless prevented by some very powerful and obvious checks." (3) "These checks, and the checks which repress the superior power of population, and keep its effects on a level with the means of subsistence, are all resolvable into moral restraint, vice and misery." In other words, no matter how great the food supply may become, human reproductive power will always adjust itself so that food will always be scarce in relation to population; the only means to deal with this is by "moral restraint" (*i.e.*, chastity or not marrying), "vice" (*i.e.*, birth-control methods), or misery (*i.e.*, starvation). More specifically, Malthus claimed that while food increases by arithmetical progression, population increases by geometrical progression. It is true that these gloomy predictions did not take place in Malthus's time largely owing to the opening up of new areas of land outside Europe, the development of new techniques in agriculture, the growth of international trade to poorer areas, the increased knowledge of birth-control, and developments in medical science which reduced the misery he had predicted. Furthermore, we now know that as a society becomes industrialised its birth-rate tends to fall. Growth in the world's population has increased from about 465 million in 1650 to over 5,500 million by 1994.

Manichaeism, an Asiatic religion which developed from Zoroastrianism (*q.v.*) and shows the influence of Buddhism (*q.v.*) and Gnosticism (*q.v.*), being founded by Mani, a Persian who was born in Babylonia, *c.* 216 A.D. Mani presented himself to Shapur I as the founder of a new religion which was to be to Babylonia what Buddhism was to India or Christianity to the West. His aspiration was to convert the East and he himself made no attempt to interfere directly with Christianity although he represented himself as the Paraclete (the Holy Ghost or "Comforter") and, like Jesus, had twelve disciples. His success in Persia aroused the fury of the Zoroastrian priests who objected to his reforming zeal towards their religion and in 276 Mani was taken prisoner and crucified.

Of Mani's complicated system little can be said here, save that it is based on the struggle of two eternal conflicting principles, God and matter, or light and darkness. Although its founder had no intention of interfering with the West, after his death his followers soon spread the religion from Persia and Mesopotamia to India and China. It reached as far as Spain and Gaul and influenced many of the bishops in Alexandria and in Carthage where for a time St. Augustine accepted Manichaeism. Soon the toleration accorded it under Constantine ended and it was treated as a heresy and violently suppressed. Yet it later influenced many heresies, and even had some influence on orthodox Catholicism which had a genius for picking up elements in other religions which had been shown to appeal to worshippers provided they did not conflict unduly with fundamental beliefs.

Maoism is the branch of communism in China that was shaped by one of the most remarkable statesmen of modern times, Mao Tse-tung (1893–1976). He set the pattern of revolution for poor peasant societies and restored pride and confidence to his fellow countrymen after years of turmoil and brutality. Although Marxist theory guided the Chinese communists in their struggle for liberation from the old, bourgeois and feudal China, it was interpreted in a manner peculiar to China and developed to fit into the Chinese way of life and the "thoughts" of Chairman Mao. As early as 1926 Mao had pointed out that the Chinese proletariat had in the peasantry its staunchest and most numerous ally. "A rural revolution," he said, "is a revolution by which the peasantry overthrows the authority of the feudal landlord class." The struggles of 1925–49 (the Long March of the Red Army, the Anti-Japanese War, the Civil War against Chiang Kai-shek) were the foundations on which present-day China has been built. Maoism is against authoritarianism and for self-reliance; against bureaucracy and for revolutionary momentum; against rivalry between individuals and for common effort. Great efforts have been made to remove poverty, ignorance, corruption and disease from China. Mao taught that struggle is necessary for the revolution to endure. "Running water does not go stale and door-hinges do not become worm-eaten," Mao reminded his comrades. "We must," he said, "make every comrade understand that the highest criterion for judging the words and deeds of the communists is whether they conform with the best interests and win the support of the broadest masses of the people." The effect of the death of Mao Tse-tung on

Chinese communism has been a huge shift towards the modernisation of China.

Marxism. The sociological theories founded by Karl Marx and Friedrich Engels on which modern communist thought is based. Marx and Engels lived in a period of unrestrained capitalism when exploitation and misery were the lot of the industrial working classes, and it was their humanitarianism and concern for social justice which inspired their work. Marx wrote his *Communist Manifesto* in Brussels in 1848 and in his great work, *Das Kapital* (1867), he worked out a new theory of society. Marx showed that all social systems are economically motivated and change as a result of technical and economic changes in methods of production. The driving force of social change Marx found to be in the struggle which the oppressed classes wage to secure a better future. Thus in his celebrated theory of historical materialism he interpreted history in terms of economics and explained the evolution of society in terms of class struggle. (*See* **Dialectical Materialism.**) "In the social production of their means of existence," he wrote, "men enter into definite and unavoidable relations which are independent of their will. These productive relationships correspond to the particular stage in the development of their material productive forces." Marx's theory of historical materialism implies that history is propelled by class struggle with communism and the classless society as the final stage when man will have emancipated himself from the productive process. Marx was the first to put socialism on a rational and scientific basis, and he foretold that socialism would inevitably replace capitalism. His prophecy, however, came to realisation not in the advanced countries as he had envisaged but in backward Russia and China. *See* **Communism, J10.**

Materialism. Any theory that tends to the view that only matter or material objects exist and that everything else, notably minds and mental experiences, can be described in material terms. Materialism is thus opposed to dualism or idealism and, in general, to any belief in God, in disembodied spirits *etc.* There is much contemporary philosophical debate as to whether "consciousness" is not a name for something mysterious, but simply a way of talking about the brain. *See also* **Mind and Matter.**

There is, of course, the popular and quite different sense of the term, which emphasizes the value of material possessions.

Mechanism. As a theory, the view that everything happens mechanically, that natural phenomena are to be explained by reference to certain laws of nature applied to the behaviour of matter in motion. Through the influence of science, there is a strong tendency in Western thought to compare the universe or parts of it, even human beings, to machines. It is a view closely connected with materialism.

Mennonites, a Christian sect rejecting infant baptism. Named after Menno Simons (1496–1559). Its members reject military service and refuse to hold public office. Hutterites share their beliefs.

Mesmerism, a rapidly vanishing name to denote the practice of hypnosis, which owes its popularity, though not its discovery, to the Austrian physician, Anton Mesmer (1733–1815). Mesmer's contribution was the realisation that a large number of what we would today call psycho-somatic or hysterical conditions could be cured (or at least temporarily alleviated) by one or another form of suggestion. Mesmer himself relied on the idea of what he called "animal magnetism," a supposedly potent therapeutic force emanating from the living body which could be controlled by the trained individual. Mesmer used wands and impressive gadgetry to dispense the marvellous force and he effected a remarkable number of cures of complaints, hitherto looked upon as incurable or totally mysterious in origin—the most typical of these being hysterical blindness, paralysis or deafness, nervous skin conditions, and so on. Hypnosis, which is a valid if very poorly understood psychological phenomenon even today, would probably have been developed much further had not efficient general anaesthetics such as ether, nitrous oxide, etc., been discovered, thus greatly diminishing its role as a pain reliever in surgery. Mesmer, who was three parts charlatan, never really troubled to think deeply about the cause of his undoubted success. The first man to treat hysteria as a formal class of illness and who made a scientific attempt to treat it with hypnosis was Ambrose Liébeault (1823–1904). He and his colleagues Hippolyte Bernheim (1840–1919) believed: (a) that hysteria was produced by suggestion, and particularly by autosuggestion on the part of the patient, and (b) that suggestion was a normal trait found in varying degrees in everyone. These conclusions are true, but as Freud showed later are far from being the whole truth.

Messianism. Most varieties of religious belief rely on the assumption that the deity is a supernatural being either permeating the universe or dwelling in some other sphere and normally inaccessible to man. Where divine intervention is necessary, the deity is traditionally believed to nominate a human being—in the case of Christianity, for example, Jesus is believed to be the actual son of God. Messianic cults introduce a novel variant on the traditional theme. In these a human being is held to be God himself. He may either nominate himself for this role, relying on his own personality or native talent to acquire the necessary following, or for one reason or another large numbers of people may alight on one individual and declare him the Messiah. While it might seem that beliefs of this kind would be confined to earlier epochs in man's recorded history, this is in fact not the case. In the past century, and even within recent decades, a number of individuals have been held by groups to be actually divine. Among these were the Dutchman Lourens van Voorthuizen, a former fisherman who declared himself to be God in 1950 and got large numbers to accept his claim; the Anglican priest Henry James Prince, who did much the same thing in 1850; and of course the famous Negro George Baker, who convinced hundreds of thousands of other Negroes that he was "Father Divine." To simple people the idea that God is to be found on earth and that one may even be personally introduced to him, is an obviously attractive one. The trouble is that all self-styled gods to this present date have eventually disappointed their supporters by performing that most human of acts—dying.

Metapsychology. Not to be confused with parapsychology (q.v.). The branch or off-shoot of psychology which goes beyond empirical and experimental studies to consider such philosophical matters as the nature of mind, the reality of free-will and the mind/body problem. It was originally used by Freud as a blanket descriptive term denoting all mental processes, but this usage is now obsolete.

Methodism, the religious movement founded by John Wesley in 1738, at a time when the Anglican Church was in one of its periodic phases of spiritual torpor, with the simple aim of spreading "scriptural holiness" throughout the land. Up to that time Wesley had been a High Churchman but on a visit to Georgia in the United States he was much impressed by the group known as Moravians (q.v.), and on his return to this country was introduced by his brother Charles, who had already become an adherent, to Peter Böhler, a Moravian minister in England. Passing through a period of spiritual commotion following the meeting, he first saw the light at a small service in Aldersgate in May 1738 "where one was reading Luther's preface to the Epistle to the Romans" and from this time forth all Wesley's energies were devoted to the single object of saving souls. He did this for fifty years and at the end of his life confessed that he had wasted fifteen minutes in that time by reading a worthless book. Even when he was over eighty he still rose at 4 a.m. and toiled all day long.

Soon Whitefield, a follower with Calvinist views, was preaching throughout the country and Charles Wesley was composing his well-known hymns; John's abilities at this time were taken up in organising the movement described as "People called Methodists." They were to be arranged in "societies" which were united into "circuits" under a minister, the circuits

into "districts" and all knit together into a single body under a conference of ministers which has met annually since 1744. Local lay preachers were also employed and to maintain interest the ministers were moved from circuit to circuit each year. These chapel services were not originally meant to conflict with the Church of England of which Wesley still considered himself a member. They were purely supplementary, and it used to be the custom (before the Methodists began to count themselves as Nonconformists) for Methodists to attend Church in the morning and Chapel in the evening.

The class-meeting was the unit of the organisation where members met regularly under a chosen leader to tell their "experiences" upon which they were often subjected to severe cross-examination. At the end of every quarter, provided their attendance was regular, they received a ticket of membership which entitled them to come to monthly sacramental services. If attendance was inadequate the name was removed from the list, without appearance on which nobody was deemed a member. The price of the ticket was "a penny a week and a shilling a quarter" but Wesley was not interested in receiving money from anyone who was not utterly devoted to the cause.

John Wesley introduced four other innovations, some of which were regarded by Churchmen who had previously been willing to commend his efforts in bringing religion to the poorer classes as dangerous: (1) He started the Sunday-school scheme and afterwards enthusiastically supported that of John Raikes, often regarded as the founder of the idea; this was of immense importance in the days before the Education Acts. (2) He reintroduced the Agapae or "love feasts" of the early Church which were fellowship meetings deepening the sense of brotherhood of the society. (3) He began to copy the open-air meetings of the eloquent Whitefield and soon unwittingly produced the most extraordinary results, finding that his sermons led to groans, tears, fainting-fits, and all sorts of emotional expression. Even his open-air lay speakers produced like results and these came to be associated with Methodism and gave significance to the proud Anglican claim that their services would be "without enthusiasm." (4) After some hesitation he ventured to consecrate Dr. Thomas Coke, who was being sent as a missionary to America, as a bishop of his church. In addition to Wesley's religious work he was a great educator of the common man. Thus he introduced the cheap book and the church magazine, publishing books of any sort which he thought would edify and not harm even when the views expressed were different from his own—e.g., Thomas à Kempis's Imitation of Christ and works of history, biography, science, and medicine in some cases written by himself. In this way the movement with its cheap books and reading rooms had an influence far beyond its actual membership. Both the Anglican Church and the Evangelical movement of Wilberforce and others profited from Wesley's work.

Methodism, especially after Wesley's death in 1791, began, like other movements, to develop schisms. These were the long-standing differences which the Baptist movement (q.v.) had shown too between Arminian and Calvinist sections—i.e., between those who did and those who did not accept the doctrine of predestination. In the case of the Methodists, this led to a complete break in 1811. Then there were differences associated with the status of the laity, or the relationship of the movement with the Anglican Church. The "Methodist New Connection" of 1797 differed only in giving the laity equal representation with the ministers but the more important break of the Primitive Methodists in 1810 gave still more power to the laity and reintroduced the "camp-meeting" type of service. In 1815 the Bryanites or "Bible Christians" were formed, and a further schism which was even brought before the law courts was ostensibly over the foundation of a theological college. The real reason, of course, was that the ministers were becoming more Tory, whilst the laity were becoming more Radical. Finally in 1932, at a conference in the

Albert Hall in London, the Wesleyan Methodists, the Primitive Methodists, and the United Methodists became one Church, the Methodist Church.

Adult Methodist membership has fallen recently, from 841,000 in 1930, to 729,000 in 1960 and now to *c.* 410,000 (1995). During 1994, leading Methodists began exploratory talks with Anglicans about reunion.

Millenarianism. The belief in a future "millenium", that is, the thousand year reign of Christ on earth. The idea however has pre-Christian roots and is reflected in Jewish and Islamic thought. It is not part of orthodox Christianity, but many sects in the 19th century, like the Plymouth Brethren and Adventists, espoused millenarianism. The idea has since broadened to mean any theory with an expectation of some transforming change: not only the Kingdom of God, but also, the just society, or harmony amongst peoples.

Mind and Matter.

Early Greek Views: Idealism and Dualism. Primitive peoples could see that there is a distinction between those things which move and do things by themselves and others, such as stones, which do not. Following the early state of **Animism** (*q.v.*), in which spirits were believed to have their abode in everything, they began to differentiate between matter or substance and a force which seems to move it and shape it into objects and things. Thus to the Greek Parmenides (fl. *c.* 475 B.C.), who was a philosopher of pure reason, thought or mind was the creator of what we observe and in some way not quite clear to himself it seemed that mind was the cause of everything. This is perhaps the first expression of the movement known as Idealism which says, in effect, that the whole universe is mental—a creation either of our own minds or the mind of God. But from Anaxagorus (488–428 B.C.) we have the clearer statement that mind or *nous* causes all movement but is distinct from the substance it moves. He does not, however, think in terms of individual minds but rather of a kind of generalised mind throughout the universe which can be used as an explanation of anything which cannot be explained otherwise. This is the position known as Dualism (*q.v.*) which holds that both mind and matter exist and interact but are separate entities.

Most people in practice are dualists since, rightly or wrongly, mind and body are thought of as two different things: it is the "commonsense" (although not necessarily the true) point of view. Plato in a much more complex way was also a dualist although he held that the world of matter we observe is in some sense not the genuine world. The real world is the world of ideas and the tree we see is not real but simply matter upon which mind or soul has imprinted the idea of a tree. Everything that exists has its corresponding form in the world of ideas and imprints its pattern upon matter. Mind has always existed and, having become entangled with matter, is constantly seeking to free itself and return to God.

Plato's pupil Aristotle had a much more scientific outlook and held that, although it was mind which gave matter its form, mind is not *outside* matter, as Plato had thought, but *inside* it as its formative principle. Therefore there could be no mind without matter and no matter without mind; for even the lowest forms of matter have some degree of mind which increases in quantity and quality as we move up the scale to more complex things.

So far, nobody had explained how two such different substances as matter and mind could influence each other in any way, and this remains, in spite of attempts to be mentioned later, a basic problem in philosophy.

Two later ideas, one of them rather foolish and the other simply refusing to answer the question, are typified by the Stoics and some members of the Sceptic school. The first is that only matter exists and what we call mind is merely matter of a finer texture, a view which as an explanation is unlikely to satisfy anyone; the other, that of some Sceptics, is that we can know nothing except the fleeting images or thoughts that flicker through our consciousness. Of either mind or matter we know nothing.

Renaissance Attitude. Christian doctrines have already been dealt with (*see* **God and Man, Determinism and Free-will**), and the past and future of the soul is dealt with under **Immortality**. Nor need we mention the Renaissance philosophers who were really much more concerned about how to use mind than about its nature. When they did consider the subject they usually dealt with it, as did Francis Bacon, by separating the sphere of science from that of religion and giving the orthodox view of the latter because there were still good reasons for not wishing to annoy the Church.

17th-cent. Views: Hobbes, Descartes, Guelincx, Spinoza, Locke, Berkeley. Thomas Hobbes in the 17th cent. was really one of the first to attempt a modern explanation of mind and matter even if his attempt was crude. As a materialist he held that all that exists is matter and hence our thoughts, ideas, images, and actions are really a form of motion taking place within the brain and nerves. This is the materialist theory which states that mind does not exist.

Thus there are three basic theories of the nature of mind and body: idealism, dualism, and materialism, and we may accept any one of the three. But, if we accept dualism, we shall have to explain precisely the relationship between body and mind. In some of his later writings Hobbes seems to suggest that mental processes are the effects of motion rather than motion itself; *i.e.*, they exist, but only as a result of physical processes just as a flame does on a candle. This theory of the relationship is known as *epiphenomenalism.*

Descartes, the great French contemporary of Hobbes, was a dualist who believed that mind and matter both exist and are entirely different entities; therefore he had to ask himself how, for example, the desire to walk leads to the physical motion of walking. His unsatisfactory answer was that, although animals are pure automatons, man is different in that he has a soul which resides in the pineal gland (a tiny structure in the brain which today we know to be a relic of evolution with no present function whatever). In this gland the mind comes in contact with the "vital spirits" of the body and thus there is interaction between the two. This theory is known as *interactionism,* and since we do not accept its basis in the function of the pineal gland, we are simply left with the notion of interaction but without the explanation of how it takes place.

One of Descartes's successors, Arnold Guelincx, produced the even more improbable theory of *psychophysical parallelism* sometimes known as the theory of the "two clocks". Imagine you have two clocks, each keeping perfect time, then supposing you saw one and heard the other, every time one points to the hour the other will strike, giving the impression that the first event causes the second, although in fact they are quite unrelated. So it is with the body and mind in Guelincx's view, each is "wound up" by God in the beginning in such a way as to keep time with the other so that when I have the desire to walk, purely unrelated physical events in my legs cause them to move at the same time. A variety of this theory is *occasionism,* which says that whenever something happens in the physical world, God affects us so that we *think* we are being affected by the happening.

The trouble about all these theories is (a) that they really explain nothing, and (b) that they give us a very peculiar view of God as a celestial showman treating us as puppets when it would surely have been easier to create a world in which mind and matter simply interacted by their very nature. Spinoza, too, believed in a sort of psychophysical parallelism in that he did not think that mind and body interacted. But since in his theory everything is God, mind and matter are simply two sides of the same penny.

John Locke, another contemporary, thought of the mind as a blank slate upon which the world writes in the form of sensations, for we have no innate or inborn ideas and mind and matter do interact although he does not tell us how. All we know are sensations—*i.e.*, sense impressions. Bishop Berkeley carried this idea to its logical conclusion: if we know nothing but sensations, we have no reason to suppose that matter exists at all. He was, therefore, an idealist.

18th cent. Views: Hume, Kant. David Hume went further still and pointed out that, if all we know are sensations, we cannot prove the existence of matter but we cannot prove the existence of mind either. All we can ever know is that ideas, impressions, thoughts, follow each other. We do not even experience a self or personality because every time we look into our "minds" all we really experience are thoughts and impressions. Hume was quick to point out that this was not the same as saying that the self did not exist; it only proved that we cannot know that it does.

Kant made it clear that, although there is a world outside ourselves, we can never know what it is really like. The mind receives impressions and forms them into patterns which conform not to the thing-in-itself but to the nature of mind. Space and time, for example, are not realities but only the form into which our mind fits its sensations. In other words our mind shapes impressions which are no more like the thing in itself than the map of a battlefield with pins showing the position of various army groups at any given moment is like the battle-field. This, of course, is true. From physics and physiology we know that the sounds we hear are "really" waves in the air, the sights we see "really" electromagnetic waves. What guarantee do we have that the source is "really" like the impression received in our brain? Kant was the leader of the great German Idealist movement of the 18th cent. which in effect said: "why bother about matter when all we can ever know is mental?"

19th and 20th cent. Views. The Englishman Bradley, and the Frenchman Henri Bergson in the 19th and early 20th cent. both held in one form or another the belief that mind in some way creates matter and were, therefore, idealists, whereas Comte, the positivist (*q.v.*), and the Americans William James and John Dewey, held that mind is a form of behaviour. Certain acts (*e.g.*, reflexes) are "mindless" because they are deliberate; others which are intended may be described for the sake of convenience as "minded" (*i.e.*, purposeful). But like the majority of modern psychologists—insofar as they take any interest in the subject—they regarded mind as a process going on in the living body. Is there any reason, many now ask, why we should think of mind as being any different in nature from digestion? Both are processes going on in the body, the one in the brain the other in the stomach and intestines. Why should we therefore regard them as "things"?

Mithraism, a sun-religion which originated in Persia with the worship of the mythical Mithra, the god of light and of truth. It was for two centuries one of early Christianity's most formidable rivals, particularly in the West since the more philosophical Hellenic Christianity of the East had little to fear from it. (Arnold Toynbee has described Mithraism as "a pre-Zoroastrian Iranian paganism—in a Hellenic dress"; Manichaeism as "Zoroastrianism—in a Christian dress".) Mithraism was a mystery-faith with secret rites known only to devotees. It appealed to the soldiers of the Roman Army which explains its spread to the farthest limits of the Roman empire and its decline as the Romans retreated. The religion resembled Zoroastrianism (*q.v.*) in that it laid stress on the constant struggle between good and evil and there are a number of parallels with Christianity. *e.g.*, a miraculous birth, death, and a glorious resurrection, a belief in heaven and hell and the immortality of the soul, a last judgment. Both religions held Sunday as the holy day of the week, celebrated 25 December (date of the pagan winter solstice festival) as the birthday of the founder; both celebrated Easter, and in their ceremonies made use of bell, holy water, and the candle. Mithraism reached its height about 275 A.D. and afterwards declined both for the reason given above and, perhaps, because it excluded women, was emotional rather than philo-

sophical, and had no general organisation to direct its course. Yet even today, from the Euphrates to the Tyne, traces of the religion remain and antiquarians are familiar with the image of the sun-god and the inscription *Deo Soli Mithrae, Invicto, Seculari* (dedicated to the sun-god of Mithra, the unconquered). Mithraism enjoyed a brief revival of popular interest in the mid-1950s when workers excavating the foundations of the skyscraper, Bucklersbury House in the City of London, found the well-preserved remains of a Roman Mithraic temple. A campaign to save the temple as a national monument resulted in its now being on open display on a site in front of the skyscraper.

Modernism. The term has two main connotations:

1. A movement in the Roman Catholic church, *c.* 1890–1910. The 19th century stress on science and the application of scientific methods in fields like history, psychology and philosophy, raised serious problems for traditional Catholic doctrine. The Modernists sought to reinterpret orthodox church teaching in the light of this modern knowledge. The movement was condemned as heresy in 1907.

2. The term is more frequently used to refer to the "modern" movement in all the arts in the period *c.* 1900–30, though defining the period it covers is only one of the problems in describing the movement. It is generally seen as an artistic response to the changes which undermined the securities on which 19th century art and literature were founded. Modernism is marked by a greater ambition for works of art themselves. As well as being novels, or paintings, or music, *etc.*, they were increasingly considered, by artists and critics alike, as representing a theoretical programme, attempts to make the audience see or understand the world in a different way. So modernist characteristics include an increased self-consciousness of the artist, and formal experiment employing a wide variety of technical innovations. In literature the prime works of modernism are T. S. Eliot's *The Waste Land* and James Joyce's *Ulysses*; the most important painters include Picasso and Matisse; and among composers Schoenberg and Stravinsky stand out (*see* **Section E).**

Mohammedanism. *See* **Islam.**

Monasticism. When in the 4th cent. A.D. Constantine in effect united state and church there were naturally many who hastened to become Christians for the worldly benefits they expected it to bring in view of the new situation. But there were others who, in their efforts to escape from wordly involvement, went into the deserts of North Africa and Syria to live as hermits and so in these regions there grew up large communities of monks whose lives of renunciation made a considerable impression on the Christian world. They were men of all types but the two main groups were those who preferred to live alone and those who preferred a community life. Among the first must be included St. Anthony, the earliest of the hermits, who was born in Egypt *c.* 250 and who lived alone in a hut near his home for fifteen years and then in the desert for a further twenty. As his fame spread Anthony came forth to teach and advocate a life of extreme austerity, until by the end of his life the Thebaid (the desert around Thebes) was full of hermits following his example. (Not unnaturally, he was constantly assailed by lustful visions which he thoughtfully attributed to Satan.) In the Syrian desert St. Simeon Stylites and others were stimulated to even greater austerities and Simeon himself spent many years on the top of a pillar in a space so small that it was only possible to sit or stand. With some of these men it is obvious that ascetic discipline had become perverted into an unpleasant form of exhibitionism.

The first monastery was founded by Pachomius of Egypt *c.* 315 and here the monks had a common life with communal meals, worship, and work mainly of agricultural type. In the Eastern part of the Empire St. Basil (*c.* 360) tried to check the growth of the extreme and spectacular practices of the hermits by organising monasteries in which the ascetic disciplines of fasting, meditation, and prayer, would be balanced by useful and healthy activities. His monasteries had orphanages and schools for boys—not only those who were intended for a monkish life. But the Eastern Church in general continued to favour the hermit life and ascetic extremes. Originally a spontaneous movement, the monastic life was introduced to the West by St. Athanasius in 339 who obtained its recognition from the Church of Rome and St. Augustine introduced it into North Africa beyond Egypt. The movement was promoted also by St. Jerome, St. Martin of Tours, who introduced it into France, and St. Patrick into Ireland. The monastery of Iona was founded by St. Colomba in 566. But it must be remembered that the Celtic Church had a life of its own which owed more to the Egyptian tradition than to Rome. Unlike the more elaborate monasteries of the Continent those of the early Celtic Church were often little more than a cluster of stone bee-hive huts, an oratory, and a stone cross. It had its own religious ceremonies and its own art (notably its beautifully carved crosses and the illuminated manuscripts such as the Lindisfarne Gospel (c. 700) and the Irish Book of Kells dating from about the same time). The Scottish St. Ninian played a major part in introducing Egyptian texts and art to Britain where, mixed with Byzantine influences and the art of the Vikings, it produced a typical culture of its own. Strangely enough, it was the relatively primitive Celts who played almost as large a part in preserving civilisation in Europe during the Dark Ages as the Italians have since. It was St. Columbanus (c. 540-615) who founded the great monasteries of Annegray, Luxeuil, and Fontaine in the Vosges country, St. Gall in Switzerland, and Bobbio in the Apennines. So, too, it was the Anglo-Saxon Alcuin (c. 735-804) who was called from York by Charlemagne to set up a system of education throughout his empire; the most famous of the monastic schools he founded was at Tours. Among those influenced by him was the philosopher John Scotus Erigena.

Meanwhile from the south, as the disintegrating Roman empire became increasingly corrupt, St. Benedict of Nursia (c. 480-c. 543) fled the pleasures of Rome to lead a hermit's life near Subiaco. Here he founded some small monasteries, but c. 520 made a new settlement, the great monastery of Monte Cassino in southern Italy, where he established a "Rule" for the government of monks. This included both study and work and emphasised that education was necessary for the continuance of Christianity. As his influence spread his Rule was adopted by other monasteries, and schools became part of monastic life. It is not possible to describe the many different orders of monks and nuns formed since, nor the mendicant orders of friars (e.g., Franciscans, Dominicans, Carmelites, Augustinians). Outside the Roman Catholic Church, both Eastern Orthodox and Anglican Christians owe much to the monastic movement. Monasticism, of course, is not peculiar to Christianity and forms a major aspect of Buddhism, especially in the form of Lamaism (q.v.) in Tibet.

Monetarism. See **Section G.**

Monophysitism, a heresy of the 5th cent. which grew out of a reaction against Nestorianism (q.v.). The majority of Egyptian Christians were Monophysites (Mono-physite = one nature)—i.e. they declared Christ's human and divine nature to be one and the same. This view was condemned at the Council of Chalcedon (A.D. 451) which pronounced that Jesus Christ, true God and true man, has two natures, at once perfectly distinct and inseparably joined in one person and partaking of the one divine substance. However, many continued to hold Monophysite opinions, including the Coptic Church (q.v.), declaring the Council to be unoecumenical (i.e. not holding the views of the true and universal Christian Church).

Montanism, a Phrygian form of primitive Puritanism with many peculiar tenets into which the early Christian theologian Tertullian (c. 150-c. 230) was driven by his extremist views that the Christian should keep himself aloof from the world and hold no social intercourse whatever with pagans. The sect had immediate expectation of Christ's second coming and indulged in prophetic utterance which they held to be inspired by the Holy Ghost but which their enemies put down to the work of the Devil.

Moral Re-Armament, a campaign launched in 1938 by an American evangelist of Lutheran background, Frank N. D. Buchman (1878-1961), founder of the Oxford Group Movement, and at first associated with the First Century Christian Fellowship, a fundamentalist Protestant revivalist movement. On a visit to England in 1920 Buchman preached "world-changing through life-changing" to undergraduates at Oxford, hence the name Oxford Group. This revivalist movement was based on Buchman's conviction that world civilisation was breaking down and a change had to be effected in the minds of men.

Two of the Group's most typical practices were group confession of sins openly and the "quiet time" set aside during the day to receive messages from the Almighty as to behaviour and current problems. In the eyes of non-Groupers the confession (often of trivial sins) appeared to be exhibitionist and there was felt to be a certain snobbery about the movement which made it strongly conscious of the social status of its converts.

The Oxford Group gave way to Moral Re-Armament, the third phase of Buchmanism. M.R.A. men and women lay stress on the four moral absolutes of honesty, purity, love, and unselfishness. They believe they have the ideas to set the pattern for the changing world and, indeed, claim to have aided in solving many international disputes—political, industrial, and racial. Theologians complained of the Groups that their movement lacked doctrine and intellectual content; M.R.A. is no different in this respect.

The peak of public interest in M.R.A. was probably reached in the 1950s. Like so many movements of its kind it relied heavily for its motive force on the dynamism of its founder and leader. With the death of Dr. Buchman and the unexpected demise at an early age of his most promising protégé and successor-designate, the journalist Peter Howard, the movement began to lose its public impact. The phrase "moral rearmament" was coined by the English scientist W. H. Bragg and appropriated by Buchman.

Moravian Church, a revival of the Church of the "Bohemian Brethren" which originated (1457) among some of the followers of John Hus. It developed a kind of Quakerism that rejected the use of force, refused to take oaths, and had no hierarchy. It appears to have been sympathetic towards Calvinism but made unsuccessful approaches to Luther. As a Protestant sect it was ruthlessly persecuted by Ferdinand II and barely managed to survive. However, in the 18th cent. the body was re-established by Count Zinzendorf who offered it a place of safety in Saxony where a town called Herrnhut (God's protection) was built and this became the centre from which Moravian doctrine was spread by missionaries all over the world. Their chief belief (which had a fundamental influence on John Wesley—see **Methodism**) was that faith is a direct illumination from God which assures us beyond all possibility of doubt that we are saved, and that no goodness of behaviour, piety, or orthodoxy is of any use without this "sufficient sovereign, saving grace".

Mormons, or **Latter-day Saints,** one of the very numerous American religious churches; founded in 1830 by Joseph Smith, the son of a Vermont farmer, who, as a youth, had been influenced by a local religious revival though confused by the conflicting beliefs of the various denominations. He said that while praying for guidance he had been confronted by two heavenly messengers who forbade him to join any existing church but prepare to become the prophet of a new one. Soon, in a series of visions, he was told of a revelation written on golden plates concealed in a nearby hillside. These he unearthed in 1827 and with the help of "Urim and Thummin" translated the "reformed Egyptian" characters into English. Described as the *Book of Mormon,* this was published in 1830 and at the same time a little church of those few who accepted his testimony was founded in Fayette, N.Y. In addition the first of Joseph Smith's "miracles"—the casting out of a devil—was performed. The *Book of Mor-*

mon purports to be a record of early American history and religion, the American Indians being identified as part of the ten Lost Tribes of Israel. Jesus Christ is believed to have appeared in America after His resurrection and prior to His ascension. Smith's eloquence was able to influence quite educated people, including Sidney Rigdon with whom he went into business for a time. *Doctrine and Covenants* is the title of another book dealing with the revelations Smith claimed to have received. Soon the sect was in trouble with the community both because its members insisted on describing themselves as the Chosen People and others as Gentiles and because they took part in politics, voting as Smith ordered them to. Smith was constantly in trouble with the police. Therefore they were turned out from one city after another until they found a dwelling-place at Nauvoo, Illinois, on the Mississippi.

In 1844 Smith was murdered by a mob, and confusion reigned for a while. Brigham Young, Smith's successor, was quite an extraordinary leader, however, and soon stamped out the warring factions and drove out the recalcitrants, though persecutions from the outside continued. There followed the famous trek of more than a thousand miles across desert country in which he led the way, reaching his journey's end in the forbidding valley of the Great Salt Lake (then outside the area of the United States) on 24 July 1847. By 1851 30,000 Mormons had reached the Promised Land. Here they held their own in a hostile environment and under the practical genius of their leader carried through a vast irrigation scheme and built Salt Lake City which still serves as the headquarters of their sect. In 1850 their pioneer settlement was made Utah Territory, and in 1896 incorporated in the Union. The church was strictly ruled by its leader who also looked after affairs of state for thirty years until his death in 1877.

"Plural marriage" (or polygamy) is one of the things for which the church is best known. Though practised in the early years—as a restoration of the Old Testament practice, as Mormons believe—it was discontinued in 1890, by a formal statement issued by Wilford Woodruff, then the President of the Church.

Membership of The Church of Jesus Christ of Latter-day Saints had reached 8·7 million by 1995, with members in over 130 nations. There are *c.* 160,000 members in Britain (1995) having grown from 6,000 in 1958.

The Reorganised Church of Jesus Christ of Latter-day Saints with its headquarters at Independence, Missouri, has been separate and distinct since 1852.

Muggletonians, one of the many sects which arose during the Commonwealth but, unlike most of the others (**Levellers** *(q.v.),* **Diggers** *(q.v.),* Fifth Monarchy Men, and the Millenarians) which tended to have a strongly political aspect, this was purely religious. Founded by two journeymen tailors, Lodowick Muggleton and John Reeve, who interpreted the Book of Revelation in their own peculiar way, it was decided that Reeve represented Moses, and Muggleton, Aaron. They also believed that the Father, not the Son, had died on the cross (an ancient heresy) but added the strange statement that He left Elijah in control during His period on earth. Rejecting the doctrine of the Trinity, they also asserted that God has a human body. Nevertheless, for a time, they had many followers.

Mystery Religions. *See* Orphism.

Mysticism, a religious attitude which concerns itself with direct relationship with God, "reality" as contrasted with appearance or the "ultimate" in one form or another. All the higher religions have had their mystics who have not always been regarded without suspicion by their more orthodox members, and, as Bertrand Russell points out, there has been a remarkable unity of opinion among mystics which almost transcends their religious differences. Thus, characteristic of the mystical experience in general, have been the following features; (1) a belief in insight as opposed to analytical knowledge which is accompanied in the actual experience by the sense of a mystery unveiled, a hidden wisdom become certain beyond the possibility of doubt; this is often preceded by a period of utter hopelessness and isolation de-

scribed as "the dark night of the soul"; (2) a belief in unity and a refusal to admit opposition or division anywhere; this sometimes appears in the form of what seem to be contradictory statements: "the way up and the way down is one and the same" (Heraclitus). There is no distinction between subject and object, the act of perception and the thing perceived; (3) a denial of the reality of time, since if all is one the distinction of past and future must be illusory; (4) a denial of the reality of evil (which does not maintain, *e.g.,* that cruelty is good but that it does not exist in the world of reality as opposed to the world of phantoms from which we are liberated by the insight of the vision). Among the great mystics have been Meister Eckhart and Jakob Boehme, the German religious mystics of the 13th and 16th cent. respectively, Acharya Sankara of India, and St. Theresa and St. John of the Cross of Spain. Mystical movements within the great religions have been: the Zen *(q.v.)* movement within Buddhism; Taoism in China; the Cabalists and Hasidim in Judaism; the Sufis within Islam; some of the Quakers within Christianity.

N

Nationalism. Devotion to one's nation and its interests. Politically, this is translated into the theory that each nationality should be organised in a sovereign state. Nationalism first developed in Western Europe with the consolidation of nation states, and brought about the reorganization of Europe in the 19th and 20th centuries, *e.g.* the unification of Italy, the rise of Germany. At first, nationalism was liberal and democratic in tone, but it has also been associated with national expansion at the expense of other nations, and was an essential element of Fascism. In the 20th century it has been important in the political awakening of Asia and Africa against colonialism, as individual states sought independence. In Europe, in recent years, the collapse of Communist regimes, which previously cut across racial, historical and linguistic barriers, has led to the rise of nationalist aspirations, most notably and violently in the former Yugoslavia and Soviet Union.

Natural Law, the philosophical doctrine which states that there is a natural moral law, irrespective of time and place, which man can know through his own reason. Originally a product of early rational philosophy, the Christian form of the doctrine is basically due to St. Thomas Aquinas who defined natural law in relation to eternal law, holding that the eternal law is God's reason which governs the relations of all things in the universe to each other. The natural law is that part of the eternal law which relates to man's behaviour. Catholic natural law assumes that the human reason is capable of deriving ultimate rules for right behaviour, since there are in man and his institutions certain stable structures produced by God's reason which man's reason can know to be correct and true. Thus, the basis of marriage, property, the state, and the contents of justice are held to be available to man's natural reason. The rules of positive morality and civil law are held to be valid only insofar as they conform to the natural law, which man is not only capable of knowing but also of obeying.

Protestant theologians criticise this notion. Thus Karl Barth and many others hold that sinful and fallen man cannot have any direct knowledge of God or His reason or will without the aid of revelation. Another theologian Niebuhr points out that the principles of the doctrines are too inflexible and that although they are the product of a particular time and circumstance, they are regarded as if they were absolute and eternal. In fact, as most social scientists would also agree, there is no law which can be regarded as "natural" for all men at all times. Nor does it seem sensible to suppose that all or even many men possess either the reason to discern natural law or the ability to obey it; whether or not we accept man's free-will (and all Protestant sects do not), we know as a fact of science that people are not always fully responsible for their actions and some not at all.

Such basic human rights as freedom of speech and religion, and freedom from fear and want, derive from natural law as later developed by John Locke.

Naturalism. 1. In general, the view that what is studied by the human sciences is all that there is, and that there is no need to go beyond or outside the universe for any explanation.

2. In ethics, the view that value terms can be defined in terms of neutral statements of fact, or derived from such statements.

Nazism, the term commonly used for the political and social ideology of the German National Socialist Party inspired and led by Hitler. The term *Nazi* was an abbreviation for *Nazional-socialistische Deutsche Arbeiterpartei*.

Neocolonialism. *See* **Colonialism**

Neo-Fascism, term used for the recent revival of Nazism (*see above*) and Fascism (*q.v.*) in France, Germany, Eastern Europe and now (1995) Russia and Italy.

Neoplatonism. Movement begun by Plotinus' interpretation of Plato and carried forward by various philosophers of the next three centuries and which had some influence in the Renaissance. Plotinus (205–270) saw reality as hierarchically ordered in a graded series from the divine to the material; man, who contains some part of the divine, longs for union with the highest level. Subsequent Neoplatonists include Porphyry, Iamblichus and Philoponus. (*See also* **Determinism and Free-will** and **God and Man**).

Nestorian heresy. The 5th cent. of the Christian Church saw a battle of personalities and opinions waged with fanatical fury between St. Cyril, the patriarch of Alexandria, and Nestorius, patriarch of Constantinople. Nestorius maintained that Mary should not be called the mother of God, as she was only the mother of the human and not of the divine nature of Jesus. This view was contradicted by Cyril (one of the most unpleasant saints who ever lived) who held the orthodox view. In addition to his utter destruction of Nestorius by stealthy and unremitting animosity Cyril was also responsible for the lynching of Hypatia, a distinguished mathematician and saintly woman, head of the Neoplatonist school at Alexandria. She was dragged from her chariot, stripped naked, butchered and torn to pieces in the church, and her remains burned. As if this were not enough Cyril took pains to stir up pogroms against the very large Jewish colony of Alexandria. At the Council of Ephesus (A.D. 431) the Western Bishops quickly decided for Cyril. This Council (reinforced by the Council of Chalcedon in 451) clarified orthodox Catholic doctrine (*see* **Monophysitism**). Nestorius became a heretic, was banished to Antioch where he had a short respite of peace, but later, and in spite of his weakness and age, was dragged about from one place to another on the borders of Egypt. Later the Nestorian church flourished in Syria and Persia and missions were sent to India and China.

New Age, a quasi-religious movement, based on a millenarian mysticism, astrology and ecology. Condemned by many Christians as pagan and heretical. It gained support in the 1980s.

Nihilism, the name commonly given to the earliest Russian form of revolutionary anarchism. It originated in the early years of Tsar Alexander II (1818–81), the liberator of the serfs, who, during his attempts to bring about a constitutional monarchy, was killed by a bomb. The term "nihilist", however, was first used in 1862 by Turgenev in his novel *Fathers and Children*. *See* **Anarchism**.

Nominalism. Early mediaeval thinkers were divided into two schools, those who regarded "universals" or abstract concepts as mere names without any corresponding realities (Nominalists), and those who held the opposite doctrine (**Realism**) that general concepts have an existence independent of individual things. The relation between universals and particulars was a subject of philosophical dispute all through the Middle Ages.

The first person to hold the nominalist doctrine was probably Roscelin or Roscellinus in the late 11th cent., but very little is known of him and none of his works remains except for a single letter to Peter Abelard who was his pupil. Roscelin was born in France, accused twice of heresy but recanted and fled to England where

he attacked the views of Anselm, according to whom Roscelin used the phrase that universals were a *flatus voci* or breath of the voice. The most important nominalist was the Englishman William of Occam in the 13th cent. who, once and for all, separated the two schools by saying in effect that science is about things (the nominalist view) whereas logic, philosophy, and religion are about terms or concepts (the Platonic tradition). Both are justified, but we must distinguish between them. The proposition "man is a species" is not a proposition of logic or philosophy but a scientific statement since we cannot say whether it is true or false without knowing about man. If we fail to realise that words are conventional signs and that it is important to decide whether or not they have a meaning and refer to something, then we shall fall into logical fallacies of the type: "Man is a species, Socrates is a man, therefore Socrates is a species." This, in effect, is the beginning of the modern philosophy of logical analysis which, to oversimplify, tells us that a statement is not just true or untrue, it may also be meaningless. Therefore, in all the philosophical problems we have discussed elsewhere there is the third possibility that the problem we are discussing has no meaning because the words refer to nothing and we must ask ourselves before going any further "what do we mean by God", and has the word "freewill" any definite meaning?

Nonconformism, the attitude of all those Christian bodies, which do not conform to the doctrines of the Church of England. Up to the passing of the Act of Uniformity in 1662 they were called "puritans" or "dissenters" and were often persecuted. The oldest bodies of nonconformists are the Baptists, Independents, and (in England) the Presbyterians; the Methodists, although dating from 1738, did not consider themselves nonconformists until some time later. The Presbyterians are, of course, the official Church of Scotland where it is the Anglicans (known as "Episcopalians") who are technically the nonconformists.

O

Occam's Razor, the philosophical maxim by which William of Occam, the 14th cent. Franciscan has become best-known. This states in the form which is most familiar: "Entities are not to be multiplied without necessity" and as such does not appear in his works. He did, however, say something much to the same effect: "It is vain to do with more what can be done with fewer." In other words, if everything in some science can be interpreted without assuming this or that hypothetical entity, there is no ground for assuming it. This is Bertrand Russell's version and he adds: "I have myself found this a most fruitful principle in logical analysis."

Occultism. *See* **Magic, Alchemy, Astrology,** and **Theosophy.**

Optimism. Originally the doctrine propounded by Leibnitz (1646–1716) that the actual world is the "best of all possible worlds", being chosen by the Creator out of all the possible worlds which were present in his thoughts as that in which the most good could be obtained at the cost of the least evil. This view was memorably mocked by Voltaire in *Candide*. The term is now more generally applied to any view which expects or hopes that there is or will be more good than evil in the world, or more pleasure than pain.

Opus Dei, a Roman Catholic organisation founded in 1928 by the Spanish priest Josemaría Escrivá de Balaguer (1902–75). Its aim is to spread, in all spheres of society, a deep awareness of the universal call to holiness and apostolate, in the fulfilment—with freedom and responsibility—of one's professional work. In 1994, the Pope named Mgr Javier Echevarria to head Opus Dei.

Orangemen, members of a society formed in Ulster back in 1795 to uphold Protestantism. Their name is taken from King William III, Prince of Orange, who defeated James II at the Battle of the Boyne (1690), hence the enormous banners depicting "King Billy on the Boyne" carried in procession on 12 July each year. The Unionist Party of Northern Ireland (the ruling political party from 1921 to 1972) is largely maintained by the Orange Order. The Order also has branches in many English-speaking countries.

Orphism. The Greeks in general thought very little of their gods, regarding them as similar human beings with human failings and virtues although on a larger scale. But there was another aspect of Greek religion which was passsionate, ecstatic, and secret, dealing with the worship of various figures among whom were Bacchus or Dionysus, Orpheus, and Demeter and Persephone of the Eleusinian Mysteries. Dionysus (or Bacchus) was originally a god from Thrace where the people were primitive farmers naturally interested in fertility cults. Dionysus was the god of fertility who only later came to be associated with wine and the divine madness it produces. He assumed the form of a man or a bull and his worship by the time it arrived in Greece became associated with women (as was the case in most of the Mystery Religions) who spent nights on the hills dancing and possibly drinking wine in order to stimulate ecstasy; an unpleasant aspect of the cult was the tearing to pieces of wild animals whose flesh was eaten raw. Although the cult was disapproved of by the orthodox and, needless to say, by husbands, it existed for a long time.

This primitive and savage religion in time was modified by that attributed to Orpheus whose cult was more spiritualised, ascetic, and substituted mental for physical intoxication. Orpheus may have been a real person or a legendary hero and he, too, is supposed to have come from Thrace, but his name indicates that he, or the movement associated with him, came from Crete and originally from Egypt, which seems to have been the source of many of its doctrines. Crete, it must be remembered, was the island through which Egypt influenced Greece in other respects. Orpheus is said to have been a reformer who was torn to pieces by the Maenad worshippers of Dionysus. The Orphics believed in the transmigration of souls and that the soul after death might obtain either eternal bliss or temporary or permanent torment according to its way of life upon earth. They held ceremonies of purification and the more orthodox abstained from animal food except on special occasions when it was eaten ritually. Man is partly earthly, partly heavenly, and a good life increases the heavenly part so that, in the end, he may become one with Bacchus and be called a "Bacchus".

The religion had an elaborate theology. As the Bacchic rites were reformed by Orpheus, so the Orphic rites were reformed by Pythagoras (c. 582–c. 507 B.C.) who introduced the mystical element into Greek philosophy, which reached its heights in Plato. Other elements entered Greek life from Orphism. One of these was feminism which was notably lacking in Greek civilisation outside the Mystery Religions. The other was the drama which arose from the rites of Dionysus. The mysteries of Eleusis formed the most sacred part of the Athenian state religion, and it is clear that they had to do with fertility rites also, for they were in honour of Demeter and Persephone and all the myths speak of them as being associated with the supply of corn to the country. Without being provocative, it is accepted by most anthropologists and many theologians that Christianity, just as it accepted elements of Gnossticism and Mithraism, accepted elements from the Mystery Religions as they in turn must have done from earlier cults. The miraculous birth, the death and resurrection the sacramental feast of bread and wine, symbolising the eating of the flesh and drinking of the blood of the god, all these are common elements in early religions and not just in one. None of this means that what we are told about Jesus is not true, but it surely does mean: (a) that Christianity was not a sudden development; (b) that the early Church absorbed many of the elements of other religions; (c) that perhaps Jesus Himself made use of certain symbols which He knew had a timeless significance for man and invested them with new meaning.

Orthodox Eastern Church. There are two groups of Eastern churches: (1) those forming the Orthodox Church dealt with here which include the ancient Byzantine patriarchates of Constantinople, Alexandria, Antioch, and Jerusalem, and the national churches of Russia, Greece, Serbia, Bulgaria, Romania, etc. (although Orthodox communities exist all over the world and are no longer confined to geographical areas); (2) the churches which rejected Byzantine orthodoxy during various controversies from the 5th to the 7th cent., notably the Coptic church (q.v.) and the Armenian church. Although all Orthodox churches share the same doctrine and traditions they are arranged as national independent bodies each with its own hierarchy. They do not recognise the pope, and the primacy of the patriarch of Constantinople is largely an honorary one. Although claiming to be the One Holy, Catholic, and Apostolic Church its alleged infallibility rests on universal agreement rather than on any one individual, and agreement over the faith comes from the Scriptures interpreted in the light of the Tradition. The latter includes dogmas relating to the Trinity, Christology, Mariology, and Holy Icons; the testimony of the Fathers (St. Athanasius, St. Basil, St. John Chrysostom, St. Cyril of Alexandria, etc.); the canons or rules as formulated by the Councils and the Fathers. The Orthodox Church did not take part in the great Western controversies about the Bible, nor, of course, in the Reformation. Attempts have recently been made to improve relations bebetween Rome and Constantinople: the two Churches agreed in 1935 to retract the excommunications cast on each other in A.D. 1054, which formalised the Great Schism. There are an estimated 250,000 Orthodox Church followers in Britain.

Ouspensky, a contemporary of Gurdjieff (q.v.), Peter Ouspensky was another obscure mystic of Eastern European origin who believed he had an occult philosophical message to bring to the West. This he embodied in a series of lengthy books which are both humourless and self-indulgent.

Oxford Group. See **Moral Re-Armament.**
Oxford Movement. See **Tractarianism.**

P

Pacifism. The belief that, because violence and the taking of life is morally wrong, war and the employment of organized armed forces cannot be justified. The word first came into use to describe movements advocating the settlement of disputes by peaceful means. Since the First World War the word has been used to describe the refusal of individuals to undertake military service. The first pacificists were minority Christian groups like the Quakers and Plymouth Brethren. In the present century the movement has broadened and many democratic nations allow their citizens to abstain from fighting on grounds of principle, often described as "conscientious objection".

Paganism, a form of worship which has its roots in the ancient nature religions of Europe. Pagans reverence the sanctity of the Earth, its people and other life forms. Paganism is still a living religion, the main forms of which include Wicca (witchcraft), Druidry, Asatru and Shamanism. The Pagan Federation was founded in 1971 to provide information and to counter misconceptions about Paganism.

Pantheism. See **God and Man.**
Panpsychism. Literally, "all-soul-ism", the view that everything that really exists in the world is a mind or consciousness. To be distinguished from "hylozoism", which claims that everything is alive. Panpsychic views can be found in Leibniz and Schopenhauer, and in the 20th century philosopher A. N. Whitehead (1861–1947).

Papal Infallibility. The basis of papal infallibility is (a) that every question of morals and faith is not dealt with in the Bible so it is necessary that there should be a sure court of appeal in case of doubt, and this was provided by Christ when he established the Church as His Teaching Authority upon earth; (b) ultimately this idea of the teaching function of the Church shapes the idea of papal infallibility which asserts that the Pope, when speaking officially on matters of faith or morals, is protected by God against the possibility of error. The doctrine was proclaimed in July 1870.

Infallibility is a strictly limited gift which does not mean that the Pope has extraordinary intelligence, that God helps him to find the answer to every conceivable question, or that Catholics have to accept the Pope's views on politics. He can make mistakes or fall into sin, his scientific or historical opinions may be quite wrong, he may write books that are full of errors. Only in two limited spheres is he infallible and in these only when he speaks officially as the supreme teacher and lawgiver of the Church, defining a doctrine that must be accepted by all its members. When, after studying a problem of faith or morals as carefully as possible, and with all available help from expert consultants, he emerges with the Church's answer—on these occasions it is not strictly an answer, it is *the* answer.

Historically speaking, the Roman Catholic Church of the early 19th cent. was at its lowest ebb of power. Pope Pius IX, in fear of Italian nationalism, revealed his reactionary attitude by the feverish declaration of new dogmas, the canonisation of new saints, the denunciation of all modern ideals in the Syllabus of Errors, and the unqualified defence of his temporal power against the threat of Garibaldi. It is not too much to say that everything regarded as important by freedom-loving and democratic people was opposed by the papacy at that time. In 1870, after a long and sordid struggle, the Vatican Council, convened by Pius IX, pronounced the definition of his infallibility. Döllinger, a German priest and famous historian of the Church, was excommunicated because, like many others, he refused to accept the new dogma. It is difficult not to doubt that there was some connection between the pronouncement of the Pope's infallibility and his simultaneous loss of temporal power.

After the humanism of the Second Vatican Council (1962-5) Pope Paul's encyclical *Humanae Vitae* (1968), condemning birth control, came as a great disappointment to the many people (including theologians, priests, and laymen) who had expected there would be a change in the Church's teaching. The Church's moral guidance on this controversial issue, however, does not involve the doctrine of infallibility. (The Roman Catholic Church teaches that papal pronouncements are infallible only when they are specifically defined as such.) That there is unlikely to be any immediate softening of the Church's line on infallibility was made clear in July 1973 when the Vatican's Sacred Congregation for the Doctrine of the Faith published a document strongly reaffirming papal infallibility. The document also reminded Catholics of their obligation to accept the Catholic Church's unique claims to authenticity.

Parapsychology, the name given to the study of psychical research (*q.v.*) as an academic discipline, and chosen to denote the topic's supposed status as a branch of psychology. The impetus behind parapsychology came from the psychologist William MacDougall who persuaded Duke University in North Carolina, U.S.A., to found a department of parapsychology under J. B. Rhine. Throughout the 1930s and 40s the work of Rhine and his colleagues, who claimed to have produced scientific evidence for the existence of E.S.P., attracted world-wide attention. Increasing reservations about the interpretation of Rhine's results and an apparent lack of any readily repeatable experiments, however, gradually eroded scientific confidence in the topic. The academic status of parapsychology is at the present time exceedingly uncertain. Rhine retired from university life in 1965 and the world-famous parapsychology laboratory at Duke University was closed. On the other hand the American Association for the Advancement of Science recently admitted the Parapsychology Association (the leading organisation for professional parapsychologists) as an affiliated member society. An American government body, the National Institute of Mental Health, has also officially supported some medical research into alleged telepathic dreams, the first "official" grant support of this kind.

Parsees. *See* **Zoroastrianism.**

Pavlovian theory. *See* **Behaviourism.**

Pelagianism. The Christian doctrine that each person has responsibility for ensuring his own salvation, apart from the assistance of divine grace. Its name is derived from Pelagius, a British lay monk who came to Rome about 400 A.D. and attacked Augustine's view that moral goodness is only possible through divine grace. Pelagius argued that if men and women were not held to be responsible for their actions, there would be nothing to restrain them from sin. His emphasis on free will and the essential goodness of human nature suggested an optimism that was at odds with doctrines of original sin. Augustine attacked Pelagius' views as heretical, a judgement that was confirmed by the church in 417, when Pelagius was excommunicated.

Pentecostalism, a religious movement within the Protestant churches, holding the belief that an essential feature of true Christianity is a vigorous and profound spiritual or mystical experience which occurs after, and seemingly reinforces the initial conversion. The origins of modern Pentecostalism appear to lie in the occasion on 1 January 1901 when a member of a Bible College in Topeka, Kansas, one Agnes N. Ozman, spontaneously began to speak in an apparently unknown language at one of the College's religious meetings. This "speaking in tongues" was assumed to be evidence of her conversion and "spirit baptism", and became a feature of most Pentecostal meetings in due course. The movement spread rapidly across America, particularly in rural communities, and also was a strong feature of Welsh religious life in the early part of the century. Pentecostal services are enthusiastic and rousing with a strong emphasis on music and participation on the part of the congregation. Pentecostalism is evangelistic in nature and seems to be gaining in strength at the present time, at the expense of more orthodox and staid versions of Christianity. Aimee Semple McPherson was one of its most prominent evangelists.

Pessimism. Philosophically this refers to the doctrine associated with Arthur Schopenhauer (1788-1860), that in this world everything tends to evil, that the amount of pain is greater than the amount of pleasure. Of course, pessimistic ideas have a long history. As the Greeks said: "Call no man happy until he is dead." They are also present in the teachings of eastern and western religions, which emphasize the corruptness of this world and the possibility of happiness only in a hereafter. Schopenhauer's pessimism had a strong influence on Nietzsche, and through him on existentialism (*q.v.*).

Peyotism. A religious movement among North American Indians centred around the *peyote*, a part of the cactus which produces hallucinogenic effects.

Phrenology, a psychological "school" founded in 1800 by two Germans, Franz Josef Gall and Johann Gaspar Spurzheim. Gall was an anatomist who believed there to be some correspondence between mental faculties and the shape of the head. He tested these ideas in prisons and mental hospitals and began to lecture on his findings, arousing a great deal of interest throughout both Europe and America, where his doctrines were widely accepted. Phrenology became fashionable, and people would go to "have their bumps read" as later men and women of fashion have gone to be psychoanalysed. Roughly speaking, Gall divided the mind into thirty-seven faculties such as destructiveness, suavity, self-esteem, conscientiousness, and so on, and claimed that each of these was located in a definite area of the brain. He further claimed that the areas in the brain corresponded to "bumps" on the skull which could be read by the expert, thus giving a complete account of the character of the subject. In fact, (a) no such faculties are located in the brain anywhere, for this is simply not the way the brain works; (b) the faculties described by Gall are not pure traits which cannot be further analysed and are based on a long outdated psychology; (c) the shape of the brain bears no specific relationship to the shape of the skull. Phrenology is a pseudo-science; there is no truth in it whatever. But, even so, like astrology, it still has its practitioners.

Physiocrats. A French school of economic thought during the 18th cent., known at the time as *Les Economistes* but in later years named physiocrats by Du Pont de Nemours, a member of the School. Other members were Quesnay, Mirabeau, and the great financier Turgot. The physiocrats held the view, common to the 18th cent., and deriving ultimately from Rousseau, of the goodness and bounty of nature and the goodness of man "as he came from the bosom of nature". The aim of governments, therefore, should be to conform to nature; and so long as men do not interfere with each other's liberty and do not combine among themselves governments should leave them free to find their own salvation. Criminals, madmen, and monopolists should be eliminated. Otherwise the duty of government is *laissez-faire, laissez passer*. From this follows the doctrine of free trade between nations on grounds of both justice and economy; for the greater the competition the more will each one strive to economise the cost of his labour to the general advantage. Adam Smith, although not sharing their confidence in human nature, learned much from the physiocrats, eliminated their errors, and greatly developed their teaching.

Physiognomy. *See* **Characterology.**

Pietism, a movement in the Lutheran Church at the end of the 17th cent.—the reaction, after the sufferings of the thirty years' war, of a pious and humiliated people against learning, pomp and ceremony, and stressing the importance of man's personal relationship with God. The writings of Johann Georg Hamann (1730–88) who came from a Pietist family of Königsberg influenced Kierkegaard. The Pietist movement was the root of the great Romantic movement of the 18th cent.

Platonism. Philosophical ideas that are inspired by the writings of Plato, usually embracing his belief in a realm of unchanging and eternal realities (specifically, abstract entities or universals) independent of the world perceived by the senses. Most working mathematicians are Platonists, in the sense that they believe that mathematical objects like numbers exist independently of our thought and hence that mathematical statements are true or false independently of our knowledge of them.

Pluralism. 1. In philosophy, any metaphysical view that the world must consist of more than one or two basic kinds of entity; these latter views would be called Monism or Dualism. Pluralists, such as William James, think of themselves as empiricists, reaffirming plain facts of experience against metaphysical extremists and pointing to the irreducible variety of things.

2. In political thought, it refers to the autonomy enjoyed by disparate groups or institutions within a society and also to the belief that such an arrangement for the distribution of political power should exist. As such it provides an alternative to collectivist doctrines, which may coerce the individual, and individualistic doctrines, which fail to provide an understanding of the individual's role in society. Pluralism is widely regarded as an ideal, but there is much argument as to how pluralism is to be interpreted in detail and how it is to be applied effectively within a modern society.

Plymouth Brethren, a religious sect founded by John Nelson Darby, a minister of the Protestant Church of Ireland, and Edward Cronin a former Roman Catholic, in 1827. Both were dissatisfied with the lack of spirituality in their own and other churches and joined together in small meetings in Dublin every Sunday for "the breaking of bread". Soon the movement began to spread through Darby's travels and writings and he finally settled in Plymouth, giving the popular name to the "Brethren". Beginning as a movement open to all who felt the need to "keep the unity of the Spirit", it soon exercised the right to exclude all who had unorthodox views and split up into smaller groups. Among these the main ones were the "Exclusives", the Kellyites, the Newtonites,

and "Bethesda" whose main differences were over problems of church government or prophetical powers. Some of these are further split among themselves. Readers of *Father and Son* by Sir Edmund Gosse, which describes life with his father, the eminent naturalist Philip Gosse, who belonged to the Brethren, will recall how this basically kind, honest, and learned man was led through their teachings to acts of unkindness (*e.g.,* in refusing to allow his son and other members of his household to celebrate Christmas and throwing out the small tokens they had secretly bought), and lack of scientific rigour (*e.g.,* in refusing for religious reasons alone to accept Darwinism when all his evidence pointed towards it).

Today, the majority of Brethren belong to the "Open Brethren" assemblies and, unlike the "Exclusives" hold that the Lord's Supper (a commemorative act of "breaking the bread" observed once a week) is for all Christians who care to join them. Baptism is required and Brethren believe in the personal premillennial second coming of Christ.

Poltergeist, allegedly a noisy type of spirit which specialises in throwing things about, making loud thumpings and bangings, and occasionally bringing in "apports", i.e., objects from elsewhere. Most so-called poltergeist activities are plain frauds, but the others are almost invariably associated with the presence in the house of someone (often, but not always a child) who is suffering from an adolescent malaise or an epileptic condition. The inference is that those activities which are not simply fraudulent are either due to some unknown influence exuded by such mentally disturbed people, or that they are actually carried out by ordinary physical means by such people when in an hysterical state—*i.e.,* unconsciously. The second hypothesis is much the more probable. *See* **Psychic Research.**

Polytheism. *See* **God and Man.**

Populism. A form of politics which emphasizes the virtues of the common people against politicians and intellectuals, who are distrusted as devious and selfish. "The will of the people" can provide sufficient guidance to the statesman. It is not restricted to any one political view and can manifest itself in left, right or centrist forms.

Positivism, also known as the **Religion of Humanity,** was founded by Auguste Comte (1798–1857), a famous mathematician and philosopher born in Montpellier, France. His views up to the end of the century attracted many and it would have been impossible throughout that time to read a book on philosophy or sociology that did not mention them, but today his significance is purely of historical interest. In his *Cours de Philosophie Positive* (1830) he put forward the thesis that mankind had seen three great stages in human thought: (1) the theological, during which man seeks for supernatural causes to explain nature and invents gods and devils; (2) the metaphysical, through which he thinks in terms of philosophical and metaphysical abstractions; (3) the last positive or scientific stage when he will proceed by experimental and objective observation to reach in time "positive truth".

Broadly speaking, there is little to complain of in this analysis; for there does seem to have been some sort of general direction along these lines. However, Comte was not satisfied with having reached this point and felt that his system demanded a religion and, of course, one that was "scientific". This religion was to be the worship of Humanity in place of the personal Deity of earlier times, and for it he supplied not only a Positive Catechism but a treatise on Sociology in which he declared himself the High Priest of the cult. Since, as it stood, the religion was likely to appear somewhat abstract to many, Comte drew up a list of historical characters whom he regarded as worthy of the same sort of adoration as Catholics accord to their saints. The new Church attracted few members, even among those who had a high regard for Comte's scientific work, and its only significant adherents were a small group of Oxford scholars and some in his own country. Frederic Harrison was the best-known English adherent and throughout his life continued to preach Comtist doctrines in London to diminishing audiences.

Postmodernism. Given that "modernism" (**J34**) is a term difficult to define, "postmodernism" is an even more elusive concept, though a very fashionable one for describing contemporary art. The modernist tradition of formal and stylistic experiment, added to our increased knowledge of the history of Western and non-Western arts, has provided a vast range of styles, techniques and technologies for the artist to choose from. This extension of choice has simultaneously created uncertainty about their use. If no one or few styles have any authority, then the artist picks and chooses with little commitment, and so tends towards pastiche, parody, quotation, self-reference and eclecticism. The post-modern style is to have no settled style. But it is always dangerous to try and pin down an artistic movement that is still taking place.

Pragmatism, a typically American school of philosophy which comes under the heading of what Bertrand Russell describes as a "practical" as opposed to a "theoretical" philosophy. Whereas the latter, to which most of the great philosophical systems belong, seeks disinterested knowledge for its own sake, the former (a) regards action as the supreme good, (b) considers happiness an effect and knowledge a mere instrument of successful activity.

The originator of pragmatism is usually considered to have been the psychologist William James (1842–1910) although he himself attributed its basic principles to his life-long friend, the American philosopher, Charles Sanders Peirce (1839–1914). The other famous pragmatist is John Dewey, best-known in Europe for his works on education (for although American text-books on philosophy express opinions to the contrary, few educated people in Europe have taken the slightest interest in pragmatism and generally regard it as an eccentricity peculiar to Americans). James in his book *The Will to Believe* (1896) points out that we are often compelled to take a decision where no adequate theoretical grounds for a decision exist; for even to do nothing is to decide. Thus in religion we have a right to adopt a believing attitude although not intellectually fully convinced. We should believe truth and shun error, but the failing of the sceptical philosopher is that he adheres only to the latter rule and thus fails to believe various truths which a less cautious man will accept. If believing truth and avoiding error are equally important, then it is a good idea when we are presented with an alternative to believe one of the possibilities at will, since we then have an even chance of being right, whereas we have none if we suspend judgment. The function of philosophy, according to James, is to find out what difference it makes to the individual if a particular philosophy or world-system is true: "An idea is 'true' so long as to believe it is profitable to our lives" and, he adds, the truth is only the expedient in our way of thinking ... in the long run and on the whole of course". Thus "if the hypothesis of God works satisfactorily in the widest sense of the word, it is true". Bertrand Russell's reply to this assertion is: "I have always found that the hypothesis of Santa Claus 'works satisfactorily in the widest sense of the word'; therefore 'Santa Claus exists' is true, although Santa Claus does not exist." Russell adds that James's concept of truth simply omits as unimportant the question whether God really *is* in His heaven; if He is a useful hypothesis that is enough. "God the Architect of the Cosmos is forgotten; all that is remembered is belief in God, and its effects upon the creatures inhabiting our petty planet. No wonder the Pope condemned the pragmatic defence of religion."

Predestination. *See* **Calvinism.**

Presbyterianism, a system of ecclesiastical government of the Protestant churches which look back to John Calvin as their Reformation leader. The ministry consists of presbyters who are all of equal rank. Its doctrinal standards are contained in the *Westminster Confession of Faith* (1647) which is, in general, accepted by English, Scottish, and American Presbyterians as the most thorough and logical statement in existence of the Calvinist creed. The Church of Scotland is the leading Presbyterian church in the British Isles.

The Reformation in Scotland was preceded by the same sort of awareness of the moral corruption of the Roman Church as had happened elsewhere, but for various political and emotional reasons, which need not be discussed here, the majority of the Scottish people (unlike the English who had been satisfied with the mere exchange of Crown for Pope) were determined on a fundamental change of doctrine, discipline, and worship, rather than a reform of manners. The church preachers had learned their Protestantism not from Luther but from Calvin and their leader John Knox had worked in Geneva with Calvin himself and was resolved to introduce the system into Scotland. In 1557 the "Lords of the Congregation" signed the Common Band (*i.e.*, a bond or covenant) to maintain "the blessed Word of God and his congregation" against their enemies, and demanded the right to worship as they had chosen. However, the real date of the Scottish Reformation is August 1500 when Mary of Guise (the regent for Mary Queen of Scots who was not yet of age) died and the Estates met to settle their affairs without foreign pressure; the *Scots Confession* was drawn up and signed by Knox and adopted by the Estates.

The ideas on which the Reformed Kirk was based are found in the *Scots Confession*, the *Book of Discipline*, and the *Book of Common Order*, the so-called Knox's liturgy. Knox's liturgy, the same as that used in Geneva but translated into English, was used until Laud's attempt to force an Anglican liturgy on the Kirk led to an abandonment of both in favour of "free prayers."

The Presbyterian tradition includes uncompromising stress upon the Word of God contained in the Scriptures of the Old and New Testaments as the supreme rule of faith and life, and upon the value of a highly trained ministry, which has given the Church of Scotland, a high reputation for scholarship and has in turn influenced the standard of education in Scotland. The unity of the Church is guaranteed by providing for democratic representation in a hierarchy of courts (unlike the Anglican Church, which is a hierarchy of persons). The local kirk-session consists of the minister and popularly elected elders (laymen). Ministers, elected by their flocks, are ordained by presbyters (ministers already ordained). Above the kirk-session is the court of the presbytery which has jurisdiction over a specified area; above that the court of synod which rules over many presbyteries; and finally the General Assembly which is the Supreme Court of the Church with both judicial and legislative powers, and over which the Moderator of the General Assembly presides. The function of the elders is to help the minister in the work and government of the kirk. The episcopacy set up by James VI and I, and maintained by Charles I was brought to an end by the Glasgow Assembly (1638), but General Assemblies were abolished by Oliver Cromwell and at the Restoration Charles II re-established episcopacy. The Covenanters who resisted were hunted down, imprisoned, transported, or executed over a period of nearly thirty years before William of Orange came to the throne and Presbyterianism was re-established (1690). Today Presbyterians no less than other Christian communities are looking at Christianity as a common world religion in the sense that the principles which unite them are greater than those which divide them. A small step in the direction of international Christian unity was made in 1972 when the Presbyterian and Congregationalist Churches in England were merged to form the United Reformed Church. *See* **Church of Scotland, Calvinism.**

Protestant, the name first applied to those who favoured the cause of Martin Luther and who protested against the intolerant decisions of the Catholic majority at the second Diet of Speyer (1529), revoking earlier decisions of the first Diet of Speyer tolerating the Reformers in certain cases (1526). In general the name "Protestant" is applied to those Churches which severed connection with Rome at the time of the Reformation. The essence of Protestantism is the acceptance by the individual

Christian of his direct responsibility to God rather than to the Church. *See* **Lutheranism, Presbyterianism, Calvinism.**

Psychic Research is a general term for the various approaches to the scientific investigation of the paranormal, in particular supposed extrasensory powers of the mind, but also manifestations such as ghosts, poltergeists, spiritualistic phenomena, etc. In recent years the word parapsychology has also come into use, particularly for the investigation of ESP in a laboratory setting, but it is really part of psychic research as the subject's fascinating history reveals.

For all recorded history, and no doubt very much earlier, man has been puzzled at his apparent ability to perceive features of the universe without the use of the normal senses—mind-to-mind contact, dreams about the future which come true, etc. He has also been intrigued by the notion that in addition to the natural world of people and things, there exists in parallel, a *supernatural* world of ghosts, spirits and other similar strange manifestations. Belief in such oddities has been tremendously widespread and still forms one of the major casual conversational topics raised when people see each other socially today. Of course, until the 19th cent. or thereabouts such phenomena, while bizarre, unpredictable and possibly frightening, were not at odds with man's view of himself and his world as revealed through basic religious beliefs. Man was supposed to be in essence a supernatural being with eternal life, and the world was seen as the happy hunting ground of dynamic evil forces which could intervene directly in the lives of humans. The rise of material science in the 19th cent. however began to shake the orthodox religious framework, and as a result in due course scientists began to question the basis of all supernatural powers and manifestations, putting forward the reasonable argument: "if such things *are* real then they should be demonstrable in scientific terms—just as all other aspects of the universe are."

Once having advanced this argument, the next step was to carry it to its conclusion and set about the systematic investigation of the phenomena to see whether they *did* conform in any way to the immensely successful framework of 19th cent. science, and from this step psychic research was born. In fact one can date its origins rather precisely—to 1882 when a group of scholars formed the Society for Psychical Research in London—an organisation which still exists today. The first experiments in this slightly eccentric field of science were haphazard and tended to be confined to spiritualistic phenomena such as table tapping, mediumistic messages, ectoplasmic manifestations, etc., which were having a great wave of popularity among the general public at the time. In fact what one might term as the first phase of psychic research—it has gone through three phases in its history—was really heavily tied up with Spiritualism. Before ridiculing it for this, it is only fair to point out that many of the most eminent figures of the time—the great physicists Sir Oliver Lodge and Sir William Crookes, Alfred Russell Wallace, co-discoverer with Darwin of the theory of evolution by natural selection, the brilliant author and creator of Sherlock Holmes, Sir Arthur Conan Doyle, and many others—became convinced Spiritualists as the result of their early experiments. Nevertheless, despite the ardent support of such intellectual giants, medium after medium was in due course detected in fraud—sometimes of the most blatant kind—and the majority of scientists gradually became more critical and less likely to be taken in by even the subtlest of trickery. As a result, interest slowly shifted from the séance room to a different realm, and as it did so the first phase of psychic research drew to a close.

The second phase was, broadly speaking, the era of the ghost hunter. With the idea of spirits materialising in laboratories seeming intrinsically less and less credible, scientists began to study what struck them at the time to be basically more "plausible" matters—haunted houses, poltergeist phenomena and so on. For some reason the idea of a house dominated by a psychic presence as the result of some tragic history seemed (at the turn of the century) *somehow* scientifically and philosophically more acceptable than did the old spiritualist notions about direct communication with the spirit world. The key figure in the "ghost hunting" era was Mr. Harry Price, an amateur magician who became the scourge of fraudulent mediums, but who staked his name and credibility on the authenticity of the alleged poltergeist phenomena at Borley Rectory in Suffolk, which became world famous through his book, *The Most Haunted House in England*. The ancient rectory's catalogue of ghosts and marvels allegedly witnessed by numerous "reliable witnesses" seemed irrefutable. Unfortunately investigations by the Society for Psychical Research some years after Price's death now make it seem certain that Price was responsible for faking some of the Borley phenomena himself, and with these disclosures scientifically "respectable" ghost hunting took a nasty tumble. Thus, with an increasingly critical attitude developing among scientists, haunted houses and poltergeists gradually began to shift out of favour to usher in the third phase of psychic research.

The date of the commencement of this phase can be identified as 1927 when the Parapsychology Laboratory at Duke University in North Carolina was formed by Dr. J. B. Rhine. Here the emphasis was on laboratory studies along the traditional lines of experimental psychology; spirit forms and poltergeists were ignored in favour of the routine testing of literally thousands of people for telepathy, precognition (the ability to see into the future), etc., almost always involving card tests which could be rigidly controlled and the results statistically analysed. By the 1940s Rhine was claiming irrefutable evidence of telepathy achieved by these means, but once again critical forces began to gather and it was pointed out that results obtained in Rhine's laboratory rarely seemed to be replicable in other scientists' laboratories in different parts of the world. In fact the failure of ESP experiments of this kind to be easily repeatable has turned out to be crucial and has led to a growing scepticism on the part of uncommitted scientists who now question whether psychic research and parapsychology have really advanced our understanding of the world of the paranormal in any way. At the present time the topic is in a highly controversial phase.

Although Rhine's university parapsychology laboratory closed with his retirement in 1965 research in the field has continued ever since, especially with the work of Dr. Helmut Schmidt who has made important contributions.

To sum up the topic one could say that in a curious way, while the third phase of psychic research is now drawing to a close, the evidence suggests that a fourth phase is appearing, and that this may well feature a return to the study of the more sensational and dramatic phenomena reminiscent of the Victorian séance room. If this is so, a century after its foundation the wheel will have turned full circle and psychic research will be back where it started, without in the opinion of most scientists, having solved any of the basic questions which it had set out to answer. *See* **Parapsychology, Poltergeist, Telepathy, Spiritualism.**

Psychoanalysis, an approach to the study of human personality involving the rigorous probing, with the assistance of a specially trained practitioner, of an individual's personal problems, motives, goals and attitudes to life in general. Often, and quite understandably, confused with psychology (of which it is merely a part), psychoanalysis has an interesting historical background and has attracted the interest of philosophers, scientists and medical experts since it emerged as a radical and controversial form of mental therapy at the turn of the century. The traditionally accepted founder is the great Austrian Sigmund Freud, but he never failed to acknowledge the impetus that had been given to his own ideas by his talented friend, the physiologist Joseph Breuer, who for most of his working life had been interested in the curious phenomena associated with hypnosis. Breuer had successfully cured the hysterical paralysis of a young woman patient and had noticed that under hypnosis the girl seemed to be recalling emotional experiences, hitherto forgotten, which bore some relationship to the symptoms of her illness. Developing this with other patients Breuer then found that the mere recalling and discussing of the emotional events under hypnosis seemed to produce a dramatic alleviation of the symptoms—a phenomenon which came to be known as *catharsis*. Breuer also noticed another curious side-effect, that his women patients fell embarrassingly and violently in love with him, and he gradually dropped the practice of "mental catharsis", possibly feeling that it was a bit too dangerous to handle. This left the field clear for Freud, whose brilliant mind began to search beyond the therapeutic aspects of the topic to see what light might be thrown on the nature of human personality and psychological mechanisms in general. The most important question concerned the "forgotten" emotional material which turned up, apparently out of the blue, during the hypnotic session. Freud rightly saw that this posed problems for the current theories of memory, for how could something once forgotten (a) continue to have an effect on the individual without his being aware of it, and (b) ultimately be brought back to conscious memory again. It must be remembered that at this time memory was considered to be a fairly simple process—information was stored in the brain and was gradually eroded or destroyed with the passage of time and the decay of brain cells. Once lost, it was believed, memories were gone for ever, or at best only partially and inaccurately reproducible. Furthermore, human beings were supposed to be rational (if frequently wilful) creatures who never did anything without thinking about it (if only briefly) beforehand and without being well aware of their reasons for so doing. It was within this framework that Freud had his great insight, one which many people believe to be one of the most important ideas given to mankind. This was simply the realisation that the human mind was not a simple entity controlling the brain and body more or less at will, but a complex system made up of a number of integrated parts with at least two major subdivisions—the conscious and the unconscious. The former concerned itself with the normal round of human behaviour, including the larger part of rational thought, conversation, etc., and large areas of memory. The latter was principally devoted to the automatic control of bodily functions, such as respiration, cardiac activity, various types of emotional behaviour not subject to much conscious modification and a large storehouse of relevant "memories" again not normally accessible to the conscious mind. Occasionally. Freud proposed, an exceedingly unpleasant emotional or otherwise painful event might be so troublesome if held in the conscious mind's store, that it would get shoved down into the unconscious or "repressed" where it would cease to trouble the individual in his normal life. The advantages of this mechanism are obvious, but they also brought with them hazards. With certain kinds of memory, particularly those involving psychological rather than physical pain—as for example a severe sexual conflict or marital problem—repression might be used as a device to save the individual from facing his problem in the "real" world, where he might be able ultimately to solve it, by merely hiding it away in the unconscious and thus pretending it did not exist. Unfortunately, Freud believed, conflicts of this kind were not snuffed out when consigned to the basements of the mind, but rather tended to smoulder on, affecting the individual in various ways which he could not understand. Repressed marital conflicts might give rise to impotence, for example, or perhaps to homosexual behaviour. Guilt at improper social actions similarly repressed might provoke nervous tics, local paralysis, *etc, etc*. Following this line of reasoning, Freud argued that if the unwisely repressed material could be dredged up and the individual forced to face the crisis instead of denying it, then dramatic allevia-

tions of symptoms and full recovery should follow.

To the great psychologist and his growing band of followers the stage seemed to be set for a dramatic breakthrough not only in mental therapy but also in a general understanding of the nature of human personality. To his pleasure—for various reasons he was never too happy about hypnosis—Freud discovered that with due patience, skill and guidance an individual could be led to resurrect the material repressed in his unconscious mind in the normal, as opposed to the hypnotic, state. This technique, involving long sessions consisting of intimate discussions between patient and therapist became known as psychoanalysis, and it has steadily evolved from its experimental beginnings in the medical schools and universities of Vienna to being a major system of psychotherapy with a world-wide following and important theoretical connotations. Psychoanalysis, as practised today, consists of a number of meetings between doctor and patient in which the latter is slowly taught to approach and enter the *territory* of his subconscious mind, and examine the strange and "forgotten" material within. A successful analysis, it is claimed, gives the individual greater insight into his own personality and a fuller understanding of the potent unconscious forces which are at work within him and in part dictating his goals.

Freud's initial ideas were of course tentative, and meant to be so. He was however a didactic and forceful personality himself, unwilling to compromise on many points which became controversial as the technique and practice of psychoanalysis developed. The outcome was that some of his early followers, notably the equally brilliant Carl Jung and Alfred Adler, broke away to found their own "schools" or versions of psychoanalysis, with varying degrees of success. Today, psychoanalysis is coming under increasingly critical scrutiny, and its claims are being treated with a good deal of reservation. Notable antagonists include the English psychologist Professor H. J. Eysenck who points out that there is little if any solid experimental data indicating that psychoanalysis is a valid method of treating or curing mental illness. Analysists respond by saying that their system is closer to an art than a craft and not amenable to routine scientific experiment. The controversy will no doubt continue for some time to come, but whatever its validity as therapy, the basic ideas behind psychoanalysis—notably the reality and power of the unconscious mind—are beyond question and have given human beings definite and major insights into the greatest enigma of all—the workings of the human mind.

Puritans were a separate sect before the accession of Edward VI, but did not become prominent till the reign of Elizabeth. Afterwards they split up into Independents and Presbyterians, and the influence of Oliver Cromwell made the former supreme. Since the Revolution the word has been replaced by 'Nonconformist' or 'Dissenter', but, of course, Roman Catholics in England and Protestant Episcopalians in Scotland are just as much Nonconformists or Dissenters as Baptists or Methodists are.

Pyramidology, a curious belief that the dimensions of the Great Pyramid at Giza, if studied carefully, reveal principles of fundamental historical and religious significance. The perpetrator of this was a Victorian publisher, John Taylor, who discovered that if you divide the height of the pyramid into twice the side of its base you get a number very similar to pi—a number of considerable mathematical importance. Later discoveries in the same vein include the finding that the base of the pyramid (when divided by the width of a single casing stone) equals exactly 365—number of days in the year. Many books have been written on the interpretation of the dimensions of the pyramid, none of which has any scientific or archaeological validity. Pyramidology is simply a classic example of the well-known fact that hunting through even a random array of numbers will turn up sequences which appear to be "significant"—always provided that one carefully selects the numbers one wants and turns a blind eye to those that one doesn't!

Pyrrhonism, a sceptical philosophy which doubts everything. (*See* **Scepticism**)

Pythagoreanism. The school of thought initiated by the followers of Pythagoras (**B49**). To be distinguished from Pythagoras himself, whose own doctrines are difficult to determine. The Pythagoreans believed that at its deepest level, reality is mathematical in nature, that is, all things can be ultimately reduced to numerical relationships. Their theory of number was applied to music theory, acoustics, geometry and astronomy. The doctrine of the "harmony of the spheres" seems to have started with them: certain parameters characterizing the planets are related to one another "harmoniously" by a mathematical rule. The revolution of each planet produces a distinct tone, and the whole set corresponds to the notes of a scale. They also held a doctrine of metempsychosis: the soul transmigrates through successive reincarnations to union with the divine.

Q

Quakers, (**Religious Society of Friends**), a religious body founded in England in the 17th cent. by George Fox (1624–91). The essence of their faith is that every individual person has the power of direct communication with God who will guide him into the ways of truth. This power comes from the "inner light" of his own heart, the light of Christ, Quakers meet for worship avoiding all ritual, without ordained ministers or prepared sermons; often there is complete silence until someone is moved by the Holy Spirit to utter his message.

In the early days Quakers gave vent to violent outbursts and disturbed church services. Friends had the habit of preaching at anyone who happened to be nearby, their denunciation of "steeple-houses" and references to the "inner light," their addressing everyone as "thee" and "thou," their refusal to go beyond "yea" and "nay" in making an assertion and refusing to go further in taking an oath, must have played some part in bringing about the savage persecutions they were forced to endure. Many emigrated to Pennsylvania, founded by William Penn in 1682, and missionaries were sent to many parts of the world. The former violence gave way to gentleness. Friends not only refused to take part in war but even refused to resist personal violence. They took the lead in abolishing slavery, worked for prison reform and better education. As we know them today Quakers are quiet, sincere, undemonstrative people, given to a somewhat serious turn of mind. The former peculiarities of custom and dress have been dropped and interpretation of the Scriptures is more liberal. Although Quakers refuse to take part in warfare, they are always ready to help the victims of war, by organising relief, helping refugees in distress, or sending their ambulance units into the heat of battle. In Britain the Quakers have (1995) some 18,000 adult members.

Quietism, a doctrine of extreme asceticism and contemplative devotion, embodied in the works of Michael Molinos, a 17th cent. Spanish priest, and condemned by Rome. It taught that the chief duty of man is to be occupied in the continual contemplation of God, so as to become totally independent of outward circumstances and the influence of the senses. Quietists taught that when this stage of perfection is reached the soul has no further need for prayer and other external devotional practices. Similar doctrines have been taught in the Moslem and Hindu religions. *See* **Yoga**.

R

Racism, the doctrine that one race is inherently superior or inferior to others, one of the bases of racial prejudice. It has no connection what ever with the study of race as a concept, nor with the investigation of racial differences, which is a science practised by the physical anthropologist (who studies physical differences), or the social anthropologist (who studies cultural differences). *See also* **Race, Section L.**

Radiesthesia, the detection, either by some "psychic" faculty or with special equipment, of radiations alleged to be given off by all living things and natural substances such as water, oil, metal, etc. The word radiesthesia is in fact a fancy modern name for the ancient practice of "dowsing," whereby an individual is supposed to be able to detect the presence of hidden underground water by following the movements of a hazel twig held in his hands. Dowsers, or water diviners, as they are sometimes called, claim also to be able to detect the presence of minerals and, hard though it may seem to believe, have actually been hired by major oil companies to prospect for desert wells—though without any notable success. The theory of dowsing is that all things give off a unique radiation signal which the trained individual (via his twig, pendulum, or whatever) can "tune in" to, a theory which, while not backed up by any data known to orthodox sciences, is at least not too fantastically far-fetched. It is when radiesthesists claim to be able to detect the presence of oil, water, or precious metals by holding their pendulum *over a map* of the territory and declare that it is not necessary for them to visit the area in person to find the required spot that the topic moves from the remotely possible to the absurdly improbable. Some practitioners of this art state that they are able to perform even more marvellous feats such as determining the sex of chickens while still in the egg, or diagnosing illness by studying the movements of a pendulum held over a blood sample from the sick individual. Such claims when put to simple scientific test have almost invariably turned out as fiascos. Yet belief in dowsing, water-divining, and the like is still very widespread.

There is an important link between radiesthesia and the pseudo-science of *radionics*, which holds that the twig or pendulum can be superseded by complicated equipment built vaguely according to electronic principles. A typical radionic device consists of a box covered with knobs, dials, etc., by which the practitioner "tunes in" to the "vibration" given off by an object, such as a blood spot, a piece of hair, or even a signature. By the proper interpretation of the readings from the equipment the illness, or even the mental state, of the individual whose blood, hair, or signature is being tested, may be ascertained. The originator of radionics seems to have been a Dr. Albert Abrams who engaged in medical practice using radionic devices in America in the 1920s and 30s. The principal exponent in this country was the late George de la Warr who manufactured radionic boxes for diagnosis and treatment of illnesses, and even a "camera" which he believed to be capable of photographing thought. In a sensational court case in 1960 a woman who had purchased one of the diagnostic devices sued de la Warr for fraud. After a long trial the case was dismissed, the Judge commenting that while he had no good evidence that the device worked as claimed, he felt that de la Warr seriously believed in its validity and thus was not guilty of fraud or misrepresentation.

Ranters, a fanatical antinomian (the doctrine that Christians are not bound to keep the law of God) and pantheistic sect in Commonwealth England. The name was also applied to the Primitive Methodists because of their noisy preaching.

Rastafarianism, a Caribbean religious movement which took root in the 1930s following the teachings of Marcus Garvey who set up the "Black Star Liner" for the repatriation of Africans abroad. Rastafarians look to Ethiopia as their spiritual and racial home since that country was the one part of Africa not to be colonised permanently (it was invaded by Mussolini in the 1930s). Reggae is their music.

Rationalism is defined as "the treating of reason as the ultimate authority in religion and the rejection of doctrines not consonant with reason." In practice, rationalism had a double significance: (1) the doctrine as defined above, and (2) a 19th cent. movement which was given to what was then known as "free-thought," "secularism," or agnosticism—*i.e.*, it was in the positive sense anti-religious and was represented by various bodies such as the Secular Society, the National Secular Society, and the Rationalist Press Association (founded in 1899).

In the first sense, which implies a particular philosophical attitude to the universe and life, rationalism is not easy to pin down although, at first sight, it would appear that nothing could be simpler. Does it mean the use of pure reason and logic or does it mean, on the other hand, the use of what is generally called the "scientific method" based on a critical attitude to existing beliefs? If we are thinking in terms of the use of pure reason and logic then the Roman Catholic Church throughout most of its history has maintained, not that the whole truth about religion can be discovered by reason, but as St. Thomas Aquinas held, the basis of religion—*e.g.* the existence of God—can be rationally demonstrated. Nobody could have made more use of logic than the schoolmen of the Middle Ages, yet not many people today would accept their conclusions, nor would many non-Catholics accept St. Thomas's proofs of the existence of God even when they themselves are religious. The arguments of a First Cause or Prime Mover or the argument from Design on the whole leave us unmoved, partly because they do not lead up to the idea of a *personal God*, partly because we rightly distrust logic and pure reason divorced from facts and know that, if we begin from the wrong assumptions or premises, we can arrive at some very strange answers. If the existence of a Deity can be proved by reason, then one can also by the use of reason come to the conclusions, or rather paradoxes, such as the following: God is by definition all good, all knowing, all powerful—yet evil exists (because it if does not exist then it cannot be wrong to say "there is no God"). But if evil exists, then it must do so either because of God (in which case He is not all good) or in spite of God (in which case He is not all powerful).

Arguments of this sort do not appeal to the modern mind for two historical reasons: (1) many of us have been brought up in the Protestant tradition which—at least in one of its aspects—insists that we must believe in God by faith rather than by logic and in its extreme form insists on God as revealed by the "inner light"; (2) our increasing trust in the scientific method of observation, experiment and argument. Thus, no matter what Aristotle or St. Thomas may say about a Prime Mover or a First Cause, we remain unconvinced since at least one scientific theory suggests that the universe did not have a beginning and if scientific investigation proved this to be so, then we should be entirely indifferent to what formal logic had to say.

The secularist and rationalist movements of the 19th cent. were anti-religious—and quite rightly so—because at that time there were serious disabilities imposed even in Britain by the Established Church on atheism or agnosticism and freedom of thought. They are of little significance now because very little is left, largely thanks to their efforts, of these disabilities.

Finally, although most people are likely to accept the scientific method as the main means of discovering truth, there are other factors which equally make us doubt the value of "pure" logic and reason unaided by observation. The first of these is the influence of Freud which shows that much of our reasoning is mere rationalising—*e.g.*, we are more likely to become atheists because we hated our father than because we can prove that there is no God. The second is the influence of a movement in philosophy which, in the form of logical positivism or logical analysis, makes us doubt whether metaphysical systems have any meaning at all. To-day, instead of asking ourselves whether Plato was right or wrong, we are much more likely to ask whether he did anything but make for the most part meaningless noises. Religion is in a sense much safer today than it ever was in the 19th cent. when it made foolish statements over matters of science that could be *proved* wrong; now we tend to see it as an emotional attitude to the universe or God (a "feeling of being at home in the universe," as William James put it) which can no more be proved or disproved than being in love.

Realism is a word which has so many meanings, and such contradictory ones, in various spheres, that it is difficult to define. We shall limit ourselves to its significance in philosophy. In philosophy, "realism" has two different meanings, diametrically opposed. (1) The most usual meaning is the one we should least expect from the everyday sense of the word—*i.e.*, it refers to all those philosophies from Plato onwards which maintained that the world of appearance is illusory and that ideas, forms, or universals are the only true realities, belonging to the world beyond matter and appearance—the world of God or mind. In early mediaeval times St. Thomas Aquinas was the chief exponent of this doctrine which was held by the scholastics as opposed to the Nominalists (*q.v.*). (2) In its modern everyday meaning "realism" is the belief that the universe is real and not a creation of mind, that there is a reality that causes the appearance, the "thing-in-itself" as Kant described it. Material things may not really be what they appear to be (*e.g.* a noise is not the "bang" we experience but a series of shock-waves passing through the atmosphere), yet, for all that, we can be sure that matter exists and it is very possible (some might add) that mind does not.

Reformation, the great religious movement of the 16th cent., which resulted in the establishment of Protestantism. John Wyclif (d. 1384), John Hus (d. 1415) and others had sounded the warning note, and when later on Luther took up the cause in Germany, and Zwingli in Switzerland, adherents soon became numerous. The wholesale vending of indulgences by the papal agents had incensed the people, and when Luther denounced these things he spoke to willing ears. After much controversy, the reformers boldly propounded the principles of the new doctrine, and the struggle for religious supremacy grew bitter. They claimed justification (salvation) by faith, and the use as well as the authority of the Scriptures, rejecting the doctrine of transubstantiation, the adoration of the Virgin and Saints, and the headship of the Pope. Luther was excommunicated. But the Reformation principles spread and ultimately a great part of Germany, as well as Switzerland, the Low Countries, Scandinavia, England, and Scotland were won over to the new faith. In England Henry VIII readily espoused the cause of the Reformation, his own personal quarrel with the Pope acting as an incentive. Under Mary there was a brief and sanguinary reaction, but Elizabeth gave completeness to the work which her father had initiated. *See* **Lutheranism, Calvinism, Presbyterianism, Baptists, Methodism.**

Relativism. Theories or doctrines that truth, morality *etc.* are relative to situations and are not absolute. The view that all truth is relative is associated with Scepticism (*q.v.*). In the area of morality, it is the view that there are no absolute or universal criteria for ethical judgements. This view is often a reaction to the differences in moral belief between different societies. It is objected against relativism that there must be standards by which to measure the correctness of judgements or beliefs.

Religious Society of Friends. *See* **Quakers.**

Renaissance is defined in the *Oxford English Dictionary* as: "The revival of art and letters, under the influence of classical models, which began in Italy in the 14th century." It is a term which must be used with care for the following reasons: (1) Although it was first used in the form *rinascita* (re-birth) by Vasari in 1550 and people living at that time certainly were aware that something new was happening, the word had no wide currency until used by the Swiss historian Jacob Burchardt in his classic *The Civilization of the Renaissance in Italy*

(1860). (2) The term as used today refers not only to art in its widest sense but to a total change in man's outlook on life which extended into philosophical, scientific, economic, and technical fields. (3) Spreading from Italy there were renaissance movements in France, Spain, Germany, and northern Europe, all widely different with varying delays in time. As the historian Edith Sichel says: "Out of the Italian Renaissance there issued a new-born art; out of the Northern Renaissance there came forth a new-born religion. There came forth also a great school of poetry, and a drama the greatest that the world had seen since the days of Greece. The religion was the offspring of Germany and the poetry that of England."

The real cause of the Renaissance was not the fall of Constantinople, the invention of printing, or the discovery of America, though these were phases in the process; it was, quite simply, money. The birth of a new merchant class gave rise to individualist attitudes in economic affairs which prepared the way for individualism and humanism. The new wealthy class in time became patrons of the arts whereas previously the Church had been the sole patron and controller. Thus the artist became more free to express himself, more respected, and being more well-to-do could afford to ignore the Church and even, in time, the views of his patrons.

It is true that art continued to serve to a considerable extent the purposes of faith, but it was judged from the standpoint of art. Mediaeval art was meant to elevate and teach man: Renaissance art to delight his senses and enrich his life. From this free and questing spirit acquired from economic individualism came the rise of modern science and technology; here Italy learned much from the Arab scholars who had translated and commented upon the philosophical, medical, and mathematical texts of antiquity, while denying themselves any interest in Greek art and literature. Arabic-Latin versions of Aristotle were in use well into the 16th cent. The Byzantine culture, though it had preserved the Greek tradition and gave supremacy to Plato, had made no move forward. But the Greek scholars who fled to Italy after the fall of Constantinople brought with them an immense cargo of classical manuscripts. The recovery of these Greek masterpieces, their translation into the vernaculars, and the invention of printing, made possible a completer understanding of the Greek spirit. It was the bringing together of the two heritages, Greek science, and Greek literature, that gave birth to a new vision. But it was not only Aristotle and Plato who were being studied but Ovid, Catullus, Horace, Pliny and Lucretius. What interested Renaissance man was the humanism of the Latin writers, their attitude to science, their scepticism.

The period *c.* 1400–1500 is known as the **Early Renaissance**. During this time such painters as Masaccio, Uccello, Piero della Francesca, Botticelli, and Giovanni Bellini were laying the foundations of drawing and painting for all subsequent periods including our own. They concerned themselves with such problems as anatomy, composition, perspective, and representation of space, creating in effect a grammar or textbook of visual expression. The term **High Renaissance** is reserved for a very brief period when a pure, balanced, classical harmony was achieved and artists were in complete control of the techniques learned earlier. The High Renaissance lasted only from *c.* 1500 to 1527 (the date of the sack of Rome), yet that interval included the earlier works of Michelangelo, most of Leonardo's, and all the Roman works of Raphael.

Ritualism, a tendency which, during the 19th cent., developed in the High Church section of the Church of England to make use of those vestments, candles, incense, etc. which are usually regarded as features of the Church of Rome. Since some opposition was aroused, a Ritual Commission was appointed in 1904 to take evidence and try to find some common basis on which High and Low Church could agree with respect to ceremonial. The report of 1906 in effect recommended the giving of greater powers to bishops to suppress objectionable practices.

Although they are often associated together, it is worth while pointing out that there was no special connection between the Oxford Movement or Tractarians (*q.v.*) and Ritualism because Pusey disliked ritual and even Newman, who eventually went over to Rome, held extremely simple services at his church of St. Mary's.

Roman Catholic Church, the Christian organisation which acknowledges the Pope as the lawful successor of St. Peter, the apostle appointed by Christ to be the head of His Church. The reforming impulse at the Second Vatican Council (1962–5), summoned by Pope John, set in train movements towards religious unity and the reform and modernisation of the Church. Pope Paul made changes in the government and liturgy of the Church but refused to allow birth control, the marriage of priests and a greater role for women in the Roman Catholic Church. Recent years have seen rapid changes in the Roman Catholic Church and the papacy has found a strong and charismatic leader in Pope John Paul II. A historic meeting took place in 1982 between Rome and Canterbury when Pope John Paul II made the first papal visit to Britain. The 1993 papal encyclical, *Veritatis Splendor,* forcefully restating the Catholic opposition to artificial birth control, has reopened Catholic divisions on this issue. The English text of the Catechism of the Catholic Church, the first complete survey of Roman Catholic teaching since the 16th century, was published in 1994. Pope John Paul's book, *Crossing the Threshold of Hope* was published the same year. Some Anglicans (opposed to women priests) have moved to join the Catholic Church. There are currently (1995) over 1,025 million Catholics worldwide.

Romantic Movement or **Romanticism** is the name given not so much to an individual way of thinking but to the gradual but radical transformation of basic human values that occurred in the Western world round about the latter part of the 18th cent. It was a great breakthrough in European consciousness and arose through the writings of certain men living during the half-century or more following, say, 1760. It arose then because both time and place were propitious for the birth of these new ideas. There was a revolution in basic values—in art, morals, politics, religion, etc. The new view was of a world transcending the old one, infinitely larger and more varied.

To understand the Romantic movement it is necessary first to take note of the climate of thought preceding the great change; then to account for its beginning in Germany where it did (*see* **Pietism**) during the latter part of the 18th cent., and finally to appraise the writings of those men whose ideas fermented the new awakening. Briefly, the shift was away from French classicism and from belief in the all-pervasive power of human reason (the Enlightenment) towards the unfettered freedom that the new consciousness was able to engender. What mattered was to live a passionate and vigorous life, to dedicate oneself to an ideal, no matter what the cost (*e.g.,* Byron).

The ideas of the Englightenment (*e.g.,* Fontenelle, Voltaire, Montesquieu) had been attacked by the Germans Hamann and Herder and by the ideas of the English philosopher Hume, but Kant, Schiller, and Fichte, Goethe's novel *Wilhelm Meister,* and the French Revolution all had profound effects on the aesthetic, moral, social, and political thought of the time. Friedrich Schlegel (1772–1829) said: "There is in man a terrible unsatisfied desire to soar into infinity; a feverish longing to break through the narrow bonds of individuality." Romanticism undermined the notion that in matters of value there are objective criteria which operate between men. Henceforth there was to be a resurgence of the human spirit, deep and profound, that is still going on.

Rosicrucians, an ancient mystical society founded in the 16th cent. by Christian Rosenkreuz which attempted to forge a theoretical link between the great Egyptian religions and the Church of Rome, drawing rituals and philosophy from both camps. The Society did not long survive the death of its founder (he managed to reach the age of 106 incidentally) but has been revived in succeeding centuries by a series of rivalling factions. Perhaps the most famous of these is the Rosicrucian Order (A.M.O.R.C) which has become well-known in the Western world as a result of its heavy advertising in the popular press. Founded by the American H. Spencer Lewis, this offers a simple and good-natured doctrine preaching the Brotherhood of Man, the reincarnation of the soul and the immense latent potential of the human mind. As with many American-based organisations of this kind, the boundary between business and religion is hard to define. It is probably best summed up as a modern secret society which serves an important function in the lives of many people of mystical inclinations.

S

Salvation Army. The religious movement which in 1878 became known by this name arose from the Christian Mission meetings which the Rev. William Booth and his devoted wife had held in the East End of London for the previous thirteen years. Its primary aim was, and still is, to preach the gospel of Jesus Christ to men and women untouched by ordinary religious efforts. The founder devoted his life to the salvation of the submerged classes whose conditions at that time were unspeakably dreadful. Originally his aim had been to convert people and then send them on to the churches, but he soon found that few religious bodies would accept these "low-class" men and women. So it was that social work became part of their effort. Practical help like the provision of soup-kitchens, accompanied spiritual ministration. Soon, in the interests of more effective "warfare" against social evils, a military form of organisation, with uniforms, brass bands, and religious songs, was introduced. Its magazine *The War Cry* gave as its aim "to carry the Blood of Christ and the Fire of the Holy Ghost into every part of the world.'

General Booth saw with blinding clarity that conversion must be accompanied by an improvement of external conditions. Various books had earlier described the terrible conditions of the slums, but in 1890 he produced a monumental survey entitled *In Darkest England and the Way Out*. From that time forward the Army was accepted and its facilities made use of by the authorities. Today (1995) the Army's spiritual and social activities have spread to over 94 countries across the world; every one, no matter what class, colour, or creed he belongs to, is a "brother for whom Christ died." Within Britain there are 60,000 active members (1995).

Scepticism. From the Greek, *skepsis*, enquiry or questioning. The philosophical attitude of doubting claims to knowledge. It springs from observations that the senses are unreliable, that the best methods often fall short of reaching the truth, and that experts often disagree. Sceptical attitudes emerge early in ancient Greek philosophy, but were only systemized into a school of thought by Pyrrhon Elis (*c.* 360–*c.* 272 B.C.). The Greek Sceptics proposed *epoche*, or suspension of belief, and aimed to achieve *ataraxia*, tranquility of mind.

Scepticism is a recurring theme in Western philosophy, for example in Montaigne (1533–92) and Bayle (1647–1706). The most powerful sceptical thinker of the modern age is David Hume (1711–76). His arguments throw doubt upon induction, the notion of causality, the identity of the self and the existence of the external world. The term is also associated with Descartes (1596–1650), though Descartes himself is not a sceptic. It refers to his "method of doubt", which attempted to put knowledge upon a sure foundation by suspending Judgement on any proposition whose truth could be doubted, until one can be found that is absolutely certain. This secure point is the famous "I think therefore I am".

Schoolmen. From the time of Augustine to the middle of the 9th cent. philosophy, like science, was dead or merely a repetition of what had gone before. But about that time there arose a new interest in the subject, although (since by

then Western Europe was entirely under the authority of the Catholic Church) the main form it took was an attempt to justify Church teaching in the light of Greek philosophy. Those who made this attempt to reconcile Christian beliefs with the best in Plato and Aristotle were known as "schoolmen" and the philosophies which they developed were known as "scholasticism." Among the most famous schoolmen must be counted John Scotus Erigena (*c.* 800–*c.* 877), born in Ireland and probably the earliest; St. Anselm, archbishop of Canterbury (1033–1109); the great Peter Abelard whose school was in Paris (1079–1142); Bernard of Chartres, his contemporary; and the best-known of all, St. Thomas Aquinas of Naples (1225–74), who was given the name of the "Angelic Doctor."

The philosophies of these men are discussed under various headings (**God and Man, Determinism and Free-will**), but being severely limited by the Church their doctrines differed from each other much less than those of later philosophical schools. However, one of the great arguments was between the orthodox Realists (*q.v.*) and the Nominalists (*q.v.*) and a second was between the Thomists (or followers of St. Thomas Aquinas) and the Scotists (followers of John Duns Scotus—not to be confused with John Scotus Erigena). The two latter schools were known as the Ancients, whilst the followers of William of Occam, the Nominalist, were known as the Terminalists. All became reconciled in 1482 in face of the threat from humanism of which the great exponent was Erasmus of Rotterdam (1466–1536).

Scientology, an applied religious philosophy dealing with the study of knowledge, which through the application of its technology, can bring about desirable changes in the conditions of life. The word Scientology comes from the Latin word *Scio* (knowing in the fullest meaning of the word) and the Greek word *Logos* (study of). Developed and founded by author, philosopher and humanitarian L. Ron Hubbard (1911–86). A world-wide organisation with approximately 600 established Churches and affiliated groups in 50 countries. Membership estimated at over 7 million (1990). In Scientology the individual is considered to be a soul or spirit of an immortal nature which goes from life to life. Although he has a mind and a body, he is himself a spiritual being called a "Thetan" (taken from the Greek letter theta, meaning thought or spirit). Scientology is traditional in its philosophical approach and although many new phenomena have been discovered, it follows the basic trend of the formal philosophies of the Egyptians, Greeks and great thinkers of the Renaissance, which consider the individual a spiritual rather than an animal being. The ultimate goal of Scientology is "a civilisation without insanity, without criminals and without war, where the able can prosper and honest beings can have rights, and where Man is free to rise to greater heights." Scientologists believe that, by helping persons achieve the State of Clear (a level of spiritual awareness and ability) they can salvage a civilisation that is otherwise doomed. Scientology technology is also used to help people improve conditions in society by dealing with community problems such as drug and alcohol abuse, problems in education, juvenile delinquency, crime and violence. Until the late 1960s the worldwide headquarters was in East Grinstead, Sussex and this is now the UK headquarters. Scientology ® is a registered trademark. Scientology has come in for criticism in recent years, particularly for its recruitment techniques. It has been attacked by one government minister as a "socially harmful pseudo-philosophical cult".

Semiology, semiotics. These two words are now used almost interchangeably. The original sense of semiotics was the study of signs and sign-using behaviour, and was propounded by the American philosopher Peirce (1839–1914). Semiotics was divided into three branches: syntactics, the study of grammar; semantics, the study of meaning; and pragmatics, the study of the purposes and effects of meaningful utterances. Under the influence of the French linguist de Saussure (1857–1913) the term has broadened to the study of any means by which human beings communicate, not only through language, but also through gestures, clothes, objects, advertisements *etc.* Societies have a multiplicity of language-like "codes" by which objects like cars and buildings have cultural meanings over and above their functions.

Shakers, members of a revivalist group, styled by themselves "The United Society of Believers in Christ's Second Appearing," who seceded from Quakerism in 1747 though adhering to many of the Quaker tenets. The community was joined in 1758 by Ann Lee, a young convert from Manchester, who had "revelations" that she was the female Christ; "Mother Ann" was accepted as their leader. Under the influence of her prophetic visions she set out with nine followers for "Immanuel's land" in America and the community settled near Albany, capital of New York state. They were known as the "Shakers" in ridicule because they were given to involuntary movements in moments of religious ecstasy. Central to their faith was the belief in the dual role of God through the male and female Christ: the male principle came to earth in Jesus; the female principle, in "Mother Ann." The sexes were equal and women preached as often as men at their meetings which sometimes included sacred dances—nevertheless the two sexes, even in dancing, kept apart. Their communistic way of living brought them economic prosperity, the Shakers becoming known as good agriculturists and craftsmen, noted for their furniture and textiles. After 1860, however, the movement began to decline and few are active today. There is now (1995) only one U.S. Shaker colony (in Maine).

Shamans, the medicine men found in all primitive societies who used their magical arts to work cures, and protect the group from evil influences. The *shaman* was a man apart and wore special garments to show his authority. Shamanism with its magical practices, incantations, trances, dances, and self-torture is still practised.

Shiites or Shia, a heretical Moslem sect in Persia, opposed by the orthodox Sunnites. The dispute, which came almost immediately after the death of the Prophet and led to bitter feuding, had little to do with matters of doctrine as such but with the succession. After Mohammed's death, there were three possible claimants: Ali, the husband of his daughter Fatima, and two others, one of whom gave up his claim in favour of the other, Abu Bakr. The orthodox selected Abu Bakr, who was shortly assassinated, and the same happened to his successor as Ali was passed over again. The Shiites maintain that Ali was the true vicar of the Prophet, and that the three orthodox predecessors were usurpers.

Shintoism, literally means "teaching of the Gods". It is a native Japanese religion, with a strong bias towards ancestor worship and the divine powers of natural forces. Unusual in that it had no recognised founder nor written dogma, Shintoism permeated Japanese life in a most vigorous way until the defeat of the country at the hands of the Allied Powers in 1945. In the 1500 years of its existence the Shinto religion produced tens of thousands of unique and beautiful shrines throughout Japan. Vast numbers of these were destroyed by bombing in the war, but a tolerant decision by the American airforce spared one Shinto centre, Kyoto, from air-attack. Shintoism was disestablished by the American occupying forces in 1945 and the Emperor Hirohito "abdicated" his divine powers. Dissatisfaction among many Japanese with the worldly extravagance of their society has led to a recent revival of interest in Shintoism. Nationalism in Japan has often made use of Shintoism.

Sikhism. The Sikh community of the Punjab, which has played a significant part in the history of modern India, came into being during a period of religious revival in India in the 15th and 16th cent. It was originally founded as a religious sect by Guru (teacher) Nanak (1469–1538) who emphasised the fundamental truth of all religions, and whose mission was to put an end to religious conflict. He condemned the formalism both of Hinduism and Islam, preaching the gospel of universal toleration, and the unity of the Godhead, whether He be called Allah, Vishnu, or God. His ideas were welcomed by the great Mogul Emperor Akbar (1542–1605). Thus a succession of Gurus were able to live in peace after Nanak's death; they established the great Sikh centre at Amritsar, compiled the sacred writings known as the *Adi Granth,* and improved their organisation as a sect. But the peace did not last long, for an emperor arose who was a fanatical Moslem, in face of whom the last Guru, Govind Singh (1666–1708), whose father was put to death for refusal to embrace Islam, had to make himself a warrior and instil into the Sikhs a more aggressive spirit. A number of ceremonies were instituted by Govind Singh; admission to the fraternity was by special rite; caste distinctions were abolished; hair was worn long; the word singh, meaning lion, was added to the original name. They were able to organise themselves into 12 *misls* or confederacies but divisions appeared with the disappearance of a common enemy and it was not until the rise of Ranjit Singh (1780–1839) that a single powerful Sikh kingdom was established, its influence only being checked by the English, with whom a treaty of friendship was made. After the death of Ranjit Singh two Anglo-Sikh wars followed, in 1845–46, and 1848–49, which resulted in British annexation of the Punjab and the end of Sikh independence. In the two world wars the Sikhs proved among the most loyal of Britain's Indian subjects. The partitioning of the continent of India in 1947 into two states, one predominantly Hindu and the other predominantly Moslem, presented a considerable problem in the Punjab, which was divided in such a way as to leave 2 million Sikhs in Pakistan, and a considerable number of Moslems in the Indian Punjab. Although numbering less than 2 per cent. of the population (*c.* 8 million) the Sikhs are a continuing factor in Indian political life. Demands for Sikh independence led to the storming by Indian troops of the Golden Temple at Amritsar on 6 June 1984. In October 1984, Mrs. Gandhi was assassinated by Sikh extremists. There are over 300,000 Sikhs in Britain (1995). There are 18·8 m. Sikhs worldwide.

Socialism, is a form of society in which men and women are not divided into opposing economic classes but live together under conditions of approximate social and economic equality, using in common the means that lie to their hands of promoting social welfare. The brotherhood of man inspires the aims of socialism in foreign, colonial, social, and economic policies alike. The word "socialism" first came into general use in England about 1834 in connection with Robert Owen's "village of cooperation" at New Lanark. About the middle of the 19th cent., Charles Kingsley and others established a form of Christian socialism, and William Morris, John Burns, and others founded a Socialist League in 1886. With the development of trade unions the socialist movement took a more practical trend. Fabianism (*q.v.*) associated in its early days with the names of Beatrice and Sidney Webb and George Bernard Shaw, aims at the gradual reorganisation of society by creating intelligent public opinion by education and legislation. The British Labour Party believes in peaceful and constitutional change to socialism by democratic methods based upon popular consent. The Labour Government of 1945–51 initiated a major period of social reform and public ownership. Though beset by economic difficulties, the 1964–70 Labour Government continued a policy of radical reform. The minority Labour Government (of February–October 1974) and the subsequent administration continued this process, particularly in the area of state intervention in industry. The election defeats of 1979, 1983 and 1987 inevitably led to a questioning of the future direction the party should take and, under the leadership of Neil Kinnock, the party became (in effect) a modernised social democratic party. It fought the 1992 election on this platform but went down to its fourth consecutive defeat. Under John Smith (until his untimely death in 1994) and subsequently under Tony Blair, the party has continued its modernisation policy.

Solipsism. The theory that nothing really exists but oneself and one's mental states. No philosopher has deliberately held this view, but it is often seen to follow from certain views, for example, the belief that all one can know is oneself and one's immediate knowledge. It is philosophically interesting in that though the theory is intrinsically absurd, it is difficult to refute. Ludwig Wittgenstein (1889–1951) argued that the fact that we have a language (in which to express this solipsism) depends on the existence of a mind-independent external world.

Spiritualism is a religion which requires to be distinguished from psychical research (*q.v.*) which is a scientific attempt carried on by both believers and non-believers to investigate psychic phenomena including those not necessarily connected with "spirits"—*e.g.*, telepathy or clairvoyance and precognition. As a religion (although for that matter the whole of history is filled with attempts to get in touch with the "spirit world") Spiritualism begins with the American Andrew Jackson Davis who in 1847 published *Nature's Divine Revelations*, a book which is still widely read. In this Davis states that on the death of the physical body, the human spirit remains alive and moves on to one or another of a considerable range of worlds or "spheres" where it commences yet another stage of existence. Since the spirit has not died, but exists with full (and possibly even expanded) consciousness, there should be no reason, Davis argues, why it should not make its presence known to the beings it has temporarily left behind on earth. In 1847, the year of the publication of Davis's book, two young girls, Margaret and Kate Fox, living in a farmhouse at Hydesville, New York, began apparently to act as unwitting mediums for attempts at such between-worlds communication. The girls were the focus for strange rappings and bangs which it was alleged defied normal explanation and which spelt out, in the form of a simple alphabetical code, messages from the spirits of "the dead." The Fox sisters were later to confess that they had produced the raps by trickery, but by that time the fashion had spread across the world and before long "mediums" in all lands were issuing spirit communications (often in much more spectacular form). In the late 19th cent. Spiritualism went into a phase of great expansion and for various reasons attracted the attention of many scientists. Among these were Sir William Crookes, Sir Oliver Lodge, Professor Charles Richet, Alfred Russell Wallace, to say nothing of the brilliant and shrewd creator of Sherlock Holmes, Sir Arthur Conan Doyle. Today many people find it astonishing that people of such brilliance should find the phenomena of the seance room of more than passing interest, but the commitment of the Victorian scientists is understandable if we realise that Spiritualists, after all, claim to do no more than demonstrate as fact what all Christians are called on to believe—that the human personality survives bodily death. Furthermore, at the time of the late 19th cent. peak of Spiritualism, much less was known about human psychology and about the great limitations of sensory perception in typical seance conditions, when lights are dimmed or extinguished and an emotionally charged atmosphere generated. Today the most striking phenomena of the seance room—the alleged materialisation of spirit people and the production of such half-spiritual, halfphysical substances as ectoplasm—are rarely if ever produced at Spiritualist meetings. Some say that the most probable explanation for this is that too many fraudulent mediums have been caught out and publicly exposed for the profes-sion to be worth the risks. The movement today, which still has a large and often articulate following, now concentrates on the less controversial areas of "mental mediumship," clairvoyance and the like, or on the very widespread practice of "spirit healing." Where people are not deliberately deluded by bogus mediums acting for monetary reward (a practice which largely died out with the "death" of ectoplasm) Spiritualism probably has an important role to play in the life of many people whose happiness has been removed by the death of a much loved relative or spouse. It does not deserve the violent attacks that are often made on it by orthodox clergy who allege that Spiritualists are communicating not with the souls of the departed but with the devil or his emissaries. *See also* **Greater World Spiritualists.**

Stalinism. The methods and policies associated with Joseph Stalin (1879–1953), leader of the USSR from 1929 until his death. This form of despotism consisted of the concentration of power in his own hands, and the ruthless suppression of dissent in any form, plus a "cult of personality", which used every means of propaganda to present Stalin as a wise and benevolent ruler fighting off "capitalist encirclement".

State and Man. Most of the early civilisations such as those of Egypt and Babylonia were theocratic, that is to say, they were arranged in a hierarchy with, at the peak, a king who was also an incarnation of the god. Needless to say, in such circumstances there was no room for philosophising about the nature of the state and the relationship which ought to exist between state and citizens. As usual, we have to turn to ancient Greece for the beginnings of thought about this problem. We do so as briefly as possible since in general it is only the later philosophers whose work has much contemporary interest and, in any case, most people today realise that the political philosophy of a particular time is bound to reflect the actual conditions prevailing then and as such is of mainly theoretical interest today.

The Greek Approach. The early pre-Socratic philosophers Democritus and the Pythagorean school for example, held that the individual should subordinate himself to the whole; they had no doubt that the citizen's first duty was to the state. The Greeks until the time of Plato were not really thinking in terms of individual rights, nor had they given much thought to what form the state should take—they simply accepted it. The first great attempt to describe the ideal state is to be found in Plato's *The Republic* which is referred to elsewhere (*see* **Education**). His pupil Aristotle did not try to form a utopia but made many comments on the nature of government. Thus, while agreeing that the state was more important than any individual person, he distinguished between good and bad states, and pointed out that to the extent that the state does not enable its citizens to lead virtuous and useful lives it is evil. A good constitution must recognise the inequalities between human beings and confer on them rights according to their abilities: among these inequalities are those of personal ability, property, birth, and status, as freeman or slave. The best forms of rule were monarchy, aristocracy, and democracy; the worst forms—tyranny, oligarchy (or rule of a powerful few), and ochlocracy (or mob-rule). The later Greek thinkers of Hellenistic times held two opposed points of view. The Epicureans (*q.v.*) taught that all social life is based upon self-interest and we become members of a group for our own convenience; therefore there are no absolute rights and laws—what is good is what members decide at that time to be good, and when they change their minds the law must change too. Injustice is not an evil in any god-given sense; we behave justly simply because if injustice became the general rule, we ourselves should suffer. The Stoics (*q.v.*), on the other hand, held that the state must dominate the individual completely and everyone must carry out, first and foremost, his social duties and be willing to sacrifice everything for it; but the state of the Stoics was no narrowly national one, but one that strove to become a universal brotherhood.

The Christian Approach. The orthodox Christian view is expressed in St. Augustine's book *The City of God.* Here it is held that the church, as the worldly incarnation of the City of God, is to be supreme over the state, and the head of the church is to be supreme over secular rulers. In addition it must be recognised that, whilst the secular ruler can make mistakes, the church does not, since it is the representative of God's kingdom on earth.

The Secular State. During the Renaissance (*q.v.*) people began to think for themselves and the results of their cogitations were not always pleasant; for it was during this time that many rulers, petty and otherwise, were seeking absolute authority. Two notable thinkers at this stage were Niccolo Machiavelli (1469–1527) in Italy and Thomas Hobbes (1588–1679) in England, where, of course, the Renaissance arrived later in history. Both supported absolute monarchy against the former domination of the church. The name of Machiavelli has become a by-word for any behaviour that is cunning and unscrupulous, but he was not really as bad as he is usually painted. It is, indeed, true that in his book *The Prince* he showed in the greatest detail the methods by which a ruler could gain absolute control and destroy civic freedom, but this despotism was intended as merely a necessary intermediate stage towards his real idea which was a free, united Italian nation wholly independent of the church. Hobbes was a materialist whose thesis was that man is naturally a ferocious animal whose basic impulse is war and pillage and the destruction of whatever stands in his way to gain his desires. But if he allowed himself to behave in this way his life would be "nasty, brutish, and short" so he creates a society in which he voluntarily gives up many of his rights and hands them over to a powerful ruler in his own interest. But having done this he must obey; even when the ruler is unjust, as he has no right to complain because anything is better than a return to his natural state. The religion of the king must be the religion of the people and the only things no ruler has the right to do is to cause a man to commit suicide or murder or to make him confess to a crime.

Views of Locke: Live and Let Live. John Locke (1632–1704) disagreed with these views. Man is naturally peaceful and co-operative and therefore social life comes readily to him. He sets up an authority in order to preserve the group and that is why laws are made; but the function of the state is strictly limited to maintaining the public good and beyond this men are to be left free. Therefore absolute power and the doctrine of the Divine Right of Kings were wrong because power ultimately rests with the people who have the right to make and break governments. It is also wrong that those who make the laws should be able to execute them. This is the important British doctrine of the separation of powers between the legislature and the executive which, in Britain and America, is regarded as one of the bases of democracy.

Rousseau's Social Doctrine. The only other views we need consider here are those of Jean-Jacques Rousseau (1712–78) and Herbert Spencer (1820–1903), since the views of the two important intervening figures, Hegel and Karl Marx, are dealt with elsewhere (*see* **Dialectical Materialism**) and after Spencer we come to a stage where political philosophy begins to merge with sociology and the social sciences. Rousseau is a puzzling figure. On the one hand he has been hailed as the prophet of freedom and on the other as the father of modern totalitarianism. His book *Social Contract* (1762) begins with the words: "Man is born free, and everywhere he is in chains." He says that he is in favour, not merely of democracy, but of direct democracy in which everyone has to give his assent to all measures as in the Greek city-states and in Geneva, of which city he was a citizen. (This method is still in force in respect of some measures in the Swiss cantons.) Natural society is based on a "social contract" or mutual agreement and Rousseau speaks of a "return to nature" which would ensure the sovereignty of the people at all times. Thus far, he seems to agree with Locke but soon we find that he is more akin to Hobbes, since (as we are learning in our own day) nothing is more tyrannical than the absolute rule of all the people. (Public opinion is more Hitlerian than Hitler.) As it turns out, then, the "social contract" consists in "the total alienation of each associate, together with all his rights, to the whole community" and "each of us puts his person and all his power in common under the supreme direction of the general will." Rousseau admired direct democracy in the small city-state, but if his doctrine is applied to large states, then the "general will" becomes absolute. It is in this sense that he is regarded as the forerunner of totalitarianism. Herbert Spencer is quoted only as an example of the inappropriate application of a biological theory to social issues. Influenced by Darwin's thesis

of natural selection, he saw in society a struggle in which the fittest survived and the less fit perished. Each individual had the right to preserve himself, but in the case of human beings this depended upon group life in which, to some extent, each individual is limited by the rights of others. But this should not go too far, and he condemned the socialism of J. S. Mill which (*a*) would give over-much protection to the unfit, and (*b*) would give the state powers which it has no right to since the best government is the least government. In accordance with Darwinism free competition was essential.

Stoics, the followers of Zeno, a Greek philosopher in the 4th cent. B.C., who received their name from the fact that they were taught in the Stoa Poikile or Painted Porch of Athens. They believed that since the world is the creation of divine wisdom and is governed by divine law, it is man's duty to accept his fate. Zeno conceived virtue to be the highest good and condemned the passions. (*See* **God and Man, State and Man, Determinism and Free-will** for a more detailed account of their beliefs.)

Structuralism. 1. *Psychology.* The name of a school of thought whose influence has not lasted. It sought to investigate the structure of consciousness through the analysis, by introspection, of simple forms of sensation, thought, images, *etc.* and then find out how these components fitted together in complex forms. The school, which is mainly identified with Edward Titchener (1867–1927), discounted the value of analysing the significance of mental experience, and of examining the functions of the mind.

2. *Linguistics.* The theory that language is best described in terms of its irreducible structural units in morphology (the study of word structure) and phonology (the study of sound systems).

3. *Social sciences.* Theories or methods of analysis characterised by a preoccupation, not simply with structures, but with such structures as can be held to underlie and generate the phenomena under observation. To use a distinction of the linguist Noam Chomsky (b. 1928), the concern is with deep structures rather than surface structures. The main influences on the movement have been the theories of the French anthropologist Claude Levi-Strauss (b. 1908). According to him, universal patterns of cultural and social systems are products of the invariant "deep" structure of the human mind. He believed that structural similarities underlie all cultures and that an analysis of the relationships between cultures could provide insight into innate and universal principles of human thought.

Structural analysis has also been applied to literary theory, notably by the French critic Roland Barthes (1915–80).

Subjectivism. In moral philosophy, the belief that all moral attitudes are merely a matter of personal taste. According to this an assertion like "Abortion is wrong" does not express an objective truth but means that the speaker or, more broadly, his society, or people in general, disapprove of abortion.

Sufism. A mystical movement within Islam. It started as a reaction against the legalistic approach of early Islam, seeking to establish a more personal relationship with Allah, or God. The objective of Sufism is perfection of the individual and union with God. Sufi orders were first established in the 12th century and some are still thriving today. Sufism has been very important in the history of Islamic faith and had a great influence on Muslim literature, and created a genre of mystical love poetry.

Sunnites, the orthodox sect of Islam as contrasted with the Shiites or Shia (*q.v.*).

Surrealism. *See* **Section L.**

Swedenborgianism. The Church of the New Jerusalem, based on the writings of Emanuel Swedenborg (1688–1772), was founded by his followers eleven years after his death. The New Church is essentially a movement bearing the same relationship to Christianity as Christianity does to Judaism. Swedenborg's many works include the 12-volume *Arcana Caelestia* (*Heavenly Secrets*) (1749–56).

Symbolism. *See* **Section M.**

Synchronicity, an attempt by the psychologist, Carl Gustav Jung, to explain the apparently significant relationship between certain events in the physical universe which seem to have no obvious "causal" link. This rather involved concept is easily understood if one realises that almost all scientific and philosophical beliefs are based on the notion that the continuous process of change which is taking place in ourselves and in the universe around us is dependent upon a principle known as causality. We can express this another way by saying that an object moves because it has been pushed or pulled by another. We see because light strikes the retina and signals pass up the nervous system to the brain. A stone falls to the ground because the earth's gravity is pulling it towards its centre, etc., etc. For all practical purposes every event can be looked upon as being "caused" by some other prior event and this is obviously one of the most important principles of the operation of the universe. Jung, however, felt that there is a sufficiently large body of evidence to suggest that events may be linked in a significant (*i.e.*, non-chance) way without there being any true causal relationship between them. The classic example he held to be the supposed predictive power of astrology by which there appears to be a relationship between the stellar configurations and the personality and life-pattern of individuals on earth. Jung was scientist enough to realise that there could be no causal connection between the aspect of the stars and the lives of people billions of miles from them, yet felt the evidence for astrology was strong enough to demand an alternative non-causal explanation. The trouble with synchronicity, which has not made much impact on the world of physics or of psychology, is that it is not really an explanation at all but merely a convenient word to describe some puzzling correspondences. The real question, of course, is whether there really are events occurring which are significantly but not *causally* linked, and most scientists today would hold that there were probably not. Still it was typical of the bold and imaginative mind of Jung to tackle head-on one of the principal mysteries of existence and come up with a hypothesis to attempt to meet it.

Syndicalism, a form of socialist doctrine which aims at the ownership and control of all industries by the workers, contrasted with the more conventional type of socialism which advocates ownership and control by the state. Since syndicalists have preferred to improve the conditions of the workers by direct action, *e.g.*, strikes and working to rule, rather than through the usual parliamentary procedures, they have been closely related to anarchists (*q.v.*) and are sometimes described as anarcho-syndicalists. Under syndicalism there would be no state; for the state would be replaced by a federation of units based on functional economic organisation rather than on geographical representation. The movement had bodies in the United Kingdom, where guild socialism (*q.v.*) was strongly influenced by its doctrines, in France, Germany, Italy, Spain, Argentina, and Mexico, but these gradually declined after the first world war. Fascism (*q.v.*) was also strongly influenced by the revolutionary syndicalism of Georges Sorel.

T

Tantra. 1. *Tantric Buddhism.* Tantra refers to a series of ritual texts said to have been originally transmitted by the Buddha himself. The tantras speak of the evocation of various gods, the pursuit of magical powers, the use of chants, and the attainment of enlightenment through meditation and yoga. Tantric theory and practice is a development within the Mahayana Buddhist tradition. It died out in India but was taken to Tibet. The most famous tantra is the *Tibetan Book of the Dead.*
2. *Tantric Hinduism.* Within Hinduism tantra refers to a group of Sanskrit texts not part of the orthodox Veda (*see* **Hinduism**). These are concerned with acquiring spiritual power and liberation in life, through practices aiming at purifying the body and controlling one's mental processes. Tantric cults have fallen into disrepute, due to the use of erotic metaphors and, it is alleged, erotic practices.

Taoism, a religion which, although in a degenerate state, is still one of the great Eastern creeds. Its alleged founder, Lao-tze, is said to have been born in Honan about 604 B.C.; he is also said to be the author of the bible of Taoism, the *Tao-te-ching,* or in English *The Way of Life,* and to have disapproved of Confucius. This, if true, would hardly be surprising; for Taoism is eminently a mystical religion recommending doing nothing and resisting nothing, whereas **Confucianism** (*q.v.*) is eminently a practical code of living and its founder insisted on intervening in everything to do with social life. But the truth as revealed by modern scholarship is rather different. We are told that the poems of the *Tao-te-ching* are anonymous and probably originated among recluses in lonely valleys long before the time of Confucius; they were collected and given form at some time late in the 3rd cent. B.C. and their authorship attributed to Lao-tze. It is entirely possible that no such peson ever existed (unlike Confucius, who certainly did), but if there were such a man he appears to have used a pseudonym since "Lao" is not a surname but an adjective meaning "old" and it was customary to attribute important works to old men on account of their supposed wisdom. Lao-tze simply means "the old philosopher", and although the *Tao-te-ching* is one of the most remarkable and instructive books ever written it is as anonymous as the Border Ballads.

It is apparent that the religion learned both from the ancient Chinese mystics and from Brahmanism: *Tao*, the Way, is impalpable, invisible, and incapable of being expressed in words. But it can be attained by virtue, by compassion, humility, and non-violence. Out of weakness comes true strength whereas violence is not only wrong but defeats its own ends. There is no personal God and such gods as men imagine are mere emanations of *Tao* which gives life to all things. *Tao* is Being. Works are worthless and internal renunciation is far better than anything that follows from the use of force because passive resistance convinces the other from within that he is in error, whereas violence only compels the external appearance of conviction whilst inwardly the individual is as before. "It is wealth to be content; it is wilful to force one's way on others."

Later Lao-tze became a divinity and indeed one of a Trinity each worshipped in the form of idols (which the founder had hated). Soon there was worship of the forces of nature: the stars, the tides, the sun and moon, and a thousand other deities among whom Confucius was one. The purest mysticism and wisdom had been utterly corrupted by contact with the world.

Telepathy and Clairvoyance. Telepathy is the alleged communication between one mind and another other than through the ordinary sense channels. Clairvoyance is the supposed faculty of "seeing" objects or events which, by reason of space and time or other causes, are not discernible through the ordinary sense of vision. Such claims have been made from time immemorial but it was not until this century that the phenomena were investigated scientifically. The first studies were undertaken by the Society for Psychical Research, which was founded in 1882 with Professor Henry Sidgwick as its first president. Since then it has carried out a scholarly programme of research without —in accordance with its constitution—coming to any corporate conclusions. In America the centre of this research was the Parapsychology Laboratory at Duke University (*see* **Parapsychology**) where at one time it was claimed clear scientific evidence for extra-sensory perception (ESP) had been obtained. These claims have been treated with great reservation by the majority of scientists but despite the belief that the study of ESP was going into eclipse, there remains a small but measurable residue of interest in scientific research in this area. It would be odd if some scientists were not interested in ESP because of the enormous weight of anecdotal evidence which has built up over centuries to support it. The weakness of the scientific as opposed to the casual evidence is however exemplified by the failure of ESP researchers to produce a reliable "repeatable" experiment.

Terrorism. A form of political violence used against governments, groups or individuals with the purpose of creating a climate of fear in which the aims of the terrorists may be fulfilled. The term derives from the "Reign of Terror" in the French Revolution. In the 20th century it is most closely associated with the violence of small political movements of both the extreme left and right, attempting to overthrow existing political institutions. It has been used as part of nationalist movements seeking to remove colonial governments, as in the expulsion of Britain from Palestine and France from Algeria. There is also what is known as "state terrorism", as practised by totalitarian regimes such as Hitler's Germany and Stalin's Soviet Union.

Theism. *See* God and Man.

Theosophy (Sanskrit *Brahma Vidya* = divine wisdom), a system of thought that draws on the mystical teachings of those who assert the spiritual nature of the universe, and the divine nature of man. It insists that man is capable of intuitive insight into the nature of God. The way to wisdom, or self-knowledge, is through the practice of **Yoga** (*q.v.*). Theosophy has close connections with Indian thought through Vedic, Buddhist, and Brahmanist literature. The modern Theosophical Society was founded by Mme H. P. Blavatsky and others in 1875, and popularised by Mrs. Annie Besant.

Totalitarianism. Totalitarian government is one which tolerates only one political party, to which all other institutions are subordinated, and which usually demands the complete subservience of the individual to the government. The Italian dictator Mussolini coined the term in the 1920s to describe the new fascist state of Italy, and the word has become synonymous with absolute and oppressive single-party government, as in Nazi Germany or Soviet Russia. *See also* **Stalinism**.

Totemism. A totem is an animal, plant or object with which a social or religious group feels a special affinity and which is often considered to be the mythical ancestor of the group. The totem is worshipped or esteemed by members of the group or clan bearing its name. Totemism is the form of social organization consisting of such clans. Membership of the clan is inherited and lifelong; but marriage is usually with a partner outside the totemic clan. Totem poles (as erected by North American Indians) are a way of representing the clan's guardian spirit. Totemism has been important in the religion and society of many primitive peoples.

Tractarianism, a Catholic revival movement, also known as the **Oxford Movement** (not to be confused with the so-called Oxford Group), which had its beginnings at Oxford in 1833. The leaders included the Oxford high churchmen E. B. Pusey, J. Keble and J. H. Newman. Through the *Tracts for the Times* (1833–41), a series of pamphlets which were sent to every parsonage in England, they sought to expose the dangers which they considered to be threatening the church from secular authority. The immediate cause of the movement was the Reform Act (1832) which meant that the state was no longer in the safe keeping of Tories and Churchmen but that power was falling into the hands of Liberals and Dissenters. They advocated a higher degree of ceremonial in worship nearer the Roman communion. In *Tract 90* (the last) Newman showed how the Thirty-nine Articles themselves, which were regarded as the bulwark of Protestantism, could be made to square with Roman doctrine. It was obvious which direction the movement was taking and the romanizing tendency was widely resented. In 1845 Newman went over to Rome. Pusey and Keble persisted in their efforts to secure recognition of Catholic liturgy and doctrine in the Anglican Church. Catholicism of the Anglican type (*i.e.*, Catholic in ritual, ceremony, and everything save submission to the Pope) is termed Anglo-Catholicism (*q.v.*).

Transcendental Meditation, popularised in the West by the Maharishi Mahesh Yogi, who achieved sensational worldwide publicity by his "conversion" of the Beatles. This is a simple meditational system which it is claimed is an aid to relaxation and the reduction of psychological and physical stress. It is a technique which can be taught in a relatively short, concentrated period of time, provided that someone trained by the Maharishi is the teacher. The pupil or would-be meditator is given a *mantra*—letting his thoughts flow freely while sitting in a comfortable position. Very many claims are made on behalf of the system. As with most cults, religious and occult systems, there is an initial psychological benefit to anyone who becomes deeply involved. Nevertheless, apart from this simple "participation-effect", there is some evidence that the body's autonomic functions (heart rate, respiratory cycle, brain waves, *etc.*) can be modified by certain individuals including yogis. The TM movement in Britain is based at Mentmore Towers in Buckinghamshire. The 'Natural Law' party contested the 1992 election. The movement recruits heavily on campuses in America, but has been the subject of many complaints by parents. More than 4 million people all over the world have learned TM, including 160,000 in this country.

Transcendentalism. 1. A term used to refer to the transcendental idealism of Immanuel Kant (1724–1804). *See* **Mind and Matter**.
2. A movement established in the United States in the 1830s, much influenced by German idealism and Platonism, which included Ralph Waldo Emerson (1803–82) and Henry Thoreau (1817–62) among its members. Transcendentalism's characteristic belief was in the supremacy of insight over logic and experience for the revelation of the deepest truths. It tended towards mysticism, pantheism and optimism about the progress of the spirit. Although the movement's followers believed that true reform must come from within the individual, they took part in contemporary reform movements.

Transcendentalism itself faded with the coming of the American Civil War, but it had a strong influence on the writings of Whitman, Emily Dickinson and Hawthorne.

Transmigration of Souls. *See* **Immortality, Buddhism, Hinduism.**

Transubstantiation, the conversion in the Eucharist of the bread and wine into the body and blood of Christ—a doctrine of the Roman Catholic Church.

Trotskyism, a form of communism supporting the views of Leon Trotsky, the assumed name of Lev Bronstein (1879–1940) who, in 1924, was ousted from power by Stalin and later exiled and assassinated in Mexico. Trotsky held that excessive Russian nationalism was incompatible with genuine international communism and that Stalin was concentrating on the economic development of the Soviet Union to an extent which could only lead to a bureaucratic state with a purely nationalist outlook. After the Hungarian uprising in 1956, which was ruthlessly suppressed by the Soviet Armed Forces, a wave of resignations from Western Communist parties took place, many of the dissidents joining the Trotskyist movement.

U

Ufology, cultish interest in the study of strange and unexplained aerial phenomena (unidentified flying objects, hence UFOs). *See* **Flying Saucers**.

Uniates, the Eastern Orthodox Churches which are in full communion with the Roman Catholic Church, recognise the authority of the Pope and in faith and doctrine are totally Catholic. However, they retain their traditional liturgies and separate canon law and permit their priests to marry.

Unitarianism has no special doctrines, although clearly, as the name indicates, belief is in the single personality of God, *i.e.*, anti-trinitarian. This general statement, however, can be interpreted with varying degrees of subtlety. Thus unitarian belief may range from a sort of Arianism which accepts that, although Christ was not of divine nature, divine powers had been delegated to him by the Father, to the simple belief that Christ was a man like anyone else, and his goodness was of the same nature as that of many other great and good men. Indeed, today many Unitarians deny belief in a personal

God and interpret their religion in purely moral terms, putting their faith in the value of love and the brotherhood of man. The Toleration Act (1689) excluded Unitarians but from 1813 they were legally tolerated in England. Nevertheless attempts were made to turn them out of their chapels on the ground that the preachers did not hold the views of the original founders of the endowments. But this ended with the Dissenting Chapels Act of 1845. In America no such difficulties existed, and in the Boston of the 19th cent. many of the great literary figures were openly unitarian in both belief and name: *e.g.*, Emerson, Longfellow, Lowell, and Oliver Wendell Holmes.

Utilitarianism, a school of moral philosophy of which the main proponents were J. S. Mill (1806–73) and Jeremy Bentham (1748–1832). Bentham based his ethical theory upon the utilitarian principle that the greatest happiness of the greatest number is the criterion of morality. What is good is pleasure or happiness; what is bad is pain. If we act on this basis of self-interest (pursuing what we believe to be our own happiness), then what we do will automatically be for the general good. The serious failing of this thesis is (1) that it makes no distinction between the quality of one pleasure and another, and (2) that Bentham failed to see that the law might not be framed and administered by men as benevolent as himself. J. S. Mill accepted Bentham's position in general but seeing its failings emphasised (1) that self-interest was an inadequate basis for utilitarianism and suggested that we should take as the real criterion of good the social consequences of the act; (2) that some pleasures rank higher than others and held that those of the intellect are superior to those of the senses. Not only is the social factor emphasised, but emphasis is also placed on the nature of the act.

Utopias. The name "utopia" is taken from a Greek word meaning "nowhere" and was first used in 1516 by Sir Thomas More (1478–1535) as the title of his book referring to a mythical island in the south Pacific where he sited his ideal society. Since then it has been used of any ideal or fanciful society, and here a few will be mentioned. (The reader may recall that Samuel Butler's 19th cent. novel, describing an imaginary society in New Zealand where criminals were treated and the sick punished, was entitled *Erewhon* which is the word "nowhere" in reverse.) It should be noted that not all utopias were entirely fanciful—*e.g.*, Robert Owen's and François Fourier's beliefs, although found to be impractical, were, in fact, tried out.

Sir Thomas More. More wrote at a time when the rise of the wool-growing trade had resulted in farming land being turned over to pasture and there was a great wave of unemployment and a rise in crime among the dispossessed. More began to think in terms of the mediaeval ideal of small co-operative communities in which class interests and personal gain played a decreasing part, a society which would have the welfare of the people at heart both from the physical and intellectual points of view. His utopia was one in which there was no private property, because the desire for acquisition and private possessions lay at the root of human misery. There was, therefore, only common ownership of land and resources. Each class of worker was equipped to carry out its proper function in the economic scheme and each was fairly rewarded for its share in production so that there was neither wealth nor poverty to inspire conflict. Nobody was allowed to idle, until the time came for him to retire when he became free to enjoy whatever cultural pleasures he wished, but since the system was devoid of the waste associated with competition, the working day would be only six hours. There was to be compulsory schooling and free medical care for everybody, full religious toleration, complete equality of the sexes, and a modern system of dealing with crime which was free from vindictiveness and cruelty. Government was to be simple and direct by democratically-elected officials whose powers would be strictly limited and the public expenditure kept under close scrutiny. It will

be seen that More was far in advance of his age, and to most democratically-minded people in advance of an earlier utopia, Plato's *Republic*, which is described under the heading of Education.

James Harrington. James Harrington published his book *The Commonwealth of Oceana* in 1656 and offered it to Oliver Cromwell for his consideration but without tangible results. Better than any other man of his time Harrington understood the nature of the economic revolution which was then taking place, and, like More, saw the private ownership of land as the main cause of conflict. He put forward the theory that the control of property, particularly in the shape of land, determines the character of the political structure of the state; if property were universally distributed among the people the sentiment for its protection would naturally result in a republican form of government. The Commonwealth of Oceana was a society "of laws and not of men"—*i.e.*, it was to be legally based and structured so as to be independent of the good or ill-will of any individuals controlling it. Thus there must be a written constitution, a two-house legislature, frequent elections with a secret ballot, and separation of powers between legislature and executive—all today familiar features of parliamentary democracy, but unique in his time.

Saint-Simon. The utopias of the late 18th and 19th cent. come, of course, into the period of the industrial revolution and of laissez-faire capitalism. Individual enterprise and complete freedom of competition formed the outlook of the ruling class. Naturally the utopias of this period tended to have a strongly socialist tinge since such theories are obviously produced by those who are not satisfied with existing conditions. Saint-Simon's *New Christianity* (1825) is one such, and by many, Claude Henri, Comte de Saint-Simon (1760–1825) is regarded as the founder of French socialism. His book urged a dedication of society to the principle of human brotherhood and a community which would be led by men of science motivated by wholly spiritual aims. Production property was to be nationalised (or "socialised" as he describes the process) and employed to serve the public good rather than private gain; the worker was to produce according to his capacity and to be rewarded on the basis of individual merit; the principle of inheritance was to be abolished since it denied the principle of reward for accomplishment on which the society was to be founded. Saint-Simon's proposals were not directed towards the poorer classes alone, but to the conscience and intellect of all. He was deeply impressed with the productive power of the new machines and his scheme was, first and foremost, intended as a method of directing that power to the betterment of humanity as a whole.

Fourier. François Marie Charles Fourier (1772–1837), although by conviction a philosophical anarchist who held that human beings are naturally good if allowed to follow their natural desires, was the originator of what, on the face of it, one would suppose to be the most regimented of the utopias. It consisted of a system of "phalanxes" or co-operative communities each composed of a group of workers and technicians assured of a minimum income and sharing the surplus on an equitable basis. Agriculture was to be the chief occupation of each phalanx and industrial employment planned and so carefully assigned that work would become pleasant and creative rather than burdensome. One of his ideas was that necessary work should receive the highest pay, useful work the next, and pleasant work the least pay. The land was to be scientifically cultivated and natural resources carefully conserved. Most of the members' property was to be privately owned, but the ownership of each phalanx was to be widely diffused among members by the sale of shares. Such "parasitic and unproductive" occupations as stockbroker, soldier, economist, middle-man and philosopher would be eliminated and the education of children carried out along vocational lines to train them for their future employment.

The strange thing was that Fourier's suggestions appealed to many in both Europe and the

U.S.A. and such men (admittedly no economic or technical experts) as Emerson, Thoreau, James Russell Lowell, and Nathaniel Hawthorne strongly supported them. An American Fourier colony known as Brook Farm was established and carried on for eight years when it was dissolved after a serious fire had destroyed most of its property.

Robert Owen. Robert Owen (1771–1858), a wealthy textile manufacturer and philanthropist, established communities founded on a kind of utopian socialism in Lanarkshire, Hampshire, and in America. Of his New Lanark community an American observer wrote: "There is not, I apprehend, to be found in any part of the world, a manufacturing community in which so much order, good government, tranquillity, and rational happiness prevail." The workers in Lanark were given better housing and education for their children, and it was administered as a co-operative self-supporting community in Scotland. Later in life Owen returned to sponsoring legislation that would remove some of the worst evils of industrial life in those days: reduction of the working day to twelve hours, prohibition of labour for children under the age of ten, public schools for elementary education, and so on. But he lived to see few of his reforms adopted.

V

Vedanta. An old-established system of Indian thought. It is expressed in commentaries on the *Brahma Sutras.* A key figure is Shankara (788–820 A.D.) who founded what is known as Advaita Vedanta.

Vegans, *see under* **Vegetarianism.**

Vegetarianism, a way of life practised by those who abstain from meat. Strict vegetarians (Vegans) also exclude all animal products (*e.g.* butter, eggs milk) from their diet.

Vitalism, the philosophical doctrine that the behaviour of the living organism is, at least in part, due to a vital principle which cannot possibly be explained wholly in terms of physics and chemistry. This belief was held by the rationalist thinker C. E. M. Joad (1891–1953) and is implicit in Henri Bergson's (1859–1941) theory of creative evolution. It was maintained by Bergson that evolution, like the work of an artist, is creative and therefore unpredictable; that a vague need exists beforehand within the animal or plant before the means of satisfying the need develops. Thus we might assume that sightless animals developed the need to become aware of objects before they were in physical contact with them and that this ultimately led to the origins of organs of sight. Earlier this century a form of vitalism described as "emergent evolution" was put forward. This theory maintains that when two or more simple entities come together there may arise a new property which none of them previously possessed. Today biologists would say that it is the *arrangement* of atoms that counts, different arrangements exhibiting different properties, and that biological organisation is an essentially dynamic affair.

W

Wahabis, members of an Arabian sect of Islam which originated in the teaching of Muhammad Ibn 'Abd-al-Wahab, born at the end of the 17th cent. He was deeply resentful of the Turkish rule which, in addition to its tyranny, had brought about innovations in the religion which Muhammad regarded as a perversion of its original form. He proceeded to reform Islam to its primitive conditions and impressed his beliefs on Mohammed Ibn Saud, a sheikh who spread them with the aid of his sword. Under the successors of Ibn Saud the power of the Wahabis spread over much of Arabia where it is dominant today in Saudi Arabia. Its particular characteristic is that it refuses to accept symbolic or mystical interpretations of the words of the Prophet and accepts quite literally the teaching of Islam. It is, in fact, a sort of Moslem fundamentalism. Although crushed by the Turks in 1811–15, the movement remains an important element in Mohammedanism.

Waldenses, a movement also known as "The Poor Men of Lyons," founded by Peter Waldo of that city about the same time, and in the same part of southern France, as the Albigenses (*q.v.*) with whom, however, they had nothing in common. Their main belief was a return to Apostolic simplicity, based on reading the Bible in their own language; their doctrines were somewhat similar to those of the Mennonites and the Quakers. However, they did not wish to separate themselves from the Church and were originally protected by several Popes until the Lateran Council of 1215 excluded them mainly for the crime of preaching without ecclesiastical permission. From this time they were subjected to persecution, yet maintained some contact with the Church until the Reformation when they chose to take the side of the Protestants. Situated mainly on the sides of the Alps, half in Piedmont and half in France, they were persecuted or not according to the contemporary political convenience of the Dukes of Savoy, and the major attempt to destroy them called forth Oliver Cromwell's intervention and the famous sonnet of Milton. In spite of torture, murder, deportation, and even the kidnapping of their children, to have them brought up in the Roman Catholic faith, the sect survived, and still exists, having been granted full equality of rights with his Catholic subjects by Charles Edward of Piedmont in 1848.

Weathermen. Far left group whose aim was to overthrow the American political system. The group's name was borrowed from the lyrics of songwriter Bob Dylan. Its membership was drawn from a well-educated social strata, and it has committed specific and well-planned acts of violence.

Witchcraft. There are various interpretations and definitions of witchcraft from that of Pennethorne Hughes who states that "witchcraft, as it emerges into European history and literature, represents the old paleolithic fertility cult, plus the magical idea, plus various parodies of contemporary religions" to that of the fanatical Father Montague Summers who says that Spiritualism and witchcraft are the same thing. A leading authority on witchcraft, however, the late Dr. Margaret Murray, distinguishes between Operative Witchcraft (which is really Magic (*q.v.*)) and Ritual Witchcraft which, she says, "embraces the religious beliefs and ritual of the people known in late mediaeval times as 'witches.'" That there were such people we know from history and we know, too, that many of them—the great majority of them women—were tortured or executed or both. Many innocent people perished, especially after the promulgation of the bull *Summis desiderantes* by Pope Innocent VIII in 1484. Himself "a man of scandalous life," according to a Catholic historian, he wrote to "his dear sons," the German professors of theology, Johann Sprenger and Heinrich Kraemer, "witches are hindering men from performing the sexual act and women from conceiving . . ." and delegated them as Inquisitors "of these heretical pravities." In 1494 they codified in the *Malleus Maleficarum* (Hammer of Witches) the ecclesiastical rules for detecting acts of witchcraft. Dr. Murray points out that there have ordinarily been two theories about witchcraft: (1) that there were such things as witches, that they possessed supernatural powers and that the evidence given at their trials was substantially correct; (2) that the witches were simply poor silly creatures who either deluded themselves into believing that they had certain powers or, more frequently, were tortured into admitting things that they did not do. She herself accepts a third theory: that there were such beings as witches, that they really did what they admitted to doing, but that they did not possess supernatural powers. They were in fact believers in the old religion of pre-Christian times and the Church took centuries to root them out. That there existed "covens" of witches who carried out peculiar rites Dr. Murray has no doubt whatever. The first to show that witch-craft was a superstition and that the majority of so-called witches were people suffering from mental illness was the physician Johann Weyer of Cleves (1515–88). His views were denounced by the Catholic Church. Few people realise how deeply the notion of witchcraft is implanted in our minds and how seriously its power is still taken. For example, the Witchcraft Act was not repealed in this country until the 1950s. *See also* Demonism.

Women's Liberation Movement. *See* Feminism (J20).

World Congress of Faiths, an inter-religious movement which aims to break down barriers between faiths. The first step was taken by the world's parliament of religions held in Chicago in 1893; similar gatherings were held subsequently at intervals in Europe; but the actual organisation was formed in 1936 by Sir Francis Young-husband; and now an annual conference is held and educational activity carried on.

World Council of Churches, a union of Christian Churches from all over the world (including the Churches of the Protestant, Anglican, and Orthodox traditions, but excluding the Roman Catholic Church), engaged in extending Christ-ian mission and unity throughout the world. This modern ecumenical movement stems from the great World Missionary Conference held at Edin-burgh in 1910. The World Council was founded in 1948 and meets for consultation from time to time. In the light of the 1975 assembly in Nairobi, the Churches have monitored the suppression of human rights throughout the world. The Salvation Army resigned in 1981 in protest at the movement's in-volvement in African liberation. The last assembly (1991) was held in Canberra.

Y

Yin and **Yang,** the two basic forces in ancient Chinese thought. Yang is associated with masculinity, heat, light, creation *etc.*, yin with femininity, coldness, dark, passivity *etc*. *See also* Confucianism, Taoism.

Yoga, a Hindu discipline which teaches a techni-que for freeing the mind from attachment to the senses, so that once freed the soul may become fused with the universal spirit (*atman* or Brah-man), which is its natural goal. This is the sole function of the psychological and physical exercises which the Yogi undertakes, although few ever reach the final stage of *Samadhi* or union with Brahman which is said to take place in eight levels of attainment. These are: (1) *Yama,* which involves the extinction of desire and egotism and their replacement by charity and unselfishness; (2) *Niyama,* during which certain rules of conduct must be adopted, such as cleanliness, the pursuit of devotional studies, and the carrying out of rituals of purification; (3) *Asana,* or the attainment of correct posture and the reduction to a minimum of all bodily movement (the usual posture of the concentrat-ing Yogi is the "lotus position" familiar from pictures); (4) *Pranayama,* the right control of the life-force or breath in which there are two stages at which the practitioner hopes to arrive, the first being complete absorption in the act of breathing which empties the mind of any other thought, the second being the ability almost to cease to breathe which allegedly enables him to achieve marvellous feats of endurance; (5) *Pratyahara* or abstraction which means the mind's complete withdrawal from the world of sense; (6) *Dharana* in which an attempt is made to think of one thing only which finally becomes a repetition of the sacred syllable OM; (7) *dhyana,* meditation, which finally leads to (8) *Samadhi* the trance state which is a sign of the complete unity of soul with reality.

Yoga is very old, and when the sage Patanjali (*c*. 300 B.C.) composed the book containing these instructions, the *Yoga Sutras,* he was probably collecting from many ancient traditions. Some of the claims made by Yogis seem, to the Western mind, frankly incredible; but in the West Yoga methods have been used at the lower levels in

order to gain improved self-control, better pos-ture, and improved health.

Z

Zen Buddhism, a Buddhist sect which is believed to have arisen in 6th cent. China but has flourished chiefly in Japan; for some reason it has of recent years begun to attract attention in the West thanks to the voluminous writings of Dr. D. T. Suzuki and the less numerous but doubtless much-read books of Mr. Christmas Humphreys. But the fact that these writings exist does not explain their being read, nor why of all possible Eastern sects this particular one should be chosen in our times. What is Zen's attraction and why should anyone take the trouble to read about something (the word "something" is used for reasons that will become evident) that is not a religion, has no doctrine, knows no God and no after-life, no good and no evil, and possesses no scriptures but has to be taught by parables which seem to be purposely meaningless? One of the heroes of Zen is the fierce-looking Indian monk Boddhidharma (fl. *c*. 516–34) who brought Buddhism to China, of whom it is recounted that when the Emperor asked him how much merit he had acquired by supporting the new creed, the monk shouted at him: "None what-ever!" The emperor then wished to know what was the sacred doctrine of the creed and again the monk shouted: "It is empty—there is nothing sacred!" Dr. Suzuki, having affirmed that there is no God in Zen, goes on to state that this does not mean that Zen denies the existence of God because "neither denial nor affirmation concerns Zen." The most concrete statement he is prepared to make is that the basic idea of Zen is to come in touch with the inner workings of our being, and to do this in the most direct way possible without resorting to anything external or superadded. Therefore anything that has the semblance of an external authority is rejected by Zen. Absolute faith is placed in a man's own inner being. Apparently the intention is that, so far from indulging in inward meditations or such practices as the Yogi uses, the student must learn to act spontaneously, without thinking, and without self-consciousness or hesitation. This is the main purpose of the *koan,* the logically insoluble riddle which the pupil must try to solve. One such is the question put by master to pupil: "A girl is walking down the street, is she the younger or the older sister?" The correct answer, it seems, is to say nothing but put on a mincing gait, to *become* the girl, thus showing that what matters is the experience of being and not its verbal description. Another *koan:* "What is the Buddha?" "Three pounds of flax" is attributed to T'ungshan in the 9th cent. and a later authority's comment is that "none can excel it as regards its irrationality which cuts off all passages to speculation." Zen, in effect, teaches the uselessness of trying to use words to discuss the Absolute.

Zen came to Japan in the 13th cent., more than five centuries after Confucianism or the orthodox forms of Buddhism, and immediately gained acceptance whilst becoming typically Japanese in the process. One of the reasons why it appealed must have been that its spontaneity and insistence on action without thought, its emphasis on the uselessness of mere words, and such categories as logical opposites, had an inevitable attraction for a people given to seri-ousness, formality, and logic to a degree which was almost stifling. Zen must have been to the Japanese what nonsense rhymes and nonsense books, like those of Edward Lear and Lewis Carroll, were to the English intellectuals. Lear's limericks, like some of the *koans,* end up with a line which, just at the time when one expects a point to be made, has no particular point at all, and *Alice in Wonderland* is the perfect example of a world, not without logic, but with a crazy logic of its own which has no relationship with that of everyday life. Therefore Zen began to impregnate every aspect of life in Japan, and one of the results of its emphasis on spontaneous action rather than reason was its acceptance by the Samurai, the ferocious warrior class, in such activities as swordsmanship, archery. Japanese wrestling, and later Judo and the Kamikaze dive-bombers. But much of Japanese art, especially landscape gardening and flower-arrangement, was influenced similarly, and Zen is even used in Japanese psychiatry. The very strict life of the Zen monks is based largely on doing things, learning through experience; the periods of meditation in the Zendo hall are punctuated by sharp slaps on the face administered by the abbot to those who are unsatisfactory pupils. Dr. Suzuki denies that Zen is nihilistic, but it is probably its appearance of nihilism and its appeal to the irrational and spontaneous which attracts the Western world at a time when to many the world seems without meaning and life over-regimented. However, it has influenced such various aspects of Western life as philosophy (Heidegger), psychiatry (Erich Fromm and Hubert Benoit), writing (Aldous Huxley), and painting (Die Zen Gruppe in Germany).

Zionism, a belief in the need to establish an autonomous Jewish home in Palestine which, in its modern form, began with Theodor Herzl (1860–1904), a Hungarian journalist working in Vienna. Although Herzl was a more or less assimilated Jew, he was forced by the Dreyfus case and the pogroms in Eastern Europe to conclude that there was no real safety for the Jewish people until they had a state of their own. The Jews, of course, had always in a religious sense thought of Palestine as a spiritual homeland and prayed "next year in Jerusalem," but the religious had thought of this in a philosophical way as affirming old loyalties, not as recommending the formation of an actual state. Therefore Herzl was opposed both by many of the religious Jews and, at the other extreme, by those who felt themselves to be assimilated and in many cases without religious faith. Even after the Balfour Declaration of 1917, there was not a considerable flow of Jews to Palestine, which at that time was populated mainly by Arabs. But the persecutions of Hitler changed all this and, after bitter struggles, the Jewish state was proclaimed in 1948. Today Zionism is supported by the vast majority of the Jewish communities everywhere. After 1990, a major exodus of Jews from Russia to Israel (made possible by the new climate of *glasnost*) introduced a new phase in the history of Zionism.

Zoroastrianism, at one time one of the great world religions, competing in the 2nd cent. A.D. on almost equal terms from its Persian home with Hellenism and the Roman Imperial Government. Under the Achaemenidae (*c.* 550–330 B.C.) Zoroastrianism was the state religion of Persia. Alexander's conquest in 331 B.C. brought disruption but the religion flourished again under the Sassanian dynasty (A.D. *c.* 226–640). With the advance of the Mohammedan Arabs in the 7th cent. Zoroastrianism finally gave way to Islam. A number of devotees fled to India there to become the Parsees. In Iran itself a few scattered societies remain.

The name Zoroaster is the Greek rendering of Zarathustra, the prophet who came to purify the ancient religion of Persia. It is thought that he lived at the beginning of the 6th cent. B.C. He never claimed for himself divine powers but was given them by his followers. The basis of Zoroastrianism is the age-long war between good and evil, Ahura Mazda heading the good spirits and Ahriman the evil ones. Morality is very important since by doing right the worshipper is supporting Ahura Mazda against Ahriman, and the evil-doers will be punished in the last days when Ahura Mazda wins his inevitable victory.

The sacred book of this religion is the *Avesta*. If Zoroastrianism has little authority today, it had a very considerable influence in the past. Its doctrines penetrated into Judaism (*q.v.*) and, through Gnosticism, Christianity. The worship of Mithra by the Romans was an impure version of Zoroastrianism. Manichaeism (*q.v.*) was a Zoroastrian heresy and the Albigensianism of mediaeval times was the last relic of a belief which had impressed itself deeply in the minds of men.

GAZETTEER OF THE WORLD

An index and guide to the maps
with up-to-date descriptive
matter. Each year the Gazetteer is
amended to include the latest
available population figures. This
current edition of *Pears* reflects
the changes created by the emergence of the newly independent
nations of Eastern Europe, the
Balkans and Central Asia.

GAZETTEER OF THE WORLD

Measurement of Geographical Phenomena.

(1) Physical Features.

In using the gazetteer the reader should note that it is impossible to make absolutely correct measurements of geographical phenomena. For example, measurement of height of land above sea-level depends, in the first instance, upon the definition of the elusive concept of sea-level itself. This is constantly changing and so an arbitrary value of *mean sea-level* is normally used, but the value adopted varies from country to country. As a result, height above sea-level has inbuilt inconsistencies and inaccuracies. Similarly, the length of a river will depend upon the scale of the survey from which measurements are made. Large-scale maps and aerial photographs can show in great detail the sinuous course of rivers, whereas a map on a smaller scale must reduce the amount of information shown and thereby the apparent length.

The gazetteer now records the heights of mountains, lengths of rivers, and land and sea areas in metric units. English equivalents will be found on p. 1 of the **Atlas**.

(2) Definition of Urban Area.

An even more difficult problem of measurement relates to the definition of the urban area of a town or city. It is possible to define the extent of urban areas in three major ways, by using (1) the administrative area, (2) the physically built-up area, and (3) the socio-geographic, metropolitan area. This latter concept is in many ways the most meaningful for it relates to the notion that a city exerts a strong influence over the population resident beyond its administrative or built-up boundary. For example, the city may provide employment opportunities or shopping and entertainment facilities for a population resident some distance away from it. In order to define "city" in these terms some means of measuring the degree of connection between it and its surrounding hinterland (the city-region) must be found and, needless to say, there is considerable disagreement among workers in this field as to what are the most suitable criteria to use. Different criteria produce different definitions and even the most recent measurements are obsolete within a short space of time. However, the real significance of this less tangible concept of "city"

may be illustrated by the fact that the reform of local government in England rests in part upon the concept of the city-region.

The population figures given in the gazetteer normally relate to the city's administrative area. In the case of some large cities two figures are given—(1) for the administrative city, and (2) for the more extensive metropolitan area which surrounds and includes the administrative city.

Place Names.

Where there have been recent changes in place names, the new name is used with the old name in brackets and a cross reference from old to new.

Chinese place names.

The romanisation of Chinese characters has long posed problems. The characters which represent sounds cannot easily be "translated" into letters. The first system adopted in Western countries was **Wade-Giles** but this is very European in its approach. In 1975 the Chinese government issued a directive to adopt an alternative system called **Pinyin** which is more Chinese in its approach. This system, which since 1977 has been more widely accepted, is the script used within the gazetteer and its maps. Cross-references are made from the Wade-Giles to the now official Pinyin version of each place name.

Population Figures.

Total population figures from a census count are no longer regarded as necessarily more accurate than estimates arrived at by other methods. The usefulness of censuses lies rather in the additional information which they provide. Even so, some countries like the Netherlands have given up censuses altogether. The gazetteer therefore no longer distinguishes between census figures and estimates but aims to include the latest reliable figures from whatever source.

This edition includes 1991 census figures for Scotland and Northern Ireland and substantial updating of figures for countries such as Argentina, Belgium, Bangladesh, Brazil, Netherlands, Egypt, India, Italy, Sweden and Germany.

ABBREVIATIONS USED IN THE GAZETTEER

GEOGRAPHICAL NAMES

Ala. = Alabama
Ark. = Arkansas
Atl. Oc. = Atlantic Ocean
B.C. = British Columbia
Brit. = British
BEF = British Expeditionary Forces
Cal. = California
CERN = European Centre for Nuclear Research
Col. = Colorado
Conn. = Connecticut
Del. = Delaware
Eng. = England
E.U. = European Union
Fla. = Florida
Fr. = French
Ga. = Georgia
ICI = Imperial Chemical Industries
Ill. = Illinois
Ind. = Indiana
Kan. = Kansas
Ky. = Kentucky

La. = Louisiana
Land = prov. (Germany)
Mass. = Massachusetts
Md. = Maryland
Me. = Maine
Mich. = Michigan
Minn. = Minnesota
Miss. = Mississippi
Mo. = Missouri
Mont. = Montana
NATO = North Atlantic Treaty Organisation
N.C. = North Carolina
N.D. = North Dakota
Neth. = Netherlands
N.H. = New Hampshire
N.J. = New Jersey
N.M. = New Mexico
N.S.W. = New South Wales
N.T. = Northern Territory (Australia)
N.Y. = New York
N.Z. = New Zealand
O.F.S. = Orange Free State
Okla. = Oklahoma

OPEC = Organization of Petroleum Exporting Countries
Ore. = Oregon
Pac. Oc. = Pacific Ocean
Penns. = Pennsylvania
R.I. = Rhode Island
R.o.I. = Republic of Ireland
S.C. = South Carolina
Scot. = Scotland
SHAPE = Supreme Headquarters, Allied Powers, Europe
S.D. = South Dakota
Tenn. = Tennessee
U.K. = United Kingdom
U.N. = United Nations
USA = United States of America
Va. = Virginia
Vt. = Vermont
Wash. = Washington
W.I. = West Indies
Wis. = Wisconsin
Wyo. = Wyoming

OTHER ABBREVIATIONS

a. = area
admin. = administrative
agr. = agriculture
alt. = altitude
anc. = ancient
arch. = archaeological
a.s.l. = above sea-level
ass. = associated
aut. rep. = autonomous republic
bdy. = boundary
bldg. = building
bor. = borough
bdr. = border
C. = cape
c. = city; circa, c. = about
can. = canton
cap. = capital
cas. = castle
cath. = cathedral
ch. = chief
cm = centimetres
co. = county
C.B. = county borough
col. = colony
colly. = colliery
comm. = commercial
conurb. = conurbation
cst. = coast
ctr. = centre
cty. = country
dep. = department
dist. = district
div. = division
E. = east or easterly
elec. = electrical
engin. = engineering
esp. = especially
exp. = exports
F. = firth

Fed. Federation
fed. = federal
fish. pt. = fishing port
fortfd. = fortified
G. = Gulf
gen. = general
G.N.P. = gross national product
gr. = great, group
ha = hectares
gtr. = greater
hgst. = highest
I. = island
impt. = important
inc. = including
indep. = independent
inds. = industries
industl. = industrial
Is. = Islands
km = kilometres
km² = square kilometres
L. = lake
l. = length
lge. = large
l. gov. dist. = local government district
lgst. = largest
lt. = light
m = metres
machin. = machinery
met. a. = metropolitan area
met. co. = metropolitan county
mftg. = manufacturing
mkg. = making
mkt. = market
mm = millimetres
mnfs. = manufactures
mng. = mining
mtn. = mountain

mun. = municipality
N. = north or northerly
nat. = national
non-met. co = non-metropolitan county
nr. = near
p. = population
par. = parish
penin. = peninsula
pref. = prefecture
prin. = principal
prod. = products
prot. = protectorate
prov. = province
pt. = port
R. = river
rep. = republic
residtl. = residential
rly. = railway
S. = south or southerly
shipbldg. = shipbuilding
sm. = small
spt. = seaport
st. = state
sta. = station
sub. = suburb
t. = town
terr. = territory
tr. = trade
trib. = tributary
univ. = university
U.D. = urban district
v. = village
W. = west or westerly
wat. pl. = watering place
wks. = works
wkshps. = workshops

A

Aachen (**Aix-la-Chapelle**), t., N. Rhine-Westphalia, **Germany**; anc. spa t. in coal-field dist.; industl., route ctr.; contains tomb of Charlemagne; p. (1990) 243,200.

Aalen, t., Baden-Württemberg, **Germany**; on R. Kocher; iron, textiles, lens mkg.; p. (1986) 62,800.

Aalst (**Alost**), t., E. Flanders, **Belgium**, 24 km N.W. Brussels; industl., comm. ctr. at rly. junc.; agr. tr.; p. (1993) 76,514.

Aarau, t., cap. of Aargau can., **Switzerland**; precision tools and instruments, shoes, textiles; hydroelectric power; p. (1980) 15,788.

Aare, R., **Switzerland**; flows through Brienz and Thun Ls., thence into Rhine; Aare gorges above Meiringen; lgst R. wholly in Switzerland, 280 km long.

Aargau, can., N. **Switzerland**; occupies lower Aare R. valley; agr. in valleys, wooded uplands; cap. Aarau; a. 1,404 km²; p. (1990) 496,300.

Aba, t., **Nigeria**; N.E. of Pt. Harcourt; mkt., palm oil processing; p. (1983) 216,000.

Abaco, Gt., I., Bahamas, W.I.; sheltered harbours, yachting; exp. crayfish; p. (1990) 10,061.

Abādān, c., **Iran**; spt., major oil terminal and refining ctr. on A.I. in Persian G.; permanently damaged by Iraqi air attack; now closed (1980); p. (1985) 294,000.

Abakan, t., **Russia**, on R. A.; recent rly.; sawmilling, food inds.; p. (1989) 154,000.

Abashiri, t., N. cst. Hokkaido, **Japan**; impt. fishing base; p. (1990) 44,416.

Abbeville, t., N. **France**; on R. Somme; connected with Paris and Belgium by canals; sugar-milling, carpets, biscuits, beer; p. (1982) 25,988.

Abbots-Langley, v., Herts., **Eng.**; birthplace of Nicholas Breakspeare (Pope Adrian IV).

Abenrå, spt., S.E. Jutland, **Denmark**; at head of A. fjord and admin, ctr. of S. Jutland prov.; vehicles, clothing, food processing; p. (1990) 21,463.

Abeokuta, t., **Nigeria**; cap. Ogun st.; N. of Lagos; palm oil, textiles; p. (1983) 309,000.

Aberaeron, t., Ceredigion, Dyfed, S. **Wales**; p. (1981) 1,446.

Abercarn, t., Islwyn, Gwent, **Wales**; tinplate, knitting pins; former colliery t.; p. (1981) 17,604.

Aberconwy, l. gov. dist., Gwynedd, **Wales**; lower Conwy valley inc. ts. Conwy, Betws-y-Coed, Llanrwst and Llandudno; p. (1993) 54,400.

Aberdare, t., Cynon Valley, Mid Glamorgan, **Wales**; on R. Cynon: wire cables; former coalmng; p. (1981) 36,621.

Aberdare Range, mtns., Nat. Park, **Kenya**; rise to 4,000 m; form a section of E. rim of Gr. Rift Valley; equable climate attractive to white settlers; camphor forests, fruit and pastoral agr. at higher alts.

Aberdeen, royal burgh, l. gov. dist., Grampian Reg., **Scot.**; between mouths of Rs. Dee and Don; impt. fishing pt. under competition from claims of rapidly growing N. Sea oil ind.; "granite-city"—much granite used in central bldgs.; univ., cath.; p. (1991) 189,707(c.), (1993) 218,200 (dist.).

Aberdeen, t., S.D., **USA**; ctr. for wheat and live-stock region; p. (1990) 24,927.

Aberdeenshire, former co., E. **Scot.** See **Grampian Region**.

Aberfeldy, burgh, Perth and Kinross, **Scot.**; in Strath Tay, 6 km below Loch Tay; mkt.; salmon and trout fishing resort; p. (1991) 1,748.

Abergavenny, t., Gwent, **Wales**; on R. Usk; scene of massacre of Welsh chiefs; light engin., concrete prods.; cattle mkt.; cas.; p. (1981) 9,390.

Aberlour, Charlestown of, burgh, Moray, **Scot.**; on R. Spey, 19 km S. of Elgin; p. (1991) 821.

Abernethy, burgh, Perth and Kinross, **Scot.**; on R. Tay, once cap. of Pictish Kings; p. (1991) 895.

Abersoch, t., Gwynedd, **Wales**; yachting resort.

Abertillery, t., Blaenau Gwent, Gwent, **Wales**; collieries, tinplate; p. (1981) 19,319.

Aberystwyth, t., Ceredigion, Dyfed, **Wales**; on Cardigan Bay at mouth of R. Ystwyth, resort; cas., univ. college; Nat. Library of Wales; p. (1981) 8,666.

Abidjan, c., replaced as cap. of Côte d'Ivoire by Yamoussoukro; pt.; exp. palm oil, cocoa, copra, hardwood, rubber; oil refining at Vridi nearby; p. (1986) 2,534,000 (met. a.).

Abilene, t., Texas, **USA**; univ.; agr. processing, oil refining; p. (1990) 106,654.

Abilene, t., on Smoky Hill R., Kansas, **USA**; childhood home of Eisenhower; p. (1980) 6,572.

Abingdon, Vale of White Horse, Oxon., **Eng.**; mkt. t. on R. Thames; cars, leather gds.; mediaeval and Georgian bldgs.; p. (1981) 22,686.

Abingdon, t., Va., **USA**; timber inds., agr. processing and tr., tobacco; tourist ctr.

Abinger Hammer, v., Surrey, **Eng.**; former centre of Weald iron industry.

Abkhazskaya, aut. rep., **Georgia**; borders Black Sea; sub-tropical crops, tourism; cap. Sukhumi; a. 8,599 km²; p. (1989) 537,500.

Abo. See **Turku**.

Abomey, t. anc. cap., former Kingdom of Dahomey, now **Benin**; former slave mkt.; cotton; p. (1982) 54,418.

Abovyan, t., **Armenia**; 16 km from Yerevan; new model t. founded 1963; p. (1990) 58,700.

Aboyne and Glentanner, par., Kincardine and Deeside, **Scot.**; on R. Dee nr. Ballater; Highland games; resort; p. (1991) 2,067.

Abraham, Plains of, nr. Quebec, **Canada**; Wolfe's victory over French under Montcalm, 1759.

Abram, t., Gtr. Manchester, **Eng.**; engin.; p. (1981) 7,083.

Abrantes, t., **Portugal**, on Tagus R.; French won battle here in Napoleonic Wars, 1807, dist. of Santarém; p. (1981) 48,653.

Abruzzo, region, central **Italy**; high limestone plateaux, narrow cstl. plain bordering Adriatic; poor agr., livestock; methane; forms part of Mezzogiorno; a. 8,513 km²; p. (1992) 1,255,549.

Abu Dhabi, I., emirate, lgst. of **United Arab Emirates**; S.E. Arabian pen.; rich oil reserves; a. 207,200 km²; p. (1985) 670,125.

Abuja, new t., **Nigeria**; became cap. of Nigeria in 1991; built from oil revenue; building slowing down with fall in oil prices; p. (1991) 378,671 (Federal Capital Territory).

Abu Qir, v. on A. Bay, **Egypt**; site of anc. Canopus; Battle of the Nile fought in the Bay 1798; offshore gasfield linked by pipeline to fertiliser plants near Alexandria.

Abu Simbel, Nile Valley, **Egypt**; anc. temples carved out of solid sandstone, one to Ramses II and the other to his Queen; saved from waters of Lake Nasser.

Abydos, anc. t. of Phrygia, Asia Minor, in present **Turkey**; resisted Philip of Macedon; famed for story of Leander and Hero.

Abydos, ruined c., Upper **Egypt**; celebrated for its temple of Osiris.

Acajutla, spt., **El Salvador**; exp. coffee; cement, oil refining, fertilisers.

Acapulco de Juárez, spt., Pac. cst., **Mexico**; major modern resort in bay surrounded by steep mtns.; exp. agr. prods.; p. (1990) 592,187.

Accra, c., cap. of **Ghana**; spt.; univ.; airpt.; consumer gds.; p. (1984) 636,067 (c.) 738,498 (met. a. inc. Tema).

Accrington, t., Hyndburn, Lancs., **Eng.**; 32 km N. of Manchester; former cotton ctr.; textile machin., more diversified new inds.; p. (1981) 35,891.

Achill I., Mayo, **R.o.I.**; mtnous.; agr., fishing, tourism at Dugort and Keal; a. 148 km²; p. (1986) 3,161.

Acireale, spt., Sicily, **Italy**; cath.; sulphur springs, p. (1981) 47,888.

Aconcagua, mtn., Andes, **Argentina**; highest peak of Western Hemisphere, alt. 6,956 m.

Aconquija, Nevada de, mtn. range, in E. Andes, N. **Argentina**; rises steeply from Chaco lowland to 5,500 m.

Acre. See **'Akko**.

Acre, st. W. **Brazil**; isolated within Amazon basin; rubber estates; major producer of coagulated rubber; cap. Rio Branco; a. 153,170 km²; p. (1991) 417,317.

Acton. See **Ealing**.

Adamawa Highlands, **Nigeria**; rise to over 5,490 m; stock rearing.

Adam's Bridge, chain of sandbanks, 35 km long, in Palk Strait, between **India** and **Sri Lanka**; construction of rail causeway mooted.

Adana, t., **Turkey**; on Seijhan R.; ctr. for fruit and cotton, impt. exp, from Turkey; cas.: cap. of A. prov.; 4th. t. of Turkey; Yumurtalik Free Trade Zone (1987); p. (1990) 972,318, 1,934,907, (prov.).

Adapazari, t., **Turkey**; rly. junction; agr. and tr. ctr., silk, linen; high-grade concentrate from low-grade iron ore deposits in Camdagi a.; p. (1985) 152,291.

Adda, R., N. **Italy;** flows through L. Como to R. Po.; agr. in wide valley above L. Como; 240 km long.

Addis Ababa, c., cap. of **Ethiopia;** at 2,440 m in central highlands; terminus of Djibouti rly.; ctr. of coffee tr., main concentration of inds. in Ethiopa; consumer gds., food processing; new cotton mill (1981); admin. ctr.; univ., palaces; p. (1991) 1,700,000.

Adelaide, c., spt., cap. of S. **Australia;** on alluvial plain of R. Torrens with Mount Lofty Range to E. and Gulf St. Vincent to W.; growth based on wheat, wool and fruit but heavy inds. since war (nearby coal and iron); cars, electrical goods, textiles, chems., oil refining; p. (1991) 1,023,617.

Adélie Land (Terre Adélie), Antarctica; French terr. and dependency of Réunion.

Adelsberg, t., Yugoslavia. *See* **Postojna.**

Aden, spt., economic and commercial cap. of **Yemen;** former Brit. col.; bay behind headlands of Aden t. and Little Aden, excellent anchorage; p. (1987) 417,366.

Aden, G. of W. **Arabian Sea;** one of most impt. shipping lanes in world; pts. of Aden, Berbera, Djibouti; length 880 km, width 480 km at mouth.

Adige, R., N. **Italy;** upper course forms impt. routeway through Alps between Italy and N.; flows via Verona to Adriatic; 360 km long.

Adirondack, mtns., **USA;** hgst. peak Mt. Marcy (1,630 m), average height 1,200 m; scenically attractive, ski resorts, sanatoria, iron-ore deposits.

Adlington, t., Lancs., **Eng.;** nr. Chorley; former cotton spinning t.; p. (1981) 5,626.

Admiralty Is., 27 km of sm. coral Is., one lge. I., S.W. **Pac. Oc.;** part of Papua New Guinea; forms part of Bismarck Archipelago; anc. civilisation; pearl fishing, coconuts; ch. t. Lorengau.; a. 2,072 km².

Adour, R., S.W. **France;** rises in Pyrenees, enters Bay of Biscay below Bayonne; 331 km long.

Adria, mkt. t., Rovigo, **Italy;** formerly on cst., now 22 km inland, old Etruscan c.; p. (1981) 21,785.

Adrianople. *See* **Edirne.**

Adriatic Sea, branch of the Mediterranean, between Italy and Balkan Peninsula; forms G. of Venice on the N.; chief trading pts., Venice, Trieste, and Ancona on the N., Brindisi and Dürres on the S.; a. 134,680 km², 720 km long.

Adullam or **Aidelma,** Judean c. of Canaanite origin, S.W. Jerusalem, **Israel,** where David hid in cave from Saul.

Adur, l. gov. dist., West Sussex, **Eng.;** lower A. valley and ts. of Shoreham-by-Sea and Southwick; p. (1993) 57,800.

Adwick le Street, t., South Yorks, **Eng.;** coal; home of George Washington's family; p. (1981) 19,162.

Adygeyskaya (Adygei), aut. region, **Russia;** in foothills of Caucasus; mainly agr. and lumbering; cap. Maykop; a. 7,599 km²; p. (1989) 432,000.

Adzharskaya, aut. rep., **Georgia;** borders Turkey; mtnous.; sub-tropical crops; cap. Batumi; a. 2,849 km²; p. (1990) 382,000.

Aegades, gr. of rocky Is. off W. cst. of Sicily, **Italy;** ch. t. Favignana on I. of that name.

Aegean Is., between **Greece** and **Turkey;** called the Grecian Archipelago, inc. Crete, Cyclades, Sporades, and Dodecanese; a. 3,901 km²; p. (1981) 428,533.

Aegean Sea, branch of the Mediterranean; studded with Is., between **Greece** and **Turkey;** connected through the Dardanelles with Sea of Marmara and thence through the Bosporus Strait with the Black Sea; rich cultural history; coral sponge fishing; recent oil finds contested between Greece and Turkey; length 640 km, width 320 km.

Afan. *See* **Por Talbot.**

Afars and Issas. *See* **Djibouti.**

Affric, Glen, Inverness, **Scot.;** 48 km S.W. of Inverness; hydroelectric power.

Afghanistan, rep. (1973), former kingdom, **Asia;** land locked, lies N. and W. of Pakistan; cap. Kabul; comm. ctrs. Kabul, Kandahar; mtnous.; ch. Rs., Kabul and Helm; intense summer heat, severe winter cold, scanty rainfall; ethnic variety, Pashtuns, Ghilzays, Uzbeks and Tadzhiks; many hill tribes; languages Pashtu and Farsi; religion Islam; geography causes fragmented settlement and slow economic progress; severe drought 1968–

72; 75 percent depend on agric.; heavily dependent on irrigation; wheat staple crop, also cotton, rice, maize; sheep, goats, horses; handicraft inds. (carpets and weaving) more impt. than modern inds.; mineral resources but poor transport hinders development; no rly.; refugees totalled 5,000,000 by 1985; hydroelectr. at Asadabad; invaded by Russian troops, Dec. 1979 but withdrew Feb. 1989; continuing civil war; a. 647,500 km²; p. (1991) 16·6 m.

Africa, third lgst. continent contains 22 per cent of world's land a. but only 11 per cent of p.; diverse physical and cultural conditions; plateaux interrupted in N. and S. by steeply folded, sharply eroded mtn. ranges and by mtn. massifs of Sahara and E. Africa; climate and vegetation vary from hot desert to equatorial rain forest and from Mediterranean woodland to tropical savannah; sparse but ethnically varied p., concentrated mainly along N.W. Mediterranean cst., Nile valley, cst. of W. Africa and N.E. of L. Victoria; little urbanisation; economic development hindered by colonial legacy and neo-colonial international companies, poorly developed transport network, poor soils, inadequate rainfall and fluctuating prices of primary prods. on world mkt.; petroleum deposits providing revenue for devel. in few ctys.; those ctys. without oil severely handicapped by high cost of imports; schemes like Volta R. multipurpose development and the Cabora Bassa dam designed to alleviate this poverty; continent contains 40 per cent of world hydroelectric potential and is storehouse of non-energy producing minerals, but many are exported in unprocessed form; agr. predominant economic activity, except in industl. enclaves of Egypt, Zimbabwe and S. Africa; 60 per cent land devoted to subsistence crops; a *c.* 30,259,000 km²; p. (1984) 536,685,000.

Agadir, spt., S. cst. **Morocco;** wrecked by earthquake, 1960; new t. built S. of former c. in a. of greater geological stability; p. (1982) 110,479.

Agana, cap. of **Guam;** reconstructed after second world war; p. (est. 1980) 3,000 (exc. armed forces).

Agen, t., cap. of Lot-et-Garonne, **France;** mkt. t.; aqueduct and bridge over Garonne R.; fruit tr. and processing; p. (1990) 32,223.

Agincourt (Azincourt), v., Pas-de-Calais, **France;** famed for battle in 1415 between English, led by Henry V and French under d'Albert.

Agra, c., Uttar Pradesh, **India;** on Jumna R., 184 km S.S.E. of Delhi; formerly cap. of Mogul Empire; famous Taj Mahal mausoleum; univ.; p. (1991) 892,000.

Agrigento, t., S. Sicily, **Italy;** spt., exp. sulphur, salt. Formerly Girgenti, founded Akragas, c. 580 B.C., famous for its temples; birthplace of Empedocles; p. (1981) 51,325.

Aguadilla, spt., **Puerto Rico;** exp. coffee and sugar.

Aguascalientes, st., **Mexico;** on central plateau at 1,800 m; agr.; mineral springs; cap. A.; a. 6,472 km²; p. (1990) 719,650.

Aguascalientes, t., cap. of A. st. **Mexico;** alt. over 1,800 m; 416 km N.W. of Mexico City; wide range of local inds.; hot springs; p. (1990) 506,384.

Agulhas, C., rocky projection, 160 km E. of C. of Good Hope, most southerly point of **Africa.**

Ahlen, t., N. Rhine–Westphalia, **Germany;** on R. Werse; coal mng., metal and engin. wks.; p. (1986) 51,900.

Ahmadabad, temporary cap. of Gujarat, **India;** Jain temple, mosques; univ.; impt. textile ctr.; oilfield at Nawagam nearby; p. (1991) 2,877,000.

Ahmadnagar, c., Maharashtra, **India;** admin. ctr.; old Bahmani cap.; lge. tr. in cotton and silk gds.; p. (1981) 143,937 (c.), 181,210 (met. a.).

Ahrewady. *See* **Irrawaddy.**

Ahvāz (Ahwāz), c., cap. of Khuzestan prov., **Iran;** airpt.; oil, aluminium, steel pipes; new steel plant; p. (1986) 589,529.

Aigues-Mortes, t., Gard dep., **France;** on Rhône delta; canal ctr., once spt., now 5 km from Mediterranean; salt works; much of mediaeval t. preserved; tourism; p. (1982) 4,475.

Aiguille d'Arves, mtn., Dauphiné Alps, S.E. **France;** 3 rock needles; hgst. alt. 3,511 m.

Aiguille du Midi, mtn., Mt. Blanc massif, S.E. **France;** rock needle, funicular rly.; alt. 3,845 m.

Aiguille Verte, mtn., Mt. Blanc massif, S.E. **France,** rock needle overlooking Chamonix; alt. 4,130 m.

Ailefroid, mtn., Dauphiné Alps, S.E. **France;** double summit; alt. 3,962 m.

Ailsa Craig, rocky I., Kyle and Carrick, **Scot.;** alt. 340 m; gannetry.

Ain, dep., **France;** in Jura; mainly agr., famous for pigs and poultry; a. 5,822 km²; p. (1990) 471,000.

Ain, R., **France;** trib. of R. Rhône, flows S.S.W. from Jura; hydroelectric power; 194 km long.

Airdrie, burgh, Strathclyde Reg., **Scot.;** 19 km E. of Glasgow; iron inds.; brick and concrete wks., steel tubes, pharmaceutics; p. (1991) 36,998.

Aire, R., West Yorks., **Eng.;** trib. of Ouse; major valley for power production; produces 20 per cent of U.K. power; length 112 km.

Aireborough, t., West Yorks., **Eng.;** woollens; p. (1981) 31,414.

Aisne, dep., **France;** borders Ardennes; forested; mainly agr., sugar-beet; sm. textile ts.; cap. Laon; a. 7,190 km²; p. (1990) 537,500.

Aisne, R., N.E. **France;** navigation improved by regularisation; 240 km long.

Aitolia and Akarnania, Greece; mtnous. prov. on N. side G. of Patras; arable cultivation on cstl. plain; cap. Missolonghi; a. 5,390 km²; p. (1991) 230,688.

Aix-en-Provence, t., Bouches-du-Rhône, **France;** 29 km N. of Marseilles; old cap. of Provence; thermal springs; cultural and comm. ctr., agr., inds.; p. (1990) 126,854 (t) 130,888 (met. a.).

Aix-la-Chapelle. *See* Aachen.

Aix-les-Bains, health resort, Savoy, **France;** p. (1982) 23,534.

Aizuwakamatsu, t. N. Honshu, **Japan;** lacquer ware, candles; p. (1990) 119,084.

Ajaccio, spt., cap. Corse-du-Sud, Corcisa, **France;** timber, flour, olive oil, tobacco; tourism; birthplace of Napoleon; p. (1990) 59,318.

Ajman, emirate, one of **United Arab Emirates;** p. (1985) 64,318.

Ajmer, t., Rajasthan, **India;** salt extraction, vegetable oils; p. (1991) 403,000.

Akhaia, prov., **Greece;** impt. currant producing a.; livestock; inc. pt. of Patras; a. 3,134 km²; p. (1991) 297,318.

Akhisar, t., **Turkey;** anc. Thyatira; in fertile agr. basin, p. (1985) 68,553

Akita, pref., **Japan;** a. 11,663 km²; contains Japan's lgst. oilfield and copper mine; mtns. and fertile lowlands; p. (1990) 1,227,000.

Akita, c., **Japan;** cap. Akita pref.; old cas. t., pt; oil refining ctr., fertilisers, wood pulp; p. (1990) 302,359.

'Akko (Acre), c., spt., **Israel;** famous for sieges during Crusades; withstood Napoleon for 61 days in 1799; pt. functions now assumed by Haifa; p. (1982) 39,100.

Akmolinsk. *See* Tselinograd.

Akola, t., Maharashtra, **India;** cotton; p. (1991) 328,000.

Akosombo, pt. **Ghana;** pt. and new t. S. of L. Volta; textile factory being built; planned p. 50,000.

Akranes, t., **Iceland;** N. of Reykjavik; lge. cement wks.; p. (1991) 5,239.

Akron, c., Ohio, **USA;** lge. rubber mftg. ctr.; maize, mills, woollens, machin., chemicals; univ.; p. (1990) 223,019 (c.), 657,575 (met. a.).

Aktyubinsk, t., N.W. **Kazakhstan;** at S. end of Ural mtns.; ferro-alloys, engin., lignite, elec. power, chemicals, copper; p. (1990) 261,100.

Akureyri, t., N. **Iceland;** herring fishery, textiles, food processing; 2nd. t. of Iceland; p. (1991) 14,436.

Akyab, *See* Sittwe.

Alabama, st., **USA;** cap. Montgomery, ch. pt. Mobile; "cotton st.", cattle-rearing; fertilisers, chemicals, mng.; lgst. c. Birmingham; settled 1702; admitted to union 1819; st. flower camelia, st. bird yellow-hammer; a. 133,667 km²; p. (1990) 4,040,587.

Alagôas, st., N.E. **Brazil;** hot, dry cattle rearing a., poor st. with low literacy rate; cap. Maceió; a. 28,648 km²; p. (1991) 2,512,515.

Alameda, spt. Cal., **USA;** on I. in San Francisco Bay; impt. naval and air base; spt. inds.; p. (1980) 63,852.

Aland Is. (Ahvenanmaa), group belonging to **Finland** at entrance of G. of Bothnia; a. 1,481 km²; p. (1991) 24,847.

Alaska, Arctic st., **USA;** separated from other sts.; bought from Russia (1868); mtnous.; furs, timber, salmon; major oil and natural gas discoveries on N. slope present difficult ecological problems for exploitation; pipeline from Prudhoe Bay to Valdez; lgst. c. Anchorage;

admitted to union 1959; st. flower forget-me-not, st. bird Willow Ptarmigan; cap. Juneau (planned cap. at Willow South never built); a. 1,518,776 km²; p. (1990) 550,043.

Alaska G. of, S. cst. A., **USA.;** semi-circular G. with precipitous csts.; oil in Cook Inlet and Controller B.; a. 5,000 km².

Alaska Highway, from Dawson Creek, B.C., **Canada,** to Fairbanks, Alaska, **USA;** 2,443 km long; built for second world war programme; main supply base and H.Q., Edmonton, Alberta.

Alaska Range, mtn. massif, S.A., **USA;** extends in arc of 640 km; separates S. cst. and N. tundra; S.E. flowing glaciers; many peaks over 3,000 m; Mt. McKinley, 6,182 m.

Alatau, mtns., bdy. of **Kazakhstan;** and Sinkiang, **China;** group of 5 ranges, outliers of Tien-Shan; alt. up to 4,600 m; highest peak Khan Tengri, 6,954 m.

Alava, Basque prov., N. **Spain;** ch. t. Vitoria; viticulture; a. 3,043 km²; p. (1991) 274,720.

Albacete, prov., S.E. **Spain;** stock-raising; a. 14,864 km². p. (1991) 339,268.

Albacete, t., cap. of A. prov., **Spain;** agr. mkt., fruit, saffron; p. (1991) 134,584.

Alba-Iulia, t., **Romania;** on R. Mures, formerly Carisburgh; union of Transylvania with Romania proclaimed here 1918; p. (1990) 73,383.

Albania, rep., **S.E. Europe;** lying along Adriatic, adjacent to Yugoslavia and Greece; Chinese economic aid and co-operation ended in 1978; food ch. ind.; petroleum reserves and refining, hydroelectric power, coal, chrome ore, copper, iron ore; first external rail link opened (1986) for ore exports; fastest growing p. in Europe but extreme poverty; cap. Tirana; a. 27,529 km²; p. (1991) 3·3 m.

Albano, crater L., **Italy;** tourist attraction 24 km S.E. of Rome; steep sides; a. 8 km².

Albany, mkt. t., Ga., **USA;** on Flint R.; agr. ctr.; cotton, food; p. (1980) 74,471.

Albany, c., cap. of N.Y. st., **USA;** R. pt. on Hudson R.; admin. and industl. ctr.; p. (1990) 101,082 (c.), 874,000 (met. a. with Schenectady-Troy).

Albany, t., **W. Australia;** pt. on King George Sound; founded (1826) as penal col.; first white settlement in W. Australia, established to counter Fr. settlement of W.; p. (1990) 15,270.

Alberta, prov., **W. Canada;** part of prairies; Rockies in W.; wheat, livestock, feed crops; coal less impt. with development of rich oil and gas resources; chemicals; timber; cap. Edmonton; a. 661,188 km²; p. (1991) 2,538,500.

Albertville. *See* Kalemie.

Albi, t., cap. of Tarn dep., **France;** cath., industl. and comm. ctr.; p. (1990) 48,707.

Ålborg, c., cap. of N. Jutland prov., **Denmark;** spt. on S. side of Lim fjord; shipping., cement, textiles; airpt.; p. (1990) 155,019.

Albula Alps, mtn. range, Rhaetian Alps, E. **Switzerland;** summits intersected by low passes; inc. several impt. Dolomitic peaks.

Albuquerque, t., N.M., **USA;** on Rio Grande; alt. 1,525 m.; univ.; food prod., engin.; resort; p. (1990) 384,736 (c.), 481,000 (met. a.).

Albury-Wodonga, t., N.S.W., Vic., **Australia;** regional urban growth ctr. (1974) on Murray R.; p. (1983) 77,970.

Alcalá de Henares, t., **Spain;** nr. Madrid; univ.; birthplace of Cervantes; p. (1991) 162,780.

Alcamo, t., Sicily, **Italy;** nr. ruins of anc. Segesta; p. (1981) 42,059.

Alcatraz, I., Cal., **USA;** San Francisco Bay; former prison.

Alcoy, t., **Spain;** textiles, paper; p. (1981) 65,908.

Aldabra Is., Seychelles Rep.; 400 km N.W. of Madagascar; leased (1971–1985) to Royal Society for wildlife research (unique animal and plant species).

Aldan, R., E. Siberia, **Russia;** flows from Stanovoy Range to Lena R. via Tommot gold-mng. dist.; coal in lower course; 2,682 km long.

Aldeburgh, spt., Suffolk Coastal, Suffolk, **Eng.;** 48 km from Ipswich; famous for annual music festival; p. (1981) 2,911.

Aldermaston, Berkshire, **Eng.;** atomic weapons research ctr.

Alderney, I., Channel Is., **Brit.;** horticulture tourism; a. 794 ha; p. (1986) 2,130.

Aldershot, t., Rushmoor, Hants., **Eng.;** bricks; lge. military camp; p. (1981) 32,654.

Aldridge, t., West Midlands, **Eng.;** plastics, packing cases; expanded t.; p. with Brownhills (1981) 87,219.

Alençon, t. cap of Orne dep., France; textiles; p. (1990) 31,139.

Aleppo, c., Syria; 2nd. c. of Syria; in limestone hills; univ.; mkt and textile ctr.; p. (1985) 1,145,117.

Alès, t., Gard dep., France; sm. coalfield; chemicals; p. (1982) 70,180 (met. a.).

Alessandria, t., N. Italy; rly. ctr. on Tanaro R.; engin.; p. (1981) 100,523.

Alesund, spt. on Giske I., W. Norway, fishing, fish processing; airpt. on I. to N.; p. (1990) 23,741.

Aletsch, glacier, Switzerland; in Bernese Alps; lgst. in Europe; length 24 km.

Aletschhorn, mtn., Bernese Alps, Switzerland; alt. 4,198 m.

Aleutian Is.; Bering Sea, Alaska, USA; chain of over 150 Is. formed from partially submerged peaks of volcanic A. mtn. range; on earthquake belt; U.S. air base.

Alexander Archipelago, S.E. Alaska, USA; dense I. system; fjord scenery; well populated; furs, lumbering, fishing; a. 33,670 km².

Alexandria, (El Iskandariyah) ch. pt. and prov., Egypt; founded by Alexander the Great, 332 B.C.; floating dock; exp. cotton, wheat, rice, gum; second lgst. c. in Africa; new steel plant at El Dikhelia; pt. being expanded and new pt. at Dikhelia; linked to offshore gas field; rapid growth, second lgst. c. in Africa; p. (1990) 3,170,000 (c.), (1991) 3,295,000 (prov.).

Alexandria, c., spt., Va., USA; on Chesapeake Bay; indust. t.; p. (1990) 111,183.

Alford, t., East Lindsey, Lincs., Eng.; mkt.; engineering, knitwear, flexographic printing; p. (1981) 2,596.

Alfreton, t., Amber Valley, Derbys., Eng.; mkt. t.; formerly coal mng.; hosiery, knitwear; p. (1981) 23,124.

Algarve, prov., anc. kingdom, Portugal; in extreme S. of cty; tourism, fishing, fruit.

Algeciras, spt., Spain; W. of Gibraltar on A. Bay; nearby Campo de Gibraltar scheme for social and economic development; p. (1991) 101,365.

Algeria, indep. st. (1962), N. Africa; former French colony; fertile cstl. plain borders Mediterranean Sea where cereal, wine, fruit and olive production and incr. mkt. garden prods. for exp.; Land reform (1980) encouraging livestock; afforestation to prevent N. spread of Sahara; exp. of high grade iron ore, phosphates, petroleum and natural gas are financing ambitious industrialisation plans; incr. tourism; new roads link Saharan oilfields to cst.; cap. El Djezair; 60 per cent of p. under 19; a. 2,373,994 km²; p. (1993) 26·6 m. Civil war since 1992 against Muslim fundamentalists.

Algiers. See El Djezair

Alicante, spt., cap of A. prov., Spain; wine, fruits; oil refinery; p. (1991) 270,951, 1,315,712 (prov.).

Alice Springs, t., N.T., Australia; ch. t., of desert a.; major cattle raising ctr.; natural gas nearby; growth of winter tourism; p. (1991) 25,586.

Aligarh, t., Uttar Pradesh, India; 128 km S.E. of Delhi; univ.; p. (1991) 481,000.

Alkmaar, t., Netherlands; impt. cheese mkt. on N. Holland canal; p. (1993) 92,421.

Allahabad, t., Uttar Pradesh, India; at confluence of Jumna and Ganges Rs.; univ.; Hindu pilgrimage ctr.; p. (1991) 806,000 (c.).

Allegheny Mtns., USA; part of Appalachian system, inc. several parallel ranges; water-shed between Atlantic and Mississippi R. drainage; forested, tourism; average alt. 1,500 m.

Allegheny R., Penns., N.Y., USA; rises in A. mtns., flows to Ohio R.; Pittsburg met. a. on lower reaches where R. entrenched 120 m below plateau making urban development difficult; used for coal and oil transport; 520 km long.

Allen, Bog of, R.o.I.; peat bogs, peat cutting, cultivation; a. 958 km².

Allentown, t., Penns., USA; coal, textiles, cement; p. (1990) 105,090 (c.), 687,000 (met. a.).

Alleppey, spt., Kerala, S. India; on sand spit coconut prods, p. (1981) 169,940.

Allerdale, l. gov. dist., Cumbria, Eng.; cstl. dist inc. Workington, Maryport, Cockermouth and Keswick; p. (1993) 96,200.

Alliance, t., Ohio, USA; iron, steel, engin.; p. (1980) 24,315.

Allier, dep., France; N. of Massif Central; coal and iron mng.; mineral springs, wine, wheat; a. 4,786 km²; p. (1990) 357,700.

Alloa, sm. burgh, Clackmannan, Scot.; on N. bank of R. Forth; bricks, tiles, glass, distilling p. (1991) 18,842.

Alma-Ata, c., cap. of Kazakhstan; in foothills of Tien-Shan mtns.; univ.; comm. agr., and ind. ctr.; food processing, machin., printing; p. (1990) 1,147,100.

Almada, t., Portugal; on R. Tagus estuary opposite Lisbon; Salazar bridge (opened 1966) links it with Lisbon; p. (1987) 42,607.

Almelo, t., Overijssel, Neth.; 40 km S.E. of Zwolle; cotton textile mnfs.; p. (1993) 63,988.

Almeria, spt. on G. of A., S.E. Spain; cap. A prov.; cath.; exp. grapes, oranges; p. (1991) 157,763, 461,938 (prov.).

Alnwick, t., l. gov. dist., Northumberland, Eng.; cas.; mkt. t.; p. (1993) 30,300 (dist.).

Alor Setar, t., cap. of Kedah, W. Malaysia; on main W. cst. road and rly.; p. (1980) 71,682.

Alost. See Aalst.

Alpes-de-Haute-Provence (Basses-Alpes), dep., S.E. France; mtnous., infertile a. bordering Italy; olives, wines; cap. Digne; a. 6,988 km²; p. (1990) 130,900.

Alpes-Maritimes, dep., S.E. France; ceded by Italy in 1860; ch. t. Nice; olives, wines, fruit; a. 3,737 km²; p. (1990) 971,800.

Alphen, t., S. Holland, Neth.; on Old Rhine, 16 km S.E. of Leiden; mkt. for dairy produce; p. (1993) 65,051.

Alps, high. mtns. in Europe; 960 km long, inc. 1,200 glaciers; separates S. and central Europe, forming a climatic divide; major tourist a., winter sports; hydroelec. power; main peaks Mont Blanc (4,814 m), Mont Rosa (4,641 m), Matterhorn (4,509 m).

Als, I., S. Denmark; in the Little Belt, a. 337 km²; linked to Jutland by bridge; p. (1990) 50,744.

Alsace-Lorraine, region, E. France; bordered to E. by W. Germany and Rhine R; incorporated into Germany at time of unification (1871), returned to France by Treaty of Versailles (1919); impt. iron-ore and iron and steel inds. in Lorraine; regional aid for economic development; well wooded; p. (1990) 1,624,400 (Alsace) See Lorraine.

Alsdorf, t., N. Rhine-Westphalia, Germany; 16 km N. of Aachen; tar-distillation plant; p. (1986) 45,900.

Alston, t., Eden, Cumbria, Eng.; in upper reaches of south Tyne in N. Pennines; limestone quarrying.

Altai Mtns., Mongolia, Russia; border China; steppes and glaciers; silver and mercury; multipurpose R. project at Kamenna-Obi; ctr. of USSR atomic ind. at Ust Kamenogorsk; stock-rearing; average alt. 3,000 m, highst. alt. 4,656 m at Tabun Bogdo.

Alta, R., N. Norway; scene of major new h.e.p. sta. fiercely opposed by Lapp residents.

Altamura, caves, N. Spain; prehistoric shelters, paintings of animals (Magdalenian).

Altamura, t., Apulia, Italy; at foot of Apennines; wines, wool; cath.; p. (1981) 51,328.

Altdorf, t., cap. of Uri can., Switzerland; rubber gds., wood workings; statue of William Tell and Tell Theatre; p. (1980) 8,200.

Altenahr, t., N. Rhine-Westphalia, Germany; site of anc. cas. of Counts von der Marck; metals, wine; p. (1983) 23,400.

Altenburg, t., Saxony, Germany; lignite mng., engin., metallurgy, mnfs. playing cards, textiles; p. (1981) 55,827.

Alton, t., East Hants., Eng.; breweries, lt. engin.; p. (1981) 14,646.

Alton t., Ill., USA; on Mississippi R.; oil refining; p. (1980) 34,171.

Altoona, c., Penns., USA; rly. t.; p. (1984) 54,600 (c.), 134,400 (met. a.).

Altrincham, mkt. t., Trafford, Gtr. Manchester, Eng.; engin.; residtl.; p. (1981) 39,641.

Alva, burgh, Clackmannan, Scot.; at S. foot of Ochil Hills, 5 km N. of Alloa; woollens, printing, fruit and fish canning; p. (1991) 5,201.

Alvsborg, co., S.W. Sweden; cap. Vänersborg; a. 11,394 km²; p. (1992) 445,921.

Alwar, c., Rajasthan, India; in hilly agr. region; former cap. of A. princely st.; fort, palace; p. (1991) 205,086.

Alyn and Deeside, l. gov. dist., Clwyd, Wales; inc. Connah's Quay, Buckley and Hawarden; p. (1993) 74,700.

Amagasaki, c., Japan; nr. Osaka; chemicals polyethylene; iron and steel; oil refining; p. (1990) 498,998.

Amalfi, spt., Italy; on G. of Salerno; tourist resort; fisheries; p. (1981) 6,052.

Amapá, fed. terr., N. **Brazil**; on equator; tropical rain forest, sparse p.; a. 137,423 km²; p. (1991) 289,050.

Amârah, Al, pt., **Iraq**; on left bank of R. Tigris 400 km below Baghdad; Arab t. and agr. mkt. at R. crossing; p. (1985) 131,758.

Amârapura, t., Myanmar; on R. Irrawaddy 10 km. S.W. of Mandalay; former cap.; craft inds.

Amarillo, t., Texas, **USA**; oil refining, creameries, meat packing; p. (1990) 157,615.

Amasya, t. and prov., **Turkey**; on Yesil-Cekerek R.; tr. ctr.; p. (1985) 53,431, (1990) 357,191 (prov.).

Amazon, gr. R., S. America; drains lgst. a. and carries more water than any other R. in world; main Andean headstreams Huarco Ucayali and Marañón from Peru unite to flow across Brazil to Atl. Oc., receiving waters of many Rs. inc. the Madeira; lgst. rain forest in world; ocean steamers penetrate to Iquitos, Peru, c. 3,680 km from mouth; a. drained c. 6 million km² of sparsely populated cty., mostly in Brazil; length 6,448 km; basin inc. 40% of S. America; ocean pt. Belém.

Amazonas, lgst. st. of **Brazil**; isolated; tropical rain forest; tree prods.; vast mineral reserves; cap. Manáus; a. 1,595,823 km²; p. (1991) 2,088,682 (mainly Indian).

Amazonas, fed. terr., **Venezuela**; cap. Puerto Ayacucho on Orinoco R., isolated, tropical rain forest; a. 181,300 km²; p. (1981) 45,667.

Amazonia, Peru, Colombia, Brazil; a. covered by Amazon R. and its tribs. and the surrounding lowland; thickly forested; underdeveloped.

Ambala, c., Haryana, **India**; cotton, flour; p. (1991) 139,889.

Ambato, c., **Ecuador**; S. of Quito, on slope of Mt. Chimborazo; alt. 2,702 m; textiles, canned fruits, leather gds.; p. (1990) 124,166.

Amberg, t., Bavaria, **Germany**; mediaeval walled t. on R. Vils; specialist steels, textiles; p. (1986) 43,300.

Amber Valley, l. gov. dist., Derbys., **Eng.**; S. of co., nr. Notts.; inc. Alfreton, Ripley, Heanor and Belper; p. (1993) 113,700.

Ambès, t., Gironde, **France**; nr. Bordeaux; oil refining; p. (1982) 2,715.

Ambleside, tourist ctr., Cumbria, **Eng.**; N. of L. Windermere.

Amboise, t., Indre-et-Loire dep., **France**; 24 km E. of Tours; famous cas, and prison; p. (1982) 11,415.

Ambon, I., Moluccas, **Indonesia**; spices, coconuts; a. 818 km²; p. 73,000.

America, the lands of the Western hemisphere, comprising the continents of North and South America, separated by narrow Isthmus of Panama; most N. point over 14,400 km from C. Horn, the extreme S. point; p. (1984) 750,000,000. *See also* **North, South,** and **Central America.**

American Samoa, Is, E.N.E. Fiji under US rule; a. 197 km²; p. (1990) 46,773.

Amersfoort, c., Utrecht, **Neth.**; walled c. on R. Eem; rapid growth of light inds.; p. (1993) 106,923.

Amersham, t., Bucks., **Eng.**; Radio chemical Ctr., renamed Amersham International after privatisation (1982); lt. inds., 17th cent. mkt. hall.

Ames, t., Iowa, **USA**; Iowa State Univ. of Science and Technology and many fed. and st. institutes; p. (1990) 47,196.

Amiens, c., cap. of Somme dep; major textile ctr. of **France,** on R. Somme; cath.; p. (1990) 136,234 (c.), 156,120 (met. a.).

Amindiui, Is, Arabian Sea; joined with Lacadive & Minicoy Is. to form Lakshadweep, Union territory, **India.**

Amirante Is., British group, **Indian Ocean**; S.W. of Seychelles.

Amlwch, t., Gwynedd, **Wales**; N. cst of Anglesey; resort; pt.; oil terminal; p. (1981) 3,690.

Amman, c., cap. of **Jordan**; N.E. of Dead Sea; site of biblical Raboth Ammon; textiles, cement, tobacco; airpt.; univ.; p. (1986) 1,160,000.

Ammanford, t., Dinefwr, Dyfed, **Wales**; brick mkg.; p. (1981) 5,711.

Amoy. *See* Xiamen.

Ampthill, Mid Beds., **Eng.**; mkt. t.; p. (1981) 5,766.

Amravati, c., Maharashtra, **India**; cotton ctr., univ.; p. (1991) 422,000.

Amritsar, c., Punjab, N.W. **India**; Golden Temple sacred to Sikhs; trade ctr. for shawls and carpets; soaps, paints, engin.; Massacre of Indian nationalists by troops under British control, 1919; p. (1991) 709,000.

Amroha, t., Uttar Pradesh, **India**; pilgrimage ctr.; p. (1991) 137.061.

Amsterdam, spt., cap. of **Netherlands**; at junction of R. Amstel and the IJ; built on 96 Is. joined by 300 bridges, harbour at terminus of N. Sea canal can hold 1,000 ships; two univs., Royal Palace, Bourse; extensive tr.; exp. dairy prod., sugar, tobacco; shipbldg., diamond polishing, aeronautical, marine, elec. machin., oil refining; p. (1993) 719,856 (c.), 1,091,338 (met. a.).

Amu-Dar'ya (Oxus), R., marks boundary between **Turkmenistan, Uzbekistan** and **Afghanistan;** flows from Pamir mtns. to Aral Sea; Kara- and Ksyl-Kum deserts on either bank; rich in fish; 1,395 km long.

Amur (Heilong Jiang), major R. of E. **Asia;** flows from Mongolia between N.E. China and E. Siberia into Pac. Oc. opposite Sakhalin I.; with tribs. Argun and Ussuri forms lgst. R. frontier in world; crossed by Trans-Siberian rly. at Khabarovsk; 2,897 km long.

Anaconda, t., Mont., **USA**; one of lgst. copper mines in world; p. (1990) 10,278.

Anaheim, t., Cal., **USA**; tourism; Disneyland; p. (1990) 266,406 (c.), 2,411,000 (met. a.).

Anahuac, plateau, **Mexico**; average alt. 2,000 m; surrounded by higher cty. inc. volcano Popocatapetl (5,456 m); contains Mexico City heartland of Aztec Mexico; a. c. 3,900 km².

Anambas Is., Indonesia; 240 km W. of W. Malaysia; little development; p. c. 12,000.

Anatolia (Asia Minor), penin. approx. coextensive with Turkey bounded by Black Sea (N.), Mediterranean (S.), Aegean (W.).

Anching. *See* **Anqing.**

Anchorage, t., Alaska, **USA**; timber, salmon fishing and canning; earthquake 28 Mar. 1964; spt.; airpt.; p. (1990) 226,338.

Ancona, spt., central **Italy**; on the Adriatic Sea; founded by Dorians, 1500 B.C.; sugar refineries, shipbldg., petrochemicals; p. (1992) 100,701.

Andalucia, region, covering southern **Spain**; Córdoba, Seville, Jaén and Granada, celebrated ctrs. in Moorish times; irrigation for wines, olives, fruits.

Andaman and Nicobar Is., Bay of Bengal; constituted a union terr., **India**, 1956; hilly remnants of drowned mtn. chain; primitive pygmy tribes; a. 8,327 km²; p. (1991) 280,661.

Anderlecht, t., residtl. and industl. sub. of Brussels, **Belgium**; p. (1983) 94,715.

Andermatt, v., Uri, **Switzerland**; at foot of Mt. St. Gotthard; tourist ctr., winter health resort.

Anderson, t., Ind., USA; car components; p. (1990) 59,459.

Andes, gr. volcanic mtn. system, **S. America**; extends over 6,400 km from N.-S.; physical and climatic divide rising to over 6,000 m; densely populated; high tropical plateaux; rich in minerals; hgst. peak, Aconcagua (6,965 m).

Andhra Pradesh, st. S.E. **India**; cap. Hyderabad; inc. valleys of lower Godavari and Krishna Rs.; sugar, rice; a. 275,278 km²; p. (1991) 66,508,008.

Andizhan, c. **Uzbekistan**; once residence of Khans of Khokan; industl. ctr.; in irrigation a.; cotton, silk; oilfields; p. (1990) 296,800.

Andorra, sm. mtn. st., E. Pyrenees; under joint suzerainty of French President and Bishop of Urgel (Spain until 1993; now virtually indep.); livestock, wines, tobacco; tourism; alt. 900–3,000 m; a. 495 km²; p. (1993) 59,000.

Andover, mkt. t., Test Valley, Hants., **Eng.**; prehistoric earthwks.; expanded t.; p. (1981) 31,006.

Andria, t., S. **Italy**; Roman remains, cath., palaces; p. (1981) 83,319.

Andropov. *See* **Rybinsk.**

Andros, lgst. I., **Bahamas**; sponges, sisal, hemp; a. 5957 km²; p. (1990) 8,155.

Andújar, t., **Spain**; on Guadalquivir R.; mineral springs, pottery, soap, textiles, uranium plant; p. (1981) 30,875.

Angara, R., Siberia, **Russia**; trib. of Yenisey; navigable almost its entire length., rises nr. and flows through L. Baykal; length 2,080 km; hydro-electric power.

Angarsk, t., E. Siberia, **Russia**; on R. Angaar 32 km N.W. Irkutsk; engin., saw milling; p. (1989) 266,000.

Angel Falls (Salto del Angel), waterfall, **Venezuela**; nr. Ciudad Bolivar; 980 m drop.

Angerman, R., N. **Sweden** rises nr. Norwegian border, falls to G. of Bothnia; timber transport; 448 km long.

Angers, t., cap, of Maine-et-Loire dep., **France**; on R. Maine; mkt. t. for local produce, fruit, vegetables, Anjou wines, Cointreau; textiles; cath., cas.; p. (1990) 146,163 (t.), 206,276 (met. a.).

Angkor, c., **Cambodia;** jungle-covered ruins of c. from Khmer civilisation; discovered 1860.

Anglesey (Ynys Môn), former co., l. gov. dist., Gwynedd, **Wales;** separated from mainland by Menai Straits; former stronghold of Druids, attacked by Romans A.D. 61; mainly agr. and tourism; p. (1993) 69,300.

Angola, People's Rep. of (Port. W. Africa), W. Africa; interior forms part of central African plateaux, bounded by transitional escarpments in W. which face on to narrow coastal plain; rainfall diminishes from N.-S. with consequent crop zoning; coffee, cotton, oil palm in N., corn, peanuts, sisal in drier interior, cattle in S., semi-desert in S.E.; economy dependent upon primary inds., especially agr.; coffee major exp., produced on plantations; newly discovered oil-fields; diamonds in remote N.E. Luanda dis.; iron-ore mng. impt. at Cassinga; little mftg.; hydroelectric scheme on Cuarza R.; pts. on natural harbours impt. transhipment points for land-locked central African ctys.; indep. 1975, followed by civil war between rival guerrilla groups resumed 1993; cap. Luanda; a. 1,246,375 km²; p. (1993) 10·77m. (inc. Cabinda).

Angoulême, mftg. t., cap. of Charente dep., **France;** on R. Charente; cognac, paper; cath.; suffered during Huguenot wars; p. (1990) 46,194 (t.), 101,108 (met. a.).

Angra do Heroismo, t., cap. admin. dist. **Azores;** pt. on Terceira I.; p. (1981) 75,010.

Angren, t., **Uzbekistan;** E. of Tashkent; lgst. ctr. of lignite mng. in central Asia; p. (1990) 133,200.

Anguilla I., Leeward Is., **W.I.;** dry climate, thin limestone soil; exp. cotton, salt; a. 91 km²; reverted to Brit. Crown after secession from St. Kitts-Nevis ass. st. 1967; status of separate Brit. dependency and withdrawal from St. Kitts-Nevis ass. statehood 1980; p. (1992) 8,960.

Angus, l. gov. dist., former co., **Scot.;** part of Tayside Reg.; a. 1,937 km²; p. (1993) 97,420.

Anhui (Anhwei), prov., E. central **China;** in delta region of Chang Jiang; a. 140,686 km²; cap. Hefei; soya-beans, rice, tea, coal and iron; p. (1992) 52,290,000.

Aniakchak, volcano, S.W. Alaska, **USA;** rich variety of flora and fauna on crater floor; alt. 1,384 m.

Anjou, former prov. of **France;** mainly S. of lower R. Loire; ch. t. Angers.

Ankara, c., cap. of **Turkey** since 1923; alt. 1,037 m; univ., cultural and admin. ctr.; p. (1990) 2,541,000, 3,236,626 (prov.).

Anklesvar, t., Gujarat, **India;** natural gas, oil; gas pipelines to Ultaran and Barodi; p. (1981) 36,123.

'Annaba, spt., **Algeria;** on fertile plain; fertiliser factory supplied by phosphates from Djebel-Onk; iron and steel complex; p. (1983) 348,322.

Annaberg-Bucholz, t., Saxony, **Germany;** in Erz Mtns.; cobalt, tin, uranium mng.; p. (1989) 25,404.

Annam, region, **Vietnam;** formerly within French Union; divided by 17th parallel bdy. (1957); a. 147,560 km²; ch. t. Hué.

Annamese Cordillera, cstl. mtn. range, **Laos, Vietnam;** N.-S. watershed between Mekong and S. China Sea; rising to 2,000 m in Ngoc Linh; forested; inhabited by hill tribes.

Annan, royal burgh, Annandale and Eskdale, **Scot.;** on R. Annan, 3 km from its mouth in Solway F.; Chapelcross reactor sta.; p. (1991) 8,930.

Annandale and Eskdale, l. gov. dist., Dumfries and Galloway, **Scot.;** close to Borders Reg. and Eng.; p. (1993) 37,130.

Annapolis, c., cap. of Maryland, **USA;** naval academy; p. (1990) 33,187.

Annapolis Valley, Nova Scotia, **Canada;** famous fruit growing a., especially for apples.

Annapurna, massif, **Nepal;** part of Himalayas; many glaciers in W. and N.W.; alt. 8,080 m.

Ann Arbor, c., Mich., **USA;** on the Huron; univ. of Michigan.; motor lorries, farm implements, scientific instruments; p. (1990) 109,592 (c.), 283,000 (met. a.).

Annecy, t., **France;** dep. of Haute-Savoie; at lower end of beautiful L. Annecy; textiles, paper, watches; resort; p. (1990) 51,143 (t.), 122,622 (met. a.).

Anqing (Anching), c., Anhui prov., **China;** R. pt. on Chang Jiang; tr. in agr. prods.

Ansbach, t., Bavaria, **Germany;** machin., metallurgy, furniture indus.; rly. ctr.; p. (1986) 37,500.

An-shan, c., Liaoning, N. **China;** at foot of

Qian Shan, 96 km S.W. of Shenyang; lgst. iron and steel complex in China (fully automated steel plant), elec., chemical and locomotive ind.; p. (1992) 1,390,000.

Antakya (Antioch), anc. c., S. **Turkey;** on R. Orontes; cap. of Hatay prov., major Roman cap. and early ctr. of Christian culture; p. (1985) 107,821.

Antalya, c., S.W. **Turkey;** freeport (1986) with shallow harbour from which Paul and Barnabas sailed to Antakya; tourism; p. (1990) 353,149, 1,132,211 (prov.).

Antananarivo (Tananarive), cap. of **Madagascar;** ctr. of commerce and communications; airpt.; lge meat preserving factories, plastics, radios, car assembly, shoes, knitted gds.; rice mills; univ.; p. (1990) 802,390.

Antarctica, plateau continent within A. circle; snow-covered, extensive ice sheets and glaciers; volcanoes and Is.; alt. 2,000-3,000 m; dependencies of U.K., Australia, N.Z., France, Norway but a. S. of 60° S reserved for peaceful international scientific research; a. 16 million km².

Antarctic Ocean, parts of Pac., Atl. and Indian Oceans, S. of 60° S.; cold and dangerous; no mammalian life other than whales.

Antibes, t., Alpes-Maritimes, N. of Cap d. A., S.E. **France;** spt. on Fr. Riviera; exp. oranges, flowers for perfume mnfs.; resort; Roman remains; p. (1990) 70,688.

Anticosti, barren I. in G. of St. Lawrence, Quebec, **Canada;** well wooded game reserve, lumbering; 224 km by 45 km.

Antigua, anc. c., **Guatemala;** 32 km W. of Guatemala c.; former cap., destroyed by earthquake 1773; comm. ctr. in coffee dist.; notable colonial ruins; tourism; p. (1989) 26,231.

Antigua and Barbuda, Leeward gr., **W.I.;** aut. st. in ass. with Gt. Britain; indep. 1981; semi-arid limestone; 75 per cent p. in N.E.; sugar, cotton, tourism; cap. St. Johns; a. (inc. Barbuda and Redonda) 440 km²; p. (1991) 65,962.

Antilles, Greater and Lesser, archipelago enclosing Caribbean Sea and G. of Mexico, **W.I.;** complex political structure, tropical climate and crops; a. c. 259,000 km².

Antioquia, mtnous. dep. **Colombia;** colonial mng.; agr. now more impt.; one of major p. clusters in Colombia inc. dep. cap. Medellin; a 65,791 km²; p. (1992) 4,467,914.

Antisana, volcano, central **Ecuador;** alt. 5,708 m.

Antofagasta, spt., **Chile;** cap., comm. and industl. ctr. of A. region; exps. copper from Chuquicamata; situated in desert, water supply 240 km by aqueduct from Andes; p. (1987) 204,577, (1992) 407,409 (prov.).

Antony, t., Hauts-de-Seine, **France;** brick wks., toys; sub. of Paris; p. (1990) 57,916.

Antrim, former co.; l. gov. dist., **N. Ireland;** fertile lowland a., arable agr.; borders L. Neagh in S.W. and A. mtns. in N.E.; p. (1991) 44,516.

Antrim, mkt. t., **N. Ireland;** on Lough Neagh; linen, nylon; p. (1991) 20,878.

Antsiranana, (Diego Suarez), t., extreme N. of **Madagascar;** oxygen plant; Fr. naval base; p. (1990) 54,418.

An-tung. See Dandong.

Antwerp, (Anvers), low-lying prov., N. **Belgium;** grain, flax; a. 2,859 km²; p. (1993) 1,619,613.

Antwerp, (Anvers), spt., **Belgium;** on Scheldt R., 88 km from sea; major transit pt. for EC, competes with Rotterdam; oil pt., refineries; diamonds; Gothic cath.; of artistic and historic interest; p. (1993) 465,102.

Anuradhapura, anc. cap., **Sri Lanka;** ctr. of Buddhism; comm. ctr. of irrigated rice-growing a. in dry zone; p. (1981) 36,248.

An-yang, c., Henan prov., **China;** coal, cotton ind.; former cap. of Shang dynasty; p. (1984) 534,400.

Anzhero-Sudzhensk, t., S.W. Siberia, **Russia;** nr. Tomsk; coal mng., mng. equipment pharmaceutics; p. (1989) 108,000.

Aomori, spt., N. Honshu, **Japan;** on A. Bay; cstl. tr. of timber, fish with Hokkaido; S. outlet of Seiken Tunnel between Honshu and Hokkaido; cap. of apple-growing A. prov.; p. (1990) 287,813.

Aosta, t., cap. of Val d'Aosta, N. **Italy;** in valley of Dora Baltea at node of trans-Alpine routes; iron inds.; Mont Blanc road tunnel links to Chamonix, Switzerland, opened 1964; cath., p. (1981) 37,682.

Apapa, spt., sub. of Lagos, **Nigeria;** on mainland opposite I. on which Lagos is situated; modern pt. terminus of W. Nigerian rly. system; exp. agr. prods.; imports industl. prods.

Apeldoorn, c., Gelderland, **Netherlands;** holiday resort; royal summer palace of Het Loo; p. (1993) 149,504.

Apennines, mtn. "backbone" of **Italy;** rich in minerals inc. Carrara marble; cultivation on lower slopes; earthquakes, in S.; barrier to E.–W. communications; hgst. alt. 2,916 m, (Grand Sasso d'Italia); length N.–S. 1,280 km; width 120 km.

Apia, spt., N. Upolu, cap. of **W. Samoa;** exp. agr. prods.; p. (1986) 32,196.

Apolda, t., Erfurt, **Germany;** ball-casting and museum; p. (est. 1989) 27,633.

Appalachian Mtns., parallel ranges between Atl. Oc. and Mississippi basin, stretching for 2,560 km from Me. to Ala., **USA;** afforestation, hydro-elec. power; coal in N., iron ore in O., region of human poverty; average alt. 900 m; Mt. Mitchell 2,039 m.

Appenzell, can., N.E. **Switzerland;** divided into the half-cans. Appenzell Inner-Rhoden, a. 174 km², cap. Appenzell; and Appenzell Ausser-Rhoden; textiles, agr.; a. 243 km², cap. Herisau; p. (1990) 65,100.

Appenzell, picturesque t., cap. of A. can., **Switzerland;** on R. Sitter; lace, embroidery.

Appian Way, anc. highway; runs from Rome to Campania and S. **Italy.**

Appleby, t., Eden, Cumbria, **Eng.;** mkt. t. on R. Eden; cas.; p. (1981) 2,384.

Appleton, c., Wis., **USA;** industl. c. in rich dairy dist.; p. (1990) 65,695 (c.), 315,121 (met. a. with Oshkosh-Neenah).

Apsheron, peninsula, E. **Azerbaijan;** on W. side of the Caspian; petroleum wells (nr. Baku) and mud volcanoes.

Apulia, region, S.E. **Italy;** hilly, cstl., pastoral plain; grain, fruits, livestock; wine, olive oil; a, 19,347 km²; p. (1992) 4,049,972.

Aqaba, t., **Jordan's** only spt. at head of G. of A., 88 km from Israeli Elat.; exp. phosphates, imports petroleum; p. (1983) 40,000.

Aqaba G., Red Sea, between **Sinai Peninsula** and **Saudi Arabia;** impt. Biblical waterway; few natural harbours, Dahab, Elat, Aqaba main pts; Elat ctr. of mng. a., and airpt.; length 160 km, width 24 km.

Aquila (L'Aquila), t., cap. of Abruzzi prov., **Italy;** on R. terrace of R. Aterno; mkt. and sm. inds. ass. with local farming; holiday resort; cath.; p. (1981) 63,678.

Aquitaine, region, S.W. **France;** inc. deps. Dordogne, Gironde, Landes, Lot-et-Garonne, Pyrénées-Atlantique; to W. and S.W. of Central Massif, to N. of Pyrenees, bordered on W. by Atl. Oc.; warm, wet, oceanic climate; rich agr. lowland; inc. Landes, reclaimed sandy area; ch. ts. Bordeaux, Toulouse; p. (1990) 2,795,800.

Arabia, peninsula, **S.W. Asia;** mainly desert plateau, lying between Red Sea and Persian Gulf; inc. Saudi Arabia, South Yemen, North Yemen, Oman, United Arab Emirates, Kuwait, Bahrain, Qatar; coffee, dates, gums, horses, camels; E. Arabia rich in oil reserves; a. 2,590,000 km²; p. 8,000,000.

Arabian Desert, E. **Egypt;** between R. Nile and Red Sea; alt. approx. 350–2,000 m; a. 207,200 km².

Arabian Mtns., ridge along W. and S.W. csts. of **Arabia;** volcanic, hgst. peaks in Yemen Arab Rep.; average alt. 1,500 m, rising to over 3,500 km.

Arabian Sea, N.W. part of Indian Oc., tr. in Arab dhows; width 2,880 km.

Aracaju, spt., cap. of Sergipe st., **Brazil;** sugar, soap, textiles, tanneries; p. (1991) 401,244.

Arad, new t. (1962) **Israel;** in Negev desert, nr. Beersheba; inds. to be based on gasfields at Zohar and Kanaim; chemicals.

Arad, t., **Romania;** industl., route ctr. on R. Mures; p. (1990) 203,198.

Arafura Sea, N. of Australia, S.W. of Papua-New Guinea, and E. of Timor.

Aragua, sm. upland cstl. st., **Venezuela;** lies in densely populated industl., agr., urban and political region of cty.; tropical climate; good road network; cap. Maracay in fertile Aragua valley; a. 7,014 km²; p. (1981) 891,623.

Araguaia, R., **Brazil;** trib. of Tocatins R.; splits into 2 parts in middle course to form Banaral I.; rapids; length 1,800 km.

Arak, t., **Iran;** mkt. and agr. processing ctr. for

surrounding region on Trans-Iranian rly.; carpets; p. (1986) 268,405.

Aral Sea (Aral'skoye More), inland sea with no outlet, **Uzbekistan/Kazakhstan;** fed by Amu-Dar'ya and Syr Dar'ya Rs.; sparse p. on shore but attempts to develop agr.; a. 63,805 km².

Aran Is.; Galway, **R.o.I.;** inc. anc. religious ctr. and I. of Inishmore; fishing; agr.; a. 47 km²; p. (1986) 735.

Arandelovac, t., Serbia, **Yugoslavia;** industl. a. based on local sources of refractory clays; tourist resort.

Aranjuez, t., **Spain;** 18th cent. planned t. on R. Tagus; mkt. gardens; strawberries, asparagus; p. (1981) 35,484.

Ararat, volcanic mtn., **Turkey;** supposed resting-place of Noah's Ark.; 5.168 m.

Ararat, t., Victoria, **Australia;** former gold rush t. on W. Highway and ctr. for Grampians; p. (1990) 8,015.

Aras (Araxes) R., flows from Bingöl Dağlari mtns. **(Turkey)** to Caspian Sea forming long sections of USSR–Iran frontier; valley in rich fruit growing a.; home of anc. civilisation; length 880 km.

Araucania, region., **Chile;** cap. Temuco; concentration of A. Indians, especially in Rio Tolten valley; a. 31,761 km²; p. (1992) 774,959.

Arbroath, royal burgh, Angus cst., **Scot.;** engin., textiles, fishing pt.; holiday resort; p. (1991) 23,474.

Arcachon, t., Gironde, S.W. **France;** on S. side of Bassin d'Arcachon, Bay of Biscay; fish. pt., oysters; resort; p. (1982) 13,664.

Arcadia, region of anc. **Greece** in Peloponnesus; tradition of pastoral agr. in dry a.; ch. c. was Megalopolis.

Arctic Ocean, almost landlocked sea extending from N. Pole to Atl. Oc.; flora and fauna of scientific interest; a. 14,089,600 km².

Ardabil, anc. c. in fertile agr. a., Azerbaijan, **Iran;** tr. and route ctr.; carpets; p. (1986) 283,710.

Ardal, t., **Norway;** on Sogne fiord; site of aluminium wks.

Ardèche, dep., S. **France;** Cevennes Mtns.; olives, wine, silk, minerals; cap. Privas; a. 55,530 km²; p. (1990) 277,600.

Ardennes, hilly wooded region, **Belgium,** N. **France, Luxembourg,** rising to over 600 m; infertile; heavy fighting in both world wars.

Ardennes, dep., N.E. **France;** farming, woollens, iron; cap. Mézières; a. 5,250 km²; p. (1990) 296,400.

Ardglass, sm. t., Down, **N. Ireland;** one of N.I.'s impt. fishing pts; p. (1991) 1,651.

Ardnacrusha, Clare, **R.o.I.;** power sta. on R. Shannon, 5 km N. of Limerick; p. (1986) 481.

Ardrishaig, sm. spt., Argyll and Bute, **Scot.;** on Loch Gilp, at entrance to Crinan canal; p. (1991) 1,315.

Ardrossan, burgh, Cunninghame, S.W. **Scot.;** resort and spt. on Firth of Clyde; oil storage, ship-bldg., road bitumen, engin.; p. (1991) 10,750.

Ards, l. gov. dist., **N. Ireland;** formerly part of Down; N. of Strangford L.; main t. Newtownards; p. (1991) 64,764.

Arecibo, spt., N. cst. **Puerto Rico;** sited in rich agr. a.; local hydroelec. power; p. (1990) 93,385.

Arendal, spt. **Norway;** on Skagerrak; wood pulp, aluminium, shipping; p. (1990) 24,985.

Arequipa, c., **Peru;** cap. of A. prov. and former Inca c.; impt. wool mkt.; alpaca wool inds.; growth point for prov. industl. development; copper mng. nearby; earthquakes frequent; p. (1990) 634,500.

Arezzo, c., cap. of Arezzo prov., Tuscany, **Italy;** hill site in basin within Apennines at junc. of valley routes; in mediaeval times ctr. of learning and the arts; birthplace of Petrarch and Vasari; Gothic cath.; mkt. for silk, wine, olives; p. (1981) 92,105.

Arfon, l. gov. dist., Gwynedd, **Wales;** borders Menai Straits and inc. Bangor and Caernarvon; p. (1993) 56,600.

Argenteuil, t., Val-d'Oise, **France;** N.W. sub. of Paris; industl., mkt. gardens; p. (1990) 94,162.

Argentina, fed. rep., **S. America;** 2nd. in a., 3rd. in p. of S. American sts.; p. predominantly of European origin and highly urbanised; varied relief and climate, inc. Andes, tropical N., Chaco, Pampas, Patagonia in S.; agr. less impt. internally than other S. American sts., yet provides most of exp., inc. meat, wool, wheat, maize, cotton; petroleum, natural gas; cap. Buenos Aires; new cap. to be built on fringe of Patagonia to decentralize power from Buenos Aires by 1989;

a. 2,797,109 km² p. (1991) 32,370,000.

Argos, c. of anc. **Greece;** N.E. Peloponnesus; leading c. in 7th cent. B.C. under King Pheidon; p. (1991) 78,884.

Argostólion, cap. of Cephalonia I., **Greece;** shipbldg.; earthquake 1953; p. (1981) 6,788.

Argyll, former co., N.W. **Scot.;** now divided between Highland and Strathclyde Regs.

Argyll and Bute, l. gov. dist., Strathclyde Reg., **Scot.;** rural a. N.W. of Glasgow conurb.; a. 6,754 km²; p. (1993) 63,260.

Århus, c., **Denmark;** prin. spt. on E. cst. Jutland; admin. ctr. of A. prov.; Gothic cath.; univ.; comm. and industl. ctr.; pt. processing inds., oil refining; p. (1987) 256,000.

Arica, spt., N. **Chile,** free zone; exp. tin, copper, sulphur mainly from Bolivia; rly. to La Paz and oil pipeline connects to Sica-Sica in Bolivia; p. (1987) 169,744.

Ariège, dep., S. **France;** Pyrenees in S., fertile lowland in N.; livestock, fruit, iron, copper; cap. Foix; a. 4,900 km²; p. (1990) 136,500.

Arizona, st., **USA;** home of Apache Indians; much desert, rainfall increasing to E.; many lge. irrigation schemes for cotton, grain, fruit, vegetables; inc. Col. Plateau and Grand Canyon to N.; copper, lead mng. and refining; prin. ts. Phoenix (cap.), Tucson; huge meteorite crater nr. Winslow; admitted to union 1912; st. flower Saguaro Cactus blossom; st. bird cactus wren; a. 295,024 km²; p. (1990) 3,665,228.

Arkansas, st., **USA;** highland in N.W., inc. Ozark, Ouachita mtns., lowland in S.E. where Arkansas R. and Mississippi alluvium; humid climate; cotton cultivation; bauxite, coal, petroleum; admitted to union 1836; st. flower Apple Blossom, st. bird Mockingbird; cap. Little Rock; a. 137,534 km²; p. (1990) 2,350,725.

Arkansas, R., **USA;** rises in Rockies, trib. of Mississippi; completion (1971) of 704 km waterway (17 dams and locks), opening Okla. and Ark. to sea; flows through impt. agr. as.; several major cs. on banks; length 2,334 kms.

Arkhangel'sk, c., major spt., **Russia;** on E. side Dvina estuary, White Sea; lge. harbour kept open in winter by ice breakers; fishery headquarters; inds. from local softwood resources; engin.; hydroelec. power; p. (1989) 416,000.

Arklow, t., spt., Wicklow, **R.o.I.;** fisheries, pottery; fertiliser plant under construction; resort; p. (1981) 8,646.

Arlberg, Alpine pass, 1,803 m; main western entry to Austria; rly. tunnel 10 km long; road tunnel (1979) 14 km long.

Arles, t., Provence, S. **France;** on Rhône delta; anc. Roman t.; historic bldgs and monuments; van Gogh and Gauguin painted here; p. (1990) 52,593.

Arlington, t., Texas, **USA;** aircraft, missiles; rapid expansion; p. (1990) 261,721.

Arlington, t., Va., **USA;** Arlington National Cemetery contains tombs of the Unknown Soldier and President Kennedy.

Arlon, t., cap. of Luxembourg prov., **Belgium;** p. (1982) 22,364.

Armadale, burgh, West Lothian, **Scot.;** 16 km S.W. Linlithgow; p. (1991) 8,958.

Armagh, former co.; l. gov. dist., N. **Ireland;** lowland in N. rising to over 450 m adjoins **R.o.I.** border; mainly rural; p. (1991) 51,817.

Armagh, c., N. **Ireland;** caths.; linen, whiskey; p. (1991) 14,265.

Armavir, c., Krasnodar Terr., **Russia** on Kuban R.; rly. junc.; engin.; food processing; p. (1989) 161,000.

Armenia, CIS, former rep. USSR; former a. divided between Turkey, Russia, Iran; mineral inds.; subtropical agr.; hydroelec. stas. under constr.; earthquake 1988; disturbances 1989; cap. Yerevan; a. 30.821 km²; p. (1992) 3·4 m.

Armenia, t., **Colombia;** coffee; p. (1992) 212,310.

Armentières, mftg. t., Nord, **France;** base of British operations against Lille in first world war; textiles; p. (1982) 55,913 (French met. a.).

Armidale, t., N.S.W., **Australia;** univ.; ctr. of New England wool producing dist.; p. (1981) 18,922.

Arnhem, c., cap. of Gelderland prov., **Neth.;** on R. Neder-Rhine; lge. tin smelter; lt. inds. using rubber and rayon; p. (1993) 133,272 (c.), 308,043 (met. a.).

Arnhem Land, N. part of N.T., **Australia;** an aboriginal reserve; bauxite worked, uranium finds.

Arno, R., central **Italy;** flows past Florence and Pisa into Mediterranean; Val d'Arno is the fruitful valley of the R.; length 120 km.

Arnold, t., Gedling, Notts., **Eng.;** almost continuous with Nottingham; hosiery, brick mkg.; p. (1981) 37,242.

Arnsberg, c. N. Rhine Westphalia, **Germany;** mftg. on R. Ruhr; p. (1989) 74,962.

Arnstadt, t., Erfurt, **Germany;** on R. Gera, 16 km S. of Erfurt; artificial silk, leather gds., engin.; p. (1989) 29,665.

Aroostook, dist., New England, **USA;** produces 12 per cent of USA potatoes.

Arran, I., Cunninghame, **Scot.;** in Firth of Clyde; contains many summer resorts; a. 427 km²; p. (1991) 4,474.

Arras, t., cap. of Pas-de-Calais dep., **France;** historic cap. of Artois; renowned for tapestry; agr. mkt.; brewing, textiles, metal inds.; almost destroyed in first world war; p. (1990) 42,715(t.), 79,607 (met. a.).

Árta, prov., Epirus, **Greece;** agr. area; Pindhos range; p. (1991) 78,884.

Artemovsk, t., **Ukraine;** industl. ctr. in Donets Basin; salt, coal, iron, mercury; p. (1990) 90,600.

Arthur's Seat, famous hill, Edinburgh, **Scot.;** 251 m.

Artois, former prov. of N. **France;** now mainly with dep. of Pas-de-Calais.

Aru Is., gr., **Indonesia;** S.W. of W. Irian; fertile; sago, rice, sugar, coconuts, tobacco; a. 8,402 km²; p. 18,139.

Aruba, I., Leeward Is., **Neth. Antilles;** closure of oil refinery (1985) which provided employment and one-third gov. receipts; shipping; guano; voted for indep. from gr. (1977) internal self-government granted 1986, (status aparte); a. 176 km²; p. (1991) 68,900.

Arun, l. gov. dist., West Sussex, **Eng.;** W. section of S. Downs and ts. of Arundel, Littlehampton and Bognor Regis; p. (1993) 133,400.

Arunachal Pradesh, new union terr. (1972), N.E. Assam, **India;** formerly N.E. Frontier Agency; in Himalayas bordering Tibet and Burma; tribal p.; cap. Itanagar; a. 81,424 km²; p. (1991) 864,558.

Arundel, t., Arun, West Sussex, **Eng.;** mkt. t. on Arun R.; Arundel Castle, seat of Duke of Norfolk; p. (1981) 2,235.

Arusha, t., **Tanzania;** S.W. of Mt. Meru; mkt. for coffee; H.Q. of E. African Common Market; airpt. at 1,388 m (W. of t.).

Aruwimi, R., **Zaïre;** trib. of R. Zaïre; route of Stanley's famous forest march in 1887; 992 km long.

Arvida, t., S. Quebec, **Canada;** aluminium plant; nearby Saguenay power development.

Arvika, t., N. of L. Vänern, **Sweden;** agr. machin. and implements, pianos, organs.

Asahikawa, c., Hokkaido, **Japan;** on Ishikari R.; industl., comm. and rly. ctr. for gr. agr. region; p. (1990) 359,069.

Asansol, t., W. Bengal, **India;** in Damodar valley; rly. junc.; coal mng., iron, steel; p. (1991) 262,000.

Ascension I., part of Brit. col. **St. Helena,** 1,216 km to S.E.; volcanic; ch. settlement Georgetown; nesting place of sooty tern; Brit. earth satellite sta. (1966); airstrip known as Miracle Mile; some arable and pastoral agr.; a. 88 km²; p. (1985) 1,700.

Aschaffenburg, t., Bavaria, **Germany;** pt. on R. Main and Trans-European waterway; cas.; synthetic fibres, scientific-based inds.; p. (1986) 59,600.

Aschersleben, t., Saxony-Anhalt, **Germany;** potash and lignite mng., chemicals, textiles, engin., horticulture; p. (1989) 33,891.

Ascoli Piceno, cath. c., central **Italy;** cap. of A.P. prov.; lies in wooded hills; agr. inds.; (1981) 54,298.

Ascot, v., Berks., **Eng.;** famous racecourse at Ascot Heath.

Ashanti, admin. region, central **Ghana;** formerly powerful native st.; timber, cocoa; growing importance of gold mines (15% Ghana's exp.); new mines opened 1984; cap. Kumasi; a. 24,390 km²; p. (1984) 2,089,683.

Ashbourne, t., Derbys. Dales, **Eng.;** nr. Dovedale; mkt. t.; quarrying, milk processing; p. (1981) 5,960.

Ashburton, t., Teignbridge, Devon, **Eng.;** old mkt. t., S. gateway to Dartmoor; anc. stannary t.; p. (1981) 3,564.

Ashburton, t., S. Island, **N.Z.;** ctr. of gr. wheat growing dist.; p. (1991) 24,435.

Ashby-de-la-Zouch, t., North West Leics., **Eng.;** hosiery; p. (1981) 11,518.

Ashby Woulds, t., North West Leics., Eng.; clay mng., pottery; p. (1981) 3,015.

Ashdod, pt., Israel; new modern deepwater pt. on Med. cst., 32 km S. of Jaffa.

Ashdown Forest, East Sussex, Eng.; heath and woodland; site of former iron industry.

Asheville, c., N.C., USA; economic and cultural ctr. of mtnous. region; winter resort; glass; p. (1984) 58,600 (c.), 165,600 (met. a.).

Ashfield, l. gov. dist., Notts., Eng.; comprises Sutton-in-Ashfield, Hucknall and Kirkby-in-Ashfield.; p. (1993) 109,800.

Ashford, t., l. gov. dist., Kent, Eng.; mkt. t., rly. works, p. (1993) 93,900 (dist.).

Ashikaga, c., Honshu, Japan; cultural ctr.; old silk-weaving ctr.; anc. school with library of Chinese classics; p. (1990) 167,687.

Ashington, t., Wansbeck, Northumberland, Eng.; coal mng., p. (1981) 27,658.

Ashkhabad, c., cap. of Turkmenistan; in foothills of Kopet-Dag mtns.; textiles, clothing, food processing; univ.; p. (1990) 407,200.

Ashland, t., Ky., USA; on R. Ohio; iron, steel, lumber, leather; p. (1980) 27,064.

Ashtabula, t., Ohio, USA; pt. on L. Erie handling iron ore, coal; many diversified inds.; p. (1980) 23,449.

Ashton-in-Makerfield, t. Gtr. Manchester, Eng.; nr. Wigan; former coal mng.; p. (1981) 29,341.

Ashton-under-Lyne, t., Tameside, Gtr. Manchester, Eng.; textiles, lt. engin., rubber, tobacco; p. (1981) 44,671.

Asia, largest continent, extends over nearly one-third of the land surface of the earth; chief mtn. ranges, Himalayas, Kunlun, Tien Shan, Altai, Tibetan plateau; ch. Rs., Ob, Yangtze, Yenisey, Lena, Amur, Hwang-ho, Mekong; deserts, Arabia, Thar, Takla Makan, Gobi; some very fertile valleys and plains; climate very varied, extreme in N., monsoonal in S. and E.; gold, coal, oil, iron, manganese, antimony, tin; principal countries in Asia: Turkey in Asia, Israel, Jordan, Iran, Iraq, Afghanistan, India, Pakistan, Sri Lanka, Burma, China, Vietnam, Indonesia, Thailand, Malaysia, Korea, Japan, Bangladesh, Kampuchea, Laos, Philippines, Korea, Syria, Lebanon, Taiwan, and Soviet Asia; industrialisation greatest in Japan, China, Korea, India, and Soviet Asia; a. c. 43,250,000 km²; p. (1984) 2,777,385,000 (58 per cent of world total).

Asia Minor. See Anatolia.

Asir, dist., S.W. Saudi Arabia; desert cstl. plain with parallel A. mtns.

Askja, volcanic crater, L. and lava plain, E. Iceland; surrounded by Dyngju-fjöll Hills; alt. 1,450 m.

Asmara, c., Eritrea; alt. 2,226 m; on rly.; textiles, matches, soap, brewing; p. (1985) 284,748.

Asnières, t., sub. N.W. Paris, Hauts-de-Seine, France; regattas; p. (1990) 72,250.

Aspra Spitia, t. central Greece; new industl. t. close to Andikira Bay; aluminium wks.

Aspull, t., Gtr. Manchester, Eng.; nr. Wigan; former coal mng.; p. (1981) 6,816.

Assam, st., India; on Brahmaputra R.; valley enclosed by mtns.; forested; extensive tea plantations; rice, cotton, coal; oil development at Rudrasagar; former cap. Shillong; since 1956 4 new sts. carved out – Nagaland (1963), Meghalaya, Manipur, Tripura (1972), and union terrs. of Arunachal Pradesh and Mizoram (1972); a. (1972) 121,973 km²; p. (1991) 22,414,322.

Assen, t., prov. cap. Drenthe, Neth.; route ctr.; food processing; p. (1993) 51,713.

Assiniboine, R., Manitoba, Canada; joins Red R. at Winnipeg; 720 km long.

Assisi, t., Umbria, central Italy; 24 km S.E. of Perugia; birthplace of St. Francis; cath. and old cas.; p. (1981) 24,440.

Assyria, gr. anc. empire, northern plain Mesopotamia (Iraq), cap. Nineveh; drained by R. Tigris; now mainly pastoral farming a.

Astara, pt., Azerbaijan; on Caspian Sea, at frontier with Iran; natural gas pipeline; p. (1990) 13,000.

Asti, t., Italy; route industl., comm. ctr.; cath.; sparkling wines; p. (1981) 77,681.

Astin Tagh, (Aerchin Shan), mtn. range, S., Sinkiang, China; N. branch of Kunlun mtn. system which separates Tibet from Turkestan; rises to 5,000 m.

Astrakhan', c., Russia; major air and sea pt. on delta of R. Volga, 80 km from Caspian

Sea; handles petroleum, timber; lge. fishing fleet; caviar; food and pt. processing inds.; astrakhan fur; cap. A. oblast; univ.; p. (1989) 509,000.

Asturias, region and former kingdom, N.W. Spain; S. of Bay of Biscay; now Oviedo prov.; isolated from rest of Spain by Cantabrian mtns.; coal mng; p. (1987) 1,115,016.

Asunción, c., cap. of Paraguay; at confluence of Rs. Paraguay and Pilcomayo; 25 per cent of p. of Paraguay in and around A.; admin., industl., comm. ctr.; cath.; p. (1990) 607,700 (met. a.).

Aswan, t. and prov., Upper Egypt; on Nile at first cataract; anc. name Syene. Aswan dam built 1902, 5 km S. of t., to control Nile flood; lge. cement plant; univ. proposed; p. (1986) 191,461 (t.), (1991) 925,000 (prov.).

Aswan High Dam (107 m high) opened 1971, on R. Nile, Egypt, 6 km S. of old Aswan dam, has harnessed R. to bring electricity and irrigation to hundreds of vs. and prevent Nile's flood from being lost into Mediterranean. See also Nile.

Asyût, major c. and prov. of Upper Egypt; nr. A. dam on Nile R.; anc. Lycopolis; noted pottery, wood, ivory carving; caravan tr. ctr.; cap. of A. prov.; p. (1986) 273,191 (c.), (1991) 2,532,000 (prov.).

Atacama, region Chile; cap. Copiapo; a. 75,705km²; p. (1992) 230,786.

Atacama Desert, N. Chile; arid coastal tract rich in nitrates; one of world's driest deserts.

Atami, t., Honshu, Japan; on Sagami Bay; seaside hot-spring resort; p. (1990) 47,291.

Atbara, t., Sudan; at confluence of Atbara R. with Nile; heavy inds.; international airpt.; p. (1983) 73,000.

Atbara R., or Black Nile, Ethiopia and Sudan; trib. of Nile; provides irrigation water for Sudan; length 1,264 km.

Athelney, hill, formerly encircled by marsh nr. Taunton, Somerset, Eng.; between the Rs. Tone and Parret; King Alfred's hiding-place.

Athens (Athínai), c., cap of Greece; on plain of Attica; admin., economic and cultural ctr.; varied mnfs., notably textiles; anc. c. of Greek art and learning; Acropolis and many splendid temples; univ.; airpt; p. (1981) 885,737 (c.) (1991) 3,096,775 (met. a.).

Athens, t., Ga., USA; univ.; cotton gds., lumber; p. (1984) 42,500 (c.), 136,600 (met. a.).

Athens, t., Ohio, USA; univ.; coal, lt. inds.; p. (1980) 19,743.

Atherstone, t., North Warwicks., Eng.; N. of Coventry; mkt. t., coal mng, footwear, granite quarrying.

Athlone, t., Westmeath, R.o.I.; on R. Shannon; radio sta.; textiles; p. (1986) 8,815.

Atholl, dist., N. Perth and Kinross, Scot.; extensive deer forests and grouse moors; a. 1,166 km².

Athos, peninsula, Khalkidhiki, N.E. Greece; Mt. Athos (2,034 m) at S. tip, known as Holy Mountain, home of monastic community; ch. t. Karyes.

Athy, t., Kildare, R.o.I.; on Grand Canal; agr. machin.; p. (1986) 4,734.

Atitlán L., S.W. Guatemala; volcanic; famed for beauty; dense p. on shore; maize, fishing; a. 137 km².

Atlanta, c., st. cap. Ga., USA; univ.; cotton, paper, farm implements, printing, clothing; p. (1990) 394,017 (c.), 2,833,511 (met. a.).

Atlantic City, c., N.J., USA; summer resort, convention c.; p. (1990) 37,986 (c.), 319,000 (met. a.).

Atlantic Ocean, 2nd lgst ocean; a. est. 82,440,000 km²; connected to Pac. Oc. by Panama Canal; central ridge of volcanic activity runs S. from Iceland to Antarctic, some peaks emerging as Is. mainly in N. (e.g. Azores, Ascension, Tristan da Cunha); S, mainly a barren waste of water; chief deeps: Milwaukee Deep (9,225 m) nr. Bahamas and Nares Deep (8,531 m) nr. Puerto Rico.

Atlas, mtn. range, N.W. Africa; extends 2,400 km through Morocco, Algeria, to Tunisia; formed of several chains; mineralised, roads across passes; long been home of Berber tribes; average height 2,500–3,000 m; hgst. peak Jebel Toubkal, 4,141 m.

Atlixco Valley, t., Mexico; 16 km S.W. of Puebla; fertile volcanic soils; wheat, fruit, vegetables; p. (1990) 104,186.

Attica, (Attiki), dep., Greece; agr., serving cap.

Athens; a. 3,761 km²; p. (1991) 3,522,769.

Attleboro, c., Mass., **USA**; founded (1669) by immigrants from English Attleborough (Norfolk); jewellery, silverware; p. (1980) 34,196.

Attock, t., **Pakistan**; on Indus R. between Peshawar and Islamabad; oil wells, oil refining; impt. crossing of R. Indus.

Atyrau, **(Guryev)** c., **Kazakhstan**; pt. on R. Ural at entrance to Caspian Sea; oil refining; pipe-line to Orsk; p. (1990) 151,400.

Aubagne, t., Bouches-du-Rhône, **France**; bricks, tiles, corks, meat processing; p. (1981) 38,571.

Aube, dep., N.E. **France**; arid, infertile chalk in ctr. and N.W.; wooded and fertile S.E.; drained by Seine and A. Rs.; cap. Troyes; a. 6,024 km²; p. (1990) 289,200.

Aubervilliers, t., Seine-St. Denis, **France**; sub. of Paris; industl.; p. (1990) 67,836.

Auburn, t., N.Y., **USA**; shoes, woollens, farm implements; st. prison; p. (1980) 32,548.

Aubusson, t., Creuse dep., **France**; sited on Creuse R.; fine tapestries and carpets; p. (1982) 6,153.

Auch, t., cap. of Gers dep., **France**; agr., mkt., tr. in Armagnac brandy; agr. processing; p. (1990) 24,728.

Auchterarder, burgh, Perth and Kinross, **Scot.**; 24 km S.W. of Perth; health resort on S. slopes of vale of Strathearn; woollen inds.; p. (1991) 3,549.

Auchtermuchty, burgh, North East Fife, **Scot.**; at S. foot of Lomond Hills, 40 km N.E. of Alloa; distilling; p. (1991) 1,932.

Auckland, spt., c., N.I., **N.Z.**; lgst. c. in N.Z.; seat of government 1845–64; univ.; extensive tr. and shipping; sawmills, sugar refinery, shipbldg., glass; steelwks. projected 40 km S. of A., in Waikato iron sand a.; p. (1991) 315,668 (c.), 855,571 (urban a.).

Aude, dep., S. **France**; mtnous.; fertile N., salt from S. cstl. lagoons; drained by A. R. to Mediterranean; cap. Carcassonne; a. 6,340 km² p. (1990) 298,700.

Audenshaw, t., Gtr. Manchester, **Eng.**; metals, leather, pharmaceuticals; p. (1981) 10,744.

Aue, t., Saxony, **Germany**; 32 km S.E. of Zwickau; uranium mng., metallurgy, textiles; p. (1989) 25,435.

Aughrim, v., Galway, **R.o.I.**; battle (1691) between William III and James II; p. (1991) 756.

Augsburg, c., Bavaria, **Germany**; at confluence of Rs. Lech and Wertach; cath.; theological institute; major industl. ctr., textiles, engin.; route ctr.; p. (1990) 258,300.

Augusta, t., Sicily, **Italy**; on E. cst. peninsula; gd. harbour used as naval base; fishing; lubricants; p. (1981) 38,900.

Augusta, c., Georgia, **USA**; pt.; on Savannah R. and boundary with S.C.; cotton, cotton-seed oil, chemicals, foundries; p. (1984) 46,000 (c.), (1990) 397,000 (met. a.).

Aulnay-sous-Bois, t., Seine-St. Denis, **France**; residtl. sub. of Paris; p. (1990) 82,537.

Aurangabad, t., admin. ctr., Maharashtra, **India**; textiles, grain tr.; p. (1991) 573,000.

Aurès, mtn. massif, **Algeria**; Berber stronghold.

Aurignac, v., Haute-Garonne, **S. France**; at foot of Pyrenees; caves, paleolithic remains.

Aurillac, t., cap., mkt. t. for dep. of Cantal, **France**; cheeses, umbrellas, leather goods; p. (1990) 32,654.

Aurora, t., Ill., **USA**; rly. wks., foundries, office equipment; p. (1990) 357,000 (met. a. with Elgin).

Auschwitz. See Oświęcim.

Aussig. See Usti Nad Labem.

Austin, st. cap., Texas, **USA**; educational and artistic ctr., st. univ.; food processing; international airpt.; p. (1990) 465,622 (c.), 782,000 (met. a.).

Australasia, div. of **Oceania**; inc. Australia, Tasmania, N.Z., New Guinea and neighbouring archipelagos.

Australia, Commonwealth of, lgst. I., smallest continent in world; forms part of **Australasia**; Cook took possession for Britain 1770; Commonwealth proclaimed 1901; fed. of N.S.W., Victoria, Queensland, S.A., W. Australia, Tasmania; inc. also Cap. Terr. (Canberra) and N.T.; p. and inds. concentrated around cst. and in st. caps.; 41 per cent live in Gtr. Sydney and Melbourne; agr. economy (sheep, wheat, dairying) giving way to mineral inds. esp. in W.A. where lge. and diverse

deposits abound; offshore petroleum deposits; N. cst. tropical, interior dry, S.E. cst. more moderate, Mediterranean climate in S.W.; mtns. in E. form Gr. Dividing Range separating E. cst. from interior, where plains drained by Murray-Darling and L. Eyre R. systems (used for hydroelec. power and irrigation); cap. Canberra; a. 7,682,300 km²; p. (1992) 7·5 m.

Australian Alps, form S. part of Gr. Dividing Range, between E. cst. and interior, **Australia**; extend for 320 km.; contain hgst. mtns. in Australia; Mount Kosciusko (2,228 m.); snow melt vital for irrigation of S.E.; popular tourist and naturalist a.

Australian Antarctic Terr., part of **Antarctica**; between 145° E. and 160° E. and S. of 60° S. excluding Adélie Land; research stas. of Mawson, Davis and Casey.

Australian Bight, Gr.; gr. cstl. indentation S. of Nullarbor Plain, **Australia**.

Australian Capital Territory, fed. terr. surrounding Canberra, seat of Fed. Govt. of **Australia**; also inc. a. around Jervis Bay, originally planned to serve as pt. p. (1991) 292,700.

Austria, rep., **Europe**; after long and glamorous history under the Hapsburg, instability between Austria and Hungary a cause of first world war; forcibly incorporated in German Reich, 1938, liberated 1945, recovered indep. 1955; almost entirely within Alps; drained mainly by Danube; continental climate; magnificent scenery generates a major tourist ind. but much food must be imported; forests and timber inds.; mineralised, iron-ore of Styria; hydro-elec.; inds. located in ts.; cap. Vienna; joined EU 1995; a. 83,898 km²; p. (1991) 7·8 m, mainly Roman Catholic.

Austria, Lower, st., **Austria**; impt. agr. a.; cap. Vienna; a. (excluding Vienna) 18,384 km²; p. (excluding Vienna) (1991) 1,480,927.

Auvergne, old prov. and present region of **France**; inc. deps. **Allier, Cantal, Haute-Loire, Puy-de-Dôme**; part of Massif Central; volcanic scenery; ch. t. Clermont-Ferrand; p. (1990) 1,321,200.

Auvergne Mtns., mtns., central **France**; in N.W. of Central Massif; highest peak Puy de Sancy in Mt. Dore, 1,887 m; volcanic landscape.

Auxerre, t., cap. of Yonne dep., **France**; comm. and industl. ctr.; wine; tr.; Gothic cath.; p. (1990) 40,597.

Ava, c., **Myanmar**; on the Irrawaddy R.; former cap.; many pagodas, now ruins; bridge over R.

Avebury, v., Wilts,. **Eng.**; mediaeval v. outside Neolithic circle and avenues, nr. Silbury Hill; lgst. prehistoric structure in England.

Aveiro, t., **Portugal**; on Vouga estuary, connected to sea by canal; fish. pt. salt from lagoons; p. (1981) 28,625.

Avellaneda, industl. sub. of Buenos Aires, **Argentina**; hides, wool; p. (1980) 330,654.

Avellino, t., cap. of A. prov., **Italy**; on motorway from Naples to W.; monastery; sulphur mng. and refining; hats; p. (1981) 56,892.

Aversa, t. **Italy**; in fertile plain of Campania; agr. and route ctr.; p. (1981) 50,525.

Avesta, t., Kopparberg, **Sweden**; on Dal R.; iron, aluminium and charcoal wks.

Aveyron, dep., **France**; on S.W. rim of Central Massif, inc. Causses limestones; extensive forests; grain, dairying, sheep; coal; cap. Rodez; a. 8,767 km²; p. (1990) 270,100.

Aviemore, t., Badenoch and Strathspey, **Scot.**; on R. Spey, 19 km S.W. of Grantown; winter sports; p. (1993) 2,214.

Avignon, t., cap. of Vaucluse, dep., **France**; anc. Roman t. at crossing of R. Rhône; Provençal tourist ctr.; diversified inds. inc. wine tr.; p. (1990) 89,440 (t.), 181,136 (met. a.).

Avila, t., cap. of A. prov., **Spain**; in Old Castile; univ., cath.; mediaeval architecture; birth-place of St. Teresa; p. (1991) 45,000, 172,656 (prov.).

Avon, non-met. co., S. **Eng.**; based on Lower Avon valley and Severnside; major ctrs. of p. at Bristol and Bath; pt. at Avonmouth; cstl. resort of Weston-super-Mare; bordered by Mendips in S.; a. 1,336 km²; p. (1993) 973,300.

Avon, R., Avon/Wiltshire, **Eng.**; flows from Cotswolds to enter Bristol Channel at Avonmouth; spectacular limestone gorge between Bristol and the sea; length 128 km.

Avon, R., Warwicks, **Eng.**; flows past Stratford-on-A., to reach Severn R. at Tewkesbury; fertile agr. valley; string of ts. along course; length 152 km.

Avon, R., Wilts./Hants./Dorset, **Eng.**; flows past Salisbury into English Channel at Christchurch; length 112 km.

Avonmouth, outport of Bristol, at mouth of R. Avon, **Eng.**; docks; seed crushing, petrol refinery, non-ferrous metal and chemical plants.

Avranches, t., Manche, **France**; Normandy mkt. t.; cider and dairy produce; p. (1982) 10,419.

Awe, Loch, Argyll and Bute, **Scot.**; 13 km W. of Inveraray, bordered by Ben Cruachan; a. 41 km², length 40 km; salmon and trout fishing; hydroelec. sta. at Cruachan.

Axholme, Isle of, flat lowland a., Bootnferry, N.W. Lincs., **Eng.**; W. of Trent R.; drained by Vermuyden in 17th cent.

Axminster, t., East Devon, **Eng.**; brushes; flour and sawmills; carpet and press tool mftg.

Ayacucho (Huamanga.) c., and prov., **Peru**; founded by Pizarro in 1539; lies in equable fertile valley; p. (1990) 101,600 (t.), 566,400 (prov.).

Aydin, t., **Turkey**; anc. Tralles; rly. and agr. tr. ctr. for surrounding a.; p. (1985) 90,449, (1990) 824,816 (prov.).

Ayers Rock, N.T., **Australia**; giant terra-cotta monolith rising abruptly to 335 m; sacred to Aborigines; major tourist attraction.

Aylesbury, co. t., Aylesbury Vale, Bucks., **Eng.**; mkt. t.; expanded t.; p. (1981) 48,159.

Aylesbury Vale, l. gov. dist., Bucks., **Eng.**; a. in N.W. of co. inc. Aylesbury and Buckingham; p. (1993) 151,600.

Aylesford, mkt. t., Kent, **Eng.**; N.W. Maidstone.

Ayr, royal burgh, Kyle and Carrick, **Scot.**; pt. on F. of Clyde, 48 km S.W. of Glasgow; Burns born nearby; p. (1991) 47,962.

Ayrshire, former co. **Scot.**; now part of Strathclyde Region.

Aysgarth, v. Richmondshire, North Yorks., **Eng.**; on R. Ure in Wensleydale; famous waterfalls.

Ayutthaya, t., **Thailand**; former cap., on Menam Chao Phraya R. delta; p. (1980) 47,189.

Azarbaijan, E. and W., provs., N. **Iran**; border Azabaijan and Turkey; cap. (E.A.) Tabriz; cap. (W.A.) Rezayeh; p. (1986) 4,180,376 (E) and 1,989,935 (W).

Azerbaijan, CIS, former rep. USSR; Transcaucasia, rep.; Caucasus and Lesser Caucasus separated by hot dry irrigated steppe; impt. oil ind.; disturbances 1989; 86,661 km²; p. (1992) 7·2 m.

Azores, gr. of physically and climatically attractive Is. in mid-Atlantic about 1,440 km W. of Lisbon, **Portugal**; partial indep. by regional gov. (1977); volcanic; fruit, wine; ch. spts: Ponta Delgada, Horta (a major whaling ctr.), Angra do Heroismo; U.S. air bases on Terceira I.; a. 2,569 km²; p. (1986) 253,500.

Azov Sea (Azouskoye More), Ukraine/Russia; joins Black Sea by Kerch strait; receives Don R.; fisheries; a. 36,000 km².

Azpeitia, t., N. **Spain**; mineral springs; local quarrying; timber inds., agr. processing; p. (1992) 12,509.

Azraq Desert Nat. Park, Jordan; first Jordanian nat. park around oasis of Azraq, 96 km E. of Amman; a. 3,900 km².

B

Baalbek, c., **Lebanon**, S.W. Asia; old Heliopolis; ruins; tourism.

Bab-el-Mandeb, strait connecting Red Sea and Indian Oc.; dangerous but impt. shipping lane; length 32 km, width 27 km.

Babergh, l. gov. dist., S. Suffolk, **Eng.**; inc. Sudbury and Hadleigh; p. (1993) 79,600.

Babylon, anc. cap. of Babylonian Empire, in Euphrates valley about 96 km S. of Baghdad, **Iraq.**

Bacau, t., E. **Romania**; on R. Bistrita; oil, sawmilling, textiles; p. (1990) 197,192.

Bacolod City, t., Negros, **Philippines**; sm. pt.; exp. sugar; p. (1990) 364,180.

Bacton, v., Norfolk, **Eng.**; terminal for S. gasfields in N. Sea.

Bacup, t., Rossendale, S.E. Lancs., **Eng.**; 32 km N. of Manchester; textiles, felts, footwear; p. (1981) 15,259.

Badagri, t., W. of Lagos, **Nigeria**; on the Bight of Benin: formerly a gr. slave pt.; coir sacks.

Badajoz, lgst. prov., **Spain**; gr. reclamation scheme in progress; a. 21,624 km²; p. (1991) 643,245.

Badajoz, c., cap. of B. prov., W. **Spain**, in Estremadura; anc. fortress c.; transit tr.; p. (1991) 129,737.

Badalona, c. nr. Barcelona, **Spain**; shipbldg.; p. (1991) 206,120.

Baden, t., **Switzerland**; health resort, mineral springs; p. (1986) 14,054.

Baden-Baden, t., Baden-Württemberg. **Germany**; fashionable spa; p. (1986) 49,300.

Baden-bei-Wien, wat. pl., **Austria**; 22 km S.W. of Vienna; p. (1991) 23,998.

Badenoch and Strathspey, l. gov. dist., Highland Reg., **Scot.**: mtn. a. S. of Inverness inc. Aviemore and Kingussie; p. (1993) 11,100.

Baden-Württemberg, *Land*, **Germany**; created 1952; bounded by Rhine in W., drained by Neckar and Donau R. systems; mtnous., inc. Black Forest and Swabian Jura; received much immigrant ind. from E. Europe, so encouraging prosperous and diversified industl. structure; several impt. industl. regions centred on Mannheim, Karlsruhe, and cap. Stuttgart; a. 35,750 km²; p. (1992) 10,002,000.

Bad Lands, S.D., **USA**; stretches of infertile badly eroded soil.

Badrinath, mtn. and t., Uttar Pradesh, **India**; pilgrim shrine of Vishnu.

Badulla, t., **Sri Lanka**; tea; anc. t.; rly. terminus; ctr. of tea estates; p. (1981) 32,954.

Badwater, salt pool, Cal., **USA**; 85 m below sea-level, lowest point in N. America.

Baeza, t., S. **Spain**; anc. Moorish c.; olives, wine; p. (1981) 12,841.

Baffin B., between **Greenland** and **Canada**; joined to Atl. Oc. by Davis Strait, to Arctic Oc. by Nares Strait; open 4 months per year; B.I., in W., ctr. of Arctic research and communications; length 1,120 km, width 100–650 km.

Bagé, t., S. **Brazil**; ctr. of cattle tr.; p. (1985) 106,300.

Baghdad, c., cap. of **Iraq**; anc. c. on R. Tigris; terminus Baghdad rly.; airport; univ.; textiles, gum, bricks, tiles, metal inds.; p. (1987) 3,841,268.

Baghdad, prov. or liwa, **Iraq**; between Iran and Syrian Desert; inc. some of the most fertile lands in the Tigris and Euphrates valleys; p. (1987) 4,648,609.

Baghlan, t., **Afghanistan**; new industl. t. in ctr. of sugar producing a.; alt. 518 m; p. (1982) 41,240.

Bagnolet, t., Seine-St. Denis, **France**; sub. of Paris; famous for "plaster of Paris" from local gypsum; textiles; p. (1982) 32,557.

Bagshot, t., Surrey Heath, Surrey, **Eng.**; heath of same name; historically old postal town, 42 km S.W. of London; residtl.

Baguio, Luzon, N.W. of Manila, summer cap. of **Philippines**, alt. 1,500 m; gold mines; p. (1990) 183,102.

Bahamas, indep. st. (1973) within Brit. Commonwealth, **W.I.**; more than 700 coral atolls; subtropical climate; infertile but valuable tourist tr.; exp. crayfish; cap. Nassau; a. 11,406 km²; p. (1992) 264,000.

Bahawalpur, t., **Pakistan**; former cap. of B. princely st.; impt. bridging point over Sutlej R.; p. (1981) 133,956.

Bahia, st., **Brazil**; cap. Salvador; cattle, cacao, sugar, coffee, tobacco; oil, extensive mineral deposits; a. 560,139 km²; p. (1991) 11,801,810.

Bahia Blanca, spt., **Argentina**; industl. ctr., oil refining; prin. shipping point of S.; exp. oil, grain, wool, hides; p. (1991) 271,467.

Bahrain Is., indep. st. (1971) in Persian G.; low sandy Is. linked by road causeway to Saudi Arabia (1985); springs allow cultivation of dates; oil wells, oil and aluminium refining; trading ctr., declining importance of agr. as incr. salinity of traditional water supplies; cap. Manamah; airpt. at Muharraq; a. 678 km²; p. (1993) 538,000.

Baia, historic v., Campania, **Italy**; beautifully situated on Bay of Naples; celebrated Roman pleasure resort; p. (1981) 2,087.

Baia-Mare, t., N.W. **Romania**; on Somesul R., in region mining copper, lead, zinc, gold, silver; mtn. resort; p. (1990) 150,403.

Baikal L. *See* **Baykal L.**

Baildon, t., West Yorks., **Eng.**; nr. Bradford; moorland resort; p. (1981) 15,904.

Baja, t., **Hungary**; impt. bridging point of R. Danube in Gr. Plain; p. (1984) 40,000.

Baja California. *See* **Lower California**.

Bakar, pt., **Croatia** (formerly Yugoslavia); S. of Rijeka; new pt. and oil harbour.

Bakersfield, c., Cal., **USA**; ctr. of oil prod. and refining; aircraft assembly; p. (1990) 174,820 (c.), 543,000 (met. a.).

Bakewell, t., Derbys Dales. **Eng.**; tourist ctr. Peak District; agr., mng.; p. (1981) 3,946.

Bakhchisaray, t., Crimea, **Ukraine**; old cap. of Tartar Khans; copper, leather; p. (1990) 25,700.

Bakhuis Gebergte mtns., W. **Suriname**; major aluminium complex based on local power and bauxite.

Bakony Wald, mtns., **Hungary**; forested; vine-yards; bauxite, manganese.

Baku, cap. of **Azerbaijan**; pt. on Caspian Sea; univ.; oil-wells; oil pipeline connects with Batumi; shipbldg.; p. (1990) 1,148,700.

Bala, t., Meirionnydd, Gwynedd, N. **Wales**; nr. Denbigh, lt. engin., resort; p. (1981) 1,848.

Bala, L., Meirionnydd, Gwynedd, N. **Wales**; drained by the Dee.

Balaklava, pt., S. Crimea, **Ukraine**; scene of the charge of the Light Brigade (1854).

Balaton, L., lgst. in **Hungary**; a. 596 km²; long history of settlement in a.; shores forested; vineyards; tourism.

Balbriggan, spt., Dublin, **R.o.I.**; hosiery; p. (1986) 5,680.

Baldock, t., North Herts., **Eng.**; on N. edge of Chiltern Hills and Gr. N. Road; hosiery, malting, lt. engin.; p. (1981) 6,679.

Baldwin, t., N.Y., **USA**; on S. Long I.; fisheries; p. (1980) 31,630.

Balearic Is., in Mediterranean Sea, **Spain**; inc. Majorca, Minorca, Ibiza, Formentera; limestone scenery and mild climate encourage tourism which has swamped Moorish influence; agr.; ch. t. Palma; a. 5,014 km²; p. (1991) 739,501.

Bali, I. off Java, **Indonesia**, in Lesser Sundas; equable climate, fertile soil, luxurious vegetation; p. mainly engaged in agr.; noted native dancers; a. (inc. Lombok) 10,196 km²; p. (1983) 2,593,900.

Balikesir, t. and prov., **Turkey**; rly. junc.; ctr. of fertile agr. region; p. (1990) 973,314. (prov), 172,570 (t.).

Balikpapan, t., Kalimantan, **Indonesia**; new oil refinery; p. (1980) 280,875.

Baliuag, t., Luzon, **Philippines**; rice, bamboo hats, mkt.; p. (1990) 89,719.

Balkan Mtns., **Bulgaria**; fine alpine meadows, forested; tourism based on Sofia; average alt. 900–1,200 m, hgst. point Botev Peak, 2,377 m.

Balkan Peninsula, the easternmost of the three gr. southern peninsulas of Europe, between the Adriatic and Ionian seas on the W., and the Black Sea, Sea of Marmara and the Aegean Sea on the E., with an area of, roughly, 500,000 km²; includes Turkey, Yugoslavia, Croatia, Slovenia, Bosnia, Bulgaria, Albania, Greece; ch. mtns.: Rodopi, Pindhus, Balkan; ch. Rs.; Danube, Maritsa, Vardar; ch. Ls.; Scutari, Okhrida.

Balkh. *See* **Wazirabad**.

Balkhash, t., **Kazakhstan**; on N. shore of L.B.; smelting, esp. local copper; vermiculite deposits nearby, salt; p. (1990) 87,400.

Balkhash, L., **Kazakhstan**; receives Ili R., but has no outlet; salt water; fishing, salt-panning; a. 17,301 km².

Ballachulish, v., Argyll and Bute, **Scot.**; on S. shore of Loch Leven, N.E. of Oban; tourism; ferry across Loch Linnhe, new road bridge; p. (1991) 557.

Ballarat, t., Victoria, **Australia**; 117 km N.W. of Melbourne, former gold-field dist.; mkt. ctr.; fine examples of 19th century architecture; 2 caths.; p. (1986) 75,210.

Ballater, burgh, Kincardine and Deeside, **Scot.**; on R. Dee, 59 km S.W. of Aberdeen; tourist resort, mineral wells; nr. the royal Highland residence of Balmoral; p. (1991) 1,362.

Ballina, t., spt., Mayo, **R.o.I.**; agr. machin. salmon fishing; p. (1991) 6,714.

Ballina, t., N.S.W., **Australia**; at mouth of Richmond R.; resort, fishing; p. (1981) 9,738.

Ballinasloe, t., Galway and Roscommon, **R.o.I.**; agr. ctr.; cattle mkt.; terminus of Grand Canal; p. (1986) 6,125.

Ballinrobe, t., Mayo, **R.o.I.**; E. of Lough Mask; trout fishing; p. (1986) 1,270.

Ballybunion, resort, Kerry, **R.o.I.**; at mouth of R. Shannon; p. (1986) 1,452.

Ballycastle, spt., mkt. t., Moyle, **N. Ireland**; abbey and cas. ruins; seaside resort; p. (1991) 4,005.

Ballyclare, t., Newtownabbey, **N. Ireland**; paper, linen, dyeing, asbestos-cement prod.; p. (1991) 7,108.

Ballymena, mkt. t., l. gov. dist., **N. Ireland**; on R. Braid; linen and dyeing; p. (1991) 28,112 (t.), 56,541, (dist.).

Ballymoney, mkt. t., l. gov. dist., **N. Ireland**; 64 km N.W. of Belfast; linen; p. (1991) 24,198 (dist), 7,818 (t.).

Ballynahinch, t., Down, **N. Ireland**; 19 km from Downpatrick; p. (1991) 4,591.

Ballyshannon, spt., Donegal, **R.o.I.**; at mouth of R. Erne; salmon fishery; resort; hydro-electric power plant; p. (1986) 2,573.

Balmoral Cas., Kincardine and Deeside, **Scot.**; royal residence, on R. Dee, 13 km W. of Ballater.

Balsas, R., and lowland, **Mexico**; R. flows E. to Pacific through rich agr. valley of Morelos; length 800 km.

Baltic Sea, an arm of Atl. Oc., opens into N. Sea by narrow channels between Denmark and Sweden; joined to Arctic by White Sea Canal; low, dune-backed cst.; shallowness, tendency to freeze reduce its importance for shipping; a. 414,000 km².

Baltic White Canal. *See* **Volga Baltic Waterway**.

Baltimore, industl. c., spt., Md., **USA**; fine harbour nr. head of Chesapeake B.; pt. processing and diversified inds.; steel wks. at Sparrow's Point; educational, cultural ctr., seat of Johns Hopkins univ.; many fine public bldgs. despite disastrous fire of 1904; p. (1990) 736,014 (c.), 2,382,172 (met. a.).

Baltoro Glacier, Karakoram Mtns., **Pakistan**; drains into tribs. of Indus; alt. 3,532 m.

Baluchistan, prov. (revived 1970), **Pakistan**; S. of Afghanistan; largely desert and rugged barren mtns.; cap. Quetta; cereals, potatoes, fruits, dates; new oil and natural gas discoveries; a. 137,011 km²; p. (1981) 4,332,349.

Bamako, cap. c. of **Mali**; impressive site at foot of escarpment on R. Niger; admin. and agr. tr. ctr.; R. pt.; univ.; main industl. ctr. of Mali; p. (1984) 740,000.

Bamberg, c., Bavaria, **Germany**; cath.; textiles, elec., leather and engin. inds.; impt. R. pt. on Trans-European waterway; p. (1986) 69,600.

Bamburgh, t., Northumberland, **Eng.**; former cap. of Bernicia and Northumbria; cas.; birthplace of Grace Darling.

Banaba I. *See* **Ocean I.**

Banagher, v., Offaly, **R.o.I.**; impt. crossing of R. Shannon; p. (1986) 1,465.

Banam, t., **Cambodia**; on Mekong R.; boat-bldg., rice milling; p. 28,000.

Banant, terr., Vojvodina, N. Serbia, **Yugoslavia**; major source of petroleum, natural gas, vineyards, but economically backward.

Banbridge, t., l. gov. dist., **N. Ireland**; on Bann R.; linen; p. (1991) 11,448 (t.), 33,482 (dist.).

Banbury, mkt. t., Cherwell, Oxford, **Eng.**; 128 km from London; aluminium ind., furniture, printing, ladies' wear; expanded t.; p. (1981) 35,796.

Banchory, burgh, Kincardine and Deeside, **Scot.**; on R. Dee, 27 km S.W. of Aberdeen; p. (1991) 6,230.

Banda Is., volcanic gr. in Moluccas, in Banda Sea **Indonesia**; nutmegs and mace; a. 103 km².

Bandama, R., **Ivory Coast**; major power and irrigation scheme at Kossou Dam; length c. 320 km.

Bandar. *See* **Masulipatnam**.

Bandar 'Abbās, spt., S. **Iran**; airport; oil exploration; deepwater harbour; p. (1982) 175,000.

Bandar-e-Būshehīr (Bushire), spt., S.W. **Iran**; on Persian G., Iran's major pt.; petrochem. complex project; p. (1982) 120,000.

Bandar-e-Torkeman, spt., N. **Iran**; on Caspian Sea, on rly. from Tehran.

Bandar Khomeynī, spt., **Iran**, on Persian G., terminus of rly. from Tehran; petrochemical plant.

Bandar Seri Begawan, t., cap. of **Brunei**; 20 km from mouth of Brunei R.; airport; p. (1981) 49,902.

Bandjarmasin, c., cap. of Kalimantan, **Indonesia**; pt. on Martapura R., nr. confluence with Barito R.; tr. ctr.; oil, timber, rubber, printing plant; p. (1980) 381,286.

Bandon, t., Cork, **R.o.I.**; on B.R.; agr. processing; p. (1986) 1,943.

Bandung, c., W. Java, **Indonesia**; industl. and tourist ctr.; tech. institute; radio sta. at nearby

Malabar; p. (1983) 1,602,000.

Banff Nat. Park, Canada; first Canadian Nat. Park; in Rocky Mtns.; variegated scenery, many tourist facilities; a. 6,695 km².

Banff, royal burgh, Banff and Buchan, **Scot.**; on Moray Firth at mouth of R. Deveron; fisheries; tourism; p. (1991) 4,110.

Banffshire, former co., **Scot.**; lge. part now forms Banff and Buchan l. gov. dist., Grampian Reg.; a. of dist. 1,525 km²; p. of dist. (1993) 88,020.

Bangalore, c., Karnataka, **India**; well-planned c., former Brit. military sta. and admin. H.Q.; route ctr.; textiles, engin.; p. (1991) 2,661,000.

Bangka (Banka), I., between Sumatra and Kalimantan, **Indonesia**; tin; a. 11,942 km²; p. 280,000.

Bangkok (Krung Thep), cap. c., **Thailand**; pt. on Menam Chao Phraya R., 32 km from sea; built originally round canals, major industl. ctr.; royal palace, univ.; p. (1989) 5,832,843.

Bangladesh (East Pakistan), indep. sov. st., S. Asia; within Commonwealth (1972); occupies former Indian prov. of E. Bengal and E. part of Ganges delta; dense rural p. engaged in intensive farming of rice and jute; illiteracy 80 per cent; poor internal communications hinder devel.; exp. textiles; susceptible to flooding and cyclones; major cyclone 1991; cstl. embankment project; open warfare between India and Pakistan (Dec. 1971) resulted in creation of indep. st.; cap. Dacca; a. 142,776 km²; p. (1993) 118·7 m.

Bangor, t., North Down, **N. Ireland**; spt. on S. shore of Belfast Lough, 16 km N.E. of Belfast; lt. inds.; carpets, hosiery; seaside resort; p. (1991) 52,437.

Bangor, t., S. Me., **USA**; pt. of entry on Penobscot R.; timber inds., shoes; p. (1980) 31,643.

Bangor, t., Arfon, Gwynedd, **Wales**; pt. on S. shore of Menai Strait; cath., univ. college; lt. engin.; tourist ctr.; p. (1981) 12,174.

Bangui, c., cap. of **Central African Rep.**; pt. on R. Ubangi; airpt.; p. (1988) 451,690.

Bangweulu, L., **Zambia**; 240 km long, 128 km wide, contains 3 islands. Dr. Livingstone died at Illala, on S. shore of this L., in 1873.

Baniyas, spt., **Syria**; terminus of oil pipeline from Kirkuk, opened 1952.

Banja Luka, t., **Bosnia-Herzegovina**, formerly Yugoslavia; caths., mosques; recent industl. development; cellulose; rly. junc.; p. (1981) 183,618.

Banjul (Bathurst), t., cap. of **Gambia**; pt. at mouth of Gambia R., exp. groundnuts; airport; p. (1983) 44,188.

Banks I., Canada, Arctic Oc.; separated by McClure Strait from Melville I.

Banks Peninsula, dist. on E. cst. of S.I., **N.Z.**; prominent feature of Canterbury cst.; p. (1991) 7,639.

Banks Strait, separating Furneaux Is. from Tasmania, **Australia**.

Bankura, t., W. Bengal, **India**; on Hooghly R.; shellac, silk; p. (1991) 114,876.

Bann, Upper and Lower R., **N. Ireland**; rises in Mtns. of Mourne, and flows through Lough Neagh to Atlantic nr. Coleraine; length 144 km.

Bannockburn, moor, nr. Stirling, **Scot.**; Bruce's victory over Edward II on June 23–24, 1314, established Scotland's independence; p. (1991) 5,799.

Banovici, basin, **Bosnia-Herzegovina**, formerly Yugoslavia; brown coal.

Banská Bystrica, region, **Slovakia**; copper and silver mng.; metal wks.; a. 9,230 km²; p. (1990) 87,000.

Banstead, Surrey, **Eng.**; dormitory t.; p. (1981) 43,163. See **Reigate**.

Bantam, t. and dist., W. Java, **Indonesia**; suffered severely from fever and volcanic eruption; former pt. and sultanate; cattle rearing.

Bantry, t., Cork, **R.o.I.**; tweed; p. (1986) 2,811.

Bantry Bay, Cork, **R.o.I.**; Atlantic inlet; natural harbour utilised mainly by oil-storage depot.

Baoding (Paoting), c., Hebei prov., **China**; on main rly. to Beijing; p. (1984) 522,800.

Baoji (Paoki), c., Shaanxi prov., **China**; ctr. of arable agr. a.; cotton weaving; nearby gorge on Huang-He used for multi-purpose dams; p. (1984) 352, 100.

Baotou (Paotow), c., Mongol Zizhiqu (Inner Mongolia), **China**; on left bank of Huang-He, on road and rly. routes to E. China; terminus of caravan routes through Gobi Desert and Tarim basin to Turkestan; tr. in non-perishable livestock prods.,

cereals; modern steel ind.; p. (1992) 1,200,000.

Bar, spt., Dalmatian cst., Montenegro, **Yugoslavia**; terminal of Belgrade-Bar rly.; p. (1981) 32,535.

Baracaldo, pt., N.E. **Spain**; rapidly growing industl. t. on Bilbão estuary; p. (1981) 117,422.

Baracoa, spt., **Cuba**; exp. bananas, coconuts.

Baranovichi, c., **Belarus**; admin. ctr. of agr. dist.; impt. rly. ctr.; p. (1990) 162,800.

Barataria Bay, S.E. Louisiana, **USA**; 56 km S. of New Orleans; ctr. of shrimp ind., petroleum extraction; picturesque stilt vs.; a. 466 km².

Barauni, t., N. Central Bihar, **India**; oil refining; oil pipelines to Gauhati, and Kanpur and from Haldia; p. (1981) 56,366.

Barbados, I., indep. sovereign st., within Brit. Commonwealth, **W.I.**; fertile soils; economy based on intensive agr. supporting dense p.; sugar, molasses, rum; fishing; tourism can and spt Bridgetown; a. 429 km²; p. (1991) 258,600.

Barbary Coast, gen. name applied to Mediterranean cst. of N. Africa between Strait of Gibraltar and C. Bon.

Barberton, t., Ohio, **USA**; S.W. of Akron; tyre mftg.; p. (1980) 29,751.

Barberton, t., Transvaal, **S. Africa**; developed from 19th cent. gold rush; ctr. of rich agr. dist.; p. (1980) 70,880 (dist.).

Barbican, dist., City of London, **Eng.**; inc. major housing scheme to attract p. back into c.; cultural amenities.

Barbizon, v., nr. forest of Fontainebleau, **France**; haunt of painters, especially those ass. with the Barbizon school.

Barbuda and Redonda, Is., Leeward Is., **W.I.**; dependencies of **Antigua and Barbuda**; sea-island cotton; a. 163 km²; p. (1991) 1,400.

Barcellona, t., N.E. cst., Sicily, **Italy**; mkt. t.; p. (1981) 36,869.

Barcelona, c., cap. of B. prov., major spt. of **Spain**; industl. and comm. ctr., textiles and varied inds.; exp. agr. prod. inc. cork; cath., univ.; p. (1991) 1,653,175, 4,605,710 (prov.).

Barcelona, t., N. **Venezuela**; cap. of Anzoátegui st.; agr. tr.; brewing; adjoins Puerto la Cruz on Caribbean cst.; joint p. (1981) 156,500.

Barcoo Creak. See **Cooper's Creek**.

Bardsey, I., Irish Sea; off cst. of **Wales**, nr. N. point of Cardigan Bay; lighthouse.

Bareilly, c., Uttar Pradesh, **India**; mkt.; sugar refining, cotton mills, bamboo furniture; p. (1991) 591,000.

Barents Sea, part of Arctic Oc., E. of Spitzbergen to N. Cape; impt. cod fisheries; oil potential; short Rs. to be diverted from Sea to Volga to carry water to Karakum Desert.

Bari, c., cap. of B. prov., Apulia, **Italy**; spt. on Adriatic handling agr. prods.; agr. processing inds., oil refinery; p. (1992) 342,129.

Barinas, t., cap. of B. st., **Venezuela**; cattle, oil in surrounding Llanos; p. (1981) 109,900.

Barisal, t., **Bangladesh**; nr. Tetulia at mouth of Ganges; river pt.; gr. damage and loss of life from cyclone 1965; p. (1991) 163,481.

Barito R, Borneo, **Indonesia**; a. of swampland in lower valley; proposals to develop valley for rice cultivation; length c. 440 km.

Barking and Dagenham, outer bor., E. London, **Eng.**; on Rs. Roding and Thames; diversified inds. inc. huge Ford motor wks.; p. (1993) 145,500.

Bar-le-Duc, t, cap. of Meuse dep., **France**; in picturesque Ornain valley; many fine old houses; varied inds.; p. (1990) 18,577.

Barletta, t., spt., **Italy**; diversified pt. processing inds.; wine tr.; p. (1981) 83,719.

Barmouth, t., Meirionnydd, Gwynedd, **Wales**; pt. on Cardigan Bay; chemicals; resort; p. (1981) 2,136.

Barnard Castle, Teesdale, Durham, **Eng.**; mkt. t., resort; woollens, penicillin; cas.; p. (1981) 5,016.

Barnaul, t., W. Siberia, **Russia**; route ctr. in cotton-growing dist. nr. industl. Kuznetsk Basin; varied inds.; p. (1989) 602,000.

Barnet, former U.D., Herts., **Eng.**; now outer bor., Greater London; comprising Finchley, Hendon, Barnet, East Barnet and Friern Barnet; p. (1993) 304,700.

Barnsley, t., met. dist., South Yorks., **Eng.**; machin., plastics; carpets; p. (1993) 225,900.

Barnstaple, North Devon, **Eng.**; mkt. t., pt. on R. Taw; seaside resort; p. (1981) 19,025.

Baroda, t., Gujarat, **India**; univ.; palaces, Hindu

temples; natural gas pipeline from Ankleshwar; oil refining nearby at Jawaharnagar; heavy water plant; p. (1987) 734,473.

Barquisimeto, t., **Venezuela**; well built c.; comm. ctr. for fertile agr. a.; p. (1981) 496,700.

Barra Is., Outer Hebrides, **Scot.**; a. 901 km²; lighthouse on Barra Head; p. (1991) 1,244.

Barrancabermeja, R. pt., **Colombia**; oilfield, oil refining, paper mkg., petrochemicals; p. (1983) 123,000.

Barranquilla, t., **Colombia**; major spt. nr. mouth of Magdalena R.; impt. industl. ctr.; international airpt.; p. (1992) 1,018,763.

Barreiro, t., Setúbal, **Portugal**; on S. bank of Tagus estuary; agr. processing; p. (1987) 50,863.

Barrow-in-Furness, spt., l. gov. dist., Cumbria, **Eng.**; iron and steel ind. once based on local haematite ores; shipbldg., submarines; p. (1993) 73,300.

Barrow I., W. **Australia**; since 1967 one of Australia's richest oilfields.

Barrow Point, most N. headland in Alaska, **USA**.

Barry, pt., Vale of Glamorgan, South Glamorgan, **Wales**; rapid growth in 19th cent. as outport of Cardiff; modern light inds., replacing coal and tinplate inds.; p. (1981) 41,681.

Barth, spt., Mecklenburg - West Pomerania, **Germany**; shipyard engin., furniture, sugar; p. (1989) 11,721.

Bartlesville, t., Okla., **USA**; oil refining, metal inds.; p. (1980) 34,568.

Barton-on-Humber, mkt. t., Glanford, Humberside, **Eng.**; anc. Eng. pt.; S. site of new Humber Bridge; p. (1981) 8,498.

Basel, c., cap. of B. can., 2nd. t. of **Switzerland**; cath., univ.; burial place of Erasmus; comm., industl, rly. ctr. at head of barge navigation on R. Rhine; p. (1990) 171,000 (c.) 358,500 (met. a.).

Basel, can., **Switzerland**; divided into 2 half cantons; (1) B.—Stadt; in immediate vicinity of B.c.; cap. B.; a. 36 km²; p. (est. 1990) 191,800; (2) B.—Land; on N. Jura slopes; watchmaking; cap. Liestal; a. 427 km²; p. (1990) 230,000.

Basford, t., Gedling, Notts., **Eng.**; outskirts of Nottingham; hosiery.

Bashkir (**Bashirskaya**) aut. rep. occupies Belaya R. basin in S.W. Urals, **Russia**; impt. mng. and metal inds., inc. major oilfield; arable agr.; cap. Ufa; a. 143,486 km²; p. (1989) 3,943,100.

Basildon, t., l. gov. dist., Essex, **Eng.**; in lower Thames valley; new t. 1949; light inds.; p. (1993) 161,700 (dist.).

Basilicata, region, S. **Italy**; comprising provs. of Potenza and Matera, mtnous. in W., drains to G. of Taranto; arable agr.; a. 9,984 km²; p. (1992) 610,821.

Basingstoke and Deane, l. gov. dist., N. Hants., **Eng.**; 80 km W. of London; expanded t.; engin., light inds.; p. (1993) 146,500.

Basle. See Basel.

Basotho ba Borwa (**S. Sotho**), Bantu Terr. Authority, O.F.S., **S. Africa**; cap. Witziesnoek; a. 52,000 hectares; p. (1969) 144,000.

Basque Provs., N. **Spain**; comprise 3 provs.: Alava, Guipuzcoa and Vizcaya where Basque language spoken; recent claims that French dep. of Pyrénées-Atlantiques should be inc. within an indep. Basque prov.; regional parliaments for provs. in Spain to help offset separatist moves (1980); lgst. c. Bilbao; p. (1981) 2,141,809.

Basra, t., cap. of B. prov.; R. pt., 64 km from mouth of Tigris R., on main rly. from Baghdad; exp. agr. prods.; p. (1985) 616,700.

Bas-Rhin, dep., E. **France**; N. part of Alsace; extends to Rhine rift valley, inc. Vosges Mtns.; impt. agr. dist.; many industl. ts.; cap. Strasbourg; a. 4,791 km²; p. (1990) 953,100.

Bass Rock, lighthouse in Firth of Forth, opposite Tantallon Cas., E. Lothian, **Scot.**; gannetry.

Bass Strait, **Australia**; between Victoria and Tasmania; length 320 km; width 224 km.

Bassano del Grappa; cap. of Vicenza prov., on R. Brenta, **Italy**; light and craft inds.; cath.; p. (1981) 64,676.

Bassein, t., **Myanmar**; on mouth of Irrawaddy R., univ.; airfield; rice tr. and milling; p. (1983) 144,000.

Basse-Normandie, region, N. **France**; inc. deps. Calvados, Manche, Orne; ch.t. Caen; p. (1990) 1,391,300. See Normandy.

Bassenthwaite, L. L. Dist., Cumbria, **Eng.**; most N. of lge. Ls.; drained to Solway Firth by R. Derwent; length 6 km; width 1·6 km.

Basses-Alpes. See Alpes-de-Haute-Provence.

Basses-Pyrénées. See Pyrénées-Atlantique.

Basse-Terre, I., cap. of Guadeloupe, **Fr. W.I.**; pt.; p. (1990) 14,107.

Basseterre, t., **St. Kitts** I., **W.I.**; cap. St. Kitts-Nevis-Anguilla ass. st.; pt.; sugar refining; p. (1980) 14,283.

Bassetlaw, l. gov. dist., N. Notts., **Eng.**; lge. a. based on Worksop and East Retford; p. (1993) 105,500.

Bastia, c. spt., cap. Haute Corse, N.E. Corsica, **France**; lgst. t. of Corsica; agr. exp. and inds.; tourism; p. (1990) 38,728

Basutoland. See Lesotho.

Bata, t., ch. spt., **Equatorial Guinea**; cap. of Rio Muni prov.; airpt.; p. (1986) 17,000.

Bataan, peninsula and prov., W. Luzon, **Philippines**; mtnous.; inc. t. of Balanga; timber inds., oil refining; p. (1990) 425,803.

Batangas, prov. and spt., S.W. Luzon, **Philippines**; oil refining; agr. tr.; p. (1990) 184,970.

Batavia. See Djakarta.

Bath, c., l. gov. dist., Avon, **Eng.**; Roman baths, hot springs, medicinal waters; fine Regency architecture; univ.; elec. engin., metal inds.; p. (1993) 83,100 (dist.).

Bathgate, burgh, W. Lothian, **Scot.**; coal mng. automobile ind.; p. (1991) 13,819.

Bathurst, t., N.S.W., **Australia**; former gold t., reliant on wool and wheat; diversifying with secondary inds.; with Orange to form site of major inland c. of 200,000; p. (1981) 19,640.

Bathurst, I., off cst. of N.T., **Australia**; separated from Melville I. by Apsley Str.; aboriginal reserve; cypress pine milling; (1981) 1,586.

Bathurst, t., N.B., **Canada**; pt. on Nipisiguit Bay; paper mill; salmon fishing; local mng.; p. (1986) 14,683.

Bathurst. See Banjul.

Bātinah, Al, fertile coastal plain, **Oman**, Arabia; produces early-ripening dates famous for flavour.

Batley, t. West Yorks., **Eng.**; heavy woollens, shoddy; p. (1981) 42,572.

Baton Rouge, st. cap., La., **USA**; on Mississippi; major tr. ctr.; univ.; oil refining, chemical plants; p. (1990) 219,531 (c.), 528,000 (met. a.).

Battambang, prov., **Cambodia**; N.W. of Phnom-Penh; rice growing, cotton mill; p. (1981) 551,860.

Battersea, dist., London, **Eng.**; S. of R. Thames; famous park; lge. power sta. now disused; part of Wandsworth.

Batticaloa, t., cap. of E. Prov., **Sri Lanka**; on E. cst.; comm. ctr.; p. (1981) 42,963.

Battle, t., Rother, East Sussex, **Eng.**; battle of Hastings 1066; abbey.

Battle Creek, t., Mich., **USA**; on Kalamazoo R.; engin., local cereal prod.; p. (1984) 54,300, (t.), 137,800 (met. a.).

Batu Arang, t., **Malaysia**; ctr. of only worked coalfield in Malaya; 45 km from Kuala Lumpur.

Batumi, t., spt. on E. shore of Black Sea; **Georgia**; oil, engin., citrus fruits, tea; oil pipeline connects with Baku; resort; airpt; p. (1990) 137,300.

Bauchi, state, **Nigeria**; cap. Bauchi; ctr. of Jos plateau; tin-mng. ctr.; p. (1991) 4,294,413.

Bauld, C., northernmost part of Newfoundland, **Canada**.

Bauru, t., São Paulo st., **Brazil**; comm. ctr.; food inds.; p. (1985) 220,900.

Bautzen, t., Saxony, **Germany**; on R. Spree; textiles, engin., iron inds.; cath.; p. (1989) 50,627.

Bavaria (**Bayern**), _land_, **Germany**; mtnous., bounded in S. by Alps, inc. Böhmerwald, Fichtelgebirge, Franconian Forest; main Rs. Danube and Main; fertile agr. valleys; forestry and agr.; economic life concentrated in ts., esp. cap. Munich, now a focus of p. immigration; rural beauty attracts tourist tr.; celebrated beer; a. 70,220 km²; p. (1992) 11,596,000.

Bavarian Alps, mtn. range, **Germany**, along Austrian border; Zugspitze (2,969 m) highest mtn.

Bavarian Forest. See Böhmerwald.

Bawdwin, t., **Myanmar**; in Shan plateau; impt. mng. ctr.; wolfram, lead, zinc, silver, rubies.

Bayamón, t., **Puerto Rico**; in fertile valley; oil refining; p. (1990) 220,262.

Baybay, t., Leyte, **Philippines**; impt. comm. pt.; p. (1990) 82,281.

Bay City, t., Mich., **USA**; comm. pt. nr. head of Saginaw B.; fishing; pt. processing inds.; p. (1980) 41,593 (c.), 119,881 (met. a.).

Bayeux, t., Calvados, **France**; mkt. t.; cath., museum, Bayeux tapestry; p. (1982) 15,237.

Baykal, L. (**Ozero Baykal**), Siberia, **Russia**; sixth largest fresh-water L. in world; basin forms deepest depression in world (1,616 m); many pts. around shores but frozen Nov.–May; skirted by Trans-Siberian rly.; sturgeon, salmon; tourism; a. 35,483 km².

Bayonne, spt., Pyrénées-Atlantique, S.W. **France**; cath.; noted for invention of bayonet; Basque Museum; p. (1990) 41,846 (t.), 136,334 (met.a).

Bayonne, t., N.J., **USA**; 10 km from New York; chemicals, oil refining; dry docks; p. (1990) 61,444.

Bayreuth, t., Bavaria, **Germany**; home of Wagner; famous for musical festivals in national theatre; p. (1986) 72,300.

Baytown, pt., S.E. Texas, **USA**; industl. t., oil refining and exp.; p. (1980) 56,923.

Beachy Head, chalk headland, S.W. of Eastbourne, East Sussex, **Eng.**; 175 m high.

Beaconsfield, t., South Bucks., **Eng.**; residtl; home of Edmund Burke; p. (1981) 10,909.

Beardmore Glacier, **Antarctica**; one of world's lgst. valley glaciers; over 176 km in length.

Bear I. (**Björnöya I.**), **Norway**; in Arctic Oc., 208 km S. of Spitzbergen; cod fisheries.

Bearsden, burgh, l. gov. dist. with Milngavie, **Scot.**; residtl.; p. (1993) 41,050 (dist.), (1991), 27,806 (burgh).

Beas (**Bias**), R., Punjab, **India**; trib. of Sutlej R.; part of irrigation scheme.; marked limit of Alexander's advance into India, 327 B.C.

Beattock, pass, S. Uplands, **Scot.**; gives access from valley of R. Clyde to R. Annan; used by main W. cst. rly. route from Carlisle to Glasgow and Edinburgh; alt. 309 m.

Beauce, region, central **France**; flat limestone plateau; arid, few surface streams; thin layer of loam (limon) permits agr.; impt. wheat growing a. ("the granary of France"); p. mainly grouped in vs.

Beaufort Sea, off N. Alaska, **USA**; part of Arctic Oc.

Beaujolais, **France**; in upper Rhône valley, N.E. Massif Central; wine-growing dist.

Beaulieu, v., Hants, **Eng.**; on Beaulieu R.; Cistercian abbey; car museum.

Beauly, t., Inverness, **Scot.**; on B. R.; ruined priory; p. (1991) 1,354.

Beaumaris, t., Anglesey, Gwynedd, N. **Wales**; pt. on Menai Strait; lt. engin.; resort; p. (1981) 2,088.

Beaumont, t.; 2nd. pt. of Texas, **USA**; ctr. of petrochemical inds.; p. (1990) 114,323 (t.), 361,000 (met. a. with Port Arthur).

Beaune, t., Cote d'Or, **France**; mediaeval walled t.; ctr. of wine tr.; p. (1982) 21,127.

Beauvais, agr. mkt. t., cap. of Oise dep., N. **France**; cath.; Gobelin tapestry removed to Paris; p. (1990) 56,278.

Bebington, Wirral, Merseyside, **Eng.**; part of pt. of Liverpool; soap, chemicals, engin.; p. (1981) 64,174.

Becancourt, t., Quebec, **Canada**; on S. bank of St. Lawrence; integrated steel mill projected.

Beccles, Waveney, Suffolk, **Eng.**; mkt. t. on R. Waveney S. of Broads; resort, agr. inds.; p. (1981) 8,903.

Béchar, dep. N.W. **Algeria**; a. 306,000 km²; p. (1987) 183,896.

Bechuanaland. *See* Botswana.

Beckum, t., N. Rhine–Westphalia, **Germany**; cement, chalk, engin. wks.; p. (1986) 36,500.

Beddington and Wallington. *See* Sutton.

Bedford, co. t., North Beds., **Eng.**; on R. Ouse, 80 km N. of London; gen. engin., inc. marine and elec., bricks, aero research; Bunyan imprisoned here; p. (1981) 74,245.

Bedfordshire, non-met. co., **Eng.**; co. t., Bedford; crossed by Chilterns; agr., mkt. gardening, brickmkg., cement, vehicles, engin.; a. 1,232 km²; p. (1993) 539,400.

Bedford Level, once over 162,000 ha. of peat marsh in S. Fenland, **Eng.**; first successful draining initiated by Earl of Bedford 1634.

Bedlington, t., Wansbeck, Northumberland, **Eng.**; nr. Blyth; coal mng.; electronics; p. (1981) 26,707.

Bedloe's I., or **Liberty I.**, N.Y. harbour, **USA**; on which the statue of Liberty stands.

Bedwas and Machen, t., Rhymney Valley, Mid Glamorgan, **Wales**; gas, coal and coke byprods.; p. (1981) 13,152.

Bedwellty, t., Islwyn, Gwent, **Wales**; elec. gds., car upholstery; p. (1981) 24,670.

Bedworth, t., Warwicks., **Eng.**; nr. Coventry; coal mng., limestone quarrying, engin., textiles; p. (1981) 41,991. *See* Nuneaton.

Bedzin, t., S. **Poland**; coalmng. t. in Upper Silesia; p. (1989) 76,883.

Beerenberg, mtn., Jan Mayen I., **Norway**, Arctic Oc.; one of lgst. volcanic cones in world; glaciated; alt. 2,546 m.

Beersheba, t., **Israel**; ctr. for development of the Negev; p. (1990) 122,000.

Beeston and Stapleford, Broxtowe, Notts., **Eng.**; sub. of Nottingham; engin., drugs, telephones; p. (1981) 64,599.

Bègles, t., Gironde, **France**; mftg.; p. (1982) 23,426.

Begovat, t., E. **Uzbekistan**; on Syr Dar'ya R.; iron and steel wks.; hydroelectric power.

Behera, prov. **Egypt**; Nile delta; cap. Damandur; a. 10,129 km²; p. (1991) 3,730,000.

Beihai, spt., Guangxi prov., **China**; seafood cultivation, fishing; food processing and machin. inds.; offshore oil development; port being rebuilt to attract foreign investment as part of new open door policy; growth centre; p. (1984) 172,000.

Beijing (**Peking**), c. and mun., cap. of **China**; cultural ctr. and c. of gr. architectural beauty; for hundreds of years seat of Chinese emperors (Mongol, Ming, Manchu); formerly surrounded by walls, Imperial and Summer palaces; seat of govt.; univ.; Catholic cath. reopened (1985); many sm. factories producing a very wide range of goods, esp. chemicals, computers, textiles, synthetic fibres, machin., precision instruments, printing, publishing; route ctr., rly. junc., airpt.; a. 8,770 km²; p. (1992) 7,050,000, (1990) 10,870,000 (prov.).

Beira, spt., **Moçambique**; airpt; rly. runs inland to Harare (Zimbabwe) and Blantyre (Malawi); exp. sugar, maize, cotton; oil pipeline to Umtali; p. (1990) 299,300.

Beirut, c., cap. of **Lebanon**; pt. on Mediterranean; anc. Phoenician c., now busy shipping and mercantile ctr.; silk, wool, fruits; 4 univs.; p. (1988) 1·5m.

Beisan (**Bet She'an**), t., **Israel**; in Jordan valley, c. 90 m below sea-level; archaeological finds date from 1500 B.C.; rebuilt since 1948 by Israelis.

Bejaia (**Bougie**), spt., **Algeria**; impt. tr. ctr.; exp. wood, hides; oil pipeline connection to Hassi-Messoud; p. (1983) 124,122.

Békéscsaba, t., **Hungary**; milling; rly. junc.; poultry processing plant; p. (1989) 71,000.

Belarus, CIS, former rep. USSR; low-lying; timber; agr. on drained marshes; peat; 209,790 km²; p. (1992) 10·28 m.

Belau, *See* Palau, **Rep. of**

Belaya Tserkov, t., N. **Ukraine**; agr. and comm. ctr.; p. (1990) 200,500.

Belém, spt., cap. of Pará st., **Brazil**; comm. ctr., ch. pt. of Amazon basin, entrepôt for riverside settlements, exp. forest prod. inc. jute, cocoa and cotton; inds. dominated by food processing and textiles; steel works; univ.; p. (1991) 1,246, 435.

Belfast, l. gov. dist., cap. of N. **Ireland**; pt. on Belfast Lough; Britain's lgst. single shipyard; freeport (1984) for air freight; linen mnf., rope, tobacco, distilling, aircraft, fertilisers, computers; oil refinery on E. side of harbour; univ.; Stormont Castle; p. (1991) 279,237.

Belfort, t., cap. of Belfort dep., E. **France**, in Alsace; fortress t. between Jura and Vosges; heavy inds., rly. wks., cotton ind.; elec. engin.; p. (1990) 51,913.

Belfort (**Territoire de**), dep., **France**; ch. t. Belfort; a. 608 km²; p. (1990) 134,100.

Belgaum, t., Karnataka, **India**; cotton; alt. 760 m; Jain temples; p. (1991) 326,000.

Belgium, kingdom, **W. Europe**, comprises 9 admin. provs.; low-lying except in Ardennes in S.E.; very high density of p., intensive agr. and highly industl.; severe social and economic problems have resulted from decline of Sambre-Meuse coalfield and associated heavy engin. inds., similar difficulties in textile inds. in N.W.; industl. expansion on Kempenland coalfield in N.E. and around Brussels, Antwerp, and Ghent; heavily dependent upon foreign tr. for economic survival; member of EU; major spt. of Antwerp competing with Rotterdam for hinterland; 2 language groups: Flemish (Dutch dialect) in N., French dialect in S. (Walloon a.); univs. at Brussels, Ghent, Liège, Louvain; cap. Brussels; a. 30,445 km²; p. (1993) 10,068,319.

Belgorod, t., **Russia**; N.W. of Kharkov, on N. Donets R.; rly. junc. in agr. region; p. (1989) 300,000.

Belgrade (**Beograd**), c., cap of Serbia and **Yugoslavia**; inland pt. on Danube at mouth of Sava R.; industl., admin. and cultural ctr.; univ.; airport; p. (1991) 1,136,786.

Belitung or **Billiton**, I., between Sumatra and Kalimantan, **Indonesia**; tin; a. 4.832 km²; p. 102,375.

Belize, indep. rep. (1981), **Central America**; formerly Brit. Honduras; almost totally underdeveloped;

heavy rainfall, hurricanes; tropical forest; only 15 percent of land is cultivated; economy hit by fall in world sugar prices; recent sale of 13 percent of land a. to clear tropical forest for citrus production; 20 per cent unemployed; lowest p. density in Central America; new cap. Belmopan; a. 22,962 km²; p. (1993) 230,000.

Belize City, c., former cap. of **Belize**; almost devastated by hurricane 31 Oct. 1961; cap. moved to Belmopan 80 km further inland; spt.; p. (1989) 43,621.

Bellary, c., Karnataka, **India**; fort; cotton processing and tr.; p. (1991) 245,391.

Bell Bay, pt., Tasmania, **Australia**; on bank of Tamar R.; modern pt. and aluminium refinery (1950s) for processing Queensland bauxite; ferry terminal; now part of Launceston.

Bell I., Newfoundland, E. **Canada**; in Conception Bay, 32 km N.W. of St. Johns; impt. Wabana iron-ore deposits outcrop on N.W. cst., smelted on Pictou coalfield, Nova Scotia; a. 31 km².

Belle Isle Strait, **Canada**; between Newfoundland and Labrador, on N. shipping route to Canada from Europe.

Belleville, pt., L. Ontario, **Canada**; agr. processing; white marble making, cement; light inds.; p. (1986) 36,041.

Belleville, t., Ill., **USA**; industl. ctr., domestic prod., coal; air force training school; p. (1980) 41,580.

Belleville, t., N.J., **USA**; machin., chemicals; p. (1980) 35,367.

Bellingham, t., spt., Wash., **USA**; agr. distribution ctr.; timber inds.; salmon canning; p. (1984) 45,100 (c.), 111,800 (met. a.).

Bellinzona, t., **Switzerland**; on R. Ticino; 22 km N. of Lugano; three castles built on hills dominating t.; rly. engin.; tourism; p. (1980) 16,743.

Bell Rock (Inchcape I.), rock and lighthouse 19 km S.E. of Arbroath, **Scot.**

Belluno, t., cap. of B. prov., Venezia, N. **Italy**; route ctr. at S. foot of Dolomites; cath.; engin.; p. (1981) 36,634.

Belmopan, new inland cap., **Belize**; (1989) 5,276.

Belo Horizonte, c., cap. of Minas Gerais st. **Brazil**; impt. inland c.; ctr. rich agr. and mng. region; steel mills, food inds., textiles, diamond cutting; oil pipeline from Guanabara; univ.; one of the fastest growing c. in Brazil, especially since building of Fiat factory; p. (1991) 2,048,861.

Beloretsk, t., Bashkir, aut. rep., **Russia**; in Ural Mtns. on Belaya R.; iron, metal inds.

Belorussia. *See* Belarus.

Belovo, t., W. Siberia, **Russia**; in Kuznetsk basin; coal mng., zinc, engin.; p. (1985) 117,000.

Belper, mkt. t., Amber Valley, Derbys., **Eng.**; hosiery, textiles, oil wks., iron foundries; p. (1981) 16,453.

Belsen, v., 24 km N.W. of Celle, **Germany**; notorious second world war concentration camp.

Belterra, t., dist., Pará st., N.E. **Brazil**; nr. confluence of Tapajós and Amazon Rs; site of Fordlandia scheme.

Beltsy, t., **Moldova**; on trib. of Dniester R.; agr. ctr., food processing; p. (1990) 164,800.

Belvoir (pronounced Beaver), Vale of, Melton Leics., **Eng.**; clay vale, cattle, sheep; Stilton cheese; recent development of coalfield.

Bembridge, v., E. cst., I. of Wight, **Eng.**; resort.

Benalla, t., dist., Victoria, **Australia**, pastoral and agr.; p. (1986) 8,490 (t.).

Benares. *See* Varanasi.

Benbecula I., Outer Hebrides, Western Isles, **Scot.**; between Is. of N. and S. Uist; airpt. in N.; fishing; a. 93 km²; p. (1991) 1,803.

Bendigo, c., Victoria, **Australia**; former goldmng. dist., gold rush 1851; mng. ceased 1955; primary prods.; impt. egg producing ctr.; p. (1983) 62,260.

Benevento, c., Campania, **Italy**; cap. of B. prov. which contains many Roman remains; cath.; agr. processing; p. (1981) 62,636.

Benfleet, t., Castle Point, Essex. **Eng.**; residtl.; p. (1981) 50,224.

Bengal, Bay of, part of **Indian Oc.** washing E. shores of India and W. shores of Burma, receives waters of Rs. Krishna, Ganges; Brahmaputra, Irrawaddy.

Bengbu (Pengpu), c., Anhui, **China**; on Kwo-Ho 168 km. NW of Nanjing; on Tianjin–Nanjing rly; p. (1984) 597,100.

Benghazi, joint cap. (with Tripoli) of **Libya**; spt. and airpt. on G. of Sirte; univ.; former Greek Hesperides; p. (1981) 368,000.

Benguela, t., Angola, S.W. Africa; rly. runs in-

land to Zaïre and Zambia; seaport now lost much tr. to Lobito.

Benha, t., **Egypt**; impt. mkt. t., rail and road ctr. in heart of cultivated a. of Nile delta 48 km N. of Cairo; airpt.; p. (1986) 115,571.

Beni, dep. **Bolivia**; drained by R. Mamoré; rubber, cattle; a. 213,564 km²; p. (1988) 215,400.

Benin City, t., **Nigeria**; cap. of Benin st.; former notorious slave ctr.; p. (1983) 166,000.

Benin, People's Republic of, (Dahomey), indep. st. (1960), **West Africa**; former French Colony; high standard of education reflected in heavy government sector and low level of productive activity in the economy; staple foods of groundnuts, palms, coffee, cocoa; intensive farming in fertile Terre de Barre; land held collectively; full potential of drier N. not yet exploited; concern about desert encroachment; oil found offshore from main pt. Cotonou; inds. process primary prods.; joint Benin-Nigerian rly; much tropical rain forest in S.; dependence on Nigeria; many joint industl. projects; cap. Porto Novo; a. 112,622 km²; p. (1993) 5·10 m.

Beni Suef, t. and prov., **Egypt**; on Nile, 96 km S. of Cairo; ctr. of fertile agr. a.; carpets, cotton; p. (1986) 151,813 (t.), (1991) 1,656,000 (prov.).

Ben Lawers, mtn., Perth and Kinross, **Scot.**; by Loch Tay; arctic and alpine flora; alt. 1,215 m.

Ben Macdhui, mtn., Kincardine and Deeside, **Scot.**; Cairngorm gr.; second highest peak in Brit. Is.; alt. 1,310 m.

Ben Nevis, mtn., Lochaber, **Scot.**; volcanic; hgst. peak in Brit. Isles; alt. 1,344 m.

Benoni, t., Transvaal, **S. Africa**; gold mng. ctr.; engin.; p. (1980) 205,420 (dist.).

Bensheim, t., Hesse, **Germany**; ctr. of fruit and wine dist. on E. edge Rhine valley; textiles, paper, metallurgy; p. (1986) 33,500.

Bentley with Arksey, t., South Yorks., **Eng.**; p. (1981) 21,786.

Benton Harbor, t., Mich., **USA**; midway along E. cst. L. Michigan; p. (1984) 14,200 (t), 163,000 (met. a.).

Benue R., **Nigeria-Cameroon**; rises in Adamawa mtns.; forms cth. trib. of Niger R.; R. pts. and agr. tr.; length 1,392 km.

Ben Vorlich. mtn., Perth and Kinross, **Scot.**; alt. 983 m.

Ben Wyvis, mtn., Ross and Cromarty, **Scot.**; nr. Dingwall; alt. 1,046 m.

Benxi (Penki), c., Liaoning prov., **China**; metallurgical ctr.; p. (1984) 810,500.

Ben-y-Gloe, mtn., Glen Tilt, Perth and Kinross, **Scot.**; alt. 1,120 m.

Beograd. *See* Belgrade.

Beppu, c., Kyushu, **Japan**; hot spring resort: p. (1990) 130,323.

Berbera, pt., **Somalia**, on G. of Aden; exp. livestock from pastoral hinterland; new deepsea pt. completed 1969; airport; p. (1987) 65,-000.

Berchtesgaden, v., **Germany**; mtn. resort 24 km S. of Salzburg; Hitler's mtn. retreat; tourism; potash.

Berck-Plage, resort, Pas-de-Calais, **France**, on Eng. Channel; p. (1982) 15,671.

Berdichev, t., **Ukraine**; ctr. of sugar a.; engin., lt. inds.; p. (1990) 92,600.

Berdyansk, c., **Ukraine**; pt. on Sea of Azov; agr. ctr.; machin.; health resort; p. (1990) 133,500.

Bere Regis, mkt. t., Dorset, **Eng.**; Saxon royal residence.

Berezina, R., **Belarus**; trib. of Dnieper; forms part of Baltic-Black Sea waterway; 608 km long.

Berezniki, t., E. European **Russia**; pt. on Kolva R., W. Urals; salt, chemicals, paper; p. (1989) 201,000.

Bergama, t., **Turkey**; anc. Pergamos, ruins; morocco leather inds.; agr. tr.; p. (1985) 38,849.

Bergamo, c., Lombardy, **Italy**; 54 km N.E. Milan; cath. and academy; silk industry; p. (1992) 114,930.

Bergen, spt., W. cst. **Norway**; univ.; most impt. comm. pt. in kingdom; shipping, fishing; mftg. inds.; birthplace of Grieg; p. (1990) 187,382.

Bergen op Zoom, t. N. Brabant, **Neth.**; sugar refining. engin.; p. (1993) 47,546.

Bergerac, t., Dordogne, S.W. **France**; impt. bridge over Dordogne R.; mkt. for wines and luxury foods; anc. Huguenot stronghold; p. (1982) 27,704.

Bergisches Land, terr., N. Rhine-Westphalia, **Germany**; specialised iron and steel prod.; chemicals machin.; inc. ts. of Solingen, Remscheid, Velbert, Wuppertal.

Bergisch-Gladbach, t., N. Rhine-Westphalia, **Germany**; 11 km E. of Cologne, paper, metallurgy, textiles; p. (1990) 104,100.

Berhampur, t., Orissa, India; admin, and educational ctr.

Bering Current (Okhotsk Current, or Oyashio), ocean current, N. Pac. Oc.; flows through Bering Strait from Arctic, along E. cst. of Kamchatka and Japanese Is. Hokkaido, Honshu; relatively cold; moderate summer temperatures along csts. causes fogs.

Bering Sea, part of N. Pac. Oc. between Aleutian Is. and B. Strait; fishing; a. 2,274,020 km².

Bering Strait, narrow sea which separates Asia from N. America, and connects Bering Sea with Arctic Oc.; 58 km wide at narrowest part.

Berkeley, v., Gloucs., Eng.; nr. R. Severn, 24 km N. of Bristol; scene of murder of Edward II; nuclear power-sta. decommissioning.

Berkeley, c., Cal., USA; univ.; chemicals; now inc. in San Francisco; p. (1990) 102,724.

Berkhamsted, Dacorum, Herts., Eng.; mkt. t., chemicals; cas. ruins, 17th cent. school; birthplace of William Cowper the poet; p. (1981) 15,461.

Berkshire, non-met. co., Eng.; chalk downland inc. Inkpen Beacon, White Horse Hills; drained by Thames and tribs.; residtl.; electronics, biscuits; dairying; Windsor Gr. Park; Ascot racecourse; a. 1,256 km²; p. (1993) 763,700.

Berlin, c., cap. of re-unified Germany; on Spree R.; formerly divided into 4 occupied zones 1945; Soviet (E. Berlin), British, American, French (W. Berlin); W. Berlin formed isolated enclave within E. Germany; focal point of escape attempts from E. to W. led to construction of "Berlin Wall", destroyed 1989; W. Berlin major industl. ctr. aided by American and W. German capital; educational, cultural and tourist ctr.; E. Berlin, former cap. of E. Germany, rebuilt as showpiece with high-rise housing, elect. manfs, machin., p. (1990) 3,437,000.

Bermuda, Brit. gr. coral Is. (360 in no. of which 20 are inhabited) N. Atlantic; about 1,120 km E. of S.C.; Hamilton, on Long I. is the ch. t.; Brit. and US air and naval stas.; favourite winter resort for Americans; inds. attracted by tax incentives; no surface water; total a. 54 km²; p. (1992) 71,950.

Bern, c., cap. of B. can. and fed. cap. Switzerland; on Aare R.; cath., univ.; textiles, musical instruments, chocolate; H.Q. of Postal Union; bear pit; p. (1990) 134,600 (c.) 298,700 (met. a.).

Bern, can., Switzerland; fertile valleys, dairying; watches; hydroelectric power; plans for separate can. in Jura reg.; a. 6,881 km²; p. (1990) 945,600.

Bernard, Great St., one of the Alps in the S. of the Valais, Switzerland; highest point 3,390 m; height of mtn. pass between Italy (Aosta) and Switzerland (Martigny), 2,477 m; famous hospice for travellers in monastery on mtn.; road tunnel completed 1962.

Bernard, Little St., one of Graian Alps, Savoy, S. of Mt. Blanc, France; pass traversed by Hannibal 218 B.C.

Bernburg, t., Saxony-Anhalt, Germany; cas.; chemicals, salt mng.; p. (1980) 46,000.

Bernese Oberland (Berner Alpen), alpine region, Switzerland; 35 peaks over 3,000 m inc. Finsteraarhorn and Jungfrau; tourist a. inc. resorts of Interlaken and Grindelwald.

Bernina Alps, Switzerland; alt. 4,050 m.

Berri, t., S. Australia; ctr. of irrigated fruit growing a. on R. Murray; wines; p. (1981) 3,419.

Berri, oilfield, Saudi Arabia; 72 km N.W. of Ras Tannura; the field extends offshore.

Berwick, l. gov. dist., former co., Border Reg., S.E. Scot.; a. of sheep rearing and woollen inds. in S. Uplands; a. 875 km²; p. (1993) 19,350.

Berwick, t., Vic., Australia; satellite of Melbourne; to be expanded to planned p. of 100,000 by 1985; p. (1983) 41,400.

Berwick-upon-Tweed, l. gov. dist., Northumberland, Eng.; spt. on mouth of Tweed; border t., changed between Eng. and Scot. 15 times in history; fishing, lt. engin., tweeds, knitwear; cas. ruins; p. (1993) 26,700 (dist.).

Besançon, t., cap. of Doubs dep., France; cath., observatory, univ.; farm implements, textiles; watch- and clock-making; birthplace of Victor Hugo; p. (1990) 119,194 (t.), 122,623 (met.a.).

Beskids, W. and E., (Beskidy Zachodnie), mtn. range, Poland, Slovakia, E. Europe; northern range of Carpathian mtn. system, seldom exceeds alt. 1,200 m, many passes; forested; tourism; length 352 km.

Bessarabia, terr., ceded to former USSR by Romania 1940, and now part of Moldova; agr. region.

Bessemer, t., Ala., USA; iron and steel; p. (1980) 31,729.

Bethany (El Azarieh), v., on Mt. of Olives 6 km W. of Jerusalem.

Bethel, anc. c., the modern Beitin, Jordan; 16 km N. Jerusalem.

Bethesda, t., Arfon, Gwynedd, Wales; slate, lt. engin; p. (1981) 4,060.

Bethlehem, t. 9 km S.W. Jerusalem; according to Matthew and Luke birthplace of Christ; p. (1980) 14,000.

Bethlehem, t., Penns., USA; 80 km N. of Philadelphia; iron-wks.; univ.; p. (1980) 70,419.

Bethnal Green, dist., London, Eng.; in E. End of London, now in Tower Hamlets.

Béthune, t., Pas-de-Calais, France; rail and canal ctr. for coalfield; mkt. t.; p. (1990) 25,261 (t.), 259,679 (met. a.).

Betteshanger, v., Kent, Eng.; on N. flank of N. Downs, 6 km W. of Deal; coal mng.

Bettws-y-Coed, t., Aberconwy, Gwynedd, Wales; waterfalls; tourism; p. (1981) 658.

Beuthan. See Bytom.

Beverley, l. gov. dist. (known as East Yorks Borough of Beverley), mkt. t., Humberside, Eng.; famous minster (13th cent.); agr. processing; p. (1993) 115,800.

Beverly, c., Mass., USA; footwear, machin.; p. (1980) 37,655.

Beverly Hills, t., Cal., USA; sub. of Los Angeles; home of many film celebrities; p. (1980) 32,367.

Beverwijk, t., nr. Haarlem, N. Holland, Neth.; agr. prods.; p. (1993) 35,523.

Bewdley, Wyre Forest, Hereford and Worcs., Eng.; mkt. t. on R. Severn; birthplace of Stanley Baldwin; residtl.; p. (1981) 8,742.

Bexhill-on-Sea, t., Rother, East Sussex, Eng.; resort; p. (1981) 35,529.

Bexley, former bor., W. Kent; now outer bor., Greater London, Eng.; inc. Sidcup, Crayford and Erith; p. (1993) 219,900

Béziers, t., Hérault, France; ctr. of wine, brandy tr. and inds.; chemicals; p. (1990) 72,362 (t.), 76,304 (met. a.).

Bezwada. See Vijayawada.

Bhadravati, t., Karnataka, India; steel; p. (1981) 77,055 (t.), 130,606 (met. a.).

Bhagalpur, t., Bihar, India; agr. tr. ctr. on R. Ganges; p. (1991) 253,000.

Bhamo, t., Upper Myanmar; on Irrawaddy; inland limit of steam boats; mkt. ctr.; ruby mines; p. 10,000.

Bhandara, cap. of Bhandara dist., Maharashtra, India; 48 km E. of Nagpur; cotton cloth, brass mftg.; p. (1981) 56,025.

Bharuch, t., Gujarat, India; world's lgst. stream urea fertiliser plant; nearby oilfield.; p. (1991) 133,102

Bhatpara, t., W. Bengal, India; on R. Hooghly; industl. t.; jute, engin.; p. (1991) 316,000.

Bhaunager, t., Gujarat, India; pt. on G. of Cambay; exp. cotton, oilseeds; p. (1991) 402,000.

Bhilai, t., Madhya Pradesh, India; steel plant; rails and rly. sleepers; p. (1981) 319,450.

Bhim-Gora, sacred pool, place of Hindu pilgrimage, Uttar Pradesh, India.

Bhopal, c., cap. of Madhya Pradesh, India; impt. tr. ctr.; varied inds.; prehistoric cave paintings nearby; 2,000 killed in world's worst chem. accident (1984); p. (1991) 1,063,000.

Bhubaneswar, t., cap. of Orissa, India; 29 km from Cuttack; admin. ctr.; Hindu temples, pilgrimage ctr.; p. (1991) 412,000.

Bhutan, kingdom, indep. mtn. st., E. Himalayas; heavy monsoon rain, rich tropical vegetation. valuable forests; N.–S. ridges and valleys result in semi-closed communities; first motor link with India opened 1962; cap. Thimphu; a. c. 46,620 km²; alt. 7,558 m (Kula Kangri); p. scattered and nomadic (1991) 1·5 m.

Biafra, Bight of. See Bonny, Bight of.

Biako, formerly Marcias Nguema (Fernando Po). I., Equatorial Guinea; in Bight of Bonny; mtnous.; coffee, cocoa, bananas, timber; p. (1984) 75,000.

Biala Podlaska, t. and prov., E. Poland; wool, furniture; p. (1989) 52,119 (t.), 304,000 (prov.).

Bialystok, t. and prov., Poland; nr. Grodno; major industl. ctr.; rly. ctr.; p. (1989) 267,670 (t),

687,800 (prov.).

Biarritz, t., Pyrénées-Atlantique dep., **France**; on Bay of Biscay; seaside resort; p. (1982) 26,647.

Biberach, t., Baden-Württemberg, **Germany**; on R. Kinzig; spa; wood, metal and engin. inds.; p. (1986) 28,000.

Bicester, Cherwell, Oxford, **Eng.**; anc. mkt. t., N.E. of Oxford; p. (1981) 14,436.

Biddulph, t., Staffs. Moorlands, Staffs., **Eng.**; coal mng., machin., textiles, furniture; residtl.; p. (1981) 19,160.

Bideford, Torridge, N. Devon, **Eng.**; pt. on estuary R. Torridge; mkt., boat-bldg.; resort; p. (1981) 12,211.

Biel (Bienne), t., Berne, **Switzerland**; nr. Lake B.; watches; impt. industl. ctr.; p. (1990) 52,736.

Bielefeld, t., Rhine-Westphalia, **Germany**; ch. ctr. of linen industry; machin., bicycles; p. (1990) 320,000.

Biella, t., Vercelli, **Italy**; textiles; p. (1981) 53,572.

Bielsko-Biala, t., and prov., S. **Poland**; textiles, engin.; p. (1989) 181,072 (t), 895,400 (prov.).

Bien-hoa, t., nr. Ho Chi-minh City, S. **Vietnam**; sugar refining; cotton mills.

Bies-Bosch, reclaimed fenland area between N. Brabant and S.W. **Neth.**; sugar refining, dairying; a. 142 km².

Biggar, sm. burgh, Clydesdale, **Scot.**; 213 m in Southern Uplands; p. (1991) 1,994.

Biggin Hill, Greater London, **Eng.**; nr. Orpington; famous airfield of Battle of Britain.

Biggleswade, t., Mid Beds., **Eng.**; in valley of R. Ivel, 14 km S.E. of Bedford; ctr. of fruit-growing and mkt. gardening dist.; hydraulic machin. tools, hosiery, caravans; p. (1981) 10,928.

Big Horn Mtns., Wyo. and Mont., **USA**; Rockies; favourite film location; attractive agr. valleys; highest alt., 3,600 m.

Bihać, t., Bosnia-Herzegovina, formerly Yugoslavia; on R. Una; industl. development; timber processing.

Bihar, st., N.W. **India**; in Ganges basin; hilly; bulk of p. in agr. N.; irrigation; minerals in S.E.: coal, iron, mica; steelwks. at Jamshedpur, oil refining at Barauni; cap. Patna, admin. ctr. Ranchi; a. 173,882 km²; p. (1991) 86,374,465.

Bihar, t., Bihar, **India**; within middle Ganges valley nr. Patna; p. (1991) 201,323.

Biisk, c., Siberia, **Russia**; ctr. of rich agr. a.; meat packing, textiles; p. (1989) 233,000.

Bijagós, Achipelago dos (Bissagos Is.), off W. cst. **Guinea-Bissau**; c. 14 Is.; coconuts, rice; ch. t. Bolama on Bolama I.; a. 1,554 km².

Bijapur, t., Karnataka, **India**; cotton tr. and inds.; ruins; former cap. of B. kingdom; p. (1991) 186,939.

Bikaner, t., Rajasthan, **India**; in Thar desert; on former caravan route; wool tr., bldg. stone, handicrafts; p. (1991) 416,000.

Bikini, atoll, **Pac. Oc.**; atomic-bomb tests (1946).

Bilaspur, t., Madhya Pradesh, **India**; silks, cottons; p. (1991) 192,396.

Bilbao, spt., N. **Spain**; cap. Basque prov. of Viscaya; formerly famous for rapier making; iron ore, smelting; pipeline from Ayoluengo oilfield; p. (1991) 372,191.

Billinge and Winstanley, t., Lancs., **Eng.**; former coal-mng. a.; p. (1981) 12,488.

Billingham, t. Cleveland, **Eng.**; on N. of Tees estuary; major petrochemical plant.

Billings, t., Mont., **USA**; agr. tr. ctr. in irrigated a.; sulphur plant; p. (1990) 81,151.

Billingsgate, London, **Eng.**; old river-gate and wharf, formerly ch. fish mkt. of England; now moved to Isle of Dogs.

Bilma (Kawar), oasis t., **Niger**; on caravan route from Tripoli to Agadés and L. Chad.

Billiton I. *See* Belitung.

Biloxi, t., Miss., **USA**; fishing, tourist ctr.; US Coast Guard air base; p. (1984) 48,700 (t.) 197,400 (met. a.).

Bilston, t., West Midlands, **Eng.**; part of Wolverhampton; iron and steel.

Bingen, t., Rhineland Palatinate, **Germany**; at S. entrance to Rhine gorge; wine; beautiful scenery; tourism; p. (1986) 22,100.

Bingerville, spt., **Côte d'Ivoire**, W. Africa; rubber processing.

Bingham Canyon, t., N. Utah, **USA**; silver, gold, lead; major open pit copper mine.

Binghamton, N.Y., **USA**; on Susquehanna R.; boot factories, aircraft components, cameras; p. (1990) 53,008 (t.), 264,100 (met. a.).

Bingley, West Yorks., **Eng.**; mkt. t. on R. Aire 26 km

N.W. of Leeds; textiles, engin., agr.; p. (1981) 28,070.

Bintan I., lgst. island of Riouw archipelago, **Indonesia**; bauxite, tin.

Bintenne, dist., **Sri Lanka**; remote a., sparse p.; lge. Gal Oya reservoir; tea and rubber estates.

Biratnagar, t., S.E. **Nepal**, in the Tarai; jute, sugar, cotton milling, stainless steel; p. (1981) 93,544.

Birbhum, dist., W. Bengal, **India**; cap. Suri; healthy climate; rice, sugar; mnfs. silk, cotton; a. 4,550 km²; p. (1981) 2,095,829.

Birkenhead, Wirral, Merseyside, **Eng.**; spt. on R. Mersey, opposite Liverpool; handles industl. goods; heavy and pt. processing inds.; ship-bldg.; p. (1981) 123,907.

Birmingham, c., met. dist., West Midlands, **Eng.**; industl. cap. Midlands, second lgst. c. Gt. Britain; metal inds.; motor vehicles, components and accessories; major growth due to Industl. Revolution; univ., cath.; freeport (1984) for air freight; p. (1993) 1,012,400.

Birmingham, t., Ala., **USA**; coal, iron, limestone, steel, aircraft, chemicals, textiles; p. (1990) 265,968 (t.), 907,810 (met. a.).

Birnam, v., Perth and Kinross, **Scot.**; location of Birnam Wood in *Macbeth*; former royal forest; p. (1991) 1,227 (with Dunkeld).

Birobidzhan, or Jewish aut. oblast, **Russia**; in Khabarovsk terr.; agr., timber and mng. inds.; a. 35,988 km²; cap. Birobidzhan City; p. (1980) 67,000 (inc. 15,000 Jews).

Birr, t. Offaly, **R.o.I.**; mkt. t. on Brosna R.; observatory; p. (1986) 3,417.

Bisbee, t., Arizona, **USA**; very rich copper deposits, gold, silver, lead; p. (1980) 7,154.

Biscarosse, Landes dep., **France**; 72 km S.W. Bordeaux; rocket and missile testing range projected; p. (1982) 8,979.

Biscay, Bay of, stormy a. of Atl. Oc., W. of France and N. of Spain, from Ushant to C. Ortegal; the Roman Sinus Aquitanicus; heavy seas.

Bisceglie, t., Apulia, **Italy**; spt. on E. cst. 35 km N.W. of Bari; tr. in wine and olives; light inds.; cath.; p. (1981) 45,899.

Bischofswerda, t., Saxony, **Germany**; quarrying, glass and iron inds.; rly. ctr.; p. (1989) 13,174.

Bishkek, (Frunze), c., cap. of **Kyrgyzstan**; univ.; engin., textiles, meat-packing; p. (1990) 624, 900.

Bishop Auckland, t., Wear Valley, Durham, **Eng.**; palace of Bishop of Durham; iron, lt. engin.; former coal mng.; p. (1981) 32,572.

Bishopbriggs, sm. burgh, Strathkelvin, **Scot.**; p. (1991) 23,825.

Bishop Rock, isolated rock, lighthouse, Scilly Is., **Eng.**; 58 km S.W. of Land's End, Cornwall; recognised internationally as E. end of trans-Atlantic ocean crossing.

Bishop's Stortford, East Herts., **Eng.**; mkt. t. on Stort R.; light inds.; Hatfield forest nearby; Norman cas.; p. (1981) 22,807.

Biskra, dep. **Algeria**; a. 109,729 km², p. (1987) 429,217.

Bisley, v., Surrey, **Eng.**; ranges of Nat. Rifle Ass. on B. common.

Bismarck, t., st. cap. N.D., **USA**; on Missouri R.; agr. mkt. ctr.; p. (1980) 44,485.

Bismarck Archipelago, volcanic gr., S.W. Pac. Oc., off New Guinea, admin. by **Australia**.

Bisotūn, t., **Iran**; in ruins; monuments to Darius I (the Great).

Bissagos Is. *See* Bijagós, Achipelago dos.

Bissau, t., cap of **Guinea-Bissau**; former ctr. of slave tr.; airpt.; plans to expand harbour; p. (1988) 125,000.

Bitola, t., **Macedonia**, formerly Yugoslavia; varied mnfs., recent industl. development; mosques; p. (1981) 137,835.

Bitonto, t., Apulia, on E. cst. 11 km N.W. of Bari; **Italy**; cath.

Bitterfeld, t. Saxony, **Germany**; lignite mng., engin. chemicals; p. (1989) 20,017.

Bitter Lakes, Isthmus of Suez, **Egypt**, utilised by Suez Canal.

Biwa-ko, lgst. lake in **Japan**, S. Honshu; 101 m a.s.l.; canal to Kyto provides hydroelectric power; superb scenery, historical associations; tourism; a. 675 km².

Biysk or Bisk, c., Altai terr., **Russia**; pt. on Biya R.; terminus of branch of Turk-Sib. rly.; p. (1989) 233,000.

Bizerte, c., N. **Tunisia**; pt. and naval sta. on Med.; the anc. Hippo Zaritus; fishing, oil refining, steel wks., tyres; p. (1984) 94,509.

Björnborg. *See* **Pori.**

Blaby, l. gov. dist. Leics., **Eng.**; sm. a. S.W. of Leicester; p. (1993) 85,000.

Black Belt, coastlands of Miss. and Ala., **USA**, where black soil prairie land is good for cotton.

Blackburn, t., l. gov. dist., Lancs., **Eng.**; once major cotton weaving ctr.; engin., lt. inds.; p. (1993) 139,500 (dist.).

Black Country, Midlands, **Eng.**; formerly impt. iron-working and coal-mng. dist. mainly in S. West Midlands; now a. of lt. engin.; c. 130 km².

Blackdown Hills, Devon and Somerset, **Eng.**; sandstone hills rising over 305 m.

Black Forest. *See* **Schwarzwald.**

Blackheath, open common, S.E. London, **Eng.**; mustering place of Wat Tyler's (1381) and Jack Cade's (1450) revolutionary peasants; now main attraction of expensive residtl. a.; a. 108 ha.

Black Hills, mtns. between S.D. and Wyo., **USA**, highest., Horney Peak, 2.208 m; form part of Nat. Park.

Black Isle, peninsula, between Cromarty and Beauly Firths, Ross and Cromarty, **Scot.**; agr., fisheries, quarrying; a. 280 km².

Black Mtn., Powys and Dyfed, S. **Wales**; rise to 802 m in Brecknock Van, sandstone plateau; moorland; valleys used for reservoirs; Nat. Park.

Black Mtns., Powys, S. **Wales**; rise to 811 m in Waun Fach.

Blackpool, t., l. gov. dist., Lancs., **Eng.**; on cst. of Fylde dist.; one of major Brit. resorts; p. (1993) 153,600 (dist.).

Black Prairie, region Texas, **USA**; extends 560 km S.W. from Ouachita Mtns. to Austin; contains very fertile Black Waxy and Grande Prairie sub-regions devoted almost entirely to cotton growing; ch. ts., Dallas, Fort Worth, Austin; a. 77,700 km².

Blackrod, t., Gtr. Manchester, **Eng.**; nr. Chorley; former cotton weaving; p. (1981) 5,628.

Black Sea, bordered by 6 sts., **Ukraine, Russia, Georgia** (N. and E.), **Turkey** (S.), **Bulgaria, Romania** (W.); receives waters of Danube, Dniester, Dnieper, Don. Bug; stagnant and lifeless below 150 m; fisheries in N. and W.; oil exploration by Turkey; a. 424,760 km² (exc. Sea of Azov).

Blacksod Bay, cst. of Mayo, **R.o.I.**

Black Volta, R., rises in Burkina Faso, flows E. and S. into L. Volta, **Ghana**; length *c.* 1,200 km.

Blackwater, R., N. Ireland; rising in Dungannon, it forms border with **R.o.I.**; enters L. Neagh; 80 km long.

Blackwater, R., R.o.I.; flows from Knockanefune to enter Atl. Oc. at pt. and resort of Youghal; chain of sm. ts. along course; 144 km long.

Blaenau Gwent, l. gov. dist., Gwent, **Wales.**; inland valley a. inc. Ebbw Vale and Abertillery; p. (1993) 77,000.

Blaenavon, t., Torfaen, Gwent, **Wales;** former coal mng.; p. (1981) 6,363.

Blagoveshchensk, t. E. Siberia, **Russia,** on Chinese bdr. and R. Amur; wat. pl.; engin., sawmilling, flour milling; on Trans-Siberian rly.; p. (1989) 206,000.

Blair Atholl, v., Perth and Kinross, **Scot.;** tourist resort; cas.; seat of Duke of Atholl.

Blairgowrie and **Rattray,** burgh, Perth and Kinross, **Scot.;** at foot of Scot. Highlands; mkt. t. in Strathmore fruit growing dist.; p. (1991) 8,001.

Blakeney, v., N. Norfolk, **Eng.;** nr. sand spit; yachting; wild fowl.

Blandford or **Blandford Forum,** North Dorset, **Eng.;** on R. Stour; pastoral mkt. t. since 13th cent.; p. (1981) 3,915.

Blantyre, c., **Malawi;** in Shire Highlands; linked by rail to Beira (Moçambique); comm. ctr.; timber processing; p. (1987) 331,588.

Blantyre, v., East Kilbride, **Scot.;** Lower B. birth-place of David Livingstone; p. (1991) 18,484.

Blarney, v., 6 km N.W. Cork, **R.o.I.;** cas. and Blarney stone; p. (1986) 1,952.

Blasket Is., Kerry. R.o.I.; rocky Is.; p. (1986) 4.

Blaydon, t. Tyne and Wear. **Eng.;** former coal mng.; p. (1981) 30,563.

Bled, glacial L., **Slovenia** (formerly Yugoslavia); tourism.

Blekinge, co. S. **Sweden;** cap. Karlskrona; a. 2,909 km²; p. (1992) 151,266.

Blenheim, t., S.I., **N.Z.;** fruit; p. (1991) 23,637 (urban a.).

Blenheim, v., **Germany;** scene of battle (1704) when English and Austrians under Marlborough defeated the French and Bavarians; **Blenheim**

Palace, Woodstock, Oxon. **Eng.;** named in honour of this victory.

Blessington, L., Wicklow, **R.o.I.;** glacial L., now serves as reservoir for Dublin.

Bletchley, Bucks., **Eng.;** expanded t.; p. (1981) 42,450.

Blida. *See* **El Boulaïda.**

Bloemfontein, t. cap. O.F.S., **S. Africa;** on plateau, alt. 1,393 m; route and tr. ctr.; univ.; p. (1985) 205,420 (met. a.).

Blois, t., cap. of Loir-et-Cher dep., **France;** historic t. on Loire R.; Renaissance château; wines; p. (1990) 51,549.

Bloomfield, t., N.J., **USA;** pharmaceuticals, metal and elec. gds.; sub. N.J. c.; p. (1990) 45,006.

Bloomington, t., Ill., **USA;** comm. ctr. and industl. t. in rich agr. and coal-mng. a.; univ.; p. (1984) 46,600 (t.), 122,800 (met. a.)

Bloomington, t., Ind., **USA;** electronic equipment, furniture, structural glass; univ.; p. (1990) 60,633.

Bloomsbury, dist., London, **Eng.;** fashionable dist. with many squares; famous for B. gr. of authors in first quarter of 20th cent.; inc. Brit. Museum, Univ. of London.

Blue Grass, dist., Ky., **USA;** area where blue grass abundant; horse breeding.

Blue Mountains, t., N.S.W., **Australia;** tourist ctr.; new t. (1981) 55,877.

Blue Mtns., Jamaica; famous for coffee; dense forest; tourism; average alt. 900–1,200 m, rising to 2,294 m in Blue Mtn. peak.

Blue Nile (Bahr-el-Azraq), R., rises in tablelands of Ethiopia, joins the White Nile at Khartoum; its seasonal flooding provides the bulk of water for irrigation in Sudan and Egypt.

Blue Ridge Mtns., S. Penn., Ga., **USA;** inc. Shenandoah valley; superb scenery, resorts; average alt. 600–1,200 m, rising to 1,737 m in Grandfather Mtn.

Bluff, S.I., **N.Z.;** 29 km from Invercargill; spt. for Southland prov., major aluminium ctr.

Blumenau, mkt. t., Santa Catarina st., **Brazil;** butter, sugar; p. (1985) 192,900.

Blyth, spt., Northumberland, **Eng.;** on coalfield; now as B. Valley forms l. gov. dist.; p. (1993) 80,700.

Bo, t., **Sierra Leone;** gold; admin. H.Q.; p. (1988) 26,000.

Boa Vista, t., R. pt., cap. Roraima st., **Brazil;** p. (1977) 25,000.

Bobbio, t., Emilia-Romagna, **Italy,** in northern Apennines; ctr. European cultural life, 9th-12th cent.; St Columban founded monastery, 612; p. (1981) 4,215.

Bobo Dioulassa, t., **Burkina Faso;** agr. tr., gold mng.; p. (1985) 231,162.

Bobigny, N.E. sub of Paris, cap. of Seine-St. Denis dep., **France;** varied inds.; p. (1990) 44,841.

Bobruysk, t., **Belarus;** pt. on R. Berezina; engin., sawmilling, paper, cellulose, grain; p. (1990) 222,900.

Bocholt, t., N. Rhine-Westphalia, **Germany;** machin., textiles, elec. gds.; p. (1986) 66,400.

Bochum, t., N. Rhine-Westphalia, **Germany;** heart of Ruhr iron and steel ind.; known since 9th cent.; Univ. of Ruhr; p. (1990) 397,400.

Bodensee (L. Constance), S.W. **Germany** and **Switzerland;** 72 km long, 14 km wide.; R. Rhine flows through; fruit and horticulture on warmer slopes of L.

Bodmin, co. t., North Cornwall, **Eng.;** on S.W. flank of Bodmin moor; china clay, lt. engin.; p. (1981) 12,148.

Bodmin Moor, upland, N.E. Cornwall, **Eng.;** lower slopes cultivated, higher slopes used for sheep pastures; average alt. 300 m, highest point, Brown Willy, alt. 419 m; major ctr. of china clay quarrying.

Bodö, t., Norway; nr. Lofoten Is.; spt., fish processing; N. rly, terminus; p. (1990) 30,252.

Bodrum, t., on Aegean cst., **Turkey;** anc. Halicarnassus; 15th cent. Crusader castle; fishing.

Boeotia, region of anc. **Greece;** scene of many battles; Thebes was the ch. c.; home of Hesiod and Pindar; p. (1991) 134,034.

Bogda Ula, massif, Sinkiang, **China;** forms N. perimeter of Turfan depression; 240 km wide, average alt. 4,000 m, rising to 5,479 m in Turpanat Targh.

Bognor Regis, t., Arun, West Sussex. **Eng.;** residtl.; seaside resort; p. (1981) 39,536.

Bogor, t., Java, **Indonesia;** rubber factory, textiles, footwear; p. (1983) 274,000.

Bogota, cap. and lgst. c. of **Colombia;** in E.

Atlas of the World

Contents

Symbols

——— Principal Railways   ═══ Internal Boundaries

═══ Motorways

——— Principal Roads   4125 Heights in Metres

▬▬▬ International Boundaries   ✧ Principal Airports

Height of Land

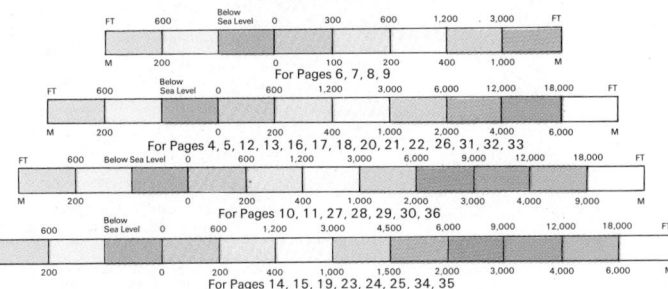

Cartography by Philip's, Copyright 1995 Reed International Books Ltd.

2

WORLD : Political

ICELAND
Reykjavik
Akureyri
Husavik
Arctic Circle
ATLANTIC OCEAN
Faroe Is. (Den.)
Shetland Is.
Orkney Is.
Hebrides
UNITED KINGDOM
SCOTLAND
Inverness
Aberdeen
Dundee
Glasgow
Edinburgh
Londonderry
N.I.
Belfast
I. of Man
REP. OF IRELAND
Galway
Limerick
Dublin
Cork
C. Clear
Carlisle
Newcastle
Manchester
Liverpool
Leeds
York
Hull
Sheffield
WALES
Swansea
Cardiff
Bristol
Birmingham
ENGLAND
Norwich
LONDON
Southampton
Portsmouth
Plymouth
Dover
Scilly Is.
English Channel
Ushant
NORTH SEA
Sogne Fd.
Bergen
Hardanger Fd.
Stavanger
Kristiansund
Trondheim
Lillehammer
Oslo
Drammen
NORWAY
Skagerrak
Kattegat
Göteborg
Vänern
Vättern
Jönköping
Örebro
Eskilstuna
Uppsala
Gävle
Östersund
Indals
Sundsvall
Narvik
Tromsø
SWEDEN
Kalmar
Karlskrona
Malmö
Aalborg
Aarhus
DENMARK
COPENHAGEN
Esbjerg
Flensburg
Kiel
Rostock
BALTIC
Gdynia
Gdańsk
Bydgoszcz
Szczecin
Poznań
Łódź
Wrocław
Katowice
POLAND
Amsterdam
The Hague
Rotterdam
Groningen
NETHERLANDS
Ostend
Calais
Antwerp
BRUSSELS
BELGIUM
Lille
LUX.
Bremen
Hamburg
Elbe
Hanover
Weser
BERLIN
Magdeburg
Oder
GERMANY
Dortmund
Essen
Bonn
Cologne
Halle
Leipzig
Chemnitz
Dresden
Wiesbaden
Mainz
Frankfurt
Würzburg
Nuremberg
Stuttgart
Munich
Freiburg
Rhine
PRAGUE
Plzeň
CZECH REP.
Brno
VIENNA
Linz
Salzburg
AUSTRIA
Innsbruck
Graz
Bratislava
BUDAPEST
HUNGARY
Cherbourg
Le Havre
Rouen
Seine
Caen
Brest
Rennes
Reims
PARIS
Le Mans
Loire
Orléans
Tours
Nantes
Metz
Strasbourg
Mulhouse
Dijon
FRANCE
Limoges
Clermont Ferrand
Périgueux
St. Etienne
Lyons
Saône
Grenoble
Rhône
Avignon
Montpellier
Perpignan
Sète
Marseilles
Toulon
Nice
Monaco
Bordeaux
Garonne
Toulouse
Andorra
BAY OF BISCAY
Basel
Bern
Zürich
SWITZERLAND
Geneva
Milan
Brescia
Trento
Turin
Genoa
La Spezia
Bologna
Venice
Trieste
Ljubljana
SLOV.
Rijeka
Zagreb
CROATIA
Ravenna
San Marino
Florence
Livorno
Ancona
ADRIATIC SEA
Split
Dubrovnik
BOSNIA-H.
Sarajevo
Corsica
Ajaccio
Sassari
Sardinia
Cagliari
Tiber
ROME
ITALY
Naples
Bari
Taranto
Brindisi
Tyrrhenian Sea
Palermo
Messina
Sicily
Reggio
Catania
Ionian
Pantelleria (Ital.)
MALTA
La Coruña
Finisterre
Oviedo
Santander
Bilbao
San Sebastian
Bayonne
Vigo
Oporto
Douro
Duero
Valladolid
Ebro
Coimbra
PORTUGAL
LISBON
Tagus
SPAIN
MADRID
Toledo
Zaragoza
Barcelona
Guadiana
Badajoz
Valencia
Balearic Is.
Minorca
Palma
Majorca
Lagos
Sevilla
Córdoba
Guadalquivir
Murcia
Alicante
Cádiz
Málaga
Granada
Cartagena
Almeria
Str. of Gibraltar
Gibraltar (Br.)
Tangier
Ceuta (Sp.)
MEDITERRANEAN SEA
Algiers
Oran
Melilla (Sp.)
Blida
Skikda
Annaba
Bizerta
Tunis
Rabat
Fès
Meknès
MOROCCO
Tlemcen
ALGERIA
Constantine
TUNISIA
Sousse
West from Greenwich
East from Greenwich

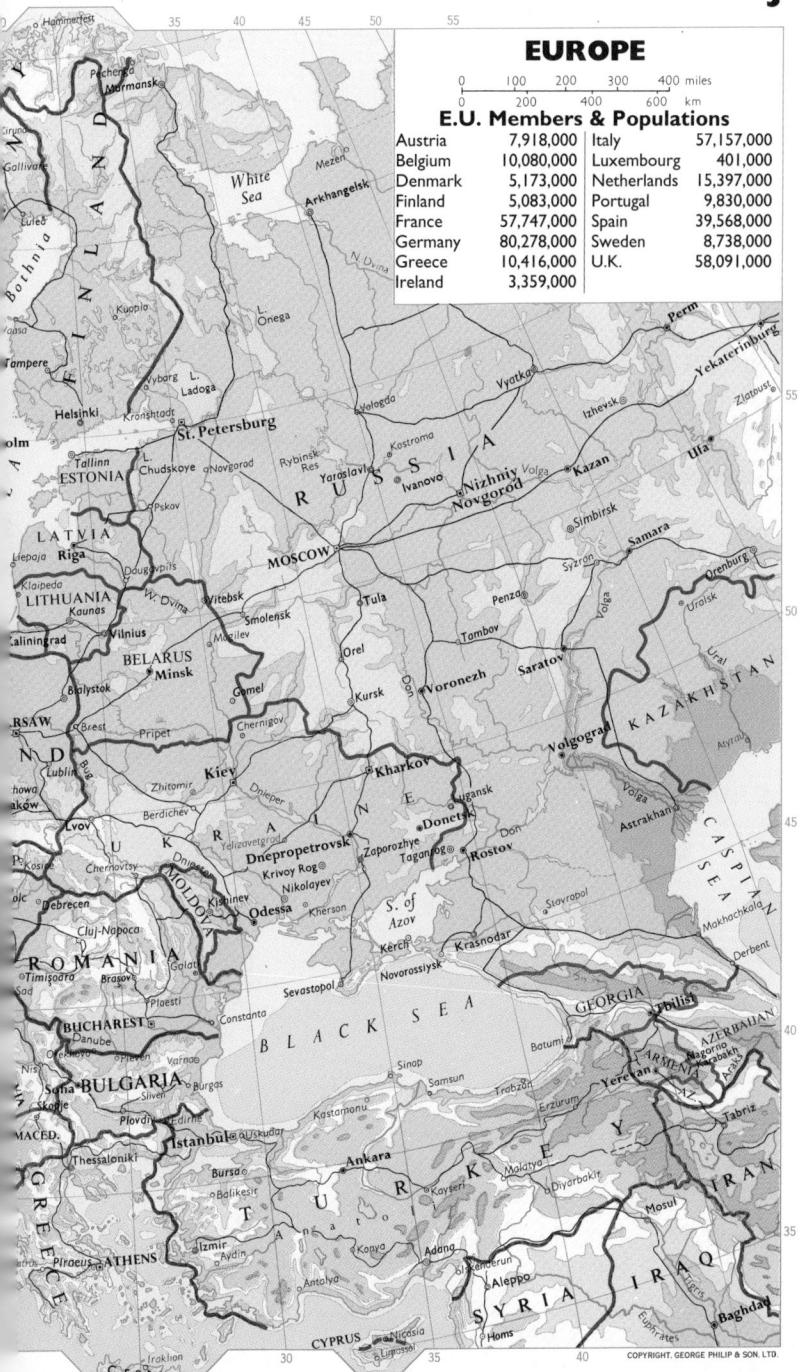

EUROPE

0   100   200   300   400 miles
0   200   400   600 km

E.U. Members & Populations

Austria	7,918,000	Italy	57,157,000
Belgium	10,080,000	Luxembourg	401,000
Denmark	5,173,000	Netherlands	15,397,000
Finland	5,083,000	Portugal	9,830,000
France	57,747,000	Spain	39,568,000
Germany	80,278,000	Sweden	8,738,000
Greece	10,416,000	U.K.	58,091,000
Ireland	3,359,000		

COPYRIGHT. GEORGE PHILIP & SON. LTD.

ENGLAND AND WALES

miles
0   20   40   60   80   100 km

0   20   40   60

NORTH SEA

Dogger Bank

IRISH SEA

Firth of Clyde

North Channel

ISLE OF MAN

Douglas
Castletown
Peel
Ramsey
Pt. of Ayre

SCOTLAND

Berwick-upon-Tweed
St. Abbs Hd.
Holy I.
Farne Is.

NORTHUMBERLAND

Morpeth
Blyth
Tynemouth
Newcastle
South Shields
Sunderland
Gateshead
TYNE AND WEAR
Durham
DURHAM
Bishop Auckland
Darlington
Stockton
Middlesbrough
CLEVELAND
Hartlepool
Redcar
Houghton-le-Spring
Richmond

P e n n i n e s

Cumbrian Mts.
Keswick
Windermere
Barrow
Walney
Whitehaven
Workington
St. Bee's Hd.
Carlisle
CUMBRIA

DUMFRIES
Dumfries
GALLOWAY
Solway Firth
Kirkcudbright
Mull of Galloway
Stranraer
Wigtown
Wigtown Bay
Luce Bay

SOUTH

Ayr
Kilmarnock
Irvine
Troon
Prestwick
Saltcoats
Ardrossan
Girvan

Glasgow
Paisley
Greenock
Port Glasgow
STRATHCLYDE
Hamilton
Wishaw
Motherwell
Coatbridge
CENTRAL
Stirling
Falkirk
Grangemouth
Ben 974

Dunfermline
Kirkcaldy
Leven
FIFE
Fife Ness
St. Andrews
Anstruther
Leuchars

TAYSIDE
Dundee
Perth
Firth of Tay

Edinburgh
Leith
Musselburgh
Dunbar

Bass Rock
North Berwick

Peebles
Selkirk
Galashiels
Hawick
Jedburgh
Cheviot

Scarborough
Whitby
Flamborough Hd.
Bridlington
Filey
Hornsea
Withernsea
Spurn Hd.
Holderness
NORTH YORKSHIRE
York
Ripon
Harrogate
Thirsk
Northallerton
Leeds
Bradford
Halifax
Huddersfield
Wakefield
HUMBERSIDE
Kingston upon Hull
Goole
Beverley
Grimsby
Cleethorpes
Mablethorpe
Louth
Lincoln Wolds
Gainsborough
Scunthorpe
Doncaster
Barnsley
Rotherham
Sheffield
Chesterfield
Retford
Worksop
SOUTH YORKSHIRE
GREATER MANCHESTER
Manchester
Salford
Stockport
Bolton
Rochdale
Oldham
Bury
Wigan
Warrington
Macclesfield
Blackburn
Burnley
Preston
Lancaster
Blackpool
Fleetwood
Southport
Formby Pt.
LANCASHIRE
Liverpool
Birkenhead
Wallasey
MERSEYSIDE
St. Helens

IRELAND

NORTHERN IRELAND
ULSTER
Belfast
Larne
Lisburn
Newtownards
Bangor
Ards Pen.
Strangford L.
Downpatrick
Newcastle
Newry
Armagh
Portadown
Lurgan
Lough Neagh
Antrim
Ballymena
Ballymoney
Coleraine
Portrush
Giant's Causeway
Ballycastle
Rathlin I.

Dublin (Baile Átha Cliath)
Dun Laoghaire
Howth Hd.
Drogheda
Balbriggan
Dundalk
Dundalk Bay
Carlingford L.
MEATH
LOUTH

Colonsay
Islay
Jura
Gigha
Kintyre
Campbeltown
Mull of Kintyre
Fair Hd.
Staffa
Iona

East from Greenwich

West from Greenwich

SCOTLAND

0   20   40   60 miles
0 20 40 60 80 100 km

SHETLAND
Unst
Yell Fetlar
Shetland Is.
Whalsay
Mainland
Rona
Foula Lerwick
Bressay
On same scale Sumburgh Hd.

ATLANTIC

OCEAN

Mainland
Sumburgh Hd.
Fair Isle

Westray
Rousay Eday
ORKNEY N. Ronaldsay
Sanday
Stronsay
Mainland Shapinsay
Kirkwall Orkney Is.
Hoy
South
Ronaldsay

NORTH

SEA

Pentland Firth
C. Wrath Strathy Pt. Dunnet Hd.
Thurso John
Duncansby O'Groats
L. Laxford Ben Hope Noss Hd.
Real Forest Wick
Eddrachillis Bay
Enard Bay L. Assynt Ben More 998
Assynt Kildonale Ord of Caithness
L. Broom Lairg Helmsdale
Butt of Lewis
Ullapool Oykel Golspie
Stornoway Broad Bay Ben Deargh 1081 Dornoch
Lewis Oykel Dornoch Firth
WESTERN Tarbat Ness
Tarbert HIGHLAND Tain
Harris L. Maree Invergordon Bonar
ISLES Ben Wyvis Cromarty Elgin Buckie Kinnairds Hd.
The Aird 1044 Fearn Forres Keith Banff Fraserburgh
North Uist Fannich Dingwall Nairn Deveron Turriff Peterhead
Monach Beauly Inverness Huntly
Is. NORTH WEST Grantown- GRAMPIAN
Benbecula S. Portree on-Spey Buchan
Ben More 619 Inner Sound Glen Affric Spey Cairn
South Uist Cuillin Loch Glen Moriston Gorm 1245
Hills Kyle 1311 Aberdeen
Barra Cuillin Sound Lochalsh Kingussie Cairngorm Mts. Banchory
Canna Mallaig Glen Lochnagar Ballater Girdle Ness
Barra Hd. Eigg L. Arkaig Ben Nevis 1310 Balmoral Castle Stonehaven
Rhum 1343 Braemar
Muck L. Maddy SCOTLAND
Ardnamurchan Fort Pass of
Point Loch Sunart William Killiecrankie Brechin
Tobermory Ardgour Grampian Mts. N. Esk
Coll MORVERN Bannoch Pitlochry Montrose
Stafa Ben Lawers Aberfeldy Blairgowrie Forfar
Tiree B. More 1214 Tummel TAYSIDE Arbroath
996 Breadalbane L. Tay Brechin
Iona Oban Crianlarich Crieff Scone Dundee
Mull 1124 Ben More Perth Firth of Tay
Colonsay Inveraray 942 Tayport
Firth of Lorne Ben Vorlich St. Andrews
Trossachs Crieff Cupar Fife Ness
CENTRAL Kinross FIFE
Rudh a' Mhail Lomond Alloa Leven Anstruther
Helensburgh Stirling Glenrothes Buckhaven
Dunoon Dumbarton Bannockburn Kirkcaldy Bass Rock
Greenock Clydebank Dunfermline Forth Dunbar
Bowmore Port Glasgow Glasgow Falkirk Edinburgh Leith
Islay Paisley Coatbridge LOTHIAN Musselburgh Haddington
Gigha Motherwell Lammermuir Hills St. Abb's Hd.
Ardrossan Hamilton Wishaw Moorfoot Holy I.
STRATHCLYDE Carstairs Hills Peebles Coldstream Farne Is.
Goat Fell Spitcoats BORDERS Berwick-upon-Tweed
Campbeltown 874 Kilmarnock Galashiels Kelso
Brodick Irvine Selkirk The Cheviot Alnwick
Rathlin I. Arran Prestwick Jedburgh Cheviot Hills
Fair Hd. Ayr Hawick Coquet
Mull of Sanquhar NORTHUMBERLAND
Giants Causeway Kintyre Uig Morpeth
Ballycastle Girvan Southern Coldstream Newcastle
Portrush Merrick DUMFRIES Blaydon Gateshead
Moville 843 AND Tyne Hexham
Coleraine Galloway Hills Gretna Green Carlisle DURHAM
Ballymoney Dumfries Annan ENGLAND Bishop
Spergin Mts. Stranraer Castle Solway Firth CUMBRIA Auckland
Sawel Kirkcudbright Maryport Cross Fell
883 Larne Portpatrick Wigtown Wigtown Bay Skiddaw 893
Ballymena Luce 931 Pennines
Antrim Bay Workington
Carrickfergus Keswick
Lough Neagh Bangor
NORTHERN Belfast
IRELAND Mull of Galloway

6   West from Greenwich   4   COPYRIGHT. GEORGE PHILIP & SON. LTD.

FRANCE

0 20 40 60 80 100 miles
0   40   80   120   160 km

FRENCH DEPARTMENTS

A.	01	Ain
Ai.	02	Aisne
Al.	03	Allier
A.H.P.	04	Alpes-de-Haute-Provence
H.A.	05	Hautes-Alpes
A.M.	06	Alpes-Maritimes
Ar.	07	Ardèche
Ard.	08	Ardennes
Ari.	09	Ariège
Aub.	10	Aube
Aud.	11	Aude
Av.	12	Aveyron
B.R.	13	Bouches-du-Rhône
C.	14	Calvados
Ca.	15	Cantal
Ch.	16	Charente
Ch.M.	17	Charente-Maritime
Che.	18	Cher
Co.	19	Corrèze
	20	Corse a) Haute-Corse
C.O.	21	Côte-d'Or b) Corse du Sud
C.A.	22	Côtes d'Armor
Cr.	23	Creuse
D.	24	Dordogne
Do.	25	Doubs
Dr.	26	Drôme
E.	27	Eure
E.L.	28	Eure-et-Loir
F.	29	Finistère Nord et Sud
G.	30	Gard
H.G.	31	Haute-Garonne
Ge.	32	Gers
Gi.	33	Gironde
H.	34	Hérault
I.V.	35	Ille-et-Vilaine
I.	36	Indre
I.L.	37	Indre-et-Loire
Is.	38	Isère
J.	39	Jura
L.	40	Landes
L.C.	41	Loir-et-Cher
Lo.	42	Loire
H.L.	43	Haute-Loire
L.A.	44	Loire-Atlantique
Loi.	45	Loiret
Lot	46	Lot
L.G.	47	Lot-et-Garonne
Loz.	48	Lozère
M.L.	49	Maine-et-Loire
M.	50	Manche
Ma.	51	Marne
H.M.	52	Haute-Marne
May.	53	Mayenne
M.M.	54	Meurthe-et-Moselle
Me.	55	Meuse
Mo.	56	Morbihan
Mos.	57	Moselle
N.	58	Nièvre
No.	59	Nord
O.	60	Oise
Or.	61	Orne
P.C.	62	Pas-de-Calais
P.D.	63	Puy-de-Dôme
P.A.	64	Pyrénées Atlantiques
H.P.	65	Hautes Pyrénées
P.O.	66	Pyrénées (Orientales)
B.R.	67	Bas Rhin
H.R.	68	Haut Rhin
Rh.	69	Rhône
H.Sa.	70	Haute Saône
S.L.	71	Saône-et-Loire
S.	72	Sarthe
Sa.	73	Savoie
H.Sa.	74	Haute-Savoie
	75	Paris
S.Me.	76	Seine-Maritime
S.M.	77	Seine-et-Marne
Yv.	78	Yvelines
D.S.	79	Deux-Sèvres
So.	80	Somme
T.	81	Tarn
T.G.	82	Tarn-et-Garonne
Va.	83	Var
V.	84	Vaucluse
Ve.	85	Vendée
Vi.	86	Vienne
H.V.	87	Haute Vienne
Vo.	88	Vosges
Y.	89	Yonne
B.	90	Belfort
Es.	91	Essonne
	92	Hauts-de-Seine
	93	Seine-St. Denis
	94	Val-de-Marne
	95	Val-d'Oise

CORSICA On same scale

COPYRIGHT. GEORGE PHILIP & SON. LTD.

NETHERLANDS

0 10 20 30 40 50 miles
0 20 40 60 80 km

ICELAND
On same scale
as general map

SCANDINAVIA

0		100		200 miles
0	100	200	300	

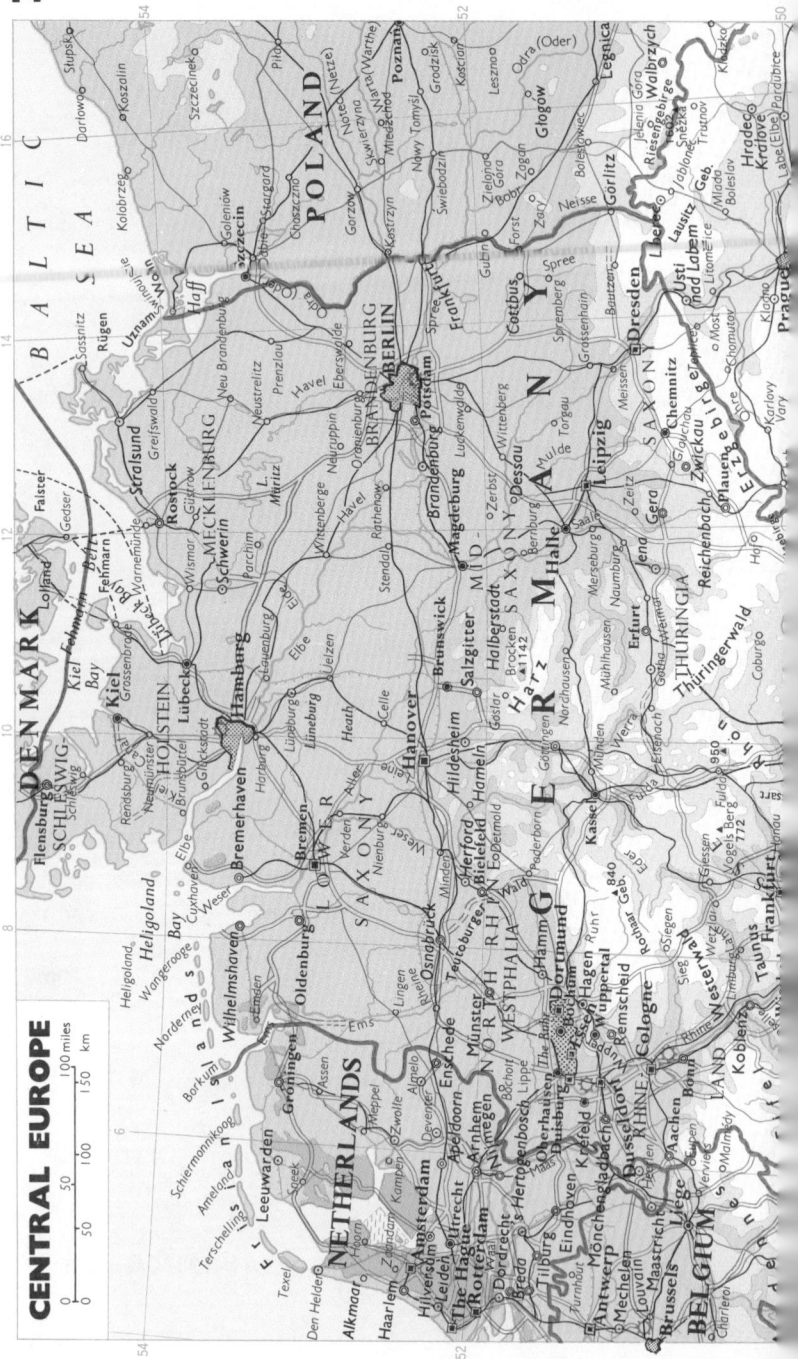

CENTRAL EUROPE

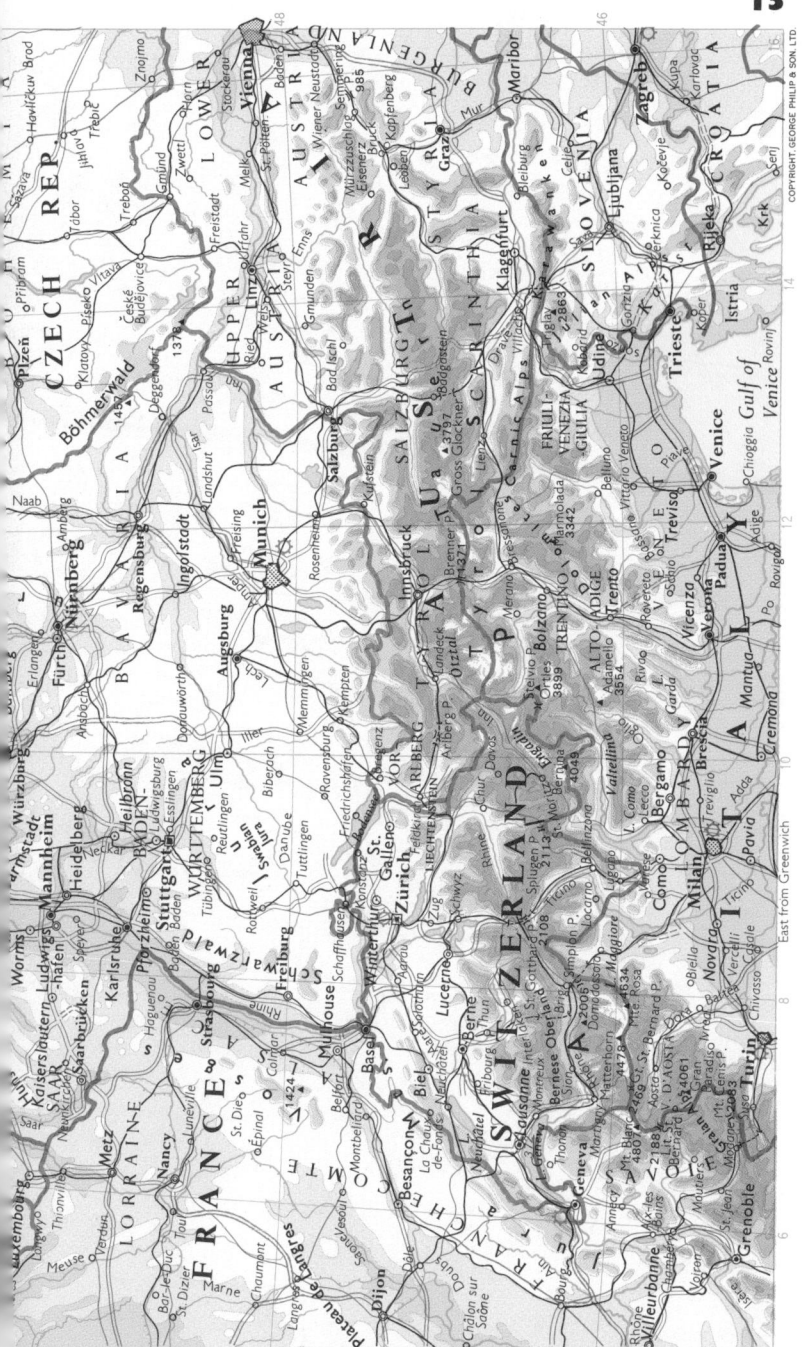

East from Greenwich

ITALY AND
S.E. EUROPE

| 0 | 50 | 100 | 150 | 200 miles |
| 0 | 100 | 200 | 300 km |

GERMANY

NUREMBERG • Plzeň • CZECH REP. • Ostrava • Jablunka

• Regensburg • Jihlava • Brno • Slavkov

Ulm • Augsburg • Linz • Bratislava

Belfort • **Munich** • Danube • VIENNA

Dijon • Besançon • Basel • L. of Constance • Salzburg • AUSTRIA • HU

• Zürich • Innsbruck • Bruck • Graz • Balaton

SWITZERLAND • TYROL • Brenner • Klagenfurt • Pécs

Berne • Gotthard • Drava • Ljubljana • SLOVENIA • Zagreb

Geneva • Simplon • Bergamo • Trento • Udine • Trieste • Rijeka • CROATIA

Lyons • Mt. Blanc • Ortler • Brescia • Vicenza • Isonzo • Pula • Brod

4802 • Como • Milan • Garda • Verona • Padua • Venice • BOSNIA &

Grenoble • Turin • Novara • Po • Reggio • Ferrara • G. of Venice • Banja Luka • HERZEGOVI

Avignon • Alessandria • Parma • Modena • Ravenna • Dinaric Alps

Genoa • Bologna • Forlì • Rimini • Zadar • Split • Mos

Cannes • Menton • La Spezia • Florence • San Marino • Šibenik • Dalmatia

Marseilles • Nice • Gulf of Genoa • Arno • Arezzo • Ancona • Vis • Lastovo • Dubrovnik

Toulon • Riviera • Livorno • Siena • Perugia • ADRIATIC SEA

Ligurian Sea • Elba • Gran Sasso • 2914

2710 • C. Corse • Sabine Mts. • Mt. Gargano

Mte. Cinta • Bastia • Civitavecchia • Tiber • **ROME** • Foggia • Barletta • **Bari**

Ajaccio • **Corsica** • Str. of Bonifacio • Caprera • Gaeta • Volturno • Ofanto

Sassari • Olbia • Naples • Vesuvius • Tarante

Sardinia • Mt. del Gennargentu • 3719 • Capri • Salerno • G. of

1834 • Tyrrhenian Sea • Taranto

• **Cagliari** • Cosenza • La Sila • Catanzaro

MEDITER • Stromboli • Lipari Is.

Skikda • Annaba • Bizerta • Trapani • **Palermo** • Messina • **Reggio** • Ion

Constantine • **Tunis** • Egadi Is. • Marsala • **SICILY** • Mt. Etna • Str. of Messina

C. Bon • Agrigento • Catania • C. Spartivento

Kairouan • Sousse • Caltanissetta • Siracusa

Tébessa • G. of Hammamet • Pantelleria (It.) • C. Passero

ALGERIA • **TUNISIA** • Gozo • Valletta • **MALTA**

Tozeur • Sfax • Lampedusa (It.) • 4135

Chott Djerid • Gabès • Kerkennah

Djerba

Cieszyn
550
Przemysl
Lvov
Vinnitsa
Yelizavetgrad
UKRAINE
Uman
Pervomaysk
Krivoy Rog
Voznesensk
Nikolayev
Kherson

G a l i c i a
Carpathians
Kolomyia
Kamenets-Podolskiy
Mogilev-Podolski
Balta
Bug

SLOVAK REP.
2655
Košice
Prut
Chernovtsy
MOLDOVA
Pripet
Banská
Štiavnica
Miskolc
Tokaj
Borosanio
Beltsy
Siret
Kishinev
Bendery
Dnestrovskiy
Odessa

HUNGARY
Tisza
Debrecen
Pietrosu
2305
Iaşi
Belgorod
Dnestrovskiy
G. of Karkinitsk

Budapest
Oradea
Cluj-
Napoca
Pietrosu
2102
Izmail
C. Tarkhankut
45

Szeged
Hódmezóvásárhely
Arad
R O M A N I A
Brašov
Galaţi
Sibiu
Nepoiu
2535
Brăila
Sulina

Subotica
Somor
Timişoara
Mureşul
Transylvanian Alps
Ploieşti
Dobrogea

Sad
Petrovaradin
Danube
Gate
Dobreta-
Turnu Severin
Pitesti
Bucharest
Constanţa

Belgrade
Smederevo
Orsova
Craiova
Danube
Silistra
B L A C K

YUGOSLAVIA
Kragujevac
Morava
Vidin
Iskur
Pleven
Ruse
Dobrich
S E A

SERBIA
Niš
Balkan Mts.
Pirnavo
Varna

Durmitor
2522
Novi Pazar
Shipka
Sliven
Burgas

MONTENEGRO
Podgorica
Cetinje
Sofia
B U L G A R I A

Shkoder
Musala
2925
Plovdiv
Zonguldak
Ereğli

2764
Skopje
Vardar
Struma
Rhodope
Edirne
Istanbul
Bosporus
Üsküdar
İzmit
Bolu

Tirane
MACEDONIA
Bitolj
Serrai
Xanthi
Tekirdağ
Sea of
Marmara
Iznik Gölü
Bilecik
Sakarya
40

Elbasan
G R E E C E
Kavalla
Komotini
Enez
Gelibolu
Bandirma
Bursa

Vlore
Aliakmon
Alexandroúpolis
Imbroz
Çanakkale
Eskişehir
Sivrihisar

Corfu
Pindus
Olympus
2917
Thessaloniki
Áthos
2033
Lemnos
Dardanelles
Balikesir
Kütahya
Afyon
Karahisar

Trikkala
Larissa
Vólos
N. Sporades
Lésvos
Ayvalik
Manisa
Turgutlu
Baiyadin
Eğridir
Gölü

Ioannina
Euboea
Chios
İzmir
Alaşehir
Menderes
Eğridir

Corfu
Corfu
Ionian Is.
Névpaktos
Levkás
Thebes
G. of Corinth
Athens
Andros
Sámos
Aydin
Denizli
Burdur
Isparta

Cephalonia
Patras
Corinth
Piraeus
Hermoupolis
Syros
Cyclades
Ikaría
Muğla
Taurus Mts.
Antalya

Zákinthos
Olympia
Peloponnesus
Náxos
Dodecanese
Elmali
3086

Kalamáta
Sparta
Milo
Ios

Pílos
5121
Thira
Rhodes
4486
Kastellórizon

C. Matapán
Cerigo
Andikithira
Khaniá
Mt. Ídhi
2456
Iráklion
Rhodes
Scarpanto

C r e t e

V E A N   S E A

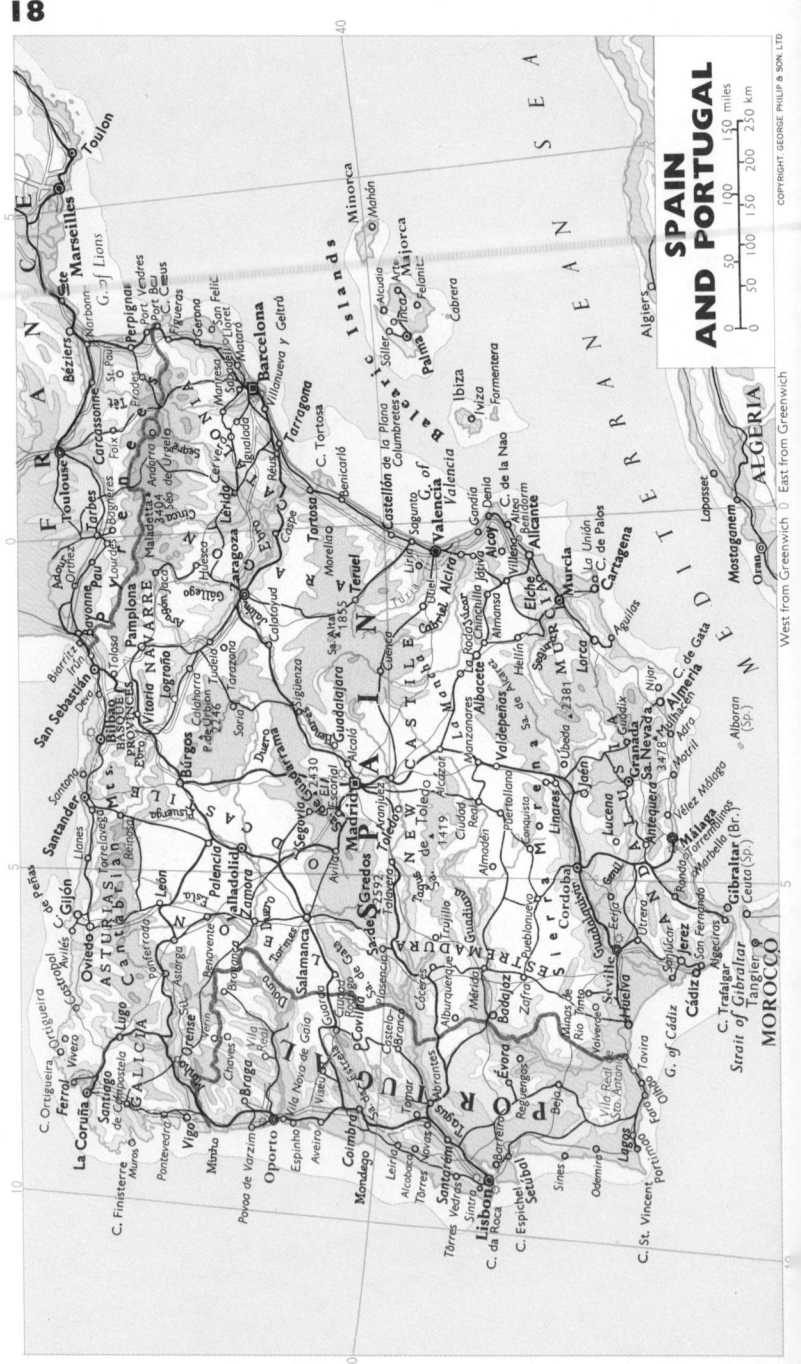

SPAIN AND PORTUGAL

0   50   100   150 miles
0   50   100   150   200   250 km

West from Greenwich   0   East from Greenwich

COPYRIGHT GEORGE PHILIP & SON LTD

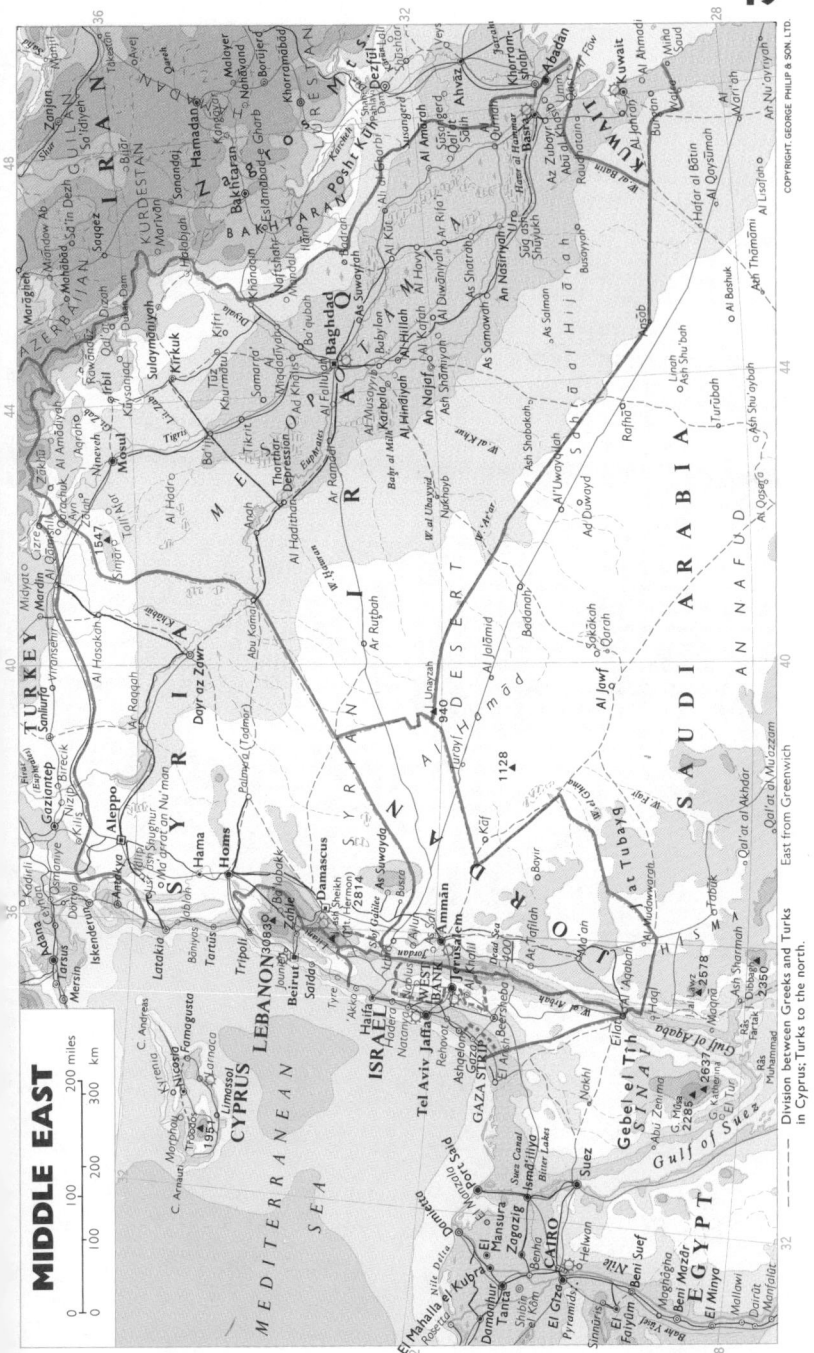

MIDDLE EAST

0 100 200 miles

0 100 200 300 km

East from Greenwich

— — — — Division between Greeks and Turks in Cyprus; Turks to the north.

COPYRIGHT GEORGE PHILIP & SON, LTD.

MEDITERRANEAN SEA

TURKEY

CYPRUS

SYRIA

LEBANON

ISRAEL

WEST BANK

GAZA STRIP

JORDAN

IRAN

IRAQ

KUWAIT

SAUDI ARABIA

EGYPT

SINAI

AZERBAIJAN

KURDISTAN

BAKHTIARAN

LURESTAN

Gulf of Suez

Gulf of Aqaba

Dead Sea

M E S O P O T A M I A

SYRIAN DESERT

An Nafūd

Şaḥrā al Ḥijārah

Al Ḥamād

Cairo, Aleppo, Damascus, Baghdad, Beirut, Amman, Jerusalem, Tel Aviv Jaffa, Haifa, Mosul, Kirkuk, Basra, Abadan, Kuwait, Al Ahmadi

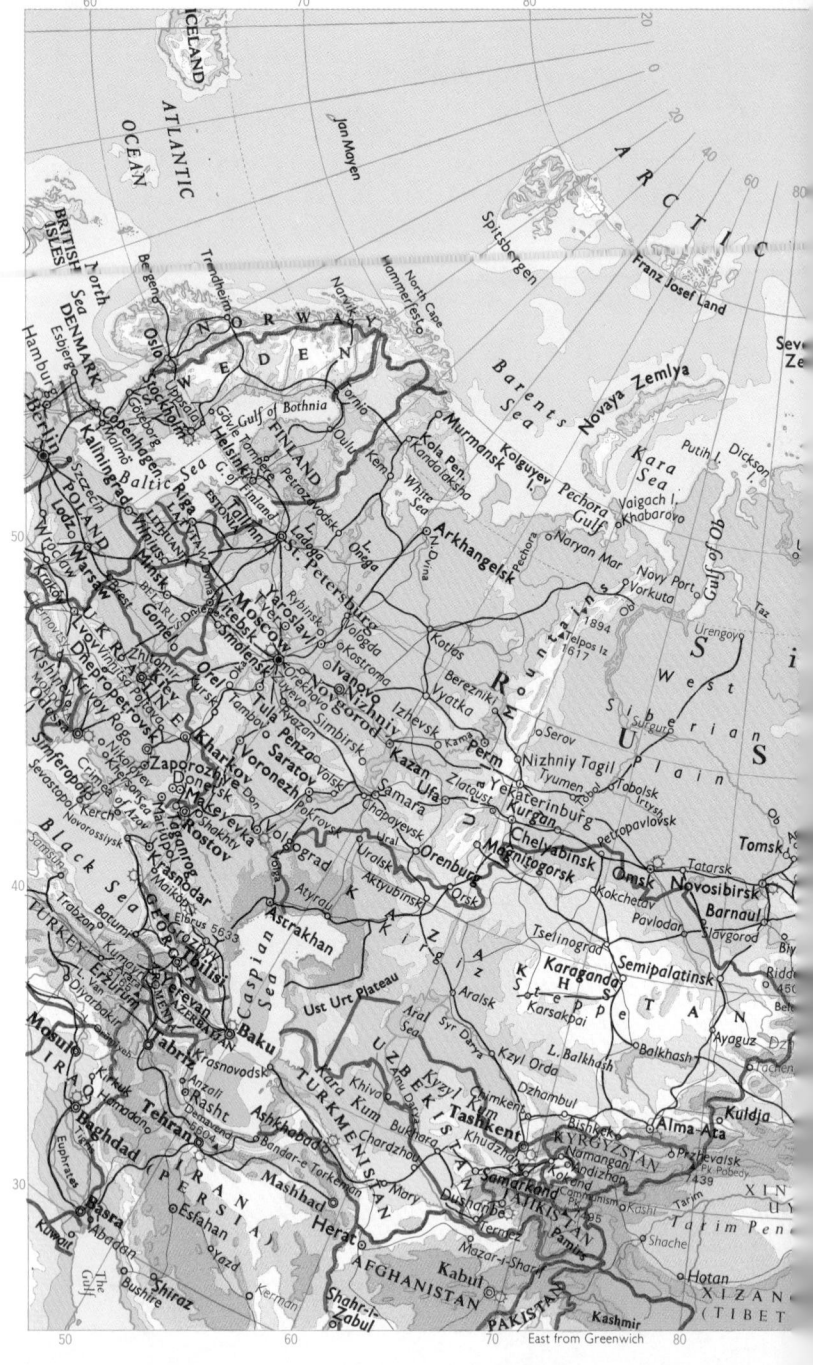

ALASKA

Bering Strait

St. Lawrence I. (U.S.A.)

Bering Sea

O C E A N

Komsomolets I.
October Revolution I.
Bolshevik I.

De Long Is.

East Siberian Sea

Chukot Sea

Wrangel I.

Chukot Range

Gulf of Anadyr

Anadyr

Komandorskiye

rrang Mts.
Taimyr Pen.
L. Taimyr

Laptev Sea

New Siberian Is.

Lyakhov Is.

Nizhne Kolymsk

Beruang I.
Amabachik

Kolyma Ra.

Gizhigo

Magadan

Kamchatka

Komandorskiye Is.

ka
Isk
a

Nordvik

Tiksi

Yana

Verkhoyansk

Sredne Kolymsk

Kolyma

Shelokhov Gulf

Ust Kamchatsko

Klyuchevsk
4750 m.

Khatanga

Kory R.

Buluno

Verkhoyansk Range

Aldan

Okhotsk

Sea of Okhotsk

Petropavlovsk Kamchatskiy

C e n t r a l

Znigansk

Lena

Dzhugdzhur Ra.

Shantar Is.

Okho

Sakhalin

Circle

Zhigansk

Vilyuisk

Yakutsk

Nikolayevsk

Aleksandrovsk

Lower Tunguska

loginsk

S i b e r i a n

Olekminsk

Aldan

Stanovoi Ra.

Gulf of Tartary

Sovetskaya Gavan

Yuzhno-Sakhalinsk
Korsakov

P l a t e a u

Lena

Skovorodino

Belogorsk

Komsomolsk

Birobidzhan

Sikhote Alin Range

Kuril Is.

Stony Tunguska

Kirensk

Bodaibo

Amur

Khabarovsk

Angara

Bratsk

Yablonovy Ra.

Sretensk

Nerchinsk

Blagoveshchensk

Sapporo

Otaru

ko
Achinsk

Krasnoyarsk

Taishet
Kansk

Nizhneudinsk

L. Baikal

Chita

Olovyannaya

Amur

Songhua

Hakodate

Vladivostok

JAPAN

vo
Kuznetskiy
znetsk

Tulun

Cheremkhovo

Angarsk

Ulan-Ude

Khilok

Petrovsk

Hailar

Harbin

Ussuriysk

Minusinsk
Munku-Sardyk
349

Irkutsk

Kyakhta

Selenga

Changchun

Shenyang

N
Wonsan

Sea of Japan

Yenisei

Ulan Bator

Ulan Bator

Dandong

Seoul

KOREA

Pusan

Hiroshima

JAPAN

nqi

Dzhibkhalantu

M O N G O L I A

Gobi Desert

Beijing (Peking)

Pyongyang

Inchon

Mokpo

Masan

Nagasaki

urpan

Baotou

C H I N A

Datong

Tianjin

Dalian

Qingdao

Kunsan

G

WALL

GREAT

Hwang

Jinan

Lianyungang

Nur

Lanzhou

Xi'an

Zhengzhou

RUSSIA AND CENTRAL ASIA

| 0 | 200 | 400 | 600 | 800 miles |
| 0 | 200 400 | 600 800 | 1000 1200 | km |

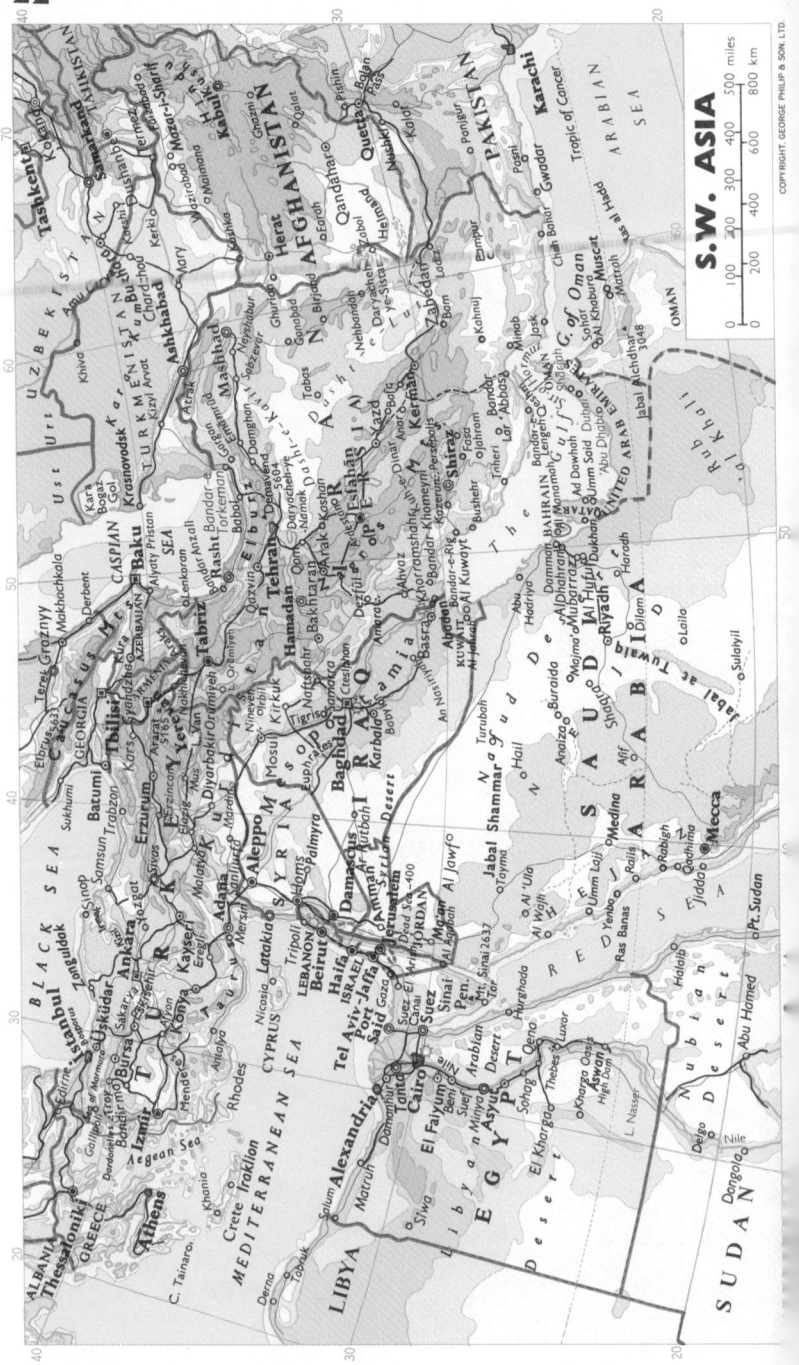

S.W. ASIA

0 100 200 300 400 500 miles
0 200 400 600 800 km

COPYRIGHT. GEORGE PHILIP & SON, LTD.

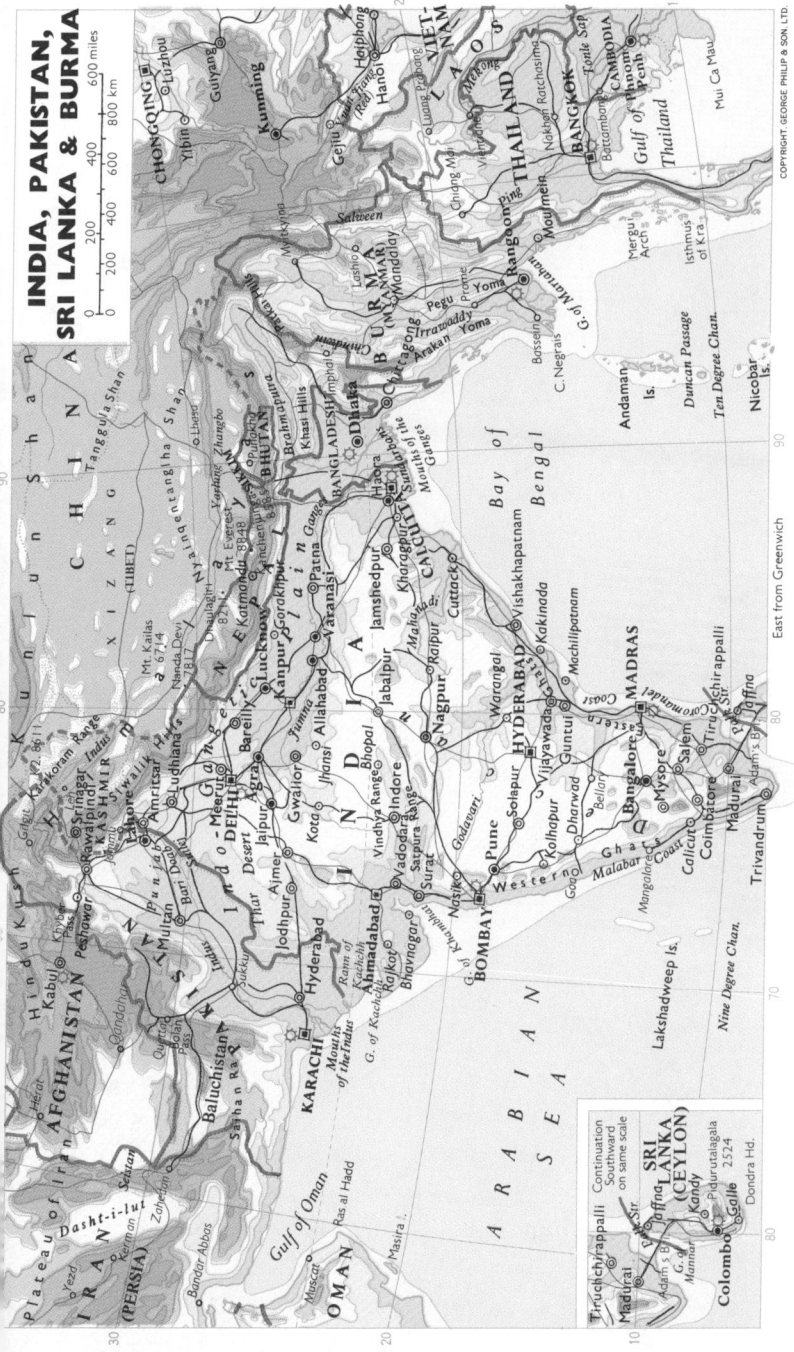

23

INDIA, PAKISTAN, SRI LANKA & BURMA

COPYRIGHT GEORGE PHILIP & SON LTD.

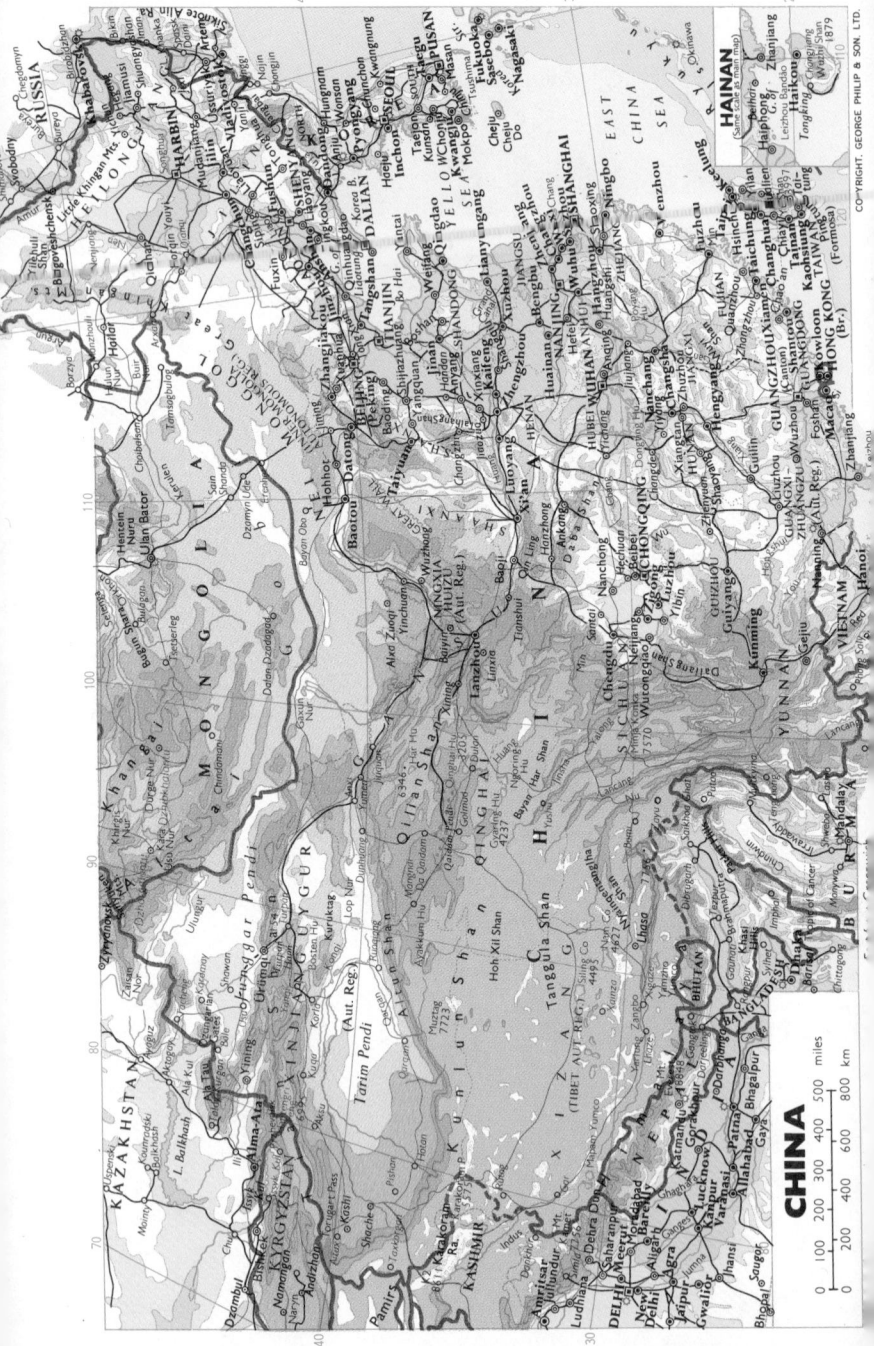

24

CHINA

| 0 | 100 | 200 | 300 | 400 | 500 miles |
| 0 | 200 | 400 | 600 | 800 | km |

HAINAN (Same scale as main map)

COPYRIGHT. GEORGE PHILIP & SON, LTD.

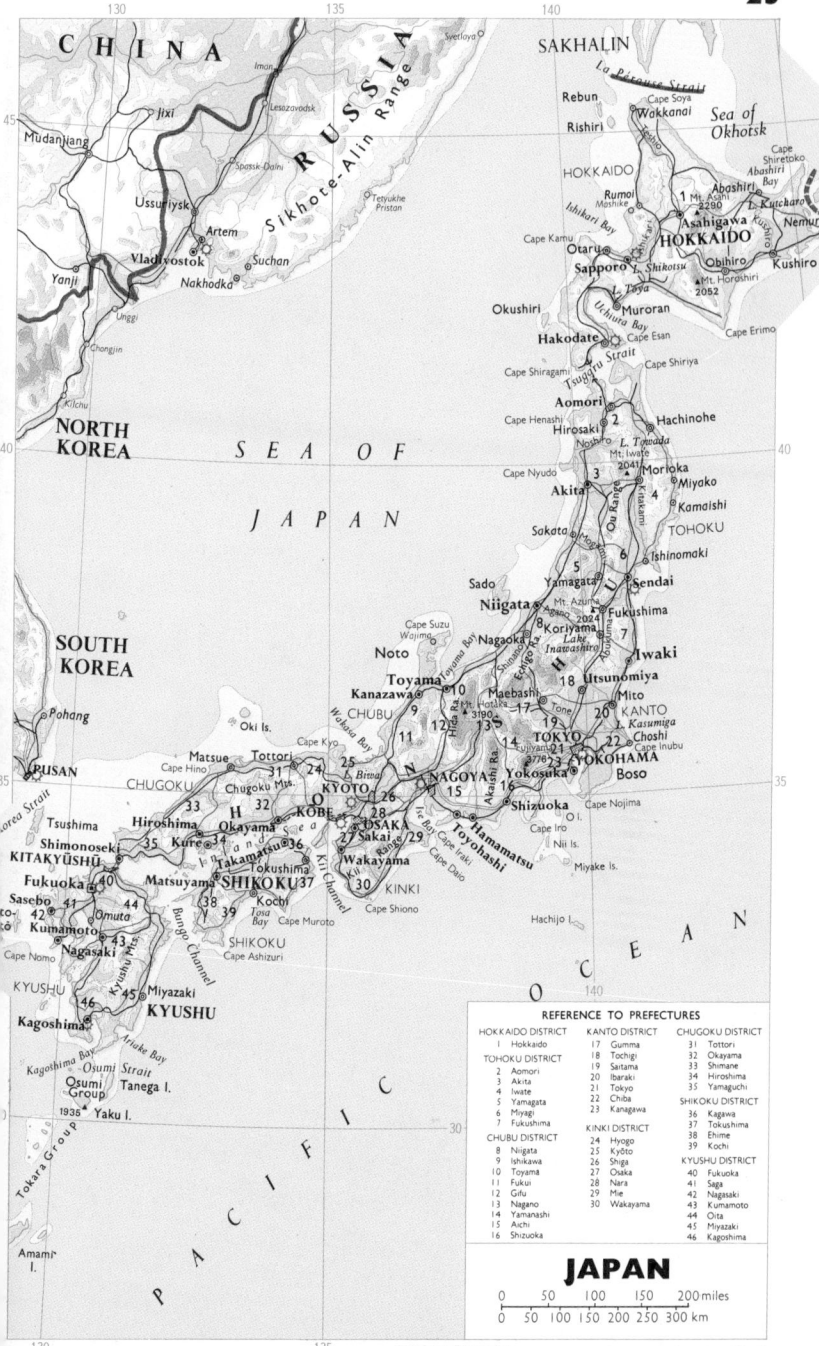

CHINA

RUSSIA

Sikhote-Alin Range

SAKHALIN

La Perouse Strait

Svetloya

Iman

Lesozavodsk

Rebun

Cape Soya

Wakkanai

Sea of Okhotsk

Jixi

Spassk-Dalni

Rishiri

Mudanjiang

Tetyukhe Pristan

HOKKAIDO

Cape Shiretoko

Abashiri Bay

Ussuriysk

Artem

Suchan

Cape Kamu

Rumoi

Mt. Asahi 2290

Abashiri

L. Kutcharo

Nemuro

Yanji

Vladivostok

Nakhodka

Otaru

Ishikari Bay

Asahigawa

HOKKAIDO

Sapporo

L. Shikotsu

Obihiro

Kushiro

Unggi

Chongjin

Okushiri

L. Taya

Uchiura Bay

Muroran

Mt. Horoshiri 2052

NORTH KOREA

Hakodate

Cape Esan

Cape Erimo

Kilchu

Cape Shiragami

Tsugaru Strait

Cape Shiriya

S E A   O F

Aomori

Cape Henashi

Hirosaki

Noshiro

L. Towada

Hachinohe

Mt. Iwate 2041

J A P A N

Cape Nyudo

Akita

Ou Range

Morioka

Miyako

Kitakami

Kamaishi

SOUTH KOREA

Sakata

TOHOKU

Ishinomaki

Sado

Yamagata

Sendai

Mt. Azuma

Niigata

Agano

Fukushima

Pohang

Noto

Nagaoka

Koriyama

Lake Inawashiro

Iwaki

Oki Is.

Cape Suzu

Wajima

Toyama

Shinano

Utsunomiya

Kanazawa

CHUBU

Maebashi

Mito

KANTO

Matsue

Tottori

Cape Kyo

Wakasa Bay

Hida Ra.

Mt. Hotaka 3190

L. Kasumiga

Cape Inubu

PUSAN

CHUGOKU

Cape Hino

Chugoku Mts.

L. Biwa

Fujiyama 3776

TOKYO

YOKOHAMA

Choshi

Boso

Tsushima

Matsuyama

KYOTO

NAGOYA

Akashi Str.

Yokosuka

Shimonoseki

Hiroshima

Kure

OSAKA

Sakai

Shizuoka

Cape Nojima

O I.

KITAKYUSHU

Okayama

KOBE

Toyohashi

Cape Iro

Nii Is.

Fukuoka

Takamatsu

Tokushima

Wakayama

Hamamatsu

Miyake Is.

Sasebo

Omuta

Matsuyama

SHIKOKU

Kochi

Cape Daio

KINKI

Kumamoto

Oita

Tosa Bay

Cape Muroto

Hachijo I.

Nagasaki

Bungo Channel

Miyazaki

Kaji Mts.

Cape Ashizuri

SHIKOKU

Cape Nomo

Cape Shiono

Kagoshima

KYUSHU

Kagoshima Bay

Ariake Bay

Osumi

O

C

E

A

N

Tokara Group

Osumi

Tanega I.

Yaku I.

1935

P

A

C

I

F

I

C

Amami I.

REFERENCE TO PREFECTURES		
HOKKAIDO DISTRICT	**KANTO DISTRICT**	**CHUGOKU DISTRICT**
1 Hokkaido	17 Gumma	31 Tottori
TOHOKU DISTRICT	18 Tochigi	32 Okayama
2 Aomori	19 Saitama	33 Shimane
3 Akita	20 Ibaraki	34 Hiroshima
4 Iwate	21 Tokyo	35 Yamaguchi
5 Yamagata	22 Chiba	**SHIKOKU DISTRICT**
6 Miyagi	23 Kanagawa	36 Kagawa
7 Fukushima		37 Tokushima
	KINKI DISTRICT	38 Ehime
CHUBU DISTRICT	24 Hyogo	39 Kochi
8 Niigata	25 Kyoto	**KYUSHU DISTRICT**
9 Ishikawa	26 Shiga	40 Fukuoka
10 Toyama	27 Osaka	41 Saga
11 Fukui	28 Nara	42 Nagasaki
12 Gifu	29 Mie	43 Kumamoto
13 Nagano	30 Wakayama	44 Oita
14 Yamanashi		45 Miyazaki
15 Aichi		46 Kagoshima
16 Shizuoka		

JAPAN

0   50   100   150   200 miles

0 50 100 150 200 250 300 km

East from Greenwich

COPYRIGHT. GEORGE PHILIP & SON. LTD.

SOUTH-EAST ASIA

0 200 400 600 miles
0 200 400 600 800 km

NORTHERN MARIANAS

P A C I F I C   O C E A N

Guam (U.S.A.)

FEDERATED STATES OF MICRONESIA

Yap Is.

BELAU

C a r o l i n e   I s l a n d s

Admiralty Is.

Bismarck Sea

New Britain

PAPUA NEW GUINEA

Owen Stanley Ra.

Port Moresby

Coral Sea

IRIAN JAYA

Torres Strait

Arafura Sea

Aru Is.

Tanimbar Is.

Kai Is.

Banda Sea

Ceram Sea

Halmahera

North C.

Morotai

Celebes Sea

Mindanao Trench

Mindanao

Davao

Davao Gulf

PHILIPPINES

Luzon

Manila

Quezon City

Cebu

Panay

Negros

Sulu Sea

Zamboanga

Sandakan

BRUNEI

Kota Kinabalu

SARAWAK

Kuching

B O R N E O

K A L I M A N T A N

Pontianak

Banjarmasin

Balikpapan

SULAWESI

Celebes

Makassar

Flores Sea

Java Sea

Banjarmasin

S O U T H

C H I N A   S E A

Natuna Is.

Anambas Is.

MALAYSIA

Kuala Lumpur

Singapore

Melaka

Ipoh

George Town

Penang

I N D O N E S I A

Sumatra

Palembang

Medan

Padang

Bengkulu

Java

Jakarta

Bandung

Semarang

Surabaya

Bali

Lombok

Sumbawa

Flores

Timor

Sumba

Mentawai Is.

Siberut

Nias

Simeulue

Str. of Malacca

I N D I A N

O C E A N

Hainan

Haiphong

Hanoi

V I E T N A M

Vinh

Hue

Da Nang

Ho Chi-Minh City

L A O S

Vientiane

THAILAND

Bangkok

CAMBODIA

Phnom Penh

Gulf of Thailand

Rangoon

Mergui Archipelago

Phuket

Andaman Is.

Gulf of Tongking

COPYRIGHT GEORGE PHILIP & SON LTD.

East from Greenwich

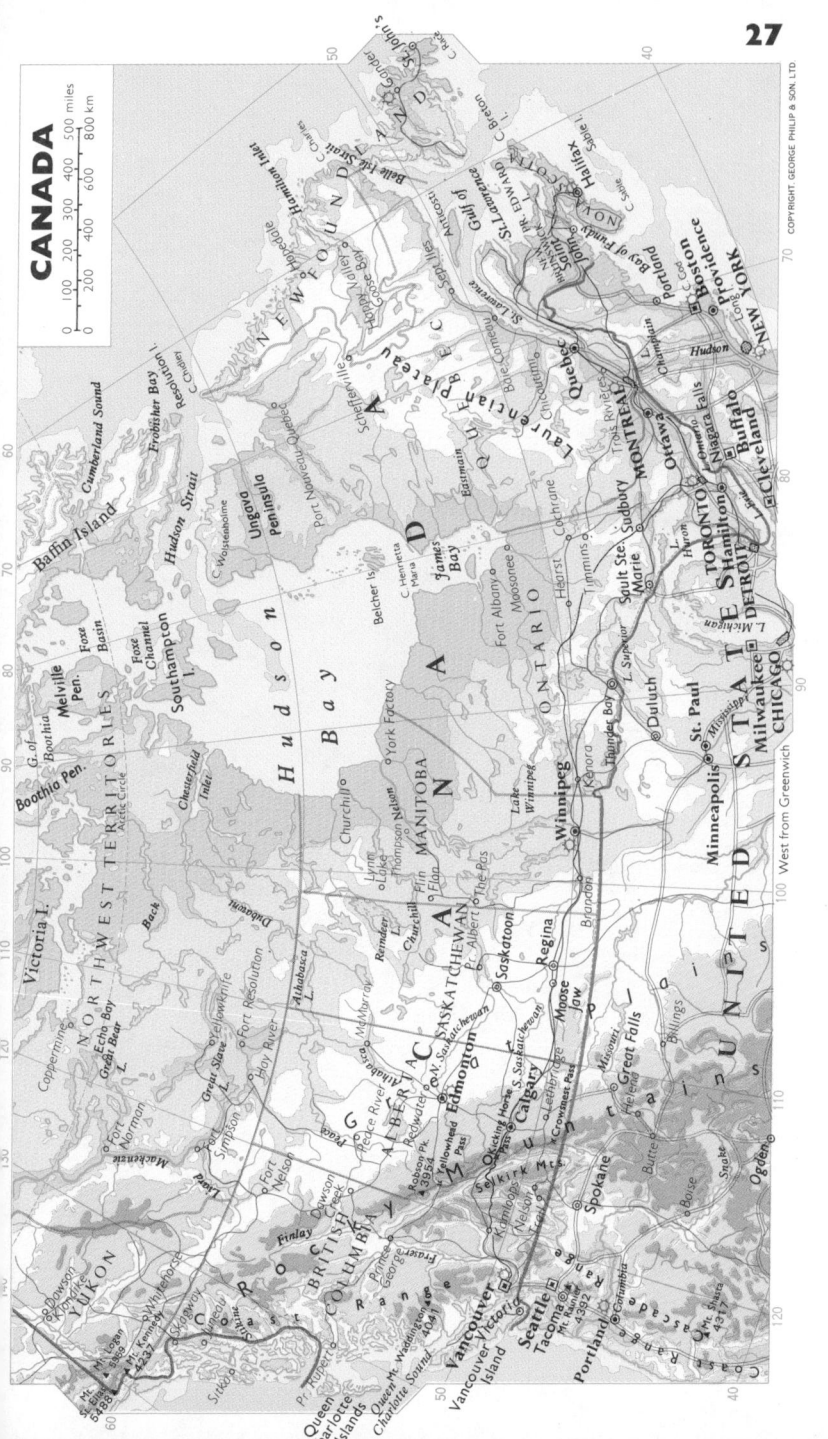

27

CANADA

0 100 200 300 400 500 miles
0 200 400 600 800 km

COPYRIGHT GEORGE PHILIP & SON, LTD.

PACIFIC

OCEAN

C. Flattery

Victoria

Vancouver

Kamloops

Red Deer

N. Battleford

Prince Albert

Saskatoon

Rosetown

Calgary

Drumheller

Moose Jaw

Regina

Portage
la Prairie

Medicine Hat

Lethbridge

Brandon

C A N

Minot

Grand Forks

Tacoma

Seattle

Everett

Sandpoint

Spokane

WASHINGTON

Mt.
Rainier 4392

Portland

Corvallis

Eugene

Columbia

Walla Walla

Gt. Falls

Missoula

Helena

Missouri

Butte

MONTANA

Yellowstone

Billings

Glendive

N. DAKOTA

Bismarck

Fargo

Aberdeen

Medford

La Grande

OREGON

Payette

IDAHO

Boise

Snake

Idaho Falls

WYOMING

Casper

Black
Hills

Rapid City

S.
DAKOTA

Sioux Fa

Klamath Falls

Mt. Shasta
4317

Twin Falls

Gt. Salt Lake

Gannett Pk.
4202

Elko

Ogden

Great

Reno

NEVADA

Basin

Sacramento

Stockton

Oakland

San
Francisco

Fresno

Mt. Whitney 4418

Salt Lake City

Provo

UTAH

Wasatch

Laramie

Cheyenne

Grand Island

NEBRASKA

Platte

Long's Pk.
4345

Denver

Grand
Junction

COLORADO

Pikes Pk.
4301

Colorado Springs

Pueblo

Kan

KANSA

Hutchinson

Wichita

Bakersfield

Santa Barbara

LOS
ANGELES

Pasadena

Long Beach

San Diego

Las
Vegas

Death
Valley

Colorado

Blanca Pk.
4364

Trinidad

Arkansas

Wich
Falls

Mexicali

Tucson

ARIZONA

Phoenix

Gila

Grand
Canyon

Colorado
Plateau

Winslow

Albuquerque

NEW MEXICO

Santa Fe

Canadian

Amarillo

Pampa

OKLA

Oklahoma
City

Clovis

Llano
Estacado

Lubbock

Fort Worth

Las Cruces

Rio Grande

Ciudad
Juarez

El Paso

Pecos

Odessa

Abilene

San Angelo

T E
X
A
S

UNITED

S

Hermosillo

Gulf of California

Guaymas

Ciudad Obregon

MEXICO

Chihuahua

Sierra Madre

Alpine

Rio Grande

Austin

San
Antonio

Nuevo Laredo

Los Mochis

Tropic of Cancer

C. San Lucas

Culiacan

Mazatlan

Torreón

Monterrey

San Luis
Potosi

Tam

Projection: Bonne

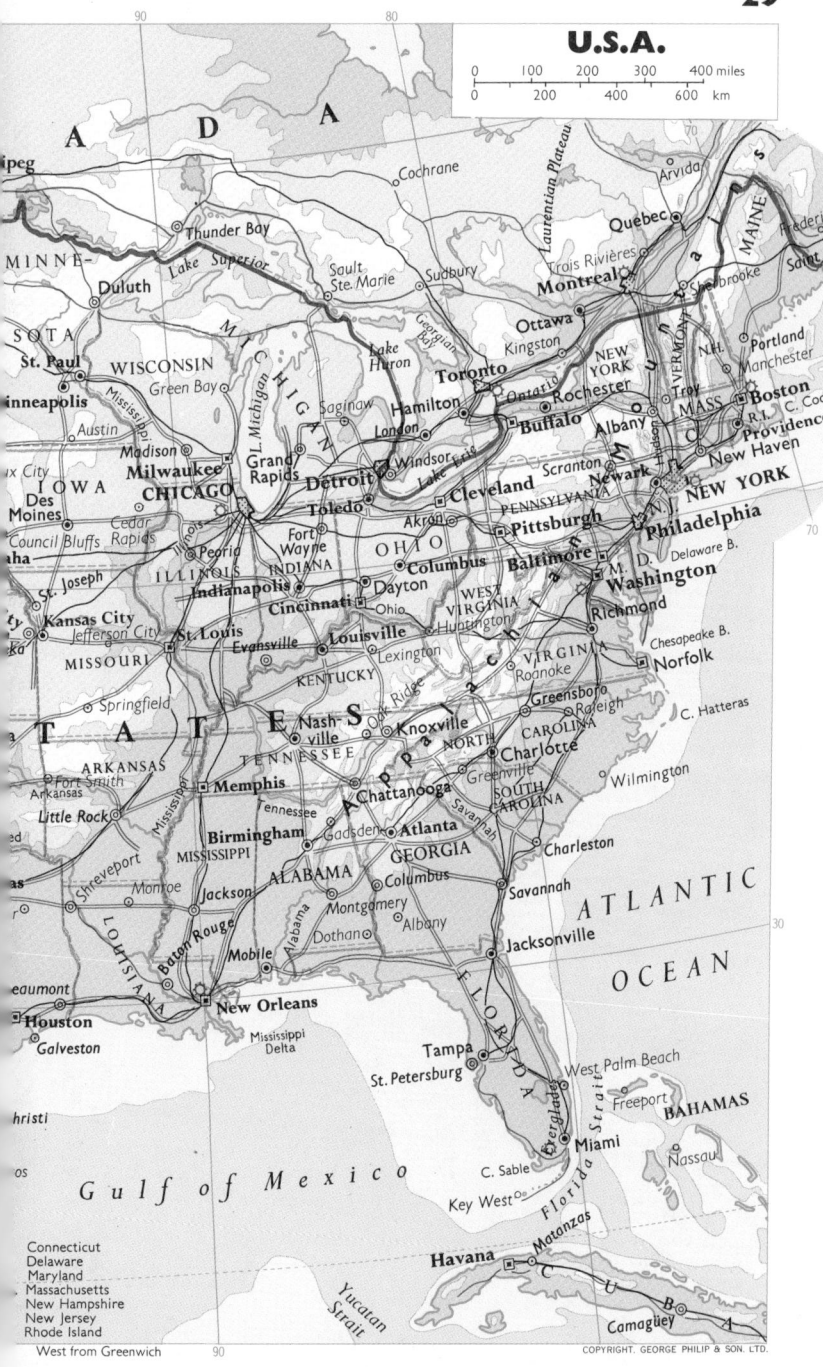

U.S.A.

0	100	200	300	400 miles
0	200	400	600 km	

Connecticut
Delaware
Maryland
Massachusetts
New Hampshire
New Jersey
Rhode Island

West from Greenwich   90

COPYRIGHT. GEORGE PHILIP & SON. LTD.

MEXICO AND THE CARIBBEAN

0 100 200 300 400 500 miles
0 200 400 600 800 km

COPYRIGHT GEORGE PHILIP & SON LTD.

ATLANTIC OCEAN

PACIFIC OCEAN

Gulf of Mexico

Caribbean Sea

Greater Antilles

Tropic of Cancer

UNITED STATES

MEXICO

Lower California

Gulf of California

Western Sierra Madre

Eastern Sierra Madre

Mexican Plateau

MEXICO CITY

Charleston
Savannah
Jacksonville
Atlanta
Columbus
Montgomery
Birmingham
Mobile
Jackson
New Orleans
Baton Rouge
Houston
Corpus Christi
Austin
San Antonio
Fort Worth
Dallas
El Paso
Ciudad Juárez
Nogales
Hermosillo
Guaymas
Chihuahua
Piedras Negras
Nuevo Laredo
Matamoros
Monterrey
Saltillo
Torreón
Durango
Mazatlán
Aguascalientes
León
Guadalajara
San Luis Potosí
Tampico
Veracruz
Puebla
Popocatepetl 5452
Oaxaca
Acapulco
Coatzacoalcos
Villahermosa
Tuxtla Gutiérrez
Mérida
Yucatan
Gulf of Campeche
Bahia de Campeche
Rio Grande
C. Corrientes
C. San Lucas
Revilla Gigedo Is. (Mexico)
G. of Tehuantepec
Golfo Cruz

Miami
Tampa
Florida
Florida Strait
C. Sable
BAHAMAS
Nassau
Turks & Caicos Is. (Br.)

Havana
Sta. Clara
Camagüey
Holguín
CUBA
Santiago de Cuba
Yucatan Strait
C. Catoche
Cayman Is. (Br.)

JAMAICA
Kingston
HAITI
DOMINICAN REP.
Santiago
Santo Domingo
Port au Prince
Hispaniola
PUERTO RICO
San Juan
Virgin Is. (Br.)
ANGUILLA
ANTIGUA & BARBUDA
ST. KITTS-NEVIS
GUADELOUPE (Fr.)
DOMINICA
MARTINIQUE (Fr.)
ST. LUCIA
ST. VINCENT & THE GRENADINES
BARBADOS
GRENADA
TRINIDAD & TOBAGO
Port of Spain

BELIZE
Belmopan
GUATEMALA
Guatemala
EL SALVADOR
San Salvador
HONDURAS
Tegucigalpa
Gulf of Honduras
NICARAGUA
Managua
Chinandega
L. Nicaragua
COSTA RICA
San José
Colón
PANAMA
Panamá
G. of Panama
C. Gracias á Dios

VENEZUELA
CARACAS
Maracaibo
Barquisimeto
Barcelona
Maracaibo
Mérida
G. of Venezuela
Orinoco
Caroni
Caura
Apure
Meta
Ciudad Bolívar

COLOMBIA
Barranquilla
Cartagena
Cúcuta
Bucaramanga
Medellín
Magdalena
Sa. Nevada de Sta. María
G. of Darién
5800

31

SOUTH AMERICA

0   200   400   600   800 miles
0 200 400   800   1200 km

COPYRIGHT, GEORGE PHILIP & SON. LTD.

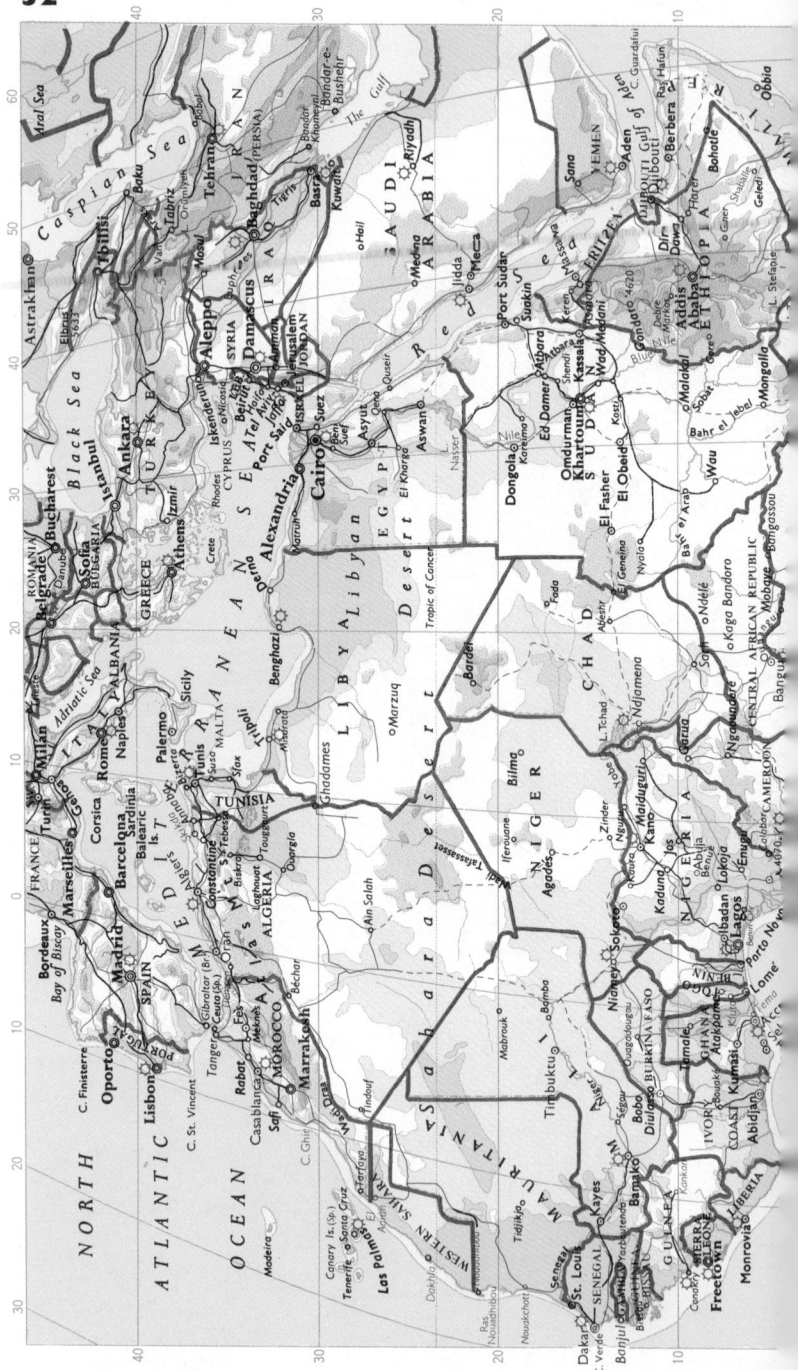

AFRICA

```
0    200   400   600   800 miles
0  200 400 600 800 1000 1200 km
```

West from Greenwich 0 East from Greenwich

COPYRIGHT GEORGE PHILIP & SON LTD.

Countries and regions: CONGO, GABON, ZAIRE, ANGOLA, NAMIBIA (SOUTHWEST AFRICA), BOTSWANA, ZAMBIA, ZIMBABWE, MOZAMBIQUE, MALAWI, TANZANIA, KENYA, RWANDA, BURUNDI, MADAGASCAR, SOUTH AFRICA, CAPE PROVINCE, ORANGE FREE STATE, TRANSVAAL, NATAL, SWAZILAND

Cities and places: Kismayu, Lamu, Malindi, Mombasa, Nairobi, Tanga, Zanzibar, Dar-es-Salaam, Arusha, Moshi, Dodoma, Tabora, Kigoma, Mtwara, Mbeya, Morogoro, Pemba, Mozambique, Mahajanga, Antananarivo, Toamasina, Fianarantsoa, Antsirabe, Morondava, C. Amber, C. Ste Marie, Quelimane, Beira, Blantyre, Harare, Bulawayo, Mutare, Inhambane, Maputo, Pietersburg, Germiston, Pietermaritzburg, Durban, Ladysmith, Pretoria, Johannesburg, Bloemfontein, Kimberley, Keetmanshoop, Windhoek, Swakopmund, Walvis Bay, Lüderitz, Namibe, Benguela, Lobito, Luanda, Ambriz, Cabinda, Pointe Noire, Brazzaville, Kinshasa, Boma, Mbandaka, Kisangani, Kananga, Kolwezi, Lubumbashi, Likasi, Lusaka, Livingstone, Gaborone, De Aar, Grahamstown, Port Elizabeth, East London, Mossel Bay, Cape Town, Simonstown, C. of Good Hope, Upington

Water bodies: INDIAN OCEAN, SOUTH ATLANTIC OCEAN, L. Victoria, L. Tanganyika, L. Malawi, L. Edward, Tropic of Capricorn, Zambezi, Orange

Islands: St. Helena, Ascension I., Aldabra, COMOROS

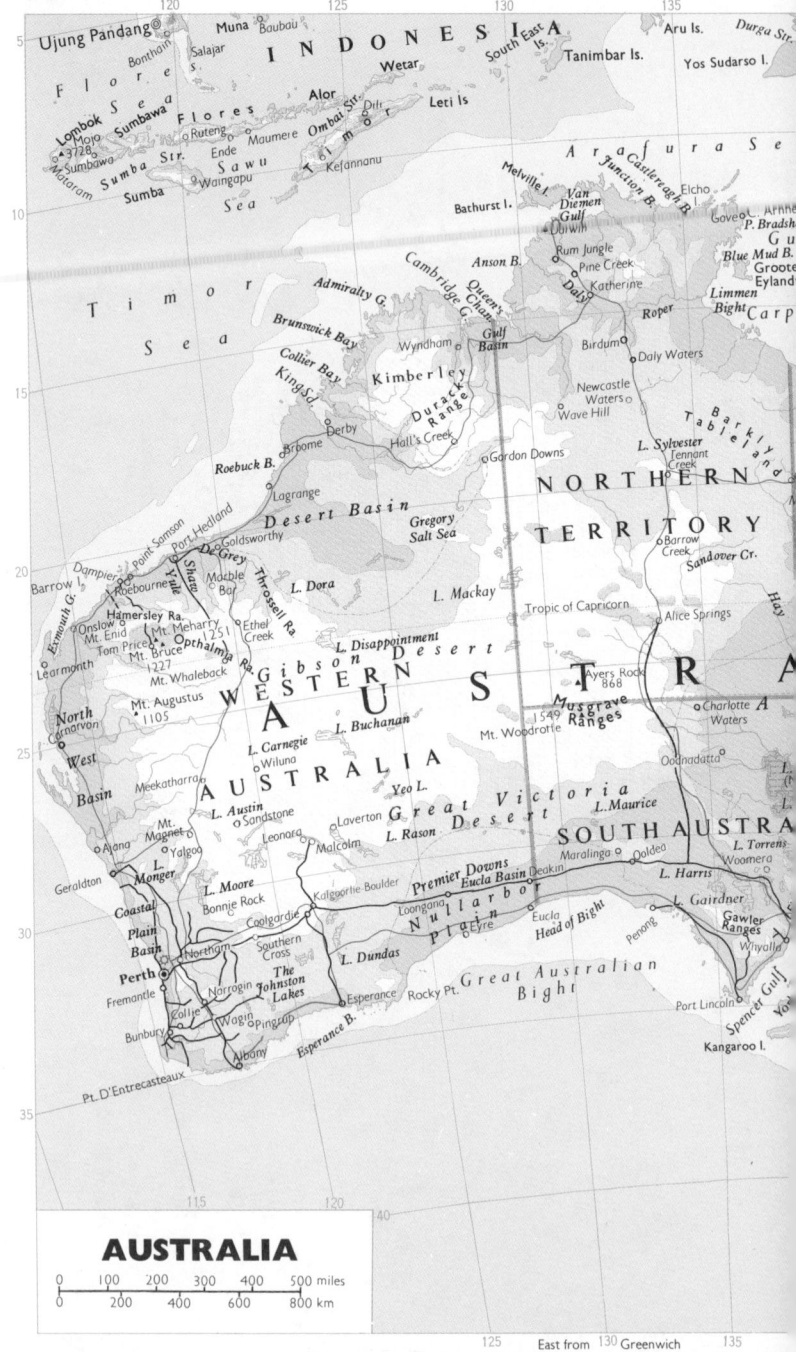

AUSTRALIA

| 0 | 100 | 200 | 300 | 400 | 500 miles |

| 0 | 200 | 400 | 600 | 800 km |

East from Greenwich

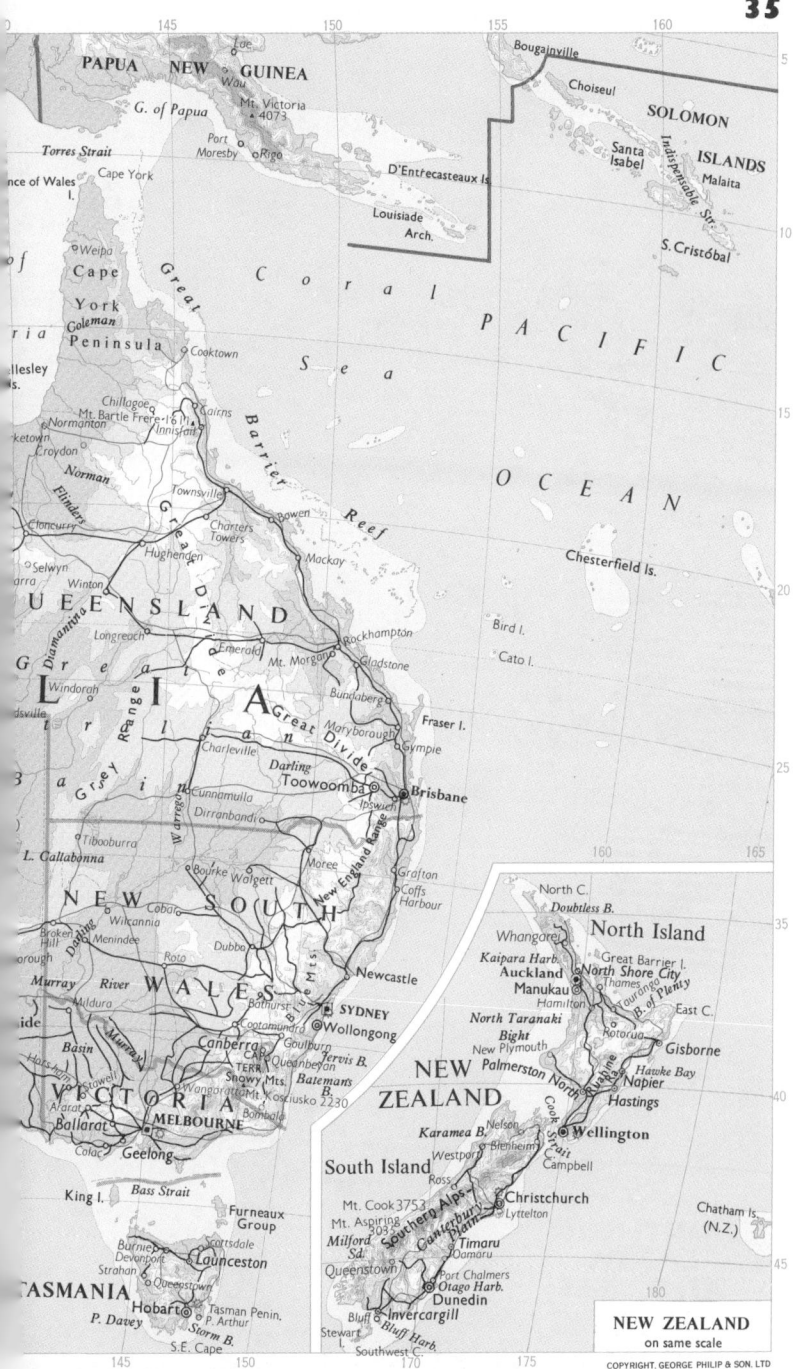

PAPUA NEW GUINEA

Mt. Victoria ▲4073
Wau
Lae
G. of Papua
Port Moresby
Rigo
Torres Strait
Cape York
nce of Wales I.

Bougainville
Choiseul
SOLOMON ISLANDS
Santa Isabel
Malaita
Indispensable Str.
D'Entrecasteaux Is.
Louisiade Arch.
S. Cristóbal

Coral Sea

PACIFIC

OCEAN

Cape York Peninsula
Weipa
Coleman
Cooktown
Chillagoe
Cairns
Mt. Bartle Frere 1611
Innisfail
Normanton
ketown
Croydon
Townsville
Bowen
Charters Towers
Mackay
Hughenden
Selwyn
Winton
Longreach
Emerald
Rockhampton
Mt. Morgan
Gladstone
Bundaberg
Maryborough
Fraser I.
Gympie
Windorah
Charleville
Darling
Toowoomba
Ipswich
Brisbane
Cunnamulla
Dirranbandi
Moree
Grafton
Coffs Harbour
L. Callabonna
Tibooburra
Bourke
Walgett
Dubbo
Newcastle
Cobar
Wilcannia
Menindee
Roto
SYDNEY
Wollongong
Broken Hill
Mildura
Canberra
Goulburn
Jervis B.
Queanbeyan
Batemans B.
Wangaratta
Snowy Mts.
Mt. Kosciusko 2230
Bombala
Ararat
Ballarat
MELBOURNE
Geelong
Colac
King I.
Bass Strait
Furneaux Group
Burnie
Scottsdale
Devonport
Launceston
Strahan
Queenstown
TASMANIA
Hobart
P. Davey
Port Arthur
Tasman Penin.
Storm B.
S.E. Cape
Southwest C.

QUEENSLAND

Great Dividing Range

NEW SOUTH WALES

Murray River

VICTORIA

Chesterfield Is.
Bird I.
Cato I.

Great Barrier Reef

Cape York

North C.
Doubtless B.
Whangarei
Kaipara Harb.
Great Barrier I.
North Shore City
Auckland
Manukau
Thames
B. of Plenty
East C.
Hamilton
Tauranga
Rotorua
North Taranaki Bight
New Plymouth
Gisborne
Palmerston North
Hawke Bay
Napier
Hastings

NORTH ISLAND

NEW ZEALAND

Karamea B.
Nelson
Westport
Blenheim
Ross
Campbell
Wellington
Cook Strait

SOUTH ISLAND

Mt. Cook 3753
Mt. Aspiring 3035
Milford Sd.
Queenstown
Southern Alps
Canterbury Plains
Timaru
Oamaru
Port Chalmers
Otago Harb.
Dunedin
Bluff
Bluff Harb.
Invercargill
Stewart I.
Christchurch
Lyttelton

Chatham Is. (N.Z.)

NEW ZEALAND
on same scale

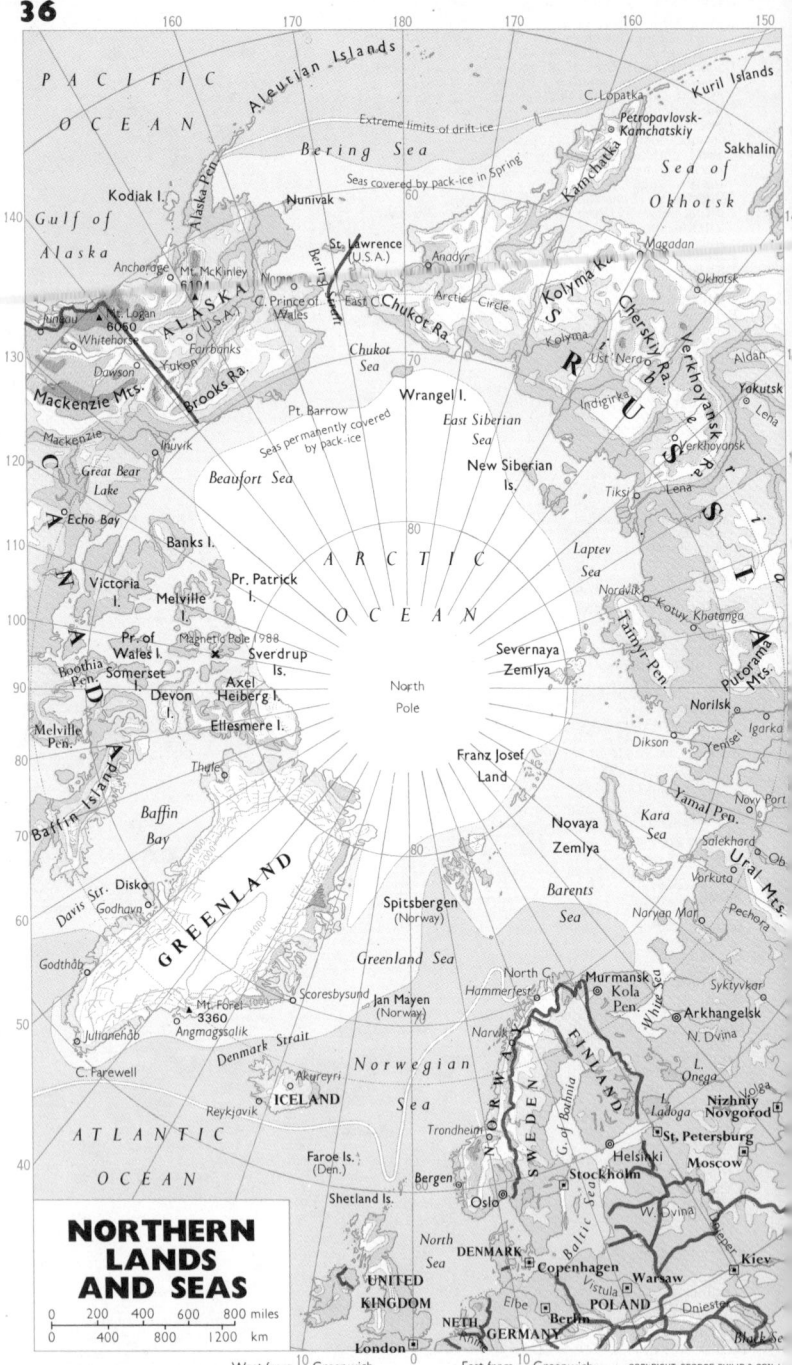

NORTHERN LANDS AND SEAS

| 0 | 200 | 400 | 600 | 800 miles |
| 0 | 400 | 800 | 1200 km |

West from 10 Greenwich   0   East from 10 Greenwich   COPYRIGHT. GEORGE PHILIP & SON. L

Cordilleras, 2,745 m a.s.l.; univ., nat. observatory, colonial architecture; political, social and financial ctr. of rep.; p. (1992) 4,819,676.

Bo Hai (Pohai), G. of, N. China; together with G. of Liaotung forms shallow expanse of water almost cut off from Yellow Sea by Liaotung and Shandong peninsulas; receives water and silt from Huang He; a. approx. 38,900 km².

Bohemia, historic region, former kingdom, Czech **Rep.;** plateau drained by R. Elbe; borders W. Germany; agr. dist.; minerals inc. lignite, graphite; textiles, sugar, pottery.

Böhmerwald (Bohemian Forest), forested range of mtns. between Czech Rep. and Bavaria, **Germany;** 240 km long; alt. 1,479 m at Aber; region of poor soils; sm. farms; some mng. and quarrying.

Bohol I., prov. **Philippines;** maize, coconuts, rice; a. 3,864 km²; p. (1990) 948,315.

Boise, t., cap. of Idaho, **USA;** financial ctr.; timber mills; hot springs; p. (1990) 125,738.

Boksburg, t., Transvaal, **S. Africa;** industl., former coal-mng.; t. p. (1980) 156,780.

Bolan Pass, Baluchistan, **Pakistan;** pass from Pakistan to Afghanistan; summit 1,800 m.

Bolbec, t., Seine-Maritime, **France;** 19 km E. of Le Havre; textiles; elec. engin.; p. (1982) 12,578.

Boldon, t., Tyne and Wear, **Eng.;** coal mng.; p. (1981) 24,171.

Boliden, t., N. **Sweden;** impt. deposits of copper and arsenic.

Bolivia, inland rep., S. **America;** land-locked, 9 deps.; cap. nominally Sucre, actual admin. H.Q. La Paz; much US investment but discouraged by nationalism from late 1960s; relief makes transport difficult; moves towards gaining access to cst. via internat. corridor; forests; savannahs; agr. in backward conditions; embryonic industl. devel. suffered from political instability; much social protest against military rule, return to democracy 1982; rubber, quinine, cattle, hides; ch. exp. gas and tin; petroleum; mafia cocaine tr.; exp. illegal narcotics; language Spanish; a. 1,331,661 km²; p. (1991) 7·61 m.

Bollington, t., Cheshire, **Eng.;** nr. Macclesfield; textile finishing; p. (1981) 6,930.

Bologna, c., N. **Italy;** cap. of B. prov. on N. flank of Apennines; impt. route ctr. commanding road and rly. across Apennines to Florence; preserved and restored in Arcadian style by Communist admin.; univ., service t.; p. (1992) 401,308.

Bolsena, L., Latium region, **Italy;** occupies lge. extinct volcanic crater in S. of Tuscan Hills 96 km N.W. of Rome; a. (approx.) 129 km²; p. (1981) 3,960.

Bolshoya Volga, t., **Russia;** 128 km N. of Moscow, at junct. of Volga and Moscow Volga Canal; Soviet Institute of Nuclear Studies.

Bolsover, t., l. gov. dist., Derbys., **Eng.;** limestone, textiles; cas.; Hardwick Hall 6 km to S., p. (1993) 71,200.

Bolton, t., met. dist., Gtr. Manchester, **Eng.;** cotton, textiles, engin.; p. (1993) 264,900 (dist.).

Bolton Abbey, North Yorks. **Eng.;** ruined Augustinian Priory.

Bolzano, t., Trentino-Alto Adige **Italy;** on R. Isarco at S. approach to Brenner Pass; resort; p. (1984) 103,009.

Boma, t., **Zaïre;** pt. on estuary of R. Zaïre; exp. timber, cocoa, palm prods., bananas.

Bombay, spt., cap. of Maharashtra st., **India;** harbour, docks, rly. ctr.; univ.; greatest cotton ctr. in republic; pt. handles nearly half of India's foreign tr.; oil refinery; film industry; univ., fine public bldgs.; new name Mumbai (1995); p. (1991) 12,596,000.

Bonaire I., Neth. Antilles; a. 287 km²; p. (1991) 11,139.

Bône. *See* Annaba.

Bo'ness, burgh, Falkirk, **Scot.;** spt. on Firth of Forth, 6 km E. of Grangemouth; foundries, timber yards; p. (1991) 14,595.

Bonifacio, spt., Corse du Sud, Corsica, **France;** opposite Sardinia, on Strait of Bonifacio; p. (1982) 2,736.

Bonin Is., Pac. Oc., **Japan;** 15 Is., volcanic; 960 km S. of Tokyo; a. 103 km².

Bonn, c., **Germany;** at confluence of Rs. Sieg and Rhine; univ.; former seat of W. German parliament; birthplace of Beethoven; founded in Roman times; varied inds. inc. printing, publishing; p. (1990) 294,300.

Bonnet a l'Eveque, mtn., **Haiti;** sheer sides, flat top; site of La Ferrière fortress, alt. 900 m.

Bonneville Dam, Ore., Wash., **USA;** across R. Columbia 64 km above Portland (Ore.), provides irrigation to valleys on Columbia-Snake Plateau; locks permit navigation and provide hydroelectric power.

Bonneville Salt Flats, Utah, **USA;** remains of anc. lake; world automobile speed test, 1937–47.

Bonny, t., S. **Nigeria;** at mouth of R. Bonny. Niger delta; oil terminal.

Bonny, Bight of (Bight of Biafra until 1975), **W. Africa;** bay lying E. of the G. of Guinea between the Niger and C. Lopez.

Bonnyrigg and **Lasswade,** burgh, Midlothian, **Scot.,** 11 km S.E. of Edinburgh, p. (1991) 13,696.

Boothferry, l. gov. dist., Humberside, **Eng.;** lowland a. of I. of Axholme and inc. Goole; p. (1993) 65,300.

Boothia, peninsula on Arctic cst., Franklin dist. **Canada;** separated from Baffin I., by G. of B.

Bootle, t., Sefton, Merseyside, **Eng.;** on E. side of entrance to Mersey estuary; shares line of docks with Liverpool; dockside inds. inc. tanning, ship-repairing; tin plant; p. (1981) 62,463.

Bophuthatswana, indep. Bantu Terr. (1977) not recognised by UN, re-incorporated in S. Africa 1994; some mineral wealth (asbestos, platinum) but land produces only 10 per cent of agricultural requirements; home of Sun City, tourist centre; cap. Mmabatho; a. 40,330 km²; p. (1985) 1,660,000.

Bor, t., Serbia, **Yugoslavia;** copper mng. and processing; p. (1981) 56,486.

Borås, t., S. **Sweden;** on R. Viske, nr. Göteborg; ctr. of textile and clothing inds.; p. (1992) 102,840.

Bordeaux, spt., cap. of Gironde, **France;** nr. mouth of R. Garonne; cath., univ.; exp. wines, liqueurs, sugar, potatoes, pit props; oil refining nearby; p. (1990) 213,274.

Borders Region, l. gov. reg., **Scot.;** occupies E. half of Southern Uplands; hilly cty. drained by R. Tweed and tribs.; rural a. interspersed by mkt. and mill ts.; a. 4,670 km²; p. (1993) 105,300.

Bordighera, t., **Italy;** Riviera winter resort.

Boreham Wood, t., Herts., **Eng.;** lt. engin.; computers, film studios.

Borinage, dist. around Mons, **Belgium;** impt. but declining coalfield.

Borislav, t., **Ukraine;** formerly Polish (1919–39); oilfield, natural gas; richest ozocerite deposits in Europe; oil pipeline links to Drogobych and Dashava; p. (1990) 40,700.

Borisov, t., **Belarus;** defeat of Napoleon, 1812; chemicals, sawmills, hardware; p. (1990) 146,800.

Borkum, I. and t., **Germany;** off Ems R. estuary; a. 36 km²; p. (1989) 5,646 (t.).

Borlänge, t., **Sweden;** iron, paper, engin. and chemical wks.; p. (1992) 47,300.

Borneo, lgst. I. in Malay archipelago and 3rd lgst. in world; high mtn. range extends from ctr. to N. rising to 4,180 m; low-lying swamp in S.; politically divided into Kalimantan (Indonesian B.), Sabah and Sarawak (E. Malaysia) and Brunei; jungle-covered and underdeveloped; scattered tribes inc. Dyaks; few nodes of development around oilfields (Sarawak and Brunei), as, of forest exploitation (Sabah); new settlement in Barito valley (Kalimantan); a. 738,150 km²; p. (1983) 7,350,000.

Bornholm, I. in Baltic Sea, **Denmark;** mostly granite with poor soils; cattle rearing; kaolin; tourism and fishing impt.; cap. Rønne; a. 543 km²; p. (1990) 45,784.

Borno, state, **Nigeria;** S.W. of L. Chad; former Moslem st.; a. 132,090 km²; p. (1991) 2,596,589.

Borobudur, Java, **Indonesia;** gr. Buddhist temple; ruins now restored.

Borrowdale, valley, Cumbria, **Eng.;** tourist resort; former graphite mines.

Boscastle, spt., Cornwall, **Eng.;** resort; pilchard fishing; sm. harbour built for slate exp.

Bosnia-Herzegovina, rep., formerly **Yugoslavia;** mtnous., forested, watered by R. Sava and tribs.; one-fourth cultivated; tobacco, cereals, fruit; cattle, sheep, pigs; mineral deposits; civil war since 1992; cap. Sarajevo; a. 51,199 km²; p. (1992) 4,365,000.

Bosporus or **Strait of Constantinople (Karadeniz Boğazi),** between Black Sea and Sea of Marmara; suspension bridge, first to link Europe and S.W. Asia, opened 1973; badly polluted by sewage from Istanbul and oil spillage from shipping.

Bossier City, t., La., **USA;** oil refineries, rly. wks., chemical and processing plants; p. (1980) 50,817.

Boston, t., l. gov. dist., Lincs., **Eng.**; sm. pt. on Witham R., agr. mkt., fruit and vegetable canning; p. (1993) 54,200 (dist.).

Boston, c., st. cap. Mass., **USA**; fine harbour and leading pt. at head of Boston Bay; cultural, comm. and financial ctr., impt. mkt. for fish and wool; 3 univs.; leading c. in 19th cent.; varied inds. inc. leather, rubber, textiles, shoes and elec. gds.; p. (1990) 574,283 (c.), 2,871,000 (met. a.).

Bosworth or **Market Bosworth**, t., Leics., **Eng.**; battle between Richard III and Henry VII, 1485; see **Hinckley**.

Botany Bay, N.S.W., **Australia**; inlet of Tasman Sea on E. cst., site of landing of James Cook, 1770; 8 km S. of Sydney; resort; first settled by Brit. in 1787; old penal colony; deep-water pt. (1961) for oil tankers supplementary to Pt. Jackson.

Botaşani, t. N. Moldavia, **Romania**; in rich pastoral a.; p. (1990) 123,857.

Bothnia, G. of, N. of Baltic; between Finland and Sweden; shallow sea, many Is.

Botswana, Rep. of, indep. sov. st. within Brit. Commonwealth (1966), **Southern Africa**; stretches from Orange R. to Zambesi R., and merges in W. with Kalahari desert; land locked; depends on rly. link to Zimbabwe and S. Africa; coal produced since 1980 to reduce dependence on S. Africa; minerals located but few mined; diamonds since 1971 (50 percent of exp.); copper, nickel; limited livestock agr.; potential arable land of Okavango chobe swamp; few inds. cap. Gaborone; a. 582,000 km²; p. (1991) 1·3 m.

Bottrop, t., N. Rhine-Westphalia, **Germany**; once a sm. t., now ctr. of Ruhr coal basin; p. (1990) 118,700.

Bouches-du-Rhône, dep., S. **France**; covers Rhône delta and inc. the Camargue and Crau; lagoon cst.; mainly agr. but inc. industl. complex ass. with cap. of Marseilles; a. 5,270 km²; p. (1990) 1,759,400.

Bougainville, I. seceded from **Papua New Guinea** to form Rep. of N. Solomons; secession ended 1977; major reserve of copper in Panguna valley; new mng. ts. of Anewa Bay and Panguna; forested; a. 10,619 km².

Bougie. See **Bejaia**.

Boulder, t., Col., **USA**; gold- and silver-mng. dist.; univ.; resort; p. (1990) 83,312 (t.), 225,339 (met. a. with Longmont).

Boulder City, t., Nevada, **USA**; nr. Hoover Dam. gr. engin. project; model t., ctr. for Nat. Park services; p. (1980) 9,590.

Boulogne-Billancourt, S.W. sub. of Paris, **France**; car, aircraft inds.; p. (1990) 101,971.

Boulogne-sur-Mer, t., Pas-de-Calais dep., **France**; on English Channel; comm. and fish. pt.; Channel port; pt. inds.; p. (1990) 44,244 (t.), 95,930 (met. a.).

Bounty I., N.Z., S. Pac. Oc.; uninhabited guano covered I.

Bourg-en-Bresse, t., cap. of Ain dep., **France**; route ctr., varied inds.; p. (1990) 42,955

Bourges, t., cap. of Cher dep., **France**; cath., univ.; industl. and transit ctr.; p. (1990) 78,773 (t.), 92,720 (met. a.).

Bourget, L., Savoie, **France**; tourist a.

Bourgogne, region, E. **France**; inc. deps Côte-d'Or, Nièvre, Saône-et-Loire, Yonne; upland region draining to the north-west into the Paris basin and to the south-east via the Saône into the Rhône; ch. t. Dijon; p. (1990) 1,609,700.

Bourkina Fasso. See **Burkina Faso**

Bourne, t., South Kesteven, Lincs., **Eng.**; home of Hereward the Wake; agr. machin. printing; p. (1981) 8,142.

Bournemouth, t., l. gov. dist., Dorset, **Eng.**; on S. cst., E. of Poole Harbour; seaside resort; conference ctr.; p. (1993) 159,900 (dist.).

Bournville, garden sub. founded by George Cadbury (1897), 6 km S.W. of Birmingham **Eng.**; chocolate and cocoa wks.

Bourton-on-the-Water, v., Gloucs. **Eng.**; tourist ctr.

Bouvet I., uninhabited island in S. Atlantic belonging to **Norway**; a. about 56 km².

Bovey Tracey, v., Devon, **Eng.**; ball clay excavating.

Bow or **Stratford-de-Bow**, Tower Hamlets, E. London, **Eng.**; 5 km from St. Paul's.

Bow, R., Alberta, N.W. **Canada**; head of Saskatchewan R., flows through Banff Nat. Park; irrigation; 504 km long.

Bowdon, t., Gtr. Manchester, **Eng.**; p. (1981) 4,925.

Bow Fell, mtn., Cumbria, **Eng.**; at head of Borrow-

dale, 6 km N.W. of West Water alt. 903 m.

Bowland, Forest of, W. offshoot of Pennines, Lancs., **Eng.**; between Rs. Lune and Ribble; designated a. of outstanding natural beauty; reservoirs.

Bowling Green, t., Ky., **USA**; tr. ctr. for agr. a. producing tobacco, livestock, limestone and dairy prods.; univ.; p. (1990) 40,641.

Bowness, v., Cumbria, **Eng.**; W. end of Hadrian's Wall.

Bowness, t., Cumbria, **Eng.**; on L. Windermere; tourist ctr.

Box Hill, nr. Dorking, Surrey, **Eng.**; E. of R. Mole gap through N. Downs; chalk; wooded, fine views; alt. 233 m.

Boyle, mkt. t., Roscommon, **R.o.I.**; on R. Boyle; dairying; p. (1986) 1,859.

Boyne, R., **R.o.I.**; flows to Irish Sea; Battle of the Boyne (1690) fought at Oldbridge, 5 km W. of Drogheda, salmon fishing; 128 km long.

Boyoma Falls (Stanley Falls), on Upper Zaïre R., **Zaïre**; nr. equator; originally named after the explorer.

Bozrah, c. of anc. Edom, probably modern Buseira **(Jordan)**, S.E. of Dead Sea.

Brabant, prov., **Belgium**; S. section of former Duchy; fertile and wooded; many breweries; mnfs, linen, cloth, paper, lace; cap. Brussels; a. 3,281 km²; p. (1993) 2,262,896.

Brabant, North. See **Noord Brabant**.

Brač, I., Adriatic Sea, off coast of **Croatia**; lgst. of Dalmatian Is.; tourism, fishing; a. 393 km².

Brackley, t., South Northants., **Eng.**; flour milling, brewing; former prosperous wool tr.; Magdalen College School (1447); p. (1981) 6,527.

Bracknell Forest, l. gov. dist., Berks., **Eng.**; on Thames Valley terrace, 16 km S. of Windsor; new t. designated 1949 to meet overspill needs from London; extends N. and W. of old v. of Bracknell; Meteorological Office H.Q.; engin., sealing compounds, plastics; p. (1993) 101,900.

Bradford, c., met. dist., West Yorks., **Eng.**; 14 km W. of Leeds; comm. ctr. of wool-textile inds.; impt. for worsted; engin. and chem. inds.; univ.; birthplace of Delius and J. B. Priestley; p. (1993) 480,000.

Bradford-on-Avon, t., West Wilts., **Eng.**; on E. flank of Cotswolds from which bldg. stone derived; former ctr. of wool ind.; p. (1981) 8,752.

Bradwell, v., Essex, **Eng.**; at mouth of R. Blackwater; Magnox nuclear power sta.

Braemar, dist. in Grampians, Kincardine and Deeside, **Scot.**; containing Balmoral estate.

Braeriach, mtn., **Scot.**; borders Badenoch and Strathspey, alt. 1,296 m.

Braga, t., cap. of B. dist., N.W. **Portugal**; agr. tr. ctr.; religious ctr.; cath.; p. (1987) 63,033.

Bragança, t., cap. of B. dist., N.E. **Portugal**; agr. tr.; p. (1981) 13,900.

Brahmaputra, one of longer Rs. in **Asia**; flows for much of its length through Himalayas and Assam; called **Tsangpo** in Tibet; fertile agr. valley subject to flooding and silting; 2,880 km long.

Braich-y-Pwll, headland, Gwynedd, **Wales**.

Brăila, t., **Romania**; R. pt. on Danube, nr. Galati; grain tr., boatbldg., reed processing; p. (1990) 247,902.

Braintree, t., Mass., **USA**; elec. machin., rubber gds., glassware; p. (1980) 36,337.

Braintree, t., l. gov. dist., Essex, **Eng.**; on Blackwater; rayon mftg., metal windows, engin.; p. (1993) 121,800 (dist.).

Brakpan, t., Transvaal, **S. Africa**; gold mng.; p. (1980) 79,800 (dist.).

Brampton, t., Ontario, **Canada**; noted for its greenhouses; p. (1986) 188,498.

Brandenburg, Land, cap. Potsdam; **Germany**, pop. (1992) 2,543,000.

Brandenburg, t., **Germany**; on R. Havel; cath.; tractors, textiles, machin.; p. (1981) 94,680.

Brandon, t., Manitoba, **Canada**; on Assiniboine R., W. of Winnipeg; comm. ctr. wheat a.; agr. equipment oil refining; p. (1986) 38,708.

Brandon, t., Suffolk, **Eng.**; ctr. of Breckland; expanded t.

Brandon and Byshottles, ts., former U.D., Durham, **Eng.**; former coal-mng. a.; p. (1981) 17,905.

Brandywine Creek, R., Penns., **USA**; Americans defeated by British 1777; length 32 km.

Brantford, t., Ontario, **Canada**; on Grand R., S.W. of Hamilton; leading mnf. t.; farm implements, cycles, bus and truck parts; p. (1986) 76,146.

Brasilia, cap. of Brazil, Goiás st., 960 km N.W. of Rio de Janeiro; ch. of many cities designed to open up interior of rep.; modern architecture; inaugurated 1960; p. (1991) 1,596,274.

Brasov, t., **Romania**; at foot of Transylvanian Alps; aircraft, engin., lge. German and Hungarian p.; p. (1990) 364,307.

Bratislava, c., cap. of **Slovakia**; pt. on Danube 48 km below Vienna; univ.; industl. and comm. ctr.; textiles, chemicals; engin., oil refining; linked to Mozyr', **Belorussia**, by oil pipeline; p. (1990) 440,000.

Bratsk, c., central Irkutsk oblast, **Russia**; on Angara R., ship-repair yards, lumber, iron-ore, wood processing, chemicals; lge. hydroelectric sta.; p. (1989) 256,000.

Braunschweig. *See* Brunswick.

Bray, t., Wicklow, **R.o.I.**; on Irish Sea cst.; popular resort; p. (1986) 24,686.

Brazil, Federative Republic of, S. America; a. 8,512,035 km²; 5th lgst. cty. in world, exceeded in size only by USSR, China, Canada and USA; covers variety of land and climate; in S., gr. Brazilian plateau, in N., Amazon R. basin (thickly forested); leading industl. nation of Latin America; agr.; coffee, cotton, sugar, cocoa, rubber, fruits, hardwoods; rapid exploitation of rainforests worries conservationists; cattle-raising; vast mineral reserves inc. manganese, iron, gold, diamonds; admin. through 22 sts., 4 terrs., and Fed. Dist.; cap. Brasilia; lgst. industl. ctr. São Paulo and Belo Horizonte; many multinational companies, inc. car mftg., chems., construction materials; p. mainly White, Negro, Indian, Mestizo; Portuguese official language; p. concentrated in coastal belt, leaving vast a. of interior relatively underdeveloped; oil shortages led to use of sugar alcohol for cars; incr. finds of oil offshore will lead to oil self-sufficiency by 1999; p. (1991) 146·2 m.

Brazos, R., Texas, **USA**; flows through agr. and industl. Young Co. via Waco to industl. Brazosport; length 1,520 km.

Brazzaville, c., cap. of **Congo Rep.**; connected by rly. with the Atlantic at Pointe-Noire; R. pt. under construction; airport; p. (1990) 760,300.

Brechin, royal burgh, Angus, **Scot.**; on S. Esk; cath.; linen, paper, whisky; p. (1991) 7,655.

Breckland, dist., S.W. Norfolk, N.W. Suffolk, **Eng.**; chalk overlain by glacial sands; heathland and coniferous plantations; lge. a. within Norfolk forms l. gov. dist., inc. Thetford, Swaffham and East Dereham; p. (1993) 110,800.

Brecknock (Breconshire), former co., **Wales**; now mostly inc. in Powys; sm. parts in Mid-Glamorgan and Gwent; now forms l. gov. dist., within Powys inc. Builth Wells, Hay on Wye and Brecon; p. (1993) 41,500.

Brecon (Brecknock), t., Powys, **Wales**; on R. Usk; agr. ctr.; p. (1981) 7,422.

Brecon Beacons, mtns., S. **Wales**; 8 km S. of Brecon; highest peak 888 m; sandstone moorland; Nat. Park.

Breda, c., N. Brabant prov., **Neth.**; mnf. ctr.; machin., foundries, canneries, refineries; historic t., 13th cent. cath.; p. (1993) 128,185 (c.), 164,512 (met. a.).

Bredbury and Romiley, ts., Gtr. Manchester, **Eng.**; paper, engin., dyeing, textiles; p. (1981) 29,122.

Bregenz, t., cap. of Vorarlberg, **Austria**; on Bodensee; hydroelec. power; textiles; resort nr. Bregenz Forest; p. (1991) 27,236.

Breidha Fjord, lge. inlet, W. cst. Iceland.

Bremen, *Land*, **Germany**; a. 404 km²; cap. Bremen; p. (1992) 684,000.

Bremen, c., cap. of *Land* B., **Germany**; old t. on right bank of Weser R., 64 km from N. Sea; new t., founded 17th cent., on left bank; leading pt., industl. and comm. ctr.; but hinterland divided by post-war division of Germany; former member of Hanseatic League; p. (1990) 522,300.

Bremerhaven, c., Bremen, **Germany**; outport of Bremen at mouth of R. Weser; docks; impt. passenger and fish. pt.; shipbldg.; united with Wesermünde 1941; p. (1990) 130,800.

Bremerton, t., Wash., **USA**; on Puget Sound; naval dockyard; elec. equipment, machin.; p. (1984) 35,200 (t.), 164,800 (met. a.).

Brendon Hills, Somerset, **Eng.**; extension of Exmoor, rising to over 400 m.

Brenner Pass, lowest Alpine pass from Bolzano (**Italy**) to Innsbruck (**Austria**); used by road and rail; frequent meeting place of Mussolini and Hitler (1940–2).

Brent, outer bor., Greater London, **Eng.**; inc. Wembley and Willesden; p. (1993) 247,600.

Brenta, R., N. **Italy**; rises in picturesque Alpine valley; forestry, silk, tourism; flows to Adriatic Sea; navigable in lower course; length 180 km.

Brentford and Chiswick. *See* Hounslow.

Brentwood, t., l. gov. dist., Essex, **Eng.**; residentl.; new R.C. cath. (1991); p. (1993) 71,200 (dist.).

Brescia, c., cap. B. prov., Lombardy, N. **Italy**; industl. ctr.; iron, steel, engin., textiles; many historic bldgs.; p. (1992) 192,883.

Breslau. *See* Wroclaw.

Bressay I., Shetland Is., **Scot**; p. (1991) 352.

Brest, naval pt., Finistère dep., N.W. **France**; base of French Atlantic fleet; used by Germans as fortfd. submarine base 1940–4; exp. agr. prods.; impt. industl. ctr.; p. (1990) 153,099 (c.), 201,480 (met. a.).

Brest (Brest-Litovsk), c., **Belarus**; nr. Polish border; route ctr. and agr. mkt.; timber, food-processing, textiles. Captured by Germans in 1915. Treaty of Brest-Litovsk signed with Soviet Russia 1918; p. (1990) 268,800.

Bretagne. *See* Brittany.

Bretton Woods, resort, N.H., **USA**; site of US monetary and financial conference, 1944, leading to establishment of the International Monetary Fund and the World Bank.

Brezhnev. *See* Naberezhnyye Chelny.

Briançon, t., Hautes-Alpes, **France**; in upper Durance R. valley; winter sports; p. (1982) 11,851.

Bridgend, t., Ogwr, Mid-Glamorgan, S. **Wales**; industl. trading estate; iron, stone, paper; coal mng.; p. (1981) 15,699.

Bridge of Allen, burgh, Stirling, **Scot.**; 3 km N. of Stirling; p. (1991) 4,864.

Bridgeport, c., Conn., **USA**; on Long Island Sound; impt. industl. c.; firearms, hardware, elec. equipment, metal products, plastics; p. (1990) 141,686.

Bridgetown, t., spt., cap. **Barbados**; deepwater harbour, comm. ctr.; exp. sugar, molasses, rum; tourism; p. (1990) 6,720.

Bridgewater Canal, Worsley–Manchester–Runcorn, Gtr. Manchester and Cheshire, **Eng.**; crosses ship canal by means of Barton swing bridge; 61 km long.

Bridgnorth, t., l. gov. dist., Shrops., **Eng.**; cas.; carpets, radio equipment; p. (1993) 50,000.

Bridgwater, t., Sedgemoor, Somerset, **Eng.**; on R. Parrett, 16 km from Bristol Channel; engin., wire rope, fibre fabrics, cellophane; p. (1981) 26,132.

Bridlington, t., East Yorks., Humberside, **Eng.**; on Bridlington Bay, S. of Flamborough Head; fishing; seaside resort; p. (1981) 28,970.

Bridport, West Dorset, **Eng.**; mkt. t.; seaside resort; p. (1981) 6,876.

Brie, region, Marne and Seine-et-Marne deps., **France**; low, level plateau of limestones and clays, S.E. of Paris; loam (limon) cover and plentiful water supply encourage agr.; grains, sugar-beet, fruit, dairy cattle; famous cheese; densely populated.

Brienz, t., **Switzerland**; resort on L. Brienz; wood carving.

Brierley Hill, t., West Midlands, **Eng.**; on W. edge of Black Cty.; cut glass, castable metal gds., firebricks, roofing and tiling, iron and steel.

Brigg, mkt. t., Glanford, Humberside, **Eng.**; ctr. of agr. dist. between Lincoln Heights and Wolds; sugar-beet, jam, seed crushing, canning; p. (1981) 5,358.

Brighouse, t., Calderdale, West Yorks., **Eng.**; on R. Calder, 5 km S.E. of Halifax; textiles and engin.; p. (1981) 35,241.

Brightlingsea, t., Tendring, Essex, **Eng.**; on R. Colne; oysters, boatbldg., yachting; p. (1981) 7,245.

Brighton, t., l. gov. dist., East Sussex, **Eng.**; 80 km S. of London on S. cst.; seaside resort and residtl. t.; Royal Pavilion (1817), univ.; lt. inds.; p. (1993) 154,400 (dist.).

Brindisi, c., Apulia, S. **Italy**; spt. on Adriatic cst., sea and air connections to Middle E.; cath.; cas.; wine, olive oil, silk, petrochemicals; oil refining; p. (1981) 89,786.

Brisbane, t., cap. of Queensland, **Australia**; third c. of A., set on winding B. river, 20 km from attractive sandy cst.; caths., univ.; consumer goods, processing of primary prods.; severe flooding 1974; rapid growth in past 30 years; p. (1991) 1,327,000 (met. a.).

Brisbane Water, t., N.S.W., **Australia**; N. of Broken Bay; rapid growth with electrification of commuting rly. to Sydney; p. (1981) 71,984.

Bristol, c., l. gov. dist., Avon, **Eng.**; pt. on R. Avon 14 km from Bristol Channel; outport at Avonmouth; cath., univ.; docks; aircraft engin., tobacco, paint, printing and lt. inds.; p. (1993)

397,600 (dist.).

Bristol, t., Conn., **USA;** foundries, ball bearings, clocks, bells; p. (1990) 79,000 (met. a.).

Bristol Channel, arm of Atl. Oc. between S. cst. of Wales and Somerset and Devon, **Eng.;** noted tidal bores.

British Antarctic Territory, Brit. col., created 1962; consists of all land and Is. S. of lat. 60° S. and between 20° and 80° W. longitude; comprising Graham Land peninsula, S. Shetlands, S. Orkneys and smaller Is., excluding S. Georgia and S. Sandwich Is.; a. 1,222,500 km².

British Columbia, W. prov. separated from rest of **Canada** by Rockies, borders Pac. Oc.; little lowland; parallel N.W.–S.E. ranges of Rockies crossed by Rs. Fraser, Columbia, Kootenay and Peace; vast coniferous forest and hydroelec. resources; salmon fishing on cst.; mng.; p. concentrated in S.W. around Vancouver; a. 948,600 km²; p. (1991) 3,244,100.

British Honduras. See Belize.

British Indian Ocean Terr., Brit. col., created 1965; consists of the Chagos Archipelago (of which Diego Garcia [Anglo-American naval communications ctr.] is lgst. I.) 1,920 km N.E. of Mauritius, and formerly Is. of Aldabra, Farquhar, and Desroches in the W. Indian Oc. now part of Seychelles Rep.; p. (1982) 3,000.

British Is., archipelago, N.W. **Europe;** comprising 2 lge. Is.; Great Britain, Ireland; and 5,000 sm. Is.; a. 315,029 km².

British Solomon Is. See Solomon Is.

British West Africa, formerly comprised Gambia, Sierra Leone, Gold Coast (Ghana), Nigeria, and parts of Togoland and Cameroons. See under their separate headings.

Briton Ferry, t., West Glamorgan, S. **Wales;** pt. at mouth of R. Neath; former ctr. for steel wks., engin., ship-breaking.

Brittany (Bretagne), region, N.W. **France;** inc, deps. Côtes-du-Nord, Finistère, Ille-et-Vilaine, Morbihan; penin. between Eng. Channel and Bay of Biscay; contrast between productive cst. lands (fishing, early vegetables, tourism) and barren moorland interior; economically depressed; p. (1990) 2,795,600.

Brive-la-Gaillarde, t., Corrèze dep., **France;** regional mkt. in fertile basin on edge of Central Massif; p. (1990) 52,677.

Brixham, S. Devon, **Eng.;** incorporated in Torbay; fishing; resort.

Brno (Brünn), c., **Czech Rep.;** cap. of Moravia; finely situated at confluence of Svratka and Svitava Rs., 109 km N. of Vienna; industl. and communications ctr. with mnfs. of machin., precision tools, textiles; annual tr. fair; p. (1990) 391,000.

Broad Haven, t., new t. planned on St. Brides Bay, **Wales.**

Broadstairs, Thanet, Kent, **Eng.;** seaside resort; 5 km N.E. of Ramsgate; p. (1981) 23,400.

Broads, The, Norfolk, **Eng.;** series of Ls. formed by mediaeval turf cutting in lower alluvial reaches of Rs. Bure, Waveney, and Yare; yachting, fishing, tourism; plans to create a Nat. Park to help relieve pollution; lge. part now forms Broadland, l. gov. dist., p. (1993) 108,500.

Brockton, c., Mass., **USA;** S. of Boston; lge. shoe and leather ind., machin.; annual tr. fair; p. (1990) 189,000 (met. a.).

Brockville, t., Ontario, **Canada;** R. pt. on St. Lawrence R. below Thousand Is.; telephone equipment, wire cables, elec. tools; p. (1986) 20,880.

Broken Hill, t., N.S.W., **Australia;** major mng. (silver, lead, zinc) ctr. in arid W. of st.; p. (1981) 26,913.

Bromberg. See Bydgoszez.

Bromley, outer bor. of London, **Eng.;** inc. Beckenham, Orpington, Penge, and Chislehurst; p. (1993) 291,800.

Bromsgrove, l. gov. dist., Hereford and Worcs., **Eng.;** mkt. t., 21 km S.W. Birmingham; wrought ironwk., lt. engin.; p. (1993) 92,800 (dist.).

Bromyard, Hereford and Worcs., **Eng.;** sm. mkt. t.

Bronx, The, one of the five bors. of New York City, **USA;** connected by bridges to bor. of Manhattan; residtl. with parks, zoological and botanical gardens, colleges and professional schools; p. (1990) 1,203,789.

Brooklyn, bor., N.Y. City. **USA;** linked with Manhattan bor. by Brooklyn, Manhattan, and Williamsburg suspension bridges across East R.; and with Staten I. by Verrazano-Narrows

bridge (longest in world); mainly residtl. with numerous mftg. and comm. interests; p. (1990) 2,291,604.

Brooks Range, mtns., N. Alaska, **USA;** forms N. section of Rocky Mtns.; Inuit p.; Arctic climate, flora and fauna; alt. 2,000 m rising to 2,818 m (Mt. Michelson).

Broom, loch on N.W. cst. of Ross and Cromarty, **Scot.**

Brora, t., Sutherland, **Scot.;** on E. cst., 19 km N.E. of Dornoch Firth; Harris Tweed ind.; tourism; p. (1991) 1,687.

Brownhills, t., West Midlands, **Eng.;** former mng. t.; expanded t.; p. (1981) 18,200.

Brownsville, t., Texas, **USA;** pt. on Rio Grande nr. Mexican border; livestock, sugar-cane, fruit processing, chemicals; p. (1984) 94,700 (t.) (1990) 260,000 (met. a. with Harlingen).

Broxbourne, t., l. gov. dist., Herts., **Eng.;** on gravel terrace to W. of R. Lea; ctr. of very intensively cultivated dist.; lt. inds.; dormitory t. linked with London; p. (1993) 82,500 (dist.).

Broxtowe, l. gov. dist., Notts., **Eng.;** made up of Beeston and Stapleford and Eastwood; p. (1993) 110,600.

Bruay-en-Artois, t., Pas-de-Calais, **France;** coal mng.; p. (1982) 23,200.

Bruchsal, t., Baden-Württemberg, **Germany;** tobacco, paper, machin.; p. (1986) 36,500.

Bruges. See Brugge.

Brugge (Bruges), c., cap. of W. Flanders prov., N. **Belgium;** mediaeval t. connected by canal to its outer pt. Zeebrugge; univ.; impt. mkt. for grain, cattle, horses; engin., ship-repairing, elec. gds., glass mkg., textiles, lace; p. (1993) 116,871.

Brühl, t., N. Rhine–Westphalia, **Germany;** 13 km S. of Cologne; cas.; lignite; p. (1986) 40,700.

Brunei, indep. st. (1984), N. **Borneo;** enclave of Sarawak; Brit. protectorate since 1888; thriving economy based on Seria and offshore oil and gas fields; oil and gas provide 95 per cent of exp.; need to diversify as reserves dwindle and prices fall; 80 percent of food is imported; agr. therefore being encouraged since only 15 per cent of land is cultivated; cap. Bandar Seri Begawan; a. 5,765 km²; p. (1992) 267,800 of whom 25 per cent are Chinese.

Brünn. See Brno.

Brunswick (Braunschweig), c., Lower Saxony, **Germany;** on R. Oker; formerly cap. of st. of Brunswick, now a comm. and industl. ctr.; mnfs. inc. canning, tinplate, optics, pianos, lorries; p. (1990) 258,500.

Brussels (Bruxelles), cap. of **Belgium** and of prov. of Brabant; impt. comm., industl. and cultural ctr.; varied mnfs., inc. pharmaceuticals, electronic equipment, machine tools; lge. oil refinery at Feluy; noted for carpets and lace; occupied by the Germans 1914–18, 1940–4; univ.; mediaeval and Renaissance monuments; H.Q. of EU; p. (1993) 950,399.

Bryan, t., Texas, **USA;** mkt. ctr., agr. college; p. (1984) 59,000 (t.), 117,400 (met. a.).

Bryansk, c., cap. of B. oblast, **Russia,** on Desna R.; rly. junc.; a fortress until 19th cent.; sawmilling, engin., textiles, chemicals, steel; oil pipeline from Kuybyshev; p. inc. Bezhitsa (1989) 452,000.

Brynmawr, t., Gwent, **Wales;** former coal-mng. a.; industl. estate; p. (1981) 5,528.

Brzeg (Brieg), t. Opole, **Poland;** on R. Oder; German until 1945; textiles, leather, chemicals; p. (1989) 38,504.

Bucaramanga, c., N. central **Colombia,** 900 m a.s.l. in E. highlands of Andes; ctr. of coffee-growing dist.; cigar and cigarette mkg.; p. (1992) 349,403.

Buchan Ness, C., nr. Peterhead, E. **Scot.**

Bucharest (Bukcresti), cap. and lgst. c. of **Romania;** "Little Paris," on the Dambovita, trib. of Danube; cath., univ.; textiles, chemicals, pharmaceuticals, oil refining, engin.; 20 per cent industl. output of rep.; badly damaged by earthquake (1977); p. (1990) 2,316,087.

Buckfastleigh, t., S. Devon, **Eng.;** wool, quarrying; nearby Benedictine abbey on site of mediaeval Cistercian abbey; p. (1981) 2,889.

Buckhaven and Methil, burgh, Kirkcaldy, **Scot.;** on N. Side of Firth of Forth, 13 km N.E. of Kirkcaldy; coal; p. (1991) 17,069.

Buckie, burgh, Moray, **Scot.;** boat- and yacht-bldg.; fisheries; p. (1991) 8,425.

Buckingham, Aylesbury Vale, Bucks., **Eng.;** mkt. t. on R. Ouse, 24 km N.W. of Aylesbury; p. (1981) 6,627.

Buckinghamshire, non-met. co., **Eng.;** crossed

by Chilterns and Vale of Aylesbury; rural and wooded, emphasis is on dairy farming; co. t. Aylesbury; mnfs. chiefly in High Wycombe; decline in traditional handicrafts (lace mkg. and furniture parts); a. 1,882 km²; p. (1993) 651,700.

Buckley, t., Alyn and Deeside, Clwyd, **Wales**; sm. castings; p. (1981) 13,386.

Budapest, cap. and lgst. c. of **Hungary**; stands on both banks of Danube (Buda on right, Pest on left); attractive townscape; univ.; varied mnfs., inc. steel, textiles, chemicals, engin., motorbuses, oil refining; employs 40 per cent industl. workers of Hungary; p. (1989) 2,115,000.

Budaun, t., Uttar Pradesh, **India**; agr. processing; ruins; p. (1991) 116,695.

Bude. See Stratton and Bude.

Budel, t., N. Brabant, S. **Neth.**; 19 km S. of Eindhoven; major zinc smelter project; p. (1991) 11,926.

Budge-Budge, t., W. Bengal, **India**; on lower Hooghly R.; hemp, rice; p. (1981) 66,424.

Budleigh Salterton, East Devon, **Eng.**; resort; birthplace of Raleigh nearby; p. (1981) 4,436.

Buena Park, t., Cal., **USA**; agr. processing mkt.; oilfields; p. (1980) 64,165.

Buenaventura, spt., **Colombia**; lumber yards, tanning, fish canning; p. (1983) 156,000.

Buenos Aires, c., cap. of **Argentina**; cap. to be rebuilt in Patagonia (by 1989) to decentralise power; B.A. now contains one third of A.'s p.; ch. spt. at head of Rio de la Plata, on E. edge of Pampa; connected to Uruguay, Paraguay, and Brazil by gr. R. system; industl. and tr. ctr. for outlying regions; p. (1991) 2,960,976.

Buenos Aires ; prov. **Argentina**; cap. La Plate, agric.; p. (1991) 12, 538,007.

Buffalo, c., N.Y., **USA**; pt. on L. Erie; focus of communications on Gr. Ls. has encouraged many heavy inds.; diversified lt. inds.; univ.; p. (1990) 328,123 (c.), 969,000 (met. a.).

Bug, R., **Ukraine**; known as S. or Ukrainian B.; flows from Volyno–Podolsh upland to Black Sea; navigable in lower course; 853 km long.

Bug, R., the western Bug rises in **Ukraine**, not far from the southern Bug and flows N. to join the Vistula below Warsaw; forms bdy. between Poland and Ukraine; 774 km long.

Buganda, prov., **Uganda**, E. Africa; located W. of L. Victoria largely at alt. between 1,300 and 1,800 m; intensive cultivation, cotton (ch. comm. crop), plantains, millets; cap. Kampala.

Builth Wells, t., Brecknock, Powys, **Wales**; on upper course of R. Wye; medicinal springs; p. (1981) 1,287.

Buitenzorg. See Bogor.

Bujumbura, t., cap. of **Burundi**; pt. on L. Tanganyika; varied inds.; airpt.; p. (1986) 272,600.

Bukavu, t., **Zaïre**; cement, quinine processing; p. (1985) 418,000.

Bukhara (Bokhara), t., **Uzbekistan**; in Amu-Dar'ya valley at W. foot of Tien Shan; agr. mkt. at W. terminus of anc. caravan route from China; modern route ctr.; local natural gas, textiles; p. (1990) 227,900.

Bukittinggi, t., Sumatra, **Indonesia**; in Padang Highlands at 1,068 m; p. 53,700.

Bukoba, t., **Tanzania**; pt. midway along W. shore of L. Victoria; exp. coffee, rice and other foodstuffs to L. pts. in Kenya and Uganda.

Bukovina, Northern; terr., formerly belonging to Romania, ceded to **USSR** in 1940; now part of Ukraine; a. 5,542 km²; ch. t. Chernovitsy; Carpathian Mtns., forested; farming, cereals; cattle.

Bulawayo, t., **Zimbabwe**; impt. rly. ctr.; major ctr. of commerce and heavy engin., airpt.; p. (1982) 413,800.

Bulgaria, Rep. of, S.E. Europe; in E. Balkans, bounded by Black Sea in E., and by Danube R. in N. which separates it from Romania; Rodopi range in S.W.; Maritsa R. basin forms central lowland a.; sharp climatic contrasts between winter and summer; fertile lowland areas organised into lge.-scale cooperative farms producing grain; impt. exp. tr. in agr. prods., inc. fruit, vegetables, tobacco; rapidly increasing industl. output; mineral and oil resources; popular tourist a. on Black Sea cst.; cap. Sofia; a. 110,911 km²; p. (1992) 8,472,724.

Bunbury, t., spt., **W. Australia**; 3rd. t. of st., exp. hardwoods, coal, mineral sands; growth since 1970 with establishment of alumina refinery and expansion of pt.; p. (1990) 27,000.

Buncrana, mkt. t., Donegal, **R.o.I.**; salmon fishing; seaside resort; p. (1986) 3,106.

Bundaberg, t., Queensland, **Australia**; on Burnett R.; ctr. of sugar refining; p. (1991) 46,195 (met. a.).

Bundoran, v., Donegal, **R.o.I.**; fish, pt. and resort; p. (1986) 3,106.

Bungay, Waveney, Suffolk, **Eng.**; mkt. t. on R. Waveney; printing, leather gds.; p. (1993), 5,250.

Bungosuido Channel, Japan; E. entrance into Inland Sea.

Bunzlau. See Boleslawiec.

Buraimi, oases lying between **Oman** and **United Arab Emirates**; rich in oil.

Buraydah (Buraida), t. Nejd., **Saudi Arabia**; oasis; tr. ctr.; p. (1988) 184,000.

Burbank, c., Cal., **USA**; airpt.; aeroplanes, film studios; p. (1980) 84,625.

Burdwan, t., W. Bengal, **India**; agr. processing and tr. ctr. in Damodar valley close to Raniganj coalfield.

Bure, R., Norfolk, **Eng.**; lower course forms part of Norfolk Broads; joins Yare at Yarmouth; 93 km.

Burg, t., Saxony-Anhalt, **Germany**; on Ihle Canal; p. (1989) 27,464.

Burgas, c., **Bulgaria**; spt. and comm. ctr. on Black Sea; ch. exp. pt. for rep.; pt. for oil tankers under construction; p. (1990) 204,915.

Burgenland, prov., **Austria**; bordered on E. by Hungary; low-lying in N., agr.; hilly in S.; cap. Eisenstadt; a. 3,962 km²; p. (1991) 273,541.

Burgess Hill, t., Mid Sussex, West Sussex, **Eng.**; bricks, tiles; p. (1981) 23,542.

Burghead, burgh, Moray, **Scot.**; fish pt., resort; p. (1991) 1,495.

Burgos, c., N. **Spain**; cap. of B. prov.; anc. cap. of Castile and cap. of Franco's regime 1936–9; cath; home of the Cid; tourism, varied inds.; p. (1991) 169,279.

Burgos, prov., Old Castile, **Spain**; cap. B.; a. 14,050 km²; p. (1991) 355,138.

Burgstädt, t., Saxony, **Germany**; textiles, machin.; p. (est. 1989) 12,968.

Burgundy, former kingdom and prov., N.E. **France**; composed largely of upper valley of R. Saône; famous vineyards; strategic position on route leading between plateau of Vosges and Jura Mtns., from Rhône valley to Rhine valley.

Burhanpur, t., Madhya Pradesh, **India**; anc. walled Mogul c.; textiles, brocades; p. (1991) 172,710.

Burkina Faso, (Upper Volta), W. Africa; landlocked st. under Fr. rule until 1960; savana and low hills, hot and dry desert in N.; p. concentrated in S. and dependent on nomadism and subsistence agr.; many migrate to Ivory Coast and Ghana for work; soil erosion and desert encroachment reduce potential; poorest cty. in Africa; low life expectancies; dependent on aid; much emigration; cap. Ouagadougou; a. 274,123 km²; p. (1991) 9,420,000.

Burlington, t., S. Ontario, **Canada**; on L. Ontario, sub., N.E. of Hamilton; in fruit-growing a.; industl.; tourism; p. (1986) 116,675.

Burlington, t., Iowa, **USA**; on bluffs of Mississippi R.; machin., furniture; p. (1990) 27,208.

Burlington, t., Vt., **USA**; on L. Champlain; pt. of entry and ch. industl. and comm. t. in st.; mnfs.; p. (1990) 39,127.

Burma. See Myanmar, Union of

Burnham Beeches, Berks./Bucks., **Eng.**; part of anc. forest acquired 1879 for public use; a. 243 ha.

Burnham-on-Crouch, t., Essex, **Eng.**; pt., yachting, boat-bldg.; p. (1981) 6,291.

Burnham-on-Sea, t., Sedgemoor, Somerset, **Eng.**; on Bridgwater Bay; resort; p. (1981) 14,920.

Burnie, spt., Tasmania, **Australia**; pulp and paper mills; impt. mineral pt. (tin); p. (1991) 20,483.

Burnley, t., l. gov. dist., Lancs., **Eng.**; textiles, engin., car accessories; p. (1993) 91,400 (dist.).

Burntisland, royal burgh, Kirkcaldy, **Scot.**; on F. of Forth; p. (1991) 5,951.

Burray, one of the Orkney Is., **Scot.**; p. (1991) 363.

Burrinjuck, t., N.S.W., **Australia**; on Murrumbidgee R., N. of Canberra; site of impt. dam providing irrigation in Riverina (dist.)

Burry Port, t., Dyfed, **Wales**; p. (1981) 5,951.

Bursa, c. and prov., N.W. **Turkey**; noted for its textiles; cap. of anc. Bithynia (3rd cent. B.C.) and later of Ottoman empire; mosques; p. (1990) 1,603,137 (prov.), 775,388 (t.).

Burslem. See Stoke-on-Trent.

Burton-on-Trent, t., East Staffs., **Eng.**; brewing, malting, rubber gds.; p. (1981) 47,930.

Burundi, rep., E. central **Africa**; high plateau on N.E. shore of L. Tanganyika; tropical climate.

irregular rainfall; economy based on agr., inc. subsistence crops of manioc. sweet potatoes, and cash crops of cotton, coffee; coffee major exp.; (89 percent of export earnings in 1980); one of poorest states in world; sm. mftg. inds. developing, but no rlys.; home of ruling Tutsi and rebel Hutu; cap. Bujumbura; a. 27,834 km²; p. (1992) 5·6 m.

Bury, t., met. dist., Gtr. Manchester, **Eng.**; on R. Irwell to S. of Rossendale Fells; cotton, textiles; birthplace of Robert Peel; p. (1993) 181,400 (dist.).

Buryat (Buryatskaya), aut. rep. **Russia**; borders L. Baykal; mtnous., forested; lge. mineral deposits; cap. Ulan Ude; a. 350,945 km²; p. (1989) 1,038,300.

Bury St. Edmunds, St. Edmundsbury, Suffolk, **Eng.**; old mkt. t., on R. Lark, abbey ruins; farm implements, sugar-beet processing; expanded t.; p. (1981) 28,914.

Bushey, t., Hertsmere, Herts., **Eng.**; residtl.; p. (1981) 23,240.

Bushir. See Bandar-e-Büshehr.

Busto Arsizio, t., Varese prov., N. **Italy**; 30 km. N.W. of Milan; cotton milling ctr., iron, steel, rayon, textile machin.; p. (1981) 79,769.

Bute, I, Argyll, Scot; p. (1991) 7,375.

Buteshire, former co., now part of Strathclyde Region, **Scot.**

Butte, t., Mont., **USA**; mng. t. (copper, zinc. silver, manganese, gold, lead, arsenic); also a farming ctr.; p. (1980) 37,205.

Buttermere, L., Cumberland, **Eng.**

Butt of Lewis, promontory with lighthouse; Lewis, Hebrides, **Scot.**

Buxton, t., High Peak, Derbys., **Eng.**; spa; lime-quarrying nearby; p. (1981) 20,797.

Buzau, t., **Romania**; rly. ctr.; cath.; wheat, timber, petroleum; p. (1990) 147,627.

Bydgoszez, prov., **Poland**; cap. B.; drained by Rs. Vistula, Brda, and Notec; formerly called Pomorze; salt and lime deposits aid chemical inds.; a. 20,800 km²; p. (1989) 1·1 m.

Bydgoszcz (Bromberg), c., N. central **Poland**; on R. Brda; R. pt., rly. ctr.; elec. equipment, machine tools, timber mnfs.; p. (1989) 380,425.

Byelorussian SSR. See Belorussiyan SSR.

Byron C., most E. point of **Australia**, Pacific cst. of N.S.W.

Bytom, c., S.W. **Poland**; formerly in Prussian prov. of Upper Silesia; ctr. of Katowice mng. a.; p. (1989) 229,991.

C

Cabinda, enclave, **Angola**; separated by Zaïre R. estuary from Angola; tropical climate encourages thick forest cover; tropical crops; offshore oil production; uranium; a. 7,236 km²; p. (1992) 152,100.

Cabot Strait, entrance of G. of St. Lawrence between C. Breton I. and Newfoundland, **Canada.**

Cáceres, c., and cap. of C. prov., W. **Spain**; in Estremadura, above Tagus valley; mkt. t. lies below the old t. topping the hill; p. (1987) 69,770; (1991) 401,956 (prov.).

Cachar, dist., Assam, **India**; tea-growing ctr.; a. 6,961 km².

Cachoeira, t., Bahia, **Brazil**; historic c.; p. (1985) 138,500.

Cachoeira do Sul, t., Rio Grande do Sul, **Brazil**; p. (1980) 112,500.

Cader Idris, mtn., Gwynedd, **Wales**; alt. 893 m.

Cádiz, maritime prov., S.W. **Spain**; cap. Cádiz; a. 7,321 km²; p. (1981) 988,378.

Cádiz, c., cap. of C. prov., S.W. **Spain**; in Andalusía; pt. on Bay of C.; fortress t., naval base; exp. sherry, cork, fruit, olive oil, tunny fish; univ., cath.; one of the most anc. ts. in Europe, built by Phoenicians, c. 1100 B.C.;

p. (1991) 156,558, 1,090,773 (prov.).

Caen, c., cap. of Calvados dep., **France**; church and abbey, tomb of William the Conqueror; univ.; iron-ore mng. and processing; severely damaged in second world war; p. (1990) 115,624 (c.), 188,799 (met. a.).

Caerleon, t., Gwent, **Wales**; on R. Usk, 5 km N.E. of Newport; Roman Isca Silurum; remains still present; agr. machin., tools, bricks; p. (1981) 6,711.

Caernarvon, t., Arfon, Gwynedd, N. **Wales**; pt. on S. shore of Menai strait; cas. where first Prince of Wales (Edward II) was christened; bricks, plastics; p. (1981) 9,506.

Caernarvonshire, former co., N. **Wales.** See Gwynedd.

Caerphilly, t., Rhymney Valley, Mid-Glamorgan, S. **Wales**, cas.; lt. inds.; former coal-mng. a.; p. (1981) 42,736.

Caesar Mazaca, anc. c., Asia Minor; residence of the Cappadocian Kings; the modern Kayeri, **Turkey.**

Caesarea Palestinae, old c., **Israel**, 32 km S. Mt. Carmel; cap. of Herod the Great.

Caeté, t., Minas Gerais st., **Brazil**; lge. iron and steel wks.; p. (1985) 35,200.

Cagliari, cap. and ch. pt. of Sardinia, **Italy**; univ., cath.; p. (1992) 180,309.

Cahir, t., Tipperary, **R.o.I.**; on R. Suir; anc. cas. and abbey; salmon fishing; p. (1986) 2,118.

Cahors, t., cap. of Lot dep., **France**; comm. ctr.; many historic bldgs., inc. cath., palace; distilleries, shoe factory; p. (1990) 20,787.

Cairngorm, mtns., Moray, Badenoch and Strathspey, **Scot.**; rise to 1,310 m (Ben Macdhui); form part of Highlands; nat. nature reserve of arctic flora and fauna; winter sports.

Cairns, spt., Queensland, **Australia**; on Trinity Bay; bulk sugar terminal; resort for Barrier Reef; p. (1991) 83,391 (met. a.).

Cairntoul, mtn., Kincardine and Deeside, **Scot.**; alt. 1,294 m.

Cairo (El Qâhira), c., cap. of **Egypt** and prov.; on E. bank of Nile, at head of delta; lgst. c. in rep.; univ.; mosques, palace; fortress of Babylon in old c.; rapid growth with rural depopulation p. (1990) 6,452,000 (c.). (1991) 6,663,000 (prov.); Greater Cairo (1987) 13·3m.

Caistor, t., West Lyndsey, Lincs., **Eng.**; site of Roman camp in Lincs. Wolds.

Caithness, l. gov. dist., former co., **Scot.**; most N. part of mainland; flat, with much moorland; herring fishery; poor agr.; quarrying; ch. ts. Wick, Thurso; a. 3,152 km²; p. (1993) 26,370.

Cajamarca, t., cap. of C. dep., **Peru**; in mtn. valley, 2,745 m; impt. in Inca times; p. (1990) 92,600.

Calabar, spt., S.E. **Nigeria**; cap. Cross River st.; exp. palm oil, kernels, rubber, ivory, cement; p. (1983) 256,000.

Calabria, region, extreme S.W. **Italy**; mtnous. pen.; highest point Mt. Pollino 2,234 m; ch. R. Crati; socially and economically under-developed; cap. Catanzaro; p. (1992) 2,074,763.

Calais, spt., Pas-de-Calais, N.E. **France**; cross-channel ferry pt. opposite to and 33·6 km distant from Dover; nearby Sangatte exit of Channel Tunnel; p. (1990) 75,836 (t.), 101,768 (met. a.).

Calama, oasis, Antofagasta prov., N. **Chile**; in Atacama desert at foot of Andean Cordillera; water from R. Loa supplies Antofagasta and used for irrigation locally.

Calatafimi, t., Sicily, **Italy**; Garibaldi defeated Neapolitans, May 1860; p. (1981) 8,159.

Calbayog, c. Samar, **Philippines**; hemp tr., fisheries; p. (1990) 115,390.

Calbe, t., Saxony-Anhalt, **Germany**; on R. Saale; p. (1989) 14,253.

Calcutta, c., cap. of W. Bengal st., **India**; pt. on Hooghly R., lgst. c. in rep. and one of most densely populated areas of world; vast tr. from Ganges plain; univ.; jute-mills, textiles, chems., engin.; exp. jute, cotton, sugar-cane, rice, tea, coal; p. (1991) 11,022,000.

Calder, R., West Yorks., **Eng.**, trib of Aire R.

Calderdale, met. dist., West Yorks., **Eng.**; chief t. Halifax; also inc. Todmorden, Brighouse, Hebden Royd, Ripponden and Sowerby Bridge; p. (1993) 193,700.

Calder Hall, Cumbria, **Eng.**; first full-scale nuclear power sta. in world (1956); now closed.

Caldy I., off Dyfed cst., **Wales**; lighthouse; Trappist monastery.

Caledonian Canal, from Moray Firth to Loch

Linnhe, Scot., connecting North Sea with Atl. Oc.; 100 km long; opened 1822.

Calf of Man, sm. I., S.W. I. of Man, **Eng.**; a. 250 ha.

Calgary, ch. t., Alberta, **Canada**; ctr. of ranching cty.; lumber mills, tanneries, oil refining, flour milling; p. (1986) 636,104 (c.), 671,326 (met. a.).

Cali, c., cap. of Valle del Cauca dep., W. **Colombia**; 1,068 m on Cauca R.; comm. and transport ctr. for rich agr. a.; p. (1992) 1,624,401.

Calicut (Kozhikade), t., Kerala, **India**; first pt. reached by Vasco da Gama (1498); gave its name to calico cloth; p. (1981) 394,447 (t.), 546,058 (met. a.).

California, st., W. USA; admitted to Union 1850; st. flower golden poppy, st. bird California Valley quail; mtnous., forested, fertile valleys; subject to earthquakes from San Andreas fault; rich in minerals, oil, natural gas, gold, silver, copper; fruits; film ind.; attractive climate and scenery; cap. Sacramento; ch. pt. San Francisco, lgst. c. Los Angeles; most populous st. in USA; a. 411,014 km²; p. (1990) 29,760,021.

California Current, E. Pac. Oc.; flows N. to S. along cst. of Ore. and Cal., **USA**; relatively cold water; reduces summer temp. and causes fog in cst. a. especially nr. San Francisco.

California, G. of, arm of Pac. Oc., N.W. **Mexico**; 1,120 km long; same rift as Imperial and Coachella valleys in S.E. Cal.

Callander, burgh, Stirling, **Scot.**; "mkt. t. on R. Teith, 24 km N.W. of Stirling; "the gate of the Highlands," tourism; p. (1991) 2,622.

Callao, c., W. **Peru**; pt. of Lima; sheltered harbour; sacked by Drake in 16th cent.; p. (1990) 588,600.

Calne, North Wilts., **Eng.**; mkt. t. on Marden R.; lge. bacon factory closed (1982); p. (1981) 10,268.

Caltagirone, t., Catania, Sicily, **Italy**; cath.; majolica ware; p. (1981) 35,682.

Caltanissetta, t., cap. of C. prov., Sicily, **Italy**; cath.; agr., sulphur ctr.; p. (1981) 61,146.

Calvados, dep., N.E. **France**; low-lying cty. and damp climate aid dairying; butter and cheese prods.; apple orchards produce Calvados brandy; cap. Caen; a. 5,690 km²; p. (1990) 618,500.

Cam (Granta), R., Cambridge, **Eng.**; trib. of R. Ouse; flows through the "backs" at Cambridge; 64 km long.

Camagüey, c., **Cuba**; comm. ctr. in rich agr. region; cattle, sugar-cane; p. (1986) 260,800.

Camargue, delta dist., Bouches-du Rhône, **France**; at mouth of R. Rhône; famous col. of flamingoes; gypsies; bull-rearing; a. 777 km².

Camberley, t., Surrey, **Eng.**; Royal Military Staff College, Royal Military Academy.

Cambodia, State of (Kampuchea), S.E. **Asia**; between Thailand and Vietnam; former ass. st. of Fr. Union; cap. Phnom-Penh on Mekong R.; mainly agr., rice, rubber, maize, pepper, kapok, livestock; Tonle Sap impt. for fishing; car assembly, cigarette mkg., textiles, plywood, paper, tyres, cement; oil refinery nr. Kompong Som; continuing civil war; a. 181,300 km²; current population estimates vary between 8.7 and 12m.

Camborne, t., Cornwall, **Eng.**; 18 km S.W. Truro; old tin and copper mines; engin., radio-television assembly; textiles, chemicals; p. (1981) 46,482 (inc. Redruth).

Cambrai, t., Nord dep., **France**; on R. Scheldt; textiles (gave its name to cambric), agr. processing; suffered in both world wars; p. (1982) 36,618.

Cambrian Mtns., Wales; collective name for mtns. of N. and Central Wales inc. Snowdonia and Cader Idris.

Cambridge, univ. c., co. t., l. gov. dist., Cambridgeshire, **Eng.**; on Cam R.; famous univ. with residtl. colleges; leading ctr. of research-based inds.; p. (1993) 113,800 (dist.).

Cambridgeshire, non-met. co., **Eng.**; low-lying, sloping from E. Anglian Heights in S.E. to Fens in N.; crossed by Rs. flowing to Wash; rich soils aid intensive agr. and mkt. gardening; inc. former cos. of Huntingdon, Peterborough and Isle of Ely; ch. t. Cambridge; a. 3,408 km²; p. (1993) 682,600.

Cambridge, c., Mass., **USA**; 5 km from Boston; seat of Harvard Univ. and MIT; mftg.; impt. research ctr.; now inc. in Boston met. a.; p. (1980) 95,322.

Camden, inner bor., N. London, **Eng.**; inc. Hampstead, Holborn, and St. Pancras; p. (1993) 181,400.

Camden, c., N.J., **USA**; pt. of entry on Delaware R., opposite Philadelphia; comm., mftg. and residtl.; iron foundries, chemicals, shipbldg.; p. (1990) 87,992; inc. in Philadelphia met. a.

Camerino, t., central **Italy**; in Apennines; univ. cath.; the anc. Camerium; p. (1981) 7,920.

Cameroon, United Rep. of, unitary st. (1972) W. **Africa**; on G. of Guinea; fed. cap. Yaoundé; dependence on primary exports of coffee and cocoa now reduced by rapid incr. in petroleum production since 1977; growing industrial sector; now graduated to middle income developing country; a. 475,500 km²; p. (1991) 12,240,000

Cameroon Mtn., volcano, massif, **Cameroon**; cstl-mtn., hgst. in W. Africa; last eruption 1959; alt. 4,072 m.

Campagna di Roma, Latium, **Italy**; malarial coastal plain around Rome; now reclaimed and used for pasture.

Campania, region, S. **Italy**; comprising provs. Avellino, Benevento, Caserta, Naples, Salerno; admin. and comm. ctr. Naples; high p. density; fertile; intensive agr.; p. (1992) 5,668,895.

Campbelltown, t., N.S.W., **Australia**; dairy and poultry ctr. for Sydney; proposed growth ctr. for 340,000; p. (1981) 91,525.

Campbeltown, royal burgh, spt., Kintyre, Argyll and Bute, **Scot.**; distilling, fishing; planned ctr. for construction of off-shore oil platforms; p. (1991) 5,722.

Campeche, spt., S.E. **Mexico**; on G. of Campeche; gives its name to prov. (a. 56,099 km²; p. (1990) 528,824); clothing; exp. timber, sisal hemp; p. (1990) 172,208.

Campina Grande, t., Paraiba, **Brazil**; inland mkt. t. industl. ctr; p. (1985) 280,700.

Campinas, t., **Brazil**; 88 km N. of São Paulo; coffee; machin.; rubber gds.; p. (1991) 846,084.

Campine or **Kempenland**, region in Limburg and Antwerp provs., **Belgium**; concealed coalfield in heathland a.

Campobasso, t., cap. of C. prov., S. **Italy**; agr. ctr.; famed for cutlery; 15th cent. cas.; p. (1981) 48,291.

Campo Belo, t., Minas Gerais st., **Brazil**; impt. cattle ctr. nr. L. formed by Furnas Dam on Rio Grande; p. (1985) 42,900.

Campo Duran, terr., **Argentina**; oilfield and refining.

Campo Grande, c., cap. Mato Grosso de Sul st. **Brazil**; p. (1990) 459,554.

Campos, c., Rio de Janeiro st., **Brazil**; ctr. for rich agr. region; sugar refining; p. (1991) 388,640.

Campos do Jordão, t., **Brazil**; alt., 1,699 m; health resort, known as the Switzerland of Brazil; p. (1985) 32,600.

Campsie Fells, range of hills, Stirling, **Scot.**; highest point, 578 m.

Canada, indep. st., within Commonwealth; occupies N. part of **N. America**; enclave of Alaska (USA) in N.W.; second lgst. cty. in world, consisting of 10 provs., 2 terrs.; coastal mtns. and Rockies in W., interior plains in ctr., Hudson Bay lowlands in N., plateau a. of Quebec and Newfoundland in E.; many Is. off Arctic cst.; continental climate, severe in interior but moderated on csts.; less than 8 per cent of total land a. classified as cultivated land but agr. prods. (especially wheat) very valuable exp.; enormous forest resources but many economically inaccessible; fur trapping in N., impt. fishing inds. on both Pac. and Atl. csts.; considerable mineral resources; lgst. world producer of asbestos, silver, nickel, zinc.; major oil and gas resources in Alberta; one of most urbanised ctys. in world; p. concentrated along E.–W. axis in S. parts of W. provs. and along Gr. Ls. and St. Lawrence lowland; economy highly integrated with USA; 80 per cent of mftg. inds. based on US investment and 78 per cent of external tr. with USA; major cultural differences between English and French communities; strong separatist movements in Quebec; both nat. languages official (30 per cent p. speak French); cap. Ottawa; a. 9,976,185 km²; p. (1992) 27.4 m.

Canada Dam, Bihar, **India**; on R. Mayurakshi, 256 km from Calcutta.

Canadian Coast Range, mtns., B.C., W. **Canada**; penetrated by deep inlets (fjords) with very little cst. plain; crossed only by R. Skeena in N., R. Fraser in S.

Canadian R., S.W. **USA;** trib. of Arkansas R., not navigable but impt. for irrigation; 1,440 km long.

Canadian Shield (Laurentian Shield), Canada; vast region of hard anc. rock surrounding Hudson Bay, deeply eroded by ice, and lake covered; mng. and forestry.

Canal du Centre, canal, **France;** links Rhône-Saône valley at Chalon-sur-Saône with R. Loire at Digoin; serves Le Creusot coalfield; length 96 km.

Canaries Current, ocean current, flows S. along N.W. coast of Africa from El Dar-el-Beida to C. Verde; relatively cold and has very marked cooling effect on Saharan coastlands.

Canary Is., or **Canaries,** N. Atl. Oc.; gr. of 7 volcanic Is. belong to Spain, 90 km off cst. Africa; dashes independence; inc. Tenerife (the lgst. I.), Gran Canaria, La Palma, Gomera, Hierro, Fuerteventura, Lanzarote; dry sunny climate and impressive volcanic landscape encourage tourism; intensive, irrigated agr. for bananas, tomatoes, oranges and vegetables; cap. Las Palmas, the "Fortunate Isles" of many myths and legends; a. 7,272 km²; p. (1981) 1,444,626.

Canberra, cap. **Australia;** midway between Melbourne and Sydney, lgst. inland c.; rapid growth since cap. established (1912); half work-force employed in government; spacious planned c. centred around L. Burley Griffin, reliant on high car ownership; p. (1991) 278,894.

Candia. See **Iráklion.**

Canea. See **Khaniá.**

Canna, sm. I., Hebrides, **Scot.;** basaltic pillars.

Cannanore, t., Kerala, **India;** exp. timber, coconuts; p. (1981) 60,904 (t.), 157,797 (met. a.).

Cannes, spt., dep. Alpes-Maritimes, **France;** 32 km S.W. Nice; famous resort; perfumes; airpt.; annual spring international film festival; p. (1990) 69,363 (t.), 335,647 (met. a.)

Cannock Chase, upland a., Staffs., **Eng.;** open a. close to Midlands conurb.; now forms l. gov. dist. based on Cannock t.; p. (1993) 90,700.

Canopus, c. of anc. **Egypt;** 19 km E. of Alexandria; here bdy. between Asia and Africa was drawn; Aboukir nr. ruins of temple of Serapis.

Cantabrians (Sierra de Cantabria), mtns., N. **Spain;** stretch from Pyrenees to C. Finisterre; form barrier between sea and central plateau; thick vegetation on lower slopes; coal, iron, hydroelec. power; hgst. peak Peña Vieja (2,673 m).

Cantal, dep., S.E. **France;** volcanic a., a part of Massif Central; hgst. peak Plomb du Cantal (1,859 m); difficult agr., sparse p.; cap. Aurillac; a. 5,778 km²; p. (1990) 158,700.

Canterbury, c., l. gov. dist., Kent, **Eng;** at foot of N. Downs on R. Stour; univ.; cath. founded A.D. 597 by St. Augustine; shrine of Thomas Becket; for centuries a place of pilgrimage; p. (1993) 132,400 (dist.).

Canterbury, region, rich grazing and wheat-growing dist., on merged alluvial fans; S.I., **N.Z.;** ch. t. Christchurch; ch. pt. Lyttelton; p. (1991) 442,392.

Can-tho, t., **Vietnam;** on Mekong R. delta, tr. ctr.; rice, fish; p. (1989) 208,326.

Canton. See **Guangzhou.**

Canton R. See **Zhujiang.**

Canton, c., Ohio, **USA;** iron and steel, pulleys, hydraulic presses; p. (1990) 84,161 (c.), 394,106 (met. a.).

Canvey I., Castle Point, Essex, **Eng.;** fronting the Thames; expanded t.; resort; radio components, bookbinding, iron and wire wks., oil storage; oil refinery projected; liquid gas terminal; p. (1981) 35,293.

Cap-de-la-Madeleine, t., S. Quebec, **Canada;** varied mnfs.; p. (1986) 32,800.

Cape Breton I., Nova Scotia, **Canada;** coalmng., steelwks; farming, timber, fishing; ch. t. Sydney; discovered in 1497 by John Cabot; a. 9,324 km².

Cape Canaveral, E. Fla., **USA;** formerly Cape Kennedy; barrier I. separating Banana R. lagoon from Atl. Oc.; military base for testing missiles.

Cape Coast, t., **Ghana;** pt. of G. of Guinea, 96 km S.W. of Accra; cap. of Gold Coast until 1876; exp. cacao; cas.; p. (1984) 51,653.

Cape Cod, low sandy penin., Mass. Bay, **USA;** resort; fishing, boat bldg.; encloses C. C. Bay where Pilgrim Fathers first arrived in America 1620.

Cape Girardeau, t., Mo., **USA;** on Mississippi R.; footwear, clothing; p. (1980) 34,361.

Cape Kennedy. *See* **Cape Canaveral.**

Cape of Good Hope, S. Africa; famous headland, S. of Cape Town; 305 m high.

Cape Province, prov., **Rep. of S. Africa;** formerly Cape of Good Hope Colony; southernmost tip of Africa; cap. Cape Town; mostly plateau; inc. Transkeian terrs. in E.; sheep raising; wheat, citrus fruits, grapes, tobacco; fisheries; diamond and copper mng. in Namaqualand; automobile assembly, textiles, food canning; a. 721,224 km²; p. (1985) 5 m.

Capernaum, in time of Christ impt. place in Palestine, on N. shore of L. Galilee; the modern Tell Hum (Israel).

Cape Town, c., cap. of Province, and legislative cap. of **Rep. of S. Africa;** spt. on Table Bay, 48 km N. of C. of Good Hope; communication by rail direct with Zimbabwe, Transvaal, O.F.S., and Natal; docks; cath.; univ.; exp. wool, gold, diamonds; oil refinery under construction at Milnerton 10 km N.E., p. (1980) 858,940 (met. a.).

Cape Verde Is., archipelago off W. cst. **Africa;** former Portuguese col.; 15 volcanic Is. and islets, divided into two grs.; windward and leeward; a. 4,040 km²; cap. Praia; agr. sugar, fruit-growing; São Vicente fuelling sta. for navigation to S. America; indep. achieved 1975; plans to develop infrastructure; irrigation and reafforestation projects; p. (1993) 350,000.

Cap-Haitien, t., N. **Haiti;** spt. on N. cst.. exp. coffee, cacao, sugar; p. (1988) 133,233.

Capraia, I., 26 km E. of Corsica, belonging to **Italy;** volcanic; part of Genoa prov.

Caprera, I., off N.E. cst. Sardinia, **Italy;** Garibaldi buried here.

Capri, I. and tourist resort in Bay of Naples, **Italy;** famous Blue Grotto; celebrated in times of Augustus and Tiberius; wines; a. 10 km²; p. (1981) 7,489.

Capua, t., Campania, S. **Italy;** on Volturno R.; founded by Etruscans, impt. ctr. under Roman rule, sacked by Gaiseric; modern t. 5 km N. of site of anc. Capua; cath.; Roman bridge; p. (1981) 18,053.

Caracas, c., cap. of **Venezuela;** in mtn. valley 921 m a.s.l.; 13 km inland from its pt. La Guaira; modern c.; contains 20 per cent of p. of rep.; cath., univs.; oil, textile mills, sugar refining; p. (1981) 1,816,900 (c.), 2,944,000 (met. a.).

Caradon, l. gov. dist., Cornwall, **Eng.;** a. between Tamar and S. cst.; inc. Looe, Saltash and Liskeard; p. (1993) 77,800.

Carbon County, N. Utah, **USA;** contains immense reserves of gd. coking coal suitable for blast furnaces; not yet developed.

Carbonia, t., Sardinia, **Italy;** built 1937–8 nr. lignite and barytes a.; p. (1981) 32,130.

Carcassonne, c., cap. of Aude dep., S. **France;** historic citadel guarding impt. routeway from Aquitaine to Rhône valley; old c. divided from new by Aude R.; tourism; p. (1990) 44,991.

Cardamom Hills, Kerala, S. **India;** highland formed where W. and E. Ghats meet; rise to over 2,400 m; hgst. land of Indian penin.; rainfall less seasonal than most of India; "China" tea plantations on middle slopes.

Cárdenas, t., W. **Cuba;** pt. on Cárdenas Bay; processes and exp. sugar.

Cardiff, c., l. gov. dist., South Glamorgan, cap. of **Wales;** at mouth of R. Taff on Bristol Channel, one of world's gr. coal-shipping pts.; univ. colls., cath., cas.; docks at Barry; iron and steel wks., flour mills; freeport (1984) to help redevelopment of docks; p. (1993) 298,700.

Cardigan, t., Ceredigion, Dyfed, S. **Wales;** at mouth of Teifi R.; former pt., now mkt. ctr.; p. (1981) 4,184.

Cardiganshire, former c., **Wales.** *See* **Dyfed.**

Caribbean Sea, part of Atl. Oc., between W.I. and Central and S. America; warm sea, entirely within tropics; a. 19,425 km².

Cariboo Range, mtns., B.C., W. **Canada;** mass of anc. crystalline rocks inside the gr. bend of R. Fraser; widespread occurrence of lode and alluvial gold; mainly above 1,500 m; hgst. point Mt. Sir Wilfred Laurier (3,584 m).

Carinthia (Karnten), prov., **Austria;** cap. Klagenfurt; contains hgst. mtn. in Austria, Grossglockner, alt. 3,801 m; many Ls.; p. (1991) 552,421.

Carlisle, c., l. gov. dist., Cumbria, **Eng.;** on Eden R.; pt. and route ctr.; Norman cas.; cath.; textiles, plasterboard, flour, bacon, biscuits, metal boxes; p. (1993) 102,900 (dist.).

Carlow, co., S.E. Leinster, **R.o.I.;** arable agr. and livestock; co. t. Carlow; a. 896 km²; p. (1986) 40,988.

Carlow, co. t., Carlow co., **R.o.I.;** cath.; mkt., agr. processing; p. (1986) 11,509.

Carlsbad, t., N.M., **USA;** tourist resort; impt. potash deposits; p. (1980) 25,496.

Carlsbad Caverns National Park, N.M., **USA;** in foothills of Guadalupe mtns.; limestone caves; a. 18,600 ha.

Carlton, t., Gedling, Notts., **Eng.;** 3 km N.E. Nottingham; hosiery; p. (1981) 46,456.

Carmarthen, t., l. gov. dist., Dyfed, **Wales;** on Towy R.; impt. agr. ctr.; cas. ruins; p. (1993) 56,400 (dist.).

Carmarthenshire, former co., **Wales.** See **Dyfed.**

Carmiel, t., N. **Israel;** new t. built built between Acre and Safad, in the Galilean hills.

Carmona, t., **Spain;** Roman walls and necropolis.

Carnac, sm. t., Brittany, N.W. **France;** famous for its megalithic monuments; p. (1982) 3,964.

Carnarvon, t., W. **Australia;** on R. Gascoyne; NASA tracking sta.

Carnoustie, burgh, Angus, **Scot.;** on N. Sea; 10 km S.W. of Arbroath; resort; p. (1991) 10,673.

Caroni, R., Venezuela; hydroelec. complex at confluence Orinoco R.; steelwks.

Carpathian Mtns., range, **E. Europe;** arc of mtns. extending from Slovakia into Ukraine and Romania; major European range; 1,288 km long; contains oilfields.

Carpentaria, G. of, N. **Australia;** between Arnhem Land and C. York.

Carpentras, t., Vaucluse, **France;** on R. Auzon; antiquities; sweetmeats; p. (1982) 25,886.

Carpi, t., central **Italy;** 16 km N. of Modena; cath.; food processing; p. (1981) 60,507.

Carrantuohill, mtn., Kerry, **R.o.I.;** 1,041 m, loftiest in all Ireland.

Carrara, t., Massa Carrara, central **Italy;** famed for white marble used by Michelangelo; p. (1981) 65,687.

Carrick, l. gov. dist., Cornwall, **Eng.;** stretches across penin. and surrounds Fal estuary; inc. Truro, Penryn and Falmouth; p. (1993) 84,500.

Carrickfergus, t., l. gov. dist., N. **Ireland;** pt. on N. shore of Belfast Lough; textiles, nylon fibres, tobacco inds.; p. (1991) 32,750 (dist.), 22,786 (t.).

Carrickmacross, mkt. t., Monaghan, **R.o.I.;** p. (1986) 1,815.

Carrick-on-Shannon, co. t., R. D., Leitrim, **R.o.I.;** on flat land in Upper Shannon valley; p. of t. (1986) 1,984.

Carrick-on-Suir, mkt. t., Tipperary, **R.o.I.;** leather prods.; N.W. of Waterford; p. (1986) 5,353.

Carron, v., Falkirk, **Scot.;** nr. Falkirk; site of first ironwks. in E. Lowlands of Scot; p. (1991) 3,605.

Carron, Loch, inlet, W. cst., Ross and Cromarty, **Scot.;** followed by rly. from Dingwall to Kyle of Lochalsh.

Carse of Gowrie, Perth and Kinross, **Scot.;** fertile coastal dist. between Perth and Dundee, S. of Sidlaw Hills; soft fruits, especially raspberries.

Carsington, reservoir opend May 1992, S. Derbyshire.

Carson City, cap. Nevada, **USA;** smallest st. cap. at 1,427 m; tourist ctr.; p. (1990) 40,443.

Carstenz Mtns., Irian Jaya, **Indonesia;** major copper and base metal deposits and mng.; slurry pipeline to pts. on Tipoeka R.

Cartagena, spt., cap. dep. Bolivar. **Colombia;** shares with Barranquilla tr. from Magdalena R. valley; platinum, coffee, chemicals, textiles, fertilisers, oil refinery; drugs summit 1990; p. (1985) 559,581.

Cartagena, c., Murcia prov., S.E. **Spain;** on Mediterranean; spt. and naval base; cath.; shipbldg., metalwkg.; p. (1991) 172,152.

Cartagena, t., port; cap. Bolivar dep., **Colombia;** founded 1533; p. (1992) 688,306.

Cartago, c., **Costa Rica;** former cap.; 1,504 m at foot of volcanic Mt. Irazu; coffee, fruits; subject to earthquakes; p. (1984) 29,564.

Cartago Basin, Meseta Central, **Costa Rica;** alt. 5,000 ft.; a. of early Spanish settlement.

Carter Fell, mtn., a summit of the Cheviot hills, on the Eng./Scot. border, 554 m.

Carthage, anc. c., N. **Africa;** on Bay of Tunis; destroyed by Romans 146 B.C.; site is sub. of Tunis.

Casablanca. See **El Dar-el-Beida.**

Casale Monferrato, t., Piedmont, **Italy;** on R. Po; cath.; cement.

Cascade Range, USA and **Canada;** extends N. and S. through B.C., Wash., and Ore. between Rocky Mtns. and Pac. cst.; timber resources, hydroelec. power; hgst. peak Mt. Rainier, 4,395 m.

Cascade Tunnel, longest rly. tunnel in N. America, Wash., **USA;** carries trunk rly. from Spokane to Seattle through Cascade Mtns.; length 12·5 km.

Caserta, t., Italy; on N.E. edge of plain of Campania; impt. route ctr. and agr. mkt.; cath.; palace; p. (1981) 66,318.

Cashel, mkt. t., Tipperary, **R.o.I.;** anc. seat of kings of Munster; ruins of cath. on Rock of Cashel; p. (1986) 2,458.

Casiquiare, R., and canal, **Venezuela;** joins Orinoco to the Rio Negro, a trib. of the Amazon.

Casper, t., Wyo., **USA;** petroleum; airpt.; p. (1990) 46,742.

Caspian Sea, salt lake, **Kazakhstan, Turkmenistan, Russia, Azerbaijan** and **Iran,** between Europe and Asia; lgst. inland sea in world; a. 422,170 km² but shrinking; 28 m below sea level; maximum depth 975 m; fed by R. Volga; agr. and dense p. on S. shore; pts.; Astrakhan, at mouth of Volga, Baku (oil ctr.).

Casquets, dangerous rocks, 11 km W. of Alderney, Channel Is., **Eng.;** lighthouse.

Cassino, t., Frosinone, **Italy;** in Apennines, on Rapido R.; t. and nearby monastery (Montecassino) destroyed 1944, now rebuilt; p. (1981) 31,139.

Castel Gandolfo, t., central **Italy;** in Alban Hills; papal summer residence; tourist centre; p. (1981) 13,348.

Castellammare del Golfo, spt., N.W. Sicily, **Italy;** wat. pl., tuna fishing.

Castellammare di Stabia, t., Campania, **Italy;** on Bay of Naples, at foot of Vesuvius; historic arsenal and dockyards; mineral springs; cath.; resort; p. (1981) 70,317.

Castellón de la Plana, prov., **Spain;** on Mediterranean, part of anc. Valencia, mainly mtns. a. 6,679 km²; cap. Castellón; p. (1991) 446,683.

Castellón de la Plana, t., **Spain;** on plain inland from Mediterranean cst.; varied agr. inds.; oil refining; p. (1991) 137,456.

Castelnaudary, t., Aude dep., **France;** in strategic gap between Central Massif and Pyrenees; captured by Black Prince 1355; mkt. for cereals; pottery; p. (1982) 11,381.

Castelo Branco, t., **Portugal,** prov. cap. Beira Baixa; agr. mkt. t.; p. (1981) 21,300.

Castelvetrano, agr. t., W. Sicily, **Italy;** wine mkg.; p. (1981) 30,577.

Castile, region in the high plateaux of central **Spain;** former kingdom; divided into Old Castile in N. (Avila, Burgos, Logroño, Santander, Segovia, Soria) and New Castile in S. (Ciudad Real, Cuenca, Guadalajara, Madrid, Toledo). Its dialect became the standard language of Spain.

Castlebar, cap. Mayo, **R.o.I.;** mkt. t.; p. (1986) 6,349.

Castleblayney, Monaghan, **R.o.I.;** nr. Dundalk; mkt. t.; shoes; p. (1986) 2,157.

Castlecary, v., Central Reg., **Scot.;** sta. on Roman wall; silica, fire clay deposits.

Castle Donington, t., Derbyshire, **Eng.;** airpt; power sta.

Castle Douglas, burgh, Stewartry, **Scot.;** nr. R. Dee; nearby cas.; stock mkt.; p. (1991) 3,697.

Castleford, t., West Yorks., **Eng.;** 16 km S.E. of Leeds at confluence of Rs. Aire and Calder; coal mng., chemical, glass, and clothing mnfs., flour milling, brick mkg.; p. (1981) 36,032.

Castle Morpeth, l. gov. dist., Northumberland, **Eng.;** based on Morpeth; p. (1993) 50,100.

Castle Point, l. gov. dist., Essex, **Eng.;** comprises Canvey I. and Benfleet; p. (1993) 86,000.

Castlereagh, l. gov. dist., N. **Ireland;** inc. S.E. outskirts of Belfast; p. (1991) 60,799.

Castleton, v., Derbys., **Eng.;** on Hope R.; tourist ctr. for the Peak District; nearby fluorspar mines.

Castletown, t., Isle of Man, **Eng.;** former cap.; pt., cas. tower; p. (1991) 3,152.

Castres, t., Tarn, **France**; on R. Agout; former Huguenot stronghold; cath.; textiles, soap, earthenware; p. (1982) 46,877.

Castries, t., cap. **St. Lucia,** Windward Is., **W.I.**; fine harbour; p. (1988) 52,868.

Castrop-Rauxel or **Kastrop Rauxel,** t., N. Rhine-Westphalia, **Germany**; part of Ruhr conurb.; industl.; coal, cement, tar prod., tiles, brandy; p. (1986) 96,100.

Catalonia, region, N.E. **Spain**; ch. industl. a.; comprises 4 provs.; Barcelona, Gerona, Lérida, Tarragona; cap. Barcelona; hilly, drained by Ebro R.; cereals, olive oil, wines; textiles, cars; hydroelec. power stas.; nuclear power sta. projected; a. 32,185 km²; p. (1981) 5,956,598.

Catamarca, t., cap. of Catamarca prov., N.W. **Argentina**; in Andean foothills 128 km S. of San Miguel de Tucumán; ctr. of irrigated oasis producing vines, apricots, cherries, cotton; thermal springs; p. (1991) 110,489 (t.), 264,940 (prov.).

Catanduanes, I., prov. off S. Luzon, **Philippines**; hilly, fertile; rice, corn, cotton, hemp, coconuts; a. 1,429 km²; p. (1990) 187,000.

Catania, c., Sicily, **Italy**; cap. of C. prov.; pt. on E. cst. at foot of Mt. Etna; rebuilt several times after earthquakes and volcanic eruption; cath., univ., cas.; p. (1992) 329,898.

Catanzaro, t., S. **Italy**; univ.; service ctr., regional cap. of Calabria; p. (1984) 101,622.

Catastrophe, C., S. extremity of Eyre Peninsula, S. **Australia.**

Catawba, R., S. and N.C., **USA**; rises in Blue Ridge Range, flows to Santee R.; extensively dammed; 480 km long.

Caterham and **Warlingham,** ts., former U.D. Tandridge, Surrey, **Eng.**; on N. Downs; residtl.; p. (1981) 33,083.

Cathay, anc. name for China and E. Tartary.

Catoche, C., N.E. point of Yucatan, **Mexico.**

Catskill Mtns., N.Y., **USA**; gr. in Appalachians, W. of Hudson R., well wooded; resort for p. of N.Y. c.; alt. c. 900 m.

Cauca, dep., **Colombia**; cap. Popayán; a. 30,191 km²; p. (1985) 674,824.

Cauca, R., **Colombia**; trib. of Magdalena; 960 km long.

Caucasia, region between Black Sea and Caspian, occupied by parts of **Russia**, **Georgia**, **Azerbaijan** and **Armenia** divided by Caucasus Mtns. into N. or Cis-Caucasia and S. or Trans-Caucasia.

Caucasus (Bol'shoy Kavkaz), mtns., separate **Russia** from **Georgia** and **Azerbaijan**; run from Black Sea to Caspian Sea; divided into 3 ranges; hgst. summits Mt. Elbruz (5,631 m) and Kasbek (5,047 m); many lofty passes and glaciers; total l. c. 1,520 km.

Caucun, I., off Yucatan penin., **Mexico**; developing tourist ctr.; airpt.

Causses, Les, limestone plateau, Aveyron, Tarn deps., S. **France**; on S.W. flank of Central Massif; caverns, gorges of Rs. Lot and Tarn; sheep provide milk for Roquefort cheese; alt. 900–1,800 m.

Cauvery, R., S. **India**; rises in W. Ghats, flows into Bay of Bengal through Karnataka and and Tamil Nadu; length 640 km; lge. irrigation and hydroelec. power project.

Caux, region of Normandy, **France**; fertile loess-covered chalk plateau adjacent to English Channel; arable agr.

Cava de' Tirreni, t., Salerno, **Italy**; summer resort; textiles; p. (1981) 50,558.

Cavaillon, t., Vaucluse, **France**; cath.; ctr. of mkt. gardening dist.; p. (1982) 20,830.

Cavan, inland co., **R.o.I.**; agr. a. with many Ls.; depopulation; borders Ulster; a. 1,932 km²; p. (1986) 53,965.

Cavan, , co. t., Cavan, **R.o.I.**; 115 km S.W. Belfast; mkt.; cath.; p. (1986) 3,381.

Cavite, spt., Luzon, **Philippines**; walled t.; oil refining nearby; p. (1990) 91,641.

Cavour Canal, irrigation canal, Piedmont and Lombardy regions, N. **Italy**; links R. Po nr. Chivassa with R. Ticino 16 km N.E. of Novara; provides water for 101,000 ha of rice-fields and meadow-land; length 128 km.

Cawnpore. See **Kanpur.**

Caxias do Sul, t., Rio Grande do Sul, **Brazil**; wines; p. (1980) 198,683.

Cayambe, volcanic mtn., Andes, **Ecuador**; alt. 5,958 m.

Cayenne, c., cap of French Guiana, at mouth of

Cayenne R.; exp. gold; gave its name to Cayenne pepper; p. (1990) 41,659.

Cayman Is., W.I.; consists of Grand Cayman, cap. Georgetown; Little Cayman; and Cayman Brac.; turtle and shark fishing; a. 259 km²; p. (1992) 29,700.

Ceará, st., N. **Brazil**; stretches from Brazilian Plateau to Atl. cst.; poor cattle rearing a. with many droughts; cap. Fortaleza; a. 148,078 km²; p. (1991) 6,353,346.

Cebu, one of Visayan Is., prov. **Philippines**; mtnous.; forested; coal, oil, gold; coconuts, maize; 4,408 km²; p. (1990) 2,645,735.

Cebu, c., Cebu I., **Philippines**; tr. ctr. of Visayan Is.; pt. for abaca and copra; p. (1990) 610,417.

Cedar Falls, t., N. Iowa, **USA**; on Cedar R.; p. (1990) 34,298.

Cedar Mountain, hill, Va., **USA**; here Stonewall Jackson defeated Banks in Civil War (second battle of Bull Run, 1862).

Cedar Rapids, c., Iowa, **USA**; distribution and rly. ctr. for agr. a.; p. (1990) 108,751.

Cegléd, t., **Hungary**; on edge of Central Plain in fruit growing a.; vehicle repair shops; p. (1984) 40,000.

Celaya, mkt. t., Guanajuato, **Mexico**; rly. junc.; ctr. of rich farming a.; many inds.; sweet-meats; p. (1990) 315,577.

Celebes. See **Sulawesi.**

Celje, t., Slovenia (formerly Yugoslavia); industl., agr. ctr., zinc refining, fertilisers; close to Austrian border; p. (1981) 63,877.

Celle, t., Lower Saxony, **Germany**; on R. Aller; cas. was residence of dukes of Brunswick-Lüneburg until 1705; oil refining, machin., textiles; p. (1986) 70,200.

Celtic Sea, a. bounded by S. Ireland, Wales, Cornwall and Brittany; rich natural gas deposits 48 km S.W. of Kinsale.

Central African Republic, indep. st., former empire until 1979; within Fr. Community, **Equatorial Africa**; formerly Fr. colony of Ubangi-Shari; land-locked upland plateau covered by savannah grassland; S.W. forest zone likely to develop with proposed rail link with Transcameroon rly.; cotton, diamonds; cap. Bangui; a. 622,984 km²; p. (1991) 3,130,000.

Central America, stretch of land between Mexico and S. America, from the Isthmus of Tehuantepec to that of Panama; includes Guatemala, Honduras, Mexico, Nicaragua, Salvador, Costa Rica, Panama, Belize; tropical climate; forests, savannahs; p. (1981) 93,000,000.

Central Asia, usually applied to regions between 30° and 40° N. lat. and 55° and 85° E. long.; the land between China and Afghanistan and the Caspian, consisting of Kazakhstan, Tajikistan, Turkmenistan, Uzbekistan and Kyrgyzstan.

Central Clydeside Conurbation, conurb., **Scot.**, based on Glasgow and includes other urban areas (Bearsden, Milngavie, Clydebank, Cumbernauld, Kilsyth, East Kilbride, Eastwood, Hamilton, Monklands, Motherwell, Renfrew and Strathkelvin); p. (1993) 1,619,960.

Central Lancashire, new t., Lancs., **Eng.**; site of 14,186 ha.; t. created from expansion of Chorley and Leyland; biggest new t. in Eng.; p. (1981) 247,224.

Central Region, l. gov. reg., **Scot.**; stretches from Grampian mtns. to Central Lowlands, inc. Forth valley; main ts. Falkirk and Stirling; a. 2,631 km²; p. (1993) 272,900.

Central Valley, Cal., **USA**; valleys of Rs. San Joaquin and Sacramento; main agr. a. of Cal.; vast scheme for irrigation, hydroelec. power, flood control and protection of wildlife.

Centre, region, **France**; inc. deps. Cher, Eure-et-Loir, Indre, Indre-et-Loire, Loir-et-Cher, Loiret; region based on the upper Loire and its tributaries; agr; vineyards; ch. ts. Orleans, Tours; p. (1990) 2,371,000.

Cephalonia (Kefalliniá), lgst. of Ionian Is., **Greece**; mtnous. with fertile valleys; impt. harbours of Argostólion and Lexourion; currant production; a. 751 km²; p. (1991) 32,314.

Ceram. See **Seram.**

Ceredigion, l. gov. dist., Dyfed, **Wales**; lge a. inc. Cardigan and Lampeter in S. and Aberystwyth in N.; p. (1993) 68,900.

Cérignola, t., Apulia, **Italy**; agr. ctr.; Spanish victory over French in Italian wars 1503; p. (1981) 50,682.

Cerigo (Kithira) I., Greece; sm. I. between Crete and Peloponnesus.

Cernauti. See Chernovtsy.

Cerro de Pasco, t., Pasco dep., Peru; mng. ctr. at 4,403 m; univ.; copper, gold, lead, zinc; p. (1990) 77,000.

Cerro Rico, mtn., Bolivia; in Andes, W. of Potosí; alt. 4,782 m; rich silver, tin, tungsten ores.

Cesena, t., Emilia-Romagna, Italy; flourished in Renaissance times; cath., Malatesta library; agr. mkt. t.; p. (1981) 89,640.

České Budějovice (Budweis), t., Czech Rep.; on R. Vitava, 128 km S. of Prague, major industl. ctr.; pencils, porcelain, brewing, anthracite; p. (1990) 99,000.

Český Těšín, t., Czech Rep.; on Olše R., trib. of Oder; part of former t. of Teschen on Czech side of frontier with Poland; coal mng.

Cessnock-Bellbird, t., N.S.W., Australia; coal mng. declining since 1968; ctr. for Hunter Valley vineyards; p. (1981) 16,916.

Ceuta, spt., Spanish N. Africa, naval base; opposite to and 26 km from Gibraltar; cath.; the anc. Abyla, one of the Pillars of Hercules; p. (1981) 65,263.

Cevennes, mtns., S. France; separating basins of Rhône, Loire, and Tarn; highest point Mt. Mézenc, alt. 1,767 m.

Ceylon. See Sri Lanka.

Chaco, prov., N. Argentina; farming and prairie land; cap. Resistencia; a. 99,632 km²; p. (1991) 799,302.

Chad, indep. st. within Fr. Community, Equatorial Africa; landlocked, focus of trans Sahara and Equatorial tr. routes; N. frontier (Aouzou Strip) rich in minerals and occupied by Libya; valuable uranium and oil reserves but no exploitation; severe droughts (1982–3) reduced cattle and restricted arable crops; cash crops of cotton and ground nuts; cap. Ndjamena; a. 1,282,050 km²; p. (1993) 6·29 m.

Chad, L., lge. sheet of water bordering Nigeria, Niger, Chad and Cameroon; a. 129,500 km² when in flood; varies in extent with season, and is drying up; shallow, many Is., lies between the wooded region of the Sudan and the steppes leading to the Sahara desert; joint project for devel. by neighbouring ctys.

Chadderton, t., Gtr. Manchester, Eng.; engin., chemicals, textiles; p. (1981) 34,013.

Chagos Is., 5 coral Is., Indian Oc.; since 1965 the British Indian Ocean Territory; fine harbour in Diego Garcia (Anglo-American naval communications ctr.).

Chainat, t., Thailand; on Menam Chao Phraya; major barrage for hydroelec. power and flood control.

Chalcis, t., Greece; resort for Athens; joined to mainland by swing bridge; p. (1981) 44,867.

Chalfont St. Giles, v., Bucks., Eng.; in London commuter belt; home of Milton.

Châlons-sur-Marne, t., cap. of Marne dep., N.E. France; comm. and industl.; cath., churches; p. (1990) 51,533.

Chálon-sur-Saône, t., Saône-et-Loire dep., E. France; R. pt., comm. ctr. for Burgundy; historic t.; p. (1990) 56,259.

Chambal, R., trib. of R. Jumna, rising in Vindhya hills, Madhya Pradesh, India; major power, irrigation and industl. scheme; agr. in lower valley causing soil erosion, major soil conservation projection; 880 km long.

Chambéry, t., cap. of Savoie dep., S.E. France; leather gds.; tourism; p. (1990) 55,603 (t.), 102,548 (met. a.)

Chambord, v., Loir-et-Cher dep., France; on R. Cosson, trib. of Loire; Renaissance château; p. (1981) 206.

Chamonix, t., Haute-Savoie, France; at foot of Mont Blanc, in valley of R. Arve; winter sports ctr., road tunnel links to Aosta; p. (1982) 9,255.

Champagne, former prov. now incorporated in Champagne-Ardenne region, France; inc. deps. Ardennes, Aube, Marne, Haute-Marne; famous for its champagne wine; wheat, sheep; Ardennes hilly and heavily wooded; ch. t. Reims; p. (1990) 1,347,800.

Champaign, t., Ill., USA; close to Urbana; univ.; foundries; food processing; p. (1984) 60,400 (t.), 170,300 (met. a.).

Champigny-sur-Marne, t., Val-de-Marne dep.,

France; E. sub. of Paris; varied inds.; p. (1990) 79,778.

Champlain Canal, N.Y., USA; follows gap between Adirondack Mtns. and Green Mtns. occupied by Hudson R.; links Albany with L. Champlain and allows through barge traffic between New York and St. Lawrence valley.

Champlain, L., USA; N. frontier of N.Y. st.; discharges by Richelieu R. into St. Lawrence; flanked by trunk route from New York to Montreal; forms link between Hudson R. and St. Lawrence waterway; a. 1,126 km².

Chañaral, spt., N. Atacama, Chile; lies in gold and copper-mng. a.

Chanda, t., Nagpur, Maharashtra, India; anc. temples.

Chandausi, t., Uttar Pradesh, India; cotton, hemp; rly. ctr.; p. (1981) 66,970.

Chandernagore, t., W. Bengal, India; on Hooghly R., N. of Calcutta; founded by French 1686; p. (1981) 101,925.

Chandigarh, union terr. (1966) and former cap. of both Punjab and Haryana sts., India; new c. designed by Le Corbusier to replace former cap. Lahore, now in Pakistan; to be sole capital of Punjab on plateau at foot of Himalayas, S.W. of Simla, (now postponed because of Sikh unrest); univ.; a. of terr. 114 km², p. (1991) 511,000 (c.), 642,015 (terr.).

Changchun, c., Jilin, China; rly. ctr.; univ.; China's biggest motor vehicle plant, machine tools; film production centre; p. (1992) 2,130,000.

Changnacheri, t., Kerala, S. India; tea, cotton-spinning, silk; p. (1981) 51,955.

Changbai Shan, mtns.; form bdy. between China and N. Korea; drained by Rs. Yalu and Tumen; hgst. point Pai-t'ou-shan, 2,442 m.

Chang Jiang (Yangtse Kiang), R., China; rises in plateau in Xizang Zizhiou (Tibet) and flows E. to E. China Sea nr. Shanghai; one of China's major Rs.; crosses 'Red Basin' of Sichuan, a deep gorge above Yichang and finally a broad level plain; many lge. cs. on its banks inc. Yichang, Nanjing, Wuhan, Zhenjiang, Chongqing; major water control project; navigable by ocean-going vessels for 2,880 km. to Yichang; total length 5,600 km.; longest river in Asia.

Changsha, c., cap. of Hunan prov., China; pt. on Xiang Jiang; univ.; tea, rice, antimony; p. (1992) 1,330,000.

Changzhou (Changchow), c., Jiangsu, China; in valley of Chang Jiang, on Grand Canal 112 km S.E. of Nanjing; mkt. for intensively cultivated dist.; silk; p. (1984) 512,600.

Channel Is., gr. of self-governing Is. belonging to the Brit. Crown off N.W. cst. France, of which the lgst. are Jersey, Guernsey, Alderney, and Sark; part of the old duchy of Normandy; vegetables, flowers, fruit, granite; two famous breeds of dairy cattle; tourist resort; impt. banking and insurance ctr. encouraged by low taxes; retirement ctr.; a. 194 km²; p. (1985) 130,000.

Chantilly, t., Oise, France; famous racecourse; formerly famous for lace and porcelain; p. (1982) 10,208.

Chao Phraya. See Menam Chao Phraya.

Chaozhou (Chaochow), c., Guandong, S. China; on Han R., 32 km N. of Shantou; ctr. of cultivated plain; rice, sugar, tea; linked to Shantou by rly.; p. (1984) 191,400.

Chapala, t. and L., Mexico; chiefly in Jalisco st.; attractive site and climate encourage tourism; pastoral agr. on shores; a. 1,080 km²; p. (1990) 35,414.

Chapelcross, nr. Annan, Annandale and Eskdale, Scot.; AEA nuclear power sta., producing electricity for nat. grid.

Chapel-en-le-Frith, mkt. t., High Peak, Derbys., Eng.; brake-linings.

Chapra, t., Bihar, India; on Ganges R.; ctr. of former saltpetre and indigo tr.; p. (1991) 136,877.

Chard, mkt. t., Somerset Eng.; lace, engin., shirt and cotton mftg.; p. (1981) 9,384.

Chardzhou, t., Turkmenistan; inland pt. on Amu-Dar'ya R.; shipyards, textiles, chemicals; major oil refinery project; p. (1990) 163,700.

Charente, dep., S.W. France; cap. Angoulême; ctr. of distilling (i.e., cognac; a. 5,970 km²; p. (1990) 342,000.

Charente, R., S.W. France; rises W. of Limoges and flows into Bay of Biscay below Rochefort; valley slopes beyond Angoulême produce celebrated grapes from which brandy is made at Cognac and Jarnac.

Charente-Maritime, dep., S.W. **France**; cap. La Rochelle; borders Bay of Biscay; wine, wheat; oysters, pilchards; a. 7,229 km²; p. (1990) 527,000.

Charleroi, t., Hainaut, **Belgium**; on R. Sambre; coal mng.; glass; p. (1993) 207,045.

Charleston, c., spt., S.C., **USA**; industl. and comm. ctr. on Atl. cst. founded 1670; scene of onset of Civil War; p. (1990) 80,414 (c.), 506,875 (met. a.).

Charleston, t., cap. W. Va., **USA**; on Kanawha R.; in bituminous coal dist.; chemicals, glass, tools, oil, natural gas, lumber, coal processing; p. (1984) 59,400 (t.), (1990) 250,000 (met. a.).

Charleville-Mézières, twin t., Ardennes dep., N.E. **France**; on Meuse R.; iron, bricks, nails, hardware; p. (1990) 59,439.

Charlotte, c., N.C., **USA**; key rly. junc.; machin., chemicals, textiles; p. (1990) 395,934 (c.), 1,160,000 (met. a. with Gastonia-Rock Hill).

Charlotte Amalie, t., cap. of Virgin Is. of **USA**; on St. Thomas I.; excellent natural harbour; former coaling sta.; p. (1985) 12,660.

Charlottesville, t., Va., **USA**; on Rivanna R.; in apple-growing region; univ.; Monticello nearby, home of Jefferson; textiles; p. (1984) 40,600 (t.), 118,300 (met. a.).

Charlottetown, t., ch. pt. Prince Edward I., **Canada**; originally named after Queen Charlotte, consort of George III; univ.; p. (1986) 15,776.

Charlton Kings, t., Cheltenham, Gloucs., **Eng.**; at foot of Cotswolds; p. (1981) 10,785.

Charnwood Forest, upland plateau, Leics., **Eng.**; to W. of Soar valley, 19 km N.W. of Leicester; composed of anc. rocks; stone-crushing; largely forests; used for recreation by industl. ts. of E. Midlands; alt. 180-275 m; now forms l. gov. dist. of **Charnwood** and inc. Loughborough and Shepshed; p. (1993) 152,500.

Charters Towers, t., N. Queensland, **Australia**; fine bldgs. remain from 1872 gold rush; ctr. of agr. dist.; p. (1984) 7,620.

Chartres, t., cap. of Eure-et-Loir dep., **France**; mkt. for cereals from Beauce region; famous Gothic cath.; p. (1990) 41,850.

Châteauroux, t., cap. of Indre dep., **France**; 96 km S.E. of Tours, on R. Indre; agr. ctr., woollens, pottery; p. (1990) 52,949.

Chateau Thierry, t., Aisne, **France**; on R. Marne; mkt. t.; cas.; precision instruments; p. (1982) 14,920.

Châtellerault, t., Vienne, **France**; 64 km S. of Tours on R. Vienne; cutlery, metallurgical and aeronautical engin. Descartes lived here; p. (1982) 36,870.

Chatham, t., Rochester upon Medway, Kent, **Eng.**; on estuary of R. Medway; lt. inds.; famous naval dockyard established by Henry VIII, now closed; p. (1981) 61,909.

Chatham, t., spt., N.B., **Canada**; lumbering, fish exporting; p. (1986) 6,219.

Chatham, c., Ont., **Canada**; on extinct L. plain on R. Thames; agr. prods.; p. (1986) 42,211.

Chatham Is., N.Z. dependency, S. Pac. Oc.; volcanic Is.; sheep rearing and fishing; a. 963 km²; p. (1991) 760.

Chatsworth, Derbys., **Eng.**; on R. Derwent; seat of the dukes of Devonshire.

Chattanooga, c. Tenn., **USA**; on Tennessee R.; univ.; rly. ctr.; cottons; iron, steel, chemicals, paper, metals; p. (1990) 152,466 (c.), 433,204 (met. a.).

Chatteris, Fenland, Cambridge, **Eng.**; mkt. t.; p. (1981) 6,180.

Chaudière Falls, on Ottawa R., above Ottawa, **Canada**; hydroelec. sta.

Chauk, t., **Myanmar**; on R. Irrawaddy; ctr. of oilfield; oil refining; fertilisers.

Chaumont, t., cap. of Haute-Marne dep., **France**; on R. Marne; gloves, leather; p. (1990) 28,900.

Chautauqua, L., N.Y. st., **USA**; summer resort; vineyards.

Chaux-de-Fonds, La, t., can. Neuchâtel, **Switzerland**; ctr. of watchmkg. ind.; p. (1990) 36,272.

Cheadle, t., Staffs. Moorland, Staffs., **Eng.**; metal mnfs.; former coal-mng. a.

Cheadle and Gatley, ts., Gtr. Manchester, **Eng.**; textile finishing and bleaching, engin.; residtl. p. (1981) 58,683.

Cheb, t., Czech Rep.; nr. Bavarian frontier; comm. ctr.; machin.; p. (1984) 31,333.

Cheboksary, c., cap. of Chuvash aut. rep., **Russia**; R. pt. on Volga; agr. ctr.; hydroelec. plant; p.

(1989) 420,000.

Chechen Republic, rep. **Russia**, formerly known as Checheno - Inguish rep; declared independence 1991; unrest 1995; a 19,300 km²; cap. Grozny; p. (1992) 1,308,000.

Cheddar, v., Somerset, **Eng.**; famous limestone caves and gorge in Mendips; cheese, strawberries.

Chefoo. See Yentai.

Cheju (Quelpart), I., off **S. Korea**, E. China Sea; extinct volcano Mt. Halla, 1,968 m.

Chekiang. See Zhijiang.

Che-ling Pass, on bdy. between Guandong and Hunan, S. **China**; historic route across Nanling mtns., now followed by Wuhan to Guangzhou trunk rly.; alt. 300 m.

Chelm, t. and prov., E. **Poland**; nr. Lublin, cath.; flour-milling; p. (1989) 64,683 (t.) 245,500 (prov.).

Chelmsford, co. t., l. gov. dist., Essex, **Eng.**; 48 km N.E. London; cath.; agr. mkt.; p. (1993) 155,700 (dist.).

Chelsea, dist., London, **Eng.**; fashionable residtl. dist. See Kensington.

Chelsea, t., Mass., **USA**; industl. sub. on Boston harbour; p. (1980) 25,431.

Cheltenham, t., l. gov. dist., Gloucs., **Eng.**; spa; educational ctr.; precision instruments; birthplace of Gustav Holst; p. (1993) 106,700 (dist.).

Chelyabinsk, t., **Russia**; major industl. ctr. on Miass R.; Siberian lowlands; steel wks.; metallurgy, machin.; on natural gas pipeline from Gazli gasfield; p. (1989) 1,142,000.

Chelyuskin, Cape, most N. point in Asia, in Krasnoyarsk Terr., **Russia**; named after Russian navigator who discovered it in 1742.

Chemnitz, c., Saxony, **Germany**; leading industl. ctr.; cotton, woollens, machin., cars, furniture, chemicals, engin.; nr. lignite mines; p. (1990) 291,400.

Chemulpo. See Inchon.

Chenab, R., W. Punjab, **Pakistan**; one of "five rivers" of Punjab; rises in Himalayas, flows S.W. into R. Sutlej; dams at Marala and Khanki; c. 1,440 km long.

Chengchow. See Zhengzhou.

Chengdu (Chengtu), c., cap. of Sichuan prov., **China**; telecommunications centre, oil refinery; chemicals, electronics, textiles, machin.; p. (1992) 2,840,000.

Chepstow, mkt. t., Gwent, **Wales**; on R. Wye, 3 km above confluence with R. Severn; Severn Bridge links to Aust (Avon); ruined cas.; p. (1981), 9,309.

Chequers, official residence of Brit. prime ministers, 3 km S. of Wendover, Bucks., **Eng.**; gift of Lord Lee of Fareham.

Cher, dep., **France**; cap. Bourges; crossed by Cher R.; a. 7,301 km²; p. (1990) 321,600.

Cher, R., central **France**; rises in Central Massif, joins Loire below Tours; length 320 km.

Cherbourg, spt., Manche, **France**; N. cst. of Contentin peninsula; opposite to and 128 km dist. from Portsmouth; naval arsenal, shipbldg.; metals, ropes, fishing; p. (1990) 28,773 (t.), 92,045 (met. a.).

Cherepovets, c., **Russia**; on Rybinskoye reservoir of R. Volga; steel, engin., sawmills, shipbldg.; p. (1989) 310,000.

Cheribon. See Tjirebon.

Cheriton, dist. near Folkestone, Kent, **Eng.**; Channel Tunnel, linked to Sangatte, Calais, France opened 1994.

Cherkassy, t., **Ukraine**; nr. Kiev, on reservoir formed by Dnieper R.; sugar, engin., sawmilling; p. (1990) 297,200.

Cherkessk, t., **Russia**; rly. terminus, industl. ctr.; p. (1989) 113,000.

Chernigov, t., **Ukraine**; on Desna R.; p. (1990) 301,100.

Chernobyl, **Ukraine**; site of world's worst nuclear accident (1986).

Chernovtsy, t., **Ukraine**; univ.; Greek cath.; wheat, dairy produce, textiles, engin., chemicals; p. (1990) 257,300.

Cherrapunji, t., Assam, **India**; in Khasi Hills; reputed wettest place in world; average annual rainfall 12,700 mm.

Chertsey, t., Runnymede, Surrey, **Eng.**; on S. bank of R. Thames, 6 km below Staines; residtl.; p. (1981) 43,265.

Cherwell, l. gov. dist., Oxon., **Eng.**; stretches from Banbury to Bicester; p. (1993) 125,100.

Cherwell, R., trib. of Thames, nr. Oxford, **Eng.**; length 48 km.

Chesapeake Bay, inlet on Atl. cst., **USA**; extending 320 km from mouth of Susquehanna R. to C. Charles; shellfish ind.; bridge-tunnel (opened 1964) spans entrance to Bay; p. of c. (1990) 151,876.

Chesham, t., Bucks., **Eng.**; in heart of Chiltern Hills; printing, textiles, lt. engin.; residtl; p. (1981) 20,655.

Cheshire, non-met. co., N.W. **Eng.**; lowland a. drained by Rs. Dee and Mersey, bounded by Pennines in E.; dairying and mkt. gardening; chemical ind. based on salt deposits around Northwich; heavy inds. in and around Warrington; attracting many high technology inds.; much of co. residtl. for Liverpool and Manchester; cap. Chester; a. 2,323 km²; p. (1993) 971,900.

Cheshunt, t., Herts., **Eng.**; in Lea valley, 11 km S. of Hertford; bricks, mkt. gardening, horticulture; p. (1980) 49,670.

Chesil Bank, Dorset, **Eng.**; shingle ridge enclosing the Fleet lagoon running from I. of Portland to Bridport.

Chester, c., l. gov. dist., Cheshire, **Eng.**; at head of estuary of R. Dee; cath., anc. walls and old timbered houses; Roman c. of Deva site of legionary barracks; engin., metal gds.; p. (1993) 120,800 (dist.).

Chester, t., Penns., **USA**; on Delaware R. S.W. Philadelphia; called Uppland by Swedish settlers 1643, renamed by William Penn; pt. of entry; shipbldg.; p. (1980) 45,794.

Chesterfield, mkt. t., colly. dist., l. gov. dist., Derbys., **Eng.**; on Rother R.; 13 km S. of Sheffield; variety of heavy inds.; 14th-cent. church with crooked spire; p. (1993) 101,200 (dist.).

Chesterfield Inlet, arm of Hudson Bay, **Canada**; 400 km by 40 km.

Chester-le-Street, t., l. gov. dist., Durham. **Eng.**; clothing, confectionery, sand wkg.; p. (1993) 53,900 (dist.).

Cheviot Hills, range between **Scot.** and **Eng.**; hgst. summit, the Cheviot, 816 m.

Cheyenne, t., cap. of Wyo., **USA**; cattle-ranching dist.; rly. ctr.; p. (1990) 50,008.

Chiana, Val di, valley, central **Italy**; separates Tuscan hills from central Apennines; occupied by upper course of R. Arno, middle course of R. Tiber; followed by main route from Florence to Rome.

Chiang Mai, c., cap of C. prov., and 3rd c. of **Thailand**; rly. terminus on Ping R.; tr. ctr.; teak; p. (1980) 101,594.

Chiapa, R., flows N. from **Guatemala** through **Mexico** to G. of Campeche; impt. routeway in lower course; length 320 km.

Chiapas, Pac. st., **Mexico**; mtnous., forested; bananas, tobacco, sugar and cocoa; cattle; oil reserves; close associations with Guatemala; cap. Tuxtla- Gutierrez; a. 74,408 km²; p. (1990) 3,203,915.

Chiasso, frontier t., S. **Switzerland**; rly. sta. on Italian border.

Chiba, c., cap. of C. pref. **Japan**; part of Keihin conurb. on Tokyo B.; tr. ctr., giant shipyard, oil refining, aluminium, chemicals, iron and steel; airpt.; p. (1990) 829,467.

Chicago, c., Ill., **USA**; on S. shore of L. Michigan; economic heart of Mid-West; comm. ctr. called "The Loop"; immense tr. by rail and Gr. Ls.; univs.; grain mills, meat packing plants, iron and steel wks., major iron-ore mkt., electronic equipment, furniture; lgst. airport in world; p. (1990) 2,783,726 (c.), 6,070,000 (met.a.).

Chichester, t., l. gov. dist., West Sussex, **Eng.**; on S. cst. plain, 18 km W. of Arundel; cath.; yachting basin; p. (1993) 102,500 (dist.).

Chickamauga Creek, **USA**; branch of Tennessee R. above Chattanooga, forming part of Tenn. Valley Authority scheme; Civil War battles; site of Nat. Park.

Chickerell, E. Dorset, **Eng.**; 5 km N.W. of Weymouth; East Fleet, a sea-fed tidal estuary, lies to the west of the village.

Chiclayo, c., Lambayeque dep., **Peru**; mkt. ctr. for irrigated desert a. between Andes and Pac. Oc. producing mainly rice and sugar; p. (1990) 426,300.

Chicopee, t., Mass., **USA**; on Connecticut R. nr. Springfield; p. (1980) 55,112.

Chicoutimi, t., Quebec, **Canada**; pt. on Chicoutimi R.; lumber, pulp, paper; hydroelectric power; p. (1986) 61,083 (t.), 158,468 (met. a. with Jonquière).

Chiemsee, L., lge. lake nr. Munich, **Germany**; c. 460 m a.s.l.

Chieti, t., cap. of C. prov., S. **Italy**; cath.; anc. Teate Marrucinorum; Europe's lgst. glass plant, using methane from Abruzzi field; p. (1981) 54,927.

Chigrik, t., **Uzbekistan**; new t. (1963) 34 km S. of Tashkent.

Chigwell, t., Epping Forest, Essex, **Eng.**; on borders of Epping Forest: Hainault Estate now incorporated in Redbridge, Greater London; resdtl.; p. (1981) 51,290.

Chihli, Gulf of. See **Pohai.**

Chihuahua, lgst. st. in **Mexico**; dry climate impedes agr.; mng., cotton, cattle, Chihuahua dogs; a. 247,024 km²; p. (1990) 2,439,954.

Chihuahua, c., cap. Chihuahua st., **Mexico**; univ., cath.; ctr. silver-mng. ind.; p. (1990) 530,487.

Chikchi, peninsula, **Russia**; world's first Arctic nuclear power sta. being built.

Chikugo, t., N. Kyushu, **Japan**; lgst. coal mines in country; p. (1990) 43,835.

Chilaw, t., **Sri Lanka**; ctr. of coconut plantations.

Chile, rep., S. **America**; extends between Andes and Pac. for 4,160 km to C. Horn, E. to W. 400 km; Atacama desert; Spanish language; Roman Catholic; similar climate to that of Argentina but lacks space for extensive agr., dairying, sheep, wool; ch. exp. nitrates, copper, iron-ore, coal, iodine, petroleum, paper; cap. Santiago; ch. pt. Valparaiso; earthquake 1960, hgst. recorded magnitude; domestic and foreign protests against human rights abuses of government; a. 738,494 km²; world's lgst. producer of copper; p. (1993) 13·44 m.

Chillán, t., cap. of Nuble prov., **Chile**; destroyed 1939 by one of world's worst recorded earthquakes; since rebuilt; agr. and comm. ctr.; p. (1987) 148,805.

Chiloé, I. and S. prov., **Chile**; cap. San Carlos, earthquakes 1939 and 1960; ch. pt. Ancud destroyed 1960; heavy rainfall, tropical forest; a. 23,460 km².

Chilpancingo de los Bravos, t., cap. of Guerrero st., **Mexico**; ctr. of pre-Aztec culture; univ.; p. (1990) 136,243.

Chiltern, l. gov. dist., Bucks., **Eng.**; inc. part of C. Hills and Chesham and Amersham; p. (1993) 90,800.

Chiltern Hills, chalk escarpment, Oxon., Bucks., Beds., and Herts., **Eng.**; cut by no. of impt. gaps used by main communications; sheep and barley; hgst. point 276 m nr. Wendover.

Chimborazo, mtn., **Ecuador**; 6,286 m; Andes; extinct volcano, first explored by von Humboldt (1802), first scaled by Whymper (1880).

Chimbote, spt., **Peru**; steel, iron-ore, coal; tinned fish, fish-meal; p. (1985) 255,000.

Chimkent, t., **Kazakhstan**; in W. foothills of Tien Shan; nearby oasis fed by Arys R.; major industl. ctr.; lead smelting; p. (1990) 400,900.

China, People's Republic of, Asia; Third lgst. cty. of world; 22 provs., 3 municipalities and 5 autonomous regions; anc. conservative civilisation overthrown by long civil war and establishment of communist régime (1949); lge. p. crowded on cultivable valleys of Hwang-ho (Yellow R.), Yangtze and Si-kiang in E.; rest of cty. either mtnous. (plateau of Tibet) or desert (Sinkiang); rapid economic growth following onset of communist régime; agr. organised on commune basis, becomes increasingly intensive in S. where climate is less extreme, employs 82 per cent of p.; vast mineral resources; esp. iron ore and coal, many underdeveloped; mineral fuels major export; recent industl. growth; heavy inds. at Wuhan, Baotou and in N.E. (Manchuria); special economic zones to attract foreign investment; poor communications except in E.; increasingly self-sufficient in petroleum; 1984 economic reform liberalised state planning system to allow mkt. forces to restructure all but key sectors; consumer goods and services to be expanded; cap. Beijing; 35 m. only children resulting from one-child family birth control policy; a. 9,595,961 km²; p. (1995) 1,200,000,000, lgst. p. of any country.

China Sea, part of W. Pacific between Korea and Philippines; divided by the narrow Formosa Strait into two areas; E. China Sea, inc. Yellow Sea, and S. China Sea.

Chinandega, mkt. t., cap. of C. dep., **Nicaragua**; sugar refining; p. (1985) 68,000.

Chincho. See **Jinzhou.**

Chindwin, R., **Myanmar**; ch. trib. of Irrawaddy;

rises in Patkai Hills, navigable in rainy season; dense p. on lower reaches; 800 km long.

Chinghai. See **Qinghai.**

Chinkiang. See **Zhenjiang.**

Chingola, t., **Zambia;** copper mng.; metal prod., printing; p. (1989) 201,000.

Chinon, t., Indre-et-Loire, central **France;** on R. Vienne, industl.; ruined cas., once a royal residency; nuclear power sta.; p. (1982) 8,873 (t.), 78,131 (met. a.).

Chinqui, volcano, **Panama;** 3,480 m.

Chinwangtao. See **Qinhuangdao.**

Chioggia, spt., cath. t., N. **Italy;** on I. in G. of Venice; fishing; p. (1981) 53,566.

Chios (Khios) I., in Aegean Sea, **Greece;** mainly agr.; wines, fruits and figs; supposed birthplace of Homer; p. (1991) 52,691.

Chippenham, North Wilts., **Eng.;** mkt. t. on R. Avon; rly. signal and brake equipment, bacon curing, tanning; p. (1981) 19,290.

Chipping Campden, v., Gloucs., **Eng.;** in Cotswold Hills; formerly impt. for woollens; tourism.

Chipping Norton, mkt. t., Oxford, **Eng.;** nr. Banbury; formerly impt. for woollens; p. (1981) 5,035.

Chipping Sodbury, mkt. t., Avon. **Eng.;** 13 km N.E. of Bristol.

Chirchik, c., **Uzbekistan;** 32 km N.E. Tashkent; engin., chemicals; hydroelec. power stas.; p. (1990) 158,600.

Chiricahua Mtns., Arizona, **USA;** form part of Coronado Nat. Forest; long inhabited by Apache Indians; spectacular volcanic scenery; alt. 2,987 m.

Chirk, t. Clwyd, **Wales;** on R. Ceriog, S. of Wrexham; slate, formerly coal-mng. a.; cas.

Chislehurst. See **Bromley.**

Chistyakovo. See **Torez.**

Chita, c., rly. ctr., Siberia, **Russia;** on upper R. Ingoda, 640 km E. of L. Baykal; coal, engin., chemicals, sawmilling; p. (1989) 366,000.

Chittagong, c., **Bangladesh;** main pt. on Karna-fuli R., nr. Bay of Bengal; exp. jute, tea; oil refining; steel mill; hydroelec. power; p. (1991) 1,363,998.

Chittaranjan, t., West Bengal, **India;** new t. on Barakhar R., in steel ctr. of Damodar valley; rly. locomotive wks.; p. (1981) 50,748.

Chkalov. See **Orenburg.**

Choisy-le-Roi, t., Val-de-Marne dep., **France,** industl. sub. of Paris on R. Seine; p. (1982) 35,531.

Cholet, t., Maine-et-Loire, **France;** textile ctr. on R. Seine; p. (1990) 56,540.

Cholon (Cho Lon), t., S. **Vietnam;** 16 km S.W. of Ho Chi-minh City; ctr. of rice tr.

Cholula, anc. c. of Puebla prov., **Mexico;** Aztec temple, pyramid of Cholula, and other remains.

Chomo Lhari, mtn., Tibet, **China** and **Bhutan;** sacred to Buddhists; part of Himalayas; alt. 7,319 m.

Chomutov, t., N. **Czech Rep.;** industl. ctr. of lignite mng. a.; coal, steel, glass; p. (1984) 57,398.

Chongqing (Chungking), c., S.E. Sichuan prov., **China;** on Chang Jiang; comm. ctr. of W. China chosen 1983 as centre for experimental economic reforms; ctr. of rich agr. dist. of Red Basin of Sichuan; coal, iron and steel, heavy machin.; lorries, vans, chemical fertilisers; textiles; former treaty pt.; p. (1992) 3,010,000.

Cho Oyu, mtn., between **Nepal** and Tibet, **China;** sixth hgst. in world; alt. 8,225 m.

Chorley, t., l. gov. dist., N. Lancs., **Eng.;** on W. flank of Rossendale Fells, 11 km S.E. of Preston; cotton, engin.; expansion as new t. with Leyland p. (1993) 97,100 (dist.). See **Central Lancashire.**

Chorleywood, t., Three Rivers, Herts., **Eng.;** nr. Watford; p. (1981) 8,415.

Chorrilos Pass, Argentina; in E. cordillera of Andes at alt. 4,470 m; used by rly. from San Miguel de Tucumán to Antofagasta.

Chorzów (Królewska Huta), t., Katowice, **Poland;** coal, iron and steel, chemicals, engin.; p. (1989) 131,850.

Chota Nagpur, plateau, Madhya Pradesh, **India;** produces lac; impt. mng. ctr.; bauxite, mica.

Chou Kou Tien, site nr. Beijing, **China;** discovery of fossil bones of Beijing (Peking) man (*Sinanthropus pekinensis*).

Christchurch, t., l. gov. dist., Dorset, **Eng.;** on S. cst. 8 km E. of Bournemouth; holiday resort, aircraft. lt. inds.; p. (1993) 42,000 (dist.).

Christchurch, c., Canterbury region, S.I., **N.Z.;** lgst. c. of S.I.; comm. ctr. for lamb, wool, and grain; cath., univ.; airpt; p. (1991) 292,858 (c), 307,179 (met. a.).

Christianshåb, Danish settlement on Disko Bay, **W. Greenland;** meteorological sta.; p. (1990) 1,712.

Christmas I., in Indian Oc., Australian terr. since 1958; a. 140 km², healthy climate, phosphate deposits; p. (1982) 3,000.

Christmas I., lge. coral atoll in Pac. Oc., one of Line Is.; discovered by Cook 1777; a. 135 km²; nuclear test site, 1957–64.

Chu, R. **Kazakhstan;** rises in Tien Shan flows N.W. for 800 km into inland drainage basin; Chumysh Dam provides hydroelectricity and water for intensive cultivation of cotton, sugar-beet, citrus fruits.

Chuanchow. See **Quanzhu.**

Chubut, R., **Argentina;** drains from Andes into Atl. Oc.; continual irrigation reducing soil fertility of valley; 640 km long.

Chubut, prov. **Argentina;** cap. Rawson; p. (1991) 356,445.

Chuchow. See **Zhuzhou.**

Chudleigh, mkt. t., Devon, **Eng.;** on R. Teign; stone quarrying.

Chu-kiang. See **Zhujiang.**

Chukotskiy, peninsula, **Russia;** extreme N.E.; rich gold deposit; hunting.

Chukyo, industl. area, Honshu, **Japan;** centred on Nagoya; textiles, ceramics, chemicals.

Chula Vista, t., Cal., **USA;** agr., aircraft; p. (1990) 135,163.

Chungking See **Chongqing.**

Chuquibamba Mtns. (alt. c. 6,400 m), **Peru.**

Chuquicamata, t., N. **Chile;** 3,050 m in Andes; lgst copper mine in world.

Chuquisaca, dep. **Bolivia;** oil, agr.; cap. Sucre; a. 51,524 km²; p. (1988) 442,600.

Chur (Coire), t., cap. Graubünden, **Switzerland;** in valley of upper Rhine; historic bldgs.; fruit, wine, tourist ctr.; p. (1990) 30,975.

Church, Hyndburn, sub. of Accrington, Lancs., **Eng.;** engin.; p. (1981) 4,332.

Churchill, R., formerly Hamilton R., flows into Hamilton inlet, cst. of Labrador, **Canada;** magnificent waterfall, Churchill Falls with lge. hydroelec. scheme.

Church Stretton, mkt. t., Shrops., **Eng.;** tourism.

Chusan I. See **Zhoushan.**

Chuvash, aut. rep., **Russia;** in middle Volga valley; arable agr., lumbering, food processing; a. 18,407 km²; p. (1989) 1,338,000.

Cibao, lowland a., **Dominican Rep.,** Central America; extends along N. side of Cordillera de Cibao for 180 km; 16–56 km wide; early a. of Spanish settlement; E. part called Vega Real; richest agr. a. of Hispaniola; cacao, tobacco, maize; dense p.; ch. t. Santiago.

Cicero, t., Ill., **USA;** adjoins Chicago; electrical appliances, hardware; p. (1980) 61,232.

Ciechanów, t. and prov., **Poland;** 78 km N.W. of Warsaw; agr. inds.; p. (1989) 43,068 (t.), 425,600 (prov.).

Cienfuegos, t., **Cuba;** sugar, tobacco; picturesque; nuclear power sta.; p. (1986) 109,300.

Cieszyn, t., Bielsko-Biala prov., **Poland;** part of former Teschen on Polish side of frontier with Czech Republic; p. (1989) 36,682.

Cimpina, t., **Romania,** in Walachia; petroleum ctr.; oil pipeline links to Ploiesti and Constanta on Black Sea.

Cincinnati, c. Ohio, **USA;** route and comm. ctr. on terraces of Ohio R.; food processing and many varied inds.; univs.; p. (1990) 364,040 (c.), 1,452,645 (met. a.).

Cinderford, t., Gloucs., **Eng.;** former ctr. of coalmng. a. of Forest of Dean; new lt. industl. estate.

Cinque Ports, confederation of anc. **Eng.** csts. on cst. of Kent and Sussex; original 5: Sandwich, Dover, Hythe, Romney, Hastings; Winchelsea, and Rye added later.

Cirencester, t., Cotswold, Gloucs., **Eng.;** the Roman Corineum; former woollen t.; p. (1981) 15,622.

Ciskei, Bantu Terr. Authority, **S. Africa;** established 1961 between Fish and Kei Rs. on S.E. cst.; indep. (1981) but only recognised by S. Africa; 40 per cent of males work outside Ciskei; new cap. Bisho; cap. Zwelitsha; p. (1985) 750,000.

Città di Castello, walled t., **Italy;** in upper Tiber valley; impt. in Roman times; Renaissance cath., palaces; p. (1981) 37,242.

Città Vecchia (Mdina), c., central **Malta;** former cap.; Roman remains; cath.

Ciudad Bolivar, c., Bolivar st., **Venezuela;** pt. on Orinoco R.; formerly called Angostura;

coffee, cattle; ctr. of new industl. development on lower Orinoco; p. (1981) 181,900.

Ciudad Guayana, c., Bolivar st., **Venezuela**; spt. on R. Orinoco; heavy inds. ctr.; p. (1981) 314,000.

Ciudad Juarez, c., **Mexico**; comm. ctr. on USA border; agr. processing; tourism; p. (1990) 797,679.

Ciudad Madero, t., **Mexico**; styrene and detergent plants, oil refining; p. (1990) 159,644.

Ciudad Obregón, t., Sonora, **Mexico**; on Yaqui R.; ctr. of irrigated agr. a.; p. (1979) 181,733.

Ciudad Presidente Stroessner, t., **Paraguay**; rapidly growing t. close to Itaipú Dam on Parana R.; p. (1984) 110,000.

Ciudad Real, c., cap. of Ciudad Real prov., **Spain**; mkt. t. founded 1255; textiles; p. (1987) 55,072.

Ciudad Real, prov., central **Spain**; mostly at 600 m; covering la Mancha dist.; agr.; cap. C.R.; a. 19,741 km²; p. (1991) 467,242.

Ciudad Rodrigo, old fortress t., Salamanca prov., **Spain**; strategic position nr. Portuguese bdy.; in Peninsular War fell to Fr. (1810) and captured by Wellington (1812).

Civitavecchia, t., Latium, **Italy**; pt. for Rome on Tyrrhenian cst., 48 km N. of mouth of R. Tiber; p. (1981) 45,836.

Clackmannan, former co., l. gov. dist., Central Reg., **Scot.**; a. 161 km²; p. (1991) 3,420 (t.), (1993) 48,660 (dist.).

Clacton-on-Sea, t., Tendring, Essex, **Eng.**; on E. cst. 19 km S.E. of Colchester; seaside resort; lt. inds.; residtl.; p. (1981) 43,571.

Clairvaux, v., Aube, **France**; Cistercian abbey.

Clamart, t., Hauts-de-Seine, **France**; sub. of S.W. Paris; p. (1982) 48,678.

Clapham, S. London rly. junction; accident 1988.

Clare, co., Munster, **R.o.I.**; cstl. co. bounded in S. and E. by R. Shannon; mainly agr. and tourism; inc. cliffs of Moher; Shannon airpt. and tax-free industl. development scheme; co. t. Ennis; a. 3,351 km²; p. (1986) 91,344.

Clare I., Clew Bay, Mayo, **R.o.I.**; p. (1986) 140.

Clarence Strait, between Melville I. and Darwin, N.T., **Australia**.

Clarksburg, t., W. Va., **USA**; industl. ctr. for coal mng. a., oil and natural gas fields; machin. glass, pottery; p. (1980) 22,371.

Clarksdale, t., Miss., **USA**; processing ctr. for rich farming a.; p. (1980) 21,137.

Clarksville, t., Tenn., **USA**; on Cumberland R.; tobacco mkt.; p. (1990) 75,494 (t.), 169,439 (met. a.).

Clay Cross, t., Derbys., **Eng.**; former ctr. coal mng. (first developed by George Stephenson 1838) iron, engin.; p. (1981) 9,725.

Clayton-le-Moors, t., Hyndburn, Lancs., **Eng.**; nr. Blackburn; textile machin., cotton and blanket weaving, bristles, soap; p. (1981) 6,309.

Clear C., southernmost point of Ireland, Clear I., **R.o.I.**; off S.W. cst. of Cork.

Cleare, c., Alaska, **USA**; site of ballistic missile early warning sta.

Clearwater, t., Fla., **USA**; citrus fruit, flowers, fish; resort; p. (1990) 98,784.

Cleator Moor, t. Cumbria, **Eng.**; former colly. t.

Cleckheaton t., West Yorks., **Eng.**; nr. Bradford; woollens, blankets, asbestos.

Clee Hills, Shrops., **Eng.**; between Rs. Severn and Teme; alt. 550 m.

Cleethorpes, t., l. gov. dist., Humberside, **Eng.**; 5 km S. of Grimsby; resort; p. (1993) 70,500 (dist.).

Clent Hills, Hereford and Worcs., **Eng.**; about 16 km S.W. of Birmingham, overlooking valley of R. Stour; recreation; maximum alt. 316 m.

Clerkenwell, industl. dist., London, **Eng.**; immediately N. of the City; noted for jewellry.

Clermont-Ferrand, c., cap. Puy-de-Dôme dep. central **France**; in Auvergne; rubber tyres, chemicals, food inds.; Gothic cath., Romanesque church; p. (1990) 140,167 (c.), 254,416 (met. a.).

Clevedon, t., Woodspring, Avon, **Eng.**; at mouth of R. Severn; seaside resort; quarrying, bricks, footwear; p. (1981) 17,915.

Cleveland, c., Ohio, **USA**; impt. Gr. Ls. pt. handling iron ore and coal which support a major iron and steel ind.; oil refining, food processing, many varied inds.; univ.; p. (1990) 505,616 (c.), 1,831,122 (met. a.).

Cleveland, non-met. co., N.E. **Eng.**; heavy industl. region centred around ts. of Tees estuary; chems., iron and steel mftg.; inc. part of N. York Moors to S.; a. 583 km²; p. (1993) 559,500.

Cleveland Hills, North Yorks./Cleveland, **Eng.**; part of N. York Moors; once mined for iron ore,

impt. potash deposit.

Clichy, t., Hauts-de-Seine, **France**; N.W. sub. of Paris; oil refining, aircraft, automobile components; p. (1982) 47,000.

Clifton, sub., Bristol, Avon, **Eng.**; on R. Avon; mineral springs; famous suspension bridge.

Clifton, t., N.J., **USA**; industl. t., nr. Passaic; p. (1990) 71,742.

Clinton, t., Iowa, **USA**; on Mississippi R.; iron and steel, machin.; p. (1990) 29,201.

Clitheroe, t., Ribble Valley, Lancs., **Eng.**; in Ribble valley; mkt. t. for rural a.; limestone quarrying nearby; p. (1981) 13,552.

Clonakilty, t., Cork, **R.o.I.**; nr. Bandon; sm. harbour; agr. prods.; p. (1986) 2,567.

Cloncurry, t., Queensland, **Australia**; rly junction and air terminal in ctr. of copper field; uranium nearby; p. (1984) 3,040.

Clones, mkt. t. on Ulster border, Monaghan, **R.o.I.**; rly. ctr.; p. (1986) 2,280.

Clonmacnoise, v., Offaly, **R.o.I.**; ecclesiastical ruins.

Clonmel, t., Tipperary, **R.o.I.**; on R. Suir; agr. ctr.; fairs; cider, footwear; p. (1986) 11,759.

Clovelly, v., Devon, **Eng.**; seaside resort.

Clowne, t., Derbys., **Eng.**; coal mng.

Cluj, c., **Romania**; in Transylvania on Somesul R.; univs., historic bldgs.; industl. ctr.; p. (1990) 329,934.

Clutha R., R. of S.I., **N.Z.**; hydroelec. power; 320 km long; gives name to district.; p. (1991) 18,303.

Clwyd, co. N. **Wales**; inc. most of Denbigh and Flintshire; mtnous. to S.; N. cstl. resorts inc. Colwyn Bay, Prestatyn and Rhyl; sm. coalfield; lgst. t. Wrexham; a. 2,424 km²; p. (1993) 415,900.

Clwyd, R., Clwyd, N. **Wales**; flows into Irish Sea at Rhyl; length 48 km.

Clydach, t., West Glamorgan, **Wales**; on R. Tawe, 8 km N.E. Swansea; steel wks., nickel refineries.

Clyde, R., Strathclyde Reg., S.W. **Scot.**; flows through industl. belt into Firth of C.; Glasgow, Greenock, Clydebank main pts.; hydroelec. stas.; twin-road tunnel under R. in Glasgow (Whiteinch–Linthouse) completed 1963; 170 km long.

Clydebank, t., l. gov. dist., Strathclyde Reg., **Scot.**; on Clyde adjoining Glasgow; tyres, biscuits; p. (1991) 29,171 (t.), (1993) 46,550 (dist.).

Clyde, Firth of, stretches from Dumbarton to Ailsa Craig, **Scot.**; Bute, Arran, Gr. and Little Cumbrae ch. Is.; 102 km long.

Clydesdale, l. gov. dist., Strathclyde Reg., **Scot.**; small dist. formerly known as Lanark; p. (1993) 58,290.

Coachella Valley, arid region, S.E. Cal., **USA**; part of G. of Cal.; dates and citrus fruits under irrigation from Imperial Valley irrigation system.

Coahuila, st., **Mexico**; 3rd st. of Mexico; lies S. of Texas, bordering Rio Grande valley; main coal deposits; mnfs. impt.; irrigated agr.; cap. Saltillo; a. 142,611 km²; p. (1990) 1,971,344.

Coalbrookdale, v., Salop, **Eng.**; old coal and iron mines; home of iron master Abraham Darby. See **Bridges, Section L.**

Coalville, t., North West Leics., **Eng.**; nr. Ashby-de-la-Zouch; coal mng., engin., elastic webbing; p. (1981) 30,832.

Coast Range, mtns., **USA**; along Pac. cst.; wooded ranges causing rain shadow to E. valleys; alt. up to 600 m.

Coatbridge, burgh, Strathclyde Reg., **Scot.**; 16 km E. of Glasgow; coal, iron and steel, prefabricated houses, tubes engin.; p. (1991) 43,617.

Coats I., S. of Southampton I. Hudson Bay, **Canada**.

Coatzacoalcos (Puerto Mexico), spt., **Mexico**; on G. of Campeche; oil refinery; chemicals, fertilisers; p. (1990) 232,314.

Cobalt, t., Ont., **Canada**; silver, cobalt, arsenic, nickel; p. (1986) 1,640.

Cobán, t. **Guatemala**, mkt. t.; coffee and Peruvian bark tr.; p. (1989) 120,000.

Cóbh (Queenstown), c., Cork, **R.o.I.**; spt. on Great I. in Cork Harbour; lge. docks; H.Q. of Royal Cork Yacht Club; seaside resort; p. (1986) 6,369.

Coburg, t., Bavaria, **Germany**; old cas.; wickerwork, furniture, metal, machines, toy inds.; p. (est. 1986) 44,400.

Cochabamba, dep., **Bolivia**; E. of Andes; lgst. p.

concentration of Bolivia in C. basin; a. 65,496 km²; p. (1988) 982,000.

Cochabamba, c., cap. of C. dep., **Bolivia**; second lgst. c. in rep.; alt. 2,559 m; univ., cath.; oil refining, shoes, rubber tyres, fruit-canning, modern milk plant; hydroelectric power; p. (1982) 403,600.

Cochin, spt., Kerala, **India**; on Malabar cst.; exp. coconut oil, tea; oil refining; silting pt.; p. (1981) 513,249.

Cockenzie and Port Seton, small burgh, E. Lothian, **Scot.**; two fishing pts. on F. of Forth; p. (1991) 4,235.

Cockermouth, t., Allerdale, Cumbria, **Eng.**; slate, shoe mftg., plywood, concrete prods.; birthplace of Wordsworth; p. (1981) 7,149.

Cockpit Country, upland a., W. **Jamaica**; classic karst landscape forming rugged upland; some cultivation in hollows; a. 500 km²; alt. 300–800 m

Ovou, R., **Honduras** and **Nicaragua**; flows to Caribbean Sea through economically impt. valley; agr., forestry, mng.; potential as routeway; 480 km long.

Cocos or **Keeling Is.**, 27 coral atolls, **Indian Oc.**; since 1955 terr. of **Australia** purchased by Australia (1978) to ensure democracy; strategic position S.E. of Sri Lanka, radio and cable sta. German cruiser *Emden* destroyed by Australian cruiser *Sydney* on N. Keeling I. in 1914; uninhabited until 1826; developed by Clunies Ross family for coconut prod.; controlled emigration since 1948 to solve problem of overpopulation; voted to integrate with Northern Territory, Australia (1984); a. 13 km²; p. (1991) 647.

Coesfeld, t., N. Rhine–Westphalia, **Germany**; textiles, machin.; p. (1986) 31,600.

Cognac, t., Charente, **France**; cognac, bottles; p. (1982) 20,995.

Coihaique, t. Chile; cap. Aysen region; p. (1982) 31,167.

Coimbatore, t., Tamil Nadu, **India**; commands Palghat Gap; varied inds. benefit from local hydroelec. power; p. (1991) 816,000.

Coimbra, t., **Portugal**; cath., oldest univ. in Portugal; wine-growing; earthenware mfns.; p. (1981) 74,616 (t.), 138,930 (met. a.).

Colchester, t., l. gov. dist., Essex, **Eng.**; pre-Roman t. of Camulodunum on R. Colne; univ.; lt. inds., engin., oyster fisheries; pt.; p. (1993) 149,100 (dist.).

Cold Fell, mtn., Northumberland, **Eng.**; 622 m.

Cold Harbour, v., Va., **USA**; battles between Grant and Lee 1864.

Coldstream, t., Berwick, **Scot.**; on Eng. border; agr. machin., knitwear; p. (1991) 1,746.

Coleraine, t., l. gov. dist., N. **Ireland**; pt. on R. Bann, 6 km from sea; univ.inen, acrilan mftg., distilling; p. (1991) 50,721 (dist.), 50,438 (t.).

Coleshill, t., l. gov. dist., North Warwickshire, **Eng.**; lurgi gasification plant.

Colima, mkt. t., **Mexico**; on Colima R. in fertile valley; univ.; agr. processing; p. (1990) 116,155.

Colima, st., **Mexico**; on Pac. cst.; cap. Colima; pt. Manzanillo; cotton, sugar, rice, coffee; a. 5,203 km²; p. (1990) 424,656.

Colima, volcano (48 km N.E. of c.), **Mexico**, alt. 3,869 m.

Coll, I. off cst. of Mull, Argyll and Bute, **Scot.**; agr. lobster fishing; p. (1991) 172.

Collie, t., W. **Australia**; impt. coal deposits supply power for much of W. Australia; p. (1981) 7,667.

Collingwood, t., Ont., **Canada**; on Georgian Bay, L. Huron; shipbldg., steel; p. (1986) 12,127.

Colmar, t., cap. Haut-Rhin dep., **France**; ctr. of Alsace textile ind.; attractive mediaeval t.; mkt. for vineyards; p. (1990) 64,889 (t.), 83,816 (met. a.).

Colne, t., Pendle, E. Lancs., **Eng.**; cotton mnfs., felts; p. (1981) 18,203.

Colne, R., **Eng.**; trib. of Thames rising in Chilterns.

Colne Valley, t., West Yorks., **Eng.**; woollens; p. (1981) 21,659.

Cologne (Köln), c., N. Rhine–Westphalia, **Germany**; on Rhine at N. end of Rhine gorge; cath., univ.; impt. R. pt., route and comm. ctr., eau-de-Cologne, electro-technical ind., machin., metallurgy, paper, chemicals, cars, oil refining, textiles; p. (1990) 955,500.

Colombes, t., Hauts-de-Seine dep., **France**; mftg. sub. of Paris on R. Seine; p. (1990) 79,058.

Colombia, rep., N.W. **S. America**; cap. Bogotá;

Andes contain most of p.; the savannahs (llanos) to S.E. are almost uninhabited; industl. employment growing; increasingly indep. of USA sphere of influence; agr. impt.; coffee, (50 percent of exports), bananas; major oil reserves discovered (1985), some exp.; eruption of Nevado del Ruiz (1985) Mount Galeras (1993); a. 1,139,592 km²; p. (1992) 33,390,000.

Colombo, c., cap. of **Sri Lanka**; on W. cst.; univ.; impt. pt. (artificial) built by British; exp. tea, rubber, coconuts; p. (1983) 623,000.

Colón, t., **Panama**; at Atl. end of Panama Canal; free tr. zone; comm. and industl. ctr.; oil refining nearby; p. (1990) 140,908.

Colonsay, I., Inner Hebrides, Argyll and Bute, **Scot.**; 13 km long; ecclesiastical antiquities; p. (1991) 349.

Colorado, st., **USA**; admitted to Union 1876; st flower Rocky Mtn. Columbine, st. bird Lark Bunting; hgst. st. in USA; in the Rockies extending up to 4,401 m (Mt. Elbert), no land below 1,000 m; drained by headwaters of Rs. Arkansas and Colorado; major stockrearing a.; many valuable minerals esp. uranium, radium and molybdenum; cap. Denver; a. 270,000 km²; p. (1990) 3,294,394.

Colorado, plateau, Arizona, Utah, Col., N.M., **USA**; arid upland with spectacular scenery, inc. Grand Canyon; alt. 1,500–3,300 m.

Colorado, R., **Argentina**; flows from Andes to Atl. Oc.; limited irrigation in pastoral valley; length 848 km.

Colorado, major R. of W. **USA**; drains 8% of USA; formed by confluence of Green and Grand Rs.; spectacular canyons inc. Grand Canyon; hydroelec. power from many dams inc. Hoover Dam; irrigation supplies intensive horticultural a. in S. section and consequent rapid decrease in volume to a sm. stream in lower course; length 2,320 km.

Colorado, R., rises N.W. Texas, **USA**; flows to G. of Mexico; irrigation and power; 1,552 km long.

Colorado Desert, Cal., **USA**; inc. Imperial Valley, a fertile irrigated a.

Colorado Springs, t., Col., **USA**; 102 km S. Denver; resort; p. (1990) 281,140 (t.), 397,014 (met. a.).

Columbia, t., Mo., **USA**; W. of St. Louis; st. univ.; flour, lumber; p. (1990) 69,101.

Columbia, t., st. cap. S.C., **USA**; in ctr. of rich farming a.; textiles, clothing; burned down in Civil War 1865; p. (1990) 98,052 (t.), 453,331 (met. a.).

Columbia, District of (D.C.); area on east bank of Potomac R., coterminus with c. of Washington, cap. of **USA**; a. 179 km²; p. (1990) 606,900.

Columbia, R., major R. of western N. **America**; rises in Rocky Mtns., B.C., flows though Washington, **USA**; power sources, inc. Grand Coulee Dam, Bonneville Dam; deepwater harbour at mouth; length 2,240 km.

Columbus, c., Ga., **USA**; at head of navigation on Chattahoochee R.; industl. and shipping ctr.; textile mills, food-processing; cotton-ginning machin.; p. (1990) 179,278.

Columbus, t., Ind., **USA**; engin.; leather gds.; p. (1980) 30,614.

Columbus, c., st. cap. Ohio, **USA**; rly. ctr.; st. univ.; machin., paper, aircraft machin., chemicals; p. (1990) 632,910 (c.), 1,377,419 (met. a.).

Colwyn Bay, t., Clwyd, N. **Wales**; on cst. 10 km E. of Llandudno; furniture; seaside resort; p. (1981) 26,278; as **Colwyn** forms basis of l. gov. dist. inc. Abergele; p. (1993) 56,800.

Comayagüela, c., former cap. of **Honduras**; twin c. of Tegucigalpa from which it is separated by Choluteca R.; both cs. administered together as Central Dist.

Combe Martin, v., Devon, **Eng.**; 8 km E. of Ilfracombe; seaside resort.

Comber, t., Ards, N. **Ireland**; linen; p. (1991) 8,333.

Commonwealth of Independent States, a community of independent states which is successor to USSR in some aspects of law and international affairs; members **Russia**, **Ukraine**, **Belorussia**, **Armenia**, **Azerbaijan**, **Moldavia**, **Kazakhstan**, **Kirghizia**, **Tajikstan**, **Turkmenistan**, **Uzbekistan.**; cap. Minsk; p. (1991) 276·65 m.

Como, c., N. **Italy**; at foot of Alps, on L. Como; oranges, olives; textiles; cath.; tourism; p. (1981) 95,571.

Como, L., N. **Italy**; beautiful mtn. scenery; tourism, villas; a. 145 km².

Comodoro Rivadavia, spt., Chubut prov., **Argentina**; on San Jorge G., 880 km S.W. of Bahia Blanca; military zone; univ.; ch. source of oil in Argentine; oil refining; p. (1980) 96,865.

Comorin, C., most S. point of **India**.

Comoro Is., arch., **Indian Oc.**; in Moçambique channel, midway between African and Madagascar; cap. Moroni; total a. 2,170 km²; turtle fishing; vanilla, copra, sisal, timber, perfume plants; indep. from France declared 1975 but rejected by Mayotte Is. whose future is still undecided; p. (1992) 497,000.

Compiègne, t., Oise, **France**; sugar mills, rope; Armistice signed between Allies and Germany 1918; Fr. surrendered to Hitler 1940; resort; p. (1982) 62,778 (met. a.).

Compton, t., Cal., **USA**; residtl. for Los Angeles; heavy engin., glass, oil refining; p. (1980) 81,286.

Conakry, c., cap. of **Rep. of Guinea**; impt. pt. on offshore islet; exp. iron-ore and alumina; experimental fruit gardens; p. (1983) 705,280.

Concarneau, pt., Finistère, **France**; 19 km S.E. Quimper; fisheries; p. (1982) 18,225.

Concepción, c., cap. Biobio region, **Chile**; shipping ctr. through its pt. Talcahuano; univ.; comm. and cultural t.; severe earthquakes 1939 and 1960; nr. to coalfield; p. (1987) 294,375.

Concepción, prov., **Chile**; cap. C.; Lota-Coronel coalfield lgst. in Chile; a. 5,701 km².

Concepción, t., cap. of C. prov., **Paraguay**; main comm. ctr. for Chaco, pt. on R. Paraguay; p. (1984) 25,607.

Conchos, R., Chihuahua prov., **Mexico**; flows N.E. from Madre Occidental to Rio Grande; cotton under irrigation in upper valley; hydro-elec. power; length 560 km.

Concord, t., Cal., **USA**; residtl. and comm. ctr. in San Francisco met. a.; p. (1990) 111,348.

Concord, t., Mass., **USA**; literary ctr.; textiles; p. (1980) 16,293.

Concord, t., st. cap., N.H., **USA**; on Merrimack R.; granite, machin., textiles; p. (1980) 30,400.

Concordia, t., **Argentina**; pt. on Uruguay R.; exp. agr. prod.; p. (1991) 138,905.

Condamine, R., Queensland, **Australia**; trib. of R. Darling; used for irrigation.

Coney I., t., N.Y., **USA**; on Long I., 8 km long, comprises Manhattan Beach, Brighton Beach, W. Brighton, and W. End.

Congleton, t., l. gov. dist., E. Cheshire, **Eng.**; on S.W. margin of Pennines; clothing, textiles; once impt. for silk; p. (1993) 85,000 (dist.).

Congo, People's Rep. of the, indep. st. within Fr. Community. Equatorial Africa; cap. Brazzaville; agr. and forestry; hardwoods; economy heavily dependent on petroleum; economy hit by fall in world oil prices; a. 342,000 km²; p. (1992) 6·69 m.

Congolese Republic. See Zaïre.

Congo R. See Zaïre R.

Conisborough, t., South Yorks., **Eng.**; limestone, bricks, tiles; p. (1981) 16,114.

Coniston, t., Ont., **Canada**; on rly. 13 km E. of Sudbury; nickel smelting; t. built by and for nickel-mng. company.

Coniston Water, L., Cumbria, **Eng.**; focus of tourism in L. Dist.; 8·8 km long.

Conjeeveram. See Kanchipuram.

Connacht, prov., **R.o.I.**; inc. Galway, Mayo, Sligo, Leitrim, Roscommon; mtnous in W.; farming, fishing; a. 17,775 km²; p. (1986) 431,409.

Connah's Quay, t., Alyn and Deeside, Clwyd, **Wales**; p. (1981) 14,801.

Connaught Tunnel (Can. Pac. Rly.), B.C., **Canada**; longest in N. America (8 km) 1,500 m under mt. Sir Donald (Selkirk Mtns.).

Connecticut, R., New Eng., **USA**; middle course forms fine agr. land; investment in navigation, irrigation and flood control; 566 km long.

Connecticut, st., New England, **USA**; one of original 13 sts.; admitted to Union 1788; st. flower mountain Laurel, st. bird robin; humid climate; arable agr.; diversified inds.; many natural harbours on cst.; cap. Hartford; lgst. c. Bridgeport; a. 12,973 km²; p. (1990) 3,287,116.

Connemara, mtns., dist., **R.o.I.**; Co. Galway; many lakes and bogs; tourist resort.

Consett, t., Derwentside, Durham, **Eng.**; on edge of Pennines, 16 km S.W. Newcastle; iron, steel closed (1980), coal mng.; p. (1981) 33,433.

Constance (**Konstanz**), c., Baden–Württemberg,

Germany; on Bodensee; cath.; textiles, machin., chemicals, elec. inds.; route ctr.; tourism; p. (1983) 69,100.

Constance, L. See Bodensee.

Constanţa, ch. spt. S.E. **Romania**; on Black Sea; oil pipeline to Ploiesti and Cimpina; Danube-Black Sea canal (1984) shortens route of Trans-European waterway to Black Sea; exp. petroleum, wheat; cement, chemicals, machin.; p. (1990) 355,402.

Constantine, c., N.E. **Algeria**; stands 650 m high on gorge of Rhumel R.; planned textile and engin. wks.; p. (1983) 449,000.

Constantinople. See Istanbul.

Conwy (**Conway**), Aberconwy, Gwynedd, spt., N. **Wales**; mediaeval walled t.; at mouth of R. Conway; sm. seaside resort; cas.; quarrying, lt. engin.; p. (1981) 12,969.

Cook, mtn., alt. 3,753 m; hgst. point in S. Alps. and **N.Z.**; 3 peaks.

Cook Inlet, S. cst. Alaska, **USA**; oil pipeline connects oilfields of Granite Point with marine terminal at Dritt R.

Cook Is., Brit. gr. (Rarotonga, lgst.) in **S. Pac.**, annexed to **N.Z.**, 1901; internal self-govt. 1965; bananas, oranges, copra; a. 241 km²; p. (1991) 18,617.

Cookstown, mkt. t., l. gov. dist., **N. Ireland**; cement wks.; p. (1991) 31,082 (dist.), 9,842 (t.).

Cook Strait, channel between N. and S. Is. of **N.Z.**; 24–29 km wide; undersea cable completed 1965.

Cooma, t., N.S.W., **Australia**; mkt. t.; tourist ctr. for Kosciusko Nat. Park; H.Q. of Snowy Mts. Authority; p. (1981) 7,978.

Coonoor, t., Tamil Nadu, **India**; in Nilgiri Hills; sanatorium c. 1,800 m a.s.l.; p. (1981) 44,750.

Cooper Creek (**Barcoo**), intermittent R., central **Australia**; rises in Warrego Range, Gr. Dividing Range, flows S.W. into marshes of L. Eyre; provides water for livestock in semi-arid region; 1,408 km long.

Copeland, l. gov. dist., Cumbria, **Eng.**; cstl. a. N. of Barrow and inc. Whitehaven and Millom; p. (1993) 71,400.

Copenhagen (**København**), ch. spt., cap. of **Denmark**; on E. cst. of Sjaelland I.; royal palace, univ., library; naval sta.; freeport; steel, metal, textiles, clothing, breweries; p. (1990) 617,637.

Copiapó, t., cap. of Atacama region, **Chile**; copper- and iron-mng. ctr.; p. (1982) 70,240.

Coquet, R., Northumberland, **Eng.**; rises in the Cheviots and flows into North Sea.

Coquimbo, region **Chile**; cap. La Serena; a. 40,656 km²; p. (1992) 502,460.

Coquimbo, spt., **Chile**; exp. iron. copper, and manganese ores; p. (1992) 105,252.

Coral Sea, Pac Oc., extends from the New Hebrides to Australia.

Coral Sea Islands Territory, Fed. terr., **Australia**; scattered Is., E. of Gr. Barrier Reef, off Queensland cst.; possibility of oil exploration.

Corbeil-Essonnes, t., Essonne, **France**; on R. Seine, 19 km S.E. of Paris; flour mills, printing, paper; p. (1982) 38,081.

Corbridge, t., Northumberland, **Eng.**; on R. Tyne, nr. Hexham; 17th cent. bridge; Roman t. nearby.

Corby, t., l. gov. dist., Northants., **Eng.**; 11 km N. of Kettering; new t.; former steel wks., shoes, clothing, lamps; p. (1993) 52,800 (dist.).

Córdoba, c. and prov., central **Argentina**; univ.; cultural and comm. ctr.; exp. wheat, cattle, lumber; health resort; local hydroelec. power from La Vina; p. (1991) 1,179,067 (c.), 2,764,176 (prov.).

Córdoba, t., Veracruz, **Mexico**; mkt. t. in coffee growing a.; p. (1990) 150,428.

Córdoba, prov., Andalusia, **Spain**; cap. Córdova; olives, vines, livestock; a. 13,724 km²; p. (1991) 753,760.

Córdoba, c., Andalusia, **Spain**; cap. of C. prov., on Guadalquivir R.; cath. originally built as a mosque in 8th cent.; tourist ctr.; p. (1991) 309,212.

Corfu (**Kérkira**), most N. of Ionian Is., **Greece**; traversed by mtns. but largely lowland producing olive oil, figs, wine, oranges; a. 637 km²; p. (1991) 105,043 (prov.).

Corinth (**Kórinthos**), t., cap. Corinthia prov., **Greece**; at end of Isthmus of C.; occupies site 5 km from anc. classic c. destroyed by earthquake 1858; raisins, wine; p. (1981) 22,658 (t.),(1991) 142,365 (prov.).

Corinth Canal, ship canal, S. **Greece**; traverses Isthmus of Corinth, links G. of Corinth and

Ionian Sea with Saronic G. and Aegean Sea; opened 1893; length 5·6 km, depth 8 m.

Corinth, Isthmus of, connects the Peloponnesus with the mainland of **Greece;** cut across by canal.

Corinto, ch. spt., N.W. **Nicaragua;** handles 50 per cent of cty's tr.; exp. hides, sugar, coffee; p. (1985) 24,000.

Cork, co., **R.o.I.;** lgst. and most S.; mtns.; dairying, brewing, agr., fisheries; cap. Cork; a. 7,485 km²; p. (1986) 412,735.

Cork, spt., Cork, **R.o.I.;** at mouth of R. Lee; cath., univ.; woollens, butter, cattle, brewing, cars, rubber; p. (1986) 133,271.

Corner Brook, c., W. Newfoundland, **Canada;** gd. harbour; iron foundries, cement, gypsum; one of world's lgst. newsprint mills; p. (1986) 22,719.

Cornwall, t., Ont., **Canada;** on St. Lawrence R.; H.Q. of Seaway Authority; textiles, pulp, paper, flour; p. (1986) 46,425.

Cornwall and Isles of Scilly, non-met. co., S.W. **Eng.;** penin. bordering Atl. Oc. and Eng. Channel; granite moorlands supply kaolin; formerly tin mining; mild maritime climate encourages tourism, dairying, and mkt. gardening; many small fishing vs.; co. t. Bodmin; a. 3,515 km²; p. (1993) 477,000.

Coro, c., Falcón, **Venezuela;** on Paraguaná penin.; agr. processing; nearby oil refineries; p. (1981) 96,339.

Corocoro, t., La Paz dep., **Bolivia;** at alt. c. 4,000 m in central Andes, 80 km S. of La Paz; impt. copper-mng. ctr.

Coromandel Coast (Carnatic region), cst. of Tamil Nadu, **India;** where earliest European settlements established; extensive a. of flat land built up by R. Cauvery.

Coronation Gulf, arm of Beaufort Sea; extreme point N. Canadian mainland; discovered by Franklin.

Coronel, spt., **Chile;** coal mng., pt. inds.; p. (1982) 49,257.

Coronel Oviedo, t., **Paraguay;** comm. ctr.; p. (1982) 21,782.

Corpus Christi, c., Texas, **USA;** cotton, oil refining, chemicals; resort; p. (1990) 257,453 (c.), 350,000 (met. a.).

Corrèze, dep., S. central **France;** part of Massif Central, mostly over 600 m; sparse p. based on livestock agr. and forestry; cap. Tulle; a. 5,884 km²; p. (1990) 237,900.

Corrib, Lough, Galway and Mayo, **R.o.I.;** drained by Corrib R. into Galway Bay; impt. brown trout fishery; a. 176 km².

Corrientes, t. and prov., **Argentina;** agr. tr. ctr. on Paraná R.; univ.; cattle, sugar, rice, cotton; river navigation reduces isolation; p. (1991) 267,742 (t.), 780,778 (prov.).

Corryvreckan, strait and whirlpool between Jura and Scarba Is., Inner Hebrides, **Scot.;** whirlpool caused by tidal movement over variable sea bed.

Corse du Sud. *See* Corsica.

Corsica (Corse), I., **France;** in Mediterranean Sea; violent history in 16th and 17th cent.; high granite peaks (Monte Cinto), mtn. torrents, fertile plains; inland and sea fishing; rapid growth of tourism with little benefit to indigenous Corsicans; split into 2 deps. to help overcome autonomist agitation (1975); Haute Corse, cap. Bastia (1990) 131,600, Corse-du-Sud, cap. Ajaccio (1990) 118,800; a. 8,721 km²; p. (1990) 250,400.

Corsicana, t., Texas, **USA;** site of first oil drilling in USA; p. (1980) 21,712.

Cortona, t., Tuscany, **Italy;** nr. Perugia; Roman remains, cath.; p. (1981) 22,281.

Corunna. *See* La Coruña.

Corvallis, t., Ore., **USA;** in fertile farming valley; lumbering; univ.; p. (1990) 44,757.

Coryton, t., Essex, **Eng.;** on Thames, oil refining; oil pipeline to Stanlow refinery.

Cos (Kos), I., Dodecanese, **Greece;** in Aegean Sea, second lgst. of gr.; gave name to Cos lettuce; birthplace of Hippocrates; p. (1981) 20,350.

Cosenza, c., S. **Italy;** ctr. for figs, oranges, olive oil, wine; cath., univ., cas.; p. (1984) 106,376.

Costa Brava, region, Catalonia, **Spain;** tourism.

Costa del Sol, region, Málaga cst., **Spain;** tourism.

Costa Rica, rep. **Central America;** over half p. in equable Meseta Central; cap. San José; forests, volcanic mtns.; agr. 40 per cent G.N.P.; coffee, bananas, cacao; high literacy and living standards; a. 50,909 km²; p. (1991) 3,029,746.

Côte d'Azur, France; Mediterranean littoral E. of Rhône R.; inc. resorts of Nice, Cannes, Monte Carlo, and St. Tropez.

Côte d'Ivoire (Ivory Coast), rep., on G. of Guinea, W. Africa; formerly a Fr. overseas terr.; hot, humid climate; coastal lagoons, interior plateau (300–1,200 m); economy based on subsistence agr. although an impt. coffee and timber producer; world's third lgst. coffee producer; half p. relies on coffee as principle source of income; underdeveloped mineral resources; poorly developed rail network but extensive road system; new pt. at San Pedro; Pt. Bouet outport of former cap. Abidjan; new cap. Yamoussoukro (1983); a. 322,481 km²; p. (1991) 13,100,000.

Côte d'Or, dep., E. **France;** heart of anc. Burgundy, traversed by R. Saône; cap. Dijon; wines, livestock, iron and steel; a. 8,783 km²; p. (1990) 493,866.

Cotentin, peninsula N. **France;** 80 km long; Cherbourg, at its extremity, 128 km from Portsmouth.

Côtes-d'Armor, dep., N. Brittany, **France;** rugged cst. and Is. and mild climate encourage tourism; mkt. gardens along cst.; many fishing ts.; cap. St. Brieuc; a. 7,218 km²; p. (1990) 538,400.

Cotonou, pt., **Benin Rep.;** new artificial pt.; fishing; lt. inds.; offshore oilfields (drilling from 1982); p. (1982) 487,020.

Cotopaxi, volcano, (alt. 5,982 m) in the Andes of **Ecuador,** nr. Quito; loftiest active volcano in the world; recent eruptions have caused great damage to Ecuador.

Cotswold, l. gov. dist., Gloucs., **Eng.;** lge a. covering C. Hills and inc. Cirencester and Northleach; p. (1993) 79,200.

Cotswold Hills, W. **Eng.;** limestone escarpment; Gloucs., Oxon.; once famous for woollens; source of Thames and tribs.; highest point Cleeve Cloud, 309 m; tourism.

Cottbus or **Kottbus,** t., Brandenburg, **Germany;** on R. Spree; rly. ctr.; textile and metal mnfs.; p. (1990) 124,900.

Cottian Alps, mtn. range on border of **France** and **Italy** crossed by Hannibal; craggy; max. alt. 2,844 m (Monte Viso).

Coulsdon and Purley. *See* Croydon.

Council Bluffs, t., Iowa, **USA;** on Missouri R. nr. Omaha; rly. ctr.; farm implements, paper, machin.; p. (1990) 54,315.

Courantyne, R., **Guyana;** rises in Serra Acari; passes through bauxite mng. region to Atl. Oc.; navigation in lower course; 720 km long.

Courtrai. *See* Kortrijk.

Cove and Kilcreggan, burgh, Dumbarton, **Scot.;** at junc. of Loch Long and R. Clyde; p. (1991) 1,586.

Coventry, c., met. dist., West Midlands, **Eng.;** 29 km E.S.E. of Birmingham; former ctr. of cycle, motor-cycle, motor-car and aircraft engines, tractors, engin.; tools; chemicals; projectiles, textiles; cath.; univ.; p. (1993) 304,100.

Covilhã, t., **Portugal;** cloth factories; p. (1981) 21,807 (c.), 60,945 (met. a.).

Covington, t., Ky., **USA;** on R. Ohio, opp. Cincinnati; machin., leather, furniture; p. (1990) 43,264.

Cowbridge, t., Vale of Glamorgan, South Glamorgan, S. **Wales;** nr. Cardiff; p. (1981) 1,224.

Cowdenbeath, burgh, Dunfermline, **Scot.;** 8 km N.E. of Dunfermline; coal; p. (1991) 12,126.

Cowes, resort and pt., Medina, I. of Wight, **Eng.;** on estuary of R. Medina; regattas and yacht bldg.; hovercraft; p. (1981) 19,663.

Cowra, t., N.S.W., **Australia;** famous wheat dist. and site of state experimental farm; p. (1981) 7,900.

Cozumel I., E. of Yucatan peninsula, **Mexico.**

Cracow. *See* Kraków.

Cradle, Mt., mtn., Tasmania, **Australia;** alt. 1,546 m; Nat. Park.

Cradock, t., Cape Prov., S. **Africa;** wool tr.; p. (1980) 39,160 (dist.).

Craigavon, c., l. gov. dist., N. **Ireland;** new "city in a garden" under construction, 16 km long, merging Portadown and Lurgan, linked by motorway, to provide major base for ind.; p. (1991) 74,986 (dist.), 9,201 (c.).

Crail, royal burgh, North East Fife, **Scot.;** cstl. resort; p. (1991) 1,449.

Craiova, c., S. **Romania,** in Wallachia; tr. ctr.; agr. processing, textiles, engin., chemicals; p. (1990) 300,030.

Cramlington, t., Northumberland, **Eng.;** 13 km N. of Newcastle; new t.; p. (1981) 25,225.

Cranborne Chase, Wilts., **Eng.;** chalk upland of over 275 m; extension of Salisbury Plain.

Cranbrook, mkt. t., Kent, **Eng.;** hops and grain; former weaving t.

Cranston, t., R.I., **USA**; machin., chemicals, textiles; p. (1980) 71,992.

Crater L., Ore., **USA**; in Nat. Park, is a body of water 600 m deep and 9·5 km across, set in a crater of an extinct volcano, c. 2,400 m high; varied flora and fauna on shore.

Craters of the Moon, dist., Idaho, **USA**; Nat. Monument of volcanic craters and cones; a. 192 km².

Crau, La, region, Bouches-du-Rhône dep., S.E. **France**; dry, pebbly area E. of Rhône delta; winter pasture for sheep.

Craven, dist., central Pennines, **Eng.**; relatively low limestone plateau, alt. mainly below 240 m; drained by R. Ribble to S.W., R. Aire to S.E.; sheep rearing in valleys, cattle for fattening, root and fodder crops; now forms l. gov. dist. based on Skipton and Settle; p. (1993) 50,900.

Crawley, t., l. gov. dist., West Sussex, **Eng.**; on N.W. flank of Weald, 14 km S. of Reigate; new t. (1947); engin., pharmaceuticals, metal, leather, wooden gds.; p. (1993) 89,300 (dist.).

Crayford. See Bexley.

Creag Meagaidh, mtn., Lochaber, **Scot.**; alt. 1,128 m.

Crediton, mkt. t., Devon, **Eng.**; p. (1981) 6,169.

Cree, R., Wigtown, **Scot.**; flows into Wigtown Bay.

Crema, industl. and agr. t., N. **Italy**; S.E. of Milan; cath.; p. (1981) 34,610.

Cremona, t., cap. of C. prov., Lombardy, N. **Italy**; famed as a ctr. of learning and later for mnf. of violins and violas; revived in last 20 years; birthplace of Stradivari; cath.; pt. on new Milan-Adriatic Waterway; p. (1981) 80,929.

Crete (**Kríti**), I., E. Mediterranean, lgst. I. of **Greece**; cradle of Minoan civilisation between 1600 and 1400 B.C.; mild climate; sm. a. of cultivable land; few minerals; part of Greece since Balkan Wars (1913); cap. Iraklion; birthplace of El Greco; a. 8,379 km²; p. (1991) 536,980 (admin. reg.).

Créteil, t., cap. Val-de-Marne dep., **France**; light inds.; p (1990) 82,390.

Creus, c., juts out into Mediterranean Sea, **Spain**; nr. Fr. border.

Creuse, dep., in Massif Central, **France**; soil infertile, harsh climate, limited agr.; a. 5,605 km² p. (1990) 131,300.

Crewe, t., Cheshire, **Eng.**; 32 km S.E. of Chester; lge. rly. wks.; impt. rly. junc.; aircraft and refrigerator wks., clothing, engin., motor vehicles; expanded t.; with Nantwich forms l. gov. dist.; p. (1993) 109,500 (dist.).

Crewkerne, mkt. t., Somerset, **Eng.**; 13 km S.W. of Yeovil; leather gds.; grammar school (1499); p. (1981) 5,330.

Criccieth, t., Dwyfor, Gwynedd, N. **Wales**; on N. shore of Cardigan Bay; seaside resort; p. (1981) 1,570.

Cricklade, t., N. Wilts., **Eng.**; on R. Thames, 13 km N.W. of Swindon; fortified Saxon township.

Crieff, t., Perth and Kinross, **Scot.**; on R. Earn; summer resort; p. (1991) 6,023.

Crimea (**Krym**) Peninsula, juts into Black Sea, **Ukraine**; wheat, tobacco, fruit; campaign 1854–55 between Russia and Allied Forces of Turkey, Britain, France, and Sardinia was chiefly fought out here (Alma, Balaclava, and Sevastopol); tourism; demands for independence (1992).

Crimmitschau, t., Saxony, **Germany**; nr. Zwickau; impt. textile ctr.; p. (1989) 23,455.

Crinan Canal, across peninsula of Argyll and Bute, S.W. **Scot.**; connects Loch Gilp with Atl. Oc.; 14 km long.

Croaghpatrick, mtns., May, **R.o.I.**; 766 m.

Croatia, formerly part of Yugoslavia, recognised as independent by EC, 1991; stretches from Istria on Adriatic cst. to Dinaric Alps; crossed by Drava and Sava Rs.; traditional agr. being replaced by new inds.; impt. aluminium wks. based on local bauxite; chemicals, shipbldg.; impt. oilfields; cap. Zagreb; a. 56,524 km²; p. (1991) 4,784,265.

Crocodile R. See Limpopo.

Cromarty, burgh, Ross and Cromarty, **Scot.**; N.E. cst. of Black Isle; offshore oil platforms at Nigg, C.Firth; p. (1991) 721.

Cromer, t., North Norfolk, **Eng.**; on N. cst. of E. Anglia; seaside resort; p. (1981) 6,192.

Cromford, v., Derbys., **Eng.**; Richard Arkwright's first waterpowered mill (1771); cotton.

Crompton, t., Gtr. Manchester, **Eng.**; 3 km S of Rochdale; cotton; engin., elec. lamps; p. (1981) 19,938. 19,938.

Crook and Willington, ts., former U.D., Wear.

Valley, Durham, **Eng.**; varied inds. to replace coal mng.; p. (1981) 21,619.

Crosby, t., Sefton, Merseyside, **Eng.**; on Liverpool Bay 5 km N. of Bootle, Seaforth container pt.; residtl.; seaside resort; p. (1981) 53,660.

Cross, R., S.E. **Nigeria**; rises in Cameroon Highlands, flows W. and S. into G. of Guinea at Calabar; useful inland waterway; 640 km long.

Cross River, state **Nigeria**, cap. Calabar; agric., cement, oil; a. 27,237 km²; p. (1991) 1,865,604.

Cross Fell, mtn., Cumbria, **Eng.**; on E. border of co.; alt. 894 m; highest point of the Pennines.

Crotone, t., S. **Italy**; pt. on E. cst. Calabria; electro-chemicals and metallurgical inds.; on site of anc. Crotona founded as Greek col.; home of Pythagoras; p. (1981) 58,281.

Crowland, t., Lincs., **Eng.**; mkt. t. in the Fens, on R. Welland; 8th-cent. abbey ruins.

Crows Nest Pass, B.C., Alberta, **Canada**; southernmost pass across Canadian Rocky Mtns.; used by rly. from Medicine Hat to Syokane (USA); summit 1,360 m.

Croydon, residtl. t., **Eng.**; now outer bor. Greater London; inc. Coulsdon and Purley; lt. inds.; major office ctr.; p. (1993) 323,300.

Crummock Water, L. Dist., Cumbria, **Eng.**; ribbon L.

Csongrad, mkt. t., agr. dist., **Hungary**; at junc. of Rs. Tisza and Körös; p. (1984) 22,000.

Cuba, I., indep. rep., **W.I.**; cap. Havana; lies within tropics; highly fertile although half land a. is mtnous.; exp. sugar, nickel, tobacco, rum, citrus fruits; revolution (1959) reoriented economic and political connections away from USA towards USSR; excellent health care and education; 88 per cent of cultivated land in state farms or cooperatives; recent attempts to diversify economy but sugar still 75 per cent of exp; a. 114,494 km²; p. (1991) 10,700,000.

Cubatão, t., **Brazil**; N.E. of Santos; rapidly growing t. from industl. expansion; hydro-electric, oil refinery, petro-chems., new integrated steel wks. to aid vehicle ind. of São Paulo; p. (1980) 66,000.

Cuckfield, mkt. t., Mid Sussex, West Sussex, **Eng.**; p. (1981) 28,254.

Cuckmere, R., Sussex, **Eng.**; passes through S. Downs in beautiful gap; length 37 km.

Cúcuta, t., cap. of Norte de Santander, **Colombia**; close to Venezuelan border; nr. oilfield; destroyed by earthquake, 1875; new planned t.; p. (1992) 450,318.

Cuddalore, spt., Tamil Nadu, **India**; nr. Pondicherry; exp. oilseeds, cottons; p. (1991) 144,561.

Cuddapah, t., Andhra Pradesh, **India**; cotton, cloth factories, millet, rice; p. (1991) 121,422.

Cudworth, South Yorks., **Eng.**; p. (1981) 9,361.

Cuenca, t., cap. of Azuay prov., 3rd. c. of **Ecuador**; in fertile agr. basin of Andes; sugar, tyres, flour mills, Panama hats; p. (1990) 194,981.

Cuenca, agr. and mng. prov., central **Spain**; furniture, leather, paper; a. 17,063 km²; p. (1991) 200,383.

Cuenca, t., cap of C. prov., **Spain**; on gorge above R. Júcar; mkt. t.; famed in mediaeval times for silver and cloth mnfs.; p. (1987) 41,407.

Cuernavaca, t., cap. of Morelos st., central **Mexico**; anc. Indian t. captured by Cortes; tourist resort; univ.; p. (1990) 281,752.

Cuiabá, t., cap. of Mato Grosso st., **Brazil**; ctr. pastoral a.; gold and diamonds produced; galena deposit nearby; p. (1985) 283,100.

Cuillin Hills, mtns., I. of Skye, **Scot.**; attaining 992 m in Sgurr Alasdair.

Culiacán, c., of Sinaloa, N.W. **Mexico**; anc. c.; Pacific pt. Altata; p. (1990) 602,114.

Culloden Moor, 10 km E. of Inverness, **Scot.**; defeat of Prince Charles Edward Stuart's highlanders by Duke of Cumberland's forces (1746).

Culross, royal burgh, Dunfermline, **Scot.**; belongs to Nat. Trust; abbey.

Culver City, t., Cal., **USA**; sub. of Los Angeles; lge. motion-picture plant; electronic equipment, machin., chemicals, tools; p. (1980) 38,139.

Cumaná, c., N.E. **Venezuela**; pt. on Caribbean; European settlement since 1510; exp. coffee, cacao; sardine canning; airpt.; p. (1981) 191,900.

Cumberland, former co., **Eng.**; now part of Cumbria non-met. co.

Cumberland, industl. t., Md., **USA**; on Potomac R.; iron and steel, tyres, glassware; p. (1990) 23,706.

Cumberland Gap, Ky., **USA**; ch. break in high E. wall of Cumberland plateau; gives access from upper Tennessee valley to Cumberland and Ohio valleys; impt. routeway in colonisation of Ky.

Cumberland Is., off cst. of Queensland, **Australia**.

Cumberland Plateau, mtn. region, Ky., Tenn., Ala., **USA**; forms S.W. zone of Appalachian mtn. system terminating abruptly towards Tennessee valley to E., Cumberland valley to W.; drained W. by tribs. of Cumberland and Ohio Rs; composed of horizontal sandstones overlying coal; thinly populated by farming communities except where mng. ts. occur in valleys cut down to coal; mainly between 360–900 m.

Cumberland R., Tenn. and Ky., **USA**; trib. of Ohio R., rises in C. plateau; upper course forested; crosses coal-mng. a. and fertile agr. valley; part of Tenn. Valley Authority scheme; hydroelec. power; 1,104 km long.

Cumbernauld, new t. (1955), Strathclyde Reg., Scot.; to house 50,000 overspill from Glasgow; mnfs. of adding machines rapidly decl. with use of computers; p. (1991) 48,762; with Kilsyth forms larger l. gov. dist.; p (1992) 60,530 (dist.).

Cumbrae, Gt. and Little, Is., in F. of Clyde, off cst. of Cunninghame, Scot.; p. (1991) 1,393.

Cumbria, non-met. co., N.W. **Eng.**; centred on L. Dist. where rugged glaciated scenery encourages tourism, sheep-farming, forestry and water storage; Cumberland coalfield on W. cst. and declining heavy inds. being replaced by new lt. inds.; major ts. Carlisle and Barrow; a. 6,809 km²; p. (1993) 490,200.

Cumbrian Mtns., L. Dist., Cumbria, **Eng.**

Cumnock and Doone Valley, t. and l. gov. dist., Strathclyde Reg., **Scot.,** hilly dist. S. of Glasgow; p. (1991) 9,607 (t.), (1993) 42,840 (dist.).

Cundinamarca, dep., **Colombia**; contains many Andean Ls. and the fed. cap Bogotá; a. 23,585 km²; p. (1992) 1,658,751 (excluding Bogota).

Cunene. See **Kunene R.**

Cuneo, prov., **Italy**; a. 7,433 km²; p. (1981) 548,452.

Cuneo, t., cap. of C. prov., Piedmont, **Italy**; mkt. for prod. of surrounding a.; withstood many sieges under the rule of house of Savoy; p. (1981) 55,875.

Cunninghame, l. gov. dist., Strathclyde Reg., **Scot.**; borders F. of Clyde and inc. I. of Arran; p. (1993) 139,020.

Cupar, royal burgh, North East Fife, **Scot.**; on R. Eden, W. of St. Andrews; p. (1991) 7,545.

Curaçao, I. (**Neth. Antilles**), off N. cst. **Venezuela**; major ctr. for refining and trans-shipping Venezuelan oil; threatened closure (1985) offset for 5 years to avoid economic collapse (provides 25 percent of C. income); picturesque Dutch archi-tecture in cap. Willemstad; a. 544 km²; p. (1991) 143,186.

Curepipe, t., central **Mauritius**; health resort; p. (1991) 74,214.

Curicó, t., **Chile**; agr. and comm. ctr.; earthquake 1928; p. (1982) 51,743.

Curitiba, c., cap. of Paraná st., **Brazil**; univ.; industl. and comm. ctr. at c. 900 m; coffee, maté, chemicals, pharmaceutical and forest prods.; foodstuffs; p. (1991) 1,290,142.

Curragh, plain, Kildare, **R.o.I.**; turf; racecourse.

Curtis I., Queensland, **Australia**; low volcanic I.; wooded; cattle.

Curzola. See **Korčula.**

Cuttack, t., Orissa st., **India**; on Mahanadi R.; long famous for gold and silver filigree work; p. (1991) 403,000.

Cuxhaven, spt., Lower Saxony, **Germany**; outport of Hamburg at the mouth of R. Elbe; fine harbour; p. (1986) 56,100.

Cuyahoga Falls, t., Ohio, **USA**; industl. and residtl.; p. (1990) 48,950.

Cuzco, dep., **Peru**; inc. Central Cordilleras, reaching c. 5,800 m; tropical climate; agr. varies with alt.; minerals; cap. C.; a. 144,304 km²; p. (1990) 1,041,800.

Cuzco, t., cap. of C. dep., S. **Peru**; in Andes at alt. 3,418 m in valley of Urubamba R.; once cap of Incas; sacked by Francisco Pizarro 1533; cath., ruins of Inca fortress; tr. ctr. for agr. prod.; p. (1990) 275,000.

Cwmamman, t., Dinefwr, Dyfed, **Wales**; on R. Loughor; p. (1981) 3,721.

Cwmbran, t., Torfaen, Gwent, **Wales**; in valley of Avon-Lwyd, 8 km N. of Newport; new t. (1949); motor accessories, wire, elec. gds., bricks, tiles, pipes; p. (1981) 44,309.

Cwm Dyli, Gwynedd, **Wales**; hydroelec. sta.

Cyclades (**Kirkádhes**), gr. of about 220 Is., **Greece**; rugged and barren csts, conceal sheltered agr. valleys; ch. t. and pt. Hermoupolis; a. 2,650 km²; p. (1991) 95,083.

Cynon Valley, l. gov. dist., Mid Glamorgan, **Wales**; inland valley inc. Aberdare and Mountain Ash; p. (1993) 65,500.

Cyprus, Rep. of, I., indep. state, E. Mediterranean, 64 km S. of Turkey; N., inc. main pt. of Famagusta, occupied by Turkey from 1974; indep. st. of Turkish Rep. of Cyprus declared (1983) but only recognised by Turkey; varied cst., limestone hills in N., forested mtns. in S., central plains of Messarois in which cap. Nicosia is situated; agr. employs 30 per cent of p.; many irrigation schemes also aid soil and water conservation; land reform programmes to reduce fragmentation of holdings; copper in Troodos mtns. but asbestos of increasing importance; lt. inds. and tourism helping to restructure economy but agr. provides over 50 per cent of exp., inc wine, citrus fruit, vegetables; split of cty. by Attila line into 2 separate parts N. dependent on aid from Turkey but S. developing rapidly since 1974; a. 9,251 km²; p. (1994) 725,000.

Cyrenaica, prov., **Libya**; impt. region in anc. times; Greek col. 7th cent. B.C., Roman prov. 1st cent. B.C., captured by Arabs A.D. 642, part of Ottoman Empire 16th cent.; animal grazing, dates, oil-wells; a. 854,700 km².

Czechoslovakia, former federal republic consisting of two nations of equal rights; landlocked country linked to sea by Elbe, Oder and Danube; socialist planned economy with coal, iron and steel; following elections in June 1992 division into **Czech Republic** and **Slovakia** took place on 1 January 1993; a. 127,897 km²; p. (1990) 15·7 m.

Czech Republic, western part of former **Czechoslovakia**, cap. Prague; 8 administrative regions; privatisation programme; a. 78,864 km²; p. (1993) 10·33 m.

Czernowitz. See **Chernovtsy.**

Czestochowa, c. and prov., S. **Poland**; on Warta R.; rly. and industl. ctr.; iron and steel, textiles; celebrated religious ctr.; monastery; p. (1989) 256,578 (c.), 773,400 (prov)

D

Dabrowa Gornicza, t., Katowice, **Poland**; coal, zinc, iron ore; p. (1989) 134,934.

Dacca (**Dhaka**), c., cap. of **Bangladesh**; on Buriganga R., old channel of Ganges; jute, muslin, paper mnfs.; medical radioisotope ctr.; univ.; p. (1991) 3,397,187.

Dachau, t., Bavaria, **Germany**; paper, elec. gds., brewing; concentration camp during last war; p. (1986) 32,900.

Dachstein, mtn., Salzkammergut, **Austria**; alt. 2,998 m.

Dacorum, l. gov. dist., Herts., **Eng.**; a. of Chilterns inc. Tring, Berkhamsted and Hemel Hempstead; p. (1993) 134,300.

Dadra and Nagar Haveli, union terr., **India**; admin. ctr. Silvassa; a. 490 km²; p. (1991) 138,477.

Dagenham, dist. former M.B., **Eng.**; now forms part of Greater London bor. of Barking; on N. bank of R. Thames with riverside Ford motor works.

Dagestan, Caucasian aut rep., **Russia**; mtnous.; cap. Makhachkala; cotton, orchards and vineyards; machin., engin. oil; a. 50,246 km²; p. (1989) 1,802,200.

Dagupan, c., Pangasiman, Luzon, **Philippines**; on Lingayen Bay; comm. ctr.; p. (1990) 122,247.

Daharki Mari, t., **Pakistan**; 560 km N.E. of Karachi; fertiliser plant.

Dahlak Archipelago, **Ethiopia**; in Red Sea; only 2 Is. inhabited; noted for pearl fishing.

Dahomey. See **Benin, People's Rep. of.**

Daimiel, mkt. t., Ciudad Real, **Spain**; cheeses, oil, wine; p. (1981) 16,260.

Dakar, spt., cap. of **Senegal,** W. Africa; S.E. of C. Verde behind Gorée I. on Atl. cst.; exp. groundnuts; some industl. development; free tr. zone, international airport; univ. and medical ctr.; p. (1985) 1,382,000.

Dakhla, oasis, Libyan Desert, **Egypt**; 272 km S.W. of Asyût; dates, olives; stage on caravan route from Cyrenaica to Upper Egypt; site of New Valley Project for irrigation.

Dalälven, R., S. central **Sweden**; length 520 km, used for timber transport.

Da Lat (Dalat), t., **Vietnam**; 224 km N.E. Ho Chiminh City; in Annamite hills; nuclear reactor (1963); airport.

Dalbeattie, burgh, Stewartry, **Scot.**; granite, dairy prod., gloves; p. (1991) 4,421.

Dalby, t., Queensland, **Australia**; 1961 oil strike of Moonie oilfield; rich volcanic soils aid grain and beef production; p. (1984) 9,590.

Dalgety, t., on Fife cst., **Scot.**; new t. proposed; p. (1991) 7,860.

Dalian, spt., Liaoning prov., **China**; seafood cultivation; shipbldg., heavy engin., elec., chemical inds.; fully mechanised pt. and another being built; designated development zone in cty.'s new open door policy; p. (1992) 2,420,000.

Dalkeith, burgh, Midlothian, **Scot.**; 10 km S.E. of Edinburgh; mkt. t.; p. (1991) 11,567.

Dallas, c., Texas, **USA**; in cotton- and graingrowing a.; machin., aircraft, petroleum prod.; univ.; scene of assassination of President Kennedy (1963); p. (1990) 1,006,877 (c.), 2,553,362 (met. a.).

Dalmatia, region of **Croatia**, N.E. Adriatic cst.; high Karst plateaux; olive oil, wine; tourism; contains many resorts; a. 12,732 km².

Daltonganj, t., Bihar, **India**; on R. Koël; coal, cement; p. (1981) 51,952.

Dalton-in Furness, t., Cumbria, **Eng.**; limestone quarrying, textiles; abbey ruins; p. (1981) 10,931.

Daman (Damão), spt., Union Territory **India**; 160 km N. Bombay; fishing, ship-bldg.; cotton; former Portuguese settlement; p. (1991), 62,101 (t.), 101,586 (terr.).

Damanhûr, t., **Egypt**; on W. margin of Nile delta, 40 km S.E. of Alexandria; mkt. for local agr. produce; p. (1986) 190,840.

Damaraland, region, **Namibia**; high plateau; pt., Walvis Bay; cattle rearing.

Damascus (Arabic **Esh-Sham**), cap. c., **Syria**; 91 km S.E. of its pt. Beirut; claims to be oldest continuously inhabited c. in world; metal-wk., glass, cement; univ.; p. (1985) 1,196,710.

Dambovitza (Dimbovita), R., **Romania**; rises in Mt. Omul (Transylvanian Alps), flows S. through Bucharest to R. Danube, via impt. oilfields; 320 km long.

Dammam, spt. on Persian G., **Saudi Arabia**; oil pt.; industry, univ.

Damodar, R., Bihar, **India**; flows through India's major coalfields; valley forms ch. industl. a. of India; multipurpose scheme for hydroelectric power, irrigation and flood control.

Dampier, spt., W. **Australia**; on Indian Oc.; ships iron ore from Mt. Tom Price and Mt. Wittenoom; pelletising plant.

Dampier Archipelago, gr. of sm. Is., off N.W. **Australia**, in Indian Oc.

Dampier Strait, **Bismarck Archipelago**, channel between W. New Britain and Umboi I.

Dampir Strait, channel between Irian Jaya and Waigeo I.

Danakil Land (Dankalia), coastal desert a., mainly in **Ethiopia**, but partly in Djibouti; includes D. depression; potash; sm. pt. and road projected.

Da-nang (Tourane), c., S. **Vietnam**; ch. pt. of Annam on S. China Sea; exp. agr. prod.; p. (1989) 370,670.

Danao, c., Cebu, **Philippines**; rice and sugar dist.; p. (1990) 73,358.

Dandenong, t., Victoria, **Australia**; 30 km E. of Melbourne; growing industl. ctr.; p. (1983) 58,200.

Dandong (Antung), c., Liaoning, **China**; pt. on Yalu R., 24 km. from mouth; Chinese frontier sta. on main rly. from China into N. Korea; mkt. for agr. prod.; lumbering; p. (1984) 560,500.

Dannemora, t., **Sweden**; 40 km N.E. of Uppsala; iron ore worked since 1579.

Danube (Donau), R., second longest R. in Europe; rises in Black Forest, Germany, and flows E. into Black Sea; forms comm. highway; Iron Gate hydro-electric and navigation project inaugurated by 1978; increased no. of dams causing concern with conservationists; linked by canals with Main, Rhine and Oder; completion of Rhine-Main-Danube canal and Danube-Black Sea canal (1984) now creates Trans-Europe Waterway of 3,500 km.; Vienna, Budapest, Belgrade, and other lge. cs. on its banks; 2,706 km long.

Danube-Tisa Canal, **Croatia**; irrigation, flood control, navigable; 261 km long.

Danville, t., Ill., **USA**; coal; mftg. tr.; p. (1980) 38,985.

Danville, t., Va., **USA**; cotton, tobacco; p. (1984) 44,700.

Danzig. *See* **Gdańsk**.

Dap Cau, t., **Vietnam**; bamboo pulp and paper factories.

Darbhanga, t., Bihar, **India**; rice, oil-seeds, grain, sugar tr.; univ.; p. (1991) 218,391.

Dardanelles, strait between European and Asian **Turkey**, connecting Aegean Sea with Sea of Marmara; (the anc. Hellespont), 64 km long.

Daresbury, v., Cheshire, **Eng.**; birthplace of C. L. Dodgson (Lewis Carroll).

Dar-es-Salaam, spt., former cap. of **Tanzania**; univ.; textile mill projected; oil refining; pipeline to Ndola, Zambia; naval base and Tanzam rly. built with Chinese aid; p. (1988) 1,360,850.

Darien, region, **Panama**; tortoiseshell, pearls, gold, but agr. is basis of economy; cap. La Palma; a. 15,540 km²; p. (1990) 43,382.

Darien, Gulf of, inlet of Caribbean Sea; separates Colombia and Panama.

Darjeeling, hill t., W. Bengal, **India**; tea, quinine; Himalayan resort; p. (1984) 63,600.

Darkhan, new t., **Mongolia**, on R. Hara; industl.

Darlaston, t., West Midlands, **Eng.**; nuts, bolts, fabricated steel mnfs., drop forgings, car components; pig iron plant closed after 100 years of production.

Darling Downs, plateau, S.E. Queensland, **Australia**; rich agr. region, fertile black soils aid wheat growing; ch. t. Toowoomba.

Darling R., N.S.W., **Australia**; longest trib. of the Murray, forming part of the Murray-Darling Rs. scheme for irrigation and flood control; 2,723 km long.

Darlington, t., l. gov. dist., Durham, **Eng.**; bridge bldg., woollen yarn mnf., engin., rly. wagons, steel wks.; p. (1993) 100,200 (dist.).

Darmstadt, c., Hesse, **Germany**; cas.; comm. ctr.; metallurgical prods., paper, machin., radio, chemicals, plastics; technical univ.; p. (1990) 139,500.

Dart, R., Devon, **Eng.**; rises in Dartmoor, flows S. into English Channel at Dartmouth; picturesque estuary; 74 km long.

Dartford, t., l. gov. dist., Kent, **Eng.**; S. side of Thames estuary; Dartford-Purfleet road tunnel (1963); road bridge (1991); engin., chemicals, quarrying, paper; mkt.; p. (1993) 82,600 (dist.).

Dartmoor, high granite plateau, S.W. Devon, **Eng.**; rough moorland; sheep, cattle, and wild ponies; granite tors; Nat. Park; tourism; granite quarries, reservoirs; prison at Princetown; china clay (Lee Moor) now extends into Nat. Park; recent discovery of tungsten, lgst. deposit in W. Europe but conflicts with conservation; a. 583 km²; hgst. point High Willays, 622 m.

Dartmouth, spt., S. Devon, **Eng.**; on W. of estuary of R. Dart; Royal Naval College; pottery; yachting, holiday resort; p. (1981) 6,298.

Dartmouth, industl. spt., sub. of Halifax, Nova Scotia, **Canada**; oil refining, shipbldg.; p. (1986) 65,243.

Darvel, burgh, Strathclyde Reg., **Scot.**; on R. Irvine, 13 km E. Kilmarnock; birthplace of Sir Alexander Fleming, discoverer of penicillin; p. (1991) 3,759.

Darwen, t., N.E. Lancs., **Eng.**; on flank of Rossendale Fells, 5 km S. of Blackburn; tile and glaze bricks, paint, wallpaper, plastics; p. (1981) 30,048.

Darwin, c., cap. N.T., **Australia**; pt. and regional ctr., invigorated in the 1950s by nearby uranium mng. (Rum Jungle); devastated by cyclone 1974, rebuilding complete by 1979; international airpt.; p. (1991) 78,139.

Daryal Gorge, Caucasus, **Georgia**; deep gorge (1,800 m) cut by Terek R.; identified as the classical Caspian or Iberian Gates from which distances were reckoned; forms part of Georgian military road.

Dashava, settlement on Lvov oblast, W. **Ukraine**; ctr. of rich natural gas field and starting point of gas pipeline to Kiev and Moscow, built after second world war.

Datia, t. Madhya-Pradesh, **India**; stone-walled, palaces; p. (1981) 60,991.

Datong (Tatung), c., Shanxi prov., **China**; impt. coalfield; steam and diesel locomotives; p. (1992) 1,110,000.

Datteln, t., N. Rhine-Westphalia, **Germany**; coal, leather, iron; p. (1983) 37,300.

Daugavpils, t., **Latvia**; on Dvina R.; textiles, engin., rly. repair wks., food prods.; p. (1991) 129,000.

Dauphiné Alps, mtn. range, S.E. **France**; 24 peaks over 3,050 m.

Daura, c., nr. Baghdad, **Iraq**; oil refining.

Davangere, t., Karnataka, S. **India**; on 600 m plateau in Indian Penin.; p. (1991) 266,000.

Davao, c., Mindanao, **Philippines**; pt. for sugar; p. (1990) 849,947.

Davenport, t., Iowa, **USA**; on Mississippi R. where it is spanned by bridges to Rock Island, Molise and East Molise; rly., comm. and industl. ctr.; p. (1990) 95,300 (t.), 351,000 (met. a. with Rock Is-Moline).

Daventry, t., l. gov. dist., Northampton, **Eng.**; 14 km S.E. of Rugby; boot-mkg., lt. engin.; radio-transmission sta.; expanded t.; p. (1993) 63,700 (dist.).

David, t., cap. of Chiriqui prov., **Panama**; timber coffee, cacao, sugar; p. (1990) 102,678.

Davis Strait, channel between Greenland and Baffin I., N.W. Terr., Canada; connects Atl. Oc. with Baffin Bay; navigable.

Davos-Platz and **Dörfli**, ts., Grisons, **Switzerland**; Alpine winter resorts; alt. 1,478 m; p. (1980) 10,468.

Dawley, t., The Wrekin, Shrops., **Eng.**; on S.E. flank of the Wrekin: ironwks., pipe, cement, roadstone, asphalt and brick wks., engin.; part of Telford new t. (1963); p. (1981) 49,137.

Dawlish, t., Teignbridge, S. Devon, **Eng.**; on S. cst. between estuaries of Rs. Exe and Teign; seaside resort; flower tr.; p. (1981) 10,755.

Dawson, t., Yukon Terr., **Canada**; on Yukon R., nr. Klondike goldfields; asbestos mng. projected 1968; p. (1986) 896.

Dayton, c., Ohio, **USA**; on Great Miami R.; univ.; aircraft, elec. machin., rubber gds.; p. (1990) 182,044 (c.), 951,270 (met. a. with Springfield).

Daytona Beach, t., Fla., **USA**; resort; shipping, ctr.; motor speed trials; p. (1984) 56,400 (t.), (1990) 371,000 (met. a.).

De Aar, t., rly. junc., Cape Prov., **S. Africa**; 500 m. from Cape Town; rlys. from N.W. (Luderitz, Walvis Bay) and S.E. (Pt. Elizabeth, E. London) join Cape Town to Johannesburg trunk rly.; p. (1980) 24,100 (dist.).

Dead Sea, salt-water L. between **Israel** and **Jordan**; surface 392 m below level of Mediterranean; a. 881 km², length 76 km, greatest width 15 km, greatest depth 399 m; receives waters of Jordan; high mineral content, very saline; Israeli plans to link to Mediterranean Sea by underground canal to generate hydro-electric power.

Deal, anc. pt., E. Kent, **Eng.**; on S.E. cst., 11 km N.E. Dover; opposite Goodwin Sands; seaside resort; lifeboat service; p. (1981) 25,989.

Dean, Forest of. See Forest of Dean.

Dearborn, t., Mich., **USA**; birthplace of Henry Ford; p. (1980) 90,660.

Death Valley, depression, Cal., **USA**; N. of Mojave Desert, 240 km N.E. of Los Angeles; completely arid; floor covered with saline deposits; tourist attraction; depth of valley floor 84 m below sea-level.

Deauville, seaside resort, Calvados dep., N. **France**; on Eng. Channel; racecourse, casino.

Debra Markos, t., cap. of Gojam prov., **Ethiopia**; vegetable oil extraction; p. (1984) 39,808.

Debrecen, t., **Hungary**; 183 km E. of Budapest; univ.; ctr. of pastoral dist.; fairs; pharmaceutics, medical instruments, furniture; ctr. of Calvinism; p. (1989) 220,000.

Decatur, t., Ala., **USA**; steel textiles; industl. development after establishment of Tenn. Valley Authority; p. (1980) 42,002.

Decatur, t., Ill., **USA**; on Sangamon R.; industl.; rly. engin., food processing; univ.; p. (1990) 83,885 (t.), 117,206 (met. a.).

Decazeville, t., Aveyron, S. **France**; ctr. of sm. coal-field (no longer worked), metallurgy; p. (1982) 9,204.

Deccan, The, upland of S. **India**, bounded by the Narbada and Kistna Rs.; coincides with Maharashtra st.; area of very fertile lava soils; impt. cotton-growing region.

Dee, R., N. **Wales** and Cheshire, **Eng.**; 144 km long; lge. silted estuary, use for water storage planned.

Dee, R., Kincardine and Deeside, **Scot.**; picturesque, tourism; 139 km long.

Dehiwala-Mt Lavina, t., **Sri Lanka**; on cst. S. of Colombo; p. (1983) 181,000.

Dehra Dun, t., Uttar Pradesh, **India**; important scientific research ctr.; sawmills; p. (1991) 368,000.

Deir-ez-Zor, t., **Syria**; on Euphrates R.; on motor route between Damascus and Baghdad.

Dej, t., **Romania**; on Somesul R., distillery; p. (1983) 38,229.

Delabole, v., Cornwall, **Eng.**; on N.W. flank of Bodmin Moor; slate quarries.

Delagoa Bay, natural harbour, **Moçambique**; ch. pt. Maputo.

Delaware, st., **USA**; admitted to Union 1787, popular name First State; st. flower Peach Blossom, st. bird Blue Hen Chicken; low-lying a. of Atl. cst. plain; agr., lumber; fertilisers, minerals, leather, chemicals, machin.; cap. Dover; ch. pt. Wilmington; a. 6,138 km²; p. (1990) 666,168.

Delaware Bay, inlet, Atl. cst., **USA**; drowned estuary of R. Delaware, extends 128 km inland from C. May into heart of highly industl. a. of Philadelphia.

Delaware, R., flows between N.Y. st., **USA** along the Penns. border, through N.J. to Delaware Bay; 504 km long.

Delft, c., pt., S. Holland, **Neth.**; on Schie R. (canalised), nr. Rotterdam; technical univ.; ceramics (delft-ware), tool mftg., precision instruments; 13th cent. Old church and 15th cent. New church; p. (1993) 91,013.

Delhi, c., cap. of **India**; on watershed between Rs. Indus and Ganges; made up of Old Delhi with walls, palace, and fort, and New Delhi with admin. ctr.; univ.; p. (1991) 301,000 (New Delhi), 7,207,000.

Delhi, union terr., **India**; hot and arid region between Indus valley and alluvial plain of Ganges; irrigation to support agr.; New Delhi and Old Delhi ch. ctrs.; a. 1,497 km²; p. (1991) 9,420,644.

Delitzsch, t., Saxony, **Germany**; 26 km E. of Halle; sugar, chemicals; p. (1989) 27,894.

Delmarva, peninsula, Del., **USA**; between Chesapeake Bay and Del. Bay; horticulture, poultry, forestry, fishing.

Delmenhorst, t., Lower Saxony, **Germany**; nr. Bremen; jute, woollens, linoleum, foodstuffs; p. (1986) 70,500.

Delphi, anc. Phocis, central **Greece**; N. of G. of Corinth; famous for Delphic oracle on Mt. Parnassus.

Del Rio, t., Texas, **USA**; pt. of entry on Rio Grande; mkt. for agr. a.; grapes; exp. wool; border t., bridge to Mexico; p. (1980) 30,034.

Delyn, l. gov. dist., Clwyd, **Wales**; W. of Dee estuary inc. Holywell, Flint and Mold; p. (1993) 70,100.

Demavend, dormant volcano, **Iran**; hgst. peak in Elburz range, c. 5,673 m.

Demerara, co., **Guyana**; between Essequibo and Demerara Rs.; exp. sugar, molasses, rum.

Demerara, R., **Guyana**; drains N. to Atl. Oc.; bauxite transport.

Denain, t., Nord dep., N. **France**; industl. ctr.; p. (1982) 21,872.

Denbigh, former co., N. **Wales**; now mostly in Clwyd; sm. part in Gwynedd.

Denbigh, t., Glyndŵr, Clwyd, **Wales**; in Vale of Clwyd, 16 km S. of Rhyl; cas.; tourism; dairy prods.; birthplace of Stanley the explorer; p. (1981) 9,040.

Denby Dale, t., West Yorks., **Eng.**; 13 km W. of Barnsley; woollen textiles; earthenware pipes; p. (1981) 13,476.

Den Helder. See Helder.

Denholme, t., West Yorks., **Eng.**; nr. Bradford; dairying, textiles; p. (1981) 2,676.

Denizli, t., **Turkey**; 75 km S.E. of Izmir; gardens — "the Damascus of Anatolia"; nr. site of Laodica; p. (1990) 190,360, 750,882 (prov.).

Denmark, kingdom, N.W. **Europe**; part of Scandinavia; member of EU; consists of Jutland peninsula, Is. of Sjaelland, Fyn, Falster, Lolland, and Bornholm, and 400 smaller Is., between N. Sea and Baltic; emphasis on dairy agr., producing butter, eggs, and bacon; increasing industrialisation; industl. prods. now account for 62 per cent of exp.; cap. Copenhagen; a. 42,932 km²; p. (1993) 5·18 m.

Denny and Dunipace, burgh, Falkirk, **Scot.**; 10 km W. of Falkirk; steel castings, precast concrete, p. (1991) 13,481.

Dent du Midi, mtn. gr., Vaud can., S.W. **Switzerland**; rises to 10,694 ft. in Haut Cime.

Denton, t., Gtr. Manchester, **Eng.**; nr. Manchester; felt-hat mkg.; p. (1981) 37,729.

Denton, mkt. t., Texas, **USA**; univs.; food processing; p. (1980) 48,063.

Denver, c., cap. of Col., **USA**; on E. slope of

Rockies, on South Platte R.; univs.; oil, electronic equipment, mng. machin., livestock, canning; tourism; p. (1990) 467,610 (c.), 1,622,980 (met. a.).

Deoghar, t., Bihar, **India**; temples, place of pilgrimage; p. (1981) 52,904.

Deptford. See Lewisham.

Dera Ghazi Khan, t., **Pakistan**; on W. bank of Indus R.; silk, brass; p. (1981) 103,000.

Dera Ismail Khan, t., **Pakistan**; on Indus R.; admin. ctr., caravan ctr.; p. (1981) 68,000.

Derby, c., l. gov. dist., Derbys., **Eng.**; on R. Derwent; general engin., aero-engines, man-made fibres; p. (1993) 228,600 (dist.).

Derbyshire, non-met. co., **Eng.**; much of a. occupied by Pennines and Peak Dist. Nat. Park.; coalfield and industl. a. in E.; forms part of Manchester met. a. in N.W.; co. t. Derby; a. 2,631 km²; p. (1993) 950,900.

Derbyshire Dales, l. gov. dist., Derbys., **Eng**; Pennine a. inc. Matlock, Bakewell and Ashbourne; p. (1993) 68,600.

Derg, Lough, in basin of R. Shannon, **R.o.I.**; separating Galway and Clare from Tipperary.

Derg, L., Donegal, **R.o.I.**, with cave on I. visited by R.C. pilgrims and known as "St Patrick's Purgatory".

Derry; l. gov. dist., **N. Ireland**; borders R.o.I. and L. Foyle; Sperrin Mtns. in S.; p. (1991) 95,371.

Derwent, lgst R. of Tasmania, **Australia**; flows to Storm Bay via Hobart; hydroelec. power; 190 km long.

Derwent, R., Derbys., **Eng.**; trib. of R. Trent; length 96 km.

Derwent, R., North Yorks, Humberside, **Eng.**; trib. of R. Ouse; length 91 km.

Derwentside, l. gov. dist., Durham, **Eng.**; inc. Consett, Stanley and surrounding a.; p. (1993) 86,900.

Derwentwater, L., Cumbria, **Eng.**; 5 km long.

Desaguadero, R., **Bolivia**; outlet of L. Titicaca; used for irrigation; 320 km long.

Desborough, t., Northants., **Eng.**; boot and shoe mnfs., iron mng.; p. (1981) 6,393.

Des Moines, c., cap. of Iowa st., **USA**; in heart of corn belt; transport and industl. ctr.; univ.; p. (1990) 193,187 (c.), 393,000 (met. a.).

Des Moines, R., Iowa, **USA**; trib. of Mississippi rising in Minn.; 880 km long.

Desna, R., main trib. of Dnieper R., **Russia/Ukraine**; navigable below Bryansk; 1,184 km long.

Des Plaines, t., Ill., **USA**; sub. of Chicago on Des Plaines R.; p. (1980) 53,568.

Dessau, t., Saxony - Anhalt, **Germany**; at confluence of Mulde and Elbe Rs.; cas.; machin., rly. carriages, paper, sugar, chemicals; route ctr.; p. (1986) 103,000.

Detmold, t., N. Rhine–Westphalia, **Germany**; cas.; paints, wood inds.; p. (1986) 66,700.

Detroit, ch. c., pt., Mich., **USA**; busy comm. and industl. ctr.; univ.; gr. grain mart; and ctr. of the Ford motor-car wks., aeroplanes, military tanks, synthetic diamonds, pharmaceutics, tools, chemicals, steel; lgst exporting t. on Great Lakes; p. (1990) 1,027,974 (c.), 4,382,000 (met. a.).

Detroit, R., channel between L. St. Clair and L. Erie (40 km) separates st. of Mich., **USA**, from Ontario, **Canada**; carries more shipping than any other inland waterway in the world.

Deurne, t., **Belgium**; nr. Antwerp, airport; p. (1982) 76,744.

Deux-Sèvres, dep., Poitou-Charentes, **France**; cap. Niort; a. 6,053 km²; p. (1990) 346,000.

Deva, t. cap. Hunedoara prov. W. central **Romania**; agr., tourism; castle; p. (1990) 82,313.

Deventer, t., Overijssel, **Neth.**; on IJssel R.; indstl. ctr., Hanse t. in Middle Ages; p. (1983) 68,529.

Devil's Island (I. du Diable), I., Atl. Oc. off **Fr. Guiana**; former penal settlement where Dreyfus was confined in 1894.

Devizes, Kennet, Wilts., **Eng.**; mkt. t., on Kennet and Avon canal at foot of Marlborough Downs; bricks, tiles, bacon-curing; p. (1981) 10,629.

Devon, non-met. co., S.W. **Eng.**; between English and Bristol Channels; attractive cstl. scenery, Nat. Parks of Dartmoor and Exmoor encourage tourism; mixed farming; modern lt. inds.; major ctrs. of p. at Plymouth, Torbay, Exeter; a. 6,713 km²; p. (1993) 1,049,200.

Devonport, spt., N. Tasmania, **Australia**; pt. for fruit dist. of R. Mersey; mnfs. primary prods.; Mersey–Forth power project p. (1991) 24,622.

Devonport, Auckland, **N.Z.**; naval base and dock-

yard; p. (1987) 10,550.

Dewsbury, t., West Yorks., **Eng.**; on R. Calder, 13 km from Leeds; heavy woollens, shoddy, coalmng.; dyewks.; p. (1981) 48,339.

Dez Dam, over Dez R., Khurzistan prov., **Iran**; opened 1963.

Dezful, t., Iran; mkt. ctr.; oil fields nearby; p. (1986) 151,420.

Dhahran, spt., **Saudi Arabia**; main oil pt. of S.A.; College of Petroleum and Minerals.

Dhanbad, t., Bihar, **India**; lead, zinc, tools, radio assembly, fertilisers; p. (1991) 151,789, (t.), 815,000 (met. a.).

Dhanushkodi, t., Tamil Nadu, **India**; on I. in Palk Strait; ferry pt. for passenger traffic from India to Sri Lanka.

Dhar, t., Madhya Pradesh, **India**; cultural and tr. ctr.; p. (1981) 48,870.

Dharmsala, hill sta., Himachal Pradesh, **India**; 160 km N.E. of Amritsar; sanatorium; c. 1,800 m; imposing mtn. scenery; p. (1981) 14,522.

Dharwad, t., Karnataka, **India**; 112 km E. of Goa; univ.; cotton mnf.; p. (1981) 13,026.

Dhaulagiri, mtn. peak, 8,172 m, **Nepal**, 4 summits in Himalayas.

Dhekélia, Cyprus; Brit. sovereign base within Rep.

Dhufar, fertile prov., **Oman**, Arabia; sugar-cane, cattle; ch. t. Salālah; ch. pt. Mirbat.

Dhulia, t., Khandesh dist., Maharashtra, **India**; cotton ind.; rly. ctr.; p. (1991) 278,000.

Diamante, R., Mendoza prov., **Argentina**; rises in Andes, flows E. to R. Salado; irrigates oasis of San Rafael; 320 km long.

Diamantina, t., Minas Gerais, **Brazil**; former diamond mng. ctr.; p. (1985) 37,200.

Dibrugarh, t., Assam, **India**; former terminus of rail communications from Calcutta; p. (1991) 125,667.

Didcot, sm. t., Oxon, **Eng.**; 16 km S. of Oxford; ordnance depots closed; Grand Prix engin.; ctr. for steam rly; p. (1981) 15,204.

Diego Garcia, I., Brit. Indian Oc. Terr.; Anglo-American naval communications ctr.: c. 1,000 islanders evacuated to Mauritius 1966–71; major US military staging base; part of Brit. Indian Oc. Terr.

Diego Suarez. See Antsiranana.

Dieppe, pt., Seine-Maritime, **France**; 56 km N. of Rouen; fisheries, shipbldg., machin.; cross-Channel ferry; p. (1982) 26,000.

Differdange, t., S.W. **Luxembourg**; iron ore; cattle; p. (1991) 15,699.

Digboi, N.E. Assam, **India**; oil fields and refinery.

Digne, t., cap. of Alpes-de-Haute-Provence, **France**; nr. Aix; cath.; p. (1990) 17,425.

Dijôn, c., cap. Côte-d'Or, E. **France**; the Roman Divonense castrum; route ctr.; Seine-Saône watershed; wine tr.; industl. ctr.; univ., cath.; p. (1990) 151,636. (c.), 226,025 (met. a.).

Dili, t., cap. of E. Timor, **Indonesia**; major spt.; exp. cotton, copra, coffee; p. (1980) 65,451.

Dimitrovgrad, t., **Bulgaria**; founded 1947; fertilisers, chemicals, superphosphate plant, iron, thermo-electric sta.

Dimitrovo. See Pernik.

Dinajpur, t., **Bangladesh**; comm. ctr.; univ.; p. (1991) 126,189.

Dinan, t., Brittany, **France**; mediaeval t. above Rance R.; hosiery, brewing; holiday resort; p. (1982) 14,157.

Dinant, t., Namur, **Belgium**; on R. Meuse: mkt. t., tourist resort; exported copperware (*dinanderie*) in Middle Ages; cath.; citadel (1040); p. (1982) 12,008.

Dinapur, t., Bihar, **India**; on Ganges R., nr. Patna; p. (1991) 126,189.

Dinard, t., Brittany, **France**; resort, especially for English; p. (1982) 10,016.

Dinaric Alps, mtn. range, extending 640 km along Adriatic; from **Albania** to **Italy**; hgst. peak Durmitor, 2,515 m.

Dindigul, t., Tamil Nadu, **India**; 40 km S. of Tiruchirapalli; cigars; p. (1991) 182,477.

Dinefwr, l. gov. dist., Dyfed, **Wales**; inland a. inc. Llandovery, Llandeilo, Ammanford and Cwmamman; p. (1993) 38,500.

Dingle B., Kerry, **R.o.I.**; long inlet of sea on Atl. cst.

Dingwall, royal burgh, Ross and Cromarty, **Scot.**; at head of Cromarty F.; rly. junc.; cattle mkt.; admin. ctr.; distilling, handloom weaving; p. (1991) 5,224.

Dinslaken, t. N. Rhine-Westphalia, **Germany**, N. of Duisburg; coal, steel, iron, footwear, timber; oil pipeline from Wesseling under construction; p. (1986) 61,300.

Diomede Is., two barren granitic islets in Bering Strait between Alaska and Siberia; accepted bdy. between Soviet and US terr.

Diredawa, t., **Ethiopia**; 40 km N. of Harar; rly. wks.; mkt and comm. ctr.; new cement wks.; p. (1984) 98,104.

Dirk Hartog I., off Shark Bay, W. **Australia**.

Disko U., off W. cst. of **Greenland** in Baffin Bay; contains harbour of Godhavn, cap. N. Greenland; rendezvous for whalers; shrimp beds; a. 8,288 km².

Dismal Swamp, morass, S. Va. and N.C., **USA**; contains L. Drummond and extends 50–65 km S. from nr. Norfolk.

Diss, South Norfolk, **Eng.**; mkt. t. on R. Waveney, 45 km S.W. of Norwich; agr. implements; p. (1981) 5,423.

Distaghil, major peak, Gr. Karakoram, N. Kashmir, **Pakistan**; two summits connected by a ridge, max. alt. 7,890 m.

Distrito Federal, federal dist., **Brazil**; inc. cap. c. of Brasilia; a. 5,815 km²; p. (1991) 1,596,274.

Ditchling Beacon, 10 km N. of Brighton, East Sussex, **Eng.**; hgst point of South Downs, 248 m.

Diu, spt., I., off S. cst. of Bombay Union Territory, **India**; oil nearby at Kayakov; p. (1991) 39,485.

Dīwānīyah, Ad, t., **Iraq**; cap. D. prov.; on Baghdad–Basra rly.; p. (1965) 60,553, (latest fig.)

Diyarbakir, c., cap. of D. prov., central **Turkey**; on Tigris R.; comm. and mnf. ctr.; flour and rice mills; the anc. Amida, old walls, gates, citadel; p. (1990) 371,038 (t.), 1,094,996 (prov.).

Djajapura (Sukarnapura), t., cap. of Irian Jaya, **Indonesia**; on Humboldt B., an inlet of Pac. Oc.

Djakarta. *See* **Jakarta**.

Djambi, dist., and t., Sumatra, **Indonesia**; on E. cst. plain 160 km N.W. of Palembang; univ.; field; a. (dist.) 44,924 km².

Djerba, t. and I., **Tunisia**, at S. entrance to G. of Gabès, joined to mainland by causeway; olives, dates, textiles, pottery; a. 510 km²; p. (1984) 92,269.

Djibouti, c. cap. of **Djibouti**; rly. terminus; main pt. free pt. (1981), container terminal (1985); p. (1991) 317,000.

Djibouti, Rep. of, indep. st. (1977) N.E. **Africa**; former French Somaliland, renamed Fr. Terr. of Afars and Issas 1967; extends inland from straits of Bab-el-Mandeb; economy based on trade through international pt. of D.; plain, mainly below 180 m; hot, dry climate; shark and mother-of-pearl fisheries; little cultivable land; a. 23,051 km²; p. (1991) 542,000, of whom over half live in cap. Djibouti.

Dneprodzerzhinsk, t., **Ukraine**; W. of Dnepropetrovsk on Dnieper R.; iron and steel, engin., chemicals; hydroelec. sta. nearby; p. (1990) 283,600.

Dneproges (abbrev. Dnieper hydroelectric sta.), **Ukraine**; nr. Zaporoz'ye, on Dnieper: lgst dam and power sta. in Europe; destroyed by Germans, rebuilt 1944–9.

Dnepropetrovsk, c., **Ukraine**; on R. Dnieper; univ.; impt. rly. and industl. ctr., using iron ore (from Krivoy Rog), coal (Dombas), manganese (Nikopol) and electric power from Dnieper dam; heavy machin., chemicals; p. (1990) 1,186,700.

Dneprorudnyy, t., **Ukraine**; new t. on S. shore of Kakhvota reservoir; p. (1990) 23,300.

Dneprostroy. *See* **Zaporoz'ye.**

Dnieper (Dnepr), gr. R. of **Russia**, **Belarussia**, **Ukraine**; 3rd longest R. of Europe; rises in Valdai hills, flows into Black Sea, 2,240 km long; connected by canals to Baltic; tribs. inc. Berezina, Pripet, Desna, Orel, Samara; since erection of Dneproges dam navigable almost entire length.

Dniester (Dnestr), R., **Ukraine**, **Moldavia**; rises in Carpathians and flows into the Black Sea; 1,403 km long.

Döbeln, t., Saxony, **Germany**; machin., metallurgy, wood, cigar and sugar inds.; p. (1989) 27,777.

Dobrich, t., N.E. **Bulgaria**; comm. and agr. ctr. of Dobruja; food-processing, textiles, furniture, agr. machin.; named **Tolbukhin** in honour of Russian soldier who took it from Germans during World War II, 1944; renamed Dobrich, 1991; p. (1990) 115,786.

Dobruja, historic region, S.E. **Europe**; along Black Sea cst., S.E. Romania, and N.E. Bulgaria; mainly agr.; ch. pt. Constanta.

Dobšiná, t., **Slovakia**; cave containing ice-field of 0·8 ha; asbestos, iron ore; p. 5,300.

Docklands, expanding area of former docks, E. London; commercial and office devt; expensive housing; light railway; Canary Wharf tallest blg. in London.

Dodecanese (S. Sporades), gr. of some 20 Greek Is. (originally 12) in S. Aegean Sea; most impt. are Rhodes, Cos, and Leros; Italian 1912–46; p. (1991) 162,439.

Dodoma, cap. of **Tanzania** since 1974; at geographical ctr. of T. in rural a.; p. (1988) 203,833.

Dodworth, t., South Yorks., **Eng.**; nr. Barnsley; coal; p. (1981) 4,922.

Dogger Bank, sandbank in N. Sea, between England and Denmark; depth varies from 6 to 37 m; valuable fishing ground.

Dogs, I. of, riverside dist., formed by bend in the R. Thames off Greenwich, London, **Eng**; Millwall and India doc̄ks.

Doha, t., cap. of **Qatar**; spt. on E. of Qatar peninsula, Persian Gulf; internat. airpt., deep sea pt.; contains 80 per cent of p.; p. (1986) 217,294.

Dokai Bay, inlet, N. Kyushu, **Japan**; landlocked bay on S. side of Shimonoseki Straits; flanked by highly industl. zone inc. Yawata, Wakamatsu, Tobata cs.; requires constant dredging; length 6 km, width 0·8–2·4 km.

Dôle, t., Jura, E. **France**; on R. Doubs, nr. Dijon; industl. ctr.; anc. cap. of Franche-Comté, ceded to France in 1678; birthplace of Pasteur; p. (1982) 27,959.

Dolgarrog, sm. t., Meirionnydd, Gwynedd, **Wales**; site of hydroelectric sta.

Dolgellau, t., Gwynedd, N. **Wales**; agr., quarrying, timber; p. (1981) 2,321.

Dollar, burgh, Clackmannan, **Scot.**; at foot of Ochil hills; p. (1991) 2,670.

Dollar Law, mtn., nr. Peebles, **Scot.**; alt. 817 m.

Dolomites, gr. of limestone mtns., S. Tyrolese Alps, N.E. **Italy**; tourist dist.; peaks assume fantastic forms; principal peak Marmolada 3,355 m.

Dominica, Commonwealth of, W.I.; indep. st. (1978); most N. of Windward Is.; 25 per cent under cultivation; volcanic soils highly suitable for bananas; N.–S. mtn. range has spectacular volcanic scenery; cap. Roseau; a. 751 km²; p. (1991) 108,812.

Dominican Rep., rep., **W.I.**; shares I. of Hispaniola with Haiti; comprises Nat. Dist. (inc. cap. Santo Domingo) and 25 admin. provs.; mtnous. with sub-tropical climate; in path of tropical cyclones; badly devastated by hurricane (1979); comm. economy mainly agr.; transport system geared to exp. of sugar (now declining with U.S. quotas on imports); decline in tobacco sales causing farmers to abandon production; govt. investment in agr. and mng.; oil refining at Nigua; exp. bauxite; 48,430 km²; p. (1991) 7,310,000.

Domodossola, frontier t., Piedmont, N. **Italy**; nr. Alpine tourist resort in Toce valley, nr. Simplon; p. (1981) 20,069.

Don, R., South Yorks., **Eng.**; trib. of R. Ouse, 112 km long.

Don, R., Gordon, **Scot.**; flows into N. Sea nr. Aberdeen; salmon; 131 km long.

Don, major R. of southern **Russia**; falls into Sea of Azov below Rostov, its ch. pt.; navigable to Voronezh; ch. trib., Donets; access to Volga by Don-Volga canal; fisheries; 1,955 km long.

Donaghadee, t., Ards, N. **Ireland**; nearest point to Scot.; spt. and seaside resort; p. (1991) 4,455.

Donauwörth, t., W. Bavaria, **Germany**; bridge t. on N. bank of Danube at Wörnitz confluence; p. (1989) 17,546.

Donbas, industl. region, **Ukraine**; in valleys of Rs. Donets and lower Dnieper; about 23,300 km²; important coalfield; adjoins Krivoy Rog ironfields; many lge. industl. ts.

Doncaster, t., met. dist., South Yorks., **Eng.**; on Don R., 27 km N.E. of Sheffield; only Harworth colliery remains; tractors, nylon mftg.; racecourse; p. (1993) 292,700 (dist.).

Donegal, spt., Co. Donegal, **R.o.I.**; on W. cst. on Donegal Bay; tweeds, carpets; p. (1986) 2,242.

Donegal (Tirconnail), co., N.W. **R.o.I.**; fishing poor agr.; cloth, hydroelectric power; co. t. Lifford; a. 4,830 km²; p. (1986) 129,664.

Donets, R., rises in uplands of central **Russia**; N.E. of Belgorod, flows S.E. to join R. Don; crosses Donets coalfield; length 1,040 km. *See* **Donbas**.

Donetsk (Stalino), t., **Ukraine**; industl. ctr. of Donets coal basin; iron, steel, engin., chemicals; p. (1990) 1,116,900.

Donges, t., Loire Atlantique, **France**; nr. St.

Nazaire; oil refinery; synthetic textiles, plastics.

Dongola (Dunqulah), t., **Sudan**; on left bank of Nile above Third Cataract; Old D. was 120 km to S.

Dong Ting (Tung Ting), lge. L., Hunan, **China**; receives water from Xi Jiang and Yuan Rs., drains N. to Chang Jiang; surrounded by flat intensively cultivated land; rice, sugar; size varies with season; max. (in late summer) 6,500 km².

Donner Pass, E. Cal., **USA**; highway pass through Sierra Nevada at 2,176 m.

Donzère-Mondragon, Vaucluse, **France**; site of Rhône barrage supplying hydroelectric power.

Dora Baltea, R., N. **Italy**; rises in Mt. Blanc, flows E. and S. through Val d'Aosta to R. Po at Chivasso; impt. routeway from N. Italy to Switzerland (through Gr. St. Bernard Pass) and France (through Little St. Bernard Pass); 152 km long.

Dorchester, co. t., West Dorset, **Eng.**; mkt. t. on R. Frome; lime, agr., engin.; Roman remains; nearby prehistoric Maiden Castle; linked with the name of Thomas Hardy; p. (1981) 14,049.

Dordogne, dep., S.W. **France**; cap. Périgueux; crossed by Dordogne R.; fertile valleys; p. (1990) 386,400.

Dordogne, R., S.W. **France**; rises in Central Massif, joins Garonne to form Gironde; vineyards; upper reaches used for hydroelectric power.

Dordrecht, c., nr. Rotterdam, **Neth.**; on R. Merwede; met. a. with Zwijndrecht; timber, shipbldg., seaplanes; p. (1993) 112,687 (c.) 212,164 (met. a.).

Dorking, t., Mole Valley, Surrey, **Eng.**; on R. Mole to S. of gap through N. Downs; mkt., residtl.; lt. inds.; p. (1981) 21,654.

Dornbirn, t., Vorarlberg, **Austria**; textiles; p. (1991) 40,881.

Dornoch, burgh, Sutherland, **Scot.**; N. of Dornoch F.; resort; p. (1991) 1,196.

Dorset, non-met. co., S. **Eng.**; borders Eng. Channel along attractive cliffed cst. formed by E.–W. limestone ridges; Portland stone quarried; many tourist resorts inc. Bournemouth; mkt. ts. serve agr. interior; a. 2,655 km²; p. (1993) 667,500.

Dorset Heights, hills, extend E. to W. across central Dorset, **Eng.**; chalk; pastoral farming, sheep; some cultivation where soil is deep enough; rise to 250–275 m.

Dorsten, t., N. Rhine–Westphalia, **Germany**; on R. Lippe; coal, iron, elec., chemical inds.; p. (1986) 74,100.

Dortmund, c., N. Rhine–Westphalia, **Germany**; on Dortmund–Ems Canal; industl. ctr. and pt. of Ruhr; coal, iron, steel; p. (1990) 599,900.

Dortmund–Ems Canal, N. Rhine–Westphalia, **Germany**; links Dortmund on Ruhr coalfield with R. Ems 8 km above Lingen; 144 km long.

Douai, t., Nord, **France**; nr. Lille on Scarpe R.; coal, iron and engin. wks.; bell founding, arsenal; p. (1990) 44,195 (t.), 199,562 (met. a.).

Douala, spt., **Cameroon**; rly. to Yaoundé; exp. hardwoods; p. (1988) 1,211,387.

Douarnenez, spt., Finistère, N.W. **France**; on D. Bay; sardine fisheries; p. (1982) 17,813.

Doubs, dep., E. **France**; traversed by Jura range and R. Doubs; mainly agr.; watchmkg., motor vehicles; cap. Besançon; a. 5,315 km²; p. (1990) 484,800.

Douglas, t., cap. of I. of Man; 120 km W. of Liverpool, **Eng.**; spt; resort; nearby freeport (1983) gaining from low tax rate; p. (1991) 22,214.

Douglas Point, on shore of L. Huron, Ont., **Canada**; nuclear power sta.

Dounreay, Caithness, **Scot.**; fast-breeder nuclear reactors.

Douro, R., **Portugal** and **Spain**; enters Atl. Oc. below Oporto; known as Duero R. in Spain; l. 776 km; famous port wine a.

Dove, R., Derbs. and Staffs., **Eng.**; trib. of Trent; flows through beautiful dales; 77 km long.

Dovedale, valley, Derbys., **Eng.**; steeply sloping limestone ravine of R. Dove; tourism.

Dover, packet pt., l. gov. dist., Kent, **Eng.**; one of old Cinque pts.; nearest spt. to France the Strait of D. being only 34 km wide; ch. pt. for passenger and mail traffic with Continent; cas.; p. (1993) 106,100 (dist.).

Dovey, R., **Wales**; flows from Cambrian Mtns. and enters Cardigan Bay by a wide estuary.

Dowlais, dist., Merthyr Tydfil, Mid Glamorgan, S. **Wales**; coal mng., iron founding, engin.

Down, former co.; l. gov. dist., **N. Ireland**; borders Strangford Lough and Dundrum

Bay; agr. and fisheries; p. (1991) 58,008.

Downham Market, t., West Norfolk, **Eng.**; on R. Ouse; flour-milling, malting, sheet-metal wks.; p. (1981) 4,687.

Downpatrick, t., Down, **N. Ireland**; on R. Quoile; linen; p. (1991) 10,113.

Downs, natural harbour of refuge for shipping between Kent cst. and Goodwin Sands in the English Channel.

Drachenfels, mtn. peak of the Rhine, **Germany**; the steepest of the Siebengebirge range, nr. Königswinter; alt. 325 m; ascended by lt. rly.; famous cave of legendary dragon.

Draguignan, t., S.E. **France**; cap. of Var. dep. until 1974; mkt. t., service ctr.; p. (1982) 28,194.

Drakensberg, mtn. chain between Natal and Orange Free State, **S. Africa**, and **Lesotho**; extending 800 km from Gt. Fish R. to Olifants R.; hgst. peak Mont-aux-Sources 3,283 m; rly. crosses range by Van Reenen Pass.

Drammen, spt., **Norway**; nr. Oslo, on the Drammen R.; shipyard; exp. timber, wood-pulp, paper; p. (1990) 58,717.

Drancy, t., Seine-St. Denis, **France**; N.E. sub. of Paris; p. (1990) 60,928.

Drava (Drau), R., trib. of Danube, **Austria** and **Yugoslavia**; flows from the Tyrol across Carinthia and Styria, joining Danube nr. Osijek; length 720 km; used for hydroelec. power.

Drax, West Yorks., **Eng.**; thermal elec. power sta. linked to new Selby coalfield.

Drenthe, prov., **Neth.**; on German frontier; cap. Assen; a. 2,663 km²; p. (1993) 448,256.

Dresden, c., **Germany**; R. pt. on Elbe, 80 km E. of Leipzig; cap. Saxony Land; impt. route ctr.; engin., chemicals, optical and photographic apparatus, porcelain, glass, brewing; fine art collections; scientific research; oil pipeline from Schwedt under construction; p. (1990) 488,000.

Driffield, t., East Yorks, Humberside, **Eng.**; on Yorks. Wolds 21 km N. of Beverley; p. (1981) 9,090.

Drin, R., N. **Albania**; rises in Yugoslavia and flows through deep gorges into Adriatic; hydro-elec. power; 288 km long.

Drina, R., trib. of Sava R., **Yugoslavia**; forming boundary between Montenegro and Bosnia-Hercegovina; source of hydroelec. power; 480 km long.

Dröbak, spt., S.E. **Norway**; winter pt. for Oslo; summer resort.

Drogheda, spt., Louth, **R.o.I.**; considerable tr. in agr. produce, salmon, etc.; stormed by Cromwell in 1649; p. (1986) 24,086.

Drogobych, t., **Ukraine**; 64 km S.W. of Lvov; ctr. of lge. oilfields, refineries; mftg.; p. (1990) 78,500.

Droitwich, t., Wychavon, Hereford and Worcs., **Eng.**; brine baths; lt. inds.; expanded t.; p. (1981) 18,073.

Drôme, dep., S.E. **France**; traversed by Alps and watered by Rs. Rhône, Drôme, and Isère; cap. Valence; agr., forestry, sericulture, textile ind.; a. 6,560 km²; p. (1990) 414,100.

Dromore, mkt. t., Banbridge, **N. Ireland**; on Lagan R.; linen; p. (1991) 3,434.

Dronfield, t., North East Derbys., **Eng.**; between Chesterfield and Sheffield; edged tools, engin. and agr. implements; p. (1981) 23,304.

Droylsden, t., Gtr. Manchester, **Eng.**; sub. of Manchester; chemicals; textiles; p. (1981) 22,513.

Drumochter Pass, Grampian Mtns., **Scot.**; carries main Perth to Inverness rly. and main road from Glen Garry into valley of R. Spey; highest alt. reached by any main rly. in Gt. Britain, 453 m.

Dschang, t., **Cameroon**; quinine processing; bauxite mng.

Dubai (Dubayy), emirate, one of **United Arab Emirates**, Arabian Gulf; recently developed as free pt. (modelled on Singapore); p. (1985) 419,104.

Dubbo, t., N.S.W., **Australia**; busy road, rail, air junction in rich agr. dist.; p. (1981) 23,986.

Dublin, co., **R.o.I.**; co. t. Dublin; a. (inc. c. of Dublin) 922 km²; p. (1981) 977,700.

Dublin (Irish *Baile Atha Cliath*), C.B., cap. of **R.o.I.**; co. t. Co. Dublin; at mouth of R. Liffey; ctr. of govt., commerce, ind., and culture; cath., univ., Abbey Theatre; brewing, distilling, food processing; Swift was buried here; p. (1986) 502,749 (c.), 1,021,449 (co.).

Dubrovnik (Ital. Ragusa), t., **Croatia** (formerly Yugoslavia); impt. pt. on Adriatic; retains much of its mediaeval architecture but damaged in civil war, 1991; tourism; airport; p. (1981) 66,131.

Dubuque, t., Iowa, **USA**; pt. on Mississippi R.;

varied inds. inc. meat-packing; p. (1990) 57,546.

Dudley, t., met. dist., West Midlands, **Eng.**; cas.; engin.; cables, chains; p. (1993) 311,500 (dist.).

Duisburg, c., N. Rhine–Westphalia, **Germany**; R. pt. on E. bank of Rhine at confluence with R. Ruhr, 16 km N. of Düsseldorf; iron and steel inds., machin., textiles, chemicals, pt. inds., route and R. tr. ctr.; p. (1990) 536,700.

Dukeries, dist., Sherwood Forest, Notts., **Eng.**; so called from ducal mansions in dist.; tourism.

Dukinfield, t., Tameside, Gtr. Manchester, **Eng.**; 10 km E. of Manchester; textiles, engin., rope and twine; p. (1981) 18,063.

Dukla Pass, 497 m. pass; anc. and easy route across Carpathians, linking Poland, Hungary and Slovakia.

Duluth, pt., Minn., **USA**; at W. end of L. Superior; gr. tr. in grain, timber and iron ore; natural gas pipeline into the Mesabi Iron Range; p. (1004) 86,600 (c.) (1990) 009,371 (met. a. with Superior).

Dulwich, residtl. sub. in bor. of Southwark, Greater London, **Eng.**; village character with lge. park and public school.

Dumaujváros, t., **Hungary**; new t. built from v. of Dunapentele; iron and steel wks.; paper inds., engin.

Dumbarton, royal burgh, l. gov. dist., Strathclyde Reg., **Scot.**; on N. bank of R. Clyde, 19 km below Glasgow; shipbldg., valve and tube-mkg., iron and brassware; p. (1991) 21,962 (t.), (1993) 78,500 (dist.).

Dum-Dum, t., W. Bengal, **India**; ammunition; impt. airpt.; p. (1991) 149,965 (N.), 232,811 (S.).

Dumfries, royal burgh, Nithsdale, **Scot.**; on R. Nith, 16 km from Solway F.; p. (1991) 32,136.

Dumfries and Galloway Region, l. gov. reg., **Scot.**; occupies W. half of Southern Uplands; drained by S. flowing rivers to Solway F.; sparse rural p.; a. 6,369 km²; p. (1993) 147,900.

Dumfriesshire, former co., **Scot.**; now part of Dumfries and Galloway Reg.

Dumyât, t., Lower Egypt; on main distributary of R. Nile delta; cotton; p. (1986) 113,000.

Dunbar, royal burgh, E. Lothian, **Scot.**; sm. fishing pt.; Cromwell's victory 1650; p. (1991) 6,518.

Dunbartonshire, former co., **Scot.**; now part of Strathclyde Reg.

Dunblane, mkt. burgh, Stirling, **Scot.**; on Allan Water, 8 km from Stirling; Gothic cath. now used as par. church; p. (1991) 7,368.

Dundalk, t., cap. of Co. Louth, **R.o.I.**; harbour, rly. ctr.; engin., footwear, tobacco, brewing; p. (1986) 26,669.

Dundee, c., spt., royal burgh, l. gov. dist., Tayside Reg., **Scot.**; on F. of Tay, 80 km N. Edinburgh; jute mnf., engin., computers, refrigerators, clocks, watches, preserves, linoleum; publishing., univ.; p. (1991) 158,981 (c.), (1993) 170,120 (dist.).

Dundonald, t. E. of Belfast, **N. Ireland**; p. (1991) 12,943.

Dunedin, c., Otago, S.I., **N.Z.**; univ.; wool and dairy produce; named after the old name of Edinburgh; p. (1991) 116,577.

Dunfermline, royal burgh, l. gov. dist., Fife Reg., **Scot.**; 22 km E. of Alloa; linen, rubber gds., synthetic fibre; birthplace of Charles I and Andrew Carnegie; cap. of Scot. 1057–93; p. (1991) 55,083 (t.), (1993) 130,150 (dist.).

Dungannon, mkt. t., l. gov. dist., **N. Ireland**; linen, bricks; p. (1991) 9,190 (t.), 45,428 (dist.).

Dungarvan, t. Co. Waterford, **R.o.I.**; spt., mkt. t.; leather processing; p. (1986) 6,849.

Dungeness, headland of shingle, Kent, **Eng.**; 16 km S.E. of Rye; two Magnox nuclear power stas.; linked by power cable to France 1961.

Dunkeld, t., Perth and Kinross, **Scot.**; on R. Tay at entrance to Strathmore; cath., ecclesiastical ctr. in 9th century; tourist resort; p. (1991) 1,227 (with Birnam).

Dunkirk (Dunkerque), spt., Nord dep., **France**; strong fort; gd. harbour and tr.; fisheries, shipbld., oil refining; steel mill; scene of evacuation of B.E.F. 1940; p. (1990) 71,071 (c.), 192,852 (met. a).

Dun Laoghaire (Kingstown), t., Dublin, **R.o.I.**; spt., mail packet sta., fishing; ferry to Eng.; p. (1986) 54,715.

Dunmanway, t., Cork, **R.o.I.**; on R. Brandon; tweeds, blankets; p. (1986) 1,382.

Dunmow, Great, mkt. t., Uttlesford, Essex, **Eng.**; on R. Chelmer; 16 km N.W. of Chelmsford.

Dunmow, Little, v., 3 km E. of Great Dunmow; Uttlesford, Essex, **Eng.**; historic Dunmow Flitch (side of bacon); bacon factory closed (1983).

Dunmurry, t. Lisburn, **N. Ireland**; engin.; p. (1991) 12,771.

Dunoon, burgh, Argyll and Bute, **Scot.**; on N. side of F. of Clyde, anc. cas.; holiday resort; p. (1991) 9,038.

Duns, burgh, Berwick, **Scot.**; agr. and allied inds.; mkt. t.; cas.; p. (1991) 2,444.

Dunsinane, hill, Sidlaws, **Scot.**; nr. Perth; alt. 309 m; referred to by Shakespeare in *Macbeth*.

Dunstable, t., South Beds., **Eng.**; on N. edge of Chiltern Hills, 6 km W. of Luton; motor vehicles, engin., cement, rubber, and plastic gds.; p. (1981) 30,912.

Duque de Caxias, t., **Brazil**; Brazil's largest oil refinery, petro-chemicals; Alfa-Romeo car plant; p. (1991) 664,643.

Durance, R., S.E. **France**; trib. of Rhône; rapid current, 347 km long; provides irrigation and hydroelec. power.

Durango, c., cap. of D. st., **México**; cath.; silver, gold, copper, iron-ore; p. (1990) 414,015.

Durango, st., N.W. **Mexico**; mng., agr., cotton, wheat; a. 109,484 km²; p. (1990) 1,352,156.

Durant, t., S. Okla, **USA**; cotton gins and compresses, cottonseed oil; p. (1980) 11,972.

Durban, c., **S. Africa**; on Durban Bay; ch. comm. c. of Natal; exp. coal, manganese, wool, hides; oil and sugar refining, chemicals, textiles, engin.; oil pipeline to Johannesburg; univ.; main pt. and seaside resort; p. (1985) 982,075.

Düren, t., N. Rhine–Westphalia, **Germany**; on R. Ruhr 37 km S.W. of Cologne; rly. ctr.; iron and steel wks., vehicles; p. (1986) 84,100.

Durgapur, t., W. Bengal, **India**; site of barrage on Damodar R.; p. (1991) 426,000.

Durham, c., co. t., l. gov. dist., Durham, N.E. **Eng.**; sited within a meander of R. Wear; cath. cas., univ.; carpets, organ mftg., confectionery; p. (1993) 88,300.

Durham, non-met. co., N.E. **Eng.**; between Rs. Tyne and Tees; stretches from attractive Pennine moorland in W. to coalfield and industl. a. with many sm. ts. in E.; borders the N. Sea; a. 2,437 km²; p. (1993) 607,500.

Durham, t., N.C., **USA**; tobacco ind., textiles; univ.; p. (1990) 136,611.

Durrës (Durazzo), ch. spt., **Albania**; on Adriatic; pt. for Tirana; tobacco ind., plastics; tourism; p. (1990) 86,900.

Dursley, t., Gloucs., **Eng.**; 21 km S.W. of Gloucester; engin., agr. machin.; 18th cent. mkt. house; p. (1981) 12,626.

Dushanbe, c., cap. of **Tajikistan**; univ.; industl. and agr. ctr.; rly. junc.; earlier called Stalinabad; 1989 ethnic unrest; p. (1986) 565,000.

Düsseldorf, c., cap. of N. Rhine-Westphalia, **Germany**; on R. Rhine, 32 km N. of Cologne; admin. and cultural ctr.; art and medical academies; iron, steel, machin., soap, cars, paper, chemical inds.; impt. trans-shipment pt.; p. (1990) 576,700.

Dust Bowl, region, **USA**; name applied to great plains on E. flank of Rocky Mtns.; subject to severe soil erosion by wind, particularly in drought years (1933, 1936) due to destruction of natural vegetation by over-grazing or by excessive ploughing.

Dutch Harbour, t., Unalaska I., Aleutian gr., N. Pac. Oc.; strategic American naval base.

Dvina or Northern Dvina, R., **Russia**; flows to White Sea at Arkhangelsk, formed by the junction of Rs. Sukhona and Vychegda at Kotlas; connected by canal with Neva and Volga; used for timber transport; 744 km long.

Dvina or Western Dvina, R., **Russia**, **Latvia**; rises in Valdai Hills nr. sources of Volga and Dnieper, flows through Latvia to G. of Riga; connected by canal to Berezina and Dnieper; c. 1,016 km long.

Dwyfor, l. gov. dist., Gwynedd, **Wales**; Lleyn penin. and ts. of Pwhelli, Criccieth and Porthmadog; p. (1993) 27,100.

Dyfed, co., S.W. **Wales**; inc. former cos. of Cardiganshire, Carmarthenshire and Pembroke; upland a. crossed by valleys of Teifi and Towy Rs.; stock rearing and fattening; tourism impt. around cst.; industl. in S.E.; a. 5,765 km²; p. (1993) 351,500.

Dzandzhikau. *See* Ordzhonikidze.

Dzerzhinsk, c., **Russia**; R. pt. of Oka; chemicals (fertilisers, explosives); p. (1989) 602,000.

Dzhalil, t., **Russia**; new t. 48 km N.E. of Almetyevsk to serve new oilfield there.

Dzhambul, c., **Kazakhstan**; on Talas R. and on Turk-Sib rly.; chemicals, food-processing; p. (1990) 310,900.

Dzhezkazgan, t., **Kazakhstan;** 560 km W. of L. Balkhash; copper-mines; manganese ore nearby.

Dzierzoniow (Reichenbach), t., Walbrzych, S.W. **Poland;** mnf. ctr.; textiles, machin., elec. equipment; formerly in Germany; p. (1989) 37,908.

Dzungaria, inland basin, Xinjiang prov., N.W. **China;** lies between Tien-Shan highlands of Soviet–Chinese frontier and Altai mtns.; former historic kingdom of Zungaria.

E

Ealing, outer bor., Greater London, **Eng.;** comprising former bors. of Acton, Ealing, and Southall; p. (1993) 285,600.

Earl's Court, residtl. a., London, **Eng.;** Bor. of Kensington and Chelsea, contains E.C. exhibition hall.

Earn R., Perth, and Kinross, **Scot.;** issues from Loch Earn (10 km long) and flows into Tay R.; 74 km long.

Easington, l. gov. dist., Durham, **Eng.;** colly. closed 1993; now part of Peterlee new t.; p. (1993) 98,700.

Easington, v., Humberside, **Eng.;** nr. Hull; natural gas terminal.

East Anglia, comprises Norfolk and Suffolk, **Eng.;** former Anglo-Saxon kingdom; one of Britain's most productive agr. regions.

East Anglian Heights, hills, extend S.W. to N.E. across N.E. Hertfordshire, N. Essex, and S.W. Suffolk, **Eng.;** chalk overlain by glacial clays and sands; smooth, rolling surface; region of lge. farms and lge. fields, mixed farms mainly grain; rarely exceed 180 m.

East Bergholt, v., Suffolk, **Eng.;** birthplace of Constable.

Eastbourne, t., l. gov. dist., East Sussex, **Eng.;** on S. cst. to E. of Beachy Head; seaside resort; p. (1993) 86,800.

East Cambridgeshire, l. gov. dist., Cambs., **Eng.;** a. N.E. of Cambridge inc. Ely; p. (1993) 62,100.

East Cape, extreme N.E. point of Asia; on Chukchi peninsula, **Russia;** Russian name Cape Dezhnova.

East Cape, extreme E. point of **N.Z.;** named by Cook on his first voyage in 1769.

East Chicago, t., Ind., **USA;** L. Michigan; iron and steel wks., oil refining; p. (1980) 39,786.

East Cleveland, t., Ohio, **USA;** residtl.; p. (1990) 33,096.

East Coast Bays, bor., N.I., **N.Z.;** series of settlements on bays N. of Auckland; amalgamated 1954; p. (1987) 31,600.

East Dereham, t., Breckland, Norfolk, **Eng.;** 22 km W. of Norwich; agr. implements; p. (1981) 11,845.

East Devon, l. gov. dist., Devon, **Eng.;** Exmouth, Sidmouth and Seaton on cst. and inland to Honiton and Ottery St. Mary; p. (1993) 120,300.

East Dorset, l. gov. dist., Dorset, **Eng.;** rural a. based on Wimborne Minster; p. (1993) 79,800.

Easter Island, S. Pac. Oc., 3,760 km W. of Chile; various theories to explain origin of gigantic statues; p. (1985) 2,000.

East Grinstead, t., West Sussex, **Eng.;** in ctr. of Weald, 14 km W. of Tunbridge Wells; famous hospital for plastic surgery; p. (1981) 22,263.

East Ham. *See* Newham.

East Hampshire, l. gov. dist., Hants., **Eng.;** stretches from Alton to Petersfield; p. (1993) 106,400.

East Hartford, t., Conn., **USA;** industl.; p. (1980) 52,563.

East Hertfordshire, l. gov. dist., Herts., **Eng.;** lge a. inc. Ware, Bishop's Stortford, Hertford and Sawbridgeworth; p. (1993) 119,600.

East Indies, name commonly applied to Is. between S.E. Asia and N. Australia, variously known as Malay archipelago, Malaysia, Indonesia.

East Kilbride, t., l. gov. dist., Strathclyde Reg., **Scot.;** 11 km S.S.E. of Glasgow; new t. 1947; lge. agr. machin., aero engines, engin., elec. gds., seawater distillation plant; knitwear, clothing; p. (1991) 70,422 (t.), (1993) 85,360 (dist.).

East Lansing, t., Mich., **USA;** residtl.; univ.; p. (1980) 51,392.

Eastleigh, t., l. gov. dist., Hants., **Eng.;** rly. engin., many new inds.; p. (1993) 109,600.

East Lindsey, l. gov. dist., Lincs., **Eng.;** lge. a. on E. cst. inc. Louth, Mablethorpe, Horncastle, Woodhall Spa, Skegness and Alford; p. (1993) 120,800.

East London, spt., C. Prov., **S. Africa;** at mouth of Buffalo R.; holiday resort; trading ctr.; inds. inc. car assembly, textiles, engin.; titanium deposits nearby; p. (1985) 193,819 (met. a.).

East Lothian (Haddington), former co., l. gov. dist., **Scot.;** part of Lothian Reg.; p. (1993) 35,640.

East Main, R., Quebec, **Canada;** flows into James Bay; 432 km long.

East Northamptonshire, l. gov. dist., Northants., **Eng.;** stretches from Oundle to Irthlingborough, Rushden, Raunds and Higham Ferrers; p. (1993) 69,300.

Easton, t., Penns., **USA;** on Delaware R.; rly. ctr., coal, steel, machin., p. (1980) 26,027.

East Orange, t., N.J., **USA;** residtl. sub. of New York; p. (1990) 73,552.

East Pakistan. *See* Bangladesh.

East Point, t., Ga., **USA;** textiles, fertilisers; p. (1980) 37,486.

East Providence, t., Rhode I., **USA;** textiles, machin.; p. (1980) 50,980.

East Retford, t., Bassetlaw, Notts., **Eng.;** on R. Idle, 10 km E. of Worksop; rubber, wire ropes, engin.; p. (1981) 19,348.

East Riding, Yorkshire. *See* Yorkshire.

East River, tidal strait about 26 km long and 180–1,200 m wide; separates the bors. of Manhattan and Bronx from the bors. of Queens and Brooklyn, N.Y., **USA.**

East St. Louis, t., R. pt., Ill., **USA;** on Mississippi R.; lge stockyards, meat-packing, aluminium, chemicals; p. (1980) 55,200.

East Staffordshire, l. gov. dist., Staffs., **Eng.;** stretches from Uttoxeter to Burton-on-Trent; p. (1993) 98,300.

East Sussex, non-met. co., S.E. **Eng.;** mainly rural, urban growth on cst., where resorts, retirement and dormitory ts. for London, inc. Brighton, Hastings and Eastbourne; crossed by S. Downs in N. terminating at Beachy Head, Ashdown Forest in N.; a. 1,795 km²; p. (1993) 722,200.

East Timor, prov., Indonesia; Port. terr. until 1975; sovereignty claimed by Indonesia and territory seized by force; mtnous; underdeveloped; cap. Dili; a. 14,693 km²; p. (1985) 2,294,000.

Eastwood, t., Broxtowe, Notts., **Eng.;** birthplace of D. H. Lawrence; coal; p. (1981) 11,700.

Eastwood, l. gov. dist., Strathclyde Reg., **Scot.;** part of Central Clydeside conurb.; p. (1993) 60,930.

East Yorkshire (formerly **North Wolds**), l. gov. dist., Humberside, **Eng.;** lge. a. inc. Pocklington, Driffield and Bridlington; p. (1993) 87,800.

Eau Claire, t., Wis., **USA;** on Chippewa R.; agr. mkt.; univ. food processing, varied mnfs.; p. (1990) 56,856.

Ebbw Vale, t., Blaenau Gwent, Gwent, **Wales;** 27 km N.W. of Newport; coal, iron, tinplate, bricks, pipes, precast concrete; some steel wks. to close; p. (1981) 24,422.

Eberswalde, t., Brandenburg, **Germany;** N.E. of Berlin; iron, wood, and cardboard wks., chemicals; p. (1981) 53,183.

Ebro, ch. R. of N.E. **Spain;** flows to Mediterranean from Cantabrian Mtns.; feeds hydroelectric plants, irrigation, esp. around Zaragoza; 928 km long.

Eccles, Gtr. Manchester, **Eng.;** 6 km W. of Manchester; chemicals, oil refining, engin.; p. (1981) 37,166.

Echo L., Tasmania, **Australia;** used to store water for hydroelectric power.

Echuca, t., Victoria, **Australia;** major inland pt. on Murray R. in mid 19th century; in 1970s original pt. and bldgs. restored.

Écija, t., Seville, **Spain;** olive oil, wine, pottery; the Roman Astigi; p. (1981) 34,619.

Ecrins, mtn. peak, S.E. **France;** hgst. point of massif du Pelvoux and Dauphiné Alps; alt. 4,106 m.

Ecuador, rep., **S. America;** on equatorial Pac. cst., bounded by Colombia to N. and Peru to W. and S.; inc. Galapagos Is. in Pac. Oc.; lowland to E. and W. of central Andes; climate temperate in Andes and hot and humid in lowlands; comm. economy mainly agr. with impt. exp. of bananas, coffee, cocoa; petroleum impt. (68 per cent of exports); pipeline across Andes to pt. of Esmeraldas; communications difficult but vital for economic development; attempts to control illegal narcotics exp.; major pts. Guayaquil and Manta; official language Spanish; cap. Quito; a. inc. Galapagos Is. 454,752 km²; p. (1991) 10,781,000.

Edam, t., N. Holland, **Neth.;** on cst. IJsselmeer; cheese, tool mftg.; p. (1993) 25,242.

Eday, I., Orkney Is., **Scot.;** the Ocelli of Ptolemy; p. (1991) 166.

Eddystone, rock with lighthouse, Eng. Channel; S.W. of Plymouth.

Ede, t., Gelderland, **Neth.;** livestock; pianos; p. (1993) 97,230.

Edea, t., pt., **Cameroon;** aluminium smelting based on nearby hydroelectric power plant.

Eden, Vale of, fertile belt in Cumbria, **Eng.;** between barren hills of Pennines and L. Dist.; occupied by R. Eden; mkt. ts. Appleby and Penrith; now forms l. gov. dist. **Eden,** inc, Penrith, Alston and Appleby; p. (1993) 46,800.

Eder, R., Germany; joins Fulda R. S. of Kassel; lldcr dain lgst. in Germany.

Edessa (Edhessa), t., N.E. **Greece;** agr. tr. ctr.; the anc. Ægae, burial place of Macedonian kings; p. (1981) 16,642.

Edgehill, ridge, 24 km S. of Warwick, **Eng.;** scene of first battle of civil war, 1642.

Edinburgh, c., cap. of **Scot.,** l. gov. dist., Lothian Reg.; royal burgh on F. of Forth; univ., cas.; palace (Holyrood); printing, publishing, brewing, electronics equipment, rubber gds.; Edinburgh Festival in August; Leith, with docks is joined to E.; p. (1991) 401,910 (c.), (1993) 441,620 (dist.).

Edirne, t. and prov., **Turkey;** in Thrace, on R. Maritsa; comm. ctr. with tr. in wine, tobacco, silk, perfume; the anc. Adrianople, named after the emperor Hadrian, later cap. of Ottoman sultans 1366–1453; p. (1985) 86,909, (1990) 404,599 (prov.).

Edmonton, c., cap. of Alberta, **Canada;** fastgrowing c. (119 km²) on both sides of N. Saskatchewan R.; high-level bridge links Strathcona; major military ctr.; univ.; international air ctr.; oilfields and farming; oil and chemical inds.; p. (1986) 573,982 (c.), 785,465 (met. a.).

Edremit, t., Balikesir, N.W. **Turkey;** cereals, opium; silverwk.; p. (1985) 30,159.

Edward, L., on frontier of Uganda and Zaire, one of the sources of R. Nile; occupies Gr. Rift Valley; alt. c. 900 m, 70km long, breadth 51km; salt, fishing, wildlife.

Eger, t., N.E. **Hungary;** mkt. t. in wine producing region; mediaeval fortress t.; p. (1989) 67,000.

Egersund, pt., S. cst. **Norway;** fishing; mentioned in Norwegian sagas.

Egham, t., Runnymede, Surrey, **Eng.;** on R. Thames, nr. Staines; contains field of Runnymede; residtl.; p. (1981) 27,817.

Egmont, mtn., N.I., **N.Z.;** extinct volcano; alt. 2,501 m.

Egremont, mkt. t., Cumbria, **Eng.;** 10 km S. of Whitehaven; limestone; former iron ore mng.

Egypt, Arab Republic of, indep. st., N.E. corner **Africa;** member of Federation of Arab Reps.; 96 per cent a. is desert except Nile valley and delta where 95 per cent of p. live; agr. depends on annual rise of Nile waters and irrigation; cereals, sugarcane, vegetables, fruit; cotton main cash crop; phosphates; oilfield in Sinai and recent finds offshore in G. of Suez and in Western Desert; nat. gas since 1974; 6 oil refineries; major port development on Red Sea to handle mineral exp.; textiles account for ⅓ of manuf. output; cap. Cairo; Aswan High Dam has produced problems; (1) silting up of reservoir (L. Nasser) behind dam; (2) reduction in fertilising silt deposits in lower Nile valley; (3) erosion of Nile delta itself; (4) reduction of fish p. in E. Med.; a. 999,740 km²; p. (1993) 56,430,000.

Eider, R., **Germany;** separates Holstein from Schleswig; flows into N. Sea; 125 m. long.

Eifel, plateau of volcanic rocks, **Germany;** lies N. of R. Moselle, forming W. edge of Rhine gorge between Koblenz and Bonn; formerly cultivated, now largely woodland and moorland; farming in valleys; rises to just over 600 m.

Eiger, mtn., one of the hgst. peaks of the Bernese Oberland, **Switzerland;** famous for steep N. wall; alt. 3,978 m.

Eigg, I., Inner Hebrides, **Scot.;** 24 km S.W. of Mallaig; basaltic rocks on cst.; rises to 393 m; p. (1991) 141.

Eilat, new spt., Negev, **Israel;** on G. of Aqaba;

growing tourist tr.; copper at Timna; oil pipeline from Ashdod (1970).

Eildon Hills, Roxburgh, **Scot.;** S. of Melrose; hgst. point 422 m.

Eindhoven, c., N. Brabant, **Neth.;** electronic equipment, motor vehicles, tobacco and textile inds.; technical univ.; p. (1993) 195,267 (c.), 390,813 (met. a.).

Eire. See **Ireland, Republic of.**

Eisenach, t., Erfurt, **Germany;** on R. Hörsel, at foot of Thuringian forest; ctr. of Werra potash field; cars, machin., textiles; birthplace of J. S. Bach; p. (1981) 50,674.

Eisenerz Alps, mtn. range, **Austria;** most N. range of Alps, overlooking Danube valley between Linz and Vienna; impt. iron-ore deposits; alt. from 1,800–2,700 m.

Eisenhüttenstadt, t., Brandenburg, **Germany;** iron smelting; terminus of Oder-Spree canal; p. (1989) 52,393.

Eisleben, t., Saxony-Anhalt, **Germany;** machin., copper and silver-mng. ctr.; birthplace of Luther; p. (1989) 26,530.

Ekibastuz, t., **Kazakhstan;** 120 km S.W. of Pavlodar; ctr. of rapidly developing mng. a. coal, gold, metals; p. (1990) 137,000.

El Aaiun, pt., **Western Sahara;** main pt. for exp. of phosphates; p. (1982) 96,784.

El Alamein, v., **Egypt;** in Libyan Desert 96 km S.W. of Alexandria, scene of Allied victory, second world war; oilfield nearby; terminal nr. Sidi Abd el-Rahman.

Elan, R. Powys, **Wales;** rises on S.E. sides of Plynlimon, flows into R. Wye; lower valley contains series of 4 lge. reservoirs, capacity 45,460 million litres; ch. source of water for Birmingham.

Eläzig, t. and prov., E. **Turkey;** dam and hydroelec. project at Keban, 48 km to N.W. at confluence of E. and W. branches of Euphrates; p. (1990) 498,225 (prov.), 218,121 (t.).

Elba, I., off Tuscan cst., **Italy;** iron ore, wine, marble, salt; ch. t. Portoferraio; Napoleon's first exile here; a. 363 km²; p. (1981) 10,755.

Elbe (Labe), R., in **Czech Rep.** and **Germany;** rises in Riesengebirge and flows into N. Sea at Cuxhaven; navigable for 840 km of total l. of 1,160 km; connected with Rhine and Weser Rs. by Mittelland canal.

Elbert, mtn., Col., **USA;** hgst. peak of Rocky Mtns. in USA, 4,401 m.

Elblag or Elbing, spt. and prov., N. **Poland;** shipbldg., machin., vehicles; p. (1989) 125,778 (t.), 475,900 (prov.).

El Boulaïda (Blida), t., **Algeria;** agr. ctr.; citrus fruits; p. (1983) 191,314.

Elbruz Mt., Caucasus, **Russia;** hgst. in Europe (5,636 m), over-topping Mont Blanc by 822 m; twin volcanic peaks.

Elburz, mtn. range, N. **Iran;** bordering on Caspian Sea; hgst. peak, Demavend, 5,642 m.

Elche, t., Alicante, **Spain;** palm groves; oil, soap, footwear; p. (1991) 181,192.

El Dar-el-Beida (Casablanca), c., **Morocco;** pt. on Atl. Oc.; artificial harbour; fish canning, textiles; exp. phosphate; p. (1982) 2,139,204.

Eldorado, radium mine, N.W. Terr., **Canada;** on E. shore of Gr. Bear Lake nr. Arctic Circle; produces 40 per cent of world's radium, sent to Pt. Hope, Ontario, for refining.

El Djezair (Algiers), pt., cap. c. of **Algeria;** old t. surmounted by 16th cent. Casbâh (fortress); univ.; exp. wine, citrus fruit, iron ore; oil refining at Maison Carrée; airpt. at Maison Blanche, 16 km E. of c.; p. (1987), 1,507,000.

Elektrenai, t., **Lithuania;** new township nr. Vievis, at site of thermal power sta. (1990) 15,800

Elektrostal, t., **Russia;** 56 km E. of Moscow; steel, engin.; p. (1989) 152,000.

Elephanta I., Bombay Harbour, **India;** Brahmanic caves with monolithic carvings.

Elephant Butte Dam, N.M., **USA;** on Rio Grande; built to control flood water; lake, a. 115 km² supplies irrigation water to 2,020 km² in N.M. and Texas, water also supplied to Mexico.

El Ferrol del Caudillo, spt., **Spain;** on N.W. cst.; fortfd., fishing; p. (1981) 91,764.

Elgin, royal burgh, Moray, **Scot.;** pt. Lossiemouth; woollens, whisky; ruins anc. cath.; p. (1991) 19,027.

Elgin, t., Ill., **USA;** watches, electrical equipment; p. (1990) 77,010.

El Giza, t. and prov., **Egypt;** on Nile, sub. of Cairo; nr.

pyramids of Khufu (Cheops), Khafra (Chephren), and the Sphinx; film ind.; p. (1990) 2,156,000 (t.) (1991) 4,182,000 (prov.).

Elgon Mt., extinct volcano, bdy. of **Kenya** and **Uganda**; 4,300 m; cave dwellings on slopes.

Elie and Earlsferry, burgh, North East Fife, **Scot.**; summer resort; p. (1991) 903.

Elisabethville. *See* **Lubumbashi.**

Elizabeth, c., N.J., **USA**; univ.; sewing machines, oil refining, cars, aircraft components; now inc. in Newark; p. (1990) 110,002.

Elk I., Nat. Park, **Canada**; animal reserve, tourism.

El Khârga, oasis, Libyan desert, **Egypt**, 136 km S.W. of Asyût; site of New Valley Project for irrigation.

Elkhart, t., Ind., **USA**; E. of Chicago; paper, machin.; elec. equipment, musical instruments; p. (1984) 43,100.

Elk Mtns., W. Col., **USA**; highest point Castle Peak, 4,305 m.

Elland, t., West Yorks., **Eng.**; on R. Calder, 5 km S.E. of Halifax; textiles; p. (1981) 18,011.

Ellesmere, agr. dist., S.I., **N.Z.**; on Canterbury Plain nr. Christchurch.

Ellesmere, mkt. t., Shrops., **Eng.**; nearby lake; tourism.

Ellesmere I., extreme N. of Arctic **Canada**; barren uninhabited; a. 106,200 km².

Ellesmere Port, t., l. gov. dist., N.W. Cheshire, **Eng.**; on Manchester Ship Canal and 14 km S.S.E. of Liverpool; metal mftg., paper, engin., oil refineries; cars; expanded t.; with **Neston** forms l. gov. dist.; p. (1993) 81,500 (dist.).

Elliot Lake, t., N. Ont., **Canada**; ctr. of uranium mines; p. (1981) 16,723.

Ellice Is. *See* **Tuvalu I.**

Ellis I., N.Y. harbour, **USA**; served as ch. immigration ctr., 1892–1943.

Ellon, burgh, Gordon, **Scot.**; on R. Ythan; p. (1991) 8,627.

El Mahalla el Kubra, t., **Egypt**; N. of Cairo on Nile delta; textile ctr.; p. (1986) 358,844.

Elmbridge, l. gov. dist., Surrey, **Eng.**; close to Gtr. London; inc. Esher, Walton and Weybridge; p. (1993) 117,300.

Elmira, t., N.Y., **USA**; rly. gds., farm implements; famous as burial place of Mark Twain; p. (1990) 33,724.

El Misti, mtn., S. **Peru**; dormant volcano with snow cap; alt. 5,846 m.

Elmshorn, t., **Germany**; N.W. of Hamburg; shipbldg.; p. (1986) 41,500.

El Paso, c., Texas, **USA**; on E. bank Rio Grande opposite Ciudad Juárez (Mexico); natural gas distribution, oil refining, metallurgy; tourism; p. (1990) 515,342 (c.), 592,000 (met. a.).

El Salvador, rep., on Pac. cst. of **Central America**; bounded by Guatemala to W. and Honduras to N. and E.; comprises 14 administrative departments; temperate volcanic uplands, hot humid coastal lowlands; comm. economy mainly agr., especially coffee, also developing comm. fisheries and iron and steel ind.; electric power from dam across Lempa R.; well-developed transport system, inc. Pan-American Highway; pt. at Acajutla and airport at Ilopango; member of Central American Common Market; protracted guerrilla warfare during much of the 1980s; cap. San Salvador; a. 21,331 km²; p. (1992) 5,047,925.

El Segundo, t., Cal., **USA**; lge. oil refinery; assembly of aircraft components; p. (1980) 13,752.

Elsinore. *See* **Helsingør.**

Elstow, v., Beds., **Eng.**; the birthplace of John Bunyan.

Elstree, t., Hertsmere, Herts., **Eng.**; 6 km W. of Barnet; residtl.; films, lt. engin., silk hosiery.

El Teniente, Andean t., central **Chile**; copper mng. and smelting; p. 11,761.

Eluru, t., Andhra Pradesh, **India**; cotton, carpets, hosiery, oil; p. (1991) 212,918.

Elvas, mkt. t., **Portugal**; on Guadiana R.; plums, olives, jams; cath.; once strongly fortfd.; p. (1981) 12,880.

Ely, t., Cambridge, **Eng.**; on S. fringe of Fens; mkt., cath.; agr. ctr.; p. (1981) 10,268.

Ely, I. of. *See* **Cambridgeshire.**

Elyria, t., Ohio, **USA**; mftg.; p. (1990) 56,746.

Emba, R., **Kazakhstan**; rises in Urals, flows S.W. to Caspian Sea; crosses productive Ural–Emba oilfield; 608 km long.

Emden, t., Lower Saxony, **Germany**; impt. N. Sea pt. nr. mouth of R. Ems and on Dortmund–Ems and Ems–Jade canals; exp. coal and iron from Ruhr; shipyards, fisheries; p. (1986) 49,600.

Emene, t., **Nigeria**; nr. Enugu; steel plant; cement.

Emilia-Romagna, region, N. **Italy**; S. of Po R.; divided into 8 provs.; fertile agr. a.; a. 22,124 km²; p. (1992) 3,920,223.

Emmen, t., Drenthe, **Neth.**; 48 km S.E. of Groningen; elec. machin., ball bearings, tinplate, iron wks.; p. (1993) 93,246.

Emmental, dist., **Switzerland**; dairy produce, especially cheese.

Empoli, t., Tuscany, **Italy**; on R. Arno; textile mnfs., glass; p. (1981) 44,961.

Ems, R., N. **Germany**; rises in Teutoburger Wald, flows N. to N. Sea at Emden; 333 km long.

Emscher, R., **Germany**; rises in Sauerland, flows W. through heart of Ruhr coalfield to enter R. Rhine at Hamborn; canalised for most of its course; very highly polluted; 88 km long.

Encarnación, pt., cap. of Itapuá dep. S.E. **Paraguay**; on Paraná R.; exp. timber, maté, tobacco, cotton, hides; p. (1984) 31,445.

Enderby Land, Australian terr., S. of C. of Good Hope, **Antarctica**.

Enfield, outer bor. Greater London **Eng**; comprising Edmonton, Enfield, and Southgate; p. (1993) 261,800.

Enfield, t., Conn., **USA**; mftg.; p. (1980) 42,695.

Engadine, **Switzerland**; upper valley of Inn R., health resort; ch. t. St. Moritz; Swiss Nat. Park.

Enggano, I., Sumatra, **Indonesia**; sparse p.; hunting, fishing, shifting cultivation.

Engels. *See* **Pokrovsk**

England, southern and lgst political div. of U.K.; bounded by Wales on W., by Scot. on N. and separated from continent of Europe by English Channel and North Sea; highly industl., circa 80 per cent of p. live in urban areas; major trading nation through main pts. London, Liverpool, Southampton; increasing contrast between prosperous S. and depressed N. and W.; very varied geology and topography produce contrasts in landscape, matched by climatic variability; increasingly attractive as tourist area although urban and agr. pressures on rural countryside cause concern in such a densely populated cty.; excellent road and rail network; rich and varied cultural heritage and numerous historic bldgs.; cap. London; a. 130,368 km²; p. (1993) 48,532,700.

Englewood, t., Col., **USA**; sub. of Denver; glasshouses; p. (1980) 30,021.

Englewood, t., N.J., **USA**; elevators, leather gds.; p. (1980) 23,701.

English Channel (La Manche), narrow sea separating England from France; extends from Strait of Dover to Land's End in Cornwall; length 480 km, greatest width 248 km.; to be crossed by Channel Tunnel (1993); *See* **Cheriton**.

Enham-Alamein, Hants., **Eng.**; rehabilitation ctr. for disabled ex-service men; 4 km N. of Andover; lt. inds.

Enid, t., Okla., **USA**; univ.; ironwks., farm implements; wheat mkt.; p. (1980) 50,363.

Enna (Castrogiovanni), t., Sicily, **Italy**; sulphurmines; famous for its connection with the Proserpine legend; p. (1981) 27,838.

Ennepetal, t., N. Rhine–Westphalia, **Germany**; t. created 1949 with merging of Milspe and Voerde; iron, machin.; p. (1986) 33,700.

Ennerdale Water, L., Cumbria, **Eng.**

Enniscorthy, mkt. t., Wexford, **R.o.I.**; cath.; p. (1986) 4,483.

Enniskillen, t., Fermanagh, **N. Ireland**; brewing, nylon mftg., meat processing; p. (1991) 11,436.

Enschede, c., Overijssel, **Neth.**; textile ctr.; technical univ.; with Hengelo forms met. a.; p. (1993) 147,349 (c.), 253,599 (met. a.).

Ensenada, t., **Mexico**; spt., exp. cotton; fishing and fish processing; p. (1990) 260,905.

Entebbe, t., **Uganda**; on L. Victoria; univ.; cotton ginning; airport; p. (1991) 41,638.

Entre Rios, prov., **Argentina**; between Paraná and Uruguay Rs.; wheat, linseed, livestock; cap. Paraná; a. 76,216 km²; p. (1991) 1,021,042.

Enugu, cap. of E. prov., **Nigeria**; coal; cloth mill; p. (est. 1983) 228,000; (1991) 3,161,255 (state).

Epernay, t., on S. bank of Marne, **France**; champagne ctr.; p. (1982) 28,876.

Ephesus, anc. Ionian c., in what is now **Turkey**, S. of Izmir; sacked by Goths A.D. 262; excavations.

Epinal, t., cap. of Vosges dep., **France**; on Moselle R.; textiles, printing, liqueur; p. (1990) 39,480.

Epirus, dist., N.W. **Greece**; a. 9,552 km²; p. (1991) 339,210.

Epping Forest, Essex, **Eng.**; forest a. N.E. of London free to public (opened by Queen Victoria 1882); formerly part of royal hunting forest; also l. gov. dist., inc. Chigwell, Waltham Abbey and Ongar; p. (1993) 118,200.

Epsom and Ewell, ts., l. gov. dist., Surrey, **Eng.**; 29 km S.W. of London; residtl., racecourse; p. (1993) 68,800.

Epworth, v., Humberside, **Eng.**; birthplace of John Wesley.

Equatorial Guinea, unitary state, W. **Africa**; former Spanish col.; indep. 1968; comprises 2 provs.; Rio Muni (mainland and ls. of Corisco, Elobey Grande, Elobey Chico) and Biako (Is. of Biako and Pagalu); narrow coastal plain and dissected upland plateau (600 m) economy almost entirely based on agr. and timber; exploration for oil; cap. Malabo on Biako I.; a. 28,051 km²; p. (1990) 417,000.

Erbil, t., **Iraq**; comm. ctr.; rly. terminus; p. (1985) 333,903.

Erebus, mtn., active volcano, Victoria Land, **Antarctica**; alt. 4,027 m.

Erewash, l. gov. dist., Derbys., **Eng.**; a. close to Nottingham inc. Ilkeston and Long Eaton; p. (1993) 107,200.

Erfurt, admin. dist., **Germany**; a. 7,322 km²; p. (1983) 1,238,200.

Erfurt, c., **Germany**; on Gera R.; cap. Thuringia *Land*; cath., ctr. of mkt. gardening and seed-growing dist., textiles, machin., foodstuffs, footwear, radios, heavy engin.; p. (1990) 207,200.

Ericht, loch, **Scot.**; in central Grampians; 25 km long; hydroelec. scheme.

Erie, c., N.W. Penns., **USA**; pt. on L. Erie; coal, iron, grain, petroleum; machin., domestic appliances; p. (1990) 108,718 (c.), 276,000 (met. a.).

Erie Canal. *See* **New York State Barge Canal**.

Erie, one of Great Lakes (the shallowest), **N. America**, separating Canada from USA; 386 km long, 48–91 km wide; polluted waters; petroleum resources.

Erith, former M.B., Kent, **Eng.**; on Thames estuary; plastics, paints, varnishes, timber, concrete; now inc. in London bor. of Bexley.

Eritrea, indep. st. N.E. **Africa** (1993); formerly prov., **Ethiopia**; tobacco, cereals, pearl fishing; demands for autonomy; secessionist rebellion crushed (1978); severe drought 1982–3; cap. Asmara, a. 118,503 km²; p. (1991) 3·5 m.

Erivan. *See* **Yerevan**.

Erlangen, t., Bavaria, **Germany**; univ.; textiles, elec. and precision engin., gloves; p. (1990) 102,600.

Ermelo, t., **Neth.**; ctr. of agr. dist.; p. (1993) 26,603.

Ernakulam, dist., Kerala, **India**; cotton, coffee, hides; p. (1991) 1,141,000.

Erne, R., N. **Ireland/R.o.I.**; links ls. in Cavan and Fermanagh; 115 km long.

Erode, t., S. Tamil Nadu, **India**; on R. Cauvery; p. (1991) 159,232.

Erzgebirge (**Ore Mtns.**), mtn. range along border of Czech Rep. and **Germany**; reaching highest peak in Mt. Klinovec (1,240 m); uranium; tourism.

Erzurum, t., **Turkey**; agr. ctr. on fertile plateau *c.* 1,890 m a.s.l.; formerly of gr. strategic importance; univ.; earthquake (1983); p. (1990) 297,544. (t.), 848,201 (prov.).

Esbjerg, spt., **Denmark**; W. cst. of Jutland; export harbour on N. Sea cst.; exp. agr. prod.; fishing; airport; p. (1990) 81,504.

Esch-sur-Alzette, t., **Luxembourg**; mng. ctr.; steel; p. (1991) 24,012.

Eschwege, t., Hesse, **Germany**; cas.; machin., textiles, leather, cigars, chemicals; p. (1986) 22,900.

Eschweiler, t., N. Rhine–Westphalia, **Germany**; N.W. of Aachen; lignite mng., steel, iron metallurgy; p. (1986) 53,100.

Esdraelon, plain, **Israel**; between Carmel and Gilboa Mtns.

Esfahān (**Isfahan**, anc. Aspadana), c., central **Iran**; prov. cap.; historic, picturesque c. noted for carpets and metal ware; tourism, airpt.; new steel mill; impt. oil refining ctr.; p. (1986) 1,001,248.

Esher, t., Elmbridge, Surrey, **Eng.**; on R. Mole, residtl.; Sandown Park racecourse; p. (1981) 61,446.

Eshowe, health resort, Natal, **S. Africa**; 64 km from Tugela R.; p. (1980) 28,680 (dist.).

Esk, R., Annandale and Eskdale, **Scot.**; Cumbria, **Eng.**; attractive agr. valley; flows into Solway F. from confluence of Black and White Esk Rs.; 37 km long.

Eskilstuna, t., **Sweden**; on R. of same name; iron, steel, machin., machin. tools; p. (1992) 89,584.

Eskisehir, t. and prov., **Turkey**; W. of Ankara, anc. Dorylaeum; rly. ctr.; p. (1990) 415,831 (t.), (1990) 641,087 (prov.).

Esmeraldas, prov., **Ecuador**; cap. E. on R. of same name; cacao, tobacco; a. 14,152 km²; p. (1990) 306,628.

Esmeraldas, pt., **Ecuador**; bananas, timber, tobacco, cacao, rubber; gold mines nearby; terminal of petroleum pipeline from Oriente; p. (1990) 98,558.

Esneh, *See* **Isna**.

Espírito Santo, st., **Brazil**; sugar, cotton, coffee, fruits, lumber, thorium; cap. Vitória; a. 40,883 km²; p. (1991) 2,598,231.

Espiritu Santo, I., **Vanuatu**; volcanic I., lgst, of gr.; depopulation.

Essaouira (**Mogador**), spt., **Morocco**; cereals, almonds, gum-arabic, crude oil; p. (1982) 42,035.

Essen, c., N. Rhine–Westphalia, **Germany**; gr. industl. c., ctr. of Ruhr conurbation; coal, steel (Krupp), electric power, engin.; canal links with Dortmund–Ems and Mittelland canals and with Rhine; minster severely damaged in second world war; p. (1990) 626,100.

Essequibo, R.; flows N. from Brazilian border draining half **Guyana**; lower course navigable, rapids; timber in upper valley; 960 km long.

Essex, non-met. co., **Eng.**; bounded on S. by Thames, on E. by N. Sea; co. t. Chelmsford; on London clay and chalk; agr.; wheat, barley, sugar-beet; mkt. gardens; S.W. of co. forms part of Greater London with mftg. subs.; oil refineries at Shell Haven; civil nuclear power sta. at Bradwell; univ. at Colchester; a. 2,637 km²; p. (1993) 1,560,300.

Esslingen, t., Baden–Württemberg, **Germany**; on R. Neckar; mach. and rly. shops; textiles, chemicals, leather gds.; Liebfrauen church (1440); p. (1986) 86,900.

Essonne, dep., **France**; S. of Paris; cap. Evry; a. 1,810 km²; p. (1990) 1,084,800.

Esteli, cap., Esteli, **Nicaragua**; on Inter-American Highway; p. (1985) 30,635.

Eston, t., Cleveland, **Eng.**; 5 km E. of Middlesbrough; shipbldg. and repairing.

Estonia (**Estoniya**), former USSR constituent rep.; borders on Baltic, G. of Finland, G. of Riga; lowland with many Ls.; farming and dairying, fishing; oil deposits; hydroelec. power; mainly Lutheran; univ.; cap. Tallinn; a. 45,610 km²; p. (1992) 1,595,000.

Estoril, wat. pl. and thermal spa, **Portugal**; N. side of Tagus estuary; holiday resort; p. (1981) 24,312.

Estremadura, maritime prov., **Portugal**; agr., tourism; cap. Lisbon; a. 5,348 km²; p. (1981) 1,064,976.

Estremadura, region, S.W. **Spain**; on the border of Portugal; largely plateau, alt. 450–900 m.; heathy moorland; sheep; less arid conditions than in remainder of central Spain allow olives, vines, cereals; irrigation in valleys of Tagus, Guadiana; govt. project to develop a. in progress.

Esztergom, t., **Hungary**; R. pt. on Danube; iron foundries, machine tools; mineral springs; cath.; p. (1984) 31,000.

Etang de Berre, lagoon, Bouches-du-Rhône, S.E. **France**; E. of Rhône delta; traversed by Rhône–Marseille canal; salt pans; oil refineries in a.; approx. a. 260 km².

Étaples, t., Pas-de-Calais, **France**; seaside resort; p. (1982) 11,310.

Etawah, t., Uttar Pradesh, **India**; textiles; p. (1991) 124,027.

Ethiopia (**Abyssinia**), indep. st. N.E. **Africa**; temperate climate as a result of high plateau terrain; coffee most impt. comm. crop, but poor communications inhibit economic development; low per capita income and rapid growth of p.; potential for hydro-electric power is lge., one sta. open on Awash R.; mftg. dominated by textiles; agr. improvements encouraged by Peasant's Association; severe drought began in 1970's and continued in 1980's, affects lowlying and Eastern regions; cap. Addis Ababa; monarchy abolished 1975; a. 1,221,900 km²; p. (1993) 51·98 m.

Ethiopian Highlands, mtns., Ethiopia; rise over 4,500 m; source of headwaters of tribs. of R. Nile.

Etna, volcano, N.E. Sicily, Italy; most recent eruptions 1971, 1979, and 1992; alt. 3,276 m.

Eton, t., Berks., Eng.; on N. bank of R. Thames opposite Windsor; public school, founded by Henry VI; p. (1981) 3,523.

Etruria, anc. dist., Italy; now forms Tuscany; home of the Etruscans and part of the Roman empire by 400 B.C.

Etruria, t., Staffs., Eng.; part of Stoke-on-Trent; seat of Josiah Wedgwood's potteries (1769).

Ettrick and Lauderdale, l. gov. dist., part of Borders Reg. in Tweed Valley, Scot.; p. (1993) 35,040.

Euboea (Evvoia), lgst. of Greek Is., Aegean Sea; mtnous. (Mt. Delphi 1,746 m); vines and olives in lowlands, sheep and goats in highlands; a. 3,864 km²; p. (1991) 209,132.

Euclid, t., Ohio, USA; electrical and agr. machin.; p. (1990) 54,875.

Eucumbene Dam and L., N.S.W., Australia; major storage of Snowy Mtns. hydroelectric scheme; holds eight times as much water as Sydney harbour.

Eugene, c., Ore., USA; univ.; mkt. ctr. for rich agr. and lumbering region; fruit-canning, sawmilling; headquarters of Willamette National Forest; p. (1990) 112,669 (c.), 283,000 (met. a. with Springfield).

Euphrates, lgst. R. in S.W. Asia; rises in Armenian uplands and joined by the Tigris enters Persian G. as the Shatt-al Arab; anc. ctr. of civilisation; modern irrigation, navigation, high dam opened 1973 and Ataturk Dam (1981) part of multi-purpose project; 2,848 km long.

Eure, dep., Normandy, France; agr., fruit, livestock, textiles; cap. Evreux; a. 6,037 km²; p. (1990) 513,800.

Eure-et-Loir, dep., N. France; mainly agr.; cap. Chartres; a. 5,934 km²; p. (1990) 396,100.

Europe, continent; W. peninsula of Eurasian land mass; no well-defined bdy. with Asia but line normally accepted runs along Ural Mtns. to Caspian Sea and Caucasus to Black Sea, Sea of Marmara and Dardanelles; after Australia, Europe is smallest continent in a., but contains 11 per cent of world's p. and even more of world's economic activity; climate varies from Arctic to Mediterranean and from temperate maritime to severe continental; major physical features inc. Alps, Pyrenees in S., Baltic Shield in N.; major political div. between E. and W. Europe along Iron Curtain; W. Europe also divided into economic grs. EU and EFTA; major concentration of p. and economic activity within Golden Triangle (q.v.), total a. c. 10,360,000 km²; p. (1984) 490,456,000 (excl. USSR).

Euro-port, name of the post-war expansion of the port of Rotterdam, Neth.; capable of handling 100,000 tonne oil-tankers; oil refining centre.

Evanston, t., Ill., USA; on L. Michigan, sub. of Chicago; univ.; p. (1980) 73,706.

Evansville, c., Ind., USA; on Ohio R.; shipping and comm. ctr. for agr. region; coal mng.; p. (1990) 116,646 (c.), 279,000 (met. a.).

Eveneki National Area, Siberia, Russia; forest and tundra covered; home of Eveneki people; cap. Tura; a. 740,740 km²; p. (1989) 24,800.

Everest, Mt. (Chomolungma = Goddess Mother of the Earth), Himalaya, on frontier of Nepal and Tibet, China; alt. 8,846 m; hgst. mtn. in the world; Hillary and Tenzing first to reach summit in 1953; within Nepal Nat. Park.

Everett, mftg. t., Mass., USA; nr. Boston; iron and steel; p. (1980) 37,195.

Everett, t., Wash., USA; on Puget Sound; harbour; comm. ctr.; timber; tourism; p. (1980) 54,413.

Everglades, Fla., USA; subtropical a.; extensive marshes; home of Seminole Indians; lge. scale drainage since 1905; early vegetables.

Evesham, mkt. t., Wychavon, Hereford and Worcs., Eng.; on R. Avon, in Vale of Evesham, 24 km S.E. of Worcester; fruit ctr.; tourism; p. (1981) 15,271.

Évora, t., cap. of Upper Alentejo prov., S. Portugal; mkt. for agr. prod.; cath.; p. (1987) 34,851.

Évreux, t., cap. of Eure dep., France; mkt. ctr.; p. (1990) 51,459.

Evros, prov., Greece; borders Bulgaria and Turkey; a. 4,191 km²; p. (1991) 143,791.

Evry, t. cap. of Essone dep., France; foundation stone laid for new cath. (1991); p. (1990) 45,854.

Exe, R., Somerset and Devon, Eng.; rises on Exmoor, flows S. via Exeter to English Channel at Exmouth; 86 km long.

Exeter, l. gov. dist., cath. c., co. t., Devon, Eng.; former Roman Isca; E. of Dartmoor on R. Exe; mkt. t.; univ.; aircraft components; airport; p. (1993) 105,100.

Exmoor, Somerset and Devon, Eng.; sandstone moorland, deep wooded valleys; Nat. Park.

Exmouth, t., East Devon, Eng.; on estuary of R. Exe; holiday resort; p. (1981) 28,787.

Exploits, R., Newfoundland, Canada; length 240 km; used for hydroelectric power.

Eye, mkt. t., Mid Suffolk, Eng.; 29 km N. of Ipswich; anc. church; p. (1981) 1,786.

Eyemouth, burgh, Berwick, Scot.; on E. cst. 14 km N. of Berwick; fishing; p. (1991) 3,473.

Eyre Lake, 2 shallow salt lakes in northern S. Australia; 12 m below sea level; receives water from flash flooding, sometimes dry; a. 7,800 km².

Eyre Peninsula, S. Australia; between Gr. Australian Bight and Spencer G.; iron-ore deposits; a. 51,800 km².

F

Fabriano, t., Marches, Italy; in Apennines; cath.; paper mills; p. (1981) 28,708.

Faenza, t., Ravenna, Italy; at foot of Apennines; majolica, textiles; p. (1981) 55,003.

Fagersta, t., Västmanland, Sweden; iron, steel smelting.

Failsworth, t. Gtr. Manchester, Eng.; N.E. of Manchester; textiles, elec. gds.; p. (1981) 21,751.

Fairbanks North Star, t., Alaska, USA; univ.; sawmilling; mng.; p. (1990) 77,720.

Fairfield, t., Conn., USA; chemicals, automobile parts; univ.; p. (1980) 54,849.

Fair I., midway between Shetland and Orkney, Scot.; bird sanctuary; famous for brightly patterned, hand-knitted articles; p. (1991) 67.

Fairmont, t., W. Va., USA; glass, machin., coal by-products; p. (1980) 23,863.

Faisalabad c. W. Punjab, Pakistan; univ. cotton chemicals, fertilizers; p. (1981) 1,092,000.

Faiyum (El Faiyûm), t. and prov. Egypt; oasis nr. L. Karun (anc. L. Moeris), fertilised by Nile water and silt; cereals, sugar-cane, fruits, cotton; archaeological finds; p. (1986) 212,523 (t.), (1991) 1,800,000 (prov.).

Faisalabad, t., Uttar Pradesh, India; rly. junc.; sugar refining; p. (1981) 101,873 (t.), 143,167 (met. a.).

Faizabad, t., Uttar Pradesh, India; mkt. t.; sugar refineries; p. (1991) 124,437.

Falaise, t., Calvados, France; birthplace of William the Conqueror; p. (1982) 8,820.

Falaise de l'Ile de France, low S.E.-facing escarpment, 80 km S.E. and E. of Paris, France; overlooks Champagne Pouilleuse; ch. vine-growing dist. for champagne-wine ind. of Reims, Epernay.

Falcón, st., Venezuela; bordering Caribbean Sea; cap. Coro; p. (1981) 503,896.

Falconara Marittima, t., Italy; nr. Ancona; spt.; oil refining, shipbldg.; p. (1981) 29,071.

Falkirk, burgh, l. gov. dist., Central Reg., Scot.; 16 km S.E. of Stirling; foundries, bricks, chemical, aluminium wks., concrete, timber yards; battles 1298 and 1746; p. (1991) 35,610 (t.), (1993) 142,610, (dist.).

Falkland, burgh, North East Fife, Scot.; 5 km S. of Auchtermuchty; mkt.; p. (1991) 1,197.

Falkland Is., Brit. Crown col., S. Atl.; comprises E. and W. Falkland and adjacent Is.; known as Malvinas by Argentina; sheep rearing (for wool); cap. Stanley on E. Falkland I.; invasion by Argentina led to Falklands War (1982); airpt. opened (1985) capable of taking long range wide bodied aircraft; a. 12,173 km²; p. (1991) 2,121.

Falkland Is. Dependencies, S. Atl.; inc. Is. of S. Georgia and S. Sandwich; a. 4,092 km²; p. (of S. Georgia) 11 males; now form part of Brit. Antarctic Terr.

Fall River, c., Mass., USA; on Mt. Hope Bay; pt. of entry; clothing, rubber gds., food prods., paper; p. (1980) 92,574.

Falmouth, t., Carrick, Cornwall, Eng.; on W. side of estuary of R. Fal. 16 km S. of Truro; sheltered harbourage; offshore oil supply base; seaside resort; fisheries, ship repairing, mng., quarrying, lt. engin.; cas.; pt.; p. (1981) 18,525.

False Bay, inlet on E. side of C. of Good Hope peninsula, S. Africa.

Falster, I., Baltic, **Denmark**; cap. Nyköbing; p. (1990) 42,846.

Falun, t., Kopparberg, **Sweden**; paper; copper mines now exhausted; p. (1992) 54,653.

Famagusta, t., spt., **Cyprus**; on E. cst.; resort; anc. crusade pt.; p. (1985) 19,400.

Famatina, t., La Rioja prov., **Argentina**; in foothills of Andes, 576 km N.W. of Córdoba; copper-mines.

Fareham, t., l. gov. dist., Hants., **Eng.**; at N.W. corner of Portsmouth Harbour; p. (1993) 101,000 (dist.).

Farewell (Kap Farvel), C., southernmost tip of Greenland.

Farewell, C., most N. point S.I., **N.Z.**

Fargo, t., N.D., **USA**; rly. ctr. and R. pt.; grain, farm machin.; p. (1984) 65,700 (t.), (1990) 157,000 (met. a.).

Faringdon, mkt. t., Vale of White Horse, Oxon., Eng.; Faringdon Folly.

Farnborough, t., Rushmoor, Hants., **Eng.**; 5 km N. of Aldershot military camp; Royal Aircraft Establishment; p. (1981) 45,453.

Farne Is., gr. of islets off Northumberland cst., **Eng.**; bird sanctuary; National Trust.

Farnham, t., Waverley, Surrey, **Eng.**; at N. foot of N. Downs, 16 km W. of Guildford; mkt.; p. (1981) 35,289.

Farnworth, t., Gtr. Manchester, **Eng.**; nr. Bolton, textiles, engin., paper; p. (1981) 24,589.

Faro, spt., cap. of Algarve prov., **Portugal**; cork, figs, oranges; p. (1981) 27,974.

Faroe Is., 320 km N.W. of the Shetlands; cap. Thórshavn (Strömö I.); Danish possession but not member of EC; impt. fisheries; a. 1,399 km²; p. (1990) 47,946.

Farrukhabad, t., Uttar Pradesh, **India**; on Ganges R.; gold, lace, brass wk.; p. (1991) 194,567.

Fars, prov., S. Iran; agr.; cap. Shīrāz; p. (1982) 2 m.

Fastnet, lighthouse in Atl. Oc., 7·2 km S.W. C. Clear, Irish cst.

Fatima, v., W. Portugal, nr. Leiria; R.C. pilgrimage.

Fatshan *See* Foshan.

Faversham, pt., Swale, N.E. Kent, **Eng.**; at head of F. creek; mkt.; fruit, hops, bricks, brushes, engin.; p. (1981) 16,098.

Fawley, t., Hants., **Eng.**; on W. shore Southampton Water; lge. oil refinery with pipeline to Staines and Heathrow Airpt.; synthetic rubber.

Fayetteville, t., N.C., **USA**; agr. processing; p. (1984) 66,100 (t.), (1990) 275,000 (met. a.).

Feather, R., N. Cal., **USA**; R. project for water supply irrigation, and hydroelectric power.

Featherstone, t., West Yorks., **Eng.**; p. (1981) 14,043.

Fécamp, sm. spt. on cst. of Normandy, **France**; fishing, tourism, 12th cent. abbey; p. (1982) 21,696.

Fedchenko, glacier, **Tajikistan**; in Pamir mtns; 80 km long; one of longest in world.

Federal German Republic. *See* Germany, **Fed. Rep. of.**

Feira de Santana, t., Bahia, **Brazil**, inland mkt. t.; p. (1991) 405,691.

Feldberg, highest peak in Black Forest, **Germany**; alt. 1,495 m.

Feldkirch, t., Vorarlberg, **Austria**; on Swiss frontier; p. (1991) 26,743.

Felixstowe, pt., Suffolk Coastal, Suffolk, **Eng.**; now one of country's best container pts.; seaside resort; p. (1981) 20,858.

Felling, Tyne and Wear, **Eng.**; Tyneside mftg. dist.; p. (1981) 36,431.

Feltham. *See* Hounslow.

Fenland, l. gov. dist., Cambs., **Eng.**; agr. a. in N. of co. inc. Wisbech, Chatteris, March, Whittlesey and North Witchford; p. (1993) 78,000.

Fens, The, low-lying dist. around the Wash, **Eng.**; artificial drainage begun in 17th cent.; impt. agr. dist.; root crops, wheat, fruit, bulbs; a. 3,367 km².

Feodosiya, t., **Ukraine**; in Crimea; major Black Sea pt., tobacco, hosiery; exp. wheat; resort and sanatoria; p. (1990) 85,000.

Ferghana, region, **Uzbekistan**; deep basin at W. end of Tien Shan Mtns.; drained W. by R. Syr Dar'ya; semi-arid but extensive irrigation system allows intensive cultivation of cotton, citrus fruits, silk, rice; ch. ts. Kokand, Namangan.

Ferghana, c., **Uzbekistan**; hydroelectric power, petroleum refining, textiles; deposits of ozocerite nearby; p. (1990) 197,800.

Fermanagh, former co.; l. gov. dist., **N. Ireland**; bisected by R. Erne and lakes; stock raising, dairying; p. (1991) 54,033.

Fermoy, t., Cork, **R.o.I.**; on R. Blackwater; cath.; woollens; p. (1986) 2,872.

Fernando de Noronha, I., fed. terr., N.E. cst. Brazil; penal settlement and met. sta.; cap. Vila dos Remédios; a. 26 km²; p. (1980) 1,279.

Fernando Po. *See* Biako.

Ferrara, c., N. **Italy**; nr. head of Po delta; cath., univ., palaces; mkt. for fertile plain; silk, hemp, wine; oil refinery nearby; petrochemicals; birthplace of Savonarola; p. (1992) 137,099.

Ferro (Hierro), most S. of the **Canary Is.**; a. 275 km²; cap. Valverde; chosen by Ptolemy (A.D. 56) for his prime meridian and used by French scientists in 17th cent.; reckoned as exactly W. 20° of Paris.

Ferryhill, v., Durham, **Eng.**; 8 km S. of Durham, in gap through limestone ridge which separates Wear valley from Tees valley; commands main N. to S. route along lowland E. of Pennines.

Fertile Crescent, an arc of fertile land from the Mediterranean Sea, N. of the Arabian Desert, to Persian G.; home of some very early civilisations and migrations.

Fez (Fès), c., **Morocco**; lies inland 160 km E. of Rabat; one of the sacred cities of Islam; univ. attached to mosque (one of lgst. in Africa); comm. ctr.; p. (1982) 448,823.

Fezzan, prov., S.W. **Libya**; desert plateau with numerous wells and inhabited oases.

Ffestiniog (Festiniog), t., Meirionnydd, Gwynedd, N. **Wales**; at head of Vale of Ffestiniog, 14 km E. of Portmadoc; contains Ffestiniog and Blaenau Ffestiniog; slate quarries; pumped-storage hydroelec. sta. (1963); cement; narrow gauge rly.; p. (1981) 5,437.

Fianarantsoa, t., **Madagascar**; rice mills, meat preserves; p. (1990) 124,489.

Fichtelgebirge, mtn. range, N.E. Bavaria, **Germany**; extending into CSSR, rising to 1,051 m in Schneeberg; forested slopes.

Fiesole, t., Tuscany, **Italy**; on summit of wooded hill overlooking Florence and the Arno; residtl.; 11th cent. cath.; p. (1981) 14,486.

Fife, l. gov. reg., former co., E. **Scot.**; occupies a. between Tay and Forth estuaries; industl. dist. based originally on coalfields; Longannet colliery remains; a. 1,305 km²; p. (1993) 351,200.

Fiji, S.W. Pac. Oc., former Brit. col., gained independence in 1970; comprises over 800 Is.; tropical climate; agr. basis of economy, especially sugar and coconut prods.; gold an impt. exp.; forestry and tourism developing; forms ctr. of communications in S.W. Pac. Oc.; international airport at Nadi, ch. pt. and cap. Suva; a. 18,272 km²; cosmopolitan p. (1993) 758,275.

Filey, t., North Yorks., **Eng.**; 8 km S.E. of Scarborough; seaside resort; p. (1981) 5,702.

Filton, Bristol, Avon, **Eng.**; aircraft wks.

Finchley. *See* Barnet.

Findhorn, v., Moray, **Scot.**; resort; 12th cent. abbey; fishing; p. (1991) 683.

Findlay, t., Ohio, **USA**; on Blanchard R.; agr. machin., tyres, beet sugar refining; p. (1980) 35,594.

Fingal's Cave, Staffa I., Inner Hebrides, W. **Scot.**; basaltic columns.

Finger Lakes, gr. of narrow glacial Ls., N.Y., **USA**; picturesque resorts and state parks.

Finistère, dep. N.W. **France**, in Brittany; cap. Quimper; fishing, tourism; a. 7,071 km²; p. (1990) 838,700.

Finland, rep., N. **Europe**; part of Scandinavia; low-lying plateau severely eroded by ice to form 60,000 Ls.; economy based on timber (forests cover 72 per cent of a.); world's leading exporter of pulp and paper; increasing importance of metal and engin. inds.; cap. Helsinki; joined EU 1995; a. 360,318 km²; p. concentrated in S.; p. (1992) 5.05 m.

Finland, G. of, E. arm of Baltic Sea, between Finland and USSR.

Finnart, Dumbarton, **Scot.**; crude oil terminal situated in Loch Long. N.W. Glasgow; pipeline to Grangemouth.

Finnmark, most N. co., **Norway**; inhabited by Lapps; whale fisheries; lge. copper deposits discovered nr. Reppan fjord; a. 48,125 km²; p. (1990) 74,590.

Finsbury. *See* Islington.

Finsteraarhorn, highest peak in Bernese Oberland, **Switzerland**; 4,277 m.

Finucane I., pt., W. **Australia**; deepwater pt. to ship ion ore and new t. projected.

Firenze. *See* Florence.

Firozabad, t., Uttar Pradesh, India; glassware; agr. tr; p. (1991) 215,128.

Firozpur, t., Punjab st., N.W. India; rly. t.; admin. ctr.; p. (1991) 61,142.

Fishguard and Goodwick, spt., Preseli, Dyfed, Wales; on S. of Cardigan Bay; steamer connection to Cork and Rosslare (Ireland); p. (1981) 4,908.

Fitchburg, t., Mass., USA; paper, machin., textiles; p. (1980), 39,580 (t.), 99,957 (met. a.).

Fitzroy, R., W. Australia; flows into King Sound; dry in winter; irrigation; 560 km long.

Fiume. *See* Rijeka.

Flamborough Head, promontory of Yorks. cst., Eng.; steep chalk cliffs; lighthouse; anc., Brit. earthwork (Danes' dyke).

Flanders, region between R. Scheldt and cst., crossed by Franco-Belgian frontier; Dunkirk, Lille ctrs. of French F.; Belgian F. divided into 2 provs., E. and W., p. (1993) 1,116,244 and 1,344,263 respectively; caps. Bruges and Ghent.

Fleet, t., Hart, Hants., Eng.; 6 km N.W. of Aldershot; p. (1981) 26,004.

Fleetwood, spt., Wyre, Lancs., Eng.; at mouth of Wyre, Morecambe Bay; deep-sea fish. pt.; fish processing; lge. chemical plant nearby; p. (1981) 28,467.

Flensburg, spt., Schleswig-Holstein, Germany; on Baltic, close to Danish border; shipbld., machin., chemicals, rum distilleries, fishing; p. (1986) 85,700.

Flevoland, prov., Neth.; estab. 1986; p. (1993) 243,441.

Flinders I., Australia; lgst I. in the Furneaux gr., Bass Strait; famous for mutton birds.

Flinders Range, chain of mtns., S. Australia; extending 400 km N.E. from head of Spencer G., reaching 1,190 m in St. Mary's Peak; named after Matthew Flinders; uranium ore at Mt. Painter.

Flint, t., Delyn, Clwyd, Wales; viscose textile yarn, cas. ruins; p. (1981) 16,454.

Flint, t., Mich., USA; motorcars, aircraft engines; p. (1990) 140,761 (t.), 430,000 (met. a.).

Flintshire, former co., N. Wales; now part of Clwyd.

Flodden, v. Northumberland, Eng.; on R. Till; battle between James IV of Scot. and the English under the Earl of Surrey 1513.

Flora, t., Norway; new t. 136 km N. of Bergen.

Florence (Firenze), c., Tuscany, Italy; on R. Arno; univ.; leather-work; famous for art treasures, cath. and churches; ruled by Medici 1421–1737; birthplace of Dante and Machiavelli; severely affected by heavy floods Nov. 1966; p. (1992) 397,434.

Florence, t., N.W. Ala., USA; on Tennessee R., nr. Wilson dam; textile, steel plants; p. (1984) 36,000 (t.), 135,700 (met. a.).

Flores, I., most northwesterly of Azores gr.; Portuguese; cap. Santa Cruz; French ballistic missiles tracking sta.; a. 142 km².

Flores, I., Indonesia; mtnous.; volcanic, densely forested; a. 22,973 km².

Flores Sea, between Sulawesi and Flores, Indonesia.

Florianópolis, spt., cap. of Santa Catarina st., Brazil; comm. ctr., fishing; p. (1985) 218,900.

Florida, st., USA; Sunshine St.; admitted to Union 1845; st. flower Orange Blossom, st. bird Mockingbird; between Atl. Oc. and G. of Mexico; low-lying, swampy, inc. Everglades; sea resorts on Atl. cst.; citrus fruit and subtropical agr.; agr. processing; cap Tallahassee; a. 151,670 km²; p. (1990) 12,937,926; hgst. percentage of p. over 65 in USA (18.3).

Florida Keys, archipelago, USA; extends in an arc from S.E. cst. Florida W.S.W. to Key West in G. of Mexico; fishing resorts.

Florida Strait, between Florida and Bahama Is.; course of Gulf Stream from G. of Mexico.

Florina. *See* Phlorina.

Florissant (St. Ferdinand), t., Mo., USA; sub. of St. Louis on Missouri R.; p. (1990) 51,206.

Flushing. *See* Vlissingen.

Fly, lgst. R. of Papua New Guinea; flows S.E. from Victor Emmanuel Range to G. of Papua; 1,280 km long.

Fochabers, v., Moray, Scot.; nr. mouth of Spey; tourist resort; food canning; p. (1991) 1,534.

Focsani, t., Romania; at foot of Transylvanian Alps; wine and grain ctr.; p. (1990) 98,645.

Foggia, cath. c., S. Italy; rly. ctr. and mkt. ctr. for plain of Apulia; site of cas. of Frederick II; p. (1992) 155,674.

Foix, t., cap. of Ariège dep., S. France; historic t.; p. (1990) 10,446.

Foligno, t., central Italy; in Apennines, on Topino R.; cath., textiles, paper; p. (1981) 52,484.

Folkestone, t., Shepway, Kent, Eng.; seaside resort; p. (1981) 43,742.

Fond du Lac, t., Winnebago L., Wis., USA; cath.; machine tools, domestic appliances; resort; p. (1990) 37,757.

Fonseca, Gulf of, Honduras; lgst. indentation along Pac. cst. of Central America; sm. pt. of Amapala, US naval base, and new deepwater pt.

Fontainebleau, t., Seine-et-Marne, France; on R. Seine, 56 km S.E. Paris; in former royal forest (a. 17,200 ha); magnificent palace; p. (1982) 18,753.

Fontenoy, v., Belgium; nr. Tournai; scene of battle (1745) when the French under Marshal Saxe defeated the English and their allies.

Foochow. *See* Fuzhou.

Fordlandia. *See* Belterra.

Foreland, N. and S., two headlands on E. cst. Kent, Eng.; between which are the Goodwin Sands and Pegwell Bay; lighthouses; sea battle between de Ruyter and Monk (1666).

Forest Heath, l. gov. dist., Suffolk, Eng.; part of Breckland inc. Mildenhall and Newmarket; p. (1993) 62,500.

Forest Hills, residtl. a., central Queen's bor., N.Y., USA; national and international matches played at West Side Tennis Club.

Forest of Dean, Gloucs., Eng.; between Wye and Severn Rs.; former Royal Forest; Forestry Commission plantations; former coal-mng. a.; tourism; new lt. industl. estates; now forms l. gov. dist.; p. (1993) 75,600.

Forfar, royal burgh, Angus, Scot.; former cty. t.; jute, linen; p. (1991) 12,961.

Forli, c., Emilia-Romagna, central Italy; route ctr. in Apennine foothills; felt, textiles, footwear; p. (1992) 109,080.

Formby, t., Merseyside, Eng.; on W. cst., 10 km S.W. of Southport; residtl.; p. (1981) 25,798.

Formosa, t. and prov., N. Argentina; bordering on Paraguay; timber; cap. Formosa; a. 72,067 km²; p. (1991) 165,700 (t.), 363,035 (prov.).

Formosa. *See* Taiwan.

Forres, royal burgh, Moray, Scot.; on Findhorn R. nr. Moray F.; agr., forestry, engin., distilleries; cas.; p. (1991) 8,531.

Forst, t., Brandenburg, Germany; on R. Neisse; E. section of t. Polish since 1945; textiles; p. (1989) 26,313.

Fortaleza, c., cap. of Ceará st., Brazil; in the dry Sertão reg. of the N.E.; terminus of cattle droving route; growth resulting from planned industl. development to revitalise region; p. (1991) 1,758,334.

Fort Collins, t., Col., USA; ctr. of rich farming a.; grain, sugarbeet, livestock; univ.; p. (1990) 87,758 (t.), 186,136 (met. a.).

Fort de France, cap. of Martinique, Fr. W.I.; landlocked harbour; exp. sugar, rum; comm. ctr.; Fr. naval base; p. (1990) 101,544.

Fort George, R., W. Quebec, Canada; rises in Labrador and flows into Hudson Bay; 880 km long.

Fort Gouraud, t., Mauritania; modern iron-ore mines.

Forth, R., Scot.; formed by two headstreams rising to N. of Ben Lomond which meet nr. Aberfoyle; takes meandering course to Alloa, whence it expands into Firth of Forth; 165 km long.

Forth, Firth of, lge. inlet, E. cst. of Scot.; submerged estuary of R. Forth; navigable by lge. vessels for 64 km inland to Grangemouth; other pts., Leith, Rosyth (naval), Bo'ness; l. (to Alloa) 80 km; the Forth rly. bridge (1890) spans the F. at Queensferry; road bridge (1964).

Forth and Clyde Canal, Scot.; links F. of Forth at Grangemouth and F. of Clyde at Glasgow; not completely navigable; 61 km long.

Fort Johnston, t., S. Malawi, on L. Malombe; new t., 1966; tobacco; airpt.

Fort Knox, Ky., USA; nation's gold bullion depository; military air-base.

Fort Lamy. *See* **Ndjamene.**

Fort Lauderdale, c., Fla., **USA**; on Atl. cst. N. of Miami; lge. marina; citrus fruits, mkt. garden prod.; holiday resort; p. (1990) 149,377 (c.), 1,255,000 (met. a. with Hollywood-Pompano Beach).

Fort Myers, t., Fla., **USA**; on G. of Mexico; resort; Edison experimented here; p. (1984) 38,200 (t.), (1990) 335,000 (met. a. inc. Cape Coral).

Fortrose, t., royal burgh, Ross and Cromarty, **Scot.**; on S. cst. of Black Isle, on Moray F.; p. (1981) 1,319.

Fort Smith, c., Ark., **USA**; on Arkansas R.; mkt. ctr. for agr. a.; varied mnfs., inc. furniture, glass; coal and zinc mined nearby; p. (1990) 72,798 (c.), 142,083 (met. a.).

Fort Victoria, (**Masvingo**), t., **Zimbabwe**, agr. and mng. ctr., cattle, historic ruins in Zimbabwe Nat. Park; p. (1982) 30,600.

Fort Wayne, c., Ind., **USA**, at confluence of 2 headstreams of Maumee R.; rly. repair shops; elec. machin. and domestic appliances, originally a Fr. fort; p. (1990) 173,072 (c.), 364,000 (met. a.).

Fort William. *See* **Thunder Bay.**

Fort William, burgh, Lochaber, **Scot.**; nr. head of Loch Linnhe, at base of Ben Nevis; aluminium factory; pulp- and paper-mill at Corpach; p. (1991) 10,391.

Fort Worth, c., Texas, **USA**; rly. and comm. ctr. on Trinity R.; livestock and grain mkt.; oil refining, meat packing, oilfield equipment; p. (1990) 447,619 (c.), 1,332,053 (met. a. with Arlington).

Fort Yukon, trading sta. on Yukon R., N.E. Alaska, **USA**.

Foshan (**Fatshan**), c., Guandong, **China**; S.W. of Guangzhou; iron and steel, textiles; p. (1984) 299,800.

Fos-sur-Mer, t., Bouches-du-Rhône, S. **France**; nr. Marseilles; new deepwater pt. and oil refinery; bauxite terminal; iron and steel plant; p. (1982) 9,446.

Fotheringhay, v., Northampton, **Eng.**; on R. Nene; Mary Queen of Scots beheaded (1587) in F. Castle.

Fougères, t., Ille-et-Vilaine, **France**; cas.; footwear, clothing; p. (1982) 25,131.

Foulness I., S. Essex, **Eng.**; at mouth of R. Crouch; owned by Min. of Defence; site of projected third London airport at Maplin, now abandoned; projected container and oil pt.

Fountains Abbey, ruined 12th cent. Cistercian abbey, North Yorks., **Eng.**; nr. Ripon.

Fowey, sm. spt., Cornwall, **Eng.**; nr. mouth of R. Fowey; exp. kaolin; resort; fishing; p. with St. Austell (1981) 36,639.

Foxe Basin and Channel, to N. of Hudson Bay, between Baffin I. and Southampton I., **Canada.**

Foyers, Falls of, Inverness, **Scot.**; E. of Loch Ness, nr. Fort Augustus; aluminium wks., the first hydroelectric plant erected in Britain (1896).

Foyle, Lough, inlet, **N. Ireland**; between Donegal (R.o.I.) and Londonderry; outlet of R. F.; Londonderry t. at head of inlet.

Foynes Is., R.o.I.; oil terminal on N. side, E. of Battery Point.

Foz do Iguacú, t., Paraná, **Brazil**; highway (coffee road) from Paranaguá; rapid growth with opening of Itaipú Dam; p. (1985) 183,400.

Framingham, t., Mass., **USA**; 32 km W. of Boston; lt. inds.; p. (1980) 65,113.

Framlingham, mkt. t., Suffolk, **Eng.**; N.E. of Ipswich; cas. remains.

Francavilla Fontana, t., Apulia, **Italy**; rly. junc.; agr. tr.; p. (1981) 32,588.

France, rep., W. **Europe**; bounded by 3 seas; Eng. Channel, Atl. Oc., Mediterranean; variety of climate and relief; leading agr. cty. of Europe; 75 per cent under cultivation; exps. grain, fruit, vegetables, wine; industl. expansion since second world war; lgst. inds. inc. iron and steel, motor vehicles, aircraft, engin., textiles, chemicals; tourism impt.; EU member; cap. Paris; 96 deps.; excessive social, economic, and political concentration around Paris promotes description of France as "Paris and the French Desert"; recent attempts to break this down using framework of 21 economic planning regions; a. 550,634 km²; p. (1994) 57·8 m.

Franceville, t., Gabon, Equatorial Africa; on R. Ogooué; lined to Libreville as part of the Trans-Gabon rly. project; manganese mines opened 1962; founded by De Brazza.

Franche-Comté, region E. **France** bordering Switzer-

land; inc. deps. Doubs, Jura, Haute-Saône, Territoire de Belfort; mainly mountainous and wooded but industrial round ch. ts. Belfort, Besançon; p. (1990) 1,097,300.

Francistown, t., **Botswana**; airpt.; butter, coppermng.; p. (1989) 52,725.

Frankenthal, t., Rhineland–Palatinate, **Germany**; in industl. dist. of Mannheim–Ludwigshafen, engin., machin.; p. (est. 1986) 44,300.

Frankfurt-on-Main, c., Hesse, **Germany**; local point in Rhine–Main urban region; rly. ctr., transit pt.; machin., cars, chemicals, elec. engin., publishing; airport; cath., univ.; birthplace of Goethe; p. (1990) 647,200.

Frankfurt-on-Oder, c., Brandenburg, **Germany**; agr. ctr., R. pt., rail junc.; machin., chemicals; E. part of t. (Slubice) Polish since 1945; p. (1981) 81,009.

Frankischer (**Franconian**) **Jura**, plateau with steep N.-facing edge, S.E. of Germany, runs 128 km S.W. from Fichtelgebirge; drained by Reg-nitz and Altmühl Rs.

Franklin, dist., N.W. Terr., **Canada**; comprising the Is. of Arctic Canada from Banks I. to Baffin I., including Boothia Peninsula and Melville Peninsula; sparsely populated; furs; a. 1,434,943 km².

Františkovy Lázne (**Franzensbad**), famous spa, W. Bohemia, **Czech Rep.**; 445 m a.s.l., between the Erzgebirge and the Fichtelgebirge.

Franz Josef Land (**Zemlya Frantsalosifa**), **Russia**; archipelago in Arctic Oc. N. of Novaya Zemlya; a. 20,720 km²; mainly ice-covered.

Frascati, t., **Italy**; 19 km S.E. of Rome; summer resort; famous villas and arch. remains; nuclear research ctr.; p. (1981) 18,728.

Fraser I. (Great Sandy I.), Queensland, **Australia**; low sandy I., timber reserve and Nat. Park; concern over ecology caused discontinuation of mineral sand exp. (1977).

Fraser, R., B.C., **Canada**; rises at *c.* 1,800 m on W. slopes Rocky Mtns.; famous salmon fisheries; routeway; Vancouver nr. delta; 1,360 km long.

Fraserburgh, spt., burgh, Banff and Buchan, **Scot.**; one of the main E. cst. herring pts.; p. (1991) 12,843.

Frauenfeld, t., cap. of Thurgau can., **Switzerland**; 11th cent. cas.; textiles; p. (1980) 18,607.

Fray Bentos, t., cap. of Rio Negro dep., **Uruguay**; pt. on R. Uruguay 80 km from mouth; meat-processing; p. (1985) 20,091.

Fredericia, t., pt., E. Jutland, **Denmark**; major rly. junc.; textiles, silver and electroplated gds., fertilisers; oil refinery; p. (1990) 46,072.

Fredericton, c., cap. of N.B., **Canada**; on St. John R.; univ., cath.; timber, shoes, plastics; p. (1986) 44,352.

Frederiksberg, sub. of Copenhagen, **Denmark**, with indep. municipal status; p. (1981) 88,167.

Frederikshåb, sm. spt. on W. cst. of **Greenland**; fish processing; p. (1990) 2,556.

Frederikshavn, fish. pt., N. Jutland, **Denmark**, on Kattegat; p. (1990) 35,500.

Frederikstad, t., **Norway**; at mouth of Glomma R.; ctr. of pulp and paper-producing ind.; electrotechnical inds., shipbldg., fish canning; p. (1990) 50,170.

Frederiksvaerk, t., Sjaelland, **Denmark**; impt. iron and steel wks.; p. (1990) 17,941.

Freetown, c., cap. of Sierra Leone; pt. on Atl. Oc.; one of lgst. natural harbours in world; humid, oppressive climate; exp. diamonds, palm oil; engin., food processing, oil refining; fishing; p. (1988) 469,776.

Freiberg, t. Saxony, **Germany**; S.W. of Dresden, at foot of Erzgebirge; mng. academy (silver discovered 12th cent.); metallurgy, textiles, glass, porcelain; p. (1981) 51,377.

Freiburg im Breisgau, c., Baden-Württemberg, **Germany**; in Black Forest; cath., univ.; cultural ctr.; tourism; p. (1990) 191,600.

Freising, t., Bavaria, **Germany**; N.E. of Munich; cath.; agr. machin., textiles, chemicals; p. (1986) 36,200.

Freital, t. Saxony, **Germany**; S.W. Dresden; glass, uranium ore processing; coalmines nearby; p. (1989) 413,588.

Fréjus, t., Var dep., S.W. **France**; cath., Roman ruins; resort on Fr. Riviera; p. (1982) 32,698.

Fréjus, Col de, Alpine pass, **France** and **Italy**, 2,083 m, under which runs the Mont Cenis tunnel (13·6 km).

Fremantle, spt., W. **Australia**; at mouth of Swan R., 19 km S.W. from Perth, principal pt. in W. Australia and first Australian pt. of call for mail steamers; part of Perth met. a.; giant industl. complex at Kwinana; p. (1981) 22,484.

French Equatorial Africa, formerly included Gabon, Congo (Brazzaville), Ubangi-Shari and Chad, sts. which are now independent.

French Guiana (Guyane), Fr. Overseas dep., on N. cst. of **S. America,** between Surinam to W. and Brazil to S. and E.; tropical climate; little developed and thinly populated; ch. ctr. of p. and spt. at cap. of Cayenne; economy based on agr., especially sugar and forestry; some gold and bauxite mng.; a. 90,650 km²; p. (1990) 114,700.

French Polynesia, Fr. overseas terr., in **S. Pac. Oc.,** comprising several archipelagos; Society Is., Marquesas Is., Tubuai Is., Tuamotu Is., and Gambier Is.; increased autonomy since 1977; cap. Papeete; a. 4,002 km²; p. (1991) 199,031.

French Somaliland. *See* Djibouti.

French S. and Antarctic Terrs., Fr. overseas terr., comprising several grs. of Is. and Antarctic terr. of Adélie Land; a. 409,220 km²; p. 132 (mainly scientists).

French West Africa, comprised former Fr. cols. of Dahomey (Benin), Ivory Coast, Mauritania, Niger, Fr. Guinea, Upper Volta, Senegal, Fr. Soudan (Mali).

Freshwater, sm. t., I. of Wight, **Eng.;** at W. end of I., 13 km W. of Newport; resort.

Fresnillo de Gonzalez Echeverria, t., Zacatecas, **Mexico;** alt. 2,227 m; mkt. t., silver mng.; p. (1990) 160,208.

Fresno, c., Cal., **USA;** ctr. of vast irrigated fruit-growing dist.; p. (1990) 354,202 (c.), 667,000 (met. a.).

Fribourg (Freiburg), c., cap. of F. can., **Switzerland;** between Berne and Lausanne; viaduct and bridges; cath., univ.; p. (1990) 34,722.

Fribourg (Freiburg), can., **Switzerland;** mainly dairy farming; cereals, sugarbeet, cheese; a. 1,671 km²; p. (1990) 207,800.

Friedrichshafen, t., **Germany;** on Bodensee; machin., boat bldg., motors; resort; p. (1986) 52,100.

Friendly Is. *See* Tonga.

Friern Barnet. *See* Barnet.

Friesland, prov., N. **Neth.;** cap. Leeuwarden; dairying, horses, cattle; natural gas on Ameland I.; a. 3,432 km²; p. (1993) 603,998.

Frimley and Camberley, ts., Surrey Heath, former U.D., Surrey, **Eng.;** 5 km N. of Farnborough; lt. engin., plastics; military training ctr.; p. (1981) 52,017.

Frinton and Walton, Tendring, Essex, **Eng.;** on E. cst., 8 km N.E. of Clacton; seaside resort; p. (1981) 14,651.

Frisches Haff, shallow freshwater lagoon, Baltic cst. of **Poland;** 85 km long, 6–18 km broad.

Frisian Is., chain of Is. stretching from Den Helder to Jutland, along csts. of Neth., Germany, and Denmark; ch. Is. are Texel, Vlieland, Terschelling, Ameland (West F. Is.), Nordeney, Borkum (East F. Is.), Sylt, Föhr, Römø (North F. Is.); severe erosion; Sylt now half size it was 500 years ago.

Friuli-Venezia Giulia, aut. reg. (created 1963), N.E. **Italy;** comprising 3 provs. Udine, Gorozia, Trieste; p. (1992) 1,195,055.

Frobisher Bay, inlet in S. Baffin I., N. **Canada,** extending 320 km between Cumberland Sound and Hudson Strait.

Frodingham, t., Humberside, **Eng.;** on W. flank of limestone ridge, Lincoln Edge; impt. iron-ore open-cast mines; mnfs. iron and steel.

Frome, mkt. t., Mendip, Somerset, **Eng.;** on R. Frome, 18 km S. of Bath; p. (1981) 14,527.

Frome, R., Dorset, **Eng.;** flows from N. Dorset Downs into Poole Harbour.

Frontignan, t., Hérault, S. **France;** oil refining; pipeline under sea from Sète; produces muscat; p. (1982) 14,961.

Frunze. *See* Bishkek.

Frýdek-Mistek, t., **Czech Republic;** on R. Ostravice on opposite banks; timber, textiles; p. (1990) 66,000.

Fuenlabrada, t. Madrid prov. C. **Spain;** rlwy, textiles; p. (1991) 144,720.

Fuerteventura, I., Canary gr.; a. 1,717 km².

Fujairah, emirate, one of **United Arab Emirates,** Persian G.; p. (1985) 54,425.

Fujian (Fukien), prov., **China;** cap. Fuzhou; intensive agr., rice and sugar-cane; shellfish raised along cst.; a. 123,103 km²; p. (1990) 30,610,000.

Fujisawa, t., Honshu, **Japan;** bearings, machin.; p. (1990) 350,330.

Fujiyama, extinct volcano, **Japan;** 96 km S.W. of Tokyo; pilgrim resort; hgst. peak of Japan; alt. 3,780 m.

Fukui, c., cap. of F. pref., central Honshu, **Japan;** synthetic fibres, paper; old silk-weaving ctr.; p. (1990) 252,743.

Fukuoka, c., N. Kyushu, **Japan;** pt. on Hakata Bay; univ. ctr., old cas. t.; textiles, dolls, shipbldg.; p. (1990) 1,237,107.

Fukushima, c., N. Honshu, **Japan;** ceramics, foods, steel; publishing; p. (1990) 277,528.

Fukuyama, c., S. Hokkaido, **Japan;** p. (1990) 365,612.

Fulda, t., Hesse, **Germany;** nr. Kassel; on R. Fulda; palace, abbey; textiles, metallurgy, rubber; route ctr.; p. (1986) 54,100.

Fulham. *See* Hammersmith.

Fulwood, t., Lancs., **Eng.;** 3 km N.E. of Preston; part of Central Lancashire New Town.

Funchal, cap. of **Madeira Is.;** pt., winter resort; cath.; p. (1987) 44,111.

Fundy, Bay of, inlet between Nova Scotia and New Brunswick, **Canada;** lge. tidal range of 21 m.

Furka Pass, Switzerland; between Valais and Uri cans.; 2,433 m.

Furneaux Is., S.E. **Australia;** in Bass Strait, belonging to Tasmania; lgst. is Flinders I.

Furness, dist., Cumbria, **Eng.;** between Morecambe Bay and the Irish Sea.

Fürstenwalde, t., Brandenburg, **Germany;** on R. Spree; metallurgy, leather, tyres; p. (1989) 35,658.

Fürth, t., Bavaria, **Germany;** nr. Nürnberg; toy and glass inds.; p. (1990) 104,400.

Fusan. *See* Pusan.

Fuse, t., Honshu, **Japan;** machin., textiles, chemicals; now part of Higashiosaka.

Fushimi, c., Honshu, **Japan;** sub. of Kyoto; p. (1990) 280,276.

Fushun, c., Liaoning, N. **China;** at foot of Changbai Shan, 35 km N.E. of Shenyang; major industl. ctr.; possesses world's thickest bituminous coal seam (127 m) worked by deep and opencast mines; oil refinery based on local oil shales; steelwks., chemicals; electronics; timber inds.; diversification planned; p. (1992) 1,350,000.

Fuskiki, spt., Honshu, **Japan;** serves Toyama c. with metals, coal.

Futa, La, pass, Tusco-Emilian Apennines, N. **Italy;** used by main road from Bologna to Florence; alt. 903 m.

Futa Jalon (Fouta Djalon), upland dist., mostly in **Guinea,** W. Africa with outliers in Liberia and Sierra Leone.

Fuxin (Fuzin), c., Liaoning, N. **China;** ctr. of lge. coalfield; p. (1984) 653,200.

Fuzhou (Foochow), c., cap. of Fujian prov., **China;** at mouth of Min R., major comm. and industl. ctr.; diverse light inds.; became impt. with tea exp.; former treaty pt.; p. (1992) 1,290,000.

Fylde, W. Lancs., **Eng.;** low plain behind coastal sand dunes; pig- and poultry-rearing dist.; ch. t. Blackpool; l. gov. dist. excluding Blackpool p. (1993) 73,700.

Fylingdales, ballistic missile early warning sta. on N. Yorks. moors, **Eng.**

Fyn, I., **Denmark;** in Baltic Sea; a. 3,419 km²; cap. Odense; dairying, sugarbeet; p. (1990) 426,106.

Fyne, loch on Argyll and Bute cst., W. **Scot.;** an arm of F. of Clyde; offshore oil platform construction: 64 km long.

G

Gabès, spt., **Tunisia;** on G. of Gabès, 320 km S. of Tunis; dates, henna, wool; p. (1984) 92,259.

Gabon, rep., W. **Africa;** Cameroon to N., Zaïre to S. and E.; tropical climate, hot, humid; much tropical rain forest; forestry main ind. but mng. increasingly impt.; petroleum exp. creating increasing prosperity; manganese at Moanda (S.), iron-ore at Mekambo (N.E.); communications geared mainly to mng. areas; major pts. Libreville (cap.), Port Gentil; Trans-Gabon rly. project to promote exploitation of timber; first part opened 1979; intense forest cover makes internal air services very impt.; airport at Libreville; agr. development limited by small size of p.; a. 266,770 km²; p. (1993) 1·01 m.

Gaborone (Gaberones), cap. **Botswana;** formerly sm. v.; chosen as cap. for new rep., bldg. began

1964; p. (1991) 138,471.

Gadag-Betgeri, t., Karnataka, **India;** cotton and silk weaving; p. (1991) 134,051.

Gaeta, t., naval pt., **Italy;** on promontory on shore of G. of Gaeta; the anc. Caietae Portus; cath.; p. (1981) 22,605.

Gafsa, t., **Tunisia;** phosphate mng. ctr.; p. (1984) 60,870.

Gaillard Cut, excavated channel, **Panama;** carries Panama Canal through Culebra Mtn. from L. Gatun to Pac. Oc.; 11 km long.

Gainesville, t., Fla., **USA;** univ.; mkt. gardening; electronics, wood prod.; p. (1990) 84,770.

Gainsborough, t., West Lindsey, Lincs., **Eng.;** on R. Trent; agr. implements, milling, packing and wrapping machin.; some R. traffic; mkt.; George Eliot's St. Ogg's in *Mill on the Floss;* p. (1981) 18,691.

Gairdner, salt L., S. **Australia;** a 4 766 km².

Gairloch, see loch and v., W. Ross and Cromarty, Scot.; resort, fishing.

Galapagos, volcanic Is., Pac. Oc.; 960 km W. of **Ecuador** (to whom they belong) on equator; flora and fauna peculiar to each I.; visited by Darwin 1835; wildlife under increased threat; a. 7,428 km²; p. (1994) 12,000.

Galashiels, burgh, Ettrick and Lauderdale, **Scot.;** on Gala River, 3 km above confluence with R. Tweed; tweeds, woollens; p. (1991) 13,753.

Galati or **Galatz,** c., E. **Romania;** major inland pt. on lower Danube; cath.; p. (1990) 326,139.

Galesburg, t., Ill., **USA;** engin., coal mng.; p. (1980) 35,305.

Galicia, historic region, S.E. **Poland** and W. Ukraine, **USSR.**

Galicia, region, N.W. **Spain;** comprising provs. La Coruña, Lugo, Orense, and Pontevedra; p. (1981) 2,811,942.

Galilee, northern div. of Palestine in Roman times, containing the ts. Cana, Capernaum, Tiberias, Nazareth; the ch. scene of Christ's ministry; now **Israel.**

Galilee, Sea of (Lake Tiberias), also known as L. Gennesaret; Biblical associations; 207 m below level of Med.; Israel plans to draw water from L. to irrigate Negev; a. 166 km².

Gallarate, t., **Italy;** nr. Milan; textiles; p. (1981) 46,915.

Galle, c., pt. on S.W. cst. of **Sri Lanka;** exp. tea, rubber, coconut oil; suffered from competition with Colombo after construction of modern harbour there; p. (1983) 88,000.

Gallego, R., N.E. **Spain;** rises in Pyrenees, flows S. to R. Ebro at Zaragoza; provides irrigation around Zaragoza; valley used by main rly. across Pyrenees from Pau (France) to Zaragoza; 176 km long.

Gallipoli. See **Gelibolu.**

Galloway, anc. dist. S.W. **Scot.;** inc. l. gov. dists. of Stewartry and Wigtown; dairying.

Galloway, Mull of, the extremity of the Rinns of G., the most southern pt. of **Scot.**

Galston, burgh, Kilmarnock and Loudoun, **Scot.;** on R. Irvine, nr. Kilmarnock; p. (1991) 5,154.

Galveston, c., spt., Texas, **USA;** on I. in Bay at entrance to G. of Mexico; gr. cotton and sulphur pt. with lge. exp. of agr. prod.; mills, foundries, food-processing, chemicals; univ., resort; p. (1990) 59,070 (c.), 217,000 (met. a. with Texas City).

Galway, co., Galway Bay, Connacht, **R.o.I.;** fishery, cattle, marble quarrying; a. 6,351 km²; p. (1986) 178,552.

Galway, co. t. and cultural ctr. Galway, **R.o.I.;** univ.; spt.; fishing; sawmills, textiles, printing; p. (1986) 47,104.

Gambia, The, W. **Africa,** on Atl. Oc.; comprises St. Mary's I. (on which is Banjul, the cap.) and narrow mainland enclave (average width 32 km) extending 320 km inland astride R. Gambia, hot all year, summer rain, but savannah inland; agr. is basis of economy, esp. groundnuts; economic aid from Taiwan; communications developed around Banjul (spt. and airpt.); union with Senegal (1982), dissolved 1989; one of Africa's smallest sts., a. 11,295 km²; p. (1991) 880,000.

Gambia, R., **Gambia,** rises in Futa Jalon Plateau, flows N. and W. into Atl. Oc. at Banjul; forms main means of communication through Gambia, 1,120 km long.

Gambier Is., Fr. Polynesia, **S. Pac. Oc.,** 4 coral Is.; a. 31 km².

Gand. See **Ghent.**

Gandhinagar, new cap. of Gujarat, **India;** on Sabarmati R., 21 km N. of Ahmadabad; under construction; p. (1991) 123,359.

Ganges (Ganga), sacred R. of **India;** rises in Himalayas and flows to Bay of Bengal via alluvial cones at foot of Himalayas and by several delta mouths, on one of which stands Calcutta; navigable for lge. ships from Allahabad; delta alone larger than Eng. and Wales; flood plain and delta very fertile and densely populated; removal of irrig. water by India causes friction with Bangladesh; agreement over division of water at Farraka barrage reached (1978); 2,400 km long.

Gangtok, t., cap. of, Sikkim st; **India;** E, Himalayas, agr. tr. ctr.; carpets; p. (1001) 23,024.

Gan Jiang (Kan R.), S. **China;** flows N. to L. Poyang; valley provides road route from Guandong to Jianxi prov.; c. 880 km. long.

Gansu (Kansu), prov., N.W. **China;** borders Inner Mongolia; cap. Lanzhou; pastoral agr., wheat, cotton, tobacco; coal reserves; rich iron ore deposits; attemps to break down isolation by attracting foreign investment; a. 391,507 km²; p. (1990) 22,930,000.

Gap, t., Hautes Alpes, S.E. **France;** textiles; p. (1990) 35,647.

Gard, dep., S. **France;** in Languedoc, on Mediterranean; cap. Nîmes; vines, olives, sericulture; a. 5,879 km²; p. (1990) 585,000.

Garda, L., between Lombardy and Venezia, **Italy;** variety of scenery, winter resort; a. 370 km²; greatest depth, 346 m.

Gardéz, t., **Afghanistan;** alt. 2,287 m; ctr. of comm. and transport; p. (1984) 10,469.

Garforth, t., West Yorks., **Eng.;** coalmng., lt. inds.; p. (1981) 28,405.

Garigliano, R. and dist., S. central **Italy;** where Liri R. joins Gari R. below Cassino; nuclear power plant.

Garmisch-Partenkirchen, t., Bavaria, **Germany;** winter sports; p. (1986) 27,700.

Garonne, R., S.W. **France;** rises at foot of Mt. Maladetta (Pyrenees), flows via Toulouse and agr. valley, and enters Gironde estuary 32 km below Bordeaux; 720 km long.

Garrigue, region, Languedoc, S. **France;** low limestone hills, run N.E. to S.W., W. of Rhône delta; semi-arid; Mediterranean vegetation to which region gives name; winter pasture for sheep; olives; Montpellier, Nîmes located on S. flank.

Garut, t., W. Java, **Indonesia,** mtn. resort, lge. spinning mill; p. 24,219.

Gary, c., Ind., **USA;** on S. shore of L. Michigan; leading producer of steel, tinplate, cement; p. (1990) 116,646 (c.), 605,000 (met. a. with Hammond).

Gascony, anc. prov., S.W. **France;** now comprises deps. along Atl. cst. and Pyrenees; Landes, Gers, Hautes-Pyrenees, and parts of Lot-et-Garonne, Tarn-et-Garonne, Haute Garonne, Gironde, and Ariège. Battleground in Hundred Years War.

Gastonia, t., N.C., **USA;** impt. textile ctr.; p. (1980) 47,333.

Gateshead, t., met. dist., Tyne and Wear, **Eng.;** on R. Tyne opposite Newcastle; engin., food-processing, pumps, paper; pt.; p. (1993) 202,900 (dist.).

Gatineau, R., **Canada;** trib. of Ottawa R., which it joins nr. Ottawa; length 480 km; hydroelec. power; forested valley.

Gatwick, West Sussex, **Eng.;** 40 km S. London; first airport in world where trunk road, main rly. line and air facilities combined in one unit.

Gaul (Lat. *Gallia*), embraced the lands inhabited by Celtic peoples in Roman times, covering what is now modern France (Gaul proper), Belgium, N. Italy, and parts of Germany, Neth., and Switzerland. South of the Alps was known as Cisalpine Gaul, north of the Alps as Transalpine Gaul.

Gauri-Sankar, mtn. in Himalayas, Nepal and Tibet, **China;** 6 km W. of Mt. Everest; alt. 7,149 m.

Gävle, spt., **Sweden;** timber, textiles, steel, porcelain; p. (1992) 89,194.

Gävleborg, co., **Sweden;** ch. t., Gävle; a. 18,544 km²; p. (1992) 289,190.

Gaya, t., Bihar, **India;** Buddhist pilgrim ctr.; cottons, silks; p. (1991) 292,000.

Gaza, ch. t. of Gaza Strip (q.v.); in ancient times the t. where Samson brought down the temple; p. (1985) 1·608 m.

Gazankulu (Machangana), Bantu Terr. Authority (1969), **S. Africa**; home of Shangana and Tsonga p.; cap. Giyana; p. (1985) 497,000.

Gaza Strip, coastal a. under Egyptian admin. since 1949; occupied by Israeli troops, Nov. 1956–March 1957, and after June 1967; now granted limited Palestinian self-rule..

Gaziantep, t. and prov., **Turkey**; S.W. of Malatya; mkt. t.; p. (1985) 573,968 (t.), 1,140,594 (prov.).

Gazli, Uzbekistan; 96 km N.W. of Gukhara; natural gas field; pipeline to Chelyabinsk opened 1963; destroyed by earthquake (1976); p. (1990) 8,900.

Gdańsk (Danzig), c., and prov., N. **Poland**; Baltic pt.; on branch of Vistula; annexed to Germany 1939, restored to Poland 1945; shipbldg., machin., chemicals, metals; Gdańsk, Gdynia and Sopot admin. as single c. (Trójmiasto = tricity). Birthplace of Solidarity trade union movement; p. (1989) 462,076 (c.), 1,417,800 (prov.).

Gdynia, spt., Gdańsk, N. **Poland**; competes with spt. of Gdańsk for Polish hinterland; impt. comm., rly. and industl. ctr.; part of the Trójmiasto; p. (1989) 251,303.

Gedling, l. gov. dist., Notts., **Eng.**; Basford, Carlton and Arnold and N.E. outskirts of Nottingham; p. (1993) 112,000.

Geelong, c., Victoria, **Australia**; spt. on Corio Bay (part of Pt. Phillip Bay); expanding comm. and industl. ctr.; improved pt. facilities in 1960s, bulk grain terminal; p. (1986) 152,800.

Gejiu (Kokiu), t., Yunnan prov., **China**; leading tin-mng. ctr. of China; p. (1984) 337,700.

Gela, t., S. Sicily, **Italy**; in cotton-growing a.; petrochemicals; p. (1981) 74,789.

Gelderland, prov., **Neth.**; E. and S. of Utrecht prov., a. 5,022 km²; cap. Arnhem; cereals, tobacco; cattle rearing; p. (1993) 1,839,883.

Geleen, with Sittard, met. a. Limburg. prov., N.E. of Maastricht **Neth.**; p. (1993) 184,097 (met. a.).

Gelibolu (Gallipoli), pt. and penin. on the Dardanelles, **Turkey**; scene of unsuccessful landing by British and Anzac troops 1915; 176 km long.

Gelligaer, t., Rhymney Valley, Mid Glamorgan, **Wales**; 6 km N.E. of Pontypridd; coal mng.; p. (1981) 34,118.

Gelsenkirchen, t., N. Rhine–Westphalia, **Germany**; in Ruhr conurb. on Rhine–Herne canal; coal, ironwks., glass, chemicals, oil refining; p. (1990) 293,400.

Geneva, c., cap of G. can., **Switzerland**; at exit of Rhône from L. Geneva; cath., univ.; former H.Q. of League of Nations; H.Q. of ILO, WHO, and Red Cross; watchmkg., jewellery, elec. gds., optical instruments; tourist resort; birthplace of Rousseau; p. (1990) 167,200 (c), 376,000 (canton).

Geneva (L. Léman), L., S.W. corner of **Switzerland**; forms a gr. crescent of water, source of poetic inspiration; 371 m a.s.l.; a. 578 km².

Génissiat, France; site of gr. barrage and hydroelec. power sta. on Rhône below Geneva.

Genk, t., Limburg, **Belgium**; stainless steel wks., petrochemicals; p. (1993) 61,765.

Gennevilliers, t., Hauts-de-Seine, **France**; N.W. sub. of Paris; R. pt.; p. (1982) 45,445.

Genoa (Genova), c., ch. pt. **Italy**; cath., univ., palaces; handles one-third of Italy's foreign tr.; pt. and airpt. expansion, shipyards, steelwks., engin., textiles, tanning; p. (1992) 667,563.

George L., N.Y., **USA**; Adirondack mtns.; picturesque resort.

Georgetown, cap., **Cayman Is.**; pt.; p. (1985) 8,900.

Georgetown (Demerara), c., cap. of **Guyana**; on Demerara R.; exp. sugar, cocoa, coffee, timber, gold, diamonds, bauxite; airpt. nearby; botanical gardens; p. (1983) 188,000, 187,056 (met. a.)

Georgetown. See **Penang**.

Georgia, st., S.E. **USA**; one of 13 original sts., admitted to Union 1788; st. flower Cherokee Rose, st. bird Brown Thrasher; on Atl. cst.; rising to Appalachians; impt. arable agr.; cotton and lumber inds.; major source of kaolin; ch. ts., Atlanta (cap.), Savannah; a. 152,489 km²; p. (1990) 6,478,216.

Georgia (Gruziya), former USSR constituent rep.; rich agr., fruit, tobacco, grain; mng. inc. manganese, gold, oil; several hydroelectric power plants; coastal and mtn. resorts; active Jewish community;

ethnic unrest 1989; cap. Tbilisi; a. 69,671 km²; p. (1990) 5,456,100.

Georgian Bay, arm of L. Huron, S. Ont., **Canada**; separated from L. by Manitoulin I. and Saugeen peninsula; c. 160 km long, c. 80 km wide; L. pts., Owen Sound, Midland, Parry Sound; Georgian Bay Is., Nat. Park.

Gera, c., cap. of G. admin. dist., **Germany**; on White Elster R.; woollens, printing; lignite mined nearby; p. (1990) 128,000.

Geraldton, spt., W. **Australia**; N. outlet for wheat belt; also exps. wool and manganese; early tomatoes; super phosphate; p. (1990) 21,386.

Germany, reunified 3 October 1990 after partition into Democratic Rep. (E. Germany) and Federal Republic (W. Germany) since 1948; N. half part of N. European Plain; rises in S. to Bavarian Alps; 2nd lgst. trading nation of world; mainly industl. with core in Ruhr conurb.; motor vehicles, chemicals, precision engin.; member of EU; tourism; 16 admin. dists. (Länder); cap. Berlin (seat. of parliament, govt. to be decided); faces economic problems after reunification; a. 357,041 km²; p. (1992) 80·28 m.

Germiston, t., Transvaal, **S. Africa**; nr. Johannesburg; gold-mng.; rly. wkshps., engin., machin., chemicals; gas pipeline from Sasolburg, p. (1980) 166,440 (dist.).

Gerona, c., cap. of G. prov., **Spain**; cath.; textiles, chemicals; p. (1987) 67,447 (c.), (1991) 504,046 (prov.).

Gerrards Cross, t., S.E. Bucks., **Eng.**; 14 km E. of High Wycombe; residtl.

Gers, dep. S.W. **France**; cap. Auch; grain, vines, brandy; a. 6,291 km²; p. (1990) 174,600.

Gersoppa Falls, Sharavati R., Karnataka, **India**; hgst. cascade 253 m; hydroelec. power.

Getalfe, t. Madrid prov. C. **Spain**; agric. ind., geog. centre of Spain; p. (1991) 140,104.

Gezira, dist., **Sudan**, N.E. Africa; between Blue and White Niles; c. 12,173 km² capable of irrigation provided by Blue Nile at Sennar Dam; lge-scale growing of high-quality cotton; total a. c. 20,200 km².

Ghadames (Ghudamis), oasis, Sahara Desert, **Libya**; at point where Tunis, Algeria, Libya converge 480 km S.W. of Tripoli.

Ghaghara (Gogra), sacred R., **India**; trib. of Ganges, rises in Tibet, flows through Uttar Pradesh; lge. catchment a. but poorly developed floodplain; 960 km long.

Ghana, rep., W. **Africa**; indep. st., member of Brit. Commonwealth; tropical monsoon climate, but rainfall decreases inland; badly affected by Sahelian drought; S. Ghana more developed than N.; agr. basis of comm. economy and cocoa (of which Ghana is world's lgst producer) 60 per cent of all exp. by value; Volta R. scheme produces power from main dam at Akosombo and an aluminium smelter plant began production in 1967; reservoir decreasing with drought in Sahel and reducing power production; oil refining and production; communications network based on Accra and Takoradi on cst., and inland ctr. of Kumasi; development of road network vital for expansion of comm. agr.; 3 univs.; pts. at Takoradi and Tema closely linked with internal economic growth; cap. Accra; a. 238,539 km²; p. (1991) 15.51 m.

Ghardaia, dep., **Algeria**; N. of Sahara; includes Mzab valley; p. (1987) 215,955.

Ghats, mtn. ranges which border the Deccan plateau in S. **India**. The **Eastern Ghats** are broken by many Rs. and rise only to 1,362 m in Northern Circars. The **Western Ghats** form an almost unbroken range, reaching 2,672 m in Dodabetta in Nilgiri hills; rainfall extremely heavy; forests; hydroelectric power.

Ghaziabad, t., Uttar Pradesh, **India**; on R. Jumna opposite Delhi; p. (1991) 454,000.

Ghazipur, t., Uttar Pradesh, N. **India**; on Ganges, E. of Varanasi; p. (1981) 60,725.

Ghazni, mtn. t., E. **Afghanistan**; once cap. of empire of Mahmud, c. A.D. 1000; now mkt. t.; p. (1982) 31,985.

Ghent, c., cap. of E. Flanders prov., **Belgium**; pt. at confluence of Rs. Scheldt and Lys; cath., univ.; textiles, steel, plastics, chemicals; oil refinery; p. (1993) 229,828.

Ghor, El, depression, **Jordan** and **Israel**, between Sea of Galilee and Dead Sea 3–24 km wide; agr. resettlement scheme.

Giant's Causeway, basaltic columns on promontory of N. cst. of Moyle, **N. Ireland**.

Gibraltar, City of, Brit. terr. at W. entrance to Mediterranean; rocky I., 426 m, joined to Spain by sandy isthmus; few natural resources; economy depends on tourism, Admiralty dockyard, services to shipping, and entrepôt tr., to close 1983; Spanish govt. lays claim to terr.; frontier with Spain opened (1985); a. 6·5 km²; p. (1992) 28,848.

Gibraltar, Strait of, connects Mediterranean with Atl., 13·6 km wide; of strategic importance.

Gidgelpha-Moomba, dist., S. **Australia**; lge. natural gas field; pipeline to Adelaide.

Giessen, t., Hesse, **Germany**; on R. Lahn; univ.; various mnfs.; p. (1986) 71,100.

Gifu, t., Central Honshu, **Japan**; cas.; fans, lanterns, textiles; tourism for cormorant fishing; p. (1990) 410,318.

Gigha, I. Argyll and Bute, **Scot.**; off W. cst. of Kintyre; 10 km by 3 km.

Gijón, spt., Oviedo, **Spain**; on Bay of Biscay; gd. harbour; tobacco, petroleum, coal, earthenware; steel wks. nearby; p. (1991) 260,254.

Gila, R., N.M. and Arizona, **USA**; trib. of R. Colorado; used for irrigation in Imperial valley; 1,040 km long.

Gilan, prov., N.W. **Iran**; on Caspian Sea, bounded by USSR; sub-tropical climate; agr., inc. cotton and rice; cap. Rasht; p. (1982) 1,581,872.

Gilbert Is. See Kiribati.

Gilgit, dist., Kashmir, **India**; mtnous., exceeding 6,000 m on N. and W.; with Ladakh links India with Tibet.

Gillingham, t., l. gov. dist., Kent, **Eng.**; 3 km E. of Chatham; on R. Medway; naval and military establishments; cement, lt. inds.; p. (1993) 96,000.

Gippsland, dist., S.E. Victoria, **Australia**; between Dividing Range and cst.; main brown coal field supplying local power plants; intensive dairying and mkt. gardens for Melbourne.

Girardot, t., **Colombia**; R. pt. and airport on upper course of Magdalena R.; linked by rly. to Bogotá; coffee, hides, ceramics.

Girgenti. See Agrigento.

Gironde, dep., S.W. **France**; vineyards, grain, fruit, wines; cap. Bordeaux; a. 10,723 km²; p. (1990) 1,213,500.

Gironde, estuary, S.W. **France**; formed by junc. of Rs. Garonne and Dordogne; navigable to Pauillac and Bordeaux.

Girvan, burgh, Kyle and Carrick, **Scot.**; on F. of Clyde, 29 km S.W. of Ayr; summer resort; p. (1991) 7,449.

Gisborne, c. and dist., spt., N.I., **N.Z.**; on Poverty Bay, 96 km N.E. of Napier; freezing-wks.; fishing; p. (1991) 44,361 (dist.).

Giuba, R. See Juba R.

Giurgiu, t., **Romania**; pt. on Danube; opposite Ruse, Bulgaria; linked by oil pipelines with Ploiesti; p. (1990) 71,875.

Givors, t., Rhône dep., **France**; on Rhône R. 16 km S. of Lyons; mnfs. inc. glass; oil refining near by at Feyzin; p. (1982) 20,554.

Gjövik, t., S. **Norway**; on L. Mjösa; furniture, footwear, lt. inds.; p. (1990) 15,514.

Glace Bay, t., Cape Breton I., Nova Scotia, **Canada**; coal; harbour; p. (1986) 20,467.

Glacier National Park, B.C., **Canada**; mtn. scenery, resorts; a. 1,349 km².

Glacier National Park, Mon., **USA**; Rocky mtns., picturesque; a. 4,040 km².

Gladbeck, t., N. Rhine–Westphalia, **Germany**; N. of Essen; coalmng; p. (1986) 76,600.

Gladstone, t., Queensland, **Australia**; spt. exports coal to Japan; alumina plant (1973), oil storage; p. (1991) 31,410.

Glamis, v., Angus, **Scot.**; G. cas. childhood home of Queen Elizabeth the Queen Mother, and featured in Shakespeare's *Macbeth*.

Glamorgan, former co., S. **Wales**; now divided into 3 cos., **South**, **West** and **Mid-Glamorgan**.

Glamorgan, Vale of. See Gwent, Plain of.

Glanford, l. gov. dist., Humberside, **Eng.**; a. S. of Humber and inc. Brigg and Barton; p. (1993) 72,700.

Glarus, can., **Switzerland**; E. of Schwyz; a. 684 km²; sheep, cheese, cottons; p. (1990) 167,200.

Glarus, t., cap. of can. G., **Switzerland**; on R. Linth, nr. Wessen; p. (1980) 5,800.

Glasgow, c., burgh, l. gov. dist., Strathclyde Reg., **Scot.**; on R. Clyde; leading spt. and 3rd lgst. c. in

Gt. Britain; major problems of urban renewal; ctr. of industl. belt; shipbldg., iron and steel, heavy and lt. engin., electronics equipment, printing; univ., cath.; p. (1991) 662,954 (c.), (1993) 681,470 (dist.).

Glas Maol, mtn., Angus, Kincardine and Deeside, **Scot.**; part of the Braes of Angus; 1,068 m.

Glastonbury, t., Somerset, **Eng.**; on R. Brue, ruins of 10th century abbey; nearby prehistoric lake villages; p. (1981) 6,773.

Glatz. See Klodzko.

Glauchau, t., Saxony, **Germany**; on R. Mulde; woollens, calicoes, dyes, machin.; p. (1989) 26,566.

Gleiwitz. See Gliwice.

Glen Affric, Inverness, **Scot.**; drained E. to Moray F.; hydroelectric scheme.

Glencoe, Lochaber, **Scot.**; S.E. of Ballachulish; scene of massacre of MacDonalds 1692.

Glendalough, Wicklow, **R.o.I.**; scenic valley with Ls. and monastic ruins; tourism.

Glenelg, t., S. **Australia**; on St. Vincent G.; sub. of Adelaide; first free settlement in Australia; p. (1984) 13,720.

Glen Garry, Perth and Kinross, **Scot.**; used by Perth to Inverness rly. on S. approach to Drumochter Pass.

Glen More, Scottish valley traversed by Caledonian canal, from Fort William to Inverness.

Glenrothes, t., Kirkaldy, **Scot.**; new t. (1948); electronics; p. (1991) 38,650.

Glen Roy, Lochaber, **Scot.**; 24 km N.E. of Fort William; remarkable terraces, remains of series of glacial lakes.

Glen Spean, Lochaber, **Scot.**; used by Glasgow to Fort William rly.

Glittertind, mtn., Opland co., S. **Norway**; highest peak in Scandinavia; alt. 2,483 m.

Gliwice (Gleiwitz), c., S.W. **Poland** (since 1945); coal mng. and steel ctr. of Katowice region; machin., chemicals; p. (1989) 212,481.

Glomma (Glommen), R., S. **Norway**; lgst. R. in Scandinavia; flows to Skaggerak; timber inds.; hydroelec. power; 400 km long.

Glossop, t., High Peak, Derbys., **Eng.**; at foot of Pennines; paper, food-canning, textile finishing; mkt.; p. (1981) 25,339.

Gloucester, cath. c., l. gov. dist., **Eng.**; on R. Severn; the Roman Glevum; cath., on site of Benedictine abbey; aircraft mftg. and repair; engin., nylon; p. (1993) 104,800 (dist.).

Gloucester, t., Mass., **USA**; pt. at head of G. Harbour; resort, fish-processing; p. (1980) 27,768.

Gloucestershire, non-met. co., W. **Eng.**; situated around lower Severn basin, Cotswolds, Forest of Dean; sheep, dairy and fruit farming; major ctrs. of p. at Gloucester and Cheltenham; a. 2,639 km²; p. (1993) 543,900.

Glyncorrwg, t., Afan, West Glamorgan, **Wales**; 6 km N. of Maesteg; coal-mng. dist.; p. (1981) 8,647.

Glynde, v., Sussex, **Eng.**; nearby Tudor manor and opera house of Glyndebourne.

Glyndŵr, l. gov. dist., Clwyd, **Wales**; lge inland a. inc. Denbigh, Ruthin and Llangollen; p. (1993) 42,200.

Gmünd. See Schwäbisch-Gmünd.

Gniezno (Gnesen), c., W. **Poland**; E. of Poznan; first cap. of Poland (11th cent.); cath.; p. (1989) 69,646.

Goa, **India**; former Portuguese enclave; statehood conferred 1987; cap. Panaji; iron pyrites, manganese, coconuts, fish, spices, cashew nuts, salt, copra; a. 3,693 km²; p. (1991) 1,169,793.

Goat Fell, mtn., I. of Arran, Cunninghame, **Scot.**; alt. 874 m.

Gobi, steppes and stony or sandy desert, **China** and **Mongolia**; divided into two principal divs.; Shamo in Central Mongolia, and the basins of the Tarim, E. Turkestan; l. about 2,400 km (E. to W.), breadth 800–1,120 km; average elevation 1,200 m; crossed by impt. Kalgan–Ulan Bator highway.

Godalming, t., Waverley, Surrey, **Eng.**; 6 km S.W. of Guildford; first public supply of elec. 1881; Charterhouse School; p. (1981) 18,209.

Godavari, sacred R., **India**; rises in W. Ghats, flows E. across Deccan through gap in E. Ghats to Bay of Bengal; forms lge. delta; used for irrigation and hydroelec. powers; c. 1,440 km long.

Godesberg, Bad, t., N. Rhine–Westphalia, **Germany**; part of Bonn; spa; meeting place of Chamberlain and Hitler 1938.

Godhavn, Danish settlement, Disco I., W. of Greenland; arctic research sta.; fish processing; p. (1990) 1,164.

Godthåb, t., admin. ctr., **Greenland;** first Danish col. 1721; sm. pt.; fish processing; p. (1990) 12,687.

Godwin-Austen Mt. or **K2,** peak (8,611 m) in Karakoram between Tibet and Sinkiang, **China,** after Everest highest in world; summit reached by Prof. Desio 1954; also named Chobrum.

Gogmagog Hills, Cambs., **Eng.;** low chalk upland, S. of Breckland; traces of Roman entrenchment.

Gora. See **Ghaghara R.**

Goiânia, t., cap of Goiás st., **Brazil;** comm. and industl. ctr.; p. (1991) 920,838.

Goiás, st., central **Brazil;** mtnous., forested; stock-raising, tobacco; gold, diamonds; cap. Goiânia, on Vermelho R.; a. 642,061 km²; p. (1991) 4,024,547.

Gökçeada I. (Imbroz I.), off W. **Turkey,** in Aegean Sea at entrance to Dardanelles; a. 280 km².

Golconda, fort and ruined c., nr. Hyderabad, S. India; famous for its legendary diamond troves.

Gold Coast, City of, Queensland, **Australia;** 40 km cstl. a. inc. 18 townships, named 1959; rapid tourist devel. inc. Surfer's Paradise; p. (1991) 274,200.

Golden Gate, strait between San Francisco Bay and Pac. Oc., Cal., **USA;** spanned by Golden Gate Bridge, opened 1937.

Golden Horn, peninsular on the Bosporus, forming the harbour of Istanbul, **Turkey.**

Golden Triangle, a. of Britain and Europe roughly bounded by Birmingham, Frankfurt, and Paris; economic core a. of **W. Europe.**

Golden Vale, dist., Limerick, Tipperary, **R.o.I.;** drained W. to Shannon and E. to Suir; rich farming a., beef and dairy cattle, pigs.

Gold River, t., B.C., **Canada;** on W. cst. of Vancouver I. at junc. of Heber and Gold Rs.; new t. 1967; p. (1986) 1,879.

Golspie, co. t., Sutherland, **Scot.;** p. (1991) 1,434.

Gomal Pass, a pass in Sulaiman ranges, **Pakistan,** leading from Indus valley to Afghanistan.

Gomel', c., S.E. **Belarus;** on R. Sozh, trib. of Dnieper; R. pt., agr. ctr.; engin., chemicals, clothing inds.; p. (1990) 506,100.

Gomera, I., Canaries; 21 km S.W. Tenerife; cap. San Sebastian.

Gondar, t. N.W. **Ethiopia;** N. of L. Tana; airport; p. (1984) 68,958.

Goodwin Sands, dangerous sandbanks off E. cst. of Kent, **Eng.;** shielding the Down roadstead.

Goodwood, v., West Sussex, **Eng.;** racecourse and motor racing; home of Dukes of Richmond.

Goole, t., Boothferry, Humberside, **Eng.;** second pt. of Hull on Humber; shipbldg., flour milling, fertilisers, alum and dextrine mftg.; p. (1981) 17,127.

Goonhilly Downs, Cornwall, **Eng.;** satellite communications sta. of Post Office.

Göppingen, t., Baden-Württemberg, **Germany;** between Ulm and Stuttgart; machin., iron, wood, chemicals; p. (1986) 51,400.

Gorakhpur, t., Uttar Pradesh, **India;** on Rapti R., N. of Varanasi; grain, timber; fertilisers; univ.; p. (1991) 506,000.

Gordon, l. gov. dist., Grampian Reg., **Scot.;** formerly part of Aberdeenshire; p. (1993) 79,650.

Gorgān, c. **Iran,** Mazandaran prov.; nr. Caspian Sea; p. (1982) 114,000.

Gori, t., central **Georgia;** at con-fluence of Bolshoy, Liakhvi, and Kura Rs.; birthplace of Stalin; p. (1990) 69,600.

Gorinchem, t., S. Holland, **Neth.;** on R. Merwede; p. (1993) 30,106.

Goring Gap, Berks./Oxon., **Eng.;** where R. Thames cuts through Chilterns and Berkshire Downs.

Gorizia (Görz), c., cap. of Gorizia prov., N.E. **Italy;** on Yugoslav border; cas.; agr. mkt., fruit, wine; textile machin.; p. (1981) 41,557.

Gorki or **Gorky** See **Nizhniy Novgorod.**

Görlitz, t. Brandenburg, **Germany;** on W. Neisse on Polish border; lignite mines; textile mills; mystic Jacob Boehme lived here; p. (1981) 80,831.

Gorlovka, t., **Ukraine;** in Donets Basin; coal, chemicals, engin.; oil pipeline connects with Grozny oilfields; p. (1990) 337,900.

Gorno-Altai, aut. region, S.E. Altai terr., **Russia;** in Altai mtns. on Mongolian border; cap. Gorno-Altaisk; forested, pastoral agr., mng. (gold, manganese, mercury); a. 92,567 km; p. (1989) 190,800.

Gorno-Altaisk, t., **Russia;** cap. of Gorno-Altai aut. region; nr. Chuya highway to Mongolia; food-processing of agr. prod. from region; p.

(1986) 39,000.

Gorno Badakhshan, aut. region, S.E. **Tajikistan;** in Pamirs, bordered by China and Afghanistan; mng. (gold, mica, salt, limestone); livestock; cap. Khorog; a. 63,688 km²; p. (1990) 164,300.

Gornyy Snezhnogorsk, t., **Russia;** new t. in Siberia Arctic on R. Hantaiki, 56 km W.N.W. Komsomolsk; tin-mng.

Gorseinon, v., West Glamorgan, S. **Wales;** nr. Loughour estuary, 6 km N.W. of Swansea; former steel-wks., zinc refineries.

Gorzów Wielkopolski (Landesberg an der Warthe), c., Gorżow prov. W. Poland (since 1945); industl. ctr.; lignite mines; p. (1989) 123,222 (c.), 497,400 (prov.).

Gosainthan (Xixabangma Feng), mtn. massif, **Nepal–Tibet (China)** border; part of Himalayas; rises to 8,091 m.

Gosford-Woy Woy, t., N.S.W., **Australia;** electric rly. connecting Sydney (80 km to S.) led to growth of commuting, dairying, mkt. gardening and tourism; p. (1981) 94,369.

Gosforth, t., sub. to Newcastle upon Tyne, Tyne and Wear, **Eng.;** coal mines closed 1948; p. (1981) 23,835.

Goslar, t., Lower Saxony, **Germany;** mng. ctr. at foot of Harz mtns.; lt. inds., tourism; p. (1986) 49,000.

Gosport, t., l. gov. dist., Hants., **Eng.;** naval depot W. of Portsmouth to which it is linked by ferry; marine engin.; p. (1993) 75,900 (dist.).

Göta, R., Sweden; flows from L. Vänern to the Kattegat; also canal connecting L. Vänern with the Baltic; the G. Canal provides a popular tourist trip from Stockholm to Göteborg.

Göteborg or **Gothenburg,** c., cap. of Göteborg and Bohus, S.W. **Sweden;** at mouth of R. Göta on Kattegat; second c. in Sweden for commerce and ind.; univ.; shipbldg., oil refining; deepwater tanker terminal; p. (1992) 433,811 (t.), 747,849 (co.).

Gotha, t., Erfurt, **Germany;** iron, machin., engin., musical instruments, textiles, porcelain, printing, cartography; p. (1981) 57,573.

Gotham, v., Notts., **Eng.;** gypsum mng. and plaster wks.

Gotland, I. in the Baltic, **Sweden;** many historic bldgs.; cap. Visby; tourism; a. 3,173 km²; p. (1992) 57,578.

Göttingen, t., Lower Saxony, **Germany;** univ.; scientific instruments, pharmaceutics, film studios; p. (1990) 122,700.

Gottwaldov. See **Zlin.**

Gouda, t., S. Holland, **Neth.;** on R. IJssel, 18 km from Rotterdam; cheese, candles, ceramics, pipes; p. (1993) 68,677.

Gough I., Atl. Oc. dependency of **St. Helena;** breeding ground of the great shearwater; guano.

Goulburn, t., N.S.W., **Australia;** commands route across Gr. Dividing Range; in agr. dist. W. of Sydney; cath.; wool, shoes; p. (1981) 21,755.

Goulburn Is., N.T., **Australia;** 2 sm. Is. off N. cst. of Arnhem Land; Methodist Mission sta.

Goulburn, R., Victoria, **Australia;** irrigation.

Gourock, burgh, Inverclyde, **Scot.;** on F. of Clyde, 3 km W. of Greenock; ferry to Dunoon; resort; p. (1991) 11,743.

Gove Peninsula, N.T., **Australia;** N.E. extremiy of Arnhem Land; giant bauxite and alumina production complex (1968); model t. of Nhulunbuy.

Gower, peninsula, W. Glamorgan, **Wales;** tourism.

Gowrie, Carse of, fertile tract N. side F. of Tay, **Scot.;** includes Dundee, Kinnoul, Perth.

Gozo, I. in Mediterranean, belonging to **Malta;** the anc. Gaulos; surrounded by perpendicular cliffs; a. 67 km²; p. (1990) 26,064.

Grado-Aquileia, t., Friuli-Venezia Giulia, N.E. **Italy;** pleasure resort and former Roman spt.; early Christian mosaics and antiquities; Grado joined to mainland by bridge.

Graengesberg, dist., Kopparberg co., **Sweden;** on S. fringe of Scandinavian mtns.; iron ore.

Grafham Water, reservoir, Camb., **Eng.**

Grafton, t., N.S.W., **Australia;** on Clarence R.; dairy prod., timber; annual jacaranda festival; p. (1981) 17,005.

Graham Land, part of British Antarctic Territory; mtnous., icebound; discovered 1832.

Grahamstown, t., C. Prov., S. **Africa;** univ. cath.; p. (1980) 25,120.

Graian Alps, mtns. between Savoie, **France,** and

Piedmount, **Italy**; hgst. point Gran Paradiso, 4,063 m.

Grain Coast, name formerly applied to cst. of Liberia, W. Africa; "grain" refers to spices.

Grammichele, t., E. Sicily, **Italy**; 37 km S.W. of Catania; planned settlement after 1968 earthquake; p. (1981) 13,607.

Grampian Region, l. gov. reg., N.E. **Scot.**; inc. former cos. of Aberdeenshire, Banff, Kincardine and Moray; highland a.; rapid devel. of cst. with N. Sea oil discoveries; a. 8,702 km²; p. (1993) 528,100.

Grampians, mtns. of **Scot.**; forming natural bdy. between Highlands and Lowlands; inc. Ben Nevis, the hgst. peak (1,344 m), the Cairngorms and Schiehallion.

Granada, t., W. **Nicaragua**; on L. Nicaragua; in rich agr. region; distilling, soap, furniture; p. (1985) 89,000.

Granada, c., cap. of G. prov., S. **Spain**; in Andalusia, at foot of Sierra Nevada; formerly cap. of Moorish kingdom of G.; univ., cath., famous 14th cent. Alhambra; tourism; p. (1991) 286,688.

Granada, prov., S. **Spain**; traversed by Sierra Nevada; wheat, olives, textiles, liqueurs, paper; a. 12,530 km²; p. (1991) 806,499.

Granby, t., Quebec, **Canada**; on Yamaska R.; sawmills, leather, textiles, rubber, plastics; p. (1986) 38,508.

Gran Chaco, extensive lowland plain, **Argentina**, **Paraguay**, and **Bolivia**, between Andes and Paraguay–Paraná Rs.; hot, wet, swampy region with forests containing quebracho trees, a source of tannin; potential for petroleum.

Grand Banks, submarine plateau, extending S.E. from Newfoundland, **Canada**; a. 1,295,000 km²; impt. cod fisheries.

Grand Bassam, t., spt., **Ivory Coast**; exp. bananas, palm-kernels.

Grand Canal, canal, N. **China**; c. 1,600 km long from Tianjin to Hangzhou; built between A.D. 605–18 and 1282–92; rebuilt for navigation and flood control.

Grand Canary, I., **Canaries**; cap. Las Palmas; tomatoes, bananas, potatoes; tourism; extinct volcanoes.

Grand Cayman I., **W.I.**; a. 220 km²; coconuts; cap. Georgetown; p. (1987) 21,500.

Grand Combin, mtn., **Switzerland**; part of Pennine Alps nr. Italian border; alt. 4,320 m.

Grand Coulee Dam, Wash., **USA**; on Columbia R., 176 km below Spokane; one of lgst. concrete dams in world, producing 1,924 mW hydroelec. power; reservoir (Franklin D. Roosevelt Lake) recreational a.; supplies irrigation water to 4,900 km² between Rs. Columbia and Snake.

Grand Falls, t., Newfoundland, **Canada**; newsprint; falls provide hydroelectric power; p. (1986) 9,121.

Grand Island, t., Nebraska, **USA**; cattle and grain t.; p. (1980) 33,180.

Grand' Mère, t., Quebec, **Canada**; pulp and paper mills; p. (1986) 15,442.

Grand Prairie. *See* Black Prairie.

Grand Rapids, c., Mich., **USA**; on Grand R.; furniture mkg., car and aircraft parts, chemicals, paper; p. (1990) 189,126 (c.), 688,000 (met. a.).

Grand R., Mich., **USA**; enters L. Mich. at Grand Haven, navigable to Grand Rapids; hydroelec. power; 400 km long.

Grand Turk, I., cap. of **Turks and Caicos Is.**; p. (1980) 3,146.

Grange, t., South Lakeland, Cumbria, **Eng.**; on N. cst. of Morecambe Bay; summer resort; p. (1981) 3,646.

Grangemouth, burgh, Falkirk, **Scot.**; on F. of Forth; shipbldg. and repair, marine engin., oil refining, projected oil tanker terminal; petroleum prods., chemicals, pharmaceutics; electronics and elec. ind.; oil pipeline to Finnart; p. (1991) 18,739.

Granite City, Ill., **USA**; iron and steel, tinplate, rly. engin., chemicals; p. (1980) 36,185.

Gran Sasso d'Italia, rugged limestone highlands, Abruzzi e Molise, central **Italy**, in highest part of Apennines, rising to 2,923 m in Monte Corno; Mussolini was rescued from here by German paratroopers 1943; Aquila at foot of Gran Sasso winter sports ctr.

Grantham, t., S. Kesteven, Lincs., **Eng.**; on Witham R.; tanning, agr. machin., engin.,

brewing, malting, basket mkg.; expanded t.; p. (1981) 30,084.

Grantown-on-Spey, burgh, Badenoch and Strathspey, **Scot.**; on R. Spey; resort; p. (1991) 2,391.

Granville, spt., Manche dep., **France**; on Golfe de St. Malo; fisheries, food-processing; p. (1982) 15,015.

Grasmere, v., Cumbria, **Eng.**; at head of Grasmere L.; home of Wordsworth; p. (1981) 1,100.

Grasse, t., Alpes-Maritimes dep., S.E. **France**, in Provence in hills above Cannes; perfumers; birthplace of Fragonard.

Graubünden. *See* Grisons.

Graudenz. *See* Grudziadz.

's-Gravenhage. *See* Hague.

Graves, Pointe de, N. point of Médoc peninsula, **France**; in famous wine dist.

Gravesend, spt., Gravesham, Kent, **Eng.**; S. bank R. Thames facing Tilbury; pilot sta. for Port of London; paper, cement; oil refinery projected; p. (1981) 52,963.

Gravesham, l. gov. dist., Kent, **Eng.**; based on Gravesend and surrounding dist.; p. (1993) 93,000.

Graz, c., cap. of Styria, **Austria**; on R. Mur at foothills of Alps; second lgst. c.; univ., cath.; machin., iron and steel, rly. wks.; p. (1991) 232,155.

Great Altai, range of mtns., lying mainly in **Outer Mongolia** but also in Western Siberia, **Russia**; rising to 4,200 m.

Great Artesian Basin, Central **Australia**; underlies plains of Queensland, N.S.W., S. **Australia**; supplies water for cattle and sheep stations; too saline for use in some a. and too hot in others (cooling towers necessary); a. 2 million km.²

Great Atlas (Haut Atlas), mtn., N.W. **Africa**; alt. c. 2,000 m; part of the Atlas mtns.

Great Australian Bight, wide inlet of **Indian Oc.**, S. cst. of **Australia**.

Great Barrier Reef, coral reef barrier off N.E. cst. of **Australia**; 1,600 km long, 120–160 km from cst.; currently being eaten away by the star fish, *Acanthaster planci*; many reef Is. form Nat. parks.

Great Basin, high plateau region between the Wasatch and Sierra Nevada mtns., **USA**; inc. most of Nevada, parts of Utah, Cal., Idaho, Ore., Wyo.; drainage ctr. Great Salt Lake; a. 543,900 km²; much desert; sparse p.

Great Bear Lake, lge. L., N.W. Terr., **Canada**; c. 280 km long; a. 36,260 km²; outlet through Great Bear R. to Mackenzie R.

Great Belt (Store Bælt), strait **Denmark**; separates Fyn I. from Sjaelland I.; sinuous shape makes navigation difficult; rly. ferry at narrowest point (18 km) between Nyborg and Korsør; 64 km long; proposed bridge.

Great Britain. *See* England, Scotland, Wales, British Isles.

Great Dividing Range, mtn. system, E. **Australia**; extends, under different local names, from Queensland to Victoria and separates E. cst. plains from interior; reaches max. alt. in Mt. Koskiusko (2,228 m), in Australian Alps, on bdy. between Victoria and N.S.W.

Greater Manchester, former met. co., pt., N.W. **Eng.**; lge. urban a. centred on major comm. ctr. of M., with former cotton spinning ts. to N., inc. Bolton, Bury and Rochdale; dormitory ts. to S.; former concentration on textile mftg. now reduced and inds. diversified; major industl. estate at Trafford Park; p. (1993) 2,578,900.

Great Falls, c., Mont., **USA**; on Missouri R.; lgst. c. in st.; mkt. for irrigated farming a.; ctr. of hydroelectric power, called the "electric city"; copper- and oil-refining, flour mills; p. (1990) 56,725.

Great Fisher Bank, submarine sandbank in N. Sea; 320 km E. of Aberdeen, 160 km S.W. of Stavanger; valuable fishing-ground; depth of water, from 45–75 m.

Great Gable, mtn., Cumbria, **Eng.**; alt. 899 m.

Great Grimsby, spt., l. gov. dist., Humberside, **Eng.**; on S. bank of R. Humber; major distant waters fish. pt.; food-processing; chemical ind. at nearby Immingham; p. (1993) 91,500.

Great Harwood, t., Hyndburn, Lancs., **Eng.**; 8 km N.E. of Blackburn; textiles, aero-engin.; p. (1981) 10,921.

Great Lake, Tasmania, **Australia**; lgst. freshwater L. in Australia.

Great Lakes, N. America; 5 freshwater Ls.; Superior, Michigan, Huron, Erie, Ontario; glacial genesis; frozen 4 to 5 months in winter; traffic in cereals, iron, coal, etc.; major ctr. of heavy inds.; resorts; serious pollution; a. 248,640 km².

Great Plains, lowland a. of central **N. America**; extending E. from Rocky mtns., and S. from Mackenzie to S. Texas.

Great Rift Valley, geological fault system extending from S.W. Asia to E. Africa, 4,800 km in l.; inc. L. Tiberias (Sea of Galilee), Jordan valley, Dead Sea, G. of Aqaba, Red Sea, and chain of Ls., notably L. Rudolf and L. Malawi; a branch runs through Ls. Tanganyika, Mobutu and Edward; used for geothermal power.

Great Salt Lake, shallow salty L., N. Utah, **USA**; in Great Basin plateau of N. America; remnant of L. Bonneville; alt. 1,286 m; varies in size and depth; receives Bear, Jordan and Beaver Rs.; many Is., no outlet.

Great Sandy Desert, W. Australia; mostly sand-hills, stony in ctr.; one of A. 3 great deserts.

Great Slave Lake, N.W. Terr., **Canada**; a. 28,490 km²; 496 km long; drained by Mackenzie R.; navigable.

Great Smoky Mtns., Tenn., **USA**; with Blue Ridge mtns. form E. zone of Appalachian mtn. system; hgst peak Clingmans Dome 2,026 m; largely preserved as Nat Park.

Great Torrington, t., Torridge, Devon, **Eng.**; on R. Torridge; mkt., processing of agr. prod.; p. (1981) 4,107.

Great Wall of China, wall built in N. **China** along S. edge of Mongolian plateau to keep out invading Mongols; length 2,400 km; begun in Ch'in dynasty by Shih Huang Ti, *c*. 220 B.C.; present form dates from Ming dynasty (1368–1644).

Great Whale R. (R. de la Baleine), Quebec, **Canada**; rises in L. Bienville, flows to Hudson Bay; difficult transport; 400 km long.

Great Yarmouth, pt., l. gov. dist., Norfolk, **Eng.**; at mouth of R. Yare; holiday resort; fish and food processing plants; base for N. Sea gas; p. (1993) 88,800 (dist.).

Greece, rep., S.E. **Europe**; mtnous. peninsula, between Mediterranean and Ægean Sea, inc. many sm. Is. to S.; lgst. Crete; inds. increasingly impt. but agr. prods. still ch. exp. (tobacco, olive oil, cotton, citrus fruit, wine); only 25 per cent a. cultivable; economy also helped by lge. merchant fleet and tourism; deposed king in exile; executive power held by military junta 1967–74; 10th member of EU (1981); cap. Athens; a. 132,561 km²; p. (1991) 10,264,156.

Green Bay, c. E. Wisconsin, **USA**; oldest settlement in Wisconsin at mouth of R. Fox; p. (1990) 96,466.

Greenland, I., between Arctic Oc. and Baffin Bay; lofty ice-capped plateau; peopled by coastal settlements of Eskimos; fisheries; whale oil, seal skins; lge. uranium deposits, potential for petroleum; first onshore drilling (1984) in Scoresby Land; some coal, lead, zinc; US base at Thule; part of Danish kingdom; internal self-government 1981; cap. Godthåb; a. 2,175,600 km² of which 1,833,720 km² are under a permanent ice-cap; p. (1993) 55,117.

Greenland Sea, Arctic Oc., between Greenland and Spitzbergen; ice-covered.

Green Mtns., Vt., **USA**; part of Appalachians reaching 1,340 m (Mt. Mansfield); Nat. Forest, tourism.

Greenock, spt., burgh, Inverclyde, **Scot.**; on S. shore of F. of Clyde, 40 km W. of Glasgow; container facilities; shipbldg., sugar refining, woollens, chemicals, aluminium casting, tin-plate inds.; birthplace of James Watt; p. (1991) 50,013.

Green River, Wyo., Utah, **USA**; rises in Wind R. Range (major watershed in Rockies); flows via spectacular scenery to Colorado R.; impt. routeway; 1,168 km long.

Greensboro', c., N.C., **USA**; cotton, tobacco, chemicals; regional financial ctr.; educational institutes; p. (1990) 183,521 (c.), 942,000 (met. a. inc. Winston-Salem-High Point).

Greenville, t., Miss., **USA**; on Mississippi R.; deep-water harbour; tr. ctr. for cotton, agr. prod.; chemicals, metal gds.; p. (1980) 40,613.

Greenville, t., S.C., **USA**; univ.; industl. and comm. ctr.; textile mills, farm prod. processing; p. (1990) 58,282 (t.), 641,000 (met. a. with Spartanburg).

Greenwich, outer bor., London, **Eng.**; inc. most of former bor. of Woolwich on S. bank of R. Thames; famous for its hospital, observatory (now moved to Cambridge) and R.N. College; longitudes conventionally calculated from Greenwich meridian; p. (1993) 214,800.

Greenwich Village, lower Manhattan, N.Y. city, **USA**; bohemian quarter.

Greifswald, spt., Mecklenburg - West Pomerania, **Germany**; on Baltic inlet; shipbldg., textiles, wood inds.; p. (1981) 61,388.

Greiz, t., Gera, **Germany**; paper, textiles, chemicals; p. (1989) 33,441.

Grenada, W.I., most S. of Windward Is.; inc. archipelago of Grenadines; known as the "spice islands" as major exp. is nutmeg; cloves and vanilla also grown; sugar and sugar prods.; cotton-ginning; cap. St. George's; former Brit. col.; achieved indep. 1974; Pt. Salinas airport opened (1984) to encourage tourism; a. 344 km²; p. (1993) 95,343.

Grenadines, dependency of Grenada I., **St. Vincent and the Grenadines, W.I.**; gr. of over 100 sm. Is., between Grenada and St. Vincent, Windward Is.

Grenoble, c., cap of Isère dep., S.E. **France**; on Isère R. at foot of Alps; univ.; thriving cultural and scientific ctr.; impt. hydroelectric ctr.; science-based inds., joint Franco-German nuclear research reactor; gloves, paper, cement, liqueurs; tourism based on skiing; p. (1990) 153,973 (c.), 400,141 (met. a.).

Gretna Green, v., Annandale and Eskdale, **Scot.**; on Eng. border; famous as place of runaway marriages until 1940; p. (1991) 3,149.

Greymouth, spt., S.I., **N.Z.**; on W. cst. at mouth of Grey R.; ch. t. prov. of Westland; grew with gold mng., now replaced by coal and timber; p. (1987) 7,530.

Grimaldi, caves, N.W. **Italy**; remains of prehistoric man, late Paleolithic, found there.

Grimsby. See Great Grimsby.

Grindelwald, v., Bernese Oberland, **Switzerland**; tourist ctr.

Gris-Nez, C., N.E. **France**; nearest point on Fr. cst. to Dover.

Grisons (Graubünden), can., E. **Switzerland**; region of glaciers and magnificent peaks; ch. resorts Davos, Arosa, St. Moritz; Swiss Nat. Park; lgst. can.; sparse p.; ctr. Romansch language; a. 7,112 km²; p. (1986) 166,000.

Grodno, c., W. **Belarus**; pt. on Neman R.; a Polish t. until 1939; machine parts, cloth; historic bldgs.; p. (1990) 277,000.

Groningen, c., cap. of G. prov., **Neth.**; univ.; impt. trading ctr.; p. (1993) 170,038 (c.), 209,376 (met. a.).

Groningen, prov., N.E. **Neth.**; agr. and dairying; major natural gas deposits at Slochteren; a. 2,157 km²; p. (1993) 555,397.

Groote Eylandt, I., G. of Carpentaria; off cst. of N.T., **Australia**; aboriginal reserve; manganese ore-mng.

Grosseto, t., cap. of G. prov., Tuscany, **Italy**; cath.; agr. mkt.; severely affected by floods 1966; p. (1981) 69,523.

Gross Glockner, mtn. (3,801 m) and pass (2,370 m), **Austria**, part of Hohe Tauern range; hgst. peak in Austria. cap. Chechersop.

Grozny, t., cap. Chechen rep. **Russia**; on R. Terek; naphtha wells, refinery, engin.; starting point of oil pipelines to Makhachkala, Tuapse and Gorlovka; fell to Russian attack 1995; p. (1989) 400,000.

Grudziadz (Graudenz), t., on R. Vistula, Torun prov., **Poland**; mftg.; p. (1989) 101,571.

Grünberg. See Zielona Góra.

Gruyères, dist., can. Fribourg, **Switzerland**; cattle; cheese.

Guadalajara, c., cap. of Jalisco st., W. **Mexico**; *c*. 1,500 m high; impt. industl. and comm. ctr.; textiles, agr. processing, traditional pottery and glassware; cath.; gas pipeline from Salamanca; health resort; p. (1990) 2,846,720.

Guadalajara, c., cap. of G. prov., **Spain**; on Henares R., N. of Madrid; palace of Mendoza family; battle of Spanish Civil War, March 1937, fought nearby; p. (1987) 59,492 (c.), (1991) 147,868 (prov.).

Guadalaviar, R., E. **Spain**; flows into Mediterranean, below Valencia; 208 km long.

Guadalcanal, volcanic I., Pac. Oc.; lgst. of Solomon Is.; jungle and mtns.; exp. copra; ch. t. Honiara.

Guadalquivir, R., S. **Spain**; flows through Andalusia via Seville to Atl.; *c*. 560 km long; hydro-elec. plants; agr.

Guadalupe Hidalgo, place of pilgrimage, N.W. Mexico City, **Mexico;** basilica and shrine; treaty ending Mexican–U.S. war signed here 1848.

Guadarrama, Sierra de, mtn. range, central **Spain;** rugged, forest covered; affects Madrid's climate; reaches 2,431 m.

Guadeloupe, overseas dep. France, **W.I.;** comprises most S. of Leeward gr., Basse-Terre, Grande-Terre, Marie-Galante and other Is.; economy based on sugar exports to France; rapidly rising p. aggravates process of econ. development; attempts to develop tourism and food-processing inds.; ch. comm. ctr. and pt. Pointe à Pitre (Grande Terre); cap. Basse-Terre; a. 1,748 km²; p. (1990) 387,000.

Guadiana, R., forms part of Spanish and Portuguese frontier; flows into G. of Cádiz; Estremadura valley reclamation scheme in progress; 816 km long.

Guam, I., U.S. air and naval base in W. **Pac.;** developing tourist ind.; free-port and tax incentives aid investment; ch. t. Agaña; a. 541 km²; p. (1990) 132,000.

Guanajuato, st., central **Mexico;** average elevation 1,800 m; mng. (silver, gold, tin, copper, iron, lead, opals); a. 30,572 km²; p. (1990) 3,980,204.

Guanajuato, cap. of G. st., **Mexico;** 1,990 m high in gorge; resort; p. (1990) 113,580.

Guangdong (Kwantung), prov., S. **China;** on S. China Sea; cap. Guangzhou; occupied by delta of Xijiang and its confluents; Hong Kong in estuary; tropical monsoon climate; densely p. on R. plains and valley slopes; intensive farming of rice, sugar, fruits; 2 Special Economic Zones to encourage foreign investment; a. 221, 308 km²; p. (1990) 63,210,000.

Guangzhou (Canton), c., cap. Guangdong prov., S. **China;** industl. and educational ctr.; mnfs. inc. steel, ships, paper, cement; univ.; former treaty pt. and major spt. of S. China but site on Zhujiang R. delta results in silting and expensive harbour wks., hence Chinese interest in Hong Kong; ctr. of revolutionary movement from days of Sun Yat-Sen; p. (1992) 3,620,000.

Guang Zhuang (Kwangsi Chuang), aut. region, S. **China;** borders on Vietnam; cap. Nanning; drained by Xijiang and tribs.; rice most impt. crop; timber from sub-tropical forests; home of the Zhuang people (over 7 million); a. 221,321 km²; p. (1990) 42,530,000.

Guantánamo, c., S.E. **Cuba;** sugar, coffee, bananas, cacao; pt. at Caimanera on G. Bay; p. (1986) 174,400.

Guaporé, R., **Brazil;** rises in Mato Grosso st., forms Brazil–Bolivia bdy. before joining the Mamoré; length 1,440 km.

Guarulhos, c., **Brazil;** N.E. of São Paulo; mechanical and electrical engin.; metals; benefits from rapid industl. growth of São Paulo; p. (1991) 781,499.

Guatemala, rep., **Central America;** straddles Central American isthmus; interior mtnous. with temperate climate; coastal lowlands hot and humid; economy based on agr.; coffee accounting for half exp.; timber exploitation, food processing; two oil refineries; trades mainly with USA, ch. pts. Puerto Barrios, San José, Santo Tomas de Castilla; 4 univs.; cap. Guatemala City; a. 108,889 km²; p. (1992) 9,742,000.

Guatemala City, c., cap. of G. rep.; cath., univ.; fruit and vegetable mkts.; coffee tr.; remains Mayan civilisation; partially destroyed by earthquake (1976); p. (1989) 2 m.

Guayama, t., **Puerto Rico;** ctr. of agr. region; sugar-milling and food-processing.

Guayaquil, ch. pt., **Ecuador;** cap. of Guayas prov. on Guayas R., nr. Bay of G.; univ., cath.; sawmills, foundries, machin., brewing, oil refinery; p. (1990) 1,508,444.

Guayas, prov., **Ecuador;** cst. lowlands; plantations for coffee, cocoa, bananas, rice; cap. Guayaquil; p. (1990) 2,515,146.

Gudbrandsdal, valley, S. **Norway;** leads S.E. from Dovrefjell towards Oslo; drained by R. Logan; used by main road Oslo to Trondheim; provides relatively lge. a. of cultivable land; hay, oats, barley, dairy cattle; 368 km long.

Guelph, t., Ont., **Canada;** on Speed R.; univ.; mkt. ctr. in rich farming a.; cloth, elec. equipment; p. (1986) 78,235.

Guernsey, I., Channel Is., between cst. of France and Eng.; tomatoes, grapes (under glass), flowers, cattle, tourist resort, t. and ch. spt.

St. Peter Port; banking; a. 6,335 ha; p. (1986) 55,482 (with ass. Is.).

Guerrero, st., S. **Mexico;** on Pac. cst.; mtnous.; cereals, cotton, coffee, tobacco; cap. Chilpancingo; ch. pt. Acapulco; a. 64,452 km; p. (1990) 2,622,067.

Guiana Highlands, plateau, **S. America;** extend c. 1,440 km from E. to W. across S. parts of Venezuela, Guyana, Surinam, Fr. Guiana; steep sides, rounded tops c. 900 m but rise to 2,852 m in Mt. Roraima; chiefly composed of crystalline rocks rich in minerals.

Guienne, former prov., **France,** partly coincides with the Aquitaine basin (q.v.); controlled by England 1154–1451.

Guildford, co. t., l. gov. dist., Surrey, **Eng.,** 45 km S.W. London' on gap cut by R. Wey through N. Downs, cath., univ.; vehicles, agr. implements, lt. inds.; residtl., cas.; p. (1993) 126,200 (dist.).

Guilin (Kweilin), c., Guangxi, **China;** on R. Li; univ.; textiles, sugar refining, timber; noted for its beautiful setting; p. (1984) 446,900.

Guinea, rep., **W. Africa;** climate hot and humid on cst. but temperate in higher interior; 95 per cent p. engaged in agr., but bauxite dominates exp. from deposits at Boké, (world's second largest producer); hydroelectric dam and aluminium smelter at Konkouré; pt. at Kamsar for mineral exp.; major spt. at cap. Conakry; a. 245,861 km²; p. (1990) 7.3 m.

Guinea, gen. name for W. African coastlands from Senegal to Angola.

Guinea-Bissau, formerly Portuguese Guinea, W. **Africa;** indep. 1974; cap. Bissau; poor econ. infrastructure; no manf. inds.; depends on agr. of rice, ground-nuts and stock raising; cst. edged by mangroves; offshore oil potential; a. 36,125 km² p. (1991) 980,000.

Guinea, Spanish. *See* Equatorial Guinea.

Guinea Current, ocean current, flows W. to E. along Guinea cst., diverted away from cst. in Bight of Benin by C. Three Points.

Guinea, Gulf of, arm of Atl. Oc. formed by gr. bend of cst. of W. **Africa** between Ivory Coast and Gabon; Bight of Benin and Bight of Bonny are inner bays.

Guipúzcoa, smallest prov. **Spain;** cap. San Sebastian; on B of Biscay and French border; a. 1,997 km²; p. (1991) 671,743.

Guisborough, t., Langbaurgh, Cleveland, **Eng.;** at foot of Cleveland hills; former ctr. of iron-mng.; 12 cent. abbey ruins; p. (1981) 19,903.

Guiyang (Kweiyang), c. and cap., Guizhou prov., **China;** univ.; comm. and industl.; coal; iron and steel, textiles, chemicals; p. (1992) 1,560,000.

Guizhou (Kweichow), inland prov., S.W. **China;** upland a. with p. concentrated in valley urban areas; cap. Guiyang; cereals, tung oil; forestry; coal, mercury; a. 176,480 km²; p. (1990) 32,730,000.

Gujarat, st., **India;** formerly part of Bombay st.; cap. temporarily Ahmedabad; new cap. Gandhinager, 21 km N. of A. under construction; oil development in Cambay area; fertiliser plant projected; a. 187,115 km²; p. (1991) 41,309,582.

Gujranwala, c. **Pakistan;** N. of Lahore; power plant, engin.; p. (1981) 597,000.

Gujrat, t., Rawalpindi, **Pakistan;** agr. ctr., handicraft inds.; p. (1981) 154,000.

Gulbarga, t., Karnataka, **India;** cotton, flour, paint; (1991) 304,000.

Gulfport, t., Miss., **USA;** pt. of entry; exp. wood, cottonseed; mnfs., textiles, fertilisers; resort; p. (1980) 39,676.

Gulf Stream, warm current of the Atl. Oc., issuing from G. of Mexico by Fla. Strait.

Guntur, c., Andhra Pradesh, **India;** on E. cst. N. of Madras; cotton mkt.; p. (1991) 273,000.

Guryev. *See* Atyrau.

Güstrow, t., Mecklenburg - West Pomerania, **Germany;** S. of Rostock; cas., cath.; mkt. t.; p. (1989) 38,527.

Gütersloh, t., N. Rhine–Westphalia, **Germany;** nr. Bielefeld; silk and cotton inds.; famous for its Pumpernickel (Westphalian rye bread); machin., furniture, publishing, metallurgy; p. (1986) 79,400.

Guwahati, t., **India;** temporary cap. of Assam being developed in E. suburb of Dispur; univ.; silk, cotton, lace, oil refinery; pipeline from Barauni; p. (1991) 577,591.

Guyana, rep., N. cst. **S. America;** former Brit.

col.; largely covered by dense jungle, p. concentrated on narrow coastal belt; economy based on agr., especially sugar and rice; forestry inds. limited by lack of transport; impt. bauxite deposits; high birth-rate creates social and economic problems, especially on overpopulated coastal belt; airport at Timehri; univ. at Turkeyen; cap. Georgetown; a. 214,970 km²; p. (1989) 990,000.

Gwalior, t., Madhya Pradesh, **India**; adjoins Lashkar (q.v.); dominated by rock of Gwalior with Jain sculptures; p. (1991) 691,000.

Gwent, co., S.E. **Wales**; inc. most of Monmouth and sm. part of Brecon; upland in N. where coalfield and former mng. ts., lowland a. bordering Severn estuary to S. where lge. industl. ts. inc. Newport; a. 1,375 km²; p. (1993) 450,300.

Gwent, Plain of (Vale of Glamorgan), lowland dist., South and Mid Glamorgan, S. **Wales**; lies S. of moorland of S. Wales coalfield, extends E. into Monmouth; fertile soils; mixed farming except in industl. areas of Cardiff, Barry.

Gweru, t. **Zimbabwe**; ctr. of farming dist.; shoes, glass, containers; p. (1982) 78,900.

Gwynedd, co., N.W. **Wales**; comprises former cos. of Anglesey, Caernarvon, most of Merioneth and a sm. part of Denbigh; mtnous. a. except cst. and Anglesey; inc. Snowdonia Nat. Park; sparse p. inland where hill farming; cstl. resorts inc. Llandudno; a. 3,867 km²; p. (1993) 240,200.

Gyandzha, (Kirovabad) c., W. **Azerbaijan**; on Gyandzha R.; industl. ctr.; textiles, agr. implements, wine; copper and manganese mines; aluminium plant; p. (1990) 281,000.

Gympie, t., Queensland, **Australia**; on Mary R., 106 m. from Brisbane; former goldfield; now dairying and pastoral dist.; tropical fruits, especially pineapples; p. (1984) 11,380.

Györ, t., **Hungary**; at confluence of Rs. Raba and Danube; cath.; textile ctr., rolling stock, chemicals, machine tools; p. (1989) 132,000.

H

Haarlem, c., cap. of N. Holland prov., **Neth.**; nr. N. Sea cst.; tulip-growing, textiles, printing; 15th cent. church; p. (1993) 149,315 (c.), 213,686 (met. a.).

Hackney, inner bor., N.E. London, **Eng.**; incorporates former bors. of Shoreditch and Stoke Newington; furniture, clothing, p. (1993) 190,900.

Haddington, burgh, E. Lothian, **Scot.**; on R. Tyne, 26 km E. of Edinburgh; woollen mnf.; grain mkt., corn mills, lt. engin., hosiery; p. (1991) 8,844.

Haderslev, t. **Denmark**; tobacco, clothing, knitted goods; p. (1990) 30,330.

Hadhramaut, dist., **Yemen**; ch. pt. and c. Al Mukalla; fertile coastal valley; frankincense, aloes, tobacco, shawls, carpets.

Hadleigh, t., Babergh, Suffolk, **Eng.**; mkt.; flourmilling; p. (1981) 5,876.

Hadrian's Wall, part of frontier barrier, N. **Eng.**; stretching across Tyne-Solway isthmus, 118 km long. *See* Roman Walls, Section L.

Hafnarijördur, t., S. of Reykjavik, **Iceland**; p. (1991) 15,623.

Hagen, t., N. Rhine-Westphalia, **Germany**; N.E. of Wuppertal; iron, steel, chemicals, textiles, paper; p. (1990) 214,100.

Hagerstown, t., Md., **USA**; machin., furniture, chemicals, aircraft; p. (1990) 35,445.

Hagersville, t., Ont., **Canada**; gypsum producer.

Hagfors, t., Värmland, **Sweden**; site of lge. iron and steel wks. since 1878.

Hague, The, or **'s-Gravenhage** or **Den Haag**, c., S. Holland, **Neth.**; seat of government; permanent court of international justice; admin. ctr.; urban inds., machin. and metal wares; engin., printing; p. (1993) 444,661 (c.), 694,319 (met. a.).

Haifa, c., ch. spt., **Israel**; on Bay of Acre at foot of Mt. Carmel; terminus of Iraq oil pipeline; oil refining and heavy inds.; p. (1990) 245,900.

Haikou (Hoihow), c., ch. pt. of Hainan I., Guangdong prov., **China**.

Hail, t., and oasis, Neid, **Saudi Arabia**; p. (1986) 92,000.

Hailsham, mkt. t., Wealden, East Sussex, **Eng.**; 8 km N. of Eastbourne; mats, rope, and twine; p. (1981) 16,508.

Hainan, I., S. cst. of **China**; densely wooded; monsoon climate; seafood cultivation; sugarcane, rubber, peanuts, sesame main crops; recent industrial development; food processing, cement, electronics; a. 36,193 km²; p. (1990) 6,420,000.

Hainaut, prov., **Belgium**, adjoining N.E. border of **France**; industl. and agr.; coal- and iron-mines; a. 3,719 km²; p. (1993) 1,285,934.

Haiphong, c., ch. pt., **Vietnam**; on Red R. delta; comm. and trading ctr.; cotton, thread, soap, glass, enamel ware, fish-canning; former naval base of Fr. Indo-China; p. (1989) 456,049.

Haiti, rep., **W.I.**, W. third of I. of Hispaniola; tropical climate modified by alt.; agr. basis of economy; coffee accounts for 45 per cent exp.; irrigation scheme in Artibonite valley; unexploited mineral resources, some bauxite mng. and exp.; sm.-scale inds.; well-developed road network and international shipping services; cap. Port-au-Prince; corrupt Duvalier dictatorship ousted in 1986. a. 27,713 km²; p. (1992) 6·76 m.

Hakodate, c., S. Hokkaido, **Japan**; Seikan rail tunnel to Honshu (Aomori) opened 1988; fishing pt.; fish food processing; p. (1990) 307,251.

Halberstadt, t., Saxony-Anhalt, **Germany**; cath.; metallurgy, rubber inds., engin., sugar refining; rly. junc.; p. (1989) 46,851.

Halden, t., S.E. **Norway**; wood-pulp, paper, footwear, cotton spinning; nuclear research reactor; p. (1990) 20,134.

Haldia, pt., W. Bengal, **India**; nr. mouth of R. Hooghly; satellite pt. for Calcutta to handle coal, ore, grain; oil pipeline to Barauni; refinery; p. (1991) 100,347.

Hale, t., Trafford, Gtr. Manchester, **Eng.**; residtl.; p. (1981) 16,247.

Halesowen, t., S.W. of Birmingham, West Midlands, **Eng.**; weldless tubes, elec. gds., stainless steel forgings, engin.; p. (1981) 57,453.

Halesworth, t., Suffolk, **Eng.**; on R. Blyth, 14 km S.W. of Beccles; p. (1981) 3,927.

Halifax, spt., cap. of Nova Scotia, **Canada**; univ.; naval sta. and dockyard, open in winter; machin., iron foundries, footwear, oil refining, food-processing; scene of explosion of munitions ship (1917); p. (1986) 113,577 (c.), 295,990 (met. a.).

Halifax, t., Calderdale, West Yorks., **Eng.**; on E. flanks of Pennines; carpets, textiles, machine tools; cast iron wks.; p. (1981) 87,488.

Halland, co. S.W. **Sweden**; cap Halmstad; a. 5,448 km²; p. (1992) 261,172.

Halle, c. Saxony - Anhalt **Germany**; on R. Saale; univ.; lignite and potash mined nearby; engin., chemicals, p. (1990) 307,200.

Hallstatt, v., Upper **Austria**; in the Salzkammergut; early Iron Age culture type site.

Halmahera, I., **Indonesia**; mtnous., active volcanoes, tropical forests; spices, pearl fisheries, sago, rice; a. 17,218 km².

Halmstad, spt., Kattegat, **Sweden**; iron and steel wks., machin. engin., cycles, textiles, leather, jute, wood-pulp; p. (1992) 81,084.

Hälsingborg. *See* Helsingborg.

Halstead, t., Essex, **Eng.**; on R. Colne, N.W. of Colchester; rayon weaving; p. (1981) 9,276.

Haltemprice, t., Humberside, **Eng.**; p. (1981) 53,633.

Halton, l. gov. dist., **Cheshire**, **Eng.**; surrounds Mersey R. and inc. Runcorn and Widnes; p. (1993) 124,100.

Haltwhistle, mkt. t., Tynedale, Northumberland, **Eng.**; on R. South Tyne; former coal-mng. dist.

Hama, c., N. **Syria**, on R. Orontes; the anc. Hamath, ctr. of Hittite culture; food tr., rural inds.; p. (1981) 176,640.

Hamadān, t., **W. Iran**; alt. c. 1,800 m; the anc. Ecbatana, cap. of Media; carpets, pottery; airport.; tomb of Avicenna; p. (1986) 274,274.

Hamamatsu, c., S. Honshu, **Japan**; on cst. plain 96 km S.E. of Nagoya; ctr. of impt. cotton-mftg. region; textiles, dyeing, musical instruments, motor cycles; p. (1990) 534,624.

Hamar, t., **Norway**; on L. Mjösa; ctr. of rich agr. dist.; tr. and mftg. inds.; p. (1990) 27,550.

Hamble, Hants, **Eng.**; popular yachting ctr.

Hambleton, l. gov. dist., North Yorks., **Eng.**; inc. Northallerton, Bedale and Thirsk; p. (1993) 81,600.

Hamburg, c., Land H., **Germany**; astride R. Elbe, nr. N. Sea; 2nd. lgst. German c. and ch. pt.; freeport since 1189; pt. to be extended by reclaiming Is. of Neuwerk and Scharhörn; diversified tr. inc. liner traffic, barge traffic down Elbe, entrepôt goods; major pt. processing inds., airpt., univ.; cultural and musical ctr.; heavily bombed in second world war; p. (1990) 1,660,700 (c.), 1,669,000 (*Land*).

Hämeenlinna (Tavastehus), c., cap. of Häme co., S.W. **Finland;** L. pt.; tourist ctr.; birthplace of Sibelius; p. (1991) 43,770.

Hameln (Hamelin), t., Lower Saxony, **Germany;** pt. on R. Weser; iron, textiles; scene of legend of the Pied Piper; p. (1986) 55,400.

Hamhung, c., **N. Korea;** industl. and comm. ctr., oil refinery, petrochemicals; coal nearby; p. (1981) 775,000.

Hamilton, spt., cap. of **Bermuda;** tourism. comm. and service ctr.; p. (1985) 3,000.

Hamilton, c., and L. pt., S.E. Ont., **Canada;** at W. end of L. Ont.; univ.; varied metallurgical mnfs.; p. (1986) 306,728 (c.), 557,029 (met. a.)

Hamilton, c. ctr. of major pastoral region; N.I., **N.Z.;** on Waikato R.; univ.; p. (1991) 101,448 (c.), 148,625 (urban. a.).

Hamilton, burgh, l. gov. dist., Strathclyde Reg., **Scot.;** in Clyde valley, 16 km S.E. of Glasgow; admin. ctr.; elec. gds., carpet mftg., cottons, woollens, knitwear; Rudolf Hess landed near Duke of Hamilton's estate 1941; p. (1991) 49,991 (t.), (1993) 107,500 (dist.).

Hamilton, t., Ohio, **USA;** on Great Miami R.; industl. ctr.; mnfs. metal prods., paper, machin.; p. (1990) 61,368 (t.), 291,000 (met. a. with Middletown).

Hamm, t., N. Rhine–Westphalia, **Germany;** on R. Lippe, in Ruhr conurb.; rly. marshalling yards, iron and steel foundries; p. (1990) 180,100.

Hammerfest, spt., **Norway;** world's most N. t., on Kvalöya I.; fishing.

Hammersmith and Fulham, Thames-side inner bor., London, **Eng.;** inc. former bor. of Fulham; industl., residtl.; p. (1993) 155,500.

Hammond, c., N.W. Ind., **USA;** on Grand Calumet R., nr. Chicago; originally slaughtering and meat-pkg. ctr., now ch. mnfs., petroleum and steel prods., soap; p. (1990) 84,236.

Hampshire, non-met. co., S. **Eng.;** inc. Hampshire basin of chalk covered in clay and sand; inc. infertile heath and New Forest; leading pts. Southampton, Portsmouth; lt. inds.; tourism, seaside resorts; co. t. Winchester; a. 3,771 km²; p. (1993) 1,593,700.

Hampstead, inc. in Greater London, **Eng.;** hilltop v. with nearby heathland. *See* **Camden.**

Hampton, Thames-side t., Richmond upon Thames, London, **Eng.;** Hampton Court Palace; Hampton Wick E. of H. Court.

Hampton, t., S.E. Va., **USA;** oldest English community in US; fishing, oyster and crab packing; p. (1990) 133,793.

Han, R., Hubei, China; rises in S.W. Shaanxi prov., flows E. to join Chang Jiang at Wuhan; ch. trib. of Chang Jiang; 1,280 km long.

Han, R., S. **China;** forms rich agr. delta nr. Shantou; c. 400 km long.

Hanau, t., Hesse, **Germany;** on Rs. Mein and Kinzig; jewellery ctr., rubber and non ferrous metals inds.; birthplace of Jakob and Wilhelm Grimm, Paul Hindemith; p. (1986) 85,200.

Hanchung. *See* **Hanzhong.**

Hangzhou (Hangchow), c., cap. of Zhejiang prov., E. **China;** picturesque setting at head of H. Bay; former treaty pt., now silted up; silk weaving, chemicals, jute cloth; tourism; p. (1984) 430,000 (c.).

Hankou, c., Hubei, China; at junc. of Han and Chang Jiang, 960 km from mouth of Yangtze but accessible to ocean-going ships; ch. comm. and mnf. ctr. of central China; former treaty pt., now part of Wuhan conurb.; machin., chemicals, cigarettes, silk. *See* **Wuhan.**

Hannibal, t., Mo., **USA;** on Mississippi R.; shoes, cement, metal gds.; boyhood home of Mark Twain; p. (1980) 18,811.

Hanoi, c., cap. of **Vietnam;** on Red R.; old Annamese fort, now modern comm. ctr.; univ.; cotton, silks, tobacco, pottery; superphosphate and magnesium phosphate nearby; bricks, concrete, rubber; p. (1989) 1,088,862.

Hanover (Hannover), c., cap. of Lower Saxony, **Germany;** route ctr.; iron, textiles, machin., paper, biscuits, cigarettes, cars, rubberprocessing, chemicals; p. (1990) 514,4000.

Hanyang. *See* **Wuhan.**

Hanzhong (Hanchung), c., S.W. Shaanxi, **China;** on Han R.; nr. Sichuan border; agr. and tr. ctr.; former Nancheng; p. (1984) 412,100.

Haparanda, spt., N. **Sweden;** salmon fishing; exp. timber, and prod. of the Lapps.

Happy Valley-Goose Bay, t., Labrador, **Canada;** on Churchill R., international airpt.; p. (1986) 7,248.

Hapur, t., W. Uttar Pradesh, **India;** tr. in sugar, timber, cotton, brassware; p. (1991) 146,262.

Harar, (Harer), t., cap. H. prov., **Ethiopia;** unique African hilltop t. with medieval walls, towers and gates; anc. c. of Islamic learning; overlooks Rift Valley; brewery; p. (1984) 62,160.

Harare (Salisbury), c., cap. of **Zimbabwe;** admin. and industl. ctr. in agr. region with gold and chrome mines nearby; tr. in agr. prods., inc. tobacco; clothing, furniture, fertilisers; univ.; airpt.; p. (1982) 656,000 (met. a.).

Harbin (Haerhpin), c., cap. of Heilongjiang prov., **China;** pt. on Sunghua Jiang; tr. and comm. ctr. of N.E. China; exp. soyabeans; food-processing, machin., paper-mills, oil refining, hydro-turbines, textiles; former treaty pt.; p. (1992) 2,840,000.

Harborough, l. gov. dist., S. Leics., **Eng.;** based on Market Harborough and Lutterworth; p. (1993) 70,000.

Hardanger Fjord, W. cst. **Norway;** 120 km long; magnificent scenery; tourism.

Hardt Mtns., **Germany;** northward continuation of Vosges on W. of Rhine rift valley; formerly forested, now largely cleared for pasture; hgst. points reach just over 600 m.

Hardwar, t., Uttar Pradesh, **India;** on R. Ganges; gr. annual fair and pilgrimage; nearby dam; p. (1991) 147,305.

Hargeisa, t., **Somalia;** comm. ctr. of livestockraising region; airport; p. (1987) 400,000.

Haringey, inner bor., Greater London, **Eng.;** comprising former bors. of Hornsey, Tottenham, and Wood Green; p. (1993) 211,900.

Hari-Rud, R., N. **Afghanistan** and **Iran;** the anc. "Arius"; length 1,040 km; (*Rud* = river).

Harlech, t., Gwynedd, **Wales;** on Cardigan Bay 16 km N. of Barmouth; farming; cas.; seaside resort.

Harlem, upper Manhattan, N.Y. city, **USA;** residtl. and business section of c. with lge. black p.; depressed economic a. with much poverty.

Harlem, R., N.Y., **USA;** separates Manhattan I. from bor. of Bronx; with Spuyten Duyvi Creek forms waterway 13 km long from East R. to Hudson R.

Harlingen, spt., S. Texas, **USA;** ctr. of productive agr. a.; p. (1980) 43,543.

Harlow, t., l. gov. dist., Essex, **Eng.;** in valley of R. Stort, 35 km N.E. of London; new t. (1947); spreads S.W. from nucleus of old mkt. t. of H.; engin., glass, furniture mkg., metallurgy; p. (1993) 73,500 (dist.).

Harpenden, t., Herts., **Eng.;** in Chiltern Hills, 8 km N. of St. Albans; Rothamsted agr. experimental sta.; residtl.; p. (1981) 27,896.

Harris, S. part of Lewis I., Outer Hebrides, **Scot.;** and several sm. Is.

Harrisburg, c., cap. of Penns., **USA;** on Susquehanna R.; iron and steel ind.; machin., cigarettes, cotton gds.; p. (1990) 588,000 (met. a. with Lebanon-Carlisle).

Harrogate, t., l. gov. dist., North Yorks, **Eng.;** in valley of R. Nidd, 22 km N. of Leeds; spa; favoured a. for retirement; p. (1993) 146,500 (dist.).

Harrow, outer bor., Greater London, **Eng.;** public school; camera mftg.; p. (1993) 206,600.

Harspränget, t., Norrbotten, **Sweden;** lge. hydroelectric plant.

Harstad, ch. t., Lofoten Is., N.W. **Norway;** herring ind., woollen gds.; p. (1990) 32,327.

Hart, l. gov. dist., N.E. Hants, **Eng.;** comprises Fleet and Hartley Wintney; p. (1993) 82,900.

Hartebeestpoort, Dam, Transvaal, **S. Africa;** on R. Crocodile (Limpopo), 40 km W. of Pretoria; supplies water for cultivation, under irrigation, of cotton, maize, tobacco.

Hartford, c., cap. of Conn., **USA;** comm. and insurance ctr.; univ.; sm. arms, typewriters, elec. machin., aircraft engin., ceramics, plastics; Mark Twain lived here; p. (1990) 139,739 (c.), 768,000 (met. a.).

Hartland Point, Barnstaple Bay, N. Devon, **Eng.**

Hartlepool, spt., l. gov. dist., Cleveland, **Eng.;** on E. cst., 5 km N. of Tees estuary; shipbldg., lt. inds.; timber, iron and steel inds., pipe making; advanced gas-cooled reactor nuclear power sta; p. (1993) 92,000 (dist.).

Harvey, t., N.E. Ill., **USA;** nr. Chicago; rolling stock, diesel engines, heavy machin.; p. (1980) 35,810.

Harwell, v. Oxon., **Eng.;** 19 km S. of Oxford; Atomic Energy Authority nuclear power research establishment.

Harwich, spt., Tendring, Essex, **Eng.**; on S. cst. of estuary of R. Stour; packet sta. for Belgium, Neth., Denmark; docks, container facilities, naval base; p. (1981) 15,076.

Haryana, st. **India**; formed 1966 from Hindi-speaking areas of Punjab; former cap. Chandigarh; Hindu speaking a. transferred from Chandigarh (1986); a. 45,584 km²; p. (1991) 16,463,648.

Harz Mtns., range, **Germany**; between the Weser and the Elbe; highest peak the Brocken; ch. t. Goslar; forested slopes; rich in minerals; tourism.

Haslemere, t., Waverley, Surrey, **Eng.**; nr. Hindhead; mkt., residtl., lt. inds.; p. (1981) 13,900.

Haslingden, t., Rossendale, Lancs., **Eng.**; on Rossendale Fells, 5 km S. of Accrington; heavy industl. textiles, waste-spinning; textile-finishing; p. (1981) 15,900.

Hasselt, t., prov., Limburg, **Belgium**; mkt. t.; gin distilleries; p. (1993) 67,080.

Hassi Massaoud, t., Algeria; lge. oilfield; pipeline to Bejaia; oil refinery.

Hassi R'Mel, t., Algeria; lge. natural gasfield.

Hastings, t., l. gov. dist., East Sussex, **Eng.**; on S. cst., midway between Beachy Head and Dungeness; seaside resort; one of the Cinque Ports; cas.; p. (1993) 82,900 (dist.).

Hastings, c. and dist., N.I., **N.Z.**; on Hawke's Bay, nr. Napier; ctr. for fruit growing dist.; fruit-canning; p. (1991) 64,693 (dist.).

Hatay (Sanjak of Alexandretta), prov. and t., S. **Turkey**; comprising Antioch (now Antakya) and its pt. Alexandretta (now Iskenderun), ceded to Turkey by France 1939; p. (1990) 1,109,754 (prov.), 118,443 (t.).

Hatfield, t., Welwyn and Hatfield, Herts., **Eng.**; 30 km N. of London; new t. (1948) which grew around old t. of Bishops Hatfield; lt. engin., aircraft; p. (1981) 25,160.

Hathras, t., Aligarh dist., Uttar Pradesh, **India**; sugar, cotton, carved work; p. (1991) 113,285.

Hatteras, Cape, promontory on I. and cays off N.C., **USA**; stormy region, marked by lighthouse.

Hattiesburg, t., Miss., **USA**; sawmilling, clothing, fertilisers; p. (1980) 40,829.

Haugesund, spt., S. **Norway**; on S.W. cst., 35 m. N. of Stavanger; ch. ctr. of herring fishery; canning inds.; p. (1987) 27,000.

Hauraki Gulf, arm of Pac. Oc.; E. cst. N.I., **N.Z.**; forming entrance to harbour of Auckland; Nat. Park; gives name to dist.; p. (1991) 16,921.

Haute Corse. See Corsica.

Haute Garonne, dep., S. **France**; in Languedoc; cap. Toulouse; a. 6,366 km²; p. (1990) 926,000.

Haute-Loire, dep., **France**; mainly in Massif Central; cap. Le Puy; cattle, fruit, vineyards; a. 4,999 km²; p. (1990) 206,600.

Haute-Marne, dep., **France**; mainly in Champagne; metallurgical inds.; a. 6,268 km²; p. (1990) 204,100.

Haute-Normandie, region **N. France**; inc. deps. Eure, Seine-Maritime; ch. t. Rouen; p. (1990) 1,737,200. See Normandy.

Hautes-Alpes, dep., **France**; mtnous.; on Italian border; sheep; cap. Gap; a. 5,641 km²; p. (1990) 113,300.

Haute-Saône, dep., **France**; inc. part of Vosges mtns.; mainly agr.; cap. Vesoul; a. 5,372 km²; p. (1990) 229,700.

Haute-Savoie, dep., **France**; borders on Italy and Switzerland; reaches highest alt. in Mont Blanc; cap. Annecy; winter sports; a. 4,595 km.; p. (1990) 568,300.

Hautes-Pyrénées, dep., S. **France**; rises in S. to steep peaks of Pyrenees, forming bdy. with Spain; Basques live on both sides of border; cap. Tarbes; Lourdes place of pilgrimage; a. 4,533 km²; p. (1990) 224,800.

Haute-Vienne, dep., **France**; entirely in Massif Central; cap. Limoges; cattle-raising; a. 5,488 km²; p. (1990) 353,600.

Haut-Rhin, dep., E. **France**; in lower Alsace; cap. Colmar; ch. industl. t. Mulhouse; a. 3,507 km²; p. (1990) 671,300.

Hauts-de-Seine, dep., **France**; W. of Paris; cap. Nanterre; a. 176 km²; p. (1990) 1,391,700.

Havana (La Habana), c., cap. of **Cuba**; ch. pt. of W.I., with lge. harbour; cigars, tobacco, sugar, rum, coffee, woollens, straw hats, iron-ore; oil refining on outskirts of c.; p. (1986) 1,993,000 (c.), 2,014,800 (met. a.).

Havant, t., l. gov. dist., **Eng.**; at foot Portsdowns Hill, 10 km N.E. of Portsmouth; p. (1993) 117,500 (dist.).

Havel, R., **Germany**; rises in Neubrandenburg L. region; flows to Elbe R.; partially canalised nr. Berlin; 354 km long.

Haverfordwest, t., Preseli, Dyfed, **Wales**; 10 km N.E. of Milford Haven; agr. mkt.; Norman cas.; p. (1981) 9,936.

Haverhill, t., St. Edmundsbury, Suffolk, **Eng.**; expanded t.; textiles; p. (1981) 17,146.

Haverhill, t., Mass., **USA**; industl.; shipping containers; p. (1990) 394,000 (met. a. with Lawrence).

Havering, outer bor., E. London, **Eng.**; inc. Hornchurch and Romford; p. (1993) 232,200.

Havířov, t. **Czech Republic**, S.E. of Ostrava; mnfs., mng.; p. (1990) 92,000.

Hawaii, I., N. central Pac. Oc.; lgst. of Hawaiian gr.; three gr. volcanic mtns., Mauna Kea (4,208 m), Mauna Loa (4,172 m), Hualalal (last erupted, 1801); ch. pt. Hilo (devastated by tidal wave, 1946); lava deserts, bamboo forests; sugar-cane, cattle, coffee; tourism; deep-sea fishing; p. (1980) 92,053.

Hawaii, st., Pac. Oc., admitted 1959 as 50th st. of **USA**; st. flower Hibiscus, st. bird Nene; chain of coral and 1959 as 50th st. of **USA**; chain of coral and volcanic Is.; cap. Honolulu on S.E. cst. of Oahu I.; tourism; ctr. of international shipping routes; sugar, pineapples; a. 16,638 km²; p. (1990) 1,108,229.

Hawarden, t., Alyn and Deeside, Clwyd, **N. Wales**; steel plant; home of Gladstone.

Hawes Water, L., Cumbria, **Eng.**; 4 km long.

Hawick, burgh, Roxburgh, **Scot.**; on R. Teviot, 28 km S.W. of Kelso; hosiery, tweed, and woollens; p. (1991) 15,812.

Hawke's Bay, region, N.I., **N.Z.**; on E. cst.; cap. Napier; a. 11,033 km²; p. (1991) 139,479.

Hawkesbury, R., N.S.W., **Australia**; impt. waterway flowing into Broken Bay; spectacular gorges.

Haworth, t., West Yorks., **Eng.**; nr. Keighley; home of the Brontës.

Hawthorne, t., S.W. Cal., **USA**; residtl.; in gas- and oil-producing a.; aircraft and electronics; p. (1980) 56,447.

Hay, t., Brecknock, Powys, **Wales**; on R. Wye; cas.; mkt.; p. (1981) 1,293.

Hay, R., Alberta, **Canada**; flows into G. Slave Lake; 560 km long.

Haydock, t., Merseyside, **Eng.**; coal mng.; inc. H. Park racecourse; p. (1981) 16,584.

Hayes and Harlington. See Hillingdon.

Hayling Island, resort, Hants., **Eng.**; E. of Portsmouth.

Hayward, t., Cal., **USA**; fruit-canning, poultry; p. (1990) 111,498.

Haywards Heath, residtl. t. West Sussex, **Eng.**

Hazel Grove and Bramhall, subs. of Stockport, Gtr. Manchester, **Eng.**; p. (1981) 41,529.

Hazleton, t., Penns., **USA**; anthracite region; textiles, iron and steel mnfs.; p. (1980) 27,318.

Headingley, sub., Leeds, West Yorks., **Eng.** mainly residtl.; county cricket ground.

Heanor, t., Amber Valley, Derbys., **Eng.**; 11 km N.E. of Derby; hosiery, pottery, prefabricated timber bldgs. mftg.; p. (1981) 24,655.

Heard, I., 4,000 km SW of Freemantle, **Australia**; volcanic, weather station.

Heathrow, London airport, **Eng.**; 24 km W. of central London, S. of M4 motorway; on Piccadilly tube line; more imports (by value) than any U.K. port.

Hebburn, t., Tyne and Wear, **Eng.**; on R. Tyne 6 km below Gateshead; shipbldg., engin.; p. (1981) 22,103.

Hebden Royd, t., Calderdale, West Yorks., **Eng.**; cotton factories, dyewks., heavy engin., woollens and worsteds; p. (1981) 8,975.

Hebei (Hopeh), prov., N.E. **China**; part of N. China plain; bounded on N. by Great Wall; cap. Shijiazhuang; wheat, kaoling, cotton, coal mng., a. 194,250 km²; p. (1990) 60,280,000.

Hebrides or Western Is., Scot.; grouped as Outer and Inner Hebrides; ch. t. Stornoway, Lewis; a. 7,382 km².

Hebron, t., **Jordan**; 26 km. S.W. of Jerusalem.

Heckmondwike, t., West Yorks., **Eng.**; wool textiles; p. (1981) 9,738.

Hedon, t., Humberside, **Eng.**; former spt.; p. (1981) 4,525.

Heerenveen, t., Friesland prov., N. **Neth.**; bicycles; p. (1993) 38,728.

Heerlen, t., Limburg, **Neth.**; 22 km E. of Maastricht; coal mng.; with Kerkrade, met. a.; p. (1993) 95,347 (c.), 269,422 (met. a.).

Heide, t., Schleswig-Holstein, **Germany;** ctr. of Ditmarschen oilfields; p. (1986) 20,700.

Heidelberg, c., Baden–Württemberg, **Germany;** on R. Neckar, nr. Mannheim; celebrated univ., cas.; tobacco, wood, leather, rly. carriages; ; p. (1990) 138,000.

Heidenheim, t. Baden–Württemberg, **Germany;** N.E. of Ulm; textiles, machin., metallurgy, furniture; p. (1986) 47,600.

Heilbronn, t., R. pt., Baden–Württemberg, **Germany;** engin., vehicles, foodstuffs; p. (1990) 116,200.

Heilongjiang (Heilungkiang), prov., N.E. **China;** separated from USSR by Amur and Ussuri Rs.; mtnous.; crossed by Songhua R. in central plain; maize, soyabeans, millets; opencast coalmines; gold; cap. Harbin; a. 466,200 km²; p. (1990) 34,770,000.

Hejaz, W prov., **Saudi Arabia;** mainly desert, very poor communications, ch. t. Mecca; a. 388,500 km².

Hekla, volcano, **Iceland;** erupted in 1970; alt. 1,554 m.

Helder (Den Helder), t., N. Holland, **Neth.;** on strait between peninsula and I. of Texel; naval base; p. (1993) 61,149.

Helena, st. cap., Mont., **USA;** grew up as gold- and silver-mng. t.; bricks, pottery; resort; p. (1990) 24,569.

Helensburgh, t., Dumbarton, W. **Scot.;** on the Clyde; resort; p. (1991) 15,852.

Helford, R., Cornwall, **Eng.;** oysters, tourism.

Helicon, mtn. gr., **Greece;** abode of classical muses.

Heligoland (Helgoländ), sm. I., N. Sea; off mouth of Elbe; ceded by Britain to Germany 1890 in return for Zanzibar.

Hellespont. See **Dardanelles.**

Helmand or **Helmund,** R., **Afghanistan;** flows c. 1,360 km from mtns. of Kabul to Hamun-i-Helmand swamp on Iranian border; cultivation in valley; major irrigation project.

Helmond, t., N. Brabant, **Neth.;** on Zuid-Willem-svaart (canal); textiles; p. (1993) 71,528.

Helmsley, mkt. t., Ryedale, North Yorks., **Eng.;** cas.

Helmstedt, t., Lower Saxony, **Germany;** E. of Brunswick; on E. German border; textiles, machin.; p. (1986) 25,500.

Helsingborg (Hälsingborg), spt., Malmöhus, **Sweden** industl. ctr.; train ferry to Elsinore, Denmark; p. (1992) 110,614.

Helsingør, t., spt., **Denmark;** shipbldg.; setting of Shakespeare's *Hamlet;* p. (1990) 56,701.

Helsinki or **Helsingfors,** c., cap. of **Finland;** spt. on G. of Finland; harbour ice-bound Jan. to Apr., channel opened by ice-breakers; cultural ctr., univ.; timber, textiles, carpets; exp. mainly timber prods.; p. (1991) 497,542.

Helston, mkt. t., Kerrier, Cornwall, **Eng.;** on R. Cober, 13 km W. of Falmouth; tourist ctr.; famous for festival of floral dance (8 May); fishing, soup-canning; p. (1981) inc. Porthleven, 10,741.

Helvellyn, mtn., L. Dist., Cumbria, **Eng.;** severely eroded by ice; alt. 951 m; sharp ridge of Striding Edge.

Helwan, t., **Egypt;** 24 km S. of Cairo; sulphur springs; iron and steel complex, recently expanded (1982); fertilisers, cement; car assembly; p. (1986) 328,000.

Hemel Hempstead, t., Dacorum, Herts., **Eng.;** new t. (1947), on S. slopes of Chilterns; scientific glass, elec. engin., cars; p. (1981) 76,257.

Henan (Honan), prov., Central **China;** traversed by Huang He; cap. Zhengzhou; densely p. in fertile E.; mainly agr.; wheat, cotton, kaolin, anthracite; a. 167,172 km²; p. (1990) 86,140,000.

Hengelo, t., Overijssel, **Neth.;** industl. ctr.; cattle mkt.; metals, textiles; p. (1993) 77,270.

Hengyang, c., Hunan, **China;** on Xiang Jiang in foot-hills to S. Chang Jiang plain; on main Guangzhau–Beijing rly.; lead and zinc mines nearby; p. (1984) 551,300.

Hénin-Beaumont, t., Pas-de-Calais, **France;** on coalfield; p. (1982) 26,212.

Henley-on-Thames, t., South Oxfordshire, Oxon., **Eng.;** 8 km N.E. of Reading; mkt. gardening, brewing; annual regatta; p. (1981) 10,976.

Hensbarrow, upland a., Cornwall, **Eng.;** granite; kaolin-mng. dist., kaolin exp. by sea from Fowey; rises to over 300 m; a. 70 km².

Henzada, t., **Myanmar,** on Irrawaddy delta; in tobacco and rice-growing dist.; p. (1983) 283,658.

Herakleion. See **Iráklion.**

Herāt, c., cap. of H. prov., N.W. **Afghanistan;** on Hari Rud R.; of historic and strategic importance, has been called "the key of India";

crude petroleum and chrome-ore nearby; tr. ctr.; textiles; p. (1982) 150,497.

Hérault, dep. S.W. **France;** in Languedoc; agr.; cap. Montpellier; govt.-sponsored tourist developments along shores of Mediterranean; a. 6,221 km²; p. (1990) 794,600.

Herculaneum, anc. c., S. **Italy;** 6 km E. of Naples; buried along with Pompeii by eruption from Vesuvius A.D. 79; rediscovered 1709; site of modern Resina and Portici.

Hereford and Worcester, non-met. co., **Eng.;** crossed by Wye and Severn valleys, separated by Malvern Hills; mainly agr.; beef, dairy and fruit farming; major ts. Hereford and Worcester; a. 3,906 km²; p. (1993) 694,800.

Hereford, c., l. gov. dist., Hereford and Worcs., **Eng.;** on R. Wye; cath., mkt., tiles, engin., timber, cider and preserves; furniture, brassware; p. (1993) 50,700 (dist.).

Herford, t., N. Rhine–Westphalia, **Germany;** on R. Werra; cotton, flax, furniture, cigars, confectionery, metallurgy; p. (1986) 59,500.

Herisau, t., cap. of Appenzell Ausser-Rhoden half-can., N.E. **Switzerland;** muslin, embroideries; p. (1980) 14,160.

Herm, sm. I. of **Channel Is.,** English Channel; 6 km N.W. Sark and N.E. of Guernsey; remarkable shell-beach; a. 130 ha.

Hermon, Mount (Jebel esh Sheikh), mtn., in Anti-Lebanon range, on **Syria–Lebanon** bdy., nr. Israel; alt. 2,862 m.

Hermosillo, c., cap. of Sonora st., N.W. **Mexico;** on San Miguel R.; oranges; agr. and mng. ctr.; p. (1990) 449,472.

Hermoupolis or **Hermopolis,** t., Syros I., **Greece;** cap. of Cyclades; Aegean pt. and comm. ctr.; p. (1981) 13,876.

Herne, t., N. Rhine–Westphalia, **Germany;** pt. on Rhine–Herne canal; industl. t. of Ruhr conurb.; p. (1990) 178,400.

Herne Bay, t., Kent, **Eng.;** on cst., 19 km W. of Margate; p. (1981) 27,528.

Herning, t., Jutland, **Denmark;** knitting ind.; p. (1990) 56,687.

Herøya, S. **Norway;** nuclear power plant; chemicals, fertilisers.

Herstal, t., **Belgium;** nr. Liège; armaments, aero-engines; p. (1993) 36,611.

Herstmonceux, v. nr. Hastings, Sussex, **Eng.;** cas.; frmr. site of Royal Greenwich Observatory.

Hertford, co. t., East Herts., **Eng.;** on R. Lea, 32 km N. of London; pharmaceutics, flour milling, rolling stock, diesels, brewing; p. (1981) 21,412.

Hertfordshire, non-met. co., **Eng.;** borders Greater London on S.; co. t., Hertford, ch. ctr. St. Albans; drained by Rs. Thames and Lea; intensive agr., lt. inds.; new ts. Welwyn, Stevenage, Hatfield, Hemel Hempstead; a. 1,637 km²; p. (1993) 999,700.

's-Hertogenbosch, t., **Neth.;** on Rs. Dommel and Aa; cap. of N. Brabant prov.; cath.; cattle mkt.; industl. development; p. (1993) 94,337 (t.), 196,202 (met. a.).

Hertsmere, l. gov. dist., Herts., **Eng.;** a. close to London, inc. Bushey, Elstree and Potters Bar; p. (1993) 92,700.

Hesse, *Land*, **Germany;** part of former Prussian prov. Hesse-Nassau; mainly upland; inds. at Frankfurt, Kassel, Darmstadt; wine produced along Rhine valley; cap. Wiesbaden; tourism; a. 21,103 km²; p. (1992) 5,837,000.

Hetch Hetchy Dam, Cal., **USA;** on R. Toulumne upstream from San Joaquin R.; ch. source of irrigation for middle San Joaquin valley; supplies water and generating power to San Francisco.

Hetton, t., Tyne and Wear, **Eng.;** 8 km N.E. of Durham; coal-mng. dist.; p. (1981) 15,903.

Hexham, mkt. t., Tynedale, Northumberland, **Eng.;** on R. Tyne, 32 km W. of Newcastle; priory; p. (1981) 9,630.

Heysham. See **Morecambe and Heysham.**

Heywood, t., Gtr. Manchester, **Eng.;** 5 km E. of Bury; chemicals, engin.; p. (1981) 30,672.

Hialeah, t., Fla., **USA;** sub. of Miami; race-course; p. (1990) 145,254.

Hidalgo, st., central **Mexico;** mtnous. with fertile valleys in S. and W.; cap. Pachuca; mng. (silver, gold, copper, lead, iron, sulphur); maguey (type of lily), tobacco, cotton, coffee; a. 20,868 km²; p. (1990) 1,880,632.

Higashiosaka, c., **Japan;** E. of Osaka; formed from amalgamation of Fuse, Kawachi, Hiraoka and many sm. ts.; p. (1990) 518,251.

Higham Ferrers, mkt. t., East Northants, **Eng.**; 5 km E. of Wellingborough; footwear and leather dressing; p. (1981) 5,189.

Highgate, residtl. dist., N. London, **Eng.**; hilltop v. in bor. of Haringay.

Highland Park, t., Mich., **USA**; sub. of Detroit; grew up with expansion of motor-car ind.; p. (1980) 27,909.

Highland Region, l. gov. reg., N. **Scot.**; rugged mtns. inland; p. concentrated around cst.; offshore oil development; stock raising, forestry, tourism; a. 25,128 km²; p. (1993) 206,900.

High Peak, l. gov. dist., Derbys., **Eng.**; a. of Pennines inc. New Mills, Glossop, Whaley Bridge and Buxton; p. (1993) 87,000.

High Point, t., N.C., **USA**; furniture ctr., hosiery; p. (1980) 63,808.

High Willhays, hgst. summit, Dartmoor, Devon, **Eng.**; 621 m.

High Wycombe, t., Bucks., **Eng.**; 13 km N. of Maidenhead; furniture, paper-mkg., egg processing; in London commuter belt; p. (1981) 60,516.

Hildesheim, t., Lower Saxony, **Germany**; at foot of Harz mtns.; cath.; machin., farm implements, textiles, ceramics; p. (1990) 105,400.

Hillah, Al, mkt. t., Iraq; on R. Euphrates; nr. anc. Babylon; food tr. rugs, leather; p. (1985) 215,249.

Hilleröd, t., **Denmark**; admin. ctr. of Frederiksborg prov.; p. (1990) 33,388.

Hillingdon, outer bor. Greater London, **Eng.**; comprising Hayes and Harlington, Ruislip and Northwood Yiewsley, W. Drayton, and Uxbridge; p. (1993) 239,600.

Hilo, t., **Hawaii**; pt. of entry and main tr. and shipping ctr. of I.; tourism; Mauna Loa volcano nearby; p. (1980) 35,269.

Hilversum, t., **Neth.**; nr. Utrecht; radio broadcasting ctr.; noteworthy modern architecture; p. (1993) 84,545 (t.), 102,427 (met. a.).

Himachal Pradesh, st., N.W. **India**; bounded by Tibet on E.; forested mtns., cultivated valleys; cap. Simla; a. 56,019 km²; p. (1991) 5,170,877.

Himalayas, vast chain of mtns. along N. border of India, between the Indus and Brahamaputra Rs., and lying in Pakistan, India, Nepal, Sikkim, Bhutan, and China; made up of several parallel ranges inc. the Siwaliks, the Hindu Kush, and the Karakorams; crossed by passes, mainly in W.; 2,560 km long; hgst. peak Mt. Everest, 8,854 m.

Himeji, c., S. Honshu, **Japan**; mkt. ctr. on shore of Inland Sea, 48 km W. of Kobe; iron and steel ind., heavy engin.; oil refining; p. (1990) 454,360.

Hinckley, mkt. t., Leics., **Eng.**; hosiery, cardboard boxes, dye-wks., engin.; nr. Watling Street; with Market Bosworth forms l. gov. dist. of Hinckley and Bosworth; p. (1993) 97,600 (dist.).

Hindenburg. See Zabrze.

Hindhead, hill common, Surrey, nr. Haslemere, **Eng.**

Hindiya Barrage, dam, Iraq; across R. Euphrates, 48 km above Al Hillah; provides flood control and irrigation in a. between Shatt al Hillah and R. Euphrates.

Hindley, t., Gtr. Manchester, **Eng.**; 3 km S.E. of Wigan; paint, knitwear, rubber, asbestos; p. (1981) 25,537.

Hindu Kush, mtn. range, mainly in N.E. **Afghanistan**; hgst peak Tirich Mir (7,755 m) in third dist., Pakistan; Salang tunnel (opened 1964) with 2-lane motor highway cuts H.K. at height of 3,300 m, runs 240 m below mtn. top, 3·2 km.

Hindustan, former name of part of N. **India** between Himalayas and Vindhya ranges.

Hinkley Point, Somerset, **Eng.**; two nuclear power-sta., one Magnox, one advanced gas-cooled reactor.

Hirfanli Dam, project on R. Kizilirmak, 144 km S.E. Ankara, **Turkey.**

Hirosaki, c., Honshu, **Japan**; mkt., lacquer-ware; cas.; p. (1990) 174,710.

Hiroshima, c., S.W. Honshu, **Japan**; on delta of Ota R.; first c. to be destroyed by atomic bomb (6 Aug. 1945); since rebuilt; motor vehicles, shipbldg.; p. (1990) 1,085,705.

Hirschberg. See Jelenia Góra.

Hispaniola, second lgst. I. of **W.I.**; lies between Cuba and Puerto Rico; divided between Haiti (Fr.-speaking) and Dominican Rep. (Spanish-speaking); complex relief, climate, and vegetation, but strong cultural differences make international bdy. a sharp divide; a. 76,498 km².

Hitchin, t., North Herts., **Eng.**; in gap through Chiltern Hills, 56 km N. of London; lt. engin., tanning, chemicals, distilling; mkt.; p. (1981) 30,317.

Hjälmaren Lake, central **Sweden**; drained into L. Malaren by Esk R.; linked by canal to Arboga; a. 474 km².

Hjörring, c., Jutland, N. **Denmark**; biscuit and clothing wks.; p. (1990) 34,558.

Hobart, cap. and ch. pt. of Tasmania, **Australia**; on R. Derwent; univ.; fruit exp.; mostly light inds.; zinc; cadmium, superphosphates, textiles; p. (1991) 181,838.

Hoboken, t., Antwerp, **Belgium**; shipbldg.; refractory metals; p. (1981) 34,563.

Hoboken, t., N.J., **USA**; on Hudson R. above Jersey City, opp. N.Y. to which it is linked by subway and ferry; pt. for ocean commerce; industl. ctr.; p. (1990) 33,397.

Ho Chi-minh City (Saigon), c., spt., **Vietnam**; former cap. of S. Vietnam; on Saigon R. to E. of Mekong Delta; tree-lined boulevards; cath., univ., modern airport; comm. ctr.; exp. rice, rubber; food processing; p. declining rapidly since reunification of Vietnam; p. (1992) 4 m (inc. Cholon).

Höchst, t., Hesse, **Germany**; industl. sub. of Frankfurt-on-Main; site of German chemical ind.

Hochstetter, mtn., S.I., **N.Z.**; in Southern Alps; alt. 3,416 m.

Hoddesdon, t., Herts., **Eng.**; in Lea valley, 6 km S. of Ware; nursery tr., tomatoes, etc.; p. (1981) 29,892.

Hodeida (Al Hudaydah), t., **Yemen**, on Red Sea; pt. and naval base; exp. dates, hides, coffee; p. (1987) 155,110.

Hódmezóvásárhely, t., S.E. **Hungary**; wheat, fruit, tobacco, cattle; natural gas pipeline from Szeged; p. (1984) 54,000.

Hof, t., Bavaria, **Germany**; on R. Saale; textiles, iron, machin., porcelain, glass, brewing; p. (1986) 50,600.

Hofei or **Hefei**, c., cap. of Anhui prov., **China**; rice-growing a.; cotton and silk, iron and steel; p. (1983) 830,000.

Hoffman, mtn. peak of the Sierra Nevada, Cal., **USA**; alt. 2,473 m.

Hofuf (Al Hufuf), t., El Hasa, **Saudi Arabia**; dates, wheat, fruit; textiles, brass- and copper-ware; oil-fields nearby; p. (1986) 101,271.

Hog's Back, Surrey, **Eng.**; steep chalk ridge; alt. 154 m.

Hohenstein-Ernstal, t., Saxony, **Germany**; textiles, metal gds.; p. (1989) 16,707.

Hohe Tauern, Alpine range, Tyrol, **Austria**; rugged crystalline rocks; highest point Gross Glockner, 3,801 m; traversed by rly. tunnel 8 km long.

Hohhot (Huhehot), c., Nei Mongol (Inner Mongolia), **China**; diesel engines; new woollen mill; p. (1984) 778,000.

Hoihow. See Haikou.

Hokkaido, lge. I., **Japan**, N. of Honshu; colder than other Is.; less dense p.; temperate agr.; skiing; tunnel link with Honshu to aid economic development; a. 88,775 km²; p. of pref. (1990) 5,643,647.

Holbaek, t., Sjaelland, **Denmark**; W. of Copenhagen; engin. and motor wks.; p. (1990) 31,151.

Holbeach, mkt. t., S. Lincs., **Eng.**; in Fens, 11 km E. of Spalding; brewing; ctr. of bulb-growing dist.

Holborn. See Camden.

Holderness, peninsula, l. gov. dist., Humberside, **Eng.**; between R. Humber and N. Sea; agr.; p. (1993) 52,200.

Holguin, t., N.E. **Cuba**; comm. ctr.; sugar, tobacco, coffee, cattle; exps. handled by pt. Gibara; p. (1985) 194,700, (1986) 927,700 (dep).

Holland. See Netherlands.

Holland, N. See Noord Holland.

Holland, Parts of. See Lincolnshire.

Holland, S. See Zuid Holland.

Hollandia, former name of cap. W. Irian, **Indonesia**; renamed Kota Baru by Indonesia, then Sukarnapura, now Djajapura.

Holloman, t., N.M., **USA**; atomic and space research ctr.; site of 1st. man-made atomic explosion.

Hollywood, t., Fla., **USA**; seaside resort on Atl. cst.; cement, furniture; p. (1990) 121,697; part of Fort Lauderdale met. a.

Hollywood, sub. of Los Angeles, Cal., **USA**; ctr. of film industry.

Holmesdale, Vale of, Kent, E. Surrey, **Eng.**; extends along foot of N. Downs escarpment; drained by Rs. Mole, Darent, Medway, Len, Stour; heavy clay soils; ch. ts. Dorking, Reigate, Sevenoaks, Maidstone, Ashford, which have grown up in gaps through hills to N. and S.

of Vale; length 96 km, average width 2 km.

Holmfirth, t., West Yorks., **Eng.**; 8 km S. of Huddersfield, textiles, engin.; p. (1981) 21,839.

Holt, mkt. t., N. Norfolk, **Eng.**; 8 km S.W. of Sheringham; 16th-cent. school.

Holt, t., Clwyd, **Wales**; on R. Dee, 11 km S. of Chester; cas. ruins.

Holyhead, spt., Anglesey, Gwynedd, **Wales**; on Holyhead I.; mail packet sta. for Ireland; lt. engin., woodwkg., clocks; site for aluminium smelter; pt. traffic reduced as result of damage to Menai Bridge; p. (1981) 10,467.

Holy I. (Lindisfarne), off cst. of Northumberland, **Eng.**

Holy I., Scot., in F. of Clyde, nr. I. of Arran.

Holy I., off cst. of Anglesey, Gwynedd, **Wales.**

Holyoke, t., Mass., **USA**; on Connecticut R., above Springfield; paper, machin.; p. (1980) 44,678.

Holywell, mkt. t., Delyn, Clwyd, N. **Wales**; woollen, rayon and paper indus.; p. (1001) 0,905.

Holywood, spt., North Down, **N. Ireland**; on S. shore of Belfast Lough; seaside resort; p. (1991) 9,252.

Homburg (Bad Homburg), c., Hesse, **Germany**; famous spa; p. (1986) 51,100.

Home Counties, term applied to the geographical counties adjoining London, *i.e.*, Middlesex, Surrey, Essex, and Kent; sometimes Hertfordshire, Buckinghamshire, and Berkshire are included, and occasionally Sussex.

Homs, t., **W. Syria**; on R. Orontes in fertile plain; anc. Emesa; steel plants, fertilisers, lt. inds.; pipeline from Kirkûk oil fields; p. (1981) 354,508.

Honan. See **Henan.**

Honda, old Spanish t., **Colombia**; on Magdalena R., at rapids; former comm. ctr.

Honduras, rep., straddles Central American isthmus with longest cst. on Caribbean; comprises 18 deps. inc. offshore Bay Is.; coastal lowlands hot and humid, more temperate in interior highlands which rise to over 2,000 m; agr. basis of economy, especially American-owned banana plantations; bananas almost half exp.; some mng.; rlys. oriented to banana-producing areas to facilitate exp.; nationalised forests; land reform; cap. Tegucigalpa; 5 airports.; a. 111,958 km², p. (1991) 5·26 m.

Honduras, British. See **Belize.**

Hong Kong, Brit. Crown Col., S.E. cst. **China**, comprises Hong Kong I., Kowloon peninsula and New Territories (on lease from China until 1997); road and rail tunnels link H.K. with Kowloon; deepwater harbour of Victoria has lost much tr. from China; industl. development rapid since second world war yet few natural resources; exp. clothing, toys, electronics, watches; dense p. increased by immigration from China and Vietnam; to return to Chinese sovereignty (1997) with status of special admin. reg.; present capitalist system to remain for 50 years after that; a. 1,068 km², p. (1993) 5·92 m.

Honiara, t., cap. of **Solomon Is.**; on Guadalcanal I.; p. (1989) 33,749.

Honiton, t., East Devon, **Eng.**; on R. Otter, 26 km E. of Exeter; mkt.; trout-fishing; once produced lace, an ind. introduced by Flemish refugees; p. (1981) 6,567.

Honolulu, c., cap. of **Hawaii**; on Oahu I.; social and comm. ctr. and ch. pt. of archipelago; gd. harbour; univ.; airport; fruit-canning, sugar-processing; tourism; p. (1990) 365,272 (c.), 836,000 (met. a.).

Honshu, lgst. i. of **Japan**; contains most of p. along E. cst. in 320 km industl. belt; Seikan tunnel links I. to Hokkaido; a. 230,300 km²; p. (1990) 99,254,000.

Hoogeveen, t., Drenthe, **Neth.**; fruit- and vegetable-canning; p. (1993) 46,524.

Hooghly, R., arm of Ganges R., **India**; flows into Bay of Bengal; used in jute-milling and navigable as far as Calcutta; 256 km long.

Hooghly Chinsura, t., W. Bengal, **India**; on Hooghly R.; rice-milling; p. (1991) 151,806 (part of Calcutta met. a.).

Hook of Holland (Hoek van Holland), spt., **Neth.**; packet sta. with steamer connections to Harwich, Eng.

Hoorn, old fishing t., N. Holland, **Neth.**; on IJsselmeer, 39 km N. of Amsterdam; cattle mkts.; birthplace of Jan P. Coen, founder of Batavia; p. (1993) 59,959.

Hoover Dam, **USA**; on Colorado R.; used for irrigation (parts of Cal., Arizona, and Mexico),

flood control and hydroelectric power; Lake Mead, 184 km long, 2–13 km wide, one of world's lgst. man-made Ls.

Hopeh. See **Hebei.**

Horbury, t., West Yorks., **Eng.**; nr. Wakefield; p. (1981) 9,136.

Horeb. See **Sinai.**

Hormuz, Strait of, between Persian G. and G. of Oman.

Horn, C., S. **Chile**, most S. point of S. America.

Horncastle, mkt. t., E. Lindsey, Lincs., **Eng.**; at confluence of Rs. Bain and Waring at foot of Lincoln Wolds; mkt.; vegetable-processing; p. (1981) 4,207.

Hornsea, t., Humberside, **Eng.**; on E. cst., N.E. of Hull; seaside resort; p. (1981) 7,204.

Hornsey. See **Haringey.**

Horsens, t., **Denmark**, E. Jutland; on inlet of Kattegat; industl. and comm. ctr.; p. (1990) 55,210.

Horsforth, t., West Yorks., **Eng.**; in Aire valley N.W. of Leeds; cloth, tanning, lt. engin.; p. (1981) 19,290.

Horsham, t., Victoria, **Australia**; on R. Wimmera; pastoral, dairying and agr. dist.; p. (1986) 12,174.

Horsham, t., l. gov. dist., West Sussex, **Eng.**; on R. Arun at W. end of forested dist. of the High Weald; agr., timber, engin., chemicals; Horsham stone once quarried here; Shelley's birthplace; p. (1993) 112,300 (dist.).

Horta, t., cap. of H. dist., **Azores**; on Fayal I.; excellent harbour and base for transatlantic flights; p. (1981) 6,910.

Horten, spt., **Norway**; nr. Oslo; naval base; shipbldg., mftg. inds.; p. (1990) 16,043.

Horton, R., N.W. Terr., **Canada**; flows into Beaufort Sea, Arctic Oc.; reindeer reserve along cst.

Horwich, t., Gtr. Manchester, **Eng.**; on W. edge of Rossendale Fells, N.W. of Bolton; rly. t.; engin.; rly. workshops closed (1983); p. (1981) 17,970.

Hospitalet de Llobregat, t., **Spain**; sub. of Barcelona, in Llobregat valley; p. (1981) 294,033.

Hotan (Khotan), c., S.W. Xinjiang, **China**; in fertile H. oasis at base of Kunlun Shan; silk, carpets, jade-ware; on anc. Silk Road; early ctr. of Buddhism; visited by Marco Polo 1274.

Hot Springs, c., Ark., **USA**; in Ouachita mtns. S.W. of Little Rock; Nat. Park since 1832; health resort; p. (1990) 32,462.

Houghton-le-Spring, t., Tyne and Wear, **Eng.**; S.W. of Sunderland; former colly. t.; coalmng. dist.; p. (1981) 31,036.

Hounslow, outer bor., Greater London, **Eng.**; inc. former bors. of Brentford and Chiswick, Heston and Isleworth, Feltham and Hounslow; rubber goods; p. (1993) 206,500.

Housatonic, R., W. Mass., Conn., **USA**; falls attracted early Puritan settlement and industrialisation; dairy farming; 240 km long.

Houston, c., spt., S. Texas, **USA**; on Galveston Bay; gr. pt., lgst. c. of S.; univ.; oil refineries, oilfield machin., steel, chemicals, paper, processing, milling and assembling plants; NASA's manned space flight ctr. and lunar science institute; p. (1990) 1,630,553 (c.), 3,301,937 (met. a.).

Houston Ship Canal, Texas, **USA**; links Houston to head of shallow Galveston Bay and continues through bay to deep water; provides site for heavy inds.; opened 1915; total length 72 km.

Hove, t., l. gov. dist., East Sussex, **Eng.**; on S. cst., contiguous with Brighton; residtl.; holiday resort; p. (1993) 91,000 (dist.).

Howrah, c., W. Bengal, **India**; on W. bank of Hooghly R., in met. a. of Calcutta; p. (1981) 744,429.

Hoy, I., Orkneys, **Scot.**; lofty cliffs along W. cst.; separated from Mainland I. by Sound of Hoy; Old Man of Hoy rock 137 m high; p. (1991) 447.

Hoylake, t., Wirral, Merseyside, **Eng.**; on N. cst. of Wirral peninsula; residtl.; golf course; p. (1981) 32,914.

Hradec Králové, t., Czech Rep.; at confluence of Elbe (Labe) and Orlice Rs.; industl. ctr.; mnfs. machin., precision instruments; 14th-cent. cath. and town hall; p. (1990) 101,000.

Huainan (Hwainan), c., Anhui prov., central **China**; ctr. of China's ch. coal mng. region; p. (1992) 1,200,000.

Huai He (Hwai-ho), R., **China**; flows E. between N. China plain and lower Chang Jiang; subject to disastrous floods and changes of course; since 1950 flood control and irrigation canal to sea; 1,224 km long.

Huamanga. See **Ayacucho.**

Huambo. See **Nova Lisboa.**

Huancayo, t., cap. of Junin dep., **Peru;** in high valley of Andes, c. 3,300 m; textiles; p. (1990) 207,600.

Huang Hai (Hwang-hai or **Yellow Sea),** arm of Pac. Oc. between Korea and China; branches into Gs. of Bo Hai and Liaotung; shallow sea rapidly infilling; named after yellow silt from Huang He; length 960 km, greatest width 640 km.

Huang He (Hwang Ho), R., **China;** the Yellow R., rises in Kunlun Shan; flows c. 4,800 km. into G. of Bo Hai; cuts through Shaanxi in a deep gorge; filled with yellow silt (loess) from this a.; floods frequently and changes course (once entered sea S. of Shandong); in lower part forms fertile plain; now part of multipurpose scheme for hydro-electric power, irrigation and flood control; lgst. dam in China opened at Liuchia in 1975; 4,640 km long.

Huangshi (Hwangshih), c., Hubei prov., **China;** main iron and steel ctr. of central China, built since 1950; p. (1984) 435,200.

Huarás or **Huaráz,** cap. of Ancash dep., **Peru;** on Santa R., c. 3,000 m; mainly agr., some mng.; avalanche 1941 killed 6,000 inhabitants; p. (1990) 65,600 (predominantly Indian).

Huascarán, extinct volcano, Peruvian Andes, nr. Huarás, 6,773 m high; avalanche 1970 killed 20,000 people.

Hua Shan (Tsinling Shan), mtn. range, central **China;** rises to over 1,830 m; watershed between Huang He and Chang Jiang basins; impt. climatic divide between temperate N. China and tropical S. China.

Hubei (Hupeh), prov., central **China;** N. of the Chang Jiang; many Ls. and Rs.; rice, wheat, cotton; iron ores; Wuhan is major industl. ctr. of prov. and central China; cap. Wuhan; a. 186,363 km²; p. (1990) 54,760,000.

Hubli, c., Karnataka, **India;** E. of Goa; textiles, rly. engin.; p. (1991) 648,000.

Hucknall, t., Ashfield, Nottingham, **Eng.;** hosiery, coal; p. (1981) 28,142.

Huddersfield, t., West Yorks., **Eng.;** on edge of Pennines, 16 km S. of Bradford; wool, textiles, chemicals, engin.; p. (1981) 123,888.

Hudson, R., N.Y., **USA;** flows from Adirondacks to N.Y. harbour; with valley of Mohawk R. makes gr. highway of tr. between Great Ls. and N.Y.; scenic beauty; hydroelec. power; 560 km long.

Hudson Bay, gr. inland sea, **Canada;** communicates by Hudson Strait with Davis Strait (Atl. Oc.); ice-free mid-July to Oct.; salmon, cod; a. 1,398,600 km².

Hué, c., Vietnam; on Hué R., 16 km from S. China Sea; pt. and tr. ctr.; former cap. of Annam; royal palace; p. (1989) 211,085.

Huelva, coastal prov., S.W. **Spain;** copper mng., vine- and olive-growing, stock-raising, fisheries, brandy distilling; a. 10,117 km²; p. (1991) 441,778.

Huelva, c., cap. of Huelva prov., **Spain;** pt. on G. of Cadiz; oil refining, chemicals, food processing; exp. of minerals from nearby Rio Tinto; p. (1991) 143,576.

Huesca, c., cap. of H. prov., N.E. **Spain;** at foot of Pyrenees on R. Isuela; cath.; agr. ctr.; wine and timber tr. with France; p. (1987) 40,949, (1991) 218, 253 (prov.).

Hugh Town, cap. of the Scilly Isles, **Eng.;** on St. Mary's I.

Huhehot. See **Hohhot.**

Hula L. See **Waters of Merom.**

Hull, t., S.W. Quebec, **Canada;** within met. a. of Ottawa; sawmills, paper; p. (1986) 58,722.

Hull or **Kingston upon Hull,** c., l. gov. dist., Humberside, **Eng.;** major spt. of U.K.; at influx of R. Hull in estuary of Humber; originally laid out by Edward I; lge. docks; premier distant water fishing pt.; inds. inc. oil-extracting, flour milling, sawmilling, chemicals, engin., univ.; p. (1993) 267,900 (dist.).

Humber, estuary of Rs. Ouse and Trent, **Eng.;** fine waterway; 2–13 km wide, 61 km long; Humber bridge opened (1981), longest single span suspension bridge in Britain.

Humberside, non-met. co., **Eng.;** inc. most of E. Riding of Yorks., and Humber estuary where growth of pt. processing and chem. inds. and

impt. pts. of Hull and Grimsby; iron and steel at Scunthorpe; cstl. resort of Bridlington in N.E.; a. 3,512 km²; p. (1993) 884,400.

Humboldt, R., N. Nevada, **USA;** rises in Ruby Mtns., flows for 480 km before disappearing by evaporation and percolation; impt. 19th cent. routeway.

Humboldt Bay, inlet, Cal., **USA;** nuclear experimental breeder reactor.

Humboldt Current. See **Peru Current.**

Hume Lake, reservoir, N.S.W., **Australia;** formed by dam where R. Murray leaves Gr. Dividing Range; supplies water for irrigation in upper Riverina dist.; capacity c. 113 million m³.

Hunan, prov., central **China;** S. of the Chang Jiang; hilly in S. and W.; rice, wheat, beans; rich mineral resources, inc. mercury, tin, tungsten; cap. Changsha; Mao Tse-tung came from Hunan peasant stock; a. 205,589 km²; p. (1990) 54,760,000.

Hunedoara, dist., **Romania;** iron mining, cap. Deva; a. 7,016 km²; p. (1990) 558,028.

Hungary, rep., **E. Europe;** bounded by Ukraine, Slovakia, Romania, Yugoslavia, and Austria; lies in basin of middle Danube (Duna), with plain in E. and Carpathian mtns. in W.; mainly agr.; exp. meat, fruit, vegetables to W. Europe; inds. increasingly impt. and now account for over 50 per cent of income; plans to make H. leading exporter of buses in Europe; cap. Budapest; a. 93,012 km²; p. (1993) 10·31 m.

Hunsrück (dog's back), forested highlands, Rhineland-Palatinate, **Germany;** between Mosel and Nahe Rs.; vineyards on S. slopes; hgst. point 816 m.

Hunstanton, t., West Norfolk, **Eng.;** S.E. shore of Wash; seaside resort; p. (1981) 4,089.

Hunter, R., N.S.W., **Australia;** rises in Liverpool range of Gr. Dividing Range, flows S. and E. into Tasman Sea at Newcastle; world famous grape growing and wine producing reg.; coal exp.; c. 400 km long.

Hunterston, Cunninghame, **Scot.;** civil nuclear power sta.; integrated iron and steel wks., engin. of oil platforms and oil terminal planned.

Huntingdon, t., l. gov. dist. **Huntingdonshire,** Cambs., **Eng.;** on R. Ouse; expanded t.; canning, engin., processed rubber, confectionery; birthplace of Cromwell and home of the poet Cowper; p. (1993) 148,800.

Huntingdon and Peterborough, former co., **Eng.;** now part of Cambridgeshire non-met. co.

Huntington, c., W. Va., **USA;** on Ohio R.; R. pt. comm. ctr.; rly. wks., steel; p. (1990) 313,000 (met. a. with Ashland).

Huntly, burgh, Gordon, **Scot.;** at confluence of Rs. Bogie and Deveron; agr. mkt.; angling resort; p. (1991) 4,230.

Huntsville, c., Ala., **USA;** textiles; rocket research ctr.; p. (1990) 159,789 (c.), 238,912 (met. a.).

Hupeh. See **Hubei.**

Huron, L., between **Canada** and **USA;** one of the Gr. Ls. of the St. Lawrence basin; a. 59,596 km²; 330 km long.

Husum, spt., Schleswig-Holstein, **Germany;** on N. Sea cst.; cattle mkt.; p. (1986) 23,800.

Hutchinson, t., Kan., **USA;** salt-mng., meat-packing, flour milling, oil refining; p. (1980) 40,284.

Huyton with Roby, Knowsley, Merseyside, **Eng.;** sub. of Liverpool; p. (1981) 57,671.

Hwai-ho. See **Huai He.**

Hwainan. See **Huainan.**

Hwang-hai. See **Huang Hai.**

Hwang-ho. See **Huang He.**

Hwangshih. See **Huangshi.**

Hyde, t., Tameside, Gtr. Manchester, **Eng.;** on R. Tame, 11 km S.E. of Manchester; paints, chemicals, food-processing, tobacco, rubber; p. (1981) 35,600.

Hyderabad, ch. c., Andhra Pradesh, **India;** on R. Musi; walled t. and impt. comm. ctr.; univ., nuclear fuel fabrication plant; p. (1991) 3,146,000.

Hyderabad, c., **Pakistan;** 5 km W. of Indus; 144 km N.E. of Karachi; old cap. of Sind; univ.; noted for silk, gold and silver embroidery; now varied mnfs.; dam at nearby Kotri; p. (1981) 795,000.

Hyndburn, l. gov. dist., Lancs., **Eng.;** inc. Colne Valley ts. of Accrington, Great Harwood, Rishton, Clayton-le-Moors, Church and Oswaldtwistle; p. (1993) 79,000.

Hythe, t., Shepway, Kent, **Eng.;** on S. cst., 5 km W. of Folkestone; one of the Cinque pts.; military canal passing through t., used for boating; p. (1981) 12,723.

I

Iasi (**Jassy**), c., **Romania**; former cap. of Moldavia; in fertile agr. region; univ., cath.; cultural ctr.; textiles, plastics, chems.; p. (1990) 346,577.

Ibadan, c., cap. Oyo st.; S.W. **Nigeria**; univ.; ctr. of rich agr. a., between the savannah and forest regions; p. mainly Yoruba; crafts, small inds.; p. (1983) 1·1 m.

Ibagué, c., cap. of Tolima dep., **Colombia**; transport ctr.; cotton, tobacco, sugar, leather gds.; p. (1992) 334,078.

Ibarra, t., **Ecuador**; alt. 2,226 m at foot of Imbabura volcano; on Pan-American highway; p. (1990) 80,991.

Iberian Peninsula, S.W. peninsula of Europe; containing sts. of **Spain** and **Portugal**; lge. a. of high tableland; interior isolation and regionalism; historical and contemporary importance for minerals; a. 593,250 km².

Ibiza. I., Balearic gr. in W. **Mediterranean**; Spanish, cath., tourism.

Iceland, rep., N. **Atl. Oc.**; volcanic I. with ice-covered plateaus; glacier fields cover 13,000 km²; only 1 per cent of a. cultivated; cold climate; hot house cultivation using thermal springs; economy dependent on fishing and fish-processing inds.; high standard of living; tourism increasingly impt.; 7 admin. dists.; cap. Reykjavik; a. 102,846 km²; p. (1992) 262,193.

Ichang. See Yichang.

Ichinomiya, c., S.E. Honshu, **Japan**; anc. Shinto shrine; textiles, pottery; p. (1990) 262,434.

Ichow. See Lin-i.

Icknield Way, prehistoric route running from near Avebury, Wilts., **Eng.**; along the Berkshire Downs, Chilterns and East Anglian Heights into Norfolk, crossing the Thames at Streatley.

Idaho, st., **USA**; Gem State; admitted to Union 1890; St. flower Syringa, St. bird Mountain Bluebird; one of the Rocky Mtn. sts.; rich in minerals; agr. mainly in irrigated Snake R. valley; cap. Boise; a. 216,413 km²; p. (1990) 1,006,749.

Idaho Falls, c., Idaho, **USA**; on Snake R.; food-processing, lumbering; silver, lead, and gold mines nearby; nuclear experimental breeder reactor; p. (1980) 39,590.

Ida Mountains, range, N.W. **Turkey**; volcanic, hot springs; max. alt. Mount Gargarus, 1,768 m.

Idle, t., West Yorks., **Eng.**; in Aire valley, 5 km N. of Bradford; woollens.

Ife, t., **Nigeria**; ctr. of the cacao tr.; univ.; p. (1983) 214,000.

Ifni, enclave, S. **Morocco**; ceded by Spain to Morocco (1969); cap. Sidi Ifni; a. 1,500 km².

Igarka, sm. t., Siberia, **Russia**; on R. Yenisey, 640 km from its mouth; graphite plant, nickel-mines, lumber mills.

Iglesias, t., Sardinia, **Italy**; N.W. of Cagliari; mng. for lead, pyrites, zinc; p. (1981) 30,117.

Iguaçu, R., trib. of Paraná; mostly in Brazil; famous falls where Argentina, Brazil, and Paraguay meet, height 20 m higher than Niagara; hydroelec. power potential.

IJmuiden, c., N. Holland, **Neth.**; on cst. at mouth of N. Sea canal; fishing; gasification plant, major iron and steel plant.

IJsselmeer (**Lake IJssel**), freshwater reservoir, **Neth.**; formerly Zuider Zee; separated from N. Sea by Wieringen–Friesland Barrage; active land reclamation in progress; Wieringermeer drained 1930, N.E. Polder 1942, E. Flevoland 1957, S. Flevoland 1968, Markerwaard to remain undrained; when reclamation complete by end of cent. a. of Neth. will have increased by some 6 per cent.; ch. c. on inlet (IJ) Amsterdam.

Ilchester, t., Somerset, **Eng.**; on R. Yeo; N.W. of Yeovil; birthplace of Roger Bacon.

Ilebo, t. **Zaire**; rlwy. terminus on Kasai R.

Ile-de-France, region, **France**; inc. deps. Paris, Seine-et-Marne, Yvelines, Essonne, Hauts-de-Seine, Seine-Saint-Denis, Val-de-Marne, Val-d'Oise; the most populous region of France, centred on Paris; p. (1990) 10,660,600

Îles d'Hyères, I. gr., **France**; in Mediterranean off Toulon; tourism.

Ilesha, t., **Nigeria**; tr. ctr., cotton weaving; p. (1983) 273,000.

Ilford. See Redbridge.

Ilfracombe, t., North Devon, **Eng.**; sm. pt. on cst. of Bristol Channel; seaside resort; p. (1981) 10,133.

Ilhéus, spt., Bahia, **Brazil**; exp. cacao, timber; losing tr. to lge. pts.; p. (1985) 146,100.

Ili, R., **Central Asia**; rises in Tienshan, China, and flows into L. Balkhash in Russia.; new t. of I. at site of hydroelec. sta.; c. 1,200 km long.

Iligan, c., Mindanao, **Philippines**; integrated steel mill; cement; p. (1990) 226,568.

Ilkeston, t., Erewash, Derbys., **Eng.**; W. of Nottingham, iron, engin., locknit fabrics, needles, plastics; p. (1981) 33,031.

Ilkley, t., spa, West Yorks., **Eng.**; on R. Wharfe, N.W. of Leeds; local mkt.; p. (1981) 24,082.

Illawara, dist., N.S.W., **Australia**; forming belt of land between S. tableland and cst.; very fertile; dairy farming; coal seams; ch. ts., Kiama, Wollongong, Bulli, Gerringong

Ille-et-Vilaine, dep. N.W. **France**; on English Channel, a. 6,990 km²; agr.; cap. Rennes; p. (1990) 798,700.

Illimani, one of the high peaks of the Cordillera Real, Andes, **Bolivia**, 6,461 m, E. of La Paz.

Illinois, st., **USA**; Prairie State; admitted to Union 1818; St. flower Native Violet; St. bird Cardinal; in Middle West; named after its principal R., a lge. trib. of Mississippi; many Rs.; cap. Springfield, metropolis Chicago; rich agr.; fuel and mineral resources; major coal-mng. st.; inds. inc. meat-processing, farm implements; a. 146,076 km²; p. (1990) 11,430,602.

Illinois, R., Ill., **USA**; glacial valley; long history of settlement; impt. routeway; 437 km long.

Illyria, region stretching along Adriatic Sea from Trieste in N. to **Albania** in S. and inland as far as Rs. Danube and Morava.

Ilmen, L., **Russia**, nr. Novgorod; drained by Volkhov R. into L. Ladoga; a. 932 km²; fisheries.

Ilminster, t., Somerset, **Eng.**; 16 km S.E. of Taunton; cutstone, concrete, collars, radio valves; p. (1981) 3,716.

Iloilo, c., cap. of I. prov., Panay, **Philippines**; ctr. of rly. network; impt. pt. exp. sugar, rice, copra, hemp; p. (1990) 309,505.

Ilorin, t., N. **Nigeria**; on Lagos–Kano rly.; agr. and caravan ctr.; govt. sugar-growing scheme at Bacita; p. (1983) 344,000.

Imabari, t., spt., N.W. Shikoku, **Japan**; on shore of Indian Sea; mnfs. cotton textiles, paper, canned fruits; p. (1990) 123,114.

Imatra, t., Kymi, **Finland**; hydroelec. power sta. supplies S. Finland; electro-metallurgy; p. (1991) 22,228.

Imbroz. See Gökçeada I.

Immingham, pt., Humberside, **Eng.**; on the Humber, N.W. of Grimsby; lge. docks; new deep-sea oil and coal terminals; chemicals engin., refinery nearby at Killingholme.

Imola, t., **Italy**; S.E. of Bologna; cath.; glass, pottery; p. (1981) 60,010.

Imperia, t., **Italy**; on G. of Genoa; sm. pt. olive-growing ctr.; resort; p. (1981) 41,609.

Imperial Valley, S. Cal., **USA**; extends 48 km S.E. from Salton Sea to Mexican bdy.; mainly below sea-level; hot, arid climate; irrigation from Colorado R. chiefly by All-American Canal nr. Yuma; total irrigated a. 405,000 ha; principal crops, fruit, dates, tomatoes, cotton, and dairy prod.

Imphal, cap. of Manipur, **India**; in rice-growing basin in hills of Assam nr. Burma bdy.; p. (1981) 156,622.

Inari L., extensive L., Lappi, **Finland**; outlet into Barents Sea; hydroelec. power; a. 1,774 km².

Ince-in-Makerfield, t., Gtr. Manchester, **Eng.**; nr. Wigan; engin.; p. (1981) 14,498.

Inchon, c., **S. Korea**; on Yellow Sea; pt. for Seoul; exp. soyabeans, rice; textile ctr., steel mill, glass, diesel engines; p. (1990) 1,818,293.

Independence, c., Mo., **USA**; E. of Kansas; oil refining; agr. machin.; p. (1990) 112,301.

India, rep., indep. st. (since 1947), S. **Asia**; second cty. of world by p.; 22 sts. and 9 union terrs.; peninsula bounded by Himalayas in N. extends in wide plateau to Indian Oc. in S.; most of p. concentrated in Indo-Gangetic Plain; unpredictable monsoon climate; heavy dependence on agr.; 70 per cent of p. farmers; few cash crops except cotton (the Deccan), tea (Himalayas), and jute (W. Bengal); 854 languages and dialects impede economic development; strong caste system; 36 per cent literate (compared with 15 per cent in 1961); new inds. expanding

rapidly; chems., engin. electronics; cap. New Delhi;
main pts. Bombay, Calcutta; a. 3,268,580 km²; p.
(1991) 846·3 m. (25 per cent growth in 10 years and
2nd most populated cty. of world).

Indiana, st., **USA**; Hoosier State; admitted to Union
1816; St. flower peony; St. bird Cardinal; in Middle
West, bounded by Mich., Ohio, Ill. and sep. from
Ky. by Ohio R.; agr.; coal, limestone, petroleum;
steel, metal prods., machin., food prod.; cap.
Indianapolis; a. 93,994 km²; p. (1990) 5,544,159.

Indianapolis, c., cap. of Ind., **USA**; on White R.;
univ.; rly. ctr.; meat-packing, jet engines,
aircraft parts, chemicals, pharmaceutics; p.
(1990) 741,952 (c.), 1,249,822 (met. a.).

Indian Ocean extends from S. of Asia and E. of Africa
to the C. of Good Hope and C. Leeuwin in Australia, separated from the Pacific by the Malay
Archipelago and Australia; a. 75,990,600 km².

Indigirka, R., Yakut ASSR, **Russia**; flows into
Arctic Oc.; hydroelec. power; 1,760 km long.

Indo-China, S.E. Asia; federation in Fr. Union
until end of hostilities July 1954; consisted
of the three sts. of Vietnam, Cambodia, and Laos.

Indo-Gangetic Plain, India, Bangladesh and **Pakistan**; name applied to flat land created by the
Indus and Ganges basins; densely populated a.

Indonesia, rep., S.E. **Asia**; former Neth. E. Indies;
made up of many sm. Is. straddling equator for
over 4,800 km; many Is. in W. volcanic and E.
coral; geothermal energy supply being developed;
lgst. Is. inc. Java, Sumatra, Kalimantan (S.
Borneo), Sulawesi, and Irian (W. New Guinea);
mostly underdeveloped except Java; intensive
agr. employs 55 per cent of p.; rapidly developing
oil and gas industry but falling oil revenues (70
per cent of exports) hindering economic development; self-sufficient in rice, stored surpluses; 63
per cent p. on Java, Madura and Bali Is.; planned
decentralisation to other Is.; cap. Djakarta; a.
1,907,566 km²; p. (1993) 187·8 m.

Indore, c., Madhya Pradesh, **India**; nr. valley of
Narbada R.; comm. ctr.; cotton-mills; p.
(1991) 1,092,000.

Indre, dep., central **France**; agr. and industl.; cap.
Châteauroux; a. 6,905 km²; p. (1990) 237,500.

Indre-et-Loire, dep., central **France**; drained by
Indre and Loire Rs.; vineyards, orchards; cap.
Tours; a. 6,156 km²; p. (1990) 529,300.

Indus, R., **Pakistan**, rises in Tibet, flows
through Kashmir, Punjab, Sind, to Arabian
Sea; 5 tribs. Jhelum, Chenab, Ravi, Beas,
Sutlej, form one of world's major R. systems,
now used extensively to irrigate the Punjab
and the Sind; impt. cotton, wheat, and sugar
dist.; hydroelec. power; supported Indus valley
civilisation 3000–1500 B.C.; 2,880 km long.

Ingleborough, mtn., near Settle, North Yorks.,
Eng.; underground caves, stalactites; made of
limestone and millstone grit; alt. 724 m.

Inglewood, t., S. Cal., **USA**; sub. of Los Angeles;
chinchilla farms; furniture, lt. engin., aircraft
parts; p. (1990) 109,602.

Ingolstadt, t., Bavaria, **Germany**; on Danube, nr.
Munich; cas.; machin., cars, tobacco, oil refining;
pipeline from Genoa; transalpine oil pipeline from
Trieste, through N.E. Italy and Austria to I.; p.
(1990) 106,400.

Inhambane, spt., **Moçambique**; sugar, copra, oilseeds, bricks, soap, tiles; p. (1980) 56,439.

Inishboffin, I., Galway, **R.o.I.**, sm. I. off Connemara; farming, fishing.

Inishmore, lgst. of Aran gr., Galway, **R.o.I.**; fishing.

Inkpen Beacon, hill, Berks., **Eng.**; highest point
reached by chalk hills in Eng.; alt. 297 m.

Inland Sea, Japan; between Honshu on N. and
Shikoku and Kyushu on S.; sheltered sea with
many Is.; ch. spts. Osaka, Amagaski, Kōbe,
Okayama, Hiroshima, Kure; Nat. Park; a. *c.*
9,500 km².

Inn, R., traversing **Switzerland**, the Tyrol,
Austria and Bavaria; enters R. Danube at
Passau; hydroelec. plants; 512 km long.

Innerleithen, burgh, Tweeddale, Borders, **Scot.**; on
R. Tweed, 8 km S.E. of Peebles; woollen cloth and
knitwear; mineral springs; p. (1991) 2,515.

Inner Mongolia (Nei Mongol), Chinese aut. region,
N.E. **China**; stretches along S. border of Mongolian
People's Rep.; vast steppelands, sparse p.; st.
farms for animal husbandry; peat beds; milk-
processing; cap Hohhot; a. 1,177,518 km²; p.
(1990) 21,110,000.

Innisfail, t., Queensland, **Australia**; ch. sugar-
producing ctr. of Australia; p. (1981) 7,933.

Innsbruck, c., cap. of the Tyrol, W. **Austria**; on R.
Inn; commands N. approach to Brenner Pass;
univ.; tourism; fortfd. 12th cent.; p. (1991) 114,996.

Inowroclaw, t., N. **Poland**; prov. Bydgoszcz; rock-
salt. iron pyrites; agr. prod.; p. (1989) 76,497.

Insterburg. See **Chernyakhovsk**.

Inter-American Highway, section of Pan-American
Highway system, from Mexico to Panama.

Interlaken, t., Bernese Oberland, Berne, **Switzerland**; on R. Aare between Ls. Thun and Brienz;
tourist resort.

Intracoastal Waterway, USA; toll-free waterway
along Atl. and Gulf of Mexico csts.; completed 1949
using bays, rivers and canals; 4,960 km long.

Inuvik, t., Arctic, **Canada**; above the permafrost;
p. (1986) 3,389.

Inveraray, burgh, Argyll and Bute, **Scot.**; nr. head
of Loch Fyne; herring fishing; p. (1991) 512.

Inverbervie, burgh, Kincardine and Deeside, **Scot.**;
on E. cst., 13 km S. of Stonehaven; linen, rayon
inds.; p. (1991) 1,879.

Invercargill, c., S.I., **N.Z.**; on S.E. cst.; sawmills,
freezing wks.; aluminium smelter; served by
Bluff Harbour; p. (1991) 56,148.

Inverclyde, l. gov. dist., Strathclyde Reg., **Scot.**; on
F. of Clyde, inc. Gourock and Greenock; p.
(1993) 89,990.

Inverell, t., N.S.W., **Australia**; 655 km N. of
Sydney; wheat and lamb cty.; tin; p. (1981) 9,734.

Invergordon, burgh, spt., Ross and Cromarty, **Scot.**;
on N. side of Cromarty F., 19 km N.E. of Dingwall; former naval pt.; whisky distillery; p. (1991)
3,929.

Inverkeithing, royal burgh, Dunfermline, **Scot.**;
on F. of Forth, nr. Dunfermline; shipbreaking,
papermkg., quarrying; p. (1991) 6,001.

Inverkip, par., v., Inverclyde, **Scot.**; 10 km S.W. of
Greenock; par. contains Gourock; resort; p.
(1991) 1,258.

Inverness, royal burgh, Inverness, N.E. **Scot.**; on
Moray F.; distilling, lt. engin., tweeds; sm. pt.
for general cargo; tourism; p. (1991) 41,234.

Inverness, former co., l. gov. dist., N.E.
Scot.; part of Highland Reg.; a. 11,269 km²; p.
(1993) 63,850.

Inverurie, royal burgh, Gordon, **Scot.**; on R.
Don, 22 km N.W. of Aberdeen; rly. ctr., mkt. t.;
tourism; p. (1991) 9,567.

Inyokern, t., E. Cal., **USA**; naval ordnance
research sta.

Ioánnina (Janina), t., Epirus, **Greece**; nr.
Albanian frontier; agr. tr.; embroidery; univ.; p.
(1981) 44,829, (1991) 157,214 (reg.).

Iona, I., off cst. of Mull, Argyll, **Scot.**; early
Scottish Christian ctr.; restored abbey; St.
Columba's burial place; anc. burial place of
Scottish kings; p. (1991) 130.

Ionian Is., gr. in Mediterranean, belonging to
Greece; comprising Corfu, Paxos, Levkas,
Cephalonia, Zakinthos, Ithake; severe earthquake
1953; total a. 1,948 km²; p. (1991) 191,003.

Ionian Sea. Mediterranean; between Greece on
E.; Italy and Sicily on W.

Iowa, st., **USA**; Hawkeye St.; admitted to Union
1846; St. flower Wild Rose, St. bird Eastern
Goldfinch; in Middle West; prairie cty.; watered
by Mississippi and Missouri; rich farm land;
maize, oats, and other grains; hogs, pigs; processing of farm prod.; flood control, reforestation;
diverse inds.; cap. Des Moines; a. 145,791 km²; p.
(1990) 2,776,755.

Iowa City, c., S.E. Iowa, **USA**; former st. cap.
(1839–56); univ.; p. (1990) 59,738.

Ipin. See **Yibin**.

Ipoh, c., cap. of Perak st., N.W. **Malaya**; tin-mng.
ctr.; Chinese rock temples; p. (1980) 300,727.

Ipswich, t., S.E. Queensland, **Australia**; nr. Brisbane; coalmng. ctr.; woollens; p. (est. 1984) 73,680.

Ipswich, co. t., l. gov. dist., Suffolk, **Eng.**; pt. on
estuary of R. Orwell; incr. impt. container pt.;
exp. timber, grain and malt; birthplace of
Cardinal Wolsey; diesel engines, gen. engin.; p.
(1993) 114,800 (dist.).

Iquique, t., N. **Chile**; pt. on Pac. Oc.; exp.
nitrates and iodine from Atacama desert;
fish-canning; p. (1987) 132,948.

Iquitos, t., N.E. **Peru**; on Amazon, 3,680 km
from mouth; comm. ctr.; exp. timber, cotton;
sawmills, oil refining; p. (1990) 269,500.

Iráklion (Candia or **Herakleion)**, t., cap. of Crete,
Greece; impt. spt. on G. of I., arm of Aegean Sea;
at foot of terraced hill slopes; wine, olive oil, fruit,
fishing; tourism; p. (1981) 102,398.

Iran, former kingdom, Islamic st. (1979), S.W. **Asia;** known as Persia until 1935; interior plateau at c. 900 km, ringed by mtn. ranges of up to c. 5,500 m; much of a. is desert; settled agr. limited to Caspian plain; heavy dependence on oil; oilfields centred on Abādān; hit by fall in world oil prices and sale losses due to Iraqi air attacks; pipeline to Iskenderun (Turkey) on Mediterranean cst. started (1986) as alternative exp. route; high quality carpets exported, esp. to USA; cap. Tehran; a. 1,626,520 km²; p. (1992) 55·8 m.

Irapuato, c., central **Mexico;** agr. tr. and processing; iron-founding; p. (1990) 362,471.

Iraq, rep., S.W. **Asia;** the anc. Mesopotamia; dominated by 2 Rs., Tigris and Euphrates; much of a. desert and semi-desert but irrigation in S. and centre enables settled agr. for barley, wheat, dates, and tobacco; only outlet to sea at N.W. end of Persian G.; oil principal source of wealth; main oilfield at Kirkūk; main oil pt. at Basra; pipelines to Lebanon and Syria; new inds. based on oil; 14 provs.; cap. Baghdad; a. 435,120 km²; p. (1993) 19·41 m.

Irazu, active volcano, 3,437 m high, **Costa Rica.**

Irbid, t., **Jordan;** comm. and agr. tr. ctr.; p. (1986) 680,200.

Ireland, I., W. of Gt. Britain, separated by Irish Sea; divided politically into R.o.I. (Eire) and N. Ireland (Ulster, part of U.K.); ch. physical features, L. Neagh in N.E., Ls. of Killarney in S.W.; Rs. Shannon, Boyne, Blackwater; mtns. of Mourne, Wicklow, and Kerry; mild moist climate; called "emerald isle" because of grasslands; pastoral agr., especially dairying; tourism; a. 83,937 km²; p. (1981) 4,888,077.

Ireland, Republic of, ind. st., W. **Europe;** comprises 26 of 32 cos. making up I. of Ireland; member of EU; ring of highlands surround central lowland basin, much of which is peat-covered; economy based on agr., especially dairying; exps. butter, cheese, bacon; new govt.-encouraged inds.; mineral resources; tourism; cap. Dublin; a. 68,894 km²; p. (1992) 3·55 m.

Irian Jaya (formerly Dutch New Guinea, later W. Irian), prov., **Indonesia;** formerly W. New Guinea and Dutch col.; part of Indonesia, 1963; inaugurated as prov., 1969; primitive agr. of rice, poultry, cocoa; few oil deposits; cap. Djajapura; a. (inc. Ternate) 412,784 km²; p. (1983) 1,268,600.

Irish Sea, Brit. Is.; between Gt. Britain and Ireland, connecting N. and S. with Atl. Oc.; 320 km long; 80–224 km wide; greatest depth 840 m; a. 18,130 km².

Irkutsk, c., cap. of I. oblast, **Russia;** on Angara R. in E. Siberia; on Trans-Siberian rly., 64 km W. of L. Baykal; univ.; engin., sawmilling, petroleum refining, chemicals, hydroelec. power sta.; p. (1989) 626,000.

Irlam, t., Gtr. Manchester, **Eng.;** engin., tar, soap, glycerine, margarine; over-spill p.; p. (1981) 19,900.

Ironbridge, t., Shrops., **Eng.;** scene of Darby's iron ind.; derives name from first cast-iron bridge (1779) which here crosses Severn; now inc. in Telford new t.

Iron Country, Utah, **USA;** vast reserves of iron ore; undeveloped due to inaccessibility.

Iron Gate (Portile de Fier), Romania; famous rapids in R. Danube; Romanian–Yugoslavian hydroelectric and navigation project, 1964–71.

Irrawaddy, R., **Myanmar;** flows S. to Bay of Bengal; navigable for lge. steamers 1,440 km; irrigation wks.; major Asian rice bowl; 2,000 km long.

Irtysh, R., W. Siberia, **Russia;** ch. trib. of R. Ob'; crossed by Turk–Sib rly. at Semipalatinsk and by Trans-Siberian rly. at Omsk; hydroelectric power stas.; ambitious plans to divert R. South now postponed; 2,960 km long.

Irvine, royal burgh, Cunninghame, **Scot.;** nr. mouth of R. Irvine; new t. (1966); cas.; hosiery, lt. engin., bottle wks., chemicals; p. (1991) 32,988.

Irvington, t., N.J., **USA;** industl. sub. of Newark; machin.; p. (1990) 61,018.

Irwell, R., Gtr. Manchester, **Eng.;** flows through Manchester to the Mersey via Manchester Ship Canal; 48 km long.

Isar, R., **Austria** and **W. Germany;** rises in Austrian Tyrol, flows N.E. to Danube; hydroelectric power stas. below Munich; 261 km long.

Isarco, R., N. **Italy;** rises nr. Brenner Pass, flows S. into R. Adige at Bolzano; 80 km long.

Isdud, anc. c. of the Philistines. *See* **Ashdod.**

Ise (Ujiyamada), t., Honshu, **Japan;** sacred c. of Shintoism; p. (1990) 104,162.

Ise Bay, inlet, S. Honshu, **Japan;** flanked by ch. textile mftg. a. of cty, with 5 million people centred on Nagoya; 64 km long, 24–32 km wide.

Iseo, L., N. **Italy;** E. of Bergamo; 124 km².

Isère, dep., S.E. **France;** drained by Rs. Isère and Rhône; cap. Grenoble; mtnous.; cereals; wine, butter, cheese; iron, coal, lead, silver, copper; gloves, silks; a. 8,231 km²; p. (1990) 1,016,200.

Isère, R., S.E. **France;** rises in Graian Alps, flows W. into R. Rhône nr. Valence; used to generate hydroelec. power; used, with trib. R. Arc, by main rly. from France to N. Italy through Mt. Cenis (Fréjus) tunnel.

Iserlohn, t., N. Rhine–Westphalia, **Germany;** S.E. of Dortmund; metal gds.; p. (1986) 89,500.

Isfahan. *See* **Esfahān.**

Ishikari, t., Hokkaido, **Japan;** on cst. of Otaru Bay, 16 km N. of Sapporo; ctr. of second lgst. coalfield in Japan; sm. petroleum production.

Ishimbay, c., Bashkir aut. rep. **Russia;** on R. Belaya; ctr. of Ishimbay oilfields; pipelines to Ufa, Orsk, and Shkaparo.

Isiro (Paulis), t., N.E. **Zaïre;** admin. offices; cotton ginneries; rly. repair shops.

Isis, R., headstream of R. Thames, **Eng.;** so named around and above Oxford.

Iskenderun (Alexandretta), spt., S. **Turkey;** recent modernisation for new Iran/Turkey rly.; new steel wks.; p. (1990) 175,998.

Islamabad, new cap. of **Pakistan,** to N. of Rawalpindi below Himalayas; nuclear power sta.; p. (1981) 201,000.

Islay, I. Inner Hebrides, Argyll and Bute, **Scot.;** a. 609 km²; farming, dairying distilleries; p. (1991) 3,538.

Isle of Grain, Kent, **Eng.;** flat promontory at confluence of Thames and Medway, once separated from mainland by a tidal estuary; lge oil refinery; pipelines to Walton-on-Thames and Heathrow Airport.

Isle of Man, Irish Sea; 43 km from Eng. (Cumbria) and N. Ireland (Down); high plateau N.E. to S.W.; ch. t. Douglas; old cap. Castletown; admin. according to own laws; tourism; freeport (1983) to take advantage of low tax rate; a. 572 km²; p. (1991) 69,788.

Isles of Scilly, archipelago, l. gov. dist., 45 km. S.W. of Land's End, Cornwall, **Eng.;** early flowers and vegetables benefit from mild winter climate; tourism; p. (1993) 2,100.

Isle of Wight, non-met. co., **Eng.;** English Channel, separated from Hampshire by Spithead and the Solent; crossed by chalk hills, terminating in the Needles; popular holiday resort; ch. ts., Newport, Ryde, Cowes; a. 381 km²; p. (1993) 128,400.

Islington, inner bor., London, **Eng.;** N. of City; incorporates Finsbury; univ.; residtl.; clocks, precision engin.; p. (1993) 175,500.

Islwyn, l. gov. dist., Gwent, **Wales;** inland ts. of Risca, Abercarn, Bedwellty and Mynyddislwyn; p. (1993) 67,200.

Ismailia (Ismāʿīliya), t. and prov., **Egypt;** at mid-point of Suez Canal on L. Timsah; rail connections with Cairo, Suez, Port Said; declined during canal closure; p. (1986) 212,567, (1991) 632,000 (prov.).

Ispra, t., Varese, **Italy;** nr. L. Maggiore; nuclear research ctr.; p. (1981) 4,629.

Israel, rep., S.W. **Asia;** occupies narrow corridor between Jordan valley and Mediterranean Sea; extends S. into the Negev desert (half a. of rep.); Mediterranean climate enables cultivation of early fruits and vegetables, especially citrus fruits; special feature of agr. is cooperative settlements (Kibbutz); main factor limiting agr. development is availability of water; diamonds hgst. exp. earner; most highly industrialised cty. of S.W. Asia, especially for textiles and clothing; petroleum of increasing impt.; tourism; Jewish rep. since 1948; until then part of the mandate Palestine; surrounded by hostile Arab sts.; difficulties of increasing Jewish immigration; cap. Jerusalem; a. 20,850 km²; nat. a. in dispute, particularly since Arab-Israeli wars of 1967 and 1973; p. (1993) 5·33 m. (75 per cent Jewish).

Issyk Kul, mtn. L., **Kyrgyzstan;** in Tien-Shan mtns., alt. 1,568 m; a. 6,216 km²; ice-free in winter.

Istanbul (Constantinople), ch. spt., former cap., **Turkey;** on Golden Horn peninsula on European cst. at entry of Bosporus into Sea of Marmara;

divided into old "Stamboul" on S. side, and dists. of Galata and Beyoglu (Pera) on N.; the anc. Byzantium; magnificent mosque of Sta. Sophia; univ.; industl. and comm. ctr.; tourism; p. (1990) 6,293,000 (t.), 7,309,190 (prov.).

Istria, peninsula, N. Adriatic, **Croatia** (formerly Yugoslavia); ch. c. Pula; agr., olives, vines, oranges, maize; p. Yugoslav and Italian; a. c. 5,200 km².

Itabira, t., Minas Gerais st., **Brazil**; on Brazilian Plateau, 96 km N.E. of Belo Horizonte; lgst. deposits of iron ore in Brazil; p. (1985) 81,800.

Itabuna, t., Bahia, E. **Brazil**; cocoa, livestock; p. (1985) 178,700.

Itajai, spt., Santa Catarina, S. **Brazil**; exp. lumber, cement, agr. prods.; (1985) 104,500.

Italy, rep., S. **Europe**; peninsula extending into Mediterranean; inc. 2 main Is. of Sicily and Sardinia; bounded by Alps to N.; central spine of Apennines; Mediterranean climate; contrast between industrialised N. and less developed agr. S. (Mezzogiorno); member of EU; agr. impt.; especially in Po basin; tourism attracted by Roman and Renaissance architecture and by climate; inds. based on hydroelectric power in N., inc. elec. engin., motor vehicles and textiles, centred at Milan and Turin; 19 admin. regions; cap. Rome; a. 301,049 km²; p. (1992) 56·96 mln.

Ithaca, t., N.Y., **USA**; on Cayuga L.; seat of Cornell Univ.; elec. clocks; machin.; p. (1980) 28,732.

Ithake, one of the Ionian Is., **Greece**; a. 96 km²; ch. t. Ithake; severe earthquake, 1953.

Itzehoe, t., Schleswig-Holstein, **Germany**; founded by Charlemagne; wood, cement, machin.; p. (1986) 31,700.

Ivano-Frankovsk (Stanislav), c., **Ukraine**; in Carpathian foothills; industl. ctr.; oilfields nearby; oil refineries, engin.; p. (1990) 219,900.

Ivanovo, t., **Russia**, N.E. of Moscow; textiles, iron and chemical wks.; peat-fed power stas.; p. (1989) 481,000.

Iviza. See Ibiza.

Ivory Coast. See Côte d'Ivoire.

Iwaki, t., Honshu, **Japan**; ctr. of apple producing dist., p. (1990) 355,817.

Iwakuni, t., Honshu, **Japan**; on Inland Sea; p. (1990) 109,530.

Iwo, t., **Nigeria**; nr. Ibadan; tr. ctr.; p. (1983) 262,000.

Izhevsk, (Ustinov), c., cap. of Udmurt aut. rep. **Russia**; steel ctr., engin.; p. (1989) 635,000.

Izmail, c., **Ukraine**; in Bessarabia, on Danube delta, nr. Romanian border; naval base of Soviet Danube flotilla; former Turkish fortress; p. (1990) 94,100.

Izmir (Smyrna), c., **Turkey**; at head of G. of I., Anatolia; exp. figs, raisins, tobacco, carpets, rugs; anc. and historic c.; ch. comm. ctr. of the Levant; Nemrut Free Trade Zone (1987); ambitous industl. project, refinery and chem. complex (1972–86); univ.; p. (1990) 2,319,188 (t.), 2,694,770 (prov.).

Izmit, c., **Turkey**; E. end of Sea of Marmara; cereals, tobacco, oil refinery and polythene plant under construction; p. (1985) 233,338.

J

Jabalpur (Jubbulpore), c., Madhya Pradesh, **India**; rly. ctr.; ordnance wks.; p. (1991) 742,000.

Jablonec nad Nisou, t., **Czech Rep.**; on R. Neisse; glassware ctr., inc. glass jewellery and imitation stones; p. (1984) 44,742.

Jáchymov, t., **Czech Rep.**; spa; uranium mines, pitchblende, lead, silver, nickel, cobalt.

Jackson, t., Mich., **USA**; on Grand R.; locomotives, motorcar accessories, electronic equipment, metal gds.; p. (1984) 37,700 (t.), 145,300 (met. a.).

Jackson, t., cap. of Miss., **USA**; comm. and industl. ctr.; p. (1990) 196,637 (c.), 395,000 (met. a.).

Jacksonville, c., Fla., **USA**; pt. on St. John's R.; impt. ctr. on Atl. cst.; chemicals, shipbldg. and repair, printing, lumber, cigar mftg.; tourism; p. (1990) 672,971 (c.), 907,000 (met. a.).

Jacobabad, t., Sind, **Pakistan**; driest and hottest place in Indian sub-continent; p. (1981) 80,000.

Jacui, R., S. **Brazil**; rises in S. edge of Brazilian Plateau, enters Atl. Oc., through lagoon, Lagoa dos Patos; 560 km long.

Jadotville. See Likasi.

Jaduguda, Bihar, **India**; uranium mine and mill to

supply India's growing nuclear power production.

Jaén, t., cap. of prov. of Jaén, S. **Spain**; in foothills of Andalusian mtns.; cath.; olive oil, wine, chemicals; p. (1991) 105,545, 624,752 (prov.).

Jaffna, spt., N. **Sri Lanka**; on J. peninsula; second t. of rep.; p. (1983) 128,000.

Jaipur, c., cap. of Rajasthan, **India**; univ.; fine fabrics, jewellery; tourism; old cap. Amber is 8 km away; p. (1991) 1,458,000.

Jajce, t., **Bosnia-Herzegovina**, formerly Yugoslavia; at junc. of Rs. Vrbas and Pliva (hydroelectric power); Fed. People's Rep. of Yugoslavia declared here by Tito (1943).

Jakarta, (Batavia), c., cap. of **Indonesia**, N.W. Java; comm. ctr.; textiles; exps. rubber, tea; printing; airport; p. (1983) 7,636,000.

Jalalabad, c., E. **Afghanistan**; on Kabul R., nr. Khyber Pass; univ.; agr. tr. ctr.; p. (1982) 57,824.

Jalgaon, t., Maharashtra, **India**; in Tapti R. valley nr. Bhusawal; p. (1991) 242,193.

Jalisco, st., **Mexico**; on Pac. Oc.; traversed by Sierra Madre; well timbered, agr.; minerals; tourism; a. 80,876 km²; p. (1990) 5,287,987.

Jalón, R., **Spain**; rises in Iberian Mtns., flows N.E. into R. Ebro nr. Zaragoza; valley forms main rly., road route from Madrid to Ebro valley.

Jalpaiguri, t., W. Bengal, **India**; frontier t.; rly. ctr.; p. (1981) 61,743.

Jamaica, rep., **W.I.**; member of Brit. Commonwealth; mtnous.; Blue Mtn. range runs E. to W. and rises to 2,258 m; tropical climate modified by alt.; economy based on agr. and mng.; major exp. crops sugar and bananas; major world producer of bauxite (recent contraction) and alumina; tourist ind. expanding; member of Caribbean Free Trade Association; 25 per cent unemployment; major pts. Kingston, Montego Bay, Pt. Antonio; international airpt.; univ. at cap. Kingston; a. 11,424 km²; p. (1992) 2·44 m, of which 22 per cent are in Kingston.

James, R. Va., **USA**; hydroelec. power in upper reaches, wide estuary in lower course; outlet to Chesapeake Bay; 544 km long.

James Bay, S. arm of Hudson Bay, **Canada**; c. 480 km long, 224 km wide.

Jamestown, spt., cap. of **St. Helena** I.; flax.

Jamestown, t., dist., Va., **USA**; nr. mouth of James R., where first English permanent settlement was founded 1607.

Jammu, t., J. and Kashmir, **India**; winter cap. of st.; univ., fort, palace; p. (1981) 206,135.

Jammu and Kashmir, st., N.W. **India**; traversed by ranges of Himalayas; wheat and rice; 1972 agreement divided state between India and Pakistan; disturbances 1989; cap. Indian sector Srinagar, cap. Pakistani sector Muzaffarabad; total a. 222,823 km²; p. (1981) 5,987,389.

Jamnagar, t., Gujarat, **India**; on G. of Kutch; p. (1991) 342,000.

Jamshedpur, c., Bihar, **India**; W. of Calcutta; major industl. ctr. of rep.; Tata iron and steel wks.; engin.; p. (1991) 461,000.

Jämtland, co. W. **Sweden**; cap. Ostersand; a. 49,857 km²; p. (1992) 135,910.

Janina. See Ioánnina.

Jan Mayen I., volcanic I. between Spitzbergen and Iceland, Arctic Oc.; annexed by **Norway** 1929; meteorological sta.; a. 373 km².

Japan, E. Asia; 4 main Is., Honshu (lgst.), Hokkaido, Shikoku, Kyushu; mtnous.; 18 active volcanoes; subject to earthquakes; only 17 per cent of land cultivable; intensive and mechanised agr.; rice, fruits, vegetables; few animals; inds. highly developed and based on imports of raw material and export of finished prods.; rapid industrialisation since second world war; economic growth has been rapid but appears to be slowing slightly; rapid technological innovation; stable labour management relationships; inds. inc. shipbldg., motor vehicles, textiles, steel, electronics, chemicals, cheap consumer gds.; cap. Tokyo, world financial ctr.; a. 370,370 km²; p. (1992) 124,450,000 (inc. Okinawa and Ryuku Is.).

Japan Current. See Kuroshio.

Japan, Sea of, portion of Pac. Oc. between Korea, USSR, and Japan.

Japurá, R., Colombia, **Brazil**; rises as Caquetá in Colombian Andes, flows S.E. through Brazil to Amazon; 2,080 km long.

Jari, new t., Amazonia, **Brazil**; ambitious project of timber and pulp plant in the rain forest; not as successful as hoped.

Jaroslaw, t., Przemyśl., prov., S.E. **Poland**; on R.

San; food-processing; founded 11th cent.; impt. tr. ctr. 16th cent.; p. (1989) 41,267.

Jarrow, t., South Tyneside, Tyne and Wear, **Eng.**; on S. bank of Tyne, 11 km below Gateshead; grew up as shipbldg. ctr.; hit by depression of 1930s; hunger march to London 1936; new enterprises introduced; steel and tube wks., oil storage; die-castings, knitting-wool-mkg. at Bede trading estate; the Venerable Bede lived and died here; p. (1981) 27,074.

Jasper National Park, Alberta, **Canada**; Rocky mtns., tourism.

Jaunpur, t., Uttar Pradesh, **India**; mkt. t.; ctr. of Moslem learning and architecture in 15th cent.; p. (1991) 136,062.

Java, I., **Indonesia**; most developed of Indonesian Is.; traversed E. to W. by forested volcanic mtns.; fertile volcanic soils aid intensive rice cultivation; over-populated; contains 70 per cent of cty.'s p. yet only 9 per cent of land a.; exps. inc. coffee, rubber, sugar, copra, teak; noted for silver craft and batik work (anc. craft of fabric decoration); a. 130,510 km²; p. (1983) 96,892,900.

Javari, R., forms bdy. between **Peru** and **Brazil**; trib. of R. Amazon.

Java Sea, part of the **Pac. Oc.** between N. cst. Java, Borneo, and Sumatra.

Jebba, t., **Nigeria**; on R. Niger.

Jebel Aulia, v., **Sudan**; S. of Khartoum; dam across White Nile R.

Jebel-Hauran, high tableland of **Syria,** alt. *c.* 1,800 m.

Jedburgh, royal burgh, Roxburgh, **Scot.**; on Jed Water, S.W. of Kelso; tweeds, woollens, rayon; abbey ruins; ctr. of Border warfare in Middle Ages; p. (1991) 4,118.

Jeddah. *See* Jiddah.

Jefferson City, st. cap. Mo., **USA**; on Missouri R.; univ.; comm. and processing ctr. of agr. a.; shoes, tiles, farm implements; p. (1980) 36,619.

Jelenia Góra (Hirschberg), t. and prov., S.W. **Poland** (since 1945), formerly in Lower Silesia; mftg.; spa; p. (1989) 93,205 (t.), 515,000 (prov.).

Jelgava (Mitau), t., **Latvia**; on Lielupe R.; textiles, foodstuffs, refractory materials; p. (1991) 74,500.

Jemappes, t., **Belgium**; 5 km W. of Mons; industl.; Fr. victory over Austria 1792; battle of Mons 1914.

Jena, c., **Germany**; on R. Saale, 72 km S.W. of Leipzig; univ., observatory; optical glass-ware, precision instruments; leading cultural ctr. late 18th and early 19th cent., defeat of Prussians by Fr. 1806; p. (1990) 101,900.

Jerez de la Frontera, t., **Spain**; in Andalusia, 22 km N.E. of Cádiz; in fertile agr. a.; sherry; p. (1991) 184,018.

Jericho, v., Jordan Valley, **Jordan**; est. through recent excavations as one of oldest towns in the world (6000 B.C.).

Jersey, I., lgst. of **Channel Is.,** 21 km W. of Fr. cst.; potatoes, tomatoes, cauliflowers, flowers, fruit. cattle; tourist resort; banking; ch. t. St. Helier; a. 117 km²; p. (1989) 82,809.

Jersey City, c., N.J., **USA**; E. of Newark, on Hudson R.; comm. and industl. ctr.; diverse inds.; p. (1990) 228,537 (c.), 553,000 (met. a.).

Jerusalem, c., **Israel** and **Jordan**; 811 m a.s.l.; between Dead Sea and Mediterranean; the "Holy City" of the Jews and the sacred c. of the Christians and Moslems; Israeli western sector and Arab eastern sector declared by Israeli parliament (1980) united c. and cap.; modern mftg.; p. (1990) 524,500 inc. E. Jerusalem.

Jervis Bay, inlet of Pac. Oc., Australian Capital Territory, **Australia**; acquired by Fed Govt. as site for establishment of pt. for Canberra 1909; plans to develop pt. and steelworks, a. 73 km².

Jesselton. *See* Kota Kinabalu.

Jhang Maghiana, t., **Pakistan**; textiles; mkt.; on R. Chenab; p. (1981) 195,000.

Jhansi, c., Uttar Pradesh, **India**; ctr. rly. ctr., mkt.; formerly of strategic importance; p. (1991) 313,000.

Jharia, t., Bihar, **India**; ctr. of most impt. coalfield in India; p. (1981) 57,496.

Jhelum, R., W. Punjab, **Pakistan**; most W. of the five Rs. of the Punjab; forms Vale of Kashmir in upper course; Mangla Dam under Indus Waters Treaty, completed 1967.

Jhelum, c., **Pakistan**; on Jhelum R.; p. (1981) 106,000.

Jiamusi (Kiamusze), c., Heilongjiang, **China**; ch. pt. on Songhua R.; p. (1984) 546,500.

Jiangsu (Kiangsu), coastal prov., **China**; on Yellow

Sea; low lying a. N. of Chang Jiang delta; rich agr., dense p.; cotton, sericulture, tea, sugar, fish (many Ls.); cap. Nanjing; a. 109,000 km²; p. (1990) 68,170,000.

Jiangxi (Kiangsi), prov., S.E. **China**; in basin of navigable Gan R. which drains through L. Poyang to Chang Jiang; ch. cs. Shanghai, Zhenjiang, Wuxi, Nanchang (cap.); rice, wheat, tea, cotton; tungsten, coking coal, kaolin; a. 172,494 km²; p. (1990) 38,280,000.

Jiddah or **Jeddah,** c., admin. cap., Hejaz, **Saudi Arabia**; on Red Sea, pt. of Mecca; pilgrims; steel mill and oil refinery; new King Faisal Port nearby; univ. (with Mecca); p. (1986) 1·4 m.

Jihlava, t., Moravia, **Czech Rep.**; on Jihlava R.; 519 m a.s.l.; timber, grain, textiles; Prague Compactata signed here 1436; p. (1004) 52,828.

Jilin (Kilin), prov., N.E. **China**; N. of Korea and Liaotung peninsula; crossed by Songhua R.; in fertile Manchurian plain; impt. industl. a.; soya beans, grain, lumber, coal, gold, lead; cap. Changchun; a. 186,998 km²; p. (1990) 25,150,000.

Jilin (Kirin), c., Jilin, N.E. **China**; former prov. cap.; on Songhua R., at outlet of Songhua reservoir; impt. position on rly. from Changchun to coastal pts.; chemical fertilisers, steel, oil refinery; p. (1992) 1,270,000.

Jimma, t., **Ethiopia**; ch. prod. Jimma coffee; connected by road with Addis Ababa; Agricultural Technical School; p. (1984) 60,992.

Jinan (Tsinan), c., cap of Shandong prov., **China**; on S. bank of Huang He, 160 km. from G. of Bo Hai; agr. ctr.; textiles, foodstuffs, chemicals, trucks; univ.; p. (1992) 2,350,000.

Jinja, t., **Uganda**; on N. shore of L. Victoria where Nile drains from L. over Ripon Falls; (now submerged by the construction of Owen Falls dam 2·4 km downstream); cotton mnfs., copper smelting, flour and maize milling; rly. to Kampala; p. (1991) 60,979.

Jinzhou (Chincho), c., Liaoning prov., **China**; cement, glass, bricks, tiles, paper, wood and pulp, oil; p. (1984) 748,700.

Jiujiang (Kiukiang), c., Jianxi prov., **China**; pt. of Chang Jiang at foot of forested mtn.; entrepôt tr.; former treaty pt.; p. (1984) 378,100.

João Pessoa, t., cap. of Paraiba st., **Brazil**; through its pt. Cabedelo expts. cotton, sugar, minerals; industl. expansion; p. (1991) 497,214.

Joban, dist., N.E. Honshu, **Japan**; third lgst. coalfield in Japan; ch. t. Fukushima.

Jodhpur, t., Rajasthan, **India**; ctr. of Thar desert; old fortress t.; p. (1991) 668,000.

Jogjakarta, c., Java, **Indonesia**; univ., cultural ctr.; handicrafts; citadel with palace; p. (1980) 342,267.

Johannesburg, c., Transvaal, S. **Africa**; univ.; gold-mng. ctr. of Witwatersrand; diamond cutting, engin., textiles, chemicals; oil pipeline from Durban; p. (1985) 1,609,408 (met. a.).

John o' Groat's House, place nr. Duncansby Head, Caithness, **Scot.**

Johnstone, burgh, Renfrew, **Scot.**; on R. Black Cart, nr. Paisley; machine tools, textiles, iron and brass foundry; p. (1991) 18,635.

Johnstown, industl. t., Penns., **USA**; on Conemaugh R.; coal-mng. and steel ctr.; machin.; p. (1984) 33,100 (t.), 259,000 (met. a.).

Johore, st., **Malaysia**; at S. end of Malaya; forested; cap. Johor Baharo; rubber, rice, copra, pineapples; tin, iron, bauxite; a. 18,985 km²; p. (1980) 1,638,229.

Joina Falls, Mali; dam projected for hydroelectric power and irrigation under auspices of Organisation of Riparian States of R. Senegal (Guinea, Mali, Mauritania, Senegal).

Joinville, t., Santa Catarina, **Brazil**; exp. timber, maté tea; textiles, machin., car parts, plastics; p. (1991) 346,095.

Joliet, c., Ill., **USA**; on Des Plaines R., S.W. of Chicago; R. pt.; coal and limestone nearby; rly. engin., oil refining; p. (1990) 76,836 (c.), 390,000 (met. a.).

Joliette, t., Quebec, **Canada**; textile mills, paper, tobacco-processing; p. (1986) 16,845.

Jönköping, t., cap. of J. co., **Sweden**; safety-matches, textiles, footwear; p. (1992) 112,802 (t.) 309,867 (co.).

Jonquière, t., S. Quebec, **Canada**; paper and pulp mills; p. (1986) 58,467. *See* Chicoutimi.

Joplin, t., Mo., **USA**; in dairy and livestock region; lead and zinc mng.; mnfs. metal and leather gds.; p. (1990) 40,961.

Jordan, kingdom, S.W. **Asia**; bounded by Israel,

Syria, Saudi Arabia, and Iraq; consists of high plateau (600 m), Jordan valley, and hill cty. to W. of R. Jordan; only 25 per cent of a. sufficiently humid for agr., much is migratory herding of animals and subsistence agr.; sm. mineral wealth; only outlet to sea Aqaba, pt. on G. of Aqaba; only one single-track rly.; new rail link built to Al-Hara phosphate mines, now major exp.; dependant on oil imports; cap. Amman; W. Bank of R. Jordan occupied by Israeli forces since June 1967; plan mooted (1972) to unify J. and W. Bank to form United Arab Kingdom; a. 101,140 km²; p. (1992) 4·01 m (80 per cent Moslem and 70 per cent under 24).

Jordan, R., Israel and Jordan; flows S. from Anti-Lebanon along sinuous course, mostly below sea-level to Dead Sea; its rapidly and variant depth render it unnavigable, and no t. of any importance has ever been built on its banks; Jesus was baptised in its waters; contemporary strife over use for irrigation; 368 km long.

Jos, t., central **Nigeria;** on Bauchi Plateau, 96 km S.W. of Bauchi; impt. tin mines; steel rolling mill; p. (1983) 149,000.

Jostedalsbre, icefield, W. **Norway,** lgst. icefield of European mainland; a. 881 km²; rises to 2,043 m.

Jotunheimen, mtn. region, central **Norway** hgst. in Scandinavia; Galdhopiggen 2,470 m, Glittertind 2,482 m.

Juan Fernández, two rocky volcanic Is., S. **Pac. Oc.,** belonging to **Chile;** a. 98 km²; the buccaneer Alexander Selkirk marooned here 1704–9 gave idea for Defoe's *Robinson Crusoe.*

Juan les Pins, resort, Alpes-Maritimes dep., S.E. **France.**

Juba (Giuba), R., Somalia; narrow fertile valley, imp. agr. a.; 872 km long.

Jubbulpore. See **Jabalpur.**

Jucar, R., E. **Spain;** rises in Montes Universales, and flows to Mediterranean; irrigation and hydroelec. power; 400 km long.

Judaea, div. of Palestine in the Roman period.

Juggernaut. See **Puri.**

Juiz de Fora, t., Minas Gerais, **Brazil;** textile ctr.; p. (1991) 385,756.

Julfa (Jolfa), c., N. **Iran;** on frontier with USSR, customs and transit ctr. on overland route from Europe.

Julian Alps, mtn. range, **Slovenia** (formerly Yugoslavia) and **Italy;** hgst. peak 2,865 m.

Julianeháb, t., S.W. **Greenland;** N.W. of C. Farewell; tr. ctr., fish. pt.; p. (1990) 3,543.

Jülich, t., N. Rhine–Westphalia, **Germany;** nuclear reactor; p. (1986) 30,200.

Jullundur, c., Punjab, **India;** rly. ctr.; st. cap. until Chandigarh was built; p. (1981) 408,196.

Jumna, R., N. India; ch. trib. of R. Ganges; rises in the Himalayas and flows past Delhi and Agra to Allahabad; 1,376 km long.

Junagadh, t., Gujarat, **India;** agr. tr. and foodprocessing; industl. ctr.; formerly cap. of principality of J.; p. (1991) 130,484.

Jundiai, t., São Paulo st., **Brazil;** industl. ctr.; nr. São Paulo; p. (1991) 312,517.

Juneau, c., cap. of Alaska, **USA;** at foot of Chilkoot mtns., lumbering; fisheries; gold settlement (1881); p. (1990) 26,751. See **Willow South.**

Jungfrau, peak, Bernese Oberland, **Switzerland;** height 4,161 m; electric rly. from Kleine Scheidegg to Jungfraujoch.

Junín, t., Argentina; agr. tr., rly. engin., pottery, furniture; p. (1980) 62,080.

Jura, dep., E. **France;** named from mtn. range on Franco-Swiss border; agr. and pastoral; cap. Lons-le-Saunier; a. 5,053 km²; p. (1990) 248,800.

Jura, I., Argyll and Bute, **Scot.;** off W. cst.; a. 378 km²; p. (1991) 196.

Jura, mtn. range, **Switzerland** and **France;** folded parallel ranges separated by deep R. valleys; hgst. peak Crêt de la Neige, 1,724 m; 240 km long, breadth 48–64 km.

Jura, canton, **Switzerland;** between Berne and Basle in a strong French speaking dist. in Jura Mtns; p. (1990) 65,700.

Juruá R., lge. trib. of Amazon; rises in E. **Peru** and flows through Acre and Amazonas sts., **Brazil;** over 3,200 km long.

Jylland (Jutland), peninsula region, **Denmark;** intensive agr. and poultry farming; sandy heath in W.; more fertile clay in E. used for dairying; a. 29,554 km²; p. (1990) 2,378,348.

Jyväskylä, t., central **Finland;** pt. on L. Päijänne; pulp. paper, plywood; univ.; p. (1991) 67,026.

K

K2. See **Godwin-Austen, Mt.**

Kabardin-Balkar, aut. rep., Transcaucasia, **Russia;** cap. Nalchik; livestock, lumber, wheat, fruit; nonferrous metals; hydro-metallurgy plant; a. 12,432 km²; p. (1989) 753,500.

Kabelega Falls (Murchison Falls), on Victoria Nile, **Uganda;** falls between L. Kioga and L. Mobutu Seso.

Kabinda. See **Cabinda.**

Kābul, c., cap. of **Afghanistan;** on Kābul R. S. of Hindu Kush; 2,104 m a.s.l.; excellent climate; univ.; comm. and cultural ctr.; textiles, leather, timber inds.; p. (1992) 2 m.

Kābul, R., flows from Hindu Kush through gorges in Khyber Pass to Indus; site of dam for hydroelec. power and irrigation; length c. 480 km.

Kabwe (Broken Hill), Zambia; comm. and mng. ctr.; lead, zinc, cadmium, silver; p. (1989) 210,000.

Kachchh, peninsula, Gujarat st., N.W. **India;** bounded on N. by Pakistan; largely barren except for fertile strip along Arabian Sea; p. (1981) 1,050,161.

Kachin State, semi-aut. st., **Myanmar;** comprising former Myitkyina and Bhamo dists.; home of Kachins; a. 89,042 km².

Kadiyevka, t., Ukraine; coal, iron and steel, synthetic rubber; p. (1990) 112,300.

Kaduna, t., N. **Nigeria;** cap of Kaduna st.; rly. junc.; aluminium wks.; spinning and weaving; new oil refinery; p. (1983) 247,100 (t.), (1991) 3,969,252 (state).

Kaffa, region, **Ethiopia;** mtnous., forested; natural habitat of coffee plant; p. (1984) 2,450,369.

Kagoshima, c., at S. end of Kyushu I., **Japan;** pt. on K. Bay; univs., cas.; porcelain, silk and cotton clothing, food-processing, publishing; rocket launching site nearby at Uchinoura; p. (1990) 536,685.

Kahoolawe, I., Hawaii; a. 117 km²; uninhabited.

Kaieteur Falls, waterfall, **Guyana;** where R. Potaro leaves Guiana Highlands; among world's hgst. falls (226 m).

K'ai-feng, c., Henan, **China;** nr. S. bank of Huang He; one of the most anc. cities in China; cottons, chemicals; p. (1984) 619,200.

Kai Islands, Is., Indonesia; between New Guinea and Timor; timber; a. 1,761 km²; p. 51,000.

Kaikoura, dist., S.I., N.Z.; on E. cst., 128 km N.E. of Christchurch; in this region are the Kaikoura ranges, in which the hgst. peaks are Tapuaenuku (2,887 m) and Alarm (2,867 m); p. (1991) 3,711.

Kailas (Kang-ti-ssu Shan), range and peak, S.W. Tibet, **China;** unclimbed sacred mtn.; source of Indus, Ganges, Sutlej and Zangbo (headstream of Brahmaputra).

Kainji Dam, Nigeria; power sta. transmission system and river transportation on R. Niger.

K'ai-ping, t., Hebei, N. **China;** second lgst. coalmng. a. (Kailan mines) in China; coal exported through Qinhuangdao.

Kairouan, holy c. of Moslems, **Tunisia;** 128 km S.S.E. of Tunis; founded A.D. 670; mosque; p. (1984) 72,254.

Kaiserslautern, c., Rhineland–Palatinate, **Germany;** nr. Mannheim; iron, textiles, machin., tobacco, wood; p. (1986) 96,800.

Kaiser Wilhelm's Land, Australian dependency, Antarctica.

Kakamega, t., Kenya; E. Africa; 48 km N. of Kisumu; ctr. of gold-mng. dist.

Kakinada, t., spt., Adhra Pradesh, **India;** cotton, oilseeds; p. (1991) 280,000.

Kalahari Desert, region of semi-desert, southern Africa; between Orange and Zambesi Rs.; mainly in **Botswana;** alt. 1,128 m; a. 51,800 km²; inhabited chiefly by Bushmen.

Kalamata, t., Peloponnesus, **Greece;** nr. Sparta; figs, currants, flour-milling, cigarette mftg.; p. (1981) 43,235.

Kalamazoo, c., Mich., **USA;** industl. and comm. ctr. in farming a.; paper, pharmaceuticals; fish hatchery nearby; p. (1984) 77,200 (c.), 215,200 (met. a.).

Kalemie (Albertville), t., Zaïre; on L. Tanganyika; rail-steamer transfer point.

Kalewa, t., Myanmar; at confluence of Irrawaddy and Chindwin Rs.; coal deposits.

Kalgan See **Zhangjiakou.**

Kalgoorlie, t., W. **Australia;** gold mng. ctr. in arid region adjacent to "Golden Mile" auriferous reef; nickel mng.; p. (1990) 27,405 (inc. Boulder).

Kalimantan (Indonesian Borneo); straddles equator; sparse p.; poor soils; lge. areas of swamp; plans for reclamation; coal, oil, diamonds, gold in sm. quantities; rice, pepper, copra; a. 539,461 km²; p. (1980) 6·7 m.

Kalinin. See **Tver.**

Kaliningrad (Königsberg), c., **Russia,** former cap. of E. Prussia; on R. Pregel, linked by canal to outer pt. Pillau; univ., cath.; shipbldg., machin., wood-pulp, chemicals, exp. agr. prods.; Kant lived here all his life; p. (1989) 401,000.

Kalisz, t. and prov., **Poland;** on R. Prosna; industl. ctr., textiles; oldest Polish t. mentioned in 2nd cent. A.D. by Ptolemy; p. (1989) 106,031 (t.), 706,500 (prov.).

Kalmar, co. and t., spt., S. **Sweden;** on I. in Kalmar Sound; cath., cas.; matches, food inds., shipbldg · p. (1992) 56,863 (t.), 241,912 (co.).

Kalmuk (Kalmytskaya), aut. rep., **Russia;** on Caspian Sea; harsh and infertile steppe; pastoral agr.; cap. Elista; a. 75,887 km²; p. (1989) 322,600.

Kalna, v., on Mt. Stara Planina, Serbia, **Yugoslavia;** uranium mine and plant; nuclear power sta.

Kaluga, c., **Russia;** pt. on Oka R.; chemicals, engin., hydroelec. power plant; p. (1989) 311,000.

Kalyan, spt., Maharashtra, **India;** nr. Bombay; bricks, tiles; p. (1991) 1,015,000.

Kalymnos, I., Dodecanese, **Greece;** mtnous.; a. 106 km²; p. 13,600.

Kama, R., **Russia;** ch. trib. of Volga which it joins below Kazan; rises in foothills of Urals; lge. hydro-electric sta. at Perm; navigable; 2,016 km long.

Kamaishi, t., spt., N.E. Honshu, **Japan;** serves Kamaishi–Sennin iron-ore field, lgst. worked deposits and reserves in Japan; impt. iron and steel ind; p. (1990) 52,484.

Kamakura, t., Honshu, **Japan;** on shore of Sagami Bay; tourism; p. (1990) 174,307.

Kamaran I., Red Sea, **Yemen;** formerly under Brit. occupation, 1915–67; a. 57 km²; p. 2,200.

Kamchatka, peninsula, E. Siberia, **Russia;** volcanic ranges; geothermal power sta.; mineral wealth, fisheries on cst., climate cold, wet and foggy; contains part of Koryak nat. okrug; cap. Petropavlovsk.

Kamenets-Podolskiy, t., **Ukraine,** on Smotrich R.; lt. inds.; mediaeval fortress t.; p. (1990) 103,300.

Kamensk-Uralsk, c., **Russia;** aluminium, iron, steel, engin.; p. (1989) 208,000.

Kamet, Himalayan peak, on border of **India** and Tibet, **China;** 7,761 m; highest mtn. climbed (Smythe, 1931) until 1953 (Everest).

Kamloops, t., B.C., **Canada;** on Thompson R.; formerly Fort Thompson; on transcontinental rlys.; suppl ctr. for mng. and grazing dist.; fruit and livestock mkts.; p. (1986) 61,773.

Kampala, c., cap. of **Uganda;** univ., ch. comm. ctr.; lt. inds., coffee-processing; p. (1991) 773,463.

Kampen, t., Overijssel, **Neth.;** on R. IJssel; cigar-mkg.; p. (1993) 32,571.

Kampot, prov., **Cambodia;** on G. of Siam; ctr. of pepper ind.; p. (1981) 337,879.

Kampuchea, Democratic. See **Cambodia.**

Kamyshin, t., **Russia;** pt. on Volga; textiles, mkt. gardening, grain; p. (1989) 122,000.

Kan, R. See **Gan Jiang.**

Kananga (Luluabourg), c., cap. of Kasai Occidental prov., **Zaïre;** on Lulua R.; comm. and communications ctr. in cotton-growing a.; p. (1985) 938,000.

Kanawha, R., W. Va., **USA;** rises in Allegheny mtns., flows into R. Ohio; runs through ch. mng. a. of W. Va. coalfield nr. Charleston.

Kanazawa, c., Honshu, **Japan;** in Kana plain, on Sea of Japan; machin., silk and cotton textiles; land-scape gardens; *No* theatre; p. (1990) 442,868.

Kanchenjunga, mtn., on Nepal–Sikkim bdy., N.E. **India;** third hgst. mtn. in world, 8,585 m.

Kanchipuram (Conjeeveram), t., Tamil Nadu, S. **India;** on plain S.W. of Madras; pilgrimage ctr.; textiles; p. (1991) 144,955.

Kandahar. See **Qandahar.**

Kandy, c., **Sri Lanka;** in mtns. in ctr. of I.; 120 km from Colombo; univ. at sub. of Peradeniya; resort in hot season; tea, cocoa; p. (1981) 97,872.

Kangaroo I., lgst. I. off S. **Australia** cst.; tourists attracted by spectacular granite scenery and varied flora and fauna.

KaNgwane, homeland, Natal, **S. Africa;** chief town Eerstehoek; pop. (1985) 392,782.

Kano, c., N. **Nigeria;** trading centre for whole of

Sudan region; impt. airport and rly. terminus; groundnut ctr.; p. (1983) 487,000 (c.), (1991) 5,632,040.

Kanpur (Cawnpore), c., Uttar Pradesh, N. **India;** on R. Ganges; impt. mftg. ctr.; textiles, chemicals, leather goods, foodstuffs; p. (1991) 1,879,000.

Kansas, st., **USA;** called the "sunflower state"; prairie; farming, maize, wheat; cattle, dairy-ing, pigs; coal, petroleum, natural gas, lead, meat packing, flour milling, aircraft, chemicals, machin.; admitted to Union 1861; st. flower sun-flower, st. bird Western Meadowlark; cap. Topeka; a. 213,095 km²; p. (1990) 2,477,574.

Kansas, R., Kan., **USA;** trib. of Missouri R., con-fluence at Kansas City; vegetable growing in valley; periodic flooding; 272 km long.

Kansas City, Kansas and Mo., **USA;** at conflu-ence of Kansas and Missouri Rs.; univ.; gr. livestock mart, car and aircraft assembly, steel prods., meat-packing, food processing; p. (1990) 149,767 (Kansas) 435,146 (Mo.); 1,566,280 (joint met. a.).

Kansu. See **Gansu.**

Kant, t., **Kyrgyzstan;** 19 km E. of Frunze; to be expanded to industl. c.; proposed p. 100,000.

Kaohsiung, spt., **Taiwan;** on S.W. cst.; industl. ctr., road and rly. terminus; oil refining, aluminium wks.; p. (1984) 1,285,132.

Kaolack, inland pt., **Senegal;** 112 km up Saloum R.; groundnut ctr., integrated textile complex; p. (1985) 132,400.

Kaposvár, t., S.W. **Hungary;** on Kapos R.; comm. ctr.; textiles, foodstuffs; p. (1989) 74,000.

Kara-Bogaz-Gol, lge. shallow bay, **Turkmenistan;** an arm of Caspian Sea; rapid evaporation allows huge quantities of salt from Caspian to be deposited along its shores (world's lgst. source of Glauber's salt); a. 18,130 km².

Karabuk, t., **Turkey;** N. of Ankara; steel wks.; p. (1985) 94,818.

Karacheyevo-Cherkesskaya, aut. region, **Russia;** in Greater Caucasus; cap. Cherkessk; livestock, grain; coal, lead, zinc; a. 14,095 km²; p. (1989) 415,000.

Karachi, c., **Pakistan;** on Arabian Sea, nr. Indus delta; former cap. of Pakistan; univ.; spt., air ctr.; oil refining, industl. gases, steel mill, natural gas from Sui; nuclear power sta.; p. (1981) 5,103,000.

Karaganda, c., **Kazakhstan;** on impt. coalfield developed since 1926; supplies industl. ctrs. of Urals; iron and steel wks., power sta.; p. (1990) 613,200.

Kara-Kalpak, aut. rep., N.W. **Uzbekistan;** inc. Ust-Urt plateau, Kyzyl-Kum desert; irrigated agr.; cap. Nukus; a. 165,553 km²; p. (1990) 1,244,700.

Karakoram Range, part of Himalayas between Kashmir and China; many lofty peaks, inc. Mt. Godwin-Austen; Karakoram highway linking Pakistan with Xinjiang prov. of China, opened 1971.

Kara-Kum, sand desert, **Turkmenistan;** E. of S.E. shore of Caspian Sea; to be irrigated with water diverted from Rs. which flow to Barents Sea. a. 349,650 km²; canal 1,440 km long across desert.

Karamay (K'o-la-ma-i), t. Xianjiang, **China;** ctr. of lge. oilfield; pipeline to Fushantzu refinery; p. (1984) 180,100.

Kara Sea, Arctic Oc.; E. of Novaya Zemlya; navigation to and from Siberian pts. July–Sept.

Karbala, c., **Iraq;** N.W. of Al Hillah; ctr. of pilgrimage; sacred c. of Moslem Shiite sect; p. (1985) 184,574.

Karelian, aut. rep., **Russia;** between Kola peninsula and Finland; lake-covered, coniferous forests; cap. Petrozavodsk; rich in timber, minerals, precious metals; granite and mica quarried; paper and pulp milling; a. 179,408 km²; p. (1989) 790,200.

Karelian Isthmus, Russia; strategic route between Finland and USSR impt. for defence of Leningrad.

Kariba Dam, in Kariba gorge of Zambesi R., on Zimbabwe–Zambia border; operated jointly by the two govts.; one of lgst. dams in world with vast artificial lake supplying hydroelectric power to Zimbabwe and the copperbelt of Zambia; badly polluted with use of D.D.T. in tsetse and malaria control; involved resettlement of Batonka peoples; completed 1960.

Karikal, former Fr. settlement on E. cst. of **India;** part of Union Territory of Pondicherry; p. (1991) 145,723.

Karkonosze. See **Riesengebirge.**

Karl-Marx-Stadt. *See* Chemnitz.

Karlovac, t., **Croatia,** (formerly Yugoslavia); S.W. of Zagreb; chemicals, textiles, food processing; p. (1981) 78,363.

Karlový Vary (Carlsbad), t., Bohemia, **Czech Rep.;** on R. Ohře; hot mineral springs; health resort; porcelain; p. (1984) 59,183.

Karlskoga, t., **Sweden;** E. of L. Vänern; seat of Bofors armament wks.; iron and steel, explosives, chemicals; p. (1983) 35,539.

Karlskrona, spt., S. **Sweden;** on Baltic Sea; main naval sta.; lighting fixtures, china; p. (1992) 59,390.

Karlsruhe, c., Baden–Württemberg, **Germany;** road and rly. ctr.; outport on Rhine; chemicals, engin., elec., tobacco inds., oil refining; nuclear reactor; oil pipeline to Lavera, nr. Marseilles; p. (1990) 276,500.

Karlstad, t., **Sweden;** on N. shore L. Väner; ironwks., engin., machin.; p. (1992) 77,290.

Karnak, t., **Egypt;** on Nile, E. of Luxor; site of the anc. Thebes; ruined temples.

Karnal, t., **Haryana, India;** clothing inds.; p. (1991) 173,751.

Karnataka (Mysore), st., S.W. **India;** borders Arabian Oc.; inc. W. Ghats where high rainfall and hydroelec. power; rainfall decreases to E.; cap. Bangalore; a. 192,203 km²; p. (1991) 44,977,201.

Karpathos, I., Dodecanese, **Greece;** Aegean Sea; between Rhodes and Crete; p. (1981) 4,645.

Karroo, W. Cape Prov., **S. Africa;** high plateau, scrub-covered; irrigated by Verwoerd dam on Orange R.

Kars, t. and prov., N.E. **Turkey;** in Armenia, alt. *c.* 1,800 m, in strategic position nr. Soviet border; p. (1985) 69,293, (1990) 662,155 (prov.).

Karst, dist., **Slovenia** (formerly Yugoslavia); in Dinaric Alps; gives name to limestone landforms which are well developed here.

Karun, R., S.W. **Iran;** mainly mtn. torrent; difficult access, sparse p.; 752 km long.

Karvina, t., **Czech Rep.;** on Polish border; ctr. of Ostrava-Karvina coalfield; p. (1990) 70,000.

Kasai, R., Angola and **Zaïre,** Central Africa; rises in Bihé Plateau (Angola) and flows over 1,920 km into R. Zaïre 192 km above Kinshasa; alluvial diamond mng. at Chicopa.

Kasai, former prov., **Zaïre;** agr.; impt. source of industl. diamonds; attempted secession 1960; now divided into E. Kasai (cap. Mbuji-Mayi), and W. Kasai (cap. Luluabourg).

Kāshān, c., central **Iran;** in agr. oasis; carpets, velvet; p. (1982) 110,000.

Kashi (Kashgar) c., Xinjiang, prov., **China;** on anc. imperial silk route through central Asia; growth rapid with irrigation; visited by Marco Polo 1275; p. (1984) 187,100.

Kashmir. *See* Jammu and Kashmir.

Kassala, t., N.E. **Sudan;** ctr. of cotton-growing dist.

Kassel, c., Hesse, **Germany;** on R. Fulda; cas.; machin., vehicles, science-based inds.; route ctr.; p. (1990) 194,800.

Kastamonu, t., N. **Turkey;** cap. of K. prov.; ctr. of dist. rich in minerals; textiles, copper gds.; p. (1985) 46,986.

Katanga. *See* Shaba.

Kathiawar, peninsula, Gujarat, **India;** between G. of Kutch and G. of Cambay; ch. pt. Bhaunagar; very dry a.

Katmai, Mount, S. Alaska, **USA;** active volcano with crater L.; alt. 2,135 m.

Katmandu (Kathmandu), cap. of **Nepal;** on Vishnumati R., 120 km from Indian frontier; highway to Kodari; hydroelec. sta.; brick and tile wks.; many palaces and temples; p. (1981) 235,160.

Katoomba, t., N.S.W., **Australia;** holiday resort at 1,017 m in the Blue Mountains; since 1947 part of City of Blue Mtns.; p. (1981) 13,942 (inc. Wentworth Falls).

Katowice, prov., S. **Poland;** in Upper Silesia; cap. K.; mng. and industl. a. drained by Warta R.; a. 9,516 km²; p. (1989) 3,953,800.

Katowice, c., S. **Poland;** cap. of K. prov.; impt. iron-mng. and industl. ctr.; heavy machin. chemicals; p. (1989) 366,077.

Katrine, Loch, S.W. Stirling, **Scot.;** beautiful woodland and moorland scenery; source of Glasgow water supply; scene of Scott's *Lady of the Lake;* 13 km long, *c.* 1·6 km wide.

Katsina, t., **Nigeria;** nr. Niger border; agr. tr. ctr., groundnuts, cotton; rural craft inds.; steel rolling mill; Hausa cultural ctr.; p. (1983) 149,000, (1991) 3,878,344 (state).

Kattegat, arm of N. Sea linked with Baltic; separates **Denmark** (Jutland) from **Sweden;** 64–112 km wide.

Katwijk, t., S. Holland, **Neth.;** on N. Sea 24 km from the Hague; resort; synthetic resins; p. (1993) 40,682.

Kaufbeuren, t., Bavaria, **Germany;** on R. Wertach; textile mnfs.; p. (1986) 41,500.

Kaunas (Kovno), c., **Lithuania;** on R. Nemen; R. pt. and comm. ctr.; univ.; 11th cent. c.; metal gds., chemicals, textiles, hydroelec. power; Jewish p. (circa 30 per cent) exterminated during German occupation 1941–4; p. (1990) 429,700.

Kavalla, c., E. Macedonia, **Greece;** on Bay of Kavalla; processes and exp. tobacco; the anc. Neapolis; p. (1981) 56,705.

Kawagoe, c., Honshu, **Japan;** in Kanto plain; silk textiles; p. (1990) 304,860.

Kawasaki, S. sub. Tokyo, Honshu, **Japan;** pt. for import of industl. raw materials; heavy inds.; p. (1990) 1,173,606.

Kawthoolei State, st., **Myanmar;** former Karen st.; extended to inc. areas in Tenasserim and Irrawaddy; a. 30,383 km².

Kayah State, semi-aut. st., **Myanmar;** on Thai border; forested plateau; tungsten mines; teak; a. 11,730 km².

Kayseri, c. and prov., **Turkey;** S.E. of Ankara; textiles, carpets, food tr.; anc. Hittite c.; p. (1990) 943,484 (prov.), 461,415 (c.).

Kazakhstan, CIS, former USSR constituent rep., located in central Asia; cap. Alma-Ata; steppe with stock-raising; lge. desert areas being made fertile by irrigation; plans to divert Ob R.; grain in N.; coal at Karaganda; asbestos at Dzhetygara; minerals inc. metaborite (richest boron mineral); oil; atomic power sta. to W. of Caspian Sea; cosmodrome at Leninsk, E. of Aral Sea; a. 2,778,544 km²; p. (1992) 16·96 m.

Kazan', c., **Russia;** cap. of Tatar aut. rep.; pt. on Volga; impt. tr. ctr. for E. Russia, Turkestan Bokhara and Iran; cath., univ. (where Tolstoy and Lenin were educated); engin., chemicals, synthetic rubber, textiles, paper, oil refining; natural gas pipeline to Minnibayevo; p. (1989) 1,094,000.

Kazanluk, t., central **Bulgaria;** in region famous for attar of roses.

Kazan-retto or **Volcanic Is.;** gr. of Is., W. Pac. Oc. S. of Tokyo; sugar plantations, sulphur; returned to Japan by USA 1968.

Kazbek, extinct volcano, N. **Georgia;** second hgst. peak of Caucasus; alt. 5,045 m.

Kāzerūn, t., S.W. **Iran;** ctr. of agr. dist. where fruit, tobacco, opium, cotton grown.

Kazvin or **Qazvin,** c., N.W. **Iran;** transit tr.; carpets, textiles; p. (1983) 244,265.

Kearsley, t., Gtr. Manchester, **Eng.;** chemicals, paper; p. (1981) 11,352.

Keban Dam, S.E. **Turkey;** at confluence of the E. and W. branches of Euphrates.

Kecskemet, c., central **Hungary;** fruit-canning and wine-distilling from locally grown prods.; 4th cent. c.; p. (1989) 106,000.

Kedah, st., **Malaysia;** on Strait of Malacca, N.W. Malaya; rice, rubber, coconuts, tungsten; cap. Alor Star; a. 9,479 km²; p. (1980) 1,116,140.

Kediri, t., E. Java, **Indonesia;** food processing; p. (1980) 221,830.

Keeling Is. *See* Cocos Is.

Keelung (Chi-lung), c., N. **Taiwan;** on E. China Sea; naval base and ch. pt.; exp. agr. prods.; chemicals; gold, sulphur, copper mined nearby; p. (1984) 352,666.

Keewatin, dist., N.W. Terr., **Canada;** barren grounds; fur a. 590,934 km².

Kegworth, v. Leics., **Eng;** scene of M1 air crash.

Keighley, t., West Yorks., **Eng.;** in Aire valley, 24 km N.W. of Leeds; engin., woollen and worsteds; p. (1981) 57,451.

Keihin, vast conurb. of Tokyo, Yokohama and Kawasaki, **Japan.**

Keith, burgh, Moray, **Scot.;** mkt. t. in agr. dist.; p. (1991) 4,793.

Kelantan, st., **Malaysia;** one of most fertile areas on E. cst. Malaya; cap. Kota Bharu; rice, coconuts, rubber; a. 14,815 km²; p. (1980) 893,753.

Kells or **Ceannanus Mor,** mkt. t., Co. Meath, **R.o.I.;** notable for monastic remains and illuminated Book of Kells, now in library of Trinity College, Dublin; p. (1986) 2,413.

Kelso, burgh, Roxburgh, **Scot.;** at confluence of Rs. Teviot and Tweed; p. (1991) 5,989.

Kemerovo, c., **Russia**; S.E. of Tomsk; coalmng. ctr.; chemicals, textiles, plastics; p. (1989) 520,000.

Kemi, t., N.E. **Finland**; spt. on G. of Bothnia; sawmills; p. (1991) 25,244.

Kemi, R., N.E. **Finland**; used for hydroelectric power and timber transport; 480 km long.

Kempten, t., Bavaria, **Germany**; nr. Bodensee; Benedictine abbey; p. (1986) 57,000.

Kendal, l. gov. dist., Cumbria, **Eng.**; mkt. ctr.; tourism; p. (1981) 23,411.

Kenilworth, t., Warwicks., **Eng.**; 6 km S.W. of Coventry; mkt.; ruined cas.; p. (1981) 19,315.

Kenitra. See **Mina Hassan Tani**.

Kennet, l. gov. dist., Wiltshire, **Eng.**; stretches from Marlborough to Devizes; p. (1993) 72,400.

Kennet, R., Wilts. and Berks., **Eng.**; trib. of R. Thames; followed by main rly. London to W. of Eng.; 70 km long.

Kennington, dist., in London bor. of Lambeth, **Eng.**; inc. the Oval cricket ground, home of Surrey C.C.

Kenosha, t., Wis., **USA**; on W. shore of L. Mich.; p. (1990) 80,352 (t.), 128,000 (met. a.).

Kensington and Chelsea, Royal Borough of, inner bor., W. London, **Eng.**; mainly residtl.; contains Kensington Palace and Gardens; p. (1993) 148,800.

Kent, non-met. co., **Eng.**; intensive agr., mkt. gardening, orchards, hops; "Garden of England"; crossed by N. Downs and Weald; industl. zone bordering Thames and Medway estuaries; tourist resorts and cross-channel ferry pts. on cst. proposed Channel Tunnel link (1993) liable to make lge impact on co.; London commuter hinterland; co. t. Maidstone; a. 3,730 km²; p. (1993) 1,539,700.

Kentucky, E. central st., **USA**; in W. foothills of Appalachians and crossed by tribs. of Mississippi; "Bluegrass" st.; mainly agr.; some coal; cap. Frankfort; lgst. c. Louisville, at falls of Ohio R.; hydroelec. power; tourism; admitted to Union 1792; st. flower Goldenrod, st. bird Cardinal; a. 104,623 km²; p. (1990) 3,685,296.

Kentucky, R., Ky., **USA**; flows from Cumberland plateau to Ohio R.; length 400 km.

Kenya, rep., E. **Africa**; member of Brit. Commonwealth; comprises 7 provs.; straddles equator but climate modified by alt.; marked contrast between sparsely populated and arid N. and well-developed S. where upland climate has attracted the European p.; economy based on prod. and processing of arable and pastoral prods., inc. dairy prod.; relatively well developed cooperative African farming; 80 per cent of p. earn living on the land; most industl. of E. African cty., mostly exp. orientated; growth in exp. of cement and fluorspar; tourism incr. impt; ch. spt. Mombasa, airports at Nairobi and Mombasa; famous for big game; univ.; cap. Nairobi; a. 582,646 km²; p. (1991) 25·91 m.

Kenya, Mt., volcano, **Kenya**; just S. of equator; snow-covered; alt. 5,197 m; 2nd hgst. peak in Africa; Nat. Park.

Kephallenia. See **Cephalonia**.

Kerala, st., **India**; cap. Trivandrum; plantations producing rubber, tea, pepper; higher proportion of literacy than in any other st.; a. 38,855 km²; p. (1991) 20,098,518.

Kerch, c., **Ukraine**; in Crimea, commanding K. strait connecting Black Sea and Azov Sea; spt. and industl. ctr.; metallurgical plant, iron and steel mills, shipbldg., fisheries; iron-ore, vanadium, natural gas nearby; p. (1990) 176,300.

Kerguelen, archipelago, S. **Indian Oc.**; part of Fr. Antarctic terr.; whaling, fishing; famous for K. cabbage (*Pringlea antiscorbutica*).

Kerkrade, t., Limburg prov., **Neth.**; coal mng.; anc. abbey; p. (1993) 53,185.

Kérkira. See **Corfu**.

Kermadec Is., volcanic gr. Pac. Oc.; 960 km N.E. of N.Z.; a. 34 km²; met. sta. on Sunday I. (Raoul I.) (lgst. of gr.); annexed to **N.Z.** 1887; p. (1986) 5.

Kerman, region, S.E. **Iran**; mtnous., much desert land; agr.; carpet-weaving; coal and iron-ore mng. being developed; recent copper find; irrigation scheme projected; p. (1982) 1,078,875.

Kermān, c., S.E. **Iran**; prov. cap.; carpet-weaving ctr.; textile mftg.; airpt.; mediaeval mosques; multi-million dollar complex for mining and refining copper; p. (1986) 254,786.

Kermānshāh, (Qahremānshahr) t., N.W. **Iran**; cap. of Kermānshāhān prov.; agr., comm. and

route ctr.; airpt.; oil refinery; p. (1986) 565,544.

Kern, R., E. Cal., **USA**; one of most impt. power-generating Rs. in st.

Kerrier, l. gov. dist., Cornwall, **Eng.**; a. inc. Lizard penin. and Helston; p. (1993) 89,100.

Kerry, coastal co., Munster, **R.o.I.**; deeply indented cst.; cap. Tralee; tourism; a. 4,703 km²; p. (1986) 124,159.

Kerulen, R., N.E. **Mongolia** and **China**; flows parallel to edge of Gobi Desert; a. designated for economic development; 1,256 km long.

Keswick, Allerdale, Cumbria, **Eng.**; on Greta R.; at N. end of L. Derwentwater; tourist ctr.; mkt.; pencils; p. (1981) 5,645.

Kettering, l. gov. dist., mkt. t., Northants., **Eng.**; nr. Wellingborough; footwear; iron mng.; p. (1993) 78,500 (dist.).

Kew, dist., London bor. of Richmond upon Thames, **Eng.**; contains Kew botanical gardens.

Keweenaw, peninsula, L. Superior, **USA**; former impt. copper deposits.

Keynsham, t., Wansdyke, Avon, **Eng.**; expanded t.; p. (1981) 20,443.

Key West, c., Fla., **USA**; on I. c. 240 km from mainland; naval sta., coastguard base; cigar-mftg.; tourism; p. (1980) 24,382.

Khabarovsk, c., **Russia**; cap. of K. terr., E. Siberia, on Amur R.; cath.; oil refining, aircraft engin., wood and paper inds.; pipeline links with oilfields in N. Sakhalin; transport ctr. of Far East; p. (1989) 601,000.

Khakass Autonomous Oblast, admin. div. of Krasnoyarsk region, **Russia**; pastoral agr., timber and mng. inds.; a. 61,784 km²; p. (1989) 566,900.

Khandwa, t., Madhya Pradesh, **India**; S. of Indore; cotton, oil-pressing; p. (1991) 145,133.

Khaniá, or **Canea**, c., Crete, **Greece**; in sheltered bay on W. cst.; historic sites; p. (1981) 47,451.

Khanka, L., **China**–**USSR** border; dairy farming, fishing; branch of Trans-Siberian rly. to W. shore; a. 4,403 km².

Khanty-Mansi, admin. div., **Russia**; in W. Siberian lowland; sparse p.; cap. KhantyMansiisk (at confluence of Ob' and Irtysh Rs.); natural gas; a. 556,850 km²; p. (1989) 1,282,400.

Kharagpur, c., W. Bengal, **India**; industl., scientific research ctr.; rly. junc.; p. (1991) 265,000.

Khārg, I., Persian Gulf, **Iran**; oil terminal for super-tankers, 48 km from mainland; repeated Iraqi air attacks resulted in total loss of terminal at Sirri island and plans for replacement terminal.

Khar'kov, c., **Ukraine**; impt. industl. ctr. in Donets coal region; cap. of K. region; univ., cath.; rly. ctr.; extensively rebuilt after second world war; p. (1990) 1,618,400.

Khartoum, c., cap. of the **Sudan**; at confluence of Blue and White Niles; univ.; famous siege under Gordon 1884–5; p. (1983) 476,218.

Khashm el Girba, t., **Sudan**; new t. on Atbara R.; between Khartoum and Ethiopian border; for p. of Wadi Halfa inundated by Aswan L.; sugar refinery.

Khasi Hills, Meghalaya, N.E. **India**; form abrupt S. edge to middle Brahmaputra valley; very heavy monsoon rains on S.-facing slopes; lower slopes forested; middle slopes impt. tea-growing region; rise to over 1,800 m.

Khaskovo, t., **Bulgaria**; woollens, carpets, tobacco; p. (1990) 95,807.

Kherson, c., **Ukraine**; 24 km up R. Dnieper from Black Sea; sea and R. pt., rly. junc.; grain, oil refining, engin., textiles, shipbldg; founded by Catherine the Great as fortress t.; p. (1990) 361,200.

Khingan, Gr. and **Little**, mtn. ranges, Inner Mongolia and Heilongjiang prov., N.E. **China**; rich timber resources; rise to over 1,800 m.

Khios or **Chios**, I., **Greece**; in Aegean Sea; wines, figs, fruits; marble; cap. Khios; supposed birthplace of Homer; p. (1981) 48,700.

Khiva, former vassal st. of Russia; now part of **Uzbekistan** and **Turkmenistan**.

Khiva, c., N.W. **Uzbekistan**; in oasis nr. Kara-Kum desert; cottons, carpets; anc. c.; p. (1990) 40,600.

Khmel'nitskiy (Proskurov), c., **Ukraine**; on R. Bug; machin. tools, textiles, food inds.; p. (1990) 241,000.

Khmer Republic. See **Cambodia**.

Khor Abdulla, Iraq; in Persian G. nr. Basra; deepwater oil-loading island terminal.

Khorāsan or **Khurasan**, prov., N.E. **Iran**; bounded by USSR and Afghanistan; sparsely p.; agr.; wool;

turquoises; cap. Mashhad; p. (1982) 3,264,398.

Khorramshahr, spt., S.W. **Iran,** leading pt. on Persian G.; increased in importance in second world war when harbour facilities expanded; handles major part of foreign trade; main exp. dates; linked by pipeline to oilfields and by road and rail to Ahvāz and Tehran.

Khotan. See Hotan.

Khovu-Aksy, t., Tuva aut. rep., **Russia;** on R. Elegest, 80 km S.W. of Kyzyl; new t. 1956; cobalt deposit being developed.

Khudzhand, (Leninabad), c., **Tajikistan;** on Syr Dar'ya R., S. of Tashkent; silks, cottons, fruit-preserving; hydroelectric power sta.; p. (1990) 163,100.

Khulna, c., **Bangladesh;** in low-lying a. in W. Ganges delta; p. (1991) 545,849.

Khunjerab Pass, Kashmir, **India;** 5,000 m. pass in Karakoram Range; links Sinkiang (China) with Pakistan and Middle East; new metal route opened (1982) making shorter route to W. for China and took 20 years to build.

Khuzestan, prov., W. **Iran;** frontier Iraq; leading petroleum ctr.; lge. dams; cap. Ahvāz; p. (1982) 2,196,920.

Khyber Pass, pass in Hindu Kush mtns., between **Pakistan** and **Afghanistan;** followed by route from Peshawar to Kabul; historically most famous route into India, used by many invaders, inc. Alexander the Great.

Kiamusze. See Jiamusi.

Kianga-Moura, dist., Queensland, **Australia;** lge. coal-field; coking coal exp. to Japan via Gladstone.

Kiangsi. See Jiangxi.

Kiangsu. See Jiangsu.

Kicking Horse Pass, mtn. pass (1,628 m), over Rocky Mtns., B.C., **Canada;** used by Canadian Pac. rly.

Kidderminster, t., Wyre Forest, Hereford and Worcs., **Eng.;** on R. Stour 6 km above its confluence with R. Severn; carpets, engin., sugar-beet refining, textile machin., elec. vehicles, drop forgings; p. (1981) 51,261.

Kidsgrove, t., "Potteries," Staff., **Eng.;** 5 km N.W. of Stoke-on-Trent; chemicals, metal wks., rayon, silk and nylon spinning, precast concrete, ceramics; p. (1981) 24,227.

Kidwelly, Dyfed, **Wales;** mkt. t.; sm. harbour; cas.; p. (1981) 3,152.

Kiel, spt., cap. of Schleswig-Holstein, **Germany;** univ.; Baltic naval pt.; shipbldg. and allied inds., elec. gds., textiles, fishing; p. (1990) 246,600.

Kiel Canal (North Sea-Baltic Canal or Kaiser-Wilhelm-Kanal) Germany; connects Elbe estuary on North Sea with Baltic; 98 km long; opened 1895, reconstructed 1914; internationalised 1919 by Treaty of Versailles, but repudiated by Hitler 1936.

Kielce, c. and prov., central **Poland;** in Swieto-krzyskie mtns.; cath., route ctr.; agr. machin., chemicals; minerals quarried in prov.; founded 12th cent.; p. (1989) 213,102 (c.), 1,123,700 (prov.).

Kielder, reservoir, Northumberland, **Eng.;** one of lgst. man-made lakes in Europe.

Kiev (Kiyev), c., cap. of **Ukraine;** on R. Dnieper; leading cultural, industl. and comm. ctr.; cath., univ.; machin., textiles; in a. of rich mineral deposits; natural gas pipeline runs from Dashava; historic c., once cap. of Muscovite empire; p. (1990) 2,616,000.

Kigali, cap. of **Rwanda;** comm. ctr.; airport; new tungsten and iron foundries; p. (1981) 156,650.

Kigoma, t., W. **Tanzania;** pt. on E. shore of L. Tanganyika; W. terminus of Central rly. to Dar-es-Salaam.

Kii, peninsula, **Japan;** highland area and inlet of same name, S. Honshu.

Kikinda, t., Vojvodina, **Serbia, Yugoslavia;** agr. tr.; rly. junc.; p. (1981) 69,854.

Kilauea, crater, 1,112 m high, on S.E. slope of Mauna Loa, **Hawaii,** one of lgst. active craters in world; over 3 km in diameter.

Kildare, inland co., Leinster, **R.o.I.;** dairying, cereals; co. t. Naas; a. 1,694 km²; p. (1986) 116,247.

Kildare, mkt. t., cap. of Kildare, **R.o.I.;** cath.; close by is the famous racecourse, the Curragh of Kildare; p. (1986) 4,268.

Kilimanjaro, volcanic mtn., N. **Tanzania;** hgst. peak in Africa, 5,895 m; international airpt. at 894 m on Sanya Plain; Nat. Park.

Kilindini, spt., **Kenya;** adjoins Mombasa; the finest harbour on E. cst. of Africa.

Kilkenny, inland co., Leinster, **R.o.I.;** cap. Kilkenny; pastoral farming, black marble; a. 2,062 km²; p. (1986) 73,186.

Kilkenny, t., cap. of Kilkenny, **R.o.I.;** on R. Nore; local mkt., caths., cas.; p. (1986) 8,969.

Killala Bay, Mayo and Sligo, **R.o.I.,** wide bay fed by R. Hoy.

Killaloe, v., Co. Clare, **R.o.I.;** crossing point for R. Shannon; cath.; p. (1986) 1,033

Killarney, t., Kerry, **R.o.I.;** local mkt.; tourist ctr. for the Ls. of K.; p. (1986) 7,837.

Killarney, Lakes of, Kerry, **R.o.I.;** Lower, Middle, and Upper, celebrated for their beauty; tourist resorts; Muckross on Middle L. site of anc. abbey.

Killiecrankie, Pass of, Scot.; on R. Garry; at S. approach to Drumochter Pass; used by main rly. Perth to Inverness; scene of battle 1691.

Killingworth, t., Tyne and Wear, **Eng.;** 6 km N.E. of Newcastle; new t.; proposed p. 20,000.

Kilmarnock, burgh, Strathclyde Reg., **Scot.,** forms l. gov. dist., with Loudoun; on R. Irvine, 17 km N.E. of Ayr.; carpet factory closed increasing unemployment to 27 per cent; p. (1991) 44,307 (t.), (1993) 80,980 (dist.).

Kilo-Moto, goldfield, **Zaïre;** in N.E. of st., 80 km W. of L. Mobutu Seso; linked by motor road to R. Zaïre (Kisangani) and L. Mobutu Seso (Kasenyi).

Kilrenny and Anstruther, t., North East Fife, **Scot.,** at entrance to F. of Forth; fishing, hosiery, oilskin mnfs; p. (1991) 3,154.

Kilrush, sm. spt., U.D., Co. Clare, **R.o.I.;** on R. Shannon; p. (1986) 2,961.

Kilsyth, burgh, Stirling, **Scot.;** at S. foot of Campsie Fells, 16 km W. of Falkirk; p. (1991) 9,918.

Kilwinning, burgh, Cunninghame, **Scot.;** 8 km E. of Ardrossan; to be incorporated in new t. Irvine; p. (1991) 15,479.

Kimberley, former goldfield dist., W. **Australia;** sparsely populated beef producing a., bauxite and iron mng.

Kimberley, t., B.C., **Canada;** on R. Kootenay; site of Sullivan mine, silver, lead, zinc; ores smelted at Trail; p. (1986) 6,732.

Kimberley, t., C. Prov., **S. Africa;** diamond-mng. dist.; asbestos, manganese, iron, cement, engin.; founded 1871; p. (1985) 149,667 (met. a.).

Kinabalu, Mount, Sabah, **Malaysia;** in Crocker mtns.; hgst. peak in Borneo, alt. 4,104 m.

Kincardine, former co., **Scot.;** with Deeside forms l. gov. dist. in Grampian Reg.; a. 2,546 km²; p. (1993) 55,960.

Kinder Scout, mtn., N. Derbys., **Eng.;** hgst. point of the Peak dist.; alt. 637 m.

Kindia, t., **Guinea;** rich bauxite deposits worked since 1974 but output restricted by poor rail links.

Kineshma, c., **Russia;** on Volga, N.W. of Gorki; pt. for Ivanovo industl. a.; textiles; dates from early 15th cent.; p. (1989) 105,000.

King George's Sound, W. **Australia;** nr. Albany; fine harbour and bay.

Kinghorn, t., Kircaldy, **Scot.;** on F. of Forth, 5 km S. of Kirkcaldy; p. (1991) 2,931.

Kingsbridge, t., South Hams, S. Devon, **Eng.;** at head of Kingsbridge estuary, 16 km S.W. of Dartmouth; mkt.; p. (1981) 4,142.

King's Lynn, spt., West Norfolk, **Eng.;** at mouth of Gr. Ouse; docks; fishing base; agr. machin., canning, chemical fertilisers, shoes; expanded t.; l. gov. dist. with **West Norfolk;** p. (1981) 33,340, (t), p. (1993) 138,600 (dist.).

Kingston, t., Ont., **Canada;** E. end of L. Ontario; univ., military college; p. (1986) 55,050.

Kingston, spt., cap. of **Jamaica;** ch. comm. ctr. for J.; landlocked harbour; agr.-processing; univ.; p. (1991) 587,798.

Kingston upon Hull. See Hull.

Kingston upon Thames, former M.B., Surrey, **Eng.;** now **The Royal Borough of Kingston-upon-Thames,** outer bor. of Greater London; inc. bors. of Malden and Coombe and Surbiton; residtl. with Richmond Park, Hampton Court, Bushey Park nearby; aircraft parts; p. (1993) 138,100.

Kingstown, spt., cap. of **St. Vincent,** W.I.; cath., botanic gardens; p. (1986) 26,542.

Kingswood, t., l. gov. dist., Avon, **Eng.;** nr. Bristol; elec. vehicles, motor cycles, boots, brushes, tools; school founded by John Wesley; p. (1993) 92,000 (dist.).

Kington, mkt. t., Hereford and Worcs., **Eng.;** 19 km W. of Leominster; p. (1981) 1,951.

Kinki, dist., S.W. Honshu, **Japan;** agr., industl. and comm. complex centred on Osaka, Kyoto, and Kōbe; p. (1990) 22,207,000.

Kinlochleven, v., Lochaber, **Scot.**; at head of Loch Leven; hydroelec. power sta.; aluminium smelting; p. (1991) 1,076.

Kinnairds Head, promontory, nr. Fraserburgh, on N.E. cst., **Scot.**

Kinross, burgh, Perth and Kinross, **Scot.**; on Loch Leven, 26 km N.E. of Alloa; textiles; resort; p. (1991) 4,552.

Kinross-shire, former co., **Scot.**; now part of Perth and Kinross l. gov. dist., Tayside Reg.

Kinsale, t., Cork, **R.o.I.**; sm. fish pt. on K. harbour; tourism; natural gas field; p. (1986) 1,811.

Kinshasa (**Leopoldville**), c., cap. of **Zaïre**; above the cataracts on R. Zaïre; univ.; textiles, shoes; founded by Stanley 1887; p. (1985) 2,796,000.

Kinta Valley, S.E. Perak, **W. Malaysia**; tin mng., rubber plantations.

Kintyre, peninsula, Argyll and Bute, **Scot.**; terminates in Mull of Kintyre; 67 km long, 16 km wide.

Kioga (**Kyoga**), L., **Uganda**; on R. Nile midway between L. Victoria and L. Mobuto Seso.

Kiölen or **Kjölen**, mtn. range, **Norway** and **Sweden**; hgst. point Mt. Sulitjelma, 1,876 m.

Kiribati (**Gilbert Is**), indep. st. (1979), former Brit. col., central **Pac. Oc.**; chain of coral Is. across equator; economy based on phosphate mng. and copra; cap. Tarawa; Ellice Is. separated 1976 and renamed Tuvalu; a. 956 km²; p. (1991) 71,000.

Kirin. See Jilin.

Kirkburton, t., West Yorks., **Eng.**; S.E. of Huddersfield; woollens; p. (1981) 21,387.

Kirkby, t., Knowsley, Merseyside, **Eng.**; p. (1981) 50,898.

Kirkby in Ashfield, t., Ashfield, Notts., **Eng.**; 16 km N.W. of Nottingham; p. (1981) 24,467.

Kirkby Moorside, t., Ryedale, North Yorks., **Eng.**; nr. Vale of Pickering; mkt.-place; sailplanes, gliders.

Kirkcaldy, royal burgh, l. gov. dist., Fife Reg., **Scot.**; spt. on N. side of F. of Forth; linoleum, engin.; birthplace of Adam Smith; p. (1991) 47,155 (t.), (1993) 148,360 (dist.).

Kirkcudbright, royal burgh, Stewartry, **Scot.**; on R. Dee at influx into K. Bay, S.W. of Dumfries; agr. ctr., hosiery; cas., abbey; p. (1991) 3,588.

Kirkcudbrightshire, former co., **Scot.**; now part of Stewartry l. gov. dist., Dumfries and Galloway Reg.

Kirkenes, t., Finnmark prov., N.E. **Norway**; on S. arm of Varanger fjord, nr. Soviet border; pt. for iron-mng. dist.

Kirkham, t., Kirklees, Lancs., **Eng.**; textiles; p. (1981) 6,289.

Kirkintilloch, burgh, Strathkelvin, **Scot.**; on Forth and Clyde canal; engin.; p. (1991) 20,780.

Kirklees, met. dist., West Yorks., **Eng.**; comprises Huddersfield, Dewsbury, Batley, Spenborough, Colne Valley, Meltham, Holmfirth, Denby Dale, Kirkburton, Heckmondwike, and Mirfield; p. (1993) 385,800.

Kirkstone Pass, mtn. pass, Cumbria, **Eng.**; used by main road between Ullswater and Windermere Lakes.

Kirkūk, t., **Iraq**; most imp. centre of Iraqi oil industry; p. (1970) 207,852 (no recent figs.).

Kirkwall, royal burgh, Mainland I., Orkneys, **Scot.**; cath.; p. (1991) 6,469.

Kirov. See Vyalka.

Kirovabad. See Gyandzha.

Kirovograd. c., **Ukraine**; on Ingul R.; cap. of K. oblast; agr. ctr.; engin.; p. (1990) 274,200.

Kirovsk, c., **Russia**; on Kola peninsula; apatite and nephelite mng.; chemicals.

Kirriemuir, burgh, Angus, **Scot.**; on N. margin of Strathmore, 8 km W. of Forfar; jute-weaving; birthplace of J. M. Barrie; p. (1991) 5,571.

Kirtland, t., N.M., **USA**; atomic and space research sta.

Kiruna, t., N. **Sweden**; inside Arctic Circle, N.W. of Luleå; linked by rly. to Narvik (Norway); impt. deposits of iron ore; p. (1983) 28,638.

Kiryu, c., Honshu, **Japan**; major textile ctr.; p. (1990) 126,443.

Kisangani (**Stanleyville**), t., **Zaïre**; on R. Zaïre nr. Boyoma Falls; airpt.; univ.; p. (1985) 557,000.

Kiselevsk, c., S.W. Siberia, **Russia**; coal-mng. ctr. in Kuznetsk basin; p. (1989) 128,000.

Kishinev, c., cap. of **Moldova**; on Byk R., trib. of Dniester; cath., univ.; industl., comm. ctr. in rich farming a.; tourism; p. (1990) 675,500.

Kislovodsk, c., **Russia**; in N. Caucasus; famous spa; p. (1989) 114,000.

Kismayu, pt., **Somalia**; new deep-water harbour; airpt.; p. (1987) 70,000

Kisumu, spt., cap. of Nyanza prov., **Kenya**; at head of Kavirondo G. on L. Victoria; handles bulk of cotton from Buganda and coffee from N. Tanzania for transhipment E. by rail; lge. brewery; p. (1984) 215,000.

Kitakyūshū, c., N. Kyushu, **Japan**; one of Japan's lgst. muns. on merging (1963) of ts. Moji, Kokura, Tobata, Yawata, and Wakamatsu, sixth c. to enjoy special aut. rights; p. (1990) 1,026,467

Kitami, c., Hokkaido, **Japan**; mkt.; food-processing; p. (1990) 107,247.

Kitchener, c., Ont., **Canada**; agr. machin., tyres, hardware, agr. processing; p. (1986) 150,604 (c.), 311,194 (met. a.).

Kithira. See Cerigo.

Kitimat, t., B.C., **Canada**; lge. aluminium smelter powered by hydroelectricity from diversion of R. Fraser trib. through the Rockies; p. (1986) 11,196.

Kitwe, t., **Zambia**; contiguous to mng. township of Nkana, ctr. of copperbelt; p. (1989) 495,000.

Kiukiang. See Jiujiang.

Kivu, L., on border of **Zaïre** and **Rwanda**; in highlands of Gr. Rift Valley; natural gas discoveries; 1,473 m high, 96 km long.

Kizil, lgst. R. of **Turkey**; rises in Kisil Dagh, flows to Black Sea via Sivas; 1,120 km long.

Kladno, t., **Czech Rep.**; 16 km N.W. of Prague; coalmng. ctr.; iron and steel wks., machin.; p. (1990) 73,000.

Klagenfurt, t., cap. of Carinthia, **Austria**; winter sports ctr.; varied mnfs.; p. (1991) 89,502.

Klaipeda (**Memel**), c. **Lithuania**; ice-free spt. on Baltic Sea; exp. timber, textiles, chemicals, paper; p. (1990) 206,200.

Klamath, mtns., N. Cal., S.W. Ore., **USA**; beautiful ranges containing Nat. Park and Indian reserve; hgst. alt. Mt. Eddy, 2,757 m.

Klamono, t., W. Irian, **Indonesia**; ctr. of oilfield; pipeline to Sorong harbour.

Klerksdorp, t., S. Transvaal, **S. Africa**; gold, diamonds; p. (1980) 238,680.

Klodzko (**Glatz**), t., Walbrzych prov. S.W. **Poland**; formerly in Prussian Silesia; rly. junc.; on R. Neisse; comm. and mftg.; p. (1989) 30,261.

Klondike, R., Yukon, **Canada**; sm. trib. of Yukon in gold-mng. region; gold rush 1896; 160 km long.

Klyuchevskaya Sopka, one of 18 active volcanoes, **Russia**; in N.E. Siberia, on Kamchatka peninsula; alt. 4,748 m.

Knaresborough, t., North Yorks., **Eng.**; 5 km N.E. of Harrogate; mkt.; cas. ruins; p. (1981) 13,375.

Knighton, t., Radnor, Powys, **Wales**; on R. Teme; mkt.; p. (1981) 2,682.

Knockmealdown Mtns., Waterford and Tipperary, **R.o.I.**; highest point 796 m; tourism.

Knob Lake. See Schefferville.

Knossos, ruined c., cap. of anc. Crete, **Greece**; S.E. of Iráklion; ctr. of Cretan bronze age culture, 1800 B.C.; archaeological source of knowledge about the Minoans.

Knottingley, t., West Yorks., **Eng.**; on R. Aire, 19 km S.E. of Leeds; engin., glass, tar distilling, chemicals; coal mng; p. (1981) 15,953.

Knowsley, met. dist., Merseyside, **Eng.**; comprises Kirkby, Prescot and Huyton with Roby; p. (1993) 155,300.

Knoxville, c., Tenn., **USA**; univ.; livestock and tobacco mkt.; textiles, marble, plastics, chemicals, aluminium; p. (1990) 165,121 (c.), 605,000 (met. a.).

Knutsford, t., N.E. Cheshire, **Eng.**; mkt.; home of Mrs. Gaskell, author of *Cranford*; p. (1981) 13,675.

Kōbe, c., spt., Honshu, **Japan**; at E. end of Inland Sea; 5th c. of Japan; developed as pt. for Osaka and Kinki plain; iron and steel, shipbldg., rubber; major earthquake January 1995; p. (1990) 1,477,423.

Koblenz (**Coblenz**), t. Rhineland-Palatinate, **Germany**; at confluence of Rs. Rhine and Moselle; fine buildings; wine, paper, machin., leather, ceramics; p. (1990) 108,800.

Kōchi, plain and c., Shikoku, Japan; early vegetables, double rice cropping; p. (1990) 317,090.

Kodiak I., lgst. of Is. of Alaska, USA; 144 km long; forested mtns.; fur-trading, salmon-fishing, canning; earthquake 1964; p. (1990) 13,309.

Kōfu, basin and c., Honshu, Japan; rice, vineyards, orchards, silk, wine; p. (1990) 200,630.

Kohat, t., Pakistan; on trib. of Indus; military t.; cement wks.; p. (1981) 78,000.

Koh-I-Baba Mtns., Afghanistan, spur of the Hindu Kush; highest point 5,380 m.

Kokand, c., Uzbekistan; in the Ferghana Valley; mftg. ctr., textiles, chemicals, engin.; p. (1990) 175,700.

Kokiu. See Gejiu.

Kokkoka (Gamla Karleby), t. Finland; on cst. of G. of Bothnia; sulphur plant; p. (1991) 34,748.

Kokomo, c., Ind., USA; on Wild Cat R.; ctr. of agr. region; car components; p. (1984) 45,400, (c.), 101,000 (met. a.).

Koko-Nor. See Qinghai Hu.

Kokura. See Kitakyūshū.

Kola Peninsula, peninsula, Russia; extension of Lapland; rich mineral deposits; hydroelectric plants and missile base.

Kolar, c., Karnataka, India; p. (1981) 144,385 (met. a.).

Kolarovgrad. See Shumen.

Kolding, c., at head of Kolding fjord, Jutland, Denmark; spt. and fishing base; lt. inds.; p. (1990) 57,285.

Kolhapur, c., Maharashtra, S.W. India; cap. of former princely st. of K.; bauxite; anc. Buddhist ctr.; p. (1991) 406,000.

Köln. See Cologne.

Kolobrzeg (Kolberg), t., Koszalin prov., N.W. Poland; spt. on Baltic cst.; comm. and fishing harbour; resort and spa; p. (1990) 44,426.

Kolomna, c., Russia; on Moskva R., nr. confluence with Oka R.; industl. ctr.; engin., locomotives, machin., synthetic rubber; p. (1989) 162,000.

Kolomyya, c., Ukraine; on Pruth R.; in Carpathian foothills; agr. tr., metal gds., oil refining, textiles.

Kolwezi, c., S. Shaba, Zaïre; comm. ctr. for mng. dist. (cobalt and copper); p. (1985) 384,000.

Kolyma, R., N.E. Siberia, Russia; flows into Arctic Oc., via Kolyma goldfields; navigable in summer; basin largely covered with tundra, sparsely p.; 2,560 km long.

Komárno, c., Slovakia; on left bank, of Danube, opposite Hungarian Komárom, on right bank; R. pt., shipbldg., oil refining; p. (1984) 35,396.

Komi, aut. rep., Russia; wooded lowland, pastoral agr.; coal from Pechora basin, oil at Ukhta and Troitsko-Pechorsk; mng. now ch. economic activity; cap. Syktyvkar, lumber ctr.; a. 415,799 km²; p. (1989) 1,250,800.

Komi-Permyak, admin. div., Russia; forestry, cellulose, paper; cap. Kudymbar; a. 31,080 km²; p. (1989) 158,500.

Komló, t., Hungary; new mng. t.; coking coal; p. (1984) 32,000.

Kompong Som (Sihanoukville) c., Cambodia; deepwater pt. on G. of Thailand; linked to Phnom Penh by modern highway; textile mills, tractors, oil refining.

Kommunarsk (Voroshilovsk), t., Ukraine; 40 km S.W. of Lugansk; ctr. of iron, steel and coking inds.; p. (1990) 125,700.

Komsomolsk, c., Russia; built by volunteer youth labour, after 1932; heavy industl. development; oil refining; pipeline connects with oilfield in N. Sakhalin; p. (1989) 315,000.

Konin, t. and prov., C. Poland; brown coal, rlwy, aluminium; p. (1989) 79,315 (t.) 465,900 (prov.).

Köniz, t. Bern canton, Switzerland; printing, rlwy, castle; p. (1990) 35,925.

Konstantinovka, industl. t., Ukraine; in heart of Donbas industl. region, 61 km N. of Donetsk; heavy engin., iron and steel, zinc smelting; p. (1990) 107,700.

Konya, c., Turkey; cap. of K. prov.; agr. tr. ctr.; mnfs. textiles, carpets, leather gds.; the anc. Iconium, fortress of the Hittite empire; p. (1990) 543,460 (c.), 1,750,303 (prov.).

Kooland I., W. Australia; rugged I. with iron-ore deposits worked since 1960 and exp. to Japan.

Koolyanobbing, mng. t., W. Australia; high-grade haematite and limonite ores mined since 1961 and t. constructed as residential and service ctr.

Kootenay or Kootenai, R., flows from B.C., Canada; through Montana and Idaho, USA, into K. L., draining it by narrow channel into Colombia R.; beautiful scenery; 720 km long.

Kopparberg , co. C. Sweden; cap. Falun; a. 28,350 km²; p. (1992) 290,245.

Korat Plateau, E. Thailand; headwaters of Mekong tribs.; cattle-rearing; tr. ctr. Korat.

Korcë (Koritsa), t., S.E. Albania; in infertile basin at 854 m nr. Greek border; mkt.; cultural ctr.; p. (1990) 67,100.

Korcula (Curzola), I., off Croatia; sm. I. in Adriatic Sea; ch. pt. K. a. 277 km².

Korea, Democratic People's Republic of, (N. Korea); occupies N. part of Korean peninsula (N. of 38th parallel), E. Asia; bounded on N. by China and USSR; continental climate; cold dry winters, hot humid summers; predominantly mtnous. with many uninhabited offshire Is.; all inds. nationalised and collective agr.; rapid mechanisation, agr. employs 43 per cent working p.; development emphasis on mng. resources of coal, iron-ore and on growth of heavy inds.; most industl. resources located in N. Korea; rapid incr. in industrialisation; transport network under reconstruction after devastation of Korean war; some R. transport, international airport at cap. of Pyongyang; longest surviving hard-line Communist ruling dynasty in Asia (Kim Il-Sung); a. 121,248 km²; p. (1991) 22·03 m.

Korea, Rep. of (S. Korea), occupies S. part of Korean peninsula (S. of 38th parallel); climate resembles N. Korea's, topography less rugged; massive US aid revitalised economy after Korean war and Korea now has one of world's largest foreign debts; 20 per cent work-force engaged in agr.; undergoing rapid industrialisation; textiles, electronics, shipbldg., vehicles; iron and steel ind. at Pusan; fishing is both source of subsistence and exp.; irrigation and power project (1971–81) for 4 Rs.—Hangang, Naktangang, Kum-Gang, and Yongsan-Gang; cap. Seoul; a. 98,992 km²; p. (1992) 43·66 m, (24 per cent in cap.).

Korea Bay, Yellow Sea; between N. Korea and North-East China (Manchuria).

Koriyama, Honshu, Japan; textiles, chemicals; p. (1990) 314,642.

Korsör, spt., Sjaelland I., Denmark; fine harbour; glass wks.; p. (1990) 20,443.

Kortrijk (Courtrai), t., W. Flanders prov., N.W. Belgium; textiles; 13th cent. Notre Dame church; battle of the Spurs 1302; p. (1993) 76,264.

Koryak, admin. div., N.E. Siberia, Russia; sparse p.; a. 393,680 km²; p. (1989) 39,900.

Kos, I. See Cos, I.

Kosciusko, Mount, N.S.W., in Australian Alps; highest peak in Australia; 2,228 m; Nat. Park popular for skiing.

Kosi, R., India; flows from Himalayas to Ganges; site of barrage for hydroelectric power and irrigation.

Košice, c., S.E. Slovakia; lies in fertile basin; major industl. ctr.; heavy inds., iron and steel plant; agr.-processing; univ., Gothic cath.; mediaeval fortress t.; p. (1990) 236,000.

Kosovo-Metohija, aut. region, S.W. Serbia, Yugoslavia; mtnous., fertile valleys; stock raising, forestry; dominant Albanian p. causing emigration of Serbs and Montenegrins; ch. t. Priština; a. 10,352 km²; p. (1981) 1,584,441.

Kostroma, c., cap. of K. oblast, Russia; at confluence of Volga and Kostroma; in flax growing a.; textiles, engin.; cath.; p. (1989) 278,000.

Koszalin (Köslin), c. and prov., N.W. Poland; nr. Baltic cst.; paper mills, textiles, building materials; p. (1989) 107,592 (c.), 502,700 (prov.).

Kota, t., Rajasthan, India; on R. Chambal; textiles; two nuclear reactors and heavy water plant; p. (1991) 537,000.

Kota Kinabalu (Jesselton), t., cap of Sabah, Malaysia; on W. cst.; main rubber pt.; rly. terminal; p. (1991) 208,484.

Köthen, t., Saxony - Anhalt, Germany; in former st. of Saxony-Anhalt; lignite mines, sugar-refining, machin., chemicals; p. (1989) 33,970.

Kotka, spt., S.E. Finland; on G. of Finland, at mouth of Kymi R.; major exp. pt. for timber, paper, pulp; p. (1991) 56,515.

Kotor, spt., S. Montenegro, **Yugoslavia**; on Bay of K., inlet of Adriatic; cath.; tourism.

Kotri, t., **Pakistan**; on R. Indus, opposite Hyderabad; barrage N. of the t., to help irrigate Sind.

Kottbus. See **Cottbus.**

Koulikoro, t., **Mali**, W. Africa; on upper course of R. Niger; mkt. for groundnuts, gumarabic, sisal; linked by R. to Timbuktu and Gao; rly. terminus, 1,216 km from Dakar.

Kovrov, c., **Russia**; on Gorki rly. line and R. Klyazma; impt. agr. exp. ctr.; engin., textiles; p. (1989) 160,000.

Kowloon, peninsula, S.E. **China**; on mainland opposite Hong Kong I.; pt. installations; major industl. and tr. ctr.; held by Britain on lease expiring 1998; p. (1986) 424,000.

Kozáni, dep., Macedonia, **Greece**; cap. K.; mainl, agr.; a. 6,143 km²; p. (1991) 150,159.

Kozhikode. See **Calicut.**

Kra Isthmus, neck of land between B. of Bengal and G. of Thailand, linking Malay peninsula with continent of Asia.

Kragujevac, t., central Serbia, **Yugoslavia**; on both banks of Lepenica R.; cath.; arsenal and garrison; route ctr., developing agr. and industl. ctr.; p. (1991) 146,607.

Krakatoa (Rakata), volcanic I., Sunda strait, **Indonesia**; between Java and Sumatra; greater part disappeared in violent eruption 1883.

Kraków (Cracow), c. and prov., S. **Poland**; pt. on Vistula; cultural ctr., univ. (Copernicus matriculated here); many historic monuments; inc. c. of Nowa Huta lgst. iron and steel ctr. of rep.; machin., chemicals, farm implements; p. (1989) 745,568, (c.), 1,223,100 (prov.).

Kramatorsk, c., **Ukraine**; in Donets basin; heavy engin., metallurgy; p. (1990) 199,300.

Kramfors, t., **Sweden**; on G. of Bothnia; papermill and sulphite pulp wks.

Krasnodar Territory, region, **Russia**; extends from Sea of Azov and Black Sea to N.W. end of Caucasus; contains Kuban steppe and Maikop oilfields; fertile black soil; main pt. Tuapse; many health resorts; p. (1989) 5,052,900.

Krasnodar, c., cap. of K. region, **Russia**; R. pt. Kuban R.; ctr. of industl. and agr. region; p. (1989) 621,000.

Krasnovodsk, c., **Turkmenistan**; pt. on Caspian Sea; oil-refining ctr.; handles agr. and oil prods.; p. (1990) 59,200.

Krasnoyarsk Territory, extensive region, **Russia**; extends across Siberia to Arctic Oc.; traversed by Yenisey and tribs.; minerals, grain from Minusinska basin and timber from coniferous forests; cap. K.; a. of labour camps in Stalin era; p. (1989) 3,605,500.

Krasnoyarsk, c., cap. of K. terr., E. Siberia, **Russia**; on Trans-Siberian rly. at crossing of Yenesey R.; hydroelectric sta.; industl. ctr.; local copper and iron-ore deposits; ctr. for grain and timber; p. (1989) 913,000.

Krefeld, t., N. Rhine–Westphalia, **Germany**; chemicals, steel, machin., textiles, soap; former ctr. of silk inds.; p. (1990) 245,000.

Kremenchug, c., **Ukraine**; on R. Dnieper; timber, engin., textiles; hydroelectric sta.; oil refining; p. (1990) 238,000.

Krems, mkt. t., **Austria**; on R. Danube; fruit processing; founded in 10th cent. as imperial fortress; p. (1991) 22,829.

Kreuznach, Bad, t., Rhineland Palatinate, **Germany**; on R. Nahe; metallurgy, leather, optical and chemical inds.; viticulture, mineral baths; p. (1986) 39,700.

Krishna (Kistna), R., S. **India**; rises in W. Ghats, flows E. across Deccan plateau into Bay of Bengal; lower valley and delta under intensive rice cultivation; densely populated; 1,360 km long.

Kristiansand, spt., S. **Norway**; on Skagerrak; shipbldg., ships, timber, paper, pulp, fish; electro-metallurgy; p. (1990) 54,267.

Kristianstad, c., cap. of K. prov., **Sweden**; on Helge R.; its pt. Ahus is on Baltic; foodprocessing, clothing, machin.; founded 1614 as fortress; p. (1992) 72,789 (t.), 292,993 (co.).

Kristiansund, spt., W. cst. **Norway**; built on 3 Is.; trawler fleet base; exp. dried fish; heavily damaged in second world war; since rebuilt; p. (1990) 17,093.

Kristinehamn, L. pt. on L. Vänern, central **Sweden**; p. (1983) 26,623.

Krivoy Rog., c., **Ukraine**; on R. Ingulets; ctr. of ch. iron-mng. a. of USSR; p. (1990) 717,400.

Krk, I., N. Adriatic Sea, off **Croatia**; S. of Rijeke; agr.; tourism; ch. t., K.; p. 14,500.

Krkonose. See **Riesengebirge.**

Kronoberg, co. S. **Sweden**; cap. Växjö; a. 8,459 km²; p. (1992) 178,961.

Kronshlot (Kronstadt), spt., on I. of Kotlin, **Russia**; at head of G. of Finland, nr. St. Petersburg; Baltic pt. and naval base; scene of naval mutiny which precipitated the Russian revolution; founded by Peter the Great 1710.

Kroonstad, t., O.F.S., **S. Africa**; on R. Vals; rly. junc.; agr. mkt.; engin., milling; p. (1980) 104,160 (dist.).

Krosno, t. and prov., S.E. **Poland**; R. Wislok; oil centre, p. (1989) 49,094 (t.), 491,500 (prov.).

Kruger Nat. Park, N.E. Transvaal, **S. Africa**; game reserve; a. 20,720 km².

Krugersdorp, t. Transvaal, **S. Africa**; gold mng., uranium, manganese; p. (1980) 153,880 (dist.).

Kuala Lumpur, c., fed. terr., **W. Malaysia**; cap. of Fed. of Malaysia and of Selangor st.; univ.; ctr. of rubber and tin dist.; outport Port Kelang; p. (1986) 1,000,000.

Kuangchow. See **Guangzhou.**

Kuantan, main t. on E. cst. **W. Malaysia**; linked to Kuala Lumpur; tin mng; p. (1980) 136,625.

Kuching, c., cap. of Sarawak, **Malaysia**; pt. on Sarawak R.; gold discovered nearby at Bau; p. (1989) 157,000.

Kucovë (Qyteti Stalin), Albania; nr. Berat; oil prod. and refining; pipeline connects to Vlore.

Kufra, oasis, **Libya**; dates, barley; on caravan route.

Kuldja. See **Yining.**

Kumamoto, c., W. Kyushu, **Japan**; 3rd c. of K.; cas., univs.; food inds.; business ctr.; p. (1990) 579,305.

Kumasi, c., cap. of Ashanti region, **Ghana**; univ., aerodrome; road and rly. junc.; ctr. of cocoaproducing a.; bauxite nearby; jute bags; p. (1984) 260,286 (c.), 345,117 (met. a.).

Kumayri (Leninakan), c., **Armenia**; nr. Turkish border; textiles, engin., rug-mkg.; earthquake 1988; p. (1990) 122,600.

Kumba Konam, t., Tamil Nadu, **India**; on Cauvery delta; silks, cotton; sacred Hindu c.; p. (1981) 132,832.

Kunene (Cunene), R., **Angola**; scheme to channel water from Angola to S.W. Africa; 1,200 km long.

Kun Lun (Kwen Lun), mtn. ranges, Xizang Zizhiou (Tibet), **China**; extend 2,900 km E. from Pamirs along N. edge of high plateau of Xizang Zizhiou; drained N. into inland drainage basin of Lop Nor; alt. frequently exceeds 5,400 m; rising to 7,729 m.

Kunming, c., cap. of Yunnan prov., S.W. **China**; univ.; comm. and cultural ctr., noted for its scenic beauty; iron and steel, milling and boring machin., textiles, chemicals; p. (1992) 1,580,000.

Kununurra Dam, Ord R., **W. Australia**; opened 1963; to irrigate 81,000 ha of semi-arid land for cotton, rice, and cattle.

Kuopio, t., **Finland**; on L. Kalki; timber inds.; tourism; p. (1991) 81,593.

Kura, R., rises in **Turkey**, chief R. of Transcaucasia, **USSR**; flows into Caspian Sea; agr., fishing, hydroelec. power; 1,504 km long.

Kurdistan (Country of the Kurds), includes parts of E. Turkey, Soviet Armenia, N.E. Iraq, and N.W. Iran; attempts at autonomy.

Kure, c., S.W. Honshu, **Japan**; spt. and naval base; engin.; shipbldg.; p. (1990) 216,723.

Kurgan, c., **Russia**; on Tobol R.; impt. junc. on Trans-Siberian rly.; tr. in cattle and foodstuffs; agr. engin.; p. (1989) 356,000.

Kuria Muria Is., 5 barren Is. in Arabian Sea off cst. of Oman; admin. by U.K. until 1967 now ceded to **Oman.**

Kurile Is., chain of volcanic Is., N. Pac., **Russia**; extend from Kamchatka to Hokkaido; mainly mtnous.; sulphur, hunting, fishing; Japan claims sovereignty over 4 Is. (Kunashiri, Etorofu, Shikotan, Habomai); a. 15,592 km².

Kurisches Haff (Kurštu Martos), shallow lagoon, Baltic cst. of **Lithuania**; receives water of R. Niemen; narrow entrance to Baltic Sea at N. end of lagoon commanded by pt. of Klaipeda (Memel).

length 92 km, maximum width 32 km.

Kurische Nehrung, sandspit, Baltic Sea; almost cuts off Kurisches Haff from Baltic Sea; 88 km long.

Kurnool, t., Andhra Pradesh, **India**; agr. comm. ctr.; p. (1981) 206,700.

Kuroshio (Japan Current), ocean current, flows N.E. along Pac. cst. of Kyushu, Shikoku and S. Honshu, relatively warm water, exerts slight warming influence on this cst. in winter.

Kursk, c., cap. of K. oblast, **Russia**; on Tuskor R.; rly. junc.; in fertile fruit-growing a.; engin., textiles, synthetic rubber; p. (1989) 424,000.

Kurume, t., W. Kyushu, **Japan**; on Chikugo plain; comm. ctr.; p. (1990) 228,300.

Kushiro, spt., S.E. Hokkaido, **Japan**; exp. lumber; local coal; fishing; p. (1990) 205,640.

Kustanay, c., **Kazakhstan**; on Tobol R.; agr.-processing, lt. inds.; p. (1990) 228,400.

Kütahya, t., cap. of K. prov., central **Turkey**; agr. mkt. ctr.; ceramics; chemical complex; p. (1990) 135,432 (t.), 578,020 (prov.).

Kutaisi, c., **Georgia**; on R. Rion (hydroelectric plant); chemicals, textiles, mng. equipment; big coal deposits being mined; mkt. gardening a.; p. (1990) 236,400.

Kut-al-Amara, t., cap. of K. prov., **Iraq**; on R. Tigris; agr. tr. ctr.; p. (1970) 58,647 (latest fig.).

Kutch, Rann of, desert region covered with salt, but flooded during monsoons; nine-tenths belongs to India; one-tenth to **Pakistan**.

Kutchan, t., S.W. Hokkaido, **Japan**; ctr. of lge. iron-ore field; ore smelted at Muroran.

Kutno, t. Plock, **Poland**; route ctr.; sm. textile ind.; p. (1989) 49,753.

Kuwait, indep. Arab st., **S.W. Asia**; under Brit. protection until 1961; invaded by Iraq, August 1990; lies at head of Persian G.; inc. mainland and 9 sm Is.; mainly desert with a few oases; imports most of food requirements; possesses 13 per cent of the proved world reserves of oil; heavily dependent on oil and natural gas exports; freshwater scarce; one of hgst. incomes per capita in world, but most of p. remains poor; a. 24,235 km²; p. (1991) 2·1 m.

Kuwait, c., cap. of **Kuwait**; pt. with natural harbour on Persian G.; univ.; p. (1985) 44,335.

Kuybyshev. *See* **Samara**.

Kuzbas (Kuznetsk Basin), industl. region, Siberia, **Russia**; lies S. of Trans-Siberian rly. in upper valleys of Rs. Ob and Tom; coal, iron and steel mftg., heavy metallurgical ind.; ch. ts., Novosibirsk, Novokuznetsk, Kemerovo, Leninsk-Kuznetsky.

Kwa Ndebele, homeland Transvaal, **S. Africa**; chief town Moutjana; pop. (1985) 235,855.

Kwangsi Chuang. *See* **Guang Zhuang**.

Kwantung. *See* **Guangdong**.

Kwanto Plain, S.E. Honshu, **Japan**; lgst. a. of continuous lowland in Japan, extends 128 km inland from Tokyo; plain devoted to intensive rice cultivation; higher, drier terraces under mulberry, vegetables, tea, tobacco; very dense rural p.; lge. number of urban ctrs., inc. Tokyo, Yokohama; a. 13,000 km².

Kwazulu, Bantu Terr. Authority (1970), E. **S. Africa**; runs 480 km from Moçambique to Cape Prov. but in 29 separate as. interspersed by white as.; cap. Nongoma in N. highland; p. (1985) 3·7 m.

Kweichow. *See* **Guizhou**.

Kweilin. *See* **Guilin**.

Kweiyang. *See* **Guiyang**.

Kwidzyn (Marienwerder), c., Elblag prov., N. **Poland** (since 1945); cath., cas.; industl. ctr. nr. Vistula R.; p. (1989) 36,409.

Kwinana, new t. (1952), pt., W. **Australia**; oil refinery and steel plant, alumina reduction, integrated steelwks.; p. (1981) 12,355.

Kyle and Carrick, l. gov. dist., Strathclyde Reg., **Scot.**; lge. dist. inc. t. of Ayr; p. (1993) 113,960.

Kyle of Lochalsh, v., Skye and Lochalsh, **Scot.**; at entrance to Loch Alsh, facing S. end of I. of Skye; terminus of rly. across Highlands from Dingwall; ch. pt. for steamers to N.W. cst.; I. of Skye, Outer Hebrides; p. (1991) 862.

Kymi, R., **Finland**; rises in L. Päijänne, flows to G. of Finland; many Ls., timber transport, hydroelec. power; 144 km long.

Kyoto, c., Honshu, **Japan**; cultural and religious ctr., without lge.-scale inds.; former cap. 794–1868; univ.; shrines, old Imperial palace; p. (1990) 1,461,140.

Kyrgyzstan, CIS, former USSR constituent rep.; S.W. of Siberia; mtnous. cty., in Tienshan and Pamir systems; livestock breeding; mineral resources, food processing; cap. Frunze; a 196,581 km²; p. (1992) 4·5 m.

Kyushu, most S. of 4 major Is. of **Japan**; mtnous.; coal mng. in Chikugo basin; heavy inds.; agr. on coastal lowlands; joined to Honshu by bridge and rly.; a. 42,007 km²; p. (1990) 13,296,000.

Kyustendil, t., **Bulgaria**; in foothills of Osogovo mtns.; lge. lead and zinc deposits; combined plant for mng. and ore dressing projected.

Kzyl Orda, R. and t., **Kazakhstan**; lge. dam to irrigate rice plantations; p. of t. (1990) 155,500.

L

Laaland I. *See* **Lolland I.**

Labrador, mainland a. of prov. Newfoundland, **Canada**; separated from I. by Strait of Belle I.; barren, severe climate; impt. cod fisheries; rich iron ore reserves nr. Quebec bdy.; Churchill R. power project; cap. Battle Harbour; a. 292,219 km².

Labrador City, t., Newfoundland, **Canada**; new t. built 1965, nr. Wabush L. to house workers of iron-ore mines; p. (1986) 8,664.

Labuan, I., Sabah, **Malaysia**; rubber, rice, coconuts; cap. Victoria; a. 81 km²; p. (1991) 54,307.

Laccadive, coral Is., Arabian Sea; about 320 km off Malabar cst. joined with Minicoy and Amindivi Is. to form union terr. Lakshadweep, **India**.

Lachine, c., Quebec, **Canada** now part of gter. Montreal; on Montreal I. where St. Lawrence R. leaves St. Louis L.; iron and steel, wire, rope; Lachine canal by-passes rapids; p. (1986) 34,906.

Lachlan, R. N.S.W., **Australia**; main trib. of R. Murrumbidgee; irrigation; 1,472 km long.

La Coruña, spt., cap. of La Coruña prov., N.W. **Spain**; fishing; p. (1991) 251,342 (c.), 1,089,810 (prov.).

Ladakh, dist., of the Upper Indus, **India**, bordering Tibet; ch. t. Leh; isolated and remote; alt. 3,600 m; p. (1981) 68,380.

Ladoga (Ladozhskoye), L., St. Petersburg, **Russia**; a. 18,389 km²; (lgst. in Europe); drained to G. of Finland by R. Neva; fishing; link in new deep-water canal between White and Baltic Seas.

Ladybank, burgh, North East Fife, **Scot.**; 8 km S.W. of Cupar; p. (1991) 1,373.

Ladysmith, t. Natal, **S. Africa**; cotton mills; besieged by Boers 1899–1900; p. (1980) 105,020 (dist.).

Lae, t., **Papua New Guinea**; pt. on Huon Gulf serving goldmng. dist.; outlet for Morobe; plywood; air ctr.; p. (1990) 80,655.

Lagan (Laggan), R., **N. Ireland**; flows into Belfast Lough; canal link to Lough Neagh; 56 km long.

Lagôa dos Patos, L., **Brazil**; drained by Rio Grande do Sul; 224 km long.

Lagôa Mirim, L., on bdy. between **Brazil** and **Uruguay**; drains N.; 176 km long.

Lagos, spt., former cap. of **Nigeria**; unhealthy and congested; cap. recently moved to Abuja; gd. natural harbour; exp. cocoa, groundnuts, palm oil and kernels, timber, hides and skins, cotton, rubber, crude oil; mnfs. textiles, confectionery, chemicals, car assembly; univ.; p. (1983) 1,097,000, (1991) 5,685,781 (state).

La Grande Chartreuse, limestone region between Chambéry and Grenoble, **France**; famous monastery and liqueur.

La Grande Rivière, N. Quebec, **Canada**; major hydroelec. scheme; mineral and timber inds.

Laguna, dist., Durango st., **Mexico**; former L. bed irrigated by Rs. Nazas and Aguanaval; ch. cotton-growing region in Mexico; ch. t., Torréon; a. 259,000 km².

Lahore, ch. c., **Pakistan**; univ., cath., temples, mosques; textiles, pottery, carpets, industl. gases; atomic research ctr.; second c. of Pakistan; p. (1981) 2,922,000.

Lahti, t., S. **Finland**; wood, plywood, brewing, textiles; p. (1991) 93,414.

Lake Champlain, N.Y., **USA**; forms lowland a. for main routes between Montreal and N.Y.

Lake Charles, c., La., **USA**; spt. at mouth of Calcasieu R.; connected to G. of Mexico by channel; exp. oil, chemicals, rice, cotton; p. (1984) 75,100 (c.), 175,000 (met. a.).

Lake District, almost circular mtnous. a., Cumbria,

Eng.; 17 major and many smaller Ls. formed by glacial erosion and deposition; increasing tourist pressure on Nat. Park as motorways improve accessibility.

Lakeland, c., Fla., **USA**; citrus fruit ctr.; holiday resort; p. (1990) 70,576 (c.), 405,000 (met. a. with Winter Haven).

Lake of the Woods, L., Ont., S.E. of Winnipeg, on bdy. between **Canada** and **USA**; in pine forest; tourism.

Lakeview, t., Ont., **Canada**; thermal elec. power plant projected; to be lgst. in world.

Lakshadweep, union terr., **India**; made up of Laccadive, Minicoy and Aminidivi Is; coir, coconuts; a. 32 km.²; p. (1991) 51,707.

La Laguna, second lgst. t., former cap. Tenerife, Canary Is; p. (1991) 116,539.

La Linea, t., **Spain**; on isthmus connecting Gibraltar with mainland; p. (1981) 55,590.

La Mancha, plain, Cuidad-Real prov., S. **Spain**; in shallow depression on central plateau, alt. between 450–900 m, drained by headstreams of R. Guadiana; semi-arid climate with hot summers, cold winters; widespread salt deposits; Merino sheep, esparto grass; Spain's lgst. grape-growing region.

Lambaréné, t., **Gabon**; site of Schweitzer's hospital on Ogooué R.

Lambayeque, prov., N.W. **Peru**; ctr. of irrigated dists.; sugar, cotton, tobacco; cap. Chiclayo, ch. pt. Pimental; a. 11,948 km²; p. (1990) 935,300.

Lambeth, inner bor., London, **Eng.**; L. palace, residence of Archbishop of Canterbury; p. (1993) 259,200.

Lammermuir Hills, E. Lothian, **Scot.**; highest peak Lammer Law, 529 m.

Lampang, t., **Thailand**; modern sugar plant; p. (1980) 42,301.

Lampedusa, lgst. of Pelagi Is., between Malta and Tunisian cst., belonging to **Italy**; barren limestone; a. 21 km²; p. (1981) 4,792.

Lampeter, t., Ceredigion, Dyfed, S. **Wales**; on R. Teifi; mkt.; univ. college of Wales; p. (1981) 1,972.

Lamu, t., **Kenya**; impt. historical and tourist ctr. on Indian Ocean.

Lanark, former co., central **Scot.**; now forms several sm. l. gov. dists. known as Clydesdale within Strathclyde Reg.

Lanark, royal burgh, Clydesdale, **Scot.**; in Clyde valley 35 km S.E. of Glasgow; hosiery; ctr. of mkt. gardening a.; nr. New Lanark model t. built by Robert Owen; p. (1991) 8,877.

Lancashire, non-met. co., N.W. **Eng.**; major growth of p. in 19th cent. based on prod. of cotton and coal; main industl. ctrs. now outside co. in Merseyside and Gtr. Manchester met. cos.; Pennines in E.; extensive lowland in W.; admin. ctr. Preston, co. t. Lancaster; a. 2,738 km²; p. (1993) 1,420,700.

Lancaster, c., co. t., l. gov. dist., Lancs., **Eng.**; 10 km up R. Lune; mediaeval cas., univ.; linoleum, vinyl, clothing; p. (1993) 133,600 (dist.).

Lancaster, c., Penns., **USA**; agr. ctr., tobacco mkt.; stockyards; mnfs. linoleum, watches; birthplace of Robert Fulton; p. (1984) 56,300 (c.), (1990) 423,000 (met a.).

Lanchow. See Lanzhou.

Lancing, v., West Sussex, **Eng.**; on S. cst., 3 km E. of Worthing; seaside resort; lt. inds.; public school.

Landau, t., Rhineland-Palatinate, **Germany**; on R. Queich; cigar mftg., wine, iron ind.; here the carriages called landaus were first made; p. (1986) 35,300.

Landes, dep., S.W. **France**; on Atl. cst.; agr., vineyards, resin; cap. Mont-de-Marsan; a. 9,334 km²; p. (1990) 306,000.

Landes, Les, region, Aquitaine, S.W. **France**; fringes Bay of Biscay from Pointe de Grave to Biarritz; coastal sand dunes and lagoons backed by low, flat plain of alternate sandy tracts and marsh; reclaimed by drainage and afforestation, now over half a. covered by pine forests; turpentine, timber; oilfield.

Land's End, extreme S.W. point of **Eng.** on Cornish cst.

Landshut, t., Bavaria, **Germany**; on R. Isar; cas.; elec. inds., glass, metallurgy, textiles, coal; rly. junc.; p. (1986) 57,100.

Landskrona, spt., **Sweden**; on the Sound; shipping and tr. ctr.; agr.-processing; on nearby I. of Ven; Tycho Brahe built his observatory; p. (1983) 35,656.

Langbaurgh-on-Tees, l. gov. dist. Cleveland, **Eng.**; a. of N. York Moors inc. Loftus, Skelton, Guisborough and Saltburn; p. (1993) 143,900.

Langdale Pikes, L. Dist., **Eng.**; 2 peaks Harrison Stickle (733 m), Pike o'-Stickel (709 m); popular rambling and climbing a.; 5 km W. of Grasmere.

Langebergen, mtns., Cape Prov., **S. Africa**; 240 km E. to W. parallel to S. cst. of Africa; form barrier to access from cst. plain to Little Karroo, broken across by valley of R. Gouritz; max. alt. exceeds 1,370 m.

Langreo, t., N. **Spain**; in Asturias, 19 km S.E. of Oviedo; coal and iron mines; p. (1981) 55,758.

Langres, t., Haute-Marne, **France**; cath., mediaeval fortifications; famous for its cutlery; birthplace of Diderot; p. (1982) 11,359.

Languedoc, former prov. now incorporated in **Languedoc-Roussillon** region, S. **France**; inc. deps. Aude, Gard, Hérault, Lozère, Pyrenées-Orientales; major sport. sponsored investment in tourist inds., along Mediterranean cst.; mono-cultural vine prod., irrigation scheme to aid agr. diversification; p. (1990) 2,115,000.

Lannemezan, region, Aquitaine, S.W. **France**; belt 80 km wide stretches over 160 km along foot of Pyrenees W. of Toulouse; consists of immense deltas of glacial gravel deeply cut by tribs. of Rs. Garonne and Adour; valleys liable to severe floods in summer, intervening plateau dry, bare; scantily populated.

Lansing, c., cap of Mich., **USA**; on Grand R. at confluence with Cedar R.; automobiles, chemicals; p. (1990) 127,321 (c.), 433,000 (met. a. with E. Lansing).

Lanzarote, I., **Canary Is.**; volcanic mtns.; developing tourist ind.; cochineal; cap. Arrecife.

Lanzhou (Lanchow), c., cap. of Gansu prov., **China**; on Huang He; tr. ctr.; oil refining, gaseous diffusion plant, woollen mills, coal mng. nearby; p. (1991) 1,530,000.

Laoag, c., N. Luzon I., **Philippines**; agr.-processing; p. (1990) 83,756.

Laoighis or **Leix Co.**, Leinster, **R.o.I.**; mtns. and bog; inland pasture and tillage; cap. Port Laoighise (Maryborough); a. 1,720 km²; p. (1986) 53,284.

Laon, t., cap. of Aisne dep., **France**; on rocky height above plain; historic fortress t.; cath.; p. (1990) 28,670.

Laois. See Laoighis.

Laos, People's Dem. Rep. of, S.E. **Asia**; kingdom until 1975; bordered by China, Vietnam, Kampuchea, Thailand and Burma; formerly part of Fr. Indo-China; under-developed and isolated cty.; considerable mineral resources but only tin exploited; disrupted by civil war, drought, crop pests; economic ctr. is Mekong valley, scene of recent Mekong R. Development Project; elsewhere thickly forested mtns.; 70 per cent of p. engaged in subsistence agr. for dry rice; now produces rice surplus; main exp., hardwoods; no rlys.; royal cap. Luang Prabang, admin. cap. Vientiane; a. 231,399 km²; p. (1993) 4·4 m.

La Paz, dep., **Bolivia**; traversed by Andes; de facto cap. La Paz, legal cap. Sucre; cocoa, coffee, rubber, tin-mng. at Catari; a. 105,377 km²; p. (1988) 1,926,200.

La Paz, c., **Bolivia**; seat of govt.; comm. ctr.; copper, alpaca wool, cinchona, textiles; highest cap. c. in world; p. (1988) 669,400.

Lapland, terr., N. **Europe**, in Norway, Sweden, Finland, and USSR, extending from Norwegian cst. to White Sea; mainly mtn. and moorland, with many lakes; Lapps are nomadic pastoralists with reindeer herds; iron-ore at Kiruna and Gällivare; a. 336,700 km²; p. of Swedish Co. of L. (1983) 118,819.

La Plata, c., spt., **Argentina**; cap. of Buenos Aires prov., univ.; mftg. ctr.; iron and steel, oil refining, refrigerated meat prods.; p. (1991) 542,567.

La Plata, Rio de. See Plata, Rio de la.

Laptev Sea (Nordenskjöld Sea), inlet of Arctic Oc.; between Severnaya Zemlya and New Siberian Is., **Russia**.

Larache, spt., **Morocco**; on Atl. cst. 64 km S. of Tangier; exp. cork, wool; p. (1982) 63,893.

Laramie, t., Wyo., **USA**; univ.; industl. ctr. for cattle and timber region; rly. engin.; p. (1990) 26,687.

Laredo, t., Texas, **USA**; frontier t. on Rio Grande; smuggling; ctr. of Chicanos; p. (1990) 122,899.

Largo, v., North East Fife, **Scot.**; fishing, holiday resort; birthplace of Alexander Selkirk.

Largs, burgh, Cunninghame, **Scot.**; on F. of Clyde

opposite Is. of Bute and Cumbrae; seaside resort, fishing; battle 1263 defeating last attempt by Norsemen to conquer Scot.; p. (1991) 10,925.

Larissa, dep., Thessaly, **Greece;** inc. infertile basin of R. Piniós; cap. Larissa; ch. pt. Volos; p. (1991) 269,300.

Larnaca, spt., **Cyprus;** the anc. Citium; grain, cotton, fruit; oil refinery; growing tourist ctr.; p. (1991) 59,600.

Larne, spt., l. gov. dist., **N. Ireland;** at entrance to Larne Lough; cross channel service to Stranraer; tourism; p. (1991) 26,419 (dist.), 17,525 (t.).

La Rochelle, spt., cap. of Charente-Maritime dep., **France;** on Atl. cst.; its deepwater pt. is La Pallice; cath.; fishing pt.; chemicals, food-processing; tourism; p. (1990) 73,744.

La Roche-sur-Yon, t., cap of Vendée dep., **France;** on R. Yon; built by Napoleon I; p. (1990) 48,518.

Larut Hills, W. Malaysia; rise to over 1,500 m; lge. tin-field.

Larvik, spt., **Norway;** S.W. of Oslo; seaside resort; engin., pulp, stone; former whaling pt; p. (1990) 20,594.

Las Cruces, t., N.M., **USA;** on Rio Grande R.; irrigated agr.; univ.; p. (1990) 62,126.

La Serena, c., cap. of Coquimbo prov., **Chile;** 14 km inland from its pt. Coquimbo; cath.; resort; p. (1987) 106,617.

Lashio, t., **Myanmar;** on R. Salween; rly. terminus; Burma road links with China; ctr. of silver-lead mines; p. 4,638.

Lashkar, c., Madhya Pradesh, central **India;** modern industl. t., adjoining Gwalior.

La Skhirra, pt. on G. of Gabès, **Tunisia;** oil; pipeline to Edjelé.

Las Palmas, prov., Canary Is., **Spain;** inc. Gran Canaria, Lanzarote, Fuerteventura and smaller Is.; intensive irrigated agr. of bananas, tomatoes, potatoes; tourism encouraged by climate and volcanic landscape; a. 4,053 km²; p. (1991) 836,556.

Las Palmas, c., N.E. Gran Canaria, ch. pt. of **Canary Is.;** exp. agr. prods.; cath.; p. (1991) 347,668.

La Spezia, spt., Liguria, N.W. **Italy;** on Bay of Spezia; ch. Italian naval sta., arsenal and docks; maritime inds., elec. machin., olive oil, oil refining; p. (1992) 100,458.

Lassen Peak, Nat. Park, Cascade Range, Cal.; only active volcano in **USA.**

Lasswade. See Bonnyrigg and Lasswade.

Las Vegas, c., Nevada, **USA;** noted for its gambling casinos; ranching and mng. a.; p. (1990) 258,295 (c.), 741,000 (met. a.).

Latacunga, t., **Ecuador;** at about 2,740 m in Andean basin, not far from Cotopaxi volcano; anc. Inca t.; ctr.; p. (1990) 39,882.

Latakia, spt., **Syria;** exp. tobacco, olive oil, sponges; p. (1981) 196,791.

Latina (Littoria), c., cap. of Latina prov., in Latium central **Italy;** in ctr. of reclaimed a. of Pontine marshes; mkt. ctr., on which planned road system converges; built since 1932; nuclear power sta. nearby; p. (1981) 93,738.

Latin America, the Spanish-, Portuguese- and Fr.-speaking countries of N. America, S. America, Central America, and the W.I., inc. the reps. of Argentina, Bolivia, Brazil, Chile, Colombia, Costa Rica, Cuba, Dominican Republic, Ecuador, Salvador, Guatemala, Haiti, Honduras, Mexico, Nicaragua, Panama, Paraguay, Peru, Uruguay, and Venezuela; sometimes Puerto Rico, Fr. W.I., and other Is. of the W.I. are included, and occasionally Belize, Guyana, Fr. Guiana, and Surinam; p. (1984) 397,138,000.

Latium (Lazio), region, central **Italy;** between Apennines and Tyrrhenian Sea, comprising provs. of Rome, Frosinone, Latina, Rieti, Viterbo; a. 17,182 km²; p. (1992) 5,162,073.

Latrobe Valley, one of most impt. economic a. in Victoria, **Australia;** major brown coal and electric power production; secondary inds. attracted by cheap power.

Latvia, former constituent rep., USSR; on dairying, stock-raising, forestry; cap. Riga; spts. Ventspils, Liepaya; a. 66,278 km²; p. (1993) 2,606,000.

Launceston, t., Tasmania, **Australia;** at head of Tamar estuary, inc. Bell Bay where many heavy inds.; p. (1991) 93,520.

Launceston, t., North Cornwall, **Eng.;** agr. mkt.; quarrying, lt. engin.; p. (1981) 6,199.

Laurencekirk, burgh, Kincardine and Deeside, **Scot.;** agr. ctr. in the Howe of Mearns; p. (1991) 1,611.

Laurion or **Laurium,** pt. on Attic peninsula, **Greece;** lead, manganese, zinc, and silver mines; silver mined 5th cent. B.C.

Lausanne, c., cap. of Vaud can., **Switzerland;** nr. L. Geneva; cath., univ.; impt. rly. junc.; seat of Swiss high courts of justice; tourism; p. (1990) 123,200 (c.), 262,900 (met. a.).

Lauterbrunnen, Alpine valley, Bern can., **Switzerland;** famous for its waterfalls, the highest of which is Staubbach 299 m; tourist and winter sports ctr.

Laval, t., cap. of Mayenne dep., **France;** Mayenne R. divides old and modern parts; cotton, paper, machin., marble; cas., church; p. (1990) 53,479.

Lavenham, t., Suffolk, **Eng.;** a ctr. of the wool tr. in 15th cent., still preserves its mediaeval character.

Lavera, pt., nr. Marseilles, S.E. **France** commencement of 752 km oil pipeline to Karlsruhe, W. Germany; oil refining.

Lawrence, t., Mass., **USA;** on Merrimac R., N.W. of Boston; textiles, paper, footwear, engin.; p. (1990) 394,000 (met. a. with Haverhill).

Lawton, t., Okla., **USA;** mnfs. cottonseed oil; p. (1984) 85,600 (t.), 119,400 (met. a.).

Laxey, v., I. of Man, **Eng.;** flour milling, woollen mills, meerschaum pipes.

Lazio. See Latium.

Lea or **Lee,** R., **Eng.;** rises in Chiltern Hills nr. Luton, flows S. and E. into R. Thames through industl. zone of N.E. London; valley to become a regional park; mkt. gardening a.; 74 km long.

Leamington (Royal Leamington Spa), t., Warwicks., **Eng.;** on R. Leam, trib. of Avon, 3 km N.E. of Warwick; fashionable spa; engin. inds.; p. (1981) 42,953.

Leatherhead, t., Mole Valley, Surrey, **Eng.;** on R. Mole to N. of gap through N. Downs; residtl.; p. (1981) 40,473.

Lebanon, mtn. range, **Lebanon,** extending to cst. of Syria; snow-capped most of year; highest peak Timarum, 3,214 m; famous in anc. times for cedar forests.

Lebanon, rep., S.W. **Asia;** at E. end of Mediterranean Sea; bordered by Syria to N. and Israel to S.; narrow coastal strip backed by mtnous. interior; free mkt. a., with economy based on transit tr.; most of p. involved in tourism, finance and commerce; oil refining based on imports; cap. Beirut; strife-torn by civil war, now being rebuilt; a. 8,806 km²; p. (1992) 2,760,000.

Le Bourget, t., N.E. of Paris, **France;** airpt.; p. (1982) 11,021.

Lebórk (Lauenburg), t. Slupsk prov., **Poland** (since 1945); in agr. dist.; timber and food inds.; p. (1980) 33,981.

Lebowa Territory, Bantu Terr., **S. Africa;** home of N. Sotho and Ndebele peoples; self-gov. Oct. 1972; cap. Seshego; p. (1985) 1·8 m.

Lecce, c., Apulia, S. **Italy;** agr. and route ctr. with ceramic and glass inds.; anc. Greek col.; baroque churches and palaces; p. (1992) 100,508.

Lecco, t., **Italy;** in Lombardy, on L. Como; iron and copper wks., agr.-processing, cheese.

Lech, R., rises in Austria and flows past Augsburg in Bavaria, **Germany,** to join Danube; 283 km long.

Le Creusot, t., Saône-et-Loire, **France;** ctr. of one of sm. coalfields bordering the Massif Central; steel, engin.; p. (1982) 32,309.

Ledbury, t., Hereford and Worcs., **Eng.;** at W. foot of Malvern hills; fruit preserving, tanning; 17th cent. mkt. hall; birthplace of John Masefield.

Leeds, c., met. dist., West Yorks., **Eng.;** on R. Aire; at E. margin of Pennines; univ.; lge. clothing ind., varied engin. mnfs., paper and printing; with Bradford forms conurb. of W. Yorks., p. (1993) 724,500 (dist.).

Leek, mkt. t., Moorland, Staffs., **Eng.;** 18 km N.E. of Stoke-on-Trent; silk mnfs., butter; expanded t.; p. (1981) 19,739.

Lee-on-Solent, t., Hants., **Eng.;** on Southampton Water.

Lees, t., Gtr. Manchester, **Eng.;** textiles; p. (1981) 4,838.

Leeuwarden, c., cap. of Friesland prov., **Neth.;** noted cattle mkt.; rly. junc.; p. (1993) 86,783.

Leeuwin, C., S.W. point of **Australia;** notorious storms; Nat. Park (1971).

Leeward Is., W.I., northern gr. of Lesser Antilles archipelago; so-called because winds in this a. generally blow from E.; inc. Virgin Is. of US; Fr. I. of Guadaloupe, Dutch Is. of St. Eustatius and Saba, and Brit. Leeward Is. (Montserrat, Virgin Is., and former cols. of Antigua, St. Kitt-Nevis, Anguilla).

Lefkosia. *See* **Nicosia.**

Leganes, t. Madrid prov., C. **Spain;** mineral springs, electronics; p. (1991) 173,043.

Legazpi, c., cap. of Albay prov., **Philippines;** spt. in S.E. Luzon; linked by rly. with Manila; p. (1990) 121,116.

Leghorn. *See* **Livorno.**

Legionowo, t., **Poland;** on outskirts of Warsaw; nr. artificial L. in R. Bug valley; p. (1989) 50,577.

Legnano, t., Lombardy, **Italy;** N.W. of Milan; textiles, machin.; p. (1981) 49,308.

Legnica (Liegnitz), c. and prov., S.W. **Poland** (since 1945); on Katzbach R., in rich agr. region; p. (1989) 103,949 (c.), 510,200 (prov.).

Leh, cap. of Ladakh, Kashmir, **India;** isolated t. in Himalayas on caravan route to Tibet; p. (1981) 8,000.

Le Havre, spt., *Seine Maritime* dep., N. **France;** at mouth of Seine on English Channel; shipbldg., engin., chemicals, ropes, cottons, oil refining; pipeline to Grandpuits; p. (1990) 197, 219 (c.), 253,627 (met.a.).

Leicester, c., co. t., l. gov. dist., Leics., **Eng.;** on R. Soar; univ.; footwear, hosiery, knitwear, textile machin.; Roman remains; p. (1993) 289,300 (dist.).

Leicestershire, non-met. co., **Eng.;** mainly rural, low-lying Midland co., but inc. Charnwood Forest; mixed agr., sm. coalfield; hosiery and footwear inds.; now inc. Rutland; ch. t. Leicester; a. 2,554 km²; p. (1993) 910,300.

Leiden or **Leyden,** c., S. Holland prov., **Neth.;** on Oude Rijn; famous univ.; printing, textiles, medical equipment; gr. weaving ctr. in Middle Ages; revolt against Spanish rule 1573–4; birthplace of Rembrandt; p. (1993) 113,838 (c.), 192,226 (met. a.).

Leigh, t., Gtr. Manchester, **Eng.;** 8 km S.E. of Wigan; mkt.; coal mng.; textiles; p. (1981) 45,341.

Leigh-on-Sea, t., Essex, **Eng.;** on N. cst. of Thames estuary, 3 km W. of Southend; holiday resort, fishing.

Leighton Buzzard, t., South Beds., **Eng.;** at N.E. end of Vale of Aylesbury; tiles, engin., sand quarrying; p. (1981) 29,772 (inc. Linslade).

Leinster, S.E. prov., **R.o.I.;** bulk of recent Irish p. increase; a. 19,637 km²; p. (1986) 1,852,649.

Leipzig, c. Saxony, **Germany;** comm., industl., and cultural ctr. at junc. of Rs. Pleisse, Elster, and Parthe; famous univ.; inds. inc. publishing, steel, textiles, chemicals, machin., cars; tr. fairs; Bach was organist at Thomaskirche; birthplace of Leibnitz and Wagner; p. (1990) 507,800.

Leiston-cum-Sizewell, t., Suffolk Coastal, Suffolk, **Eng.;** on cst. 6 km E. of Saxmundham; agr. implements; nuclear power sta.; p. (1981) 5,133.

Leith, t., Edinburgh City, **Scot.;** shipbldg., timber, whisky; outport for Edinburgh.

Leith Hill, Surrey, **Eng.;** nr. Dorking; alt. 294 m; Lower Greensand crest.

Leitmeritz. *See* **Litoměřice.**

Leitrim, co., Connacht, **R.o.I.;** agr.; cap. Carrick-on-Shannon; a. 1,588 km²; p. (1986) 27,035.

Leix. *See* **Laoighis.**

Leixões, the modern harbour of Oporto, **Portugal;** oil refinery.

Lek, R., **Neth.;** one of the branches of the Neder Rijn; from Wijk-bij-Duurstede to Krimpen nr. Rotterdam; 64 km long.

Le Locle, t., Neuchâtel, **Switzerland;** ctr. of watch-mkg. ind.; p. (1986) 10,900.

Léman L. *See* **Geneva, L.**

Le Mans, t., cap. of Sarthe dep., N.W. **France;** cath.; linen, ironmongery, chemicals, motor cars, aeroplanes; motor-racing; p. (1990) 148,465 (t.), 189,107 (met.a.).

Lemnos, Greek I., Aegean Sea, **Greece;** 64 km S.W. of Dardanelles; ch. t. Kastro (the anc. Myrina); tobacco, wine; a. 466 km²; part of Lesvos dep.

Lena, one of gr. Siberian Rs., **Russia;** rises in Oc.; navigable; 4,480 km long.

Leninabad. *See* **Khudzhand.**

Leninakan. *See* **Kumayri.**

Lenin Dam (Dnieper Dam). *See* **Zaporozh'ye.**

Leningrad. *See* **St. Petersburg.**

Leninogorsk. *See* **Ridder.**

Lenin Peak (Mt. Kaufmann); Trans-Altai Range, **Tajikistan-Khirghizia;** adjoining glacier; salt. 7,132 m.

Leninsk-Kuznetski, t., **Russia;** in W. Siberia on Inya R.; coalfield in Kuznetsk basin; heavy engin., power sta.; p. (1989) 134,000.

Lenkoran, c., pt. **Azerbaijan;** on Caspian Sea, nr. Iranian border; rice, citrus fruits, tea, fisheries, food-processing; p. (1990) 45,500.

Lennoxtown, t., Stirling, **Scot.;** alum. wks.; p. (1991) 4,524.

Lens, t., Pas-de-Calais dep., N. **France;** industl. ctr. in coal a.; p. (1990) 35,278 (t.), 323,174 (met.a.).

Leoben, t., Styria, **Austria;** lignite mng. ctr.; p. (1991) 28,504.

Leominster, mkt. t., l. gov. dist., Hereford and Worcs., **Eng.;** 19 km N. of Hereford; once famed for woollen ind.; p. (1993) 40,500 (dist.).

León, c., central **Mexico;** at c. 1,700 m; comm., agr. and mng. ctr. (gold, copper, silver, lead, tin); textiles, leather; p. (1990) 872,453.

León, c., cap. of León dep., N.W. **Nicaragua;** cath., univ.; ctr. for agr. and industl. prods.; footwear, textiles; p. (1985) 101,000.

León, cap. of L. prov., N.W. **Spain;** gothic cath.; craft inds.; p. (1991) 146,720, 517,176 (prov.).

Léopoldville. *See* **Kinshasa.**

Lepontine Alps, major gr., **Switzerland-Italy;** alt. over 3,300 m.

Le Puy, t., cap. of Haute Loire dep., **France;** lace, liqueurs; cath. sited on old volcanic plug; tourism; p. (1990) 23,434.

Lérida, t., cap. of L. prov., **Spain;** on R. Segre; 2 caths.; textiles, leather, glass; p. (1991) 119,167 (t.), 358,123 (prov.).

Lerwick, t., Shetland Is., **Scot.;** on Mainland; fishing; p. (1991) 7,336.

Lesbos. *See* **Lesvos.**

Les Causses. *See* **Causses, Les.**

Leskovac, t., Serbia, **Yugoslavia;** on Morava R.; in economically backward a.; textiles, soap, furniture, tobacco-processing; p. (1991) 61,693.

Les Landes. *See* **Landes, Les.**

Leslie, burgh, Kirkcaldy, **Scot.;** 11 km N. of Kirkcaldy; paper, bleaching; p. (1991) 3,062.

Lesotho (Basutoland), kingdom, southern **Africa;** surrounded by Rep. of S. Africa; at head of Orange R. and enclosed by Drakensberg mtns.; economy mainly agr., especially pastoral farming; exp. livestock, wool, mohair, diamonds; 50 per cent revenue from U.K. grants; poor communications; many workers migrate to S. Africa (23 per cent in 1981); inds. encouraged by tax concessions becoming increasingly impt.; Highlands Water Project started (1986) to export water from Orange R. to S. Africa and generate hydro-electr. from 6 dams; cap. Maseru; a. 30,344 km²; p. (1991) 1,825,000.

Lesser Antilles. *See* **Antilles.**

Lesvos (Lesbos, Mytilene), I., off Turkey, Aegean Sea, belonging to **Greece;** highest point 939 m; agr., antimony, marbles; cap. Mytilene; a. 1,601 km²; p. (1991) 103,700 (dep.).

Leszno, t. and prov., W. **Poland;** engin., distilling, tobacco; p. (1989) 57,673 (t.) 383,300 (prov.).

Letchworth (Garden City), t., North Herts., **Eng.;** at foot of Chiltern Hills, 3 km N.E. of Hitchin; first garden c., founded by Sir Ebenezer Howard 1903; engin., office equipment; expanded t.; p. (1981) 31,835.

Lethbridge, c., Alberta, **Canada;** in foothills of Rockies; ctr. of lge. coal-mng. dist. and of irrigated wheat-growing a.; p. (1986) 58,841.

Le Touquet-Paris Plage, fashionable resort, W. cst. **France;** S. of Canche estuary.

Letterkenny, t., Co. Donegal, **R.o.I.;** on Lough Swilly; tourist ctr.; p. (1986) 6,691.

Leuna, t., Saxony - Anhalt, **Germany;** 5 km S. of Merseburg; synthetic chemical ind.; oil pipeline from Schwedt; p. (1989) 8,647.

Levant, French and Italian name for E. cst. of Mediterranean.

Leven, burgh, Kirkcaldy, **Scot.;** on N. side of F. of Forth; resort; p. (1991) 8,317.

Leven, L., Perth and Kinross, **Scot.;** ass. with escape of Mary Queen of Scots from Castle I. 1568.

Leverkusen, t., N. Rhine–Westphalia, **Germany;** on R. Rhine, N. of Cologne; iron, machin., textiles, chemicals; p. (1990) 161,000.

Levkás or **Santa Maura,** one of Ionian Is., off W. **Greece;** wine, olive oil, currants; p. (1991) 20,900.

Lewes, t., l. gov. dist., East Sussex, **Eng.;** on R. Ouse at N. entrance to gap through S. Downs; mkt., cas., printing, light inds.; p. (1993) 88,600 (dist.).

Lewis, I., Outer Hebrides, **Scot.;** fishing, tweeds; ch. t. Stornoway; a. 1,994 km²; p. (1991) 21,731 (with Harris).

Lewisham, inner bor., London, **Eng.;** inc. Deptford; residtl.; industl.; p. (1993) 240,400.

Lewiston, t., Maine, **USA**; power for textile mill supplied by waterfall since early 19th cent.; p. (1980) 40,481.

Lexington-Fayette, c., Ky., **USA**; in heart of Blue Grass region; univ.; ch. tobacco mkt. and horse-breeding ctr. of USA; p. (1990) 225,366 (c.), 348,000 (met. a.).

Lexington, t., Mass., **USA**; nr. Boston; residtl.; first battle in war of independence 19 Apr. 1775; p. (1980) 29,479.

Leyburn, t., Richmondshire, North Yorks., **Eng.**; in lower Wensleydale; mkt.

Leyden. See **Leiden.**

Leyland, t., Lancs., **Eng.**; 8 km S. of Preston; motor vehicles, rubber; p. (1981) 26,567. See Central Lancashire.

Leyte, one of Visayan Is., prov. central **Philippines**; maize, abaca, rice; Japanese fleet defeated by US in battle of Leyte Gulf 1944; a. 7,213 km²; p. (1990) 1,368,510.

Leyton. See **Waltham Forest.**

Lhasa (**Lasa**), c., cap. of Tibet, **China**; "forbidden" c.; Buddhist ctr., temple, monasteries, shrines; caravan tr. in carpets, silk, lace, gold, tea; pharmaceutical factory, turbine pumps, fertilisers; much hotel bldg. and restoration of Buddhist sites to encourage tourism and break down isolation; p. (1982) 343,200.

Lhotse, mtn., Tibet, **China-Nepal**; 4th hgst. mtn. in world; alt. 8,506 m.

Lianyungang, spt., Jiangsu, **China**; impt. fishing and tea centre; rapid industrial development, esp. mineral processing, chemicals and motors; univ.; attracting foreign investment as 'open' c. under China's new economic policy; p. (1984) 450,000.

Liao-ho, R., Liaoning, N.E. **China**; flows into G. of Liaotung, Yellow Sea; navigable for last 640 km of course; c. 1,600 km long.

Liaoning, prov., N.E. **China**; inc. lower course and delta of Liao-ho; part of N.E. China (formerly called Manchuria); maize, millets, soyabeans; lge. mineral reserves of coal and iron ore; cap. Shenyang; a. 150,220 km²; p. (1990) 39,980,000.

Liaotung, peninsula, N.E. **China**; nr. G. of same name.

Liaoyang, c., E. Liaoning prov., N.E. **China**; in fertile valley of Liao-ho; cotton-growing; textile mills; p. (1984) 565,300.

Liao-yuang, c., S.W. Jilin, **China**; lge. coal-mng. ctr.; p. (1984) 375,600.

Liberec, t., Czech Rep.; on R. Neisse; univ.; textiles, chemicals, tr. ctr.; p. (1990) 104,000.

Liberia, rep., **W. Africa**; founded (1847) by free slaves from USA; tropical climate; 72 per cent of p. involved in agr.; few cash crops, inc. rubber and cocoa; rich iron deposits provide main exp.; world's lgst. merchant fleet as result of "flag of convenience"; cap. and ch. pt. Monrovia; a. 99,068 km²; p. (1992) 2·83 m.

Libourne, t., Gironde, **France**; on R. Dordogne, 35 km N.E. of Bordeaux; wine tr.; p. (1982) 23,312.

Libreville, c., cap. of Gabon; pt. on G. of Guinea; exp. tropical hardwoods, rubber, cacao; Trans-Gabon rly. project to link L. to Booué to promote timber exploitation; p. (1983) 350,000.

Libya, or **Popular Socialist Libyan Arab Jamahiriyah** (since 1977), rep., N. **Africa**; on Mediterranean cst.; desert conditions prevail; radical attitude towards oil companies as oil accounts for 99 per cent of exp. earnings and forms basis of new-found wealth; petro-chemical inds.; over half working p. are foreigners; most of p. engaged in subsistence agr. (nomadic pastoralism; most food and mnfs. imported; plans for unity with Chad; joint caps. Tripoli (site of government deps.), Benghazi; a. 1,759,537 km²; p. (1990) 4·5 m.

Libyan Desert, part of the Sahara, **Africa.**

Licata, t., Sicily, **Italy**; spt.; sulphur-processing; p. (1981) 40,050.

Lichfield, c., l. gov. dist., Staffs., **Eng.**; cath.; agr. and lt. inds.; expanded t.; birthplace of Dr. Samuel Johnson; p. (1993) 94,000 (dist.).

Lickey Hills, gr. of hills, Hereford and Worcs., **Eng.**; 6 km S.W. of Birmingham; reveal anc. rocks underlying younger sediments; rise to 292 m, largely wooded.

Liechtenstein, principality, between Austria and Switzerland; official language German; economy based on sm.-scale inds. and tourism in picturesque Alpine scenery aided by mild climate; wine; cap. Vaduz; a. 161 km²; p. (1992) 29,797, one-third foreign born.

Liège (**Luik**), industl. c. and prov., E. **Belgium**; on R. Meuse nr. confluence of Ourthe; cath., univ.; conurb. inc. Herstal, Bressoux, Ougrée, Angleur, Grivegnée; metallurgy, armaments, vehicles, chemicals, textiles, glassware, tyres; p. (1993) 196,632 (c.), 1,011,368 (prov.).

Liepaja (**Libau**), c., **Latvia**; ice-free pt. on Baltic Sea, second to Riga; shipyards, steel-wks., paper mills, chemicals; exp. timber, grain; p. (1991) 114,900.

Liestal, t., cap. of the half-can. Baselland, **Switzerland**; p. (1980) 12,158.

Liffey, R., **R.o.I.**; rises in Wicklow Mtns. and enters Irish Sea at Dublin; water supply for Dublin; inds. along estuary.

Liguria, region, N.W. **Italy**; inc. provs. of Genoa and Porto Maurizio; a. 5,411 km²; p. (1992) 1,667,896.

Ligurian Sea, Mediterranean; N. of Corsica.

Likasi (**Jadotville**), t., **Zaïre**; ctr. for copper mng. and refining; p. (1985) 194,000.

Lille, c., cap. of Nord dep., N. **France**; on R. Deûle; mftg., comm. and cultural ctr.; former cap. of Fr. Flanders (1668); textiles (the term lisle derived from earlier spelling of city's name), metallurgy, engin.; univ., art museums; p. (1990) 178,301 (c.), 950,256 (met.a.).

Lilongwe, c., main ctr. of Central Region, **Malawi**; replaced Zomba as cap. 1975; p. (1987) 233,973.

Lima, c., cap. of **Peru**; 13 km from its pt. Callao; dominates comm., industl. and social life of cty.; cath., univ., imposing architecture; seaside subs. Miraflores, Barranco, Chorillos; shanty ts. on outskirts; p. (1990) 6,707,300 (10 times bigger than next c., Arequipa).

Lima, t., Ohio, **USA**; on Ottawa R.; rly. wks., oil, car bodies, refrigerators; p. (1990) 45,549.

Limassol, t., S. **Cyprus**; spt. on Akrotiri Bay; new artificial harbour; ctr. of admin. dist.; wine, agr.-processing; exp. foodstuffs; tourism; p. (1991) 129,700.

Limavady, t., l. gov. dist., **N. Ireland**; mkt.; linen; p. (1991) 29,567 (dist.), 10,350 (t.).

Limbach, t., Saxony, **Germany**; hosiery, textiles, machines; p. (1989) 22,526.

Limbe. See **Blantyre-Limbe.**

Limbourg, prov., N.E. **Belgium**; bordering Neth.; mainly agr.; coal-mng. in Campine region; cap. Hasselt; a. 2,409 km²; p. (1993) 763,565.

Limburg, prov., S.E. **Neth.**; bordering on Belgium and W. Germany; drained by R. Maas; former coalmng.; new inds. to relieve unemployment; a. 2,191 km²; p. (1993) 1,119,942.

Limeira, t., São Paulo, **Brazil**; ctr. of orange cultivation; hats, matches; p. (1985) 187,800.

Limerick, co., Munster, **R.o.I.**; agr., livestock, fishing; a. 3,385 km²; p. (1986) 164,569.

Limerick, cap. of Limerick, **R.o.I.**; spt. at head of Shannon estuary; bacon, tanning, shipbldg.; p. (1986) 56,279.

Limmat, R., **Switzerland**; trib. of R. Aare; flows through c. of Zürich; 128 km long.

Lim Fjord, shallow strait, Jutland, **Denmark**; connects N. Sea with Kattegat; contains I. of Mors.

Limoges, c., cap. of Haute-Vienne dep., **France**; to N.W. of Central Massif; anc. t., celebrated in middle ages for goldsmith's work, later for enamel ware and porcelain; cath.; p. (1990) 136,407 (c.), 170,065 (met.a.).

Limón, spt., **Costa Rica**; on Caribbean; oil refining nearby; p. (1984) 67,784 (dist.).

Limousin, region and former prov., central **France**; to W. of Auvergne; inc. deps. Corrèze, Haute-Vienne, Creuse, plateau, average alt. 300 m, composed of old crystalline rocks; exposed damp climate; infertile, some pastoral agr.; kaolin; ch. t.; Limoges; p. (1990) 722,900.

Limpopo or **Crocodile R., S. Africa, Moçambique**, and **Zimbabwe**; lower R. forms a fertile valley 1,600 km long.

Linares, prov., central **Chile**; thermal springs in Andes; cereals and vineyards in valleys; cap. Linares; a. 9,816 km².

Linares, t., Jaén prov., **Spain**; silver-lead mines; metallurgical inds.; p. (1981) 51,278.

Lincoln, c., co. t., l. gov. dist., Lincs., **Eng.**; on R. Witham in gap through Lincoln Edge; impt. Roman t.; cath., cas.; heavy engin., iron foundries, bricks, lime, seed milling, malting; p. (1993) 85,500 (dist.).

Lincoln, c., cap. of Nebraska, **USA**; univ.; educational ctr.; grain and cattle mkt.; flour mills, agr. machin., cars, chemicals, rubber gds.; p. (1990) 191,972.

Lincoln Edge, limestone ridge, Lincs. and Humberside, **Eng.**; runs N. from Ancaster through Lincoln to Humber; narrow ridge with steep scarp slope to W., broken by R. Witham at Lincoln; iron-ore deposits worked in N. nr. Scunthorpe; sheep, barley; rarely exceeds 90 m alt.

Lincolnshire, non-met. co., **Eng.**; between Humberside non-met. co. and the Wash; fertile soil on low-lying fenland; intensive agr., arable crops, bulbs, market gardening; food-processing; formerly divided into 3 admin. parts: Holland, Kesteven, and Lindsey; a. 5,884 km²; p. (1993) 601,400.

Lincoln Wolds, low plateau, Lincs. and Humberside, **Eng.**; runs N. 72 km from Wash to Humber; chalk covered with glacial deposits; mixed farming, grains, roots, sheep; lge. farm units; scantily populated; rise to approx. 135 m

Lindau, t. Baden-Württemberg, Germany; on I. in Bodensee; tourist resort; p. (1986) 23,100.

Lindisfarne or **Holy I.,** off cst. of Northumberland, **Eng.**; connected to mainland by stretch of sand and causeway at low tide; abbey founded 635 A.D. as first establishment of Celtic Christianity in Eng.

Lindsey. See Lincolnshire.

Line Is., Pac. Oc., coral gr. admin. by U.K., except Palmyra, Kingman and Jarvis, which belong to USA; coconuts; airfields, meteorological stas.

Lin-i (formerly **Ichow**), t., Shandong, **China**; at foot of Shandong Highlands.

Linköping, t., S.E. **Sweden**; aero-engin., pianos, furniture; cath.; p. (1992) 126,377.

Linlithgow, burgh, W. Lothian, **Scot.**; distilling, brewing, paper, shoes; birthplace of Mary Queen of Scots; p. (1991) 11,866.

Linnhe, Loch, Lochaber, Argyll and Bute, **Scot.**; 21 m. long; entrance to Caledonian canal.

Linslade. See Leighton Buzzard.

Linz, c., cap. of Upper **Austria**; pt. on Danube; comm. and industl. ctr. with iron and steel wks.; cath.; p. (1991) 202,855.

Lipa, c., Luzon, **Philippines**; sugar, tobacco, cocoa, maize; processing; p. (1990) 160,117.

Lipari Is. or **Aeolian Is.,** volcanic gr. between Sicily and toe of **Italy**; inc. Stromboli (927 m), Lipari, Vulcano, Salina; olives, grapes, currants, pumice; p. (1981) 10,208.

Lipetsk, c., **Russia**; on Voronezh R.; ctr. of iron-ore mng. a.; engin., steel, ferro-alloys; health resort; p. (1989) 450,000.

Lippe, R., **Germany**; trib. of Rhine; paralleled by L. canal; forms N. bdy. of Ruhr industl. dist.; 176 km long.

Lippstadt, t., N. Rhine–Westphalia, **Germany**; on R. Lippe; metallurgy, textiles rly. ctr.; p. (1986) 60,100.

Liri, R., central **Italy**; rises in Alban Hills, flows S.E. to Cassino and then S.W. to G. of Gaeta; valley followed by main road from Rome to Naples; length 168 km.

Lisbon (**Lisboa**), c., cap of **Portugal**; on R. Tagus, 14 km from mouth; spt. with fine natural harbour; cas., cath., univ.; admin., comm., and industl. ctr.; expanding inds., airpt.; attracts p. from rural areas; p. (1987) 830,500.

Lisburn, t., l. gov. dist., **N. Ireland**; on R. Lagan, 10 km S.W. of Belfast; p. (1991) 99,458 (dist.), 42,110 (t.).

Lisieux, t., Calvados dep., N. **France**; historic t., severely damaged in second world war; cath.; Camembert cheese; p. (1982) 25,823.

Liskeard, mkt. t., Caradon, Cornwall, **Eng.**; on R. Looe at S. edge of Bodmin Moor; p. (1981) 6,316.

Lismore, t., N.S.W., **Australia**; pt. on Richmond R.; dairying, sugar refining, maize, potatoes, textiles, engin., bacon; p. (1981) 24,033.

Lismore, mkt. t., Waterford, **R.o.I.**; on Blackwater R.; cas.; p. (1986) 703.

Listowel, t., Kerry, **R.o.I.**; on R. Feale; cas. ruins; p. (1986) 3,494.

Litherland, t., Sefton, Merseyside, **Eng.**; N. sub. of Liverpool; p. (1981) 21,946.

Lithuania, former constituent rep., USSR; borders Baltic Sea; agr. development on reclaimed marshland; dairy farming, stockraising, fishing, timber inds., food-processing, ship bldg., textiles, machin.; cap. Vilnius; a. 65,201 km²; p. (1994) 3·74m.

Litoměřice, t., **Czech Rep.**; in Bohemia on R. Elbe (Labe); cath.; brewing, agr. ctr.; p. (1984) 28,844.

Little Belt (**Lille Bælt**), strait, **Denmark**; separates Fyn I. from Jutland; too shallow for lge. ships; road/rly., motorway bridges cross narrow N. section nr. Frederidicia; 48 km long.

Little Bighorn, R., Wyo, Mont., **USA**; Custer's last battle on ridge overlooking R. (1876); 144 km long.

Littleborough, t., Gtr. Manchester, **Eng.**; textiles and textile finishing; p. (1981) 13,861.

Littlehampton, t., Arun, West Sussex, **Eng.**; on S. cst. at mouth of R. Arun; holiday resort, sm. spt.; p. (1981) 22,181.

Little Lever, t., Gtr. Manchester, **Eng.**; 5 km S.E. of Bolton; residtl. and industl.; p. (1981) 11,439.

Little Rock, c., cap. of Ark., **USA**; N.E. of Hot Springs, on Ark. R. opposite N. Little Rock; comm. and mnf. ctr. in rich cotton and dairy farming a.; bauxite nearby; p. (1990) 175,795 (c.), 513,117 (met. a. with N. Little Rock).

Littoria. See Latina.

Liuchow, See Liuzhou.

Liuzhou (**Liuchow**), c., Guangxi, S. **China**; on trib. of Xijiang; route ctr. and R. pt.; p. (1984) 446,900.

Liverpool, c., spt., met. dist., Merseyside, **Eng.**; on N. bank at entrance to Mersey estuary; deep-sea container berths at Seaforth; shipping and ship-repairing; elec. mnfs. and engin., flour milling, sugar refining, seed and rubber processing, cars; cath., univ.; second Mersey tunnel opened 1971; freeport (1984) to help revive docks; p. (1993) 477,000.

Liverpool, t., N.S.W., **Australia**; within met. a. of Sydney; major source of poultry, vegetables and dairy prods. for Sydney.

Livingston, new t. (1962), W. Lothian, **Scot.**; p. (1991) 41,647.

Livingstone, t., **Zambia**; on Zambesi R. where rly. bridges R.; stands at c. 900 m; former cap.; sawmilling ctr.; p. (1989) 102,000.

Livorno (**Leghorn**), spt., cap. of L. prov., **Italy**; on Ligurian Sea; shipbldg., machin., chemicals, iron and steel wks., oil refining; exp. wine, olive oil, textiles, marble; p. (1992) 166,394.

Lizard, The, C., Cornwall, **Eng.**; S. point of Eng.

Ljubljana, c., cap. of **Slovenia** (formerly Yugoslavia); on trib. of Sava R.; industl. ctr., local coal, hydroelectric power; route ctr.; airport; univ., mediaeval fortress; ctr. of Slovene nat. movement in 19th cent.; p. (1981) 305,211.

Llanberis, pass, Gwynedd, N. **Wales**; between Snowdon and Clyder Fawr; road carries heavy tourist traffic; summit 356 m; nearby tourist resort of Llanberis.

Llandarcy, v., West Glamorgan, S. **Wales**; on cst. Swansea Bay, Bristol Channel; lge. oil refinery; pipeline to Angle Bay, Pembroke.

Llandeilo, mkt. t., Dinefwr, Dyfed, **Wales**; in vale of Towy, E. of Carmarthen; cas.; p. (1981) 1,614.

Llandovery, t., Dinefwr, Dyfed, **Wales**; on R. Bran, nr. confluence with Towy; mkt. ctr. for rural a.; p. (1981) 1,691.

Llandrindod Wells, t., Radnor, Powys, **Wales**; medicinal waters; p. (1981) 4,186.

Llandudno, t., Aberconwy, Gwynedd, **Wales**; between Gr. Ormes and Little Ormes headlands; resort; p. (1981) 18,991.

Llanelli, l. gov. dist., Dyfed, **Wales**; pt. on Burry inlet, 18 km N.W. of Swansea; industl. and comm. ctr.; coal mng., steel, and tinplate wks., mng. machin.; cas.; p. (1993) 74,000 (dist.).

Llanfairfechan, t., Aberconwy, Gwynedd, **Wales**; at foot of Penmaenmawr mtn.; seaside resort; granite quarrying; p. (1981) 3,780.

Llanfyllin, t., Powys, **Wales**; anc. mkt. t.; p. (1981) 1,207.

Llangefni, t., Anglesey, Gwynedd, **Wales**; in ctr. of the I.; mkt. and agr. t.; p. (1981) 4,265.

Llangollen, t., Glyndwr, Clwyd, **Wales**; on R. Dee; vale of L., tourist ctr.; annual Eisteddfod; p. (1981) 3,058.

Llanidloes, t., Powys, **Wales**; on R. Severn; surrounded by hills; anc. mkt. house; p. (1981) 2,416.

Llanos, lowland region, **Venezuela** and **Colombia**, S. America; drained by R. Orinoco and tribs.; high temperatures throughout year, but rain chiefly in summer; ch. vegetation, coarse grass which withers during dry season (Dec. to May).

Llanos de Urgel, upland region, Lérida, N.E. **Spain**; semi-arid; formerly steppe-land, now irrigated by R. Segre; vine, olive, maize, tobacco.

Llanrwst, mkt. t., Aberconwy, Gwynedd, **Wales**; on R. Conway; tourist ctr.; p. (1981) 2,931.

Llanstephan, v., Dyfed, **Wales**; at mouth of R. Towy; ruins of Norman cas.

Llantrisant, new t., Taff-Ely, Mid Glamorgan, S. Wales; iron-ore quarrying; Royal Mint.

Llantwit Major, t. s. Glamorgan, **Wales**; famous centre of learning in Celtic times.

Llanwrtyd Wells, t., Brecknock, Powys, **Wales**; once a spa; resort; p. (1981) 488.

Lleyn, peninsula, Gwynedd, N. **Wales**; from Snowdonia to Bardsey I.; crystalline rocks form hills in E., otherwise low, undulating; pastoral farming, sheep, cattle; sm. seaside resorts; ch. t. Pwllheli; a. 466 km².

Lliw Valley, l. gov. dist., West Glamorgan, **Wales**; comprises Pontardawe and Llwchwr; p. (1993) 64,600.

Llwchwr, t., Lliw Valley, West Glamorgan, S. **Wales**; p. (1981) 26,864.

Llwchwr or **Loughor**, R., S. **Wales**; in lower course forms bdy. between Dyfed and West Glamorgan, empties into Burry inlet.

Loanhead, burgh, Midlothian, **Scot.**; 8 km S.E. of Edinburgh; coal, engin.; p. (1991) 5,659.

Lobito, spt., **Angola**; on Atl. Oc.; 29 km N. of Benguela; fine natural deepwater harbour; rly. terminus; varied exps.; oil-refinery.

Locarno, t., **Switzerland**; on L. Maggiore; tourist ctr.; L. treaty 1925; p. (1986) 14,341.

Lochaber, mtnous. l. gov. dist., Highland Reg., **Scot.**; bounded by Loch Linnhe and Loch Leven; inc. Ben Nevis; hydroelec. power; a. 4,465 km²; p. (1993) 19,369.

Lochalsh. *See* Kyle of Lochalsh.

Lochgelly, burgh, Dunfermline, l. gov. dist., **Scot.**; nr. Dunfermline; p. (1991), 7,044.

Lochgilphead, co. t., Argyll and Bute, **Scot.**; at head of Loch Gilp, 3 km N. of Ardrishaig; tourist ctr.; p. (1991) 2,421.

Lochmaben, burgh, Annandale and Eskdale, **Scot.**; in Annandale, 11 km N.E. of Dumfries; p. (1991) 2,024.

Lockerbie, burgh, Annandale and Eskdale, **Scot.**; in Annandale, 16 km E. of Dumfries; sheep mkt.; air disaster 1988, caused by terrorist bomb; p. (1991) 3,982.

Lockport, t., N.Y., **USA**; on N.Y. st. barge canal, 38 km N.E. of Buffalo; power from Niagara falls supplies paper, metal, and other inds.; p. (1980) 24,844.

Lodi, t., **Italy**; on R. Adda, S.E. of Milan; cath.; scene of Napoleon's victory over Austrians 1796; p. (1981) 42,873.

Lodore Falls, waterfalls, Cumbria, **Eng.**; in Watendlath beck at foot of Derwentwater.

Łódź, c. and prov., central **Poland**; second c. of rep. and ctr. of textile ind.; machin., elec. equipment, chemicals, metals; univ.; cultural ctr.; problems of water-supply; p. (1989) 849,204 (c.), 1,139,400 (prov.).

Lofoten Is., storm-swept chain of Is. off N.W. cst. **Norway** within Arctic Oc., stretching 240 km; cod and herring fisheries among richest in world.

Loftus, t. Langbaurgh, Cleveland, **Eng.**; on N.E. flank of Cleveland Hills; p. (1981) 8,477.

Logan, Mount, S.E. Yukon, **Canada**, E. of Alaska; alt. 5,959 m.

Logroño, t., N. **Spain**; on Ebro R.; in wine growing a.; industl. and agr. ctr.; p. (1991) 126,760.

Loire, R., **France**; longest in cty., flows from Cevennes mtns. to Atl. Oc. at St. Nazaire; vineyards and many castles in attractive valley; 1,000 km long.

Loire, dep., E. central **France**; in part of the former provs. of Beaujolais and Lyonnais; agr.; coal mng., cattle raising; cap. St. Etienne; a. 4,799 km²; p. (1990) 746,300.

Loire-Atlantique, dep., W. **France**; mainly agr., salt-marsh on cst.; inds. at cap. Nantes; a. 6,980 km²; p. (1990) 1,052,200.

Loiret, dep., N. central **France**; agr., vineyards, distilling, mftg.; cap. Orléans; a. 6,812 km²; p. (1990) 580,600.

Loir-et-Cher, dep., central **France**; contains fertile a. of Beauce; cap. Blois; a. 6,421 km²; p. (1990) 305,900.

Lokeren, industl. t., **Belgium**; between Ghent and Antwerp; textiles, chemicals, tobacco; p. (1993) 35,435.

Lokoja, t. **Nigeria**; at confluence of Rs. Niger and Benue; R. pt.; iron-ore nearby.

Lolland or **Laaland**, Danish I. part of **Denmark** in Baltic Sea; a. 1,241 km²; agr. forests; ch. ts. Maribo, Nakshov; p. (1990) 73,191.

Lomami, R., central **Zaire**; trib. of Zaïre R., rich coal-bearing strata at confluence; 1,812 km long.

Lombardy, Plain of, N. **Italy**; extensive low-land flanked by Alps, Apennines, Adriatic Sea; built up by alluvium from R. Po, its tribs. and R. Adige; intensively cultivated; rice, maize, flax, clover, lucerne, wheat, apples, dairy cattle; densely populated; many industl. ts.; Milan, Novara, Pavia, etc.; p. of region (1992) 8,882,408

Lombok, one of the lesser Sunda Is., **Indonesia**; mtnous. volcanic terrain; Wallace's Line passes between Lombok and Bali; ch. t. Mataram; p. 1,300,000.

Lomé, spt., cap. of **Togo**, W. Africa; on G. of Guinea; deepwater pt.; exp. cacao, cotton, palm prods.; phosphates; p. (1987) 500,000.

Lomond, Loch, Stirling, lgst. loch in **Scot.**, stud-ded with Is., surrounded by hills with Ben Lomond on E. side; a. 70 km².

Łomża, t. and prov., **Poland**; on Narew R., metal inds., foodstuffs; p. (1989) 57,976 (t.), 344,500 (prov.)

London, cap. of UK, **Eng.**; at head of Thames estuary; seat of govt., world ctr. of finance and communication; cultural and artistic ctr.; comprises the City, 12 inner and 20 outer bors.; Port of London; upstream docks now closed; main pt. downstream at Tilbury; currently losing p. and inds. to outer met. a.; univs. (London, Brunel, City), caths., many historic bldgs., thea-tres, museums, galleries, libraries, and parks; p. (1993) 3,900 (City of London), 2,647,400 (Inner London), 6,933,000 (Greater London).

London, t., Ont., **Canada**; on R. Thames, 104 km W. of Hamilton; industl. ctr.; univ.; p. (1986) 269,140 (c.), 342,302 (met a.).

Londonderry or Derry, N. **Ireland**; on left bank of R. Foyle, 6 km upstream from Lough Foyle; shirt mftg.; textiles; acetylene from naphtha; training ctr. for ind.; p. (1991) 21,485.

Londrina, c., Paraná, **Brazil**; industl. and agr. ctr.; coffee, maize, cotton, livestock; p. (1991) 540,982.

Long Beach, c., Cal., **USA**; Pac. cst. resort and industl. suburb of Los Angeles met. a.; p. (1990) 429,433 (c.). *See* Los Angeles.

Longbenton, t., Tyne and Wear, **Eng.**; 5 km N.E. of Newcastle; former coal mng.; expanded t.; p. (1981) 50,646.

Long Eaton, t. Erewash, Derbys., **Eng.**; on R. Trent, 8 km S.W. of Nottingham; former ctr. for lace mftg., elec. cables, flexible tubing, hosiery; p. (1981) 32,895.

Longford, co., Leinster, **R.o.I.**; peat bogs; dairy farming; co. t. Longford; a. 1,090 km²; p. (1986) 31,496.

Longford, co. t., Longford, **R.o.I.**; cas., cath.; mkt. t.; p. (1986) 6,457.

Long Forties Bank, submarine sandbank, N. Sea; 128 km E. of Aberdeen; valuable fishing-grounds; depth of water, from 45–75 m.

Long I., part of N.Y., **USA**; separated from mainland by East E.; contains Queens and Brooklyn bors. of N.Y. City; mkt. gardening, fisheries, oysters, holiday resorts; a. 4,356 km².

Longreach, t. Queensland, **Australia**; in ctr. of Gr. Australian (artesian) basin; collecting ctr. for cattle and wool.

Longridge, t., Ribble Valley, Lancs., **Eng.**; 10 km N.E. of Preston; p. (1981) 7,161.

Longview, t. Texas, **USA**; oil, chemicals, plastics; p. (1984) 73,300 (t.), 168,400 (met. a.).

Longwy, t., Meurthe-et-Moselle dep., N.E. **France**; on Belgian–Luxembourg frontier; upper part fortfd.; lower part industl. with iron and steel ind.

Lons-le-Saunier, cap. of Jura dep., E. **France**; saline springs; agr. ctr.; p. (1990) 20,140.

Looe, t. Caradon, Cornwall, **Eng.**; on Looe estuary; holiday resort; p. (1981) 4,499.

Lopburi, t., **Thailand**; ctr. of haematite iron deposits; former cap.

Lop Nor, marsh, Xinjiang, W. **China**; in Tarim Basin at foot of Altun Shan; ctr. of inland drainage, receives water from R. Tarim; atomic testing grounds.

Lorain, t., Ohio, **USA**; on L. Erie; shipbldg., steelwks., fisheries; p. (1990) 71,245 (c.), 271,000 (met. a. with Elyria).

Lorca, t., Murcia, **Spain**; agr. prod., woollens, chemicals; bishop's palace; p. (1981) 60,627.

Lord Howe I., forested volcanic I., S. Pac. Oc., 698 km N.E. of Sydney; palm seed ind.; admin. by N.S.W. **Australia;** p. (1981) 287.

Lorient, spt., Morbihan dep., N.W. **Fance;** on Atl.; naval shipyard, fishing harbour; p. (1982) 64,675.

Lorraine, region and former prov., N.E. **France;** inc. deps. Moselle, Meurthe-et-Moselle, Meuse, and Vosges; ch. t. Nancy; rich iron-ore deposits; impt. but declining industl. a.; mkt. gardening, vineyards; with Alsace long disputed between Germany and France; p. (1990) 2,305,700.

Los Alamos, t., N.M., **USA;** site of research for first atomic bomb; p. (1980) 11,039.

Los Angeles, c., S. Cal., **USA;** booming modern c. ("the valley of angels"), busiest in Cal.; fine harbour; riots 1992; many prosperous inds., inc. aircraft, missiles, chemicals, machin., electronic equipment, food-processing oil refining; film ctr.; earthquake 1994, p. (1990) 3,485,398 (c.), 8,863,000 (met. a. with Long Beach).

Lossiemouth, burgh, Moray, **Scot.;** on Moray F., 8 km N. of Elgin; birthplace of Ramsay MacDonald; fishing; p. (1991) 7,184.

Lostwithiel, mkt. t. Cornwall, **Eng.;** on R. Fowey S.E. of Bodmin; anc. Stannary t.

Lot, dep., S.W. **France;** livestock, wine, cereals, coals, iron; a. 5,227 km². cap. Cahors; p. (1990) 155,800.

Lot, R., S. **France;** trib. of Garonne R., 435 km long.

Lota, pt., **Chile;** coal-mng. ctr.; ceramics, copper smelting; p. (1982) 62,662.

Lot-et-Garonne, dep., S.W. **France;** agr. (cereals, vines, fruit); cap. Agen; a. 5,385 km². p. (1990) 306,000.

Lothian Region, l. gov. reg., central **Scot.;** borders F. of Forth, and inc. a. around Edinburgh; mainly industl.; a. 1,753 km². p. (1993) 753,900.

Lötschental, picturesque valley, Valais, Switzerland; ch. v. Kippel.

Loughborough, t., Charnwood, Leics., **Eng.;** on R. Soar 16 km N. of Leicester; engin., elec. gds., chemicals, textiles; univ.; former hosiery t.; bell foundry; p. (1981) 47,647.

Loughrea, mkt. t., Galway, **R.o.I.;** cotton mill; p. (1986) 3,360.

Louisiana, southern st., **USA;** Pelican St.; admitted to Union 1812; st. flower Magnolia, st. bird Eastern Brown Pelican; leading producer of rice, sugarcane, sweet potatoes, also cotton, maize, tobacco, oil, natural gas, lumber; cap. Baton Rouge; New Orleans major pt.; a. 125,675 km². p. (1990) 4,219,973.

Louisville, c., Ky., **USA;** on Ohio R.; univ.; lgst. tobacco mkt. in world; chemicals, paints, cars, machin., elec. gds., synthetic rubber; p. (1990) 269,063 (c.), 953,000 (met. a.).

Lourdes, t., **France;** on R. Pau; Catholic pilgrim centre.; slate, marble; p. (1982) 17,619.

Lourenço Marques. See Maputo.

Louth, t., East Lindsey, Lincs., **Eng.;** on E. edge of Lincoln Wolds; abbey ruins; cattle mkt., farm implements, plastic bags, corrugated board; p. (1981) 13,296.

Louth, maritime co., Leinster, **R.o.I.;** mtns., bog and barren land; salmon fishing; cap. Dundalk; a. 818 km². p. (1986) 91,810.

Louvain (Leuven), c., Brabant prov., **Belgium;** on R. Dyle; univ. (Erasmus taught here); brewing ctr., bell foundries; p. (1983) 85,592.

Low Archipelago. See Tuamotu Is.

Low Countries, name for Belgium and the Neth.

Lowell, c., Mass., **USA;** at junc. of Merrimac and Concord Rs.; 48 km N. of Boston; textiles, machin., chemicals, carpets; birthplace of Whistler; p. (1990) 103,439 (c.), 273,000 (met. a.).

Lower California (Baja California), peninsula, N.W. **Mexico;** separating G. of Cal. and Pac. Oc.; isolated, arid; divided into 2 sts., Baja California (cap. Tijuana) p. (1990) 1,657,927, and Baja California, Territorio Sur (cap. La Paz) p. (1990) 317,326; a. 143,963 km².

Lower Hutt, c., N.I., **N.Z.;** rapid industl. devel. in last 45 years; engin., plastics, textiles, vehicle assembly; p. (1991) 94,540.

Lower Saxony (Nieder Sachsen), Land, **Germany;** inc. Lüneburg heath and Harz mtns.; cap. Hanover; a. 47,205 km². p. (1992) 7,476,000.

Lowestoft, fish pt., Waveney, Suffolk, **Eng.;** on E. Anglian cst. 14 km S. of Gr. Yarmouth; holiday resort, nr. Broads; food processing plants; base for N. Sea gas; p. (1981) 55,231.

Lowther Hills, mtns., between Strathclyde and Dumfries and Galloway Regs., **Scot.;** hgst. point 733 m.

Loyalty Is., S. **Pac. Oc.;** included in Fr. administration of New Caledonia; copra; lgst. Is. Maré, Lifou, Uvéa; a. c. 2,100 km².

Lozère, dep., S.E. **France;** traversed by Cevennes mtns.; cap. Mende; a. 5,170 km². p. (1990) 72,800.

Lualaba, R., **Zaïre,** central **Africa;** rises nr. Lubumbashi in Shaba prov., flows N. circa 800 km to Kikondja, where joined by R. Lufira to form R. Zaïre; name also applied to main stream of R. Zaïre as far downstream as Ponthierville.

Luanda, c. cap. of **Angola;** pt. on Atl. Oc.; exp. coffee, cotton, palm prod.; industl. ctr.; foodstuffs, tobacco, plastics; oil refining; hydro-electric power; p. (1988) 1,200,000.

Luang Prabang, c., N.W. **Laos;** at confluence of Mekong and Kahn Rs.; rubber, rice, teak; former royal cap.

Lubbock, c., N.W. Texas, **USA;** on Double Mountain fork of Brazos R.; ctr. of cotton-growing a.; p. (1990) 186,206.

Lübeck, c., pt. of Schleswig-Holstein, **Germany;** on Baltic Sea at mouth of Trave R.; cath.; shipbldg., machin., chemicals, textiles, iron, foodstuffs; birthplace of Thomas Mann; p. (1990) 215,200.

Lublin, c. and prov., E. **Poland;** motor vehicle and elec. engin.; agr. tr. and processing; cultural ctr., univ.; cas.; p. (1989) 348,881 (c.), 1,010,600 (prov.).

Lubumbashi (Elizabethville), t., Shaba, **Zaïre;** copper-mng. ctr.; p. (1985) 795,000.

Lucca, c., cap. of L. prov., Tuscany, **Italy;** cath., churches, palaces; noted for olive oil, pasta, wine; silk, cotton, jute, tobacco inds.; p. (1981) 91,246.

Lucena, t., Córdoba, **Spain;** olive oil, ceramics, gilt metals, wine; p. (1981) 29,717.

Lucenec, t., Czech Rep.; on Hungarian border; magnesite, textiles, sawmilling; p. (1984) 27,477.

Lucerne (Luzern), can., **Switzerland;** agr., pastoral, vineyards; oil refinery projected at Schötz/Ettiswil; cap. Lucerne; a. 1,492 km². p. (1990) 319,500.

Lucerne (Luzern), c., cap. of L. can., **Switzerland;** at N.W. end of L. Lucerne; aluminium gds., sewing machin.; tourist ctr.; p. (1990), 60,035 (c.), 161,000 (met. a.).

Lucerne, L., Switzerland; also known as L. of the Four Cantons; length 37 km; a. 70 km².

Luchon or **Bagnères-de-Luchon,** resort in Fr. Pyrenees, Haute-Garonne dep., S. **France;** warm sulphur springs; winter sports ctr.

Luchow. See Zuzhou.

Luckenwalde, t., **Germany;** on R. Nuthe; textiles, footwear, machin., wood and metals, chemicals; p. (1989) 26,552.

Lucknow, c., cap. of Uttar Pradesh st., N. **India;** on R. Gumti (trib. of Ganges); educational and cultural ctr. with textile inds.; rly. ctr.; scene of 1857 mutiny; p. (1991) 1,619,000.

Lüda, special mun., S. Liaoning prov., **China;** comprising Port Arthur Naval Base District and the pts. of Port Arthur and Talien (Dairen); chemicals, machin., shipbldg., textiles; p. (1984) 1·59 m.

Lüdenscheid, t., N. Rhine–Westphalia, **Germany;** metal mngs., domestic hardware; supplied structures for first Zeppelins; p. (1986) 73,400.

Lüderitz, t., **Namibia;** rly. pt. on desert cst.; diamonds, fishing; p. (1990) 6,000.

Ludhiana, t., Punjab st., N.W. **India;** S. of Sutlej R.; industl. ctr.; hosiery, knitwear; p. (1991) 1,043,000.

Ludlow, t., South Shrops., **Eng.;** agr. mkt.; agr. engin.; cas.

Ludwigsburg, t. Baden-Württemberg, **Germany;** N. of Stuttgart; cas.; textiles, foodstuffs, machin., toys; p. (1986) 76,900.

Ludwigshafen, t., Rhine-Palatinate, **Germany;** on R. Rhine, opposite Mannheim; chemicals, marine diesel engines, metallurgy, glass; R. pt. and rly. junc.; oil pipeline from Rotterdam under construction; p. (1990) 163,700.

Lugano, t., Ticino can., **Switzerland;** on L. Lugano; tourist resort; p. (1980) 27,815.

Lugano, L., lies at S. foot of Alps between **Switzerland and Italy;** attractive scenery, tourism; a. 49 km².

Lugansk (Voroshilovgrad), industl. t., **Ukraine**; S. of R. Donets in Donbas Region; impt. rly. engin. factories; textiles; p. (1990) 501,100.

Lugnaquilla, mtn., loftiest summit in Wicklow, **R.o.I.**; 927 m.

Lugo, c., cap. of L. prov., N.W. **Spain**; in Galicia, on Miño R.; in fertile agr. a.; cath.; p. (1987) 77,043, (est. 1991) 379,077 (prov.).

Lukuga, intermittent outlet of L. Tanganyika, **Zaïre**, linking with R. Zaïre.

Luleå, spt., N. **Sweden**, cap. of Norrbotten co.; on Lule R. at head of G. of Bothnia; iron ore; smelting plant, engin.; p. (1992) 68,924.

Luluabourg. See **Kananga**.

Lulworth Cove, sm. inlet, Dorset, **Eng.**; formed by sea breaching limestone cliffs and eroding clay behind; tourism.

Lund, t., S. **Sweden**; 16 km N.E. of Malmö; 11th cent. Romanesque cath.; univ.; publishing ctr.; p. (1992) 92,027.

Lundy I., Bristol Channel, N. Devon, **Eng.**; 19 km N.W. of Hartland Point; wildlife sanctuary; about 5 km long and 1 km wide.

Lune, R., Cumbria, **Eng.**; flows 72 km to Irish Sea; attractive valley.

Lüneburg, t., Lower Saxony, **Germany**; on Ilmenau R., S.E. of Hamburg; rly. junc., R. pt.; iron wks., chemicals; dates from 8th cent.; p. (1986) 59,500.

Lüneburg Heath, Lower Saxony, **Germany**; lies to S. of Lüneburg; glacial outwash plain of sands and gravels; heather, scrub; some agr. but infertile acid soils.

Lünen, t., N. Rhine–Westphalia, **Germany**; in Ruhr conurb.; coal, metallurgy, glass, wood; R. pt. and rly. ctr.; p. (1986) 84,400.

Lunéville, t., Meurthe-et-Moselle dep., N.E. **France**; in Lorraine, on R. Meurthe; 18th cent. château.

Lungi, t., **Sierra Leone**, W. **Africa**; nr. Freetown; only civil airport in st.

Luoyang (Loyang), c., Henan prov., **China**; industl.; ball bearing and mng. machin.; lge. car and tractor plant, oil refinery, textiles; p. (1992) 1,190,000.

Lupata Gorge, Moçambique, E. Africa; narrow pass occupied by R. Zambezi.

Lurgan, t., Craigavon, **N. Ireland**; textiles, tobacco mftg.; merging with Portadown to form new c. of Craigavon; p. (1991) 21,905.

Lusaka, c., cap. of **Zambia**; comm. and admin. ctr.; at junc. of routes to Tanzania and Malawi; motor assembly, footwear, metal prods., clothing; p. (1989) 921,000.

Lushun. See **Lüda**.

Luton, t., l. gov. dist., Beds., **Eng.**; in Chiltern Hills nr. source of R. Lea; motor vehicles, engin., hat mkg., aircraft, gear instruments, chemicals; expanded t.; p. (1993) 178,600 (dist.).

Lutong, main oil pt. of Sarawak, E. **Malaysia**; oil refining.

Lutsk, c., **Ukraine**; pt. on Styr R.; one of oldest ts. in Volhynia; coal mng., machin.; architectural monuments; p. (1990) 204,100.

Lutterworth, t., Leics., **Eng.**; church with relics of John Wyclif, religious reformer; engin.

Luxembourg, prov., S.E. **Belgium**; on Fr. border; wooded and hilly; a. 2,784 km²; cap. Arlon; p. (1993) 236,850.

Luxembourg, grand duchy, W. **Europe**; lies between Belgium, W. Germany, and France; divided into 12 admin. cans.; official language French though German frequently used; well wooded, most of a. over 300 m; economic prosperity based upon iron and steel inds. and lge. deposits of iron-ore; agr. and cattle raising impt.; sm. size of home market makes L. keen member of EU and cap. of L. contains many European organisations; tourist ind. based upon scenery and cas. ts.; a. 2,587 km²; p. (1993) 395,200.

Luxembourg, c., cap. of grand duchy of **Luxembourg**; historic t., perched above valleys of Alzette and Petrusse Rs.; cath.; seat of European Court of Justice; p. (1991) 75,377.

Luxor, t., Upper **Egypt**; on E. bank of Nile; site of Thebes; tomb of Tutankhamun; p. (1986) 138,000.

Luxulyan, St. Austell, Cornwall, **Eng.**; proposed site for nuclear power sta., fiercely opposed.

Luzon, I., lgst. and most N. of **Philippines**; mtn. ranges; fertile Cagayan valley; rice, sugar cane, cotton, coffee, hemp, tobacco; mineral deposits; cap. Manila; a. 104,688 km²; p. (1990) 28,289,866.

L'vov, c., **Ukraine**; founded 13th cent.; univ., caths.; major industl. ctr.; petroleum refining; natural gas nearby; p. (1990) 797,800.

Lyalpur, See **Faisalabad**.

Lydd, Shepway, Kent, **Eng.**; anc. t. on Romney marsh, at edge of Dungeness shingle; name given to explosive lyddite mnf. here; airport; p. (1981) 4,721.

Lydda, c., **Israel**, S.E. of Tel Aviv; major airport.

Lydney, t., Gloucs., **Eng.**; in Forest of Dean; spt. on Severn estuary; timber imports; new lt. inds.

Lyme Regis, spt., West Dorset, **Eng.**; on bdy. between Devon and Dorset; holiday resort; p. (1981) 3,447.

Lymington, t., Hants., **Eng.**; on the Solent; ferry to I. of Wight; abbey; p. (1981) 38,698.

Lymm, t., Cheshire, **Eng.**; 8 km W. of Altrincham; mainly residtl.; p. (1981) 10,364.

Lynchburg, c., Va., **USA**; on James R. in foothills of Appalachians; tobacco ctr.; p. (1984) 67,300 (c.), 142,600 (met. a.).

Lyndhurst, v., Hants., **Eng.**; recognised as cap. of New Forest; tourism.

Lynemouth, nr. Blyth, Northumberland, **Eng.**; aluminium smelter.

Lynn, industl. c., Mass., **USA**; on Mass. Bay; footwear, elec. appliances; Mary Baker Eddy lived here; p. (1980) 78,471.

Lynton, t., North Devon, **Eng.**; 27 km W. of Minehead on Bristol Channel; tourist ctr. for Exmoor; sm. harbour of Lynmouth 130 m below; devastating flood of R. Lyn 1952; p. (1981) 2,037.

Lyons, c., cap. of Rhône dep., **France**; at confluence of Rs. Saône and Rhône; silk, rayon, chemicals, engin., heavy lorries; oil refinery nearby; univ.; world ctr. for cancer research; p. (1990) 422,444 (c.), 1,262,223 (met.a.).

Lytham St. Annes, t., N. Lancs., **Eng.**; on N. cst. of Ribble estuary, 6 km S. of Blackpool holiday ctr.; p. (1981) 39,707.

Lyttleton, spt., S.I., **N.Z.**, on N. cst. of Banks peninsula; imp. pt.

M

Ma'an, t., S. **Jordan**, terminus of rly. through Amman to Beirut; Hijaz rail line to Medina; p. (1989) 108,300.

Maas, R., Dutch name for the R. Meuse after it has entered the Neth.

Maastricht, t., cap. of Limburg prov., **Neth.**; on R. Maas; pottery, glass, textiles, brewing; p. (1993) 118,285 (c.) 164,080 (met. a.).

Mablethorpe, t., East Lindsey, Lincs., **Eng.**; holiday resort; p. (1981) 7,456.

Macao, Portuguese col., S.E. **China**; increased indep. since 1975; to be returned to China in 1999; gambling, tourism, recreation for Hong Kong; new deep water port; rapid recent industl. growth (toys, textiles and transistors) with influx of capital resulting from uncertainty over the future of Hong Kong; oldest European col. in Far East (1557); a. 17 km²; p. (1990) 452,300.

Macapá, c., cap. of Amapá st., **Brazil**; at mouth of R. Amazon; rubber, cattle tr.; p. (1985) 169,600.

Macclesfield, t., l. gov. dist., Cheshire, **Eng.**; at foot of Pennines, 16 km S. of Stockport; on R. Bollin; mkt., textiles, clothing, paper prods., engin.; expanded t.; p. (1993) 151,400 (dist.).

Macdonald Is., terr. of Australia, **Antarctica**.

Macdonnell Range, mtns., N.T., **Australia**; highest part of desert tableland, centrally situated within the continent; some gold and mica mines, but development hampered by aridity and isolation; highest alt. 1,500 m.

Macduff, spt., burgh, Banff and Buchan, **Scot.**; 3 km E. of Banff; fishing; p. (1991) 3,894.

Macedonia, region of Balkan peninsula, covering parts of Greece, Yugoslavia, and Bulgaria.

Macedonia, dist., **Greece**; mtnous.; cereals, tobacco; chromium; cap. and pt. Salonika; a. 33,945 km²; p. (1981) 2,121,953.

Macedonia, rep., formerly Yugoslavia; agr., chromium; cap. Skopje; a. 27,436 km²; p. (1992) 2·06 m.

Maceio, spt. cap. of Alagôas st., **Brazil**; cotton, sugar, tobacco, soap, sawmills, distilleries; p. (1991) 628,209.

Macerata, t., cap. of M. prov., **Italy**; cath., univ.; terracotta, glass, chemicals; p. (1981) 43,782.

Macgillicuddy's Reeks, mtns., Kerry, **R.o.I.**; highest peak, Carantuohil, 1,041 m.

Machala, t., Tibet, **China**; hgst. coalmine in world.

Machilipatnam (Bandar, Masulipatnam), spt., Andhra Pradesh, **India**; on Coromandel cst.; cotton mftg., rice; p. (1991) 159,007.

Machynlleth, t., Powys, **Wales**; on R. Dovey; clothing; tourism; p. (1981) 1,768.

Macintyre, R., N.S.W., **Australia**; forms border between Queensland and N.S.W.; trib. of R. Darling; 645 km. long.

Mackay, spt., Queensland, **Australia**; sugar, artificial deep-water pt. for sugar exp.; p. (1991) 51,023 (met.a.)

Mackenzie, R., N.W. Terr., **Canada**; lgst. in N. America; rises in Rocky mtns. as Athabaska, flows into Athabaska L., leaves as Slave R., thence into Gr. Slave L., below which it is known as Mackenzie R., across arctic plains to Beaufort Sea; 4,000 km. long.

Mackenzie Mtns., N.W. Terr., **Canada**; range of Rockies, still much unexplored; game preserve; max. alt. 2,760 m.

Mâcon, t., cap. of Saône-et-Loire dep., **France**; on R. Saône; Burgundy wines; p. (1990) 38,508.

Macon, c., Ga., **USA**; on Ocmulgee R.; industl. and shipping ctr. for agr. a., cotton, livestock; cotton mftg.; p. (1990) 106,612 (c.), 281,000 (met. a. with Warner Robins).

Macquarie, I., Australian I., **S. Pac.**; 1,440 km S.E. of Tasmania; rich in wildlife, Tasmanian st. reserve (1972).

Macquarie, R., N.S.W., **Australia**; trib. of R. Darling; 960 km long.

Macroom, t., Cork, **R.o.I.**; on R. Sullane; agr., fishing; p. (1986) 2,449.

Madagascar (formerly **Malagasy Rep.**), I. off Moçambique; former Fr. col.; distinctive evolution of flora and fauna; p. engaged in agr.; rice staple food, coffee and cloves main exp.; inds. based on processing; offshore petroleum deposits; new refinery at ch. pt. of Toamasina; cap. Antananarivo; a. 587,041 km.²; p. (1991) 12·37 m.

Madang, t., **Papua New Guinea**; entrepôt pt. on N. cst.; international airpt.; p. (1990) 27,057.

Madeira, R., **Brazil**; trib. of Amazon; with Mamoré R., c. 3,200 km long.

Madeira Is., volcanic archipelago, Atl. Oc., part of met. **Portugal**; partial autonomy by regional gov. (1977); wine, sugar, fruits; tourism; cap. Funchal on Madeira I., lgst. of gr.; a. 790 km²; p. (1986) 269,500.

Madhya Pradesh, st., **India**; absorbed sts. Bhopal, Vindhya Pradesh, Madhya Bharat, 1956; rice, jute, pulses, oilseeds, cotton; forests; manganese, coal, marble, limestone; cotton textile mftg.; cap. Bhopal; a. 443,452 km²; p. (1991) 66,181,170.

Madinat ash Sha'b (Al Ittihad), t. **Yemen**; cap. of Democratic Rep. of Yemen; N.W. of Aden.

Madison, c., cap. of Wis., **USA**; educational and admin. ctr.; univ.; mnfs. agr. tools, footwear; p. (1990) 191,262 (c.), 367,085 (met. a.).

Madiun, t., Java, **Indonesia**; agr. and comm. ctr.; engin.; p. (1980) 150,502.

Madras, c., cap. of Tamil Nadu st., **India**; spt. on Bay of Bengal, on Coromandel cst.; cath., univ.; comm. and mftg. ctr.; textile mills, tanneries, potteries, chemical plants; oil refinery projected; p. (1991) 3,841,000.

Madras. *See* Tamil Nadu.

Madre de Dios, R., **Bolivia**; trib. of R. Madeira; rises in Peru; 960 km long.

Madrid, c., cap. of **Spain**; and of M. prov. on Manzanares R.; stands at 665 m (highest cap. in Europe) in vast open plains; although remote with relatively few inds. is ctr. of Spanish admin. and communications; univ., cath., Prado gallery; printing, publishing; p. (1991) 2,984,576 (c.), 4,935,642 (prov.).

Madura, I., **Indonesia**; off N.E. Java; dry climate, limestone soils; arable and pastoral agr.; salt; a. 4,584 km²; p. c. 2,000,000.

Madurai, t., Tamil Nadu, **India**; univ., impt. textile ctr.; p. (1991) 941,000.

Maebashi, c., central Honshu, **Japan**; N.W. Kanto

plain; silk textile ctr.; p. (1990) 286,261.

Maelstrom, tidewater whirlpool, in Lofoten Is., **Norway**.

Maentwrog, v., Gwynedd, N. **Wales**; in Vale of Ffestiniog, 3 km E. of Ffestiniog; hydroelectric power sta. run by Nuclear Electric.

Maesteg, t., Ogwr, Mid Glamorgan, **Wales**; dormitory t. for steel wks. at Pt. Talbot; coal mng., cosmetics; p. (1981) 20,888.

Mafeking, **(Mafikeng)** t., N.E. Cape Prov., **Bophuthaswana S. Africa**; famous siege at outbreak of Boer War 1899–1900; p. (1980) 6,500.

Magadan, spt., **Russia**; on N. side of Sea of Okhotsk; marine engin.; fishing; p. (1989) 152,000.

Magadi, L., **Kenya**; in Gr. Rift valley; carbonate of soda extracted.

Magdalena, R., **Colombia**, forms basis of inland navigation system, opening up interior; 1,600 km long.

Magdeburg, cap., Saxony - Anhalt *Land*, **Germany**; on R. Elbe; cath.; beet-sugar ctr., sugar-refineries; chemicals, steel, mng. machin., heavy engin.; route ctr. and lge. inland pt.; p. (1990) 277,200.

Magelang, t., Java, **Indonesia**; tr. ctr.; tannery; p. (1980) 123,484.

Magellan, strait, between Tierra del Fuego and Chile, separates Atl. and Pac. Ocs.

Maggiore, L., N. **Italy**–**Switzerland**; a. 212 km²; contains Borromean Is.; tourist resort.

Magherafelt, l. gov. dist., centred on t. of M., **N. Ireland**; agr. a. bordering L. Neagh; (1991) 36,293 (dist.), 6,682 (t.).

Maghreb, collective name given to Arabic-speaking countries bordering Mediterranean in N. Africa, inc. Algeria, Morocco and Tunisia.

Magnet Mtn., S. Urals, **Russia**; very rich deposit of magnetite iron ore; smelted at Magnitogorsk, and in Kuzbas region.

Magnitogorsk, c., **Russia**; in S. Urals, on R. Ural; sited on magnetite deposits; metallurgical ctr.; oil pipeline from Shkapovo in Bashkira; p. (1989) 440,000.

Mahajanga (Majunga), t., **Madagascar**; second t. and pt.; meat conserves, sacks, cement; p. (1990) 121,967.

Mahalla El Kubra. *See* El Mahalla el Kubra.

Mahanadi, R., **India**; flows from Orissa to Bay of Bengal; forms extensive delta; sugar and rice growing; 832 km long.

Maharashtra, st., W. **India**; on Arabian Sea; ch. ts. Bombay (cap.), Poona, Nagpur; fertile lava soils; impt. cotton-growing dist. of Deccan; a. 307,477 km²; p. (1991) 78,937,187.

Mahé, former Fr. prov., S. **India**; united with India 1954; cap. Mahé part of Union Territory of Pondicherry; p. (1991) 33,425.

Mahon, spt., cap. of Minorca, Balearic Is., **Spain**; p. (1981) 21,624.

Maidenhead, t., Windsor and Maidenhead, Berks., **Eng.**; on R. Thames, 14 km above Windsor; residtl.; p. (1981) 49,038; *See* **Windsor**.

Maidens, The, gr. of dangerous rocks off Larne cst., **N. Ireland**.

Maidstone, co. t., l. gov. dist., Kent, **Eng.**; on R. Medway; regional ctr.; brewing, paper, agr. tools, confectionery, timber inds.; p. (1993) 138,500. (dist.).

Maiduguri, t., **Nigeria**; cap. Bornu st.; on rly. from Bornu; mkt.; p. (1983) 231,000.

Maikop, c. cap. of Adygei aut. oblast, Krasnodar terr., **Russia**; oilfields nearby; oil-refineries, woodwkg., food-processing; p. (1989) 149,000.

Main, R., **Germany**; joins Rhine opposite Mainz; linked with Danube via Ludwig canal; and newer Rhine-Main-Danube canal creating waterway from N. Sea to Black Sea of 3,500 km; 448 km long.

Main Range, central mtns. of **W. Malaysia**; rise to over 2,100 m.

Maine, st., New England, **USA**; Pine tree St.; admitted to Union 1820; st. flower White Pine Tassel, st. bird Chickadee; mtnous., with much forest; potatoes, paper, pulp, metals, woollens, shoes, processed foods; cap. Augusta; ch. spt. Portland; a. 86,027 km²; p. (1990) 1,227,928.

Maine-et-Loire, dep., **France**; agr. vineyards; cap. Angers; a. 7,280 km²; p. (1990) 705,900.

Mainland, I., lgst. of Shetlands, **Scot.**; p. (1991) 17,596.

Mainland, I., lgst. of Orkneys, *see* **Pomona**.

Mainz, c., cap of Rhineland-Palatinate, **Germany**; at confluence of Rs. Rhine and Main; R. pt.; cath., univ., cas.; cement, engin., optical glass, food-processing; p. (1990) 180,800.

Maisons-Alfort, t., **France**; S.E. sub. of Paris; p. (1990) 54,065.

Maitland, t., N.S.W., **Australia**; on R. Hunter, nr. Newcastle; ctr. for fertile Hunter Valley; coal mng. decreasing; p. (1981) 38,865.

Majes, R., S. **Peru**; valley a. site of projected irrigation scheme; 240 km. long.

Majorca (Mallorca), lgst. of Balearic Is., **Spain**; major tourist ctr.; ch. t. and pt. Palma; a. 3,639 km²; p. (1981) 561,215.

Majunga. *See* **Mahajanga.**

Makalu, mtn., Nepal and Tibet, **China**; fifth hgst. mtn. in world; part of Himalayas; alt. 8,486 m.

Makasar. *See* **Ujung Pandang.**

Makassar, strait, **Indonesia**; separates Kalimantan from Sulawesi; 384 km wide.

Makeyevka, c., **Ukraine**; in Donets basin; metallurgical and coal-mng. ctr.; p. (1990) 426,700.

Makhachkala, c., cap. of Dagestan aut. rep., **Russia**; pt. on Caspian Sea; comm. and industl. ctr.; oil refineries linked by pipeline to Grozny fields; p. (1989) 317,000.

Makó, t., **Hungary**; on Maros R., nr. Romanian bdy.; comm. and agr. ctr.; p. (1984) 30,000.

Makran, dist., **Pakistan** and **Iran**; coastal dist.; lowland route between India and Middle E.

Makurdi, t. **Nigeria**, W. Africa; on R. Benue; mkt. for palm prod., groundnuts; rly. bridge across R. Benue.

Makwar, v., **Sudan**, N.E. Africa; on Blue Nile; site of Sennar Dam.

Malabar Coast, India; name applied to W. cst. of India from Goa to southern tip of peninsula at C. Comorin; sand dunes backed by lagoons; coastlands intensively cultivated, rice, spices, rubber, coconuts; ch. pt. Cochin.

Malabo (Santa Isabel), cap of **Equatorial Guinea**; on Marcias Nguema I.; ch. pt. for I., exp. cacao; comm. and financial ctr.; p. (1986) 10,000.

Malacca, st., S.W. **W. Malaysia**; originally part of Brit. Straits Settlements (*q.v.*); cap. M.; a. 1,658 km²; p. (1980) 464,754.

Malacca, strait, separates Sumatra, **Indonesia**, from **W. Malaysia**; 38 km wide at narrowest point; international routeway but attempts by Malaysia and Indonesia to claim it as territorial water.

Maladetta, with Pic d'Anéto, hgst. point in Pyrenees, **Spain**; alt. 3,408 m.

Malaga, c. cap. of Malaga prov., **Spain**; in Andalusia on Bay of M.; impt. spt.; olive oil, wine, fruit; oil pipeline from Puertollano; winter resort; cath., citadel; birthplace of Picasso; p. (1991) 524,748 (c.), 1,177,259 (prov.).

Malagasy Rep. *See* **Madagascar.**

Malang, t., Java, **Indonesia**; ctr. of fertile agr. basin; p. (1983) 560,000.

Mälar, L., S.E. **Sweden**; connected with Baltic by Södertelge canal; 1,260 ls.; length 128 km; a. 1,235 km².

Malatya, c., cap. of M. prov., central **Turkey**; at foot of Taurus mtns.; ctr. of rich agr. a.; fruit, opium; p. (1990) 304,760 (c.), 702,055 (prov.).

Malawi, land locked rep., Central **Africa**; L. Malawi to S. and E.; tropical climate modified by alt.; few natural resources; economy based on agr.; one of most fertile soils in Africa but only 50 per cent cultivated; exp. tobacco and tea; new cap at Lilongwe (old cap. Zomba); a. 117,614 km²; p. (1991) 8,560,000.

Malawi, L., central **Africa**; southward extension of the Gr. Rift valley; *c.* 450 m a.s.l.; 560 km by 64 km; drains by R. Shire into R. Zambezi; petroleum under L. bed.

Malaya. *See* **Malaysia, West.**

Malay Archipelago, lge. gr. of Is. extending 7,680 km from Nicobar Is. in Bay of Bengal to Solomon Is. in Pac.; inc. Sumatra, Java, Kalimantan, Sulawesi, Philippines, New Guinea, Bismarck archipelago.

Malaysia, East, part of **Fed. of Malaysia**; inc. Sarawak and Sabah (formerly Brit. N. Borneo); less developed than W. Malaysia; p. concentrated on cst; hill tribes engaged in hunting in interior; diversification of Malaysian agr. has introduced cocoa as a major crop; oil major exp., exploration off cst.; separated from W. Malaysia by S. China Sea; a. 200,971 km²; p. (1980) 2,318,628.

Malaysia, Federation of, indep. federation (1963), S.E. **Asia**; member of Brit. Commonwealth; inc. W. Malaysia (Malaya) and E. Malaysia (Borneo sts. of Sarawak and Sabah); cap. Kuala Lumpur; a. 329,293 km²; p. (1993) 19·03 m.

Malaysia, West (Malaya), part of **Federation of Malaysia**; consists of wide peninsula S. of Thailand; most developed in W.; world's leading producer of natural rubber; worlds leading exporter of tin; but decline in world prices of both these prod. has encouraged economic diversification; timber exports also declining due to efforts to conserve rainforest; palm oil, petrol, electrical and electronic machin. now impt. export; new gas discoveries, attempts to convert palm oil into diesel fuel; free port at Pasir Gudang to divert exports from Singapore; 35 per cent of p. Chinese; a. 131,588 km²; p. (1985) 15,557,000.

Malbork (Marienburg), t., Elblag prov., **Poland**; R. pt. on Nogat R.; p. (1989) 39,016.

Malden, t., Mass., **USA**; mftg. sub. of Boston; rubber gds., hosiery, furniture; p. (1980) 53,386.

Maldive Is., indep. rep. (1968) former Brit., prot., **Indian Oc.**; chain of coral atolls *c.* 640 km S.W. of Sri Lanka; 1,067 Is., 193 inhabited; economy based on fishing (bonito and tuna); dried fish main exp.; modernisation of fishing with Japanese aid; coconuts, copra, coconut oil, coir, cowrie shells; cap. Male; former Brit. air base on Gan. I. (until 1976); a. 298 km²; p. (1993) 238,363.

Maldon, t., l. gov. dist., Essex, **Eng.**; sm. pt. at head of Blackwater estuary; agr. machin., steel window-frames, flour-milling; p. (1993) 53,100 (dist.).

Malegaon, t., Maharashtra, **India**; in Satmala Hills N.E. of Bombay; p. (1991) 342,000.

Malham Cove, North Yorks., **Eng.**; in Craven dist. of N. Pennines, 16 km N.W. of Skipton; semi-circular amphitheatre limestone cliffs from base of which emerges R. Aire.

Mali, Rep. of, W. Africa; landlocked st.; former Fr. col. of Soudan; dry semi-desert climate in S.; extends into Sahara desert in N.; badly affected by Sahelian drought since 1971; few natural resources; nomadic pastoralist p. in N.; only 20 per cent of a. cultivable; livestock basis of inds. (hides, wool, etc.) and exps.; many minerals but not exploited; cap. Bamako; a. 1,204,350 km²; p. (1990) 9,362,000.

Malinda, t., **Kenya**; growing tourist resort on Indian Ocean cst.

Malin Head, Donegal, **R.o.I.**; most N. point.

Malines (Mechelen), t., **Belgium**; on R. Dyle; cath.; rly. ctr., textiles, furniture; once famous for lace; p. (1993) 75,740.

Malling, t., Kent, **Eng.**; 5 km W. of Maidstone; fruit, chemicals. *See* **Tonbridge.**

Mallow, mkt. t., Cork, **R.o.I.**; on R. Blackwater; agr. fishing, flour mills, tanneries, condensed milk, dehydrated foods; p. (1986) 6,488.

Malmesbury, t., North Wilts., **Eng.**; anc. hilltop t. in Cotswolds; mkt.; abbey; elec. engin.; birthplace of Thomas Hobbes; p. (1981) 2,552.

Malmö, c., spt., S. **Sweden**; on the Sound opposite Copenhagen; third lgst. c. in cty.; naval and comm. pt.; former ctr. for shipbldg., textiles, machin.; founded in 12th cent.; car and aerospace engin. plant to relieve unemployment; proposed bridge across Öresund Str. to Denmark; p. (1992) 236,684.

Malta, indep. st. within Br. C. (1964), rep. (1974); I. in Mediterranean, 93 km S. of Sicily; strategic location; former British naval and military base; agr. ch. occupation with ship-repairing at dry-docks of Valletta; sm.-scale inds. growing; tourism exploits Mediterranean climate; major airport at Luqa; awarded George Cross for bravery in second world war; cap. Valletta; a. 316 km²; p. (1993) 364,593. (inc. Gozo and Comino).

Maltby, t., Ryedale, South Yorks., **Eng.**; mine still open 1994; p. (1981) 16,749.

Malton, mkt. t., North Yorks., **Eng.**; on R. Derwent, in S.W. of Vale of Pickering; brewing; p. (1981) 4,143.

Malvern, t., Hereford and Worcs., **Eng.**; at E. foot of Malvern hills; spa; annual dramatic festival; Elgar lived here; p. (1981) 30,187.

Malvern Hills, narrow ridge forming bdy. between Worcs. and Hereford, **Eng.**; rises very abruptly from Severn valley to over 300 m between Malvern and Bromsberrow; moorland, woodland on lower slopes; now forms l. gov. dist.; p. (1993) 89,300.

Mammoth Cave, Ky., **USA**; to S. of Green R. in hilly forested parkland; spectacular limestone formations (stalactites, stalagmites), lakes and rivers (e.g. Echo R., 110 m below surface) in avenues aggregating 240 km long; included in Nat. Park.

Mamoré, R., N. **Bolivia** and **Brazil;** rises in Andes; 1,920 km long.

Mam Soul, mtn., Kyle of Lochalsh and Inverness, **Scot.;** alt. 1,178 m.

Manacle Rocks, dangerous reef off cst. of Cornwall, **Eng.;** 12 km S. of Falmouth.

Manacor, t., Majorca, **Spain;** artificial pearls, wine, stalactite caves of Drach and Hams; p. (1981) 24,153.

Managua, c., cap. of **Nicaragua;** on S. shore of L. Managua; industl. and comm. ctr.; oil refining, agr. processing, textiles, steel; univ.; 48 km from pt. Puerto Somoza; violent earthquake Dec. 1972; p. (1985) 682,111.

Managua, L., **Nicaragua;** second lgst. L. in Central America.

Manámah, Al, cap. and ch. pt. **Bahrain,** Persian G.; free pt., comm. ctr.; declining pearl-fishing ind.; linked by causeway to internat. airpt.; p. (1988) 151,500.

Manáus (Manaos), c., cap. of Amazonas st., N.W. **Brazil;** on Rio Negro nr. confluence with Amazon; impt. R. pt., airport.; oil refinery; former rubber ctr.; in free zone (10,360 km²) recently set up to encourage development in Amazonas; new inds. include steel wks., oil refinery; boom now far exceeds 19th century rubber boom; tourism; internat. airpt.; p. (1991) 1,010,558.

Manche, dep., N.W. **France;** on English Channel; agr. and dairying; cap. Saint Lô; ch. pt. Cherbourg; a. 6,410 km²; p. (1990) 479,600.

Manchester, c., Gtr. Manchester, **Eng.;** on R. Irwell; terminus of Manchester Ship Canal; but only 1 dock out of 8 left open; ctr. of cotton and man-made fibre textile inds.; heavy, lt., and elec. engin., machine tools, petro-chemicals, dyestuffs, pharmaceutical gds.; univ.; comm., cultural and recreational cap. of N.W. Eng.; p. (1993) 432,000 (met. dist.), 2,578,900 (Greater Manchester).

Manchester, t., Conn., **USA;** textiles (silk); p. (1980) 49,761.

Manchester, c., N.H., **USA;** at Amoskeag falls, on the Merrimac R.; textiles, footwear, machin.; p. (1984) 94,900 (c.), 136,400 (met. a.).

Manchester Ship Canal, ship canal, Cheshire/Merseyside/Gtr. Manchester, **Eng.;** joins Manchester to Mersey estuary at Eastham; 57 km long.

Manchuria. See **North-East China.**

Mandalay, c., **Myanmar;** on R. Irrawaddy, 640 km N. of Rangoon; former cap.; lost importance with rise of Irrawaddy delta; many temples, palaces; p. (1983) 532,895.

Manfredonia, mkt. t., Foggia, **Italy;** fish. pt.; cath.; p. (1981) 52,674.

Mangalore, spt., Karnataka, **India;** exp. coffee, coconuts, rice, spices, fertiliser; p. (1991) 273,000.

Mangere, N.I., **N.Z.;** 21 km S. of Auckland; international airport (opened 1965).

Mangla Dam, Pakistan; world's lgst. earth-filled dam, on Jhelum R., part of Indus Basin irrigation scheme.

Manhattan, I., N.Y., **U.S.A.;** at mouth of Hudson R.; a. 57 km²; forms major part of bor. of Manhattan of N.Y. City; p. (1990) 1,487,536 (bor.).

Manila, c., S.W. Luzon, **Philippines;** cap. and ch. pt. of Is.; entrepôt tr.; modern skyscrapers; univ.; cath.; airpt.; p. (1990) 7,928,867.

Manipur, new st. (1972), E. **India;** borders Burma; former princely st.; cap. Imphal; a. 22,274 km²; p. (1991) 1,837,149.

Manisa, c., cap. of M. prov., W. **Turkey;** agr. ctr.; mineral deposits nearby; p. (1990) 158,426, 1,154,418 (prov.).

Manitoba, prov., **Canada;** wheat, rich mineral deposits, fisheries; diverse inds.; cap. Winnipeg; a. 650,090 km²; p. (1991) 1,096,700.

Manitowac, c., Wis., **USA;** on L. Mich.; shipbldg., aluminium wks., flour mills; p. (1980) 32,547.

Manizales, c., cap. of Caldas, **Colombia;** at 2,155 m in the Central Cordillera; in rich coffee a.; route ctr.; p. (1992) 327,115.

Mannar, G., with Palk Strait separates **India** from **Sri Lanka.**

Mannheim, c., Baden-Württemberg, **Germany;** major R. pt. at confluence of Rs. Neckar and Rhine, opposite Ludwigshafen; heavy and lt. inds., notably precision instruments, machin., vehicles; p. (1990) 312,000.

Manono, t. Zaïre; ctr. for tin-mng.; foundries.

Manresa, industl. t., N.E. **Spain;** in Catalonia; textiles; associated with Ignatius of Loyola; place of pilgrimage; p. (1981) 64,745.

Mansfield, t., l. gov. dist., Notts., **Eng.;** on E. flank of Pennines, 19 km N. of Nottingham; 2 remaining coal mines; sand-quarrying, textiles, footwear, metal boxes, machin.; p. (1993) 102,100 (dist.).

Mansfield, t., Ohio, **USA;** machin. farm tools, paper, rubber gds.; p. (1990) 50,627.

Mansfield Woodhouse, t., Notts., **Eng.;** 3 km N. of Mansfield; stone quarries; Roman remains; p. (1981) 26,725.

Mansûra, c., Lower **Egypt;** pt. on Nile; cotton mftg.; univ. p. (1986) 316,870.

Mantua, c., cap. of M. prov., N. **Italy;** on R. Mincio; comm. and agr. ctr.; old fortfd. c.; p. (1981) 60,866.

Manukau, c., N I , **N.Z.,** new c. (1965) formed from amalgamation of suburban communities around Auckland; p. (1991) 226,147, now lgst. c. of N.Z.

Manukau Harbour, N.I., **N.Z.;** lge. shallow inlet on W. cst. of Auckland peninsula; provides additional harbour facilities for spt. of Auckland; recreational sailing; fishing.

Manych, R., **Russia;** trib. of R. Don; 480 km long; canal being built through R. to Caspian to provide through connection with Black Sea.

Manzala (Menzala), lagoon, Mediterranean cst., **Egypt;** extends E. from Damietta mouth of Nile to Pt. Said; fringed by salt marsh; a. 2,072 km².

Manzanillo, spt., S.E. **Cuba;** exp. sugar, rice, tobacco.

Manzanillo, c. Colima, W. **Mexico;** ch. pt. on Pac. Oc.; exp. coffee, timber, minerals; p. (1990) 92,168.

Maputo (Lourenço Marques), spt., cap. of **Moçambique;** at head of Delagoa Bay; rly. terminus; oil refining, deposits of bentonite worked nearby; ore terminal, main transit tr.; second lgst. pt. in Africa; p. (1991) 1,098,000.

Maracaibo, spt. cap. of Zulia st., **Venezuela;** deepwater harbour; on W. of narrow entrance on L. Maracaibo; univ.; oilfields and refineries; exp. coffee, cocoa; p. (1981) 888,800.

Maracaibo, G., and L., Zulia st., **Venezuela;** brackish lake, 192 km long, 96 km wide; oilwells on fringes and drilled into lake floor.

Maracay, c., N. **Venezuela;** on L. Valencia, 112 km from Carácas; p. (1981) 440,000.

Maragheh, t., **Iran;** on N. end of L. Urmia; comm. and fruit ctr.

Marajó, I., at mouth of the Rs. Amazon and Pará, **Brazil;** a. 38,850 km².

Maralinga, S. **Australia;** 320 km N.E. Eucla; joint U.K.–Australian atomic testing ground, first weapon exploded here 27 Sept. 1956.

Maranhão, st., N.E. **Brazil;** rice, cotton, sugar, tobacco, coffee, cattle, gold, copper; oil in the Barrierinhas a.; cap. São Luiz; a. 334,812 km²; p. (1991) 4,922,339.

Marañon, R. See **Amazon, R.**

Maras, t. and prov., S. central **Turkey;** tr. in Kurdish carpets; p. (1985) 210,371, (1990) 892,952 (prov.).

Marathon, v. and plain, **Greece;** 32 km N.E. of Athens; here the Athenians defeated the Persians 490 B.C.

Marazion, mkt. t., Cornwall, **Eng.;** on Mount's Bay, nr. St. Michael's Mount; pilchard fisheries.

Marble Bar, t., W. **Australia;** 136 km inland by rail from Pt. Hedland; ctr. of Pilbara goldfields.

Marburg on Lahn, t., Hesse, **Germany;** univ., cas.; noted for optical instruments; p. (1986) 77,100.

March, mkt. t., Fenland, Cambs., **Eng.;** on R. Nene in Fens; rly. junc.; farm tools; p. (1981) 14,475.

Marches, The, region, central **Italy;** extending from eastern slopes of Apennines to Adriatic cst.; embracing provs. of Macerata, Ascoli-Piceno, Ancona, and Pesaro e Urbino; a. 9,697 km²; p. (1992) 1,433,994.

Marchfeld, plain, Lower **Austria;** between Rs. Danube and Morava which here forms bdy. between Austria and ČSSR.

Marcias Nguema. See **Biako.**

Mar del Plata, c., **Argentina;** on C. Corrientes; Atl. cst. resort; p. (1991) 407,024.

Maree, L., Ross and Cromarty, **Scot.;** 21 km long, c. 3 km wide; rocky shores; studded with wooded islets.

Maremma, coastal region along Tyrrhenean Sea, S. Tuscany, **Italy;** once malarial, now drained with wide fertile areas.

Mareotis or Birket-et-Mariut, L., Lower **Egypt;** separated from Mediterranean by ridge of sand on which stands Alexandria; 80 km long, 32 km wide.

Margam, t., in Pt. Talbot, West Glamorgan, S. **Wales;** on cst. of Swansea Bay; lge. new steel-wks.; lgst. steel-rolling mill in Europe.

Margarita, I., in Caribbean off N. **Venezuela;** tourism; formerly pearl-fishing ctr.; cap. Asunción; a. 1,166 km².

Margate, t., Kent, **Eng.;** W. of N. Foreland, in the Isle of Thanet; seaside resort; p. (1981) 53,280.

Margolan, t., E. **Uzbekistan;** in Ferghana Valley; noted for silk ind.; p. (1990) 124,900.

Mari, aut. rep., **Russia;** timber, paper inds.; p. (1984) 729,000.

Maribor, t., **Slovenia** (formerly Yugoslavia); on Drava R., nr. Austrian border; metallurgical inds.; ctr. of agr. a.; p. (1981) 185,699.

Marilia, t., São Paulo st., **Brazil;** coffee, cotton, oil peanuts; p. (1985) 136,500.

Mariinsk Canal. See **Volga Baltic Waterway.**

Marion, c., Ind., **USA;** mkt. ctr. within corn belt; varied inds.; p. (1980) 35,874.

Marion, t., Ohio, **USA;** agr. ctr., with varied agr. mnfs.; p. (1990) 34,075.

Maritime Provinces, group of provs. in **Canada—** Nova Scotia, New Brunswick, Prince Edward I.

Maritsa, R., **Bulgaria** and **Greece;** used for irrigation and hydroelectric power; 416 km long.

Mariupol, (Zhdanov), spt., S.E. **Ukraine;** on Sea of Azov; metallurgical ctr., chemicals; fishing and fish-processing; p. (1990) 519,900.

Market Drayton, t., North Shrops., **Eng.;** on R. Tern, 21 km S.W. of Newcastle-under-Lyme; agr. implements, nylon mftg.

Market Harborough, t., Harborough, Leics., **Eng.;** on R. Welland, 13 km N.W. of Kettering; elec. engin., foodstuffs, corsetry; p. (1981) 15,934.

Market Rasen, t., West Lindsey, Lincs., **Eng.;** agr. ctr.; racecourse; p. (1981) 2,689.

Markinch, burgh, Kirkcaldy, **Scot.;** 13 km N. of Kirkcaldy; paper mftg., whisky blending and bottling factory closed 1983; p. (1991) 2,176.

Marl, t., N. Rhine–Westphalia, **Germany;** in Ruhr; coal mng.; chemicals; p. (1986) 87,800.

Marlborough, t., Wycombe, Wilts., **Eng.;** on R. Kennet in heart of Marlborough Downs; public school; p. (1981) 5,771.

Marlborough, dist., S.I., **N.Z.;** pastoral; a. 10,930 km²; cap. Blenheim; p. (1991) 36,765.

Marlborough Downs, hills, Wilts., **Eng.;** chalk; highest point, Milk Hill, 298 m.

Marlow, t., Bucks., **Eng.;** on R. Thames; mkt., tourist ctr.; home of Shelley; p. (1981) 14,132.

Marmara, Sea of, separates Europe from Asia; connected with Black Sea through the Bosporus, with Aegean Sea through Dardanelles; shores belong to **Turkey.**

Marne, dep., N.E. **France;** in Champagne; ctr. of champagne ind.; cap. Châlons-sur-Marne; a. 8,205 km²; p. (1990) 558,200.

Marne, R., central **France;** rises in Plateau de Langres, flows across Champagne Humide, Champagne Pouilleuse, and Beauce, joins R. Seine just above Paris; with Marne–Rhine and Marne–Saône canals forms impt. inland waterway linking Seine with Rhine and Rhône valleys; c. 520 km. long.

Marple, t., Gtr. Manchester, **Eng.;** 5 km. E. of Stockport; engin., residtl.; p. (1981) 23,899.

Marquesas Is., volcanic gr. in central **Pac. Oc.,** part of Fr. Polynesia; lgst. Nukuhiva and Hivaoa; mtnous., fertile; exp. copra, vanilla, tobacco, cotton; a. 1,274 km²; p. (1983) 6,548.

Marrakesh, c., **Morocco;** tourist ctr.; leather gds., carpets; p. (1982) 439,728.

Marsa el-Brega, new pt., G. of Sirte, **Libya;** oil pipeline from Zelten; gas liquefaction plant opened 1970; airport.

Marsala, pt., Sicily, **Italy;** on site of anc. Carthaginian settlement; wine ctr.; p. (1981) 79,093.

Marseille, c., spt., cap. of Bouche-du-Rhône dep., S. **France;** on Provence cst.; passenger and gds. traffic; pt. inds., marine engin., oil refining; oil pipeline to Karlsruhe; industl. expansion at G. of Fos; cath., univ., palace; founded as Massilia by Phocaean Greeks of Asia Minor 600 B.C.; p. (1990) 807,726 (c.), 1,087,376 (met.a.).

Marshall Is., Rep. of, gr. of coral Is., central **Pac. Oc.;** internal self-government (1978); comprising 34 atolls; exp. copra, sugar, coffee; admin. ctr. Jaluit I.; joined UN 1991; nuclear bomb tests; a. 181 km²; p. (1990) 45,630.

Martha's Vineyard, I., S.E. Mass., **USA;** state forest; summer resort; ch. ts., Vineyard Haven, Oak Bluffs, Edgartown; summer resort.

Martigny, t., Valais, **Switzerland;** linked by road tunnel to Aosta, Italy; p. 6,572.

Martin, t. **Slovakia,** S. E. of Zilina; rly.; p. (1990) 66,000.

Martina Franca, t., S. **Italy;** in Apulia; wine, olive oil; summer resort.

Martinique, I., Fr. overseas dep., Windward Is., **W.I.;** dominated by volcanic peak Mt. Pelée which erupted 1902 destroying t. of St. Pierre; hurricanes, earthquakes; economy based on sugar-cane and fruit prod.; much emigration to France; cap. Fort de France; a. 1,088 km²; p. (1990) 359,600

Martos, t., Jaen prov., Andalusia, **Spain;** castled hilltop t.; wines, sulphur springs; mftg.; p. (1981) 21,672.

Mary (Merv), c., **Turkmenistan;** in oasis in Kara-Kum desert; anc. c. founded 3rd cent. B.C.; textile ctr.; p. (1990) 93,800.

Maryborough, t., Queensland, **Australia;** pt. on Mary R.; exp. fruit, sugar, timber, coal; p. (1991) 23,286.

Maryborough. See **Port Laoighise, Ireland.**

Mary Kathleen, t., Queensland, **Australia;** new t., nr. uranium field in Cloncurry a.

Maryland, one of original 13 sts. of **USA;** Old Line St.; admitted to Union 1788; st. flower Black eyed Susan, st. bird Baltimore Oriel; on shores of Chesapeake Bay; humid continental climate; arable agr. and mkt. gardening; sea-fishing; cap. Annapolis; lgst. c. Baltimore; a. 27,394 km²; p. (1990) 4,781,468.

Maryport, t., Allerdale, Cumbria, **Eng.;** former pt.; modern lt. inds. in industl. estate to S. of t.; p. (1981) 11,598.

Masaya, t., W. **Nicaragua;** comm. ctr. in rich agr. a.; p. (1985) 75,000.

Masbate, I., prov. **Philippines;** gold mng.; a. 3,269 km²; p. (1990) 599,915.

Mascarene Is., collective name of **Mauritius, Rodriguez and Réunion, in Indian Oc.**

Maseru, t., cap. **Lesotho;** nr. border with S. Africa on Caledon R.; two new industl. estates to encourage light inds.; tourists from S. Africa; p. (1986) 109,382.

Masham, t., North Yorks., **Eng.;** on R. Ure; 14 km N.W. of Ripon; mkt.

Mashhad, c., N.E. **Iran;** cap. of Khorassan prov.; linked by oil pipeline to Esfahan and rly. to Turkmenistan; p. (1986) 1,466,018.

Mashonaland, dist., **Zimbabwe;** a. inhabited by the Mashona tribe; ch. t. Salisbury.

Masjid-i-Sulamain, t., **Iran;** impt. oilfield and refinery; p. (1982) 117,000..

Mask, L., Mayo and Galway, **R.o.I.;** 19 km long 3–6 km wide.

Mason City, t., Iowa, **USA;** on Sheel Rock R.; tr. ctr. of lge. agr. a.; p. (1990) 29,040.

Mason–Dixon Line. See **Section L.**

Massachusetts, st., New England, **USA;** Bay St.; admitted to Union 1788; st. flower Mayflower, st. bird Chickadee; on Atl. cst.; humid continental climate; hilly interior severed by N.–S. Connecticut valley; major fishing ind.; replacement of traditional textile inds. by modern science-based inds., especially around M. Institute of Technology; impt. arable gr. a.; cap. Boston; a. 21,386 km²; p. (1990) 6,016,425.

Massa di Carrara. See **Carrara.**

Massawa. See **Mits'iwa.**

Massif Central, upland a., **France;** variable geology and scenery inc. volcanic Auvergne and limestone Causses; much rural depopulation, pastoral agr.; industl. ts. inc. St. Etienne based on sm. coalfields in N.E.; others ts. inc. Limoges and Clermont-Ferrand.

Masterton, dist., N.I., **N.Z.;** meat-packing; dairy prods., woollen mills; p. (1991) 22,947.

Masulipatnam. See **Machilipatnam.**

Masvingo. See **Fort Victoria.**

Matabeleland, dist., **Zimbabwe;** a. inhabited by Matabele tribe; ch. t. Bulawayo.

Matadi, spt., **Zaïre;** on R. Zaïre; main pt.; exp. forest prod.; proposed Inga power project nearby; p. (1985) 216,000.

Matagalpa, t., **Nicaragua;** ctr. of agr. a., food processing; second lgst. t. of Nicaragua; p. (1985) 37,000.

Matamoros, irrigated region, **Mexico;** around t.

of M. on Rio Grande delta; Mexico's leading producer of cotton.

Matamoros, t., **Mexico**; on Rio Grande; livestock tr. ctr.; p. (1990) 303,392.

Matanzas, spt., cap. of M. prov., **Cuba**; exp. sugar, cigars; rayon plant; p. (1985) 105,400, (1986) 599,500 (prov.).

Matarani, new spt., S. **Peru**; oil refinery.

Mataró, spt., **Spain**; nr. Barcelona; fisheries, textiles, chemicals, paper; p. (1991) 101,172.

Matera, t., cap. of M. prov., S. **Italy**; stands on limestone ridge cleft by canyon; agr. ctr.; 13th cent. cath. and cas.; p. (1981) 50,712.

Mathura (**Muttra**), t., Uttar Pradesh, **India**; sacred t. on R. Jumna; Hindu pilgrimage ctr.; textiles; p. (1991) 226,691.

Matlock, t., Derbys. Dales, **Eng.**; on R. Derwent; 24 km N. of Derby; tourist ctr., limestone quarrying, lt. inds.; p. (1981) 20,610

Mato Grosso, st., **Brazil**; cap. Cuiabá; a. 1,232,081 km²; p. (1991) 2,020,581.

Mato Grosso, plateau, Mato Grosso st., **Brazil**; average alt. 900 m, acts as divide between Amazon and Paraná–Paraguay R. systems; reserves of gold, diamonds, manganese but largely undeveloped; lge. areas of tropical rain forest.

Mato Grosso do Sul, st. Brazil; cap. Campo Grande; separated from Mato Grosso state in 1979; a. 350,548 km²; p. (1991) 1,778,494.

Matosinhos, t., **Portugal**; fish. pt. at mouth of Leca R.; seaside resort; p. (1981) 43,488.

Matsue, c., S.W. Honshu, **Japan**; on L. Shinji; old cas.; p. (1990) 142,956.

Matsumoto, c., central Honshu, **Japan**; machin., food-processing, paper; once impt. for silk; remains of 16th cent. cas.; p. (1990) 200,723.

Matsuyama, c., **Japan**; pt. based inds. of oil refining and petrochemicals; univ., feudal cas.; p. (1990) 443,317.

Matterhorn (Fr. **Mt. Corvin**. It. **Monte Cervino**); alt. 4,477 m; Pennine Alps, **Switzerland**.

Mauchline, mkt. t., Strathclyde Reg., **Scot.**; associated with Robert Burns; p. (1991) 3,931.

Mauna Kea, volcano, **Hawaii**; alt. 4,208 m; now dormant.

Mauna Loa, volcano, **Hawaii**; alt. 4,172 m; one of the world's lgst. volcanoes.

Mauritania, Islamic Rep. of, **W. Africa**; desert in N., S. more fertile; Senegal R. forms main artery of transport; mainly pastoral agr. (nomadic); severe effects of Sahelian drought since 1971 caused p. to become settled and move to ts.; urban p. 35% (1984); deposits of iron ore (Fort Gouraud) and copper (Bakel Akjouit); fishing; new pt. development at Nouadhibou; cap. Nouakchott; a. 1,085,210 km²; p. (1992) 2,114,000.

Mauritius, I., rep. within Brit. Commonwealth; **Indian Oc.**; volcanic I., surrounded by coral reefs, 800 km E. of Madagascar; subtropical climate, prone to cyclone; racially mixed; dependent on sugar for 95 per cent of exps.; attempts to decr. this dependence by Export Processing Zone (tax-free industrial zone), and incr. tea output; dense p. and unemployment cause social tension; former residents of Chagos Arch. resettled on 2 of Agalega Is.; tourism incr. impt.; cap. Port Louis; a. (inc. Rodriguez and Agalega) 2,038 km²; p. (1992) 1,092,384.

Mawson, national research base for Australia, Antarctica.

Mayagüez, c., spt., **Puerto Rico**; ctr. of fertile region producing sugar, coffee, tobacco; cultural and educational ctr.; p. (1990) 100,371.

Maybole, burgh, Kyle and Carrick, **Scot.**; 13 km S. of Ayr; commuter centre for Ayr etc; cas.; p. (1991) 4,737.

Mayenne, dep., N.W. **France**; pastoral and agr.; cap. Laval; a. 5,146 km²; p. (1990) 278,000.

Mayfair, dist., City of Westminster, London, **Eng.**; fashionable residtl. and comm. a., to E. of Hyde Park; clubs and hotels.

Mayo, maritime co., Connacht, **R.o.I.**; broken cst., much barren mtn. land, many lge. lakes; agr., fishery; co. t. Castlebar, a. 5,506 km²; p. (1986) 115,184.

Mayotte, ch. I., **Fr. terr.**, Comoro Archipelago, Moçambique Channel; rejected indep. to remain Fr. dep. (1975); sugar-cane, vanilla, cacao; a. 363 km²; p. (1993) 104,185.

Mazandaran, prov., N.E. **Iran**; Caspian Sea, borders USSR; subtropical climate; agr.; cap. Sari; p. (1982) 2,375,994.

Mazar-i-Sharif, c., **Afghanistan**; chemical fertil-

isers from natural gas; textiles, bricks, flour-milling; noted mosque; p. (1982) 110,367.

Mazatlán, c., N.W. **Mexico**; major spt. on Pac. cst.; comm. and industl. ctr.; exp. metals, hides, fish prods., woods; oil refinery; fishing, tourism; p. (1990) 314,249.

Mbabane, cap. of **Swaziland**; stands at c. 1,160 m; admin. ctr.; tin mng.; p. (1986) 38,290.

M'Bao, **Senegal**, W. Africa; oil refinery.

McMurdo Sound, ice-locked channel, Antarctica; base for many expeditions.

Mead, L., Arizona/Nevada., **USA**; on R. Colorado behind Hoover Dam; one of world's lgst. reservoirs; stores water for irrigation in Imperial Valley and Yuma dist.; tourist attraction; 184 km long, 2-13 km wide.

Meath, maritime co., Leinster **R.o.I.**; pastoral; co. t. Trim; a. 2,347 km²; p. (1986) 103,881.

Meaux, t., Seine-et-Marne dep., **France**; on R. Marne; cath.; comm. and industl. ctr.; p. (1982) 55,797 (met. a.).

Mecca, holy c. of Islam, cap. of **Saudi Arabia**; birthplace of Mohammed; pilgrimage ctr.; Gr. Mosque enclosing the Kaaba; univ. (with Jidda); p. (1986) 618,000.

Mechelen. See Malines.

Mecklenburg-West Pomerania, **Land**, **Germany**; part of N. European plain, bordering Baltic Sea; cap. Schwerin; a. 22,947 km²; pop. (1992) 1,892,000.

Medan, c., cap. of N. Sumatra prov., **Indonesia**; ctr. for rubber, tobacco, tea; printing; univ.; pt. is Belawan; p. (1983) 1,966,000.

Médéa, t., 80 km S. of El Djezair, **Algeria**; projected industl. complex; p. (1983) 84,292.

Medellin, c., cap. of Antiquia prov., **Colombia**; at 1,533 m in Central Cordillera; second c. of rep.; univ.; ctr. of drug trade; coffee; textiles, steel, sugar refining, glass; coal, gold, silver mined nearby; hydroelec. power; p. (1992) 1,581,364.

Medicine Hat, t., Alberta, **Canada**; on S. Saskatchewan R.; rly. junc.; coal, natural gas, flour mills; p. (1986) 41,804.

Medina, c., Hejaz, **Saudi Arabia**; 352 km N. of Mecca; tomb of Mohammed; place of Moslem pilgrimage; univ.; harbour at Yanbu' on Red Sea; p. (1986) 500,000.

Medina, l. gov. dist., I. of Wight, **Eng.**; N.E. part of I. inc. Ryde, Newport and Cowes; p. (1993) 71,800.

Medinipur, t., W. Bengal, **India**; mkt. for agr. prods.; (1981) 86,118.

Mediterranean, gr. inland sea, almost tideless, dividing Europe from Africa; communicating with Atl. by Strait of Gibraltar and Black Sea by Dardanelles, Sea of Marmara and Bosporus, E. part touches Asia in the Levant; total length W. to E. 3,520 km; greatest width of sea proper c. 1,120 km; water a. 2,331,000 km²; greatest depth 4,482 m; ch. Is.; Corsica, Sardinia, Sicily, Crete, Cyprus, and the Balearic, Lipari, Maltese, Ionian grs., also Greek arch.

Médoc, region, Gironde, **France**; extending for about 77 km along Garonne R.; noted for wines.

Medway, R., Kent, **Eng.**; flows N.E. past Tonbridge, Maidstone and Rochester (where it becomes estuarial) to mouth of Thames; 112 km long; Medway Bridge completed 1962.

Medway, former l. gov. dist., Kent, **Eng.**; now Rochester upon Medway.

Meekatharra, t., W. **Australia**; Flying Doctor and School of the Air ctr.

Meerut, c., Uttar Pradesh, **India**; scene of outbreak of Indian mutiny 1857; p. (1991) 850,000

Meghalaya ("Home of the Clouds"), new st. (1970), India; former Khasi-Jaintia Hills and Garo Hills dists. of Assam; cap. Shillong; a. 22,549 km²; p. (1991) 1,774,778.

Meiling Pass, on bdy. between Guandong, Jianxi, S. **China**; provides historic routeway across Nanling mtns., followed by old imperial highway from Nanjing to Guangzhou; alt. c. 300 m.

Meiningen, t., **Germany**; on R. Werra; cas.; machin., chemicals, timber inds.; drama ctr. in second half 19th cent.; p. (1989) 25,474.

Merionnydd, l. gov. dist., Gwynedd, **Wales**; based on former co. of Merioneth; stretches from Ffestiniog and Bala to Tywyn and Dolgellau; p. (1993) 32,800.

Meissen, t., Saxony, **Germany**; on R. Elbe; cath.; famous porcelain popularly known as Dresden china; p. (1981) 39,276.

Meknès, t., **Morocco**; one of the caps. of M.; agr. ctr., olives; p. (1982) 319,783.

Mekong, R., S.E. **Asia**; rises in Tibet, flows through China, Laos, Kampuchea, and S. Vietnam, entering China Sea in extensive swampy delta; used for sm. boats but many rapids; 4,000 km long; new R. project for flood control, irrigation and hydroelectric power.

Melanesia, archipelago, S.W. **Pac. Oc.**; inc. Admiralty, Solomon, Santa Cruz, New Hebrides, Loyalty, New Caledonian, and Fiji Is.; New Guinea is sometimes included; ethnic region.

Melbourne, c., cap. of Victoria, **Australia**; at mouth of Yarra R. and N. head of Port Phillip Bay; focal point of trade, transport and inds.; produces 30 per cent of total factory output in Australia; varied inds. inc. car and aircraft assembly, petrochemicals, foodstuffs; internat. airport; 2 univs., 2 caths.; p. (1991) 3,153,500 (met. a.), 71 per cent of st. p.

Melilla, spt. and enclave in **Morocco**, on Mediterranean cst., belonging to Spain; exp. iron ore; p. (1981) 53,593.

Melitopol, c., **Ukraine**; on Molochnoy R.; ctr. of rich fruit-growing a.; heavy machin., food-processing; p. (1990) 175,800.

Melksham, t., West Wilts., **Eng.**; on R. Avon, 8 km N.E. of Bradford-on-Avon; rubber wks., engin., flour mills, creameries, rope and matting; p. (1981) 9,621.

Melrose, burgh, Ettrick and Lauderdale, **Scot.**; on R. Tweed; 6 km E. of Galashiels; ruined abbey; p. (1991) 2,270.

Melton Mowbray, t., Leics., **Eng.**; on Lincoln Heights, 24 km N.E. of Leicester; mkt., hunting dist.; famous pork pies; footwear, pet foods, Stilton cheese; with surrounding a. forms l. gov. dist. of **Melton**; p. (1993) 46,200 (dist.).

Melun, t., cap. of Seine-et-Marne dep., N. **France**; on R. Seine; agr. tools and prod.; Romanesque church; p. (1990) 36,489 (t.), 92,459 (met.a.).

Melville I., off N. cst., Arnhem Land, **Australia**; Aboriginal settlement; a. 4,350 km².

Melville I., N.W. Terr., Arctic **Canada**; natural gas; a. 41,958 km².

Memaliaj, t., **Albania**; new mng. t. on banks of R. Vjosa.

Memel. See **Klaipeda.**

Memmingen, t., Bavaria, **Germany**; rly. junc.; machin., textiles; p. (1986) 37,300.

Memphis, anc. c., **Egypt**; on R. Nile; 19 km S. of Cairo; nearby are Saqqara ruins.

Memphis, c., Tenn., **USA**; on R. Mississippi; rly. ctr., pt. of entry, lgst. c. in st.; mkt. ctr. for cotton and hardwoods; cottonseed oil, textiles, farm machin.; natural gas and hydroelectric power; univ.; Martin Luther King assassinated here (1968); p. (1990) 610,337 (c.), 981,747 (met. a.).

Menado, t., Sulawesi, **Indonesia**; second t. of I.; pt. for transit tr.; p. (1980) 217,159.

Menai Strait, separates Isle of Anglesey from mainland, **Wales**; crossed by Telford's suspension bridge (1825) and Britannia rly. bridge (1850).

Menam Chao Phraya, R., **Thailand**; main R. of cty.; dense p. in valley; lge. multi-purpose scheme for hydroelectric power and irrigation; 1,120 km long.

Mendip Hills, Avon/Somerset, **Eng.**; limestone range containing many karst features inc. Cheddar gorge and Wookey Hole; a. of outstanding natural beauty; quarrying; motorway; hgst. point. 325 m; now forms l. gov. dist. **Mendip** within Somerset, inc. Frome, Wells, Shepton Mallet, Glastonbury and Street; p. (1993) 98,100.

Mendoza, prov., W. **Argentina**, on Chilean border; Andean peaks Aconcagua and Tupungato; oilfields; alfalfa, vines, olives, fruit, peppermint; cap. M.; a. 148,783 km²; p. (1991) 1,400,142.

Mendoza, c., cap. of M. prov., W. **Argentina**; stands at c. 730 m in oasis known as "garden of the Andes"; starting point of Transandine rly.; univ.; wine, fruit; petroleum, agr. processing; p. (1991) 121,696.

Mendoza, R., **Argentina**; enters L. Guanacache; used for hydroelectric power; 320 km long.

Menin (**Meenen**), t., **Belgium**; on R. Lys on Fr. border; mediaeval cloth ctr.; tobacco tr., textiles, rubber gds., soap; scene of fierce fighting in first world war; p. (1981) 33,542.

Mentawei Is., S.W. Sumatra, **Indonesia**; hilly and forested; fishing, shifting cultivation.

Menteith, Lake of, Stirling, **Scot.**; contains 3 Is.; 2·4 km by 1·6 km.

Menton, t., Alpes-Maritimes dep. S. **France**; Riviera resort; p. (1982) 25,449.

Meppel, t., Drenthe, **Neth.**, 21 km N. of Zwolle; shipbldg.; p. (1993) 24,217.

Merauke, t. W. Irian, **Indonesia**; pt. on S. cst.; ctr. of livestock raising region.

Mercedes, t., S.W. **Uruguay**; livestock ctr., E. of its pt. Fray Bentos; p. (1985) 37,110.

Mergui, archipelago, Tenasserim cst., S. **Myanmar**; teak, rice, pearl fishing.

Mérida, c., cap. of Yucatan st., S.E. **Mexico**; sisal-hemp; Spanish colonial architecture; tourism; Mayan ruins; p. (1990) 557,340.

Mérida, c. Badajoz prov., S.W. **Spain**; on Guadiana R.; comm. ctr. of Estremadura; impt. Roman remains; p. (1981) 41,783.

Mérida, t. cap. of M. st., **Venezuela**; in Andes; univ., cath.; tourist ctr.; world's highest cable rly. to Espejo peak (4,690 m); p. (1981) 142,800.

Meriden, t., Conn., **USA**; hardware mftg.; p. (1980) 57,118.

Meridian, t., Miss., **USA**; mkt. ctr. in cotton, livestock, lumber a.; rly. and route ctr.; textiles, clothing; p. (1980) 46,577.

Merioneth, former co., **Wales.** See **Meirionnydd.**

Merksem, industl. t., Antwerp, **Belgium**; p. (1982) 41,782.

Merrick, mtn., Wigtown, **Scot.**; hgst. peak in S. Uplands of Scot.; alt. 843 m.

Mersea, I., at mouth of R. Colne, Essex, **Eng.**; oysters; holiday resort; 8 km long, 3 km wide.

Merseburg, c., Saxony - Anhalt, **Germany**; on R. Saale; ctr. of gr. lignite field; paper mills, chemical wks.; historic c.; p. (1981) 50,932.

Merse of Berwick, region, S.E. **Scot.**; lower valleys of Rs. Tweed and Teviot; glacial clays; arable agr. for barley, wheat; dairy cattle; ch. t. Berwick-on-Tweed; a. 570 km².

Mersey, R., Cheshire/Gtr. Manchester/Merseyside, **Eng.**; enters Irish Sea by fine estuary at Liverpool; 109 km long.

Merseyside, former met. co., N.W. **Eng.**; a. around lower Mersey estuary inc. N. Wirral penin., pts. of Liverpool, Birkenhead and Bootle; many chem. and pt. processing inds.; p. (1993) 1,440,900.

Mersin, c., S. **Turkey**; freeport (1986), on Mediterranean cst.; oil refinery; dates from c. 3,600 B.C.; p. (1980) 216,308.

Merthyr Tydfil, t., l. gov. dist., Mid Glamorgan, S. **Wales**; in narrow valley of R. Taff, 35 km N.W. of Cardiff; former coal-mng. ctr.; hosiery, aircraft, bricks, elec. domestic gds.; p. (1993) 59,700 (dist.).

Merton, outer bor., Greater London, **Eng.**; inc. former bors. of Mitcham, Wimbledon, and Merton and Morden; p. (1993) 175,100.

Meru, mtn., **Tanzania**, E. Africa; extinct volcano overlooking E. arm of Gt. Rift valley; coffee plantations at alt. 1,500–1,800 m, some rubber below 1,200 m; alt. summit 4,560 m.

Merv. See **Mary.**

Mesa, t., Arizona, **USA**; in Salt River Valley, founded by Mormons 1878; agr. ctr., helicopter mftg.; p. (1990) 288,091.

Mesa Central, plateau, **Mexico**; part of Mexican plateau, major a. of comm. agr. (maize, wheat, agave); contains cap. Mexico City; dense p. and industl. comm. ctrs.

Mesa del Norte, plateau, **Mexico**; northern part of Mexican plateau.

Mesabi Range, hills, N.E. Minn., **USA**; vast iron ore deposits, now running out.

Mesa Verde National Park, S.W. Col., **USA**; Indian cliff dwellings.

Mesopotamia, anc. region, S.W. **Asia**; between Tigris and Euphrates Rs.; a. of early civilisation.

Messenia, anc. region, Peloponnesus, **Greece**; corresponding to present Messinia, densely p. agr. dep.; cap. Kalamata; a. 3,406 km²; p. (1991) 167,292.

Messina, c., spt. Sicily, **Italy**; opposite Reggio; univ.; exp. fruit, wine, oil; p. (1992) 232,911.

Messina, strait, between Sicily and Italian mainland; length 35 km, minimum width 5 km.

Mesta, R., **Bulgaria**, **Greece**; rises in Rodopi mtns., flows S.E. into Aegean Sea 24 km E of Kavalla; valley famous for tobacco; known in Greece as Nestos; c. 280 km long.

Mestre, t., **Italy**; on lagoon at landward end of causeway linking Venice to mainland.

Meta, R., **Colombia** and **Venezuela**; navigable for 640 km; trib. of R. Orinoco; 1,200 km long.

Metz, c., cap of Moselle dep., N.E. **France**; on

R. Moselle 40 km N. of Nancy; cultural and comm. ctr. of Lorraine; impt. iron mines; wines, preserved fruits; mediaeval bldgs.; birthplace of Verlaine; p. (1990) 123,920(c.), 193,117 (met. a.).

Meudon, t., Hauts-de-Seine, **France**; S.W. sub. of Paris; observatory; glass, linen, ammunition; p. (1982) 49,004.

Meurthe, R., N.E. **France**; rises in Vosges and joins Moselle N. of Nancy.

Meurthe-et-Moselle, dep., N.E. **France**; borders on Belgium and Luxembourg; cap. Nancy; a. 5,276 km²; p. (1990) 711,800.

Meuse, dep., N.E. **France**; borders on Belgium; cap. Bar-le-Duc; a. 6,237 km²; p. (1990) 196,300.

Meuse (**Maas**), R., **France**; rises in Haute-Marne, flows past Verdun into Belgium past Namur, and Liège into the Neth. and joins the Waal, left arm of the Rhine; impt. routeway; 919 km long.

Mexborough, t., South Yorks., **Eng.**; on R. Don, 16 km above Doncaster; potteries; p. (1981) 15,683.

Mexicali, c., Baja Cal., **Mexico**; border resort; p. (1990) 602,390.

Mexican Plateau, central plateau, **Mexico**; between the branches of the Sierra Madre; highest point over 2,400 m; impt. landform and a. of human settlement.

Mexico, fed. rep., **Central America**; inc. 31 sts., and fed. dist. of Mexico City; mtnous.; Sierra Madre covers most of rep.; variety of climate according to alt.; W. mostly desert; one of world's fastest-growing p.; agr. requires irrigation; major world exporter of cotton, fruit, sulphur, silver, oil; 14 oil refineries, new petrochemical complex at Cosoleacaque; rapid industl. expansion for consumer gds.; attempts to decentralise inds. from Mexico City not very successful; tourism for Americans; cap. Mexico City; a. 1,972,360 km²; p. (1992) 84,439,000.

Mexico, st., **Mexico**; encircles fed. dist. of Mexico City; cap. Toluca; a. 21,412 km²; p. (1990) 9,815,901.

Mexico City, c., cap. of **Mexico**; lgst. c. in Latin America; on plain at 2,275 m; altitude and basin site trap pollutants; many note-worthy bldgs.; cath., univ.; admin., comm. and industl. ctr.; nuclear reactor nearby; lge. earthquake (1985) destroyed many parts of c.; surrounded by shanty ts.; p. (1990) 8,236,960 (fed. dist.).

Mexico, Gulf of, lge. inlet of Atl. Oc. (1,600 km E. to W. by 1,280 km N. to S.) lying S. of USA and E. of Mexico; communicates by Florida strait with Atl. and by Yucatan strait with Caribbean Sea; submarine oil drilling.

Mexico, Valley of, Meseta Central, **Mexico**; major industl. zone; over 60 per cent by value of Mexican mngs. produced; wide range of inds.; major ctr. Mexico City; attempts to decentralise p. and economic activity throughout Mexico; once ctr. of Aztec p.

Meyrin, t., **Switzerland**; H.Q. of CERN Organisation Européené pour la Recherche Nucléaire; nr. Geneva.

Mezhdurechensk, t., **Russia**; W. Siberia, on R. Rom'; new coal-mng. ctr.; p. (1989) 107,000.

Mezzogiorno, lge. underdeveloped region, southern **Italy**; comprising Abruzzo and Molise, Campania, Basilicata, Apulia, Calabria and the Is. of Sicily and Sardinia; major govt. attempts to develop a.; agr. reforms and industl. growth, oil refining, iron and steel, petrochemicals; contains 35 per cent of p. of Italy, much emigration; much devastated by earthquake (1980); p. (1981) 20,053,334.

Miami, c., Fla., **USA**; on Biscayne Bay, at mouth of Miami R.; famous resort and recreational ctr.; varied inds.; international airport; world's 5th lgst. cargo airpt.; 3rd container pt. on U.S. East cst.; lge. freeport; M. beach across Biscayne Bay; ctr. of Cuban exiles; p. (1990) 358,548 (c.), 1,937,000 (met. a. with Hialeah).

Miass, c., **Russia**; in Urals, 90 km S.W. of Chelyabinsk; gold-mng. ctr.; cars; p. (1989) 168,000.

Michigan, st., **USA**; Wolverine St.; admitted to Union 1837; st. flower Apple Blossom, st. bird Robin; in valley of Gr. Ls.; industl.; cars, iron and steel gds., chemicals, minerals; some agr.; cap. Lansing; a. 150,779 km²; p. (1990) 9,295,297.

Michigan Lake, 3rd lgst of Gr. Ls. and the only one wholly in **USA**; in basin of St. Lawrence R., enclosed by two peninsulas of the st. of Mich. and by Wis., Ill., and Ind.; a. 61,901 km²; discharges by Straits of Mackinac to L. Huron.

Michipicoten, R., Ont., **Canada**; flows 200 km to L. Superior; iron ore deposits in valley.

Michoacan, st., **Mexico**; on Pac. Oc.; mtnous., rich in minerals; cap. Morelia; a. 60,088 km²; p. (1990) 3,534,042.

Michurinsk, t., **Russia**; N.W. of Tambov; engin., textiles, food inds.; agr. exp. ctr.; p. (1989) 109,000.

Micronesia, Federated States of, Is., W. Pac. Oc. of Yap, Truk, Ponape and Kosrae; status of free association with **US**; p. (1990), 107,900.

Mid Bedfordshire, l. gov. dist., Beds., **Eng.**; a. N. of Luton and inc. Biggleswade, Sandy and Ampthill; p. (1993) 113,500.

Mid Devon, l. gov. dist., Devon, **Eng.**; based on Tiverton; p. (1993) 65,600.

Middleburg, t. cap. of Zeeland prov., **Neth.**; on Walcheren I. nr. Flushing; margarine, timber, optical instruments; cloth ctr. in mediaeval times; p. (1993) 40,105.

Middlesbrough, t., l. gov. dist., Cleveland, **Eng.**; expanded t.; pt. on S. side of Tees estuary; impt. iron and steel ind., heavy engin., chemicals; p. (1993) 145,800.

Middlesex, former co., S.E. **Eng.**; N. of R. Thames; largely absorbed in Greater London 1964.

Middleton, t., Gtr. Manchester, **Eng.**; in valley of R. Irk; textiles, engin., chemicals, foam rubber; p. (1981) 51,696.

Middletown, t., Ohio, **USA**; on Miami R. and canal; steel, paper; p. (1990) 46,022.

Middlewich, t., Cheshire, **Eng.**; on Rs. Dane, Wheelock and Croco, 8 km N. of Crewe; salt, chemicals, clothing; p. (1981) 8,170.

Mid Glamorgan, co., S. **Wales**; upland in N. dissected by deep R. valleys containing former coal-mng. settlements; Tower colliery remains; lowland to S. borders Bristol Channel; a. 1,018 km²; p. (1993) 544,300.

Midhurst, t., West Sussex, **Eng.**; on R. Rother; famous polo grounds; birthplace of Richard Cobden.

Midi-Pyrénées, region, S.W. **France**; inc. deps. Ariège, Aveyron. Haute-Garonne, Gers, Lot, Hautes-Pyrénées, Tarn, Tarn-et-Garonne; mountainous region on Spanish border descending to agricultural lowlands north-eastwards; p. (1990) 2,430,700

Midland, t., Texas, **USA**; oilfield ctr., cotton ginning, natural gas; p. (1990) 89,443.

Midlands, region, **Eng.**; comprises non-met. cos. of Staffs, Derbys., Notts., Leics., Warwicks., Northants., and met. co. of West Midlands; impt. a. for lt. engin.

Midlothian, former co., l. gov. dist., Lothian Reg., **Scot.**; adjoins Edinburgh; a. 357 km²; p. (1993) 79,910.

Mid Suffolk, l. gov. dist., Suffolk, **Eng.**; rural a. inc. Eye and Stowmarket; p. (1993) 78,400.

Mid Sussex, l. gov. dist., West Sussex, **Eng.**; a. inc. Cuckfield and Burgess Hill; p. (1993) 125,000.

Midway Islands, I., Pac. Oc.; calling-place on air-routes betweeen San Francisco and Asia, midway between Asia and **USA** (to which it belongs); p. (1981) 453 (excl. military personnel).

Mieres, t., Oviedo prov., N. **Spain**; in Asturias; coal-mng. ctr., iron and steel inds.; p. (1981) 58,098.

Mikkeli, c., cap. of M. prov., **Finland**; L. pt. in Saimaa L. region; p. (1991) 32,158.

Milan, c., cap. of M. prov., N. **Italy**; route ctr. in Lombard plain; second lgst. c. in rep.; ctr. of commerce and ind.; textiles, chemicals, printing, publishing, machin., cars, aircraft, porcelain; cath., univ.; p. (1992) 1,358,627.

Mildenhall, t., Forest Heath, Suffolk, **Eng.**; on R. Lark; 13th cent. church; R.A.F. sta. nearby; expanded t.

Mildura, t., Victoria, **Australia**; on R. Murray; irrigation ctr.; wine, citrus fruits, tomatoes; ctr. for dried fruit; p. (1986) 18,382.

Milford Haven, spt., Preseli, Dyfed, **Wales**; magnificent deepwater harbour recently developed; major tanker terminal (250,000 tonnes); 2 refineries; pipeline from Angle Bay to Llandarcy (nr. Swansea); major white fish pt.; trawlers built and repaired; net mkg.; p. (1981) 13,934.

Milford Sound, inlet, at S. of S.I., **N.Z.**; tourist resort; noted for scenery and rare birds.

Millau, t., Aveyron, **France**; on R. Tarn; glove mnfs.; p. (1982) 22,256.

Millom, t., Copeland, Cumbria, **Eng.**; on N.W. cst. of Duddon estuary; ironwks. (closed 1968 after 100 years); hosiery; declining p.

Millport, burgh, Cunninghame, **Scot.**; on Gr. Cumbrae I., in F. of Clyde; resort; cath.; quarries; p. (1991) 1,340.

Milngavie, burgh, Bearsden and M., Strathclyde

Reg., **Scot.**; 8 km N.W. of Glasgow, textiles; p. (1991) 12,592.

Milnrow, t., Gtr. Manchester, **Eng.**; sub. of Rochdale; cotton and waste spinning engin., brick mkg., paper and tub mftg.; p. (1981) 11,759.

Milo or **Melos,** I., Cyclades, **Greece**; cap. Plaka, nr. site of anc. c.; famous statue of Venus of Milo (now in Louvre) found here in 1820.

Milton Keynes, t., l. gov. dist., Bucks., **Eng.**; a. 9,000 ha; new c. for London overspill comprising Bletchley, Wolverton and Stony Stratford; Open University; p. (1993) 184,400 (dist.).

Milwaukee, c., Wis., **USA**; lgst. c. and ch. pt. of st.; on L. Mich.; 112 km N. of Chicago; univ.; major mftg. ctr. with numerous inds., notably machin. and transport equipment, meat-canning, beer; p. (1990) 628,088 (c.), 1,432,149 (met. a.).

Min, R., Fujian, S. **China**; descends steeply on S.E. course to enter S. China Sea nr. Fuzhou, length 480 km, navigable.

Min, R., Sichuan, W. **China**; flows S., diverted into irrigation channels; joins Chang Jiang at Yibin; length 800 km, navigable.

Mina Hassan Tani (Kenitra), spt., **Morocco**; exp. grain; p. (1981) 450,000.

Minas Gerais, st., **Brazil**; vast iron ore reserves; gold, diamonds, manganese, uranium, aluminium; cotton, coffee; hydroelec. power sta.; cap. Belo Horizonte; heavy inds.; a. 585,472 km²; p. (1991) 15,746,200.

Minas Novas, t., Minas Gerais, **Brazil**; p. (1985) 28,400.

Mina Sulman, free transit pt., **Bahrain**; deepwater pt., dry dock for OPEC super-tankers, entrepôt.

Minatitlán, t., E. **Mexico**; petroleum refineries; petrochemicals; p. (1990) 199,840.

Minch, The, channel between the mainland of **Scot.** and the N. portion of Outer Hebrides, 38–64 km wide; very rapid current.

Minch, The Little, channel between I. of Skye, **Scot.**, and the middle portion of Outer Hebrides, 22–32 km wide.

Minchinhampton, t., Gloucs., **Eng.**; in Cotswolds, 6 km S.E. of Stroud.

Mindanao, second lgst. I. of **Philippines**; forested mtns., volcano Mt. Apo; exp. pineapples, hemp, coconuts, coffee; iron, gold, copper mined; plywoods and veneer, paper, pulp; ch. ts. Zamboanga, Davao; a. of govt. sponsored immigration; lge. Moslem p.; greatest ocean depth Mindanao Deep, off Philippines, 11,524 m; a. 94,628 km²; p. (1990) 14,297,462.

Minden, c., N. Rhine–Westphalia, **Germany**; on R. Weser at crossing of Mittelland canal; pt., rly. junc.; cath. (12th–14th cent.) destroyed in second world war; p. (1986) 75,400.

Mindoro, I., **Philippines,** S. of Luzon; mtnous., thickly forested; rice, coconuts grown on cst., a. 9,376 km²; p. (1990) 832,642.

Minehead, t., West Somerset, **Eng.**; at N. foot of Exmoor, on Bristol Channel cst.; mkt., holiday resort; shoe factory closed 1981; p. (1981) 11,176.

Minho, R., separates Portugal from Spain in N.W.; length 272 km.

Minicoy Is., Arabian Sea; joined with Laccadive and Amindivi Is. to form union terr. of Lakshadweep **India.**

Minneapolis, c., Minn., **USA**; on Mississippi R., at falls of St. Anthony; lgst. c. of st., pt. of entry, rly. terminus; wheat mkt., comm. and industl. ctr.; wide range of inds.; univ.; p. (1990) 368,383 (c.), 2,464,124 (met. a. inc. St. Paul which it faces).

Minnesota, st., **USA**; North Star St,; admitted to Union 1858; st. flower Lady's Slipper, st. bird Common Loon; W. of L. Superior; studded with Ls., many Rs.; iron ore; maize, wheat, livestock, dairying; cap. St. Paul; a. 217,736 km²; p. (1990) 4,375,099.

Minorca (Menorca), I. off **Spain**; 2nd lgst. of Balearic Is.; Mediterranean agr.; developing tourism; cap. Mahón; a. 733 km²; p. (1981) 58,727.

Minsk, c., cap. of **Belarus**; lge. rly. junc.; cultural and industl. ctr.; univ.; engin., computers; rebuilt since second world war; p. (1990) 1,612,800.

Minya, c. and prov., central **Egypt**; on Nile; cotton tr. ctr.; p. (1986) 179,136 (c.), (1991) 3,003,000 (prov.).

Minya Konka, mtn., S.W. Sichuan prov., **China**; in Himalayas; highest peak in China; 7,570 m.

Mirfield, t., West Yorks., **Eng.**; on R. Calder, 5 km S.W. of Dewsbury; woollens; p. (1981) 18,686.

Miri, t., Sarawak, E. **Malaysia**; impt. oil ctr.;

---

p. (1989) 91,000.

Mirzapur, t. Uttar Pradesh, **India**; on R. Ganges; carpets, brassware; p. (1991) 169,336.

Miskolc, c., N.E. **Hungary**; impt. industl. ctr.; iron ore, lignite nearby; varied inds., inc. textiles, porcelain, engin., bricks, refrigeration plants; p. (1989) 208,000.

Mississauga, c., Ontario, **Canada**; lies to W. of Toronto; part of T. met. a.; p. (1986) 374,005.

Mississippi, st., S. **USA**; Magnolia St.; admitted to Union 1817; st. flower Magnolia, st. bird Mockingbird; in lower M. valley; bounded on S. by G. of Mexico; cotton, sweet potatoes, pecan nuts, rice, sugar-cane, sorghum-cane, fruit, livestock raising; petroleum, natural gas; cotton textiles, chemicals, fish-processing; cap. Jackson; a. 123,584 km²; p. (1990) 2,573,216.

Mississippi, principal R. of **USA**; rises in N. Minn. nr. L. Itasca; drains c. 3,170,000 km²; enters G. of Mexico in lge. delta nr. New Orleans; navigable, flood control problems; length 3,760 km (Mississippi–Missouri–Red Rock 6,176 km).

Missolonghi, t., **Greece**; on inlet of G. of Patras; fish, tobacco; Byron died here 1824; p. (1981) 11,375.

Missoula, t., Mont., **USA**; on Klark R.; univ.; rly. wks., agr., fruit, oil refinery; tourism; p. (1990) 42,918.

Missouri, st., central **USA**; Show-me St.; admitted to Union 1821; st. flower Hawthorn, st. bird Bluebird; dominated by Mississippi and Missouri Rs.; predominantly agr.; livestock, maize; coal, iron; transport equipment; cap. Jefferson City; ch. t. St. Louis; a. 180,456 km²; p. (1990) 5,117,073.

Missouri, longest R. of **USA**; 3,942 km; trib. of Mississippi R.; main headstream Jackson R.; flood, power and irrigation schemes.

Missouri Coteau, hill ridge, N. **America**; runs N.W. to S.E. across prairies of Saskatchewan (Canada), N. and S. Dakota (USA); rises abruptly from 480–600 m.

Mistassini, L., Quebec, **Canada**; 160 km long.

Misurata, t., Tripolitania, **Libya**; on cst. of Mediterranean, 176 km E. of Tripoli; mkt. for local agr. produce; p. (1984) 117,000.

Mitau. *See* Jelgava.

Mitchelstown, t., Cork, **R.o.I.**; nr. Fermoy; dairy prods.; p. (1986) 3,210.

Mitidja, plain, **Algeria,** N. Africa; borders Mediterranean; intensive cultivation of vine; ch. ts. Algiers, Blida.

Mito, c. Honshu, **Japan**; cas., comm. ctr.; famous for lime trees; site of two nuclear power plants nearby; p. (1990) 234,970.

Mits'iwa (Massawa), spt., Eritrea on Red Sea; fine harbour; fishing; fish meal; p. (1980) 32,977.

Mittelland Canal, inland waterway system, **Germany**; system of canals and canalised Rs.; links Dortmund–Ems canal nr. Rheine through Minden, Hanover, Magdeburg, Berlin to R. Oder at Frankfurt-on-Oder; makes use of natural E.–W. troughs across the N. German plain.

Mittweida, t., Saxony, **Germany**; metallurgy, textiles; p. (1989) 17,633.

Miyazaki, c., Kyushu, **Japan**; famous shrine; ctr. of sandy plain with lagoons; p. (1990) 287,367.

Mizoram ("Land of Highlanders"), union terr. (1972); new st. (1986); Assam, N.E. **India**; former Mizo Hills dist. of Assam; 80 per cent p. Christian; 44 per cent literate, higher proportion than any other a. except Kerala; new cap. Aizawl; a. 21,238 km²; p. (1991) 689,756.

Mjosa, lgst. L., **Norway**; 88 km long.

Mladá Boleslav (Jungbunziau), t., Bohemia, **Czech Rep.**; vehicles, agr. machin., textiles; once ctr. of Bohemian Brethren (followers of John Hus); p. (1984) 47,686.

Moanda, spt. at mouth of Zaïre R., **Zaïre**; oil refinery, aluminium smelter.

Mobutu Sese Seko, L., (L. Albert), Zaïre, Uganda; on floor of Gt. Rift Valley; crocodile farming; tourism; main pt. Kasenyi; 160 km long, 32 km wide; alt. 640 m; a. 5,346 km².

Mobile, c., spt., Ala., **USA**; on R. M.; shipbldg. pt. inds.; exp. cotton; p. (1990) 196,278 (c.), 476,923 (met. a.).

Moçambique, former Portuguese prov., indep. st. (1975), **E. Africa**; wide cstl. plain rising inland to 2,100 m; crossed by Zambesi R.; few exp. inc. cashew nuts, cotton, sugar, tea; deposits of coal and bauxite; Beira and Maputo (cap.) serve as import pts. for transit tr.; 40% GNP from tourism and transport; Cabora Bassa Dam in Tete dist.;

severely hit by drought since 1984; civil war against Renamo rebels ended 1992; a. 771,820 km²; p. (1991) 16·11m.

Moçambique Channel, strait, **Indian Oc.**; separates Madagascar from mainland of Africa; 1,600 km long, 400–960 km wide.

Moçambique Current, ocean current, flows N. to S. along E. cst. of Moçambique and Natal, E. Africa; relatively warm water.

Moçâmedes. *See* Namibe.

Modane, t., S.E. Savoie, **France**; commands routes via Mont Cenis Pass and tunnel; electro-metallurgy; p. (1982) 4,877.

Modena, t., cap. of M. prov. **Italy**; cath.; univ.; textiles, leather, engin.; p. (1992) 176,972.

Modesto, t., Cal., **USA**; fruit (especially peaches), vegetable-processing; p. (1990) 164,730 (t.), 371,000 (met. a.).

Modica, t., S.E. Sicily, **Italy**; agr. ctr.; limestone grottoes, cave dwellings, Cava d'Ispica; p. (1981) 45,769.

Moe. *See* Yallourn.

Moers, t. North Rhine-Westphalia, **Germany**; W of Duisburg in the Ruhr; ind. coal; p. (1990) 105,000.

Moffat, burgh, Annandale and Eskdale, **Scot.**; 24 km N.W. of Lockerbie; resort; p. (1991) 2,342.

Moffat Tunnel, Col., **USA**; carries trunk rly. from Chicago to San Francisco under Rocky mtns. between Denver and Salt Lake City; 10 km long; alt. 2,774 m.

Mogadishu, c., cap. of **Rep. of Somalia**; on Indian Oc.; modernised deep-sea pt., airpt.; p. (1987) 1,000,000.

Mogador. *See* Essaouira.

Mogi das Cruzes, t., São Paulo, **Brazil**; agr.; bauxite mng.; p. (1985) 234,900.

Mogilev, c., **Belarus**; on R. Dnieper; industl.; rly. and route junc.; p. (1990) 362,600.

Mohács, t., S. **Hungary**; on Danube; impt. R. pt.; strategic site; battle 1526; p. (1984) 22,000.

Mohammedia, t., Morocco, N. Africa; oil refining; p. (1982) 105,120.

Mohawk, R., N.Y., **USA**; trib. of Hudson R.; followed by impt. road, rly. and canal routes across Appalachian mtns.; 280 km long.

Mojave or **Mohave**, S. Cal., **USA**; desert region of mtns. and valleys; a. 38,850 km².

Moji, spt., Kyushu, **Japan**; exp. coal, cement, timber; linked by bridge to Honshu. *See* Kitakyushu.

Mokpo, spt., W. cst. **S. Korea**; ctr. of food-processing and cotton-ginning; p. (1983) 228,000.

Mol, t., N.E. **Belgium**; nuclear energy research ctr.; p. (1983) 29,970.

Mold, t., Delyn, Clwyd, N. **Wales**; on R. Alyn; chemicals, roadstone; p. (1981) 8,589.

Moldau. *See* Vltava.

Moldova, CIS former constituent rep., USSR; fertile fruit growing a. especially for vines; inds. based on fruit; cap. Kishinev; a. 34,188 km²; p. (1992) 4·4m.

Mole Valley, l. gov. dist., Surrey, **Eng.**; based on Mole R. ts. of Leatherhead and Dorking; p. (1993) 79,100.

Mole R., Surrey, **Eng.**; rises in central Weald, flows N. into R. Thames nr. Molesey; cuts impt. gap through N. Downs between Dorking and Leatherhead; 80 km long.

Molenbeek-Saint-Joan, t., **Belgium**; nr. Brussels; lge mftg. ctr.; p. (1983) 71,181.

Molfetta, spt., Apulia, **Italy**; olive oil, macaroni, wine, caths.; p. (1981) 65,951.

Moline, t., Ill., **USA**; on Mississippi R.; agr. implements, ironwks., flour; p. (1980) 46,278.

Molise, region, central **Italy**; subsistence arable and pastoral farming; a. 4,437 km²; p. (1992) 331,494.

Mollendo, t., S.W. **Peru**; pt. on Pac. Oc.; former outlet for Arequipa; replaced by Matarani; wool textiles, fishing.

Mölndal, t., S.W. **Sweden**; paper, textiles; margarine; p. (1992) 52,423.

Moluccas or **Spice Is.**, prov. **Indonesia**; gr. of Is. between Sulawesi and W. Irian; mtnous., fertile; spices, sago, timber, pearls, rice, copra, ch. t. Ternate; attempts at secession by S. Moluccans; a. 496,454 km²; p. (1983) 1,534,300.

Mombasa, spt., **Kenya**; ch. harbour, Kilindini; rly. terminus; oil refinery; exp. tropical produce (ivory, hides, rubber, etc.); fertiliser plant, sheet glass, steel rolling mill; p. (1984) 425,634.

Møn, I., off cst. of Sjaelland, **Denmark**; a. 233 km²; cap. Stege; p. (1990) 10,132.

Monaco, principality on Mediterranean cst. between France and Italy, W. **Europe**; economy based on tourism; benefits from climate and amenities, inc. famous casino; tax laws attract p. and shortage of land causes M. to build out into sea; much revenue derived from transactional laws, sales of tobacco and postage stamps; cap. Monte Carlo; a. 146 ha; p. (1990) 29,972.

Monadhliath Mtns., Badenoch and Strathspey, **Scot.**; between Spey R. and Loch Ness; hgst. peak Carn Mairg 1,216 m.

Monadnock Mt., peak, 965 m high, N.H., **USA**; name used as a term for the geomorphological feature of an isolated hill which has successfully resisted erosion.

Monaghan, co., **R.o.I.**; mainly pastoral and agr.; a. 1,295 km²; p. (1986) 52,379.

Monaghan, co. t., Monaghan, **R.o.I.**; on the Ulster canal; cath.; p. (1986) 6,075.

Mona Passage, strait, Caribbean Sea; separates Hispaniola from Puerto Rico.

Monastir. *See* Bitola.

Mönch, peak, Bernese Alps, **Switzerland**; 4,101 m.

Mönchengladbach, t., N. Rhine-Westphalia, **Germany**; 26 km W. of Düsseldorf; rly. ctr. textiles; p. (1990) 260,700.

Monchique, t., Algarve, **Portugal**; spa; wine, oil, chestnuts; p. (1981) 9,609.

Moncton, t., N.B., **Canada**; rly. ctr., textiles; oil nearby; p. (1986) 55,468.

Monfalcone, t., N.E. **Italy**; on Adriatic; modern industl. t.; shipbldg., oil refining; p. (1981) 30,277.

Monferrato, low hills, Piedmont, N. **Italy**; S. and S.E. of Turin between valleys of Po and Tanaro; celebrated vineyards, produce Asti Spumante wines; alt. never exceeds 460 m.

Mongla, pt., **Bangladesh**; on Pussur R.; shipping pt. under construction.

Mongolia, vast elevated plateau in heart of Asia between China and USSR. *See* Mongolian People's Rep. and Inner Mongolia.

Mongolia, Inner. *See* Inner Mongolia.

Mongolia, People's Rep. of (Outer Mongolia), central Asia; land-locked, extensive plateau at 1,200 m bordering Gobi desert in S.; dry continental climate with extremely cold winters; pastoral agr. collectively organised for horses, sheep, camels, oxen, and goats; extensive state farms for cereals; cap. Ulan Bator; incr. mechanisation; food processing, livestock prods.; a. 1,564,360 km²; p. (1992) 2,260,000.

Monklands, l. gov. dist., Strathclyde Reg., **Scot.**; part of Central Clydeside conurb. inc. Airdrie and Coatbridge; p. (1992) 102,590.

Monmouth, t., l. gov. dist., Gwent, **Wales**; at confluence of Rs. Wye and Monnow; mkt. ctr.; timber, crushed limestone, wrought ironwk.; p. (1993) 78,400 (dist.).

Monmouthshire, former co., S. **Wales**; mostly inc. in Gwent; parts in South and Mid Glamorgan.

Monongahela, R., W. Va., **USA**; joins Allegheny R. at Pittsburgh to form Ohio R.; impt. waterway.

Monopoli, spt., Apulia, **Italy**; oil, wine, fruit, flour tr.; p. (1981) 43,424.

Monroe, t., La., **USA**; cotton ctr., natural gas, paper, printing ink; p. (1984) 56,000 (t.), 142,700 (met. a.).

Monrovia, c., cap. of **Liberia**, W. Africa; free port and industl. free zone on Atl. at mouth of St. Paul R.; exp. rubber, palm oil; ship registration; p. (1984) 425,000.

Mons, c., cap. of Hainaut prov., W. **Belgium**; nr. Fr. border; cath.; inds. linked with Borinage coal-mng. dist.; varied mnfs.; scene of many battles; NATO (SHAPE) H.Q. nearby at Casteau; p. (1993) 92,533.

Montana, st., N.W. **USA**; Treasure St.; admitted to Union 1889; st. flower Bitterroot, st. bird Western Meadowlark; in Rocky mtns. region; cap. Helena; lgst. c. Great Falls; copper, silver, gold, zinc, lead, manganese; coal, petroleum, natural gas; pastoral agr.; Glacier Nat. Park, tourism; a. 377,456 km²; p. (1990) 799,065.

Montauban, t., Tarn-et-Garonne dep., **France**; on R. Tarn; cath., agr. prod., wines; p. (1990) 53,278.

Montbéliard, t., Doubs dep., **France**; S. of Belfort; textiles, watches, typewriters, vehicles; p. (1990) 30,639(t.), 117,510 (met. a.).

Mont Blanc, mtn., Alps; on confines of **Italy** and **France**; alt. 4,814 m; longest road tunnel in world (opened to traffic 1965) linking Courmayeur (Italy) and Chamonix (France), length 12 km.

Montceau-les-Mines, t., Saône-et-Loire dep., **France**; coal, textiles, metal-working; p. (1982) 51,290 (met. a.).

Mont Cenis Pass and Tunnel, W. Alps; on bdy. between France and Italy; approached from W. by Isère-Arc valleys, from E. by Dora Riparia; alt. 2,097 m; tunnel carries main rly. from Lyons to Turin under Col de Fréjus; opened 1871; 12 km long.

Montclair, t., N.J., **USA;** residtl. sub. of N.Y.; paper gds. manfs.; p. (1990) 37,792.

Mont-de-Marsan, t., Landes dep., **France;** mkt. ctr.; p. (1990) 31,864.

Mont-Dore, spa, Puy-de-Dôme dep., **France;** 48 km S.W. of Clermont-Ferrand; Puy de Sancy (1,887 m) hgst. peak of Mont-Dore mtn. gr.; p. (1982) 2,394.

Monte Bello Is., gr. off N.W. cst., **Australia;** about 136 km N. of pt. of Onslow; first Brit. atomic weapon exploded here 3 Oct. 1952.

Monte Carlo, t., **Monaco;** tourist resort, casino; p. (1985) 12,000.

Monte Corno, mtn., **Italy;** in Central Apennines; alt. 2,923 m.

Monte Cristo, Italian I., 42 km S. of Elba, in Tyrrhenian Sea; famed by novel by Dumas.

Monte Gargano, peninsula, S. **Italy;** projects into Adriatic Sea nr. plain of Foggia; formed by limestone plateau, alt. over 900 m; pasture on upper slopes, woodland on lower slopes; a. 1,030 km².

Montego Bay, spt., **Jamaica;** main ctr. for tourism; p. (1991) 83,446.

Montélimar, t., Drôme dep., **France;** bricks, tiles, nougat; hydroelectric barrage on R. Rhône; p. (1982) 30,213.

Montenegro, constituent rep., S.W. **Yugoslavia;** agr., pastoral; cap. Titograd; a. 13,812 km²; p. (1981) 584,310.

Monterey, t., Cal., **USA;** S. of San Francisco, resort of artists and writers; sardine ind., fruit and vegetable canneries; p. (1980) 27,558.

Monteria, c., cap. of Cordoba prov., **Colombia;** tobacco, cacao, cotton, sugar; p. (1992) 265,754.

Monte Rosa, hgst. peak, 4,637 m, Pennine Alps, on border of **Italy** and **Switzerland.**

Monte Rotondo, hgst. mtn., Corsica, **France;** 2,767 m.

Monterrey, t., cap. of Nuevo León prov., **Mexico;** third lgst. c.; cath.; textiles, brewing, ironwks., minerals; thermoelec. plant; sheet metal; p. (1990) 1,064,197.

Monte Sant'Angelo, hilltop t., **Italy;** on Gargano promontory; notable ctr. of pilgrimage; p. (1981) 16,500.

Montevideo, c., cap. **Uruguay;** major pt. on Rio de la Plata; dominates life of rep. as financial, comm. and industl. ctr.; fisheries, oil-refining, food-processing, tourism; cath. univ.; p. (1992) 1,383,660.

Montgomery, t., l. gov. dist. Montgomeryshire, Powys, central **Wales;** in upper Severn valley, 13 km N.E. of Newtown; agr. mkt.; cas.; p. (1993) 54,100 (dist.).

Montgomery, c., cap. of Ala., **USA;** at head of Alabama R.; cotton, livestock, timber, dairying, fertilisers; hydroelec. power; p. (1990) 187,106 (c.), 292,517 (met. a.).

Montluçon, t., Allier dep., **France;** on R. Cher; terminus of Berry canal, linking Commentry coalfields with Loire; iron foundries, glassmaking; cas.; p. (1982) 51,765.

Montmartre, dist., N. Paris, **France;** on Butte de M. (101 m), commands superb view S. over Paris; picturesque square, frequented by artists; basilica of Sacré Coeur.

Montparnasse, dist., Paris, **France;** on left bank of Seine R.; haunt of artists and writers.

Montpelier, st. cap., Vermont, **U.S.A.;** sm. t. in Green Mtns. and on Winooski R.

Montpellier, t., cap. of Hérault dep., **France;** 8 km N. of Mediterranean cst. on coastal lowland route to S.W. France; comm. and cultural ctr.; univ.; wines, fruit tr.; silk, chemicals; many anc. bldgs. inc. cath.; p. (1990), 210,866(t.), 236,788 (met. a.).

Montreal, c., spt., Quebec, **Canada;** at confluence of Ottawa and St. Lawrence Rs.; caths., univs.; major industl., comm. and financial ctr.; extensive harbour installations, lge. grain exp.; diverse mnfs.; lgst. c. and spt. in Canada; p. mainly French-speaking; p. (1986) 1,015,420 (c.), 2,921,357 (met. a.).

Montreuil-sous-Bois, E. sub. Paris, **France;** hothouse flowers and fruit for Paris mkt.; peach growing; mnfs.; p. (1990) 95,038.

Montreux, t., **Switzerland;** on L. Geneva; tourist ctr.; Chillon cas.; p. (1980) 19,685.

Montrose, spt., burgh, Angus, **Scot.;** on E. cst. at mouth of S. Esk R.; chemicals, rope wks., vegetable-canning, boat-bldg., fishing; supply base for N. Sea oil; p. (1991) 11,440.

Mont-Saint-Michel, rocky granite I., in English Channel, off Normandy cst., **France;** tourist ctr. with Benedictine abbey; connected to mainland by causeway; surrounding marshland reclaimed for agr.; alt. 79 m.; p. (1982) 80.

Montserrat, volcanic I., **Leeward Is., W.I.;** chiefly agr.; exp. sea-island cotton, limes, sugar-cane and tomatoes; cap. Plymouth; a. 101 km²; p. (1987) 11,900.

Montserrat, mtn., Catalonia, **Spain;** Benedictine monastery, alt. 1,236 m.

Monument Valley, Utah and Arizona, **USA;** home of Navajo Indians.

Monza, c., Lombardy, N. **Italy;** 14 km from Milan; cath.; textiles, leather, hats; former royal residence; motor-racing circuit; p. (1992) 120,054.

Moonie, t., Queensland, **Australia;** 320 km W. of Brisbane; oilfields; pipeline to Lytton, at mouth of Brisbane R.

Moose Jaw, c., Saskatchewan, **Canada;** rly. junc.; agr. ctr.; agr. implements, oil refining, p. (1986) 35,073.

Moradabad, c., Uttar Pradesh, N. **India;** rly. junc.; cotton mills, brassware; mosque; p. (1991) 444,000.

Morava, R., **ČSFR** and **Austria;** trib. of R. Danube; navigable in lower course; 339 km long.

Morava, R., Serbia, **Yugoslavia;** formed from W. Morava and S. Morava, flows N. into Danube 80 km below Belgrade to Istanbul; 560 km long.

Moravia, region, **Czech Rep.;** part of Bohemian plateau, drained by Morava R.; inc. fertile agr. a.; mineral resources and industl. ts.

Moray, former co., l. gov. dist., Grampian Reg., **Scot.;** borders M. Firth; arable agr. benefiting from glacial soils; a. 2,230 km²; p. (1993) 88,250.

Moray Firth, arm of N. Sea; on Scottish E. cst., between Highland and Grampian Regs.; plans for lge.-scale industl. expansion; offshore oil platforms at Arderseir; valuable inshore oilfield.

Morbihan, dep., N.W. **France;** on Bay of Biscay; agr., fishing; cap. Vannes; a. 7,094 km²; p. (1990) 619,800.

Mordovia, aut. rep., **Russia;** forested steppe between Rs. Oka and Volga; pastoral agr., lumbering; food processing; a. 25,493 km²; p. (1989) 963,500.

Morea. *See* **Peloponnesus.**

Morecambe and Heysham, t., N. Lancs., **Eng.;** on S. shore of M. Bay; M. holiday resort; H., pt. for N. Ireland and oil refinery; two advanced gas-cooled reactor nuclear power stas.; p. (1981) 41,187.

Morecambe Bay, between Lancs. and Cumbria, **Eng.;** isolates Furness dist. of Lancs.; many proposed barrages across Bay, now project increasingly probable as water shortage in N.W. Eng. grows; discoveries of nat. gas.

Morelia, c., cap. of Michoacán st., W. **Mexico;** on rocky hill, 1,891 m in fertile valley; cath.; textiles, pottery; p. (1990) 489,758.

Morelos, inland st., **Mexico;** mtns., forested; arable agr.; cap. Cuernavaca; a. 4,962 km²; p. (1990) 1,195,381.

Morez, t., Jura dep., **France;** precision instruments, optical equipment; winter sports.

Morgan, t., R. pt., S. **Australia;** transhipment ctr.; from here water pumped from R. Murray and sent by pipeline to Whyalla.

Morgantown, c., W. Va., **USA;** univ.; coal, oil, gas fields; chemicals, heavy ind.; p. (1980) 27,605.

Morioka, c., N. Honshu, **Japan;** textiles, ironwks.; p. (1990) 235,440.

Morlaix, spt., Finistère, **France;** tobacco, paper, brewing, agr.; p. (1982) 19,541.

Morley, t., West Yorks., **Eng.;** 5 km S.W. of Leeds; woollens, stone quarrying; p. (1981) 44,134.

Morocco, kingdom, N.W. **Africa;** csts. on Atl. Oc. and Mediterranean Sea; rises to Atlas mtns. inland; leading world producer of phosphates; other minerals inc. iron-ore, lead and manganese; agr. main occupation, provides 30 per cent of exp.; fishing and tourism well developed; cap. Rabat; a. 466,200 km²; p. (1991) 25·7 m.

Morogoro, t., **Tanzania**, E. Africa; on E. edge of Central African plateau, alt. *c.* 900 m, 176 km by rail W. of Dar-es-Salaam; ctr. of sisal-and cotton-growing a.

Moron, t., **Venezuela**; on cst. nr. Puerto Cabello; industl.; natural gas, oil refining.

Morón de la Frontera, t., S.W. **Spain**; agr. tr. ctr.; ruined Moorish cas.; p. (1981) 27,311.

Morpeth, t., Castle Morpeth, Northumberland, **Eng.**; finely situated in valley of Wansbeck; coal mng., iron-founding; mkt.; Norman cas. remains; p. (1981) 14,545.

Morro Velho, gold mng. dist., Minas Gerais, **Brazil**; in Serra do Espinhaco; ch. t. Nova Lima.

Mors, I., N. Jutland, **Denmark**; in Lim fjord; a. 357 km²; p. (1990) 23,774.

Morwell, t., Victoria, **Australia**; ctr., for brown coal extraction and briquetteg inds. attracted by cheap power; p (1986) 16,387.

Moscow, c., cap. of **Russia**; leading cultural, political, comm., industl. and route ctr.; on Moskva R.; served by several airpts., R. and canal pts.; contains Kremlin in c. ctr. with Red Square; caths., univs., palaces, many famous theatres and art galleries; p. (1989) 8,771,000 (c.), 8,970,000 (met. a.).

Moscow Sea (Ucha Reservoir), artificial L., **Russia**; created behind dam on R. Volga at Ivankovo; supplies water to Moscow, maintains level on Moscow-Volga canal, and supplies water to 8 hydroelec. power-stas.; a. 329 km².

Moscow-Volga Canal, **Russia**; links R. Volga at Ivankovo with Khimki sub. of Moscow; forms part of St. Petersburg-Moscow inland waterway; opened 1937; 128 km long.

Moselle, dep., N.E. **France**; iron-ore, coal mng.; metal inds.; cap. Metz; a. 6,224 km²; p. (1990) 1,011,300.

Moselle, R., **France** and **Germany**; trib. of R. Rhine; canalised between Thionville and Koblenz (269 km); lower valley forms famous wine dist.; 525 km long.

Moshi, t., N. **Tanzania**; on southern slope of Mt. Kilimanjaro; ctr. of coffee-growing dist., airpt. at 854 m (S.W. of t.).

Mosi-oa-Toenja. *See* **Victoria Falls.** The local name means "Smoke of the Thunders."

Mosjoen, t., N. **Norway**; recent aluminium wks; p. (1990) 9,391.

Moskva, R., central **Russia**; trib. of R. Oka; Moscow stands on its banks; linked with upper Volga by Moscow-Volga canal (128 km long); 400 km long.

Mosonmagyarórvár, t., **Hungary**; aluminium wks.; agr. machin.; p. (1984) 30,000.

Mosquito Cst., lowland, E. cst. **Nicaragua**; 400 km N.-S., 192 km E.-W.; lumbering, bananas; ch. t. Bluefields; sparse p.

Moss, spt., **Norway**; pulp, paper, machin., textile inds.; p. (1990) 29,363.

Mossamedes. *See* **Moçâmedes.**

Mossel Bay, pt. and seaside resort, Cape Prov., **S. Africa**; between Cape Town and Port Elizabeth; p. (1980) 33,240 (dist.).

Mossley, t., Tameside, Gtr. Manchester, **Eng.** 5 km E. of Oldham; mkt. t., textiles; p. (1981) 10,224.

Most, t., Czech Rep.; lignite, chemicals; Druzhba crude oil pipeline extended to chemical wks.; p. (1990) 71,000.

Mostaganem, t., **Algeria**; spt. on Mediterranean cst., E. of Oran; exp. wine and fruits; gas pipeline from Hassi Messoud; p. (1982) 169,526.

Mostar, t., **Bosnia-Herzegovina**, formerly Yugoslavia; on R. Naretva; bauxite, lignite; inds., wine, food processing, aluminium plant; devastated in civil war 1993; p. (1981) 110,377.

Móstoles, t. Madrid prov. C. **Spain**; agr. ctr.; p. (1991) 193,056.

Mosul, t., N. **Iraq**; on R. Tigris; in region producing cereals, citrus fruit, cattle; impt. oilfields nearby; metal works; impt. during crusades; p. (1985) 570,926.

Motala, t., on L. Vättern, **Sweden**; radio sta.; engin., woollen gds.; p. (1992) 42,264.

Motherwell, burgh, l. gov. dist., Strathclyde Reg., **Scot.**; in Clyde valley, 24 km S.E. of Glasgow; Iron, steel, machin., engin., textiles; p. (1991) 30,717 (t), (1993) 143,730 (dist.).

Moulins, c., cap. of Allier dep., **France**; on Allier R.; leather gds., clothing; cath., ruined château, art treasures; p. (1990) 23,353.

Moulmein, spt., **Myanmar**, on R. Salween; exp. teak, rice; p. (1983) 219,991.

Mountain Ash, t., Cynon Valley, Mid Glamorgan, **Wales**; in narrow valley 5 km S.E. of Aberdare; coal-mng. a.; p. (1981) 26,231.

Mount Adams, mtn., S. Wash. **USA**; beautiful volcanic scenery in Cascade Range; pine forests; alt. 3,803 m.

Mount Alberta, mtn., W. Alberta, **Canada**; in Canadian Rockies and Jasper Nat. Park; alt. 3,622 m.

Mount Assiniboine, mtn., Alberta, B.C., **Canada**; "Matterhorn" of Canadian Rockies; alt. 3,620 m.

Mount Carmel, mtn., N.W. **Israel**; rises to 554 m and extends 10 km as penin. into Mediterranean Sea, forming S. limit to Bay of Acre; ass. with prophets Elijah and Elisha.

Mount Gambier, t., S. **Australia**; at foot of extinct volcano; forestry, sawmilling of radiata pine; p. (1991) 21,156.

Mount Goldsworthy, t., W. **Australia**; new t. being developed in iron ore mng. a.

Mount Isa, t., W. Queensland, **Australia**; in Selwyn Range 128 km W. of Cloncurry; copper, silver, lead mng.; p. (1991) 23,935.

Mount Lofty Range, mtn. range, S. **Australia**; forms barrier to routes leaving Adelaide; lower slopes support vineyards and outer suburbs of Adelaide; rises to over 700 m.

Mount Lyell, Tasmania, **Australia**; impt. copper mines, and refinery.

Mount McKinley, Alaska, **USA**; in Alaska Range and Nat. Park; highest point in N. America, c. 6,191 m.

Mountmellick, t., Laoighis, **R.o.I.**; p. (1986) 2,789.

Mount Newman, W. **Australia**; t. built 1967 to exploit nearby iron ore.

Mount of Olives, **Jordan**; ridge (817 m), E. of Jerusalem; Garden of Gethsemane on lower slopes.

Mount's Bay, inlet, S. cst., Cornwall, **Eng.**; 32 km wide; fishery grounds.

Mount Tom Price, t., W. **Australia**; new t., being developed in iron ore mng. a.

Mount Vernon, c., N.Y., **USA**; on Bronx R.; sub. of N.Y.; residtl.; takes name from George Washington's house on Potomac, Va., 24 km S. of Washington D.C.; varied inds., notably electronic equipment; p. (1990) 67,153.

Mourenx, t., Pyrénées-Atlantique, **France**; nr. Lacq; new t., in oil dist.; p. (1982) 9,036.

Mourne Mtns., Newry and Mourne, **N. Ireland**; hgst. peak, 853 m.

Mouscron, t., **Belgium**; textile ctr. nr. Fr. border; p. (1993) 53,606.

Moyle, l. gov. dist., **N. Ireland**; borders N.E. cst.; inc. Rathlin I., Giants Causeway; main t. Ballycastle; p. (1991) 14,789.

Mozambique. *See* **Moçambique.**

Mudanjiang (Mutankiang), c., Heilongjiang prov., **China**; pulp, paper, machin., flour milling; site of dam on Mudan R.; oil shale found locally; p. (1984) 603,300.

Mühlhausen, t., Erfurt, **Germany**; on R. Unstrut; textiles, machin., tobacco; p. (1981) 43,348.

Mukden. *See* **Shenyang.**

Mulhacén, mtn., Sierra Nevada range, **Spain**; 3,483 m (hgst. peak Europe, outside Alps).

Mülheim-an-der-Ruhr, t., N. Rhine-Westphalia, **Germany**; on R. Ruhr; cas.; coal mng., iron, steel., tobacco, engin., elec., oil refining; airpt.; p. (1990) 177,200.

Mulhouse, t., Haut-Rhin dep., **France**; impt. textile ctr.; potash deposits to N. supply chemical inds.; p. (1990) 109,905(t.), 223,856 (met.a.)

Mull, I., Argyll and Bute, **Scot.**; included in Hebrides; a. 925 km²; pastoral farming, fishing, tourism; ch. t. Tobermory; p. (1991) 2, 708.

Mullet, The, peninsula, W. cst. Mayo, **R.o.I.**

Mullingar, c., t., Westmeath, **R.o.I.**; on Brosna R.; mkt., agr. ctr.; cath.; p. (1986) 8,077.

Mull of Galloway, S. point of Wigtown, **Scot.**

Multan, t., W. Punjab, **Pakistan**; on R. Chenab; carpets, silks, pottery, steel, thermal sta.; import gas pipeline to Lyallpur; nuclear fuel enrichment plant based on Pakistan's main uranium deposits nearby; p. (1981) 730,000.

Mumbai. *See* **Bombay.**

Muncie, t., Ind. **USA**; on White R.; iron, steel, glass and paper; p. (1990) 71,035.

Munger, t., Bihar, **India**; on R. Ganges; mkt. ctr.; p. (1981) 129,260.

Munich or **München**, c., cap. Bavaria, **Germany**; on R. Isar; cultural ctr. with univ., cath., many old bldgs.; inds. varied, notably scientific instruments, brewing, elec. engin., chemicals; famous film studios; annual beer festival; p. (1990) 1,236,500.

Münster, c., N. Rhine–Westphalia, **Germany**; pt. on Dortmund–Ems canal; heavy machin., with varied mnfs.; cath., univ. and mediæval bldgs. damaged or destroyed in second world war; p. (1990) 261,400.

Munster, prov., S.W. **R.o.I.**; includes cos. Waterford, Kerry, Cork, Limerick, Clare, Tipperary; a. 24,540 km²; p. (1986) 1,020,577.

Muonio, R., part of bdy. between **Finland** and **Sweden**; flows into G. of Bothnia.

Murano, t., Venice, **Italy**; famous since Middle Ages for glass ind.

Murchison Falls. See **Kabelega Falls**.

Murchison, R., W. **Australia**; flows to Indian Oc., spectacular gorge, Nat. Park; length 1,280 km.

Murcia, prov. and former Moorish kingdom, S.E. **Spain**, on Mediterranean, irrigated agr., cereals and fruit; cap. Murcia; a. 8.467 km²; p. (1991) 1,046,561.

Murcia, c., cap. of Murcia prov., S.E. **Spain**; on R. Segura; cath., univ.; textiles and food inds.; p. (1991) 328,847.

Murgab or **Murghab**, R., **Afghanistan**; flows 400 km to desert swamps.

Murmansk, spt., **Russia**; on Kola peninsula; ice-free throughout year; engin., elec. power; fishing, shipbldg.; submarine base; marine power sta. utilising tidal energy projected; p. (1989) 468,000.

Murom, t., **Russia**; pt. on Oka R.; anc. t.; textiles, engin.; p. (1989) 124,000.

Muroran, spt., Hokkaido, **Japan**; on W. cst.; impt. iron and steel ctr.; p. (1990) 136,209.

Murray, R., separates N.S.W. and Victoria, **Australia**; major irrigation schemes support intensive agr.; hydro-electric power; 2,560 km long; length Murray-Darling system 3,696 km.

Murrumbidgee, R., N.S.W., **Australia**; trib. of R. Murray; used extensively for irrigation; 2,160 km long.

Mururoa, coral Is., S. Pac.; used by **France** as nuclear testing site; p. (1985) 3,000.

Musa Jebel, mtn., **Egypt**; 2,249 m; identified with the biblical Sinai.

Muscat, t., cap. of **Oman**, Arabia; on S. cst. of G. of Oman; gd. harbour; dates, mother-of-pearl; terminal of oil pipeline; p. (1990) 380,000 (met. a.).

Muscat and Oman. See **Oman**.

Musgrave Range, mtns., on bdy. between S. Australia and N.T., **Australia**; isolated highland in ctr. of continent; arid; rise to 1,520 m.

Muskingum, R., Ohio, **USA**; trib. of Ohio R.; canalised for navigation; 384 km long.

Musselburgh, burgh, East Lothian, **Scot.**; on F. of Forth at mouth of R. Esk; wire, cables, nets, twine; paper mkg.; golf course; p. (1991) 20,630.

Mutankiang. See **Mudanjiang**.

Mutari. See **Umtali**.

Mutrah, t., **Oman**; ch. comm. ctr.; agr. tr.; site of Port Qaboos, deep water pt.; p. (1980) 15,000.

Muttra. See **Mathura**.

Muzaffarnagar, t., Uttar Pradesh, **India**; N.E. of Delhi; p. (1991) 240,609.

Muzaffarpur, t., Bihar, **India**; in middle Ganges valley N. of Patna; p. (1991) 241,107.

Mwanza, t., N. **Tanzania**; pt. on L. Victoria; rly. term.; gold and diamonds mined; p. (1988) 233,013.

Mweelrea, mtn., Mayo, **R.o.I.**; 820 m.

Mweru, L., between **Zaïre** and **Zambia**; a. 6,993 km² at c. 900 m.

Myanmar, Union of, until 1989 Burma; rep., S.E. **Asia**; Irrawaddy R. basin, developed by British in 19th cent., forms major cluster of p., routeways and source of rice of which M. is one of few exporters; surrounding mtns. relatively underdeveloped, although they are a source of teak and hardwood exps.; almost self-sufficient in petroleum from deposits in N.; natural gas prod. increasingly impt.; monsoon climate; p. mainly Buddhist; secessionist moves in Moslem Arakan st., ch. ts., Mandalay, cap. Rangoon; a. 676,580 km²; p. (1993) 42·33m.

Mycenae, anc. c., N.E. Peloponnesus, **Greece**; excavations by Schliemann.

Myingyan, t., **Myanmar**; on R. Irrawaddy, S.W. of Mandalay; cotton spinning mill, zinc smelting, chemicals, fertilisers.

Myitkyina, t., **Myanmar**; on R. Irrawaddy; terminus

of caravan route to China.

Mymensingh, t., **Bangladesh**; rice, jute; p. (1991) 185,517.

Mynyddislwyn, t., Islwyn, Gwent, **Wales**; in narrow valley of W. Ebbw R., 11 km N.W. of port; elec. gds., kerb- and flagstones; p. (1981) 15,547.

Mysłowice, t., Katowice, **Poland**; ctr. of coal-mng. dist.; technical porcelain; p. (1989) 92,009.

Mysore. See **Karnataka**.

Mysore, t., Karnataka, **India**; univ.; new inds. based on hydroelec. power; p. (1991) 481,000.

Mytilene, pt. Aegean Sea, **Greece**; ch. c. of I. of Lesvos (sometimes called Mytilene); p. (1981) 24,991.

N

Naantali, t., S.W. **Finland**; pt. for Turku, on Baltic Sea; oil-refining, chemicals; founded 15th cent.

Naas, co. t., Co. Kildare, **R.o.I.**; former cap. of Leinster prov.; p. (1986) 10,017.

Naberezhnyye Chelny, t. S. Urals, **Russia**; S. shore of Nizhnekamsk reservoir; named Brezhnev for a time after Soviet leader; p. (1989) 500,000.

Nabeul, governorate, **Tunisia**, N. Africa; p. (1984) 461,405.

Nablus, t., **Jordan**, N. of Jerusalem; nr. site of anc. Schechem and Jacob's Well.

Nadiad, t., Gujarat, **India**; S. of Ahmadabad; p. (1991) 167,051.

Nagaland, st., **India** formerly part of Assam; separate st. since 1963; many border disputes; incorporates Naga Hills and Tuengsang; tribal a., cap. Kohima; a. 16,488 km²; p. (1991) 1,209,546.

Nagano, c., central Honshu, **Japan**; on R. Sinanogawa, 160 km S.W. of Nigata; cultural ctr.; publishing, machin., food-processing; textiles; site of 1998 Winter Olympics. p. (1990) 347,036.

Nagaoka, t., N.W. Honshu, **Japan**; lge. oil production ctr.; p. (1990) 185,938.

Nagapattinam, t., Tamil Nadu, **India**; spt. at mouth of R. Vettar; exp. cotton, tobacco, groundnuts; rly. terminus; p. (1981) 82,828.

Nagasaki, c., spt., Kyushu, **Japan**; on narrow peninsula; second c. destroyed by atomic bomb in second world war; impt. shipbldg. ctr. and associated engin.; p. (1990) 444,616.

Nagercoil, t., Tamil Nadu, **India**; extreme S. of Indian peninsula; coconut-processing; p. (1991) 190,084.

Nagh Hamadi (**Nag' Hammâdi**), t., Upper Egypt; on R. Nile 256 km above Asyût; site of barrage (opened 1930) to regulate Nile flood and ensure irrigation of Girga prov.; barrage carries Cairo–Shellal rly. across Nile.

Nagorno-Karabakh, aut. oblast, S.W. **Azerbaijan**; on E. of Lesser Caucasus; forested mtns.; unrest 1990; cap. Stepanakert; a. 4,403 km²; p. (1990) 192,400.

Nagoya, third c. of **Japan**; on Ise Bay, central Honshu; major pt. and industl. ctr.; univ.; textile mills, ceramic ctr., oil-refining; 16th cent. fortress t.; p. (1990) 2,154,664.

Nagpur, c., Maharashtra st., **India**; univ.; admin. ctr.; textiles; Hindu temples; p. (1991) 1,625,000.

Nagy Banya. See **Baia-Mare**.

Nagykanizsa, t., S.W. **Hungary**; industl. ctr.; heavy equipment, glasswks., beer; p. (1984) 56,000.

Nagykörös, mkt. t., N. **Hungary**; in fruit-growing region; wine, food-processing; p. (1984) 27,000.

Nagymáros, t., **Hungary**; on Danube R. between Budapest and Austrian border; site of hydro-electr. dam built jointly with Austria.

Naha, spt., cap. of Okinawa I., Ryuku Is. **Japan**; p. (1990) 304,896.

Nailsworth, t., Gloucs., **Eng.**; in Cotswold Hills 6 km S. of Stroud; p. (1981) 5,086.

Nairn, former co., l. gov. dist., Highland Reg. **Scot.**; on Moray F., agr. a.; a. 420 km²; p. (1993) 10,850.

Nairn, royal burgh, Nairn, N.E. **Scot.**; fishing ctr.; cas.; p. (1991) 7,892.

Nairobi, c., cap. of **Kenya**; stands at c. 1,500 m on edge of Kenya highlands; modern c., 528 km from Mombasa; univ.; tourist ctr.; lt. inds.; steel rolling mill; inland ctr. for containers; wildlife game reserve; p. (1984) 1,103,554.

Naivasha, L., Kenya; on floor of Gt. African Rift Valley; alt. 1,800 m.

Najaf or Nejef, c., Iraq; in Euphrates valley; Shiite Moslem pilgrimage ctr.; p. (1985) 242,603.

Nakhichevan, c. Azerbaijan; food and wine inds.; ctr. of Nakhichevan aut. region; p. (1990) 60,100.

Nakhicheva, aut. rep. Azerbaijan; borders Iran and Turkey; cotton, tobacco, rice, wheat in irrigated lowlands; salt and mineral deposits; a. 5,439 km²; p. (1990) 300,400.

Nakhodka, t., Russia; outpt. for Vladivostok on Sea of Japan; p. (1989) 160,000.

Nakhon Pathom, t., Thailand; in central plain, S.W. of Bangkok; mkt. t.; p. (1980) 45,242.

Nakhon Ratchasima, t., Thailand; on Mun R., in Korat plateau; rly. junc.; copper deposits nearby; p. (1982) 87,371.

Nakhon si Thammarat, t., Thailand; in S. of Isthmus of Kra, on G. of Siam; anc. t.; mkt.; p (1980) 102,123.

Nakskov, spt., Lolland I., Denmark; sugar-refining; p. (1990) 16,037.

Nakuru, t., Kenya rift valley (1,837 m), E. Africa; protected bird sanctuary (flamingoes) on L. Nakuru; wool-processing, fertilisers; p. (1979) 92,851 (latest fig.).

Nalchik, c., cap. of Kabardino-Balkar aut. rep., Russia; in foothills of N. Caucasus; food-processing; tourist resort; p. (1989) 235,000.

Namangan, c., Uzbekistan; on Syr Dar'ya R., in Ferghana Valley; textiles, leather; p. (1990) 312,000.

Namaqualand, region, S.W. cst. of Africa; divided by Orange R. into Gr. N. in S.W. Africa, and Little N. in Cape Prov., Rep. of S. Africa; semi-arid; a. 259,000 km²; copper, diamonds.

Nam Co (Nam Tso), L., Tibet, China.

Namhol. *See* **Foshan.**

Namib Desert, desert a. along S.W. coastal strip of Africa for 1,200 km; very dry a., and almost unused.

Namibe (Moçâmedes) pt. Angola, S.W. Africa; rail link to Cassinga mines; p. (1981) 100,000.

Namibia, indep. st. (1990); formerly mandated territory under S.Af. rule; became (1990) 50th member of Commonwealth; scanty rainfall; stock rearing; alluvial diamonds from Lüderitz on Orange R.; copper, lead, zinc mng. in Grootfontein dist.; coal and offshore natural gas discovered; minerals provide 60 per cent exp. earnings; ch. pt. Walvis Bay; cap. Windhoek; summer cap. Swakopmund; a. 824,296 km²; p. (1992) 1·51m.

Namsos, spt., central Norway; on Folda fjord; lumber, fish canning; textiles; copper; p. (1990) 8,437.

Namur, c., cap. of N. prov., Belgium; at confluence of Meuse and Sambre Rs.; agr. processing, cutlery, glass; p. (1993) 104,372 (c.), 429,536 (prov.).

Nanaimo, t., B.C., Canada; pt. on Vancouver I.; timber and allied inds.; fisheries; boating and yachting; tourism; p. (1986) 49,029.

Nanchong, c., Sichuan, China; on Kan R.; major transportation and industl. ctr.; textiles, machin., chemicals, paper; tractor wks.; dates from Sung dynasty (12th cent.); p. (1984) 231,700.

Nancheng. *See* **Hanzhong.**

Nancy, c., Meurthe-et-Moselle dep., France; industl. and admin. ctr.; univ., cath.; chemical ind. (based on local salt); anc. cap. of duchy of Lorraine; p. (1990) 102,410 (c.), 310,628 (met. a.).

Nanda Devi, mtn., Uttar Pradesh, India; in Himalayas, 7,822 m; first scaled, 1936.

Nanded, t., Maharashtra, India; p. (1991) 275,000.

Nanga Parbat, mtn., N.W. Kashmir, India, in W. Himalayas; alt. 8,131 m.

Nanjing (Nanking), c., Jiangsu, China; on Chang Jiang; cap. of China during Kuomintang régime 1928–49; famous seat of learning; tombs of founders of Ming dynasty; lge. motor vehicle plant, electronics, precision instruments, insecticides, cotton cloth, oil-refining; road-rail bridge over lowest reaches of Chang Jiang opened 1969; p. (1992) 2,520,000.

Nanling, mtns., S. China; form divide between Rs. flowing N. to Chang Jiang and S. to Xi R.; crossed by historic Cheling and Meiling Passes; alt. mainly below 1,800 m.

Nanning, c., cap. of Guangxi prov., China; on Yu R.; ch. mkt. on S. frontier; rice transplanter factory; p. (1992) 1,070,000.

Nan Shan, mtns., central China; branch range of Kunlun; rise to over 3,600 m.

Nanterre, N.W. sub. of Paris, France; cap. of Hauts-de-Seine dep.; aluminium mftg.; p. (1990) 86,627.

Nantes, spt., cap. of Loire-Atlantique dep., W. France; on R. Loire; ocean pt. St. Nazaire; impt. industl. and shipping ctr.; univ., cath., cas.; p. (1990) 252,029 (c.), 492,255 (met. a.).

Nantong (Nantung) c., Jiangsu, China; on N. bank of Chang Jiang estuary; cotton; p. (1984) 402,700.

Nantucket, I., Mass., USA; official W. end of trans-Atlantic sea-crossing; summer resort; fishing; p. (1980) 3,229.

Nantung. *See* **Nantong.**

Nantwich, mkt. t., Crewe and N. Cheshire, Eng; on R. Weaver, 5 km S.W. of Crewe; brine baths; clothing, food prods.; p. (1981) 11,958; *see* **Crewe.**

Nantyglo and Blaina, t., Blaenau Gwent, Gwent, Wales; in narrow valley 3 km N. of Abertillery; footwear, rubber prods.; p. (1981) 9,862.

Napier, c., N.I., N.Z.; pt. and ch. c. of Hawke's Bay prov. dist.; exp. frozen meat; timber processing, fishing; p. (1991) 51,645.

Naples (Napoli), c., Campania, S. Italy; spt. on Bay of N., at foot of Vesuvius, opposite anc. Pompeii; exp. food prods.; impt. industl. ctr.; shipbldg., oil refining, food-processing; cultural and artistic ctr.; univ., cath.; tourism; earthquake, 1980; p. (1992) 1,071,744.

Nara, c., S. Honshu, Japan; anc. religious ctr. and place of pilgrimage; colossal image of Buddha (16·3 m high); cap. of Japan A.D. 710–84; tourism; p. (1990) 349,356.

Nara Basin, Honshu, Japan; agr. dist. serving the Kinki plain; intensive rice and vegetable cultivation.

Narayanganj, c., Bangladesh; S. of Dacca in middle Ganges delta; p. (1991) 268,952.

Narbeth, mkt. t., South Pembrokeshire, Dyfed, Wales; nr. head of Milford Haven; p. (1981) 1,072.

Narbonne, t., Aude dep., S. France; in Languedoc; nr. Mediterranean cst.; in wine-growing a.; impt. in Roman times; cath., palace (now town hall); p. (1982) 42,657.

Narew, R., Poland and USSR; flows to R. Vistula nr. Warsaw, c. 432 km long; ch. trib. W. Bug.

Narmada, R., central India; flows W. through Madhya Pradesh and Gujarat to G. of Cambay; 1,280 km long.

Narrabri, t., N.S.W., Australia; 570 km N.W. Sydney; observatory with stellar interferometer.

Narrandera, t., N.S.W., Australia; on R. Murrumbidgee; collecting ctr. for wool, mutton, wheat, fruits produced in irrigated a.

Narrogin, t., W. Australia; major ctr. of wheat belt; p. (1981) 4,969.

Narva, t., N.E. Estonia; textiles, machin., sawmills; hydroelectric power; founded by Danes 1223; p. (1991) 87,900.

Narvik, pt., N.W. Norway; sheltered by Lofoten Is.; ice-free; linked by rly. to iron-ore fields in N. Sweden; scene of fierce sea-battles between British and Germans 1940; p. (1990) 13,873.

Naseby, v., Northants., Eng.; battle where parliamentarians under Fairfax and Cromwell beat royalists under Charles I and Prince Rupert 1645.

Nashville, c., st. cap. Tenn., USA; pt. on Cumberland R.; rly. ctr.; impt. shipping, industl. and educational ctr.; food and tobacco prods., cellophane, rayon; univs. and colleges; p. (1990) 487,973 (c.), 985,026 (met. a. with Davidson).

Nasik, t., Maharashtra, India; on R. Godavari; Hindu pilgrimage ctr.; metal work; p. (1991) 657,000.

Nassau, spt., cap. Bahamas, W.I.; exp. forest, sea and agr. prods.; resort; p. (1980) 3,233 (t.), 135,437 (met. a.).

Nassau, I., Cook Is., S. Pac. Oc.; N.Z. terr.; uninhabited; radio telegraph sta.

Nasser City, t., Egypt; rural development at Kom Ombo, N. of Aswan, for resettlement of 50,000 Nubians before formation of Lake Nasser behind the High Dam.

Natal, spt., cap. of Rio Grande do Norte st., Brazil; above mouth of Potengi R.; exp. sugar, cotton, salt, carnauba wax, hides; industl. expansion ; textile mills; airport on main routes from Africa to S. America; p. (1991) 606,541.

Natal, prov., S. Africa; subtropical coastal climate; sugar-cane, tea, cereals; coal; cap. Pietermaritzburg; a. 91,385 km²; p. (1985) 2,145,018.

Natanya or Nathania, t., Israel; resort on Mediterranean cst.; food-processing.

Natauna Is., Indonesia; I. gr. in S. China Sea, N.W. of Borneo; little developed; a. 2,113 km²; p. 27,000.

Naucratis, anc. c., **Egypt**; between Cairo and Alexandria; excavated by Flinders Petrie and Gardiner.

Naumburg, t., Saxony - Anhalt, **Germany**; on R. Saale; cath.; textiles, leather, toys, chemicals; p. (1989) 30,706.

Nauplia (Gr. **Nauplion**), pt. and comm. ctr., on E. cst. Peloponnesus, **Greece**; the anc. Argos; first cap. of indep. Greece 1830-4, when it was superseded by Athens; p. (1981) 10,611.

Nauru, I., indep. rep. (1967), central **Pac. Oc.**; formerly admin. by Australia; coral I., heavily dependent on phosphate-mng.; 80% uninhabitable because of this; a. 21 km²; p. (1990) 8,100.

Navan (**An Uamh**), t., Meath, **R.o.I.**; carpets; lead and zinc ores; p. (1986) 3,660.

Navarre, prov., N. **Spain**; bounded by Pyrenees; thickly wooded; cap. Pamplona; sugar-beet, cereals, cattle, hardwoods, vineyards; former kingdom; p. Basque; p. (1991) 521,940.

Naver, R., Sutherland, **Scot.**; flows N. to Pentland Firth; valley once densely p., cleared early 19th cent. to make room for sheep.

Naxos, I., **Greece**; in Aegean Sea, lgst. of the Cyclades; famous for wine and fruit; a. 425 km²; p. 19,000.

Nayarit, st. W. **Mexico**; agr.; cap. Tepic; a. 26,979 km²; p. (1990) 816,112.

Nazareth, t., **Israel**; 34 km S.E. Acre; home of Jesus Christ.

Naze, The, headland in Essex, 5 m. s. of Harwich.

Nazilli, t., S.W. **Turkey**; on R. Menderes; agr., especially olives; p. (1985) 77,627.

Ndjamena (**Fort Lamy**), c., cap. of **Chad Rep.**; at confluence of Shari and Logone Rs.; isolated but ctr. of caravan tr.; airpt.; p. (1992) 687,800.

Ndola, t., **Zambia**; nr. bdy. with Zaïre, 176 km by rail N. of Kabwe; ctr. of rich copper-mng. a., less impt. lead- and zinc-mng.; minerals despatched by rail E. to Beira and W. to Lobito Bay; oil refining nearby; international airpt. being built; p. (1989) 467,000.

Neagh, Lough, L., **N. Ireland**; lgst. freshwater I. in Brit. Is.; a. 396 km²; drained by R. Bann.

Neath, t., l. gov. dist., West Glamorgan, **Wales**; 10 km up R. Neath from Swansea Bay; coal, aluminium inds., oil refining; cas., abbey; p. (1993) 65,900 (dist.).

Nebraska, st., **USA**; Cornhusker St.; admitted to Union 1867; st. flower Golden rod, st. bird Western Meadowlark; mainly prairie; cap. Lincoln; farming, meat-packing, wheat, maize, hay, potatoes, sugar-beet, apples, wool, livestock, petroleum, cement; a. 200,147 km²; p. (1990) 1,578,385.

Neckar, R., **Germany**; rises between Swabian Jura and Black Forest; flows through Baden-Württemberg to Rhine at Mannheim; 384 km long.

Needles, chalk stacks in English Channel, off W. cst. of I. of Wight, **Eng.**

Neftyne Kamni, t., **Russia**; built on piles over Caspian Sea for Russian oil workers.

Negev, desert, region, S. **Israel**; new a. of irrigated agr.; oil and natural gas.

Negombo, t., S.W. **Sri Lanka**; at mouth of Negombo lagoon; ctr. of coconut belt; metalware, ceramics; p. (1981) 61,376.

Negril Beach, Jamaica; 40 km W. of Montego Bay; new resort to further Jamaica's tourist tr.

Negri Sembilan, st., W. **Malaysia**; on Strait of Malacca; tin and rubber; cap. Seremban; a. 6,682 km²; p. (1980) 573,578.

Negro Rio, R., **Argentina**; flows into G. of St. Mathias, Atl. Oc.; used for irrigation, partly navigable.

Negro Rio, R., **Brazil**; one of ch. tribs. of R. Amazon; rises in Colombia, joins Amazon nr. Manaus; c. 1,520 km long.

Negro Rio, R., **Uruguay**; flows from Brazil border to Uruguay R.; major multi-purpose project at Rincon del Bonete; 800 km long.

Negros, I., **Philippines**; S. of Mindanao; impt. sugar producing I.; copper deposits; a. 12,704 km²; p. (1990) 3,182,219.

Neheim-Hüsten, t., N. Rhine-Westphalia, **Germany**; at confluence of Rs. Möhne and Ruhr; chemicals; part of Arnsberg.

Neijiang (**Neikiang**), c., Sichuan prov., **China**; on To R.; agr. ctr.; p. (1984) 289,100.

Neisse or Nisa, two tribs. of R. Oder, (1) Western or Glatzer Neisse, frontier between Poland

and E. Germany, 224 km long; (2) Eastern or Lausitzer Neisse, E. Silesia, Poland, 192 km long.

Neiva, t., **Colombia**; at head of navigation of R. Magdalena; tr. in cattle and coffee; panama hats; p. (1992) 232,610.

Nejd, C. prov.; with Hejaz, forms kingdom of **Saudi Arabia**; mainly desert; impt. oil wells, horses, camels, dates, various fruits; cap. Riyadh; a. 1,087,800 km²;

Nellore, t., Andhra Pradesh, **India**; admin. ctr.; p. (1991) 316,000.

Nelson, R., **Canada**; drains L. Winnipeg to Hudson Bay; length (with its gr. trib. the Saskatchewan) 2,320 km.

Nelson, t., Pendle, Lancs., **Eng.**; on N. flank of Rossendale 5 km N.E. of Burnley; cotton, iron and brick wks., lt. engin., paper; p. (1981) 30,435.

Nelson, c., S.I., **N.Z.**; pt. nr. head of Tasman Bay; fishing, fruit-packing, timber; coalfield; cath.; p. (1991) 37,943.

Neman (Pol. **Nieman**, Ger. **Memel**), R., **Lithuania** and **Belorussia**; rises S.W. of Minsk and flows c. 920 km into Kurisches Haff (Courland Lagoon), Baltic Sea, forming sm. delta.

Nene, R., Northants., **Eng.**; rises nr. Naseby and flows 144 km to the Wash.

Nepal, indep. kingdom, S.E. **Asia**; on S. slopes of Himalayas and inc. Mt. Everest; isolated from India by malarial forested zone of Terai; N. mostly tropical forest and jungle; home of Gurkhas; poor infrastructure hinders development; only 5,000 km of road; agr. in fertile valleys, rice, wheat, maize; forestry impt. but deforestation a problem; plans to incr. cottage inds.; cap. Katmandu; a. 141,414 km²; p. (1991) 19·36 m.

Nerbudda. See Narmada.

Ness, Loch, L., Inverness, **Scot.**; occupies N.E. end of Glenmore; forms link in Caledonian Canal; very deep; 36·4 km long.

Neston, t., Cheshire, **Eng.**; on N. side of Dee estuary; residtl.; sea bed engin.; p. (1981) 18,415; See Ellesmere Port.

Nestos, R. See Mesta.

Netherlands, kingdom, N.W. **Europe**; bounded by N. Sea, Belgium and W. Germany; comprises 11 provs.; since second world war has taken advantage of location at mouth of Rhine, opposite Thames estuary, to develop lge.-scale coastal inds., inc. iron and steel at IJmuiden, oil refining, petrochemicals at major European pt. complex of Rotterdam–Europort; similarly major industl. growth in conurbation of Randstad Holland in steering economy far away from formerly predominant agr. basis; agr. still impt. and major sea-flood control schemes around IJsselmeer and Rhine estuary are creating valuable land for intensive agr. in a densely populated cty.; recent discoveries of natural gas in Groningen have also turned cty. into major supplier of energy for European mkts.; practises advanced policy of social welfare; EU member; cap. Amsterdam; seat of govt. at The Hague; a. 36,175 km²; p. (1993) 15,240,000.

Netherlands Antilles (**Curaçao**), 2 gr. of Is. in Caribbean Sea, part of Lesser Antilles; main gr. off Venezuela inc. Curaçao, Bonaire and formerly Aruba; 2nd gr. inc. volcanic Is. of St. Eustatius, Saba, and St. Maarten (S. part only); agr. of sm. importance as a result of low rainfall; benefits from Venezuelan oil ind.; oil refineries in Curaçao; petrochemical inds.; indep. planned; Aruba separated (1986) with full internal self-government; cap. Willemstad; a. 1,020 km²; p. (1991) 191,311.

Netze. See Notec.

Neubrandenburg, c., Brandenburg, N. **Germany**; fibreglass, machin., chemicals; p. (1982) 620,600 (dist.).

Neuchâtel, can., **Switzerland**; in Jura mtns.; forested with some pastures; cattle, cheese, wine; watches, cutlery, cottons, hosiery; asphalt from Val de Travers; a. 800 km²; p. (1990) 160,600.

Neuchâtel, cap. of Neuchâtel can., **Switzerland**; on N. slope of Lake Neuchâtel; cas.; univ.; watches, jewellery, condensed milk; p. (1990) 33,060.

Neuchâtel, L., **Switzerland**; at S.E. foot of Jura mtns.; drains N.E. to R. Aare; vineyards on S. facing slopes; remains of lake dwellings, anc. Celtic site of La Tène culture.

Neuilly-sur-Seine, sub., W. of Paris, Hauts-de-Seine, **France**; fine bridge and cas.; engin.; p. (1990) 62,033.

Neumünster, t., Schleswig-Holstein, **Germany**; rly.

ctr.; leather, paper and textile inds.; p. (1986) 77,900.

Neunkirchen, t., Saarland, **Germany**; iron and steel mngs.; coal mng.; p. (1986) 49,500.

Neuquén, prov., S. **Argentina**; natural gas reserves; pipeline planned to feed urban ctrs. of Pampas; p. (1991) 385,606.

Neuquén, t., cap. of N. prov., **Argentina**; at confluence of Rs. Limay and Neuquén, in ctr. of fruit-farming dist.; p. (1980) 90,037.

Neusalz. See **Nowa Sól.**

Neusandetz. See **Nowy Sacz.**

Neuss, c., N. Rhine–Westphalia, **Germany**; rly. junc., canal pt.; nr. Rhine, opposite Düsseldorf; metal gds., food-processing; p. (1990) 147,200.

Neustadt, t., Rhineland-Palatinate, **Germany**; on R. Haardt; agr. machinery; impt. wine tr.; p. (1990) 147,200.

Neustadt. See **Wiener-Neustadt.**

Nentitsehehu. See **Nový Jičin.**

Neva, R., **Russia**, on which St. Petersburg stands; drains L. Ladoga to G. of Finland; navigable but liable to flooding; 74 km long.

Nevada, st., **USA**; Silver St.; admitted to Union 1864; st. flower Sagebrush, st. bird Mountain Bluebird; in Rocky mtns., continental climate; mng. basis of economy gold, silver, copper, tungsten, gypsum, iron, lead; livestock agr., timber; tourism; ts. inc. Las Vegas and cap. Carson City; a. 286,299 km²; p. (1990) 1,201,833.

Nevers, c., cap. of Nièvre dep., **France**; on R. Loire; anc. iron and steel ind.; porcelain and faience; cath., historic bldgs.; p. (1990) 43,889.

Nevis, I., Leeward Is., W.I.; cotton, sugar; ch. t. Charlestown; part of ind. country of St. Christopher-Nevis; a. 130 km²; p. (1980) 9,428.

New Albany, c., Ind., **USA**; on R. Ohio; domestic glassware, furniture, leather, iron and steel, car bodies; p. (1980) 37,103.

New Amsterdam, spt., **Guyana**; on Berbice R.; processes agr. prods. from surrounding lowland.

New Amsterdam, Dutch settlement, Manhattan I., **USA**; taken by English 1664, and renamed New York.

Newark, mkt. t., l. gov. dist. **Newark and Sherwood**, Notts., **Eng.**; on R. Trent 27 km N.E. of Nottingham; ball bearings, brewing and malting; cas.; coal mining at Bilsthorpe; p. (1993) 104,400 (dist.).

Newark, c., N.J., **USA**; meat-packing, printing, elec. gds., paints, chemicals, cars, aircraft, leather; route ctr.; p. (1990) 275,221 (c.), 1,824,000 (met. a.).

New Bedford, c., spt., Mass., **USA**; on estuary of R. Acushnet; whale-fishery ctr.; mnfs. cottons, cordage, glass, shoes; resort; p. (1984) 97,700 (c.), 167,700 (met. a.).

Newbiggin-by-the-Sea, t., Wansbeck, Northumberland, **Eng.**; sm. seaside resort; coal mng.; p. (1981) 12,132.

New Brighton, t., Merseyside, **Eng.**; at entrance to Mersey estuary; residtl. dist. of Wallasey, resort.

New Britain, lgst. I., Bismarck Archipelago, **Papua New Guinea**; volcanic mtns.; exp. copra, cacao; a. (with adjacent Is.) 37,814 km²; p. (1990) 311,955.

New Britain, t., Conn., **USA**; iron and brass mnfs.; p. (1990) 148,000 (met. a.).

New Brunswick, maritime prov., **Canada**; forest-clad mtns.; impt. timber inds.; fishing and fish-processing; many minerals; road and rail link with Prince Edward I.; cap. Fredericton; a. 72,481 km²; p. (1991) 727,300.

New Brunswick, t., N.J., **USA**; on Raritan R.; chemicals, motor lorries, leather, hosiery and hardware; univ.; p. (1980) 596,000 (met. a.).

Newburgh, burgh, North East Fife, **Scot.**; on S. side of F. of Tay, 13 km E. of Perth; fish. pt.; linoleum; p. (1991) 1,401.

Newburn, t., Tyne and Wear, **Eng.**; on R. Tyne. 5 km W. of Newcastle; pure graphite for nuclear reactors; p. (1981) 43,700.

Newbury, t., l. gov. dist., Berks., **Eng.**; on R. Kennet, 27 km S.W. of Reading; engin., furniture, paper, cardboard boxmaking; mkt.; racecourse; p. (1993) 141,000 (dist.).

New Caledonia, overseas terr. of **France**; volcanic I. in S. Pac. Oc.; nickel and chrome deposits; nickel processing; cap. Nouméa; independence movements to establish separate Melanesian reg. in S. Pacific and much unrest since 1984; referendum on full independence to be held in 1998; a. 22,139 km² p. (1989) 164,173.

Newcastle, c., N.S.W., **Australia**; spt. at mouth of

R. Hunter; second c. of st.; lgst. exporter of coal in Australia; iron and steel based on coal resources; new inds. on reclaimed land; mineral sand mng. (rutile, zircon); p. (1991) 432,600 (met. a.).

Newcastle, spt., on Dundrum Bay; Down, **N. Ireland**; resort; p. (1991) 7,214.

New Castle, t., Penns., **USA**; tinplate, glass, steel wire, iron, coal, limestone; p. (1980) 33,621.

Newcastle Emlyn, t., Dyfed, **Wales**; on R. Teifi; p. (1981) 664.

Newcastle-under-Lyme, t., l. gov. dist., Staffs., **Eng.**; 3 km W. of Stoke-on-Trent, on Lyme Brook; coal mng.; brick and tile mnfs.; p. (1993) 123,000 (dist.).

Newcastle-upon-Tyne, c., met, dist, Tyne and Wear, **Eng.**; snt on N. bank of Tyne R., 16 km from N. Sea; shipbldg., heavy engin., chemicals; connected by bridges across Tyne to Gateshead; univ., cath., many fine public bldgs., partially preserved in redevelopment of c. ctr.; airport; new metro system; p. (1993) 285,300 (dist.).

New Delhi. See **Delhi.**

New England, N.S.W., **Australia**; dist. of N. Tablelands; pastoral cty. for sheep and beef; ch. ts. Armidale, Glen Innes, and Tenterfield.

New England, the six N.E. Atl. sts. of **USA**; Me., N.H., Vt., Mass., R.I., Conn.; humid-continental climate, infertile soils, poor agr. conditions; fishing; recent industl. metamorphosis as traditional inds. are replaced by modern science-based, high-value inds.; tourism; ch. t. Boston; p. (1990) 13,206,943.

Newent, mkt. t., Gloucs., **Eng.**; 13 km S. of Ledbury.

New Forest, forest and heathland, Hants., **Eng.**; relic of Royal Forest; now partly owned by Forestry Commission; pasture, ponies, tourism, residtl.; oil reserves but no drilling yet as conflicts with conservation; ch. t. Lyndhurst; now forms l. gov. dist.; p. (1993) 164,500.

Newfoundland, I., with Labrador, prov., of **Canada**; E. of the G. of St. Lawrence; in E. low; in W. rugged mtns., many Ls.; coniferous forest; fishing, cod, salmon, halibut, lobster, seal; lumber, wood-pulp, paper; iron ore, lead, zinc, copper, asbestos; hydroelec. power; climate is severe; cap. St. John's; a. prov. 404,519 km² (I. 112,300 km², Labrador 292,219 km²); p. (1991) 575,600.

New Galloway, burgh, Stewartry, **Scot.**; on R. Dee; nearby Clatteringshaws hydroelec. sta..

New Guinea, I., S.W. Pac. Oc.; N. of Australia; equatorial climate; dense forest; central mtn. chain; lge. a. of lowland in S.; divided politically between Irian Jaya in W. (Indonesia) and Papua New Guinea in E.; economically underdeveloped; a. 831,390 km². See **Papua New Guinea, Irian Jaya.**

Newham, inner bor. Greater London, **Eng.**; W. of R. Lea; contained Royal group of London docks (now all closed); p. and industl. decentralisation from a.; p. (1993) 226,300.

New Hampshire, st., New England, **USA**; borders on Canada; Granite St.; admitted to Union 1788; st. flower Purple Lilac, st. bird Purple Finch; forested mtns.; agr., fruit-growing; paper and forest prods.; textiles, shoes; granite; cap. Concord; ch. spt. Portsmouth; ch. mftg. ctr. Manchester; a. 24,097 km²; p. (1990) 1,109,252.

Newhaven, t., East Sussex, **Eng.**; on S. cst. at mouth of R. Ouse, 14 km E. of Brighton; passenger pt. for Dieppe; boat-bldg. and lt. indus.; p. (1981) 9,857.

New Haven, c., pt., Conn., **USA**; on inlet of Long I. Sound; Yale Univ.; firearms, clocks, hardware, radiators, rubber gds.; p. (1990) 130,374 (c.), 530,000. (met. a. with Meriden).

New Hebrides. See **Vanuatu.**

New Holland, v., rly. terminus, ferry pt. for crossing to Hull, Humberside, **Eng.**

New Ireland, volcanic I., **Papua New Guinea**, in Bismarck archipelago; mtnous.; ch. pt. Kavieng; exp. copra; a. (with adjacent Is.) 9,842 km²; p. (1990) 87,194.

New Jersey, st., **USA**; Garden St.; admitted to Union 1787; st. flower Purple Violet, st. bird Eastern Gold Finch; on Atl. cst. plain, adjacent to N.Y. C.; intensive agr., mkt. gardening; heavily industrialised; oil refining, glass sand, zinc, iron ore, clay, chemicals, motor vehicles; cap. Trenton; ch. cs. Newark, Jersey City; a. 20,295 km²; p. (1990) 7,730,188.

Newmarket, t., Forest Heath, Suffolk, **Eng.**; at

foot of E. Anglian Heights; horse racing centre; p. (1981) 16,235.

New Mexico, st., **USA**; popular name 'Land of Enchantment'; admitted to Union 1912; st. flower Yucca, st. bird Road Runner; N. of Mexico, S. of Col. st.; traversed by Rocky mtns.; dry climate; agr. dependent upon irrigation; dry farming, arable crops, livestock; uranium, potash salts, pumice, beryllium, copper, petroleum; ch. ts., Albuquerque and cap. Santa Fé; a. 315,115 km²; p. (1990) 1,515,069.

New Mills, industl. t., High Peak, Derbys., **Eng.**; at W. foot of Pennines; textile printing, bleaching and dyeing; rayon, paper; confectionery; p. (1981) 9,084.

Newmilns and Greenholm, burgh, Kilmarnock and Loudoun, **Scot.**; on R. Irvine, 19 km E. of Kilmarnock; muslin and lace curtain mnf.; p. (1991) 3,436.

New Mirpir, t., **Pakistan**; new t. 3 km. from old Mirpur submerged by Mangla L. 1967; planned p. 40,000.

New Orleans, c., spt., La., **USA**; on delta of Mississippi R.; the gr. cotton mart of America, busy comm., mftg. and cultural ctr., home of jazz; sugar refining, oil refining; p. (1990) 496,938 (c.), 1,238,816 (met. a.).

New Plymouth, dist., N.I., **N.Z.**; on W. cst. at N. foot of Mt. Egmont; oil and natural gas deposits; dairy-farming; p. (1991) 67,951.

Newport-on-Tay, burgh, North East Fife, **Scot.**; on S. side of F. of Tay, opposite Dundee; p. (1991) 4,343.

Newport, Medina, cap. I. of Wight, **Eng.**; on R. Medina, in gap through central chalk ridge; mkt.; brewing, joinery, bait mnfs.; prison; p. (1981) 23,570.

Newport, mkt. t., The Wrekin, Shrops., **Eng.**; 13 km N.E. of Wellington; p. (1981) 8,983.

Newport, spt., **Vietnam**; on N. outskirts of Ho Chi-minh City; lge. pt. inaugurated 1967.

Newport, t., **R.I.**, **USA**; on Narragansett Bay; fashionable seaside resort; precision instruments; p. (1980) 29,259.

Newport, t., l. gov. dist., Gwent, **Wales**; on R. Usk, 8 km from its mouth; timber terminal and deepwater berth; engin., iron and steel, aluminium, paperboard, confectionery, chemicals, plastics; p. (1993) 137,000 (dist.).

Newport News, c., spt., Va., **USA**; on N. shore of estuary of James R. on Hampton Roads; lge. harbour; shipbldg.; outlet for Virginian tobacco and Appalachian coal; p. (1990) 170,045 (c.), 1,396,000 (met. a. with Norfolk-Virginia Beach).

Newport Pagnell, mkt. t., Bucks., **Eng.**; on R. Ouse; mnfs. Aston Martin cars; p. (1981) 10,810.

Newquay, t., Restormel, Cornwall, **Eng.**; on N. Cornish cst.; seaside resort; p. (1981) 16,050.

New Quay, t., Ceredigion, Dyfed, **Wales**; on cst. of Cardigan Bay; fishing; resort; p. (1981) 766.

New Radnor, t., Powys, **Wales**; on slope of Radnor Forest, 10 km S.W. of Presteign.

New Rochelle, t., N.Y., **USA**; on Long I. Sound; residtl.; p. (1990) 67,265.

New Romney, t., Shepway, Kent, **Eng.**; nr. S. cst. to E. of Dungeness; in rich agr. dist. of Romney Marsh; Cinque pt.; old harbour silted up by shingle, now a mile from sea; p. (1981) 4,563.

New Ross, mkt. t. Wexford, **R.o.I.**; brewing and malting; p. (1986) 5,343.

Newry, t., Newry and Mourne, **N. Ireland**; pt. at head of Carlingford Lough; machin., rope, brewing, granite; p. (1991) 21,633.

Newry and Mourne, l. gov. dist., **N. Ireland**; surrounds t. of N., borders R.o.I., Irish Sea; inc. Mtns. of Mourne; p. (1991) 82,943.

New South Wales, st., S.E. **Australia**; first col. established by Brit. in A.; much mineral wealth in tablelands and mtns.; climate equable and well suited to both arable and pastoral agr.; leading agr. st. in Australia; major irrigation schemes in drier E. plains of Murray, Murrumbidgee, and Lachlan Rs.; coal mng. and heavy inds. at Newcastle, Port Kembla, Wollongong; hydroelectric power from Snowy mtns. scheme; lge. concentration of p. in cap. c. of Sydney; a. 801,431 km² (excluding Cap. Terr. of Canberra); p. (1991) 5,940,800.

Newton, t., Mass., **USA**; on R. Charles; in met. a. of Boston; lt. inds.; p. (1980) 83,622.

Newtonabbey, t., l. gov. dist., **N. Ireland**; sub. of Belfast, textiles, lt. inds.; p. (1991) 74,035 (dist.), 56,811 (t.).

Newton Abbot, mk. t., Teignbridge, Devon, **Eng.**; at head of Teign estuary; rly. junc.; pottery, lt. engin.; agr. processing; p. (1981) 20,927.

Newton Aycliffe, t., Durham, **Eng.**; 10 km N.W. of Darlington; new t. (1947); engin., textiles, plastics, paint; p. (1981) 24,720.

Newton-le-Willows, t., Merseyside, **Eng.**; engin., printing, sugar-refining; p. (1981) 19,723.

Newton-Stewart, burgh, Wigtown, **Scot.**; on R. Cree, 8 km N. of Wigtown; mkt.; wool, creameries and agr. inds.; p. (1991) 3,673.

Newtown and **Llanllwchaiarn**, mkt. t., Powys, **Wales**; on R. Severn 13 km S.W. of Montgomery; precision instruments, machine tools; plan for expansion as growth-pole for central Wales; p. (1981) 8,660.

Newtownards, spt., mkt., Ards, **N. Ireland**; 11 km E. of Belfast; textile and engin. inds.; p. (1991) 23,869.

Newtown St Boswells, burgh, Ettrick and Lauderdale, **Scot.**; cap. Borders region; p. (1991) 1,108.

New Waterway. See **Nieuwe Waterweg**.

New Westminster, t., B.C., **Canada**; spt. on estuary of R. Fraser; exp. timber; agr. ctr., food-processing and canning; fishing; oil refining; forms part of Vancouver met. a.; p. (1986) 39,972.

New York, st., N.E. **USA**; popular name 'Empire St.'; admitted to Union 1788; st. flower Rose, st. bird Bluebird; one of 13 original sts., borders Canada on N., faces Atl. Oc. in S.; Adirondack mtns. in N., with lowland in E. alongside L. Ontario; Hudson valley impt. routeway; humid-continental climate; second lgst. st. in p. size and despite p. movement to W., remains major a. of urbanisation (megalopolis) with comm. and industl. activity; ch. ts. inc. Buffalo, Rochester, Syracuse; st. cap. Albany, metropolis New York city; decline of N. ts. offset by inds. from Quebec, leaving Canada because of separatist moves; dairy farming and intensive agr. serve urban mkts.; a. 128,402 km²; p. (1990) 17,990,455.

New York, c., spt., N.Y., **USA**; on N.Y. Bay at mouth of Hudson R.; lgst. c. in USA and one of lgst. in world; comprises 5 bors., Manhattan, Bronx, Queens, Brooklyn, Richmond; originally founded by Dutch settlers as New Amsterdam on Manhattan I.; gr. comm. ctr. and cultural cap.; univ.; fine parks, bridges, skyscrapers, and deepwater harbour; varied inds., inc. clothing, food-processing, printing and publishing, shipbldg.; despite p. and industl. decentralisation concentration of socially needy in c. causing financial difficulties to c. govt.; 2 intern. airports; p. (1990) 7,322,564 (c.), 8,546.846 (met a.).

New York State Barge Canal (Erie Canal), N.Y. st., **USA**; links Tonawanda on Niagara R. with Hudson R. via the Mohawk gap through Appalachian mtns.; provides through water route from N.Y. to Gr. Ls.; opened as Erie Canal 1825, improved 1918; length 542 km (with branches 840 km), depth 4 m.

New Zealand, indep. sov. st. within Brit. Commonwealth, S. Pac. Oc.; 1,920 km E. of Sydney. Australia; consists of two major Is., N.I. and S.I., separated by Cook Strait, and several smaller Is., inc. Stewart I. to S.; mtnous., glaciated, volcanic; landscapes with superb scenery; dependent upon pastoral prods., taking advantage of equable climate and excellent grass growing conditions, but mainly reliant on Brit. mkts.; economic diversification; expansion of lt. indus., inc. car assembly, pulp and paper, textiles; hydroelec. potential being developed; oil and natural gas recently discovered; advanced social services; cap. Wellington; ch. pt. Auckland; a. 268,676 km²; p. (1994) 3·49 m.

Neyland, t., Preseli, Dyfed, **Wales**; on Milford Haven; rly. terminus and sm. pt.; p. (1981) 3,097.

Ngami, L., Botswana, S.W. Africa; swamp, the remnant of a much larger L.

Ngauruhoe, mtn., N.I., **N.Z.**; an active volcano; 2,292 m.

Niagara, R., forms part of boundary between **Canada** and **USA**; flows from L. Erie to L. Ontario; rapids and famous falls utilised by gr. hydroelec. power sta. heavily polluted with toxic waste; 56 km long.

Niagara Falls, waterfall, Niagara R., on bdy. of **USA** and **Canada**; in two sections, American (51 m high) and Canadian (48 m high), separated by Goat I.; major tourist attraction and hydroelec. power sta.

Niagara Falls, t., Ontario, **Canada**; opposite the falls; hydroelectric power sta.; timber and agr., inds., tourism; p. (1986) 72,107.

Niagara Falls, c., N.Y., **USA**; extends along summit of cliff for 5 km; paper, flour, aluminium, chemicals, hydroelectric power stas.; univ.; p. (1990) 61,840 (c.), 221,000 (met. a.).

Niamey, t., cap of **Rep. of Niger,** W. Africa; one of the termini (the other is Zinder) of the trans-Sahara motor routes; agr. tr. ctr.; p. (1988) 398,265.

Nicaragua, rep., Central America; civil war (1970), lies across isthmus with Pac. Oc. to W., Caribbean Sea to E.; sparsely populated; central mtn. range, marshy E. cst.; tropical rain forest and climate; limited a. of fertile soils but 70 per cent. p. farmers; main exps. coffee, cotton industl. growth was based on US investment, gold and silver mng.; food shortages caused by war and US trade embargo; declining coffee exports, cotton hit by disease; cap. Managua; a. 148,006 km²; p. (1991) 3·87m.

Nicaragua, Lake, S.W. Nicaragua; lgst. L. in Central America; 24 km from Pac. Oc., but discharges into Caribbean via San Juan R.; fisheries; 160 km N.W. to S.E., 67 km S.W. to N.E.

Nicaraguan Depression, lowland, **Nicaragua**; contains Ls. Maragua and Nicaragua.

Nice, c., spt., cap. of Alpes Maritimes dep., **France**; on Mediterranean cst., at foot of Alps; pleasant climate and surroundings; adjoins anc. t. of Cimiez; ceded to France 1860 by Sardinia; resort; fruit and flower exp., perfume mftg.; attracting science-based inds.; major airport; p. (1990) 345,647 (c.), 475,507 (met.a.).

Nicobar Is. See **Andaman and Nicobar Is.**

Nicosia, c., cap. of **Cyprus**; agr. tr. ctr.; textiles, cigarettes, leather, pottery mnfs.; remains of Venetian fortifications; mosques; airport; cap. of admin. dist. of Nicosia; tourism; new name Lefkosia (1995); p. (1991) 166,500.

Nidd, R., trib. of R. Ouse, North Yorks., **Eng.**; 80 km long.

Nidwalden. See **Unterwalden.**

Nieder Sachsen. See **Lower Saxony.**

Nieuwe Waterweg, ship canal, S. Holland, **Neth.**; connects R. Lek 11 km below Rotterdam with N. Sea cst. at Hook of Holland.

Nieuwveld Range, mtns., Cap Prov., **S. Africa**; part of S. terminal escarpment of African tableland; overlooks Gr. Karroo to its S.; forms impenetrable barrier to routes; mainly over 1,500 m. max. alt. 1,914 m.

Nièvre, dep., central **France**; traversed by Morvan mtns., forests, arable agr.; cap. Nevers; a. 6,887 km²; p. (1990) 233,300.

Nigel, t., Transvaal, **S. Africa**; gold mng.; industl.; p. (1980) 76,700 (dist.).

Niger, landlocked rep., W. **Africa**; 90 per cent p. dependent upon agr. but only 3 per cent of land cultivated; livestock (cattle, sheep, goats), cotton; exp. of groundnuts main source of wealth; rainfall diminishes to N. giving way to Sahara Desert; discovery and exploitation of uranium (1967), 75 per cent of exp. earnings in 1980 but now declining; fishing in L. Chad; game hunting; close economic ties with France; cap. Niamey; a. 1,253,560 km²; p. (1991) 8·04m

Niger, R., W. **Africa**; rises nr. sea in outer mtn. zone of W. Africa as R. Tembi, sweeps round by Timbuktu to delta in G. of Guinea, on circuitous course of 4,160 km, receiving its gr. trib., the R. Benue, about 400 km from the mouth; navigable for 1,600 km; Kainji (Nigeria) hydroelec. plant and dam opened 1969; now organised by international Niger Basin Authority.

Nigeria, fed rep., W. **Africa**; within Brit. Commonwealth; federation of 19 sts.; climate, wet, tropical in S., increasingly dry to N.; main economic development in S.; exp. agr. prods., especially cocoa; exp. hardwoods; economic growth based on cstal. oil deposits (sulphur free); fall in oil prices causing decline in production and exp.; 2nd oil producer in Africa; 6th in world; former cap. Lagos, lgst. c. Ibadan; cap. Abuja; a. 923,773 km²; p. (1991) 88,514,501.

Niigata, c., Honshu, **Japan**; pt. on W. cst. exp. locally produced petroleum; chemical inds.; p. (1990) 486,097.

Niihama, c., N. Shikoku, **Japan**; on cst. of Inland Sea, 32 km S.E. of Imabari; refines copper obtained from Besshi mines 19 km to the S.; petrochemicals; p. (1990) 129,151.

Nijmegen, c., E. **Neth.**; on R. Waal, nr. German bdr., 18 km S. of Arnhem; Hanse t. in Middle Ages; historic bldgs., univ.; p. (1993) 146,993 (c.), 246,885 (met. a.).

Njni-Novgorod. See **Gorki.**

Nikko, t., Honshu, **Japan**; famous temples and shrines; tourist resort; p. (1990) 20,128.

Nikolayev, c., cap. of N. oblast, **Ukraine**; major spt. at head of Dnieper-Bug estuary on Black Sea; shipbldg., ctr.; exp. minerals, grains; founded 1784 as fortress; p. (1990) 507,900.

Nikolayevsk, R. pt., Khabarovsk terr., **Russia**; on R. Amur; shipyards; fishing, canning, lumbering, oil refining.

Nikopol, c., **Ukraine**; on Dnieper, manganese mng. ctr.; steel mnshn.; p. (1990) 158,000.

Nikšić, t., Montenegro, **Yugoslavia**; N. of Cetinje; bauxite mng., growing industl. ctr.; p. (1981) 72,299.

Nile, longest R. in Africa (see **White Nile** (Bahr-el-Abiad) and **Blue Nile** (Bahr-el-Azrek);); flows through a longer stretch of basin (over 3,920 km in a direct line) than any other R., and along all its windings measures 6,670 km; on Upper Nile navigation is hindered by sudd (floating vegetation); R. rises April, overflows Sept.; formerly cultivation entirely dependent on annual floods, but now assisted by dams, at Asyût, Aswan, Sennar, for regulating flow and navigation; Aswan High Dam completed 1970, but complex problems of delta erosion and dam-lake silting. See also **Egypt.**

Nilgiri Hills, Tamil Nadu, S. **India**; tea-growing dist.; resort a.

Nîmes, c., cap. of Gard dep., S. **France**; in Cevennes; Roman antiquities, notably Maison Carrée; silk, cotton, carpets, wines; tourism; p. (1990) 133,607.

Nineveh, celebrated anc. c., **Iraq**, stood on E. bank of upper R. Tigris, opposite modern Mosul.

Ningbo (Ningpo), c., spt., Zhejiang, **China**; 160 km from Shanghai; leading fish, pt., comm. and mnf. ctr.; exp. agr. and fish prods.; c. opened to foreign investment under new economic reforms; p. (1992) 1,090,000.

Ningxia Hui, aut. region, N.W. **China**; bounded on N. by Inner Mongolia; dry a. but modern irrigation projects allow growth of spring wheat and rice; coal reserves, salt; cap. Yingchuan; a. 66,408 km²; p. (1990) 4,660,000.

Niobrara, R., **USA**; trib. of Missouri R.; flows from Wyoming to Nebraska; 960 km long.

Niort, c., cap. of Deux-Sèvres dep., W. **France**; noted for mkt. gardens and leather gds. (gloves); birthplace of Mme de Maintenon; p. (1990) 58,660.

Nipigon, Lake, in Thunder Bay dist., Ont., **Canada**; 106 km long, 74 km wide; studded with Is.; discharges by Nipigon R. to L. Superior.

Nipissing, Lake, S. Ont., **Canada**; 855 km²; drained by French R. to Georgian Bay.

Niš, t., Serbia, **Yugoslavia**; on R. Nishava; route ctr.; rly. engin., developing mftg.; univ.; p. (1991) 175,555.

Nišava, R., Serbia, **Yugoslavia**; flows N.W. into R. Morava nr. Niš; valley used by trunk rly. from Belgrade to Istanbul; length over 160 km.

Nishapur, mkt. t., N.E. **Iran**; S.W. of Mashhad; in fertile a.; cotton, fruits; famous turquoise mines nearby; birthplace of Omar Khayyám; impt. archaeological finds dating 9th and 10th cent.

Nishinomiya, c., S. Honshu, **Japan**; produces famous liquor called saké; machin., chemicals; p. (1990) 426,919.

Niterói, t., cap. of Rio de Janeiro st., **Brazil**; shipbldg.; residtl. sub. of Rio de Janeiro c. to which it is linked by bridge; p. (1991) 416,123.

Nith, R., S.W. **Scot.**; flows to Solway F., S. of Dumfries; followed by main rly. from Carlisle to Kilmarnock and Glasgow; 114 km long.

Nithsdale, t. gov. dist., Dumfries and Galloway, **Scot.**; a. based on Dumfries; p. (1993) 57,220.

Nitra, t. **Slovakia**, on R. Nitra N.E. of Bratislava; first Christian church in region there; agric. industries; p. (1990) 91,000.

Niue or **Savage I., Pac. Oc.**; one of Cook Is., formerly part of N.Z., self government 1974; ch. pt. Alofi; copra, plaited basketware, sweet potatoes; a. 259 km²; p. (1991) 2,239.

Nivernais, former prov. of **France**, now forming Nièvre prov. and part of Cher.

Nizamabad, t., Andhra Pradesh, **India**; road and rly. ctr. N. of Hyderabad; p. (1991) 240,924.

Nizhneudinsk, t., W. Irkutsk, **Russia**; new mftg. t.

Nizhniy Novgorod, (Gorki), c., **Russia;** cap. of forested region, on Rs. Oka and Volga; univ., churches, 13th cent. kremlin; gr. industl. ctr. with heavy engin., steel, textiles, chemicals, oil refining, cars, glass, timber inds.; birthplace of Maxim Gorky; p. (1989) 1,438,000.

Nizhniy Tagil, t., **Russia;** in Ural mtns.; metallurgical ctr. using ore from Mt. Visokaya; rly. cars, iron, and steel plants, chemicals; p. (1989) 440,000.

No, Lake, Bahr-el-Ghazal prov., **Sudan;** N.E. Africa; vast swamp a., 906 km S.W. of Khartoum; flow of water blocked by papyrus reed and floating weed (sudd).

Nobeoka, t., Kyushu, **Japan;** on E. cst.; p. (1990) 130,615.

Nobi Plain, S. Honshu, **Japan;** at head of Ise Bay; consists of low, badly drained alluvial plain on W. under intensive rice cultivation, with higher, drier, terraces on E. under mulberry, vegetables, pine-woods; very dense urban and rural p.; ch. textile and pottery mftg. a. in Japan; inc. cs. Nagoya, Gifu, Yokkaichi; a. 1,865 km².

Nocera Inferiore, t., **Italy;** nr. Naples; vegetable-canning, textile mnfs.; p. (1981) 47,698.

Nogales, Sonora, **Mexico;** mng. and agr. ctr.; p. (1990) 107,119.

Noginsk, t., **Russia;** nr. Moscow; textiles, metals; natural gas pipeline from Central Asia projected; p. (1989) 123,000.

Nola, c., **Italy;** at foot of Vesuvius, 19 km N.E. of Naples; ctr. of fertile arable agr. a. in Campania plain; anc. c., home of Giordano Bruno; p. (1981) 30,979.

Nome, c., W. Alaska, **USA;** on Seward peninsula; gold rush (1900); now admin. and route ctr.; airport; tourism; p. (1990) 8,288.

Noord Brabant, prov., **Neth.;** s. of Gelderland; N. half former Duchy; cattle, grain, hops; cap. 's-Hertogenbosch; a. 4,973 km²; p. (1993) 2,243,546.

Noord Holland, prov., **Neth.;** a. 2,722 km²; cap. Haarlem; natural gas in Schermer Polder nr. Alkmaar; p. (1993) 2,440,165.

Noordoostpolder, Overijssel, **Neth.;** land reclaimed from Zuider Zee, 1942; now used for intensive agr.; a. 479 km²; p. (1993) 39,053.

Nord, dep., N. **France;** borders on Belgium and N. Sea; flourishing agr., mng. iron and coal, textile and chemical mnfs.; cap. Lille; a. 5,773 km²; p. (1990) 2,531,900.

Nordenham, pt. on Lower Weser R., Lower Saxony, **Germany;** lead and zinc smelting; fishing; p. (1986) 28,800.

Norderney, one of the E. Frisian Is., **Germany;** low-lying sand-dunes; resort at Nordseebad.

Nordhorn, t., Lower Saxony, **Germany;** nr. Neth. frontier; textiles; p. (1986) 48,000.

Nordkyn, Cape, northernmost pt. of European mainland, Finnmark prov., N. **Norway.**

Nordland, co., N. **Norway;** fjord cst.; p. on cst. lowlands; fishing, livestock; iron-ore, electro-chemical and metallurgical inds. based on local hydroelec. power; spt. Narvik; a. 38,146 km²; p. (1990) 238,345.

Nord-Pas-de-Calais, region, N.E. **France;** inc. deps. Nord, Pas-de-Calais; north-eastern corner of France, bordering Belgium; inc. ports of Boulogne, Calais, Dunkirk and southern end of Channel Tunnel; p. (1990) 3,965,100.

Norfolk, non-met. co., E. **Eng.;** low-lying fens in W.; low sandy cst. suffers from erosion; intensive arable agr. on lge. farms; wheat, barley, root crops; inds. based on agr. processing and provision of agr. requisites; tourism intensively developed on Norfolk Broads; cap. Norwich; a. 5,354 km²; p. (1993) 765,100.

Norfolk, c., Va., **USA;** naval base on Hampton Roads; fine deepwater harbour; exp. coal, industl. prods.; shipbldg., car assembly, food-processing, timber inds., fertilisers; p. (1990) 261,229 (c.), 1,396,107 (met. a. with Virginia Beach-Newport News).

Norfolk I., remote dependency of Australia; **Pac. Oc.;** volcanic I., 1,676 km N.E. of Sydney; unique ecology; fertile agr.; discovered by Cook 1774; penal settlement 1788–1853; tourism; a. 34 km²; p. (1986) 1,977.

Norilsk, t., Krasnoyarsk terr., **Russia;** in N. Siberia; northernmost t. in Russia; mng. of coal, uranium, nickel, copper; natural gas pipeline from W. Siberia; p. (1989) 175,000.

Normandy, historic prov. of **France;** on English Channel; now divided into deps. Manche, Calvados, Eure, Seine-Maritime and part of Orne; Rouen was cap.; Channel Is. were part of the old duchy; conquered England 1066; allied invasion of Europe 1944.

Normanton, t., West Yorks., **Eng.;** 5 km N.E. of Wakefield; coal mng.; p. (1981) 17,256.

Norman Wells, t., N.W. Terr., **Canada;** at confluence of R. Mackenzie and Gr. Bear R., 112 km W. of Gr. Bear L.; ctr. of rich oil-field; p. (1986) 627.

Norrbotten, prov., N. **Sweden;** rich iron deposits at Kiruna; ore exp. via ice-free Narvik on Norwegian cst.; many Ls. and Rs., highest peak in Sweden, Kebnekaise; cap. Pitea; a. 105,553 km²; p. (1992) 266,089.

Norris Dam, Tenn., **USA;** across R. Clinch at confluence with R. Tennessee, N.W. of Knoxville; lgst. dam Tenn. Valley Authority (TVA); built for flood control and hydroelectric power.

Norrköping, c., S.E. **Sweden;** nr. inlet of Baltic Sea; industl. and shipping ctr.; ocean-going shipping through Lindö canal; p. (1992) 120,798.

Northallerton, mkt. t., Hambleton, North Yorks., admin. ctr., **Eng.;** in broad gap between Cleveland hills and Pennines; in dairy farming and agr. dist.; p. (1981) 9,622.

North America, northern continent of W. hemisphere; comprises Greenland (on N. American continental shelf), Canada, USA, Mexico; high W. Cordilleras, inc. Rocky mtns., run N. to S. from Alaska to Mexico; lower range of Appalachian mtns. in E. with vast interior basin, inc. Gr. Ls., Saskatchewan, St. Lawrence, and Miss.-Mo. R. systems; gr. variation in climate and vegetation from subtropical in S. and Mediterranean in W. to Arctic in N. and continental in interior; enormous endowment of natural resources provide basis for vast economies of USA and Canada, but contemporary public concern for natural environment of continent; formerly inhabited by Indians, now mainly occupied by a white p. with lge. European minorities, and an African-based, black p.; p. (1994) 373 m. (inc. Hawaii).

Northampton, t., l. gov. dist., Northampton, **Eng.;** on R. Nene; footwear, engin., leather gds.; new t. designation; p. (1993) 187,200 (dist.).

Northamptonshire, non-met. co., **Eng.;** E. Midlands; chiefly agr.; iron mng. and mftg.; footwear, engin., leather; co. t. Northampton; a. 2,367 km²; p. (1993) 591,900.

North Atlantic Drift, drift of surface waters of Atl. Oc. N.E. from Gulf Stream towards Europe; relatively warm; supplies prevailing S.W. winds with warmth and moisture to modify climate of Brit. Is. and N.W. Europe.

Northavon, l. gov. dist., Avon, **Eng.;** a. N. of Bristol, inc. Sodbury; p. (1993) 138,100.

North Bay, t., Ont., **Canada;** on L. Nipissing; air base; tourism; route ctr.; p. (1986) 50,623.

North Bedfordshire, l. gov. dist., Beds., **Eng.;** a. inc. Bedford and surrounding rural a.; p. (1993) 137,300.

North Berwick, royal burgh, E. Lothian, **Scot.;** on S. of F. of Forth, 32 km E. of Edinburgh; seaside resort; golf course; fishing pt.; p. (1991) 5,687.

North Beveland, I., **Neth.;** in Scheldt estuary; arable agr.; a. 91 km².

North Carolina, st., S.E. **USA;** Tarheel St.; admitted to Union 1789; st. flower Flowering Dogwood., st. bird Cardinal; bounded on E. by Atl. Oc.; one of 13 original sts.; sandy, indented cst., rising in W. to Appalachian mtns.; humid subtropical climate, modified by alt.; agr. impt.; maize, cotton, tobacco; mica; textiles; ch. pt. Wilmington; cap. Raleigh; a. 136,524 km²; p. (1990) 6,628,637.

North Channel, gives access from Atl. Oc. to Irish Sea between **S.W. Scotland** (Galloway) and **N.E. Ireland** (Larne); length 96 km; narrowest width 24 km.

North China Plain, China; alluvial lowland of Huang-He basin; notorious floods but R. now controlled; wheat and millets; very dense p.

North Cornwall, l. gov. dist., **Eng.;** lge. a. on N. cst. stretching from Bodmin to Bude; p. (1993) 75,600.

North Crimean Canal, Ukraine; links R. Dnieper with Black Sea and Sea of Azov, crossing steppes of S. Ukraine and Crimea, terminating at Kerch; first section (123 km long) opened 1963; when completed will be 352 km long, 200 km of which will be navigable.

North Dakota, st., N.W. **USA;** Flickerhill St.; admitted to Union 1889; st. flower Wild Prairie Rose, st. bird Western Meadowlark; rolling prairie, rising from E.-W.; drained by Missouri R., controlled by multi-purpose Garrison Reservoir; arable agr., mainly grains, but eroded "Badlands" in S.; coal mng., petroleum; a. 183,022 km²; p. (1990) 638,800.

North Devon, l. gov. dist., **Eng.**; inc. Exmoor and ts. of Barnstaple, Ilfracombe and Lynton; p. (1993) 86,700.

North Dorset, l. gov. dist., Dorset, **Eng.**; mainly rural but inc. ts. of Shaftesbury, Sturminster Newton and Blandford Forum; p. (1993) 54,700.

North Down, l. gov. dist., **N. Ireland**; borders Belfast Lough; main ts. Bangor, Holywood; p. (1991) 71,823.

North Downs, Surrey/Kent, **Eng.**; chalk escarpment running E. to W. across S.E. Eng.; form "white cliffs of Dover"; followed in part by Pilgrim's Way; Box Hill 900 m.

North-East China, formerly known as Manchuria, comprising provs.—Liaoning, Jilin, Heilongjiang; mtnous., N.W. and E.; drained to N. by Songhua Jiang and S. by Liao Rs.; forested; soya-beans, wheat, coal, iron; impt. a. for iron and steel; occupied by Japanese in 1931 and returned to **China** in 1947.

North East Derbyshire, l. gov. dist., Derbys., **Eng.**; industl. a. of Clay Cross and Dronfield; p. (1993) 99,100.

North East Fife, l. gov. dist., Fife Reg., **Scot.**; a. between F. of Forth and F. of Tay; impt. ts. St. Andrews and Cupar; p. (1993) 72,420.

North-East Frontier Agency. See **Arunachal Pradesh.**

North East Passage, along N. cst. Europe and Asia between Atl. and Pac. See **Section L.**

Northern Ireland, part of **U.K.**; occupies N.E. a. of Ireland, consisting of 26 l. gov. dists.; mild, temperate climate, exploited by dairy farming using excellent grass; arable agr. inc. barley, potatoes; traditional inds. inc. linen, shipbldg., food-processing, tobacco; modern inds. encouraged by extensive government aid inc. artificial fibres, carpets, elec. and aero-engin.; heavily dependent upon Brit. mkt.; serious social disturbance since 1969, based upon long-standing religious differences between Roman Catholic and Protestant as a result of discrimination against minority; Stormont Parliament replaced by Assembly (suspended 29 May 1974 and direct rule resumed); returns 12 members to Westminster; a. 14,121 km²; p. (1991) 1,577,836.

Northern Marianas, chain of Is., **W. Pac.**; former US Trust Terr. now a commonwealth in union with USA; a. 479 km²; p. (1991) 45,200.

Northern Territory, self governing st. (1978) N. **Australia**; variable rainfall decreasing inland from N. to S.; land rises generally N. to S. and reaches over 1,800 m in Macdonnell ranges; lge. semi-nomadic Aboriginal agr.; livestock agr. dependent upon rail, road access to mkt.; mng.; newly opened uranium mines abuse aborigine terr.; ch. ts. Darwin on N. cst., Alice Springs; a. 1,356,176 km²; p. (1991) 167,800.

Northfleet, l. Kent, **Eng.**; on S. bank of R. Thames, adjoining Gravesend; cement, paper, rubber, tyres, cables; p. (1981) 26,250.

North Foreland, E. Kent, **Eng.**; chalk headland.

North Hertfordshire, l. gov. dist., Herts., **Eng.**; stretches from Baldock, Letchworth and Hitchin to Royston; p. (1993) 113,700.

North Island, I., **N.Z.**; one of the two major Is. of N.Z., separated from S.I. by Cook Strait, volcanic mtns., Waikato R. drains L. Taupo, cap. Wellington, spt. Auckland, oil deposits on E. and W. csts.; a. 114,688 km²; p. (1991) 2,553,413.

North Kesteven, l. gov. dist., Lincs., **Eng.**; rural a. based on Sleaford; p. (1993) 81,200.

Northleach, t., Cotswold, Gloucs., **Eng.**; once impt. woollen tr.

North Little Rock, t., Ark., **USA**; agr. processing, engin.; p. (1990) 61,741.

North Norfolk, l. gov. dist., Norfolk, **Eng.**; cstl. a. inc. Wells-next-the-Sea, Cromer, Sheringham, Walsingham and North Walsham; p. (1993) 93,700.

North Ossetian, aut. rep., **Russia** on N. slope of Gr. Caucasus; cap. Vladikavkaz; agr. in valleys; lead, silver, zinc, and oil deposits with metallurgical and food-processing inds.; a. 8,029 km²; p. (1989) 632,400.

North Platte, t., Nebraska, **USA**; on N. Platte R.; p. (1980) 24,509.

North Platte, R., **USA**; rises N. Col., flows 1,088 km through Wyo., across W. Nebraska to join S. Platte at c. of North Platte; extensive power and irrigation developments.

North Rhine–Westphalia, Land, **Germany**; highly industrialised, coal mng., iron and steel, textiles; cap. Dusseldorf; a. 34,066 km²; p. (1992) 17,510,000.

North River (Beijiang), Guandong, S. **China**; rises in Nanling mtns., flows S. into Xi Jiang delta; 480 km long.

North Sea, arm of the Atl., E. of Gr. Brit., W. of Norway, Sweden, and N. Germany, and N. of Holland, Belgium, and France; length 960 km, width 640 km; gd. fisheries; major natural gas, coal and oil deposits.

North Sea Canal, ship canal, N. Holland Neth.; connects Amsterdam to N. Sea at Ijmuiden; depth 14 m, length 26 k.

North Shields, t., Tyne and Wear, **Eng.**; Tyne pt.; major new fishing pt. planned; marine engines, chain cables, anchors, rope; mkt.; p. (1981) 41,608.

North Shropshire, l. gov. dist., Shrops., **Eng.**; a. N. of Shrewsbury and inc. Market Drayton; p. (1993) 93,900.

North Solomons, Rep. of, formed 1975 when Bougainville I. seceded from Papua New Guinea.

North Tonawanda, t., N.Y., **USA**; on Niagara R.; timber tr., paper mnfs.; p. (1990) 34,989.

North Tyneside, met. dist., Tyne and Wear, **Eng.**; comprises Tynemouth, Whitley Bay and Wallsend; p. (1993) 194,800.

Northumberland, non-met. co., N. **Eng.**; on border of Scot., along Cheviots and R. Tweed; drained by Tyne, Blyth, Coquet Rs.; pastoral agr., especially sheep; coal mng., with former impt. exp. to London and S.E. Eng.; industl. a. now inc. in Tyne and Wear met. co.; isolation and wild landscape attractive as tourist resort; a. 5,032 km²; p. (1993) 307,200.

Northumberland Straits, separate Prince Edward I. from Nova Scotia and New Brunswick, **Canada**; 14 km combined road and rail tunnel, bridge and causeway to link provs. projected.

Northumbria, Anglo-Saxon kingdom stretching from the Humber to the Forth; conquered by the Danes 9th cent.

North Walsham, mkt. t., North Norfolk, **Eng.**; 22 km N. of Norwich; former wool-weaving ctr.; p. (1981) 7,944.

North Warwickshire, l. gov. dist., Warwicks., **Eng.**; close to Midlands conurb., based on Atherstone; p. (1993) 61,800.

North West Leicestershire, l. gov. dist., Leics., **Eng.**; inc. Ashby de la Zouch, Ashby Woulds, Coalville and Castle Donington; p. (1993) 82,800.

North-West Passage, between Atl. and Pac. along Arctic cst. of **Canada**; potentially of gr. importance as a W. outlet for Alaskan oil; sovereignty claimed by Canada but disputed by U.S.A. who claims it is an internat. strait. See **Section L.**

Northwest Territories, N.W. region and terr. of **Canada**; N. of 60° Lat. N., between Yukon (W.) and Hudson Bay (E.); comprises 3 dists., Franklin, Mackenzie, Keewatin; varied physical geography, inc. vast areas of lowland with some of highest peaks in E.N. America; tree-line marks physical bdy. between N. and S.; drained in W. by Mackenzie R.; major inds. gold and silver mng. around cap. Yellowknife, zinc and lead in the High Arctic; petroleum, fur-trapping, fisheries; incr. indep. since 1983; a. 3,379,711 km²; p. (1991) 55,000 (two-thirds Inuit and Indians).

Northwich, t., Cheshire, **Eng.**; on R. Weaver; impt. chemical inds. based originally upon local salt deposits, now much subsidence in a. due to salt extraction; p. (1981) 17,126.

North Wiltshire, l. gov. dist., Wilts., **Eng.**; rural a. inc. ts. of Calne, Chippenham and Malmesbury; p. (1993) 116,700.

North Wolds. See **East Yorkshire.**

North York Moors, limestone plateau, North Yorks./Cleveland, **Eng.**; lies S. of estuary of R. Tees, heather moorland; some pastoral farming on lower slopes; alt. varies from 300–450 m; formerly impt. iron-ore quarrying along N. edge in Cleveland dist.

North Yorkshire, non-met. co., N. **Eng.**; inc. much of former N. Riding; stretches from Pennines (W.) to Vale of York (central), N. York Moors and Yorks. Wolds (E.); crossed by R. Ouse and tribs.; mainly rural, mixed agr.; major ctrs. of

p. at York, cstl. resort of Scarborough and spa of Harrogate; a., 8,316 km²; p. (1993) 721,800.

Norton-Radstock, t., Avon, **Eng.**; footwear, sm. coalfield; p. (1981) 18,338.

Norwalk, t., Cal., **USA**; oil refining; p. (1980) 85,286.

Norwalk, t., Conn., **USA**; gd. harbour on Long I. Sound; lt. inds., clothing; formerly impt. oyster ind. diminished by industl. pollution; p. (1990) 127,000 (met. a.).

Norway, kingdom, W. Scandinavia, N. **Europe**; long fjord cst. stretches from Arctic to N. Sea; mtnous.; cool damp climate, influenced by prevailing W. winds; excellent conditions for hydroelectric power and electro-inds.; sm. p. makes N. heavily dependent upon foreign tr., especially exp. of aluminium, wood-pulp, paper, fish; now possesses lge. deposits of petroleum in N. Sea; arable agr. limited to fjord lowlands and a. around cap. Oslo; pastoral transhumance in mtnous. interior; a. 322,600 km², p. (1992) 4·3 m.

Norwich, c., co. t., l. gov. dist., Norfolk, **Eng.**; on R. Wensum just above confluence with R. Yare; univ.; cath., cas.; cult. and agr. ctr.; food mnfs., footwear, printing; decentralization of office employment from London; p. (1993) 128,100 (dist.).

Norwich, t., Conn., **USA**; sm. pt. on Thames R.; machin., textiles; p. (1980) 38,074.

Notec (Netze), R., **Poland**; trib. R. Warta; partially navigable; 224 km long.

Notodden, t., S. **Norway**; nr. Tinnfoss falls which provide hydroelectric power; iron smelting, nitrates; p. (1990) 8,275.

Nottingham, c., co. t., l. gov. dist., Nottinghamshire, **Eng.**; a bridging pt. over Trent R.; lace, hosiery, tobacco, pharmaceutical and cycle inds., all based upon local capital; univ., cas., p. (1993) 282,600 (dist.).

Nottinghamshire, non-met. co., Midlands, **Eng.**; contains part of productive E. Midlands coalfield serving many power stas. along Trent R.; urban growth concentrated mainly on coalfield; ch. and co. t. Nottingham; engin., hosiery; wheat, barley, cattle, roses; brilliantly characterised in writings of D. H. Lawrence; a. 2,165 km²; p. (1993) 1,028,400.

Nouadhibou, pt., **Mauritania**; new pt. for bulk carriers to exp. iron ore; fish processing plants; pelletizing plant; p. (1988) 59,198.

Nouakchott, t., cap. of **Mauritania**, W. Africa; comm. ctr. on caravan route; tr. in agr. prods.; planned industl. zone; rapid growth with mass migration of nomadic p. to shanty ts. as response to Sahelian drought; p. (1988) 393,325.

Nouméa (Port de France), t., cap. of Fr. New **Caledonia**; ch. pt. of Is.; exp. nickel, chrome; p. (1983) 60,112.

Nouvelle Amsterdam, I., **Indian Oc.**; part of Fr. Southern and Antarctic Terrs.; volcanic; ctr. of meteorological research; a. 65 km².

Nova Frilburgo, t., Rio de Janeiro, **Brazil**; health resort; p. (1985) 144,000.

Nova Iguaçú, t., Rio de Janeiro, **Brazil**; steel, tyres, chemicals; p. (1991) 1,286,337.

Nova Lima, t., Minas Gerais st., **Brazil**; in Serra do Espinhaço, 16 km S. of Belo Horizonte; adjacent to impt. gold-mines of Morro Velho; p. (1985) 47,400.

Nova Lisboa (Huambo), central **Angola**, Africa; E. of Benguela; rly. repair shops; agr. comm. ctr.

Novara, c., cap. of N. prov., N. **Italy**; agr. and mnf. ctr., textiles, chemicals, cheese; Romanesque church; p. (1992) 102,029.

Nova Scotia, maritime prov., **Canada**; mainly fertile upland and rich valleys with agr. aided by temperate maritime climate; fruit, livestock, dairying; forested uplands along cst. nr Bay of Fundy give rise to impt. timber inds. with many pts. along indented cst.; fishing and fish-processing; local coal supplies, iron and steel ind.; cap. Halifax; a. 54,556 km²; p. (1991) 903,700.

Novaya Kakhovka, c., **Ukraine**; built (1951) on K. Sea nr. hydroelec. power sta. on Dnieper R.; tourism; p. (1990) 57,700.

Novaya Zemlya, archipelago, Arctic Oc. **Russia**; 2 main Is.; lofty and rugged, severe climate; nuclear testing a.; a. 90,750 km².

Novgorod, c., **Russia**; on Volkhov R. nr. exit from L. Ilmen; food and timber inds., engin.; in mediaeval times gr. comm. and cultural ctr., cap. of an indep. rep.; architectural monuments;

damaged by Germans in second world war; p. (1989) 229,000.

Novi Sad, c., Serbia, **Yugoslavia**; R. pt. on Danube R., formerly royal free c.; almost destroyed by Austrians 1849; tr. in fruit, wine, vegetables, corn; p. (1991) 178,896.

Novoknybyshevsk, t., **Russia**; S.W. of Kuybyshev; lge. oil processing plant; p. (1989) 113,000.

Novo Kuznetsk, c. **Russia**; grew up as iron and steel ctr. of Kuznetsk Basin; engin., chemicals, aluminium, ferro-alloys; p. (1989) 600,000.

Novomoskovsk, c., **Russia**; on R. Don; lignite, fertilisers, p. (1989) 146,000.

Novorossiisk, spt., **Russia**; on N.E. cst. of Black Sea; engin., textiles; lgst. cement producer in USSR; exp. industl. prods.; p. (1989) 186,000.

Novoshakhtinsk, c., **Russia**; on Rostov–Kharkov highway; coal mng., chemicals; p. (1989) 108,000.

Novosibirsk, c., **Russia**; on Ob R. and Trans-Siberian rly.; lgst. industl. ctr. of Siberia, nr. Kuznetsk Basin; hydroelec. power; varied inds., uranium nearby; univ.; p. (1989) 1,437,000.

Novo Troitsk, t., **Russia**; in Urals, 18 km S.W. of Orsk; cement, special steels; p. (1989) 106,000.

Novovoronezh, **Russia**; on R. Don, S. of Voronezh; nuclear power sta.

Nowa Huta, t., **Poland**; 10 km S.E. Kraców on Vistula R.; newly developed Lenin metallurgical combine and modern residtl. a. within c. of Kraców; p. (1989) 224,386.

Nowa Sól (Neusalz), t., Zielona Góra, **Poland**; pt. on R. Oder; metal-working, food and timber inds.; p. (1989) 43,053.

Nowgong, t., Assam, **India**; agr. and comm. ctr.; rice, tea.

Nowra-Bomaderry, t., N.S.W., **Australia**; on E. cst. at mouth of Shoalhaven R.; expanded (1979) into c. of Shoalhaven; collecting ctr. for coastal agr. prod.; powdered milk, paper mill; p. (1981) 17,887.

Nowy Sącz, t. and prov., S. **Poland**; on Dunajec R.; lignite nearby; rly. engin., mftg.; ctr. of a. renowned for beauty and tourist attractions; p. (1989) 76,658.

Noý Jičin (Neutitschein), t., Moravia, **Czech Rep.**; farm machin., and eng.

Nubia, anc. region, N.E. **Africa**, extending on both sides of Nile from first cataract at Aswan to Khartoum, Sudan; largely desert, some irrigation alongside Nile.

Nuble, prov., **Chile**; borders on Argentina; comprehensive attempt to develop agr.; most industl. development and agr. mkt. at cap. Chillán; a. 14,204 km².

Nueva Esparta, st., **Venezuela**; consists of over 70 Is.; impt. fisheries; cap. La Asunción; a. 1,150 km²; p. (1981) 197,198.

Nueva San Salvador, t., **El Salvador**; agr. comm. ctr. in coffee-growing and livestock region; p. (1992) 116,575.

Nuevo Laredo, c., N.E. **Mexico**; entry point for American tourists driving to Mexico; tr. ctr. in pastoral and arable agr. a.; p. (1990) 217,912.

Nuevo Léon, st., N.E. **Mexico**; arable agr. needs irrigation in arid climate; impt. iron and steel inds.; cap. Monterrey; a. 65,097 km²; p. (1990) 3,086,466.

Nuku'alofa, cap. of Polynesian kingdom of **Tonga**; p. (1986) 28,899.

Nukus, c., cap. of Karakalpak aut. rep., **Uzbekistan**; on Amu Dar'ya R. in Khorezm oasis; clothing inds.; p. (1985) 139,000.

Nullarbor Plain, S. **Australia**; low, level, limestone plateau fringing Gr. Australian Bight; arid; treeless, salt-bush scrub; crossed by Trans-continental rly. between Naretha (W. Australia) and Ooldea; rly. is dead straight, dead level for 477 km.

Numazu, t., Honshu, **Japan**; nr. Tokyo; ctr. of industl. dist. with varied mnfs. inc. machin.; p. (1990) 211,731.

Nuneaton, t., with Bedworth forms l. gov. dist., Warwicks., **Eng.**; on Anker R.; coal mng., textiles, lt. inds.; mkt.; birthplace of George Eliot; p. (1993) 118,500 (dist.).

Nunivak, I., Alaska, **USA**; lge. reindeer herds.

Nunjiang, former prov., N.E. **China**; crossed by Nen Jiang, trib. of Songhua Jiang; now part of Heilung-kiang prov.

Nürnberg (Nuremberg), c., Bavaria, **Germany**; historic c. of architectural beauty; indust.. ctr. with elec. mnfs., machin., heavy vehicles, precision instruments, chemicals, toys, pencils and crayons; rly. junc.; inland pt. on Rhine–Danube waterway; p. (1990) 494,900.

Nusa Tenggara, Is., **Indonesia;** part of Lesser Sunda Is.; p. (1980) 5,461,830.

Nuwara Eliya, hill t., (c. 1,800 m), **Sri Lanka;** health resort; p. (1981) 20,471.

Nyasa, L. See **Malawi L.**

Nyasaland. See **Malawi.**

Nyíregyháza, t., N.E. **Hungary;** ctr. of reclaimed agr. a.; mkt. for tobacco, wine, fruits; domestic ware; p. (1989) 119,000.

Nyborg, pt., **Denmark;** on Fyn I.; terminal of train-ferry across Gr. Belt; shipyards; textile ind.; p. (1990) 18,207.

Nyköbing, spt., Falster I., **Denmark;** varied inds.; admin. ctr. of Storstrøms prov.; p. (1990) 25,214.

Nyköping, spt., **Sweden;** at head of inlet on Baltic cst.; comm. and industl. ctr.; p. (1992) 68,093.

Nystad. See **Uusikaupunki.**

O

Oadby, t., Leics., **Eng.;** 5 km S.E. of Leicester; footwear; with Wigston forms small l. gov. dist., S. of Leicester; p. (1993) 53,500 (dist.).

Oahu, I., **Hawaii,** Pac. Oc.; sugar, pineapples; tourist tr.; cap. Honolulu; a. 1,564 km²; p. (1988) 838,500.

Oakengates, t., The Wrekin, Shrops., **Eng.;** 24 km N.W. of Wolverhampton; iron and steel, pre-cast concrete, engin.; now part of new t. of Telford; p. (1981) 17,663.

Oakham, t., Rutland, Leics., **Eng.;** mkt.; hosiery, footwear; p. (1981) 7,996.

Oakland, c., Cal., **USA;** on San Francisco Bay; residtl. sub.; cars, shipbldg., fruit canning, elec. machin., clothing, tanneries, chemicals; p. (1990) 372,242 (c.), 2,083,000 (met. a.).

Oak Park Village, t., Ill., **USA;** now included in Chicago; birthplace of Ernest Hemingway; p. (1980) 54,887.

Oak Ridge, t., Tenn., **USA;** Atomic Energy Commission's major research ctr.; p. (1990) 27,310.

Oamaru, bor., spt., S.I., **N.Z.;** wool, frozen meat; exp. agr. prods.; p. (1987) 12,550.

Oaxaca, st., Pac. cst., S. **Mexico;** mtnous., subsist-ence agr. in fertile valleys; comm. prod. of coffee, cotton, tobacco; stock-raising; mng. in mtns.; cap. Oaxaca; a. 94,201 km²; p. (1990) 3,021,513.

Oaxaca, c., cap. of O. st., S. **Mexico;** stands at c. 1,500 m; coffee; gold and silver mines; handi-craft mkt.; table linen weaving, wool zarapes; tourist ctr.; p. (1990) 212,943.

Ob', R., W. Siberia, **Russia;** one of the world's lgst. Rs., flows from Altai mtns. to G. of Ob'; crossed by Turk-Sib. rly. at Barnaul and by Trans-Siberian rly. at Novosibirsk; ch. trib. Irtysh; hydroelec. power; navigable; oilfields in middle section; outlet of Ob basin Novy-Port (Gdansk); plans to divert waters to irrigate Kazakhstan by 2,500 km canal; 4,160 km long.

Oban, t., burgh, Argyll and Bute, **Scot.;** on F. of Lorne; resort; ctr. for local shipping; woollens, tartans; p. (1991) 8,203.

Obed, Alberta, **Canada;** 240 km W. of Edmonton; major natural gas a.

Obeid, El, t., Kordofan, **Sudan;** economically dependent upon rly. link to Khartoum; agr. tr. ctr.; p. (1983) 140,024.

Oberammergau, v., Upper Bavaria, **Germany;** scene of decennial Passion Play; winter sports; p. (1989) 4,980.

Oberhausen, t., N. Rhine–Westphalia, **Germany;** industl. ctr. of Ruhr conurb.; rly. junc., canal pt.; p. (1990) 224,000.

Obihiro, t., Hokkaido, **Japan;** mkt; sugar-beet re-fining, flax, dairy prods.; p. (1990) 167,389.

Obuasi, t. **Ghana,** W. Africa; ctr. of gold mng.; lge. deep-level mine, modernised 1984.

Obwalden, demi-canton, **Switzerland;** a. 492 km²; p. (1990) 28,800.

Ocaña, t., Magdalena st., **Colombia;** coffee, hides; isolated by difficult transport conditions.

Ocean City, t., N.J., **USA;** seaside resort founded by the Methodists; p. (1980) 13,949.

Ocean I. (Banaba), Kiribati, Pac. Oc.; high grade phosphate (guano) worked by Brit.; p. (1990) 284.

Oceania, name given to the Is. of the Pacific; comprising Australasia, Polynesia, Melanesia, Micronesia; p. (1984) 24,460,000.

Ochil Hills, volcanic hill-range, **Scot.;** stretching 40 km N.E. to S.W. from F. of Tay to nr. Stirling; loftiest Ben Cleugh 721 m; beautiful glens and valleys.

Odawara, t., **Japan;** pt. with rail connections to Tokyo, 48 km to N.E.; p. (1990) 193,417.

Odemis, t., Asiatic **Turkey;** N.E. of Aydin; to-bacco, cereals, silk, cotton, flax, olives, raisins, figs; minerals; p. (1985) 47,475.

Odense, spt., **Denmark;** admin. ctr. of Fyn prov.; varied inds.; exp. dairy prod.; birthplace of Hans Andersen; p. (1990) 176,133.

Odenwald, forested hills, Hesse and Baden-Württemberg, **Germany;** highest point Katzen-buckel 626 m.

Oder (Pol. **Odra**), R., central **Europe;** flows from Moravia to Baltic through Silesia and Pomer-ania forming from junc. with Neisse R. fron-tier between Poland and E. Germany; ch. trib. Warta R.; impt. comm. waterway below Wroclaw; 896 km long.

Odessa, t., Texas, **USA;** impt. oil ctr., chemicals, foundry prod., livestock tr.; p. (1990) 89,699.

Odessa, spt., **Ukraine;** on Black Sea; cultural, industl. ctr.; cath., univ.; gr. grain exp.; engin., oil refining, chemicals; ice-bound for a few weeks in winter; p. (1990) 1,106,400.

Offaly, co., Leinster, **R.o.I.;** much marshy land (inc. Bog of Allen), barren uplands (inc. Slieve Bloom); pastoral agr., wheat; p. mainly rural; sm.-scale domestic prods. and agr.-processing inds. in ts.; co. t. Tullamore; a. 1,999 km²; p. (1986) 59,835.

Offa's Dyke, earthwork constructed by Offa, king of Mercia (757–96) as bdy. between the English and the Welsh; still forms part of border between the two countries; long-distance footpath along the Welsh marches, 269 km.

Offenbach, t., Hesse, **Germany;** on R. Main; cas., leather museum; machin., chemicals, leather gds., metals; p. (1990) 115,200.

Offenburg, t., Baden–Württemberg, **Germany;** on R. Kinzig; textiles, glass, rly. junc.; cas.; p. (1986) 50,500.

Ogaden, arid region, S.W. **Ethiopia;** on border of Rep. of Somalia; oil exploration with Soviet assistance.

Ogaki, t., Honshu, **Japan;** route ctr. in lowland em-bayment, 40 km N.W. of Nagoya; p. (1990) 148,281.

Ogbomosho, t., S.W. **Nigeria;** ctr. of agr. dist.; cotton weaving; p. (1983) 527,000.

Ogden, c., Utah, **USA;** stands at 1,324 m., nr. Gr. Salt L.; rly. ctr.; beet-sugar, meat-packing, flour-milling, clothing, cement; p. (1980) 64,407.

Ogdensburg, c., pt., N.Y., **USA;** on St. Lawrence R., opposite Prescott; impt. R. pt.; p. (1980) 12,375.

Ogmore and Garw, t., Ogwr, Mid Glamorgan, **Wales;** in narrow valley, 10 km N. of Bridgend; industl.; cas.; p. (1981) 18,220.

Ogooué, R., **Gabon,** Congo; site of Schweitzer's hospital at Lambaréné; 800 km long.

Ogwr, l. gov. dist., Mid Glamorgan, **Wales;** inc. Ogmore, Maesteg and Bridgend inland and Porthcawl on cst.; p. (1993) 134,900.

Ohau, Lake, S.I., **N.Z.;** in Mt. Cook dist.; fed by glaciers; 19 km by 35 km; hydroelectric power potential.

Ohio, R., trib. of Mississippi R., **USA;** formed in Penns., by junc. of Monongahela and Alleg-heny Rs. at Pittsburgh, thence navigable for 1,560 km to Cairo in Ky.; an impt. comm. waterway for industl. raw materials; flood pro-tection schemes.

Ohio, st., N. **USA;** Buckeye St.; admitted to Union 1803; st. flower Scarlet Carnation, st. bird Cardinal; gr. agr. and industl. region; maize, wheat, cattle; major deposits of coal form basis of heavy inds., especially in major ts. of Cleveland, Cincinnati, Toledo, Akron, Dayton, Youngstown; petroleum; timber inds.; cap. Columbus; a. 106,508 km²; p. (1990) 10,847,115.

Ohre (Eger), R., Bohemia, **Czech Rep.;** rises in Fichtelgebirge, flows N.E. into Labe (Elbe) and through Karlovy Vary; 224 km long.

Ohrid or Ochrida, L., forms part of bdy. between **Albania** and **Macedonia;** alt. c. 850 m; deepest L. in Balkans; scenic tourist a.; monasteries on shores.

Ohrid or Ochrida, t., Macedonia, **Yugoslavia;** on N.E. shore of L.; airport and tourist ctr.; p. (1981) 64,245.

Oich, Loch, L., Gr. Glen, Inverness, **Scot.;** forms part of Caledonian Canal.

Oise, dep., N. **France;** traversed by R. Oise;

fertile, forested; cap. Beauvais; a. 5,884 km²; p. (1990) 725,600.

Oise, R., trib. of R. Seine, **France**; canalised navigable to Chauny; 298 km long.

Oita, c., spt., N.E. Kyushu, **Japan**; on Beppu Bay; wire, carbon, iron, and steel; oil refinery; p. (1990) 408,502.

Ojos del Salado, mtn., N.W. **Argentina**; alt. 6,884 m.

Oka, R., Kursk, **Russia**; rises S. of Orel, flows past Kaluga, Serpukhov, Kolomna, Ryazan, Murom, to become trib. of Volga at Gorki; navigable, carrying grain and timber; 1,520 km long.

Oka, R., Irkutsk, Siberia, **Russia**; joins Angara R. below Bratsk; 800 km long.

Okayama, c., Honshu, **Japan**; textiles; lt. inds.; p. (1990) 593,730.

Okazaki, t., Honshu, **Japan**; nr. G. of Ovari; industl. ctr.; textiles, chemicals, machin.; p. (1990) 306,821.

Okeechobee, L., S. Fla., **USA**; drains to Atl. Oc. via Everglades; tourist attraction especially for fishing; also comm. fisheries.

Okefenokee, swamp, Ga./Fla., **USA**; forms O. Nat. Wildlife Refuge.

Okehampton, mt. t., West Devon, **Eng.**; on N. flank of Dartmoor; granite quarries; p. (1981) 4,181.

Okha, spt., E. cst. Sakhalin I., **Russia**; exp. petroleum; lge. refinery.

Okhotsk, Sea of, N.E. **Asia**; 1,600 km by 800 km; enclosed by the Siberian mainland, Kamchatka, the Kurils and Sakhalin I.

Oki Is., off cst. of Honshu, **Japan**; a. 350 km².

Okinawa, I., **Japan**, under U.S. control until 1972; lgst. and most impt. of Ryuku Is. US air bases at Kadena and cap. Naha; a. 1,500 km²; p. (1990) 1,222,398.

Oklahoma, st., **USA**; Sooner St.; admitted to Union 1907; st. flower Mistletoe, st. bird Scissor-tailed Fly-catcher; prairie, plains and mtns.; continental climate; cereals, cotton, stock-raising; petroleum, gas, zinc, coal, gypsum, lead; ch. ind. petroleum refining; cap. Oklahoma City; a. 181,090 km²; p. (1990) 3,145,585.

Oklahoma City, c., cap. of Okla. st., **USA**; univ.; livestock mkt.; tr. and processing ctr.; oil and by-prods., field machin., flour mills, meat-packing; scene of horrific extremist bombing, April 1995; p. (1990) 444,719 (c.), 959,000 (met. a.).

Okovango, R.; rises in **Angola**, flows to Ngami depression, **Botswana**, where it forms swampy delta; 1,600 km long.

Oktyabrsky, t., Bashkir aut. rep., **Russia**; on R. Ik; in new oil-mng. dist., the "New Baku"; p. (1989) 105,000.

Öland, I., Baltic Sea; off E. cst. **Sweden**; connected by Europe's longest bridge to mainland; agr., limestone quarries; ch. t. Borgholm; seaside resorts; a. 1,341 km²; p. (1983) 23,874.

Oldbury. *See* **Warley.**

Oldbury-on-Severn, Avon, **Eng.**; nuclear power sta.

Old Castile, historical div., **Spain**; now divided into Santander, Soria, Segovia, Logrono, Avila, Valladolid, Palencia, and Burgos provs.

Oldenburg, c., Lower Saxony, **Germany**; on R. Hunte nr. Hunte-Ems canal; rly. junc.; mkt. for horses and cattle; lt. inds.; natural gas nr. to cst.; p. (1990) 143,800.

Old Fletton, Cambs., **Eng.**; on R. Nene opposite Peterborough; bricks, engin.; beet sugar, fruit and vegetable canning; p. (1981) 13,657.

Oldham, c., met. dist., Gtr. Manchester, **Eng.**; on R. Medlock, 11 km N.E. of Manchester; manmade fibre and cotton textiles, machin.; recent industl. diversification inc. electro- and aero-engin., leather, paints; p. (1993) 220,500 (dist.).

Oldmeldrum, burgh, Gordon, **Scot.**; 6 km N.E. of Inverurie; p. (1991) 1,976.

Olenek, R., **Russia**; N. Siberia; flows W. of Lena R. into Laptev Sea, Arctic Oc.; abounds in fish; 2,160 km long, 960 km navigable.

Oléron, Ile d', I., Charente-Maritime dep., **France**; lies off estuary of Charente, Bay of Biscay; oysters, early vegetables; a. 176 km².

Olifant, R., Transvaal, **S. Africa**; trib. of Limpopo; irrigation scheme for intensive agr. in valley.

Olinda, c., Pernambuco st., **Brazil**; seaside resort; phosphates; p. (1991) 340,673.

Oliva, t., Valencia, **Spain**; nr. Alicante; wine dist., ducal palace; p. (1981) 19,232.

Olivos, sub., Buenos Aires, **Argentina.**

Olmütz. *See* **Olomouc.**

Olney, t., Bucks., **Eng.**; mkt., dairy produce; annual Shrove Tuesday pancake race.

Oloibiri, S. **Nigeria**; oilfields; pipeline to Pt. Harcourt, 128 km W.

Olomouc (Olmütz), Czech Rep.; industl. ctr., steel wks., elec. equipment, textiles, food prod.; cath., univ.; formerly one of ch. fortresses of Austria; p. (1990) 107,000.

Oloron-Sainte-Marie, t., Pyrénées-Atlantique, **France**; in Pyrenean foothills; caths.; p. (1982) 12,237.

Olsztyn (Allenstein), t., and prov. N.W. **Poland**; on R. Alle, 160 km N. of Warsaw; cas.; machin., wood inds.; p. (1989) 160,956 (t.) 746,200 (prov.).

Olten, t., N. **Switzerland**; rly. junc., on R. Aare; p. (1986) 18,025.

Olympia, anc. c., Peloponnesus, S. **Greece**; at confluence of Alphaeus and Cladeus Rs.; site of gr. temple of Zeus and scene of Olympic games; modern v. of O. nearby; museum.

Olympia, cap. of Washington st., **USA**; spt. on Puget Sound; exp. timber; machin., agr.-processing inds.; p. (1984) 29,200 (c.), 138,300 (met. a.).

Olympus, Mt., highest mtn. in **Greece**; on border of Thessaly and Macedonia, nr. Aegean cst.; alt. 2,975 m; regarded by anc. Greeks as home of the Olympian gods.

Omagh, t., l. gov. dist., N. **Ireland**; on R.; Stule agr. mkt.; tourist ctr.; p. (1991) 45,809 (dist.), 17,280 (t.).

Omaha, c., Nebraska, **USA**; on Missouri R.; one of lgst. livestock and meat-packing ctrs. in US, gold and silver smelting and refining, steel fabrication, industl. alcohol prod.; univ.; p. (1990) 335,795 (c.), 618,000 (met. a.).

Oman (Muscat and Oman until 1970), sultanate, S.W. **Asia**; fertile coastal plain, interior desert plateau; irrigated agr., especially impt. for dates; fishing; oil discovered 1964, now main exp.; a. 212,380 km²; p. (1991) 2,070,450.

Oman, G. of, Arabian Sea; connected through strait of Kormuz to Persian G.; length 480 km, width 208 km.

Omaruru, t. and dist. **Namibia**; creamery; aero-drome; p. (1991) 7,446 (dist).

Omdurman, c., central **Sudan**, on Nile, opposite Khartoum; site of Mahdi's tomb; here Kitchener defeated the dervishes 1898; native mkts.; p. (1983) 526,287.

Ometepe, I., L. Nicaragua, **Nicaragua**; volcanic; alt. 1,753 m.

Omsk, c., W. Siberia, **Russia**; at confluence of Irtysh and Om Rs.; major R. pt. on Trans-Siberian rly.; in agr. region; engin., chemicals, textiles, oil refining, food processing; cath.; founded as fortress 1716; p. (1989) 1,148,000.

Omuta, t., W. Kyushu, **Japan**; on Amakusa Sea; local coal at Miike giving rise to chemical inds.; pt. exp. coal; p. (1990) 150,461.

Onega, Lake, Russia; between L. Ladoga and White Sea; second lgst. L. in Europe (L. Ladoga is lgst.); a. 9,751 km²; ch. c. Petro-zavodsk; Onega canal forms part of Volga-Baltic waterway.

Onega, R., **Russia**; flows to G. of Onega; 640 km long.

Onitsha, t., **Nigeria**; on R. Niger; agr. tr. ctr.; p. (1983) 269,000.

Ontario, prov., **Canada**; bounded on N. by Hudson Bay, on S. by Gr. Ls.; extreme continental climate in N., milder in S. peninsula; extensive coniferous forest in N.; temperate agr. in S.; leading mineral producer, nickel, uranium, copper, gold; well-developed inds. using plentiful hydroelectric power; agr.-processing, machin., engin.; cap. Toronto; contains fed. cap. of Ottawa; a. 1,068,587 km²; p. (1991) 9,961,200, concentrated in S.E.

Ontario, L., N. America; smallest of the Gr. Ls. of the St. Lawrence basin, separating the Canadian prov. of Ont. from N.Y., **USA**; navigable, carries industl. raw materials; polluted waters; a. 19,425 km²; depth 226 m.

Ontario, t., Cal., **USA**; aircraft components; fruit comm. ctr.; p. (1990) 133,179.

Onteniente, t., Valencia, **Spain**; on R. Clariano; woollen gds., paper mills; p. (1981) 28,123.

Oosterhout, t., N. Brabant, **Neth.**; nr. Breda; footwear, tobacco; p. (1993) 49,655.

Ootacamund, t., Tamil Nadu, **India**; in Nilgiri hills, *c.* 2,100 m; summer H.Q. of st. govt.; sanatorium.

Opatija (It. Abbazia), t., **Croatia** (formerly Yugoslavia); tourist resort, known as the Nice of the Adriatic; p. (1981) 29,274.

Opava (Troppau), t., N. Moravia, **Czech Rep.**; nr. Polish border; industl. ctr. in agr. a.; p. (1984) 60,961.

Opland or **Oppland**, co., central **Norway**; mtnous. N. inc. alpine region of Jotunheimen; forestry prods.; a. 24,885 km²; p. (1990) 182,593.

Opole (Oppeln), c. and prov., S. **Poland**; on R. Oder; R. pt., rly. junc.; cement, metals, furniture; 3 univ. schools; cap. Prussian prov. of Upper Silesia 1919–45; p. (1989) 126,962 (c.), 1,010,400 (prov.).

Oporto (Porto), c., spt., **Portugal**; second c. of rep., built high above Douro R.; ctr. of port wine tr.; cath., univ., historic bldgs.; sardine fisheries, cotton and wool textiles, sugar refining, distilling, oil refining; outer harbour at Leixões; p. (1981) 327,368 (c.), 1,562,287 (met. a.).

Oradea t., **W. Romania**, on Crisul Repede R., nr. Hungarian border; cap. Bihor prov.; baroque architecture; p. (1990) 228,956.

Öraefa Jokull, hgst mtn., **Iceland**; alt. 1,955 m.

Oran. See **Ouahran.**

Orange, t., N.S.W., **Australia**; in fertile fruit growing a., agr. processing; tourism; with Bathurst is planned growth ctr.; p. (1981) 27,626.

Orange, historic t., Vaucluse, **France**; title founded by Charlemagne passed to William the Silent of the house of Nassau; Roman amphitheatre; tourism; p. (1982) 27,502.

Orange, R., Cape Prov., **S. Africa**; flows from Lesotho to Atl.; part forms S. bdy. between Cape Prov. and Orange Free State; Verwoerd dam (1972) for power, irrigation, flood control; Highlands Water Project (1986) to export water from Lesotho to S. Africa; 2,080 km long.

Orange Free State, prov., **Rep. of S. Africa**; plateau land, Drakensberg to N.E., Rs. Orange, Vaal and Caledon; sheep, cattle, horses, wheat, maize, fruit, tobacco, coal, diamonds; cap. Bloemfontein; a. 128,586 km²; p. (1985) 1·8 m.

Oranienburg, t., Potsdam, **Germany**; on R. Havel; industl.; chemicals, metals, machin.; p. (1989) 28,978.

Ord of Caithness, hill, headland, nr. Helmsdale, Scot.; alt. 366 m.

Ordos, desert region, Inner Mongolia, **China**; lies S. of Huang He; mean alt. 1,000 m; dry cropping, especially millets; pastoral farming.

Ord, R., W. **Australia**; in Kimberley dist.; since 1972 Ord Irrigation Project; hydroelectric power.

Ordu, spt. and prov., **Turkey**; on Black Sea; exp. manganese; p. (1985) 80,828 (t.), (1990) 850,105 (prov.).

Ordzhonikidze. See **Vladikavkaz.**

Örebro, c., cap. of Örebro prov., **Sweden**; on R. Svartå at entrance to Hjälmar L.; anc. t., cas.; footwear, biscuits; p. (1992) 123,188 (t.), 274,325 (prov.).

Oregon, st., N.W. **USA**; Beaver St.; admitted to Union 1859; st. flower Oregon Grape, st. bird Western Meadowlark; borders Pac. Oc.; ch. physical features, Coast ranges, Cascade mtn. region, Blue mtns., Columbia R. and tribs., Willamette valley; rainy cst., drier interior (agr. with irrigation); cereals, sugar-beet, fruit, cattle; gold, silver, copper, coal, uranium; fisheries, canning, meat-packing, timber, milling; cap. Salem; a. 250,948 km²; p. (1990) 2,842,321.

Orekhovo-Zuyevo, t., **Russia**; E. of Moscow, on R. Klyazma; textile inds.; p. (1989) 137,000.

Orel, c., **Russia**; on R. Oka; univ.; rly. junc.; engin., textile mills, food prods.; birthplace of Turgenev; p. (1989) 337,000.

Orenburg (Chkalov), c., cap. of Orenburg oblast, **Russia**; on Ural R.; rly. junc.; food processing, agr. machin.; oil and natural gas in region; p. (1989) 547,000.

Orense, t., cap. of Orense prov., **Spain**; on R. Minho; flour, leather, iron; p. (1991) 107,247, 351,529 (prov.).

Ore Sound, strait, between Sjaelland, Denmark, and S. Sweden; protected by agreement of adjacent countries; freezes occasionally; proposed bridge (1988).

Orford Ness, coastal sandspit, Suffolk, **Eng.**; cas. keep at Orford.

Oriente, terr., **Peru/Ecuador**; for long in dispute between the two ctys., partially settled by treaty (1942); lies E. of Andes, between Putumayo and Marañon Rs.; mainly dense forest, reputedly rich in minerals.

Orihuela, t., Alicante, **Spain**; on R. Segura; leather, textiles, wine; univ., cath.; p. (1981) 49,851.

Orinoco, R., **Venezuela**; rises in Parima mtns., flows to Atl., connected to Rio Negro and Amazon; impt. industl. development on lower O., based on hydroelec. power and iron ore; experimental scheme to reclaim delta for agr.; 2,368 km long.

Orissa, st., **India**; agr. with few ts.; Hirakud dam across Mahanadi R.; Paradeep being developed as pt.; rice; cap. Bhuvaneshwar; a. 155,825 km²; p. (1991) 31,659,736.

Orizaba, t., Veracruz, **Mexico**; textiles, paper mills, breweries; resort; p. (1990) 113,516.

Orizaba, mtn., Veracruz, **Mexico**; volcanic; called Citlatepetl in Aztec times; alt. 5,704 m.

Orkney, l. gov. reg., **Scot.**; gr. of 68 Is. in N. Sea inc. Pomona, Sanday, Westray; 20 inhabited; antiquarian remains, stone circles; farming, fishing; North Sea oil; cap. Kirkwall; total a. c. 932 km²; p. (1993) 19,760.

Orlando, c., Fla., **USA**; winter resort; inds. based on citrus fruit and mkt. garden prods.; p. (1990) 164,693 (c.), 1,073,000 (met. a.).

Orléannais, region and former prov., **France**; inc. deps. of Loire-et-Cher, Loiret, and parts of Eure-et-Loire and Yonne.

Orléans, c., cap. of Loiret dep., **France**; on R. Loire; cath., univ.; regional tr. ctr.; wine, textiles, chemicals, farm implements; statue of Joan of Arc; p. (1990) 107,965 (c.), 243,153 (met. a.).

Ormoc, c., W. Leyte, **Philippines**; pt. and agr. ctr., exp. hemp, rice; disastrous floods Nov. 1991; p. (1990) 129,456.

Ormskirk, t., West Lancs., **Eng.**; 22 km N.E. of Liverpool; in mkt. gardening a.; lt. engin., clothing; p. (1981) 27,753.

Orne, dep., N. **France**; agr., dairying, stock-keeping, fruit-growing. Camembert cheese; cap. Alençon; a. 6,143 km²; p. (1990) 293,200.

Orontes, R., rises in **Lebanon**, flows through **Syria** past Hama into **Turkey** past Antioch to Mediterranean; unnavigable but used for irrigation; part of valley followed by rly.; irrigated areas intensively cultivated; c. 400 km long.

Orpington. See **Bromley.**

Orsha, c., **Belarus**; impt. industl. and transport ctr. on R. Dnieper; textiles, metal wks., food-processing; once a frontier fortress; p. (1990) 124,000.

Orsk, c., **Russia**; in Ural mtns. on Ural R.; inds. based on surrounding mng. a.; oil pipeline terminus; oil refining; hydroelectric power sta. nearby; p. (1989) 271,000.

Orta, L., Italy; W. of Lago Maggiore; a. 18 km².

Orthez, t., Pyrénées-Atlantique, **France**; scene of Wellington's victory over Soult (1814); Bayonne hams; p. (1982) 11,542.

Orumiyeh. See **Rezaiyeh.**

Oruro, t., Bolivia; cap. of O. prov. at alt. 3,709 m; once impt. ctr. for silver mng.; now other minerals impt.; tin smelter; p. (1988) 176,700 (t.), 388,300 (dep.).

Oruwala, t., Sri Lanka; steel rolling mill.

Orvieto, t., Umbria, **Italy**; on R. Paglia; cath., Etruscan antiquities; wines, olive oil, cereals; pottery.

Osaka, c., Honshu, **Japan**; ctr. of Kinki plain; built on delta in shallow O. Bay; comm. ctr.; banking, heavy industry, metals, machin., clothing; p. (1990) 2,623,831.

Osasco, t., São Paulo st., **Brazil**; industl. satellite of São Paulo with traditional and new inds.; p. (1991) 563,419.

Osh, t., **Kyrgyzstan**; textiles, food-processing; one of oldest ts. in central Asia; p. (1990) 217,500.

Oshawa, t., Ont., **Canada**; pt. on L. Ont.; motor vehicles; p. (1986) 123,651 (c.), 203,543 (met. a.).

Oshima, I., Tokyo Bay, **Japan**; lgst. and most N. of Izu-shichito gr.; site of volcanic Mt. Mihara (755 m).

Oshkosh, t., Wis., **USA**; on Fox R.; meat packing, flour, motors; p. (1990) 55,006 (c.), 315,000 (met. a. Appleton-Oshkosh-Neenah).

Oshogbo, t., **Nigeria**; comm. and educational ctr.; serves agr. dist.; cotton-ginning; new steel rolling mill; p. (1983) 345,000.

Osijek, t., **Croatia** (formerly Yugoslavia); on Drava R.; growing industl. ctr. for textiles and leather; p. (1991) 104,761.

Osinniki, t., **Russia**; W. Siberia; new ctr. of coal mng.; thermal power sta.

Osipenko. See **Berdyansk.**

Oslo (Christiania), c., cap. of **Norway**; at head of Oslo Fjord; ch. spt., comm., industl., and cultural ctr.; ice-free harbour, cath., univ.; exp. timber, fish, matches; wood pulp, paper; p. (1990) 461,644.

Osnabrück, c., Lower Saxony, **Germany**; on R. Hase; stands on a branch of the Mittelland canal; inland pt. and industl. ctr.; iron and steel mills; mach., textile and paper mnfs.; p. (1990) 164,000.

Osorno, t., **Chile**; agr. ctr.; in beautiful forested cty.; Germanic influence; food-processing; tourism; p. (1987) 122,462.

Ossett, t., West Yorks., **Eng.**; 5 km W. of Wakefield; woollens, shoddy-processing, engin.; p. (1981) 20,416.

Ostend, spt., **Belgium**; passenger route between Britain and continent of Europe; popular resort; casino, fisheries, shipbldg., textiles, tobacco; p. (1993) 69,148.

Östergötland, co., **Sweden**; on Baltic cst.; rises to uplands of Småland in S. where p. declining; lowland, a. crossed by Gota canal; cap. Linköping; a. 11,050 km²; p. (1992) 408,268.

Östersund, t., Jämtland, **Sweden**; on Storsjön L.; p. (1992) 59,019.

Östfold, co., S.E. **Norway**; hilly a. crossed by R. Glomma; dairy prods. for Oslo; a. 4,178 km²; p. (1990) 238,345.

Ostia, anc. c., **Italy**; once pt. of Rome, at mouth of R. Tiber, founded 4th cent. B.C.; layout revealed by excavations; modern v. of O. nearby on plain reclaimed from salt marsh.

Ostrava, c., **Czech Rep.**; at junc. of Oder and Ostravice Rs.; industl. ctr. of Ostrava–Karvinna coalmng. region; iron and steel, machin., chemicals, oil refining; p. (1990) 331,000.

Ostrołęka, t. and prov., N.E. central **Poland**; on R. Narew; cellulose, paper; p. (1989) 49,032 (t.), 393,400 (prov.).

Ostrow Wielkopolski, t., Kalisz prov., **Poland**; agr. machin., clothing; p. (1989) 72,085.

Ostrowiec Swietokrzyski (**Ostrovets**), t., Kielce, **Poland**; on R. Kamienna; ceramic and metallurgical inds. p. (1989) 77,466.

Oswaldtwistle, t., Hyndburn, Lancs., **Eng.**; at N. foot of Rossendale Fells; chemicals, textiles; p. (1981) 14,519.

Oswego, t., N.Y., **USA**; pt. on L. Ontario; mnfs. hosiery, matches, textiles, boiler engines; paper; p. (1980) 19,793.

Oswestry, t., l. gov. dist., Shrops., **Eng.**; at foot of Welsh mtns., cas.; engin.; p. (1993) 34,200 (dist.).

Oświecim (Ger. **Auschwitz**), t., Bielsko prov., **Poland**; at confluence of Rs. Iola and Vistula; lge. chemical wks.; German concentration camp (1940–44); p. (1989) 45,402.

Otago, reg., S.I., **N.Z.**; forested mtns.; gold; farming, sheep, fruit; lge. deposit of jade found at head of L. Wakatipu; coalfields; cap. Dunedin; a. 65,320 km²; p. (1991) 186,067.

Otago Harbour, Otago dist., S.I., **N.Z.**; Dunedin and Port Chalmers are ports on this harbour.

Otanmäki, **Finland**; rich deposit of magnetite-ilmenite ore.

Otaru, reg., Hokkaido, **Japan**; herring fisheries; coal mng., lumbering; p. (1990) 163,215.

Otley, t., West Yorks., **Eng.**; on R. Wharfe; printing, machin., wool, paper mkg., leather, furnishings; birthplace of Thomas Chippendale; p. (1981) 13,806.

Otranto, t. S. **Italy**; on Strait O.; once a flourishing c., fine mosaic pavement, cath., cas.; submarine cable sta.; bauxite exp., fishing; p. (1981) 4,811.

Otsu, t., Honshu, **Japan**; on L. Biwa; p. (1990) 260,004.

Ottawa, c. Ont. cap. of **Canada**; on R. Ottawa; univ.; caths., parliament bldgs.; hydroelec, power, lumbering, sawmills, paper, flour, leather, matches, machin., ironware; p. (1986) 300,763 (c.), 819,263 (met. a. with Hull).

Ottawa, R., **Canada**; trib. of St. Lawrence; forming bdy. between Ont. and Quebec; timber transport, hydroelec. power; 1,000 km long.

Ottery St. Mary, mkt. t., East Devon, **Eng.**; 16 km E. of Exeter; birthplace of Coleridge; p. (1981) 7,069.

Ottumwa, t., Iowa, **USA**; on Des Moines R.; in coalfield and agr. dist.; iron and steel, meat-packing; p. (1990) 24,488.

Ötzal, valley, **Austria**; longest side valley of R. Inn; tourist dist.

Ouachita or **Washita**, R., Ark., **USA**; trib. of Red R.; 880 km long.

Ouachita National Forest, Ark., Okla., **USA**; part of forested O. highlands.

Ouagadougou, cap. of **Burkina Faso**; tex., soap, comm.; p. (1985) 442,223.

Ouahran (**Oran**), spt., N. **Algeria**; founded by Moors 10th cent.; occupied by French 1831–1962; handles wines, wool, cereals, meat, skins; fine roadstead at Mers-el-Kebir; former French naval and military sta.; p. (1983) 663,504.

Oudenaarde (**Audenarde**), t., **Belgium**, on R. Scheldt; textile ctr.; scene of Marlborough's victory over French 1708; p. (1981) 27,318.

Ouenza, c., **Algeria**; 75 per cent of Algerian iron-ore produced in dist.

Oujda, t., N.E. **Morocco**; comm. ctr.; phosphate, lead and zinc-mng. dist.; p. (1982) 260,082.

Oulton Broad, L., Suffolk, **Eng.**; nr. Lowestoft. *See* **Broads.**

Oulu, spt., cap. of Oulu prov., N.W. **Finland**; on G. of Bothnia at mouth of R. Oulu; univ.; p. (1991) 102,280

Oundle, mkt. t., East Northants., **Eng.**; on R. Nene; public school; p. (1981) 3,290.

Ouro Prêto, old colonial t., **Brazil**; former cap. of Minas Gerais st.; as gold mng. ctr.; founded 1711; school of mines.

Ouse or Great Ouse, R., **Eng.**; rises in S. Northamptonshire and flows N.E. via the Fens to the Wash; 250 km long.

Ouse, R., East Sussex, **Eng.**; flows to English Channel at Newhaven; 48 km long.

Ouse, R., North Yorks./Humberside, **Eng.**; formed by Rs. Swale and Ure, flows to Humber estuary; 208 km long.

Ovalle, t., Coquimbo prov., **Chile**; ctr. of fruit and pastoral dist.

Overijssel, prov., **Neth.**; dairying, fishing; ch. ind. textiles; a. 3,364 km²; p. (1993) 1,039,083.

Oviedo, coastal. prov., N. **Spain**; agr., fruit, sardine, and other fisheries; cap. O.; a. 10,888 km²; p. (1991) 1,096,155.

Oviedo, c., cap. of O. prov., **Spain**; on R. Nalón; cath., univ.; industl. and comm. ctr. for agr. and mng. dists. of Asturias; p. (1991) 203,189.

Owenus, pt., **Liberia**, deepwater pt. built to serve iron ore mines at Belinga.

Owen Falls, Uganda; dam inaugurated 1954 to supply Uganda with hydroelectric power; also converts L. Victoria into reservoir for irrigation of Egypt.

Owensboro', t., Ky., **USA**; petroleum; ctr. for stock raising and tobacco growing a.; p. (1990) 53,549.

Owens, L., S. Cal., **USA**; on E. flank of Sierra Nevada, 32 km S.E. of Mt. Whitney; water taken by 360 km-long aqueduct to Los Angeles; a. 311 km².

Owen Sound, t., L. pt., Ont., **Canada**; on S.W. cst. of Georgian Bay, L. Huron; E. terminus of lgst. wheat-carrying L. steamers; linked by rly. to Toronto (200 km) and Montreal; p. (1981) 19,883.

Oxelösund, spt., E. **Sweden**; on Baltic cst., S. of Stockholm; steelwks., glass.

Oxford, c., l. gov. dist., Oxon., **Eng.**; between R. Thames and R. Cherwell; 13th cent. univ. and residtl. colleges; printing, cars, elec. engin.; p. (1993) 132,000 (dist.).

Oxfordshire, non-met. co., **Eng.**; formed by Chilterns and Cotswolds, drained by R. Thames and tribs.; mainly agr. with lge. arable farms; being prospected for new coalfield; ch. t. Oxford; a. 2,611 km²; p. (1993) 585,800.

Oxnard, t., Cal., **USA**; citrus fruits, sugar beet, oil refining; p. (1990) 142,216 (t.), 669,000 (met. a. with Ventura).

Oxus, R. *See* **Amu Dar'ya.**

Oyashio. *See* **Bering Current.**

Oyo, t., **Nigeria**; cotton weaving; mkt.; p. (est. 1983) 185,000, (1991) 3,488,789 (state).

Ozark Mtns., Okla. and Ark., **USA**; lead, zinc; ch. t, Joplin; forested.

P

Paarl, t., Cape Prov., **S. Africa**; summer resort extending along Gt. Berg R.; wines, fruit, tobacco; flour, saw and textile mills; p. (1980) 108,860 (dist.).

Pabianice, t., Poland; nr. Lodz; textiles, farming implements, paper; p. (1989) 74,755.

Pabna, t., and dist., Bengal, Bangladesh; dist. is a fertile alluvial plain; t. serves as trading, industl. and admin. ctr. for a.; hosiery, carpets; p. (1991) 104,479 (t.), 4,305,000 (dist.).

Pachitea, R., Peru; rises in Andes, flows N. to R. Ucayali; sm. German immigrant colonies in upper valley; 512 km long.

Pachmarhi, Madhya Pradesh, India; summer cap., tourist ctr.

Pachuca, cap., Hidalgo st., Mexico; silver mnfs. and mng.; woollen and leather gds.; p. (1990) 179,440.

Pacific Islands, Trust Terr. of, external terr. of USA held under U.N. trusteeship; consists of Mariana Is. (except Guam), Caroline and Marshall Is., W. Pac. Oc.; inc. ? 141 Is., grouped into 6 admin. dists., cap. (provisional) Saipan, Mariana Is.; total land a. c. 1,800 km²; p. (1985) 154,000.

Pacific Ocean, a. 176,120,000 km²; lgst. ocean in the world; extends from W. cst of America to E. cst. of Asia and Australia and the S. Ocean in the S.; enters Arctic Oc. via Bering Strait; greatest length N. to S. 1,280 km; breadth, 16,000 km; mean depth 3,830 m, 11,524 m in the Mindanao trench; many coral and volcanic Is. in S.W.

Padang, spt., W. cst. Sumatra, Indonesia; exp. agr. prods., coffee, copra, rubber and coal; cement mnfs.; univ.; p. (1983) 726,000.

Paddington. See Westminster, City of.

Paderborn, c., N. Rhine–Westphalia, Germany; cath. and other historic bldgs. severely damaged in second world war; foodstuffs, textiles, metals; p. (1990) 122,700.

Padiham, t., Lancs., Eng.; at N. foot of Rossendale Fells, textiles, engin., gas appliances; p. (1981) 9,246.

Padstow, mkt. t., Cornwall, Eng.; on W. side of Camel estuary in which silting has caused pt. of P. to decline; lt. inds.; seaside resort.

Padua (Padova), c., cap. of P. prov., N.E. Italy; cath., arcades, anc. bridges; univ. founded 1222 (Galileo taught here); flourished as artistic ctr.; birthplace of Livy; machin., chemicals, cloth, distilling; agr. ctr.; p. (1992) 213,656.

Paducah, c., Ky., USA; pt. on Ohio R.; saw-mills, tobacco, railway wks.; atomic energy plant; p. (1990) 27,256.

Paestum, anc. c., S. Italy; S.E. of Salerno; founded by the Greeks 600 B.C.; ruins of temples, Roman forum and amphitheatre.

Pagan, ruined c., central Myanmar; on Irrawaddy R.; founded circa 849, sacked 1299; in ctr. of a. covered with pagodas, place of Burmese pilgrimage; lacquer work.

Pago Pago, spt., cap. of American Samoa, S. Pac.; on Tutuila I., magnificent harbour; US naval and radio sta.; airport; p. (1990) 46,773.

Pahang, st., Malaysia, central Malaya; isolated from rest of Malaya, less economically developed; largely covered with forest; some rubber production, gold, tin mng.; cap. Kuala Lipis; a. 34,395 km²; p. (1980) 798,782.

Pahlevi. See Bandar-e-Pahlevi.

Paignton, t., S. Devon, Eng.; incorporated in Torbay; resort; p. (1981) 40,820.

Painted Desert, Arizona, USA; a. of bare multicoloured shale and sandstones; arid; a. c. 19,400 km².

Paisley, burgh, Renfrew, Scot.; 8 km W. of Glasgow; anc. abbey; shipbldg., chemicals, engin., preserves, car bodies, cotton thread; p. (1991) 75,526.

Paita, pt., Peru; exp. cotton, wool, flax, panama hats; lge. whaling sta. to S.; p. 37,000.

Pakistan, Islamic Rep. of, forms part of Indian subcontinent, S. Asia; formerly split into two separate units, E. Pakistan (cap. Dacca) and W. Pakistan, (cap. Lahore), 1,600 km apart; politically separate since 1972; W. part now forms Pakistan; rejoined Commonwealth 1989; E. part indep. st. of Bangladesh; dry semi-desert, irrigated by Indus R. and tribs.; cash crops, sugar, wheat, cotton; natural gas fields; new cap. Islamabad; main spt. Karachi; a. 803,944 km²; p. (1992) 119·11 m (+3.1 per cent. a year).

Paknampoh, t., Thailand; on R. Menam, at upper limit of navigation; terminus of private rly.; fish breeding in L. created from swamp.

Pakokku, t., Upper Myanmar; pt. on Irrawaddy R.; shipping ctr. for a. producing sugar, tobacco, peanuts, teak, petroleum; Yenangyaung oilfields nearby.

Paktia, prov., Afghanistan; mtnous., forested; difficult to govern, inhabited by sm. and indep. tribes, but sparse p.; livestock basis of agr.; timber exp; a. c. 12,950 km²; p. (1984) 525,000.

Palau Rep. of, formerly Western Carolines; group of Is. 300 km. E. of Philippines; renamed 1981; part of U.S. Trust Terr. of Pacific Is.; p. (1991) 15,105.

Palawan I., prov. Philippines; elongated I., rising to 1,731 m; coffee, resin, timber; prov. a. 11,784 km²; p. (1990) 528,287.

Palembang, cap. of G. Sumatra prov., Indonesia; R. pt. of Musi R., 80 km from sea; terminus of S. Sumatran rly. systems; exp. coffee and petroleum prods. from nearby oilfields; inds. based on agr. processing and oil refining; p. (1981) 903,000.

Palencia, t., cap. of P. prov., N.W. Spain; industl. ctr.; rly. engin.; cath.; p. (1987) 75,951; (1991) 183,908 (prov.).

Palermo, spt., Sicily, Italy; cath., univ.; shiprepairing; processes agr. prod. from surrounding fertile Conca d'Oro; p. (1992) 696,735.

Palestine or The Holy Land, historic region, bounded by Syria and Lebanon on the N., Jordan on the E., the Egyptian prov. of Sinai on the S., and the Mediterranean on the W.; a. when under Brit. mandate 2,701 km². See Israel.

Palghat, t., Kerala, India; commands Palghat gap through W. Ghats; p. (1981) 117,986.

Palitana, t., Gujarat, India; t. of Jain temples inhabited by priests and their servants; p. (1981) 34,449.

Palk Strait, separates India from Sri Lanka.

Palma de Mallorca, spt., Mallorca I, Spain; cath.; palaces, varied inds.; agr. exp.; well-known tourist resort; p. (1991) 308,616.

Palm Beach, t., Fla., USA; Atl. coastal resort; permanent p. (1980) 9,729.

Palmerston North, c., N.I., N.Z.; rly. junc. at ctr. of Manawatu R. lowlands; sheep and dairy prod.; univ.; p. (1991) 70,318.

Palmira, t., W. Colombia; agr. ctr. in Cauca valley; p. (1983) 179,000.

Palm Springs, Cal., USA; resort; p. (1980) 32,366.

Palmyra, anc. c. in Syrian desert, 192 km. N.E. of Damascus; extensive ruins.

Palmyra Is. See Line Is.

Palo Alto, t., sub. development 48 km S.E. San Francisco, Cal., USA; attractive wooded site of variable relief; on shore of San Francisco Bay peninsula; Stanford Univ.; science-based inds.; p. (1980) 55,225.

Palomar, Mount, peak, 1,868 m high, S. Cal., USA; observatory with 5,080 mm reflecting telescope.

Palos de la Frontera, t., Huelva, S.W. Spain; on Rio Tinto; starting point for Columbus in 1492; pt. now silted up; p. (1981) 4,014.

Palua, pt., Venezuela; pt. of shipment for iron mines at El Pao; nearby Caroni hydroelec. plant built to serve steel wks. and aluminium plant.

Pamir Mtns., high mtn. plateau ("roof of the world"), Tajikistan, Central Asia; Mt. Communism (7,400 m) climbed by Russo-British team 1962; name derives from high mtn. valleys known as pamirs.

Pampas, Argentina; vast plains stretching from the Rio Negro on the S. to the Gran Chaco in the N., and E. from the Andes to the Atl.; woodless, level country; rich pastures in E., supporting countless numbers of sheep and cattle, a major influence upon the Argentinian economy, source of livestock exps.; W. mostly barren.

Pamplona, t., Norte de Santander, Colombia; agr., comm. and tr. ctr.; inds. based on agr. processing.

Pamplona, c., cap. of Navarre, N. Spain; at foot of Pyrenees, anc. Baxque c.; cath., fortress, univ.; industl. ctr. with varied mnfs.; p. (1991) 191,112.

Panaji, cap. of Goa state, India; p. (1981) 77,226.

Panama, rep., Central America; narrow strip of terr. at S. end of isthmus separating N. and S. America; mtnous. and tropical, thickly forested; 9

prov. and 1 autonomous Indian reservation; split by Canal Area from which rep. earns 25 per cent of revenue; shipping registration and other services impt.; subsistence agr.; exp. bananas, shrimps, sugar, coffee; rich copper deposits found 1975; poor communications; Cap. Panama City; a. 74,009 km²; p. (1990) 2,329,329.

Panama Canal Area, Panama; strip of land 82 km long 16 km wide on either side of Canal; 1979 former Canal Zone transferred by US to Panamanian sovereignty; a. 1,675 km².

Panama City, c. spt., cap. of **Panama**; free pt. at S. entrance to Canal; cath.; oil refining, steel rolling mill, cement plant, lt. inds.; contains 25 per cent p. Panama rep.; p. (1990) 584,803.

Panama City, t., Fla., **USA**; pulp and paper mill; resort; p. (1984) 34,100 (t.), 108,500 (met. a.).

Pan American Highway, international road project, not yet fully complete, from Alaska to Chile, down W. csts. of continents; section between USA and Mexico is called Central American Inter-American Highway.

Panay, I., Philippines; between Negros I. and Mindoro I.; coconuts, maize grown in E., fertile lowland; ch. t. Iloilo; a. 11,515 km²; p. (1990) 8,031,271.

Pančevo, t., N.E. Serbia, **Yugoslavia**; agr. ctr. for grain growing a., flour-milling; developing industl. ctr., fertilizers, oil refining; p. (1991) 72,717.

Pangalanes Canal (Canal Des Pangalanes), Madagascar; follows E. cst from Farafangana to Tamatave, through series of lagoons; 480 km long.

Panipat, t., Haryana, N.W. **India**; on Jumna R.; on route from Afghanistan to central India; scene of battles; p. (1991) 191,212.

Panjim, cap. of Goa, **India**; pt.; old cap. (Velha Goa) in ruins; p. (1981) 43,165.

Panjsher Valley, Afghanistan; silver and mica mines.

Pantelleria, volcanic I., Mediterranean, **Italy**; midway between W. Sicily and Tunisia; figs, raisins, vines, capers, cereals; fishing; a. 150 km²; ch. t. P.; p. (1981) 7,917.

Pantin, N.E. sub., Paris, Seine-St. Denis, **France**; glasswks., sugar refining, tobacco factories, chemicals, leather, tallow; p. (1982) 43,553.

Paoki. *See* Baoji.

Paoting. *See* Baoding.

Paotow. *See* Baotou.

Papakura, dist., N.I., **N.Z.**; residtl. a. for Auckland; p. (1991) 36,553.

Papaloa, R., **Mexico**; agr. and industl. development; Papaloan project for flood control and electricity generation.

Papal States, Italy, areas ruled by the Pope until 1870; comprised Latium, Umbria, the Marches, and Emilia-Romagna.

Papatoetoe, c., N.I., **N.Z.**; residtl. ctr. close to Auckland; p. (1987) 21,900.

Papeete, t., pt., **Tahiti I.**, Pac. Oc.; cap. Tahiti and of Fr. Settlements in Oceania; exp. copra, vanilla, phosphates and mother-of-pearl; p. (1983) 78,814.

Paphos (Pafos), admin. dist., W. cst. **Cyprus**; anc. c.; Old P. dates from 3000 B.C., New P. impt. spt.; rich deposits of copper and iron pyrites, sulphur in Vretsia a.; scene of ambitious project (completed 1983) to grow tropical fruits (mango, avocado, papaya) with irrigation; p. (1991) 30,900 (c.).

Papua New Guinea, E. New Guinea, S.E. Asia; indep. st. (1975); mtnous., thickly forested; under-developed; copra, rubber and timber prods.; many valuable reserves of gold and copper; cap. Pt. Moresby; a. 461,693 km²; p. (1992) 3·85 m.

Pará, st., **Brazil**; densely forested; rubber, fruits, cacao, Brazil nuts; massive iron ore deposits in Serra do Carajás with new road and rail access; cap. Belem; a. 1,228,061 km²; p. (1991) 5,084,726.

Paracel Is., S. China Sea; claimed by China, Taiwan and Vietnam.

Paraguay, landlocked rep., **S. America**; undulating cty.; swamps, forest; hot summers, warm winters, high but seasonal rainfall; sm. densely populated areas, lge. areas with no p.; most economically developed in E.; in and around cap. Asunción 25 per cent p.; economy based on agr., decline of meat and timber but agr. expansion in other prods.; cereals, livestock, fruit, cotton, oil-seeds, but food imported; aid from USA for rural development; few fuel resources (a few oilfields in the Chaco Borea) and low energy consumption; hydroelectric plant on Paraná (Itaipu dam), Paraguay Rs. and at Guaira Falls; electricity exp. to Brazil; new inds. with cheap power; first steel mill (1982); some agr. based inds.; a. 406,630 km²; p. (1993) 4·5 m.

Paraguay, R., S. America; rises in plateau of Mato Grosso, flows S. and joins R. Paraná nr. Corrientes; forms bdy. between Brazil and Bolivia, Brazil and Paraguay; impt. navigable waterway to Cáceres (Brazil); 1,920 km long.

Paraíba, st., N.E. **Brazil**; livestock, cotton, sugar cane; tin, scheelite; cap. João Pessoa; a. 56,462 km²; p. (1991) 3,200,620.

Paraíba do Sul, R., S. **Brazil**; rises in São Paulo st., and flows between Rio de Janeiro and Minas Gerais to Atl. N.E. of Rio de Janeiro; forms routeway between São Paulo and Rio de Janeiro; 1,040 km long.

Paramaribo, spt., cap. of **Suriname**; on Suriname R.; exp. bauxite, timber, rubber, rice, fruit; is. built on grid pattern with canals and tree-lined streets; p. (1990) 200,000.

Paraná, c., cap. of Entre Rios prov., N.E. **Argentina**; pt. of P. R. for grain, cattle, sheep; road tunnel to Santa Fé; p. (1991) 277,338.

Paraná, R., S.W. **Brazil**; formed by junc. of Rs. Rio Grande and Paranaíba; flows W. between Paraguay and Argentina; flows into Rio de la Plata; navigable to Brazil frontier nr. Iguaçu Falls; forms part of international inland waterway system; hydroelec. power, Itaipú lgst. sta. in world; joint hydroelec. scheme between Paraguay, Brazil and Argentina; 3,280 km long; rapid rise in p. with indust. expansion from electricity.

Paraná, st., S. **Brazil**; between Paraná R. and Atl. Oc.; extensively forested; maté, timber, coffee; cap. Curitiba; a. 201,287 km²; p. (1991) 8,415,659.

Paranaguá, spt., Paraná st., **Brazil**; ch. pt. for Paraná; in lagoon harbour; modern highway links with Asunción (Paraguay); p. (1986) 94,800.

Pardubice, t., Czech Rep.; univ., cath.; rly. junc.; industl. ctr.; distilling, oil refining; p. (1990) 96,000.

Paricutin, Mt. Michoacán, **Mexico**; volcano formed between 1943 and 1952, 2,501 m high; of great interest to scientists.

Paris, c., cap. of **France**; dominates rep. politically, economically, and socially, partly as result of extreme centralisation of political power in cap.; on R. Seine, 176 km from mouth, in ctr. of Paris Basin; forms major ctr. of communications; planning of Haussmann gives spacious appearance, 12 boulevards radiate from Arc de Triomphe; many historic bldgs., especially on and around Ile de la Cité, an I. on R. Seine, site of cath. of Notre Dame; major cultural and tourist ctr.; univs.; comprises 20 admin. arrondissements; major ctr. of inds. with concentration of modern science-based inds. hindering planned attempts at decentralisation; p. (1990) 2,152,400 (c.), (1982) 9,060,257 (met. a.).

Paris Basin, concentric limestone escarpments form saucer-shaped depression with Paris at ctr.; impt. agr. dist., wheat, dairy prod. and wines.

Parkersburg, t., W. Va., **USA**; on Ohio R.; iron- and steel-wks., oil and natural gas, coal, glassware, rayon, porcelain; p. (1984) 39,400 (t.), 157,900 (met. a.).

Parkes, t., N.S.W., **Australia**; mkt.; rly. junc.; radio telescope; p. (1981) 9,047.

Parma, c., cap. of P. prov., **Italy**; between Apennines and Po R.; tr. ctr. rly. junc.; food-processing, wine, Parmesan cheese, precision instruments, agr. machin.; Roman remains, many historic bldgs., univ., cath.; p. (1992) 170,555.

Parma, t., Ohio, **USA**; motor vehicle parts; residtl.; p. (1990) 87,876.

Parnaiba, spt., Piauí, **Brazil**; agr. comm. ctr., cotton, cattle; exp. agr. prods.; p. (1986) 116,206.

Parnaiba, R., rises in Brazil; flows into N. Atl. Oc., forms bdy. between Maranhão and Piauí; 1,200 km long.

Parnassus, mtn. ridge, **Greece**; 133 km N.W. of Athens, nr. the anc. Delphi, the modern Llakhura; hgst. peak Licoreia, 2,461 m.

Parnu or **Pyarnu**, spt., S.W. **Estonia**; pt. of G. of Riga; exp. timber flax; health resort; p. (1991) 58,600.

Páros, I., Grecian Archipelago; W. of Naxos; source of Parian marble; cap. P.; a. 163 km².

Parramatta, c., N.S.W., **Australia**; pt. nr. head of Parramatta R. in met. a. of Sydney; 2nd Brit. settlement in Australia.

Parrett, R., Somerset, **Eng.**; flows to Bristol Channel, nr. Bridgwater; 56 km long.

Pasadena, c., Cal., **USA**; N. of Los Angeles; in fruit-growing region, base of San Gabriel mtns.; 5,080 mm telescope on Mt. Palomar; famous for its carnival; p. (1990) 131,591.

Pasco, t., Wash., **USA**; on Snake R.; atomic energy plant; p. (1980) 18,425.

Pasco. See **Cerro de Pasco.**

Pas-de-Calais, dep., N. **France**; impt. heavy industl. a. based upon local extensive coal deposits; heavy inds. inc. iron and steel, but many ts. in decline as importance of coal diminishes; prosperous agr. based on arable farming; N. cst. faces English Channel and inc. pts. of Calais and Boulogne; severe devastation in both world wars; cap. Arras; a. 6,750 km²; p. (1990) 1,433,200.

Pasir Gudang, free port, Malaysia, across Jahore Str. from Singapore; opened (1984) to divert M.'s exports from Singapore.

Passage West, t. Cork, **R.o.I.**; declining pt., fishing; p. (1986) 3,511.

Passaic, c., N.J., **USA**; rubber gds., springs, steel cabinets, tin cans; p. (1990) 58,041.

Passau, c., **Germany**; at confluence of Rs. Danube, Inn and Ilz, nr. Austrian frontier; trans-shipment base, inds. inc. leather, porcelain, tobacco and brewing; cath., picturesque tourist ctr.; p. (1986) 52,700.

Passchendaele, t., **Belgium**; strategic point in first world war; battle 31 July–6 Nov. 1917.

Passero I., Mediterranean Sea; off S.E. cst. of Sicily, **Italy.**

Passy, residtl. part of W. Paris, **France**; between Bois de Boulogne and right bank of Seine; residence of Balzac.

Pasto, t., cap. of Narino dep., **Colombia**; on flank of Pasto volcano; univ.; agr. comm. ctr.; gold nearby; p. (1992) 303,401.

Patagonia, extensive region, E. of Andes, Argentina/Chile; elevated plateau, arid, sterile; prin. Rs. Colorado, Río Negro, and Chubut; impt. source of oil at Commodoro Rivadavia; lge. tracts of grazing for livestock; much of p. Welsh descendants; plans to decentralise cap. of A. to small Ts. of Viedma and Carmen de Patagones.

Patan, c. **Nepal**; impt. ctr. of Buddhism; gold and silver gds.; p. (1981) 79,875.

Patani or **Pattani,** pt., S. **Thailand**; on E. cst. of Malay peninsula; spices, rubber, coconuts; tin mng.; former Malay sultanate.

Paterno, t., Sicily, **Italy**; N.W. of Catania; cath., cas.; mineral springs, wines; p. (1981) 45,144.

Paterson, c., N.J., **USA**; on Passaic R. whose falls provide hydroelectric power for gr. silk mnf. ind.; now inds. diversified; in addition to textiles and textile machin., aeroplane engines, metallurgical inds., electronic equipment; p. (1990) 140,891.

Patiala, t., Punjab, **India**; metal gds., flour; cement; p. (1981) 206,254.

Patino Mines. See **Unicia.**

Pátmos, I., one of the Dodecanese, **Greece**; in Aegean Sea; St. John wrote the Revelation here; a. 34 km²; p. 3,000.

Patna, c., cap. of Bihar, **India**; univ.; rly. junc.; agr. tr., rice, oilseeds, cotton; handicraft inds.; p. (1991) 917,000.

Patras (**Pátrai**), spt., cap. of Akhaia, **Greece**; citadel and cas., exp. currants, raisins, figs, olive oil; inds. based on agr. processing; p. (1981) 141,529.

Pau, c., cap. of Pyrénées-Atlantique dep., **France**; on Gave-de-Pau; impt. mkt. and regional ctr.; summer and winter resort; linen, chocolate, hams, wine; natural gas nearby; p. (1990) 83,923 (c.), 134,625 (met. a.).

Pauillac, t., Gironde dep., **France**; pt. on Gironde estuary; ships, wines, timber; oil refinery, natural gas; p. (1982) 6,359.

Paulo Affonso, falls, São Francisco R., **Brazil**; 79 m; Tres Marias dam and power sta. opened 1960; in Nat. Park.

Pavia, c., prov. cap., N. **Italy**; on R. Ticino; route ctr. and agr. mkt. in Po valley; olives, wine, Parmesan cheese; oil refining at Spineto; walled c.; battle 1525; birthplace of Lanfranc; p. (1981) 85,029.

Pavlodar, pt., **Kazakhstan**; on R. Irtysh; chemicals, sulphates, agr. machin., locomotives, aluminium, oil processing; food prod.; p. (1990) 336,800.

Pawtucket, c., R.I., **USA**; on Pawtucket R. at head of navigation; first water-power cotton

spinning factory in USA 1790; textiles remain most impt. ind.; p. (1990) 329,000 (met. a. with Woonsocket–Attleboro).

Paysandú, dep., W. **Uruguay**; rich pastoral a.; ranching, cattle, sheep; arable agr., cereals, mkt. gardening around c. of P.; a. 13,406 km²; p. (1985) 103,487.

Paysandú, cap. of P. dep., W. **Uruguay**; pt. on Uruguay R. with meat-packing, soap and footwear inds.; p. (1985) 74,014.

Pays de la Loire, region, W. **France**; inc. deps. Loire Atlantique, Maine-et-Loire, Mayenne, Sarthe, Vendée; region based upon lower reaches of R. Loire; ch. ts. Le Mans, Nantes; p. (1990) 3,059,100.

Pazardzhik, t., **Bulgaria**; on main rly. line to Istanbul; industl. hemp spinning and weaving; p. (1990) 87,277.

Paz de Rio, t., Boyacá, **Colombia**; iron and steel wks.; iron ore, coal, limestone nearby.

Peace, R., **Canada**; one of ch. headstreams of Mackenzie R.; rises in Rocky mtns., and flows generally N. to Gr. Slave R. nr. L. Athabaska; a. of very mild climate in lower course, fertile agr. valley; 1,680 km long.

Peak Dist., Pennine hill dist., mid-**Eng.**; extends from Chesterfield to Buxton, and Ashbourne to Glossop; composed of limestone with typical karst features; within P.D. Nat. Park, tourist and recreation a. for cities to E. (Sheffield) and W. (Manchester); limestone quarrying for cement; Kinder Scout 634 m.

Pearl Harbor, landlocked harbour, Oahu I., **Hawaii,** one of finest natural harbours in E. Pac.; US naval base; attacked by Japanese without warning 7 Dec. 1941 (7.55 a.m., local time), precipitating U.S. entry into Second World War.

Pearl Is., archipelago, G. of Panama; sea fishing, pearls.

Pearl R. See **Chu-kiang.**

Pechenga (**Petsamo**), spt., **Russia**; on inlet of Barents Sea; formerly Finnish, ceded to USSR Sept. 1944; ice-free throughout year; exp. nickel, timber, cobalt.

Pechora, dist., **Russia**; E. of Urals; coalfields; coking coal; ch. ts., Vorkuta and Inta.

Pechora, R., **Russia**; rises in Urals and flows N. into Arctic Oc.; 1,120 km navigable between June and Sept. for transport of timber from its basin; fishing; 1,792 km long.

Pecos, R., N.M. and Texas, **USA**; trib. of Rio Grande; water control schemes provide irrigation for lge. a.; 1,482 km long.

Pécs, c., S.W. **Hungary**; on Yugoslav border; one of oldest and most pleasantly situated ts. of Hungary; cath., univ., airport; in coal-mng. a.; coke, chemicals, majolica, leather gds., engin., brewing; p. (1989) 183,000.

Peebles, royal burgh, Tweeddale, **Scot.**; on upper course of R. Tweed; woollen cloth, knitwear; mkt., tourist ctr.; p. (1991) 7,065.

Peeblesshire, former co., S. **Scot.**; now part of Borders Reg.

Peel, t., I. of Man, **Eng.**; resort, fishing pt. midway along W. cst.; cas., cath.; p. (1991) 3,829.

Peel Fell, mtn. Northumberland, Eng.; 1,964 ft.

Pegu, c., Pegu prov., S. **Myanmar**; R. pt., rly. junc.; many temples, notably Shwe May Daw Pagoda; once cap. of Burmese kingdom; came under Brit. rule 1852; p. (1983) 150,447.

Pegu Yoma, mtns., **Myanmar**; between valleys of Rs. Irrawaddy and Sittang; thickly forested with teak which is comm. exploited and forms impt. exp.

Peine, t., Lower Saxony, **Germany**; N.W. of Brunswick; iron, furniture, textiles; p. (1986) 45,600.

Peipus, Lake, Estonia; drained by Narva R. into G. of Finland; Pskov lies to S.; scene of Alexander Nevsky's victory over the Germans 1242; a. 3,626 km².

Pekalongan, t., N. cst. Java, **Indonesia**; exp. sugar, rubber; p. (1980) 132,558.

Peking. See **Beijing.**

Pelagi, gr. of Italian Is., inc. Lampedusa and Linosa, between Malta and Tunisian cst.

Pelée, mtn., **Martinique**; active volcano, devastated town of St. Pierre 1902; alt. 1,342 m.

Pella, dep. of Macedonia, **Greece**; mtnous.; cotton, wheat, tobacco; cap. Edessa; a. 2,802 km²; p. (1991) 138,261.

Peloponnesus (**Peloponnisos**), peninsula, S. **Greece**; separated from mainland by G. of Corinth, but joined in N.E. by Isthmus of Corinth; mtnous.; livestock agr., drought-resistant sheep and goats; ch. ts., Kalamata, Tripolis; a. 21,642 km²; p. (1991) 605,663.

Pelotas, t., Rio Grande do Sul, **Brazil**; pt. on lagoon S.S.W. Pôrto Alegre; meat-packing and industl. ctr.; p. (1985) 278,400.

Pemba, I., part of **Tanzania**; cloves, copra, coconuts; exp. mangrove bark for tannin; a. 984 km²; p. (1985) 257,000.

Pemba (Port Amelia), spt., **Moçambique**; sisal, coconuts, cotton, maize, groundnuts; p. (1980) 41,166.

Pembroke, mkt. t., South Pembs., Dyfed, **Wales**; on S. side of Milford Haven; sm. pt.; dock facilities; cas., ruins of Monkton priory; birthplace of Henry VII; p. (1981) 15,618.

Pembroke Dock, Dyfed, **Wales**; site of government dockyard (1814) with consequent growth of a new t.

Pembrokeshire, former co., **Wales**. *See* **Dyfed**.

Penang, I., st. W. **Malaysia**; cap. Georgetown, pt. for N. Malaya handling rubber and tin; paper mill; the first Brit. Straits Settlement (*q.v.*); linked by bridge (1985) to mainland; longest bridge (13 km.) in Asia; a. 1,036 km²; p. (1980) 954,638.

Penarth, t., Vale of Glamorgan, South Glamorgan, **Wales**; former sm. pt. on Severn estuary, 3 km S. of Cardiff; seaside resort; p. (1981) 24,000.

Pendle, l. gov. dist., Lancs., **Eng.**; ts. of Barrowford, Colne and Nelson; p. (1993) 85,900.

Pengpu. *See* **Bengbu**.

Penicuik, burgh, Midlothian, **Scot.**; on R. Esk; paper; p. (1991) 17,173.

Penistone, t., South Yorks., **Eng.**; on R. Don; steel; mkt.; p. (1981) 8,990.

Penki. *See* **Benxi.**

Penmaenmawr, t., Aberconwy, Gwynedd, **Wales**; 6 km. S.W. of Conway; resort; p. (1981) 3,903.

Pennine Alps, Switzerland; div. of Alpine system; ch. peaks; Mont Blanc (4,814 m) Monte Rosa (4,637 m), Matterhorn (4,477 m); winter sports.

Pennine Range, mtn. range, "backbone of England," extends 224 km southwards from Cheviot hills to Derbyshire; limestone, millstone grit; moorland sheep, dairying in valleys, quarrying, tourism; inc. Peak Dist. Nat. Park and Pennine Way long distance route; water supply, forestry; Cross Fell, 895 m.

Pennsylvania, st., **USA**; 'Keystone St.'; admitted to Union 1787; st. flower Mountain Laurel, st. bird Ruffed Grouse; originally proprietary colony of Penn family, later one of the 13 original sts. in the Union; traversed N.E. to S.W. by Appalachians; ch. Rs.: Delaware, Susquehanna, Allegheny, and Monogahela; major industl. st.; iron and steel, coal (bituminous and anthracite), natural gas, petroleum; maize, wheat, oats, rye; textiles, machin., motor cars, tobacco; cap. Harrisburg; ch. ts.: Pittsburgh, Philadelphia; a. 117,412 km²; p. (1990) 11,881,643.

Penrith, t., N.S.W., **Australia**; in Sydney met. a.; ctr. for mkt. gardening.

Penrith, mkt. t., Eden, Cumbria, **Eng.**; at N. foot of Shap Fell, 29 km S.E. of Carlisle; agr. mkt.; tourist ctr.; p. (1981) 12,205.

Penryn, t., Carrick, Cornwall, **Eng.**; on R. Fal estuary; sm. pt., boat repairs; once ctr. of granite quarrying; p. (1981) 5,090.

Pensacola, t., Fla., **USA**; on N. shore of P. Bay; originally a Spanish settlement, retaining much Spanish influence in squares, bldgs., street names; fishing, sea food inds.; univ.; naval air training school; p. (1984) 62,000 (t.), 318,700 (met. a.).

Penticton, B.C., **Canada**; comm. fruit ctr.; p. (1986) 23,588.

Pentonville, dist., London, **Eng.**; prison; birthplace of John Stuart Mill.

Pentland Firth, strait, between Orkney Is. and Caithness, **Scot.**; connecting N. Sea and Atl. Oc.; dangerous tidal currents.

Pentland Hills, range, **Scot.**; extend from Lanark to Edinburgh; Scald Law, 878 m.

Penwith, l. gov. dist., Cornwall, **Eng.**; S.W. tip of Cornwall inc. Penzance, St. Just and St. Ives; p. (1993) 59,700.

Pen-y-Ghent, peak, Pennines, North Yorks., **Eng.**; alt. 680 m.

Penza, c., cap. of P. oblast, **Russia**; on Sura R.; rly. junc.; agr. ctr., especially for grain tr. to

Moscow; food-processing and wide range of mnfs.; oil pipeline from Mozyr'; p. (1989) 543,000.

Penzance, t., Penwith, Cornwall, **Eng.**; on Mount's Bay; tourist ctr.; ferry to Scilly Isles; engin.; birthplace of Sir Humphrey Davy; p. (1981) 19,521.

Peoria, t., Ill., **USA**; machin., domestic gds.; grain tr.; univ.; p. (1990) 113,504 (t.), 339,172 (met. a.).

Perak, st., **W. Malaysia**; ch. tin-dredging a., in basin of Perak R.; rubber; cap. Taiping; a. 20,668 km²; p. (1980) 1,805,198.

Pereira, t., Caldas, **Colombia**; cath.; comm. ctr. for coffee; p. (1992) 335,960.

Perekop, Isthmus of, connects Crimea with **Ukraine**.

Pergamino, t., Buenos Aires, **Argentina**; road and rail focus in maize-growing dist.

Périgord, dist., S.W. **France**; limestone plateau crossed by Dordogne R.; famous for truffles.

Périgueux, t., cap. Dordogne, **France**; on R. Isle; cath.; famous for pâté de foie gras; engin., china; p. (1990) 32,848.

Perim, I. in strait of Bab-el-Mandeb at S. entrance to Red Sea; part of **Yemen**; former coaling sta.; a. 13 km²; p. 1,700.

Perlis, st., **W. Malaysia**; agr. dist. for rice and coconuts; tin; a. 803 km²; p. (1980) 148,276.

Perm, oblast, **Russia**; major mng., timber, and paper dist.; produces oil (Krasnokamsk), coal (Kizel), hydroelectricity, and potash (Solikamsh); cap. Perm.

Perm (Molotov), c., cap. of P. oblast, **Russia**; on Kama R.; machin., chemicals, oil refineries; univ.; p. (1989) 1,091,000.

Pernambuco, st., N.E. **Brazil**; mtnous. interior, cst. fertile; cap. Recife; sugar, cotton, manioc, tobacco, fruits; a. 98,322 km²; p. (1991) 7,109,626.

Pernik (Dimitrovo), c., **Bulgaria**; iron and steel inds.; p. (1990) 99,643.

Pernis, t., opposite Rotterdam, **Neth.**; lge. oil refinery; pipeline to Wesserling (nr. Cologne).

Perovo, t., **Russia**; nr. Moscow; engin., chemicals; agr. research institute; p. inc. in Moscow.

Perpignan, c., cap. of Pyrénées-Orientales dep., **France**; nr. Spanish border and Mediterranean; on Paris–Barcelona rly.; mkt. and comm. ctr. for wines and fruits; cath.; tourism; p. (1990) 108,049 (c.), 138,735 (met. a.).

Persepolis, anc. c., **Iran**; former cap. of Persian empire, now in ruins; tourism.

Pershore, t., Wychavon, Hereford and Worcs., **Eng.**; on R. Avon; ctr. of fruit-growing a.

Persia. *See* **Iran**.

Persian Gulf, inlet from Indian Oc. through G. of Oman and Strait of Kormuz, between Iran and Arabia; oilfields in surrounding land and now in G. itself; ch. pts. Bandar-e-Bushehr, Abadan, Kuwait, Dubai; Bahrain, lgst. I.

Perth, c., cap. of W. **Australia**; on R. Swan; well planned garden c.; univ., cath., airport; many employed in services; inds. moving to Fremantle (pt.) or to Kwinana; p. (1991) 1,143,265 (met. a., 73 per cent of st. p.).

Perth, c., royal burgh, Perth and Kinross, **Scot.**; on R. Tay; rly. junc.; cap. of Scot. until assassination of James I, 1437; dyeing, textiles, whisky distilling; cath., historical associations; p. (1991) 41,453.

Perthshire, former co., **Scot.**; now part of Perth and Kinross, l. gov. dist., Tayside Reg.; p. (1993) 127,660.

Peru, Andean rep., **S. America**; consists of 3 N.W.–S.E. regions; Costa (cst.) Sierra (Andes, rising to over 6,100 m) and Selva (interior *montaña* and R. basins); 40 per cent p. in Costa, 60 per cent in Sierra, yet Selva covers 70 per cent total a.; ch. Rs. Ucayali, Marañon; L. Titicaca shared with Bolivia; El Misti volcano in S.; cap. Lima on Pac. cst. with 20 per cent p.; agr. diversified and being extended by irrigation schemes; fishing main single ind.; mng. impt. in Andes; major world producer of silver, phosphates, potash, copper, petroleum; social, economic and political problems provoking guerrilla insurgents; inflation 103 per cent; a. 1,249,048 km²; p. (1993) 22·13 m.

Peru Current (Humboldt), ocean current, S. Pac. Oc.; flows N. along cst. of N. Chile and Peru; causes clouds and fog.

Perugia, t., Umbria, **Italy**; on R. Tiber; univ.,

observatory; woollens, silks, lace; foodstuffs, furniture, pottery, chemicals, agr. machin.; p. (1992) 146,160.

Pervouralsk, t., **Russia**; in Urals; metallurgical ctr.; p. (1989) 142,000.

Pesaro, c., central **Italy**; on Adriatic cst.; agr. ctr., seaside resort; birthplace of Rossini; p. (1981) 90,412 (inc. Urbino).

Pescadores Is. (P'eng-hu Lieh-tao), archipelago, between Taiwan and mainland **China**; fishing, fish-processing; a. 132 km².

Pescara, c., cap. of P. prov., S. **Italy**; on estuary of R. Aterno; fish. pt., olive oil, soap, pasta, pottery; resort; birthplace of D'Annunzio; p. (1992) 121,424.

Peshawar, c., cap. of North-West Frontier Prov., **Pakistan**; 18 km E. of Khyber pass, commanding route to Afghanistan; military sta.; univ.; handicrafts, textiles, furniture; p. (1981) 555,000.

Petah Tikva, oldest modern Jewish settlement in **Israel** (1878); ctr. for oranges; mnfs. inc. textiles; p. (1990) 144,000.

Petaling Jaya, t., **W. Malaysia**; industl. estate nr. Kuala Lumpur; tyres, aluminium rolling mill.

Peter I., uninhabited I., **Antarctic Oc.**, belonging to Norway, a. c. 243 km².

Peterborough, t., Ont., **Canada**; flour-milling, elec. machin., trailers, agr. equipment, plastics, textiles, paper; p. (1986) 61,049.

Peterborough, c., l. gov. dist., Cambs., **Eng.**; on R. Nene on margin of Fens; cath.; rly ctr.; ctr. of brick ind. (Oxford clay around Fletton); diesel engines, agr. machin., gen. engin.; expanding t.; p. (1993) 156,400, (53,471 in 1951).

Peterborough, Soke of. See **Cambridgeshire**.

Peterhead, spt., burgh, Banff and Buchan, **Scot.**; on E. cst., 43 km N.E. of Aberdeen; herring fisheries, leading U.K. fish. pt. by value of fish landed (1982); fish-processing, granite quarrying; supply base for N. Sea oil; p. (1991) 18,674.

Peterlee, new t. (1948), Durham, **Eng.**; coal-mng. dist.; textiles, science-based inds.; p. (1981) 22,756.

Petersfield, t., East Hants., **Eng.**; on R. Rother, N.W. of Chichester; mkt.; p. (1981) 10,001.

Petra, anc. c., **Jordan**; temples, rock tombs and Roman ruins; called Sela in Bible (2 Kings 14. 7); rediscovered by Burckhardt 1812.

Petropavlovsk, t., **Kazakhstan**; on Ishim R.; rly. junc.; flour, leather, meat canneries, furs, engin.; p. (1990) 245,200.

Petropavlovsk-Kamchatsky, t., **Russia**; spt. on Pac. cst.; shipyard, timber mills, engin.; fishing and whaling fleet; p. (1989) 269,000.

Petrópolis, t., Rio de Janeiro, **Brazil**; health resort, c. 700 m a.s.l.; cath.; p. (1985) 275,100.

Petsamo. See **Pechenga**.

Petten, t., **Neth.**; 48 km N.W. of Amsterdam, on cst.; atomic research ctr.

Petworth, mkt. t., West Sussex, **Eng.**; in Rother valley, 19 km N.E. of Chichester; associated with Turner.

Pevensey Levels, marshy a., East Sussex, **Eng.**; lie behind coastal sand-bars between Eastbourne and Bexhill, extend 8 km inland to Hailsham; now largely drained, cattle pastures; a. 62 km².

Pforzheim, t., Baden-Württemberg, **Germany**; S.E. of Karlsruhe; gold, silver, metal wks., jewellery; p. (1990) 113,600.

Phetburi, t. and prov., **Thailand**; on Isthmus of Kra crossed by Phetburi R.; p. (1980) 366,612 (prov.).

Philadelphia, c., pt., Penns., **USA**; on Delaware R.; comm., industl. and cultural ctr.; univ., R.C. cath., masonic temple, mint, academy of fine arts; shipbldg., locomotives, machin., surgical instruments, carpets, woollens, cottons, worsteds; sugar, and petroleum refining; ctr. of War of Independence 1775–1783; founded as Quaker col. by William Penn 1682; p. (1990) 1,585,577 (c.), 4,857,000 (met. a.).

Philippeville. See **Skikda**.

Philippines, Rep. of, S.E. **Asia**; chain of 7,100 Is. in Pac. Oc., stretching over 1,760 km; ch. Is. Luzon, Mindanao, Negros, Cebu, Mindoro, and Palawar; lie in track of cyclones; tropical climate; mtnous., agr. aided by intricate terracing system; most Is. underdeveloped except Luzon where p. concentrated; subsistence agr. rice and maize; 60 per cent of households live below the poverty line; coconuts major export crop; sugar impt. once but falling world prices have curtailed production; electronics and garments also exported; income generated by Filipinos working abroad sending wages home; geothermal energy used; coconut shells burnt for fuel; cap. Manila; a. 299,681 km²; p. (1993) 65·65 m.

Phlorina (Florina), t., Macedonia, **Greece**; in basin at 900 m, 16 km from Yugoslav border; agr. ctr.; p. (1981) 12,573.

Phnom-Penh, c., cap. of **Cambodia**, S.E. Asia; pt. on Mekong R.; handles ships up to 2,500 tonnes; linked to Kompong Som by modern highway; multi-purpose dam to W.; univ., royal palace; airport; p. (1990) 800,000.

Phoenix, c., Arizona, **USA**; on Salt R., ctr. of Salt River Valley irrigated region; electronics research, steel, aircraft, clothing; p. (1990) 983,403 (c.), 2,122,101 (met. a.).

Phoenix Group, Is., **Pac. Oc.**; part of Kiribati; a. 41 km²; US have some rights over Canton and Enderbury; Canton used as international airport; p. (1985) 24.

Phuket I., **Thailand**; off Kra Isthmus; main alluvial tin-working region of Thailand; ch. t. Phuket where a tin-smelting plant is to be established; a. 534 km².

Piacenza, c., cap. of P. prov., **Italy**; in Emilia-Romagna, on R. Po; agr. and comm. ctr.; cath., palaces, arsenal; cars, chemicals, cement; p. (1992) 102,161.

Piatra-Neamt, t., Moldavia, **Romania**; timber, pharmaceuticals, soap; oil refineries; p. (1990) 118,216.

Piaui, st., **Brazil**; semi-arid, underdeveloped dist.; thorn scrub; livestock rearing; cap. Teresina; a. 249,319 km²; p. (1991) 2,581,054.

Piave, R., N.E. **Italy**; flows to Adriatic, 200 km long.

Picardy (Picardie), former prov. and region inc. deps. Aisne, Oise, Somme, **France**; old battle sites, Agincourt and Crécy; rich agr. a.; textiles; p. (1990) 1,810,700.

Pichincha, prov., **Ecuador**; p. concentrated in Andes; many natural resources inc. lime, gypsum, silver; tropical hardwoods; cattle raising; cap. Quito; a. 16,105 km²; p. (1990) 1,756,228.

Pickering, mkt. t., Ryedale, North Yorks., **Eng.**; on N. margin of Vale of P.; church with murals; cas.; gas terminal; p. (1981) 5,942.

Pickering, Vale of, North Yorks., **Eng.**; wide, flat-floored vale, once occupied by glacial lake; bounded to N. by N. York Moors, to S. by York Wolds; drained W. by R. Derwent, alluvial soils, marshy in ctr.; crop farming along margins, cattle grazing in damper meadows in ctr., ch. ts. Pickering, Malton, Helmsley.

Picos de Europa, mtn. massif, N. **Spain**; hgst. massif in Cantabrian mtns., rising to 2,650 m; partially inc. in Nat. Park.

Picton, t., S.I., **N.Z.**; freezing wks.; tourist and fishing ctr.; pt.

Pictou, t., Nova Scotia, **Canada**; on Northumberland Strait; founded by Scottish settlers; p. (1986) 4,413.

Pidurutalagala, mtn., **Sri Lanka**; alt. 2,530 m; hgst. peak in rep.

Piedmont, region, N. **Italy**; rice, wheat, vines, fruits; cottons, woollens; a. 25,416 km²; p. (1992) 4,303,830.

Pietermaritzburg, c., cap. of Natal, **S. Africa**; named after Piet Retief and Gerhardus Maritz, two Boer leaders; lt. inds.; tanning; iron-ore mng. in a.; part of univ. of Natal; 2 caths.; p. (1985) 192,417 (met. a.).

Pietersburg, t., Transvaal, **S. Africa**; gold, asbestos, tin; comm. ctr. for cereals, tobacco, cotton, citrus fruits; p. (1980) 115,480 (dist.).

Pila (Schneidemühl), t. and prov., N.W. **Poland** (since 1945); formerly in Prussian prov. of Pomerania; tr. ctr., lignite mines nearby; p. (1989) 71,109 (t.), 476,000 (prov.).

Pilar, t., **Paraguay**; impt. R. pt.; sawmills; textiles; p. (1984) 26,352.

Pilbara, dist., W. **Australia**; extensive iron mng.;

other minerals inc. salt, oil, nat. gas; rapid growth of p.

Pilcomayo, R., northernmost R. of **Argentina**; rises in Bolivian Andes, flows across the Gran Chaco, to enter Paraguay, joining the Paraguay R. nr. Asunción; hydroelec. power; 1,120 km long.

Pilibhit, t., Uttar Pradesh, N. **India**; admin. ctr.; sugar-refining; p. (1991) 106,605.

Pilsen. See **Plzeň.**

Pinar del Rio, c., prov. cap., **Cuba**; tobacco; p. (1985) 100,900 (1986) 681,500 (prov.).

Pinatubo, volcano **Philippines**; erupted June 1991.

Pinawa, t., Manitoba, **Canada**; 88 km N.E. of Winnipeg; nuclear research; p. (1986) 2,078.

Pindus, mtn. chain, between Thessaly and Albania, **Greece**; hgst. peak 2,455 m.

Pingxiang, c., Jianxi, **China**; supplies coking coal to Wuhan. p. (1984) 1,270,400.

Pinneberg, t., Schleswig-Holstein, **Germany**; N.W. of Hamburg; rose cultivation, metals, leather; p. (1986) 35,600.

Pinsk, c., **Belarus**; in Pripet Marshes, pt. on Pina R.; paper, wood-working inds., matches; Jewish residents exterminated during German occupation second world war; p. (1990) 121,600.

Piombino, t., **Italy**; mainland pt. for island of Elba; steel wks.; p. (1981) 39,389.

Piotrkow Trybunalski, t. and prov., **Poland**; cas.; timber and glass inds.; new textile combine; p. (1989) 80,598 (t.), 638,900 (prov.).

Piqua, t., Ohio, **USA**; N. of Dayton: ironwks., woollens; nuclear reactor; p. (1980) 20,480.

Piracicaba, t., São Paulo, **Brazil**; ctr. of agr. dist.; sugar-refining, brandy, flour; p. (1985) 252,900.

Piraeus, c., **Greece**; pt. of Athens and prin. pt. of Greece; major industl. and comm. ctr.; p. (1981) 196,389.

Pirmasens, t., Rhineland-Palatinate, **Germany**; S.W. of Mannheim; footwear, leather gds.; p. (1986) 46,100.

Pirna, t., Saxony, **Germany**; on R. Elbe; textiles, paper, glass; p. (1989) 43,486.

Pirot, t., Serbia, **Yugoslavia**; nr. Bulgarian border; in economic development a.; p. (1981) 69,653.

Pisa, c., **Italy**; at head of Arno delta, 19 km N.E. of Livorno; famous leaning tower, cath., univ.; textiles, chemicals, engin.; airport; tourism; p. (1984) 103,894.

Pistoia, t., Tuscany, **Italy**; on Arno plain, N.W. of Florence; iron and steel gds., macaroni; p. (1981) 92,274.

Pit, R., Cal., **USA**; rises in Goose L.; cuts spectacular gorges in the Cascades; used for hydroelectric power.

Pitcairn I., E. **Pac. Oc.**, Brit. col.; inc. atolls of Ducie and Oeno and I. of Henderson; sweet potatoes, bananas, oranges, coconuts; a. 5 km²; p. mostly descendants of mutineers of the *Bounty*; p. (1993) 65.

Pitch Lake, **Trinidad**, W.I.; S. of I., 16 km S.W. of San Fernando; natural deposit of asphalt; tourism; a. 86 ha.

Pitea, spt., N. **Sweden**; on G. of Bothnia; sawmills; p. (1992) 40,766.

Pitesti, t., **Romania**; on Arges R.; petroleum, fruit, grain; lge. automobile plant; oil refinery; p. (1990) 174,790.

Pitlochry, burgh, Perth and Kinross, **Scot.**; on R. Tummel, 6 km S. of Pass of Killiecrankie; summer resort; distilleries, hydros; p. (1991) 2,541.

Pittenweem, burgh, North East Fife, **Scot.**; at entrance to F. of Forth; fisheries; p. (1991) 1,561.

Pittsburgh, c., Penns., **USA**; univ.; R.C. cath.; pt. on Ohio R.; ctr. of richest American coalfield; natural gas, petroleum, iron and steel, machin., metal gds., meat-packing, glass, aluminium, chemicals, p. (1990) 369,379 (c.), 2,057,000 (met. a.).

Pittsfield, c., Mass., **USA**; textiles, paper, plastics, elec. machin.; resort; p. (1980) 51,974.

Piura, t., N. **Peru**; on Piura R.; oldest Spanish t. in Peru; cotton mkt. and processing, p. (1990) 324,500.

Pladju, t., S. Sumatra, **Indonesia**; oil refining; linked by pipeline with Tempino and Bejubang.

Plata, Rio de la (Plate R.), estuary between **Argentina** and Uruguay; receives waters of Rs. Paraná and Uruguay; cst. provides sites for lge. spts., Buenos Aires, La Plata, Montevideo.

Platte, R., Nebraska, **USA**; formed by union of

N. Platte and S. Platte Rs.; total length 2,240 km; irrigation, hydroelec. power.

Plauen, t., Saxony, **Germany**; textiles, machin., cable, leather, paper, radios; rly. junc; p. (1981) 78,800.

Plenty, Bay of, reg. and bay, N.I., **N.Z.**; on E. cst.; 208 km wide; p. (1991) 208,163.

Plettenberg, t., N. Rhine–Westphalia, **Germany**; on R. Lenne; iron wks.; p. (1986) 27,600.

Pleven, mkt. t., **Bulgaria**; many mosques; famous siege 1877; textiles, wines; p. (1990) 138,323.

Plitvička Jezera, lakes, W. **Croatia** (formerly Yugoslavia); beautiful scenery; tourism; fishing.

Ploče, new spt., **Croatia** (formerly Yugoslavia); on Dalmatian cst.; industl. and rly. ctr.

Plock, t. and prov., **Poland**; on R. Vistula, nr. Warsaw; agr.; oil refinery and petrochemical plant; food processing; agr. machin.; p. (1989) 120,933 (t.), 512,600 (prov.).

Ploiesti, t., Prahova dist., **Romania**; petroleum, engin.; p. (1990) 259,014.

Plovdiv (Philippopolis), c., **Bulgaria**; on R. Maritsa; univ., Greek cath.; second c. of rep.; agr. processing, clothing, metals, engin.; p. (1990) 379,083.

Plymouth, c., spt., l. gov. dist., S. Devon, **Eng.**; on Plymouth Sound; comprises the "three towns" of Plymouth, Devonport, and Stonehouse; Brit. fleet faced Armada 1588; R.C. cath., guildhall, museum; Naval dockyard; seaside resort; fishing and fish-canning, lt. inds.; recently discovered deposit of tungsten, thought to be lgst. in W. Europe but lies within Dartmoor Nat. Park; p. (1993) 259,000 (dist.).

Plymouth, ch. t., **Montserrat** I., W.I.; p. (1985) 3,500.

Plymouth, spt., Mass., **USA**; on Plymouth Bay, S.E. of Boston; here Pilgrim Fathers landed 1620 from *Mayflower* to form first English col.; Pilgrim Hall, Pilgrim Rock; textiles, cordage, machin.; tourism; p. (1980) 7,232.

Plynlimmon, mtn., Powys and Dyfed, **Wales**; alt. 753 m; source of R. Severn.

Plzeň (Pilsen), c., W. Bohemia, **Czech Rep.**; ctr. of coal-mng. region; famous for beer and Lenin (former Skoda) armament wks.; p. (1990) 175,000.

Po, R., **Italy**; flows from Monte Viso, through Piedmont and Lombardy to the Adriatic; valley forms a major component of N. Italian lowland; natural gas deposits in valley; liable to flooding; 648 km long.

Pocklington, mkt. t., East Yorks., Humberside, **Eng.**; foot of York wolds, 19 km E. of York; ctr. of agr. dist.; 16th cent. grammar school.

Podgorica, (Titograd) t., cap. of Montenegro, S. **Yugoslavia**; nr. Albanian frontier; anc. t. but now mainly modern with growing industl. activity; agr. processing, aluminium smelting; airport; p. (1991) 118,059.

Podolsk, t., **Russia**; on main rly. from Moscow to S.; engin., tin-smelting, food-processing; p. (1989) 209,000.

Pohai. See **Bo Hai.**

Point-à-Pierre, Trinidad; oil refinery; natural gas pipeline from Forest Reserve field.

Point-à-Pitre, ch. t. and pt. **Guadeloupe**, Fr. W.I.; on Grande Terre I.; exp. agr. prods., bananas, sugar; p. (1982) 25,310.

Pointe-des-Galets or **Le Port**, ch. pt., **La Réunion** (Fr.), Indian Oc.

Pointe-Noire, spt., **Congo Rep.**; airport, rly. to Brazzaville; agr. exp.; potash deposits nearby; linked to deepwater terminal for bulk carriers but mine closed due to flooding; petroleum refinery (1982); gas reserves; p. (1990) 387,774.

Point Fortin, t., **Trinidad**; oilfield and refinery.

Poitiers, c., cap. of Vienne dep., **France**; many attractive bldgs., cath.; agr. tr.; mnfs. chemicals, hosiery; Black Prince defeated Fr. 1356; p. (1990) 82,507 (c.), 105,268 (met. a.).

Poitou-Charentes, region, **France**; on western seaboard inc. deps. Charente, Charente-Maritime, Deux-Sèvres, Vienne; agr., vineyards; p. (1990) 1,595,100.

Pokrovsk, (Engels), c., **Russia**; on Volga; R. pt., mftg. and food-processing ctr.; engin., petroleum refining, textiles; p. (1989) 181,000.

Poland, Rep. E. **Europe**; history of country dominated by constantly changing sovereignty between E. and W. powers; strong national identity, based esp. on Catholic church; mainly lowland; continental climate; economy retarded by history of political fluctuation; growth of export-based inds. almost halted in 1980s depression; major ctr. of mng. and heavy inds. in conurb. of Upper Silesia, agr. land remains largely in private ownership, but govt. attempts to rationalise farm structure, major pts. at Gdynia, Gdansk, and Szczecin, international airport at cap. Warsaw, 17 historic provs. to be replaced by 49 large dists.; border with Germany fixed along Oder-Neisse line; a. 311,700 km²; p. (1993) 38·31 m.

Polotsk, c., **Belarus;** cath.; gasoline prod., oil refining; pipeline to Latvian pt. of Ventspils; food processing; p. (1990) 77,800.

Polotskiy, t. **Belarus;** 13 km W. of Polotsk; oil.

Poltava, c., **Ukraine;** industl. and food-processing ctr. in rich agr. dist.; countryside described in Gogol's work; textiles, synthetic diamond plant; battle 1709 between Swedish and Russian armies, p. (1990) 317,000.

Polynesia, ethnic region, **Oceania;** I. grs. in Pac. Oc. within 30° N. and S. of equator; between longitude 135° E. and W.; p. (1984) 498,000.

Pomerania, former prov., N. Germany; in post-war redivision part E. of R. Oder to **Poland;** part W. of R. Oder incorporated in Mecklenburg, **E. Germany;** farming, shipbldg., fishing.

Pomona (Mainland), lgst of the Orkney Is., **Scot.;** Kirkwall (cap.) and Stromness on I; p. (1991) 15,128.

Pomorze. See Bydgoszcz.

Pompeii, ruined c., **Italy;** stood 21 km S.E. of Naples, at foot of Vesuvius; destroyed A.D. 79 by volcanic eruption, site re-discovered 1748; many interesting excavations; also modern c. nearby; fine church with famous collection of silver and gold plate; p. (1981) 22,896.

Ponape, volcanic I., Caroline Is., W. **Pac. Oc.;** copra, ivory, nuts, starch, bauxite; a. 334 km².

Ponce, c., **Puerto Rico;** recently improved harbour on S. cst.; well connected with other ts. in rep.; ctr. of fertile, irrigated sugar-cane a.; industl. ctr.; p. (1990) 187,749.

Pondicherry, spt., Tamil Nadu st., **India;** on Coromandel cst.; cap. of P. Union Territory.; tr. ctr. for local prod.; p. (1991) 203,065 (c.), 807,785 (terr.).

Ponta Grossa, t., Paraná, **Brazil;** rly. junc.; comm. ctr.; maté, rice, timber, tobacco, bananas, cattle, jerked beef; p. (1985) 224,000.

Pontardawe, t., Lliw Valley, West Glamorgan, S. **Wales;** on R. Tawe, N.E. of Swansea; zinc smelting and refining.

Pontchartrain, Lake, shallow L., lower Mississippi flood plain, **USA;** connected by canal to New Orleans 10 km to S., and by deltaic channels to G. of Mexico.

Pontefract, mkt. t., West Yorks., **Eng.;** 11 km E. of Wakefield; coal, furniture, confectionery, mkt. gardening; cas. ruins; p. (1981) 31,971.

Pontevedra, prov., **Spain;** on deeply indented Atl. cst.; transatlantic pt. Vigo; scenery and fiesta attractions for tourists; agr., livestock, timber, fisheries; cap. P.; a. 4,390 km²; p. (1991) 879,872.

Pontevedra, c., cap. of P. prov., N.W. **Spain;** fish. pt., handicrafts, agr. tr.; p. (1987) 67,314.

Pontiac, t., Mich., **USA;** on Clinton R.; fishing and shooting, motor cars, rubber gds., machin., varnish; p. (1980) 76,715.

Pontianak, t., cap. of Kalimantan, **Indonesia;** exp. rubber, copra; rubber processing; p. (1983) 355,000.

Pontine Is., off W. cst. of **Italy;** in Tyrrhenian Sea; a. 11·6 km²; p. 6,000.

Pontine Marshes, region, Latium, S. **Italy;** coastal zone S.E. of Rome extending from Velletri to Terracina; formerly highly malarial fens, largely drained and colonised 1930–35; 3,200 new farms, 4 new ts.; ch. t. Littoria; a. 647 km².

Pontresina, t., Grisons, **Switzerland;** E. of St. Moritz; tourist resort.

Pontypool, t., Torfaen, Gwent, **Wales;** coal, steel, glass, bricks, tin galvanising, nylon at Manhilad; p. (1981) 36,761.

Pontypridd, t., Taff-Ely, Mid Glamorgan, **Wales;** on R. Taff, 19 km N.W. of Cardiff; coal, iron-founding; p. (1981) 32,992.

Pool Malebo (Stanley Pool), Congo and **Zaïre;** lake formed by expansion of R. Zaïre; length 40 km.; width 26 km.

Poole, t., l. gov. dist., Dorset, **Eng.;** spt. on Poole Harbour, 6 km W. of Bournemouth; imports

clay for local pottery inds. petroleum production began 1979; tourism, yachting, marine engin., chemicals; p. (1993) 137,200 (dist.).

Poona. See Pune.

Poopó, salt L., Oruro dep., **Bolivia;** fed from L. Titicaca by R. Desaguadero, which flows over saline beds; no outlet; c. 3,600 m a.s.l.; a. 2,600 km².

Popayan, c., S.W. **Columbia;** 1,677 m above Cauca R.; cath., univ.; food processing, coffee, flour; mng. nearby; p. (1992) 203,722.

Poplar. See Tower Hamlets.

Popocatepetl, volcano, nr. Puebla, **Mexico;** alt. 5,456 m; dormant since 1702.

Porbander, spt., Gujarat, **India;** exp. silk cotton, imports coal, dates, timber, machin., petroleum; birthplace of Mahatma Gandhi; p. (1991) 116,671.

Pori (Björneborg), spt., S. **Finland;** at mouth of R. Kokemäen; copper refinery, rolling mills, match, paper and pulp wks.; p. (1991) 76,432.

Porirua, c., Wellington, N.I., **N.Z.;** dormitory for Wellington; p. (1991) 46,601.

Porjus, t., Norrbotten, N. **Sweden;** on R. Lulea, hydroelectric plant supplies power to iron-ore mng. dists. of Gallivare and Kiruna, also to Narvik rly.

Porsgrunn, spt., **Norway;** timber, shipping, engin., porcelain, explosives; p. (1990) 35,172.

Port Adelaide, main pt., S. **Australia;** serves Adelaide; exp. agr. prods. from hinterland; imports bulk cargoes (petroleum, phosphate, limestone).

Portadown, t., Craigavon, **N. Ireland;** on R. Bann, 40 km S.W. of Belfast; linen, food processing; merged with Lurgan to form new c. of Craigavon; p. (1991) 21,299.

Portaferry, spt., Ards, **N. Ireland;** shipping fisheries; p. (1991) 2,324.

Portage la Prairie, t., Manitoba, **Canada;** sm. pt. on Assiniboine R.; grain and potato tr.; p. (1986) 13,198.

Port Alberni, spt., Vancouver I., B.C., **Canada;** exp. timber; fisheries; timber inds.; p. (1986) 18,241.

Port Alfred, pt., **Canada;** upper St. Lawrence R.; imports bauxite for smelting at Arvida.

Port Amelia. See Pemba.

Portarlington, mkt. t., Offaly, **R.o.I.;** farming; first place to have elec. power-sta. using local peat fuel; p. (1986) 3,295.

Port Arthur. (Canada) See Thunder Bay.

Port Arthur (China). See Lushun.

Port Arthur, t., Texas, **USA;** pt. on L. Sabine; exp. petroleum, chemicals, grain; p. (1980) 61,251.

Port Arzew, pt., **Algeria;** world's first plant to liquefy natural gas (1964); oil pipeline from Haoud el Hamra; oil refinery.

Port Augusta, t., spt., S. **Australia;** at head of Spencer G.; fine harbour; salt field; exp. wheat, fruit; impt. rly. junction; p. (1991) 14,966.

Port-au-Prince, c., cap. of **Haiti;** spt. on bay in G. of La Gonave; cultural and political ctr.; univ., cath.; food processing and exp.; oil refinery; p. (1984) 462,000 (c.), (1988) 1,143,626 (met. a.).

Port Blair, spt., cap. of Andaman and Nicobar Is., **India;** p. (1991) 74,955.

Port Chalmers, t., bor., S.I. **N.Z.;** container pt., timber exp.

Port Colborne, t., Ont., **Canada;** pt. on L. Erie; iron smelting; nickel and copper refining; power from Niagara falls; p. (1986) 18,281.

Port Elizabeth, spt., Cape Prov., **S. Africa;** on Algoa Bay; bilingual univ.; exp. skins, wool, ostrich feathers, mohair; foundries, soap, chemicals, car assembly, food preservation, sawmills; p. (1985) 651,993 (met. a.).

Port Erin, v., I. of Man, **Eng.;** on S.E. cst.; seaside resort, fisheries.

Port Essington, N. point, of Coburg peninsula, N.T., **Australia;** pearl culture experiments.

Port Etienne, See Nouadhibou.

Port Franqui, See Ilebo.

Port Gentil, spt., **Gabon,** Eq. Africa; exp. palm-oil, mahogany, ebony; sawmills, fishing, centre of Gabon's main oil reserves, oil refining; p. (1983) 123,300.

Port Glasgow, burgh, spt., Inverclyde, **Scot.;** on S. bank of R. Clyde, 27 km below Glasgow; shipbldg. and repairing, textiles, rope, canvas mftg.;

p. (1991) 19,693.

Port Harcourt, spt., **Nigeria**; 48 km from sea on E. branch of Niger delta; terminus of E. Nigerian rly. system; tin, palm oil, groundnuts; bitumen plant, tyres; oil refining; p. (1983) 296,000.

Porthcawl, t., Ogwr, Mid Glamorgan, **Wales**; on cst. 16 km S.E. of Pt. Talbot; resort; p. (1981) 15,566.

Port Hedland, sm. spt., **W. Australia**; new t. being built 8 km inland to absorb impact of Mt. Newman ore project; twin ts. linked by industl. belt; exp. iron ore to Japan; p. (1990) 13,707.

Porthmadog (**Portmadoc**), t. Dwyfor, Gwynedd, **Wales**; pt. on Tremadoc Bay; terminus of Ffestiniog lt. rly.; p. (1981) 3,927.

Port Hope, t., Ont., **Canada**; midway along N. shore of L. Ont., fruit, dairying, radium refining; p. (1986) 10,281.

Port Huron, t., Mich., **USA**; on L. Huron; summer resort, dry docks, grain elevators; motor-car parts; p. (1980) 33,981.

Portici, spt., Campania, **S. Italy**; on Bay of Naples; dockland sub. of Naples; p. (1981) 79,259.

Portile de Fier. *See* **Iron Gate.**

Portishead, pt., Woodspring, Avon, **Eng.**; on Severn estuary 5 km S.W. of Avonmouth; shipping; p. (1981) 11,331.

Port Jackson, N.S.W., **Australia**; deep natural harbour used by Sydney and crossed by Sydney bridge.

Port Kelang (**Port Swettenham**), major spt. of **Malaysia**; 48 km W. of Kuala Lumpur; exp. primary prods. inc. tin, rubber, fruit; imports mnfs.; p. 11,300.

Port Kembla, spt., N.S.W., **Australia**; part of Wollongong; artificial pt. built to exp. coal; many expansion programmes; integrated steelworks; p. (1981) 208,651 (inc. Wollongong).

Portknockie, burgh, Grampian Reg., **Scot.**; on N. Buchan cst., 8 km E. of Buckie; sm. fish. pt.; p. (1991) 1,296.

Portland, t., Weymouth and P., Dorset, **Eng.**; 6 km S. of Weymouth on sheltered N.E. side of I. of Portland; lge artificial harbour; naval base closing, prison; p. (1981) 10,915.

Portland, t., spt., Me., **USA**; comm. cap. of Me.; lge fisheries; paper, pulp, lumber, processed food, clothing; p. (1984) 61,800 (t.), 201,200 (met. a.).

Portland, c., Ore., **USA**; gr. wheat and wool tr.; flour milling, shipbldg., fishing and canning, aluminium, lumber; p. (1990) 437,319 (c.), (1990) 1,240,000 (met. a.).

Portland Canal, fjord, N.W. cst of America, forming bdy. between Alaska and B.C.

Portland, I. of, Dorset, **Eng.**; limestone mass, linked to mainland by shingle spit, Chesil Bank, terminates S. in Portland Bill; naval base, Borstal institution; limestone quarrying; masonry wks.

Portlaoighise, mkt. t., Laoighis, **R.o.I.**; flour, malting; p. (1986) 3,773.

Port Louis, c., cap., of **Mauritius**; pt. on Indian Oc.; exp. sugar; contains 42% of Mauritius p. in met.a.; port extension and bulk sugar terminal; p. (1991) 142,505.

Port Macquarie, t., N.S.W., **Australia**; former penal settlement on Hastings R.; resort; p. (1981) 19,581.

Port Moresby, t., cap. of **Papua New Guinea**, 2,880 km from Sydney; spt., airpt.; univ.; p. (1990) 193,242.

Port Nelson, spt., Manitoba, **Canada**; on cst. of Hudson Bay at mouth of R. Nelson; linked by rly. to trans-continental systems; exp. wheat, minerals; closed by ice for 7 months each year.

Port Nolloth, spt., Cape Prov., **S. Africa**; serves copper- and diamond-mng. dists.; declining crayfish pt.

Pôrto Alegre, c., cap. of Rio Grande do Sul st., **Brazil**; exp. lard, preserved meats, rice, timber, tobacco; textiles, chemicals, furniture, brewing, metallurgy; oil refinery under construction; pipeline connects with Rio Grande; 2 univs.; p. (1991) 1,262,631.

Portobello, resort, **Scot.**; on F. of Forth, 5 km E. of Edinburgh; bricks, pottery, paper.

Port of Spain, c., cap. of **Trinidad**; attractive c. with squares; 2 caths., mosque; spt. exp. cocoa, sugar, asphalt, oil; natural gas pipeline from Penal; food processing; p. (1988) 58,400.

Porto Marghera, spt., Venezia, **N. Italy**; the modern pt. of Venice, reached by ship canal dredged through shallow lagoon; oil refineries; chemicals, metal refining.

Porto Novo, t., cap. of **Benin Rep.**; on coastal lagoon; spt.; fishing; many old colonial bldgs.; p. (1982) 208,258.

Pôrto Velho, c., cap of Rondônia st., **Brazil**; in a. producing maize, rice, rubber, tin; p. (1985) 202,000.

Portoviejo, t., **Ecuador**; mkt. and comm. ctr. for agr. dist.; p. (1990) 132,937.

Port Philip, lge. inlet., Victoria, **Australia**, landlocked bay, Melbourne on N., Geelong on W.

Port Pirie, t., spt., **S. Australia**; major pt. on Spencer Gulf; refines zinc and lead from Broken Hill; exp. wheat; p. (1991) 14,398.

Port Radium, t., N.W. Terr., **Canada**; on Gr. Bear L.; pitchblende deposits.

Portree, spt., v., I. of Skye, **Scot.**; landlocked harbour on P. Bay, Sound of Raasay; fishing; tweed mill; p. (1991) 2,126.

Portrush, spt., Coleraine, **N. Ireland**; 8 km N. of Coleraine; tourism; p. (1991) 5,598.

Port Said, (**Bur Sa'id**), spt. and prov., **Egypt**; at N. end of Suez Canal; free tr. a.; impt. fuelling sta.; entrepôt tr.; p. (1991) 449,000, (1990) 461,000 (prov.).

Port St. Mary, v., I. of Man, **Eng.**; on S.E. cst.; resort; fisheries, boat-bldg.

Portsdown Hill, chalk ridge, Hants., **Eng.**; extends E. to W. behind Portsmouth from Havant to Fareham.

Portsea I., fortfd. I., between Portsmouth and Langston harbours, Hants., Eng.

Portslade-by-Sea, t. East Sussex, **Eng.**; W. of Hove; p. (1981) 18,128.

Portsmouth, c., naval pt., l. gov. dist., Hants., **Eng.**; opposite I. of Wight; naval establishment; Portsmouth is the garrison t.; Portsea has the naval dockyards, Landport is residtl., and Southsea is a popular resort; naval dock yard closed (1984) fleet maintenance and repair; across the harbour is Gosport; shipbldg.; gen. mnfs.; birthplace of Dickens and I. K. Brunel; p. (1993) 189,100 (dist.).

Portsmouth, t., N.H., **USA**; summer resort, naval dockyard, cotton; the 1905 Peace Treaty between Japan and Russia was negotiated here; p. (1984) 27,800 (t.), 206,500 (met. a.).

Portsmouth, t., Ohio, **USA**; iron and steel gds., aircraft, boots, shoes, bricks; p. (1980) 25,943.

Portsmouth, spt., Va., **USA**; naval dockyard; farm produce, cotton, rly. wks.; p. (1990) 103,907.

Portsoy, burgh, Banff and Buchan, **Scot.**; spt. 8 km W. of Banff; fisheries and meal milling; p. (1991) 1,822.

Port Stanvac, **S. Australia**; 24 km S. of Adelaide; oil refining.

Port Sudan, spt., **Sudan**; 48 km N. of Suakin; linked by rail to Atbara and Khartoum; oil refining; p. (1983) 206,727.

Port Sunlight, Merseyside, **Eng.**; garden v. founded 1888 by Lord Leverhulme for the employees of the Port Sunlight factories.

Port Swettenham. *See* **Port Kelang.**

Port Talbot, t., l. gov. dist. West Glamorgan, **S. Wales**; on E. side of Swansea Bay; impt. iron and steel ind., copper, coal; new deep-water harbour serves as ore terminal; p. (1993) 51,400 (dist.).

Portugal, rep., Iberia, **W. Europe**; member of EU (1986); mild temperate climate on cst., drier and hotter in interior; economy based on an inefficient agr. sector, located in wide fertile valleys, and associated processing inds.; major exp. of cork, but few industl. raw materials; textiles; post-war growth of tourist inds.; cap. and airport Lisbon; a. 91,945 km²; p. (1991) 9,858,600.

Portuguesa, st., **Venezuela**; inc. llanos plains; livestock raising; cap. Guanare; a. 15,200 km²; p. (1981) 424,984.

Portuguese Guinea. *See* **Guinea-Bissau.**

Portuguese Timor. *See* **East Timor.**

Porvoo, spt., S. **Finland**; on G. of Finland; exp. ctr. for forest prods.

Porz, t., N. Rhine-Westphalia, **Germany**; on R. Rhine, part of Cologne; glass, metals, paper.

Posadas, c., cap. of Misiones prov., N.E. **Argentina**; on upper Paraná R.; on border of Paraguay; yerba-maté, tobacco, cereals; connection for Iguaça falls; p. (1991) 219,824.

Posen. *See* **Poznań.**

Pössneck, t., Gera, **Germany;** S.E. of Weimar; porcelain, textiles, leather; p. (1989) 17,410.

Postillon Is., Lesser Sunda Is., **Indonesia;** coconuts.

Postojna (Ádelsberg,) t., **Slovenia** (formerly Yugoslavia); 32 km N.E. of Trieste; extensive grotto and stalactite cavern.

Potchefstroom, t.., Transvaal, **S. Africa;** on Mooi R.; univ.; agr.; malt, timber, engin.; p. (1980) 141,000 (dist.).

Potenza, t., cap. of P. prov., **Italy;** on hill 220 m above Basento R.; agr. and industl. ctr.; univ.; p. (1981) 64,358.

Poti, spt., **Georgia;** exp. manganese; fish processing, timber-milling, engin.; p. (1990) 137,300.

Potomac, R., **USA;** divides Va. from Md.; flows past Wash., to Chesapeake Bay; 464 km long.

Potosi, dep., **Bolivia;** famous for silver- and tin-mines; zinc ore; cap. Potosi; a. 110,000 km²; p. (1988) 667,800.

Potosi *o.,* **Bolivia;** on slope of Cerro Gordo de Potosi, 4,072 m a.s.l.; tin, silver, copper, lead mng.; p. (1982) 103,183.

Potsdam, c., cap. of Brandenburg *Land,* **Germany;** on R. Havel, 29 km S.E. of Berlin; beautiful parks and gardens, many palaces; scene of conference between Allies on bdy. questions, 1945; motor and locomotive wks., engin.; precision instruments; p. (1990) 139,500.

Potteries, The, dist., N. Staffs., **Eng.;** ctr. of earthenware ind., comprising ts. Burslem, Hanley, Fenton, Tunstall, Stoke and Longton.

Potters Bar, t., Hertsmere, Herts., **Eng.;** residtl.; in London commuter belt; p. (1981) 23,159.

Poulton-le-Fylde, t., Lancs., **Eng.;** ctr. of mkt. gardening, poultry rearing dist.; p. (1981) 17,608.

Powys, co., central **Wales;** mtnous. a. made up of former cos. of Radnorshire, Montgomery and most of Brecon and bordering Eng.; forestry, stockraising and water catchment for Eng.; crossed by Rs. Wye and Severn; sparse p.; a. 5,076 km²; p. (1993) 119,900.

Powys, Vale of, Powys, **Wales;** drained by R. Severn; cattle-rearing; ch. t. Welshpool.

Poyang Hu, lge. L., Jiangxi, **China;** on S. margin of Chang Jiang plain; surrounded by flat, intensively cultivated land, rice, sugar, mulberry; size varies greatly with season, max. a. (in late summer) 4,662 km².

Poznań, prov., W. **Poland;** drained by Warta and Notec Rs.; mainly agr.; stock-raising; mnfs. inc. locomotives; a. 26,705 km²; p. (1989) 1,323,400.

Poznań, c., cap. of P. prov., **Poland;** on Warta R.; route ctr., industl. and educational ctr.; cath. univ.; engin., iron-founding, chemicals; anc. c., once cap. of Poland; p. (1989) 586,908.

Pozzuoli, t., **Italy;** 3 km W. of Naples; anc. Puteoli; mineral baths, ordnance wks.; Roman ruins; p. (1981) 70,350.

Prague (Praha), c., cap. of **Czech Rep.;** picturesque, anc. c. on R. Vltava; comm. and cultural ctr.; univ. (founded 1348); outstanding architecture; extensive mnfs.; machin., sugar, leather, milling, chemicals; p. (1990) 1,215,000.

Prahova, R., Walachia, **Romania;** rises in Transylvanian Alps, flows S. into R. Ialomita; p. 176 km long.

Prato, t., **Italy;** 13 km N.W. of Florence; cath., mediaeval cas. and fortifications; cottons, woollens, machin.; p. (1992) 166,108.

Predeal Pass, Romania; carries main road and rly. across Transylvanian Alps from Bucharest to Brasov; alt. over 1,200 m.

Pregel, R., **Poland;** flows to Frisches Haff, nr. Kaliningrad; 200 km long.

Prek Ihnot, Cambodia; power and irrigation development project on lower Mekong R.

Prerov, t., **Czech Rep.;** S.E. of Olomouc; hardware, textiles; p. (1984) 50,241.

Presall, t., Wyre-Lancs., **Eng.;** N. of Blackpool; p. (1981) 4,608.

Prescot, mftg. t., Knowsley, Merseyside, **Eng.;** 6 km. S.W. of St. Helens; mkt., elec. cable ind.; p. (1981) 10,992.

Preseli Pembrokeshire, l. gov. dist., Dyfed, **Wales;** W. penin. with ts. of Fishguard, Haverfordwest and Milford Haven; p. (1993) 70,900.

Prešov, mkt. t., **Slovakia;** linen mnfs.; p. (1990) 89,000.

Prestatyn, t., Rhuddlan, Clwyd, **Wales;** on N. cst., 5 km E. of Rhyl; seaside resort; p. (1981) 16,439.

Presteign, mkt. t., Radnor, Powys, **Wales;** on R. Lugg, 16 km N.W. of Leominster; p. (1981) 1,213.

Preston, t., l. gov. dist., Lancs., **Eng.;** pt. on R. Ribble; textiles, engin., aircraft wks.; p. (1993) 132,200 (dist.).

Prestonpans, burgh, E. Lothian, S.E. **Scot.;** on F. of Forth, 14 km E. of Edinburgh; scene of Jacobite victory 1745; p. (1991) 7,014.

Prestwich, t., Gtr. Manchester, **Eng.;** in valley of R. Irwell, 6 km N.W. of Manchester; cotton bleaching and dyeing, soap, furnishings; p. (1981) 31,198.

Prestwick, burgh, Kyle and Carrick, **Scot.;** on F. of Clyde, 5 km N. of Ayr; golfing ctr. and transatlantic airpt. and freeport (1984); resort; p. (1991) 13,705.

Pretoria, c., Transvaal, admin. cap. of **Rep. of S. Africa;** univ., tr. ctr., inds. inc. engin., chemicals, iron, and steel; p. (1985) 822,925 (met. a.).

Preveza, ch. pt. and t. of P. dep. of Epirus, N.W. **Greece;** guards G. of Arta; p. (1981) 13,624 (c.), (1991) 58,910 (dep.).

Pribilof Is., off S.W. Alaska, **USA;** seal fur; a. 168 km².

Pribram, t., Bohemia, **Czech Rep.;** impt. lead and silver mines, zinc, barium and antimony; p. (1984) 38,787.

Prijedor, t., **Bosnia-Herzegovina,** formerly Yugoslavia; on E. flank of Dinaric Alps, 104 km S.E. of Zagreb; rly. junc.; iron-ore mines.

Prilep, t., **Macedonia,** formerly Yugoslavia; mkt.; refractory materials, tobacco processing; p. (1981) 99,770.

Primorskiy Kray, terr., **Russia;** S.E. Siberia, on Sea of Japan; coal, iron ore, and various metals in vicinity; fisheries; millet and rice; slow economic development results from isolation; wants economic links with China; ch. cs., Vladivostok (cap.), Ussuriysk; a. 168,350 km²; p. (1989) 2,256,100.

Prince Albert, t., Saskatchewan, **Canada;** lumbering, furs; p. (1986) 33,686.

Prince Edward I., prov., **Canada;** sm. I. in G. of St. Lawrence; physically poorly endowed; rocky, with thin soils; pastoral agr., furfarming, fishing; cap. Charlottetown; a. 5,657 km²; p. (1991) 129,100.

Prince George, t., B.C., **Canada;** oil refining; lumbering, mng., fur tr.; p. (1986) 67,621.

Prince Rupert, t., B.C., **Canada;** Pac. pt. of Canadian National rly.; service ctr., fishing and fish-processing; p. (1986) 15,755.

Princeton, bor., N.J., **USA;** seat of Princeton Univ.; p. (1980) 12,035.

Principe. *See* São Tomé.

Pripet Marshes, Belarus; forested swampy region crossed by Pripet R. and its streams; greater part reclaimed; coal and petroleum; a. 46,620 km².

Pripet (Pripyat), R., **Belarus;** trib. of R. Dnieper; 560 km long.

Privas, t., cap. of **Ardèche** dep., **France;** p. (1990) 10,490.

Pristina, c., cap. of Kossovo aut. region, S.W. Serbia, **Yugoslavia;** on Sitnic R.; admin. ctr.; many mosques; p. (1981) 210,040.

Prokopyevsk, t., S.W. Siberia, **Russia;** in Novosibirsk dist.; one of the main coalfields of Kuznetsk Basin; mng. machin., metallurgy; p. (1989) 274,000.

Prome, c. **Myanmar;** pt. on R. Irrawaddy; connected by rail and road to Rangoon; tr. in rice, cotton, tobacco; one of oldest cs. in Burma, founded 8th cent.

Proskurov. *See* Khmel'nitskiy.

Prostejov, t., N. Moravia, **Czech Rep.;** rly. junc.; agr. machin., textiles; historic bldgs.; p. (1984) 51,100.

Provence, former prov. now incorporated in **Provence-Alpes-Côte d'Azur, France;** inc. deps. Alpes-de-Haute-Provence, Hautes-Alpes, Alpes-Maritimes, Bouches-du-Rhône, Var, Vaucluse; mkt. gardening, tourism esp. along coast; ch. city Marseille; p. (1990) 4,257,900.

Providence, c., R.I. **USA;** at head of Narragansett Bay; univ.; jewellery, textiles, silverware, rubber gds., machin., oil, coal; p. (1990) 160,728 (c.), 655,000 (met. a.).

Provo, t., Utah, **USA;** at base of Wasatch mtns., nr. shore of Utah L.; univ.; flour, bricks, blast furnaces; p. (1990) 264,000 (met. a. with Orem).

Prudhoe, Tynedale, Northumberland, **Eng.;** former coal mng. t.; chemicals, paper; p. (1981) 11,820.

Prudhoe Bay, N.E. Alaska, **USA;** ctr. of recent extensive oil finds; arctic conditions make extraction and transport of oil difficult and ecologically dangerous but despite opposition from environmentalist groups 1,262 km pipeline to ice-free pt. of Valdez.

Prussia, former kingdom (1701–1806); former st. (1806–1945), **Germany**; consisted of 13 provs., cap. Berlin; formally abolished 1947; E. Prussia partitioned between USSR and Poland.

Pruszkow, t., **Poland**; nr. Warsaw; elec. plant; engin.; p. (1989) 53,889.

Prut, R., rises in **Ukraine** and then forms the boundary between **Romania** and **Moldova** as it flows from the Carpathian mtns. to the Danube R.; 576 km long.

Przemysl, c. and prov., S.E. **Poland**; on San R. (trib. of Vistula) nr. bdy. between Poland and Ukrainian SSR; anc. fortress t.; sewing machin.; p. (1989) 68,121 (c.), 404,200 (prov.).

Pskov, c., **Russia**; on R. Velikaya, nr. entry to L. Peipus; rly. junc.; flax tr.; historic bldgs.; scene of abdication of Nicholas II, March 1917; p. (1989) 204,000.

Pudsey, t., West Yorks., **Eng.**; between Leeds and Bradford; woollens; p. (1981) 38,977.

Puebla, c., cap. of P. st., **Mexico**; one of oldest and most impt. cs. of rep.; fine cath., theatre, univ.; cotton mills, onyx quarries, glazed tiles; p. (1990) 1,054,921.

Puebla, st., **Mexico**; on interior plateau at 2,400 m; fertile valleys for coffee and sugar; mng. impt.; dense p.; a. 33,991 km²; p. (1989) 4,118,059.

Pueblo, c., Col., **USA**; on R. Arkansas, in foothills of Rockies; iron and steel ctr.; coal and various metals nearby; p. (1990) 98,640 (t.), 123,051 (met. a.).

Puente-Genil, t., Córdoba, **Spain**; olive oil, quince pulp; p. (1981) 25,615.

Puerto Barrios, pt., **Guatemala**; rly. terminus; oil refining; p. (1989) 338,000.

Puerto Cabello, spt., N. **Venezuela**; on Caribbean nr. Valencia; excellent harbour; linked by rail and highway to Carácas; asbestos, vegetable oils, soap, candles, meat-packing; p. (1980) 94,000.

Puerto Cortés, spt., N.W. **Honduras**; on Caribbean; exp. bananas, hardwoods; p. (1988) 43,300.

Puerto de Santa Maria, El, spt., S.W. **Spain**; on Bay of Cadiz; exp. mainly sherry; p. (1981) 45,933.

Puerto la Cruz, t., **Venezuela**; 16 km from Barcelona; oil refining; p. with Barcelona (1981) 156,500.

Puerto Limón. *See* Limón.

Puerto Montt, spt., **Chile**; cap. Los Lagos region; in sheep-farming dist.; S. terminus of rlys.; devastated by earthquake 1960; p. (1987) 113,488.

Puerto Ordaz. *See* Santo Tomé de la Guayana.

Puerto Rico, I., terr. of **USA**, W.I.; since 1952 free commonwealth ass. with USA; democratic economic growth aided recently by falling birth-rate; mtnous., eroded soils, alt. modifies tropical climate; exp. mnfs., but agr. impt. internally; 80 per cent land under cultivation, sugar, tobacco, coffee; tourism; cap. San Juan; a. 8,866 km²; p. (1990) 3,522,037.

Puerto Saurez, R. pt., **Bolivia**; on R. Paraguay; collecting ctr. for rubber, coffee, Brazil nuts.

Puerto Varas, t., **Chile**; tourist ctr. in Chilean "Switzerland".

Puget Sound, Wash., **USA**; inlet of Pac. Oc.

Puket. *See* Phuket.

Pula, spt., **Croatia**, (formerly Yugoslavia); on Adriatic; industl. ctr. with shipyards, docks, and various inds.; ch. naval base of Hapsburg empire; tourism; Roman remains; p. (1981) 77,278.

Pulia. *See* Apulia.

Puna, cold, bleak, and barren plateau of Andes in **Peru** and **Bolivia**, 3,600–5,500 m.

Pune (**Poona**), c., Maharashtra, **India**; in W. Ghats; temperate pleasant climate; cultural, educational (univ.) and political ctr.; military base; agr. tr. ctr.; cotton gds., paper; p. (1991) 1,567,000.

Punjab, region N.W. Indus plains, Indian sub-continent; extensive irrigation from the "five rivers"—Jhelum, Chenab, Ravi, Bias, Sutlej; now divided politically between **India** and **Pakistan**; impt. cotton, wheat, and sugar dist.; coal deposits.

Punjab (**East**), former st., **India**; partitioned on linguistic basis 1966; Punjab-speaking Punjab st. (a. 50,375 km²; p. (1981) 16,788,915 inc. 55 per cent Sikh); and Hindi-speaking Haryana st. (a. 44,056 km²; p. (1991) 20,281,969; joint cap. Chandigarh.

Punjab (**West**), prov., **Pakistan**; old prov. revived 1970; p. (1981) 47,292,441.

Punta Arenas, c., cp. of Magallanes prov., S. **Chile**; most S. c. in world; mutton, wool;

coal nearby; natural gas pipeline from Kimiri-Aike; p. (1987) 111,724.

Puntarenas, spt., **Costa Rica**, on G. of Nicoya; fishing; fish-processing; resort; p. (1984) 37,390 (dist).

Purbeck, I. of, sm. peninsula, Dorset cst., **Eng.**; anc. v. of Corfe Castle in ctr.; limestone ("Purbeck marble") quarries; site of Britain's lgst. onshore oilfield; once a royal deer forest; now forms l. gov. dist. inc. Wareham and Swanage; p. (1993) 43,800.

Puri, t., Orissa, **India**; famous for its temple and festival of the god Vishnu and his monster car, Juggernaut; p. (1991) 125,199.

Purley; rail accident 1989 *See* Croydon.

Purus, R., **Peru** and **Brazil**; rises in Andes, flows to Amazon R. through underdeveloped a.; 3,360 km long.

Pusan, main pt. of **S. Korea**; on Korean Strait at head of Naktong R. basin; textiles; steel mill at Pohang nearby; Korea's first nuclear power sta.; p. (1990) 3,797,566.

Pushkin, c., **Russia**; nr. St. Petersburg; summer palaces of Tsars; Pushkin museum; Pulkovo observatory nearby.

Puteaux, sub. Paris, **France**; woollens, dyes, engin., printing; p. (1982) 36,143.

Putney, sub. of London, **Eng.**; residtl.; Thames-side dist.

Putrid Sea. *See* Sivash.

Putumayo, R., trib. of R. Amazon; rises in Colombia, forming bdy. with Ecuador and Peru; here in wild-rubber region, Roger Casement exposed cruel exploitation of native labour; 1,600 km long.

Puy-de-Dôme, extinct volcano, Massif Central, **France**; hgst peak of Auvergne mtns., 1,466 m.

Puy-de-Dôme, dep., **France**; in Auvergne; cap. Clermont-Ferrand, industl. ctr. Thiers; a. 8,003 km², p. (1990) 598,200.

Puymorens Tunnel, Pyrenees, on bdy. between **France** and **Spain**; carries main rly. between Toulouse and Barcelona.

Pwllheli, t., Dwyfor, Gwynedd, N. **Wales**; sm. pt. on S. cst. Lleyn peninsula; seaside resort; inshore fishing, boat-bldg.; p. (1981) 3,989.

Pyatigorsk, c., N. Caucasus, **Russia**; ctr. of Caucasian mineral water springs; Lermontov shot here in duel 1841; p. (1989) 129,000.

Pylos, pt., S.W. Peloponnesus, **Greece**; shipbldg. and repair yard, heavy metal wks. projected; sea-battles 1827 (Navarino), 425 B.C.

Pyongyang, c., cap. of **N. Korea**; stands high above Taedong R.; major industl. ctr. with coal and iron ore deposits nearby; univ.; many historic relics; p. (1984) 2·6 m.

Pyrenees, range of mtns., S.W. **Europe**; dividing France from Iberian Peninsula; 432 km long; hgst peak Pic d'Anéto (Maladetta) 3,408 m.

Pyrénées-Atlantiques, dep., S.W. **France**; mainly agr., sheep and cattle raising; ch. ts. Pau (cap.), Bayonne, Biarritz; a. 7,713 km²; p. (1990) 578,500.

Pyrénées-Orientales, dep., S. **France**; on Mediterranean; wine, fruit, olives; cap. Perpignan; a. 4,141 km²; p. (1990) 363,800.

Pyrgos, t., Elis, S.W. **Greece**; has suffered from earthquakes; p. (1981) 21,958.

Q

Qaidam (**Tsaidam**), depression, Qinghai prov., China; a. of salt marsh and Ls.; rich deposits of oil; state farms for intensive animals husbandry.

Qacentina (**Constantine**), c., N. E. **Algeria**; 650 m. alt. on gorge of R. Rhumel; textile and engin. wks.; lge tractor and diesel engine complex; p. (1983) 448,578.

Qandahar, c., former cap of **Afghanistan**; alt. 1,037 m.; fruit preserving and canning; airpt. built with U.S. aid; textiles; p. (1982) 191,345.

Qarun (**Birker el Qarum**). *See* Karun.

Qatar, emirate, indep. st. (1971), **Arabia**; crown prince appointed (1979); peninsula on Persian G.; economy based on oil; inland production declining, but increasing offshore drilling; political stability less certain after withdrawal of Brit. military protection (1971); cap. Doha; a. 10,360 km²; p. (1992) 453,000, of whom 75 per cent are foreign nationals.

Qattara Depression, N. **Egypt**; 134 m below sea level, salt marsh produced by seepage and evaporation of artesian water; marshes; few inhabitants; scheme to flood depression with sea water to generate electricity now under construction.

Qenâ, t. and prov., central **Egypt**; on R. Nile; water jars and bottles; agr. tr., cereals, dates; p. (1986) 119,794 (t.). (1991) 2,598,000 (prov.).

Qingdao (Tsingtao), c., Shandong prov., **China**; spt. with excellent harbour at head of bay; tourism impt.; mnfs. locomotives, cement, textiles, machin., chemicals; special development zone to attract high technology inds.; oil jetty for Shengli oil field; p. (1992) 2,060,000.

Qinghai (Tsinghai), prov., W. **China**; between Xinjiang and Xizang Zizhou (Tibet), inc. c. plateau; local coal and iron ore but exploitation hindered by isolation; two new iron and steel plants; new rly.; massive hydro-electricity plant; international airpt. link with Hong Kong, attempts to increase economic development; oil exploration; a. 721,004 km²; p. (1990) 4,430,000.

Qinghai Hu (Koko Nor), salt L., Qinghai prov., **China**; at over 3,000 m. in Tibetan highlands; a. 5,957 km²; no outlet.

Qinhuangdao (Chinwangtao), c., spt., former treaty pt., Hebei, N. **China**; on Yellow Sea cst. 240 km N.E. of Tianjin; only good natural harbour on N. China cst.; exp. coal from Gailan mines; machin., textiles, chemical inds.; designated a development zone to attract foreign investment; p. (1984) 425,300.

Qiqihar (Tsitsihar), c., Heilongjiang prov., N. **China**; on Vladivostok portion of Trans-Siberian rly.; food processing and tr., chemicals; potential oilfield; p. (1992) 1,380,000.

Qisil-Qum, desert region, **Central Asia**; covering dried-up a. of extended Pleistocene Aral Sea.

Qizan, spt., **Saudi Arabia**; cereals, pearl-fishing, salt.

Qom (Qum), c., **Iran**; pilgrimage ctr., shrine of Fatima; rly. junction; p. (1986) 550,630.

Qornet es Sauda, mtn., Lebanon range, Levant, **Lebanon**; max. alt. 3,050 m.

Quantock Hills, Somerset, **Eng.**; S. of Bridgwater Bay; hgst. pt. 385 m.

Quauzhu. See **Zhengzhou**.

Queanbeyan, t., N.S.W., **Australia**; rapid growth as commuter ctr. as only 13 km from Canberra; pastoral, dairying dist.; mkt. and service ctr.; p. (1981) 19,056.

Quebec, c., cap. of Q. prov., **Canada**; spt. with fine harbour on St. Lawrence R. at mouth of St. Charles; cultural cap. of French Canada; inds. based on local raw materials of timber, agr. prods.; oil refining at St. Romauld; historic c. with many fine bldgs., univ., tourism; p. (1986) 164,580 (c.), 603,267 (met. a.).

Quebec, prov., **Canada**; mainly within Canadian Shield; continental climate; forests and timber inds.; agr. in S.; hydroelectric power and abundant minerals; p. mainly French-speaking; ch. cs., Quebec (cap.), Montreal; strong separatist movements causing decline in investment and movement of some inds. to USA; a. 1,540,687 km²; p. (1991) 6,872,600.

Quebec-Labrador Trough, Canada; geological formation extending through central Quebec prov. to Ungava Bay, Hudson Strait; immense reserves of iron-ore (locally "red-gold").

Quedlinburg, t., Saxony-Anhalt, **Germany**; at foot of Harz mtns.; cas., cath.; aniline dyes, metals, engin., horticultural mkt. t.; p. (1989) 29,096.

Queen Charlotte's Is., archipelago, N. of Vancouver I., off cst. B.C., **Canada**; halibut fishing, lumbering.

Queen Charlotte Sound, strait, separating Vancouver I. from B.C. mainland **Canada**; a continuation of Johnstone Strait.

Queen Elizabeth Is., **Canada**; I. gr. in Canadian Arctic; most N. land of N. America; a. 349,443 km².

Queen Maud Land, Norwegian sector of **Antarctica**; ice crystal mtns., 3,050 m high for 160 km along cst.

Queens, bor., N.Y. City, **USA**; residtl. dist.; lgst. bor. of N.Y. c.; p. 1,951,598.

Queensbury and Shelf, t., West Yorks., **Eng.**; textiles; p. (1981) 11,658.

Queensferry, royal burgh, Edinburgh City, **Scot.**; at S. end of Forth road and rail bridges; p. (1991) 8,887.

Queensland, st., N.E. **Australia**; sub-tropical a. rising from cst. to Gt. Dividing Range and Western Plains (inc. Gt. Artesian Basin); Barrier Reef off cst.; p. concentrated on cst. where

sugar cane and tropical fruits grown, popular all year tourist resorts and retirement ctrs.; all year mkt. gardening replaced by extensive cattle and sheep ranching in W.; coal, copper, uranium, bauxite; oil at Moonie; mftg.; cap. Brisbane; a. 1,727,200 km²; p. (1991) 2,999,900.

Queenstown. See **Cobh**.

Queenstown, t., Tasmania, **Australia**; copper mng. t.; prosperity depends on continuation of mng. at Mount Lyell.

Queenstown, S.I., **N.Z**, tourist ctr. on L. Wakatipu in S. Alps; p. (1991) 15,123.

Queenstown, t., Cape Prov., **S. Africa**; in agr. region producing wool and wheat; p. (1980) 48,860 (dist.).

Quelimane, pt., **Moçambique**; at head of estuary; rly. terminus; exp. copra, sisal, tea; notorious in 18th and 19th cent. as slave mkt.; p. (1980) 60,151.

Quelpart. See **Cheju**.

Quemoy, gr. of Is. off Chinese mainland nr. Amoy.

QueQue, t., **Zimbabwe**; major new steel works has attracted many ancillary inds.; p. (1982) 47,600.

Querétaro, t., cap. of Q. st., **Mexico**; site of pre-Aztec settlement at 1,881 m; cath., many colonial bldgs.; old cotton ind.; p. (1990) 454,049.

Querétaro, st., **Mexico**; in Central Plateau; arid with fertile valleys; variety of crops; mng. impt.; famous for opals; cap. Q.; a. 11,479 km²; p. (1990) 1,044,227.

Quetta, t., cap. of Baluchistan, **Pakistan**; at 5,000 ft., commands routes to Bolan Pass; ctr. of irrigated agr. a.; military ctr.; coal mng. nearby; damaged by severe earthquake (1935); p. (1981) 285,000.

Quezaltenango, t., S.W. **Guatemala**; second c. of rep.; at 2,333 m at foot of Santa Maria volcano; univ.; comm. ctr. for rich agr. region; textiles, handicrafts; p. (1989) 246,000.

Quezon City, c., **Philippines**; new city within metropolitan Manila; univ.; p. (1990) 1,666,766.

Quibdó, t., **Colombia**; in forested a. on R. Atrato; platinum, gold mng.; p. (1992) 119,027.

Quillon, t., Kerala, **India**; on Malabar cst., ctr. of coconut tr. and processing; p. (1981) 137,943 (t.), 167,598 (met. a.).

Quimes, t., Buenos Aires, **Argentina**; on Rio de la Plata estuary; English public school; resort; oil refining, textiles, glass; p. (1980) 441,780.

Quimper, t., cap. Finistère dep., **France**; tourist ctr. for S. Brittany; Breton pottery; Gothic cath.; p. (1990) 62,541.

Quincy, t., Ill., **USA**; at bridging point of R. Mississippi; agr. machin., clothing, footwear, food inds.; p. (1980) 42,554.

Quincy, t., Mass., **USA**; in Mass. B., 13 km S.E. of Boston; shipbldg. ctr.; p. (1980) 84,743.

Quindio, pass, **Colombia**; provides impt. routeway through Cordillera Central; 11,099 ft.

Qui Nhon, t., S. **Vietnam**; on E. cst.; tr. in coconut prods.; fishing.

Quintana Roo, st., S.E. **Mexico**; on Caribbean; low-lying swamp, underdeveloped; cap. Chetumal; a. 50,344 km²; p. (1990) 493,605.

Quito, c., cap. of **Ecuador**; in Andes at 2,852 m, 24 km S. of equator; anc. Inca c., cath., univ., slower growth than coastal ts.; impt. textile ctr.; p. (1990) 1,100,847.

Quorndon or Quorn, sm. t., Leics., **Eng.**; on R. Soar, 5 km S. of Loughborough; ctr. of fox-hunting dist.

Qwaqwa, homeland, **S. Africa**; p. (1985) 181,559.

R

Raake, t., N. **Finland**; spt.; iron wks.

Raasay, I., E. of Skye, Skye and Lochalsh, **Scot.**; 21 km long, 5·6 km wide; p. (1991) 163.

Rab I., at head of Adriatic, off **Croatia**; tourism; a. 192 km².

Rabat, c., cap. of **Morocco**; spt. at mouth of Bu Regreg R. on Atl. cst.; cath., univ.; textiles, carpets, rugs; p. (1982) 518,616.

Rabaul, spt., New Britain, **Papua New Guinea**; ch. pt., exp. copra; damaged by volcanic eruption (1937) former cap. of New Guinea; p. (1990) 17,022.

Raciborz (Ratibor), t., Upper Silesia, **Poland** (since 1945); on R. Oder; textiles, metals, wood engin.; p. (1989) 62,733.

Racine, c., Wis., **USA**; sm. pt. on L. Mich., 16 km S. of Milwaukee; agr. machin., tractors, car parts; p. (1990) 84,298 (c.), 175,034 (met. a.).

Radcliffe, t., Gtr. Manchester, **Eng.**; N.W. of Manchester; paper, rubber, paint, engin.; p. (1981) 30,501.

Radebeul, t., Saxony, **Germany**; on R. Elbe; satellite of Dresden; p. (1989) 32,011.

Radium Hill, v., S. **Australia**; ctr. for radium mng. 1920–30 and uranium later; mines now closed (since 1961).

Radnorshire, former co., Central **Wales**; gov. dist., Powys, inc. Knighton, Presteigne and Llandrindodd Wells; p. (1993) 24,200.

Radom, t. and prov., **Poland**; in Radomska Plain; route ctr.; metal and chemical inds.; lge. tobacco factory; p. (1989) 226,025 (t.), 745,400 (prov.).

Radomosko, t., Piotrków, **Poland**; on edge of Lodz Upland; metallurgical wks., food inds.; bentwood chairs for exp.; p. (1989) 50,059.

Ragaz, **Bad**, spa, St. Gall can., **Switzerland**; at mouth of Tamina R.; hot springs from nearby v. of Pfäfers.

Ragusa. See **Dubrovnik.**

Ragusa, t., Sicily, **Italy**; oil and asphalt production; p. (1981) 64,492.

Rahway, t., N.J., **USA**; on R. Rahway; residtl. suburb for N.Y.; p. (1980) 26,723.

Raichur, t., Karnataka, **India**; comm. ctr.; agr. processing; p. (1991) 157,551.

Rainford, t., Merseyside, **Eng.**; nr. St. Helens; former coal-mng. a.; p. (1981) 8,941.

Rainier, mtn., Wash., **USA**; 4,432 m; forms Nat. Park.

Rainy, L., on border of Canada and Minn., **USA**; drained by Rainy R. to L. of the Woods.

Raipur, t., Madhya Pradesh, **India**; ctr. of fertile rice growing a.; p. (1991) 439,000.

Rajahmundry, t., Andhra Pradesh, **India**; on delta of Godivari R.; agr. tr.; p. (1991) 325,000 .

Rajasthan, st., **India**; dry a. inc. Thar desert; sparse p. where primitive irrigation; agr., millets, pulses, cotton; impt. gypsum deposits; cap. Jaipur; a. 342,274 km²; p. (1991) 44,005,990.

Rajkot, t., Gujarat, **India**; p. (1991) 559,000.

Rajshahi, t., Rajshahi dist., **Bangladesh**; on R. Ganges; univ.; silk inds.; p. (1991) 299,671.

Raki-Ura I. See **Stewart I.**

Raleigh, c., cap. of N.C., **USA**; educational ctr. univ.; printing, cotton tr. and processing; p. (1990) 207,951 (c.), 735,000 (met. a. with Durham).

Ralik, W. chain of Is., Marshall gr., **Pac. Oc.**; lgst. atoll Kwajalein; parallel with Ratak chain.

Ramat Gan, t., **Israel**; in plain of Sharon; univ.; lt. inds.; p. (1990) 119,500.

Rambouillet, t., Yvelines, **France**; nr. Versailles; anc. château; p. (1982) 22,487.

Rameswaram, t., Tamil Nadu. **India**; on Rameswaram I., Palk Strait; contains Dravidian temple, Hindu holy place of pilgrimage; p. (1981) 27,928.

Ramla, t., **Israel**; S. of Lydda; former cap. of Palestine; ass. with crusaders.

Rampur, t., Uttar Pradesh, **India**; N.W. of Bareilly; agr. tr.; sugar refining; chemicals; cap. of former princely st. of R.; p. (1991) 243,742.

Ramree I., **Myanmar**; in Bay of Bengal, off Arakan cst.; 80 km long.

Ramsbottom, t., Lancs., **Eng.**; on R. Irwell, 6 km N. of Bury; engin., paper, textiles; p. (1981) 17,799.

Ramsey, mkt. t., Cambs., **Eng.**; on edge of Fens, 11 km N. of St. Ives; engin.; abbey ruins; p. (1981) 5,828.

Ramsey, t., spt., I. of Man, **Eng.**; on N.E. cst.; holiday resort; p. (1991) 6,496.

Ramsgate, t., Kent, **Eng.**; on S. cst. of I. of Thanet; seaside resort; p. (1981) 39,642.

Rancagua, t., cap. Libertador region, **Chile**; ctr. of fertile valley in Andean foothills; tractors, agr. processing; p. (1982) 172,489.

Rance, R., Brittany, **France**; world's first major tidal hydroelectric power sta. (opened 1966).

Ranchi, t., Bihar, **India**; hot season seat of govt. in Chota Nagpur plateau; univ.; heavy engin.; p. (1991) 599,000.

Rand. See **Witwatersrand.**

Randers, pt., **Denmark**; on Randers Fjord, inlet of Kattegat; machin., foundries; exp. dairy prod.; mediaeval monastery; p. (1981) 61,020.

Randfontein, t., Transvaal, **S. Africa**; gold-mng. ctr.; uranium plant; p. (1980) 91,460 (dist.).

Randstad, conurb., **Neth.**; Dutch "urban ring." inc. Rotterdam, The Hague, Leiden, Amsterdam

and Utrecht, contained within radius of 16 km; a. of rapid industrialisation.

Rangitaiki, R., N.I., **N.Z.**; flows into Bay of Plenty; 192 km long.

Rangoon, c., cap. of **Myanmar**; on E. arm of Irrawaddy delta; 2 caths., many mosques, temples and pagodas; replaced Mandalay as cap.; ctr. of rice tr. and exp.; oil refining; teak collecting ctr.; p. (1983) 2,458,712.

Rangpur, t., **Bangladesh**; on R. Ghaghat; jute; p. (1991) 203,931.

Raniganj, t., W. Bengal, **India**; coalfield in Damodar basin; engin.; p. (1981) 48,702 (t.), 119,101 (met. a.).

Rannoch, Loch, Perth and Kinross, **Scot.**; 14 km long, 1·6 km wide; drained to R. Tay.

Raoul I. See **Sunday I.**

Rapallo, t., Liguria, N.W. **Italy**; on G. of Genoa, 35 km E. of Genoa; most celebrated resort on Italian Riviera di Levante; p. (1981) 28,318.

Rapanui. See **Easter I.**

Rapid City, t., S.D., **USA**; second t. of st.; comm. ctr. for agr. and mng. a.; p. (1990) 54,523.

Rarotonga, volcanic I., Pac. Oc.; lgst. of **Cook Is.**; fruit canning; ch. t. and pt. Avarua; p. (1981) 9,530.

Ra's al Khaimah, emirate, member of the **United Arab Emirates**; p. (1985) 116,470.

Rasht (Resht), c., **Iran**; cap. of Gilan prov., in a. producing rice, cotton, silk; carpets; nearby Pahlevi serves as pt.; p. (1986) 293,881.

Ras Lanug, oil terminal, on G. of Sidra, **Libya**; pipeline from Hofra oilfield.

Ras Tannura, spt., Nejd, **Saudi Arabia**; lge. oil refinery; oil exp.

Ratak, E., chain of Is., Marshall Group, **Pac. Oc.**; ch. I. Majuro; parallel with Ralik chain.

Rathenow, t., Brandenburg, **Germany**; on R. Havel; optical and precision instruments; p. (1989) 30,935.

Rathlin, I., off Fair Head, Moyle, **N. Ireland**; 8 km by 1·6 km.

Ratibor. See **Racibórz.**

Ratingen, t., N. Rhine–Westphalia, **Germany**; N.E. of Düsseldorf; textiles, machin., glass; famous for Blue L.; p. (1986) 89,200.

Ratisbon. See **Regensburg.**

Ratlam, t., Madhya Pradesh, **India**; rly. junc. in Malwa Plateau; p. (1991) 195,776.

Ratnapura, t., **Sri Lanka**; former ctr. of gem mng.; p. (1981) 37,354.

Rauma, spt., S.W. **Finland**; on Baltic Sea; p. (1991) 29,858.

Raunds, t., East Northants., **Eng.**; 8 km N.E. of Wellingborough; p. (1981) 7,401.

Raurkela, t., Orissa, **India**; steel, tinplate, iron, fertilisers; p. (1991) 398,864.

Ravenglass, t., Cumbria, **Eng.**; nr. mouth of R. Esk; old pt.; Roman remains.

Ravenna, c., cap. of Ravenna prov., Emilia-Romagna, **Italy**; on reclaimed plain nr. Po delta; connected to Adriatic by canal; ctr. of fertile agr. dist., agr. processing; new inds. aided by discovery of methane N. of c.; oil refineries, chemicals, fertilisers; cath., mausoleum, famous mosaics; p. (1992) 136,009.

Ravenna, prov., Emilia-Romagna, **Italy**; N. Italian plain rising to Apennines; fertile agr. a.; cap. R.; a. 1,852 km²; p. (1981) 358,654.

Ravensburg, t., Baden-Württemberg, **Germany**; nr. Konstanz; engin., textiles; p. (1986) 43,200.

Ravenscraig, t., nr. Motherwell, Strathclyde Reg., **Scot.**; hot strip steelmill; cold reduction mill at Gartcosh 13 km away; steel wks. now closed.

Ravi, R., Punjab, **India**; trib. of Chenab; used for irrigation; 720 km long.

Rawalpindi, c., **Pakistan**; seat of govt. until completion of Islamabad; admin. comm. and rly. ctr.; foundries, oil refining, industl. gases; p. (1981) 928,000.

Rawmarsh, t., South Yorks., **Eng.**; 3 km N.E. of Rotherham; engin.; p. (1981) 18,985.

Rawtenstall, t., Rossendale, Lancs., **Eng.**; on R. Irwell in ctr. of Rossendale Fells; felts; footwear, textiles; p. (1981) 22,231.

Rayleigh, t., Rochford, Essex, **Eng.**; 8 km N.W. of Southend; lt. inds.; dormitory for London; p. (1981) 29,146.

Ré, Ile de, I., W. cst. of Charente-Maritime dep. **France**; off La Rochelle; citadel (built 1681) at St. Martin de Ré is now a prison.

Reading, t., l. gov. dist., Berks., **Eng.**; at confluence of Rs. Thames and Kennet; univ.;

biscuits, engin., electronics, mkt. gardening, tin-box mftg. printing; p. (1993) 137,700 (dist.).

Reading, c., Penns., **USA**; on Schuylkill R.; steelwks. using local coal, optical gds.; p. (1990) 337,000 (met. a.).

Recife, spt., cap. of Pernambuco st., N.E. **Brazil**; fine natural harbour; univ.; processing and exp. of sugar from surrounding a.; "Venice of Brazil" because of I. and peninsula site; lge. petrochemical wks. nearby; recent industl. expansion and diversification; engin., chem., electrical and telecommunications equipment; integrated steel wks.; p. (1991) 1,290,149 .

Recklinghausen, t., N. Rhine–Westphalia, Germany; nr. Dortmund; collieries, iron, machin., textiles, chemicals; p. (1990) 125,500.

Recôncavo, dist., Bahia st., N.E. **Brazil**; surrounds bay at mouth of R. Paraguassu; intensive cultivation of sugar cane, cotton, tobacco rice by Negro farmers; oil production; ch. ts. São Salvador, Cachoeira.

Redbridge, outer bor., E. London, **Eng.**; incorporates Ilford, Wanstead and Woodford, Chigwell (Hainault Estate), Dagenham (N. Chadwell Heath ward); mainly residtl.; p. (1993) 232,700.

Redcar, t., Cleveland, **Eng.**; lge. iron and steel wks.; p. (1981) 84,931.

Redcliff, t., **Zimbabwe**; iron-mng.; iron and steel wks.; fertilisers.

Red Deer, t., Alberta, **Canada**; on Red Deer R.; mkt. t. in farming a.; lge. natural gas processing plant nearby; p. (1986) 54,425.

Redditch, t., l. gov. dist., Hereford and Worcs., **Eng.**; 19 km S. of Birmingham; needles, fishing tackle, cycles, springs, aluminium alloys; new t. (1964); p. (1993) 78,500 (dist.).

Redlands, t., Cal., **USA**; univ.; citrus fruit packing and canning; p. (1980) 43,619.

Redonda, I., Leeward gr., **Antigua and Barbuda**; between Montserrat and Nevis; uninhabited.

Redondo Beach, t., Cal., **USA**; residtl.; tourism; p. (1980) 57,102.

Red R. (China and Vietnam). *See* Song-koi.

Red R., USA; southernmost of lge. tribs. of Mississippi R.; derives name and colour from red clay in upper course; dammed for flood control and hydroelec. power; 2,560 km long.

Red R. of the North, USA; rises in Minn., flows N. into Canada to empty into L. Winnipeg; 1,040 km long.

Redruth, t., Cornwall, **Eng.**; once major ctr. of tin mng.; most mines now closed, although recent revival of some; p. (1981) 46,482 (inc. Camborne).

Red Sea, arm of sea separating Arabia from Africa; connects with Indian Oc. by Straits of Bab-el-Mandeb; extension of Great African Rift Valley which further N. encloses the Dead Sea; 2,240 km long.

Redwood City, t., W. Cal., **USA**; timber tr.; electronics; p. (1980) 54,951.

Ree, Lough, L., **R.o.I.**; between Roscommon, Longford and Westmeath, an extension of R. Shannon; 27 km long.

Regensburg (Ratisbon), c., R. pt., Bavaria, **Germany**; N.E. of Munich on R. Danube; timber processing, chemicals; p. (1990) 122,300.

Reggio di Calabria, spt., Calabria, **Italy**; on Strait of Messina; cath.; fishing, ferry to Sicily; mkt. for citrus fruit; tourism; agr. processing; rebuilt after 1908 earthquake; p. (1992) 178,312.

Reggio nell' Emilia, c., cap. of prov. of same name, in Emilia-Romagna, N. **Italy**; at foot of Apennines; Renaissance church of the Madonna della Ghiara; locomotives, aircraft, agr. engin.; birthplace of Ariosto; p. (1992) 133,191.

Regina, t., cap. of Saskatchewan, **Canada**; ctr. of wheat growing dist. of Prairies; connected by pipeline to Alberta oilfields; oil refining, chemicals, agr. machin.; p. (1986) 175,064 (c.), 186,521 (met. a.).

Rehovoth, Israel; t., in citrus fruit dist.; Weizmann Institute of Science.

Reichenbach, t., Saxony, **Germany**; at foot of Erzgebirge; p. (1989) 25,663.

Reichenberg. *See* Liberec.

Reigate, t., Surrey, **Eng.**; at foot of N. Downs, 8 km E. of Dorking; dormitory for London; with Banstead forms l. gov. dist.; p. (1993) 118,800 (dist.).

Reims, c., Marne dep., N.E. **France**; on R. Vesle; famous Gothic cath.; univ.; champagne ctr., textiles; p. (1990) 185,164 (c.), 206,362 (met. a.).

Reindeer L., Saskatchewan, Manitoba, **Canada**; Indian settlement on shore; a. 6,475 km².

Rejang R., Sarawak; **Malaysia**; navigable for 72 km by ocean boats; main R. of Sarawak.

Rembang, pt., N. cst. Java, **Indonesia**; in dry limestone R. plateau; proposed nuclear power plant.

Remscheid, t., N. Rhine–Westphalia, **Germany**; nr. Düsseldorf; iron and steel ctr.; machin. tools; p. (1990) 123,400.

Renaix. *See* Ronse.

Rendsburg, t., Schleswig-Holstein, **Germany**; on Kiel Canal; shipbldg., elec. gds.; p. (1986) 30,600.

Renfrew, royal burgh, Renfrew, **Scot.**; nr. R. Clyde, 8 km W. of Glasgow; p. (1991) 20,764.

Renfrewshire, former co., central **Scot.**; now reduced in size and forms l. gov. dist. within Strathclyde Reg.; a. of l. gov. dist. 308 km²; p. (1993) 201,150.

Renkum, t., Gelderland, **Neth.**; 13 km W. of Arnhem; paper mnfs.; p. (1993) 32,867.

Rennes, c., cap. of Ille-et-Vilaine dep., **France**; only major inland t. of Brittany, in fertile agr. basin; univ., comm. ctr.; cars, engin.; p. (1990) 203, 533 (c.), 245, 065 (met. a.).

Reno, lgst. t. of Nevada, **USA**; univ.; st. agr. college; famous for easy divorce procedure and gambling; p. (1990) 133,850 (t.), 255,000 (met. a.).

Repton, t., South Derbyshire, **Eng.**; famous public school in priory; former Saxon cap. of Mercia.

Resende, t., Rio de Janeiro st., **Brazil**; chemicals, rly. junc.; univ.; p. (1985) 102,900.

Resht. *See* Rasht.

Resina, t., S. **Italy**; on Bay of Naples at W. foot of Vesuvius; nr. site of anc. Herculaneum; resort.

Resistencia, t., cap. of Chaco terr., **Argentina**; served by R. pt. of Barranqueras on R. Paraná; tr. in cattle, timber, cotton; agr. processing; p. (1991) 218,438.

Resita, t., Banat region, **Romania**; steel inds. based on local iron ore; heavy engin.; p. (1990) 110,519.

Restormel, l. gov. dist., Cornwall, **Eng.**; inc. N. and S. cst. and ts. of Newquay and St. Austell; p. (1993) 88,300.

Retalhuleu, dep., **Guatemala**; ctr. for coffee, sugar; a. 1858 km²; p. (1991) 238,857.

Réunion (Ile de Bourbon), I., overseas terr. of **France**; in Indian Oc., between Mauritius and Madagascar; volcanic I.; impt. sugar producer; cap. St. Denis; a. 2,512 km²; p. (1990) 597,800.

Reus, t., Tarragona, prov., **Spain**; textiles; agr. tr.; p. (1981) 75,987.

Reuss, R., **Switzerland**; flows N. from the St. Gotthard Pass through L. Lucerne, joining Aare R. nr. Brugg; 157 km long.

Reutlingen, t., Baden–Württemberg, **Germany**; S. of Stuttgart; textiles, metals, machin., leather; p. (1990) 104,300.

Reval. *See* Tallin.

Revelstoke, t., B.C., **Canada**; rly. junc.; in timber producing a.; ctr. for R. Nat. Park; p. (1986) 8,279.

Revillagigedo Islands, archipelago, Pac. Oc., off S.W. **Mexico**; ch. Is., Socorro, San Benedicto (volcano suddenly arose on I. 1952).

Reykjavik, c., cap. of **Iceland**; on S.W. cst.; impt. fish. pt.; fish exp. and processing; water piped from geysers; airport; univ.; 2 caths.; p. (1991) 99,623.

Rezayeh, (Orūmiyeh) c., **Iran**; cap. of W. Azerbaijan prov.; comm. ctr. of agr. region; p. (1986) 304,823.

Rheidol, R., Dyfed, **Wales**; flows from Plynlimmon in deeply incised valley (Devil's Bridge) to Aberystwyth; hydroelec. power; 38 km long.

Rheine, t., N. Rhine–Westphalia, **Germany**; on R. Ems; textiles, machin.; p. (1983) 71,200.

Rheingau, dist., **Germany**; famous wine a. on right bank of Rhine from Biebrich to Assmanshausen.

Rheinhausen, t., Rhine–Westphalia, **Germany**; on left bank of Rhine opposite Duisburg; coal mng., iron, textiles.

Rhin (Bas). *See* Bas Rhin.

Rhine, R., rises in Switzerland, can. Grisons, passes through L. Constance, skirts Baden, traverses Hesse, Rhineland, and the Neth., flowing to N. Sea by two arms, Oude Rijn and the Waal (the latter discharging finally by the Maas); famous for its beauty, especially between Bonn and

Bingen; ch. falls at Schaffhausen; once a natural barrier between E. and W. Europe spanned by 30 rly. bridges; linked to Rhône by 1985 and Rhine-Main-Danube canal allows navigation from N. Sea to Black Sea for 3,500 km. (Trans European waterway); very polluted; 1,280 km long.

Rhine-Hern, canal, **Germany**; impt. Ruhr waterway, part of Mitelland Canal; 38 km long.

Rhineland Palatinate (Rheinland-Pfalz), *Land*, **Germany**; borders France, Luxembourg and Belgium; drained by Rhine and Moselle, inc. Hunsrück and Eifel mtns.; arable agr. in Rhine valley; vineyards; cap. Mainz; a. 19,852 km; p. (1992) 3,821,000.

Rhode Island, st., New England, **USA**; 'Little Rhody'; admitted to Union 1790; st. flower violet, st. bird R.I. Red; washed by Atl. Oc., surrounded by Mass. and Conn.; divided by Narragansett Bay, with many Is. lgst. being that from which the st. takes its name; smallest and most densely populated st.; famous for poultry; major ind. textiles; cap. Providence; a. 3,144 km²; p. (1990) 1,003,464.

Rhodes (Rhodos), I., Dodecanese Is.; off S.W. cst., Anatolia, belonging to **Greece**; cap. R.; p. (1981) 87,831.

Rhodes, cap. of I. of Rhodes, **Greece**; on N.E. cst.; picturesque; p. (1981) 41,425.

Rhodesia. *See* **Zimbabwe**.

Rhodope Mtns. *See* **Rodopi Mtns.**

Rhondda, t., l. gov. dist., Mid Glamorgan, **Wales**; in narrow R. valley; former coal-mng. ctr.; lt. inds. introduced since 1930s depression; picturesque a. in upper R. valley; p. (1993) 78,500 (dist.).

Rhône, dep., S.E. **France**; drained by R. Rhône, and its trib. R. Saône, which unite at Lyons; agr. grain, potatoes, wine; vine-growing, many mnfs., silks, textiles; cap. Lyons; a. 2,859 km²; p. (1990) 1,509,000.

Rhône, R., **Switzerland** and **France**; rises in Rhône glacier of St. Gotthard mtn. gr., and flows through L. of Geneva and E. France to G. of Lyons in Mediterranean; power stas. at Sion and Geneva; canals, dams, locks and power stas. form part of Fr. Rhône Valley project (1937–72); linked to Rhine by 1985; 811 km long.

Rhône-Alpes, region, S.E. **France**; inc.deps. Ain, Ardèche, Drôme, Isère, Loire, Rhône, Savoie, Haute-Savoie; based on the upper Rhône valley, inc. important industrial ctrs. of Lyon and Grenoble; p. (1990) 5,350,700.

Rhône-Saône Corridor, routeway, **France**; impt. transport artery using Rhône, Saône R. valleys as a means for linking Paris, Lorraine and Rhine rift valley with Mediterranean cst.; rlys., roads, with major pt. of Marseille serving the S. terminus.

Rhuddlan, l. gov. dist., Clwyd, **Wales**; cstl. a. of Rhyl, Prestatyn and St. Asaph; p. (1993) 55,000.

Rhyl, t., Rhuddlan, Clwyd, N. **Wales**; at entrance Vale of Clwyd; resort developed from sm. fishing v.; serves Lancs. conurbs.; p. (1981) 22,714.

Rhymney, t., Mid Glamorgan, **Wales**; on R. Rhymney, E. of Merthyr Tydfil; former colly. and iron founding ctr.; engin.; p. (1981) 7,360.

Rhymney Valley, l. gov. dist., Mid Glamorgan, **Wales**; based on Rhymney and inc. Caerphilly, Bedwas and Gelligaer; p. (1993) 104,300.

Ribble, R., North Yorks., Lancs., **Eng.**; rises in Pennines, flows W. to Irish Sea nr. pt. of Preston; 120 km long.

Ribble Valley, l. gov. dist., N. Lancs., **Eng.**; inc. Forest of Bowland and ts. of Clitheroe and Longridge; p. (1993) 51,800.

Ribe, mkt. t., Jutland, S. **Denmark**; admin. ctr. of R. prov.; impt, mediaeval c.; Romanesque cath.; many fine bldgs.; p. (1990) 17,872.

Ribeirão Prêto, t., São Paulo st., **Brazil**; mkt. in rich agr. a., coffee, cotton, sugar; p. (1991) 430,805.

Richard's Bay, Natal, **S. Africa**; new pt. to supplement congested Durban; on natural harbour; silting problem but designed for bulk carriers; plans to attract ass. industl. development.

Richborough, pt., Kent, **Eng.**; at mouth of R. Stour; Caesar's ch. pt., Roman remains; pt. has been privately redeveloped; chemicals.

Richmond, t., North Yorks., **Eng.**; at E. foot of Pennines on R. Swale; mkt. t., agr. tr.; 14th cent. grammar school; Norman cas.; now as Richmondshire forms l. gov. dist. with surrounding a. of Aysgarth and Leyburn; p. (1993) 45,800 (dist.).

Richmond, c., Cal., **USA**; deepwater pt.; oil refining; car assembly, chemicals, electronics; p. (1980) 74,676.

Richmond, c., cap. of Va., **USA**; on falls on R. James; pt. at head of navigation; financial, and tr. ctr.; tobacco inds., and mkt.; chemicals, iron and steel; p. (1990) 203,056 (c.), 866,000 (met. a. with Petersburg).

Richmond upon Thames, outer bor., Greater London, **Eng.**; inc. Barnes, Richmond and Twickenham; industl. and residtl.; park and Kew Gardens; p. (1993) 166,600.

Rickmansworth, t., Three Rivers, Herts., **Eng.**; residtl. sub of London; p. (1981) 29,408.

Ridder, (Leninogorsk), c. **Kazakhstan**; in Altai mtns.; lead, zinc, and silver mines; metallurgical plants; p. (1990) 69,200.

Rideau Canal, Ont., **Canada**; from Ottawa R. at Ottawa to Kingston on L. Ontario; 211 km long.

Riesa, t., Saxony, **Germany**; R. pt. on Elbe R. nr. Meissen; p. (1981) 51,857.

Riesengebirge, mtn. range, between Silesia **(Poland)** and Bohemia **(ČSSR)**; highest peak Schneekoppe (Czech Snežka, Polish Sniezka), 1,604 m.

Rieti, Latium, **Italy**; an anc. Sabine c. with mediaeval townscape, in fertile Apennine basin; route ctr. and cap. of R. prov.; chemicals, sugar refinery, textiles; p. (1981) 43,079.

Riff or Rif, mtns., **Morocco**, N.W. Africa; extend along N. African cst. for 320 km from Straits of Gibraltar; inaccessible and economically unattractive, terr. of semi-nomadic tribes; rise to over 2,100 m in many places.

Riga, cap. of **Latvia**; Baltic pt.; exp. wheat, flax, hemp, dairy produce; industl. ctr., diesel rly. engin., furniture; univ.; local bathing beaches; p. (1991) 910,200.

Rigi, mtn., nr. L. Lucerne, **Switzerland**; viewpoint reached by rack and pinion rly.; 1,801 m.

Rijeka-Susak, c., **Croatia** (formerly Yugoslavia); formerly Fiume, ceded to Yugoslavia by Italy after second world war; rival pt. to Trieste on Adriatic Sea; oil refining, shipbldg., tobacco, chemicals; hydroelectric power; p. (1991) 167,364.

Rimac, R., Lima dep., **Peru**; rises in W. cordillera of Andes and flows W. to Pac. Oc.; provides water for irrigation and for c. of Lima; 120 km long.

Rimini, c., Emilia-Romagna, **Italy**; on Adriatic cst. at junc. of Via Emilia and Via Flaminia; mkt. for fertile agr. a.; sm. inds.; bathing resort; p. (1992) 129,876.

Ringerike, t., Buskerud, **Norway**; new t., 40 km N.W. of Oslo and inc. former t. of Hönefoss; p. (1990) 27,433.

Riobamba, t., Chimborazo, **Ecuador**; on R. St. Juan; woollens, cotton gds., cement, ceramics; Inca palace ruins; p. (1990) 94,505.

Rio Branco, R., flows c. 560 km from Guiana Highlands through Brazil to join Rio Negro.

Rio Branco, t., cap. of Acre st., **Brazil**; p. (1985) 145,900.

Rio Cuarto, t., Cordoba prov., **Argentina**; agr. ctr.; p. (1991) 217,717.

Rio de Janeiro, c., spt., S.E. **Brazil**; cap. of Guanabara st., on G. Bay, Alt. Oc.; former fed. cap.; beautiful natural harbour, many fine bldgs., Sugar Loaf mtn., Copacabana beach; flourishing tr. and inds.; mnfs. inc. textiles, foodstuffs, pharmaceutics, china, sheet glass; oil refining; p. (1991) 5,336,178 .

Rio de Janeiro, st., S.E. **Brazil**; on Atl. Oc.; consolidated with Guanabara (1975); consists of cst. plain, central Sero do Mar escarpment, fertile Paraíba R. basin in W.; coffee, sugar, fruit; ctr. of heavy ind.; cement, textiles, sugar refineries at Campos, steel wks. at Volta Redonda; offshore oil finds in Campos basin; cap. Niterói; a. 42,735 km²; p. (1991) 12,584,108.

Rio Grande, headstream of R. Paraná., **Brazil**; Furnas dam, Estreito dam for hydroelec. power; 1,040 km long.

Rio Grande, R., flows from st. of Col. through N.M. to G. of Mexico; forms bdy. between Texas, **USA** and **Mexico**; Elephant Butte, Caballo, and Falcon multi-purpose dams; known also as Rio Grande do Norte and Rio Bravo; c. 3,016 km long.

Rio Grande do Norte, st., N.E. **Brazil**; cst. plain rising to S. plateau; climate semi-arid; cotton, sugar, salt, scheelite; cap. Natal; a. 53,038 km²; p. (1991) 2,413,618.

Rio Grande do Sul, st., S. **Brazil**; grassy plains, rolling plateaux; cool climate; stock-raising, meat-processing, wheat, wine, wool; lge. coal deposits at São Jeronimo; cap. Pôrto Alegre; a. 267,684 km²; p. (1991) 9,127,611.

Rioja, region and prov., N. **Spain**; upper Ebro valley; famous for wines and orange groves; ch. ctr. Logroño; p. (1991) 265,823.

Riom, t., Puy-de-Dôme dep., **France**; former cap. of Auvergne; old bldgs. built of lava; p. (1982) 18,901.

Rio Muni, terr., **Equatorial Guinea**; former Spanish terr., on cst. between Cameroon and Gabon, inc. offshore Is. of Corisco, Elobey Grande, Elobey Chico; with Biako forms Equatorial Guinea; equatorial forest; exp. tree prods. of cacao, coffee, hardwood; ch. t. Bata; a. 26,003 km²; p. (1983) 240,804.

Rion, R., **Georgia**; flows from Caucasus to Black Sea; lower half navigable; hydroelec. sta. at Kutaisi. (In Greek mythology the R. Phasis of the Argonauts.)

Rio Negro, prov., **Argentina**; in N. Patagonia, irrigated agr. in R. valley, fruits, grain crops; elsewhere stock-raising; cap. Viedma; a. 201,010 km²; p. (1991) 506,314.

Rio Negro, dep., **Uruguay**; livestock fattening from N. Uruguay; grain crops; ch. t. and cap. Fray Bentos; a. 8,466 km²; p. (1985) 48,241.

Rio Tinto, t., **Spain**; at W. end of Sierra Morena 64 km N.E. of Huelva; major world ctr. of copper production.

Riouw-Lingga Archipelago, I. gr., **Indonesia**; S. of Malaya; Bintan lgst. I. where bauxite mng.; pepper and rubber cultivation; a. 5,905 km².

Ripley, mkt. t., Amber Valley, Derbys., **Eng.**; 11 km N.E. of Derby; coal, iron, heavy engin., bricks, agr. implements; p. (1981) 18,691.

Ripon, c., North Yorks., **Eng.**; on R. Ure; cath.; old mkt. square; old custom of wakeman; tourism; p. (1981) 11,952.

Risca, t., Gwent, **Wales**; on R. Ebbw; former coal-mng. dist.; limestone quarrying; bricks, plastics; p. (1981) 14,860.

Risdon, t., Tasmania, **Australia**; first white settlement in Tasmania, opposite Hobart; electrometallurgy.

Rishton, t., Hyndburn, Lancs., **Eng.**; at N. foot of Rossendale Fells, 6 km N.E. of Blackburn; p. (1981) 6,212.

Rive-de-Gier, t., Loire dep., **France**; on R. Gier, nr. Lyons; coal mng.; iron and steel, glass; p. (1982) 15,850.

Rivera, dep., **Uruguay**; on Brazilian border; noted for cattle and sheep ranches; cap. R.; a. 9,824 km²; p. (1985) 88,800.

Rivera, t., cap. of R. dep., **Uruguay**; on Brazilian frontier opposite Santa Ana; agr. mkt.; p. (1985) 56,335.

Riverina, pastoral cty., N.S.W., **Australia**; between Lachlan-Murrumbidgee and Murray Rs.; merino sheep in W., good wheat yields in E.; gtr. crop variety with irrigation; a. 68,894 km².

River Rouge, t., Mich., **USA**; ctr. of Ford car mnf.; many heavy inds.; rapidly growing t. p. (1980) 12,912.

Riverside, t., Cal., **USA**; ctr. for citrus fruit packing and tr.; resort; p. (1990) 226,605 (t.), 2,589,000 (met. a. with San Bernardino).

Riviera, the belt of cst. between the Alps and the Mediterranean from Spezia to Hyères, **France** and **Italy**; picturesque scenery, sheltered, mild climate; fashionable health resorts.

Riyadh, t., royal cap. of **Saudi Arabia**; 368 km inland from Persian G.; palace; univ.; route and tr. ctr., linked by rail with pt. of Zahran; p. (1988) 2 m.

Rizaiyeh (**Urmia**), c., cap. of Azerbaijan prov., **Iran**; nr. L. Urmia; comm. ctr.; birthplace of Zoroaster; p. (1983) 262,588.

Rizal, prov., central Luzon, **Philippines**; rapidly growing prov. in fertile Central Plain; new inds. developing; cap. Pasig; a. 2,049 km²; p. (1990) 980,194.

Rize, t. and prov., **Turkey**; nr. Trabzon, on Black Sea; ctr. of Turkish tea inds.; p. (1985) 50,221 (t.), (1990) 348,776 (prov.).

Road Town, spt., Tortola; cap. of the Brit. Virgin Is.; tr. in fish, poultry; p. (1991) 6,330.

Roanne, t., Loire dep., **France**; on R. Loire; château ruins; textiles; p. (1990) 42,848 (t.), 77,160 (met.a.).

Roanoke, R., Va., and N.C., **USA**; flows into Albemarle Sound; hydroelec. power; 656 km long.

Roanoke, c., S.W. Va., **USA**; between Blue Ridge and Allegheny mtns.; rly. junc.; engin. p. (1984) 100,700 (c.), 222,700 (met. a.).

Roanoke I., off cst. N.C., **USA**; attempted settlement of colony by Raleigh.

Roaring Creek, Belize, Central America; site of new cap. 80 km inland, at junc. of W. highway with Hummingbird highway.

Robben I., at entrance of Table Bay, Cape Prov., **S. Africa**; penal settlement and former leper colony.

Robin Hood's Bay, v., North Yorks., **Eng.**; picturesque site in inlet; tourism, fishing.

Robson, Mt., Canada, on B.C. and Alberta border; alt. 3,956 m; in Nat. Park.

Rocha, dep., **Uruguay**; borders Atl. Oc.; a. of cattle and sheep rearing; cap. R.; a. 11,850 km²; p. (1985) 66,440.

Rochdale, t., met. dist., Gtr. Manchester, **Eng.**; at S. foot of Rossendale Fells, on R. Roch; textiles, engin., asbestos; co-operative movement started here 1844; p. (1993) 206,800.

Rochefort, t., Charente-Maritime dep., **France**; fishing pt.; former impt. naval base; p. (1982) 27,716.

Rochester-upon-Medway, t., l. gov. dist., Kent, **Eng.**; on R. Medway, adjoining Chatham; cath., cas.; many associations with Dickens; aeronautical, elec. and mechanical engin., paint, varnish, cement; p. (1993) 146,200 (dist.).

Rochester, t., Minn., **USA**; famous for Mayo clinic, and Mayo medical research ctr.; p. (1980) 57,890.

Rochester, c., N.Y., **USA**; on Genesee R.; univ.; cameras, films, optical instruments, thermometers, electronic equipment; hydroelectric power; p. (1990) 231,636 (c.), 1,002,000 (met. a.).

Rochford, l. gov. dist., Essex, **Eng.**; cstl. a. inc. Rochford and Rayleigh; p. (1993) 75,900.

Rock, R., Wis., Ill., **USA**; formerly home of native Indians; focus of white settlement since 1830; 456 km long.

Rockall, sm. I., **Atl. Oc.**; lies 320 km W. of Outer Hebrides; forms hgst. part of submarine bank which forms gd. fishing grnds.; uninhabited; annexed by Britain 1955; formally incorporated into Inverness-shire (1972) to ensure control of oil and natural gas deposits; claimed also by Ireland and Iceland; rock samples aged 1,000 million years place it with some Canadian rocks.

Rockall Deep, submarine trench, N. **Atl. Oc.**; between N.W. Ireland and Rockall I.; suspected oil and natural gas reserves.

Rockford, c., Ill., **USA**; serves agr. dist.; agr. machin., machin. tools; p. (1990) 139,426 (c.), 283,719 (met. a.).

Rockhampton, t., pt., Queensland, **Australia**; on Tropic of Capricorn; outlet for vast pastoral and mng. a.; comm. cap. of central Queensland; meat-preserving; p. (1991) 62,475.

Rockingham, t., W. **Australia**; satellite of Perth; major pt. planned to serve Kwinana; p. (1981) 24,932.

Rock Island, c., Ill., **USA**; on R. Mississippi; former site of US arsenal; agr. machin., timber and agr. processing; p. (1980) 46,928.

Rocky Mtns., vast mtn. chain, N. **America**; extend from Alaska, through Canada, USA to Mexico; made up of several parallel ranges separated by intermontane basins and plateaux; barrier to spread of settlers to W. cst. in 19th cent.; climatic barrier; extensive snow and glacier fields in N.; dry desert landscapes in S.; many Nat. Parks; sparse p.; hydroelectric power; hgst. peak Mt. Logan (6,054 m); length 5,120 km.

Rodez, t., cap. of Aveyron dep., **France**; on R. Aveyron; cath.; woollens; p. (1990) 26,794.

Rodopi (Rhodope) Mtns., range S. **Bulgaria**; rise to 3,100 m.

Rodosto. See Tekirdag.

Rodriguez, I., Brit. dependency of **Mauritius**, Indian Oc.; 560 km N.E. of Mauritius; mainly agr. and fishing; cap. Port Mathurin; a. 109 km²; p. (1991) 34,379.

Roermond, t., Limburg prov., **Neth.**; on R. Maas; minster; textiles; p. (1993) 42,744.

Roeselare, (Roulers) t., W. Flanders, **Belgium**; on R. Lys, nr. Kortrijk, textile ctr.; p. (1993) 53,455.

Rogerstone, t., Gwent, **Wales**; on R. Ebbw; lge. aluminium wks.

Rohtak, t., Haryana, **India**; N.W. of Delhi; p. (1991) 216,096.

Roissy-en-France; 26 km N.E. of Paris, **France**; site of Charles de Gaulle airport; p. (1982) 1,411.

Roman, t., **Romania**; on R. Moldava; cath.; agr. processing; p. (1983) 67,962.

Romania (Rumania), Rep. of, S.E. **Europe**; country bounded by Ukraine, Moldavia, Hungary, Yugoslavia, Bulgaria, and Black Sea; Carpathian mtns., Transylvanian Alps, wide Walachian plain, Moldavian plateau; drained by Danube and its tribs.; cold winters and hot summers; since second world war transformation of economy from agr. to industl. basis, although agr. still impt., contributing many exps., especially timber, wine, fruit; major pt. Constanta on Black Sea; oilfields at Ploiesti; cap. Bucharest; ch. tr. partners former USSR and E. Europe; Danube used for navigation; Iron Gates power and navigation system being constructed in co-operation with Yugoslavia; tourism from W. Europe and N. America encouraged; measures to stimulate birth rate; revolution 1989, popular uprising against Ceaucescu dictatorship; a. 237,428 km²; p. (1992) 22·76 m.

Rome (Roma), cap. of **Italy**, and of Latium and Rome prov.; on R. Tiber, 24 km from sea; in Roman legend founded by Romulus 753 B.C.; once cap. of anc. Roman empire; inc. Vatican c., ctr. of Roman Catholic Church; situated on original "seven hills," and along the R.; leading cultural ctr.; St. Peter's church, Colosseum, Pantheon; univ.; admin. ctr.; tourism; created cap. of United Italy 1871; p. (1992) 2,723,327.

Romford. *See* **Havering.**

Romney Marsh, coastal marsh, Shepway, Kent, **Eng.**; formed by blocking of R. Rother by shingle spit of Dungeness which extends from Rye to Hythe; largely drained; pastures for special Romney Marsh breed of sheep; a. 129 km².

Romsey, t., Test Valley, Hants., **Eng.**; on R. Test, 14 km N.W. of Southampton; mkt. ctr.; Norman abbey; p. (1981) 12,941.

Ronaldshay, North, most N. of Orkney Is., **Scot.**; p. (1991) 92.

Ronaldshay, South, most S. of Orkney Is. **Scot.**; p. (1991) 943.

Roncesvalles, mtn. pass in Pyrenees, Navarre, **Spain**; 32 km N.E. of Pamplona; defeat and death of Roland 778.

Ronda, t., Málaga, **Spain**; in Andalusia; anc. Moorish t., divided by deep gorge crossed by bridge; p. (1981) 31,383.

Rondônia, st., **Brazil**; on Bolivian border; forest covered; forest prods.; nomadic Indian tribes; cap. Pôrto Velho; a. 243,071 km²; p. (1991) 1,130,400.

Rønne, t., **Denmark**; cap. of Bornholm I.; fish. pt.; shipyards, ceramics; p. (1990) 15,187.

Ronse (Renaix), t., **Belgium**; nr. Ghent; textile ctr.; p. (1982) 24,287.

Roodepoort-Maraisburg, t., Transvaal, **S. Africa**; ctr. Witwatersrand goldfields; p. (1980) 165,315.

Roosendaal, t., S.W. of N. Brabant, **Neth.**, sugarrefining; p. (1993) 62,115.

Roosevelt Dam (1903–11), Arizona, **USA**; on R. Salt in canyon E. of Phoenix on edge of Col. plateau; used for irrigation and hydroelectric power; part of Salt river project.

Roquefort-sur-Soulzon, t., S.E. Aveyron, **France**; caves in limestone cliffs used for ripening cheese; p. (1982) 880.

Roraima, mtn., at junc. of boundaries of **Brazil**, **Guyana,** and **Venezuela**; 2,852 m, hgst. point of Guiana Highlands.

Roraima (Rio Branco), fed. terr., **Brazil**; underdeveloped rain forest; cap. Boa Vista; a. 214,320 km²; p. (1991) 215,790.

Rosa Monte, Pennine Alps, Swiss-Italian border; alt. 4,637 m.

Rosario, t., Santa Fé, **Argentina**; second t. of rep.; R. pt. on Paraná R.; agr.-processing, iron and steel, lt. inds.; univ., cath.; p. (1991) 1,078,374.

Roscommon, co. t., Roscommon, **R.o.I.**; mkt.; cas., priory; p. (1986) 1,673.

Roscommon, inland co., Connaught, **R.o.I.**;

extensive peat bog and Ls.; pastoral agr., cap. R.; a. 2,458 km²; p. (1986) 54,592.

Rosetta (Rashid), t., Lower **Egypt**; nr. Rosetta mouth of Nile; Rosetta stone found nearby gave key to Egyptian hieroglyphics.

Roskilde, t., spt., Sjaelland, **Denmark**; former cap.; cath. contains tombs of kings; admin. ctr. of R. prov.; p. (1990) 49,081.

Ross and Cromarty, former co., l. gov. dist., Highland Reg.; **Scot.**; extends from N. Sea to Atl. Oc.; most of a. over 300 m, lake-covered; cattle breeding, fishing, tourism; a. 4,999 km²; p. (1993) 50,260.

Rossendale Fells (or Forest), upland, S.E. Lancs./ Gtr. Manchester, **Eng.**; extension of Pennines between Rs. Mersey and Ribble; millstone grit moorland used for reservoirs; alt. mainly above 360 m; now forms l. gov. dist. **Rossendale,** in Lancs. inc. ts. of Haslingden, Rawtenstall, Bacup and Whitworth; p. (1993) 65,800.

Ross Dependency, Antarctica; N.Z. sector; inlet of Ross Sea; a. 414,400 km².

Rosslare, spt., Wexford, **R.o.I.**; on extreme S.E. of Ireland; steamer connections to Fishguard; p. (1986) 704.

Ross-on-Wye, t., South Herefordshire, Hereford and Worcs., **Eng.**; mkt., tourism; p. (1981) 7,182.

Ross Sea, sea extending to 85° S. in **Antarctic**.

Rostock, c. Mecklenburg - West Pomerania, **Germany**; pt. nr. Baltic cst., outport of Warnemünde; shipbldg., fish-processing, chemicals; univ.; mediaeval t.; p. (1990) 246,600.

Rostov, c., **Russia**; pt. on R. Don, nr. Azov Sea (Black Sea); one of Russia's finest and oldest cs.; ctr. of agr. dist.; grain mkt.; agr.-processing; univ.; p. (1989) 1,019,000.

Rosyth, t., Dunfermline, **Scot.**; naval dockyard.

Rothamsted, v., Herts., **Eng.**; in Chiltern Hills, S. of Harpenden; famous agr. research sta.

Rother, l. gov. dist., East Sussex, **Eng.**; rural a. inc. Rye, Bexhill and Battle; p. (1993) 84,800.

Rother, R., Derbys. and South Yorks., **Eng.**; flows to R. Don at Rotherham; 34 km long.

Rother, R., East Sussex and Kent, **Eng.**; rises in the Weald, flows S.E. into English Channel at Rye; 50 km long.

Rotherham, t., met. dist., South Yorks., **Eng.**; on R. Don, 6 km N.E. of Sheffield; coal mining, iron, steel, wire, springs, glass; p. (1993) 255,700.

Rothes, burgh, Moray, **Scot.**; on R. Spey 19 km S.E. of Elgin; p. (1991) 1,345.

Rothesay, royal burgh, Argyll and Bute., **Scot.**; on E. cst. of I. of Bute in F. of Clyde; tourism; p. (1991) 5,264.

Rothwell, West Yorks., **Eng.**; on R. Aire, suburb of Leeds; coal-mng. ctr., engin.; p. (1981) 29,142.

Rotorua, c., leading spa of **N.Z.**; on volcanic plateau, Auckland, N.I.; hot springs; p. (1991) 65,096.

Rotterdam, c., spt. **Neth.**; Europe's lgst. spt., on Nieuwe Maas, part of Rhine-Maas-Scheldt delta; linked to outport Europoort (*q.v*) by New Waterway; serves hinterland of Rhine valley and central Europe; freeport; processing of imports, especially oil refining and petrochemical inds.; badly damaged in second world war; p. (1993) 596,623 (c.), 1,069,356 (met. a.).

Roubaix, t., Nord dep., **France**; nr. Lille; on Roubaix canal close to Belgian frontier; major textile ctr., especially for woollens; p. (1990) 98,179.

Rouen, c., Seine-Maritime dep., **France**; gr. R. pt., 125 km up R. Seine; oil refining, textiles, chemicals; cath.; birthplace of Joan of Arc burned here; birthplace of Corneille and Flaubert; badly damaged in second world war; p. (1990) 105,470 (c.), 380,161 (met. a.).

Rousay, Orkney Is., **Scot.**; p. (1991) 291.

Roussillon, former prov., S. **France**; now part. of Pyrénées-Orientales; irrigated by many sm. streams; olives, wine, fruit; historical cap. Perpignan.

Rovaniemi, t., **Finland**; on Kemi R.; timber and saw mills; p. (1991) 33,954.

Rovigo, prov., Venetia, **Italy**; part of N. Italian plain extending to Adriatic; impt. agr. dist.; cap. R.; a. 218 km²; p. (1981) 253,508.

Rovigo, t., cap. of R. prov., **Italy**; on R. Adige, cath., cas. ruins, palace; p. (1981) 52,218.

Rovno, c., cap. of R., oblast, **Ukraine**; rly. junct.; industl. ctr.; ruins of mediaeval palace; p. (1990) 232,900.

Roxburgh, former co., S. **Scot.**; sheeprearing

hilly cty. with wool-based inds.; now forms l. gov. dist. in Borders Reg.; a. 1,538 km²; p. (1993) 35,350.

Royal Oak, t., Mich., **USA**; residtl.; Detroit zoological park here; p. (1980) 70,893.

Royston, mkt. t., North Herts., **Eng.**; at N. foot of E. Anglian Heights, 11 km N.E. of Baldock; p. (1981) 11,799.

Royton, t., Gtr. Manchester, **Eng.**; 13 km N.E. of Manchester; textiles; p. (1981) 21,233.

Ruanda-Urundi. See Rwanda and Burundi.

Ruapehu, highest mtn., N.I., **N.Z.**; volcanic peak at S. extremity of central volcanic dist.; crater L. at summit; alt. 2,798 m; gives name to dist.; p. (1991) 18,104.

Rubicon, R., central **Italy**; flows to Adriatic; crossed by Julius Caesar and his armies 49 B.C.; has been identified with the Fiumicino or the Uso.

Ruhtsowsk, t., W. Siberia, **Russia**; agr. engin.; p. (1989) 172,000.

Ruby Mines, dist., Mandalay, Upper **Myanmar**; hilly region of Shan plateau, once famous for rubies.

Ruda Slaska, t., Katowice, **Poland**; coal-mng. ctr.; iron and steel wks.; p. (1989) 169,017.

Rudnyy, t., **Kazakhstan**; t. 48 km S.W. of Kustanay; iron-ore mng. and dressing plant supplying Magnitogorsk; p. (1990) 126,200.

Rudolf, L., N.W. **Kenya**; in Great Rift Valley; a. 9,065 km²; ctr. of semi-arid region; renamed **Turkana**.

Rudolph I., N. of Franz Josef Land Arctic Oc.; **Russia** naval base; met. sta.

Rudolstadt, t., **Germany**; on R. Saale, in former st. of Thuringia; seat of counts of Schwarzburg-Rudolstadt (1584–1918); tourism; porcelain; p. (1989) 31,776.

Rueil-Malmaison, sub. of Paris, **France**; château; tomb of the empress Josephine; p. (1990) 67,323.

Rufiji, R., **Tanzania**; E. Africa; flows to Indian Oc.; 720 km long.

Rufisque, t., **Senegal** sm. spt. nr. Dakar; growing industl. ctr. for consumer gds.

Rugby, mkt. t., l. gov. dist., Warwicks, **Eng.**; on R. Avon, 18 km E. of Coventry; famous public school; elec. and gen. engin., motor and aircraft patterns; p. (1993) 86,200 (dist.).

Rugeley, mkt. t., Staffs, **Eng.**; on R. Trent, 14 km S.E. of Stafford; coal, iron, tanning; expanded t.; p. (1981) 24,340.

Rügen, I., **Germany**; in Baltic Sea, off Stralsund; ch. t. Bergen; pt. Sassnitz, terminus of train ferry; steamer services to Trelleborg, Sweden.

Ruhr, industl. dist., **Germany**; lies to E. of R. Rhine, on either side of R. Ruhr; rich coalfield; impt. iron and steel, heavy engin. inds. based on local coal and iron ore from Luxembourg, Spain, Sweden; water communications to N. Sea along R. Rhine and Dortmund–Ems Canal; ch. ts. Essen, Duisburg, Düsseldorf, Dortmund, Bochum.

Ruhr, R., **Germany**; trib. of Rhine; flows S. of Ruhr conurb.; 232 km long.

Rukwa, L., E. **Africa**; between L. Tanganyika and L. Malawi in the rift valley; 48 km by 19 im, a. increasing.

Rum, I., Inner Hebrides, Lochaber, **Scot.**; nature reserve, highland ecology; a. 168 km².

Rumaila, **Iraq**; oilfield; pipeline links to the Zubair–Fao system.

Rum Jungle, N.T., **Australia**; 64 km S.E. of Darwin; site of Australia's first major uranium project; ceased operation in 1970.

Runcorn, t., Halton, Cheshire, **Eng.**; on S. side of Mersey estuary; new t. (1964); chemicals; pipeline carrying petrochemical feedstock from Teeside; new Runcorn–Widnes bridge over Mersey and Manchester Ship Canal opened 1961 (lgst. span arch in Europe); p. of new t. (1981) 63,813.

Rungis, Paris, **France**; site of major new mkt. to replace Les Halles; nr. Orly airpt., Val de Marne dep.; p. (1982) 2,650.

Runnymede, l. gov. dist., Surrey, **Eng.**; comprises Egham and Chertsey; p. (1993) 75,100.

Ruse, t., **Bulgaria**; on R. Danube, opposite Giurgiu in Romania; univ.; Roman t.; agr. processing; p. (1990) 192,365.

Rushcliffe, l. gov. dist., Notts., **Eng.**; a. S.E. of Nottingham inc. West Bridgeford; p. (1993) 101,500.

Rushden, t., East Northants., **Eng.**; 5 km E. of Wellingborough; shoes; p. (1981) 22,253.

Rushmoor, l. gov. dist., Hants., **Eng.**; small a. of Farnborough and Aldershot; p. (1993) 85,600.

Rüsselsheim, t., **Germany**; impt. car factory; p. (1986) 57,300.

Russia, CIS former constituent rep., USSR; lgst. rep. by a. and p.; economic development; inds. centred on St Petersburg and Moscow with new inds. being developed in Urals and Kuznetz basin; extends from Baltic to Pac. Oc. (8,000 km), from Arctic to Caspian Sea (4,000 km); part of N. European plain in W. and Siberian plain in E., separated by Ural mtns.; major Rs. Volga, Don, Ob, Yenisey, Lena, Amur; gr. variety in climate and p. density; major agr. region for wheat, sugarbeet, livestock; vast mineral deposits have aided economic growth; oil around Volga valley; metal lic ores from Ural and Black Sea, hydroelectric power from Volga, Yenesey and Ob Rs.; cap. Moscow; a. 16,838,885 km²; p. (1992) 148·7 m.

Rustavi, t., **Georgia**; t., 32 km S.E. Tbilisi; iron and steel; lge. metallurgical plant; p. (1990) 160,400.

Rustenburg, t., Transvaal, **S. Africa**; on N.W. edge of High Veld, 96 km W. of Pretoria; local mkt. for agr. produce; agr.-processing.

Rutbah, t., **Iraq**; on oil pipeline from Iraq to Haifa; impt. ctr. on trans-desert routes.

Rutherglen, royal burgh, Strathclyde Reg., **Scot.**; on R. Clyde, S.E. of Glasgow; chemicals, tubes, paper, wire ropes, bolts.

Ruthin, t., Glyndwr, Clwyd, **Wales**; Vale of Clwyd, 13 km S.E. of Denbigh; p. (1981) 4,430.

Rutland, former Midland co., **Eng.**; sm. co. of 394 km², now part of Leics. and l. gov. dist. based on Oakham; p. (1993) 33,400.

Rutland Water, reservoir, Leics., **Eng.**

Ruwenzori mtn. range, on **Uganda-Zaïre** border; overlooking W. arm of Gt. Rift Valley, midway between L. Mobutu Seso and L. Edward; hgst. peaks, Mt. Margherita (5,123 m), Mt. Alexandra (5,109 m); lower slopes covered in equatorial rain forest, coffee plantations on middle slopes above 1,500 m.

Rwanda, indep. rep., **Central Africa**; former kingdom of Ruanda, part of UN trust terr. of Ruanda-Urundi under Belgian admin. (until 1962); sm., landlocked st., S. of equator, consisting of upland plateau at 1,200 m; mainly subsistence agr. under gt. strain with rapid p. growth; coffee (ch. exp.), cotton, pyrethrum (3rd lgst. world producer); cattle; tin, tungsten and natural gas discoveries; little ind.; cap. Kigali; a. 26,338 km²; p. (1991) 7·43 m. The country was locked in bitter tribal warfare in 1994.

Ryazan, c., cap. of R. oblast, **Russia**; on Oka R.; food inds., agr. machin., footwear, chemicals; mediaeval architecture; p. (1989) 515,000.

Rybinsk, c., cap. of R. oblast, **Russia**; on Upper Volga; tr. and shipping ctr. since 16th cent.; site of hydroelectric power sta.; shipbldg., engin.; renamed Andropov 1984 to honour dead General Secretary; p. (1989) 251,000.

Rybinsk Sea (**Rybinsk Reservoir**), **Russia**; artificial L.; created behind dams on R. Volga and R. Sheksna at Rybinsk; part of scheme to regulate flow of R. Volga and to incorporate it in a vast inland waterway system; opened 1945; a. 3,885 km.

Rybnik, t., Katowice prov., S.W. **Poland**; ctr. of coal-mng. dist.; p. (1989) 142,059.

Rydal Water, L., nr. Ambleside, Cumbria, **Eng.**; adjacent v. contains Rydal Mount, home of Wordsworth.

Ryde, t., Medina, I. of Wight, **Eng.**; on N.E. cst.; yachting ctr. and seaside resort; boat and yacht bldg.; steamer connection across Spithead to Portsmouth; p. (1981) 24,346.

Rye, t., Rother, East Sussex, **Eng.**; at mouth of R. Rother to W. of Dungeness; one of the Cinque pts.; Ypres cas.; tourist ctr.; p. (1981) 4,293.

Ryedale, l. gov. dist., North Yorks., **Eng.**; lge. a. inc. Malton, Pickering, Norton, Kirby Moorside and Helmsley; p. (1993) 92,600.

Ryton, t., Tyne and Wear, **Eng.**; on R. Tyne, W. of Newcastle; p. (1981) 15,023.

Ryukyu Is., archipelago, between Kyushu I., **Japan**, and Taiwan; ch. t. Naha on Okinawa I.; following second world war Is. S. of Lat. 30° N. occupied by USA; Amami and Tokara grs. returned to Japan 1953; American military installations on Okinawa withdrawn 1972; lge. Is. mtnous., volcanic; sweet potatoes, sugarcane, pineapples; 3 lge. oil refineries; a. 2,196 km²; p. (1990) 1,222,398.

Rzeszów, c. and prov., S.E. Poland; at foot of Carpathian highlands; route ctr.; growing industl. t.; p. (1989) 150,702, (c.), 716,300 (prov.).

S

Saale, R., **Germany**; rises in Fichtelgebirge flows N. through Thuringia to Elbe; attractive, well wooded valley; irrigation; hydroelec. power; 360 km long.

Saalfeld, t., Gera, **Germany**; on R. Saale; famous cas., iron-mng.; machin., chocolate; p. (1989) 34,037.

Saarbrücken, c., cap. of Saarland, **Germany**; on R. Saar, nr. Fr. border; cas.; rich coalfield; iron and steel wks., textiles, leather, paper, oil refining at Klarenthal nearby; p. (1990) 191,500.

Saaremaa (**Osel**), I., Baltic Sea; at entrance to G. of Riga, **Estonia**; low plateau, bleak and barren; ch. t. Kingisepp (Kuressaare); a. 2,720 km².

Saarland, *Land*, **Germany**; heavy inds. based on lge. coalfields; drained by R. Saar; cap. Saarbrücken; admin. by League of Nations 1919-35, returned to Germany after plebiscite; economic attachment to France after second world war; reunited politically with W. Germany 1957; a. 2,567 km²; p. (1992) 1,077,000.

Saarlouis (**Saarlautern**), Saarland, **Germany**; on R. Saar; coal mng.; wood and metal inds.; founded by Louis XIV; birthplace of Marshal Ney; p. (1986) 37,400.

Sabadell, t., **Spain**; N.W. of Barcelona; textiles, fertilisers, paper; p. (1991) 184,190.

Sabah, E. **Malaysia**; attempted secession 1975; formerly N. Borneo; underdeveloped; tropical forest; forest prods., inc. rubber, the major exp.; main pt. Sandakan; cap. Kota Kinabalu; a. 76,112 km²; p. (1991) 1,736,902

Sabahiyah, t., **Kuwait**; new t. being built between Ahmadi and Fahahil.

Sabara, t., Minas Gerais, **Brazil**; historic c.; museum of gold.

Sabine, R., Texas and La., **USA**; flows through S. Lake (an expansion of the R. 29 km long) to G. of Mexico; 936 km long.

Sable I., off S.E. cst. Nova Scotia, **Canada**; sandy I., scene of many shipwrecks.

Sacramento, c., st. cap. Cal., **USA**; on R. Sacramento; shipping and industl. ctr.; rly. wk.-shps., smelting, meat and fruit packing, flour, lumber, metal prods., rocket and missiles ind.; p. (1990) 369,365 (c.), 1,481,102 (met. a.).

Sacramento, R., Cal., **USA**; forms N. section of Central Valley projected for irrigation, hydro-electric power and flood control; 624 km long.

Saddleback (**Blencathara**), mtn., Cumbria, **Eng.**; nr. Keswick; alt. 868 m.

Saddleworth, t., Gtr. Manchester, **Eng.**; in Pennines, 8 km N.E. of Oldham; woollens, paper mkg., engin.; p. (1981) 21,851.

Saffron Walden, mkt. t., Uttlesford, Essex, **Eng.**; on E. Anglian heights; cas.; abbey ruins; saffron crocus once cultivated here; p. (1981) 12,515.

Safi, spt., **Morocco**; on Atl. Oc.; linked by rail to phosphate deposits at Youssoufia; pottery, fish-processing; resort; p. (1982) 197,616.

Saga, c., cap. of S. pref., Kyushu, **Japan**; coal-mng. ctr., textiles, ceramics; p. (1990) 169,964.

Saganoseki, t., N.E. Kyushu, **Japan**; on Bungo strait; impt. gold, copper, and silver mines; smelting.

Sagar, t., Karnataka, **India**; nr. Krishna R. valley; p. (1991) 195,346.

Saginaw, c., Mich., **USA**; on R. Saginaw; former fur and lumbering region; coal; beans, sugarbeet; various mnfs.; p. (1990) 399,000 (met. a. with Bay City-Midland).

Saguenay, R., Quebec, **Canada**; trib. of St. Lawrence R.; outlet of L. St. John; used for hydroelec. power; tourism; length c. 176 km.

Sagunto, t., **Spain**; nr. Valencia; integrated steelwks. projected; anc. t., sieged by Hannibal; p. (1981) 54,759 (met. a.).

Sahara, the gr. N. African desert between the Sudan and the Barbary sts., extending from the Atl. to the Nile, inc. Tripoli and Fezzan; a. 16,835,000 km²; numerous oases with ts. and tr. ctrs.; oil pipelines to Algerian and Tunisian

csts.; nomadic Arab and Berber tribes.

Saharan Arab Democratic Rep. *See* **Western Sahara**.

Saharan Atlas, S. range of Atlas mtns. in **Algeria**; ch. peaks., Jebel Aurès, 2,331 m. J. Aissa, 2,242 m, J. Ksel, 2,011 m.

Saharanpur, c., Uttar Pradesh, N.W. **India**; wood-carving, furniture, agr.-processing inds.; p. (1991) 375,000.

Sahel, region of W. **Africa**, inc. Chad, Mali, Mauritania, Niger, Senegal and Bourkina Fasso, which suffered severe famine and drought 1972-4 and 1984-5 caused by desertification of an area marginal to Sahara Desert.

Saïda (**Sidon**), t., **Lebanon**; on Mediterranean, S. of Beirut; terminus of oil pipeline from Saudi Arabia; refinery; p. (1988) 38,000.

Saigon. *See* **Ho Chi-minh City**.

Saimaa, L. system, **Finland**; a. of water which forms basin of R. Vuoksi; canal connects with C. of Finland and runs partly through Russian terr.; a. 1,699 km².

Saingdin Falls, **Myanmar**; on Kaladan R.; site of new hydroelec. power sta.

St. Abb's Head, rocky promontory, lighthouse, Berwick, **Scot.**

St. Albans, c., l. gov. dist., Herts., **Eng.**; on N. margin of Vale of St. Albans, 32 km N.W. of London; faces remains of Roman Verulamium across R. Ver; lt. inds., electronics, instrument mkg.; cath.; residtl.; p. (1993) 127,700 (dist.).

St. Amand, t., Cher dep., **France**; on R. Cher; Roman remains; new recreational park; p. (1982) 12,801.

St. Andrews, royal burgh, North East Fife, **Scot.**; seaside resort; univ.; famous golf course; p. (1991) 11,136.

St. Anthony, waterfalls, on R. Mississippi; **USA**; predominant factor in site of Minneapolis.

St. Asaph, t., Rhuddlan, Clwyd, N. **Wales**; on R. Clwyd.

St. Austell with **Fowey**, mkt. ts., Restormel, Cornwall, **Eng.**; on S. flank of Hensbarrow; ctr. of Cornwall's china clay ind.; p. (1981) 36,639.

St. Barthélemy, Fr. I., **W.I.**; dependency of Guadeloupe; crops of sugar, bananas, cacao; cap. Gustavia; p. (1982) 3,059.

St. Bees Head, promontory, 4 km N.W. of St. Bees, Cumbria, **Eng.**; freestone quarries, anhydrite.

St. Bernard Pass, Great, on Italian-Swiss bdy., W. Alps; carries main road from W. Switzerland to Plain of Lombardy; 2,477 m a.s.l.; road tunnel (5·6 km) constr. 1958-62 links Cantine de Proz (Valais can., Switzerland) and St. Rhémy (Italy); under tunnel will run projected 416 km pipeline from Genoa to Aigle.

St. Bernard Pass, Little, on French-Italian bdy. W. Alps; links Isère valley with Val d'Aosta; alt. 2,190 m.

St. Boniface, t., Manitoba, **Canada**; sub. of Winnipeg; meat-packing, petroleum prods.

St. Bride's Bay, Dyfed, **Wales**.

St. Brieuc, t., cap. of Côtes-du-Nord dep., N.W. **France**; sm. fish. pt.; iron and steel wks.; cath.; p. (1990) 47,340 (t.), 83,661 (met.a.).

St. Catharines, c., Ont., **Canada**; on Welland Ship Canal; mkt. for Niagara fruit-growing region; agr. implements, textile, paper and flour mills, vehicle components; resort; p. (1986) 123,455 (c.), 343,258 (met. a. with Niagara).

St. Chamond, t., Loire, **France**; nr. St. Etienne; ribbons, rayon; rly. wks.; coal mng.; p. (1990) 39,262 (t.), 81,795 (met. a.).

St. Clair, L., **Canada-USA**; part of link between L. Huron and L. Erie; a. 1,191 km².

St. Clair, R., **N. America**; flows from L. Huron through L. of St. Clair into L. Erie; forms bdy. between Mich. (USA) and Ont. (Canada); impt. link in Gr. Ls. waterway; length 136 km, depth dredged to 6 m.

St. Clair Shores, t., Mich., **USA**; residtl. sub. of Detroit; p. (1980) 76,210.

St. Cloud, W. sub. of Paris, **France**; fine park; porcelain; p. (1982) 28,760.

St. Cloud, t., Minn., **USA**; on R. Mississippi; granite quarries; st. college; p. (1984) 42,100 (t.), 171,300 (met. a.).

St.-Cyr-l'Ecole, t., Yvelines, **France**; once famous for military school founded by Napoleon; bldgs. destroyed second world war; p. (1982) 16,380.

St. Davids, c., Dyfed, **Wales**; 24 km S.W. of Fishguard; on site of anc. Minevia; cath., ruins of Bishop Gower's palace (1342); p. (1981) 1,800.

St. David's Head, promontory, Dyfed, **Wales**.

St. Denis, t., N. sub., Paris, **France**; on R. Seine; abbey, burial place of Fr. kings; chemicals., machin.; p. (1990) 90,086.

St. Denis, spt., cap. of Ile de la Réunion (Fr.), Indian Oc.; p. (1990) 122,875.

St. Dié, t., Vosges, **France**; on R. Meurthe; cath.; textile ctr., hosiery; p. (1982) 24,816.

St. Dizier, t., Haute-Marne, dep. **France**; on R. Marne; metallurgy; p. (1982) 37,445.

St. Edmundsbury, l. gov. dist., Suffolk, **Eng.**; based on Bury St. Edmunds and inc. Haverhill; p. (1993) 92,700.

St. Elias, mtns., Alaska, **USA**; and Yukon, **Canada**; inc. Mt. McKinley (5,780 m); source of world's lgst. icefield outside polar regions

Saintes, t., Charente-Maritime dep., **France**; cath.; Roman antiquities; suffered in Huguenot wars; agr. implements; earthenware; p. (1982) 27,486.

St. Etienne, t., cap. of Loire dep., **France**; nr. Lyons; in sm. coal basin on edge of Central Massif; famous for firearms; modern inds. inc. engin., dyes, chemicals, textiles, glass; p. (1990) 201,569 (t.), 313,388 (met.a.).

St. Gall (St. Gallen), t., cap. of can. St. G., **Switzerland**; founded around Benedictine monastery (7th–8th cent.); embroidered cottons; p. (1990) 74,136.

St. Gall (St. Gallen), can., **Switzerland**; borders L. Constance, rising to S.; mainly industl.; ch. ind. textiles; cap. St. G.; a. 2,012 km²; p. (1990) 420,300.

St. George's Channel, part of Irish Sea, separating **Wales** from Ireland.

St. George's, t., cap. of Grenada, **W.I.**; ch. spt.; built around submerged volcanic crater forming St. G. Bay; p. (1989) 35,742.

St. Germain-en-Laye, t., Yvelines, **France**; on R. Seine; outer sub. of Paris; residtl.; popular resort; birthplace of Debussy; p. (1982) 40,829.

Saint Gotthard, mtn. gr., Alps, S. central **Switzerland**; crossed by St. G. pass (2,115 m); rly. passes through St. G. tunnel (14·8 km, max. alt. 1,155 m); road tunnel (16·3 km) opened 1980, longest in world; motorways link pass with Zürich, Basle, and Lugano.

St. Gowan's Head, promontory, Dyfed, **Wales**.

St. Helena, I., Brit., col., **Atl. Oc.**; 1,920 km from W. cst. Africa; spt. and only t. Jamestown; Napoleon imprisoned 1815–21, and Boer captives 1900; famous for its wirebird, species of plover peculiar to I.; a. 122 km²; p. (1992) 5,700.

St. Helens, t., met. dist., Merseyside, **Eng.**; 19 km E. of Liverpool; connected by canal with R. Mersey; coal, iron, alkali; copper smelting, glass, fibreglass, plastics; p. (1993) 180,200 (dist.).

St. Helier, spt., Jersey, Channel Is., **Eng.**; resort; cas.; tr. in early vegetables.

Saint-Hyacinthe, t., spt., Quebec, **Canada**; on Yamaska R.; cath.; famous for organs; lt. inds.; p. (1986) 38,603.

St. Ives, t., Penwith, Cornwall, **Eng.**; at entrance to St. Ives Bay; fishing, holiday resort; p. (1981) 10,985.

St. Ives, t., Camb., **Eng.**; on R. Ouse, 6 km E. of Huntingdon; borders the Fens; R. Ouse crossed by 16th cent. bridge containing a chapel; p. (1981) 12,278.

Saint-Jean, t., Quebec, **Canada**; on Richelieu R.; timber, grain exps.; textiles, sewing machines, p. (1986) 34,745.

Saint John, c., spt., N.B., **Canada**; lgst. c. of N.B.; ice-free pt.; lge. dry docks; rly. terminus; impt. inds. inc. sugar- and oil-refining, paper, textiles; p. (1986) 76,381 (c.), 121,265 (met. a.).

St. John, L., Quebec, **Canada**; on Saguenay R.; tourism; a. 971 km².

St. John, R., Maine, N.B., **Canada**, **USA**; flows to B. of Fundy forming section of international boundary; 720 km long.

St. John's, t., cap. of Antigua, **W.I.**; pt., airpt.; cath.; ch. comm. ctr. of I.; p. (1982) 30,000.

St. John's, c. spt., cap. of Newfoundland, **Canada**; on E. cst.; first English settlement in America early 16th cent.; gr. tr. in fish with allied inds.; univ., 2 caths.; p. (1986) 96,216 (c.), 161,901 (met. a.).

St. Johns, R., **USA**; drains swamps of central Fla., 21 km from Atl. Oc.; 560 km long.

St. John's Wood, residtl. dist., Westminster London, **Eng.**; contains Lord's Cricket Ground,

home of English cricket.

St. Joseph, t., Mich., **USA**; pt. on L. Mich.; ctr. of fruit-growing a.; resort; p. (1980) 9,622.

St. Joseph, t., Mo., **USA**; declining pt. on R. Mississippi; agr. tr. and processing; p. (1990) 71,852.

St. Just, t., Penwith, Cornwall, **Eng.**; nr. Lands End, 10 km W. of Penzance; former tin-mng. ctr.; p. (1981) 4,047.

St. Kilda, rocky I., west W. of the Hebrides, **Scot.**; 5 km long; bird sanctuary, famous for its wren, a sub-species.

St. Kitts-Nevis, Leeward gr. of Is., **W.I.**; aut. st. in association with Gt. Britain; indep. (1983); sugar, sea island cotton, molasses; a. 262 km²; cap. Basseterre; p. (1991) 40,618.

Saint-Laurent, t., Quebec, **Canada**; industl. t. on Montreal I., W. of Montreal; p. (1986) 67,002.

St. Lawrence, G. of Canada, arm of Atl. Oc., partly enclosed by Newfoundland and Nova Scotia; impt. fisheries.

St. Lawrence I., Alaska, **USA**; in Bering Sea; 160 km long.

St. Lawrence, R., Canada; major outlet from Gr. Lakes; forms bdy. between USA and Canada; ch. tribs. Ottawa, Richelieu, St. Maurice, Saguenay Rs.; with St. L. Seaway forms a major waterway facing Europe; grain, timber, oil, iron-ore traffic; used for hydro-electric power; total length from source (St. Louis) 3,360 km.

St. Lawrence Seaway, N. America; joint Canada–USA project links head of the Gr. Lakes with Atl. Oc.; providing channel for lge. ocean-going vessels to reach American continent; provides major source of hydroelectric power to industl. a.; opened 1959.

St. Lô, t. cap. of Manche dep., N.W. **France**; built on rocky hill overlooking R. Vire; cath.; p. (1990) 22,819.

St. Louis, t., Réunion, overseas territory of France, Indian Ocean.

St. Louis, t., Senegal, W. Africa; at mouth of R. Senegal; cath.; former cap.; comm. ctr.; impt. fish. pt.; p. (1985) 91,500.

St. Louis, c., Mo., **USA**; on R. Mississippi 16 km below confluence of Rs. Mississippi and Missouri; two univs.; impt. rly. and river junc.; mkt. for furs, livestock, grain, farm prod.; banking and fin. ctr.; varied mnfs.; machin., cars, aircraft, leather gds., beer, chemicals; p. (1990) 396,685 (c.), 2,444,099 (met. a.).

St. Lucia I., indep. st. (1979) within Commonwealth; Windward Is., **W.I.**; volcanic, forested, fertile valleys; exp. bananas and other tropical agr. prod.; airpt.; cap. Castries; a. 616 km²; hurricane disaster 1980; p. (1993) 136,000.

St. Malo, spt., Ile-et-Vilaine dep., N.W. **France**; on Normandy cst.; cath.; once fortfd.; shipping, fishing, and tourist inds.; p. (1982) 47,324.

St. Martin, I., Leeward Is., **W.I.**; N. part Fr. dependency of Guadeloupe, S. part belongs to Neth. Antilles; divided since 1648; ch. exp. salt; total p. (1981) 13,156.

St. Marylebone. *See* Westminster, City of.

St. Mary's I., Scilly Is., **Brit. Isles**.

St. Maur-des-Fossés, residtl. garden sub. of Paris, Val-de-Marne dep., **France**; p. (1990) 77,492.

St. Maurice, v., Valais, **Switzerland**; nr. Martigny; 6th-cent. abbey; once a leading Burgundian t.; p. c. 10,000.

St. Maurice, R., Quebec, **Canada**; trib. of St. Lawrence R.; used for timber transport and hydroelec. power; 520 km long.

St. Mawes, t., Cornwall, **Eng.**; on E. cst. of estuary of R. Fal; cas.; holiday resort, fishing.

St. Michael's Mt., castled rock, Cornwall, **Eng.**; the anc. Ictis; alt. 70 m.

St. Monance, burgh, North East Fife, **Scot.**; resort; p. (1991) 1,373.

St. Moritz, resort and winter sports ctr., **Switzerland**; in the Upper Engadine; alt. 1,857 m.

St. Nazaire, t., Loire-Atlantique dep., W. **France**; spt. at mouth of R. Loire, outport for Nantes; growing pt. and industl. ctr.; shipyds., iron and steel, fertilisers, aircraft, oil refining; p. (1990) 66,087 (t.), 131,511 (met.a.).

St. Neots, mkt. t., Cambs. **Eng.**; on R. Ouse, 16 km N.E. of Bedford; brewing, milling, paper-mkg.; expanded t.; p. (1981) 21,185.

St. Niklaas, mftg. t., E. Flanders, **Belgium**; nr. Antwerp; textile ctr., carpets; p. (1993) 68,472.

St. Omer, t., Pas-de-Calais dep., N. **France**; ctr. of mkt.-gardening a.; textiles, food inds.;

cath., abbey ruins; p. (1982) 53,748 (met. a.).

St. Ouen, N. sub. of Paris, Seine-St. Denis dep., **France**; on R. Seine at base of Butte de Montmartre; metals, chemicals, glues, tanning; p. (1982) 43,743.

St. Pancras. See Camden.

St. Paul, spt., **Réunion**, French territory, Indian Ocean; p. (1990) 71,952.

St. Paul, c., cap. of Minn., **USA**; faces Minneapolis across Mississippi; cath.; univ.; ctr. of agr. dist.; agr. mkt. and processing; car assembly, oil refining, electronics; p. (1990) 272,235 (c.), 2,464,000 (met. a. with Minneapolis.)

St. Paul, I., **Indian Oc.**; bare volcanic islet rising to 493 m; part of Fr. Southern and Antarctic Terr.; uninhabited.

St. Peter Port, spt., cap. of Guernsey, **Channel Is.**; exp. fruit, flowers, vegetables; resort.

St. Petersburg, c., formerly Leningrad, **Russia**; at mouth of Neva R.; cultural ctr. with many fine bldgs., inc. winter palace, Hermitage museum, cath., admiralty bldg.; former cap. of Russia; major pt. and industl. ctr.; exp. timber, furs, and raw materials; ice-bound December–March; founded (1703) by Peter the Great as St. Petersburg; p. (1989) 4,460,000 (c.), 5,024,000 (met. a.).

St. Petersburg, c., Fla., **USA**; resort on Tampa Bay; p. (1990) 238,629.

St. Pierre, t., Martinique I., Fr. **W.I.**; utterly destroyed and all inhabitants save one by eruption of Mt. Pelée 1902; tourism.

St. Pierre, t., **Réunion**, French Territory, Indian Ocean; sm. artificial harbour.

St. Pierre and Miquelon, Fr. dep., consisting of 8 sm. Is. off S. cst. of Newfoundland; a. of St. Pierre gr. 26 km²; a. of Miquelon gr., 215 km²; ch. t. St. Pierre, fisheries; p. of St. P. and M. (1987) 6,300.

St. Pölten, cap. of Lower **Austria**; nr. Vienna; founded round an abbey; textiles, machin.; p. (1991) 49,805.

St. Quentin, t., Aisne dep., **France**; on R. Somme; impt. textile ctr.; p. (1990) 62,085.

St. Raphaël, t., Var dep., S.E. **France**; resort on Fr. Riviera, S.W. of Cannes; marina; p. (1982) 24,310.

St. Rémy, t., Bouches-du-Rhône dep., **France**; Roman antiquities; p. (1982) 8,439.

St. Thomas, t., Ont., **Canada**; ctr. of agr. dist.; rly. ctr.; lt. inds.; p. (1986) 28,851.

St. Thomas, I., Atl. Oc.; main economic ctr. of **USA Virgin Is.**; tourism; p. (1990) 48,166.

St. Thomas I. See São Tomé.

St. Trond, t., Limburg, **Belgium**; impt. fruit mkt.; p. (1982) 36,591.

St. Tropez, t., Var dep., S.E. **France**; on Fr. Riviera; popular, expanding tourist resort; marina; p. (1982) 6,248.

St. Vincent, C., S.W. **Portugal**; Spanish fleet defeated by British 1797.

St. Vincent, Gulf of, lge. inlet, S. **Australia**; penetrates 160 km inland, max. width 65 km; Pt. Adelaide is on E. side.

St. Vincent, I., ind. st. (1979) within Commonwealth; **St. Vincent and the Grenadines**; one of Windward gr., **W.I.**; volcanic; exp. bananas, arrowroot from alluvial soils in S.W. which has majority of p.; subsistence agr. on hill slopes; cap. Kingstown; inc. 5 Is. in Grenadines; a. 389 km²; p. (1991) 107,578.

Sakai, sub. of Osaka, Honshu, **Japan**; industl. ctr., engin., chemicals, textiles, electricity generation; p. (1990) 807,859.

Sakhalin, I., off cst. of Siberia; with Kuriles forms Sakhalin oblast of **Russia**; herring fisheries, coal, naphtha, alluvial gold, oil, timber, natural gas; oil pipelines connected to Komsomolsk and Khabarovsk refineries; a. c. 63,610 km².

Sakashima Is. See Ryuku.

Sakura-jima, peninsula, S. Kyushu, **Japan**; former I. joined to mainland by lava flows; famed for fruit and vegetables.

Sala, t., Västmanland, **Sweden**; silver mine worked for over 400 years, now to limited extent; lime, bricks.

Salado, R., N.W. **Argentina**; impt. Andean trib. of Paraná R.; 800 km long.

Salamanca, t., Guanajuato st., **Mexico**; oil refining; ammonia plant; natural gas pipeline to Guadalajara; p. (1990) 206,275.

Salamanca, t., cap. of S. prov., **Spain**; on R. Tormes; old univ., 2 caths., many convents; p. (1991) 185,992, 370,624 (prov.).

Salamis, I., **Greece**; opposite harbour of Athens; spt. and ch. t. S.; famous naval battle 480 B.C.; p. (1981) 20,807.

Salar de Uyumi, windswept, dry, salt flat, S.W. **Bolivia**.

Salavat, t., **Russia**; in Bashkiria, 144 km S. of Ufa; ctr. of oilfield; glass factory; became t. in 1954; p. (1989) 150,000.

Sala-y-Gomez, barren, uninhabited volcanic I., **Pac. Oc.**; belonging to Chile, 328 km E.N.E. of Easter I.

Salazar, Mexico; nr. Mexico City; alt. 2,897 m; nuclear reactor for radioisotopes for medical, industl. and agr. purposes.

Salcombe, t., South Hams, S. Devon, **Eng.**; mkt.; fishing; resort; p. (1981) 2,374.

Saldanha Bay, inlet on W. cst. C. of Good Hope, **S. Africa**; whaling, fishing; fish-canning at t. of S.B.

Sale, t., Victoria, **Australia**; tr. of lge. irrigated agr. a.; gas processing and crude oil stabilisation plant (1969); p. (1986) 13,559.

Sale, t., Trafford, Gtr. Manchester, **Eng.**; residtl. sub. of Manchester; p. (1981) 57,824.

Sale or Salch, spt., Fez, **Morocco**; former pirate headquarters; fishing, fish-processing, carpets; p. (1982) 289,391.

Salekhard, t., R. pt., N.W. Siberia, **Russia**; on R. Ob; fisheries, collecting ctr. for furs; exp. timber.

Salem, t., Tamil Nadu, **India**; industl. ctr., rly. junc. in picturesque valley; local iron ore, manganese mng.; mineral processing, textiles; p. (1991) 367,000.

Salem, t., Mass., **USA**; 24 km from Boston; one of oldest New England ts.; many fine bldgs.; textiles, leather prods., machin., electronics; p. (1990) 264,000 (met. a. with Gloucester).

Salem, t., st. cap. Ore., **USA**; on Willamette R.; univ.; fruit packing, flour milling and canning; p. (1990) 107,786 (t.), 278,000 (met. a.).

Salemi, t., Sicily, **Italy**; the anc. Halicyæ; famous Norman cas., terracotta vases; p. (1981) 12,289.

Salerno, c., cap. of Salerno prov., in Campania, S. **Italy**; on G. of S.; fishing pt. and comm. ctr.; machin., textiles, food processing; univ.; famous for Allied landing 1943; p. (1992) 147,564.

Salford, c., met. dist., Gtr. Manchester, **Eng.**; on R. Irwell, adjoining Manchester; inc. terminal docks of Manchester Ship Canal; univ.; varied inds.; p. and industl. decentralization; p. (1993) 229,300.

Salgótarján, t., N. **Hungary**; coal mng., agr. machin., tools, glass; p. (1989) 49,000.

Salina, t., Kan., **USA**; on Smoky Hill R.; univ.; flour milling, cattle mkt., farm implements; p. (1980) 41,843.

Salinas, t., Cal., **USA**; comm. tr. and processing ctr. for fertile Salinas valley; birthplace of John Steinbeck; p. (1990) 108,777 (t.), 356,000 (met. a. with Seaside–Monterey).

Salinas, R., Cal., **USA**; rises in US Coast Range, flows N.W. into Bay of Monterey, Pac. Oc.; fertile valley floor irrigated to produce hard and stone fruits, mkt. garden produce (especially lettuce), alfalfa; 166 km long.

Salinas-Grandes, Las, gr. salt marsh region, **Argentina**; provs. Santiago del Estero and Cordoba; dry, no Rs.

Salisbury, t., South **Australia**; part of Adelaide; research ctr. for long-range weapons.

Salisbury (**New Sarum**), cath. c., historic county town and l. gov. dist., Wilts., **Eng.**; on S. edge of Salisbury Plain at confluence of Rs. Avon, Nadder, Wylye and Bourne; Old Sarum to N. was the Roman Sorbiodunum and present site represents a move (1220) to a more sheltered and better watered in. valley; cath. pure Early English with tallest spire in Eng. (123 m); ctr. mediaeval woollen ind.; engin. ind.; p. (1993) 109,800 (dist.).

Salisbury. See Harare.

Salisbury Plain, Wilts., **Eng.**; chalk upland, N. of Salisbury; Stonehenge; army training a.; a. 777 km².

Salonika. See Thessaloniki.

Salmon, R., Idaho, **USA**; canyon c. 1·6 km deep and 16 km wide in places; rapids navigable downstream only, thus its name of River of No Return; l. c. 680 km.

Salop. See Shropshire.

Salsette, I., **India**; connected by bridge and

causeway with Bombay; popular seaside resort of Juhu; a. 624 km².

Salt, R., Arizona, **USA**; rises in Colorado plateau, flows into Gila R. below Phoenix; rich, irrigated fruit growing valley in lower course; many multipurpose schemes in Salt River Valley project; length 384 km. *See also* **Roosevelt Dam**.

Salta, c., cap. of Salta prov., **Argentina**; on R. Salta; picturesque c. with colonial atmosphere, cath.; comm. ctr. for rich agr. a.; p. (1991) 373,857 (c.), 863,688 (prov.).

Saltash, mkt. t., Caradon, Cornwall, **Eng.**; on W. side of Tamar estuary; lowest bridging point of Tamar by Brunel's rly. bridge (1859) and toll road bridge; p. (1981) 12,659.

Saltburn and Markse-by-the-Sea, t., Langbaurgh, Cleveland, **Eng.**; seaside resort; 16 km E. of Middlesbrough; p. (1981) 19,989.

Saltcoats, burgh, Cunninghame, **Scot.**; on Firth of Clyde 2 km S. of Ardrossan; sm. harbour; hosiery; mainly residtl.; p. (1991) 11,865.

Saltillo, c., cap. of Coahuila st., **Mexico**; comm., industl., and mng. ctr.; p. (1990) 440,845.

Salt Lake City, c., cap. of Utah, **USA**; nr. Gr. Salt L., H.Q. of Mormonism; temple and univ.; agr. comm. ctr. for irrigated a.; meat packing; p. (1990) 159,936 (c.), 1,072,227 (met. a. with Ogden).

Salto, c., cap. of S. dep., **Uruguay**; on Uruguay R., nr. Concordia (Argentina); rly. and tr. ctr. for agr. a.; citrus fruit, grapes, wine; p. (1985) 80,787.

Salton Sea, L., S. Cal., **USA**; 80 m below sea-level in depression which extends N.W. from head of G. of Cal.; ctr. of inland drainage; a. 699 km². *See also* **Imperial Valley.**

Salvador, spt., cap. of Bahia, **Brazil**; Brazil's first cap.; many years of economic stagnation now replaced by rapid growth; Brazil's first oil strike here in 1939; refining less impt. than petrochemicals at Camaçari complex (started 1972); new pt., naval base; hydro-elect. from Paulo Afonso encouraging many new light inds.; cement, aluminium, laminated timber, special alloys; p. (1991) 2,056,013 .

Salween, R., S.E. **Asia**; rises in E. Tibet, crosses Yunnan, descending into Burma to empty in G. of Martaban; many rapids; navigable to Moulmein; hydroelec. scheme; 2,880 km long.

Salzburg, c., cap. of Salzburg prov., **Austria**; on R. Salzach; cath., cas.; birthplace of Mozart; tourist resort; annual music festival; p. (1991) 143,971.

Salzburg, prov., **Austria**; adjoins Bavaria and the Tyrol, on N. slope of E. Alps; pastoral agr.; timber and some mineral wealth; hydro-electric power; cap. Salzburg; a. 7,154 km²; p. (1991) 483,880.

Salzgitter, t., Lower Saxony, **Germany**; S.W. of Brunswick; steel, engin., wagon bldg., fertilisers; p. (1990) 144,800.

Salzkammergut, lake dist., Upper **Austria**; saline baths at Aussee and Ischl; tourist region; stock-raising forestry.

Samar, I., **Philippines**; separated from Leyte by narrow strait; mainly forested mtns.; hemp, rice in lowlands; cap. Catbalogan; typhoons; a. 13,080 km²; p. (1990) 1,246,722.

Samara, (Kuybyshev), c., cap. of S. oblast, **Russia**; on R. Volga; major R. pt., rly. junc. on Moscow-Siberian line, airport; hydroelectric power sta.; comm. ctr. with varied mnfs., inc. cars, aircraft, textiles, synthetic rubber; oil refining; grain and livestock exp.; p. (1989) 1,254,000.

Samarkand, c., **Uzbekistan**; one of cs. in world, sited in productive oasis on Zeravshan R.; many historical associations and anc. bldgs; agr. tr. ctr.; food processing; cotton, silk; univ.; p. (1990) 369,900.

Samarra, t., **Iraq**; on Tigris R., N. of Baghdad; holy c. of Shiite sect; p. (1970) 62,008 (latest fig.).

Sambalpur, t., Orissa, **India**; on Hirakud reservoir of Mahandi R.; p. (1991) 131,138.

Sambhar, salt lake, Rajasthan, **India**; exploited on lge. scale; a. 233 km².

Sambre, R., trib. of R. Meuse at Namur; crosses Franco-Belgian coal basin; part of N. Fr.-S. Belgian waterway system; 176 km long.

Samnan, t., N. **Iran**; in foothills of Elburz mtns.; iron, sulphur ores, petroleum.

Samoa, archipelago, S. **Pac. Oc.**; volcanic mtns.,

tropical climate; agr., fishing; divided into two parts. *See* **Western Samoa, American Samoa.**

Sámos, I., Aegean Sea, off W. cst. Anatolia. belonging to **Greece**; mtnous., fine climate, fertile soils; wine, tobacco, Med. crops; ch. t. Vathy; a. 466 km²; p. (1991) 41,850.

Samothrace, I., Aegean Sea, **Greece**; barren, mtnous.; sparse p.; goats, grain, olives, sponge fishing; a. 184 km²; p. c. 4,000.

Samsö, I., Kattegat, **Denmark**; a. 109 km².

Samsun, spt., Trabzon, **Turkey**; on Black Sea cst.; exp. tobacco, grain, timber, wax, wool, skins, copper gds., antimony, chemical complex; p. (1990) 277,222 (t.), 1,158,400 (prov.).

San, R., S.E. **Poland**; trib. of R. Vistula; bdy. between Poland and Ukraine; navigable in lower course; 442 km long.

Sana'a, c., cap. of **Yemen**; walled c. at 2,217 m. tr in oills, sottons, hides, grapes; handicraft inds.; Islamic cultural and educational ctr.; p. (1990) 500,000.

San Andreas Fault, Cal., **USA**; shearing plate bdy. which extends from G. of Cal. to San Francisco; stress liable to cause sudden sharp earthquakes.

San Angelo, t., Texas, **USA**; on R. Concho; cattle, wool, mohair mkt.; dairy produce, petroleum, machine-shop prod.; p. (1990) 84,474.

San Antonio, sm. coastal t., **Angola**, Africa; at mouth of R. Zaïre; serves as occasional pt. of embarkation for travellers from lower regions of Zaïre.

San Antonio, spt., **Chile**; nearest pt. for Santiago; holiday resort; agr. prods.; exp. copper; p. (1982) 65,174.

San Antonio, C., most W. point of **Cuba.**

San Antonio, c., cap. of Bexar co., Texas, **USA**; in fertile San Antonio valley; serves farming and livestock a.; oil refining, food processing, meat packing; military installations in a.; warm climate attracts winter tourist tr.; Mexican atmosphere; siege of Alamo (1836); p. (1990) 935,933 (c.), 1,302,099 (met. a.).

San Bernardino, c., Cal., **USA**; founded and planned by Mormons (1852) rly. ctr.; citrus fruit packing and tr.; p. (1990) 164,164.

San Bruno, t., Cal., **USA**; 16 km S. of San Francisco; site of international airpt.; printing, mainly residtl.; p. (1980) 35,417.

San Carlos, t., Luzon, **Philippines**; p. (1990) 124,529.

San Cristóbal, c., cap. of Táchira st., **Venezuela**; at 830 m nr. Colombian bdy.; mng. and comm. ctr.; coffee, cacao, sugar; food-processing, cement; cath.; p. (1981) 198,600.

Sancti Spiritus, t., Las Villas, **Cuba**; comm. ctr. in grazing dist.; tr. in sugar tobacco; agr. processing; p. (1986) 75,600.

Sandakan, t., Sabah, **Malaysia**; fine natural harbour on N.E. cst.; exp. agr. prods., timber, rubber; sawmilling, fishing; p. (1990) 223,432.

Sanday, I., Barra Is., Orkney, **Scot.**; flat, many shipwrecks; agr., fishing; p. (1991) 533 .

Sandbach, mkt. t., Cheshire, **Eng.**; 8 km N.E. of Crewe; salt, chemicals, comm. vehicles; p. (1981) 14,747.

Sandefjord, t., Vestfold prov., S.E. **Norway**; whaling pt. nr. mouth of Oslo Fjord; ship-yds., whale-processing; chemicals; p. (1990) 32,718.

Sandhurst, v., Berkshire, **Eng.**; 16 km S.E. of Reading; Royal Military Academy, National Army Museum.

Sandia, t., N.M., **USA**; atomic research ctr.

San Diego, c., Cal., **USA**; first Spanish settlement in Cal. 1542; on Pac. cst., 16 km N. of Mexican border; fine natural harbour, naval base; fish-canning, aircraft; comm. ctr. for fruit-and vegetable-growing dist.; p. (1990) 1,110,549 (c.), 2,498,016 (met. a.).

Sandlings, The, S.E. Suffolk, **Eng.**; a. of glacial sands, forming heathland; difficult agr. conditions.

Sandown-Shanklin, t., South Wight, I. of Wight, **Eng.**; on Sandown Bay; resort; p. (1981) 16,852.

Sandringham, v., Norfolk, **Eng.**; Royal residence since 1861.

Sandusky, c., Ohio, **USA**; on S. cst. L. Erie; tr. in coal, fruit, foodstuffs; paper, farm implements, chemicals; summer resort of Cedar Point nearby; p. (1980) 31,360.

Sandviken, t., Gävleborg, **Sweden**; impt. steel inds.; p. (1986) 40,000.

Sandwell, met. dist., West Midlands, **Eng.**; comprises Warley and West Bromwich; p. (1993) 294,200.

Sandwich, t., Kent, **Eng.**; Cinque pt. at mouth of Stour R.; harbour silted up 16th cent.; mkt. lt. inds.; p. (1981) 4,227.

Sandwich Is., dependency of Falkland Is., Brit. Crown col. S. **Atlantic.**

Sandy, t., Mid Beds., **Eng.**; 5 km N.W. of Biggleswade; mkt. gardening; p. (1981) 8,048.

Sandy Hook, peninsula, N.J., **USA**; projects into lower bay of N.Y.; government reservation.

San Felipe, cap. of Aconcagua prov., **Chile**; 72 km N. of Santiago; agr., copper and gold-mng. ctr.; p. (1982) 38,254.

San Felipe, cap. of Yaracuy st., **Venezuela**; ctr. of agr. dist. producing coffee, sugar and other tropical prods.; p. (1981) 57,526.

San Fernando, N.W. sub. of Buenos Aires, **Argentina**; spt. on Rio de la Plata; industl. ctr., footwear, furniture, fish canning.

San Fernando, cap. of Colchagua prov., **Chile**; agr. mkt. ctr.; p. (1982) 38,871.

San Fernando, t., Bay of Cadiz, S. **Spain**; pt. has naval arsenal; salt mftg.; much of surrounding marshland now reclaimed; p. (1981) 78,048.

San Fernando, spt., **Trinidad,** W.I.; on W. cst. 40 km S. of Port of Spain; exp. sugar, asphalt, petrol; p. (1988) 34,200.

San Fernando, t., **Venezuela**; ctr. cattle ranching region of upper Llanos; oil; p. (1981) 57,308.

San Francisco, c., Cal., **USA**; spt. on S. F. Bay; entrance spanned by Golden Gate Bridge; attractive hilly site; cosmopolitan c. with several immigrant quarters; comm. and financial ctr. with many varied inds.; univ.; sudden earthquake (1906) destroyed much of c. (*see* **F9**); p. (1990) 723,959 (c.), 1,604,000 (met. a.).

Sangihe Is., **Indonesia**; volcanic archipelago between Kalimantan and Philippines; sago, nutmeg, copra; ch. t. and spt. Tahuna; a. 813 km²; p. *c.* 90,000.

San Gimignano, hill t., Tuscany, **Italy**; overlooks Val d'Elsa; 13th cent. mediaeval t., preserved as national monument; tourist ctr.; p. (1981) 7,377.

San Giovanni in Fiore, t., Calabria, **Italy**; agr. ctr. at 1,006 m nr. confluence of Neto and Arvo Rs.; p. (1981) 20,154.

Sangli, t., Maharastra, **India**; nr. Miraj on Karnataka border; p. (1991) 193,197.

Sangre de Cristo Mtns., part of Rocky mtns. **USA**; name (Span.—Blood of Christ) derives from reddish hue seen at sunset; highest summit Blanca Peak 4,367 m.

San Joaquin, R., Cal., **USA**; forms part of Central Valley project for irrigation of farmlands of R. valley; 512 km long.

San José, prov., **Costa Rica**; bauxite mng. nr. San Isidro del General projected with road to Punta Uvita where sm. pt. will be built; cap. San José; a. 4960 km²; p. (1984) 1,105,844.

San José, c., cap. of **Costa Rica**; sited at *c.* 1,160 m in S. J. basin; cath., univ., observatory, theatre, park; ch. industl. and comm. ctr. of rep.; oil refining, agr. processing; major route ctr., international airport; p. (1984) 296,625.

San José, t., cap. of San José prov., **Uruguay**; impt. mkt.; flour-milling; p. (1985) 1,105,844.

San José, c., Cal, **USA**; in fertile Santa Clara valley; fruit and vegetable canning and processing, chemicals, paper, electronics; p. (1990) 782,248 (c.), 1,498,000 (met. a.).

San Juan, prov., **Argentina**; at foot of Andes; gold, copper mng.; cap. S. J.; a. 89,179 km²; p. (1991) 526,263.

San Juan, c., cap. of San Juan prov., **Argentina**; comm. ctr. of agr. a., tr. in wine, fruit, cattle; p. (1991) 119,399.

San Juan, c., cap of **Puerto Rico**; built in part on I.; major spt. on N.E. cst.; exp. agr. prod. to USA; agr. processing; modern inds. inc. oil refining, cement, metallurgy, pharmaceuticals; cath., univ.; p. (1990) 437,745.

San Juan, R., **Central America**; divides Nicaragua and Costa Rica; plans made for its canalisation, which would give both countries a clear waterway from Caribbean to Pac.; 144 km long.

San Juan, R., Col., N.M., and Utah., **USA**; flows in goose-neck incised meanders; Navajo Dam part of Colorado River storage project, bringing irrigation to Navajo Indian reservation; 640 km long.

San Juan del Norte (Greytown), pt. on Caribbean cst. of **Nicaragua**; silting; sm. exp. of bananas, hardwoods.

San Juan del Sur, spt., on Pac. cst., **Nicaragua**; exp. ctr. for coffee, sugar, cocoa, balsam.

Sankt Ingbert, t., Saarland, **Germany**; N.E. of Saarbrücken; coal mng.; iron, glass, machin., textiles, leather; p. (1986) 40,500.

San Leandro, t., Cal., **USA**; food processing; Portuguese residents have annual religious festival; p. (1980) 63,952.

Sanliurfa, (Urfa), t., **Turkey**; nr. Syrian bdr.; handicrafts, local agr. tr.; p. (1990) 239,604.

San Lorenzo, t., **Argentina**; 22 km N. Rosario; lge. chemical wks., oil refining.

Sanlúcar de Barrameda, pt., Cadiz prov., **Spain**; nr. mouth of R. Guadalquivir; wines and agr. prod.; mediaeval cas.; bathing resort; p. (1981) 48,496.

San Luis, c., cap. of S. L. prov., **Argentina**; ctr. of cattle, grain, wine producing dist.; rich mineral deposits in surrounding a.; hydro-electric power sta. and irrigation dam nearby; p. (1991) 121,146 (c.), 286,379 (prov.).

San Luis Potosí, st., **Mexico**; leading mng. st.; metals melting, food-processing; cap. San Luis Potosí; a. 63,235 km²; p. (1990) 2,001,966.

San Luis Potosí, t., cap. of San Luis Potosí st., **Mexico**; industl. and comm. ctr.; metallurgy textiles; cath.; palace; p. (1990) 525,819.

San Marino, sm. indep. rep., **Italy**; in Apennines nr. Rimini; has kept its independence since 4th cent. A.D.; exp. wine, textiles, building stone; cap. San Marino; a. 62 km²; p. (1993) 24,003.

San Marino, t., cap. of **San Marino**; on slope of Mt. Titano, 19 km. S.W. of Rimini; tourism; p. (1987) 4,179.

San Miguel, c., **El Salvador**, at foot of San Miguel volcano; sisal-fibre, coffee, cattle, cotton, indigo; cath.; p. (1992) 182,817.

San Miguel Allende, t., Guanajuato st., **Mexico**; picturesque hilly site; famous art institute; p. (1990) 110,057.

San Miguel de Tucumán, c., cap. Tucumán prov., **Argentina**; on R. Salí; univ.; breweries, sawmills, flour, sugar; p. (1991) 473,014 (c.), 1,142,321 (prov.).

San Millán de la Cogolla, Spain; oldest (6th cent.) monastic foundation in Spain; in Cárdenas valley (Logrono prov.); p. (1981) 298.

San Nicolas, R. pt., **Argentina**; on Paraná R.; cattle, flour, agr. prod., distillery, steel plant; p. (1980) 96,313.

Sanniya Hor, shallow L., **Iraq**; linked to R. Tigris; acts as flood control reservoir.

Sanok, t., Krosno prov., S.E. **Poland**; site on steep banks of San R.; industl. ctr., comm. vehicles, rubber gds.; p. (1989) 15,481.

San-Pedro, spt., **Côte d'Ivoire**; new pt. (1970) linked with development of timber production in hinterland and to Bangolo iron ore deposits; iron pelletizing plant; p. (1980) 50,000.

San Pedro, spt., a. of Los Angeles, Cal., **USA**; shipyds., oil refining, fruit canning.

San Pedro de Macoris, spt., **Dominican Rep.**; on Caribbean; exp. sugar, sugar prods.; clothing, soap; p. (1982) 115,000.

San Pedro Sula, t., **Honduras**; ctr. for banana and sugar inds.; food processing; p. (1988) 460,600.

Sanquhar, burgh, Nithsdale, **Scot.**; coal mng., brick mkg.; p. (1991) 2,095.

San Rafael, t., W. **Argentina**; comm. ctr. for agr. a.; food processing, meat, wine, fruit; p. (1980) 70,477.

San Remo, sm. pt., **Italy**; winter resort on Italian Riviera; flower mkt., olive oil, lemons, wine; 12th cent. church; p. (1981) 60,787.

San Salvador (Watling's I.), Bahama Is., **W.I.**; discovered by Columbus 1492, his first sight of the New World; a. 155 km²; p. (1990) 539.

San Salvador, c., cap. of **El Salvador**; stands *c.* 600 m a.s.l.; ch. comm. and industl. ctr.; food processing, textile and tobacco inds.; univ., observatory; oil refining; liable to earthquakes; p. (1992) 422,570.

Sansanding, t., **Mali,** W. Africa; lge. barrage across R. Niger.

San Sebastian, c., cap. of Guipúzcoa prov., N. **Spain;** spt. on Bay of Biscay, at foot of Mt. Urgull; seaside resort; fishing, textiles, paper, glass; captured by Wellington 1813; p. (1991) 174,219.

San Severo, mkt. t., S. **Italy;** hilltop site, 24 km N.W. of Foggia, Apulia; cath.; wine ctr., cream of tartar, bricks; p. (1981) 54,273.

Santa Ana, c., W. **El Salvador;** second lgst. c. of rep.; coffee, sugar, cattle; Santa Ana volcano nearby; p. (1992) 202,337.

Santa Ana, c., Cal., **USA;** S.E. of Los Angeles; in fruit farming a.; fruit pkg., walnuts, oranges; p. (1990) 293,740.

Santa Barbara, c., Cal., **USA;** resort on Pac. cst., picturesque setting, mild climate; p. (1990) 370,000 (met a with Santa Maria Lompoc).

Santa Barbara Is., **USA;** along S. cst. of Cal.; inc. Santa Catalina I., a favourite resort.

Santa Catarina, st., **Brazil;** between Atl. and Argentina; tobacco, manioc, fruit, hogs; impt. coal producer; cap. Florianópolis; a. 95,830 km²; p. (1991) 4,536,433.

Santa Clara, c., **Cuba;** attractive site at over 360 m; agr. and comm. ctr. for sugar and tobacco; decisive victory for guerrilla army of Fidel Castro 1959; p. (1986) 178,300.

Santa Clara, c., W. Cal., **USA;** citrus fruit pkg.; electronics, plastics, chemicals; univ.; p. (1980) 87,700.

Santa Clara Valley, Cal., **USA;** extends S. from San Francisco Bay; intensive fruit-growing under irrigation, prunes; ch. t. San José.

Santa Cruz, c., cap. of S.C. dep., **Bolivia;** alt. 457 m; agr. mkt. for sugar, coffee, rice, cattle; oil refining; gas pipeline planned; international airport; impt. reserves iron ore; univ.; p. (1988), 529,200; 1,110,100 (dep.).

Santa Cruz de Tenerife, pt. on Tenerife I., **Canary Is.;** cap. of S.C. de T. prov.; Spain; gd. harbour, oil refinery; exp. agr. prods.; developing resort in attractive a. with mild climate; p. (1991) 191,974, 765,260 (prov.).

Santa Cruz Is., volcanic gr., S. Pac. Oc.; part of **Solomon Is.;** exp. copra.

Santa Fé, c., cap. of S.F. prov., **Argentina;** impt. R. pt. on I. in Salado R.; comm. ctr. for surrounding grain and livestock a.; food processing; univ., cath.; p. (1991) 442,214 (c.), 2,782,809 (prov.).

Santa Fé, t., N.M., **USA;** at base of Sangre de Cristo range; oldest capital in US founded by Spaniards 1610; tourist and comm. ctr.; p. (1990) 55,859.

Santa Isabel. See Malabo.

Santa Maria, t., Rio Grande do Sul, **Brazil;** rly. junc., rly. engin., agr. tr. and processing; p. (1985) 197,200.

Santa Maria de Garoña, **Spain;** nr. Burgos; nuclear power plant being built.

Santa Marta, spt., cap of Magdalena dep., **Colombia;** banana pt. on deep bay at mouth of Manzanares R., serving local plantations; p. (1992) 286,471.

Santa Monica, c., Cal., **USA;** W. of Los Angeles; attractive site on Santa Monica Bay; aircraft, plastics, cosmetics; p. (1980) 88,314.

Santander, c., cap. of Santander prov., N. **Spain;** spt. and seaside resort on Bay of Biscay; exp. iron and zinc ore, agr. prods.; heavy inds., shipbldg., oil refining, chemicals; former summer resort of Spanish court; cath.; p. (1991) 194,214, 526,866 (prov.).

Santarém, t., Pará, **Brazil;** rubber, cacao, Brazil nuts, sugar; p. (1985) 227,400

Santarém, t., cap. of Ribatejo prov., **Portugal;** on slope of hill overlooking Tagus R.; Moorish cas.; mkt. for agr. prod.; p. (1981) 52,138.

Santa Rosa, t., cap. of La Pampa terr., **Argentina;** p. (1980) 51,689.

Santa Rosa, t., Cal., **USA;** tr. and industl. ctr. for Somona Valley fruit-growing a.; p. (1990) 113,000 (t.), 388,000 (met. a. with Petaluma).

Santiago, c., cap of **Chile** and S. prov.; planned t. ctr. in broad valley of Mapoche R., one of lgst. and most attractive cs. in S. America; cultural, comm., political and financial ctr., focus of routes; univ.; textiles, chemicals, paper, iron and steel; rapidly growing p.; p. (1992) 4,858,342.

Santiago de Compostela, c., La Coruña, Spain; on

R. Sar, surrounded by hills; univ., palace, cath. (with tomb of St. James); famous place of pilgrimage; agr. tr., food processing, tourism; p. (1991) 105,527.

Santiago de Cuba, c., **Cuba;** spt. on S. cst., exp. minerals, agr. prods., sugar, tobacco; oil refining, cigars, soap; cath., univ.; p. (1986) 358,800.

Santiago del Estero, c., cap. of S. del E. prov., **Argentina;** transportation ctr. of Argentine Chaco; agr. tr. ctr., cattle, food processing; p. (1991) 201,709 (c.), 670,388 (prov.).

Santiago de los Caballeros, t., **Dominican Rep.;** comm. agr. ctr. in fertile a.; food processing, coffee, rice, tobacco; cigars, cigarettes; p. (1982) 394,000.

Santis, mtn., on border cans. St. Gallen and Appenzell, **Switzerland;** alt. 2,506 m. Europe's hgst. television transmitter on summit.

Santo Andre, c., **Brazil;** part of industl. complex built to S.E. of São Paulo to relieve congestion; specialises in metalware and chems., p. (1991) 613,672.

Santo Domingo, cap. **Dominican Rep.;** pt. on S. cst. exp. agr. prods.; reputed burial place of Columbus; univ.; p. (1981) 1,313,172.

Santorine. See Thira.

Santos, c., spt., São Paulo, **Brazil;** world's ch. coffee pt.; also exp. oranges, bananas, cotton, and industl. prod. from modern harbour; p. (1991) 428,526.

Santo Tomé de la Guayana (Puerto Ordaz) c., S.E. **Venezuela;** new industl. c. nr. confluence of Orinoco and Caroni Rs.; iron mines, steel, hydroelec. power and aluminium plants in a.; industl. complex.

San Vicente, t., cap. of S.V. dep., **El Salvador;** ctr. for coffee, sugar, tobacco; mnfs. leather gds., shawls, hats; p. (1992) 45,842.

São Bernardo, c., **Brazil;** part of industl. complex built to relieve congestion in São Paulo which lies to N.W.; p. (1991) 565,171.

São Caetono, c., **Brazil;** ctr. for metalwk. built to S.E. of São Paulo to relieve congestion; p. (1985) 171,200.

São Carlos, t., São Paulo st., **Brazil;** 192 km N.W. of São Paulo; ctr. of coffee-growing a.; textiles, refrigerators, furniture; p. (1985) 140,400.

São Francisco, R., **Brazil;** flows from Minas Gerais prov. to Atl.; navigable for 1,440 km of middle course; used for hydroelectric power at Paulo Afonso falls and Três Marias dam; 2,560 km long.

São Goncalo, c., Rio de Janeiro, **Brazil;** fast-growing c.; p. (1991) 747,891.

São Jeronimo, t., Rio Grande do Sul, **Brazil;** low-grade coal; p. (1985) 30,600.

São João do Meriti, c., Rio de Janeiro, **Brazil;** industl. and comm. ctr.; p. (1991) 425,038.

São José dos Campos, c., São Paulo, **Brazil;** ctr. of Brazil's aircraft ind.; synthetic fibres, telecommunication equipment, chems., motor vehicle components; p. (1991) 442,728.

São Leopoldo, t., Rio Grande do Sul, **Brazil;** 32 km N. of Porto Alegre; mkt. t.; p. (1985) 114,100.

São Luis, pt., cap. of Maranhão st., **Brazil;** on São Luis I.; noted cultural ctr. in 19th cent.; aluminium plant; p. (1991) 695,780.

São Miguel, I., **Azores;** lgst. and most productive I. of archipelago; ch. t. and spt. Ponta Delgada, exp. agr. prods., pineapples; volcanic landscape a tourist attraction; p. (1981) 131,908.

Saône, R., **France;** rises in Vosges and flows to R. Rhône at Lyons; navigable, canalised; 451 km long.

Saone-et-Loire, dep., **France;** mtnous.; noted vineyards; cap. Mâcon; a. 8,627 km²; p. (1990) 559,400.

São Paulo, st., **Brazil;** on Atl. cst.; major industl. a. of S. America; coffee, cotton, sugar, rice, maize; vehicles, elec. gds., chemicals, textiles, telecomm. equipment, metal-wkg. plants; cap. São Paulo; Santos lgst pt. in Brazil; a. 247,226 km²; p. (1991) 31,192,818.

São Paulo, c., cap. of São Paulo st., **Brazil;** fast-growing c., comm. and industl. ctr. of rep. and leading c. of S. America; vehicles, machin., elec. gds., textiles, pharmaceuticals; aluminium refinery; nearby pt. Santos ships rich agr. prod. from hinterland; univs., cath.; p. (1991) 9,480,427.

São Roque, Cape of, Rio Grande do Norte, N.E. Brazil; most N.E. point of S. America.

São Tomé, cap. **São Tomé and Principe**; p. (1985) 30,000.

São Tomé and Principe, former Port. col.; **W. Africa**; volcanic Is. in G. of Guinea; cocoa, coffee; cap. São Tomé; a. 963 km²; airpt. extended to encourage tourism; indep. achieved as democratic rep. 1975; p. (1991) 124,000.

São Vicente, c., S.E. São Paulo, **Brazil**; first Portuguese settlement in Brazil (1532), on I. off mainland; sub. of Santos; fashionable beach resort; p. (1985) 240,800.

Sapele, t., Benin st., **Nigeria**; S. of Benin; lge. lumber mill and plywood plant.

Sapporo, c., Hokkaido, **Japan**; main t. of Hokkaido; planned t.; univ.; brewing, dairy processing, sawmills; p. (1990) 1,671,765.

Saqqara, v., **Egypt**; necropolis of anc. Memphis; step pyramids.

Sarajevo, c., cap. of Bosnia-Herzegovina, formerly Yugoslavia; major route ctr., airport; ctr. of Yugoslav Moslems; mosques, caths.; diversified mnfs., metallurgy, elec. prods., textiles, tobacco, pottery; assassination 28 June 1914 of Archduke Francis Ferdinand precipitated First World War; under siege in civil war, 1992; p. (1981) 448,500.

Saransk, c., Mordovian aut. rep., **Russia**; 232 km S.E. of Gorki; univ.; elec. equipment, engin., agr. processing; p. (1989) 312,000.

Sarapul, c., **Russia**; pt. on R. Kama; radio equipment, machin., footwear, gloves; p. (1989) 110,000.

Sarasota, Fla., **USA**; exp. fruit, veg.; resort; p. (1990) 278,000 (met. a.).

Saratoga Springs, N.Y., **USA**; summer resort at foot of Adirondack mtns., mineral springs; horse-racing; casino; p. (1980) 23,906.

Saratov, c., **Russia**; pt. on R. Volga; regional ctr. for agr. prod. of lower Volga valley and oil from Baku; univ.; engin., ball-bearings, textiles, oil refining, sawmilling; p. (1989) 905,000.

Sarawak, st., **E. Malaysia**; mtnous. inland with sparse a.; rubber, sago, pepper grown along coast.; oil; cap. Kuching; a. 121,914 km²; p. (1992) 1,583,000.

Sardinia, I., aut. region, **Italy**; mtnous., dry climate; fertile Campidano plain with fruit, wines, sheep; zinc and lead mng.; tourism; fishing; major petrochemical complex at Ottana; part of former kingdom of Sardinia belonging to house of Savoy; a. 24,002 km²; p. (1992) 1,651,902.

Sargasso Sea, zone S.W. of N. Atl. Oc.; relatively still sea within swirl of warm ocean currents; noted for abundance of gulf-weed on its surface, rich in marine life; named by Columbus.

Sari, c., cap. of Mazandaran prov., **Iran**; p. (1983) 124,663.

Sark, I., **Channel Is.**; 10 km E. of Guernsey; picturesque scenery; tourist ctr.; farming; a. 516 ha; p. (1986) 550.

Sark, R., forms extreme W. bdy. between **Scot.** and **Eng.**

Sarnia, c., and pt., Ont., **Canada**; on St. Clair R.; connected to Port Huron by rly. tunnel; oil refineries, petrochemical inds., agr. tr.; p. (1986) 49,033.

Sarno, t., Campania, **Italy**; spa at foot of mtns. on E. edge of fertile Sarno plain; agr. mkt., textile ctr.; cas.; p. (1981) 30,583.

Šar-Planina, mt. range on border of Macedonia and Serbia, **Yugoslavia**; impt. chrome deposits; ctr. of mtn. tourism.

Sarpsborg, t., **Norway**; on R. Glommen; lgst. pulp and paper concern in kingdom; hydro-electric power sta.; p. (1990) 39,772.

Sarreguemines, t., Moselle dep., **France**; in Lorraine; potteries based on local clay; coal mng.; p. (1982) 25,178.

Sarthe, dep., N.W. **France**; undulating surface; farming, apples, livestock; coal, linen, potteries; cap. Le Mans; a. 6,247 km²; p. (1990) 513,700.

Sarthe, R., **France**; trib. of R. Loire; 265 km long.

Sasebo, spt., Kyushu, **Japan**; ctr. of coalfield; engin., shipbldg.; p. (1990) 244,693.

Saskatchewan, prov., **Canada**; coniferous forests and plains; Rs. Saskatchewan and Churchill; many lge. Ls.; extreme climate; hydroelec. power; gr. wheat prov.; livestock, dairying; oil, copper, uranium, helium plants, furs, fisheries; cap. Regina; a. 651,903 km²; p. (1991) 994,900.

Saskatchewan, R., Canada; flows from Rocky

mtns. through L. Winnipeg and thence by R. Nelson to Hudson Bay; 2,320 km long.

Saskatoon, c., Saskatchewan, **Canada**; grew rapidly after arrival of rly. (1890); comm. ctr. for grain producing a.; meat packing and tr.; varied inds., cement, oil refining; univ.; p. (1986) 177,641 (c.), 200,665 (met. a.).

Sasolburg, t., O.F.S., **S. Africa**; oil from coal production; gas pipeline to Germiston a. p. (1980) 77,680 (dist.).

Sassari, t., Sardinia, **Italy**; nr. G. of Asinara; cath., univ., palaces; tobacco and macaroni wks., cheese; p. (1992) 121,961.

Sattahip, pt., **Thailand**; new pt. inaugurated 1967.

Satu-Mare, t., N.W. **Romania**; agr. machin., handicraft inds. based on local prods., food-processing; cath.; p. (1990) 137,723.

Saudi Arabia, kingdom, Arabian peninsula, S.W. **Asia**; mainly desert, agr. in oases and S.W. upland region of Asir; lgst. producer of oil in Middle East; oil sales account for 85 per cent govt. revenue; steel inds. and oil refinery at Jiddah, petrochemicals at Dammam; Moslem holy cs. Mecca and Medina; cap. Riyadh (royal), Mecca (religious), Jiddah (admin.); main pt. King Faisal Port.; a. 2,400,930 km²; p. (1992) 16·9 m. (1,500,000 foreign workers).

Sauerland, dist., N. Rhine–Westphalia, **Germany**; plateau, alt. from 150–450 m E. of Rhine; agriculturally poor, largely forested; crossed by R. Wupper, with which are associated industl. ts. Wuppertal (textiles), Solingen and Remsched (cutlery and special steel); supplies hydroelectric power to Ruhr.

Sault Ste. Marie, t., Ont., **Canada**; pt. on St. Mary's R., opposite Sault Ste. Marie, Mich., to which it is connected by bridge; pulp, paper, iron and steel; tourist ctr. for L. and forest region; p. (1986) 80,905.

Sault Ste. Marie, t., Mich., **USA**; pt. on St. Mary's R.; opposite Sault Ste. Marie, Ont.; calcium carbide; tourist ctr. for fishing, hunting a.; p. (1980) 14,448.

Sault Ste. Marie Canals (Soo), **Canada and USA**; twin canals on Canadian and American side of shallow channel linking L. Superior and L. Huron; traversed by all wheat and iron-ore traffic from L. Superior pts.; length (Canadian) 2 km; depth 5 m.

Saumur, t., Maine-et-Loire dep., **France**; on R. Loire, 48 km S.W. of Tours; sparkling wines, brandy; flower, vegetable mkt.; cas.; p. (1982) 33,953.

Sauternes, v., Gironde, **France**; name applied to white wines of dist.

Sava, R., Slovenia, **Yugoslavia**; joins Danube at Belgrade; used for hydroelectric power; agr. in valleys; transport axis; 928 km long.

Savage or Niue, Cook Is., **Pac. Oc.**; under **N.Z.**; ch. exp. native plaited ware, bananas, copra, and sweet potatoes; ch. pt. Alofi; a. 259 km²; p. (1986) 3,000.

Savaii I., lgst. is. of **Samoa**, Pac. Oc.; volcanic, mtnous., fertile; exp. bananas, copra, cocoa; a. 1,821 km²; p. (1986) 44,930.

Savannah, c., Ga., **USA**; spt. nr. mouth of Savannah R.; rly., fishing and comm. ctr. for Sea Is., Savannah valley and surrounding plantations; mkt. for naval stores; sugar refining, paper, oil refining, diverse mnfs.; tourist ind. stimulated by mild climate; p. (1990) 137,560.

Savannah, R., **USA**; flows between Ga. and S.C., to Atl. Oc.; used for hydroelectric power; 720 km long.

Saverne, Col de, low pass, N.E. **France**; carries trunk rly. from Paris to Strasbourg and the East between Vosges and Hardt mtns.; gradual approach from W., steep descent to E. into Rhine valley.

Savoie (Savoy), dep., **France**; borders Italy in Savoy Alps; part of former duchy; dairying and vineyards; hydroelectricity forms basis of metallurgical inds.; first Fr. National Park (Vanoise Park); cap. Chambéry; a. 6,188 km²; p. (1990) 348,300.

Savona, spt., Genoa, **Italy**; cath.; iron, shipbldg., glass and tinplate wks.; exp. preserved fruits and tomatoes; imports coal, oil, iron-ore; p. (1981) 75,353.

Savonlinna, t., Mikkeli, E. **Finland**; in Saimaa L. region; route ctr.; timber inds.; p. (1991) 28,557.

Sawankalok, t., Thailand; impt. teak collecting ctr.

Sawbridgeworth, t., East Herts., Eng.; on R. Stort, 6 km S. of Bishops Stortford; malting, fruit preserving; p. (1981) 7,777.

Saxham, t., Suffolk, Eng.; agr. machin.

Saxmundham, mkt. t., Suffolk Coastal, Suffolk, Eng.; 29 km N.E. of Ipswich; p. (1981) 16,235.

Saxony, Land, Germany; turbulent political and territorial history, now comprises admin. dists. of Leipzig, Dresden, Chemnitz inc. Erzgebirge; kaolin deposits basis for porcelain ind. at Meissen; industrialised in 19th and 20th cent. with notable textile ind.; coal mng. nr. Zwickau; inds. concentrated around Chemnitz; cap. Dresden; comm. ctr. at Leipzig; a. 16,996 km²; pop. (1992) 4,679,000.

Saxony-Anhalt, Land, Germany; inc. Halle and Magdeburg; cap. Magdeburg; pop. (1992) 2,823,000.

Sayan Mtns., range of mtns.; between Rs. Yenisey and Angra, Russia; form part of Sino-Russian border; mineral resources.

Scafell Pike, mtn., Cumbria, Eng.; in Cumbrian Mtns, Lake Dist.; highest in Eng.; alt. 979 m.

Scalby, t., North Yorks., Eng.; 5 km N.W. of Scarborough; p. (1981) 9,228.

Scalloway, Shetlands, Scot.; on W. cst. of Mainland; the anc. cap.; ruined cas.; fish. pt.; p. (1991) 1,056.

Scalpay, I., off E. cst. of Skye, Scot.

Scalpay, I., Harris, Outer Hebrides, Scot.; p. (1991) 382.

Scandinavia, name given to lge. peninsula in N.W. Europe; comprises kingdoms of Sweden and Norway; sometimes inc. Denmark, Finland and Iceland; rugged a. of anc. peneplained rocks; climate varies from arctic (N.) to humid maritime (S.W.); rich in timber and mineral ores. esp. iron and copper; W. cst. waters valuable fishing grounds.

Scapa Flow, strait, N. Scot.; between Pomona and Hoy, Orkney Is.; surrendered German fleet scuttled 1919; Brit. battleship Royal Oak sunk at anchor 1939.

Scarba, I., Argyll and Bute, Scot.; off N. end of Jura, red deer in woods and moorlands; p. (1991) 547.

Scarborough, c., Ontario, Canada; part of Toronto met. a.; p. (1986) 484,676.

Scarborough, t., l. gov. dist., North Yorks., Eng.; on E. cst.; seaside resort; cas.; former spa; p. (1993) 108,700 (dist.).

Scarpanto. See Karpathos.

Schaffhausen, most. N. can., Switzerland; on R. Rhine; pastoral, forested; cereals, fruit, vegetables, wine; hydroelectric power from S. falls on Rhine; cap. S.; a. 298 km²; p. (1990) 71,700.

Schaffhausen, c., cap. of S. can., Switzerland; on Rhine below I. Constance; falls to S.W. of c.; hydroelectricity supplies power for electrochemical ind. and aluminium wks.; p. (1990) 34,324.

Schefferville, t., Canada; 576 km N. of St. Lawrence estuary and connected to it (at Seven Islands) by rly.; ctr. of iron-ore mines in Quebec-Labrador trough; p. (1986) 322.

Scheldt (Dutch Schelde, French Escaut), R., France, Belgium, Neth.; rises in Aisne, France, flows to N. Sea forming extensive delta with Rhine (Rijn) and Meuss (Maas) in Netherlands; navigable; 432 km long; network of canals.

Schenectady, c., N.Y., USA; on Mohawk R., N.W. of Albany; electrical plants, locomotive wks.; p. (1990) 65,556.

Scheveningen, seaside resort, Neth.; 3 km N.W. of The Hague; fish. pt.

Schiedam, t., Neth.; on Nieuwe Maas, 4 km downstream from Rotterdam; forms part of Rotterdam-Europort; diverse pt.-based inds.; gin; p. (1993) 71,875.

Schiehallion, mtn., Perth and Kinross, Scot.; alt. 1,082 m.

Schio, t., Veneto, Italy; at foot of Alps on Leogra R.; woollens, textiles, machin.; p. (1981) 35,596.

Schleswig, t., Schleswig-Holstein, Germany; fish. pt. on Schlei inlet; lt. inds.; p. (1986) 23,300.

Schleswig-Holstein, Land, Germany; occupies S. part of Jutland peninsula; a. disputed between Denmark and Prussia in 19th cent.; mainly agr.; many sm. pts.; crossed by Kiel Canal; cap. Kiel; a. 15,664 km²; p. (1992) 2,649,000.

Schneidemühl. See Pila.

Schönebeck, t., Saxony - Anhalt, Germany; pt. on R. Elbe; metals, chemicals, machin.; p. (1989) 44,660.

Schoonebeek, v., Drenthe, Neth.; S. of Emmen; lge. oilfield.

Schouten I., W. Irian, Indonesia; in Geelvink Bay; p. 25,487.

Schouwen-Duiveland, I., Zeeland prov., Neth.; cap. Zierikee; formerly 2 separate Is.,

Schuylkill, R., Penns., USA; flows into Delaware R.; navigable; length 208 km.

Schwäbish-Gmünd, t., Baden-Württemberg, Germany; at foot of Swabian Jura, E. of Stuttgart; clocks, glass, optical, precious metal and jewellery inds.; mediaeval and baroque bldgs.; p. (1986) 56,100.

Schwarzwald (Black Forest), forested mtn. range, Baden-Württemberg Germany; highest peak Feldberg 1,496 m; tourism; famous for clock and toy inds.

Schwedt, t., Brandenburg, Germany; on R. Oder; lge. oil refinery; pipeline from Mozyr' (USSR); paper, fertilisers; p. (1981) 52,291.

Schweinfurt, t., Bavaria, Germany; on R. Main, N.E. of Würzburg; metals, machin., ball bearings, dyes, brewing; p. (1986) 50,600.

Schwelm, t., N. Rhine–Westphalia, Germany; E. of Wuppertal; metals machin., textiles; p. (1986) 29,800.

Schwenningen, t., Baden-Württemberg, Germany; clocks, precision instruments, optical apparatus; p. with Villingen (1986) 76,200.

Schwerin, c., cap. of Mecklenburg-West Pomerania, Land, Germany; on Schwerin L., surrounded by smaller Ls.; comm. and industl. ctr. of agr. dist.; food processing, engin., furniture; cath., cas.; p. (1990) 126,800.

Schwyz, can., Switzerland; mtnous. in S.; forested; dairying impt.; original member of confederation; cap. S.; a. 907 km²; p. (1990) 110,500.

Schwyz, c., of Schwyz can., Switzerland; tourist ctr. nr. Lucerne; p. (1980) 12,100.

Sciacca, sm. pt., Sicily, Italy; nr. Agrigento; mineral springs; p. (1981) 34,294.

Scilly Is., See Isles of Scilly.

Scioto, R., Ohio, USA; joins Ohio at Portsmouth; 400 km long.

Scone, par., Perth and Kinross, Scot.; place of residence and coronation of early Scottish kings; from here Edward I removed Stone of Destiny to Westminster Abbey 1297; tourist ctr.; civil aerodrome.

Scoresbysund, E. Greenland; lgst. fjord system in the world; length 304 m; fishing and hunting; onshore oil drilling (1984); p. (est. 1990) 554.

Scotland, Brit. Is., N. part of Gt. Britain; 12 Gov. Regs.; home affairs admin. by Dept. of Sec. of State for Scot.; physically divided into 3 parts; (1) the Highlands and Is., an upland a. suffering from depopulation, economically reliant on stock-rearing, tourism, hydroelec. power, whisky and fishing; intrusive impact of N. Sea oil on N.E. cst.; (2) the Central Lowlands, containing most p., based in industl. ts. on sm. coalfields, inc. lgst. c. Glasgow and cap. Edinburgh; (3) the S. Uplands, a stock-rearing a. bordering Eng.; a. 78,772 km²; p. (1993) 5,120,200.

Scott Base, main base Ross Dependency, Antartica; staffed throughout the year with about 12 people in winter.

Scrabster, pt. nr. Thurso, Scotland; main ferry terminal for Orkneys.

Scranton, c., Penns., USA; on Lackawanna R.; anthracite ctr.; chemicals, shoes, textiles; univ.; p. (1990) 734,000 (met. a. with Wilkes-Barre).

Scunthorpe, t., l. gov. dist., Humberside, Eng.; on Lincoln Edge, 10 km S. of Humber; iron, limestone mng. and major iron and steel ind.; p. (1993) 60,800 (dist.).

Scutari (Albania). See Shkodër.

Scutari (Turkey). See Usküdar.

Seaford, t., East Sussex, Eng.; 5 km E. of Newhaven; seaside resort; declined as a pt. with shift of Ouse R. channel to Newhaven; p. (1981) 17,785.

Seaforth, Loch, Lewis, Outer Hebrides, Scot.; 22 km long.

Seaham, spt., Durham, Eng.; Seaham Harbour on E. cst. 6 km S. of Sunderland; modern colly. workings extend under sea, closed 1993; p. (1981) 21,130.

Sea Islands, USA; chain of Is. off Atl. cst. of S.C., Ga. and Fla.; formerly impt. for sea-island cotton but since 1919 infested with boll weevil.

Seathwaite, v., Cumbria, **Eng.**; 11 km from Keswick, close to Styhead (436 m); exceptionally heavy annual rainfall (above 3,800 mm).

Seaton, t., East Devon, **Eng.**; on Lyme Bay at mouth of R. Axe, seaside resort; freestone quarries; p. (1981) 4,974.

Seaton Carew, t., Cleveland, **Eng.**; site for nuclear power sta. nr. mouth of R. Tees; seaside resort.

Seaton Valley, t., Blyth Valley, Northumberland, **Eng.**; coal mng.; expanded t.; p. (1981) 46,141.

Seattle, c., Wash., **USA**; spt. between Puget Sound and L. Wash.; S.E. is Mt. Rainier, N.E. Mt. Baker; tr. with Far East and Alaska from wooded, agr. hinterland; fishing and fish exp.; lgst. c. of Wash., a major industl. and comm. ctr.; aircraft (home of Boeing), shipbld., food processing; univs., cath.; p. (1990) 516,259 (c.), 1,973,000 (met. a.).

Secunderabad, t., Andhra Pradesh, **India**; now incorporated within Hyderabad; comm. ctr., rly. junc.; p. (1981) 135,994.

Sedan, t., Ardennes dep., **France**; on R. Meuse; machin., metal ware, woollens, flour; Napoleon III surrendered to Prussians 1870; p. (1982) 24,535.

Sedbergh, mkt. t., South Lakeland, Cumbria, **Eng.**; woollen ind., public school.

Sedgefield, t., l. gov. dist., S.E. Durham, **Eng.**; in fertile agr. a.; cattle mkt.; racecourse; p. (1993) 91,400 (dist.).

Sedgemoor, l. gov. dist., Somerset, **Eng.**; based on Bridgwater, Burnham and surrounding a.; p. (1993) 100,700.

Sefton, met. dist., Merseyside, **Eng.**; comprises Crosby, Bootle and Litherland; p. (1993) 294,300.

Ségou, t., R. pt., **Mali**; W. Africa; on R. Niger; ctr. of irrigation scheme; cotton, hides, cattle; cap. of former kingdom; p. (1984) 99,000.

Ségou Canal, Mali, W. Africa; leaves R. Niger 6 km below Bamako, extends 208 km N.E. to Segou; irrigates 7,770 km² on right bank of Niger and assists navigation.

Segovia, c., cap. of S. prov., Old Castile, **Spain**; on rocky hill above Eresma R.; Roman aqueduct, cath.; p. (1991) 55,000, 1,606,357 (prov.).

Segovia, R., rises in N.W. Nicaragua, flows N.E. to Caribbean; forms part of S. limit of Mosquito cst., and bdy. between **Honduras** and **Nicaragua**; 480 km long.

Segre, R., Lérida, N.E. **Spain**; rises in E. Pyrenees flows S.W. into R. Ebro; water irrigates the a. around Lérida, the lgst. block of irrigated land in Spain; c. 272 km long.

Segura, R., **Spain**; flows to Mediterranean at Guardamar; 288 km long.

Seibersdorf, Austria; ENEA experimental food irradiation project.

Seikan Tunnel, Japan; links Honshu with Hokkaido under Tsugaru strait; 37 km long.

Seine, R., **France**; rises in Côte d'Or dep. and flows past Paris and Rouen to English Channel at Havre; navigable, part of French waterway network; 757 km long.

Seine-et-Marne, dep., N. **France**; agr., stockraising, dairying; impt. source of food for Paris mkts.; Brie cheese; cap. Melun; a. 5,892 km²; p. (1990) 1,078,200.

Seine-Maritime, dep., N. **France**; undulating and fertile; grain, dairying; heavy inds. at cap. Rouen; oil refineries; beach resorts; p. (1990) 1,223,400.

Seine-Saint Denis, dep., N.E. Paris, **France**; mkt. gardens; cap. Bobigny; p. (1990) 1,381,200.

Seistan and Baluchistan, twin prov., **Iran**; co. ts. Zabol, Zahedan; rly. terminus Pakistan rly. from Quetta through Mirjaveh.

Sekondi-Takoradi, t., S.W. **Ghana**; spt. on G. of Guinea; developed after construction of rly. (1903) to tap mineral, agr. and forest wealth of hinterland; deepwater harbour at Takoradi constructed 1928; fisheries, saw milling; p. (1984) 91,874 (c.), 160,868 (met. a.).

Selangor, st., central Malaya, **W. Malaysia**; former sultanate; economically well developed; chemicals, rubber, tin, coal, pineapples; ch. pt., Pt. Swettenham; fisheries; new st. cap. designated at Klang to relieve congestion of Kuala Lumpur; p. (1980) 1,515,536.

Selby, mkt. t., l. gov. dist., North Yorks., **Eng.**; on R. Ouse, 20 km. S. of York; anc. abbey church; flour milling, flax, oil-cake; development of major coalfield since 1983 linked to bldg. of power sta. in Aire Valley; p. (1993) 91,800 (dist.).

Sele, R., S. **Italy**; rises in S. Apennines, flows W. into G. of Salerno; headwater carried E. through gr. Apennine tunnel (11 km) to irrigate plateau of Apulia in S.E. Italy.

Selenga, Asiatic R., rises in **Mongolia**, enters **Russia** nr. Kiachta from where it is navigable to its delta in L. Baykal; c. 1,100 km long.

Selkirk, royal burgh, Etterick and Lauderdale, **Scot.**; on Etterick Water; 6 km S. of Galashiels; mkt. t.; tartans, tweeds; p. (1991) 5,922.

Selkirk Mtns., B.C. Canada; run N.W. to S.E. parallel with Rocky mtns.; anc. rocks, highly mineralised; rise to over 2,700 m.

Selkirkshire, former co., S. **Scot.**; now part of Borders Reg.

Sellafield, nuclear power plant, Cumbria, **Eng.**; formerly Windscale; reprocesses nuclear waste.

Selma, t., Ala., **USA**; on Alabama R., in cotton, dairying, lumbering region; food processing, fertilisers; p. (1980) 26,684.

Selsey Bill, peninsula between Bognor Regis and Portsmouth, West Sussex, **Eng.**

Selukwe, t., **Zimbabwe**; alt. 1,444 m; gold mng., chrome ore, molybdenum; ranching.

Selwyn Range, mtns., Queensland, **Australia**; extend 560 km W. from Gr. Dividing Range.

Semarang, spt., Java, **Indonesia**; exp. sugar, tobacco, tapioca, kapok; shipbldg., rly. repairs, cement, sawmills, tyres, elec. equipment; univ.; p. (1983) 1,269,000.

Semipalatinsk, t., **Kazakhstan**; on R. Irtysh; lge. meat-packing plant; textiles, engin.; rich gold deposit found in a. 1965; p. (1990) 338,800.

Semmering Pass, low pass, **Austria**; provides route across E. Alps for rly. from Vienna to Venice; scenic resort; alt. below 915 m.

Semnan, t., Central Prov., **Iran**; comm. ctr. for tobacco growing region; p. (1986) 418,152.

Sena, t., **Moçambique**; on R. Zambesi; iron-ore mng.

Sendai, t., Honshu, **Japan**; cas.; univ.; metallurgy, food processing, lacquer ware; p. (1990) 918,378.

Senegal, rep., W. cst. Africa; union with Gambia (1982), dissolved 1989; flat savannah; tropical climate with long dry season; agr. main occupation, groundnuts accounting for 72 per cent exp.; production hit by severe drought (1982–3); groundnut and agr. processing provide industl. basis; bauxite, phosphate, titanium, zirconium mng.; oil refinery at cap. Dakar; a. 197,109 km²; p. (1993) 7·97 m.

Senegal, R., W. **Africa**; flows from Kong mtns. W. and N.W. to Atl. at St. Louis, above Cape Verde; lower valley forms fertile agr. land; partially navigable; plans for economic development of valley; joint water scheme with 3 dams to relieve water shortages, improve navigation and provide hydro-electric power for Mali, Senegambia and Mauritania; 1,600 km long.

Senegambia, former rep., W. cst Africa; formed (1982) from unification of Senegal and Gambia following attempted coup (1981); union dissolved, 1989. *See* **Senegal** and **Gambia**.

Senftenberg, t., Brandenburg, **Germany**; inds. based on local lignite deposits; glassware, tiles; p. (1989) 31,580.

Senigallia, t., **Italy**; resort and spt. on Adriatic; fishing and agr. ctr., food processing, agr. machin.; p. (1981) 40,108.

Senlis, t., Oise dep., **France**; Gallo-Roman wall; tourist ctr. in forested region, 43 km N.E. of Paris; mkt. t., furniture, rubber gds.; p. (1982) 15,280.

Sennar, t., **Sudan**; on Blue Nile, on rly. route to Khartoum, Suakin, Pt. Sudan; dam for irrigation, flood control and hydroelectric power; p. c. 8,000.

Sens, t., Yonne dep., **France**; on R. Yonne; known to Romans as Agedincum; Gothic cath.; agr. tr., food processing, farm implements, boots, chemicals, cutlery; p. (1982) 27,501.

Sensuntepeque, t., **El Salvador**; pottery, distilling; p. (1992) 38,073.

Senta, t., Serbia, **Yugoslavia**; pt. on Tisa R.; agr. ctr.; food processing, agr. machin., chemicals.

Seoul, c., cap. of **S. Korea**; in Han R. valley; food processing, textiles, rly. engin.; univs., anc. walls; international airport, connected by rly. to out-port of Inchon; host of 1988 Olympic games; p. (1990) 10,627,790.

Sepik, R., N. **Papua New Guinea**; flows E. to Bismarck Sea; drains vast mtn. a.; very fast flow; navigable by shallow craft; 800 km long.

Sept-Îles (**Seven Islands**), pt., on St. Lawrence, Quebec, **Canada**; iron brought by rail from Schefferville; airline service but no highway; p. (1986) 25,637.

Sequoia National Park, Cal., **USA**; sequoia trees.

Seraing, t., Liège, **Belgium**; on R. Meuse; coal mng.; iron and steel heavy inds.; seat of famous Cockerill iron wks. (1817) and glass wks. (1825); p. (1993) 61,225.

Seram (**Ceram**), I., Moluccas, **Indonesia**; W.-E. mtn. range rising to 3,357 m; tobacco; sago; a. 17,143 km².

Serampore, t., W. Bengal, **India**; former Danish settlement; cotton and silk weaving, pottery, jute and paper mills; p. (1991) 137,028.

Serbia, constituent rep., N.E. **Yugoslavia**; lgst. and most impt. rep., "bread basket" of Yugoslavia; grain, fruit; mng. copper and antimony; cap. Belgrade; a. 87,879 km²; p. (1981) 9,313,676.

Seremban, t., cap. of Negri Sembilan st., **W. Malaysia**; on Linggi R.; linked by rly. to Pt. Dickson; comm. ctr. for rubber and tin a.; p. (1980) 136,625.

Sereth, R., rises in Carpathians, W. **Ukraine** and enters **Romania** to join Danube above Galati; 720 km long.

Sergipe, cst. st., **Brazil**; sandy cst. rising to undulating plateau in interior; well wooded and cropped for sugar, cotton; drier interior devoted mainly to stock-raising; oil deposits; a. 21,054 km²; p. (1991) 1,492,400.

Sergiyev Posad, (**Zagorsk**) c., **Russia**; 70 km N.E. of Moscow; woodcarving, toy mkg.; site of famous Troitse-Sergiyeva Lavra monastery, converted into museum 1920; p. (1989) 115,000.

Sergo. See **Kadiyevka**.

Seria, t., **Brunei**; coastal t., protected from sea by 8 km dyke; oil ctr., linked by pipeline with Lutong; p. (1988) 23,415.

Serov, t., **Russia**; in Urals; iron and steel; natural gas pipeline from Ingrim; p. (1989) 104,000.

Serowe, t., **Botswana**; Southern Africa; seat of Bamanguato tribe; mkt. ctr.; lge coal reserves widening economic base of Botswana and reducing dependence on S. Africa; p. (1989) 95,041.

Serpukhov, t., R. pt., **Russia**; on R. Oka, planned canal link to Moscow; p. (1989) 144,000.

Serra da Mantiqueira, mtn. range, hgst. in **Brazil**.

Serra do Espinhaco, mtns., **Brazil**; highest peak, Itambe, 2,045 m; iron-ore deposits.

Serra do Mar, mtns., **Brazil**; form steep E. edge of Brazilian Plateau S. from Rio de Janeiro.

Serrai (**Seres**), dep., Macedonia, N. **Greece**; N. mtns. form frontier with Bulgaria in gorge of Struma R. valley; lower Struma R. basin fertile agr. a., producing cotton, tobacco; mkt. ctr. at cap. Serrai; a. 4,053 km²; p. (1981) 46,317 (t.).

Sertão, semi-arid hinterland. N.E. **Brazil**; stock-raising, but drought causes migration to Amazon basin; hydroelectric power and irrigation schemes.

Sesto San Giovanni, sub., Milan, **Italy**; machin., glass, chemicals, plastics; p. (1981) 94,738.

Sète, spt., Hérault dep., **France**; on Med. cst.; chemicals, fisheries; exp. oysters, brandy, wine; oil pipeline under sea to Frontignan; importance originally based upon canal network, now supplanted by rlys.; tourism of growing importance; p. (1982) 58,865 (met. a.).

Setesdal (**Saetersdal**), Aust-Agder, S. **Norway**; remote valley retaining traditional social customs; arable pastoral agr.

Sétif. See **Stif**.

Seto, t., central Honshu, **Japan**; porcelain ctr. (since 13th cent.); based on local deposits of kaolin; p. (1990) 126,343.

Setouchi, dist., S.W. Honshu, **Japan**; rice, mandarin oranges, reeds, salt, textiles; part of Japan's industl. belt.

Setté Cama, spt., **Gabon**, Equatorial Africa; open roadstead, landing difficult owing to swell; exp. timber; oil nearby.

Settle, mkt. t., Craven, North Yorks., **Eng.**; on R. Ribble in heart of Craven dist.; tourist ctr. for limestone cty. of N. Pennines; textiles.

Settsu Plain, S. Honshu, **Japan**; at head of Osaka Bay at E. end of Inland Sea; intensively cultivated alluvial lowlands, ch. crops, rice, vegetables, oranges; gr. industl. belt extends

along cst. through Kobe, Osaka, Kishiwada; engin., chemicals, textiles; a. 1,295 km².

Setubal, t., Estremadura, S. **Portugal**; impt. pt. on Sado R., estuary; exp. cork, wine, oranges; fishing, fish processing, shipyds.; p. (1987) 77,885.

Sevan (**Gokcha**), lge. L., **Armenia**; alt. 1,934 m; never freezes; surrounded by high barren mtns.; drained by Razdan R.; several hydroelectric power stas.

Sevastopol, spt., **Ukraine**; built on ruins left after famous siege 1855; Black Sea resort; rebuilt after second world war; one of most beautiful Crimean cs.; p. (1990) 361,400.

Sevenoaks, mkt. t., l. gov. dist., Kent, **Eng.**; in Vale of Holmesdale; residtl.; agr., lt. inds.; Knole Park; public school founded in 1432; p. (1993) 109,400 (dist.).

Severn, R., Ont., **Canada**; flows to Hudson Bay; tr. post at mouth; 560 km long.

Severn, R., W. of **Eng.** and N. **Wales**; rises in Powys and flows to Bristol Channel; suspension bridge at estuary opened 1966; several proposals for major economic development around shores of estuary; 344 km long.

Severn Tunnel, **Eng.**; under estuary of R. Severn between Pilning (Avon) and Severn Tunnel Junction (Gwent); carries main rly. from London to S. **Wales**; longest main-line rly. tunnel in Brit. Is.; 7 km long.

Severodvinsk, t., **Russia**; on Dvina Bay, White Sea; metals, bldg. materials; p. (1989) 249,000.

Seville, c., cap. of Seville prov. and of Andalusia, **Spain**; spt. on Guadalquivir R., canal link with Atl. Oc.; exp. agr. prod., imports industl. raw materials; major industl., comm. and cultural ctr.; diverse mnfs.; beautiful c. with Moorish influence, prominent in narrow streets of ctr. a.; Alcázar palace; Gothic cath.; bullfighting, tourist ctr.; p. (1987) 655,435.

Sèvres, t., Hauts-de-Seine, dep., N. **France**; S.W. sub. of Paris on Seine R.; celebrated porcelain mnfs.; headquarters of International Bureau of Weights and Measures; p. (1982) 20,225.

Seward, t., S. Alaska, **USA**; rly. terminal, airfield and ice-free harbour make it an impt. supply ctr. for interior Alaska; p. (1980) 1,843.

Seychelles Is., indep. rep. (1976) within Commonwealth, **Indian Oc.**; consists of 86 Is. (37 granitic, 49 coralline), among most beautiful in world; lgst. I. Mahé; cap. Victoria; fishing, heavy dependence on tourism pays for dependence on imported food; petroleum exploration; exp. copra, cinnamon bark; famous for species of nut; total a. 404 km²; p. (1991) 70,438.

Seyne, or La Seyne-sur-Mer, t., Var dep., **France**; nr. Toulon; shipbld.; p. (1982) 58,146.

Sfax, spt., **Tunisia**; admin. ctr.; exp. phosphate, olive oil, salt, esparto grass, cereals, dates, hides; imports food, coal, textiles, soap; sponges; fishing; natural gas found in a.; surrounded by irrigated gardens and olive groves; p. (1984) 231,911.

Sgurr Mor, mtn., Ross and Cromarty, **Scot.**; alt. 1,109 m.

Shaanxi (**Shensi**), prov., N. **China**; Great Wall runs nr. N. border with Inner Mongolia; from N.-S. four main regions: (1) dry, fertile loess plateau, notorious famine region, but increasingly irrigated; (2) fertile Wei R. valley, ctr. of p. and agr.; (3) Hua Shan (4) agr. a. of upper Han R.; grain, livestock; coal, petroleum; developing transportation network aiding economic development; cap. Xi'an; a. 188,860 km²; p. (1990) 32,470,000.

Shaba (**Katanga**), prov., **Zaïre**; many varied mineral deposits inc. copper, tin, iron-ore, cobalt, radium; cap. Lubumbashi; a. 466,200 km²; (1984) 3,874,019.

Shache (**Yarkand**), c., Xinjiang prov., **China**; tr. ctr. in S. oasis; tr. in wheat, rice, beans, fruit, carpets, textiles; p. (1985) 60,000

Shache (**Yarkand**), R., Xinjiang prov., **China**; trib. of Gan R.; 800 km long.

Shaftesbury, mkt. t, North Dorset, **Eng.**; Saxon hilltop t., abbey ruins; ctr. for agr. a.; p. (1981) 4,942.

Shahjahanpur, t., Uttar Pradesh, **India**; on Deoha R.; agr. mkt. t. and rly junc.; grain, sugar tr. and processing; p. (1991) 237,717 .

Shakhty (**Alexandrovsk Grushevski**), t., **Russia**; anthracite mng. in Donets Basin; leather, textiles, metal wkg., food inds.; p. (1989) 226,000.

Shamaldy-Say, t., **Kyrgyzstan**; new t. on site of Uch-Kurgan hydroelectric power sta.

Shandaken Tunnel, N.Y. st., **USA**; carries water under Catskill mtns. to augment water supply of c. of N.Y.; 29 km long.

Shandong (Shantung), coastal prov., N. **China**; S. of fertile plain of Huang He; dense p. but agr. potential limited by dry climate; wheat, millet, maize, soyabeans, cotton, hemp, fruits; E. mtns. contain coal, iron, bauxite, kaolin; iron and steel inds. and cotton mills at main industl. ts. of Jinan and Qingdao; special economic zones to encourage foreign investment; birthplace of Confucius at foot of sacred peak Tai; cap. Jinan; a. 146,198 km²; p. (1990) 83,430,000.

Shanghai, c. and mun., **China**; major spt. on left bank of Huangbu; its strategic location developed, largely by Brit. businessmen, as ctr. for imperialist trading; rich agr. region; handles major share of Chinese shipping but dredging required; machin., chemicals, electronics, cars, steel, shipbldg., are main inds.; major educational and research ctr.; open to foreign investment, esp. for high technology inds.; a. 6,186 km²; 3rd most populous c. in world; p. (1990) 13,510,000 (prov.), (1992) 7,860,000 (c.).

Shannon Airport, Clare, **R.o.I.**; N.W. of Limerick; on main transatlantic air route; ctr. of customs-free industl. estate built (1958) to compensate for decline in air traffic with larger planes; p. (1981) 7,998 (t.).

Shannon, R., **Ireland**; separates Connaught from provs. of Leinster and Munster, flows to Atl. at Loop Head; hydroelectric power sta. at Ardnacrusha; 358 km long.

Shan State, div., **Myanmar**; elevated plateau through which flows Salween R.; impt. mng. dist., lead, zinc, silver at Bawdwin, smelters at Namtu; also tungsten, tin, antimony, manganese; home of Shan people; former Shan and Wa sts.; cap. Taunggyi; a. 155,801 km².

Shantou (Swatow), c., spt., S.E. Guandong, **China**; at mouth of Han R.; mftg. and exp. tr.; univ.; special economic zone to attract foreign inds. and new dock being built; p. (1984) 899,900.

Shanxi (Shansi), prov., N. **China**; bounded W. and S. by Huang He; mainly high plateaux; fertile loess deposits, but drought conditions limit agr. potential; dry crops and livestock; coal, iron-ore, petroleum; cap. Taiyuan; a. 156,420 km²; p. (1990) 28,180,000.

Shaohing. *See* Shaoxing.

Shaoxing (Shaohing), c., N. Zhejiang prov., S.E. **China**; agr. ctr. on Hangzhou Bay; rice, wheat, cotton; p. (1984) 244,100.

Shaoyang, c., Hunan prov., **China**; coal and iron mng.; timber; p. (1984) 416,500.

Shap, mkt. t., Cumbria, **Eng.**; nearby in Shap Fell 279 m, an impt. pass traversed by rly. and by a main road; granite quarries.

Shapinsay, Orkney Is., **Scot.**; p. (1991) 322.

Shari, R., central **Africa**; formed by several head-streams in Central African Rep., flows across Chad Rep. into L. Chad in wide delta; navigable.

Shārjah, emirate, member of the **United Arab Emirates** (1971), Persian Gulf; international airport at cap. Shārjah (p. 25,000); natural harbour at Khawr Fakhan; oil exploration, fishing; p. (1985) 268,722.

Sharon, plain, **Israel**; citrus fruits, vines, poultry.

Shashi, t., S. Hubei prov., **China**; agr. mkt. ctr. and canalised R. pt.; tr. in cotton, grain; flour milling, textiles; p. (1984) 246,800.

Shasta Dam, Cal., **USA**; dams water of Rs. Pit, McCloud, Sacramento for hydroelectric power; irrigation, flood control and reclamation of lower Sacramento valley.

Shatt-al-Arab, R., **Iraq**; formed by union of Tigris and Euphrates, flows thence to head of Persian G.; swampy delta in rich agr. a.; deepest-water line of R.'s estuary defined (1975) as new Iraq/Iran bdy.; 192 km long.

Shawinigan Falls, c., Quebec, **Canada**; pulp and paper, chemicals, aluminium inds., powered by hydroelectric power from falls on St. Maurice R.; p. (1986) 24,470.

Shawnee, c., Okla., **USA**; rly. and tr. ctr. for rich agr. a.; electronics, aircraft components; p. (1980) 26,506.

Sheaf, R., South Yorks., **Eng.**; rises in S.E. Pennines, flows N.E. to join R. Don at Sheffield; 18 km long.

Shebelinka, natural gas fields nr. Kharkov, **Ukraine**; pipelines to Kharkov-Bryansk and Dnepropetrovsk-Odessa.

Sheboygan, t., Wis., **USA**; on L. Michigan; ctr. for dairy farming and resort a.; cheese, leather gds., hardware; p. (1990) 49,676.

Sheerness, Kent, **Eng.**; on I. of Sheppey at entrance to estuary of R. Medway; former royal dockyard and garrison; deepwater comm. pt.; electronics, furniture, coach bldg.

Sheffield, c., met. dist., South Yorks., **Eng.**; on cramped site at confluence of Rs. Sheaf and Don; univ.; heavy engin. ctr., famous for high quality steels, cutlery, tools; major post-war redevelopment of c. ctr.; p. (1993) 531,900.

Sheksna, R., **Russia**; rises in L. Beloye and flows S. to Rybinsk Reservoir; forms part of Volga–Baltic waterway; 160 km long.

Shellhaven, oil refineries, Essex, **Eng.**; on N. side of Thames estuary, nr. Standord-le-Hope.

Shenandoah National Park, Va., **USA**; extends along forested Blue Ridge mtns.; views of Shenandoah valley and Allegheny mtns.

Shenandoah, R., Va., **USA**; trib. of Potomac R.; picturesque valley noted for rich apple orchards and pastures; scene of several campaigns in Civil War; 272 km long.

Shensi. *See* Shaanxi.

Shen-yang (Mukden), c., cap. of Liaoning prov., N.E. **China**; on Hun R. in narrowest part of lowland with hilly country on both sides; impt. rly. junc. with main routes N. to Harbin and Trans-Siberian rly., S. to Beijing, Luta and into Korea; comm. and educational ctr.; impt. textile ctr., heavy inds., cement, chemicals, machin.; agr. tr.; univ.; p. (1992) 4,580,000.

Shenzhen, special economic zone, Guandong, **China**; a. selected (1980) to encourage foreign investment; close to Hong Kong; soft drinks, cement, electronic equipment, petrochems. relocated from Hong Kong; spt.; univ.; planned nuclear power plant to supply Hong Kong; p. (1984) 337,000 (146,000 temporary workers).

Shepparton-Mooroopna, t., Victoria, **Australia**; ctr. of vegetable and orchard a. of Goulburn valley irrigation; p. (1986) 37,056.

Sheppey, I. of, Kent, Swale, **Eng.**; in Thames estuary E. of mouth of R. Medway; cereals, sheep-raising; new steel wks.; ch. t., Sheerness; a. 117 km².

Shepshed, t., Charnwood, Leics., **Eng.**; 5 km W. of Loughborough; hosiery; p. (1981) 11,151.

Shepton Mallet, mkt. t., Mendip, Somerset, **Eng.**; at foot of Mendip Hills, 8 km S.E of Wells; old woollen ctr.; bacon curing, brewing; p. (1981) 6,303.

Shepway, l. gov. dist., S.E. Kent, **Eng.**; cstl. a. of Folkestone, Hythe, New Romney and Lydd; p. (1993) 95,100.

Sherborne, mkt. t., West Dorset, **Eng.**; 6 km E. of Yeovil; famous abbey and school; Norman cas. ruins; glass fibre; p. (1981) 7,572.

Sherbrook, t., S.E. Quebec, **Canada**; comm. and mkt. ctr. for surrounding agr. region; inds. based on local sources of hydroelectric power from Magog R.; textiles, paper mills, machin., flour milling; deposits of asbestos nearby; p. (1986) 74,438 (c.), 129,960 (met. a.).

Sheringham, t., North Norfolk, **Eng.**; on cst. 6 km W. of Cromer; resort; fishing; p. (1981) 5,515.

Sherwood Forest, anc. royal woodland, Notts., **Eng.**; now restricted to infertile Bunter Sandstone ctr.; inc. several estates and parks, notably the Dukeries.

Shetland Is., l. gov. reg., **Scot.**; 80 km N.E. of the Orkneys; about 100 in gr., ch. I., Mainland; lge. number of rainy days, but climate mild and tourism attracted by isolation, scenery and wildlife; Fair Isle famous for knitted clothes; fishing, livestock, agr.; potatoes; rapid growth with oil drilling in N. Sea; lge oil terminal of Sullum Voe; wreck of oil tanker Braer, Jan 1992; ch. t. Lerwick; a. 1,428 km²; p. (1993) 22,830.

Shibin el Kôm, Menûfiya, **Egypt**; rly. and mkt. ctr. in agr. a. of Nile delta; tobacco, textiles; p. (1986) 132,751.

Shigatze. *See* Zigaze.

Shijiazhuang (Shihkiachwang) c., Hebei prov., **China**; cotton milling, glass mftg.; grew rapidly with coming of rly.; p. (1992) 1,320,000.

Shikarpur, t., N. Sind, **Pakistan**; tr. ctr. for grain, precious stones; engin., food processing; p. (1981) 88,000.

Shikoku, I., **Japan;** S. of Honshu; smallest of Japan's 4 main Is.; sparsely populated, mtnous. interior, heavily forested; arable agr. in lowlands; ch. cs., Matsuyama, Kochi, Tokushima; a. 18,772 km²; p. (1990) 4,195,000.

Shilka, R., E. Siberia, **Russia;** trib. of R. Amur; 552 km long.

Shillelagh, v., Wicklow, **R.o.I.;** oak forest, gave its name to oak or blackthorn cudgel; p. (1986) 334.

Shillong, c., cap. Meghalaya, former cap. of Assam, **India;** at alt. 1,372 m in Khasi hills; ctr. of impt. tea-growing dist.; admin. technical education; pleasant climate attracts summer tourists; p. (1981) 109,244 (c), 174,703 (met. a).

Shimizu, spt., **Japan;** exp. tea, oranges; fishing; p. (1990) 241,524.

Shimoda, spt., Honshu, **Japan;** between Nagoya and Yokohama; fishing; p. (1990) 30,081.

Shimoga, t., Karnataka, **India;** on Tunga R.; cotton-ginning, rice milling, p. (1991) 178,882.

Shimonoseki, spt., Honshu I., **Japan;** at extreme S.W. of I.; tunnel and bridge links island of Kyushu; rly. ctr.; engin., chemicals based on local coal; fishing; p. (1990) 262,635.

Shin, Loch, Sutherland, **Scot.;** 26 km long; drained by R. Shin to R. Oykell.

Shipka Pass, Bulgaria; over the Balkan mtns., 75 km N.E. of Plovdiv.

Shipley, t., West Yorks., **Eng.;** on R. Aire, 13 km N.W. of Leeds; worsted mnfs.; inc. model v. of Saltaire, built by Titus Salt (1851) to house his alpaca mill workers; p. (1981) 27,894.

Shiraz, c., cap. of Fars prov., **Iran;** beautifully sited in vine-growing dist.; textiles, rugs, metal wks., lt. elec ind., tourist ctr.; tombs of mediaeval poets Saadi and Hafez; known as "city of roses and nightingales"; pleasant winter climate; univ., airpt.; oil refinery; petrochemical complex; fertilisers; p. (1986) 848,011.

Shire, R., flows out of L. Malawi south through **Malawi** and **Moçambique** to Zambesi; lge. hydroelect. potential; 592 km long.

Shirwa or **Chilwa,** shallow L., **Malawi;** 64 km long, 22 km wide; has 4 Is.

Shizuoka, c., cap. of S. pref., Honshu, **Japan;** pt. on Suruga Bay; impt. ctr. for tea and oranges; lacquerware, textiles; p. (1990) 472,199.

Shkodër (Scutari), c., N. **Albania;** stands at foot of L. Scutari, 26 km from Adriatic; mkt. ctr., tobacco, cement, textiles; enjoyed greatest comm. prosperity after Ottoman conquest; several mosques; rail link to Titograd, Albania's first external rail link, used mainly for metal ore export; p. (1990) 83,700.

Shkodër (Scutari), L., on borders of Montenegro **(Yugoslavia)** and **Albania;** outlet via R. Boyana into Adriatic, 46 km long.

Sholapur, c., Maharashtra, **India;** between Hyderabad and Poona; rly. junc., impt. textile ctr.; p. (1991) 604,000.

Shoreham-by-Sea, t., Adur, West Sussex, **Eng.;** at mouth of R. Adur, 6 km E. of Worthing; spt. and mkt. t.; oil jetty; boat bldg., chemicals, soap, preserves; p. (1981) 20,827.

Shoshone Falls, on Snake R., Idaho, **USA;** height 61 m, used for irrigation projects.

Shott el Jerid, Algeria and Tunisia; deep depression in the desert.

Shotts, plateau, N. **Africa;** upland region with salt Ls., within Atlas mtns.

Shreveport, c., La., **USA;** industl. ctr. in cotton-growing dist.; petroleum; p. (1990) 198,525 (c.), 334,000 (met. a.).

Shrewsbury, co. t., Shrops., **Eng.;** on R. Severn 19 km above Ironbridge gorge between the Wrekin and Wenlock Edge; agr. and dairy equipment, machin., elec. gds.; cattle and sheep mkt.; public school; with Atcham forms l. gov. dist.; p. (1993) 93,700 (dist.).

Shropshire (Salop) non-met co., **Eng.;** on Welsh border, crossed by R. Severn; fine pastoral cty.; with hills and woodland, agr. and dairying; industl. activity at co. t. Shrewsbury; a. 3,489 km²; p. (1993) 413,900.

Shumen, c., cap. of S. prov., N. E. **Bulgaria;** agr. tr., leather; Moslem architecture; p. (1985) 100,122.

Shusha, t., **Azerbaijan;** health resort; silk spinning, rug making; Armenian p. massacred by Tartars 1926; p. c. 6,000.

Shustar, t., **Iran;** carpets, woollens, pottery; shallow-draught boats can reach Shallili, nr. S. by R. Karun.

Sialkot, t., **Pakistan;** N.E. of Lahore; sports gds., musical and surgical instruments, paper; agr. tr. and processing ctr.; p. (1981) 296,000.

Siam. See **Thailand.**

Sian. See **Xi'an.**

Siangtan. See **Xiangtan.**

Siauliai, t., **Lithuania;** 184 km N.W. of Vilna; rly. junc.; food and leather inds.; p. (1990) 147,600.

Sibenik, t., **Croatia** (formerly Yugoslavia); Adriatic spt.; exp. timber, bauxite; aluminium, chemical and textile inds.; p. (1981) 80,148.

Siberia, terr., **Russia;** extends from Urals to Sea of Okhotsk and Bering Strait, bounded by Arctic on N. and by Mongolia and Turkestan on S.; climate mostly severe; ch. ts., Novosibirsk (cap. W. S.) and Irkutsk (cap. E. S.); rich in coal, iron, minerals; oil and gas in W. Siberian lowland; liquified coal pipeline under construction to Moscow, p. and economic activity clustered around rlys., esp. Trans-Siberian rly.; a. c. 12,950,000 km²; p. (1983) 29,587,000.

Sibiu, t., central **Romania;** picturesque site at foot of Transylvanian Alps; retains mediaeval character despite being an impt. industl. ctr.; lge. German minority p.; caths.; p. (1990) 188,385.

Sibu, t., Sarawak, E. **Malaysia;** 128 km up R. Rejang; comm. ctr. at head of ocean navigation; airport; p. (1989) 114,000.

Sichuan (Szechwan) prov., S.W. **China;** mostly occupied by Chang Jiang; known as Red Basin because of colour of its sandstone; fertile a. with mild climate; rice, tea, citrus fruits, tobacco, sugar-cane; lge coal reserves; exp. tung oil; silk producing a.; most populous prov.; cap. Chengdu; a. 568,977 km²; p. (1990) 106,370,000.

Sicily, lgst. I., Mediterranean Sea; former kingdom and now aut. region of **Italy;** pleasant climate, mtnous.; fertile lowlands, especially plain of Catania, but gr. hampered by primitive methods, absentee landlords and need for irrigation; lge. range of Mediterranean crops; fishing; sulphur; petroleum reserves, refining and petrochemical inds.; volcanic Mt. Etna erupted in 1971; a. 25,708 km²; p. (1992) 4,997,705.

Sidi-bel-Abbès, t., W. **Algeria;** old fortress t., became H.Q. of Fr. Foreign Legion; agr. mkt. ctr. for region producing grain, grapes, olives, livestock; p. (1983) 186,978.

Sidlaw Hills, low mtn. range, Tayside Reg., **Scot.;** max. alt. 455 m.

Sidmouth, mkt. t., East Devon, **Eng.;** on S. cst., 24 km S.E. of Exeter; seaside resort; retirement ctr.; p. (1981) 12,446.

Sidon. See **Saida.**

Siebengebirge, sm. wooded range of seven hills, **Germany;** of volcanic origin rising to 457 m on right bank of Rhine; famous for Drachenfels association with the Siegfried saga.

Siedlce, t. and prov., **Poland;** E. of Warsaw; rly. junc.; agr. inds.; p. (1989) 70,529 (t.), 648,100 (prov.).

Siegburg, t., N. Rhine–Westphalia, **Germany;** on R. Sieg; Benedictine abbey; dyes, iron, ceramics; p. (1986) 34,100.

Siegen, t., N. Rhine–Westphalia, **Germany;** on R. Sieg; 2 cas.; iron mng. and smelting, machin., leather; p. (1990) 109,800.

Siemianowice Slaskie, t., **Poland;** nr. Katowice; ctr. of mng., industl. region; iron and steel, machin.; cas.; p. (1989) 80,412.

Siena, hill-town, Tuscany, **Italy;** 51 km S. of Florence; spreads over three hilltops with Piazza del Campo in between where celebrated Palio festival (horse-races) are held; 13th- and 14th-cent. arch., cath.; agr. mkt., tanning, glass, textiles, bricks; *panforte* confectionery; tourist ctr.; p. (1981) 61,989.

Sieradz, t. and prov., central **Poland;** R. Warta; old mediaeval t.; tourism; p. (1989) 42,041 (t.), 408,100 (prov.).

Sierra Leone, rep., W. cst. **Africa;** mangrove swamps on cst., high plateau, with peaks over 1,800 m in interior; climate hot, humid; economy based on subsistence agr. with rice, coffee and cocoa for exp.; iron ore mng. at Marampa; main exp. diamonds, notorious smuggling problem; fishing along cst.; cap. Freetown; a. 72,326 km²; p. (1991) 4·26 m.

Sierra Madre Occidental, mtn. range, **Mexico;** volcanic, forms W. edge of Mexican plateau; average alt. 2,100 m.

Sierra Madre Oriental, mtn. range, **Mexico;** limestone, forms E. edge of Mexican plateau; average alt. 2,400 m.

Sierra Maestra, mtn. range, Oriente prov., S.E. **Cuba**; rises abruptly from cst.; rich in minerals.

Sierra Morena, mtn. range, **Spain**; between Guadalquivir and Guadiana basins, highest point 1,677 m; rich in minerals.

Sierra Nevada, mtn. range, Granada, **Spain**; highest summit Mulhacén 3,483 m.

Sierra Nevada, mtn. chain, Cal., **USA**; highest peak Mt. Whitney 4,544 m; nat. parks.

Sierra Nevada de Mérida, mtn. range, W. Venezuela; extends N.E. from San Cristóbal to Barquisimeto; extension of E. range of Andes, alt. over 4,880 m; impt. coffee plantations from 900–1,800 m on slopes.

Sierra Pacaraima, mtn. range, **Brazil, Venezuela**; forms part of international bdy. and watershed between Amazon and Orinoco basins.

Sighet, frontier t., N. **Romania**; on R. Tisa, on border with USSR; extreme, continental climate; timber, agr. and livestock tr.; cotton textiles.

Siglufjörd, spt., N. **Iceland**; impt. herring fisheries; p. (1991) 1,795.

Sigtuna, t., Stockholm, **Sweden**; on Mälaren L.; first cap. of Sweden; educational ctr., tourist resort; p. (1983) 28,681.

Sihanoukville. *See* **Kompong Som.**

Sikhote-Alin, mtn. range, S.E. Asiatic **Russia**; rises to 1,800 m and extends for 1,200 km parallel to Pac. cst.; hinders access to W. basins; forestry, minerals.

Si-Kiang. *See* **Xi Jiang.**

Sikkim, st., **India**; on S. slopes of Himalayas; incorporated as 22nd st. 1975; forest covered; economically underdeveloped; scene of rivalry between India and China; cap. Gangtok; a. 7,110 km²; p. (1991) 406,457.

Sila, La, massif, Calabria, S. **Italy**; granite mass occupying full width of peninsula; alt. over 1,060 m, max. 1,930 m.

Silchester, par., Hants., **Eng.**; ruins of Roman t., Calleva Atrebatum; impt. ctr. of Roman communications network.

Silesia (Polish **Slask**, Czech **Slezsko**, German **Schlesien**), geographical region, **Central Europe**; since 1945 divided between Poland, Czech Republic and Germany; extends along both banks of Oder R.; bounded in S. by Sudeten mtns.; forested mtns., fertile arable agr. in lowlands; major concentration of economic activity based on coalfield of Upper Silesia (ceded to Poland 1922); complex territorial history; now forms highly urbanised industl. conurb. mainly in Poland, admin. by Katowice, Opole, Wroclaw, Wroclaw (c.), and part of Zielona Gora; Czech Republic portion forms part of N. Moravia; Germany retains sm. part of Lower Silesia W. of Neisse R.; total a. 46,600 km².

Silistra, t., **Bulgaria**; on Danube opposite Romanian t. of Calarasi; cereals and timber tr.; mnfs. foodstuffs, ceramics, furniture; mosques.

Silkeborg, t., Jutland, **Denmark**; tourist resort in beautiful forest and lake region; p. (1990) 48,280.

Silsden, t., West Yorks., **Eng.**; wool textiles; p. (1981) 6,742.

Silver Spring, t., Md., **USA**; sub. N. of Washington, D.C.; science-based inds. and research laboratories; p. (1990) 76,046.

Simbirsk (**Ulyanovsk**), c., cap. of S. oblast, **Russia**; industl. ctr. of middle Volga region; birthplace of Lenin whose real name was Ulyanov; p. (1989) 625,000.

Simcoe, L., S. Ont., **Canada**; several resorts; boating, fishing; 48 km by 42 km.

Simeulue, I., S.W. of Sumatra, **Indonesia**; primitive islanders; fishing and shifting cultivation.

Simferopol, t., **Ukraine**; on R. Salghir nr. Sevastopol; industl. ctr. in rich agr. a., fruit-canning, tobacco, machin.; p. (1990) 348,900.

Simla, t., Himachal Pradesh, **India**; famous hill-station c. 2,158 m high on forested ridge of Himalayas, 280 km N. of Delhi.

Simonstown, W. Cape Prov., **S. Africa**; naval sta, docks; p. (1980) 48,520 (dist.).

Simplon, mtn., **Switzerland**; alt. 3,567 m; the pass over the Simplon (alt. 2,011 m) from Domodossola, Italy, to Brig in the Rhône valley, Switzerland, was originally made by Napoleon I. The Simplon rly. tunnel leads from Brig on the Swiss side to Iselle in the Val di Vedro on the Italian and is the longest in the world, 19.7 km.

Simpson Desert, Central **Australia**; uninhabited arid a. covered in ridge dunes and spinifex; a. 77,000 km².

Sinai, peninsula, easternmost part of **Egypt**; between Gs. of Aqaba and Suez, at head of Red Sea; mainly desert in N., granitic ridges in S. rising to 2,592 m at Jebel Katrun; Jebel Musa or Mt. Sinai (2,244 m) is one of numerous peaks; mineral resources; coal mine at Maghâra; occupied by Israeli troops, Nov. 1956–March 1957, and since June 1967; phased Israeli withdrawal began 1979, completed 1982; prov. N. Sinai and S. Sinai; a. 28,632 km²; p. (1991) 223,000 (N.), 41,000 (S.).

Sinaia, t., S. **Romania**; health and winter sports resort in Transylvanian Alps; until 1947 summer residence of Romanian kings; palaces.

Sinaloa, st., **Mexico**; on G. of Cal.; agr. and mng., rich in gold, silver, copper, iron and lead; cereals on uplands; sugar, cotton on lowlands; cap. Culiacán; a. 48,482 km²; p. (1990) 2,210,766.

Sind, prov. (revived 1970), **Pakistan**; lower Indus valley; dry climate; E. part reaches edge of Thar desert; agr. depends on irrigation; irrigated by Sukkur and Kotri systems; wheat, rice, cotton, oilseeds, sugar-cane, fruits; handicraft inds. in ts.; ch. ts., Karachi, Hyderabad, Sukkur, Shikarpur; a. 129,500 km²; p. (1981) 19,028,666.

Singapore, rep., S.E. **Asia**; I. separated from Malaysian mainland by Johore Strait and linked by causeway; equatorial climate; cap. Singapore on S. cst. has fine natural harbour; p. (1991) 2·69 m, second largest port in the world; world ctr. of rubber and tin mkts.; tr. in machinery, petrol prods., mnfs., with Japan, Malaysia and USA; increasingly impt. as regional financial centre; oil refining, shipbldg., but industl. development slowing down since 1985; only 20 per cent of land cultivated; fruit, mkt. gardening; second hst. standard of living in Asia; reduction in Brit. military presence from base on N. cst. of I.; a. 620 km²; p. (1992) 2·82 m (rep.).

Singhbhum, dist., Bihar, **India**; iron and steel wks. based on local iron mng.; a. 13,445 km²; p. (1981) 2,861,799.

Sinhailon. *See* **Lianyungang.**

Sining. *See* **Xining.**

Sinkiang-Uighur. *See* **Xinjiang Uygur.**

Sinop, cap. of S. prov., **Turkey**; sm. pt. with gd. harbour on Black Sea but poor communications with hinterland; p. (1985) 23,148 (t.), (1990) 265,153 (prov.).

Sintra (**Cintra**), t., **Portugal**; summer resort, 29 km from Lisbon; Moorish castle, royal palace; p. (1981) 126,010 (met. a.).

Sinuiju, c., W. **N. Korea**; spt. at mouth of Yalu R. on Yellow Sea; linked by bridge to Antung (China); industl. ctr.; chemicals, aluminium inds., using power from Supung Dam; p. (1984) 500,000.

Sinyang. *See* **Xinyang.**

Sion, t., cap. of Valais can., **Switzerland**; on R. Rhône; built on two castled hills; cath.; horticultural mkt. ctr.; hydroelectric power stas. and coal mines nearby; p. (1980) 22,877.

Sioux City, Iowa, **USA**; on R. Missouri; meat-packing, foundries, elec. gds., cement; p. (1990) 80,508.

Sioux Falls, t., S.D., **USA**; on Big Sioux R.; in rich wheat region; machin., cars, farming implements; nuclear reactor; p. (1990) 100,814.

Siping (**Szeping**), c., Jilin prov., **China**; agr. distributing ctr.; cement; p. (1984) 353,300.

Siret, R., **Romania, Ukraine**; flows S. from Carpathians to Danube; steep forested left bank, fertile terraced right bank; hydroelectric power and irrigation schemes; 448 km long.

Sisak, t., Croatia (formerly Yugoslavia); developing indust. ctr. and R. pt.; iron and steel, oil refining.

Sistan and Baluchistan, twin prov., **Iran**; bounded by Afghanistan and Pakistan; cap. Zahedan; much desert land; arid, very hot; p. (1982) 664,292.

Sitapur, t., Uttar Pradesh, **India**; rly. junc.; agr. tr. ctr.; eye hospital; p. (1991) 121,842.

Sitra, I., Persian G.; forms part of st. of **Bahrain**, 5 km long and 1·6 km wide; oil pipeline and causeway carrying road extends out to sea for 5 km to deep-water anchorage; oil refinery; power sta. and desalinisation plant.

Sittang, R., **Myanmar**; rises in Pegu Yoma, flows S. to. G. of Martaban through delta; valley intensively cultivated, delta forested; irrigation project; 976 km long.

Sittard, mkt. t., Limburg, **Neth.**; tanning; p. (1993) 46,578, 184,097 (met. a. with Geleen).

Sittingbourne and Milton, mkt. t., Swale, Kent, **Eng.**; on Milton Creek, 14 km E. of Chatham; paper mills, brick wks.; cement; insecticides;

ctr. of fruit-growing dist.; p. (1981) 33,645.

Sittwe (Akyab), spt., **Myanmar**; at mouth of Kaladan R.; exp. rice; (1983) 107,907.

Sivas, c., cap. of S. prov., **Turkey**; impt. tr. and agr. ctr. in Kizil Irmak valley; cement, rugs; copper mng. nearby; foundations of modern Turkey laid here by Atatürk 1919; p. (1990) 219,949 (c.), 767,481 (prov.).

Sivash Sea or **Putrid Sea**, lagoon on N.E. cst. of Crimea, **Ukraine**; 20 per cent salt; a. 2,590 km².

Siwa, oasis, **Egypt**; in Libyan Desert, *c.* 480 km S.W. of Alexandria; dates, olives; remains of temple of Zeus Ammon (visited by Alexander the Great); 32 km long, 1·6 km wide.

Sizewell, Suffolk, **Eng.**; Magnox nuclear power sta.; Britain's 1st pressurised water nuclear reactor sta. under construction.

Sjaelland, I., **Denmark**; lgst. I., separated from Fyn I. by the Gr. Belt; fertile glacial clays but rapidly spreading ts., ch. c. Copenhagen; a. 7,356 km²; p. (1990) 1,972,711.

Skagerrak, arm of N. Sea, giving access to the Kattegat, between Norway and Denmark, 112–144 km wide.

Skagway, sm. spt., Alaska, **USA**; at head of Lynn Canal inlet, 640 km N.W. of Prince Rupert; linked by rly. to Whitehorse on upper R. Yukon; boomed in gold rush (1898), p. (1990) 4,385 (inc. Yakutat and Angoon).

Skåne (Scania), old prov. and peninsula, extreme S. of **Sweden**; corresponds approx. to cos. Malmöhus, Kristianstad; most favoured part of Sweden in relief, soil, climate; intensive farming, wheat, barley, sugar-beet, fodder crops, dairy cattle; ch. ts. Malmö, Lund, Hälsingborg; a. 10,939 km².

Skaraborg, co., **Sweden**; between Ls. Vänern and Vättern; dairy agr.; a. 8,467 km²; p. (1992) 278,860.

Skara Brae, prehistoric v., Mainland, Orkneys, **Scot.**; v. excavated from under sand dunes.

Skarzysko-Kamienna, t., Kielce, **Poland**; ctr. of metallurgical ind.; p. (1989) 50,455.

Skaw The (Grenen), C., at extreme N. of **Denmark**.

Skeena, R., B.C., **Canada**; rises in N. Rocky mtns., flows S.W. to Pac. Oc. at Prince Rupert; lower valley used by Canadian National Rly.; 640 km long.

Skegness, t., East Lindsey, Lincs., **Eng.**; on E. cst.; resort; lt. engin.; p. (1981) 14,425.

Skelleftea, t., N. **Sweden**; on Bothnia G.; growing since discovery of Boliden ores nearby; iron and copper ore smelting; p. (1992) 73,734.

Skelmersdale, t., West Lancs., **Eng.**; coal, bricks, drainpipes; new t. (1961); p. (1981) 39,144.

Skelton and Brotton, t., Langbaurgh, Cleveland, **Eng.**; at N. foot of Cleveland hills, 16 km E. of Middlesbrough; steel flooring; p. (1981) 16,208.

Skiddaw, mtn., Cumbria, **Eng.**; E. of Bassenthwaite L.; alt. 931 m.

Skien, spt., Bratsberg, **Norway**; on R. Skien; saw-mills, timber tr.; birthplace of Ibsen; p. (1990) 29,328.

Skierniewice, t. and prov. central **Poland**; fruit and vegetables, elec. engin; p. (1989) 43,963 (t.), 416,700 (prov.).

Skikda (Philippeville), t., spt., **Algeria**; exp. prods. from Saharan oases; oil pipeline to Mesdar; vast petrochemical plant; p. (1983) 141,159.

Skipton, t., Craven, North Yorks., **Eng.**; on R. Aire; cotton and rayon inds.; cas.; p. (1981) 13,246.

Skopje, t., cap. of Macedonia, formerly Yugoslavia; anc. Scupi, one of oldest ts. in Balkans; oriental appearance; destroyed by massive earthquake (1963); food processing, iron and steel wks.; new oil refinery; airpt., route ctr.; p. (1981) 506,547.

Skòvde, t., **Sweden**; between Ls. Vänern and Vättern; garrison t., chemicals, cement; p. (1992) 48,460.

Skye, I., lgst. of Inner Hebrides, l. gov. dist. Skye and Lochalsh, **Scot.**; mtnous.; sheep-farming and fisheries; tourism; only t. Portree; a. 1,417 km²; p. (1991) 8,868 (I.), (1993) 11,870 (dist.).

Skyros, I., Sporades, **Greece**; in Aegean Sea; mainly agr.; a. 199 km².

Slagelse, t., Sjaelland, **Denmark**; food inds.; iron wks.; 11th cent. church; p. (1990) 34,279.

Slave Coast, name given to the Guinea cst. of W. Africa between the Volta and Niger deltas where slaves were shipped from 16th to 19th cent.

Slave, R., N.W. Terr., **Canada**; flows into Gr. Slave L.; length 416 km.

Slavonia, historic region, Croatia (formerly Yugoslavia); between Drava R. (N.) and Sava R. (S.); ch. t. Osijek.

Slavyansk, t., **Ukraine**; in Donets basin; chemicals, engin.; p. (1990) 136,000.

Sleaford, mkt. t., North Kesteven, Lincs., **Eng.**; 19 km N.E. of Grantham; agr. and agr. implements; p. (1981) 8,523.

Sleat, Sound of, Lochaber, Skye and Lochalsh, **Scot.**; separates I. of Skye from the mainland; 11 km wide.

Slezsko. *See* Silesia.

Sliema, t., **Malta**; E. of Valletta; resort; p. (1983) 20,123.

Slieve Bloom, hill range, Offaly and Laoghis cos., **R.o.I.**; highest point 529 m.

Slieve Donard, mtn., N. Ireland, highest of the Mourne mtns.; alt. 835 m.

Sligo, co., Connacht, **R.o.I.**; borders Atl. Oc.; rises to Ox Mtns. over 600 m; pastoral agr., fishing; co. t. S.; a. 1,909 km²; p. (1986) 56,046.

Sligo, co. t., Sligo, **R.o.I.**; on S. Bay; pt., exp. agr. prods.; abbey ruins; cath.; p. (1986) 17,259.

Slioch, mtn., Ross and Cromarty, **Scot.**; 981 m.

Sliven, t., **Bulgaria**; in Balkan mtns.; impt. woollen mnf. ctr.; carpets; p. (1990) 112,220.

Slough, t., l. gov. dist., Berks., **Eng.**; on river terrace N. of R. Thames, 37 km W. of London; many lt. inds.; p. (1993) 103,500 (dist.).

Slovakia, formerly eastern part of Czechoslovakia, cap. Bratislava; extends from Carpathians to Danube valley; mainly agricultural, depressed industry; a. 49,035 km²; p. (1992) 5,296,768.

Slovenia, former constituent rep., Yugoslavia; independence recognised by EC, 1991; mtnous., but many minerals inc. coal; highly developed region; cap. Ljubljana; a. 16,229 km²; p. (1992) 2 m.

Slupsk (Stolp), t. and prov., N.W. **Poland** (since 1945); formerly in Pomerania; on R. Stupia, nr. Baltic Sea; cas.; wood, metal, food processing; p. (1989) 100,127 (t.), 410,000 (prov.).

Småland, historic prov., S. **Sweden**; barren upland a. S. of L. Vättern; moorland, deciduous forest; contrasts greatly with remainder of S. Sweden; a. 29,322 km².

Smederevo, t., Serbia, **Yugoslavia**; nr. Belgrade; pt. on R. Danube; walled t.; steel wks.; p. (1991) 64,257.

Smethwick. *See* Warley.

Smolensk, c., cap. of S. oblast, **Russia**; on upper Dnieper; anc. c. damaged in many wars; route ctr.; vehicles, machin., food processing; p. (1989) 344,000.

Smyrna. *See* Izmir.

Snaefell, highest mtn., **I. of Man**; alt. 620 m.

Snake R., or **Lewis Fork**, trib. of Columbia R., flows from Wyo. to Wash., **USA**; gorges; hydroelectric power; 1,680 km long.

Sneek, t., Friesland, **Neth.**; butter, cheese mkt.; yachting ctr.; p. (1993) 29,234.

Sneeuwbergen, mtn. range, Cape Prov., **S. Africa.**

Snowdon, mtn., Gwynedd, **Wales**; highest in Eng. and Wales, alt. 1,086 m; forms part of Snowdonia Nat. Park.

Snowy Mtns., N.S.W., **Australia**; part of Australian Alps inc. Australia's hgst. peak (Mount Kosciusko); rise to over 2,000 m; S.M. scheme (1950) diverts water from headstreams in tunnels through mtns. to provide water for irrigation and hydroelectric power; completed 1972.

Snowy, R., N.S.W. and Victoria, **Australia**; rises in Mt. Kosciusko, flows S. into Bass strait 128 km W. of C. Howe; part of Snowy Mtn. scheme; 432 km long.

Soar, R., Leics., Notts., **Eng.**; rises S. of Leics., flows N.W. to join R. Trent; 69 km long.

Sobat, R., Sudan and Ethiopia; made up of several sm. Rs.; trib. of White Nile; 800 km long.

Soche. *See* Yarkand.

Sochi, t., **Russia**; on Black Sea at foot of main Caucasian range; health resort with subtropical climate and sulphur springs; developed since 1933; p. (1989) 337,000.

Society Is., Fr. Polynesia, S. Pac. Oc.; comprise Windward Is. (Tahiti, Moorea, Mehetia, etc.) and Leeward Is. (Huahune, Raiatea, etc.); visited by Captain Cook; main prods. phosphate and copper; cap. Papeete; a. 1,647 km²; p. (1983) 142,129.

Socotra, I., G. of Aden, Indian Oc.; since 1967 part of **Yemen**; under Brit. protection 1886–1967; lofty tableland; myrrh, frankincense, aloes; cap. Tamrida; a. 3,626 km².

Sodbury, t., Northavon, Avon. **Eng.**; former coalmng. ctr.; expanded t.

Söderhamn, spt., **Sweden**; on G. of Bothnia, N. of Gavle; timber, wood-pulp; p. (1983) 30,736.

Södermanland, co., **Sweden**; between Baltic cst. and L. Mälar; cattle-rearing; mng.; a. 6,822 km²; p. (1992) 257,858.

Södertälje, t., **Sweden**; on S. canal linking L. Mälar with Baltic cst.; vehicles, chemicals, tobacco; p. (1990) 81,770.

Soest, c., N. Rhine–Westphalia, **Germany**; one of oldest ts., member of Hanseatic league; suffered heavily in second world war; soap, textile machin., engin.; p. (1993) 41,785.

Soest, t., Utrecht, **Neth.**; residtl., agr. ctr.; p. (1987) 41,000.

Sofia, c., cap. of **Bulgaria**; Roman Serdica, and Triaditsa of Byzantine Greeks; nr. Yugoslav border; impt. route ctr. and ch. industl. ctr. of rep.; machin., textiles, chemicals, elec. engin.; cath., univ., and many historic bldgs.; p. (1990) 1,141,142.

Sogne Fjord, **Norway**; longest fjord in Norway; length 176 km; tourism.

Sogn og Fjordane, co., W. **Norway**; borders Atl. Oc., indented by Sogne Fjord; lge. hydroelectric power resources; tourism; a. 18,480 km²; p. (1990) 106,614.

Sohag, t. and prov., **Egypt**; on R. Nile; cotton processing; p. (1986) 132,965 (t.), (1991) 2,763,000 (prov.).

Soho, dist., London, **Eng.**; settled by Fr. Huguenots 16th cent.; high proportion of foreign residents, sometimes known as London's "Latin quarter"; night-clubs, theatres, restaurants, filmcompany offices.

Soissons, t., Aisne dep., **France**; anc. Augusta Suessionum; commands N.E. approaches to Paris; cath.; agr. tr.; p. (1982) 32,236.

Sokoto, t., **Nigeria**, W. Africa; founded 1809 as cap. of native st. of S., p. mainly Hausa and Fulani; tr. ctr.; p. (est. 1983) 148,000, (1991) 4,392,391 (state).

Solent, The, strait separating I. of Wight from Hampshire mainland, **Eng.**;

Solihull, t., met dist., West Midlands, **Eng.**; 8 km S.W. of Birmingham; residtl.; motor vehicles chemicals; p. (1993) 200,400 (dist.).

Solikamsk, t., **Russia**; on R. Kama; chemicals from local potash; rapidly growing t.; p. (1989) 110,000.

Solingen, t., N. Rhine–Westphalia, **Germany**; 24 km E. of Düsseldorf; cutlery ctr.; p. (1990) 165,600.

Solnechnyy. *See* **Gornyy Snezhnogorsk**.

Solomon Is., S. Pac. Oc.; internal self-gov. (1976); full independence (July 1978); archipelago of volcanic Is.; N. Is. form part of Papua New Guinea; remainder Brit.; dependent on exp. of copra, timber, fish; threatened by insect pests; a. 29,785 km²; p. (1993) 349,500 (mostly Melanesian).

Solothurn (Soleure), can., N.W. **Switzerland**, crossed by Jura mtns., and R. Aare; 97 per cent cultivated; dairying; many industl. ts.; cap. S.; a. 793 km²; p. (1990) 226,700.

Solothurn (Soleure), t., cap. of S. can., **Switzerland**; on R. Aare; anc. t.; cath.; watches, motor mnf.; p. (1980) 15,778.

Solway Firth, arm of **Irish Sea**, Dumfries and Galloway Reg., Scot., and Cumbria, **Eng.**; 6 km long.

Somalia (Somali Democratic Rep.), E. cst. **Africa**; narrow cst. plain in N., widens in S., interior plateau reaching c. 2,400 m; dry, hot climate; 75 per cent. p. nomadic; livestock herding; permanent agr. in irrigated R. valleys; sugar, banana plantations in Webi Shebeli and Juba Rs. in S.; potential for mineral exploitation; continuing civil war, famine; UN intervention 1992; cap. Mogadishu; a. 637,658 km²; p. (1990) 7.56 m.

Somaliland, French. *See* **Djibouti**.

Sombor, t., Serbia, **Yugoslavia**; cattle, grain tr.; textiles; p. (1981) 99,168.

Somersby, v., Lincs., **Eng.**; the birthplace of Tennyson.

Somerset, non-met. co., S.W. **Eng.**; inc. part of Exmoor, Mendips, Quantocks and Blackdown hills; to N. is drained marshland of Somerset levels; dairying; coastal resorts; co. t.

Taunton; a. 3,458 km²; p. (1993) 474,100.

Somme, dep., N. **France**; borders Eng. Channel; crossed by R. Somme; low-lying agr. a.; textile inds.; cap. Amiens; a. 6,327 km²; p. (1990) 547,800.

Somme, R., **France**; flows in deps. Aisne and Somme to English Channel; scene of battles 1916; linked to Rs. Oise and Scheldt by canal 186 km long.

Somport Tunnel, on bdy. **France–Spain**; carries main rly. from Pau to Zaragoza under Pyrénées; 8 km long.

Sönderborg, spt., S. Jutland, **Denmark**; older part of c. on Als I.; palace; textiles; p. (1990) 28,291.

Sondrio, t., cap. of S. prov., **Italy**; commands the Adda valley, impt. routeway through Alps; agr. mkt.; textiles; p. (1981) 22,747.

Songhua R., **(Sungari R.)**, N.E. **China**; trib. of R. Amur; length 1,840 km.; hydroelectric power.

Songkhla, t., **Thailand**; most S. t.; ctr. of rubber growing dist.; third t. of cty.; p. (1980) 172,604.

Song-koi (Red R.), R., rises in Yunnan plateau, S.W. **China**, flows S.E. through N. **Vietnam**, enters G. of Tongking; Hanoi is nr. head of delta; Haiphong nr. one of R. mouths; lower valley densely populated and intensively cultivated; c. 1,280 km long.

Sonora, st., **Mexico**; on G. of Cal.; crossed by Sierra Madre Occidental; irrigated agr.; ch. producer of wheat, cattle; fish exp.; cap. Hermosillo; a. 182,535 km²; p. (1990) 1,822,247.

Sonoran Desert, Arizona, **USA**; alt. 900 m; enclosed basins and salt marshes.

Sonsonate, t., **El Salvador**; old t. with cath.; comm. ctr. of richest agr. region of rep., famed for coffee and dairy prod.; nr. Isalco volcano; p. (1992) 76,200.

Soo Canals. *See* **Sault Ste. Marie Canals**.

Soochow. *See* **Suzhou**.

Sopot, spt., Gdansk, **Poland**; on Gdansk Bay; resort, spa; part of Trójmiasto; p. (1989) 46,874.

Sopron, t., N.W. **Hungary**; nr. Austrian border; textiles, chemicals; p. (1983) 55,000.

Sorau. *See* **Zary**.

Soria, t., cap. of prov. of Soria, **Spain**; on R. Duero at c. 900 m; agr.-processing; retains mediaeval appearance; p. (1987) 31,507; (1991) 93,950 (prov.).

Sorocaba, t., São Paulo st., **Brazil**; textiles, food processing; p. (1991) 377,270.

Sorrento, cst. t., S. **Italy**; nr. S. extremity G. of Naples; popular resort, celebrated for its wines in anc. times; p. (1981) 17,301.

Sosnowiec, t., Katowice prov., **Poland**; coal-mng. ctr., iron wks.; metal and textile inds.; cas.; p. (1989) 259,318.

Soufrière, volcano, St. Vincent, **W.I.**; alt. 1,235 m.

Sound, The, channel between Kattegat and Baltic, 5 km across at narrowest part; proposed tunnel between Denmark and Sweden.

Sousse (Susa), spt., **Tunisia**; exp. olive oil, phosphates; resort; p. (1984) 83,509.

South Africa, Republic of, lies in most S. part of **Africa** between Atl. and Indian Ocs.; comprises 4 provs., Cape Prov., Natal, O.F.S., Transvaal; narrow cst. plain, several interior plateaux (600–1,800 m) with upland grasslands (Veld) and fringed by escarpments; climate warm and sunny; most highly developed cty. in Africa, based on mineral resources of gold and diamonds, and more recent successful economic diversification; coal in Witbank and Vryheid dists. serves iron and steel ind. at Pretoria; growing textile, foodprocessing inds. at pts. Cape Town, Durban and rubber at Pt. Elizabeth; agr. dependent upon water supply; rich fruit growing a. around Cape Town, extensive grain growing and pastoral areas extended by irrigation; caps. Pretoria (admin.), Cape Town (legislative), Bloemfontein (judicial); a. 1,224,254 km²; p. (1993) 32·59 m. (including homelands).

South America, S. continent of Western Hemisphere; inc. all ctys. S. of Panama. *See* **Latin America**.

Southampton, c. spt., l. gov. dist., Hants., **Eng.**; at head of Southampton Water on peninsula between estuaries of Rs. Test and Itchen; univ.; decline of passenger liners, now one of Britain's biggest container pts.; ship repairing, oil refining, cable mkg., electronics, synthetic rubber; freeport (1984); p. (1993) 209,200 (dist.).

Southampton Water, inlet, Hants., **Eng.**; comprises drowned estuaries of Rs. Itchen and Test; gives access from Solent and Spithead to spt. of Southampton; 14 km by 1·6–2·4 km.

South Australia, st. of the **Australian Commonwealth**; the "desert state"; barren undulating interior forms part of central plateau of continent but inc. mtns. in S. and S.E. and L. Eyre basin 12 m below sea level; Nullarbor Plain in S.W.; sheep in S.E., intensive agr. in Murray R. valley; some interior mng. inds. but st. cap. of Adelaide contains most inds. and 69 per cent of p.; a. 984,381 km²; p. (1991) 1,454,000.

South Bedfordshire, l. gov. dist., Beds., **Eng.**; close to Luton and inc. Dunstable and Leighton-Linslade; p. (1993) 110,000.

South Bend, c., Ind., **USA**; on St Joseph R., ctr. of fruit and dairy region; motorcars, aircraft, agr. machin.; p. (1990) 105,511.

South Buckinghamshire, l. gov. dist., Bucks., **Eng.**; based on Beaconsfield; p. (1993) 63,400.

South Cambridgeshire, l. gov. dist., Cambs., **Eng.**; rural a. surrounding Cambridge; p. (1993) 123,600.

South Carolina, st., **USA**; 'Palmetto St.'; admitted to Union 1788; st. flower Carolina Jessamine, st. bird Carolina Wren; level in E., mtns. in W.; subtropical climate; part of cotton belt; pigs and maize also impt.; cotton textiles; cap. Columbia; a. 80,432 km²; p. (1990) 3,486,703.

South Dakota, st., **USA**; 'Cayote St.'; admitted to Union 1889; st. flower Pasque flower, st. bird Ring Necked Pheasant; lies in Gt. Plains; crossed by R. Missouri; irrigated agr.; part of spring wheat belt, but now more diversified crops; agr. processing; cap. Pierre; a. 199,552 km²; p. (1990) 699,004 (inc. 25,000 Indians).

South Derbyshire, l. gov. dist., Derbys., **Eng.**; a. S. of Derby and inc. Repton and Swadlingcote; p. (1993) 74,300.

South Downs, chalk escarpment, East and West Sussex and Hants., **Eng.**; stretch from Chichester to Eastbourne; rise to over 240 m.

Southend-on-Sea, t., l. gov. dist., Essex, **Eng.**; on N. side of Thames estuary; varied lt. inds.; air ferry terminal; resort; dormitory for London; p. (1993) 167,500 (dist.).

Southern Alps, mtns., S.I., **N.Z.**; alt. 3,000 m.

Southern Ocean, surrounds Antarctica; pack ice.

Southern Uplands, region, S. **Scot.**; broad belt of hilly cty., N. part bleak moorland, S. part deeply cut by glens; sheep-rearing; dairying in valleys.

South Georgia, Brit. I., S. Atl. Oc.; dependency of Falkland Is.; former whaling ctr; no permanent population; a. 4,144 km².

South Glamorgan, co., S. **Wales**; mostly lowland borders Bristol Channel; inc. lge. industl. ts. and pts. of Cardiff and Barry; a. 417 km²; p. (1993) 413,200.

South Hams, l. gov. dist., S. Devon, **Eng.**; a. between Torquay and Plymouth inc. Totnes, Kingsbridge and Salcombe; p. (1993) 78,500 (dist.).

South Herefordshire, lge rural a. inc. Ross-on-Wye; **Eng.**; lge rural a. inc. Ross-on-Wye; p. (1993) 53,600.

South Holland, l. gov. dist., Lincs., **Eng.**; fenland a. around Spalding; p. (1993) 69,300.

South I., lge I., **N.Z.**; inc. S. Alps (highest Mt. Cook, 3,764 m), Canterbury Plains, impt. sheep-rearing dist.; cool climate; considerable hydroelectric power resources; tourism; a. 150,461 km²; p. (1991) 881,537.

South Kensington, dist., W. London, **Eng.**; contains Victoria and Albert Museum, Geological and Science Museums, British Museum of Natural History, Commonwealth Institute, Albert Hall.

South Kesteven, l. gov. dist., Lincs., **Eng.**; rural a. and ts. of Grantham and Bourne; p. (1993) 112,700.

South Lakeland, l. gov. dist., Cumbria, **Eng.**; lge. a. surrounding Morecambe Bay and inc. Ulverston, Grange, Kendal and Sedbergh; p. (1993) 99,600.

South Norfolk, l. gov. dist., Norfolk, **Eng.**; lge. a. inc. Diss and Wymondham; p. (1993) 103,700.

South Northamptonshire, l. gov. dist., Northants., **Eng.**; inc. Brackley and Towcester; p. (1993) 71,900.

South Orkney Is., Antarctica; S.W. of S. Georgia; part of **Brit. Antarctic Terr.** (1962); meteorological sta.

South Ossetian, aut. oblast, **Georgia**; in Caucasus

mtns.; goat and sheep rearing dist.; a. 3,898 km²; p. (1990) 99,200.

South Oxfordshire, l. gov. dist., Oxon., **Eng.**; Wallingford, Thame and Henley-on-Thames; p. (1993) 121,800.

South Pembrokeshire, l. gov. dist., Dyfed, **Wales**; from Pembroke and Tenby on cst. to Narbeth inland; p. (1993) 42,900.

Southport, t., Sefton, Merseyside, **Eng.**; on S. side of Ribble estuary; 29 km N. of Liverpool; leisure centre; residtl.; p. (1981) 89,745.

South Ribble, l. gov. dist., Lancs., **Eng.**; a. S. of Preston and inc. Walton-le-Dale; p. (1993) 103,500.

South Sandwich Is., Antarctica; dependency of **Falkland Is.**; sm. volcanic Is.; a. 337 km².

South Shetland, archipelago, S. Atl. Oc.; 640 km S. of C. Horn; part of **Brit, Antarctic Terr.** (1962).

South Shields, t., Tyne and Wear, **Eng.**; pt. on S. bank at mouth of R. Tyne; holiday resort; marine engin., new lt. inds.; p. (1981) 87,203.

South Shropshire, l. gov. dist., Shrops., **Eng.**; S. of Shrewsbury and inc. Ludlow; p. (1993) 39,400.

South Somerset, l. gov. dist. including Yeovil; p. (1993) 146,300.

South Staffordshire, l. gov. dist., Staffs., **Eng.**; a. bordering W. Midlands conurb.; p. (1993) 105,900.

South Tyneside, met. dist., Tyne and Wear, **Eng.**; comprises Jarrow, Hebburn and South Shields; p. (1993) 157,200.

Southwark, inner bor., London, **Eng.**; S. of R. Thames, incorporating former bors. of Bermondsey and Camberwell; cath.; site of former Globe theatre; p. (1993) 229,400.

South West Africa. See **Namibia**.

Southwick, t., Adur, West Sussex, **Eng.**; on S. cst. 6 km W. of Brighton; p. (1981) 11,388.

South Wight, l. gov. dist., I. of Wight, **Eng.**; inc. Ventnor and Sandown-Shanklin; p. (1993) 53,000.

Southwold, spt., Waveney, Suffolk, **Eng.**; on E. cst. 13 km S. of Lowestoft; fishing; resort; p. (1981) 1,795.

South Yorkshire, former met. co., **Eng.**; mainly industl. a. E. of Pennines; inc. productive coalfield nr. Barnsley and Doncaster and steel producing ts. of Sheffield and Rotherham; p. (1993) 1,306,200.

Sovetsk (Tilsit), t., **Russia** (since 1945); on R. Niemen, formerly in E. Prussia; timber and paper inds.; famous for Treaty of Tilsit between Napoleon and Russia 1807.

Sowerby Bridge, t., Calderdale, West Yorks., **Eng.**; on R. Calder, 5 km W. of Halifax; woollens; p. (1981) 15,546.

Spa, t., Liège, **Belgium**; mineral springs, resort; gave name to "spas"; p. (1981) 9,619.

Spain, indep. sov. st., Iberia, S.W. **Europe**; member of EU (1986); lge. land a. takes up 80 per cent of Iberian peninsula and helps to make climate continental; mtnous. interior and narrow coastal strip encourages regional isolation and development of regional culture; civil war 1936–9 hindered modern economic growth; economy based on agr., but much of land is arid and an oil refinery under construction at Bilbao, economic development has depended largely upon the spectacular growth of tourism; 42 million visitors each year; Europe's biggest car exporter; inds. attracted by cheap labour; monarchy revived 1975; cap. Madrid; a. 504,747 km²; p. (1992) 39·68 m.

Spalding, mkt. t., South Holland, Lincs., **Eng.**; in Fens, 16 km up R. Welland from Wash; agr., bulb mkt., agr. machin., sugar-beet, fruit canning; p. (1981) 18,223.

Spandau, t., Potsdam, **Germany**; previously gr. military ctr.; at confluence of Rs. Havel and Spree; now part of Berlin.

Spanish Guinea. See **Equatorial Guinea**.

Spanish Sahara (Spanish West Africa). See **Western Sahara**.

Sparrows Point, t., Md., **USA**; situated on Chesapeake Bay; impt. iron and steel inds.

Sparta (Spárti), famous anc. c., **Greece**; on R. Eurotas, in Peloponnesus; passed under Roman rule 146 B.C.; modern c. dates from 1834; p. (1981) 14,388.

Spelthorne, l. gov. dist., Surrey, **Eng.**; close to Gtr. London; inc. Staines and Sunbury-on-Thames; p. (1993) 91,600.

Spencer Gulf, lge. inlet, S. **Australia**; penetrates

384 km inland, many impt. pts. along cst. (Whyalla, Pt. Pirie, Pt. Augusta).

Spennymoor, t., Durham, **Eng.;** growing industl. t. S. of Durham; p. (1981) 20,630.

Sperrin Mtns., Strabane, **N. Ireland;** peat-covered schists; Sawell, 683 m.

Spey, R., Moray, Badenoch and Strathspey, the most rapid in **Scot.,** flows N.E. to Moray Firth; used for hydroelec. power; 171·2 km long.

Speyer, t., Rhineland-Palatinate, **Germany;** Roman origin; Romanesque cath.; famous Diet 1529 condemning Reformation gave rise to term "Protestant"; cas; publishing, engin.; p. (1986) 42,900.

Spitalfields, par., E. London, **Eng.;** formerly noted for silk weaving, introduced by Huguenots 17th cent.; name derives from spital or hospital of St. Mary, founded 12th cent.

Spithead, roadstead, between Portsmouth and I. of Wight, **Eng.;** used by ships of Royal Navy.

Spitsbergen (Svalbard), I. gr. belonging to **Norway;** within Arctic; mtnous.; sealing and whaling; coal mng.; asbestos, copper, gypsum; a. 62,921 km²; p. (1990) 3,405.

Split (Spalato), t., **Croatia** (formerly Yugoslavia); spt. on Adriatic; airport; food processing; p. (1991) 189,388.

Spokane, c., Wash., **USA;** on R. Spokane at falls used for hydroelec. power; timber tr. impt.; flour and saw mills, elec. gds.; lge. aluminium wks.; p. (1990) 177,196 (c.), 361,000 (met. a.).

Spoleto, c., Umbria, central **Italy;** cath., many Roman remains; textiles; p. (1981) 36,839.

Sporades, scattered Is. belonging to **Greece** in Aegean Sea, inc. Skyros, Skiathos and Skopelos.

Spratley Is., S. China Sea; cluster of about 50 reefs and sand bars, thought to contain petroleum; ownership disputed by China, Taiwan, Philippines, and Vietnam.

Spree, R., **Germany;** flows W. past Berlin to the Havel at Spandau; 363 km long.

Spremberg, t., Brandenburg, **Germany;** on R. Spree; cas., older part of t. on I.; glass, textiles; p. (1989) 24,547.

Springfield, c., cap. of Ill., **USA;** in rich agr. and coal mng. a.; farming and elec. machin., food processing; home of Abraham Lincoln; p. (1990) 105,227 (c.), 189,550 (met. a.).

Springfield, c., Mass., **USA;** varied mnfs.; US armoury establ. 1794; p. (1990) 156,983 (c.), 530,000 (met. a.).

Springfield, c., Mo., **USA;** agr. ctr.; flour milling, engin.; p. (1990) 140,494.

Springfield, t., Ohio, **USA;** agr. mach., motor lorries; p. (1990) 70,487.

Springs, t., Transvaal, **S. Africa;** E. of Johannesburg; gold mng., engin., cars, elec. gds.; uranium plant; p. (1980) 170,180 (dist.).

Spurn Head, Humberside, **Eng.;** sand spit at mouth of Humber estuary.

Sri Lanka (Ceylon), indep. rep. (1972) within Brit. Commonwealth (1948); in **Indian Oc.;** S.E. of India; fertile plains with cash crops of coconuts and rubber (S.W.) but dry in N.; mtnous. interior ameliorates climate where tea cultivation; varied p. composition inc. Sinhalese (70 per cent of p.), Tamils, Burghers (Portuguese and Dutch); agitation for Tamil independence; dependent on exp. of primary produce; inds. growing; cap. and ch. spt. Colombo; a. 65,610 km²; p. (1992) 17·4 m.

Srinagar, t., cap. of Kashmir, **India;** in vale at c. 1,600 m. on Jhelum R. in W. Himalayas; beautiful surrounding cty.; summer resorts; mnfs. silks, woollens, carpets; tourism; p. (1991) 595,000.

Srirangam, t., Tamil Nadu, **India;** on R. Cauvery; temple dedicated to Vishnu; pilgrimage ctr.; p. (1981) 64,241.

Stade, t., Lower Saxony, **Germany;** nr. Hamburg; pt. on R. Schwinge; leather, wood, textiles; p. (1986) 43,000.

Staffa, I. on Inner Hebrides, **W. Scot.;** 10 km N. of Iona, off W. cst. Mull; grand basaltic caverns, inc. Fingal's Cave, 69 m long, 13 m wide, 20 m high.

Stafford, co. t., l. gov. dist., Staffs., **Eng.;** on R. Sow, 24 km N. of Wolverhampton; heavy elec. and other engin.; expanded t.; p. (1993) 121,500 (dist.).

Staffordshire, non-met. co., W. Midlands, **Eng.;** plain drained by R. Trent and tribs.; N. Staffs.

coalfield inc. a. of Potteries; S. Staffs. coalfield now inc. in W. Midlands met. co.; a. 2,717 km²; p. (1993) 1,053,600.

Staffordshire Moorlands, l. gov. dist., Staffs., **Eng.;** borders S. Pennines and inc. Leek, Biddulph and Cheadle; p. (1993) 95,700.

Staines, mkt. t., Spelthorne, Surrey, **Eng.;** on R. Thames, 6 km S.E. of Windsor; linoleum, machin.; nr. birthplace of Matthew Arnold; p. (1981) 53,823.

Stainmore, pass, North Yorks./Durham, **Eng.;** crosses N. Pennines from Greta valley into upper Eden valley; used by main road; alt. 418 m.

Staithes, v., North Yorks., **Eng.;** potash mng.

Stalin. See Brasov.

Stalinabad. See Dushanbe.

Stalingrad. See Volgograd.

Stalino. See Varna.

Stalino. See Donetsk.

Stalinogorsk. See Novomoskovsk.

Stalinsk. See Novo Kuznetsk.

Stalybridge, t., Gtr. Manchester, **Eng.;** on R. Tame, 13 km E. of Manchester; cotton and wool engin., plastics, rubber, gds., elec. cables; p. (1981) 26,396.

Stamboul. See Istanbul.

Stamford, mkt. t., Lincs., **Eng.;** old bldgs., one of 5 Danelaw ts.; agr. inds., elec. gds., plastics; p. (1981) 16,153.

Stamford, c., Conn., **USA;** on shore of Long I. Sound; chemicals, engin.; p. (1990) 108,056 (c.), 203,000 (met. a.).

Stanislav. See Ivano-Frankovsk.

Stanley, t., Derwentside, Durham, **Eng.;** former colly. dist.; p. (1981) 41,210.

Stanley, spt., cap of **Falkland Is.;** former whaling port., contains over half p. of Falklands; p. (1991) 1,557.

Stanley Falls. See Boyoma Falls.

Stanley Pool. See Pool Malebo.

Stanleyville. See Kisangani.

Stanlow, Ches., **Eng.;** petrol refinery, oil storage, docks, chemicals, linked to Anglesey by pipeline.

Stanovoi Mtns., range of mtns., **Russia;** extending from N. of R. Amur to nr. Sea of Okhotsk.

Stara Zagora, t., central **Bulgaria;** textiles, agr. processing; educational ctr.; p. (1990) 164,553.

Stargard Szczecinski, t., N.W. **Poland** (since 1945); formerly in Pomerania; rly. junc.; metal chemical, and food inds.; devastated in second world war; p. (1989) 69,852.

Start Point, C., nr. Dartmouth, Devon, **Eng.**

Stassfurt, t., Saxony - Anhalt, **Germany;** in gr. potash mng. region; chemicals, machin., metals; p. (1989) 26,466.

Staten I., the most S. point N.Y. st. **USA;** shipyds.; linked with Brooklyn by Verrazano-Narrows bridge (opened 1964); residtl; p. (1990) 378,977.

Staten I., off Tierra del Fuego, **S. America.**

Stavanger, spt., cap. of Rogaland prov., S.W. **Norway;** comm. and industl. ctr.; fish curing and canning; oil refinery at Sola; cath., airport; p. (1990) 97,328.

Staveley, t., Derbys., **Eng.;** 5 km N.E. of Chesterfield; iron, chemicals, concrete and iron pipes; p. (1981) 17,828.

Stellenbosch, t., Cape Prov., **S. Africa;** 40 km. E. of Cape Town; univ.; wines, saw milling, brick and tile mkg.; p. (1980) 64,100 (dist.).

Stelvio Pass, between **Italy** and **Switzerland;** road pass, alt. 2,762 m.

Stendal, c., Saxony - Anhalt, **Germany;** impt. rly. junct.; sugar, metal and food inds.; cath.; Stendhal (Henri Beyle) took his name from the c.; p. (1989) 50,717.

Stepney. See Tower Hamlets.

Sterlitamak, t., Bashkir aut. rep., **Russia;** on S.W. flank of Ural mtns.; impt. oil refineries on "second Baku" oilfield; linked by pipeline to Togliatti; p. (1989) 247,000.

Stettin. See Szczecin.

Stettiner Haff, lagoon, **Germany** and **Poland;** separated from Baltic Sea by Is. Usedom and Wollin; receives R. Oder; 56 km long.

Stevenage, t., l. gov. dist., Herts., **Eng.;** 6 km S.E. of Hitchin; first new t. to be designated under the New Towns Act 1946; old t. known in Domesday as Stevenach; agr., lt. engin., elec. goods., chemicals, aircraft parts; p. (1993) 75,700 (dist.).

Stevenston, burgh, Cunninghame, **Scot.;** explosives factory; p. (1991) 10,153.

Steventon, v., Hants., **Eng.;** birthplace of Jane Austen.

Stewart I., S. of S.I., **N.Z.**; a. 1,735 km²; rises to over 900 m; famous for oysters.

Stewarton, burgh, Kilmarnock and Loudoun, **Scot.**; woollens, carpets; p. (1991) 6,481.

Stewartry, l. gov. dist., Dumfries and Galloway, **Scot.**; replaces old co. of Kirkcudbright; p. (1993) 23,690.

Steyning, v., West Sussex, **Eng.**; on R. Adur, 6 km N. of Shoreham at entrance to gap through S. Downs; residtl.

Steyr, t., Austria; at confluence of Rs. Enns and Steyr; industl. ctr.; historic bldgs.; p. (1991) 39,542.

Stif (Sétif), t., N.E. Algeria; agr. ctr. for surrounding plateaux; grain, livestock; phosphates in a.; p. (1983) 186,978.

Stilton, v., Cambs., **Eng.**; 10 km S.W. of Peterborough; famous for cheese.

Stirling, royal burgh, Stirling, **Scot.**; on R. Forth in gap between Campsie Fells and Ochil hills; gas univ., coal mng., engin., concrete, wool, rubber gds.; p. (1991) 30,515.

Stirlingshire, former co., central **Scot.**; on S. edge of Grampians; now forms l. gov. dist. within the Central Reg.; a. of l. gov. dist. 2,168 km²; p. (1993) 81,630.

Stockholm, c., cap. of **Sweden**; freeport; on I. at outlet of L. Malar; called the "Queen of the Baltic" for the beauty of its surroundings; comm. ctr.; machin., textiles, leather, sugar, chemicals; univ. and many academic institutions; p. (1992) 684,576.

Stockport, t., met. dist., Gtr. Manchester, **Eng.**; on R. Mersey, S.E. of Manchester; cotton manmade fibres, engin.; p. (1993) 291,400 (dist.).

Stocksbridge, t., South Yorks., **Eng.**; iron and steel; p. (1981) 14,015.

Stockton, t., Cal., **USA**; R. pt. on San Joaquin R.; agr. processing, farm implements; p. (1990) 210,943 (t.), 481,000 (met. a.).

Stockton-on-Tees, mkt. t., l. gov. dist., Cleveland, **Eng.**; 6 km W. of Middlesbrough; impt. iron and steel inds., plywood; first rly. for passenger traffic opened 1825 between Stockton and Darlington; 18th cent. town hall; racecourse; p. (1993) 177,800 (dist.).

Stoke Newington. *See* **Hackney.**

Stoke-on-Trent, c., l. gov. dist., Staffs., **Eng.**; at S.W. foot of the Pennines; formed in 1910 by union of the five towns of Arnold Bennett's novels, Hanley, Burslem, Tunstall, Longton, and Fenton (with Stoke-upon-Trent); ceramics, iron and steel, engin., brick and tile works, precast concrete, rubber gds.; p. (1993) 252,900 (dist.).

Stolberg, t., N. Rhine–Westphalia, **Germany**; E. of Aachen; metals, glass, wood, chemicals; p. (1986) 56,400.

Stolp. *See* **Slupsk.**

Stone, mkt. t., Staffs., **Eng.**; on R. Trent, 11 km S. of Stoke-on-Trent; footwear, tiles, porcelain, scientific glassware; p. (1981) 12,115.

Stonehaven, t., burgh, Kincardine and Deeside, **Scot.**; fish. pt. on E. cst., 22 km S. of Aberdeen, distilling, net mftg.; p. (1991) 9,445.

Stonehenge, prehistoric gr. of monumental stones, on Salisbury Plain, Wilts., **Eng.**; date of erection est. between 2100–1600 B.C.

Stornoway, spt., burgh, **Scot.**; on E. cst. of I. of Lewis, Outer Hebrides; ctr. Harris Tweed ind.; fishing ctr.; p. (1991) 5,975.

Stour, R., Kent, Eng.; flows past Canterbury to Pegwell Bay; 64 km long.

Stour, R., Somerset, Dorset, **Eng.**; trib. of R. Avon; 88 km long.

Stour, R., Suffolk and Essex, **Eng.**; flows E. to sea at Harwich; 67 km long.

Stour, R., Hereford and Worcs./West Midlands, **Eng.**; trib. of R. Severn; 32 km long.

Stourbridge, t., West Midlands, **Eng.**; on R. Stour; 14 km W. of Birmingham; brick and glass wks.; p. (1981) 54,661.

Stourport-on-Severn, mkt. t., Wyre Forest, Hereford and Worcs., **Eng.**; at confluence of Rs. Stour and Severn; carpets, iron and steel gds., porcelain, ceramics; old canal and R. pt.; p. (1981) 19,092.

Stowmarket, t., Mid Suffolk, **Eng.**; on R. Gipping, 18 km N.W. of Ipswich; I.C.I. paint factory; p. (1981) 10,910.

Strabane, t., l. gov. dist., **N. Ireland**; agr. ctr., shirt mkg.; p. (1991) 36,141 (dist.), 11,670 (t.).

Straits Settlements, former Brit. crown col. of Penang, Malacca, and Singapore, established 1867, dissolved 1946. *See* **Malaysia, West.**

Stralsund, spt., Mecklenburg - West Pomerania, **Germany**; opposite Rügen I.; grain tr., machin., metals, fish smoking, shipbldg.; p. (1981) 74,421.

Strangford Lough, arm of sea, Down and Ards, **N. Ireland**; 29 km long, 10 km wide at entrance.

Stranraer, royal burgh, Wigtown, **Scot.**; at head of Loch Ryan; steamer service to Larne, N. Ireland; creameries, brewing, knitwear; cas.; mkt.; p. (1991) 11,348.

Strasbourg, c., cap. of Bas-Rhin dep., E. **France**; impt. pt. in Rhine valley on Ill R., 16 km S. of confluence with Rhine; terminus of Marne–Rhine and Rhône–Rhine canals; industl., comm. and cultural ctr. of economically impt. Alsace region; food processing and varied mnfs.; historic c., with many fine bldgs., inc. cath., univ., imperial palace; surrendered to Germany 1871, reoccupied 1919; meeting-place of European Parliament; p. (1990) 255,937 (c), 388,483 (met.a.).

Stratford. *See* **Newham.**

Stratford-on-Avon, t., l. gov. dist., Warwicks., **Eng.**; on R. Avon; birthplace of Shakespeare; memorial theatre, library; many bldgs. ass. with Shakespeare; tourist ctr. in attractive setting; lt. inds.; p. (1993) 108,600 (dist.).

Strathclyde Region, l. gov. reg., Central Scot.; indust. dist. formed around Glasgow, inc. ts. on Ayr and Lanarkshire coalfields; borders the F. of Clyde; a. 13,794 km²; p. (1993) 2,286,800.

Strathkelvin, l. gov. dist., Strathclyde Reg., **Scot.**; part of Central Clydeside conurb.; p. (1993) 85,670.

Strathmore, lowland belt, central **Scot.**; flanked to N. by Grampians, to S. by Sidlaw and Ochil hills; drained by Rs. Earn, Tay, Isla, S. Esk; famous for cereals and small fruits; length 96 km, width 11–16 km.

Strathspey, valley of the Spey, **Scot.**; 112 km long.

Stratton and Bude, North Cornwall, **Eng.**; 19 km S. of Hartland Point; resort; p. (1981) 6,783.

Straubing, t., Lower Bavaria, **Germany**; agr. mkt. ctr.; machin.; p. (1986) 41,600.

Strawberry, R., Utah, **USA**; on E. slopes of Wasatch mtns. 128 km S.E. of Salt Lake City; dammed to supply irrigation water led through tunnel under Wasatch mtns. to 259 km² cultivable land round L. Utah.

Street, t., Mendip, Somerset, **Eng.**; at foot of Polden Hills, 11 km S.W. of Wells; footwear, leather; p. (1981) 8,803.

Stretford, t., Gtr. Manchester, **Eng.**; borders Manchester Ship Canal; inc. Trafford Park industl. estate; residtl.; Lancashire co. cricket ground, Manchester United football ground at Old Trafford; p. (1981) 47,600.

Stromboli, I., Lipari Is., Tyrrhenian Sea, N. of Sicily, **Italy**; active volcano, alt. 927 m.

Stromness, burgh, Mainland, Orkney Is., **Scot.**; 21 km W. of Kirkwall; mkt., fish. pt.; p. (1991) 1,890.

Stronsay, Orkney Is., **Scot.**; p. (1991) 382

Stroud, mkt. t., l. gov. dist., Gloucs., **Eng.**; on R. Frome, in Cotswolds; former ctr. of impt. cloth ind. in W. Eng.; woollens, dyes, plastics, engin.; p. (1993) 105,400 (dist.).

Sturminster Newton, t., North Dorset, **Eng.**; impt. cattle mkt. on Stour R.; creameries.

Sturts Stony Desert, a. N.W. of S. **Australia**; named after Charles Sturt, explorer.

Stuttgart, c., cap. of Baden–Württemberg, **Germany**; on Neckar R.; cas., cath., rly. junc.; industl. and comm. ctr.; publishing, science-based inds.; oil refinery nearby; p. (1990) 583,700.

Styria, prov., **Austria**; borders Slovenia on S.; mtnous. with forests and pastures; lignite and iron mng., inds. around cap. Graz; grain, wine, fruit, stock-rearing; tourism; p. (1991) 1,184,593

Suakin, former pt., **Sudan**, N.E. Africa; on Red Sea; now used only for pilgrim traffic to Jeddah; replaced by Pt. Sudan.

Subotica, t., Serbia, **Yugoslavia**; univ.; agr. ctr. with Hungarian culture; agr. processing; expanding industl. ctr.; p. (1991) 100,219.

Suceava, t., S. Bukovina, N.E. **Romania**; mkt. t. on Suceava R.; once the residence of Moldavian princes; p. (1990) 107,988.

Suchow. *See* **Zuzhou.**

Sucre, c., cap. of Chuquisaca dep. and *de jura* cap. of **Bolivia** (La Paz is *de facto* cap.); in valley of Andes at 2,600 m; agr. ctr., oil refining; p. (1988) 105,800.

Sucre, st., **Venezuela;** on Caribbean cst.; coffee and cacao; fishing impt.; fish canning at cap. Cumaná; a. 11,800 km²; p (1981) 585,698.

Sudan, The, rep., N.E. **Africa;** climatic transition from N. desert to rainy equatorial S.; mainly plateaux, dissected by Nile R. system; sporadic conflict between N. and S.; 3 southern provs. now form an autonomous reg.; long staple cotton, grown in irrigated areas, provides most valuable exp.; gum arabic from lge. forest areas; food processing; dams constructed on Atbara and Blue Nile Rs.; suffering from drought in 1980s; Khartoum; a. 2,530,430 km²; p. (1993) 30·83 m.

Sudbury, t., Ont., **Canada;** nickel, copper mng.; refining; p. (1986) 88,717 (c.), 148,877 (met. a.).

Sudbury, t., Babergh, Suffolk, **Eng.;** on R. Stour, 19 km N.W. of Colchester; p. (1981) 15,524.

Sudene, terr., N.E. **Brazil;** government sponsored economic development.

Sudetenland, region of **Czech Rep.** bordering Germany, until 1945 German-speaking; annexed by Hitler 1938, recovered by Czechoslavakia 1945; named after Sudeten mtns.

Sudeten Mtns. or **Sudetes,** mtn. range along borders of **Czech Rep.** and **Poland;** separating Bohemia and Moravia from Silesia; mineral resources.

Suez (Es-Suweis), spt. and prov., **Egypt;** the anc. Arsinoë; at head of G. of Suez (arm of Red Sea) and S. entrance of Suez canal, which crosses the isthmus of Suez to the Mediterranean at Port Said; Port Tewfiq adjoining has quay and docks; declined during closure of canal 1967–75; oil refining, fertilisers; p. (1990) 392,000 (c.), (1991) 376,000 (prov.).

Suez Canal, ship canal, **Egypt;** connects Mediterranean Sea (Pt. Said) with Red Sea (Suez) through Ls. Manzala, Timsah, and Bitter; length 162 km; closed after Arab-Israeli war of June 1967; reopened 1975; tunnel links Egypt and Israel (1980); widening and deepening of canal to accommodate larger oil tankers, complete (1980).

Suez, G., Red Sea; N.W. arm of Red Sea between Arabian desert and Sinai peninsula, **Egypt;** southern approach to Suez canal; length 304 km., width varies from 19–40 km.

Suffolk, non-met. co., E. Anglia, **Eng.;** bounded on E. by N. Sea, drowned coastline; rises to 90 m in E. Anglian Heights in W.; impt. agr. a., lge. farms, mixed farming; inds. based on agr.; many expanded ts. in S.; formerly divided into 2 admin. parts; co. t. Ipswich; a. 3,800 km²; p. (1993) 646,200.

Suffolk Coastal, l. gov. dist., E. Suffolk, **Eng.;** lge. rural a. inc. ts. of Leiston-cum-Sizewell, Saxmundham, Aldeburgh, Woodbridge and Felixstowe; p. (1993) 110,500.

Suhl, t., Suhl, **Germany;** once famous for armaments; motor-cycles; p. (1981) 49,849.

Sui, Baluchistan, **Pakistan;** natural gas; pipeline to Karachi.

Sukhumi, spt., **Georgia;** agr. processing; resort; p. (1990) 121,700.

Sukkur, t., **Pakistan;** major bridging point of R. Indus; 368 km N.E. of Karachi; dam for irrigation; thermal sta.; p. (1981) 193,000.

Sula Is., I. gr. in Molucca Sea, E. of Sulawesi, **Indonesia;** little developed.

Sulawesi (Celebes), I., **Indonesia;** mtnous., lge. forests; copra, coffee, gold, nickel, copper, asphalt; ch. pts. Menado, Makasar; a. 189,484 km²; p. (1983) 11,112,200.

Sulaymāniyah, t., **Iraq;** in hill dist. nr. Iran border; p. (1985) 279,424.

Sullum Voe, Shetland Is., **Scot.;** oil terminal and receiving ctr. for N. Sea oil.

Sultanabad. *See* **Arak.**

Sulu Is., prov. **Philippines;** archipelago between Borneo and the Philippines; inc. over 400 volcanic Is. and coral islets; a. 2,461 km²; under US control 1899–1940; p. (1990) 469,971.

Sumatra, I., **Indonesia;** relatively underdeveloped; sparse p.; main development in Cultuurgebied, rubber, oil palm, sisal, tobacco; impt. oil deposits and new oil refineries; a. 473,607 km²; p. (1981) 30,928,500.

Sumba or **Sandalwood I.,** S. of Flores, **Indonesia;** horse-breeding; rice, maize, tobacco, timber, cinnamon; cap. Waingapu; a. 11,150 km².

Sumbawa, I., **Indonesia;** between Flores and Lombok; wet climate, sparse p.; a. (inc.

nearby Is.) 13,572 km²; p. (1980) 320,000.

Sumgait, t., **Azerbaijan;** on Caspian Sea; 40 km N.W. of Baku; metallurgical ind.; chemicals; p. (1990) 234,600.

Sumy, t., **Ukraine;** engin., chemicals, textiles, agr. processing; p. (1990) 296,000.

Sunbury-on-Thames, t., Spelthorne, Surrey, **Eng.;** W. of London; residtl., water wks., gravel pits; petrol research establishment; p. (1981) 39,075.

Sunda Is., **Indonesia;** between S. China Sea and Indian Oc.; form two grs., Greater Sunda Is., inc. Java, Sumatra, Borneo, Sulawesi, Banka, and the Lesser Sunda Is. (renamed Nusa Tenggara 1954) inc. Bali, Lombok, Sumbawa, Timor.

Sundarbans, The, tract of forest and swamps, fringing the delta of the Ganges, **India/Bangladesh;** 130 km wide; rice grown in N.; tigers and crocodiles found in S.

Sunda Strait, between Java and Sumatra, **Indonesia;** 21 km wide, contains the volcanic I. of Krakatao.

Sunday I. or **Raoul I.,** lgst. and only inhabited of Kermadec Is., **N.Z.;** 32 km in circuit; meteorological and radio sta.

Sundbyberg, t., **Sweden;** adjoins Stockholm; chemicals, paper; p. (1983) 26,985.

Sunderland, c. (1992), spt., met. dist., Tyne and Wear, **Eng.;** at mouth of R. Wear; precision and aero-engin., clothing, glass, shipbldg.; car plant; p. (1993) 297,800.

Sundsvall, spt., Västernorrland, **Sweden;** on a wide bay of the Baltic nr. Hernösand; timber and wood-pulp inds.; p. (1992) 94,329.

Sungari. *See* **Songhua R.**

Sunnyvale, t., Cal., **USA;** ctr. of fruit-growing a.; lt. inds.; p. (1990) 117,229.

Superior, t., Wis., **USA;** at head of L. Superior; tr. in grain, timber, coal; shipbldg. and flour mills; oil refining; p. (1980) 29,571.

Superior, L., N. America; lgst. sheet of fresh water in the world; lies between **Canada** and **USA;** one of chain of gr. Ls. in St. Lawrence system; outlet to L. Huron by St. Mary's R., receives waters of St. Louis, Pigeon and Nipigon; impt. waterway; a. 82,880 km².

Surabaya, spt., Java, **Indonesia;** ch. naval base; handles nearly half Indonesia's tr.; shipbldg., oil refining, food processing; p. (1983) 2,289,000.

Surakarta (Solo), Java, **Indonesia;** on Solo R.; tr. ctr. for agr. region; former sultan's palace; p. (1980) 469,888.

Surat, c., Gujarat, **India;** on R. Tapti; gold and textile ctr.; notable as first English trading post 1612; plague (1994); p. (1991) 1,499,000.

Surbiton, Gtr. London, **Eng.;** on R. Thames, inc. in Royal Borough of Kingston-upon-Thames; residtl.; lt. engin., bricks, tiles, elec. components.

Suresnes, t., Hauts-de-Seine dep., **France;** sub. of Paris; cars, chemicals; p. (1982) 35,744.

Suriname (Dutch Guiana), former self-gov. terr. of Neth.; indep. 1975; **S. America;** sub-tropical climate; p. concentrated on cst. where rice, sugar, and citrus fruits grown; great agr. potential; main exp. bauxite (80 per cent of total exp. though recently declining); iron ore, timber, hydroelectr. oil; cap. Paramaribo; a. 163,265 sq. km; p. (1991) 404,310.

Surinumu Dam, 48 km from Port Moresby, **Papua New Guinea;** part of hydroelectric scheme; opened 1963.

Surrey, non-met. co., S. **Eng.;** S. of R. Thames inc. part of N. Downs; serves as dormitory a. and recreational dist. for London; mkt. gardening, dairying; co. t. Guildford; a. 1,655 km²; p. (1993) 1,037,900.

Surrey Heath, l. gov. dist., Surrey, **Eng.;** based on Bagshot, Frimley and Camberley; p. (1993) 81,300.

Susa. *See* **Sousse.**

Susquehanna, R., N.Y., Penns., and Md., **USA;** flows to Chesapeake Bay through highly industl. a.; routeway W. from Philadelphia and Baltimore across Appalachian mtns.; not navigable; hydroelectric power; 675 km long.

Sussex. *See* **East Sussex,** and **West Sussex.**

Susten Pass, alpine road, alt. 2,225 m between Hasli Tal and Reuss valley, links Bernese Oberland with Gotthard road, **Switzerland.**

Sutherland, l. gov. dist., former co., Highland Reg.,

Scot.; stretches from Atl. Oc. to Moray F.; sparsely p. reg.; a. 3,152 km²; p. (1993) 13,190.

Sutlej, R., Pakistan; rises in the Himalayas and flows to the R. Indus; used for lge. scale irrigation; 1,600 km long.

Sutton, outer bor., Greater London, **Eng.;** inc. former bors. of Beddington and Wallington, Sutton and Cheam, and Carshalton; residtl.; p. (1993) 173,300.

Sutton Coldfield, t., West Midlands, **Eng.;** 10 km N.E. of Birmingham; residtl.; hardware, plastics; p. (1981) 86,494.

Sutton-in-Ashfield, t., Ashfield, Notts., **Eng.;** 5 km S.W. of Mansfield; lt. engin.; hosiery; former coalmng. dist.; p. (1981) 41,270.

Suva, c., cap. of Fiji Is.; on Viti Levu I.; fine harbour; exp. coconut prods., sugar; international airport; p. (1986) 71,608.

Suwalki, t. and prov., N.E. **Poland;** nr. Lithuanian bdy.; timber, grain, woollens; p. (1989) 59,684 (t.), 467,100 (prov.).

Suwannee, R., Fla., and Ga., **USA;** flows to G. of Mexico; known as Swanee River, 400 km long.

Suzhou (Soochow), c., Jiangsu, **China;** nr. Shanghai; former treaty pt.; textile ctr.; p. (1984) 695,500.

Svendborg, spt., Fyn, **Denmark;** exp. dairy prods.; textiles, machin.; p. (1990) 41,030.

Sverdlovsk *See* Yekaterinburg.

Svir, R., **Russia;** flows between L. Onega and L. Ladoga; hydroelectric power; navigable; 200 km long.

Svishtov (Sistova), t., N. **Bulgaria;** R. pt. on Danube in vine-growing dist., nr. Romanian bdr.; cath., univ.

Swabia, historic region, mediaeval duchy, **Germany;** now forms part of Baden–Württemberg and Bavaria; contains Black Forest.

Swabian Alps, mtns., Baden–Württemberg, **Germany;** inc. the Swabian Jura range between valleys of Neckar and Danube.

Swadlincote, t., South Derbys., **Eng.;** 5 km E. of Burton-on-Trent; potteries, engin., clothing; p. (1981) 23,388.

Swaffham, mkt. t., Breckland, Norfolk, **Eng.;** fruit canning; p. (1981) 4,776.

Swale, R., North Yorks., **Eng.;** joins R. Ure to form R. Ouse, 96 km long.

Swale, l. gov. dist., mid Kent, **Eng.;** nr. Thames estuary inc. Sittingbourne, Faversham and I. of Sheppey; p. (1993) 117,200.

Swanage, mkt. t., Dorset, **Eng.;** on bay, E. cst. I. of Purbeck; seaside resort; p. (1981) 8,647.

Swansea, c., spt., l. gov. dist., West Glamorgan, **Wales;** on Swansea Bay; univ.; grew with exp. of coal; now imports minerals; copper and zinc refining; steel, aluminium, wire, plastics; p. (1993) 189,300 (dist.).

Swatow. *See* Shantou.

Swaziland, indep. kingdom, S. **Africa;** within Brit. Commonwealth (1968), govt. based on tribal communities; bordered by S. Africa on S., W., and N. and by Moçambique on E.; four north–south regions; high, middle, low veld and Lebombo escarpment; rainfall increases with alt.; agr. basis of economy and sugar impt. exp., but iron-ore major exp.; asbestos mng., food processing inds.; cattle raising main internal activity; cap. Mbabane; a. 17,363 km²; p. (1990) 800,000.

Sweden, kingdom, Scandinavia, N.W. **Europe;** divided for admin. purposes into 24 cos.; cap. c. Stockholm; mtnous. in N. and S. with central lowland belt containing major agr. a. and lge. proportion of p.; sm. home mkt. makes for dependency on exps., especially of mftg. products and minerals; inc. high-grade iron-ore from Kiruna and Malmberget, N. of Arctic circle; development of high-value science-based inds.; furniture, porcelain and glass mnfs. have international reputation; social democratic st. since 1932; remained neutral in second world war; highly advanced system of social security; joined EU 1995; a. 449,792 km²; p. (1992) 8·7 m.

Swidnica (Schweidnitz), t., Walbrzych, **Poland** (since 1945); formerly in Lower Silesia; metals, elec. machin., leather, textiles; p. (1989) 62,424.

Swilly, Lough, N.E. Donegal, **R.o.I.;** arm of Atl. Oc. between Fanad Point and Dunaff Head; extends 40 km inland.

Swindon, t., Thamesdown, Wilts., **Eng.;** in upper Thames Valley (Vale of White Horse), 43 km S.W. of Oxford; impt. rly. junc.; rly. workshops closed (1986); mkt. for local dist.; heavy engin., textiles, tobacco; expanded t.; growing ctr. for micro-electronics inds.; p. (1981) 91,136.

Swinoujście (Swinemünde), spt., N.W. **Poland** (since 1945); formerly in Pomerania; on I. of Usedom (Uznam), Baltic Sea; spt. for Szczecin; spa and summer resort; fishing; p. (1989) 42,932.

Swinton and Pendlebury, ts., Gtr. Manchester, **Eng.;** 8 km W. of Manchester; cotton spinning, coal, engin.; p. (1981) 39,621.

Switzerland, confederation, central **Europe;** landlocked mtnous. st. with major physical features dominated by Alpine mtn. system; divided into 26 cantons and half-cantons for purposes of govt.; 3 official languages; German (72 per cent), French (20 per cent), Italian (6 per cent) in addition to Romansch; like Norway, major natural resource is water power; industl. specialisation on precision engin., especially watch and clock mnfs.; agr. in valleys with impt. output of dairy prod., transhumance between mtn. pastures and valley bottoms; tourism provides valuable source of income; neutral; voted to remain non-member of U.N. (1986); cap. Berne; a. 41,310 km²; p. (1993) 6·9 m.

Sydney, c., cap. of N.S.W., **Australia;** pt. and c. built around natural harbour of Pt. Jackson, crossed by S. Harbour Bridge and bordered by many impt. bldgs. and parks (Opera House, Government bldgs.); one of best harbours on E. cst., pt. developed with improved transport; site of first European settlement; contains 61 per cent of state p., 22 per cent of Australia's p.; covers vast a. as suburbs grow rapidly; caths., 3 univs., airpt. on Botany Bay where heavy inds. developing; services most impt. employment, vast range of inds.; p. (1991) 3,698,500 (met. a.).

Sydney, spt., Cape Breton I., Nova Scotia, **Canada;** coal mng. and exp.; steel, chemicals; p. (1986) 27,754.

Syktyvkar, c., Komi, aut. rep., **Russia;** R. pt. on Vychegda R.; shipyds., sawmilling, engin.; cultural ctr. of Komi people; p. (1989) 232,000.

Sylhet, t., **Bangladesh;** on Surma R. in tea growing dist.; fertilisers; p. (1981) 168,371.

Syracuse, c., S.E. Sicily, **Italy;** old t. on Ortygia I., off E. cst., modern t. on mainland, connected by bridge; founded c. 734 B.C.; ctr. of anc. Greek culture; exp. olive oil, oranges, lemons, wine; chemicals at Priolo; many Greek and Roman remains; p. (1992) 126,800.

Syracuse, c., N.Y., **USA;** on Erie Barge canal; impt. industl. ctr. for chemicals, electronics, machin.; formerly salt-producing ctr.; univ.; p. (1990) 163,860 (c.), 650,000 (met. a.).

Syr Dar'ya, one of main Rs. of central Asia; formed in Ferghana Valley in **Uzbekistan;** flows through **Tajikistan** and **Kazakhstan** to Aral Sea; not navigable but used for irrigation and hydroelectric power; 2,400 km long.

Syria (Syrian Arab Rep.), S.W. **Asia;** on E. cst. Mediterranean; much of a. mtnous. and semi-desert; climate hot, but cold winters in highland interior; 32 per cent p. engaged in agr. which provides 20 per cent nat. income; mainly pastoral, but grains, fruit and cotton grown in well watered Euphrates R. valley and along cst.; oil exp. since 1968; phosphate mines in Palmyra a.; textiles, food processing in Aleppo and cap. Damascus; a. 187,088 km²; p. (1993) 13·4 m (inc. Palestinian refugees).

Syriam, t., **Myanmar;** nr. Rangoon; main oil refining ctr. of cty.

Syros or **Syra,** I., one of Cyclades, Aegean Sea, S. **Greece;** heath-covered; most populous of Cyclades; ch. t. Hermoupolis.

Syzran, c., **Russia;** impt. R. pt. on Volga nr. confluence with Syzran R.; rly. ctr.; engin., oil refining; p. (1989) 174,000.

Szazhalombatta, t., **Hungary;** on Danube, 24 km S. of Budapest; lgst. oil refinery in rep.; oil supplied through Druzhba pipeline.

Szczecin (Stettin), c., N.W. **Poland** (since 1945); formerly cap. of Prussian prov. of Pomerania; impt. spt. at mouth of R. Oder; deep-sea fishing base; shipbldg., metallurgy, engin., chemicals, technical univ.; p. (1989) 411,275.

Szczecin, prov., **Poland;** borders Baltic Sea; drained by R. Oder; mainly agr.; a. 31,339 km²;

p. (1989) 964,300.

Szechwan. *See* **Sichuan.**

Szeged, t., **Hungary;** nr. confluence of Rs. Tisza and Maros; anc. R. pt. destroyed by floods 1879, since rebuilt; univ.; tr. in cereals, paprika; textiles; p. (1989) 189,000.

Szekesfehérvár, t., **Hungary;** nr. Budapest; mkt. t., with aluminium and metal inds., food processing; known since Roman times; once cap. of Hungarian kings; p. (1989) 114,000.

Szeping. *See* **Siping.**

Szolnok, t., **Hungary;** pt. on R. Tisa, E. of Budapest; route ctr.; machin., paper, cellulose, chemicals; p. (1989) 82,000.

Szombathely, t., W. **Hungary;** rly. ctr.; agr. machin., shoes; birthplace of St. Martin of Tours (c. A.D. 316); p. (1989) 88,000.

T

Tabasco, coastal st., **Mexico;** on Bay of Campeche; low-lying; rapid development with drainage of swamps; cash crops of cacao, coffee, sugar, tobacco; major petroleum deposits aiding industl. development; cap. Villa Hermosa; a. 25,335 km²; p. (1990) 1,501,183.

Table Bay, inlet of Atl., cst. of C. of Good Hope, **S. Africa;** site of Cape Town.

Table Mountain, Cape Prov., **S. Africa;** nr. Cape Town; alt. 1,082 m.

Tabor, t., **Czech Rep.;** S. of Prague, on R. Luznice; rly. junc.; textiles, tobacco; p. (1984) 33,757.

Tabora, t., central **Tanzania,** E. Africa; at junc. of rlys. from Dar es Salaam and L. Victoria; p. (1985) 134,000.

Tabriz, c., **Iran;** cap. of Azerbaijan; metal inds., carpets, leather, soap; famous blue mosque; univ.; impt. oil refining ctr.; p. (1986) 994,377.

Tachira, st., **Venezuela;** mtnous. inland st. bordering Colombia; coffee; cap. San Cristobal; a. 11,100 km²; p. (1981) 660,234.

Tacna, t., cap. of Tacna prov., **Peru;** in fertile valley of mtnous. region; agr. t.; p. (1990) 150,200.

Tacna, prov., **Peru;** mtnous. and arid, some irrigated valleys; transferred from Chile by treaty 1929; subject to earthquakes; a. 12,769 km²; p. (1990), 209,800.

Tacoma, spt., Wash., **USA;** on Puget Sound; shipping, fishing; grew with Alaskan and Pac. tr.; port inds. and agr. processing; p. (1990) 176,664 (c.), 586,000 (met. a.).

Tacuarembo, dep., **Uruguay;** N. of Rio Negro R., which provides hydroelectricity; mainly agr.; cap. T.; a. 15,812 km²; p. (1985) 82,809.

Tadoussac, v., Quebec, **Canada;** on R. Saguenay, where it enters St. Lawrence R.; tourist ctr.; settlement dates from 1599; p. (1986) 838.

Taegu, c., **S. Korea;** textiles, agr. processing; p. (1990) 2,228,834.

Taejon, t., **S. Korea;** S. of Seoul; fish, petroleum; p. (1990) 1,062,084

Taff, R., Powys, South and Mid Glamorgan, **Wales;** rises in Brecon Beacons, flows S.E. across coalfield to Bristol Channel at Cardiff; 64 km long.

Taff Ely, l. gov. dist., Mid Glamorgan, **Wales;** inland ts. of Pontypridd and Llantrisant; p. (1993) 101,400.

Tafilalet, Morocco, N. Africa; oasis of the Sahara, E. of Atlas; dates.

Tagab, c., **Afghanistan;** in Panjshir R. valley N.W. of Kábul.

Taganrog, c., **Russia;** spt. on Sea of Azov; iron and steel, engin.; site of fortress founded by Peter the Great 1698; birthplace of Chekhov; p. (1989) 292,000.

Tagliamento, R., N.E. **Italy;** rises in Carnic Alps, flows W. into Adriatic; 160 km long.

Tagus, R., **Spain** and **Portugal;** rises in E. Spain and flows across the Meseta to Atl. Oc. at Lisbon where there is a magnificent bridge; its estuary forms one of the finest harbours in Europe.

Tahiti, ch. I., Society Is., **Fr. Polynesia;** contains Papeete, main admin. ctr. of Fr. Oceania; fer-

tile alluvial belt; exp. copra, phosphates, vanilla; tourism; a. 1,041 km²; p. (1983) 115,820.

Taichow. *See* **Taizhou.**

Taichung, t., **Taiwan;** agr. mkt.; food processing; p. (1984) 655,196.

Taif, t., Hejaz, **Saudi Arabia;** 80 km E. of Mecca; 1,800 m a.s.l.; summer resort.

Tai Hu, L., Jiangsu, **China;** focus of intensive system of small canals and waterways, 96 km N. of Shanghai; a. c. 260 km².

Taimyr Peninsula, N. cst., Siberia, **Russia;** terminates with C. Chelyuskin; occupies most of Taimyr National Area, inhabited by nomadic Samoyeds; p. (1986) 54,000.

Tainan, t., S.W. cst. of **Taiwan;** former cap.; univ.; p. (1985) 622,000.

Taipei, c., cap. of **Taiwan;** on cst. plain in N. Taiwan, nucleus of major industl. a.; major transport ctr.; international airpt.; univ.; p. (1986) 2,560,000.

Taiwan (Formosa), I., off cst. of S.E. **China;** beautiful I. with intensive agr. on W. cst.; most densely populated cty. in the world; part of Japan 1895–1945; returned to China 1945; occupied by Nationalist government since 1949; growing political isolation; USA aid has built growth economy, textiles, plastics, electronics exp. to USA esp.; cap. Taipei; a. 35,975 km²; p. (1991) 20·6 m.

Taiyüan, c., cap. of Shanxi prov., N. **China;** on Fen R.; walled c.; univ.; ctr. of rapid industl. development; integrated iron and steel plant; chemicals, machin., paper, textiles; p. (1992) 1,980,000.

Taiz, t., **Yemen;** in fertile valley; former cap.; p. (1987) 178,043.

Taizhou (Taichow), c., Jiangsu prov., **China;** rice ctr.; p. (1984) 161,300.

Tajikistan, CIS former constituent rep., USSR; borders China and Afghanistan; mainly mtnous., inc. Pamirs and Turkestan and part of highly cultivated Ferghana Valley; cattle breeding; cotton main cash crop; impt. oil and hydroelec. power resources; cap. Dushanbe; a. 144,263 km²; p. (1992) 5·5 m.

Takamatsu, t., **Japan;** N. cst. Shikoku; ferry terminal; univ.; tourism; p. (1990) 329,684.

Takaoka, t., Honshu, **Japan;** ctr. of rice tr.; lacquer wk.; cars; p. (1990) 175,466.

Takapuna, c., N.I., **N.Z.;** connected by motorway to Auckland; residtl. ctr.; p. (1987) 70,000.

Takasaki, t., Honshu, **Japan;** radiation chemistry research ctr.; textiles; p. (1990) 236,463.

Taklimakan Shamo, desert, W. **China;** basin of inland drainage; home of the Turko people; surrounded by a ring of oases.

Takoradi. *See* **Sekondi-Takoradi.**

Taland I., Indonesia; N.E. of Sulawesi; copra; underdeveloped; a. 1,279 km².

Talavera de la Reina, t., Toledo prov., central **Spain;** on Tagus R.; ceramics; scene of battle 1809; p. (1981) 69,307.

Talca, t., cap. of Maule region., **Chile;** S. of Santiago; lge. mftg. ctr.; matches, footwear, paper, and flour mills, foundries; p. (1987) 164,482.

Talcahuano, spt., **Chile,** nr. Concepción; naval sta.; steel plant at Huachipato; fish processing, oil refining; p. (1987) 231,356.

Talien. *See* **Lushun.**

Tallahassee, t., Fla., **USA;** univ.; timber-based inds.; p. (1990) 124,773.

Tallinn, spt., cap. of **Estonia;** on G. of Finland; diverse inds. inc. radio equipment; mediaeval architecture; p. (1991) 502,400.

Tamale, t., cap. of Kaduna st., **Ghana,** W. Africa; admin. ctr.; cotton milling, peanut processing; p. (1984) 83,653.

Tamar, R., Tasmania, **Australia;** formed at confluence of N. Esk and S. Esk at Launceston, flows into Bass Strait nr. George Town.

Tamar, R., Devon and Cornwall, **Eng.;** flows S. to Plymouth Sound; 72 km long.

Tamatave. *See* **Toamasina.**

Tamaulipas, st., **Mexico;** on G. of Mexico, S. of Texas; petroleum is main resource; fishing along lagoon cst.; cotton, livestock; cap. Ciudad Victoria; a. 79,593 km²; p. (1990) 2,244,208.

Tambao, t., **Bourkina Fasso;** rich deposits of manganese could diversify economy and provide valuable exports; development depends on railway extension.

Tambov, c., cap. of Tambov oblast, **Russia;** on

Tsna R.; regional ctr. serving agr. dist.; engin.; p. (1989) 305,000.

Tameside, met. dist., Gtr. Manchester, **Eng.**; comprises Dukinfield, Ashton-under-Lyne, Hyde and Mossley; p. (1993) 221,600.

Tamil Nadu (formerly **Madras**), st., **India**; on S.E. cst. of peninsula; home of Tamils; crossed by R. Cauvery; dry crops; acute water shortages relieved by water and sewerage development plan; ch. ts. Madras, Madura; a. 130,357 km²; p. (1991) 55,858,946.

Tampa, c., Fla., **USA**; popular winter resort, cigar factories, phosphates, electronics; fruit growing and canning; p. (1990) 280,015 (c.), 2,067,959 (met. a. with St. Petersburg-Clearwater).

Tampere (Tammerfors), t., S. **Finland**; on rly. between Helsinki and Vaasa; textiles, leather, paper, based on local hydroelec. power; cath.; p. (1991) 173,797.

Tampico, spt., Mexico, on R. Panuco, 14 km from G. of Mexico; exp. petroleum; oil refining, fish processing, chemicals; tourism; p. (1990) 271,636.

Tamworth, t., N.S.W., **Australia**; impt. service and shopping ctr. for N. Tablelands; p. (1981) 29,657.

Tamworth, t., l. gov. dist., Staffs., **Eng.**; on R. Tame, 8 km S.E. of Lichfield; anc. cas.; lt. engin.; expanded t.; p. (1993) 71,600 (dist.).

Tana, lge. freshwater L., N.W. **Ethiopia**, nr. Gondar; source of Blue Nile, surrounded by marsh, papyrus swamp.

Tana, R., **Kenya**; rises nr. Mt. Kenya and flows to Indian Oc.; impt. elephant habitat in valley; 5 major hydro-elect. sta.,; 800 km long.

Tananarive. *See* Antananarivo.

Tandridge, l. gov. dist., Surrey, **Eng.**; S. of Gtr. London, inc. Caterham and Godstone; p. (1993) 76,600.

Tanga, spt., **Tanzania**, E. Africa; on plateau overlooking Tanga Bay; rly. terminus; new plywood plant; p. (1988) 187,634.

Tanganyika, gr. L., E. **Central Africa**; lies in Gt. Rift Valley; c. 672 km long, 24–32 km wide; second lgst. L. in Africa and except for L. Baykal deepest L. in world; c. 823 m a.s.l.; discovered by Burton and Speke 1858, explored by Livingstone and Stanley 1871.

Tangier, free pt., **Morocco**, N. Africa; on Strait of Gibraltar; no longer internationalised zone but integral part of kingdom of Morocco; summer cap.; shipyard; cigarettes, fishing; p. (1982) 266,346.

Tangshan, c., Hebei prov., **China**; impt. industl. ctr.; steel, machin.; textiles, cement, oil refining; devastated by a series of earthquakes (1976); p. (1990) 1,500,000.

Tanimbar Is., Indonesia; gr. of Is. in Banda Sea, S. Moluccas; forests, swamps; maize, rice, coconuts, sago.

Tanta, t., Lower **Egypt**; 88 km N. of Cairo; impt. rly. junc.; religious fairs; cotton processing; univ. proposed; p. (1986) 334,505.

Tanzania, rep., E. cst. **Africa**; inc. Is. of Zanzibar and Pemba, united since 1964; narrow coastal plain rises to inland plateau (Mt. Kilimanjaro, 5,895 m, hgst. peak in Africa); climate varies with alt., tropical in Zanzibar, temperate inland; predominantly subsistence agr., maize, millet, groundnuts, livestock; comm. crops inc. sisal, sugar, cotton, coffee; cloves on Is., especially Pemba; food processing, textile inds.; 5-year planning system to assist economic development especially in rural a.; old cap. Dar es Salaam; new cap. Dodoma (since 1974); a. 939,706 km²; p. (1991) 25.09m.

Taormino, resort, E. Sicily, **Italy**; 230 m above sea at foot of Mt. Etna; magnificent scenery and anc. ruins.

Tapachula, c., Chiapas st., S. **Mexico**; on Pac. cst. lowlands; comm. ctr. for agr. dist.; p. (1990) 222,282.

Tapti, R., W. **India**; flows W. to G. of Cambay from Betul dist., Madhya Pradesh; 702 km.

Tarai, marshy, jungle tract at foot of Himalayas, **India, Nepal**; barrier to economic development of Nepal, now much modified and reduced in area by human occupation.

Taranaki, reg., N.I., **N.Z.**; impt. stock rearing and dairying a.; offshore oil and gas fields; a. 9,713 km²; p. (1991) 107,222.

Taranto, t., Lecce, **Italy**; on G. of Taranto,

inlet of Ionian Sea; maritime arsenal with gr. comm. and industl. interests; strong cas.; steel wks.; cement; oil refinery; famous for its oyster and mussel fisheries; p. (1992) 230,207.

Tarapacá, region, N. **Chile**; cap. Iquique; hot, arid desert; nitrate deposits; a. 55,270 km²; p. (1989) 341,112.

Tarascon, t., Bouches-du-Rhône dep., **France**; connected by bridges with Beaucaire on opposite bank of R. Rhône; old cas., famous festival; p. (1982) 11,024.

Tarawera Mtn., volcanic peak, N.I., **N.Z.**; 305 m; in Hot Springs dist.; eruption 1886 destroyed L. Rotomahana (water later returned to form bigger and deeper L.).

Tarbes, t., cap. of Hautes-Pyrénées dep., **France**; on R. Adour; cath.; p. (1990) 50,228.

Tarifa, t., Spain, on Gibraltar Strait; most S. point of mainland of Europe; fish tr., cereals, oranges, wines; p. (1981) 15,220.

Tarija, dep. **Bolivia**; part of Gran Chaco rising to W.; extensive agr. and forests; cap. T.; a. 64,196 km²; p. (1988) 246,600.

Tarija, t., cap. of T. prov., **Bolivia**; alt. 1,906 m; cath., univ.; mkt. t.; p. (1988) 66,900.

Tarim Basin, depression, Xinjiang, **China**; desert with oases; crossed by Silk Road; anc. civilisation; state farms for wheat, millet, maize, cotton.

Tarn, dep., S. **France**; watered by Tarn and its tribs.; between Central Massif and basin of Aquitaine; mainly agr.; cap. Albi; a. 5,781 km²; p. (1990) 342,700.

Tarn, R., **France**; trib. of R. Garonne; rocky gorge 50 km long in its upper course; 376 km long.

Tarn-et-Garonne, dep., W. **France**; alluvial plain formed by Rs. Tarn, Garonne and Aveyron; mainly agr.; cap. Montauban; a. 3,730 km²; p. (1990) 200,200.

Tarnobrzeg, t. and prov., S.E. **Poland**; sulphur mng. and processing; p. (1989) 45,702 (t.), 594,200 (prov.).

Tarnow, t. and prov., **Poland**; E. of Kraków; industl. ctr.; lge. nitrogen factory; synthetic fibres, metallurgy; cath.; p. (1989) 120,639 (t.), 664,900 (prov.).

Tarpon Springs, t., Fla., **USA**; pt.; main source of sponges in USA.

Tarragona, prov., **Spain**; on Mediterranean; vineyards and agr.; cap. Tarragona; a. 6,283 km²; p. (1991) 540,360.

Tarragona, spt., cap. of T. prov., **Spain**; at mouth of R. Francoli; exp. agr. prod. of Ebro valley; cath.; many Roman remains, inc. aqueduct; liqueur; p. (1991) 112,655.

Tarsus, anc. c., S. **Turkey**; nr. Adana; orange and citrus groves; ruined Roman temple; birthplace of St. Paul; p. (1990) 168,654.

Tartu c., **Estonia**; pt. on Emayygi R.; rly. junc.; famous univ. founded 1632; agr. machin., tobacco ind.; p (1991) 115,300.

Tashkent, c., cap. of **Uzbekistan**; cultural, industl. and scientific ctr. of central Asia; on Trans-Caspian rly. in fertile Ferghana valley; univ.; diverse inds.; terminus of gas pipeline; p. (1990) 2,093,900.

Tasman Bay, lge inlet, S.I., **N.Z.**; penetrates N. cst., between Separation Point and D'Urville I.; enclosed by mtns., sheltered, fertile, coastal fringe; ch. ts. Nelson, Motueka; gives name to dist.; p. (1991) 36,416.

Tasman Glacier, S.I., **N.Z.**; one of the lgst. in the world.

Tasmania (formerly **Van Diemen's Land**), I., st., **Australia**; smallest and least populous st. of Australia, second to be colonised (in 1803); mountainous with rugged cst.; temperate climate aids hydro-electric development and consequent rapid industl. expansion; plans for hydro-electric sta. on Franklin R. to help relieve high unemployment but fiercely opposed because of region's rare and striking natural beauty; 9 Nat. Parks; mng.; pastoral agr.; forestry; cap. Hobart; a. 67,897 km²; p. (1991) 469,200.

Tasman Sea, Australia; part of Pac. Oc. between Australia and New Zealand.

Tatabánya, t., N. **Hungary**; lignite mng. ctr.; aluminium refining, chemicals; p. (1989) 77,000.

Tatar, aut. rep., **Russia**; in middle Volga valley; wooded steppeland; extensive oil deposits and natural gas fields; cap. Kazan; a. 67,988 km²; p. (1989) 3,641,700.

Tatra Mtns., highest mtn. gr. of W. Carpathians, on border of **Slovakia** and **Poland**; highest peak Gerlach in Slovakia, 2,664 m; mountaineering and winter sports.

Tatung. *See* **Datong.**

Taubaté, t., São Paulo st., **Brazil**; industl. ctr.; p. (1985) 205,900.

Taunton, co. t., Somerset, **Eng.**; on R. Tone at W. end of Vale of Taunton; old cas.; with Wellington forms l. gov. dist. of **Taunton Deane**; p. (1993) 97,500 (dist.).

Taunton, t., Mass., **USA**; cotton, iron foundries, machin., plastics; p. (1980) 45,001.

Taunus, mtn. range, Hesse, **Germany**; between Rs. Lahn and Rhine and Main; forests, vineyards and spas.

Taupo, L., N.I., **N.Z.**; lgst. L. in N.Z.; geysers, hot springs in vicinity; 40 km by 27 km; gives name to dist.; p. (1991) 30,721.

Tauranga, t. and dist., N.I., **N.Z.**; spt. on Bay of Plenty; tourism; fishing; p. (1991) 67,333 (dist.).

Taurus Mtns., range, S. **Turkey**; rise to over 3,660 m.

Tavastehus. *See* **Hämeenlinna.**

Tavistock, mkt. t., West Devon, **Eng.**; on R. Tavy; anc, stannary t.; Drake born nearby.

Taw, R., Devon, **Eng.**; flows from Dartmoor to Barnstaple Bay; 80 km long.

Taxco, t., **Mexico**; alt. 1,700 m; gold- and silver-mng.; tourist ctr.; anc. Aztec t.; p. (1990) 86,811.

Taxila, ruined c., **Pakistan**; nr. Rawalpindi; anc. seat of learning; ruins of Buddhist univ.

Tay, R., **Scot.**; flows S.E. from Loch Tay in Perth and Kinross, to Firth of Tay; longest R. in Scot., 188 km; salmon fisheries.

Tay, Firth of, lge. inlet, E. cst. **Scot.**; extends inland almost to Perth.

Tayeh, t., Hupeh, **China**; lies to S. of Yangtze R., 67 km S.E. of Wuhan; impt. iron-ore deposits; supplies Hwangshih; iron and steel inds., heavy engin.

Tayport, burgh, North East Fife, **Scot.**; at entrance to Firth of Tay; opposite Broughty Ferry; linen, jute; p. (1991) 3,346.

Tayside, l. gov. reg., **Scot.**; inc. former cos. of Perth and Angus bordering the Highlands; a. 7,500 km²; p. (1993) 395,200.

Tbilisi (Tiflis), c., **Georgia**; route ctr. on Kura R.; major admin., economic and cultural ctr. of Transcaucasia; machin., textiles, tanneries, furniture, food processing; power from hydroelectric power stas.; anc. tr. ctr.; some mediaeval fragments in c. ctr.; p. (1990) 1,267,500.

Tczew (Dirschau), t., Gdansk prov., N. **Poland**; pt. on Vistula; rly. junc.; agr. implements; p. (1989) 58,887.

Team Valley, Tyne and Wear, **Eng.**; impt. trading estate.

Tebessa, t., N.E. **Algeria**; in Atlas mtns., at 851 m; mkt.; carpets; phosphate deposits nearby.

Tees, R., N. **Eng.**; rises on Cross Fell, Cumbria, flows E. to N. Sea between Hartlepool and Redcar; heavy inds. in lower section; 112 km long.

Teesdale, l. gov. dist., Durham, **Eng.**; Pennine a. inc. Barnard Castle; p. (1993) 24,300.

Teesport, oil refinery, between Redcar and Middlesbrough, Cleveland, **Eng.**

Teesside, former admin. dist., Cleveland, **Eng.**; inc. Middlesbrough, Redcar, Thornaby-on-Tees, Stockton-on-Tees, Billingham, and Eston; p.(1981) 382,689.

Tegal, spt., Java, **Indonesia**; textiles, sugar refining; lge. dam nearby; p. (1980) 131,728.

Tegucigalpa, c., cap. of **Honduras**; on R. Choluteca at 976 m; inter-ocean highway connects with Caribbean and Pac. Oc.; former ctr. of silver mng.; inc. Comayagüela, the modern part of c., where the nat. univ. is situated; p. (1988) 678,700.

Tehran (Teheran), c., cap. of **Iran**, 112 km S. of Caspian Sea; mftg. and comm. ctr.; modern bldgs.; gas pipeline to USSR; international airpt.; univ.; car assembly, textiles, chemicals, glass; new oil refinery; ctr. for more than 90 per cent of all industl. firms in Iran; p. (1986) 6,022,078.

Tehuantepec, Isthmus of, separates G. of Mexico

from Pac. Oc. at narrowest point of **Mexico**; width 200 km.

Teifi, R., S. **Wales**; rises in Cambrian mtns., flows S.W. to Cardigan Bay; 150 km long.

Teign, R., Devon, **Eng.**; flows to sea at pt. of Teignmouth from Dartmoor; picturesque estuary; 48 km long.

Teignbridge, l. gov. dist., S. Devon, **Eng.**; lower T. valley and ts. of Dawlish, Teignmouth, Newton Abbot and Ashburton; p. (1993) 112,100.

Teignmouth, t., Teignbridge, Devon, **Eng.**; at mouth of R. Teign, 21 km S. of Exeter; resort; revival of pt. with ball clay exp.; p. (1981) 13,264.

Tekirdag, t. and prov., **Turkey**; on Sea of Marmara, W. of Istanbul; former Greek settlement; p. (1985) 63,215 (t.), (1990) 468,842 (prov.).

Tel Aviv-Jaffa, c., **Israel**; on Mediterranean; lgst. c. of cty.; financial and cultural ctr.; univ.; founded by Zionists 1909; p. (1990) 339,400.

Telemark, co., **Norway**; borders Skagerrak; mtnous., lake-covered, much forested; hydro-electric power forms basis for electrochemical inds.; a. 15,118 km²; p. (1990) 162,869.

Telford, new t. (1963), Shropshire, **Eng.**; 32 km W. of Wolverhampton; p. (1981) 103,411.

Tellicherry, t., spt., Kerala, **India**; exp. pepper; lge. college; furniture; p. (1981) 75,561.

Telok Betong, spt., Sumatra, **Indonesia**; exp. pepper, agr. products.

Tema, pt. (opened 1962), nr. Accra, **Ghana**; deepwater harbour, oil refinery, aluminium smelter; impt. industl. development; p. (1984) 60,767.

Teme, R., on border of Wales and Hereford and Worcs., **Eng.**; trib. of R. Severn; 112 km long.

Temir-Tau, c., **Kazakhstan**; on Nura R.; industl. ctr.; iron, steel, synthetic rubber, soda; lge. thermal power sta.; p. (1990) 213,100.

Temuco, c., cap. of Araucania region., **Chile**; cath.; tr. in cereals, apples, timber; Araucanian Indian mkt.; p. (1987) 217,789.

Tenali, t., Andhra Pradesh, **India**; nr. Guntur in Krishna delta; p. (1991) 143,836.

Tenasserim, div., lower **Myanmar**; on Thailand border; extends along Isthmus of Kra; tin and rubber; a. 92,945 km². p. (1983) 917,628.

Tenby, mkt. t., S. Pembs., Dyfed, **Wales**; on W. side of Carmarthen Bay, Bristol Channel; seaside resort; walled cas. t.; p. (1981) 4,814.

Tendring, l. gov. dist., E. Essex, **Eng.**; inc. cstl. ts. of Harwich, Frinton, Clacton and Brightlingsea; p. (1993) 128,700.

Tenerife, I., Canary Is.; volcanic landscapes and mild climate attracts tourists; cap. Santa Cruz; a. 2,025 km².

Tennessee, R., Tenn., Ky., **USA**; lgst. and most impt. branch of Ohio R.; valley once liable to flooding, now controlled by dams, and improved by the Tenn. Valley Authority; 1,251 km long.

Tennessee, st., **USA**; 'Volunteer St.'; admitted to Union 1796; st. flower Iris, st. bird Mockingbird; rises to Appalachians in E., crossed by Tennessee R. and tribs.; a. of heavy rainfall and severe soil erosion necessitated the public Tenn. Valley Authority scheme of conservation, dam bldg., and afforestation; cap. Nashville; a. 109,412 km²; p. (1990) 4,877,185.

Tenterden, mkt. t., Kent, **Eng.**; 13 km N. of Rye; grew with wool tr., church with famous tower; p. (1981) 6,209.

Teófilo Otoni, t., Minas Gerais, **Brazil**; semi-precious stone polishing; p. (1985) 126,200.

Tepic, c., cap. of Nayarit st., **Mexico**, comm. ctr. for agr. dist.; nr. Sanguaney volcano; p. (1990) 238,101.

Teplice, watering pl., Czech Rep.; N.W. of Prague; textile and hardware inds.; mineral springs; p. (1984) 53,508.

Teramo, c., cap. of T. prov., **Italy**; 24 km from Adriatic; route and agr. ctr.; cath.; textiles; the anc. Interamnium; p. (1981) 51,092.

Terek, R., N. Caucasia, **Russia**; flows to Caspian Sea; used for irrigation and hydroelectric power in lower course; 592 km long.

Teresina, t., cap. of Piaui st., **Brazil**; comm. ctr.; lt. inds.; p. (1991) 598,449.

Terezopólis, t., Rio de Janeiro, **Brazil**; health resort; textiles; p. (1985) 115,900.

Terneuzen, t., **Neth.**; on W. Schelde R.; pipeline

from Pernis; p. (1993) 35,429.

Terni, t., Perugia, **Italy**; among the Apennines; iron and steel wks., arms factory; cath.; p. (1992) 108,150.

Ternopol (Tarnopol), t., **Ukraine**; E. of Lvov; rly. junc., mkt.; agr. machin., food inds.; p. (1990) 211,600.

Terrassa, t., Barcelona, **Spain**; textile ctr.; p. (1991) 153,519.

Terre Adélie, part of Fr. Antarctic terr., S. **Indian Oc.**; research stn.; est. a. 424,400 km².

Terre Haute, t., Ind., **USA**; coal, natural gas, flour, paper, glass, foundries; p. (1990) 57,483.

Teruel, t., cap. of Teruel prov., **Spain**; on R. Turia; walled t., cath.; p. (1987) 27,475, (1991) 141,006 (prov.).

Test Valley, l. gov. dist., W. Hants., **Eng.**; stretches from Andover to Romsey; p. (1993). 105,000.

Tete, t., central **Moçambique**; on R. Zambesi; ctr. of coalfield, iron-ore, graphite, radioactive materials.

Tetovo, t., **Macedonia**, formerly Yugoslavia; chemicals, electro-metallurgy, textiles.

Tetuan, ch. spt., **Morocco**, N. Africa; walled t. p. (1982) 199,615.

Teviot, R., Roxburgh, **Scot.**; trib. of R. Tweed; 59 km long.

Tewkesbury, mkt. t., l. gov. dist., Gloucs., **Eng.**; on R. Avon, close to confluence with R. Severn; Norman abbey; p. (1993) 72,200 (dist.).

Texarkana, t., Texas and Ark., **USA**; bdy. passes down middle of main street; timber and cotton region; total p. (1984) 32,900 (t.), 118,500 (met. a.).

Texas, st., S.W. **USA**; 'Lone Star St.'; admitted to Union 1845; st. flower Bluebonnet, st. bird Mocking bird; second lgst. st. by a.; borders Mexico; dry plains in W., humid cst. in E.; problems of soil erosion yet leading agr. st.; leading producer of petroleum and natural gas; cap. Austin; a. 692,408 km²; p. (1990) 16,986,510.

Texel, one of the W. Frisian Is., **Neth.**; scene of several naval battles; p. (1991) 12,726.

Thailand (Siam), kingdom, **S.E. Asia**; 4 main regions; parallel N.–S. hill ranges (2,400 m) and valleys in N. producing teak; rice growing, fertile plain of Chao Phraya R. in ctr.; thinly populated E. plateau, drained by Mekong; S. coastal strip on G. of Siam; monsoon climate; predominantly agr., accounting for 60 per cent of p. and 60 per cent of exports; fifth lgst. exporter of foodstuffs in the world, mainly rice, tapioca, rubber and maize to U.S.A., Japan & Singapore esp.; desire to conserve rainforest now resulting in the intensification of agr.; recent offshore gas discoveries; mnfg. development centres on cap. Bangkok; tourism and fishery increasingly impt.; a. 519,083 km²; p. (1993) 57·8 m.

Thailand, G. of, lge. inlet, S. China Sea; sheltered with shallow water; length 616 km N.W. to S.E.

Thal Desert, Pakistan; W. of Punjab; now irrigated for wheat and cotton.

Thame, mkt. t., South Oxford, **Eng.**; on R. Thame, 11 km S.W. of Aylesbury; p. (1981) 8,533.

Thames, R., **Eng.**; rises in Cotswold hills and flows past Oxford, Reading, Windsor, and London to the N. Sea; tribs. inc. Windrush, Cherwell, Thame, Kennet, Colne, Lea, and Roding; estuary impt. industl. a. with many oil refineries; flood barrier at Silvertown in Woolwich (1983), 336 km long.

Thamesdown, l. gov. dist., N.E. Wilts., **Eng.**; based on Swindon; p. (1993) 173,800.

Thameshaven, lge. oil refinery, Essex, **Eng.**; on N. cst. of Thames estuary 13 km below Tilbury.

Thana, t., Maharashtra, **India**; textiles, chemicals; p. (1991) 803,000.

Thanet, I. of, lge. promontory, N.E. extremity of Kent, **Eng.**; formed by bifurcation of R. Stour; now also l. gov. dist. which contains Margate, Ramsgate, and Broadstairs; p. (1993) 125,500.

Thanjavur, t., Tamil Nadu, **India**; silks, carpets, jewellery, inlaid metals; impt. Brahman ctr.; p. (1991) 202,013.

Thar Desert, on bdy. of **India** and **Pakistan**; covers slopes between N.W. Deccan and R. Indus; barren, lack of Rs. or level land prevents irrigation; crossed by caravan routes.

Thebes, c., of Boeotia, in anc. **Greece**; Mycenaean site; destroyed by Alexander the Great 335

B.C.; modern c. of Thivai occupies site; p. (1981) 18,712.

Thebes, c. of anc. **Egypt**; on banks of Nile; site now partly occupied by vs. Karnak and Luxor; archeological discoveries in Valley of the Kings 1922, inc. tomb of Tutankhamun.

The Entrance, t., N.S.W., **Australia**; tourist resort on waterway from L. Tuggerah to Tasman Sea; fishing; p. (1981) 37,891.

Thermopylae, celebrated pass between Mt. Oeta and the sea, N.E. **Greece**; heroic battle between Spartans and Persians 480 B.C.

Thessaloniki, c., **Greece**; spt. at head of G. of T.; with fiscal free zone; second c. of Greece; impt. route and industl. ctr.; univ.; p. (1981) 406,413.

Thessaly, prov., central **Greece**; fertile plain drained by R. Piníos; mainly agr.; a. 13,489 km²; p. (1991) 731,230.

Thetford, t., Breckland, Norfolk, **Eng.**; on Little Ouse; industl. estate for London overspill; fruit and vegetable canning, pulp mftg., engin.; p. (1981) 19,591.

Thetford Mines, t., Quebec, **Canada**; asbestos mng. ctr.; p. (1986) 18,561.

Thienen (Tirlemont), t., Brabant prov., **Belgium**; ctr. of Belgian beet-sugar refining; captured by Marlborough 1705; p. (1981) 32,620.

Thiès, t., **Senegal**; rly. ctr. and wkshps.; aluminium, phosphate quarrying; p. (1985) 156,200.

Thimphu, t., cap. **Bhutan**; hydroelectric plant; 176 km road link to Phuntsholing (Sikkim) 1968; p. (1991) 27,000.

Thionville, t., Moselle dep., N. **France**; in Lorraine ironfield conurb.; metallurgical and chemical inds.; p. (1990) 40,835 (t.), 132,413 (met.).

Thira (Santorine), volcanic I., Cyclades, **Greece**; wine prods.; max. alt. 567 m; a. 75 km².

Thirlmere, L., Cumbria, **Eng.**; 5 km long; furnishes part of water supply of Manchester.

Thirsk, mkt. t., Hambleton, North Yorks., **Eng.**; in wide gap between Pennines and Cleveland hills, 11 km S.E. of Northallerton; racecourse.

Thompson, t., B.C., **Canada**; trib. of R. Fraser; forms impt. routeway through Rocky mtns.; 448 km long.

Thon Buri, c., **Thailand**; on R. Menam opposite Bangkok; second c. of T.; former cap., "Temple of Dawn".

Thorez (Chistyakovo), **Ukraine**; coal mng.; p. (1990) 88,200.

Thornaby-on-Tees. *See* Teesside.

Thornbury, mkt. t., Avon, **Eng.**; 16 km N. of Bristol; aircraft mftg.; expanded t.; Oldbury Magnox nuclear power sta.

Thornton Cleveleys, t., Wyre, Lancs., **Eng.**; 6 km N.E. of Blackpool; resort; p. (1981) 26,139.

Thórshavn, c., on Stromo I.; cap. of **Faroe Is.**; fish. pt.; anc. fortress; lighthouse; p. (1986) 15,287.

Thousand Isles, gr. of over 1,500 Is. in St. Lawrence R. which extend up-river for c. 48 km from Brockville to Gananoque, at junc. of L. Ont. and St. Lawrence R.; partly in N.Y. st. and partly in Canada.

Thrace, anc. name of terr. in S.E. Europe, part of which has been added to **Greece**; successively under Macedonian, Roman, Byzantine, and Turkish rule, before passing to Greece; tobacco; a. 8,586 km²; p. of dep. (1981) 345,220.

Three Rivers, l. gov. dist., S.W. Herts., **Eng.**; close to London and inc. Rickmansworth and Chorleywood; p. (1993) 82,600.

Thule, N.W. **Greenland**; 1,600 km from N. Pole; American air base and site of ballistic missile early warning sta.; spt. open 2–3 months per annum; p. (1990) 846.

Thumba, Kerala, **India**; space science and technological ctr.

Thun, L., Berne can., **Switzerland**; occupies valleys of R. Aare where it leaves Alpine region; separated from L. Brienz by deltaic neck of land on which is Interlaken; a. 98 km².

Thun, t., Berne, **Switzerland**; on N.W. end of L. Thun; cas. on hill above t.; tourism; p. (1990) 38,124.

Thunder Bay, t., **Canada**; formed from Port Arthur and Port William; pt. on N.W. cst. of L. Superior; grain exp. ctr.; p. (1986) 112,272 (c.), 122,217 (met. a.).

Thurgau, can., N.E. **Switzerland**; on L. Constance, bordered by R. Rhine; prosperous agr. a.; inds. ass. with textiles; cap. Frauenfeld; a. 1,005 km²; p. (1990) 205,900.

Thuringia, *Land,* **Germany;** bordered by Bavaria, Saxony-Anhalt, Lower Saxony, and Hesse; drained by Rs. Saale and Werra; crossed by Thüringer Wald and extending to Harz mtns.; fertile arable agr. a.; cap. Erfurt; pop. (1992) 2,572,000.

Thuringian Forest or **Thüringer Wald,** forested range of hills **Germany;** rising to 982 m in Beerberg; famous for romantic scenery and legends; resorts.

Thurles, mkt. t., Tipperary, **R.o.I.;** on R. Suir; agr. processing; cath., cas.; p. (1986) 7,049.

Thurrock, t., l. gov. dist. Essex, **Eng.;** on Thames, nr. Tilbury; oil refining, metal refining, cement, paper board; p. (1993) 131,200 (dist.).

Thurso, burgh, Caithness, **Scot.;** nr. Dounreay; anc. stronghold of Vikings; p. (1991) 8,488.

Tianjing (Tientsin) c. and mun., **China** 112 km S.E. of Beijing; impt. pt. using poor harbour on Hai R.; industl. ctr., oil refining, textiles, elec. instruments, steel rolling mills, machine tools, chemicals, tobacco, food processing; univ.; p. (1990) 8,830,000 (met. a.), (1992) 5,090,000 (c).

Tiaret, t., **W. Algeria; N.** Africa; in strategic pass; walled; agr. mkt.; cereals, wool, cattle.

Tiber, R., Italy; flows from Apennines to Mediterranean, passing through Rome; 352 km long.

Tiberias, t., **Israel;** on Sea of Galilee (L. Tiberias); agr. ctr.; health resort with medicinal springs.

Tibesti, mtns., on bdy. between **Libya** and **Chad,** Equatorial Africa; barren in spite of slight rainfall; mainly above 1,800 m max. alt. 3,401 m.

Tibet (Xizang Zizhiqu), aut. region, **China;** lofty plateau called "the roof of the world" its lowest plains being 3,660 m a.s.l.; semi-desert; network of roads inc. one across Himalayas to Katmandu; pastoral agr. sheep; arable agr. in R. valleys, especially Zangbo valley, wheat, barley, fruit, vegetables; tr. of wool, musk, gold, skins, drugs traditionally carried by yaks which can stand intense cold; salt, alluvial gold, radioactive ores; recent liberalisation by China encouraging restoration of Buddhist temples and monastries, tourism and incr. in economic contact with outside world. cap. Lhasa; a. 1,217,308 km²; p. (1990) 2,220,000.

Ticino, R. Switzerland and **Italy;** trib. of Po; forms S. approach to St. Gotthard Pass; irrigation in lower course; length 240 km.

Ticino, can., **Switzerland;** on S. slopes of central Alps, bordering Italy; contains parts of Ls. Maggiore and Lugano; mainly pastoral agr., but wine, corn, tobacco in valleys; industl. a., in S. based on hydroelectric power, chemicals, metallurgy; many tourist resorts inc. Locarno, Lugano; cap. Bellinzona; a. 2,813 km²; p. (1990) 286,700.

Ticonderoga, V., N.E., N.Y., **USA;** resort between Ls. George and Champlain; L. George falls provide hydroelectric power for paper mill; local graphite used in pencil ind.; p. (1980) 2,938.

Tideswell, t., Derbys., **Eng.;** tourist ctr.; limestone quarrying in a.; lge. 14th cent. church known as "cath. of the Peak." p. c. 1,500.

Tidore I., Moluccas, **Indonesia;** volcanic; densely populated; coffee, tobacco, spices, fruit; a. 78 km².

Tien Shan (Celestial Mtns.) mtn. chain, central Asia, along **China–USSR** border; highest peak 7,320 m; source of Syr-Dar'ya, Chu, Ili and many other Rs.

Tierra del Fuego, archipelago, southernmost part of **S. America;** separated from Patagonia by Strait of Magellan; W. Chile and E. prov. Argentina; timber, pastoral agr. sheep; oilfield at Rio Grande; mng.; a. prov. 21,571 km²; p. (1991) 69,450.

Tigre, st., **Ethiopia;** formerly an independent kingdom; cap. Adua; severe drought 1982–3.

Tigris, R., S.W. Asia; rises in Taurus mtns. S. Turkey, flows through Iraq where it is joined by the Euphrates and proceeds to Persian G.; comm. routeway; dams for flood control and irrigation; many of the earliest cs. located in valley; 1,840 km long.

Tijuana, t., Baja Cal. st., **Mexico;** resort catering for Americans; casinos, race-tracks, bull-fights; p. (1990) 742,686.

Tiksi, t., **Russia;** Arctic spt., at mouth of Lena R.; local coal deposits; linked by air and R; to Yakutsk.

Tilburg, c., N. Brabant, **Neth.;** nr. Breda; woollens, textiles, tobacco, leather; p. (1993) 162,398 (c.), 235,681 (met. a.).

Tilbury, pt., Essex, **Eng.;** on N. Bank of R. Thames 32 km E. of London; within Port of London; major container terminal.

Tilimsen (Tlemcen), t., N. W. **Algeria;** picturesque medieval t.; agr. ctr. in fertile region; textiles, furniture, handicrafts; p. (1983) 146,089.

Tillicoultry, burgh, Clackmannan, **Scot.;** on Devon R.; woollen and worsted fabrics, paper; p. (1991) 5,269.

Tilsit. *See* **Sovetsk.**

Timaru, c. and dist., S.I., **N.Z.;** E. cst. spt., exp. frozen foods; fishing; regional ctr. for S. Canterbury; p. (1991) 34,208 (dist.).

Timbuktu. *See* **Tombouctou.**

Timisoara, c., W. **Romania;** comm., industl. and educational ctr.; univ., 2 caths., cas.; once a frontier fortress; p. (1990) 351,293.

Timmins, t., Ont., **Canada;** gold mng. declining; vast deposits of copper, zinc, silver, discovered 1964; timber inds., brewing; p. (1986) 46,657.

Timok Basin, Serbia, **Yugoslavia;** industl. region; coal mng., copper smelting, chemicals, glass, food processing; arable agr., vines.

Timor, lgst. of Lesser Sunda Is., **E. Indies;** divided politically until 1975 into W. Timor part of Indonesia and Port Timor; now both part of Indonesia; a. 33,748 km²; p. (1980) 3,292,516.

Timor Sea, that part of the Indian Oc. N.W. of W. Australia, and S. of Timor I.

Tinogasta, t., Catamarca prov., **Argentina;** in E. foothills of Andes, 192 km N.W. of Catamarca; impt. copper mines.

Tintagel, v., Cornwall, **Eng.;** ruined Norman cas.; reputed birthplace of King Arthur; tourism.

Tintern, v., Gwent, **Wales;** Cistercian abbey.

Tinto, R., Huelva prov., S.W. **Spain;** in Andalusia; flows W. to Alt. Oc.; gives its name to Rio Tinto copper mng. region which it crosses; 104 km long.

Tipperary, inland co., Munster, **R.o.I.;** drained by Rs. Suir and Shannon; mtnous., Knockmealdown and Galty mtns.; fertile Golden Vale in S.W.; dairying, sugar-beet; divided into N. and S. Ridings; co. t. Clonmel; p. (1986) 59,522 (N.R.), 77,097 (S.R.).

Tipperary, t., Tipperary, **R.o.I.;** 46 km S.E. Limerick; dairy processing; p. (1986) 5,033.

Tiranë, t., cap. of **Albania;** agr. processing, engin., clothing, glass; univ.; airport; p. (1991) 251,000.

Tiraspol, c., S.E. **Moldova;** on R. Dniester; agr. processing ctr.; heat and power sta. recently constructed; p. (1990) 183,700.

Tiree, I., Inner Hebrides, **Scot.;** off cst. of Mull; 22 km long, up to 10 km wide; sm. freshwater lochs and prehistoric forts; p. (1991) 768.

Tirgu-Mures, c., **Romania;** on R. Mures; ch. t. of Magyar aut. region in Transylvania; old fort, Gothic Calvinist cath.; agr. tr. and processing; p. (1990) 172,470

Tiruchirapalli (Trichinopoly), c., Tamil Nadu, S.E. **India;** on R. Cauvery; rly. ctr.; textiles, cigars, goldsmithery; p. (1991) 387,000.

Tirunelveli (Tinnevelly), c., Tamil Nadu, S.E. **India;** agr. tr. ctr. with sugar refinery; p. (1991) 135,825.

Tiruppur, t., Tamil Nadu, **India;** nr. Coimbatore; p. (1981) 165,223 (t.), 215,859 (met. a.).

Tisa (Tisza), R., **E. Europe;** rises in E. Carpathians, W. Ukraine, flows across Hungary into Yugoslavia where it joins the Danube 72 km below Novi Sad; ch. tribs. Koros and Mures; length c. 960 km; navigable in part.

Titicaca, L., **S. America;** between two ranges of Andes, on borders of Bolivia and Peru; 3,812 m a.s.l.; highest lge. L. in world; max. depth 300 m; crossed by steamers; fishing; a. c. 8,300 km².

Titograd, *See* **Podgorica.**

Titov Veles, t., central **Macedonia,** formerly Yugoslavia; on R. Vardar, and main rly. to Belgrade; recent industl. growth; textiles; p. (1981) 64,799.

Tiverton, mkt. t., Mid Devon, **Eng.;** 22 km N. Exeter; once famous for lace; textiles, engin.; p. (1981) 16,539.

Tivoli, the anc. Tibur, nr. Rome, **Italy;** on Aniene R., magnificent situations; hydroelec. power;

resort; remains of Hadrian's villa; p. (1981) 50,969.

Tjirebon (Cheribon), spt., Java, **Indonesia**; on N. cst. 192 km E. of Djakarta; rice, tea, coffee tr.; ctr. of irrigation scheme; oil refining.

Tlaxcala, smallest st., **Mexico**; on Mesa Central; dense p.; mainly agr.; cap. T.; a. 4,027 km²; p. (1990) 763,683.

Tlemcen. See Tilimsen.

Toamasina (Tamatave), t., **Madagascar**; lge seapt. on Indian Oc., handles 70 per cent of M. tr.; industl. complex, car assembly, oil refinery; p. (1990) 145,431.

Tobago, southernmost I., Windward Is., **W.I.**; volcanic, forested, picturesque, irregular topography; resorts utilising pleasant climate; exp. coconuts, copra, cacao, limes; ch. t. Scarborough; seeks internal self-gov.; a. 300 km²; p. (1980) 40,700. See Trinidad and Tobago.

Tobata. See Kitakyushu.

Tobermory, burgh, Argyll and Bute, **Scot.**; on I. of Mull at N. entrance to Sound of Mull; fish. pt., resort; p. (1991) 825.

Tobol, R., W. Siberia, **Russia**; trib. of R. Irtysh; navigable in lower course; 800 km long.

Tobolsk, t., W. Siberia, **Russia**; R. pt. on Irtysh R.; shipbldg., sawmilling, fishing.

Tobruk, spt., Libya, N. Africa; on cst. 352 km E. of Benghazi; exp. oil, served by pipeline from Libyan oilfields; p. (1984) 94,006.

Tocantins, R., central **Brazil**; rises in Goias prov., flows N. across plateau of Brazil through Pará estuary to Atl. Oc.; navigation interrupted by rapids 320 km above Pará; ch. trib. Araguaya R.; 2,560 km long.

Toce, R., N. **Italy**; rises in Lepontine Alps, flows S. and S.E. into L. Maggiore; valley used by trunk rly. from Milan to Berne as S. approach to Simplon Tunnel; 86 km long.

Tocopilla, spt., **Chile**; exp. nitrate, copper ore, sulphates, iodine; p. (1982) 26,123

Todmorden, mkt. t., Calderdale, West Yorks., **Eng.**; nr. source of R. Calder, 10 km N.E. of Rochdale; cottons, machin.; p. (1981) 14,665.

Togo, Rep. of, W. Africa; narrow strip between Ghana (W.) and Benin (E.); N. and S. lowlands separated by mtns. (1,000 m); climate hot and humid, but drier savannah conditions in N.; coffee on slopes of central mtns., cacao, copra in S., maize in N.; phosphate mng., major iron ore deposits in N. now form ch. exp.; developing food-processing inds.; cap. Lomé; a. 54,960 km²; p. (1991) 3·5 m.

Tokaido, Japan, one of gr. feudal highways, along S. cst. Honshu, now forms main line of modern communications network.

Tokaj, t., Hungary; at confluence of Bodrog and Tisa Rs.; nearby slopes of Hegyalia produce Tokay wine.

Tokat, t., cap. of T. prov., **Turkey**; copper refining, leather mnfs.; p. (1985) 73,008 (t.), (1990) 719,251 (prov.).

Tokelau or Union Isles, gr. of 3 coral atolls, S. **Pac.**, N. of W. Samoa, belonging to N.Z.; Fakaofo, Nukunono and Atafu; natives are Polynesians; subsistence economy; copra; a. 10 km²; p. (1991) 1,577.

Tokoroa, co. t., N.I., **N.Z.**; kraft paper, pulp, and sawn timber; p. (1987) 17,400.

Tokushima, t., Shikoku, **Japan**; spt. on E. cst.; mkt. ctr., cotton mnfs.; p. (1990) 263,356.

Tokyo, c., cap. of **Japan**; spt. with deepened harbour handling mainly S. coastal tr.; major industl. ctr. with diverse mnfs. and major problems of pollution; built on marshy site with much expensive reclamation from sea; planned decentralisation of p. and economic activity in progress; with Osaka–Kobe-Kyoto conurbs. (480 km long ribbon development) spoken of as Tokaido (q.v.) megalopolis; major educational ctr. with many univs.; p. (1990) 8,163,127 (c.).

Tolbukhin. See Dobrich.

Toledo, prov., **Spain**; mtnous.; agr., vineyards, stock-raising; a. 15,346 km²; p. (1987) 487,867.

Toledo, anc. c., cap. of T. prov., **Spain**; in New Castile; on hill above Tagus R.; Gothic, Moorish, and Castillian architecture; picturesque narrow streets; Alcázar citadel; associated with El Greco; sword mkg. still flourishes; sm. arms; tourism; p. (1987) 58,297, (1991) 489,640 (prov.).

Toledo, c., Ohio, **USA**; rly. ctr. and L. pt. with natural harbour on Maumee R.; exp. mnfs.,

oil, coal, agr. prod.; imports iron-ore; glass mkg., shipbldg., car components and many varied mnfs.; p. (1990) 332,943 (c.), 614,128 (met. a.).

Tolentino, t., in the Marches, central **Italy**; on R. Chienti; mediaeval walls and houses; cath.; sm. handicraft inds.; spa and tourist ctr.; p. (1981) 17,984.

Toliary, spt. S.W. **Madagascar**; cap. T. prov.; p. (1990) 61,460.

Tolosa, t., Guipúzcoa prov., **Spain**; in the Basque cty.; mediaeval bldgs., and armour; paper mills; (p. (1981) 18,894.

Tolpuddle, v., Dorset, **Eng.**; 11 km N.E. of Dorchester; famous for Tolpuddle martyrs, agr. labourers condemned to transportation for trying to form a trade union (1834).

Toluca, c., cap. of Mexico st., central **Mexico**; stands at 2,672 m; brewing, flour, cottons pottery, especially noted for basket weaving; p. (1990) 487,630.

Tol'yatti, c., **Russia**; on R. Volga 56 km W.N.W. of Kuybyshev; engin., motor wks., natural gas pipeline to Moscow; chemicals; p. (1989) 631,000.

Tom, R., Siberia, **Russia**; flows through Kuznetsk Basin and joins R. Ob; 704 km long.

Tomaszow Mazowieki, t., Piotrków prov., central **Poland**; industl. t. on Pilica R., surrounded by forests; textile ind., artificial silk; p. (1989) 69,579.

Tombigbee, R., Miss., **USA**; flows S. to join Alabama R. to form Mobile and Tensaw Rs.; navigable, partially canalised; length 654 km.

Tombouctou, formerly Timbuktu, **Mali**, W. **Africa**; nr. Niger R. on border of Sahara; salt tr., handicraft inds.; flourished as comm. mart and Moslem ctr. 14th–16th cent.; p. (1987) 453,032 (reg.).

Tomsk, c., cap. of marshy T. oblast, **Russia**; one of few lge. ts. in N. Siberia; major pt. on R. Tom; rly. junc. on Trans-Siberian rly.; educational ctr.; univ., cath.; engin., chemicals; p. (1989) 502,000.

Tonawanda, t., N.Y. st., **USA**; on Niagara R. at terminus of Erie Barge Canal; steel, plastics, chemicals; power from Niagara Falls, adjacent to N. Tonawanda; p. (1980) 18,693.

Tonbridge, t., Kent, **Eng.**; on R. Medway; food processing; lt. inds., inc. cricket balls; Norman cas. gatehouse; public school; with Malling forms l. gov. dist.; p. (1993) 102,100 (dist.).

Tone, R., Honshu, **Japan**; flows E. across Kanto Plain to Pac. Oc., N. of Tokyo; longest R. in Japan.

Tonga, I. gr., S. **Pac. Oc.**; Polynesian kingdom, gained independence 1970; 158 coral and volcanic Is.; 50 per cent. p. on Tongatabu I.; exp. copra, bananas; fishing; oil discovered 1969; airport; cap. Nuku'alofa; a. 699 km²; p. (1991) 103,000.

Tongariro, volcanic peak, N.I., **N.Z.**; nat. park in ctr. of volcanic dist.; alt. 1,970 m.

Tongeren (Tongres), t., Limburg prov., N.E. **Belgium**; mkt. ctr. for fertile Hesbaye region; historic bldgs.; p. (1982) 29,765.

Tonghua (Tunghwa), c., S.W. Jilin, **China**; rly junc.; soya bean processing; local iron and coal reserves; p. (1984) 363,400.

Tonkin, region, N. **Vietnam**; mtns. in N. and W., alluvial plain in E. around delta of Red R., containing most p. and lge. cs.; fertile agr.; ch. t. Hanoi; ch. pt. Haiphong; a. 104,973 km².

Tonle Sap, L., **Cambodia**; major comm. fishing a.; L. acts as natural reservoir to control floods of Mekong R.

Tönsberg, c., Vestfold prov., S.E. **Norway**; one of oldest Norwegian cs. on Skagerrak at entrance to Oslo fjord; ctr. of whaling fleet; oil mills; p. (1990) 38,333.

Toowoomba, t., S.E. Queensland, **Australia**; regional ctr. for Darling Downs, a rich wool and beef a.; planned with parks and gardens; agr. based inds., engin.; p. (1991) 82,438.

Topeka, c., cap. of Kansas st., **USA**; on Kansas R.; impt. tr. ctr. in rich agr. region; food processing, rly. ctr. and engin.; p. (1990) 119,883.

Torbay, l. gov. dist., S. Devon, **Eng.**; formed by amalgamation of Torquay, Paignton and Brixham; located around Tor Bay; tourism; p. (1993) 121,100.

Torcello, I., with anc. Byzantine cath., on lagoon nr. Venice, Italy.

Torfaen, l. gov. dist., Gwent, **Wales**; based on Pontypool, Cwmbran and Blaenavon; p. (1993) 90,700.

Torgau, t., **Germany**; R. pt. on Elbe; industl. ctr.;

American and Soviet armies met here 1945; p. (1990) 22,742.

Torne, R., N. **Europe**; rises in Sweden, drains L. Tornetrask and flows S.W. to G. of Bothnia, forming Finno-Swedish bdy.; rich in salmon; 512 km long.

Torness, East Lothian, **Scot.**; site of advanced gas cooled nuclear power sta.

Toronto, c., cap. of Ont. prov., **Canada**; major Gt. Ls. pt., on L. Ont.; spacious harbour; exp. lge. quantities of wheat; comm., financial, industl. and educational ctrs.; many varied mnfs., univ.; notable bldgs., parks; a. 622 km²; p. (1986) 612,289 (c.), 3,427,168 (met. a.), lgst. c. of C.

Torpoint, t., Cornwall, **Eng.**; on Plymouth Sound; p. (1981) 8,423.

Torquay, t., S. Devon, **Eng.**; incorporated in Torbay; on N. side of Tor Bay; seaside resort with all-year season.

Torre Annunziata, Campania, **Italy**; at foot of Vesuvius; spt., spa, bathing resort on Bay of Naples; arms factory, pasta mnf.; p. (1981) 57,097.

Torre del Greco, t., Campania, **Italy**; spt. and resort on Bay of Naples at foot of Vesuvius; coral fishing; pasta mnf.; p. (1992) 100,688.

Torremolinos, cst. resort, **Spain**; S. of Malaga; p. (1981) 22,535.

Torrens, L., S. **Australia**; 2nd lgst. salt L. in A.; varies from brackish lake to salt marsh.

Torreon, c., Coahuila, N. **Mexico**; cotton in surrounding Laguna dist.; cotton mills, rubber, smelting, food processing; rly. connection with ts. in S. Mexico; p. (1990) 459,809.

Torres Strait, between C. York, Queensland, **Australia**, and **New Guinea**; 144 km wide, strong tidal currents endanger navigation; contains volcanic and coral Torres Strait Is., 20 of which are inhabited by Australian Melanesians; p. (1986) 4,837.

Torridge, R., Devon, **Eng.**; flows from Hartland dist. to a confluence with the Taw at Bideford Bay; 85 km long.

Torridge, l. gov. dist., N.W. Devon, **Eng.**; inc. N. cst. ts. of Northam and Bideford and stretches inland to Great Torrington; p. (1993) 54,100.

Tortona, t., Piedmont, N. **Italy**; on Scrivia R.; textiles, metallurgy, engin., wines; cath.; the Roman Dertona; p. (1981) 28,806.

Tortosa, c., Tarragona prov., N.E. **Spain**; pt. on Ebro R., 35 km from mouth; food processing, soap, pottery; cath.; impt. Moorish t.; p. (1981) 31,445.

Tororo, t., **Uganda**; lge. chemical wks., cement, fertilisers.

Tortuga or **Ile de la Tortue**, I., Caribbean Sea; off N. cst. **Haiti**; provides shelter from N.E. tr. winds for Port-de-Paix; private development to convert I. into free pt. with tax incentives for inds.; scenic attractions being tapped to develop tourist tr.; airport under construction; subsistence agr. fishing; a. c. 65 km².

Torun (Ger. **Thorn**), c. and prov., **Poland**; rly. junc., pt. on Vistula; industl. ctr.; chemicals, elec. gds., clothing, metallurgy, engin., food processing; univ. bears name of Copernicus who was born here; p. (1989) 200,800 (c.), 656,400 (prov.).

Tory I., off N.W. cst., Donegal, **R.o.I.**; lighthouse; fishing; p. (1986) 136.

Totnes, t., South Hams, Devon, **Eng.**; on R. Dart 10 km N.W. of Dartmouth; mediaeval t.; agr. mkt., food processing; p. (1981) 5,627.

Tottenham. *See* **Haringey**.

Tottori, c., Honshu, **Japan**; spt. on Sea of Japan; exp. lumber, raw silk, fruit; industl. ctr.; p. (1990) 142,477.

Touggourt or **Tuggurt**, t., S. **Algeria**; on edge of Sahara; rly. terminus; dates.

Toulon, c., Var dep., S.W. **France**; reinstated as cap. of Var dep. (1974); on Mediterranean cst.; base of Fr. navy; fine natural harbour; comm. pt. and industl. ctr.; many fine bldgs.; Port-Cros Nat. Park nearby; p. (1990) 170,167 (c.), 437,553 (met.a.).

Toulouse, c., cap. of Haute-Garonne dep., S. **France**; in Languedoc on Garonne R. and Canal du Midi, commanding route through Gate of Carcassonne; industl. and agr. tr. ctr.; food processing, varied mnfs.; many fine bldgs., notably mediaeval univ., basilica, Gothic cath.; p. (1990) 365,933 (c.), 608,430 (met.a.).

Touraine, former prov. of **France**, of which Tours was the cap.; now occupied by Indre-et-Loire dep. and part of Vienne dep.; known as the "garden of France."

Tourcoing, c., Nord dep., N. **France**; 16 km N.E.

of Lille; with twin t. of Roubaix forms major wool textile ctr.; p. (1990) 94,425.

Tournai, c., Hainaut prov., W. **Belgium**; on R. Scheldt, nr. Mons; historic c.; famous cath.; textiles, carpet mftg., ctr. of cement ind.; p. (1993) 67,875.

Tours, c., cap. of Indre-et-Loire dep., **France**; in Touraine, on R. Loire; tourist ctr. for the châteaux of the Loire; route ctr.; agr. inds.; printing, engin.; Gothic cath.; p. (1990) 133,403 (c.), 271,927 (met.a.).

Towcester, mkt. t., South Northants., **Eng.**; 14 km S.W. of Northampton; "Eatanswill" of *Pickwick Papers*.

Tower Hamlets, inner bor., E. London, **Eng.**; inc. former bors. of Bethnal Green, Stepney and Poplar; undergoing rapid economic and social change as p. and inds. are decentralised; site of lge. a. of London Docks (now all closed) with allied dockland inds. now dev. as Docklands; clothing, brewing; p. (1993) 169,600.

Townsville, spt., Queensland, **Australia**; coastal outlet for rich dairying, pastoral and mng. a. along Great Northern Rly; artificial harbour; univ.; copper refining; p. (1991) 115,600.

Towton, v., North Yorks., **Eng.**; nearby Towton field, scene of bloodiest battle of Wars of the Roses 1461: Lancastrians under Henry VI defeated by Yorkists under Edward IV.

Towy, R., S. **Wales**; flows S.W. of Carmarthen Bay; 104 km long.

Toyama, c., Honshu, **Japan**; on Etchu plain to E. of Noto peninsula; regional admin. and comm. ctr.; patent medicines, aluminium smelting, machin.; p. (1990) 321,254.

Toyohashi, t., Honshu, **Japan**; food processing, textiles; p. (1990) 337,988.

Trabzon or **Trebizond**, spt., **Turkey**; on Black Sea; exp. tobacco, food prods., carpets; once a gr. tr. ctr. on caravan route between Persia and Europe; founded 8th cent. B.C. by Greek colonists; p. (1990) 173,354 (t.), 795,849 (prov.).

Trafalgar, C., S.W. cst., Cadiz, **Spain**; Nelson's famous victory 1805.

Trafford, met. dist. Gtr. Manchester **Eng.**; comprises Sale, Hale, Altrincham, Urmston and Stretford; p. (1993) 217,800.

Trail, t., B.C., **Canada**; lgst. metallurgical smelter in Commonwealth using local non-ferrous metals; chemicals; p. (1986) 7,948.

Tralee, mkt. t., spt., Kerry, **R.o.I.**; on R. Lee; exp. grain, butter; p. (1986) 17,109.

Trani, spt., N. Apulia, **Italy**; on Adriatic; mkt. t. for fertile coastal a.; fishing, food processing; cath., cas.; p. (1981) 44,235.

Transbaykal, region, Siberia, **Russia**; E. of L. Baykal; mineral wealth; ch. t., Chita.

Transcaucasia, region between the Black Sea and the Caspian Sea; comprising the constituent reps. of Georgia, Armenia, and Azerbaijan; ch. t. Tbilisi.

Transkei, former indep. Bantu Terr. (1976), S. **Africa**; agr., maize and livestock; heavily dependent on S. Africa; p. mainly employed in mines in Transvaal and Orange Free State; cap. Umtata; a. 42,849 km²; p. (1985) 2·9 m.

Transvaal, prov., **Rep. of S. Africa**; high veld plateau (900–1,200 m) with Kruger Nat. Park in N.E.; hot summers, temperate winters; livestock on grasslands, grains, citrus fruits and temperate crops on irrigated land; lge. mineral wealth, especially gold in Witwatersrand; diamonds, uranium, platinum; inds. in ch. cs., Johannesburg and cap. Pretoria; a. 286,066 km²; p. (1985) 7·5 m.

Transylvania, historic region and prov., central **Romania**; high plateau surrounded by Carpathians; forested; mineral wealth not yet fully realised; arable agr. in valleys; ch. ts. Cluj, Brasov.

Transylvanian Alps, range of mtns., **Romania**.

Trapani, t., cap. of T. prov. W. Sicily, **Italy**; spt. on promontory, sheltering natural harbour; exp. wine, pasta, tuna fish caught locally; p. (1981) 71,927.

Traralgon, t., Victoria, **Australia**; industl. growth based on Yallourn brown coal; tourism; p. (1986) 19,233.

Trasimeno, L., Umbria, central **Italy**; occupies lge. extinct volcanic crater; drained S. to R. Tiber; a. c. 155 km².

Tras-os-Montes e Alto-Douro, prov., N. **Portugal**; high, bleak plateau, cultivated valleys; climate cold except in S.; port wine cty. of Douro R.; remote, sparsely populated; a. 11,834 km².

Trawsfynydd, Gwynedd, **Wales**; within N. Wales Nat. Park; nuclear power sta. decommissioning 1993.

Trebizond. *See* Trabzon.

Tredegar, t., Blaenau Gwent, Gwent, **Wales**; in narrow valley 5 km W. of Ebbw Vale; engin.; home of Aneurin Bevan; p. (1981) 16,446.

Treforest, t., Mid Glamorgan, **Wales**; on R. Taff; lge. trading estate established in 1930s to alleviate unemployment in primary inds. of S. Wales; aircraft accessories, electronics, chemical, pharmaceutical, rayon, metal wks.

Trelleborg, spt., S. **Sweden**; on Baltic Sea; most impt. rubber factory in cty.; p. (1983) 34,146.

Trengganu, st., **Malaysia**; N.E. Malaya; rice, rubber, coconuts; tin, iron; cap. Kuala Trengganu; a. 13,080 km²; p. (1980) 540,627.

Trent, R., **Eng.**; rises in N. Staffs, flows round S. Pennines and joins the Ouse to form estuary of the Humber, many power stas. along its banks; polluted waterway, especially between Humber and Nottingham; 240 km long.

Trentino-Alto Adige, aut. region, N.E. **Italy**; between Austrian and Swiss Frontiers and L. Garda; embraces provs. Trento and Bolzano; cap. Trento; formerly called Venetia Tridentina; a. 13,598 km²; p. (1992) 896,722.

Trento, t., cap. of Trento prov. and ch. t. of Trentino-Alto Adige, N. **Italy**; on R. Adige and route to Brenner Pass; chemicals, cement, elec. engin.; picturesque t.; cath.; p. (1981) 99,179.

Trenton, c., cap. N.J. st., **USA**; on Delaware R.; transport and industl. ctr.; noted for its wire-rope and pottery inds., established mid-19th cent.; crockery, machin., metal and rubber gds.; p. (1990) 88,675 (c.), 326,000 (met. a.).

Trèves. *See* Trier.

Treviso, c., cap. of T. prov., Venetia, N.E. **Italy**; on R. Sile; agr. ctr. on fertile Venetian plain; silk mills, paper, furniture, fertilisers, pottery; p. (1981) 87,696.

Trichinopoly. *See* Tiruchirapalli.

Trichur, t., Kerala, **India**; comm. and educational ctr.; p. (1981) 77,923 (t.), 170,122 (met. a.).

Trier (**Trèves**), c., Rhineland-Palatinate, **Germany**; on R. Moselle; Roman origin. (Augusta Trevorum, the Rome of the North), cath., Porta Nigra; ctr. of Moselle wine reg.; textiles, leather goods; birthplace of Marx; p. (1986) 93,100.

Trieste, spt., cap. of T. prov., Friuli-Venezia Giulia, N.E. **Italy**; shipbldg., fishing, oil refining; pipeline to Schwechat, nr. Vienna; cath., cas., Roman antiquities; univ.; p. (1992) 228,398.

Trieste Free Territory, former free st. on the Adriatic; constituted by Peace Treaty with Italy, 1947, as compromise between conflicting Yugoslav and Italian claims; a. 743 km²; Zone A handed over to Italy, Zone B to Yugoslavia 1954. Yugoslav/Italian agreement 1975 settled border dispute and established free industl. zone on both sides of border in region of Sezana-Fernetti.

Trikkala, t., cap. of T. dep., W. Thessaly, N. **Greece**; mkt. t. for pastoral prods.; damaged by earthquake 1954; p. (1981) 45,160, (1991) 137,819 (dep.).

Trim, co. t., Meath, **R.o.I.**; mkt. t. on R. Boyne; anc. seat of Irish Parliament; p. (1986) 1,967.

Trincomalee, t., N.E. cst. **Sri Lanka**; excellent natural harbour; formerly a British naval base; p. (1981) 44,913.

Tring, mkt. t., Dacorum, Herts., **Eng.**; in gap through Chiltern hills, 14 km N.W. of Hemel Hempstead; p. (1981) 10,683.

Trinidad, t., cap. of Beni dep., **Bolivia**; exp. beef by air, but development hampered by isolation.

Trinidad, I., **W.I.**; N. of Venezuela; climate warm and humid; oil, natural gas, asphalt, sugar, rum, coconut oil, molasses, citrus fruits; tourism; cap. Port of Spain; a. 4,828 km². *See* **Trinidad and Tobago.**

Trinidad, t., central **Cuba**; picturesque old t. of colonial period declared a national monument.

Trinidad and Tobago, indep. st. within Commonwealth (1962), rep. (1976), **W.I.**; main exps. crude oil and petroleum prods. which with natural asphalt represent over 20 per cent national income; lge. offshore gas deposits with rising production; oil refining; tropical crops and food processing; sugar, molasses, rum, fruits, textiles; cap. and major spt. Port of Spain; internal self-gov. sought by Tobago; a. 5,128 km²; p. (1991) 1,250,000.

Trinity, R., Texas, **USA**; flows S.E. to Galveston Bay; used for reservoirs; valley contains lge. p. and much economic activity; 800 km long.

Trino, Piedmont, N. **Italy**; 18 km S.S.W. of Vercelli; nuclear power sta.; p. (1981) 9,067.

Tripoli, c., **Lebanon**; spt. on Mediterranean; admin. ctr. for N. Lebanon; terminus of oil pipeline from Iraq; oil refining; exp. agr. prods.; p. (1988) 160,000.

Tripoli, c., joint cap. of **Libya** (with Benghazi), on Mediterranean; stands on edge of palmoasis, site of anc. Oea; tourist, comm, and mnf. ctr.; gd. harbour; p. (1981) 858,000.

Tripura, st. **India**; N.E. Ganges delta, bordering Assam and Bangladesh; cap. Agartala; rice, jute, cotton, sugar-cane; a. 10,360 km²; p. (1991) 2,757,205.

Tristan da Cunha, sm. gr. S. Is., S. **Atl. Oc.**; dependency of Brit. col. (t. Helena, ch. t. Tristan); evacuated 1961 volcanic eruption) but resettled 1963; weather sta. (Gough I.); a. 117 km²; p. (1984) 315.

Trivandrum, c., cap. of Kerala st., S.W. **India**; pt. on Arabian Sea; textiles coconut processing; univ.; p. (1981) 483,086 (c.), 520,125 (met. a.).

Trnava, c., W. **Slovakia**; mkt. t. in fertile agr. region on Vah R.; food processing, steel wks.; cath., monasteries, called "little Rome"; p. (1990) 73,000.

Trnovo or **Tirnovo**, c., **Bulgaria**; on Jantra R.; food processing, textiles, leather; anc. cap. of Bulgaria.

Trogir, t., **Croatia** (formerly Yugoslavia); sm. pt. and seaside resort, partly sited on I. of Čiovo; mediaeval bldgs., inc. cath., palaces; p. c. 20,000.

Trois Rivières, t., Quebec, **Canada**; industl. ctr. on St. Lawrence R.; noted for newsprint; hydroelectric power from St. Maurice R.; p. (1986) 50,122 (c.), 128,888 (met. a.).

Trojmiasto (Tri-City), **Poland**; name given to the three municipalities of Gdansk, Gdynia, and Sopot, a loosely-knit conurb.

Trollhättan, t., S.W. **Sweden**; on Göta R., nr. T. falls which generate power for metallurgical and chemical inds.; car and aircraft components; p. (1992) 51,673.

Trombay, I., off Bombay, **India**; oil refining; atomic reactor; uranium processing and nuclear waste reprocessing plant; zirconium metal produced; fertilisers.

Troms, co., N. **Norway**; deep fjords, offshore Is.; fishing, livestock, boat-bldg.; cap. Tromsö; a. 25,916 km²; p. (1990) 146,816.

Tromsö, t., cap. of Troms prov., N. **Norway**; spt. on sm. I. of T. in Norwegian Sea; arctic fishing, sealing; fish processing; p. (1990) 41,651.

Trondheim, c., spt., **Norway**; on W. cst. on S. side of T. fjord; shipbldg., engin.; exp. timber and wood-pulp, butter, fish, copper; anc. cath., burial place of early Norwegian kings and place of coronation of recent sovereigns; p. (1990) 130,522.

Troon, burgh, Kyle and Carrick, **Scot.**; on F. of Clyde, 10 km N. of Ayr; gd. harbour and graving docks; shipbldg., hosiery; seawater distillation research ctr. project; resort; p. (1991) 15,231.

Troppau. *See* **Opava.**

Trossachs, Stirling, **Scot.**; picturesque wooded glen; tourist resort.

Troste, nr. Llanelly, **Wales**; steel strip mill, tin plate.

Trouville, t., Calvados dep., N. **France**; popular seaside resort and fishing pt. on Normandy cst.; p. (1982) 6,012.

Trowbridge, mkt. t. and county admin. ctr., West Wilts., **Eng.**; cloth wks., bacon curing, dairying, engin.; p. (1981) 22,984.

Troy, c., N.Y., **USA**; at confluence of Rs. Hudson and Mohawk; gr. shirt-mftg. ctr.; p. (1990) 54,269.

Troyes, c., cap. of Aube dep., N.E. **France**; on R. Seine; once cap. of Champagne; hosiery, textile machin., food processing; magnificent cath.; site of mediaeval fairs which standardised Troy weight; p. (1990) 60,755 (c.), 122,763 (met.a.).

Trucial States. *See* **United Arab Emirates.**

Trujillo, c., N.W. **Peru**; comm. and mkt. ctr. for irrigated agr. region, on Moche R., in foothills of Andes; sugar, cocaine; univ., cath.; p. (1990) 532,000.

Trujillo, t., cap. of T. st., W. **Venezuela**; on Transandean highway at 805 m; agr. mkt. for region producing coffee, cacao, tobacco, maize; p. (1980) 42,000.

Truro, t., Nova Scotia, **Canada**; on Salmon R.; hosiery, lumber mills, printing, metallurgy, machin.; p. (1986) 12,124.

Truro, c., Carrick, Cornwall, **Eng.**; at confluence of Rs. Kenwyn and Allen; mkt. t. and former sm. pt.; admin. ctr. of Cornwall; cath.; p. (1981) 16,277.

Tselinograd, c., **Kazakhstan**; cap. Virgin Lands terr.; on Ishim R., nr. Karaganda coalfield; chemicals, agr. machin.; p. (1990) 281,400.

Tskhinvali, c., N. **Georgia**; elec. prods., lumber mills, fruit canning; p. (1990) 43,300.

Tsu, t., Honshu, **Japan**; textiles; p. (1990) 157,178.

Tsugaru Strait, **Japan**; separates Is. Hokkaido and Honshu; links Sea of Japan with Pac. Oc.; 72 km long, 24–32 km wide.

Tsuruga, spt., **Japan**; on W. cst. Honshu; rayon textiles, cotton, atomic power plant; p. (1990) 68,041.

Tuam, mkt. t., Galway, **R.o.I.**; sugar refining; p. (1986) 4,109.

Tuamotu, coral archipelago, Fr. Polynesia. S. **Pac. Oc.**; pearl fisheries; p. of gr. (1983) 11,793.

Tuapse, c., S. Krasnodar terr., **Russia**; at foot of Caucasus on Black Sea; major petroleum pt. at W. end of pipeline from Baku and Makhachkala; oil refineries.

Tübingen, t., Baden-Württemberg, **Germany**; on R. Neckar; 15th cent. univ., cas.; mediaeval c. ctr.; birthplace of Hölderlin, p. (1986) 76,200.

Tubuai, archipelago, Fr. Polynesia. S. **Pac. Oc.**; a. 163 km².

Tucson, c., S.E. Arizona, **USA**; mkt. and distribution ctr. on Santa Cruz R.; cultural ctr. and winter resort based on Spanish heritage and warm dry climate; food processing, missile components; p. (1990) 405,390 (c.), 667,000 (met. a.).

Tucumán. See **San Miguel de Tucumán**.

Tudela, t., Navarre, N. **Spain**; mkt. ctr. for fertile fruit-growing dist. and I. of La Majana in Ebro R.; fine cath., Roman bridge; p. (1981) 24,629.

Tula, c., cap. of T. oblast, **Russia**; mnf. ctr. in Moscow industl. region; local iron and lignite mng.; Yasnaya Polyana, home of Tolstoy, nearby; p. (1989) 540,000.

Tulare, L., S. Cal., **USA**; ctr. of inland drainage 64 km S. of Fresno; streams feeding it used for irrigation; in drought years L. dries up completely; a. 233 km².

Tullamore, mkt. t., Offaly, **R.o.I.**; on Grand Canal; farming, distilling, brewing; p. (1986) 8,484.

Tulle-sur-Mer, t., cap. of Corrèze dep., **France**; firearms, textiles; p. (1982) 20,642.

Tulsa, c., Okla., **USA**; impt. oil ctr., based on lge. local deposits; machin., aeroplanes; well laid out with many parks; p. (1990) 367,302 (c.), 709,000 (met. a.).

Tumaco, t., S.W. **Colombia**; spt. on Pac. Oc., on sm. I. off cst.; exp. agr. prods.; climate hot and humid.

Tummel, R., Perth and Kinross, **Scot.**; trib. of R. Tay; used by Perth to Inverness rly. as S. approach to Drumocheter Pass; hydroelec. scheme nr. Pitlochry; 88 km long.

Tunbridge Wells (officially **Royal Tunbridge Wells**), t., l. gov. dist., Kent, **Eng.**; on border of East Sussex; chalybeate waters; attractive 17th cent. promenade known as "The Pantiles"; p. (1993) 101,800 (dist.).

Tunghwa. See **Tonghua**.

Tung Ting Hu. See **Dong Ting**.

Tunguska, Upper, Stony and Lower, Rs., Siberia, **Russia**; all rise in Sayan mtns. nr. L. Baykal and flow N.W. through forested cty. into R. Yenisey.

Tunguska Basin, coalfield between Yenisey and Lena Rs., **Russia**; main ts., Norilsk, Igarka, Yeniseysk.

Tunis, c., cap. of **Tunisia**, N. Africa; spt. on inlet of Mediterranean; exp. raw materials; base for fishing fleets; univ.; notable mosques; tourist ctr.; ruins of anc. Carthage to N.E.; p. (1984) 596,654.

Tunisia, indep. st., N. **Africa**; bounded by Algeria on W., by Libya on E., indented Mediterranean cst.; Atlas mtns. penetrate into N.; temperate cst. climate, hot and dry in S. desert; agr. and mng. basis of economy; wheat, olive oil, wine, fruits, limited to wetter coastal areas and irrigated valleys; phosphates

around Ghafsa; iron ore and lead in N.W.; steelwks. at Menzel Bourguiba; chemical and paper inds. based on local phosphates; economy hit by fall in world oil prices and lower remittances from Tunisians working abroad (immigration controls in France); cap. Tunis; a. 164,108 km²; p. (1992) 8·37 m.

Tunja, c., cap. of Boyacá dep., **Colombia**; route and agr. tr. ctr.; p. (1992) 112,360.

Turda, t., Transylvania, **Romania**; local salt mines and quarrying aid chemical and ceramic inds.; p. (1983) 59,695.

Turfan, depression, E. Xinjiang prov., **China**; on S. slopes of Tien Shan mtns.; desert a. irrigated by wells and canals for animal husbandry, fruit, cotton, grain; 275 m below sea level; ch. t. Turfan; archaeological finds.

Turgutlu (**Kassaba**), t., Manisa prov., **Turkey**; 48 km E.N.E. of Izmir; lignite, cotton, melons; p. (1985) 65,740.

Turin or Torino, c., cap. of T. prov., N. **Italy**; on R. Po at confluence with the Dora Riparia; former cap. of Piedmont and kingdom of Sardinia; univ., cath., many historic monuments; headquarters of Italian motor ind.; clothing, machin., furniture, chemicals; oil refinery nearby; p. (1992) 952,736.

Turkana, L. See **Rudolf, L.**

Turkestan E., terr. included in Xinjiang, **China**; separated from W. or former Russian Turkestan by Pamir plateau; mainly desert.

Turkestan W., terr. inc. **Turkmenistan, Uzbekistan, Tajikistan, Kyrgyzstan**, and part of **Kazakhstan**.

Turkey, rep., S.W. **Asia** and E. **Europe**; occupies mtnous. Anatolian penin.; equable climate on coastal margins, continental severity in interior; economy predominantly agr. but hampered by poor land resources; grain grown on Anatolian plateau and a Mediterranean variety of crops around cst.; noted for tobacco; industl. development based on mng. resources and oil in S.E.; lge cities in W. act as magnet for the poorer areas of E.; 30 percent of p. in 5 cities; many migrate to Europe & Middle East as migrant workers; cap. Ankara; a. 814,578 km²; p. (1993) 59,869,000.

Turkmenistan, CIS former constituent rep., USSR; borders on Afghanistan, Iran, and the Caspian Sea; much of a. in Kara-Kum desert; agr. based on irrigation; fruit, cotton, wool; sulphates, petroleum; p. concentrated in oases and industl. ctrs. of cap. Ashkhabad, Mary-Chadzhou, along Trans-Caspian rly.; a. 491,072 km²; p. (1992) 3·8 m.

Turks and Caicos, Is., Caribbean Sea, **W.I.**; about 30 sm. Is., geographically S.E. continuation of Bahamas; dry climate, poor limestone soil; exp. salt, crawfish; cap. Grand Turk; a. 430 km²; p. (1990) 11,696.

Turku (**Abo**), spt., S.W. **Finland**; on Baltic Sea; ctr. of fertile agr. a.; exp. agr. prods.; industl. ctr.; shipbldg., steel, machin., textiles; Finnish and Swedish univs.; p. (1991) 159,403.

Turnhout, t., N.E. **Belgium**; nr. Antwerp, on Campine canal; textiles, lace, printing; p. (1993) 38,419.

Turnu Severin, c., S.W. **Romania**; R. pt. on Danube below Iron Gate cataracts; grain, salt, petroleum tr., shipbldg.; p. (1990) 107,460.

Tuscaloosa, c., Ala., **USA**; on Black Warrior R.; rly. and industl. ctr. based on local coal, iron, cotton, timber; univ.; p. (1990) 77,759 (c.), 150,522 (met. a.).

Tuscany, region, central **Italy**; inc. provs. Arezzo, Firenze, Livorno, Siena, Grosseto, Lucca, Pisa, Massa and Carrara, Pistoia; mainly mtnous., drained by Arno R. system; wines, olive oil, cereals; iron ore from Elba, marble from Apuan Alps around Carrara; pt. at Livorno (Leghorn); cap. Firenze (Florence); a. 22,989 km²; p. (1992) 3,528,735.

Tuticorin, t., Tamil Nadu, S.E. **India**; on G. of Manaar; fertiliser plant; declining cotton and tea pt.; heavy water plant; p. (1991) 199,854.

Tuttlingen, t., Baden-Württemberg, **Germany**; on R. Danube; surgical instruments; footwear; p. (1986) 30,800.

Tuva aut. rep., **Russia**; bounded by Siberia and Mongolia; mtn. basin, forested; timber inds., coal mng., asbestos, pastoral agr.; cap. Kyzyl; a. c. 165,800 km²; p. (1989) 308,600.

Tuvalu Is., formerly Ellice Is., until 1975 part of

Gilbert and Ellice Is., W. **Pac. Oc.**; indep. (1979); p. mainly Polynesian; cap. Funafuti; coconut cultivation in high temps on poor coral soils; exp. copra; a. 25 km²; p. (1991) 10,090.

Tuxtla Gutiérrez, c., cap. of Chiapas st., **Mexico**; in fertile valley at 450 m; ctr. for sisal, tobacco, coffee, cattle; on Inter-American Highway; Mayan ruins nearby; p. (1990) 295,615.

Tuz, L., **Turkey**; salt L.; a. 1,619 km² in winter, much reduced in summer.

Tuzla, t., **Bosnia-Herzegovina,** formerly Yugoslavia; salt, lignite, coal; hydroelectric power in a.; agr. mkt. ctr.; textiles; civil war 1992 onwards; p. (1981) 121,717.

Tver, (Kalinin), c., **Russia**; on upper Volga; diversified inds.; 17th cent. cath. and cas.; p. (1989) 451,000.

Tweed, R., S.E. **Scot.**; rises in Tweeddale and reaches sea at Berwick; salmon fisheries; length 155 km.

Tweeddale, l. gov. dist., Borders reg., **Scot.**; based on upper Tweed valley around Peebles; p. (1993) 15,560.

Twelve Pins, star-shaped mtn. range, Galway, **R.o.I.**; Benbaum, 730 m.

Twickenham. See **Richmond-upon-Thames.**

Tychy, t., Katowice prov., **Poland**; on edge of Upper Silesian industl. a.; surrounded by forest; brewing; p. (1989) 189,816.

Tyler, c., Texas, **USA**; oil ctr. on E. Texan field; agr. ctr. for local mkt. gardening; famous for rose growing; p. (1990) 75,450.

Tyne, R., Tyne and Wear, Durham and Northumberland, **Eng.**; formed by confluence of N. Tyne and S. Tyne at Hexham; flows E. to sea at Tynemouth and S. Shields; valley gives easy route across mtns. from Newcastle to Carlisle; lower course forms harbour (with shipbldg. and other wks.) from Newcastle to Tynemouth; road tunnel between Wallsend and Jarrow; 128 km long.

Tynedale, l. gov. dist., W. Northumberland, **Eng.**; lge. inland a. inc. Haltwistle, Hexham and Prudoe; p. (1993) 57,500.

Tynemouth, t., North Tyneside, Tyne and Wear, **Eng.**; pt. on N. bank of Tyne R.; ruined priory and cas.; residtl., resort; p. (1981) 60,022.

Tyne and Wear,former met. co., N.E. **Eng.**; mainly industl. a. around lower T. and W. Rs.; inc. Newcastle-upon-Tyne, Tynemouth, Gateshead, South Shields and Sunderland; traditionally ass. with shipbldg. and coal mng., but inds. incr. diversified; p. (1993) 1,137,900.

Tyre (Sur), **Lebanon**; anc. Phoenician c. and spt., founded c. 15th cent. B.C.; now sm. comm. t., tr. in cotton, tobacco; p. (1988) 14,000.

Tyrol, Alpine region, **Europe**; falls within Austria and Italy, linked by Brenner Pass; embraces highest peaks of Austrian Alps, culminating in Ortler Spitz; two-fifths forest, timber inds.; mtn. pasture; tourism; Austrian prov. of Tyrol; cap. Innsbruck; a. 12,650 km²; p. (1991) 630,358.

Tyrone, former co., **N. Ireland**; now replaced by Strabane, Omagh, Dungannon and Cookstown l. gov. dists.

Tyrrhenian Sea, part of Mediterranean between Italy and Corsica, Sardinia and Sicily.

Tyumen, c., **Russia**; one of oldest Siberian ts., rly. ctr. on Trans-Siberian rly., R. pt. on Tura R.; many heavy inds.; ctr. of oil and natural gas region; p. (1989) 477,000.

Tywyn, mkt. t., Meirionnydd, Gwynedd, **Wales**; on cst. of Cardigan Bay, 5 km N.W. of Aberdovey; major floods 1990; p. (1981) 4,551.

Tzekung. See **Zigong.**

Tzepo. See **Zibo.**

U

Ubangi, major R., **Central Africa**; trib. of R. Zaïre, rises on bdr. of Central Africa Emp. and Zaïre flows W. and S. to join Zaïre R. at Irebu; partially navigable; 2,240 km long.

Ube, spt., S. Honshu, **Japan**; coal mng. and industl. ctr.; machin., synthetic petroleum; p. (1990) 175,053.

Ubeda, t., Jaén prov., **Spain**; on plateau between Guadalquivir and Guadalimar; food processing, olive oil, soap; p. (1981) 27,441.

Uberaba, t., Minas Gerais, **Brazil**; ctr. of cattle rearing and arable agr. region; sugar milling, mnfs. lime; p. (1985) 245,900.

Uberlandia, t., Minas Gerais st., **Brazil**; rail junc., agr. processing; p. (1991) 366,711.

Ucayali, R., **Peru**; headstream of R. Amazon; over 2,240 km long, navigable for 1,600 km.

Uckfield, mkt. t., East Sussex, **Eng.**; 13 km N.E. of Lewes; a. ctr. of former Sussex iron ind.

Udaipur, c., Rajasthan, N.W. **India**; in picturesque valley at 760 m a.s.l.; cap. of former princely st. of U.; maharajah's palace; p. (1991) 309,000.

Uddevalla, spt., S. **Sweden**; N. Göteborg; former shipyds., prefab. houses, timber, granite quarrying, textiles; p. (1992) 48,178.

Udi, t., S. **Nigeria,** W. Africa; 160 km N. of Pt. Harcourt; impt. mng. ctr. on Enugu coalfield; linked by rail to Kaduna and Pt. Harcourt.

Udine, c., cap. of U. prov. Friuli Venezia Giulia, N.E. **Italy,** between Alps and G. of Venice; route and industl. ctr. in agr. region; textiles, chemicals, engin., leather, woodwork; cath., many attractive bldgs., piazzas; severe earthquakes (1976); p. (1984) 101,179.

Udmurt aut. rep. **Russia**; part of Urals industl. a.; two-fifths forested, timber inds.; arable agr., flax; steel inds. at cap. Izhevsk, Votkinsk, Sarapul; p. (1989) 1,605,700.

Udokan Khrebet, mtns., **Russia**; world's lgst. reserve of copper.

Ufa, c., cap. of Bashkir aut. rep. **Russia**; in Urals industl. a., at confluence of Rs. Belaya and Ufa; p. (1989) 1,082,000.

Uganda, rep., E. **Africa**; dictatorship overthrown (1979); 4 regs. established for economic devel.; equatorial cty., climate modified by alt.; forms part of E. African plateau (1,200 m); well-developed economy; coffee, tea, tobacco, cotton for exp.; developing pastoral economy, fishing on L. Victoria; copper at Kilembe, tin; hydroelectric power from Owen Falls, second project at Kabelega Falls; electricity exp. to Kenya; savannah areas contain abundant wildlife in Nat. Parks and Game Reserves; cap. Kampala; a. 235,887 km²; p. (1991) 16·6m.

Uist, N. and **S.,** Is., Outer Hebrides, N.W. **Scot.**; indented csts.; N. Uist boggy in E., hilly in W.; S. Uist smaller but mtnous.; crofting, fishing; p. (1991) 1,404 (N.), 2,106 (S.).

Uitenhage, t., Cape prov., **S. Africa**; fruit, wool, rly. wks., tyres, car assembly, textiles; summer resort; p. (1980) 134,640 (dist.).

Ujiji, t., in sm. terr. same name (a. 2,383 km²) on E. shore L. Tanganyika, **Tanzania**; where Stanley found Livingstone 1871.

Ujiyamada. See **Ise.**

Ujjain, t., Madhya Pradesh, **India**; sacred c. and formerly cap. of Malwa; univ.; p. (1991) 362,000.

Ujpest, industl. sub., Budapest, **Hungary**; elec. engin., leather, shoes, textiles, furniture, pharmaceuticals.

Ujung Pandang (Makasar), c., Sulawesi, **Indonesia**; in dist. of rich volcanic soils; major spt. and airpt., entrepot tr.; p. (est. 1983) 888,000.

Ukhta t., **Russia**; ctr. of natural gas field in Pechora Basin; p. (1989) 111,000.

Ukraine, CIS former constituent rep., USSR; in Eastern Europe; of dominating importance in Soviet economy; drained by Rs. Dnieper Dniester, S. Bug, Donets; Pripet Marshes in N., wooded steppes in ctr., fertile black-earth a. in S.; major wheat-growing a. of Europe; highly mineralised, many industl. raw materials and ctrs. of metallurgical and heavy inds.; cap. Kiev; a. 582,750 km²; p. (1992) 52·1 m.

Ulan Bator, c., cap. of **Mongolian People's Rep.**; in stock-raising region; industl. ctr. of cty.; woollen gds., saddles, knitwear; new indust. ctr. at Darkhan nearby; rly. link to China and USSR; contains one-quarter of p. of rep.; p. (1990) 575,000.

Ulan-Ude (Verkhneudinsk), t., Siberia, **Russia**; major route and mnf. ctr.; pt. on R. Ude, junc. on Trans-Siberian rly., linked by rail to Peking; engin., textiles, glass, leather; p. (1989) 353,000.

Ullapool, v., Ross and Cromarty, **Scot.**; fish. pt. (herring landings), on L. Broom, 72 km N.W. of Inverness; landed more fish in 1981 than any other British pt.; attractive mtn. and cst. scenery in a.; p. (1991) 1,231.

Ullswater, L., Cumbria, **Eng.**; 13 km long; supplies water to Manchester; attractive tourist a.

Ulm, c., Baden-Württemberg, **Germany**; route ctr. at limit of barge navigation on Danube, although navigable limits being extended by canalisation; food-processing, metal gds., textiles, cement; p. (1990) 111,000.

Ulsan, t., **South Korea;** oil refining, fertilisers; nuclear power sta. (1983) built to reduce oil imports; p. (1990) 682,978.

Ulster. anc. prov of **Ireland.** consisting of counties of Cavan, Donegal, Monaghan and the six counties now **N. Ireland.** Prov. Ulster, part of consists of Cavan, Donegal and Monaghan; p. (1986) 236,008.

Ulúa-Chamelhcón, R. basin, N. cst. **Honduras;** major banana region of Central American cst.

Ulva, I., Argyll and Bute, **Scot.;** off W. cst. of Mull; 8 km long.

Ulverston, mkt. t., South Lakeland, Cumbria, **Eng.;** nr. Morecambe Bay; antibiotics, elec. gds., tanning; p. (1981) 11,963.

Ulyanovsk. *See* **Simbirsk.**

Uman, c., **Ukraine;** at confluence of Kamenka and Umanka Rs.; rly. junc.; agr.-processing; p. (1990) 91,300.

Umanak, t., W. **Greenland;** hunting and fishing base on arm of Baffin Sea; marble mng.; p. (1990) 2,677.

Umbria, region, central **Italy;** comprising provs. of Perugia and Terni, crossed by Apennines and upper Tiber; agr. mainstay of economy; inds. based on hydroelectric power at Terni; chemicals; tourist tr.; cap. Perugia; a. 8,472 km²; p. (1992) 814,796.

Ume, R., **Sweden;** flows S.E. to the G. of Bothnia; length 400 km.

Umeå, c., cap. of Västerbotten prov., N.E. **Sweden;** on G. of Bothnia at mouth of Ume R.; cultural ctr.; woodpulp; p. (1992) 94,912.

Umm-al-Quaywayn, emirate, member of **United Arab Emirates;** p. (1985) 29,229.

Umm Qasr, t., **Kuwait;** on Iraq border; new deepwater port planned.

Umtali (Mutare), t., **Zimbabwe;** comm. ctr. for rich agr. a.; oil refinery at Feruka; pipeline to Beira; paper milling, food processing, vehicle assembly; p. (1982) 69,600.

Umtata, t., Cape Prov., **S. Africa;** admin. ctr. for Transkei terrs.; cath.; p. (1976) 24,805 (latest fig.).

Uncia, t., Oruro dep., **Bolivia;** alt. 3,900 m in E. Cordillera of Andes, 96 km S.E. of Oruro; site of impt. Patino tin mines.

Ungava Bay, arm of Hudson Strait, projecting into Labrador, N.E. **Canada;** minerals abundant, recent exploitation of impt. medium and low-grade iron deposits.

Union of South Africa. *See* **South Africa, Rep. of.**

Union of Soviet Socialist Republics (USSR), E. **Europe,** N. **Asia;** until 1991 major world economic and political power; ctr. of European communist bloc; extended over 9,600 km W.–E., 4,800 km N.–S.; continental climate with marked regional variations; centrally planned economy emphasised development of heavy inds. at major sources of natural resources, and development of new resources in E.; timber inds. and textiles impt. with lge.-scale, mechanised agr. with planned prod. reflecting regional variations in physical conditions; cap. Moscow; a. 22,272,290 km²; p. (1991), 290 m.

United Arab Emirates (Trucial Sts.), indep. sov. st. on Persian G., S.W. **Asia;** formed (1971) from Trucial Sts. (Abū Dhabi, Ajmān, Dubai, Al Fujayrah, Ra's al Khaimah, Shārjah, Umm-al-Quaywayn) after withdrawal of Brit. forces and termination of special defence treaty (1820–1971); p. immigration from Middle and Far East as oil-based economic growth proceeds, esp. in Abu Dhabi; a. 82,880 km²; p. (1993) 2·1 m.

United Kingdom, cty., N.W. **Europe;** separated from continent of Europe by English Channel; consists of Gr. Britain (Eng., Wales, Scot.) and N. Ireland; member of EU; a. 244,022 km²; p. (1992) 58 m.

United States of America, fed. rep., **N. America;** world's major economic power; variety of climatic and physical conditions (*see* **N. America**); economically self-supporting, but imports petroleum, coffee, machin., textiles; extremely diversified mnfs.; exp. capital goods, industl. supplies, vehicles and food; consists of 50 sts. and Dist. of Columbia, co-extensive with cap. of Washington; outlying dependencies inc. Puerto Rico, U.S. Virgin Is., Panama Canal Zone, Guam, American Samoa, Trust Terr. of the Pac. Is.;

assertive foreign policy; a. 9,363,169 km²; p. (1995) 261,653,000.

Unst, I., Shetlands, **Scot.;** most N. of gr.; length 20 km; p. (1991) 1,055.

Unterwalden, can., **Switzerland;** divided into Obwalden and Nidwalden; dairying, fruit and livestock; cap. Stans; a. 767 km²; p. (1986) 58,000.

Upernavik, t., W. **Greenland;** on sm. I. in Baffin Bay; sealing and whaling base; meteorological sta.; p. (1990) 2,375.

Upper Austria, prov., **Austria;** borders on W. Germany and Slovakia; hilly and forested; drained by Danube R. system; inc. Salzkammergut resort a.; agr., forestry; inds. centred on Linz (cap.), Steyr and Wels; a. 11,979 km²; p. (1991) 1,340,076

Upper Hutt, c., N.I., **N.Z.;** shares rapid industl. growth of Hutt Valley; p. (1991) 37,092.

Upper Volta. *See* **Bourkina Fasso.**

Uppingham, mkt. t., Leics., **Eng.;** 16th cent. school.

Uppsala, c., cap. of U. prov., **Sweden;** on R. Sala, 72 km from Stockholm; historic ctr. of anc. Sweden; cultural ctr., famous univ. (Linnaeus taught there); cath.; lt. inds.; p. (1992) 174,554 (t.), 278,610 (prov.).

Ur, anc. Chaldean c., **Iraq;** 208 km W.N.W. of Basra; ruins; flourished about 3,000 B.C.

Ural, R., **Russia;** flows S.W. and S. to Caspian Sea; used for domestic and industl. water supply; navigable; 2,400 km long.

Ural Mts., Russia; mtn. system, forms bdy. between Europe and Asia and separates Russian plain from W. Siberian lowlands; extends N.-S. for 2,400 km; highest peaks Narodnaya and Telpos-Iz; rich mineral resources have given rise to huge ctrs. of heavy ind., inc. Sverdlovsk, Chelyabinsk, Magnitogorsk.

Uralsk, N.W., **Kazakhstan;** on R. Ural; grain-trading and cattle-mart ctr.; flour, leather, woollens, iron-ware; p. (1990) 206,700.

Uranium City, N. Saskatchewan, **Canada;** nr. N. shore of L. Athabasca, ctr. of Beaverlodge uranium-mng. a.; founded 1951; p. (1986) 2,748.

Urawa, t., Honshu, **Japan;** sub. of Tokyo; p. (1990) 418,267.

Urbino, t., in the Marches, central **Italy;** agr. mkt. and route ctr.; picturesque tourist ctr.; cath., univ., palace; p. with Pesaro (1981) 15,918.

Ure, R., North Yorks., **Eng.;** flows E. and S.E. to the Swale to form the Ouse; upper part of valley known as Wensleydale; 80 km long.

Urengoy, dist., Siberia, **Russia;** lge. natural gas field with 5,400 km. pipeline to W. Europe.

Urfa, prov. S.E. **Turkey;** a. 18,584 km²; p. (1990) 1,001,455.

Urgench, t., cap. of Khorezm oblast, **Uzbekistan;** pt. on Amu Dar'ya R. in Khiva oasis; cotton, food-processing; p. (1990) 128,900.

Uri, can., **Switzerland;** S. of L. of Lucerne; forest and mtns.; traversed by St. Gotthard rly. and R. Reuss; sparse p., German speaking; cap. Altdorf; a. 1,075 km²; p. (1990) 33,700.

Urmia, L., nr. Tabriz, N.W. **Iran;** 136 km by 48 km; salt and shallow; no outlet.

Urmston, Trafford, Gtr. Manchester, **Eng.;** residtl. sub. of Manchester; inc. part of Trafford Park industl. estate; p. (1981) 44,009.

Uruapan, t., Michoacán, W. **Mexico;** mkt. ctr. for semi-tropical mtnous. a.; famous handicrafts; parks, gardens; p. (1990) 217,142.

Urubamba, R., **Peru;** rises in E. Cordillera of Andes; forms one of headstreams of R. Amazon; length 560 km.

Urubupunga, t., **Brazil;** new. t. for 10,000, at site of hydroelectric power sta.

Uruguaiana, t., **Brazil;** on R. Uruguay; cattle ctr.; jerked beef, soap, candles; p. (1985) 105,900.

Uruguay, rep., **S. America;** smallest of S. American reps.; situated on N. bank of Rio de la Plata estuary; low hills in N.; temperate climate; 60 per cent land a. devoted to livestock rearing, especially cattle, sheep, based on extensive natural grasslands; arable land in S., grains; ch. t. Montevideo, cap. and main ctr. of inds.; food processing, leather, metallurgy, textiles, rubber; inflation 83 per cent; a. 186,925 km²; p. (1992) 3,116,802.

Uruguay, R., **S. America;** rises in S. Brazil,

flows 1,360 km to Rio de la Plata; forms bdy. between Argentina and Uruguay and part of bdy. between Argentina and Brazil.

Ürümqi (**Wulumuchi**), c., cap. of Xinjiang Aut. Reg., N.W. **China**; admin., comm. and industl. ctr.; iron and steel, cement, textiles, nitrogenous fertilisers, agr. machin.; local coal, tin, silver mng.; p. (1992) 1,160,000.

Usak, t. and prov., **Turkey**; connected by rail with Izmir; noted for pile carpet-weaving; p. (1985) 88,267 (t.), (1990) 290,283 (prov).

Usambara, mtns., N.E. **Tanzania**; scene of early European settlement (1902); lumber, tea, coffee produced on slopes; max. alt. 2,560 m.

Usedom (**Uznam**), I., Baltic Sea; off mouth of R. Oder; since 1945 E. part belongs to **Poland**, W. (the larger part) to Germany; a. 445 km²; p. 45,000.

Ushant, I., off cst. of Finistère, **France**; at entrance to English Channel; it was off Ushant that Lord Howe gained his gr. naval victory on the "glorious first of June" 1794; lighthouse, fishing; p. 2,000.

Ushuaia, t. cap Tierra del Fuego prov., **Argentina**; most S. t. in world; sheep farming, timber, furs; freezing plant; p. (1980) 11,000.

Usk, mkt. t., Gwent, **Wales**; 13th cent. cas.; p. (1981) 1,907.

Usk, R., Gwent, S. **Wales**; flows S. past Newport to Bristol Channel; picturesque, gd. fishing; 91 km long.

Üsküdar (**Scutari**), t., **Turkey**; on Bosporus, opposite Istanbul; mkt. ctr.; new bridge to European side of Bosporus; Crimean memorial cemetery for Brit. troops; Muslim cemeteries.

Uspallata Pass, 3,800 m high over Andes between Mendoza, **Argentina**, and Santiago, **Chile**; monument "Christ of the Andes" marks international bdy. settlement; used by Mendoza–Valparaiso rly.

Ussuri, R., rises in Maritime prov. of **Russia**, flows c. 800 km to R. Amur; final 480 km forms Sino-Russian bdy.

Ussuriysk (**Voroshilov**), t., **Russia**; 112 km N. of Vladivostok; rly. junc. of Trans-Siberian and Chinese Eastern rlys.; engin., agr. prod.; p. (1989) 158,000.

Ustica, I., Palermo, **Italy**; basalt; agr., fishing, handicrafts; a. 8 km²; p. (1981) 1,157.

Usti-nad-Labem (**Aussig**), c., Bohemia, **Czech Rep.**; R. pt. on Elbe; route and industl. ctr.; chemicals, textiles, machin.; p. (1990) 106,000.

Ustinov. See Izhevsk.

Ust Kamenogorsk, c., **Kazakhstan**; on Irtysh R.; mng. ctr.; food processing, clothing, furniture; hydroelectric power sta. nearby; p. (1990) 329,900.

Usumbura. See Bujumbura.

Utah, st., **USA**; 'Beehive St.'; admitted to Union 1896; st. flower Sego Lily, st. bird Sea Gull; Rocky mtns. in E.; forms part of Gr. Basin in W.; Gr. Salt L. in N.W.; dry continental climate; poor agr. conditions, soil erosion; copper, gold; tourism; Nat. Parks; cap. Salt L. City; a. 219,932 km²; p. (1990) 1,722,850.

Utica, c., N.Y., **USA**; on Mohawk R. and Barge Canal; in rich dairying region; textiles, electronics, tools, firearms; p. (1990) 68,637 (c.), 317,000 (met. a. with Rome).

Utrecht, c., **Neth.**; on Old Rhine (Oude Rijn); univ., cath.; chemical and cigar factories; printing, machin., woollens, silks, velvets; major transport and financial ctr.; picturesque; p. (1993) 234,170 (c.), 543,372 (met. a.).

Utrecht, prov., **Neth.**; between Gelderland and N. and S. Holland; fertile agr., cattle rearing, horticulture; a. 1,362 km²; p. (1993) 1,047,035.

Utsunomiya, t., Honshu, **Japan**; ctr. for Nikko Nat. Park; p. (1990) 426,809.

Uttar Pradesh, st., **India**; Himalayas on N. bdy., drained by Ganges and Jumna; irrigation; wheat, rice, millet, barley, maize, cotton, sugar, oil-seeds; ch. ts. Allahabad, Lucknow (cap.), Varanasi, Kanpur, Agra, Meerut; a. 293,732 km²; p. (1991) 139,112,287; (p. increasing by 2 million a year).

Uttlesford, l. gov. dist., Essex, **Eng.**; inc. Saffron Walden and Dunmow; p. (1993) 66,600.

Uttoxeter, t., East Staffs., **Eng.**; on R. Dove; machin., biscuit mftg.; expanded t.; p. (1981) 10,012.

Uusikaupunki (Swed. **Nystad**), spt., Abo-Bjorneborg, S.W. **Finland**; on G. of Bothnia.

Uzbekistan, CIS former constituent rep., USSR;

crossed by Rs. Amu Dar'ya and Syr Dar'ya; contains part of fertile Ferghana Valley; intensive farming based on irrigation; rice, cotton, fruits, silk, cattle, sheep; ch. cs. Tashkent (cap.), Samarkand; alluvial gold deposits and bauxite in Kizil-Kum desert; a. 412,250 km²; p. (1992) 21·2 m.

Uzhgorod, c., **Ukraine**; economic and cultural ctr.; friendship pipeline from Kuybyshev; univ.; p. (1990) 119,600.

V

Vaal, R., S. **Africa**; rises in Drakensberg mtns., flows between the Transvaal and Orange Free State to John the Orange R. nr. Kimberley. V. dam irrigates lge. a. of Witwatersrand; 896 km long.

Vaasa, c., cap. of Vaasa prov., W. **Finland**; pt. on G. of Bothnia; exp. timber and timber prods.; agr. ctr.; food processing, textiles, timber inds.; p. (1991) 53,764.

Vác, t., **Hungary**; on R. Danube; comm. ctr.; summer resort for Budapest; cath.; p. (1984) 36,000.

Vadso, cap. of Finnmark prov., N.E. **Norway**; ice-free Arctic pt. on N. side of Varangar fjord; whaling and fishing base.

Vaduz, mkt. t., cap. of **Liechtenstein**; nr. Rhine; sm. tourist resort; p. (1991) 4,887.

Vaigach, sm. I., between Novaya Zemlya and mainland of **Russia**; geological extension of Urals; low-lying reindeer pasture; seal fishing.

Valais, can., **Switzerland**; in upper valley of R. Rhône; surrounded by mtns., forested on slopes; vines and cereals in valleys; ch. resort Zermatt, cap. Sion; a. 5,234 km²; p. (1990) 248,300.

Valdai Hills, morainic ridges between Leningrad and Moscow, **Russia**; rise to c. 348 m and form ch. watershed of E. European Rs., Vlga, Dvina and Dniester.

Val d'Aosta, aut. region, N.W. **Italy**; high Alpine cty., borders France and Switzerland; cap. Aosta; agr., hydroelectric power; winter resorts; a. 3,263 km²; p. (1992) 117,204.

Val-de-Marne, dep., S.E. of Paris, **France**; cap.. Créteil; a. 243 km²; p. (1990) 1,215,500.

Valdez, t., Alaska, **USA**; ice-free pt., fishing; terminal of oil pipeline from North Slope; p. (1990) 9,952 (with Cordova).

Valdivia, c., S. **Chile**; on R. Callecalle nr. the sea (pt. Corral); damaged by earthquake and tidal wave 1960; univ.; metal, wood and leather gds.; paper, flour, brewing; p. (1987) 117,205.

Val d'Oise, dep., N.W. of Paris, **France**; cap. Pontoise; a. 1,248 km²; p. (1990) 1,049,600.

Valdosta, t., Ga., **USA**; rly. and tr. ctr. for region producing tobacco, cotton, timber; p. (1980) 37,596.

Valence, t., cap. of Drôme dep., S.E. **France**; on R. Rhône; silks., hosiery, vineyards; agr. mkt.; p. (1990) 65,026 (t.), 107,965 (met. a.).

Valencia, region, E. **Spain**; on Mediterranean; comprises provs. of Alicante, Castellón de la Plana and Valencia; mtnous., with densely populated, fertile coastal plain; irrigation makes a. a major producer of Mediterranean fruit and crops; a. 23,305 km² p. (1991) 2,135,846.

Valencia, c., cap. of V. prov., E. **Spain**; pt. on Mediterranean at mouth of R. Turia; one of most impt. agr. ts. of cty., and active industl. and comm. ctr.; univ., cath.; resort; p. (1991) 777,247.

Valencia, c., N. **Venezuela**; nr. L. Valencia; ctr. of agr. a., sugar-cane, cotton; leading industl. t.; cattle mart; cotton mills, meat packing; cath.; p. (1981) 616,000.

Valenciennes, c., Nord dep., N. **France**; in Hainaut cty. on R. Escaut (Scheldt); metallurgical and chemical inds.; once famous for hand-made lace; birthplace of Froissart and Watteau; p. (1990) 39,276 (c.), 336,481 (met. a.).

Valentia, I., S.W. Kerry, **R.o.I.**; in Dingle Bay; agr., fishing; 10 km by 3 km.

Vale of Glamorgan, l. gov. dist., South Glamorgan, **Wales**; inc. cstl. ts. of Penarth, Barry and Cowbridge; p. (1993) 114,500.

Vale of White Horse, l. gov. dist., Oxon., **Eng.**; based on Abingdon, Faringdon and Wantage; p. (1993) 113,200.

Vale Royal, l. gov. dist., Ches., **Eng.**; a. in ctr. of co. and inc. saltfield ts. of Northwich and Winsford; p. (1993) 114,600.

Valladolid, c., cap. of V. prov., **Spain**; on R. Pisuerga (trib. of Douro); grain tr.; route, industl. and comm. ctr.; food processing, textiles; cath., univ.; p. (1991) 345,259 (c.), 505,309 (prov.).

Valle del General, upland, S.W. **Costa Rica**; pioneer subsistence agr., maize, tropical fruit, cattle; improving transport.

Vallejo, t., Cal., **USA**; at mouth of Napa R. on San Pablo Bay; pt. and processing ctr. for farm prod.; naval shipyard; p. (1990) 109,199 (t.), 451,000 (met. a. with Fairfield-Napa).

Vallenar, t., Atacama prov., **Chile**; agr. ctr.; dried fruit, wines; iron ore nearby; p. (1982) 42,309.

Valletta, c., cap. of **Malta**; ch. spt. on rocky penin. of Mt. Scebarras, E. cst.; formerly naval base; cath., univ.; p. (1990) 9,199, 101,749 (urban harbour area.).

Valli di Comacchio, lagoon a., N.E. **Italy**; ctr. of an impt. eel industry; a. 259 km².

Valparaiso, c., central **Chile**; leading pt. on Pac. cst. of S. America; attractive c. with backdrop of steep hills; mftg., comm. and industl. ctr. of rep. with textile mills, sugar refineries, paint, shoe and chemical factories; univ.; p. (1987) 278,762, (1992) 1,373,967 (region).

Valtellina, fertile valley, **Italy**; in Lombard Alps above L. Como; impt. for vine cultivation; hydroelectric power resources; tourism.

Van, c., cap. of Van prov., S.E. **Turkey**; stands at 1,726 m on shore of salty L. Van; tr. ctr. of wheat-growing a.; new Turkish-Iranian rail link; p. (1990) 126,010 (t.), 637,433 (prov.).

Vancouver, c., B.C., **Canada**; Pac. cst. spt. with excellent natural harbour; international airport and terminus of transcontinental rly.; timber inds., shipbldg., fishing, oil and sugar refining; exp. prod. from these inds.; protection by mountains and mild climate make c. a major tourist ctr.; univ.; p. (1986) 431,147 (c.), 1,380,729 (met. a.).

Vancouver, I., B.C., **Canada**; off W. cst.; mtnous., forested; woodpulp, paper; indented cst. provides many natural harbours; fishing; cap. Victoria; a. 33,797 km².

Vancouver, t., Wash., **USA**; spt. on Columbia R. opposite Portland (Ore.); exp. grain, timber; food processing; p. (1990) 238,000 (met. a.).

Vandellos, Tarragona, **Spain**; nuclear power sta.; p. (1981) 3,838.

Vanderbijlpark, t., Transvaal, **S. Africa**; on Vaal R.; ctr. for steel wks.; p. (1980) 294,082 (dist.).

Vänern, lge. L., **Sweden**; W.N.W. of L. Vättern, with which it is connected by canal (and thence with the Baltic); a. 5,566 km².

Vänersborg, L. pt., **Sweden**; on tongue of land between R. Göta and the Vasobotten (southernmost bay of L. Väner); footwear, wood and sulphite pulp; p. (1983) 34,976.

Vannes, t., cap. of Morbihan dep., N.W. **France**; sm. pt. on S. cst. Brittany; cath.; dates from Roman times; p. (1982) 45,397.

Vanuatu, (**New Hebrides**), former Anglo-French condominion, S. **Pac. Oc.**; between New Caledonia and Fiji Is.; indep. st. 1980; strong separist moves in Santo I.; mostly subsistence agr.; few cash crops; ch. crop coconuts; no worked minerals; thickly forested; cap. Vila; a. 14,763 km²; p. (1992) 154,000.

Var, dep., S.E. **France**; in Provence, on Mediterranean; mainly agr. with some inds. at Draguignan and Toulon (cap. since 1974); bauxite at Brignoles; rapid growth of p.; inc. many coastal resorts; a. 6,042 km²; p. (1990) 815,400.

Varanasi (**Benares**), c., Uttar Pradesh, **India**; famous holy c. on Ganges, 640 km N.W. of Calcutta; place of annual pilgrimage; univ.; handicrafts, brasses, brocades, embroideries; p. (1991) 932,000.

Varanger Fjord, inlet of Arctic Oc. into Finnmark, **Norway**; iron mng. on S. shore.

Vardar, R., flows through Yugoslav and Greek Macedonia into Aegean Sea nr. Salonika; inc. V. agr. region; hydroelectric power; routeway; 448 km long.

Varde, t., W. Jutland, **Denmark**; agr. and route ctr.; food processing; steelwks; p. (1990) 19,134.

Vardö, t., Finnmark prov., N.E. **Norway**; sm. ice-free pt. on Vardoy I. with fish and oil interests; p. (1990) 3,008.

Vares, t., Bosnia-Herzegovina, formerly Yugosla-

via; iron mng.; developing mnfs.

Varese, t., Lombardy, **Italy**; in Alpine foothills; resort and industl. ctr.; engin., furniture, paper, textiles, wines; p. (1981) 90,527.

Värmland, prov., **Sweden**; agr., iron mng. and processing, timber inds.; cap. Karlstad; a. 19,236 km²; p. (1992) 284,691.

Varna, t., **Bulgaria**; spt. on Black Sea; industl. ctr. of heavy inds.; summer resorts on cst. nearby; p. (1990) 314,913.

Varnsdorf, t., **Czech Rep.**; rly. junc. on German bdr.; impt. textile ctr.

Västerås, c., cap. of Västmanland prov., **Sweden**; on L. Mälar; impt. elec. and metallurgical inds.; power sta.; impt. mediaeval c., cath., cas.; p. (1992) 120,889.

Västerbotten, prov., **Sweden**; forested; timber inds.; cap. Umeå; a. 59,153 km²; p. (1992) 255,987.

Västernorrland, prov., **Sweden**; forests and timber inds.; cap. Harnosand; a. 25,706 km²; p. (1992) 260,829.

Vastervik, t., Kalmar prov., **Sweden**; on Baltic cst. engin., chemicals, paper; p. (1992) 39,731.

Västmanland, prov., **Sweden**; N. of L. Mälar; mkt. gardening in S.; iron and silver mng. in N.; iron and steel inds.; cap. Västerås; a. 8,363 km²; p. (1992) 260,096.

Vasto, t., Abruzzi e Molise, **Italy**; agr. ctr. on steep-sided, vine-producing plateau; sm. Adriatic fishing pt.; p. (1981) 30,036.

Vatican City, indep. sov. Papal st., **Italy**; forms an enclave in Rome; inc. Papal residence, St. Peter's cath.; a. 44 ha; p. (1993) 1,000.

Vatna Jökull, mtn., **Iceland**; elevated snowfield; active volcano; alt. 2,120 m.

Vättern, L., **Sweden**; 40 km S.E. L. Vänern; a. 1,898 km².

Vaucluse, dep. S.E. **France**; in Provence; cap. Avignon; a. 3,577 km²; p. (1990) 467,100.

Vaud, can., W. **Switzerland**; N. of L. Geneva; forests and vineyards; cap. Lausanne; a. 3,209 km²; p. (1990) 583,600.

Växjö, t., S. **Sweden**; engin., timber wks., hosiery; p. (1992) 70,704.

Vejle, spt., Jutland, **Denmark**; admin. ctr. V. prov.; industl.; p. (1990) 51,263.

Velbert, t., N. Rhine–Westphalia, **Germany**; N.W. of Wuppertal; metal ind., locks and keys; p. (1986) 88,600.

Vélez-Málaga, t., Málaga prov., S. **Spain**; famous for wine, raisins, sugar, olive oil; Moorish cas.; p. (1981) 41,776.

Velletri, t., central **Italy**; at foot of Alban hills overlooking Pontine marshes; noted for its wine; Garibaldi routed Neapolitans here 1849; p. (1981) 41,114.

Vellore, t., Tamil Nadu, **India**; agr. mkt. t.; scene of Sepoy mutiny 1806; p. (1991) 175,061.

Velsen, t., N. Holland prov., **Neth.**; nr. entrance to N. Sea Canal, inc. IJmuiden iron and steel wks.; lge. paper mill; met. a. with Beverwijk; p. (1993) 62,828 (c), 132,479 (met. a.).

Veluwe, dist., Gelderland, **Neth.**; between Arnhem and IJselmeer; low hills of glacial sands and sand-dunes; heathland and pinewoods; relatively low p. density.

Venda, Bantu homeland, Transvaal, **S. Africa**; 3rd homeland granted "independence" (1979); nr. Zimbabwe border; p. (1985) 459,986.

Vendée, dep., W. **France**; on Bay of Biscay; fish. pts., beach resorts, agr. pasturage, vineyards; cap. La Roche-sur-Yon; a. 6,972 km²; p. (1990) 509,400.

Vendôme, t., Loir-et-Cher dep., **France**; on R. Loire; leather gds., cottons; mediaeval cas.; p. (1982) 18,218.

Venetia (**Veneto**), region, N.E. **Italy**; between the Alps and the Adriatic; embraces provs. Vicenza, Verona, Venice, Udine, Treviso, Padua, Belluno, and Rovigo; mtnous. in N., inc. Dolomite Alps; fertile plain of Po R. in S.; intensive arable agr.; ch. c. Venice; a. 18,384 km²; p. (1992) 4,395,263.

Venezia Giulia. See Friuli-Venezia Giulia.

Venezuela, fed. rep., N. cst. **S. America**; wealth derived from long-established oil ind. (90 per cent of exp. are oil); tropical climate, with temperate uplands, tropical forests and tall grass savannah lands (llanos); most economically advanced a. around cap. Carácas and oilfield a. of L. Maracaibo; counter pole of development based on hydroelectric power resources and iron ore in Caroní R. region; growing steel inds., government investment in lge. agr. areas, esp. maize and cereals; coffee from highlands main comm. agr. crop and exp.; large foreign debt; a. 912,050 km²; p. (1993) 20·41 m.

Venice (Venezia), c., cap. of V. prov. and ch. c. of Venetia, N.E. **Italy**; built on gr. of islets within lagoon in G. of V., at head of Adriatic; splendid architecture, rich in art treasures and historic associations; extensive canal network, inc. Grand Canal, intensive use leading to erosion of bldgs.; gradually sinking into Adriatic, lge.-scale projects to preserve c.; industl. zone on landward side in subs. of Porto Marghera and Mestre; craft and heavy inds.; p. (1992) 305,617.

Venlo, t., **Neth.**; on R. Maas; agr. mkt. and rly. junc.; chemicals, optical instruments, electric lamps; p. (1993) 65,172.

Ventimiglia, t., Liguria, N.W. **Italy**; on Medi terranean cst on Fr. border; cath.; flower mkt.; tourism; p. (1981) 26,373.

Ventnor, t., South Wight, I. of Wight, **Eng.**; on S. cst. 18 km S. of Ryde; mild climate, tourist and health resort; p. (1981) 7,941.

Veracruz, st., E. **Mexico**; narrow coastal plain rising to Sierra Madre Oriental; contains volcano Orizaba; recent agr. improvements; growth of petroleum inds.; cap. Jalapa; a. 71,836 km²; p. (1990) 6,215,142.

Veracruz, c., V. st., E. **Mexico**; spt. on G. of Mexico; comm. and industl. ctr. of oil region; nearby Laguna Grande, Mexico's first nuclear power sta. (1984); nr. site where Cortés landed 1519; p. (1990) 327,522.

Vercelli, c., cap. of V. prov., N. **Italy**; in Piedmont, on Sesia R.; rice mkt. for lge. irrigated plain textiles, machin., aircraft parts; p. (1981) 52,488.

Verde, Cape, most W. part of **Africa**; site of Dakar, cap. of Senegal.

Verdun, t., Quebec, **Canada**; sub. of Montreal; p. (1986) 60,246.

Verdun, t., Meuse dep., N.E. **France**; in Lorraine, on R. Meuse; strategic ctr. with varied mnfs.; 12th cent. cath.; scene of famous battle 1916; p. (1982) 24,120.

Vereeniging, c., Transvaal prov., **S. Africa**; on Vaal R.; coal, iron and steel, bricks; Treaty of Vereeniging 1902 ended Boer War; p. (1985) 177,220 (dist.).

Verkhneudinsk. *See* Ulan-Ude.

Verkhoyansk, t., Yakutsk, aut. rep., **Russia**; in N.E. Siberia; coldest permanently inhabited place in world; mean Jan. temp. of −59° F.; ctr. of fur trapping a.

Vermont, st., New England, **USA**; 'Green Mtn. St.'; admitted to Union 1791; st. flower Red Clover, st. bird Hermitt Thrush; traversed by the Green mtns.; farming, dairying, stock-raising, lumbering, quarrying, machine tool and textile mftg.; traditional inds. revitalised by new inds. coming from neighbouring Quebec; cap. Montpelier; famous for autumn colours; a. 24,887 km²; p. (1990) 562,758.

Verona, c., cap. of V. prov., N.E. **Italy**; on R. Adige; commands route from central Europe to Brenner pass and from Venice to Milan; cath. and notable monuments; active agr. tr. and inds., printing; p. (1992) 255,492.

Versailles, c., cap. of Yvelines dep., N. **France**; S.W. sub. of Paris; famous royal palace; mkt. gardening, distilleries; Treaty of Versailles 1919; p. (1990) 91,029.

Verviers, t., **Belgium**; nr. Liège; ctr. of textile ind. in Ardennes; p. (1993) 53,731.

Vesoul, t., cap. Haute-Saône dep., **France**; p. (1990) 19,404.

Vestmannaeyjar or **Westman Is.**, archipelago, S. W. **Iceland**; impt. cod fishing ind. based on Heimaey I; p. (1991) 4,933.

Vesuvius, famous active volcano, S. **Italy**; on shore of Bay of Naples; alt. c. 1,186 m; its eruption in A.D. 79 destroyed Pompeii and Herculaneum, and frequent eruptions have since been recorded; observatory founded 1844; funicular rly. from base of mtn. to rim of crater existed from 1880 to 1944 (destroyed by eruption).

Veszprem, c., **Hungary**; in fruit-growing dist., 96 km S. of Budapest; cath., univ. for chemical ind.; p. (1989) 66,000.

Vevey, t., Vaud can., **Switzerland**; on N. shore of L. Geneva; beautiful situation; chocolate, watches; resort; p. (1986) 15,149.

Viareggio, beach resort, Tuscany, **Italy**; on

Tyrrhenian Sea, nr. Pisa; monument to Shelley; p. (1981) 58,136.

Viborg, t., Jutland, **Denmark**; admin. ctr. V. prov.; comm. and route ctr.; anc. cath.; textiles, machin., food processing; p. (1990) 39,395.

Vicenza, c. cap. of V. prov., N.E. **Italy**; in Venetia; mkt. ctr. for surrounding fertile agr. plain; textiles, iron and steel; many examples of Palladian architecture; p. (1992) 107,481.

Vichy, t., Allier dep., **France**; on Allier R.; famous spa; hot mineral springs; lge. exp. of V. water; seat of Pétain govt. during German occupation 1940–3; p. (1982) 63,501 (met. a.).

Vicksburg, t., Miss., **USA**; R. pt., on bluffs of Mississippi at junc. of Yazoo canal; shipping and mftg. ctr. in cotton and timber region; prominent in American Civil War; Confederate surrender 1863; p. (1980) 25,434.

Victoria, st., **Australia**; settled rapidly in 19th century with gold rush; now most densely populated yet smallest mainland st.; Latrobe brown coal, offshore natural gas, hydroelectric power encourage rapid industrialisation; dominated by cap. Melbourne; rural a. of Great Dividing Range produces wheat, sheep and dairy prods.; a. 227,516 km²; p. (1991) 4,439,400.

Victoria, c., cap. of B.C., **Canada**; spt. on Vancouver I.; fishing and fish-processing; sawmills, chemicals, cement; beautiful scenery; tourist ctr.; p. (1986) 66,303 (c.), 255,547 (met. a.).

Victoria, main pt. and harbour between **Hong Kong I.** and Kowloon; built on reclaimed land; admin. ctr. of Hong Kong.

Victoria, t., cap. of Labuan I., Sabah, **Malaysia**; fine harbour; p. 3,213.

Victoria, t., cap. of **Seychelles**, Ind. Oc.; harbour on lgst. and most impt. I. of Mahé p. (1987) 59,500 (island).

Victoria, t., S. Texas, **USA**; comm. ctr. in prosperous agr. a.; local oilfields; p. (1980) 50,695.

Victoria Falls (Mosi-oa-Toenja), on R. Zambesi, **Zambia**; discovered by Livingstone 1855; falls are 1,674 m wide and broken by islands and rocks.

Victoria, Lake, lgst. L. of **Africa**; bordered by Kenya, Uganda, Tanzania; in depression of Gt. Rift Valley, at alt. 999 m. a. c. 67,340 km²; discharges into Victoria Nile; impt. fisheries; discovered by Speke 1858.

Victoria Land, region, **Antarctica**; discovered by Ross in 1841.

Victoria Nile, R., **Uganda**; E. Africa; name of R. Nile from its source at L. Victoria until it enters L. Mobuto Seso.

Vienna (Wien), c., cap. of **Austria**; R. pt. on branch of Danube; surrounded by Wiener Wald (Vienna forest) and Carpathian foothills; major industl., comm. and transport ctr.; many fine blds., inc. univ., cath., parliament bldgs., magnificent Prater park; influential ctr. of music, cultural and scientific ctr.; home of Haydn, Mozart, Beethoven, Schubert, Mahler, Brahms, and Freud; p. (1991) 1,533,176.

Vienne, dep., W. **France**; drained by R. Vienne; mainly agr. dist.; cap. Poitiers; a. 7,021 km²; p. (1990) 380,000.

Vienne, t., Isère, **France**; nr. Grenoble, on R. Rhône; textiles, metallurgical inds.; Roman remains; overshadowed by Lyons 27 km to N.; p. (1982) 372,000.

Vienne, R., **France**; trib. of the Loire; rises in Massif Central; 354 km long.

Vientiane, admin. cap., **Laos**; pt. and comm. ctr. on Mekong R.; p. (1985) 377,409.

Viersen, t., N. Rhine–Westphalia, **Germany**; S.W. of Krefeld; textiles, machin., furniture, paper ind.; p. (1986) 78,100.

Vierzon, t., Cher dep., **France**; on R. Cher; bricks, tiles, porcelain from local sands; clay; agr. machin.; p. (1982) 34,886.

Vietnam, Socialist Rep. of, S.E. **Asia**; comprises regions of Cochinchina and Tonkin in former French Indo-China; from 1954–1976 two separate countries, N. and S. Vietnam, based on two rivers, Song-koi and Mekong respectively, and separated by the high Annamite chain of mtns.; long period of civil war resulted in reunification; intensive agr. based on rice cultivation now largely collectivised; monsoon climate and river irrigation aid high yields; coffee, tea, rubber, sugar, main comm. crops but much devastation as result of war; minerals mainly concentrated in the N. with impt. anthracite deposit at Quang-Yen; industl. devel. also mainly in N. around Hanoi and ch. pt. Haiphong; hill tribes practising subsistence agr. inhabit the intervening Annamite mtns.; since reunification ts. declining rapidly; a. 335,724 km²; p. (1992) 66·3 m.

Viet-Tri, t., N. **Vietnam**; 128 km N.W. of Hanoi; chemicals, paper mill, sugar refining.

Vigevano, t., Lombardy, **Italy**; on R. Ticino; impt. agr. and industl. ctr.; footwear, plastics, textiles; cath.; p. (1981) 65,228.

Vigo, spt., **Spain**; transatlantic pt. on V. Bay; processing of imports; oil refining; p. (1981) 261,329.

Vijayanagar, ruined c., S.E. **India**; once cap. c. of Hindu empire in S. Deccan; 96 km in circumference; destroyed by Moslem forces at battle of Talikota 1565.

Vijayavada, t., Andhra Pradesh, **India**; rly. junc., comm. ctr.; irrigation dam, Kistna R.; p. (1991) 702,000.

Vila, t. cap. of **Vanuatu**, on S.W. coast of Efate I; p. (1989) 19,400.

Vila Real de Santo António, pt., Faro, **Portugal**; on W. bank of Guadiana R.; exp. copper ore, fish, fruit; p. (1981) 7,390.

Villach, t., Carinthia, S. **Austria**; junc. of Gail and Drava Rs.; impt. route ctr.; tourism; p. (1991) 55,165.

Villahermosa, c., cap. of Tabasco, S.E. **Mexico**; agr. mkt.; sugar processing; rich local petroleum deposits; p. (1990) 390,161.

Villa Maria, t., **Argentina**; rly. junc.; ctr. of grain, timber, dairying dist.; p. (1980) 67,490.

Villarrica, t., S.E. **Paraguay**; agr. tr. ctr. for cattle, tobacco, fruit; wines, yerba-maté grown in surrounding a.; p. (1982) 21,203.

Villavicencio, t., E. **Colombia**; in foothills of Andes; comm. ctr. for the *llanos*; cattle tr.; p. (1992) 233,026.

Villaviciosa, t., Oviedo prov., N.W. **Spain**; major fishing pt. on Bay of Biscay; p. (1981) 15,703.

Villeurbanne, t., Rhône dep., **France**; forming part of Lyons agglomeration; metallurgy, chemicals, leather, textiles; p. (1990) 119,848.

Vilnius, (Pol. **Wilno**), c., cap. of **Lithuania** on Vilija R. (trib. of Niemen); cultural ctr., cath., univ., historic bldgs.; held by Poland 1920–39; lt. inds., food processing; p. (1990) 592,500.

Vilvoorde, t. Brabant, **Belgium**; on Willebroek Canal NE of Brussels; p. (1993) 33,253.

Vilyui, R., Yakut aut. rep., **Russia**; flows E. from Siberian uplands into Lena R.; R. basin impt. agr. and mng. a.; fishing; 2,400 km long.

Vimy, t., Pas-de-Calais dep., N. **France**; nearby Vimy Ridge, site of Allied victory led by Canadians 1915; p. (1982) 3,621.

Viña del Mar, seaside t., central **Chile**, nr. Valparaiso: fashionable S. American resort; oil and sugar refining, textiles; p. (1987) 297,294.

Vincennes, t., Val-de-Marne dep., **France**; sub. of Paris; famous cas. and Bois; industl. and residtl.; p. (1982) 43,068.

Vindhya Hills, mtn. range, central **India**; separating the Deccan from the Ganges basin; c. 640 km long.

Vinnitsa, t., **Ukraine**; on R. Bug 192 km S.W. of Kiev; agr. mkt. t.; engin. chemicals, textiles; p. (1990) 378,800.

Virginia, st., **USA**; one of original 13 sts.; 'Old Dominion' St.; admitted to Union 1788; st. flower Dogwood, st. bird Cardinal; wide Atl. coastal plain rising inland to Blue Ridge; famous for high quality "Virginia Leaf" tobacco; industl. ts. of Norfolk, Richmond, Portsmouth and Newport News; cap. Richmond; a. 105,711 km²; p. (1990) 6,187,358.

Virgin Is. (Brit.), **W.I.**; gr. of Is. E. of Greater Antilles; most impt. Tortola, Virgin Gorda, Anegada; water scarcity, semi-subsistence agr. economy; livestock, fish, fruit, vegetables; a. 153 km²; p. (1991) 16,749.

Virgin Is. (**USA**), **W.I.**; external terr. of USA E. of Greater Antilles, 64 km E. of Puerto Rico; 3 main Is., St. Thomas, St. John, St. Croix; bought from Denmark 1917; favourite tourist a. in Caribbean; cap. Charlotte Amalie on St. Thomas; livestock, sugar; rum distilling; a. 344 km²; p. (1990) 101,809.

Vis (Lissa), I., off **Croatia**, Adriatic; fish-canning ctr.; a. 91km²; anc. remains; resort; sea battle 1866 between Italian and Austrian ironclads; p. 3,000.

Visby, old spt., **Sweden**; on Gotland I. in Baltic

Sea; rich in historic interest; resort; p. (1984) 20,000.

Vishakhapatnam, spt., Andhra Pradesh, **India**; deepwater harbour on Bay of Bengal; exp. manganese and oilseeds from Madhya Pradesh; shipbldg.; p. (1991) 752,000.

Vistula, R., **Poland**; rises in Beskids range of Carpathians, flows through Poland past Krakow to Baltic Sea nr. Gdansk; forms major link in E. European waterway system; coal and timber transport; 1,056 km long.

Vitebsk, c., **Belarus**; R. pt. on W. Dvina and impt. rly. junc., in agr. region; textiles, machine tools, food processing; p. (1990) 356,400.

Viterbo, c., cap. of V. prov., **Italy**; N. of Rome; agr. ctr., food-processing; 12th cent. cath. and historic bldgs.; p. (1981) 57,632.

Vitim, R., E. Siberia, **Russia**; flows to R. Lena; navigable for 5 months of year; coal and grain tr.; 1,400 km long.

Vitória, spt., Espirito Santo, **Brazil**; new ocean terminal capturing tr. from Rio de Janeiro; exp. coffee, cocoa, fruit, iron ore; sugar refining, shoes, textiles, cement; p. (1985) 254,400.

Vitoria, c., cap. of Alava prov., **Spain**; in Basque cty.; stands on hill at 534 m; furniture mnf.; defeat of Fr. by Wellington 1813; p. (1991) 208,569.

Vitry-le-François, t., Marne dep., N.E. **France**; on Marne R.; industl., textiles, earthenware; agr. mkt. for Champagne Pouilleuse; p. (1982) 18,829.

Vitry-sur-Seine, S.E. sub., Paris, **France**; flower growing on sand and gravel terraces of Seine R., acreage being reduced by competition from housing and inds.; p. (1990) 82,820.

Vittoria, t., Sicily, **Italy**; mkt. for wine; p. (1981) 50,220.

Vittorio Veneto, t., **Italy**; N. of Venice; resort; textiles; p. (1981) 30,028.

Vizcaya, Basque prov., N. **Spain**; on Bay of Biscay; iron mng.; iron and steel inds.; dense p.; cap. Bilbao; a. 2,165 km²; p. (1991) 1,153,515.

Vlaardingen, t., S. Holland prov., **Neth.**; 8 km W. of Rotterdam, on Nieuwe Maas; leading fish. pt.; p. (1993) 73,774.

Vladikavkaz (**Ordzhonikidze**), c., cap. of N. Ossetian aut. rep., **Russia**; on R. Terek at foot of Caucasus, ind. ctr., metallurgical inds.; natural gas pipe-line to Tbilisi; hydroelec. power sta.; p. (1989) 300,000.

Vladimir, c., cap. of V. oblast, **Russia**; between Gorki and Moscow, on trib. of Oka R.; founded 12th cent.; caths., historic bldgs.; machine tools, agr. machin., textiles; p. (1989) 350,000.

Vladimir-Volynski, c., N.W. **Ukraine**; one of oldest Ukrainian settlements, founded 9th cent.; agr. mkt. ctr.; p. (1990) 38,400.

Vladivostok, c., spt., **Russia**; ch. pt. and naval base on Pac.; terminus of Trans-Siberian rly. and airline from Moscow; ch. cultural ctr. of Far East; shipyards, fisheries, oil refining, engin., chemicals; economic development in hinterland hindered by distance from major ctrs. of p. and ind.; p. (1989) 634,000.

Vlieland, Friesian I., at entrance to IJsselmeer, **Neth.**; resort, nature reserve.

Vlissingen or Flushing, spt., Zeeland prov., S.W. **Neth.**; on Walcheren I.; shipyards, oil refining, fishing; resort; birthplace of Admiral de Ruyter; p. (1993) 44,147.

Vlonë, spt., S.W. **Albania**; on Strait of Otranto, Adriatic Sea; salt; oil pipeline connects from Kucovë nr. Berat; p. (1990) 76,000.

Vltava or Moldau, R., Bohemia, **Czech Rep.**; rises in Sumava mtns. (Bohemian Forest) and flows to R. Elbe below Prague; used for hydro-electric power; c. 416 km long.

Voghera, t., Lombardy, **Italy**; rly. junc. and agr. mkt.; textiles, machin. engin.; cas., cath.; p. (1981) 42,639.

Voi, t., **Kenya**, E. Africa; 144 km N.W. of Mombasa on rly. to Nairobi; branch connection with Tanzania rly. system allows agr. prod. from Arusha and Moshi dists. to pass through Mombasa as alternative to Tanga; shoe factory.

Voiron, t., Isère dep., **France**; on Morge R., 24 km N.W. of Grenoble; textiles, paper; p. (1982) 19,658.

Vojvodina, aut. prov., N. Serbia, **Yugoslavia**; impt. and fertile agr. dist. crossed by Danube R.; intensive agr., prosperous and dense p.; fruit, vegetables, livestock, food processing; ch. c. Novi Sad; a. 22,489 km²; p. (1981) 2,034,772.

Volcano Is., Japan; 3 volcanic Is. in Pac. Oc., S. of Japan, admin. by USA until 1968, now Japanese.

Volga, R., Russia; rises in Valdai hills, flows in serpentine course to Caspian at Astrakhan in wide delta; ch. tribs., Oka, Sura, Vetluga, Kama, Samara; major waterway linked to Baltic Sea, Azov, and Black Seas, and to Moscow; hydroelectric developments reducing sturgeon in Caspian Sea and caviar prod. declining; longest R. in Europe, 3,720 km.

Volga Baltic Waterway (Mariinsk Waterway), Russia; inland deepwater navigation network linking Black Sea and Caspian Sea in S. with Baltic Sea and White Sea in N.

Volgograd (Stalingrad), c., Russia; R. pt. on Volga and major rly. ctr.; exp. raw materials, fish; industl. ctr. for steel, engin., chemicals, oil refining; hydroelectric power sta.; fierce siege and successful defence 1942 turning point of second world war; p. (1989) 999,000.

Volhynia, historic region, **Ukraine;** on Polish frontier; rich agr. lowland; coal mng. at Novovodinsk; cap. Lutsk.

Volkhov, R., Russia; flows from L. Ilmen to L. Ladoga; navigable; hydroelectric power sta. and aluminium smelting plant at Volkhov (St. Petersburg oblast); 208 km long.

Volkingen, t., Saarland, **Germany;** on Saar R., 13 km W. of Saarbrücken; coal mng., iron and steel; p. (1986) 43,100.

Vologda, c., Russia; R. and rly. junc. on upper Sukhona R.; in dairying a.; engin., textiles, sawmilling, paper, dairy inds.; cath., historic bldgs.; p. (1989) 283,000.

Volos, spt., Greece; at head of G. of V.; impt. transport, industl., comm. ctr.; exp. agr. prods.; car mnfs.; p. (1981) 71,378.

Volsk, c., Russia; R. pt. on Volga R.; cement, tanneries, metallurgy, food processing.

Volta (White Volta), major R., **W. Africa;** drains extensive terr. in Niger bend, flows S. through Ghana to delta on Guinea cst., 112 km E. of Accra; main means of communication but rapids make through navigation impossible; Volta R. project for industrialisation of Ghana; dam and power plant at Akosombo, aluminium smelter at Tema; power decr. with decline in reservoir size from drought in Sahel; 1,520 km long. *See also* **Black Volta.**

Volta Redonda, t., Rio de Janeiro, **Brazil;** state-owned steel plant; p. (1985) 220,100.

Volterra, hill t., Tuscany, **Italy;** Etruscan and mediaeval walls; alabaster, salt; p. (1981) 14,080.

Volzhsky, t., Russia; industl. t. on Volga R.; aluminium smelting, chemicals; p. (1989) 269,000.

Voorburg, t., Neth.; industl. ctr. E. of the Hague; p. (1993) 39,734.

Vorarlberg, prov., **Austria;** forestry, dairying, tourism; inds. based on hydroelectric power; textiles; cap. Bregenz; a. 2,600 km²; p. (1991) 333,128.

Vorkuta, ctr. of Pechora coal basin, **Russia;** beyond Arctic circle, which supplies entire European N. Russia; p. (1989) 116,000.

Voronezh, c., Russia; R. pt. on Voronezh R. nr. junc. with Don; impt. comm. ctr. in fertile agr. dist.; machin., rubber, oil refining, food processing; nuclear power sta.; univ., cath.; p. (1989) 887,000.

Voroshilovgrad, *See* **Lugansk.**

Voroshilovsk. *See* **Kommunarsk.**

Vosges, dep., E. **France;** on Franco-German frontier; dairying, vineyards, stone quarrying, textiles; cap. Epinal; a. 5,970 km²; p. (1990) 386,300.

Vosges, highlands, E. **France;** structurally similar to Black Forest, from which they are separated by Rhine rift valley; forested slopes, vineyards; source of Meurthe, Moselle, Sarve, Ill, and Saône Rs.; highest summit Ballon de Guebwiller, 1,425 m.

Votkinsk, t., Russia; 61 km N.E. of Izhevsk; lge. engin. plant; hydroelectric power sta.; birthplace of Tchaikovsky; p. (1989) 104,000.

Vranja, t., Croatia (formerly Yugoslavia); flax and hemp culture and mnf.; developing industl. ctr. based on handicrafts.

Vratsa, t., Bulgaria; on R. Vratcanska; jewellery, wine, silk, tanning; p. (1990) 85,272.

Vrsac, t., Yugoslavia; milling, wine, brandy; p. (1981) 61,005.

Vulcano, I., Lipari gr., **Italy;** off N.E. cst. Sicily; active volcano; gave its name as generic title for this type of mtn.

Vyatka, (Kirov), c., Russia; pt. on Vyatka R.; rly. junc.; engin., saw milling, chemicals, leather inds.; cath.; p. (1989) 478,000.

Vyatka, R., Russia; rises in foothills of Urals, flows past Vyotka into Kama R.; timber transport, fishing; c. 1,360 km long.

Vyborg (Viipuri), c., Russia; spt. on G. of Finland, occupies strategic site on Karelian Isthmus, N.W. of Leningrad; Finnish until 1945; exp. timber; shipyards, engin., food processing.

Vychegda, R., Russia; rises in Urals, flows W. to N. Dvina R.; timber transport; 1,120 km long.

Vyrnwy, L., reservoir, Powys, **Wales;** with dam 360 m long supplies water for Liverpool; a. 454 ha.

W

Waal, R., Neth.; S. arm of R. Rhine.

Waco, c., Texas, **USA;** in Brazos valley; route ctr., airport; regional cultural ctr.; univ.; textiles, leather; p. (1990) 103,590.

Waddenzee, stretch of shallow water between W. Frisian Is. and Neth. mainland.

Wadebridge, spt., Cornwall, **Eng.;** at head of Camel estuary, 10 km N.W. of Bodmin; agr. mkt.

Wadi Halfa, t., Sudan; on R. Nile at second cataract; rly. terminus of Sudan rlys.; inundated by Aswan L.; new t. Khashm el Girba for inhabitants.

Wadi Medani, t., cap. of Blue Nile prov., **Sudan;** ctr. of cotton growing dist.; p. (1983) 141,065.

Wagadugu. *See* **Ouagadougon.**

Wagga Wagga, t., N.S.W., **Australia;** on R. Murrumbidgee; ctr. of agr. and pastoral dist.; p. (1981) 36,837.

Wahiawa, t., Oahu I., **Hawaii;** pineapples.

Waikaremoana, L., N.I., **N.Z.;** hydroelectric power.

Waikato, R., N.I., **N.Z.;** rises in L. Taupo and flows N.W. into Tasman Sea; coalfields, hydroelec. power stas.; longest R. of N.Z.; 422 km long; gives name to dist. and region; p. (1991) 37,556 (dist.), 338,959 (region).

Wairakei, N.I., **N.Z.;** on L. Taupo; health resort; geothermal power sta.

Waitemata, c., N.I., **N.Z.;** part of Auckland on picturesque inlet; p. (1987) 98,500.

Wakamatsu. *See* **Kitakyushu.**

Wakatipu, L., Otago, S.I., **N.Z.;** 83 km long, 5 km wide, 360 m deep, 320 m a.s.l.

Wakayama, spt., Honshu, **Japan;** textiles; new iron and steel plant; p. (1990) 396,553.

Wakefield, c., met. dist., West Yorks., **Eng.;** on R. Calder; 13 km S. of Leeds; cath.; former ctr. of coal-mng. a.; woollen and worsted gds., chemicals, engin.; p. (1993) 317,500 (dist.).

Wakefield, t., Va., **USA;** on Potomac R., nr. Fredericksburg; birthplace of George Washington; p. (1980) 1,355.

Wake I., coral atoll, **Pac. Oc.;** between Marianas and Hawaii; comm. and naval base on route to Far East, belonging to **USA.**

Walachia, region, S. **Romania;** wide plain bounded by Transylvanian Alps and separated from Yugoslavia by Danube; rich agr. a., "the bread-basket of Romania"; Ploiesti oilfields; inds. nr. ch. c. Bucharest; a. 76,563 km²;

Walbrzych (Waldenburg), c. and prov., S.W. **Poland** (since 1945); formerly in Lower Silesia; industl. and mng. ctr. at 427 m; porcelain, machin., engin.; p. (1989) 141,504 (c.), 738,100 (prov.).

Walchensee, Lake, Bavaria, **Germany;** a. 16 km²; hydroelectric power sta.

Walcheren, I., Zeeland prov., S.W. **Neth.;** in N. Sea at entrance to Scheldt estuary; mainly agr.; ch. ts., Vlissingen, Middelburg; flooded 1944 to stop German advance; tourism.

Waldenburg. *See* **Walbrzych.**

Wales, principality, **Great Britain;** mostly mtnous.; Cambrian mtns. rise to 1,085 m at Snowdon; contrast between N. and Central Wales (pastoral farming, forestry, water supply, tourism, rural depopulation) and S. Wales (coalfield, metal-based inds., lge. ts.); cap. Cardiff; a. 20,761 km²; p. (1993) 2,906,500 (26 per cent Welsh speaking).

Wallasey, t., Wirral, adjoining Birkenhead, Merseyside, **Eng.**; residtl., seaside resort (New Brighton); p. (1981) 90,057.

Wallensee, L., **Switzerland**; 18 km long.

Wallingford, t., South Oxon., **Eng.**; on R. Thames, to N. of its gap between Chilterns and Lambourn Downs; p. (1981) 6,328.

Wallis and **Futuna Is.,** gr. of coral Is., S. **Pac. Oc.**; overseas terr. of **France**; copra; a. 275 km²; p. (1990) 13,705 (mostly Polynesians).

Wallsend, t., Tyne and Wear, **Eng.**; on N. bank of Tyne, 6 km below Newcastle; Tyne tunnel links with Jarrow; shipbldg., engin., iron, plywood; at end of Hadrian's Wall; p. (1981) 44,699.

Walmer, t., Kent, **Eng.**; 3 km S. of Deal; holiday resort; cas., residence of Warden of Cinque Ports.

Walney, I., off cst. of Cumbria, **Eng.**; opposite Barrow.

Walsall, t., met. dist., West Midlands, **Eng.**; 8 km E. of Wolverhampton; leather and iron gds., engin., steel tubes; p. (1993) 264,700 (dist.).

Walsingham, v., North Norfolk, **Eng.**; many old bldgs., priory ruins, abbey; mediaeval pilgrimage ctr.

Walsum, t., N. Rhine–Westphalia, **Germany**; at confluence of Rhine and Emscher canal; R. pt. for Oberhausen steelwks.

Waltham, c., Mass., **USA**; nr. Boston; science-based inds.; univ.; p. (1980) 58,200.

Waltham Abbey, t., Epping Forest, Essex, **Eng.**; 21 km N.E. London, on edge of Epping Forest; glasshouses (tomatoes); Norman nave of abbey part of parish church; p. (1981) 19,432.

Waltham Forest, outer bor., E. London, **Eng.**; incorporating former bors. of Chingford, Leyton, Walthamstow; industl. and residtl.; p. (1993) 219,800.

Walthamstow. See **Waltham Forest.**

Walton and **Weybridge,** ts., Elmbridge, Surrey, **Eng.**; on R. Thames, 27 km S.W. of London; eng., aircraft; p. (1981) 49,237.

Walton-le-Dale, t., South Ribble, N.E. Lancs., **Eng.**; on R. Ribble, 3 km E. of Preston; mkt. gardening, cottons, timber; p. (1981) 29,009.

Walvis Bay, spt., **South Africa,** enclave in **Namibia**; on Walvis Bay, Atl. Oc.; fishing, fish processing; impt. base for **S. Africa** who wishes to keep it separate from Namibia; p. (1980) 20,740 (dist.).

Wandsworth, inner bor., S.W. London, **Eng.**; inc. Battersea; on R. Wandle at influx into Thames; oil mills, metal wks., paper, brewing; p. (1993) 265,700.

Wanganui, c. and dist., N.I., **N.Z.**; pt. on R. Wanganui; tr. ctr. for wool, grain, meat, dairy prod.; agr. processing, steel-pipes, fertilisers; iron ore deposits; p. (1991) 45,082.

Wanganui, R., N.I., **N.Z.**; famous for its beauty; 265 km long.

Wangaratta, t., Victoria, **Australia**; 232 km from Melbourne; ctr. of varied agr. dist. supplying prods. (milk, wool) for processing; p. (1986) 16,598.

Wankie, t., **Zimbabwe**; site of coal-mng. ind.; 344 km N.W. of Bulawayo; new coal fired power sta.; p. (1982) 39,200.

Wanne-Eickel, t., N. Rhine–Westphalia, **Germany**; pt. on Rhine–Herne canal; coal-mng. ctr. of Ruhr.

Wansbeck, R., Northumberland, **Eng.**; flows E. from Pennines into N. Sea 5 km N. of Blyth.

Wansbeck, l. gov. dist., Northumberland, **Eng.**; inc. Newbiggin, Ashington and Bedlington; p. (1993) 61,900.

Wansdyke, l. gov. dist., S. Avon, **Eng.**; inland a. inc. Keynsham, Bathavon and Clutton; p. (1993) 80,400.

Wantage, mkt. t., Oxon., **Eng.**; in Vale of the White Horse; birthplace of King Alfred; p. (1981) 8,765.

Wapping, Thames-side dist., London, **Eng.**

Warangal, t., Andhra Pradesh, **India**; textiles, carpets; p. (1991) 448,000.

Ware, mkt. t., East Herts., **Eng.**; on R. Lea; 3 km N.E. of Hertford; p. (1981) 14,203.

Wareham, mkt. t., Purbeck, Dorset, **Eng.**; on R. Frome, on N. of I. of Purbeck, 13 km S.W. of Poole; agr. machin., pipes; p. (1981) 4,577.

Warley, t., Sandwell, West Midlands, **Eng.**; inc. Smethwick, Oldbury and Rowley Regis; varied inds.; p. of dist. (1981) 163,567.

Warminster, t., West Wilts., **Eng.**; on Wylye watershed at edge of Salisbury Plain; agr. mkt., gloves; p. (1981) 15,065.

Warnemünde, spt., **Germany**; ferry pt. for rail traffic between Berlin and Copenhagen; shipbldg.; outport for Rostock; resort.

Warrego, R., Queensland, N.S.W., **Australia**; trib. of R. Darling; 640 km long.

Warren, t., Ohio, **USA**; on Mahoning R.; iron and steel mftg.; p. (1990) 50,793.

Warrenpoint, spt., Newry and Mourne, **N. Ireland**; at head of Carlingford Lough; p. (1991) 5,408.

Warrington, t., l. gov. dist., Cheshire, **Eng.**; on R. Mersey and Manchester Ship Canal; metal inds. (wire-drawing), chemicals, brewing, paper; expanded as new c. (to take people from Manchester); attracting high technology inds.; p. (1993) 185,000 (dist.), (1981) 134,327 (t.).

Warrnambool, t., spt., Victoria, **Australia**; former pt. on Lady Bay; wool processing, rugs, blankets; p. (1986) 22,706.

Warsaw (Warszawa), c., cap. of **Poland**; on R. Vistula; devastated in second world war; facsimile rebuilding based on Canaletto's paintings; cath., univ.; rly. ctr.; iron, steel, engin., textiles, chemicals; p. (1989) 1,651,255 (c.), 2,415,900 (prov.).

Warsop, t., Notts., **Eng.**; 6 km N.E. of Mansfield; limestone, gravel; p. (1981) 13,675.

Warta, R., **Poland**; trib. of R. Oder; connected to R. Vistula by canal; 720 km long.

Warwick, t., Queensland, **Australia**; sawmilling, agr. processing; p. (1992) 9,540.

Warwick, co. t., l. gov. dist., Warwicks., **Eng.**; on R. Avon, 13 km S.W. of Coventry; cas.; agr. implements, brewing, malting; p. (1993) 118,600 (dist.).

Warwick, c., R.I., **USA**; on Narragansett Bay; textile ctr.; p. (1980) 87,123.

Warwickshire, non-met. co., W. Midlands, **Eng.**; undulating, drained by tribs. of Rs. Severn and Trent, crossed by Cotswolds to S.; sm. coalfield to N.; potential new coalfield in S.; much of industl. N. now inc. in West Midlands met. co.; a. 1,981 km²; p. (1993) 493,600.

Wash, The, bay, N. Sea between Lincs. and Norfolk, **Eng.**; 35 km long, 24 km wide; partly reclaimed to form the Fens; proposed barrage to aid further reclamation and water storage.

Washington, t., Tyne and Wear, **Eng.**; 8 km S.E. of Gateshead; coal, iron and steel, stone quarrying, chemicals; new t. 1964; p. (1981) 47,445.

Washington, c., cap. of **USA**; in Dist. of Columbia on Potomac R.; c. planned as national seat of Government; White House, Capitol, 5 univs.; over half p. Black; p. (1990) 606,900 (c.), 3,923,574 (met. a.).

Washington, st., **USA**; 'Evergreen St.' admitted to Union 1889; st. flower Western Rhododendron, st. bird Willow Goldfinch; in extreme N.W., stretching from Pac. Oc. into Rocky mtns.; over half a. forested; Colombia R. and tribs. provide hydroelectric power; timber, fishing, tourism; cap. Olympia; a. 176,617 km²; p. (1990) 4,886,692.

Wassatch Mtns., range of Rocky mtns., Utah and Idaho, **USA**; alt. 3,600 m.

Wast Water, L. Dist., deepest L. in **Eng.**; 5 km long, 79 m deep.

Watchet, t., West Somerset, **Eng.**; sm. pt. on cst. of Bristol Channel; paper mkg., fishing; p. (1981) 3,050.

Watenstedt-Salzgitter. See **Salzgitter.**

Waterbury, c., Conn., **USA**; on Naugatuck R.; ctr. of brass ind. and metal gds.; p. (1990) 108,961.

Waterford, co., Munster, **R.o.I.**; mtnous. co. in S.E.; mainly agr., dairying, pigs; fishing; co. t. Waterford; a. 1,867 km²; p. (1986) 91,151.

Waterford, co. t., spt., Waterford, **R.o.I.**; on R. Suir; cath.; brewing, fishing, glass mnfs.; p. (1986) 39,529 (t.).

Waterloo, t., Brabant prov., **Belgium,** nr. Brussels; battle nearby 1815; p. (1982) 24,936.

Waterloo, t., Ont., **Canada**; industl. sub. of Kitchener; p. (1986) 58,718

Waterloo, c., Iowa, **USA**; on Cedar R.; agr. prod. and tools; p. (1990) 66,467.

Waters of Merom (L. Hula), Upper Galilee, **Israel**; extensive drainage completed 1957; a. 14 km².

Waterton Glacier International Peace Park,

Albert and Mont., **Canada** and **USA**; glacial and lake scenery; a. 596 km².

Watertown, t., Mass., **USA**; on Charles R.; textiles, clothing; p. (1980) 34,384.

Watertown, t., N.Y., **USA**; on Black R.; engin., paper; p. (1990) 29,429.

Watford, t., l. gov. dist., Herts., **Eng.**; on R. Colne, 26 km N.W. of London; mkt.; varied inds., inc. lt. and elec. engin., paper, printing; p. (1993) 75,600 (dist.).

Wattenscheid, t., N. Rhine–Westphalia, **Germany**; E. of Essen; coal, metals, footwear; p. (1980) 67,653.

Waukegan, c., Ill., **USA**; on L. Michigan; summer resort; steel, brass, motors, sugar refining; p. (1980) 67,653.

Wauwatosa, t., Wis., **USA**; sub. of Milwaukee; metals, concrete, chemicals; p. (1990) 49,366.

Waveney, R., Norfolk and Suffolk, **Eng.**; 80 km long.

Waveney, l. gov. dist., Suffolk, **Eng.**; based on Lowestoft, Beccles and Bungay; p. (1993) 107,700.

Waverley, l. gov. dist., Surrey, **Eng.**; inc. Farnham, Godalming and Haslemere; p. (1993) 115,100.

Wayatinah, hydroelectric commission v., Tasmania, **Australia**; dam, lagoon and power sta. at confluence of Rs. Nive and Derwent.

Wazirabad (Balkh), t., **Afghanistan**; anc. Bactra, cap. of Bactria, called the "mother of cities", destroyed by Genghiz Khan 1221; textile plant projected; p. c. 13,000.

Weald, The, wooded and pastoral tracts S.E. **Eng.**; extending from Folkestone, Kent, through Surrey, Hants., and Sussex to the sea at Beachy Head; former a. of iron working; name derived from German *Wald* = forest.

Wealden, l. gov. dist., East Sussex, **Eng.**; stretches from Uckfield to S. cst.; p. (1993) 133,700.

Wear, R., Durham/Tyne and Wear, **Eng.**; rises in Pennines, flows through Durham to N. Sea at Sunderland; 96 km long.

Wear Valley, l. gov. dist., Durham, **Eng.**; Pennine a. inc. Bishop Auckland, Crook and Willington; p. (1993) 63,800.

Weaver, R., Cheshire, **Eng.**; industl. trib. of R. Mersey; 72 km long.

Weddell Sea, arm of S. Atl. Oc., **Antarctica**; whaling and sealing.

Wednesbury, t., West Midlands, **Eng.**; former metal wkg. t.

Wednesfield, t., West Midlands, **Eng.**; metal tubes, materials handling engin.; expanded t.

Wei, R., Shaanxi prov., W. **China**; rises in highlands of Kansu, flows E. between highlands of Shaanxi and Hua Shan to join Yellow R; valley contains very fertile loess soils; formed cradle of Chinese civilisation; c. 800 km long.

Weifang, c., Shandong prov., **China**; coal-mng. ctr.; tobacco processing; p. (1984) 1,033,200.

Weihai, spt., Shandong prov., **China**; naval base; fishing; vegetable-oil processing, textiles; p. (1984) 216,400.

Weimar, t., Erfurt, **Germany**; on R. Ilm; ctr. of music and culture in 19th cent., associated with Goethe, Schiller, Nietzsche, Liszt, Herder; scene of establishment of German rep. 1919; elec. and metal inds., textiles, musical instruments, glass; p. (1981) 63,725.

Weipa, Queensland, **Australia**; Aboriginal community t., since 1965 taken over by Queensland to overcome opposition to bldg. of new t., pt., and alumina plant; bauxite nearby at Aurukin.

Weisshorn, mtn. peak, **Switzerland**; alt. 4,505 m.

Wejherowo, t., Gdansk, **Poland**; on R. Reda; mediaeval stronghold; palace; p. (1989) 46,465.

Welkom, t., O.F.S., **S. Africa**; ctr. of O.F.S. goldfields; p. (1980) 187,660 (dist.).

Welland, t., Ont., **Canada**; on Welland Canal; industl. t.; p. (1986) 45,054.

Welland, R., Northants. and Lincs., **Eng.**; rises in Northampton heights and flows N.E. into the Wash; 112 km long.

Welland Ship Canal, Ont., **Canada**; connects Ls. Erie and Ont.; 43 km long; 2-lane waterway.

Wellingborough, t., l. gov. dist., Northants., **Eng.**; on R. Nene, 14 km N.E. of Northampton; mkt.; footwear; expanded t.; p. (1993) 68,300 (dist.).

Wellington, mkt. t., The Wrekin, Shrops., **Eng.**; brewing, sugar refining, timber, toys; name derived from "Watling Town" (stood on Watling Street); with Dawley and Oakengates forms new t. of Telford; p. (1981) 15,699.

Wellington, mkt. t., Somerset, **Eng.**; 10 km S.W. Taunton, anc. woollen ind. still survives; dairy prod.; p. (1981) 10,567.

Wellington, c., spt., N.I., cap. of **N.Z.**; univ.; impt. exp. ctr. for dairy prod., wool, meat; new inds. developing in Hutt valley with vehicle assembly, rubber, oil refineries; p. (1991) 150,301, 356,682 (urban a.).

Wellington, prov., N.I., **N.Z.**; mtnous., pastoral and dairy farming; a. 28,153 km²; p. (1985) 587,700.

Wells, cath. t., Mendip, Somerset, **Eng.**; on S. flank of Mendip hills; cath., bishop's palace; paper mftg.; tourism; p. (1981) 8,374.

Wels, t., Upper **Austria**; on Traun R.; mkt. for agr. a.; cas.; p. (1991) 53,042.

Welshpool, mkt. t., Powys, **Wales**; on R. Severn; nearby is Powys cas.; p. (1981) 7,030.

Welwyn Garden City, t., Welwyn-Hatfield, Herts., **Eng.**; 34 km N. of London; founded by Sir Ebenezer Howard (1920) as first satellite t. of London; new t. 1948; pharmaceuticals, plastics, radio, and electronics, lt. inds.; p. (1981) 40,496.

Welwyn Hatfield, l. gov. dist., Herts., **Eng.**; comprises Welwyn Garden City and Hatfield; p. (1993) 95,300.

Wembley, former M.B., Middx., **Eng.**; now inc. in Brent outer bor. Greater London; lt. inds., sports ctr.; British Empire Exhibition 1924–5.

Wenlock Edge, narrow ridge, Shrops., **Eng.**; extends 29 km S.W. from Much Wenlock to Craven Arms; limestone; moorland, mainly above 290 m.

Wensleydale, North Yorks., **Eng.**; valley in N. Pennines drained E. by R. Ure; cattle reared for fattening on lowland farms; some dairying (cheese); length 56 km.

Wenzhou (Wenchow), c., spt., Zhejiang prov., **China**; pt. on estuary of Wu R., E. China Sea; fishing, coastal tr.; exp. wood, tea, agr. prod.; univ.; textile, leather and medicine inds.; designated an economic development zone, communications being improved; p. (1984) 519,100.

Wernigerode, t., Saxony - Anhalt, **Germany**; on N. slopes of Harz mtns.; mediaeval cas.; tourism; p. (1989) 36,778.

Wesel, t., N. Rhine–Westphalia, **Germany**; R. pt. at confluence of Rs. Lippe and Rhine, Ruhr conurb.; p. (1986) 54,600.

Weser, R., **Germany**; formed by confluence of Fulda and Werra Rs. at Münden; flows N. to N. Sea at Bremerhaven; linked by Mittelland canal to Rhine, Ems, and Elbe; navigable for entire length of 330 m.

Wesermünde. *See* **Bremerhaven.**

Wessex, anc. kingdom, S. **Eng.**; inc. Berks., Hants., Wilts., Dorset, Somerset and Devon.

West Bengal, st., N.E. **India**; W., mainly Hindu section of former presidency of B. (Muslim E.B. now Bangladesh); on Ganges delta and flood plain; humid sub-tropical climate; very dense p.; rice, jute; ch. c. Calcutta; a. 87,617 km²; p. (1991) 68,077,965.

West Bridgford, t., Rushcliffe, Notts., **Eng.**; at junc. of Grantham canal with R. Trent; residtl. sub. of Nottingham; p. (1981) 28,073.

West Bromwich, t., Sandwell, West Midlands, **Eng.**; on R. Thame, 8 km N.W. of Birmingham; heavy engin. and allied inds., chemicals, springs, oil refining; p. (1981) 154,930.

West Derbyshire. *See* **Derbyshire Dales.**

West Devon, l. gov. dist., Devon, **Eng.**; rural W. of Dartmoor and ts. of Tavistock and Okehampton; p. (1993) 46,700.

West Dorset, l. gov. dist., Dorset, **Eng.**; inc. Lyme Regis, Bridport, Sherborne and Dorchester; p. (1993) 87,700.

Western Australia, st. of the **Australian Commonwealth**; cut off from the rest of A. by desert; lgst. st., nearly a third of continent with only 9 per cent of p. concentrated in S.W. around st. cap. of Perth in fertile Mediterranean-like a.; diversity of relief, Hammersley range in N.W., Kimberley range in N.E., Gibson desert in interior; rich but irregularly distributed mineral deposits; intensive agr. in S.W., wheat and sheep in interior; a. 2,525,500 km²; p. (1991) 1,650,600.

Western Desert, Egypt; part of Libyan Desert; inc. Qattara depression; coastal road from Cairo to Tripoli; fighting in second world war.

Western Isles, l. gov. reg., **Scot.**; remote a. of Outer

Hebrides where pastoral farming and fishing have been the traditional livelihood for some time; p. (1993) 29,410.

Western Pacific High Commission Territories, inc. Solomon Is. and Kiribati and Tuvalu Is.

Westernport, inlet, Vic., **Australia;** major heavy industl. a. close to Melbourne, rapidly growing.

Western Sahara (Spanish Sahara), N.W. African cst.; comprising Rio de Oro and Sagui el Hamra; desert; rich phosphate mines at Bou Craa connected to El Aaiun pt. by rly.; upon decolonisation terr. split between Morocco and Mauritania (1976) but declared Saharan Arab Democratic Rep. by Algerians (Polisario) and still disputed; UN peace resolution 1991; a. 265,993 km², p. largely nomadic (1993) 214,000.

Western Samoa, indep. sov. st., S. **Pac. Oc.;** member of Commonwealth (1970); gained independence from N.Z. 1962; consists of 2 lge Is. (Savai'i, Upolu) and 7 sm. Is.; 70 per cent p. in agr.; c. 30 per cent is. devoted to bananas; exp. bananas, copra, cacao beans; ch. spt. Apia on Upolu I.; a. 2,841 km²; p. (1988) 168,000.

Westerwald, plateau of old volcanic rocks, **Germany;** ending in steep slope E. of R. Rhine; fertile soil; pastureland or deciduous woodland; sm. quantities of iron ore in Siegerland.

West Glamorgan, co., S. **Wales;** borders Bristol Channel; inc. Gower Penin. and lge. industl. ts. of Swansea, Neath and Port Talbot; impt. metal refining and engin. inds.; a. 816 km²; p. (1993) 371,200.

West Ham, former C.B., Essex, **Eng.;** sub. to E. of London; bordered by Rs. Thames and Lea; now inc. in Newham bor., Greater London.

West Hartford, t., Conn., **USA;** residtl. sub. of Hartford; metal gds., ctr. for dairying, tobaccogrowing dist.; p. (1980) 61,301.

West Indies or **Antilles,** I. grs., **Atl. Oc.;** extend between csts. of Fla. and Venezuela, separating Caribbean Sea and G. of Mexico from Atl.; inc. Cuba, Haiti, Dominican Rep., Bahamas, Barbados, Jamaica, Leeward Is., Trinidad and Tobago, Windward Is., Guadeloupe, Martinique, Curaçao, Puerto Rico, Virgin Is.; mostly volcanic and coral Is.; former colonial terrs. developed for plantation agr. worked by W. African slaves; most of indigenous Indians killed.

West Irian. *See* **Irian Jaya.**

West Lancashire, l. gov. dist., Lancs., **Eng.;** N. of Merseyside, inc. Skelmersdale and Ormskirk; p. (1993) 109,700.

West Lindsey, l. gov. dist., Lincs., **Eng.;** lge. a. N. of Lincoln and inc. Market Rasen and Gainsborough; p. (1993) 77,600.

West Lothian, l. gov. dist., former co., Lothian Reg., **Scot.;** industl. dist. in Central Lowlands close to Edinburgh; a. 417 km²; p. (1993) 146,730.

Westmeath, co., Leinster, **R.o.I.;** low-lying, drained by R. Shannon, many Ls.; dairying; co. to Mullingar; ch. t. Athlone; a. 1,834 km²; p. (1986) 63,379.

West Mersea, t., Essex, **Eng.;** on Mersea I.; p. (1981) 5,514.

West Midlands, former met. co., **Eng.;** mainly industl. a. centred around Birmingham and the S. Staffs. coalfield (Black Country) and Coventry and the Warwicks. coalfield; many forms of engin. and light inds. inc. vehicle mftg.; p. (1993) 2,633,700.

Westminster, City of, inner bor., London, **Eng.;** on N. bank of R. Thames; W. of City of London; incorporates former bors. of Paddington and St. Marylebone; contains Houses of Parliament, Westminster Abbey, Government offices, Royal Palaces (Buckingham Palace and St. James's); p. (1993) 189,000.

Westmorland, former co., **Eng.;** now part of **Cumbria** non-met. co.

Weston-super-Mare, t., Woodspring, Avon, **Eng.;** on Bristol Channel, 32 km S.W. of Bristol; holiday resort; expanded t.; p. (1981) 57,980.

West Orange, t., N.J., **USA;** elec. equipment; home of T. A. Edison; p. (1980) 39,510.

West Oxfordshire, l. gov. dist., Oxon., **Eng.;** in Cotswolds and ts. of Chipping Norton, Witney and Woodstock; p. (1993) 93,700.

West Pakistan. *See* **Pakistan.**

West Palm Beach, Fla., **USA;** domestic hardware; spt.; tourism; p. (1990) 864,000 (met. a. with Boca Raton-Delray Beach).

Westphalia. *See* **North Rhine-Westphalia.**

West Point, military sta., N.Y., **USA;** on Hudson R.; military academy.

Westport, spt., Mayo, **R.o.I.;** on Clew Bay; fishing; mkt.; p. (1986) 3,456.

Westray, I., Orkney Is., **Scot.;** 16 km long; p. (1991) 704.

West Somerset, l. gov. dist., Somerset, **Eng.;** inc. Exmoor and cstl. ts. of Watchet and Minehead; p. (1993) 31,500.

West Sussex, non-met. co., S.E. **Eng.;** crossed by E.-W. chalk ridge of S. Downs and forested Weald; diverse agr.; dormitory, retirement and tourist ts. on cst. inc. Bognor Regis and Worthing; Crawley new t. in N.; a. 2,015 km²; p. (1993) 717,700

West Virginia, st., **USA;** 'Mountain St.' admitted to Union 1863; st. flower Big Rhododendron, st. bird Cardinal; inc. Allegheny plateau; impt. mng. st. for coal; fruit farming; many industl. ts.; cap. Charleston; a. 62,629 km²; p. (1990) 1,793,477.

Westward Ho!, v., N. Devon, **Eng.;** named after Kingsley's novel.

West Wiltshire, l. gov. dist., Wilts., **Eng.;** stretches from Melksham, Bradford-on-Avon and Trowbridge to Warminster; p. (1993) 110,300.

West Yorkshire, former met. co., **Eng.;** industl. and mainly built-up a. E. of Pennines; traditionally ass. with woollen textile mftg.; inc. major ctrs. of Bradford and Leeds; p. (1993) 2,101,600.

Wetar I., Indonesia; N. of Timor I.; mtns.; underdeveloped; sparse p.; a. 31,080 km².

Wetherby, t., West Yorks., **Eng.;** on R. Wharfe; mkt., t.; racecourse.

Wethersfield, t. Conn., **USA;** oldest settlement (1634) in Conn.; aircraft parts, agr. implements.

Wetterhorn, mtn., **Switzerland;** alt. 3,710 m.

Wetzlar, t., Hesse, **Germany;** on R. Lahn; metallurgical and optical inds.; p. (1986) 50,300.

Wexford, coastal co., Leinster, S.E. **R.o.I.;** mixed farming, fishing; cap. Wexford; a. 2,334 km²; p. (1986) 102,552.

Wexford, t., cap. of Wexford; Leinster, S.E. **R.o.I.;** on R. Slaney; agr. processing; outport at Rosslare; p. (1986) 10,336.

Wey, R., Hants., Surrey, **Eng.;** rises in W. Weald, flows N. into R. Thames nr. Weybridge; cuts impt. gap through N. Downs at Guildford; length 56 km.

Weybridge. *See* **Walton and Weybridge.**

Weymouth and Portland, t., l. gov. dist., Dorset, **Eng.;** on Weymouth Bay, 13 km S. of Dorchester; torpedo and boatbldg., bricks, tiles, engin.; holiday resort; p. (1993) 62,400.

Whaley Bridge, t., High Peak, Derbys., **Eng.;** textile bleaching and finishing; p. (1981) 5,501.

Whangarei, c. and dist., N.I., **N.Z.;** deep harbour; oil refining; natural gas pipelines from Kapuni; fertilisers, sheet glass; p. (1991) 62,644.

Wharfe, R., West and North Yorks., **Eng.;** trib. of R. Ouse; 96 km long.

Wheeling, c., W. Va., **USA;** pt. on Ohio R.; comm. and mftg. ctr. in coal and natural gas a.; iron, steel, and metal plants; p. (1984) 42,100 (c.), 183,200 (met. a.).

Whickham, t., Tyne and Wear, **Eng.;** nr. Gateshead; chemicals, paper; p. (1981) 31,543.

Whitburn, burgh, W. Lothian, **Scot.;** 32 km S.W. of Edinburgh; coal, limestone; p. (1991) 11,511.

Whitby, t., North Yorks., **Eng.;** at mouth of R. Esk, 27 km N.W. of Scarborough; anc. spt. and fishing t.; residtl. and coastal resort; abbey; famous for jet ornaments; potash to be mined nearby; p. (1981) 13,763.

Whitchurch, t., Shrops., **Eng.;** 21 km S.W. of Crewe; dairy prods.

White, R., Ark. and Mo., **USA;** trib. of Mississippi; hydroelectric power; 1,104 km long.

Whiteadder, R., Berwick, **Scot.;** trib. of R. Tweed; 54 km long.

Whitehaven, spt., Copeland, Cumbria, **Eng.;** on Solway F. 5 km N. of St. Bees Head; coal, methane gas, cement, chemicals; p. (1981) 26,714.

Whitehead, t., Carrickfergus, **N. Ireland;** at entrance to Belfast Lough; seaside resort; p. (1991) 3,761.

Whitehorse, t., cap. of Yukon terr., **Canada;** ctr. coal and copper mng., hunting and fur trapping; once a gold "boom town"; H.Q. Royal Canadian Mounted Police; end of Alaska highway linking Edmonton, Alberta; p. (1986) 15,199.

White Mtns., part. of Appalachian system, N.H., **USA;** highest summit Mt. Washington, 1,918 m.

White Nile (Bahr-el-Abiad), R., **Sudan;** N.E. Africa; strictly, name applied to stretch of R. Nile between L. No and Khartoum; 800 km long.

White Plains, t., N.Y., **USA**; on Bronx R.; residtl.; battle 1776; p. (1990) 48,718.

White Russia. See **Belorussia.**

White Sea or **G. of Arkangelsk**, inlet of Barents Sea, **Russia**; frozen for 6 months of year; connected to Baltic Sea by deep-water canal; impt. fisheries.

Whitley Bay, t., North Tyneside, Northumberland, **Eng.**; 5 km N. of Tynemouth; seaside resort; plastics; p. (1981) 37,079.

Whitstable, spt., Kent, **Eng.**; on Thames estuary 10 km N. of Canterbury; holiday resort, oysters; p. (1981) 27,896.

Whittlesey, t., Fenland, Cambs., **Eng.**; in the Fens, 13 km W. of March; bricks, mkt. gardening; p. (1981) 11,812.

Whyalla, t., spt., S. **Australia**; t. on N.W. shore of Spencer Gulf developed by Broken Hill Co in 1901 as terminal for Iron Knob iron exp.; major iron and steel wks.; shipbldg. now in difficulties; p. (1991) 25,740.

Wichita, c., Kan., **USA**; in Arkansas valley; rly. wks., oil refineries and equipment, meatpacking ctr. in agr. and stock-raising region; univ.; p. (1990) 304,011 (c.), 485,000 (met. a.).

Wichita Falls, c., Texas, **USA**; oil refining, ctr. in agr. and ranching a.; p. (1990) 92,259.

Wick, spt., sm. burgh, Caithness, **Scot.**; on E. cst., 22 km S. of John O'Groats; airport to Orkneys and Shetlands; herring fishing ctr.; p. (1991) 7,681.

Wicklow, coastal co., Leinster, **R.o.I.**; crossed by Wicklow mtns.; pastoral agr. and tourism; cap. Wicklow; a. 2,033 km²; p. (1986) 94,542.

Wicklow, t., cap. of Wicklow, Leinster, **R.o.I.**; on S.E. cst., 56 km S. of Dublin; mkt.; sm. seaside resort; p. (1986) 5,304.

Wicklow, mtns., Wicklow, **R.o.I.**; highest summit Lugnaquillia, 927 m.

Widecombe, v., Devon, **Eng.**; Dartmoor tourist ctr.; famous through ballad "Widecombe Fair."

Widnes, t., Halton, Cheshire, **Eng.**; on R. Mersey 19 km E. of Liverpool; impt. chemical inds.; expanded t.; p. (1981) 54,411.

Wiener Neustadt, t., Lower **Austria**; rly. and industl. ctr.; heavy machin.; founded 1192; anc. bldgs., cas., cath.; education ctr.; p. (1991) 35,268.

Wieringermeer Polder, reclaimed a., N. Holland, **Neth.**; N.W. of IJsselmeer; a. 202 km².

Wiesbaden, c., cap. of Hesse, **Germany**; on Rhine, at S. foot of the Taunus; famous spa.; cas.; ctr. for Rhine wines; chemicals, metal gds.; p. (1990) 261,800.

Wigan, t., met. dist., Gtr. Manchester, **Eng.**; 26 km. N.E. of Liverpool; engin., chemicals, 1992 312,400 cement, food processing, paper; former coal-mng. ctr.; p. (1993) 313,200 (dist.).

Wigston, t., Leics., **Eng.**; 6 km S. of Leicester; engin., hosiery; p. (1981) 31,900. See **Oadby.**

Wigtown, l. gov. dist., former co., Dumfries and Galloway Reg., **Scot.**; along N. cst. of Solway F.; impt. dairying reg.; a. 1,712 km²; p. (1993) 29,860.

Wigtown, sm. burgh, Wigtown, **Scot.**; on W. Bay, Solway F.; shares admin. with Newton Stewart; p. (1991) 1,117.

Wilhelmshaven, c., Lower Saxony, **Germany**; on inlet of N. Sea, 64 km N.W. of Bremen; ch. German naval base until 1945; industl. ctr. with heavy machin., elec. equipment, textiles, furniture; oil pipeline; p. (1986) 94,900.

Wilkes-Barre, c., Penns., **USA**; on Susquehanna R.; industl. ctr. in rich anthracite mng. a.; p. (1980) 51,551.

Wilkes Land, **Antarctica**; featureless plateau, alt. 2,900 m; immense glaciers; U.S. base taken over by Australia 1959.

Willamette, R., Ore., **USA**; rises in Cascade mtns., flows N. into Columbia R. below Portland; valley gives rich agr. land, wheat, rootcrops, dairy prod., hard and soft fruits; ch. ts. Eugene, Salem, Oregon City, Portland; used for hydroelectric power; 480 km long.

Willemstad, pt., cap. of Neth. Antilles; on Curaçao I.; oil refining; tourism; p. (1983) 50,000.

Willenhall, t., West Midlands, **Eng.**; locks and keys, drop forgings.

Willesden, former M.B., Middx., **Eng.**; now inc. in Brent outer bor., Greater London impt. rly. junc., residtl. and industl.

Williamsburg, c., Va., **USA**; between James and York Rs.; historic t., settled 1632; rebuilt in 1920s to original plan; in Colonial Nat. Historical Park; p. (1980) 9,870.

Williamsport, t., Penns., **USA**; on Susquehanna R.; rly. ctr., timber, machin.; summer resort; p. (1984) 32,300 (t.), 117,100 (met. a.).

Willow South, was to be new cap. (1977), Alaska, **USA**; replacing Juneau; closer to ctr. of p.; lack of finance halted construction.

Wilmington, t., spt., Del., **USA**; on Delaware R.; shipbldg., machin., iron and steel wks.; chemicals; leather, cork, rubber gds.; p. (1990) 71,592 (t.), 579,000 (met. a.).

Wilmington, spt., N.C., **USA**; exp. cotton, tobacco, timber, fertilizers, shipbldg., textiles, chemicals; p. (1984) 44,800 (t.), 110,400 (met. a.).

Wilmslow, t., Cheshire, **Eng.**; on R. Bollon, 10 km S.W. of Stockport; residtl.; pharmaceuticals; p. (1981) 30,207.

Wilton, t., Wilts., **Eng.**; on R. Wylye, 5 km W. of Salisbury; agr. mkt., carpets, felt; anc. cap. of Wessex; many old bldgs.; p. (1981) 4,005.

Wilton, industl. estate, Cleveland, **Eng.**; on S. side of Tees estuary; heavy organic- and petro-chemicals; nylon polymer plant.

Wiltshire, non-met. co., **Eng.**; crossed by chalk downland and Salisbury Plain; barley, wheat, dairying, pigs; co. t. Salisbury; a. 3,484 km²; p. (1993) 583,000.

Wimbledon, dist., London, **Eng.**; lge. open common; site of international tennis tournament; part of London Bor. of Merton.

Wimborne Minster, mkt. t., Dorset, **Eng.**; on R. Stour; Roman settlement and home of early Saxon kings; Badbury Rings earthworks nearby; p. (1981) 5,531.

Winchcomb, t., Gloucs., **Eng.**; nr. Cheltenham; old mills; pottery, paper; nearby cas.

Winchelsea, anc. t., East Sussex, **Eng.**; 3 km S.W. of Rye; once impt. walled spt. and Cinque port; now 3 km inland.

Winchester, cath. c., l. gov. dist., Hants., **Eng.**; on R. Itchen, 19 km N. of Southampton; anc. Anglo-Saxon cap.; meeting place of parliaments until time of Henry VII; magnificent cath., famous public school; p. (1993) 100,500 (dist.).

Windermere, lgst. English L., in Cumbria; outlet to Morecambe Bay; supplies water to Manchester; 16 km long, 1·6 km wide.

Windhoek, t., cap. of **Namibia**; in hills at 1,700 m; comm. ctr., agr. processing; tr. in karakul (Persian lamb); p. (1989) 158,609.

Windrush, R., Oxford, Gloucs., **Eng.**; trib. of R. Thames.

Windscale. See **Sellafield.**

Windsor, c., pt., Ont., **Canada**; on Detroit R., linked to Detroit, USA, by tunnel, bridge and ferry; ctr. for car mftg., salt wks., chemicals, paints; univ.; p. (1986) 193,111 (c.), 253,988 (met. a.).

Windsor and Maidenhead, l. gov. dist., Berks., **Eng.**, on R Thames, 32 km W. of London; Windsor has famous royal cas. (founded by William the Conqueror) and park, St. George's Chapel and the Royal Mausoleum; p. (1993) 136,700.

Windward Is., W.I.; extend S. from Leeward Is.; consist of Fr. Martinique and former Brit. cols. of Grenada, St. Vincent, St. Lucia and Dominica with their dependencies (the Grenadines divided between Grenada and St. Vincent) which attained associated statehood 1967; sm. limited resources, economically depressed; volcanic; p. (1984) 419,000.

Windward Passage, channel, 96 km wide, between Cuba and Haiti.

Winnebago, L., Wis., **USA**; 43 km long; lgst. L. in Wis.

Winnipeg, c., cap. of Manitoba, **Canada**; at junc. of Red and Assiniboine Rs.; cath., univ.; rly. ctr.; ch. world wheat mkt.; meat packing and food processing; lgst. garment mnf. ctr. in cty.; oil refining; p. (1986) 594,551 (c.), 625,304 (met. a.).

Winnipeg, L., Manitoba, **Canada**; 64 km N. of Winnipeg; 416 km long, 49–96 km wide; contains several lge. Is. (Reindeer, 181 km²; Big I., 155 km²); used for hydroelectric power.

Winnipegosis, L., Manitoba and Saskatchewan, **Canada**; a. (exclusive of Is.) 5,180 km²; 80 km W. of L. Winnipeg, into which it drains.

Winsford, t., Cheshire, **Eng.**; on R. Weaver; 6 km S. of Northwich; ctr. of salt inds., chemicals; expanded t.; computer peripherals; p. (1981) 26,915.

Winston-Salem, t., N.C., **USA**; formed 1913 from union of 2 adjacent ts.; tobacco ctr.; p. (1990) 143,485.

Winterthur, t., Zurich, **Switzerland**; on Eulach R.; rly. ctr., locomotives, machines, cottons; p. (1990) 86,143.

Wirksworth, t., West Derbys., **Eng.**; in Pennines, 8 km S. of Matlock; limestone, fluorspar wks.; ctr. of Derbys. former lead mng.; p. (1981) 5,492.

Wirral, penin., met. dist., Merseyside, **Eng.**; between estuaries of Dee and Mersey; residtl.; comprises Wallasey, Birkenhead, Bebington and Hoylake; p. (1993) 334,100.

Wisbech, t., Fenland, Cambs., **Eng.**; on R. Nene, 18 km from its mouth in the Wash; mkt. gardening, fruit growing and canning, agr. implements; p. (1981) 17,332.

Wisconsin, st., **USA**; 'Badger St.'; admitted to Union 1848; st. flower Wood Violet. st. bird Robin; bounded by Gr. Ls.; low lying; leading dairying st.; industl. ts. around Gt. Ls.; cap. Madison; ch. t. Milwaukee; a. 145,439 km²; p. (1990) 4,891,769.

Wisconsin, R., Wis., **USA**; trib. of R. Mississippi; used for hydroelectric power; 960 km long.

Wismar, spt., Mecklenburg West Pomerania, **Germany**; on Baltic Sea, N. of Schwerin; oil pt. and industl. ctr. with shipyards and food processing inds.; p. (1981) 57,718.

Witbank, t., Transvaal, **S. Africa**; leading coalmng. dist. with power sta. and carbide and cyanide factories; p. (1980) 154,400 (dist.).

Witham, t., Essex, **Eng.**; 14 km N.E. of Chelmsford; ctr. of mkt. gardening a.; expanded t.; p. (1981) 25,373.

Witham, R., Leics. and Lincs., **Eng.**; flows into the Wash; cuts impressive gap through Lincoln.

Witney, t., Oxford, **Eng.**; on R. Windrush, 16 km W. of Oxford; woollens, blankets, gloves; p. (1981) 14,109.

Witten, t., N. Rhine–Westphalia, **Germany**; on R. Ruhr; glass, machin., metals, chemicals, optical inds.; p. (1990) 105,300.

Wittenberg, t., Saxony - Anhalt, **Germany**; on R. Elbe; ctr. of Reformation and burial place of Luther (Schlosskirche); cas.; machin., textiles; p. (1981) 53,874.

Wittenberge, t., Mecklenburg - West Pomerania, **Germany**; on R. Elbe; rly. junc., repair wkshps., machin.; p. (1989) 29,572.

Witwatersrand, dist., Transvaal, **S. Africa**; goldmng. dist. producing over quarter of world's gold.

Wivenhoe, t., Essex, **Eng.**; on R. Colne; boatbldg., oysters, lt. inds.; p. (1981) 6,470.

Wloclawek, t. and prov., river pt., N. **Poland**; on R. Vistula; impt. paper mnfs., ceramics; p. (1989) 120,680 (t.), 427,400 (prov.).

Woburn, t., Beds., **Eng.**; 8 km N.E. of Leighton Buzzard; Woburn Abbey (seat of Dukes of Bedford).

Woking, t., l. gov. dist., Surrey, **Eng.**; 6 km N. of Guildford; residtl.; p. (1993) 88,200 (dist.).

Wokingham, mkt. t., l. gov. dist., Berks., **Eng.**; 8 km S.E. of Reading; agr. tr. and machin., bricks; p. (1993) 142,900 (dist.).

Wolds, The, chalk downland, Lincs., Humberside, **Eng.**; extend S. to E. Anglian Heights; traditional pastoral agr. changing to extensive arable farming; 72 km long.

Wolfenbüttel, t., Lower Saxony, **Germany**; on R. Oker, 11 km S. of Brunswick; noted for ducal library, founded 17th cent., of which Leibnitz and Lessing were librarians; p. (1986) 48,600.

Wolf Rock, isolated rock with lighthouse, at approach to English Channel from Bay of Biscay; 14 km S.W. of Lands End, Cornwall.

Wolfsburg, t., Lower Saxony, **Germany**; on R. Aller, N.E. of Brunswick; Volkswagen wks.; p. (1990) 129,200.

Wolin, I., Baltic Sea; off mouth of R. Oder, Szczecin, **Poland**; Nat. Park; fishing, tourism; a. 344 km²; p. (1989) 4,495.

Wollongong Greater, t., N.S.W., **Australia**; 7th. c. of A.; heavy inds. attracted by local coal especially at Pt. Kembla; iron, steel, chems.; Australia's only tinplate plant; p. (1991) 239,900.

Wolsingham, t., Durham, **Eng.**; on R. Wear; impt. steel wks.

Wolverhampton, t., met. dist., West Midlands, **Eng.**; heavy inds. and lt. engin., boilers, rayon, elec.

engin. and apparatus, iron wks., aircraft and motor components, hollow-ware, tools, strongrooms and safes, paints; p. (1993) 246,400.

Wolverton, t., Bucks., **Eng.**; on R. Ouse, 24 km S.W. of Bedford; rly.-carriage wks.; p. (1981) 22,249.

Wombwell, t., South Yorks., **Eng.**; at E. foot of Pennines, 11 km N. of Sheffield; coal mng., bricks; p. (1981) 16,628.

Wonsan, spt., **N. Korea**; on Sea of Japan; major pt. and rly. ctr.; Japanese naval base in second world war; oil refining; p. (1984) 350,000.

Woodbridge, t., Suffolk Coastal, Suffolk, **Eng.**; on R. Deben; engin., brush mkg.; p. (1981) 7,224.

Wood Green, former M.B., Middx., **Eng.**; now inc. in Haringey outer bor., Greater London.

Woodhall Spa, t., East Lindsey, Lincs., **Eng.**; 6 km S.W. of Horncastle; former spa, bromoiodine springs; resort; p. (1981) 2,445.

Woodspring, l. gov. dist., Avon, **Eng.**; S. of Bristol and inc. Clevedon, Portishead, and Westonsuper-Mare; p. (1993) 182,100.

Woodstock, t., Ont., **Canada**; on R. Thames; ctr. of agr. dist.; lt. mnfs. based on hydroelectric power; p. (1986) 26,603.

Woodstock, t., Oxford, **Eng.**; on Glyme R., 11 km N.W. of Oxford; glove mnfs.; Blenheim Palace; p. (1981) 2,036.

Wookey Hole, cave, Mendip Hills, Somerset, **Eng.**; at foot of limestone hills, 3 km N.W. of Wells; R. Axe emerges from the cave.

Woolwich, dist. former met. bor., London, **Eng.**; on either side of R. Thames; impt. Tudor dockyard, now closed; now part of Greenwich and Newham bors.

Woomera, S. **Australia**; c. 432 km N.W. of Adelaide; base for joint U.K.–Australian guided-weapon testing range extending N.W. across the continent; established 1947; p. (1981) 1,658.

Woonsocket, t., R.I., **USA**; on Blackstone R.; textiles, rubber gds.; p. (1980) 45,914.

Worcester, c. and l. gov. dist., Hereford and Worcs., **Eng.**; on R. Severn, 38 km N. of Gloucester; cath.; machin., porcelain, glove mkg.; birthplace of Elgar; p. (1993) 87,600.

Worcester, t., Cape Prov., **S. Africa**; viticultural and industl. ctr.; Goudini spa nearby; p. (1980) 95,100 (dist.).

Worcester, c., Mass., **USA**; univ.; cultural ctr.; machine tools, elec. engin.; p. (1990) 169,759 (c.), 437,000 (met. a.).

Worcestershire, former Midland co., **Eng.**; now part of Hereford and Worcs. non-met. co. and West Midlands met. co.

Workington, t., Allerdale, Cumbria, **Eng.**; sm. spt. on Solway F. at mouth of Derwent R., first Bessemer steel plant, heavily dependent upon iron and steel wks. closed (1981), engin.; industl. diversification on nearby industl. estates, inc. bus wks.; p. (1981) 27,581.

Worksop, t., Bassetlaw, Notts., **Eng.**; 24 km S.E. of Sheffield; coal-mng. dist.; brewing, knitwear, glass, flour; p. (1981) 36,893.

Worms, t., Rhineland-Palatinate, **Germany**; on left bank of Rhine; historic ctr.; famous imperial diet 1521 when Luther refused to retract; scene of *Nibelungenlied*; ctr. for Liebfraumilch wines; chemical, textile, leather and metal inds.; p. (1986) 72,000.

Worms Head, promontory, on West Glamorgan cst., Gower peninsula, **Wales**.

Worsley, t., Gtr. Manchester, **Eng.**; ctr. of coalmng. dist.; p. (1981) 49,021.

Worthing, t., l. gov. dist., West Sussex, **Eng.**; on S. cst., 16 km W. of Brighton; holiday resort, retirement ctr. in mkt. gardening dist.; p. (1993) 97,500 (dist.).

Woy Woy, t., N.S.W., **Australia**; resort and commuter t. for Sydney; clothing; p. inc. in Gosford.

Wrangel I., Arctic Oc., off Khabarovsk terr., **Russia**; weather sta.

Wrath, C., N.W. Sutherland, **Scot.**

Wrekin, hill, Shrops., **Eng.**; alt. 403 m.

Wrekin, The, l. gov. dist., Shrops., **Eng.**; inc. Newport, Wellington, Oakengates and Dawley; p. (1993) 142,700.

Wrexham, t., Clwyd, **Wales**; 18 km S.W. Chester; tyres, synthetic fibres, clothing; as **Wrexham Maelor** forms l. gov. dist.; p. (1993) 117,100 (dist.).

Wrocław (Breslau), c., Silesia, **Poland**; on R. Oder; impt. route ctr. and R. pt.; univ., cath.;

rapid industl. development; ctr. of electronics inds.; p. (1989) 640,557.

Wrocław (Breslau), prov., Lower Silesia, **Poland**; until 1945 part of Germany; heavy inds. based on local minerals; cap. Wrocław; a. 24,740 km²; p. (1989) 1,122,800

Wroxeter, v., Shrops., **Eng.**; on R. Severn, 8 km S.E. Shrewsbury; Roman sta. Uriconium.

Wuchow. See **Wuzhou.**

Wuhan, c., Hubei prov., **China**; formed by union of Hankan, Hanyang and Zhifang; major metropolis on Chang Jiang; integrated iron and steel wks., machine tools, walking tractors, textiles, shipbldg.; univ.; p. (1992) 3,790,000.

Wuhu, c., Anhui prov., **China**; former treaty pt. on Chang Jiang; textiles; p. (1984) 491,700.

Wupper, R., **Germany**; trib. of Rhine; industl. concentration along middle course; 64 km long.

Wuppertal, t., N. Rhine–Westphalia, **Germany**; formed by amalgamation of Barmen and Elberfeld, textiles, rubber gds., paper, metals, pharmaceuticals; p. (1990) 383,900.

Würzburg, c., Bavaria, **Germany**; on R. Main; univ., cath.; historic bldgs., engin., chemicals, printing; p. (1990) 128,000.

Wurzen, t., Saxony, **Germany**; on R. Mulde; cath., cas.; machin., furniture, leather, foodstuffs; p. (1989) 18,830.

Wuxi (Wusih), c., Jiangsu prov., **China**; on N. shore of Tai L., 120 km W. of Shanghai; univ.; industl. ctr. with cotton mills, chemical wks.; former treaty pt.; p. (1984) 825,100.

Wuzhou (Wuchow), c., R. pt., Guangxi, **China**; on Xijiang; tr. ctr.; exp. tung oil, hides; p. (1984) 256,500.

Wyandotte, t., Mich., **USA**; on Detroit R.; salt deposits; chemical ind.; p. (1980) 34,006.

Wychavon, l. gov. dist., Hereford and Worcs., **Eng.**; inc. Vale of Evesham and Pershore in S. and Droitwich in N.; p. (1993) 104,900.

Wycombe, l. gov. dist., Bucks., **Eng.**; close to Oxon. and inc. High Wycombe and Marlow; p. (1993) 161,400.

Wye, R., Bucks., **Eng.**; rises in Chiltern hills, flows S.E. to R. Thames at Cookham.

Wye, R., **Eng.** and **Wales**; rises in Plynlimmon, flows S.E. into R. Severn at Chepstow; forms deeply incised valley at Symond's Yat; 208 km long.

Wye, t., Kent, **Eng.**; nr. Ashford; impt. agr. college (Univ. of London).

Wylfa Head, Anglesey, Gwynedd, N. **Wales**; Magnox nuclear power sta.

Wymondham, t., South Norfolk, **Eng.**; 14 km S.W. of Norwich; mkt.; Benedictine abbey founded 1107; p. (1981) 9,811.

Wyoming, st., **USA**; 'Equality St.'; admitted to Union 1890; st. flower Indian Paintbrush, st. bird Meadowlark; inc. areas of Rocky mtns. and great plains; Yellowstone Nat. Park; scant rainfall; irrigation; cattle and sheep ranching; petroleum; sparse p.; cap. Cheyenne; a. 253,597 km²; p. (1990) 453,588.

Wyre, R., Lancs., **Eng.**; rises in Pennines, flows W. into Lancaster Bay at Fleetwood; 45 km.

Wyre, l. gov. dist., Lancs., **Eng.**; inc. Preesall, Fleetwood and Thornton Cleveleys; p. (1993) 103,900.

Wyre Forest, l. gov. dist., Hereford and Worcester, **Eng.**; inc. Bewdley, Kidderminster and Stourport; p. (1993) 96,800.

X

Xalapa, c., cap. of Veracruz st., **Mexico**; c. 1,370 m. a.s.l.; luxuriant vegetation; agr. ctr.; tourism; p. (1990) 288,331.

Xanthi, t. and dep. Thrace, **Greece**; on R. Mesta; ctr. of tobacco-growing a.; p. (1991) 90,450 (dep.).

Xanthus, ruined c., **Turkey**; on R. Xanthus; destroyed 43 B.C.; tourism.

Xauen, t., Morocco, N. Africa; holy t. founded 15th cent.

Xiamen (Amoy), c., Fujian, **China**; rail link to Jianxi; tea, fruit, machin., chemicals, textiles, electronics, tourism; univ.; formerly treaty pt.; in special Economic Zone to encourage foreign investment; p. (1984) 532,600.

Xi'an (Sian), cap. of Shaanxi prov., **China**; impt. route and industl. ctr.; machin.; tourism; research ctr.; iron and steel, textiles, chemicals; p. (1992) 2,790,000.

Xiangtan (Siangtan), c., Hunan prov., **China**; on navigable Xijiang; regional tr. ctr., tea, cotton, electrical goods, machin., textiles; Mao Tse Tung born nearby; p. (1984) 501,700.

Xi Jiang (Si Kiang), ch. R., S. **China**; headstreams rise in Yunnan plateau, R. then flows E. enters S. China Sea through lge delta nr. Hong Kong; lower valley intensively cultivated, rice, sugar cane, tea; tropical climate permits continuous cultivation of most crops through year; valley densely populated; c. 2,000 km. long.

Xingu, R., **Brazil**; trib. of Amazon; navigable in its lower course; Nat. Park and Indian reserve threatened by new cattle ranches, 1,920 km long.

Xinhailion. See **Lianyungang.**

Xining (Sining), cap. of Qinghai prov., **China**; ctr. of spring wheat a.; woollen mills, iron and steel; new rly. completed to help reduce isolation; p. (1984) 576,400.

Xinjiang Uygur (Sinkiang-Uighur), aut. region, N. W. **China**; very dry climate; remote until new roads and rlys. penetrated a.; ethnic minority p. of Turkish background and Islamic faith; many attempts to develop natural resources and industry by Chinese government; pastoral agr.; sheep, goats; new st. arable farms, wheat, maize, millet; lge. oil reserves; cap. Ürümqi; a. 1,646,800 km²; p. (1990) 15,370,000.

Xinyang (Sinyang), t., S. Henan, **China**; regional ctr. for S. Henan and Hubei; p. (1984) 226,600.

Xizang Zizhiqu. See Tibet.

Y

Yablonovy, mtn. range, Siberia, **Russia**; E. of L. Baykal; highest peak, Sokhondo, 2,510 m; crossed by Trans-Siberian rly.

Yaila Mtns., Ukraine; form S.E. margin of Crimea penin., extend from Sevastopol to Kerch; form marked climate barrier between Black Sea littoral and N. part.

Yakima, t., Wash., **USA**; agr. ctr. of irrigated valley, noted for fruit; p. (1984) 48,900 (t.), 179,500 (met. a.).

Yakima, R., Wash., **USA**; trib. of Columbia R.; used for irrigation; 333 km long.

Yakut, aut. rep., **Russia**; borders Arctic Oc.; home of Yakuts; tundra and forest region, isolated; fur trapping, diamond and gold mng., state farms; a. 3,963,355 km²; p. (1989) 1,094,100.

Yakutsk, t., cap. of Yakut, aut. rep., **Russia**; pt. on Lena R.; univ.; airport; p. (1989) 187,000.

Yallahs Valley, **Jamaica**; severe soil erosion; govt. improvement scheme of afforestation and new crops; a. 181 km².

Yallourn, t., Victoria, **Australia**; ctr. of lignite mng. a.; p. (1983) 18,220 (inc. Moe).

Yalta, spt., **Ukraine**; sub-tropical resort on Black Sea, sheltered by Yaila mtns.; conference between Churchill, Roosevelt, and Stalin 1945; p. (1990) 88,800.

Yalu, R., forms bdy. between N.E. **China**, and N. **Korea**; flows into Yellow Sea; used for hydroelectric power.

Yamagata, t., Honshu, **Japan**; ctr. of ricegrowing a.; cas.; p. (1990) 249,487.

Yamaguchi, t., cap. of Y. prov., S.W. Honshu, **Japan**; cas.; comm. ctr., chemicals; p. (1990) 129,461.

Yamal-Nenets National Okrug, **Russia**; inc. Yamal penin.; permafrost; hunting, fishing; cap. Salekhard; lge. natural gas finds; a. 670,810 km²; p. (1989) 494,800.

Yambol, t., **Bulgaria**; on R. Tunja; ruined mosque; agr. tr.; recent inds. inc. canning, farm machin., textiles, ceramics; p. (1990) 99,225.

Yamethin, dist., Upper **Myanmar**; teak forests, rice; ch. t. Yamethin; site of irrigation project; p. 9,291.

Yamoussoukro, t., **Côte d'Ivoire**; cap. replaced Abidjan (1983) to relieve congestion; p. (1986) 120,000.

Yana, R., Siberia, **Russia**; flows into Arctic Sea; navigable; 1,600 km long.

Yangchow. *See* Yangzhou.

Yangchuan. *See* Yanqan.

Yangi-yer, t., **Uzbekistan**; founded 1957 as ctr. for new irrigated cotton lands of E. Uzbekistan.

Yangon, *See* Rangoon.

Yangtze River. *See* Chang Jiang.

Yangzhou, c., Jiangsu, **China**; in valley of Chang Jiang, N.W. of Shanghai; mkt. for local agr. prods.; p. (1984) 382,200.

Yanqan (**Yangchuan**), c., Shaanxi prov., **China**; iron working ctr.; p. (1982) 477,600.

Yantai, spt., Shangdong prov., **China**; anc. c.; food processing, light ind., textiles, cement, steel; exp. foodstuffs esp. prawns & wines; pt. being enlarged as c. declared an economic development zone to attract foreign investment, esp. high technology; p. (1984) 699,400.

Yaoundé, t., cap. of **Cameroon Rep.**, W. **Africa**; lt. inds. inc. beer, cigarettes, textiles; p. (1988) 775,729.

Yapura, R., **Brazil** and **Colombia**, S. America; trib. of R. Amazon; length 2,400 km.

Yaracuy, st., **Venezuela**; crossed by Y. valley impt. agr. a. for bananas, coffee, sugar, tobacco; crossed by Pan-American Highway; cap. San Felipe; a. 7,099 km²; p. (1981) 300,597.

Yare, R., Norfolk, **Eng.**; flows E. to N. Sea at Gorlestown; forms part of Norfolk Broads navigable waterways; 80 km long.

Yarkand. *See* Shache.

Yarmouth, spt., Nova Scotia, **Canada**; fisheries; p. (1986) 7,617.

Yarmouth. *See* Great Yarmouth.

Yaroslavl, c., cap. of Y. oblast, **Russia**; on upper Volga in Moscow industl. region; founded 1010; comm. and industl. ctr.; mnfs. inc. textiles, motor vehicles, synthetic rubber, agr. machin.; Volkov theatre, 12th cent. monastery, churches; p. (1989) 633,000.

Yasan, N., **Bulgaria**; lge. refinery and petrochemicals complex.

Yatsushiro, t., Kyushu, **Japan**; p. (1990) 108,135.

Yazd, c., Isfahan prov., **Iran**; in desert a. at 1,190 m; fine silks, carpets; p. (1986) 248,874.

Yazoo, dist., Miss., **USA**; flood plain of R. Mississippi and R. Yazoo; very fertile alluvial soil, but subject to disastrous floods; one of ch. cotton-growing dists. in USA.

Yegoryevsk, t., **Russia**; 115 km S.E. of Moscow; lge textile ind.; phosphorite deposits.

Yekaterinburg, (**Sverdlovsk**), c., cap. of Y. oblast, **Russia**; on R. Iset in E. foothills of Ural mtns.; on Trans-Siberian rly.; industl. expansion during second world war; heavy machin., metallurgical and chemical plants; univ.; p. (1989) 1,365,000.

Yeletz, t., **Russia**; on R. Sosna; grain and cattle tr.; cultural ctr.; rly. junc.

Yelizavetgrad. *See* Kirovograd.

Yell, I., Shetlands, **Scot.**; 27 km long; covered in peat moorland; p. (1991) 1,075.

Yellowhead Pass, B.C., Alberta, **Canada**; most N. and lowest of main passes across Rocky mtns.; carries Canadian Nat. rly. on route from Edmonton to Vancouver and Prince Rupert; summit alt. 1,130 m.

Yellowknife, t., N.W. Terr., **Canada**; on N. shore of Gr. Slave L.; ctr. of impt. gold-mng. dist.; linked by air to Edmonton, Alberta; p. (1986) 11,753.

Yellow R. *See* Huang He.

Yellow Sea. *See* Huang Hai.

Yellowstone, L., Wyo., **USA**; 32 km long, 24 km wide; alt. 2,360 m; in Y. Nat. Park.

Yellowstone National Park, N.W. Wyo., **USA**; volcanic scenery, geysers; a. 8,956 km².

Yemen, rep. of S.W. Arabian peninsula; cap. Sana'a, economic and commercial cap. Aden; divided since 1967 into Yemen Arab Republic (N. Yemen) and People's Democratic Rep. of Yemen (S. Yemen); reunification May 1990; climate hot and humid coastal strip, summer rainfall on high plateau and desert interior; agr. millet, maize, sorghum, oats (fruit, Mocha coffee; oil (1984); rich fishing grounds; British withdrawal and closure of Suez canal led to ec. decline in south; a. 540,000 km²; p. (1993) 13 m.

Yenangyaung, t., R. pt., **Myanmar**; on left bank of R. Irrawaddy, 448 km N. of Rangoon; ctr. of Burma oilfields.

Yenisey, R., Siberia, **Russia**; rises in Sayan mtns., flows N. into Arctic Oc.; ch. tribs., Angara, Stony Tunguska, Lower Tunguska; hydroelectric power sta. at Krasnoyarsk; linked to Ob R. by canal; middle course navigable; 5,280 km long.

Yentai (**Chefoo**). *See* Yantai.

Yeo or Ivel, R., Dorset, Somerset, **Eng.**; trib. of R. Parrett; 38 km long.

Yeovil, mkt. t., Somerset, **Eng.**; on R. Yeo; glove mnf., aero-engin., agr. machin., dairy processing; p. (1981) 36,597.

Yerevan or Erivan, c., cap. of **Armenia**; on Zanga R. in deep valley of Caucasus mtns.; earthquake 1988; major science-based, industl. ctr.; earthquake 1988; p. (1990) 1,201,500.

Yes Tor, second highest summit, Dartmoor, Devon, **Eng.**; 618 m.

Yevpatoriya or Eupatoria, spt., Crimea, on Black Sea, **Ukraine**; popular resort; children's sanatoria; chemicals, leather, tools, dried fish; new pt. being built; p. (1990) 108,900.

Yezd. *See* Yazd.

Yibin (**Ipin**), c., Sichuan prov., **China**, at junction of Chang Jiang and Min Jiang.

Yichang (**Ichang**), c., S.W. Hubei, **China**; on Chang Jiang; site of famous gorges; terminus of lge. vessels from Shanghai.

Yiewsley and West Drayton, former U.D., Middx., **Eng.**; now inc. in Hillingdon outer bor. Greater London; varied lt. inds.

Yingchuan, t., cap. of Ninxia, aut. region, **China**; on Huang He; ctr. of fertile agr. a.; new lt. inds.; p. (1982) 576,000.

Yingkou (**Yingkow**), c., Liaoning prov., N.E. **China**; 32 km upstream from mouth of Liao R.; soyabean prods.

Yining (**Kuldja**), c., Xinjiang prov., **China**; on highway to Turkestan; coalfield; recent industl. development inc. iron and steel.

Ynys Môn. *See* Anglesey.

Yokkaichi, c., spt., S. Honshu, **Japan**; on Ise Bay, 37 km S. of Nagoya; textiles, petrochemicals, synthetic rubber, porcelain; p. (1990) 274,184.

Yokohama, leading spt., Honshu, **Japan**; on W. shore of Tokyo Bay; steel, chemicals, cars, oil refining, shipyards; univs.; with Tokyo and Kawasaki forms conurb. of Keihin; p. (1990) 3,220,350.

Yokosuka, spt., Honshu, **Japan**; S. of Tokyo; holiday resort; thermal power sta.; p. (1990) 433,358.

Yonkers, c., N.Y., **USA**; on E. bank of Hudson R.; residtl.; lt. inds., textiles; p. (1990) 188,082.

Yonne, dep., **France**; in S.E. of Paris basin, inc. Champagne, Burgundy, Orléanais; drained by R. Yonne; cap. Auxerre; agr., Chablis wines; a. 7,495 km²; p. (1990) 323,100.

Yonne, R., **France**; major trib. of R. Seine; 288 km long.

York, c., co. t., l. gov. dist., North Yorks., **Eng.**; on R. Ouse; in central position in Vale of York; anc. part of c. enclosed by walls; minster, cas., univ.; chocolate, confectionery, rly. wkshps.; p. (1993) 104,000 (dist.).

York, c., Penn., **USA**; ctr. of fertile agr. region; varied inds., inc. agr. tools, machin., textiles, metal gds.; p. (1990) 437,000 (met. a.).

York, C., Queensland, **Australia**; most N. point on mainland of Australia.

York, Vale of, broad lowland, North Yorks., **Eng.**; between Pennines and N. Yorks. Moors and Yorks. Wolds; drained to Humber by R. Ouse and tribs.; glacial and alluvial soils have required draining; crop farming, wheat, barley, root-crops, associated with fattening of beef cattle; settlement mainly marginal; ch. t. York; length 96 km, width from 16 km in N. to 48 km in S.

Yorke, penin., S. **Australia**; separates Spencer G. and G. of St. Vincent; 160 km long, 48 km wide.

Yorkshire, former co., **Eng.**; formerly divided into 3 separate admin. parts (Ridings) N., E., and W.; now split into 3 non-met. cos., Cleveland, North Yorks., and Humberside and 2 met. cos. West Yorks. and South Yorks.

Yorkshire Moors, hills, North Yorks. and Cleveland, **Eng.**; inc. N. Yorks. Moors, Cleveland hills and Hambleton hills; bounded to N. by Tees valley, S. by vale of Pickering, W. by Swale valley, E. by sea; composed of oolitic limestone; gd. sheep pastures; impt. iron-ore deposits worked in Cleveland hills; max. alt. 454 m.

Yorkshire Wolds, hills, Humberside, **Eng.**; extend N.E. from Humber and terminate in Flamborough Head; chalk; gd. sheep pasture; average alt. 180 m.

Yorktown, v., Va., **USA**; scene of surrender by Lord Cornwallis to Washington 1781.

Yosemite National Park, Cal., **USA**; in Sierra Nevada; contains Yosemite creek and canyon with three famous cataracts.

Yoshkar-Ola, t., Mari, aut. rep., **Russia**; 128 km N.W. of Kazan; cultural ctr.; wood processing, food inds.; p. (1989) 242,000.

Youghal, spt., Cork, **R.o.I.**; on estuary of the Blackwater; resort; p. (1986) 5,706.

Youngstown, c., Ohio, **USA**; on Mahoning R.; 91 km N.W. of Pittsburgh; ctr. of one of most impt. iron and steel dists. in USA; heavy engin.; univ.; p. (1990) 95,732 (c.), 492,619 (met. a. with Warren).

Yoyang. *See* **Yueyang.**

Ypres (Ieper), t., W. Flanders prov., N.W. **Belgium**; textiles and textile machin.; ctr. of cloth ind. in middle ages; scene of battles 1914–17; p. (1981) 34,426.

Ypsilanti, t., Mich., **USA**; on Huron R.; residtl., agr. mkt., mnfs.; univ.; p. (1980) 24,031.

Ystwyth, R., Dyfed, **Wales**; flows 40 km to join R. Rheidol at Aberystwyth.

Yuan, R., N.W. Hunan prov., **China**; flows into Dongting Hu and Chang Jiang R.; rapids; 640 km long.

Yucatán, st., S.E. **Mexico**; limestone lowlands poor soils; henequen (sisal hemp), chicle (resin from which chewing gum is made); cap. Mérida; a. 61,968 km²; p. (1990) 1,363,540.

Yueyang (Yoyang), t., Hunan, **China**; at outlet of Dongting Hu and Chang Jiang; p. 4,800.

Yugoslavia, Socialist Fed. Rep., S.E. **Europe**; comprises reps. of Serbia, Montenegro, and aut. regions of Kosovo and Vojvodina; former constituent reps. of Croatia and Slovenia recognised as independent by E.U. 1991; Bosnia-Herzegovina and Macedonia have declared independence, but civil war continues; long W. cst. on Adriatic Sea with well-developed limestone karstic topography; hilly interior; climate Mediterranean on cst., continental in interior; distinctive political development after second world war; refused to accept Soviet hegemony; well-developed links with W.; with major attempts to industrialise, based on energy, heavy and consumer inds. less p. engaged in agr.; economic decision-making increasingly freed from central control; developing tourist tr., especially with countries of W. Europe, based on climate and attractive Adriatic littoral, with many sm. Is.; cap. Belgrade; a. 255,698 km²; p. (1992) (including now independent republics) 10·46 m.

Yukon, R., **Canada** and Alaska, **USA**; flows N.W. and W. into Bering Strait; navigable for 1,920 km; 3,200 km long.

Yukon Territory, prov., N.W. **Canada**; mtnous. (Mt. Logan 6,050 m); gold, silver, lead, zinc; Alaska Highway links with B.C. and Alberta; ch. ts. Dawson, and Whitehorse (cap.); incr. indep. since 1983; a. 536,327 km²; p. (1991) 27,300.

Yuma, t., Arizona, **USA**; at confluence of Rs. Gila and Colorado, nr. Mexican bdr.; ctr. of irrigated agr. region; p. (1980) 42,481.

Yumen, t., N.W. Gansu prov., **China**; leading petroleum ctr.; drilling equipment, precision instruments; on Old Silk Road to Xinjiang; p. (1984) 158,100.

Yunnan, prov., S. **China**; adjoins Burma; mtnous. a. of minority groups; rice, tobacco, tea, cotton; copper, tin; cap. Kunming; a. 420,466 km²; p. (1990) 36,750,000.

Yuzhno-Sakhalinsk, t., **Russia**; at S. end of Sakhalin I.; paper, lt. inds.; p. (1989) 159,000.

Yvelines, dep., **France**; W. of Paris; cap. Versailles; a. 2,271 km²; p. (1990) 1,307,200.

Yverdon, t., Vaud, **Switzerland**; typewriters; p. (1980) 20,802.

Z

Zaanstadt, t., N. Holland **Neth.**; industl. dist.; food processing p. (1993) 131,785.

Zabrze, t., Upper Silesia, Katowice, **Poland**; impt. coal-mng. ctr. with associated heavy inds.; cultural ctr.; p. (1989) 202,824.

Zacapa, t., cap. of Z. prov., **Guatemala**; mkt. t. at rly. junc.; tobacco tr. and processing; sulphur springs; p. (1989) 35,769.

Zacatecas, st., **Mexico**; on central plateau at 2,100 m; dry, agr. dist.; sm. mng. ctrs.; a. 72,836 km²; p. (1990) 1,278,279.

Zacatecas, t., cap. of Z. st., **Mexico**; cath.; ctr. of silver mng., pottery, clothing; p. (1990) 108,528.

Zacatecoluca, t., **El Salvador**; cigar mkg., hand looms; coffee, cotton, sugar, vanilla in a.; p. (1992) 57,032.

Zadar (Zara), t., **Croatia** (formerly Yugoslavia); spt. on cst. of Adriatic Sea; formerly Italian (1920–47); Roman remains; cath.; car ferry to Pesaro (Italy); tourism; p. (1981) 116,174.

Zagan (Sagan), t., Zielona Gora, W. **Poland** (since 1945); on R. Bober; cas.; textiles, paper, lignite mines; p. (1989) 27,333.

Zagazig, t., **Egypt**; on Nile Delta; tr. ctr. of fertile agr. a. producing cotton, grains; cotton mills; p. (1986) 255,000.

Zagorsk. *See* **Sergiyev Posad.**

Zagreb, c., cap. of **Croatia** (formerly Yugoslavia); on Sava R.; cath., univ.; tr. fair; many inds., notably petrochemicals based on local petroleum reserves, elec. engin.; airport; second c. of rep., p. (1991) 706,770.

Zagros, mtns., **Iran**; inc. Iran's major oilfield; highest peak Zardesh Kuh, 4,551 m.

Zahedan, c., **Iran**; cap. of Sistan and Baluchistan prov.; airport; terminus of rly. from Pakistan; p. (1982) 165,000.

Zahle, t., **Lebanon**, S.W. Asia; on slopes of L. mtn.; p. (1988) 45,000.

Zaire, Rep. of, Central Africa; comprises eight provs. (caps. in brackets): Bas-Zaïre (Matadi), Bandundu (Bandundu), Equateur (Mbandaka), Haut-Zaïre (Kisangani), Kivu (Bukavu), Shaba (Lubumbashi), Kasai Oriental (Mbuji-Mayi), Kasai Occidental (Kananga); lies in vast basin of Zaïre R., mtns. on E. and S. borders; climate equatorial in N., tropical in S.; agr. exp. inc. palm oil, cotton, coffee, but economy based on mng., diamonds (Kasai), cobalt, non-ferrous metals (Shaba), major world producer of copper; radium deposits nr. Lubumbashi; extensive navigation on Zaïre R.; main pt. Matadi on estuary linked by rail to cap. Kinshasa; a. 2,345,457 km²; p. (1991) 38·55 m.

Zaïre, gr. R. of **Equatorial Africa**; numerous tribs., drains 3,885,000 km²; navigable from sea to Matadi for ocean steamers, from Matadi to Pool Malebo interrupted by rapids and falls, again navigable to Boyoma Falls; proposed power project to be lgst. in Africa; estuary 11–16 km wide; c. 4,800 km long.

Zakinthos (Zante), Ionian I., **Greece**; cap. Zakinthos (Zante); devastated by earthquake 1953; currants, wine, olives; a. 717 km²; p. (1981) 30,014.

Zakinthos (Zante), t., Zakinthos I., **Greece**; spt. on E. cst.; agr. tr. and processing; p. (1981) 9,764.

Zakopane, t., Nowy Sącz prov., **Poland**; in High Tatra mtns.; base for mountaineering and winter sports; health resort; tourism; p. (1989) 28,417.

Zalaegerszeg, t., **Hungary**; in Göcsej dist.; oil refining; mkt. t. for grain and livestock; p. (1989) 64,000.

Zambesi, R., S.E. **Africa**; flows E. to Moçambique Channel, Indian Oc.; forms frontier between Zambia and Zimbabwe; inc. Victoria Falls and Kariba and Cabora Bassa dams; navigable but impeded by rapids; 3,520 km long.

Zambia, rep., **Central Africa**; member of Commonwealth; tropical climate, modified by alt.; plateau (1,200 m); subsistence agr.; livestock on uplands free from tsetse fly; mng. basis of economy, especially in copperbelt; world's 4th lgst copper producer; exp. disrupted by Rhodesian U.D.I. (1965); falling copper output as mines near exhaustion; need to develop alternative routes to cst.; pipeline from Ndola to Dar-es-Salaam; construction of Tan-Zam rly. financed by Chinese aid; cap. Lusaka; a. 752,618 km²; p. (1991) 8·78 m.

Zamboanga, c., Mindanao, **Philippines**; spt. on Basilian Strait, exp. prod. timber; p. (1990) 442,345.

Zamora, prov., **Spain**; borders Portugal; drained by R. Duero; cereals, wine, merino sheep; cap. Zamora; a. 10,559 km²; p. (1991) 210,822.

Zamora, t., cap. of Zamora prov., **Spain**; on R. Duero; cath.; agr. tr. and processing ctr.; developing mnfs.; p. (1987) 60,708.

Zamosc, t. and prov., Lublin, **Poland**; Renaissance planned t. in valley of Lubianka R.; industl., comm. and cultural ctr.; p. (1989) 60,565.

Zanesville, t., Ohio, **USA**; textiles, pottery, machin.; p. (1990) 26,778.

Zangbo (Tsangpo), R., Tibet, **China**; one of head-streams of R. Brahmaputra; 1,350 km. long.

Zanjan, c., **Iran**; cap. of Gilan prov.; cotton, woollen gds.; p. (1986) 215,458.

Zanzibar, terr., E. **Africa**; comprises Is. of Z. and Pemba; joined Tanganyika to form **Tanzania** (1964); major world source of cloves; coconut and coconut prod. major exp. and basis of processing inds.; cap. Zanzibar; a. 2,642 km²; p. (1988) 604,578.

Zanzibar, spt., Zanzibar I., **Tanzania**; on W. cst. 35 km from E. Africa; outlet for clove exp., entrepot tr.; former slave mkt.; p. (1985) 133,000.

Zaporozh'ye, t., **Ukraine**; on R. Dnieper, nr. dam and hydroelec. power sta.; metal inds. based on Donets coal and Krivoi Rog iron ore; p. (1990) 891,000.

Zaragoza, prov., **Spain**; largely barren plain suffering from climatic extremes; a. 17,122 km²; cap. Z.; p. (1991) 852,766.

Zaragoza, cap. Z. prov., **Spain**; on R. Ebro; 2 caths., univ.; former cap. of Aragon; rly. junc.; comm. ctr.; p. (1987) 575,317.

Zarate, t., Entre Rios, **Argentina**; paper wks., agr. ctr., meat packing; p. (1980) 65,504.

Zaria, c., N. **Nigeria**; founded 15th cent., old part surrounded by walls; univ., cotton ctr.; rly. ctr., p. (1983) 274,000.

Zarga, t. **Jordan**; ind. ctr., phosphates; p. (1986) 404,500.

Zary (Sorau), t., Zielona Gora, **Poland** (since 1945); textiles; p. (1989) 39,172.

Zawiercie, t., **Poland**; industl. ctr.; coal, iron, textiles, glass; p. (1989) 56,017.

Zdunska Wola, t. Sieradz, **Poland**; nr. Lodz; textiles, engin.; p. (1989) 44,686.

Zealand. See **Sjaelland**.

Zeebrugge, spt., **Belgium**; 14 km N. of Bruges; exp. coal, chemicals; oil refining; linked by canal to Bruges.

Zeeland, prov., **Neth.**; a. covering part of Scheldt estuary and Is.; low-lying; dairying; cap. Middelburg; a. 1,787 km²; p. (1993) 361,195.

Zeist, t., Utrecht, **Neth.**; chemicals, toys; p. (1993) 59,096.

Zeitz, t., Saxony - Anhalt, **Germany**; textiles, chemicals; p. (1991) 59,357.

Zelten, **Libya**, N. Africa; oilfield; 320 km S. of Benghazi; pipeline to Mersa al-Brega.

Zenica, t., **Bosnia-Herzegovina**, formerly Yugoslavia; lge. iron and steel wks.; ctr. of Z. basin; rly. junc.; p. (1981) 132,733.

Zeravshan, R., **Tajikistan** and **Uzbekistan**; flows for 736 km before evaporating in desert region N. of Chardzhou.

Zetland. See **Shetland**.

Zgierz, t., Lodz. prov., central **Poland**; nr. source of R. Bzura; textiles, chemicals, textile machin.; p. (1989) 58,836.

Zhangjiakou (Kalgan), c., Hebei, **China**; nr. Great Wall, 160 km N.W. of Beijing; a main route to Mongolia; tea wool, hides; p. (1984) 607,900.

Zhangzhou (Chuangchow), c., Fujian prov., **China**; former pt. now silted up; p. (1984) 210,600.

Zhanjiang (Tsamkong), c., Guandong prov., **China**; spt. on Liuzhou peninsula; machin., chemicals, elec. inds.; designated economic development zone; cotton, milling, leather mnfs.; p. (1984) 899,500.

Zhdanov. See **Mariupol**.

Zhengzhou, (**Quauzhu**), c., cap. Henan prov., **China**; 24 km. S of Huang He where it emerges on to N. China Plain; impt. route ctr. and rly. junc.; p. (1992) 1,730,000.

Zhenjiang (Chinkiang), c., Jiangsu, **China**; former treaty pt. on Chang Jiang, 77 km. below Nanjing; tr. ctr.; p. (1984) 397,300.

Zhijiang (Chekiang), coastal prov., S.E. **China**; cap. Hangzhou; impt. rice growing a.; major natural gas field; a. 102,269 km²; p. (1990) 40,840,000.

Zhitomir, t., **Ukraine**; engin., clothing; route ctr.; p. (1990) 295,900.

Zhousan (Chusan), I., and archipelago off E. cst. of China and Chang Jiang delta; ch. ctr. Dinghai on Zhousan I.; valuable fishing grounds.

Zhuhai, special economic zone, **China**, N. of Macau; selected (1983) to attract foreign investment; new pt.; p. (1984) 144,400.

Zhujiang (Chukiang or Pearl R.), Guandong, S. **China**; one of most impt. waterways of China; 176 km. long from Guangzhou to Hong Kong; fertile delta known as "land of fish, rice and fruit"; around Guangzhou network of elec., drai-

nage and irrigation stas; built since 1959; estuary now silting.

Zhuzhou (Chuchau), c., Hunan prov., **China**; on Xiang Jiang; rly.; p. (1984) 487,800.

Zibo (Tzepo), c., Shandong, **China**; formed by merging of several coal mng. ts. in the 1950s; p. (1991) 2,460,000.

Zielona Gora (Grünberg), c., W. **Poland** (since 1945); in valley surrounded by wooded hills; admin. and industl. ctr., cap. of Z.G. prov.; textiles, food processing, machin.; viticulture; p. (1989) 113,108.

Zielona Gora, prov., **Poland**; borders E. Germany; glacial sands, wooded; brown coal deposits; cap. Z.G.; a. 14,514 km²; p. (1989) 655,000.

Zigaze (Shigatze), t., Tibet, **China**; on R. Zangbo; tr. ctr. on main caravan routes.

Zigong (Tzekung), c., Sichuan, **China**; petroleum, natural gas, salt wks.; p. (1984) 899,700.

Ziguinchor, t., **Senegal**; pt. on R. Casamance; exp. groundnuts; p. (1979) 79,464 (latest fig.).

Zilina, t., **Slovakia**; on R. Vah; paper, fertilisers; p. (1990) 97,000.

Zimbabwe, **Central Africa**; former Brit. col. (Rhodesia); indep rep. 1980; landlocked st.; much of land high veld above 900 m covered in savannah; impressive economic growth with removal of sanctions and end of warfare; manuf. limited by lack of skilled labour; still heavy dependence on agr., maize and tobacco; mng. also impt.; Wankie coal mine lgst. in world; also asbestos, chrome and copper; power from Kariba dam encourages lt. inds.; cap. Harare; a. 389,329 km²; p. (1992) 9·9 m.

Zimbabwe National Park; site nr. Victoria, Mashonaland, of ruined t. built c. 15th cent. A.D. by a Bantu people; discovered 1868.

Zinder, t., **Niger**, W. Africa; terminus of trans-Saharan motor route; tr. ctr.; former cap.; second t. of Niger; p. (1988) 120,900.

Zion National Park, Utah, **USA**; contains Z. canyon; a. 596 km².

Zipaquirá, t., **Colombia**; 48 km N. of Bogotá; salt mng., chemicals; cattle-rearing a.

Zistersdorf, t., Lower **Austria**; recently developed oilfields.

Zittau, t., Saxony, **Germany**; on R. Mandau; woollens, linens, machin., cars, chemicals; p. (1989) 36,246.

Zlatoust, t., S.W. **Russia**; in Ural mtns.; metallurgical ctr.; steel, chemicals, sawmilling; p. (1989) 208,000.

Zletovo, tern., N.E. **Macedonia**, formerly Yugoslavia; oil shales, lead, zinc deposits.

Zlin (Gottwaldov), t., **Czech Rep.**; 64 km E. of Brno; footwear, leather and domestic woodware inds.; home of Bata footwear; p. (1990) 87,000.

Znojmo or Znaim, t., **Czech Rep.**; anc. t., cas.; ctr. of fertile agr. dist.; p. (1984) 38,321.

Zomba, t., former cap. of **Malawi**, 884 m a.s.l. on slopes of Zomba mtn., 67 km N.E. Blantyre; Malawi's univ. t.; p. (1983) 46,000.

Zonguldak, t. and prov., **Turkey**; spt. on Black Sea; coal-mng. a.; p. (1990) 124,862 (t.), 1,073,560 (prov.).

Zorita De Los Canes, Guadalajara, **Spain**; on R. Tagus; nuclear power plant.

Zrenjanin, t., Vojvodina, Serbia, **Yugoslavia**; pt. on R. Begej; ctr. of agr. dist.; agr. processing; p. (1991) 81,328.

Zuetina, oil pt. (1968), **Libya**; pipeline links shore storage sta. with offshore berths.

Zug, smallest can., **Switzerland**; drained by R. Reuss; contains part of L. Z.; dairying, fruit; cap. Z.; a. 241 km²; p. (1990) 84,900.

Zug, t., cap. of Zug can., **Switzerland**; on L. Z.; elec. engin., printing; p. (1980) 21,609.

Zugspitze, mtn., Bavarian Alps, on Bavarian–Austrian bdr.; highest peak in **Germany**, 2,965 m; connected by rack-and-pinion to Garmisch-Partenkirchen at foot.

Zuider Zee. See **IJsselmeer**.

Zuid Holland, prov. **Neth**; crossed by R. Rhine; mkt gardening; a. 2,927 km²; p. (1993) 3,295,522.

Zulia, st., **Venezuela**; centred on L. Maracaibo, producing 70 per cent of Venezuelan oil; timber reserves; cap. Maracaibo; a. 63,902 km²; p. (1981) 1,674,252.

Zürich, c., cap. of Z. can., **Switzerland**; on L. Z. and R. Limmat; cath., univ.; leading world banking ctr.; inds. inc. textiles, paper; p. (1990), 341,300 (c.), 840,000 (met. a.).

Zürich, can., **Switzerland**; forested and agr. a. stretching N. from L. Z.; inds. at cap. Z. and Winterthur; a. 1,728 km²; p. (1990) 1,150,500.

Zürich, L. Z., **Switzerland**; drained by R. Limmat; length 40 km.

Zutphen, t., Gelderland, **Neth.**; on R. Ijssel; textiles, paper; Sir Philip Sidney died here 1586; p. (1993) 31,117.

Zuzhou (**Suchow**), c., Jiangsu, **China**; at junct. of N. China plain and Chang Jiang basin; rly. junct.

Zuzhou (**Luchow**), c., Sichuan, **China**; coal, iron, kaolin; synthetic ammonia plant.

Zweibrücken, t., Rhineland-Palatinate, **Germany**; nr. Saarbrücken; cas.; machin., footwear, textiles; p. (1986) 32,700.

Zwickau, c., Saxony, **Germany**; on R. Mulde; cas.; coal, motors, machin., textiles; birthplace of Schumann; p. (1990) 113,600.

Zwolle, t., Overijssel, **Neth.**; canal ctr.; cattle mkt.; p. (1993) 98,318.

Zyrardow, t., Skierniewice, **Poland**; nr. Warsaw; specialised textile ctr.; p. (1989) 42,068.

Zyryanovsk, t., **Kazakhstan**; lead, zinc; p. (1990) 53,400.

GENERAL
INFORMATION

This section contains some three thousand entries, arranged alphabetically, including a number of scientific terms and explanations. Entries range across a wide spectrum of human knowledge, from the animal kingdom and medieval history to such contemporary topics as the Internet. Cross references direct the reader to fuller information elsewhere in the book.

MEASUREMENTS ARE GIVEN IN METRIC UNITS

Abbreviations

mm	= millimetre	m²	= square metre
cm	= centimetre	km²	= square kilometre
m	= metre	ha	= hectare
km	= kilometre	m³	= cubic metre
km/h	= kilometres per hour	s	= second
g	= gram	min	= minute
kg	= kilogram	h	= hour
tonne	= metric ton		

Equivalents

Length		*Reciprocal*
1 cm	= 0·394 in	2·540
1 m	= 1·094 yd	0·914
1 km	= 0·621 mile	1·609

Area		
1 m²	= 1·196 yd²	0·836
1 km²	= 0·386 mile²	2·590
1 hectare	= 2·471 acres	0·405

Volume		
1 m³	= 1·308 yd³	0·765
1 litre	= 0·220 gallon	4·546

Mass		
1 kg	= 2·205 lb	0·454
1 tonne	= 0·984 ton	1·016

Temperature

$$C = (F - 32) \div 1·8$$
$$F = (1·8 \times C) + 32$$

See also **Metric Equivalents, F66–70**

GENERAL INFORMATION

A

Aard-vark (Dutch *aarde* = earth + *vark* = pig), a large nocturnal mammal found only in Africa. It feeds on termites and ants.

Abacus, a device for making arithmetical calculations, consisting of parallel bars on which are strung movable coloured beads. The earliest form of this instrument was used in Mesopotamia about 3000 B.C., and its use spread westwards throughout the Graeco-Roman world and eastwards to China. An efficient form of the abacus is still used in parts of Asia.

Abdication. The term usually refers to the renunciation of the royal office by a reigning monarch. Both Edward II (1327) and Richard II (1399) were forced to abdicate, James II left the throne vacant without waiting for a formal deposition, and the abdication of Edward VIII was effected by the Declaration of Abdication Act, 1936. Since 1688 when Parliament declared James II to have abdicated by reason of desertion and subversion of the constitution, no British monarch can abdicate without the consent of Parliament.

Aberration, in astronomy, is the apparent displacement of a star due to the speed of the observer with the earth (*see* **Parallax**). In optics (i) spherical aberration is when there is blurring of the image and fringes of colour at its edges, due to failure of lens to bring light to a single focus; (ii) chromatic aberration is due to the refractive index of glass being different for light of different colours. For instance, violet light is bent more than red.

Abiogenesis, or spontaneous generation; the origination of living from non-living matter. The term is applied to such discredited ideas as that frogs could be generated spontaneously by the action of sunlight on mud, or maggots arise spontaneously in dead meat without any eggs from which the maggots hatch being present. Spallanzani (1729–99) upset the hypothesis of spontaneous generation; Pasteur dealt it a death-blow.

Abominable Snowman. *See* Yeti.

Aborigines, a term first applied to an ancient mythical people of central Italy, derives from the Latin *ab origine* = from the beginning. It now signifies the original inhabitants of any country, in particular the aboriginal tribes of Australia. In contrast to their highly complex social and religious customs, the material culture of Australian aboriginals is very low and ill adapted to stand up to contact with European civilisation. Originally estimated at 300,000, their number has dropped in the last 200 years to some 225,000. The 1988 Australian bicentenary focused attention on their lack of legal right to ancient tribal lands and their welfare problems. The passage of the Native Rights Act in 1993 may redress some of their grievances.

Absolute Temperature, Absolute Zero. This is a refined notion requiring some study of thermodynamics for its full understanding. For setting up an absolute temperature scale one must first assign a numerical value to one fixed temperature. At present the triple point of water has been chosen, *i.e.*, the temperature at which solid, liquid, and gaseous water are all in equilibrium. The triple point is defined to be 273·16 K where K is read for kelvin (after Lord Kelvin). This temperature is 0·01°C on the Celsius scale (*q.v.*) and is thus very close to the melting point of ice. Suppose the pressure and volume of a mass of gas are measured (i) at the triple point of water, giving (pV)tr as the product of the pressure and volume; and (ii) at any unknown temperature T K, giving (pV) as the product. Then the absolute temperature, T K, is defined by

$$T\,\mathrm{K} = 273\cdot16\,\frac{(pV)}{(pV)\mathrm{tr}}$$

It is to be understood that the gas pressure is very low. The nature of the gas is immaterial. More subtly, it can be shown that the temperature so defined is identical with that derived in a rather abstract way in the science of thermodynamics. The absolute scale is therefore also called the thermodynamic scale. Absolute temperatures can be obtained from Celsius temperatures by adding 273·15; thus the absolute temperature of melting ice is 273·15 K. Conversely, absolute zero is a temperature 273·15 K below the temperature of melting ice, *i.e.*, −273·15°C. Theory shows that absolute zero is unattainable, but it has been approached to within about 1 millionth of a degree. Within ten or so degrees of absolute zero, matter develops some remarkable properties. *See* Kelvin, Cryogenics, Superconductor, Helium.

Abstract Art, a term applied to 20th cent. plastic arts in which form and colour possess aesthetic value apart from the subject. Usually represented as a modern movement beginning with Cézanne. The idea is ancient, abstract design being found in the Neolithic period, in folk-art, and particularly in Moslem art (which forbids naturalistic representations especially of the human figure). Among those in the tradition are Kandinsky, Braque, Mondrian, Calder.

Acetic Acid, an organic acid produced when ordinary (ethyl) alcohol is fermented by the organism called *Acetobacter aceti*. The same oxidation process yields vinegar: this is a weak and crude solution of acetic acid obtained by trickling dilute alcoholic liquor over beechwood shavings at 35°C. The souring of wine is due to the same process. Acetic acid is used as a food preservative and flavouring material, and in the manufacture of cellulose acetate and white lead.

Acetylene (also called ethyne), a compound of carbon and hydrogen prepared from calcium carbide and water. A very reactive gas, it is used industrially on a large scale to prepare acetaldehyde, chlorohydrocarbon solvents, and many intermediates for plastics manufacture. Burns in air with a highly luminous flame, formerly used for lighting purposes, but is now widely used, with oxygen, in welding. For safe storage and transportation it is dissolved in acetone.

Acid Rain is the name given to rain, snow or sleet contaminated with acid substances so that its acidity is greater than the limit expected by normal concentrations of carbon dioxide dissolving in the rain to give carbonic acid (pH 5·5–5·6). The pH (*see* **L95**) of acid rain therefore is less than about 5·5. The increased acidity is caused by larger concentrations of a number of contaminants, principally the strong acids, nitric and sulphuric, which arise from industrial effluents containing oxides of nitrogen and sulphur. The European emission of sulphur dioxide doubled between 1940 and 1980. In some European and North American areas such contamination can give a rain pH as low as 3 (which is 100 times more acid than pH 5). The acid rain can mark fruit and leaves, and adversely affect soil but its main effect is on the aquatic ecosystems especially in regions which cannot naturally buffer acidic inputs such as those with thin soils and granite rocks. It is likely that the disappearance of fish from many Scandinavian lakes has been the result of pollution by acid rain.

Acids, substances having a tendency to lose a positive ion (a proton). This general definition overcomes difficulties of earlier views which merely described their properties and asserted that they are chemically opposite to bases. As a whole acids contain ionisable hydrogen, replaceable by a metal, to form a salt. Inorganic acids are compounds of non-metals or metalloids, *e.g.*, sulphuric, phosphoric acid. Carboxylic acids contain the group –COOH. *See* **F25.**

Actinides, the fourteen metallic elements from thorium (no. 90) to lawrencium (no. 103). All known isotopes of these elements are radioactive and those with atomic number greater than 92 (uranium) have been produced only in significant quantities artificially. Plutonium (no. 94) is obtained from uranium during the course of nuclear reactor operation and the higher transuranic elements can be made from it by the successive capture of neutrons or nuclei of light atoms. The availability of only minute quantities of short-lived isotopes makes the determination of the physical and chemical properties of the higher actinides very difficult. Claims for the discovery of new elements can therefore be controversial and since the discoverers can name the elements their naming is also controversial. There were three different reports for Nobelium (no. 102). Lawrentium (no. 103) is called Jolistium by Russian authors. Element no. 104 was reported in 1964 by a Russian group and called Kurchatovium but is called Rutherfordium (Rf) in the West. Element no. 105 is called Hahnium (Hn).

Advent, a period devoted to religious preparation for the coming celebration of the Nativity (Christmas). It includes the four Sundays immediately preceding the festival.

Advocatus Diaboli ("the devil's advocate"), a Roman Catholic functionary who presents opposing evidence in regard to the life of any deceased person it may be proposed to canonise.

Aerodynamics, the science of gases (especially air) in motion, particularly in relation to aircraft (aeronautics). The idea of imitating the birds by the use of wings is of ancient origin. Leonardo da Vinci first carried out experiments in a scientific manner. The invention of the balloon in 1783 and the researches of scientists and engineers in the 19th cent. ultimately led to the development of the aeroplane.

Aerolites, the name given to the class of meteorites composed chiefly of heavy silicates. The other two main classes are *siderolites* (nickel–iron and silicates) and *siderites* (nickel–iron).

Aerosol, a suspension of a liquid in a gas; for example, a fog is very small drops of water suspended in air. Formed by spraying the liquid in air, aerosols are used to disperse liquid over a wide area in crop spraying, air freshening and pest control. *See also* **Fluorocarbons.**

Afrikander, type of cattle bred in South Africa.

Afrikaner, an Afrikaans-speaking South African, usually of Dutch descent.

After-damp occurs in a mine after an explosion, causing suffocation. It is composed mainly of carbon dioxide and nitrogen and contains water vapour and carbon monoxide (produced by the burning, in a restricted supply of air, of fine coal dust).

Agaric, large fungi of the family *Agaricaceae*, which includes the mushroom and what are popularly called "toadstools", though the idea that these two lay terms sharply differentiate between edible and poisonous fungi is an incorrect one. Characteristic of the agarics is the presence of a cap or *pileus* (bearing underneath the spore-shedding gills) and a stalk or *stipe*.

Agave, the American aloe or Century Plant which sometimes does not attain to flowering maturity under sixty or seventy years, and then dies. The flower spray may reach a height of 6 m and in its development the rush of sap is so great that the Mexicans collect for brewing the strong spirit called mescal. 1,000 litres of sap can be obtained from a single plant. Some species of agave yield sisal used for making cord and rope.

Aggression. After many years of consideration a definition of aggression was agreed at the United Nations in 1974. It is the use of armed force by a state against the sovereignty, territorial integrity, or political independence of another state or in any other manner inconsistent with the Charter of the UN. Iraq's invasion of Kuwait in 1990 was one recent example.

Air, a mixture of gases in the earth's atmosphere, the main constituents being nitrogen, oxygen and argon. Dry air contains these gases in the following proportions by volume: nitrogen 78·06%, oxygen 21%, argon 0·94%. Other gases are also present in small amounts. Of particular importance are water vapour and carbon dioxide. Water vapour is not only critical for life forms on land but also a major

factor in the behaviour of the atmosphere—weather and climate. Carbon dioxide is utilised by green plants in photosynthesis (**F32**). Air also contains traces of ammonia, nitrogen oxides, hydrogen, sulphur dioxide, ozone, and of the rare gases, helium, krypton, neon and xenon. Near cities and industrial areas there are also large quantities of dust and smoke particles (up to 100,000 particles per cc), and traces of other gases from industrial processes. A litre of air at 0°C and 760 mm pressure weighs 1·2932 g. *See also* **Atmosphere, Pollution.**

Air Glow is the general name given to a large number of relatively weak optical emissions from the earth's upper atmosphere in the height range 70 to 400 km (approx.). It is distinct from the aurora polaris *(q.v.)* which is usually much brighter and normally only observable at high latitudes. Air glow is produced by a combination of photochemical reactions in the upper atmosphere, excitation by photoelectrons, or by solar ultra-violet light. In the latter case it is more correctly called "dayglow." These emissions occur in the ultra-violet and infra-red spectral regions as well as in visible light.

Air Passenger Duty, tax levied on airline tickets from 1 November 1994 at a rate of £5 for most European destinations (including those in Britain) and £10 for airports further afield.

Alabaster, a soft crystalline form of sulphate of lime, or granulated gypsum, easily worked for statuary and other ornamental articles, and capable of being highly polished. Volterra, in Tuscany, yields the finest; that in highest ancient repute came from Alabastron in Egypt, near to the modern Antinoë.

Alb, white vestment reaching to the feet, worn by priests in religious ceremonies.

Albatross, a large sea-bird of almost pure white, black and white, or brown plumage. It nests in colonies on remote islands, but at other times rarely approaches land. Of the thirteen species, nine are found in the southern oceans, one in the tropics, three others in the North Pacific. Modern fishing methods are threatening the albatross with extinction.

Albert Memorial, a large Gothic monument designed by Sir George Gilbert Scott, and embellished with sculptures by eminent artists. Erected in memory of Prince Albert in Kensington Gardens at a cost of £120,000.

Alcázar the palace at Seville, famed for the beauty of its halls and gardens, in ancient days the residence of the Moorish kings.

Alchemy. *See* **Section J.**

Alcohols. A class of organic compounds of general formula R–OH, where R is an aliphatic radical. "Alcohol" is the name used for ethyl alcohol (ethanol); this is produced by distilling fermented liquors, and synthetically from ethylene, a product of petroleum cracking. Industrially ethyl alcohol is used in the manufacture of chloroform, ether, perfumes, etc. Diluted with wood alcohol or other denaturants ethyl alcohol is called "methylated spirits"; the denaturants are varied according to the industrial purposes for which it is required, the methylated spirits then being largely exempt from duty. Wood alcohol (methyl alcohol or methanol) can be obtained by distilling wood or synthetically from water gas.

Alcoholic Strength. In 1980 Great Britain adopted the OIML (International Organisation of Legal Metrology) system of spirit strength measurement in metric units as required by EEC directive. The alcoholic strength of wine is expressed in percentage volume ("% vol") terms, *i.e.*, the number of volumes of pure alcohol in 100 volumes of the product at 20°C. For spirits the quantity for duty is the litre of alcohol at 20°C. For example, a case of 12 bottles of 75 cl each = 9 litres; at 40% volume 9 litres = 9 × 40% = 3.60 litres of alcohol. The alcoholic strength of spirits and liqueurs appearing on bottle labels is increasingly shown in % vol. terms (*e.g.*, "40.5% vol"). The USA continues to use the US proof gallon (1.37 US proof gallons = 1 British proof gallon).

Aldehyde, the generic term for a class of chemical compounds of general formula R–CHO, where R is an organic radical. Except for formaldehyde, which is a gas, aldehydes are volatile liquids. They are produced by oxidation of primary alcohols. Most important aldehyde is formaldehyde (methanal) used in making the plastics described as formaldehyde resins. Formalin (formaldehyde solution in water) is much used for preserving zoological specimens.

Alder, a river-side tree of the genus *Alnus*, including some 30 species and found in north temperate regions and the Andes. The only species native to Britain is *A. glutinosa*, which has been described as "guardian of river-banks" because of the way its roots bind together the sand and stones, and so slow down erosion. The wood is used for furniture and charcoal.

Aldine Editions are the beautiful books printed in Venice by the Renaissance printer Aldo Pio Manuzio and his family between 1490 and 1597. Italics were first introduced in these books.

Algae, flowerless plants living mostly in water. Seaweeds and the green pond scums are the best known algae. The green powder found on trees is a microscopic alga (*Protococcus*). See **F42(1).**

Algebra, a branch of mathematics in which symbols are used in place of numbers. Sir Isaac Newton styled it the "universal arithmetic". The Chinese were able to solve the quadratic equation before the Christian era but it was Al-Khowarizmi, an Arab mathematician of the early 9th cent., who introduced algebra to Europe.

Alhambra, the ancient palace of the Moorish kings at Granada in Spain, built in the 13th and 14th cent. Though part of the castle was turned into a modern palace under Charles V, the most beautiful parts of the interior are still preserved—the graceful halls and dwelling-rooms grouped round the Court of Alberca and the Court of Lions, with their fountains, arcades, and lovely gardens.

Aliphatic describes derivatives of hydrocarbons having chains of carbon atoms, as distinct from rings of carbon atoms as in benzene (*see* **Aromatic**). The gas butane is aliphatic.

Alkali, the general name given to a number of chemicals which are bases (*q.v.*). The term should be limited to the hydroxides of metals in the first and second group of the periodic table and of ammonia, *e.g.*, NaOH, KOH. They are used commercially in the manufacture of paper, glass, soap, and artificial silk. The word comes from the Arabic *al-kali* meaning calcined wood ashes. Alkalis are extremely soluble in water and neutralise acids to form salts and water.

Alkaloids, a large group of natural products which contain nitrogen; they are usually basic. Isolated from plants and animals, they include some hormones, vitamins, and drugs. Examples are nicotine, adrenalin, and cocaine. Many alkaloids are made synthetically for medicinal use, *e.g.*, morphine, quinine. Their function in plants is not well understood. *See* **Belladonna.**

Alligator, the crocodile of America, found in the lower Mississippi and adjacent lakes and marshes. There is also a Chinese species. Alligators have broader snouts than other crocodiles.

Allotropy. Depending on the temperature, pressure or method of preparation, an element may exist in one of several forms, each having different physical properties (crystal structure, electrical conductivity, melting point, etc.). This is known as allotropy and the different forms of the element are called allotropes Many elements exhibit allotropy, *e.g.*, sulphur, phosphorus, oxygen, tin and carbon, the most well-known allotropes of carbon being diamond and graphite.

Alloys are combinations of metals made for their valuable special properties, *e.g.*, durability, strength, lightness, magnetism, rust-resistance, etc. Some well-known ones are brass (zinc + copper), coinage bronze (copper + zinc + tin), steels (iron + carbon + various other materials), soft solder (tin + lead), dental fillings (mercury + various ingredients).

All Saints' Day (Nov. 1) is common to both the Anglican and Roman Catholic Churches, and is in commemoration of the saints generally, or such as have no special day set apart for them. Instituted by Pope Boniface IV, early in the 7th cent., this ecclesiastical festival was formerly called "All Hallows".

All Souls' Day (Nov. 2) is a festival of the Roman

Church, intended for the mitigation by prayer of the sufferings of souls in purgatory. The commemoration was enjoined by Abbot Odilo of Cluny during the 11th cent. upon the monastic order over which he presided, and was afterwards adopted generally throughout the Roman Communion.

Allspice, a flavouring obtained from a West Indian tree of the myrtle family, *Pimenta officinalis*, likened to the flavour of cinnamon, nutmeg and cloves combined. The berries resemble peppercorns and are used as a spice in mincemeat, etc.

Alluvium, river transported deposits of sand, mud and gravel which accumulate to form distinctive features such as levées, flood plains and deltas. The frequent renewal of alluvium by flooding causes riverine lands to be some of the most fertile. In Asia alluvial lands support high densities of population, *e.g.*, The Hwang-ho plains and the Ganges delta.

Almond, the fruit of the *Amygdalus communis*, originally indigenous to Persia, Asia Minor and N. Africa; now cultivated in Italy, Spain, France, the USA and Australia. It yields both bitter and sweet oil. Bitter almond oil is obtained by macerating and distilling the ripe seeds; it is used for flavouring and scenting purposes, its fragrant odour being due to the presence of benzaldehyde and hydrogen cyanide. When the seeds are pressed sweet almond oil results: this is used in perfumery, and also as a lubricant for very delicate machinery.

Almuce, a fur stole worn by certain canons.

Aloe, large plants of the lily family, with about 180 species found mainly in the S. African veldt and karroo. The bitter purgative drug (aloes) is prepared by evaporating the plant's sap. *See* **Agave.**

Alpaca, a South American ruminant related to the llama whose long, fine wool is woven into a soft dress fabric known by the same name. Sir Titus Salt first manufactured alpaca cloth (1836). Saltaire, near Bradford, remains to evidence the success which for many years attended the enterprise.

Alpha Particle, or alpha-ray, fast-moving helium nucleus ejected by some radioactive atoms, *e.g.*, polonium. It is a combination of 2 neutrons and 2 protons. *See* **F12.**

Alphabet (so called from the first two letters of the Greek alphabet—alpha, beta) is the term applied to the collection of letters from which the words of a language are made up. It grew out of the knowledge that all words can be expressed by a limited number of sounds arranged in various combinations. The Phoenicians were the first to make use of an alphabetic script derived from an earlier Semitic alphabet (earliest known inscriptions *c.* 1500–950 B.C.) from which all other alphabets have sprung. The stages in the development of the alphabet were mnemonic (memory aids), pictorial (actual pictures), ideographic (symbols), and lastly phonetic. All the ideographic systems died out, with the exception of that of the Chinese.

Altimeter, an instrument used in aircraft to estimate altitude; its usual essential feature is an aneroid barometer which registers the decrease of pressure with height. Roughly 1 millibar corresponds to 9 m. To read an aircraft altimeter correct for its destination, the zero setting must be adjusted for difference of ground height and difference of surface pressure, especially when pressure is falling or when flying towards low pressure.

Altitude, an astronomical term used to signify the angular elevation of a heavenly body; this is measured with a quadrant or sextant. In aeronautics it is the height above sea-level.

Alto-Relievo, a term applied to sculptured designs which are depicted in prominent relief on a flat surface, technically signifying that the projections exceeds one-half the true proportions of the objects represented. Basso-relievo is carving kept lower than one-half such projection.

Alum is a compound salt used in various industrial processes, especially dyeing, its constituents being the sulphate of one univalent metal or radical (*e.g.*, potassium, sodium, ammonium, rubidium, caesium, silver, thallium) and the sulphate of a tervalent metal (*e.g.*, aluminium, iron, chromium, manganese), and water of crystallisation.

Alumina is the oxide of aluminium. Very valuable as a refractory material. The ruby is almost 100 per cent. alumina; so also are the emerald, oriental amethyst, etc. An hydrated aluminium oxide is bauxite, chief ore of aluminium from which the metal is extracted electrolytically.

Aluminium, element no. 13, symbol Al, is a light metal which conducts electricity well. Its specific gravity at 20°C is 2·705. Melting point of aluminium is 660·2°C. It is made commercially by electrolysing bauxite dissolved in cryolite (double fluoride of aluminium and sodium). Aluminium alloys are being increasingly used for construction purposes.

Amadavat, a popular cage bird of the weaver family, mainly crimson with spots, so named because the first specimens came from Ahmadabad in India about 1700.

Amalgam is the term applied to any alloy of which mercury forms a part.

Amber, a brittle resinous substance; in origin, fossilised resin. Obtained mostly from the Baltic coasts, and used for ornaments, pipe mouth-pieces, etc.

Ambergris is a waxy substance produced in the intestines of the sperm whale, and generally found floating on the sea. It is a valuable perfumery material.

Amblyopsis, a species of fish, practically sightless, and with inoperative organs of hearing and feeling, that inhabit the Mammoth Cave of Kentucky. A remarkable illustration of the failure of senses not brought into use.

America's Cup. In 1851 the Royal Yacht Squadron put up for competition a silver cup that has become the most famous trophy in yachting. In that year the New York Y.C. sent the schooner *America* across the Atlantic to compete in a 53-mile (85 km) race round the Isle of Wight; it captured the trophy which now bears its name. Until 1983 none of the many challenges by yachtsmen from Great Britain, Canada, and latterly, Australia, had been successful. In that year, however, in Rhode Island Sound *Australia II*, skippered by John Bertrand, won on the 25th challenge. The triumph was short-lived. The 1992 winner was Bill Koch's *America*[3] which claimed the 141-year-old trophy 4-1. In 1995 the New Zealand yacht *Black Magic* achieved a sensational 5-0 victory over the Americans – for only the second time in its history the Cup had left America.

Amethyst, the violet variety of quartz, used as a precious stone, containing traces of manganese, titanium and iron. The finest coloured specimens come from Brazil and the Urals.

Amice, a white linen vestment worn by Roman Catholic and many Anglican priests when officiating at Mass or Holy Eucharist.

Amines, organic chemicals composed of carbon, hydrogen and nitrogen. They are derived from ammonia, which they resemble in smell and chemical characteristics. The smell of bad fish is due to the presence of amines. Important industrially as intermediates in a wide variety of products, for example, the synthesis of dye-stuffs and man-made fibres such as nylon.

Amino acids, organic compounds containing an amine group and a carboxylic acid group. They are the "building bricks" of proteins (*q.v.*).

Ammeter, an instrument for measuring the current flowing in an electric circuit. A contraction of ampere-meter. *See* **Ampere**.

Ammonia, a colourless gaseous compound comprising three atoms of hydrogen to one of nitrogen. Formerly it was made by heating the horns and hoofs of deer, acquiring the name of spirits of hartshorn. The ammonia of commerce is now procured by coal decomposition in the course of gas-making and by direct synthesis. In the very important Haber process of ammonia production by fixation of atmospheric nitrogen, the nitrogen is made to combine with hydrogen and the ammonia so prepared is converted into nitric acid, ammonium nitrate or ammonium sulphate. The Haber process made Germany self-sufficient in nitrates in the first world war.

Ammonites, extinct animals related to the Nautilus. The chambered shell is coiled, usually in a plane spiral. They are confined to Mesozoic rocks.

Ammonium, the basic radical of ammonium salts,

Composed of one atom of nitrogen and four of hydrogen, it behaves chemically like an ion of a monovalent alkali metal. Ammonium chloride is known as "sal ammoniac". "Sal volatile" is ammonium carbonate.

Amnesty, an act of grace by which a ruler or governing power pardons political offenders.

Amnesty International is the world's largest human rights organisation. It seeks to secure the release of prisoners of conscience, works for fair and prompt trials for all political prisoners, and campaigns against torture and the death penalty.

Amorphous, a term used to indicate the absence of crystalline form in any body or substance.

Ampere, unit of electric current in the SI system of units; named after André Marie Ampère, who in the 1820s helped to lay the foundations of modern electromagnetism. Defined as that constant current which, if maintained in two parallel rectilinear conductors of infinite length, of negligible circular cross section, and placed at a distance of one metre apart in a vacuum, would produce between these conductors a force which is equal to 2×10^{-7} newton per metre.

Amphioxus *or* **Lancelet**, a primitive chordate (**F36**(2)), occurring in sand-banks around British shores and elsewhere.

Anabolism. *See* **Catabolism**.

Analysis is one of the major branches of modern pure mathematics and includes the theories of differentiation, integration, differential equations and analytic functions.

Anchor, an instrument used for keeping ships stationary. Great improvements have been introduced in recent years, stockless anchors being now chiefly used, consisting of a shank and a loose fluke. Lloyd's rules prescribe the number and weight of anchors which must be carried by merchant ships.

Anchorite is a religious person who retires into solitude to employ himself with holy thoughts. Among the early Christians, anchorites were numerous, but in the Western Church they have been few. Their reputation for wisdom and prescience was high, and kings and rulers in olden days would visit their cells for counsel. An anchorite or "ankret" was in mediaeval times a source of fame and profit to the monastic house within which he was voluntarily immured.

Anchovy, a fish of the herring family, distinguished by its large mouth and projecting snout, plentiful in the Mediterranean and much esteemed when cured.

Ancient Lights are rights of light enjoyed by a property owner over adjoining land. Such a right is obtained either by uninterrupted enjoyment for twenty years, or by written authority, and once legally established cannot be upset, no building being permissible that would seriously interfere with the privilege.

Anemometer, an instrument for measuring the strength of the wind. In the most widely used pattern the rotation, about a vertical axis, of a group of hemispherical or conical cups gives a measure of the total flow of air past the cups, various registering devices being employed. The Dines anemograph provides a continuous record of the variation in both velocity and direction; changes of pressure produced in a horizontal tube, kept pointing into the wind by a vane, cause a float, to which a pen is attached, to rise and fall in sympathy with the gusts and lulls. The hot-wire anemometer, depending upon the change of electrical resistance experienced by a heated wire when cooled, enables very gentle air currents to be investigated.

Aneroid is the kind of barometer which does not depend upon atmospheric support of a mercury (or other liquid) column. It consists of a metallic box, partially exhausted of air, with a corrugated lid which moves with atmospheric changes. A lever system magnifies the lid movements about 200 times and atmospheric pressure is read from a dial. The construction of the vacuum chamber provides automatic compensation for temperature changes. An aneroid barometer is the basic component of an altimeter.

Angelica, an aromatic plant of the Umbelliferae order, *Angelica officinalis*, valuable as a flavouring and possessing medical properties. In olden times supposed to protect against poison.

Angelus, a church bell rung in Roman Catholic countries, at morn, noon, and sunset, to remind the faithful to say their Angelic Salutation.

Angevin Dynasty includes the Plantagenet kings from Henry II to Richard II. The name was derived from Henry II's father, Geoffrey, Count of Anjou.

Angles, a northern tribe originally settled in Schleswig, who with the Saxons and Jutes invaded Britain in the 5th cent.

Angström, a unit of wavelength, named after the Swedish physicist A. J. Angström (1814–74), equal to one hundred-millionth of a centimetre (10^{-8} cm). It is used to measure wavelengths of light, X-rays, etc.

Aniline, a simple aromatic compound ($C_6H_5NH_2$) related to benzene and ammonia. It is obtained from coal-tar. The name recalls the fact that it was first prepared by distilling indigo (anil is Portuguese for indigo). In 1856 W. H. Perkin (1838–1907) discovered the first aniline or coal-tar dye, mauve, and thus founded the modern dyestuff industry.

Animal Kingdom. See **F36**.

Anise, an umbelliferous plant (*Pimpinella anisum*) found in Egypt and the Levant, and valued for its fruit, aniseed, possessing certain medicinal properties and yielding an aromatic, volatile oil, Also used in cooking. The anise of the Bible is *Anethum graveolens*, i.e., dill.

Annates were acknowledgments formerly paid to the Popes by way of fee or tax in respect of ecclesiastical preferment and consisted usually of a proportion of the income ("first-fruits") of the office. Introduced into England in the 13th cent.; annexed to the Crown under Henry VIII; transferred to a perpetual fund for the benefit of the poorer clergy in 1704. See **Queen Anne's Bounty.**

"Annual Register", a yearly record of political and literary events, founded by Edmund Burke (as editor) in 1759 and Robert Dorsley, the bookseller.

Annunciation, Feast of the (March 25), is a Church festival commemorating the message of the incarnation of Christ brought by the angel Gabriel to the Virgin Mary, hence the title Lady Day.

Anointing is the pouring of consecrated oil upon the body as a mark of supreme honour. In England it is restricted chiefly to the ceremony of the monarch's coronation, and the spoon with which the oil is applied forms part of the English regalia. In the Roman Catholic Church anointing represents the sacrament of extreme unction.

Ant. There are about 6,000 species of ants, which belong to the same order (Hymenoptera) as the bees, wasps and ichneumon flies. They are social in habit, living in communities of varying size and development. There are three basic castes in ants—the females or *queens*, the *males*, and the *workers* (the last-named being neuter), although specialised forms of workers are sometimes found, e.g., the *soldiers* of the harvesting ants. In the communities of those species of ants which evolved most recently there is a highly complex social life and well-developed division of labour. Some species of these ants make slaves of other species, stealing the cocoons before the adult forms emerge. Many ants "milk" green-flies, which they protect for their honey-like secretion, and most ants' nests contain many "guests", such as beetles and silver fish. Some ants harvest grains of corn, and others, from S. America, live on fungi which they cultivate in underground "mushroom beds".

Antarctic Exploration. In earlier centuries it was thought that a great continent must exist in the southern hemisphere, around the South Pole, to balance the known land masses in the north. Its supposed extent was greatly reduced in the 18th cent., particularly when Capt, Cook sailed for the first time south of the Antarctic Circle and reached the edge of the ice-pack. A portion of the ice-covered continent—the coast of Graham Land—was first sighted by Lieut. Edward Bransfield in 1820. Explorers of several other nations sighted portions of the coast-line in other quarters, but the first extensive exploration was made by Capt. James Clarke Ross, who with the *Erebus* and *Terror* penetrated into the Ross Sea in 1841, and discovered the great Ross Ice Barrier in 78° South lat. Interest in the Antarctic did not revive until after 1890, when an international scheme

of research was drawn up. A Norwegian, C. E. Borchgrevink, in 1898–1900, was the first to winter in the Antartic and to travel on the ice barrier. The British share in this work was carried out by Capt. R. F. Scott's expedition in the *Discovery*, 1901–4. Scott's party sledged across the barrier to 82° 17′ South, then a record "farthest south". A little later, Ernest Shackleton beat this by travelling to within 160 km of the South Pole. The Scottish polar explorer William Spiers Bruce led the Scottish national Antarctic Expedition of 1902 in the *Scotia* and discovered Coats Land and founded a meteorological observatory on the South Orkneys. In 1910 Scott organised his second expedition in *Terra Nova*, and became engaged against his will in a "race for the Pole" when, after his departure, the Norwegian Arctic explorer, Roald Amundsen, suddenly announced that he was sailing for the Antarctic. Amundsen set up his base at the eastern end of the Barrier, and, relying on dog teams for hauling his sledges, reached the Pole on 14 December 1911. Meanwhile Scott and his party, their start delayed by adverse weather, were marching southwards, man-hauling their sledges, for Scott was against the use of dogs. After an arduous journey they reached the Pole one month after Amundsen. The return was a struggle against the weather and increasing weakness, probably due to scurvy, until at last they perished within a few kilometres of their base. After the first world war the development of the whaling industry greatly stimulated further exploration. Outstanding expeditions included that of Admiral R. E. Byrd, 1929, when he flew over the South Pole; the British Graham Land expedition, 1934, which carried out the first extensive mapping of any part of the Antarctic continent; and the US Navy's Antarctic Expedition of 1940, when the whole continent was circumnavigated and great areas photographed from the air. In recent years valuable work has been done by the first International expedition, the Norwegian–British–Swedish Expedition to Queen Maud Land, and by the French in Adélie Land. The Falkland Island Dependencies Survey, set up during the war, has continued the scientific exploration of Graham Land. The Antarctic was the scene of high adventure during the International Geophysical Year (1957–58), when scientists from many countries participated in the explorations. The Commonwealth Trans-Antarctic Expedition set out from opposite sides of the continent and met at the South Pole, the UK party, led by Sir Vivian Fuchs, from the Falklands, and Sir Edmund Hillary and his party from New Zealand. The UK party accomplished the first crossing of the White Continent in 99 days. Their scientific work included the marking of seismic and complementary gravimetric studies at frequent intervals along the 3,540 km traverse. In 1993, the explorers Sir Ranulph Fiennes and Dr Michael Stroud completed the first unsupported crossing of the Antarctic land mass and the longest unsupported polar journey—both world records. In December 1994, Liv Arnesen (Norway) became the first woman to reach the South Pole alone.

Anteaters, a small family (the Myrmecophagidae) of mammals from Central and South America. They feed on ants, termites and other insects which they gather with a long tongue covered with sticky saliva.

Antennae, paired feelers of insects and crustaceans, In radio, the term "antenna" is equivalent to "aerial".

Anthem, a choral composition, with or without instrumental accompaniment, usually sung after the third collect in the Church of England services. The words are from the Scriptures, and the composition may be for solo voices only, for full choir, or for both. Among the chief British composers of anthems are Tallis, Purcell, Croft, Boyce, Goss and Stainer.

Anthracite is a black coal with a brilliant lustre. It contains 92 per cent. and over of carbon and burns slowly, without smoke or flame. See **Coal.**

Anthropoid, meaning "resembling man", a sub-order of the primate mammals including man and also the gibbon, chimpanzee, orang-utan, and gorilla.

Anthropology. *See Section F, Part V.*

Antibiotics, a collective name for any substance derived from micro-organisms or fungi which is capable of destroying infections, *e.g.*, penicillin.

Anticyclone, a region where barometric pressure is greater than that of its surroundings. Such a system is distinguished on weather charts by a pattern of isobars, usually circular or oval-shaped, enclosing the centre of high pressure where the air is calm. In the remaining areas light or moderately strong winds blow spirally outwards in a clockwise direction in the Northern Hemisphere (and in the reverse direction in the Southern Hemisphere), in accordance with Buys Ballot's law (an observer with back to wind in Northern Hemisphere has lower pressure to left; in Southern to right). Over the British Isles anticyclonic weather is generally quiet and settled being fair, warm, and sunny in summer and either very cold and often foggy or overcast and gloomy in winter. These systems move slowly and sometimes remain practically stationary for days at a time, that over Siberia being particularly well defined. Extensive belts of almost permanent anticyclones occur in latitudes 30° N and 30° S. Persistent anticyclonic weather with easterly winds during the months December to March, 1962–3, brought the coldest and hardest winter to Britain since 1740.

Antimony. Metal element, no. 51, symbol Sb. In group 5 of the periodic table. Exists in various forms, the stable form being a grey metal with a layer structure. The other forms are non-conductors. On being burned, it gives off dense fumes of oxide of antimony. By itself it is not of special utility; but as an alloy for hardening other metals, it is much used. As an alloy with lead for type-metal, and with tin and copper or zinc for Britannia-metal, it is of great value. Most important antimony ore is stibnite (antimony sulphide).

Anti-Pope, one elected in opposition to one held to be canonically chosen; applied to the popes Clement VII and Benedict XIII, who resided at Avignon during the Great Schism (1378–1417).

Anti-proton, the "negative proton", an atomic particle created in high energy collisions of nuclear particles. Its existence was confirmed in Oct. 1955. *See Section F.*

Antisemitism. *See Section J.*

Antlers are the branched horns of deer, the branches being called tines. Antlers originate as outgrowths of the frontal bone, and are usually shed once a year. Except in the reindeer and caribou they are restricted to the male.

Aotearoa, meaning 'Long White Cloud', the Maori name for New Zealand.

Apartheid. *See Section J.*

Ape, a term applied to the gorilla, chimpanzee, orang-utan and gibbon—the anthropoid apes.

Aphelion, the point in the orbit of a planet farthest from the sun; the opposite of perihelion. At aphelion the earth is $1 \cdot 52 \times 10^8$ km from the sun.

Aphids, green-flies or plant lice, a numerous species of destructive insects living on young shoots and foliage, some on roots. Reproduction is by parthenogenesis (virgin birth).

Apis, the sacred bull worshipped by the ancient Egyptians; also the scientific name for the bee.

Apocalyptic writings are those which deal with revelation and prophecy, more especially the Revelation of St. John.

Apocrypha (hidden writings), the books which were included in the Septuagint (Greek) and Vulgate (Latin) versions of the Old Testament but ex- cluded from the sacred canon at the Reformation by the Protestants on the grounds that they were not originally written in Hebrew nor re- garded as genuine by the Jews. The books include: 1 and 2 Esdras, Tobit, Judith, additions to Esther, Wisdom of Solomon, Ecclesiasticus, Baruch, Song of the Three Holy Children, History of Susannah, Bel and the Dragon, Prayer of Manasses, 1 and 2 Maccabees. The term is usually applied to the additions to the Old Testament, but there are also numerous Christian writings of the same character. *The New English Bible,* which contains the Apocrypha, was published in 1970.

Apogee, that point in the orbit of a heavenly body which is farthest from the earth; used in relation to the sun, moon and artificial satellites.

The sun's apogee corresponds to the earth's aphelion. *See Perigee.*

Apostasy is a revolt, by an individual or party, from one form of opinions or doctrinate to another. Julian, the Roman Emperor (331–63), brought up as a Christian, became converted to paganism and on coming to the throne (361), proclaimed religious toleration. Hence his name, Julian the Apostate.

Apostles. The twelve apostles who were disciples of Jesus were: Simon Peter and Andrew (his brother), James and John (sons of Zebedee), Philip, Bartholomew, Thomas, Matthew, James, Thaddaeus, Simon, and Judas Iscariot. After the Ascension Matthias was chosen to take the place of Judas. St. Paul was the leading apostle in the mission to the Gentiles, though he was not one of the twelve. St. Barnabas has also been called an apostle.

Apostles' Creed, the name of the most ancient of the Church's statements of its belief: "I believe in God the Father Almighty; and in Jesus Christ his only Son our Lord, who was born of the Holy Ghost and the Virgin Mary...." A later version is used in the Church of England at morning and evening prayer.

Apostolic Fathers were the immediate disciples or followers of the apostles, especially such as left writings behind. They included Barnabas, Clement of Rome, Ignatius of Antioch, Hermas, Papias of Hieropolis and Polycarp.

Appeasement Policy. The name of the policy during 1937 and 1938 of yielding to the demands of Hitler and Mussolini in the hope that a point would be reached when the dictators would co-operate in the maintenance of peace. The policy culminated in the Munich Agreement (which was the subject of much criticism) after a series of concessions including the recognition of the Italian conquest of Abyssinia and the German annexation of Austria. The policy was finally demonstrated as futile when Hitler seized Czechoslovakia in March 1939.

Appian Way, the oldest and finest of the Roman roads originally laid by Appius Claudius (312 B.C.) from Rome to Capua and thence to Brundisium (Brindisi).

Approved Schools were residential schools, subject to Home Office inspection, for the training of young persons under 17 who, because of disturbed behaviour as a result of unfavourable influences such as bad environment or parental neglect, were guilty of offences or in need of care and protection and had been sent to them by magistrates from juvenile or other courts. The approved school order was abolished by the Children and Young Persons Act 1969. Such young people may now be committed to the care of a local authority and accommodated in a system of community homes ranging from children's homes to borstal type institutions.

April, the fourth month of the year, from the Roman *Aprilis* derived from *aperire* "to open" —the period when the buds begin to open.

Apse is a semicircular recess, arched or dome-roofed, at the end of the choir, aisles, or nave of a church.

Aqueducts are conduits in which water flows or is conveyed from its source to the place where it is to be used. Most famous builders were the Romans and the oldest Roman aqueduct was the Aqua Appia, which dates from about 310 B.C. Among modern aqueducts may be mentioned that of Glasgow, which brings water to that city from Loch Katrine; that of Manchester, which taps Thirlmere; that of Liverpool, with Lake Vyrnwy in North Wales as its source, and the Fron Aqueduct, Powys, which carries water from the Elan Valley to Birmingham.

Arabian Nights Entertainment or **Book of a Thousand and One Nights,** a collection of fascinating tales of the Orient, of mixed Indian, Persian, Arabic, and Egyptian origination, and first made known in Europe by Antoine Galland's French translation (1704–17) from Arabian texts. The "master" tale tells how the princess Shahrazad so beguiles the king through the telling of the tales over one thousand and one nights that her life was spared. English translators include E. W. Lane (1840), Sir Richard Burton (1885–8), John Payne (1882–4).

Arabic Numerals. The modern system of numbering, 0, 1, 2, 3, 4, 5, 6, 7, 8, 9, in which the digits depend on their position for their value is called the Arabic numerical notation. The method is, in fact, of Indian origin. By the 9th cent. Hindu science was available in Arabic, and the Persian mathematician Al-Kwarizimi (c. 830) in his *Arithmetic* used the so-called "Arabic" system of numbering. Gradually the method spread to Europe, taking the place of the Roman system which was useless for calculation. The West is indebted to the Arabs for the zero symbol, the lack of which had been a serious drawback to Greek mathematics. It made the invention of decimal fractions possible.

Aragonite, the unstable form of calcium carbonate found as a mineral in some young deposits. It crystallises in the orthorhombic system but tends to revert to calcite.

Aramaic Languages, the Semitic dialects current in Mesopotamia and the regions extending southwest from the Euphrates to Palestine from about the 12th cent. B.C. until after the rise of Islam, when Aramaic was superseded by Arabic. Both Aramaic and Greek were spoken in Palestine during the time of Christ.

Archaeopteryx, a fossil bird providing a connecting link between reptiles and birds. It had feathers, jaws with teeth, no bill, reptilian bones and skull, a long tail, and it probably used its fore-limbs for gliding flight. The first specimen, found in 1861, in the Solenhofen limestone of Bavaria, is in London's Natural History Museum.

Archbishop, the chief of the bishops of an ecclesiastical province in the Greek, Roman, and Anglican churches. In the Church of England there are two archbishops, the Archbishop of Canterbury, called the Primate of *all* England, and the Archbishop of York, styled the Primate of England.

Archimedes' Principle. When a body is weighed in air and then in any fluid, the apparent loss in weight is equal to the weight of fluid displaced. This scientific fact was noted by the Syracusan philosopher Archimedes (287–212 B.C.) and is often used as a basis for density measurements.

Architecture, the art and science of building. The provision of shelter for mankind by the orderly arrangement of materials in a manner which expresses man's attitude to living. The forms which buildings take are the outcome of the function for which they are to be used, of the architect's aesthetic sensibility and the structural method adopted. Until the last hundred years structural methods were limited to timber frames, and columns, lintels, load-bearing walls, arches, vaults, and domes in brick or stone. From these few basic elements have evolved the great variety of historic styles of building to be found throughout the world. To give but one example, the Greeks created those systems of decorated columns and beams, known as the Orders, which were adapted by the Romans, revived decoratively rather than structurally during the Renaissance and are still used in debased form on the more presumptuous type of modern building. In recent years, however, architecture has taken on a new meaning. Once confined to the rich, in the form of Church, State or Commerce, it is now, with the coming of democracy, recognised as an essential social service for all. This, and the development of new structural techniques and materials (steel, aluminium, sheet glass, reinforced concrete, plastics and plywoods, to name a few), have made the interest in historic styles, the mainstay of the older architect, of secondary importance. Modern architecture is the creation of buildings with the highest possible standards of functional performance in terms of efficient planning and structure, good artificial and natural lighting, adequate heating or cooling, and proper acoustic conditions.

Arctic Exploration. Modern exploration of the Arctic begins in the 16th cent. when men sought to reach the East Indies by sailing through the Arctic to the Pacific Ocean. The North-east Passage, via the shores of northern Asia, was the first attempted. In 1553 and 1554 the English navigators Sir Richard Chancellor and Stephen Burrough sailed into the White Sea, but were prevented by storms and ice from advancing farther eastwards. The project was later revived by the Dutch; Barendts in 1594 discovered Spitsbergen, but also failed to get beyond Novaya Zemlya. It was not, in fact, until 1879 that the Swede, A. E. Nordenskjöld, in the *Vega*, succeeded in reaching the Pacific. The attempts to find a North-west Passage were more numerous and determined. In 1585 John Davis penetrated Davis Strait and coasted along Baffin Island. Hopes ran high when Henry Hudson discovered Hudson Bay in 1610, but a practicable passage continued to elude explorers. The problem was to find a navigable route through the maze of channels in the short summer season, and to avoid being frozen in with supplies exhausted. After the Napoleonic Wars the Admiralty sent out many naval expeditions which culminated in Sir John Franklin's expedition with the *Erebus* and *Terror* in 1845. The ships were beset by ice in Victoria Channel and, after Franklin's death, were abandoned by their crews, who perished from scurvy and starvation on their march southwards. To ascertain their fate, several further expeditions were despatched, and the crew of the *Investigator*, commanded by R. J. M'Clure, sailing eastwards from Bering Strait, were the first to make the Passage, though in doing so they were obliged to abandon their ship. It was thirty years before the Norwegian, Roald Amundsen, succeeded in sailing the *Gjoa* from the east to west. In the meantime, the North Pole had become the goal of explorers. Nansen, in 1893, put the *Fram* into the ice-pack to drift across the Polar basin, and himself made an unsuccessful attempt on the Pole across the pack. This was eventually achieved by the American explorer Robert E. Peary, who after several expeditions in the North Greenland region, sledged to the Pole with Eskimo companions in 1909. The next phase was the employment of airships and aeroplanes in Arctic exploration. In 1926 Admiral Byrd made the first flight over the Pole, and in the same year Amundsen and Lincoln Ellsworth flew the airship *Norge* from Spitsbergern to Point Barrow Alaska. Two years later, the *Italia*, commanded by the Italian, Nobile, was wrecked on a return flight from the Pole, and Amundsen lost his life in an attempt to rescue the survivors. With modern developments in aircraft and navigation, flights over the Polar basin are almost a routine matter. The first voyage under the North Pole was made in 1958 by the American nuclear-powered submarine *Nautilus*. In 1995 scientists reported that a part of the Arctic ice-cap the size of Norway had melted in the previous 16 years.

Arenaceous Rocks, the rocks composed of grains of sand, chiefly sandstones; quartz is the most abundant mineral in these rocks.

Argillaceous Rocks are a sedimentary group, including the shales and clays.

Argon, chemical element no. 18, symbol A. This was the first of the inert gases (**F14**) to be isolated from air by Rayleigh and Ramsay in 1894. Argon is used for filling gas-filled metal filament electric lamps. In gas discharge tube it gives a blue glow. *See also* **Rare Gases.**

Arithmetic, the branch of mathematics that deals with numerical calculations as in counting, measuring, weighing. The early civilisations used simple arithmetic for commercial purposes, employing symbols and later letters of the alphabet as numerals. When Hindu-Arabic numerals replaced Roman numerals in the Middle Ages it meant a great step forward and led to rapid developments—the invention of logarithms, slide-rule, calculating machines.

Arithmetic Progression, a sequence of numbers in which the successor of each number is obtained by adding or subtracting a fixed number, for example 2, 5, 8, 11, . . . or 100, 95, 90, 85. . . .

Ark of the Covenant was the sacred chest of the Hebrews and symbolised God's presence. It was overlaid with gold inside and outside. It accompanied the Israelites into battle and was once captured by the Philistines. Eventually it found a resting-place in Solomon's Temple.

Armada, Spanish, the naval expedition fitted out by Philip II of Spain in 1588 against England, commanded by the Duke of Medina Sidonia. It comprised 129 ships, was manned by 8,000 sailors and carried 19,000 soldiers and more than 2,000 cannon. Against this formidable force Elizabeth had only 80 ships, manned by 9,000 sailors, under Lord Howard of Effingham, under whom served Drake, Hawkins and Frobisher. The British Fleet awaited the Armada off Plymouth, and at Tilbury there was a considerable defensive land force under the command of the Earl of Leicester. On 19 July the ships of the Armada were sighted off the Lizard, disposed in a crescent 11 km long from horn to horn. The excellent manoeuvring of the English, their fire-ships and a gale from the N.W. combined so effectively to cripple the Spanish ships that the Armada was scattered, only 63 of the original fleet of 129 reaching home via the North of Scotland. It was impossible to embark the army of Parma waiting in the Netherlands. Elizabeth had a medal struck bearing in Latin the inscription, "God blew and they were scattered".

Armadillo, a genus of animals related to the sloths and anteaters, belonging to South America, and carrying a hard bony covering over the back, under which one species (*Tolypeutes*) can completely conceal itself when attacked, rolling itself up like a hedgehog.

Armageddon, according to the Revelation of St. John, the great battle in which the last conflict between good and evil is to be fought.

Armillary Sphere, an early form of astronomical apparatus with a number of circles representing equator, meridian, ecliptic, etc. Used by Hipparchus and Ptolemy and up to the time of Tycho Brahe for determining the position of the stars.

Aromatic. A term used by chemists, originally to describe compounds like benzene, having a characteristic smell. It is a term which implies a collection of chemical characteristics, the salient features being a flat ring structure and a general similarity to benzene.

Arsenic, a metalloid element, no. 33, symbol As in group 5 of the periodic table usually met with as a constituent of other minerals, sometimes by itself. Its compounds are very poisonous. Lead arsenate is a powerful insecticide used for spraying fruit trees. The more stable allotropic form (grey) has a layer structure, and conducts electricity.

Art Deco, the name given by modern collectors to the decorative style of the 1920s and 1930s; it is derived from the long official name of the Paris Exhibition of 1925, which was almost exclusively devoted to "les Arts Décoratifs". Art Deco runs parallel in time with Functionalism (*q.v.*) but unlike that austere and philosophical style, Art Deco is gay, elegant and even frivolous, being a creation of fashionable Paris. It is related superficially to Cubism, using squares, circles and triangles in interesting combinations for ornament. Another popular motif is the modern girl with her shingled head dancing the tango or drinking cocktails. The style is brash and worldly, but in its best expressions full of charm and vitality. Famous names within the style are the glassmaker Rene Lalique (1860–1945), the fashion designers Gabrielle Chanel and Elsa Schiaparelli, and the decorator and illustrator Erte (Roman de Tirtoff, b. 1829). There has been a nostalgic revival of Art Deco, *e.g.*, in films like "Bonny and Clyde" (1967) or "The Great Gatsby" (1974) based on F. Scott Fitzgerald's novel (1925).

Artesian Wells take their name from Artois in France, where the first wells of this kind were constructed in 1126. They are to be found only when a water-bearing bed is sandwiched between two impervious beds. When a boring is made to the lower part of the bed, the pressure of water is sufficient to cause the water to overflow at the surface. Artesian wells were known to ancient Egypt and China, and have existed in the Sahara since the earliest times. The fountains in Trafalgar Square were once fed by artesian wells sunk through the London clay into the chalk about 250 m.

Articles. The *Six Articles* are those contained in an Act of Henry VIII, and were of Roman Catholic origin. The *Thirty-nine Articles* were drawn up for the English church at the Reformation. They are printed at the back of the Prayer Book. Candidates for holy orders in the Church of England are required to subscribe to them, though the form of assent has been modified.

Art Nouveau (German *Jugend Stil*) was prevalent in architecture and decoration in Europe and the USA *c*, 1885–1910. It was rooted in the thoughts of Ruskin and William Morris. In reaction against the impersonal uniformity of industrial products which were flooding the market, artists turned to Nature for their inspiration, choosing organically growing forms, flowers or animals, as motifs for decoration or even for shaping whole objects. Another favourite motif was Romantic Woman with long robes and flowing hair, as interpreted so beautifully by Aubrey Beardsley. The sharply undulating line with a whiplash rhythm is a recurring theme. Famous names are the glass-makers Emile Gallé in France and Louis Comfort Tiffany in New York, the English goldsmith Charles Robert Ashbee (1863–1942), Henry Van de Velde (1867–1942) in Belgium and Charles Rennie Mackintosh (1868–1928) in Scotland, both architects and interior decorators, and in pure architecture Antonio Gaudí of Barcelona (1852–1926) and Victor Horta of Brussels (1861–1946).

Arts and Crafts Movement, the English revival of decorative art which began about 1875 as a revolt against the existing vulgarity of internal decoration and furnishings and the pettiness of academic art. Inspired by William Morris and Burne-Jones together with Rossetti, it was strongly influenced by the former's mediaeval-ism, his hatred of industrialism, and his own version of socialism which included the regeneration of man by handicrafts. His firm of Morris & Co. produced wallpapers, tapestries, furniture, stained-glass windows, carpets and fabrics in a style totally different from that of contemporary Victorian decoration. Morris's Kelmscott Press did much to raise the standards of book design and printing. *See* **Art Nouveau** (above).

Arum, a genus of plants of the *Araceae* family of which there is but one British species, the wake-robin or cuckoo-pint, sometimes also styled "Lords and Ladies".

Arundel Marbles, a collection of ancient Greek sculptures formed by Thomas Howard, Earl of Arundel in the 17th cent. and presented to Oxford University by his grandson, Henry Howard, who became Duke of Norfolk.

Aryans, nomadic peoples who made their way in successive waves from the Eurasian steppes to the Indus and the Nile during the first half of the 2nd millennium B.C. They crossed the Hindu Kush into N.W. India and settled in the valleys of the Indus and Ganges, where an earlier Indus civilisation had flourished, *c*. 3240–2750 B.C. Their religious ideas are reflected in the Veda (oldest Hindu scriptures, written down many centuries later in Vedic, parent language of Sanskrit). Those who made their way to Syria and Egypt founded the Hyksos empire (*c*. 1720–1550 B.C.). The Aryans introduced the horse-drawn chariot and spoke a language from which the great Indo-European family of languages is derived, with one group in India and Iran, and another in Europe. Because of the misuse of the term by the Nazis, Aryan is now referred to as proto-Indo-European.

Asafoetida, an acrid, strong-smelling gum resin exuded from the stem of umbelliferous plant, *Ferula foetida*, found in Iran and Afghanistan. Formerly used medicinally to treat hysteria; still used in cooking in India, Iran and France.

Ascension Day, or Holy Thursday, is the 40th day after Easter.

Ascot Races are an annual fashionable function dating from 1711 and taking place on Ascot Heath, only 10 km from Windsor, in June. These races have always had royal patronage. The course is *c*. 3 km long.

Ash, a familiar deciduous tree of the genus *Fraxinus*, of over 60 species, native to North temperate regions. The ash held an important place in Norse mythology, as it was supposed to support the heavens with its roots in Hell. The species native to Britain, and to Europe, is *F. excelsior*, a tall tree with compound leaves, greenish flowers, winged seeds, and black buds in winter. It is a valuable timber tree, tough and elastic, and largely used for wheels and handles. The rowan, or mountain ash, *Sorbus aucuparia*, with similar leaves and orange berries, belongs to a different family. *F.*

pendula or weeping ash is a strain which makes an ideal natural summer house.

Ashes, The, the symbol which distinguishes the winning cricket team in the Australian Test Matches. In 1882 the Australians won at the Oval by 7 runs. After the match the following epitaph appeared in the *Sporting Times*: "In affectionate remembrance of English Cricket which died at the Oval on 29 Aug. 1882, deeply lamented by a large circle of sorrowing friends and acquaintances. R.I.P. NB. The body will be cremated and the ashes taken to Australia." When the English Eleven went to Australia the same winter it was said that they had come to recover the "ashes". England won two out of three matches, and after the third match the ashes of what is now generally believed to have been a stump were presented in an urn to Ivo Bligh, later Lord Darnley. He bequeathed the urn to the M.C.C. It is now in the Memorial Gallery at Lord's. The Ashes are currently (1995) held by Australia.

Ash Wednesday, first day of Lent, the seventh Wednesday before Easter.

Assassination, treacherous murder for political ends, usually of a ruler or distinguished person. Among the most notable: Julius Caesar, 44 B.C.; Thomas Becket, 1170, David Rizzio, 1566; William the Silent, 1584; Henry IV of France, 1610; Jean Paul Marat, 1793; Abraham Lincoln, 1865; Alexander II of Russia, 1881; Archduke Francis Ferdinand of Austria, 1914; Dr. Dollfuss, 1934; King Alexander of Yugoslavia, 1934; Mahatma Gandhi, 1948; King Abdullah of Jordan, 1951; Liaquat Ali Khan, 1951; King Feisal of Iraq, 1958; Mr. Bandaranaike, 1959; President Kennedy, 1963; Malcolm X, 1965; Dr. Verwoerd, 1966; Dr. Martin Luther King, 1968; Senator Robert Kennedy, 1968; Mr. Tom Mboya, 1969; King Faisal, 1975; Lord Mountbatten, 1979; John Lennon, 1980; Pres. Sadat, 1981; Indira Gandhi, 1984; Olof Palme, 1986; Rajiv Gandhi (1991); President Premadasa of Sri Lanka (1993); and (1994) the Presidents of Rwanda and Burundi.

Asteroids or the minor planets are relatively small objects which move in orbits mainly between those of Mars and Jupiter. The first to be discovered (by Piazzi in 1801) was Ceres. Many thousands more have since been discovered, of which nearly 2,000 now have well-determined orbits and have been named. The largest are Ceres (800 km), Pallas (500 km), Vesta (530 km) and Juno (240 km). Few others have diameters of more than 80 km, while those of the majority are less than 5 or 10 km. Of particular interest are the Trojan group, located at the two stable "Lagrangian" points in Jupiter's orbit round the sun, where their locations make isosceles triangles with the sun and Jupiter. Also, a number of asteroids have orbits like that of Icarus which at perigee (*q.v.*) comes close to the sun.

Astrolabe, a mediaeval scientific instrument for taking altitudes, observing the sun by day and the stars by night, and used for telling the time and finding the latitude. Used by the ancient Greeks, later by the Arabs and Persians, and introduced into Europe by way of Spain in the 14th cent. Chaucer is said to have sent his son Lois, a ten-year-old student at Oxford, an astrolabe with a treatise on its use in 1391.

Astronaut, a person who travels in space.

Astronomical Unit, the mean distance between the centres of the sun and earth, or the semi-major axis of the earth's orbit, has a value of about $1\cdot495979 \times 10^8$ km (149,597,900 km). This value has been constantly improved over the past 300 years, first using observations of the planets, later transits of Venus across the sun's disc, then observations of minor planets such as Eros as they came near the earth, and now by the transit time of a radar beam bounced off the planet Venus. The astronomical unit is fundamental for astronomers.

Astronomy. The Pythagoreans believed the stars and planets moved with uniform circular velocity in crystalline spheres, centred round the earth (the "harmony of the spheres"). Hipparchus (190–120 B.C.) made the first star catalogue, discovered the precession of the equinoxes and introduced the idea of epicyclic motion. His planetary system, in the form it was presented by Ptolemy 200 years later, held until the Renaissance when Copernicus revived the heretical view first put forward by Aristarchus of Samos (310–230 B.C.) that the sun and not the earth was at the centre. Galileo, accurate observer and experimenter, went beyond Copernicus; helped by the contributions of Tycho Brahe, Giordano Bruno, Kepler and others, he was able to overthrow the Ptolemaic system of the heavenly spheres and Aristotelian philosophy and pave the way for Newton and modern astronomy. To Galileo we owe the conception of acceleration; to Newton the theory of universal gravitation; they showed that the same laws govern both celestial and terrestrial physics. Three landmarks in more recent times were the discovery of Uranus by Herschel in 1781 which extended the solar system as then recognised; the estimation by Hubble in 1924 of the distance of Andromeda, which showed that our Galaxy was just one of many; and Einstein's theory of relativity which improved on Newton's theory of the solar system by bringing gravitation into the domain of space-time. Today radiotelescopes and space probes are advancing astronomical knowledge and making it possible to explore regions beyond the scope of optical telescopes. The following have held the position of **Astronomer Royal** (period of office in brackets): John Flamsteed (1675–1719), Edmund Halley (1719–42), James Bradley (1742–62), Nathaniel Bliss (1762–65), Nevil Maskelyne (1765–1811), John Pond (1811–35), Sir George Airy (1835–81), Sir William Christie (1881–1910), Sir Frank Dyson (1910–33), Sir Harold Spencer Jones (1933–55), Sir Richard Woolley (1956–72), Sir Martin Ryle (1972–82), Professor Sir Francis Graham Smith (1982–90), Professor Sir Arnold Wolfendale (1991–95) and Professor Sir Martin Rees (1995–). *See* **F5–7,** *also* **Radio Astronomy.**

Astrophysics, a branch of astronomy concerned with the physical nature and constitution of the various objects within the universe. Recent developments in radio astronomy and in space research technology, opening up gamma-ray, X-ray, ultra-violet and infra-red parts of the spectrum, have all advanced this science.

Athanasian Creed, one of the three ancient creeds of the Christian Church, often referred to as the *Quicunque Vult*, is a statement of the doctrine of the Trinity and the Incarnation, and though named after St. Athanasius, it is thought to be the work of St. Ambrose (339–97).

Atmosphere is the gaseous envelope of the earth, and consists of a mixture of gases (*see* **Air**) and water vapour, the variability of the latter being of great importance meteorologically. The ozone layer, which absorbs solar ultra-violet radiation which would be lethal to plant life if it reached the ground lies between 12 to 50 km above the earth. The lower level of the atmosphere up to a height of about 12 km (10 km at the Poles and 16 km at the Equator) is known as the *troposphere*, and it is in this region that nearly all weather phenomena occur. This is the region of most interest to the forecaster studying temperature, humidity, windspeed, and the movement of air masses. Temperature falls with height by about 1°C per 152 m in this layer. The *tropopause* is the boundary between the troposphere and the *stratosphere*. Temperature varies little in the lower levels of this region: it is mainly cloudless, and has no vertical currents. Strangely enough, the lowest temperatures of the atmosphere are to be found not at the Poles, but at about 18 km above the Equator, where a temperature as low as −80°C has been recorded! Temperatures begin to rise about 32 km from the earth's surface at about the same rate as they fall in the troposphere owing to the absorption of solar radiation by the concentration of ozone. The stratospheric air is extremely dry. Near the 100 km level a number of important atmospheric phenomena occur. Above this level the oxygen becomes predominantly monatomic in contrast to the normal diatomic form at lower altitudes. This is the *ionosphere* (*q.v.*). This layer acts as an electrical radio mirror which makes long-distance radio transmission possible. The region of the

L12

Van Allen belts (*q.v.*) above the earth is called the magnetosphere (*q.v.*). The auroras are most frequently observed at altitudes between about 100 and 400 km but do extend at times far higher. Many aspects of the upper air can only be studied through space-research techniques. These include the composition and temperature of the charged particles in the ionosphere, the location of the electric currents in the ionosphere which produce the regular variations of the compass needle, as well as those which circulate during magnetic storms, the variation of the intensity of different radiation in the air-glow (*q.v.*) with height, the composition of the air at heights above 32 km, and so on. In addition, the pressures, density, temperatures, and wind distribution of the neutral atmosphere can be studied more directly, in much greater detail, and up to much greater altitudes than is possible if one is confined to the use of equipment on the ground. Instruments outside the atmosphere can make systematic observations on a world-wide basis of the atmospheric circulation, through observation of cloud cover and of the thermal radiation into space from the atmosphere. Such observations are of great importance for meteorology. The atmospheres of the other planets are vastly different to our own. For example, the Venusian atmosphere is considerably denser than the Earth's and is composed primarily of carbon dioxide. Carbon dioxide is also the main constituent of the Martian atmosphere, although this is much thinner than that of the Earth. Titan, the largest satellite of Saturn, has a nitrogen-rich atmosphere. *See also* **Ionosphere.**

Atmospherics are electrical impulses which are believed to originate in atmospheric electrical discharges such as lightning. They give rise to crashing background noises in the loudspeakers of radio sets, interfering with reception at distances of up to 6,400 km from the centre of the disturbance. The location of atmospherics with the aid of radio direction-finding methods gives warning of thunderstorms.

Atom. *See* **F10–17, F23.**

Atomic Pile, an apparatus containing a fissionable element and a moderator, such as heavy water or graphite, in which a self-sustaining fission process proceeds at a controllable rate. The first atomic pile, constructed on a squash court at Chicago, was operated for the first time on 2 December 1942, under the direction of Enrico Fermi. The pile contained 12,400 lb (5,580 kg) of uranium. *See* **Nuclear Reactors.**

Augsburg Confession, name given to the doctrine of faith of the Lutheran churches, drawn up by Melanchthon and endorsed by Luther for the Diet of Augsburg (1530).

August, named after the Emperor Augustus, because it was his "lucky" month.

Auks, duck-like sea-birds, black and white, with short, narrow wings, compact bodies and legs set well back. Breed in colonies on rocky coasts of N. Europe (incl. British Isles) and spend most time in coastal waters. Migrate south in winter. The Auk family includes the Razorbill, Little Auk, Guillemot and Puffin. The Great Auk became extinct in the 19th cent. after ruthless hunting for its feathers.

Aurora polaris. This wonderful phenomenon of the night sky is a common sight at high northern and southern latitudes, where it is called the aurora borealis and the aurora australis respectively. It is visible less often at temperate latitudes, and only rarely in the tropics. The auroral ovals, or zones of maximum frequency of aurora, surround both of the earth's geomagnetic poles, and the northern auroral oval includes the northern parts of Scandinavia, Canada and Alaska. The aurora is the visible manifestation of complex plasma processes occurring within the earth's magnetosphere (*q.v.*), whereby streams of high-energy electrons and protons (mainly) are accelerated and dumped via the earth's magnetic field lines into the upper atmosphere. This mechanism produces the light emission of the aurora. The brightest aurora, which may also extend to lower latitudes, occurs during geomagnetic storms, which are complex and large-scale plasma instabilities within the magnetosphere triggered by fluctuations in the solar wind (*q.v.*)

—usually ascribed to "M" regions on the sun associated with coronal holes, flares and active sunspot groups. Auroral displays may take several forms—a faint glow, a diffuse ribbon of light crossing the heavens, great folded waving curtains or draperies, or the entire sky may be flooded with a rapidly varying brilliant panoply of light. Specially instrumented spacecraft which can directly explore the magnetosphere and high-latitude ionosphere have provided a great deal of our knowledge about this fascinating and complex phenomenon. The aurora is a kind of light essentially different from that of the rainbow which is a partly subjective phenomenon. Each beholder sees his own rainbow, whose light is sunlight refracted and reflected by many raindrops. The raindrops that produce his rainbow depend on his position as well as on the direction of the sun. The aurora, on the contrary, is a light as objective as that of a candle, though produced differently. It is a self-luminescence of the air in particular regions of the atmosphere that lie far above the clouds.

Austerlitz, Battle of, was fought near Brünn, in Moravia, on 2 December 1805. Napoleon defeated the Russians and Austrians under Kutuzov.

Auto-da-Fé, or Act of Faith, was the ceremony connected with the sentencing of heretics under the Inquisition of Spain and Portugal, the persons found guilty being imprisoned or burned alive. The ceremony took place in some public square, often in the presence of the king and court.

Automation is a modern word used to designate the adoption of methods of automatic control either of manufacturing processes or of any business process involving a large mass of routine work. The word is used in broader and narrower senses. In its broadest sense it covers any form of mechanisation which largely replaces human labour by the work of automatic or semi-automatic machines, such as has been in progress continuously since the Industrial Revolution; but it it better kept to a narrower meaning, in which it is confined to the recent development of electronic or similar devices, involving feedback (automatic detection and correction of malfunction). Human labour is eliminated save for that needed for watching and maintaining the elaborate machines used.

Autumn, the third season of the year, begins with the autumnal equinox, and ends with the winter solstice, but the term is generally understood as covering the period from mid-August to mid-November.

Auxins, "plant hormones", organic substances produced by plants to regulate growth. Synthetic auxins are now widely used, *e.g.*, for promotion of root formation in cuttings, differential weed control, prevention of premature dropping of fruit, in storage of potatoes *etc.* and to overcome frost damage to fruit buds.

Average is a single number designed to give a typical example of a set of numbers, *e.g.*, a cricketer's batting average for a season gives an idea of his typical score. There are several kinds of average and their uses are studied in the science of statistics (*q.v.*). A statement that "so and so is the average value" can be misleading if one does not know which average is meant. Three common averages are: the arithmetic average (or mean), the mode, and the median. The arithmetic average of *n* numbers is found by adding them together and dividing by *n*; this is a very common method of averaging. The mode of *n* numbers is the most frequently occurring number. The median is the middle number, *i.e.*, the number which is smaller than just as many of the other numbers as it exceeds. Of the numbers 1, 2, 2, 2, 3, 4, 5, 6, 8, 9, the arithmetic means is 4, the mode is 2, the median is 3.

Avocet, a graceful wading bird related to the stilts, of black-and-white plumage, bluish legs, and slender upturned bill. There are four species. Avocets nest in colonies. There are now over 200 breeding pairs, mainly in E. Anglia.

Avogadro's Hypothesis. This is a fundamental concept of chemistry. Equal volumes of all gases under the same conditions of temperature and pressure contain the same number of molecules. This law was instrumental in assigning the formulae of molecules. The hypothesis was put

L13

forward in 1811, but was not generally accepted until 1860.

Avogadro's Number. See **F24.**

Ayers Rock. See **K14.**

Aztecs, the name of a powerful race found in Mexico when the Spaniards first discovered that country, and with difficulty subdued.

B

Babiroussa, a ferocious, long-legged wild pig, native of Sulawesi, sometimes called the horned-hog, because of the long upper tusks in the male, which are developments of the canine teeth which grow upwards, piercing the upper lip, and curving backwards, often broken in fighting.

Baboon, monkeys belonging to the African genus *Papio.* They are considered the lowest of the Old World (Catarrhine) monkeys, and walk on all fours. In the main terrestrial, but take to trees after food. The mandrill is closely related.

Babylonian Captivity, the period spent by the Jews in Babylon after Jerusalem was captured by Nebuchadnezzar, the Babylonian emperor, in 586 B.C. Traditionally the captivity lasted 70 years, but when Babylon was in turn taken by Cyrus in 538 B.C., the exiles were permitted to return to Jerusalem. The term is also applied in church history to the period 1309–78 when the papacy moved to Avignon, into the control of the French monarchy.

Bacteria. See **F41.**

Bacteriophage (Phage), literally "bacteria eater", *i.e.,* a virus which specifically infects bacteria. In common with viruses which attack animal or plant cells, isolated phages are inert, and can only reproduce by making use of the chemical apparatus of a more sophisticated host cell (in this case a bacterium). However phages may be of two types, virulent or temperate. Virulent phages completely disrupt the normal functioning of the infected bacterium and adapt its reproductive mechanism to produce more phage. This eventually kills the bacterium and the newly assembled phages are released. Temperate phages on the other hand may enter into a remarkable symbiotic relationship with the bacterium, known as lysogeny. The phage genetic material is incorporated into that of the bacterium and is reproduced each time the still functioning bacterium subsequently divides. Furthermore the bacterium is immune from attack by potentially virulent phages of the same type. When such lysogenic bacteria die, phage particles may again be released. Phages carried in lysogenic bacteria are in a state known as prophage and it is often difficult to obtain pure, prophage-free strains of bacteria. Because of their relatively simple structure, phages have been extensively used in research on genetics and molecular biology.

Badger, a carnivorous mammal related to the weasel, of nocturnal and burrowing habits, inoffensive, subsisting chiefly on roots and insects, though sometimes mice, young rabbits and eggs form part of its diet. Badger-baiting was a favourite sport in Britain until it was prohibited in the middle of 19th cent. The badger does little harm and quite a lot of good; badger digging is to be condemned as a cruel sport. In Britain the badger is partly protected by an Act passed in 1973, but the Ministry of Agriculture officials may destroy the animal in areas where bovine tuberculosis has been found.

Bagpipe. Once popular all over Europe, this instrument is still played in Scotland, Ireland, Brittany and elsewhere. The bag acts as a reservoir of air and, when squeezed by the player's arm, forces air through the pipes. One of these, the Chanter pipe, provides the tune and is played by the fingers as in a flageolet. The remainder, the Drone pipes, give a continuous, unvarying note.

Bailey Bridge, invented by Sir Donald Bailey and first used in the N. African campaign 1942–3. Built up of prefabricated girders, it can be easily transported and erected.

Bailiwick, a feudal term denoting the limits of a bailiff's jurisdiction. The term has survived in the Channel Islands, where Jersey and Guernsey are Bailiwicks.

Balance of Power was the doctrine in British policy whereby European groups should be so balanced as to prevent the emergence of a dominating Power. Thus the balance was maintained between the Triple Alliance (Germany, Austria and Italy) and the Triple Entente (Great Britain, France and Russia) and preserved peace from 1871 to 1914. After the first world war there was tentative support of Germany's recovery to counterweigh the possible French hegemony; but when Germany's power grew under Hitler leading to the second world war, Britain, France and Russia again became allies.

Baldachin (It. *Baldachino*), a canopy usually supported by four pillars over throne, altar, or other sacred object. The name is also applied to the silken canopy used in processions by the priest who carries the Host.

Balearic Crane, the crowned crane of the Balearic Islands and the North African mainland, distinguished by its yellowish, black-tipped occipital tuft and by its trumpet note.

Baleen *or* "whalebone" the name given to a series of horny plates growing from the roof of the mouth in those whales classified as Whalebone or Baleen Whales (*Mystacoceti*). There are 300–400 or so plates on each side, and their inner edges are frayed, the whole system constituting a filter for collecting minute organisms used for food. The Baleen Whales include the Right-Whales, the Pacific Grey-Whale and the Rorquals. See **Whales.**

Ballet is a combination of four arts; dancing, music, painting, and drama, each of which is ideally of equal importance. The movement of the individual dancers and the "orchestration" of the whole group is in the hands of the choreographer. The dancer's training follows certain basic rules but save in classical ballet there is considerable freedom of movement. Ballet as we know it today developed professionally at the Court of King Louis XIV of France, though it owes its origins to Italy and in the earliest times to Greece and Rome. Its movements were made up from the dances of courtiers, country folk and tumblers. Technique grew more complex as costume became modified, the body gaining complete freedom with the invention of tights. A succession of great dancers—French, Italian and latterly Russian left their imprint on the art. Contemporary ballet reflects the aesthetics of the Russian, Sergei Diaghilev. In England Dame Ninette de Valois has laid the foundation of a national ballet, at Sadler's Wells and Covent Garden, with a personality that reflects the national character. A Royal Charter was granted in 1957 setting up the Royal Ballet to co-ordinate the activities of the Sadler's Wells group.

Ballistics, the science dealing with the motion of projectiles, especially shells, bombs and rockets. Great advances have been made in this science.

Balloon, the modern balloon consists of a bag of plastic material inflated with a gas lighter than air. The first ascent by man in a hot-air balloon was made on 21 November 1783, and in a hydrogen balloon on 1 December 1783. The most famous of the early scientific flights by manned balloons were those of the Englishmen Coxwell and Glaisher, in 1862, when a height of 11 km was reached. The first aerial crossing of the English Channel by Blanchard and Jeffries was made on 7 January 1785. Piccard's ascent to 16 km, in 1931, marked the conquest of the stratosphere. Four years later the American balloon *Explorer II,* inflated with nearly 112,000 m³ of helium, carried a team of scientists with their floating laboratory to an altitude of 23 km. In 1957 a pressurised balloon carrying an American doctor rose 31 km above the Earth. Captive kite-balloons were widely used in the war as defensive measures against air attack. Meteorologists send their instruments up in balloons to collect data about the upper atmosphere, and of recent years physicists have learned much about cosmic radiation from the study of photographic plates sent to the upper regions in balloons. Ballooning as a hobby is carried on by a number of enthusiasts.

Balsam, a big genus (140 species) of flowering plants. Many species are cultivated for their showy flowers, *e.g.*, *Impatiens noli-me-tangere*, the yellow balsam or "touch-me-not", so called because the fruit explodes when touched, slinging out the seeds. Balsam fir is a conifer (*Abies balsamea*) from which Canada balsam gum is obtained.

Bamboo, a genus of strong grasses, some species growing to over 36 m in height; much used by oriental peoples for all kinds of purposes. The young shoots of some species are tender and esculent.

Banana (family *Musaceae*), a large herbaceous plant cultivated in moist regions of the tropics, and one of the most productive plants known. The main areas of commercial cultivation are in tropical America, the Canary Islands and West Africa. Europeans currently (1995) eat £2 billion worth of bananas each year and the market is rapidly growing.

Bandicoots, Australasian marsupial mammals, of the size of a large rat or rabbit. They are burrowing animals living largely on insects. The rabbit-eared bandicoot, restricted to Australia, has shrew-like snout, long ears like a rabbit, long crested tail, and a silky coat. The long-nosed bandicoot has a spiny coat and comes from E. Australia. The pig-footed bandicoot has two functional toes on the foot, like a pig.

Bank of England. Founded by Royal Charter on 27 July 1694. Known as "The Old Lady of Threadneedle Street". Prior to 1759 the lowest denomination note issued was £20.

Bank Rate, the rate at which the Bank of England is prepared to lend to the clearing banks. If raised it has the immediate effect of raising the rate of discount on Treasury Bills. Known as the Minimum Lending Rate from Oct. 1972 to Aug. 1981. *See* **Section G.**

Bantu (native word = people), term loosely used for large family of Negro races of Southern Africa.

Baobab, a tropical African tree. The species *Adansonia digitata* is one of the largest trees known, though not the tallest; the trunk can reach 9 m in thickness. The fruit is woody, but its juice provides a cooling beverage. The bark yields a fibre used for making rope and cloth.

Barbary Ape, a large monkey belonging to the genus *Macaca*. It is the only monkey living in relative freedom in Europe, a small colony existing on the Rock of Gibraltar. It has no tail.

Barberry, a genus of berry-producing shrubs containing a hundred species. Several species are cultivated for their flowers and bright berries. Has an interesting pollination mechanism; the base of each stamen is sensitive to touch, and insects probing for nectar cause top of stamen to spring inwards, so dusting visitor's head with pollen which can then be carried to the next flower visited. The common barberry (*Berberis communis*) harbours one stage of the fungus that causes rust of wheat.

Barbican, a fortified entrance to a castle or city, with projecting towers. In the London area called Barbican there was formerly a barbican in front of the city gates.

Barbiturates. A group of drugs derived from a parent compound called barbituric acid: phenobarbitone is the best-known example. They induce sleep and are used in the manufacture of sleeping pills and sometimes as anaesthetics, but they can be habit forming.

Barbizon School, a school of mid-19th-cent. landscape painters whose main tenet was a return to nature with an exact rendering of peasant life and country scenery painted on the spot. It was named after the village of that name in the Forest of Fontainebleau, where its chief members—Millet, Theodore Rousseau, Daubigny and Diaz—made their home. Their practice of painting direct from nature, made them the precursors of Impressionism (*q.v.*).

Barcarolle, a Venetian gondolier's song applied to instrumental as well as vocal compositions.

Bard, among the ancient Celts a poet or minstrel whose mission was to sing of heroic deeds. He was supposed to have the gift of prophecy, and was exempt from taxes and military service.

Barilla, soda carbonate or soda ash obtained by burning certain salt-marsh plants (*e.g.*, the saltwort, *Salsola kali*). It used to be in great demand, until the product of the Leblanc and then the Solvay ammonia-soda process was made available by the chemical industry.

Barium, metal element, no. 56, symbol Ba. In group 2 of the periodic table. The metal is soft and easily cut. It occurs as the sulphate and carbonate in nature. It was first prepared by Sir Humphry Davy in 1808, as an amalgam, by electrolysis of barium chloride. The pure metal was not isolated until 1901.

Barium meal. Barium sulphate is opaque to X-rays and before X-ray pictures of the alimentary canal radiologists give a "barium meal" to the patients so that the alimentary canal shows up more clearly.

Barnacles constitute a sub-class (*Cirripedia*) of the Crustacea. The barnacle fouling the bottom of ships is the Goose Barnacle, which has a long muscular stalk and a shell composed of five plates. The Acorn Barnacles, which cover rocks, breakwaters, etc. just below high-water mark are similarly constructed, but have no stalk. The manner of feeding of barnacles was vividly described by T. H. Huxley, who said the barnacle is "a crustacean fixed by its head kicking the food into its mouth with its legs". It was a naval surgeon, J. Vaughan Thompson, who discovered in 1830 that barnacles have a free-swimming larva (or nauplius). In the Middle Ages a curious myth grew up to the effect that the Barnacle changed into a sea-bird called, for that reason, the Barnacle Goose.

Barnard's Star. A star discovered by the American astronomer Edward Emerson Barnard in 1916 and which has the largest stellar proper motion known. Barnard's Star is one of the closest stars to us and also one of the intrinsically faintest stars known.

Barometer is an instrument for measuring atmospheric pressure, invented at Florence by Torricelli, pupil of Galileo, in 1644. The standard method consists of balancing the air column against a column of mercury, used on account of its high density. The mercury is contained in a long glass tube, closed at one end, and inverted in a cistern also containing mercury. The height of the mercury column, supporting the air column, is taken as the pressure at the time, and can be read off very accurately by means of a vernier scale. Present-day tendency is to express the readings in units of pressure instead of length, the millibar being adopted (1 mb = 1,000 dynes per sq. cm.; 1,000 mb $\equiv$ 75 cm of mercury approx.). The standard instrument is correct for pressures at 0°C in Lat. 45°, so that corrections have to be applied for temperatures and latitudes other than these. Also a correction has to be made for reducing the pressure to mean sea level. *See* **Aneroid.**

Baron, title given in feudal England to a man who held his land directly from the king by military or other honourable service. The first baron created by letters patent was John Beauchamp de Holt, Baron of Kidderminster, in 1387. A baron is a member of the fifth and last grade of the peerage of the United Kingdom and is addressed as "Lord". Life peers and life peeresses rank with hereditary barons and baronesses according to the date of their creation. In Scotland the term baron is used of the possessor of a feudal fief, or the representative by descent of such a fief. The equivalent of the English baron, as a rank of the Scottish peerage, is Lord of Parliament.

Baronet, the lowest hereditary title, instituted by James I to provide funds for the colonisation of Ulster. The first baronet was Sir Nicholas Bacon. Between 1964 and 1983 no recommendations for hereditary honours were made. In 1990 the Queen bestowed the title on Denis Thatcher.

Baroque, a term used for the art style of the period *c.* 1600–1720 which was the artistic accompaniment of the Jesuit counter-Reformation. Its most obvious characteristics are: (*a*) its emotional appeal and dramatic intensity both related to its deliberate intention as propaganda ("a good picture makes better religious propaganda than a sermon" said one of its exponents); (*b*) in architecture, a style which is heavily and sometimes almost grotesquely ornate, plentifully covered with voluptuous sculpture on which draperies float rather than hang, with twisted and spiral instead of plain or fluted columns, and unnecessary windows or recesses added for ornament rather than use; (*c*) its emphasis on the whole at the expense of the parts such that a building's sculpture merges into its architecture and both into its painting (Baroque paintings are as closely knit as a jigsaw puzzle so that one cannot isolate individual figures as would be possible in a Renaissance one). Baroque architecure owing to its origin is found mainly in the Catholic countries; Italy, France, Austria, Bavaria, e.g., the Barberini Palace, Rome, designed by its greatest exponent Bernini and others; the Church of the Invalides, Paris. Baroque artists include Caravaggio, Guido Reni, Murillo and Rubens the greatest Northern Baroque painter. The Baroque style merges gradually into **Rococo** (q.v.).

Barque, a small sailing vessel with three or four masts. A three-masted barque has fore- and mainmasts square-rigged, the mizzenmast fore- and aft-rigged.

Barrow is an ancient artificial mound of earth or stone raised over the site of a burial. In Britain barrows were built from 2500 B.C. until the late Saxon period, but the Egyptian are the earliest barrows known, the great pyramids being a spectacular development of the custom of ceremonial burial. Silbury Hill, south of Avebury, is the biggest artificial mound in Europe, 512 m in circuit at the base, 96 m at top, and 41 m high.

Bartholomew, Massacre of St., occurred in Paris on the night of 24 August 1572, when over two thousand Huguenots were massacred by order of the Catholic French Court.

Baryons, the group of heavier subatomic particles which includes the proton, neutron, lambda and omega-minus particles (and their corresponding anti-particles, called anti-baryons). Baryons interact by means of all the known forces of nature (strong, weak, electromagnetic and gravitational). However, in any closed system the total baryon number (i.e., the number of baryons minus the number of anti-baryons) is constant. This means that the proton, being the lightest known baryon, must be stable against spontaneous decay. Unlike the lighter leptons (q.v.), baryons are now thought to have internal structure reflecting the fact that they are composed of quarks (q.v.) See **F15.**

Basalt Rocks are fine-grained, dark coloured, of igneous origin and occur either as lava flows as in Mull and Staffa, or as intrusive sheets, like the Edinburgh Castle Rock and Salisbury Crags. One of the best examples of columnar basalt is the Giant's Causeway in Ireland.

Basanite, a smooth black siliceous mineral, or flinty jasper; a crypto-crystalline quartz used as a touchstone for testing the purity of gold, etc., by means of the mark left after rubbing the metal with it. Sometimes styled the Lydian stone.

Base, a substance having a tendency to accept a proton (H^+). This is a wide definition and covers unconventional types of compounds. In aqueous solution bases dissolve with formation of hydroxyl ions, and will neutralise an acid to form a salt. In non-aqueous solvents, like liquid ammonia or hydrogen fluoride, compounds classically regarded as salts can be bases, e.g., sodium fluoride is a base in hydrogen fluoride solution.

Basilisk, is a lizard of aquatic habits, with an elevated crest (which it can erect or depress at will) down the centre of its back.

Basques, people of N. Spain and S.W. France, oldest surviving racial group in Europe, who have preserved their ancient language which is unrelated to any other tongue.

Bas-Relief ("low relief"), a term used in sculpture to denote a class of sculptures the figures of which are only slightly raised from the surface of the stone or clay upon which the design is wrought.

Bastille, a castle or fortress in Paris, built in the 14th cent., and used as a state prison, especially for political offenders. Its bad repute as an instrument of despotism excited the hatred of the populace, who stormed and demolished it on 14 July 1789, at the start of the Revolution.

Bastinado, an oriental punishment, by beating with a pliable cane on the soles of the feet.

Bats. These mammals fly by means of a membrane stretched between each of the long fingers of the hand and between the fifth finger and the body. Another membrane stretches between the legs and the tail. Most British bats, including the pipistrelle, long-eared bats, noctules, belong to the family Vespertilionidae (with the exception of the horseshoe bats which belong to the family Rhinolophidae). These all feed on insects which they catch on the wing. The problem of how bats can detect their insect prey and avoid obstacles when flying in total darkness has interested zoologists for a very long time. The problem was solved with the advent of sensitive ultrasonic recording devices. Blindness does not affect this ability but deafness leave bats comparatively helpless. One of the most interesting types of bat is the fishing bat (Noctilio) found in central America, which can detect fish by being able to receive echoes from the ripples they make on the water surface. New European legislation to protect bats came into force in 1994. There are 15 species of bat in Britain. See also **Ultrasonics.**

Bath, Order of the, Britain's second oldest order of knighthood. Exclusive to men since its institution by Henry IV in 1399, women became eligible for admission to the order in 1971. The order has three grades: Knight Grand Cross (G.C.B.), Knight Commander (K.C.B.), and Companion (C.B.). Women members of the order are known as Dame Grand Cross, Dame Commander and Companion.

Battery, Electric, the common term for an electric cell but really meaning a combination of two or more cells. A cell is a device for converting stored chemical energy into electricity which can then be used for heat, light, traction, or any desired purpose. A primary cell will do this until the chemical action is completed and the cell is then useless. In a secondary cell, the chemical actions are reversible and the cell can be returned to its initial condition and used again. This is done by passing an electric current through—a process called recharging. A common primary cell is the Leclanché dry cell; used in torches. This works by the action of sal-ammoniac on electrodes made of zinc and carbon. About a century after it came into common use it is still the chief source of power for portable equipment in armed forces. A common secondary cell is the lead and sulphuric acid accumulator used in cars. Many other types of cell are known and some are under development because the demands of space travel, medicine, warfare, etc., call for batteries of lighter weight, greater reliability, or special properties. See **Fuel Cell, Energy Conversion.**

Bauhaus, a German institution for the training of architects, artists and industrial designers founded in 1919 at Weimar by Walter Gropius, (d. 1969). It was closed by Hitler in 1933 and re-opened at Chicago. The Bauhaus doctrine held that there should be no separation between architecture and the fine and applied arts; that art, science and technology should co-operate to create "the compositely inseparable work of art, the great building". Thus it was an organisation with a social purpose. The original institution, at the instigation of Gropius, included on its teaching staff not only architects and technicians but also such noted artists as Paul Klee and Wassily Kandinsky.

Bauxite, the chief ore of aluminium. Chemically it is aluminium oxide. Aluminium metal is made industrially by electrolysing purified bauxite dissolved in fused cryolite. Chief producing areas; Jamaica, Australia, Surinam, Russia, Guyana, France, Greece, Guinea, USA, Hungary and ex-Yugoslavia.

Bayeux Tapestry, a famous tapestry representing the conquest of England by William the Conqueror. It is embroidered on a band of linen 70 m long and 51 cm wide in blue, green, red and yellow, divided into 72 scenes ranging over the whole story of the conquest. The accepted view is that the tapestry was commissioned for Bayeux Cathedral, but a new interpretation is that it is an Anglo-Norman secular work of art, much influenced by the contemporary chansons de geste (songs of deeds), executed by English embroiderers for a Norman patron. A representation can be seen in the Victoria and Albert Museum in London.

Beagle, a small hound that tracks by scent, and extensively used for hare hunting.

Bears belong to the Ursidae family of the Carnivora. They are plantigrade mammals, walking (like man) on the soles of their feet. Found in most parts of the world except Australia. The common Brown Bear was once spread over the whole of Europe; it became extinct in England about the 11th cent.; 2–2·5 m in length, and stands 1 m or more at the shoulder. The Grizzly Bear of N. America is larger, and the coat is shorter and greyer. The Polar Bear is remarkable in having a white coat all the year round; it spends much time in water, and unlike other bears is entirely carnivorous. Bear-baiting was made illegal in England in 1835.

Beaufort Scale of wind force is used to specify numerically the strength of the wind. Since the introduction of anemometers to measure the actual velocity, equivalent values of the ranges in miles per hour at a standard height in the open have been agreed. *See* **Section Z.**

Beaver, a genus of mammals of the Rodentia order, with short, scaly ears, webbed hind feet, and a long broad scaly tail. They grow up to 1·2 m long, and live in communities, constructing dams and lodges where they breed. A campaign was launched in 1977 to bring back beavers to Britain where they have been extinct for several hundred years after being mercilessly hunted for their valuable pelt.

Bedlam (a corruption of Bethlehem) was a priory in Bishopsgate, afterwards converted into a hospital for lunatics. The asylum was transferred to St. George's Field, Lambeth, in 1815. The term "bedlamite" came to be applied to any person behaving like a madman.

Beech, a deciduous tree belonging to the genus *Fagus* of some eight or nine species found in north temperate regions. The common beech, *F. sylvatica*, is believed to be native to Britain and is one of our finest trees, with massive trunk, long, pointed winter buds, and smooth, grey bark. There is little undergrowth under its dense shade. It is shorter-lived than the oak taking about 200 years to reach full size and then declining. The timber of beech has a variety of uses, *e.g.*, spoons, handles, tools, and chairs.

Bee-eater, name of a family of brilliantly coloured birds closely related to the rollers and kingfishers inhabiting the tropical and sub-tropical parts of Africa, Asia and Europe. The European species successfully nested in Britain for the first time in 1955 and a pair nested in Alderney in 1956. With their long curved beaks they catch insects on the wing, especially bees and butterflies, and lay their eggs in dark tunnels.

Beefeater, *See* **Yeomen of the Guard.**

Beeswax, the secretion of the bee, used for the formation of the cells or honey-comb of the hive; when melted it is what is commercially known as yellow wax, white wax being made by bleaching. Being impervious to water, it acts as a good resistant and is an article of much utility.

Beetles (Coleoptera) constitute one of the biggest orders of insects, numbering over 200,000 species. There are two pairs of wings; the hind pair are used for flight, while the front pair are hardened to form a pair of protective covers (elytra). Some beetles have lost the power of flight and then the elytra are joined together.

Bel and the Dragon is the title of certain supplementary chapters to the "Book of Daniel" of an apocryphal character. First appeared in the Septuagint, but the Jewish Church did not accept it as inspired. In 1546 the Council of Trent declared it to be canonical.

Bell, a hollow body of metal used for making sounds. Bells are usually made from bell-metal, an alloy of copper and tin. Small bells used for interior functions are often made of silver, gold or brass. Ordinary hand-bells are of brass. From the 7th cent. large bells have been used in England in cathedrals, churches and monasteries. The greatest bell in the world is the "King of Bells" in the Kremlin at Moscow which weighs about 198 tonnes, is 627 cm high and 691 cm in diameter. It was cast in 1733 but cracked in the furnace (the broken part weighed 11 tonnes) and is now preserved as a national treasure. Other large bells in Russia include the 171 tonne one at Krasnogvardersk, near St Petersburg, and the one of 110 tonnes at Moscow. The Great Bell

(Great Paul) at St. Paul's, cast in 1881, weighs nearly 17 tonnes and is the largest in the United Kingdom. Other gigantic bells are the Great Bell at Peking (53 tonnes); Nanking (22 tonnes); Cologne Cathedral (25 tonnes); Big Ben, Westminster (over 13 tonnes); Great Peter, York Minster (10 tonnes). The Curfew Bell is rung in some parts of England to this day, notably at Ripon. The number of changes that can be rung on a peal of bells is the *factorial* of the number of bells. Thus four bells allow 24 and eight bells 40,320.

Belladonna or **Deadly Nightshade** (*Atropa belladonna*), a well-known poisonous wild plant found in Southern Europe and Western Asia. The alkaloid atropine it contains is valuable in medicine, although a large dose is poisonous.

Bell, Book and Candle. To curse by "bell book, and candle" was a form of excommunication in the Roman Church ending with the words: "Close the book, quench the candle, ring the bell".

Benedicite, the canticle in the Book of Common Prayer, known also as "The Song of the Three Holy Children".

Benedictines are monks and nuns of the Benedictine Order who live under the rule of St. Benedict—the monastic code whose influence on the religious and cultural life of the West has been so powerful. The rule is marked by an absence of extravagant asceticism. The greatest of the early Benedictines was Pope Gregory I (590–604) who sent St. Augustine of Canterbury to Anglo-Saxon England. Gregorian plainsong is named after him.

Benzene. An aromatic hydrocarbon obtained from coal tar and some petroleum fractions. It is a volatile inflammable liquid with a characteristic smell. The molecule consists of a flat ring of six carbon atoms, each bound to one hydrogen atom. Benzene is the parent member of many aromatic organic compounds and is widely used in industry to synthesise intermediates for fibres, dyestuffs, explosives and pharmaceutical chemicals.

Berlin Wall, construction dividing Berlin. Symbol of the Cold War. Built 13 August 1961. Dismantling began in 1989.

Beryl, a mineral, of which the emerald is a grass-green variety. Composed of beryllium and aluminium silicates. The pure mineral is colourless; the colour of most beryl comes from traces of impurities, notably iron and chromium. Otherwise it is yellowish, greenish-yellow, or blue, and is found in veins which traverse granite or gneiss, or embedded in granite, and sometimes in alluvial soil formed from such rocks.

Beryllium. Metallic element, no. 4, symbol Be. Very similar to aluminium, it is stronger than steel and only one-quarter its weight. It is not very abundant, its main source is the mineral, beryl. Copper containing 2 per cent. beryllium is used for making springs. Because of its special properties the metal is used as a component in spacecraft, missiles and nuclear reactors. This accounts for its recent development on a technical scale. The metal powder is toxic.

Bessemer Process for making steel depends on the forcing of atmospheric air into molten pig iron to burn out the impurities. Ousted by the oxygen converter. *See* **Steel.**

Betel, the leaf of an Indian climbing plant, of pungent, narcotic properties. It is destructive to the teeth, and reddens the gums and lips.

Bhang, the Indian name for the hemp plant *Cannabis sativa*, the leaves and seed-capsules of which are chewed or smoked. The drug which comes from flowers of the female plant is called hashish in Arabia and marihuana in the U.S.A.

Bible (Greek *biblion* = scroll of paper; pl. *biblia* = writings) includes the Hebrew sacred Scriptures (Old Testament) and those held sacred by the Christians (New Testament). The Old Testament—the prehistoric portion—consists of 39 books, and is divided into three parts: (1) the Law, (2) the Prophets, (3) Miscellaneous Writings. The Old Testament was written in Hebrew except for parts of Ezra and Daniel, which were in Aramaic. It was not until the 9th cent. A.D. that a complete Hebrew text was made, the so-called Massoretic text. Before that the main versions were the Alexandrian Greek translation (Septuagint) made in the 2nd cent. B.C. and St.

Jerome's Latin Vulgate of the 4th cent. A.D. (It was Jerome who used the Latin word "testament" (formed from *testis* = a witness).) Portions were translated into the Anglo-Saxon in the 8th cent. and the Venerable Bede put the greater part of St. John's gospel into English, but it was not until 1535 that a complete, printed English version appeared—the Coverdale Translation. The Authorised Version dates from 1611 in the reign of James I, and its beautiful phraseology has given it a lasting appeal. The Revised Version dates from 1885. *The New English Bible*, with the Apocrypha, was published in 1970. It is a new translation in plain English prose of the earliest Hebrew, Aramaic, and Greek manuscripts. The finding of the Dead Sea Scrolls (since 1947) has added to our knowledge of Scripture. By the mid-1990s the complete Bible had been translated into 322 languages, the New Testament alone into 695.

Biedermeier, style in interior decoration and the decorative arts developed from Empire (*q.v.*). It was created in Vienna *c.* 1815 and the name was derived from a fantasy figure in Viennese writing personifying all that which is sedate and bourgeois. Biedermeier furniture is less austere and grandiose than Empire's predecessors, more intimate and homely. A most important creation is the large circular table on a stem-like foot, which became the centre of family life, around which chairs could be grouped freely, not formally against walls as previously. In Vienna itself the style died out *c.* 1830, but in other Continental countries it survived well into the second half of the 19th cent. Its English equivalent is Early Victorian.

Billion, formerly in English usage a million million; now a thousand million or 10^9.

Bill of Rights, or Declaration of Rights, was the document setting forth the conditions upon which the British throne was offered to William and Mary in 1688. This was accepted and ultimately became an Act of Parliament. The pressure group Charter 88 currently campaigns for a Bill of Rights to enshrine civil liberties.

Binary Notation, for numbers, is a way of representing numbers using only two digits, 0 and 1. Electronic digital computers handle numbers in this form and many people these days are having to learn it. Many school children find it both easy and fascinating—as did the great philosopher and mathematician Leibniz. The ordinary, or decimal numbers, 0, 1, 2, 3, 4, 5, 6, 7, 8, 9, 10 are written in binary notation as follows: 0, 1, 10, 11, 100, 101, 110, 111, 1000, 1001, 1010. The reader might divine the rules from this. The point is you "carry 1", *i.e.*, move the digit 1 a place to the left, when you reach 2. In decimal notation you move 1 a place left when you reach 10. In other words, instead of columns for units, tens, hundreds, thousands, etc., the columns are for units, twos, fours, eights, etc. In binary notation: "1 + 1 = 0 with 1 to carry". Since every digit in binary notation is either 0 or 1 it requires one bit of information to specify a binary digit.

Biological Clock. All living organisms undergo cyclical changes in activity of some sort. These are linked to the changes in their environment which are produced by the alternation of night and day, the phases of the moon and the tides, and the cycle of the seasons. These cycles of activity frequently persist if the organism is put into a constant environment in which there appear to be no external clues as to what time or what season it is. A squirrel, for example, wakes up at about the same time each evening even when it is put into constant darkness. It is usual to refer to these activity patterns as being driven by a biological clock inside the organism. But very little is known about how these biological clocks work.

Biological Warfare, is the use for warlike purposes of bacteria, viruses, fungi, or other biological agents. These can be used to spread distress, incapacity, disease or death among the enemy's people or livestock. One of the strange uses to which mankind puts its science is to make naturally infective organisms even more virulent for military use. This sort of research can be done in many countries; it is much cheaper and easier to hide than nuclear weapons research.

Biosensors, micro-electronic or optoelectronic devices used to sense the presence of chemicals. This new technique for diagnosis and analysis could have a host of applications in medicine (*e.g.* blood analysis), industry *etc*.

Biosphere, that part of the earth in which life exists—a very thin layer near the surface bounded by regions too hostile for life processes to occur. The upper limit is at about 9,000 m above sea level and the lower limit at about 10,000 m in the deep oceans. Ample supplies of solar energy, liquid water and places where liquid, solid and gas all meet seem to be requirements for a biosphere to exist and for all the biological cycles of water, oxygen, mineral, nitrogen, *etc.*, to function.

Birch, a genus of deciduous trees including about 40 species and found only in northern regions. Birches native to Britain, and to Europe generally, are of two species—the silver birch, *Betula pendula*, with its graceful, drooping branches and triangular leaves, and the white birch, *Betula pubescens*, which has erect branches and soft oval leaves. Birch timber is an important plywood timber, the bark is used for tanning leather, and wintergreen oil comes from the bark of black birch, *Betula lenta*, a North American species. The birch is not a long-lived tree.

Birds, or Aves, are, next to mammals, the highest class of animal life. There are two kinds of modern birds—*Carinatae*, possessing keeled breast-bones and having power of flight; *Ratitae*, having raft-like breast-bones, and incapable of flight; and a sub-class of fossil birds, Archaeornithes, including *Archaeopteryx*. Estimates of the total number of birds breeding in the British Isles vary, but there are 229 breeding species. Of these the commonest are wrens, of which there are 10 million breeding pairs, house sparrows, blackbirds and chaffinches with up to 7 million pairs each, robins with 5 million and starlings with 3·5 million pairs.

The wheatear is usually the first of the migratory birds to return, often reaching Britain at the end of February and always before the middle of March; the sand martin is the first of the "early swallows" to return, followed by the house martin. The first cuckoo arrives about the middle of April, and the whinchat, garden warbler, and sedge warbler during the last week in April. The nightjar, spotted flycatcher, and red-backed shrike are not seen until the first week in May. The swift is among the last to return from Africa and the earliest to depart. Bird-nesting is illegal in Britain. With the passing of the Wildlife and Countryside Act in 1980 the trapping and caging of robins, nightingales, larks, kingfishers, cuckoos, owls, martins, fieldfares, flycatchers, ravens and other birds was made illegal in Britain. *See also* **F36**(2).

Birds of Paradise, over 40 species of tropical birds inhabiting the dense forests of New Guinea and neighbouring islands. The male birds are remarkable for their brilliant plumage, long tail feathers, and ruffs on wings and neck, which are displayed to advantage during courtship. Related to the Bower Birds of Australia.

Biretta, a four-cornered head-covering worn by ecclesiastics of the Roman Church and varying in colour according to the rank of the wearer. A cardinal's biretta is red, a bishop's purple, a priest's black.

Bise, a keen dry north wind prevalent in Switzerland and South France.

Bishop is a Christian ecclesiastic, a person consecrated for the spiritual government of an area, a diocese or province, to the spiritual oversight of which he has been appointed (diocesan bishops), or to aid a bishop so appointed (suffragan bishops). In the Church of England there are forty-three diocesan bishops, all nominated by the Crown. Two, Canterbury and York, are archbishops having primacy in the respective provinces. The archbishops of Canterbury and York and the bishops of London, Durham and Winchester and twenty-one other diocesan bishops in order of seniority are spiritual peers, and sit in the House of Lords. The (Disestablished) Church of Ireland has two archbishops and twelve bishops; the (Disestablished) Church of Wales an archbishop and five bishops and the Episcopal Church in Scotland seven bishops. *See also* **Cardinal.**

Bismuth, metallic element, no. 83, symbol Bi, in group 5 of the periodic table. Like antimony, the stable form is a grey, brittle, layer structure; electrical conductor. It is readily fusible, melting at 264°C and boiling at about 1420°C. Wood's metal, an alloy with one of the lowest melting points (under 65°C, so that a spoon made of it will melt when placed in a cup of hot tea), contains four parts bismuth, two parts lead, one part tin, one part cadmium.

Bison, a genus of wild cattle, distinguished from the ox by its shorter, wider skull, beard under the chin, high forequarters, and, in winter, a great mane of woolly hair covering head and forequarters. There are two species, the European and the American bison, both now protected in game reserves.

Bit, formerly the word often referred to the metal piece in the mouth of a bridled horse, now more likely to be a technical expression in the mouth of a computer expert. A bit is a unit of information; it is the information that can be conveyed by indicating which of two possibilities obtains. Any object that can be either of two states can therefore store one bit of information. In a technical device, the two states could be the presence or the absence of a magnetic field, or of an electric voltage. Since all numbers can be represented in the binary system (*see* **Binary Notation**) by a row of digits which are *either* 0 *or* 1, it takes one bit of information to specify a binary digit. Bit is short for binary digit.

Bittern, a bird of the heron genus, with long, loose plumage on the front and sides of the neck. It is a solitary bird inhabiting marshes, but rare in Britain.

Bivalves, shell-fish whose shell consists of two hinged valves, lying one on each side of the body, such as mussels, oysters and cockles.

Blackbird, or Merle, a member of the Thrush family, a familiar song bird in Britain. Male is all-black with orange bill; female is mottled brown with brown bill; the young are spotted brown.

Blackcock and Greyhen (as the female is called) are closely related to the Capercaillies but smaller. They nest on the ground and prefer wooded country to open moors. Found in northern half of northern hemisphere. Polygamous, they perform excited courtship dances; the male is a handsome blue-black bird with white undertail, the female dark brown mottled.

Black Death, the plague which swept across Europe in the years 1348–50, beginning in the ports of Italy, brought in by merchant ships from Black Sea ports. It was the worst scourge man has ever known; about a quarter of the European population was wiped out in the first epidemic of 1348. It reached England in the winter of that year. The disease was transmitted to man by fleas from black rats, though this was not known at the time, the specific organism being *Bacillus pestis*. The disease continued to ravage Europe in recurrent outbreaks up to the late 17th cent. The epidemic which raged in England in 1665 wiped out whole villages and one-tenth of London's population, then estimated at 460,000. Samuel Pepys wrote a grim account of it in his *Diary. See also* **Labourers, English Statute of.**

Black Hole of Calcutta, the name given to the place where a captured British garrison was confined in 1756, during the struggle for India between the French and British. Into a noisome space, about 6 m square, 146 persons were driven and only 23 were found alive the next morning. The authenticity of the story has been called into question, but after sifting the evidence Professor H. H. Dodwell, in the *Cambridge History of the British Empire,* believes it to be substantially true.

Black Holes. *See* Astronomy, Section F, Part I.

Black-letter, the Old English or Gothic type first used in printing blocks.

Black Woodpecker (*Dryocopus martius*), a black bird about the size of a rook, with slightly crested scarlet crown, found in parts of Europe.

Blenny, a group of marine fishes with spiny rays part of the fin running along the back. Several species are found around the British coast.

Blood Groups. *See* Index to Section P.

Bloody Assizes, the assizes conducted in 1685 by George Jeffreys, Lord Chief Justice, at which participants in the Duke of Monmouth's rebellion against King James II were tried. They were marked by relentless cruelty.

Bluebird, a migratory bird of North America, deriving its name from its deep blue plumage, it has a pleasant warbling song and is a familiar sight in the woods from early spring to November. In India and Malaya there is the Fairy Blue-bird; the male is black with shiny blue upper parts. Used as the symbol of happiness by Maeterlinck in his play *The Blue Bird.*

Blue Peter, a blue flag with a white square in the centre, is hoisted 24 hours before a ship leaves harbour (the letter P in the alphabet of the International Code of Signals).

Blue Ribbon, a term in general use to denote the highest honour or prize attainable in any field or competition. Thus the Derby is the blue ribbon of the turf. The expression is derived from the highest Order of Knighthood in the gift of the British Crown, the insignia of which is a garter of blue velvet.

Blue Stocking, a term used to describe a learned or literary woman, particularly if pedantic and undomesticated. It is said that the term derives from the Bas-Bleu club of Paris, which was attended by the literary savantes of the 17th cent. In England a similar literary club was formed about 1780, whose members were distinguished by their blue stockings.

"Blue" Sun, Moon, etc., a phenomenon caused by the scattering of sunlight by transparent particles suspended in the atmosphere, the effect being that blue light is transmitted, and red light extinguished to direct vision. The dust from the Krakatoa eruption in 1883 and the drifting layer of smoke from the forest fires in Alberta, Canada, in September 1950 gave rise to "blue" moons and suns, phenomena sufficiently rare to be described as occurring "once in a blue moon". In the cold climatic conditions of the Pamirs and the far north, vegetation is said to look "blue" on account of the rays of high calorific value (red, yellow, green) being absorbed, while only the blue and violet are transmitted. It was Tyndall who first explained the blue colour of the sky.

Boa, a term applied to a family of snakes of large size, some attaining a length of 9 m. They are not poisonous, but kill their prey by crushing —constriction—hence the name "boa constrictor". They occur both in the Old World and the New, but are more abundant in the latter. Most Boas retain the eggs within the body until young are fully developed, whereas the Pythons almost all lay leather-shelled eggs.

Boar, or Wild Hog, an animal largely distributed over the forest regions of Europe, Asia, Africa and South America. It has a longer snout and shorter ears than its descendant the domestic hog, and is provided with tusks. Having to forage for itself, it is a more active and intelligent animal than the pig of the sty, and offered good sport to the hunter.

Boat, an open vessel, propelled by oars or sails, or both. The boats of a ship of war are the launch, barge, pinnace, yawl, cutters, jolly boat and gig; of a merchant vessel, the launch, skiff, jolly boat or yawl, stern boat, quarter-boat and captain's gig. Every ship is compelled to carry adequate, fully provisioned and equipped lifeboats.

Bode's Law, a numerical relationship formulated by Bode in 1772 (though pointed out earlier by J. D. Titius of Wittenberg), which states that the relative mean distances of the planets from the sun are found by adding 4 to each of the terms 0, 3, 6, 12, 24, 48, 96, and dividing each number by 10. The gap between Mars and Jupiter caused Bode to predict the existence of a planet there, which was later confirmed by the discovery of Ceres and other minor planets. The law breaks down however, for Neptune and Pluto.

Boer War lasted from 11 October 1899, when the Boers invaded Natal, to 31 May 1902, when the Treaty of Vereeniging ended hostilities. At first the operations of the British troops in Cape Colony were unsuccessful and disastrous reverses were sustained. Lord Roberts was then sent out as Commander-in-Chief, with Lord Kitchener as Chief-of-Staff, and from February 1900, when Kimberley was relieved and Cronje was compelled to surrender and Ladysmith and Mafeking were relieved, the struggle was practically over.

Boiling-point is the temperature at which a liquid boils. At that point the pressure of the vapour is equal to the pressure of the atmosphere. Under increased pressure the b.p. rises and under less pressure, as on the top of a mountain, it is lower. At standard atmospheric pressure (760 mm of mercury) the b.p. of water is 100°C; alcohol 78·4°C; ether 35·6°C.

Book of Hours, the most widespread devotional work of the Middle Ages. Most surviving copies are 15th century, but the earliest (the de Brailes Hours) dates from c.1240.

Books, Classification of. All libraries are classified to facilitate reference, but the favourite system is the Dewey Decimal System, which divides the whole field of knowledge into ten Main Classes. Each of these Main Classes is again subdivided into ten main divisions. As an example: the main class of Sociology receives the number 300. This range 300 to 400 (the next main class) is graduated into tens, and Economics is 330. The range 330 to 340 is again graduated, and the subject of Labour and Capital is 331. This process is carried on by decimals so that 331·2 deals with Remuneration for Work, 331·22 with Wage Scales, and 331·225 with Extra Pay.

Borax (Sodium Pyroborate) is a white, soluble, crystalline salt. It is widely and diversely used, e.g., as a mild antiseptic, in glazing pottery, in soldering, in the making of pyrex glass, as a cleansing agent and sometimes as a food preservative. Borax occurs naturally in the salt lakes of Tibet, where it is called tincal.

Bore. In physical geography, an almost vertical wall of water which passes upstream along certain estuaries. Its formation requires special conditions of river flow, incoming high tide, and shape of river channel. It can be spectacular and dangerous on some rivers. In Britain the best known is the Severn bore which can be over a metre high and move at 16–19 km/h. In parts of Britain the bore is called an eagre.

Boron. A metalloid element, no. 5, symbol B. There are two forms, one crystalline, the other amorphous. It is not very abundant in nature but occurs in concentrated deposits. It is best known in boric acid, which is used as a mild antiseptic (called boracic acid) and borax (q.v.). Boron compounds are essential to some plants, e.g., beans. Used in the preparation of various special-purpose alloys, such as impact resistant steel. Compounds of boron and hydrogen are used as rocket fuels.

Borstal, an institution where young offenders under 21 on conviction were sent for detention and reform. Emphasis was placed on vocational training in skilled trades. The first was opened in 1902 at Borstal, near Rochester in Kent. Borstals were abolished by the 1982 Criminal Justice Act. Young offenders' are now referred to the Young Offenders' Institution (q.v.).

Boston Tea Party, an incident which occurred on 16 December 1773, on board some tea-ships in Boston Harbour. High taxation imposed by the British Parliament under George III had caused bitter feelings, and instigated by popular meetings, a party of citizens, disguised as Indians, boarded the tea-ships and threw the tea overboard. This incident was a prelude to the American War of Independence (1775–83) which resulted in Britain's loss of her American colonies.

Bounds Beating, an old Anglo-Saxon custom. The parish clergyman and officials go round the parish boundaries accompanied by boys who beat the boundary stones with long sticks of willow. The ceremony takes place on the Rogation days preceding Ascension Day.

Bourgeoisie, a term used by Marxists to indicate those who do not, like the proletariat, live by the sale of their labour. They include, on the one hand, industrialists and financiers or members of the liberal professions and, on the other, small artisans and shop-keepers who, although their standard of living may not be appreciably higher (and today is often lower) than that of the proletariat, are described as the "petty bourgeoisie". According to the Marxist view of history, the bourgeoisie arose with modern industrialism after it had overthrown the old feudal aristocracy and thus replaced it as the ruling class.

Bovine Spongiform Encephalopathy (BSE), see **Mad Cow Disease.**

Bow, an instrument for propelling arrows, and, in the days when it was a weapon of war, was usually made of yew or ash, and was about 2 m long, with an arrow c. 1 m long. It was the weapon with which Crécy, Poitiers and Agincourt were won. The cross-bow was Italian and was adopted in France, but did not become popular in Britain.

Bow Bells is the peal of the London church of St. Mary-le-Bow, Cheapside, within sound of which one must be born to be entitled to be called a "cockney". Bow Bells had not been heard since 1939, but they once again rang out over the City of London on 20 December 1961.

Bowdlerise, to expurgate a book. Derived from Thomas Bowdler (1754–1825), the editor of the Family Shakespeare, in which "those words and expressions are omitted which cannot with propriety be read aloud in a family". He treated Gibbon's *History of the Decline and Fall of the Roman Empire* in the same way, omitting "all passages of an irreligious and immoral tendency". Such prudery met with ridicule and hence the words "bowdlerism" "bowdlerist", etc.

Bower Bird, native to Australia and New Guinea and related to the Bird of Paradise, though often less striking in appearance. In the mating season the male builds a "bower" of sticks and grasses for courtship displays and as a playground. The Gardener Bower Bird of Papua makes a lawn in front of his bower and adorns it with bright coloured pebbles and flowers which are replaced as they wither. The female builds her nest away from the bower.

Boycott, a term used in connection with a person that the general body of people, or a party or society, refuse to have dealings with. Originally used when Captain Boycott (1832–97) was made the victim of a conspiracy by the Irish Land League which prevented him making any purchases or holding any social intercourse in his district. He had incurred the League's hostility by a number of evictions.

Brass, an exceedingly useful alloy of copper and zinc. Much brass is about two-thirds copper but different proportions give different properties. It is harder than copper and easily worked. Brass in the Bible (Matt. x, 9) probably refers to bronze.

Breadfruit Tree (*Artocarpus altilis*), a native of the South Sea Islands; the fruits are a brownish green, about the size of a melon, and contain a white pulpy substance which is roasted before being eaten. The tree grows 12 m or more. Captain Bligh's ship *Bounty* was on a voyage to Jamaica carrying a cargo of 1,000 breadfruit trees when the mutiny occurred.

Breeder Reactor, a kind of nuclear reactor (q.v.) which besides producing energy by the fission process also produces ("breeds") more nuclear fuel at the same time. A typical reaction is: a neutron induces fission of a U-235 nucleus which breaks up into two medium-sized nuclei and some neutrons; one of the latter then enters a U-238 nucleus turning it into U-239 which then decays radioactively via neptunium into plutonium which is useful fuel. There are technical problems in breeder reactors which have delayed their practical use.

Breviary (Lat. *breviarium* = abridgment), the short prayer-book of the Roman Catholic Church which gives the Divine Office, i.e., the services to be said daily. The directions for Mass are in the Missal. The current Roman breviary is a simplified version of the one decreed by the Council of Trent, 1568. See also **Matins.**

Bridges are structures for continuing a road, railway, or canal across a river, valley, ravine, or a road or railway at a lower level. From early times bridges were made of timber, stone, or brick, and it was not until the 19th cent. that wrought- and cast-iron were used. Today the materials mostly used are steel and reinforced concrete. Among the most famous of ancient bridges is that of S. Angelo at Rome, built by Hadrian as the Pons Aelius, A.D. 134. The Rialto bridge at Venice dates from 1588.

The Ponte Santa Trinita at Florence, one of the finest Renaissance bridges and deemed the most beautiful in the world, was destroyed by German mines in 1944 but has now been reconstructed just as it was before. The first stone bridge across the Thames was begun in 1176. It had 19 arches and was lined with houses and stood until 1831 when it was replaced by the granite bridge designed by Sir John Rennie which stood until 1972. This has been replaced by a three-span concrete bridge with a six-lane carriageway and two footways. The first cast-iron bridge (recently repaired) was built by Abraham Darby at Coalbrookdale, Shropshire, in 1779. Telford's Menai suspension bridge (1825) has since been enlarged, the original design maintained. Another example of Britain's supremacy in constructional iron-work was Robert Stephenson's tubular bridge across the Menai Straits (1850), the prototype of all modern plate girder railway bridges. Other famous bridges are the Niagara (suspension), Forth railway bridge (cantilever), London Tower bridge (suspension), Tay railway bridge, Victoria Jubilee bridge across the St. Lawrence at Montreal (an open steel structure), Sydney Harbour bridge, Lower Zambesi bridge, Storstrom bridge in Denmark, Auckland Harbour bridge, and Verrazano-Narrows bridge spanning New York's harbour from Brooklyn to Staten I., exceeding by 18 m the centre span of San Francisco's Golden Gate bridge.

British bridges include the road suspension bridge across the Firth of Forth, completed 1964, the Severn suspension bridge (from which the design principles for the new bridge across the Bosporus were taken) and the Tay road bridge, both completed 1966, the Tinsley viaduct, near Sheffield, opened 1968 and the Humber suspension bridge, linking Hull and Grimsby, opened in 1981. When completed, it was the longest single-span suspension bridge in the world (1,410 m). The M25 'Dartford' bridge (opened 1991) is the largest cable-stayed bridge in Europe. The second Severn bridge is due to open in 1996.

Bridleway. In English law (sec. 27(6) of the National Parks and Access to the Countryside Act 1949) a highway over which the public have the following, but no other, rights of way: that is to say, a right of way on foot and a right of way on horseback or leading a horse, with or without a right to drive animals of any description along the highway.

Britannia Metal, an alloy of tin, antimony and copper, harder than pure tin, corrosion-resistant, used for teapots, jugs (often electro-plated).

British Association for the Advancement of Science, The, was founded in 1831 by a group of British scientists under the leadership of Charles Babbage (1792–1871) to stimulate scientific inquiry and promote research in the interest of the nation. Its meetings are held annually.

British Legion, see Royal British Legion.

British Museum, was created by an Act of Parliament in 1753, when the Sir Hans Sloane collection, which the British Government had acquired for £20,000, was added to the Cottonian Library and the Harleian Manuscripts. It was opened to the public in 1759 at Montague House Bloomsbury. The acquisition of the library of George III (known as the King's Library) in 1823 led to the construction of the present building with the new wing (1829), quadrangle (1852), domed reading room (1857), and later additions. The books and the reading room are now part of the British Library (see Libraries). The Natural History Department was transferred to South Kensington in the 1880s. As a museum it is perhaps the most famous in the world, since it has many priceless collections. It attracted 6·2 million visitors in 1992. Its treasures include the Elgin Marbles (q.v.), the Rosetta Stone (q.v.), the Portland Vase (q.v.).

British Rail (British Railways). The name under which the railways of Britain were unified on 1 January 1948. Instead of the former four main railway systems six regions were formed: London Midland region (former L.M.S.R.), Western (former G.W.R.), Southern (formerly S.R.), Eastern (southern area of former L.N.E.R.), N.E. region (N.E. of former L.N.E.R.), Scottish region (Scottish system of the former L.M.S.R. and L.N.E.R.). Under the Transport Act 1962 the British Railways Board was set up to manage railway affairs. The most far-reaching change in the modernisation and re-equipment programme since 1955 has been the replacement of steam traction by electric and diesel locomotives. Under the chairmanship of Lord (then Dr.) Richard Beeching the British Railways Board planned a viable railway system by closing uneconomic branch lines, by developing new services on the liner train principle, and by utilising a more limited trunk route system. Under the Transport Act 1968 some railway passenger services became eligible for grants on social grounds, including urban railways and unprofitable rural services. High-speed inter-city passenger services came into operation in 1976 and in 1985 it was announced that the Advanced Passenger Train (the Electra) would go into production. Following the passage of the 1993 Railways Act, the privatisation of British Rail began on 1 April 1994 when a new company, Railtrack, took over the management of the track, signalling and other infrastructure. In November 1994, the government announced its intention to privatise Railtrack, which owns 2,500 stations and 11,000 miles of track. The first 8 routes to be privatised will include the Gatwick Express, InterCity East Coast, Great Western, the Midland Main Line and the London, Tilbury and Southend.

British Standard Time, The British Standard Time Act of 1968 put Britain an hour ahead of Greenwich Mean Time (GMT) throughout the year for an experimental 3 years. This brought Britain into line with countries in Western Europe where Central European Time is observed. In 1970 Parliament called for the restoration of the previous position—BST in the summer months and GMT in the winter months—as from 31 October 1971.

Brocken-spectre or Glory. The series of coloured rings which an observer sees around the shadow of his own head (or an aeroplane in which he is travelling) as cast upon a bank of mist or thin cloud. This effect is produced by reflection and refraction of sunlight in minute water-droplets in the air just as in a rainbow.

Bromine. A non-metal element, no. 35, symbol Br, member of the halogen family (q.v.). It is a red, evil-smelling liquid (Greek bromos, a stink). It is an abundant element. In the USA bromide is extracted from sea-water on a large scale. It unites readily with many other elements, the products being termed bromides. Its derivatives with organic compounds are used in synthetic chemistry. Bromoform is a liquid resembling chloroform. Bromides are used in medicine to calm excitement.

Bronze is primarily an alloy of copper and tin, and was one of the earliest alloys known, the Bronze Age (began c. 4,000 B.C. in Middle East) in the evolution of tool-using man coming before the Iron Age (c. 2,000 B.C.) Some modern bronzes contain zinc or lead also, and a trace of phosphorus is present in "Phosphor-bronze".

BSE, see Mad Cow Disease.

Bubble Chamber. An instrument used by physicists to reveal the tracks of fast fundamental particles (e.g., those produced in large accelerating machines) in a form suitable for photography; closely related to the Wilson cloud chamber (q.v.), but the particles leave trails of small bubbles in a superheated liquid (often liquid hydrogen) instead of droplets of liquid in a supersaturated gas; invented in 1952 by the American physicist, Dr. D. Glaser, Nobel Prizeman, 1960, and developed by Prof. L. W. Alvarez, Univ. of California, Nobel Prize, 1968.

Buckingham Palace, London residence of British sovereigns since 1837. Originally built for the Duke of Buckingham (1703); bought by George III in 1762 and remodelled by Nash 1825–36. Part of the palace was opened to visitors in 1993.

Buntings, name of a group of finches, seed-eating birds, usually found in open country. The Yellowhammer, Reed Bunting, Corn Bunting and Cirl Bunting are resident in Britain; the Snow Bunting (which breeds in small numbers in Scotland) and Lapland Bunting are regular winter visitors. The Ortolan is a rare visitor.

Bustard, type of bird, related to the crane.

Butane, a colourless inflammable gas made of carbon and hydrogen; formula C_4H_{10}. Found in natural gas and made as a by-product of oil refining. Butane, like propane (*q.v.*), can easily be liquefied and moved safely in cans and tanks. It is thus useful as a "portable gas supply"; also used in internal combustion fuels.

Byzantine Art developed in the eastern part of the Roman empire after Constantine founded the city of Constantinople (A.D. 330). It has many sources—Greek, Syrian, Egyptian and Islamic —and reached its zenith in the reign of Justinian (527–65). The major art form was ecclesiastical architecture, the basic plan of which was Roman—either basilican (symmetrical about an axis) or centralised (symmetrical about a point). Arched construction was developed, and the dome became the most typical feature, although, unlike the Roman dome which was placed on a round apartment, the Byzantine dome was placed on a square one on independent pendentives. Frequently small domes were clustered round a large one as in the case of the great church of Santa Sophia (537), the climax of Byzantine architecture. Usually the churches were small and include those of SS. Sergius and Bacchus, Sta. Irene (in Constantinople), S. Vitale in Ravenna, and the much later and larger St. Mark's in Venice. Byzantine art also took the form of miniatures, enamels, jewels, and textiles, but mosaics, frescos, and icons (*q.v.*) are its greatest treasures.

C

Cacao, Theobroma cacao, is an evergreen tree, from 4–6 m high, growing abundantly in tropical America, West Africa, the West Indies, Sri Lanka, etc., yielding seeds, called cocoa beans from which cocoa and chocolate are manufactured. The fruit is 17–25 cm long, hard and ridged; inside are the beans, covered with a reddish-brown skin, which are first fermented, then dried. The trees mature at five to eight years and produce two crops a year.

Cactus, a family of flowering plants numbering about a thousand species adapted to living in very dry situations. The stem is usually fleshy, being composed of succulent tissue, remarkably retentive of water; commonly equipped with sharp thorns which deter animals from eating them. The roots are generally very long, tapping soil water over a large area; a "prickly pear" cactus may have roots covering a circular area 7 m or more in diameter. The leaves are commonly insignificant or absent, and the stem takes over the photosynthetic leaf function and becomes accordingly flattened to expose greater area to sunlight and air. In some kinds of cactus (*e.g.*, *Echinocactus*) the stem is shaped almost like a sea-urchin.

Cadmium. A metallic element, no. 48, symbol Cd, chemically similar to zinc and mercury. Used in alloys to lower the melting point, as in Wood's metal with bismuth and tin. Alloyed with copper to make electric cables. Like zinc, it is a protective metal and is used in electroplating. The cadmium-vapour lamp gives a characteristic frequency used in measuring wavelength.

Caesium, also spelt **Cesium,** is an alkali metal element, no. 55, symbol Cs, in first group of the periodic table. It resembles rubidium and potassium and was discovered by Bunsen and Kirchoff in 1860. It was the first element whose existence was discovered spectroscopically. The caesium atom consists of a heavy nucleus surrounded by 55 electrons, 54 of which are arranged in stable orbits, and one of which, known as the valency electron, is in a less stable orbit surrounding them. Used in the construction of photo-electric cells and as an accurate time standard (atomic clock).

Calcium, a silvery-white metallic element, no. 20, symbol Ca. It melts at 810°C and is very reactive. It was discovered by Sir Humphry Davy in 1808, but not until 1898 was it obtained pure, by Moissan. Does not occur as metal in nature, but calcium compounds make up a large part of the earth's crust. Most important calcium sources are marble, limestone, chalk (all three are, chemically, calcium carbonate); dolomite, which is the double carbonate of calcium and magnesium; gypsum, a hydrated calcium sulphate; calcium phosphate and calcium fluoride. Igneous rocks contain much calcium silicate. Calcium compounds are essential to plants and are used in fertilisers. Animals require calcium and phosphorus for bone and teeth formation; deficiency is treated by administration of calcium phosphate. Strontium is chemically similar to calcium, and the radioactive strontium 90 from atomic "fall-out" is therefore easily assimilated by the body.

Calendar, a collection of tables showing the days and months of the year, astronomical recurrences, chronological references, etc. The Julian Calendar, with its leap year, introduced by Julius Caesar, fixed the average length of the year at 365¼ days, which was about 11 minutes too long (the earth completes its orbit in 365 days 5 hours 48 minutes 46 seconds of mean solar time). The cumulative error was rectified by the Gregorian Calendar, introduced in Italy in 1582, whereby century years do not count as leap years unless divisible by 400. This is the rule we now follow. England did not adopt the reformed calendar until 1752, when she found herself 11 days behind the Continent. The Gregorian Calendar did not come into use in Russia until 1918. Old Style and New Style dates are identified as "O.S." "N.S.".

Calends, the first day of the month in the Roman calendar.

Calorie. Unit of quantity of heat. The "small" or fundamental calorie is the amount of heat required to raise the temperature of 1 gram of water from 14·5° to 15·5°C and is equal to 4·185 joules. This is the gram-calorie used in physics and chemistry. The large Calorie (written with a capital C), commonly used in nutritional connotations, is equal to 1000 small calories and is called the kilogram-calorie.

Calvinism. See Section J.

Calypso, West Indian song in the form of a doggerel lampoon composed spontaneously and sung to a guitar.

Cambridge University had a sufficiently good teach-ing reputation to attract Oxford students in 1209, when lectures at their own university were suspended. In 1226 it had a Chancellor who was recognised by King and Pope. The first college to be founded was Peterhouse in 1284. The university was reorganised and granted a Charter of Incorporation by an act of Elizabeth in 1571. The colleges with their dates of foundation are Christ's (1505), Churchill (1960), Clare (1326), Clare Hall (1966), Corpus Christi (1352), Darwin (1964), Downing (1800), Emmanuel (1584), Fitzwilliam (1966), Gonville and Caius (1348), Jesus (1496), King's (1441), Magdalene (1542), Pembroke (1347), Peterhouse (1284), Queens' (1448), Robinson (1977) St. Catharine's (1473), St. Edmund's House (1896), St. John's (1511), Selwyn (1882), Sidney Sussex (1596), Trinity (1546), Trinity Hall (1350), Wolfson (1965). The women's colleges are: Girton (1869), Newnham (1871), New Hall (1954), Hughes Hall (formerly Cambridge T. C.) (1885), and Lucy Cavendish Collegiate Society (1965) (for women research students and other graduates; took undergraduates in 1970s). Women were admitted to degrees (though not allowed to sit for examination) in 1920, and to full membership of the University in 1948. All colleges now admit both men and women.

Camel, a large ruminant quadruped, inhabiting Asia and Africa, where it is largely used as a beast of burden. There are two species—the Arabian camel or dromedary, with only one hump; and the Bactrian, or double-humped camel. There are no wild dromedaries, and the only wild bactrians occur in the Gobi Desert. The camel is able to go for long periods without water, not, as was formerly believed, because it stored water in its hump, but because of the unique mechanism of its physiology which enables it to conserve water at the expense of not sweating until 40°C is reached.

Campanile, or bell-tower, is separate from but usually adjoining its parent church. The most famous are in Italy. Giotto's tower at Florence, adjoining the cathedral of Santa Maria del Fiore, is architecturally the finest in the world. Others are at Cremona, the loftiest in Italy (110 m) and Pisa (the leaning tower). The magnificent pointed campanile of St. Mark's, Venice, which collapsed in 1902 and has since been rebuilt in its original form, was begun in 902.

Canal, an artificial watercourse used for navigation which changes its level by means of locks. The completion of the Bridgewater Canal in 1761 to take coal from Worsley to Manchester marked the beginning of canal building in industrial Britain. There are over 4,000 km of navigable inland waterways in Great Britain today, c. 3,220 km of which are under the control of British Waterways The English network is based on the four great estuaries, Mersey, Humber, Severn and Thames. Many canals are now being developed for boating, fishing and other leisure pursuits.

Candela unit of luminous intensity, symbol cd. An idea of the value which this unit represents may be gained from the fact that light obtained from a 40 W filament-type electric lamp or bulb is approximately the same as would be given by a point source of luminous intensity 30 cd. See **S.I. units, F66.**

Candlemas, an English and Roman Church festival in celebration of the Purification of the Virgin Mary. The date is 2 February.

Cannabis, a bushy plant found wild in many parts of the world. A 'soft drug', its use is illegal in Britain.

Canon, a term applied to signify a recognised rule for the guide of conduct in matters legal, ecclesiastical and artistic, or an authoritative ordinance: thus we have Canonical Scriptures, Canon Law, etc. A Canon is also a dignitary of the Church, usually a member of a cathedral chapter in the Anglican communion, or in the Roman Church a member of an order standing between regular monks and secular clergy.

Canonical Hours were seven in number in the Western Church; Matins and Lauds, before dawn; Prime, early morning service; Terce, 9 a.m.; Sext, noon; Nones, 3 p.m.; Vespers, 4 p.m.; Compline, bed-time.

Canonisation, the entering of one of the faithful departed on the list of saints of the Roman Catholic Church. The rules governing canonisation were simplified by papal decree in 1969. The forty English martyrs, of whom Edmund Campion was one, executed between 1535 and 1679 and beatified long ago, were canonised in 1970. Beatification, by which a person is called blessed, is usually followed by canonisation, but not necessarily.

Canticles, the name given to the scriptural passages from the Bible sung by the congregation in the various Christian liturgies. They are the *Benedicite, Benedictus, Magnificat, Nunc Dimittis.*

Capercaillie, the largest of the grouse family, found in the Scottish highlands and the pine forests and mountainous regions of Northern and Central Europe and Asia. The bird was reintroduced to Scotland in 1874. Now (1994) its numbers are down to 2,000.

Capet, the family name of the royal house of France, founded by Hugh Capet in 987, with its collateral branches. The main line of the dynasty came to an end in 1328 with the death of Charles IV when the throne passed to the related house of Valois. The direct Valois line ended in 1498 with the death of Charles VIII. The first of the Bourbon line was Henry IV whose descendants ruled France (except during the Revolution and the Napoleonic era) until 1848.

Capitalism. See **Section J.**

Capuchins are members of a mendicant order of Franciscans, founded in the 16th cent. with the aim of restoring the primitive and stricter observance of the rule of St. Francis, so called from the capuce (pointed cowl) worn by them.

Carat, a term used in assessing the value of gold and precious stones. In connection with gold, it represents the proportion of pure gold contained in any gold alloy, and for this purpose the metal is divided into 24 parts. Thus 24-carat indicates pure gold, and any lesser number of carats shows the proportion of gold contained in the alloy. The carat as a measure of weight is now obsolete, having been replaced by the *metric carat* of 0·2 grams.

Caravan, a band of travellers or traders journeying together for safety across the Eastern deserts, sometimes numbering many hundreds. There are several allusions to caravans in the Old Testament. The great caravan routes of this period from Egypt to Babylon and from Palestine to Yemen linked up with the Syrian ports and so with Western sea commerce. Many wars have been fought in the past over their control.

Carbohydrates. See **Diet, Section P.**

Carbon, a non-metallic chemical element no. 6, symbol C, which occurs in crystalline form as diamonds and graphite; amorphous forms of carbon include charcoal and soot, while coke consists mainly of elementary carbon. The biochemistry of plants and animals largely hinges upon carbon compounds. The study of carbon compounds is called Organic Chemistry. **Carbon 14.** A radioactive isotope of carbon, with a half-life c. 6,000 years, used in following the path of compounds and their assimilation in the body. Also used in determination of the age of carbon-containing materials such as trees, fossils and very old documents.

Carbonari, members of a secret political society originating in Naples, and at one time very numerous. Their chief aim was to free Italy from foreign rule, and they exerted considerable influence in the various revolutionary movements in the first half of the 19th cent. Their name was adopted from the charcoal-burners (*carbonari*), and their passwords, signs, etc., were all in the phraseology of the fraternity.

Carbon dioxide. Commonest of the oxides of carbon. It is formed when carbon and its compounds are burnt with abundant supply of air, and when carbon compounds are oxidised in the respiration process of animals. The atmosphere contains carbon dioxide to the extent of about 325 ppm and is increasing by about 1 ppm per year, principally because of the burning of fossil fuels and possibly because of deforestation which not only leaves more oxidisible material but lowers the amount of carbon dioxide removed by photosynthesis (**F32**).

Carbon monoxide is a colourless gas with no taste or smell. It is formed when coal and coke are burnt with a restricted supply of air; the blue flame to be seen in a coke brazier, for instance, is the flame of carbon monoxide. This gas is very poisonous, forming with the haemoglobin of the blood a compound which is useless for respiration and cherry red in colour, which gives a visible sympton of poisoning by carbon monoxide. With nickel it forms a volatile compound, called nickel carbonyl, and this reaction is the basis of the Mond process for extracting nickel.

Cardinal, one of the chief dignitaries of the Roman Catholic Church who constitute the Pope's council, or Sacred College, and when the papal chair is vacant elect by secret ballot a Pope from among themselves. There are three orders: cardinal bishops, members of the Roman Curia (the central administration of the Church) and bishops of sees near Rome; cardinal deacons, also members of the Curia, holding titular bishoprics; and cardinal priests who exercise pastoral duties over sees removed from Rome, though some are members of the Curia. Pope John Paul I, who had been elected in Aug. 1978 to succeed Pope Paul VI, died suddenly after only 33 days. He was succeeded by Pope John Paul II (Cardinal Karol Wojtyla, Archbishop of Cracow). Pope John Paul II created 30 new cardinals in 1994. The College of Cardinals comprises 120 members eligible to elect a new pope. Papal insignia were trimmed of embellishment by papal decree in 1969 with the abolition, subsequently revoked, of the famous red hat (the galero) and the shoes with buckles. Cardinals must now retire at 80.

Cardinal Virtues, according to Plato these were justice, prudence, temperance, fortitude—*natural* virtues as distinct from the *theological* virtues of the Roman Catholic Church, faith, hope, charity. The phrase "seven cardinal virtues", combining the two, figures in mediaeval literature. *See* Sins, Seven Deadly.

Caribou, the reindeer (*see* **L104**) of North America.

Carmelites, a body of mendicant friars taking their name from Mount Carmel, where the order was first established in the 12th cent. The original rule of the order required absolute poverty, abstinence from meat and a hermit life. The rigidity of the rule of the order was mitigated by Innocent IV. They wear a brown habit with white mantle, hence their name of White Friars. The order of Carmelite nuns was instituted in the 15th cent.

Carolingians, dynasty of Frankish rulers founded in the 7th cent. The family was at its height when represented by Charlemagne. It ruled, with interruptions, until 987 when the Capetian dynasty succeeded.

Carp, a well-known fresh-water fish, found in plenty in most European and Asiatic still waters; reaches a length of about 60 cm and under favourable conditions lives for about 40 years. Familiar British members of the family are the roach, rudd, dace, chub, gudgeon, tench, minnow, barbel, bream and bleak. The goldfish, popular in ornamental ponds, is the domesticated variety of a Far Eastern member of the carp family.

Carthusians, an order of monks founded in 1084 by St. Bruno at the Grande Chartreuse near Grenoble, and introduced into England about a century later. They built the Charterhouse (corruption of Chartreuse) in London in 1371. The chief characteristics of the order are a separate dwelling-house in the precincts of the charterhouse for each monk, and the general assembly in the Church twice in the day and once at night. They wear a white habit, with white scapular and hood. The liqueur *Chartreuse* was invented by the order and is still their valuable secret. The order of Carthusian nuns dates from the 12th cent.

Casein, the chief protein in milk and cheese. It is coagulated by the action of rennet or acid. An important class of plastics ("casein plastics") are produced from it, and these plastics are converted into buttons, kitting-needles, etc. 36,000 litres of milk yield about 1 tonne of casein.

Cassowary, a genus of ostrich-like birds which, together with the emu, forms a separate order found only in Australasia. All species are black, with brightly coloured necks, and with a horny crest on the head. Noted for fleetness.

Castor-oil Plant (*Ricinus communis*), an African shrub now cultivated in most tropical countries. It has broad palmate leaves and bears a spiny fruit containing seeds which when pressed yield the well-known oil.

Cat, the general name for all members of the class *Felidae* of the carnivorous order, from the lion down to the domestic cat. The latter is believed to be descended from the European and African wild cats. Egypt is credited with being the first country in which the cat was domesticated.

Catabolism, Anabolism, are the terms used to describe the two types of metabolic pathway. Catabolic pathways are routes by which large organic molecules are broken up by enzymes into their simpler constituents *e.g.*, starch into glucose. The anabolic pathways are the routes by which complex molecules are synthesised from simple sub-units, *e.g.*, proteins from amino acids.

Catalyst. A substance which alters the rate of reaction without itself being chemically changed. Various aluminium and titanium compounds are catalysts in the formation of polythene from ethylene. Palladium catalyses the reaction of hydrogen with oxygen (hence its use in gas lighters). Enzymes in the body hasten the breakdown of carbohydrates and proteins by catalytic action. *See* **F26**.

Cataracts are gigantic waterfalls. The most famous are those of Niagara in North America, the Orinoco in South America, the Victoria Falls on the Zambesi in Africa, and the Falls of the Rhine at Schaffhausen.

Catechism, an elementary book of principles in any science or art, but more particularly in religion, in the form of questions and answers. There is a great variety of these, including the Lutheran, prepared by Luther in 1529, Calvin's Geneva (in 1536), and the Anglican, in the Book of Common Prayer.

Caterpillar, the larva of a butterfly or moth, worm-like in its segmented body, with 3 pairs of jointed true legs, often curiously marked and coloured, and frequently more or less hairy.

Cathedral, the chief church of a diocese, so called from its containing a Bishop's seat, or episcopal chair. The town in which it is situated is a cathedral city. Some celebrated cathedrals are St. John Lateran of Rome, Notre Dame of Paris, the cathedrals of Cologne and Milan, St. Paul's in London, Canterbury Cathedral, York Minster, and the cathedrals of Durham, Bristol, Gloucester, Peterborough, Exeter, Liverpool, and Coventry (destroyed by bombs, now rebuilt),

Catholicism. *See* Section J.

Cat's eye, a kind of quartz, much valued as a gem, opalescent, and of various shades.

Cavalier, a name adopted during the troubles of the Civil War to designate the Royalist party; it is also used generally in reference to a knightly, gallant or imperious personage.

Caves, natural hollow places in the earth, frequently found in Carboniferous limestone areas. The underground caves are formed by the action of rainwater carrying carbon dioxide, a dilute acid which slowly attacks the limestone rocks. The main caves in the British Isles are in the Mendips, Derbyshire, Yorkshire, S. Wales and in County Clare. Many British inland caves are thought to have been formed at the end of the Ice Age when there was a rise in the water table. The floods of September 1968 moved masses of débris in some of the British caves, redistributing it in a major way; new routes were blocked and old passages reopened. The scientific study of caves is known as spelaeology.

Caviar. *See under* Sturgeon.

Cedar, a dark-leaved, cone-bearing, horizontal-branched evergreen tree that grows to a considerable height and girth, the best known species in Britain being the Cedar of Lebanon, which was introduced in the 17th cent.

Celluloid, one of the first synthetic thermoplastic materials, discovered by Alexander Parkes in 1865 when he was attempting to produce synthetic horn. It is made by treating cellulose nitrate with camphor and alcohol. Photographic film is made of a similar, but less-inflammable material, formed by the use of cellulose acetate instead of the nitrate.

Cellulose, a carbohydrate, and a constituent of nearly all plants. Cellulose occurs in an almost pure state in the fibres of linen (flax), absorbent cotton, jute, and filter-paper (used in laboratories).

Celsius was an 18th cent. Swedish scientist (**B13**) after whom the modern Celsius temperature scale is named. Since 1954, °C stands for "degree Celsius" instead of "degree Centigrade" but this is only a change in name. Both symbols refer to the temperature scale which calls the melting point of ice 0°C and the boiling point of water at one atmosphere pressure 100°C. *See* Absolute Temperature.

Celts, an ancient race found late in the third millennium B.C. in S.W. Germany, united by a common language and culture, who spread westward into Spain, northward into Britain, eastward to the Black Sea, reaching Galatia in Asia Minor. The "La Tène" iron-age Celts invaded Britain *c.* 250 B.C. After Britain was conquered by the Romans and invaded by the Angles and Saxons there remained as areas of Celtic speech only Wales (Brythonic speakers), Ireland, Scotland, the Isle of Man (Gaelic speakers), and in Cornwall. The late Celtic period in Britain produced a distinctive Christian art (*e.g.*, the Lindisfarne Gospel *c*, 700, and the Irish Book of Kells, dating from about the same time). Surviving Celtic languages are Welsh, Irish, Breton, Scots Gaelic and a tiny Cornish tradition. Manx Gaelic is on the point of extinction.

Centrifuge, a machine which produces large accelerations by utilising the radial force caused by rotating a body about a fixed centre. Centrifuges have found extensive application in modern science. They can be used for the separation of one size of particle from another in biochemistry or in the training of astronauts where the accelerations occurring during rocket lift off can be simulated in a centrifuge on the ground.

Ceramics, are substances in which a combination of one or more metals with oxygen confers special and valuable properties. These include hardness, and resistance to heat and chemicals. Ceramic comes from the Greeek word for pottery, and pottery materials of mud and clay were probably the first man-made ceramics. Nowadays the range is enormous and growing; apart from all the pottery materials, there are fire-bricks, gems, glasses, concretes, nuclear reactor fuel elements, special materials for electronic devices, coloured pigments, electrical insulators, abrasives, and many other things. The scientific study of ceramics is part of materials science (*see* **Materials Science**). The need to design ceramic objects has inspired great art, and the production of ceramics has become a major industry.

Cerium, a scarce metallic element, no. 58, symbol Ce, discovered by Berzelius in 1803. A mixture of cerium and thorium nitrates is used in the manufacture of gas mantles, which owe their incandescent property to the deposit of cerium and thorium oxide with which they are coated.

Cern, French acronym for the European Laboratory for Particle Physics in Geneva. In 1989, the Large Electron Positron collider (LEP) was opened there. It recreates the swirl of matter just after the 'Big Bang' which scientists believe created the universe 15 billion years ago.

Chain reaction. *See* **F13(1).**

Chalcedony, a mixture of crystalline silica and amorphous hydrated silica, *i.e.*, of quartz and opal. It has a waxy lustre, and is much used by jewellers for necklaces, bracelets, etc. Commonly it is white or creamy. Its bright orange-red variety is called carnelian; its brown variety, sard. Chrysoprase, plasma, bloodstone are varieties which are respectively pale apple-green, dark leek-green, green with red spots.

Chalk, a white limestone, calcium carbonate, found in the Upper Cretaceous deposits (formed from the shells of minute marine organisms). As chalk is porous, few streams form on its surface and consequently it is eroded slowly, although generally speaking it is a soft rock. Its juxtaposition with soft impervious clay in some areas results in its forming steep ridges known as escarpments, *e.g.*, N. and S. Downs and Chilterns. In contrast to the dry upland surfaces of chalk, lower levels are frequently saturated with water which emerges as springs.

Chamberlain, Lord, the senior officer of The Royal Household who is responsible for all ceremonial within the palace (levées, courts, garden parties, entertainment of foreign royalties and heads of state) but not the coronation or state opening of parliament. He is also in charge of appointments to The Royal Household. His office as censor of plays was abolished in 1968.

Chamberlain, Lord Great, one of the great officers of state whose duties are now mainly ceremonial. He attends the monarch at the state opening of parliament and at the coronation and is custodian of the Palace of Westminster (Houses of Parliament). The office is hereditary, dating from Norman times, and is held for one reign in turn by the descendants of the De Veres, Earls of Oxford. The present Lord Great Chamberlain is the Marquess of Cholmondeley.

Chameleon, a family of lizards with numerous species. Their ability to change colour is well known, but exaggerated, and is due to the movement of pigment cells beneath the skin. They are slow in movement, arboreal, and mainly insectivorous. Found in Africa, India, Sri Lanka, Madagascar and Arabia.

Chamois, a species of antelope, native of Western Europe and Asia. About the size of a goat, it lives in mountainous regions, and possesses wonderful leaping power, so that it is very difficult to capture. Its flesh is much esteemed, and from its skin chamois leather is made, although today sheep and goat skins are usually substituted. The mating season is October-November and the fawns are born in May or June. Live to be 20–25 years old.

Channel Tunnel, a scheme to bore a tunnel through 32–48 km of chalk under the sea between Dover and Calais has been a subject for discussion ever since Albert Mathieu first conceived the idea as a practical possibility in 1802. In the 1830s proposals for a bridge were made. In the 1980s plans for a cross channel fixed link

began to surface again although it was stated clearly that the project would have to be entirely financed from private capital. The British and French Governments called for the submission of plans for a fixed link by November 1985.

The announcement in January 1986 of the intention by Britain and France to construct a 31-mile tunnel under the Channel between Cheriton, Kent and Frethun in northern France has brought the idea of a Channel Tunnel very close to realisation. According to the original plans, by May 1993 a direct "fixed link" would be ready for travellers. Delays have put back this date. Bitter controversy has surrounded the route of the proposed high-speed rail link (finally announced in March 1993, with St Pancras as the proposed terminal). The tunnel (which is the longest underwater tunnel in the world) was officially opened on 6 May 1994 by the Queen and President Mitterrand but fare-paying passenger services did not start until 14 November 1994.

Chapel Royal, the church dedicated to the use of the Sovereign and Court. There are, among others, chapels royal at St. James's Palace, Buckingham Palace, Windsor, Hampton Court, the Tower, and Holyrood. *See also* **E4(2).**

Charcoal, a term applied to wood that has been subjected to a process of slow smothered combustion. More generally it refers to the carbonaceous remains of vegetable, animal, or combustible mineral substances submitted to a similar process. Charcoal from special woods (in particular buckthorn) is used in making gunpowder. Bone charcoal finds use in sugar refining, as it removes dark colouring matter present in the crude syrup.

Charter '88, pressure group working for major constitutional reform, including a Bill of Rights, fair electoral system, democratic Upper House *etc.*

Chasuble, a sleeveless vestment worn by ecclesiastics over the alb during the celebration of Mass (to symbolise the seamless coat of Christ).

Cheese, an article of food made from the curd of milk, which is separated from the whey and pressed in moulds and gradually dried. There are about 500 varieties differing with method of preparation and quality of milk. They used to be made in the regions after which they are named but nowadays many of them are massproduced, *e.g.*, Cheddar is made not only in all parts of Britain but in Canada, New Zealand, Australia, Holland and the USA. Cheeses may be divided into 3 main classes: (1) soft, *e.g.*, Camembert, Cambridge, l'Evêque; (2) blue-veined, *e.g.*, Stilton, Gorgonzola, Roquefort (made from ewe's milk), (3) hard-pressed, *e.g.*, Cheddar, Cheshire, Gruyère, Parmesan, Gouda.

Cheetah or "hunting leopard", the large spotted cat of Africa and Southern Asia, the swiftest four-footed animal alive.

Chemical Warfare. This term is usually restricted to mean the use in war of anti-personnel gases, aerosols and smokes, although explosives, napalm, herbicides and defoliants are also chemical agents that are used in war.

The first occasion when poison gas was used on a large scale was in the first world war; more than 100,000 fatalities resulted from the use of principally chlorine, phosgene and mustard gas. Worldwide revulsion at the hideous effects of chemical weapons and their potential as indiscriminate weapons of mass destruction resulted in the Geneva Protocol of 1925 which prohibited the use of both chemical and bacteriological weapons. It has now been ratified by over 90 nations including all the major powers (although Japan and America are only recent signatories). The Protocol has been generally well observed although notable violations have been by the Italians in Abyssinia (1935–6), the Japanese in China during the second world war, the Americans in S.E. Asia in the 1960s and Iraq (against the Kurds in the 1980s).

Chemistry is the science of the elements and their compounds. It is concerned with the laws of their combination and behaviour under various conditions. It had its roots in alchemy and has gradually developed into a science of vast magnitude and importance. Organic chemistry deals with the chemistry of the compounds of carbon; inorganic chemistry is concerned with the chemistry of the elements; physical chemistry is concerned with the study of chemical reactions and with the theories and laws of chemistry. *See* **F23–8.**

Chernobyl Disaster Site in the Ukraine of 1986 Soviet nuclear disaster, which caused major radioactive fallout across many countries. The scale of the disaster (the Atomic Energy Authority estimated in 1991 that it would cause 40,000 cancer deaths world-wide) was kept from the Russian people.

Chestnut, the fruit of trees of the genus *Castanea*, members of the family *Fagaceae*. C. *sativa* is the sweet or Spanish chestnut, C. *dentata* the American chestnut and C. *crenata* the Japanese chestnut. The nut is edible. The wood is used in carpentry and fencing. *See also* **Horse Chestnut.**

Chiaroscuro, a term used in painting to denote the disposition of light and shade. Rembrandt is unrivalled as a painter for his contrasts of light and shadows.

Children Act (1989) was the outcome of numerous child-abuse scandals (*e.g.* Cleveland). It has two main elements, namely parents' rights and responsibilities and children's rights and welfare. The child's welfare is of paramount concern.

Chiltern Hundreds, three hundreds—Stoke, Burnham and Desborough—the stewardship of which is now a nominal office under the Chancellor of the Exchequer. Since about 1750 the nomination to it has been used as a method of enabling a member of Parliament to resign his seat on the plea that he holds an office of honour and profit under the crown. An alternate symbolic post for an M.P. giving up his seat is the stewardship of the Manor of Northstead in Yorkshire.

Chimpanzee, a large anthropoid ape, a native of tropical Africa, of a dark brown colour, with arms reaching to the knee, and capable of walking upright. Its brain is about a third of the weight of the human brain, but is anatomically similar. The animal has considerable intelligence and powers of learning.

Chinchilla, a South American burrowing rodent. Grey in colour, and white underneath. It is greatly esteemed for its beautiful fur.

Chippendale Furniture was introduced in the reign of George I by Thomas Chippendale, a cabinetmaker from Yorkshire who migrated to London and set up for himself in St. Martin's Lane, Charing Cross. He was fonder of inventing designs for furniture than of making it, and in 1752 published a book of patterns; the London furniture-makers of the day soon began to model their work upon it.

Chivalry an international brotherhood of knights formed primarily during the 13th cent. to fight against the infidels in the Crusades. For the French the major battle was against the Moslems in the Holy Land and North Africa, the Spaniards fought the same enemy in their own country, and the Germans were concerned with the heathen of Baltic lands, but Chaucer's "very perfect gentle knight" had fought in all these areas. One did not easily become a knight who had to be of noble birth and then pass through a period of probation, beginning as a boy page in the castle of some great lord, serving his elders and betters humbly while he was taught good manners, singing, playing musical instruments, and the composition of verse. Probably he learned Latin, but he certainly learned French, which was the international language of knights as Latin was of scholars. At fourteen he became a squire and learned to fight with sword, battle-axe and lance, and to endure conditions of hard living while carrying out his duties of waiting on his lord, looking after his horses, and in time accompanying him in battle. Only if he showed himself suitable was he finally knighted by a stroke of the hand or sword on the shoulder from the king or lord. Knighthood was an international order and had its special code of behaviour; to honour one's sworn word, to protect the weak, to respect women, and defend the Faith.

Chlorine, a gaseous element, no. 17, symbol Cl, of the halogen family, first isolated in 1774 by Scheele by the action of manganese dioxide in hydrochloric acid. It unites easily with many other elements, the compounds resulting being termed chlorides. The gaseous element is greenish-yellow, with a pungent odour. It is a suffocating gas, injuring the lungs at a concentration as low as 1 part in 50,000, and was used during the first world war as a poison gas. Has a powerful bleaching action, usually being used in form of bleaching powder, made by combining lime and chlorine.

Chloroform, a volatile colourless liquid, compounded of carbon, hydrogen, and chlorine. It is a powerful solvent, not naturally occurring but synthesised on a large scale. When the vapour is inhaled it produces unconsciousness and insensibility to pain. It owes its discovery to Liebig, and its first application for medical purposes to Sir James Young Simpson.

Chlorophyll, the green pigment contained in the leaves of plants, first discovered by P. J. Pelletier (1788–1829) and J. B. Caventou (1795–1877) in 1818. Enables the plant to absorb sunlight and so to build up sugar. The total synthesis of chlorophyll was reported in 1960 by Prof. R. B. Woodward. This was an outstanding achievement in the field of organic chemistry. *See* **Photosynthesis, F32(1).**

Chouans, the name given to the band of peasants, mainly smugglers and dealers in contraband salt, who rose in revolt in the west of France in 1793 and joined the royalists of La Vendée. Balzac gives a picture of the people and the country in which they operated in his novel *Les Chouans*. They used the hoot of an owl as a signal—hence the name.

Chough, a member of the crow family, of glossy blue-green-black plumage, whose long curved bill and legs are coral red. It used to be abundant on the cliffs of Cornwall, but its haunts are now restricted to the rocky outcrops of the western coasts and in the mountains near by. It nests in cleft rocks and caves. The Alpine chough with yellow bill inhabits the mountainous districts of Europe and Asia and is not found in Britain. It was found at *c.* 8,200 m on Everest.

Christmas means "mass of Christ" from the old English *Cristes maesse*, which is celebrated by the Western church on 25 December. The actual day on which Christ was born is not known and there is some uncertainty about the year. 25 December as the day of Nativity was not generally observed until the 5th cent. A.D., though, as the winter solstice, it had long been observed as a pagan festival of *sol invictus* (unconquered sun). The first Christmas card dates from about 1843 and the Christmas tree, of pagan origin, was introduced into England from Germany where it had been a tradition since the Middle Ages. Santa Claus is a corruption of Santa Nikolaus (St. Nicholas) patron saint of children, whose feast day is on 6 December.

Chromium, a very hard, bluish-white metal element, no. 24, symbol Cr, melting at very high temperature (above 1,900°C). Its chief ore is chromite or chrome iron-ore (ferrous chromite). "Ferro-chrome" is produced by heating chromite and anthracite in an electric furnace, and chrome steels are prepared by adding the pre-calculated amount of ferro-chrome to melted steel. Best known chrome steel is stainless steel first made by Brearley in 1912 and since then developed greatly at Sheffield. A typical formula is 18 per cent. chromium, 8 per cent, nickel, 74 per cent. iron. Equally important are Stellite alloys, containing chromium, cobalt, tungsten (or molybdenum), which have made possible modern high-speed cutting tools. Dies used in manufacture of plastics are commonly of chrome steel. The elementary metal finds little use alone except in chromium-plating for motor cars, etc.

Chromosomes, the structures contained within the nucleus of every animal and plant cell by which genetic information is transmitted. The chromosome number in somatic (body) cells is constant for each species of plant and animal, *e.g.*, man (46), cat (38), mouse (40) honey bee (16), fruit fly *Drosophila* (8), potato (48). Chromosomes are long molecules composed of deoxyribonucleoproteins (*i.e.*, proteins and DNA). Human chromosomes have been the subject of much recent research since it has been found that certain disorders are associated with chromosomal aberration, *e.g.*, in Mongolism an extra chromosome is present. *See also* **Genes, Chromosome Theory (F31), Cell Division (F34).**

Church Commissioners. The Church Commissioners were established in 1948 by the amalgamation of Queen Anne's Bounty (established

1704) and the Ecclesiastical Commissioners (established 1836) to administer Church revenues and to manage Church property.

Cid, El, a famous Spanish hero of the 11th cent., Don Rodrigo Diaz de Vivar, also called Cid Campeador, whose exploits, against Christians and Moors alike, are celebrated in poem and play.

Cilia, minute hair-like projections on the surface of some cells, which beat together in wavelike movements like the wind over a corn-field. These movements can be used as a means of locomotion as in the aquatic organism paramecium. Cilia are also found on the outer layers of the human trachea where they waft particles upwards to the throat, thus protecting the lungs. See **F37, Index to Section P** and **Flagella.**

Cinque Ports, a number of seaport towns on the coast of Kent and Sussex, originally five; Hastings, New Romney, Hythe, Dover and Sandwich. Winchelsea and Rye were added later. These ports were required to furnish a certain number of ships, ready for service, and in return they were granted many privileges. The official residence of the Lord Warden is Walmer Castle, near Dover. The holder of the office is the Queen Mother, the first-ever woman to be appointed.

Cistercians, an order of monks and nuns taking their names from Citeaux, near Dijon, where their first monastery was established in 1098. The order was noted for the severity of its rule. They were famous agriculturists. The habit is white, with a black cowl or hood.

City Technology Colleges (CTCs), new concept of educational institute introduced by the Conservative Government after 1987. The first three to be opened were at Solihull, Nottingham and Middlesbrough.

Civil List is the estimate of the expenses to be incurred by the Sovereign in conducting her official business and engagements and those of the members of her family during each year. The amount is granted by Parliament upon the recommendation of a Select Committee and has to be settled afresh in the first six months of a new reign. The Civil List of Queen Victoria was £385,000; Edward VII and George V, £470,000; Edward VIII and George VI, £410,000; Elizabeth II £475,000. In 1990, a fixed 10-year Civil List arrangement was agreed for all the Royal Family. This was changed in 1992 so that only the Queen (£7·9m), the Queen Mother (£643,000) and Prince Philip (£359,000) continued to receive annual Civil List payments.

The Prince of Wales does not receive a Civil List payment but derives his revenue from the Duchy of Cornwall. Other resources available to the Queen include (1) the sums which Parliament votes to government departments each year, e.g., upkeep of palaces (Dept. of the Environment) royal yacht Britannia and the royal flight (Min. of Defence); (2) privy purse (revenues of the Duchy of Lancaster); (3) personal fortune, the size of which is not disclosed. In 1992 the Queen agreed to pay tax on her private income and meet the working expenses of most junior members of the Royal Family. The system under which annual payments are made by the Government to the Queen was changed by the Civil List Act 1975; payments are now included in the annual estimates in the same way as the expenditure of a government department, and subject to scrutiny in the House of Commons.

Cleopatra's Needle on the Thames Embankment is of the time of Tuthmosis III (1500–1450 B.C.). The monolith had nothing to do with Cleopatra, as it only came to Alexandria after her death. It was first erected at the Biblical On (Greek Heliopolis), sacred City of the Sun. It was presented to the British Government by Mehemet Ali in 1819, but not brought to this country until 1878. Weight c. 183 tonnes; height, 20·8 m.

Climate has been defined by Professor H. H. Lamb as the total experience of the weather at any place over some specific period of time. Not only averages but extremes of temperature, variation of humidity, duration of sunshine and cloud cover, amount of rainfall and frequency of snow, frost, gales, etc., are amongst the data normally investigated. The interiors of great land masses are characterised by large ranges of temperature and low rainfall (continental climate), while proximity to oceans has an ameliorating effect with increase in rainfall (oceanic climate). Presence of mountain ranges and lakes and configuration generally produce local modifications of climate, also apparent between the centre and the outlying suburbs of a city. Latitude introduces zones of climate, e.g., tropical rain, subtropical steppe and desert, temperate rain and polar. The climate is always changing in greater or less degree. Every year, every decade, every century brings a somewhat different experience. The tendency between 1880 and 1940 was for most parts of the world to become warmer. See also **Section Y** for such issues as the 'greenhouse' effect.

Clock, a device for measuring the passage of time. The earliest timekeeper was the shadow-clock, a primitive form of sundial, used in Ancient Egypt about 1500 B.C. To find the time at night the water clock or clepsydra was used. The sand-glass dates from the 15th cent. No one knows when the first mechanical clocks were invented, but it is known that a complicated mechanical clock driven by water and controlled by a weighbridge escarpment was built in Peking in 1090. The Dover Clock in the Science Museum is not the earliest surviving clock in England, as was once believed, but early 17th cent. The Salisbury Cathedral clock dates from 1386 and that of Wells Cathedral from 1392. The pendulum clock was invented by the Dutch scientist Christiaan Huygens (1625–95). The first watches were made in Nuremberg shortly after 1500. The marine chronometer is a high-precision timepiece used at sea for giving Greenwich mean time. The quartz-crystal clocks are accurate to one thousandth of a second a day, and the improved atomic clock, developed at the British National Physical Laboratory, which makes use of the natural vibrations of the caesium atom, is an almost absolute measure of time. Its accuracy of 1 sec. in 300 years has been improved to 1 sec. in 1,000 years.

Cloud Chamber, an apparatus invented by C. T. R. Wilson in which the tracks of atomic particles can be made visible. Just as the vapour trails tell of the track of an invisible aircraft high up in the air, so the vapour trails of an unseeable particle can tell of its behaviour. The rays under investigation pass through a chamber containing a gas, e.g., air thoroughly cleansed of dust, supersaturated with water, or alcohol-vapour. As the particle passes through it forms a track of tiny water droplets which can be photographed. After a long and honourable history this wonderful instrument is now virtually obsolete. A later ingenious device for tracking fast fundamental particles is the Bubble chamber (q.v.).

Clouds are formed by the cooling of moist air, the type depending on the way the air cools and the height at which condensation occurs. There are three main classes: (1) high cloud (about 6,100 m)—cirrus (delicate and fibrous), cirrostratus (thin white veil), and cirrocumulus (delicately rippled) consisting of ice crystals; (2) medium cloud (above 2,100 m)—altostratus (dense, greyish veil) and altocumulus (broken flattened cloudlets)—chiefly water particles, often supercooled; (3) low cloud (from near ground to 2,100 m)—cumulus (fair weather, broken, dome-topped), cumulominbus (heavy, towering to great heights), stratocumulus (layer of globular masses or rolls), stratus (like fog but off the ground), nimbostratus (low, rainy cloud). The highest clouds of all, and the rarest, are the noctilucent, seen only on summer nights in high latitudes. They form at about 80 km above the earth and consist of ice-coated dust from meteors.

Clover, plants of the *Trifolium* genus, family *Leguminosae*, with about 250 species. These are "nitrogen fixing" plants and include red clover, white clover, alsike clover and crimson clover. They are of great importance in agriculture because in a good pasture they supply directly or indirectly most of the protein available to the animals. Seed of "wild white" clover has been accepted since about 1939 as the indispensable plant of good United Kingdom grassland, largely through the efforts of pioneers like D. A. Gilchrist (1859–1927).

Coal. Until recently the most important single fuel has been coal. It is a mineral of organic origin, formed from the remains of vegetation which over millions of years has changed to coal by the effects of heat and pressure from overlying rock or water. All coal contains moisture, inflammable volatiles, mineral impurities (some of which remain as coal ash after the coal is burnt), and fixed carbon (the coke that is left after the volatiles have been driven off). The relative proportions vary—from Anthracite, a hard coal containing the highest proportion of fixed carbon, to Lignite or brown coal which is little more than a hard peat. World reserves of bituminous coal have been estimated at 7.5×10^{12} tonnes. If one adds the reserves of brown coal and lignite, this figure is increased by about 15 per cent. The proportion of the reserves that could be economically recovered varies from country to country and estimates vary from 50 to 100 per cent of the reserves. The reserves are highly localised—over half being located in the former Soviet Union. In the United Kingdom coal has formed the basis of past industrial prosperity. Peak output occurred in 1913 when 290 million tonnes were mined one third of which was exported. At the end of the second world war production had fallen to 186 million tonnes and was far below demand. In 1947 the British coal industry was brought under public ownership and all its assets were vested in the National Coal Board. During the next ten years great efforts were made to increase coal output but, quite suddenly in 1956, demand for coal fell as oil became a popular fuel. The fall in demand was accompanied by increasing productivity, both mines and miners having been cut in their numbers by over half. Then as a result of the high cost of oil in 1973 came expansion of the industry. From 1984 the coal industry faced a bitter strike over plans to make large-scale pit closures. The defeat of the miners weakened the NUM and its leader, Arthur Scargill. The Government decision (in 1992) to close many of the remaining collieries and to privatise the industry created a bitter political controversy. By the beginning of 1995 the last pits had been privatised and the workforce reduced to 7,000 (compared to 700,000 on nationalization in 1947).

Coat of Arms, in heraldry, a device containing a family's armorial bearings. In mediaeval times the coat upon which such device was embroidered; knights wore it over their armour.

Cobalt, element no. 27, symbol Co, a white metal melting at 1490°C. Two main ores are *cobalt glance* (in which the element is combined with arsenic and sulphur) and *smaltite* (cobalt arsenide). The principal sources are Ontario and Zaïre. Various cobalt alloys are important, *e.g.*, stellite, ferrocobalt and carboloy. Its monoxide is an important colouring medium, and is used for colouring glass and porcelain blue.

Cobra, hooded and very venomous snakes. The best known species are the Indian Cobra, the Egyptian Cobra, and the Black-necked Cobra. Their food consists chiefly of small rodents. The King Cobra is almost exclusively a snake-eater. "Spitting" Cobras (or Ringhals) of S. Africa are a related genus, capable of spitting their venom several yards.

Coca, a S. American shrub, *Erythroxylon coca*, also cultivated in Java. The leaves yield cocaine, classified as a dangerous drug. When the natives chew the leaves they are enabled to withstand hunger and fatigue, as cocaine acts both as a mental stimulant and as an anaesthetic on the mucous lining of the stomach.

Cochineal *or* **Carmine,** a dyestuff consisting of the dried bodies of the female scale insect (*Dactylopius coccus*) which feeds on cacti. Of ancient origin, the dye was well known to the Aztecs, and was used widely in the Middle Ages. The scarlet tunics worn by the English during the Napoleonic wars owed their colour to carmine.

Cockatoo, a member of the parrot family, bearing a crest of feathers on the head, native to Australia and adjacent regions. Predominant colour is white tinged with yellow or scarlet while some species have dark plumage. The cockatoo of New Guniea is slaty black with pale red cheeks and can crack Kanary nuts which require a hammer to break them open.

Cockchafer (*Melolontha*), one of the most destructive of beetles, the larvae feeding on roots. It is about 2·5 cm in length, of a brownish colour, and emits a loud whirring sound when flying.

Cockle, the popular name of the bi-valve shell-fish of the genus *Cardium*, found in sandy bays.

Cockroach, inaccurately called the "black beetle"; a pest of bakeries and kitchens. In Britain two species are commonly found; the Common Cockroach (*Blatta orientalis*), resident since the time of Elizabeth I, dark brown, about 2·5 cm long, with the wing covers long in the male and short in the female; and the German Cockroach (*Blatta germanica*), now the most common, half the size, dark yellow, with both sexes fully winged. All species have long antennae and flattened, leathery, shiny bodies. They are nocturnal and omnivorous.

Coconut Palm (*Cocos nucifera*), a tropical tree, growing to a height of 30 m, with a slender trunk surmounted by giant feather-like leaves. One of the most important sources of food and raw material for people living in the tropics. The juice of the fruit, or coconut, is drunk; the kernel is eaten fresh or dried to form copra, which yields animal feeding stuffs and oil, used in the manufacture of soap, margarine, cosmetics, synthetic rubber, etc.; leaves are used for thatching; leaf stalks for canes, fence posts, needles, etc., and the trunk for houses and bridges. Main producing areas: Indonesia, Philippines, Malaysia, Sri Lanka and S. India.

Codes, a term used to designate a system of laws properly classified. The Code of Hammurabi, king of Babylon, *c.* 1751 B.C., had extensive influence over a long period. The Romans formulated several codes of historic importance including the Theodosian Code which summarised the Roman laws from the time of Constantine to 438 A.D. The final codification was made under order of the Emperor Justinian by his chief minister Tribonian and published in 529 with a new edition in 534. The most important of modern codes is the *Code Napoléon*, compiled between 1803 and 1810, and still in force. It has been used as an example for the codification of the laws of a number of countries from America to Japan. Under Frederick the Great the law of Prussia was codified. English law has never been codified, although the law on certain subjects has been gathered up into a single statute. The Law Commission Act, 1965, was passed to consolidate and codify the law.

Codex, a manuscript volume of the Scriptures comprising the Sinaiaticus of the 4th cent., the Vatican codex of the same period, the Alexandrine codex of the 5th cent., and others. The British Museum, in 1933, purchased the *Codex Sinaiticus* from the Soviet Government for £100,000. The Sinaiaticus was written on 347 vellum leaves some fifteen to sixteen hundred years ago and the binding into 2 volumes was completed by Douglas Cockerill and his son in 1936. It was sold to an American in 1981 for $5·2 million.

Coffee, a shrub found originally in Arabia and Ethiopia, but now extensively grown in Brazil, Colombia, Ivory Coast, Uganda, Angola and Central America. It yields a seed or berry which after undergoing the necessary preparation, is ground and used in most countries as a breakfast beverage. The best coffee is the Mocha, an Arabian variety. The stimulating effect of coffee is due to the caffeine, which is also present in tea. The beverage was introduced into Europe in the 17th cent., and the first London coffee shop was opened in 1652.

Coke is the solid residue remaining when coal is carbonised and nearly all the volatile constituents have been driven off. Used as fuel, and as an agent for reducing metallic oxides to metals, *e.g.*, iron ore to iron, in the manufacture of steel.

Colorado Beetle, a serious pest of potato crops. Both adults and larvae feed on the foliage where the orange eggs are laid. The grub is reddish, with two rows of small black spots on each side. The adults are about 1·2 cm long with yellow and black striped wing cases. The beetle is avoided by birds because of its nasty taste, and is controlled by arsenical sprays.

Colosseum, the name of the Flavian amphitheatre at Rome, begun by Vespasian and finished by Titus A.D. 80. In general outline it still remains one of the most magnificent ruins in the world. In the arena of this great building the famous gladiatorial displays and mimic naval battles used to be given, and about 50,000 spectators could be accommodated.

Colossus is the name which the ancients gave to any statue of gigantic size. The Colossus at Rhodes, which was a bronze statue of the sun god, Helios, was the most famous, and reckoned among the seven wonders of the world. It stood over 30 m high at the mouth of the harbour. There is no truth in the legend that ships could pass between its legs. It fell in an earthquake in 224 B.C.

Colugo, also known as "flying lemur", caguan or kubuk, a remarkable mammal which may be regarded as an aberrant insectivore or an aberrant form of the earliest ancestor of the bats. It has nothing to do with lemurs. There are two genera, one inhabiting the Philippines and one inhabiting Malaya. They have a parachute-like membrane which covers them from the neck to the tip of the tail, by means of which they can glide from treetop to ground, a distance of up to 64 m.

Column, in architecture, is an upright solid body serving as a support or decoration to a building. Columns consist of a pedestal, a shaft, and a capital, over which the supported entablature rises. They are named according to the styles of architecture of which they form part, being Doric, Tuscan, Ionic, Corinthian or Composite as the case may be.

Comets are celestial bodies which generally move about the solar system in elongated elliptical or nearly parabolic orbits. Most comets are in the latter category, having extremely long orbital periods, up to millions of years, and have therefore only been seen once in recorded history. They spend most of their lifetimes at extremely large distances from the sun, far outside Pluto's orbit. Those in elliptical orbits appear periodically and a few have been observed regularly. Halley's comet, named after Edmund Halley, who first correctly predicted that this comet would reappear in 1758, was first observed in Roman times and is one of the brightest of the periodic comets. The nucleus of a comet, which appears as a faint star when the comet is very far from the sun, is believed to be a frozen mixture of dust and materials called "ices"—CO_2, H_2O, NH_3 and CH_4, frozen at the low temperatures in the outer solar system. Approaching the sun, the comet is heated by sunlight and the surface "ices" are first vaporised and later photo-dissociated and ionised by sunlight, also freeing the surface dust. The dust, gases and ions produce the fuzzy appearance of the coma of the comet. Under the influence of sunlight acting on dust, and the solar wind and interplanetary field acting on the ions, the cometary tail (often multiple) is produced. This may stretch up to 200 million km, pointing away from the sun. Donati's comet (1858) was possibly the most spectacular of all and was visible even in daylight. Kohoutek's comet (1975) was the first to be observed from space, by the American Skylab and Russian Soyuz, and many exciting new space studies were conducted during the last return of Halley's comet in 1985. *See also* **F4(1).**

Commons are the remnants of the mediaeval open fields round villages in which the villagers had rights in common, *e.g.*, (i) estover—the right of taking wood for house building or firewood; (ii) pasture—the right of grazing beasts; (iii) turbary—the right of digging turf; (iv) piscary—the right to fish. Many of these common lands were enclosed during the agrarian revolution which went on steadily in England from the 15th cent. onwards, and with their enclosure common rights vanished. A Royal Commission on Common Land described the commons in 1965 as the "last reservoir of uncommitted land" which provide, as far as the public is concerned, by far the largest part of the accessible open spaces of the country. Under the Commons Registration Act, 1965, it was the duty of County Councils and County Borough Councils to make a register of all common land and all town and village greens in their areas.

Commons, House of, the Lower House of the British Parliament. *See* **Section D.**

Commune of Paris has twice played a dramatic part in the history of France. In 1792 it was able, through its control of the administrative organisation of Paris, to override the National Assembly. In 1871, after the withdrawal of the Prussian troops, it tried to assert its authority. Public buildings were destroyed by members of the Commune and civil war raged during April and half May, but Government troops savagely suppressed the rising.

Community Charge, *see* Poll Tax (**L98**).

Compass *or* **Mariner's Compass.** It has been known since very early times that an iron needle, suspended freely to hang horizontally when not magnetised, comes to rest roughly along the geographical north south line when magnetised. Further, it generally does not hang horizontally. This is the essential behaviour of the *compass*, a navigational instrument whose invention is obscure but which seems to have been known to the Chinese 4,500 years ago. That the behaviour of the compass shows the existence of a *magnetic field* associated with the Earth was first fully recognised by William Gilbert in 1600. Aircraft and ships now largely employ gyrostatic compasses which are not affected by electrical and magnetic disturbances. Sperry, Brown and Anschutz are three important types of gyroscopic compass.

Composite Materials, or more simply composites, are materials which derive useful properties by combining the virtues of two or more components. Combining clay with straw to make tougher bricks is an ancient example in which fibres (straw) are embedded in a matrix or body (the clay). A modern example is fibreglass in which glass fibres are embedded in a plastic matrix. Nature also uses composites as in bamboo in which a lignin matrix binds together the fibres of cellulose to make a light strong structure. Composites may contain flakes or particles embedded in the matrix instead of fibres—it depends on the application. Although the idea is not new composite technology has made rapid strides in the last few decades guided by scientific insight into the nature of solids and the origin of their stengths and weaknesses. The motivation had been that scientifically designed composites offer materials with exceptional strength/weight ratio, desirable magnetic properties and other technological advantages which meet the extreme demands of a variety of industries. For example, composite aluminium containing boron fibres or resin containing graphite fibres can have strength/weight ratios over twice that of highstrength solid aluminium. Composites of many kinds are now widespread in industrial use and are attracting much research and development.

Computer, a technical device for accepting an input of information, processing this information according to some prescribed programme of operations and supplying an output of processed information. Many types of operation can be performed on many types of information and computers are now indispensable in science, business, warfare, government and other activities. Early thinkers in this field were Pascal (17th cent.), Babbage (19th cent.) and Turing (1930s), but electronic computers as we know them appeared during the second world war and the first commercial machine was on sale in 1950. Computers are millions of times faster than human beings at computing; and the introduction of computers into an organisation does more than just speed up the calculations, it tends to transform the whole nature of the organisation. The possibilities for future developments seem enormous. Analogue computers and digital computers are two different kinds stemming from the difference between *measuring* and *counting*. Analogue types handle data that is represented by physical quantities of continuously variable size such as voltages or lengths. These quantities can be made to vary like the quantities in a problem which the computer is set to solve; the problem is thus solved by analogy. A slide rule is a rudimentary analogue computer in which numbers are represented by lengths of rule. Digital computers handle actual numbers expressed in digits and the quantities in the problem are represented by discrete numbers. These can all be expressed in binary form and thus stored or handled in bits. *See* **Bit, Binary Notation.**

Conclave, an assembly of Roman Catholic cardinals met together to elect a pope. The last Conclave was held in the Vatican in Oct. 1978 when Cardinal Wojtyla, Archbishop of Cracow, was elected Pope John Paul II.

Concordat, an agreement of convention between the Pope and a secular government regarding ecclesiastical matters. The Concordat of Worms in 1122 between Calixtus II and the Emperor Henry V was famous as deciding a long struggle in regard to investiture. In 1801, Napoleon concluded a concordat with Pius VII defining the restored relations between the head of the Church and the French Roman Catholics.

Condor, a large eagle of brilliant black plumage with a circlet of white feathers round its neck. It is a native of the Andes.

Confederation is a free association of sovereign states united for some common purpose. It s to be distinguished from a Federation, which is a union of states with one central government, each state relinquishing its sovereignty, though retaining some independence in internal affairs.

Confucianism. *See* **Section J.**

Coniferae are cone-bearing trees, including firs, pines, cedars, cypresses, junipers, yews, etc., and are widely distributed in temperate regions.

Conservatism. *See* **Section J.**

Constellation, a grouping of stars that forms a pattern when seen from Earth. There are a total of 88 constellations in use on modern star charts, some of which are much larger than others. The stars within a particular constellation are not necessarily close to each other in space. In most cases they only appear close together due to their lying in more or less the same line of sight as seen from Earth.

Constitution, the fundamental organic law or principles of government of a nation, state, society, or other organisation, embodied in written documents, or implied in the institutions and customs of the country or society. The government of the USA, unlike Great Britain, works upon a written Constitution. It was framed when the USA came into existence as a republic out of a federation of thirteen states, based on representative government. The constitution was adopted in 1789, and its strength has been tested by the fact that, substantially unchanged, it is the groundwork for a federation which now comprises fifty states. *See also* **Section D.**

Continent, a word used in physical geography to denote the larger continuous land masses in contrast to the great oceans of the earth. They are: Eurasia (conventionally regarded as 2 continents, Europe and Asia), Africa, North America, South America, Australia and Antarctica. (Australasia is Australia, New Zealand and adjacent islands. Oceania is Australasia and the many islands of the S.W. Pacific.)

Continental Drift. The hypothesis of drifting continents is due to F. B. Taylor, an American geologist who published his theory in 1908, and to the Austrian meteorologist Alfred Wegener in 1910. The latter was impressed by the matching coasts of South America and Africa, which seemed to him to fit together like the pieces of a jigsaw puzzle. Since then many other people have taken up and developed the idea. According to Wegener, at one time there were two primary super-continents. Laurasia and Gondwanaland. The one in the northern hemisphere consisted of North America, Europe, and the northern part of Asia. Its southern counterpart included Antarctica, Australia, India, Africa and South America. These super-continents broke up, and their various bits moved apart. In particular, the southern hemisphere continents drifted radially northwards away from the south pole, and the two Americas shifted westwards from Europe and Africa. What would have been the leading edges of the land masses on this hypothesis, are now heavily buckled up into mountain belts, such as the Cordillera and the Alpine-Himalayan chain. The resistance afforded to drifting by

the strong ocean floors may well have been the cause of such structures. Despite the wealth of geological facts which have a bearing on the problem of continental drift, none of these has been able to decide the issue in a conclusive manner. Further studies of rock magnetism (*q.v.*) and of fossil climates should ultimately establish the concept of continental drift on a firm basis. *See also* **Earth, F8.**

Conurbation, a term used in reference to an extensive and continuous area of urban land-use. Conurbations are frequently formed by the physical coalescence of several formerly freestanding towns. They may themselves coalesce to form a higher order of physical urbanisation, known as a megalopolis.

Convention is an assembly of delegates, representatives, members of a party met to accomplish some specific civil, social, political, ecclesiastical or other important object.

Convention Parliaments, terms used to describe the Parliaments of 1660 (after the dissolution of the Long Parliament) and 1689, (summoned by William of Orange).

Convocation, an assembly called together to deliberate ecclesiastical affairs. In the Church of England the provinces of Canterbury and York each have their convocation. The term is also applied to assemblies of the graduates of certain universities.

Coot. A very widely distributed bird of the rail family and a common resident of the British Isles. The adult is black with a conspicuous white bald shield on the forehead and a white bill. The juvenile is brownish grey with whitish breast and throat. The coot flies heavily, but swims well. It dives frequently and can remain submerged for a considerable time. It is pugnacious and in winter gregarious. The food is chiefly vegetable. The large nest is usually built among aquatic vegetation and the young are fed by both parents. Another species, the Crested Coot, occurs in S. Europe.

Copper, one of the most familiar of metals, element no. 29, symbol Cu, used in ancient times as an alloy with tin in producing bronze, and preceding iron as an industrial material. Copper ores are most abundant in the USA, Chile, Canada, Zambia and Zaire. All copper compounds are poisonous.

Copyright. Under the Copyright Act, 1956, copyright subsists in every original literary, dramatic musical, and artistic work if the author is a British subject or a citizen of the Republic of Ireland or resident in the United Kingdom, or if the work is first published in the United Kingdom. The Act provides that, except in certain special cases, the author of the work shall be the first owner of the copyright, and there are no formalities, such as registration or payment of fees, to be accomplished. Copyright includes the right to reproduce the work in any material form, to perform the work in public, or, if the work is unpublished, to publish the work. The Act also protects sound recordings, films and television and sound broadcasts. Literary, dramatic, musical and artistic works which enjoy the protection of the Act are automatically protected in those countries which are parties to the Berne Copyright Convention or the Universal Copyright Convention. In general, copyright in literary, dramatic, musical and artistic works is vested in the author for the period of his lifetime and 50 years following after which it passes into the public domain and becomes freely available to any who wish to make use of it. The Copyright Libraries, entitled to receive copies of books published in the United Kingdom are given under **Libraries.** The Berne Copyright Convention and the Universal Copyright Convention were revised at a diplomatic conference held in Paris in 1971. The effect of the revisions allows any national of a developing country to obtain, under certain conditions, a compulsory licence to translate and publish a copyright work for the purpose of teaching, scholarship and research, upon payment of compensation to the copyright owner of the original work. The Government Department responsible for matters in connection with copyright is the Industrial Property and Copyright Department, State House, 66–71 High Holborn, London WC1R 4TP.

Coral, an order of small marine animals closely related to the sea-anemone, but differing from it in their ability to develop a limy skeleton. They multiply sexually and by budding. The structure of the coral secretions assumes a variety of forms, fan-like, tree-like, mushroom shape, and so forth. Red coral (the skeleton of *Corallium rubrum*) is mainly obtained from the Mediterranean. The coral reefs of the Pacific and Indian Oceans are often many miles in extent. Living corals occur only in warm seas at about 23°C.

Cordite, a smokeless explosive adopted for small arms and heavy artillery by the British Government in the naval and military services in 1889, and composed of 58 parts of nitro-glycerine, 37 of gun-cotton, and 5 of vaseline. It is a jelly or plastic dough, and used in the form of sticks. Invented by Sir Frederick Abel and Sir James Dewar in 1889.

Cork, the bark of a species of oak, *Quercus suber*, grown largely in the South of Europe and North America. The cork tree is said to yield bark every six to ten years for 150 years, and grows to a height of from 6–12 m. Its lightness, impermeability, and elasticity enable it to be used for a variety of commercial purposes, especially for stoppers of bottles.

Cormorant, a large, long-billed water-bird which captures fish by diving. The common cormorant has bronze-black plumage with white cheeks and sides and is found round the sea coasts of most parts of the world, including the British Isles. It nests in colonies on sea cliffs and rocky ledges. The Shag or Green Cormorant is a smaller bird with green-black plumage and a crest.

Corncrake. See **Landrail.**

Corn Laws were statutes intended for the benefit of British agriculture, and restricted import and export of grain. From the 14th to the mid-19th cent. such laws were in force, and were often of a stringent nature. They became so oppressive and caused corn to reach so high a price that the poorer classes were plunged into distress. A powerful anti-corn law agitation was organised of which Cobden, Bright and Villiers were the leaders, and Sir Robert Peel, in 1846, at the time of the Irish potato famine, carried through free trade. The repeal of the Corn Laws marked an important phase in the transformation of an agricultural to an industrial Britain.

Corona or **Solar Corona,** the outer atmosphere of the sun. This glows by virtue of light emitted by the sun and scattered by electrons and dust particles at various heights in the sun's atmosphere and also by light emitted from ionised atoms in the corona itself. Corona light is much fainter than the bright disc of the sun and is invisible against the normal blue of the sky. During total solar eclipses, the corona can be seen by the human eye as a faint glow extending irregularly outwards a few solar diameters from the sun. The sun's atmosphere extends much further than this but is invisible to the eye at large distances from the sun. The corona gases are thought to be very hot (millions of degrees) and in complex violent motion; the gross structure of the corona is connected with the sunspot cycle.

Cortes, the Parliaments of Spain and Portugal.

Cosmic Rays are a form of radiation coming from outer space, of deep penetrating power and of great scientific interest. The rays consist of extremely energetic atomic particles—protons, electrons and some heavier nucleons—travelling at speeds very close to that of light. A complex series of events result from their collision with the atmosphere, giving rise to showers of secondary high-energy particles containing many of those listed on **F16.** Cosmic rays are now investigated with instruments buried in deep mines, as well as those in satellites, and the great interest is because we now believe their origin to be in, or associated with, some of the most interesting objects in the universe—supernovae, neutron stars, pulsars and perhaps some gigantic galactic nuclei. See **F3**(2).

Cosmology is the science which studies the whole universe, its origin, its nature, its size, age and evolution. It is presently a very active science because of many new discoveries of radio astronomy and space astronomy (X-ray, ultraviolet and infra-red) of extremely distant and luminous objects whose radiation has taken many thousands of millions of years to reach us, and whose explanation is taxing many of the world's best theoretical scientists. See **F3–8.**

Cosmonaut, the Russian term for a space traveller.

Cotton, the name of a plant of several species bearing large yellow flowers with purple centres. These centres expand into pods, which at maturity burst and yield the white fibrous substances known as cotton. The raw cotton contains a large proportion of seeds which are removed by "ginning". Long before the Christian era, cotton had been grown and used with great skill in India to make fabrics. The industry was not introduced into England until the middle of the 17th cent. when Protestant refugees from Flanders came to settle in the wool textile districts of East Anglia and Lancashire. With improvements in machinery and expansion of overseas trade in the 18th and 19th cent., Lancashire became the centre of the world's cotton industry but now man-made fibres have taken the place of cotton.

Coulomb, a unit of electric charge, named after the French naval engineer, Charles Augustin de Coulomb (1736–1806), equal to the quantity of electricity transferred in one second by a current of one ampere.

Council Tax. See **Section H.**

County. Since the 1972 reorganisation of local government in the United Kingdom the distinction between *administrative* counties and *geographical* counties no longer exists. Certain geographical counties have disappeared (*e.g.,* Rutland and Pembroke), new counties have appeared (*e.g.,* Avon and Gwynedd), while former counties have been modified (*e.g.* Glamorgan and Yorkshire). In 1991 a new Local Government Commission was established to make proposals for the reform of local government.

Coup d'Etat, a violent change in the government of a state carried out by force or illegally. Examples are the overthrow of the French Republic in 1851 by Louis Napoleon, who then became Emperor, and, since 1945, the military *coups* in the Middle East (*e.g.* Egypt in 1952, Iraq in 1958). The 1991 attempted *coup* in the Soviet Union helped precipitate the collapse of the USSR.

Court Leet, a court of record held annually before the steward of any particular manor or lordship; originally there was only one court for a manor, but in the time of Edward I it branched into two, the court baton and the court leet.

Coypu or **Nutria rat,** a large beaver-like rodent found in S. America; it became wild in E. Anglia, where it caused damage to dykes and crops, having escaped from farms where it is bred for its fur. Eradicated in E. Anglia by 1989.

Crane, a large, graceful wading-bird with elegant long legs and neck, greyish plumage, superficially resembling the heron and related to the bustard. They migrate in V or W formation and have trumpet-like voices. There are several species, found in all continents except S. America, including the Crowned Crane with golden coronet and the Demoiselle with tuft-like crest of white feathers. The Common Crane nested in East Anglia in mediaeval times.

Credit is an advance of money or of goods or services in consideration of a promise of payment later. Trade credit is such an advance from trader to customer; bank credit is an advance of money by a bank to a client, whether a business firm or a private person, in consideration of an interest payment by the borrower.

Creed (Latin *credo* = I believe), a formal statement of belief. The three orthodox Christian creeds are the Apostles' Creed (a summary of their teaching), the Nicene Creed (drawn up by the Church Council at Nicaea in A.D. 325 to define its theological doctrines), and the Athanasian Creed (concerning the nature and divinity of Christ). *See also* under individual headings.

Cremation, the ancient custom, revived in modern times, of burning the dead. Cremation was first legalised in Great Britain in 1885 and the first crematorium opened at Woking in that year. Application for cremation must be accompanied by two medical certificates.

Cricket, a genus of insects of the grasshopper order which move by leaps. The male produces a chirping noise by rubbing its wing-covers together. Just as the males inherit the nerve machinery for emitting the song of the species, so the females receive and respond to that song and to no other.

Crimean War (1853–56). This war between Russia and the allied powers of Turkey, Britain, France and Sardinia, was connected with the Eastern Question (q.v.) and the desire of Russia for a port on the Mediterranean. Chief engagements were the Alma, Balaclava and Inkerman. Fighting virtually ceased with fall of Sevastopol in September 1855. The Treaty of Paris was signed 30 March 1856.

Criminal Justice Act. A controversial measure whose main proposals limit a defendant's right to silence, gives powers to the police to establish a DNA database, extends offences for which 10-13 year olds can be given custodial offences etc.

Crocodiles and their allies (alligators, caimans and gavials) are the largest of modern reptiles. They are well equipped for a predatory life in shallow waters, having powerful tails and strong jaws. Their eggs are laid on land, in sand or decomposing vegetation.

Crop circles (corn circles) are unusual landmarks in fields, ranging from small rings to circles with a diameter of up to 200 feet. They are frequent in the Marlborough area, and around the Hampshire–Berkshire border. The earliest reported case was in 1810. Amidst many fanciful explanations, local wind factors have been considered. Crop circles have been reported in Japan, Italy, France, Brazil, Australia and the USA.

Crow, a family of birds including many well-known species such as the rook, raven, jackdaw, carrion crow, hooded crow, magpie, nutcracker, jaw and chough.

Crusades were military expeditions undertaken by some of the Christian nations of Europe with the object of ensuring the safety of pilgrims visiting the Holy Sepulchre and to retain in Christian hands the Holy Places. For two centuries nine crusades were undertaken: First, 1095–99, under Godfrey of Bouillon, which succeeded in capturing Jerusalem; Second, 1147–49, led by Louis VII of France, a dismal failure, which ended with the fall of Jerusalem; Third, 1180–92, in which Richard I of England took part, making a truce with Saladin; Fourth, 1202–4, led by French and Flemish nobles, a shameful expedition, resulting in the founding of a Latin empire in Constantinople; Fifth, 1217–21, led by John of Brienne; Sixth, 1228–29, under the Emperor Frederick II; Seventh, 1248–54, under St. Louis of France; Eighth, 1270, under the same leadership, but cut short by his death on an ill-judged expedition to Tunis; Ninth, 1271–72, led by Prince Edward of England, which accomplished nothing. Millions of lives and an enormous amount of treasure were sacrificed in these enterprises and Jerusalem remained in the possession of the "infidels". The chief material beneficiaries were the Italian maritime cities; the chief spiritual beneficiary was the Pope; but in literature and the arts both Europe and the Levant benefited enormously.

Crux. See under **Southern Cross**, L113.

Cryogenics (Greek roots: productive of cold) is the science dealing with the production of very low temperatures and the study of their physical and technological consequences. "Very low" is often taken to mean below about −150°C. The growth of cryogenics (essentially a 20th-cent. science) is connected with the discovery of how to liquefy all gases including even helium which resisted liquefaction until 1908. Scientifically, cryogenics is important partly because special phenomena (e.g., superconductivity (q.v.)) appear at lower temperatures and partly because more can be learned about ordinary properties by studying them in the absence of heat. Technologically, cryogenics is becoming more and more significant, for example, liquefied gases are rocket propellants, superconductors make valuable magnets, tissue-freezing techniques (using very cold liquids) have been introduced into surgery. See **Absolute Temperature.**

Crystal, in everyday usage, a solid chemical substance bounded by plane surfaces which show a regular geometrical arrangement as, e.g., quartz crystals, rock salt, snow flakes. In physics the term means any substances whose atoms are arranged in a regular three-dimensional array. This includes most solids, even those not particularly crystalline in appearance, e.g., a lump of lead. See **Glass** and **Liquid Crystals.**

Cubism, the name of a revolutionary movement in art created in the years 1907–9 by the two painters Picasso and Braque. Rejecting purely visual effects, they approached nature from an intellectual point of view, reducing it to mathematical orderliness. Its respectable grandparent was Cézanne who had once written: "you must see in nature the cylinder, the sphere, and the cone"—a concept which, together with the contemporary interest in Negro sculpture, moved the two founders of the movement to experiment with the reduction of natural forms to their basic geometrical shapes. In practice, this meant combining several views of the object all more or less superimposed in order to express the idea of the object rather than any one view of it. The name Cubism was derisive and the movement aroused the same opposition as Impressionism, Fauvism and the later Futurism. Picasso's *Les Demoiselles d'Avignon* (1907; Museum of Modern Art, New York) was his first Cubist painting. Three phases are recognised: (1) Cubism under the influence of Cézanne; (2) high or analytical Cubism (c. 1909–12) concentrating on the breaking-down of form to the exclusion of interest in colour; (3) synthetic Cubism (c. 1913) making use of *collage* in which pieces of pasted-on paper (illustrations, wallpaper, newspaper) and other materials were used in addition to paint. Amongst other early cubist painters were Metzinger, Gleizes, Gris and Léger.

Cuckoo, a well-known migratory bird which is found in Great Britain from April to July, hawk-like in shape, with a very characteristic note, uttered during the mating season only by the male. The hen has a soft bubbling call. It lays its eggs in the nests of other birds, e.g., the meadow pipit and hedge sparrow, but only one egg in each nest. Feeds mainly on insects, particularly hairy caterpillars.

Cuneiform, (Latin = *wedge-shaped*), an ancient method of writing by impressing wedge-like strokes into tablets of damp clay which when dried and hardened formed a permanent script, Cuneiform writing developed from its original pictographic form into a phonetic writing and can be traced back to the non-Semitic Sumerians of ancient Mesopotamia, the earliest civilisation known to us. It passed to the Semitic Accadians of Babylonia in the 3rd millennium B.C. who adapted it to their own language. Decipherment by Sir Henry Rawlinson, 1835.

Curfew (Old F. *covre-feu* = cover fire), a regulation common throughout Europe in mediaeval times by which, at a fixed hour in the evening, the church bell was rung as a signal that fires were to be put out and the people were to go to bed. The custom originated in the fear of fire when buildings were built of timber. Nowadays a curfew is imposed by the military in areas where riots or disturbances are expected, compelling the civilian population to remain indoors after nightfall.

Curia, the central government of the Roman Catholic Church. By the reform which came into force on 1 January 1968, its twelve Sacred Congregations or "ministries" were reorganised and reduced to nine.

Curie, a measure of the rate at which radioactive material emits radiation. One curie is a disintegration rate of 3.7×10^{10} disintegrations per second.

Curlew, a wading-bird of which there are several species. It frequents marshy places, feeds on worms, insects, molluscs and berries and possesses a very long, down-curved bill.

Currency is the name given to the types of cash money—metal or paper—in use in an area (e.g. pound, sterling, dollar, franc). It also designates the actual coins or notes issued. Its amount is usually subject to regulation by the Government, or by a Central Bank acting on the Government's behalf. Britain changed over to a £-based decimal currency in February 1971. On 1 January 1985, ½p coins ceased to be legal tender. The old 'halfpenny' first appeared in 1280. See also **National Currencies, Section Z.**

Cybernetics, the science concerned with the automatic control and communication processes in both animals and machines. Thus it is concerned with brain function, information theory, electronic computers, and automation.

Cyberspace. *See* Internet (Special Topic, L132).

Cyclone, a term usually applied to a tropical revolving storm. Cyclones often occur towards the end of the hot seasons and are mainly confined to tracks in the western areas of the oceans, being known as hurricanes (Caribbean and Pacific), cyclones (Indian Ocean) and typhoons (China Seas). The circulation of air in a cyclone is similar to that in the *depression* of temperate latitudes, but the region of low pressure is much more localised and the pressure gradients steeper. Winds of hurricane strength and torrential rain occur generally, although at the centre of the storm there is a small area, known as the "eye", where fair, calm weather prevails. Hurricane Andrew, which hit Florida in August 1992, left 250,000 people homeless and was America's costliest natural disaster.

Cyclotron, a machine for accelerating charged particles such as protons to very high energies. Devised by E. O. Lawrence in California in 1930, it uses a magnetic field to make the particles traverse nearly circular paths and an electric field to give them an additional pulse of energy each time round. The accelerated particles impinge on targets, and the resulting events are a basic source of information for nuclear physicists. The cyclotron is obsolescent and has led to the development of other machines, *e.g.*, betatrons, synchrotrons. Britain has two major national high-energy machines: a 7 GeV proton synchroton (to be closed and replaced by a "spallation neutron source"), and a 5 GeV electron synchrotron. The European Organisation for Nuclear Research (CERN), carries out research at higher energies. *See* L24.

D

Dactylopterus, a fish of the gurnard family, with wing-like pectoral fins; sometimes known as the flying fish, though that appellation is more generally given to *Exocaetus exiliens*.

Dadaism (French *Dada* = hobby-horse) was a hysterical and nihilistic precursor of **Surrealism** (*q.v.*) resulting from the shock produced by the first world war. Beginning in Zurich about 1915, it spread to other continental cities, such as Berlin and Paris, dying out in 1922. The movement was deliberately anti-art, destructive, and without meaning; it intended to scandalise by such tricks as "compositions" made out of anything that came to hand—buttons, bus tickets, pieces of wire, bits of tin, etc. Other excesses included incoherent poetry, Dada night-clubs, plays, and short-lived newspapers. Many Dadaist painters became Surrealists at a later stage, but where Surrealism is a deliberate attempt to present dreamlike images, Dadaism was sheer anarchism. Leading Dadaists were Hans Arp, Marcel Duchamp, André Breton, Kurt Schwitters and Max Ernst.

Daddy Longlegs, or **Crane-fly,** a slender long-legged fly of the family Tipulidae. The larvae which do damage to lawns and plants are called leather-jackets. The Americans call Harvestmen (*q.v.*) daddy longlegs.

Daguerreotype, the first practical photographic process, invented in Paris by M. Daguerre during the years 1824–39. The light-sensitive plate was prepared by bringing iodine in contact with a plate of silver. After exposure a positive image came to development of the plate in mercury vapour. Even for openair scenes the first daguerreotypes involved exposure of 5–10 minutes. The picture came in one copy and the process was therefore of limited use. The wet collodion process (1851) rendered the technique obsolete.

Dail Eireann, the name of the national parliament of the Irish Republic.

Dalai Lama, the temporal and religious leader of Tibet. The present Dalai Lama, Tenzin Gyabo (b. 1935), the 14th reincarnation, fled to India in 1959. Awarded the 1989 Nobel Peace Prize.

Damaskeening, the art of inlaying one metal upon another, largely practised in the East in mediaeval times, in the decoration of sword blades.

Dandies, the name given to a class of exquisites prominent in early Victorian days, and who attracted attention by excessive regard for dress.

Danegeld, a tax imposed in England in Anglo-Saxon times to raise funds for resisting the Danes or to buy them off. Edward the Confessor abolished the tax, but it was revived by the Conqueror and subsequently retained, under another name, after the danger from the Danes was past. It is the basis of all taxation in this country. Domesday Book (*q.v.*) was originally drawn up for the purpose of teaching the State how to levy the tax.

Danelaw, the law enforced by the Danes in the kingdoms of Northumbria, East Anglia, and in the districts of the five (Danish) boroughs—lands grouped round Leicester, Nottingham, Derby Stamford and Lincoln—which they occupied during the Viking invasions of the 9th and 10th cent. The country occupied was also called the Danelaw or Danelagh.

Darter, 1. Snakebirds, a genus of the pelican family, with long, pointed bill and serpent-like neck and resembling cormorants in appearance. There are 5 species. 2. Numerous species of small freshwater fish belonging to the perch family, found in N. America.

Date Palm. *Phoenix dactylifera,* one of the oldest known food plants widely cultivated in N. Africa and W. Asia. It grows to 30 m and continues to bear for 2 or 3 centuries, its fruit being of great value as a food. From the leaves the Africans make roofs for their huts; ropes are made from the fibrous parts of the stalks; and the sap furnishes a stimulating beverage.

Dauphin, the title borne by the eldest sons of the Kings of France from 1349 to 1830.

Day is the most natural unit of time and may be defined as the period of rotation of the earth relative to any selected heavenly body. Relative to the sun it is called the *solar day.* Relative to a fixed star it is called the *sidereal day.* Owing to irregularities in the earth's movements, the time taken for the earth to rotate through 360° relative to the sun is variable, and so the *mean solar day* of 24 hours has been introduced, which is the average throughout the year. The *mean solar day* is our standard, used for purposes of the calendar, and astronomers use *sidereal* clocks to check mean solar time. In practice, for convenience, the sidereal day is determined by the earth's rotation relative to the vernal equinox or first point of Aries, and is equal to 23 hours 56 minutes and 4·091 seconds of mean solar time (*i.e.*, about 4 minutes shorter than a solar day). The lengths of day on other planets can differ greatly to that of the Earth. Jupiter spins once every 10 hours or so while the length of a day on Venus is equal to 243·01 Earth-days, longer than its year of 224·7 days. *See* Time.

D-Day, the allied invasion of Normandy on 6 June 1944 which began the liberation of France in World War II.

DDT (dichloro-dephenyl-trichloroethane). A very powerful insecticide which has had wide success in the control of diseases, such as malaria and typhus which are carried by insects. Mosquito swamps are sprayed with DDT to kill the carriers. Because this toxic chemical breaks down very slowly it builds up in birds and animals and its use is now banned in Britain. Its detection in Antarctic wild life confirmed that DDT pollution was virtually worldwide.

Deacon, an ecclesiastical official, who assists in some of the smaller ministerial duties in church or chapel.

Dead Languages are such as the ancient Greek and Roman tongues, which are no longer spoken but are preserved in literature.

Dead Sea Scrolls, a group of ancient Jewish documents, consisting of scrolls and fragments which have been recovered since 1947 in the vicinity of Qumran near the Dead Sea and which represent one of the most important finds ever made in the field of biblical archaeology and Christian origins. The scrolls written in Hebrew or Aramaic, were found in caves, the first by chance by an Arab shepherd in 1947. These consisted of biblical texts older by a thousand years than the earliest Hebrew manuscript of the Old Testament (A.D. 895). Many fragments have since been discovered, comprising the whole of the Old Testament with the exception of Esther. In addition there are commentaries and other non-biblical writings, including one called "The War of the Sons of Light with the Sons of Darkness". The writing on the scrolls indicates that they were written over a period of two centuries, the greater proportion before the birth of Christ. A nearby ruin is believed to have been the home of a religious sect called the Essenes (**J17**), to whom the scrolls belonged. By the aid of the latest scientific techniques, including radiocarbon tests, the age of the scrolls has been confirmed as between the second century B.C. and first century A.D. Readers may wish to refer to R. Eisenman and M. Wise, *The Dead Sea Scrolls Uncovered* (1992).

Dean, a Church of England dignitary, ranking below a bishop, and the head of the chapter of a cathedral. A Rural Dean supervises a *deanery* or group of parishes. There are also Deans of Faculties in some universities, and at Oxford and Cambridge the Dean is in charge of chapel services and disciplinary arrangements.

Death Watch Beetle (*Xestobium rufovillosum*), a wood-boring beetle, larger than the common furniture beetle, found chiefly in the old oak beams of churches and other historic buildings. The grub bores from 4–12 years. The name "death watch" comes from the superstition that the ticking sound, made by the beetle striking its head against the wood, is a sign of approaching death. The death watch beetle found in the roof of Westminster Hall was smoked out by means of an insecticide called gamma benzine hexachloride. *See also* **Furniture Beetle, Woodworm**.

Decalogue, the name given to the Ten Commandments of the Old Testament. There are two versions of them, differing in detail: Exodus xx. 2–17 and Deuteronomy v. 6–21. They are of Hebrew origin and are recognised by Jews and Christians as the divine law given by God to Moses on Mt. Sinai. Most of them are prohibitions in contrast to the beatitudes (pronounced by Christ in the Sermon on the Mount) which are positive, *e.g.*, Blessed are the merciful.

December, the last month of the year in our calendar, and the tenth in the old Roman.

Deciduous Trees are such as shed their leaves at certain seasons as distinguished from evergreens or permanent foliaged trees or shrubs.

Declaration of Independence was an Act by which the American Congress, on 4 July 1776, declared the American colonies to be independent of Great Britain. "Independence Day" is a holiday in the United States.

Defender of the Faith (*Defensor Fidei*), a title conferred upon Henry VIII by Pope Leo X in 1521 for entering the lists against Luther with his pamphlet in defence of the Seven Sacraments. After Henry assumed headship of the Church of England the Pope withdrew the title but it was confirmed to him by Parliament in 1544 and has been used ever since by English monarchs.

Deflation. *See* **Section G.**

Dehydrate, to eliminate the water from a substance. The process of dehydration is now used in the food industry, as a result of wartime research, in making such things as dried egg and packet soups. Most vegetables contain over 90 per cent of water, and much of this can be removed under vacuum at low temperatures without appreciably impairing the flavour. The lightness of the dehydrated products is an advantage when supplies have to be transported.

Deliquescence, the process of dissolving by the absorption of moisture from the atmosphere. For instance, chromic acid crystals on exposure to the air quickly deliquesce.

Deluge, a flood, commonly applied to the story of the Deluge in the Bible, in which Noah and the Ark figure. A similar tradition lingers in the mythologies of all ancient peoples.

Democratic Party, one of the two great American political parties, originated about 1787, advocating restrictions on the federal governments and in opposition to the federalists. It was in 1825 that a group who were in favour of high tariffs seceded, later to become the Republican Party. The Democratic Party was split again over slavery before the Civil War (1861–65), and in the main the southern states have been supporters of the Democrats. The economic depression helped the Democrats to power in 1932 (*see* **New Deal**) and they held office until 1953 when Eisenhower became President. In 1960 Kennedy narrowly won the Presidency and in 1964 Lyndon Johnson swept in with a landslide victory over the Republican candidate. In 1968 and 1972 the Democratic candidates were beaten by Nixon. In 1976 Jimmy Carter won an easy victory, but after that the Democrats lost three successive presidential elections (1980, 1984, 1988) before winning a narrow but convincing victory under Bill Clinton in the 1992 election. However, the party suffered severe reverses in the 1994 mid-term elections. The symbol of the party is a donkey, invented, like the Republican's elephant, by the cartoonist Thomas Nast. *See* **Section C.**

Dendrite, a stone or mineral on or in which tree-like tracery appears, the result of the action of the hydrous oxide of manganese.

Density, a measure of the mass per unit volume of a material, usually expressed in grams per cubic centimetre. *Specific gravity* is the ratio of the density of a material at the termperature under consideration to that of water at the temperature of its maximum density (4°C). In grams per cubic centimetre the density of gold is $19 \cdot 3$, silver $10 \cdot 5$, lead $11 \cdot 3$, water $0 \cdot 99997$, air $0 \cdot 00129$.

Depreciation of a currency is a fall in its relative value in terms of gold or of other currencies. *See* **Section G.**

Depression, a region where barometric pressure is lower than that of its surroundings. These areas of low pressure are usually less extensive than anticyclones (*q.v.*) and may vary from hundreds to thousands of kilometres in diameter. The winds, often of gale force where the depression is deep, blow round the system in an anticlockwise direction in the Northern Hemisphere (in the reverse direction in the Southern Hemisphere). Well above the earth's surface the winds blow along rather than down the pressure gradient but near the surface, friction causes the winds to blow slightly (*c.* 15°) across the isobars. The depression exists only as long as more air diverges out of its upper parts than converges into its lower parts. The majority of depressions which cross the British Isles travel from the Atlantic, sometimes in series or families at rates from a few kilometres to a thousand kilometres a day, bringing their generally unsettled weather with them.

Desalinisation, the process of removing minerals, chiefly salt, from sea or brackish water to provide pure water for drinking or industry. Small-scale desalinisation by distillation has been practised for many years on ships and small islands. By the 1960s, many large-scale distillation plants were in operation, many of them in hot dry countries as in the Middle East. Kuwait, for example, used oil revenues to buy desalination plant and powers the plant with natural gas. As water for large population centres becomes more precious and desalinisation techniques more efficient, the process may be more and more used though it is expensive in capital outlay and in the cost of heating required to distil the water. Methods other than distillation are under investigation but not as yet much used.

Deserts, vast, barren, stone or sandy wastes where there is almost no rainfall and little or no vegetation. These regions are found in the interior of the continents Africa, Asia and America between 20° and 30° north and south of the equator. Europe is the only continent without deserts. The most famous are the Sahara, the largest in the world, the Gobi desert of central Asia, the Kalahari desert of southwest Africa and the great Australian desert. The marginal extension of deserts (desertification) is a topic of considerable debate. The increasing size of deserts is thought to result from either climatic change or the interference by man.

Detention Centres in Britain were for young people (boys and girls) over 14 but under 21 who have been found guilty of an offence for which an adult could be sent to prison. They have now been replaced by Young Offenders' Institutions.

Determinism and Free-will. *See* **Section J.**

Deuterium or "heavy hydrogen". The second isotope of hydrogen; the third is called tritium. Deuterium atoms have in their nuclei a neutron as well as a proton; tritium nuclei have two neutrons and one proton. In ordinary hydrogen gas about one out of every 5,000 atoms is a deuterium atom. Deuterium was discovered in 1932 by Professor Harold Urey. The oxide of deuterium corresponding to water is called "heavy water". The nucleus of the deuterium atom is called a deuteron. An anti-deuteron consisting of anti-proton and anti-neutron was produced at Brookhaven in 1965, the first compound anti-nucleus ever to be produced.

Devaluation is a definite, official downward valuation of a country's currency in terms of its exchange value with other currencies. The £ was devalued in 1949, when an official exchange rate of £1 = $2.8 was established, and again in 1967, to a rate of £1 = $2.4. Since 1972 there has been greater flexibility in exchange rates and national currencies have been allowed to "float". *See* **Section G, Part IV**.

Devonian System in geology refers to the strata between the Silurian and the Carboniferous formations. It includes the Old Red Sandstone formation. The fauna of the Devonian include the group of fishes known as the Rhipidistra (on the evolutionary route towards the amphibians), Actinistia (coelacanth), and the Dipnoi or lung fishes. *See* **F48**.

Dew, moisture deposited by condensation of water vapour on exposed objects especially during calm, cloudless nights. The loss of heat from the ground after sunset, by radiation, causes the layer of atmosphere close to the surface to be chilled below the temperature, known as the dew-point, at which the air is saturated with vapour. Part of the vapour condensed may be transpired from blades of grass and foliage of plants.

Dew Pond is a shallow artificial pond which is on high ground and rarely dries up, even during prolonged droughts, despite being used by cattle and sheep as a drinking source. The name arose from the belief that dew deposits at night provided the moisture for replenishment. Drainage of rain-water and mist condensed on neighbouring trees and shrubs are probably more important factors.

Dialectical Materialism. *See* **Section J**.

Diamond, a mineral, one of the two crystalline forms of the element carbon (the other is graphite), the hardest known substance, used as a gem and in industry. India was the first country to mine diamonds (the Koh-i-noor, which means "mountain of light", known since 1304, came from Golconda near Hyderabad and came into British possession when the Punjab was annexed in 1849). The celebrated diamond mines of South Africa were discovered in the 1870s. Other important diamond producing countries are Zaïre, USSR, Congo, Ghana, Sierra Leone, Namibia, Angola, Tanzania. The world's biggest diamond is the 3,106-carat Cullinan, discovered near Pretoria, South Africa, in 1905. Diamonds can be made artificially by subjecting carbon to very high temperatures and pressures; many industrial diamonds are made this way. Antwerp is the main diamond centre of the world, London the main marketing centre, Amsterdam the main diamond cutting centre.

Diatoms. One-celled algae, common in fresh and salt water. Distinctive feature is the siliceous wall which is in two halves, one fitting over the other like the lid of a box. These walls are often very finely and beautifully sculptured. The diatoms constitute a class of the plant kingdom known as the Bacillariophyta. *Diatom ooze* is a deep-sea deposit made up of diatom shells. *Diatomite* or *diatomaceous earth* is the mineral form that such diatom oozes assume (sometimes known as kieselguhr which mixed with nitroglycerine yields dynamite).

Diesel Engine, an engine in which the liquid fuel is introduced into a compressed or partially compressed charge of air, and which does not need an extraneous source of ignition. The modern oil engine has been evolved mainly from the principles enunciated by Herbert Akroyd-Stuart in his patent of 1890 and, like the steam and other inventions, represents the improvements achieved by many men, including those by Rudolf Diesel of Germany, in respect of high compression pressures and greater fuel economy.

Diet, in German history, an assembly of

dignitaries or delegates called together to debate upon and decide important political or ecclesiastical questions. The most famous imperial Diets were those held at Worms (1521), Speyer (1529), and Augsburg (1530), all of which dealt with matters of religious conflict arising from the Reformation.

Diffusion is the process of mixing which occurs when two liquids or gases are in contact. It is most rapid between gases, and, as laid down by Graham's law, "the rates of diffusion of different gases are in the inverse proportion to the square roots of their relative densities". Diffusion arises through the continual movement of molecules. Even in solids diffusion can occur. If a block of gold and a block of silver are welded together, after some time particles of gold are found in the silver, and *vice versa*.

Dimensions in common speech are the magnitudes of length, breadth and thickness giving, the size of an object, thus a line has only one dimension: length; a plane surface two: length and breadth; and a solid three: length breadth and thickness. In mathematics, hypothetical objects with any number of dimensions are considered. In physics and mechanics, dimensions are numbers which relate the units in which any quantity is measured to the so-called fundamental units. The latter are usually but not necessarily those of length, mass and time. "Dimensional analysis" is an important technique of scientific reasoning.

Dimorphism, the quality of assuming two distinct forms. For instance, carbon, which is graphite in one form, is the diamond in another.

Dinosaur, the name given to a group of extinct reptiles of the Mesozoic period, some of which were of immense size—much larger than crocodiles. *See* **Diplodocus**.

Dip Needle. Instrument for measuring the *dip* or inclination of the earth's magnetic field.

Diplodocus, one of the best known of the extinct mammoth dinosaurs. Fossil remains have been discovered in the Jurassic rocks of the United States. Some reached a length of over 24 m.

Dipnoi *or* **Lung Fishes**. These have the air bladder adapted to function as a lung, and they can remain alive when the stream or marsh in which they live dries up. Species of lung fish occur in Australia, Africa and S. America.

Diptera, an order of insects. Their main characteristic is that they are two-winged, and the common house-fly is the best-known example. There are at least 50,000 species of these insects, including gnats, blow-flies, mosquitoes, tsetses.

Diptych was a folding two-leaved tablet of wood, ivory, or metal, with polished inner surfaces, utilised for writing with the style by the ancient Greeks and Romans. The same term was applied to the tablets on which the names of the persons to be commemorated were inscribed in the early Church. In art any pair of pictures hinged together is styled a diptych, a set of three, a triptych.

Discus, a circular piece of metal or stone about 30 cm in diameter, used in athletic contests by the ancient Greeks and Romans. Throwing the discus was a very favourite game, which was deemed worthy of celebration in Myron's famous *Discobolus* (*c.* 460 B.C.–450 B.C.), the best copy of which is in Rome.

Disk, an astronomical term denoting the seemingly flat surface of celestial bodies as seen by the eye.

Distillation, a process used to separate liquids of different boiling points. This is effected by placing the mixture in a distillation apparatus and heating. The liquid with the lower boiling point distils over first, the vapour being condensed and collected, forming the first *fraction*. With continued heating the second liquid reaches its boiling point, distils over and the mixture is said to be *fractionated*. Mixtures of liquids with close very high boiling points require more elaborate apparatus. Fractional distillation is a common process in the chemical industry, particularly in the refining of petroleum.

Diwali, the festival of light, marking the triumph of good over evil, celebrated by Hindus, Sikhs and Jains. Sweets and gifts are exchanged.

DNA (Deoxyribonucleic acid), a polymer molecule

in the form of a double-strand helix containing many thousands of sub-units. Contains the genetic information coded in sequences of sub units called bases. The Nobel Prize for medicine was awarded in 1962 for the discovery of the structure of DNA; that for 1968 for interpreting the genetic code and its function in protein synthesis. See **Nucleic Acids**. and **Special Topic, end Section F**.

DNA Database. The world's first police DNA database was established at the Forensic Science Laboratory, Birmingham in April 1995. The database, which will eventually hold up to 5 million samples, will allow police to compare genetic material from crime scenes with DNA profiles of convicted criminals. DNA profiling has been developed from genetic fingerprinting, an earlier technique created in the mid 1980s by Sir Alec Jeffreys of Leicester University.

Docks are enclosed water spaces where ships rest while being loaded or unloaded, repaired, or waiting for cargo. There are three main types: the wet dock in which water is maintained at the level of high tide so that vessels remain afloat while loading and unloading; the tidal dock, with open entrance to permit free ebb and flow of tide (e.g., Glasgow, Southampton (which has double tides)); and the dry dock, or graving dock, for overhauling and repairing vessels, so constructed that, after a ship has been docked, the water can be drawn off (e.g., Southampton, Tilbury). The floating dock is a type of dry dock. Technological advances in the handling of cargo, e.g., containers (sealed boxes of cargo), have led to modernisation of the docks. Under the 1991 Ports Act, many ports have faced the prospect of privatisation.

Dodo, an extinct bird, giant and flightless, which lived on the island of Mauritius up until 250 years ago. Another species, the white dodo, lived on Réunion. Some reached exceptional sizes. By the end of the 17th cent. Mauritius, Rodriguez, and Réunion had all been colonised, and the dodo along with many other birds vanished forever because of their inability to stand up to man and the animals imported by him.

Dog-days, a period of 40 days (3 July–11 August) when Sirius rises and sets with the sun. The ancient superstition, which can be traced back in Greek literature to Hesiod (8th cent. B.C.), was that this star affected the canine race.

Doge, the chief magistrate in the old republics of Venice (697–1797) and Genoa (1339–1797, 1802–5).

Dogfish, a large family of small sharks, seldom more than 1 m in length. The flesh is sold as "rock salmon". The eggs are contained in horny cases called "mermaid's purses". The commonest of the British dogfishes are the spurdogs.

Doldrums, a nautical term applied to those areas of the Atlantic and Pacific within a few degrees of the Equator towards which the trade winds blow and where the weather is calm, hot and sultry. Pressure is low and the air often rises to produce heavy tropical rainfall and squalls, rendering navigation difficult.

Dolomite, a name applied to a limestone containing appreciable magnesium; also the mineral dolomite, a double carbonate of magnesium and calcium.

Dolphin, a mammal of the whale order, from 2–2·4 m long, with a long, sharp snout, and of an active disposition. They abound in most seas and swim in shoals. A few species live in large rivers (Ganges and Amazon). They can cruise for long periods at around 15 knots and produce bursts of speed in the region of 20 knots, the water apparently flowing smoothly past their bodies. Dolphins are some of the most intelligent of mammals and are currently the subject of scientific experiments in communication. Name also for the fish, dorado. In 1990, a virus (linked to the one which killed 18,000 North Sea seals) was held responsible for dolphin deaths in the Mediterranean.

Domesday Book is the famous register of the lands of England framed by order of William the Conqueror. According to Stowe, the name was derived from *Domus dei*, the name of the place where the book was deposited in Winchester Cathedral; though by others it is connected with doom in the sense of judgment. Its compilation was determined upon in 1085, in order that William might compute what he considered

to be due to him in the way of tax from his subjects. William sent into each county commissioners to make survey. They were to inquire the name of each place, the possessor, how many hides of land were in the manor, how many ploughs were in demesne, how many homagers, villeins, cottars, serving men, free tenants, and tenants in soccage; how much wood, meadow, and pasture; the number of mills and fish ponds; what had been added to or taken away from the place; what was the gross value at the time of Edward the Confessor. So minute was the survey that the Saxon chronicler of the time reports "there was not a single hide, nor one virgate of land, nor even, it is shame to tell, though it seemed no shame to do, an ox, nor a cow, nor a swine was left that was not set down". The record, which did not take in Northumberland, Cumberland, Durham and parts of Lancashire and Westmorland, was completed in 1086, and was comprised in two volumes—one a large folio, sometimes called the Little Domesday, which deals with Essex, Norfolk and Suffolk, the other a quarto, sometimes called the Great Domesday. The first is written on 384 double pages of vellum in one and the same hand, and in a small but plain character, each page having a double column. The quarto is written on 450 pages of vellum, but in a single column and in a large, fair character. The original is preserved in the Public Record Office. *See also* **Danegeld**.

Dominicans, an order of mendicant preaching friars founded by St. Dominic in Languedoc in 1215 and confirmed by the Pope in 1216. The rule of the order was rigorous. The dress was a white habit and scapular with a long black mantle. This gave them the name of Black Friars. Their official name is Friars Preachers.

Donjon, the keep, or inner tower of a castle, and the strongest and most secure portion of the structure. This was the last refuge of the garrison, and there was usually a prison on the lower floor, hence the name *dungeon*.

Don Juan, the legendary hero of many famous works, supposedly based on the life and character of the unscrupulous gallant Don Juan Tenorio of 14th-cent. Seville. The first dramatisation of the legend and the most famous is Tirso de Molina's *El Burlador de Sevilla*. Don Juan was also the subject of Molière's *Le Festin de Pierre*, Mozart's *Don Giovanni*, Byron's *Don Juan*, and José Zorilla's *Don Juan Tenorio*. The latter is played on All Saints' Day throughout Spanish-speaking countries.

Don Quixote, the "knight of the doleful countenance", the hero and title of Cervantes' classic novel of 16th-cent. Spain. Don Quijote de la Mancha, a gentle country gentleman of lofty but unpractical ideals, having read many chivalric romances, believes he is called upon to redress the wrongs of the world. Mounted on his nag Rosinante and accompanied by his companion Sancho Panza, a hard-headed and practical peasant, he sets out on his journeys of knight-errantry.

Dormouse, a family of small, squirrel-like rodents widely distributed throughout Europe and Asia, and living mainly on fruit and nuts. It is of nocturnal habits and sleeps through the winter. One of nature's most secretive creatures, it is now making a comeback in Britain after nearly becoming extinct.

Dot, a French term indicating the property which a wife brings to her husband on marriage and is usually settled on the woman, being her separate property, though the income from it may go towards the general household expenses.

Dotterel, a handsome bird of the plover family found in northern Europe and Siberia.

Doukhobors. *See* **Section J**.

Drachm (or **Drachma**), an ancient Greek silver coin and weight. One drachma was equivalent to six obols. The word has survived as the name of a weight: Avoirdupois, one-sixteenth part of an ounce; Apothecaries' Weight, one-eighth part of an ounce.

Drag. Term used in mechanics for resistance offered by a fluid to the passage of a body moving through it. When speed of sound is reached drag increases abruptly. The lift/drag ratio gives the aeroplane designer his measure of aerodynamic efficiency.

Dragon, a fabulous monster common to folk-lore in most countries; generally represented as a winged reptile with fiery eyes and breath of flame. A dragon guarded the garden of the Hesperides; in the New Testament there is mention of the "dragon, that old serpent, which is the devil"; St. George, England's patron saint, is supposed to have overcome the dragon; mediaeval legend abounds in dragons; in heraldry the dragon has also a conspicuous place; and in China it was the imperial emblem.

Dragonet, the name of the fish of the *Callionymus* genus, beautifully coloured, and about 30 cm in length. They are common on the British coast and in the Mediterranean.

Dragon Fly, the common name of a well-known order of insects having two pairs of membraneous wings, and often of very brilliant colours. They are swift of flight and may be seen hovering over sheets of water in the sunshine all through the summer. Their chief food is mosquitoes.

Dragon's Blood, a dark-red resinous substance obtained from the fruit of a Malay palm, and possessing medicinal virtues. In a special technique used for making line blocks in printing, dragon's blood is used.

Drawbridge, a bridge that can be lifted up so that no passage can be made across it. It was a usual feature of a fortified castle in the Middle Ages, and was raised or lowered by chains and levers. It spanned the fosse, and on the approach of an attacking party was raised and formed a special barricade to the gate. Modern drawbridges are such as are raised to allow of the passage of boats up and down a river or estuary. The Tower Bridge is a famous London bridge of this type.

Drongo. The King Crow or Indian Black Drongo is frequently seen in India perched on branches or telegraph wires, darting suddenly to catch insects and to attack crows and hawks. Other members of the family are found in Asia, Africa and Australia. Its plumage is black with steel-blue gloss.

Drosophila or **Fruit Fly.** More has been learnt by geneticists from breeding experiments with this insect than with any other.

Dross, the name generally applied to the refuse of molten metal, composed of slag, scales and cinders.

Drought occurs when there has been an absence of rain for a long period or a marked deficiency of precipitation over a much longer period in a climatic zone where precipitation is ordinarily adequate for vegetation or agriculture, river flow and water supplies. It is different from aridity which refers to the extreme dryness of desert or arid regions where rainless periods characterise the climate. Hitherto in the British Isles "an absolute drought" was defined as "a period of at least 15 consecutive days without measurable rainfall", but arbitrary definitions of this type are not now normally used. In the British Isles droughts occur from time to time but very long rainless spells at a place are rather rare. The longest recorded spell in the British Isles with no measurable daily rainfall lasted 61 days at Liss (Hants) from 16 March to 15 May 1893. Over the country as a whole the 12-month period beginning 1 May 1975 was the driest such period since records began. The South of England's longest drought this century was ended by rain at the end of November 1992. As 1995 opened, Australia was experiencing its worst recorded drought, whilst in Andalucia in the south of Spain no significant rain had fallen for four years.

Druidism. *See* **Section J.**

Drupe is the scientific term for stone fruit. The stone forms the inner part (endocarp) of the fruit, and encloses a seed or kernel which is liberated after the flesh part (pericarp) has rotted.

Dry-rot, the term was first used about 1775 to describe the fungal decay of timber in buildings. Creosote distilled from coal tar is the standard material for preservation of timber, and pentachlorophenol and copper naphthenate are two compounds now extensively used. Dry wood always escapes dry-rot. Chief fungi causing dry-rot are *Merulius* and *Poria.*

Duck, water bird smaller than the related goose and swan, which together form the family Antidae. Duck refers to the female, drake to the male. The duck family falls into two separate groups: the river or freshwater (surface feeding) ducks, such as the mallard, pintail, wigeon, shoveler, mandarin, teal, garganey; and the sea (diving) ducks, such as the goldeneye, pochard, scoter, eider, and the fish-eating mergansers or "sawbills". The ancestor of all domestic breeds, with the exception of the muscovy, is the mallard.

Duckbill, *Ornithorhynchus anatinus,* also duck-billed platypus, a fur-covered, egg-laying, nest-building mammal inhabiting Australia and Tasmania. It has webbed feet and a muzzle like a duck's bill and is about 50 cm long.

Ductility is a property possessed by most metals which renders them capable of being stretched without breaking. Gold is the most, and lead the least ductile of metals, the order being gold, silver, platinum, iron, copper, palladium, aluminium, zinc, tin, lead. In animated nature the spider and the silkworm produce secretions of notable ductility.

Dugong. A marine mammal, belonging to the order Sirenia (sea-cows). Inhabits Red Sea and Indian Ocean; also found as far East as the Philippines and Australia. Lives on sea-weed. Related to the Manatee.

Duke, the highest rank in the British peerage. Edward, the Black Prince, eldest son of Edward III, who died before his father, was the first English duke, being created Duke of Cornwall in 1337. Since then all Princes of Wales have held that title.

Dukeries, a stretch of English woodland and park country, mainly in Nottinghamshire, comprising the adjacent demesnes of several English dukes and nobles. The Dukeries include Sherwood Forest and the estates of Welbeck Abbey, Clumber Park, Worksop Manor and Thoresby Hall.

Dunes. Sand dunes are elliptical or crescent-shaped mounds of loose sand produced by wind action. The dune has a gentle slope on windward side; a steep slope on the leeward side.

Dunlin, very common small wading-bird of the Sandpiper family nesting in Britain. Its range extends to other areas where it also breeds.

Dunmow Flitch, a custom which originated in the parish of Little Dunmow, Essex, in the reign of Henry III, which was that the husband who was prepared to swear before the prior, convent, and townsfolk of Dunmow that he had not repented of marriage or quarrelled with his wife for a year and a day, should be rewarded with the gift of a flitch of bacon. The custom has frequently been revived.

Dunnock (*Prunella modularis*), a small bird of rich brown and dark grey plumage common in gardens and hedgerows. Sings a cheerful song all the year round. Called hedge-sparrow in southern England. Another member of the same family, the larger Alpine Accentor (*Prunella collaris*), is found on rocky mountain slopes of Europe and Asia.

Duodecimo, a sheet of paper folded into twelve leaves, written "12mo".

Durbar, a term used in India from the Persian word *darbár* meaning "court" or "audience". The word was applied to great ceremonial gatherings like Lord Lytton's durbar for the proclamation of the Queen-Empress in 1877 and the Delhi durbar of 1911.

Dust, solid particles of matter floating in the atmosphere, produced chiefly by volcanic eruptions, sand-storms in desert regions, and industrial and domestic smoke. When the island of Krakatoa erupted in 1883, more than 4 km² of dust was thrown into the air and carried three times round the earth by the explosive wave. The particles in dust-storms are much finer than those in sand-storms and are swept up to far greater heights. The local whirlwinds which form over loose dry soils are termed dust-devils.

Dutch Elm Disease. *See under* **Elm, L39.**

Dyke. A wall-like intrusion of igneous rock which cuts across the bedding or other layered structure of the country rock; the word also signifies in alternative usage, a sea-wall and an open drain.

Dynamite, a powerful explosive whose chief element is nitro-glycerine. It was discovered by Nobel in 1867, who absorbed nitro-glycerine in kieselguhr; has a disruptive force of about eight times that of gunpowder.

Dynamo. Machine for transforming mechanical energy into electrical energy. Depends on principle of electromagnetic induction whereby a current is produced in a conductor (*e.g.*, copper wire) traversing a magnetic field. The two essential parts of a dynamo are the conductors or *armature* and the *field magnets*.

Dynasty, a succession of monarchs of the same family, as the Carolingian dynasty, the Bourbon dynasty, the Plantagenet dynasty, *etc.*

E

Eagle, large bird of prey with huge hooked bill, related to the buzzard, kite, hawk, harrier, falcon and vulture, together forming the family Falconidae. There are many species to be found throughout the world, the Golden, Imperial, Tawny, Spotted and Lesser Spotted being found in Europe. The Golden Eagle, a magnificent-looking bird, nests in the Scottish Highlands, and the White-tailed Sea Eagle, which used to breed in Britain, is now only an occasional visitor. The eagle has been the symbol of royal power since the earliest times, and the American or Bald Eagle is the emblem of the United States.

Earl, a British title of nobility of the third rank, duke and marquis coming first and second. The title dates from Saxon times, and until 1337 ranked highest in our peerage.

Earl-Marshal, in England ranks as the eighth of the great officers of state, is head of the College of Arms, attends the sovereign in opening and closing the session of Parliament, arranges state processions (especially coronations) and assists in introducing newly created peers in the House of Lords. The office is hereditary in the family of the Dukes of Norfolk.

Earth, our habitable globe, is the third of the planets of the solar system in order from the sun and on an average throughout the year takes 24 hours to turn completely round relative to the sun, the whole earth revolving round the sun in a slightly elliptical orbit once in a year of 365·2564 days. The mean distance of the earth from the sun is 149,597,900 km. Recent earth satellite studies have shown that small variations of the surface gravity field (or geoid) occur which are believed to be related more to the structures deep within the earth's mantle than to the location and dimension of crustal features, such as oceans, continents and mountain ranges. The crust consists of a skin, 30 km thick under the continents, but only about 6–8 km thick under the ocean bed, comprised of rocks and sediments or soil. At the base of the crust is a sharp discontinuity (the Mohorovičić Discontinuity) to denser rocks of the mantle. This region, nearly 3,000 km thick, is in a process of slow but inexorable change, one of convection responding to heat sources (due mainly to radioactivity of the materials within the earth). This slow convection is responsible for many changes in the surface of the earth—continental drift (*q.v.*), earthquakes and volcanic activity. The core is a region of very high density and temperature, comprised of heavy elements such as iron and nickel. The crustal rocks are mainly comprised of oxygen, silicon, aluminium, sodium, potassium, iron, calcium and magnesium, with traces of many other elements. The mass of the earth is about 6,000 million million million tonnes, and it was formed about 4,600 million years ago. The earth has one natural satellite, the moon. *See also* **F8–10.**

Earthquake, a sudden violent disturbance of the earth's crust; the region of the surface immediately above the "focus", or source where the earthquake originates, is termed the "epicentre". On account of their destructive power

earthquakes have attracted attention from the earliest times, but accurate study dates only from the last century and the development of a world-wide network of recording stations from the present one. The majority of severe earthquakes result from fractures, usually along existing faults, in underlying rock strata subjected to great strains, the shearing movement sometimes extending to the surface. These dislocations set up vibrations which are propagated as waves throughout the bulk of the earth or round the crust. Frequently the main shock is followed by a series of smaller aftershocks. Minor local earthquakes may be attributed to the effects of volcanic activity, but most of the larger ones originate in non-volcanic regions along well-marked lines of weakness in the earth's crust. Generally the ground is felt to tremble, undergoing oscillations which may gradually or suddenly increase to a maximum and accompanied by sounds. When there is movement of the sea-bed a tsunami (*q.v.*) may result. One of the greatest of historic times was that which destroyed and flooded Lisbon in 1755. Among the notable shocks of the present century rank those of San Francisco (1906), Messina, Italy (1908), China (1920), Japan (1923), Napier, New Zealand (1931), Ionian Is. (1953), Morocco (1960), Chile (1960), Iran (1962), Yugoslavia (1963), Alaska (1964), E. Turkey (1966), W. Sicily (1968), Peru (1970), China (1976), S. Italy and North Africa (1980), Mexico (1985) Armenia (1988), N.W. Iran (1990), west central India (1993), Los Angeles (1994) and Kobe (Japan), 1995. The most devastating earthquake in recorded history hit Shanxi (China) in 1556, killing 830,000 people. The Kobe earthquake of January 1995 in central Japan left over 5,000 dead. *See* **Richter Scale** and **F9(2).**

Earthworm, of which there are several species, has a cylindrical body, tapering at both ends and segmented into rings. It moves by contraction of its rings, aided by retractive bristles; is eyeless, but has a mouth, gullet and stomach. Earthworms exist in immense numbers, and perform an important part in the scheme of nature by loosening the soil and rendering it more amenable to tillage. They also form a valuable food for birds and many mammals, and are unequalled as bait for certain kinds of fish. The New Zealand flatworm (now spreading in Britain) is devouring native earthworms.

Earwig, a genus of insects possessing two pairs of wings and anal forceps. It is nocturnal, lives on vegetable matter, and hides by day under stones or in flowers, *e.g.*, dahlias. The old belief that it deliberately creeps into people's ears is altogether unfounded.

Easter, the annual Christian festival in commemoration of the resurrection of Christ, the English name being derived from Eostre, goddess of Spring. The date cannot fall earlier than 22 March nor later than 25 April. Many disputes arose among the early Christians as tt the proper time to celebrate this day which governs all other movable feasts. It was eventually ruled at the Council of Nicaea in 325 that Easter Day should be the first Sunday after the full moon following the vernal equinox. If this happens to be a Sunday, then Easter Day is the Sunday after. *See also* **Section Z.**

Eastern Front, the battlefront between Russia and Germany in both World Wars.

Eastern Question, a term formerly applied to the problems arising from the instability of the Mohammedan power of Turkey and its relations with the other nations of Europe. Later connected with other problems of the Near East such as the possession of Constantinople and the position of the Balkan states.

East India Company was incorporated by Elizabeth in 1600. In 1613 the Company set up a factory at Surat, India, and in 1662 Bombay came under the Company's influence and developed into an important trading port. Dupleix wanted to establish French power in India and a struggle for supremacy took place. Clive gained the victory for England and thenceforward British dominion in India remained undisputed except by native princes. In 1772 Warren Hastings was appointed the first Governor-General and in 1784 Pitt's India Act established a Board of Control for the India Company. A great increase of trade resulted, and this rule continued down to 1858, when, as a result of the mutiny, the Crown assumed the sovereignty. British dominion ended in 1947.

Eau-de-Cologne, a popular distilled perfume first manufactured at Cologne in the 18th cent. by Johann Maria Farina, an Italian, and since made in large quantities in Cologne and elsewhere.

Ebony, a name applied to various hard black woods, the best of which are grown in Mauritius and Sri Lanka. There are also Indian and American varieties. Only the inner portions, the heartwood, of the trees are of the necessary hardness and blackness. Ebony is largely used in ornamental cabinet work, for piano keys, *etc.*

Ecce Homo ("Behold the Man!"), used in reference to the pictures and sculptures representing Christ crowned with thorns.

Ecclesiastical Courts, courts for administering ecclesiastical law and maintaining the discipline of the Church of England. Introduced by the Normans. Originally they had jurisdiction over both clergy and laity.

Eclipse, the partial or complete obscuring of one heavenly body by another. An eclipse of the sun occurs when the moon, which is 1/400th of the diameter of the sun and about 1/390th as far away, obscures some portion of the sun as seen by an observer on the earth. A total eclipse occurs when the whole of the sun's disc is covered by the moon. Astronomers travel many thousands of miles to observe the outer layers of the sun and its corona, which is only possible when the light from the sun is totally obscured by the moon during the few minutes of an eclipse. The total solar eclipse of 7 March 1970, as seen from Mexico, was watched by millions on their television screens. Total solar eclipses have occurred over parts of the British Isles in the years 1424, 1433, 1598, 1652, 1715, 1724, 1927, 1954 (visible from the Shetland Is.), and the next will be seen only from near Land's End on 11 August 1999. An eclipse of the Moon occurs when the Moon moves into the Earth's shadow. When this happens, the sunlight is cut off and the lunar surface becomes quite dark until it emerges from the shadow again. Lunar eclipses can be either partial or total, depending on whether all or part of the Moon moves into the Earth's shadow. They are more common than solar eclipses. *See also* **Z11.**

Ecliptic is the sun's apparent path in the sky: the great circle described by the sun from west to east in the course of a year. The sun is exactly on the equator on approx. 21 March, and 23 September, and the points where the celestial equator and ecliptic intersect on these days are called the *equinoctial points.* On approx. 21 June and 22 December the sun reaches its greatest and least midday elevation and its greatest distance north and south of the equator, and the points on the ecliptic on these days are called the *solstices* (*see* **Seasons, Section Z**). These four points are equidistant from each other by 90°. The angle of the ecliptic to the earth's equator is called the obliquity of the ecliptic. Due to the gravitational perturbations of the other planets, both the equinoctial point and the obliquity of the ecliptic change with time. The value of the obliquity is *c.* 23·5.

Ecology, a term first described by the German biologist Haeckel in the 19th cent., is the study of the inter-relationships between living organisms and their environment. **Autecology** is the study of the environmental relationships of *individual* plants and species. **Synecology** is the study of plant and animal *communities* living together as groups and their relationship to their environment. *See also* **F44**-7 and **Section Y.**

Ecotourism is the form of tourism based on the natural ecological attractions of a country.

Ecumenical Council, a general council of the Christian Church summoned when important questions of Church doctrine and policy are to be decided. The early councils were predominantly Greek and convoked by the emperor. Those summoned by the pope when they meet at the Lateran Palace in Rome are called Lateran Councils; others have met at Constance, Florence, Trent and the Vatican. Their decisions are not binding on the rest of Christendom. Only 21 Ecumenical Councils have been held in the history of Christendom. The first

was held at Nicaea in 325 when the mystery of the Trinity was defined. The 21st (known as the 2nd Vatican Council), convened by Pope John, opened in October 1962 in St. Peter's, Rome, and ended in December 1965. Two of the principal themes were the reunion of all Christians with the Church of Rome and the Church's place in the modern world. At the last session of the Council the Pope announced his decision to establish for the first time an international synod of bishops in Rome for consultation and collaboration in the government of the Roman Church. This Senate of Bishops provides the balancing factor alongside the Curia, which represents the Papacy and not the episcopacy.

Edda, the name given to two important collections of early Icelandic literature—*the Elder or Poetic Edda,* poems handed down from the 9th and 10th cent., probably Norwegian in origin, and the *Younger* or *Prose Edda* of Snorri Sturluson compiled about 1230. They treat of legends of an early Scandinavian civilisation.

Eddystone Lighthouse, 21 km south of Plymouth, is one of the most isolated in the world. The tower is 51 m high, and its light can be seen for 28 km. The present structure is the fourth that has occupied this dangerous position. The first was of wood, completed by Winstanley in 1698, but it was destroyed by storm in 1703. In 1708 a second and stronger lighthouse was built by Rudyerd. This lasted until 1755, when it was destroyed by fire. Smeaton built the third lighthouse of granite and this withstood storm and tempest for over a hundred years, 1759–1881. The present lighthouse, also of granite, was built 1879–81 on a nearby rock by Sir James Douglass.

Eels, edible fishes of the order Apodes, with snakelike body covered with minute scales embedded in the skin. The common or freshwater eel *Anguilla anguilla* is found in the Atlantic coastal areas of N. America and Europe and in the Mediterranean, and breeds S.E. of Bermuda. The electric eel of S. America is able to cause electric shocks.

Egghead, a term used derogatively to describe the more intelligent people. Frequently applied in USA to the late Adlai Stevenson.

Egret, a slender, graceful bird of the heron family, of pure white plumage, famed for its beautiful silky plumes (aigrettes), which appear in the breeding season, and for which it was ruthlessly hunted and would have been exterminated had not international action been taken to protect it. The Little Egret with black bill, black legs, and yellow feet breeds in Mediterranean lands.

Eider, a large diving duck, found along the rocky coasts of northern latitudes, well known for the beautifully warm soft down, called "eider down", which the female bird plucks from her breast to line her nest. In Norway and Iceland the haunts of the eider are preserved and the birds protected by law on account of the much prized "eider down", which is collected from the nests just before the breeding season. "Eider down" is so elastic that a kilogram of it will fill an ordinary bed covering.

Eiffel Tower, built by the French engineer Alexandre Gustave Eiffel (1832–1923) for the Paris Exhibition of 1889. The tower which is made of iron is 300 m high and weighs about 7,000 tonnes.

Eisteddfod (a sitting) was originally a congress of Welsh bards and minstrels, and dates from before the 12th cent. These assemblies, discontinued for a long period, were resumed in 1819, and have been held yearly since, each lasting three or four days. Their object is to foster the Welsh patriotic spirit; they are devoted to orations and competitions in poetry, singing and harp-playing. Prizes are awarded.

Eland, largest species of antelope, native of Africa; large pointed horns, stands 1·5 m high at the withers, and weighs several hundred kg.

Elder, small trees of the *Sambucus* genus, with pinnate leaves, and clusters of white flowers and, later, small purplish-black berries. The black elder, the best known, thrives in Britain. A wine is made from its berries.

El Dorado, a "golden land", was an idea much favoured in the days of the early Spanish explorers. It was believed that somewhere on the South American continent there was a country abounding in gold and precious stones. Many expeditions were fitted out to discover it. Sir Walter Raleigh also went forth on this illusive quest.

Electret, a piece of solid matter which retains a permanent electric polarisation analogous to the magnetic polarisation of a permanent magnet. There are various recipes for making them; carnauba wax is a common constituent.

Electricity. See **F21,** also **Energy Conversion.**

Electric Telegraph may be said to date from 1836, when Sir Charles Wheatstone and his co-inventor Cooke introduced their Single-Needle instrument, which was soon followed by the Double-Needle apparatus, Morse, in 1837, invented his famous recording instrument. The first electric cable was between Dover and France, and was laid in 1850. The first Atlantic cable was laid in 1858, and the second in 1866. It was in 1899 that the first Marconi wireless telegraph messages were sent between England and France.

Electroencephalograph, an instrument which records the minute voltages produced by the electrical activity of the brain by means of electrodes taped to the scalp. The record of brain waves, known as EEG, shows that there is a general cycle of activity in the brain that underlies both sleep and wakefulness.

Electrolysis is the condition established when an electric current passes through a conducting substance, between electrodes, resulting in decomposition and separation into constituents. Water thus becomes decomposed into hydrogen and oxygen.

Electromagnetic radiation. Radiation consisting of oscillating electronic and magnetic fields travelling together through space. Including visible light, the speed of travel is around 300,000 kms per second. Together with visible light, many different types exist including gamma rays, X-rays, ultraviolet and infrared radiation, microwaves and radio waves.

Electromagnetic waves. See **F14.**

Electron. See **F11, 16.**

Electronic Mail. See **Special Topic, L132.**

Electronic News Gathering (ENG), also known in the United States as Electronic Journalism (EJ) or Electronic Camera Coverage (ECC), is a system for obtaining television pictures by means of very lightweight, portable electronic cameras. ENG is highly suited to the coverage of news events. It is usually operated by a crew of two—cameraman and engineer—who are also equipped with a van or field car serving as a mobile base. Pictures from the unit can be used in three ways: they can be transmitted "live", beamed back by radio link to the studio, or recorded on to a videotape cassette on site and taken back to headquarters for editing and transmission. The chief advantage of ENG lies in its speed, as the use of electronic equipment avoids the delay which occurs in the chemical processing of film before it can be transmitted.

Electronics. The science which deals with the behaviour and control of free electrons. It started with the discovery of the electron by Sir J. J. Thomson in 1897. The practical applications, constituting electronic engineering, have given us radio, radar, photo-electric cells, cathode-ray oscillographs, electronic microscopes, television. Nowadays electronics uses devices like transistors such that the electrons move inside solid matter instead of *in vacuo.* This is sometimes referred to as "solid state electronics". *See also* **Microelectronics.**

Electron Microscope. A microscope in which beams of electrons are focused by magnetic lenses in a manner analogous to the focusing of light beams in the ordinary optical microscope. Modern electron microscopes have very high resolving power and can magnify up to 1,500,000 times, making it possible to explore the cell and the virus. A development of the electron microscope is the scanning electron microscope (stereoscan), developed at Cambridge, which can examine an essentially thick object, giving a very large depth of focus.

Electronvolt, unit of energy used in nuclear physics. It is the amount of energy required to move one electronic charge through a potential difference of one volt. It is very small—$1·6 \times 10^{19}$ joules—and therefore suited to atomic physics. 1 MeV = a million electronvolts; 1 GeV = a thousand million electronvolts; these larger units are used in high energy physics.

Elementary Particle, one of the basic constituents of the material universe. The idea that matter consists of tiny particles goes back to classical times but the modern concept of the atom grew out of the chemistry and physics of the 19th cent. With the discovery of the electron in 1897 and the rise of nuclear physics in the 20th cent., the chemical atom was understood to be a structure built of even more fundamental particles—the electron, the proton and the neutron. In the last few decades, many more particles have been discovered, especially in the study of cosmic rays and by the use of large accelerating machines like those at CERN (Geneva) and Brookhaven National Laboratory (Long Island, New York). Among the later discoveries are the neutrino, the positron, the antiproton, the muon, the pion. These differ in electric charge and mass and other intrinsic properties and many have only a very short lifetime before they change into something else. Whether there is a small number of really elementary particles out of which all the others can be constructed is an unanswered question of contemporary physics. See **F15–17.**

Elements. In chemistry, substances which cannot be separated into two or more simpler chemical substances. 91 elements are found naturally on the earth, some are observed spectroscopically in the stars and planets, and a further fourteen have been made artificially. Between them these elements can appear in some 1,200 different isotopes, of which 317 occur in Nature. (There are 274 stable isotopes among 81 stable elements.) See **F6, F23,** and **F64.**

Elephant, a proboscidian mammal of which only two species survive—the Asiatic, in India, and the African elephant. No other animals possess a trunk. Both males and females have large ivory tusks, of considerable commercial value. The Indian elephant is usually about 2·7 m high and weighs about 3 tonnes; African elephants are larger, weighing about 6 tonnes, and are usually much fiercer. Several fossil elephants of still larger bulk have been discovered, including the mammoth and the mastodon. The Indian elephant is domesticated and used as a beast of burden, and may live 70 years. The ivory trade (banned in 1989) was responsible for the mass slaughter of perhaps 700,000 elephants. This evil trade still continues clandestinely.

Eleusinian Mysteries, festivals common throughout ancient Greece, agricultural in their symbolism.

Elgin Marbles, a collection of ancient Greek sculptures and architectural fragments got together by the 7th Earl of Elgin and brought to England between 1802 and 1812. These celebrated treasures had originally formed part of the Parthenon at Athens, and were probably carved by pupils of the sculptor Phidias. Lord Elgin expended over £70,000 upon them, and they were purchased for £35,000 for the British Museum. The Greek government is pressing for their return.

Elk, the largest animal of the deer family, possessing enormous antlers, and standing, when mature, about 2 m high. The American moose is of the same family.

Elm, a stately, wide-spreading tree having some 20 species spread over north-temperate regions, several of which are native and peculiar to Britain. The grandest of the field elms is the English elm, *Ulmus procera,* which may reach a height of *c.* 42 m and a girth of 8 m. The wych elm, *U. glabra,* or Scots elm, is a valuable hardwood and used in boat-building. The fungus that causes Dutch elm disease is carried from tree to tree by a bark beetle. The fungus came from infected veneer logs from central Europe. Ironically the disease was named after the Dutch workers who discovered its cause! Since re-entering Britain in 1963, Dutch elm disease has caused the death of 12 million trees.

Elzevir, the name of a celebrated family of Dutch printers, who produced editions of Latin, French and German classics, which were highly valued for their beauty of type and accuracy of printing. They flourished in the 17th cent.

E-Mail. See **Special Topic, L132.**

Ember-days are set apart for fasting and prayer in the Western Church, at the periods appointed for ordination, viz., the Wednesday, Friday and Saturday after the first Sunday in Lent, Whit-Sunday, 14 September (Holy Cross Day), and 13 December (St. Lucia's Day); of very ancient origin.

Embossing, the art of stamping in relief, letters or designs upon pliant substances.

Emerald. The rich green variety of beryl (beryllium aluminium silicate). The colour is due to the presence of chromium oxide.

Empire, the style created in France during the reign of Napoleon in architecture and all the arts. It is austerely classical, making much use of columns, pediments and the like in buildings as well as furniture, with eagles and sphinxes, reminiscent of Napoleon's campaigns, as ornaments. The style is heavy, grandiose and with a strong element of the heroic. A typical monument is the *Arc de Triomphe* in Paris (begun 1806), almost a repetition of a Roman model. In painting Jacques Louis David interpreted the style with heroic subjects taken from classical mythology or from Napoleon's career. The style was transmitted to the rest of Europe, remaining magnificent and rich at all the Bonaparte courts. In bourgeois surroundings in Germany and Scandinavia it became simple and domesticated but retained its essence of classical dignity.

Encaenia, a festival commemorating a dedication; at Oxford University the annual commemoration of benefactors, accompanied by the conferring of honorary degrees, is held in June.

Encyclical Letters, a term used in reference to letters addressed by the Pope to his bishops upon matters of doctrine or discipline.

Encyclopaedists, a term first applied to the eminent writers who collaborated in the French *Encyclopédie* (1751-65). They included Diderot, D'Alembert, Voltaire, Helvetius; their writings generally were sceptical as to religion, destructive as to politics and had great influence in popularising the social ideas which afterwards resulted in the French Revolution.

Energy. One of the most fundamental concepts of science. A body in motion possesses *kinetic energy* as a result of the *work* done by the forces creating the motion. But a force which does work to stretch a spring does not create motion. Instead, the work is stored up in the spring and is one example of *potential energy*. A raised body also possesses potential energy which turns into kinetic when the body falls. The *heat energy* contained in a body is the sum of the kinetic and potential energy of the constituent atoms which are vibrating all the time. Heat and motion are obtainable from electrical, magnetic, chemical, atomic, and other sources, and physicists therefore define corresponding forms of energy. The vital point is that all forms of energy are transferable into one another *without loss or gain*. This is the Law of Conservation of Energy. It is one of the most fundamental laws of science, and its general validity is the reason why energy is an important idea. Since Einstein, it has been recognised that mass also is interchangeable with energy. *See* **F18,** *also* **Nuclear Energy.**

Energy Conversion. For practical purposes it is frequently necessary to change energy from one into another of its many forms; indeed almost every activity does this in one way or another. The primary sources of energy are the sun, uranium and other elements from which nuclear energy can be drawn, and the tides. The sun is not much used *directly* because its heat is intermittent and not very intense, but solar cookers and refrigerators have been invented and solar batteries (*q.v.*) are used in spacecraft. The sun can be used *indirectly* because it has produced, *via* living processes, fossil fuels like coal and oil and still continues to generate winds, rain and rivers and hence hydroelectric and wind power. Commonly both fossil fuels and the energy of river or tidal waters are converted into electricity. Windmill type electricity generators are also quite common. The bulk of electricity production is a two-stage process: first fossil or nuclear fuel is used to create heat (*see* **Nuclear Reactors**); then the heat is used to raise steam and drive generators. Efforts are being made to convert heat into electricity more directly, *e.g.*, by using thermoelectric or thermionic effects (*q.v.*), but

these have not been used for large-scale production. Once electrical energy is available, factories can make chemical batteries in great numbers and these can then be used as portable energy sources, as can petrol and other refined forms of fossil fuel. *See* **Battery, Fuel Cell, Solar Battery.**

Engraving is the art of cutting or otherwise forming designs of pictures on wood, stone, or metal surfaces for reproduction by some method of printing. Wood-engraving was the earliest in the field, dating from the 15th cent. Later, engraving on steel and copper plates was introduced, and mezzotint, lithography, stipple, aquatint, etc. Most modern methods of reproduction are based on photography.

Entablature, that portion of a building which surmounts the columns and extends to the roof of the tympana of the pediments; it comprises the architrave, the frieze and the cornice.

Enthalpy, another name for the heat content (H) of a system in thermodynamics. If a system generates heat it is presumed that the heat comes from the enthalpy of the system which by the 1st law of thermodynamics (**F20**) thus falls. It can be combined with the entropy (S) in an equation which defines the important thermodynamic quantity called the Gibbs Free Energy: $G = H - TS$ where T is the thermodynamic temperature. G is important in the prediction of chemical change (**F26**).

Entropy, one of the most important quantities in thermodynamics, symbol S. According to Clausius' statement of the Second Law (**F20**) the entropy of an isolated system cannot decrease. Although introduced by Clausius it arose from a consideration of Carnot's studies of the limitation of the convertibility of heat into work. It is most easily viewed as disorder in the statistical approach introduced by Boltzmann. This may be illustrated by considering the separate sets of coloured balls in a box. This is an ordered arrangement (of low entropy). The natural tendency is for the balls to mix and for the colours to become disordered (of higher entropy). We do not expect the opposite process for the balls to spontaneously separate, *i.e.*, we do not expect the entropy to decrease. In the context of energy changes, say in heat engines, the entropy change is equal to the heat change divided by the (thermodynamic) temperature (*see* **L3**).

Environment Agency, new government body proposed in 1994 to police emissions to air, land, rivers and coastal waters. It will merge the powers of the National Rivers Authority, Her Majesty's Inspectorate of Pollution and local waste regulation authorities. The chairman designate is Baron De Ramsey, an East Anglian landowner.

Enzymes. Organic catalysts which accelerate chemical processes occurring in living organisms. There are a large number present in the cell, and most have a high degree of specificity. Enzyme mechanisms are the key to basic biological processes. *See* **F32(1).**

Ephemoptera or **May-flies,** an order of insects. In the larval condition they exist from two to three years aquatically, but no sooner do they arrive at maturity than their lives are hurried to a close. They rise up in pyramids on warm summer nights, take no food, propagate and perish. The Latin name expresses the fact that the adults have an ephemeral existence.

Epiphany, a Christian festival celebrated on 6 January, originally an old solstice festival, celebrating the birth of light.

Equator, the imaginary great circle of the earth, every point of which is 90 degrees from the earth's poles, and dividing the northern from the southern hemisphere. It is from this circle that the latitude of places north and south is reckoned. The celestial equator is the circle in which the plane of the earth's equator meets the celestial sphere (the imaginary sphere, in which the observer is at the centre, used for representing the apparent positions of the heavenly bodies).

Equinox, the time when the sun crosses the plane of the earth's equator, making day and night of equal length.

Eras are distinctive periods of time associated with some remarkable historical event or personage. *The Christian era* is computed according to a 6th-cent. reckoning to begin with Jesus's birth, AD. 1. The date is placed some years too late. Scholars now believe that Jesus was born *c.* 4 B.C. The *Jewish era* dates from 3761 B.C.; the *Julian era* from the alteration of the calendar by Julius Caesar 45 B.C.; the *Mohammedan era* from the date of the *Hejira*, or the flight of Mohammed from Mecca to Medina, which is A.D., 622, 16 July, in the Julian Calendar.

Erbium, belongs to the group of rare-earth metals discovered by Mosander in 1842. Element no. 68, symbol Er.

Erg, the unit of work and energy in the centimetre-gram-second system; the energy involved when a force of 1 dyne moves its point of application through a distance of 1 cm.

Ernie, the name given to the "electronic random number indicator equipment", the electronic machine which selected the prizewinning numbers in the first Premium Bond draw, June 1957.

Eros. This asteroid is 24–32 km in diameter. It comes closer to the earth than any other member of the solar system with the exception of the moon and several very small asteroids. Determination of solar parallax based on observations of Eros in 1930–31 yielded until then the most accurate estimate of the distance of the sun from the earth. *See* **Astronomical unit.**

Erse, a term used by Lowland Scottish, and English writers for the Gaelic language spoken in the Highlands of Scotland. Sometimes erroneously applied to Irish, the Gaelic language as spoken in Ireland and revived as an official language in recent times. Dr. Johnson, Sir Walter Scott, and other writers used "Erse" to signify Scottish Gaelic. The language of the Scottish Lowlands (that used by Robert Burns) is related to the English language and not to Gaelic and is variously termed Scots, Braid Scots, the Doric, the Scottish vernacular, and fashionably of late, Lallans.

Escurial or **Escorial,** Spanish monastery built in the mountains near Madrid by Philip II to commemorate the victory over the French at Saint-Quentin (1557). A palace was added later and it also includes a church, library and royal mausoleum. Built in granite in sombre style, it is one of the finest buildings in Europe.

Eskimo. Popular name for the Inuit peoples of the Arctic, living in Canada, Greenland, Alaska and the northern territories of Russia. Canada has recently agreed to grant self-government to an Arctic Eskimo territory (Nunavut).

Esperanto, an artificial international language created by Ludwig Zamenhof of Warsaw and first published in 1887. It does not seek to replace national languages but to serve as a second language for international communication. It is based on the internationality of many words in the principal modern languages, and is entirely phonetic in spelling and pronunciation. In 1995 there are *c.* 10,000 British speakers of the language. Other artificial languages are Volapuk, Ido and Glosa, a grammar-free international language based on Latin and Greek. Today (1995), Esperanto is estimated as being spoken by six to eight million people in 120 countries. Over 100 magazines and newspapers are published in Esperanto.

Estates of the Realm in Great Britain are the Lords Spiritual, the Lords Temporal and the Commons. They are the great classes invested with distinct political powers, and whose concurrence is necessary to legislation.

Esters. Organic chemicals formed by combining an alcohol with an acid. They have a pleasant smell, and occur naturally in plants as the scent of flowers. Manufactured for use in the perfumery industry, and as flavourings in food. Some esters are used as solvents, notably amyl-acetate ("pear drops") in quick-drying paints. The polymeric fibre "Terylene" consists of chains of molecules containing many ester groups, formed by reacting an alcohol having two alcoholic (OH) groups with an acid having two acid (COOH) groups.

Etching, a technical method for producing graphic work and works of art. A plate, traditionally of copper, is covered with wax; the design or picture desired is drawn with a sharp implement which penetrates the wax. When the plate is exposed to the action of an acid this will etch into the copper where the lines have been drawn.

The wax is then removed, ink is applied to the plate with its engraving, and the design or picture can be printed on to paper in many copies. Rembrandt, Goya and others made great and original works of art in the technique, but it was also widely used for reproductive purposes before the invention of photography. Hogarth painted his famous pictures in oil and reproduced them graphically.

Ether, in chemistry, is a volatile inflammable liquid composed of carbon, hydrogen and oxygen. It is a valuable anaesthetic obtained by heating alcohol with sulphuric acid. In physics, in the 19th cent., all space was supposed to be filled with a substance called ether, the chief property of which was to carry light waves, *i.e.*, light was supposed to be waves in this all-pervading medium known as the ether. Speculation and experiment concerned with the ether were very fruitful in advancing physics. Ultimately the attempts by Michelson and Morley to detect the motion of the earth through the ether were unsuccessful in this respect but profoundly successful in stimulating the theory of relativity. The ether concept has now been abandoned. *See also* **F17(2).**

Ethylene (also called ethene). A gas compounded of carbon and hydrogen, it is related to acetylene and ethane. Industrially it is obtained as a by-product in petroleum refining. It has wide uses as a starting material in the industrial manufacture of intermediates, especially alcohol. Its most important application is in the production of polythene (poly-ethylene). *See* **Catalyst.**

Etruscans, people believed to have come from Asia Minor who colonised Italy about 900 B.C., settled in what is now Tuscany and part of Umbria, reached the height of their civilisation about 500 B.C., and were ultimately absorbed by the Romans. They were skilled technitians in bronze, silver and goldwork.

Euro-dollar Market. An international financial market, located mainly in Britain and Europe, for lending and borrowing dollars, *i.e.*, titles to dollar deposits in United States banks.

European Space Agency was created in 1975 with headquarters in Paris. Examples of space research which it has undertaken include the Giotto probe to Halley's Comet, involvement with the Cassini mission to Saturn and the space station Spacelab, which is carried into space in the cargo bay of the Space Shuttle.

Europium, element no. 63, symbol Eu, discovered by Demarcay in 1906. A member of the rare-earth metal group.

Evaporation is the process by which a solid or liquid is resolved into vapour by heat. The opposite process is condensation. Wherever a liquid or solid surface is exposed, evaporation takes place into the space above. If the vapour is continually removed the solid or liquid vanishes into vapour; the higher the temperature the quicker the process. If the vapour is confined, then it collects, getting more concentrated until as many atoms of vapour are condensing as are evaporating. The vapour is then said to be saturated. Evaporation of water from sea, soil, plants, skin, *etc.*, is continuously in progress.

Everest Expeditions. For many years after Mt. Everest had been shown to be the highest mountain in the world, political conditions in Nepal, lying south of the summit, and in Tibet, to the north, prevented mountaineers from attempting an ascent. At last in 1921 the Tibetan authorities gave permission, and the first expedition, organised, as were all subsequent British expeditions, by a joint committee of the Royal Geographical Society and the Alpine Club, and led by Col. C. K. Howard-Bury, was sent out. This was primarily a reconnaissance; besides mapping the northern flanks, it found a practicable route up the mountain. By 1939, six further expeditions had climbed on the northern face. Some were baulked by bad weather, others by problems previously little known, such as the effect of high altitudes on the human body and spirit. Nevertheless, notable climbs were accomplished. In 1924, for example, Col. E. F. Norton reached 8,589 m, and it was on this expedition that G. L. Mallory and Andrew Irvine were seen going well at about the same height. They never returned, however, and what disaster befell them is not known. When the British 1953 Expedition led by Col. John Hunt (now Lord Hunt), was being organised, stress was laid on three main points; proper acclimatisation of the climbers; use of oxygen for the final stages; and the establishment of very high altitude camps, so that the final assault parties would set out fresh and unencumbered. Great attention was also paid to recent developments in diet, clothing and equipment. In all these matters the 1953 expedition was able to draw on the accumulated experience of its predecessors. By the end of April, a base camp had been established below the ice-fall, and with the aid of thirty-four Sherpa porters supplies had been carried up into the Western Cwm. The next critical stage was the ascent of the steep head of the cwm, the Lhotse face, with the threat of avalanches always present. D, most strenuous efforts, a camp was established on the South Col (7,869 m) on 21 May. From this camp on 26 May, T. D. Bourdillon and R. C. Evans climbed the South Peak of Everest (8,760 m), then the highest altitude ever attained. On 28 May Edmund Hillary and the Sherpa leader, Tenzing Norgay, spent the night at the highest camp (8,510 m) and on the following day, 29 May, climbed to the South Summit, negotiated the difficult final ridge, and reached the summit of Everest. On 17 May 1993 (exactly 40 years later) Rebecca Stephens became the first British woman to conquer Everest.

Evolution, in the words of Sir Julian Huxley (d. 1975), "a natural process of irreversible change which generates novelty, variety and increase of organisation". The theory, as laid down by Darwin, is that all existing species, genera and classes of animals and plants have developed from a few simple forms by processes of change and selection. Up to the time of Darwin a large part of the civilised world believed that life had been created suddenly at the beginning of the world which God had created, according to Archbishop Usher, on 22 October 4004 B.C. The evidence of the rocks, however, has given a more convincing theory of creation, and by studying the fossils preserved in the various layers of the earth's crust the past history of the earth's life has been pieced together. Darwin has been called the Newton of biology. *See also* **Section F.**

Exchequer, which derives its name from the checkered tablecloth on which accounts were calculated in early Norman times, is a term connected with the revenues of the Crown. In former times it had jurisdiction in all revenue matters. The term Exchequer is now applied to the Governmental department which deals with the public revenues, the working head of which is the Chancellor of the Exchequer.

Existentialism. *See* **Section J.**

Exploration. Modern exploration began in the second half of the 15th cent. with the voyages of the great Portuguese and Spanish discoverers. They were followed by sailors of other European nations, who profited from their developments in navigation and from their charts, and in less than one hundred years the coastlines of much of the Americas, Africa and South-west Asia had been revealed and the globe circumnavigated. The motives of these early explorers were mixed: they were seeking adventure, trade, plunder, national power and the conversion of the heathen. Few if any were directly interested in advancing scientific knowledge. But from the reports of their voyages and travels, scholars at home compiled descriptions of the strange new world which stimulated their successors to undertake more systematic enquiries. One of the earliest English expeditions to be despatched for scientific research was that of William Dampier on the *Roebuck*, which was sent out by the Admiralty in 1699 to examine the coasts of North-west Australia. In the 18th cent. British explorers were at work mainly in the Pacific Ocean, with the object of breaking the Spanish monopoly of trade. Capt. James Cook sailed thither in 1769 to observe first the transit of Venus at Tahiti, and then to search for the alleged great southern continent. On this voyage he discovered and charted much of the coasts of New Zealand and the east coast of Australia. On his second voyage he was the

first to sail across the Antarctic Circle, and he showed that the southern continent was much smaller than had been supposed. By 1800 the general outlines of the continents, except for Antarctica were known, and explorers in the 19th cent. were largely engaged in opening up the interiors. In Africa British explorers solved two problems which had puzzled men for centuries: Mungo Park and Richard Lander established the true course of the River Niger, and Sir Richard Burton, J. H. Speke, Sir Samuel Baker and others revealed the true sources of the Nile. The greatest African explorer of that age was undoubtedly David Livingstone, the missionary, who in three great journeys explored the Zambesi and the region of the Great Lakes, spreading the Gospel, fighting the slave trade, and opening up the interior to settlement and trade. In North America Alexander Mackenzie was the first to cross the main breadth of the continent from sea to sea. In Asia motives were also mixed; men like Charles Doughty, who explored in Arabia, and Sir Francis Younghusband, who journeyed from China to India across the Gobi and the Himalayas, were impelled by a love of adventure and the quest for knowledge, but political considerations were often involved.

Explosives, substances which burn violently to produce gases in such volume that an explosion is induced. Gunpowder was the first explosive to be used; Roger Bacon's powder, consisting of charcoal, sulphur and saltpetre, was the only effective explosive until the 19th cent., but it was difficult to control. Nitroglycerine (glyceryl trinitrate) was first compounded in 1847 by adding glycerine to a mixture of sulphuric acid and nitric acid. In 1866 Alfred Nobel discovered how to make dynamite by absorbing nitroglycerine in the fine sand kieselguhr. Cordite was the joint invention of Sir Frederick Abel and Sir James Dewar (1889). It came into general use as a propellant. High explosives, providing bursting charge for shells and bombs, include TNT (trinitrotoluene), picric acid, cyclonite (RDX) and many others. Slurry explosives can be pumped on to the site and therefore offer advantages in transportation and safety; they are also waterproof. Chemical explosives have been eclipsed by nuclear explosives which have developed from the first atom bomb (dropped on Hiroshima 6 August 1945) to the 100-megaton hydrogen bomb.

Expressionism, a modern art movement confined primarily to the non-Latin countries of Europe which sought to give expression to intimate and personal emotions by means of distortions of line and colour and simplified style which carried a greater impact in terms of feeling. Broadly speaking, this has been characteristic of northern art in general. (*See* **Gothic.**) The term is usually used of the modern movement which influenced the Post-impressionists and subsequent movements in France. Tired of the naturalism of the Impressionists, such artists as van Gogh, Gauguin, Matisse and Rouault, together with the Fauvists (*q.v.*) made use of simple outlines and strong colours. Apart from Toulouse-Lautrec, the principal Expressionists were Norwegian, like Munch, or German, like the painters of *Die Brücke* and *Der Blaue Reiter* groups. Individual artists were Ensor, Kokoschka, Nolde, Rouault and Soutine.

F

Fabian Society. *See* **Section J.**

Fables are fictitious narratives intended to enforce some moral precept, and may be either in prose or verse, and deal with personified animals and objects or with human beings. Aesop in ancient times and Hans Christian Andersen and the Brothers Grimm (in many of their stories) in later days, have given fables. Mention must also be made of La Fontaine's and Krylov's fables.

Fairs were established in mediaeval times as a means of bringing traders and customers together at stated periods, and formed the chief means of distribution. The great English fairs of early times were those of Winchester and Stourbridge near Cambridge. Traders from the Netherlands and the Baltic gathered there with the great merchants of London, and goods of every kind, wholesale and retail, were sold. One of the biggest trade fairs was at Nijni-Novgorod, founded in the 17th cent.; other big continental fairs were those of Leipzig (founded in the 12th cent.), Lyons and Prague. Expositions of advanced industrial products are still popular today.

Fairy Rings are the circles caused in grassland by certain fungi. The circles expand outwards as the fungus spreads, the fruiting bodies being at the periphery. Farther inward where the fungi are decaying the grass grows more strongly, fertilised by the nitrogen released from the rotting fungi. In olden times these rings were held to be the scene of fairy dances.

Falcon, name given to diurnal birds of prey which belong to the same family, *Falconidae*, as the hawk, eagle, buzzard, kite and harrier. They are swift of wing and feed on birds and small mammals. These birds have long, pointed wings, strong, hooked and notched bill, long, curved claws and an eye of great power. They are found all over the world. Those that breed in Britain are the Kestrel (the most common), Hobby (one of the swiftest of European birds), Merlin and Peregrine, a swift and magnificent bird with slate-grey back, blackish crown, black "moustache" and whitish breast. Other members of the family are the Gyr Falcon from northern latitudes, Iceland and Greenland, which is a winter visitor to Britain, the Lanner, Saker, Eleonora's falcon, Red-footed falcon and the Lesser Kestrel. The Gyr Falcon and the Peregrine were used in the sport of falconry in olden times. Because of its fearlessness and larger size, the female bird was used. When the quarry was sighted, the bird was unhooded, set free, and after mounting high into the air would dart swiftly down to strike the prey. The heron was the usual victim.

Fall-out. Radioactive material produced by nuclear explosions which may cause bodily and genetic damage. (1) *Local fall-out*, due to the return to earth of larger particles, occurs locally, and within a few hours after the explosion; (2) *Tropospheric fall-out*, due to particles which remain in the troposphere and come down within a month or so, possibly all over the world, but within the altitude in which the explosion occurred; (3) *Stratospheric fall-out*, which comes from fragments taken up into the stratosphere and then deposited, in the course of many years, uniformly all over the globe. The two radioactive materials which have given rise to the greatest concern for the health of the individual are strontium-90 and iodine-131. Both these materials are liable to become concentrated in certain parts of the human body, strontium-90 in bone and iodine-131 in the thyroid gland. Radiation exposure may produce genetic effects, that is effects which may show up in succeeding generations. An extensive survey was carried out by scientists of the US Atomic Energy Commission on the islands of Bikini atoll, site of some 23 nuclear tests, 1946–58. Their records, published in 1969, revealed that the intensity of radioactivity underneath the point of explosion was still exceedingly high. Most of the radiation remaining was due to the radioactive isotope caesium-137. The variation in intensity from one place to another seemed to be correlated with the variations of vegetation: where there was little vegetation weathering had been rapid. (The nuclear test ban treaty, 1963, applies to all nuclear tests except those held underground.)

Fantail, a variety of the domestic pigeon; also a genus of Australian birds of the *Muscicapidae* family. A small New Zealand bird is called a fantail.

Fan Tracery, a complicated style of roof-vaulting, elaborately moulded, in which the lines of the curves in the masonry or other material employed diverge equally in every direction. It is characteristic of the late Perpendicular period of Gothic architecture, and may be seen in St. George's Chapel at Windsor and the Chapel of Henry VII at Westminster Abbey.

Farmer-General, the name given to the financiers who in the days of the old French monarchy farmed certain taxes, contracting to pay the Government a fixed sum yearly, on condition that the unspecified taxes were collected and appropriated by themselves. The revolution of 1789 swept the Farmer General away.

Fascism. *See* **Section J.**

Fata Morgana, the name given to a curious mirage often observed over the Straits of Messina, attributed to the magic of the fairy Morgana, half-sister of King Arthur, who was fabled to live in Calabria.

Fathers of the Church were early writers who laid the foundations of Christian ritual and doctrine. The earliest were the Apostolic Fathers (*q.v.*). The Four Fathers of the Latin Church were St. Ambrose, St. Jerome, St. Augustine and St. Gregory the Great. The Four Fathers of the Greek Church were St. Basil, St. Gregory Nazianzen, St. John Chrysostom and St. Athanasius.

Fathom, a nautical measure, the six-foot stretch (1·8 m) of a man's arms. Replaced by the metre on British Admiralty charts, but continued on yachtsmen's coastal charts.

Fatigue, a condition leading to breakage when a solid component, *e.g.*, an axle, is subjected to a large number of fluctuating repetitive stresses. Fatigue is the cause of most failures in service of metal engineering components though fatigue is not confined to metallic materials alone. Fatigue failures result from the *repetition*, not simply from the *size* of the stresses; indeed, fatigue breakage can result from stresses much lower than the material could stand if the load were applied steadily. Fatigue causes minute cracks, usually at the surface, which grow and spread. Early detection is difficult and fatigue, discovered by the railway engineers of the 19th cent., remains a severe engineering problem.

Fats are important foodstuffs. In physiology they constitute a valuable form of reserve food. They contain carbon, hydrogen and oxygen; chemically they are described as esters of glycerol (glycerine). Commonest fats are stearin, palmitin and olein, esters formed by the combination of glycerol with stearic, palmitic and oleic acid respectively. Fats are converted into soap by alkali; this process (saponification) also releases glycerol.

Fatwa, an edict issued by a Moslem religious leader (*e.g.* the death threat to Salman Rushdie issued in 1989 by Ayatollah Khomeini).

Fault, a term designating a breakage coupled with displacement of geological strata. *See* **F9**(2).

Fauvism (French *Fauve* = wild beast), a term used, at first contemptuously, to describe the work of a group of French painters who first exhibited at the Salon d'Automne in Paris in 1905. The most prominent among them was Henri Matisse. Forms are freely distorted and colours are selected and applied for their emotive power with no necessary reference to the "real" colour of the object in question. Other famous *Fauves* were Derain, Vlaminck and Rouault. By 1908 the group had lost its cohesion and its members went their separate ways.

February, the second month of the year, contains in ordinary years 28 days, but in leap years 29 days. When first introduced into the Roman calendar by Numa, *c.* 700 B.C. it was made the last month of the year, preceding January, but in 452 B.C. the position of the two months was changed, February following January.

Federation. *See* **Confederation.**

Félibrige, a movement founded in 1854 to revive the ancient glories of Provence, initiated by the French poet Frédéric Mistral.

Felspar, the name given to a group of minerals, silicates of aluminium with some calcium and sodium, or potassium, which make up probably more than half of the earth's crust. It is formed in granite and other rocks, both igneous and metamorphic.

Fenestella, the niche set apart on the south side of the altar for the piscina in Roman Catholic churches.

Fermentation, the action of chemical ferments or *enzymes* in bringing about chemical changes in the materials of living animals and plants, *e.g.*, the breaking-down of sugar by yeast into alcohol.

Ferret, a domesticated polecat. It is about half the size of a cat and is bred in captivity to hunt rats and rabbits. It has a long sinuous body and short legs which enable it to enter rabbit and rat holes and chase the quarry out to guns or into nets. Such ferreting is a popular country sport.

Ferrites are compounds containing iron, oxygen, and one or two of a certain range of other possible metallic elements. Ferrites have recently become very important technically, because, unlike ordinary magnetic materials, they combine strong magnetism with electrical insulating properties. Ferrite-rod aerials are now common in portable radios, and ferrite devices are used in radar. *See* **F22**(2).

Feudalism. *See* **Section J.**

Fieldfare, the largest member of the thrush family, a regular winter visitor to Britain from Scandinavia. It is brown in colour with a lighter spotted breast and a grey head.

Field-Marshal, the highest ranking title in the British army, and only bestowed on royal personages and generals who have attained great distinction. The first British Field-Marshal was created in 1736, when John, Duke of Argyll, had the title conferred upon him by George II.

Fifth Column. When Franco, the Spanish dictator, revolted against the Spanish Republic in 1936 and attacked Madrid with four armies, his commander, General Mola declared that a group of fascists within the city was assisting the besiegers. The term is used to describe a body of spies behind a fighting front.

Fighting-Fish, small pugnacious Siamese fish with long caudal and ventral fins. They are kept in glass globes in Siam, and when brought into contact will fight to the death, these encounters being the occasion of much gambling.

Filibuster, a name first given to pirates and buccaneers in the 17th cent. who took possession of small islands or lonely coast lands, and there maintained themselves apart from any governing authority. In later times the term was used to specify men taking part in expeditions whose object was to appropriate tracts of country, and settle upon them in disregard of international law. The most notable expeditions of this kind in modern times were those of Narciso Lopez against Cuba in 1850-51, and of William Walker against Nicaragua, between 1855 and 1860. Both leaders were captured and executed. The term is also used to express the right of a minority in the United States Senate for unlimited debate, which is used on occasions to delay legislation.

Finches, a large family of small birds belonging to the Passerine or perching order of birds. There are about 200 species, including greenfinch, hawfinch, chaffinch, goldfinch, siskin, bullfinch, crossbill, linnet, twite and bunting.

Fir, a cone-bearing tree with small evergreen leaves and of considerable use as timber. There are two types: the Silver Firs and the Douglas Firs numbering about 25 species. All these firs attain to a considerable height, and all yield turpentine or other resinous material.

Fire-damp. *See* **Methane.**

Fire-Fly, a small winged insect of the *Eleteridae* family, is able to throw out a strong phosphorescent light in the dark. There are some remarkable specimens in tropical countries.

Fire of London, of 1666, extended from East to West, from the Tower to the Temple church, and northward to Holborn Bridge. It broke out in a baker's shop in Pudding Lane, and lasted four days, and destroyed 87 churches, including St. Paul's Cathedral, and many public buildings, among them the Royal Exchange, the Custom House and the Guildhall. In the ruins were 13,200 houses and 400 streets. About 100,000 people were made homeless yet in about 10 years all the houses had been rebuilt. The plague had not disappeared from London when the fire occurred.

Firkin, a former measure of capacity, the fourth part of a barrel, now only used in reference to a small cask or tub for butter, lard, allow, etc.

Fischer-Tropsch Process. A process for making synthetic petrol from carbon monoxide and hydrogen. The synthesis is accelerated by cobalt-thoria and nickel-thoria catalysts.

Fish Louse. Parasitic crustacea found on marine and fresh-water fishes and whales.

Fission, Nuclear. A nuclear reaction in which the nucleus of an atom (*e.g.*, uranium 235, plutonium) captures a neutron, and the unstable nucleus so produced breaks into two nearly equal fragments and throws out several neutrons as well. In biology the term fission is applied to reproduction by fragmentation of a single-cell organism, as in amoeba. *See* **F13**(1).

Flagella, single hair like projections found on many micro-organisms. Their sole function is, by complicated motion, to move the organism about. They are longer and less versatile than cilia (*q.v.*).

Flag Officer, a British naval officer who enjoys the right of carrying a flag at the mast-head of his ship, and is of the rank of Admiral of the Fleet, Admiral, Vice-Admiral or Rear-Admiral.

Flagship, the ship that flies the Admiral's flag, and from which orders proceed.

Flamingo, a strangely beautiful, extremely slender wading bird of white and rose-pink plumage with long, slender legs and neck and a long, down-curved bill with which it rakes the mud and obtains its food of worms and molluscs. The wings are bright crimson, bordered with black, and a flock in flight is a picture of singular beauty. There is a large and famous colony in the Camargue, S.E. France.

Flash-Point. This is found by heating an oil in a special cup and taking the temperature at which sufficient vapour is produced to ignite when a small flame is applied. It is an index of the inflammability of oils.

Fleas. Fleas are small parasitic insects belonging to the order *Aphaniptera* (so called because these creatures have no wings). They obtain their food by sucking blood from their host. They are laterally compressed, which immediately distinguishes them from lice. The human flea (*Pulex irritans*) is able to jump vertically a distance of over 18 cm.

Fleet Prison, a noted debtors' prison that stood on the east side of Farringdon Street, London. It was notorious for the cruelties inflicted on prisoners, particularly under the wardenship of Thomas Bainbridge who took charge in 1728. It was pulled down in 1846.

Fleet Street, a famous thoroughfare in London, until 1990 the centre of journalism and newspaperdom, though it was long celebrated for its taverns where the literary coteries of the day were wont to meet. It takes its name from the Fleet stream which used to run from Hampstead through Holborn to the Thames at Blackfriars.

Flemings, the Dutch-speaking people of Flanders, whose ancestors of mediaeval times excelled in the textile arts: England owes its early eminence as a manufacturing nation to the migration of numbers of Flemings to this country in the 16th and 17th cent. *See also* **Walloons.**

Fleur de Lis, the former national emblem of France, the flower of the lily. It was superseded by the Tricolour in 1789, but is still adhered to by the supporters of the old French royalties.

Flint, consists of granular chalcedony with some opaline silica, and occurs as nodules and bands in the Chalk. It is hard and has a conchoidal fracture, so enabling it to be used in making cutting implements in prehistoric times. Before the invention of lucifer matches, it was used along with steel for striking lights.

Flint implements are objects found in the younger geological strata, and constituting evidence of the condition and life of the period. They include knives, clubs, arrow-heads, scrapers, etc., used as weapons, tools and possibly as surgical instruments and in religious ceremonies. Similar to prehistoric specimens are the flint and obsidian implements of some of the primitive peoples of today. Ritual weapons and sacrificial knives continued to be made of stone long after the introduction of metals for practical purposes.

Flounder, one of the most familiar of the smaller

flat fishes common round the British coasts, and seldom attaining a weight of over 1·3 kg.

Fluoridation, the process of adding the element fluorine, in the form of suitable compounds, to something deficient in it. Commonly met with as a proposal to add fluorides (fluorine compounds) to drinking water to combat dental decay, especially in children. Some toothpastes are fluoridated and fluoride can also be taken as tablets and in other ways. In 1976 a working party of the Royal College of Physicians recommended that water supplies should be fluoridated when the natural fluoride level is below 1 mg/litre. This recommendation drew on many investigations throughout the world giving evidence for the effectiveness of fluoride in the prevention of decay without harmful side-effects. There is, however, a body of opinion unconvinced by this and opposed to adding fluoride to drinking water, one argument being that to take or not to take fluoride should be a personal decision.

Fluorine, chemical element, no. 9, member of the halogen family, symbol F, it is found in combination with calcium in fluorspar, and occurs in minute quantities in certain other minerals. Discovered by Scheele in 1771, it was first obtained by Moissan in 1886. A pale yellow gas, it is very reactive and combines with most elements except oxygen. Its acid, hydrogen fluoride, etches glass, the fluorine combining with the silicon to form volatile silicon fluoride. Organic fluorine compounds have found use as very stable polymers which resist a wide variety of chemical actions.

Fluorescent Lamp. *See* **Electric Light and Ultra-Violet Rays.**

Fluorocarbons are hydrocarbons in which some or all of the hydrogen atoms have been replaced by atoms of chlorine or fluorine. They are non-toxic, non-flammable and chemically inert gases or low boiling point liquids. These properties make them very suitable for use as refrigerants, and propellants in fire-extinguishers and aerosols. The most widely used fluorocarbons are the chlorofluoromethanes (CCl_3F, CCl_2F_2, CCl_2F and $CHClF_2$). In 1974 it was first suggested that the vast release of fluorocarbons into the atmosphere due to the greatly increased use of aerosols could cause a significant depletion of the protective ozone (*q.v.*) layer in the upper atmosphere. The mechanism for this involves the decomposition of fluorocarbons at high altitudes as a result of intense solar irradiation. The chlorine atoms so released can then catalyse the conversion of ozone into ordinary molecular oxygen. The degree of ozone depletion that will result is a matter of considerable current controversy. Similarly, opinions differ as to the detrimental effect ozone depletion might have on the incidence of skin cancer and on the climate.

Fluorspar, a mineral; chemically calcium fluoride. Can be colourless, green or yellow, but is most commonly purple. Blue fluorspar under the name of Derbyshire "blue John" has been used for ornamental purposes.

Fly, the popular name for a large number of insects with one pair of wings and a proboscis terminating in a sucker through which fluid substances can be drawn up. The best-known species are the common house-fly, the blue-bottle and the blow-fly. In the larval form flies are maggots, and feed upon decaying substances, animal flesh, etc. Flies are able to walk upon ceilings or upright surfaces by having suckers at the soles of their feet. *See* **Diptera.**

Flycatcher, member of a large family of small birds, the Muscicapidae. They are insect feeders, catch their food in the air, and are distributed over most countries of the world. The spotted and the pied nest in Britain, which they visit from April to September.

Flying Fish are frequently to be seen in southern waters, and are capable of gliding considerable distances without touching the water. To build up speed for its "take-off" the fish swims rapidly, to break the surface at 24–32 km/h. Maximum air speed is about 64 km/h.

Flying Fox, a member of the bat family, but of much larger size, and confined to the tropical and sub-tropical Old World. Like the bats, it is nocturnal, but it feeds entirely on fruits.

Flying Lemur. *See* **Colugo.**

Flying Lizard, or *Draco*, an Asiatic lizard, possessing wing-like projections from each side which enable it to make flying leaps through the air, though not sufficient for continuous flight.

Flying Saucers, the name given to certain saucer-like shapes which have on occasion been seen travelling through the atmosphere. For some time speculation was rife, especially in America, but it is now believed that when not hallucinations, meteorological or cosmic-ray balloons, they are nothing more than atmospheric phenomena like mirages or mock suns caused by unusual atmospheric conditions. Described by Dr. Menzel, astrophysics professor at Harvard, "as real as rainbows are real, and no more dangerous". *See also* **Section J.**

Flying Squirrel, rodents of which there are several species in Europe, Asia and America. It possesses a parachute-like fold of skin by means of which it projects itself through the air. In appearance they are much like ordinary squirrels, to which they are related. The African flying squirrels belong to a different family.

Fog is caused by the presence of particles of condensed water vapour or smoke in the surface layers of the atmosphere, the term being applied meteorologically when the resulting obscurity is such as to render objects invisible at distances of up to 1 km. Fogs are frequently formed when the air near the ground is cooled below its dew-point temperature by radiation on a still, cloudless night; by flowing over a relatively cold land or water mass; or by mixing with a colder air stream. An accumulation of smoke over a large city may cause a high fog cutting off the daylight and producing gloom. *See* **Pollution, Aerosol.**

Foliation, a geological term applied to rocks whose component minerals are arranged in parallel layers as the result of strong metamorphic action.

Folio, a printing term for a sheet of paper folded once, a half sheet constituting a leaf.

Folklore concerns itself with the mental and spiritual life of the people—both civilised and primitive—as expressed in the traditional beliefs, customs, institutions and sayings that have been handed down from generation to generation by word of mouth and with the observation, recording and interpretation of such traditions. (The word *folklore* itself was first suggested and used—as two words *Folk Lore*—by W. J. Thoms in the *Athenaeum* of 22 August 1846, and was at once absorbed into the English language.) Traditional lore of the kind included in the term folklore takes many forms and ranges from omens of good and bad luck (spilling the salt, breaking a mirror, dropping an umbrella, etc.) and the wearing of amulets or the possession of talismans (such as the horseshoe) as protection against misfortune, to elabor-ate ceremonial dances such as the Abbots Bromley Horn Dance, the Hobby horses of Padstow and Minehead the Northern sword-dances and the Christmas mummers' plays. Especially important are the beliefs and customs associated with birth, babyhood, marriage and death such being occasions when the individuals concerned require special protection or when unusual happenings can be used for foretelling their future. The child born on a Sunday will be the luckiest; rocking on an empty cradle will ensure the speedy arrival of a new baby; throwing an old shoe after a newly-married couple brings them luck; the bride should be carried over the threshold of the new home; on the sea-coast, death is believed to take place at the ebb-tide; the bees must be told of the death of the master of the house, or they will leave the hive. Another very large section of the subject deals with the traditional sayings and practices associated with particular days and seasons of the year—calendar customs, as they are called. The eating of pancakes on Shrove Tuesday; Mother Sunday customs and the simnel cake; Good Friday as the right day for planting potatoes, but emphatically the wrong day for washing clothes or cutting one's finger-nails; the necessity of wearing something new on Easter Sunday; the children's maypole dances and May garlands; midsummer fires; All Hallowe'en as the most favourable occasion for divining the future—especially in respect of marriage—and for games and sports such as apple-bobbing; the numerous practices accompanying the harvest. All these are examples of calendar customs; their full story would occupy several volumes. Folklorists are interested in all such oral tradition because they think that to a large extent it represents what folk have mentally stored up from the past and transmitted to their descendants throughout the centuries, and because therefore it is able to assist other historic methods—ethnographical, linguistic, archaeological, etc.—in the elucidation of the early story of man. In those countries with a great diversity of peoples in all stages of culture, a knowledge of folklore and what it can teach of the mind of man is of great importance to administrators. The Folk-Lore Society was founded in 1878, and that part of the subject represented by song and dance has now its own organisation in the English Folk Dance and Song Society.

Footpath. In English law a highway over which the public have a right of way on foot only, other than such a highway at the side of a public road. *See also* **Long-Distance Walks.**

Force, as a term in physics, signifies an influence or exertion which, when made to act upon a body, tends to move it if at rest, or to affect or stop its progress if it be already in motion. In the c.g.s. system, the unit of force is the dyne; in the foot-pound-second system, the poundal; in the SI system, the newton.

Formaldehyde. Chemically it lies between methyl alcohol and formic acid; oxidation of methyl alcohol yields formaldehyde, and oxidation of formaldehyde produces formic acid. It is used as a disinfectant, in silvering mirrors, and in the manufacture of phenolformaldehyde plastics (of which bakelite is the best-known example). Solutions of formaldehyde in water, formalin, are used to preserve biological specimens.

Forme, a body of letterpress type, composed and secured for printing from; or a stereotype or electrotype. The former is used more for newspaper formes and the latter in good book work.

Formic Acid can be obtained from a colourless fluid secreted by ants and other insects and plants. It is a strong irritant. Commercially it is obtained from sodium formate, which is synthesised by the absorption of carbon monoxide in caustic soda. It is used in the electroplating, tanning and textile industries.

Fossils. Remains of animals and plants, or direct evidence of their presence, preserved in rocks. They include petrified skeletons and shells, leaf imprints, footprints, etc.

Four Freedoms, a phrase coined by President Roosevelt in January 1941, embodying what should be the goal of the Allies. They were (1) Freedom of speech and expression; (2) Freedom of every person to worship God in his own way; (3) Freedom from want; (4) Freedom from fear.

Fox, carnivorous animal of the canine family, found in considerable numbers in most parts of the world. The common fox *Vulpes vulpes* of Europe is a burrowing animal of nocturnal habits, living upon birds, rabbits and domestic poultry, in the capture of which it displays much cunning. The fox in Britain is preserved from extinction chiefly for hunting purposes. Among other notable species are the Arctic fox and the red fox of North America, of which the valuable silver fox, coveted for its fur, is a variety.

Fox-Shark *or* **Thresher Shark,** a large species of shark common in the Atlantic and in the Mediterranean. It is very destructive to small fish, but although it attains a length of 4·5 m it is not dangerous to man.

Franciscans. *See* **Friars.**

Franco-German War (1870–71) was opened by a declaration of war by Napoleon III, but the Germans who were better prepared than the French, won victory after victory. On 12 September Napoleon with 104,000 men were made prisoners at Sedan, a republic was then pro-

claimed, and Paris sustained a four months' siege. In the end France ceded Alsace and part of Lorraine to Germany, who claimed a war indemnity of £200 million.

Frankincense is of two kinds, one being used as incense in certain religious services and obtained from olibanum, an Eastern shrub, the other is a resinous exudation derived from firs and pines, and largely used in pharmacy.

Franklin, the name given in feudal times to a country landowner who was independent of the territorial lord, and performed many of the minor functions of local government, such as serving as magistrate.

Freeport, a port exempt from customs duties and regulations. The north German towns of the Hanseatic League (**L56**) were among the earliest and most famous freeports.

Freira, small grey and white sea bird. Extremely rare, it nests on the island of Madeira. Likely to become the first European species to face extinction since the Great Auk in 1844.

Fresco, a painting executed upon plaster walls or ceilings, a technique which has remained unchanged since it was practised by the great Renaissance artists.

Friars, members of certain mendicant orders of the Roman Catholic Church. The four chief orders are the Franciscans or Grey Friars, the Dominicans or Black Friars, the Carmelites or White Friars and the Augustinians (Austin Friars).

Friday, the 6th day of the week, named after Frigga, the wife of Odin. It is the Mohammedan Sabbath, a general abstinence day of the Roman Catholic Church, and according to popular superstition, an unlucky day.

Friends, The Society of. *See* **Quakers, Section J.**

Frigate-Bird, a web-footed bird widely distributed over tropical latitudes, and deriving its name from its great expanse of wing and forked tail, resembling the shape of a swift vessel. It feeds on flying fish mostly, being unable to dive and also steals from other birds. A frigate-bird was found dying on the Hebridean island of Tiree in July 1953; only twice previously had one been recorded in Europe—the first on the German coast in 1792, and the second on the coast of France in 1902.

Frog, a familiar amphibian, breathing through gills in the earlier (tadpole) part of its existence and through lungs later. It remains three months in the tadpole stage. The frog hibernates underwater in the mud during the winter.

Frost occurs when the temperature falls to, or below, 0°C, which is freezing point. Hoar frost is applied to the needles or feather-like crystals of the ice deposited on the ground, in the same manner as dew. Glazed frost is the clear icy coating which may be formed as a result of rain falling on objects whose temperatures are below the freezing point. These layers of ice, often rendering roads impassable for traffic, damaging overhead power and communication systems and endangering aircraft, can also be caused by condensation from warm, damp winds coming into contact with very cold air and freezing surfaces.

Froth-Hopper *or* **Frog-Hopper.** A family of bugs (belonging to the insect order *Hemiptera*) which in the larval stage surround themselves with a protective mass of froth ("cuckoo spit"). These insects, which suck the sap of plants, bear a faint resemblance to frogs, and the adults possess great leaping powers.

Fuel Cells. A recent development is a type of battery into which the active chemicals are fed from external fuel tanks. This is the *fuel cell*, which is being developed in a number of versions in several countries. One was demonstrated in action when in 1959 Bacon of Cambridge University used his fuel cell to drive a fork-lift truck and a welding machine. The Bacon fuel cell consists of two electrodes of porous nickel dipping into a solution of caustic potash in water. One electrode is supplied with hydrogen gas from an outside cylinder and the other with oxygen. These gases, forming layers on the nickel, are the active chemicals. The oxygen combines with water to make two negatively charged ions, each consisting of an oxygen and a hydrogen atom joined together (a hydroxyl ion). The hydroxyl ions travel through the solution to the hydrogen electrode, where they combine with hydrogen to form neutral water. Their negative charge (one electron per ion involved) has now arrived at the hydrogen electrode and is ready to flow back to the other electrode through any outside circuit that is provided. This flow constitutes the useful electric current, and it has been provided at the expense of creating water out of the original hydrogen and oxygen. The water can be removed in the form of steam. What is the advantage of all this? In the first place the fuel gases are easy to make and to store in cylinders. Supplying a new gas cylinder is easier and quicker than recharging an ordinary accumulator. Furthermore, a fuel cell is lighter for a given power than an accumulator; satellite designers have found them useful. The fuel cell is not damaged by heavy overloading, and this is valuable for application to vehicle driving. Fuel-cell-driven buses could combine the advantage of diesel buses and trolleybuses. Fuel cells are still in the development stage. It is not certain how they will compete with combustion engines or, in an oil-less future, with improved ordinary batteries.

Fulani, a non-Negro people of Hamitic stock widely distributed in N.W. Africa, chiefly in Nigeria. There are two main branches: the dark-skinned Fulani, settled farmers and city dwellers, Moslem in religion; and the light-coloured Bororo'en who are semi-nomadic herdsmen. The Fulani are different from any tribe in W. Africa though they resemble in some ways the Masai of E. Africa. The Fulani conquered the Hausa states at the beginning of the 19th cent. which passed under British suzerainty after 1903. Sokoto, built in 1810, was capital of the Fulani empire.

Fuller's Earth, a special kind of clay or marl possessing highly absorbent qualities, originally used in the "fulling"—that is, cleansing and felting—of cloth. Now used in clarifying oils. Deposits in America and in south of England.

Function. In mathematics, one quantity y is said to be a function of another quantity x, written $y = f(x)$, if a change in x results in some corresponding change in y. Thus $\sin x$ or $\log x$ are functions of x. If y depends not only on x but on several other quantities as well, y is called a function of many variables.

Functionalism, in architecture, a movement originated by Le Corbusier, Swiss-born French architect and town-planner, who applied the austere principles of the Purist movement in painting to his own art. From about 1924 he designed in concrete, steel and glass, buildings in which every part had a significance in terms of function on the theory that objects created to carry out their particular function to perfection cannot help being beautiful. "A house is a machine for living in." The style was in vogue between the two wars, and although its severity became somewhat modified, it is still the basis of most modern architecture.

Fungi, a class of simple plants, which reproduce from spores and lack the green colouring matter *chlorophyll.* It includes moulds, rusts, mildews, smuts, mushrooms, etc. Potato blight is a fungus disease which caused the failure of the potato crop in Ireland in 1846. 50,000 different fungi are known. See also **F42(1).**

Furniture Beetle (*Anobium punctatum*). The common furniture beetle is responsible for 80 per cent of all woodworm damage and is the great pest of the comparatively modern house, causing damage in the main to softwood roofing and flooring timbers. Adults are 3 mm long. The grub tunnels for about 33 months. See also **Woodworm, Death Watch Beetle.**

Futurism, an Italian school of art and literature initiated by Marinetti, an Italian writer and mountebank friend of Mussolini at a later period. Its origin took the form of a manifesto published in Paris in 1909 in which Marinetti glorified violence, war and the machine age. In its aggression it favoured the growth of fascism. One of the distinctive features of Futurist art was the use of the principle of "simultaneity" in which the same figure (*e.g.*, a woman descending a flight of stairs) is represented in successive positions like film "stills" superimposed on each other. In spite of two further manifestoes

it was not until 1911 that the first examples of Futurist painting and sculpture appeared by the artists Severini, Balla and Boccioni. Apart from the principle of simultaneity, Futurism derived from Cubist and Post-impressionist techniques. The movement faded out early in the first world war.

G

Gabardine, a long, loose, coarse, over-garment, worn by men of the common class in the Middle Ages, and prescribed by law as the distinctive garment of the Jews. The name is now given to a closely woven cloth of wool and cotton used to make raincoats.

Gabbro, a kind of igneous rock, often very coarse-grained, containing a good deal of plagioclase felspar, and monoclinic pyroxene; it may occasionally also include biotite, magnetite, ilmenite and hornblende. A gabbro containing nickel at Sudbury in Canada is one of the richest sources known of that metal.

Gadfly, a widely distributed family of flies with only one pair of wings, including the horse fly. The females are very voracious, being able to bite through the skin and suck the blood of animals. The males are harmless.

Gadolinium. An element, no. 64, symbol Gd, belonging to the rare-earths metals discovered in 1886 by Marignac. It is strongly magnetic.

Gaelic, relating to the Gaels and their language, a term now applied only to the Celtic people inhabiting the Highlands of Scotland, but formerly also to the Celts of Ireland and the Isle of Man.

Galago, "Bush Babies", related to the lemur, native to Africa, large-eyed, in keeping with its nocturnal characteristics.

Galaxy *or* **Milky Way Galaxy** is the huge disk-shaped cloud of gas and stars (some 100,000 million, one of which is the sun) that is turning in space like a great wheel, with a diameter of about 100,000 light years. The Milky Way (that part of the heavens in Milton's words "powdered with stars") is really only a small part of this disk, and every star in the galaxy is moving round the centre under the gravitational control of the whole. The sun and planets lie near the edge of the disk, and it takes them about 250 million years to travel once round. The number of stars that can be seen with the unaided eye is about 3,000, and they all belong to the Milky Way Galaxy, as do most of the stars that can be seen with anything but the greatest telescopes. With the large modern optical and radar telescopes many other systems, similar in size and weight to our galaxy, have been discovered, scattered more or less uniformly through space, and the universe is known to include at least 10,000 million such galaxies. See also **F4(2).**

Gale, a high wind now technically defined as one of at least Beaufort force 8. Between thirty and forty gales a year occur on the north and west coasts of the British Isles and only about half of this number in the south-east. At St. Ann's Head, Dyfed, the anemometer registered a gust of 113 mile/h (182 km/h) on 18 Jan. 1945, which is a record for these islands. Gusts exceeding 113 km/h are rarely experienced in London. Gale warnings are issued for specified areas by the Meteorological Office, the warnings taking the form of radio broadcasts and the hoisting of storm signals at certain points on the coast. See **Beaufort Wind Scale, Section Z.**

Gall, abnormal vegetable growths caused by insects, mites, bacteria, or fungi, found on all parts of the plant. Oak-apples, Robin's pin-cushion (on wild rose), "witches' brooms" (on trees) are examples. Some are useful commercially, *e.g.*, oak apples yield tannic acid and the black oak gall is used in America as animal food.

Galleon, the name given to the old three-decked Spanish treasure vessels employed in conveying the precious minerals from the American colonies to Spain. The term is often applied to any large, especially stately, sailing vessel.

Galley, an oar-propelled sea-boat used by the ancient Greeks and Romans for transport purposes, manned by slaves. They were also used as warships from classical to relatively modern times, e.g., Lepanto 1571. When so used the sides were raised to protect the rowers.

Gallic Acid, obtained from gall nuts, sumach, tea, coffee, and the seeds of the mango, is used in the manufacture of inks and as an astringent in medicine. It was discovered by C. W. Scheele (1742–86), a Swedish chemist.

Gallium, metallic element, no. 31, symbol Ga, related to aluminium, but which can be cut with a knife. It was discovered spectroscopically by L. de Boisbaudran in 1075. Long before Mendeleyev had predicted that an element with its properties would be found to fill the then existing gap in the Periodic Table; this gap came immediately below aluminium, so he suggested the name "eka aluminium" for it.

Gallup Poll, a system, introduced by Dr. Gallup in the United States, for testing public opinion on topical subjects by taking a test poll on questions framed to elicit opinions.

Galvanised Iron is iron coated with zinc. The name comes from the fact that such a coat protective against rust could be deposited electrolytically. Electrodeposition is sometimes used, but the cheaper and more common process depends on dipping the iron in a bath of molten zinc.

Gamboge, a resinous gum obtained from the sap of *Garcinia morella*, a tree native to Thailand, Cambodia and Sri Lanka, and used as a yellow pigment in paints and also as a purgative.

Game is the term applied to wild animals which are protected from indiscriminate slaughter by Game Laws. In the United Kingdom game comprehends deer, hares, pheasants, partridges, grouse, black game, moor game, woodcocks, bustards and certain other birds and animals of the chase. Game can only be killed (with few exceptions) by persons holding game licences. Occupiers of land and one other person authorised by them in each case are allowed to kill hares and rabbits on their land without licence. Game cannot be sold except by a person holding a proper licence. There is a "close time" prescribed for the different classes of game; for instance, the selling or exposing for sale of any hare or leveret during March, April, May, June or July is prohibited by law. Grouse cannot be shot between 11 December and 11 August; partridges between 2 February and 31 August; pheasants between 2 February and 30 September; and black game between 11 December and 10 August. In regard to foxes and stags, custom prescribes a certain law which sportsmen observe. Game reserves are legally protected areas where natural vegetation and wild life are allowed to remain unmolested by sportsmen or those who might destroy for economic ends.

Gaming, *or* **Gambling**—*i.e.*, staking money on the chances of a game—differs from betting in that it depends upon the result of a trial of skill or a turn of chance. The Betting and Gaming Act of 1959, passed by the Macmillan administration, replaced all the old laws on gaming, which went back to an Act of 1541 entitled "An Acte for Mayntenance of Artyllarie and debarringe of unlauful games", under which some games were unlawful if played for money in any circumstances. Roulette and any game of dice were among such games. Under the 1959 Act any game was lawful, subject to certain conditions. Since then the Betting, Gaming and Lotteries Act, 1963, and the Gaming Act, 1968, have been passed, to deal with unlawful gaming and to prevent the exploitation of gaming by commercial interests. The playing of bingo is now restricted to clubs licensed for bingo only. Sunday betting on dogs and horses became legal in January 1995. The government is currently (May 1995) considering further proposals to liberalise the gambling laws. See also **National Lottery.**

Gammexane, a powerful insecticide, used particularly to kill the tsetse fly and mosquito.

Gangue. Useless minerals associated with metallic ores.

Gannet, a fish-eating bird which dives on its prey from a great height, swallowing it under water, is found in large numbers off the coast of Scotland, and has breeding stations in the Hebrides, St. Kilda, Ailsa Craig, the Bass Rock, Grassholme Island and on Ortac and Les Etacs (rocks off Alderney). It is a bird of white plumage, black tips to long narrow wings and wedge-shaped tail, and weighs about 3 kg. The gannet breeds in colonies on ledges of steep, rocky, island cliffs. Related to the cormorants, pelicans and frigate-birds.

Garden Cities in England were founded by Ebenezer Howard (1850–1900), and his ideas were put forward in his book *Tomorrow—A Peaceful Path to Real Reform* (later re-issued as *Garden Cities of Tomorrow*). New towns should be so placed and planned as to get the best of town and country life, an adaptation of the model villages of certain industrial philanthropists such as Salt, Richardson, Cadbury, Leverhulme and others. The Garden City Association (later the Town and Country Planning Association) was formed in 1899, and the first garden city was begun at Letchworth in 1903 and successfully established. Welwyn Garden City (1919) was Howard's foundation.

Gardener-Bird, a bird possessing many of the characteristics of the bower bird, found only in Papua–New Guinea. *See also* **Bower Bird.**

Gargantua, the giant hero of Rabelais' satire, of immense eating and drinking capacity, symbolical of the greed of the Church.

Gargoyle, a projecting spout for carrying off water from the roof gutter of a building. Gargoyles are only found in old structures, modern waterpipe systems having rendered them unnecessary. In Gothic architecture they were turned to architectural account and made to take all kinds of grotesque forms—grinning goblins, hideous monsters, dragons and so forth.

Garlic, a bulbous plant of the same genus as the onion and the leek, and a favourite condiment among the people of Southern Europe. It possesses a very strong odour and pungent taste and its culinary use is agelong.

Garnet, a group of minerals; chemically they are orthosilicates of the metals calcium, magnesium, titanium, iron, aluminium. Garnets can be coloured yellow, brown, black, green or red; the blood-red garnet is an important gemstone.

Garrotte, a method of strangulation used as capital punishment in Spain, and consisting of a collar which is compressed by a screw that causes death by piercing the spinal marrow. Garrotting was also applied to a system of highway robbery common in England in 1862–63, the assailants seizing their victims from behind, and by a sudden compression of the windpipe disabling them until the robbery was completed.

Garter. The Most Noble Order of the Garter was founded (c. 1348) by King Edward III, and is the premier order of knighthood in Great Britain. The traditional story associating the garter and the motto with the Countess of Salisbury, who it was said dropped her garter while dancing with the King, who remarked "honi soit qui mal y pense" cannot be accepted. The order was originally limited to the Sovereign and 25 knights, but the number has been extended, and it may now be bestowed on royal personages and leading representatives of the British peerage. The insignia of the order are the garter of dark-blue velvet with the motto in letters of gold, the mantle of dark-blue velvet lined with white silk, the surcoat and hood, and the gold-and-enamel collar. The garter is worn on the left leg below the knee and by women as a sash over the left shoulder. Recent recipients have been James Callaghan (1987), Sir Edward Heath (1992), the Princess Royal (1994), Sir Edmund Hillary and Baroness Thatcher (1995). *See* **Knighthood.**

Gas is an elastic fluid substance, the molecules of which are in constant rapid motion, and exerting pressure. The technique whereby gases are liquefied depends on increasing pressure and diminishing temperature. Each gas has a critical point; unless the temperature is brought down to this point no amount of pressure will bring about liquefaction. Last gas to be liquefied was helium (1908) which boils at −209°C.

Gas from coal was first used as an illuminating agent by William Murdoch towards the end of the 18th cent. in Birmingham, and about 1807 was introduced in London, one side of Pall Mall being lighted with it. It became widely used as an illuminant, and for space heating and cooking. In the U.K. increasing attention has been paid to the use of a primary fuel—natural gas—instead of producing gas from coal or oil.

Gas, Natural, natural mixture of gases often present with deposits of petroleum, found issuing from the ground in many parts of the world—in the oilfields of Venezuela and the Caucasus, in China, Saudi Arabia, but chiefly in North America. Its chief component is methane. Large industrial centres have made use of this gas since the latter part of the 19th cent., but much of this valuable fuel still goes to waste. Pipelines have been constructed to deliver the gas to where it is wanted. Britain began to ship liquid methane from the Saharan oilfield in 1964. Some of the world's largest natural gas fields have recently been discovered in the North Sea and are being actively exploited. Domestic gas appliances have to be modified if the natural product is substituted for town gas because the burning characteristics are different. Oil production from the North Sea fields began in 1975 and the main single source of gas in the UK is now natural gas.

Gas Turbine. In this kind of engine mechanical movement is produced by a jet of gas impinging on a turbine wheel; used in aeroplanes, locomotives and ships. These engines are mechanically simple compared with internal combustion engines, and require less maintenance.

Gauge, a standard dimension or measurement, applied in various branches of construction. Thus the standard railway gauge is 4 ft 8½ in (143·5 cm) in the UK, USA and most European countries. The former Soviet Union used the broader gauge of 5 ft (152 cm). Narrow railway gauges of different standards are in use on very steep inclines in various countries. Other standard gauges are fixed in building and gun-boring.

Gauls were inhabitants of ancient Gaul, the country which comprised what is now France, Belgium and parts of the Netherlands, Switzerland and Germany.

Gault, a stratum of blue clay between the Lower Greensand and the Chalk. A typical section of the Gault can be seen at Folkestone.

Gauss, a unit of magnetic induction in the c.g.s. system, named after the great German mathematician and astronomer, K. F. Gauss.

Gavelkind, an old English custom of land tenure in Kent and other places in England, whereby on the death, intestate, of a property owner his property is divided equally among his children and not according to the law of primogeniture.

Gazelles, a group of small, graceful antelopes which live in the drier regions of Africa and Asia. They can run very fast: speeds of over 64 km/h have been recorded.

GCSE, (General Certificate of Secondary Education), the new school-leaving examination, introduced in 1988, which replaced the existing GCE and CSE.

Gegenschein. A faint oval-shaped glow situated at the point in the sky directly opposite the Sun and caused by the reflection of sunlight from tiny interplanetary dust particles.

Geiger Counter, an electrical device, invented by Geiger, which can detect individual atomic particles, e.g., electrons, protons, etc. It often consists of a tube of gas at a few cm Hg pressure, fitted with two electrodes—a cylinder and an axial wire. A high voltage is kept across the electrodes, and the passage of a charged particle through the gas releases ions which permit a momentary discharge between the electrodes. Electronic circuits register this discharge as a "count". Geiger counters are used to detect and measure radioactivity and cosmic rays both for technical and research purposes.

Gelatine, a transparent, tasteless, organic substance obtained from animal membranes, bones, tendons, etc., by boiling in water. It is of various kinds, according to the substance used in making it. Isinglass, the purest form of it, is made from air-bladders and other membranes of fish, while the coarser kind—glue—is made from hoofs, skin, hides, etc. Its constituents are carbon, hydrogen, oxygen and nitrogen. Gelatine is applied to an immense variety of purposes, from the making of food jellies to photographic materials.

Gemsbok, a large South African antelope of the open dry plains, sandy coloured with black and white markings on its face, and with long straight horns.

General, a military title next in rank to that of Field-Marshal, the highest officer in the army.

Generation, a time-measure reckoned at about 30 years when children are ready to replace parents; also the body of persons existing at the same time or period. In the 1990s, the generation gap is now even fewer years apart.

Generation, Spontaneous. See **Abiogenesis.**

Genes, the elementary units of heredity. They exist as highly differentiated regions arranged along the length of the chromosomes which the nuclei of cells carry. A chromosome may carry hundreds or even thousands of genes, each with its own particular structure and specific properties. The position of a particular gene on a chromosome is called its locus. The material of the gene is DNA (q.v.). See **F34.**

Genesis, the first book of the Pentateuch, compiled in the 5th cent. B.C. from earlier documents, which carries the scriptural narrative from the creation to the death of Joseph. Sometimes there is disagreement, as in the story of the creation, Gen. i and ii. Gen. i reflects the views of the ancient Greek scientist Thales (c. 640–546 B.C.) and may be said to be the first scientific account of the creation of the world. The conditions described around the figures of Abraham, Isaac, Jacob and Joseph have a genuine historical basis.

Genetic Code. The elucidation of the structure of DNA (q.v.) for which Crick, Wilkins and Watson were jointly awarded the 1962 Nobel Prize for medicine, revealed the code or chemical dictionary out of which messages serving as blueprints for living structures can be made. See **Protein synthesis, F34** and **F70-76.**

Genetic Engineering is the name given to the introduction of human choice and design criteria into the construction and combination of genes. This refers not to breeding by selection, a traditional process, but to the biochemical alteration of the actual DNA in cells (see **Section F, Part IV**) so as to produce novel self-reproducing organisms. Such manipulations became possible when techniques were recently discovered for severing and rejoining DNA molecules and inserting sections into them. Many people regard this development as fraught with enormous significance. Like nuclear power, it can lead to good, to evil, and to accidental hazards, not all of which can be foreseen. Thus when biologists realised they could create new lifeforms, e.g., bacteria, with novel genes, they appreciated that, as well as medically beneficial strains, new virulent forms might by accident be produced and escape into the world. Ultimately, not imminently, men may be able to design the genes of higher animals and even of man himself and thus consciously influence biological evolution. Many scientists have been brought by these possibilities up against an old problem: is science going too far too fast?

Genetics. See **F30(2)** and **F70-76.**

Geneva Convention, an agreement made by the European Powers at Geneva in 1864, establishing humane regulations regarding the treatment of the sick and wounded in war and the status of those who minister to them. All persons, hospitals, hospital ships are required to display the Geneva cross—a red cross on a white ground. A second conference held at Geneva in 1868 drew up a supplementary agreement. An important result of this Convention was the establishment of the Red Cross Society in 1870.

Genocide is an international crime, defined by the General Assembly of the United Nations in 1948 as "acts committed with intent to destroy, in whole or in part a national, ethnic, racial or religious group as such". The UN Convention came into force in 1951.

Genus, a term applied in biology to designate a group of similar species. A group of similar genera is called a family. *See* **F35**(2).

Geodesy, the science of calculating the configuration and extent of the earth's surface, and determining exact geographical positions and directions, with variations of gravity etc. Land-surveying is a branch of geodesy.

Geography, science concerned with the spatial organisation of natural features and life and man-made artifacts upon and immediately above the surface of the earth. It is increasingly concerned with the processes by which such patterns are generated and this concern is leading to both a greater degree of specialisation within the subject and the merging of its constituent parts with related disciplines of economics, sociology, political science, geology, biology and meteorology.

Geology, the science which deals with the condition and structure of the earth, and the evidence afforded of ancient forms of life. The geological strata are classified in the following categories: *Primary* or *Palaeozoic* (the oldest fossil-bearing rocks including the Cambrian, Ordovician, Silurian, Devonian, Carboniferous, Permian); *Secondary* or *Mesozoic* (Triassic, Jurassic, Cretaceous); *Tertiary* or *Cainozoic* (Eocene, Oligocene, Miocene, Pliocene, Pleistocene); *Post tertiary* (most recent rocks). *See* **F48**.

Geometrical Progression is a term used to indicate a succession of numbers which increase or decrease at an equal ratio—as 3, 9, 27; or 64, 16, 4.

Geometry is the branch of mathematics which demonstrates the properties of figures, and the distances of points of space from each other by means of deductions. It is a science of reason from fundamental axioms, and was perfected by Euclid about 300 B.C. The books of Euclid contain a full elucidation of the science, though supplemented in modern times by Descartes, Newton and Carnot. Of recent years non-Euclidean geometry has been developed.

Geophysics, the branches of physics which are concerned with the earth and its atmosphere. Meteorology, geomagnetism, aurora and airglow, ionosphere, solar activity, cosmic rays, glaciology, oceanography, seismology, nuclear radiation in the atmosphere, rockets and satellites—all these are geophysical subjects. The object of the International Geophysical Year, 1957-58, was to investigate the physical phenomena occurring on and around the earth by means of carefully co-ordinated observations made simultaneously all over the globe.

Geothermal Energy. Some of the heavy elements within the earth's crust are radioactive and this gives rise to a temperature rise towards the centre of the earth. The practical exploitation of this geothermal energy comes about when there are hot springs or geysers. It is believed that these are caused by rainwater slowly percolating down to the hot rocks and blowing out as steam. The homes of people living in Reykjavik are heated by geothermal steam and there are a number of small power stations in various parts of the world. Although the costs in the few cases where geothermal power has actually been exploited are remarkably low, the expense of drilling, etc., required when attempting to exploit the heat in the rocks where surface manifestations do not occur, is likely to limit the use of this source of power.

Geothermal Heating. The earth's interior is hot and in certain localities, often adjacent to volcanic or earthquake-prone regions, reservoirs of hot water or steam exist at accessible depths. Natural hot geysers occur in many such places and people, *e.g.*, the ancient Romans and present-day Japanese, use natural hot water for bathing, cooking and laundry. Occasionally the subterranean reserves permit large-scale power generation by drilling for hot steam and passing it into turbines to produce electricity. Pioneering work on this was done at Lardarello in Italy which can produce hundreds of megawatts. Other sites are in New Zealand, California, Japan and Iceland. There are possibilities in S.W. England.

Germanium. A grey, hard, brittle chemical element, no. 32, symbol Ge, chemically related to silicon and tin. Discovered by Winkler in 1886. Its richest ore is germanite containing 6% of the metal. Coal is also a relatively rich source. Since 1948 it has assumed great importance as a semi-conducting material for making transsistors (*q.v.*). Because of this it has been so intensively studied that more is known about its physical properties than about those of any other element.

Gesta Romanorum (Latin = deeds of the Romans), a mediaeval collection of Latin stories of unknown authorship which circulated widely in Europe during the Middle Ages. First printed in the 15th cent. The stories were used by Chaucer, Shakespeare and other writers who found many romantic incidents and legends which they were able to turn to good account.

Gestation, the carrying of young in animals during pregnancy, varies considerably in its length. In the case of an elephant, the period is 21 months; a camel, 12 months; a cow, 9 months; a cat, 8 weeks; a horse, 48 weeks; a dog, 9 weeks; and a pig, 16 weeks. Hens "sit" for 21 days; geese, 30; swans, 42; turkeys, 28; pigeons, 18.

Geysers, hot springs of volcanic origination and action, are remarkable for the fact that they throw out huge streams of boiling water instead of lava as in the case of a volcano. The most famous geysers are those of Iceland, which number over a hundred, the principal one having an opening of 21 m in diameter and discharging a column of water to a height of 61 m. There are also geysers in the Yellowstone region of America, and some in New Zealand.

Ghost-Moth or **Ghost Swift,** an interesting nocturnal insect (*Hepialus humuli*) common in England, possessing in the male a white collar and known for its habit of hovering with a pendulum-like action in the twilight over a particular spot where the female is concealed.

Gibbon, the name of a long-armed ape mainly inhabiting S.E. Asia. It is without tail, and possesses the power of very rapid movement among the trees of the forests.

Gin, a well-known spirit distilled from malt or barley and flavoured with the juniper berry. The principal varieties are the English and American, known as "Gin" or "Dry Gin", and the Dutch, referred to as "jenever" or "Hollandse jenever". In Germany and Austria it is called "Schnapps". The word "Gin" is an abbreviation of "Geneva", both being primarily derived from the French *genièvre* (juniper).

Giraffe, the tallest of existing animals, reaching a height of from 5–6 m when full grown. Its sloping back and elongated neck seem to be the natural evolution of an animal that has to feed on the branches of trees. It is a native of Africa, is of a light fawn colour marked with darker spots and has a prehensile tongue.

Giralda, a beautiful and remarkable example of Arabian art, erected in 1195 at Seville, still in existence.

Glaciers form in the higher Alpine ranges, and are immense consolidated masses of snow, which are gradually impelled by their force down the mountain-sides until they reach a point where the temperature causes them to melt, and they run off in streams. From such glaciers the five great rivers, the Rhine, the Po, the Rhône, the Inn and the Adige, have their source. The longest of the Swiss glaciers is the Gross Aletsch, which sometimes extends over 16 km. Some of the glaciers of the Himalayas are four times as long. The Muir in Alaska is of enormous magnitude, and that of Justeldals Brae in Norway is the largest in Europe.

Gladiators were professional athletes and combatants in ancient Rome, contesting with each other or with wild beasts. At first they were drawn from the slave and prisoner classes exclusively, but so much were the successful gladiators held in esteem that men came to make a profession of athletics, and gladiatorial training schools were established. When a gladiator was vanquished without being killed in combat, it was left with the spectators to decide his fate, death being voted by holding the hands out with the thumb turned inward, and life by putting forth the hands with the thumb extended.

Gladiatorial shows were the chief public displays in Rome from the 3rd to the 4th cent. A.D.

Glass is an amorphous, man-made substance, fluid when hot, solid, though fragile, when cooled. It is made of sand mixed with an alkaline flux, usually soda or potash. While hot, glass can be formed into almost any shape by moulding, blowing or, since the early 19th cent., by machine pressing. Unrefined glass normally has a greenish tinge, due to the iron content of most sands, but it is transparent or at least translucent. To make truly colourless glass is a difficult and expensive process, and such glass resembling the natural mineral, rock crystal, is given the name crystal. Glass can be tinted by the addition of various metallic oxides, cobalt producing blue, manganese mauve, etc. Because it is at once solid and transparent, glass is the perfect material for windows for which it has been used since Roman times. And since it can be made cheaply and is easy to clean, it has been used for containers in homes, shops and pharmacies, again since Roman days. Glass can also be made into things of beauty, by the use of coloured glass and by cutting, engraving, painting and gilding. The earliest vessels of glass so far found come from Egypt and date back to c. 1500 B.C. With the invention of glass-blowing in the 1st cent. A.D., the use of glass spread throughout the Roman empire. Many varieties were made, including superb art glass like the Portland vase (q.v.) The Arabs were great glassmakers from the 7th to 15th cent. During the Renaissance the Venetians created luxurious art glass, rich in colour and often manipulated into fantastic forms, Bohemia's 17th-cent. glass is wonderfully engraved with pictures and cut into glittering facets. During the 1670s in England George Ravenscroft invented a new, heavy, water-clear crystal, with an addition of lead as the magic ingredient, and English lead glass is still the basis for all modern crystals.

Glass-Snake, genus, *Ophisaurus*, of legless lizards with long fragile tails capable of re-generation when broken. Six species are known; in S.E. Europe, S.W. Asia, Indo-China and N. America. Attains a length of about 60 cm; main colouring, green, with black and yellow markings.

Glauconite. A green mineral, chemically a hydrated silicate of potassium and iron. Commonly found in marine sands (hence these rocks are known as "greensands") and sandstones.

Glaucus is a curious genus of sea slugs often called the Sea Lizard belonging to the molluscs. It is without shell and has a soft body, with horny mouth and four tentacles. It is a native of the Atlantic, and is not more than 30 cm in length.

Glee, an unaccompanied piece for three or more voices. Glee-singing was popular in England during the 18th and early 19th cent. and glee-clubs are still in existence.

Globigerina, an oceanic unicellular animalcule with a perforated shell, and occurring in certain parts of the Atlantic in such vast numbers as to form a bed of chalk ooze with their empty shells.

Glockenspiel, an instrument composed of metal bars each of which is tuned to a note. The bars are struck by hand-hammers and give forth chiming sounds.

Glow-worm, a beetle, possessing the power (much stronger in the female than the male) of emitting phosphorescent light from the hind end of the body. The female is wingless.

Glucinium. See Beryllium.

Glucose, Dextrose or **Grape Sugar** is a carbohydrate (q.v.). It is produced by hydrolysis from cane sugar, dextrine, starch, cellulose, etc., by the action of reagents. It also occurs in many plants, fruits and honey. For brewing purposes glucose is prepared by the conversion of starch by sulphuric acid. Malt also converts starch into glucose.

Glutton or **Wolverine**, the biggest animal of the weasel family, inhabits the northernmost parts of Europe and America. In build it resembles the bear, and is rather larger than a badger. Its fur is of a brown-black hue, but coarse.

Glycerine or **Glycerol**, occurs in natural fats combined with fatty acids, and is obtained by decomposing those substances with alkalis or by superheated steam. It is colourless and oily and sweet, and is put to a variety of commercial uses, being widely utilised for medicaments, for lubricating purposes, and in the manufacture of nitro-glycerine.

Glycols. Organic compounds containing two alcohol groups. Ethylene glycol is the most widely known example; it is used as an anti-freeze in motor-car radiators on account of its property of greatly reducing the freezing point of water. Also used in the manufacture of "Terylene". See Esters.

Glyptodon, an extinct species of gigantic armadillo, fossil remains of which have been discovered in S. America. It was some 2·7 m long, carried a huge tortoise-like shell and had fluted teeth.

Gneiss, a metamorphic rock usually containing quartz, felspar and mica. It is banded, the light-coloured minerals being concentrated apart from the dark minerals.

Gnosticism. See Section J.

Gnu or **Wildebeest**, a large antelope from Africa south of the Sahara, distinguished by its excessively short thick neck and large head with a pronounced roman nose. There are two species; the white-tailed gnu is almost extinct, the brindled gnu is still common and migrates in large herds.

Goat-Moth (*Cossus cossus*), a large moth of the *Cossidae* family, common in Britain, evil-smelling and very destructive in the larval stage to trees of the poplar and willow genus, into the wood of which the caterpillar bores during its three years' period of development.

Goats are horned ruminant quadrupeds, indigenous to the Eastern Hemisphere, but now domesticated in all parts of the world. Though related to the sheep, they are a much hardier and more active animal. The male has a tuft of hair under the chin. Many species, including those of Cashmere and Angora, are valuable for their hair, which is used for fine textile fabrics. The milk of the goat is nutritive, and goat-skins are in demand for leather for gloves, shoes, etc.

God and Man. See Section J.

Gog and **Magog**, two legendary City of London giants, supposed to be the offspring of certain wicked daughters of the Emperor Diocletian and a band of demons. They were brought captive to London and made to serve as prisoners at the Palace of Brute, which stood on the site of Guildhall. Effigies of the giants have stood in Guildhall since the time of Henry V. They were destroyed in the Great Fire of 1666, replaced in 1672 and used to be carried through the streets of London in the Lord Mayor's Show. The present figures replaced those carved in 1708 by Richard Saunders, which were destroyed in an air raid during the last war.

Gold. Metallic element, no. 79, symbol Au (Latin *Aurum*) related to silver and copper, the coinage metals. The greatest amount of gold is obtained by treating gold-bearing quartz by the cyanide process. The gold is dissolved out by cyanide solution, which is then run into long boxes filled with zinc shavings when the gold is precipitated as a black slime. This is melted with an oxidising agent which removes the zinc.

Gold-Beaters' Skin is the outside membrane of the large intestine of the ox, specially prepared and used by gold-beaters for placing between the leaves of gold while they beat them. Thin membrane is of great tenacity, and gets beaten to such extreme thinness that it is used to put on cuts and bruises.

Gold Standard. Under the gold-standard system which was widely prevalent up to 1941, each gold-standard country fixed the value of its currency in terms of a weight of gold of a certain fineness and was, broadly speaking, ready to exchange its currency freely for gold, which could then be exported without restriction. This involved keeping a gold reserve big enough to meet all likely demands and also to serve as a backing for the issue of notes. The gold standard had to be given up during the first world war; and though it was in substance restored in Great Britain in 1925 (when Churchill was Chancellor), the restoration was never complete, as the gold reserve remained too small for complete freedom to export to be practicable. Sterling had to be devalued in the finan cial crisis of 1931 (which brought about the fall of the Labour Government) and Great Britain was forced off the gold standard. Imbalance in payments between countries is financed by transfers of gold or foreign exchange. Such reserves are known as international liquidity. See also **Section G, Parts II and IV.**

Goldeneye, a species of wild duck, widely distributed over Arctic regions. It is a passage-migrant and winter-visitor to the British Isles. Has nested in Cheshire. Distinguished by a large white spot in front of each eye on a dark ground.

Golden Dawn. See **Section J.**

Golden Number, the number of any year in the metonic cycle of 19 years, deriving its name from the fact that in the old calendars it was always printed in gold. It is found by adding 1 to the number of the year A.D. and dividing by 19, the remainder being the Golden Number; or, if no remainder, the Golden Number is 19. The only use to which the Golden Number is put now is in making ecclesiastical calculations for determining movable feasts.

Goldsmiths Company, one of the richest London City Companies; the official assayers of gold and silver, invested with the power of "hall-marking" the quality of objects made from these metals. First charter granted in 1327.

Gondola, the old regulation black boats so common on the canals of Venice, propelled by a gondolier with one oar who stands at the stern. The covered part in the centre (*felze*) is rarely seen nowadays as most passengers are tourists who want to see the city.

Gonfalon, the pennon affixed to a lance, spear or standard, consisting usually of two or three streamers and made to turn like a weather-cock.

Gophers. Rodent mammals. The pocket gophers are stout-bodied burrowers common in the USA. The slender burrowing gophers, also called "ground squirrels", occur in central and western USA. The sisel or suslik is a related European species. They are a great pest among grain crops.

Gordon Riots of 1780 were an anti-popery agitation fomented by Lord George Gordon. Called also "No-Popery Riots".

Gorilla, the largest of the anthropoid apes, found in the forests of Equatorial Africa, and at maturity standing from 1·2–1·5 m high.

Goshawk (*Accipiter gentilis*), a diurnal bird of prey, fearless and extremely agile; loves wooded country and is very destructive of poultry and game-birds. It resembles the peregrine falcon in appearance, but has shorter, rounded wings. This bird was a great favourite of falconers in mediaeval times. A few have now been reintroduced from Scandinavia.

Gospels are those portions of the New Testament which deal with the life, death, resurrection and teachings of Christ. They are the gospels of Matthew, Mark, Luke and John, all probably compiled in the later part of the 1st cent. The first three are called the *synoptic gospels* because of their general unity of narrative. Mark was probably the first to be written and John the last, and it is to Mark that scholars have turned for the most reliable source of knowledge of the life of Jesus. The word *gospel* comes from two Anglo-Saxon words *gode* (good) and *spell* (tidings), a translation of the Greek *evangelion* = evangel, evangelist. Recent research (1995) suggests Matthew could have been written much earlier than previously thought.

Gothic, the predominant style of architecture in northern Europe from 12th–15th cent. Its most striking characteristic is the extensive use of the pointed arch, but this is really a mere external reflection of the important structural invention of the 12th cent., that of the rib vault, whereby the whole pressure of the stone vaulting is supported on slim ribs which cross each other at a rising centre. On the outside of the building, the pressure from the vaults is caught up and supported by flying buttresses. A complete Gothic construction gives a marvellous effect of airy lightness, also of something striving upwards, towards the heavens, and this is further accentuated when the churches are crowned by lofty towers and spires. The vital structural elements of Gothic architecture were first put into use in the abbey church of St.

Denis in Paris *c.* 1140. The style was further developed in a glorious sequence of cathedrals in northern France: Notre Dame in Paris, Rheims, Amiens, Beauvais and others. When, as in Chartres, the windows are filled with stained glass of glowing colours and the doorways flanked with magnificently carved life-size figures of saints and apostles, the whole effect is one of unsurpassed solemnity and grandeur. From France the style spread to other lands in each of which it developed its own characteristics; thus the English churches tended to have massive towers and delicate spires and, as at Salisbury, were often set in open grounds surrounded by lawns; Flemish and Dutch churches were sometimes built of brick as were those in north Germany and Scandinavia; in Spain the Flamboyant style was followed. The main Gothic cathedral in Italy, that of Milan, although begun in 1386 was not completed until the early 19th cent. Late English Gothic is seen, for example, at King's College Chapel, Cambridge, Henry's Chapel at Westminster and St. George's Chapel at Windsor (all *c.* 1500). Gothic is also found in secular buildings, *e.g.*, Little Wenham Hall in Suffolk, the castle at Ghent, the town halls of Louvain and Middelburg and the streets of Gothic houses in Bruges still in use today. Virtually Gothic as a style (excluding the "Gothic revival" of 19th cent. England) ended at the close of the 15th cent. Gothic art is best seen in the illuminated manuscripts of the 13th and 14th cent. and in the church sculpture. Its characteristic is a complete departure from the cool, perfectionist realism of classical times with distortion to produce emotional effects. The human figures are not ideal forms but recognisable as people we might meet in the street: yet there was also the element of wild imagination, intricate design and a wealth of feeling which might be grotesque, humorous, macabre, or even obscene. Gothic style also found expression in the decorative arts, retaining its architectural character even in small-scale works like caskets, chalices and the like in metalwork and ivory.

Goths. A Teutonic people who originally came from southern Sweden (Gotland) and by the 3rd cent. were settled in the region north of the Black Sea. They began to encroach on the Roman Empire and early in the 4th cent. split into two divisions: the "wise" Goths or Visigoths between the Danube and the Dniester (referred to as the West Goths), and the "bright" Goths or Ostrogoths in southern Russia on the Dnieper (referred to as the East Goths). The Ostrogoths were conquered by the Huns *c.* 370, while the Visigoths under Alaric devastated Greece and sacked Rome in 410. Eventually the Visigoths spread to France and Spain and their last king Roderick fell in battle against the Moors in 711. The Ostrogoths regained their independence on the death of Attila in 453 and under king Theodoric the Great conquered Italy in 493. They lost their identity after Justinian regained Italy, 525–552.

Gourd Family *or* **Cucurbitaceae.** This family of about 650 species of flowering plants includes the gourds, pumpkins, cantaloupes, cucumber, gherkin, water-melon and squashes. Most abundant in the tropics, the cucurbits are mainly climbing annuals with very rapid growth. The bathroom loofah is the skeleton of one cucurbit fruit, *Luffa cylindrica*. The squirting cucumber is another member of the family.

Governor. A device attached to an engine, turbine, compressor, etc., which automatically controls the engine's speed in accordance with power demand. Most governors depend upon the centrifugal action of two or more balls which are thrown outwards as their speed of rotation increases and actuate a throttle valve or cut-off. The centrifugal governor was invented by Thomas Mead, patented by him in 1787. Watt adapted it to the steam engine.

Grail, Legend of the Holy, a tale of Celtic origin which became part of Arthurian legend and the subject of many mediaeval quest-romances. According to the Christian version the grail was the cup which Christ used at the Last Supper, brought to England by St. Joseph of Arimathea.

Grand Prix, the "French Derby" was established by Napoleon III, in 1863. It is the chief

French race and is an international competition of three-year-olds.

Granite is a coarsely crystalline igneous rock consisting of quartz and alkali felspars plus mica or hornblende. It is a much used ornamental and building stone; it forms the high ground of Dartmoor and Bodmin Moor.

Graphite *or* **Plumbago**, commonly called blacklead, is a form of carbon occurring in foliated masses in marble, schist, etc. It is soft, will make black marks on paper or other plain surfaces, and is mainly used for lead pencils. It is also a valuable lubricant. Pure graphite has found a new use with the construction of atomic piles. Important deposits occur in Siberia, Sri Lanka, Malagasy, Canada and USA.

Graphology, the science which interprets and analyses the way letters are formed and shaped.

Graptolites, fossil animals confined to Cambrian, Ordovician and Silurian strata. Once classified as hydrazoa but now considered more likely to be hemichordates.

Grasshopper. There are many species of these leaping insects which are related to the locusts and crickets. Most are vegetarians; some eat flies and caterpillars also. The chirping sound they make is made by scraping the hind legs against the wings; in some species a noise is produced by rubbing the wings together.

Gravitation. One of the four, possibly five, types of force known to physics. The others are electromagnetic, nuclear (two types) and colour forces. Gravitational forces are an attraction that one piece of matter has for another; they dominate astronomical phenomena, but inside the atom they are negligible compared with the other types of force. Einstein's General Theory of Relativity is the only theory at present extant which attempts to interpret gravitational forces in terms of more fundamental concepts. *See* **F15**(1), **18**(2).

Graylag, the ordinary wild grey goose of Europe, the species from which domestic geese are derived; frequents fens and marshes; breeds in Iceland, Scandinavia and Scotland; distinguished by pinkish legs and feet and lack of black markings on bill.

Great Barrier Reef. *See* **K62.**

Grebe, a diving bird of beautiful plumage found over a great part of the world on lakes and oceans. The two species familiar in Great Britain are the Dabchick or Little Grebe and the large and handsome Great Crested Grebe, which has a feathery tuft, lost in the autumn, on each side of the head. Grebes have remarkable courtship displays. The breast feathers are of a downy softness and silver lustre, for which they were formerly much hunted.

Greek Art. *See* **Hellenic Art.**

Greek Fire, a combustible supposed to have been composed of sulphur, nitre, naphtha and asphalt, used with destructive effect by the Greeks of the Eastern Empire in their wars.

Greek Kalends, equivalent to never, as only the Romans, not the Greeks, had kalends.

Green Revolution. *See* **Section G, Part III.**

Greenwich Mean Time. The first Nautical Almanac, for the use of navigators and astronomers, was published by the Astronomer Royal in 1767. It was based on the meridian at Greenwich, with longitude measured east and west of 0°. A master clock, which still exists, was built at Greenwich Observatory in 1852 to control the railway station clocks and Greenwich Mean Time, or Railway Time as it was sometimes called, prevailed. In 1884 Greenwich was chosen as the prime meridian of the world and GMT became known as Universal Time. The timekeeping role is now done by the International Bureau of Weights and Measures. GMT has become CUT (Coordinated Universal Time). Recently, the Daylight Extra Now group has campaigned to abolish GMT and have an extra hour of daylight in the evening. It argues that this would make British industry more competitive, reduce road accidents, cut crime, and give more time for sport and hobbies such as gardening. *See also* **British Standard Time** and **F68.**

Gregorian Calendar. *See* **Calendar.**

Gresham's Law states that if money, *i.e.*, money with the higher intrinsic value, and bad money are in circulation together, the bad money will tend to drive out the good money from circulation. For instance, the good money is more likely to be melted down or demanded in payment by foreign creditors.

Gretna Green, a celebrated village in Annandale and Eskdale, just over the border from England, where runaway marriages were performed from 1754 to 1856, though only completely stopped during present century.

Griffin, in ancient mythology, a winged creature with an eagle's head and the body of a lion, found in ancient sculptures of Persia and Assyria. Its origin is traced to the Hittites.

Grilse, a young salmon that has only been once to the sea.

Grimm's Law, formulated by Jacob Grimm, an eminent German philologist, lays down a principle of consonantal change in the Germanic languages. For instance, Lat. *pater*, Eng. *father*, Ger. *Vater*; Lat. *frater*, Eng. *brother*, Ger. *Bruder*; Lat. *decem*, Eng. *ten*, Ger. *zehn*.

Grogram (French = *gros grain*), a kind of rough fabric made of wool and some other fibre, such as silk, mohair or cotton, formerly much used for commoner kinds of wearing apparel.

Grotto, a natural or artificial cave. Among the most famous are the blue grotto of Capri and the grotto of Antiparos (Cyclades, Aegean).

Ground Wave, that part of the energy emitted by a radio transmitter which travels along the ground; as opposed to the sky wave which is reflected back to earth by the ionosphere. With the lower radio-frequencies, the ground wave can be picked up over several thousand miles; in the broadcasting band, over a hundred or so miles; it is virtually useless at high frequencies.

Grouse, game bird of the northern latitudes where some 20 species occur. They are stout, compact, ground-dwelling birds, protectively plumaged (the willow grouse turns white in winter), the male usually being larger and more brightly coloured than the female. The red grouse of the British moorlands has been introduced into Belgium and W. Germany. Of the same family are the blackcock, ptarmigan, capercaillie, American prairie-hen and the partridge. Grouse shooting begins in Britain on Aug. 12.

Guanaco, a large species of llama, common to South America, and utilised as a beast of burden.

Guano, the excrement of sea-birds, found in large quantities on the rocky islands of the western coasts of South America and Nauru Is. It forms a useful fertilising agent, being rich in phosphate and ammonia, and first came into use in 1841, since which time Peruvian guano has been a recognised article of commerce. Beds of guano from 15–18 m in thickness are not uncommon. Fish guano and bat guano from caves in South America and the Bahamas are also used as fertilisers.

Gudgeon, a small fresh-water fish of the carp family with 2 small barbels on the upper lip.

Guelph and Ghibelline, italianised forms of the German words "Welf" and "Waiblingen", the names of two rival princely families whose conflicts made much of the history of Germany and Italy during the Middle Ages. The feuds between these two factions continued in Italy during the campaigns of Emperor Frederick I, and later developed into the fierce struggles of the 13th cent. between emperor and pope. In Italy the Ghibellines supported the side of the German emperors and the Guelphs the cause of the Pope. The present Royal Family of England and other Northern monarchies are descended by different routes from the Guelph George I, Duke of Brunswick-Lüneburg of the House of Hanover.

Guildhall, the place of assembly of the members of a guild, and at one time, when guilds were in full strength, was practically the Town Hall. The London Guildhall is today the hall of meeting for the City of London Corporation.

Guilds for the fostering and protection of various trades have existed in England since Anglo-Saxon times, and from the 12th to the 16th cent. exercised great influence and enjoyed many privileges. There were trades' guilds and craftsmen's guilds, and in all large cities and towns there was a guild hall. Their successes in the Middle Ages led to many monopolistic abuses, and in the end it became necessary to free the country from their restrictive power. The City Guilds (Livery Companies of the City of London) derive their name from the distinctive dress assumed by their members in the 14th cent.

Guild Socialism. *See* **Section J**.

Guillemot, a genus of sea-birds of the auk family, common in Northern Europe, two species—the Common Guillemot and the Black Guillemot—being natives of our own sea coasts, nesting on the cliffs. Brünnich's Guillemot, an Arctic species, is a rare straggler in the British Isles.

Guinea, an English gold coin of the value of twenty-one shillings, current from 1663–1817, and deriving its name from the first guinea coinage having been struck from gold obtained on the coast of Guinea.

Guinea-Pig, a rodent of the cavy family about 25 cm in length and with a tail so short that it does not project outside the body. It makes an excellent pet, though easily frightened. Its ancestors were species of the wild cavy of S. America said to have been domesticated by the Incas of Peru.

Gules, a heraldic term, denoting a rose of red tincture, indicated by vertical lines drawn or engraved without colour.

Gulf Stream is confined entirely to the western side of the N. Atlantic and is the warm-water current flowing through the Straits of Florida from the Gulf of Mexico parallel to the American coast up as far as Cape Hatteras. From there it continues north-eastwards as a slower, broader, cooler (yet even so, relatively warm) drift of water, merging with the North Atlantic Drift and losing its identity about 40° N. Lat., 60° W. Long. It is a common error to attribute the warmth of the British Isles and Western Europe generally to the Gulf Stream but this has no influence whatever except in so far as it feeds the North Atlantic Drift. Both the Gulf Stream and the North Atlantic Drift owe their movement to the direction of the prevailing winds, and it is the south-westerly airstream coming from warmer regions and passing over the surface waters of the Atlantic Drift that brings the warmth inland to influence the climate of Western Europe.

Gull. An extremely well-known, long-winged sea-bird with rather short legs and webbed feet. In almost all adults the body and tail are white whilst the back and most of the wings are grey or black. In the majority of cases the plumage of juveniles is partly or entirely dusky. Gulls are omnivorous, and are very useful as scavengers. They follow ships and quickly seize upon any refuse which may be thrown overboard. There are 44 species, which vary in size from moderately small to large. With certain exceptions, such as the Kittiwake in the North Atlantic, they are not found very far from land. They are sociable and mostly breed in colonies on cliff-ledges, on islands, beaches and sandhills and among vegetation in swamps, sometimes a long way from the sea. The nest is usually substantial, and the eggs generally number from two to three. Of the 29 species breeding in the northern hemisphere, 14 occur in the British Isles. The pure white Ivory Gull is the most northerly of birds. Sabine's and the Swallow-tailed Gull have forked tails. Ross's Gull has a black ring round the neck and one species, Franklin's Gull, migrates from the North, where it breeds, to pass the winter in the Southern hemisphere.

Gums are glutinous compounds obtained from vegetable sources, soluble in cold or hot water, but not in alcohol. There are innumerable varieties. Gum Arabic is exuded from a species of acacia grown in Senegal, the Sudan, Arabia, India and other countries, and is a valuable commercial product, used in dyeing, ink-making, as a mucilage, and in medicine. India-rubber is an elastic gum. Gums are also made from starch, potatoes, wheat, etc., from seeds, bark, roots and weeds. Many so-called gums are resins.

Gun-Cotton, a powerful explosive manufactured by subjecting a prepared cotton to the prolonged action of a mixture of three parts sulphuric acid and one part of nitric acid. It burns without explosion on ignition, but by percussion explodes with a force five times greater than

gunpowder does.

Gunpowder, also called "black powder", the oldest of explosive mixtures, consists of saltpetre, sulphur and charcoal, intimately mixed, the proportions being varied for different intended uses.

Gunpowder Plot was a conspiracy by a desperate band of Roman Catholics in the reign of James I to avenge the harsh treatment to which Catholics were subjected. Barrels of gunpowder were secreted in the vaults underneath the Houses of Parliament, and it was proposed to fire these when the King and his Ministers assembled on 5 November 1605. The plot was betrayed and Guy Fawkes and his co-conspirators were arrested and executed. The date serves to perpetuate the ancient custom of burning the effigy of Fawkes.

Gurnard, a sea-fish, with large, bony head and diminutive body, of which there are some forty species. They are plentiful in British waters.

Gymnasium, originally the name given in ancient Greece to the public places where Greek youth used to exercise and receive instruction. Plato, Aristotle and other great teachers lectured there. The Greek institution was never very popular with the Romans, and it was not until the 18th and 19th cent. that the cult of combining physical with intellectual activity again found a place in educational systems. In Germany the name was applied to the classical grammar school; in this country and America to the halls where gymnastics were practised.

Gypsies, a nomadic race, believed to be of Indian origin; their language, Romany, is related to the languages of N.W. India. The Rom are spread over many parts of the world, but are most common in Europe where they appeared towards the end of the Middle Ages. The English name *gypsy* comes from the Spanish *gitano* = Egyptian; other European names are *Zigeuner* (Ger.), *zingaro* (It.), *tzigany* (Magyar), all resembling the Persian *singar* = a saddler. Their history has been one of persecution. Hitler treated them like the Jews. In Britain since the war they have been kept increasingly on the move, but in 1968 Parliament passed a Bill to make the provision of sites a duty of local authorities. However, the 1994 Criminal Justice and Public Order Act will make it much easier to move on unwelcome gypsies. Economic pressure has largely removed their traditional crafts of tinkering, basket-making and peg-making. The majority now deal in scrap-iron.

Gypsum, a whitish mineral consisting of hydrated sulphate of calcium. The finest gypsum is alabaster. When heated gypsum is converted into the powder called Plaster of Paris; the water it loses can be taken up when the plaster is wetted, and the reconversion of Plaster of Paris into gypsum accounts for the way in which the former sets hard. The name "Plaster of Paris" came from the location of important gypsum quarries in the Montmartre district of Paris. It was found after the flood disasters of January 1953 that gypsum could undo the effect of sea-water. By spreading it for the rain to wash into the soil, thousands of acres of farmland in Holland and Britain were made productive again.

Gyroscope is a symmetrical rapidly rotating object, typically wheel-like, which because of its mass and rotation possesses a lot of the dynamical property known as angular momentum. Basic dynamical laws tell us that angular momentum is conserved and a consequence of this is that the axis of rotation tends to stay pointing in the same direction. Disturbing influences make a gyroscope's motion complicated but the general effect of the presence of a gyroscope attached to any body is to help to stabilise the body's motion. This is made use of in reducing the rocking of ships and in compasses and control systems in aircraft, torpedoes and missiles.

H

Habeas Corpus, the name given to a writ ordering the body of a person under restraint or imprisonment to be brought into court for full inquiry into the legality of the restraint to be made. The first Habeas Corpus Act was passed in 1679, though nominally such a right had existed from Magna Carta, but some of the more despotic kings had disregarded it. In times of public peril the privilege of *habeas corpus* is sometimes temporarily suspended, many instances occurring in the history of Ireland and during the first and second world wars.

Haber–Ostveldt Process, the important industrial process for synthesising ammonia from atmospheric nitrogen. Nitrogen and hydrogen are combined at high pressure (*c*. 350 atmospheres) and moderately high temperature (500°C) using a catalyst (made largely of iron). A yield of 30% is obtained. The majority of the world's ammonia is produced in this way or from methods derived from it.

Habsburg (Hapsburg), the ruling house of Austria, 1282–1918; held title of Roman Emperor, 1438–1806, except for 1740–5. The aggrandisement of the Hapsburg family was mainly brought about by a series of fortunate marriages. In 1521 when the Hapsburg power was at its zenith, Charles V divided his dominions into two branches—Austrian Hapsburg and Spanish Hapsburg. The Hapsburg Danubian Monarchy dates from 1526 when the Hungarian and Bohemian crowns were united with the Austrian patrimony of the Hapsburg. The triple union lasted 400 years. The murder of the heir to the Hapsburg thrones, Francis Ferdinand, at Sarajevo in 1914, provoked the outbreak of the first world war. Francis Joseph's great-nephew, Charles, went into exile in 1918.

Haddock, one of the best-known fishes abounding in northern seas and averaging about 1·8 kg in weight. Related to the cod. Largely used for curing, and sold as "finnan haddies".

Hade of veins, a mining term indicating the particular inclination that any vein, seam or strata may have from the perpendicular; thus, in Weardale the veins mainly "hade" to the north.

Hadrian's Wall. *See* **Roman walls.**

Haematite, ferric oxide, one of the principal iron ores, containing about 70% of the metal. It is usually found in kidney-shaped masses, and is specular, red or brown, in thin fragments but greyish in bulk.

Haemocyanin, the respiratory pigment of crustaceans and molluscs. It functions like haemoglobin, from which it differs in containing copper instead of iron and being blue when oxidised instead of red. *See* **F39**(1).

Haemoglobin, the pigment containing iron which gives red blood corpuscles their colour. It is a respiratory pigment, having the property of picking up oxygen when the blood passes through the lungs to produce the compound known as oxyhaemoglobin. In other parts of the body the oxyhaemoglobin breaks down, liberating oxygen, which is used in the oxidation process (respiration) that the body tissues carry on. *See* **F38**(2).

Hafiz, besides being the pseudonym of a famous Persian poet, is a title conferred upon any Mohammedan who has committed the whole of the Koran to memory.

Hafnium, a metallic element, no. 72, symbol Hf, discovered by Coster and Hevesy in 1922 and important in the atomic-energy field. It occurs in most zirconium minerals to the extent of about 5%.

Hagiology, a branch of literature that is wholly given up to the history of the saints, and the setting forth of the stories and legends associated with their names.

Hail, hard, roughly spherical balls of ice, consisting of white cores covered by layers of both transparent and opaque ice, frequently falling during thunderstorms. They usually do not exceed 2·5 cm in size, but hailstones as large as tennis balls have been observed. The general theory of a hailstone is that near the top of a cumulonimbus cloud a raindrop becomes frozen, grows in size by condensation and through collisions with snow particles, and eventually becomes so weighty as to overcome the ascending air currents in the cloud. Falling, it first encounters supercooled water drops, immediately freezing on it, increasing the white core,

and then at lower levels ordinary water drops, freezing more slowly, producing a layer of clear ice. Before the hailstone arrives at the ground gusts and lulls may transport it several times up and down both regions, adding alternate coatings of soft white and hard clear ice.

Halcyon, a term associated in olden times with the kingfisher and days of soothing calm, "halcyon days" being a frequently used expression. The legend was that the kingfisher laid its eggs on the surface of the sea at the time of the winter solstice when the sea was unruffled. (Halcyon is the Greek for kingfisher.)

Halibut, one of the largest of the flat fishes, averaging when full grown from 1·2–1·8 m in length, and highly esteemed for the table. Specimens of still larger size occasionally occur. It is plentifully distributed. Its two eyes are on the right side of the head.

Hallmark. A mark or group of marks, impressed by an assay office on gold or silver articles (and on platinum since 1974) guaranteeing the standard of fineness of the precious metal used in them. These marks, which have been applied to silver made in London since the beginning of the 14th cent. and perhaps earlier, make it possible to establish the year and place of assay and also the name of the maker. English pieces of silver usually have not less than four marks, viz., (1) town mark; (2) maker's mark; (3) date letter; (4) sterling mark.

The town mark is rarely changed; in London a crowned leopard's head was used from the earliest days until 1820 with only minor modifications, except for the period 1697–1720 when a lion's head erased was substituted; since 1820 the crown has been omitted.

Until the late 17th cent. a symbol was often used as a maker's mark, from 1696–1720 the first two letters of the maker's surname, and subsequently the maker's initials. Owing to the destruction of the earlier mark plates at Goldsmiths' Hall no maker's name prior to the late 17th cent. can be identified with certainty.

The London date letter is changed at the end of May each year, so each letter covers seven months of one year and five months of the following. The London date cycle has usually consisted of twenty letters: the alphabet of each cycle is of different style, and the letters are enclosed in shields of different shape.

The sterling mark, the lion passant, was introduced in 1544 and continued in use until 1697, when the higher Britannia standard was introduced in order to discourage the practice current amongst goldsmiths of melting down coin of the realm to make plate. The leopard's head crowned and the lion passant were then replaced by a figure of Britannia and a lion's head erased. Though the regulation imposing a higher standard was withdrawn in 1720, a small amount of Britannia standard silver continued to be made and still is made.

From 1784 until 1890 a plate tax was levied on all silver assayed in Great Britain and an additional duty mark, the sovereign's head, was used during this period. A Jubilee mark bearing the head of George V and of Queen Mary was used between the years 1933 and 1935, and in 1953 a coronation mark with the head of Queen Elizabeth was introduced.

Under the Hallmarking Act 1973 the hallmarking of platinum is now compulsory; the hallmark symbol is an orb surmounted by a cross and encompassed by a pentagon; assay offices London and Birmingham.

Halloween (31 October), the eve of All Saints' Day, a time associated, especially in Scotland, with certain traditions attractively set forth in Burns's famous poem "Hallowe'en". It is the night when young men and maidens are supposed, by observing certain rites, to have their future wives and husbands disclosed to them.

Hallucinogen, a drug which acts upon the brain to create sensory illusions or hallucinations with a variety of emotional effects. One of the most widely studied is LSD (*q.v.*) which will produce symptoms very similar to those found in some mental disorders.

Halo, a luminous circle usually of 22° radius, surrounding sun or moon, produced by the refraction and reflection of light by ice crystals of high cirrus cloud. It is a very common occurrence, in the British Isles almost one day in three. The inner side is red and the outer a whitish-yellow colour. "Mock suns", *i.e.*, patches of light at the same elevation as the sun are much rarer occurrences, sometimes being of great beauty and brilliance. Halo is the Greek for threshing-floor. *See* **Corona.**

Halogens, the group name for the five non-metallic elements fluorine, chlorine, bromine, iodine and astatine. The term "halogen" means "salt-producer".

Halteres, the modified hind-wings of the two-winged flies or *Diptera* (*e.g.*, the house-fly). The equilibrium in flight of these insects depends on the halteres, which are commonly called "balancers".

Hampton Court Conference, presided over at Hampton Court Palace by James I in 1604 and which brought about his authorised translation of the Bible, had an important bearing on the religious differences of the time. James refused to grant tolerations to the Puritans. This sowed the seeds of civil war. Following the conference three hundred English Puritan clergy were ejected from their livings.

Hanaper Office, a former Chancery office, deriving its name from the fact that its writs and papers were kept in a hanaper (hamper). The Chancellor's office thus came to be known as the Hanaper. The Comptrollers of the Hanaper were abolished in England in 1842.

Hand, a measure of 4 in (10 cm), the average size of the palm; used in reckoning height of horses.

Handfasting, an informal marriage custom once prevalent in Scotland, whereby a man and woman bound themselves to cohabit for a year and a day, and at the end of that period either confirmed their contract by a regular marriage or separated.

Hanoverians, Royal dynasty which ruled Great Britain and Ireland, from 1714 to 1901. From the Brunswick-Luneburg branch of the Guelph family, they took their name from the German state of Hanover where they were Electors of the Holy Roman Empire. Their succession to the English, and later British, crown was secured by the 1710 Act of Settlement. In 1837 the crown of Hanover went to the uncle of Queen Victoria, Ernest, Duke of Cumberland and the personal union of the Hanoverian and British crowns ceased.

The British Hanoverian monarchs were George I (ruled 1714–27); his son George II (1727–60); George III, grandson of George II (1760–1820); his eldest son George IV (1820–30 and Prince Regent from 1812); William IV, third son of George III (1830–37) and Queen Victoria, granddaughter of George III (1837–1901).

Hansard, the title given to the official reports of Parliamentary debates, so named after Luke Hansard who in 1774 became partner in a firm of printers to the House of Commons. His son T. C. Hansard was first the printer and then the publisher of an unofficial series of parliamentary debates inaugurated by William Cobbett in 1803. In 1909 production was taken over by H.M. Stationery Office and today's volumes contain full, substantially verbatim, reports of what is said in both Houses of Parliament.

Hanseatic League was a confederation of North German towns established about 1241 for purposes of mutual protection in carrying on international commerce. The League became so powerful that it was able to dominate the foreign trade of Norway, Sweden, Denmark, and even to some extent of London. A branch was established in London and had its guild hall in Cannon Street for hundreds of years. The League existed down to the middle of the 17th cent. Hamburg, Lübeck and Bremen are the only cities which, as free ports, still by commercial courtesy retain the name of Hanse towns. *Hansa* is Old High German for Association or Merchants' Guild. *See also* **Freeport.**

Hapsburg, *see* **Habsburg.**

Hara-kiri, the custom of suicide, as formerly practised in Japan, when in disgrace.

Hardware, the electrical, electronic, magnetic and mechanical parts of a computer or data-processing system. *See also* **Software.**

Hare, a rabbit-like animal with longer ears and legs. There are many kinds of hare distributed over the northern hemisphere and in Africa

south to the Cape. They do not burrow as do rabbits but rely on camouflage, speed and mobility for safety. *See* **Game.**

Harleian MSS. comprise some thousands of volumes of MSS. and documents, collected by the first Earl of Oxford (1661–1724) and his son Edward. After the death of the latter, his widow handed the MSS. over to the nation for £10,000, and they are deposited in the British Museum.

Harlequin, the buffoon of ancient Italian comedy. As adapted to the British stage, however, harlequin is a pantomime character only, in love with Columbine, appearing in parti-coloured garments and carrying a wand, by which he exercises a magic influence in thwarting the fantastic tricks of the clown and pantaloon.

Harmattan, a dry wind which may blow between January and May across the Sahara to the Gulf of Guinea. Although affording relief from the tropical heat, vegetation withers because of its extreme dryness and much irritation is caused by the clouds of fine dust which it carries.

Harmonic Motion, regular periodic motion of the kind exemplified by a ball bobbing up and down at the end of a spring, and by the piston in a steam engine. It may be simple (simple harmonic motion) or composed of two or more simple harmonic motions. In simple harmonic motion the acceleration is proportional to the distance of the moving body from its original rest position.

Harp-seal, the ordinary Greenland seal, with a dark harp-shaped marking on its back, hence its name. It abounds in Newfoundland waters and further northward towards the Arctic.

Harpy Eagle, a large bird of prey named from the winged monsters of Greek mythology, inhabiting the forest regions of Central and South America. There are eight species, one with handsome grey plumage and large crest which attacks and kills animals much larger than itself, and was called by the Aztecs "winged wolf".

Harrier, a bird of prey of the falcon family; of the various species distributed over the world, three breed in Britain: the moorland Hen harrier, the Marsh harrier and Montagu's harrier. They are large birds with long tails, long legs, long wings and gliding flight. They nest on the ground and eat small mammals, frogs, lizards and small birds.

Hartebeest, common African antelope of a grey-brown colour, with ringed and knotted horns bending backward and tapering to sharp points; gregarious, of large size. There are several species.

Harvest Bug, a very small insect, of a dark red colour, which appears in large numbers in the fields in autumn, and is peculiarly irritating to animals and man by the tenacity with which it attaches itself to the skin and burrows underneath. Probably the larvae of spinning mites (Trombidoids). In the USA they are called "chiggers".

Harvest Moon, the full moon that occurs nearest to the autumn equinox, in September. It rises for several nights running about the same time, and yields an unusually brilliant series of moonlight nights.

Harvestmen are, like spiders, members of the arachnid class but belong to the distinctly different order of Phalangida. They are common in the countryside in autumn and have small oval bodies and eight long slender legs which besides being mere organs of locomotion also act as sense organs. Known as "daddy longlegs" in America and Britain.

Hashish, an Arabic word for the narcotic substance prepared from the hemp plant (*Cannabis sativa*). It is known by a variety of names, *e.g.*, bhang in India and marijuana in America.

Hatchment, in heraldry, is a square board, in vertical diagonal position, placed outside a house or on the tomb at the death of a member of a family and so arranged that it indicates the sex and condition of the deceased.

Hawfinch, a well-known European bird of the finch family, having a variegated plumage, a sturdy bill and black-and-white tail. In England it is found in the Midland and Eastern counties, and locally in Scotland.

Hawk. This name is applied to almost any diurnal bird of prey other than eagle, falcon or vulture, but in its strict sense applies only to the *Accipiter* genus—the small Sparrow Hawk and the larger Goshawk, round-winged, long-tailed birds with barred under-parts. They prey upon small birds captured in flight and small mammals.

Hawk-moths, large species of moths, thick of body and strong of wing, which fly with rapid swooping motion, hence the name. There are numerous handsome species in Britain.

Hearth-Money was a tax laid on hearths (in all houses paying the church and poor rates). Charles II introduced it in 1662, and it was repealed in the reign of William and Mary.

Heat, after prolonged controversy over whether or not heat is a "substance" (formerly called "caloric"), it was established in the 19th cent. that heat is a form of energy; it is in fact the combined kinetic and potential energy of the atoms of which a body is composed. Heat can be turned into other forms of energy, *e.g.*, a red hot body loses heat by radiating it in the form of electromagnetic waves ("radiant heat"—chiefly infra-red rays). Heat may also be transferred from one place to another by conduction and, in fluids, by convection. All three processes occur when a glowing fire heats a room. A unit quantity of heat is the calorie, which is the amount of heat sufficient to raise the temperature of 1 g of water by 1°C. In general, adding heat to a body raises its temperature. The number of calories required per gram of material to raise the temperature 1°C is called the *specific heat* of the material. However, adding heat may not raise the temperature-but may instead cause a change of state, *e.g.*, from solid to liquid (melting) or liquid to gas (evaporation). The amount of heat required to melt 1 gram of a solid is called the latent heat of melting. Similarly, there is a latent heat of evaporation. Strictly speaking, the specific and latent heats of a substance depend on how much its pressure and volume are allowed to vary during the measurements. Water has a high specific heat, and this makes the oceans a vast heat reservoir, a factor of great meteorological significance. The science of heat is called thermodynamics, and is of great importance in physics and chemistry. **F20(1).**

Heat Pump, essentially a refrigerator working in reverse, *i.e.*, a device which warms up one place, say, a house by releasing into it heat transferred from another place, say, the air or earth outside the house. The idea is attributed to Lord Kelvin (1852) and later Haldane used a heat pump to heat his house in Scotland. In Summer, a house could be cooled by operating the device in reverse. As in a domestic refrigerator, the heat is transferred by a suitable fluid whose circulation has to be driven by an external supply of energy, *e.g.*, by running a mechanical compressor. With good design and favourable conditions, the energy required to run the heat pump is considerably less than would be required to produce the same warming effect directly. Since the 1930s heat pumps have been produced commercially for domestic and industrial use but, as always, careful consideration is needed to decide whether in a particular application they are cheaper to run than alternative methods of heating.

Heath, flowering plants of the *Ericaceae* family. Heaths are widely distributed over uncultivated spaces of Europe and Africa. In Britain they are represented by heather (of which there are several species) and ling (*Calluna vulgaris*), which cover thousands of acres of moorland. Some of the African or Cape heaths are very beautiful and much prized by florists. One species of heath (*Erica arborea*) which grows in S. Europe and N. Africa has close-grained woody rootstock used for making briar pipes. In N. Europe acid heathlands, dominated by heather and ling, form one of the most widespread vegetation areas created by man through the destruction of former oak forests, grazing and burning.

Heathrow Airport, originally called London Airport (Heathrow) and named after a village where Terminal 3 now stands, opened on 1 January 1946. The airport handles more than 90 airlines from 85 countries and offers direct flights to more than 200 destinations. Every day the airport's

catering facilities serve the public more than 23,500 cups of tea and coffee. A proposed new Terminal Five is currently (1995) the subject of a public inquiry.

Hegira, an Arab term signifying departure or flight, used in reference to Mohammed's departure from Mecca, A.D. 622, from which date the Mohammedan era is reckoned.

Helicopter, heavier-than-air aircraft which obtains its lift from blades rotating above the fuselage in windmill-fashion. The first successful helicopters were the Focke-Wulf 61, a German machine (1936), and the VS-300, designed by Igor Sikorsky, flown in 1937. Helicopters can hover, and rise and descend vertically, in addition to being capable of horizontal flight.

Heliotrope, a favourite sweet-scented flowering plant, common in tropical and sub-tropical countries; the Peruvian heliotrope is the "cherry pie" of our summer garden borders.

Helium, a gaseous element, no. 2, symbol He, first discovered by means of the spectroscope in the sun's atmosphere. This discovery, made in 1868 by the astronomer Sir Norman Lockyer, was followed in 1895 by Sir William Ramsay's proof that the element existed on earth. He found it in the uranium ore, clevite. Later it was established that helium is formed by the radioactive decay of many elements which emit *a*-particles (nuclei of helium atoms) and is contained in all radioactive minerals. The largest source of helium is natural gas, the richest in helium being the gas from certain wells in Utah, USA. Next to hydrogen, helium is the lightest gas known, has a lifting power equal to 92% of hydrogen and the advantage that it is inert and non-inflammable. It is used for inflating airships. Ordinary air contains 1 part in 200,000 of helium. It was the last gaseous element to be liquefied, this being achieved by Onnes in 1908 in Leyden. Liquid helium has many remarkable properties only imperfectly understood. As well as being scientifically fascinating it is indispensable in cryogenics (*q.v.*) as a medium for cooling other substances to temperatures near absolute zero. Hydrogen fusion in the "H bomb" produces helium.

Hellebore, a plant of the *Ranunculaceae* (buttercup) family. The best-known British examples are the green and stinking varieties. There is also a garden kind which flowers in December called the Christmas Rose. Hellebore yields a bitter substance which forms a drastic purgative, but is now little used.

Hellenic Art. The art of ancient Greece may be roughly divided into three periods: the prehistoric period (c. 1500–1000 B.C.) of the bronze age Mycenaeans; the archaic period (c. 600–500 B.C.); and the classical period (c. 500–300 B.C.). Of the first period centred on Mycenae in Peloponnesus but extending to the coasts of Asia and the city of Troy we can mention only the massive stone gateways and the shaft graves of Mycenae, where the archaeologist Schliemann discovered painted vases, gold cups, bronze swords and ornaments of what had once been a great, if primitive, civilisation. During the archaic period sculpture was the principal form of art expression. The magnificent male and female figures are reminiscent of Egyptian art, but are distinctive in liveliness of facial expression. The vase-paintings of this period became more elaborate, depicting scenes from mythology or ceremonial events. Typical of classical Greek art is the representation of the beautiful and healthy human body deliberately posed and often carrying out heroic or athletic acts. The vast majority of these statues are known to us only through Roman copies. The *Hermes* of Praxiteles (born c. 385 B.C.) is possibly the only existing statue which can be assigned with any degree of certainty to an individual artist. Almost the whole of the Greek genius in architecture was expended on temples which are all basically similar in design—a rectangle with a low-pitched gabled roof resting on side walls. The three orders Doric, Corinthian and Ionic mainly referred to the type of column used, but naturally the whole building was influenced thereby. Some of the main buildings are on the Acropolis, a hill outside Athens, on which stand the Parthenon (from the outer frieze of which the Elgin marbles (*q.v.*), now mostly in the

British Museum, were taken), the Erechtheum, famous for its Porch of Maidens, and the gateway known as the Propylaea with its broad flight of marble steps. Apart from that on vases, no Greek painting has come down to us, although Greek painters existed and were noted in their time. All we have are copies in mosaic and fresco made by the Romans, at Naples and Pompeii. Of Greek literature in prose, verse and the drama little can be said here. To the early period (*i.e.*, the archaic age) belong Homer's *Iliad* and *Odyssey*. Hesiod's long poem *Work and Days* and Sappho's love poems, and Pindar's Odes. The period of Pericles in the 5th cent. B.C. produced more great literature than any comparable period in history: the philosophical writings of Plato and Aristotle, the tragedies of Aeschylus, Euripides and Sophocles, the comedies of Aristophanes—all these are still part of the European tradition, and together with Greek architecture played a major part in the Renaissance (*see* Section J).

Hellenistic Art, the age of the period of Greek civilisation which began with the conquests of Alexander the Great (356–323 B.C.) and lasted until his former empire (which encompassed most of the Middle East and part of North Africa) was conquered by the Romans in 146 B.C. Culturally it was an important period because it spread Greek culture far beyond its original boundaries—even as far as the north of India, and its centres spread from Athens to the cities of Alexandria in Egypt, Antioch in Syria and Pergamum in Asia Minor. But equally Eastern culture spread to the West: democracy was replaced by absolute monarchy, cosmopolitanism took the place of the Greek tendency to believe that all who were not Greeks were barbarians, and mystical philosophies took the place of Greek rationalism. This was a sensuous, secular, pleasure-loving, rootless society, and these tendencies were reflected in its art. Hellenistic sculpture was sensual, effeminate and violently emotional, depicting individuals not always noble or beautiful ones. (Classical Greek sculpture was idealistic, showed types rather than individuals and appealed to the intellect rather than the emotions.) Some of the best examples came from the school at Pergamum and later from the island of Rhodes, and the titles themselves speak of their nature: *The Dying Gaul, Gaul Slaying his Wife and Himself* and the famous *Laocoön* (representing Laocoön and his two sons being crushed by two enormous serpents). All these date from about 240 to 50 B.C.—for the culture did not immediately end with the Roman conquest. The enormous frieze of the altar of the temple in Pergamum depicts a battle between gods and giants with tremendous realism and brutal violence far removed from the serene art of classical times. Portrait sculpture is typical of Hellenistic art, where it may almost be said to have been invented, since such ventures in the past had been idealistic rather than realistic. The great Hellenistic cities were geometrically planned and fine public buildings made their appearance in which the slender and graceful Ionic of the ornate Corinthian columns took the place of the more austere and heavy classical ones. Alexandria was celebrated for its vast libraries and was the centre of a brilliant intellectual life (the Septuagint or Greek translation of the Bible was prepared here). Here too worked the mathematicians Euclid and Archimedes, the physicians Erasistratus and Herophilus, and the geographer Pytheas. But Hellenistic literature was a pale reflection of the glories of the past and we mention only the comedies of Menander and the pastoral verse of Theocritus of Syracuse.

Hemiptera, the order of insects to which belong the true bugs. Their wing structure is in most species incomplete, hence the term hemiptera (half-wing). This order includes the familiar water insects, the water boatman and water skater, also the aphids, cicadas, leaf hoppers, scale insects.

Hemlock, a plant of the *Umbelliferae* family, growing in all parts of Britain, and containing a strong alkaloid poison. Used medicinally, this alkaline substance is of considerable service, being a powerful sedative. According to Pliny,

hemlock was the poison used by the Athenians in putting criminals to death.

Hemp (*Cannabis sativa*), name of a plant native to Asia, now cultivated widely for the valuable fibre contained in the stalk or in some species in the leaves. Hemp fibre has been replaced by cotton for textiles and by jute for sacks and is now chiefly used for cordage and twine. It contains a resinous substance from which the narcotic hashish is made. The seed yields a valuable oil. The term hemp is also used for other fibre plants, including manila hemp from the Philippines, sunn hemp from India, sisal from W. and E. Africa and phormium from New Zealand.

Henbane, a plant found in Britain and other parts of Europe and Northern Asia. It belongs to the potato family *Solanaceae*, grows mostly on waste ground and bears yellow-brown flowers veined with purple. The leaves yield a poisonous alkaloid substance which, medicinally prepared and administered, is of great use. Tincture of henbane is often preferred to laudanum.

Heptarchy, a word derived from the Greek *hepta*, seven, and denoting the seven kingdoms (*archai*) into which Anglo-Saxon England was divided before 900. The seven were Kent, Essex, Sussex, Wessex, Mercia, East Anglia and Northumbria.

Heracleum, a plant of the *Umbelliferae* family, common in southern and central Europe, though only one species, the cow parsnip, grows in England. It has a bitter root, and from the juice of the stem an intoxicating liquor is occasionally prepared.

Herald, an officer of state empowered to make formal proclamations and deliver messages from the sovereign or other high personage whom he serves. In the developments which took place in armorial bearings, the herald was the functionary charged with the duty of their proper depiction.

Heraldry, the knowledge of armorial bearings, was mainly the outcome of the love of outward distinction which prevailed in mediaeval times, "Heraldry," says Stubbs, "became a handmaid of chivalry, and the marshalling of badges, crests, coat-armour, pennons, helmets and other devices of distinction grew into an important branch of knowledge." The *shield*, or *escutcheon*, is the ground upon which armorial signs are traced, the colour of the shield being called the *tincture*, the signs recorded the *charges*. There are seven *tinctures*—or (gold), *argent* (silver), *gules* (red), *azure* (blue), *vert* (green), *purpure* (purple) and *sable* (black). The *charges* are classed as "Honourable" and "Subordinate" ordinaries, comprising lines and geometrical forms; and "Common" ordinaries, which latter includes all representations of natural objects. There is also a system of external signs, such as crowns, coronets, mitres, helmets, mantlings, wreaths and crests, each having its distinctive significance. For other distinguishing marks *see* **Hatchment, Quartering, Rampant.**

Heralds' College or College of Arms, was incorporated by Richard III in 1483. Its head is the Earl Marshal (an office hereditary in the family of the Dukes of Norfolk), and there are three Kings of Arms, six Heralds and four Pursuivants. The business transacted is wholly connected with the tracing of genealogies and the granting of armorial bearings. In Scotland the Heraldic functions are performed by the Lord Lyon King of Arms.

Herbarium, a systematically classified collection of preserved plants. One of the largest in the world is at the Royal Botanic Gardens at Kew.

Heredity is the study of the transmission of physical and mental characteristics from one generation to another. Gregor Mendel (1822–84), a great experimenter in the field of inheritance, established the principle embodied in Mendel's law in his work published in 1866. The ideas which he then put forward were forgotten until the early years of this century, but today they form the basis of the modern study of genetics. Genes are the units of heredity; they are contained in the chromosomes of the cell nucleus. In human cells there are 46 chromosomes—22 pairs of characteristic shape, and a 23rd (the sex chromosomes) similar in women and dissimilar in men, which unite in the process of fertilisation. An individual can only develop, even under the most favourable surroundings, as far as his inherited characteristics, *i.e.*, his genes will allow him to do. It is in the development of personality that the interplay between heredity and environment becomes most apparent. *See* **Evolution, Section F, Part IV.**

Hermaphrodite, animals or plants possessing both male and female reproductive organs, *e.g.*, snail, earthworms, most flowering plants.

Hermit Crab, a decapod, with a soft asymmetrical body which it protects by thrusting it into an empty gastropod shell, *e.g.*, whelk, which it carries about, only abandoning it when necessary for a larger one. Found in all seas, many live in commensal relationship with sea anemones etc.

Heron, a large wading bird with long curved neck and pointed bill, is a member of the *Ardeidae* family, of which there are many species. Egrets and bitterns are included as herons. Herons are to be met with in marsh lands and near rivers and lakes, where they feed on fish and frogs. They nest in trees in large numbers, these colonies being called heronries. The common heron is native to England, and other species from the Continent are frequent visitors.

Herring (*Clupea harengus*), an important food-fish inhabiting the North Sea which has been subjected to overfishing. In Britain the herring industry is based on the Shetlands and the coastal ports of E. Scotland and N.E. England. Marine biologists have recently reported on its unique structure for hearing which makes it receptive to sound frequencies over a very wide range and able to determine distance, direction and sound of a source of sound.

Hibernation, the dormant condition in which numerous mammals, reptiles, amphibians, insects, plants, *etc.*, pass the winter. The rate of metabolism slows down, and the body temperature drops to that of the surroundings. Work on these low temperatures and their physiological effect has led to improved surgical techniques. Animals of the torrid regions pass through an analogous period (aestivation) during the hot season, when the sources of food are dried up.

Hickory, several species of American tree of the walnut family, remarkable for its very hard, solid, heavy white wood, and bearing an edible, four-lobed nut.

Hieratic Art, a type of art (typified by the major part of the art of ancient Egypt) which is (*a*) exclusively religious and (*b*) conventionally based on earlier forms and traditions.

Hieroglyphics are the earliest form of pictured symbolic expressionn, and are supposed to have been introduced by the ancient Egyptians. They consist of rude depictions of animals, plants, signs and objects, and in their later examples express, in abridged form, ideas and records from which significant historical information has been gleaned. The deciphering of Egyptian hieroglyphics long formed an ardent study, but gradually the key to the riddle was discovered, and most of the ancient records can now be understood. Besides the Egyptian there are also Hittite, Minoan and Mayan hieroglyphic scripts. *See* **Rosetta Stone.**

Hi-Fi means high fidelity and refers to gramophones, tape recorders and similar apparatus which will *faithfully* reproduce sounds. It is not too difficult these days to amplify electrical signals without distorting them much; it is more difficult to turn electrical impulses into exactly equivalent sound waves (with a loudspeaker, for example) or *vice versa* (with a microphone or gramophone pick-up). Pick-up and loudspeakers are therefore often the weak links in domestic hi-fi and faults in their design, deficiencies in the electronic amplifiers, imperfect gramophone motors can all contribute to audible results ranging from the tolerable to the execrable.

Hindi, the official language of India.

Hinduism. *See* **Section J.**

Hindustani, the spoken form of Hindi (written in Devanagari script) and Urdu (written in Arabic characters).

Hippogriff, a fabulous animal like a horse in body, but with the head, wings and front legs and claws of an eagle. The monster frequently appears in the romances of the Middle Ages.

Hippopotamus or "river-horse" the largest living representative of the hippopotamidae family, widely distributed over Africa, where it lives in herds. It is of immense bulk, attaining a length of 3·6 m and a weight of 4 tonnes and stands about 1·5 m high. Its skin is hairless and about 5 cm thick, and it has a pair of tusks often weighing as much as 2·7 kg. It leads an amphibious way of life, and lives entirely on vegetation, both aquatic and terrestrial. The pigmy hippopotamus, which occurs in forests and swamps in W. Africa, is only half the size.

Histology is the study of the structure of plant and animal tissues. These mainly consist of groups of cells with similar functions, *e.g.*, muscle, brain tissue.

Hittites, an ancient race (often mentioned in the Old Testament) who inhabited Cappadocia (region of Eastern Asia Minor) from the third to the first millennium B.C. Excavations have revealed that they attained a high level of civilisation round about 1350 B.C. The Hittites were rivals of Egypt, disputing with the Pharaohs the mastery of the Middle East. They were the first to smelt iron successfully.

Hobby, a bird of the falcon family, 30–35 cm long. Local breeding visitor to England and Wales, April–September; irregular visitor to Scotland and Ireland. They winter in Africa.

Hog, the common name of animals of the Suidae family, including the wild boar, pig and sow. The wild boar, *Sus scrofa*, is the common ancestor. The skin of the hog is covered with bristles, the snout truncated and each foot has four hoofed toes. Hogs are omnivorous feeders and eat almost anything that is given them.

Hogmanay, the Scottish New Year's Eve festival and a national holiday of the country. The custom of demanding Hogmanay bread is still upheld in many parts of Scotland.

Hogshead, a cask of varying capacity, also a specific measure. In the old English measure a hogshead was 63 old gallons of wine (=52½ imperial gallons = 238·6 litres). Of beer 54 old gallons make a hogshead.

Holly, a hardy evergreen shrub, largely grown in England. Its bright dark green prickly curved leaves and clusters of red berries are familiar in all parts of the country, and used as house decoration between Christmas Eve and Twelfth Night, probably a relic from Roman and Teutonic customs. Its wood is white and hard, valued for carved work, while its bark yields a gummy substance which is converted into bird-lime.

Hologram, a photographic record, taken under special optical conditions, of light reflected from a scene or object. The hologram is typically a piece of film. However it is nothing like a photographic negative of the ordinary kind; for one thing it will show an unintelligible pattern of light and dark patches. Nevertheless if it is illuminated (again under special optical conditions) the light coming through it will form a *three dimensional* image of the original object. Another radical difference between a hologram and an ordinary film is that if the hologram is cut up, each fragment can be used to construct the entire image. Holography, as a method of recording and reproducing photographic information, was conceived by Gabor in 1947 but was only fully realised in practice after the invention of the laser (*q.v.*), which made available powerful sources of coherent light. The use of laser light is one of the "special conditions" referred to above. Technical applications are being explored in many laboratories. Gabor received the 1971 Nobel prize for his discovery and invention.

Holy Alliance, an alliance ostensibly for conserving religion, justice and peace in Europe, but used for repressing popular tendencies towards constitutional government. Formed by Alexander I of Russia, Francis I of Austria and Frederick William III of Prussia, at Paris on 26 September 1815. Subsequently joined by all the sovereigns of Europe, except the Pope and the King of England. It ended after the 1830 revolution in France.

Holy Coat of Trèves, a garment preserved in the Cathedral of Trèves and said to have been worn by Christ. It was brought from Jerusalem by the Empress Helena in the fourth century.

Holy Roman Empire, the title traditionally given (although the term "Holy" does not appear in a document until 1157) to the revived Empire when the German king Otto I was crowned in Rome by Pope John XII in 962. It endured until Napoleonic times (1806) two years after Francis II had assumed the title of Emperor of Austria.

Holy Rood, an annual Roman Catholic festival held on 14 September to celebrate the Elevation of the Cross in commemoration of its re-erection in Jerusalem by the Emperor Heraclius in 628 after retaking it from the Persians. Also included in the Church of England calendar.

Holyrood, the ancient royal palace at Edinburgh, dating from the 15th cent., and inhabited by many Scottish sovereigns, notably Mary Stuart, the rooms occupied by her (including the one in which Rizzio was murdered) being still shown. It is now known as Holyrood House and is still used as a royal residence.

Holy Water, water blessed by a priest and kept in small fonts at the entrance to Roman Catholic and some Anglican churches, and used by worshippers going in, and out, or by priests in sprinkling.

Holy Week is the week preceding Easter Sunday, and embraces the days of the Sufferings of Christ. It includes Good Friday and Holy Saturday.

Homoeopathy. *See* **Section J.**

Honey, the sweet syrup formed by bees from the nectar of flower, the sucrose in the nectar being converted into a mixture of the simple sugars, glucose and fructose. Hybla, an ancient town of Sicily, on the southern slope of Mt. Etna, was famous for its honey.

Honey-eater, an Australian bird (of which there are many species) provided with a long curved bill and tufted tongue. It lives by sucking the nectar from the flowers which abound in rural parts of Australia and New Zealand.

Hookah, an Oriental pipe for tobacco smoking, the smoke being drawn through the water of a goblet (commonly a coconut shell) by means of a long flexible tube.

Hoopoe, a remarkably handsome bird with vivid black and white-barred wings and tail and black-tipped crest which opens like a fan. Ranges over Europe, Asia and Africa. It has bred in England and Wales and occurs in the British Isles in small numbers at all seasons. Other species are confined to Africa, Madagascar and India.

Hops, the female "cones" of the hop plant used in brewing; their essential oils give beer an aromatic flavour, and their tannin and resin act as a preservative as well as accounting for the bitter taste desired. The hop is a perennial climber belonging to the mulberry family. The male and female organs are on separate plants; as only the female flower-heads are commercially useful, female plants predominate in a hop garden, only a very few male plants being grown so that the female flowers can be fertilised.

Horizon, the limit of vision, the apparent line where sea and sky, or land and sky meet. This is termed the visible horizon. An ordinary person at the height of 1·5 m can see for 4·8 km, at 6 m 9·6 km, at 15 m 14·8 km and at 305 m 67·5 km. The figures are approximate.

Hormone, a chemical substance which is released by one part of the body and produces a response in other parts after having been carried there by the bloodstream or some other transport system. Prolactin, for example, is a hormone produced by the pituitary gland of nursing mothers and serves to stimulate and maintain the milk supply.

Horn *or* **French Horn,** a brass instrument of the trumpet family (*i.e.,* played by three valves) whose tube is very thin and long (Horn in F = 12 ft). In consequence the tube is curled in a complicated manner. Owing to the sweet tone it is capable of producing, the Horn sometimes plays as part of the wood-wind.

Hornbill, large bird found in Africa and oriental regions. Some species have a casque or a horny growth above the very powerful beak. It feeds on fruits. When the female has laid her eggs in the hollow of a tree, the male bird stops up the entrance, and keeps her imprisoned until the hatching is completed and the young ones are able to fly. There are about 45 species.

Hornblende, the commonest member of the amphibole group of minerals, a silicate of calcium, magnesium, iron and aluminium, of a dark green colour. It is a constituent of numerous rocks, including diorite, syenite and hornblende schist.

Horned Viper, any of a number of species of African viper which have scales over each eye resembling horns. Their bite is usually very poisonous. The significance of the horns is not known.

Hornet, a general name for many of the bigger wasps. It usually nests in hollow trees, and despite its rather fiercesome appearance does not sting unless unduly provoked.

Horology, the science of time-measurement, including the construction and management of clocks, watches, etc. Instruments of this kind are not known to have existed before the 12th cent. and until the introduction of the pendulum in the 17th cent., clocks were ill-regulated and inaccurate. The time-recording mechanisms of the present day include (*a*) the *clock*, which shows the hours and minutes by hands, and strikes the hours, and sometimes quarters; (*b*) the *timepiece*, which is not generally a fixture and shows the time, but does not strike; (*c*) the *watch*, which is a pocket time-keeper; (*d*) the *chronometer*, which indicates the minutest portions of times; (*e*) electric timepieces, mains electric clocks; (*f*) the highly accurate quartz-crystal and atomic clocks used for astronomical purposes. *See* **Clock.**

Horse Chestnut, one of the large forest trees, with ample branches, and full foliage, and much esteemed for parks and ornamental grounds. The flowers, which appear in May, are white tinged with red and yellow. The tree is native to the mountainous regions of northern Greece. *See also* **Chestnut.**

Horse Guards, the building in Whitehall which until 1872 was the headquarters of the Commander-in-Chief of the British Army. The archway is still sentinelled by mounted guards.

Horse Latitudes, the latitudes of the sub-tropical high pressure systems, between the trade winds and the prevailing westerlies, characterised by light variable winds and low humidity.

Hospitallers, Knights, were of the order of St. John of Jerusalem, at first devoted to the aid of the sick, but afterwards military monks, who became prominent figures in the Crusades of the 12th cent. They adopted the Benedictine black habit with the eight-pointed cross worn by the modern St. John's Ambulance Brigade. In 1309 they took Rhodes, but were expelled by the Ottomans in 1522. In 1530 the emperor Charles V gave them the island of Malta, which as Knights of Malta, they held until 1798, when they were dislodged by Napoleon. The Knights still survive as a sovereign order, with headquarters in Rome. *See* **Templars** and **Teutonic Order.**

Hottentots, name given to certain African natives by Dutch settlers in the 17th cent. They used to occupy the greater part of Cape Colony and though driven out a number still survive in Namibia. They appear to be related to the Bushmen, though their culture is more advanced. In addition to herding, they practise some farming and know how to smelt iron.

Hounds are dogs that were originally bred and trained for hunting, such as the greyhound, fox-hound, bloodhound, wolfhound, deerhound, beagle, harrier, etc., but now often kept also as domestic dogs. The greyhound, deerhound and wolfhound hunt by sight, the others, with the bloodhound first in order, track by scent.

House Flies are world-wide and prolific. Their eggs are hatched within 24 hours of being laid, and full maturity is attained in a month. They feed on decayed animals and vegetable matter.

Hovercraft, or air cushion vehicle, is a craft which is lifted on a pad of air underneath it. This pad or cushion must be at a pressure higher than that of the atmosphere and it is made by sucking in air above the craft and ejecting it in a downward stream all round the lower edge. The stream is guided by a flexible skirt and the high pressure air pad is contained partly by the skirt and partly by the air stream itself which forms a continuous air curtain all round the vehicle. Hovercraft are being intensively developed and there are variations in the basic scheme just described and also in the means of propulsion which can be by air or water jets or propellers. Hovercraft were devised by Cockerell in the 1950s and a full-scale example appeared before the British public in June 1959. The air pad support means that hovercraft can move over land, water or marsh. Cross-Channel hovercraft were introduced in 1966.

Howler Monkey, a genus of South American monkey noted for a laryngeal conformation which enables it to emit a loud reverberant noise something between a yell and a howl, as the name suggests.

Huanuco-bark, a medicinal bark, brought from the Peruvian town of that name, and derived from the *Cinchona micrantha* tree.

Huguenots, a name applied to the French Protestant communities of the 16th and 17th cent. Henry of Navarre, by the Edict of Nantes in 1598, granted them religious freedom, but more than a quarter of a century before—24 August 1572—thousands had been put to death in the massacre of St. Bartholomew. The revocation of the Edict of Nantes by Louis XIV in 1685 drove thousands into exile in England, Holland, Germany and America.

Human Genome Project, a 15-year £2 billion global effort launched in the 1990s to unravel the human genetic blueprint.

Humanism. *See* Section J.

Humble-bee or **Bumble-bee,** the common name of the insects of the genus *bombus,* of the Hymenoptera order. They live in small communities comprising males, females and drones, their habitations being underground. They do not have one queen bee only like the hive bee, but several females occupy the same nest, and these alone live through the winter, breeding and forming new colonies in the spring. Their sting does not have a barb like the honey bee's.

Humidity, the state of the atmosphere with respect to the water-vapour it contains. "Absolute humidity" is defined as the density of the vapour present, while "relative humidity", more frequently employed indicates the degree of saturation, *i.e.,* the ratio of the actual vapour pressure to the saturation vapour pressure at the particular temperature, expressed as a percentage.

Humming Birds are so called because of the humming noise made by the vibration of their wings in flying. They are of radiant plumage, and are among the smallest birds. The smallest bird in the world is the Fairy or Princess Helen's humming bird of Cuba, whose body is only 5·7 cm long. There are from four to five hundred species, and they are confined wholly to North and South America, being most numerous in the tropical latitudes. They have long, slender bills and tubular tongues which reach down into flowers to suck up the nectar on which they feed.

Hummum, the original name for what is now called the Turkish Bath in this country. One of the first of these baths to be established in London was the Hummums in Covent Garden.

Hundred, the ancient divisonal name given to a portion of a county for administration or military purposes. It is supposed to imply the territory occupied by a hundred families; or the space of a hundred hides of land, or the capacity of providing 100 soldiers. Each hundred had its hundred court, with powers similar to those of a manor court, but this was abolished in 1867 by County Court Act.

Hundred Days, the interval of time between Napoleon Bonaparte's entry into Paris after his escape from Elba and his departure after his abdication, extending from 20 March 1815 to 28 June. During this period occurred the battle of Waterloo, 18 June. *See* **L128.**

Hundred Years' War, a term applied to the almost incessant contest between England and France, lasting from 1338 to 1453, including such famous battles as Crécy, Poitiers and Agincourt, and engaging successively Edward III, Henry V and Henry VI, among English kings.

Huns, a fierce Asiatic race which swept over eastern Europe in the 4th cent. Under Attila about the middle of the 5th cent, they obtained control of a large portion of central and eastern Europe, forcing even Rome to pay tribute. Their defeat at Châlons-sur-Marne in 451 by a mixed army of Romans, Goths and Teutonic tribes, and the death of Attila in 453, terminated their empire.

Hurdy-Gurdy, an Italian rustic musical stringed instrument of the lute order, the sounds of which are produced by the action of a rosined wheel turned by the left hand, the notes being made by the fingering of the right hand.

Hussites. *See* Section J.

Hurricane. *See* **Cyclone, Wind.**

Hydra, an aquatic animal of simple structure, whose body is in the form of a cylindrical tube, with a disc-shaped base by which it attaches itself to any shifting substance. Its mouth is surrounded by tentacles by which it catches its food. The Hydra has the power of reproducing lost parts.

Hydrates are compounds containing water of crystallisation.

Hydraulic Ram, a form of automatic pump, used to raise water to a height by the action of its own falling velocity.

Hydraulics, the science of applied hydrodynamics, or water-machine engineering, ranging from pumps to marine engines.

Hydrocarbons are compounds of carbon and hydrogen. They include the *paraffins,* which are saturated compounds (*e.g.,* methane); the ethylene, acetylene and other series which are unsaturated; compounds with ring structures, *e.g.,* benzene, naphthalene and anthracene. Petroleum is composed almost entirely of hydrocarbons.

Hydrochloric Acid, a solution of hydrogen chloride gas in water, and resulting in considerable quantities as a by-product of the soda-ash or salt-cake manufacture. Its solution forms the common hydrochloric or muriatic acid of commerce. It is present to the extent of nearly half a per cent, in the digestive juice secreted by the stomach.

Hydrocyanic Acid, cyanide of hydrogen or prussic acid; very poisonous, and of the odour of bitter almonds. It is formed by the action of acids on sodium or potassium cyanide. Used to kill wasps (and in the gas chamber in the USA). It is a very important chemical on account of the reactions of its derivatives in many synthetic fields. Discovered by Scheele in 1782.

Hydroelectric Schemes. The sun's energy has been indirectly exploited in the past by harnessing the energy of the winds and rain. The climate is due, essentially, to differential heating of the earth. The resulting convection currents in the air (the motion of which is complicated by the rotation of the earth) give rise to winds. Moisture is collected from the sea and deposited high up on mountains as rain. Some of the gravitational energy may be collected as hydropower. Simple windmills or waterwheels are so undependable that they have not been used to any extent since the beginning of the Industrial Revolution. However, the modern form of the waterwheel—the hydroelectric generation plant—is extensively used in mountainous countries and about a third of the world's electricity is produced by this means. The essential requirements for a modern hydroelectric scheme are a river with a sufficient flow of water to provide the required power, a large "head" of water so that a cheap, compact turbine can be used and a dam so that water can be stored until it is required. In some cases a hydroelectric scheme is made economic by being associated with an irrigation or drainage scheme. Such multi-purpose schemes are especially important in India and Pakistan, where most hydro projects are of this type. Other well-known examples include the Snowy Mountains scheme in Australia and the Aswan High Dam in Egypt.

Although over 90 per cent of the electricity in certain individual countries, notably Norway, Sweden, Portugal, Switzerland and Uganda is produced from hydroelectric schemes, only a relatively small fraction of the total potential has been exploited. This fraction varies from about a third in Western Europe to a quarter in the United States to a very small fraction in Alaska, Canada, Africa and the hinterland of Asia.

Hydrofluoric Acid is obtained by distillation of fluorspar with sulphuric acid, and is a compound of fluorine and hydrogen. Its action is highly corrosive; a valuable agent in etching on glass, and a rapid decomposer of animal matter.

Hydrogen, symbol H, the simplest element, atomic number (**F11(2)**) of 1, colourless, and the lightest of all substances. Cavendish in 1766 was the first to recognise that it was an element. It is 14·4 times as light as air, and is found in a free state in volcanic regions. It can be obtained by the action of metals on acids, and forms an explosive mixture with air, burning with oxygen to form water. Commercially it is used to produce the very hot flame of the oxy-hydrogen blowpipe for cutting metals; to fill balloons and airships; to harden certain oils and render them suitable for margarine- and soap-production. The gas can be liquefied, and the presence of the isotope deuterium was detected by Urey in 1931 in the residue of the evaporated liquid. The third isotope, tritium, is very rare. *See also* **Deuterium, Tritium.**

Hydrography, the science of water measurement, as applied to seas, rivers, lakes, currents, rocks, reefs, *etc.*, and embracing the whole art of navigation.

Hydrometer, an instrument for measuring the specific gravity of liquids, especially for ascertaining the strength of spirituous liquors and solutions. It is usually in the form of a glass bulb, to the lower end of which a smaller bulb, containing mercury, is attached which forces the instrument to sink into the liquid which it is to test. The larger bulb has a scale fixed to it, and the indication on this scale of the sinking point shows the specific gravity. There are many varieties: Twaddell's—a pear-shaped bulb containing mercury: Beaumé's, of similar construction, but applicable to liquids both heavier and lighter than water: Sykes', largely employed for determinining the strength of alcohol: and Nicholson's, used for taking the specific gravities of solids.

Hydropathy, the method of treating disease with water, either by bathing or drinking. Natural springs of special chemical and therapeutic properties, such as sulphur springs, and other mineral sources, have been used since prehistoric times for this purpose. It is probably one of the most ancient methods of cure. Recently the beneficial effects of pure water treatment have been advocated. Hydropathic establishments have been set up in many health resorts.

Hydroponics, or soilless growth, is the craft and science of growing plants in liquid nutrients instead of soil. Originally a laboratory technique, hydroponics has become since the 1930s a practical method of vegetable, fruit and flower production on both small and large scale. Basically, the growing plants have their roots in troughs of nutrient solution, either in or out of doors. Advantages include: much higher crop yields; the close control of weeds and diseases; quicker growth; and, very important, the possibilities of growing food in places where ordinary agriculture would be impracticable, *e.g.*, deserts and stony land, city roofs, in houses and in remote situations like Antarctic stations. Hydroponics is widely practised and contributes usefully to agriculture and horticulture in many countries, including the USA, Britain, India and France. Its value in spaceships and planetary colonies has often been pointed out by technological prophets.

Hydrostatics, the science of the pressure and equilibrium of liquids that are non-elastic.

Hydrozoa are a class of water animals of the *Coelenterata* phylum to which hydra (*q.v.*) belongs. In one order of the hydrozoa, free-swimming colonies showing marked division of labour between the individual units occur; this order includes the Portuguese man-of-war.

Hyena, a nocturnal carnivore with powerful jaws. The striped hyenas inhabit N. Africa and S.W. India. The brown hyenas with long shaggy hair are natives of S. Africa. The spotted, or laughing hyena, noted for the peculiar cry from which its name is derived, is also confined to Africa.

Hygrometer, an instrument for measuring the amount of water vapour in the atmosphere. A simple form of hygrometer, known as the wet-and-dry bulb, consists of two vertical thermometers affixed to a frame. One bulb is exposed to the air, and the other is covered with muslin which dips into a water-bath to keep it moist. If the air is saturated, it takes up no moisture from the wet bulb and the two thermometers read the same. If the air is not saturated, evaporation takes place from the wet bulb, latent heat is absorbed from the air and the temperature of the wet bulb is lower than that of the dry bulb. Relative humidity and dew-point of the air can then be derived from suitable tables. Hygrometers depending upon the expansion of human hair and gold-beater's skin and the deposition of dew on a polished surface, when cooled sufficiently, are also in general use. *See* **Humidity.**

Hymenoptera, the order of insects to which bees, wasps, hornets, ants and sawflies belong. They have a well-defined waist, two pairs of membranous wings coupled together, mouth parts modified for biting or sucking; the females possess an ovipositor used for depositing eggs and is sometimes modified for stinging. There are about 70,000 species in this order and many live in highly organised communities. *See also* **Ichneumon Fly.**

Hyperbola. A curve described by certain comets that go round the sun and never return.

Hypsometer, an instrument formerly used by mountaineers to find the height above sea-level by indirectly measuring the atmospheric pressure by determining the boiling point of water at the particular height. Based on the fact that as pressure decreases with height so the boiling point is lowered. Superseded by the aneroid barometer.

I

Ibex, wild goats of several species found in the mountain regions of Europe, Asia and Africa. The male has exceedingly large curved ridged horns. The species that lives in the Alps is called the Steinbock or bouquetin.

Ibis, belongs to a family of birds related to the stork. The sacred ibis of ancient Egypt is now extinct in Egypt but is found in the lakes and swamps of the Sudan near the Upper Nile. It has white and black plumage and a long curved beak. Other species are found elsewhere, the Glossy Ibis (black plumage glossed with purple and green) occasionally visiting England.

Ibo (properly Igbo), a large tribe of S.E. Nigeria, numbering between 5 and 6 million. After the end of British rule they were active in their struggle for national independence and under their leader, Ojukwu, embarked upon the secessionist state of Biafra and the unsuccessful civil war against Federal forces. The Hausa and the Yoruba are the other main Nigerian groups.

Ice is frozen water. It is a colourless, crystalline and brittle solid. Being only 92% as dense as water, it floats on the latter; the expansion which occurs as water changes into ice causes the fracture of water-pipes, though the fracture only becomes obvious when the ice melts and leaks out through the crack. The temperature at which ice forms is 0°C, 32°F. Ice can be melted by pressure, and the ease and smoothness with which one is able to skate on ice depends on this phenomenon.

Ice Ages. Periods during which the continents were partly or largely covered by ice-sheets and glaciers. The present-day ice-sheets of Greenland and Antarctica are relics of the most recent ice age (one of the eight major ones during the past 700,000 years), which began in the Pleistocene and ended about 10,000 years ago. During this last great glaciation ice sheets covered the northern part of Europe, Asia and North America. There is strong evidence that periodic changes in the earth's orbit around the sun caused the ice ages. The earth is now in one of its warm periods though there are signs that a moderate cooling trend has begun.

Icebergs are detached masses of glacier which subside into the sea and float as wind or current may take them. About one-ninth of an iceberg is above sea-level. The North Atlantic is the chief home of icebergs, which reach the ocean from the ice-clad plateaux of Greenland. Some of these floating masses of ice are of enormous proportions, and constitute in the spring and early summer seasons a great menace to the safety of ships, as was disastrously shown in the *Titanic* catastrophe of 1912. For some years past these menaces to N. Atlantic shipping have been kept under close observation by vessels specially detailed for this work.

Ice-breaker, a special heavy bow-plated ship for forcing a way through ice and used especially at ports of the Baltic Sea and the Great Lakes region of Canada which freeze during the winter months. The Soviet atomic ice-breaker *Lenin,* the first of its kind in the world, launched in December 1957, was designed to cut a channel through ice of any thickness. Her performance allowed the sea-route to the north of Siberia to be kept open throughout the year. Russia has now several nuclear-powered icebreakers.

Icelandic Literature, the old Norse literature, centred about Iceland, which includes numerous works of poetry, mythology and history of interest and importance. Much of this literature is in the saga form. *See also* **Edda.**

Iceland Moss, a kind of lichen (*Cetrario islandica*) which grows in great quantities in the mountain regions of Iceland and other Northern countries. It possesses certain nutritive qualities and is of some value in medicine.

Iceland Spar, a colourless form of calcite (calcium carbonate), frequently found in association with metallic ores; it has the power to produce strong double refraction of light so that two images are seen of an object viewed through a piece of Iceland spar. It was formerly used in optical apparatus for producing polarised light.

Iceni, an ancient British race who in early times lived in Norfolk and other parts of Eastern England. Their most famous ruler was Queen Boadicea, who led her people against the Romans in A.D. 61.

Ice Plant, also called "dew plant" and "diamond plant". A South African mesembryanthemum commonly grown in British gardens. Introduced in 1690.

Ice Saints, St. Mamertus, St. Pancras and St. Servatius, so called because of the legendary cold on these Saints' Days, namely, 11–13 May.

Ichneumon, the Egyptian mongoose, popularly known as "Pharaoh's Rat". It is of great use in checking the multiplication of reptiles. It is frequently domesticated.

Ichneumon Fly, a numerous group of parasitic hymenopterous insects abounding in many lands, and all having the peculiarity of depositing their eggs in the bodies of other insects. It destroys swarms of caterpillars, which become the unwilling hosts of its progeny.

Ichthyology, the natural history of fishes.

Ichthyosaurus was a gigantic marine reptile of the Mesozoic age. The fossils are mostly found in the lias formation. Some were over 9 m.

Icon, an image of a sacred personage used in the home or in churches for devotional purposes by Christians of the Eastern Orthodox faith. Icons can be painted on wood, perhaps with the figures picked out against a golden background, or they can be cast in bronze, in the form of a crucifix, diptych (*q.v.*) or triptych with details in coloured enamels. Subjects are taken from the life of Christ or of the Saints. In churches several icons are sometimes placed together on a screen (the iconostasis, which divides the altar and sanctuary from the main body of the church). The earliest preserved icons date from the 12th cent. Icons were venerated in Russia until the Revolution and remain, still in their archaic stylised form of mediaeval origin, a characteristic feature of the Orthodox Church to this day.

Ides, in the ancient Roman Calendar, the 15th of March, May, July, October, and the 13th of all other months; always the eighth day after the Nones.

Idiom, an expression characteristic of a country, district, dialect or language, which usually gives strength and force to a phrase or sentence. The idioms of a language are its distinctive marks, and the best writers are the most idiomatic.

Idris, a famous giant belonging to the myths of Wales, commemorated by a chair of rock on the top of the Cader Idris mountain in Gwynedd.

Igneous Rocks are such as have been molten under conditions of great heat at some stage in their history: *e.g.*, granite, basalt. *See* **F9**(1).

Ignis Fatuus *or* **"Will-o'-the-wisp",** a phosphorescent light which may often be seen on summer and autumn evenings hovering over marshy ground or graveyards. Its nature is hardly understood, though it is generally believed to be the result of the spontaneous combustion of the gases from decaying organic matter. In olden times when marshy grounds were more common than now, this "dancing light" was very frequently visible and was regarded with superstition.

Iguana, large South American lizard, with a long tail, a scaly back and head, a thick fleshy tongue and a prominent dew-lap in the throat. Specimens of the different species average 1·2–1·5 m in length, and they live mostly in trees, though they are equally at home on land or in the water. The flesh of some species is good eating, as are also the eggs.

Iguanodon, a genus of extinct dinosaurs, whose fossils are found in the Jurassic and Cretaceous rocks. Iguanodons were 4·5–7·6 m long, and walked on their hind legs, the front legs being small and adapted for grasping the branches of trees on the leaves of which they fed.

Ilex, mentioned by classical authors, the holm- or holly-oak, which flourishes round the Mediterranean. To botanists Ilex is the genus to which the holly and maté plant belong.

Iliad, the great epic poem of ancient Greece attributed to Homer (*c.* 700 B.C.). It consists of ancient folk tale and saga, welded into an artistic unity, having as plot the carrying off of Helen by Paris to Troy and the subsequent siege of Troy.

Illuminated MSS. of great value and beauty of decoration exist in most public museums and in many private collections, some of them being of great antiquity, especially those of ancient Egypt executed on papyri. Greek and Latin specimens are also numerous, and the British Museum contains fine examples of all these kinds and also an extensive collection of mediaeval English MSS.

Illuminati. *See* **Section J.**

Ilmenite, a mineral widespread in igneous rocks: chemically it is an oxide of iron and titanium. Rich deposits have recently been found in the Allard Lake area of Quebec: the Travancore sands are also a source of ilmenite.

Immortality. *See* **Section J.**

Immortelles are wreaths, crosses or other designs made from what are called everlasting flowers, which are obtained from certain plants of the Composite order, and retain their colours and compactness for a long time. Immortelles are largely used as mementoes for decorating graves, especially in France.

Impeachment, a special arraignment, usually before Parliament or other high tribunal, of a person charged with some offence against the State. The custom in England was for the impeachment to be made in the House of Commons, and the trial to be before the House of

Lords. The first instance occurred in 1376 when Lord Latimer was impeached. With present parliamentary procedure, impeachment is no longer necessary, since the Cabinet is responsible for the individual actions of its ministers, who, acting as a team, must carry the Commons with them, or resign, when it falls to the Leader of the Opposition to form a new Cabinet. Other famous impeachments were those of the Lord High Chancellor Francis Bacon (1621), Earl of Strafford and Archbishop Laud (1640), Warren Hastings (1788), the last being that of Lord Melville (1805). Under the constitution of the United States public officials may be impeached by the House of Representatives and tried by the Senate. A famous case was that of President Andrew Johnson who was saved from impeachment in 1868 by one vote. Had President Nixon not resigned in 1974 he would have been impeached for the affair of the tapes and his abuse of executive privilege.

Imperialism. *See* **Section J.**

Impressionism, the most important and influential movement in 19th cent. European painting. It gained its name, at first contemptuously, in 1874 from a picture painted by Claude Monet and named by the artist *Impression: soleil levant,* which showed the play of light on water with the observer looking straight into the rising sun. Although intended to be the ultimate form of naturalism the inspiration of the school had been the scientific study of light with an attempt to render the play of light on the surface of objects. Feeling that putting a line around a form was bound to cause it to look unnatural, they used bright colours corresponding to the spectrum and unmixed on the palette, and noted that an object of any given colour casts a shadow tinged with the complementary one (*e.g.,* red-green, yellow-blue). Hence bright sunlight was represented in clear yellows and orange with violet shadows. The first Impressionist exhibition held in Paris in 1874 aroused derision with its paintings by Monet, Renoir, Sisley, Pissaro, Cézanne and Degas among others. Impressionism subsequently led to the entirely artistic and anti-naturalist movement of Post-impressionism. Cézanne, who felt that he wanted to produce "something solid and durable, like the art of the museums" was only dubiously impressionist, as were also Degas and Renoir. Of course, in the wider sense of the word (*i.e.,* the recording of an ephemeral impression of a scene), Whistler, Turner and even Rembrandt used the technique.

Impressment, the forced seizure of persons for military service resorted to by many countries before the establishment of conscription. Press gangs forcibly recruited men for British war-ships especially during the Napoleonic wars, but such measures were abandoned after about 1850.

Imprimatur, originally an official licence to print and an important formula in the early days of printing. The term is now used in the wider significance of authority, or endorsement.

Incas, an Indian people who inhabited ancient Peru, founded a great empire and reached a high level of civilisation; overthrown by the Spaniards in 1533.

Incense, an aromatic resinous substance which, under combustion, exhales a pungent odour, and is used, mixed with certain fragment perfumes, in the celebration of Mass in Roman Catholic churches. Olibanum or frankincense is ordinarily the leading ingredient.

Incisors, the sharp-edged cutting teeth at the front of mammalian jaws. Rodents have long, sharp incisor teeth. Elephant tusks are modified incisors.

Independence Day, commemorates the adoption of the Declaration of Independence on 4 July 1776. 4 July is celebrated as a holiday in the USA.

Index. The name given to a list of books, prepared by papal authority, which are declared to be dangerous to faith and morals, and therefore forbidden to Roman Catholics, called the *Index librorum prohibitorum.* One of the reforms of the Vatican Council was the closing in 1966 of the Curia office which judged writings for the Church's Index of forbidden books, though the Index itself still remains. The Pope ordered that nothing should be placed on the Index until the author had been given a chance of explaining his views. The first Index was issued by Pope Pius IV, in 1559.

Indian Mutiny. This turning-point in the history of modern India occurred in 1857–58. The ostensible cause was the serving out to the native troops of cartridges greased with animal fat, for contact with this was forbidden both by the Hindu and Mohammedan faiths. A rebellious feeling, however, had long been developing, and when the Sepoys at Meerut in May 1857 refused to obey the English officers, overpowered and put them to death, the mutiny spread like wildfire. The rebels took Delhi and Lucknow, and for many months terrible massacres and atrocities were committed; men, women and children were slain in thousands. Order was re-established in the autumn of 1858 when the governing power was transferred from the East India Company to the Crown.

Indicators, substances which by a marked change in colour are used to indicate the course of a chemical reaction. Litmus paper, for instance, is red with acids and blue with alkalis. In biological work some radioactive substances are used as tracer elements.

Indigo, the substance obtained from the plant *Indigofera tinctoria,* a native of S. Asia, India being the chief producing country. The colouring matter is the result of the decomposition and fermentation of a glucoside contained in the plant. This is afterwards dried and becomes the caked indigo of commerce. Natural indigo has been eclipsed by artificial indigo, a coal-tar dye which came into commercial production at the end of the last century, and which is cheaper and more uniform in quality.

Indium, a scarce lead-coloured metallic element, no. 49, symbol In, found in zinc blende in Saxony and certain other ores. Discovered in 1863 by Reich and Richter. It is an important material in the manufacture of transistors.

Indulgence. In the Roman Catholic Church the remission granted by ecclesiastical authority to a repentant sinner of the temporal punishment still due after the guilt of sin has been forgiven by God. The indiscriminate sale of Indulgences by Tetzel and other Papal agents in the 16th cent. was one of the grievances which led to the Reformation (*see* **Section J**); the Council of Trent made such traffic unlawful.

Indulgence, Declaration of, was the proclamation by which James II suspended the penal laws against Roman Catholics and Dissenters. It was issued in 1688, but the clergy as a body refused to obey, and the trial of the Seven Bishops and their acquittal by a jury followed. An invitation was thereupon sent to William of Orange to become King.

Industrialisation is simply a name for industrial development. It is customarily used in particular to designate the course of events in a hitherto underdeveloped country which is seeking to increase its wealth and productivity by the introduction of more advanced techniques and by the establishment of industries previously not carried on within it. The word usually covers not only the development of modern industrial production but also the provision of electric power-stations, irrigation works and transport and other developments designed to improve production in any field by methods involving large capital investments. The outstanding example in our time of rapid industrialisation has been the Soviet Union, which, unable to get the capital from abroad, had to carry it through by ruthless restriction of the people's consuming power so as to achieve an unprecedentedly high ratio of investment to total production. Industrialisation has in practice meant a high concentration on the expansion of the basic heavy industries and of power supply, coupled with much slower development of the industries supplying consumer goods and of agricultural production; but there is no reason why this should always be the case. It may well be that in most underdeveloped countries development can but be devoted largely to the industries making consumers' goods and to measures designed to increase agricultural production and productivity.

Industrial Revolution. The name, first given by Engels in 1844, to describe the radical changes that took place in Britain during *c.* 1730–1850 to transform a mainly agricultural country into one predominantly industrial. It began with the mechanisation of the textile industry (Hargreave's spinning jenny, 1764, Arkwright's water-frame, 1769, Crompton's mule, 1770, and Watt's steam-engine, 1785), with subsequent major developments in mining, transport and industrial organisation. It was based on Britain's rich mineral resources, particularly coal and iron ore. With the use of the steam-engine as power, industry became concentrated round the coalfields and the great new industrial towns developed—Birmingham, Manchester, Newcastle and Glasgow. Britain became supreme in constructional ironwork (Telford, George and Robert Stephenson). Canals, bridges, railways and ships were built, and great advances were made in the practical application of scientific principles. Aided by colonial exploitation Britain became the most prosperous country in the world. The new industrial capitalists began to replace the country squires as ruling class. But the great accumulation of wealth at one pole of society was matched at the other by poverty and misery, for child labour, long working hours, low wages and slums were features of the industrial revolution in its infancy. As with all great technological developments, the industrial revolution produced related changes in all fields of social life—in politics, art, religion, literature and morals, and with the rise of democracy, social reforms.

Inertia, a term used in mechanics for the property of matter by which it offers resistance to a change in its state of rest or in its state or direction of motion.

Inertial Navigation, an automatic method of dead-reckoning which at present finds its chief application in guided missiles, submarines and aircraft. Navigation by this means is carried out with reference to inertial space (*i.e.,* space which is stationary with respect to the fixed stars) and not to the surface of the earth as in normal navigation (latitude and longitude). This is done by means of high-accuracy gyroscopes combined with highly sensitive accelerometers in an apparatus known as the Ship's Inertial Navigation System. The American nuclear-powered submarine *Nautilus* pioneered the new north-west passage under the polar ice pack by this method of dead-reckoning in August 1958.

Inflorescence, a flowering shoot. Many arrangements of the flowers are possible and there are many kinds of inflorescence; *e.g.,* the spike, catkin, umbel, capitulum (in composites).

Inflation. *See* Section G.

Information Superhighway. *See* **Special Topic,** L132.

Infra-red Rays *or* **Radiation.** This is the range of rays which come between the visible red rays and the ultra-short Hertzian radiation. The wavelengths involved range between 0·75 micron (0·75 × 10⁻⁶m) and 100 micron (1 millimetre). Infra-red rays penetrate haze; hence landscapes obscured by haze or cloud can be photographed using plates sensitive to infrared. Many substances strongly absorb these rays and thereby become hot; this happens in toasting bread. Many industries use infra-red lamps for drying paints and lacquers. Very important to chemists, as a tool in the investigation of the structure of compounds, since various groups of elements absorb infra-red radiation at a characteristic frequency. Infrared astronomy has developed in recent years.

Infula, a sacred fillet, of woollen material, worn on the forehead by priests, magistrates and rulers in Roman times, also by persons fleeing for protection to sanctuary. Later, each of the two lappets of a bishop's mitre.

Ingoldsby Legends, a series of whimsical metrical tales full of droll humour written by the Rev. R. H. Barham, and first published in *Bentley's Miscellany* in 1837. The best known is the *Jackdaw of Rheims.*

Ink, a liquid pigment ordinarily made from an infusion of nut-galls, copperas and gum arabic. Shumac is substituted for nut-galls for inferior inks. An acid is sometimes added to prevent oxidation, and for the blue-black inks a small quantity of solution of indigo serves for colouring. Copying ink contains glycerine or sugar, which keeps the ink moist. Lampblack used to be the leading ingredient in printer's ink but now new methods of manufacturing have been developed. Marking ink is composed of a solution of nitrate of silver, gum, ammonia and carbonate of soda. For red, blue and other coloured inks, colouring solutions are used, *e.g.* Prussian blue. The earliest examples of ink writing (on wooden tablets) ever found in Britain were recovered from the well of a Roman villa (3rd cent. A.D.) at Chew Stoke, Somerset in 1954.

Ink Sac, a glandular organ found in squids and other cephalopods which contains an inky solution. When roused the animal discharges the contents of the ink sac into the water, to make a cloud through which its enemies cannot see. The pigment, sepia, comes from the ink sac of the cuttlefish.

Inns of Court, the four bodies in London which enjoy the privilege of calling candidates to the bar after they have studied for a certain number of terms and passed certain examinations. The Inns are: the Inner Temple, the Middle Temple, Lincoln's Inn and Gray's Inn.

Inquisition, a Roman Catholic ecclesiastical court which became a formidable weapon of the Church in the 13th cent. under Pope Innocent III in dealing with charges of heresy. It was effectively set up in the various Catholic countries of the Continent, obtaining its fullest and most sweeping organisation in Spain in the days of Ferdinand and Isabella, when Torquemada was made Grand Inquisitor, and used its powers with terrible severity. *See* **Auto-da-fé.** In the 18th cent. its influence began to wane, and the jurisdiction of the Congregation of the Holy Office at Rome was limited to the suppression of heretical literature (*see* Index). Recently, the Congregation for the Doctrine of Faith (CDF), as it is now called, called into question the orthodoxy of two of the Roman Catholic Church's most respected theologians.

Insectivorous Plants, plants which trap insects with special mechanisms. Plant enzymes or bacteria digest the prey, providing the plants with nitrogen usually scarce in the soil in which they grow. The most common British species are the Sun-dew and the Bladderwort.

Insects. This huge class of invertebrate animals (*see* **Arthropods** **(F36)**) includes about 100,000 species. Insects are ubiquitous except in the sea, only a very few species being adapted to marine existence. Characteristic features are: the body is divided into three parts, head, thorax and abdomen: the head carries a pair of antennae, the thorax three pairs of legs and usually two pairs of wings. The most primitive insects constituting the sub-class *Apterygota* are wingless. The other sub-class, *Pterygota,* is divided into the *Exopterygota* (*Hemimetabola*), which have a simple metamorphosis, *e.g.,* cockroach, and the *Endopterygota* (*Holometabola*), with a complex metamorphosis, *e.g.,* butterfly, bee. Although many are parasitic on man, animals and plants, innumerable animals and some plants use them as food, and many flowering plants are dependent on a variety of insects for pollination leading to the development of seeds and fruits. *See* **F36(1), 41(1).**

Insignia, marks or badges of office or honour, such as stars, ribbons, crosses, medallions or other designating objects, worn by members of special Orders or holders of prominent offices.

Instinct. *See* **F40(2).**

Institut de France was formed in 1795, and after various modifications was in 1832 organised on its present basis. Its five academies are—the Académie Française, Académie des Inscriptions et Belles-Lettres, Académie des Sciences, Académie des Beaux-Arts, and the Académie des Sciences morales et politiques. It is restricted to 40 members.

Instruments, Musical. Musical instruments may be classified in a number of ways, but in general they fall into one of the three main classes, String, Wind and Percussion, according to how the sound in produced. **Stringed Instruments** are those which produce the sound by the vibration of a string: (a) by plucking, as in Harp, Lyre, Psaltery, Zither, Lute, Guitar, Balalaika, Ukelele, Harpsichord; (b) by friction (bowed), as in Crwth, Rebec, Viol, Violin, Marine Trumpet, Hurdy-Gurdy; (c) by striking (hammered), as in Dulcimer, Pianoforte, Clavichord; (d) by wind (blown), as in the Aeolian Harp. **Wind Instruments** are those in which the air in the instruments is set in vibration: (a) by blowing into a tube (flue-voiced), as in Recorder, Pandean Pipe, Flute, Organ; (b) by means of reeds (reed-voiced), as in Oboe, Clarinet, Saxophone, Bagpipe, Cor Anglais, Bassoon, Organ reed-stops; (c) those in which the sound is produced by the vibration of the player's lips against the mouthpiece (lip-voiced), as in Bugle, Horn, Trumpet, Tuba, Trombone, Saxhorn, Flügelhorn, Cornet. In a modern orchestra these are known as the *Brass* instruments of the flute, oboe and clarinet families as the *Woodwinds*. Then there are the **Percussion Instruments,** which include the Drums, Cymbals, Tambourines, Castenets.

Insulator, a substance that will not conduct electric current. Many solids, liquids and gases are important insulators—rubber, cotton, silk, plastics, porcelain, glass, air, oil. If the applied voltage is too high, all insulators will "break down", *i.e.,* conduct electricity perhaps with resulting breakage, puncture or charring. Thermal insulators will not conduct heat; they are usually the same kinds of substance as electrical insulators.

Insulin is a hormone which controls the supply of sugar from the blood to muscles. The breakdown of sugar provides energy. In diabetes there is a lack of insulin, causing a build-up of blood sugar which can be released by the injection of insulin. It is secreted by the islet tissue of the pancreas, from which it was isolated in 1922 by Banting and Best. Dr. F. Sanger of Cambridge won the 1958 Nobel Prize in Chemistry for isolating and identifying its amino acid components. Prof. Dorothy Hodgkin and her team at the Dept. of Molecular Biophysics at Oxford succeeded in determining the structure of insulin, a task which would not have been possible without the electronic computer. In 1980 insulin became the first product of genetic engineering techniques to reach clinical trials.

Intelligence. Intelligence has been variously defined as the innate potential of a person to learn and understand; to make appropriate judgments; to see the relationships between things; to profit from experience; or to meet adequately new problems and conditions in life. There are many lines of evidence to show that intellectual capacity is closely related to heredity and influenced by environmental factors. The idea of intelligence testing was first devised by the French psychologist Binet at the beginning of this century. He was asked by the French government to invent a test which would weed out backward children in state schools, and thus save public money and avoid holding back the work of the class by teaching children who were incapable of learning at a given standard. Briefly, a series of problems are given to a large number of children and it is thus found out which series can be solved by the average child of a given age-group; if a child of 7 can only pass the tests suitable to the average child of 6, then his mental age is 6. The intelligence quotient or I.Q. is discovered by dividing his mental age by his chronological age and multiplying by 100. A gifted child can usually be spotted at an early age. Although I.Q. tests are the standard method of estimating intelligence, they are not universally accepted as a criterion; a teacher's general judgment may be the best assessment. High intelligence may be inherited, but fail to develop to the full because facilities for education are not available. Recent research suggests that the growth of the brain may be permanently affected by under-nutrition at the time of its fastest growth (the last weeks before birth and, to a lesser extent, the first weeks after birth). At this vulnerable period even quite minor deprivation can affect the rate and ultimate extent of growth of the brain. This has significance not only for the severely under-nourished babies in the poor

parts of the world, but for babies of low birth weight in our own communities in the Western world.

Interest is the payment made for the use of borrowed money over time. The rate of interest is the rate per cent per annum charged for such loans. There are many such rates, varying with the plenty or scarcity of borrowable money, with the length of time for which the loans are made, and with the degree of risk, if any, that the loans will not be duly repaid. Short-term loans are usually cheaper than long-term: the lowest rates are usually for "call money" repayable immediately on demand. These are used principally in short-term financial transactions, such as bill discounting. Bank loans, though usually made for fairly short terms, command higher rates. Long-term loans are made chiefly to public authorities, or as bonds or debentures to business concerns. The rates obtained vary with the demand and the supply of such accommodation.

Interferon, identified in 1957 as a defence protein produced in animal cells, is also produced in human immune systems. Its use as a possible anti-cancer agent as well as for other complaints has been limited by extraction problems. Modern production is likely to be by genetic engineering. In 1980 the amino acid sequence was determined for the 150 residues in human interferon.

International Date Line, a line along the 180° meridian marking the difference in time between E. and W. For the westward-bound traveller crossing the line the date would be put forward one day, for the eastward-bound, back one day. To avoid difference of date in adjacent land areas, the line deviates from the 180° meridian where this crosses land.

Internet. *See* **Special Topic, L132.**

Introit, the psalm sung by the choir as the priest approaches the altar to celebrate the Eucharist.

Inuit. *See under* **Eskimo, L41.**

Invention of the Cross, a Roman Catholic festival held on 3 May, to celebrate the finding of the alleged True Cross at Calvary by the Empress St. Helena in 326. Also included in the Church of England calendar. *See* **Holy Rood.**

Iodine, a non-metal element, no. 53, symbol I, member of the halogen family (*q.v.*), a substance formerly exclusively obtained from the ribbon-wrack seaweeds (kelp) extracted with water. After concentrating the iodides, these were distilled with manganese dioxide and sulphuric acid to yield iodine vapour which was condensed in stoneware bottles. Nearly all iodine now in use is derived from the iodine salt present in Chile saltpetre (natural sodium nitrate). Iodine is used in photography, as an antiseptic solution in alcohol or potassium iodide (tincture of iodine), and in medicine. Discovered by Courtois in 1812.

Ionosphere. Although a certain degree of ionisation occurs at all levels of the atmosphere due to cosmic rays and the radioactivity of rocks, etc., the ionosphere is normally denoted as the region above about 70 km where the ultra-violet component of sunlight is able to ionise a significant fraction of the atoms and molecules present. This ionisation causes the reflection of radio waves by which the ionosphere was initially discovered and for many years, explored. The nomenclature of the ionospheric layers—"D" region up to about 95 km, "E" region 95 km to about 180 km, and "F" region above 180 km—is due to the historical observations of radio wave reflections from "layers". Satellite and rocket observations have shown that the structure is in fact more continuous. Solar flares and aurora cause enhancements of the electron density in the ionosphere, which may result in the disturbance of radio communications over large distances (radio blackouts). *See also* **Atmosphere, Aurora, Magneto-sphere.**

Ions, electrically charged atoms, or groups of atoms. Atoms of the metals lose electrons to become positively charged ions, *e.g.,* the sodium ion (Na^+) has one electron less than the atom. The non-metal ions are negatively charged, *e.g.,* the chloride ion (Cl^-) has one electron more than the atom. Similarly, a group like the sulphate ion $(SO_4{}^{2-})$ has more electrons than the constituent atoms. Thus, the hydrogen atom without its electron is a hydrogen ion or *proton* and the helium atom without its two electrons is a helium ion or *alpha-particle*. When an electric force is applied to certain solutions, the ions into which molecules of the dissolved substance are broken up are attracted to the oppositely charged electrodes, their movements constituting an electric current through the solution. In the same way gases, including air, conduct electricity by virtue of free ions (*see* **F14(1)**). Combustion, radioactivity and ultra-violet and cosmic radiations produce ionisation. *See* **F23**.

Iridium, a white and very hard metallic element, no. 77, symbol Ir, discovered by Tennant in 1804. It occurs naturally as an alloy with platinum or osmium; tips for fountain-pen nibs have been made from the former native alloy. The former standard metre was composed of platinum–iridium alloy (*see* **Metre**) as are parts of scientific apparatus and surgical tools that must be non-corrodible.

Iris, the typical genus of the botanical order *Iridacae*, with tuberous rhizomes and swordshaped leaves, many of the family having beautiful flowers. About 100 species of Iris are recorded from the northern temperate zone, the most common species wild in Britain being the yellow flag. Orris root, used in perfumery, comes from another iris species.

Iron is a metallic element, no. 53, symbol Fe (Latin *ferrum*), occurring widely in nature in such ores as haematite, loadstone (magnetic iron oxide), spathic ore and iron pyrites. It is extracted by a process known as smelting, with coke and limestone in a furnace. Its many uses are familiar, the most important being in the manufacture of cast- and wrought-iron products and of steels, which are alloys mainly of iron with added carbon and various metals. Iron rust is formed by the action of oxygen and water, and is a coating of iron oxide. *See* **Smelting.**

Ironclads, ships of war cased in iron or steel plates of sufficient thickness to resist projectiles. They were first introduced (1858) in the French Navy, and in 1860 the first British ironclad, the *Warrior,* was launched.

Iron Curtain. In a speech at Fulton, USA, on 5 March 1946, Sir Winston Churchill used this phrase to describe the dividing line behind which, he said, lie all the capitals of the ancient States of Central and Eastern Europe—Warsaw, Berlin, Prague, Vienna, Budapest, Belgrade, Bucharest and Sofia. The Iron Curtain was symbolised by the Berlin Wall (dividing that city in half) and the rival military groupings of NATO and the Warsaw Pact. The dramatic changes in Eastern Europe since 1989 and the collapse of the Soviet Union in 1991 have ended all this as many former Communist countries increasingly look to the West.

Ironsides were Cromwell's special troopers, so called because of their solidity and firmness in battle.

Irrational Number, a number such as the square root of two, or pi, which cannot be expressed as the ratio of two whole numbers. *See* **Rational Number,** and *Pi.*

Irredentists, a political party organised in Italy about 1878 with the object of incorporating within Italy neighbouring regions. Also a person, group or party advocating policies for the restoration to their country of territory formerly belonging to it but later lost.

Irrigation, an artificial method of providing water for the growth of plants on lands where the natural supply of water is deficient. For many hundreds of years techniques of irrigation have been slow and primitive (*e.g.*, tanks, inundation canals and the Archimedes screw) and consequent inefficiencies include large water losses by evaporation and seepage, and the watering of only a small area. New developments in perennial irrigation, using barrages, large reservoirs and pumping stations, permit vast tracts of land to be irrigated. Yet these are not without their problems as witnessed after the construction of the Aswan High Dam on the Nile where complex problems of delta erosion and dam lake silting ensued. Irrigation also serves the pur-

pose of supplying *warmth* in winter; *e.g.*, in the English water-meadows, and in the more highly developed Italian *marcite* and winter-meadows, where the water is mostly applied in winter when there is plenty of rain. There are several other functions of irrigation; *e.g.*, washing out of excess salts and the renewing of fertility by the addition of alluvium.

Islam. *See* **Section J**.

Isobars are the lines drawn on charts linking together points of equal barometric pressure.

Isochasms, lines connecting places at which there is an equal probability of seeing an aurora, taking the average over a number of years, based on the auroral catalogue of Fritz.

Isomers are chemical compounds having the same composition but different structural arrangements, and consequently different physical and chemical properties. For example, ethyl alcohol and methyl ether are isomers, since the molecules of both are built up of two atoms of carbon, six of hydrogen and one of oxygen, *viz.*, C_2H_6O; ethyl alcohol, C_2H_5OH; and methyl ether, CH_3OCH_3.

Isotherms are lines drawn on charts through points of equal temperature.

Isotopes. When one talks of an element, say, uranium or lead, the name of the element is a generic name for a collection of uranium species and lead species. The different species are called isotopes. For any particular element, the number and arrangement of electrons around the nucleus are the same in all the isotopes, so all the isotopes have the same chemical properties. Soddy has described isotopes as "elements, the atoms of which have similar outsides but different insides". For example, in the nucleus of the uranium isotopes, U 235, U 238 and U 239, there are respectively 143, 146 and 147 neutrons, but all have 92 protons. The isotopes have different atomic weights, in this instance respectively 235, 238 and 239. But all have the same chemical properties. *See* **F12(1)**.

Ivory, the dentine substance of which the tusks of the elephant, hippopotamus, walrus, etc., are composed. The tusks of the African elephant sometimes weigh as much as 45 kg, and reach a length of 2·4–2·7 m.

Ivory Gull, a small, beautifully shaped sea-bird with striking all-white plumage and black legs which breeds on the rocky shores of the Arctic, being found farther north than any other bird; it occasionally wanders south in the winter.

J

Jabiru, the Brazilian name for the giant stork of South America.

Jacamar, from *Jacameri*, the Brazilian name for a smallish bird with long, sharply pointed bill and brilliant plumage which inhabits the tropical regions of South America east of the Andes. These birds are seen sitting motionless on trees, darting off at intervals, like flycatchers, to catch insects on the wing.

Jacanas, small water birds with immensely long toes which enable them to walk on water lily leaves. They are sometimes called "lily-trotters" and are found in tropical Africa and America. They live in swamps and feed on seeds and insects. Sometimes brilliantly coloured.

Jack, a small schooner-rigged vessel, used in the Newfoundland fisheries; a pike; an oscillating lever; a device used in roasting meat.

Jackal, *Canis aureus,* a small wild dog related to the wolf and resembling a fox. The Common Jackal is found in S.E. Europe, India and Sri Lanka; other species inhabit Africa and Egypt. The jackal is a well-known scavenger. It hunts singly or in pairs, unlike the wolf, which usually hunts in packs.

Jackdaw, one of the smaller members of the Crow family. This European bird is typically black with grey collar. It is easily tamed, makes an amusing pet and delights in making off with and taking to its nest bright objects, such as silverware.

Jacobins, a French revolutionary club or party, formed in 1789, and accustomed to meet at a Jacobin convent, hence the name. It became a controlling force in the Revolution, especially in the movement which led to the Terror. Robespierre was its chief spokesman.

Jacobites, adherents of the Stuart cause after the abdication of James II. First James himself, then his son (the Old Pretender), and later his grandson (the Young Pretender) tried to fan the flame of rebellion in Scotland and Ireland, but after the defeat at Culloden on 16 April 1746 the cause was lost. Also the name of the monophysite heretics of Syria, so named after their leader Jacobus Baradaeus in the 6th cent. A.D.

Jade, an exquisite kind of hardstone, ranging in colour from a whitish green to a deep mauvish brown. It can be translucent or opaque and sometimes it is veined. Jade is the common name for two minerals—the rarer *jadeite* (found in Burma, Tibet and China), a sodium–aluminium–silicate, and *nephrite* (found in New Zealand, China, Turkestan and Siberia), a calcium-magnesium silicate. The presence of small quantities of other chemicals accounts for the wide range of shades. In China jade has for centuries been looked upon with great veneration, magical powers have been ascribed to it, and it has been fashioned into ritual objects, also into miniature sculptures of animals or even whole landscapes, charming to look at and incredibly skilfully made. The Chinese word for jade is *yü*, used as a symbol for all that is noble, beautiful and pure.

Jaguar, a South American carnivorous animal resembling the leopard, but larger and more powerful. It preys on other animals but rarely attacks man.

Jainism. See **Section J.**

Janeite, a devotee of Jane Austen and her writings.

Janissaries, an élite band of Ottoman foot soldiers who acted as the Sultan's bodyguard. They were conscripts, raised by the "tribute of children" from conquered Christian countries, mainly Serbia and Albania. First recruited under Murad I (14th cent.). They were not allowed to marry. They gained great power under the Ottoman Empire. In 1826 the Sultan Mahmud II had them massacred.

January, the first month of the year, named after Janus, the two-faced god of the Romans. It was the *Wolf monath* and *Aefter Yule* of the Saxons.

Jasmine, a graceful climber belonging to the olive family with odoriferous blossom, originally a Persian plant, but now acclimatised in many varieties in almost all parts of the world. Two species of jasmine (the common jasmine and the Spanish jasmine) yield oils used in perfumery.

Jasper, a precious stone of the chalcedony variety, opaque, and coloured red, brown, yellow and sometimes green. It was greatly esteemed by the ancients, the Bible having numerous allusions to it.

Jay, a gaily-coloured bird of the Crow family, of many species—the Blue jay of N. America, the Canada jay, sometimes called "whisky jack", the Siberian jay and the British jay, fawn-coloured with black and whitish crest and bright blue feathers in the wings. It lives in woods and like the magpie, takes the eggs and young of small nesting birds.

Jazz, a rhythmical syncopated music characterised by a strong element of improvisation in the performance, probably originating among the Negro population of the Southern States of the USA. It became popular during the first world war and, in a commercialised form, has held the popular field ever since. Modern dance music and popular songs are based on the jazz idiom, which has also had a profound effect upon more serious contemporary music.

Jean, a stout kind of twilled cotton cloth much worn in olden times, and resembling fustian.

Blue jeans, adopted by American city youngsters from farmworkers, are now the fashion elsewhere and worn not only as overalls by workmen but by both sexes in leisure time.

Jelly-fish. The jelly-fishes, which have gelatinous, translucent bodies fringed at the margin with delicate tentacles, constitute the coelenterate order *Scyphozoa*. The mouth, with a squarish opening, is seen on the underside, and there are four horseshoe-shaped sex organs.

Jerboa, small jumping mammals of the Rodent order. These mice-like animals have long tufted tails and very long hind legs, the front legs not being used for locomotion.

Jeremiad, any utterance or writing in which sorrow or complaint is the chief characteristic, so named as recalling the style of the "Lamentations of Jeremiah", in the Old Testament.

Jerusalem Chamber, a room in Westminster Abbey, deriving its name from the circumstance of its having originally been decorated with a view of Jerusalem. Henry IV died in this chamber, and the Committee for the Revision of the Bible met there in 1870 and later.

Jesuits, members of the Roman Catholic religious order founded by Ignatius Loyola in 1540. A long and vigorous course of study is prescribed before they are admitted into the privileges of full membership. They are required to take the vows of voluntary poverty, perfect chastity, perfect obedience and complete submission to the Pope with regard to the Mission of the Order. Pope Paul VI gave them the particular mission of initiating a dialogue with atheists.

Jet, a deep black fossil substance admitting of a high polish and much used for jewellery, ornaments and trimming. It is a form of lignite, the most important British deposit being found near Whitby, where jet manufacture has been an established industry for a long period.

Jet Engine, an aeroplane engine which derives its thrust from the high velocity of the gases it ejects. The essential units in a jet engine are a rotary compressor and a gas turbine, the latter driving the compressor. The first reliable, high-performance jet propulsion engine for aircraft was invented by Sir Frank Whittle.

Jet Stream, a meteorological term coined in 1946 to describe the relatively narrow belt of strong winds (160–320 km/h) at levels in the atmosphere from 5–11 km. These winds are important in forecasting weather, and can be a valuable aid to aircraft. From the ground, where there may be little wind, the jet stream can sometimes be seen as high cirrus cloud moving across the sky at high speed.

Jew's Harp. The name is believed to be a corruption of "jaws harp". This instrument consists of a metal frame with a central tongue of spring steel. The frame is pressed against the teeth, and the tongue of the harp is twanged with the finger, the mouth acting as a resonating chamber. By altering the shape of the mouth the resonant frequency and therefore the note can be varied.

Jockey Club, the governing body that, although possessing no legal status, frames rules and laws by which horse-racing and turf matters are regulated. The club-house is at Newmarket.

John Bull, the typical figure of an Englishman, bluff, big and burly. Arbuthnot's *History of John Bull* is supposed to have originated the character.

John Dory, a fish found in most temperate seas and common in British waters. It is of a golden-yellow colour (*jaune doré*), has a high dorsal fin with long filaments projecting from the spines, very protractile jaws and is much valued as a table fish. According to legend the dark spot on each side of its body is the thumbprint of St. Peter who took a coin from the fish's mouth (Matt. XVII 24–7).

John o' Groat's House, W. of Duncansby Head, Caithness, popularly named as the northernmost point of Scotland. According to legend the house, which has now disappeared, was built in octagonal form by a Dutchman Jan de Groot who came to live there in the 16th cent. The site is marked and an inn was erected near it in 1876.

Jongleurs were minstrels and jesters who wandered from town to town singing songs, playing

musical instruments, dancing and giving entertainments in mediaeval France and Norman England. Jongleurs were low-born in contrast to the Troubadours, who were often of the nobility.

Joule, a unit of energy in the SI system of units, defined as the work done when the point of application of a force of one newton is displaced through a distance of one metre in the direction of the force. Named after J. P. Joule (1818–89). The relationship between mechanical energy and heat energy is called the mechanical equivalent of heat and was found by Joule to be 778 ft lbf in lb °F units, or 4·18 × 10⁷ ergs in gram °C units, or 1 Nm in SI units. *See* **F20(1).**

Julian Calendar, named after Julius Caesar, who in 45 B.C., finding the Roman year 90 days in advance of the real time, was the first to adopt the calculation of time by the solar year, the average length being fixed at 365¼ days. There was still an overplus of a few minutes every year, and this was rectified by the Gregorian Calendar, introduced in Italy in 1582 and adopted in England in 1752, from which date what is called the "New Style" begins.

July, the seventh month of the year, named after Julius Caesar. It was the *Maed monath* (Meadmonth) of the Saxons.

June, the sixth month of the year, containing 30 days and deriving its name from Juno. It was the *Sear* (Dry) *monath* of the Saxons.

Jupiter is the largest of the planets, 11 times the diameter of the earth, 318 times its mass but only one fourth its density. It is the fifth farthest from the sun and is the second brightest. Our knowledge of Jupiter, its sixteen moons, its ring and its magnetosphere was enormously increased in 1979 by data from the Voyager 1 and 2 space-probes which passed the planet at distances of 349,000 km and 722,000 km on March 5 and July 9 respectively. Jupiter is a gaseous planet composed mainly of hydrogen and helium like the sun, possibly with a small molten core of silicates. The centre is presumed to be at a very high temperature (30,000°C) and enormous pressures—a hundred million earth atmospheres—which make hydrogen not only liquid but metallic. This metallic flux leads to intense magnetic fields. Jupiter's large magnetosphere is distorted by the solar wind and contains trapped high energy particles in radiation belts which would be lethal to man. Its existence was first inferred from its radio emissions and was confirmed by Pioneer 11 in 1974. Jupiter's outer gaseous surface is very cold (−120°C) and consists of three layers of crystal clouds (ice ammonium hydrogensulphide and ammonia) interspersed with gaseous hydrogen and helium. It shows massive persistent features like the swirling high pressure Red Spot (larger when first seen in 1664 but which could hold two earths) and the neighbouring white oval formations. All these features are in relative motion, some moving east and others west which account for Jupiter's banded appearance. The persistence of the features arises because Jupiter has no terrain to break them up and because the surface temperature is low. Lightning continuously flashes over the Jovian surface and at the poles there are large auroras caused by an electric current of five million amperes which flows from the poles out to Io, one of the four moons discovered in 1610 by Galileo. The others are Europa, Ganymede and Callisto. The fourteenth moon was discovered in 1979 by Voyager 2 at the outer edge of the thin ring of particles discovered by Voyager 1, which also discovered high plumes due to volcanic activity on Io, the first seen beyond earth (although a recent suggestion is that the plumes are caused by the electric current). Io's sulphurous surface shows no meteoric craters and Europa's smooth ice surface shows only a few impacts and is probably young, unlike the older Ganymede and Callisto whose ice-crust surfaces have many. Ganymede's crust has been reworked, however, by extensive tectonic movements. Ganymede is now known to be the largest moon in the solar system, larger than the planet Mercury. In 1994, Jupiter was struck by the Shoemaker-Levy-9 comet whose impact sent seismic waves across the planet, providing astronomers with the "fireworks of the millennium". In 1995, the Hubble

telescope found oxygen on Europa, one of Jupiter's moons. *See* **F8.**

Jurassic Formation, a series of rocks (the evidences of which are most marked in the Jura Mountains) coming between the Cretaceous and Triassic groups and including the Oolite and the Lias. It is a formation rich in fauna, abounding in echinoids, lamellibranchs, ammonites and belemnites; large reptiles, marine and land, are common, as are the plants called cyads. In Britain the Jurassic outcrop extends from the Dorset coast to the Yorkshire moors.

Jury, a body of private citizens chosen and sworn to hear and pass verdict upon evidence brought forward at a trial, inquest or inquiry. The origin of the English jury is obscure but it is thought to have been introduced by the Normans. The jurors are the sole judges of the true facts upon the evidence laid before them. Under the Criminal Justice Act of 1967 their verdicts in criminal courts in England and Wales no longer have to be unanimous but may be by a majority of 10 to 2. The age limit has been reduced from 21 to 18 and raised from 60 to 65. In Scotland 45 jurors are summoned in criminal cases, of whom 15 are chosen by ballot, and majority verdicts are accepted: not guilty, not proven and guilty.

Jute, the name given to the fibre of a plant grown largely in Bangladesh in the Ganges delta and used for the manufacture of coarse cloths, cordage and sacks. Calcutta is the biggest jute-manufacturing centre of the world, as Dundee was in the 19th cent.

Jutes, a Low German race who in the 5th cent. invaded the south-eastern part of England, establishing themselves in Kent and making Canterbury their capital.

Juvenile Court, (now called Youth Court). This is a special kind of Magistrates' Court to deal with persons under the age of 18 accused of criminal offences. The Magistrates chosen are specially qualified for the work, and the court normally contains at least one man and at least one woman. The Court is held in private away from the ordinary court room. The object of the Youth Court is to introduce into the trial a plan to reform the offender by providing for the care and protection which he may need, by removal from undesirable surroundings, and by subsequent education or training. In these objectives the Court has the co-operation of social workers, including Probation Officers (*q.v.*). The court's former civil jurisdiction (care proceedings) no longer exists – such proceedings are now the concern of Family Proceedings Courts (at Magistrates' level) and the High Court and County Courts.

K

Kangaroo, pouched (marsupial) mammals of Australia and adjacent islands. There are over 20 species, the smaller ones being known as "wallabies". Kangaroos leap in a succession of springy bounds 3–6 m long, the forefeet not touching the ground. They can reach a height of over 2 m and a weight of 90 kg. First seen by white men when Capt. Cook's expedition visited Australia in 1770. Related genera include the tree kangaroos, rat kangaroos and the Tasmanian Jerboa kangaroo.

Kaolin or **China Clay** is an essential ingredient in hard-paste porcelain (*q.v.*). It results from the decomposition of felspar, and is widely found in China, Japan and the USA. The richest deposits in Europe are in Cornwall, near Limoges in France, and in the Czech and Slovak Republics.

Kelvin. Lord Kelvin, an important 19th-cent. physicist, gave his name to the kelvin, symbol K, a measure of temperature on the absolute scale. The Kelvin scale is a development of the scale invented by Celsius (*q.v.*) for everyday use, long known as the "centigrade" scale; the degree interval on both scales is the same. The conversion formula for the absolute or Kelvin scale is K = C + 273·15. *See* **Absolute Temperature.**

Kernewek. The native language of Cornwall which died out *c.* 1770 but is now being revived.

Kestrel, the most common British falcon, well known for its habit of hovering for minutes at a time with vibrating wings and then swooping down to attack mice and insects. The male has spotted chestnut-brown back, greyish head and tail, which has a broad black band near tip.

Ketones. A class of organic compounds, related to aldehydes, of general formula R_2CO (where R is an organic radical). The simpler ketones, especially acetone, are widely used as solvents for lacquers, synthetic rubber and polymers, such as cellulose acetate and perspex. More complex ketones occur in nature, and some are used in the perfumery industry, muscone (from the musk deer (q.v.)) is an example.

Kew Gardens, officially known as the Royal Botanic Gardens, are among the most celebrated gardens in the world. They were started in 1759 by Princess Augusta of Saxe-Gotha, widow of Frederick, Prince of Wales, and mother of George III. They remained private property until 1841, when control passed to the Commissioners of Woods and Forests. They now cover 121 hectares and are administered by the Min. of Agriculture, Fisheries and Food. Since 1841 the gardens have been open to the public, and form one of the most attractive resorts near London. They suffered severe damage in the 1987 hurricane.

Keys, House of, is the Manx representative assembly. See **Tynwald.**

Keystone, the stone which occupies the centre and highest point of an arch and is usually the last to be inserted.

Khaki, a clay-coloured cloth adopted for uniforms in the British Army in the time of the war with the Boers, and used in the first and second world wars. First used by Indian regiments.

Kilderkin, once a common liquid measure in England, representing 18 gallons or 82 litres.

Kilogram, unit of mass, defined as the mass of the international prototype kilogram of platinum-iridium kept at the International Bureau of Weights and Measures at Sèvres. A remeasurement of Avogadro's Number (**F24(1)**) may lead to an atomic standard of mass (the second and the metre are already defined in atomic terms), but this will depend on the precision with which atoms can be counted.

Kilowatt. Unit of power, equal to one thousand watts. See **Watt.**

Kinetic Art denotes works of art which actually move or give the illusion of so doing. An early exponent of kinetic art was the American sculptor Alexander Calder (1898–1976) when he launched his famous "mobiles" in the early 1950s. Since then, constructions which rotate, jump, blink with lights, etc. have been made by many artists and the genre is being further elaborated upon today. Kinetic painters give a visual illusion of movement to their pictures by the use of particular colour contrasts or by a skilful play with spirals, squares, etc. in black and white, sometimes with colours blended in. An interesting exponent of the style is the English artist Bridget Riley (b. 1931).

Kinetic Energy, the energy (q.v.) possessed by a particle or body in virtue of its motion. If the motion is destroyed, e.g., by the impact of the body with an obstacle, the kinetic energy vanishes, being turned into some other form of energy such as heat and sound. If the body has mass m and speed v its kinetic energy (leaving out corrections due to relativity) is $\frac{1}{2}mv^2$.

King Crab, remarkable arthropods now classified separately from both Arachnids and Crustacea which they resemble, inhabiting the sea coasts of America, Japan, India and Malay Peninsula, carrying a shield-shaped shell, and having a long pointed spine projecting from the posterior. The body comprises three separate sections articulated together. These crabs—in America known commonly as the horseshoe crab because of their shape—are from 45–60 cm in length. Fossil king crabs are found as far back as the Silurian. There are about six living species.

Kingfisher, a well-known family of brilliant-plumaged birds, found in all continents, comprising some 250 species and sub-species. The British kingfisher, *Acedlo atthis*, haunts the rivers and streams, and is one of the most beautiful of native birds, having iridescent

blue-green, white and rich chestnut in its plumage and bright-red feet. All kingfishers have long, dagger-shaped bills. In the Malayan region, New Guinea, the Moluccas and Australia, the varieties are very numerous. The quaint *Laughing Jackass* of Australia is among the largest of the kingfisher family. The European kingfisher is the bird of the Greek legend of the Halcyon.

King-of-Arms, the name of the chief officials of the Heralds' College. There are several in England —the principal being those of the Garter, Norroy and Ulster, Clarenceux. See **Heralds' College.**

Kiosk, a word of Turkish origin meaning a small open pavilion of light construction much used in Eastern countries as a place of shade and rest. Similar structures are common in the streets of Paris as news and advertisement stands, and in London as telephone boxes.

Kirimon (*Kiri no go Mon*) and **Kikumon** (*Kiki no go Mon*), the two Japanese imperial crests, the first a design of leaves, stems and flowers of the Paulownia plant, and the other representing the sixteen-petalled chrysanthemum.

Kite, name of several birds of prey, widely distributed, related to the hawks and eagles, graceful in flight, and distinguished by their long wings and deeply forked tails. The red kite, light chestnut brown, once the most familiar bird of prey in Britain, seen scavenging the streets of London, is now the rarest, and found only in Wales. The Egyptian kite and the pariah kite of India, notorious for their daring thefts, are closely related to the black kite, a smaller European species, with less forked tail and blackish-brown plumage.

Kittiwake, a beautiful white and pearl-grey gull with black legs, dark eyes and greenish-yellow bill. Its range is wide, and includes the British Isles, where it is a local resident. The flight of this only truly oceanic gull, which except in the breeding-season is generally found off-shore, is graceful, swift and buoyant. A triangular black patch, noticeable on the ends of the wings when open, is characteristic of the species, as is the call kitti-wake, from which the bird derives its name. It nests in colonies on the ledges of caves and steep cliffs.

Kiwi, flightless, stoutly-built birds of New Zealand now very rare and carefully protected by the Government. They are little larger than a domestic hen, and lay astonishingly large eggs for their size. Incubation and care of chicks fall to the male bird. They have rudimentary wings concealed by the plumage, and the feathers are hair-like. They are nocturnal.

Knighthood is a degree of honour or title common in Europe since the Middle Ages, and was at first exclusively a military order. In Great Britain the four main orders of knighthood are those of the Garter, the Bath, the Thistle and St. Patrick; in addition to which there are several other orders, such as the Order of St. Michael and St. George, the Star of India, *etc.* There are also Knights Bachelors not associated with any special order. The title is not hereditary, and therefore ranks below that of a baronet, though both are entitled to the prefix "Sir".

Knot, a nautical measure of speed (1 sea mile per hour), and formerly measured by a log-line, divided by knots at equal distances $\frac{1}{120}$ of a geographical mile. The number of knots travelled by the ship in a half a minute corresponded to the numbers of sea miles it travelled per hour. A sea mile is equal to about 1¼ of a statute mile or 1·9 km. Also, a grey and white wading bird, usually a winter visitor to Britain found in flocks on the coast.

Knout, a whip of many thongs, often fatal in its effects, formerly used in Russia for flogging criminals.

Koala, the Australian arboreal marsupial mammal that looks like a toy teddy-bear, with ashy-grey fur, bushy ears and rudimentary tail. It feeds on the leaves and shoots of certain eucalyptus trees, and is not more than 60 cm in length.

Kohl, a powder prepared from antimony or burnt almond shells, and in common use by the women of the East for darkening the eyelids.

Koto, a musical instrument in general use in Japan consisting of a series of 13 silken strings stretched across a curved wooden surface, and played with the fingers. Each string is 1·5 m long, and has a separate bridge so fixed as to give the vibration necessary for the note it has to produce. It is a sort of horizontal harp, and in the hands of an expert player is capable of giving forth excellent music.

Kremlin, the citadel or walled city within a Russian city which during the Middle Ages served as an administrative and religious centre and offered protection. That of Moscow, now the headquarters of the Russian government, contains the cathedral where the Tsars were crowned, an imperial palace and the "King of Bells" (*see* **Bells**). Its walls which are topped with towers were built in the 15th cent.

Krypton, one of the rare gas elements, no. 36, symbol Kr, occurring in the air to the extent of 1 part in 20 million. It was discovered in 1898 by Ramsay and Travers. It is used in gas-filled electric lamps.

Kumara. *See* **Sweet Potato, L117.**

Kurds, an Arab people with no homeland of their own. Persecuted by Saddam Hussein in Iraq. *See* **Section C** (under Iraq).

Kusti, the sacred cord or girdle of the Parsees, consisting of 72 threads—the number of the chapters of the *Yasna*—and two branches, each branch containing six knots, together standing for the 12 months of the year.

Kyrie Eleison ("Lord, have mercy"), the name of a common form of prayer in the Anglican, Roman Catholic and Greek Churches; also applied to the English Church responses after the recital of the commandments.

Kyrle Society, named after Pope's "Man of Ross", John Kyrle, founded by Miss Miranda and Miss Octavia Hill in 1875, and having for its object, the decoration of workmen's clubs, hospitals, etc. and the promotion among the poor of a taste for literature, music and outdoor re-creation.

L

Labarum, the standard of Constantine the Great, adopted after his conversion to Christianity, marked with his seal and represented upon the coinage.

Labourers, English Statute of, was passed 1350–51, with the object of compelling labourers to accept a certain rate of wages and not leave their employers' service, the Plague having rendered labourers so scarce that they were in great demand and had been insisting on higher pay. These enactments were bitterly opposed and led to the "Peasants' Revolt", headed by Wat Tyler.

Labradorite, a felspar rich in calcium and of a pearly lustre on cleavage, found in masses in igneous rocks, the best samples of which come from Labrador.

Labyrinth, or **Maze,** a combination of roads and passages so constructed as to render it difficult for anyone ignorant of the clue to trace the way to the central part. The Egyptian labyrinth near Lake Moeris had 3,000 rooms, half of them subterranean and the remainder above ground. The labyrinth in Crete, according to Greek myth, was built by Daedalus to house the Minotaur. There was one at Lemnos, renowned for its stalactite columns; and another at Clusium constructed by Porsenna, King of Etruria, about 520 B.C. The labyrinth in which Fair Rosamond was concealed was at Woodstock. Hampton Court maze dates from the 16th cent.

Labyrinthodonts, gigantic fossil amphibians which get their name from the curious labyrinthine structure of their teeth, probably an evolutionary link between fishes and reptiles. They occur in the Carboniferous, Permian and Triassic formations, and remains have been found in Britain and other parts of Europe. Their heads were long, and their footprints, by which they were discovered, closely resemble the prints of the human hand.

Lac, a resinous matter deposited on the branches of a number of tropical trees by the females of the lac insect, the exudation including eggs and a viscous covering. At the gathering time the twigs are broken off and dried in the sun, when the insects die, and the lac that remains is termed *stick-lac*. From this, by the removal of extraneous accretions and dissolving, *seed-lac* is produced. *Shell-lac* is seed-lac after it has been melted and otherwise prepared, and this is the best known of the lacs, being used in printing and the manufacture of varnishes and sealing-wax, and for other commercial purposes.

Lace, a delicate fabric of linen, silk or cotton threads, made by hand or machinery, and worked in various ornamental designs. The kinds of lace are many, deriving their distinctive names either from the method employed in production or from the place where any special variety was originally made. The best-known makes are pillow or bobbin-lace, woven and plaited by hand; needle-point lace, worked by the needle over a traced design; and machine lace, which practically dates from Heathcote's invention of the early part of the 19th cent. Some of the most famed laces are the following: *Alençon*, a needle-point lace; *Brussels*, a very fine kind, with needle-point sprigs and flowers; *Chantilly*, a silk variety with flowers and open-work; *Cluny*, a netlace with darned stitch; *Honiton*, a delicate kind with dainty sprigs and figures; *Mechlin*, generally made in one piece and very varied in design; and *Valenciennes*, or bobbin lace, of great durability, the pattern and ground of which are made at the same time, being one of the best and most costly of laces, now manufactured mainly in Belgium. Nottingham is famous for its lace.

Lace-Wings, insects with frail, transparent and much-veined wings whose grubs eat large numbers of insect pests such as aphids. The eggs are borne at the ends of threads attached to plants.

Ladybird, the common name of a large family of beetles—the *Coccinellidae*. The insect is usually of a red or yellow colour with small black or coloured spots. Ladybirds are of good service to the gardener because their larvae feed on aphids. There are about 2,000 species.

Lady-Day, the day of the festival of the Annunciation of the Virgin Mary, 25 March. One of the four English quarter days.

Lake Dwelling, the name given to certain prehistoric habitations which were thought to have stood on platforms over lakes, like villages in certain Pacific islands. Recent excavations at the Lake of Burgäschi in Switzerland show that the prehistoric Swiss pile dwellings probably stood on the shores of lakes, not on platforms over the water. Also found at Mere and Glastonbury, Somerset.

Lakes are bodies of water collected in depressions of the earth's surface. The most notable lakes are the Great Lake series of North America, including Superior, Michigan, Huron, Erie and Ontario, all discharging into the St. Lawrence River. Africa has an enormous area of lakes, including the Mobutu Seso and the Victoria, forming the sources of the White Nile. Smaller lakes are numerous in other countries—Switzerland, Finland, Italy, England, Ireland, Scotland, all having their lake regions, where the scenery is invariably beautiful and romantic. The Kariba Dam (Zimbabwe–Zambia border) and the Nasser (Egypt) are the largest man-made lakes in the world.

Lake School, the name given, at first in ridicule, to a distinguished trio of poets—Wordsworth, Coleridge and Southey—who made their homes in the English Lake District.

Lamellibranchs (Pelecypods), the class of aquatic, bi-valve molluscs to which the oysters, cockles, mussels, clams and scallops belong. In these animals the body, which is compressed laterally, is enclosed in two hinged shells held together by muscular action. The gills are thin plates hence the name "lamellibranchs". *See* **F36(1), 41(1).**

Lamination, stratification on a very fine scale, as in shales.

Lammas Day is one of the oldest of the Church festivals, probably derived from the loaf-mass (*hlafmaesse*) of the Anglo-Saxons. It occurs on 1 August. In the olden times it was the day when loaves were given in place of first-fruit offerings.

Lammergeyer, the bearded vulture of alpine regions, resembling an eagle in appearance. It has a white head with black tufts at base of the bill, and its general plumage is dark brown, nearly black. It is found in the remote mountain ranges from southern Spain and parts of Africa to China, and is becoming scarce.

Lampblack, a carboniferous pigment obtained from flame-smoke, and now produced in specially constructed furnaces in which bodies rich in carbon, such as tar, resin, petroleum, etc., are burned. The smoke or soot resulting is collected from the sides of the furnace, and forms lampblack. It finds use in making printer's ink, black paint, etc. Being a very pure form of carbon, it is also utilised in the manufacture of dynamo brushes and arc-lamp carbons.

Lamprey. Eel-like fish having no scales, bones, paired fins or jaws. They attach themselves by their mouths to fish whose blood they suck. Together with the hagfishes, the lampreys are placed in a special class—the Cyclostomes. There are three British lampreys.

"Lancet", the name of a noted English medical journal, established in 1823 by Dr. Wakley.

Land Crab, a family of crabs (*Gecarcinidae*) which live mainly on land, though migrating to the seas to deposit their eggs.

Land League, an association formed in 1879, with Parnell as president, for compelling a reduction in the rents of land, and a reconstruction of the land laws in Ireland, and in case of non-compliance refusing to pay rent. For a time this League exercised great political influence and was an important aid to the Home Rule agitation.

Landrail, popularly known as the Corncrake, was a regular summer visitor to Britain two generations ago, but no longer. Its harsh and piercing note was a familiar sound in English cornfields. It is decreasing almost everywhere and international efforts were launched in 1994 to try and save it from extinction.

Landslip, a sudden downward sliding under gravity of large masses of rock, soil, etc.; often set off by earthquake shock or saturation of a particular stratum with water. Many serious landslides have occurred from time to time. In 1618, an earthfall happened at Plurs, on Lake Como, involving the destruction of many buildings and the loss of numerous lives. In 1806 a portion of Rossberg mountain in Switzerland slipped from its position, and falling into the valley below buried many villages and hamlets and over 800 people. A chalk cliff 30–45 m high and 1·2 km long fell at Lyme Regis, in Dorset, in 1839, doing great damage. Over 200 people were killed by a landslip in Naini Tal, in India, in 1880; and at Quebec, in 1889, a rocky eminence called Cape Diamond gave way, many buildings being destroyed and lives lost. Notable landslips in recent times have occurred at Amalfi (Italy) in 1924, at Murchiston (New Zealand) in 1929, at Aberfan (Wales) in 1966 and near St. Gervais (France) in 1970.

Langue d'oc and Langue d'oïl, the two principal mediaeval French dialects, *oc* and *oïl* being their respective words for the affirmative particle (modern French *oui*). *Langue d'oc*, spoken south of the Loire, was the language of the troubadors. Provençal, one of its dialects had a literary revival in the 19th cent. under the influence of the poet Frédéric Mistral. *Langue d'oïl* was spoken in northern France, and it was the dialect of the Paris region which developed into modern French.

Lantern Fly, bugs belonging to the family *Fulgoridae* in which the head is drawn out to form a lantern-like structure. In no instance is the "lantern" luminous, though naturalists used to think it was.

Lanthanides, the fourteen metallic elements following lanthanum in the Periodic Table, i.e., the elements cerium (no. 58) to lutetium (no. 71). They are also known as the rare-earth metals, though they are in fact all more terrestrially abundant than, for instance, mercury or arsenic (with the exception of the unstable radioactive element promethium, no. 61). The lanthanide atoms are distinguished by having an incomplete inner electron sub-shell (the 4f level), this feature giving them interesting magnetic properties. For instance, gadolinium, holmium and dysprosium are ferromagnetic (see **F22**) at low temperatures. Chemically, the lanthanides behave similarly, being highly reactive metals usually forming trivalent salts. See **Periodic Table, F65**.

Lapis Lazuli, an azure-blue mineral, being a silicate of aluminium and sodium. The pigment ultramarine is made by grinding it, though artificial ultramarine has largely superseded it. The mineral (also called *lazurite*) has been used as a gemstone since ancient times.

Lapwing or **Green Plover**, familiar British bird on moors and marshlands with iridescent greenish-black plumage, white underparts and black crest. Often called "peewit" from its cry. Protected under Protection of Birds Act, 1967.

Larboard is the old nautical term indicating the left-hand side of a ship, and changed by Admiralty order to "port" in 1844. Starboard is the right-hand side.

Larch, a familiar coniferous tree in the mountain regions of northern Europe, and though not native to Britain, the Common Larch is successfully cultivated in various parts of the kingdom. It is one of the best of all turpentine-yielding trees, and the bark is valued for tanning. The larch is an unusual conifer in being deciduous.

Lark, a family of song birds (*Alaudidae*) of many species, some of which—notably the skylark—are famed for their habit of soaring into the air, singing all the while. They build their nests on the ground in the open country and, except for the black lark of Russia, have streaked brown plumage. The skylark and woodlark are the best known British species, while the crested lark and shore lark are among the occasional visitors. Africa has the greatest number of larks; America has only one species, the horned lark.

Larkspur, the common name of the genus *Delphinium*, a favourite flower introduced into British gardens from Switzerland in 1573. The common larkspur is *D. consolida*.

Larva, the undeveloped form of any animal which, before maturity undergoes metamorphosis, usually different from the adult in structure and habits.

Laser. A remarkable kind of light source that was discovered in 1960. With the laser it is possible to probe the behaviour of matter under the influence of enormous energy densities, range and survey vast distances to microscopic accuracy and send millions of telephone and television messages between any two points that can see each other with telescopes. Laser light, in contrast to natural light, is coherent and can be expressed as a regular progression of waves carrying energy along a particular path. Thus the essential difference is that laser light is an orderly sort of wave motion in contrast to ordinary light which is inherently unsteady and therefore an inefficient carrier of information in time. The name *maser*, which is the microwave parent of the laser, derives from the expression "microwave amplification by the stimulated emission of radiation". Upon application to light wavelengths the microwave part of the name lost its meaning and the term maser became generally descriptive of any device in which stimulated emission dominates.

Laser Fusion is a method by which it has been proposed that thermonuclear reactions may be controlled and exploited as a source of energy (see **Nuclear Fusion**). The idea is to irradiate a millimetre-sized pellet of a mixture of frozen deuterium and tritium with a short ($\sim 10^{-9}$ s) but very intense pulse of energy in the form of laser light. This has the effect of both compressing the pellet by a factor of at least a thousand and heating it to about $10^8 \,^\circ$C. Under these conditions, thermonuclear reactions (principally $^2D + ^3T \rightarrow ^4He + ^1n$) proceed sufficiently fast that a net output of energy is obtained before the pellet explosively separates. Formidable technical problems need to be solved before laser fusion can become a practical proposition. These include the development of efficient high-powered lasers and the design of a suitable reactor that can withstand up to 100 micro-hydrogen bomb explosions per second. It is still not clear whether this method of controlling nuclear fusion is more practical than the more conventional approach involving the magnetic confinement of plasmas.

Latent Heat is the quantity of heat required to convert 1 gram of a substance from one form into another. For example, when a solid changes into a liquid or a liquid into a gas, the addition of heat to bring about the change produces no rise in temperature, the energy being absorbed in the form of latent heat. An equal amount is released when the process is reversed. The latent heat of fusion of ice is about 79·6 calories per gram, that of the vaporisation of water about 539 calories per gram.

Lateran Councils were the religious conventions held in the Lateran basilica at Rome for deciding important questions of Church doctrine. The most brilliant was that of 1215 which pronounced in favour of a Crusade.

Lateran Treaty, 1929, between Italy and the Vatican established the Vatican City as an independent sovereign state.

Laterite refers to any tropical soil or soil horizon rich in hydrated ferric and aluminium oxides which harden when exposed to the atmosphere. It is difficult to cultivate and is commonly used for bricks and road metal. Laterite buildings have been known to withstand the weathering for many centuries and a number of fine examples are found in India and S.E. Asia.

Latin America. The Spanish-speaking, Portuguese-speaking and French-speaking countries of N. America, S. America, Central America and the W. Indies. *See* **Section K.**

Latitude of a point on the earth's surface is its angular distance from the equator, measured on the surface of the earth in degrees, minutes and seconds. Thus the equator is 0° Lat. and the poles 90° Lat. (N. or S.). First determined by Hipparchus of Nicaea about 160 B.C. Latitude introduces zones of climate, *e.g.*, tropical rain, subtropical steppe and desert, temperate rain and polar.

Laughing Gas. *See* **Nitrous oxide.**

Launce *or* **Sand Eel,** a family of eel-like sea fishes found in large numbers on the coasts of North America and Europe. There are two species common to British waters. These fishes are of a bright silvery hue, and live much in the sand underneath the water. They are prized as human food and as bait.

Laurentian Shield refers to the Pre-Cambrian rocks in the region of the Upper Lakes of Canada, nearly 5 million sq km in extent. Of enormous importance to Canada on account of the mineral wealth, forests yielding valuable timber and wood-pulp, and water-power.

Lava, the molten rock which is erupted from a volcanic vent or fissure. Also the same material which has cooled and solidified.

Lawn, very fine sun-bleached linen, in olden time called "cloth of Rheims".

Lead, a soft malleable metallic element, no. 82, symbol Pb (Latin *plumbum*), occurring in numerous ores, which are easily smelted. Its most important source is the mineral galena which consists chiefly of lead sulphide; rarely is it found free. Lead is largely used in plumbing on account of its pliability, and in nuclear reactors as a shield against radiation because of its very high density. As an alloy element it combines in the formation of type metal, stereo metal, shot metal, pewter and many other compounds. Oxides of lead are used in some types of glass and in the manufacture of paints (red lead). All lead compounds are poisonous. Leading producers of lead are the United States (Missouri), Australia (Broken Hill) and the Russian Federation.

Leaf Miners, insect larvae which tunnel between the upper and lower skins of leaves. Most leaf miners are caterpillars of tiny moths; some sawfly larvae have the same habit.

Leagues, or combinations of kings, countries, communities, have been frequent since the kings of Canaan united against the Israelites. Among the most famous leagues may be mentioned the Holy or Catholic League, which prevented the recognition of Henry IV as King

of France until he became a Roman Catholic; and the League of Augsburg against Louis XIV of France in 1686.

League of Nations, was founded on 10 January 1920, with the object of promoting international peace and security. The original members were the signatories to the Peace Treaties at Versailles, and membership grew to fifty-three as new nations and ex-enemy States were admitted. Two notable absentees were the United States and Soviet Russia, the latter not being represented until 1934. Germany was a member from 1926 to 1933. The League had an Assembly which met at Geneva every year and a Council which met five or six times a year. The Permanent Court of International Justice (now under the UN) sits at The Hague. The League held its last Assembly at Geneva in April 1946. Its place was taken by the United Nations. The International Labour Organisation, set up by the League of Nations, met in April 1944 at Philadelphia and resumed its work at Geneva under the UN in 1946.

Leap Year *or* **Bissextile,** was fixed by Julius Caesar, 45 B.C., the addition of one day in every four years bringing the measure of the calendar year even with the astronomical year with three minutes per year over. The Gregorian Calendar corrected this by dropping leap year at the centuries not divisible by 400. For instance, 1700, 1800 and 1900 were not leap years.

Learning. *See* **F40**(2).

Leather was made in ancient Egypt, Greece and Rome, and has through succeeding centuries played an important part in the service of man. It consists of the dressed hides or skins of animals after the process of tanning has been gone through. Untanned skins are known as pelts. Leather is classed either according to the skins from which it is made or the system of preparation employed. The best-known kinds are morocco, kid, Russian, chamois, Cordovan, grained, patent, russet, tan, calf, Hungarian.

Leech, an aquatic blood-sucking worm, mostly found in fresh-water ponds. Each end of the body is provided with a sucker, but that at the head end has jaws and teeth. The medicinal leech has three jaws. The leech attaches itself with avidity to animal bodies and sucks until glutted. Its saliva contains an anti-coagulant.

Leeward, a nautical term, meaning the sheltered side of a vessel—that is, the opposite side to that from which the wind is blowing.

Legion, a body of Roman troops, varying in numbers at different periods. A legion was divided into 10 cohorts, and every cohort into three maniples. Three legions composed the Roman army of occupation in Britain.

Legion of Honour, the French order for distinguished services, military or civil, was instituted by Napoleon I in 1802, and confirmed and modified under later rules. There are five grades—Grands Croix, Grands Officiers, Commandeurs, Officiers and Chevaliers.

Legume, the fruit typical of the pea, bean family, or *Leguminosae.*

Lemming, small light-brown rodents with dark spots, abounding in Scandinavian countries and in Siberia, about 12 cm long, with a short stump of a tail. The migrations of the lemming are famous, probably caused by overbreeding when food is plentiful. So insistent is the urge to keep moving that these animals will march on into the sea in their thousands and be drowned.

Lemur, almost the most primitive member of the primate order of mammals (to which man, apes and monkeys also belong). They are noted for having strong pliant toes enabling them to use their feet as hands, and also well-developed thumbs on the hands. They have long squirrel-like tails, fox-shaped heads and large staring eyes. True lemurs are confined to the Malagasy Rep.; closely related are the "bush-babies" of S. Africa.

Lend-Lease. During the earlier phases of the second world war the bulk of British investments in the USA had to be either sold or pledged to Americans in payment for dollar supplies. After the United States entered the war this drain was stopped by the Lend-Lease arrangement, under which Great Britain met the costs of American consumption in Great Britain, while the United States paid for British supplies from America. This arrangement was abruptly terminated on the ending of hostilities; and Great Britain and other belligerent countries found themselves without means of paying in dollars for indispensable American supplies, including the foodstuffs, materials and capital goods needed for economic reconstruction. In these circumstances Great Britain negotiated with the United States and also with Canada a large loan, which was used for buying dollar supplies and played an inportant part in helping the West European economies to maintain themselves and feed their people while they were carrying through the earlier stages of postwar reconstruction. These loans involved larger charges for interest and amortisation in future years, but proved far too small to meet the dollar deficit for more than a short period. In face of this situation the United States launched the Marshall Plan.

Lenses, pieces of transparent material designed to focus an image of an illuminated object. Usually of glass, but plastic lenses are common, and quartz, etc. are used for special purposes. The surfaces of the simplest lenses are parts of spheres. Lenses which are thickest, or thinnest, at the centre are called convex and concave respectively. Lenses of complex shape are often used in microscopes, etc. Electron lenses are arrangements of electric or magnetic fields which focus beams of electrons, *e.g.*, on to T.V. screens.

Lent, the forty days' period of fasting that precedes Easter.

Lepidoptera, the order of insects with scaly wings and bodies, to which the 90,000 butterflies and moths belong.

Leptons. A group of particles which include electrons, neutrinos and muons. All are much lighter than protons or any baryons (*q.v.*). See **F16**.

Lepus, the constellation of the Hare, situated under the Orion group, and one of the constellations with which the ancients were familiar.

Lettres de Cachet, sealed letters which the kings of France issued to their agents to secure the imprisonment of distrusted or disliked persons without trial. Abolished in 1789.

Levée, a State reception held by the Sovereign or his representative and attended by men only.

Lewis, a contrivance for stone-lifting, the principle of which was known to the ancient Romans; it consists of two dovetail tenons of iron or other metal, expanded by an intervening key in a dovetail-shaped mortice in the stone, and shackled by a ringed bolt to the hoisting chain.

Leyden Jar, the earliest form of electrical condenser. Its invention is usually credited to Muschenbroeck of Leyden (1745). It consisted of a jar coated inside and out with tinfoil for about two-thirds of its height and having its inner coating connected with the top by a brass knob and chain. The jar was charged by connecting it to an electrostatic machine.

Lias, a geological term referring to the lower section of the Jurassic group, and mainly comprising shales and limestones.

Liberalism. *See* **Section J.**

Libraries, before the invention of printing, were few, and collected together at enormous cost. At Nineveh remains of libraries, consisting of tablets of baked clay, have been discovered. There were two libraries at Alexandria containing a vast collection of rolls or volumes, founded by Ptolemy I Soter (367–382 B.C.) and established by Ptolemy II Philadelphus (309–246 B.C.). Among the great libraries of later times may be mentioned the Vatican Library at Rome, moved to its present premises in 1588; the Royal Library in Paris which later became the Bibliothèque Nationale; The Astor Library, New York; and in England, the Bodleian Library, Oxford, and the British Library (*see below*). Since 1850 public libraries have been established in all the chief cities and towns of the kingdom. The first lending library was opened in Edinburgh in 1726. The British Library in London, the National Library of Scotland, in Edinburgh, that of Wales in Aberystwyth, the Bodleian Library of Oxford, Cambridge University Library and Trinity College Dublin comprise the "copyright" libraries, entitled to receive a copy of each new book and journal published in Britain. The British Library Act 1972 brought together into a single organisation

(a) the former British Museum Library (the books remaining in the Museum) and the Science Reference Library in Holborn and Bayswater, the whole now being known as the British Library, Reference Division; (b) the former National Lending Library for Science and Technology and its arts and humanities counterpart, the National Central Library, together now known as the British Library, Lending Division and located at Boston Spa, Yorkshire. It is intended eventually to rehouse Reference Division in a single new building in London, near Euston Station. Lending Division remains in Yorkshire. In 1994 the government commissioned a full-scale review of public libraries to decide who should run them, the services they should offer *etc.*.

Libretto (It. booklet), the literary text of an opera or oratorio. Usually the composer and the librettist collaborate in the writing of an opera, but several composers (*e.g.*, Wagner) wrote their own librettos. Boito, librettist to Verdi for *Otello* and *Falstaff*, himself composed two operas *Mefistofele* and *Nerone*. Most famous of Italian opera librettists was the poet and dramatist Metastasio (1698–1782). His librettos were set to music by many composers, including Gluck, Handel, Mozart, Rossini.

Licence is a permission given to do some act, which without such permission, it would be unlawful to do. Licences are required for keeping dogs, for operating a television receiving set, for driving a motor vehicle, for killing game, for setting up as a bookmaker, for selling beer, wines and spirits, tobacco, etc. and for importing certain items such as arms, ammunition, radioactive materials, animals, plants, drugs and explosives.

Lichens. In every lichen, two plants are associated, one being an alga and the other a fungus. The fungus derives its food from the alga; probably the alga gains too from the association, being protected against desiccation by the fungus (an example of symbiosis). Lichens are the first plants to colonise bare rocks.

Life-Boats were invented by three men, Lionel Lukin who converted a coble into a boat for saving life in 1785; William Wouldhave, who discovered how to make a boat right herself if she capsized; and Henry Greathead, who built a life-boat, partly from Wouldhave's model, in 1789. This boat was stationed at South Shields, although the earliest recorded reference to a lifeboat station was in 1770 at Formby, Lancs. It was not until 1851 that the first lifeboat able to self-right was built, and a motor was first installed in a life-boat in 1904. Mersey class lifeboats, introduced in 1988, have twin turbo-charged diesel engines with maximum speed of 17·5 knots. Most coastal life-boats in this country are maintained by the Royal National Lifeboat Institution founded by Sir William Hillary in 1824. It is supported entirely by voluntary contributions, and has saved over 125,000 people. Its headquarters are in Poole, Dorset. In 1995, it costs over £50m. to maintain the service. The last traditional double-ended lifeboat was phased out of service in 1993, ending 200 years of tradition. There are 213 lifeboat stations around the UK and Ireland.

Light, a particular kind of electromagnetic disturbance capable of travelling through space, and some kinds of matter, and of affecting our eyes to cause vision. Its finite speed was first demonstrated by O. Römer, using observations of the eclipses of Jupiter's satellites in 1675. In 1860 Maxwell showed that light waves are electromagnetic. Since Einstein's theory of relativity (1905) it has been generally realised that the speed of light is a fundamental natural constant. Visible light with wavelengths between about 4 and 7×10^{-5} cm is only a small part of the electromagnetic spectrum. The speed of light in vacuum is about $2·997925 \times 10^8$ m/s.

Light Year, a measure of astronomical distance, equal to the distance light travels in a period of one year. A light year is $9·463 \times 10^{12}$ km but the unit parsec is now preferred. (1 pc = 3·2616 l.y.).

Lighthouses, to warn ships of dangerous places and indicate coasts, points, harbours, etc., have existed since the building of the Pharos, a tower of white marble 183 m high, built by

Ptolemy II Philadelphus at Alexandria about 280 B.C. In early lighthouses the lights were simple fires. The most famous and one of the earliest British lighthouses is the Eddystone (q.v.). Dungeness lighthouse, opened in 1960, is very modern in design, capable of automatic operation and the first of its kind to incorporate the xenon electric arc lamp as a source of illumination. The electric fog signal consists of sixty loud-speaker units built into the tower just below the lantern, giving a honeycomb effect. The lighthouses of England and Wales, the Channel Islands and Gibraltar are under the control of Trinity House; Commissioners of Northern Lighthouses control those of Scotland; and the Commissioners of Irish Lights control the coasts of Ireland. Particulars of lights in all parts of the world are published for the guidance of navigation in the *Admiralty Lists of Lights*, compiled annually by the British Admiralty. Under the 1987 Pilotage Act, responsibility for pilotage now rests with harbour authorities.

Lightning, the flash of a discharge of electricity between two clouds, or between a cloud and the earth, when the strength of the electric fields becomes so great as to break down the resistance of the intervening air. With "forked" lightning the actual path, often branched, is visible, while with "sheet" lightning the flash is hidden by the clouds which themselves are illuminated. "Ball" lightning or fireballs is the name given to the luminous balls which have been seen floating in the air during a thunderstorm. The Boys camera has provided much information regarding the sequence of events in a lightning discharge. It is found that a flash consists of a number of separate strokes, usually four or five, and that the discharge of electricity to earth begins with a faintly luminous "leader" moving downwards and branching at intervals. As the ground is approached a much brighter luminosity travels back along the conducting channels, lighting up with several branches. The multiple strokes which follow in fractions of a second have the same "return" nature and are rarely branched. Lightning flashes to earth damage structures, cause loss of life and endanger overhead power systems, often interrupting electricity supply. Such storms generally affect radio transmissions and present hazards to aircraft. Thunderclouds may develop energy far exceeding that of our largest power generating stations.

Lightning Conductor, a metal rod, the upper part of which is of copper with a conical point, the lower portion being iron, which extends into the earth. Its effect is to gather to itself the surrounding electricity and discharge it into the earth, thus preventing its falling upon the protected building. In ships, lightning conductors are fixed to the masts and carried down through the ship's keel-sheathing. Benjamin Franklin was the first to realise the possibilities of lightning protection and, in 1752, carried out his famous experiment of drawing electricity from thunder-clouds, with the aid of a sharp-pointed conductor fixed to a kite.

Lillibulero, an old marching song arranged by Purcell. With words by Wharton, it is said to have "sung James II out of three kingdoms". Used by the B.B.C. during the second world war as a station identification signal preceding news bulletins.

Lily Family (Liliaceae), one of the largest families of flowering plants, with 200 genera and 2,500 species. It includes the true lilies (*Lilium*), tulips and hyacinths. Vegetables belonging to the family are the onion and asparagus.

Limes, trees of the genus *Tilia*, including some 30 species spread over north temperate regions. The word is a corruption of "linden". Limes native to Britain are the small-leaved *T. cordata* and the broad-leaved *T. platyphyllos*. The hybrid *T. vulgaris* was introduced into Britain from the Continent during the 17th cent. and is frequently seen in streets and parks. Lime-wood was used by Grinling Gibbons for his fruit, flower and bird decorations.

Limestones, sedimentary rocks composed wholly or largely of calcium carbonate and formed by two main processes, (1) organic (skeletal remains of organisms), *e.g.*, chalk (q.v.) and (2) chemical (precipitation of calcium carbonate), *e.g.*,

oolite (q.v.). Marble is limestone that will polish after cutting.

Linen, a textile fabric manufactured from flax fibre, known to the ancient Egyptians, and first manufactured in England under Henry III by Flemish weavers. The greatest linen-manufacturing region in the world is Northern Ireland (largely yarns and the lighter types of fabrics); Scotland produces coarse linens and canvas as well as household linens.

Ling, a sea-fish common on the coasts of Britain, and abounding in more northern waters. It averages about 1 m in length, and is a voracious feeder, living chiefly on small fish. Ling is also the name applied to *Calluna vulgaris*, the plant commonly called "heather".

Linseed, the seed of the flax plant, containing, apart from its fibrous substance, certain oily and nitrogenous matter of considerable commercial value. This yields linseed oil, and some of the residue is used to make cattle food.

Lion, the most impressive of the Cat family. It is chiefly found in open bush country in Africa, being comparatively rare in Asia. Its large square head, its flowing mane (in the males only) and its tufted tail distinguish it. From tip to tip it can reach a length of 3m; a weight of 225 kg.

Lion and Unicorn, the supporting figures of the royal arms of Great Britain, date from the union of Scotland with England (1603) at the accession of James I (James VI of Scotland), the lion representing England and the unicorn Scotland.

Liqueurs are essences combined with alcoholic liquid, and are of many kinds, named according to their flavouring or place of production, and include Cointreau, Chartreuse, Curaçao, Benedictine, Tia Maria, Drambuie *etc.*

Liquid, the name given to matter in such state that it takes its shape from the containing vessel. The volume it occupies is independent of the container, however. *See* **F20(2).**

Liquid Crystals form a special class of substance and are true liquids in that they flow easily and can be poured. However, unlike ordinary liquids, liquid crystals have their molecules arranged with geometrical regularity in one or two dimensions, so that they have a certain internal structure similar to that of solid crystals. They are fairly complicated chemicals with somewhat elongated molecules. Liquid crystals are of interest to biologists as well as to chemists and physicists, and not just because they account for the iridescence of beetles. Some body fluids are in fact liquid crystals. There are also technological applications because of their unique electrical and optical properties. They are receiving increasing attention for these reasons.

Litanies were first used in church processions in the 5th cent. The first English litany was commanded to be recited in the Reformed churches by Henry VIII in 1544.

Lithium, a soft metallic element, no. 3, symbol Li, similar to sodium. It is very reactive and is stored under paraffin oil. It is the lightest metal element.

Lithography, the art of drawing on stone and printing therefrom, was discovered by Alois Senefelder about 1796, and was introduced into England a few years later. Many improvements in the art have been made, especially in chrome-lithography and photo-lithography.

Litre, a metric measure, was abolished in 1964 as a scientific unit of volume, but remains as a special name for the cubic decimetre and as an everyday unit, *e.g.*, a litre of petrol.

Liturgy, the name given to the Church ritual, though strictly applying only to the portion used in the celebration of the Eucharist or Lord's Supper. The Anglican liturgy is laid down in the Book of Common Prayer (1662). Temporary powers granted by Parliament in 1965 to the Church to make changes in the form of worship were made permanent in 1974. The Alternative Service Book was introduced in 1980.

Liverworts (Hepatics), a class of simple green plants related to the mosses. Liverworts are most common in damp situations, such as the banks of ditches. The majority of British species are leafy, only some are thalloid.

Lizard, the name given to a diversified order of reptiles, of which there are about 1,600 species. They include the geckos, chameleons, glass snakes, skinks and blind worms.

Llama, mammals related to the camels, from which they differ in small size, absence of the humps, and more woolly coat. The domestic llama of S. America is used as a beast of burden, also providing wool, meat and milk. *See also* **Alpaca, Guanaco.**

Loadstone or **Lodestone,** an oxide of iron, found chiefly in Sweden and Norway. Its scientific name is magnetite. It has the power of attracting pieces of iron and served as the first magnets used in compasses. One of the class of non-metallic magnetic materials nowadays known as "ferrites" (*q.v.*).

Lobby Correspondents are political correspondents of newspapers who do not report the actual proceedings of Parliament—this is done by Parliamentary Correspondents—but interpret political news and events.

Lobsters are marine crustacean animals existing in large numbers in the northern seas of Europe and America and in fair proportion on some parts of the British coasts, especially in the neighbourhood of the Channel Islands.

Locarno, Treaty of, 1925, whereby Germany, France and Belgium undertook to maintain their present frontiers and to abstain from the use of force against each other. Hitler broke the pact by re-occupying the Rhineland, the demilitarisation of which had been recognised by Germany.

Locust, insects of the grasshopper family, but much more powerful. They are inhabitants of hot countries, and often make their appearance in untold millions, like clouds, devastating all the vegetation that comes within their course. The locust-tree (*Ceratonia siliqua*) is supposed to have furnished food to St. John the Baptist in the wilderness, and its "beans" have accordingly been styled "St. John's Bread".

Loess, a deposit of silt or marl laid down by wind action. The biggest loess deposits are in Asia, the source of the dust of which they are composed probably being the deserts of Central Asia. Large deposits in Europe are thought to have originated from the edge of ice sheets during the Ice Age.

Logarithms, a system of calculation invented by John Napier in 1614, and developed by Henry Briggs a few years later. Thus if a number is expressed as the power of another number, *i.e.*, if $a = b^n$, then n is said to be the logarithm of a to base b, written $\log_b a$. Common logs are to base 10 and Napierian to base $2{\cdot}7182818\ldots$, expressed as e.

Lombards, a German people, originating on the Elber, who settled in Italy in the 6th cent., occupying northern and central regions, and establishing a kingdom with Pavia as capital. They were conquered by Charlemagne in 774, but left their name to the region of Lombardy. Lombard Street, London, takes its name from the Lombard merchants and bankers who came to settle there in the 12th cent.

London Clay, geological stratum which occupies much of the London Basin and part of the Hampshire Basin. It represents the lower stratum of the Eocene. Outside the metropolis, brickfields utilise the clay for brickmaking. Water held down in the Chalk by this impervious stratum is tapped by a number of artesian wells in London. The tunnels of the underground run through the London Clay.

London University is recognised as one of the great universities of the world. Originated in the foundation of a non-sectarian college in Gower Street in 1828. Among the chief colleges are: University College London, King's College, (inc. former Chelsea College and Queen Elizabeth), Imperial College of Science and Technology, London School of Economics, School of Oriental and African Studies, Queen Mary and Westfield, Birkbeck, together with Royal Holloway and Bedford New College. London University was the first to throw open all degrees to women (1878). In 1995 the London School of Economics (LSE) celebrated its centenary.

Long Distance Walks. The National Parks and Access to the Countryside Act 1949 provided for the establishment in England and Wales of Long Distance Footpaths and Bridleways. The following walks have been opened: Pennine Way (the first long-distance footpath, a magnificent hill walk of 270 miles from Edale in Derbyshire along the Pennines over the Cheviots and the Scottish border); Pembrokeshire Coast Path (from St. Dogmael's to Amroth, 170 miles); Offa's Dyke Path (176 miles along the marches of Wales, one of the most important remaining earthworks of its kind in northwestern Europe); South Downs Way (Beachy Head to Buriton in Hants, 80 miles); South-West Peninsula Coast path (Minehead to Poole Harbour, 520 miles); Coast to Coast Walk from Robin Hood's Bay to St. Bee's (190 miles); Ridgeway (Avebury to Ivinghoe Beacon, 90 miles); Pilgrim's Way (Winchester to Canterbury, 116 miles); Cotswold Way (Bath to Chipping Campden, 95 miles); West Highland Way (Glasgow to Fort William, 95 miles). In 1987 plans were announced for a 180-mile Thames footpath. Recently opened paths include (1989) the 83-mile Centenary Way from York to the North Sea at Filey, the 278-mile Icknield Way, reputed to be the oldest road in Britain (1993), the 147-mile Grand Union Canal walk (1993), the 88-mile Jurassic Way from Banbury to Stamford (1994) and the 225-mile Midshires Way (which will link with the proposed Pennine Bridleway). *See also* **National Parks.**

Longitude of a point on the earth's surface is the angle which the meridian through the poles and that point makes with some standard meridian. The meridian through Greenwich is usually accepted as the standard meridian and the longitude is measured east or west of that line. As the earth revolves through 360° in 24 h, 15° longitude represent 1 hour's difference in apparent time.

Long Parliament (1640–60), marked the end of Charles I's 11-year attempt to govern without Parliament. It carried through what has come to be called "the English Revolution" and was the parliament of the civil war (1642–49).

Lord Lieutenant is the Queen's representative in the county, and his office is now largely ceremonial. On his recommendation the magistrates or J.P.s are appointed by the Lord Chancellor. The office was created in 1549 to take over the military duties of the sheriff.

Lords, House of, the Upper House of the British Parliament composed of Lords Spiritual and Lords Temporal. The former consist of the two Archbishops and twenty-four English Bishops and the latter of hereditary Peers, Peeresses and Life Peers. The right of the Lords to veto Bills passed by the Commons is restricted by the Parliament Acts of 1911 and 1949. The Lord Chancellor presides over the House of Lords. Under the Peerage Act 1963 a peerage may be disclaimed for life. *See* **Section D.**

Louse, parasitic insect found on the skin of birds and mammals. The two sub-species that parasitise man are the body louse and the head louse. Typhus can be transmitted by lice.

Louvre, one of the old royal palaces of Paris, was built in its present form partly by Francis I and added to by later monarchs, Louis XIV completing the edifice. Napoleon I turned it into a museum and enriched it with the plunder of many foreign art galleries. The great extension to the Louvre building begun by Napoleon I was completed under Napoleon III in 1857. Much injury was done to the building during the Commune of 1871. Amongst other famous treasures it houses the Venus de Milo and Leonardo da Vinci's masterpiece, *La Gioconda*.

LSD (d-lysergic acid diethylamide). This hallucinogenic drug has achieved wide notoriety because of its use by certain people to give themselves abnormal mental experiences. Doctors have frequently warned against the dangers of its use. It is active in extremely small quantities and a dose as small as a fifty-millionth part of a gram can cause marked disturbances of the mental function in man. LSD has been used in the study of mental disease because it produces symptoms very similar to mental disorders such as schizophrenia.

Luddites, a combination of workmen formed in 1811, in a period of great distress, with the object of destroying the new textile machinery then being largely adopted, which they regarded as the cause of their troubles. Their first outbreak was at Nottingham, and was stated to have been started by a young apprentice named Ned Ludd. Afterwards, serious Luddite riots occurred in various parts of the country, especially in West Yorkshire, where many people were killed, mills were destroyed and numbers of rioters were tried and executed. Charlotte Brontë used the period in her novel, *Shirley*.

Lunatic Fringe, term used by Theodore Roosevelt to characterise adherents of reform movements who refuse to recognise the difficulty of practical administration and insist upon immediate fulfilment of an extreme programme.

Lutecium, element (no. 71) of the rare-earth metal group discovered in 1907 by Urbain. Symbol Lu.

Lutheranism. *See* **Section J.**

Lynx, cats of sturdy build, with tufted ears and spotted fur, inhabiting many parts of the world, including Northern and Central Europe. They commit serious ravages among sheep and goats.

Lyon King of Arms, the President of the Scottish Lyon Court, and head of the heraldic organisation for Scotland.

Lyre-Bird, a remarkable family of Australian birds, the males of which possess a beautiful lyre-shaped tail. The bird is not more than 38 cm long, but its tail, displayed during its remarkable courtship dance, is 58 cm in length. There are two species: the Superb and Albert's Lyrebird.

M

Macaque. A family of monkeys which includes the Barbary ape (specimens of which live on Gibraltar), the Rhesus macaque (the organ grinder's monkey and the one used for experimental work in the investigation of disease), the Bonnet monkey of southern India and Sri Lanka, the Crab-eating and the Pig-tailed monkeys of south-eastern Asia.

Macaw, a genus of large parrots with brilliant scarlet and sky-blue plumage, with inter-minglings of green. Native to South and Central America.

McCarthyism, the term given to the wave of anti-Communist hysteria, associated with the name of Senator McCarthy (1908–57). The campaign lasted from early 1947 to late 1954.

Mace, originally a weapon of offence, now an ensign of authority borne before officers of state and other dignitaries. In the House of Commons the mace is handed to an official of the Crown by the Sergeant-at-Arms at the close of a parliamentary session.

Mach Number. Unit of flight speed. The ratio of speed of flight to speed of sound under same conditions of pressure and density. Speed of sound at sea-level is 762 mile/h (1,226 km/h), so flight speed of 381 mile/h (613 km/h) is equivalent to a Mach Number of ½. At supersonic speeds the Mach Number is greater than 1; subsonic speeds, less than 1.

Mackerel, a sea-fish existing in large numbers in the northern Atlantic off America and Europe. They are beautiful fish with a streamlined body and among the fastest fish in the sea.

Macromolecules are very large molecules about 10,000 times or more as heavy as ordinary small molecules like hydrogen. Most are built up from a large number of simple sub-units, *i.e.*, are polymers (*q.v.*). The term macromolecule is often used in biology, *e.g.*, starch and cellulose are biological macromolecules, both built from glucose sub-units. Other important ones are proteins and nucleic acids. The properties of macromolecules depend on the sub-units of which they are composed.

Mad Cow Disease, popular name for Bovine Spongiform Encephalopathy (BSE). A fatal brain disease in cattle rather similar to scabies in sheep. New cases of BSE are currently running at 35,000 per year. The first case among cats was reported in May 1990.

Madder, one of the most important of dye-stuffs, largely used in producing Turkey-red dye, but now superseded by synthetic alizarin. Natural madder is the root of the *Rubia tinctorum*.

Maelstrom, a great whirlpool. The most famous is that off the coast of Norway, between the islands of Moskenës and Mosken, of the Lofoten group the power of which has been much exaggerated.

Mafia. A term which is connected with Italo-American organised crime. Historically, remoteness from the central government of Italy encouraged the growth in Sicily in the 19th cent. of *mafiosi*, key-men who gained power through fear and violence. Contemporary police records give details of *mafia* behaviour in defending their authority. Emigration of vast numbers of southern Italians to the United States led to a new type of urban *mafioso* who became connected with gangsterism and vice. Sometimes called the *Cosa Nostra*, the organisation has infiltrated city governments and is reputed to be in control of drug smuggling and other illegal operations. In Italy neo-fascist groups have made use of the *mafia* in acts of terrorism, especially in the north.

Magellan, Clouds of, the name given to a pair of small galaxies, satellite systems of our own galaxy, visible only from the southern hemisphere. On account of their relative nearness to the earth (186,000 light-years), they are receiving much attention from astronomers.

Magenta, a blue-red aniline dye discovered in 1859 by Sir W. H. Perkin, and named after the battle of that year between the French and Austrians.

Magic. *See* **Section J.**

Magistrates *or* **Justices of the Peace** preside over petty sessional and Youth Courts (as well as Family Proceedings Courts, liquor licensing committees *etc.*), and are appointed by the Lord Chancellor on the recommendation of the Lord Lieutenant of the County. Most J.P.s are laymen and are unpaid. In certain big towns a legally-qualified, paid, full-time magistrate is appointed, known as a stipendiary magistrate. In London stipendiaries are known as Metropolitan Stipendiary Magistrates. J.P.s are no longer appointed over the age of 60 and they must retire when they reach 70. The judicial office of Justice of the Peace derives from a statute of 1361. Magistrates, though mostly laymen and unpaid, are now subject to compulsory training.

Magma, molten rock material rich in volatile constituents prior to its eruption at the surface. With the loss of volatiles it becomes lava.

Magna Carta was sealed by King John at Runnymede on 15 June 1215, in obedience to the insistent demands of the barons and has been confirmed many times by later monarchs. It was not a revolutionary document. It laid down what the barons took to be the recognised and fundamental principles for the government of the realm and bound king and barons alike to maintain them. Its main provisions were that no man should be punished without fair trial, that ancient liberties generally should be preserved, and that no demands should be made by an overlord to his vassal (other than those recognised) without the sanction of the great council of the realm.

Magnesium, a metallic element, no. 12, symbol Mg, first isolated in 1808 by Sir Humphry Davy, who prepared it by electrolysing the chloride. Its chief ores are magnesite and dolomite. Industrially it is obtained by electrolysis. Many important light alloys contain magnesium. The metal burns with a very bright light, and for this reason it is used in photographers' flash bulbs and also in firework manufacture.

Magnetic Storms. These are the effects of magnetospheric storms observed world-wide at ground level as fluctuations of as much as 5% in the earth's magnetic field. The largest effects are observed at high latitudes, in the auroral ovals, and are due to electric currents flowing in the ionosphere and between the ionosphere and the magnetosphere. There may be concurrent disruption of radio communications. *See* **Magnetosphere.**

Magnetism, originally the name given to the quality of attraction for iron possessed by lodestone (*q.v.*). Now known to be a phenomenon inseparably connected with electricity (**F21**). Strong magnetic attraction is possessed by a comparatively small class of substances; iron, nickel and cobalt are the most common elements, but there are several less well known, *e.g.*, gadolinium. Many alloys have valuable magnetic properties which make possible numberless technical devices. New magnetic substances are always being developed (see **Ferrites**). The earth acts like a huge magnet with its axis inclined at about 11° to the axis of rotation, the magnetic poles being on the Boothia Peninsula (North Canada) and South Victoria Land (Antarctica). The magnetic field at the surface consists of the regular field of a magnetised sphere with an irregular field super-imposed upon it. Variation in the magnetic forces occurs from place to place and from time to time, and maps showing the distribution over the globe of points of the same declination (i.e., the angle which the magnetic meridian makes with the geographical one) are of the utmost importance in navigation. Little is known regarding the origin of the main (regular) field of the earth, but it is believed that the irregularities are due to the presence of intense electric currents in the upper atmosphere and local magnetisation of rock strata. In 1967 the discovery was claimed of isolated magnetic poles, i.e., north and south magnetic poles existing separately, just as positive and negative electrical charges exist separately. If this is confirmed it will probably rank as one of the most important experimental results of the 20th cent., because of its significance for the theory of electromagnetism and fundamental particles. Magnetic field strengths are measured in gauss (c.g.s.) or tesla (S.I.) units.

Magnetohydro-dynamics. A current-carrying wire always experiences a force if it is in a magnetic field. This is the well-known electrodynamic force, and electric motors work because of it. If the current is carried in a fluid, e.g., a liquid metal or a plasma, these forces cause bodily movements to the fluid, which are in general very difficult to calculate. The forces are then called *magnetohydro-dynamic forces*. Now magnetic fields are themselves produced by electric currents; so a current flowing in a fluid produces a magnetic field, which then reacts on the fluid itself by means of the magnetohydro-dynamic forces. In the Harwell machine Zeta, used in studying the technical problems of thermonuclear reactions, this effect acts so as to constrict the electric discharge on to the axis of the tube and thus keeps it away from the walls. This action is assisted by an extra magnetic field produced by a separate current flowing in metallic conductors outside the tube. Thus the hot plasma is contained by magneto-hydro-dynamic forces and not at all by the material tube wall. In practical devices of the future magnetic forces may have to sustain plasma pressure of 60 atmospheres—a pressure for which a thick steel wall would normally be used! See also **Plasma Physics**.

Magnetosphere. The magnetic field of the earth prevents the plasma of the solar wind from directly impinging on the earth's upper atmosphere and ionosphere. The cavity thus maintained within the solar wind is known as the magnetosphere. The tenuous plasma within this cavity is partly of solar and partly of terrestrial origin, from the solar wind and the ionosphere respectively. These plasmas are subject to large perturbations, known as magnetospheric storms, triggered by fluctuations within the solar wind. These storms generate intense auroral displays, magnetic field fluctuations at ground level, and often major disturbances of the upper atmosphere and ionosphere which may result in disruption of radio communications. The inner parts of the magnetosphere contain the Van Allen radiation belts (q.v.). On the sunward side the magnetosphere extends to between 12 and 20 earth radii. However, on the side of the earth away from the sun it extends, like a comet tail, for many millions of km. Jupiter's large magnetic field produces a large magnetosphere, one of the largest features in our planetary system being as large as the sun itself.

Magnificat, the hymn of the Virgin Mary, given in Luke 1, 46 beginning in the Vulgate with the words "Magnificat anima mea Dominum" ("My soul doth magnify the Lord").

Magnitude in astronomy is a measure of the apparent brightness of a star, which is inversely proportional to the square of its distance. A low number indicates a bright star, and a high

one a faint star. The *absolute magnitude* is a measure of *real* brightness, i.e., the brightness a star would have at a standard distance away of 10 parsecs (32·6 light years). The distance can be calculated if the apparent and absolute magnitudes are known. Another magnitude system used by astronomers is bolometric magnitude, which is a measure of the total radiation emitted by a star at all wavelengths.

Magpie, a well-known bird of the crow family, of glossy black and white plumage, famed for its mischievous propensities.

Magyars, the Hungarian race who came to eastern Europe from S.W. Asia and settled in Hungary in the 10th cent. Their language belongs to the Finno-Ugrian group.

Mahdi an Arab leader of great influence, invested with powers akin to those of a Messiah in the Mohammedan mind. The title was taken by Mohammed Ahmed, who overran the Egyptian Sudan, and in 1885 captured Khartoum.

Maidenhair Tree or **Ginkgo.** This tree takes its name from the shape of its leaves, which resemble those of the maidenhair fern. Widely cultivated in China and Japan. It is the only survivor of an order of gymnosperms which flourished in Mesozoic times. Botanically interesting because the male gametes are motile.

Malmaison, château at Rueil-Malmaison, a western suburb of Paris. It derives its name from having been inhabited in the 11th cent. by the Norman brigand Odon, and afterwards, according to the tradition, by evil spirits, exorcised by the monks of St. Denis. It was the residence of Napoleon and of the Empress Josephine after her divorce. She died there in 1814. In 1900 it was given to the nation.

Mamluks, commonly known as Mamelukes, were originally—in the 13th cent.—a bodyguard of Turkish and Circassian slaves in the service of the Sultan of Egypt, and attained such influence that in 1250 they were strong enough to appoint one of their own body to the throne of Egypt. After that a succession of Mamluk Sultans reigned down to 1517. Then the Turks annexed Egypt, and the Mamluks were taken into the service of the Beys. They again came to the front after Napoleon's conquest of Egypt, but in 1811 they were massacred by order of Mehemet Ali.

Mammoth, extinct elephants of gigantic size. In 1799 the first perfectly preserved specimen was found in Siberia in a block of ice. It was in prehistoric times found in Britain and other parts of Europe, as well as in Asia and America.

Mammoth Cave of Kentucky, one of the largest known limestone caverns in the world, with subterranean passages at different levels, lakes and rivers (the Echo R. flows 110 m below the surface); stalactites and stalagmites abound.

Manatee, an aquatic mammal of the sea cow (Sirenia) order of mammals, averaging when full grown from 3–3·6 m in length, with shovel-shaped tail, and forelimbs and nails which almost give the appearance of arms and hands. Gentle and trusting they are under threat from man. Protected in Florida. In spite of their ungainly aspect, they are believed to have given rise to the legend of mermaids.

Manchus, originally nomads inhabiting northern Manchuria who invaded China early in the 17th cent. A Manchu dynasty occupied the imperial throne of China from 1644 to 1911.

Mandarin, the name given to a powerful Chinese official, civil or military, under the old régime, whose rank was shown by the wearing of a button on the cap. Mandarin is the major language of N. China.

Manganese, a metallic element, no. 25, symbol Mn, discovered by Scheele, 1774. It is silver-white, not very hard (it forms a hard alloy with carbon), brittle, and tarnishes when exposed to air. Its chief ore is pyrolusite (manganese dioxide). Steels containing manganese are very tough, used for making machine parts.

Maniple, eucharistic vestment worn over left arm.

Manna, a tree of the ash genus, *Fraxinus ornus*, growing in the South of Europe and in the East and exuding a sweet substance which is gathered, boiled and eaten.

Manometer, instrument used to measure gas pressure. Usually a U-tube containing water or mercury, one end open to the atmosphere, the other to the gas whose pressure is to be measured. More sensitive for small pressures than the Bourdon gauge.

Mansion House, the official residence of the Lord Mayor of London, stands opposite to the Bank of England, and was erected in 1739–53 from the designs of George Dance.

Mantis. Large insects belonging to the same order as the locusts and grasshoppers. The manner in which the forelegs are held, as though in suppliance, has gained for these insects the common name of "praying mantis". They are distributed throughout the warmer countries.

Manx, the Celtic dialect (Manx Gaelic) of the Isle of Man, now on the point of extinction.

Maoism. *See* **Section J.**

Maoris, the race living in New Zealand at the time it was first visited by Captain Cook in 1769. They are believed to have migrated from Polynesia about 1350. Up to 1871 they were frequently in arms against the European settlers but their high intelligence and stamina enabled them to adapt themselves and the New Zealand laws have encouraged equal citizenship. They number *c.* 322,000 (1995). In 1994 Maoris in the upper North Island were offered land and money in compensation for land seized in the 19th century.

Maple, trees native to the northern hemisphere. There are over 100 species. The sycamore is the best-known species growing in Britain. The sugar maple abounds in Canada and the eastern parts of the United States. The sugar is tapped by boring holes in the tree in February and March, and the juice that escapes is collected and evaporated. The maple-leaf is the Canadian national emblem.

Maquis, name of the dense scrub in Mediterranean France and Corsica, providing good cover for bandits and outlaws. The French resistance movement, 1940–45, adopted the name Maquis.

Marble is limestone in its hardest and most crystalline form. There are many varieties—33 were used in the building of the Paris Opera House—but white is the purest and rarest. White marble was used by the ancient Greeks for their temples and statues. Among the famous marbles of Italy are the Carrara and Siena marbles, which were used by Renaissance sculptors. Devonshire and Derbyshire yield some beautiful marbles and Connemara furnishes a serpentine-marble.

March, the third month of the year, and the first of the old Roman Calendar. It was named after the god Mars, and was the *Hlyd* (storm) *monath* of the Anglo-Saxons.

Mardi Gras, the last day of the Carnival in France, Shrove Tuesday.

Marine Nature Reserve (MNR), sea areas within territorial waters, established by English Nature or the Countryside Council for Wales, to conserve marine fauna, flora and seabed features. The only MNRs so far are Lundy Island (England) and Skomer Island (Wales).

Marionettes are puppets moved by strings. They originated in the *Fantoccini* of the 15th cent. which had such a vogue in Italy and elsewhere on the Continent. The English *Punch and Judy* is a version of Punchinello.

Marmoset, small monkeys confined to the New World. Very squirrel-like in appearance, with long bushy tails, and thick woolly fur, they are pretty little animals and the smallest of all monkeys. There are claws, not nails, on their digits, the big toe excepted.

Maronite, Christian sect living mainly in Lebanon and Syria. Now part of the Catholic Church.

Marprelate Tracts, seditious pamphlets written with great maliciousness by a group of Elizabethan puritans about 1586, and intended to discredit the episcopacy, caused a great sensation in their time, and led to the execution of their supposed author, John Penry.

Marquess *or* **Marquis,** the title next in precedent to that of duke. The first English marquess was Rovery de Vere, Earl of Oxford, who was honoured by Richard II, in 1385.

Mars, the fourth nearest planet to the sun (*see* **F8**). The enormous amount of new information from the pioneer visits to Mars, primarily by the US *Mariner* and *Viking* spacecraft, in 1971 and 1976 respectively, has revolutionised our understanding of the planet. Where the brief glimpses of the planet by the early *Mariner 4, 6* and *7* missions showed a dead, barren world, not unlike the moon, the 1971 and 1976 missions showed that the planet's surface displayed many contrasts—the ancient crated terrains glimpsed previously, enormous volcanos, far larger than any on earth, vast wastelands, particularly near the polar regions, scoured by wind-blown dust over many aeons, and most tantalising, in many regions water had set unmistakable marks. We see the plains which have been subject to torrential deluges of rain in, probably, a number of different episodes over hundreds of millions of years. Other regions, extending over hundreds of km, show great gorges and canyons cut by catastrophic floods, when some natural dam has burst, releasing the pent-up waters of a gigantic lake or sea. This pictorial evidence, and more detailed information of the atmosphere and surface obtained from the *Viking* spacecraft tell us that there must have been episodes in the planet's history when its climate was quite different from that observed today. The atmosphere, if only for brief interludes, must have been much denser, and warmer, and rain must have been able to fall. Mars is today too cold and dry for water but there are polar ice caps, and the nature of the meteoric craters suggests that the surface is rock over ice and solid carbon dioxide. The search for life carried out by *Viking* produced much new information, but no traces of organic compounds as evidence, or precursors, of life. Mars has two small moons, Phobos and Deimos.

Marseillaise, the French national hymn, written and composed by Rouget de L'Isle, a French engineer officer, who was inspired to write it in 1792 to encourage the Strasburg conscripts. It immediately became popular, and received its name because it was sung by the Marseillaise troops while marching into Paris.

Marshalsea, a former prison in Southwark, London, closed 1849. It existed as early as Edward III's time and was used as a jail for royal servants convicted of offences. In its later days it became a debtors' prison. Dickens described it in *Little Dorrit.*

Marston Moor, near York, was the scene of the famous battle between Prince Rupert and Cromwell on 2 July 1644. Cromwell's victory was the turning-point in the Civil War.

Marsupials, members of the order of pouched mammals. Except for the opossums of America, all marsupials occur in Australasia, and include kangaroos, wallabies and wombats.

Martello Towers, circular forts erected on the coasts of England, Ireland and the Channel Isles early in the 19th cent. as defences against the threatened Napoleonic invasion. So called from the circular fort at Mortella (Corsica), which resisted an English sea attack in 1794.

Marten, carnivorous animals of the weasel family; one species (the Pine Marten) was once common in Britain. Most famous for their fur are the Siberian Sable and the American Marten.

Martial Law is a term loosely employed to indicate the suspension of the administration of normal civil law and its replacement by military authority.

Martin, a well-known bird-visitor to Britain. It belongs to the swallow family, and the two species that spend their summers here are the house-martin, which makes its nest of mud under the eaves of houses, and the sand martin, which builds in sandy banks.

Martinmas *or* **St. Martin's Day,** falls on 11 November, and is one of the Scottish quarter days. St. Martin was a popular Saint with our ancestors and Martinmas was a busy time for the mediaeval housewife. It was the date when "Martlemas Beef" was dried in the chimney, and enough bacon and mutton cured to last until the spring, because, owing to the scarcity of winter fodder, fresh meat could seldom be obtained. This diet of dried meat without vegetables caused scurvy. St. Martin (c. 316–400) was regarded as the patron saint of drinking and jovial meetings, as well as of reformed drunkards. The late spell of fine weather sometimes occurring at Martinmas is called St. Martin's Summer.

Martyrs. People who suffer death in testimony to their faith. Stephen (Acts 6; 7) was the first Christian martyr in 39. The first English martyr was St. Alban, 286, and in Tudor times many eminent churchmen went to the stake. The Smithfield martyrs' memorial church used to be St. Peter's, St. John Street, Clerkenwell. After its demolition the memorial moved to the Church of St. James, Clerkenwell Green.

Mary Rose, the flagship of Henry VIII's navy. A 700-ton carrack, she sank in July 1545. Raised from the silt of the Solent 437 years later.

Marxism. *See* **Section J.**

Mason and Dixon Line, boundary line between Pennsylvania and Maryland, for long a source of dispute, drawn up by two English surveyors, Charles Mason and Jeremiah Dixon, between 1763 and 1767. It came to designate the boundary dividing the slave states from the free states of America, and is still used in distinguishing the "North" from the "South".

Masques were light dramatic compositions set to music and performed on special occasions. One famous example is Milton's "Comus", which was given at Ludlow Castle in 1634.

Mass, the service in the Roman Catholic Church defined as the Propitiary Sacrifice of Calvary, reoffered by the Priest acting *in persona Christi.* It was first celebrated in Latin in the 4th cent., and was introduced into England in the 7th cent. The use of a vernacular language was sanctioned by the 2nd Vatican Council (1965).

Mass Spectrograph, an instrument for separating isotopes. It works by sorting electrified particles according to their masses; the particles stream through a magnetic and possibly an electric field, and the lightest particles undergo the greatest deflection.

Massorah, a collection of criticisms on the Hebrew text of the Scriptures, and rules for its correct interpretation.

Mast, a long round piece of timber or tubular steel or iron, standing upright in a vessel, and supporting the yards, sails and rigging in general. The earliest ships had only one mast, carrying a simple sail. The number increased until there were 4 or 5, or even more. Above the lower mast of a sailing-ship comes the topmast, and above that, the topgallantmast and royalmast. The position of each mast is indicated by a prefix, as foremast, foretopmast, foretopgallantmast, foreroyalmast, mainmast, maintopmast, etc. The foremast is in the fore of the ship, the mainmast in the centre and the mizzen nearest the stern. In large vessels nowadays the mast does not extend to the keel, as it formerly did, but is usually stopped at the second deck.

Master of the Revels was an important Court official upon whom devolved the arrangement of Court festivities. The office is at least as old as the time of Edward III. By 1737 it seems to have died.

Master of the Rolls, one of the English judges, formerly a judge of Chancery, but since 1881 a judge of the Court of Appeal only. He has charge of the rolls or records of Chancery and ranks next to the Lord Chancellor and Lord Chief Justice.

Mastodon, an extinct order of quadruped closely resembling the elephant, but larger.

Materials Science is a blend of science and technology; it is the use of scientific research methods to study and improve materials for practical use. The deeper understanding so obtained enables scientists to design new substances with hitherto unknown combinations of properties that are useful in engineering, aircraft, nuclear power, surgery, etc. Materials science institutes or university departments will usually contain an assortment of chemists, physicists, metallurgists, ceramicists, engineers and others because materials science brings to bear on materials a great many specialised techniques. The scientific study of materials is bringing continual improvement in metals, ceramics, plastics, fibres and many valuable combinations of these.

Mathematics is a body of knowledge expressed in a language of symbols. *Pure* mathematics studies the propositions that can be deduced in this language by applying definite rules of reasoning to sets of axioms. In *Applied* mathematics, the mathematical language is used, often with great effect, to discuss problems of the real world, such as mechanics, statistics and science generally. In range, subtlety, complexity and depth mathematics is unsurpassed among the intellectual disciplines and its study has attracted some of the most brilliant men in history.

Matins, the first of the canonical hours or services of the day in the Roman Catholic Church and Morning Prayer in the Anglican Church. The daily service in the Roman breviary (*q.v.*) used to consist of eight offices or "hours", fixed by canon, for prayer and devotion but since the second Vatican Council the structure has been simplified. Formerly, Matins was recited or sung at midnight, Lauds at sunrise, Prime at 6 a.m., Terce at 9 a.m., Sext at midday, Nones at 3. p.m., Vespers at sunset and Compline before retiring for the night. Lauds are now commonly joined to Matins.

Matrix, a rectangular array of numbers considered as a single mathematical object. There are special rules for multiplying and adding matrices and they are often used in mathematics, physics and elsewhere to simplify calculations and as a notational device.

Mau-Mau, a secret, anti-European, terrorist movement which agitated the Kikuyu tribe of Kenya during the years 1953–57. Mau-Mau was a symptom of native insecurity and discontent; emergency powers were lifted in November 1959, and large-scale reforms were instituted. Kenya attained independence in 1963 with Mr. Jomo Kenyatta as the Prime Minister.

Maundy Thursday, the day before Good Friday, commemorates the Last Supper. "Maundy" derives from Christ's command (mandatum) to his disciples on that day to love one another. It was the custom in the monasteries for the monks to wash the feet of the poor on this day, and for many centuries the sovereigns of England, through their almoners, have distributed money, food and clothing to "as many old men and as many old women as the Sovereign is years of age". The Royal Maundy ceremony is still observed, maundy coins being struck from standard silver.

Mausoleum, a special place of sepulture, generally for the reception of the remains of members of a royal or other family of distinction. The name is derived from the tomb of King Mausolus at Halicarnassus, erected 352 B.C., and forming one of the seven wonders of the ancient world. Another mausoleum of antiquity is that of Hadrian in Rome.

Mauve, a colouring matter produced from lichens by Dr. Stenhouse in 1848, but in 1856 obtained from aniline by William Perkin (1838–1907), who gave it the name Mauveen. This was the first synthetic organic dyestuff ever to be produced, which led to the building up of the great synthetic dyestuffs industry (which Germany dominated before the first world war).

May, the fifth month of the year, but the third of the ancient Roman calendar. Supposed to be named after Maia, the mother of Mercury, to whom sacrifices were offered on the first day of this month. In England in former days May Day was made the occasion of many festivities, including the crowning of the May Queen, dancing round the Maypole, etc.

"Mayflower", the name of the ship which in 1620 conveyed the Pilgrim Fathers, 101 in number, from England to America. *See* **Pilgrim Fathers.**

May Fly. *See* **Ephemeroptera.**

Mazarin Bible, an edition of the Latin Vulgate, acknowledged as the masterpiece of the Gutenberg press (1456). It was the first book completely printed from movable types. It is called the Mazarin Bible because the first copy to capture the attention of scholars was found in the library of Cardinal Mazarin, in Paris. Also called the Gutenberg or the 42-line Bible.

Mean. In statistics and mathematics generally understood to be the arithmetic mean. The geometric mean between two quantities is the square root of their product. *See* **Average.**

Mechanical Equivalent of Heat. *See* **Joule.**

Medals, as decorations for military service, were first issued in this country by Charles I, who ordered medals for gallantry to be distributed to certain soldiers in 1643. Medals were also issued to officers and men who were victorious against the Dutch fleet in 1653. After Lord Howe's victory in 1794 a naval medal was instituted. Medals were also struck for the victory of Waterloo, and since that time special medals have been issued in connection with all our wars. The Victoria Cross, a special reward for personal gallantry, was instituted in 1856. The George Cross for gallantry instituted in 1940 ranks next to the Victoria Cross. The Military Cross was instituted in 1914.

Megalith, a prehistoric monument, consisting of a large single stone or a group of such stones, in a circle as at Stonehenge or in burial chambers as at New Grange, Ireland. Megalithic monuments have been constructed by different peoples in different parts of the world since the third millennium B.C.

Meiosis, special type of cell division by which the gametes or sex cells are generated, resulting in the sperm or ovum receiving only half the number of chromosomes found in a somatic cell. *See* **Mitosis.**

Mendelian Law. *See* **F30(2).**

Mendicant Friars, certain religious orders which spread over Europe in the 13th cent., and comprised the Franciscans, Dominicans, Augustines and Carmelites. Originally they depended entirely on alms.

Mercator's Projection, a method of indicating meridians and parallels of latitudes on maps, introduced by Mercator in the 16th cent., and still universally used in navigators' charts.

Mercury, the second smallest of the planets (c. one-twentieth of the earth's mass) is the closest to the sun at little more than one-third of the earth's average distance. It appears to resemble the earth in its interior and has about the same density but its surface resembles the moon and is heavily cratered. Mercury was visited by Mariner 10 which passed within a few hundred kilometres in March 1974 and which relayed pictures on the two following passes in September 1974 and March 1975 before control of its altitude was lost. It nevertheless continues to revisit Mercury every 176 days (two mercurian years). Mariner 10 was guided to Mercury by the gravitational field of Venus before it became a satellite of the smallest planet. The relayed pictures showed that the planet has an approximately 59-day rotation period exactly two thirds of its orbital period of 88 days. This relationship means that unlike on earth the seasonal variations are with longitude not latitude. Surface temperatures vary from 400°C to –200°C and there is virtually no atmosphere except a thin envelope of helium gas. Mariner 10 measured a small magnetic field at the surface about 1% of the earth's but much stronger than for Venus or Mars.

Mercury *or* **Quicksilver,** element no. 80, symbol Hg (Latin *hydrargyrum*) is one of the oldest-known metals, whose chief ore is the sulphide, cinnabar, found in certain parts of Spain, China, Japan and South America. It is liquid at ordinary temperature and is used in the construction of barometers and thermometers. Alloys of mercury are called amalgams. It is also of great value in medicine. The metal is used in the mercury-vapour (or "sunlight") lamp, since the vapour gives a bright yellow-white glow in an electric discharge.

Mercy-killing, taking the life of a person suffering from a painful and incurable disease. The killer is often actuated by a good *motive*—the desire to relieve hopeless suffering; but the *intention* is to kill, and the act, in English law, is therefore a crime. (It is not necessary for the prosecution to prove any motive.)

Meridian, an imaginary circle extending through the North and South Poles and any given place. When the sun is at its midday height at any place it is "on the meridian"; hence the terms ante-meridian (a.m.) and post-meridian (p.m.). *See also* **Greenwich Mean Time.**

Merino Sheep were imported into England from Spain in 1788 and had great influence in improving native breeds, especially in regard to the quality of the wool.

Merit, Order of, founded by King Edward VII in 1902 as a special distinction for eminent men and women without conferring a knighthood upon them. The Order has twenty-four British companions in addition to foreign honorary members limited in number, as the choice of members is, by the Sovereign's pleasure. Lord Kelvin was the founder companion. Florence Nightingale (1907), Professor Dorothy Hodgkin (1965), Dame Veronica Wedgwood (1969), Mother Theresa of Calcutta (honorary member, 1983) and Margaret Thatcher (1990) are the only women to have received this coveted decoration. Nelson Mandela was appointed an honorary member in 1995.

Merovingians, the name given to the family that ruled over France from about 500 to 750. Clovis was first of the line and Childeric the last. The "long-haired kings" have become the centre of much recent speculative history.

Mesons (from Greek *meso* = middle), a family of unstable particles of mass between that of an electron and that of a proton. Some are positive, some negative, some neutral. No stable meson is known, the longest-lived particle having a lifetime of only two-millionths of a second. The first of these particles was discovered in cosmic radiation in 1937 and called the mu-meson or *muon*. In 1947 a heavier type was discovered called the pi-meson or *pion* which behaved like the meson predicted on theoretical grounds by Yukawa in 1935. The pion is connected with the theory of nuclear forces. *See also* **F15, 16.**

Mesozoic. The geological era, including the Triassic, Jurassic and Cretaceous rocks.

Metamorphic Rocks are such geological deposits as have undergone alterations of structure and mineral reorganisation. The most active agents in producing these metamorphic changes are heat, water and pressure. *See* **F9(1).**

Metamorphosis, period of development from egg to adult, during which the animals have different forms, as found, *e.g.,* in the life histories of frog and butterfly.

Meteorites are small bodies, asteroids, or fragments of asteroids, which survive their fiery passage through the earth's atmosphere and hit the ground. The present surfaces of the moon, Mars and Mercury tell us that all the planets have been subjected since their formation to bombardment by meteorites. Though some large craters are still to be found on the earth, most have disappeared due to extensive weathering over thousands of millions of years. In some meteorites iron and nickel are the chief metals (siderites), others are like rock (aerolites). The iron meteorites are more common amongst those which have been preserved, but falls of rock-like meteorites occur more frequently. At L'Aigle in France in 1803 from 2000 to 3000 meteorite stones fell; this fall is famous because it convinced scientists that meteorites really came from outside our atmosphere. The largest meteorite stone actually known to have fallen to earth is one which descended in Emmott County, Iowa, in 1870, weighing 197 kg. A meteorite weighing no less than 37 tonnes found in Greenland is now in New York. On 30 June 1908, an enormous object fell in Siberia in a sparsely-inhabited region. A hot blast destoyed all trees within a radius of about 8–16 km. There is still controversy about the Siberian meteorite, whether it was an asteroid or the nucleus of a small comet.

Meteoroid, a tiny solid object in space. When meteroids are drawn into the atmosphere at high speed by the Earth's gravity they burn up producing a meteor.

Meteorology, the science of the atmosphere considered as a heat engine. Deals with weather, climate, optical phenomena, atmospheric electricity, physical processes such as radiation and precipitation, the dynamics and structure of cyclones, anticyclones, etc. Wide application to problems of aviation, agriculture, commerce and shipping. Meteorological observing stations are in operation all over the world, and on the simultaneous or synoptic reports of their instrument readings and estimates of pressure, temperature, humidity, speed and direction of wind, rain, character and amount of cloud, visibility, etc., forecasts, gale, snow and frost warnings are based. Instruments carried by earth satellites (*e.g., Tiros, Nimbus*) outside the atmosphere can make systematic observations on a worldwide basis of the atmospheric circulation, through observation of cloud cover and of the thermal radiation into space from the atmosphere. Such observations together with the use of computers are of great importance for weather analysis and forecasting. The main communications centre for the UK is at the headquarters of the Meteorological Office at Bracknell, Berkshire, where the collection, editing and re-transmission of weather messages continue according to strict schedules day and night throughout the year.

Meteors or more commonly, "shooting stars", are small objects which enter the upper atmosphere to burn up in a bright streak of light. Their origin is mainly in the dust particles ejected in large quantities from comets. Some, particularly the larger and more brilliant ones, called fireballs, are debris of asteroids. Those which reach the earth's surface are called meteorites (q.v.).

Methane. The simplest hydrocarbon, compounded of one carbon atom and four hydrogen atoms. This gas occurs over marshes and swamps, where it is liberated in the decay of vegetable matter. It is the main constituent of natural gas, and also occurs in coal-mines, where it is called "fire-damp" because of the explosive character of its mixture with air. Formerly this natural gas was removed from the coal seams and ran to waste; now in many countries (including Britain) it is being used for commercial purposes.

Methylated Spirit, a mixture of 90 parts by volume ethyl alcohol, 9¼ parts wood naphtha (methyl alcohol), ¼ part crude pyridine, together with small amounts of petroleum oil and methyl violet dye. Industrial methylated spirit consists of a mixture of 95 parts by volume ethyl alcohol and 5 parts wood naphtha. It is used as a solvent and a fuel.

Metre, the rhythmical pattern of Verse.

Metre, unit of length in the metric system; since 1983 has been redefined as "the length of the path travelled by light in vacuum during a time interval of 1/299 792 458 of a second". This definition replaces that adopted in 1960 which used the wavelength of the orange-red line of krypton-86. Before that the "international prototype metre" was the distance between marks on the platinum-iridium bar placed at Sèvres in 1889.

Metric System, the system of weights and measures based on the gram and the metre, smaller and larger units being decimals and multiples of the primary units respectively. A decimal currency was adopted in France in 1795 and the metric system of weights and measures in 1799. (In that year the quadrant of the earth was surveyed and the standard metre adopted.) Nevertheless the change was accepted slowly, and as late as 1837 the French Government had to pass a law forbidding the use of the old measures. Since then the metric system has been adopted in most of the continental countries and is used universally in scientific work. Although there have been many attempts to get the system adopted in Britain, it was not until 1965 that the Government encouraged the adoption of the metric system of weights and measures. The changeover to decimal coinage was made in 1971; the system of weights and measures in industry is now mainly metric. See **F66–69** for **SI** units.

Mezzotint, a technical method for producing graphic work and works of art. A copper plate is made rough by close cross-hatching, so that a print from it produces an even black. When parts of the cross-hatching are scraped away, these areas will come out white when printed. By skilful use of his tools, the artist or technician can produce pictures finely graded from black to white and with a velvety black as background. The principles of the method were known and practised, for instance, by Rembrandt, but mezzotint became most popular for the reproduction of famous paintings from the end of the 18th cent.

Mica. The mica of commerce is a nearly transparent mineral, which has great heat-resisting power, and can be split into thin plates. The most important micas are muscovite (potassium mica), the commoner variety, phlogopite (magnesium mica) and biotite (the magnesium and iron mica).

Michael, St., and George, St., an order of knighthood originally founded for the Ionian Isles and Malta in 1818, and reorganised in 1869, so as to admit Crown servants connected with the Colonies. The Earl of Derby, Earl Russell and Earl Grey were the first of the new knights.

Michaelmas Day, the festival day of St. Michael and All Angels, 29 September, one of the English quarter days.

Microbe, a term proposed by Sédillot in 1878 to denote any microscopic organism, vegetable or animal, or found on the borderland between the two great natural kingdoms. The term is commonly used, but not by scientists.

Microelectronics, a rapidly developing technology of the 1960s which reduces entire electronic circuits to minute size and embeds them in tiny chips of solid material. These are then called integrated circuits. A circuit, consisting of, say, a dozen transistors and fifty resistors can be built into a small piece of semiconductor (q.v.) measuring not more than a couple of millimetres in any direction. Hundreds of these circuits can be made simultaneously in penny-size wafers of silicon about one-hundredth of an inch thick. There are great advantages in cheapness, reliability, robustness and speed of electronic performance. The small size is in itself an advantage in space vehicles and medical instruments. Applications to missile control systems, computers and communications equipment are no doubt only the first fruits of this new achievement of the current technological revolution.

Micrometer, an instrument for measuring minute distances; usually attached to the eye-pieces of a microscope or telescope, and consisting of two very fine hairs or wires stretched across the field of view, one fixed, the other movable. It was invented by William Gascoigne in the 17th cent. and improved by later inventors. Sir Joseph Whitworth made one in 1858 designed to measure the millionth part of an inch.

Micro-organisms, the collective term applied to several types of organism, the most important of which are fungi, viruses, bacteria and protozoa. It is a classification of convenience in biological studies. These organisms are generally simple in their environmental requirements (e.g., have simple nutritional needs) and in cellular organisation. This makes them very suitable for modern biological research. Much of the information on the nature of the genetic code (**F32(2)**) was obtained from experiments on these organisms.

Microphone, device for converting the acoustic energy of sound waves into waves of electrical energy, used in sound amplifying systems. Developed independently by Edison (1877) and Hughes (1878).

Microscope, invented about 1590 by Janssen, and improved by Galileo, Fontana and others, is an instrument which by a lens system magnifies minute objects. Microscopes are simple, compound and binocular. See also **Electron Microscope.**

Middle Ages (c. A.D. 400–1500), usually considered to be the period between the decline and fall of the Western Roman Empire and the fall of Constantinople to the Turks in 1453. The period covers (a) an earlier part ending with the 12th cent. (sometimes called the Dark Ages) when science was dead, when theology was the main preoccupation, and when the language of the learned West was Latin; and (b) a later age of Arabian influence when alchemy and astrology (at that time indistinguishable from astronomy) were central interests, technology was advancing, and Greek learning was transmitted by Arab scholars. Characteristic features of the mediaeval scene were monasticism (**Section J**), the Crusades (q.v.), Gothic art (q.v.), feudalism (**Section J**), and the supremacy of Islam in the field of learning. The period came to an end with the general decline of Christendom and the ushering in of the Renaissance (**Section J**). The term "Middle Ages" was coined by the 17th-cent. German historian Christoph Keller.

Midrash, name given to the homiletical interpretation of some of the Hebrew Scriptures in which allegory and legendary illustration were freely used. Compiled by Jewish rabbis from c. A.D. 200.

Milky Way. See **Galaxy, L47.**

Millenary Petition was presented to James I in 1603, on behalf of nearly 1000 Puritan Ministers against certain of the rites and ceremonies of the Church of England. The Hampton Court Conference was the outcome of this petition.

Millennium, a period of a thousand years. The term is specifically used of the period of a thousand years during which, according to Rev. xx. 1–5, Christ will reign in person on earth. The Millenarians are a sect that interprets the "Millennium" as beginning with the commencement of the 6001st year from the Creation, which, according to Archbishop Ussher (1581–1650), was in 4004 B.C.

Millipede. Arthropods (**F36**) allied to the centipedes, from which they differ in having two pairs of legs to each body segment (except the first three) instead of one pair. Worm-like in shape but with a pair of antennae on the head, they can do much harm to garden plants, unlike centipedes which are beneficial.

Millstone-Grit, a series of grits and sandstones of deltaic origin underlying the coal measures of the Carboniferous system and attaining in England a thickness in parts of 1,525 m. It is from this rock that millstones have been made from time immemorial.

Mimicry, protective similarity of an animal to another animal or to inanimate objects. Examples of the former are the hover flies, which mimic wasps and bees; of the latter, leaf insects, stick insects and caterpillars that look like dead twigs.

Mink. Semi-aquatic mammals closely related to polecats. There is one American species and one European. The fur, which varies light to dark brown, is soft and thick, and is among the most valuable of commercial furs. They are now well-established in the wild in the British Isles.

Minnesingers were minstrel poets of Germany who, during the 12th and 13th cent., composed and sang verses of heroism and love. They were of knightly rank, the counterpart of the French troubadours.

Minnow, a small fresh-water fish of the carp family, abounding in all the waters of Europe; it has a mottled back and silvery belly, and forms a popular bait for trout.

Minor Planets. *See* **Asteroids, L11**

Minstrels were originally specially appointed instrumentalists and singers—pipers, harpers and gleemen—engaged by barons and manorial lords to amuse their tenants. Later, minstrels assumed nomadic habits, made their way into the houses of the great and were generally welcome. By Elizabeth's time, however, they were too numerous, and were classed as "rogues and vagabonds", along with actors.

Miracle Plays, mediaeval verse plays, popular in England in the 15th cent., were usually religious in character, representing some of the dramatic incidents of the Bible.

Mirage, an optical illusion caused by unequal temperatures in different layers of the atmosphere near the earth's surface. These temperature variations alter the refracting power of the air and cause light rays to be curved, making the air act as a huge distorting lens. This can happen at sea, in deserts and elsewhere and various types of mirage are known. A common kind in deserts curves light from the sky so that it appears to come from the ground, deceiving the observer into thinking that the sky is reflected in a lake of water. Inverted images of hills, trees, etc. also look as if reflected in the non-existent lake.

Mishna, the first part of the Talmud, setting forth the "Oral Law" of the Jews.

Missal, the name of the mass-book of the Roman Church compiled 492–96 by Pope Gelasius I. The missal used until modern times was sanctioned by the Council of Trent, 1546–63, but the current missal was authorised by Pope Paul VI in 1969 after the Second Vatican Council. In the Anglican Communion the Book of Common Prayer superseded the Missal in 1549.

Mistle Thrush receives its name from its partiality to the mistletoe-berry. Larger than the song-thrush, with spotted breast rather than speckled.

Mistletoe, a parasitic evergreen with white berries used as a decoration at Christmas-time. The familiar mistletoe of Europe is the *Viscum album*, which grows on the boughs of lime,

willow, apple, poplar, maple, ash, hawthorn but seldom on oak-trees. It was sacred to the Druids, and in Norse mythology it was a mistletoe dart that killed the god Baldur.

Mistral, a cold, dry, northerly wind peculiar to the French coast of the Mediterranean.

Mitosis, cell division whereby each daughter cell receives the same number of chromosomes as the parent cell. When the gametes (sex cells) are formed a special type of division occurs (meiosis) in which the number of chromosomes is halved. *See* **F34(1).**

Mitre, the twofold pointed head-dress of bishops and certain abbots of the Western Church and occasionally of other ecclesiastics.

Moa, the name for several species of ostrich-like extinct birds related to the New Zealand kiwi. The largest species, *Diornis maximus*, stood 2·6 m high, the smallest, *Anomalopteryx parva*, was nearer the size of a turkey. This wingless bird became extinct several centuries ago because of hunting by the Maoris from whom the name comes.

Moabite Stone, a stone of the 9th cent. B.C. containing the earliest known inscription in Phoenician characters, and discovered in the highlands of Moab in 1868. It is now in the Louvre, Paris. It records the campaign between Moab and Israel (c. 850 B.C.), an account of which is given in the Old Testament (2 Kings 3:27).

Moderator, a material used to slow down neutrons in an atomic pile. Examples of moderators are pure graphite and heavy water. *See* **Nuclear Reactors.**

Mohole Project, a scheme to bore through the earth's crust to take samples of the mantle rocks beneath. Drilling trials, led by an American team of geophysicists, began in 1961 near the island of Guadalupe off the Mexican coast in the Pacific. The project, however, was cancelled in 1966 on account of the escalating cost. Russian geophysicists started on a similar experiment, boring through land rocks where the digging is much deeper and higher temperatures are met with. The name "Anti-Cosmos" was given to the project. The boundary between the earth's crustal and mantle rocks is known as the Mohorovičić Discontinuity, or, more simply, as the Moho. The technology of deep sea drilling came from this project.

Molasses, sugar-cane juice in its uncrystallised form after boiling. The crystallised part is the raw sugar. Used to make rum.

Mole, a small burrowing animal with long, sensitive nose, about the size of a small rat, with short legs and forefeet armed with strong claws for digging in the earth. Their subterranean dwellings are of curiously ingenious construction, and they do not often leave them except to make raids on mice, frogs, snails, etc. The earth-worm, however, is the mole's chief item of food. Not to be confused with the vole which has a blunt nose.

Mole, or gram molecular weight. *See* **F24(1).**

Molecular Biology, a rapidly expanding branch of science mainly concerned with cell structure and function at a molecular level, in particular with genes and enzymes and the interaction between the two. Research work in Britain led to the unravelling of the structure of DNA, the hereditary substance of the genes, and played a major part in uncovering the molecular mechanism of the transfer of hereditary information and the nature of the genetic code. Crystallisation of the first enzyme (urease) took place in 1929; the gene as a definite chemical entity was discovered in 1943. *See* **F29(1).**

Molecule. A group of atoms held together by chemical forces. *See* **F14, F23,** *also* **Macromolecule.**

Molybdenum, element no. 42, symbol Mo, a fairly hard white metal with properties resembling those of chromium. Its commonest ore is the sulphide, molybdenite. The chief use of the metals is in the manufacture of alloy steels.

Monasticism. *See* Section J.

Monazite, a cerium mineral containing some thorium. Occurs as grains, often as sand ("monazite sands"), derived from granites. Deposits occur in India (Travancore), Russia, Norway, Malagasy Rep., S. Africa, Brazil, USA.

Monday, the second day of the week, called by the Anglo-Saxons *Monandaeg* (moon-day).

Mongoose, species of mammals related to the civets, feeding on vermin and reptiles. These animals, which have long tails and short legs, occur in Africa and Asia (especially India). The biggest mongoose is the Egyptian ichneumon, and this has been introduced into the W. Indies because of its ability to kill large poisonous snakes.

Monitor, a family of lizards most resembling dragons. There are about 30 species widely distributed over the tropical parts of Asia, Australia and Africa.

Monroe Doctrine, a principle of American policy declining any European intervention in political affairs of the American continent, outlined by President Monroe in 1823. At the same time interference was disclaimed with existing European colonies in the Western Hemisphere. The American Civil War hampered the application of the doctrine for some time, but afterwards the United States firmly insisted on it. The Doctrine is not international law, but a national policy of the USA.

Monsoons, regular persistent winds which blow at certain seasons in middle latitudes, mainly in South and East Asia. Their occurrence is related to the great changes of pressure which take place between summer and winter over the land mass. In India the south-west monsoon (June–October) is moisture-laden from its long passage over the sea and in the higher regions, especially, there is heavy rainfall. Sudden reversal of the wind results in the cold north-east monsoon (October–March) which is dry on account of the shelter afforded by the mountain ranges to the north. Frequently the term "monsoon" is applied to denote the associated rainfall without reference to the actual winds.

Monstrance, an ornamental transparent receptacle in which the Sacred Host is carried in procession or exposed for adoration.

Month, the 12th part of the calendar year. A lunar month is the interval of new moon to new moon or full moon to full moon; mean length, 29 days, 12 hours, 44 minutes, 2·87 seconds. A sidereal month represents the time of the moon's revolution from a given star back to the same again, 27 days, 7 hours, 43 minutes, 11·5 seconds. In English law, since 1926, a month, unless otherwise expressed, means a calendar month.

Monument of London, a 202 ft (61·6 m) column, overlooking Billingsgate, designed by Wren and erected (1671–77) to mark the starting-point of the Great Fire of London (1666). The original inscription upon it ascribed the fire to "the treachery and malice of the popish faction", which stood until 1831, when the words were erased as objectionable. The black marble staircase has 345 steps (311 to the balcony).

Moon, the earth's satellite, 3,475 km in diameter and 384,400 km distant from the earth. It rotates in the same time as it revolves round the earth (27 days 7 hours 43 minutes), so that the same face is always presented to the earth. The lunar surface is pockmarked by innumerable collisions with solid particles of all sizes. Unlike the earth, it is unprotected by any atmosphere and for aeons of time has been exposed to every kind of cosmic influence, including the parching effect of solar radiation. All moonlight derives from the sun but on the whole it is a pretty poor reflector. The exploration of the moon by means of rockets began in 1959 when the Russian *Luna 2* crashlanded on the plains of the *Mare Imbrium*. 1969 will be remembered as the year of the U.S. *Apollo* triumphs when man first set foot on the moon. The samples of lunar rock and dust brought back to earth by the *Apollo* astronauts and the Soviet *Luna* unmanned automatic stations are being studied by lunar scientists. Samples date back further than any found on Earth as yet. The most famous, known as the Genesis Rock, is 4,100 million years old. The exploration of the moon at close range by means of spacecraft was made possible only by parallel developments in several branches of technology—rocket propulsion, long-range radio and television transmission, electronic computer control.

Moorhen, a widely distributed bird of the rail family, a common resident in the British Isles. The adult is blackish with white under tail coverts, a white line on the flanks and a yellow-tipped bill. The frontal shield and the base of the bill are vermilion. It bobs its head, flirts its tail and dives well. The nest is usually placed close to the water's edge or on an overhanging branch. In feeding the young the parents are sometimes helped by their offspring of a previous brood of the season. In N. America the bird is known as the Florida Gallinule.

Moors, the name given to the Moslems who live in N.W. Africa and to those who once lived in Spain. In 711 Moorish Arabs invaded Spain and spread beyond the Pyrenees into France, where they were driven back by the end of the century. Spain, however, remained virtually under Moorish domination until the 11th cent. and during that period was the most civilised and prosperous part of Western Europe. In the arts and sciences the impact of Moorish culture was profound and lasting. Examples of the brilliant splendour of Moorish architecture are still to be seen in Toledo, Córdoba, Seville and Granada. During the long struggle for the Christian reconquest thousands were killed and expelled, and in 1492 Granada, their last remaining kingdom, was forced to surrender. They were virtually exterminated by the Inquisition, and the last were expelled in 1609.

Moose, the largest members of the deer family. The N. American Moose stands 1·6–2 m high, and has huge palmate antlers. There is another New World species, occurring in Alaska. The European species is known as the elk.

Morse Alphabet, a system of dots and dashes intended to be used in combination with the indicator in telegraphy; but usually read by sound, the receiving operator writing down the words in the system as transmitted. This system of signals was invented by the American inventor and artist Samuel Finley Breese Morse (1791–1872) of Charlestown, Massachusetts.

Mosaic, art of arranging small pieces of coloured glass, marble, or other materials in such a fashion as to produce a decorative pattern. Some of the best examples of Byzantine mosaics are to be seen at Ravenna, Rome, Venice and Sicily.

Mosque, a Mohammedan church, the greatest being that of Santa Sophia at Istanbul, now converted into a museum of Byzantine art.

Mosquito, small two-winged flies with long legs and slender body. Their larvae are aquatic. The females of some species are blood-suckers, and thus come to transmit the blood parasites which cause malaria and yellow fever, for example. *See* **DDT** and **Gammexane.**

Mosses. With liverworts, mosses comprise an important group of relatively simple non-vascular land plants, the bryophytes (**F42**). In the main they are small plants, the largest between 30–70 cm high, having been recorded in the Southern Hemisphere. Mosses rarely occur singly, but usually form cushions or small colonies on moist soil, bark, wood, rock or walls. The genus *sphagnum* known as "peat" or "bog moss" is of commercial value in horticulture. In Lancashire and Cheshire lowland moors in which sphagnum is common are known as "mosses". Reindeer moss is a lichen and Spanish moss a seed plant.

Moths, of the insect order, *Lepidoptera*, differing from butterflies which have clubbed antennae, in having feathery, sometimes thin, pointed antennae, rarely clubbed. Most are nocturnal, and the pupae are usually brown and enclosed in a cocoon unlike those of the butterfly, which are usually naked. *See* **Lepidoptera.**

Motion, Laws of. According to Newton: (1) A body continues in its state of rest or uniform motion in a straight line except in so far as it is compelled by external forces to change that state. (2) Rate of change of momentum is proportional to the applied force, and takes place in the direction in which the force acts. (3) To every action there is an equal and opposite reaction. These laws are the basis of almost all engineering and everyday mechanics. Corrections to them have been made by relativity and the quantum theory. *See* **F17, 19.**

Mule, a cross between a male ass and a horse

mare; a hinny is a cross between an ass mare and a horse stallion. Also the name of the spinning machine invented by Crompton in 1779 which combined the principle of Hargreaves' spinning jenny with the machine invented by Arkwright.

Mullions, the vertical bars dividing the lights in a window, forming a highly decorative feature in the Tudor period of English Gothic architecture. The cross-beam or horizontal bar of wood or stone in a mullioned window is styled a transom. *See* **Windows.**

Munich Agreement. In September 1938 Mr. Neville Chamberlain and M. Daladier, British and French Premiers, reached agreement with Hitler at Munich for the dismemberment of Czechoslovakia, primarily for the benefit of Germany. Czechoslovakia itself was not consulted, nor Russia who with Britain and France had jointly pledged themselves to uphold the independence of Czechoslovakia. Mr. Chamberlain declared on return that he had secured "Peace in our Time".

Muscles. *See* **F37**(1).

Musk Deer, a small deer of the Himalayas, standing about 51 cm high. It is grey in colour, slightly brindled, and carries a small pouch in the abdominal region, containing what is commercially known as musk, an article which is of great value in the manufacture of various perfumes. The active constituent of musk, muscone, is now made synthetically. The species has become rare on account of its slaughter for its musk.

Mutton Bird, an Australian name of controversial origin for a shearwater or petrel, *e.g.,* the Short-tailed and Sooty Shearwaters and the Great-winged, Kermadec, and White-headed Petrels. The young are taken by hand from their burrows for human food.

Myrrh, a resinous substance obtained from a tree of the natural order *Amyridaceae,* growing plentifully in Ethiopia and Arabia. Its use for embalming, medical and aromatic purposes may be traced back to the most remote times.

Mysteries, Greek, secret mystic ceremonies of the ancient Greeks, religious drama accompanied by dancing, the most well known being the Eleusinian and Orphic ceremonies.

Mystery Plays were mediaeval religious dramas performed at great ecclesiastical festivals, particularly in France and Bavaria, staging the Nativity, Passion and Resurrection stories.

N

Nadir, one of the two poles of the horizon, the other being the zenith. The nadir is the pole vertically below the observer's feet.

Nahum, one of the books of the Minor Prophets of the Old Testament. It is a prophecy of doom on the approaching sack of Nineveh which fell in 612 B.C. to the Medes and Babylonians.

Nantes, Edict of, was a decree promulgated by Henry IV of France in 1598, giving full freedom of worship to the Protestants of the country. It was the revocation of this edict in 1685 by Louis XIV that drove hundreds of thousands of French Huguenots to this country.

Naphtha, a liquid combustible believed to have been one of the ingredients of "Greek fire". Naphtha is a light, highly inflammable oil obtained by distilling petroleum, shale oil, or coal tar. The petroleum naphtha consists of a mixture of paraffins; that from shale contains olefines as well as paraffins. Coal-tar naphtha contains xylol.

Naphthalene is an aromatic hydrocarbon; it is obtained from coal tar, and its derivatives are much used in the manufactures of colours for dyers and printers. "Moth balls" are made of naphthalene.

Narcotic, a medical dictionary definition is that a narcotic is a drug that produces stupor; complete insanity or sleep. In terms of drug addiction, it has been defined as altering the user's perception of himself and of the external

world, being taken primarily for that purpose.

Nardus, a genus of coarse grasses, growing on bleak upland heaths and hill slopes. *Nardus stricta,* known as "mat-weed", is a British species.

Narghile, an oriental tobacco pipe so constructed that smoke passes through water and up a long flexible tube before reaching lips of the smoker.

Narrative Art, a type of art popular during the late 19th cent. based on the principle: "every picture tells a story"—*e.g.,* such paintings as the little Royalist boy surrounded by his anxious family and confronted across a table by the Roundheads bearing the title: "When did you last see your father?" The term, although often applied derisively, suitably describes many works of considerable artistic merit: *e.g.,* Hogarth's *Marriage à la Mode,* the Bayeux Tapestry, *etc.*

Naseby, Battle of, was fought on 14 June 1645, between the Royalists under the command of Prince Rupert and the King, and the Parliamentarians under Fairfax and Cromwell. Charles I was decisively defeated.

National Anthem, a musical composition with words, officially adopted for ceremonial use as an expression of patriotism and loyalty to a national cause. The national anthem of the United Kingdom, "God save the King (Queen)", probably dates from the late-17th cent, to mid-18th cent. It was sung in 1745, the year of the landing of the Young Pretender. It had no one composer and was probably a recasting of folk-tunes and plainsong. Resemblances can be traced in pieces by Purcell and John Bull.

National Assembly, the name taken by the body responsible for the opening stages of the French Revolution and subsequently by other sovereign bodies in France and elsewhere.

National Covenant, an oath and declaration subscribed to by the Scottish Presbyterians in 1638 to maintain their religion against Charles I.

National Curriculum. The Education Reform Act (1988) originally provided for a national curriculum in state schools in England and Wales with three *core subjects* – maths, English and science – and seven *foundation subjects* – history, geography, technology, music, art, physical education, and a modern language. The compulsory curriculum has now been reduced (history and geography are no longer compulsory after 14) and attempts to reduce teachers' workloads have been made.

National Forest, a new forest given approval by the government in 1994. The National Forest area covers 194 sq. miles in Derbyshire, Leicestershire and Staffordshire. The aim is to plant one-third of the area with trees.

National Gallery, established in 1824 at Pall Mall, London, with the Angerstein Collection of 38 pictures, purchased for £60,000, as a nucleus. The existing building which was opened in 1838 has been enlarged several times. The National Gallery at Millbank, the Tate Gallery, was given to the nation by Sir Henry Tate in 1897.

Nationalisation is the taking over by the State of the ownership and operation of an industry or service—*e.g.,* coal-mining, railways, transport, gas and electricity. The administration of the nationalised service is usually by a publicly appointed Board or Corporation acting, with greater or lesser autonomy, under the direction of a Minister responsible to Parliament. Many nationalised industries have now been privatised.

National Lottery, proposed in 1992 Budget. The first National Lottery draw was on 19 November 1994. It hopes to raise £2 billion annually to support sport, buy art treasures, restore churches *etc.* The last previous national lottery in Britain was in 1826. All European countries (except Albania), and 22 U.S. states, have similar schemes. Oflot is the Office of the National Lottery whose director is Peter Davis.

National Marine Reserves *See* **Marine Nature Reserves.**

National Parks. Under the National Parks Act 1949 a National Parks Commission was set up to create National Parks in England and Wales. Ten have been established: Peak District, Lake District, Snowdonia, Yorkshire Dales, Exmoor, Brecon Beacons, Dartmoor, Pembrokeshire Coast, North York Moors and Northumberland. They cover an area of some 13,618 km², or 9 per cent of the total area of England and Wales. It is not intended to change the character of these territories but to control their development so as to harmonise with the two dominant principles: (a) that the characteristic beauty of the landscape within the Park area shall be preserved and (b) that the visiting public shall have ample access and facilities for recreation and enjoyment. The establishment of a new national park has been proposed for mid-Wales. The Commission also has power to designate areas in England and Wales outside the national parks as "areas of outstanding natural beauty". Thirty-three areas had been designated by 1977. Under the Countryside Act, 1968, the National Parks Commission was reconstituted as the Countryside Commission. In 1988, a special authority was established to manage the 120 miles of waterways constituting the Norfolk Broads and in 1991 national park status was granted to the New Forest. Pressure is now (1995) growing for National Parks to be established in Scotland (e.g. in the Cairngorms, Loch Lomond, Ben Nevis and Wester Ross). A new National Parks Bill was introduced in 1994. See also **Long Distance Walks** and **Marine Nature Reserves**.

National Physical Laboratory, situated at Teddington, is one of the world's largest and best-equipped laboratories. It conducts research in its three main groups: Measurement, Materials and Engineering Sciences, and maintains British primary standards and physical units. First established in 1900 and managed by the Royal Society. Under privatisation it became an Executive Agency in 1990.

National Portrait Gallery, established in 1856, and now located in a building in St. Martin's Lane adjoining the National Gallery. Contains portraits of eminent people in British history and a valuable collection of medals and autographs.

National Rivers Authority (NRA), established in July 1989, has overall responsibility for the management of rivers, water resources and water environment. It operates via 10 regional units. In April 1996 the NRA is set to become part of the new Environment Agency.

National Trust, founded in 1895. "A non-profit-making organisation incorporated by Act of Parliament for the purposes of promoting the permanent preservation of lands and buildings of historic interest or natural beauty for the benefit and access of the people." As a consequence of gifts and public-spirited individuals the Trust now owns many hectares of magnificent scenery and property. Since 1946 lands and houses may be given to the National Trust in lieu of death duties. The Trust celebrated its centenary in 1995, with a membership of 2·2m.

Nativity. There are three nativity festivals of the Christian Church: Christmas, 25 December, festival of birth of Christ; birthday of the Virgin Mary (8 Sept.); and St. John the Baptist (24 June).

NATO, the North Atlantic Treaty Organisation, established 4 April 1949. A defence grouping of Western European states, America and Canada. Britain is a member. The Russian equivalent was the Warsaw Pact (signed 1955, disbanded, 1991). NATO's Secretary-General is Willy Claes. Its first offensive action was in Bosnia in March 1994.

Natterjack, a curious warty, prominent-eyed, brown toad (Bufo calamita), having a bright yellow line down the middle of its back. It utters a muttering sort of croak, hence its name.

Naturalism in painting has been defined as "a direct and spontaneous approach to nature" —to landscape primarily. Constable, Turner and Boudin were among the great naturalist painters of the 19th cent.

Natural Numbers, the counting numbers 1, 2, 3, 4, 5, . . .

"Nautical Almanac", published under the authority of the Admiralty, is always issued four years in advance, and contains information specially prepared for the use of navigators and astronomers. It first appeared in 1767.

Nautilus, a term now applied only to the pearly-shelled nautilus, the sole surviving example of the four-gilled section of the Cephalopoda. Its fossil relatives are called Ammonites. The spiral shell is divided into a number of compartments, the animal living in the last and largest chamber. There are three or four species, all living in tropical seas. The Paper Nautilus is not related to the Pearly Nautilus, belonging to the same order as the octopus.

Nave is the body or main open portion of a cathedral or church, and extends from the chief entrance to the choir, or chancel, and is usually flanked by aisles.

Neanderthal, the name of the valley lying between Düsseldorf and Wuppertal, where in a limestone cave a skull of a very early species of prehistoric man was discovered in 1856.

Nebula, a cloud of gas and dust in space. There are three basic types; emission nebulae create their own light, shining through the effects of very hot stars embedded within them; dust particles within reflection nebulae simply reflect the light from accompanying stars; dark nebulae contain no stars and appear as dark patches against a brighter background.

Nekton, term used to differentiate actively swimming aquatic organisms (e.g., fishes) from the "drifters" or plankton.

Nelson Column, in Trafalgar Square, London, designed by Mr. William Railton, was chosen from among a number of designs—temples, obelisks and various sculptural groups—sent in as a result of a competition held in 1839. The erection of the column was begun in 1840. Twenty-six years later the lions designed by Landseer were set up at the foot of the completed column. The statue of Nelson himself was made by E. H. Bailey and the bronze reliefs at the base executed by Carew, Woodington, Ternouth and Watson, representing the Battles of the Nile, St. Vincent, Copenhagen and Trafalgar. Height 52 m, executed in Dartmoor granite from Foggin Tor quarries, at a cost of £46,000.

Néné or **Hawaiian Goose**. At the Severn Wildfowl Trust at Slimbridge Sir Peter Scott saved this bird from extinction.

Neo-Classical Style, term applied to the revival of classical logic and order after the extravagances of Rococo (q.v.), beginning in France in the mid-18th cent. and finding expression in architecture and the decorative arts. The style retains some of the daintiness of Rococo, furniture is on a small scale, often gilt, and silks and porcelain favour pastel shades. Straight lines take the place of the wild curvatures of Rococo and classical details like festoons and urn forms are used in many contexts and materials. Its English version is closely associated with the name of the architect Robert Adam whose light and graceful adaptations of Greek and Roman forms were introduced into English country houses. In France the style is sometimes called Style Louis XVI. Eventually the Neo-Classical style merges into Empire (q.v.).

Neodymium, element no. 60, symbol Nd, belonging to the rare earth metals. Discovered 1885. Named after the Greek word for 'new twin', from twin lines in its spectrum.

Neo-Impressionism, a development of Impressionism (q.v.) by Seurat and Signac during the 1880s who devised the method of painting known as pointillism (the application of pure colours in minute touches to form a composite whole, based on a knowledge of the laws of colour and optics). One of the best-known examples of this technique is Seurat's Sunday Afternoon on the Grand Jatte.

Neon, inert gas present in air to the extent of about 1 part in 65,000. The crimson glow produced when an electric discharge passes through the gas is familiar in advertising signs. Element no. 10, symbol Ne.

Nepotism, the bestowal of patronage by reason of relationship rather than of merit.

Neptune. Apart from Pluto this is the most distant of the planets, estimated to be about $4,497 \times 10^{6}$ km from the sun, and taking about 165 years to revolve around it. Discovered by the German astronomers Galle and D'Arrest in Sept. 1846, after its existence had been predicted by Leverrier and Adams. The planet was visited by Voyager 2 in 1989, its last planetary stop. This revealed Neptune had eight moons (not just Triton and Nereid as previously thought) and a ring system. Its diameter is 49,528 km. A huge Earth-sized storm has been observed, which has been named the 'Great Dark Spot'.

Neptunium, element no. 93, symbol Np, one of the

four new elements discovered during the progress of the atomic bomb project in the second world war, Neptunium is formed when a neutron enters nucleus of Uranium 238, and it decays radioactively to yield plutonium.

Neutrino, a neutral particle which carries energy and spin and although possessing little or no mass plays an important part in the interaction of other fundamental particles. The discovery that there are in fact two distinct neutrinos, each with its counterpart, was discovered in 1962 as a result of an experiment made with the 30,000 million-electronvolt proton accelerator at Brookhaven. *See* **F16.**

Neutron, a neutral particle present in all atomic nuclei except the hydrogen nucleus which is a single proton. In the development of nuclear science and technology the neutron has played a most important role and neutrons produce the radioisotopes now widely used in medicine, agriculture and industry. Neutrons and protons are termed nucleons. *See* **F11(2), 16.**

Neutron Bomb, a thermonuclear fusion weapon which produces increased lethal radiation while the destructive blast and fallout are significantly less than for a fission weapon of equivalent yield; it kills organic life while sparing property, except within a small radius. In 1978 President Carter reserved his decision on production; in 1981 the new Reagan administration decided to go ahead and stockpile the weapon. *See also* **F13(2).**

New Deal. The measures taken by President Roosevelt in USA in 1933 to overcome the great economic crisis which broke out at the end of 1929 and to restore the social security threatened by it. The measures were drawn up by a group of experts called a Brains Trust and they provided for recovery by a programme of public works, including large-scale construction of houses and large-scale assistance to farmers. Loans were granted and authorities formed to stimulate activities which reduced the workless from 17 millions to between 7 and 10 millions. Unemployment relief was regulated and enlarged; and social insurance (which for decades had been a subject of dispute, being held to be contrary to American principles of self-help) was introduced.

Newgate Prison was situated at the western end of Newgate Street, opposite the Old Bailey at the site of one of the old London city gates. There is a record of a prison upon this spot in the 13th cent. Later a new one was built by the executors of Richard Whittington, but this was destroyed by the Great Fire in 1666. Still another new prison on this site was erected between 1778 and 1780. In the Gordon Riots of the latter year it was destroyed by fire and re-erected. It was not used as a prison after 1880 and was demolished in 1902–3.

Newspapers. The first news-books to be published at regular intervals in Britain appeared in 1662 with news of what was going on abroad translated from German and Italian news-sheets. Licence to print was obtained from the Star Chamber, which until its abolition in 1641 allowed only the printing of foreign news. With the lifting of the ban on domestic news the Press became free. In the reign of Queen Anne English newspapers employed writers of great intellectual power and versatility. Despite the newspaper tax introduced in 1712, the number of newspapers published in London in 1776 had increased to 53, though the standard of writing was below that of earlier times. The development of the Press was greatly assisted in the 19th cent. by the abolition of the "taxes on knowledge", by the introduction of the cheap postal system and by improvements in printing, distribution, collection of news and advertising. The *London Gazette*, founded in 1665 (and still appearing twice weekly as the official organ of the Government), is the oldest newspaper living. *The Times*, known throughout the world, began as the *Daily Universal Register* in 1785, and adopted its present title in 1788. The *Manchester Guardian* (renamed *Guardian* in 1959), began as a weekly in 1821, and became a daily in 1855. The *Scotsman*, founded as a weekly in 1817 and established as a daily in 1855, and the *Glasgow Herald*, which began as the *Glasgow Advertiser* in 1783, are the leading Scottish newspapers. The first evening newspaper, the *Star and Evening Advertiser* was published in London in 1788. During 1989, the last national newspapers left Fleet St. In 1993 *The Guardian* acquired *The Observer*.

Newt, amphibian of lizard shape and mottled markings. There are three British species, the largest being the Great-Crested Newt (*Triturus cristatus*), which attains a length of 15 cm.

Newton, the unit of force in the SI system of units. Under its influence a body with a mass of 1 kilogram will accelerate at a rate of 1 metre per second each second.

Newton's Rings. Concentric circular rings, due to the phenomenon of interference, which are seen around the point of contact of a slightly convex lens with a flat plate of glass.

New Towns. Under the New Town Act 1946 and subsequent Acts some 33 new towns were designated in Britain; 23 are in England and Wales, five in Scotland and four in Northern Ireland. They are: Basildon, Bracknell, Crawley, Harlow, Hatfield, Hemel Hempstead, Milton Keynes, Northampton, Peterborough, Stevenage and Welwyn (to relieve housing problems in the Greater London area); Aycliffe, Corby, Cwmbran, Peterlee and Washington (to serve the special needs of their areas); Newtown (to help stem rural depopulation in mid-Wales); Runcorn and Skelmersdale (to meet the overspill needs of Liverpool and north Merseyside); Telford and Redditch (to take population from Birmingham); Warrington (expanded to take people from Liverpool and Manchester); Central Lancashire New Town (new regional city based on existing towns of Preston, Leyland and Chorley). The five Scottish new towns are Cumbernauld, East Kilbride, Glenrothes, Irvine and Livingston. In Northern Ireland Craigavon is being developed as a new city; Antrim and Ballymena are becoming centres of economic growth; Londonderry and the surrounding district have been designated as an area of special development. A major reversal in Government policy was announced in 1976 to the effect that development resources in future were to be directed towards inner-city areas.

New Year's Day, 1 January. The first New Year's festival of which we have record is that constituted by Numa 713 B.C., and dedicated to Janus.

Nibelungenlied, the German epic of the early 13th cent. comprising numerous mythical poems or sagas. Wagner's *The Ring of the Nibelungs* was based on Norse legends and the Nibelungenlied.

Nicene Creed, a summary of the principles of Christian faith, first issued in 325 by the Council of Nicaea (summoned by the emperor Constantine the Great) for the purpose of thwarting the Arian heresy and asserting the godhead of Christ. Date of Easter fixed at Council of Nicaea.

Nickel, silver-coloured metallic element, no. 28, symbol Ni, fairly soft though harder than iron. Chief source of the metal is the nickel sulphide in iron-copper pyrites deposits in Ontario. Chief uses are: in electroplating, in coins, as an element in alloy steels. A novel method of making pure nickel (by treating the metal with carbon monoxide and heating the resulting liquid, nickel carbonyl) was developed in 1890 by Mond. This discovery led to many technical advances in industrial chemistry, one of which is the production of catalysts. Discovered by Crondstedt in 1751 as an impurity in copper ore. Substituted for silver in French coinage in about 1882.

Night Heron, a stocky, short-legged heron of black and white plumage, red eyes and yellowish legs, crepuscular except in breeding season, and an occasional visitor to Britain.

Nightingale, a familiar singing bird which visits the southern counties of England every summer, and is sometimes found as far north as Yorkshire. It is a shy, brown bird, not often seen, but the song of the male, usually heard in the late evening or at early morn, is of remarkable sweetness and variety. After its wooing period is over its song ceases.

Nightjar, nocturnal, insectivorous bird, owl-like in appearance, with mottled brown plumage of "dead leaf" pattern, and a churring song. It is a common breeding visitor to the British Isles,

April to September, laying its eggs on bare ground.

Niobium is a metal element, no. 41, symbol Nb, related to vanadium. Technical development has been slow because of its rare occurrence, although niobium is now used in ferrous alloys to increase resistance to corrosion and produce steel which can be used at high temperatures.

Nitre or **Saltpetre,** is now mostly manufactured by the double decomposition of sodium nitrate and potassium chloride. Its chief use is the manufacture of gunpowder and fireworks. It has been manufactured in England since 1625.

Nitrogen, a non-combustible gaseous element, no. 7, symbol N, devoid of taste or smell, and constituting nearly four-fifths of the atmospheric air. Nitrogen compounds are essential to plants and animals, and are used in fertilisers.

Nitro-Glycerine, an explosive yellow fluid produced by mixing small quantities of glycerine with a combination of one part of nitric acid and two parts of sulphuric acid. By itself it is a dangerously explosive substance to handle. In 1867, Nobel produced dynamite, a safe explosive made by absorbing nitro-glycerine in kieselguhr.

Nitrous Oxide, a compound of nitrogen and oxygen possessing mild anaesthetic power. Termed "laughing gas" on account of its exhilarating effect. It is still used in dentistry, and for minor operations and has proved useful in a new technique for finding leaks in water mains.

Nobel Prizes. The Nobel Foundation was established at the beginning of the century to give effect to the wishes expressed by Alfred Nobel in his Will. By the terms of the Will the judges are the Swedish Academy of Science, the Caroline Medico-Surgical Institute, the Swedish Academy and five members of the Norwegian Storting. The award of a Nobel Prize is accepted as the highest form of international recognition in the field in which it is given: physics, chemistry, medicine, literature, peace and, since 1969, economics.

Nones were dates of the Roman calendar which fell on the 5th of each month, excepting March, May, July and October, when they fell on the 7th.

Norman Architecture is English Romanesque (q.v.), which flourished from the time of the Norman Conquest and was gradually superseded through a transition period (c. 1175–1200) by the introduction of the pointed arch characteristic of the Early English (first Gothic style). Typical of Norman churches are the round arches, thick walls, massive cylindrical columns, with throughout the basic pattern of the square and the circle. Some churches (e.g., the Temple church in London or the chapel at Ludlow Castle) were wholly circular. Roofs in the early days were flat and towers, usually placed at the "crossing", were square but occasionally round; the spire of all these towers have perished, but it seems likely that they were squat and pyramidal.

North-East Passage, from the North Atlantic to Bering Strait has been rapidly developed by the USSR in recent years as a northern sea route to render accessible vast areas of northern Siberia. Attempts to find a North-East passage were made by Englishmen and Dutchmen in the 16th cent. but they were always defeated by the ice, for the sea is completely frozen for some 4,800 km for 9 months of the year. A Swede succeeded in sailing from Europe to Japan via the Arctic in the late 19th cent. See also **Arctic Exploration.**

North-West Passage, from the Atlantic to the Pacific through the Arctic Seas, has been the dream of navigators for centuries. Attempts to find it were made in the 16th and early 17th cent. by John and Sebastian Cabot, Frobisher, Gilbert, Davis, Hudson and Baffin. Two centuries later Ross, Parry, Franklin and others made the attempt; but it was not until 1903-5 that Amundsen, discoverer of the South Pole, made the complete voyage in the *Gjoa.* The Canadian icebreaker *Labrador* was the first deepdraft vessel to traverse the North-West Passage (1954) and the US tanker *Manhattan* was the first commercial vessel to do so (1969).

Notre Dame, the famous Paris cathedral, was founded in 1163, and is one of the finest specimens of Gothic architecture in Europe.

November, the 9th month of the year originally, but from c. 700 B.C., when Numa added January and February, it became the 11th month.

Nuclear Energy. Atomic nuclei consist of protons and neutrons joined in various proportions (**F11**). The heaviest naturally occurring nucleus contains 238 particles (92 protons, 146 neutrons) and is uranium 238 (U^{238}); the lightest is hydrogen, which consists of 1 proton. Neutrons and protons attract one another by very strong forces which are not at all well understood; they are called *nuclear forces.* Consequently it requires energy to be supplied if a nucleus is to be pulled apart into its constituent particles. The energy is required to overcome the attractions of the nuclear forces. Conversely, when the particles rush together to form a nucleus energy is released in the form of heat or radiation. The energy released when protons and neutrons coalesce to form a nucleus is called *Binding Energy.* The binding energy of a nucleus divided by the number of particles involved is called the binding energy per particle, which we will call B. It is very difficult to overestimate the importance of B to the human race. B varies from nucleus to nucleus, and the exact form of its variation is only roughly understood at the present time. But the most significant thing is that B is greatest for elements of medium atomic weight and lowest at the heavy (uranium) and light (hydrogen) ends of the periodic table. This means that if middleweight nuclei can be formed either from heavy ones or from light ones, B increases and energy is released in either case.

Nuclear Fission. See **F13**(1).

Nuclear Fusion. If light nuclei are hurled at high speeds into intimate contact they sometimes coalesce and release binding energy (*see* **Nuclear Energy**). This has been studied in laboratories where powerful and energy-consuming machines accelerate small numbers of particles for purely experimental purposes. If useful amounts of energy are to be gained these fusion reactions will have to occur on a bigger scale in an apparatus from which the resulting heat can be extracted in a controlled way. The one "useful" fusion device so far made is the thermonuclear bomb ("H-bomb"). Thermonuclear is the important word. If a suitable gas can be raised to a very high temperature the nuclei are stripped of their electrons and all particles move with very high speeds. The gas is then called a plasma. High enough temperatures will make speeds great enough for fusion reactions to occur and nuclear energy to be released. This is a thermonuclear reaction. For example, in deuterium gas, at temperatures over a million degrees Centigrade, the deuterium nuclei (i.e., heavy hydrogen nuclei consisting of 1 proton joined to 1 neutron) interact to produce helium nuclei. To obtain a net gain in energy from this process, the temperature must be raised to about 100 million degrees C and maintained long enough; otherwise the energy released is less than that required to heat the fuel and to make up for heat losses. Many attempts to study the staggering technical problems are being made, and fusion research is very active in Britain, the USA, Japan and the Russian Federation. The joint European Torus (JET) fusion research project sited at Culham near Oxford aims to develop a new source of energy for the generation of electricity for the 21st cent. In 1991, the JET project achieved a two minute successful nuclear fusion, bringing nearer the prospect of new energy sources.

Nuclear Power Stations. In 1994 Britain generated some 22 per cent of her electricity for public supply in nuclear power stations. There are 13 nuclear power stations which produce electricity for the national grid controlled by the electricity authorities and four controlled by the Atomic Energy Authority or British Nuclear Fuels plc. Seven of the 13 nuclear power stations are operated by the electricity authorities are at Bradwell, Essex (1962), Hunterston "A", Scotland (1964), Hinkley Point "A", Somerset (1965), Dungeness "A", Kent (1966), Sizewell, Suffolk (1966), Oldbury, Avon (1968) and Wylfa, Anglesey (1970).

They have all been developed from the classic Calder Hall type, burning natural uranium inserted in a graphite moderator and cooled by carbon dioxide gas. They are called Magnox stations because the fuel elements of natural uranium rods are encased in magnesium alloy cans. A second nuclear power programme is based on the advanced gas cooled reactor (AGR) at Windscale, and include the reactors at Dungeness "B", (1983) and those at Hinkley Point "B", Hunterston "B", Hartlepool (Cleveland) and Heysham (Lancashire). In 1987, after the Layfield Report, the Government gave approval for the Sizewell B project which will be Britain's first pressurised water reactor. Closure of the Berkeley (Gloucs) nuclear power station, built in 1962, began in 1989. In November 1989, AGRs and the Sizewell B PWR were withdrawn from planned privatisation. In 1994 the Government gave the go-ahead for the controversial Thorp nuclear reprocessing plant at Sellafield. The Sizewell B PWR became Britain's latest (and possibly last) nuclear power station in February 1995. In May 1995, the Government published a White Paper setting out proposals for the partial privatisation of the nuclear power industry.

Nuclear Reactors are pieces of apparatus designed to permit nuclear chain reactions to occur under controlled conditions. (Uncontrolled chain reactions are dangerous, *e.g.* atomic bombs.) The success of a reactor depends on the neutrons reaching the U^{235} nuclei to produce more fissions and not being wasted in irrelevant processes or simply escaping through the wall of the apparatus (neutrons are quite difficult to contain). The neutrons leaving the scene of fission are rapidly moving, and they stand more chance of causing another fission if they are slowed down. Consequently a material other than the uranium has to be present to facilitate this, and it is called a moderator. A useful moderator is pure graphite. Thus a reactor may consist of alternate blocks of uranium and graphite. If the reactor is too small so many neutrons escape that there are not enough to keep the chain reaction going. The reactor must therefore be greater than a certain *critical size*. In order to intensify or damp down the chain reaction it is arranged for pieces of neutron-absorbing material, such as cadmium, to be inserted or withdrawn as required. While the chain reaction is proceeding countless numbers of fissions are occurring, each one liberating energy which turns into heat. The temperature therefore increases, and to prevent a catastrophic rise, cooling has to be provided. The reactor therefore has cooling pipes through which a fluid coolant is pumped. The coolant carries the heat away and, in a reactor designed to produce electrical power, the heat is taken to steam-raising boilers which the high-pressure steam is led to turbines which drive the electric generators. What has been briefly described is the type of reactor first used for serious power production at Calder Hall (1956). This is a graphite-moderated, gas-cooled reactor using as fuel natural uranium (*i.e.*, fissile U^{235} greatly diluted with U^{238}). Other thermal types of nuclear reactor are the advanced gas-cooled reactor (AGR), the high temperature reactor (HTR), the steam-generating heavy-water (SGHWR) and the light-water reactor (LWR). It is also possible to make reactors work without slowing the neutrons with a moderator; these are called *fast reactors*. The design of the prototype fast reactor (PFR) at Dounreay was based on experience gained with the Dounreay experimental fast breeder reactor (closed 1977 after 17 years' safe operation) which was the first to produce electricity on a commercial scale (1962) and achieved the highest power output of any of its type in the world. These fast reactors can produce new nuclear fuel in the course of their operation and therefore offer great economies; but they are more difficult to develop than thermal reactors. The fuel is made from the mixed oxides of plutonium and uranium and the coolant is liquid sodium metal.

Environmental considerations are likely to be increasingly topical. Most of the products of the fission process are of necessity radioactive isotopes: they could be gaseous, like krypton, xenon and tritium or solid like strontium, caesium, zirconium and ruthenium. There are also present the new radioactive elements plutonium, curium,

actinium, etc. Further, in both the nuclear reactor and in the plant which is used to chemically treat and reprocess the nuclear fuel, radioactivity will be induced in associated structural materials, to varying degrees. In this latter case, unlike the former, the radioactive waste with which one is left can to a great extent be selected and is largely overshadowed in importance by the waste arising from the fission and breeding processes. Even if the whole of the UK electrical power was produced by nuclear means, the volumes of such wastes would be relatively small and need in principle tens of acres of storage area. Much of the activity would decay in a decade, a great deal more in a century, but that associated with the elements bred from uranium, would be present for thousands of years: Pu^{239} has a half-life of 25,000 years. Segregation of the various types of activity is feasible; their incorporation into physically and chemically stable form has received a great deal of study so that storage, readily monitored even for many generations, seems entirely possible. The radioactive properties of these wastes can only be changed by nuclear reactions. Bombardment with neutrons or other highly energetic particles can bring about such reactions so that forms of "nuclear incineration" are feasible but are not yet fully explored.

Nucleic Acids. Living matter is built up of cells each of which has a nucleus surrounded by cytoplasm. Cell nuclei are composed chiefly of substances called nucleoproteins, which consist of a protein attached to a nucleic acid (this original name is still used, although nucleic acids are found in the cytoplasm as well as the nucleus). Nucleic acids are complex organic structures made up of chains of compounds called nucleotides (**F32**(2)). Nucleotide molecules have a sugar group attached to a nitrogenous base and a phosphate group. Only two sugar groups are found in the nucleotides, ribose, giving rise to ribonucleic acids (RNAs, found mainly in the cytoplasm) and deoxyribose, which forms deoxyribonucleic acids (DNAs, found mainly in cell nuclei). Seven different nitrogenous bases have been isolated, so that a number of different nucleotides are possible. A repeating, regular pattern of nucleotides is linked by the phosphate groups, forming nucleic acids. The functions of nucleic acids are of fundamental importance. They are concerned in the process of transmission of inherited qualities in reproduction and in building up body proteins. *See* **F34**.

Nuremberg Trial. On 21 November 1945, an International Military Tribunal, consisting of one American, one British, one Russian and one French member, began the trial of twenty-four Nazi leaders. Twelve were condemned to hanging of whom ten were hanged on 16 October 1946. Goering committed suicide; Bormann is now dead; Papen, Schacht and Fritsche were acquitted. The rest received varying terms of imprisonment.

Nuthatch, name of a number of tree-creeping birds, plump, with a short tail, bluish-grey plumage and black stripe under eye. Nest in holes and wedge nuts in bark of trees, hammering them to get a kernel. There are three European species, one, *Sitta europaea*, resident in England.

Nylon, a generic term for any long-chain synthetic polymeric amide which has recurring amide groups as an integral part of the main polymer chain, and which is capable of being formed into a filament in which the structural elements are orientated in the direction of the axis. The first nylon of commercial interest was made in 1935, and the world's first nylon factory—in the United States—began production in 1940.

O

Oak, a tree of the genus *Quercus*, including some 300 species distributed over the northern hemisphere and into the tropics. Two species are native to Britain, where the oak is the commonest tree (1 in 3)—*Q. petraea*, more common in the west and north on shallower, lighter soils, and *Q. robur*, more common in the south on deeper, heavier soils. Oak timber is much prized for its strength and durability, and from the time of the Spanish Armada to Nelson's day was in great demand for naval construction. It has always been used for building, flooring, furniture and cabinet work. The oak is attacked by many insects, the round nut-like oak galls, or oak-apples, being produced by the sting of certain minute gall wasps.

"Oaks", a famous race for three-year-old fillies run at Epsom three days after the "Derby".

Obelisk, a tapering monolithic column, square at the base and pyramidal at the top, regarded by the ancient Egyptians as a sacred stone and usually found at the entrance to the sun temples. Many were transported from Egypt and set up at various times; there is one in the Place de la Concorde in Paris, and one on the Embankment in London—Cleopatra's Needle—originally erected at Heliopolis, centre of the sun-cult, by Tuthmosis III *c.* 1500 B.C.

Observatories. *See* Astronomy *and* Telescope.

Occam's Razor. *See* Section J.

Occultation, the passage of one celestial object in front of another, where the closer object has a larger apparent diameter than the more distant one and which, therefore, temporarily hides it from view. An example is the passage of the Moon across the Sun during a total solar eclipse.

Ocean, comprises the great body of water which covers seven-tenths of the surface of the earth, and has an average depth of 3·2 km. The principal oceans are the Pacific, Atlantic, Indian and Arctic. The greatest ocean depth is in the Pacific, in the Mindanao Deep, 37,782 ft (11,524 m).

Ocean Currents are well-defined streams running over certain portions of the ocean and caused mainly by wind-friction, slope of the sea surface and differences in density of the water, all movements being influenced by the deflective forces due to the earth's rotation. The climatic importance of the great ocean currents is that they constitute one means whereby heat is transferred from lower to higher latitudes.

Oceanography is the scientific study of the world ocean, *i.e.*, the single connected body of water that covers 70·8 per cent of the earth's surface. Modern oceanography dates from the voyage of HMS *Challenger* (1872–6) during which wideranging observations of the ocean were made, for the first time going well beyond what was directly required to assist shipping. Since then oceanography has matured into a highly technical and interdisciplinary science which may be roughly divided into: biological oceanography (the study of marine organisms and marine ecology); chemical oceanography (concerned with the composition of sea-water); physical oceanography (the study of ocean currents, tides and waves and the role played by the oceans in climate and weather); and geological oceanography (concerned with the formation, composition and evolution of the ocean basins). Oceanographic knowledge is essential to allow exploitation of the enormous food, mineral and energy resources of the ocean with the minimum damage to the ocean environment.

Ocelot, the most common wild cat of S. America. It is about 1·2 m in length, including tail, and of a grey or tawny colour and spotted. Closely related to the Leopard cats.

Octane Number, the index of the knock-rating of petrol. It is based on the arbitrary scale in which iso-octane (which does not cause "knocking") has a value of 100, and normal heptane (which is prone to "knocking") has a value of 0. A good fuel for modern cars must have an octane number greater than 80.

Octarch, the kings of the English heptarchy, Hengist (455) being the first, Egbert (800) the last.

October, the 10th month, but the 8th in the old Roman calendar. It was held sacred to Mars.

Octopus, a genus of marine molluscs with eight tentacles that bear suckers.

Odin, the chief god of Scandinavian mythology.

Odyssey, Homer's epic setting forth the incidents of the wanderings of Odysseus on his way back to Ithaca after the Siege of Troy.

Oersted, a unit of magnetic-field intensity in the c.g.s. system.

Offa's Dyke, largest remaining earthwork in Britain, supposed to have been built by Offa (A.D. 757–96) as a defensive boundary line between the English settlers and the dispossessed Welsh of Gwynedd, Powys and Gwent.

Ohm's Law, propounded by G. S. Ohm in 1826, is expressed in the equation: electromotive force (in volts) = current (in amperes) × resistance (in ohms). The ohm is the unit of electrical resistance in the metre-kilogram-second system.

Oil. The great expansion in energy demand over recent years has been met to a large extent by petroleum oil. This contains a wide range of hydrocarbon molecules of varying complexity. The various components are separated from each other by making use of their different boiling points. Crude oil is heated in the base of a fractionating tower; the various components condense at different temperatures in trays at different levels of the tower. The fraction of a given composition can be increased by "cracking" or breaking down the heavier hydrocarbons into lighter ones. The total world reserves of petroleum oil are still uncertain since large parts of the world are still not fully prospected. The cutback and the rise in the price of Middle Eastern oil following the 1973 Arab-Israeli war has now been succeeded by a glut of oil and falling prices. In 1993, British offshore oil production was 94·1m tonnes, down from the peak in 1985. A new UK oil boom is predicted. as development begins of oil production in the Atlantic (there are huge reserves in the Foinaven field west of the Shetland Islands). The first British North Sea field (the Argyll) dried up in 1992 having produced 97m barrels.

Okapi, nocturnal ruminant mammal, smaller than the giraffe, chestnut brown in colour with zebra-striped legs, native to the African Congo.

Olbers' Comet was discovered in 1815 by Olbers the German astronomer. Olbers also discovered the asteroids Pallas and Vesta (1802–07).

Old Red Sandstone, the continental rocks formed during the Devonian. *See* **F48**.

Olefines, a series of hydrocarbons, in which the hydrogen atoms are double the number of carbon. The first member of the series is ethylene.

Oléron Laws *or* **Judgments**, were a code of maritime laws, introduced into England in the reign of Richard I in the 12th cent. Oléron is an island off the west coast of France, opposite the mouth of the Charente.

Olive. This small tree, whose fruit yields olive oil, is a native of the eastern Mediterranean countries, but has been introduced into cultivation elsewhere. The green unripe fruit is pickled in brine for table olives.

Olympiads were periods of four years which elapsed between each celebration of the Olympic games, held at Olympia in honour of Zeus. These festivals included competitions in literature, art, drama, rhetoric, music and gymnastics, and they were continued, with intervals, from 776 B.C. to A.D. 394. Modern Olympics have taken place at Athens 1896, Paris 1900, St. Louis 1904, London 1908, Stockholm 1912, Antwerp 1920, Paris 1924, Amsterdam 1928, Los Angeles 1932, Berlin 1936, London 1948, Helsinki 1952, Melbourne 1956, Rome 1960, Tokyo 1964, Mexico City 1968, Munich 1972, Montreal 1976, Moscow 1980, Los Angeles 1984, Seoul 1988 and Barcelona in 1992. Atlanta, Georgia, has been chosen for the 1996 Olympic Games. The first Winter Olympics were held at Chamonix in 1924. The next will be in 1998 at Nagano in Japan. Sydney will host the 2000 Olympics.

Onomasticians are scientists who study the fascinating subject of names—names of places and names of people—to find out their origins. They tell us, for example, that Cambridge is an Anglo-Norman corruption of *Grantabrycg* = bridge over the Granta; that Harrow-on-the-Hill was an early Anglo-Saxon settlement—"heathen temple on the hill"; that we owe the ridings of Yorkshire to the Vikings (Old Norse *thrithungr* = third part); that in Scotland *-ton* and *-toun* indicate not a town but a hamlet or village. Onomasticians are also concerned with international standardisation of place names.

Onyx *or* **Sardonyx**, a variety of chalcedony built up of different-coloured layers, which are parallel and straight (not curved as in agate).

Oolite, a geological term for the Jurassic oolitic

limestones existing through a long stretch of country extending from Yorkshire to Dorset. It abounds in fossils of molluscs and reptiles. The term "oolite" derives from the fact that these rocks are made of egg-shaped particles of calcium carbonate.

Opal, a mineral consisting of hydrous silica, occurring in numerous varieties and colours. Opals have been prized as gems since at least 400 B.C. but the secret of their unique internal "fire" or opalescence has only recently been learned. It is a result of the diffraction of light by a regular array of tiny silica spheres, about 100 nm in diameter, of which gem opals are now known to be composed. Opal miners are called gougers. Chief source—the Andanooka and Coober Pedy fields of South Australia.

Opium was known to the ancients, and used by them as a medicine. It is obtained from the poppy (*Papaver somniferum*), the unripe "head" or seed capsule of that flower yielding a juice which when dried becomes the opium of commerce. The poppy is cultivated in India, Iran, Turkey, Afghanistan and China for the sake of this juice, which yields various alkaloids, such as morphine, narcotine, codeine, *etc.* These days the drug is rarely used medicinally.

Opossum, marsupial mammals found in the more southerly of the United States, South America and Australasia. They are arboreal except for the water-opossum, which eats fish.

Optics, the branch of physics which investigates the nature and properties of light and the phenomena of colour. Burning lenses were known to the ancient Greeks and Ptolemy wrote a treatise on optics A.D. 150. Lenses as visual aids were known in ancient China but eyeglasses were not in use until the 13th cent. Spectacles were in more general use after the invention of printing in the 15th cent. The camera obscura was invented in the 16th cent. and the telescope and microscope early in the 17th cent.

Oracles were in ancient times supposed to be words spoken by the gods, and it was the custom on important occasions to consult them about the future. The Greeks had the Oracles of Zeus at Dodona, and Apollo at Delphi, while the Romans consulted the Oracles of Mars, Fortune and others.

Orange, a fruit growing in most sub-tropical climates and in universal demand. It is grown on an evergreen tree that attains a height of about 6 m at maturity.

Orang-utan, one of the largest of the anthropoid apes, found only in the swampy forests of Borneo and Sumatra. When full-grown it stands over 1·2 m in height and weighs c. 67 kg.

Orbit, is the path of one celestial object around another. For example, the path of the Earth around the Sun. Also applied to the path of an artificial satellite around the Earth.

Orchestra, a group of instruments and instrumentalists whose playing is under the direction of a conductor. The composition of a typical symphony orchestra is as follows: STRINGS: 1st Violin (16), 2nd Violin (16), Viola (12), Violoncello (12), Double Bass (8). WOODWIND: Flute (3–4), Piccolo (1), Oboe (3), Cor Anglais (1), Bass Oboe (1), Clarinet (3), Bass Clarinet (1), Bassoon (3), Contra-bassoon (1). BRASS: Horn (6), Trumpet (5), Trombone (3–4), Tuba (2). PERCUSSION: Timpani (3–6), Side Drum (1), Bass Drum (1), Cymbals (1), Harp (2).

Orders in Council are issued by the sovereign on the advice of a few selected members of the Privy Council. They must not seriously alter the law of the land. Another class of Orders in Council are issued by authority of an Act of Parliament for the carrying out of its provisions.

Ordination, the ceremony of installing ministers or clergymen in clerical offices, has existed from the earliest times. In the Anglican and Roman Catholic Churches the rites of Ordination are performed by bishops; among Nonconformists it is done by the governing bodies. The first women were ordained Anglican priests in Bristol Cathedral in March 1994.

Organ is a musical wind instrument of ancient origin whose tones are produced by the vibrations of air in pipes of varying length. Basically, an organ consists of a number of pipes grouped in rows or ranks according to their special tone-character. The air is fed by bellows or, in modern organs, by a rotary fan electrically driven. Each rank is controlled by a slider, and the knob that controls the slider is called a stop. The organist pulls out the stops to give the tones he wants, the other pipes being kept out of action by the slider. When a particular note on the keyboard is depressed the player may hear, by pulling out the appropriate stop, not only the normal pitch but the note in several octaves. A stop of which the notes are of normal pitch is called an 8-foot stop, a 16-foot stop would give an octave lower, a 4-foot stop an octave higher and a 2-foot stop two octaves higher. The hand keyboard is called a manual, and the foot keyboard the pedal board. The basic tone of an organ is its diapason tone, and is normally of 8-foot length and pitch. Most large organs have four manual keyboards and one pedal board. The most important manual is the great organ which comprises the majority of basic stops. The next in importance is the swell organ, so called because the pipes are enclosed in a box fitted with movable shutters operated by a swell-pedal. The effect provides a controlled crescendo or diminuendo. The tone of a typical English swell has a reedy character. The third manual controls the choir organ—a collection of stops suitable for vocal accompaniment. The fourth manual controls the solo organ—a group of stops which, singly or in combination, may provide a solo melody which the remainder of the organ accompanies. The pedal keyboard controls most of the bass stops. In some very large organs there is a fifth manual controlling the echo organ. This is a small group of stops usually set high in the roof of the building to give the effect of distant music. Most church organs have two or three manuals.

Organic Chemistry. The chemistry of compounds containing carbon and usually associated with living organisms. See **F23**.

Organic Farming, rapidly expanding area of British agriculture. Cereals are the main organic crop in Scotland, livestock predominates in Wales. In 1990 there were 576 organic farms in Britain. Organic farming means the production of food or other farm produce without artificial fertilisers or chemical pesticides.

Oriel Window is a window projected from the front of a building, rectangular, triangular, or pentagonal. The ordinary bay window and bow window are varieties of Oriel. When an Oriel window does not reach to the ground it usually rests upon moulded sills supported by corbels.

Oriflamme, the name of the original banner of the abbey of St. Denis, and adopted by Louis VI as his standard. It remained the national emblem of France for three centuries. The flag was of red silk, the outer edge being cut in the form of flames.

Original Sin, according to Christian doctrine the corruption that is born with us, as a result of Adam's fall.

Orimulsion, an emulsified bitumen fuel which comes from Venezuela.

Orioles, brilliantly coloured birds, members of the passerine family *Oriolidae,* found in the tropical regions of Asia, Africa and Australia. The golden oriole, perhaps the most beautiful of them all, with brilliant yellow plumage, black wings and tail, winters in Africa, visits England and is known to have nested here.

Orion, a famous constellation of the heavens, comprising nearly a hundred stars, all visible to the naked eye. It contains three stars of the second magnitude in a line, and these are called "Orion's Belt".

Ormer, a shellfish (*Haliotis tuberculata*) which occurs in the Channel Islands and on parts of the French coast. It is a great delicacy.

Ornithology, the scientific study of birds.

Ornithorhynchus. See **Duckbill.**

Orogeny, large-scale earth movements, including faulting and folding and sometimes igneous activity, which produce a linear belt of mountains, *e.g.,* the Alpine orogeny in Europe which produced the Alps.

Orphism. See **Section J.**

Orphrey, the name of an ornamental strip richly embroidered on ecclesiastical vestments.

Orrery, an instrument used in the 18th and early 19th cent. which showed the motions of the planets round the sun and the satellites round their primaries. The first orrery made was named after Charles Boyle, Earl of Orrery.

Orthodox Eastern Church. *See* **Section J.**

Osborne House, near Cowes, in the Isle of Wight. Queen Victoria's favourite winter-residence, and where she died.

Osier, a species of willow growing in damp soils and yielding branches utilised in basket-making.

Osmium, a very hard, bluish-white metallic element, no. 76, symbol Os, of the platinum group and one of the heaviest of known metals. It is obtained from certain sands of S. America, California, Australia and Russia. The alloy of osmium and iridium (osmiridium) provides tips for gold fountain-pen nibs. Discoved by Tennant in 1803.

Osmosis, the process by which absorption of liquids through semi-permeable membranes takes place. A solution exerts osmotic pressure (O.P.) or suction in proportion to concentration but also depending on kind of dissolved substance. The roots of the higher plants are covered with fine root-hairs, within the cell-walls of which the sap is normally of a higher concentration than the dissolved matter in the surrounding soil. The root-hairs, therefore, draw into themselves these weaker salt-solutions. (The explanation of water and salt exchanges is complicated by the selective ability of some cells (*e.g.*, roots) to accept or reject particular dissolved substances along with the water. The absorption of salts by a plant is selective, each plant selecting through the semi-permeable membranes of its root-hairs those substances which are most suited to it.)

Osprey (*Pandion haliaëtus*), a large and magnificent bird of prey, dark brown above and nearly white below. The head is whitish with a dark band from eye to nape. To the British Isles it is a rare passage migrant. In 1955, thanks to the energy and vigilance of the Royal Society for the Protection of Birds, a pair nested in a Scots pine in Inverness-shire and reared three young. Since then more young ospreys have been safely fledged in this sanctuary. The food consists almost entirely of fish, which the bird seizes with its talons. The so-called osprey plumes in fact come from the egret.

Ostrich, the largest living bird, related to the rhea, emu and extinct moa, now found only on the sandy plains of Africa and parts of S.W. Asia. The male has beautiful white plumes on wings and tail. The wings are useless in flight, but the birds have a speed exceeding that of the swiftest horse. An ostrich's egg weighs 1·3 kg.

Otary, any seal which has external ears (as opposed to the *true seals* which lack them). The eared seals make up the family *Otariidae*, which includes the Sea-lion and the Fur-seal.

Otter, an aquatic carnivorous mammal widely distributed over Europe, and until the 1950s very common in England and Wales. The otter averages about 60 cm in length, exclusive of tail, has web-feet and is a very expert swimmer. Otters are harmless and their hunting is a cruel and senseless blood sport. Having almost disappeared by 1980, the otter is now protected by the 1981 Wildlife and Countryside Act.

Ounce or **Snow Leopard,** a very beautiful pale spotted cat from the Himalayas the size of a labrador retriever but with a long furry tail.

Outcrop. Where a bed of rock appears at the surface of the ground, there is an outcrop of the particular rock. The mining of outcrop coal is called open-cast mining.

Oviparous, a zoological term referring to animals which lay eggs to be hatched outside the body of the parent.

Ovipositor, the organ by means of which female insects lay their eggs.

Owls, nocturnal birds of prey, distributed over the greater part of the world. Their forward-looking eyes, embedded in rings of feathers, give them a characteristic "owl-like" appearance, and their plumage, usually a mottled blend of browns and greys, is so soft that their flight is almost noiseless. Owls live on small mammals, reptiles, birds, insects and fish, and are very valuable birds to the farmer. British owls include the barn owl (screech owl), short-eared owl, long-eared owl, tawny owl, little owl. In many English counties the barn owl is nearly extinct.

Ox, the popular name of the mammals included

in the genus *Bos*. They are hollow-horned ruminants and hoofed quadrupeds, and include the various classes of domestic cattle as well as the different wild species. The adult male is called a bull, the female a cow and the young a calf. The best-known breeds of domesticated cattle are the Durham or Shorthorn, the Angus, the Jersey, Ayrshire, Suffolk and Hereford.

Oxalic Acid, an organic acid obtained from numerous plants, such as sorrel and rhubarb, and produced artificially for commercial purposes from sawdust, treated with caustic potash or caustic soda. It combines with metals to form oxalates; used in the manufacture of ink.

Oxford Clay, a geological formation consisting of a bed of blue clay *c.* 200 m thick, and forming the lower portion of the Upper Jurassic. It makes good bricks.

Oxford Movement. *See* **Tractarianism, Section J.**

Oxford University. The early history of the university is obscure. There was a school at Oxford as early as 1115 and it is known that Robert Pullen, a theologian from Paris, lectured there in 1133. Allusions to Oxford as the most celebrated centre of learning in England occurred in a work of Gerald of Wales in 1184–5. The earliest colleges to be founded were University College (1249), Balliol (about 1263), Merton (1264). In 1571 the university was reorganised and granted a Charter of Incorporation by an Act of Elizabeth. Other colleges and halls with their dates of foundation incude: All Souls (1438), Brasenose (1509), Christ Church (1546), Corpus Christi (1517), Exeter (1314), Hertford (1874), Jesus (1571), Keble (1868), Linacre (1962), Lincoln (1427), Magdalen (1458), New College (1379), Nuffield (1937), Oriel (1326), Pembroke (1624), Queen's (1340), St. Anthony's (1950), St. Catherine's (1962), St. Cross (1965), St. Edmund Hall (1270), St. John's (1555), St. Peter's (1929), Trinity (1554), Wadham (1612), Wolfson (1965), Worcester (1714), Campion Hall (1962), St. Benet's Hall (1964), Mansfield (1886), Regent's Park (1958), Greyfriar's Hall (1953), Manchester and Harris College (1990) and Rewley House (1990, now renamed Kellogg College). The most recent foundation is the postgraduate Green College. The original women's colleges were:— Lady Margaret Hall (1878), Somerville (1879), St. Hugh's (1886), St. Hilda's (1893), St. Anne's (1952). Women were not admitted to degrees (though allowed to sit for examination) till 1920. The last remaining women only college is St Hilda's.

Oxygen is the most abundant of all terrestrial elements, no. 8, symbol O. In combination, this gaseous element forms about 46% of the earth's crust; one-fifth of the atmosphere; eight-ninths by weight of all water. Discovered independently by Scheele (*c.* 1773) and Priestley (1774). It is colourless, tasteless and odourless, and forms the chief life-supporting element of animal and vegetable life.

Oyster, a bivalve mollusc, of the genus *Ostrea*, having very numerous species and abounding in nearly all seas. The shell is rough and irregular. Oysters are exceedingly prolific, spawning in May and June. In England and Scotland deep-sea oysters are not allowed to be sold between 15 June and 4 August, and other kinds between 14 May and 4 August. In Ireland, no oysters may be taken between 1 May and 1 September, except in certain waters. The Whitstable oyster beds have existed since pre-Roman times.

Oystercatcher, a wading bird with black and white plumage and long, orange bill, inhabiting estuaries and sea-shores. Feeds on mussels, shell fish, *etc.*, but not oysters.

Ozone, a modified form of oxygen, containing three atoms of oxygen per molecule instead of two. It is prepared by passing oxygen through a silent electric discharge. When present in air to the extent of 1 part in 4 million parts of air it kills bacteria, and has been used for this purpose in ventilating systems, *e.g.*, that of underground railways. It is present in extremely small quantities in the lower atmosphere (*q.v.*) but is comparatively plentiful at heights between 12 and 50 km. As ozone absorbs ultraviolet light of certain wavelengths spectroscopic methods, involving the analysis of sunlight, are chiefly used in ozone determination.

L93

P

Paca, a genus of large rodents found in Central and South America, and resembling the guinea-pig. It is of nocturnal habits, has streaked and spotted fur and lives on fruits and plants.

Pacific Ocean. The first European to recognise the Pacific as distinct from the Atlantic was the Spanish explorer, Vasco Nuñez de Balboa, who discovered its eastern shore from a peak in Panama in 1513. The first European to sail upon it was Magellan, who entered it by the strait that bears his name in 1520. Sir Francis Drake was the first Englishman to sail upon it in 1577. The world's greatest known ocean depth is in the Mindanao Trench, off the Philippines, 37,782 ft (11,524 m).

Pagan, a person who does not worship God; a heathen. The word is derived from the Latin *paganus* (a countryman or uncultivated person). In the Middle Ages the term was used largely to describe Mohammedans (Moors, Saracens, *etc.*). *See* **Paganism, Section J.**

Pagoda, the name given in China, India *etc.* to a high pyramidal tower, usually, but not necessarily, connected with a temple.

Pahlevi, family name of the last Shahs (rulers) of Iran.

Palaeontology, the science which is devoted to the investigation of fossils: animal (palaeozoology) and plants (palaeobotany). By studying the markings and fossils of living things in the stratified rocks, palaeontologists have been able to establish with astonishing accuracy a record of the evolution of life through geological time. The geologist at the same time with the evidence of the fossils has been able to work out the order and the age of the rocks. *See also* **Section F.**

Palatinate, a term formerly applied to two German regions, historically related, the Upper and Lower Palatinates. Now provinces of Bavaria.

Pale, the name given to the part of Ireland colonised by the English and comprising portions of the counties of Louth, Dublin, Meath and Kildare. The Anglo-Norman rulers were styled "Lords of the Pale".

Palimpsests are ancient MSS. or parchments which have been partly effaced and used for fresh writings. Many valuable MSS. were thus lost, but sometimes the second writing has been washed out, enabling the original writings to be deciphered. Among such restorations are a dialogue of Cicero's, a part of a book of Livy.

Palladium, a scarce metallic element, no. 46, symbol Pd, similar to platinum, with which it is usually found. It is an expensive metal, with desirable properties as a catalyst in reactions involving hydrogen, since it has a remarkable capacity for absorbing this gas; for example, coal gas and air will inflame in the presence of palladium at room temperature. It forms a silver-white alloy with gold, and this is used in some kinds of jewellery. It is used in expensive watches to make non-magnetic springs.

Pallium, a vestmental ornamentation of white wool presented by the Pope to archbishops on their appointment, and the sign of Papal confirmation.

Palm, a large straight-trunked plant or tree common to tropical countries, and usually fruit yielding, such as dates, coconuts, etc. Many commodities useful to man are obtained from plants of the Palm family (*Palmaceae*).

Palm Sunday, the Sunday before Easter, upon which occasion it is customary to carry palms to the churches in some countries, in commemoration of Christ's entry into Jerusalem for the Feast of the Passover, when the people went forth to greet Him with palm branches.

Panama Canal. In 1903 the United States signed a treaty with Panama (which had previously seceded from Columbia) which gave the United States rights in perpetuity over a 16 km-wide strip of land extending across the isthmus for the purposes of building and running the canal. The canal connects the Atlantic and Pacific Oceans, is just over 80 kilometres long (with sea approaches) and the depth varies from 12 to 26 m. It is constructed above sea-level, with locks, and has been available for commercial shipping since 3 August 1914. Agreement was reached in 1978 for the waterway to be turned over to Panama by the end of the century.

Panda, *or* **Cat-Bear,** is related to the Raccoon. There are two kinds, the Red or True Panda, resembling a large domestic cat, which lives in the eastern Himalayas and S.W. China, and the Giant Panda, which is more like a bear in appearance and inhabits the mountains of western China. Both frequent the dense bamboo forests of those regions.

Pangolin, the scientific name of the "scaly ant-eater", a toothless mammal, found in W. Africa and S.E. Asia. It has a long extensible tongue which it uses in catching ants and termites, its chief food. When attacked the pangolin rolls itself into a ball, and its scales assume the form of sharp spikes. Pangolins have an Order of their own—the Pholidota, the scale-bearers.

Pantagruel, the leading character in one of the satires of Rabelais.

Pantheon, the famous temple in Rome, originally consecrated to the gods, built by Agrippa in 27 B.C. and rebuilt in the 2nd cent. by Hadrian. Its splendid dome and portico make it one of the most interesting architectural monuments of ancient days. Since the 7th cent. it has been used as a Christian church.

Panther, another name for the leopard, *Panthera pardus*, related to the lion, carnivorous, active climber, found in India, and other parts of Asia, also in Africa.

Papal Infallibility. *See* **Section J.**

Paper has been known in one form or another from very early times. The papyrus reeds of the Nile swamps served the ancient Egyptians for sheets upon which to inscribe their records. The Chinese and Japanese, centuries later, were using something more akin to modern paper in substance, an Asiatic paper-mulberry, yielding a smooth fibrous material, being utilised. With the spread of learning in Western Europe the necessity of a readier medium made itself felt and paper began to be manufactured from pulped rags and other substances. The first known English paper-mill was Sele mill near Stevenage, built about 1490, which produced the paper for an edition of Chaucer in 1498. Other mills were set up under Elizabeth, using linen and cotton as raw material. Other papermaking staples were later introduced, such as surat, esparto grass and wood-pulp. The chief raw material in the world paper industry is wood-pulp, the main exporters being the timber-growing countries of Canada, Sweden and Finland. Canada is the world's chief producer of newsprint.

Papyrus, the earliest known paper made in Egypt at a very remote period from a large species of reed, *Cyperus papyrus*. This plant is to be found all over tropical Africa, especially in the "sudd" region of the White Nile.

Parachute, the umbrella-shaped safety device used in emergency by the crew and passengers of aircraft. The first parachute descent from a great height was made in 1797 by André Garnerin who dropped 915 m from a balloon. Rate of descent for a parachute jump is about 5 m/s.

Paraclete (the Holy Ghost, or Comforter), the name used in the English translations of St. John's Gospel, and adopted by Abelard to designate the convent in Champagne founded by him, of which Héloïse became the abbess.

Paradise, a Persian word used by the translators of the Old Testament to designate the Garden of Eden, and since meaning any place of happiness.

Paraffin, a mixture of hydrocarbons of higher boiling point than petrol. Paraffin was first obtained by distillation of coal, the process being discovered about 1830. About 1848, Mr. James Young procured it from mineral oil, and Irish peat also yielded it. The main source of paraffin supply today is crude petroleum. Used in the manufacture of candles, for waterproofing and numerous other purposes.

Parakeets, various small parrots of vivid plumage native to Australia, Polynesia, Asia and Africa. One of the loveliest of the parakeets is the budgerigar of Australia.

Parallax, the change in direction of a body caused by a change in position of the observer. If the parallax is measured (in degrees of angle) and the distance between the two observation points is known the distance of the observed body can be calculated. The distance of heavenly bodies has been found this way. The first stellar distances were so obtained in 1838 by Henderson, Struve and Bessel. Stellar distances are so great that even when the two observations are made at opposite points of the earth's orbit round the sun, the parallax is always less than 1·0″ of arc. See **Aberration.**

Parameter, a number which is fixed for the application of a theory to one particular situation but may be different for other situations. For example, in a theory of motion near the surface of a planet the acceleration due to gravity may be regarded as a parameter constant for a particular planet but differing from planet to planet. The word is often used in a similar way in discussions of economic affairs.

Parapsychology. See **Section J.**

Parchment, made chiefly from the skins of animals, usually of goats and sheep, was employed in olden times before printing was invented and superseded papyrus as writing material. Vegetable parchment, invented by W. E. Gaine in 1853, though not equal in strength and durability to skin parchment, is about five times stronger than ordinary paper. Vellum is parchment made from the skins of young calves or lambs.

Paris University, of which the Sorbonne forms a part was founded in the 12th cent. and is one of the greatest educational institutions of Europe.

Parliament, is the name given to the supreme legislature of the United Kingdom. It consists of the Queen, the Lords spiritual and temporal and the Commons. It meets in two houses: the House of Lords (the Upper or Second Chamber) and the House of Commons. It derives from the Anglo-Saxon *Witans* (*see* **Witan**). The Statute of Westminster (1275) first uses "parlement" of the Great Council in England, which comes from the French word meaning discourse. See **Section D.**

Parliamentary Correspondents sit in the Press Gallery of the House of Commons and describe its proceedings for the news media either by impressions or a summary of the debate.

Parquetry, the name of a style of flooring consisting of small rectangular wooden blocks laid down according to geometrical pattern.

Parrot, the popular name of a widely distributed family of tropical birds, including the African grey parrot, the green parrot of South America —both familiar cage pets in this country—and the various parakeets, cockatoos, macaws, lories, etc. Many of these birds possess a remarkable gift of imitating sound, especially human voices.

Parsec, modern unit of astronomical distance, the distance at which the diameter of the earth's orbit subtends an angle of 1 arc second. 1 parsec (pc) = $3·0857 \times 10^{13}$ km.

Parthenogenesis. The development of animals from unfertilised eggs. The drones of the honey bee are parthenogenetic, and the phenomenon is also common among aphids.

Parthenon, the famous Temple of Athena on the Acropolis at Athens, was built under the rule of Pericles between 447 B.C. and 432 B.C. It was made wholly of marble without mortar. The famous sculptured friezes, known as the Elgin Marbles, are now in the British Museum.

Partridge, a well-known British game-bird. Close time: 2 February to 31 August. Two species are common in Britain.

Passport is an official document issued to a person by his own government, certifying to his citizenship and permitting him to travel abroad. Passports to British subjects issued by the United Kingdom Passport Agency (an Executive Agency of the Home Office) authorise bearer to leave the country and guarantee him the state's protection. Passports now (1995) cost £18—and are issued for a period of 10 years. Children over 16 require separate passports. Parents of children under 16 who require passports should make application on form (B). For those making frequent visits abroad a 94-page passport was first issued in 1973, which costs £30 (1995). From July 1988, British citizens began using a common wine-coloured EU passport. Existing blue passports will remain valid until they expire. They will disappear entirely after 31 December 1999. The old one-year British visitor's passport and the British Excursion Document (used by short-stay visitors to France) are to be abolished from early 1996. The government is planning to allow travel agents, banks and post offices to issue application forms and collect fees for full ten-year passports.

Patricians, the aristocracy of ancient Rome.

Paul's Cathedral, St., is the third cathedral church to be built on the site. It was preceded by a Norman building which was practically destroyed by the Great Fire in 1666. This followed a Saxon church which was burnt in 1086. The present building was designed by Sir Christopher Wren. The foundation stone was laid in 1675 and the structure was completed in 1710. It cost a little under £748,000. Its central feature is the dome, crowned by its cupola and lantern with the golden ball and cross. It escaped serious damage during the air raids of the second world war.

pC Value, introduced by Dr. C. L. Whittles in 1935 as a measure of salinity of aqueous solutions (soil extract, irrigation water, etc.); defined as the negative logarithm of specific electrical conductivity in reciprocal ohms. Alone or joined with **pH** (*q.v.*) is useful as an index of osmotic pressure (*see* **Osmosis**) and related hindrance to plant growth resulting from excess of fertiliser or soil salts. If manuring is balanced, growth is best about **pC** 3.3.

Peacock, a bird of large size and beautiful plumage, its characteristic feature being a tail of brilliant "eyed" feathers, which it can erect and spread out, the males possessing resplendent feathering to a much greater extent than the females. It is related to the pheasant; one species is found wild in the forests of India, and another inhabits Burma and the Malaysian regions. In Africa there is the Congo Peacock.

Peanut, Groundnut *or* **Monkey Nut.** A member of the pea family native to S. America, but now cultivated in many parts of the world. After pollination, the flower stalk bends down and buries the pod containing the peas ("nuts") in the ground. The oil from these "nuts" can be used for margarine manufacture.

Pearl is produced by certain shelled molluscs, chiefly the oyster. The inner surface of the shells of the pearl oyster yield "mother-ofpearl", and distinct pearls are believed to be morbid secretions, caused by some external irritation. Many fine pearls are found in the actual body of the oyster. The Persian Gulf, Sri Lanka, the northwest coast of Western Australia, many Pacific islands and the Gulf of Mexico are among the most productive pearlfishing grounds. In ancient times Britain was renowned for its pearl fisheries, the pearls being obtained from a species of freshwater mussel. Western Australia has produced a 40-grain pearl, the finest the world has seen. The largest pearl ever found was the "Beresford-Hope Pearl", which weighed 1,800 grains, over six times as much as the oyster that produced it.

Peat, decayed vegetable matter found mostly in marshy positions, and common in Ireland and Scotland. Peat is coal in its first stage of development; burnt for fuel in many cottages.

Peccary, a pig-like animal native to the Americas. There are two species: the collared peccary and the white-lipped peccary, the latter being a vicious and dangerous animal.

Pelican, a genus of bird with long depressed bill pouched underneath, thus able to hold fish in reserve. It has immense wings and webbed feet. Eight species.

Pemmican, venison or other meat, sliced, dried, pounded and made into cakes, used by explorers and others when out of reach of fresh meat.

Penguin, a genus of flightless, fish-eating seabirds of the southern hemisphere. They are stoutbodied, short-necked and of small, moderate or large size. The Emperor and King Penguins make no nest but protect and incubate the single egg by carrying it in the down feathers between the feet and the body. Other species brood in the usual way and may lay as many as three eggs. Penguins use their flippers for swimming under water. All 17 species are bluish-grey or blackish above and white below. They are very sociable and breed in colonies.

Penicillin. An antibiotic drug produced by the

mould *Penicillium notatum*, and discovered by Sir Alexander Fleming in 1928. It is one of the most effective chemotherapeutic agents known. The mould produces a number of penicillins, all of which are effective antibiotics. *See* **P9**(1), **22**(2).

Peninsular War lasted from 1808 to 1814. Fought in Spain and Portugal (the Iberian peninsula) by the British, Spanish and Portuguese forces, chiefly under Wellington, against the French. The latter were defeated.

Pentagon, government office in Washington (the largest in the world), housing many thousands of military and civilian workers in the War Department of the United States (Army, Navy and Air Force).

Pentateuch, the first five books of the Old Testament—Genesis, Exodus, Leviticus, Numbers and Deuteronomy. Referred to in the Gospel of Mark as "the book of Moses".

Penumbra, the half shadow of the Earth or Moon during an eclipse. The term is also used to describe the lighter, outer part of a sunspot.

Pepys Diary, by Samuel Pepys, was first published in 1825. It gives a picture of the social life of the period 1 January 1660 to 31 May 1669. He bequeathed the manuscript, together with his library, to Magdalene College, Cambridge.

Perch, a well-known family of fresh-water fish, with dark striped sides. The common perch of British rivers and lakes falls an easy prey to the angler because of its voracity.

Perfumes are essences or odours obtained from floral and other substances. The chief flower perfumes are those obtained from rose, jasmine, orange flower, violet and acacia. Heliotrope perfume is largely obtained from vanilla and almonds. Among the aromatic herbs which yield attractive perfumes are the rosemary, thyme, geranium, lavender, *etc.*, while orange peel, citron peel, musk, sandalwood, patchouli and other vegetable products are largely drawn upon. In recent times chemistry has been called into play in aid of the perfumer, and many of the popular perfumes of today are chemically prepared *See* **Musk Deer.**

Perigee, the closest point of the orbit of an object such as a satellite to the earth. The opposite of apogee (*q.v.*).

Perihelion. That point in a planet's orbit when it is nearest to the sun; opposite of aphelion. The earth is at perihelion ($1 \cdot 47 \times 10^8$ km) in midwinter, about 3 January.

Peripatus, an animal which stands as a link between the annelid worms and the arthropods. Wormlike with short unjointed legs it breathes by a system of air tubes like those in insects. Certain other points of internal structure point to a relationship with annelid worms. There are some fifty species, the best known being the S. African *Peripatus capensis*.

Perjury, the offence of giving false evidence. The ancient Romans threw the perjurer from the Tarpeian Rock, and after the Empire was Christianised, those who swore falsely upon the Gospel had their tongues cut out. The usual punishment in England from the 16th to the 19th cent. was the pillory, fine and imprisonment.

Permian Formation, a group of rocks lying between the Trias and the Carboniferous strata. It has three subdivisions, Upper, Middle and Lower Permian. *See* **F48.**

Per Procurationem signature means that the subject of the correspondence has been put into the writer's care by his principal for him to use his personal judgment in the matter, and that he is authorised to sign on behalf of his principal. Normally contracted to *per pro* or *p.p.*

Peruke, the name given to the wigs worn by men in the latter half of the 18th cent. The custom of wearing wigs was gradually superseded by powdering the natural hair. Wigs are still worn by the Speaker of the House of Commons, judges and barristers.

Petrel, the name given to a member of a large, widely-distributed family of sea-birds of great diversity of size and colouring and distinguished by tube-like external nostrils. They usually skim low over the waves, and some, for this reason, are known as shearwaters. The storm petrel or Mother Carey's chicken occasionally patters along the surface, and is often called Little Peter—a reference to St. Peter walking

on the water. Except when breeding, petrels are always at sea. They mostly nest in holes and crevices on islands and lay one egg, which is invariably white. The storm petrel, Leach's petrel, Manx shearwater and the fulmar petrel are resident in the British Isles. *See also* **Mutton Bird.**

Petroleum. *See* **Oil.**

Pewter, alloy of tin and lead formerly used for making household utensils and ornaments.

pH Value. Introduced in 1909 by the Danish chemist Sørensen to indicate hydrogen-ion concentration on the basis of electrical conductivity and a view of ionisation since discarded; is now taken as a logarithmic scale of acidity or alkalinity of aqueous solutions: acidity 0–7, neutrality at $7 \cdot 0$, alkalinity 7–14. The *pH* of blood is about $7 \cdot 6$ (faintly alkaline).

Phalanger, pouched marsupial mammals. They are arboreal and superficially resemble squirrels. There are two genera of flying phalangers or flying squirrels, which have a remarkable membrane along each side of the body enabling the animals to glide through the air. The members of the phalanger family are confined to the Australasian and oriental regions.

Phalangid, a member of the arachnid family Phalangida: popularly known as "harvesters".

Phalanx, a name applied by the ancient Greeks to a body of pike-men drawn up in close array, with overlapping shields, and eight, ten or more rows deep. The Macedonians stood sixteen rows deep. As many as 500 men could be in the front row.

Pharisees and Sadducees, two ancient Jewish sects. *See* **Judaism, Section J.**

Pharmacopoeia, an official publication containing information on the recognised drugs used in medicine. Each country has its own pharmacopoeia. The British Pharmacopoeia (B.P.) is published under the direction of the General Medical Council. The Pharmaceutical Society issues the British Pharmaceutical Codex (B.P.C.); there is also an International Pharmacopoeia (2 vols.) issued by the World Health Organisation.

Pharos, the name of the first lighthouse, built by Ptolemy II about 280 B.C., on the Isle of Pharos, at the entrance to the harbour of Alexandria. It was said to be 180 m high but this is doubtful. One of the "seven wonders".

Pheasant, game birds related to the partridges, quails, peacocks, chickens and turkeys, males distinguished by their brilliant plumage and long tapering tail. First found by the Greeks in Georgia where the River Phasis flows through to the Black Sea. Close time: 2 February to 30 September.

Phillippics, the oration delivered by Demosthenes, 352–341 B.C., against Philip of Macedon—remarkable for their bitter invective. The word was also used for Cicero's speeches against Antony. In modern use, any impassioned invective.

Philosopher's Stone. *See* **Alchemy, Section J.**

Phosphorus is a non-metal element, no. 15, symbol P. Most familiar as a waxy, yellow solid which is spontaneously inflammable in air. It has chemical similarities to arsenic, like which it is very poisonous. It was discovered by Brandt in urine in 1669. It is found in most animal and vegetable tissues. It is an essential element of all plants and of the bones of animals. In combination with various metals it forms different phosphates, which are largely utilised as manures. The chief commercial use of phosphorus is in the preparation of matches.

Photoelectric Cell, a device which gives a useful electrical response to light falling on it. There are several kinds depending on the different effects which light may have on a suitably chosen solid (usually a semiconductor), viz., the emission of electrons from the surface ("photo-emissive cell"); change in electrical resistance ("photoconducting cell"); generation of electric current from a specially designed sensitive structure ("barrier layer" or "photovoltaic cell", "solar battery"). Different cells respond differently to lights of various wavelength and must be chosen for each application. *See also* **Solar Battery.**

Photogrammetry, the science of measurement from photographs taken from an aircraft. Aerial photography has many uses and is of great value to military intelligence and for mapmaking.

Photon. When light behaves like a stream of discrete particles and not like waves, the particles are called photons. *See* **F14, 16.**

Photosynthesis. *See* **F32(1), 43(2).**

Phrenology. *See* **Section J.**

Phylloxera, a genus of plant-lice related to the aphids, which attacks the grape vine. Many vineyards of France, in common with the rest of Europe, were replanted with native vines grafted on immune stocks from California in 1879 after being ravaged by the insect (which came from America). Curiously enough, the remedy also came from America, the vine stocks there being immune to *phylloxera*.

Pi is the unique number denoted by the Greek letter π and obtained by dividing the length of the circumference of any circle by its diameter. Its value is approximately 3·14159.

Picts, inhabitants of Scotland in pre-Roman times, are held by some historians to be a branch of the old Celtic race, by others to have been of Scythian origin. They occupied the north-eastern portion of Scotland, and were subdued by the Scots in Argyll in the 9th cent., Kenneth MacAlpin becoming king of a united kingdom of the Picts and Scots—the kingdom of Alban.

Pike, a familiar fresh-water fish abundant in the temperate regions of both hemispheres. It forms good sport for the angler in rivers and lakes, and sometimes attains a weight of from 9–13 kg. It is extremely voracious, is covered with small scales and has a ferocious-looking head.

Pilchard, a fish of the herring family, but with smaller scales and more rounded body. It appears off the Cornish coasts in vast shoals every summer.

Pilgrimage. The undertaking of a journey to a distant place or shrine to satisfy a religious vow or secure spiritual benefit, was resorted to in early Christian times. The first recorded pilgrimage is that of the Empress Helena to Jerusalem in 326. In the Middle Ages pilgrimages became common, and were undertaken by monarchs and people of rank in all Christian countries. Moslems have been making pilgrimages to Mecca since the death of the Prophet, such duty being enjoined by the Koran. Among the great centres of Christian pilgrimages are Jerusalem, Rome, the tomb of Becket at Canterbury and the holy places of Lourdes and La Salette in France.

Pilgrimage of Grace (1536), the rising in Lincolnshire and Yorkshire in the reign of Henry VIII against religious innovations and the dissolution of the smaller monasteries, which overlapped with discontents caused by taxation, rising prices, enclosures and land speculation. The insurrection was followed by many executions.

Pilgrim Fathers, the 101 English Puritans who, after living some years in exile in Holland, to escape persecution in their own country, set sail for America in the *Mayflower*, 6 September 1620, landing at Plymouth, Mass., 4 December. They founded the settlement of Plymouth, and are regarded as the pioneers of American colonisation although 13 years earlier a small Virginian colony had been established.

Pillory, a wooden instrument of punishment in use in England until 1837. It consisted of a pair of movable boards with holes through which the culprit's head and hands were put, and was usually erected on a scaffold. While a person was undergoing this punishment the mob generally pelted him with stones and rubbish, sometimes to his serious injury. People convicted of forgery, perjury or libel were often condemned to the pillory, but from 1816–1837 the only offence for which it could be inflicted was perjury.

Pine, a conifer of the genus *Pinus*, which flourishes all over the northern hemisphere and includes 80–90 species, which afford valuable timber and yield turpentine and tar. The Scots Pine, *Pinus silvestris*, with its blue-green, short needles, set in pairs, and its rosy-orange branches, is native to Britain, as it is to the whole of Europe. It provides the red and yellow deal in everyday use.

Pitcairn Islanders were originally the mutineers of the *Bounty*. They took possession of the island in 1790, and it was not until 1814 that their whereabouts was ascertained, accidentally, by a passing ship. The mutineers, under their leader, Adams, had settled down to a communal existence, married Tahitian women and increased so in numbers that in the course of years they were too many for the island to support, and in 1856 they were removed to the British Government to Norfolk Island. A small number returned to Pitcairn.

Pitchblende *or* **Uraninite,** a relatively scarce mineral. It is nearly all uranium oxide, but lead, thorium, etc., are also present. Pitchblende from Joachimstal in Czechoslovakia was the material in which radium was discovered by the Curies. Other major sources are the Great Lakes region of Canada and Zaïre.

Placebo, medical treatment that the therapist uses deliberately although he knows it is without any specific effect on the condition being treated. There may be various medical reasons for using placebos, *e.g.*, for the beneficial psychological effect on people who like to feel something is being done for them; for differentiating during clinical trials of a new treatment between those persons given the real thing and a control or comparison group of persons given a placebo or inactive imitation.

Plainsong, a style of musical composition sung in unison (all voices singing the same tune without harmony), familiar in the Western Church from very early times and still performed, principally in the Roman Catholic Church. Though restrained and contemplative in spirit, it is capable of expressing deep emotion. *See* **E3(2).**

Planetarium, a complex optical system which projects into the interior of a dome a replica of all the phenomena of the sky that can be seen by the naked eye, *e.g.*, sun, moon, planets, stars, comets, meteors, aurora, eclipses and clouds. There is a planetarium in the Marylebone Road, London. The world's largest (opened in 1987) is at Miyazaki, Japan.

Planets, the name given to such celestial bodies as revolve round the sun in elliptical orbits. The name was first used by the Greeks to indicate their difference from the fixed stars. There are nine major planets, Mercury, Venus, Earth, Mars, Jupiter, Saturn, Uranus, Neptune and Pluto. There are also a large number of minor planets or asteroids. Saturn, Uranus and Jupiter are ringed. Many important questions can be answered by means of probes sent to the neighbourhood of the planets. These include the measurement of the magnetic field, if any, of the planets, the study of their atmospheres, much of which can be done without actually penetrating to the surface. With instruments landed gently on the surface it is possible to investigate surface conditions and composition by many methods. Even without a soft-landing information on these questions can be obtained by photography and subsequent transmission of the picture back to earth by some form of television scanning. The US Mars probe *Mariner IV* transmitted pictures of the Martian surface in 1965, the Russian *Venus IV* in 1967 made a soft-landing on Venus, and the US *Pioneer 11* came within 43,000 km of Jupiter in December 1974. Two US *Voyager* spacecraft were launched in 1977 flying by Jupiter (1979), Saturn (1980, 1981) Uranus (1986) and Neptune (1989), sending back exciting new data. *See under* their names for further details.

Plankton, a word which first came into biological use in 1886 to describe the usually microscopic plants and animals floating, swimming and drifting in the surface waters of the sea. To be distinguished from *nekton* (swimming animals like fishes and squids) and *benthos* (plants and animals living on the sea bottom, like fixed algae, sponges, oysters, crabs, etc.). Of great economic importance, providing food for fish and whales.

Plantagenets, the kings who reigned in England between 1154 and 1485 and included the Houses of Lancaster and York. More correctly they are styled Angevins, from Anjou, of which Geoffrey, father of Henry II, was Count, and whose badge was a sprig of broom (*Planta genista*).

Plasma Physics is the physics of wholly ionised gases, *i.e.*, gases in which the atoms initially present have lost practically the whole of the electrons that usually surround their nuclei, so that the gas consists of a mixture of two components, positively charged ions and negatively charged electrons. The physical properties of a *plasma* are very different from those of an unionised gas. In particular, a plasma has a high electrical conductivity and can carry large currents. *See also* **Nuclear Fusion.**

Plastics, a broad term covering those substances which become plastic when subjected to increased temperatures or pressures. The Plastics Industry is based on synthetic organic examples of this group. There are two classes of plastics: the *thermoplastic*, which become plastic every time they are heated (*e.g.* cellulosic plastics) and *thermosetting*, which undergo chemical change when heated, so that once set they cannot be rendered plastic again (*e.g.*, Bakelite). Plastics are composed of long-chained molecules, *e.g.*, polyethylene.

Plate Tectonics, the contemporary and by now well-developed theory of the movements of the earth's crust. The view is that the surface of the Earth consists of about a dozen rigid plates. Some larger than continents, some much smaller, all in ceaseless motion relative to one another. Their separation and approach and their friction and collision are closely related to the evolution of mountain ranges, oceans and rift valleys and to phenomena like earthquakes and volcanoes. *See* **F9**

Platinum, a metallic element, no. 78, symbol Pt. It is a scarce white metal generally allied with iridium, osmium, ruthenium and palladium. It can only be melted in an oxyhydrogen or electric furnace, but can be rolled out into a film-like sheet, or drawn out to the finest wire; being resistant to acids it is termed a noble metal. Named after the Spanish for 'silver-coloured' –platina. First found in the sands of the River Pinto in S. America.

Platonic Solids, five regular solid figures known to the ancient world. They are: the tetrahedron (4 triangular faces), cube (6 square faces), octahedron (8 triangular faces), dodecahedron (12 five-sided faces), icosahedron (20 triangular faces). All the faces and angles of each solid are identical.

Pleiades, famous cluster of stars in the constellation of Taurus. Of the seven principal stars in the group, one is rather faint, and many myths have sprung up about this "lost Pleiad". *See also* **I23.**

Pleistocene, the geological period that succeeded the Pliocene. During the Pleistocene, also known as the *Great Ice Age*, there were four cold periods, when the ice sheets covered northern Europe and N. America, separated by warm periods when the glaciers drew back into the mountains. From recent studies based on rock magnetic measurements the transition to Pleistocene took place *c.* 1,850,000 years ago.

Pliocene, the geological period preceding the Pleistocene, and the last major division of the Tertiary strata. It began about fifteen million years ago. *See* **Section F.**

Plough Monday, the first Monday after the Epiphany, when in olden times the rustic population returned to work after the Christmas festivities.

Plover, wading birds, widely distributed over marshy places of Europe. Several species occur in Britain, including the Golden-plover, which breeds on the moors of Devon, Somerset, Wales, N.E. Yorkshire and Scotland, and the Ringed plover, Kentish plover and Dotterel.

Pluto, the last planet to be discovered was searched for following the 1914 predictions of P. Lowell and discovered by C. W. Tombaugh at the Flagstaff Observatory in Arizona in January 1930. Generally the most distant of the planets its orbit is much more elliptical than the other planetary orbits and so it sometimes approaches the sun closer than Neptune. It was thought to be different from the other outer Jovian planets which are gaseous and to consist of rock covered in frozen methane gas. Recently the size of Pluto has been revised downwards by interferometric measurement of its diameter. The diameter of Pluto is currently (1994) estimated to be 2250 km. It is the only planet in the solar system not yet visited by spacecraft, but NASA plans a probe in 2001. Pluto's own moon, Charon, was also detected by earth-based telescopes using special photometric measurements. It is made almost entirely of ice. *See* **F8.**

Plutonium, a chemical element, no. 94, symbol Pu,

capable of nuclear fission in the same way as Uranium 235. Not until after it had been synthesised in atomic piles during the second world war was it shown to occur in infinitesimally small traces in nature. Its synthesis in the atomic pile depends on the capture by Uranium 238 nuclei of neutrons; immediate product of this reaction is the element neptunium, but this undergoes rapid radioactive disintegration to plutonium.

Poet Laureate is the poet attached to the royal household, an office officially established in 1668, though its origins go back to the early Middle Ages, when minstrels were employed at the courts of English kings. Chaucer, Skelton and Spenser, though not court poets, were all unofficial poets laureate. Ben Jonson has been called the first "official laureate" (1616), but the office was not officially recognised until 1668, when Dryden was formally granted the office. It is customary for the poet laureate to write verse in celebration of events of national importance. Ted Hughes (*see* **B33**) became Poet Laureate in December 1984. Previous holders of the title are John Dryden 1668–1689, Thomas Shadwell 1689–1692. Nahum Tate 1692–1715, Nicholas Rowe 1715–1718, Laurence Eusden 1718–1730, Colley Cibber 1730–1757, William Whitehead 1757–1785, Thomas Warton 1785–1790, Henry Pye 1790–1813, Robert Southey 1813–1843, William Wordsworth 1843–1850, Alfred Tennyson 1850–1892, Alfred Austin 1896–1913, Robert Bridges 1913–1930, John Masefield 1930–1967, Cecil Day-Lewis 1968–1972, John Betjeman 1972–1984 and Ted Hughes 1984–.

Pogrom. Russian word meaning "destruction". First used to describe the Czarist attacks on the Jews in 1881 in Russia. In 1938 Hitler ordered a general pogrom in Germany; which led on to the holocaust.

Poitiers, Battle of, was fought on 19 September 1356, during the Hundred Years' War, when Edward the Black Prince gained a complete victory over John, King of France, who was taken prisoner and brought to London.

Polecat, an animal of a dark-brown colour, about 46 cm in length, exclusive of tail; the ears and face-markings are white or light brown. It is carnivorous and belongs to the weasel family.

Pole-Star is of the second magnitude, and the last in the tail of the Little Bear constellation. Being near the North pole of the heavens—never more than about one degree from due north—it always remains visible in the Northern hemisphere; hence its use as a guide to seamen.

Police, a regular force established for the preservation of law and order and the prevention and detection of crime. The powers they have vary from country to country and with the type of government; the more civilised and democratic the state, the less police intervention. England, compared with countries abroad, was slow to develop a police force, and it was not until 1829 that Sir Robert Peel's Metropolitan Police Act established a regular force for the metropolis, later legislation establishing county and borough forces maintained by local police authorities throughout England and Wales. Up to that time police duties were discharged by individual constables and watchmen appointed by local areas in England and Wales. The police service in Great Britain today has recently (March 1993) seen the most radical review since 1966. Many forces will be amalgamated and radical changes implemented. At present, however, the structure is:

1. County forces (43 in 1995) under a police committee consisting of local councillors and magistrates.
2. Combined forces, covering more than one county, also under a police committee consisting of local councillors and magistrates and representatives from constituent areas.
3. The Metropolitan Police Force, covering an area within a 15-mile (24-km) radius of Charing Cross, but excluding the City of London (under the Home Secretary).
4. The City of London force under the Court of Common Council.

In Scotland the police authority is the regional or island council. Police ranks are: chief constable, assistant chief constable, chief superintendent, superintendent, chief inspector, inspector, sergeant and constable. In the Metropolitan Police area the chief officer is the Commissioner of Police of the Metropolis. Central authority rests with the Home Secretary in England and Wales and the Secretary of State for Scotland in Scotland. In the present troubles in Northern Ireland responsibility for law and order is retained at Westminster. Great opposition faced the Sheehy Report when it proposed fixed-term contracts and performance-related pay. Likewise recent attempts by the Home Secretary to decrease local control of the police have met all-party opposition.

Poll Tax, common name for the Community Charge, which replaced the rates. It was replaced by the Council Tax from 1993. *See* **Section H.**

Pollution. *See* **Section Y.**

Polonium, a radioactive element, no. 84, symbol Po, discovered by Madame Curie in 1898, and named after her native land of Poland.

Polymerisation is the linking together of small molecules to make a large long-chain molecule. The general name for polymers of ethylene is Polythene, a wax-like plastic solid.

Polytheism. *See* **God and Man, Section J.**

Pomology, the science of fruit-growing.

Pontifex, the title assigned in ancient Rome to members of the college of pontifices. "Pontifex maximus" was the official head of Roman religion. It was as "pontifex maximus" that Julius Caesar revised the calendar in 46 B.C., and when after the rise of Christianity the Popes took over the title the revision fell to them.

Pope, The, the head of the Roman Catholic Church, recognised by that Church as the lawful successor of St. Peter. He is elected by the body of Cardinals. Since 1870, when the King of Italy deposed the holder from temporal power, no Pope had left the Vatican between appointment and death until 1929, when peace was made between the Church and State in Italy and compensation was paid to the Holy See for the loss of temporal power. Cardinal Karol Wojtyla, Archbishop of Cracow, was elected Pope John Paul II in 1978.

Porcelain. The word is thought to be derived from the Italian *porcellana,* indicating the texture of a piglet. The majority of porcelain made on the continent was of "hard-paste", or true porcelain, similar to that discovered by the Chinese as early as the T'ang Dynasty (A.D. 618–907). It was composed of *kaolin* (china-clay) and *petuntse* (china-stone) which when fired in a kiln at a temperature of *c.* 1300°C became an extremely hard and translucent material. The recipe of "hard-paste" porcelain remained a secret of the Chinese until 1709, when it was re-discovered in Europe by Johann Böttger of the Meissen factory (popularly known as Dresden). Aided by disloyal Meissen workmen, factories were later established at Vienna, Venice and in many parts of Germany. Plymouth and Bristol were the only English factories to produce this type of porcelain, from 1768 to 1781. Elsewhere, both in England and France, the material manufactured was known as "soft-paste" or artificial porcelain which was made by blending varying white-firing clays with the ingredients of glass. The French factory of Sèvres began to make some hard-paste porcelain by 1768 and by the 19th cent. such porcelain was the only type being made throughout the whole of the continent. In England Josiah Spode is credited with the introduction of "bone-china" about 1794. This hybrid-paste was quickly adopted by many other factories and remains the most popular type of English porcelain.

Porphyry, a form of crystalline rock of many varieties that in ancient Egypt was quarried and used for the decorative portions of buildings and vessels. The term is applied generally to the eruptive rocks in which large well-formed crystals of one mineral are set in a matrix of other minerals.

Porpoise, a highly intelligent marine mammal of the dolphin and whale family, and a common inhabitant of northern seas. Porpoises travel in shoals, their progression being marked by constant leapings and plungings. Their average length is from 1·2–1·5 m. There are several species, nearly all being confined to northern oceans.

Port, a special kind of red Portuguese wine, taking its name from Oporto. It was little known in England until the Methuen Treaty of 1703, when it could be imported at a low duty.

Portland Vase, one of the most renowned specimens of ancient art, long in the possession of the Portland family. In 1810 it was loaned to the British Museum. Here it was shattered in 1845 by a stone from a maniac's hand, but has been skilfully restored. It is said to have been found in the 17th cent. in an ancient tomb near Rome. It was purchased from the Barberini family in 1770 by Sir Wm. Hamilton, subsequently sold to the Duchess of Portland. The vase, which is actually a two-handled urn, stands about 25 cm high, is of transparent dark blue glass, ornamented with figures cut in relief in overlaid white opaque glass. It was purchased by the British Museum in 1945. *See also* **Glass.**

Portreeve in olden times was an official appointed to superintend a port or harbour, and before the name of mayor was used the chief magistrate of London was styled the Portreeve.

Positivism. *See* **Section J.**

Positron, the "positive electron", an atomic particle having the same mass but an electric charge equal but opposite to that of an electron. It was discovered in 1932. *See also* **F16.**

Post-Impressionism, a term introduced by Roger Fry to describe the exhibition of paintings sponsored by himself in London (1910–11) officially entitled "Manet and the Post-Impressionists". The exhibition included paintings by Manet, Cézanne, Gauguin, Van Gogh, Seurat, Signac, works by Matisse, Rouault and the *Fauves* (*q.v.*), and sculpture by Maillol. In a second exhibition, held in 1912, Picasso and the Cubists were also represented. The term therefore refers to the movement in modern art which reacted against the transient naturalism of the Impressionists by concerning itself primarily with colour, form and solidity. Most artists today would include Cézanne, Van Gogh and Gauguin as the main Post-Impressionists and maintain that it prepared the way for Fauvism, Cubism and Expressionism.

Post Office, The, is made up of three separate companies, Royal Mail, Parcelforce and Post Office Counters. There are 20,000 post offices in Britain. The Royal Mail with 150,000 employees, handles 63 million letters daily (collected from 120,000 post boxes). Britain is the only country with two urban deliveries daily. Recent government attempts to privatise the Post Office have collapsed in the face of public opposition.

Potassium, a metal, no. 19, symbol K (German *Kalium*). It is similar to sodium, reacting violently with water. It was discovered by Sir Humphry Davy in 1807, and is now generally obtained by the electrolysis of fused potassium hydroxide or chloride/fluoride mixture. Its principal minerals are carnallite and kainite, and it is relatively common in rocks, accounting for about 2½% of the earth's crust. An essential element for healthy plant growth; the ashes of plants are relatively rich in potassium.

Potsdam Agreement was signed by Truman, Stalin and Attlee in August 1945. By this Agreement a Council of Foreign Ministers was established, representing the five principal Powers: China, France, Soviet Russia, the United Kingdom and United States of America, with the task of drawing up the peace treaties for submission to the United Nations. It laid down, *inter alia,* that German militarism and Hitlerism should be destroyed; that industrial power should be so reduced that Germany would never again be in a position to wage aggressive war; that surplus equipment should be destroyed or transferred to replace wrecked plant in allied territories; that Germany should be treated as an economic whole; and that local self-government should be restored on democratic lines as rapidly as was consistent with military security. The Potsdam Agreement became a dead letter with the creation of a communist régime in the Russian zone of Germany, and marked the beginning of the "cold war".

Prado Gallery, the great public picture collection of Madrid, containing a superb collection of paintings by Velasquez, Murillo, Raphael, Titian, Dürer, Van Dyck, Rubens and Goya.

Pragmatism. *See* **Section J.**

Prefect, chief magistrates in ancient Rome. The

title is now applied to the chiefs of administration of the departments of France.

Pre-Raphaelite Brotherhood was the name given to their school of thought by three British artists, Dante Gabriel Rossetti, J. E. Millais and W. Holman Hunt, who in 1848 revolted against the academic art of their time and advocated a return to the style of the Italian painters prior to Raphael—the simple naturalism of the Primitives, such as Botticelli, Fra Angelico and Filippo Lippi. Thus they avoided the use of heavy shadows and painted on a white ground in bright colours—a technique which aroused the ire of those used to the dark and murky canvases of the contemporary romantic artists. Although they held these principles in common the three members of the "P.R.B.", as it was popularly called, were really quite different in other respects. Thus Rossetti (who for some reason is always thought of as the typical Pre-Raphaelite) produced works of a highly romanticised mediaevalism which, apart from certain aspects of technique, bear not the slightest resemblance to the sentimental naturalism of Millais or the much more dramatic realism of Holman Hunt (*e.g.*, in *The Scapegoat*). The Brotherhood was later joined by a number of lesser artists, but its works are not commonly accepted with enthusiasm today when the general feeling is that they are sentimental and religiose rather than the product of deeply-felt emotions. Ruskin in his writings defended their work but the movement ended in 1853.

Presbyterianism. *See* Section J.

Press-Gang, a body of sailors employed to impress men into naval service, frequently resorted to in England, especially during the war with France in the early 19th cent. Press gangs were not used after about 1850.

Primitive Art. The word "primitive" has a number of different meanings: (1) the art of prehistoric communities (*e.g.*, the famous animal cave-drawings of the Aurignacians, *c.* 25,000 B.C., at Altamira in Spain); (2) the art of modern primitive communities (*e.g.*, Bushman rock-paintings; (3) child art; (4) peasant art which springs from a spontaneous desire to impart beauty to objects of daily use and shows a tendency towards abstraction. Peasant art has many features in common the world over, the woodcarving of the Norsemen being almost indistinguishable from that of the Maoris; (5) the modern school of primitive painting in which naïveté of presentation is either the aim of a highly sophisticated mind (*e.g.*, the self-taught French painter Le Douanier Rousseau (d. 1910), or arises naturally from a simple one (the American "grandma" Moses (d. 1961) who began to paint in her seventies).

Printing by movable types was first used in Europe in 1454 by Johann Gutenberg, a citizen of Mainz. The invention is also claimed for Laurens Koster of Haarlem. It was introduced into England by Caxton, who set up a printing press in Westminster in 1476. Gothic characters were first used, being superseded by Roman letters in 1518. In 1798 Earl Stanhope replaced the wood printing press by one of iron. In 1814 Friedrich Koenig applied the principle of steam power to the press. Mr. John Walter, of *The Times* newspaper, was the first to use the steam press. Improvements were introduced by Applegarth and Cowper in 1828 and great strides were made in 1858 when the Hoe machine was put on the market. Then came the Walter press in 1866 which printed on continuous rolls of paper from curved stereotyped plates. The Monotype machine casts single letters and the Linotype whole lines. The term letterpress is used for all printing methods using plates where the characters stand in *relief*. The other main printing methods are *intaglio* and *planographic*. The development of computer technology using electronic methods has introduced a new era in printing.

prion, a tiny micro-organism, one hundred times smaller than a virus.

Privatisation, selling of state-owned industries to private businesses and individuals, encouraged by the government after 1979 as part of its free market policies, to reduce the role of the state, and to raise money. Among the industries partly or wholly sold off were British Aerospace and

Britoil (1983), British Telecom (1984) and British Gas (1986). Others included British Airways, British Coal and the Trustee Savings Bank. A further aspect of privatisation was the requirement of local authorities to contract out activities to private companies and the introduction of "internal markets" in the National Health Service.

The Privy Council is the Sovereign's own council, consisting of about 300 persons who have reached eminence in some branch of public affairs (Cabinet ministers must be Privy Counsellors), on whose advice and through which the Sovereign exercises his or her statutory and a number of prerogative powers. From it have sprung many organs of the constitution and many of our government departments have grown from committees of the Privy Council. For example the Judiciary or courts of justice have grown from the Sovereign's Council sitting as a Court of Justice, and today the Judicial Committee of the Privy Council is a body of distinguished lawyers acting as a Court of Appeal from courts of the Commonwealth.

Probation Officers are attached to particular Courts, sometimes a Magistrates' or a higher court. Sometimes an offender is not sentenced to punishment, but is released "on probation", that is on the condition that he behaves well and follows directions given by the Court or by a probation officer. Such an officer is a trained man (or woman) who advises, assists and befriends people who are placed under his supervision by a court of law. The probation officer, by his assessment of the social background of the offender, can advise the court upon the wisdom of putting the offender on probation. The probation officer by his understanding can so befriend an offender as to provide a basis for his rehabilitation. He undertakes the "after care" of those released from prison or Young Offenders' Institutions.

Productivity. Physical productivity is the output of products during a time unit, *e.g.*, so many products per man hour, or day, or year. Total productivity is the sum of all the units of product created during the given time. Labour productivity is the part of the total that is attributed to labour as a factor of production. Productivity of capital is the element attributed to capital as a factor. Productivity of land is the element attributed to the natural powers of the soil, as distinct from what is contributed by the application to it of capital or labour.

Propane, a colourless inflammable gas made of carbon and hydrogen; formula C_3H_8. It is easily liquefied and transported liquid in cylinders and tanks. In this form it is familiar as a "portable gas supply" for domestic and industrial uses. It is sometimes mixed with butane (*q.v.*) for this purpose. Propane occurs in natural gas and is a by-product of oil refining.

Proteins are the main chemical substances of living matter: they are a part of every living cell and are found in all animals and plants. All proteins are basically constructed of carbon hydrogen, oxygen and nitrogen, and some contain sulphur, phosphorus (nucleoproteins) and iron (haemoglobin). Proteins are built up of very long chains of amino-acids connected by amide linkages (the synthetic polymers such as "nylon" and casein plastics (from milk) are built up of the same linkages). The structure of protein molecules allows a variety of function. Enzymes, which bring about chemical reactions in living cells, are proteins having specific properties. *See* **F32–3**, *also* Diet, **Section P.**

Proton, a basic constituent of the atomic nucleus, positively charged, having a mass about 1836 times that of the electron. It is a positive hydrogen ion. *See* **F13**(2), **16.**

Prout's hypothesis. The English chemist William Prout (1785–1850) advanced the idea that all atoms are made of hydrogen, and their weights are exact multiples of the weight of a hydrogen atom. With the modification that neutrons as well as protons occur in the nucleus, Prout's belief, though rejected for many years, has been substantially vindicated.

Provost, a Scottish official similar in rank to an English mayor. The Provosts of Edinburgh, Glasgow, Aberdeen, Perth and Dundee are styled Lords Provost. The title of provost is also given to the heads of certain colleges.

Prud'hommes (Prudent Men), **Councils of,** were French trade tribunals, of masters and workmen, formed to decide on disputes. Originally mediaeval, they were revived by Napoleon in 1806, and carried on by the Third Republic.

Psalms, Book of, for many years attributed to David, but present-day scholars are of opinion that the psalms were written by a series of authors at different times and for different purposes, and that few, if any, were written by David. The Holy Scriptures contain 150.

Psychic Research. See **Section J.**

Psychoanalysis. See **Section J.**

Ptarmigan, birds of the grouse family, one species of which inhabits the Scottish Highlands. In the winter the bird assumes a white plumage.

Ptomaines, amino acids produced during the putrefaction of proteins of animal origin. Not a cause of food poisoning, as was once generally supposed, which is almost invariably due to certain specific bacteria.

Publicans, under the Roman Empire, were people who farmed the public taxes. It is this class of officials that is alluded to in the "publicans and sinners" phrase in the New Testament.

Public Corporations, statutory bodies which operated major industries and services in the public interest, e.g., UK Atomic Energy Authority, Bank of England, B.B.C., Electricity Authorities, Gas Council, British Coal Corporation, British Steel Corporation, British Railways Board, the Post Office, British National Oil Corporation, British Nuclear Fuels, British Airports Authority. They were accountable to Parliament but their staffs were not civil servants. Conservative Governments after 1979 have pursued a policy of privatisation of most of these bodies, and many (e.g. British Gas plc) are now public companies. Others (such as British Rail) are currently in the process of being privatised.

Public Record Office. See **Record Office.**

Public Schools. The Public Schools Act of 1864 named nine "public" schools: Eton, Harrow, Rugby, Winchester, Westminster, Shrewsbury, Charterhouse, St. Paul's and Merchant Taylors'. Today the term embraces many more, and can be applied to all those schools which are financed by bodies other than the State and whose headmasters belong to the Headmasters' Conference as distinct from the Headmasters' Association. There are very many such schools in Britain, including among others: Bedford School (founded 1552); Bradfield College, Berks. (1850); Charterhouse, Godalming (1611); Cheltenham College (1841); Christ's Hospital, Horsham (1553); City of London (1442); Clifton College, Bristol (1862); Dulwich College (1619); Eton College (1440); Felsted, Dunmow, Essex (1564); Haileybury College (1862); Harrow (1571); King Edward's, Birmingham (1552); King's School, Canterbury (600); Malvern College (1865); Manchester Grammar School (1515); Marlborough College (1843); Merchant Taylors' (1561); Mill Hill (1807); Oundle (1556); Radley College, Abingdon (1847); Repton, Derbyshire (1557); Rugby School (1567); St. Albans (948); St. Paul's (1509); Sevenoaks School (1418); Sherborne (1550); Shrewsbury School (1552); Stonyhurst College (1593); Stowe School, Bucks. (1923); Tonbridge (1553); Uppingham, Leics. (1584); Warwick (914); Wellington College (1859); Westminster (1560); Winchester College (1382). Public schools for girls include: Christ's Hospital, Hertford (1552), Cheltenham Ladies' College (founded by Miss Beale in 1853), North London Collegiate School (founded by Miss Buss in 1850), Roedean (1885), Wycombe Abbey (1806). Many public schools have become coeducational. Public Schools are now known as Independant Schools.

Pulsars, cosmic objects discovered in 1967 by the Radio Astronomy group at Cambridge; of great scientific interest, since they are probably neutron stars, and extremely dense. Unlike quasars (q.v.) they are nearby objects within our own galaxy. See **F5.**

Puma, mountain-lion or cougar, a large wild cat found throughout the Americas. It looks like a lean greyish lioness.

Puritans. See **Section J.**

Pyramidology. See **Section J.**

Pyramids of Egypt, on the west bank of the Nile, are vast stone or brick-built structures with inner chambers and subterranean entrances, built by the Pharaohs as royal tombs and dating from about 2700 B.C. The most celebrated are at Gizeh built during the 4th dynasty. The largest, originally 147 m high, is called the Great Pyramid, one of the seven wonders of the world, built by the Pharaoh Khufu, better known as Cheops, and there he was buried, 100,000 men, according to Herodotus, being employed for 20 years upon it. Chephren, successor of Cheops, erected the second pyramid, and the third was built by Mycerinus, a son of Cheops. The pyramid at Meidum built by King Snefru, founder of the 4th dynasty, is the most imposing of all.

Pythons, large snakes, non-poisonous and destroying their prey by crushing it. Some species may reach 9 m in length, and prey upon deer and other small mammals. Found in Asia, Africa and Australia. They lay eggs.

Q

Quadrant, an astronomical instrument for measuring altitudes, superseded for navigational purposes in modern times by the sextant. It consists of a graduated arc of 90° with a movable radius for measuring angles on it.

Quai d'Orsay. An embankment in Paris where the French Foreign Office is situated.

Quail, an edible bird of the partridge family, of which only one species, the Common Quail, is found in England. It is not more than 20 cm long. It is found in most of the warmer regions of the world. In England and Wales the Quail is covered by the Wild Bird Protection Acts.

Quantum Theory. The rapid development of quantum theory has been almost entirely due to the experimental and theoretical study of the interactions between electromagnetic radiation and matter. One of the first steps was taken when it was discovered that the electrons emitted from metals due to the action of ultra-violet radiation have an energy which is not related to the intensity of the incident radiation, but is dependent on its wavelength. Einstein showed in 1905 that this could only be explained on the basis that energy is transferred between radiation and matter in finite amounts, or quanta, which are inversely proportional to wavelength. See **F17(2).**

Quarks were hypothetical subnuclear particles which were postulated by theoretical physicists concerned with the so-called elementary particles. There are believed to be six kinds of quarks. Quarks carry electrical charges which are fractions of those carried by familiar particles like electrons and protons. This and other special properties of quarks make them suitable for explaining the existence of the large number of other particles referred to on **F16–17.** The physical existence of quarks may be demonstrated by experiment at any time and if this happens it will be an exciting triumph for theoretical physics. See **F15(2).**

Quartering, in heraldry, is the disposition of various escutcheons or coats of arms in their proper "quarters" of the family shield, in such order as indicates the alliances with other families.

Quartermaster, a military officer charged with the provisioning and superintendence of soldiers in camp or barracks, and holding the equivalent rank to a lieutenant. The Quartermaster-General is an officer who presides over the provisioning department of the whole army. A Quartermaster in the Navy is a petty officer responsible to the Officer of the Watch; at sea for the correct steering of the ship and in harbour for the running of the ship's routine.

Quarto, a sheet of paper folded twice to make four leaves, or eight pages; abbreviated to "4to".

Quartz is a common and usually colourless mineral, occurring both crystallised and massive. In the first form it is in hexagonal prisms, terminating in pyramids. When pure its specific gravity is 2·66. It is one of the constituents of granite, gneiss, etc. Among the quartz varieties are *rock crystal* (colourless), *smoky quartz* (yellow or brown), *amethyst* (purple), *rose quartz* (pink) and *milky quartz* (white). Quartz veins in metamorphic rocks may yield rich deposits of gold. Mining for gold in the rock is termed quartz-mining.

Quasars, or in preferred terminology, quasi-stellar radio-sources, form a new class of astronomical objects, first identified in the period 1960 to 1962. They have enormous energy output, and are at vast distances. Many are strong sources of radio waves and fluctuate in intensity. There is still controversy over the nature of these objects. We presently consider that the intense emission comes from a relatively small region at the centre of peculiar galaxies. While a plausible explanation would be the existence of a gigantic black hole formed by the gravitational collapse of the nucleus of the galaxy, dragging in surrounding material, including entire star systems, our information is not yet conclusive, and has been further questioned by the findings of the Hubble telescope. *See* **F5**.

Queen Anne's Bounty, established by Queen Anne in 1704 for the augmentation of the maintenance of the poor clergy. Since 1 April 1948 Queen Anne's Bounty and the Ecclesiastical Commissioners ceased to exist and became embodied in the Church Commissioners for England.

Queen's (or **King's**) **Speech** is the speech prepared by the Government in consultation with the Queen and delivered by Her Majesty in person or by her deputy, at the opening or closing of a Parliamentary session.

Quinine, a vegetable alkaloid obtained from the bark of several trees of the *Cinchona* genus. It is colourless and extremely bitter. The drug, sulphate of quinine, is one of the most valuable medicines, forming a powerful tonic. It is anti-periodic, antipyretic and antineuralgic. In cases of malaria it is the most efficacious remedy of natural origin known.

Quirinal, one of the seven hills of Rome.

Quisling, term which came into use during the second world war to denote traitor, collaborator or fifth-columnist. After Vidkun Quisling, who became head of the puppet government after the German invasion of Norway in 1940.

Quorum, the number of members of any body or company necessary to be present at any meeting or commission before business can be transacted. The House of Commons needs a quorum of 40, the Lords a quorum of 3.

R

Rabbi, a Jewish term applied to specially ordained officials who pronounce upon questions of legal form and ritual, and also generally accorded to any Jewish scholar of eminence.

Raccoon, plantigrade carnivorous mammals common to the American continent. There are several species. The common Raccoon (*Procyon lotor*) is about 60 cm long, with a bush ringed tail and sharp snout. Its skin is valuable.

Race. In the old text-books anthropologists were much concerned with the differences between the various races of Man; they described the Black Man (Negro), the Yellow Man (Mongol), the Red Man (American Indian), the Brown Man (Indian), and the White Man (European). Those who study Man from this point of view further subdivide each group into others. Thus White Man may be divided into Nordic, Alpine and Mediterranean; Black Man into Hamitic, Bushman and so on. Each of these groups tends to have physical traits which its members hold in common, although, of course, there are no *pure* racial types. All existing races have been fairly thoroughly mixed. What, in view of recent experience, is really important, is that races or even nations do not have psychological traits—at least not *innate* traits. Anthropology dismisses all theories of a superior race as unscientific: there is not the slightest evidence that one race differs in any way from another in its psychological potentialities; Jews, Irish, Scots, Italians do differ: but their differences are due to their situation and not to anything inborn. *See* **Racism, Section J**.

Raceme, an inflorescence in which the main stem bears stalked flowers, *e.g.*, lupin, foxglove. The youngest flowers at the tip of this axis.

Radar. The basic principle of radar is very similar to that of sight. We switch on a light in the dark, and we *see* an object because the light waves are reflected from it and return to our eye, which is able to detect them. Similarly, the radar station *sees* an object because the invisible radio waves sent out from the transmitter are reflected from it and return to the receiver, which is able to detect them. Thus radar is the use of radio signals that man broadcasts.

The utilisation of radio waves for the detection of reflecting surfaces began with the classical experiment of the late Sir Edward Appleton in 1925, which he conducted in order to demonstrate the existence of the Heaviside layer in the upper atmosphere. During the course of the last war developments took place which tremendously improved the methods and instruments used. As in the case of so many of the inventions primarily developed for the purpose of waging war, many useful applications have been found for radar in times of peace, and, in particular, it has proved of great service as an aid to aerial and marine navigation, and in meteorology and astronomy. Radar astronomy investigates the solar system with the echoes of signals sent out from the Earth.

Radiation, energy emitted in the form of a beam of rays or waves, *e.g.*, acoustic (sound) radiation from a loudspeaker, radiant heat from a fire, β-radiation from a radioactive substance. The radiation of electromagnetic waves from a body depends on its temperature, the amount of energy radiated per second being proportional to the fourth power of the absolute temperature. The hotter the body, the shorter the wavelengths of the radiation; thus the colour of a glowing body depends on its temperature. Of paramount importance to us is radiation from the sun. Amongst other radiations, the sun sends ultra-violet, visible and infra-red (heat) waves. The principal gases of the atmosphere are transparent to practically all of the solar and sky radiation and also that which the earth re-transmits to space. Carbon dioxide and water vapour, however, strongly absorb certain types, the latter, as clouds, playing an important rôle in regulating the temperature of the globe. The cooling of the ground on a clear night is a result of the outgoing long-wave radiation exceeding that coming down from the sky; at sunrise cooling ceases as the incoming radiation becomes sufficient to compensate for the loss of heat.

Radiation, Cosmic. *See* **F3**(2).

Radio. The theory of electromagnetic waves—of which the radio wave is one—was originated by the British physicist James Clerk Maxwell (**F14**). He showed that both electrical and optical phenomena in space are essentially similar in character, and that the waves if short in wavelength are those of light, and if of longer wavelength those of radio waves. Heinrich Hertz made many useful discoveries about the waves themselves, and about their behaviour under differing conditions, and also about the apparatus for producing them. Marconi developed the use of radio waves as a practical means of communication.

Radio methods are vital for the transmission of observed data from space vehicles back to earth, a process known as "telemetering". This is done by converting the observations into electrical pulses which actuate a suitable radio transmitter so that it radiates a signal, in coded form, which can be received at a ground station and decoded. The transmission of such a signal can also be remotely controlled by means of signals from the earth. Photographic and television techniques may also be employed for obtaining the desired information and sending it back to earth, as in the case of the Russian picture of the reverse side of the moon and the American pictures of the lunar surface. The information may be stored within the spacecraft for a time, and then, upon receipt of a particular radio signal from the earth transmitted by the spacecraft at a time convenient for its reception. Soviet scientists, by a special technique, were able in the case of their *Venus IV* probe (October 1967) to parachute an instrumented canister from the spacecraft so that it could descend slowly to the surface of the planet. Another breathtaking achievement was the transformation of the faintest of signals from a billion miles away into superb pictures of the planet Saturn and its rings (*see* **Voyagers 1 and 2**). *See also* **Radio Astronomy, Telemetry.**

Radioactivity is the spontaneous transformation of atomic nuclei, accompanied by the emission of ionising radiations. It was discovered in 1896 by Becquerel, who noticed that salts containing uranium sent off radiations which, like X-rays, can blacken a photographic plate. Two years later Marie and Pierre Curie discovered several new chemical elements which possessed the same property, but many times more intense than uranium; the most important of these was radium. Shortly afterwards it was established, mainly by Rutherford, that three types of radiations called *a-*, *β-* and *γ-* rays, are emitted from radioactive substances. It was also Rutherford who, jointly with Soddy, deduced that the emission of the radiations is associated with the spontaneous disintegration of atoms which result in the transformation of one radioactive substance into another. A series of such transformations ends when a stable element is produced. All of the heavy radioactive elements can be arranged in three radioactive series, called, the uranium, thorium and actinium series. Initially, radioactivity was thought to be a property confined only to a few elements occurring in nature. In 1934, however, Irene and Frederick Joliot-Curie discovered that ordinary elements can be transformed into radioactive forms by subjecting them to bombardment with *a*-particles. Following this, it was found that beams of other fast particles produced in accelerators can also render ordinary substances radioactive. Nowadays it is known that radioactivity is a general property of matter; any chemical element can be produced in one or more radioactive forms, or isotopes. *See* **F12**(1).

Radio Astronomy. The science of radio astronomy makes use of radio apparatus and techniques for the observation of events occurring in far distant parts of the universe, and, in so doing, is able to enlarge upon the observational field of optical astronomy in a remarkable way. By means of radio telescopes it is possible to observe parts of the universe so far distant that the radio waves received have taken thousands of millions of years to travel from their source to the earth, and thus to observe happenings which may have occurred near the beginning of the history of the universe. Thus radio astronomy works with signals that are broadcast by objects in space.

There are two main types of radio telescope. The first, known as the interferometer, uses aerials spaced at large distances to obtain very high angular resolution. Indeed, the so-called very long baseline interferometers (VLBI) use receivers with separations of many thousands of km to obtain higher resolution than any optical telescope. The second, and "steerable", type, is that of the radio telescope at Jodrell Bank, Cheshire, which consists of an enormous concave metal bowl, with the radio aerials at its centre. This, though it has a lower "resolution", can be directed or "steered" on to any

part of the sky which is above the horizon. The interferometers, particularly the VLBI, have been used to examine the fine structure of many objects, including the nuclei of large and unusual galaxies. The jet-like structures recently found in several galaxies are of particular interest. As well as exploring the structure of gas clouds and clusters in our own galaxy and in more distant ones, several of the large steerable telescopes have been used as radar antennae, for example to explore the surface of the cloud-covered Venus, and to locate suitable landing sites for the *Viking* spacecraft exploring Mars. Increasingly the radio telescope is used as one of an armoury of instruments available to explore the nature of objects of astronomical interest, such as pulsars or quasars.

Radiocarbon Dating is a method of dating the origin of organic materials or objects by observing their radioactivity. It is of great importance to archaeology because it enables prehistoric dates back to about 50,000 B.C. to be established for animal and vegetable remains. It works because cosmic rays (*q.v.*) entering the atmosphere create neutrons which convert nitrogen in the air to radioactive carbon. This forms radioactive carbon dioxide and gets incorporated into animals and vegetables throughout the world along with ordinary carbon dioxide in a definite ratio, approximately 1 radio carbon atom to 0.8×10^{13} ordinary carbon atoms. When the tissue dies it stops interchanging its carbon with the atmosphere, *e.g.*, by breathing, and the radioactive carbon in it gradually turns into nitrogen emitting a *β*-particle (*see* **F12**(1)). The radiocarbon content decreases by about 1% in 88 years. By measuring the proportion of radioactive carbon left in, say, dead wood, and comparing it with living wood, the age of the dead sample can be calculated. This needs careful laboratory experiments. It is now believed that the proportion of radioactive carbon in the atmosphere varied from time to time in the past because changes in the earth's magnetic field affected the cosmic rays. This has to be allowed for in calculating the radiocarbon date. One use of radiocarbon dating has been to trace the spread of agriculture through the world from its origin in the Near East *c.* 7000 B.C. *See also* **Tree rings.**

Radiosonde, a weather station in miniature carried aloft by a free balloon to heights normally in the neighbourhood of 16 km. Signals representative of values of atmospheric pressure, temperature and humidity are transmitted simultaneously by radio to ground receiving apparatus. The position of the balloon at any instant can be determined by radar, enabling the speed and direction of the upper winds to be deduced.

Radium, a radioactive metallic element, no. 88, symbol Ra, discovered by Marie and Pierre Curie in 1898. Atomic weight 226. Radiotherapy (use of X-rays from radium) is used in the treatment of cancer.

Radon, a radioactive gaseous element, no. 86, symbol Rn, formed by radioactive decay of radium. Its discovery completed the series of elements known as the inert (or rare) gases.

Railways. *See under* **British Rail.**

Rain. When moist air rises into lower temperatures and becomes saturated, condensation takes place on the numerous hygroscopic particles present in the atmosphere. If the temperature is above freezing a cloud of small droplets is formed. These droplets may then grow larger by coalescing with each other as they pass through the cloud until their weight is great enough to make them fall to the earth as rain. In clouds which extend above freezing level, snow and rain both form from the prefer-ential growth of ice crystals at the expense of liquid water droplets. If the resultant ice particle melts as it falls to earth, it gives rain: if not it gives snow. *See also* **Acid Rain.**

Rainbow, a beautiful colour effect visible to an observer with back to the sun and facing a rain shower, caused by the refraction and reflection of sunlight in minute water-droplets in the air. From high in the air it would be possible to see a rainbow as a complete circle, but from the ground the most that can be seen is a semi-circle when the sun is just on the horizon; the higher the sun is, the smaller the arc of the rainbow. When conditions are suitable two bows are seen, the secondary with the colours of the spectrum reversed. The colours the rainbow are seven; red, orange, yellow, green, blue, indigo and violet—the colours of the spectrum. See *also* **Aurora.**

Raingauge, an instrument consisting of a deep metal funnel whose stem dips into a graduated glass jar from which the depth of the rain water collected can be read. Continuous records of rainfall are provided by self-registering instruments.

Rain Making is a facility long desired by mankind, especially in the drought-ridden regions, and attempted throughout history by numerous non-scientific means. Since the second world war it has been proved that clouds can sometimes be made to rain or snow by dropping into them from an aeroplane very cold particles of solid carbon dioxide or by burning a solution containing silver iodide. This makes the moisture of the cloud form tiny ice crystals which grow big and finally fall out of the cloud. The process is quite complicated and not fully understood. The practical exploitation is somewhat chancy at present, but experiments have been made in many countries and the United States has a considerable programme of study. As well as scientific there are commercial and legal problems; premature commercial exploitation has resulted in disillusionment in some cases.

Ramblers' Association, an organisation formed with 1,200 members in 1935 and which now numbers 93,000. It has played a decisive influence on the creation of new long-distance paths (*see* **L76**) and the improvement of the footpath network.

Rambouillet, a royal French château (14th cent., rebuilt 18th cent.), near Paris, and the official summer residence of the President of the French Republic. Also the name of the literary salon of the Marquise de Rambouillet (1588–1665).

Rampant, in heraldry, is a term applied to the figure of an animal with forelegs elevated, the dexter uppermost. When the animal is shown side-faced it is *rampant displayed*, when full-face, *rampant guardant*; when looking back *rampant reguardant*; and when in sitting position *rampant sejant.*

Rape, a cruciferous plant yielding coleseed or rapeseed, extensively grown in all parts of Europe and India. Rape oil is made from the seeds and as oilcake is a valuable animal feeding-stuff.

Rare Gases (also called **Inert Gases**). These are a group of elements which are chemically inert, comprising helium, neon, argon, krypton, xenon and radon. Cavendish in 1785 noticed that there was in air some gas which was not oxygen, nitrogen or carbon dioxide, but it was not until 1894 that the first of the rare gases was found by Rayleigh and Ramsay. This they called argon (inert). After the discovery of helium in 1895 Kayser, Rayleigh and Travers soon isolated the other gases except radon, which was later detected as a radioactive decay product of radium. Some of these inert gases are used to fill electric-light bulbs, and helium is used in balloons, since it is very light and non-inflammable.

Rat, a well-known group of rodent embracing many species. The *brown rat* appeared in Europe early in the 18th cent., coming from the East and entering by way of Russia; now it is widespread and met with in Britain and all parts of the Continent. The *black rat*, which was the common rat before the arrival of the brown species, is a smaller animal and now comparatively scarce. There are numerous other kinds, all of them gross feeders, and existing in such numbers in many places as to constitute a pest.

Rational Number, a number which can be expressed as a ratio of two whole numbers. Examples are 2, $\frac{1}{4}$, 0·3, −8. *See* Irrational Number.

Rationalism. *See* **Section J.**

Rattlesnake, venomous snakes which obtain their name from the possession of a rattle in the end of their tail, consisting of horny pieces so arranged that when vibrated they make a rattling sound. They are only found in N. and S. America.

Raven, a black-plumaged bird of the crow family, with raucous voice and massive bill. Occurs in many parts of Europe, Asia and America. Ravens

are easily domesticated and form interesting pets. Dickens had one which he described in *Barnaby Rudge.*

Ray, fish with a very flat body and broad and fleshy pectoral fins, related to the sharks. There are about 140 species. In Britain they are generally called *skate.*

Razorbill, a sea-bird of the auk family, having a high, furrowed bill and black-and-white plumage. It inhabits rocky cliffs during the breeding season, and at other times is mostly out on the open sea.

Realism is a vague term. As a movement in art it can be said to have started with Gustave Courbet in the mid-19th cent. in his revolt against the classicism of Ingres and the romanticism of Delacroix. He was a man of strong radical views, and like Zola, Balzac and Flaubert in literature, turned to the actuality of everyday life, recording it with frankness and vigour. Some young English painters, notably Bratby, of the "kitchen sink" school, practise what some describe as social realism. In another sense, realism is an attitude concerned with interpreting the essential nature of the subject, revealing truths hidden by the accidentals of ordinary visual appearance. Thus form becomes more significant than content. Beginning with Cézanne and Van Gogh this trend passes on to Cubist and Abstract painting. *See also* **Section J** (philosophy).

Record Office, in Chancery Lane, London, the place where the Public Records of England were preserved, including Domesday Book. Most of these records are currently being moved to Kew. Modern records are subject to at least a 30-year restriction on access. Some records may be closed for 100 years. Since 1992 the PRO has been an Executive Agency.

Rectifier, an electrical device which will allow electric current to flow in one direction only and can therefore be used for turning alternating current into direct current. Since electricity is usually supplied in alternating form and frequently needed in direct form, rectifiers are of very common use in both industry and the home, for example in radio and television and for battery chargers. Rectifying properties are possessed by a number of different devices, one of which is a thermionic diode (*see* **Valve**). Very large valves filled with mercury vapour are often used for rectifying heavy currents for industrial purposes. Many other rectifiers use semiconductors in close contact with metals or with other semiconductors because such junctions have the property of passing electric current easily only in one direction.

Recusants, people who refused to attend the Anglican Church or to acknowledge the ecclesiastical supremacy of the Crown in the 16th and 17th cent.

Recycling, the process of sorting and re-using waste products. By no means a new idea, and already much used in industry and by the whole community in war-time, recycling assumes prominence when materials are scarce and prices high. There is much evidence from several countries that the public responds well to properly organised schemes for the collection, sorting and re-use of paper, plastic, *etc.*

Redstart, a small bird of the Thrush family of handsome plumage and striking song. Two species visit Great Britain: the Common Redstart, with bright chestnut rump and tail, white forehead and black cheeks, favours wooded country, and the Black Redstart, with black breast and throat, chestnut tail and white wing bars, prefers rocky ground or ruins, and breeds in S. England.

Redwing, a bird of the Thrush family which finds its way to this country for the winter. Resembles the song thrush, but distinguished by smaller size, buffish-white eye-stripe, chestnut flanks and underwings. It has bred in Scotland and on Fair Isle.

Redwood *or* **Sequoia.** This genus of coniferous tree comprises two species of Redwoods occurring in N.W. America. Specimens of one species, the Giant Redwood, reach a height of over 90 m and a thickness of 11 m. The age of the largest, the General Sherman tree, is put at 3,500 years.

Referendum and Initiative, two methods by which the wishes of electors may be expressed with regard to proposed legislation. It is developed to the highest extent in Switzerland. In a *Referendum* some specific matter is referred to the electors. The *Initiative* is the means by which electors can compel their representatives to consider a specific issue. Gen. de Gaulle made use of the referendum in seeking the consent of the French nation for his policies. The British Labour Government held a referendum in June 1975, asking voters whether they wanted to remain in or withdraw from the European Economic Community. An Act of Parliament was required to authorise the referendum (which was something new in British constitutional history). The result was for continued membership. More recently Norway rejected membership of the European Union in a referendum in 1994.

Reformation. See **Section J**.

Reform Bills. The principal Bills have been passed for the reform of the Parliamentary franchise. The first was the great Reform Bill of 1832, introduced by Lord John Russell and enacted under the Whig administration of Lord Grey. In addition to a sweeping redistribution of seats, this Act greatly extended the franchise but still left many people without the right to vote. The second Bill, passed by Disraeli in 1867, by giving the vote to workers in towns, established household suffrage. A third Bill, passed in 1884 under a Gladstone ministry, removed the distinction between borough and county franchise, enfranchised agricultural workers, and thus gave the vote to all men over 21. Women had to wait until 1918 to get the vote at the age of 30. The Representation of the People (Equal Franchise) Act, 1928, gave them the right to be registered as Parliamentary electors at the age of 21, thus making England into a true democracy. The Representation of the People Act, 1948, abolished the representation of the universities and the separate representation of the City of London and the business-premises vote. The Representation of the People Act, 1969, reduced the voting age to 18.

Refraction. The change of direction which light rays undergo when passing from one medium to another. The phenomenon is due to the fact that in different media light (and other forms of radiation) has different speeds.

Refractory, a substance capable of standing high temperatures and therefore useful for making furnaces and allied apparatus. Some insulating refractories are fire-clay, alumina, porcelain, carborundum, graphite and silica. Some refractory metals are platinum, molybdenum, tungsten, tantalum and the alloys nichrome, chromel, alumel.

Regency Style is the English version of the French Empire (*q.v.*) and approximately covers the period of the regency of Prince George, later George IV, from 1810 to 1820. It is somewhat less austere than the French style, and contains elements of the fantastic and exotic absent from Empire. The most famous monument of Regency style is the Royal Pavilion at Brighton, built for the Prince Regent by John Nash. (Regency style should not be confused with the *Régence* style in France, fashionable during the regency period between the death of Louis XIV in 1715 and the ascent to the throne of Louis XV in 1723. Here the English equivalent is Queen Anne style.)

Reindeer, a genus of deer horned in both sexes, occurring only in northerly regions. It has an average height of 1·3 m, is very fleet of foot and the Laplanders utilise it for draught purposes and for food.

Relativity. The laws of relativity have been substantially proved and have revolutionised our ideas as to the nature of space, time, matter and energy and forced us to think along new lines. In 1949 a new theory by Einstein was announced which sets forth in a series of equations the laws governing both gravitation and electromagnetism, which is said to bridge the gap that separates the universe of the stars and galaxies and the universe of the atom. At present the one is explained by relativity, the other rests on the quantum theory. See **F17–19**.

Relief in sculpture is of three kinds—high relief (*alto-relievo*), in which the figures stand out to the extent of one-half of their natural proportions, low-relief (*basso-relievo*) when the figures project but slightly; and middle-relief (*mezzo-*

relievo), when the projection is intermediate.

Renaissance. See **Section J**.

Republican Party of the United States was born by the fusion in 1854 of the group who called themselves National Republicans, having split from the Democrats over tariffs in 1825, and the northern Democrats, both of them being opposed to slavery. It came to power when Abraham Lincoln was elected President in 1860 and won 14 of the 18 presidential elections held between 1860 and 1932. It was defeated in 1932 largely as a result of the economic depression and reached its lowest ebb in the years of Roosevelt's New Deal (*q.v.*) The Party went on being defeated every four years until Eisenhower's victory in 1952. Nixon narrowly failed to defeat Kennedy in 1960 and Goldwater was decisively beaten by Lyndon Johnson in 1964. In 1968 and again in 1972 Nixon was successful in winning the Presidency. His fall from power in the aftermath of Watergate made 1974 a bad year for the Republican Party. In 1980 and in 1984, Ronald Reagan won landslide victories. George Bush completed a trio of Republican victories in 1988. However George Bush faced a more difficult campaign in 1992, against a background of economic recession, and was defeated by Bill Clinton. In the 1994 mid-term elections, however, Republicans won landslide victories. The symbol of the Party is an elephant, the invention of Thomas Nast, a cartoonist, in 1874.

Requiem. Properly a mass for the dead, the term is extended to cover musical settings by Palestrina, Mozart, Verdi and others.

Reredos, the ornamental screen at the back of the altar or communion table. It is often of a highly decorative character and is an architectural feature in many churches in Spain. Other examples are to be found in the following cathedrals in England: Southwark, St. Albans, Winchester, Durham and Liverpool.

Resins, natural resins are vegetable compounds largely employed in the industrial arts. They comprise india-rubber, amber, mastic, copal, etc. "Synthetic resins" is a term sometimes used as a synonym for "plastics".

Reuter, an international news agency, founded by Baron J. de Reuter in 1849. Reuters became a private trust in 1916 and a public company in 1984.

Rhea, a large flightless bird, the "ostrich" of S. America, distinguished from the ostrich proper by smaller size, longer beak, larger wings, no tail and 3 toes instead of 2. There are 2 species.

Rheology, science of flow. See **F21**(1).

Rhesus Factor. See **Index to Section P**.

Rhinoceros, a large almost hairless animal related to the horse. Two kinds in Africa and several others in Asia. They have a horn, sometimes two, over the snout composed of modified hair. Most are leaf eaters but the largest species, the white rhino of South Africa, is a grazer. They have been much hunted for their horns. The numbers of African white rhinos have fallen from 100,000 in 1962 to less than 2,500 in 1995.

Rhodium, a metallic element, no. 45, symbol Rh, discovered by Wollaston in 1804. It is found in platinum ores in small amounts, generally less than 2 per cent. With platinum it gives a very hard and durable alloy. It is also used, instead of silver, in putting the reflecting layer on a mirror.

Ribbon Fish or **Oarfish,** a deep-sea fish, deriving its name from its ribbon-like shape. Though fairly long, it is only a few centimetres thick. The ribbon fish is rarely met with because of its habitat, and most of what is known about it has been learnt from specimens cast ashore.

Rice, a grain-yielding grass, of which thousands of strains are known today, extensively cultivated in China, India, S.E. Asia and certain parts of America, and forming the main food of the peoples of China, Japan, India and S.E. Asia. Some 95 per cent. of the world's rice is produced and consumed in the Orient. The grain with the husk is known as "paddy". Arrack, an alcoholic liquor, is made from fermented rice seeds. There are over 70,000 varieties of rice, including long grain, Basmati, Italian risotto rice and Japanese sticky rice.

Richter Scale, a series of numbers used to record the relative magnitude of earthquakes. Devised by F. Richter of the California Institute of Technology. An earthquake is given a number on the scale by measuring the amplitude of earth movements, *i.e.*, the size of the to and fro motion in an earthquake wave, with a special instrument called a seismometer. The reading is corrected by calculation to allow for the distance of the instrument from the earthquake and the corrected results by observers at different places agree quite well. The scale is logarithmic, *i.e.*, earthquakes differing by one unit on the Richter scale are a factor 10 different in amplitude. An earthquake allotted zero on the scale would give a reading of 10^{-6} m on a standard seismometer 100 km from the centre of the earthquake. Smaller disturbances would have negative values on the scale. The largest known earthquakes had Richter values between $+8$ and $+9$, *i.e.*, they had 10^{+8} to 10^{+9} bigger amplitudes than earthquakes of magnitude zero. It is a widespread misconception that the scale has an upper limit of 10; there are no upper or lower limits to the scale.

Rime, a crystalline deposit of ice formed on objects exposed to wet fog at the same time as frost.

Rinderpest *or* **Cattle Plague,** is a highly contagious disease affecting cattle, sheep and other ruminants. In Europe the disease has been eradicated, but it was formerly very widespread and caused great loss of life among cattle. The disease is caused by a filtrable virus, and is attended by fever and congestion of the mucous membranes.

Ring Dove *or* **Wood Pigeon,** a blue-grey bird, distinguished from other pigeons by larger size (41 cm), white wing-bar, glossy green-and-purple neck and white half-collar. It is very common in Britain.

Rituale, the book of rites used in the Roman Catholic Church for the administration of certain sacraments and other church ceremonies.

RNA (Ribonucleic Acid). *See* Nucleic Acids.

Roaring Forties, name applied to the prevailing westerly winds over the oceans in the temperate latitudes of the Southern Hemisphere. Because unimpeded by large land areas the winds are more regular and stronger than the westerlies in the Northern Hemisphere.

Robin (or **Redbreast**). A small bird with olive-brown upper parts and orange-red forehead, throat and breast; both sexes look alike. The young are speckled, lacking the red breast. Its wide European distribution includes the British Isles, where it is the national bird. It also occurs in N. Africa and W. Asia. The nest is placed in a great variety of situations including holes in banks, trees and walls; in sheds, amongst ivy and sometimes in old tins. Nesting-boxes are readily adopted, but care should be taken to ensure that the entrance-hole is small enough to exclude starlings. Robins are pugnacious and defend their territories with vigour. Their attractive appearance, trustful disposition, engaging ways and sweet song make them extremely popular. Robin numbers declined 24% in 1992 (over 1 million birds) because of cold and rain, habitat loss and pollution. The name robin is also applied to a number of very different birds, one of which, the American Robin, occasionally wanders to Europe.

Rock Dove, the grey pigeon *Columbia livia* of Europe and Asia, ancestor of the domestic pigeons as Darwin was the first to show.

Rockets for use in war were first studied by Sir William Congreve early in the 19th cent., and proved very destructive in siege operations. They were invented by the Chinese as long ago as the 11th cent. The Germans devised the huge V2 rocket, carrying a ton of explosive, which was used near the end of the war to bombard London. Rockets are propelled by the burning of fuel (*e.g.*, oxygen or nitric acid), the exhaust, being ejected at high velocity, thrusts the rocket forward. For the study of the properties of the atmosphere vertical sounding rockets are used. Rocket flight in outer space was first presented as practicable by the Russian rocket expert, K. E. Tsiolkovsky, in 1903. The provision of sufficient launching velocity involves the use of rocket motors with adequate thrust. To launch a satellite into an orbit circulating within a few hundred kilometres of the surface a velocity of 29,000 km/h must be imparted. This may be done by using a multi-stage launching system. When the first-stage

motor has burned out it drops off, so that, when the second-stage motor ignites, it does not have to support the weight of the first-stage, and so on. If the launching velocity is increased to 40,000 km/h the vehicle will not return to the neighbourhood of the earth but pass out of the range of the earth's gravitational pull completely. Unless the launching velocity reaches 161,000 km/h it will not escape from the sun and will become an artificial planet.

Rock Magnetism. The study of naturally occurring magnetism in rocks is a subject which has gained considerable importance in recent years. There are two principal reasons for this. One is that this so-called "fossillised magnetism" may be able to tell us more about the past history of the earth's magnetic field. The other is that after many years of heated dispute between geologists rock magnetism promises to settle once and for all the controversy as to whether or not the continents have changed their relative positions in past times (continental drift theory (*q.v.*)). This branch of geophysical research, in addition to its academic interest, may well have important economic consequences. It might, for instance, become possible to locate mineral deposits once accumulated under special conditions at certain latitudes but now drifted to other places. Salt and similar deposits formed by the continuous evaporation of solutions in hot countries are one example; oil may well be another. There has been a *steady* change in rock magnetisation direction with geological time. It is known with some accuracy that the most recent reversal took place 700,000 years ago. It has been found that the older the rock, the farther removed is its fossil magnetisation from the present field.

Rococo, an architectural style which was, in effect, the final stage of **Baroque** (*q.v.*). The name first came into use about 1830 to describe the period 1720–70 and means "shell-shaped" (French *Rocaille*), since the shell was a favourite motif in Rococo ornamentation. At about the beginning of the 18th cent. the heavy older type of Baroque began to show even less restraint than had characterised it in the past; it became still less utilitarian, and showed a kind of playful lighthearted vitality which manifested itself in a wealth of ornamental invention. Baroque was flamboyant and robust, Rococo dainty, graceful and smiling. Its ornaments are frequently asymmetrical, and in this Rococo is unique among the historical styles of Europe. In architecture Rococo is naturally found in those areas where the Baroque had flourished, *i.e.*, Munich, Prague, Vienna and Dresden. In painting, the best expressions of Rococo are to be seen in the works of the French painters Watteau (d. 1721), Boucher (d. 1770), a favourite of Mme de Pompadour, and famous as a decorator of boudoirs, and Fragonard (d. 1806). (As with Baroque, it was typical of Rococo that the sculpture, painting and decorative arts of a building all expressed the same spirit.)

Roe, popular name given to organs in fish which produce eggs and sperms. "Hard roe" is that of the female and consists of eggs; that of the male is the soft roe or milt.

Roe Deer (*Capreolus capreolus*) deer native to Europe and found in England and Scotland but not Ireland. "Roebuck" is the name of the male adult.

Roller, a tropical Old World bird of the *Coraciidae* family, related to the hoopoe, kingfisher and bee-eater, of strikingly brilliant blue, chestnut, greenish-blue plumage. There are fifteen species, one of which breeds in the far north and visits the British Isles on its migrations to and from its winter quarters in Africa.

Romanesque Architecture, prevailed throughout Europe from the mid-10th to the 13th cent., and implies an art which developed from that of the Romans. Notable in Romanesque style were the rounded arch and masonry vaulting. Romanesque led to the graceful and more complex Gothic (*q.v.*). The Italians never regarded Gothic highly and Romanesque churches, generally based on the basilican plan (oblong with double colonnades and a semi-circular apse at the end), continued to be built there until the beginning of the 15th cent. Some of the best examples can be seen at Pisa (11th cent.), Florence (San Miniato, 1013), Lucca (12th cent.) and Milan (the 12th cent. San Ambrogio, most famous of all). In Germany Romanesque architure flourished longer than in France or England; the most famous churches are in the valley of the Rhine, at Cologne (completely destroyed during the second world war), Mainz and Speyer. In France Romanesque churches are found in Burgundy, Provence and Normandy. See **Norman Architecture.**

Roman Roads, highways constructed by the Romans. They were of great durability. The best known British roads were Ermine Street (London, Lincoln, York), Fosse Way (Lincoln through Leicester, Cirencester, Bath, Exeter), Watling Street (Channel Ports, London to Shropshire).

Romanticism, a term for a movement in the arts—whether in music, painting, sculpture or literature—which seeks to give expression to the artist's feelings about his subject rather than to be concerned with form or reality. The romantic view is that art is nature seen through a temperament; the realist view is that art is a slice of life. In painting Delacroix (1798–1863) is the romantic artist *par excellence* with his uncontrolled expression of the passions and love of the exotic. In literature the Romantic movement reached its finest form in the works of Goethe, Schiller and Heine; in the poetry of Byron, Keats, Wordsworth, Shelley and Blake; and in the writings of Victor Hugo. Since Romanticism is partly a matter of temperament in the artist just as Classicism is, it may be found at all times and places, although whether or not it becomes predominant depends on contemporary taste. Cubism, for example, with its attention to form is classical whereas Surrealism with its attention to content is romantic. See also **Romantic Movement, Section J.**

Roman Towns, among Roman towns were Aquae Sulis (Bath), Durovernum (Canterbury), Eboracum (York), Londinium (London), Ratae Coritannorum (Leicester), Venta Belgarum (Winchester) and Verulamium (St. Albans).

Roman Walls were built as frontier barriers under the Emperors Hadrian (76–138) and Antoninus Pius (86–161). Hadrian's works, linking Wallsend-on-Tyne with Bowness-on-Solway, comprised a twenty-foot stone wall, ditches, turrets, "milecastles", fortresses and a double earthen mound, or "Vallum". Impressive ruins are still visible at Chesters and Housesteads. Antoninus Pius, Hadrian's successor, made a further advance, but the turf wall which he built between Forth and Clyde was soon abandoned. Septimius Severus (146–211) restored Hadrian's wall after the assassination of Commodus and the subsequent civil wars. It was finally abandoned between 380 and 390.

Rood Screen, an ornamental partition, separating the choir from the nave in a church, and supporting a crucifix or rood.

Rook, a member of the crow family, abounding in most parts of the British Isles and found in Europe, Asia and N. Africa. It has been introduced into New Zealand. Rooks usually nest in colonies in tall trees. They are highly intelligent birds, and their ways have long been the subject of much careful study.

Rosary, a circular chain of beads, used by Catholics when reciting a particular form of prayer. Each bead represents an entire prayer, and the combined prayers constitute the Rosary.

Roses, Wars of the (1455–85), between the rival houses of York and Lancaster, for the possession of the English crown, began in the reign of Henry VI and ended with the death of Richard III on Bosworth Field. The emblem or badge of the Lancastrians was the red rose and of the Yorkists the white rose. All rivalry between The Roses ended by the marriage of Henry VII, the Lancastrian, with the Princess Elizabeth, daughter of Edward IV, the Yorkist.

Rosetta Stone, discovered in 1799 by the French at Rosetta in Egypt, and deposited in the British Museum. It is a piece of black basalt about 91 cm long, and contains a decree of the Egyptian priests of Ptolemy V Epiphanes (205–181 B.C.) in (1) hieroglyphics, (2) demotic and (3) Greek

characters. It was the three different inscriptions on the same stone that enabled hieroglyphic writing to be deciphered.

Rotten Row, a corruption of *route de roi* (king's drive), the riding resort in Hyde Park.

Rouge et Noir, a well-known gambling card game played on a table divided into two sections and marked with two black and two red lozenges. Any number of players can take part, and the money is staked on the red or black spaces. The cards are dealt out, first to Noir, until the pips aggregate more than 30; then in like manner to the Rouge, and the packet coming nearest to 31 wins the stakes.

Roulette, a gambling game played on a table carrying a revolving wheel divided into 37 compartments. Each compartment bears a number, 0 (zero) and 1 to 36. The numbers are mixed and do not follow any particular order. Of these 37 numbers 18 are black and 18 are red, whereas zero is green. The players stake their money on any compartment, colour or combination of numbers they please. The wheel is whirled round and a ball is set rolling in the opposite direction, dropping finally into one of the compartments, thus deciding the winning number and colour.

Roundhead. In the reign of Charles I and later, a Puritan or member of the Parliamentary party who wore his hair cut short. It was originally a term of derision applied by the Royalists, who usually wore ringlets.

Round Towers, high circular towers with conical roof and massive masonry walls, built during the early Middle Ages (c. 10th cent.). It is believed that they served as refuges and lookouts. These buildings are numerous in Ireland, and two remain in Scotland, at Brechin, which is attached to the church, and at Abernethy.

Royal Academy of Arts was founded in London in 1768, under the patronage of George III. The early exhibitions of the Academy were held first in Pall Mall, and later in Somerset House where the exhibitions continued to be held until 1836, when the National Gallery being built, the Academy moved its quarters to that building. In 1869 the present Royal Academy at Burlington House was opened. List of presidents: Sir Joshua Reynolds (1768), Benjamin West (1792), James Wyatt (1805), B. West (1806), Sir Thomas Lawrence (1820), Sir M. A. Shee (1830), Sir C. Eastlake (1850), Sir F. Grant (1866), Lord Leighton, (1878), Sir J. E. Millais (1896), Sir E. J. Poynter (1896), Sir Aston Webb (1919), Sir F. Dicksee (1924), Sir William Llewellyn (1928), Sir E. Lutyens (1938), Sir A. J. Munnings (1944), Sir Gerald F. Kelly (1949), Sir A. E. Richardson (1954), Sir Charles Wheeler (1956), Sir Thomas Monnington (1966), Sir Hugh Casson (1976), Sir Roger de Grey (1984) and Sir Philip Dowson (1993). The Academy holds an exhibition of pictures, designs *etc.* every summer.

Royal British Legion, the ex-servicemen's welfare organization founded by Earl Haig in 1921. A non-political organization, it organizes the sale of poppies on Remembrance Day.

Royal Hospital, Chelsea, built by Wren, was opened in 1694 as an institution for invalid soldiers.

Royal Institution, established 1799, and incorporated by Royal Charter in 1800 for "the promotion, extension and diffusion of Science and of Useful Knowledge". It was in the building of the Institution that Faraday conducted his experiments. Today it has extensive research laboratories. Famous also for its Christmas lectures designed for a juvenile audience.

Royal Society was founded in 1660 and incorporated by Royal Charter in 1662. Viscount Brouncker being named the first president. Its *Philosophical Transactions* date from 1665. Among those who served as president of the Royal Society are Sir Christopher Wren, Pepys, Sir Isaac Newton, Sir Joseph Banks, Sir Humphry Davy, Prof. T. H. Huxley, Lord Rayleigh, Sir Archibald Geikie, Sir J. J. Thomson, O.M., Prof. Sir C. Sherrington, O.M., G.B.E., Lord Rutherford, O.M., Sir William Henry Bragg, O.M., Sir Henry Dale, O.M., Sir Robert Robinson, O.M., Lord Adrian, O.M., Sir Cyril Hinshelwood, O.M., Lord Florey, O.M., Lord Blackett O.M. (1965), Sir Alan Hodgkin, O.M. (1970), Lord Todd O.M. (1975), Sir Andrew

Huxley (1980) and Lord Porter (1990).

Rubber, substance obtained from the milky juice (latex) exuded by certain tropical trees and shrubs after tapping. Demand spread so rapidly in the 19th cent. that plantations were established wherever the tree would grow. Seeds of the Para rubber tree (*Hevea brasiliensis*) native to the Amazon basin were obtained by Kew, the young plants shipped to Ceylon and it was from these cultivated trees that the vast plantations of Malaysia and Indonesia developed. Recent years have seen great advances in the production of synthetic rubber.

Rubicon, a small river falling into the Adriatic, and forming one of the Italian boundaries, the crossing of which anciently involved decisive action and constituted a declaration of war. Thus the phrase "crossing the Rubicon", denoting an act from which there is no withdrawal.

Rubidium, a metallic element, no. 37, symbol Rb, most closely resembling potassium. It is silver-white and very soft, and was discovered in 1861 by Bunsen and Kirchhoff, using the spectroscope. It is rare, occurring in small amounts in the mica called lepidolite and in potash salts of the Stassfurt deposits in Germany.

Rubrics are instructions in regard to the ceremonies of the Church, appearing in red in the Prayer Book.

Ruby is a deep red variety of Corundum (aluminium oxide); one of the most valued of precious stones. Burma yields some of the finest, and rubies of inferior colour are found in Thailand, Sri Lanka, South Africa and Brazil.

Rudd, a fresh-water fish of wide distribution, plentiful in the rivers of Britain. It is of a reddish-gold colour, with a greenish-blue beard.

Ruff, a bird related to the common sandpiper, at one time common in the Fen districts. The males have a ruff of feathers round the neck in the breeding season. The female is the Reeve.

Ruffe *or* **Pope,** a small fresh-water fish common in most parts of central Europe, and similar in appearance to the ordinary perch. It is found in British rivers.

"Rule, Britannia!" the national sea-song of England, was written by James Thomson (1700–48), the author of the "Seasons", and set to music by Dr. Arne about 1740. The poet's words were "Britannia, rule the waves!" but it is usually rendered "Britannia rules the waves."

Rum, a ardent spirit distilled from molasses, and containing from 40 to 50 per cent. of alcohol. It is chiefly manufactured in the West Indies, and derives its special flavour from a volatile oil.

Ruminants, animals that chew the cud, being provided with a compartmented stomach, enabling them to swallow food, and later to bring it back to the mouth for mastication; *e.g.*, sheep, goats, oxen, etc. While in the rumen some digestion of food, especially cellulose, takes place by bacterial action.

Runcible spoon, a kind of fork used for pickles having three broad prongs. The word was used by Edward Lear about 1870 as a nonsense word and may be derived from *Rouncival* meaning large or huge from the bones said to have been dug up at *Roncesvalles* where Roland fell. Rouncival peas are the large peas called "marrowfats".

Runes, certain characters of an alphabet found in inscriptions in the Germanic languages, found cut into buildings and implements of stone or wood in many parts of northern Europe, including Britain. The runic alphabet originally had 24 letters. Scholars agree that some of the runes derive from Greek and others from Latin.

Ruskin College, the first residential college for working people, founded at Oxford in 1899 by the American Walter Vrooman.

Rusts, parasitic fungi, some common species of which have reddish spores which in a mass have a rusty appearance. A well-known species is the Wheat Rust (*Puccinia graminis*), which has an alternative host in the barberry.

Ruthenium, a greyish-white metallic element, no. 44, symbol Ru, discovered by Claus in 1845. It is harder and more brittle than platinum, in whose ores it occurs.

Rutile, mineral titanium dioxide. It is found in many igneous rocks, and in gneisses and schists, Its commonest colour is reddish-brown.

S

Sabaoth, a Hebrew word, meaning an army or host, and applied sometimes to the Supreme Being, *e.g.*, "the Lord of Hosts" (Rom. ix. 29).

Sabbath and Sunday. Sunday, or the Lord's Day, is the first day of the week in the Christian year. It was substituted for the Jewish Sabbath in the 1st cent. A.D. as the Christian day of worship in commemoration of the Resurrection. The Sabbath, in the Jewish system, was the last day of the week (Saturday in the Christian calendar), designated as the day of religious rest in the fourth commandment of the Decalogue. It was the Puritans at the time of the Reformation who applied the term Sabbath to the Christian Sunday and the two terms have been used indiscriminately ever since.

Sabbatical Year was instituted by the Jews in ancient times for the purpose of giving the soil a rest from cultivation. This was every seventh year. In universities a sabbatical year is a year of absence from duty for the purpose of study and travel, granted to professors at certain intervals.

Sable, a furred mammal of the weasel family mainly inhabiting Siberia. It is bright brown in colour, and has a long, bushy tail. American sable is a marten.

Saccharin, a white crystalline solid manufactured from toluene, 550 times as sweet as cane sugar. It is used as a sweetening agent; as a substitute for sugar when sugar is forbidden, as in certain diseases, or when there is a shortage. It has no value as a food.

Safety Lamp, as used in coal-mines, was invented by Sir Humphry Davy in 1816. The flame is enclosed in a cage of fine-meshed wire which allows air to enter and promote burning, but conducts away the heat generated in combustion so that no product of combustion escapes at a temperature high enough to ignite explosive gases in the mine.

Saffron, a plant similar to a purple crocus. It is used for orange flavouring and colouring.

Sainfoin, a widely cultivated forage plant, especially adapted for sheep. It is of strong, leafy growth and bears bright red flowers. It belongs to the same family of flowering plants as peas and beans.

St. Elmo's Fire, a glowing brush-like discharge of electricity which takes place from sharp-pointed objects on mountains or the masts of ships exposed to the intense electric fields of thunder-clouds.

Saints' Days. In the liturgy of the Roman Catholic church a saint is commemorated and his intercession sought on a special day (saint's day), usually the anniversary of his death. Pope Paul decreed that from 1 January 1970 the following saints were to be dropped from the calendar; Christopher, Catherine of Alexandria, Alexis, Pudenzia, Susan, Margaret, Viviana, Eustace, Martina, Venantius and Domitilla. Many others, including our own Saint George, and Nicholas (Santa Claus) have been demoted though they may be venerated locally. There are now only 153 saints' days in addition to those in honour of the Apostles, Saint Joseph and the Virgin Mary. The festival of All Saints is on 1 November.

Salamanders are amphibia superficially resembling lizards, from which they differ in having a moist skin and no scales.

Salic Law was probably instituted in France in the 5th cent. for the purpose of excluding females from inheriting the Crown. The Bourbons introduced the same law into Spain, but this was abolished by decree in 1830 to enable Isabella II to succeed.

Salmon, a fish notable for its habit of returning from the sea to spawn in the river where it was itself hatched. Their origin can be inferred from the chemical composition of certain blood proteins. Salmon from the two sides of the Atlantic migrate to communal feeding grounds off Greenland.

Saltpetre. *See* **Nitre.**

Salvarsan, the organic arsenical compound asphenamine, which Ehrlich discovered was able to kill inside the human body the spirochaete germ that causes syphilis. Also known as

"606". It has been superseded by neosalvarsan.

Salvation Army. *See* **Section J.**

Samarium, metallic element, no. 62, symbol Sm, one of the lanthanides (**L72**). Discovered in 1879 by Boisbaudran

San Andreas Fault, is the dividing line between the North American plate and the North Pacific Ocean plate where "plate" means one of the rigid sections of the earth's crust as conceived in the theory of plate tectonics (*q.v.*). The fault runs roughly north-west-south-east in California passing near San Francisco. The Pacific Ocean bed and the North American continent are sliding past each other along this fault at about 5 cm per year. As at all plate-to-plate boundaries—another is the Western Pacific coast—the San Andreas fault is the scene of great earthquake activity. Between 1934 and 1970 there were over 7,000 earthquakes severer than magnitude 4 on Richter scale (*q.v.*) in and near southern California. Because of large population centres, the activity of San Andreas region is studied with great care and some apprehension about a repeat of the San Francisco earthquake of 1906 which caused displacements of up to 6·4 m along the San Andreas Fault. *See also* **F9.**

Sandering, small wading bird of sandpiper family; breeds in tundra regions of far north, and is seen on sandy beaches of Britain as a winter visitor, Conspicuous white wing stripe and, like Curlew, Sandpiper, Knot, Dunlin and other members of sandpiper family, has marked change of plumage between winter and summer.

Sandpiper, small- to medium-sized wading birds of several species whose migratory powers are so great that they are found in most parts of the world. They include the Common Sandpiper, a bird about 18 cm long, greenish-brown head and back, white under-parts, beak long and slender; Purple, Wood and Curlew-Sandpipers.

Sans-culottes (French = without knee breeches), a term applied by the French aristocrats to the revolutionary leaders during the French Revolution who wore long trousers instead of knee breeches.

Sanskrit is the language of ancient India, spoken by the Brahmins, and existing in early Oriental literature. It was the language of literature and government and is now confined to temples and places of learning. Its relationship to the modern Indian languages is rather like that of Latin and Greek to modern European languages.

Saponin. The term is a generic one applied to a range of organic compounds which produce frothy, soapy solutions. Saponins are extracted from the soapwort root, horse chestnut seeds, etc. Saponin is the basis of the "foam" used for fire fighting; it can be used like soap to make insecticides and fungicides adhere to the leaves of plants. Also used as detergents.

Sapphic Verse, a form of verse said to have been invented by Sappho, the lyric poetess of Lesbos, who flourished about 600 B.C.

Sapphire, a valuable deep blue variety of Corundum (aluminium oxide) found mostly in India, Sri Lanka and Northern Italy. Synthetic sapphire is often used for gramophone styli.

Saracen, the name given in classic times to the Arab tribes of Syria and adjacent territories. In the Middle Ages the current designation among the Christians for their Muslim enemies.

Sarcophagus, the name given to a stone coffin, such as was used by the ancient Egyptians, Greeks, and Romans, for receiving the remains of their famous dead. These sarcophagi were often decorated with rich carvings and sculptures.

Sassanides were a dynasty of Persian rulers descended from Artaxerxes from 226 to 625.

Satellite Communication, the system for transmitting telephone and television signals over long distances. Satellites orbiting the earth at a height of *c.* 35,700 km above the Atlantic, Pacific and Indian oceans provide a global coverage. They take exactly 24 h to complete one orbit and so appear to stay in the same place. *Telstar,* launched in the summer of 1969, took only 2·5 h and was therefore within range of the earth stations on each side of the Atlantic for very short periods. The global satellite system Intelsat (International Telecommunications Satellite Organisation) was founded in 1964 to establish a world-wide system on a commercial basis. The first generation of Intelsat satellites to be launched from Florida was *Early Bird,* which went into service in June 1965. Further series have been introduced since then. For example, in 1981 Intelsat had five satellites covering the Atlantic, Indian and Pacific oceans. The Intelsat 5 type of satellite weighs nearly 2,000 kg and can handle two television channels and 12,000 telephone calls simultaneously. Post may now be sent by satellite through Intelpost which began operating in 1980.

Satrap, the name given to the governor of a province (satrapy) in the ancient Persian monarchy.

Saturday, the seventh day of the week (the Jewish Sabbath) derived name from planet Saturn.

Saturn, the sixth planet in order from the sun, from which it is distant 1427 × 10⁶ km and around which it makes a revolution in 29.46 years (**F8**). It is 120,200 km in diameter or 9.42 times as large as the Earth and rotates on its axis in 10h 14 min. Saturn is noted for its magnificent ring system which is composed of myriads of ice-covered particles. Among the planet's 18 moons are Mimas, Enceladus, Tethys, Dione, Titan, Rhea, Hyperion, Iapetus and Phoebe. Titan is the largest (radius 2,575 km), being the second largest satellite in the solar system, about the size of the planet Mercury. Galileo was the first to observe that Saturn was ringed; Christiaan Huygens the first to study the nature of the rings; and Jacques Cassini the first to suggest that they were composed of myriads of particles. Our knowledge of the planet and its moons and rings has been greatly increased by the camera observations of the spacecrafts Pioneer 11 (flyby Sept 1979), Voyager 1 (flyby autumn 1980) and Voyager 2 (flyby Aug 1981). *See* **Voyager 1 and 2, L127.**

Saturnalia, festivals held in ancient Rome in honour of the god Saturnus.

Sawfly. These insects are considered to be the most primitive members of the order (*Hymenoptera*) to which the bees and wasps belong. In appearance they resemble somewhat the latter, but there is no waist separating thorax and abdomen. The ovipositor is never used as a sting; usually it is saw-like so that the female can use it to make incisions into tissues of plants where the eggs are laid. The larvae look like caterpillars of butterflies and moths.

Saxons, a Teutonic race originally inhabiting what is now Holstein. By the 7th cent. they had, with the Angles and Jutes, conquered and colonised most of England.

Scallop, marine bivalve molluscs of the genus *Pecten,* which is widely distributed. The scalloped edge to the shell results from a pattern of radiating groves. Related to the oyster.

Scandium, a metallic element, no. 21, symbol Sc. It was discovered in 1879 by Nilson, and occurs in small quantities in certain rarer minerals such as wolframite.

Scarabaeidae, a family of beetles (Scarabs) widely distributed through Africa and Asia and the inner parts of Europe. It is to this genus that the "Sacred Beetle" of the Egyptians belongs, and numerous representations of it are found on ancient monuments.

Sceptre, the staff or rod used since ancient times to symbolise supreme authority. The sceptre used for the coronation of Queen Elizabeth II is the one made for Charles II. It is about 90 cm long and tipped with a jewelled cross.

Schism, an ecclesiastical term for division in a church. The East–West Schism was the separation of the Greek Church from the Latin, finally established in 1054. The Great Schism was the division in the Roman Catholic Church from 1378 to 1415, when there were two lines of popes, one at Rome and one at Avignon.

Schist, the geological name of certain metamorphic rocks composed for the most part of mineral with thin plate-like crystals (*e.g.*, mica) so that the layers of a schist are closely parallel. Quartz occurs in schists, and where it preponderates the term "quartz schist" is applied.

Schoolmen, the great scholastic philosophers of the Middle Ages who devoted themselves to the study and exposition of questions of religious inquiry, and attempted to reconcile the teaching of the Church with that of Aristotle. The chief Schoolmen were Archbishop Anselm, Albertus Magnus, Thomas Aquinas, Peter Lombard, Duns Scotus. *See also* **Section J.**

Scientific Units. The International Bureau of Weights and Measures at Sèvres near Paris, is the custodian of accurate scientific measurement in terms of internationally agreed units. Methods of measurement are continually being improved and measurements of new kinds coming into use. In defining units certain principles have evolved which can be expressed as a statement of priorities:

> (i) units should be so defined that measurements made in one laboratory should be reproducible in another with as much consistency as possible;
> (ii) units of all kinds should, so far as practical, form an interrelated system based on as few fundamental units as possible;
> (iii) the fundamental units adopted should have a natural basis, independent of particular man-made objects such as metal bars or weights. An invariable universal natural standard was achieved for the metre in 1958 when it was defined in terms of the wavelength of a line in the spectrum of krypton-86. This was changed in 1983. *See* **L82** and **S.I. Units.**

Scorpion. The scorpions constitute an order of the arthropods. Distinctive features are the pair of powerful claws at the head and a "sting" at the tail, which curves over the back in attack or defence so that it points forwards. The poison injected by the sting is potent, causing instant death in spiders, centipedes, etc., and acute discomfort to humans. The idea that a cornered scorpion can sting itself to death is a myth; scorpions are immune to their own poison.

Scorpion Fly. The scorpion fly, of which there are less than 500 species, constitute a separate order of insects, the *Mecoptera.* They have 2 pairs of membranous wings, and gain their popular name because in some species the end of the abdomen is turned up, though it does not function as a sting.

Scree *or* **Talus,** the mass of loose, angular rock fragments which accumulate towards the bottom of hill-sides and mountain-sides. These fragments have been detached by weathering processes, in particular frost action.

Scythians, nomadic conquerors and skilled horsemen (9th—3rd cent. B.C.) who inhabited much of Southern Europe and Asiatic Russia.

Sea Anemones *or* **Actinaria,** an order of marine animals of the coelenterate class *Antozia.* They form a large and varied group of about 1,100 species and occur in many beautiful colours, flower-like in form.

Seaborgium, 106th element in the periodic table, named in 1994 after Nobel laureate Glenn T. Seaborg.

Sea Butterfly, marine molluscs which propel themselves by two "wings", or side expansions of the foot. They constitute the order *Pteropoda.*

Sea Cow. *See* **Manatee** and **Dugong.**

Sea Cucumbers *or* **Holothurians.** These animals constitute the class of echinoderms called *Holothuroidea.* They are elongated and worm-like, with a ring of about twenty tentacles round the mouth. There are about 500 species.

Sea Eagle, a genus of flesh-eating birds related to the true eagles, kites and other birds of prey. Examples are the Bald Eagle, emblem of the USA, White-tailed Eagle (Grey Sea Eagle), and Steller's Sea Eagle of the Pacific coast of Asia. Last known in Britain in 1911, but successfully reintroduced from Norway in 1976 to the coast of Scotland.

Sea Elephant *or* **Elephant Seal,** a curious genus of seal, the males of which possess a proboscis of *c.* 30 cm in length that suggests an elephant's trunk. They are found on the coast of California and in certain parts of the Southern Ocean; their blubber has a commercial value.

Sea Gravimeter, an instrument to determine the density of the earth's crust beneath the oceans of the world. Designed by Dr. A. Graf of Munich and Dr. J. Lamar Worzel of Columbia University, it can detect changes of one-millionth of the value of gravity at the earth's surface.

Sea Hare, a genus of molluscs (*Aplysia*), so-called because of resemblance to a crouching hare. The shell is thin curved plate largely sunk in the animal's body. They have four tentacles, occur in Britain in the laminaria or ribbon wrack zone, and discharge a purple fluid when molested.

Sea Horse, sea-fish (*Hippocampus*), very numerous in the tropics and comprising some twenty species. Their bodies are ringed and they have prehensile tails. Their heads are horse-shaped, and they swim in a vertical position.

Seal, a marine mammal of the *Phocidae* family. They are found in the cold seas of the world, including the waters around Britain. In 1988, over 17,000 perished in the outbreak of deadly seal distemper.

Sea Lily. A class of echinoderms, the sea lilies may be roughly described as "stalked starfishes". There are about 400 living species and several thousand extinct species are known. Otherwise called Crinoids.

Sea Mouse, a genus of marine worms called *Aphrodite*, oval in shape, 20–23 cm long, iridescent, covered with fine bristles.

Seasons comprise the four natural divisions of the year, and are due to the inclinations of the earth's axis to the plane of the ecliptic (*q.v.*). *See* **Z10.**

Sea Squirts *or* **Tunicates.** These animals are placed in the sub-phylum called *Urochorda*; found growing in rounded, jelly-like masses on rocks near low-water level. They get their name through the water jets they discharge.

Sea Urchin, species forming the class *Echinoidae.* The body is globular and covered with spines which may be used for both defence and locomotion. The main organs of locomotion are, however, the tube feet, as in starfishes.

Secondary Sexual Characters, characters of animals which are distinctive of sex, but have no direct connection with the reproductive process. Examples are: the mane of the lion and the antlers of some deer.

Secretary Bird, so called because of the quill-like plumes about its ears, is a bird of prey related to the eagles and vultures; common in Africa, and of considerable service as an exterminator of snakes. It is a large bird about 1·2 m in height.

Sedimentary Rocks. *See* **F9(1).**

Seismology, the branch of geophysics devoted to the study of earthquakes and other earth movements. The instruments used for the registration of earth tremors are termed seismographs and consist in principle of a pendulum system, the supporting framework following the ground movement and the bob remaining at rest, thus setting up a relative movement between two parts. In order to record the displacements completely, at one station, three seismographs are necessary to show the two horizontal and the vertical components of the motion. Apart from detection and study of waves from earthquakes, sensitive seismographs are now widely used in geophysical prospecting, particularly in the search for oilfields. *See also* **Richter Scale.**

Selenium, a non-metallic element, no. 34, symbol Se; related to sulphur it is a dark red colour, and solid, found associated with sulphur, iron, pyrites, etc., though only in small quantities. It is a semiconductor (*q.v.*) and its special electrical properties have led to its use in photo-electric cells and rectifiers. Selenium is widely used in the chemical industry as a catalyst (*q.v.*) in producing aromatic hydrocarbons from less useful hydrocarbons. Also used in making some types of glass.

Semiconductors, substances with numerous special and useful electrical properties. These include:

> (i) they conduct electricity much better than do insulators, but much less well than metals (hence their name);
> (ii) their power to conduct depends strongly on their temperatures—which makes them useful for temperature sensitive devices;
> (iii) they are sensitive to light—hence their use in photoelectric cells and solar batteries;
> (iv) when in contact with metals, or with other suitable semiconductors, they form a boundary layer which conducts electricity much better one way than the other—this is

the basis of many rectifiers some of which, called crystal diodes, are an important component in radios and electronic devices;

(v) their electrical properties can be greatly influenced by putting in minute amounts of impurity, this enables semiconductor devices, especially transistors, to be made with carefully selected properties.

Semiconductors were known to Faraday, but the semiconductor age really arrived with the invention of the transistor (q.v.) in 1947. The ubiquitous transistor is only one of very many semiconductor devices which perform a variety of functions in technical apparatus of all kinds. Semiconductors used in technology are usually small crystals, frequently of germanium or silicon, and their robustness and small power consumption often make them superior to other devices, such as thermionic valves, which they often replace. Other semiconducting materials are cadmium sulphide, selenium lead telluride, indium antimonide. *See also* **F22**(1).

Senate, the higher governing Assembly of a Legislature. The word, applied primarily to the Roman council, is also used to denote the upper chamber in the legislatures of France, the United States, and other countries. In certain universities the governing body is also called the Senate.

Sensitive Plant. A species of Mimosa (*Mimosa pudica*), whose leaves are extremely sensitive to touch, shaking and burning.

Sepia, the "ink" of the cuttlefish. *See* **Ink Sac.**

September, the ninth month of the year, and the seventh of the old Roman calendar; hence the name, from Septimus. The designation was several times changed by the Emperors, but none of the new names survived for long.

Septuagesima Sunday, the third Sunday before Lent.

Septuagint, the Greek translation of the Old Testament made by Alexandrian Jews between 250 B.C. and 100 B.C. from Hebrew texts now lost. There are many differences between the Septuagint and the Massoretic version (A.D. 900), and therefore it is of great value for textual criticism. The symbol for the Septuagint is LXX.

Serfs, the name given to the peasants formerly existing in Russia, who answered to the condition of the feudal "villeins" of England. They were attached to the soil and were transferred with it in all sales or leases. Serfdom existed in Prussia until 1807 and in Russia until 1861.

Serpentine, a mineral: chemically a hydrous silicate of magnesium. Green serpentine is used as an ornament stone. Fibrous serpentine is called asbestos.

Serval, a collie-dog-sized cat, long-limbed and spotted, from Africa. Preys on a variety of animals, from lizards to small antelope. Black servals occur mainly in mountainous regions.

Set, both in everyday speech (as in tea set, chess set) and in mathematics, a set is a collection of things. The members of the set can be specified by listing them or by describing the properties necessary for membership of the set, *e.g.*, the set of ginger-haired boxers. Set theory is a very important branch of mathematics founded by a great mathematician, Georg Cantor (1845–1918). Its development has influenced many other branches of mathematics. Perhaps one reflection of its fundamental nature is to be found in the fact that many schoolchildren, even of tender age, are now learning set theory and confounding parents who did not hear of it at school when they were there.

Settlement, Act of, passed in 1701, assigned the Crown to the House of Hanover in case of Anne's death without children. The decision represented the determination of the squires and the Anglican Church never again to trust themselves to a Roman Catholic king.

Seven Champions of Christendom, as set forth in mediaeval literature, were St. George of England, St. Andrew of Scotland, St. Patrick of Ireland, St. David of Wales, St. James of Spain, St. Denis of France, and St. Antony of Italy.

Seven Churches of Asia, referred to in the Revelation of St. John, were those of Ephesus, founded by St. Paul in 57, Smyrna, Pergamos, Thyatira, Sardis, Philadelphia (Lydia) and Laodicea (Phrygia), all in W. Asia Minor.

Seven Wonders of the World were: 1. The Pyramids of Egypt; 2. the tomb of Mausolus, King of Caria (hence the word mausoleum); 3. the Temple of Diana at Ephesus; 4. the Walls and Hanging Gardens of Babylon; 5. the Colossus at Rhodes; 6. the Ivory and Gold Statue of Jupiter Olympus; and 7. the Pharos, or Watch Tower, built at Alexandria by Ptolemy Philadelphus, King of Egypt.

Seven Years War was waged by Frederick the Great and England against Austria, France, and Russia, from 1756 to 1763. It resulted in the retention of Silesia by Prussia, the breaking of French power in India and the strengthening of the British Indian Empire.

Severn Barrage, a barrier across the River Severn estuary proposed with a view to extracting useful electrical energy from tidal power. Essentially the idea is to let the tidal water flow into a reservoir upstream from the barrage and then to flow seaward under gravity through specially designed hydroelectric generators situated on the barrage. Tidal power has been harnessed in a French project and there is little doubt that the Severn scheme is technically feasible. However, environmental, economic and social factors enter the matter and are influencing consideration of its overall desirability. *See also* **Tidal Power.**

Sexagesima Sunday is the 2nd Sunday before Lent.

Sextant, a reflecting instrument for measuring the angular distances of objects. It is of special importance in navigation and surveying, and contains 60 degrees described on a graduated arc. A small telescope is attached and there are also a couple of mirrors which reflect the distant objects so as to enable them to be accurately observed. The invention is attributed to John Hadley, and to Thomas Godfrey independently, about 1780. The principle had been foreseen, and its application described, at earlier dates by Newton, Halley and Hooke.

Shad, a marine fish belonging to the same genus as the herring. It is found along the Atlantic Coast of the USA, and ascends rivers to spawn.

Shagreen, shark's skin: also untanned leather of peculiar grain made from skins of wild asses, camels and horses.

Shalloon, a kind of cloth manufactured from wool and worsted, and used chiefly for women's dresses and coat linings. It gets its name from the fact that it was originally made at Châlons-sur-Marne. It was called "chalouns" by Chaucer and "shalloons" by Swift.

Shamrock, the three-leaved clover-like plant native to Ireland and its national emblem.

Shark, a large and powerful ocean fish, comprising many species, very widely distributed, but most numerous in tropical seas. They have formidable teeth and are the most carnivorous of all fishes. They usually attain a large size, the whale-shark being often of a length of 15 m. Commercially the shark yields shagreen from its skin, the fins are made into gelatine, and an oil is obtained from the liver.

Sheep, a well-known family of ruminants of great utility as wool-producers, and for food. From the earliest times sheep have been a source of wealth to England. So much were they valued in the 15th and 16th cent., that their exportation was frequently prohibited. Sheep are classified under (1) longwools; (2) shortwools; and (3) mountain breeds. Most of the longwools carry Leicester blood in their ancestry and the shortwooled Down breeds carry the blood of the Southdown. The Southdown produced the present Suffolk, one of the most popular breeds. Cheviot is an important mountain breed. Of the foreign breeds the most valued are the Merino sheep of Spain, which yield a fine long wool. Australia, China, New Zealand, India, Argentina, South Africa, Turkey, Iran and Great Britain are among the chief wool-producing countries in the world.

Shelduck, a handsome genus of surface-feeding ducks, one of which, the common shelduck, is an inhabitant of Great Britain. It is a beautiful white-and-chestnut plumaged bird with dark-green head and neck and red bill. Another species, the ruddy shelduck, appears in Britain only occasionally.

Shellac. This resin is the secretion of the lac

insect (*Coccus lacca*), which occurs in forests of Assam and Thailand. It is used for making varnish and in the manufacture of gramophone records. *See also* **Lac.**

Sherardizing. Process for coating steel or iron parts with zinc to prevent corrosion; this is done by heating the parts in a closed rotating drum containing zinc dust.

Shilling has been an English coin from Saxon times, but it was not of the value of 12 pence until after the Conquest. It is interchangeable with the 5 new pence decimal piece which came into circulation in 1968. A new, smaller 5p coin was introduced after 1991.

Ships have existed from prehistoric times. There is mention of one that sailed from Egypt to Greece in 1485 B.C., and in 786 B.C. the Tyrians built a double-decked vessel. No double-decked ship was known in England, however, before the *Royal Harry* was built by Henry VII, and it was not until the 17th cent. that ship-building was carried on in Great Britain as a prominent industry.

Shoddy, the name given to a kind of cloth mainly composed of woollen or worsted rags, torn up and re-fabricated by powerful machinery. It was first made at Batley in Yorkshire about 1813, and became a very important industry at Batley and the neighbouring town of Dewsbury.

Shooting Star, the popular name for a meteor.

Shot, the name given to solid projectiles fired from guns. In the time of Henry V stone shot was used, later leaden shot, then iron shot, and finally steel shot, introduced by Sir Joseph Whitworth.

Shrike, a large and varied family of birds of hawk-like behaviour found in all continents except S. America. The Red-backed Shrike, which winters in Africa, is a breeding visitor to England and Wales. It is commonly called the "Butcher Bird" from the way it impales its prey (small birds and insects) on thorn-twigs. The other species on the British list are the Great Grey Shrike, the Lesser Grey Shrike, the Woodchat Shrike, and the Masked Shrike.

Shrove Tuesday, the day before the first day of Lent, receiving its name from the old custom of shriving, or making confession, on that day. In England the day has always been associated with the making of pancakes.

Sicilian Vespers, the term applied to the terrible massacre of French people in Sicily in 1282. The French under Charles of Anjou were then in occupation of the island and had been guilty of many cruelties. It began at Palermo on Easter Monday at the hour of vespers and resulted in the expulsion of the French king and the introduction of Spanish rule.

Silence, Tower of, or *dakhma*, a tower about 8 m high, built by the Parsees for their dead. The corpse is taken inside by professional corpse-bearers and left to be consumed by vultures. Parsees do not burn or bury their dead, and the *dakhma* is to protect the living and the elements from defilement.

Silicon, an important non-metallic element, no. 14, symbol Si, it is related to carbon. Next to oxygen, it is the most abundant constituent of the earth's crust (27% by weight). It occurs in many rocks, and its oxide occurs in many forms (*e.g.* quartz, sand, flint, agate, chalcedony, opal, etc.). Principally used as a semi-conducting material for making transistors and similar devices. The circuitry of the computer is etched on a chip of silicon.

Silicones are synthetic organic derivatives of silicon which because of their high resistance to heat and moisture have special uses, *e.g.,* lubricants, heat-resistant resins and lacquers, and water-repellent finishes. Silicones are compounds in which the molecules consist of chains of atoms of silicon and oxygen alternately. Silicones were developed in the United States from discoveries first made by Prof. F. S. Kipping at Nottingham University. Manufacture began in Britain in 1950, and in the form of fluids, resins, rubbers and greases they find wide use in industry. The largest plant in Europe is in Glamorgan.

Silk, the name given to a soft glossy fabric manufactured from the fine thread produced by the silkworm. It was known to, and highly prized

by the ancients, being at one time paid for, weight for weight, with gold. The manufacture of silk was carried on in Sicily in the 12th cent., later spreading to Italy, Spain and France, where Lyons has been the great centre of production from 1450 to this day. It was not manufactured in England before 1604; but when certain French refugees established themselves at Spitalfields in 1688, the industry was developed and became of importance. In the 18th cent. the Lombes of Derby achieved great success in this industry. Japan, China, Italy, and Korea are the chief silk-producing countries.

Silkworm, the larva of a species of moth, *Bombux mori*. It is native to China, and has been cultivated with success in India, Iran, Turkey and Italy. The silkworm of commerce feeds on mulberry leaves and produces a cocoon of silk varying in colour from white to orange. The cocoon is the silken habitation constructed by the worm for its entrance upon the pupal condition, and to obtain the silk the pupa is killed by immersing in hot water.

Sill, a sheet-like mass of igneous rock which has been intruded parallel with the stratification of the country rock, cf. a dyke.

Silurian. This geological period is one of the major subdivisions of the Palaeozoic era. Its beginning is estimated at 440 million years ago, and the period lasted about 40 million years. Maximum thickness of the Silurian strata in Britain measures 4,575 m. *See* **F48.**

Silver, a white precious metallic element, no. 47, symbol Ag (Latin *argentum*) found in a free state, also in certain combinations, and in a variety of ores. The chief silver-producing regions are the Andes and Cordilleras. Peru, Bolivia and Mexico have yielded vast supplies of the metal since the 16th century, and Colorado and Nevada in the United States have also been very prolific in silver yield. In England standard silver (that used for coinage) formerly contained 92½ per cent. fine silver and 7½ per cent. alloy, but when the price rose to 89½d. per oz and the coins became worth more than the face value, the Coinage Act of 1920 was passed, reducing the fineness to half. To provide silver bullion for industry and for a fund towards the redemption of our silver debt to America, it was decided in 1946 to replace the United Kingdom silver coinage by one made of cupro-nickel (75 per cent. copper, 25 per cent. nickel). Maundy money, however, is of the original silver standard. Silver chloride and bromide are light-sensitive compounds and are used in photography.

Simony, the offence of trading in church offices, has been contrary to English law since the time of Edward VI. Elizabeth also promulgated laws against simony. In 1879 a Royal Commission reported on the law and existing practice as to the sale, exchange and resignation of benefices. The position is now controlled by the Benefices Act 1898, the Amendment Measure 1923, and the Benefices Rules 1926.

Sinn Fein (*Irish* = ourselves alone), Irish nationalistic movement founded in 1905 which developed into a mass republican party and triumphed in the establishment of the Irish Free State. A continuing group has survived which represents politically the outlawed IRA. In Northern Ireland Sinn Fein was legalized in 1974.

Sins, The Seven Deadly or Capital sins are pride, avarice, lust, anger, gluttony, envy, sloth.

Sirius, the dog-star, so called because of its situation in the mouth of the Dog (Canis Major): it is the brightest star in the sky, and is also one of the nearest to us.

Sirocco, a warm, southerly, often dust-laden, wind blowing across Mediterranean lands from the Sahara, in advance of an eastward-moving depression over the Mediterranean.

Siskin, a small bird of the finch family, common in Northern regions, nesting in Britain. The common Siskin has a yellow-green colour and is a lively, swift-flying bird with a stout bill.

Sistine Chapel, the chapel of the Pope in the Vatican, renowned for its frescoes by Michelangelo.

S.I. Units (*Système International d'Unités*) form an internationally recognised system of metric units for scientific and technical quantities. The basic units of length, time, mass, electric current, temperature, amount of substance, and luminous intensity are, respectively the metre, second, kilogram, ampere, kelvin (*see* **Absolute Temperature**) mole (*see* **F24**) and candela. The S.I. was recommended for general adoption by a number of international organisations such as the General Conference on Weights and Measures (1960). Many countries have made or are making the S.I. the only legally recognised set of Units. Gt. Britain's decision to "go metric" has brought general use of S.I. units in its train. These units command the widespread though not absolutely unanimous support of industrialists, technologists, and scientists. Many have urged their adoption to end the confusing multiplicity of units on the world scene. *See also* **F66–69.**

Six Articles, The Statute of the, was passed in 1539 for compelling adhesion to the chief doctrines of Roman Catholic faith: transubstantiation, communion in one kind only for the laity, vows of chastity, celibacy of the clergy, private masses and auricular confession; those who refused to subscribe to the Articles were treated as heretics. The Act was repealed in 1547.

Skink. The skinks constitute a large family of lizards with large smooth scales, under each of which is a bony plate. The largest species, found in Australia, is about 61 cm long. Some skinks have adopted a burrowing habit and degeneration of the limbs is associated with this. The Common Skink is a small species *c.* 12 cm long, living in deserts of N. Africa.

Skua, falcon-like marine birds related to the gulls found throughout the world. Known as "Robber Birds" because they steal not only the young and eggs of other birds (including penguins) but also their food, which they force them to disgorge in mid-air. The Arctic Skua breeds as far south as Scotland. The Great Skua breeds in both Antarctica and Arctica. Other species are the Pomarine, the Long-tailed, and McCormick's Skua.

Skunk, a North American mammal of the weasel family, with short legs and long bushy tail. All fifteen species are black and white, some being striped and the rest spotted. It secretes and ejects at will a foul-smelling fluid.

Sky. The blue colour of the sky on a summer's day is the result of the scattering of light waves by particles of dust and vapour in the earth's atmosphere. Blue light having almost the smallest wavelength in the visible spectrum ($0·00004$ cm) is scattered laterally about 10 times as much as the red ($0·00007$ cm).

Skyscraper. Owing to lack of ground space, increasing cost of land, and growth of modern cities, buildings are being made higher than broader; hence the name. The structures are constructed of steel framework usually clothed in concrete or reinforced concrete. The first modern skyscraper of steel skeletal construction was the Home Insurance Building in Chicago, designed (1883) by William Le Baron. The New York skyscrapers include the World Trade Center building (110 stories), Empire State building (102 stories), Chrysler (77 stories), Rockefeller Center (70 stories), and 60 Wall Tower (67 stories). Even taller than any New York skyscraper is the Sears Tower, Chicago (447m). The Petronas Towers, now being built in Kuala Lumpur, will reach 450 m (1477ft). The tallest building in Britain is the 50-storey Canary Wharf tower (243·7m), visible from 20 miles away in Kent. It has overtaken the National Westminster Bank tower (183m) and the BT radio tower (177m). The tallest *structure* in Britain is the IBA mast at Belmont, Lincs., (387·1m).

Slate, fine-grained clayey rocks which have undergone metamorphism. They cleave easily, and it is this property of cleavage which makes them a valuable source of roofing material. Important quarries producing mainly green slate are in the Coniston–Ambleside area of the Lake District.

Slavery. In its earlier forms, as in the times of ancient Greece and Rome, in the feudal ages, when vassalage and villeinage existed, and in the serfdom of Russia and other northern nations, slavery was attended by many inhumanities and evils; but perhaps in the negro slavery system which prevailed in the British colonies for upwards of 200 years and in certain parts of the United States up to 1865, it attained its highest point of cruelty. In 1833 the Act of Emancipation was passed, emancipating all slaves in British territories, though slavery

continued to be tolerated in northern Nigeria, Sierra Leone and in the Anglo-Egyptian Sudan long after that date. Even today slavery and forced labour are still to be found.

Slide Rule, an instrument which consists of two logarithmic scales sliding alongside each other. By its use multiplication, division, extraction of roots, etc., are speedily carried out.

Sloth, a curious family of mammals, only found in Central and South America. They dwell almost entirely in the trees, proceeding from branch to branch with their bodies hanging downwards, their weight being supported by their large hook-like claws. They eat foliage.

Slow-Worm, a species of lizard found in Britain which lacks legs. Silver with longitudinal brown stripes, it lives almost entirely on slugs.

Smelting. The process of heating an ore with a reducing agent to convert ore into metal, and with a flux to convert rocky impurities into a slag that will float on top of the molten metal. Slag and metal can then be tapped separately. An example is iron smelting; the reducing agent is coke, and limestone is added as the flux; the smelting is carried out in a blast furnace.

Snake. The snakes constitute the important reptilian order *Ophidia.* Snakes have a scaly, cylindrical, limbless body, lidless eyes, forked tongue, and the upper and lower jaws joined by an elastic ligament. All snakes have teeth used for seizing prey, and the poisonous varieties are furnished with poison fangs in the upper jaw. These fangs are hollow modified teeth and the venom passes into them from a special gland situated behind the angle of the mouth. Some 2,500 species of snakes are known, divided into 13 families. There are 3 British species—the grass-snake, smooth-snake, and adder.

Snipe, a wading bird, long-legged, with long, slender, straight bill, brown plumage, and zig-zag flight. The Common Snipe breeds locally throughout Britain; the Great Snipe and small Jack Snipe are occasional visitors. The close season is February 1 to August 11.

Snow. When water vapour condenses at high levels at a temperature below freezing (sublimation), a cloud of ice particles is formed. If these frozen droplets are small, they fall slowly and gradually assume a feathery crystalline structure, reaching the earth as snowflakes if the temperature remains below freezing.

Soda, carbonate of sodium, is now mainly obtained by certain processes of manufacture from common salt. It was formerly obtained from the ashes of plants. Bicarbonate of sodium is the primary product in the Solvay or Ammoniasoda method for commercial manufacture of soda; it is also formed when carbon dioxide is passed into strong soda solution. The bicarbonate is used in medicine and in the preparation of baking powder.

Sodium, a metallic element, no. 11, symbol Na (Latin *Natrium*), first obtained by Sir Humphry Davy in 1807 from caustic soda by means of the electric battery. Its chloride is *common salt*; the deposits of salt (*e.g.*, in Cheshire and at Stassfurt) have come into existence through the drying up of inland seas. Salt occurs in sea-water to the extent of about 3 per cent.; the Dead Sea contains about 22 per cent. The blood of animals is maintained at a level of about 0·6% sodium chloride. That there is sodium in the sun's atmosphere was confirmed in 1859 by Kirchhoff from his spectroscopic observations. Liquid sodium metal has properties which make it suitable as a coolant in some nuclear reactors; a technique of handling this very reactive liquid has had to be developed.

Software, the internal programmes and operating procedures of a computer as opposed to its hardware. This includes system software designed to make the computer usable as well as programmes intended for particular applications (*e.g.* commercial or scientific calculations).

Soil Erosion occurs when the soil is removed from an area at a faster rate than soil formation. This situation usually occurs as a result of man's interference with the natural balance of the environment by the removal of natural vegetation, overgrazing or by poor farming techniques. Soil thus exposed is then removed by the wind (as in the Dust Bowl in the 1930s) or by rain in the form of gully or sheet erosion (as in the Tennessee Valley, USA). Methods introduced to stop soil erosion include contour ploughing, afforestation and dry farming techniques.

Solar Battery, one of the innumerable devices made possible by the development of semi-conducting materials, notably germanium and silicon. This device creates an electric current from light falling on it. The current can be put to use or stored in storage batteries. The energy of the current is derived from the sunlight. The solar battery is thus an *energy converting* apparatus. Solar batteries have provided power for the instruments in satellites.

Solar System, the system dominated by the Sun, containing the nine major planets and their satellites, the asteroids, comets, meteoroids and interplanetary gas and dust. *See also* **Section F.**

Solar Wind, a continuous stream of electrically charged particles blowing outwards from the sun, supplemented from time to time by intense outbursts from particular regions of the sun's surface. These streams of protons and electrons on encountering the earth's magnetic field distort it and cause magnetic storms (*q.v.*) and aurorae (*q.v.*).

Soldering is a means of joining together two pieces of material, usually metals, by melting a third metal (the solder) into the joint. The solder solidifies in the pores of the other metals and holds them together. The materials to be joined are not themselves melted so the technique requires less heat than welding. Solders are alloys; there are many kinds depending on the materials to be joined and the strength of joint desired. *See* **Welding.**

Solstice, an astronomical term indicating the point at which the sun is most distant from the equator. *See* **Seasons, Section Z.**

Soundings at sea, to determine depth at any point, have been taken in all seas, and with considerable accuracy. A deep reading was that of the *Challenger* expedition in 1873, near St. Thomas's in the North Atlantic, when 3,875 fathoms (7,091 m) were sounded. In 1851 H.M.S. *Challenger* recorded the then maximum ocean depth in the Marianas Trench (W. Pacific) by echo-sounding as between 5,882 and 5,950 fathoms (10,764 and 10,800 m). Another deep was located in the S. Pacific in 1952–53 of 5,814 fathoms (10,640 m) in the Tonga Trench, 290 km S. of Tonga Tabu. Since then greater depths have been recorded, in the Marianas Trench and the Mindanao Deep. *See* **Pacific Ocean.**

Southern Cross, popular name of *Crux,* is the smallest constellation in the entire sky and can be observed from latitudes below + 30°. Its four brightest stars form a conspicuous Latin cross. The constellation is a vital guide to seafarers.

South Sea Bubble, the name given to a series of financial projects which began with the formation of the South Sea Company in 1711 and ended nine years later in disaster after a mania of speculation. The idea behind the parent scheme was that the state should sell certain trading monopolies in the South seas in return for a sum of money to pay off the National Debt (which stood at £51,300,000 in 1719 when the scheme started). The idea fascinated the public, fabulous profits being dreamt of, and the price of the stock rose out of all proportion to the earnings of the Company. Many dishonest speculative ventures sprang up in imitation with the inevitable result that thousands were ruined. All classes had joined in the gamble and a Committee of Secrecy set up by the House of Commons in December 1720 to investigate the affairs of the Company proved that there had been fraud and corruption on a large scale in the affairs of the Company. Sir Robert Walpole, an opponent of the scheme from the outset, dealt with the crisis.

Space Flight. The Soviet Union was the first country to launch a man into space and bring him safely back to earth. This epoch-making event took place on 12 April 1961, when Yuri Gagarin, tragically killed in an air crash in 1968, circled the earth in a spaceship weighing about 4,826 kg. It was launched by rocket in an elliptical orbit with greatest height 300 km and least 175 km. The inclination of the orbit to the equator was 65° 4′, and the period of revolution was 89 min. 6s. Since then, the Russian *Vostok* cosmonauts Titov (17 orbits), Nikolaev (64 orbits), Popovich (48 orbits), Bykovsky (81 orbits), Tereshkova, the first woman space traveller (48 orbits), the *Voskhod*

cosmonauts Komarov, Feoktistov and Yegorov (16 orbits), Belyaev and Leonov (17 orbits), the American *Mercury* astronauts Glenn (3 orbits), Carpenter (3 orbits), Schirra (6 orbits), Cooper (22 orbits), the *Gemini* astronauts Grissom and Young (3 orbits), McDivitt and White (62 orbits), Cooper and Conrad (120 orbits), Borman and Lovell (206 orbits), Schirra and Stafford (15 orbits), Armstrong and Scott (6·6 orbits), Stafford and Cernan (44 orbits), Young and Collins (43 orbits), Conrad and Gordon (44 orbits), Lovell and Aldrin (60 orbits) were among the first to complete successful missions in space. Leonov was the first to perform the extra-vehicular (EVA) experiment (1965), *i.e.,* to leave an orbiting spaceship and float in space. Russia was the first to achieve an automatic docking (link-up) between two unmanned spacecraft in orbital flight (October 1967), and of two unmanned spacecraft (January 1969). The American *Apollo* mission was accomplished when Armstrong and Aldrin became the first men to set foot on the moon (July 1969). A joint Soviet-American project culminated in a *Soyuz–Apollo* link-up 225 km up on 17 July 1975. On 11 January 1978 two Soviet spacecraft docked with an orbiting laboratory, the first triple link-up in space. The longest endurance record is held by Valentin Lebedev and Anatoly Berezovoy (211 days in space aboard *Salyut 7* in 1982). The first free walk in space was made by two American astronauts on 7 February 1984 from the space shuttle *Challenger.* The *Challenger* disaster in January 1986 disrupted America's space programme. *Challenger* has been succeeded by *Endeavour,* the most technologically advanced shuttle yet developed.

In 1991, Helen Sharman became the first Briton in space. In 1995, Michael Foale became the first Briton to walk in space. In 1995, the Russian cosmonaut Valeri Poliakov broke the record for the longest time spent in space when he completed 438 days aboard the Mir space station.

Space Research. By space research we mean scientific research work which can only be carried to otherwise inaccessible observing locations by rocket propulsion. Such propulsion does not rely on the presence of an atmosphere to provide oxygen so that it is capable in principle of conveying objects to unlimited distances. The subject of space research is, therefore, one which is concerned with scientific applications in various fields of a single highly specialised and powerful technique. It is not a single discipline, but can provide data of great importance for many, such as the physics of the earth, the sun, moon and other bodies of the solar system, astronomy, geodesy and the study of gravitation. The prospect of investigating the biological conditions on different planets such as Mars and Venus is also opened, as well as that of experimental biological studies under conditions of zero gravity. The technical problems involved are:

 (*a*) Launching of the instrument-containing vehicle with the necessary velocity.
 (*b*) Guidance and control of the vehicle so it pursues the desired path.
 (*c*) Tracking the vehicle to determine its actual path and the position on the path at any time.
 (*d*) Transmission of the data, recorded by the instruments, back to the earth.
 (*e*) Satisfactory operation of scientific instruments within the vehicle.
 (*f*) Provision of adequate power supplies to operate the equipment within the vehicle.

It is important to distinguish three distinct types of vehicle—the vertical sounding rocket, the artificial earth satellite, and the deep space probe. The track of a vertical sounding rocket is mainly vertical, and the whole path to the highest point and back is traversed in a few minutes only. An earth satellite circulates in an orbit round the earth in the same way as does our natural satellite, the moon. If it approaches the earth at any point within 160 km of the surface the air resistance causes the path to spiral in so rapidly that the vehicle is eventually burnt up by air friction within the dense atmosphere after an orbital life of a few months only. It follows that artificial satellite vehicles are only useful as instrument containers if the distance of closest approach (the perigee distance) is not much less than 160 km. For the study of the properties of the atmosphere at lower altitudes down to the limit (32 km) attainable by balloons, vertical sounding rockets must be used. It is a great advantage for work at higher altitudes to use satellites, as it is then possible to make systematic observations for months at a time from a great number of positions relative to the earth. During recent years both the American and Russian space programmes have developed the concept of space stations for providing facilities for continuous manned observatories and laboratories in the future. There have now been successful soft landings on Mars and Venus, and "fly by" visits to Jupiter and Saturn. Voyager 2 left Saturn in Aug. 1981 visiting the planets Uranus (1986) and Neptune (1989) and continuing beyond. *See also* **Voyagers 1 and 2.**

Space Shuttle. The first reusable manned space vehicle, *Columbia*, was launched on 12 April 1981 from Cape Canaveral, Florida. It orbited the earth 36 times and returned on 14 April landing in California after a flight of 34 h 22 min with its two crew members controlling its landing. The 1986 *Challenger* disaster was a severe blow.

Spanish Civil War, 1936 to 1939. The war began with a revolt by the Fascist General Franco against the Republic which had succeeded the Monarchy in 1931. Germany and Italy aided the rebels who besieged Madrid for over 2 years. An International Brigade was formed to help the Republic, but the Spanish Government was faced by the greater part of the Army, and very effective assistance from Italy and Germany. Those powers seized the opportunity to have a curtain-raiser to the world conflict which they intended to precipitate. After a total loss of a million men the Fascists overpowered the Republic.

Sparrow, name given to finch-like birds found in most parts of the world, of which the House Sparrow *Passer domesticus*, is the most familiar of British birds. Also native to Britain is the rural Tree Sparrow, distinguished from the male House Sparrow by its chestnut crown. Other European species are the Italian, Spanish and Rock Sparrows.

Specific Gravity, defined as the ratio of the mass of a particular volume of a substance to the mass of an equal volume of water at 4°C. *See* **Hydrometer.**

Spectroscopy. Newton's arrangement with the prism was the first spectroscope; its function was to separate out the colour components of a source of light. Two hundred years elapsed before this apparatus was developed into a precise scientific instrument, capable of measuring both the wavelength and intensity of each colour component. In this form it is called a spectrometer. All atoms and molecules have well defined characteristic spectra which can be used to recognise them. In order to produce emission spectra it is necessary to energise the material under investigation by some means, such as by heating in a flame. The resulting radiation then consists largely of sharp bright lines, characteristic of the material. Absorption spectra are produced by interposing the experimental material between a white light source and the spectrometer. Then dark lines are seen, corresponding to absorptions of energy, in exactly the same places as the bright lines are observed in the emission spectra. Spectroscopic techniques have now been developed to such an extent that accurate measurements of wavelength and intensity are possible not only in the visible region, but over almost the whole of the electromagnetic spectrum. Two of the most useful types for the chemist are infrared spectroscopy which reveals absorption characteristic of the type of chemical bonds because of their different bond vibration frequencies and nuclear magnetic resonance spectroscopy which operates in the radiofrequency region. It reveals the structure environments of atoms containing particular nuclei. Not only does spectroscopy play an important rôle in probing the structure of matter, but it can be applied in the field of astronomy. The use of radio wave spectroscopy has led to the discovery of several new types of stellar object, and this data has produced a major reappraisal

of our understanding of the universe. *See* **F14**(2).

Sphinx, in Greek mythology, a winged creature with a woman's head and a lion's body. The sphinx of ancient Egypt represented the pharaoh in a divine form.

Spiritualism. *See* **Section J.**

Spirituals, negro melodies with religious inspiration and which are still spontaneously created, but have also passed into art-music.

Sponge. *See* **Porifera, F36**(1).

Spoonbill, a long-legged, marsh bird, closely related to the ibis and stork, remarkable for its snowwhite plumage and broad, flat, spoon-shaped bill. The European species has not bred in England since the beginning of the 17th cent., but is still a regular summer visitor from the Netherlands, where it nests in colonies in reed beds and islets.

Sputniks, the name of the Russian earth satellites first launched during the period of the international Geophysical Year. *Sputnik I*, launched 4 October 1957, became the first man-made earth satellite. *Sputnik II*, launched a month later carried a dog as passenger. *Sputnik III*, launched in May 1958, and weighing well over 2 tonnes, became the first fully-equipped laboratory to operate in space. The father of space travel with rockets was a Russian—Konstantin Eduardovich Tsiolkovsky.

Stalactites are deposits of calcium carbonate formed on the roofs and sides of limestone caves, and in tunnels, under bridges, and other places where the carbonic acid of rain-water percolates through and partly dissolves the limestone, resulting in the growth of icicle-like forms that often assume groupings. The water that drops from these may deposit further calcium carbonate, which accumulates and hardens into the sharp mounds or hillocks called stalagmites.

Standard Deviation. In statistics it is often desirable to compare the variability or "spread" of different sets of data. For example, two kinds of light bulb could have the same average life but one kind could be more uniform or consistent than the other. The standard deviation is one of the commonest measures of spread. It is found as follows. If x is one of the data and $\bar{x}$ is the mean of all the x's, then $x - \bar{x}$ is called the deviation. Every deviation is now squared and the average squared deviation calculated. The standard deviation is then the square root of the average squared deviation. The lifetimes of the more uniform kind of light bulb would have a smaller standard deviation than those of the more erratic one.

Star, a luminous ball of hot gas which produces its own light and energy through thermonuclear reactions. *See* **Section F.**

Star Chamber, an ancient tribunal of state in existence in 1487 and possibly earlier, charged with the duty of trying offences against the government, unfettered by the ordinary rules of law. It was in effect a Privy Council entrusted with judicial functions. Under Charles I the Star Chamber was used by the King and his party to persecute opponents; and in 1641 a Bill carried in both Houses abolished it.

Starling (*Sturnus vulgaris*), a well-known European bird now common in many parts of the world. It has handsome iridescent blackish plumage and nests in holes and crevices. Flocks of starlings are often seen wheeling in the air; thousands roost on buildings in the heart of London. Other European species are the Spotless and Rose-coloured starlings. The latter sometimes wanders to the British Isles.

States-General, national assembly in which the chief estates of the realm were represented as separate bodies. The name, though not the institution, has survived in the Netherlands, where the two houses of parliament are known as states-general. In France the states-general consisted of three orders, clergy, nobility and commons. Philip IV first summoned it in 1302 to support him in his quarrel with Pope Boniface VIII. While absolute monarchy was establishing itself it met rarely, and not at all from 1614 until 1789, when it was convoked as a last resort by Louis XVI. But when it met it declared itself the National Assembly which marked the beginning of the revolution.

Statistics is a science that deals with the collection of numerical facts and the evaluation of their significance. The word is also used to refer to the facts themselves as in "trade statistics". This important science gives precise meanings to words like "average" and to statements like "this set of data is significantly different from that". *See* Average.

Statute of Westminster 1931. An Act of parliament which gave a basis of equality to the British Dominions. The Dominions as well as the United Kingdom were defined by the Balfour Memorandum of 1926 as "autonomous communities within the British Empire, equal in status, in no way subordinate one to another in any aspect of their domestic or external affairs, though united by a common allegiance to the Crown, and freely associated as members of the British Commonwealth of Nations". The Statute was the sequel. The Dominions are sovereign States governed solely by their own Parliaments and Governments.

Steam Engine, a machine whereby steam becomes the active agent of the working of machinery, and of very wide application. The leading types of steam engine are: (*a*) condensing, or low-pressure engines, where the steam is generated by a boiler; (*b*) non-condensing, in which the cylinder exhausts its steam into the open air. Engines of the latter type are used where portable engines are required.

Steam-hammer, invented (1839) by the Scottish engineer James Nasmyth. Consists basically of a vertical steam cylinder atop two legs with piston-rod passing through cylinder base and attached to a tup (hammer) of from 100 kg to 15 tonnes which rests on an anvil. The tup slides in V grooves on inside of legs. Length of stroke and therefore weight of blow can be accurately controlled from a light tap to a massive punch. It made possible the forging in one piece of multi-throw crankshafts for marine engines, etc. and the mass production of high-class axles and wheels, con rods and buffers, etc. for locomotives and rolling stock.

Stearin is the portion of fatty matters and oils which remains solid at an ordinary temperature, and is a compound of stearic acid with glycerine. It is largely used in the manufacture of candles. With caustic soda stearin forms a soap (sodium stearate), which is present in most commercial soaps which contain sodium palmitate and oleate in addition.

Steel, an alloy of iron and carbon, with varying proportions of other minerals. The famous blades of Damascus and steels of Toledo were made by the cementation and crucible method. The metal produced by the "Bessemer process" (*q.v.*) is of the highest value for structural purposes, rails, etc. In recent years the technique known as continuous casting has been developed which bypasses some major steps in the conventional process of steel-making.

Stereophonic Broadcasting. A person having normal hearing is able to determine the direction from which a sound reaches him by virtue of the fact that he has two ears, and, therefore, the sound will reach one of them a fraction of a second before it reaches the other. This difference in arrival time allows the brain to calculate direction. It will, therefore, be apparent that if the same person listens to, say, an orchestral concert in a large hall he will be able to determine—even with his eyes shut—the approximate position of a particular instrument with respect to the rest of the orchestra. If, however, he listens at home to a broadcast of the same concert, then, due to the fact that he hears the music after it has been picked up by a single microphone located at one point and radiated over a single-channel transmission system, he will be unable to allocate a definite position to any instrument. The aim of stereophonic broadcasting, or sound reproduction therefore, is to restore the listener's ability to locate the position in space of the various sources of sound and to follow movement. To do this it is necessary to use two microphones in the studio—to simulate the two human ears—and to transmit their outputs, through two similar, but separate, chains of equipment, to two radio receivers and their two loudspeakers, which must be placed some distance apart, in the listener's home. The fundamental work on

two-channel stereophony was done by A. D. Blumlein (1903–42), an electronics engineer and inventor of E.M.I. Ltd., his original patent being dated 1931.

Stereotype, a metal cast taken from movable type which has been set up in the ordinary way. The first to introduce the process in practical form in this country was William Ged, of Edinburgh, who made stereotype plates in 1730. An impression of the type matter is first taken by means of a mould of prepared plaster of Paris or moistened sheets of specially prepared paper and when molten stereo metal is poured upon the mould and allowed to cool and harden, the stereo plate is formed, and can be printed from as a solid block for some time.

Steroids. A class of structurally related compounds, based on a system of condensed rings of carbon and hydrogen, which are widely distributed in animals and plants. Included in the steroid family are sterols, found in all animal cells, vitamin D, sex hormones, bile acids and cortisone, a drug used in the treatment of rheumatic fever.

Stickleback, a family of small spiny-finned fish widely distributed in both fresh and salt water. Male constructs roofed nest held together by sticky secretion from glands near kidneys. Several females deposit eggs therein which he jealously guards until after young are hatched.

Stirrup, a loop of metal U-shaped strap suspended from the sides of the saddle, used for mounting and to support the horseman's foot. Some authorities allege their use as far back as the early Iron Age, and it is generally believed that they were used in battle in A.D. 378, when the Gothic cavalry defeated the legionaries of the Emperor Valens at Adrianople. Stirrups relieved the tension of the rider's knees and so enabled him to be armed from top to toe.

Stoat, a slender, carnivorous mammal with short legs, related to the weasels. The stoat is distinguished from the latter by its longer tail, which has a black tip. The black tip is retained even in the winter when the animal turns white, the fur then being known as "ermine". It is found in northern latitudes, and is abundant in Arctic America.

Stoma (pl. **stomata**), microscopic pores on the surfaces of leaves through which gaseous exchanges take place and water is lost. It has been estimated that a single maize plant bears 200 million stomata, usually closed at night.

Stone-Flies, comprise the order of insects called *Plecoptera*, which includes some 700 species, of which about thirty occur in Britain. The wings are membranous, and two long, thread-like feelers protrude at the tail end. The larvae are aquatic.

Stonehenge, a remarkable collection of Bronze Age monuments on Salisbury Plain. The site which contains ditches, earthwork-banks and megaliths (large stones) has long been recognised for its architectural innovations (the trilithon or free-standing arch and the circle of dressed and lintelled stone blocks) and for its astronomical, numerical and geometrical properties. The building and rebuilding, according to modern archaeological research, lasted from about 2100 to 1600 B.C.

Stork, a family of heron-like birds with long bills, freely distributed over Europe, Asia, Africa and S. America. The White Stork is an occasional visitor to England, and, more rarely, the Black Stork; these are the only two European storks.

Stratosphere, a layer of the earth's atmosphere which lies between the tropopause (*c.* 12 km above the earth) and the stratopause (*c.* 50 km). The ozone layer lies within the stratosphere and is responsible for the relatively high temperature there. The region is less turbulent than the troposphere, and is usually clear of clouds and other "weather", making it attractive for air transport.

Stratum (pl. **strata**), a bed or layer of rock.

Strontium. This silver-white metallic element, no. 38, was discovered by Hope and Klaproth in 1793, and isolated by Sir Humphry Davy in 1808. The chief strontium minerals are celestite (sulphate) and strontianite (carbonate). Compounds of strontium give a brilliant colour to fireworks and signal flares. Radioactive isotopes of strontium (strontium-90) are formed as fission products in nuclear explosions and tend to collect in bone on account of the chemical similarity of strontium and calcium (q.v.). This hazard is a cause of great alarm. See **Fall-out.**

Sturgeon, a large fish found in northern seas and rivers with five rows of bony plates along the back and sides and pointed mouth with four barbels. Caviar is prepared from sturgeon ova.

Sublimation, when a solid substance is heated and turns into vapour without passing through the liquid stage and then condenses as a solid on a cold surface, it is said to "sublime" and the process is called "sublimation". Iodine behaves in this way, and sublimation is used as a method of purifying it.

Submarine, the first submarine, the *Nautilus,* was designed by Robert Fulton and tried out in the river Seine and in the sea off Brest in 1801. The idea was too revolutionary to find acceptance and it was not until electricity for under-water propulsion became available that the submarine underwent extensive development. Britain became interested about 1900 and the Germans developed it and made it into an instrument of warfare. The first voyage under the North Pole was made in 1958 by the American nuclear-powered submarine *Nautilus* (q.v.). The Royal Navy's nuclear submarine fleet includes 4 Polaris vessels—HMS *Resolution* (1968), *Renown* (1969), *Repulse* (1969), *Revenge* (1970), each armed with 16 missiles with thermonuclear warheads. The Government in March 1982 decided to replace the Polaris force with a new fleet of Trident II submarines at a cost of £7,500m. The Labour Party opposed this decision. The first Trident submarine, HMS *Vanguard,* was launched in 1992. Four Trident submarines will be in action by the mid-1990s.

Suez Canal, connecting the Mediterranean and the Red Sea, was built by the French engineer Ferdinand de Lesseps and opened in 1869. An Egyptian company, *Canal Maritime de Suez,* was formed in 1866 with a capital of 200 million francs. The British Government acquired 176,602 shares out of a total of 400,000 for £4 million (value 31 March 1956, £28,982,544). Under the Convention of 1888 all nations were granted freedom of navigation without discrimination in peace or war. The right was recognised by Egypt in the Anglo-Egyptian Agreement of 1954, under which Britain agreed to give up the Suez base. The Suez Canal Company was nationalised by the Egyptian Government without warning in 1956, since when it has been widened and deepened and the average time of transit reduced.

Suffragette, member of the Women's Suffrage Movement who in the early part of this century agitated to obtain the parliamentary vote. The movement ended in 1918, when women of 30 were given the vote. In 1928 a Bill was passed which granted equal suffrage to men and women. The leaders of the Women's Suffrage Movement were Mrs. Pankhurst and her two daughters, Sylvia and Dame Christabel, Mrs. Fawcett, Annie Kenney and others.

Sugar, to the chemist the term is a generic one covering a group of carbohydrates, including cane sugar (sucrose), glucose, fructose, and maltose. In ordinary parlance sugar means sucrose, which is obtained from the sugar cane, sugar beet or sugar maple.

Sulphur, element no. 16, is a brittle, crystalline solid, symbol S, abounding in the vicinity of volcanoes. It is yellow in colour. It occurs in combination with other elements, as sulphates and sulphides, and allied with oxygen, hydrogen, chlorine, etc., is of great commercial utility. Used in its pure state it constitutes the inflammable element in gunpowder; it is also used for matches and for making sulphuric acid.

Sulphuric Acid, a compound of great commercial importance, used in many manufactures, and composed of sulphur, oxygen and hydrogen. Extremely corrosive, and is present in acid rain (q.v.).

Sun, the centre of our solar system, is only one of millions of stars in our galaxy. The earth orbits the sun, which has a diameter of 1·39 million km, at a distance of 149·6 million km.

The sun thus has a volume a million times that of the earth. At the surface, the gravitational field is 28 times that at the earth's surface. It rotates on its axis from east to west, though not as a solid, the solar equator turning once in about 25½ days and the poles in about 34 days. Large spots are observed on the sun which form and disappear at irregular intervals. The area of the disc covered by the spots, however, reaches a maximum roughly every 11 years, when the sun's heat seems rather greater than usual and magnetic storms more frequent (sunspot cycle). Spectrum analysis shows that the sun is composed of many elements found in the earth. Its surface temperature is about 6,000°C. Observations made in 1964–65 (Year of the Quiet Sun) complemented those obtained during the International Geophysical Year 1957–58, when the sun was remarkably active. The earth is in the outer atmosphere of the sun and subject to its winds and storms. The apparently inexhaustible heat of the sun, which has maintained life on the earth for millions of years, is derived from the destruction of matter, involved in the transmutation of hydrogen nuclei into helium nuclei, in which process about four million tonnes of matter are destroyed every second. At this rate of conversion the sun will go on radiating for 30,000 million years. The Soviet space rocket *Lunik I,* fired on 2 January 1959, became the first artificial planet of the sun. *See also* **F8.**

Superconductor, a metal in a state in which its electrical resistance has entirely vanished so that electric currents can flow indefinitely without generating heat or decreasing in strength. The superconducting state of metals was first discovered in mercury by Onnes in Leiden in 1911. There are many magnetic and thermal properties associated with superconductivity and the phenomenon as a whole has proved to be of great scientific interest: it resisted explanation till about 1957. In the meantime many metals and alloys were found to show the property but only at very low temperatures— below c. −260°C. There is a growing number of practical applications, e.g., coils of super-conducting wire (kept very cold by liquid helium) can be made to carry enough electric current to produce strong magnetic fields. Such fields are very constant and do not require the large supply of electrical power that ordinary electromagnets need. By 1990, scientists seemed on the point of developing a revolutionary material that would superconduct (i.e. lose all electrical resistance) at *room temperature.* Such a development would revolutionise computers, power transmission and medicine.

Supersonic Speed, a speed greater than the speed of sound (in air at sea-level sound waves travel at about 1223 km/h). When a body travels at a speed which is greater than the speed at which disturbances themselves can travel, a mechanism exists for the generation of waves of enhanced intensity. Thus aircraft travelling at supersonic speeds produce shock waves in the air somewhat analogous to the bow waves of fast-moving ships. These shock waves are regions of intensely disturbed air which produce the sonic boom effect so distressing to people living near supersonic routes. *Supersonic* is not to be confused with *ultrasonic* (q.v.).

Surface Tension. The surfaces of fluids behave in some respects as though they were covered by a stretched elastic membrane. This property is called "surface tension". The action of detergents may be attributed in part to a reduction in the surface tension of water, allowing it to wet the surface of dirty articles.

Surrealism. The aim of the Surrealist school of painting and sculpture is to overcome the barriers between conscious and unconscious mind, the real and unreal worlds of waking and dreaming. As such it has a long and respectable ancestry, although the term was not in use until 1922 when it was picked by André Breton from Guillaume Apollinaire who had used it in connection with certain works by Chagall. However, Bosch in the 15th cent., Fuseli and Goya in the 18th, and many other purveyors of the weird and fantastic were the forerunners of modern Surrealism. The modern movement has broadly speaking taken two different directions: the first was towards complete fantasy and absurdity which took the form of "found objects"—*e.g.* a bird-cage filled with sugarcubes and a thermometer, a bottle-dryer, a bicycle wheel, or abstract works with strange and apparently irrelevant titles such as Paul Klee's *Twittering Machine*; the second towards highly detailed and realistic paintings of objects placed in strange juxtapositions—*e.g.*, Salvador Dali's trees with limp watches drooping over their branches or Georgio de Chirico's deserted and classical-looking streets with long arcaded perspectives and a lone statue or a bunch of bananas in the foreground. On the whole Surrealism has spent its initial force and become almost respectable; its idea of strange juxtapositions, now widely commercialised, finds a place in advertisement illustrations and in the more sophisticated forms of window-dressing.

Swans, large, graceful birds which together with the ducks and geese form the family Anatidae. There are three European species with white plumage; the Mute Swan distinguished by its orange bill with black knob (less prominent in female), a familiar sight on the rivers and ornamental lakes of Great Britain. Two wild swans are winter visitors here, the Whooper and Bewick's Swan. The "pen" (female) and "cob" (male) mate for life and the young swans are called "cygnets".

Swan-upping. The annual marking of the Thames swans which takes place during the third week of July. This ancient ceremony dates back to the 15th cent. when all the Thames swans were declared to be Royal birds owned by the Crown. Two city guilds—the Vintners' and Dyers' Companies—own about a third of the 200 swans now on the Thames. This privilege was granted to them by King Edward IV in return for money grants. Vintners' birds are marked with a nick on each side of the bill, the Dyers' with a nick on the right side only. The Queen's birds are unmarked.

Sweet Potato. This plant (*Ipomoea batatas*), which is a climbing perennial belonging to the convolvulus family, has thick roots that are rich in starch, and are eaten like potatoes. A native of the W. Indies and Central America, new varieties of sweet potato have been bred which stand cooler climates and can be grown as far north as Cape Cod. The sweet potato of New Zealand is called the Kumara.

Swift, a bird so-called from the extreme speed of its flight, resembling a swallow but related to the humming-bird. It has long, scythe-like wings, sooty-black plumage and greyish-white chin. There are several species inhabiting most parts of the world, particularly the tropics. The British breeding bird is among the latest to return from Africa and the earliest to go. Swifts are the only birds to use saliva for their nests. One oriental species builds its nest entirely from saliva.

Sword, hand weapon of metal used in open combat, characterised by a longish blade. During the Middle Ages the most famous blades were those made by the Arabs at Damascus and those made at Toledo.

Symbiosis. When two organisms live together and both derive mutual benefit from the association, the partnership is known as symbiosis. An example is the symbiosis of an alga and a fungus in lichens; another is the ordinary pea plant and the bacteria which live in the nodules on the pea's roots.

Synapse is the point of association between one nerve cell and another. The nervous impulse travelling along one nerve has to be transmitted to the next across a minute gap. This is the synaptic gap. The mode of transmission is chemical though it was at first thought to be electrical. The impulse arriving at the synapse releases a chemical transmitter which diffuses across the gap and stimulates an impulse in the adjacent nerve cell.

Syndicalism. *See* **Section J.**

Synod, an assembly of the clergy of a particular church, state, province, or diocese. The Synod of Whitby (664) settled the dispute between the Celtic and the Roman churches in the matter of Easter in favour of the Roman system of reckoning.

Synoptic Charts. These are meteorological charts used in forecasting on which weather conditions at a network of stations, at a standard hour of observation, are recorded, using symbols of the international weather code. Surface weather maps have been drawn regularly for more than a hundred years and the modern advance is the drawing of other maps showing conditions in the upper air. The plotting is done quickly by computer.

Synoptists. The writers of the first three Gospels whose narratives in the main agree, though Matthew and Luke add material not found in Mark; all three differ from John's Gospel.

T

Taiping Rebellion, 1850–64, most famous of China's many peasant uprisings. It took place in Hunan (the province where Mao Tse-Tung was born) and was savagely suppressed with the help of foreign powers.

Taj Mahal, the white marble mausoleum built at Agra by Shah Jehan in memory of his favourite wife who died 1629. Over 20,000 men were occupied for over 20 years in its erection.

Takahe or Notornis, large New Zealand bird of the rail family which for many years was believed to be extinct. Small colony found in 1948 in remote valley of mountainous part of the S. Island. The bird is strictly protected.

Take-Over Bid describes an offer made to all the shareholders of a company to purchase their shares at a named price and conditional upon acceptance by the holders of a named proportion of the total share issue. If accepted the purchaser thus gains control of the company.

Tallage, in Norman times, were taxes levied by the Crown upon lands of the royal demesnes. The levying of tallage was taken away by a statute of 1340 which required the consent of Parliament for all direct taxes.

Tammany, an organisation founded in New York (*c.* 1786) and formed from a benevolent society named after an Indian chief. It came to exert a powerful influence over political movements in that city. The leaders of the organisation used their power when their party was successful at the polls to appoint their nominee to every prominent office, and exacted bribes for concessions and privileges, and generally Tammany rule has meant wholesale corruption. Of this there was ample evidence in the disclosures of the Tween and other Tammany frauds, and in the fact that the "Boss" usually contrived to make himself wealthy.

Tantalum, a scarce bluish metallic element, no. 73, symbol Ta, discovered by Ekeburg in 1802. Chemically related to vanadium and niobium, it is usually associated with the latter in nature. For several purposes it can be used in place of platinum, and it finds application in the making of surgical instruments. Tantalum is very hard, and resistant to acids (other than hydrofluoric acid); it is used in alloys.

Taoism. *See* **Section J.**

Taoiseach, the name for the Prime Minister of the Republic of Ireland.

Tapestry, a fabric largely used in former times for wall decoration and hangings. It was known to the ancient Greeks, but in its modern form came into prominence in the 15th and 16th cent., when it was manufactured in a marked degree of excellence by the weavers of Flanders, especially those of Arras. The manufacture was introduced into England early in the 17th cent., and was attended by considerable success. At the present day the term is applied to worsted cloths for furniture coverings, and there are also various kinds of tapestry carpets now made. The most famous tapestries of olden times were the Aubusson Tapestry and the Savonnerie. The Gobelin Tapestry factory, originated in Paris in the reign of Francis I, is still a national establishment. *See also* **Bayeux Tapestry.**

Tapirs. The tapirs constitute a family close to the horse family and the rhinoceros in the Ungulate order. They have four toes on the front feet and three on the hind. The snout is drawn out into a short trunk. The largest tapir is the Malayan tapir, which stands 1 m at the

shoulder. Four species occur in C. and S. America.
Tar is a dark viscid product obtained from the destructive distillation of wood, coal, peat, etc. Wood tar is acid owing to the presence of acetic acid ("pyroligneous acid"). The highest proportion of coal tar goes into road making. Distillation of coal tar yields many valuable compounds, including benzene, phenol (carbolic acid), naphthalene and creosote; the final residue after distillation is pitch. Based on the chemical manipulation of compounds from coal tar is the preparation of many perfumes, food essences, drugs, antiseptics and plastics.

Tarpeian Rock at Rome received its name from the tradition that Tarpeia, the daughter of the Governor of the Citadel who betrayed the fortress of the Sabines, was crushed to death by their shields and buried beneath the rock. From this height persons guilty of treason were hurled to death.

Tate Gallery, named after its founder, Sir Henry Tate, at Millbank, S.W., was opened in 1897; Sir Henry Tate bore the cost of the building (£80,000) and also gave the nucleus of the present collection. "The Turner Wing", the gift of Sir Joseph Duveen, was added in 1910. In 1990, 2·2 m. people visited the Tate.

Tayberry, a high-yielding fruit, which is a cross between a raspberry and a blackberry.

Tay Bridge spans the Tay at Dundee, opened for rail traffic on 20 June 1887. A previous bridge, completed in 1877, was blown down on 28 December 1879, as a train was passing over it. A new bridge was opened on 18 August 1966 for road traffic, 2,244 m in length, the longest road bridge in Britain.

Tea was introduced into England about the middle of the 17th cent., when it was a great luxury, and fetched from £6 to £10 a pound. It is an Asiatic plant, native properly to China, Japan and India. Up to c. 1885 most of the tea imported into this country came from China. The bulk now comes from India and Sri Lanka.

Teal, the smallest of the European ducks and next to the Mallard the commonest British species. It is handsome and a very swift flier, but not as swift as the Garganey or Summer Teal.

Telecommunications. The sending of messages over a distance. The term is generally applied to the sending of messages by telegraph, telephone, radio, television or radar. The first submarine telegraph cable between England and France was laid in 1850 and, following Hertz's investigations into electric waves, Marconi's invention led to Britain being linked with Europe by wireless telegraphy in 1899. The first permanently successful telegraph cable across the Atlantic was laid in 1866. The first telephone service between London and Paris was opened in 1891. The electromagnetic telephone was invented by Alexander Graham Bell, a Scottish-born American, in 1876. The first submarine telephone cable to span the Atlantic was laid in 1956 connecting Britain with Canada and the United States, and many submarine telephone cables have since been laid including the Commonwealth cable system completed in 1967. The spectacular advances in space research depended on the new tools of work provided by parallel developments in telecommunications, e.g., long-range radio and television transmis-sion, electronic computer control. See also **Satellite Communication, Radar, Radio Television.**

Telemetry, measurement at remote distances by means of a radio-link from the object (missile or satellite) to the ground. The third Russian sputnik, for instance, carried apparatus for measuring, among other things, the pressure and composition of the atmosphere, and the intensity of different kinds of radiation from the sun. Its radio transmitter, powered by solar-energy batteries, sent out the information in coded form by means of uninterrupted signals at 20·005 megacycles with a duration of 150–300 milli-seconds. Radio telemetry from inside the body is increasingly used in medical and biological research; miniature radio transmitters can be swallowed or implanted in man or animal to detect physiological conditions.

Telepathy and Clairvoyance. See Section J.

Teleprinter, a telegraph transmitter with a typewriter keyboard, by which characters of a message are transmitted electrically in combinations of 5 units, being recorded similarly by the receiving instrument, which then translates the matter mechanically into printed characters. The telex service provides direct person-to-person transmission of written messages.

Telescope, an optical instrument for viewing objects at a distance, "the astronomer's intelligencer". Lippershey is credited with construction of the first in 1608; Galileo constructed several from 1609 and Newton was the first to construct a reflecting telescope. The ordinary telescope consists of an object-glass and an eye-lens, with two intermediates to bring the object into an erect position. A lens brings it near to us, and the magnifier enlarges it for inspection. A refracting telescope gathers the rays together near the eyepiece and is necessarily limited as to size, but the reflecting telescope collects the rays on a larger mirror, and these are thrown back to the eyepiece. The world's largest reflectors are at Mount Pastukhov, Caucasus (6 m), Mount Palomar, California (200 in), Mount Wilson, California (100 in), the McDonald Observatory at Mount Locke, Texas (82 in), and the Victoria B.C. Observatory (183 cm). The Hale 200 in telescope at Mount Palomar has revealed objects never before photographed; it is able to probe space and photograph remote galaxies out to a limiting distance of 2,000 million light years. The Schmidt telescope at Mount Palomar has been used to make a huge photographic map of the universe. The 98 in Isaac Newton telescope has been moved from the Royal Observatory at Herstmonceux, Sussex, to La Palma, Canary Is. The giant steerable radio telescope built by Manchester University at Jodrell Bank, Cheshire, has a 250 ft reflector. The largest single radio dish in the world is the non-steerable 300 m instrument at Arecibo in Puerto Rico. Another instrument of radio astronomy is the interferometer which consists of spaced aerials. The biggest of these is in New Mexico. In 1990, the project to put the Hubble Space Telescope into space became reality, but the telescope suffered initial malfunctions. The Hubble uses gravity to magnify distant galaxies and its findings are casting doubt on theories of the age of the universe. The world's biggest radio telescope, the Very Long Baseline Array, (VLBA), a series of linked instruments stretching from the Caribbean to Hawaii, is now operational. See also **F3, Astronomy, Radio Astronomy.**

Teletext, the system of displaying printed information and simple diagrams on domestic television screens. Two public services are available in Britain—CEEFAX (Seeing Facts), broadcast by the BBC, and ORACLE (Optical Reception of Announcements by Coded Line Electronics), by the Independent Broadcasting Authority. Teletext makes use of some of the spare lines available in the ordinary 625-line television picture, the signals being translated into written display on the screen by means of a special decoding adaptor built into the set or attached to it. User access to the information, broadcast as separate "pages", is obtained by using a pocket calculator-sized keypad. Teletext services in Britain at present offer a wide range of subject material, including weather forecasts, news headlines, sport and financial statistics, in six colours plus white. It is also possible to superimpose news flashes over ordinary programmes. All the information is provided by specially created editorial units and the pages are transmitted in rapid rotation, a one-hundred page "magazine" taking up to 25 seconds in all. CEEFAX and ORACLE pages are made up of a maximum of 24 lines of 40 characters, the same standard format as that of Viewdata. Viewdata links the television set with computerised information via the telephone and is regarded as almost limitless in application as it would be possible to make use of data offered via the global communications satellite system.

Television, or the transmission of images of moving objects by radio. To understand the problems of television it is necessary to consider the action of the human eye. Basically the eye consists of a lens which projects an image of the scene before it upon the retina, a light-sensitive screen at the back of the eye. The retina is made up of several millions of tiny light sensitive elements, each quite separate and distinct from its neighbours, and each separately connected to the brain by an individual fibre in the optic nerve. Thus the eye is a very complex organ, and it is able to pick out numbers of tiny details from a scene and convey each detail separately and simultaneously to the brain. It does not send a blend of different points of light and shade in the same way that the ear sends a blend of different sounds; if it did the brain would receive a completely unintelligible blur. From this it is clear that a television system which transmitted a mixture of detail would be useless; it must transmit all the details in a scene separately, yet almost simultaneously, and re-assemble them at such a speed that the eye cannot observe the building-up process. A means of doing this was provided by Nipkow in 1884, when he invented his famous scanning disc, and later Weiller invented the mirror drum for the same purpose. Such mechanical devices as these held the field for many years and in 1923 Baird in this country and Jenkins in America were both using them for the experiments which, in 1925, led to the successful transmission of shadows and simple outlines. It was not until 1926, however, that the first practical demonstration of television, as we understand it, took place when Baird transmitted by radio moving pictures of living human faces over a short distance. The B.B.C. began televised broadcasts in 1930; the I.T.A. in 1955. The first television exchange across the Atlantic was made in July 1962 by way of the *Telstar* satellite.

Tellurium, a relatively scarce element, no. 52, symbol Te, discovered in 1782 by von Reichenstein. Chemically it behaves rather like sulphur; its salts are known as tellurides. It occurs chiefly combined with metals in ores of gold, silver, copper and lead. It is a semiconductor, and some of its compounds (also semiconductors) are coming into use in technical devices.

Templars were soldier knights organised in the 12th cent. for the purpose of protecting pilgrims in their journeyings to and from Jerusalem, and obtained their name from having had granted to them by Baldwin II a temple for their accommodation. At first they were non-military, and wore neither crests nor helmets, but a long wide mantle and a red cross on the left shoulder. They were established in England about 1180. During the crusades they rendered valuable service, showing great bravery and devotion. In the 12th cent. they founded numerous religious houses in various parts of Europe and became possessed of considerable wealth. It was this that caused their downfall. Kings and Popes alike grew jealous of their influence, and they were subjected to much persecution, and Pope Clement V abolished the Order in 1312. Edward II in 1308 seized all the property of the English Templars. The English possessions of the Order were transferred to the Hospitallers of St. John, afterwards called the Knights of Malta. *See also* **Hospitallers, Knights, Teutonic Order.**

Temple, a building dedicated to the worship of a deity or deities. Those built by the ancient Greeks at Olympia, Athens and Delphi were the most famous. The Temple of Diana at Ephesus was another. The Temple of Solomon at Jerusalem was destroyed and rebuilt several times; Herod's Temple was destroyed by the Romans in A.D. 70.

Temple Bar, an historic gateway (designed by Sir Christopher Wren in 1672) that until 1877 stood at the junction of the Strand and Fleet Street, London, dividing the City from Westminster. It was re-erected at the entrance to Theobald's Park, near Cheshunt, Herts., in 1888.

Terbium, an element, no. 65, symbol Tb, discovered in 1842 by Mosander, belonging to the group of rare-earth metals.

Teredo, the scientific name of the ship-worm, a peculiar bivalve mollusc, which lodges itself when young on the bottoms of wooden ships and bores its way inwards, causing much injury.

Termites, also known as *White Ants,* though they are not related to the true ants and are placed in an entirely different insect order (*Isoptera*). They abound in the tropics and also occur in temperate countries, though only two species are common in Europe. There is no British species. They live in colonies and their nests take the form of mounds of earth and wood, cemented together with saliva, and up to 6 m in height. Five separate castes are recognised, three of them being capable of reproduction, and the other two are sterile.

Tern. This slender, gull-like bird has long pointed wings, a deeply-forked tail, pale grey and white plumage, black cap, and is a very graceful flier. There are several species, some of which are summer migrants to Britain. The Arctic tern winters in the Antarctic, returning to find a nesting place in the spring.

Terracotta Army, the thousands of life-sized figures in fired clay of soldiers who were to guard China's Emperor Qiu Shihuangdi after his death in the 3rd century B.C. Discovered by peasants digging a well in 1974, at Xian, it is often referred to as the Eighth Wonder of the World.

Terrapin, a kind of fresh-water tortoise. There are several species widely distributed in the Northern Hemisphere.

Tertiary Rocks, in geology the rocks formed during the Caenozoic era comprising the Eocene, Oligocene, Miocene and Pliocene periods. *See* **F48.**

Teutonic Order, of German military knights, was founded in the Holy Land at the end of the 12th cent. for succouring the wounded of the Christian army before Acre. They were dispersed in the 15th cent. but the Order continued to exist until 1809, when Napoleon I confiscated its properties. In 1840 the order was resuscitated in Austria as a semi-religious knighthood. *See also* **Hospitallers, Knights, Templars.**

Textured Vegetable Protein, often referred to as TVP, is an edible protein material given a fibrous texture in the course of its manufacture from agricultural products. Nutritionally the material resembles meat and the extent to which it also resembles meat in succulence, flavour, feel in the mouth, suitability for chewing, etc. depends on the sophistication of the manufacturing technique and on the skill of the cook. The common starting material is the soya bean which is rich in protein and oil. The latter is removed, also for use in the food industry, and the residue is further processed to concentrate the protein and to remove unwanted flavours. A paste of suitable consistency is then forced under pressure through small holes and solidified as fibres. Bound together with a suitable binder and appropriately flavoured, these fibres form a lump of protein substance analagous to meat.

Thallium, a blue-grey metallic element, no. 81, symbol Tl, discovered by Crookes in 1861. It is obtained from the flue dust resulting from the burning of pyrites for sulphuric acid manufacture.

Thanksgiving Day, a national holiday in the United States, observed on the fourth Thursday in November: instituted by the Pilgrim Fathers in 1621 to celebrate their first successful harvest.

Theodolite. The instrument used by surveyors for measuring angles in the horizontal and vertical planes; also used in meteorology for following balloons to measure windspeed etc.

Therm. The charges for gas for lighting and heating (formerly reckoned at per cubic foot) are now based on the calorific, or heat, value of the gas, and the unit used is termed a therm. The therm is 100,000 British thermal units.

Thermionic Emission is the departure of charged particles from matter under the influence of heat. The higher the temperature the greater the flow of escaping particles. The most common example is the emission of electrons from red-hot electrodes—this is the basic phenomenon made use of in thermionic valves (*see* **Valve**). If the hot electrode (the cathode) is enclosed in an evacuated or gas-filled bulb, the emitted electrons can be collected at another electrode (the anode) and will flow through an external circuit back to the emitter. Thus an electric current has been generated by heat.

Thermodynamics, a term first applied by Joule to designate that branch of physical science which treats of the relations of heat to work. What is called the first law of thermodynamics is thus stated by Clerk Maxwell: "When work is transformed into heat, or heat into work, the quantity of work is mechanically equivalent to the quantity of heat." In one of its many formulations, the second law asserts that "the heat tends to flow from a body of hotter temperature to one that is colder, and will not naturally flow in any other way". *See* **F20**.

Thermo-electric Devices. If two wires of different materials are formed into a loop and if the two joins are kept at different temperatures a current flows in the loop. This was discovered by Seebeck in 1822, and the device is called a thermocouple. The electric current could in principle be made to drive some useful machine, and the energy comes from the heat that is absorbed by the thermocouple—if one part of the thermocouple is not hotter than the others it will not work. It has long been realised that this is a device that converts heat directly into electricity without raising steam and driving dynamos as in a power-station. However, until recently nobody has used thermocouples for much besides temperature measurement, for which they are exceedingly useful. The new development is the manufacture of semiconductors (*q.v.*); for the thermo-electric effects of these new materials are much greater than those of metals. A material much studied in this connection is a compound of bismuth and tellurium, bismuth telluride. It now seems practicable to generate useful electricity from suitably designed thermocouples. For example, the USSR produces a thermo-electric device which uses the heat from the chimney of a domestic oil-lamp to produce enough electricity to work a radio. Presumably this is very useful in remote parts with no electricity supply. But the possibilities do not stop there. Indeed, an eminent Russian authority has stated that thermocouples could produce electricity direct from the warmth of sunlight on a scale and at a cost comparable with conventional fuel-burning power-stations. Even if solar energy cannot be so used, it might be possible to use the heat of nuclear reactors, but this means that the thermo-electric devices would have to stand up to very heavy radioactivity and still work.

Thermometer, an instrument by which the temperature of bodies is ascertained. The most familiar kind of thermometer consists of a glass tube with a very small bore, containing, in general, mercury or alcohol. This expands or contracts with variation in the temperature, and the length of the thread of mercury or alcohol gives the temperature reading on a scale graduated in degrees. *See also* **F66–69**.

Thermonuclear Reactions. *See* Nuclear Fusion.

Thirty-nine Articles. *See* Articles.

Thistle, Order of. *See* Knighthood.

Thorium, a scarce, dark grey, metal element, no. 90, symbol Th, discovered by Berzelius in 1828. All substances containing thorium are radioactive. Chief source of thorium is monazite sand, big deposits of which occur in Travancore (India), Brazil and the USA. Important as a potential source of atomic energy since the discovery that it can be transmuted into U^{233}, which is capable of fission like U^{235}.

Thrush, a large family of song-birds of the *Passeriform* order, distributed all over the world. The British species include the robin, redstart, nightingale, song-thrush (or mavis), blackbird, mistle-thrush, ring-ouzel of the mountains and large numbers of migrant fieldfares and redwings from northern Europe are winter visitors.

Thunder, the sound heard after the occurrence of a lightning flash. It is due to vibrations of the air along the path of the flash, which are set up by the sudden heating (and expansion) followed by the rapid cooling (and contraction) to which the air is subjected. It is unusual for thunder to be heard more than 16 km away, the distance being estimated roughly by allowing 1 km for every 3 seconds which elapse between seeing the flash and hearing the thunder. Continued rolling of thunder results from the zig-zag nature of the flash and the multiple strokes of which it is composed, variations in the energy developed along the path, and echo effects. Thunderstorms are caused by powerful rising currents of air within towering cumulonimbus clouds and are most frequent during the afternoons and evenings of sunny summer days.

Thursday, the 5th day of the week, named after Thor, the Scandinavian deity. To the Romans Thursday was *dies Jovis*, or Jupiter's day.

Tiananmen Square, central square in Beijing (Peking). Scene of 1989 massacre. *See* **Section C**.

Tidal Power. The principle of exploiting the energy of the tides is similar to hydro-power since it involves the harnessing of falling water. A barrage across a bay or estuary is filled during flow tide and closed during ebb tide creating a difference in level. When the water is allowed to fall towards the lower side of the barrage it operates a turbine which drives a generator. More sophisticated schemes would incorporate pumped storage facilities. An essential requirement is a large tidal range in order to get a sufficient head of water. *See also* **Hydroelectric Schemes** and **Severn Barrage.**

Tides, the periodical rise and fall of the waters of the ocean and its arms, are due to the gravitational effect of the moon and sun. Newton was the first to give a general explanation of the phenomenon of the tides. He supposed the ocean to cover the whole earth and to assume at each instant a figure of equilibrium, under the combined gravitational influence of earth, sun and moon, thus making and controlling the tides. At most places there are two tides a day, and the times of high- and low-water vary according to the positions of the sun and moon relative to the earth. When earth, moon and sun are in line (at full moon and new moon) the gravitational pull is greatest and we get "spring" tides. When sun and moon are at right angles (first and third quarters of the moon's phases) we get the smaller "neap" tides.

Tiers Etat, the lowest of the three estates of the realm as reckoned in France—nobility, clergy and commons (*tiers état*)—prior to the Revolution.

Tiger, a powerful carnivorous animal of the cat family, which occurs in India and certain other parts of Asia. Its skin is of a tawny yellow, relieved by black stripings of great beauty of formation. Some tigers attain a length of from 3 to 3·6 m. There are now (1995) fewer than 5,000 tigers left in China, South-East Asia and Siberia, a decline of 20% since 1990.

Tilapia, alternative name for St Peter's fish, now readily available at supermarkets.

Time. The measurement of time has become of increasing importance to man with the advance of civilisation. It was at first almost inevitably based on the succession of night and day, the waxing and the waning of the moon, and on the changing seasons of the year, and the astronomical observation of these three periodic effects has served as the basis of time measurement until recent years. The precision of the observations has continually increased, and clocks have been developed for dividing the day into smaller units. The clocks were adjusted so as to keep in step with the rotation of the earth on its axis, but during recent years an atomic standard of time has been developed, and clocks are now adjusted so as to keep in step with the natural period of an atomic vibration. *See* **Clock, Greenwich Mean Time, British Standard Time.**

Tin is a white, metal element, no. 50, symbol Sn (Latin *Stannum*), whose commonest ore is cassiterite (tin oxide), which occurs in Malaya, Indonesia, Bolivia, Zaïre, Nigeria and Cornwall. It protects iron from rusting, and the tin coating on tinplate is applied by dipping the thin steel sheet in molten tin or by electrolysis. Tin alloys of importance include solder, bronze, pewter and Britannia metal. South Crofty, the last tin mine in Europe, was saved from closure in 1994, thus preserving a 2,500 year tradition of tin mining in Cornwall.

Tit *or* **Titmouse,** a small insectivorous bird of the woodlands and forests, bright of plumage and very active and agile, often seen hanging upside down searching for food. There are over fifty species, eight of which occur in Britain: the Great and Blue Tits, familiar in gardens and countryside, the Cole Tit, Marsh Tit, Willow Tit, Bearded Tit, Long-tailed or "Bottle" Tit and the Scottish Crested Tit.

Titanium, a scarce metallic element, no. 22, symbol Ti, difficult to extract from ores, found in association with oxygen in rutile, anatase and brookite, as well as with certain magnetic iron ores. It combines with nitrogen at a high temperature. Discovered by the Rev. William Gregor in 1791. Titanium alloys, being very resistant to stress and corrosion, and combining strength with lightness, and finding wide application not only in marine and chemical engineering but in the building of aircraft, rockets, and the nuclear-energy field. Titanium dioxide is now widely used in making paints.

Tithes, an ecclesiastical tax consisting of a tenth part of the annual produce known to the ancient Jews, and first imposed by Christian authorities in the 4th cent., although not made compulsory in England before the 9th cent. Tithes derived from land are termed "praedial", those derived from cattle being styled "mixed", while others are personal. After the passing of the Tithes' Commutation Act of 1836, tithes were gradually converted into rent charges, and to-day the old form of tithes exists only to a small degree. For details, consult Tithe Act of 1936.

TNT (Trinitrotoluene). A high explosive formed by the action of a mixture of nitric and sulphuric acids on toluene. Not highly sensitive to shock, it can be used in shells without danger, and is exploded by a time, or detonator, fuse. Apart from wartime applications, it is used in blasting in quarries and mines.

Toad, an amphibian, differing from the frog in having a dry, warty skin, a heavier, squat build and shorter limbs. It has a similar metamorphosis, is largely nocturnal, and will wander far from water after the breeding season. Two toads occur in Britain, the Common Toad and the Natterjack. The latter have a narrow light stripe running down the middle of the back.

Tobacco is made from the leaves of various narcotic plants of the *Nicotiana* family, which contain a volatile oil and an alkaloid called nicotine. Tobacco is largely grown in America, India, Japan, Turkey, Greece, Canada, Italy, Indonesia, Bulgaria, Philippines, France, Zaïre, China, Zimbabwe, Zambia, S. Africa, S. America and other countries of a warm climate. It undergoes various processes of preparation. The leaves are first dried, then cut into small pieces, moistened and compressed, and in this form it is known as cut or "shag" tobacco; when moistened with syrup or treacle and pressed into cakes, it is Cavendish; when twisted into string form, it is "twist" or "pig-tail". For cigars the midribs of the dry leaves are removed, and what is left is moistened and rolled into cylindrical shape. For snuff, the tobacco leaves are moistened and allowed to ferment, then dried, powdered and scented. *See* **Section P (Respiratory System)** for the connection between smoking and lung cancer.

Tolls. Payments for privileges of passage were first exacted in respect of ships passing up rivers, tolls being demanded on the Elbe in 1109. Tolls for land passage are said to have originated in England in 1269, toll-bars being erected at certain distances on the high-roads in the 17th cent., where toll had to be paid for all vehicles passing to and fro. After about 1825 they began to disappear, but still linger on some country roads and bridges. Tolls on London river bridges ceased in 1878–79. Today, tolls are a feature of motorways and major bridges (*e.g.* Severn) and tunnels (*e.g.* Dartford).

Tonic Sol-Fa, a system of musical notation in which monosyllables are substituted for notes. Thus the major diatonic scale is represented by Doh, Ray, Me, Fah, Soh, La, Te, Doh. The system was invented by a Miss Glover of Norwich in about 1840 and has proved of great assistance in the teaching of music in schools.

Tonsure, the shaven part of the head of a Roman Catholic ecclesiastic, dates from the 5th or 6th cent. In the Roman Catholic Churches only a circle, or a crown, is shaved, while in the Greek Church shaving is forbidden.

Topaz, a transparent mineral gem, being a silicate and fluoride of aluminium and generally found in granite rocks. Its colour is yellow, but it also occurs in pink and blue shades. The best kinds come from Brazil.

Topiary, the art of clipping and trimming trees, shrubs, etc., into ornamental shapes. In Britain this art goes back before Elizabethan times when gardens were formal and the shapes simple and symmetrical. By the end of Queen Anne's reign topiary had become much more elaborate, and all kinds of fanciful shapes were produced. Pliny in his *Letters* tells how box hedges were clipped into different shapes in Roman times.

Topology is a branch of mathematics which studies geometrical objects from the point of view of their general shape rather than their precise measurements. For example, from the point of view of topology a ring doughnut and a picture frame have the same shape because they both have one single hole through them. Topology is used, for example, to deduce geometrical facts about an irregularly shaped object such as the Earth from the geometry of a regular object such as a perfect sphere of the same general shape. Topology is an important tool in other parts of mathematics.

Tornado, a violent whirlwind, characterised by a black, funnel-shaped cloud hanging from heavy cumulonimbus and travelling at speeds up to 60 km/h. Tornadoes vary in diameter from less than a metre to a kilometre and occur frequently in the Mississippi region of the USA, where it has been estimated that the circling winds of the vortex may reach a velocity of 600 km/h. In West Africa the term is applied to thundery squalls.

Tortoises and Turtles, are cold-blooded reptiles, four-footed and encased in a strong shell protection, the shells of some species being of beautifully horny substance and design, once in much demand for combs, spectacle frames and ornamental work. It is the custom to designate the land species as tortoises and the aquatic kinds as turtles. The green turtle, so called because its fat has a green tinge, is in great demand for soup. Together the tortoises and turtles make up the reptilian order called *Chelonia,* the biggest representatives of which are the giant land tortoises of the Galapagos Islands, reaching a weight of 225 kg and living a century. Some of these giant tortoises are even said to have lived 200 or 300 years.

Toucan, a South and Central American family of brilliantly coloured birds, remarkable for their huge bills. Toucans live on fruit, are of arboreal habits, and nest in holes. There are about 37 species.

Touchstone, a kind of jasper called by the ancients "Lydian stone", of economic value in testing the quality of metal alloys, especially gold alloys. The testing process is very simple. The alloy is drawn across the broken surface of the Touchstone, and from the nature of the mark or streak it makes the quality of the alloy can be ascertained.

Tourmaline, a mineral occurring in different colours in prismatic crystals. It is a well-known example of a pyro-electric crystal, *i.e.*, one that has a permanent electric polarisation. A double silicate of aluminium and boron, it occurs in S.W. England, S. America and Asia.

Tournaments were equestrian contests between military knights and others armed with lances, and frequent in the Middle Ages. The Normans introduced them to England.

Tower of London was built as a fortress by William the Conqueror. It was a royal palace in the Middle Ages and later used as a garrison and prison. Many distinguished prisoners were executed there, or on the neighbouring Tower Hill, including Anne Boleyn, Catherine Howard, Lady Jane Grey, the 2nd Earl of Essex, and the Duke of Monmouth. The Chapel Royal of St. Peter ad Vincula in the Tower was built in 1105 and took its present shape in the reign of Henry VII. The Crown Jewels are kept at the Tower, and in the Armoury a fine collection of armour is preserved. The staff (in Tudor dress) are called Yeomen Warders of the Tower.

Trademark, a mark used in relation to goods for the purpose of indicating a connection in the course of trade between the goods and some person having the right, either as a proprietor or registered user, to use the mark. Trade marks can be registered, the registration holding good for 7 years and being renewable thereafter indefinitely for periods of 14 years. Infringement of a registered trademark renders the infringer liable to damages. In 1994, a new law was brought in to harmonise British trademark law with the EU. Owners of registered trademarks will now also be able to have their sign protected in international law.

Trade Winds form part of the circulation of air round the great permanent anticyclones of the tropics and blow inwards from north-east (Northern Hemisphere) and south-east (Southern Hemisphere) towards the equatorial region of low pressure. Atlantic trades are more regular than those of the Pacific. The belts may extend over 2,400 km of latitude and, together with the Doldrums, move north and south in sympathy with the seasonal changes in the sun's declination, the average annual range being about 5 degrees of latitude.

Trafalgar, Battle of, was fought off Cape Trafalgar on 21 October 1805, between the British under Nelson and the French and Spanish under Villeneuve and Gravina. It was a complete victory for the British, but Nelson was killed.

Trafalgar Square. The site has often been referred to as the finest in Europe. It was conceived originally as a square by John Nash (1752–1835) when the project was considered of linking Whitehall with Bloomsbury and the British Museum. It was to be named after the new monarch as King William the Fourth's Square but on the suggestion of George Ledwell Taylor (a property owner near the site) alteration to the more popular name Trafalgar Square was agreed to by the King. On the north side the National Gallery was planned by Nash and erected by William Wilkins on the place of the Royal Mews—a work of William Kent a century before. The layout was the idea of Charles Barry but he did not approve the erection of the Nelson column (which see). His place for the square to have a grand flight of steps from the north side with sculptural figures of Wellington and Nelson but the Commons decided otherwise and the column as designed by William Railton was begun in 1840. The two fountains by Barry were supplanted in 1948 by ones designed (1938) by Sir Edwin Lutyens. Executed in Portland stone they are flanked by some bronze sculptures. In the same year memorial busts of Lords Jellicoe and Beatty were placed by the north wall.

Transept. The cross aisles of a church, projecting at right angles from the nave or choir.

Transistor. An electronic device consisting of a small piece of semiconducting solid (usually germanium or silicon) to which contact is made at appropriate places by three wires. The three parts resemble in function (not construction or behaviour) the cathode, anode, and grid of a thermionic valve, and transistors can perform many of the operations that valves have hitherto been used for in radio, television, etc. They possess several advantages over valves since there is no need for evacuated glass bulbs nor for a heated emitter to give off electrons. This leads to much greater compactness and economy as well as to a much longer life. Nevertheless, there are certain limitations to their use, and they are not yet suitable as substitutes for valves in all cases. The device was invented by the Americans Bardeen, Brattain and Shockley in 1948.

Transubstantiation. See **Section J.**

Treasure-Trove, a legal term applying to treasure (coin, bullion, gold or silver articles) found hidden in the earth or other place, for which no owner can be discovered. The treasure legally belongs to the Crown, but it is the practice to return to the finder all articles not required for national museums and to reward him with the full market value of such as may be retained. It is the duty of the finder to report to the Coroner for the district in which the find is made who holds an inquest to find whether the discovery be treasure-trove or no. In England concealment is a criminal offence. *See also* **Wreck.**

Tree Council, an organisation founded in 1974 whose aim is to promote the improvement of the environment by the planting and conservation of trees and woods throughout the United Kingdom. Its address is 35 Belgrave Square, London, SW1X 8QN.

Tree Frog, occurs most commonly in America and Australasia. The common European tree frog is a brilliant green animal, the adhesive discs at the tips of its fingers and toes enabling it to cling to trees, *etc.*, with ease.

Tree Rings as Natural Calendar. The approximate relationship between radiocarbon dating (*q.v.*) and true calendar age for the past 7,000 years has been established from measurements on tree-rings. Because one tree-ring is formed annually and its thickness is characteristic of the climatic conditions during its growth, it is possible, by comparing distinctive groups of rings, to date a series of trees. By using the long-lived Bristle Cone pines, tree-rings dating back to 500 B.C. have been obtained. It has been found that the radiocarbon age around, say, 3000 B.C. is too young by *c.* 600 years and because of short-term fluctuations near, say, 2000 B.C., a particular radiocarbon age can correspond to more than one true calendar age. These corrections are far less than those proved necessary after the publication of the first radiocarbon dates. Tree-rings (based on the measurement of deuterium in wood) can also show the pattern of temperature fluctuations over hundreds of years and thus make it possible to trace climatic changes before written records began. The term for tree-ring dating is dendrochronology.

Tree Shrew, an arboreal insectivorous mammal of Asia belonging to the family *Tupaiidae*. Tree shrews are related to the shrews, though in appearance they resemble squirrels except for their sharply pointed snout. They occur in Borneo, Thailand, China and Malaya.

Trees. See *under* **Ash, Elm, Oak** *etc.*

Trent, Council of, the longest and one of the most important in the history of the Roman Catholic Church, was convened to combat the doctrines of Martin Luther. It first sat in 1545, the last sitting being in 1563. At this Council general policy, principles and dogmas of the Roman Catholic Church were settled.

Triassic *or* **Trias,** the earliest geological period in the Mesozoic era, which began some 225 million years ago. Triassic formations 7,600 m thick occur in the Alps. Modern insects were appearing, and also small reptile-like mammals. Other important Triassic animals were: dinosaurs, ichthyosaurs (marine reptiles), and pterosaurs (flying reptiles). *See* **Section F.**

Tribunes, name assigned to officers of different descriptions in ancient Rome. The original tribunes were the commanders of contingents of cavalry and infantry. The most important tribunes were the tribunes of the plebs, first elected in 494 B.C. as the outcome of the struggle between the patrician and the plebeian orders. They held the power of veto and their persons were sacred.

Trichoptera. This is the insect order comprising the Caddis-flies. These are moth-like insects having hairs on the wings. They are usually found fluttering weakly near water. The larvae are aquatic and are remarkable for the cases (caddis cases) which they build out of sticks, small stones, sand grains, and shells.

Tricolour, the flag of the French Republic since 1789, consisting of three nearly equal vertical bands of blue, white and red (ratio 90:99:111).

Trilobites, extinct marine arthropods, most abundant in the Cambrian and Ordovician systems. Their appearance may be roughly described as resembling that of a woodlouse, and like that animal the trilobites were capable of rolling their bodies up into a ball.

Trinity. The Christian doctrine that God exists in three persons, all co-equal, and indivisible, of the same substance—God the Father, God the Son (who became incarnate as Jesus), begotten of the Father, and God the Holy Ghost, proceeding from Father and Son. The system denying the Trinity is Unitarianism. *See* **Section J.**

Trinity House, on Tower Hill, London, was incorporated in 1514 as an association for piloting ships, and has ever since been entrusted with various matters connected with the regulation of British navigation. Since 1854 the lighthouses of the country have been under its supervision. The acting Elder Brethren act as Nautical Assessors in Marine cases which are tried by the High Court of Justice. Under the 1987 Pilotage Act, Trinity House lost its responsibility as the principal pilotage authority in Britain to local harbour authorities.

Trireme, an ancient vessel with three rows of oars of great effectuality in early naval warfare. Mentioned by Thucydides. It was a long, narrow vessel propelled by 170 rowers. The Romans copied it from the Greeks.

Tritium, a radioactive isotope of hydrogen which has three times the weight of the ordinary

L123

hydrogen atom. It is produced by bombarding an isotope of lithium with neutrons and has a half-life of 12½ years, decaying with the emission of β-particles (electrons).

Triumvirate, a term used to denote a coalition of three persons in the exercise of supreme authority. The first Roman triumvirate was that of Pompey, Julius Caesar, and Crassus, 60 B.C.: the second was that of Mark Antony, Octavus and Lepidus, 43 B.C.

Tropic-Bird, a long-tailed sea bird, of which there are 3 species (the Red-billed, the White-tailed, and the Red-tailed), frequenting the tropical regions of the Atlantic, Pacific and Indian oceans. They are commonly called Bo'sun Birds.

Troposphere. The atmospheric layer which extends from the earth's surface to the stratosphere. As a general rule temperature falls as altitude increases. *See* **Atmosphere.**

Troubadours, lyric poets who flourished from the 12th to the end of the 13th cent., chiefly in Provence and the north of Italy. They were often knightly amateurs, and cultivated a lyrical poetry intricate in metre and rhyme and usually of a romantic amatory strain, written in the *langue d'oc.* They did much to cultivate the romantic sentiment in days when society was somewhat barbaric and helped considerably in the formation of those unwritten codes of honour which served to mitigate the rudeness of mediaeval days. *See also* **Jongleurs.**

Trouvère *or* **Trouveur,** mediaeval poet of northern France, whose compositions were of a more elaborate character—epics, romances, fables, and chansons de geste—than those of the troubadour of the south. The poetry was written in the *langue d'oïl.* Flourished between the 12th and 13th cent.

Truffles are subterranean edible fungi much esteemed for seasoning purposes. There are many species, and they are found in considerable quantities in France and Italy, less commonly in Britain. They are often met with under beech or oak trees, and prefer calcareous soils, but there are no positive indications on the surface to show where they are, and they are not to be cultivated. Hogs, and sometimes dogs, are used to scent them out, the former, by reason of their rooting propensities, being the most successful in the work.

Tsetse, an African dipterous fly belonging to the same family as the house-fly. It is a serious economic pest as it transmits the protozoon causing African sleeping sickness when it pierces human skin in order to suck blood.

Tsunami, a seismic sea wave originating from any one of several submarine geological phenomena such as volcanic explosions, landslides or earth movements. Tsunamis are extremely long wavelength waves which travel in the open ocean at speeds up to 640 km/h. In deep water their height is only barely perceptible, but on reaching shallow coastal water they may attain heights of up to 30 m and can cause devastation to low-lying areas. The Pacific Ocean, whose rim is a seismically active area, is particularly susceptible to tsunamis. Tsunamis are often incorrectly referred to as tidal waves.

Tuatara *or* **Sphenodon,** a reptile of great antiquity, the sole surviving species of the *Rhynchocephalia,* found in New Zealand. It has a rudimentary third eye on the top of the head; this is called the pineal eye and corresponds to tissue which in mammals forms the pineal gland.

Tube Foot, the characteristic organ of locomotion of starfishes and kindred animals. They are arranged in pairs along the underside of the arms, and their sucker-like ends can grip a surface very tightly. The action of the suckers depends on hydraulic pressure.

Tudor Period extends from 1485 to 1603. The first Tudor sovereign was Henry VII, descended from Owen Tudor; then followed Henry VIII, Edward VI, Mary and Elizabeth, the last of the line.

Tuesday, the third day of the week, named from the Saxon deity Tuisto, Tiw or Tuesco. To the Romans it was the day of Mars.

Tuileries, a French royal and imperial palace dating from 1564. It was attacked by insurgents during the outbreaks of 1792, 1830 and 1848, and was burned down during the Commune of Paris in 1871.

Tumulus, a mound of earth raised over the bodies of the dead. The mound of Marathon, enclosing the bodies of the Athenians who were killed in the famous battle with the Persians, is a celebrated tumulus. Such mounds were commonly raised over the tombs of the distinguished dead in ancient times, and sometimes enclosed heavy structures of masonry. The Roman "barrows" were tumuli. Evidence of such mounds are frequent in prehistoric remains.

Tuna *or* **Tunny,** a large marine fish belonging to the mackerel family, frequenting the warm waters of the Atlantic, Pacific and Mediterranean. Tuna fisheries are an important industry.

Tundra, the vast treeless plains lying in northern N. America and northern USSR where long severe winters and permanently frozen subsoils (permafrost) have resulted in specially adapted plant communities. The summer thaw and impervious permafrost cause waterlogging of lowland areas and marsh plants occur on these sites. In summer the ground cover of lichens and mosses with some flowering plants is distinctive. Stunted willows and birches occur in certain sites.

Tungsten, a hard, brittle metallic element, no. 74, symbol W (it was formerly called wolfram), silver to grey in colour. Its chief ores are wolframite (iron and manganese tungstate) and scheelite (calcium tungstate). Tungsten is alloyed in steel for the manufacture of cutting tools; also in the non-ferrous alloy stellite. Electric lamp filaments are made from tungsten. Tungsten carbide is one of the hardest substances known and is used for tipping tools.

Turbines propelled by steam provide power for the propulsion of many ships, and on land steam turbines are a principal source of power, being used in large central electricity stations, for instance, to convert heat energy into electrical energy. Gas turbines have recently come into use in aeroplanes, and gas-turbine railway locomotives are being developed. The first gas-turbine ship had its trials in 1947, just half a century after the first steam-turbine ship.

Turbot, a large flat fish, highly valued as food. It often attains from 13 to 18 kg in weight. Its flesh is white and firm. It is confined to European waters, and is caught by line or trawl.

Turkey, a fowl of American origin, brought to Europe from America soon after the discovery of that country. It was a domesticated bird in England in the first half of the 16th cent.

Turpentine, an oily substance obtained from coniferous trees, mostly pines and firs. It is widely used especially in making paints and varnishes, and also has medicinal properties.

Turquoise, formerly called Turkey-Stone, is a blue or greenish-blue precious stone, the earliest and best specimens of which came from Persia. It is composed of a phosphate of aluminium, with small proportions of copper and iron. India, Tibet, and Silesia yield turquoises, and a variety is found in New Mexico and Nevada. It derives its name from the fact that the first specimens were imported through Turkey.

Turtle Dove, a summer visitor from Africa to southern England. It is a small, slender bird with reddish-brown upper parts, pinkish throat, black tail with white edges, and a repeated purring note.

Tweed. A rough-surfaced fabric of the twilled type, usually all-wool, though cheaper kinds may include cotton. Of a soft, open, flexible texture, it may have a check, twill or herring-bone pattern. Harris, Lewis, Bannockburn and Donegal tweeds are well known. "Tweeds" is said to have been written in error by a clerk for "twill".

Twelfth Night is the eve of the feast of the Epiphany, and in olden times was made the occasion of many festivities. It was the most popular festival next to Christmas, but is now little observed.

Twilight. There are several different classifications of twilight, each of which is based on the angular distance of the Sun below the observer's horizon. Civil twilight begins or ends when the centre of the solar disc is 6° below the horizon, nautical twilight beginning and ending when the centre is 12° below. The brightest stars are visible during nautical twilight. The third is astronomical twilight, at which time stars of 6th magnitude are visible provided the sky is clear. Astronomical twilight starts and finishes when the centre of the Sun is 18° below the horizon.

Tyburn, a former small tributary of the Thames, which gave its name to the district where now stands the Marble Arch, Hyde Park. Here public executions formerly took place.

Tycoon, the title by which the commander-in-chief of the Japanese army (virtually the ruler of Japan) was formerly described by foreigners. (In Japanese *taikun* means great lord or prince.) The term is now applied, usually in a derogatory sense, to an influential business magnate.

Tympanum is, in architectural phraseology the triangular space at the back of a pediment, or, indeed, any space in a similar position, as over window or between the lintel and the arch of a doorway. In ecclesiastical edifices the tympanum is often adorned with sculpture.

Tynwald, the title given to the Parliament of the Isle of Man, which includes the Governor and Council (the Upper House), and the House of Keys, the representative assembly. This practically constitutes Home Rule, the Acts passed by the Tynwald simply requiring the assent of the Sovereign.

U

Uhlan, a light cavalry soldier armed with lance, pistol, and sabre and employed chiefly as skirmisher or scout. Marshal Saxe had a corps of them in the French Army; and in the Franco-German war of 1870 the Prussian Uhlans won fame.

Ultramarine, a sky-blue pigment obtained from *Lapis lazuli,* a stone found in Tibet, Iran, Siberia and some other countries. A cheaper ultramarine is now produced by grinding and heating a mixture of clay, sulphur, carbonate of soda and resin.

Ultrasonics, sound waves of frequency so high as to be inaudible to humans, *i.e.,* above 15,000 Hz (Hz is SI unit for cycle per sec.). Ultrasonic waves are commonly produced by causing a solid object to vibrate with a suitable high frequency and to impart its vibrations to the air or other fluid. The object may be a quartz or other crystal in which vibrations are excited electrically, or a nickel component which is magnetically energised. There are numerous technical applications, *e.g.* submarine echo soundings, flaw detection in castings, drilling glass and ceramics, emulsification. Ultrasonic waves are an important tool of research in physics. Bats produce very loud sounds when they are flying, but at ultrasonic frequencies (20,000 to 150,000 Hz), so that we cannot ourselves hear them.

Ultra-Violet Rays. These are invisible electromagnetic rays whose wavelengths are less than 3900 Å. (Angstrom = one hundred-millionth of a centimetre.) The sun's radiation is rich in ultra-violet light, but much of it never reaches the earth, being absorbed by molecules of atmospheric gases (in particular, ozone) as well as by soot and smoke particles. One beneficial effect of ultra-violet light on human beings is that it brings about synthesis of vitamin-D from certain fatty substances (called sterols) in the skin. The wavelengths which effect this vitamin synthesis also cause sun tan and sun burn. Ultra-violet lamps (which are mercury-vapour discharge lamps) are also used for sterilising the air inside buildings, their rays being lethal to bacteria. Many substances fluoresce under ultra-violet light; for instance, zinc silicate glows green, while cadmium borate throws out red light. This phenomenon is applied practically in fluorescent lamps, the light of requisite hue being secured by judicious mixture of the fluorescent materials which coat the lamp.

Umbra, the full shadow of the earth or moon during an eclipse. The term is also used to describe the darker, cooler central region of a sunspot.

Unciae. The Romans took over the Egyptian cubit and divided it into 16 digits as well as into 12 parts called *unciae,* the *uncia* being the origin of the inch.

Underdeveloped Countries are those in which economic structure and development are held back, or, as some would have it, countries which are underdeveloped in the transitive sense of the word. The causes of the condition of underdevelopment are complex but two opposing sets of theories dominate discussion. On the one hand there are those theories that attribute underdevelopment to the internal characteristics of the underdeveloped countries themselves. This is the doctrine of original underdevelopment as it implies that such countries are responsible for their own underdevelopment. On the other hand there are the theories that ascribe underdevelopment directly to the distortions of economic structure and the exploitation involved in the relations between the developed and underdeveloped countries. The expansion of capitalism from its birthplace in Western Europe has created a world-wide production system and market (*i.e.,* a world economy from which no country is completely isolated) structured and determined by the imperatives of capital accumulation in the developed countries. This view implies that the state and process of underdevelopment in one part of the world is inevitable as long as there is development in another. Development and underdevelopment are then mutually interdependent. *See also* **Section G, Part III.**

Unicorn, a fabulous single-horned animal. In heraldry its form is horse-like, with the tail of a lion and pointed single horn growing out of the forehead. In the Middle Ages the unicorn was a symbol of virginity.

Union of Great Britain and Ireland was proposed in the Irish Parliament in January 1799 after the 1798 Rebellion and came into force on 1 January 1801. The troubled history of Ireland, associated with the question of self-government, nationalism, land and religion, culminated in the Easter revolution of 1916. A treaty giving the 26 southern counties independence in 1921, as the Irish Free State, was followed by a period of internal dissension. In 1937 a new constitution was enacted in Ireland in which no reference was made to the Crown. This, however, left in force the External Relations Act of 1936 and with its repeal in 1948, Ireland separated itself from the British Crown and thus severed the last constitutional link with the Commonwealth, and became an independent Republic.

Union, Treaty of, was the treaty by which Scotland became formally united to England, the two countries being incorporated as the United Kingdom of Great Britain, the same Parliament to represent both, Scotland electing sixteen peers and forty-five members of the House of Commons. Uniformity of coins, weights, and measures was provided for, Scottish trade laws and customs were assimilated to those of England, and as regards religion and the practices of the law, Scotland was to continue as before. This Act was ratified on 1 May 1707.

Universe in astronomy means not only the star system (of which the sun and planets are a small part) but all the countless star systems or nebulae which may be separated from each other by millions of light-years. *See* **F3–8.**

Universities are institutions of higher education whose principal objects are the increase of knowledge over a wide field through original thought and research and its extension by the teaching of students. Such societies existed in the ancient world, notably in Greece and India, but the origin of the University as we know it today lies in mediaeval Europe, the word *universitas* being a contraction of the Latin term for corporations of teachers and students organised for the promotion of higher learning. The earliest bodies to become recognised under this description were at Bologna and Paris in the first half of the 12th cent.; Oxford was founded by an early migration of scholars from Paris, and Cambridge began with a further migration from Oxford. Other Universities sprang up all over Europe, including three in Scotland—St. Andrews (1411), Glasgow (1451) and Aberdeen (1494)—which were followed by Edinburgh in 1582. These six bodies remained the only Universities in Great Britain until the foundation in 1826–29 of University and King's Colleges in London (resulting in the establishment of the University of London in 1836) and of the University of Durham in 1832. The 34 old-established universities in England are: Aston, Bath, Birmingham, Bradford, Bristol, Brunel, Buckingham, Cambridge, The City, Durham, East Anglia, Essex, Exeter, Hull, Keele, Kent, Lancaster, Leeds, Leicester, Liverpool, London, Loughborough, Manchester, Newcastle, Nottingham, Open, Oxford, Reading, Salford, Sheffield, Southampton, Surrey, Sussex, Warwick and York. Other old institutions of university standard are the University of Manchester Institute of Science and Technology; the Manchester Business School; the London Graduate School of Business Studies; Cranfield Institute of Technology; and the Royal College of Art. Formed from colleges of technology, art and design, commerce and other institutions, over thirty polytechnics were established in England and Wales as centres of higher education (see below). Wales used to have one University (The University of Wales with colleges at Aberystwyth, Bangor, Cardiff and Swansea) in addition to the Welsh National School of Medicine, the Institute of Science and Technology, and St. David's, Lampeter. Scotland had eight: Aberdeen, Dundee (1967), Edinburgh, Glasgow, Heriot-Watt (1966), St. Andrews, Stirling (1967), and Strathclyde (1964), Britain's first technological University. Northern Ireland has two: Queen's University, Belfast and the New University of Ulster at Coleraine. The Open University received its charter in 1969; it provides degrees and other courses together with radio and television programmes and began its broadcasts in January 1971. The Republic of Ireland has the University of Dublin (Trinity College, Dublin), and the National University of Ireland with colleges at Dublin, Cork and Galway. In the USA the development of higher education has left the Universities less sharply defined than in Europe and the Commonwealth, among the best known being Harvard (1636), Yale (1701), Princeton (1746), Columbia (1754), Cornell (1865), California (Berkeley), Massachusetts Institute of Technology. In 1972 the European University Institute was established with headquarters in Florence. In Britain, universities receive aid from the State mainly in the form of grants from the Higher Education Funding Council which oversees the distribution of state finance. But they are selfgoverning institutions free from State control. Since 1992, the distinction between the former polytechnics and the 34 older universities has ended. The former polytechnics have now adopted university names (e.g. Leicester Polytechnic is now the De Montfort University).

Uranium, a metallic element, no. 92, symbol U, discovered by Klaproth in 1789 in pitchblende. It is a white metal which tarnishes readily in air. Great developments have followed the discovery that the nucleus of the uranium isotope U^{235} undergoes fission, and uranium minerals have become very important since it was found that atomic energy could be released controllably by taking advantage of fission. Before atomic energy work began to take the major part of the world's output of uranium minerals, the chief users of uranium compounds were the ceramics and textile industries. See also **Nuclear Reactors, Nuclear Fission, F13(1)**.

Uranus. This planet was discovered by Herschel in March 1781. Its diameter is 51,118 km and its mean distance from the Sun is $2,871 \times 10^6$ km. When Voyager 2 visited Uranus in January 1986, it raised the number of known moons orbiting the planet from five to 15. The number of known rings surrounding Uranus was also increased to 11. Uranus has a large axial tilt which means that it rotates on its side. Each pole faces the Sun every half-revolution around the Sun, i.e. every 42 years. See **F8 and Voyager**.

Urea, the final product in mammals of the breakdown of nitrogenous waste, e.g., excess aminoacids. It is very soluble in water and is excreted in urine. In 1828 Wohler synthesised urea from inorganic matter. This was the first laboratory synthesis of an organic substance and refuted the idea that living creatures or

life force are needed to create such substances.

Ursa Major and **Ursa Minor** ("Greater Bear" and "Lesser Bear"), two celebrated constellations, each of seven stars, in the northern celestial hemisphere, familiar since ancient times. Ursa Major has also been called "the Plough", "Charles's (Charlemagne's) Wain" or "the Wagon". The "Pointers" in this group of bright stars point to the brightest star in Ursa Minor, the Pole Star. Called the Big Dipper and the Little Dipper in the USA.

V

Valency. A term used by chemists to describe the combining ability of an element with respect to hydrogen. Thus oxygen, which forms water, H_2O, with hydrogen is said to have a valency of two, nitrogen (forms ammonia, NH_3) three, and carbon (forms methane, CH_4) four. Chlorine forms hydrogen chloride, HCl, and is said to be monovalent. This empirical approach cannot account for valency in such compounds as carbon monoxide, CO, which appears to require both elements to have the same valency. With the discovery of the electron it was realised that the concept of valency and chemical bonds is intimately concerned with the electronic structure of atoms, and theories have been advanced to explain why the same element can have different valencies in different compounds. Iron, for example, can have a valency of two ($FeCl_2$, ferrous chloride) or three ($FeCl_3$, ferric chloride). See **F11(1), F24(2)** and **Table of Elements (F64)**.

Valentine's Day (14 February), is a festival in celebration of St. Valentine, one of the Christian martyrs of the 3rd cent. A sweetheart or Valentine is chosen on that day and letters or tokens sent secretly to the object of affection.

Valhalla, in Scandinavian mythology, is the special Paradise to which the souls of warriors slain in battle were transported.

Valkyries, the chosen handmaidens of Odin, appointed to serve at the Valhalla banquets. Their most important office, however, according to the Norse mythology, was to ride through the air at a time of battle and point out the heroes who were to fall. One of these Valkyries is made the heroine of Wagner's opera "Die Walküre".

Valve, an electronic device consisting of two or more metal plates (electrodes) usually enclosed in an evacuated glass bulb. One of the electrodes is heated causing electrons to be emitted. If a positive voltage is applied to the other electrode, the electrons will move towards it and the valve must conduct electricity. The current will only flow in one direction as the electrons are emitted only from one electrode. A valve with two electrodes is called a diode, but by putting in one or more intermediate electrodes the flow of current can be sensitively controlled and the valves are then called triodes, pentodes, etc., according to the total number of electrodes in them. Valves have found extensive applications in amplifiers, rectifiers, oscillators and many electronic devices, but have now been superseded by transistors in many applications where it is advantageous to have greater reliability, smaller power consumption and smaller size.

Vanadium, a scarce metallic element, no. 23, symbol V, whose chief ores are carnotite and patronite. Some iron ores contain it. Most of the vanadium commercially produced finds its way into vanadium steels, which are used for tools and parts of vehicles, being hard, tough and very resistant to shocks. The oxide is used as a catalyst in industry, especially in making sulphuric acid.

Van Allen Belts. One of the most remarkable discoveries made during the IGY, 1957–58, was that the earth is surrounded by a great belt of radiation. Evidence came from Sputnik II (which carried the dog Laika) and from the American satellites, Explorers I and III. The American scientist, J. A. van Allen, was able to explain the puzzling data collected from these satellites. Subsequent observations with deep space-probes showed that there are in fact two zones of high intensity particle radiation surrounding the earth, one concentrated at a distance of about 1,600 km, the other at about 24,000 km. A close relation exists between the shapes of the zones and the earth's magnetic field. Recent evidence suggests that Jupiter also is surrounded by a dense belt of trapped high-energy particles.

Vatican, the Papal residence at Rome, a famous palace on the hill adjacent to St. Peter's. Its museum is a rich treasure-house of literary and artistic objects. Works of Michelangelo glorify the Sistine Chapel.

Vauxhall Gardens, a famous London pleasure resort from the early part of the 18th to the middle of the 19th cent. It was here that many great singers appeared and where the earliest balloon ascents were made.

Ventriloquism, the art of projecting or throwing the voice so that it seems to come from a different source.

Venus, the brightest of all the planets, whose orbit lies between the orbits of Mercury and Earth, is second in order from the sun (see **F8**). It approaches the earth to within 40 million km. It moves around the sun in the same direction as Earth and the other planets but rotates in the opposite sense. It has been visited by a number of American and Russian probes, some flybys, some soft-landings, others atmospheric probes. Venus has 100 times the atmospheric pressure of the earth and temperatures of 500°C. It is covered in a very thick cloud mainly of carbon dioxide which some scientists believe acts like a greenhouse trapping the heat from the sun. Complex reactions occur in the atmosphere and the rain consists mainly of sulphuric and hydrochloric acid. The cloud rotates about six times faster than Venus rotates and swirls into the polar regions like giant whirlpools. The terrain has been studied by radar, much of it ground-based, but a vast amount of information has come from both the Pioneer Venus orbiter and the recent successful Magellan probe, which between them have mapped nearly the entire Venusian surface. There are two major continents, Aphrodite Terra, is about the size of Africa, and the smaller Ishtar Terra, about the size of Australia, which consists of a very high plateau (c. 3,300 m) and a mountain range dominated by Maxwell Montes (at 10,600 m higher than Everest). Aphrodite Terra has a deep trench 2,900 m below "sea level". Most of the planet (60 per cent) is relatively flat. The Magellan probe (1990) revealed a carbon dioxide atmosphere, 100 times thicker than Earth's, with sulphur escaped from volcanoes as well as the longest channel (4,200 miles) in the solar system. It also found that there are no asteroid impact craters bigger than 5 miles across. See also **Special Topic, F76–78.**

Venus Fly-trap, a well-known insectivorous plant (*Dionaea muscipula*) occurring in Carolina in damp mossy places. It is related to the Sundew. The leaf is the organ that catches the insects. The leaf blade is in two halves, hinged along the centre line. Each half bears three sensitive hairs called "trigger hairs". When an insect touches a trigger, the two halves of the leaf clap together, trapping the insect between them, when it is digested by a secretion (digestive enzymes) from the leaf, which afterwards absorbs the soluble products.

Vernalization. Seeds which, after being exposed to a low temperature, produce plants that flower earlier than usual are said to have been "vernalized". This technique of seed treatment devised by Lysenko is called vernalization. It is claimed to have been widely used in Russia to obtain cereal crops in places where climatic conditions are favourable for only a short season.

Versailles, Treaty of. The Peace Treaty, 1919, ending the first world war. The first half was devoted to the organisation of the League of Nations. Among the territorial changes Germany ceded Alsace-Lorraine to France, Posen and the Corridor to Poland. Germany undertook to disarm, to abolish universal military service, to keep only a small army of 100,000 and a small navy. Her colonies were to be shared out among the Allies under League Mandates. Reparations were to be paid, but were gradually reduced and entirely ceased in 1932. Hitler took unilateral action against the Treaty especially in regard to rearmament and the annexation of Austria.

Victoria and Albert Museum, in Kensington, London, was begun in 1852 as the Museum of Ornamental Art at Marlborough House. The present building was completed in 1909. It has the following departments: Architecture and Sculpture, Conservation, Ceramics, Paintings, Prints and Drawings, Oriental Library Metalwork, Museum Services (inc. Information and Slide Loan Service), Textiles, Furniture and Woodwork. Education (into which the old Circulation Dept., has been absorbed), and Theatre Museum. A controversial restructuring of these departments is now (1989) taking place. The V. & A. also administers the Wellington Museum (Apsley House, Piccadilly), Ham House (Richmond, Surrey), and Osterley Park House (Middx). The Bethnal Green Museum (The Museum of Childhood) is a branch of the V. & A.

Victoria Cross, an order of merit for conspicuous valour, awarded to members of the Army, Navy and Air Force, was established in 1856.

Videotape recording (VTR), technique for recording television programmes on to magnetic tape. The original means of storing programmes for broadcast or library purposes was by filming productions from high-quality monitors, an expensive and slow process, since the film had to be chemically developed and edited in the conventional way. The difficulty in establishing an instant play-back system along the lines of the sound tape recording system lay in the high speed and large amount of tape needed to accommodate the picture signal. The BBC experimented with a machine called VERA (Vision Electronic Recording Apparatus), but it was an American machine, the Ampex VR100, which provided the breakthrough. This recorded the picture across a wider tape rather than along it, and moving at a slower speed. Tapes, in colour or black and white, now run for *c.* 90 minutes and can be used many times by erasing and re-recording, accuracy of editing is achieved by re-recording chosen sequences on to a second machine.

Vienna Congress, sat at Vienna from September 1814 to June 1815, and settled the delineation of the territories of the various European nations after the defeat of Napoleon. The Treaty of Vienna which resulted gave Sri Lanka, Mauritius, Cape Colony, Heligoland, Malta and part of Guyana to England; Belgium, Holland and Luxemburg were united in the Kingdom of the Netherlands; Austria took Lombardy-Venetia; Russia took part of Poland; and Prussia, part of Saxony and the Rhenish province. Except for one or two changes the clauses of the treaty were maintained for over forty years.

Vikings. Scandinavian pirates who from the 8th to the 10th cent. were the terror of northern waters. Sometimes the Viking raids reached south to the Mediterranean and east to the White Sea. Their leader Rurik founded the first Russian kingdom of Novgorod in A.D. 862. The Icelandic Vikings under Eric the Red discovered Greenland in A.D. 982 and a warm period in world climate allowed many to settle there. Their expeditions took them to Labrador and Newfoundland. They excelled in shipbuilding, were fine sailors and craftsmen. The name may derive from *vik*, a sheltered deep-water bay now called a *fjord*.

Vinyl Plastics are polymers made from derivatives of ethylene, examples are polyvinyl chloride (PVC), which is used in making plastic pipes and kitchen utensils, among other things; polyvinyl acetate used in the paint industry and in bonding laminated articles like plywood; and polystyrene (polyvinyl benzene) used in making electrical fittings and for lenses.

Viper, a family of poisonous snakes in which the venom-conducting fangs hinge forward when the snake bites. One species is found in Britain, the common viper or adder.

Virus. See Index to P and **F31(2).**

Visibility is defined by the distance at which the farthest of a series of objects, specially selected to show against the skyline or in good contrast with their background, can be distinguished. Visibility depends chiefly upon the concentration of water or dust particles suspended in the air. Instruments are available to measure the obscurity of the atmosphere more directly, including that at night.

A large lapse rate of temperature and a strong wind are favourable to good visibility; a small lapse rate, calm or light wind favourable to bad visibility. Fog is when the visibility is less than 1,000 m; mist or haze when it is between 1,000 and 2,000 m. See **Pollution**.

Viscount, a title of rank coming between that of Earl and Baron. The title originally stood for deputy-earl. The first English Viscount was Viscount Beaumont, created in 1440.

Vitamins, name of a group of organic substances found in relatively minute amounts in certain foodstuffs, essential for growth and the maintenance of normal bodily structure and function. The Hungarian biochemist Szent-Györgyi, who first isolated vitamin C or ascorbic acid, defined the vitamin as "a substance that makes you ill if you don't eat it!" See **F32(1).**

Volcanoes are vents through which magma reaches the surface as lava flows, or as the solid products, e.g., ashes and bombs, of explosive eruption. The vent may be cylindrical or it may be a long fissure. The former type usually builds up cones, e.g., Vesuvius. Notable active volcanoes are Etna, Vesuvius and Stromboli, in Italy; Hekla in Iceland; and Mont Pelée in Martinique. The last-named was in violent eruption in 1902, when the chief town of St. Pierre was completely destroyed. Volcanic eruptions are sometimes linked with brilliant sunset phenomena, e.g., the Indonesian island of Krakatoa (1883), whose atmospheric and tidal effects were recorded all over the world, and Agung on the island of Bali (1963), which had been dormant for 120 years. A new fissure volcano (Surtsey) developed off the coast of Iceland in 1963. In 1991, the eruption of Mt Pinatubo in the Philippines killed 500 people.

Vole, a small rodent with blunt nose, round face and short tail. Three kinds occur in Britain: the field, the bank and the water vole.

Volt, the electromotive force unit, named after Alessandro Volta (1745–1827), and defined in terms of the coulomb, the second and the joule.

Voyagers 1 and 2. These spacecraft were launched from Earth on 5 Sept. 1977 and 20 Aug. 1977 respectively as a follow-on mission to the earlier and successful Pioneer 10 and 11 spacecraft. Both were targeted initially to swing by Jupiter (q.v.), with Voyager 1 on the faster trajectory, to make the next phase of investigation of Jupiter and its moons, before continuing to Saturn (q.v.) and beyond, using the enormous gravitational field of Jupiter to assist them in their journeys. (It was this planet's gravitational field that flung Pioneer 10 (launched 1972) into space in June 1983 to make it the first man-made object to leave the solar system.) Voyager 1, in flying through the Jovian system in 1979, discovered the unique features of Io, the most volcanically active object yet found in the solar system, photographed the ice-covered moons—Europa, Ganymede and Callisto—and made many new discoveries of Jupiter, the largest and most massive planet of the solar system. Voyager 1 began surveying Saturn in Aug. 1980, and continued sending back a vast amount of new data, including some 18,000 pictures of the planet, its moons and, perhaps most spectacularly, its fascinating and complex system of rings. The measurements included infra-red and ultra-violet measurements of the structure of the planet's atmosphere, as well as data on the magnetic field and charged particle environment of the planet. When the spacecraft passed through one of the "gaps" of the ring system on 12 Nov. 1980, it made a series of fascinating revelations. The flyby of Saturn by Voyager 2 in Aug. 1981 was carefully planned to obtain the maximum of new information to complement that obtained from Voyager 1 to help understand some of the perplexing new phenomena, and revealed even more new features of this beautiful and still enigmatic planet. Even after its Saturn flyby, the work of Voyager 2 was far from complete: its swing by Saturn redirected it toward Uranus, on which it provided our first close-up data in Jan. 1986, and from there it continued to Neptune in 1989, taking maximum advantage of a unique arrangement of all four of the outer planets, Jupiter, Saturn, Uranus and Neptune, which only occurs once every 200 years. Voyager 1, which would not pass particularly close to any planet after Saturn, carries a multi-lingual goodwill message as well as musical selections to far outside our solar system. It will not reach its nearest star, Sirius, for 360,000 years. In March 1990, Voyager 1 beamed back its last colour photographs before leaving the solar system for outer space. By then it was 3,500 million miles from Earth, travelling at 37,000 mph.

Vraic, a name for seaweed in the Channel Islands, where it is extensively used as a manure.

Vulgate, a term used to designate the Latin version of the Scriptures sanctioned by the Council of Trent. The work of St. Jerome in the late 4th cent. A.D. and still the official Bible of the Roman Catholic Church.

Vulture, a famous bird of prey of two distinctive groups; that of the Old World, whose nostrils are separated by a bony partition, and the New World vulture, which has no such division. Vultures feed on carrion and are the great scavengers of tropical regions. The European species are the Egyptian vulture, Griffon vulture, Black vulture and Bearded vulture. Vultures have no feathers on the head and neck.

W

Wading Birds, Charadriiformes, an order of migratory, long-legged, long-billed birds, frequenting marshes and shallow waters. They include the plovers, avocets, stilts, oystercatchers, curlews, phalaropes, godwits, dunlins, sandpipers, redshanks, greenshanks, snipe, woodcocks, the pratincole of the Mediterranean and the sun bittern of tropical America. Many species breed in Britain.

Wagtails, familar long-tailed small birds, the most common British species being the Pied or Water (with sub-species White) Grey and the Yellow (sub-species Blue). Wagtails nest in holes and are active of habit.

Walloons, name given to the French-speaking population of the southern provinces of Belgium, in contrast to the Flemings or Dutch-speaking population of the northern provinces. The Walloon areas contain the mining and heavy industries of the country.

Walpurgis Night, the night before 1 May, when witches and creatures of evil are supposed to have liberty to roam. Named after St Walpurgis, an English nun, who went on a mission to Germany in the 8th cent.

Walrus, a very large marine mammal, related to the seals having in the upper jaw two large curved tusks, which average in length from 38 to 60 cm. It lives on bi-valve molluscs, and inhabits the Arctic seas. An adult walrus can exceed 4 m in length and weigh over a tonne.

Wankel Engine or **Rotary Engine,** is an internal combustion engine invented by Felix Wankel in the 1930s and greatly developed since by large automobile firms in several countries. The ordinary internal combustion engine has to convert reciprocating motion of the pistons into rotary motion. In the Wankel engine the explosion of the fuel and air mixture drives a moving part (the rotor) directly into rotatory motion, and the rotor itself opens and closes the fuel inlet and exhaust ports. The three spaces between the triangular rotor and its specially shaped housing act successively as intake, compression, explosion and exhaust chambers as the rotor revolves. There are no valves and far fewer moving parts than in an ordinary piston engine. The Wankel engine is claimed to have many advantages in that it is smaller and lighter for a given horse-power, relatively simple, quieter and freer from vibration, and could contribute to pollution control. There are cars now on sale with the Wankel engine and continuous research and development will no doubt test in practice the claim of some protagonists that this engine is the agent of a technological revolution in the automobile.

Wapentake, the ancient name given in the northern countries to territorial divisions corresponding to the Hundreds of southern counties.

Warblers, a family of small, lively song-birds closely related to the flycatchers and thrushes. Represented in Britain by about 36 species, including the chiffchaff, one of the earliest spring visitors, willow-wren, wood-warbler, blackcap, garden-warbler, whitethroat, sedge and grasshopper-warbler.

Warsaw Pact. *See under* **NATO, L86.**

Water is the simplest compound of hydrogen and oxygen. It is formed when an electric spark is passed through a mixture of the gases, and is a product of combustion of all hydrogen-containing compounds, *e.g.*, petrol, coal, coal gas and wood. Water is essential to living matter, and is the medium which carries food to animals and plants. Salts in hard water may be removed by distillation of the water or by a process known as ion-exchange (water softening). Pure water freezes at 0°C and boils at 100°C and is used as a standard of temperature on this scale. It has a maximum density at 4°C. Heating water above 100°C converts it into steam, which is used under pressure to convert heat energy into useful work, as in electrical power stations and steam engines. Water gas is a mixture mainly of carbon monoxide and hydrogen formed by blowing steam and oxygen through red-hot coke: it is used as a fuel. Water is one of the very few compounds which freezes from the surface down rather than from the bulk of the liquid up. This property has important consequences on the preservation of life in rivers and lakes when they are frozen. The Drinking Water Inspectorate set up in January 1990 has responsibility for checking that water supplied by the water companies is wholesome and fit to drink when it reaches your home. *See also* **Section Y.**

Water Hyacinth (*Eichhornia crassipes*), a beautiful aquatic plant native to Brazil which has spread to other favourable equatorial regions of the world causing havoc on account of its abnormal rate of reproduction away from its natural environment. In recent years it has invaded the Nile and the Zaïre, forming vast floating carpets which block the channels, clog the paddles of river craft and deoxygenate the water, killing the fish. It is being held in check by spraying with the herbicide 2,4-D.

Waterloo, Battle of, was fought on 18 June 1815. The Allies (British, German and Dutch) under Wellington and Blücher defeated the French under Napoleon, ending Napoleon's career.

Waterloo Bridge, crossing the Thames, was built by Rennie, and opened in 1817. It had nine arches, each 120 ft (36 m) span, was built of granite, and had a length (including approaches) of 2,456 ft (749 m). The present bridge, completed in 1942, and formally opened 10 December 1945, is a fine example of reinforced concrete construction. (Architect, Sir Giles Gilbert-Scott.)

Watling Street, the name of the old Roman road which ran from the Channel ports by way of London to Shropshire. *See also* **Roman Roads.**

Watt. A unit of electrical power equivalent to 1 joule of work per second, named after James Watt (1736–1819). *See* **F66–69.**

Waxbill, a small Oriental and African bird of the *Estrildidae* family, with wax-like bill and beautifully variegated plumage. The Java sparrow, and the Blue-breasted waxbill are attractive, and often find their way into cages.

Wayz-Goose, the name given to a festive gathering of people employed in printing and other works, so called from the fact that in earlier times a goose was the principal dish of the feast.

Weasel. A carnivore mammal found in Britain, smallest member of the group including the Stoat, Polecat, and Pine-marten, about 20 cm long. Its fur is reddish on the upper side of the animal, white on the under side; it may all turn white in winter with the exception of the tail.

Weather is generally accepted as being the current state of the atmosphere, particularly as regards its pressure and temperature, wind, cloud and precipitation. Many other features such as fog, sunshine duration, humidity, pressure tendency, may be added to the list, all items of which are routinely observed by specially instrumented stations usually sponsored by the national meteorological services. Day-to-day changes in the weather as experienced by the individual are due to the passage of circulation systems, many of which bring clearly recognisable areas of "good" (*i.e.*, calm and sunny) weather as frequently occurs in anticyclones and "bad" (*i.e.*, cold, windy, cloudy and rainy) weather. Clearly, the weather in any place at any time is primarily determined by the frequency and intensity of synoptic-scale weather circulation

systems (*c.* 3,000 km across). Local weather (over areas of *c.* 100 km) may be heavily influenced by topography, *e.g.*, valley fogs, frost hollows.

Weather Lore. Before instruments were invented to measure atmospheric conditions, man relied on his own observation of wind and sky, behaviour of birds and animals, and came to associate certain phenomena with types of weather. Many popular weather rhymes have survived the centuries, and as long as forecasting is confined to the next 24 hours there is perhaps something to be said for them, particularly those dealing with the winds. What is very unlikely is that next year's summer can be predicted from this year's winter, or that one month's weather is related to that of another. The study of past records reveals too many exceptions for firm future predictions.

Weaver Bird, the popular name for a large group of finch-like birds belonging to the family *Ploceidae*, found principally in Africa but also in Southern Asia, Australia, and Europe and remarkable for their habit of building nests formed of blades of grass dexterously interwoven and suspended from the boughs of trees.

Weaving. The interlacing of two or more threads at right angles to form a fabric is a craft that has been practised since ancient times. The main principle of the weaving loom is the same to-day as it was thousands of years ago; a warp extends lengthwise through the loom, the threads being held in separate regular order by being passed through a reed or "slay", while the weft is crossed through alternating threads of the warp by means of a shuttle which holds the weft. Thus the fabric is built up. Weaving was done by hand up to the early part of the 19th cent., when Cartwright's steam-power loom was introduced. The Jacquard loom for weaving figured designs dates from 1801.

Wedding Anniversaries are: first, Cotton; second, Paper; third, Leather; fourth, Fruit and Flowers; fifth, Wooden; sixth, Sugar; seventh, Woollen; eighth, Bronze; ninth, Pottery; tenth, Tin; twelfth, Silk and Fine Linen; fifteenth, Crystal; twentieth, China; twenty-fifth, Silver; thirtieth, Pearl; thirty-fifth, Coral; fortieth, Ruby; forty-fifth, Sapphire; fiftieth, Golden; fifty-fifth, Emerald; sixtieth, Diamond; sixty-fifth, Platinum or Blue Sapphire; seventieth, Platinum; seventy-fifth, Diamond or Gold.

Wednesday, the 4th day of the week, derived its name from Woden or Odin, the Norse god of war.

Weights and Measures. *See* **F66–69.**

Welding is a means of joining together two pieces of material, often metals, by heating the joint until the substances melt locally, run together, and then solidify. The heating can be by burning gas (*e.g.*, oxy-acetylene welding) or electric current (electric arc welding). Techniques exist for welding anything from hair-like wires to massive steel plates. *See* **Soldering.**

Werewolf, a man or woman, who according to mediaeval belief, could be turned by witchcraft or magic into a wolf, eat human flesh or drink human blood and turn into himself again. This belief was widely held in Europe, and similar superstitions prevail among most primitive peoples, *e.g.*, the "leopard man" of certain African tribes. Lycanthropy (from Gr. = wolf-man) is a form of madness in which the patient imagines himself a beast.

Westminster Abbey stands on the site of an old church and Benedictine foundation of the 7th cent. It was rebuilt under Edward the Confessor, and again under Henry III, and important additions were made by Edward II, Edward III, Richard II, Richard III and Henry VII, the latter erecting the beautiful eastern chapel in the perpendicular style which bears his name. The west towers and gable were designed by Hawksmoor (1661–1736). The Abbey contains tombs of many sovereigns, of the Unknown Warrior, and many other illustrious persons are commemorated by monuments.

Westminster Cathedral, seat of the Roman Catholic Archbishop of Westminster. It was designed by J. F. Bentley and built betwen 1895 and 1910. It is of red brick, in early Christian Byzantine style with a domed campanile, 283 ft (86 m) high, and a decorative interior.

Westminster Hall, adjoining the House of Parliament, was built as a Banqueting Hall by

William Rufus, and many courtly festivals were held there in succeeding centuries. King John established the Law Courts there. It now forms a gigantic hallway, leading to the Houses of Parliament. Charles I, Sir Thomas More, and Warren Hastings were tried there.

Whale, a completely aquatic mammal; the forelimbs are modified to form fin-like paddles and there is virtually no external trace of the hindlimbs. There are two major groups of whales—the *Toothed Whales*, including the Sperm-whale (Cachalot), Dolphin, Killer-whales and Porpoises; and the *Whalebone Whales*. In the latter a series of whalebone plates grow down from the roof of the mouth, and, being frayed at their edges into a hairy fringe, together constitute a filtering mechanism. The animal takes in sea water containing minute organisms on which it feeds; the mouth is then closed and the tongue raised when the water is forced out through the filter, on which is left the food. As the tongue is lowered, the whalebone plates straighten up, flicking the food on to the tongue, which transfers it to the gut. Most whale oil is obtained from the thick layer of fat under the skin (blubber), but in the Sperm-whale there is a large reserve of oil in the head. One of the major users of sperm oil is the leather industry. Ambergris used in perfumery comes from the intestine of whales. The number of whales that may be killed in a season is limited by International Convention. Today the three main whaling nations are Japan, Norway and Russia. In 1994 a whale sanctuary around Antarctica was established by the International Whaling Commission. The sactuary bans commercial whaling in the Southern Ocean for at least 10 years.

Whiskers in physics and materials science (*q.v.*) are tiny rods of crystal, thinner than human hair and perhaps 1 cm long. Their importance lies in the fact that such crystals are free from the defects described on **F21.** They are also free from surface cracks and steps. This means they are immensely strong because failures of strength in ordinary solids are due to imperfections and cracks of one kind or another. Large numbers of whiskers of strong solids like graphite, silicon, or silicon carbide embedded in a matrix of softer matter such as plastic or metal would make a very strong new material. Laboratories are developing. such substances.

White Elephant, a term in common use to designate a gift that causes the recipient more trouble or cost than it is worth; derived from an old-time custom of the Kings of Thailand who presented a white elephant to a courtier whom it was desired to ruin.

Whitehall Palace, built within sight of Westminster by Hubert de Burgh, Earl of Kent, round about 1240, was the residence of the Archbishops of York until Wolsey presented it to Henry VIII in 1530. From then until 1697, when it was burned down, it continued to be the favourite town residence of royalty, and to the Stuarts especially it was a great centre of court festivities. In those days, with its grounds, it extended from the Strand to the river. The only portion of Whitehall Palace now standing is the Banqueting Hall built by Inigo Jones, on a scaffold projected from the front of which Charles I was beheaded. A block of government buildings has been built on part of the site of the old Palace.

White House, the official residence at Washington of the President of the United States. It was built in 1792, having been designed by an Irishman, James Hoban. In 1814 British troops captured Washington and set fire to the White House.

Whitsuntide, the festival celebrating the descent of the Holy Ghost and occurring seven weeks after Easter.

Widow Bird, certain species of African weaver birds with predominantly black plumage. In the breeding season the male birds are strikingly beautiful, with scarlet and buff markings and long tail feathers. They are social parasites and trick other birds into rearing their young.

Wigeon, a surface-feeding duck of northern Europe, known in Britain more as a winter visitor than a nesting bird. It feeds in flocks in the muddy estuaries and has a characteristic "whee-oo" call.

Willow, a water-side-loving tree of the genus *Salix*, to which the osiers belong. The best cricket-bat blades are made from a white willow, *S.*

alba var. *caerulea*, a fine tree with bluish-green leaves, mostly found in Essex. Willow is also used for polo balls. Weeping willow, *S. babylonica*, is native to China and is the willow seen on Old China willow-pattern plates.

Wind, air set in motion by special atmospheric conditions, is of various degrees, from a slight rustling breeze to a hurricane. Winds are *constant*, as in trade winds or anti-trade winds; *periodic*, as in monsoons and other windvisitations occurring according to influences of season; *cyclonic* and *anti-cyclonic*, when their motion is spiral: *whirlwinds*, *hurricanes*, and *tornados*, when high temperature and great density induce extreme agitation. Ordinarily, a wind is named from the point of the compass from which it blows, or it may be expressed in degrees from true north. The *sirocco*, the *mistral*, and the *simoom* are local forms of winds of great velocity. A *blizzard* is a biting blast of icy temperature. *See also* **Beaufort Scale, Section Z.**

Windmills were in use in the East in ancient times, but were not much seen in Europe before the 13th cent. Wind sawmills were invented by a Dutchman in the 17th cent., and one was erected near the Strand in London in 1633. Great improvements have been made in these mills, especially in the United States, where, by the application of the windshaft principle, much space is saved and the mills can be used for pumping, grinding and other purposes.

Windows (Old Norse *vindauga* = wind-eye), an opening in a wall of a building to admit light and air, and to afford a view of what is outside. In northern Europe windows, as the derivation of the word implies, were first used for ventilation and glass was not used in private houses before the end of the 12th cent. In early Gothic (12th cent.) windows were still small and narrow, with rounded heads. In Early English (13th cent.) they became longer and the heads pointed. In the Decorated period (14th cent.) windows were mullioned (divided by slender bars into panes) and the pointed heads often traceried. In Tudor times when the Renaissance had found its way to England, windows were larger and the bay-window (projecting from the wall) and the oriel window (*q.v.*) were much in vogue; in the late 18th cent. curved bays (called bow-windows) became fashionable. Sash windows (invented by the English) with wooden frames and divided into equal rectangular panes were used in Queen Anne and Georgian houses. Their design was influenced by a passion for symmetry; they were very efficient ventilators. The French window reaches to the floor and has double casements opening as doors. A Dormer window is a vertical window set on the sloping side of a roof. One of the main features of modern architecture is the large area devoted to windows, a development made possible by improved heating systems.

Windsor Castle, the famous British royal residence on the banks of the Thames, as it now stands, was mainly built by Henry III, though a royal residence had existed there from the time of the Conqueror. Additions were made by Henry VIII, Elizabeth and Charles II. Windsor Park and Forest comprise over 5,200 ha. A serious fire in 1992 caused very extensive damage, destroying St. George's Hall and gutting the Queen's Chapel.

Wine, the fermented juice of the freshly-gathered grape. There are innumerable varieties, each obtaining its distinctive character from the species of wine producing the grape, the locality of the vineyard, method of cultivation, etc. Wines are of three main kinds: *sparkling*, as in champagne, due to their having been bottled before fermentation is complete; *beverage*, when the must has been fermented out before bottling. Such wines include the famous red and white wines of Burgundy, Bordeaux and the Rhône valley and the white wines of the Rhine, Moselle and Loire valleys. Wines are *fortified* by the addition of alcohol either after fermentation is complete (*e.g.*, Sherry) or during fermentation (*e.g.*, Port). The principal wine-producing countries are: France, Italy, Spain, Portugal, Romania, Australia, Argentina, USA, Russia, Greece, Germany and Hungary. Wine drinking in Britain has increased nearly 60 per cent in the past ten years with £4·2 billion spent on 928 million bottles in 1993.

Witan *or* **Witenagemot,** the name given to the king's council of "wise men" in Anglo-Saxon times, composed of the archbishops, bishops, abbots of the greater abbeys, earldormen and influential thanes.

Witchcraft. *See* **Section J.**

Woad, a plant (*Isaatis tinctoria*) that in olden days was largely used in England for the blue dye obtained from the leaves. It is a biennial plant belonging to the same family (*Cruciferae*) as the wallflower.

Wolves, well-known carnivorous animals still found in many parts of Europe, but not existing in Britain since the middle of the 17th cent. They usually hunt in packs.

Women's Liberation Movement. *See* **Feminism, J20.**

Woodcock, a wading bird, valued for its flesh. It is a member of the snipe family, and breeds in Britain. The parent bird is able to carry its young between its thigh and body when flying to and from the feeding spots. It is one of the birds protected by the Game Laws.

Woodpecker, a familiar tree-climbing, insectivorous bird of conspicuous plumage, of which four species are found in Britain, the green woodpecker or yaffle (because of its harsh cry), the great spotted, the lesser spotted, and the wryneck. They build in the hollows of trees. Yaffle has a long sticky tongue for licking up ground insects, especially ants. The great and lesser woodpeckers obtain insects by digging into tree trunks with strong, chisel-like bills, spearing the insects with a sharp tongue. The metallic drumming sound made by the birds in spring is thought to be caused by their beaks hammering away at some hard resounding substance.

Wood's Metal, an alloy with a very low melting point (65°C, which is under 150°F) so that a spoon made of it will melt when used to stir a cup of tea. Contains bismuth 4 parts, lead 2 parts, tin 1 part, cadmium 1 part. Its use as a heat exchanger has now been largely superseded by silicone oils, which have a wider temperature range.

Woodworm. Four beetles are mainly responsible for woodworm damage: common furniture beetle (*Anobium punctatum*), powder post beetle (*Lyctus brunneus*), death watch beetle (*Xestobium rufovillosum*), and house longhorn beetle (*Hylotrupes bajulus*). Particular attention should be paid to wood in damp, dark and out-of-the-way places, and the backs and underneaths of furniture. The most frequent cause of woodworm damage is the common furniture beetle (*q.v.*).

Wool is a fibre, made up of very long protein molecules. It has been largely grown and used in the manufacture of cloth in England since before the Roman invasion. It is grown on the backs of sheep, and is of various kinds, according to the breed of sheep from which it is derived. Wool differs from hair in that it has a wavy, serrated fibre, its curl being a notable characteristic, whereas hair has a smooth surface comparatively free from serratures. Long wools are mostly used for the manufacture of worsted goods, and short wools for woollen cloths, though the improvements in machinery in recent years have enabled manufacturers to utilise short wools to a great extent for dress fabrics as well as for woollens. The finest wools are obtained from the fleece of the Spanish merino sheep. Australia, the former USSR, New Zealand, Argentina and South Africa are the greatest wool-producing countries.

Woolsack, the name given to the seat occupied by the Lord Chancellor in the House of Lords. It is a large square bag of wool, without back or arms, covered with red cloth. At the time when it was first used, in the reign of Edward III, wool was the great staple commodity of the country and, it is said, chosen for the seat of judges as a constant reminder of the main source of the national wealth. The Lord Chancellor is "appointed to the woolsack".

World Population. According to United Nations sources world population in 1995 had passed 5,660 million. More than half the total live in Asia. Different countries are at different stages in a demographic transition from the stability provided by a combination of high birth rate and high death rate to that provided by a combination of low birth rate and low death rate. Their recent

population history and current trend of growth, the age-structure of their population, and consequently their population potential for the near future are all widely different. Most rapid growth is in Africa with rates of over 3 per cent in some countries. In most European countries the rate is less than 1 per cent. A baby girl born in Norway may expect to live the longest (77·6 years) and a baby boy in Sweden (72·1 years), but a baby born in some African countries may not live to reach 40 years. It is estimated that about one in 25 of all human beings who have ever lived are alive today. It took 115 years for the world's population to rise from one to two thousand million; in a further 35 years it rose from two thousand million to three; in only 15 more years from four to five thousand million. It is estimated to reach over 6·25 billion by 1999 and over seven billion by 2010. Life expectancy in Britain today (1995) is 74 for men and 79 for women (compared to 48 and 51 in 1906). Life expectancy is increasing in Britain. Women are expected to live until the age 80 and men to 74½ by the year 2000. Already Britain has the oldest population in the EU. One in 5 Britons are now over 60 and nearly 2 million are over 80. There were 7,159 centenarians in Britain at the 1991 census. Highest life expectancies in the world (1990 figures) are Japan (78·8), Iceland and Switzerland (78·0) and Sweden (77·6).

Wreck, the name given to trove found under water, usually from a maritime wreck. Finds must be brought to the notice of the Official Receiver of Wrecks, an officer of H.M. Customs and Excise.

Wren, a family of small passerine birds possessing upturned tails and most abundant in South America. The British species is an interesting singing bird with a surprising loud note for its size.

X

Xenon a rare gaseous element, no.54, symbol Xe, occurring in minute quantities in the atmosphere, discovered by Sir William Ramsay and M. W. Travers in 1898. *See* **Rare Gases.**

X-Rays were discovered in 1895 by Professor Röntgen, of Wurzburg. X-rays are produced when heavy metal atoms (*e.g.* tungsten) are struck by electrons of sufficient energy. X-rays are now commonly used to examine the internal structure of many opaque objects. In medicine, industry and for security, examination may be conducted without physical invasion. X-rays may also be used to probe the structure of matter, for example the atomic structure of crystals. The discovery in the 1960s that cosmic objects emitted intense X-rays has led to many important new astronomical phenomena being discovered. *See* **F12.**

Xylem, the woody tissue of higher plants whose function is to conduct water and mineral salts upwards, and to provide mechanical support.

Y

Yacht, a light vessel now much used for pleasure trips and racing. The first yachting club was the Cork Harbour Club, started about 1720; and in 1812 the Royal Yacht Squadron was founded at Cowes. The Royal Thames Yacht Club dates from 1823. The most famous international yachting trophy is *The America's Cup* (**L6**).

Yak, a curious, long-haired ox, found in Tibet. Used as a beast of burden, and also kept for milk and meat.

Yard, a standard measure of 36 in, the word being derived from the Saxon gryd, or rod. The yard and pound are now defined by reference to the metre and the kilogram: yard = 0·9144 of a metre; pound = 0·45359237 of a kilogram.

By international agreement the metre is defined by reference to the wavelength of krypton-86 light.

Yardies. Jamaican criminal gangs, in some ways similar to the Chinese Triads or Italian mafia.

Yellowhammer, a common British bird of the bunting family, of lemon-yellow and brown plumage. Nests on or near the ground.

Yeomen of the Guard are a body of Foot Guards established in the reign of Henry VII for the protection of the Royal Person. Yeomen are now about 100 in number, and their duties consist in being present on ceremonial State occasions, the yearly distribution of Maundy Money, and the searching of the vaults of the Houses of Parliament on Guy Fawkes' day. "Beefeater" is the nickname of both Yeomen of the Guard and Yeomen Warders of the Tower, and they both wear the style of dress of the Tudor period, but with one distinction, the Yeomen of the Guard wear a cross belt, the Warders do not.

Yeti, opinions differ as to whether this is a mythical inhabitant of the Himalayas, a primitive primate or bear. Evidence to date is inconclusive.

Yoga. *See* Section J.

York Minster, one of the oldest and finest of English cathedrals, is 160 m long, its nave is 73 m broad, and the central tower is 66 m high. The present edifice, in parts, dates back to the 12th cent., but a church stood on the site in the 7th cent. In 1829 it was set on fire by a lunatic named Jonathan Martin. In July 1984, a serious fire caused by lightning wrought severe damage to the south transept.

Youth Courts. *See* Juvenile Courts (**L69**).

Ytterbium, a chemical, no.70, symbol Yb, element discovered by Urbain in 1907; one of the group of rare earth metals.

Yttrium, a chemical element, no.39, symbol Y, discovered by Mosander in 1842. It is found in a few rare minerals such as gadolinite, xenotime, fergusonite and euxenite. One of the group of rare earth metals.

Z

Zamboni Pile, a dry galvanic battery, which can provide small amounts of high-voltage current over a very long time. At Oxford a couple of Zamboni piles have kept a bell ringing for over a hundred years. These piles in the second world war were perfected and produced in quantity, being the most convenient source of current for infra-red signalling devices.

Zebra, an African quadruped of whitish-grey colour, with regular black stripings, perhaps the most beautiful member of the Equine family. Rather larger than an ass and smaller than the horse, it has a tufted tail, is of light build, wild and fleet of foot. The Zebra may be threatened with extinction—already the fate of the Quagga species—because of its slaughter by man for its beautiful skin.

Zen Buddhism. *See* Section J.

Zenith, the highest point in the heavens above an observer's head, the opposite pole to the nadir.

Zero, the cypher signifying nothing originally came from China. The West is indebted to the Arabs for it, who themselves obtained it from India and passed it to European mathematicians towards the end of the Middle Ages. The zero has also been found in Babylonian cuneiform. The Greeks had no such symbol, which hindered the development of their mathematics. The use of zero led to the invention of decimal fractions and to the

later developments in astronomy, physics and chemistry. For absolute zero on the temperature scale *see* **Absolute Temperature.**

Zinc, a familiar metallic element, no.30, symbol Zn, known to the ancients, and used by them in the making of brass. It occurs as the sulphide, carbonate, etc. The ores of zinc are crushed, roasted and reduced with coal. In combination with copper it constitutes the familiar alloy called brass, and zinc itself is much used for roofing and other protective purposes, Zinc ores are mined in Canada, the USA, Mexico, Poland, Australia, Russia, Italy, Spain and many other parts of the world. Zinc smelting is carried on in most industrial countries.

Zionism. *See* Section J.

Zirconium, metallic element, no.40, symbol Zr, was discovered by Klaproth in the sand of the rivers of Sri Lanka in 1789. The crystalline metal is white, soft and ductile; in its amorphous condition it is a blue-black powder. Zirconium is used in atomic reactors as containers for fuel elements, since it does not absorb neutrons.

Zodiac, an imaginary zone or belt of the sky enclosing the circuit over which the principal planets travel. It is divided into 12 equal spaces of 30 degrees each, comprising respectively the 12 signs of the zodiac—Aries, Taurus, Gemini, Cancer, Leo, Virgo, Libra, Scorpio, Sagittarius, Capricornus, Aquarius and Pisces. The idea of the zodiac originated with the Babylonians about 2000 B.C. and passed by way of the Greeks to the Western world. The traditional 12 signs of the zodiac were thrown into turmoil recently when a 13th sign – Ophiucus – was added by astronomers.

Zodiacal Band, a very faint band of light sometimes seen stretching along the ecliptic joining the Zodiacal Light to the Gegenschein and, like them, caused by the reflection of sunlight from interplanetary dust particles.

Zodiacal Light, a faint cone of light occasionally seen stretching along the zodiac from the western horizon after evening twilight or the eastern horizon before morning twilight. It is believed to be due to the scattering of the sun's light by dust particles in orbit round the sun and extending beyond the earth. Recent observations at the high altitudes station at Chacaltaya in the Andes suggest that the dust is travelling round the sun in regular planetary orbits.

Zonda, a warm moist wind in Argentina of great velocity blowing from the north or northwest, and, like the Sirocco in Southern Europe, causes much discomfort. It happens when a depression is moving across the pampas, bringing with it a mass of air from the humid tropics. It is followed by a refreshing wind from the south east.

Zoological Gardens of London were opened in 1828, and belong to the Zoological Society of London. They contain one of the largest and most varied collections of living animals in the world. The Society maintains an open-air zoo at Whipsnade, on the edge of Dunstable Downs; this was opened in 1931. The future of London Zoo was (at least temporarily) secured in 1992 by a £1·7 million cost-cutting programme and many generous donations.

Zoology, the branch of science concerned with animal life, embracing many aspects such as anatomy, behaviour, classification, distribution and ecology. *See* **Section F, Part IV.**

Zoroastrianism. *See* Section J.

Zulus, one of the peoples of South Africa. Prior to white rule, the Zulus were ruled by a succession of paramount chiefs, reaching the zenith of their powers under King Shaka in the 1820s. Their power was crushed by the British at Ulundi in 1879 (after the Zulus had earlier routed the British at Isandlwana).

SPECIAL TOPIC

THE INTERNET REVOLUTION

The Background.

The Internet is a world-wide communications Network for computers. The number of computers able to communicate with or "access" the Internet is estimated at over 20 million, and is expected to rise to 200 million within twenty years. The Internet was developed by the American defence agencies as a means of ensuring that many routes were available between a computer in one location and another elsewhere so that, during a war, information could be passed through the Network even if parts of it were damaged. The Internet is one of the products of the close relationship between America's universities and its defence agencies, which dates back to the Manhattan Project which developed the atomic bomb.

With the thawing of the cold war the defensive use of the Internet became less important, and it became the primary means of communication between universities throughout the world. The increasing ownership of personal computers (or PCs) outside of academic institutions has meant a further expansion of "The Net" as it is more commonly called.

Use for Electronic Mail.

The primary uses of the Net are: electronic mail or E-mail – electronic communication between one individual or group and another; and the general dissemination of information in the form of text, graphics, video, sound, music or software.

E-mail is perhaps the mundane side of the Net, although the ability to send a message to one or more addresses world-wide within minutes for the cost of a short local telephone call makes normal postal methods (called "Snail Mail" by Net people) seem primitive. Generally in E-mail messages are delivered to specific addresses and will be read on the next occasion the addresses are accessed. "Bulletin Boards" or "BBSs" are where individuals can leave messages for others accessing the BBS. It is also possible to access "Talk-Request" places on the Internet which allow one to talk in "real-time" to other individuals or groups. A similar facility is available at some BBSs.

Dissemination of Information.

The dissemination of information occurs through special interest "conference sites" (NewsNet or UseNet). These often have a magazine-like quality about them. The range of topics is vast. There seems to be no subject too trivial or obscure to grace the Net. The authors of these range from institutions such as NASA, with pictures of the recent Shoemaker-Levy comet impact on Jupiter, through fans of pop groups, to individuals who believe that pyramids keep razor blades sharp. It is hard to convey how much information is available; but it is far more than any individual could ever access in many lifetimes.

The use of the Net as a publishing and broadcasting medium is becoming more commonplace. Some authors have placed their creative output on the Net in preference to conventional publishers, while the band Future Sound of London has broadcast "live" concerts featuring guitarist Robert Fripp over the Net. This tendency has caused some alarm in the traditional publishing media, as it is hard to see how such events can be commercially exploited.

Accessing "The Net".

Accessing the Net is achieved in a number of ways. Most expensive is to establish a direct or "leased-line", a high speed connection providing the maximum throughput of information. This is the choice of corporations who require such volume and can afford it. Individuals with a computer and modem – a device which allows digital information to be transmitted as a set of pitches through a telephone "voice" line – need not go to this expense,

as companies with leased-lines often share them amongst individuals on a commercial basis. These are the "service providers" that most people use to gain access to the Net via the SLIP and PPP Internet protocols, which effectively connect the individual's computer directly to the Net – any information accessed is delivered straight to the computer.

It is possible to connect to the Net through "on-line" services such as CIX, CompuServe and Delphi as well as some Bulletin Boards. However these can be limiting, as they involve indirect connection to the Net. Information accessed is first delivered to a storage area in the on-line service and then downloaded to the computer. The time taken to access very large files can be longer than a direct link and this may be reflected in increased cost.

The Net can be difficult to use for the less computer-literate. Until recently access was achieved using a "Command Line Interface" or CLI which the Net has due to its UNIX origins. This is similar to MSDOS and relies on the user's ability to remember a large vocabulary of abbreviations and acronyms, as well as an associated hierarchy of punctuation marks which are used as commands to control access to the Net.

The World Wide Web (WWW).

The recent, almost exponential, increase in the number of users on the Internet is in part due to the World Wide Web (WWW, The Web or W³). The web was developed at CERN to simplify and improve access to the Net by using a "hypertext" system, whereby intelligent links exist between one item of text (or an image) and another related item, even if these items are on separate computers. For example, a web version of this article would have such links for each of the jargon words which appear in it. Selecting a word would call up a definition of it, or display a related article from elsewhere in *Pears Cyclopaedia*. The definitions which are currently embedded in the text would then not be necessary.

The web relies on a "graphic user interface", which allows users to choose options by selecting icons (pictures) on the screen with a mouse, instead of using the UNIX-like CLI. For those familiar with IBM-type PCs the effect is much like the replacement of MSDOS by Windows. Two such interfaces (or "browsers") are called "Mosaic" and "Cello".

The Net's Culture and Language.

The Net has its own culture and language. Net people "surf" the Internet. The Net is "Cyberspace" – a term invented by the American author William Gibson in 1981. In fact the word cyber is used *ad nauseam* as a prefix –cybergames, cyberwork, cyberfunk, cyberpunk, cyberschool *etc*. Real world things become cyberthings in the "virtual" world of the Net. Reducing on-line time (and cost) and the "techie" background of some of the Net's users has led to the dominance of abbreviations and acronyms in e-mail and interactive chats. Examples of these include: FAQ – Frequently Asked Questions; IMHO – In My Humble Opinion; ROFL – Roll On Floor Laughing; TANJ – There Ain't No Justice; TTBOMK – To The Best Of My Knowledge, *etc*.

Punctuation marks used to create face-like figures with emotive qualities ("Smileys" or "Emoticons") also reduce the amount of sensible text in Net dialogues. Thus:-)means "happy" :-(means "sad" :'-(means "crying" :-& means the user is speechless (though one wonders why the user has taken the trouble to access the Internet in this condition). Similarly the use of capitals is the Internet equivalent of shouting and is discouraged.

Internet culture has an ethics or taboo system, sometimes called "Netiquette". Commercialism is frowned upon, as is "spamming" – sending messages to several sites or users – named after the Monty Python song which consists of the single word spam repeated. Spamming commercially or junk e-mail is a most heinous offence. Perpetrators get "flamed" – hundreds of irate users will send abusive e-mail.

L133

Flaming may result in a logjam of messages in the spammer's system, and this may prompt their service provider to take action. A legal firm which advertised its services to a large number of Internet sites was subsequently flamed and the service provider suspended the legal firm's access for a while.

Problems of Internet.

Despite the hyperbole in the media about the "information superhighway" or "infobahn" of which the Internet is part, there are problems. One of these is the question of jurisdiction. Within which legal framework does a system without national frontiers operate? If a pornographic image is legally made available on the Internet in one country, could it be illegal to access it from another? Would such access constitute illegal "importation"?

Related to this is the issue of censorship. The attempts by one American university to block students' access to an Internet site containing pornography led to a storm of protest from the wider net community. Appeals to the first amendment of that country's constitution guaranteeing freedom of expression, the threat of a legal action on this basis and adverse publicity in the media had the university reversing its decision within a few days.

Were an authority minded to censor the Internet, would it be able to? The answer may be no. It is a relatively trivial matter for a computer to encrypt a file before it is transmitted so that the file cannot be understood by unauthorised users, and in principle Internet users could conceal the nature of material from government enforcers by encrypting it. A number of such encryption systems exist. Usually these are based on the Data Encryption Standard or DES.

The Data Encryption Standard (DES).

The DES was developed by the US National Security Agency during the late 1960s and has recently been declassified and published as a National Standard. It is an extremely effective system. However, some are concerned that there is an unpublished "back door" into DES which allows government agencies to decrypt any Internet files which use it. For this reason other systems have been developed independently. One of these, "Pretty Good Privacy" or PGP, has landed its developer before a Grand Jury, Philip Zimmerman, PGP's author, is charged with supplying a "US Munitions List" item (encryption standards other than DES appear to fall under the category of

restricted weapons). The apparent zeal of the government in prosecuting Zimmerman for producing a non-DES encryption standard is confirmation for some that the government does indeed retain access to DES encrypted files.

Another unresolved question is whether material made available on the net is subject to copyright, *i.e.* is such material in the Public Domain? This issue has very significant ramifications for those who are planning commercial exploitation of the net.

The Problem of Hacking.

The Internet would seem to be a hacker's playground. No one knows whether hacking (the access and abuse of computer systems by unauthorised individuals) is a widespread problem. Much consideration has been given to the security of the Internet, especially given its defence origins. The Internet has in-built software "firewalls" between the network and the computers which administer it. These are supposed to restrict the activities of unrecognised computers and were considered to be effective. Tsutomu Shimomura, an expert on computer security at the San Diego Supercomputer Center, has now discovered to his cost that they are not. His computer, believed to be safe behind a firewall, was recently hacked and a number of files on computer security systems were stolen. Vandals have also placed "worms" – programs which replicate themselves – onto the network. The replication is exponential and within a short time the entire network can be clogged up.

Another problem is more fundamental. In the past information has been at a premium: "information is power". How are we to fare in a world where there is a glut of information? And where information is dross?

Future Prospects.

The Internet is still in its infancy. It has shrugged off its origins with the development of the web, leading to a dramatic improvement in its usability. The next stage is for a more complete integration into the domestic environment. Increasingly the television could recover its position as the information centre in a home by combining the technologies of TV and PC. The British technology company ARM has just announced a deal to develop their RISC chips into just such products. The processing power available will make voice control a possibility. Once the Internet has a friendly graphic interface, which is as easy to use as a TV remote control, the promises of the information superhighway may well be delivered.

CALENDAR 1996

CHRONOLOGICAL CYCLES AND ERAS

Dominical Letter		GF
Epact		10
Golden Number (Lunar Cycle)		II

Julian Period (year of)		6709
Roman Indiction		4
Solar Cycle		17

Era	Year	Begins		Era	Year	Begins
Byzantine	7505	14 Sept		Grecian (Seleucidae)	2308	14 Sept
Roman (A.U.C.)	2749	14 Jan				(or 14 Oct)
Nabonassar	2745	24 Apr		Indian (Saka)	1918	21 Mar
Japanese	2656	1 Jan		Diocletian	1713	11 Sept

RELIGIOUS CALENDARS

Epiphany		6 Jan		Low Sunday		14 Apr
Septuagesima Sunday		4 Feb		Rogation Sunday		12 May
Quinquagesima Sunday		18 Feb		Ascension Day—Holy Thursday		16 May
Ash Wednesday		21 Feb		Whit Sunday—Pentecost		26 May
Quadragesima Sunday		25 Feb		Trinity Sunday		2 June
Palm Sunday		31 Mar		Corpus Christi		6 June
Good Friday		5 Apr		First Sunday in Advent		1 Dec
Easter Day		7 Apr		Christmas Day		25 Dec
Passover, First day of (Pesach)		4 Apr		Day of Atonement (Yom Kippur)		23 Sept
Feast of Weeks (Shavuot)		24 May		Tabernacles, First day of (Succoth)		28 Sept
Jewish New Year (5757) (Rosh Hashanah)		14 Sept				
Ramadan, First day of		22 Jan		Islamic New Year (1417)		19 May

All Jewish and Islamic dates above are tabular dates, which begin at sunset on the previous evening and end at sunset on the date tabulated. In practice, Islamic fasts and festivals are determined by an actual sighting of the appropriate New Moon.

CIVIL CALENDAR—UNITED KINGDOM

Accession of Queen Elizabeth II		6 Feb		Coronation Day		2 June
St David (Wales)		1 Mar		The Queen's Official Birthday		8 June
Commonwealth Day		11 Mar		Birthday of Prince Philip,		
St Patrick (Ireland)		17 Mar		Duke of Edinburgh		10 June
Mothering Sunday		17 Mar		Remembrance Sunday		10 Nov
Birthday of Queen Elizabeth II		21 Apr		Birthday of the Prince of Wales		14 Nov
St George (England)		23 Apr		St Andrew (Scotland)		30 Nov

LITERARY
COMPANION

This section is arranged in three parts. The first provides a concise introduction to the history of the English Novel. The second contains a glossary of literary terms whilst the third section features special topics, including in this edition articles on the British romantic poets and the modern French novel.

TABLE OF CONTENTS

LITERARY COMPANION

I. THE ENGLISH NOVEL

INTRODUCTION

Definition

A novel is a fictitious prose narrative, usually of more than 50,000 words in length. It often deals with characters and actions that give readers an illusion of reality, but it can also be fanciful or fantastic. Its elements conventionally include a plot or story, personages, dialogue and a setting. Some novels contain such poetic elements as symbol, metaphor and rhythmical construction. Just as the content and general approach of novels show many variations, so the techniques in their writing greatly differ: narratives told in the first or third persons, in the form of letters and from different points of view are amongst the devices of presentation that have been used.

Types

Certain types can be defined, although they cannot always be clearly distinguished from one another.

The *picaresque novel* has a *picaro* (Spanish: "rogue") at the centre of its action, but sometimes this main character is an innocent or foolish person. Many adventures, described comically, satirically or realistically, befall him and influence him. A famous example is Lesage's *Gil Blas* (1715, 1724, 1735). Fielding's *Tom Jones* (1749) and Dickens' *Pickwick Papers* (1836–7) are in this tradition, which has been widely followed in England.

The *Bildungsroman* (German: "formation novel") relates the upbringing and education of the hero, as in Goethe's *Wilhelm Meister's Apprenticeship* (1795–6) and Dickens' *David Copperfield* (1849–50).

Psychological novels, exploring character, motives and relationships, were first established in France, with Madame de La Fayette's *La Princesse de Clèves* (1678) and the Abbé Prévost's *Manon Lescaut* (1731). Richardson's *Pamela* (1740) belongs to this category of fiction, which is often considered the most significant of all the kinds, reaching great profundity in the work of Dostoevsky (1821–81), Tolstoy (1828–1910) and Henry James (1843–1916).

Social novels, with the aim of exposure and reform of abuses and injustice, were prominent in the nineteenth century. Examples are Mrs Gaskell's *Mary Barton* (1848) and Charles Kingsley's *Alton Locke* (1850). Balzac's numerous novels, collected as *La Comédie humaine* (1842–8), and many by Dickens (*e.g. Little Dorrit*, 1855–6) are social novels in a more comprehensive sense, depicting characteristics of French and English society respectively.

The *novel of manners* is a sophisticated presentation of social codes of behaviour, especially amongst the leisured classes. Meredith's *The Egoist* (1878) partly belongs to this type.

Naturalistic novels, like those in Emile Zola's series, *Les Rougon-Macquart* (1871–93), and many by George Gissing (1857–1903), emphasise the power of environment in moulding human character.

Regional novels, by Thomas Hardy (1840–1928) and Arnold Bennett (1867–1931), amongst others, place importance on the traditions and influences of particular areas of a country.

In *adventure* and *detective novels*, the story or plot is a principal feature, as in Wilkie Collins' *The Moonstone* (1868) and Robert Louis Stevenson's *Treasure Island* (1883). The thriller, a variation of this type, is marked by excitement and violence, as in the James Bond novels of Ian Fleming (1908–64).

The *historical novel* deals with the past, sometimes mixing fact and fiction, such as the novels of Sir Walter Scott (1771–1832), Flaubert's *Salammbô* (1862) and Tolstoy's *War and Peace* (1863–9).

Fantasy has become increasingly popular, especially in the form of *science fiction*; Jules Verne (1828–1905) was one of the earliest and most widely read writers of this genre. English writers who have used this kind of fiction include H. G. Wells (1866–1946) and John Wyndham (1903–69). J. R. R. Tolkien (1892–1973) created a new "legendary" world in *The Lord of the Rings* (1954–5).

Purpose

The purpose of a novel varies with its type. Anthony Trollope's statement, made in his study of Thackeray (1879), has a fundamental validity: "the object of a novel should be to instruct in morals while it amuses." At one extreme, some novels are expressly meant to teach, such as some Victorian children's novels and social novels (*e.g.* many written by Charles Kingsley). At the other, some novels are meant simply as entertainment, such as detective stories and much science fiction. Trollope's term, "morals", is difficult to define, but one can say that the aim of most novels is to reveal and stimulate thought about aspects of human behaviour both individually and in personal and social relationships. Apart from these generalisations, the specific purposes of some English novels are described separately in the following survey.

Rise and popularity of the novel

Though stories in verse and prose are as old as human life itself, the novel, as we know it today, became established in the late seventeenth and early eighteenth centuries. Its rise is related to changes in the climate of ideas during that period, with its increasing emphasis on the rational and the actual. Influenced by such thinkers as Sir Isaac Newton (1642–1727) and John Locke (1632–1704), philosophers investigated the ordinary, physical world rather than the world of metaphysical speculation. At the same time, the reading public had increased in numbers, especially amongst the middle classes. This public wanted to read about the behaviour of realistic people in credible surroundings. One result in England was the publication of novels by Defoe, Richardson, Fielding and Smollett in the first half of the eighteenth century.

THE EIGHTEENTH CENTURY

Daniel Defoe

Daniel Defoe (*c.*1661–1731) is regarded as the first notable English novelist. After many years as a political pamphleteer, he published *Robinson Crusoe* (1719), based on accounts of the actual adventures of the mariner, Alexander Selkirk. The book is written with convincing, detailed realism. Robinson Crusoe's practical approach to his predicament and his powerful individualism make him an admirable character who can be seen to have a universal significance. We are shown a man confronted by adversity and yet overcoming it by means of his resourcefulness and holding to his belief in a providential God. The basic idea of a person shipwrecked on an island had a wide appeal, which was reflected in many imitations, including *The Swiss Family Robinson* (1813) by Johann Rudolf Wyss. Defoe's other novels include *Captain Singleton* (1720), *Moll Flanders* (1722), *Colonel Jack* (1722) and *Roxana* (1724). He claimed that *Moll Flanders* had a moral purpose, in that from every part of it "something may be learned, and some just and religious inference is drawn." But it survives because of its lively and uninhibited representation of the personality and doings of its disreputable, resilient heroine, who (like Robinson Crusoe) tells her own story. Formally, Defoe is an unsophisticated writer, who relies mostly on his invention of incident to keep his narrative in motion. His strength lies in his powers of observation and in his rendering of particulars, conveyed in so straightforward prose, so that readers feel that they are experiencing things that actually happened.

Richardson, Fielding, Smollett and Sterne

The first great period of the English novel is 1740–71, when four important novelists flourished: Samuel Richardson (1689–1761), Henry Fielding (1707–54), Laurence Sterne (1713–68) and Tobias Smollett (1721–71). George Saintsbury, in *The English Novel* (1913), aptly called them the "remarkable exponents of a new kind of Human Comedy."

Richardson was a printer who was compiling a

collection of model letters to suit various occasions when he thought of writing an epistolary novel. The outcome was *Pamela* (1740), in which the letters reveal the story of Pamela, a servant girl, who resists her master's attempts to seduce her but finally agrees to marry him. *Clarissa* (1747–8), also written in the form of letters, tells of the tragedy of its heroine, who dies after her rape by the libertine, Lovelace. Containing a million words, it is probably the longest novel in English. Richardson's third and last epistolary novel, *Sir Charles Grandison* (1754), centres upon the scrupulously gentlemanly conduct of its hero. These are not novels of external action but are explorations of human psychology, especially of the thoughts and emotions of the young women involved. Their main theme is sexual passion and the moral problems that arise from it. The novels are admired for their sensitive portrayals of emotional and mental processes, realistically presented by means of the letters written by the characters.

Henry Fielding's first novel, *Joseph Andrews* (1742), was conceived partly as a satire on *Pamela*, which he thought hypocritical and sentimental. In picaresque style, he relates the adventures of Joseph Andrews, who is supposedly Pamela's brother, and his companion, Parson Adams. His intention in this "comic epic in prose", as he called it, was to expose the ridiculous. He therefore displays and comments upon hypocritical and affected behaviour in several walks of life. Parson Adams is one of the great humorous characters of English literature and yet he epitomises a true Christian goodness. Fielding's ironic approach reached an extreme in *Jonathan Wild* (1743), in which he treats the villainous thief who is the hero as if he were a great man. *Tom Jones* (1749), his masterpiece, gives us in an ingenious plot the history of a young man of unknown birth: his boyhood in the country, his journey to London and his escapades when he gets there. The book is full of vivid characters and episodes and contains much moral comment from the author himself. *Amelia* (1751) is concerned with the misfortunes of the heroine and her husband and with her patience and virtue. An experienced playwright, Fielding uses dramatic devices and events, sometimes involving physical action. His comedy is occasionally coarse and boisterous but often drily ironical. The reader is frequently aware of his authorial presence and he intervenes directly in the narrative. Like many of his contemporaries, he acknowledges the influence of the classics of Greek and Latin literature and here and there writes in a mock-heroic style. He is the opposite of Richardson, as Dr Johnson said to Boswell: "there was as great a difference between them as between a man who knew how a watch was made (*i.e.* Richardson), and a man who could tell the hour by looking on the dial-plate (*i.e.* Fielding)."

Tobias Smollett is superficially reminiscent of Fielding in his novels: *Roderick Random* (1748), *Peregrine Pickle* (1751), *Ferdinand, Count Fathom* (1753), *Sir Lancelot Greaves* (1760–61) and *Humphry Clinker* (1771). All of them recount the wanderings and adventures of their heroes and can therefore be described as picaresque, although *Humphry Clinker* is an epistolary novel. Smollett depicts an often brutal world with a mixture of relish and repulsion and his novels have a remarkable vivacity of invention. The episodes on board ship in *Roderick Random*, for example, give an unforgettable picture of the cruelties and rigours of eighteenth-century seafaring life.

Laurence Sterne stands apart from the novelists of his time and indeed can still be regarded as unique. *Tristram Shandy* (1760–67) is an eccentric, digressive composition. Chronological order and the sequence of cause and effect do not apply to Sterne's handling of his subject-matter—the hero is not born till half way through the novel, for instance. The personages talk of this and that, the author intervenes at will, a chapter may break off suddenly or may be blank, and so on. Despite this whimsicality and the flux of ideas and impressions, characters, such as My Uncle Toby and the Widow Wadman, are fully realised and an atmosphere of gentle humanity prevails.

Although one cannot draw clear lines of influence, it is possible to see these four novelists—Richardson, Fielding, Smollett and Sterne—as representatives of kinds of approaches to fiction that were apparent in the next two centuries. Richardson displays the interest in psychological introspection characteristic of the work of many twentieth-century writers. The emphasis laid by Fielding and Smollett upon external action has its counterpart in the broad humour and simple characterisation of some nineteenth-century novels. Modern experiments in the form of the novel remind us of Sterne's rejection of the rational development of narrative.

Later Eighteenth-Century Novelists

After the middle of the century, no outstanding English novelist emerged until Scott and Jane Austen started to write fiction at its end. But a few memorable novels appeared, including Oliver Goldsmith's *The Vicar of Wakefield* (1766) and Fanny Burney's *Evelina* (1778). Horace Walpole's *The Castle of Otranto* (1765) is important as the first Gothic novel. This type contained mystery and terror, often associated with the supernatural and a medieval setting. Its famous exponents came later: Mrs Ann Radcliffe, who wrote *The Mysteries of Udolpho* (1794) and Matthew Gregory ("Monk") Lewis, who wrote *The Monk* (1796). The most celebrated is Mary Shelley's *Frankenstein* (1818).

THE EARLY NINETEENTH CENTURY

Sir Walter Scott

The Gothic novels just mentioned are typical of Romantic literature, of whom one of the principal representatives in Britain and Europe in the early years of the nineteenth century was Sir Walter Scott (1771–1832). In his own time and for long afterwards, Scott was regarded as akin to Shakespeare in his comprehensive renderings of human life and his powers of imagination. He was a prolific author, who wrote poems, dramas, short stories, biographies and histories as well as the following novels: *Waverley* (1814), *Guy Mannering* (1815), *The Antiquary* (1816), *The Black Dwarf* (1816), *Old Mortality* (1817), *Rob Roy* (1818), *The Heart of Midlothian* (1818), *The Bride of Lammermoor* (1819), *A Legend of Montrose* (1819), *Ivanhoe* (1820), *The Monastery* (1820), *The Abbot* (1820), *Kenilworth* (1821), *The Pirate* (1822), *The Fortunes of Nigel* (1822), *Peveril of the Peak* (1822), *Quentin Durward* (1823), *Saint Ronan's Well* (1824), *Redgauntlet* (1824), *The Betrothed* (1825), *The Talisman* (1825), *Woodstock* (1826), *The Fair Maid of Perth* (1828), *Anne of Geierstein* (1829), *Count Robert of Paris* (1832) and *Castle Dangerous* (1832). These are mostly historical novels, set in many places and periods. *Waverley* takes place in Scotland during the 1745 Jacobite Rebellion; *Ivanhoe* in the England of Richard I; and *Quentin Durward* in fifteenth-century France during the reign of Louis XI.

Scott presents a great range of characters, from the lowliest peasants to monarchs, and mingles actual and fictional personages convincingly together. He enables us to see in their adventures, attitudes and relationships the forces of history at work. Their private lives are affected by public events. He imaginatively recreates history in his novels, which also show his sympathy for—and understanding of—all kinds of people, whatever their religious and political beliefs. His narratives are vigorously inventive, with colourful and dramatic scenes, as adaptations for opera, films and television have demonstrated. Having once read them, the reader will recall such things as Waverley's journeyings in the Highlands of Scotland, the battles in *Rob Roy*, Jeanie Deans' interviews with the Duke of Argyll and Queen Caroline in *The Heart of Midlothian*, and Meg Merrilies' roadside curses upon the Laird of Ellangowan in *Guy Mannering*. His memorable characters are often Scots, such as Jeanie Deans, Meg Merrilies, Dominie Sampson (in *Guy Mannering*) and Jonathan Oldbuck (in *The Antiquary*), but also noteworthy are Caleb Balderstone (in *The Bride of Lammermoor*) and Diana Vernon (in *Rob Roy*). His portrait of King James I in *The Fortunes of Nigel* is a remarkably convincing representation of an historical personage. But some of his heroes and women characters tend to be colourless and commonplace. Scott was not greatly concerned with psychological probings or with profound moral or religious issues. He used a huge canvas on which he portrayed the actions of people of every kind and degree in specific places and historical periods. He rendered "the being of the age" (in George Lukács' phrase) and the richness and variety of human life within that age.

Jane Austen

No novelist could be more different from Scott than Jane Austen, as he himself recognised. In an admiring comment on her work, he wrote: "The big bow-bow strain I can do myself like any now going, but the exquisite touch which renders ordinary commonplace things and characters interesting from the truth of the description and sentiment, is denied to me." Jane Austen (1775–1817) wrote only six novels, which were published as follows: *Sense and Sensibility* (1811), *Pride and Prejudice* (1813), *Mansfield Park* (1814), *Emma* (1816), *Northanger Abbey* and *Persuasion* (both 1818). The dates of composition are sometimes different: for example, *Northanger Abbey*, which was published posthumously, was one of her earliest books, begun in 1798. She also wrote shorter stories and fragments, which are conveniently collected in one volume in the *Oxford Jane Austen*.

She based her novels on the people and places with which she was familiar: the upper middle-class society of southern England, particularly Hampshire, the county in which she was born and lived for most of her life. Her work, she modestly wrote, was "that little bit (two inches wide) of ivory, in which I work with so fine a brush as produces little effect after much labour." Her subject-matter is the relationships between men and women, especially those concerned with love and marriage, and she accepts the social code of her class and period. She uses no exciting or ingenious plots, no startlingly dramatic incidents. She ignores doings and people outside the small circle in which her characters move. Yet working within these conventions of subject-matter and social code, she illuminates wider areas of human conduct. In *Persuasion*, for example, she tells the story of Anne Elliot, who had rejected the suit of Captain Wentworth, the man she truly loved, because she yielded to the well-meant advice of Lady Russell, a close friend of her family. Anne and Captain Wentworth, who have met again seven years afterwards, slowly but surely re-establish their loving relationship and eventually marry. Questions raised include the rights and wrongs of persuasion, the place of love and money in marriage, the pressures of family vanity, and motives of men and women respectively when they fall in love. Moral issues like these are treated by Jane Austen with irony and wit as well as sympathy.

Her dialogue and passages of description contain much that is subtle and drily amusing, revealing her as an author who views folly and pretension with amused disfavour and who values the qualities of prudence and tolerance. Elizabeth Bennett in *Pride and Prejudice* comes close to her ideal of what a person should be like and some words that she gives to her can represent the novelist's own approach: "I hope I never ridicule what is wise and good. Follies and nonsense, whims and inconsistencies do divert me, I own, and I laugh at them whenever I can."

Jane Austen's characters come alive through their dialogue and reflections and through the novelist's observations. She constructs her novels neatly and with a feeling of inevitability so that they have an effortless artistic unity. Although she wrote at the time of the Romantic Movement, she remained cool and rational; it is significant that Charlotte Brontë attacked her for lacking warmth and enthusiasm. But her clarity of style and form, her comedy and wit and, above all, her penetrating analyses of behaviour and motive have led to her justifiably being regarded today as one of the greatest of English novelists.

Minor Novelists of the 1820s and 1830s

Between the time of Scott and the time of Dickens, who shot to fame in 1836, there flourished many minor novelists. The most enduring of these is Thomas Love Peacock (1785–1866), who wrote *Headlong Hall* (1816), *Melincourt* (1817), *Nightmare Abbey* (1818), *Maid Marian* (1822), *The Misfortunes of Elphin* (1829), *Crotchet Castle* (1831) and *Gryll Grange* (1860). These were mostly comic, satirical novels of ideas, wittily satirising fashionable thinkers and intellectual tendencies of the age. Peacock's usual device is to place his characters round a dinner-table and to record their conversation. In this way, he could poke fun at the Gothic Novel, Byronic gloom and German romanticism (in *Nightmare Abbey*), modern trends in education and agriculture (in *Crotchet Castle*) and Rousseau's views on natural

man (in *Melincourt*). Some of his characters are caricatures of living people: Scythrop is Shelley (in *Nightmare Abbey*) and Mr Fax is Malthus (in *Melincourt*). His is a rational voice, puncturing what he considered to be the pretensions and affectations of the Romantic Movement. The elegance and polish of his dialogues at the dinner-table make his novels a permanent delight.

Humour of a more obvious sort is present in the once-popular novels of Theodore Hook (1788–1841), such as *Sayings and Doings* (1826–9), but these are now forgotten. They are worth mentioning if only because some critics have seen Hook as a precursor of Dickens. "Fashionable" or "silver-fork" novels, relating the intrigues, customs and speech of high society, were also widely read at this time. Amongst the authors of these were Mrs Catherine Gore (1799–1861) and Edward Bulwer-Lytton (1803–73), whose *Pelham* (1828) still has a little amusing life in it. Bulwer-Lytton achieved fame, too, with his "Newgate Novels", such as *Paul Clifford* (1830) and *Eugene Aram* (1832), which depicted criminal life in a romanticised and even glamorous manner. Scott's prestige and influence led to the production of historical novels. Bulwer-Lytton's *The Last Days of Pompeii* (1834) and some by William Harrison Ainsworth (1805–82)—for example, *The Tower of London* (1840)—are readable, but those by G. P. R. James (1799–1860) have fallen into oblivion. These minor comic, "fashionable", "Newgate" and historical novels have little intrinsic interest for most readers today, although the student of the period will find them valuable for the insights they give, sometimes unwittingly, into the tastes and prejudices of the 1830s.

Undeserving of neglect, however, are the energetic novels of Captain Frederick Marryat (1792–1848). Like several naval officers of the period, he wrote seafaring fiction, beginning with *Frank Mildmay* (1829). *Peter Simple* (1834) and *Mr Midshipman Easy* (1836) were amongst the novels that followed. *Snarleyyow* (1837) is a macabre comedy about an apparently immortal dog. Towards the end of his writing career, Marryat turned to juvenile fiction, which included *Masterman Ready* (1841–2), *The Settlers in Canada* (1844) and *The Children of the New Forest* (1847). His novels are extrovert entertainments, full of vigour and knockabout comedy, written in an unpretentious prose style. Parts of them are reminiscent of Smollett and, more interestingly, of Dickens, who was one of his closest friends.

Some distinctively Scots novels were published at this time. John Galt (1779–1839) wrote *The Annals of the Parish* (1821), which chronicles the doings of a country parish in Scotland, and *The Entail* (1823), a tragicomedy of protracted disputes about an inheritance. Outstandingly original in form and content is *The Private Memoirs and Confessions of a Justified Sinner* (1824) by James Hogg (1770–1835). This story of evil and damnation, a narration followed by a confession, is centred upon the "sinner", who is encouraged in his wickedness by a friend, who—it becomes clear—is the Devil.

This period between Scott and Dickens was therefore productive of novels of great variety. If one had to choose amongst so many writers of fiction (and they have not all been named here), one could point to Peacock, Galt, Hogg and Marryat as novelists worth remembering, with Bulwer-Lytton and Ainsworth not far behind them. All were suddenly outshone, however, in 1836 by the dazzling appearance of Dickens on the scene.

THE EARLY VICTORIAN NOVELISTS

Charles Dickens

Charles Dickens (1812–70), who first came to public notice with sketches and articles in periodicals (collected as *Sketches by Boz* in 1835–6), achieved fame with *Pickwick Papers* (1836–7). This was rapidly followed by *Oliver Twist* (1838), *Nicholas Nickleby* (1838–9), *The Old Curiosity Shop* (1840–41), *Barnaby Rudge* (1841), *A Christmas Carol* (1843) and *Martin Chuzzlewit* (1843–4). These early books were exuberant and original in invention of every kind: colourful characterisation, vivid episodes, extravagant humour, pathos and evocation of the macabre, and an unfailingly fluent, fresh prose style. Many of Dickens' fictional personages immediately became household words: Mr Squeers, Little Nell, Scrooge and Mrs Gamp, to name only four from the books just listed. Similarly, sayings and phrases entered the English language, such as Oliver Twist's asking for more and Mrs Gamp's remarks about her imaginary friend, Mrs Harris. Dickens' tragic powers, especially those displayed in *The Old Curiosity Shop*, were found deeply moving. His evident concern for children, the poor and the deprived appealed to the humanitarian instincts of many of his contemporaries. On the other hand, his comedy made a tremendous impact, as in the *Pickwick Papers*, where Mr Pickwick's adventures and Sam Weller's sayings gave great joy to thousands of readers.

Dombey and Son (1846–8) seems to mark a turning-point in Dickens' career. It is more carefully unified than its predecessors and it relies less on exaggeration of plot and feelings; its central theme of pride is all-important. Dickens' next novel, *David Copperfield* (1849–50), with its suggestions of autobiography, is written in a calmly flowing manner, although it contains characters and incidents as striking as anything he invented: Mr Micawber, Uriah Heep, the storm at Yarmouth. Its subject-matter, concerned chiefly with the private and domestic affections, is, we feel, the product of mature contemplation.

The later novels of Dickens are *Bleak House* (1852–3), *Hard Times* (1854), *Little Dorrit* (1855–7), *A Tale of Two Cities* (1859), *Great Expectations* (1860–61), *Our Mutual Friend* (1864–5) and *The Mystery of Edwin Drood* (unfinished, 1870). They are more sombre than the earlier books. They are constructed with some care and they often deal with specific themes and subjects: the intricacies and deceits of the law (*Bleak House*), the opposition of utilitarian and imaginative values (*Hard Times*), the inefficiencies, irresponsibilities and materialism of mid-Victorian society (*Little Dorrit* and *Our Mutual Friend*) and snobbery (*Great Expectations*).

As we read a Dickens novel, we enter a self-sufficient imaginative world. He has many of the characteristics of a poet. This impression of a fertile, comprehensive imagination is enhanced in his later books by his use of motifs and symbols, such as the fog in *Bleak House*, the prisons in *Little Dorrit* and the dust-heaps and the River Thames in *Our Mutual Friend*. Although he has often been said to draw caricatures rather than characters, the people he creates spring to life on the page. In any case, some of his characters have a convincing truth about them—for example, his self-tormented people, like Miss Wade in *Little Dorrit* and Bradley Headstone in *Our Mutual Friend*. He has an amazing ability to distinguish his numerous characters from one another by their idiosyncrasies of speech. His plots are over-complicated, in a melodramatic mode, but they help to increase the tensions and mysteries that are so important in his stories and also help to hold together the many elements of his complex narratives. It should be remembered that his novels were written and published as serials, which partly accounts for some of his repetitions and exaggerations.

Dickens has astonishing powers of observation, seeing people and things as no one had seen them before, especially their peculiarities and strange resemblances. Allied to these powers is his ability to animate everybody and everything, so that even the furniture in a room can seem to have an active life of its own. He conveys all of this in vital prose, which is capable of expressing a wide range of particulars and moods. His purpose in writing, apart from sheer entertainment, is to put forward a message of hope and love, which he trusts will triumph over evil and over the vices and narrow-mindedness of materialism and a mechanical, uncaring social system.

Dickens' strengths as a novelist include his striking characterisation, his versatile prose, his power to evoke laughter, tears and fears, and his fundamental, positive "message". In the force and extent of his imagination, he stands next to Shakespeare.

William Makepeace Thackeray

William Makepeace Thackeray (1811–63) wrote miscellaneous prose and verse in the 1830s. *Catherine* (1839–40) and *Barry Lyndon* (1844), his first novels, were written partly to satirise the contemporary vogue for "Newgate Novels". *Vanity Fair* (1847–8) established him as major novelist. This book, set mostly in the Regency period, tells the related stories of two contrasted women, Amelia Sedley and Becky Sharp. One of its principal purposes is to expose the shams and pretensions of high society, as is indicated by its title, which Thackeray took from Bunyan's *Pilgrim's Progress*. *Pendennis* (1848–50), like *David Copperfield*, is coloured by autobiographical reminiscence. Its eponymous hero encounters temptations during his youth in the country, at Oxbridge and in the London literary world. Thackeray turned to the eighteenth century, his favourite historical period, for the background of *Henry Esmond* (1852), whose melancholy, meditative hero is tormented by his love for Beatrix Esmond and is also active in military and political affairs, including an unsuccessful attempt to put the Old Pretender on the English throne. *The Newcomes* (1853–5) is a chronicle of the loves, intrigues, successes and disappointments of the Newcome family, centred upon Clive and his father, Colonel Newcome. Thackeray's last important novel was *The Virginians* (1857–9), which continues the story of the Esmond family into later generations, set mostly in America during the War of Independence. His career as a novelist ended with *Philip* (1861–2) and the unfinished *Denis Duval* (1864).

During his lifetime and for long afterwards, Thackeray was frequently contrasted with Dickens. Unlike the latter, he avoided complicated plots and caricatures. His narratives flow smoothly from one incident or tableau to another. Thackeray's aim was to be as truthful as possible in his portrayal of people. He disliked the falsities he detected in such novelists as Bulwer-Lytton. His characters, therefore, are often ambiguously conceived, since he refused to simplify what he saw as complexity. A good man like Dobbin in *Vanity Fair* can be ridiculous on occasions; a man as honourable as Henry Esmond can love a woman as fickle and hard-hearted as Beatrix; a schemer like Becky Sharp is sometimes sympathetically described by the author. Like Fielding, whom he admired, Thackeray sought to reveal and mock hypocrisy and cant, especially in the middle and aristocratic classes, from which his fictional personages invariably came. One topic that engaged his attention was snobbery, which he deplored. Yet gentlemanliness was all-important to him, as personified in Colonel Newcome.

Thackeray has been called both cynical and sentimental. On one hand, he shows that conduct is not always what it appears to be; on the other, he depicts some people, especially when they are female, with fulsome affection. In all his work he is a moralist, relating the behaviour, thoughts and motives of his characters to those of his readers and people in general. Commentary, description, dialogue and story-telling are blended in his novels. Furthermore, the novels connect with one another, since characters recur; Pendennis, for example, tells the story of the Newcomes. This fact increases that sense of an actual, fully realised world which many critics have found to be characteristic of Thackeray's fiction.

The Brontës

Charlotte Brontë (1816–55) wrote *Jane Eyre* in 1847. Its second edition, by the way, was dedicated to Thackeray. This novel, which has never lost its power to enthrall the reader, uses a melodramatic plot, coincidence and exaggeration. But these devices, poetically and imaginatively realised by the author, intensify the reality of the passion that informs the book: Jane's sufferings, anger, independent spirit and feelings of love. These are brought close to us by the first-person narration. Her two great temptations, first towards an illicit relationship with Rochester and secondly towards the loveless religious life that St John Rivers offers her, are necessary, we feel, so that she can deserve the final, hard-won happiness that she finds. It is therefore a convincing psychological and moral novel as well as one of dramatic impetus.

Charlotte Brontë's second published novel was *Shirley* (1849), set in the north of England during the Napoleonic Wars and Luddite Riots. In it, we read of the fortunes of Caroline Helstone and Shirley Keeldar. One of its themes is the independence of women, though the book ends conventionally with the happy marriage of each of the heroines. *Villette* (1853) is a strangely-constructed novel, to the point of clumsiness, although its mysterious opening and conclusion are remarkable. But more importantly, its love story of Lucy Snowe, the English teacher in Villette (*i.e.* Brussels), and Paul Emanuel, the

Belgian schoolmaster she meets there, is one of the most sincere and moving in English fiction. *The Professor*, Charlotte Brontë's first novel (written in 1846), was published posthumously in 1857. Basically, it has the same story as *Villette*, though roles and sexes are reversed: an English schoolmaster in Brussels falls in love with a Swiss pupil. It is a novel not to be underrated, since it has a calm air of truthfulness.

Charlotte Brontë was essentially a Romantic novelist, dealing with emotional issues. As already noted, she had a low opinion of Jane Austen's coolness. Her sister, Emily Brontë (1818–48), was even more intense in her treatment of passion. *Wuthering Heights* (1847), her only novel, concerns two generations of the Linton and Earnshaw families in Yorkshire and how they are tormented by the ferocity of Heathcliff, who was brought into their lives as a boy found in the streets of Liverpool. The love between him and Catherine Darnshaw is all-consuming, destructive and yet immortal. *Wuthering Heights*, which has been called a dramatic poem, is full of the most violent emotions, paradoxically made even more intense by the perspective in which they are placed by the various narrators of the story. The construction of the novel—its points of view and its time-shifts—is notable, as are its imagery and passages of poetic description. As in *Jane Eyre*, the settings are important: the interiors of the houses, the Yorkshire moors and the changing seasons.

Anne Brontë (1820–49) echoes some of the themes explored by her sisters. *Agnes Grey* (1847) is about a governess's life and *The Tenant of Wildfell Hall* (1848) is a tale of mystery, drunkenness and love.

Anthony Trollope

Anthony Trollope (1815–82) wrote forty-seven novels, of which the best-known are contained in two "series". The Barsetshire Novels, dealing with the lives of the clergy and others in a fictional country district, are *The Warden* (1855), *Barchester Towers* (1857), *Doctor Thorne* (1858), *Framley Parsonage* (1860–61), *The Small House at Allington* (1862–4) and *The Last Chronicle of Barset* (1866–7). The Palliser Novels, which are mostly political, are *Can You Forgive Her?* (1864–5), *Phineas Finn* (1867–9), *The Eustace Diamonds* (1871–3), *Phineas Redux* (1873–4), *The Prime Minister* (1875–6) and *The Duke's Children* (1879–80). Other novels worth noting are *The Three Clerks* (1858), *Orley Farm* (1861–2), *The Vicar of Bullhampton* (1869–70) and *The Way We Live Now* (1875).

His novels are firmly constructed and written plainly and explicitly, without the poetic imagination of Dickens and the Brontës or the elegant subtlety of Thackeray (whom he admired above all contemporary novelists). Nathaniel Hawthorne, the American novelist, wrote that Trollope's novels were "solid and substantial, written on the strength of beef and the inspiration of ale, and just as real as if some giant had hewn a great lump out of the earth and put it under a glass case, with all its inhabitants going about their daily business, and not suspecting that they were being made a show of." If you want to have an accurate impression of what daily life was like amongst the upper middle-classes of England in the 1850s, then a reading of *Barchester Towers*, for example, will supply you with details of customs, dress, furniture and manner of speech. Apart from this characteristic, Trollope provides the reader with interesting and entertaining plots. The accusations of theft made against the Reverend Josiah Crawley and the ensuing complications make *The Last Chronicle of Barset* a fascinating novel. *The Eustace Diamonds* is another well-constructed tale of intrigue, about Lizzie Greystock's determination to retain an heirloom, a diamond necklace.

Trollope is especially skilful in working out the conflicts between public and private lives, in clerical and political matters above all: the disputes over the wardenship of Hiram's Hospital in *The Warden* and *Barchester Towers* and the jockeyings for power and influence in the Palliser novels. No other English novelist has so comprehensively treated this perpetually relevant subject, though C. P. Snow's *The Masters* (1951) is a modern example influenced by Trollope. He draws his characters with humour and sympathy but he occasionally disconcertingly interrupts his narration with authorial comments, as Henry James noted disapprovingly. He unques-

tioningly accepts Victorian standards of morality and conduct and sees everything from the standpoint of an upper-middle class English gentleman. Trollope was proud of his craftsmanship and almost without exception his novels are carefully constructed. They remain reliably readable and amusing without being too demanding. The Prime Minister, John Major, unveiled a memorial tablet in Westminster Abbey in March 1993.

Benjamin Disraeli, Mrs Gaskell and Charles Kingsley

Three novelists who flourished in the mid- nineteenth century were Benjamin Disraeli (1804–81), Mrs Elizabeth Gaskell (1810–65) and Charles Kingsley (1819–75). Like many of their contemporaries, they were perturbed by the social conditions of England brought about by industrialisation. As a result, they wrote influential novels that highlighted the problems of capital and labour and the sufferings of the poor.

Disraeli's first novels (*e.g. Henrietta Temple*, 1837) were of the "fashionable" kind already discussed but in the 1840s he produced three that were concerned with politics and society: *Coningsby* (1844), *Sybil* (1845) and *Tancred* (1847). Disraeli, who at that time was already prominent as a politician, developed his theories of Conservatism in the first of these, using the education, career and ideas of its hero, Coningsby, as the basis of his story. The alternative title of *Sybil* is *The Two Nations*, by which Disraeli denotes the rich and the poor. He dramatises the issues by means of the love between Sybil, the daughter of a Chartist, and Charles Egremont, a member of the aristocracy. In *Tancred*, the hero, the son of a Duke, journeys to the Holy Land to seek guidance towards true belief and conduct.

Mrs Gaskell's social novels were *Mary Barton* (1848) and *North and South* (1854–5). The first, which is set in Manchester, vividly evokes the appalling conditions of the working class, which Mrs Gaskell knew at first hand. She sensationalises the problem by using a melodramatic plot, involving murder committed by the heroine's father, but there is no escaping the fact that it is a gripping novel that not surprisingly made a considerable impression upon readers in mid-Victorian England. *North and South* contrasts two regions of England, as its title implies, through the medium of its heroine, Margaret Hale, who leaves southern England to live in the industrial north. Mrs Gaskell sympathetically presents a balanced view of social problems, indicating some of the virtues as well as the shortcomings of the employers, personified in John Thornton, with whom Margaret falls in love. Mrs Gaskell's other novels include *Cranford* (1851–3), a quiet and charming account of life amongst genteel middle-class ladies in a northern village in the 1830s; *Ruth* (1853), a harrowing tale of seduction and desertion; *Sylvia's Lovers* (1863); and *Wives and Daughters* (1864–6, unfinished), about the characters and family relationships in a provincial town.

Charles Kingsley's interests as a clergyman and Christian Socialist inspired *Alton Locke* (1850), which is about working-class London and Chartism, and *Yeast* (1851), which is concerned with problems of rural England. As in all his books, Kingsley writes with enthusiasm and commitment, not hesitating to preach his social sermons when the occasion prompts. For the student of political and religious ideas of the period, these two novels are valuable sources. Kingsley also wrote historical novels: *Hypatia* (1853), *Westward Ho!* (1855) and *Hereward the Wake* (1866). *The Water Babies* (1863) is a lively, didactic story for children.

George Eliot

George Eliot (the pseudonym of Mary Ann Evans, 1819–80), wrote three long short stories, *Scenes of Clerical Life* (1857) and then the following novels: *Adam Bede* (1859), *The Mill on the Floss* (1860), *Silas Marner* (1861), *Romola* (1862–3), *Felix Holt, the Radical* (1866), *Middlemarch* (1871–2) and *Daniel Deronda* (1876). The first three novels are set in rural England, recalling the Warwickshire where she was born and brought up. *Adam Bede* is the tragic story of Hetty Sorrel, a village girl who is seduced, bears an illegitimate child and is convicted of infanticide. *The Mill on the Floss* is concerned mainly with the life, loves and emotional vicissitudes of Maggie Tulliver, who has some of the characteristics of the author herself. *Silas Marner* tells of an unhappy, miserly weaver, who regains his love of humanity after bringing up a child who has found her way to his cottage door. All, then, are about comparatively humble people and all sympathetically render the seasons, scenes, activities and speech of country life.

For her fourth novel, George Eliot turned to a completely different setting and period, as if to challenge her powers of invention: *Romola* is an historical novel, set in late fifteenth-century Florence, at the time of Machiavelli and Savonarola. It is a moving and exciting account of the conflicts of personal and public issues and of treachery and love. *Felix Holt* has the political events of 1832 as its background, although its principal interest lies in Esther's personal relationships and in the disputes over the ownership of an estate. By general agreement, *Middlemarch* is George Eliot's masterpiece. This long, complex novel has four interwoven plots revealing various themes: love and marriage, ambition, religious hypocrisy and the pressures exerted by a provincial environment. *Daniel Deronda* has two plots and themes, again interrelated: the character and unhappy marriage of Gwendolen Harleth and the revelation of Daniel's Jewish parentage.

George Eliot brought great seriousness of purpose to the novel. Like the other Victorian novelists, she made moral teaching an essential part of her fiction. Although she had lost her belief in orthodox Christianity, she held to the ideals of duty and personal responsibility. She explores these fundamental doctrines of hers through her characters and plots and through much authorial comment. In *Silas Marner*, for example, she shows how Godfrey Cass tries to ignore his past actions that have caused distress to himself and others and how instead he hopes that Chance will come to his aid. To make the point clear to her readers, she writes a long passage, almost like a sermon, on the error of not facing the consequences of one's actions and of trusting to Fortune. Nevertheless, she constantly shows sympathy and tolerance towards her characters. She can express her pity for such people as Casaubon, Rosamond Vincy and Bulstrode in *Middlemarch* whereas a novelist who saw personality in simpler terms would deplore or condemn their faults. Perhaps more than any previous novelist, she describes and analyses the sheer complexity of character, with the result that her portraits, especially of women, have great profundity—Maggie Tulliver in *The Mill on the Floss*, Mrs Transome in *Felix Holt*, Dorothea in *Middlemarch* and Gwendolen Harleth in *Daniel Deronda*. Some of her personages, especially rural folk in her earlier novels, are presented with humour—Mrs Poyser in *Adam Bede* and Maggie's aunts and uncles in *The Mill on the Floss*.

George Eliot was scrupulous in the construction of her novels, allowing few digressions or inessential characters. The villagers' "chorus" in *Silas Marner*, for example, is necessary for our understanding of their opinions of the main characters and of the kind of existence, past and present, amongst which those characters must live. By the standards of the time, she avoids exaggeration and highly coloured incidents. Because of her wise moral concern, her understanding of psychology, and her care over the structure of her novels, George Eliot is regarded nowadays as one of the greatest English novelists.

Charles Reade, Wilkie Collins, and Sensation Novels

From about 1860 onwards, "sensation novels" were enormously popular. Their ingredients could include crime, detection, and passionate and illicit love-affairs; they had, too, a highly emotional atmosphere. Two of the best-known were *Lady Audley's Secret* (1862) by Mary Elizabeth Braddon (1837–1915) and *Uncle Silas* (1864) by J. Sheridan Le Fanu (1814–73).

Dickens, Charles Reade and Wilkie Collins have sometimes been called "sensation novelists" although that is too limiting a description of them. Charles Reade (1814–84), an original and lively author, wrote two famous historical novels: *Peg Woffington* (1853), recounting an episode in the life of the eighteenth-century actress, and *The Cloister and the Hearth* (1861), a romance set in fifteenth-century Europe. His novels dealing with contemporary social abuses include *It is never too late to Mend* (1853), in which he exposes brutalities in the prisons, and *Hard Cash* (1863), in which he describes conditions in a lunatic asylum. Wilkie Collins (1824–89), a friend and associate of Dickens, was a prolific

writer. His most enduring novels, with ingenious plots, are *The Woman in White* (1859–60), *No Name* (1862) and *The Moonstone* (1868), which is often called the first English detective story.

THE LATE VICTORIAN PERIOD

George Meredith

George Meredith (1828–1908) was a substantial poet as well as a novelist. After writing an Oriental fantasy, *The Shaving of Shagpat* (1856), he wrote *The Ordeal of Richard Feverel* (1859), *Evan Harrington* (1860), *Emilia in England* (1864, retitled *Sandra Belloni*, 1886), *Rhoda Fleming* (1865), *Vittoria* (1867), *The Adventures of Harry Richmond* (1870–1), *Beauchamp's Career* (1874–5), *The Egoist* (1879), *The Tragic Comedians* (1880), *Diana of the Crossways* (1885), *One of our Conquerors* (1890–1), *Lord Ormont and his Aminta* (1894) and *The Amazing Marriage* (1895). Of these novels, *The Ordeal of Richard Feverel*, *The Egoist* and *Diana of the Crossways* are generally accounted the best.

Richard Feverel is brought up by his father, Sir Austin, according to a System, which should train him to be a perfect English gentleman, who would avoid making the kind of disastrous marriage that the baronet had suffered. The fine plans break down. Richard marries a girl of unsuitable birth and quickly becomes corrupted in London society. Not unexpectedly, there is a tragic end to everything. But the novel is remarkable for its disparate elements: its irony and satire, not only in situation but also in the wry comments of Adrian Harley; its passages of poetic description; the melodramatic turns of the plot; its humour and its pathos. *The Egoist*, in contrast, is perfectly organised, reminiscent of a comedy of manners in the theatre, especially in its denouement. Its comedy lies in the exposure of the egoism of the central character, Sir Willoughby Patterne, but the play of wit is modified by the sympathetic portrayal of Clara Middleton, to whom Sir Willoughby is engaged to be married, and the delightfully fresh portrayal of Crossjay Patterne, a twelve-year-old boy. *Diana of the Crossways* is about a witty, attractive young woman, involved in divorce proceedings and a love affair.

Like Fielding, Meredith set great store by the ability of comedy to reveal and rectify affectation. "Comedy is the foundation of good sense," he wrote in his *Essay on Comedy* (1877). Another relevant definition comes at the beginning of *The Egoist*: "Comedy is a game played to throw reflections upon social life, and it deals with human nature in the drawing-room of civilized men and women." His theory is brilliantly put into practice in the final chapters of *The Egoist*, when devices and revelations of different kinds bring about Sir Willoughby's humiliation.

His handling of his characters' psychology is occasionally elusive, but he has meaningful insights to offer and can be seen to be anticipating the "stream of consciousness" in parts of *The Egoist*, notably in "Clara's Meditations". Amongst his main themes are the tensions between appearance and reality (as in Evan Harrington's social position contrasted with his humble birth) and the independence of women (as shown in the fortunes of Clara and Diana).

Meredith was lionised towards the end of his life, but he is unjustly neglected today. At the least, he should be read for the new possibilities he found in the novel-form and for the risks he took. Apart from his importance in the history of the English novel, there is much in his writing that the modern reader will find intrinsically rewarding.

Thomas Hardy

The career of Thomas Hardy (1840–1928) divides into two parts. In the nineteenth century, up to 1896, he published novels. He then abandoned the writing of prose fiction and for the rest of his life concentrated wholly on poetry. He divided his novels into three groups. First, there are "Novels of Character and Environment", which comprise *Under the Greenwood Tree* (1872), *Far from the Madding Crowd* (1874), *The Return of the Native* (1878), *The Mayor of Casterbridge* (1886), *The Woodlanders* (1887), *Tess of the D'Urbervilles* (1891) and *Jude the Obscure* (1896). Secondly, there are the

"Romances and Fantasies": *A Pair of Blue Eyes* (1873), *The Trumpet-Major* (1880), *Two on a Tower* (1882) and *The Well-Beloved* (1892). Thirdly, there are the "Novels of Ingenuity": *Desperate Remedies* (1871), *The Hand of Ethelberta* (1876) and *A Laodicean* (1881). Hardy's major works are those in the first of these categories, with the possible additions of *A Pair of Blue Eyes*, *Desperate Remedies* and *The Trumpet-Major*. As well as these novels, Hardy wrote a considerable number of short stories.

His novels are set in Wessex, by which Hardy means Dorset and the adjacent counties of southwest England. This was the region where he was born and where he lived for most of his life. The scenery, occupations, customs, traditions and speech of Wessex all play vital parts in his narratives. One subject of his is the contrast between the rural world and the world outside, seen most dramatically when an outsider comes into the community or a former inhabitant returns. Fancy Day's coming to Mellstock in *Under the Greenwood Tree*, Sergeant Troy's arrival in *Far from the Madding Crowd* and the return of Clym Yeobright and Grace Melbury from the Continent to their native English villages in *The Return of the Native* and *The Woodlanders* respectively are examples of this kind of conflict. Hardy's great respect for traditional custom is evident in his loving rendering of typical country tasks and events: cider-making, tending sheep, felling trees, cutting furze, threshing wheat, lighting bonfires on 5 November, marriage ceremonies, and so on. Following George Eliot's practice, he uses conversation of village people as sources of commentary and local history. A setting can take on a symbolic function, as Egdon Heath does in *The Return of the Native* or the woods do in *The Woodlanders*. A character can become symbolically identified with his occupation and surroundings, like Diggory Venn in *The Return of the Native*.

Hardy's view of life was fatalistic, since he believed that the human situation was, in Lord David Cecil's words, "a struggle between man on the one hand and, on the other, an omnipotent and indifferent fate." One of his most forthright statements of this belief occurs at the end of *Tess of the D'Urbervilles* when he reports the execution of the heroine: " 'Justice' was done, and the President of Immortals, in Aeschylean phrase, had ended his sport with Tess." His novels therefore contain much that is pessimistic and melancholy. The last two, *Tess of the D'Urbervilles* and *Jude the Obscure*, are the most tragic of all. Jude and Sue Bridehead, the central characters of the last novel, find all their aspirations concerning love, marriage, education and religious belief confounded and defeated and their story ends with the death of Jude and the resignation of Sue to unhappiness.

As an aspect of Hardy's deterministic view of life, he believed in the importance of chance, accident and coincidence. A trivial or thoughtless action, such as Bathsheba Everdene's throwing up a hymn book to see whether it falls open or shut (in *Far from the Madding Crowd*), can have unforeseen, appalling consequences. "Life's Little Ironies" and "Satires of Circumstance", titles of collections of his short stories and verse respectively, can be appropriately applied to much that he wrote. His novels are full of strange, striking episodes, in line with his theory that the artist was justified in using exaggeration and distortion to make his points effectively. Readers of Hardy always remember such things as the slaughter of the pig in *Jude the Obscure*, the sale of Henchard's wife in *The Mayor of Casterbridge*, the death of Mrs Yeobright on the heath in *The Return of the Native* and Sergeant Troy's first encounter with Bathsheba in *Far from the Madding Crowd*. Such scenes and events are there for their emotional impact and for the illumination they shed on key motives and developments in the novels.

Hardy's stories are mostly about the tragedies and disappointments of love between men and women. A favourite plot of his depends on the relationship of a woman with two or three men (e.g. Fancy Day, Eustacia Vye, Anne Garland and Tess). Women play a dominant part in his novels. He draws them with sympathy and understanding and he is especially interested in the personalities and actions of strong-willed women or women striving for independence and a life of their own (Sue Bridehead is a famous example). Amongst his men characters, those who are tortured by misgivings, remorse and disappointment are dramatically presented, as witness Henchard, Boldwood and Jude.

Henry James

The importance of Henry James (1843–1916) in the history of the English and American novel is very great indeed. His practice and the theories he expounded in his essay, "The Art of Fiction" (1884), and in the Prefaces to his novels, have been widely influential in this century. An American by birth, James lived and worked in England for most of his life, writing short stories, travel books, essays and numerous novels.

It is convenient to divide the novels into three groups, corresponding to three stages in his career. A favourite theme of his early work is the mutual influences of European and American culture. Principal works of this period are *Roderick Hudson* (1875), *The American* (1877), *The Europeans* (1878), *Daisy Miller* (1879), *Washington Square* (1881), *The Portrait of a Lady* (1881), *The Bostonians* (1886) and *The Princess Casamassima* (1886). His middle period, in which his technique becomes more complex and his subject-matter frequently concerned with English topics, includes *The Tragic Muse* (1890), *The Spoils of Poynton* (1897), *What Maisie Knew* (1897), *The Turn of the Screw* (1898), *The Awkward Age* (1899) and *The Sacred Fount* (1901). James's most difficult novels, which show a return to his interest in the tensions between English and American values, are the final three: *The Wings of a Dove* (1902), *The Ambassadors* (1903) and *The Golden Bowl* (1904).

As a man who had experienced life in the United States and Europe, James was fascinated by the differences in culture between the Old and the New Worlds. On the one hand were the newness, potentiality and democracy of America (wonderfully evoked in the opening chapter of *The Europeans*) and on the other hand were the history and achievements of Europe. In his opinion, expressed in his study of Nathaniel Hawthorne, "it takes a great deal of history to produce a little literature" and "it needs a complex social machinery to set a writer in motion." His most famous treatment of the issues involved in this opposition of two ways of life is *The Portrait of a Lady*, which many critics think is his most fully accomplished work of fiction. Isabel Archer, an American girl, comes to England and Europe. She is attractive, frank and eager for adventure and experience. Having rejected two suitors and having inherited a fortune from her uncle, she makes a disastrously ill-judged marriage with an expatriate American but finally decides to endure the consequences of her error. The novel is rich in characterisation: apart from Isabel, the most intriguing personages are Ralph Touchett (her cousin, an invalid) and Madame Merle (a cosmopolitan woman, who arranges Isabel's marriage). James reveals, with understanding, tenderness and wit, the virtues and the weaknesses of Isabel. Moreover, he gives a wise and analytical picture of many aspects of human behaviour, relating them where appropriate to the society and culture of the United States, Europe and England. The theme of the young American woman who visits Europe with tragic consequences is repeated in *The Wings of a Dove*, with Milly Theale as the girl in question. *The Europeans*, one of James' earliest books, is a brief, elegant but searching presentation of the same basic subject; in that novel the scene is the United States, which the Europeans visit.

James was also interested in exploring the problems and corruptions of contemporary English society, as embodied in the contents of the house and the avarice for them displayed in *The Spoils of Poynton*. Or there are what the critic F. R. Leavis has called the "egotistic squalors" revealed in the comings and goings of the divorced people and spouses in *What Maisie Knew*. His fascination for observing the effects of corruption of a directly personal kind, irrespective of social pressures, is memorably realised in *The Turn of the Screw*.

He believed intensely in the importance of technique and form for the novelist, who held a "sacred office", in his view. The novelist had a duty, he maintained, to tell the truth and to impart to his fiction an "air of reality". In order to accomplish that aim, the writer had to ensure that the novel was an organic whole, with each of its parts contributing to the totality. James called some nineteenth-century novels "large, loose, baggy monsters" and sought in his own work to practise a strict control over his material. His novels are accordingly tautly constructed and written in the most meticulous prose style. This style in the later novels is difficult and subtle and some critics have thus accused him of sacrificing life and warmth for the sake of brilliant intellectual structures. Meredith and Hardy in their different ways broke with some of the conventions of the Victorian novel; but James departed radically from many of its features and can be regarded as the first of the modern novelists.

Robert Louis Stevenson and the Adventure Novel

Robert Louis Stevenson (1850–94), essayist, poet, travel-writer and novelist, achieved fame with *Treasure Island* (1883) and *Dr Jekyll and Mr Hyde* (1886). His subsequent novels include *Kidnapped* (1886), *The Black Arrow* (1888), *The Master of Ballantrae* (1889), *Catriona* (1893), *Weir of Hermiston* (unfinished, 1896) and *St. Ives* (completed by A. Quiller-Couch, 1898). With Lloyd Osbourne, his stepson, he wrote *The Wrong Box* (1889), *The Wrecker* (1892) and *The Ebb-Tide* (1894).

Stevenson was as scrupulous a writer as Henry James, one of his friends and correspondents. His novels are precisely and elegantly shaped and are expressed in clear, economical prose. He wrote that the artist's "one main and necessary resource" was his compulsion to "omit what is tedious or irrelevant, and suppress what is tedious and necessary." Action and the revelation of character through action form the main material of his novels. *Treasure Island*, written for boys, is a masterpiece of construction, beginning quietly but ominously, building up suspense with the discovery of Long John Silver's true nature and coming to a climax on the island with the battles between the pirates and Jim Hawkins and his friends. It has incidents and devices that stick in the mind (the black spot, the pirates' chorus) and colourful personages (Long John Silver, Ben Gunn). *Kidnapped* is admirable adventure fiction with an authentic feeling for place and period: Scotland in the years just after the '45 Jacobite Rebellion. Both books gain in immediacy through their first-person narration.

The Master of Ballantrae, set in post-1745 Scotland, is a remarkable tale of evil and persecution, personified in its leading character, the Master. It has a relentless urgency and a number of unforgettable scenes, such as the duel between the Master of Ballantrae and his brother by candlelight out-of-doors on a frosty night. Although Stevenson emphasised action rather than psychology, at least two of his characters have become household words: Long John Silver and Dr Jekyll, alias Mr Hyde.

The adventure novel or "romance" became popular towards the end of the nineteenth century. With Stevenson's successful *Treasure Island* in mind, Rider Haggard (1856–1925) wrote *King Solomon's Mines* (1885), followed by *She* (1887) and many other books of the same kind. G. A. Henty (1832–1902) wrote prolifically, producing some eighty novels for boys. Other adventures and romances were Conan Doyle's Sherlock Holmes stories (beginning in 1887 with *A Study in Scarlet*) and novels of exciting action, Stanley Weyman's historical novels from 1893 onwards, Anthony Hope Hawkins' *The Prisoner of Zenda*, George du Maurier's *Trilby* (1894), Bram Stoker's *Dracula* (1897) and E. W. Hornung's *Raffles* stories from 1899 onwards. The adventure novels of John Buchan (1875–1940) include *Prester John* (1910), *The Thirty-Nine Steps* (1915), *Greenmantle* (1916) and *Mr Standfast* (1919).

Naturalism: Gissing and Moore

Naturalism, which is sometimes used as a synonym for realism, was a literary movement associated mostly with the novels of Emile Zola (1840–1902). Writers who held the doctrine maintained that novels should be as physically detailed as possible, that novelists should use scientific methods of description and analysis and that they should emphasise the importance of environment. The subject-matter of naturalistic novels tended to be about the harsh realities of the lives of the poor and to concentrate on the least ideal aspects of human nature.

George Gissing (1857–1903) was one exponent of naturalism in England, writing about the poverty and miseries of working-class existence in novels such as *Workers in the Dawn* (1880), *The Unclassed* (1884), *Demos* (1886), *Thyrza* (1887), and *The Nether World* (1889). *New Grub Street* (1891) surveys writers' lives, contrasting the success of the unprincipled Jasper Milvain with the wretched life and death of the uncompromising Edwin Reardon. *The Private Papers of Henry Ryecroft* (1903) is a series of semi-autobiographical reflections. George Moore (1852–1933), strongly influenced by Zola and Maupassant, wrote *Esther Waters* (1894), as well as a variety of other novels. In an objective and yet poignant manner, he relates the hardships suffered by Esther from the time she goes into domestic service as a seventeen-year-old girl. Samuel Butler (1835–1902), who wrote the fantasies, *Erewhon* (1872) and *Erewhon Revisited* (1901), achieved a high posthumous reputation with *The Way of All Flesh* (1903; written 1872–5), a satirical treatment of Victorian beliefs and values. Conventional moral ideas were also questioned by Oscar Wilde (1856–1900) in his "aesthetic" novel, *The Picture of Dorian Gray* (1891).

Naturalism: Arnold Bennett

Arnold Bennett (1867–1931) also modelled his novels on those of the French naturalists. Flaubert, the Goncourt brothers, Zola and Maupassant had established aesthetic ideals for him in their objectivity and precision of language. A writer of dogged productivity, he wrote over thirty novels, beginning with *A Man from the North* (1898). The first of importance was *Anna of the Five Towns* (1902), the title of which makes clear its setting in the Potteries, the midland region of England which is the environment of most of his best fiction. His reputation was established with *The Old Wives' Tale* (1908), a long, detailed study of Sophia and Constance Baines, two sisters, from youth to age. His achievement here is his skilful handling of Time, which E. M. Forster declared was the "real hero" of the book. *Clayhanger* (1910), *Hilda Lessways* (1911) and *These Twain* (1915) are collectively known as *The Clayhanger Family*. Set in the Five Towns, the first two deal respectively with the young lives of Edwin Clayhanger and Hilda Lessways and the third with their married life together. *The Card* (1911) is a lighter story about the agreeable rogue, Denry Machin. *Riceyman Steps* (1923) is a grim novel about a miserly second-hand bookseller in Clerkenwell; it is a tale of meanness, squalor, illness and death and is one of the most powerful of all Bennett's novels.

Bennett is meticulously realistic, supplying explicit details of the environment, thoughts and actions of his characters. He is a regional novelist, who shows us panoramic and close-up pictures of the places where his personages live. *The Old Wives' Tale* opens with a description of the county of Staffordshire, which surrounds his heroines, as he points out. The focus moves to the Five Towns, to St Luke's Square, to the Baines's shop and finally to the showroom. Bennett slowly completes his picture of the two girls, the shop and the town. Similarly, Edwin at the beginning of *Clayhanger* is shown standing on a canal bridge in a precisely depicted location in the Five Towns. Such accumulation of detail, leaving little to the imagination, was adversely criticised by later novelists, notably Virginia Woolf. But it gives a photographic verisimilitude to Bennett's stories. He is not an idealist or moralist; he is content to display to us his personages and their doings. He is not without sympathy and humour, he is inventive, he can give meaning to trivial and mundane happenings and he constructs his novels solidly.

THE TWENTIETH CENTURY

Rudyard Kipling

Rudyard Kipling (1865–1936) was another author sensitive to the aesthetic shaping of his work. He was primarily a poet and writer of short stories, but two novels of his are *The Light that Failed* (1890) and *Kim* (1901). The former, with its tragic account of the blindness that overcomes Dick Heldar, may be melodramatic and sentimental, but it has a compelling emotional drive that makes it hard to put down. *Kim* evokes the India of the Raj, which Kipling knew intimately as a child and young man. Its central character, the boy Kim, travels through India with a Tibetan lama and becomes involved in espionage organised by the British Secret Service. He is therefore torn between the demands of two ways of life: the contemplative and the active. The novel can be appreciated on several levels: as an adventure story, as an unrivalled description of the peoples, customs and scenes of India, as a glorification as well as a criticism of British imperialism, and as a presentation of conflicts of ideas and loyalties.

H. G. Wells

H. G. Wells (1866–1946) was a prolific and versatile writer whose abiding interests were science and socialist politics. He made his name with scientific romances, which include *The Time Machine* (1895), *The Island of Dr Moreau* (1896), *The Invisible Man* (1897), *The War of the Worlds* (1898) and *The First Men on the Moon* (1901). Although Jules Verne's books were known in England, these were the first thoroughgoing examples of science fiction in English. Based on the sound scientific knowledge he had acquired as a London University student, his stories were daringly imaginative but convincing and still rank among the best of their kind. Their startling subject-matter includes travelling into the future, the coming of Martians to England and journeying to the moon, all realised in credible detail. Wells also wrote social comedies, typically featuring a "little man" of the lower middle class: *Love and Mr Lewisham* (1900), *Kipps* (1905) and *The History of Mr Polly* (1910). He explored social problems in a more serious manner in a third group of novels, including *Tono-Bungay* (1909), *Ann Veronica* (1909) and *The New Machiavelli* (1911). Apart from *Mr Britling Sees It Through* (1916), his later novels lack the vigour and imagination of his earlier novels.

Unlike James, Stevenson, Bennett and Kipling, Wells was impatient with the novel as an art-form, since for him its entertainment value and message were of prime importance. In his science fiction, he wanted to make his readers aware of the potentialities of technological discovery. His social novels had clear lessons to impart. *The History of Mr Polly* is an enjoyable story of the misfortunes and eventual happiness of its hero, with Dickensian humour in its characterisation (*e.g.* Uncle Pentstemon), Mr Polly's pathetically comic aspirations and actions (*e.g.* his conversation with the schoolgirl sitting on a wall and his attempted suicide) and his misuse of language. At the same time, Wells is making serious points about a system of society and education that can starve Mr Polly's imagination and stunt any possibilities of a fulfilled existence for him. The main purpose of *Ann Veronica* is an argument for women's liberation. *Tono-Bungay* is concerned with the world of commerce and *The New Machiavelli* with the world of politics, with relevance to the corruptions which Wells saw in Edwardian England.

Psychological subtlety and experiments with formal techniques have little part in Wells' novels, which succeed in their intention of giving much pleasure blended with instruction. His prose style is spontaneous and lively, sweeping the reader along. His instinctive skills and many-sidedness make him a novelist of considerable achievement.

Joseph Conrad

In contrast to the novels of Bennett and Wells, those by Joseph Conrad (1857–1924) are innovatory in a number of respects. Although he was Polish by birth, he served in the British Merchant Navy for many years and wrote all his novels in English. The principal ones are *Almayer's Folly* (1895), *An Outcast of the Islands* (1896), *The Nigger of the Narcissus* (1897), *Lord Jim* (1900), *The Heart of Darkness* (1902), *Typhoon* (1902), *Nostromo* (1904), *The Secret Agent* (1907), *Under Western Eyes* (1911), *Chance* (1913), *Victory* (1915) and *The Rover* (1923). Conrad also wrote short stories and some books in collaboration with Ford Madox Ford (1873–1939), who was a considerable novelist in his own right.

Conrad's experience as a seaman is reflected in the settings he uses: Malaysia and the Indian Ocean (as in *Lord Jim*), the Congo (*The Heart of Darkness*) and South America (*Nostromo*). London, however, is the setting of *The Secret Agent*. In such places a typical Conrad hero confronts dangers and is compelled to make immediate choices. Conrad concerns himself not so much with the relationships between people as the relationships between an individual person and circumstances. Questions of moral decision, heroism and cowardice, loyalty and treachery are therefore basic to his novels. In *Lord Jim*, Jim jumps overboard from the *Patna*, which he mistakenly thinks is about to sink. Tormented by self-accusations of despicable conduct, he seeks to redeem himself. But after achieving a measure of redemption as the respected "Lord Jim", he makes another error of judgment, which brings about his death. Conrad may show us, too, how a sensitive man may be inferior at a moment of crisis to one of little imagination. A solid and stupid man like Captain MacWhirr in *Typhoon* triumphs over the terrible storm and brings his ship to safety.

To demonstrate the complexity of arriving at a true account of happenings and motives, Conrad disrupts chronology and uses various narrators. *Lord Jim* begins with Jim as a water clerk, recounts how the *Patna* hit something below the surface of the sea, and continues with the court of enquiry. At this point, Marlow (a narrator Conrad uses in several books) intervenes. Largely through him, we are given a vivid sense of the way Jim feels defeated and only then do we arrive at the crucial event: the desertion of the *Patna*. Thus chronological order is replaced by a dramatic, significant order. Perspective and shades of meaning are gained by Conrad's using the memories and prejudices of different story-tellers. In *Nostromo*, the events are narrated by the omniscient novelist and also by Captain Mitchell, Decoud (in a letter), Dr Monyghan (in his reflections) and Nostromo. Readers have to work hard at piecing together the mosaic of action and thought and are consequently made aware of the ambiguities and subtleties of human behaviour. Unity is derived from central themes: Jim's agonies of conscience in *Lord Jim*, the storm in *Typhoon* and the silver mine in *Nostromo*.

Conrad's use of English has its awkwardnesses, especially in colloquial speech, but these are outweighed by the scrupulous way in which he expresses shades of meaning and realises people and things in concrete detail. His novels have great depth and integrity, as well as sensibility.

Ford Madox Ford and Dorothy Richardson

The principal novels of Ford Madox Ford (1873–1939), who influenced Conrad and collaborated with him (*see above*), are *The Good Soldier* (1915), *Some Do Not* (1924), *No More Parades* (1925), *A Man Could Stand Up* (1926) and *The Last Post* (1928). The last four are known as the Tietjens tetralogy, after their principal character. In the interests of what he saw as truthful presentation, Ford used experimental techniques in his fiction, including time-shifts, different viewpoints and "*progression d'effet*" (*i.e.*, carrying on the story faster as it progresses). Together with authorial "invisibility" and irony, these methods give his narratives a sense of elusiveness and open up fascinating possibilities of interpretation. His psychological depictions (of Tietjens and Dowell, the protagonist of *The Good Soldier*, for example) are subtle and complex. Ford was concerned to explore such moral issues as honour and fidelity and also the codes and assumptions of society and class.

Dorothy Richardson (1873–1957) was one of the first English novelists fully to use the technique of the "stream of consciousness", which is associated particularly with the work of Virginia Woolf and James Joyce (*see below*). Her sequence of twelve novels, published between 1915 and 1938 and collectively known as *Pilgrimage*, has the "consciousness" of her heroine, Miriam, at their centre.

John Galsworthy, Hugh Walpole and Somerset Maugham

Three novelists who achieved immense popularity and yet who never rose high in critical esteem (at least in England) were John Galsworthy (1867–1933), Sir Hugh Walpole (1884–1941) and W. Somerset Maugham (1874–1965).

Galsworthy, who was also famous as a playwright, is remembered for *The Forsyte Saga* (1922), which consists of *The Man of Property* (1906), *In Chancery* (1920) and *To Let* (1921). The Forsyte story continues in two more trilogies: *A Modern Comedy* (1929) and *End of the Chapter* (1934). The substance of these novels is the relationships and intrigues of a wealthy upper-middle class family from the 1880s to the 1920s. The books have a comforting readability and a documentary value in their charting the outlook, habits and possessions of the family. Galsworthy was awarded the Nobel Prize for Literature in 1932.

Walpole's books have proved to be less durable. *Mr Perrin and Mr Traill* (1911), about the cruel rivalry of two schoolmasters, still has vitality. But once-favoured novels, such as *Jeremy* (1919), *The Cathedral* (1922) and the four known as *The Herries Chronicle* (1930–33) are little read today.

Somerset Maugham began in naturalistic style with *Liza of Lambeth* (1897). Equally successful as a playwright and a short-story writer, Maugham wrote *Of Human Bondage* (1915), *The Moon and Sixpence* (1919), *Cakes and Ale* (1930), *The Razor's Edge* (1944) and many other novels. His range is wide and he is always a supreme entertainer. His sardonic attitude may disturb some, but most readers find that this gives an edge to his clear, fluent narratives. Although he has been called superficial, no one can deny his sheer readability.

E. M. Forster

Besides Conrad, four novelists of the first half of the twentieth century extended the possibilities of the form: E. M. Forster, Virginia Woolf, James Joyce and D. H. Lawrence.

E. M. Forster (1879–1970) wrote *Where Angels Fear to Tread* (1905), *The Longest Journey* (1907), *A Room with a View* (1908), *Howards End* (1910) and *A Passage to India* (1924). *Maurice* was written in 1914, but because of its homosexual theme was not published till 1971. After 1924, Forster wrote no more novels.

In all his writings, fiction and nonfiction, Forster is liberal and humanist in outlook. He always set great store by loving personal relationships and was suspicious of conceptions of duty, patriotism and imperialism. In a notorious statement in his essay, "What I Believe" (1939), he said: "I hate the idea of causes, and if I had to choose between betraying my country and betraying my friend, I hope I should have the guts to betray my country." Later in the same essay, he declared that he distrusted Great Men and believed in an aristocracy of the "sensitive, the considerate and the plucky".

His novels are elegant, drily humorous and witty, but at the same time they contain elements of the poetical and the mystical. The motto, "Only connect", which appears on the title page of *Howards End*, expresses one of his tenets. To bring out its implications, he will place two sets of ideas in opposition and show the tensions and connections between them. In *Where Angels Fear to Tread*, Lilia, an English girl from the conventional middle-classes, outrages her family when she marries Gino, an Italian dentist. After her death, they make attempts to "rescue" her baby. The comedy and the message of the novel, therefore, derive from the interactions between English and Mediterranean ways of life. The opposition in *Howards End* is that between the world of "telegrams and anger" and the world of culture and the finer feelings.

Forster's most ambitious novel, *A Passage to India*, is concerned with the mutual misunderstandings between the Indians and the ruling English in the India of 1910–20. The narrow-minded English community is angered by Dr Aziz' apparent assault on Adela Quested in the Marabar Caves. The principal characters are Fielding, the well-meaning and humane schoolmaster; Dr Aziz, impulsive and warm-hearted; Mrs Moore, the elderly, visionary Englishwoman; and Adela herself, who—like Fielding—has good intentions but is bewildered by her encounter with India. Forster carefully patterns his novel, writes amusing and lively description and dialogue and conveys a sense of the incomprehensibility and fascination of India felt by English people. As always, he seeks to inculcate the truth that love and understanding at the personal level are vital in all circumstances.

In *Aspects of the Novel* (1927), Forster deplored the need to tell a story in the novel. But his novels contain much that is amusing and thought-provoking: surprises in the plot, realistic dialogue, economical but convincing characterisation and unexpected authorial generalisations. Altogether, we get the impression of a sharp but tolerant perception of the virtues and frailties of mankind.

Virginia Woolf

E. M. Forster was associated with the Bloomsbury Group, although he was never a fully committed member of it. The relations and friends who formed the Group between 1905 and the 1930s (Lytton Strachey, Maynard Keynes, Virginia Woolf and her sister Vanessa Bell, Clive Bell, Duncan Grant, Roger Fry and others) saw themselves as rational, enlightened people who rejected the intolerance and narrow-minded morality of the Victorians. They valued love, friendship and the arts.

One of the central figures of the Bloomsbury Group was Virginia Woolf (1882–1941), whose career as a novelist began with two fairly conventional books: *The Voyage Out* (1915) and *Night and Day* (1919). She proceeded to experiment in both form and content and all her subsequent novels are works of originality, breaking with traditional approaches and methods: *Jacob's Room* (1922), *Mrs Dalloway* (1925), *To the Lighthouse* (1927), *Orlando* (1928), *The Waves* (1931), *The Years* (1937) and *Between the Acts* (1941).

Virginia Woolf was opposed to the technique of such Edwardian novelists as Bennett, Wells and Galsworthy. In her opinion, they were materialists, who were "concerned not with the spirit but with the body". Their painstaking renderings of a solid, exterior world meant, she argued, that the inner meaning of life escaped them. What she attempted to do, on the other hand, was to capture the transience and subtlety of experience and thought. In a famous statement, she said that "Life is not a series of gig lamps symmetrically arranged; life is a luminous halo, a semi-transparent envelope surrounding us from the beginning of consciousness to the end." Modern authors should therefore "record the atoms as they fall upon the mind in the order in which they fall" and "trace the pattern, however disconnected and incoherent in appearance, which each sight or incident scores upon the consciousness." To achieve these ends, she uses as a means the "stream of consciousness" technique. She takes us inside her characters' minds, revealing the flow of their thoughts and emotions, past, present and future. The trivial and the grand are fused; the exterior world impinges now and then; repetitions, allusions, memories blend together.

A typical example of this technique is the scene of the dinner-party in *To the Lighthouse*. Outwardly, Mrs Ramsay, the hostess, is serving the food and making unremarkable conversation with her guests. But we are witnesses of the interior lives of these people. The reflections of Mrs Ramsay, Lily Briscoe, Charles Tansley and William Bankes make a delicately woven texture of thoughts and emotions, adding to what we have already learned earlier in the novel.

Realising the difficulty of giving a clear shape to the intangible, Virginia Woolf uses repeated phrases and objects as focal points, such as the royal car in *Mrs Dalloway* and the lighthouse and Lily Briscoe's painting in *To the Lighthouse*. Her prose is supple and quietly rhythmical and contains memorable and beautiful imagery. Her novels have a refined artistry—too rarefied in the opinion of some, who have criticised her for narrowness of social range and for creating people who all share her own delicate sensitivity. But she is one of the most discerning and subtle of psychological novelists.

James Joyce

James Joyce (1882–1941), an exact contemporary of Virginia Woolf, was the most far-reaching innovator in the English novel of this century. His comparatively small output began with a collection of short stories, *Dubliners* (1914), economically realistic evocations of the frustrated lives of ordinary inhabitants of the Irish city. *A Portrait of the Artist as a Young Man* (1916) is an autobiographical novel. This was followed by his masterpiece, *Ulysses* (1922). His last book was *Finnegans Wake* (1939).

Joyce used the stream of consciousness technique, carrying it to greater lengths than Virginia Woolf. It can be seen in its purest form in Molly Bloom's soliloquy at the end of *Ulysses*, where her drifting mental processes as she lies half-asleep are rendered in unpunctuated prose that moves from one apparently disconnected thought to another. His most astonishing innovations were linguistic. *A Portrait of the Artist* begins with childish-sounding language mirroring the boy's immaturity. Throughout the book, his stages of development are recorded in appropriate levels of prose. *Ulysses* is written in widely varied styles of English, most obviously in the scene where Stephen and Bloom await the birth of a baby. The conception and growth of the child are reflected in Joyce's imitations of English prose from Anglo-Saxon times to the end of the nineteenth century. His most extreme linguistic innovation is in *Finnegans Wake*, a book of such intensive verbal coinage and word-play that it can be said to be written in a new language, for which a key is necessary.

Joyce also employs allusions and symbols, which enrich his meaning once they are interpreted (which again can be a difficult process). *Ulysses* has indirect allegiances to Homer's epic poem, the *Odyssey*, but it is filled with the actuality of one day in Dublin: 16 June 1904. It contains numerous other emblems, references and echoes, making it a fascinatingly complex picture of human experience. His psychological explorations of character are associated with the life and traditions of Ireland, for although Joyce exiled himself from his native country as a young man its politics, religion and customs are inseparable from his work.

Stephen Daedalus, the hero of *A Portrait of the Artist as a Young Man*, is the fictional equivalent of Joyce. His education, temptations and artistic credo make the main subject-matter of the book. Stephen reappears as one of the central characters of *Ulysses*, in which his companion during the day's adventures is a middle-aged Jew, Leopold Bloom. Using their particular situations in early twentieth-century Ireland, Joyce creates a universal impression of the emotions and problems of humanity, by means of interior monologue, sensuous description, individualised dialogue and allusion. In *A Portrait of the Artist*, Stephen said that the highest form of literature is the dramatic. In that form, "the artist, like the God of creation, remains within or behind or beyond or above his handiwork, invisible, refined out of existence, indifferent, paring his fingernails." By fully and uncompromisingly presenting his characters' innermost thoughts and by withholding authorial moral judgement, Joyce aimed to achieve the ideal that Stephen desired.

D. H. Lawrence

D. H. Lawrence (1885–1930) differed in many remarkable aspects from James Joyce and Virginia Woolf in his approach to writing novels. He brought an urgency and spontaneity and, above all, a poetic sense to prose fiction. He was a prolific author, who produced numerous short stories, travel books, poems, plays and essays besides novels. His principal novels are *The White Peacock* (1911), *Sons and Lovers* (1913), *The Rainbow* (1915), *Women in Love* (1920), *The Lost Girl* (1921), *Aaron's Rod* (1922), *Kangaroo* (1923), *The Plumed Serpent* (1926) and *Lady Chatterley's Lover* (1928).

As a novelist, Lawrence considered himself "superior to the saint, the scientist, the philosopher, and the poet", since in his opinion the novel dealt with the complete human being instead of a particular aspect. "The novel," he declared, "is the one bright book of life." His main theme is the tensions, joys and sorrows that exist in personal relationships: those between parents and children, husbands and wives, and other people in love. *Sons and Lovers*, his most famous book, centres upon the semi-autobiographical hero, Paul Morel, whose attachment to his mother inhibits his love for Miriam. The novel is also deeply concerned with the opposition between Paul's sensual coal-mining father and his refined, sensitive mother. *The Rainbow*, to which *Women in Love* is a kind of sequel, shows three generations of the Brangwyn family: the conflict and mutual understanding inherent in passionate marriages and love-affairs and the disputes and reconciliations between parents and children are revealed as repeating themselves through a long period of time. But no summaries can convey the subtleties of Lawrence's handling of the psychological and moral issues involved.

For Lawrence, "blood" and instinct were the dominating forces of life, superior in strength to the dictates of reason, and he saw his task as a novelist to transmit these forces through the medium of words. The result is that his novels lack conventional form. What matters is the internal lives of his characters and not their external actions, except when these actions reveal significant behaviour. He therefore concentrates on episodes of intensity and he will, where necessary, ignore the reader's expectations of an even time-scale and the clear development of plot and character. "You mustn't look into my novel for the old stable *ego* of character," he wrote. "There is another *ego*, according to whose action the individual is unrecognisable, and passes through, as it were, allotropic states which it needs a deeper sense than any we've been used to exercise, to discover and are

states of the same single radically unchanged element." His writing consequently has a great emotional impact and gives the feeling of complete fidelity to life as it actually is, with its contradictions and uncertainties. But Lawrence's uncompromising frankness and refusal to conform to literary and social conventions led to the censorship and banning of some of his books, notably *Lady Chatterley's Lover*, which was too sexually explicit for contemporary English standards—it was not published in Britain in unexpurgated form until 1960.

Lawrence's descriptions of the physical appearance of his characters and their surroundings are direct and sensuous; his prose rhythms and choice of words remind us that he was a poet. Places he lived in inspired many of his settings: the Midlands countryside in *The White Peacock*, Australia in *Kangaroo*, Mexico in *The Plumed Serpent*. His imagery is rich in suggestion and is typically drawn from natural and religious sources. In *The Rainbow*, for example, the rainbow itself, doorways, archways and rural scenery and occupations evoke important aspects of the characters' lives and motives and give unity to the novel.

It has been argued that Lawrence was not always in touch with reality because the intense level at which his personages live lacks credibility. Some critics have deplored his preaching, his lack of humour and his repetitiveness. Some of these criticisms are justified only if the criterion of naturalism is rigorously applied. Most people will agree that his great novels—*Sons and Lovers*, *The Rainbow* and *Women in Love*—are masterpieces of psychological insight and moral profundity.

Other Novelists of the 1920s and 1930s

Although Ronald Firbank (1886–1926) began publishing his work in 1905, his slight, artificial novels seem to represent the frivolous side of the 1920s. Amongst them are *Vainglory* (1915), *Caprice* (1917), *Valmouth* (1919), *The Flower beneath the Foot* (1923), *Prancing Nigger* (1924) and *Concerning the Eccentricities of Cardinal Pirelli* (1926). The wit and fantasy of these books can also be related to the aestheticism of the 1890s.

One of the most influential writers of the two decades was Aldous Huxley (1894–1963). An intellectual and polymath, Huxley wrote satirical, comic novels of ideas, which have affinities with those of Peacock. They include *Crome Yellow* (1921), *Antic Hay* (1923) and *Those Barren Leaves* (1925). *Point Counterpoint* (1928) consists mainly of brilliant conversation pieces, in which the participants (e.g. Rampion, who is based on D. H. Lawrence) exchange ideas on philosophy, politics, religion, the arts and society. Of Huxley's later novels, the most important are *Brave New World* (1932), which is set six hundred years hence, *Eyeless in Gaza* (1936) and *Island* (1962).

Evelyn Waugh (1903–66) made his reputation with comic, witty, mocking novels: *Decline and Fall* (1928), *Vile Bodies* (1930), *Black Mischief* (1932), *A Handful of Dust* (1934), *Scoop* (1938) and *Put Out More Flags* (1942). Waugh's books of this period are characterised by an air of satirical detachment, black comedy and farce, the fertile invention of entertaining personages and episodes and a pointed prose style. They remain freshly amusing, though some readers dislike their apparent heartlessness. *Brideshead Revisited* (1945), with its nostalgic recollections of events centred upon a great country house, is, in contrast, a romantic and even sentimental novel. *The Loved One* (1948), a satire on American funeral customs, marked a return to his earlier manner. Waugh's last considerable work, which some consider to be his masterpiece, was a trilogy: *Men at Arms* (1952), *Officers and Gentlemen* (1955) and *Unconditional Surrender* (1961), later united as *Sword of Honour* (1965). Though this book contains much comedy, it is a sympathetic portrayal of the doubts and anxieties during the Second World War of its central figure, Guy Crouchback, a Roman Catholic and army officer.

The first novels of George Orwell (pseudonym of Eric Blair, 1903–50) reflect the period: *Burmese Days* (1934), *A Clergyman's Daughter* (1935), *Keep the Aspidistra Flying* (1936) and *Coming up for Air* (1939). His most celebrated were his last two: *Animal Farm* (1945), which is a short fable satirising revolution and dictatorship, and *Nineteen Eighty-Four* (1949), which is a grim picture of a future authoritarian world.

Christopher Isherwood (1904–86) wrote *All the Conspirators* (1928), but made his reputation with the plays he wrote with W. H. Auden in the 1930s and with his two novels about Germany in the last days of the Weimar Republic: *Mr Norris Changes Trains* (1935) and *Goodbye to Berlin* (1939). The narrator of these says "I am a camera" and consequently records his experiences in a spare, objective manner, which nevertheless evokes the emotions of himself and the other characters. Isherwood's other novels, which are varied in content, include *Prater Violet* (1946) and *Down There On A Visit* (1962).

Much of the fiction of Firbank, Huxley, Waugh, Orwell and Isherwood therefore reflects the spirit of the age. But other novelists of the time were free from contemporary preoccupations. The two most famous novels of John Cowper Powys (1872–1963) are *Wolf Solent* (1929) and *A Glastonbury Romance* (1932), which are conceived on a grand scale and are full of a metaphysical awareness of the forces of Nature. His brother, T. F. Powys (1875–1953), is best known for *Mr Weston's Good Wine* (1927). The novels of Ivy Compton-Burnett (1892–1969) are set at the end of the nineteenth century in a stylised world of middle-class families in country houses. Their titles, whose similarities denote the unchanging nature of the novels, include *Pastors and Masters* (1925), *Men and Wives* (1931), *A House and its Head* (1935), *A Family and a Fortune* (1939), *Manservant and Maidservant* (1947), *Two Worlds and their Ways* (1949), *A Father and his Fate* (1957), *The Mighty and their Fall* (1961) and *A God and his Gifts* (1963). Through the medium of mannered conversation, Ivy Compton-Burnett presents stories of wrongdoing, sin and crime. Aspects of evil are coolly exposed by means of her highly artificial narration.

J. B. Priestley (1894–1984) wrote *The Good Companions* (1929), which was a huge success, and followed with his numerous realistic, entertaining novels, including *Angel Pavement* (1930).

Graham Greene

Graham Greene (1904–91) was a writer of novels for over sixty years as well as short stories, plays, autobiography, essays and criticism. He began with *The Man Within* (1929) and his subsequent novels are *Stamboul Train* (1932), *It's a Battlefield* (1934), *England Made Me* (1935), *A Gun for Sale* (1936), *Brighton Rock* (1938), *The Confidential Agent* (1939), *The Power and the Glory* (1940), *The Ministry of Fear* (1943), *The Heart of the Matter* (1948), *The Third Man* (1950), *The End of the Affair* (1951), *Loser Takes All* (1955), *The Quiet American* (1955), *Our Man in Havana* (1958), *A Burnt-Out Case* (1961), *The Comedians* (1966), *Travels with my Aunt* (1969), *The Honorary Consul* (1973), *The Human Factor* (1978), *Doctor Fischer of Geneva* (1980), *Monsignor Quixote* (1982), *The Tenth Man* (1985; written 1944) and *The Captain and the Enemy* (1988).

Greene's novels are gripping and exciting, since they contain the basic features of such popular fiction as thrillers, adventure stories and spy stories. Their settings are dangerous or exotic places, such as Mexico (*The Power and the Glory*), West Africa (*The Heart of the Matter*), the Congo (*A Burnt-Out Case*), Haiti (*The Comedians*) and Argentina (*The Honorary Consul*). His vivid descriptions of places and people and his fast-moving pace are cinematic and many of his novels have been turned into successful films. Enmeshed in challenging circumstances, his characters are compelled to make moral choices and, in doing so, to face problems of loyalty and faith. As Greene was a Roman Catholic, these problems are generally related to religious belief. Pinkie, the young Roman Catholic criminal in *Brighton Rock*, is dedicated to evil but is opposed by the warm-hearted Ida, who has firm ideas of Right and Wrong, untroubled by theological considerations. Scobie in *The Heart of the Matter*, a self-tormented Catholic, chooses to commit the sin of suicide as a result of his entanglements in unhappy relationships with women. In his novella, *Doctor Fischer of Geneva*, Greene uses memorable, macabre events and strange—even grotesque—characterisation to stimulate thought about profound issues: greed, power, love, revenge and death.

Greene's settings, characters and themes, especially from *Brighton Rock* onwards, are fused into complete statements about the springs of human conduct. The environment, which has sometimes been called "Greeneland", can symbolise and emphasise the dangers experienced by the characters.

Because of the quantity and quality of his achievement, Graham Greene is widely considered to be the outstanding English novelist of the past fifty years. He was appointed a Companion of Honour in 1966 and awarded the O.M. in 1986.

THE NOVEL SINCE 1940

Novelists of the 1940s

Some writers who began their literary careers in the 1930s became more prominent in the war and post-war years. Joyce Cary (1888–1957) began by writing novels set in Nigeria, where he had worked as a government official: *Aissa Saved* (1932), *An American Visitor* (1933), *The African Witch* (1936) and *Mister Johnson* (1939). He followed these with two books about childhood: *Charley is my Darling* (1940) and *A House of Children* (1941). Then there came a trilogy centred upon three characters, Gulley Jimson, Sara Monday and Wilcher: *Herself Surprised* (1941), *To Be a Pilgrim* (1942) and *The Horse's Mouth* (1944), which is generally accounted his best novel. Another trilogy, centred upon Chester Nimmo, was *Prisoner of Grace* (1952), *Except the Lord* (1953) and *Not Honour More* (1955). A further notable novel is *A Fearful Joy* (1949). Cary's most famous works, *Mister Johnson* and *The Horse's Mouth*, are exuberant, inventive and full of *joie de vivre*, largely owing to their central characters, Mister Johnson, an African clerk, and Gulley Jimson, a painter and rogue.

L. P. Hartley (1895–1972) wrote a trilogy dealing with the fortunes of a brother and sister in the early years of this century: *The Shrimp and the Anemone* (1944), *The Sixth Heaven* (1946) and *Eustace and Hilda* (1947). *The Go-Between* (1953) is a vivid, delicate evocation of a boy's being caught up in adult sexual intrigue and of Edwardian country house life.

The sensitive, psychologically penetrating novels of Elizabeth Bowen (1899–1973) include *The House in Paris* (1935), *The Death of the Heart* (1938), *The Heat of the Day* (1949)—usually said to be her greatest achievement, *A World of Love* (1955) and *Eva Trout* (1969).

Henry Green (pseudonym of Henry Yorke, 1905–73) wrote *Blindness* (1926), *Living* (1929), *Party Going* (1939), *Caught* (1943), *Loving* (1945), *Back* (1946), *Concluding* (1948), *Nothing* (1950) and *Doting* (1952). He explores personal relationships in rhythmical prose, much dialogue, imagery and symbols. His novels are some of the most imaginative works of the period.

In contrast, the novels of C. P. Snow (1905–80) are heavily realistic, often dealing with people in the midst of public affairs (in, for example, government and university circles). His best-known novels form the *Strangers and Brothers* sequence: *Strangers and Brothers* (1940), *The Light and the Dark* (1947), *Time of Hope* (1949), *The Masters* (1951), *The New Men* (1954), *Homecomings* (1956), *The Conscience of the Rich* (1958), *The Affair* (1960), *Corridors of Power* (1964), *The Sleep of Reason* (1968) and *Last Things* (1970). The novels of Elizabeth Taylor (1912–75) include *At Mrs Lippincote's* (1945), *A View of the Harbour* (1947), *A Wreath of Roses* (1949), and *Mrs Palfrey at the Claremont* (1971).

Samuel Beckett

As a young man, Samuel Beckett (1906–89) was a friend and associate of James Joyce, whose stream-of-consciousness technique influenced his writing. He first came into prominence in England in 1955 when his English version of his play, *Waiting for Godot*, originally written in French, was performed in London. His first novel, *Dream of Fair to Middling Women* (1932), was published posthumously in 1992. His novel, *Murphy* (1938), set in London, is written in a fairly traditional manner. *Watt*, completed about 1944, was published in 1953. Three short novels, first written in French and in the form of monologues, comprise a trilogy: *Malone Dies* (1951; English version, 1956), *Molloy* (1951; English version, 1955) and *The Unnamable* (1953; English version, 1958). Like much of Beckett's work, which includes plays, short prose pieces and poems, these three novels are characterised by moods of negation, despair and hopelessness but also by elements of grim humour. Beckett was awarded the Nobel Prize for Literature in 1969.

The 1950s: Anthony Powell, Lawrence Durrell, Sir Angus Wilson and Barbara Pym

Anthony Powell (b. 1905) wrote some amusing novels in the 1930s, rather like those of Evelyn Waugh: *Afternoon Men* (1931), *Venusberg* (1932), *From a View to a Death* (1933), *Agents and Patients* (1936) and *What's Become of Waring?* (1939). His major work, a sequence called *A Dance to the Music of Time*, began to appear in the 1950s: *A Question of Upbringing* (1951), *A Buyer's Market* (1952), *The Acceptance World* (1955), *At Lady Molly's* (1957), *Casanova's Chinese Restaurant* (1960), *The Kindly Ones* (1962), *The Valley of Bones* (1964), *The Soldier's Art* (1966), *The Military Philosophers* (1968), *Books Do Furnish A Room* (1971), *Temporary Kings* (1973) and *Hearing Secret Harmonies* (1975). Its subject is the relationships of a large circle of friends and acquaintances spanning a period of sixty years and including about three hundred characters. it is written with gentle irony and sharp observation of psychology, manners and social class. Powell has also written *O, How the Wheel Becomes It!* (1983) and *The Fisher King* (1986).

Lawrence Durrell (1912–90) published his best-known novels in this decade. *The Alexandria Quartet* consists of *Justine* (1957), *Balthazar* (1958), *Mountolive* (1958) and *Clea* (1960). These complex, erotic and exotic novels are notably experimental in their treatment of time. Durrell's other novels include *Tunc* (1968), *Nunquam* (1970), *Monsieur* (1974), *Livia* (1978), *Constance* (1982), *Sebastian* (1983) and *Quinx* (1985). The last five were later published as *The Avignon Quintet* (1992).

Sir Angus Wilson (1913–91) achieved success with two collections of short stories, *The Wrong Set* (1949) and *Such Darling Dodos* (1952). His novels are *Hemlock and After* (1952), *Anglo-Saxon Attitudes* (1956), *The Middle Age of Mrs Eliot* (1958), *The Old Men at the Zoo* (1961), *Late Call* (1964), *No Laughing Matter* (1967), *As If By Magic* (1973) and *Setting the World on Fire* (1980). An admirer of Dickens, Dostoevsky, Proust and Virginia Woolf, Angus Wilson writes in a realistic, detailed manner with convincing renderings of conversation, although this air of realism does not preclude him from using fantasy and symbolism, especially in his later work. The people and milieux he deals with are predominantly middle-class. His subject-matter is personal relationships, often amongst middle-aged men and women. Class is an important element in his varied work.

Barbara Pym (1913–80) wrote quiet fiction typically dealing with the lives of single, middle-class women in a sympathetic, observant manner, tinged with comedy. Her novels include *Some Tame Gazelle* (1950), *Excellent Women* (1952), *Jane and Prudence* (1953), *Less than Angels* (1955), *A Glass of Blessings* (1958), *No Fond Return of Love* (1961), *Quartet in Autumn* (1977), *The Sweet Dove Died* (1978), *A Few Green Leaves* (1980), *An Unsuitable Attachment* (1982; written 1961–63); *Crampton Hodnet* (1985; written 1939–40); *An Academic Question* (1986; written 1970–71) and *Civil to Strangers and Other Writings* (1987; written 1936, 1940–41).

Sir Kingsley Amis, John Wain and Northern Working-Class Novelists

Other novelists of the 1950s took a disillusioned, ironical look at the postwar world, just as many of the new poets and playwrights of the period did. Distrusting anything grandiose and experimental, they wrote in wryly amusing and observant ways about people of no particular privileges, wealth or pretensions. William Cooper's *Scenes of Provincial Life* (1950), with its significant title, was a forerunner of the disrespectful, non-metropolitan stance which they adopted.

The most famous of these writers is Sir Kingsley Amis (b. 1922), whose novels are *Lucky Jim* (1954), *That Uncertain Feeling* (1955), *I Like It Here* (1958), *Take a Girl Like You* (1960), *One Fat Englishman* (1963), *The Anti-Death League* (1966), *I Want It Now* (1968), *The Green Man* (1969), *Girl, 20* (1971), *The Riverside Villas Murder* (1973), *Ending Up* (1974), *The Alteration* (1976), *Jake's Thing* (1978), *Russian Hide-and-Seek* (1980), *Stanley and the Women* (1984), *The Old Devils* (1986), *Difficulties with Girls* (1988), *The Folks That Live on the Hill* (1990), *We Are All Guilty* (1991), *The Russian Girl* (1992) and *You Can't Do Both* (1994). As a moral novelist, Amis writes with economy, precision, wit and cynical commonsense, constantly puncturing affectations and falsity. *Lucky Jim*, with its account of the fortunes and misfortunes of a provincial university teacher, has become one of the classic comic novels.

Another versatile novelist is John Wain (1925–94), whose *Hurry on Down* (1953) achieved the same kind of status and popularity as *Lucky Jim*. His other novels include *Living in the Present* (1955), *The Contenders* (1958), *A Travelling Woman* (1959), *Strike the Father Dead* (1962), *The Young Visitors* (1965), *A Winter in the Hills* (1974), *Young Shoulders* (1982) and the trilogy; *Where the Rivers Meet* (1988), *Comedies* (1990), and *Hungry Generations* (1994).

Novelists writing of life amongst the working classes, especially in the north of England, also came to the fore in the 1950s. John Braine (1922–86) wrote *Room at the Top* (1957) about a go-getting young man, Joe Lampton. His subsequent novels, which vary in theme, include *The Vodi* (1959), *Life at the Top* (1962), *The Crying Game* (1964), *Stay With Me Till Morning* (1970), *The Queen of a Distant Country* (1972), *Waiting for Sheila* (1976), *One and Last Love* (1981) *The Two of Us* (1984) and *These Golden Days* (1985). Alan Sillitoe (b. 1928) made his reputation with *Saturday Night and Sunday Morning* (1958) and went on to write novels of different kinds, including *The General* (1960), *Key to the Door* (1961), *The Death of William Posters* (1965), *A Start in Life* (1970), *Travels in Nihilon* (1971), *Raw Material* (1972), *A Flame of Life* (1974), *The Widower's Son* (1976), *The Storyteller* (1979), *The Second Chance* (1981), *Her Victory* (1982), *Down from the Hill* (1984), *Life Goes On* (1985), *Out of the Whirlpool* (1988), *The Open Door* (1989), *Last Loves* (1990), *Leonard's War* (1991) and *Snowstop* (1993). Stan Barstow (b. 1928) wrote *A Kind of Loving* (1960); the best-known of his other novels is *A Raging Calm* (1968); his latest are *Give Us This Day* (1989) and *Next of Kin* (1991). The first novel by David Storey (b. 1933) was *This Sporting Life* (1962), about Rugby League football. His other books include *Radcliffe* (1963), *Pasmore* (1972), *Saville* (1976), *A Prodigal Child* (1982) and *Present Times* (1984). *Room at the Top*, *Saturday Night and Sunday Morning*, *A Kind of Loving* and *This Sporting Life*, are the most famous novels of northern working-class life of the 1950s.

Fantasy and Experiment

Amis, Wain, Braine, Sillitoe, Barstow and Storey are mainly realistic novelists writing without linguistic experimentation or poetic devices. Their subject-matter, point of view and style are down-to-earth. Others of their contemporaries and near-contemporaries used new fictional forms or explored more imaginative areas. J. R. R. Tolkien (1892–1973) wrote *The Lord of the Rings* (1954–5), a trilogy about an imaginary world that for many has the power and attraction of genuine mythology. Mervyn Peake (1911–68) created a fantastic, grotesque world in *The Gormenghast Trilogy*: *Titus Groan* (1946), *Gormenghast* (1950) and *Titus Alone* (1959).

Sir William Golding (1911–93) achieved great success with *Lord of the Flies* (1954), his story of shipwrecked boys who revert to a primitive, savage state. His other novels are *The Inheritors* (1955), *Pincher Martin* (1956), *Free Fall* (1959), *The Spire* (1964), *The Pyramid* (1967), *Darkness Visible* (1979) and *The Paper Men* (1984). *Rites of Passage* (1980), *Close Quarters* (1987) and *Fire Down Below* (1989) were later published in one volume as *To the Ends of the Earth: a Sea Trilogy* (1991). In complex, imaginative ways, Golding explores profound questions of morality, especially the nature of sin and evil. His novels are often difficult but original in technique and content. He was awarded the Nobel Prize in 1983.

Muriel Spark (b. 1918) has written *The Comforters* (1957), *Robinson* (1958), *Memento Mori* (1959), *The Bachelors* (1960), *The Ballad of Peckham Rye* (1960), *The Prime of Miss Jean Brodie* (1961), *The Girls of Slender Means* (1963), *The Mandelbaum Gate* (1965), *The Public Image* (1968), *The Driver's Seat* (1970), *Not to Disturb* (1971), *The Hothouse by the East River* (1973), *The Abbess of Crewe* (1974), *The Takeover* (1976), *Territorial Rights* (1979), *Loitering with Intent* (1981), *The Only Problem* (1984), *A Far Cry from Kensington* (1988) and *Symposium* (1990). Her novels are wittily written and sometimes fantastic. She presents the reader with provocative studies of moral and metaphysical issues. Her characterisation is vivid (*e.g.* Miss Brodie). There is occasionally an element of the fairy tale or myth (*e.g. The Ballad of Peckham Rye*).

Doris Lessing (b. 1919), a novelist deeply concerned with psychological, political and social tensions (especially in Africa), has also experimented with techniques of fiction. Her novels include *The Grass is Singing* (1950), the *Children of Violence* series (1952–69), *The Golden Notebook* (1962), *The Good Terrorist* (1985) and *The Fifth Child* (1988).

One of the most prolific and inventive of postwar English novelists is Iris Murdoch (b. 1919). Her novels are *Under the Net* (1954), *The Flight from the Enchanter* (1956), *The Sandcastle* (1957), *The Bell* (1958), *A Severed Head* (1961), *An Unofficial Rose* (1962), *The Unicorn* (1963), *The Italian Girl* (1964), *The Red and the Green* (1965), *The Time of the Angels* (1966), *The Nice and the Good* (1968), *Bruno's Dream* (1969), *A Fairly Honourable Defeat* (1970), *An Accidental Man* (1971), *The Black Prince* (1973), *The Sacred and Profane Love Machine* (1974), *A Word Child* (1975), *Henry and Cato* (1976), *The Sea, The Sea* (1978), *Nuns and Soldiers* (1980), *The Philosopher's Pupil* (1983), *The Good Apprentice* (1985) *The Book and the Brotherhood* (1987), *The Message to the Planet* (1989) and *The Green Knight* (1993). A professional philosopher as well as a novelist, Iris Murdoch raises philosophical issues in her fiction by implication, although she maintains that she writes primarily to entertain her readers. Her books contain numerous characters and incidents and often have complicated plots. Their surface attractions are considerable: narrative pace, lively descriptions of people and places, striking episodes and realistic, entertaining dialogue. She uses symbols (the bell and the sea in the appropriately titled novels, for example) and mysterious happenings and coincidences. She stimulates thought about such problems as intentions, appearance and reality, truth and falsity and the part played in life by contingency and chance.

The 1960s and after

Anthony Burgess (1917–93) became well known in this decade with *A Clockwork Orange* (1962). He is a productive, versatile and experimental novelist, whose many other works include *Inside Mr Enderby* (1963), *The Napoleon Symphony* (1974), *Earthly Powers* (1980), *The End of the World News* (1982), *Enderby's Dark Lady* (1984), *The Kingdom of the Wicked* (1985), *The Pianoplayers* (1986), *Any Old Iron* (1989) and *A Dead Man in Deptford* (1993).

Paul Scott (1920–78) is concerned in his principal novels with the English in India. These are the *Raj Quartet*—which consists of *The Jewel in the Crown* (1966), *The Day of the Scorpion* (1968), *The Tower of Silence* (1971) and *A Division of the Spoils* (1976)—and *Staying On* (1977).

John Fowles (b. 1926) is an ingenious and innovatory novelist, whose books include *The Collector* (1963), *The Magus* (1966, revised 1977), *The French Lieutenant's Woman* (1969), *Daniel Martin* (1977), *Mantissa* (1982) and *A Maggot* (1985).

A number of African and West Indian novelists writing in English established themselves at this time. Chinua Achebe (b. 1930), a Nigerian, wrote *Things Fall Apart* (1958), followed by various novels and collections of short stories. V. S. Naipaul (b.1932), a Trinidadian, became acknowledged as one of the leading novelists of the period. His novels include *The Mystic Masseur* (1957), *A House for Mr Biswas* (1961), *Mr Stone and the Knights Companion*

(1963), *The Mimic Men* (1967), *In a Free State* (1971), *Guerrillas* (1975), *A Bend in the River* (1979) and *The Enigma of Arrival* (1987). He was knighted in 1990.

Edna O'Brien (b. 1932) began her career in this decade with three novels that humorously and poignantly portrayed the lives and loves of young Irish women: *The Country Girls* (1960), *The Lonely Girl* (1962) and *Girls in their Married Bliss* (1964). Her other books include *August is a Wicked Month* (1965), *Johnny I Hardly Knew You* (1977), *The High Road* (1988), *Time and Tide* (1992) and *House of Splendid Isolation* (1994). After the publication of *Wide Sargasso Sea* (1966), interest revived in the novels of Jean Rhys (1894–1979), including *Good Morning, Midnight* (1939). *Wide Sargasso Sea* is a sympathetic, brilliantly imaginative account of the early life in the West Indies of Mr Rochester's first wife, Charlotte Brontë's fictional character in *Jane Eyre*. The prevalent tone of Jean Rhys's novels is one of sadness and anguish, as experienced and expressed by a lonely suffering woman.

Margaret Drabble (b. 1939) has written novels that subtly explore human relationships, often with women at their centre. These are *A Summer Bird-Cage* (1963), *The Garrick Year* (1965), *The Millstone* (1965), *Jerusalem the Golden* (1967), *The Waterfall* (1969), *The Needle's Eye* (1972), *The Realms of Gold* (1975), *The Ice Age* (1977), *The Middle Ground* (1980), *The Radiant Way* (1987), *A Natural Curiosity* (1989) and *The Gates of Ivory* (1991).

Beryl Bainbridge (b. 1934) is a comically observant, ironical novelist who made her name with *The Bottle Factory Outing* (1974). Her other novels include *Harriet Said* (1972), *Sweet William* (1975), *A Quiet Life* (1976), *Injury Time* (1977), *Young Adolf* (1978), *Another Part of the Wood* (1979), *Winter Garden* (1980), *Watson's Apology* (1984), *Filthy Lucre* (1986), *An Awfully Big Adventure* (1989) and *The Birthday Boys* (1991).

Malcolm Bradbury (b. 1932) and David Lodge (b. 1935), both teachers and critics of literature, became well-known in the 1970s as novelists. They are associated particularly with "campus novels" dealing with the academic life. Bradbury's novels include *Eating People is Wrong* (1959), *Stepping Westward* (1965), *The History Man* (1975), *Rates of Exchange* (1983), *Cuts* (1987) and *Doctor Criminale* (1992). Lodge's include *The British Museum is Falling Down* (1965), *Changing Places* (1975), *How Far Can You Go?* (1980), *Small World* (1984), *Nice Work* (1988) and *Paradise News* (1991).

For details of other present-day novelists, *see* Fiction in the 1990s (**M25–26**).

THE ENGLISH NOVEL IN PERSPECTIVE

This survey has been confined to the English novel, which should be seen in the perspective of the great European and American novels of the past two or three centuries. Its qualities—its particular strengths and weaknesses—can be truly judged only by considering it in relation to the work of such acknowledged masters as Cervantes; Stendhal, Balzac, Flaubert, Zola and Proust; Tolstoy and Dostoevsky; Goethe and Thomas Mann; Hawthorne, Melville and Mark Twain; Manzoni and Svevo. Comparisons are especially important when we look at modern novelists, since much of today's most significant fiction in English comes from the United States. It is necessary, therefore, to realise that this survey of the English novel deals with just one area of an extensive field.

II. GLOSSARY OF LITERARY TERMS

acatalectic. Having the complete number of syllables in a line of verse. *See* **catalectic** *and* **hypercatalectic**.

accentual verse. Verse (like most English verse) which is measured by the number and pattern of stresses in a line and not by the number or quantitative value of syllables. *See* **metre** *and*

syllabic verse.

act. Principal division of a dramatic work, sometimes subdivided into scenes.

aestheticism. A movement that flourished in the 1880s and 1890s and that considered beauty, not morality, as the most important principle in literary and artistic work. Its key phrase was "Art for art's sake." Two of its chief exponents in England were Walter Pater and Oscar Wilde.

affective fallacy. A phrase coined by M. C. Beardsley and W. K. Wimsatt (1946), who contended that it was false to criticise a poem on the basis of its psychological effects on the reader because as a result "the poem itself, as an object of specifically critical judgement, tends to disappear." See **Intentional fallacy** and **New Critics**.

alexandrine. A line of verse containing six iambic feet. See **metre**.

alienation. The principle, propounded by Bertolt Brecht (1898–1956), that actors and audience should remain detached from a dramatic performance and not become identified with the rôles and action.

allegory. A narrative or description in prose or verse with a hidden meaning or moral message, e.g., Spenser's *Faerie Queene* and Bunyan's *Pilgrim's Progress*.

alliteration. The use of the same consonants in close proximity, often in verse, for the sake of euphony, memorability or emotional effect, e.g.,

"the low last edge of the long lone land"
(Swinburne, "A Forsaken Garden").

See **assonance**.

ambiguity. Unclear or contradictory meaning. Positively, complexity of meaning and tone, as analysed in William Empson's *Seven Types of Ambiguity* (1930).

amphibrach. See **metre**.

anabasis. The progress of an action to a climax, especially in a drama.

anacoluthon. An inconsistency of construction in a sentence, so that the latter part does not grammatically fit with the earlier part, e.g., "One of the prettiest touches was *when*, at the relation of the queen's death . . . *how* attentiveness wounded his daughter" (Shakespeare, *The Winter's Tale*, V, ii).

anacreontic. Applied to light-hearted poetry praising such pleasures as wine, women and song, e.g., Abraham Cowley's *Anacreontics*. (From Anacreon, Greek poet of the sixth century B.C.)

anacrusis. An additional syllable or half-foot at the beginning of a line of verse, e.g.,

"Cóld / and cleár- / cút faće / why come / yōu so crú- / ĕllý méek?"
(Tennyson, "Maud").

anagnorisis. The discovery or recognition, originally by the protagonist of a Greek tragedy, of a truth that leads to the resolution of the drama, e.g., Othello's discovery of Desdemona's innocence. (Term from Aristotle's *Poetics*.)

anapaest. See **metre**.

anaphora. The repetition of a word or phrase at the beginning of consecutive phrases or sentences, e.g.,

"*For gold* his sword the hireling ruffian draws,
For gold the hireling judge distorts the laws"
(Johnson, *The Vanity of Human Wishes*).

anti-hero. A principal character who has no traditional heroic qualities but who is diffident, cowardly, foolish and not particularly estimable, e.g., the eponymous hero of Kingsley Amis's *Lucky Jim*.

anti-novel. Loosely used for some twentieth century novels (by Beckett and Robbe-Grillet, for example) with minimal regard for such conventional features as plot and development of character. See **nouveau roman**.

antistrophe. In the Greek *chorus* (q.v.) the *Pindaric Ode* (q.v.) the response to the *strophe* (q.v.), written in the same metrical form.

antithesis. The balanced juxtaposition of words or phrases for the sake of emphasis or contrast, widely used in eighteenth-century prose and verse, e.g.,

"But sometimes Virtue starves, while Vice is fed"
(Pope, *Essay on Man*).

apocope. The omission of the final letter, syllable or sound of a word, e.g., the poetic use of "th'" for "the."

aposiopesis. Breaking off a sentence, usually for dramatic effect, e.g.,

"I will have such revenges on you both
That all the world shall—I will do such things—
What they are yet I know not"
(Shakespeare, *King Lear*, II, iv).

apostrophe. Address to a person or a personified quality, place or thing, e.g., "Ye distant spires, ye antique towers" (Gray, "Ode on a Distant Prospect of Eton College"); "Stern Daughter of the Voice of God!" (Wordsworth, "Ode to Duty").

apron stage. A stage, like that in the Elizabethan theatre, which projects beyond the proscenium arch into the audience.

art for art's sake. See **aestheticism**.

assonance. The use of the same vowel-sounds in close proximity, often in verse, for the sake of euphony, memorability or emotional effect, e.g., 'And deep-asleep he seemed" (Tennyson, "The Lotus-Eaters"). See **alliteration**.

asyndeton. The omission of a conjunction between words, phrases or clauses, .e.g.,

"And dreams of home,
Waving from window, spread of welcome,
Kissing of wife under single sheet"
(W. H. Auden, "The Wanderer").

See **ellipsis**.

Augustan. Referring to the reign of the Emperor Augustus (27 B.C.–14 A.D.), when Virgil, Horace and Ovid wrote, or to the neo-classical period in English literature between c. 1670 and 1790, when such writers as Dryden, Addison, Pope, Swift and Johnson conformed to the Augustan principles of reason, order and decorum. See **classical** and **neo-classicism**.

ballad. A narrative poem (often anonymous) telling of heroic or tragic deeds, typically written in quatrains of alternating four and three stresses and rhyming abcb or abab, e.g., "Sir Patrick Spens." See **quatrain**.

ballade. A poem of three eight-line stanzas (rhyming ababbcbc) and one four-line envoi (bcbc) with a refrain at the end of each of its four sections, e.g., those written by Hilaire Belloc. See **envoi**.

bathos. An anticlimax or sudden descent from the sublime to the commonplace, intentional or unintentional, e.g., the last two lines of Tennyson's "Enoch Arden":

"And when they buried him the little port
Had seldom seen a costlier funeral."

belles-lettres. Elegant, polished prose writing, especially essays, e.g., those written by Max Beerbohm.

Bildungsroman. Literally, "formation novel" (German), i.e., one that relates the upbringing, education and development of its hero, e.g., Goethe's *Wilhelm Meister's Apprenticeship*. See **M4**.

black comedy. Comedy that finds amusement in what are conventionally regarded as tragic, sick or pessimistic people and situations, e.g., Joe Orton's *Loot*.

blank verse. Unrhymed iambic pentameter (see **metre**), as used in Shakespeare's plays, Milton's *Paradise Lost* and Wordsworth's *Prelude*.

bouts-rimés. Literally, "rhymed ends" (French), i.e., rhyming words supplied in advance to which lines must be fitted.

bowdlerise. To expurgate, from the Rev. Thomas Bowdler (1754–1825), who removed what he considered to be coarse expressions from the plays in his *Family Shakespeare*.

burlesque. A ludicrous, mocking imitation in prose or verse of a literary or dramatic work, e.g., the Duke of Buckingham's *The Rehearsal*, a burlesque of seventeenth-century heroic plays. See **heroic tragedy**.

caesura. A break in a line of poetry, often towards the middle, sometimes used to emphasise an antithesis or comparison, e.g.,

"Willing to wound, / and yet afraid to strike"
(Pope, *Epistle to Arbuthnot*).

See **antithesis**.

canon. Authentic works of an author or standard works of literature (as studied on academic courses, for example).

canto. A division of a long poem, perhaps consisting of many **stanzas** (q.v.), as in Byron's *Don Juan*.

catachresis. A misuse or incorrect application of a word, e.g., "chronic" to mean "severe".

catalectic. Describing a line of verse with one or more syllables missing in the final foot, e.g.,

"Rúiń / seíze thée, / rúthlěss / kíńg!"
(Gray, "The Bard").

See acatalectic, hypercatalectic *and* metre.

catalyst. A substance that alters the rate of a chemical reaction but itself remains unchanged. T. S. Eliot used the term as an analogy in his theory of the poet's impersonality: "the more perfect the artist, the more completely separate in him will be the man who suffers and the mind which creates" ("Tradition and the Individual Talent," 1919).

catastrophe. The tragic climax of a drama or narrative.

catharsis. The purgation of pity and terror by means of the representation of those emotions in tragedy (Aristotle, *Poetics*). *See* tragedy.

character. A seventeenth-century genre of writing illustrating individual and social human types ("a modest man", "a shopkeeper", etc.), e.g., John Earle's *Microcosmography*. More widely, a fictional personage, defined by E. M. Forster in *Aspects of the Novel* (1927) as either "flat" ("constructed round a single idea or quality") or "round" (with the "incalculability of life about it").

chiasmus. A "laying crosswise" of elements in a sentence, *i.e.*, the order of words in one of two parallel clauses or phrases is inverted in the other, e.g.,

"Love without end, and without measure grace"
                    (Milton, *Paradise Lost*).

chorus. A group of actors in Greek drama providing a commentary on the action; a device adapted, for example, by Shakespeare in *King Henry V* and T. S. Eliot in *Murder in the Cathedral*.

classical. Showing a regard for the values and forms of Ancient Greek and Latin literature and so having qualities of order, restraint, reason and precision. *See* Augustan *and* neo-classical.

clerihew. Comic biographical poem in the form of a *quatrain* (*q.v.*) with lines of various length, rhyming *aabb*, named after its inventor Eric Clerihew Bentley (1875–1956).

comedy. A literary or dramatic work, or aspect of it, that is amusing in various ways. More particularly, a work with a happy ending, e.g., a comedy by Shakespeare. *See* black comedy.

comedy of ideas. A play (or novel) that is entertainingly and wittily concerned with ideas, problems and theories, e.g., the novels of Thomas Love Peacock and the plays of Bernard Shaw.

comedy of manners. A play concerned with the behaviour and intrigues of elegant, sophisticated society, e.g., Congreve's *The Way of the World* and Wilde's *The Importance of Being Earnest*.

conceit. An ingenious or highly fanciful example of imagery, perhaps using elaborate figures of speech and word-play, often associated with the *Metaphysical Poets* (*q.v.*), e.g., Donne's comparison of two lovers' souls with a pair of compasses ("A Valediction: Forbidding Mourning").

couplet. Two successive rhyming lines. *See* heroic couplet *and* rhyming couplet.

dactyl. *See* metre.

decasyllable. A line of verse of ten syllables, often synonymous with the iambic pentameter. *See* metre.

deconstruction. A theory and method of textual analysis that emphasises the infinite number of uncertainties and ambiguities that exist in any literary work. *See* post-structuralism.

defamiliarisation. A conception of artistic technique held by the Russian Formalist, Victor Shklovsky, who maintained that art enables us to experience the world afresh by means of making things unfamiliar and thus increasing "the difficulty and duration of perception". *See* formalism.

diaeresis. The separation of a diphthong into two sounds, sometimes indicated by a mark (¨) placed over the second vowel, e.g., "Noël".

dialogue. Conversation between two or more people in a literary or dramatic work. Also, a separate genre often used for the discussion of ideas, e.g., Landor's *Imaginary Conversations*.

didactic. Applied to a literary work in prose or verse that aims to instruct the reader lightly or seriously, e.g., Pope's poem, *An Essay on Criticism*.

diegesis. The process of authorial explanations, commentaries and narrative in a fictional work as distinct from the direct display of characters and action by such means as dialogue. Sometimes used in criticism as the opposing term to mimesis (*q.v.*). (From Plato's *Republic*.)

dirge. A funeral song or poem, e.g., Shelley's "Autumn: A Dirge". *See* elegy *and* threnody.

dissociation of sensibility. T. S. Eliot's term (in "The Metaphysical Poets," 1921) to explain the failure of post seventeenth-century poets to amalgamate "disparate experience" to form "new wholes". There was a separation of feeling from thought in their work.

distich. Two lines of verse expressing a complete idea.

dithyramb. A passionate, rapturous poem, e.g., Dryden's "Alexander's Feast".

doggerel. Rough, technically incompetent verse, often comic, vulgar or abusive, e.g., some of the street ballads of the nineteenth century.

donnée. A situation or idea given or suggested to an author, who then bases a literary work on it, e.g., an anecdote at the dinner-table led to Henry James's *The Spoils of Poynton*.

dramatic irony. Words or a situation on the stage understood by the audience in a different way from the way the characters understand them, e.g., Duncan's speech, "This castle hath a pleasant seat . . .", spoken on the eve of his murder there (Shakespeare, *Macbeth*, I, vi).

dramatic monologue. Poem with one speaker addressing a listener or listeners and revealing, knowingly or unknowingly, important aspects of his character and situation, e.g., Browning's "Fra Lippo Lippi."

eclogue. A fairly short pastoral poem often in the form of a dialogue, e.g., the ten *Eclogues* of Virgil.

elegiac stanza. Quatrain of four iambic pentameters rhyming *abab*, as used in Gray's "Elegy in a Country Churchyard".

elegy. A poem of mourning or lament, e.g., Milton's "Lycidas" and Shelley's "Adonais". *See* dirge *and* threnody.

elision. The suppression of a vowel or syllable in verse for the sake of metrical correctness, e.g., "ta'en" for "taken".

ellipsis. The omission of words, especially in poetry, to achieve compression, complexity or surprise, e.g., in passages of T. S. Eliot's *The Waste Land*. *See* asyndeton.

emblem. A symbolic picture with a motto and explanation, associated with allegorical and figurative writing in such seventeenth century works as Francis Quarles' *Emblems*, a collection of religious poems.

end-stopped. Describing a self-contained line of verse that ends with a punctuation mark, e.g.,

"Black is the beauty of the brightest day!
The golden ball of Heaven's eternal fire,
That danced with glory on the silver waves,
Now wants the glory that inflamed his beams"
          (Marlowe, *Tamburlaine*, 2nd Part, II, iv).

See enjambment.

enjambment. The running-on of one line of verse into another without a grammatical break, e.g.,

"Nay, but this dotage of our general's
O'er flows the measure . . ."
          (Shakespeare, *Antony and Cleopatra*, I, i).

envoi. The short final stanza of a poem, especially a *ballade* (*q.v.*), addressed as parting words to a person or persons, emphasising the subject of the poem.

epic. A long narrative poem in an elevated style celebrating heroic personages and deeds, e.g., Homer's *Iliad* and *Odyssey*.

epic simile. A long, elaborately developed comparison, as found in some epic poems. Sometimes termed *Homeric simile*. *See* simile.

epigram. A pointed, witty saying or verse that can be sarcastic, complimentary or amusing, e.g.,

"Swans sing before they die; 'twere no bad thing
Did certain persons die before they sing"
          (Coleridge).

epigraph. A quotation or motto at the beginning of a work or of a section of it, e.g., 'Mistah Kurtz—he dead" (quotation from Conrad's *Heart of Darkness* prefixed to T. S. Eliot's *The Hollow Men*).

epilogue. The final section of work, serving such purposes as pointing a moral or summarising, e.g., Rosalind's concluding speech in Shakespeare's *As You Like it*.

epiphany. James Joyce's term for a significant moment of revelation that a writer should record: "a sudden spiritual manifestation, whether in the vulgarity of speech or of gesture or in a memorable phase of the mind itself'' (Joyce, *Stephen Hero*).

epistolary novel. A novel written in the form of letters, *e.g.*, Samuel Richardson's *Clarissa* and Laclos' *Les Liaisons dangereuses*.

epode. In the Greek *chorus* (*q.v.*) and the *Pindaric Ode* (*q.v.*), the third and last section, coming after the *antistrophe* (*q.v.*).

essay. A fairly short discussion in prose (or, more rarely, in verse) of any topic, light-hearted or serious in tone and formal or informal in style, as written by Bacon, Addison and Lamb.

euphemism The use of a mild, pleasant term to express something disagreeable, harsh or vulgar, *e.g.*, "And lo, he had answered to his name, and stood in the presence of The Master'' (Thackeray, *The Newcomes*), meaning "He had died''; "visually challenged'' meaning "blind'' or "partly blind''.

euphony. Agreeable sound in verse or prose achieved by such means as metre, rhyme, alliteration and assonance, enhanced by the meanings and associations of the words chosen, frequently found, for example, in the poems of Tennyson.

euphuism. Highly elaborate prose style, as found in John Lyly's *Euphues* (1579–80).

eye-rhyme. A rhyme that is visually correct but orally incorrect, *e.g.*, "love'' and "rove'', though in considering older poetry changes in pronunciation must be borne in mind. Also, Spenser's practice of adjusting spelling to make a rhyme clear to both eye and ear.

fable. A short prose or verse narrative, often with animals as characters, intended to convey a moral lesson, as written, for example, by Aesop, La Fontaine and John Gay.

fabula. In Formalist criticism, a story as it would actually have happened chronologically and objectively, as distinct from its literary treatment in a specific text, which is termed the *sjuzet*. See **formalism**.

farce. A comedy of broad, absurd and slapstick humour, often of frantic pace and technical ingenuity, *e.g.*, Ben Travers' *Rookery Nook*.

fashionable novel. A novel about life in high society written in an inflated, sentimental style, popular in the 1820s and 1830s, *e.g.*, Disraeli's *The Young Duke*. See **M6**.

foot. *See* metre.

foregrounding. Emphasis and prominence achieved in literary work by such means as linguistic deviation from normal usage.

formalism. A critical theory and method developed by critics in Russia *c.* 1913–30 (*e.g.*, Shklovsky and Jakobson) that concentrated on the analysis of literary works as self-sufficient structures and paid little or no attention to biographical and social influences.

fourteener. A line of verse containing fourteen syllables arranged as seven iambic feet. *See* metre.

free verse. Verse with no regular metrical pattern or length of line but with its form sometimes determined by its meaning, *e.g.*, D. H. Lawrence's "Snake''. Also known as *vers libre*.

genre. A kind or type of literary work defined by its form and/or its purpose, *e.g.*, comedy, satire, ode.

Georgian poetry. Poetry written between *c.* 1910 and 1925, during the reign of George V, in short, lyrical forms and of easy comprehensibility, typically dealing with English rural subjects in an affectionate and nostalgic manner. The principal poets included W. H. Davies, Walter de la Mare, James Stephens, Edward Thomas and Edmund Blunden.

Gothic novels. Melodramatic novels of the late eighteenth and early nineteenth centuries dealing with terror, mystery and the supernatural, often in medieval settings, *e.g.*, M. G. Lewis's *The Monk*. See **M5**.

grand style. A plain, natural and noble style of poetry, as found in Homer (termed thus by Matthew Arnold).

great tradition. Phrase used by the critic F. R. Leavis to denote certain novelists "significant in terms of that human awareness they promote'', *i.e.*, Jane Austen, George Eliot, Henry James and Joseph Conrad (*The Great Tradition*, 1948). Leavis would later have added Dickens and D. H. Lawrence to the tradition.

haiku. Japanese verse form of seventeen syllables in three lines of five, seven and five syllables, conveying a single, sharp impression of an image or mood.

half-rhyme. Rhyme in which the consonants are the same but the vowels are different, *e.g.*,

"leaves''/ "lives'', "simmer''/"summer'' (taken from Wilfred Owen's 'Miners'').

hamartia. The flaw or defect in a tragic hero that leads to his downfall (Aristotle, *Poetics*).

hemistich. Half a line of verse, divided at the *caesura* (*q.v.*).

hendecasyllabic. A line of verse of eleven syllables, as used by the Latin poet, Catullus, but rarely found in English.

hendiadys. Expression of a compound notion by two elements co-ordinated by "and'' instead of by one element subordinated to the other, *e.g.*, "waving to him *white hands and courtesy*'' (Tennyson, "Gareth and Lynette'') for "courteous white hands.''

heptameter. *See* metre.

heroic couplet. A pair of rhyming iambic pentameters, so called because the metre was used in seventeenth century 'heroic' plays and poems by Dryden and others. (*See* heroic tragedy.) The prevalent metrical form in the eighteenth century. *See* metre *and* rhyming couplet.

heroic tragedy. Late seventeenth-century type of drama, dealing in an elevated manner with themes of love and honour, written in *heroic couplets* (*q.v.*), *e.g.*, John Dryden's *The Conquest of Granada*.

hexameter. *See* metre.

historical novel. A novel set in past times, sometimes mixing fictional and factual characters and events, *e.g.*, Sir Walter Scott's *Ivanhoe*. See **M4**.

Homeric simile. *See* epic simile *and* simile.

homonym. A word having the same sound and sometimes the same spelling as another but a different meaning, *e.g.*, "fast'': "rapid''; "fast'': "abstinence''; "fast'': "fixed''.

homophone. A word having the same pronunciation as another but a different meaning and spelling, *e.g.*, "son'' and "sun''.

hubris. In Greek tragedy, the arrogance of a hero or heroine who ignores divine commands and who is therefore brought to ruin, e.g., the behaviour of Creon in Sophocles' *Antigone*.

hypallage. Transference of epithet from the normal substantive to an unexpected one, *e.g.*, "Who sees his true love in her *naked bed*'' (Shakespeare, *Venus and Adonis*).

hyperbaton. Transposition of words out of normal order or separation of words usually associated together, *e.g.*,

"So much I hate a *breaking* cause to be
Of *heavenly oaths*''
          (Shakespeare, *Love's Labour's Lost*, V, ii).

hyperbole. Exaggeration for the sake of emphasis or comedy, *e.g.*,

"There emerged from scores of by-streets, lanes,
and nameless turnings, innumerable people,
carrying their dinners to the bakers' shops''
          (Dickens, *A Christmas Carol*).

hypercatalectic. Describing a line of verse with an extra syllable, *e.g.*,

"Thĕ slĭngs / ănd ar̆- / rŏws ŏf / oŭtra̅ge-/ oŭs
fŏr-/ tŭne''
          (Shakespeare, *Hamlet*, III, i).

See acatalectic, catalectic *and* metre.

hysteron proteron. Reversal of normal or temporal order, *e.g.*,

"Take, eat; this is my body''
          (*St. Matthew*, ch. 26)

"Th'Antoniad, the Egyptian admiral,
With all their sixty, fly and turn the rudder''
          (Shakespeare, *Antony and Cleopatra*, III, x).

idyll. A poem, pleasing and contented in tone, on an innocent, rural subject, of the type written by the Ancient Greek poet, Theocritus. More widely, a poem conveying a feeling of calm happiness.

imagery. Figures of speech and other devices of language used to convey sensuous and imaginative impressions to the reader.

Imagism. A poetic movement and theory, flourishing *c.* 1909–14, which emphasised direct treatment of subject-matter, concreteness, extreme economy of language and the rhythm of phrases rather than the rhythm of regular metres. The principal Imagist poets were Richard Aldington, H.D. (*i.e.*, Hilda Doolittle), F. S. Flint, Amy Lowell and Ezra Pound.

imitation. In particular, the practice, commended

in the eighteenth century, of copying and adapting classical models (*e.g.*, Pope's *Imitations of Horace*). More generally, synonymous with *mimesis* (*q.v.*).

inscape. Gerard Manley Hopkins' term for the particular, unique, distinctive identity of a thing, an identity which the poet should capture in his work. *See* **instress**.

instress. Hopkins' term for the natural energy that determines an *inscape* (*q.v.*) and that maintains its existence: "the blue [of the sky] was charged with simple instress" (Hopkins' *Journal*, 1871).

intentional fallacy. A phrase coined by M. C. Beardsley and W. K. Wimsatt (1946), who argued that the "design or intention of the author is neither available nor desirable as a standard for judging the success of a work of literary art." *See* **affective fallacy** *and* **New Critics**.

interlude. In the sixteenth century a play performed in the midst of festivities. It could be farcical, romantic or religious and was sometimes indistinguishable from a *morality play* (*q.v.*). John Heywood's interludes are amongst the best-known.

internal rhyme. The rhyming of two or more words within one line of verse, *e.g.*,

"When you're lying *awake* with a dismal *headache*,
and repose is taboo'd by anxiety"
(Gilbert, *Iolanthe*).

See **rhyme**.

inversion. The reversal of normal syntax, usually by putting the verb before the subject, as in poetic language imitating Latin word-order, *e.g.*, the opening six lines of Milton's *Paradise Lost*: "Of Man's first disobedience . . . sing heavenly Muse". *See* **Latinism**.

irony. The use of words (verbal irony) or situations (situational irony) to convey the opposite of what is really meant or what might naturally be expected. It can be comic, tragic or satirical, *e.g.*, Fielding's description of Blifil as "this worthy young man" (*Tom Jones*), the remark made by Jane Austen's Mr Bennet about Mr Collins' "talent of flattering with delicacy" (*Pride and Prejudice*) and Thomas Hardy's portrayal of Jude's death in the midst of student festivities at Christminster (*Jude the Obscure*). *See* **dramatic irony**.

Johnsonian. In the literary style and manner of Dr Samuel Johnson (1709–84), *e.g.*, using weighty, well-balanced sentences and a Latinised vocabulary and expressing a pragmatic, common-sense attitude to life and literature.

Lake Poets. The English Romantic poets, Wordsworth, Coleridge and Southey, who lived in the Lake District.

lampoon. A personal satire, often malicious and coarse in tone, *e.g.*, Henry Carey's "Namby-Pamby" (a poem on the poet, Ambrose Philips). *See* **satire**.

langue. A language considered as a whole, abstract system, which all its speakers have in common. (Term used by the linguist, Ferdinand de Saussure.) *See* **parole**.

Latinism. Word, phrase, idiom or construction that imitates a Latin one. Characteristics can include sentence-inversion (*see* **inversion**), placing adjectives after and around substantives (see the first example below) and the use of many words (often learned and abstract) derived from Latin (see the second example), *e.g.*,

"I come to pluck your *berries harsh and crude*,
And with *forc'd fingers rude*
Shatter your leaves before the mellowing year"
(Milton, "Lycidas").

"A *doctrine* so *extraordinary* and so *sublime* must *inevitably* command the *veneration* of the people" (Gibbon, *Decline and Fall of the Roman Empire*).

lay. A narrative or lyrical poem recounting romantic or adventurous deeds, *e.g.*, Scott's *Lay of the Last Minstrel*.

Leavisite. Pertaining to the ideas and followers of F. R. Leavis (1895–1978), whose rigorous literary criticism was informed by a serious moral concern. *See* **great tradition**.

lexis. The vocabulary of a language, which therefore consists of lexical items (which can include words and brief phrases).

limerick. A comic five-line verse-form in anapaests (*see* **metre**), rhyming *aabba*, ideally with a surprising last line.

litotes. An understatement, particularly one that

uses the negative, often made for the purposes of irony or emphasis, *e.g.*, "Mrs Blifil was not over and above pleased with the behaviour of her husband" (Fielding, *Tom Jones*); "No little band of yet remembered names" (Wordsworth, *The Prelude*, I). *See* **meiosis**.

loose sentence. A sentence with the main clause first, followed by subordinate clauses, *e.g.*, "*There can be no doubt* that this remarkable man owed the vast influence which he exercised over his contemporaries at least as much to his gloomy egotism as to the real power of his poetry" (Macaulay, *Byron*). *See* **periodic sentence**.

lyric. A short poem of a song-like nature, expressing a single—often personal—mood. For numerous examples, *see* Palgrave's *Golden Treasury*.

macaronic. Describing comic or burlesque verse written in mixed languages or languages adapted and distorted, *e.g.*, "Charmer virumque I sing, Jack plumigeramque Arabellam" (first line of "Narrative Macaronic Verses" by Frank Sidgwick).

malapropism. A word used in the wrong sense, sometimes for comic effect, *e.g.*, "I would have her instructed in *geometry*, that she might know something of the *contagious* countries" (Mrs Malaprop in Sheridan's *The Rivals*, I, ii).

masque. A courtly entertainment, popular in the late sixteenth and early seventeenth centuries, consisting of artificial, fantastic dramatic action, dancing, songs, and elaborate costumes and settings, *e.g.*, Ben Jonson's *Masque of Oberon*.

meiosis. An understatement, often used for purposes of emphasis or comedy, *e.g.*, "A small accident had happened, which somewhat disconcerted them; and this was no other than the thief's escape"
(Fielding, *Joseph Andrews*)

"But she is in her grave, and, oh,
The difference to me!"
(Wordsworth, "She dwelt among the untrodden ways").

See **litotes**.

melodrama. Extravagant drama of heightened emotions, characterised by sentimentality and sensationalism, *e.g.*, Leopold Lewis' *The Bells*, in which Henry Irving gave a famous performance.

metaphor. A figure of speech of comparison stating an identity rather than a likeness, *i.e.*, something is said to be that which it only resembles, *e.g.*, "I fall upon the thorns of life" (Shelley, "Ode to the West Wind"); "the very honey of earthly joy" (Cowley, "The Wish").

Metaphysical Poets. Seventeenth century poets, including John Donne, George Herbert, Henry Vaughan, Richard Crashaw and Andrew Marvell, whose subject-matter was usually love or religion. Their poems contain striking imagery, wit, intense passion and powers of argument and persuasion. (Term first used by Dr Johnson, who may have been influenced by a phrase of Dryden's.)

metonymy. The application of the name of an attribute to that of the thing meant, *e.g.*, "Dickens" for "the works of Dickens"; "the Bench" for the magistrates".

metre. The measure of lines of verse, which in English is basically **accentual** (*q.v.*). Each group of syllables (usually two or three) is a **foot**. These feet of stressed syllables (marked with ΄) and unstressed syllables (marked with ˘) are often classified as follows: iambus (˘΄); trochee (΄˘); spondee (΄΄); pyrrhic (˘˘); anapaest (˘˘΄); dactyl (΄˘˘); amphibrach (˘΄˘). The number of feet in a line is indicated as follows: monometer (1); dimeter (2); trimeter (3); tetrameter (4); pentameter (5); hexameter (6); heptameter (7). An *iambic pentameter*, for example, is therefore a line of five iambic feet, *e.g.*,

"Bĕlín- / dă smiléd, / ănd áll / thĕ wŏrld / wăs gáy"
(Pope, *The Rape of the Lock*).

Metrical variation, however, is a common feature of English verse.

Miltonic. Pertaining to the work of John Milton (1608–74), with reference to his Latinised syntax and vocabulary, his blank verse, his sonnets and his Protestant theology and outlook.

mimesis. Plato's term for artistic imitation or representation, which he thought necessarily false. Aristotle saw it as a basic function of art, stating that the "objects of imitation are the actions of men". The term can also denote more particularly the direct representation of speech and action in a literary work. See **diegesis**.

miracle plays. Fourteenth and fifteenth century plays, sometimes known as Mystery Plays, consisting of dramatised episodes from the Bible, from the Creation to the Day of Judgement, acted by members of trade guilds, usually on Corpus Christi day. Cycles survive from York, Coventry, Wakefield and Chester.

mock heroic. The satirical or comic application of heroic or epic styles, conventions, situations and characters to trivial or vulgar subjects, *e.g.*, Pope's *The Rape of the Lock.*

monodrama. A dramatic work for one character or performer, *e.g.*, Tennyson's poem, "Maud".

monologue. A prose or verse composition spoken by one character or performer, either as a separate work or as part of a work, *e.g.*, Beckett's *Krapp's Last Tape.* See **dramatic monologue, monodrama** *and* **soliloquy.**

morality plays. Allegorical dramas of the late fifteenth and early sixteenth centuries, in which personified virtues and vices contend for a man's soul, *e.g.*, *Everyman.*

morpheme. The smallest linguistic unit which has a grammatical function and an independent meaning, *e.g.*, sang, bread, -ing, -ed.

mystery plays. See **miracle plays.**

myth. Story of unknown origin expressing and explaining universal and religious experience (*e.g.*, fertility and seasonal change) often by means of the deeds of a hero or god. See **Section I Classical Mythology.**

Naturalism. Originating in nineteenth century France, a literary movement that aimed at presenting the reality of life, with an emphasis on environment, objectivity and amorality. Prominent naturalistic novelists included Zola, Gissing and Bennett. See **realism** *and* **M11.**

negative capability. John Keats' phrase (in a letter, 1817) for the quality, found in such great poets as Shakespeare, "of being in uncertainties, mysteries, doubts, without any irritable reaching after fact and reason".

neo-classicism. The theory and application, particularly in the eighteenth century, of the classical values and rules of reason, order and decorum, as shown in the work of Dryden, Pope and Johnson, who emulated Homer, Virgil, Horace, Juvenal and other writers of Ancient Greece and Rome. See **Augustan** *and* **classical.**

neologism. A new word or phrase, or an old word used in a new sense, *e.g.*, "agnostic" (coined by T. H. Huxley) and "prestigious" (meaning "having prestige" instead of "juggling").

New Critics. American group of critics, including Cleanth Brooks, R. P. Blackmur, Robert Penn Warren, John Crowe Ransom and W. K. Wimsatt, who were active in the late 1930s and the 1940s and who advocated close textual analysis, free of biographical and contextual associations. See **affective fallacy** *and* **intentional fallacy.**

Newgate novels. Crime novels of the 1820s and 1830s that tended to romanticise criminals and highwaymen, *e.g.*, Bulwer Lytton's *Paul Clifford* and W. H. Ainsworth's *Rookwood.* See **M6.**

nouveau roman. Type of French novel that began in the 1950s and that rejected conventional characterisation and plot, as written by Alain Robbe-Grillet. See **anti-novel.**

novel. See **M4–M17** for definitions, types and history.

novella. A short novel, *e.g.*, Conrad's *Typhoon* and D. H. Lawrence's *The Fox.*

objective correlative. T. S. Eliot's term (in his essay on *Hamlet*, 1919) for "a set of objects, a situation, a chain of events which shall be the formula" of a particular emotion expressed in art.

octave. See **sonnet.**

ode. A lyrical poem of elaborate structure and elevated diction written to celebrate or commemorate a noble, beautiful or admirable subject or theme, *e.g.*, Keats' "Ode to a Nightingale" and Tennyson's "Ode on the Death of the Duke of Wellington." See **Pindaric Ode.**

onomatopoeia. The use or invention of words to imitate sounds, *e.g.*, "buzz", "hiss", "swish", or the imitative effect of such word usage as Tennyson's "murmuring of innumerable bees" ("Come down, O maid").

ottava rima. Eight iambic pentameters (*see* **metre**) rhyming *abababcc*, as in Byron's *Don Juan.*

oxymoron. Combination of two contradictory terms in one expression, *e.g.*, "fearful joy" (Gray) and "sweet unrest" (Keats).

palindrome. A word, sentence or verse that reads the same backwards or forwards, *e.g.*, "level", "A man, a plan, a canal—Panama."

parable. A short, often realistic story told to exemplify a doctrine or moral, as told by Christ in the New Testament, *e.g.*, "The Sower" and "The Good Samaritan".

paradox. An apparent contradiction or absurdity often designed to upset conventional opinion and to indicate a truth, *e.g.*, G. K. Chesterton's "If we are to be international we must be national" and "The subtle man is always immeasurably easier to understand than the natural man."

parataxis. Arrangement of clauses without conjunctions, *e.g.*, "After a painful struggle I yielded to my fate: I sighed as a lover, I obeyed as a son; my wound was insensibly healed by time, absence, and the habits of a new life" (Gibbon, *Autobiography*).

parody. A comic or satirical imitation of an original work or of the characteristic style of a writer or literary movement, *e.g.*, Max Beerbohm's "Scruts" (a parody of Arnold Bennett) and Henry Reed's "Chard Whitlow" (a parody of T. S. Eliot's *Four Quartets*).

parole. An actual, individual utterance of language, as distinct from *langue* (*q.v.*). (Term used by the linguist, Ferdinand de Saussure.)

paronomasia. A play on words. See **pun.**

pastoral poetry. Poetry dealing in an idealised way with rustic life, especially the lives and emotions of shepherds and shepherdesses, *e.g.*, Spenser's *Shepherd's Calendar.*

pathetic fallacy. The false belief that human emotions exist in non-human things and phenomena. Such appearances are "entirely unconnected with any real power or character in the object, and only imputed to it by us", *e.g.*, "the cruel, crawling foam" (Ruskin, *Modern Painters*, where he coined, discussed and illustrated the term, 1856).

pentameter. See **metre.**

periodic sentence. A sentence that begins with subordinate clauses and ends with the main clause, *e.g.*, "Since then the imaginary right of vengeance must be at last remitted, because it is impossible to live in perpetual hostility, and equally impossible that of two enemies, either should first think himself obliged by justice to submission, *it is surely eligible to forgive early*" (Samuel Johnson, essay in *The Rambler*). See **loose sentence.**

peripeteia. In drama, a sudden change of fortune, "the reverse of what is expected from the circumstances of the action" (Aristotle, *Poetics*), as in Sophocles' *Oedipus Tyrannus*, where the messenger, meaning to make Oedipus happy, reveals the secret of his birth, with tragic consequences.

periphrasis. Roundabout speech or circumlocution, *e.g.*, Mr Micawber's speeches in Dickens' *David Copperfield.*

persona. A character or narrator who can in some cases be thought to be the author in disguise, *e.g.*, Stephen Daedalus in Joyce's *Portrait of the Artist as a Young Man.*

personification. Representation of a thing or quality as a person, *e.g.*, "There Honour comes, a pilgrim grey" (William Collins, "Ode").

Petrarchan sonnet. See **sonnet.**

phoneme. The minimum significant sound-unit in language, either consonant-type or vowel-type, *e.g.*, "meat," "boy".

picaresque novel. A novel with a rogue as its hero, undergoing many adventures, *e.g.*, Smollett's *Peregrine Pickle.* See **M4.**

Pindaric Ode. An ode modelled on the Greek odes of Pindar (518–438 B.C.) consisting of a **strophe, antistrophe** and **epode** (qq.v.) in complex stanzas, this three-part structure often being repeated at least once, *e.g.*, Thomas Gray's "Progress of Poesy". See **ode.**

pleonasm. Using more words than are needed, either unconsciously or deliberately for emphasis, *e.g.*, 'at this moment of time" (for "now") and "most unkindest cut of all" (Shakespeare, *Julius Caesar*).

plot. The sequence or complex of connected events in a fictional narrative or drama, with (in Forster's definition in *Aspects of the Novel*, 1927) "a sense of causality" to distinguish it from *story* (*q.v.*).

poetic diction. Words, phrases and syntax prescribed specifically for poetic use, especially in the eighteenth century, and including *periphrasis* (*q.v.*) (*e.g.*, "the finny tribe" for "fish"), personification and Latinised structures and expressions.

poetic prose. Prose using such devices as rhythm, elaborate imagery, figures of speech and symbols, conventionally associated with poetry, to be found, for example, in some of George Meredith's descriptive passages in his novels.

portmanteau word. One word formed by combining two or more words, *e.g.*, "smog," a combination of "smoke" and "fog". (Term coined by Lewis Carroll in *Through the Looking-Glass*.)

poststructuralism. A development of *structuralism* (*q.v.*), which concentrates on the power of language as a creative force within itself and the indeterminate number of possibilities of meaning and interpretation. *See* **deconstruction**.

practical criticism. Exercises in the close analysis of texts, as advocated and practised by the critic and teacher I. A. Richards (in *Practical Criticism*, 1929).

prolegomenon. An introduction, sometimes of a learned nature, *e.g.*, R. B. McKerrow's *Prolegomena for the Oxford Shakespeare*.

prolepsis. Anticipatory use of an epithet, *e.g.*, "the two brothers and their murder'd man" (Keats, "Isabella") and " 'I'm killed, Sire!' " (Browning, "Incident in the French Camp").

prologue. The introductory section of a work with such functions as setting the scene, whetting the appetite of audience or reader and giving preliminary explanations, *e.g.*, the opening Chorus of Shakespeare's *Romeo and Juliet*.

prosody. The study of versification, including rhythm, rhyme and stanza forms, as in George Saintsbury's *History of English Prosody*.

pun. A play on words, *e.g.*,

"I cannot say *'whore'*:
It does ab*hor* me now I speak the word"
        (Shakespeare, *Othello*, IV ii)

"They went and *told* the sexton, and
The sexton *toll'd* the bell"
        (Thomas Hood, "Sally Brown").

pyrrhic. *See* metre.

quatrain. A four-lined **stanza** (*q.v.*).

realism. In the nineteenth century, the theory and practice of a belief that art (*e.g.*, the novel) should be a precise, truthful representation of life, associated in France with Balzac and the Goncourt brothers, amongst others. Sometimes synonymous with **naturalism** (*q.v.*).

Revenge Tragedy. Popular seventeenth century type of drama, derived from Seneca's plays (1st century A.D.), in which revenge, ghosts and terror are prominent, *e.g.*, Kyd's *The Spanish Tragedy*.

rhetorical question. A question which does not require an answer but which is put for purposes of emphasis, *e.g.*, "Were they again to advance their money on pledges which had been forfeited over and over again?" (Macaulay, "Milton").

rhyme. Identity of sound from the last stressed vowel to the end, sometimes used in conventional patterns, such as **rhyming couplets**, **sonnets** and the **Spenserian stanza** (*qq.v.*).

rhyme royal. A stanza of seven iambic pentameters rhyming *ababbcc*, used, for example, in Chaucer's *Troilus and Criseyde*. *See* **metre**.

rhyming couplet. The same as **heroic couplet** (*q.v.*), but rhyming couplets in iambic tetrameter (*not* known as heroic couplets) are also frequently used, *e.g.*, in Swift's poems. *See* **metre**.

rhythm. Regular recurrence of stress or of long or short sounds, especially in poetry, analysed by the process of **scansion**. *See* **metre**. More widely, patterns of event or motif in various literary compositions, including novels.

roman à clef. A novel about actual people disguised as fictional personages, *e.g.*, Aldous Huxley's *Point Counterpoint*.

roman-fleuve. A long series of inter-related novels, *e.g.*, Proust's *A la Recherche du temps perdu*.

romance. A term of many meanings, including a medieval poetic or prose story of chivalry and love (*e.g.*, Malory's *Morte Darthur*); later, a work dealing with adventures in a fanciful and unrealistic manner (*e.g.*, Shakespeare's *The Winter's Tale*); in modern times, a glamorous, sentimental story of love (*e.g.*, the "romantic novels" published by Mills and Boon).

Romanticism. In literature, the movement at the end of the eighteenth and the beginning of the nineteenth centuries identified with individual expression, sensibility, imagination, emotion, the love of Nature and "simple" people (such as peasants and children) and a wide variety of literary forms. In part the movement was a reaction against **neo-classicism** (*q.v.*). Leading Romantic writers in English literature were Scott, Wordsworth, Coleridge, Byron, Shelley and Keats.

rondeau. A form of verse, originally French, in which lines are repeated at regular intervals. A typical pattern is *aabba*; *aab* and refrain; *aabba* and refrain, all octosyllabic. Written by some minor nineteenth century English poets, *e.g.*, Austin Dobson.

run-on line. *See* **enjambment**.

saga. An ancient Icelandic or Scandinavian prose tale of heroes and great deeds, mostly oral in origin.

samizdat. Self-published, typescript, underground literature, in the former Soviet Union, expressing opinions unacceptable to the government.

sapphics. A classical, quantitative metre consisting of three longer lines and one shorter.

satire. Prose or verse composition ridiculing and criticising vice and folly by such means as **irony** (*q.v.*), sarcasm, the **mock-heroic** (*q.v.*), **parody** (*q.v.*) and invective. John Dryden said that "the true end of satire is the amendment of vices by correction" (*Absalom and Achitophel*, "To the Reader"). Famous examples include Swift's *Modest Proposal* and Pope's *Dunciad*.

scansion. The process of analysing **metre** (*q.v.*).

semiology. The science of studying signs, especially those used in systems of communication (including objects, gestures and clothes as well as language). *See* **semiotics**.

semiotics. The study of patterns of behaviour in communication, particularly through the use of linguistics. More broadly, synonymous with *semiology* (*q.v.*).

sensation novel. Mid-nineteenth century English novels of crime, detection and passion, with an atmosphere of excitement, suffering and suspense, *e.g.*, M. E. Braddon's *Lady Audley's Secret*. *See* **M9**.

sestet. *See* **sonnet**.

sestina. Elaborate verse-form of six six-line stanzas ending with a three-line **envoi** (*q.v.*).

Shakespearean sonnet. *See* **sonnet**.

signified and **signifier.** Saussure's terms for the concept and its oral or written verbal "sound image", indissolubly but arbitrarily connected to each other.

simile. A figure of speech in which two things or actions are likened to each other, usually by means of "as" or "like", *e.g.*,

"Your face, my Thane, is as a book where men
May read strange matters"
        (Shakespeare, *Macbeth*, I, v)

"From the earth thou springest
Like a cloud of fire"
        (Shelley, "To a Skylark").

sjuzet. *See* **fabula**.

soliloquy. A solo utterance often by a character in a play talking to himself or thinking aloud, as if there were no audience, *e.g.*, Hamlet's "To be or not to be . . .".

sonnet. Poem of fourteen iambic pentameters. The two main forms are the Petrarchan (after Petrarch, 1304–74), consisting of an **octave** (eight lines usually rhyming *abbaabba*) stating the theme and a **sestet** (six lines using different rhymes in various patterns) commenting on the theme or modifying it; the Shakespearean, consisting of three quatrains (usually rhyming *ababcdcdefef*) presenting the theme and a final **rhyming couplet** (*gg*) summarising or clinching the theme. *See* **metre**, **quatrain** *and* **rhyming couplet**.

Spenserian stanza. Eight iambic pentameters followed by one iambic hexameter (or **alexandrine**, *q.v.*) rhyming *ababbcbcc*, as used in Spenser's *Faerie Queene*. *See* **metre**.

spondee. *See* **metre**.

sprung rhythm. Gerard Manley Hopkins' metrical system, dependent on measuring stresses and not on regular numbers of feet and syllables; hence, like the rhythms of common speech, written prose, music and folk poetry.

stanza. A formal arrangement of a group of lines of poetry, usually in a rhyming pattern.

stichomythia. Interchange of short, one-line speeches in dramatic verse, *e.g.*, some of the dialogue between King Richard and Queen Elizabeth in Shakespeare's *King Richard III*, IV, iv.

story. A tale, or the general, complete action of a narrative work, ranging more widely than the **plot** (*q.v.*).

stream of consciousness. Term coined by the philosopher William James (1890) to denote the unending, formless flow of human thoughts and emotions. Some novelists, *e.g.*, James Joyce and Virginia Woolf, have conveyed this "stream" by various techniques (*e.g.*, loose syntax and light punctuation) in order to explore the consciousness of their characters.

strophe. The first section of the Greek **chorus** or the **Pindaric Ode** (*q.v.*).

structuralism. As applied to literature, a complex form of textual analysis concentrating on formal linguistic and thematic patternings, as practised, for example, by Roland Barthes.

sub-plot. A plot of lesser importance but sometimes used as a parallel or foil to the main plot, *e.g.*, the Falstaff-Prince Hal sub-plot in Shakespeare's *King Henry IV, Part 1*. See **plot**.

syllabic verse. Poetry written in metre measured by the number of syllables in each line, *e.g.*, some of W. H. Auden's later verse.

syllepsis. A figure of speech in which one word has the same syntactical relationship to two or more other words but different meanings, *e.g.*, The nymph may "lose her heart, or necklace, at a ball" (Pope, *The Rape of the Lock*). Sometimes synonymous with **zeugma** (*q.v.*).

symbolism. Artistic movement of the 1890s, mostly originating amongst French writers (*e.g.*, Mallarmé and Valéry), using mystical, occult and magical images and musical, evocative language. More widely, the use of objects, actions, scenes and structures to represent or suggest significant themes and ideas in a literary work, *e.g.*, the dust heaps and the Thames in Dickens' *Our Mutual Friend* and the rose, the tower, Troy and swans in Yeats' poetry.

synaesthesia. Combination of different sense impressions, as described in Baudelaire's sonnet, "Correspondances". They are often evoked in a single phrase, *e.g.*, "dark music" (Isaac Rosenberg, "Louse Hunting") and "squealing light" (Edith Sitwell, "Gold Coast Customs").

syncope. The cutting short or contraction of a word, especially in poetic usage, *e.g.*, "e'er" for "ever".

synecdoche. A figure of speech in which the part represents the whole or the whole represents the part, *e.g.*, "the multitude of Coketown, generically called 'the Hands'" (*i.e.*, the factory-workers, Dickens, *Hard Times*) and "England" for "the English cricket team".

tercet. A three-lined stanza, particularly as used in **terza rima** (*q.v.*).

terza rima. Verse-form of three-lined stanzas rhyming *aba, bcb, cdc*, etc., as used in Dante's *Divina Commedia* and Shelley's "Ode to the West Wind".

tetrameter. *See* **metre**.

theme. The central idea or topic of a literary work.

threnody. A poem of lamentation. *See* **dirge** *and* **elegy**.

touchstones. Criteria of excellence in poetry provided by the "lines and expressions of the great masters", *e.g.*, Homer, Dante, Shakespeare and Milton (Matthew Arnold's term and definition, "The Study of Poetry," 1880).

tragedy. "An imitation of some action that is important, entire, and of proper magnitude ... effecting through pity and terror the correction and refinement of such passions' (Aristotle, *Poetics*). A drama that ends sadly, especially with the downfall of a flawed hero *See* **catharsis, hamartia** *and* **peripeteia**.

tragi-comedy. A drama that mixes elements of tragedy and comedy, *e.g.*, Shakespeare's *Measure for Measure*.

trimeter. *See* **metre**.

triolet. Verse-form of eight lines and two rhymes, in which the fourth line repeats the first and the eighth line repeats the second, popular with some late nineteenth century minor poets, including Austin Dobson.

triplet. Three rhyming lines, usually iambic pentameters, sometimes used for variation or emphasis in a poem of **rhyming** or **heroic couplets**.

trochee. *See* **metre**.

trope. A figure of speech in general.

unities. Theory partly deriving from Aristotle's *Poetics* and fully formulated by Castelvetro (1505–71) that a drama should conform to the three unities of Action (*i.e.*, there must be no digressions), Time (*i.e.*, the action in performance should correspond as nearly as possible to the duration of the action in real life) and Place (*i.e.*, its scene should not change).

ut pictura poesis. "As a picture, so a poem", *i.e.*, "a poem is like a picture," a much-discussed formulation by the Latin poet, Horace, in his *Art of Poetry*.

vers de société. Light, elegant verse dealing with people and behaviour in polite society, *e.g.*, the poems of W. M. Praed.

vers libre. The same as **free verse** (*q.v.*).

verse. Originally a metrical line; more commonly, a stanza or versification and verse composition in general.

villanelle. Verse-form of five **tercets** (*q.v.*) and one **quatrain** (*q.v.*) with two rhymes. The first line ends the second and fourth tercet; the third line ends the first, third and fifth tercets; the first and third lines then end the final quatrain, *e.g.*, William Empson's "Missing Dates."

zeugma. A figure of speech in which a single epithet or verb is applied to two substantives but is appropriate to only one of them, *e.g.*, "See Pan with flocks, with fruits Pomona crowned" (Pope, *Windsor Forest*). Sometimes used to mean the same as **syllepsis** (*q.v.*).

III. SPECIAL TOPICS

FICTION IN THE 1990s

Introduction

When we consider fiction in the 1990s, the first fact to bear in mind is that well over 7,000 titles, including reprints, translations and new editions, are published annually in the United Kingdom. About 3,500 of these are new works. Among these are many bestsellers, which receive little or no critical attention. Literary historians and critics discuss "serious" novels; it is these works of fiction that receive literary awards and prizes and that eventually appear on school and college syllabuses. Meanwhile, the modern authors who are read most widely include Jeffrey Archer, Jean M. Auel, Barbara Taylor Bradford, Agatha Christie, Jackie Collins, Catherine Cookson, Jilly Cooper, Frederick Forsyth, Dick Francis, Arthur Hailey, Jack Higgins, Stephen King, Robert Ludlum, Rosamund Pilcher, Terry Pratchett, Sidney Sheldon, Wilbur Smith, and Sue Townsend. These popular novels, which make immense fortunes for their authors, are of various types: thrillers and detective stories, tales of adventure, espionage, sex and horror, historical romances, comedies, and science fiction. They are easy to read and they emphasise intrigue, suspense, action and immediacy of emotion rather than the complexities of psychology and morality that are traditionally the marks of the "serious" novel. "Graphic novels" (*i.e.*, stories in the form of comic strips) are increasingly popular. Recent examples are Art Spiegelman's *Maus* (1986) and *Maus II: And Here My Troubles Began* (1991) and Frank Miller's *Batman: The Dark Knight Returns* (1986). All these kinds of fiction constitute an important sociological phenomenon since they indicate not only popular taste but also commercial factors in the world of authors and publishers.

Upsurge in Serious Fiction

At the same time, there has been a boom in serious fiction in the past few years. This may have been due partly to the proliferation of literary prizes—over 200 of these now exist in Britain and Ireland. The Booker Prize is especially well publicised and its award is an annually televised event. In 1994, it went to James Kelman's *How Late It Was, How Late*. As a result of the award of the 1994 Nobel Prize for Literature to Kenzaburo Oe, the Japanese novelist and short story writer, the sales in Britain of his fiction (*e.g.*, *The Silent Cry*) immediately increased. It is debatable whether the various conditions attached to the award of prizes for novels have any influence on technique and content. But it is possible that the attention paid to literary theory in the past decade by academic critics and teachers has had an effect on modern novelists and their readers. There has been widespread discussion of narrative, structure and the ways in which language works. A prominent Italian scholar in this field is Umberto Eco, whose novel, *The Name of the Rose* (1983), a mystery story set in a medieval monastery, was composed with careful, self-conscious artistry; it was a highly successful book, which was filmed in 1986 with Sean Connery in the leading role. This novel was followed by *Foucault's Pendulum* (1989), another complex, fascinating narrative.

Another Italian writer whose innovatory style has been widely admired is the late Italo Calvino, whose *If on a Winter's Night a Traveller* (1981) is recognised as an outstanding achievement in contemporary fiction; his *Under the Jaguar Sun* appeared here in 1992. As well as the novels by Oe, Eco and Calvino, other translated works have made an impact, in different ways widening horizons, which have tended to remain narrow in the English novel. Recent examples, with the nationalities of the authors and the dates of publication of the English translations in parentheses, include Isabel Allende's *The Infinite Plan* (Chilean; 1993), Marguerite Duras's *Yann Andrea Steiner* (French; 1994),

Carlos Fuentes' *The Orange Tree* (Mexican; 1994), Günter Grass's *The Call of the Toad* (German; 1992), Bohumil Hrabel's *Cutting It Short* and *The Little Town Where Time Stood Still* (Czech; 1993), Vlady Kociancich's *The Last Days of William Shakespeare* (Argentinian; 1990), Milan Kundera's *Immortality* (Czech; 1991), Mario Vargas Llosa's *Conversation in the Cathedral* (Peruvian; 1993) Gabriel Garcia Marques' *Strange Pilgrims* (short stories; Colombian; 1993), Milorad Pavic's *Dictionary of the Khazars* (Yugoslav; 1989), Georges Perec's *Life: A User's Manual* (French; 1988) and *A Void* (1994), Abel Posse's *The Dogs of Paradise* (Spanish; 1990), Christoph Ransmayer's *The Last World* (Austrian; 1990), Alina Reyes' *The Butcher* (French; 1991), Jean Rouaud's *Fields of Glory* (French; 1992; Prix Goncourt winner), Françoise Sagan's *Evasion* (French; 1993), José Saramago's *The Year of the Death of Ricardo Reis* (Portuguese; 1992), Joseph Skvorecky's *The Republic of Whores* (Czech; 1994). and Banana Yoshimoto's *N. P.* (Japanese; 1994).

It is impossible to make satisfactory generalisations about such a variety of novels, but it can be said that many of them, by English standards, are unconventional or even daring in technique (those by Perec and Pavic, for example) and subject-matter (Ransmayer imagines Ovid in exile in 8 AD and in modern times). Others, particularly those from South America, dramatise and illuminate unfamiliar social and political issues (*e.g.*, the novel by Vlady Kociancich). The experimental and imaginative treatment of subject-matter in a good deal of South American fiction has frequently been termed "magic realism".

Recent Commonwealth and American Fiction

Much stimulating fiction has been produced in past and present Commonwealth countries by such writers as V. S. Naipaul and Wilson Harris (West Indies), Robertson Davies, Mordecai Richler and Margaret Atwood (Canada), Anita Desai (India), Patrick White and Peter Carey (Australia), Chinua Achebe and Buchi Emecheta (Nigeria), and Nadine Gordimer (South Africa). Major American novelists have continued to produce challenging work: John Barth's *The Last Voyage of Somebody the Sailor* (1991), Saul Bellow's *Something To Remember Me By* (1992), E. L. Doctorow's *The Waterworks* (1994), Joseph Heller's *Closing Time* (1994), John Irving's *A Son of the Circus* (1994), Norman Mailer's *Harlot's Ghost* (1991), Thomas Pynchon's *Vineland* (1990), Philip Roth's *Operation Shylock: A Confession* (1993), John Updike's *Brazil* (1994), Gore Vidal's *Live from Golgotha* (1992), and Kurt Vonnegut's *Hocus Pocus* (1990). Other recent American fiction includes Robert James Waller's *The Bridges of Madison County* (1993) Jeffrey Eugenides' *The Virgin Suicides* (1993) and Nicholson Baker's *The Fermata* (1994).

United Kingdom Fiction

When we turn to fiction in the UK, we see that many interesting novels come from writers writing in English but not of English descent. The most controversial example is Salman Rushdie's *The Satanic Verses* (1988), which provoked world-wide anger among Moslems, who considered it blasphemous. His latest book, *East, West* (1994), is a collection of short stories. Rushdie made his reputation with *Midnight's Children*, which won the Booker Prize in 1981 and the "Booker of Bookers" in 1993. Kazuo Ishiguro's novels include *An Artist of the Floating World* (which won the Whitbread Book of the Year award in 1986) and *The Remains of the Day* (Booker Prize, 1989). Timothy Mo's *Sour Sweet* was awarded the Hawthornden Prize in 1982; *An Insular Possession* came out in 1986. Hanif Kureishi's first novel, *The Buddha of Suburbia*, was published in 1990 (televised 1993). Ahdaf Soueif's *In the Eye of the Sun* (1992), Ben Okri's *Songs of Enchantment* (1993) and Vikram Seth's *A Suitable*

Boy (1993) are other notable examples.

Some long-established English novelists continued to produce significant work: Anthony Powell, William Golding, Kingsley Amis, John Wain, Graham Greene, Iris Murdoch, Muriel Spark, Anthony Burgess, Margaret Drabble, Beryl Bainbridge and others all wrote novels in the past few years, as reference to **M15–17** will show. Among the younger generation, Julian Barnes first came to notice with *Metroland* (1980). His subsequent novels include *Flaubert's Parrot* (1984), which is like a collection of reflective essays on the 19th century French novelist; *Staring at the Sun* (1986), *A History of the World in 10½ Chapters* (1989), *Talking It Over* (1991), and *The Porcupine* (1992). D. M. Thomas became famous with the publication of *The White Hotel* (1981), which combines the themes of psychoanalysis and the Holocaust in a dazzling display of styles and with some direct and vivid description. Other novels of his, also original in form, are *Ararat* (1983), *Swallow* (1984), *Sphinx* (1986), *Summit* (1987), *Lying Together* (1990), *Flying in to Love* (1992) *Pictures at an Exhibition* (1993) and *Eating Pavlova* (1994). Martin Amis, who achieved instant success with *The Rachel Papers* (1973), went on to write *Dead Babies* (1975), *Success* (1978), *Other People* (1981), *Money* (1984), *Einstein's Monsters* (1987), *London Fields* (1989), *Time's Arrow* (1991) and *The Information* (1995). The striking feature of his work is linguistic and structural virtuosity (*e.g.*, the reversal of time in *Time's Arrow*), revealing human behaviour and social attitudes in the contemporary world in startling prose.

Two writers of novels and short stories with the power to disturb readers with their perception of the darker and more macabre aspects of life are Angela Carter (1940–92) and Ian McEwen. One of Angela Carter's more remarkable books is *Nights at the Circus* (1984); others are *The Passion of New Eve* (1977), *The Bloody Chamber* (1979), *Black Venus* (1985), *Wise Children* (1991) and *American Ghosts and Old World Wonders* (1993). Ian McEwen's books include *The Cement Garden* (1978), *The Comfort of Strangers* (1981; filmed in 1990, with a screenplay by Harold Pinter), *The Child in Time* (1987), *The Innocent* (1990), *Black Dogs* (1992) and *The Daydreamer* (children's stories; 1994). A. N. Wilson is a prolific writer of fiction, biography, criticism and miscellaneous journalism. His novels include *The Sweets of Pimlico* (1977), *Unguarded Hours* (1978), *Lead Kindly Light* (1979), *The Healing Art* (1980), *Who was Oswald Fish?* (1981), *Wise Virgin* (1982), *Scandal* (1983), *Gentlemen in England* (1985), *Incline Our Hearts* (1988), *A Bottle in the Smoke* (1990), *Daughters of Albion* (1991) and *The Vicar of Sorrows* (1993). In contrast to many of the novelists surveyed so far, Wilson is traditional in approach, writing comic, entertaining novels, reminiscent of those by Evelyn Waugh.

Another novelist whose work has something of a conventional form is William Boyd: *A Good Man in Africa* (1981), his highly successful first novel, has been followed by *An Ice-Cream War* (1982), *Stars and Bars* (1984), *The New Confessions* (1987), *Brazzaville Beach* (1990) and *The Blue Afternoon* (1993). The innovative novels of Peter Ackroyd, characterised by literary pastiche and evocation of the past, include *The Great Fire of London* (1982), *The Last Testament of Oscar Wilde* (1983), *Hawksmoor* (1985), *Chatterton* (1987), *First Light* (1989), *English Music* (1992) *The House of Doctor Dee* (1993) and *Dan Leno and the Limehouse Golem* (1994). Basing her story on her own experiences as a young married woman in Venezuela, Lisa St. Aubin di Teran wrote *Keepers of the House* (1982). Her subsequent novels include *The Slow Train to Milan* (1983), *The Tiger* (1984), *The Bay of Silence* (1986), *Black Idol* (1987), *Joanna* (1990) and *Nocturne* (1992). Fay Weldon, a versatile and combative author, writes entertainingly, putting the woman's point of view, at a time when feminist literary and cultural criticism has become influential. Thanks partly to a memorable television adaptation (and a 1989 film), *The Life and Loves of a She-Devil* (1984), a fantastic and disturbing serio-comedy, has enjoyed wide popularity. Her *Affliction* appeared in 1993. Another feminist writer is Jeanette Winterson, whose first novel, *Oranges Are Not the Only Fruit* (1985), is a partly autobiographical account of her childhood in a strict, evangelical household. Her other novels are *Boating for Beginners* (1986), *The Passion* (1987), *Sexing the Cherry* (1989) *Written on*

the Body (1992) and *Art and Lies* (1994). In quiet vein, Anita Brookner's *Hotel du Lac* (1984), which won the Booker Prize, sensitively conveys the feelings of a single woman involved in a disappointing love affair. Her other novels include *A Family Romance* (1993) and *A Private View* (1994). A notable event of 1993 was the twentieth anniversary of Virago Books, the publishers of women's writing. We turn now to some authors who cannot easily be classified as either "popular" or "serious", to use these imprecise terms. Richard Adams' *Watership Down* (1972) made him a bestselling author on a huge scale; he subsequently wrote *Shardik* (1975), *The Plague Dogs* (1977), *The Girl on a Swing* (1980), *Maia* (1984) and *Traveller* (1989). One of the most subtle thriller writers, John Le Carré, who made his name with *The Spy Who Came in from the Cold* (1963), continues to produce his scrupulously crafted books. The most recent are *The Honourable Schoolboy* (1982), *The Little Drummer Girl* (1983), *A Perfect Spy* (1986), *The Russia House* (1989) *The Secret Pilgrim* (1991) and *The Night Manager* (1993). Connoisseurs of the detective story admire the work of Peter Dickinson, Dick Francis, P. D. James (who was given a Life Peerage in the 1991 New Year's Honours List), H. R. F. Keating and Ruth Rendell.

One continuing trend is the writing of sequels to novels of the past, Susan Hill's *Mrs de Winter* (a sequal to Daphne du Maurier's *Rebecca*) was a sucess in 1993. 1994 titles include Emma Tennant's *An Unequal Marriage* (*Pride and Prejudice*) and Suleika Dawson's *The Forsytes* (*The Forsyte Saga*). Novels by celebrities in other fields appeared in 1994: Naomi Campbell's *Swan*, Martina Navratilova and Liz Nickles's *The Total Zone*, and Tim Renton's *The Dangerous Edge* are examples. Other notable novels of 1994 were Stephen Fry's *The Hippopotamus*, Alan Hollinghurst's *The Folding Star*, and Hilary Mantel's *A Change of Climate*.

A Prolific Scene

In 1993, twenty "Best Young British Novelists" were chosen by Salman Rushdie, A. S. Byatt, Bill Buford and John Mitchinson, the Marketing Director of Waterstone's bookshops: Iain Banks, Louis de Bernières, Anne Bilson, Tibor Fischer, Esther Freud, Alan Hollinghurst, Kazuo Ishiguro, A. L. Kennedy, Philip Kerr, Hanif Kureishi, Adam Lively, Adam Mars-Jones, Candia McWilliam, Lawrence Norfolk, Ben Okri, Caryl Phillips, Will Self, Nicholas Shakespeare, Helen Simpson and Jeanette Winterson.

Fiction today is probably more prolific and varied than it has ever been. In addition to the writers just considered, many more are worthy of inclusion—for example, Penelope Fitzgerald, Margaret Forster, Penelope Lively, Brian Moore, P. H. Newby, V. S. Pritchett, Simon Raven, William Trevor and Mary Wesley. But no particular English novelists seem to predominate in the current literary scene, though when we are so close to so many different books it is difficult to see things in proportion.

THE PLAYS OF SHAKESPEARE

Introduction

Shakespeare's plays are as alive and popular today as they have ever been with numerous productions by the Royal Shakespeare Company in Stratford-on-Avon and London, at the National Theatre, and at many theatres in all parts of the United Kingdom. Recent films include Franco Zeffirelli's *Hamlet* (1991) and Kenneth Branagh's *King Henry V* (1989) and *Much Ado About Nothing* (1993). Star-studded productions have been broadcast on BBC Radio 3: *Hamlet* (1992), *Romeo and Juliet* (1993), and *King Lear* (1994). Many different, excellent editions are in print (the Oxford *Complete Works* (1988), for example, radically reconsidered textual matters), critical controversies are keenly pursued, and the discoveries in 1989 of remains of the Rose and Globe theatres in London added significantly to our knowledge of the Elizabethan theatre.

Life and Background

William Shakespeare, the third child and eldest son of John and Mary Shakespeare, was born in

April 1564 in Stratford-on-Avon, where his father was a prominent citizen. He may have attended the grammar school in the town. In 1582, he married Ann Hathaway. They had three children: Susanna (b. 1583), and twins, Hamnet and Judith (b. 1585). Little is known about Shakespeare's youth, but in the early 1590s he established himself in London as an actor, poet and playwright. After about twenty years in the world of the London theatre, he seems to have retired to Stratford-on-Avon, where he died on 23 April 1616.

Shakespeare wrote and acted in a period of remarkable dramatic creativity. Among his contemporaries and near-contemporaries were Christopher Marlowe, Thomas Kyd, Ben Jonson, John Webster, John Ford, Francis Beaumont and John Fletcher. The London theatres at that time included the Rose, the Swan, the Globe and the Blackfriars, in which several actors' companies performed—Shakespeare was a member of the Lord Chamberlain's Men (later, the King's Men). The principal actors of the time were Richard Burbage (who acted the part of Hamlet, among many other Shakespearean roles), Will Kemp (a comedian, who acted Dogberry), Edward Alleyn (famous in Marlowe roles), and Richard Tarlton.

Publication and Chronology of the Plays

No authorial manuscripts of Shakespeare's plays exist although some scholars contend that part of the manuscript of *Sir Thomas More*, a late sixteenth-century play of unknown authorship, is in his hand. Eighteen of his plays were printed in separate Quarto volumes in his lifetime; a nineteenth, *Othello*, appeared in 1622. A few of these are called "Bad Quartos" because they print texts that are usually thought to be corrupt. *Romeo and Juliet* and *Hamlet* were printed in both "Bad" and "Good" quartos. In 1623, John Heminges and Henry Condell, two of Shakespeare's fellow-actors, collected thirty-six of his plays in the so-called First Folio, "truly set forth, according to the first Original." They grouped the plays into three categories: Comedies, Histories and Tragedies. They omitted *Pericles* and *The Two Noble Kinsmen*, which were both partly written by Shakespeare. Editorial problems arise when discrepancies occur between the Quarto and Folio versions of a play (*e.g., King Lear*) and when Shakespeare is thought to have collaborated with other playwrights (*e.g.,* in the two omitted plays and in *King Henry VI, Part 1* and *King Henry VIII*). Some editors and scholars have refined the three groups that Heminges and Condell made in the First Folio and have put some of the plays into more precise sub-groups. These are the "romantic comedies" (*The Merchant of Venice, Much Ado about Nothing, As You Like It,* and *Twelfth Night*); the "problem comedies" (*All's Well that Ends Well, Measure for Measure* and *Troilus and Cressida*); the "Roman Plays" (*Titus Andronicus, Julius Caesar, Antony and Cleopatra* and *Coriolanus*); and the "Romances" (*Pericles, The Winter's Tale, Cymbeline* and *The Tempest*).

The exact chronology of Shakespeare's plays cannot be determined because of the lack of evidence about their dates of composition but most scholars would agree that they could be roughly grouped as follows. The letters, C, H and T in brackets denote Comedy, History or Tragedy.

1592–4: *King Henry VI, Parts 1, 2, and 3* (H); *King Richard III* (H); *The Comedy of Errors* (C); *The Two Gentlemen of Verona* (C); *The Taming of the Shrew* (C); *Titus Andronicus* (T); *Love's Labour's Lost* (C).

1594–7: *Romeo and Juliet* (T); *King Richard II* (H); *A Midsummer Night's Dream* (C); *King John* (H); *The Merchant of Venice* (C).

1597–1600: *King Henry IV, Parts 1 and 2* (H); *King Henry V* (H); *Much Ado About Nothing* (C); *The Merry Wives of Windsor* (C); *As You Like It* (C); *Julius Caesar* (T); *Troilus and Cressida* (T).

1600–08: *Hamlet* (T); *Twelfth Night* (C); *Measure for Measure* (C); *All's Well That Ends Well* (C); *Othello* (T); *King Lear* (T); *Macbeth* (T); *Timon of Athens* (T); *Antony and Cleopatra* (T); *Coriolanus* (T).

After 1608: *Pericles* (C); *Cymbeline* (C); *The Winter's Tale* (C); *The Tempest* (C); *King Henry VIII* (H); *The Two Noble Kinsmen* (T).

It can be seen that up to 1600 Shakespeare wrote mostly comedies and histories (though *Romeo and*

Juliet is one exception) and that his great tragedies appeared in the following eight years or so. As already noted, the first four plays in the post-1608 group are often called Romances. This term is used to denote their themes of loss, reunion and reconciliation and their use of "fantastic" elements. Some commentators have seen possible autobiographical significance in the different phases of Shakespeare's career but it is likely that changes in taste, literary fashion and theatrical conditions were also influential.

Form and Style

With the exception of *Much Ado about Nothing* and *The Merry Wives of Windsor*, Shakespeare's plays are written mainly in blank verse (*see* Glossary of Literary Terms **M18**). He also uses rhyme (especially to round off scenes, to convey axioms and moral advice and for songs). As time went on, he tended to use less rhyme and he developed more complex and varied blank verse. He generally uses prose for the speech of lower-class people (such as servants) and for reports of off-stage events, letters, and rapid exposition (*e.g.,* the three gentlemen's account of the identification of Perdita in *The Winter's Tale*, Act 5, Scene 2). His vocabulary of 20,000 words ranges from the learned to the vulgar and from the grand to the simple, often in juxtaposition (as in "...my hand will rather / The multitudinous seas incarnadine / Making the green one red" in *Macbeth*, Act 2, Scene 2). An outstanding feature of Shakespeare's language is his use of word-play and imagery, which can sometimes reveal important themes in the drama (as, for example, images of sickness and disease in *Hamlet*). Soliloquies are important (*see* **M23**) for the revelation of character and motive, especially in the tragedies (for example, those spoken by Brutus in *Julius Caesar*, Hamlet and Macbeth).

The plays vary in length, from *The Comedy of Errors* (which is the shortest, with 1,778 lines) to *Hamlet* (the longest, with 3,931 lines). Many of them are "mixed" in action, containing subplots (as in *King Henry IV, Parts 1 and 2*) and *King Lear*) and both comic and tragic elements (*e.g.,* the porter in *Macbeth* and the melancholy expressed in *Twelfth Night*). They can also freely range in place and time (*e.g.,* Egypt and Rome in *Antony and Cleopatra* and the sixteen years that elapse in *The Winter's Tale*). The plays were often not divided into Acts and Scenes when they were first printed and stage-directions were minimal, and so the form in which we read the plays is largely the work of later editors. The convention is division into five Acts, with a climactic point reached at the end of Act 3. Most editors modernise the spelling and punctuation of the Quarto and Folio texts.

Shakespeare used various sources for his plays. Holinshed's *Chronicles* (1577), for example, supplied him with material for the Histories, *King Lear, Macbeth* and *Cymbeline* and he drew on Sir Thomas North's translation of Plutarch's *Lives* (1579) for the Roman plays. He sometimes combined sources, as in *A Midsummer Night's Dream*, where he seems to have used Plutarch, Ovid, Lucius Apuleius's *Golden Ass*, Chaucer, Spenser, Robert Greene and others. But he always transforms this material into his own imaginative creations.

Ten Favourite Plays

1. *Romeo and Juliet*

Written in 1594 or 1595, this tragedy was immediately popular, as shown by its appearance in Quarto editions in 1597, 1599 and 1609 (when two were published). The background to the play is the enmity between the Montague and Capulet families. Romeo, a Montague, falls in love with Juliet, a Capulet, and secretly marries her. Through a series of tragic happenings and misunderstandings, Romeo, who thinks the drugged Juliet is dead, poisons himself. Consequently, she stabs herself. But the feuding families are reconciled over the dead bodies of the young lovers. A notable feature of the play is Shakespeare's use of a Chorus, who at the outset tells us that the "pair of star-crossed lovers" will meet their deaths and that this event, originating in the family feud, "is now the two-hours' traffic of our stage." The lyrical speeches of love and Mercutio's description of Queen Mab are celebrated passages of poetry. The Nurse is a vivid flesh-and-blood character who provides a down-to-earth contrast to the idealistic young lovers.

2. A Midsummer Night's Dream

This play was written at about the same time as Romeo and Juliet and printed as a Quarto in 1600. It is a comedy of love and misunderstanding set in a wood near Athens. Three plots are blended: the confusions experienced by four young lovers (Lysander, Hermia, Demetrius and Helena); the comic doings of Bottom, the weaver, and his fellow workmen; and the quarrel between Oberon and Titania, the Fairy King and Queen. These plots are framed by the nuptial ceremonies of Theseus and Hippolyta. Puck, the mischievous sprite, is an important agent in the action and speaks the Epilogue, which delicately indicates the dreamlike qualities of the play. As in Romeo and Juliet, musical, romantic poetry abounds (e.g., Oberon's "I know a bank where the wild thyme blows" and the Fairies' song, "You spotted snakes with double tongue").

3. The Merchant of Venice

Probably written in 1596 or 1597, the play had "been divers times acted by the Lord Chamberlain his servants" before its publication as a Quarto in 1600. In order to lend money to his friend Bassanio, Antonio, the Merchant of Venice, borrows 3,000 ducats from Shylock, the Jew, agreeing to sacrifice a pound of his flesh if he cannot repay the loan. Bassanio needs the money to go to Belmont to try to win the hand of Portia. His mission is successful and subsequently Portia, disguised as a male lawyer, defeats Shylock's attempt to claim his "pound of flesh" from Antonio. Shakespeare's characterisation of Shylock is complex, since he is seen as both a cruel usurer and a man whose humanity transcends a racial stereotype ("If you prick us, do we not bleed?" as he himself asks). Portia has the independence and teasing wit that typify several Shakespearean heroines. The device of her man's disguise reminds us that only men and boys were allowed to act at that time (and also see the use of this device in Twelfth Night, **M28**).

4. King Henry IV, Parts 1 and 2

These plays were written in 1597 and 1598 and were published as Quartos in 1598 and 1600. In both, the King (who himself was seen leading a rebellion in King Richard II) is contending with rebellion from dissident noblemen and is ultimately successful through battle in maintaining his regal authority. His son, Prince Hal (later King Henry V), consorts with disreputable companions, the chief of whom is Sir John Falstaff, the fat and cowardly knight who is one of the most famous of all Shakespeare's characters (he reappears in The Merry Wives of Windsor). The Prince has resolved, however, to reform and to renounce his friends. Loyalty (of subject to monarch and son to father) and honour, considered in various aspects, are underlying themes. The plays combine serious history, humorous and sardonic comments and events, and occasional poignancy. Besides Falstaff, the Prince and the King, the striking characters are Hotspur (in Part 1), Mistress Quickly, and Justice Shallow (in Part 2).

5. Hamlet

Three versions exist of the play, which was probably written in 1600: Quartos of 1603 and 1604 and the Folio text. It is basically a "revenge tragedy" but its profundity and ambiguities arise from Hamlet's prolonged hesitations and reflections concerning the revenge he has been urged to take by the Ghost of his father, crystallised in his soliloquy, "To be or not to be". Fascinating interpretative problems include Hamlet's "madness", his not killing the King (his father's murderer) when at prayer, his treatment of Ophelia, and the scene of the "play within the play". These issues, along with Shakespeare's prolific invention of varied incidents, speeches and characters (e.g., Claudius, the Queen, Ophelia, Polonius, Horatio and the First Gravedigger) have made the play perennially and universally popular. Above all, the character of Hamlet continues to intrigue us, perhaps because "it is we who are Hamlet," as William Hazlitt said.

6. Twelfth Night

It seems as if Shakespeare wrote the play in 1601, perhaps for a performance on Twelfth Night (6 January) that year. In this romantic comedy, which is tinged with sadness, Viola, disguised as a man, falls in love with her employer, Orsino, the Duke of Illyria, who is in love with Olivia. Malvolio, Olivia's Puritan steward, is tricked into believing that she is in love with him. Throughout these and other misunderstandings, runs a vein of deeply-felt love (as in Viola's self-description of a woman who "sat like Patience on a monument, / Smiling at grief" and in one of Feste's sad songs, "O mistress mine") and the tensions between appearance and reality. Broader humour is supplied by Sir Toby Belch and Sir Andrew Aguecheek.

7. Othello

Performed on 1 November 1604 before King James I in the Banqueting House at Whitehall, the play was probably written in the preceding twelve months. It is a tragedy based on the consuming power of jealousy and on the presence of apparently "motiveless malignity" (to use the words of Coleridge). Othello, a Moor, convinced by Iago that Desdemona, his wife, is guilty of infidelity with Cassio, smothers her in her bed. On discovering her innocence, he kills himself with a sword. Shakespeare's use of a compressed time-scheme, his portrayal of a black man as a noble and yet susceptible human being, and his disturbingly vivid personification of evil in Iago are among the technical and ethical problems raised by this unforgettable drama.

8. King Lear

This play, the most intense and overwhelming of Shakespeare's tragedies, was written in 1606 and printed in Quartos of 1608 and 1619. A different version appears in the First Folio. The aged King Lear, who impetuously disinherits his virtuous daughter, Cordelia, divides his kingdom between his other daughters, Goneril and Regan, who malevolently cast him out. Broken-hearted and accompanied by his Fool, he loses his reason on a storm-swept heath. Parallel to his evil treatment is that of the Duke of Gloucester, who is blinded by Cornwall, Regan's husband. By the end of the play, all the principal characters, except Edgar, Gloucester's son, have died. Lear's impassioned speeches, full of pity as well as bitterness, and Gloucester's expression of fatalism ("As flies to wanton boys are we to the gods; / They kill us for their sport") represent the profoundly tragic nature of King Lear.

9. Macbeth

The shortest of Shakespeare's tragedies, this is usually dated 1606. Influenced by the Three Witches' prophecies and urged on by his wife, Macbeth embarks on a course of murder in order to gain the crown of Scotland and then to establish his power. He is eventually killed by Macduff, and Malcolm, one of the murdered King Duncan's sons, succeeds to the kingdom. This is a play of relentless pace (sometimes acted without a break) that dramatises issues of ambition, kingly qualities, self-deception, the influence of the supernatural, and the nature of evil and conscience (revealed, for example, in Macbeth's soliloquies and in Lady Macbeth's sleepwalking scene).

10. The Tempest

Traditionally regarded as Shakespeare's farewell to the stage, the play was probably written in 1611. Unusually, it observes the unities of time and place. The exiled Prospero lives on an island with his daughter, Miranda, the airy spirit, Ariel, and the beast-like Caliban. Through his magical powers, he contrives the shipwreck of Alonso, the King of Naples, and others who belonged to his former courtly world and who were implicated in his banishment. After various complications and machinations, forgiveness and reconciliation ensue. Miranda will marry Ferdinand, the King's son, and Prospero renounces his magic. This is a romantic, supernatural and endlessly fascinating play, which blends coarse and delicate humour, resentment and love, and which finally instils feelings of satisfaction and happiness (as expressed in Miranda's exclamation, "O brave new world, / That has such people in it!")

ROMANTIC POETRY IN BRITAIN

Introduction

About two hundred years ago some books of verse were published in Britain that broke new ground: collections by William Blake (1757–1827) and Robert Burns (1759–96) and *Lyrical Ballads* by William Wordsworth (1770–1850) and Samuel Taylor Coleridge (1772–1834). These marked the beginning of the Romantic Movement in British literature, which lasted until the 1830s. Romanticism emphasised emotion and the imagination, the individual personality, liberty, Nature, children and "simple" people. Other features were medievalism and the "Gothic," the supernatural, mystery and exoticism. The language and forms of this poetry and prose became varied and often colourful and elaborate. These characteristics contrasted with those of eighteenth century literature with its classical ideals of rationality, restraint and formality.

This article surveys poetry, but the prose of the period is typically Romantic. Besides "Gothic" novels and Scott's novels (*see* **M5**), we have William Hazlitt's essays (mostly 1817–26), Charles Lamb's *Essays of Elia* (1820–33), and Thomas De Quincey's autobiographical *Confessions of an English Opium Eater* (1821) and other essays, which record their authors' personal feelings, experiences and responses.

Blake and Burns

Blake's *Poetical Sketches* (1783) contain work imitative of Spenser and Milton but also fresh, lyrical verse, such as the song, "How sweet I roamed from field to field" and the "Mad Song". *Songs of Innocence* (1789), like most of Blake's works, was issued as an "illuminated" book, with the text and designs etched, printed and coloured by him, to form an integrated whole of words and pictures. This collection of lyrics was followed by *Songs of Experience* (1794), the complete book "showing the two contrary states of the human soul", to use Blake's own description. Using simple words, rhythms and stanza-forms, Blake sings in *Songs of Innocence* of love, tenderness and joy, as in "The Echoing Green," "The Lamb" and "Nurse's Song". This feeling is summarized in the first stanza of "The Divine Image":

To Mercy, Pity, Peace and Love
All pray in their distress;
And to these virtues of delight
Return their thankfulness.

In *Songs of Experience*, the emotions are those of anger, sorrow and suffering, epitomised in "The Sick Rose":

O Rose, thou art sick!
The invisible worm
That flies in the night,
In the howling storm.

Has found out thy bed
Of crimson joy,
And his dark secret love
Does thy life destroy.

Instead of the lamb, Blake now writes of "The Tyger". Blake's "prophetic books", including the *Book of Thel* (1789), *Milton* (1804–08) and *Jerusalem* (1804–20), are largely inaccessible to the general reader because of their mythology and symbolism devised by the poet, although some passages can be appreciated for intrinsic power and beauty. The prefatory lyric to *Milton*, "And did those feet in ancient time/Walk upon England's mountains green?" is familiar as a hymn in Parry's setting. Blake conceived poetry as a religious and imaginative medium of expression.

Burns's poetry is based on Scottish literary conventions and traditions and owes something to such forebears as Allan Ramsay (1685–1758) and Robert Fergusson (1750–74) and to popular songs and ballads. *Poems Chiefly in the Scottish Dialect*

appeared in 1786. Much of Burns's subsequent career consisted in his writing and adapting Scott's songs. His narrative, satirical and epistolary poems are vigorous in metre and language; they are full of a delight in life and express a comic view of pretension and hypocrisy. "Tam O'Shanter", for example, in rhyming iambic tetrameters, is about the pursuit of the tipsy Tam riding home from the inn by a crowd of witches including "'ae winsome wench and wawlie", to whom he had gleefully roared out, "Well done, Cutty-sark!" "Holy Willy's Prayer," in Burns's favourite six-line stanza, is a satirical portrait of a smug Calvinist. His hundreds of lyrical poems, often meant to be sung to Scottish airs, include "My luve is like a red, red rose", "Comin' thro' the rye", "A man's a man for a' that" and "Auld Lang Syne". Burns's poetry is popular in all senses of the word, dealing with the lives, loves, thoughts and desires of ordinary people, based on late eighteenth century Scottish life but also on an instinctive understanding of life in general.

Wordsworth and Coleridge

William Wordsworth and Samuel Taylor Coleridge brought out *Lyrical Ballads* (1798), one of the key books of the English Romantic Movement. Most of the poems in the collection were by Wordsworth; the most famous of Coleridge's contributions was the "Rime of the Ancient Mariner". Wordsworth's aim, stated in his Preface, "was to choose incidents and situations from common life, and to relate or describe them, throughout, as far as was possible, in a selection of language really used by men." He writes, for example, of children in such poems as "We are Seven" and "The Idiot Boy", using a style of extreme simplicity. "Tintern Abbey", in which he reflects on the power of Nature, is written in blank verse with a more formal vocabulary. In the ten years between 1797 and 1807, Wordsworth produced most of his best poetry. Although he modified the simple language of *Lyrical Ballads*, he invariably wrote in a plain style, with few ornaments and no extraneous musical effects. Matthew Arnold said that "Nature herself seems ... to take the pen out of his hand, and to write for him with her own bare, sheer, penetrating power." An example is the opening stanza of "Resolution and Independence" (1807):

There was a roaring in the wind all night;
The rain came heavily and fell in floods;
But now the sun is rising calm and bright;
The birds are singing in the distant woods;
Over his own sweet voice the stock-dove broods;
The jay makes answer as the magpie chatters;
And all the air is filled with pleasant noise of waters.

For Wordsworth, "Nature" meant partly the "rocks and stones and trees", the sky, the wind and the sea, animals and plants, particularly of the Lake District, and partly human nature, particularly as seen in unsophisticated people. The relationship between Nature and the human mind was the constant theme of his poetry:

One impulse from a vernal wood,
May teach you more of man,
Of moral evil and of good,
Than all the sages can.

("The Tables Turned", 1798). In "Michael" (1800), the old shepherd of the title had lived for more than eighty years among the mountains, valleys and fields, which "had impressed/So many incidents upon his mind/Of hardship, skill or courage, joy or fear". The growth of the poet's own mind is traced in *The Prelude* (first version, 1805; revised and published posthumously, 1850), a poem in 13/14 books written in blank verse, intended as a preliminary to a philosophical poem, *The Recluse*, which was never completed, though *The Excursion*, its second part, was published in 1814. In the first two books especially, Wordsworth recalls scenes and moments which inspired him with a feeling that there was a vital force in the universe. Whilst skating on the frozen lakes, for instance, he sensed Presences and Visions that haunted him.

He wrote many sonnets in the Petrarchan form,

ranging over many subjects. These sonnets include "Composed upon Westminster Bridge" (1802), "The world is too much with us" (1807), "Personal Talk" (1807) and "Surprised by joy" (1815). His "Ode: Intimations of Immortality from Recollections of Early Childhood" (1807), in elaborate stanzas, celebrates the innocence and visionary powers he associated with childhood, the beginning of our earthly life, when "trailing clouds of glory" we come "From God, who is our home". The "Extempore Effusion upon the Death of James Hogg" (1835) is written in memory of Hogg, Scott, Coleridge, Lamb, Crabbe and Mrs Hemans.

Wordsworth is a philosophical poet, who sought to communicate with people in general and not with a privileged few, since for him the definition of a poet was "a man speaking to men". Two people who influenced him were his sister, Dorothy Wordsworth (1771–1855), and Coleridge.

In his *Biographia Literaria* (1817), Coleridge recalled his co-operation with Wordsworth in *Lyrical Ballads*, pointing out that his own "endeavours should be directed to persons and characters supernatural, or at least romantic", but that he should treat them so truthfully that he would "procure for these shadows of imagination that willing suspension of disbelief for the moment, which constitutes poetic faith." The "Rime of the Ancient Mariner", his principal contribution to the collection, is an imitation of a traditional ballad, narrating the tale of the mariner's wanton killing of an albatross, the consequent fate that befell the ship and his companions, and his involuntary blessing of the beautiful water-snakes, which led to the lifting of the curse and his compulsion to tell everyone of the lesson he had learned: "He prayeth well, who loveth well/Both man and bird and beast." The vivid, economical depictions in the poem are much admired:

All in a hot and copper sky,
The bloody sun, at noon,
Right up above the mast did stand,
No bigger than the moon.

"Christabel" (written 1797–1800; published 1816), an unfinished "Gothic" narrative of magical powers, moonlight, castles and beautiful ladies, is written in rhyming lines of varying lengths, with four stresses in each line – the variations, Coleridge explained, are "in correspondence with some transition in the nature of the imagery or passion". "Kubla Khan" (written 1798; published 1816) is also unfinished. In his introductory remarks, Coleridge says that he dreamt the poem during a three hours' sleep, but was interrupted while writing it down by "a person on business from Porlock". Its fifty-four lines give a sensuous picture of a "pleasure-dome", its gardens, a "deep romantic chasm", a river, caverns and ocean, and end with a vision of "an Abyssinian maid" playing "on her dulcimer". All three of these poems, therefore, represent the kind Coleridge agreed to write for *Lyrical Ballads*, though the last two were published later and independently. Amongst his other poems, three meditations on human relationships and Nature should be mentioned: "This Lime-Tree Bower My Prison" (1797), "Frost at Midnight" (1798) and "Dejection: an Ode" (1802).

Scott and Southey

Sir Walter Scott (1771–1832) achieved great fame with his verse narratives: the *Lay of the Last Minstrel* (1804), *Marmion* (1808), the *Lady of the Lake* (1810), *Rokeby* (1813), and others. They are historical stories of adventure, heroism and love, told in vigorously rhythmical, rhyming lines, usually iambic tetrameters. Though popular in Scott's time and for long afterwards, they are little read today. Scott also wrote songs and lyrics, including "Lochinvar" (in *Marmion*), "Proud Maisie is in the wood" (in the *Heart of Midlothian*, 1818) and "Look not thou on beauty's charming" (in the *Bride of Lammermoor*, 1819).

Robert Southey (1774–1843) also wrote a number of long narrative poems, such as *Thalaba* (1801) and the *Curse of Kehama* (1810), but as a poet is remembered nowadays only for a few ballads and lyrics: the "Holly Tree" (1798), the "Battle of Blenheim" (1798), "God's Judgement on a Wicked Bishop" (1799), the "Inchcape Rock" (1803) and

the "Cataract of Lodore" (1823). His verse has unobtrusive qualities of precision of observation and expression and has suffered some undeserved neglect.

Byron, Shelley and Keats

George Gordon, Lord Byron (1788–1824) became the archetypal Romantic figure in Britain and Europe, not just because of his poetry but also because of his aristocratic birth, his looks, his unconventional morals, his identification with the cause of Greek independence and his early death. His narrative poems of adventures, travel and love, sometimes partly autobiographical, brought him enormous popularity. These include *Childe Harold's Pilgrimage* (1812, 1816, 1818), *the Giaour* (1813), the *Bride of Abydos* (1813), the *Corsair* (1814), *Manfred* (1817), *Beppo* (1818), *Mazeppa* (1819) and *Don Juan* (1819–24). The central figure in many of them is a Byronic hero – a man at odds with the world, melancholy, heroic and defiant. The settings and events are highly coloured and the moods are those of excitement and passion, as in the description of the eve of the Battle of Waterloo in *Childe Harold's Pilgrimage*:

There was a sound of revelry by night,
And Belgium's Capital had gathered then
Her Beauty and her Chivalry, and bright
The lamps shone o'er fair women and brave
men;
A thousand hearts beat happily; and when
Music arose with its voluptuous swell,
Soft eyes looked love to eyes which spake
again,
And all went merry as a marriage bell;
But hush! hark! a deep sound strikes like a rising knell!

Satire, cynicism and disrespect are also characteristic of his verse, jauntily expressed in strong rhythms and unexpected rhymes, shown fully in *Don Juan*, where he indulges in sharp, amusing authorial comments, achieving the sense of a personal, speaking voice in the medium of the *ottava rima*. The " Vision of Judgement" (1822), written in the same metre, is a satire on Southey, the Poet Laureate, and on the recently-dead King George III. Byron wrote lyrics, the best-known of which is "So, we'll go no more a-roving" (1817). The *Prisoner of Chillon* (1816), in rhyming iambic tetrameters and told in the first person, is an affecting account of the prisoner's sufferings, partly alleviated by the "carol of a bird" that said "a thousand things" to him in his incarceration. Byron's prolific output of verse is fluent and encompasses a wide range of emotions.

Byron's friend, Percy Bysshe Shelley (1792–1822), was predominantly a lyrical poet, though he wrote some satire and politically committed verse. *Queen Mab* (1813), in blank verse interspersed with lyrics, is an attack on tyranny, religion, selfish commercialism and war, with a prophecy of their destruction. Much of his poetry is inspired by a love of freedom and idealism, for example, his poetic drama, *Prometheus Unbound* (1820). His sonnet, "Ozymandias", ironically portrays the ruined statue of a "King of Kings". Shelley's lyrical poetry has a rapidity of movement and a sense of lightness and grace. Its imagery is typically of the wind, clouds, sky and water. Favourite descriptive words of his include "blue" and "azure". The "Ode to the West Wind" (1819), the "Ode to a Skylark" (1820) and "The Cloud" exemplify this characteristic. The delicacy of his verse is shown in a poem like the following:

Music, when soft voices die,
Vibrates in the memory;
Odours, when sweet violets sicken,
Live within the sense they quicken.

Rose leaves, when the rose is dead,
Are heaped for the beloved's bed;
And so thy thoughts, when thou art gone,
Love itself shall slumber on.

Some of Shelley's poetry is marked by a tender and occasionally self-pitying melancholy, for example, "Stanzas written in Dejection Near Naples" "Rarely, rarely comest thou/Spirit of Delight!" and

"A Lament" (all published posthumously, 1824). "Adonais" (1821), in Spenserian stanzas, is an elegy on the death of John Keats. Critical opinion is divided on Shelley's achievement. Some commentators see his poetry as vague and diffuse, whereas others see it as representing the high point of English lyricism.

The poetry of John Keats (1795–1821) is, in contrast, rich and sensuous. In a letter to Shelley, he advised him to "load every rift of [his subject] with ore". He published three volumes of verse: *Poems* (1817), *Endymion* (1818) and *Lamia, Isabella, The Eve of St Agnes, and Other Poems* (1820). The first line of *Endymion*, " A thing of beauty is a joy for ever", is the key to the main theme of his work. "Beauty" for Keats was associated with a passionate appreciation of flowers and lush vegetation, music and bird song, sweet scents and tastes, cool water in summer heat, and so on. He presents such experiences in descriptive, concentrated language, as in the description of the meal in the narrative poem, the "Eve of St Agnes":

> And still she slept an azure-lidded sleep,
> In blanched linen, smooth, and lavender'd.
> While he from forth the closet brought a heap
> Of candied apple, quince, and plum, and gourd;
> With jellies smoother than the creamy curd,
> And lucent syrops, tinct with cinnamon;
> Manna and dates, in argosy transferr'd
> From Fez; and spiced dainties, every one,
> From silken Samarcand to cedar'd Lebanon.

His Odes, written in complex stanza-forms, explore the implications of beauty in our lives: in the "Nightingale" and "Grecian Urn" Odes, the contrasts between human mortality and the immortality of the bird's song and the work of art respectively; in "Melancholy", the relationship between sad and joyful feelings; in "Autumn", the affirmation explicit in the fruition of the season. Keats attempted a Miltonic style of poetry in "Hyperion" (in the 1820 volume) and the "Fall of Hyperion" (published posthumously), but left both poems unfinished. A spontaneous apprehension and presentation of experience was the principle he sought to put into practice, expressed in his phrase, "negative capability" (*see* the Glossary of Literary Terms, M22). Many would consider Keats to be the quintessential Romantic poet because of the worlds of beauty and emotion he evokes in highly-charged words and imagery.

Other Poets

The works of George Crabbe (1754–1832) include *The Village* (1783), *The Borough* (1810), *Tales* (1812) and *Tales of the Hall* (1819). Mainly using rhyming couplets, Crabbe realistically portrays scenes and tales of rural life. "Peter Grimes", one section of *The Borough*, tells the tale of the fate of a fisherman, a "lost, lone man, so harassed and undone", tormented by the memories of the cruelty and murder he had committed. Familiar today in Benjamin Britten's operatic version (1945), the poem has a disciplined pathos typical of the author. Though Crabbe's best work belongs to the nineteenth century and is contemporary with Romantic poetry, its language and form can be called Augustan. On the other hand, his detailed descriptions and his sympathies for the poor make it possible to relate him to the Romantic movement.

Thomas Moore (1779–1852) wrote a widely-read Oriental poem, *Lalla Rookh* (1817). Between 1807 and 1834, he wrote *Irish Melodies*, lyrics intended to be sung to Irish airs. These include such popular songs as "Believe me, if all those endearing young charms" and "Oft in the stilly night".

John Clare (1793–1864) wrote *Poems Descriptive of Rural Life and Scenery* (1820), the *Village Minstrel* (1821), the *Shepherd's Calendar* (1827) and the *Rural Muse* (1835), followed by other poems published posthumously. As the titles of his volumes suggest, his subjects were mainly rural; the seasons, flowers, birds and animals. His later poems especially also deal with the joys and pains of love and often have a melancholy tone. Clare's style is clear and simple, with sharp and original perceptions.

Other Romantic poets are Thomas Campbell (1777–1844), Leigh Hunt (1784–1859), and Felicia Dorothea Hemans (1793–1835). Two excellent anthologies are Geoffrey Grigson's *The Romantics* (1942) and Jerome J. McGann's *New Oxford Book of Romantic Period Verse* (1993).

THE MODERN FRENCH NOVEL

Introduction

The modern French novel begins with the publication in 1678 of *La Princesse de Clèves*. Previous to this, fiction largely consisted of long pastoral romances (the French term for a novel is *roman*): the loves and exploits of Arthurian knights, princes disguised as shepherds, usually set in distant epochs and places, with frequent supernatural interventions. The most popular example of this genre was Honoré d'Urfé's *Astrée*, 1607–27. The novelty of *La Princesse de Clèves* lay in its conciseness, but also in its concentration on the character and actions of the heroine, which has led to the novel being long recognised as the first narrative of psychological analysis. On first publication it created a sensation. The author, Madame de La Fayette (1634–93) was part of a distinguished literary circle and had published two conventional romances before her masterpiece. It is a story of unconsummated love. The heroine, the princess of the title, is married but falls in love with the handsome and distinguished Duc de Nemours. She confesses her love to her husband but remains faithful. When her husband dies, the princess refuses to marry Nemours and enters a convent. The novel is a remarkable work of art and possesses the classical virtues of the century: clarity, economy and insight into the human heart.

The Novel of Manners

The fiction written at the beginning of the eighteenth century is usually characterised as the novel of manners, with its greater stress on social life. Alain-René Lesage (1688–1747) was the most successful novelist of the period, and his best known work is *L'Histoire de Gil Blas* (1715–35), a rambling picaresque story of its hero's rise in society. The novel best remembered from this period, and the only work for which its prolific author is remembered is *Manon Lescaut* (1731) by the Abbé Prévost (1697–1763). This story, of a weak-willed and sentimental young man who throws his life away in his passion for the charming and amoral Manon, is a striking blend of romance and realism.

This increasing preoccupation with emotion reached its peak with *Julie: ou La Nouvelle Héloïse* (1761) by Jean-Jacques Rousseau. He was one of the greatest thinkers of the age and wrote highly original works in a number of genres. In this work, his one novel, the heroine falls in love with her tutor, but marries an elderly suitor. She settles down to married life, but when the tutor reappears he is invited by her husband to live with them. On her deathbed, Julie realises that she has loved her former tutor all along. The emphasis on sensibility coupled with an appreciation of the beauties of nature made the work a bestseller.

Fiction at the end of the eighteenth century is dominated by one novel, *Les Liaisons Dangereuses* (*Dangerous liaisons*, or *Dangerous acquaintances*) by Pierre Choderlos de Laclos (1741–1803). It was his first novel and his one masterpiece. It is written in the form of letters, and is a brilliantly crafted novel. Two experienced seducers, the Vicomte de Valmont and the Marquise de Merteuil seduce and corrupt two young innocents, Cecile Volanges and the chevalier de Danceny (who are, incidentally, in love with each other). Valmont also seduces a virtuous married woman, and then abandons her. But Valmont and Merteuil fall out and bring each other down, Valmont is killed in a duel, Merteuil has to flee the country, her evil nature exposed. The theme of sexual intrigue has always been considered shocking, but few novels show such sharpness of insight into human motivation or such cool precision of style.

The 19th Century

Until this period the most successful French novels had tended to be individual works, 'one-offs'. But after the Revolution the novel developed

M32

very quickly and became the most important literary genre, taking over from drama and poetry. There arose a new generation of novelists, writers who worked consistently in the form.

Stendhal is the pseudonym of Marie-Henri Beyle (1783–1842). From early in his life he had literary ambitions. On first arrival in Paris at the age of 16 he wanted to be a playwright. But his first book, *Vies de Haydn, Mozart et Metastasio*, was not published until 1814. He published a travel book on Italy, a country he loved passionately, a study of love, a critical work *Racine et Shakespeare*, and a biography of Rossini. His first novel, *Armance*, came in 1827. His first masterpiece, *Le Rouge et le Noir* (*The Red and the Black*) followed shortly, in 1830.

This is the story of a poor but intelligent and ambitious young man, Julien Sorel. The Red and the Black refer to the two main routes to success available—the red is the army and the black the church. The story is, however, concerned with his relationship with two women. He seduces and falls in love with the wife of his first employer, Madame de Renal; then seduces the aristocratic daughter of his second employer, Mathilde. The book ends with Julien's execution for the attempted murder of Mme de Renal after she had jeopardised his plans for marriage to Mathilde. His second great novel *La Chartreuse de Parme* (*The Charterhouse of Parma*) was published in 1839. It takes place in his beloved Italy and centres on another young and Romantic hero, Fabrice, set against a background of the intrigues of the small court of Parma. Both these works present the gifted hero trying to make his way within a nonheroic society. In both these novels Stendhal raises questions about the nature of happiness, the nature of the self, of love, and the relationship of the individual to society.

Two other novels he left uncompleted: *Lucien Leuwen* and *Lamiel*. He died in 1842. Although not taken very seriously as a writer in his lifetime he has since come to be recognised as a great writer. Romantic but ironic, he employed a plain but incisive style, which is remarkable for its swiftness and lightness, and its capacity to convey a wide range of emotion. The characters of the novels, especially the women, are vividly presented. His autobiographical works are also fascinating.

Honoré de Balzac

Honoré de Balzac (1799–1850) is generally considered one of the greatest of all novelists. Certainly he was one of the most prolific; there are some 80 titles (including short stories) in what he came later to call his *Human comedy*.

Early attempts at writing (plays, Gothic thrillers, humorous novels) having failed, he took a partnership in a printing-firm which went bankrupt. Left at thirty with a huge debt which he would never shake off, he returned to writing with *Les Chouans* (*The Chouans*) (1829) the story of a royalist rising during the Revolution, and so embarked on twenty years of labour which ended only in his death from overwork. He would write all night, kept going by endless cups of black coffee.

The novels came in a steady stream. By 1835 he had produced over 20 including *La Peau de Chagrin* (1831; *The Wild Ass's Skin*), *Le Chef d'oeuvre inconnu* (1831; *The Unknown Masterpiece*), *Le Curé de Tours* (1832), *Eugenie Grandet* (1832), *Le Medecin de campagne* (1833; *The Country Doctor*), *Louis Lambert* (1834), *Le Père Goriot* (1835; *Old Goriot*). About 1834 Balzac realised he had been writing piece-meal a panorama of contemporary French society. He now consciously constructed a vast plan to continue this design, by dividing his novels into categories. The two main headings were *Studies of manners* and *Philosophical studies*. The first category was further divided into 'scenes' of private, provincial, Parisian life *etc*. At this time Balzac also hit upon the idea of connecting different novels by using the same characters from one to another. But it was not until 1842 that he came up with the overall title, the "*Human comedy*".

Books continued to pour forth. These included *Illusion perdues* (1837–43; *Lost Illusions*), *Cesar Birotteau* (1837), *Une Ténébreuse Affaire* (1841; *A shady business*), *Splendeurs et Misères des courtisanes* (1843–47; *A harlot high and low*), *Cousin Bette* (1847) and *Cousin Pons* (1847).

With his great curiosity about virtually all spheres and aspects of life and his fascination with money,

ambition and love, Balzac was able to give a realistic account of most of French society. He was the first great novelist to give meticulous attention to the material background of his characters. At the same time his novels are distinguished by large casts of vivid, fascinating characters, great narrative drive, a strong sense of drama (not to say melodrama), and immense versatility. He had an immense influence on the novel and not only in France.

The Work of Flaubert

Gustave Flaubert (1821–80) continued the trend of French fiction towards greater realism. He was a far more careful writer than Balzac and had a very high conception of the novel as a work of art. His first and most famous novel was *Madame Bovary*, published in 1857. It had taken him five years of hard labour. It is the story of an undistinguished young woman living in a provincial town, whose head is turned by reading too much romantic literature. In trying to escape the banality of ordinary life, she falls into adultery, financial ruin and finally suicide.

After *Madame Bovary* came *Salammbô* (1862), a novel about ancient Carthage. This was followed by two works which he had started well before *Madame Bovary*. Both *L'Education sentimentale* (1870; *A sentimental education*) and *La Tentation de Saint Antoine* (1874; *The temptation of Saint Antony*) had gone through several versions. The first is a story of a young man with modest ambitions whose Romantic ideals gradually wither. It is the story of Flaubert's own generation. The second presents the parade of temptations to which the saint was exposed.

Trois contes (1877; *Three tales*) contains three long stories. At his death he left unfinished *Bouvard et Pécuchet*, the novel he had been working on for eight years. It is the story of two retired clerks who set out to explore all the branches of knowledge, with farcical results.

Flaubert was probably the most conscientious of all novelists. He always sought exactly the right word to convey his meaning and paid great attention to the overall construction of his novels. At the same time he was a master of precise observation, controlling his Romantic tendencies by attention to detail and objective description of people and events.

Emile Zola

Emile Zola (1840–1902) developed the realist tradition of the nineteenth century novel, best exemplified by Balzac and Flaubert, into 'naturalism'. This aimed to apply the methods of the experimental sciences, and resulted in an emphasis on heredity and the physical and social influences upon character. His major work is the 20 volume cycle of novels under the overall title The Rougon-Macquart, a natural and social history of a family under the rule of Napoleon III, from 1852 to 1870. The first was published in 1871, and the others followed at the rate of almost one a year. It was the success of the seventh novel in the series, *L'Assommoir* (*The Drunkard*) in 1877 that made him into a best-selling novelist. He became the best known writer in France. The others that followed included *Nana*, (1880) the life of a courtesan, and *Germinal*, (1885) a harsh story of mines in the north of France—his greatest success. Other outstanding novels in the cycle are *L'Oeuvre* (1886; *The Masterpiece*), a study of a painter, partly based on the life of Cezanne; *La Terre* (1887; *Earth*), on the brutality of peasant life; and *La Bête humaine* (1890; *The Beast in man*) describing the lives of railway workers.

Although his scientific theories cannot be taken seriously, Zola had a powerful imagination which succeeds in bringing alive the atmosphere of places and the character of crowds. His novels have a strong documentary nature and concentrate on the lives of working people, but are animated by his poetic vision.

Guy de Maupassant

Guy de Maupassant (1850–93) was, in a short life, a highly prolific writer. In ten years, from 1880–90, he published some 300 short stories, 6 novels, three travel books and various other miscellaneous works. His career as a successful writer was established by the publication in 1880 of "Boule de suif" (Ball of fat), one of his finest stories, and it is as a writer of stories that he did his best work. They tend to deal with the peasantry of Normandy (where he was brought up), the Franco-German war of 1870 (in which he served), bureaucracy (he spent his twenties working in the French civil service) and life on the banks of the Seine. His most successful novels are *Une vie* (1883; *A woman's life*), *Bel-ami* (1885) and *Pierre et Jean* (1888). He became a bestseller in several countries.

Although he is associated with the naturalism of Zola, he served an apprenticeship with Flaubert. He is an acknowledged master of the realistic short story. He sought what he called "the humble truth", and succeeded in creating, with remarkable objectivity and great simplicity of style, an exact and economical portrait of ordinary life.

The 20th Century

In the present century the novel became more strongly established as the leading genre and ever more varied. French novelists have won the Nobel Prize several times. Two writers who bridge the turn of the century are Romain Rolland (1866–1944) and Anatole France (1844–1924) who won the prize in 1915 and 1921 respectively. Rolland's best known work is the story of a musical genius, *Jean-Christophe*, published in several volumes (1903–12). Anatole France was very popular in his day, but he is now much less read. More modern than either of these is André Gide (1869–1951) who won the Nobel Prize in 1947. His reputation was first established by the short novels *La Porte étroite* (1908; *Strait is the gate*) and *La Symphonie pastorale* (1919; *The Pastoral Symphony*). His most complex work is *Les Faux-monnayeurs* (1926; *The counterfeiters*), but he also wrote travel books, plays, criticism, an autobiography and published his *Journals* in several volumes.

Marcel Proust

Marcel Proust (1871–1922) did not win the Nobel Prize, but he is the greatest of modern French novelists. His masterpiece is the immensely long novel, known in English as *Remembrance of things past*, though the French title *A la recherche du temps perdu* means 'in search of lost time'. The first volume, *Du Côté de chez Swann* (*Swann's Way*) was published in 1913, to be followed by *A l'ombre de jeunes filles en fleurs* (*Within a budding grove*) in 1918. This won the most prestigious literary award in France, the Prix Goncourt. Two more volumes were published in his lifetime; *Le Côté Guermantes* (1920; *The Guermantes way*) and *Sodome et Gomorrhe* (1922). After his death in Paris of pneumonia there were three more volumes: *La Prisonnière* (1923; *The prisoner*), *La Fugitive* [*1925; The sweet cheat gone*] and *Le Temps retrouvé* (1927; *Time regained*). The work begins with a memory of the narrator's childhood, suddenly aroused by the taste of a piece of cake in a cup of tea. The author senses the value of this involuntary memory and through it and other memories is led to recreate and meditate on his own life—holidays on the Normandy coast, playing along the Champs-Elysées, his entry as a young man into high society and his love for Albertine, who comes to live with him. The work's great originality is that it is both the history of an epoch (high society in decline before the First World War) and the history of an individual soul, seeking its true destiny. Proust's rich style, with its long and complex sentences, enables him to convey the subtleties and nuances of sensations and emotions. He portrays too a wide range of characters. The narrator's mother and grandmother, the dilettante Swann, artists like the painter Elstir and the musician Vinteuil, his friend the aristocrat Saint-Loup, the homosexual Baron de Charlus and the ladies of high society all come vividly to life.

The Inter-War Years

A prominent writer of the years between the wars

was Roger Martin du Gard (1881–1958) who won the Nobel Prize in 1937. His major work is a cyclical novel in eight parts, *Les Thibault* (1922–40; *The World of the Thibaults*). François Mauriac (1885–1970) established his reputation in the twenties and went on to a long career as a novelist of Catholic themes, winning the Nobel Prize in 1952. His novels include *Thérèse Desqueyroux* (1927) and *Le Noeud de vipères* (1932; *The Nest of Vipers*). One of the most original French novelists is Louis-Ferdinand Céline (1894–1961). His first novels were *Le Voyage au bout de la nuit* (1932; *Journey to the end of night*) and *Mort á credit* (1936; *Death on the installment plan*). These works, written in a colloquial, angry style, attack the follies of mankind and yet are full of vitality.

Two writers who led very active lives are André Malraux (1901–76) and Antoine de Saint-Exupéry (1900–44). Malraux was involved in revolutionary movements in China, the civil war in Spain and also the Resistance, before becoming a politician. His best known novel is *La Condition humaine* (1933; *Man's Estate*) which won the Prix Goncourt. Saint-Exupéry was a pilot in Europe, Africa and South America, before being killed in the war. His best novel is *Vol de nuit* (1931; *Night Flight*). He also wrote the still popular children's story *The little prince* (1945).

Jean-Paul Sartre

The most prominent literary figure since the war has undoubtedly been Jean-Paul Sartre (1905–80). His published work contains much more philosophy and criticism than fiction, but he reached a wide public with his early novels: *La Nausée* (1938; *Nausea*), and the trilogy *Les Chemins de la liberté* (*Roads to freedom*), which consists of *L'Age de raison* (*The age of reason*) and *Le Sursis* (*The reprieve*) both published in 1945, and *La Mort dans l'âme* (1951; *Iron in the soul*). Sartre later turned more to drama for creative work. He was awarded the Nobel Prize in 1964 but declined to accept it. Like Sartre, Albert Camus (1913–60) was a man of wide literary interests, writing plays, essays, and philosophical works. He is, however, best known for his novels: *L'Etranger* (1942; *The Stranger*), *La Peste* (1947. *The Plague*) and *La Chute* (1956; *The Fall*). He was awarded the Nobel Prize in 1957.

Samuel Beckett

Samuel Beckett (1906–89) was born in Ireland and settled in Paris in 1937. After World War II he gave up his native English and began writing in French, first as a novelist, later as a playwright. *Molloy* (1951) was immediately hailed as a highly original novel, and this was followed by *Malone meurt* (1951; *Malone dies*) and *L'Innommable* (1953; *The Unnameable*). In this trilogy, Beckett strips away all non-essential aspects of his characters in search of the basic human self. His later prose works become ever briefer and more concentrated. He won the Nobel Prize in 1969.

Beckett was a Pioneer of the 'nouveau roman', (the new novel), a movement which began in the early 1950s. This school rejected traditional fictional techniques, like plot and character, and focused on the detailed impressions of a single observer. Writers in this group are Alain Robbe-Grillet, Michel Butor, Nathalie Sarraute and Claude Simon, who won the Nobel Prize in 1985 for *Les Georgiques* (1981; *The Georgics*).

Two of the most interesting novelists in France of recent years are Michel Tournier (b. 1924) and George Perec (1936–82). Tournier is a highly imaginative writer, whose novels are full of challenging ideas. The first was a retelling of the Robinson Crusoe story under the title of *Vendredi* (1967; *Friday; or, The Other Island*). The second, *Le Roi des aulnes* (1970; *The Erl King*) is set in Nazi Germany and won the Prix Goncourt. Perec was a more experimental writer. He made his name with his fourth novel *La Disparition* (1969; *The Disappearance*) which as well as being an entertaining novel is written without once using the letter "e", the commonest letter in French. His most complex work is *La Vie mode d'emploi* (1978; *Life: a user's manual*), a minute description of all the objects and events in a block of flats.

The French Contribution

Overall, French novelists have contributed a large number of masterpieces to world literature, as well as exercising a large influence on other writers. It is difficult to generalise about such a varied tradition, but the predominant qualities of French fiction are realism, clarity, wit and a taste for ideas. French writers are rarely afraid to appeal to the reader's intelligence.

For more information on French fiction, there is no single guide to the subject. There are interesting and useful chapters in *A New History of French Literature*, published by Harvard University Press in 1989. Many books have been published on most of the authors discussed in this article. Two recent series may be mentioned: *Macmillan Modern Novelists*, which has volumes on Flaubert, Proust, Gide, Camus and Sartre; and Longman's *Modern Literature in Perspective* with, so far, volumes on Stendhal and Claude Simon.

MEDICAL
MATTERS

Here we give a brief summary of up-to-date medical knowledge for a wide variety of the most common illnesses. The section also includes new developments in areas such as transplant surgery, radiography and hormone replacement therapy. It must not be allowed to replace your doctor, who should be consulted immediately if you are worried. An index at the end of the section ensures easy reference.

TABLE OF CONTENTS

MEDICAL MATTERS

PART I. INTRODUCTION.

In earlier editions of Pears the Medical Section took the form of a dictionary. More recently we have attempted something different: a small medical textbook for the layman. We have two reasons for this. Firstly, we feel that there are some readers who would like to have an overall picture of modern medicine and learn something of the progress in its various fields. They may like to read the section through as a continuous narrative. Secondly, there are always readers (probably the majority) who simply want to use the section as a ready-reference guide and to that end, rather than have an alphabetically arranged collection of snippets of information (which can be unsatisfying), we have grouped diseases under bodily 'systems'. We have made no attempt to produce a *dictionary* of symptoms because self-diagnosis is foolish. However, we have retained an alphabetical index (Part IV) for easy reference.

The plan in this section is to deal with diseases according to either (a) their cause (*e.g.*, the infections due to bacteria or viruses) or (b) the body system affected (*e.g.*, the nervous system, the heart and blood vessels, the lungs and so on). We cannot emphasise too strongly that this section is not intended as a substitute for seeking medical advice. It is one thing to satisfy curiosity or try and solve a puzzle about a disease, condition or collection of symptoms by "looking it up" but quite another to try and diagnose one's own disease, condition or collection of symptoms in the same way. In other words, this section is no substitute for a doctor and when you are ill, unless you know it to be a trivial, or relatively trivial, self-limiting condition, you must get medical advice. It is easy to listen to and believe unqualified opinions and to take and act on advice from unqualified persons. However, it is unwise to do so because although doctors are sometimes wrong (just as are lawyers, architects, judges and veterinary surgeons) the unqualified are much more likely to be wrong. So choose a doctor you can trust, and then believe what he tells you and carry out his advice. There is no use in complaining about the whole medical profession just because you are dissatisfied with your own G.P. If you are, you should sign on with another.

Of recent years there has been a veritable explosion in medical information for the layman through newspapers, magazines, books, radio and television (collectively referred to as "the media") and among the more intelligently perceptive of doctors' patients there is now a much greater understanding of "how the body works" and how it can go wrong. Progress in treatment of some diseases has been rapid and, with the more ready access to specialist medical journals in which reports of drug and other trials appear which journalists now have, such news gets into a patient's hands very quickly, albeit often prematurely. The G.P. simply cannot keep up with advances in all fields and is therefore occasionally confronted by a patient who asks him why he cannot have this "new drug" for his rheumatoid arthritis, for example, a new drug which may not at that stage even have reached the market place.

Modern Medicine.

Much in medicine which is now taken for granted (that for the majority of diseases caused by identifiable organisms there is a specific drug treatment, for example) was undreamed of even as recently as 50 years ago. Progress in diagnosis, in preventive medicine and in treatment, both medical and surgical, has been so rapid as to be almost breathtaking. A doctor retiring from active practice in 1993 will have seen smallpox completely eradicated, poliomyelitis practically banished (at least from the U.K.), tuberculosis become curable, coronary artery disease relievable surgically and he will have witnessed the dramatic progress in the field of molecular biology and in the research by immunologists and geneticists into their efforts to control parasitic diseases like bilharzia, malaria and river blindness that affect millions of people in the Third World. One aspect of medicine and medical thinking still resistant to progress in understanding in spite of continued research is the effect of mind on body. Many of us still like to think that our bodies are just something we have got into, like cars, that ill-health is simply something that has "gone wrong" in one system or another and that therefore provided we find the appropriate expert (a chest physician, a gastro-enterologist or an ophthalmic surgeon, for example) to correct the fault, we will recover. Whereas that idea holds good for a broken leg, for instance, with many diseases the idea that mind can be totally separated from the "defective" part just isn't good enough. You cannot simply divorce your stomach, your bowels, your liver or your heart from your "self". They are all part of you and react, as you yourself react, to all the stresses and anxieties, fears and worries and the hundred and one other factors that are part and parcel of modern living. It is true that most of your stomach can be removed, your gall-bladder entirely so and with the aid of a dialysing machine or a transplant you can get by without your kidneys. As with your car, old or diseased parts can be repaired or totally replaced; even your heart, conventionally the very "seat" of the emotions.

Mens sana in corpore sano—a sound mind in a sound body. Your body and its many parts may be helped to normal function by modern medicines and surgery but, in general, it will only stay that way if you can rid yourself of all those emotional blemishes—anger, frustration, fear, worry and anxiety—which trouble you. Easier said than done, of course, but a good physician can help with good advice, with medicines if necessary—or simply with his ear. Emotional stress can not only inhibit healing of such things as duodenal or gastric ulcers but may even *cause* them. There are many diseases now recognised which are known to be associated with stress factors if not actually caused by them. Mainly these are diseases of the digestive tract or of the heart and blood vessels and you will find some of them discussed in the appropriate sections.

The state of the mind has more influence on bodily functions than you might think and recovery from many serious conditions can be slowed or hastened, depending on your state of mind. Every doctor has had experience of the patient who "loses the will to live", a situation which is unfortunately commoner than the reverse.

A word about preventive medicine—or helping yourself to health. A great deal of nonsense has been talked about the healthy life; at one time we were told to take eighteen chews to each bite, to do deep breathing, to take plenty of exercise, to get lots of fresh air, to eat regularly (or to indulge in peculiar diets). But more recently eminent doctors have cast doubt on most of these fancies. Moderate exercise is necessary to health, but athletes who indulge in violent exercise have not always been noted for longevity. Fresh air is pleasant and stimulating, but, where actual breathing is concerned, it is no better than the air in most rooms, though secondary smoking is now considered to be harmful. Certainly, one of the problems of our time is air pollution, but at present we are considering ordinary fresh air in comparison with the air indoors, and, in this case, the experts say there is little difference so far as health is concerned.

A balanced diet containing correct amounts of the basic food substances is essential, but there is no evidence that when, or at what intervals, you eat makes the slightest difference—unless you are a sufferer from stomach ulcer, in which case it is necessary that the intervals between meals should not be too long. The whole business of having meals at fixed intervals is nothing but a social convention, and in modern life obviously a matter of convenience. (*See* **Diet, P39**).

Sleep, too, is a necessity. But different people require different amounts of sleep. Some manage on as little as three hours, others need ten or more.

In a number of studies of men and women who lived to a ripe old age it was found that the only factors in common between them were that they had a good balanced diet of healthy food, that they had contented minds, and that they were interested in something which gave them an aim in life. They also came of long-lived families—for living a long and healthy life depends partly upon heredity.

So the main rules of health are:
(1) Don't abuse your body—*i.e.*, exercise it, feed it sensibly and in moderation and don't poison it with cigarette smoke (yours or anyone else's), with alcohol or with other drugs

(2) Think positively about health—make it a purpose for living

(3) Turn your thoughts away from those bodily functions (digestion, circulation, breathing and so on) which can look after themselves. Introspection leads to hypochondriasis, and

(4) Choose your parents for *their* longevity!

The Development of Medicines

A great surgeon, the first of the moderns, was Ambroise Paré, who died in 1590, and one of his best known sayings was: "I apply the dressing, but God heals the wound." He was quite right; for until about sixty years ago, or even less, all the physician could do was to put the patient in as favourable a state as possible to enable his body to cure itself. That is to say, there were hardly any specific drugs—drugs that had a direct effect on the disease. There was quinine, discovered by the Spaniards in America, which was specific for malaria, and there were iron (specific for anaemia) and digitalis (specific for certain types of heart disease), but otherwise nothing until the nineteenth century, when Paul Ehrlich discovered salvarsan, which is specific for syphilis. Ehrlich died in 1914, having conceived the brilliant idea of drugs, which he described as "magic bullets"—*i.e.*, drugs which, like bullets, would be aimed at the real cause of the disease. They would, that is to say, be specific.

Since then a large number of such drugs have been discovered. For example, the antibiotics, such as penicillin, discovered in 1928 by Fleming at St. Mary's Hospital, Paddington. Later, Florey and Chain in Oxford, helped in the war years by the vast resources of the American pharmaceutical industry, were able to make penicillin available to the public in sufficient quantities by new techniques of production. Penicillin is practically non-poisonous (although it is possible to become allergic to it, sometimes with serious results). It can kill some germs in a dilution of one part of penicillin to one million parts of water; it is effective against streptococci, the cause of blood-poisoning, sepsis in wounds, and many other diseases; and also against the germs of anthrax, gonorrhoea, meningitis of some types, syphilis—penicillin is typically active at 1–10 ug/ml *i.e.* 1–10 parts per million. Blood-poisoning, whether from wounds or childbirth, used to be almost incurable—now the rate of cure is 80–90 per cent.; anthrax and gonorrhoea have an almost 100 per cent. rate of cure. In pneumonia the rate is 90 per cent., and early syphilis can be cured in a week, instead of the previous two to three years.

But that was only the beginning. Other antibiotics—streptomycin, tetracycline, erythromycin, and many others—have greatly reduced the terrible scourges of the human race, in particular, in the case of streptomycin, tuberculosis. The sulpha group of drugs—sulphadiazine, sulphadimidine, etc.—have also proved a great boon. Then there are the new drugs which have created a revolution in psychiatry—the tranquillisers which relieve anxiety, the drugs which clear up certain types of depression, and substances such as chlorpromazine which make it possible to nurse formerly violent patients in the wards of a general hospital. The antihistamine drugs help in allergies, anticoagulants are of value after heart attacks and levodopa mitigates some of the distressing features of Parkinson's Disease.

No drug, old or new, is completely safe—if we define "safe" as meaning having absolutely no potential for harm. The household aspirin, widely used in a variety of conditions for its analgesic (pain-relieving) and antipyretic (fever-reducing) qualities, can cause bleeding from the stomach and small intestine. Phenacetin, at one time a component of compound codeine tablets but now withdrawn, can—with prolonged use—damage the kidney. Chloramphenicol, a powerful antibiotic effective in typhoid fever, typhus and whooping cough, can damage the blood-forming cells of the bone marrow producing an agranulocytosis which can be fatal.

Clearly, in any one case, the doctor must weigh up the advantages and disadvantages of this or that drug before prescribing. Minor, self-limiting illnesses do not require potent, potentially toxic remedies. Chloramphenicol is rarely justified in whooping cough, but would never be withheld from a patient with typhoid fever.

Man is a unique species. A new chemical compound promising in animal experiments, for example, as an anti-inflammatory agent, apparently safe when given, say, to mice in a dose 100 times that required to produce that anti-inflammatory effect may, over a long period of time in man, not only have no effect but make his hair fall out or perhaps cause retention of urine. Nevertheless, some animal species do react like man, or vice versa, and it is possible to make reasonably accurate extrapolations from animals to man in terms of drug effect. It is also possible to estimate the toxicity of a drug for man from its toxicity in certain animal species but the ultimate test, both of the effectiveness and the toxicity of a new drug, comes only when it is given to man.

Thalidomide was unique. In every animal test used throughout the drug industry at that time—it was introduced in the late 1950s—it had a clean bill of health. It was chemically related to other drugs which had been in use for a long time. Overdosage with other sedatives such as the barbiturates was common at that time, although less so now. Overdosage with thalidomide was unlikely to prove fatal. It was marketed in Europe and in Britain as a "safe sedative". The tragic results that followed its ingestion by women in the early weeks of pregnancy are now well known. Babies were born with severe deformities of limbs, internal organs or both. That effect could not have been foretold from any animal tests then in use. Since that date new drugs have been subjected to rigorous testing in various animal species to check the effect on foetal development as a statutory requirement, along with the older tests for toxicity which had always been undertaken by reputable drug companies.

The thalidomide disaster of the early 1960s led directly to the setting up of regulatory drug agencies in most countries of the world. In Britain the introduction and clinical testing of new compounds is controlled by the Medicines and Environmental Health Division of the Department of Health and Social Security, statutory machinery set up by the Medicines Act 1968, which followed the purely voluntary scheme of control under what was known as the Dunlop Committee after Sir Derrick Dunlop, its first chairman.

The development and introduction of new drugs is now very strictly controlled. No new drug can be marketed in Britain without the Medicines Commission being satisfied about its efficacy and its safety. We would need space in this edition almost the size of the complete Medical Section to describe fully the workings of the Commission and the limitations that the requirements of the Medicines Act inevitably place on the development and introduction of new remedies. The time from the initial synthesis of a novel compound likely to be of value to its eventual appearance in the pharmacy on prescription is now eight to 10 years. The cost is measured in millions of pounds because, for each successful drug, there will have been many thousands of unsuccessful ones.

Briefly, no new drug or modification of an old one can be sold, whether or not on prescription, unless it has been granted a product licence by the Department of Health and Social Security through its Medicines and Environmental Health Division. Many stages have to be passed to acquire that licence, from the granting of certificates to allow the drug to be tested initially in a limited way in patients in a strictly controlled manner by investigators approved by the Commission, to permission for extension of those trials at a later date to include larger numbers of patients or more investigators, to perhaps a "monitored release"—that is, to enable its use in, say, hospitals only—to the final release on the granting of a full product licence. Thus, the Medicines Commission has control at all stages.

Furthermore, all the stages are dependent on production of evidence relating to the safety and efficacy of the drug, evidence which may take the drug company months, sometimes years, to produce and which, of course, must be acceptable to the Commission. Trials may be stopped at any time, for example, if evidence of side effects of an undesirable nature come to light during clinical testing, or when evidence from some other similar compound indicates a likely risk in the use of the drug in question. Of course, "acceptable" means that the strict criteria which have been laid down by the specialist committees appointed to deal with all the various aspects of drug development, such as toxicology, adverse reactions and so forth, have been met. Experts serve on these committees which meet regularly, but the day-to-day running of the Medicines Commission is in the hands of full-time medically qualified personnel as well as pharmacists, pharmacologists and toxicologists. In addition, outside consultant opinion can be sought.

As well as all these rigid controls on development and testing in the early stages, there is also a scheme of surveillance for untoward side effects. These are the action, or actions, of a drug apart from its main one. Take the well-known side effect of drowsiness which occurs with certain antihistamine drugs: the main action, the one for which the drug is prescribed, is the mitigation of the effects of allergy, such as urticaria. Drowsiness would be an unwanted effect if the patient is not incapacitated and is able to do his usual job. On the other hand, some antihistamines have an appetite-stimulating effect which could, of course, be a useful attribute in certain situations or even allow the drug to be used solely for that purpose, the anti-allergic effect then being incidental.

An adverse reaction is a type of side effect which by definition, is unwanted and potentially harmful. The intestinal bleeding associated with aspirin, or the depressive effects of some of the earlier drugs used to lower blood pressure, such as reserpine and methyldopa, are good examples. When new drugs first become licensed for marketing and are prescribed by doctors on a gradually increasing scale it is important that adverse reactions such as those are reported. Every doctor in the National Health Service, whether in general practice or in hospital, has access to a stock of special record cards on which he can record in a standard way the details of any untoward reaction occurring in his patient during the prescribing of a new or existing drug, and which he has good reason to believe is associated with the taking of that drug. These record cards are posted to the DHSS which has a special unit to deal with them. A doctor noticing, for example that one of his patients developed, say, double vision during treatment with a new antidepressant could not assume in the absence of other firm evidence that the two events were necessarily connected. However, if 100 cards are received by the DHSS reporting the same kind of event, there is good circumstantial evidence that those events are likely to be connected with drug administration. This adverse reaction reporting system, although voluntary, is working well and is an effective "early warning system" for drug toxicity

We have come a long way since thalidomide, but have had to steer between the Scylla of stifling innovation in drug research by excessive control of development and the Charybdis of the free-for-all, profit-motivated bonanzas of the pre-thalidomide era. No system can be perfect, and it is fair to say that had it been necessary, for example, for aspirin, penicillin and streptomycin to be put through the system as we have set it up now they would probably never have reached the market and thence the patient.

Mention must of course be made of the surgical advances and progress in anaesthesia. Hardly a week goes by without operations being undertaken which seemed inconceivable even as short a time as 40 years ago. Transplantation and re-plantation (the re-attachment of severed limbs) are regularly reported; haemodialysis (the 'cleansing' of blood in patients with irreversibe kidney disease) is now often undertaken in the patient's own home where, with appropriate adaptation and the modern kidney machine, he or she can run the procedure—single-handed in many instances—and still keep his or her job; and the laser beam is used to deal with detached retinas or to obliterate tiny, microscopic blood vessel 'bubbles' (aneurysms) in the back of the eye while the patient is conscious and cooperative. The list grows daily.

Social Medicine.

Medicine has passed through many phases from the time when disease was regarded as a punishment from the gods or a sign of devil possession to the present era, when increasingly there is a tendency to look on society as the patient. Indeed, one commonly hears doctors and sociologists nowadays talking about "the sick society."

The early primitive stage came to an end—at least in one part of the world—when in Greece, five centuries before Christ, Hippocrates and others began to teach that all diseases were due to natural causes. But after the first ray of hope the outlook began to deteriorate when, during the Middle and Dark Ages (that is, from the fall of the Roman Empire right up to the fifteenth century), there was a return to the belief in devil possession and supernatural causes.

Eighteenth-century medicine in Europe was materialistic, regarding the body as a machine. It was founded upon a sort of pseudo-science—although, of course, there were always individual exceptions, physicians such as Sydenham in England, who, avoiding all theories, based their work on observation of the patient. This mechanistic approach persisted right through the nineteenth century, but medicine became more and more truly scientific, and the century saw the most rapid advances in the field ever known until our own times: the discovery of germs by Pasteur, of antiseptics to combat them by Lister, of vaccination by Jenner and anaesthetics by the American Wells and the Scot Simpson. The use of the microscope by Virchow, who was a German, brought great advances in the understanding of disease and Ehrlich, another German, conceived, as we have already seen, the idea of "magic bullets" which would attack the germs at the root of a disease without harming the patient. But one of the greatest of all these great men is perhaps the least known. His name was Edwin Chadwick.

From the earliest period of recorded history human communities had been constantly ravaged by great plagues which swept over their lands year after year, killing untold millions. The Black Death of 1348–9 wiped out almost half the population of Europe. But, even in the first quarter of the nineteenth century in London, tens of thousands died from typhus, typhoid, and small-pox—and not only these, for periodically cholera would be brought into the country by travellers from abroad.

In the face of these terrible visitations the individual physician was helpless. He could not treat each one of the many sick even had he known how, and Chadwick's claim to fame rests on the fact that he was the first man to think in terms of *social* control of diseases, by so dealing with their causes that they were prevented from arising at all. In order to wipe out typhoid and cholera, he argued, we must ensure clean water supplies; for these diseases are caused by germs carried in polluted water. In order to attack typhus and plague, one must get rid of the lice which carry the germs of typhus and the rat-fleas which carry the germs of plague (including, of course, the rats, which, in turn, carry the fleas).

Chadwick was born in a Lancashire farmhouse where the children were washed every day all over, and he ruthlessly drove an obsession with cleanliness into the heads of his countrymen until, later in the century, it was possible for the German philosopher Treitschke to tell his class in Berlin: "The English think soap is civilisation." Although this remark was meant cynically, there is little doubt that soap, if it is not civilisation in itself, has played a greater part in making civilisation possible than many more elaborate remedies. A population riddled with chronic infectious illness has neither the time nor the energy to apply to the arts or sciences, and soap did a great deal to reduce infection.

One of the first public health measures was introduced by Chadwick and others when they brought in legislation to purify the water supply of London. Previously, the citizens had used water from the Thames (they still do, but only after it has been filtered and sterilised at the waterworks!), and from filthy, refuse-laden ponds and springs. Later, Chadwick helped to found the Poor Law Commission, and produced a Report in 1842, the principal suggestions of which were: a municipal water supply for all towns; scientific drainage both in town and country; and an independent health service with large powers for dealing with those who endangered the lives of others by polluting water or causing nuisances. He also proposed a national service for interment of the dead; for in those days bodies often remained for days in the overcrowded homes of the poor without burial.

What has the twentieth century contributed to the concept of social health? Well, of course, there has been a great deal of legislation along the lines initiated by Chadwick to control disease, and a great many other measures have been introduced concerned with the idea of positive health—not merely preventing bad health, but trying to bring about the highest possible state of good health.

Orange juice, milk, and good meals for school-children brought about a transformation in child health which became apparent to the least observant. And the National Health service is in the direct line of descent from early nineteenth-century legislation.

But in future years it is probable that the main achievement of the twentieth century will prove to be its extension of the term "social health" to cover every aspect of community life, not only in such subjects as bodily health and its control of social means, but also such problems as mental illness, crime, delinquency, drug addiction, and so on. What we are now asking ourselves is how far are these problems produced by society itself, and if this is the case, how far can we go in preventing them by social means?

Community medicine takes the view that these problems can never be dealt with solely by moral-ising and retribution, but only by dispassionately analysing causes and dealing with them. In this century we have developed a social con-science. Not always, it is true, a very well-informed social conscience, but at least this is a good beginning. There are organisations for dealing scientifically with delinquency, for dealing with problem children, for spreading knowledge about cancer in order to show people that it can be successfully treated if taken in time. We can well say with John Donne, who died in 1631, that "no man is an island ... every man's death diminisheth me; for I am involved in mankind." This is the attitude of twentieth-century com-munity medicine.

Summary. Perhaps we can sum up our pro-gress in the past century and a half more dramatically in terms of hard facts.

Before that time a surgical operation was never undertaken except under the gravest circum-stances. There were no anaesthetics and no anti-septics, and the operation was carried out by a surgeon in a filthy tail-coat, stained with the con-gealed blood of countless operations (indeed the surgeons of that time took pride in the dirty condi-tion of their coats as showing how much experience they had previously had). Germs and the part they play in producing disease were unknown, and Paul Ehrlich had not yet been born, so there were no "magic bullets" to attack syphilis, or sera for diphtheria and other diseases. The mentally ill were simply locked up with little treatment and subjected to such indignities as the strait-jacket and the padded cell; now they are given treatment which becomes more effective each year, the padded cell and strait-jacket have gone, and in very few hospitals are the ward doors locked.

In the earlier years of this century you would very likely have died if you had developed pneumonia, "childbed fever" after the birth of a child, men-ingitis, dysentery, typhoid, or tuberculosis. With such infections as blood-poisoning you would have had practically no chance at all. Today, the sulpha drugs and the antibiotics have changed all that. Syphilis and gonorrhoea were lifelong tragedies both to the patient and his family, but now they, too, can be conquered. With scientific research and its application proceeding at a brisk pace many diseases are now being brought under control.

The National Health Service has brought the possibility of good treatment equally to all, and it is up to us to see that all these facilities are used to the full by all who need them.

PART II. DISEASES ARRANGED BY CAUSE OR BODY SYSTEM AFFECTED

THE INFECTIOUS DISEASES.
INTRODUCTION.

INFECTIOUS diseases are those which are caused by an invasion of the human body by organisms from outside (the word "organism" simply means living things, and we are using this word because, as will be seen later, it is not only what are known as

"germs" which can cause infection. We know, too, that what is generally typical about this group is: (a) that the disease can be passed on from one person to another, and (b) that it is usually accompanied by a raised temperature or fever. Now (a), of course, is always true, because the definition of an infectious disease is one that can be passed on to others, but (b) is not always true, because a few infections produce little or no temperature, and also because it is possible to have a raised temperature (again in only a few cases) without any infection. For example, certain types of brain injury, tumour, or haemorrhage can produce a raised—or lowered—temperature, and so can the injection of some foreign substance such as milk into the muscles. This is known as "protein shock," and was at one time used in the treatment of certain illnesses. Finally, solutions of dead germs, such as the antityphoid vaccine given to protect troops during the War, may lead when injected to very high temperatures. But, by and large, we are entitled to suppose that the patient with a raised temperature is probably suffering from an infection.

Types of Infection.

As we have seen, it is not only germs which cause infections—so from now on we shall give germs their proper name of "bacteria." Here is a list of the chief offenders which are liable to attack our bodies: bacteria, viruses, fungi, amoebae, worms and other parasites.

Bacteria are tiny living things which can be seen only under a fairly powerful microscope. Some are grouped like bunches of grapes (staphylococci) or in strings or chains (streptococci). They are given these names because "staphylos" is the Greek word for a bunch of grapes, and "streptos" means a chain. Yet others are comma-shaped (such as the cholera vibrio), or shaped like a drumstick—a rod with a small knob at the end (the tetanus bacillus, which causes lockjaw).

It would be a mistake to think that all bacteria are harmful; for without some species we could not survive for long. Bacteriologists divide them according to their behaviour in the human body into three groups: saprophytic, parasitic or pathogenic, and symbiotic. The *saprophytic* organisms are the bacteria normally found in the skin, mouth, and intestines; they do us neither harm nor good. The *parasitic*, or as they are more usually called, pathogenic (*i.e.*, disease-producing) organisms, are the harmful ones with which we are naturally more concerned. Lastly, there are the *symbiotic* organisms, which, whilst taking something from the body, give something in return. For example, cattle would not be able to digest the cellulose of the grass they eat were it not for helpful bacteria in the lower parts of the intestines, and there are certain bacteria in the large intestine of man which produce vitamins.

Bacteria have two peculiar characteristics: each reproduces by splitting into two separate individuals as often as every twenty minutes in favourable circumstances like an open wound. If no bacterium were destroyed, one individual could produce a mass of bacteria larger than the whole world in a matter of a few weeks (since each of the offspring also divides into two, which in turn divide again—the progression goes: one gives birth to two, these two to four, the four to eight, eight to sixteen, sixteen to thirty-two, and so on—you will see, if you work it out, that in a short period the figure becomes astronomical. Fortunately, most bacteria do not find themselves in ideal conditions, so for the present the world is safe! The other curious thing about bacteria is that, barring accidents, they are potentially immortal. Under ideal conditions in which no bacteria were killed, none would die; for a bacterium there is no death from old age, no corpse except when it is actively destroyed. It simply goes on dividing, dividing, and subdividing for ever.

How, then, are bacteria destroyed? Briefly, the answer is that most are destroyed by the natural defences of the body of whatever host they are preying on; others are destroyed by antiseptics and the new drugs; and many are destroyed when they are excreted from the body in the sputum or through the bowels and land in places where they are dried up and cannot survive —although some bacteria in such circumstances can form what are called "spores," rather like the seeds of plants, so making it possible for them to survive in a state of suspended animation for months on end until picked up accidentally by another unfortunate host. Finally, bacteria, in addition to all these possibilities, face another danger: they may themselves develop disease. This disease is caused by even more minute organisms known as bacteriophages (viruses which affect bacteria), discovered by F. W. Twort in 1915. Attack by bacteriophage causes whole groups of bacteria (known as "colonies") to disintegrate and become harmless.

Although bacteriophage have been used in the treatment of some diseases in human beings, this method has now been largely given up, since the new drugs are infinitely more effective.

Other Spirochaetes, like bacteria, are minute organisms, but differ in being shaped somewhat like a corkscrew and in being able to move. Their progress is produced by a sideways wriggling motion. The two main diseases caused by spirochaetes are syphilis and spirochaetal jaundice. Spirochaetal jaundice is carried by rats, and is common in those who work in mines. It is now rare in Britain, but still occurs in Japan, Egypt, and Malaysia; the infection is passed through the skin where the excreta of infected rats mingles with water on damp ground in the mine where miners kneel. Infection may also occur through eating infected food.

Viruses. Unlike bacteria, viruses are too small to be seen under an ordinary microscope. They can, however, be photographed in some cases under an electron microscope, which uses a magnetic field instead of a glass lens and a stream of electrons in place of a beam of light. Viruses cause such diseases as measles, mumps, poliomyelitis, smallpox, and chickenpox—not to mention such plant and animal diseases as tobacco mosaic disease and foot-and-mouth disease, which often have serious economic consequences. Other virus diseases are swine fever in pigs, influenza in Man, and myxomatosis in rabbits. They also cause the common cold.

The main characteristics of viruses are, first, that they can only grow in living cells—unlike bacteria, which readily grow in the laboratory on plates containing a jelly made from meat, broth, gelatin, milk, and other delicacies. The scientist, therefore, must keep them in portions of living tissue kept alive outside the body. Secondly, many are so small that they pass through the pores of the finest filter. Thirdly, a first attack usually produces immunity for life. Second attacks of the common virus diseases mentioned above are very rare; but unfortunately, this rule does not apply to influenza or the common cold. Fourthly, there is reason to believe that viruses represent an extraordinary intermediate stage between the living and non-living; they can, for instance, be produced in crystalline form and yet are just as dangerous when "thawed out." Lastly, the virus diseases have proved for the most part to be little affected by the new antibiotics and other drugs, although vaccination in smallpox and the injection of sera from infected patients in other infections may give immunity for longer or shorter periods, and progress has been made in developing drugs to combat some viruses, such as herpes viruses and the AIDS virus.

The two great practical problems that doctors face with viruses are: (i) many viruses are unknown because of the difficulty of growing them outside the body in suitable tissue culture. They cannot therefore be conveniently identified in specimens from the patient, as bacteria can; and (ii) most are unaffected by antibiotics like penicillin. It has been a great step forward to grow viruses artificially in tissue culture, in which they are identified indirectly by the effects they have on the cultured *cells*. But since we do not know exactly how to grow some viruses (like those of infective hepatitis) many have still not been seen.

When we recover from a viral illness like chickenpox, we probably do so by producing virus-killing substances such as interferon inside our own cells. Scientists are currently searching for these substances in case they can be used, like penicillin, to cure viral disease.

Fungi. Some infections are caused by fungi— that is to say organisms belonging to the same group as moulds, mushrooms, and toadstools. Penicillin and some other antibiotics are produced from moulds, so, as in the case of bacteria, some fungi are helpful; they even help to destroy each other, as bacteria do. For example actinomyces, which can cause infection of the jaw and other tissues, is destroyed by penicillin.

Most fungal infections are trivial and limited to the skin. But, although trivial, they can be unsightly and uncomfortable. Ringworm of the scalp, dhobie itch—an infection of the groin spread by infected underclothing—and so-called "athlete's foot" are caused by a fungus.

Amoebae. Amoebae are small, single-cell organisms, the largest of which (a harmless type found in stagnant ponds in Britain and elsewhere) is just visible to the naked eye. It is about the size of the head of a pin. Amoebae move, in the species which are capable of moving, by pushing forward a part of the cell in the appropriate direction and causing the rest to flow into the advancing portion. Like bacteria, they reproduce by dividing into halves, each of which becomes a new amoeba.

The main human disease caused by amoebae is amoebic dysentery (not to be confused with bacillary dysentery).

Parasites. These may live on the skin like lice (which can carry typhus) or fleas (carriers of plague) or the parasites of scabies which burrow into the skin, or they may live part of their time in the blood or other tissues, like malaria. They often have complicated life-cycles involving other hosts (like mosquitoes) at certain stages of development.

Worms. Worms are intestinal parasites, but the only common types found in Britain are threadworms, the tiny thread-like worms which cause irritability and itching in the skin of children, less often in adults; round-worms, somewhat resembling the ordinary garden earthworm, which seldom lead to symptoms; and tapeworms, which may reach a length of 3 or even 6 m. Many parasitic worms (like parasites elsewhere) lead a double life—they spend part of their life in the human intestine and the other part in the muscles of another animal. The tapeworm, for example, whilst in the human intestine, lays eggs which pass out of the body in the excreta, and are then swallowed by pigs, especially in those parts of the world where human excreta are used as manure in the fields. In the pig, the eggs form cysts in the muscles—meat infected in this way is known as "measly pork"—and when, in turn, the meat is eaten by man, the process in the intestine begins all over again.

Less common types, from our point of view, are the Russian tape-worm (which, as befits a Russian, grows to nearly 9 m!); this type is spread by caviare or undercooked infected fish. The small, leaf-shaped liver fluke lays eggs which are passed into canals or pools in tropical countries in the urine of infected people, hatch out and enter a water snail, and finally leave the snail in the form of small parasites which pierce the skin of bathers, whence they pass to the liver and subsequently the bladder and rectum. This is a serious condition, as is also filariasis (another tropical disease), for which, unlike bilharzia—caused by the liver fluke—no cure is known. The tropical disease known as loa-loa is caused by a variety of filaria.

How the Infection is Spread.

Infection is spread in many ways, some of which have already been mentioned. In the common fevers found in Europe and elsewhere one of the most frequent ways is by *droplet infection*—that is to say, by minute drops carrying the germs which are coughed or sneezed into the air by someone already suffering from the disease. Such droplets can be projected into the air for 3m or more, and when breathed in by someone within range infection may result. Next commonest mode of spread is perhaps by *infected food, water*, and the dirty hands of those who prepare food: cholera, dysentery, food-poisoning, and typhoid are spread in this way. Spread by *direct contact* is found in the venereal diseases (usually, but not

always, spread by sexual intercourse with someone who already has the disease), and, of course, lice, fleas, and other parasites, including the scabies mite, are spread by contact with the infested individual—or sometimes with his clothes or bed linen. Spread through an *intermediary host*, whether it be lice, fleas, or mosquitoes carrying infection, or the various means adopted by worms, has already been described above, so no more need be said. Lastly, the infection may result from *bacteria already within the body*; for example, Escherichia coli, which lives in the large intestine is harmless there, but if it gets into the bladder or the ureters (the tubes leading from kidney to bladder) a quite unpleasant result may follow in the form of cystitis or pyelitis.

How the Body Deals with Infection.

The body has many mechanisms of defence against intruders; these can generally be divided into two types. First, non-specific defence substances such as lysozyme, an enzyme that digests bacterial cell walls, are present in many body fluids, and a system of blood proteins known as the complement cascade punches holes in bacteria to kill them. Interferons and other so-called cytokines are produced when the body's cells are damaged by infection and help other cells to resist infection. A class of blood cell, known as macrophages, responds to infection and other damage by migrating to the affected part of the body and swallows bacteria and cell debris for destruction by the powerful enzymes that they contain. Secondly, specific defences are stimulated by infection: one class of lymphocytes produces antibodies, which recognise particular parts of bacteria and viruses, neutralising them and marking them out for destruction. Another class of lymphocytes hunts for foreign cells and kills them by a variety of methods, bursting them open and leaving debris for the macrophages to clear away.

Immunity can be induced by immunisation, which can be active or passive. In active immunisation, a vaccine is injected into the body to simulate the first time the body is infected with a disease-causing agent. Vaccines are made either from dead bacteria or viruses or from specially adapted strains which have lost their ability to cause disease. Passive immunisation is used when a person has already been exposed to a disease or when an effective vaccine is not available, and consists of injections of specific gamma-globulin obtained from the blood of a patient who has recently recovered from the disease concerned.

Immunology is one of the fastest-growing areas of medical research, as there are still many infectious diseases which are difficult to treat with antibodies, and manipulation of the immune system has great potential in the fight against cancer.

Antiseptics.

The earliest antiseptic was carbolic acid, used by Lister in his operating-theatre in the form of a fine spray directed throughout the operation on the wound, or sometimes in the form of steam from a kettle containing a solution of carbolic. But carbolic is dangerous, and since Lister's time many more useful antiseptics have been discovered. Acriflavine, thymol, and other old favourites have been discarded too. The various forms of carbolic are still used to disinfect drains, but, to tell the truth, the use of antiseptics nowadays is very limited. In surgery the *antiseptic* method has given way to the *aseptic* method—instead of fighting sepsis we see to it that no possibility of sepsis is present before operating; all instruments, the surgeons' and nurses' hands, the skin, are sterilised—the instruments by boiling, the dressings by dry heat, the hands by soap and water, and almost the only antiseptic used is to clean the patient's skin in the area to be operated on.

Antiseptics are used as first-aid treatment for cuts and wounds, but should be applied only once as a general rule—that is, when the wound is first received. The trouble with antiseptics is that as well as killing germs they also kill the surrounding tissues, which antibiotics never do.

Antiseptic sprays to purify the air of a room or to destroy germs lurking in the dust on the sick-room floor—or any other floor—are practically useless. To quote the *British Medical Journal:* "There is no good scientific evidence that any of the chemical air-disinfectants can control the spread of infection in places such as schools, offices, or cinemas. Nor is there good evidence that any substantial effect on the spread of illness can be obtained by disinfection of dust."

Neither is there any good reason to believe that mouth-washes and gargles have any effect other than making the mouth feel fresher and (temporarily) removing mouth odour—by covering it up with the scent of the antiseptic. Mouth-washes are in contact with the bacteria for far too short a time to have any damaging result, and, in the case of tonsillitis and other diseases, all the important bacteria are hidden far out of any danger from gargles.

Antibiotics.

Some antibiotics—penicillin, streptomycin, erythromycin and so on—have already been mentioned (*see* **P4**). In recent years many others have been introduced—ampicillin, gentamicin, cephalexin. Indiscriminate use of these drugs (*e.g.* for trivial complaints) has led to problems, the most important being the development of resistance by previously sensitive organisms. It is not always convenient or possible to be able to identify the particular germ responsible for an infection and determine to which drug it is sensitive, but if there is an initial clinical response, it can be assumed that the "right" drug has been used. It is important to have a full course of treatment—which usually means ten days minimum.

Other problems are hypersensitivity (allergic) reactions which can take many forms. Once hypersensitivity to one of the antibiotics has been identified (penicillin hypersensitivity is not rare) the patient must be made aware of this, and so protect himself from unwitting prescribing by another doctor. Hospital and GP records are clearly marked in such instances but it is very important that the patient himself knows.

Antibiotics are only available on prescription, at least in the U.K., but medicine cupboards are full of them, accumulated from unfinished courses. Self-prescribing is tempting but ill-advised; antibiotics must always be given under medical supervision. Side effects are common and some are dangerous. Repeated use may lead to rapid overgrowth of fungi *e.g.* thrush (Candida albicans) normally present in harmless numbers in the alimentary tract with serious, sometimes fatal results.

General Treatment of Fevers.

Fevers are ordinarily heralded in by a rise in temperature which is noticeable either by a flushed face or by alternate sensations of heat and cold. A patient with a high temperature may have shivering attacks known as "rigors." Tell the doctor.

A high temperature does not necessarily (especially in a child) mean that the trouble is serious but the lay person should always treat it as such and certainly call a doctor if the patient is a child or an elderly person. The majority of fevers are of a viral origin and usually self limiting. The patient tends to improve rapidly once the temperature is controlled.

Even the trained physician finds it difficult to tell one fever from another in the early days; for most of the common fevers begin in more or less the same way. It is only when a rash or some other more definite sign becomes evident that a certain diagnosis can be made, and these may not show themselves until the patient has been feeling "run-down" and fevered for some days. A clinical thermometer is a useful tool and inexpensive to buy. The more recent fever scans applied directly to the forehead also give an immediate and fairly accurate temperature reading. Control of temperature is important, especially in young children, where a high fever may produce a convulsion. A febrile convulsion is a frightening experience for any parent, particularly as their child may have seemed quite well a few minutes previously. High temperature, twitching, and increased irritation may herald the onset. Emergency management involves keeping the child on its side to avoid inhalation of vomit,

clearing debris around his mouth, removing his clothes and sponging him with lukewarm water. Get someone to summon medical help, but never leave an unconscious child alone. Above all, do not panic as the initial episode will usually soon pass.

Briefly, then, the way to treat a fever in the early stages before the doctor comes, and before one knows exactly what is wrong, is as follows:

(1) Put the patient to bed. The child is probably better on the living room sofa where he will feel less isolated and is more easily observed.

(2) Give plenty of clear fluids; water, water and fruit juice, weak tea or lemonade.

(3) Give small amounts of easily digested food but only if the patient requires it.

(4) Aspirin is no longer recommended for the treatment of feverish children, and should not be given to children under 12 years of age. This is because it has been linked to the development of "Reye's Syndrome", an acute encephalopathy or inflammation of the brain with delirium, convulsions and coma. Although very rare, "Reye's Syndrome" carries a high mortality.

Adults with a history of peptic ulcer or chronic indigestion should also avoid aspirin because of the possible risk of a gastrointestinal bleed.

Paracetamol is now the treatment of choice to reduce temperature and relieve headache and elixir preparations are available for children. The dose may be repeated 4/6 hourly and there are no gastro-intestinal side effects.

Medicines containing Paracetamol should be stored in a safe place as overdosage, accidental or otherwise, may cause liver damage without initial drowsiness or loss of consciousness. Symptoms may not be apparent for a number of days.

Other methods of cooling a feverish patient involve removing excess clothing, administering tepid baths or sponging with lukewarm water. Simply standing at an open door and allowing the cool outside air to waft around the feverish child, can have an immediate effect.

THE INFECTIOUS FEVERS.

The remarks made above apply to the management of *any* fever, and we are now going to discuss particular infectious diseases, beginning with the common childhood fevers, then passing on to less common ones, tropical diseases, and worm and parasitic infestations.

The common infectious fevers are caused by bacteria or viruses, and it is useful to know the meaning of the following terms: *incubation period* is the time which elapses between being infected and developing symptoms; *prodromal period* is the time which elapses between the end of the incubation period and the appearance of a rash; *quarantine period*, the maximum time during which a person who has been in contact with the infection may develop the disease—it is usually two days more than the incubation period; *isolation period* the time a patient is supposed to be isolated.

Virus Diseases.

First, we shall take the common virus diseases, measles, chickenpox, and rubella or German measles, then the other virus diseases, mumps, infective hepatitis, viral pneumonia, and some less common conditions which do not always produce a typical rash as in the case of the first three.

In nearly all of these fevers there is a long incubation period, and one infection gives immunity for life.

Measles. The incubation period is 10–11 days. The first sign is the appearance of symptoms rather like a severe cold. The eyes become red, and exposure to light is unpleasant, the nose runs, the throat becomes inflamed, and a dry, harsh cough develops. There may be headache and the temperature rises to 39°C or more. Usually the patient is a child, and especially typical is the development of so-called Koplik's spots, which are small, bluish-white, raised spots seen on the inside of the cheek at the back of the mouth. The rash begins on the fourth day of the prodromal period, i.e., 14 days after the initial infection. It shows on the forehead and behind the ears, spreading within a day downwards over the whole body; in another two days it starts to disappear, but often leaves behind a sort of brownish staining which may last for one to two weeks.

Measles can be serious, especially in very young children because of its complications, such as bronchopneumonia and infection of the ear, which can now be treated with antibiotics. These drugs have no effect on the measles virus, but only on the secondarily invading bacteria which have invaded the lungs and ear during the illness. The illness can be attenuated or lessened by injection of antibodies (gamma globulin) from an immune adult, and this is often worth while in the very young. Effective vaccination is now available.

Rubella or German Measles. Incubation period 14–19 days. A mild fever, similar to measles except that the rash is usually the first sign that anything is wrong, and the temperature is rarely above 38°C. The eyes may be pink, and there are enlarged glands at the back of the neck. The rash disappears completely in thirty-six hours. There are no complications.

German measles, in itself, is harmless, but if a woman gets the disease in the early months of pregnancy malformations in the child may appear at birth. Vaccination is advised if a girl has not contracted the disease by the time she reaches puberty. There is no special treatment except the general rules for fevers given above.

Chickenpox. Incubation period 14–15 days, but may be more variable. In children chickenpox is a mild fever which begins with the appearance of tiny blisters on the chest and back. These later spread outwards to the legs, arms and face, and cause itching. Treatment is the general one for fevers already described. Calamine lotion or dusting powder will be helpful for the irritation, and the child's nails should be cut short to prevent scratching and infection of the spots. Whereas children are usually little bothered by chickenpox, young adults may be much more drastically affected—a temperature of 40°C is not uncommon, and then there may be severe headache. Shingles is a disease that sometimes follows chickenpox – usually by many years, and results from reactivation of the chicken pox virus which 'hides' in the spinal cord after a childhood infection.

Mumps. Incubation period 17–18 days. The typical appearance of mumps is a swelling in the salivary glands in front of the ears which makes the face look full. This causes pain later on, and it may be difficult to open the mouth. Temperature is not usually high (about 38°C). Although uncomfortable, mumps is rarely dangerous, but orchitis—swelling of the testicles—is sometimes a complication, especially if the infection occurs beyond childhood. Fluid diet should be given if eating is painful, with mouth-washes, and rest in bed.

Infective Hepatitis. "Hepatitis" means inflammation of the liver, and infective hepatitis, which is much the commonest cause of jaundice in young adults, is a viral infection of the liver. The main symptoms are fever, followed by jaundice, which is first noticed in the whites of the eyes as yellow staining, then in the skin. The urine becomes coloured also, and this is most easily noticed if, on shaking in a bottle, the froth shows coloration. If the froth remains white, no jaundice is present. Treatment is a matter for the doctor, but great care should be taken, both by the patient and those in contact with him, to wash the hands thoroughly after urinating or defaecat-

ing, after handling utensils from the sickroom, and both before and after eating; for the disease is very infectious.

Viral Pneumonia. Pneumonia is usually caused by bacteria, and when we speak of pneumonia, that is the type we ordinarily refer to. Viral pneumonia can be caused by a variety of viruses. There is no specific treatment so far, and since diagnosis is a specialist matter little more need be said except that the symptoms in general resemble those of ordinary pneumonia. Although there is no specific treatment for virus infections of the lungs, it is always worth while trying antibiotics in view of the possibility that the lung condition may be caused by a secondary invasion of bacteria.

Influenza. While serious epidemics of influenza take the form of a very dramatic and often fatal disease—for example, the epidemic of "Spanish 'flu" which followed the First World War killed more people than the actual fighting— the milder type more usually seen is difficult to distinguish from the common cold. In fact, many people who complain of "a dose of the 'flu" are suffering from simple colds.

However, a sudden onset, aching in the muscles of the back and legs, and redness of the eyes, would suggest influenza, and especially typical is the depression and weakness which follow influenza but not a cold. The measures suggested above for the general treatment of fever should be applied; but the depression and weakness which follow influenza may need special treatment by the doctor. Effective vaccines are now available, and are particularly recommended for the elderly, though immunisation must be carried out each year to overcome the propensity of influenza viruses to change the proteins in their "coats."

Colds. Although everyone thinks he, or she, knows what a "cold" is, the issue is not so simple; for the symptoms of fever, running nose, and a rundown, "headachy" feeling are found in many illnesses. They may be observed, as we have seen, in the early stages of measles before the arrival of the rash, or in a number of other fevers, such as whooping cough. Mild attacks of influenza (see above) may resemble the common cold, and blocking of the nose with discharge and fever may be due to sinusitis—although here there is usually pain above, between, or below the eyes. Colds can be caused by any one of 113 (in 1993) different viruses known as "rhinoviruses" This is why a single cold does not confer immunity on the sufferer. It is probable that you will not catch a cold from the same virus, at least for the rest of the year, but there are all those others waiting to infect you with other colds in buses, tubes, and other crowded places. Like all infections, do not forget that the best way to avoid them is to keep generally well, and in a good nutritional state. Do not spend money on injections or other vaccines. They do not work, probably because of the multiplicity of viruses involved. It is unlikely that adding vitamins or mineral supplements to normal diet will do any good at all provided you are eating sensibly. The vogue for prophylactic or therapeutic treatment of colds with massive doses of vitamin C has recently received much attention from scientists attempting, with little success, to prove the effect by controlled clinical trial and to find a rational basis for its use.

Poliomyelitis.

Polio, or infantile paralysis as it used to be known, is caused by a virus which has a particular affinity for the nerve cells of the spinal cord and which results in paralysis of those muscles under the control of the particular group of cells infected. Rarely, the infection is widespread in the nerve tissue causing paralysis of muscles of swallowing and respiration as well as those of the trunk and limbs. The usual pattern is for a single muscle group to be affected, for example, the muscles controlling the movements of the arm at the shoulder. Such paralysis may be transient with complete recovery, partial with some residual weakness, or total, leaving a "flail limb" which is wasted and powerless.

At one time in this country epidemics of polio-myelitis were common, mainly affecting children and young adults. There is no doubt that mild forms of the disease were always occurring in very young children, forms never diagnosed as such but conferring a natural immunity in later life.

In common with other infections, poliomyelitis begins with a mild or moderate fever, with a sore throat, headache, nausea and perhaps actual vomiting, some five to 10 days after contact with the virus. There may be rigidity of the neck muscles. Paralysis, if it occurs, will become apparent about the second or third day of illness. This stage may last two or three weeks, by which time the temperature will have subsided and the paralysis started to improve. There is no specific treatment and medical care is confined to sympto-matic relief. Difficulty with swallowing and breathing calls for special nursing measures. In severe cases, artificial means of maintaining respiration may have to be continued for months, or for the rest of the patient's life. Many severely paralysed polio victims of the post-war epidemics —the self-styled "responauts"—depend for their lives on artificial respirators ("iron lungs").

With the development of the oral vaccine early in the 1960s, and its introduction into the im-munisation schedule in this country, the disease has now virtually disappeared from Great Britain.

Smallpox. In previous editions we stated that "since the introduction of vaccination it (small-pox) is comparatively rare in industrialised coun-tries." In the 88th edition we reported that small-pox (*variola major*) had now been eradicated throughout the world. The less serious form of the disease, variola minor, is still found in some parts of Africa, but all the signs are that it, too, will soon be eradicated. The last case of *variola major* occurred in Bangladesh in 1975, except for at least one accidental infection in England in the 1980s. With the disappearance of the disease vaccination will become unnecessary; however, the World Health Organisation is planning to store vaccine (which can be done almost indefinitely at a temperature of $-20°C$) in sufficient quantities to vaccinate many millions of people should the need ever arise again. We made no excuse therefore for leaving out of that edition of *Pears*, for the first time in its long history, the detailed description of the disease.

Glandular Fever. Sometimes called infectious mononucleosis, since one of its features is an in-crease in a certain type of white cell—the monocyte—and a change in its microscopic charac-teristics. It is caused by a virus (the Epstein-Barr), predominantly affects young children and adults and although often taking a protracted course, it is not in itself a serious infection. The main symptoms are fever, enlargement of lymph glands in the neck and a sore throat. A transient body rash may be seen occasionally, particularly during or after the treat-ment of the sore throat with penicillin or one of its synthetic cousins such as ampicillin. Diagnosis without laboratory tests on the blood (the Paul-Bunnel test) may not be easy although the com-bination of sore throat, swollen neck glands and a rash is highly suspicious. The disease is self-limiting and there is no treatment.

Rabies. Finally, we shall deal very briefly with a number of less common virus diseases, beginning, as is appropriate, with *hydrophobia* or *rabies*, since it was in this infection that the great French scientist Louis Pasteur (1822–95) showed the possibility of prevention by vaccination. Unlike Jenner, with his ready-made cowpox virus, which is probably the virus of smallpox weakened by natural passage through cows, Pasteur had to weaken the rabies virus by passing it through rabbits. The rabbits were infected, and after death the spinal cord was dried and powdered, and a solution passed through another rabbit, and so on until the virus was sufficiently weakened.

Rabies is spread by the bite of infected animals, usually dogs, cats, or wolves, who are driven mad

by the disease; in Trinidad, however, it has been spread by vampire bats. Those who are bitten usually show no symptoms for six weeks or more, but sooner or later convulsions and delirium arise, which within four to five days are fatal.

There is no cure once the symptoms have developed, but antirabies serum, followed by anti-rabies inoculation as soon as possible, prevents illness in the majority of cases. Dogs should be muzzled in areas where the disease is common, but quarantining imported dogs has made the infection almost unknown here. Effective immunisation is now available.

Sandfly Fever, or phlebotomus fever, *Dengue,* or breakbone fever, and *Trench Fever* are all somewhat similar conditions in that they resemble influenza and are rarely fatal. They are all due to viruses, spread in the first case by sandflies in tropical climates; in the second by mosquitoes in tropical climates; and in the third by lice in temperate climates. They are all typical 'soldiers' diseases''; the first two were common in the Middle East and Far East during the last War, the third during the First World War in France.

Yellow Fever. Yellow fever is carried by a mosquito known as Aedes, common in South and Central America and in African ports. For its spread, it therefore needs: a hot climate, the Aedes mosquito, and an infected person.

In 1898 the United States was at war with Spain in Central America, where yellow fever was a serious problem. Following this war the United States, by this time acutely aware of this terrible disease, asked a Dr. G. E. Waring to deal with it in Havana, where it was rife. But Waring died of yellow fever, as had many millions before him, without knowing its cause, and it was left to Walter Reed, who died in 1902, to prove the con-nection between the mosquito and yellow fever. By a vigorous war on the mosquito, the disease has been eradicated from Havana and the West In-dian islands, and Reed's discovery made possible the building of the Panama Canal.

In yellow fever there is a sudden high tempera-ture, aching of limbs and head, jaundice, and black vomit; the pulse-rate falls as the fever rises. Previous vaccination seems to be preventive if undertaken in time.

AIDS. AIDS stands for acquired immunodefi-ciency syndrome, and is caused by the human immunodeficiency virus (HIV). AIDS seems to be a new affliction for the human race, and was first described in 1981, after which its frequency increased so that there were nearly 9000 in England and Wales by March 1994. Infection occurs by inter-course, the anal variety apparently being the more dangerous, by direct transmission through infected blood, and congenital transmission from mother to baby. Thus, the major risk factors for AIDS are male homosexuality, needle sharing by intravenous drug abusers, haemophilia, and having an infected mother. Heterosexual intercourse is also an impor-tant mode of spread, especially among prostitutes, who are the most promiscuous members of communi-ties. AIDS can be avoided by restricting sexual relations to the one you trust, and by avoiding *any* contact with other people's blood.

HIV damages the T-lymphocytes that are respon-sible for protecting the body against infection. with the result that the sufferer becomes prey to a variety of otherwise rare infections such as *Pneumocystis carinii* pneumonia, as well as some rare tumours, particularly Kaposi's sarcoma and lymphomas. The incubation period can be very long, and the first signs are often lethargy, weight loss and swelling of the lymph glands. There is as yet no effective vaccine; a number of drugs have been and are being tested, though the results of these tests are accompanied by a great deal of controversy.

Conclusion.

There is no specific cure for most viral diseases, though several can be prevented by immunisation or by social control of the creatures carrying the virus and by the use of common day-to-day hygiene, and drugs are beginning to be introduced against a few viruses. Incubation periods are generally of the order of days, though in the case of the AIDS virus can be measured in years. Where active immunisation is not available, passive protection with gamma globulin is often an effective alternative.

Bacterial Diseases.

Bacterial diseases differ from virus infections in a number of respects; their incubation period tends to be shorter: having the disease once does not often confer lifelong protection; and unlike virus diseases, most bacterial diseases respond to one of the antibiotics or sulphonamides. In some cases it is possible to inoculate against the disease to prevent it occurring, as is possible with some of the virus diseases.

Scarlet Fever and Other Streptococcal Infections. In the days, not so long ago, before the arrival of chemotherapy (sulphonamides and antibiotics), streptococci were very much feared and even caused a high mortality, particularly in such susceptible groups as children, and mothers and babies in maternity hospitals. They are still taken very seriously in the latter and rightly so, although one wonders how much of the mystique is simply a hangover from the days, fifty years ago, when many mothers died from "childbed fever." All signs of infection, such as fever, during the puerperium (the period following childbirth) must be promptly dealt with by a doctor, and only occasionally now is there real cause for anxiety provided treatment is prompt and rigorous.

Scarlet fever is much less common and very much less serious an illness than it used to be, partly because of the effective treatments available today, but also because of a definite but unexplained reduction in its severity. Perhaps the streptococcus has changed, and certainly the improved physical condition of people who are now much better fed and housed than they were, has helped to ward off the terrors of this disease as of so many other infections. The classical picture of signs and symptoms is now so rarely seen that it will not be further described. However, there is some evidence that streptococci are changing again, and becoming more pathogenic and difficult to treat.

The importance of streptococcal infections has shifted from the initial infection, such as a sore throat, to some serious conditions which occasionally arise as a result of some form of delayed sensitivity to the bacteria. Acute rheumatism or rheumatic fever (not to be confused with ordinary aches and pains nor with rheumatoid arthritis) occasionally arise in people who have had a sore throat a few weeks before. Since the streptococcus is not the direct cause of the damage which may consequently occur in the heart or kidney, the antibiotics are no answer except sometimes to keep off further streptococcal invasions.

Diphtheria. This used to be an extremely serious disease, but immunisation has made it almost unknown; it is important, therefore, that all children should be immunised. There are many modern and up-to-date doctors who have qualified since the war who have never seen a case because it has become so rare, and in spite of the propaganda of certain ill-informed people, this saving of children's lives is entirely the result of nationwide inoculation during the war and since. The following description is of historic interest only, and will remain so if a high level of inoculation is kept up by parents.

In a typical case of diphtheria the incubation period is about three days; the patient is a child who becomes ill and pale-looking (*i.e.,* the onset is not sudden, as in many fevers, but insidious); the temperature is only slightly raised to, perhaps, 37° or 38°C, and although there may be no complaint of sore throat, examination will reveal inflammation with—and this is typical of diphtheria —a grey membrane spread over the tonsils, the palate, and the back of the mouth generally. The diphtheria germ does not spread within the body. It stays at the place where it entered (in this case the throat) and sends its toxins throughout the body.

Even after the acute phase is over the patient must not be allowed to walk, because the diphtheria toxin is particularly poisonous to the heart. The ordinary rule is at least one or two months in bed.

Diphtheria also occurs in the larynx—in pre-inoculation days many children choked to death with this form of the infection; in the nose; and, although this is not generally known, wounds can be infected. The so-called "Desert sores" of the North African campaign seem to have been caused by diphtheria-like organisms.

Diphtheria may lead to paralysis of the throat, with difficulty in speaking or swallowing, and paralysis of the eyes or limbs; these are due to neuritis caused by the influence of the toxin on the nerves.

Whooping Cough. For many years whooping cough has been regarded merely as a bother to the patient and a nuisance to others, as, in fact, a trivial disease. Unfortunately, this is not so; because statistics show that it caused more deaths than polio, diphtheria, scarlet fever, and measles put together.

Whooping cough begins in a child as an ordinary cold with cough and slight fever, and this stage lasts for a week or ten days. Then the "paroxysmal stage" begins as a series of coughs following in rapid succession, during which time the patient is unable to breathe. The "whoop" is caused by the noisy indrawing of breath when the fit stops. The face may become blue and congested. Bronchitis is usually present, and bronchopneumonia may result as a complication, so inoculation of all children before the disease has a chance to strike them is most important.

Once whooping cough has begun, there is no specific treatment, although modern drugs can reduce the frequency of the fits of coughing. The antibiotic chloramphenicol has been used for this disease, but the general opinion is that it is ordinarily of little benefit. Chinese physicians once described whooping cough as the "hundred-days cough," and the cough may, indeed, continue for at least a hundred days. There is an effective vaccine.

Typhus. This disease used to be known as "jail fever," because it was frequent in prisons; but overcrowding, poverty, and bad hygienic surroundings anywhere are suitable conditions for epidemics of typhus. Improved conditions in industrialised countries have made it unusual, since typhus is carried from one person to another by infected body lice. It is due to the organism *Rickettsia prowazekii*, a very small type of bacterium.

Typhus comes on suddenly with a rise in temperature to about 39°C, but within four days it may be as high as 42°C. There may, or may not, be a rash at this time, and in the second week, when the temperature is at its highest, there is delirium, weakness, and a feeble pulse. The typical typhus rash appears about the fifth day as reddish blotches on the chest, abdomen, and wrists.

Typhus is, needless to say, very serious but responds to modern antibiotics. Preventive measures are directed towards eradicating lice.

Psittacosis. This disease which is of interest mainly in that it is spread by birds of the parrot group, such as parrots, lovebirds, macaws, and the rest is caused by chlamydia, which are similar to bacteria. It occasionally occurs here in people who have been in contact with birds of this type, and is serious both to the bird and to its owner. Quarantine regulations greatly reduced the risk of infection in Britain. Concern over renewed outbreaks, not only of psittacosis but a number of economically important diseases such as fowl pest, led to their reintroduction in 1976.

The symptoms of psittacosis are fever, cough, and bronchitis. The disease is especially dangerous to old people, but it responds to the same antibiotics as typhus.

Tuberculosis. No disease causes more public concern, and no disease is more difficult to describe, than tuberculosis; for, like the Streptococcus or the Staphylococcus, the tubercle germ can attack many different parts of the body and manifest itself in many ways. Furthermore, it is a widely spread disease, infecting not only humans but also cattle, birds and reptiles. But here we shall be concerned with those types common to man—the human and bovine (*i.e.*, the type occurring in cattle which can be spread to man by infected milk).

The tubercle bacillus is particularly hardy, so that when coughed or spat out on the ground it continues to be infectious for a long time. Infection is therefore caused by: (*a*) drinking infected milk; (*b*) droplet infection from aerosols produced by coughing; (*c*) breathing in infected dust. In other words, tuberculosis is caused by absorption through either the lungs or the intestines; the former is common in adults, the latter in children.

But there is a good deal more to the problem than this; we know, for example, that over 90 per cent. of people in industrial countries have been infected with T.B. in early life and have conquered the infection. So the question arises: what conditions predispose to T.B.—why do some people get over the early infection and others not? There are two answers to this question: one is certain—that those who are impoverished and do not get enough food are liable to T.B.; the second is not so certain—that mental stress plays some part. Stress causes a general reduction in immunity, predisposing the body to several infections including T.B.

In children, lung tuberculosis is not common, but tuberculosis of the bones and glands is, as is also infection in the abdomen, the kidney or spine, and, worst of all, tuberculous meningitis. These are often of the bovine type from infected milk. Ordinarily, T.B. in children is less serious than adult infections; but tuberculous meningitis used to be almost invariably fatal until streptomycin was discovered.

Adult tuberculosis usually occurs in the lungs or the pleura—the thin membrane surrounding the lungs. In younger people miliary tuberculosis, which is a form of T.B. blood-poisoning or septicaemia, is a very serious condition, and the infection spreads throughout the whole body in a few weeks.

Lung infection begins gradually in someone who has previously felt unwell. There may be cough, and later blood-stained sputum (although blood which is coughed up does not necessarily prove that T.B. is present). Whatever means of treatment is used, the struggle between disease and patient is likely to be fairly long, but the outlook is now good. The closure of the Swiss sanatoria is due partly to modern disbelief that air in one place is better than that in another, but mainly to improved treatment.

Prevention depends on legal action ensuring tuberculosis-free herds of cattle; on control of spread of the disease by those "open" cases who carry germs in their sputum; on the use of vaccination in childhood with B.C.G. vaccine (which you can ask your doctor about).

Many methods are used in treatment: drugs, such as streptomycin, isoniazid, and P.A.S., lung surgery, rest, and so on. T.B is now a fairly rare disease in developed countries, but there are worries that the emergence of antibiotic resistant strains will lead to an upsurge in its frequency. There are skin tests to show whether there is susceptibility to T.B.

Septicaemia. Commonly known as "blood-poisoning." This is one of those diseases of which textbooks prior to the Second World War used to say: "death usually occurs."

Blood-poisoning occurs generally by spread from some septic area such as a wound (or even a small prick), after childbirth, or any place where certain germs have got admission to the body. The most usual germ is the Streptococcus, although the pneumococcus—which ordinarily causes pneumonia—and the Staphylococcus may also cause septicaemia.

Fever comes on suddenly and rises rapidly with headaches, sweating, and shivering. The patient is obviously very ill, and later there is wasting and delirium. The white blood cells increase in number. Septicaemia sometimes occurs without any apparent local infection in those who are weak and debilitated.

Pyaemia is a type of septicaemia which leads to the formation of numerous abscesses throughout the body. Its symptoms are the same as described above, except that the causative germ is usually the Staphylococcus, and abscesses are found which may need surgical treatment.

However, in both conditions the state of affairs has been revolutionised by the use of the sulpha drugs and antibiotics; cure is now the rule rather than the exception.

Septicaemia should be suspected when any small wound or cut is followed by high temperature and the symptoms described above.

The word "*Toxaemia*" is used when the germs stay in their original position and produce symptoms by spreading their toxins throughout the body. Tetanus, diphtheria, and some kinds of childbirth infection come into this category; the symptoms may vary from mild disturbance to severe illness.

Meningitis means inflammation of the meninges, the covering which, like a layer of plastic, lies over the brain and spinal cord, just as the pleura covers the lungs and the peritoneum covers internal organs in the abdomen. (Hence inflammation of the pleura is known as pleurisy, and inflammation of the peritoneum as peritonitis.)

Various germs may cause meningitis, for example, some viruses, the bacillus of tuberculosis, the pneumococcus, which ordinarily causes pneumonia, and the Streptococcus or Staphylococcus, but ordinarily the word refers to *cerebrospinal meningitis* or "spotted fever" caused by the meningococcus and occurring at times as an epidemic. It is commonest in the years from infancy to the early twenties, and begins suddenly with headache, vomiting, and fever. The temperature rises quickly, and pain develops in the back and legs; on the second or third day a rash appears on the body, and particularly on the inside of the thighs. Later there is stiffness of the neck, the head may be drawn back, vomiting persists, and the headache can be so severe as to cause the patient to scream with pain.

Fortunately, this type of meningitis (and most of the others) respond to treatment with antibiotics or the sulpha drugs, so the risks are very much less than formerly.

Pneumococcal meningitis is an unusual complication of pneumonia, and the septic types (*streptococcal* or *staphylococcal*) arise either following an infected fracture of the skull or from infection of the ear or mastoid.

Tuberculous meningitis has already been mentioned; originally always fatal, it is now treatable with streptomycin.

All these diseases are very much a matter for specialist and hospital treatment, but it is worth while mentioning viral meningitis, in which, although all the symptoms of meningitis are present, recovery without specific treatment is invariable.

Tetanus is usually known as "lockjaw" because there may be difficulty in opening the mouth, although this is simply part of a spasm of all the muscles of the body. The tetanus bacillus is found in rich soil—hence the disease is less common in desert areas—and tetanus resembles rabies in that: (*a*) it enters at a wound; (*b*) it affects the nervous system; (*c*) it results in fits and ultimately death.

However, active immunisation with T.T. (tetanus toxoid) has resulted in the disease becoming uncommon, and even when developed, treatment with antitoxin, sedatives, muscle relaxants, and antibiotics may lead to cure.

The bacillus is anaerobic (*i.e.*, does not use oxygen) and is most likely to occur in such situations as when a man digging manure or working in his garden sticks a fork through his foot, or, in war-time, when he is wounded in soil contaminated with manure.

Undulant fever, also known as Malta fever, abortus fever or brucellosis, falls into two types: melitensis, which infects goats, and abortus, cattle and pigs. Man gets the disease by reason of close contact with or drinking the milk of infected animals. (The name abortus is given because abortion is produced in cattle and sows.)

In undulant fever, as one would suppose, the fever goes up and down for two to three weeks; it may then go down and rise again, persisting for many months. The disease may occur in Britain, but modern drugs are on the whole successful in dealing with it. A striking feature of the disease is the combination of a high temperature with an appearance of relative well-being.

Another disease carried by mammals is *Glanders* or *Farcy*, spread by horses. In glanders there is discharge from the nose and sometimes pneumonia. Occasionally the disease is fatal. In farcy abscesses form, usually along the lymph vessels. Both conditions are very contagious, and treatment is a matter for a specialist; infected horses should be destroyed.

Cholera. Cholera could be classified under the head of food-poisoning, because it is mainly spread by infected water (however, like typhoid, it can also be spread by flies, infected food, and carriers); it could also be classified as a tropical disease, since, although it used to be found in Europe, it is now mainly rife in India.

Cholera is caused by a vibrio, which is a spiral bacterium, and can be prevented by early inoculation and care over food supplies—boiling water and milk, washing uncooked foods in chlorinated water, and keeping flies away.

The fever begins in the usual way with a short incubation period, followed by abdominal pain, severe vomiting, and diarrhoea. Later with the loss of fluid from the body there may be cramps in the muscles, diarrhoea increases, and the motions become of the typical "rice-water" type—*i.e.*, there is no solid matter, and the appearance is that of water to which a little milk has been added. This stage is followed by collapse, with low pulse and cold hands and feet. Death, if adequate treatment is not available, results in about 70 per cent. of cases. Cholera can generally be survived simply by replacing the water and salts lost in the diarrhoea, along with antibiotic therapy.

Anthrax. The bacillus of anthrax, like that of tuberculosis, can exist outside the body for long periods, and, like that of tetanus, then takes the form of spores or seed-like bodies. It is spread by infected cattle and horses, which get the disease from eating grass containing spores.

In human beings the form the disease takes depends on where the germ alights; sometimes it comes from infected shaving-brushes, when it causes a large sore, like a boil, on the face, known as "malignant pustule"; sometimes it develops in those who inhale the dust from infected hides or wool (hence the name "wool-sorters' disease," which is a form of bronchitis with blood-stained sputum); lastly it may arise through eating infected meat, when the result is intestinal anthrax.

In all cases the outlook was serious. Death was often common, preceded by a high temperature, skin symptoms in the first instance, lung symptoms in the second, and food-poisoning symptoms in the third. Penicillin or tetracycline is now increasingly effective.

Food Poisoning Diseases.

Strictly speaking there is no such thing as "food poisoning" if one is thinking of "poisoning" in terms of anything apart from germs. But not so long ago it used to be thought that decomposition of food in itself produced poisons known as "ptomaines" which were deadly to those who swallowed them. All food poisoning is caused by infection of food with bacteria and by no other cause—unless of course, we are thinking of the kind of poisoning which is the concern of the lawyer rather than the doctor!

Here we are considering those diseases which are commonly spread by contaminated food or drink. The classification is not scientific, but then no scientific classification has as yet been devised. First, we shall deal with typhoid, paratyphoid, and dysentery—uncommon here in Britain, although Sonné dysentery is fairly frequent. Then there is gastro-enteritis (which means irritation of the stomach and intestines), which is caused by staphylococci and the germs of the salmonella group, and lastly botulism, which is rare.

Typhoid and Paratyphoid. These diseases are spread by infected water, food, or hands—especially uncooked food, such as milk, salads, oysters, and shellfish. Flies, too, play some part in spreading the disease. Some people are "carriers" and carry and excrete the germs without being themselves affected; for example, "Typhoid Mary," a carrier in the United States in the early years of this century, spent a large part of her life in custody as a public danger, although she did not show any symptoms of typhoid. Nevertheless, this woman caused a great deal of illness in others in her chosen profession of cook.

The influence of Chadwick's propaganda for pure water supplies is shown by the fact that deaths from typhoid, still 332 per 1,000,000 in 1870, fell to 198 per 1,000,000 at the beginning of this century. In the 1920s the death-rate was only 25 per 1,000,000, and now it is even less.

Typhoid fever begins like most fevers with headache, raised temperature, and general feeling of unwellness. This stage lasts about a week, and then the rash appears in the form of rose-red spots on the front of the chest and abdomen and on the back. In the second week there is great weakness, sometimes diarrhoea, flatulence, and mental dullness, together with dry and cracked lips and tongue. The third week is the week, in hopeful cases, of gradual decrease in temperature and other symptoms, and the fourth week is the week of convalescence.

Complications are perforation of the intestine (which needs surgical treatment), delirium, and bronchitis.

Paratyphoid fever is a milder form of typhoid (there are two forms, A and B); ordinarily it can be diagnosed only by scientific tests. The main thing is to inoculate contacts with T.A.B. vaccine and to protect food supplies; treatment is with chloramphenicol.

Dysentery. Dysentery may be caused either by a bacterium or an amoeba; the first type is known as bacillary dysentery, the latter as amoebic dysentery (which is dealt with under tropical diseases). Infection is spread in much the same way as in typhoid. There is high fever, abdominal pain, and diarrhoea, at first consisting of faecal matter, then blood and mucus. In severe cases the death-rate used to be over 20 per cent.

Dysentry is caused by several species of bacteria of the genus *Shigella*.

However, in all these infections sulphaguanidine, ampicillin or tetracycline bring rapid relief, but care must be taken to avoid infection of other people.

Diarrhoea and Vomiting. Leaving out typhoid and paratyphoid fevers and dysentery, there is a group of infections known as "D. and V."—diarrhoea and vomiting. In Britain D. & V. is mostly due to:

(1) Salmonella infection.
(2) Staphylococcal infections.
(3) Other bacteria, ordinarily harmless, such as Escherichia coli, when present in sufficient numbers.
(4) Various viral infections, particularly rotavirus.

Salmonella Infections are the most serious of this group; they affect the small intestine and produce vomiting, severe abdominal pain, and diarrhoea. These symptoms occur about one day after eating infected food and usually clear up within about two weeks, but occasionally death results. Salmonella bacteria are most likely to be found in meat, egg powder, vegetables, and ducks' eggs.

Staphylococcal Food Poisoning has greatly increased in recent years, so it is important to know what circumstances are likely to cause it. Staphylococci are liable to grow in milk products, such as ice-cream and cream buns. Food poisoning from staphylococci is seldom severe, and recovery takes place in about a week. Nevertheless, it is extremely infectious, and causes a great deal of lost time in industry and temporary illness in institutions; for it is in such situations that it is most likely to occur.

The reason for the increase in staphylococcal food poisoning has nothing to do, as many people suppose, with greater use of canned foods, but it has much to do with the greater use of communal feeding and canteen meals. It is *possible* for bacterial toxins in infected food to bring about illness even when the canning process has killed the bacteria, but it is certainly extremely rare. Canned foods, in fact, are much safer than so-called "fresh" foods in this respect—except when they have been opened, left about, and then re-heated. The same applies to the re-heating of any kind of food.

The real enemy is the canteen worker with a boil, a discharging nose, dirty hands, or a septic finger. Occasionally food may be infected in the larder by rats or mice, but the sort of canteen or restaurant where this can happen has little to commend it. Frankly, these infections are caused by dirty or stupid people who do not realise that their sore finger or boil can become someone else's diarrhoea and vomiting. Where children are concerned, the outlook is potentially more serious, and in the early part of this century the Summer-time "procession of baby coffins" was all too familiar. Infection is much more common in artificially fed babies or in older children who eat infected ice-cream. However trivial the condition may seem, diarrhoea and vomiting with fever in a child should never be ignored. Those in charge of canteens or restaurants must ensure that staff is supervised, that anyone with a septic infection is put off duty, and that all know about washing after visiting the lavatory and absolute cleanliness.

Bacilli normally present in the intestine, such as Escherichia coli, can cause infections if absorbed in large amounts, or if of a different strain from those in the patient's intestine. They are not usually serious.

Botulism. Now uncommon, this is the disease which used to be known as "ptomaine poisoning" on the theory that it was caused by poisons produced by bad food apart from germs. In the 1920s a party of picnickers at Loch Maree in the Scottish Highlands developed botulism and a number died, with the result that the disease attracted much public attention. Botulism is caused by a germ, clostridium botulinum, which is peculiar in that, like tetanus, its poison attacks the nervous system rather than the intestines, resulting in fits, double vision, paralysis beginning in the face and spreading downwards, and difficulty in swallowing. It is found in tinned fruits or vegetables containing the toxin even when the germ has been killed, but, as we have already seen, the toxin comes from the bacilli, not from decomposition of food as such (in fact, food does not decompose in the absence of germs). Death is common in botulism, but an antitoxin is now available which, if used in time, can cure the disease.

Diseases Caused by Fungi.

Numerous fungi are pathogenic, and fungal diseases may be primary or secondary to other diseases; allergies to fungi are also important. The most common fungal disease is candidiasis, which is infection with the imperfect yeast-like fungus *Candida* albicans; this frequently infects the feet (athlete's foot), the mouth and the vagina, producing local itching as the main symptom. Ringworm or tinea, despite its name, is not caused by worms but fungi which cause ring-shaped pigmented patches on the skin, sometimes covered with vesicles or scales. Actinomycosis, a disease caused by bacteria which superficially resemble fungi, is a serious but treatable condition with inflamed lymph glands around the jaw or ulcerating sores on the skin; it can also affect the lungs, intestines and brain.

The Venereal Diseases.

The venereal diseases are those caused—or at least that is what the name means—by the goddess of love, Venus. Venus, of course, causes a great deal of trouble, but venereal disease is not necessarily the worst she can do. Venereal disease is spread by sexual intercourse with an infected person.

Gonorrhoea is the result of an infection by the gonococcus (*Neisseria gonorrhoeae*) and ordinarily comes on after an incubation period of three to seven days. However, babies can get an infection of the eyes, known as ophthalmia neonatorum, from their mother if she is infected, and gonorrhoea in young children is often the result of being in contact with infected towels or clothes. The disease in adults is evident when there is a thick, creamy discharge from the sexual organs and sometimes pain on passing water; in infants ophthalmia is prevented by the use of silver nitrate eye-drops at birth. Gonorrhoea is fairly easily cured by the use of sulpha drugs or penicillin; but unfortunately venereal disease is increasing in recent years and drug-resistant forms are becoming more common.

Syphilis is a serious venereal disease caused by a spirochaete (*Treponema pallidum*). Stories about lavatory seats are simply stories, although it is occasionally possible to get syphilis by other than sexual means: for example, it has happened that a man playing football has been infected through his hand being grazed by the teeth of someone with syphilis. But this is very unusual, although kissing can spread the disease. Children, too, can be born with syphilis (the so-called congenital syphilis).

Adult syphilis begins with a sore, known as a hard chancre, at the point where the spirochete of syphilis has entered; this may be on the lips, through kissing; on the sexual organs, through intercourse; and very rarely, as explained above, elsewhere. In a short time the chancre disappears and all may seem to be well, but this primary stage is followed by a secondary stage with sore throat, a rash, headache, and enlargement of glands. This, if left alone, also clears up, but is followed by the tertiary stage, in which a chronic infection develops in some part of the body which, presumably, is most susceptible in the particular individual. Thus there may be chronic syphilis of the skin, the bones, the heart, liver, or nervous system.

In the nervous system, the commonest forms are the two diseases of *tabes dorsalis*, in which the spinal cord is infected, and G.P.I. (general paralysis of the insane), in which the brain and mind are affected. These will be discussed under Nervous Diseases.

In congenital syphilis the pregnant mother gives her child syphilis. Such infants are often stillborn or premature, they look wizened, like little old men, and amongst other symptoms are eye disease, "snuffles," a flattened nose, and when the adult teeth appear the front ones may be notched at the biting surface.

The treatment, of course, is very much a matter for a specialist, but diagnosis is usually made through the Wassermann blood test. It was for syphilis that Ehrlich produced his "magic bullet"—an arsenical drug, known as salvarsan, which could attack the organism selectively without harming the body and was the first of the modern specific drugs. Present-day treatment is with penicillin. G.P.I. was once treated with malarial therapy with some success. Penicillin alone is often adequate.

It is important to understand that venereal disease can only be transmitted during sexual intercourse (or with intimate acts associated with it—*e.g.*, "oral sex"), that promiscuity therefore increases the risk, that not all lesions in, on or around the genitals are necessarily venereal disease and that *fear* of contracting it is widespread in many communities. If in doubt consult your own doctor or attend one of the many special clinics which can be found in most cities. Their location is usually advertised in conveniences and other public places. Delay is certainly dangerous.

Chancroid produces small septic ulcers around the sex organs, with swelling of the local glands in the groin, which may suppurate. It is caused by a bacillus, and can usually be cleared up by sulpha drugs within a week. Scabies and lice often pass from one body to another during sexual intercourse, but are not usually thought of as venereal in origin, although in many cases they are.

Tropical Diseases.

Nothing is more difficult than to define the term "tropical diseases." One might define them as the diseases which occur in tropical climates—but then measles occurs there too; and if they are defined as those diseases which are found *only* in the tropics, the solution is no easier, since leprosy, cholera, smallpox, and typhus are usually listed as tropical diseases, yet were found in this country until fairly recently—and the odd case still is.

But what a story could be told about the conquest of those infections which were—and many still are—the scourge of humanity! One day when generals and dictators are forgotten we shall remember that great international army of physicians and bacteriologists who have saved millions of lives and infinitely reduced human suffering: Koch and Ehrlich of Germany, Pasteur and Roux of France, Ross and Jenner of Britain, Reed of America, Noguchi of Japan, and many others. We shall remember how the Jesuit priests brought quinine from Peru to Europe in 1638, the first drug to save people from malaria; how in tropical heat Ronald Ross (1857–1932) peered for hours through his microscope to discover the connection between malaria and the mosquito until the sweat running from his brow rusted the instrument; how Major Walter Reed's work in Havana (1851–1902) made possible the building of the Panama Canal, and think, too, of the American soldiers who died in helping him to find the cause of yellow fever. In mentioning Jenner once more, we should recall Lady Mary Montagu (1689–1762), who brought the practice of vaccination to England from Turkey—or, rather, the practice of "variolation," which meant inoculating with the pus from smallpox cases. This was, of course, a dangerous practice, but the idea was there.

Relapsing Fever, common in India and Africa, may be louse- or tick-borne; the germ is a spirochaete, similar to that of syphilis, but the disease is non-venereal. Relapsing fever gets its name from the fact that the temperature remains high (39°–41°C) for about a week, returns to normal for a week, and rises again. There may be three to five relapses of this sort. Penicillin is effective; lice or ticks must be eradicated.

Epidemic Jaundice (also known as Weil's disease or—if you prefer it—ictero-haemorrhagica spirochaetosis), is also caused by a spirochaete, and spread by rats. Now it is rarely found in Europe, although it occurred in the trenches during the First World War, in men working in sewers, and in the women who worked in the fish market of Aberdeen, which at one time was rat-infested. It is rarely fatal, but leads to high fever and jaundice. Penicillin in high dosage or tetracycline may help.

Yaws is also a spirochaetal disease, common in the tropics and particularly in children. It is unpleasant, but not serious, and tends to clear up in a year or so. There are raspberry-like growths on the skin, which disappear with the drugs used in syphilis (although the condition is non-venereal). The Wassermann reaction, positive to syphilis, is also positive in yaws.

Leprosy. Whereas syphilis, relapsing fever, epidemic jaundice, and yaws are caused by spirochaetes, leprosy is caused by a bacillus resembling the bacillus of tuberculosis. Apart from the difficulty of classification, many popular beliefs about the disease are untrue. It is *not* the oldest disease afflicting man; *not* a disease confined to tropical countries; it is *not* very catching; *not* hereditary, *not* incurable; in leprosy the fingers and toes do *not* drop off; it is *not* a divine punishment for wrongdoing.

Leprosy is a serious disease not because of disfiguring light-coloured skin patches and lumps, but because it destroys peripheral nerves. Leprosy may disappear spontaneously, or it may progress until the face is lion-like and the hands and feet wasted and ulcerated. The disease rarely kills, but it is the world's greatest crippler.

Leprosy was once fairly common in colder Western countries, though its extent was exaggerated. The great majority of the millions of people who suffer from leprosy live in tropical countries, but it still exists in Iceland, Japan, Korea and some of the southern states of the United States. Prolonged and intimate contact with an "open" case is said to be the main mode of infection, but only one infected husband in twenty passes leprosy to his wife.

The cheap synthetic drug dapsone is highly effective in leprosy, but problems in delivery to third-world settings has resulted in the emergence of resistant strains, so that much more expensive drugs now have to be used. The WHO has launched an ambitious "multi-drug therapy" programme in an attempt to bring this disease under control. Established deformity (such as claw hand, drop foot, paralysed eyelids) can be mitigated by reconstructive surgery, although lost sensation cannot be restored.

In the past, only Christian missions were concerned with the plight of the leprosy sufferer. Now, non-sectarian voluntary agencies, Governments and the World Health Organisation have joined in the fight against the disease. Enough is known to control the disease, but not enough is being done, as only one victim in five is at present getting treatment.

Plague is another disease caused by bacteria, common in Europe at one time, but now largely restricted to Asia. Nevertheless, it caused millions of deaths in Europe during the years 1348–49 and 1665 and was the "Black Death," which, indeed, changed the course of history.

Plague is carried by the bite of the rat flea, but, once people become infected, spread may occur from one to the other by droplet infection—*i.e.*, by coughing and sneezing. After an incubation period of two to ten days, fever develops, rather like severe influenza, and in a day or two the glands in the groin begin to swell, followed perhaps by swelling of the glands elsewhere. This is the usual type of plague, but it is also possible to get disease of the lungs from droplet infection and blood-poisoning from infection of the blood-stream. Both the latter types are almost invariably fatal, and even the glandular type (bubonic plague) has a mortality of about 80 per cent. The vaccine has given place to streptomycin and sulpha drugs which are also used on contacts.

Although we have little space to discuss the subject of plagues and epidemics in general, it is worth noting that serious epidemics have almost always followed wars, revolutions, and economic and political collapse. Thus the Black Death followed the break-up of the Roman Empire, and, in the fourteenth century, accompanied the end of mediaeval civilisation. The Napoleonic wars were followed by other epidemics, and the wars of the 1830s in Europe were followed by influenza. In the most widespread outburst of influenza after the First World War, more people were killed by the disease than in all the fighting of four years. It is a reflection on the peculiar mentality of man that this devastating epidemic, which affected almost the whole world, occupies little space in his history books. Yet 20 million men, and women, and children died from influenza, and no cure has, as yet, been found! Later we shall see that many millions of people die yearly from starvation or vitamin deficiencies. But these facts—the real facts of life—we rarely hear about.

Protozoal Diseases.

Nearly all the diseases caused by protozoa are tropical diseases, although one of the best-known protozoans is the harmless amoeba found in British ponds. Protozoal diseases are caused by these organisms, large in comparison with bacteria, which should really be thought of as one-celled animals. Viruses are neither animals nor plants, are much smaller than the other two groups, and have some distinctive characteristics described elsewhere.

Among the diseases caused by protozoa are sleeping sickness or trypanosomiasis, malaria, and amoebic dysentery (as contrasted with bacillary dysentery), another disease, leishmaniasis—also known by the numerous names of kala-azar, dum-dum fever, and, in milder form, Delhi boil, Oriental sore, or Baghdad sore—will also be mentioned briefly. These infections are few, but important in their influence on man; for, as Dr. Clark-Kennedy has pointed out, malaria until recently was responsible for one-fifth of all human sickness, sleeping sickness not so long ago caused a large part of Central Africa to be uninhabitable, and in some areas of the tropics there are probably more people with, than without, amoebic dysentery.

Malaria. The word, of course, means "bad air," just as "influenza" means "influence"—in Italian *influenza di freddo*—the influence of cold. Human beings have a natural tendency to suppose that, when two events occur together, then one must be caused by the other. Yet, although malaria and "bad air" may often go together, and influenza and cold, it does not follow that bad air (whatever that may be) causes malaria nor that cold causes influenza. In fact, the Anopheles mosquito carries the amoeba of malaria, and the mosquito prefers climates which some people might describe as "bad," but it is the amoeba, not the air, which causes the disease. Anyhow, the unfortunate mosquito might well use the phrase honoured by many generations of schoolmasters: "It hurts me more than it hurts you!" For the mosquito, too, is sick, and passes on its sickness to the person it bites.

There are several types of Plasmodium—which is the scientific name for this amoeba—producing attacks of fever varying in severity and frequency: benign tertian, quartan, and malignant quartan. Entering the body from the mosquito bite, the parasites penetrate the blood cells, multiply there, and finally burst into the blood stream. When this happens the temperature rises, and then they return to the cells to carry out once more the same procedure. Depending on the type, the attacks of fever may be at intervals of three or four days, severe or milder. When someone with malaria is bitten by a mosquito the infection can be transmitted to the next person it meets, but malaria is not infectious from one person to another directly. Quinine, of course, is the time-honoured remedy, but many other drugs are now available: mepacrine, primaquine, chloroquine and some sulpha drugs. The drug must be taken long enough for the infection to die out, otherwise relapses can occur even after leaving a malarial country (but it is only fair to say that, just as some people continue to give themselves the title of "Major" when they have left the army, so others long in Britain continue to describe attacks of cold or 'flu as "my old malaria again," when, to say the least of it, they are exaggerating).

Important as are the drugs used in the treatment of malaria, even more so is the control of the parasite-bearing mosquito. The eggs of mosquitoes hatch in water, and there the young or larval forms can be attacked by pouring oil on the surface of pools so that they are unable to breathe, or by introducing small fish which have a partiality for them. Adult mosquitoes can be killed by insecticides or kept away by repellent creams or nets over beds. Prophylaxis with antimalaria before entering and while living in known malarial zones is important.

Blackwater Fever is a sequel to malaria in tropical Africa and some parts of India. Rather illogically, it is described as "Blackwater," although the urine is red and the skin is yellow but the result is due to breaking down of the red blood cells by some malarial toxin. Possibly too much quinine may help in producing the illness. Treatment is to give plenty of fluids and no quinine or any other anti-malarial drugs in the early stages. The death-rate is about 25 per cent.

Trypanosomiasis or sleeping sickness—not to be confused with *sleepy* sickness—is essentially an African disease (although also found in tropical America) spread by the tsetse fly. Its cause is the type of protozoan known as a trypanosome, almond-shaped with vibrating membranes at the sides which enable it to move through the blood-stream, rather like a flat fish in the water.

There are three stages of the disease: first, the stage of fever with enlarged glands and a rapid pulse; which may continue off and on for three years; secondly, the stage of trembling hands, legs, and tongue, vacant expression, and slow and stumbling speech; thirdly, and lastly, the stage of low temperature, apathy, wasting of the muscles, and possibly death.

Treatment is with pentamidine, suramin or melarsoprol—which give good results in early cases. Preventive measures in infected areas include the destruction of tsetse flies by insecticide, the cutting down of forests near rivers which are inhabited by tsetse flies, and some authorities have suggested the shooting of big game which may form a "reservoir" of the parasities, whence tsetse flies can carry them to human beings. For similar reasons infected people should not be allowed to move to noninfected areas.

Amoebic Dysentery, also known as *Amoebiasis*, is caused by the *Entamoeba histolytica*, an amoeba whose cysts are found in food and water, or spread by infected fingers or flies. There is mild fever and diarrhoea which contains blood. The disease may become chronic, and can cause abscesses, usually in the liver but sometimes in the lungs. Amoebiasis is treated with chloroquine or nitroimidazoles.

Leishmaniasis, kala-azar, or dum-dum fever, is another amoebic disease, probably spread in this instance by the bite of sandflies. It is also known as tropical splenomegaly—enlargement of the spleen in ordinary language—since infection results in enlargement of the spleen and liver, low, irregular fever, and death within a year or so. A milder form, affecting the skin, is known as Delhi boil, Oriental sore, or Baghdad sore, does not lead to kala-azar, and is fairly readily cured. The cure for both conditions is to give injections of antimony compounds which reduce the death-rate from kala-azar from 80 per cent, to about 5 per cent.

Diseases Caused by Parasitic Worms.

Many types of worms infest human beings and other animals. They are interesting for such reasons as their size (which may range from the almost invisible to 9 m or more), their life histories, and their serious or trivial consequences on their hosts. We shall mention only a few groups here, and mainly the ones likely to be met with in Europe—the tapeworms, the roundworms, and the threadworms—although some tropical types will be described briefly.

Tapeworms, as we have seen earlier, like many other types of intestinal worm, lead a double life. What usually happens is that the worm breeds in the human intestine, the eggs pass out in the faeces, and are then swallowed by animals eating contaminated material. In the animal the eggs hatch out into larvae—primitive forms which penetrate the muscle, forming cysts—and man is infected in turn by eating its meat. Thus *Taenia solium* gets into the flesh of pigs, which, if imperfectly cooked (measly pork), causes infestation of the intestine in man. It reaches a length of about 3 m. *Taenia saginata*, which reaches a length of about 6 m, is spread in imperfectly cooked beef, and in Baltic countries *Dibothriocephalus latus* gets into the human intestine from caviare or undercooked fish. It reaches the awesome length of 9 m.

Now all the worms we have mentioned so far are found in the human intestine, and the cysts, which are much more dangerous and unpleasant, in the animal's muscles. But in some worms the reverse happens, with the adult in the animal's intestines and the cysts in man. Thus in Australia the dog tapeworm (*Taenia echinococcus*) produces cysts in both sheep and man. This is known as hydatid disease, and may remain unsuspected until cysts in the lungs, liver, or elsewhere become infected or rupture. *Trichinella spiralis* is similar in action, being found in the intestines of pigs and getting into the muscles or other organs of man. The main difference is that this worm migrates from the pig's intestines into its muscles, whence it reaches man in undercooked pork meat or sausages. The muscular cysts cause swellings and sometimes pain. There are changes in the blood, swelling of the face and leg in the early stages, and fever. A minor epidemic occurred in England in 1941. *Taenia echinococcus* and *Trichinella spiralis* are small—not more than 0·5 cm in length—but are more serious in their consequences than the large worms. Treatment is very difficult, and ordinarily all that can be done is to deal with individual cysts when they make themselves apparent.

The large tapeworms, *Taenia solium* and *saginata* and *Dibothriocephalus latus*, produce varying symptoms or none at all. Usually they are not discovered until some segments of the worm are excreted, but there may be mild indigestion, excessive hunger, and occasionally anaemia. However, when the worm is discovered the patient, not unnaturally, is likely to become anxious and uncomfortable at the thought of "having" a tapeworm; these symptoms are caused by the worry rather than the worm.

Treatment is, of course, a matter for a doctor, who now has a number of very effective drugs to choose from. One has to make sure that the head of the worm has been removed, otherwise it will continue to grow.

Roundworms are similar both in appearance and size to ordinary earth-worms and the eggs reach man, not from an animal, but from the contaminated fingers of someone else who handles food. They give rise to no symptoms, and are noticed only when discharged in the faeces or occasionally vomited up. Piperazine is an effective treatment.

Threadworms, as the name suggests, are like small 0·5–1 cm long pieces of white thread. They are very common in children, and live mainly in the caecum—*i.e.*, the part of the large intestine near the appendix. The males, which are the smaller ones, remain there, but the females pass down towards the rectum at night-time and lay their eggs in the area around the anus. Infection is by contaminated hands handling food—especially uncooked food—and water. Threadworms are not serious, and cause few symptoms other than itching around the anus and between the legs, but heavily infected children may show symptoms of anaemia. The nervousness often shown by such children is usually the result of the irritation produced by the worms in the anal region. Infection is not common in adults, and in children tends to disappear at puberty.

Treatment is, in theory, simple; for the worms are easily destroyed by a number of drugs, such as piperazine and other, more modern drugs. Ointment is applied to the itching area, and the child should be prevented from scratching. However, since the eggs may lie about the house for some time, reinfection often happens, especially if there are several small children in the home who may pass the disease from one to another.

The idea that intestinal worms in general are likely to cause loss of weight by absorbing food eaten by the patient is largely mistaken; for although it is true that they do live on this food, the amount taken is certainly not enough to be significant.

Tropical Worms. Bilharzia has been mentioned before in connection with its frequency in Egypt, although it is also found in other parts of Africa, Arabia, and Iraq. There are two main types: one infecting the bladder (*Schistosoma haematobium*), the other the rectum (*Schistosoma mansoni*). *Bilharzia* is more correctly known as *schistosomiasis*.

The parasite's fantastic life-history begins when a man bathes in infected water, and the small swimming forms known as cercariae pierce and enter his skin—or they may enter the body by drinking infected water. From the skin they pass to the portal vein below the liver, remain there six weeks until they become adult and then swim against the blood-stream down to the pelvis, where the female lays eggs which have a sharp spine. The eggs penetrate into the bladder or rectum—depending on the type of fluke—and pass out in the faeces or urine. If they enter water they hatch out into small moving forms which seek out a water-snail, develop further in its body, and leave it in the form of cercariae ready to find a new human victim. The female fluke is slender and round, about 2·5 cm in length, the male, flat and leaf-shaped, is about 2 cm long, and, as we have seen, their grisly courting takes place in the portal vein, whence the impregnated female passes to the bladder (*haematobium*) or rectum (*mansoni*) to lay her eggs.

Infection results in raised temperature and, in the urinary type, blood in the urine; in the intestinal type blood is found in the faeces, and there are symptoms resembling dysentery—*e.g.*, diarrhoea. Treatment in both cases is with antimony tartrate or niridazole. Needless to say, attempts should be made at prevention by telling people to avoid infected canals (usually easier said than done), and by periodically cutting off the water supply to the canals to kill the snails.

Hookworm Disease, or ankylostomiasis, is found in many parts of the world, especially in miners who work on damp ground. The tiny worm enters the body usually through the feet, passes through the blood-stream to the lungs, eats through into one of the bronchial tubes, climbs the windpipe, and passes down the oesophagus into the stomach to end up in the duodenum. It causes anaemia, can be fairly readily cured, but is occasionally fatal.

Elephantiasis. Some types of parasitic worm are spread by insects. Thus in *Filiarisis* mosquitoes inject by their bites the infantile forms of a tiny worm which enters the lymphatic channels; there the blockade they cause leads to the swelling of the legs and the lower part of the body, known as elephantiasis.

PHYSICAL INJURIES AND FIRST AID.

This section which lists emergencies in alphabetical order is designed for rapid reference. Yet it would be wise to make sure now of knowing very thoroughly the parts dealing with bleeding, burns, resuscitation, shock and unconsciousness, situations which are immediately life threatening.

Nothing can teach first aid as effectively as attending one of the many courses organised by the three main organisations:

St. John Ambulance Association, 1, Grosvenor Crescent, London, S.W.1.
British Red Cross Society, 9, Grosvenor Crescent, London, S.W.1.
St. Andrew's Ambulance Association, Milton Street, Glasgow, C.4.

Their local addresses are in the telephone directory; enquiry will get details of classes held at various hours of the day.

Purpose of First Aid.

First aid is not treatment proper (which is "Second Aid"). It aims to save life, to prevent further harm or suffering and to keep the victim in the best condition until taken over by a doctor or a nurse.

Under ordinary circumstances attempts to do more can be detrimental. If you limit your help to what is outlined here you cannot go wrong.

General Principles.

There are two priorities:

1. That the patient must breathe.
    (—*see* Choking, Resuscitation, Unconsciousness)
2. That severe bleeding is controlled.
    (—*see* Bleeding)

In any accident scene try to judge quickly which person most needs immediate attention. Treat a victim where he is; do not move him unless the surroundings suggest immediate danger (*e.g.*, fire, fumes, collapsing building).

Handle the patient with gentleness and sympathy yet achieve an atmosphere of reassurance and confidence by firm instructions and methodical actions.

Clear away a crowd (always demoralising to the victim) and use likely bystanders to telephone for an ambulance when necessary. Let your message be clear and written if possible. Let it clearly state the exact locality, the number of patients and the nature of their troubles. Always guard against shock (*q.v.*).

Asthma Attacks.

Breathing becomes very difficult, harsh and wheezing, fighting against air passages narrowed in spasm. Fear aggravates and relaxation relieves spasm. Show calm confidence.

1. Allow fresh air ventilation. Loosen tight clothes.
2. Help the mechanics of breathing by telling the patient
    to sit upright with a straight back but all the rest of the body relaxed;
    to direct breathing movements from the lower part of the chest.
3. Give him medicines he has prescribed for the emergency but avoid overdose.

Bleeding.

Treat mild bleeding as for wounds (*q.v.*).
For severe bleeding aim to let the blood clot by stopping or slowing the flow.

1. Immediately firmly press the edges of the wound together between fingers and thumb or press the palm of the hand hard down on it. (Maintain this at least ten minutes.)
2. Lay the patient down: elevate a bleeding limb (unless you suspect it to be fractured).
3. Slip a thick pad (handkerchief, gauze, wool) under your hand. Replace the hand pressure with a firmly bound bandage (stocking, belt, scarf).
4. If blood still leaks out add another pad and bandage.
5. Protect against shock (*q.v.*).

Nose Bleeding.

1. Have the patient sit up.
2. Get him to pinch between finger and thumb the whole lower half of the nose and maintain this for at least ten minutes. Repeat another ten minutes if necessary.
3. Tell him not to sniff or blow his nose.

Ear Bleeding.

1. Bandage or tape a loosely covering dressing (gauze, handkerchief) over the ear.
2. Lay the patient down towards the injured side.—*Nose or ear bleeding which follows a blow to the head may signify a fractured skull which needs immediate medical attention.*

Tooth Socket Bleeding.

This may follow after a dental extraction. Get the patient to bite hard on to a big pad (gauze, bunched-up handkerchief) placed over the bleeding area. He maintains pressure at least ten minutes sitting with a hand under his chin and the elbow on a table.

Blood Vomited.

This could appear black due to the effect of stomach acids.

1. Lay the patient down, on his side, with his head low.
2. Give him nothing to eat or drink.
3. Get a doctor or ambulance.
4. Guard against shock (*q.v.*).

Blood Coughed Up (*see also* Chest Injury).
Blood from the Back Passage.
Blood in the Urine.

However slight and brief the loss, always seek a doctor's opinion.

Blisters.

Leave them intact and protect them with a simple dressing. But if they are so big as to be in the way and need flattening:—

1. Boil a needle for ten minutes: leave it in the water until needed.
2. Wash the blister area with soap and water.
3. Holding the needle by one end pierce the blister at two opposite points. Press down with clean cloth to squeeze the fluid out.
4. Dress it like a wound (*q.v.*).

Burns (*see also* Chemical Burns).

1. Put out flames the quickest way: a douche of water; smothering with cloth (rug, coat, blanket).
2. Remove burnt clothes, but leave on what is adherent to the skin.
3. Cool the burnt part with cold water for at least ten minutes, longer if pain persists. Plunge a limb in a bucket or sink. Cover other parts with a thick cloth soaked in water; renew it if it dries.
4. Lay the patient down; keep a burnt limb elevated; remove possibly constricting things (rings, bracelets) from a burnt region before it swells.
5. Dress the burn as a wound (*q.v.*).
6. Guard against shock (*q.v.*).—in severe burns give to drink half a cupful of tepid water with a pinch of salt and sugar every ten or fifteen minutes.

Car Accidents.

1. Urgently stop severe bleeding (*q.v.*) or give resuscitation (*q.v.*) where this is needed; treat choking (*q.v.*). Unless they are at risk from fire or fumes leave the injured where they are. Look for victims thrown into ditches or over walls and hedges.
2. Minimise risks by forbidding smoking (petrol leak), by switching off the ignition and applying the brakes.
3. Set your own car off the road if possible; at night have its light shining on the scene.
4. Detail bystanders (wearing or carrying white objects at night) to stop approaching traffic some 200 yards on either side.
5. Send a message for help (written down) detailing the exact place, the number injured and the injuries.
6. Give other first aid to those in the cars without trying to move them: attempts to pull them out, especially from a distorted car, can do great harm. Leave to the rescue services.

Chemical Burns.

Rapidly wash away the chemical with copious free-flowing water. Remove any contaminated clothing.
The contaminated eye, closed in painful spasm, may need gently forcing open; let the water flow on it without force and bend the patient towards the affected side so that the washings flow off at once.

Chest Injury.

Where there has been a severe blow or deep wound to the chest, possibly followed by blood being coughed up:

1. Clear the mouth of any obstruction (blood, vomit, dentures).
2. If there is an open wound at once close it with the palm of your hand firmly applied. While you keep it there, improvise a thick pad

(towel, cloth, handkerchief, sock) to replace your hand. Tape or bandage it securely to make an air-tight seal.

3. Loosen tight clothing.

4. Lay the patient down *towards* the injured side. If he has difficulty in breathing have him half propped up with head and shoulders raised.

5. Cover him loosely.

6. Get ambulance urgently.

Choking.

1. With your fingers try to clear any obstruction (food, toy, dentures) from the back of the throat.

2. If this fails tell the patient to relax, to bend well forward; give a hard slap between the shoulder blades. This may loosen the obstruction so that the patient can cough it out. A small child you place head down over your arm or your bent knee. Try up to four separate slaps.

If back slapping fails try to force the matter out by pressure:

1. Patient standing: stand behind him; put both your arms round his waist. Patient lying: turn him on his back; kneel astride him.

2. Place your fist (thumb side first) on his abdomen *between his navel and the lower end of his breast bone*; cover your fist with your other hand.

3. Make firm thrust inwards and upwards. This may propel the obstruction out of his windpipe. Try up to four separate thrusts. If these fail continue alternating four slaps and four thrusts. After each of these be ready to remove immediately any matter propelled into the mouth.

After receiving thrusts the patient must be checked by a doctor lest internal damage has occured.

If an obstruction is not cleared and the patient ceases breathing and collapses begin resuscitation (*q.v.*).

Always remember that in the unconscious the tongue may fall back and be an obstruction. *See* Unconsciousness.

Cold Effects. *See* Exposure and Hypothermia.

Cramp.

Cramps may follow severe loss of body fluid and minerals—as with severe repeated diarrhoea, vomiting or sweating. Slowly give tepid drinks containing a small pinch of table salt to each cupful or with diluted meat or yeast extracts.

Sudden cramp in a single muscle can be stopped by having the patient strongly stretch the muscle. In the front of the arm; straighten the elbow and swing the arm back. In the front of the thigh bend the knee and swing the leg back. In the back of the thigh: straighten the knee and swing the leg forward. In the calf: bend the foot up at the ankle while straightening the leg.

Diabetes.

Under certain circumstances a diabetic treated with insulin may suddenly collapse through sugar deficiency. Passing through phases of weakness, vagueness, sweating, tremor, uncoordinated actions and slurred speech he may go into a coma.

If he is conscious give him two teaspoonfuls (or lumps) of glucose or sugar in water. Failing this, give anything sweet; jam, honey, chocolate. This should clear him rapidly but repeat the dose after ten minutes.

If he is unconscious send for medical help urgently. Give nothing by mouth and put the patient in the recovery position (*q.v.*).

Ear—object in.

Do not try to poke it out.

A small object (*e.g.*, insect) can sometimes be floated up and out by lying the patient down with the ear uppermost and pouring in a little water or olive oil. But do not try this if the ear drum is possibly damaged or the ear is painful.

Electric Shock.

At once disconnect the current (at the switch or by pulling a plug out). If you cannot do this do not touch the patient but knock him away from his contact with dry non-conducting material; wooden stick, light furniture, folded thick garment.

He may need resuscitation (*q.v.*). He may have sustained a fracture (*q.v.*) or a burn. He may recover, only to collapse later; keep watch and send him to hospital.

Beware of very high voltage currents, as from wires of electric pylons: keep at least 20 feet away and do not try to rescue until the electricity authority has cut the current.

Epileptic Attack.

The patient may suddenly become unconscious, fall and soon begin convulsive jerkings, and sometimes frothing at the mouth.

1. Do not try to stop the jerking, but protect him from banging against furniture. Move the furniture or push cloth in position as buffer.

2. Clear froth from the mouth.

3. Once the convulsions stop put him in the recovery position (*q.v.*)—but beware lest he sustained a fracture (*q.v.*) in falling.

A succession of closely following attacks is dangerous: get medical aid at once.

Exposure.

A hill climber or a worker inadequately dressed against cold weather becomes slow, inefficient, clumsy, drowsy. Eventually he collapses and if not properly treated may die.

1. Put him to rest.

2. If you can, get him into a warm shelter. Otherwise protect him with screens of clothes or blankets and poles.

3. If he is conscious give warm drinks (cocoa, chocolate, tea). On no account give alcohol.

4. Get wet cold clothes off him if possible and put him in warm dry covers (sleeping bag, blankets). A plastic sheet over those helps to retain heat. Include the head, leaving only the face free. Well-prepared walkers will equip themselves with a special survival bag, now widely available.

See also Hypothermia.

Gradual rewarming is given when the patient has become cold gradually. When exposure has been sudden, as with falling in extremely cold water, you can warm up the patient fast in a bath at about 40° C. (103° F.).

Eye Injury.

Fix a loosely covering pad over the eye and get medical aid.—Do NOT use drops or ointments.—If the wound is severe and painful keep the patient on his back and cover both eyes (since movement of the good eye entails that of the injured one).

Eye—Object In.

Have the patient seated in a good light and stand behind him. If you can see the object on the white of the eye try to lift it off gently with the rolled-up and moistened twist of a handkerchief. If it does not come easily it may be embedded; leave it alone.

If it is within the coloured part of the eye leave it for a doctor to treat.

If you cannot see it look under the lids. The lower lid you pull down as he looks upwards. The upper lid you must evert as he looks down; lay a matchstick along the "hinge" of the lid; firmly grasp the edge of the lid and roll it up over the matchstick.

Fainting.

Lay the patient down with his legs higher than his head (if this is not possible, get him seated with his head bent low between his knees); loosen any tight clothes: tell him to breathe deeply and slowly. He should soon recover. A drink of water (provided he is conscious) will help. If he has fainted fully treat as for unconsciousness (*q.v.*).

Fractures.

Always suspect a broken bone where a blow or crush near a bone is followed by pain, swelling, deformity, weakened or restricted movement. Not all these features are always present: sometimes relatively slight pain is the only one.

Your task is to prevent movement which could worsen the condition by shifting a broken edge of bone into an important organ, or by making it pierce hitherto unbroken skin (with a risk of infection). No one will blame you for undue caution—but all will hold you responsible if you allow a fractured bone to do more damage by movement which could have been avoided.

When a fracture is suspected:—

1. Warn the patient not to move and bystanders not to try to lift him.
2. At once control any severe bleeding (q.v.). Dress any wound (q.v.) temporarily.
3. Now immobilise the fractured area including the joint at either end. The best splint is the patient's own body; e.g., injured arm secured against chest, injured leg against good leg (move the good leg up to the injured one). Or a thin board or rolled-up newspaper, well buffered with cloths and towels tied round it can be slipped under a fore-arm and wrist. Between the injured part and the splinting surface fill any hollows with firm padding of wool, or bunched-up cloth, socks, handkerchiefs. Tie the whole firmly with bandages (or stocking, thin towels) making the knots over the splint (not the hurt part) and avoiding bandage directly over the level at which you suspect the fracture. Work gently; do not lift or move the injured part.
4. Help to reduce shock (q.v.).

These are the general principles. How best to apply them for individual fractures you can learn from first aid courses.

If you expect expert help (doctor, nurse, ambulance) to arrive soon, then omit step 3 above and keep the patient lying still.

The fractured spine. When a blow or fall gives a painful back or neck, the vertebral column may be fractured. Inexpert moving may possibly drive a bone fragment into the spinal cord of nerves, causing paralysis or loss of feeling. It is most important to let the patient lay still until experienced first aiders take over. Keep him warm with a loose covering of blanket or coat.

Frostbite.

Do not heat the area directly or put it in hot water. Do not rub it.

1. Remove any wet cover (e.g., glove).
2. Remove any tight object (garter, ring, bracelet).
3. Cover the area loosely with dry material and let it warm up slowly. Fingers can be tucked under clothes into the opposite armpit. Nose, chin or ear can be covered with a dry hand.

Hanging.

Support the victim by his legs. Get the cord cut and be prepared to receive his weight as he falls. Loosen the cord round the neck. Act fast. Get medical help.

See also **Choking** *and* **Resuscitation.**

Head Injuries.

Blows to the head can cause fracture of the skull and also brain damage.

Fracture of the skull is not always obvious. Skin may swell over the site. Sometimes a fracture of the base of the skull (the body platform within the head at eye and ear level which supports the brain) may show up by bruising round an eye or by blood loss from ear or nose (see **Bleeding**).

Brain Damage may be of two kinds:—

Concussion, a temporary "shaking up" of brain tissue causing immediate "knock-out" unconsciousness. Recovery is in anything from a few seconds to several hours.

Compression of the brain develops from bleeding within the skull, from displacement of a fractured bone or from general swelling of the damaged brain tissues within the hard unyielding skull. The patient gradually (minutes or hours) becomes comatose and perhaps unconscious. This condition is dangerous.

The patient is unconscious—see unconsciousness.

The patient is dazed: put him in the recovery position (q.v.) and watch him closely while awaiting help.

The patient recovers after a knock-out (concussion). He may yet develop features of compression as well. However much he wants to carry on, keep him at rest, under observation and get medical advice.

In all cases remember that head injuries are often accompanied by injuries to other parts of the body.

Heart Attack.

Sudden heart attacks may produce:—

severe gripping pain in the centre of the chest, sometimes spreading to the neck, shoulder or arm; fast weak pulse; breathlessness; pallor and blueness; sweating.

or sudden painless breathlessness with slight cough and very wet bubbly breathing.

In either case send urgently for medical help. Get the patient to rest (in bed if possible). If he is very breathless it will be easier for him to be in a sitting position, against banked-up pillows. Otherwise have him laying down.

Loosen tight clothes. Keep him warmly but loosely covered. Mop any sweat from the face.

Heat Effects.

Heat Exhaustion. Anyone working in an unusually hot atmosphere is helped to remain cool by copious sweating which extracts heat from the body as it evaporates off the skin. But this loss of fluid also carries with it essential minerals from the body. The patient may collapse with his temperature normal or just a little raised; his skin is pale, moist and sunken, his pulse fast and weak. Muscles depleted of minerals go into cramp.

Let him rest in a cool place and give him (slowly) fruit juices or water with half a teaspoonful of salt added to each pint.

Heat Stroke happens in unusually hot and moist areas in rare industrial circumstances and in some tropical zones. Evaporation of sweat cannot take place in an atmosphere already saturated with water vapour. The patient becomes burning hot with a red dry skin and a fast forceful pulse. He may suddenly collapse and go into coma.

He must rest, have his clothes removed and be fanned or sponged down with cold (but not iced) water. The condition is dangerous and needs medical help.

Hypothermia.

Small babies and the elderly are specially susceptible to cold, e.g., overnight in a poorly heated bedroom. They become lethargic, comatose and then unconscious. Extremely cold to touch, even under bedclothes, the skin is white (though in babies it may be deceptively pink). Death may follow.

Cover the patient well including the head, leaving the face free. Put him in the recovery position (q.v.). Warm him GRADUALLY by warming the whole room and by giving slowly warm (not hot) drinks. Do NOT give alcohol. Do NOT use electric blankets or hot-water bottles.

Insect Bites.

Cool with water or (better) smooth in anti-histamine cream.

If a bee sting has been left in the skin pull it out with fine tweezers: apply these well down near the skin so that they do not squeeze in any venom left at the free top of the sting.

Lightning.

As for electric shock (q.v.) except that the patient can be touched at once as he bears no electric charge. Put a dry dressing over any skin burns.

Nose Bleed. *See* Bleeding.

Nose—Object in.

Do not try to probe it. Unless GENTLE nose blowing gets it out consult a doctor.

Poisoning.

Do not try to administer antidotes. Do not give salt solutions.

If the patient is unconscious.

Treat as for unconsciousness (*q.v.*).

If he is conscious.

Give, slowly, soothing drinks to dilute the poison (water, barley water, milk and water).
Put him in the recovery position (*q.v.*) while awaiting the ambulance. He may lose consciousness.

In all cases.

Get the patient urgently to hospital.
Send with him any remaining poison or empty container and a sample of any vomit.
Keep a close watch on him all the time you are with him.

Poisoning by pesticides (weed or insect killers).

The patient must be at complete rest. If his clothes and skin are contaminated with the poison (splashes, spray droplets) remove clothes and wash the skin copiously with water (avoid contaminating yourself). If he is conscious give sweetened drinks.

Poisoning by gases.

Get the victim rapidly out of the contaminated atmosphere, but do not venture within this unless you have a lifeline and respirator, with others to safeguard you.

Recovery Position.

This safeguards the patient's comfort and breathing if he is unconscious, or comatose, or likely to lose consciousness. It consists in having him—
  laying on his side;
  with lower arm and leg stretched out straight behind him;
  upper leg and arm bent forward at right angles at hip, knee, shoulder, elbow;
  face tilted slightly downwards and head bent backwards (no pillow).

This ensures a clear airway and lets any fluid in the mouth (saliva, blood, vomit) flow out and not choke the patient.
To get him in position:

1. Empty his pockets; remove items like bracelet or wrist watch. Put his belongings away safely. Loosen tight clothing.
2. Kneel alongside him.
3. Straighten his arms alongside his body; tuck the nearer hand below his hip.
4. Put one of your hands under his face to protect it as your other hand pulls him at the hip over towards you, on his side.
5. Adjust the limbs.
6. Cover him with a blanket or coat.

However, do not move the patient if circumstances suggest he received a heavy blow to the backbone. In that case ensure free breathing by keeping his head bent well back (never sideways). Be ready to clear immediately any vomit from his mouth.

Resuscitation.

This is the attempt to restore life to someone who has stopped breathing. Never try it unless this really is the case; you will do harm if the patient has collapsed but is still breathing. Do not try it if the problem is that of fighting against choking (*q.v.*).
In cases of drowning do not try to tip the patient up to drain out water; this wastes valuable time.
(It is best to have learnt the technique in organised first aid classes, practising only on a manikin.)

Artificial Respiration.

Act very quickly:—

1. Get the patient on his back.
2. Bend his head fully backwards and keep it thus all the time.

3. With fingers rapidly clear out any obstructing matter from mouth and throat.
4. Hold his mouth open (keep your fingers clear of his lips) and pinch his nose shut.
5. Take a deep breath in: open your mouth wide and seal your lips round his mouth: breathe firmly into his mouth. The air going in should make his chest rise. Do not blow more forcibly than is needed to achieve this.
6. Lift your mouth off. His chest will now sink as air comes out. Meantime you take another breath in.
7. Continue by repeating the breathing processes of steps 5 and 6.

The first four breaths you give quickly. Thereafter time yourself by the rise and the natural fall of the patient's chest.
With small children you need not pinch the nose, but let your mouth seal over both the nose and mouth of the patient. Much gentler blowing is needed, and quite small puffs are right for babies.
Keep on until medical authority takes over.
If patient vomits turn his head to one side and clear out the mouth. Then resume artificial respiration, with the first four breaths quick ones.
Successful artificial respiration should soon improve the patient's colour, and later you may find he begins to breathe for himself, even if only weakly. Watch this closely, for he may cease again.

Heart Compression.

If there is no improvement it may be necessary to add heart compression to artificial respiration. This, however, cannot be safely learnt except from first aid class teaching and demonstration. (See the Introduction to this section.)

Shock.

Failure of the heart and of the circulation of the blood may follow any serious injury (bleeding, wounds, burns, fractures). This can happen in minutes or hours according to the severity of the lesion.
In first aid terms this dangerous physical condition is called Shock. The patient is pale, cold, sweating, faint or comatose, with weak and fast pulse and breathing.

Try to prevent or to minimise the development of shock before it appears by applying the following simple but valuable measures to every badly hurt patient.

1. At once stop severe bleeding (*q.v.*).
2. Treat the patient where he is (unless you both are in an area of danger).
3. Lie him down: keep his head low and his legs raised (but avoid movement where a fracture is suspected).
4. Loosen tight clothing.
5. Keep him warm by covering below and loosely above him—but do not use hot-water bottles.
6. Gently dress any wounds—with the minimum of disturbance.
7. Guard his mental state. Be sympathetic but as optimistically reassuring as possible. Never whisper to others. Never assume that because the patient appears unconscious he cannot hear and understand what is said near him.

Do not give the badly injured patient anything to drink. This could worsen his condition and risk vomiting and choking, especially if he becomes unconscious or needs an anaesthetic. If he is very thirsty let him refresh himself by sucking a moistened handkerchief.

Snake Bite.

The adder is the only dangerous snake in Britain. Its bite can cause collapse and great pain, but only very rarely is it fatal.

1. Lay the patient down.
2. Wipe or wash the bite area. Put on a dry dressing.
3. Cover the area with a thick pad and bandage it in position so that it presses down very firmly.

4. Immobilise the bitten part as if it were a fracture (q.v.).
5. Get the patient rapidly to hospital.
6. Reassure him about his recovery. Give aspirin or paracetamol to minimise pain.

You NEVER cut or suck the bite, or apply chemicals. You NEVER use a tourniquet.

Sprains.

These are stretched and torn ligaments at a joint. Immediately after it happens you can reduce the swelling and pain which will follow by applying a cold compress—a cloth soaked in cold water and then wrung out to be just moist. Keep it in position half an hour, and renew it if it gets dry.

Otherwise support the joint firmly with layers of cotton wool interleaved between turns of crepe bandaging. Beware of making it so tight that it interferes with circulation in the limb.

A severe sprain may be difficult to distinguish from a fracture. If in doubt treat as for the latter.

Strains.

A strain is an overstretching of muscle fibres, and is very like a sprain except that it does not necessarily happen at a joint. Treat it as a sprain.

Strokes.

Some part of the brain has sudden damage of its blood supply. The results are as variable as are the functions of the brain: e.g., poor feeling or power in hand, arm or leg, altered speech, loss of bladder control, paralysis of one side, or unconsciousness.

A mild effect may be the forerunner of more serious damage. Get the patient to bed, if necessary in the recovery position (q.v.), and keep him under observation until the doctor arrives.

Unconsciousness.

In first aid finding the cause of unconsciousness is less important than protecting the patient's breathing. The unconscious patient lying on his back and with head straight or bent towards the chest is at risk of choking from his lax tongue, flopping against and obstructing his throat. Correct positioning prevents this. Act methodically:—

1. Has the patient stopped breathing? He will urgently need resuscitation (q.v.).
2. Is his airway blocked making breathing difficult? Clear any material from his mouth. Bend his head straight back at the neck (but do not twist or turn it), and keep it there (see Choking).
3. Arrest any severe bleeding (q.v.).
4. Dress any wounds (q.v.).
5. Consider the possibilities of fractures (q.v.). If you suspect they might be present do not move him (specially important if he might have injured the backbone); stay by his head to ensure its proper position and to clear out immediately any fluid (saliva, blood, vomit) which threatens to choke.

If he can be moved:—

6. Turn him into the recovery position (q.v.)

Two other important points are that you NEVER try to give anything by mouth to the unconscious or comatose, and that you realise how much you must guard your speech, since these patients may overhear and understand what is spoken near them.

Wounds.

The general treatment is simple, and should avoid the use of antiseptics or ointments.

1. At once control any severe bleeding (q.v.).

2. Sit or lay the patient down.
3. Put a clean temporary dressing on the wound.
4. Wash your hands. Prepare dressings and bandages.
5. Wash *around* the wound (but not the open wound itself) with swabs or clean material moistened with soap and water. Use a fresh swab or material area for each stroke.
6. Cover the wound with a large dry dressing. Over this place a thick soft pad. Bandage firmly.
7. Put the injured part at rest.
8. Take measures against shock (q.v.).

Dressings. Gauze from freshly opened pack. Or improvise from clean handkerchief or small towel, held by corners, allowed to fall open and then refolded so that inside surface comes to outside. A leg or arm can be slipped inside a pillowcase.

Padding. Cotton wool. Or improvise from bunched clean handkerchief, sock.

Bandages can be improvised from stockings, necktie, belt.

Object embedded in wound. Do not try to remove it. Cover it with a clean dressing and over this place a "frame" of padding to surround the side of the object and protect above it. You can now apply further padding and bandages without pressing on the object.

Tetanus (lockjaw) is a risk in wounds contaminated with soil or from animals or thorns. Get medical advice.

St. John Ambulance Brigade.

Readers of *Pears* will be interested to know that the Brigade celebrated its centenary in 1987. From its origins over a century ago, the organisation now boasts some 62,000 volunteers who deal with over 300,000 casualties each year. These casualties can range from minor upsets such as nose bleeds to victims of heart attacks and broken limbs. The work of the St. John Ambulance is divided into two aspects: the Brigade, which provides volunteers to give first-aid at public meetings *etc.*, and the Association, which is engaged in the task of spreading first-aid education.

THE BLOOD.

INTRODUCTION.

Doctors who have made a special study of the blood are known as haematologists. Haematology itself is a complex subject because blood itself is complex and its many functions are not easy to describe and only a brief account will be given here. A few basic facts to begin with:

Blood consists of a fluid, called plasma, in which are suspended red and white blood cells and platelets and in which are dissolved many substances from the simple ones like glucose to the complex like hormones, proteins and fats. Total blood volume amounts to about five litres; the blood donor gives about half a litre at a session and feels no ill effects. Loss of a litre or more induces surgical shock (q.v. **Physical Injuries and First Aid**). Red cells are red because they carry a protein called haemoglobin which is capable of carrying oxygen. There are about five million red cells for each cubic millimetre of blood (that is an average sized drop), a total of 25 million million circulating in the body at any one time. The life of a red cell is about 120 days; new ones are constantly replacing old ones which are "buried" by the spleen.

The haemoglobin from dead cells is recycled; new cells are generated in the marrow of bones, including the breast bone, from which samples of marrow can be taken by a technique known as sternal puncture. Such samples are studied with a microscope to establish diagnoses of various blood disorders. White cells are of five basic types, the names of which need not concern us here. Each type has a specific function—some act as bacterial scavengers, some are concerned with antibodies (q.v.) and some with the general defence system of the body which is concerned with the development and maintenance of immunity to various diseases both bacterial and viral. There are also non-cell particles derived from large cells which the marrow produces. These are platelets, which are concerned with blood clotting. They have the capacity to "stick" to any gaps in blood vessels (such as may be caused by injury or, in the minutest of blood vessels, "wear and tear") and initiate blood clotting. All these types of cells can be studied in the test tube after taking a sample from the patient. This is known as venipuncture, a simple and virtually painless procedure, carried out by doctor or nurse or trained "phlebotomist", by inserting a needle on the end of a syringe into a dilated vein in the crook of the arm. Marrow samples can also be taken, as we have said, from the breast bone—but that is a very different procedure, requiring local anaesthetic and much more skill. For the patient it is not a comfortable procedure either.

The fluid part of the blood, plasma, is more the province of the biochemist than the haematologist. The immunologist is also interested in plasma and all three disciplines tend to overlap to some degree. Plasma can be studied in the same way as whole blood. A venipuncture is carried out, a chemical added to stop clotting and the cells can then be removed in a centrifuge. If blood is allowed to clot in the test tube, the cells are all caught up in the clot and the plasma remains liquid and can be poured off. It is then known as serum. Plasma contains substances which are either dissolved, that is, in solution, or are held "in suspension". By this is meant that the plasma forms an emulsion because fat particles and some proteins are not soluble and can only form suspensions in this way. The protein and fat particles are in suspension in a like manner. The substances both in solution and in suspension are much too numerous to be dealt with here.

The functions of blood are manifold, but essentially blood is a transport medium, concerned with moving gases (oxygen and carbon dioxide), moving food (protein, carbohydrate, fat, minerals and vitamins), eliminating waste products and protecting and repairing the body.

Red Cell Diseases.

These are of two main groups leading to a shortage of red cells (anaemia), or an excess (polycythaemia). The former is much the more common and there are many different kinds. In all of them the shortage of red cells results in a depletion of the capacity of the blood to carry oxygen. This means that the heart must work harder to send more blood than usual to the tissues, and even so the tissues will often go short. The patient will be persistently tired and listless, and if the anaemia is severe the action of the brain and heart will be seriously impeded, even leading to fainting, cardiac pain, and breathlessness on exertion. All these symptoms, however, can be caused by many other conditions. The only way to be sure they are due to anaemia is by a proper examination of the blood, and even this will not lead to the truth if the picture has been spoilt by the patient taking iron tonics and other remedies of his own accord. Therefore do not dose yourself with tonics, in case you really have anaemia. You may make it impossible to arrive at a proper diagnosis later.

Haemorrhagic Anaemia. Anaemia, a shortage of red cells, may be due to a variety of causes, singly or in combination. One very obvious cause is loss of blood or haemorrhage. Following the sudden loss of a half-litre of blood or more, the red-cell-producing bone marrow "factory" will step up its production; but even if it is adequately supplied with all the raw materials such as iron,

it may well take many weeks to build up the numbers to normal. A very severe degree of haemorrhagic anaemia is usually treated by blood transfusion. Milder degrees can be treated by taking extra iron, often over a long period of time. The supply of iron for making new red-cell pigment is nearly always the bottle-neck which limits production. Haemorrhagic anaemia can commonly occur, however, without a sudden severe haemorrhage. From what has been said about the constant replacement of red cells as they wear out, it must be obvious that even if there is only a slight failure to keep pace with the numbers lost, several months of such a failure can eventually deplete the numbers to the level of very severe anaemia. This situation is common when small amounts of blood are being continuously or repeatedly lost, and here again it is a shortage of dietary iron which is the usual cause of the failure to replace the lost red cells. Normal menstrual loss in women and girls whose diet is on the border-line of iron deficiency is a common cause of progressive tiredness and lack of energy. Where the menstrual flow is heavier than usual, or where it is frankly excessive in older women due to the various common gynaecological disorders, serious anaemia is surprisingly common. During pregnancy a great deal of iron is lost by the mother to the baby, and this, together with the inevitable blood loss at delivery, often makes for a very tired mother indeed, just at the time when there is an enormous amount of work to be done to manufacture milk and attend to all the extra household tasks of baby care. For these reasons it is almost routinely advisable to build up stocks of iron throughout the pregnancy by remembering to take the pills provided. Men as well as women can lose small amounts of blood continuously in later life from gastro-intestinal conditions such as piles, ulcers, and tropical infestations such as hookworm; and here again the anaemia may be just as severe in the long run as that which inevitably follows a sudden, massive haemorrhage. One extra word of warning. Do not assume because you are pale that you are anaemic. Pallor is a very poor guide, because it is dependent on so many other things, like the blood vessels in your skin, and its thickness and translucency. Nothing but a blood test (which is so easy for your doctor to do) can really tell you if you are anaemic. And if your anaemia is due to a blood-losing condition, then that too must be treated. So do not be tempted to treat yourself, and never delay seeing your doctor about any unexplained bleeding.

Haemolytic Anaemia occurs when for any reason, there are more blood cells than usual being destroyed in the body. This may be because the cells are abnormally fragile, or because normal cells have been attacked by something to which you are allergic, or rarely because you have become sensitive to your own red cells. Sometimes unborn babies have severe haemolytic anaemia, due to an incompatibility of blood group (Rh factor) between the mother and the baby, and the same sort of thing happens if incompatible blood is given by mistake in blood transfusion. Up to a point, in mild haemolytic anaemia, the bone marrow can keep pace with the increased loss of cells, but beyond this point anaemia develops. After incompatible blood transfusions a very dangerous situation results from the effects of the destruction of red cells and the liberation of their products into the blood. One form of jaundice is often produced in haemolytic anaemia, the patient becoming yellow because of the breakdown products of red cells circulating in excess as bile pigments. These latter are normally always present to a small extent due to the normal, comparatively small, rate of destruction of effete red cells.

Aplastic Anaemia is the term given to anaemia due to a virtually total failure of the bone marrow red-cell factory. Sometimes this occurs for no obvious reason. It is sometimes due to a heavy dose of radioactivity or X-rays knocking out the cells of the "factory." It may even be due to cancer cells growing in the bone marrow cavity and not leaving sufficient room for the red marrow cells. It is fortunate that aplastic anaemia is very rare, because it can only be treated by blood transfusions every few weeks for the rest of the patient's life. Very occasionally there have been exceptions to this rule, when the patient's marrow has re-awakened for no apparent reason and suddenly begins to make red cells again. Rapid progress has been made in the treatment of marrow disease with bone marrow grafts.

Pernicious Anaemia. This is a fairly uncommon anaemia, which has a very interesting story. The processes by which red cells are manufactured are many and complex, and depend, like so many other bodily activities, on the supply of a vitamin containing cobalt, called vitamin B_{12}. This is nearly always present in more than adequate quantities in the diet, but in order for it to be absorbed from the intestine, there must also be a substance called "intrinsic factor" which is normally made by the lining of the stomach. People with pernicious anaemia have suffered a degeneration of the lining of their stomachs, probably because, for some reason, they have become "sensitive" to this part of their own tissue. This kind of civil war within the body is known as an "auto-immune" disease, and is comparable in type with some forms of haemolytic anaemia. In other words they destroy their own stomach lining, fail to produce "intrinsic factor," and as a result fail to absorb vitamin B_{12} into the body. Faced with a failure in the supply of this essential substance, the bone marrow produces too few red cells, and the few that are produced are deformed, much too large, and very fragile. In addition to its role in blood formation, vitamin B_{12} is essential to the normal functioning of the spinal cord, and in long-standing cases of untreated pernicious anaemia, there is often a neurological disability.

Nowadays pernicious anaemia is treated by small occasional injections of the vitamin, whose other name is cyanocobalamin. A similar molecule, without the cyanideion, is now used. This is called hydroxycobalamin.

Polycythaemia. Too many red cells per cubic millimetre of blood can be found without there being an increase of the total number of red cells in the body. This occurs in dehydration, when there is a loss of plasma without a comparable loss of cells, and is called haemo-concentration. Alternatively, the bone marrow can manufacture more cells than usual as a response to living for long periods at high altitudes. The beneficial result can be that the blood can carry normal amounts of oxygen, even though the supply (in the rarefied air) is reduced. Finally there is a red cell disease in which the bone marrow factory gets out of control and produces too many cells with no beneficial results. The number in the blood can be double the normal and the blood becomes so thick that the heart has difficulty pumping it round the body. This disease (*polycythaemia rubra vera*) used to be treated by repeatedly bleeding the patient to reduce the numbers of cells. It is now treated very successfully with carefully judged amounts of radioactive phosphorus or certain other "antimitotic" chemicals which reduce the rate of multiplication of bone marrow cells.

White Cell Diseases.

Diseases of the white cells are very much less common but are inevitably serious.

Agranulocytosis. In this condition the number of those white cells which are responsible for phagocytosis of bacteria falls precipitously. The result is that one of the main bodily defences against infection fails, and the patient may die from an overwhelming invasion of germs and the accompanying high fever. The usual cause is an abnormal sensitivity to a variety of drugs, often those which are in widespread use and only give trouble in the occasional case. One example among hundreds is the antibiotic chloramphenicol which specifically kills typhoid bacteria and is used for that purpose. It is believed that about one patient in 60,000 becomes sensitive to it and agranulocytosis often fatally follows, though appropriate treat-

ment of infections has greatly reduced the likelihood of death. The fact that almost any drug *can* do this to some people and yet be quite safe for the majority, is one good reason not to dose yourself unnecessarily with over-the-counter medicines.

Leukaemia. Leukaemia comprises a spectrum of diseases which involve the abnormal production of white blood cells. Immature or blast cells are produced at an increased rate and tend to infiltrate various areas of the body, for example, bone marrow, lymph nodes and spleen. They are also found in the peripheral blood and cerebrospinal fluid. In spite of their large numbers these cells, because of their abnormality, are unable to deal effectively with infection and anaemia, sepsis and fever can result. The cause of this type of cancer is open to some speculation but we know there is an increased incidence in those with Down's Syndrome and other chromosomal abnormalities. Viral infections may also be implicated and there is almost certainly an association with ionising radiation. This latter fact was proved by the increased incidence of leukaemia in those who survived the atomic explosion in Japan at the end of the Second World War. Pregnant women should not be subject to X-Rays as this may cause an increased incidence of leukaemia in their children.

Cases of leukaemia are known to occur in clusters or small groups in certain areas. Sometimes this is thought to be associated with natural radiation arising from rock structures. However, it is also suspected that there is an increased incidence around atomic power stations and plants which reprocess nuclear waste. In particular, a great controversy has raged about the incidence of leukaemia around the Sellafield reprocessing plant with some authorities insisting that the rate of occurrence is no greater than normal. However, those working and living in the area have always felt this to be untrue and recent research has suggested that workers exposed to small amounts of radioactive material may suffer abnormal spermatic development so that the tendency to leukaemia may be passed on to their unborn children who may be prone to the disease later in life.

The outcome of the illness largely depends on the specific type. Chronic lymphatic leukaemia for example, which tends to affect older people, may have no clinical signs or symptoms. In fact, it can run a very indolent course, require no treatment and be compatible with a normal lifespan. On the other hand, acute myeloid leukaemia which tends to affect younger adults is a very serious disease with an acute onset and which if not treated can prove to be rapidly fatal.

In childhood, leukaemia is the most common form of malignant disease but nevertheless, it is quite rare with an incidence of approximately 25 per 1,000,000 children. Over 85% of all cases involve the type known as acute lymphoblastic leukaemia. With modern treatment, a remission (that is to say, a disease free period) can be induced in over 90% of children and cure rates are very high. Presenting features of acute leukaemia are tiredness, lethargy, abnormal susceptibility to infection, excessive bruising and occasionally bone or joint pain. A blood count usually helps in the diagnosis but this needs to be confirmed by examination of the bone marrow. Treatment involves repeated courses of cytotoxic drugs, sometimes combined with radiotherapy. For those with more resistant forms of the illness, bone marrow transplantation can often provide a cure. Treatment is best performed in specialist centres where the expertise is available to deal with the complicated drug regimes. With modern treatment the outlook for all forms of leukaemia has improved. For children, in particular, the outlook has been dramatically transformed and in a great many cases a cure can be successfully achieved. The address of the Leukaemia Care Society is 14 Kingfisher Court, Venny Bridge, Pinhoe, Exeter, Devon EX4 8JN.

Hodgkin's disease, Lymphosarcoma and Reticulosarcoma. These are diseases which are in some ways akin to *leukaemia.* Abnormal cells are found in the reticulo-edothelial system and proliferate in a disorganised manner, causing enlargement of lymph nodes (glands), spleen and sometimes the liver.

Hodgkin's disease, named after a 19th cent. Guy's physician, has been the subject of much research and therapeutic trial. At special centres in London and elsewhere, earlier diagnosis and new methods of ascertaining the extent of the disease process have led to advances in surgical and medical treatment which show much promise. If treated early the disease can be apparently halted or even eradicated.

Hæmorrhagic or Bleeding Diseases.

Whenever blood vessels are damaged by injury, there is a remarkable series of mechanisms which automatically come into operation to stem the flow of blood. There is a constriction of all the smaller vessels in the locality. Platelets stick together and release substances which help the vessels to stay constricted as well as others necessary to blood clotting, and yet others which help to bind the clot tightly together. Later, materials appear to prevent too much clotting, and eventually the clot is removed altogether as healing proceeds. There are some very complicated diseases of this blood-conserving mechanism which can lead to abnormal bleeding, sometimes beneath the skin to produce bruising or even smaller leaks; sometimes leading to a greater loss of blood, particularly following a wound. In some kinds of *purpura* (bleeding tendency) the blood vessels are the cause of the trouble, having become fragile and leaky for a number of reasons. This happens in old age (*senile purpura*), in scurvy, or vitamin C deficiency, as an occasional accompaniment to infective diseases, or as an immunological effect on the lining of blood vessels when the patient becomes sensitised to certain substances (*Schönlein-Henoch* or *anaphylactoid purpura*). The latter often follows a streptococcal sore throat, just as rheumatic fever and acute nephritis do; and as well as the purpura there may be joint pains and nephritis. Just as almost any drug or chemical will cause agranulocytosis in some people, so it can also cause anaphylactoid purpura.

Purpura may also be due to a lack of platelets, known as thrombocytopenia (a shortage of thrombocytes or platelets). This can happen if the bone marrow factory is depressed, since this is where platelets too are made. It is therefore a common accompaniment of leukaemia or aplastic anaemia. Or there can be increased destruction of platelets in some diseases of the spleen. Platelets normally last eight to ten days, but their lifespan can be shortened in heart failure, and following massive transfusions, or often for no apparent reason ("idiopathic" thrombocytopenia), when removal of the spleen can sometimes help.

Finally, defects of the *clotting mechanism* will lead to a bleeding tendency, and since the mechanism itself is very complex, so is the variety of things which can upset it. The liver provides the blood with many of the substances required for clotting, so it is not surprising that a clotting defect commonly accompanies liver disease. One necessary substance for blood clotting is called "antihaemophilic factor" and is missing from those people who have inherited the disease *haemophilia*. These people may die of haemorrhage from quite small cuts or minor surgical procedures.

THE HEART AND BLOOD-VESSELS.

INTRODUCTION.

The heart consists of about 350g of muscle which makes up the walls of its four chambers. Anatomically the human heart closely resembles the sheeps' hearts to be found in a butcher's shop. Indeed it would be an instructive exercise to dissect one of these in the order described below, since there is no other way of properly appreciating what the chambers, valves, etc., are really like. There are two quite separate pumps in the heart—one on the owner's right (or on your *left* if you are looking at the front of someone else), and one on his left. The right heart collects spent, deoxygenated, "venous" blood which returns there from the whole of the body, and gives it the comparatively small push required to drive it through the adjacent lungs. The left heart collects the revitalised, oxygenated "arterial" blood as it leaves the lungs, and gives it the enormous push required to build up the arterial blood pressure, so that it can be forced through all the tissues of the body. As may be expected, the right heart chambers have much thinner walls than the left, since their muscle has less work to do. This will help you get your bearings with the sheep's heart. The tip, or apex, is the lowest part. The thick-feeling side is the left, the thin right; and the great vessels are at the top.

The upper chamber on the right, or right atrium, has two large openings into it through which all the spent blood arrives from the upper and lower great veins (the superior and inferior venae cavae). Cut open the thin wall of the right atrium with scissors between these two holes to lay open the interior of the chamber, noting the "auricle" or "dog's ear" that forms a small cul-de-sac. The whole chamber is sometimes, inaccurately, called the auricle. You should be able to push a finger downwards into the lower chamber—the right ventricle—through a communicating hole guarded by the three thin cusps of the *tricuspid valve*. These will not obstruct your finger, since they are designed to permit blood flow in the same direction. When the atrium is full of blood, it squeezes its contents through the tricuspid valve into the right ventricle; and when, a split second later, the ventricle is full and contracts, the three cusps come together to prevent the blood from flowing backwards into the atrium again. Instead the spent blood is driven onwards through the *pulmonary valve* (in the upper part of the right ventricle), through the pulmonary artery, to be delivered to the lungs. The pulmonary valve has three very well-defined cusps which prevent blood from coming back into the ventricle as it relaxes to receive more blood from the atrium before the next contraction or beat. It is possible to pass a blade of the scissors from the opened-out right atrium, through the tricuspid valve towards the tip of the heart, and cut along the right border of the heart through the thickness of the ventricular muscle. Then cut upwards again, passing the scissors blade through the pulmonary valve and open up the *pulmonary artery*. If you have done this successfully you will have followed the path taken by the spent blood through the right heart to the lungs. Notice the thick round bands of muscle lining the ventricle, and notice too that you have not entered the left heart, which has no connection with the right except in some congenital malformations (see later). The same dissection can now be made of the left heart. Open up the *left atrium*, noting its "dog's ear" or "auricle," pass the scissors down into the *left ventricle* through the two rather flimsy cusps of the *mitral valve*. Notice how much thicker is the muscle of the left ventricle, and cut upwards through the three well-formed cusps of the *aortic valve* into the main artery of the body—the *aorta*. The aorta as it leaves the left heart is distinguishable from the pulmonary artery as it leaves the right, partly by the extreme toughness of the aortic wall (it has to withstand so much more blood-pressure); and partly by the entrances or orifices of the two small branches given off by the aorta, just beyond the valve cusps, which go to supply the heart muscle itself with blood. These are the *coronary arteries* which are so necessary for the heart's own survival.

The amount of blood pumped in unit time, or the *cardiac output*, can be varied a great deal, according to the needs of the moment. This is accomplished by altering both the heart rate and the stroke volume, the amount expelled per beat. Every minute, the healthy adult man at rest shifts about 5 litres of blood through the heart—an amount equivalent to all the blood he possesses. When exercise is taken, or in response to anxiety or fear, this is stepped up many times, so that the muscles can receive a greatly augmented supply of the materials required for action. The controlling mechanisms which allow these changes to be made automatically are partly organised in the brain by the so-called *cardiac centre*; and partly by local mechanical and chemical stimuli to the heart muscle itself. The cardiac centre is continuously receiving information through nerves about the physical and chemical state of the circulation, and also from the mind; which is partly how certain emotions make the heart beat faster. All the information is integrated, and a cardiac output continuously arranged which is appropriate for current demands.

Cardiac Neurosis. In ordinary circumstances at rest, most healthy people are not conscious of their heart-beat. However, there are many perfectly healthy people whose hearts slip in an extra beat occasionally. Sometimes their owners are aware of this and become unnecessarily alarmed. Their fear causes palpitations (a pounding of the heart) and the tension mounts. An undue anxiety about the tricks played by a healthy heart sometimes leads people to interpret minor pains in the chest, or even indigestion, as grave symptoms of heart disease, and the consequent anxiety leads to still worse symptoms. If you are one of these worried people, take your worries to your doctor, and let him decide for you whether there is anything wrong. A hundred to one there isn't, and then you will have to find something else to worry about, or better still give up the habit altogether. Many people secretly worry about heart disease and high blood-pressure for years, when very often they are worrying unnecessarily. Even if there is cause for worry, so much can be done for these conditions (as it can for cancer) provided medical advice is taken early in the course of the disease. Remember, too, that the slight feeling of giddiness when you get up suddenly from having been lying down, is often experienced by most normal people; but if you get frightened by it you will begin to breathe more quickly and deeply; and this in itself will make you feel even more faint—and so on.

Heart Failure. When the cardiac output of blood is too little for the requirements of the body, a state of *circulatory failure* has arisen, and when this is due primarily to the heart itself being at fault, it is more properly called *heart failure.* As will be seen, heart failure is not a disease, but the common result of a large number of different diseases. The signs and symptoms produced are caused by two sorts of process: (*a*) tissues of the body have too little blood flow through them and are therefore undersupplied; (*b*) blood accumulates and stagnates in tissues, causing congestion, since the failing heart cannot move forward the amount of blood presented to it in the great veins. Often the left or right side of the heart fails disproportionately. In *left heart failure* the lungs are congested because they are the territory from which the left heart is failing to move blood. The patient has great difficulty with his breathing, and in advanced cases may not be able to breathe when he lies down, because the lungs become so congested and waterlogged. In *right heart failure* the main veins are congested and the other parts of the body become swollen with excess tissue fluid, mainly in the lower parts such as the legs and ankles. This swelling with fluid is called oedema, and in heart failure is only partly due to the mechanics of the failing heart. It is mainly due to a poorly understood retention of sodium in the body, a situation in which excess water is also retained. Whatever the type of heart failure it is always likely to be a changing condition, since the amount of failure will depend as much on the demands being made as on the state of the heart. For instance, in mild cases at rest when the required cardiac output is small, there may be no signs or symptoms. These may only appear on exertion. Heart failure will be referred to again later under the various conditions which cause it.

Treatment of heart failure is quite logical. It is aimed at correcting the imbalance between supply and demand of blood, and at the removal of the accumulated excess fluid. We can therefore (*a*) reduce the body's demand for blood; (*b*) increase the supply or cardiac output; and (*c*) promote the excretion of sodium and fluid. Demand for blood is reduced by rest, both physical and mental, and by reduction of weight, since obesity (being overweight) is an additional demand on the cardiovascular system. The cardiac output can be increased by administering a "tonic" to the heart muscle in the form of *digitalis,* which is a powerful heart stimulant derived from fox-

glove leaf. Fluid (and hence salt) accumulation can be helped by restricting the intake of salt and by giving drugs which promote its excretion by the kidneys (diuretics). Very occasionally, very large accumulations of fluid in the legs, abdomen, or thorax, are tapped and drained physically, with needles. These remarks on treatment, as elsewhere in the Medical Section, are of course very general and must not encourage anyone to treat himself for such a potentially serious condition as heart failure. Even such a simple measure as doing without salt can be practised quite unnecessarily by many people for years, simply as a result of reading a paragraph like the above. If you need to reduce salt intake you should be in your doctor's care, and so please let him decide.

Congenital Heart Disease. It has been estimated that of all the babies born who survive at least one month, there will be about one in every two hundred with some form of congenital heart disease; that is to say that the heart will have failed to develop properly in embryonic life. In some cases this is associated with a virus disease of the mother (commonly rubella, or German measles) or with certain drugs taken by the mother (e.g. thalidomide) at a time, very early in pregnancy, when organs are assuming their adult shape. Parents should see to it that their daughters get German measles or the vaccine before they grow up; and drugs of all kinds should be avoided where possible during early pregnancy. In most cases of congenital heart disease, however, there is no known cause, and it seems that the manner of formation of the embryonic heart is so delicate that it can be thrown out of gear very easily, perhaps even by chance. Scores of different types of defect occur, singly and in combination. Any of the valves may be anatomically defective—either failing to close properly (*incompetence*) or being too tight (*stenosis*); the great vessels (pulmonary artery and aorta) may be switched round, or *transposed,* so that they emerge from the wrong ventricle; there may be defects in the wall (*septum*) which separates the atria or the ventricles on each side (*septal defect,* or "hole in the heart"); or there may be a persistence of the vessel which in the foetus normally by-passes the lungs by joining the pulmonary artery to the aorta (*patent ductus arteriosus*). This vessel normally closes at the time of birth when the first breaths are taken, and subsequently disappears, so that the whole output of the heart is then sent round the lungs. Detecting congenital heart disease early is one of the purposes of routine post-natal check-up examinations of the baby. Exact diagnosis requires very complicated techniques, and sometimes the structural defect can be corrected by surgery, with almost miraculous results.

Rheumatic Heart Disease. Acute rheumatic fever is not to be confused with other forms of rheumatism. Many tissues of the body (particularly the heart) are attacked, as well as the joints, and the trouble is due to a sensitivity which has developed to certain bacteria (*haemolytic streptococci*) which have probably caused a sore throat about three weeks before the onset of the disease. Why acute rheumatism only rarely follows streptococcal sore throat is poorly understood, but this is no consolation to the one per cent or so of the population whose hearts bear its scars. During the acute phase of the illness which usually occurs before the age of fifteen, inflammatory damage occurs to the valves, the heart muscle, and the sac in which the heart lives, the *pericardium.* So there is a *valvulitis* or *endocarditis,* a *myocarditis* and a *pericarditis.* There may be acute heart failure at this stage if the heart is severely affected. The better-known results of rheumatic heart disease, however, are caused in the ensuing years by scarring of the healed valves. The valves are thickened and deformed. They may have lost their elasticity and stretch, so that they do not close properly (*incompetence*); or they may contract and tighten (*stenosis*). In both cases the heart chamber situated next to the affected valve has to work progressively harder, either because it gets no rest in between beats (in *incompetence*); or it has to force the blood through too narrow a hole (in *stenosis*). The end result is some variety of heart failure (*q.v.*). Other causes of heart disease may be syphilis, congenital valvular anomaly, healed bacterial endocarditis, atherosclerosis, and mechanical injury.

The most commonly affected valve is the mitral, usually causing *mitral stenosis*, in which the opening between the left atrium and the left ventricle will sometimes only admit one finger-tip instead of three fingers as it should. In time the left atrium becomes much enlarged as it overworks to force blood through this narrow orifice. Later still a back pressure develops in the lungs causing congestion and breathlessness; and even later the right ventricle is strained as it tries to force blood into the already congested lung. This is a classic example of the march of trouble backwards from the site of the damaged valve involving first the chamber "behind" it (the left atrium), then the territory "behind" that (the lungs), then the pulmonary arteries taking blood to the lungs, and finally the right ventricle trying to send blood to the pulmonary artery. This steady march of events is usually very slow, and can commonly take twenty years or longer from the initial attack of acute rheumatism to the severer symptoms of advanced mitral stenosis. Treatment is both medical and surgical. The heart failure is treated medically as already described. These days surgical reopening of the valve is almost commonplace, either by inserting a finger through the left auricle and breaking down the constriction, or by opening up the heart and re-shaping the valve under direct vision. The latter involves the additional problem of by-passing the heart by the use of some sort of external pump and poses additional problems, even though from other points of view it is obviously more convenient. As always with major surgical procedures much of the problem is in selecting the patients who will benefit from the operation and in whom it is feasible. Quite often there are other valves involved, mainly the aortic or tricuspid or both, and the hydrostatic or "plumbing" problems can be extremely complex. With luck, however, combined with good judgement and good surgery, the lives of incapacitated patients can be transformed by mitral, and other valvular, surgery. Recently a great deal of progress has been made in designing new "ball-in-basket" valves of manmade materials to replace damaged natural valves. The *aortic valve* is stenosed or narrowed by other degenerative processes besides rheumatism. *Tricuspid stenosis* is nearly always rheumatic in origin.

Coronary Heart Disease. This is the term used whenever the blood supply to the heart muscle (through the coronary arteries) is reduced to such an extent that the heart muscle suffers from a lack of supplies. It has a number of causes, but the only really common one is partial obstruction of the coronary arteries by a condition known as *atheroma* or *atherosclerosis*, and sometimes inaccurately called *arteriosclerosis*. This arterial disease is described later (**P29**). It takes the form of swellings or lumps on the lining of the artery which, if they become large enough to interfere seriously with the flow of blood, produce a blood starvation or *ischaemia* of the tissue being supplied. Obviously, the smaller the artery, the more easily will a lump of given size impede the flow. Equally obviously the greater the demand for blood, as in exercise, the more blood "starvation" there will be. There are two degrees of coronary artery disease: one in which the blood flow is reduced to the point where the increased demands of hard work cannot be met, and this results in *angina pectoris* due to *coronary insufficiency*; the other is when the coronary artery becomes completely blocked, preventing the flow of blood altogether, usually by a *thrombus* or clot of blood, and this is *coronary thrombosis*, or heart attack.

Angina Pectoris. Whenever activity is increased in any muscle, the demands for oxygen and nutriments from the blood-stream increase, and as these are used up there is an increased production of waste products known as metabolites. To meet the demands for a greater supply and a more efficient waste-disposal, the blood flow through the exercising muscle must always be increased. If sufficient increase does not occur, not only will there be a shortage of supplies, but there will also be a pile-up of metabolites in the muscle which cannot be carried away. It is mainly because of these latter that pain is caused in ischaemic, or blood-starved muscle, and pain is one of the chief symptoms when heart muscle becomes ischaemic. One important mechanism for increasing blood flow normally to exercising muscle is by automatically dilating the vessels concerned. Diseased vessels, such as coronary arteries when they are affected by atheroma, are not so easily dilated, although certain drugs which are powerful dilators of arterioles can accomplish a great deal, albeit temporarily. The measures taken to relieve the pain and blood-starvation of angina are twofold. The patient can reduce the demands of the heart by a few minutes' rest, and a drug (usually nitroglycerin) can be taken to dilate the coronary vessels of supply. Another obvious long-term way to reduce demands is for the overweight patient to eat less, and reduce the load of extra body weight on his circulation. It is very frustrating, to say the least, that such an incapacitating and often lethal condition should be caused by the narrowing or blockage of only 5 or 8 cm of narrow piping about 3·5 mm wide. Coronary bypass operations in which the blocked segment is replaced with a piece of blood vessel taken from another part of the body, are now fairly routine.

Heart Attack or *Coronary Thrombosis.* It should readily be understood from the above description that heart attacks will vary in their severity according to the amount of heart muscle deprived of blood; and this in turn will depend on where in the coronary artery the obstruction occurs. Most usually it is the left ventricular muscle which is cut off from supplies and dies, either in part or in all of its thickness. Since it is the left ventricle which does most of the work of pumping blood to the body, serious heart failure (**P27**) is to be expected. If too much muscle is killed, the heart will simply stop, and the patient will suddenly die. It is much more usual, however, for enough muscle to be left for survival, albeit with a greatly reduced cardiac efficiency. A heart attack is usually accompanied by severe pain, similar to the pain of angina but more severe, and unrelieved by rest or by the patient's usual drugs. Very occasionally the event occurs apparently without pain, or with so little that it is ignored. These so-called "silent" coronary attacks can make diagnosis extremely difficult. Since the doctor depends very considerably with heart attacks on an exact, spontaneous description of symptoms for his diagnosis, no description will be given here. There are many over-anxious people who will read these words and could be misled into an unspontaneous description of their own symptoms, and this could make the task of treating them such a problem that they could even be mis-diagnosed as a result. If you have the smallest worry that your chest pain is due to your heart, take your anxiety to your doctor without delay. He will almost certainly be able to reassure you; and if it happens to be your heart after all, you will have taken the first sensible step towards proper treatment. Dangerous as heart attacks are, they are by no means the death warrant that many lay people think, any more than cancer is. The treatment for a true heart attack is urgent and prolonged. Patients must be at complete rest and their pain relieved quickly. The area of heart muscle they have lost must be allowed to heal with a good, firm scar, and this can take three months of rest, often in hospital.

You can help to avoid a heart attack by not smoking, avoiding obesity and living a physically active life. Avoid sudden exercise, however, when you are not in training.

Blood pressure. The blood is normally under great pressure in the arterial system, since it is this which forces it into all the tissues of the body.

It is therefore no more meaningful to say you have "blood pressure" than to say you have a temperature. You would be very badly off without. Blood pressure which is too high, however, can give rise to problems, though not always. It is another of those conditions like angina and cancer, which engender much anxiety among people even when they do not suffer from them. For this reason doctors are often unwilling to disclose a patient's blood pressure and because of this they unjustifiably earn a reputation for unreasonable secrecy. They are themselves to blame for the general public anxiety as the following true story shows. Some years ago a lady in her fifties wished to accompany her husband to a post abroad which was to last four years. All arrangements had been made—the husband resigned his previous job, sold the house, etc.—when it was discovered at a routine medical examination that she had a high blood pressure, and she was very solemnly advised by the rather elderly doctor not to go. There was great consternation and emotional upheaval, not least because of the inconvenience involved. Eventually she was allowed to go at her own risk. The husband's job lasted eight years instead of four, during which the lady was in no way inconvenienced by her blood pressure; except that she worried interminably about it. On returning home to retire she began to think she had angina, and elaborate hospital investigation revealed that, as might be expected, her arteries were not as young as they used to be. She was undoubtedly suffering from mild angina, but not as badly as she thought. The opportunity then arose, in her late sixties, to go abroad yet again, and this she did, living a quite strenuous life, and one which she enjoyed. She returned home again, twenty years after she had gone abroad for the first time, able to run a home and still with very little inconvenience from her blood pressure. There is no doubt that it had been very high all that time, and it is also certain that she will die one day, although it may well not be of her blood pressure. How much better it would have been for her not to have been told it was high in the first place and to have avoided all these years of anxiety. It is not being suggested here that high blood pressure is a trivial condition, but that it is for doctors to worry about rather than patients! If you ever find out your own blood pressure, never try to work out for yourself what the figures mean. It is much too complicated. Finally, it should be mentioned that high blood pressure may occasionally be associated with, or "secondary to," certain kidney diseases (*nephritis*) including a strange condition known as *toxaemia of pregnancy*, which lasts only as long as the pregnancy, provided great care is taken. Most high blood pressure is, however, "primary", and without any known association or cause.

Low Blood pressure. Some people seem normally to have surprisingly low blood pressure all the time. There is nothing whatever wrong with this; indeed it may even be beneficial. At least they are unlikely ever to suffer the effects of high blood pressure. The sudden low blood pressure of circulatory failure or shock (**P27**) is another matter and must be urgently treated.

Irregularities of the Heart beat. How quickly or how slowly the heart beats is largely under the control of the cardiac centre in the brain and the level of certain hormones in the blood. The *regularity* of the beat, however, is controlled by the so-called pace-maker in the wall of the right atrium, and by the way impulses from the pace-maker travel through specialised conducting heart cells (the bundle of His and its branches) to the ventricles. When any part of this elaborate mechanism is upset, either by altering the biochemical or electrical conditions of these specialised tissues, or by killing some of them off by deprivation of blood supply in the course of a heart attack, disordered rhythm can result. Increase (*tachycardia*) or decrease (*bradycardia*) in rate is nearly always a normal response to exercise, or anxiety. Very occasional irregularity, such as the mis-timing of an occasional beat is also quite normal in some people, although many are alarmed by it. Persistent irregularity, however, is abnormal. Its true nature can usually be elucidated by making an electrical record of the heart beat—

an electro cardiogram. The commonest causes are varieties of coronary artery diseases or rheumatic heart disease.

Pericarditis. The heart beats inside a bag or sac. At every beat its outer surface slides against the lining of the sac, lubricated by a small amount of fluid. This is the pericardial sac, the *pericardium* being strictly the lubricated membrane which lines the sac and which also covers the outer surface of the heart. Sometimes inflammation occurs—*pericarditis*—and the sliding surfaces become roughened and even separated by a fluid effusion. Very occasionally, so much fluid accumulates that the heart's action is seriously impeded. Pericarditis may be due to infection or to rheumatic fever, and it usually overlies the area of damaged muscle after a heart attack. This illustrates something which people rarely appreciate—that inflammation is not by any means always due to infection by bacteria. The last two varieties of pericarditis are quite free from germs (sterile).

Myocarditis. A term loosely applied to disorders affecting the heart muscle. There are lots of very rare causes. The really common ones are due to acute or chronic rheumatic causes or to coronary artery disease, both of which are described above.

Endocarditis or inflammation of the lining of the heart is a term loosely applied to any disorder of the valves or heart lining. All varieties of rheumatic valvular disease (**P27**) are included. Bacterial endocarditis in its several forms usually involves valves already damaged by rheumatic disease. It is a complication which is still much to be feared, though somewhat less so now that antibiotic drugs are available.

Atheroma or *Atherosclerosis.* This is the condition referred to above in which lumps arise on the lining of arterial blood-vessels. Although it is therefore a disease of the arteries, its importance lies in the way blood flow is held up, either by the lumps themselves, or by thrombosis ultimately blocking the narrowed portion of the pipework. The effects on the body are therefore those of depriving the tissues of blood. It is an astonishing fact that in England and America, more people die of the consequences of atheroma than of any other single disease, including all forms of cancer put together. Furthermore, cancer is mainly a disease of old age, whereas many of the effects of atheroma on men occur in early middle age. If narrowing of the artery is going to do significant harm it is easy to see that it will be of more consequence in those parts of the body where small-bore vessels are supplying tissues whose functions are necessary for life. Exactly such a situation exists in the heart and in the brain. An additional factor is that the arrangement of the blood supply in these tissues is such that any particular area has only one vessel leading to it. This is unusual among the tissues generally, where several alternative, or "collateral" vessels usually supply an area, and where others can take over if one becomes obstructed. We have, therefore, a situation in which perhaps the most important tissues —the heart and the brain—run the greatest risk of deprivation, and this leads to angina and coronary thrombosis on the one hand, and cerebral thrombosis and haemorrhage ("stroke illness") on the other, accounting jointly for about one death in every five. In addition, the effects of atheromatous narrowing are often felt in the legs, where the blood supply to the muscles is inadequate for exercise, leading to intermittent pain comparable with that in the heart in similar circumstances. This is called *intermittent claudication*, or intermittent closing of the leg arteries. In its most severe forms, it leads to the need for amputation, although in most cases early treatment can avoid this. It is small wonder that there is intensive research into the causes of atheroma, as with cancer, but it is probably true to say that we still know rather more about cancer. A lot of attention has been given to the amounts of certain fats in the circulating blood, particularly cholesterol. This fat is found in larger amounts in the blood of sufferers from atheroma, and is also found in the arterial lumps themselves.

Efforts have therefore been made to reduce blood cholesterol by modifications of the diet, but it has been extremely difficult to prove that this has done any good. Many other factors are known to contribute to atheroma, and hence to heart attacks and strokes, some of which can be reduced and others not. Such factors are age, obesity, high blood pressure, and smoking cigarettes. People who lead an active life, like bus conductors, seem to have less trouble than others who are less active, like bus drivers. Sudden severe exercise, however, is bad if you are not used to it. It is better, and life saving, to take regular, moderate exercise. Women have less atheroma than men, until the menopause when they begin to catch up, so that hormones have something to do with it. Serious starvation, such as occurred in the German-occupied territories of Holland and Scandinavia and in the concentration camps conferred one benefit a freedom from atheroma, but obviously we cannot all starve, and the puzzle remains. Like many of the more important outstanding medical puzzles, there is no single factor responsible, and this is what makes it difficult to solve.

Aortic Disease. The aorta, the main artery of the body, running from the left ventricle down through the chest and abdomen, also suffers from atheroma, but is too wide (about 2·5 cm across) to become obstructed. However, weaknesses occur in the thickness of its wall, sometimes due to syphilis but nowadays much more usually due to atheroma, which results in a ballooning out of a part of the vessel, rather like you sometimes see in an old bicycle inner tube. In days gone by these *aneurysms*, as the dilations are called, reached an enormous size, and would wear away the breastbone and ribs, to appear as large pulsating masses on the chest. Now that advanced syphilis is less common, atheromatous aneurysm, with a predilection for the abdominal aorta, is the one most commonly seen; and these days it is treated by replacement of the diseased portion of vessel. *Dissecting aneurysms* of the aorta are another variety in which the blood, under high pressure, somehow finds its way in between the layers of the aortic wall and then suddenly rips up and down the whole length of the vessel, separating (or dissecting) one layer from another in its path. Sometimes it tracks back towards the heart and suddenly fills the pericardium with blood to stop the heart's action altogether.

Embolism. This term refers to any foreign object travelling in the circulation and becoming impacted when it reaches a vessel too small for it to pass through. It may be a thrombus (**P30**), a collection of cancer cells, a group of bacteria, a chunk of infected pus from an abscess, a collection of fat droplets or even a bubble of air. If it originates in a vein it travels to the right heart and to the lungs. If it comes from the left heart or an artery, it will impact in any part of the arterial tree. Reasonably enough an arterial embolus will commonly end up in those parts of the body with the richest blood supply, like the brain, the kidneys, the liver or the bone marrow. A thrombotic embolus will cause death of the tissue in the area previously supplied by the blocked vessel, a condition known as *infarction.* Perhaps the commonest source of thrombotic embolism is the lining of the heart chambers where a thrombus has occurred at the site of muscle damaged by a heart attack. Massive pulmonary (lung) embolism is usually the result of the thrombosis of the leg veins in people kept immobile following surgery or childbirth. That is why postoperative patients are got out of bed for a while as soon as the first day after the operation. The cells of a cancer embolus usually die; but if they survive, a new cancer deposit begins to grow where the embolus impacts, and this is one of the ways cancer may spread. An infected embolus may infect the vessel wall when it impacts, producing a weakness which may give way. Air embolism, if enough insoluble gas enters the circulation, can kill by making so much froth in the heart chambers as to impede the normal pumping action. If bubbles pass the lungs and enter the brain, all sorts of neurological disorders like scores of tiny strokes arise. The same sort of thing happens all over the body in the *"bends"* or *"caisson" disease*,

in which nitrogen dissolved in the blood at high pressure, usually in deep-sea diving, bubbles out of solution if decompression is too rapid. Fat embolism sometimes occurs after fractures, due to marrow fat entering damaged veins and being carried away to the lungs.

Thrombosis. This is not quite the same as clotting. It is the mass which arises when platelets adhere to the lining of blood-vessels or heart chambers. Blood clot accumulates among layers of deposited platelets and the thrombus therefore has structure, unlike pure blood clot. Thrombosis usually occurs when the lining of the vessel or chamber is damaged by atheroma or inflammation, or when the circulation becomes very stagnant. One danger is that it will become dislodged and travel as an embolus during the first week or ten days of its existence. After this time it is usually firmly incorporated into the vessel walls by cells which migrate into it from the surrounding tissue. The other danger is, of course, that the tissue previously supplied by the blocked vessel will die before a collateral circulation can be established. As previously explained, this is called infarction. All the technical terms in this section are used elsewhere and can be looked up.

Varicose Veins. When veins become swollen they also often become tortuous (wriggly), and particularly on the surface of the leg look very unsightly. They are, however, a sign of a sluggish circulation, and are often due to disease in small valves within the veins which normally prevent the blood from pooling backwards, down towards the feet. They are often a normal maternal accompaniment of pregnancy and disappear after the child is born. If allowed to persist, the sluggish circulation allows the formation of unpleasant ulcers, mainly in elderly people. Treatment is according to severity. In the early stages they are helped by supportive stockings. Later, often as an out-patient, the sufferer may have to have them removed or obliterated by a surgeon.

Raynaud's Disease. This is a strange condition in which the finger tips and in severe cases all the fingers or the whole hand respond in an exaggerated way to cold. The vessels supplying the hand are constricted and the fingers go white as the blood drains from them. Then the capillaries dilate and become distended and filled with blood. But owing to stagnation it is venous and blue, and the fingers are therefore blue. Now we have all experienced this in very cold weather, but sufferers from Raynaud's disease, nearly always women, respond even to very slight cold, like putting their hands into cold water. Even emotional stress will start the process off. In very severe cases the fingers will be so deprived of blood for so long, that sores will develop and fingers can even be lost, but this is very rare, and can be avoided by an operation to cut the nerves which supply the circular muscle of the vessels concerned. In most cases it is sufficient to avoid getting the hands cold.

Frostbite. Strictly speaking, this is literally a freezing of the tissues and usually only occurs at temperatures below −13° C. The patient may feel a pricking feeling at first, and feel an area of firmer, pale skin on the cheeks, nose, ears, fingers, or toes. If these parts are numb with cold, the onset of frostbite may not be felt, and will often only be noticed by others. In countries where extreme cold is prevalent, it is usual for complete strangers to stop each other in the street and point it out when they see it. It is important not to rub the affected part nor to apply direct heat in any form. Rapid warming can be harmful; rewarming by close application of body temperature is good treatment, *e.g.*, fingers can be firmly held in the armpit or a warm hand closely applied to an ear or a nose.

THE RESPIRATORY SYSTEM.

INTRODUCTION.

When air is drawn in during the process of breathing, it is brought into very close contact with the blood passing through the lungs. In this way the air we breathe in, which contains 21 per cent oxygen, is confronted with "spent" blood returning from the tissues which contains much less, and oxygen therefore diffuses into the blood from the air. At the same time, the waste gas, carbon dioxide, passes by diffusion in the reverse direction from the blood into the air, because there is much more carbon dioxide in the returning "spent" blood than the tiny amount in the air we breathe. The blood is therefore continually circulating through the lungs and exchanging carbon dioxide for oxygen from the air we breathe in. When we breathe out, we disperse the carbon dioxide into the atmosphere.

When the air enters the nose or mouth, it passes into the windpipe or *trachea*, through the vocal cords in the pharynx. The trachea is held open all the time by rings of cartilage and is lined by a mucus-secreting membrane covered by millions of tiny "hairs" or cilia. These continuously waft a sheet of sticky mucus upwards, which traps any dust or other small particles we may have inhaled, until a collection of this material in the pharynx stimulates us to cough and expel the phlegm, usually to be swallowed. At its lower end, the trachea or windpipe divides into two, the right and left main *bronchus*. Each main bronchial tube enters a lung, one on each side, and proceeds to divide repeatedly within the lung until the air is being carried by more and more smaller and ever smaller tubes called *bronchioles*. There are many millions of these on each side, and each one ends in a collection of very small balloon-like structures —the air sacs or *alveoli*. If you were to cut across a lung and examine the cut surface in a good light, you would see that it is a spongy tissue, with many millions of tiny holes, each one just visible to the naked eye. These are the air sacs. In their walls run the blood capillaries, each one of which is a branch of the vessels carrying "spent" blood from the right side of the heart. At this stage, the blood is only separated from the air in the sacs by the walls of the capillaries and of the air sacs themselves. Both structures are extremely thin, making for easy diffusion of the gases between blood and air.

The action of breathing is accomplished by two muscular mechanisms. One is by the muscles which move the ribs, and the other by the diaphragm, a sheet of muscle which runs across the body, separating the chest cavity from the abdominal cavity. These muscles are all actuated by nerves, just as all other muscles are. Those running to the muscles of breathing are organised by a mechanism in the brain known as the *respiratory centre*. It is this centre—one of the so-called vital centres of the brain—which receives information from many different sources, and translates it into instructions for the breathing mechanism. Thus, when you run for a bus, you will automatically breathe more deeply and more quickly because the respiratory centre has been informed about all the extra carbon dioxide in your blood which has been produced by the exercising leg muscles. Even the conscious instructions involved when you blow a trumpet, inflate a balloon, or during speaking, all pass first to the respiratory centre. It is the death of the cells of this and other vital centres of the brain that is the ultimate cause of death in everyone who dies.

Bronchitis may be acute or chronic. It is an inflammation of the lining mucous membrane of the larger air passages or bronchi, and results in much more secretion than the amount normally produced, mixed with some pus. The acute form is often caused by viruses, with "secondary" infection from bacteria. It may sometimes be caused by irritant gases, like the sulphur dioxide in smog. The chronic, or long-standing form of bronchitis is often associated with *emphysema*, in which the small air sacs of the lung architecture are destroyed or distorted, leaving larger spaces than normal, often surrounded by fibrous scar tissue. Such an arrangement makes the normal gaseous exchange difficult between air and blood. While the exact cause of chronic bronchitis is

difficult to discover, because it is such a mixture of causes, it is mainly associated with older age groups, particularly men, in damp foggy climates like ours in Britain, with polluted town air and especially with smoking. Smoking also makes any existing bronchitis much worse. Bronchitis can cause even more trouble than lung cancer, since instead of dying in a short time, the bronchitic lives for many years in chronic sickness. About 6100 (in 1992) people die of bronchitis each year. It isn't smart to smoke. Patients cough, and produce varying amounts of sputum, or phlegm. They often wheeze like asthmatics. This may go on for many years before the right side of the heart begins to fail (**P27**). Gradually, during this time, the chest tends to become barrel-shaped. Treatment consists of getting the patient to stop smoking or otherwise contaminating his lungs, preventing infection, particularly during winter months, with germ-killing antibiotics, and breathing exercises. The outlook for chronic bronchitis and emphysema is nevertheless not good, although many patients continue with their disease for many years, provided they take constant care to obey instructions and stop smoking.

Bronchial Asthma is a condition in which the finer air passages become constricted due to an allergic response. In addition, an increased secretion tends to obstruct them and the patient wheezes. In many cases it can be shown that he is allergic to a particular component of dust, or, less commonly, a foodstuff. This is the same sort of thing as occurs in the upper respiratory passages in hay fever, but the effect is on a different, lower part of the respiratory system. Many other cases are due to respiratory infection of some sort, probably combined with an allergy to the bacteria causing it. A predisposition to asthma is often inherited. Once a patient has become asthmatic, his attacks will be triggered off by such additional things as emotional stress, changes in temperature (particularly sudden cold), irritating fumes or smoke, and physical exertion. These are secondary factors, and although much of the treatment is concerned with them, it is unlikely that any of them is a sole cause of the condition. Treatment is directed at the relief of the breathing difficulty and of the wheezing, as well as the control of the causative factors. Many useful drugs are available to dilate the contracted air passages and reduce the obstructing secretions. Asthma in children often gets better as the patient grows up. Asthma is another condition made much worse by smoking.

A tiny living mite about 0·3 millimetres long exists in large numbers in nearly all mattresses and floor dust. This is the cause of much asthma, and in such cases it is often very helpful to vacuum-clean mattresses and floors frequently.

Bronchiectasis. In this condition the bronchial air passages are abnormally and permanently dilated, and the normal structure of the walls destroyed. It is thought to be caused by obstructions of the tubes which lead to dilatation of the parts beyond. Secretions accumulate, and since they cannot easily drain away, they become infected. The infection helps to complete the process of destruction of structures in the bronchial wall. The patient has a chronic cough which often produces large quantities of purulent sputum, and there are often recurrent episodes of pneumonia. Diagnosis is made by a special X-ray examination—a bronchogram—in which a material, opaque to X-rays, is dropped into the air passages. This shows up the dilated and distorted tubes. In some cases, where the disease is localised to one part of the lung, it is often a good idea to cut out that portion, and this is particularly true in young people. Vigorous physiotherapy, involving drainage of the lungs by placing the patient in a suitable posture, together with antibiotic drugs for the infection, are other forms of treatment.

Cystic Fibrosis is an inborn disease which affects chiefly the lungs and the digestive system. It is sometimes called *Fibrocystic disease of the Pan-*

creas, and sometimes "mucoviscidosis". Until it was medically recognised forty years ago, children affected usually died from pneumonia in the first year of life. This, of course, was before antibiotics were available for the treatment of infections. Today, cystic fibrosis is known to be the commonest genetically determined disorder affecting children in Britain. One child in 2,000 receives one of the abnormal genes from each parent. Such a child therefore has a double dose of the harmful gene, and will have the disease from birth. One person in 25 of the general population carries only one of these abnormal genes, and such an individual will not have the disease, but will be a carrier of the abnormal gene. If such a seemingly normal carrier marries another carrier, there is a one in four chance of each of their children being affected. The children, therefore, who actually develop cystic fibrosis have inherited the disease *equally* from both parents, who are carriers, but are themselves unaffected by the disease. The disease is inherited recessively and involves a defect in pumping salt across cell membranes, particularly in glands. The prospects for survival into reasonably healthy adult life are steadily improving, but they depend upon early diagnosis and careful management through childhood. In cystic fibrosis most of the damage is caused by the excessive viscidity, or stickiness, of the mucus which is produced in the breathing tubes as a lubricant, and also in the ducts of the pancreatic gland which provides enzymes to help digestion. Being thick and sticky, instead of thin and slimy as in the normal, this mucus tends to block the passages instead of keeping them clear. The pancreatic cells are permanently destroyed. The gland cannot secrete pancreatic enzymes, and the food, especially protein and fat, is not properly absorbed. This deficiency can be compensated fairly well by giving pancreatic extract by mouth with every meal, and by dietary care.

The major clinical problem is in the lungs. The lung passages normally have a thin coating of mucus which is propelled steadily upwards, and is completely renewed in less than one hour. It moves more suddenly on coughing. In cystic fibrosis this upward movement is slowed down and interrupted. There is difficulty in keeping the passages clear, especially when infection with bacteria or viruses greatly increases the amount of mucus. This results in intermittent blocking of the air passages, difficulty in breathing, incomplete use of the lungs, and persistent local pockets of infection. If such infectious processes are not controlled, areas of lung will be destroyed, chronic infection will persist, and multiple lung cavities will develop. These predispose to further infection, interfering with the natural development of the lung—a process not normally complete until halfway through childhood—thus adding to the respiratory problems which the child will face in later life. Unless a correct diagnosis is made and proper treatment instituted before the first serious lung infection has occurred, the resulting lung damage may well be permanent.

Pneumonia. This is an infection of the lung tissue, rather than of the air passages. The lung is the only internal organ which is directly exposed to the air, and since there are germs of all kinds in the air, it is a source of surprise that pneumonia is not a much more common event in all of us. The answer lies, as with all infections, in the fact that it is not simply (or even mainly) bacteria which cause disease, but our own lack of resistance to them. If we allow germs to thrive and multiply by being unhealthy or run down or undernourished, infective disease will occur. If we are fit, the entry of those same harmful germs into the body causes us no inconvenience, unless we are very young, or very old, or unless the invasion of germs is abnormally overwhelming. This helps to explain why pneumonia is so often quoted as a cause of death. In most cases it is merely a terminal event occurring in the elderly sick, whose normal resistance is so far reduced by their illness that they succumb to an invasion which they would normally not notice. There are two main kinds of pneumonia, and in both the air sacs become filled with inflammatory secretions,

making the normally porous lung tissue as solid as liver. In *lobar pneumonia*, a whole segment (or lobe) of the lung becomes solid. In *bronchopneumonia*, areas of lung tissue surrounding the smaller bronchioles become consolidated, leaving normal porous lung tissue in between. Bronchopneumonia is the one which occurs in the rather stagnant lungs of people who are already ill or bedridden. Both forms respond to treatment with the appropriate antibiotics, provided any underlying debility does not interfere with the patient's own resistance. In the terminal bronchopneumonia of fatal illness, it is sometimes considered kinder not to treat the additional pneumonia. *Pleurisy* is a natural complication, and before the days of antibiotic drugs *lung abscess* was very much feared. Another form of pneumonia—*viral pneumonia*—is referred to in **P9(2)**.

Pneumoconiosis. This is a term which refers to a large group of different diseases, all of which are caused by breathing in some form of dust over a very long period of time. It is therefore an occupational hazard of certain trades. We have already mentioned the mechanisms of mucus secretion in the air passages which normally trap small particles from the air, and prevent them reaching the lung. However, in some occupations there is so much dust breathed in over the months and years that these normal barriers are defeated. About a quarter of the earth's crust consists of silicon, in quartz, flint, or sand. *Silicosis* occurs in people who have worked for many years in trades like mining, stone crushing, sandblasting, or metal grinding, who are often breathing silicon dust in high concentration. When the particles arrive in the air sacs, they set up an irritant chemical reaction which produces nodules of scar tissue. Silicosis for some reason predisposes to tuberculosis. Emphysema also occurs and there is a general impairment of respiratory function. Coalminer's pneumoconiosis is similar to silicosis but not identical with it. It is more prevalent in some coalfields than others, owing to the different composition of the dust to which these unfortunate men are daily exposed. It is hoped that modern mining methods will help to reduce this dread disease. Asbestos is a complex silicate of magnesium, calcium, and iron. *Asbestosis* is caused by inhaling its fine fibres, and often leads to the appearance of a type of lung cancer called mesothelioma. *Berylliosis* is caused by compounds of beryllium, used in the manufacture of fluorescent lamps. *Farmer's lung* is a pneumoconiosis caused by inhaling hay and grain dust, and is similar to *bagassosis* and *byssinosis* caused by sugar cane and cotton dust respectively. The newest pneumoconiosis to be reported is *mushroom worker's lung*, caused by something in the compost in which mushrooms are commercially grown.

Pulmonary Embolism. This catastrophic, yet quite common condition has already been briefly referred to (**P30(1)**). It is a cause of tragic, sudden death in people who have had operations or have given birth to babies some days previously, or who have been bedridden for any other cause. The first event is that the blood in the veins of the legs becomes stagnant, due to the lack of exercise; and together with the tendency to clot which often follows surgery or childbirth, the whole length of a leg vein may be obstructed for twelve inches or more by an elongated clot of blood. This does little harm to the circulation of the leg, since there are plenty of other veins for returning blood to the heart. The danger is that the clot will become dislodged and be swept upwards towards the heart by the flow of returning blood. When this happens it is carried by way of the right atrium and ventricle into the pulmonary vessels which normally carry spent blood to the lungs. Here, for the first time, it enters vessels which are getting smaller as they divide, and it then impacts in the main pulmonary artery. The patient, who may have been recovering very well, suddenly collapses and not unusually dies there and then. At autopsy a long coiled-up mass of clot is found obstructing the pulmonary vessels. It often can be seen to form a cast of the leg vein and even bears the marks of the small venous valves which are present at its site of origin. With the dramatic advances being made in chest surgery, it is now sometimes possible in selected cases to operate to remove the clot. Success clearly depends on the patient's surviving long enough to be taken to the operating theatre for the major operation of *pulmonary embolectomy*. Three quarters of all cases of pulmonary embolism die within two hours, and therefore the best hope would be to prevent the occurrence altogether. This is not at present possible, but clotting in leg veins can be discouraged by early exercise following surgery and childbirth. Patients often resent having to get up the next day because it is so uncomfortable. Herein, however, lies their best hope of avoiding pulmonary embolism.

Haemoptysis. This means coughing up blood or blood-stained material. It must be distinguished from *haematemesis*, in which the blood is vomited from the stomach. It must always be taken seriously because of the underlying lung disease which may be present. No one who coughs up blood, in however small a quantity, should neglect to inform their doctor so that its source can be determined. Haemoptysis occurs in a variety of lung disease, some of which is not serious but much of which must be treated immediately if it is not to become so. This is a suitable place to repeat our general rule that you should see your doctor without delay if you have any unexplained bleeding from any part of the body, however well you feel. And this includes haemoptysis.

Fat Embolism. Liquid fat sometimes enters the bloodstream following extensive crush injuries to soft tissue and bone. It splits up into millions of small globules which are carried to the lungs, and impact in small blood vessels there, producing obstruction of the lung circulation and consequent difficulties in breathing.

Lung Cancer. This is one of the commonest, nastiest and most incurable forms of cancer which can occur. It is also probably the easiest to prevent. Each year about 35,000 people die of lung cancer in Great Britain, all but 5,000 of them men. Every year the toll goes on. There has been no reasonable doubt for several years now that it is associated with cigarette smoking, and the evidence is overwhelming. However, in spite of this certain knowledge, smoking continues to increase, and every year there are more and more people dying unpleasantly of lung cancer. It seems that nothing the health authorities can do is able to stop it. Intensive campaigns of public advertising of the dangers, and well organised instruction in schools have so far made little impression whatever on the smoking habits even of people who accept the evidence. The only group of people who are known to have stopped smoking are British doctors, very many of whom have given it up, and it is easy to show that giving it up has saved them from the disease. Their colleagues who have not done so have continued to die. Undoubtedly a large factor contributing to the failure of anti-smoking propaganda is the enormous expenditure by the tobacco manufacturers on very clever advertising, amounting to many millions of pounds each year. Moreover they spend a pitiful fraction of this amount on their own research into the harmful effects of their own product, which has so far discovered nothing which was not already known by research doctors many years ago. Another problem is that it takes a number of years to get cancer. It is not like an infectious disease which is caught a few days after exposure to the bacteria concerned. It may be fifteen or twenty years before the cancer begins, and many smokers are apparently unwilling to look so far ahead. Furthermore, not everyone who smokes dies this way; and so a smoker can gamble with his life and hope it will not be him. The present writer once had to perform a series of post-mortem examinations on people who died of lung cancer, and this helped him to stop smoking completely, having smoked more than twenty cigarettes a day for several years. Not everyone can have this incentive. The main

encouragement to smoke probably comes from other people. Schoolboys are easily impressed when their teachers and parents stop smoking. They are not likely to fear the habit when these same people smoke openly. The smoking doctor is also a powerful stimulus to people to carry on smoking.

Lung cancer grows in the wall of a main bronchial air passage. If it grows inwards it can obstruct the airway, choking that part of the lung it is supplying with air. This causes collapse and infection of the lung and may lead to *lung abscess*. The patient will then cough up blood-stained infected and purulent material. Such a case is comparatively lucky, since the disease declares itself early by producing symptoms. In others, the lump may grow outwards into the surrounding lung and produce no symptoms at all in the early stages. Indeed, it may spread to other parts of the body, like brain or bone or liver before causing any trouble to the patient. If this happens he may go to his doctor because of fits, changes of personality, or fracture, only to discover that the origin of the trouble is in the lung.

Cure rates are low, although much can be done to relieve the pain and suffering of the last stages of the illness. Survival rates vary from 16–53% at 5 years, depending on the type and severity of disease. Surgery, by removing the lung, and irradiation of the growth are the standard palliative treatment. It is not the practice of the Medical Section to alarm the reader unnecessarily, but if only a few are induced to stop giving themselves such a horrible disease, then writing in this way will have been justified.

Secondary Cancer of the Lung. In nearly all forms of cancer, the big problem is that it spreads to other parts of the body. If this were not so it could be eradicated by surgical removal more often than it is. One common way in which it spreads from any part of the body is by entering the bloodstream and being carried as clumps of living cancer cells to distant parts. When these come to rest in smaller blood vessels, they begin to grow and colonise the new environment. Such new colonies are called *secondary deposits* or *metastases*. It so happens that all veins (except portal veins of the liver) lead to the right heart and thence directly to the lungs, and for this reason the lungs are a very common site of *secondary* cancer, which may have begun in the bowel, or breast, or indeed anywhere else in the body. Other common sites of secondary, blood-borne cancer are the brain, liver, bone marrow, and kidney, since all of them have an abundant blood supply, and there is therefore a high chance of the travelling cells arriving there. Secondary cancer of the lung usually consists of several lumps scattered throughout the lung. Lung cancer itself is usually only one growth. One of the main reasons for the success of early diagnosis is that treatment may be possible before blood-borne and other means of spread have occurred. Unfortunately, in the case of primary cancer of the lung, even early diagnosis is of little avail, but in many other common cancers permanent cure is possible if treatment is begun early enough.

Pleurisy. The chest is lined by one layer of a thin membrane called the *pleura*. The lungs are covered and enclosed by a second, continuous layer of this same membrane. When the lungs move during respiration, the pleura covering the lungs rubs against the pleura lining the chest, lubricated by a very thin layer of pleural fluid separating the two pleura. Whenever the pleural surface becomes inflamed, this is known as *pleurisy*. It is nearly always due to inflammatory disease of the adjoining lung, and is therefore not strictly a disease in its own right. For example, pneumonia, tuberculosis, lung cancer, or a lung infarct will produce a pleurisy if the area of diseased lung adjoins the lung surface. Sometimes the area of inflamed inner pleura will tend to stick to its outer layer or rub painfully against it, producing a sharp pain when the patient breathes. Sometimes a large effusion of fluid is produced which separates the two layers and collapses the lung by occupying space in the chest which the lung should be occupying. This latter is more usual in tuberculosis or cancer.

The lung can be collapsed by the entry of anything between the normally adjacent layers of pleura. For example, air can be introduced, either deliberately to rest the lung in tuberculosis, or by accidental penetrating wounds of the chest wall, or by accidental rupture of the emphysematous lung (*q.v.*). This condition is called *pneumothorax* or "air in the chest." Bleeding into the cavity between the pleura is called *haemothorax*.

THE DIGESTIVE TRACT AND LARGE INTESTINE.

INTRODUCTION.

The digestive tract consists of the mouth, pharynx, oesophagus (or gullet), stomach, small intestine, large intestine (or colon), rectum, and anus. The small intestine is very long, and is subdivided into the duodenum, jejunum, and ileum. It ends at the junction of the ileum with the caecum, where there is a small blind side-tube, the appendix. The caecum leads into the colon. The whole tract has two main mechanical functions and two main biochemical ones. Mechanically, food has to be chewed in the mouth and further minced up by muscular squeezing, mainly by the stomach. It has also to be propelled along by an orderly series of squeezing movements known as *peristalsis*. While it is still in the digestive tract, food has to be digested. That is to say, it has to be broken down chemically into suitable materials for absorption into the system, and secondly, it has to be absorbed across the wall of the intestine into the blood stream, itself a highly complex biochemical process. The blood stream it now enters is a special part of the circulation, the "portal" system, which travels directly to the liver without first passing to the heart. In the liver the broken-down foods are processed and issued in their new form into the general, or "systemic" circulation, by which they are finally carried to all the tissues of the body.

As the food passes along the digestive tract (or, as it is sometimes called, the alimentary canal), it is mixed with various secretions which are either made in the wall of the tract, or by organs outside the wall connected to the main pathway by small tubes. Examples of the latter are bile, manufactured by the liver and sent into the duodenum through the bile ducts; and pancreatic juice, which comes from the pancreas down the pancreatic ducts, also into the duodenum. These secretions are either digestive juices concerned with splitting up the foodstuffs so that they can be absorbed, or they have a lubricant so that the gut contents slide along easily under the influence of peristalsis. Roughly speaking, it may be said that digestive juices give place to lubricant secretions at the junction between the small and large intestine.

The constituents of the diet are dealt with in a later section. The principal classes with whose digestion we are now concerned are carbohydrates, proteins, and fats.

Carbohydrates are sugars and starches. There are many sugars, which may exist alone, in pairs, or with lots of them stuck together. Alone they are such things as glucose or fructose. Common table sugar is a substance called sucrose, formed by sticking one glucose molecule to one fructose molecule. Starch is lots of glucose molecules all stuck together. Digestion of carbohydrates consists of splitting up sugars and starch into single sugars like glucose, since only single sugars can be absorbed into the system. The splitting is done by digestive *enzymes* which are found in the juices secreted into the digestive tract. Sugar-splitters are found in the saliva of the mouth, in the pancreatic juice of the duodenum, and in the duodenum's own juice from its own wall. On the face of it, you might think it would be better to eat glucose which needs no digestion and can be absorbed in

this form, than to eat starch which has first to be split; and so a lot of money has been made out of a gullible public by the sale of glucose drinks and powder. In fact digesting starch is no problem whatever, even for the sick, who can obtain their carbohydrate energy just as easily (and much more cheaply) from potatoes as from expensive glucose. The end result of eating both is the same. The starch-splitting enzyme in saliva is mixed with the food as it is chewed, and it is therefore probably a good idea to chew it well. However, even if the food is bolted it does not seem to matter very much. People without teeth (neither their own nor dentures) seem to digest their carbohydrate quite well, presumably by means of their pancreatic juice at a later stage.

Proteins, which are found in meat, cheese, and eggs, are very large molecules consisting of lots of small ones strung together. Unlike starch, in which all the component glucose molecules are identical, the amino acids of which proteins are composed come in many different types. They all contain nitrogen, and there are about twenty-seven varieties. One protein differs from another in the proportions of the mixture and the order in which they are stuck together. Only single amino acids can be absorbed from the food, and so protein digestion again consists of splitting the material down into its building bricks. There is a strong protein-splitting enzyme in the gastric (or stomach) juice called pepsin, whose job it is to split the long amino-acid chains into shorter chains. Several other protein-splitters in the duodenal and pancreatic juice contrive to break the smaller chains into individual amino acids which are then absorbed and sent to the liver for processing.

Fats mainly consist of glycerol to which are attached three fatty acid molecules for each molecule of glycerol. An enzyme in pancreatic juice splits the fatty acids off the glycerol, but would have some difficulty penetrating the globules of fat without the help of bile. One of the constituents of bile (bile salts) has detergent properties like washing-up powder and breaks the fat globules up into a very fine emulsion so that the enzyme can get at the fat. Some fat particles of this size can even be absorbed as such, without preliminary splitting.

The processes by which all these enzymic secretions are produced are very finely controlled. They are very expensive to make in terms of energy and raw materials, and so it would be very wasteful to produce them all the time, even when there was no food to digest. And so the body has some very well designed automatic arrangements for sampling the foods as they are eaten and passed on, which ensure that exactly the right kind of juice is waiting in every part of the digestive tract for whatever food arrives. As soon as the food is digested the supply of enzymes is automatically switched off, so that there is very little waste of precious materials. It is, of course, beyond the scope of this account to describe the control mechanisms. Suffice it to say that they are operated partly by nerve reflexes which signal the imminent arrival of food, and partly by special hormones produced in various parts of the gut wall. The best secretion is affected even by psychological factors, so that pleasant company and surroundings, attractive appearance of the food, and an eager anticipation of it all make for good digestion and good health. These psychological factors are all capable of proper scientific investigation and proof. The poor health of those who habitually and irregularly bolt unpalatable food is probably due to such factors as these. So is the failure of appetite in the depressed, the anxious adult, or the scolded child.

Nearly all the digestion which has been described occurs in the stomach and upper part of the small intestine (the duodenum, jejunum, and upper ileum). Almost all absorption of the products of digestion occurs in the small intestine which is long and intricately folded to give it a large surface area for this purpose. The colon, or large intestine, is adapted for conserving water, by removing it from the residual waste material. This has then to be eliminated, and being rather dry its passage has to be lubricated by suitable secretions of mucus.

Constipation. Here, perhaps we had better mention the morbid question of constipation, about which so many people are obsessed and hold such pronounced views. First of all, what is it? For some people it is entirely normal only to pass motions about once or twice a week. For others the normal frequency is once or twice a day. What is abnormal? The answer is that the only thing worth worrying about is only pronounced change of bowel habit, particularly in middle-aged and older people. By a change is meant a change from that individual person's normal routine. Such a pronounced change—either in the direction of constipation or diarrhoea—is worth consulting your doctor about if it persists for more than a week or two. Otherwise, forget your bowels and leave them to work naturally as they know best. Many believe that constipation is the root of all evil, that it causes a mysterious condition known to them (although, alas, not to doctors) as "auto-intoxication." Sedulously fostered by the manu-facturers of patent medicines, their beliefs range from the notion that headaches, spotty skin, muddy skin, and tiredness are caused by con-stipation, to the more extreme idea that the whole system is being poisoned and that, if the bowels do not work, the individual will shortly die. Of course, all this is the merest rubbish; for, as Professor Samson Wright, whose *Applied Physiology* is one of the most famous of medical text-books, has pointed out, there is no such thing as absorption of poisonous products from the bowel. There is no such thing as "auto-intoxica-tion." "The symptoms of constipation," he writes, "are largely due to distension and mechanical irritation of the rectum." It has been shown that an enema removes these symptoms *immediately*, which would not be the case if they were due to poisons in the blood, and exactly the same symptoms can be produced by packing the rectum with cotton-wool. Wright mentions the case of a man who went for just over a year with-out bowel motion, and at the end of that time, although his abdomen was distended and he felt some discomfort, he was not noticeably ill. Need-less to say, telling these facts to the purgative addict will only make him annoyed, but it is as well to note that if no known diseases are due to constipation (although constipation may be a symptom of another disease), the regular use of purgatives *can* cause disease.

Constipation should be treated first by diet containing plenty of roughage—bran and oatmeal are excellent—plenty of stewed and fresh fruits, and at least 1½ litres of fluid should be taken daily. Failing that, one of the best things to take is a proprietary product prepared from senna pods. Never to be taken regularly are liquid paraffin, castor oil, preparations of aloes, Epsom salts, and all the other dreadful stuff that people swill down.

Oesophagus.

The oesophagus, or gullet, is more than a simple tube for taking the food from the mouth to the stomach. It is normally closed except when swallowing, and the act of swallowing is very complicated. When the material to be swallowed arrives in the back of the throat there is an auto-matic mechanism which opens the top end of the oesophagus to receive it, and from then onwards everything happens automatically. The next portion of the tube opens and the top closes strongly, so that the food (or drink) is propelled forcibly down the next segment. Then the part below this relaxes and the material is squeezed further downwards and so on until it arrives in the stomach. This squeezing (or milking) action is akin to the action known as peristalsis which propels contents in other parts of the gut. Thus when you see someone swallowing a glass of beer very quickly in warm weather, it is not going "down the hatch" under the influence of gravity, however much it may look like it. It is perfectly possible to swallow the same, or any other liquid, standing on your head. Getting into that position is the only difficult part. Sometimes this compli-cated swallowing mechanism gets out of order, leading to difficulties of swallowing, or *dysphagia*. Another disorder known as *hiatus hernia* occurs at the lower end of the oesophagus as it meets the stomach. At this point the oesophagus has to pass through the diaphragm, the sheet of muscle which separates the chest from the abdomen. The muscular fibres of the diaphragm are normally arranged in a ring around the oesophagus. These help to keep the lower end shut, so that the acid contents of the stomach do not regurgitate up-wards, causing inflammation (*oesophagitis*) or heartburn. A hiatus hernia is when muscle fibres get slack, and the upper end of the stomach can even slide upwards into the chest. People with hiatus hernia get heartburn after meals, and particularly when they bend down or lie down. Except for very severe forms, which need surgical repair, the treatment is to eat less at a time, reduce the acidity with a suitable antacid and reduce weight so that the weight of the abdomen does not press upwards so much. The other disease of the oesophagus, quite unrelated to the above, is *cancer of the oesophagus*, the cause of which is still un-known in most cases. When cancer occurs in the wall of any tube, it will often encircle the tube and gradually narrow the way through. This is what happens in the oesophagus, leading to difficulty in swallowing, particularly solids. It is a condition usually, of rather elderly men, although it is some-times associated with a special form of severe anaemia in women. Treatment is in some way to keep the passage open, either by transplanting a new tube, or more usually, by removing the con-stricted piece and joining up the remainder.

The Stomach and Duodenum.

By far the commonest diseases of the stomach and duodenum are *gastric ulcer* and *duodenal ulcer.* They are actually the same condition in two different sites and are often classed together as *peptic ulcer* or *acid-peptic disease.* The ulcers, which are rather like sores on the lining of the stomach or duodenum, may be "acute" or "chronic." Acute ulcers tend to be small and there are often several of them. Chronic ulcers are usually single. They may be small, or they may be several centimetres across. Chronic ulcers smoulder for months and even years, like a sore which will not heal, and a great deal of scar tissue forms in their depths. Thus they may in time erode their way right through the wall of the stomach, destroying all its layers, and begin to eat into surrounding structures like the pancreas or liver. The fact that they do not perforate more frequently is due to all the fibrous scar tissue which is formed during the slow eroding process. Healing of such a destructive ulcer is nevertheless common, and the great problem is how to help the natural healing process to win against the ulcer's tendency to erode. Ulcers are very commonly associated with the bacterium Helicobacter pylori, which may be the cause of ulcers. Appropriate treatment to eradicate this organism is an important part of ulcer therapy. This extremely common affliction is confined to the human species and has been known since the earliest times. It does not vary very much with diet or with social class. Although occurring at all ages, it usually begins between the ages of twenty and forty, and is most commonly found in men between forty-five and fifty-five. Gastric ulcer is four times, and duodenal ulcer ten times more common in men than in women. It is always due to an inability of the lining to stand up to the normal digestive activity of the stomach contents. These are normally acid and contain a powerful enzyme for digesting proteins. Again it is perhaps more surprising that we all do not digest our own stomachs, rather than that some unfortunate people do digest small areas slowly. In certain abnormal conditions when the stomach stops making acid, ulcers always heal. However, some ulcers occur without excessive secretion of acid and many heal without the acid being neutralised with antacids. All this points to the main trouble being in the response of the lining to acid rather than to the acid itself. Nevertheless, the most effective treatment at present known involves regulating gastric secretion, and particularly its acidity. It is also known that peptic ulcers are more common in people whose occupations involve administrative and professional responsibility, competitive effort and nervous tension, long periods of anxiety or frustration. Presumably the higher nervous system influences these events by the same nerves, which normally help to control secretion.

The main symptom of peptic ulcer is pain, and this usually responds well to proper doses of antacids. Many different varieties are available and a lot of money is made from selling them. When indigestion persists for longer than a few days it is always better to see your doctor so that a proper diagnosis can be made and the best remedies begun. Many other causes exist for similar pains, and you should not try to make the diagnosis yourself. It may be necessary to analyse your gastric secretions in the hospital laboratory. Almost certainly you will have a special X-ray examination, and since the stomach cannot easily be seen on a normal X-ray, they will have to show it up by making you drink a white material containing barium. This will be seen as a silhouette of the stomach and duodenal contents. Searching for an ulcer this way is a highly skilled matter and is performed by doctors specially trained in radiology.

Until recently, no drugs capable of influencing the course of peptic ulcer in any significant manner were available and the physician had to rely on general measures, such as rest, diet and the administration of antacids to relieve pain and discomfort: episodes of acute haemorrhage were not uncommon and required surgical intervention if life were threatened.

However, recent advances in our knowledge of gastric and duodenal pathology have led to the development of at least two therapeutic agents of which the newest, *cimetidine*, is highly effective. Developments in fibre-optic technology have contributed greatly to progress in peptic ulcer treatment. The gastro-enterologist can now pass a *flexible* instrument, the *gastroduodenal endoscope* (the gastroscope is a *rigid* tube), under mild sedation through the patient's gullet and into the stomach and duodenum and view the lesions directly. Once an ulcer is diagnosed, the time has come to stop treating yourself with antacids from the chemist's counter, and to take the ones your doctor decides are best. Smoking should be stopped by ulcer patients (as, indeed, by everyone else, but that is another matter) because it inhibits healing. Alcohol tends to increase acid secretion and should be avoided. It is also *extremely important* to avoid taking any form of aspirin, even in quite small amounts, since this can lead to very serious bleeding from the ulcer. The ulcer patient should be warned that hundreds of proprietary preparations contain aspirin and all of them are dangerous for him. Search for the formula in small print on the label before taking any remedy, looking particularly for acetylsalicylic acid—the systematic name for aspirin. Even some widely sold "hang-over" remedies which are sold for "upset stomach" contain large quantities of aspirin. Some of the patients with "upset stomach" are, of course, ulcer patients, and some even die of haemorrhage following the ingestion of aspirin.

The main complications of peptic ulcer are bleeding, perforation, and a narrowing of the pylorus, or lower part, known as *pyloric stenosis*. Bleeding is caused by the eroding ulcer eating away at one of the many blood vessels in the stomach or duodenal wall. It leads to the passing of "altered" blood in the stool (*melaena*), or to the vomiting of blood (*haematemesis*). When the initial bleeding occurs, the patient may feel suddenly faint, and a little later will notice the black, tarry colour of his stool. This is sometimes confused with a similiar colour when the patient is taking iron. Peptic ulcer is not the only cause of this very serious haemorrhage, which constitutes a hospital emergency whatever its cause. The treatment, like that of every large haemorrhage, is blood transfusion which must be continued until the bleeding stops, or until the patient is sufficiently fit for surgery, should that be deemed necessary. Perforation is perhaps the most serious complication of peptic ulcer, leading to the spilling of stomach contents within the abdominal cavity. Treatment is invariably surgical, either the closure of the perforation or the partial removal of the stomach.

Surgical removal of part of the stomach is often the only way to treat a peptic ulcer which has had its chance to heal in other ways. It is tempting for the patient to "have it out and done with," but the time for surgery is a matter of fine judgment. So many ulcers heal by medical means if you give them a chance, and operations are for those which persistently refuse, or which become complicated.

Stomach Cancer. The stomach is a fairly common site for primary cancer. There is no known reason for this, and it is particularly important to stress that we know of no connection whatever between the peptic ulcers which have just been discussed and cancer. Stomach cancer used to be the commonest cancer of men, but the current rise of lung cancer has pushed it into second place. There are some strange geographical differences in its distribution. For example, it is much commoner in Japan and Scandinavia than in England or the U.S.A. It is difficult to see any reason for this in dietary habits. In Wales it causes three times as many deaths as in South-East England. All this is very puzzling, as is so much of our information about cancer generally. One of the main problems with stomach cancer is that it often causes the patient no inconvenience and thus produces no symptoms of note until the disease is far advanced and it is difficult to do much. Treatment is by surgical removal of the growth, and even in the most advanced cases a great deal can often be done to make the patient more comfortable.

The Small Intestine.

The small intestine runs from the stomach to the caecum and comprises the duodenum, jejunum, and ileum in that order. On a more cheerful note it may be remarked that it is very rarely the site of cancer. Its main problems arise in connection with defects in absorption mechanisms, with obstructions, and with a strange inflammatory condition known as *regional enteritis*. Most obstructions are due not to blockages of the tube, but to failures of peristaltic propulsion, the process which is briefly described above under "oesophagus." Such a failure is called *ileus*. When peristalsis stops for any reason, the result is severe dehydration and loss of important chemicals like sodium and chloride from the body. This is because about 9 litres of fluid enter the small intestine each day in the form of digestive juices, and all of this has to be pushed onwards to be reabsorbed into the system at lower levels. If peristalsis fails, this bulk of fluid remains in the small intestine, or is vomited. In both cases it is lost to the body itself, leading to serious dehydration and illness. Treatment is by very careful replacement by transfusion of the fluid and the chemicals lost, and by removal of the trapped fluid within the intestine through a tube threaded down through the mouth.

Regional enteritis or *ileitis* is sometimes known as *Crohn's disease*. It is a very mysterious condition in which the normally supple wall of the small intestine becomes inflamed and gradually replaced by thick fibrous scar tissue, so that it looks and feels like a thick garden hose. Loops of inflamed gut stick together, and channels open between them, and if the disease progresses a mass of adherent, thickened intestine results to which everything in the neighbourhood also adheres. However, for some unknown reason some cases do not progress downhill in this way and get better spontaneously. Surgical treatment is necessary for the majority, however, particularly those with advanced disease leading to complications such as obstruction or perforation. Sometimes an early case can be resolved by cutting out the length of affected gut, although recurrences are unfortunately common.

Appendicitis. This must be one of the best-known surgical diseases of the intestinal tract.

The appendix is a narrow, blind-ended side tube attached to the caecum near the end of the small intestine, Appendicitis is when it becomes obstructed, or infected, or both. From its position it is almost predictable that it will get obstructed sooner or later by pieces of faecal matter which pass its entrance and which are normally infected. The surprising thing is that it does not happen more often. Once this has occurred, however, a closed abscess forms, and as the abscess distends the appendix, first weakens its wall, making it gangrenous, and then bursts into the abdominal cavity causing *peritonitis* (see later). It would be useless and misleading to describe the symptoms of acute appendicitis in detail, since it is difficult even for experienced doctors to distinguish them from those of several other conditions. Suffice it to say that any severe, persisting pain in the abdomen, whether continuous or intermittent, whether associated with diarrhoea or not, should lead the sufferer to a doctor for a quick diagnosis. Germ-killing antibiotics are useless against appendicitis, and any laxative is extremely dangerous as it may cause an acutely inflamed appendix to perforate.

The Large Intestine or Colon.

The two main serious diseases of the colon are ulcerative colitis and cancer in its various forms. *Ulcerative colitis* is yet another mysterious disease in which severe ulceration of the lining of the colon gives rise most frequently to diarrhoea with the passage of blood and mucus. In fact it can be like dysentery, and it has often been considered to be due to some form of infection. Unfortunately no particular germ can routinely be found in these cases, and the situation is endlessly confused by the presence in the normal bowel of lots of different germs anyway. Nevertheless the ulcerated lining of the bowel certainly does get infected by the germs normally present, and this makes the disease worse. Therefore germ-killing antibiotics are often helpful in alleviating symptoms and can lead to an earlier settling down of the condition, although not to a cure. It has long been known that certain kinds of psychological upset are often associated, but here again the disease is so unpleasant for the sufferer that he is to be forgiven some despondency as a result of, rather than as a cause of, his troubles. It is also suspected that ulcerative colitis may be an auto-immune disease; that is it may represent rejection by the patient of his own colonic lining in a manner somewhat comparable to the tissue rejection which often follows organ transplantation. Some of the more alarming complications are perforation through the wall of the ulcerated bowel, and sometimes massive haemorrhage occurs. The mainstay of medical treatment is the drug *sulphasalazine* together with dietary measures and the occasional use of other drugs to minimise symptoms. Surgery may be required to relieve obstruction, deal with perforation, remove chronically affected parts of the bowel, etc.

Cancer of the Colon and Rectum. This is another very common form of cancer, which can often be completely cured by surgical removal of the growth provided it is caught in the early stages before it has spread. The commonest symptom is a change in bowel habit, either towards constipation or, more often, towards diarrhoea, in the second half of life. There may be rectal bleeding, or the passage of mucus, and there may be abdominal pain. We cannot too often repeat that any such change of bowel habit, or any unexplained bleeding from any site should lead the patient promptly to his doctor.

Diverticulitis. Some people have small pockets or sacs in the wall of the colon known as diverticula. A minority of these sometimes get inflamed, and this is *diverticulitis*. Occasionally perforation occurs.

Hernia or Rupture. This is a condition in which abdominal contents, usually a loop of intestine, protrude forwards through the muscular wall of the abdomen. The wall consists of a sheet of muscle fibres running in several directions. They normally become tense when we cough, or strain, or in getting up from a recumbent position. There are places in the groin on each side where there is a way through the muscle for the spermatic cord in the male. In many men a weakness can arise at this point, and if it persists, the way through may enlarge and allow loops of bowel to emerge from behind the muscle sheet to appear as a lump under the skin of the groin. On relaxation the lump can be made to disappear by pushing the contents back the way they came; and they will re-emerge when the patient strains. This is an extremely common complaint in men, and it should be treated by an operation in which the muscle wall is repaired. Some men, however, neglect to have their rupture treated until one day it proceeds to "strangulate." This is the term used when the muscle tightens around the neck of the protruding loop of bowel, cutting off its blood supply. From then onwards the loop becomes gangrenous and the intestine is obstructed by having a part of itself nipped outside the abdominal wall. The patient is in severe pain, vomits continuously, and quickly is liable to get into such a poor condition that surgical relief is difficult. It is therefore a surgical emergency, and it would have been better to have had the relatively simple repair operation earlier and at leisure. Hernia in the region of the groin is of two types: *inguinal hernia* and *femoral hernia*, the difference between them being technical and of no consequence to the patient. They nearly always occur in men. Other types of hernia less frequently occur in both sexes. *Incisional hernia* is when the muscle wall has been weakened at the site of an old abdominal operation and has failed to heal properly. *Umbilical hernia* occurs owing to the natural weakness of the abdominal wall at the navel, and is so common in babies as to be almost normal. When a baby cries and thereby puts a strain on his abdominal wall, a lump often appears in the region of the navel, and this can be very alarming for the parents. They should of course show it to their doctor who will nearly always be able to reassure them. It is self-healing without operation in the majority of cases.

Peritonitis. The cavity of the abdomen in which the intestines and other organs lie is called the peritoneal cavity, and it is lined by a thin membrane called the peritoneum. When this becomes inflamed the condition is a serious one and is called *peritonitis*. Inflammation may be bacterial, as occurs following a burst appendix and the spillage of bacteria and pus in the cavity. It may be a sterile peritonitis as often follows perforation of a peptic ulcer, when the inflammation is caused by the acid contents of the stomach. It is always very dangerous, probably because of the large surface area afforded by the peritoneum for the absorption of inflammatory toxins.

Haemorrhoids are simply varicose veins in the rectal and anal regions. They are very common, and are caused probably in about equal degrees by inherited weakness of the veins, strain such as heavy lifting, and constipation (this is one of the very few conditions in which constipation may do some damage, due to the mechanical pressure of hardened faeces in the rectum on the veins). Pregnant women are liable to develop haemorrhoids or "*piles*," as they are commonly called, owing to the pressure of the baby's head in the pelvis. Haemorrhoids may be external or internal, the former being in the anal region below the sphincter, the latter in the rectum; the two usually go together. There may be no symptoms, but the veins are liable to bleed, to get thrombosed (*i.e.*, a clot forms within) or to become infected. When clotting or infection occurs the piles enlarge and tend to be pushed out through the anus during defaecation, when they form extremely painful external swellings. Treatment in simple cases may be by the use of suppositories—cones which are inserted in the rectum—in other cases the veins may be injected, as with varicose veins of the leg, in order to close them, but when there is much bleeding, thrombosis, infection, or interference with bowel movements they should be removed surgically.

THE LIVER.

The liver is the largest organ and has such a wide variety of known functions (to say nothing of the unknown) that it is also one of the most complicated. Nearly all of its functions are biochemical, and it is often called the laboratory of the body. Medical students, when asked to enumerate the functions of the liver, usually stick at about twenty-five, nearly all of them to do with general metabolism: that is the biochemical processing of substances taking part in structure or as body fuel. For example, the liver makes proteins from the amino acids absorbed from the gut, and breaks down amino-acids and manufactures a waste product (urea) from them. It stores carbohydrates as glycogen, and conducts many of the processes necessary to turn carbohydrates into energy. It manufactures prothrombin with the help of vitamin K, and this is essential for blood clotting. It makes bile and secretes it into the gall bladder and bile ducts (see later). The three main constituents of bile (cholesterol, bile pigment or bilirubin, and bile acids) all have to be processed, or metabolised, in the liver during the production of bile. Vitamin B_{12} and iron are also stored and dealt with there, and these are involved in preventing various forms of anaemia (q.v.); and in addition to all these things the liver is the place where harmful substances, both from within the body and from outside it, are dealt with and rendered harmless. This last function of "detoxication" is often accomplished by making the offending molecules suitable for rapid excretion by the kidneys, or by altering their chemical shape to make them harmless.

Nearly all of these very different things are done by one single type of cell: the liver cell, and it is one of the remarkable features of the design that this cell can be so versatile. There also have to be some very efficient transport systems in the liver, in addition to the usual blood supply and venous drainage possessed by all other tissues.

One of these is the "portal venous system." Whenever a substance is absorbed across the gut wall from any part of the intestine into the interior of the body it enters the special draining blood vessels of the portal system, which are arranged throughout the length of the digestive tract. All these veins eventually unite in the main portal vein which enters the liver. Everything absorbed from the gut is therefore taken first to the liver to be processed. After this the products are carried away from the liver in the ordinary veins to the heart, and are distributed to the rest of the body by the arterial system. The liver has arteries of its own by which it receives oxygen and nutriment like any other tissue. The fourth transport system collects the bile as it is formed within the liver and delivers it to the gall bladder and bile ducts, which eventually drain it into the duodenum.

Portal Hypertension means high blood pressure in the portal venous system, and is the usual accompaniment to *cirrhosis* (see later). When the terminations of the portal veins in the liver are strangled and obstructed by cirrhotic disease, this tends to blow them up, or dilate them with blood. There is a natural escape route for the portal blood where the lower end of the oesophagus or gullet joins the upper end of the stomach. At this place some of the portal veins draining the stomach are connected with the ordinary veins draining the oesophagus so that when pressure rises in the portal system, blood tends to be diverted into these connecting veins, and they in turn become dilated, or varicose. Trouble begins when these dilated connecting veins, which bulge inwards into the oesophagus, are damaged by food particles passing across them and bleed severely into the stomach. The patient vomits large quantities of blood (*haematemesis*) or passes tarry altered blood in the stool

(*melaena*). The other main cause of these is the bleeding which occasionally accompanies peptic ulcer (q.v.).

A second complication of portal hypertension (and hence of cirrhosis) is *ascites*, in which large amounts of a lymph-like fluid accumulate in the abdominal cavity. The fluid contains a great deal of precious protein and salt which is lost to the body economy. Ascites also sometimes accompanies cancerous deposits in the abdomen.

Jaundice means being yellow because there is too much yellow bile pigment circulating in the blood, and there are three main possible causes for this. The term "yellow jaundice," like "gastric stomach" is therefore unnecessarily redundant: there is no other kind.

Bile pigment comes from broken-down red blood cells, which normally come to the end of their time after existing for about 120 days. The breakdown products of red cells can always be found in the blood of normal people, but there is normally insufficient colour to show. Abnormal amounts of colour build up quite logically in any of the following three circumstances:

(1) If too many red cells are being destroyed and even the normal liver cannot deal with the amount of bile pigment produced, it piles up in the blood, and *haemolytic jaundice* is the result. The expression simply means jaundice due to (abnormally large) red-cell destruction.

(2) If the liver cells are themselves sick and unable to cope even with the normal amounts of pigment from normal red-cell destruction. Here too the pigment will pile up and cause *hepatocellular jaundice*, or liver-cell jaundice.

(3) If the bile ducts carrying bile away from the liver are blocked, then bile will pile up behind the blockage and re-enter the blood stream, causing *obstructive jaundice*. In this case the rate of red-cell breakdown is normal, and the liver cells are normal: at least for a time.

It is enormously important for the treatment of jaundice for the doctor to diagnose its type correctly, since the treatment varies from surgical relief of obstruction to the medical treatment of viral infection or of excess red-cell destruction. The so-called differential diagnosis of jaundice is often exceptionally difficult, and sometimes requires some very sophisticated laboratory tests and X-rays. At other times it is extremely easy and is obvious from a cursory glance at the urine and the stool. In any case all jaundice is a highly technical matter for the doctor who must be consulted early.

There is a special jaundice of newborn babies which resembles haemolytic jaundice and can occasionally have serious consequences for the developing brain (*kernicterus*) if it is allowed to become too severe. When this is threatened, steps are taken to reduce the level of circulating bile pigment by replacement of the baby's blood or by other means.

The commonest cause of hepatocellular jaundice is infective or viral hepatitis. Obstructive jaundice is usually due either to blockage by gallstones (q.v.) or by a lump pressing on the bile ducts from an adjacent cancer. This can often be quite satisfactorily relieved by surgery.

Infective Hepatitis. There is a group of disorders affecting the liver which are caused by viruses. The incubation period is often very long, and the sickness and other debility caused is often quite severe and prolonged. One variety, known as serum sickness, is now much less common than a few years ago. It used to be transmitted by using the same needle for injections into several different people, or from transfusing contaminated blood. A greater awareness of the problem, and the use of disposable needles and syringes has cut down the incidence.

Cirrhosis. There are many different kinds of cirrhosis, the commonest of which has already

P39

been mentioned under *portal hypertension* above. In all cases, liver cells are slowly poisoned and are killed off over a long period of time. In response to this, the surviving liver cells undergo cell division, trying to make good the numbers lost, and at the same time fibrous scar tissue replaces the damaged tissue throughout the organ. The result is a hard, knobbly liver. The many "knobs" are spherical areas of regenerated new cells, and they are separated by thickened bands of scar tissue. All of this destroys the normal architecture and leads to the portal hypertension and ascites mentioned above. In some countries (*e.g.*, France and the United States) excessive alcohol is the main cause of the original liver damage which starts it all off. In others (*e.g.*, Bantu South Africa) it seems to be nutritional starvation of the liver. In England much less than half the cases are due to alcohol, and many are thought to be due to a previous episode of infective hepatitis (*q.v.*), but this is not certain. Infective hepatitis is quite common but cirrhosis is comparatively rare. So that the great majority of people do not progress from one to the other. One treatment for advanced cirrhosis is to replace the liver by transplantation, but there are still problems to overcome before this can become routine.

Cancer of the Liver. Cancer of the liver is quite common, but it is nearly always cancer which has spread in the blood stream from other parts of the body. The liver is a favourite site for such secondary deposits, since it has a large blood supply and will receive a generous helping of anything being carried. It is also a very "fertile soil" for the cancer seedlings to grow in. Primary cancer of the liver is uncommon, and only occurs in a few cases of pre-existing cirrhosis.

Gallstones. These are "stones" formed by some of the major constituents of bile coming out of solution and forming solid bodies. They are very common, and often cause no trouble at all. When they do, it is usually a colicky intermittent severe pain. This is due to the muscular walls of the bile passages contracting in an effort to expel an obstructing stone into the duodenum. The second common trouble arising from gallstones is obstructive jaundice, described above. It is small consolation to gallstone sufferers that the stones are often very pretty, often being composed of beautiful cholesterol crystals coloured by varying shades of bile. If they contain calcium they will be visible on an X-ray. Otherwise they are not seen. Stones often occur in conjunction with inflammation of the gall bladder, known as *cholecystitis.* The treatment for gallstones is to remove them surgically together with the gall bladder if they are causing persistent symptoms. Ways of avoiding surgery by dissolving them in substances taken by mouth are under investigation.

The Pancreas.

This is a soft, elongated gland lying behind the stomach; it is about 12·5 cm long and 5 cm wide. Within its tissues lies the duct, which, when it leaves the pancreas, passes into the duodenum near the point of entry of the bile-duct. This duct transmits the juices containing enzymes which aid in the digestion in the small intestine. The pancreas, however, has two main functions: not only does it manufacture these important digestive juices, but in certain specialised areas, known as the islets of Langerhans, it manufactures insulin, the hormone which makes it possible for the body to utilise sugar. *Diabetes mellitus* or ordinary diabetes is a chronic disorder usually caused by a deficient secretion of insulin. The unused sugar accumulates in the blood and acts as a poison, which, in extreme cases, sends the patient into coma and may—indeed, in former times, usually did—result in death. The treatment of diabetes was revolutionised by the discovery of the hormone insulin by Banting and Best in 1921. On the whole, diabetes is more severe in young people than in the elderly, but with correct treatment it is possible for all cases to lead a perfectly normal life except for dietary restrictions and insulin injections. Not to be confused with *Diabetes insipidus* (**P43**(1)). The main problem with diabetes mellitus now is that the wrong (albeit slightly) blood sugar levels that are found even with good therapy eventually damage small blood vessels, leading to problems with the eyes, peripheral nerves and kidneys.

DIET.

When considering diet, and the effect it has on our health and well-being, there is more to it than just the things we eat. We must also know about what our body does with the food, and it would be unscientific not to acknowledge the effects of our psychological make-up and our nutritional beliefs on what we eat, what we do with it, and how well (or ill) we feel as a result.

For example, a deep-rooted conviction that brown eggs or free-range poultry are better for us than white eggs or intensively reared birds is entirely unsupported by any evidence. However, if we believe such a thing sufficiently, we will not only eat the "better" ones, but we will feel happier and more secure afterwards, and this is likely to make us healthier. Food fads can occasionally be dangerous, as when extreme vegetarians become ill through lack of certain vitamins (*e.g.* B_{12}) which are present only in the foods they exclude. But this is so rare, even among strict vegetarians, that such danger can virtually be ignored. On the whole (and vegetarianism is probably a good example of this) food faddism often leads to a sense of health and well-being in the believer, and should not be attacked by the rest of us for that. It is an accepted fact that personal misfortune, even when it is severe, is more easily withstood by those with strong religious conviction than by others. In the same way, a firm attachment to a theory of what is good for you can produce a feeling of well-being and genuine good health, when another person on exactly the same food intake will not feel so fit. These factors—religious belief, food faddism, or the bedside manner of a kind or persuasive doctor—are commonly dismissed by free-thinking people because they are not "true" or "real." All three, however, can materially affect our health just as can a shock, a personal tragedy or being in love.

The basic constituents of any diet are protein, fats, carbohydrates, water, vitamins, minerals, salts, and indigestible roughage. All are chemicals whose structure and function are reasonably well understood. Even the mystical differences between fine table wines, so beloved of the connoisseur and gourmet, are reasonably well understood in chemical terms. Perhaps that is a pity.

Much nonsense is talked, especially by nutritionists, about minimal daily requirements. In general terms, however, requirements can be described in terms of how many calories there are in the total intake of proteins, fats, and carbohydrates per day, and how these are distributed between the three classes of food. The other substances mentioned above are only required in trace or small amounts except for water; and roughage is only required as a mechanical stimulus to bowel movement.

During the process of digestion (described on **P34-5**) all proteins are split into their constituent amino acids; all carbohydrates are split into their constituent simple sugars and most fats are converted into fatty acids and glycerol. At this stage, and not until this stage, all these simpler building bricks derived from the three classes of food are absorbed into the body proper, and taken to the liver and other tissues. Here they are "metabolised." That is to say they are either burned as fuel for the various processes of the body; or they are built up again into proteins, fats, and carbohydrates of the special kinds the body needs. They will either be used to rebuild structures suffering ordinary wear and tear or they will be stored. Many of them will be converted into a different class from the one they came from when they entered the body. For example, excess carbohydrate is converted into fat; or if there is a shortage of carbohydrate, some will be made out of the protein amino-acids which would normally have been used for tissue growth and repair. Thus it is only a generalisation to say that dietary carbohydrates are fuel and proteins are for building bodily structure. The body can convert one into the other, and spoil the calculation.

There is a great deal of confusion in people's minds about *energy*, and that is why the word *fuel* has been used above in connection with carbohydrates. The lay person uses energy as a term meaning something which allows us to leap about, running and jumping and skipping and dancing, and which keeps us from getting tired and run down. Thus, the food industry tells us, we need potatoes or breakfast cereals for these activities or for a hard day's work. This is a deliberate commercial confidence trick, and the scientist is largely to blame. He originally handed out the word energy to an eager food industry and an unsuspecting public, forgetting to explain that he meant it in the strictly scientific sense of fuel for bodily processes. It simply is not true that more potatoes, or more cornflakes will make you more active. Indeed the reverse is the case, and after a certain point they will only be converted into fat and reduce your activity. The nutritionist measures energy as calories, which are units of heat, and it is certainly true that you must eat enough of these each day if you wish to remain alive, let alone active.

All the three main classes of food provide calories, and in an ordinary well-balanced diet about 15% are provided by protein. Carbohydrates produce most of the remainder. Each gram of fat contains about twice the calories of a similar quantity of carbohydrate. We simply eat less fat than carbohydrate, because fat has a "high satiety value." It takes away the appetite for more. Proteins are mostly found in meat, fish, eggs, cheese, and milk. However, there is quite a lot of protein in many predominantly starchy foods like bread, and such grains as wheat, rice, and corn. Carbohydrates are mainly found in bread, potatoes, sugar, pastry, sweets, and so forth. That is one of the words which fortunately seems to be used by both scientists and laymen in much the same sense.

Some substances are absolutely essential to the body if life is to continue, even if they are only needed in trace amounts. These are substances which the body's own factories (like the liver) cannot make for themselves, even if they are provided with the correct ingredients.

One group of such substances are the *vitamins*. Some of these are found in predominantly fatty foods (milk, butter, cheese and so on) and are known as the fat-soluble vitamins—Vitamins A, D, E and K; the others are water-soluble—the Vitamin B group and Vitamin C. All have now been chemically identified, are manufactured and can be bought over a pharmacist's counter. The myth has grown up that if a little is good for one then a lot more will be better and there are a great many vitamin enthusiasts who consume vast quantities of such manufactured products in the belief that by doing so they will induce extra vitality and energy. Unless your diet is unbalanced in some way (a vegetarian diet may be grossly deficient in Vitamin B_{12}) you will not need extra vitamins.

Fortunately, most people buy food because they like it, not because it does them good; and provided they have normal dietary tastes they will usually get a perfectly adequate selection of the things we have spoken of as necessary for good health. The main danger in England is to have a surfeit and become overweight. In addition there are certain times of life when conscious attention should be paid to what is necessary. For example babies and nursing mothers have special dietary needs and will hear about them from their Health Visitor or from their Welfare Clinic or Doctor. Elderly people living alone are also prone to dietary deficiencies for reasons ranging from poverty to loss of appetite or inability to look after themselves properly.

Recent surveys have revealed some interesting facts about people's attitude to food and their knowledge of it. For example, half the people asked knew that meat was a source of protein, a third mentioned eggs and a fifth cheese, fish, and milk. But practically no one knew there was protein in bread. Yet in England about a fifth of our daily protein intake comes from bread, and nearly a third from cereals as a whole. Fish is well known as a source of protein, but did you know that on average we only obtain 4% of our daily protein from fish—less than we get from

potatoes (5%)? No one seems to know that potatoes are an important source of vitamin C, although fruit and vegetables are well-known sources. Calcium is recognised in milk, but most people forget its presence in cheese. Most people are very confused about iron. Why does everyone think it is mainly in green vegetables, when these are really such a poor source? For our daily requirement of iron we would each have to eat 1 kg. spring greens or peas; or 2 kg. of sprouts! In fact meat provides one of our best sources, and one-fifth of our daily needs is contained in bread.

Since most of the people who read *Pears* live in Britain let us return finally to our commonest nutritional disease, or our commonest form of malnutrition in these islands: obesity. Call it "being overweight" if you like, but acknowledge that it means being fat. Being fat is not only unattractive and unsightly but it is dangerous to health and carries a high mortality. Ask any life insurance company how they view your chances if you are overweight and you will find they are as worried about it as if you had high blood pressure, or smoke heavily. It is a particularly important cause of heart disease. However, it is very important to know exactly what we mean by fatness. Many girls who are not at all fat think they are, and this leads them to diet unnecessarily. On the other hand there are people who do not appreciate they are overweight. Here is a table which shows what your weight should be according to your height.

DESIRABLE WEIGHTS FOR MEN AND WOMEN ACCORDING TO HEIGHT AND FRAME, AGES 25 AND OVER

Men Height (in shoes 2·5 cm heels)	Weight in kilograms (in indoor clothing)		
	Small frame	Medium frame	Large frame
157	51–54·5	53·5–59	57–64
160	52–56	55–60·5	59–65·5
162	53·5–57	56–62	60–67
165	55–59	58–63	61–69
167	56–60·5	59–65	63–71
170	58–62	61–67	64·5–73
172	60–64	63–69	67–75·5
175	62–66	64·5–71	68·5–77
177	63·5–68	66–72·5	70·5–79
180	65·5–70	68–75	72–81
183	67–72	70–77	74–83·5
185	69–73·5	72–79·5	76–86
188	71–76	73·5–82	78·5–88
190	72·5–77·5	76–84	81–90·5
193	74·5–79·5	78–86	82·5–93

Women Height (in shoes 5 cm heels)	Weight in kilograms (in indoor clothing)		
	Small frame	Medium frame	Large frame
147	42–44·5	43·5–48·5	47–54
150	43–46	44·5–50	48–55·5
152	43·5–47	46–51	49·5–57
155	45–48·5	47–53	51–58
157	46–50	48·5–54	52–59·5
160	48–51	50–55·5	53·5–61
162	49–53	51–57	55–63
165	50·5–54	53–59	57–64·5
167	52–56	54·5–61	59–66
170	53·5–58	56–63	60·5–68
172	55·5–59·5	58–65	62–70
175	57–61	60–67	64–72
177	59–63·5	62–68·5	66–74
180	61–65·5	63·5–70·5	68–76
183	63–67	65·5–72	69·5–78·5

If you are overweight according to these tables you need to slim, and the question is how? Answer: by will-power. There is no other satisfactory method than to decide to eat less. For the time being eat as much fruit, and green vegetables, as you like, but no sugar, starch, sweets, cakes, pastry, or biscuits, and no eating between meals. And cut down on beer and other alcoholic drinks. In case you are tempted to eat "slimming" foods, be aware that there is no such thing. There is nothing you can eat which will cause you to lose weight, in spite of what the advertisement says. In special cases doctors will prescribe tablets to suppress appetite, but they are too dangerous for general use without supervision, and they do not work as well as will-power. At the same time take more exercise. Walk to work. If you make a real and genuine effort for three months without success, you should ask your doctor for advice. Almost certainly you will have to admit you have not really tried. Good luck!

NUTRITIONAL DISORDERS.

Nutritional Deficiency and Malnutrition.—Until quite recently a consideration of malnutrition would have merely led to an account of how too little food, or a deficiency of certain articles in the diet, produced deficiency diseases at the time of the restriction. For example lack of vitamins of various kinds gives rise to such diseases as rickets, scurvy, beri-beri, and pellagra; and an overall shortage of food to general starvation. These may be considered the immediate or concurrent effects of a poor diet. Modern nutritionists, however, are beginning to be concerned with two more kinds of nutritional disorders; and although the study of both kinds is in its infancy, both will be introduced in this account.

The first deals with the effects of comparatively small amounts of harmful constituents in our diet, introduced either voluntarily or involuntarily, and consumed for a long period of time; and the second with the lasting effects on our adult well-being of nutritional deficiencies in early life even though they have long since been corrected.

When viewed in this light, one or other of these three kinds of nutritional disorder may at this moment be affecting almost every individual in every part of the world, "privileged" or "under-privileged." Let us first define some terms.

Undernutrition, strictly speaking, means a state of affairs in which the quality of the diet is perfectly good. There is the correct balance of the various dietary constituents and all the necessary components are present: but there is simply too little of it. Many hundreds of millions of people throughout the underprivileged world are suffering and dying from this kind of under-nutrition, and the simplicity of the problem must be appreciated: they simply need more food of the kind they are at present getting, and which can often be produced locally.

Malnutrition means an imbalance of the various constituents: a relative lack or excess of one or more of them. It usually leads to conditions which are, from the point of view of medical treatment, much more difficult to deal with. And therefore doctors often class them as "more serious."

The diseases of malnutrition range from the widespread protein deficiencies in other parts of the underprivileged world to *obesity* in our own better-off industrial countries, which is usually due to excess carbohydrate. Make no mistake about it: obesity (or being overweight) is a wide-spread disease of nutritional imbalance, and it kills. It is the commonest form of malnutrition in (for example) England and America today, and is a consequence of the sophistication of our diet in modern times. Between one-fifth and one-tenth of the population of the United States is more than 20% overweight, and to be 10% or 15% overweight is almost the rule nowadays in people over thirty. There are high authorities in the world of nutritional science who attribute all this overfed malnutrition to the consumption of refined sugar, or sucrose. They say it is not only the amount of refined sugar we put in our tea or on our breakfast cereals, but also the amount in sweet cakes, biscuits, drinks, chocolates and sweets, and so forth. For some people it adds up to a phenomenal quantity each day. According to this school of thought we are not so

much suffering from a surfeit of carbohydrates or starches, but from this single sugar, sucrose. It is interesting to reflect on the recent banning of the artificial sweetener, cyclamate, by many governments. This substance, having been used extensively throughout the world as an apparently harmless non-fattening substitute for sugar, was suddenly banned in America because in very large doses (equivalent to the amount taken in hundreds of cups of coffee per day for a long time) it was found to produce cancer in rats. It has never been shown to do humans any harm, whereas the effects of sugar in producing an overweight population, thereby indirectly kill tens of thousands of British people each year. This is a fascinating example of the difficulties confronting our legislators in making balanced judgments when deciding to ban a foodstuff, a drug, or an artificial fertiliser.

Much the most widespread form of malnutrition, however, is a variety protein-lack which is part of a collection of nutritional diseases known as *Protein-Calorie Deficiency.* In very large under-privileged areas of the world, the childhood population receives such an inadequate diet that children live continuously on the brink of nutritional disaster. It only requires a small extra restriction or stress to topple them over into one of the clinical conditions to be described. At this stage they cease to be merely hungry. They become nutritionally ill. Sometimes the force which produces the disaster is a community catastrophe like a famine, an earthquake, or a war. Sometimes it is a family catastrophe like the loss of a lactating mother or a parental delinquency. Parents abandon young children as often in Africa as anywhere else. Sometimes the clinical nutritional disease is unmasked by a common childhood illness like measles, or gastro-enteritis which the well-fed child would have overcome. The starved child reveals his malnutrition instead and frequently dies. When the precipitating cause of the "epidemic" of malnutrition is a war or other national calamity, our newspapers and television screens carry distressing pictures of thin skeletal, pot-bellied children, and the conscience of a few is touched. It is insufficiently realised that these scenes can be witnessed anywhere in the continents of Africa and Asia, and in large parts of Central and South America any day of the week in normal times. The war has not been the cause, but is only the precipitating factor which has revealed the chronic malnutrition in more children than would normally exhibit it openly.

Protein-Calorie Deficiency is a collection of different kinds of childhood malnutrition. Some are due predominantly to deficiency of protein and are collectively called kwashiorkor, a West African word meaning "red-haired boy" (see below). Others are mainly due to a severe deficiency of overall foodstuffs and are called *marasmus.* But in any real-life situation the severe *mal*nutrition of kwashiorkor exists side-by-side with all gradations between itself and the severe *under*nutrition of marasmus, so that many intermediate forms of "marasmic kwashiorkor" are described. In kwashiorkor the child is typically listless, apathetic, whining, with a reddish discoloration of the hair, a peeling, scaly skin, and with much extra fluid in his tissues causing oedema. He is so listless as not even to be hungry. In marasmus the child is ravenously hungry. He is extremely thin and "starved" looking and is quite a different picture.

There is good reason to believe that even when protein-calorie deficiency is successfully treated, there will always be some lasting restriction of mental function, particularly if the malnutrition occurred as early as the first year of life. This is especially true in situations of appalling poverty in towns, where thousands of babies are not breast-fed because their mothers are at work. Many of them die. Some of them are no heavier than their birth weight at one year of age. Breast feeding in an underprivileged community is an essential insurance for childhood health and survival.

Two new avenues of nutritional inquiry were mentioned at the beginning of this section. The impact of very long continued intake of refined sugar over many years on our bodily health is an example of one of them. Scientists and others are also becoming alarmed at the effects of modern food additives when taken, even in small amounts, over a long period. These additives include colouring matter, decolorising chemicals, taste "enhancers," and so forth, which are present in everyone's diet in a "civilised community." We are as unable to avoid a constant dosage with them as if they had been added to our water supply. It is, however, difficult to strike a balanced attitude. It is one thing to suspect that these additives are harmful and quite another to prove it. Naturally if any of them are shown to produce harm in animals given reasonable quantities they are invariably withdrawn. But in practice it is extremely difficult for animal experiments to mimic the conditions of human intake, especially as the human life span involves eating the substance concerned in small quantities for several decades. Thus it is easy to postulate the harmful effects of monosodium glutamate (a very common taste enhancer) but practically impossible to prove the question either way. It is not sufficient to condemn "chemicals." All natural foods consist of chemicals, and so do we.

The other new topic in nutrition is more soundly based on animal experiment. It has been repeatedly found that if animals do not grow quickly enough at certain early periods of life, they not only become small, but they remain smaller than they should be even when they are subsequently given as much as they like to eat. This is true of all animals and birds so far studied. For example, if rats are suckled in large families it is found that they are smaller by the time they are weaned (3 weeks of age) than those suckled in small families. The interesting thing is that if they are then given as much as they want to eat for the rest of their lives, the small animals from the larger families never catch up to the others. Whereas if their growth is not restricted until later in their "childhood," full "catch-up" is possible soon after normal diet is resumed. In other words there is a critical time in early life when growth can be permanently affected. At the moment it is difficult to know whether the same is true of humans and, if so, when is our period of vulnerability. There is some suggestion that the corresponding critical period in humans is during the last part of gestation in the uterus, and the first year or so of postnatal life. This new idea may turn out to be very important for world nutrition. Since there will not be enough food for all the children all the time, it may become important to concentrate our aid to underprivileged countries on certain sections of the population only. It may be a good idea to see that pregnant mothers and small babies are specially fed. In this way we may be able to put off the periods of inevitable malnutrition until a time of life when it is recoverable. Such a plan would also go a long way to safeguarding the development of the brain which also occurs mostly at the same early time of life.

We shall now describe some of the better-known nutritional deficiencies, bearing in mind that vitamin deficiencies are virtually unknown in the better-off countries. No one in England need spend money buying vitamins, as has been emphasised in the preceding section. Vitamin deficiency can still occur, however, in elderly people living alone and not having a well-balanced diet. It also occurs for similar reasons in alcoholics, vagrants, etc., and very occasionally in small children.

Beri-beri is a group of diseases usually confined to the Far East where a diet of polished rice results in a poor intake of vitamin B, (thiamine). In one form there is oedema (*q.v.*); in another the peripheral nerves are affected leading to tingling and numbness. A similar condition is occasionally seen in alcoholics and diabetics. Treatment is with thiamine, and with other vitamins too, since most sufferers are going short of more than one.

Pellagra is found among maize-eating populations and is due to a deficiency of several vitamins including niacin, another member of the B group of vitamins. There is dermatitis on exposed skin, and soreness of the mouth and tongue, with gastro enteritis.

Scurvy is due to vitamin C deficiency. In children bone growth is affected. At all ages there is bleeding into the skin (bruising), impaired wound healing, mental depression, and anaemia. Most fresh fruit and vegetables contain vitamin C and a diet containing these prevents the disease.

Vitamin A deficiency is commonly found in children in some underprivileged countries. It causes permanent blindness, with thickening opacity and dryness of the whites of the eyes leading to ulceration of the eye. Beyond a certain stage, therefore, a child's sight cannot be saved. The only real hope is prevention, with an adequate diet.

Rickets, another disease of early childhood, is caused by deficiency of vitamin D. Bones are not properly calcified, and their softness leads to deformities of the legs and many other bones. Vitamin D can either be eaten in the diet or produced under the skin under the influence of sunlight. Therefore rickets commonly occurs when both the diet and the sunlight are inadequate. It was once very common in industrial England, and is still to be seen very occasionally there and in impoverished urban communities in the United States.

THE ENDOCRINE GLANDS.

Glands are structures or organs which manufacture secretions (except for *lymph glands* which are not glands at all and should be called *lymph nodes*). The secretions are of two main kinds. The first are passed down tubes, or ducts, or are secreted directly into the hollow organs, and act locally. Good examples are the salivary glands which make saliva and pass it down ducts into the mouth for digestion of its contents and lubrication. These are *exocrine glands*. The second kind have no ducts, and secrete their product straight into the blood stream. This secretion is called a *hormone* and it is carried to all parts of the body by the blood where it acts at a distance on some remote part. These are the *endocrine glands* or *ductless glands*, and a number of them will be discussed in this section.

The first hormone, or "chemical messenger," was discovered by the British physiologist Starling in 1904, but the effects of removing some of the endocrine glands were known centuries before when removal of the male testes (castration) was practised to procure a form of manpower safe for the harem, to salvage a good male alto voice for the church choir, or to convert a rooster into a more eatable capon.

Anterior Pituitary.—Many of the endocrine glands do not act as separate autonomous organs in spite of their great differences. They are organised into a well-disciplined band by a "master-gland" called the anterior pituitary. Somebody once called it the "conductor of the endocrine orchestra" and the phrase is still repeated *ad nauseam* in students' examination papers. The pituitary, consisting of its two parts, anterior and posterior, is not much bigger than a pea and it sits right in the middle of the skull, centrally beneath the brain and joined to the brain by a short stalk. This astonishing tiny nodule of tissue produces at least eight important hormones.

One of these is *growth hormone*, which is necessary for normal growth, and also has an influence on insulin. An excess causes *gigantism* and *acromegaly*, often coinciding with diabetes, and too little results in a form of dwarfism. Three others, known as *gonadotrophic hormones* regulate the cyclical and other activities of the reproductive organs and lactating breast. Another, *thyrotrophic hormone*, regulates thyroid activity, *Adrenocorticotrophic hormone*, or *ACTH*, as its name implies, looks after the activities of another important endocrine gland, the adrenal cortex. And there are several others.

Hypopituitarism, including *Simmonds' disease* and *Sheehan's disease*, results from destruction of the anterior pituitary. It is extremely rare, and is usually associated with difficult childbirth involving very severe bleeding. There are disturbances of all the functions mentioned above, particularly thyroid and adrenal failure (*q.v.*) with upset sexual function. Treatment is by replacing the lost hormones.

Hyperpituitarism, including *gigantism* and *acromegaly*, results from over-activity of the anterior pituitary, and is usually due to a tumour or overgrowth of the gland. In acromegaly the growth hormone is produced in excess over a long period of time in an adult. This results in overgrowth of all the organs except the brain, and it is characteristic to find enlarged extremities—feet, hands, and jaw. In gigantism the same has occurred during childhood before the bones have stopped growing and the result is a person who may be 2 m tall or more.

Posterior Pituitary. The posterior part of the gland is really a quite separate gland. The main hormone it produces is concerned with the excretion of urine by the kidney (antidiuretic hormone). Deficiency of the hormone results in *diabetes insipidus*, not to be confused with *diabetes mellitus* or "sugar diabetes." In diabetes insipidus, the patient produces enormous quantities of dilute urine. He consequently has a prodigious thirst and consumes astonishing quantities of fluids. Treatment is by replacing the missing hormone.

Thyroid. The thyroid gland in the neck secretes an iodine containing hormone called thyroxine. Excess of it causes *hyperthyroidism*, *thyrotoxicosis*, or *Graves' disease*. Lack of it produces *cretinism* in the growing child or *myxodoema* in the adult. Thyroxine is concerned with the metabolic rate of cells throughout the body, or the rate at which they work, as well as with the proper growth of developing tissues, especially the brain. Too much thyroxine as in thyrotoxicosis leads to over-activity, warm sweatiness in an over-excitable patient whose pulse is rapid and who is eating ravenously to try to replace the wasted energy. In spite of his appetite he is very thin, and he often has bulging eyes for a reason not understood. Treatment is by drugs which neutralise the thyroxine or by cutting out some of the gland. A *cretin* is a child usually born with insufficient thyroid. He is destined to grow poorly, and to mental subnormality of a permanent and distressing kind. If the condition is diagnosed soon after birth treatment with thyroxine can avert most of the trouble. In myxoedema, thyroxine is deficient in an adult. They become slow in all their bodily processes, the hair thins and their flesh is puffy with a dry, wrinkled skin. Treatment is by thyroid replacement. *Goitre* simply means enlargement of the gland. It may be accompanied by overactivity or underactivity, or with little functional change. One variety (Derbyshire neck) occurs in areas short of iodine in the soil and drinking water.

Adrenal Cortex. The adrenal or suprarenal glands sit, as the name implies, one on top of each kidney. There are two distinct parts: the cortex or outside which secretes steroid hormones, and the *adrenal medulla*, or core, which secretes adrenalin. There are many different steroid hormones in the adrenale cortical secretion, which look after such diverse matters as sodium and potassium balance, sexual function, the reaction of the body to stress, and the regulation of sugar levels. *Addison's disease* (not to be confused with Addisonian anaemia) results from adrenal cortical insufficiency, and is often due to destruction of the gland by tuberculosis. There is weariness, malaise, pigmentation of skin creases and mucous membranes. They are short of sodium and have excess potassium. Treatment is with cortisone or synthetic steroids to replace the missing hormone, and by extra salt by mouth for the lack of sodium. *Cushing's* disease is due to excessive adrenal cortical function, and sometimes also occurs in patients treated with steroids for other purposes. They have a striking redistribution of fat in the face, neck, and trunk, with stretch marks similar to those acquired by most women during pregnancy. The facial obesity makes them "moon-faced," and female patients may suffer masculinisation with deepening of the voice and hirsutism.

Testis. The male testes, as well as producing sperm are also endocrine glands producing steroid hormones known as androgens. They are mainly concerned with maintaining secondary sex characteristics. At the time of puberty the controlling secretions from the anterior pituitary begin to appear and androgens are produced. There is a whole range of rare disorders, resulting in everything from precocious puberty to delayed puberty. It should be borne in mind that the normal time of puberty can vary by several years from one boy to another.

Ovary. The human ovary has two functions: to produce ova, or eggs; and to produce two hormones, oestrogen and progesterone. These functions begin at puberty, one of whose features in the female is the onset of menstruation, or menarche. Just as in boys, the timing of normal puberty is very variable, but on the average, girls achieve puberty before boys. As social conditions improve, the age of menarche is getting younger generation by generation. All the secondary sex characteristics are under the control of the ovarian hormones which are released in response to the appropriate anterior pituitary hormones. The changes which occur in the womb and elsewhere in the intervals between menstrual periods and the periods themselves are controlled by a cyclical or rhythmic secretion, first of oestrogen and then of progesterone, by the ovary. This cycle is upset by pregnancy to allow the development of the embryo. It can also be upset by taking certain combinations of the two hormones by mouth. These can prevent the formation of ova, and are a popular form of contraception. In late middle age, the ovaries lose their function, the menstrual cycles cease to occur, and reproductive life is at an end. This is called the *menopause* or "change of life," and is sometimes accompanied for a time by distressing symptoms due to a temporary imbalance between oestrogen and progesterone. Many sexual functions, however, continue well after the menopause into old age, and these can include a continuing libido or sexual desire.

Parathyroid. Four tiny parathyroid glands are buried behind the thyroid gland and are responsible for regulating the body calcium and phosphate. They are therefore particularly important for the building and maintenance of bones and teeth. Since a proper calcium level in the blood is necessary for muscle (including heart muscle) contraction, and for correct functioning of nerves, disorders of the parathyroids can give rise to muscular spasms as well as loss of bone calcium. The latter can result in fragility and fractures. Overactivity of the glands leads to too much calcium and the formation of stones especially in the kidney.

Pineal. We end this section with a mystery gland. Like the pituitary it is small—about the size of a pea—and sits well back at the base of the brain. It was endowed in ancient times with metaphysical properties all of which remain speculative. In fish and lizards and certain lower vertebrates it is a kind of third eye, and receives light. In higher mammals, like ourselves, it is so far from any source of light that it could scarcely do so. It can be removed without harm. Indeed it normally becomes calcified and inactive about the time of puberty, and its position seen on X-rays of the skull can be a good guide to whether the brain is being pushed to one side by an abnormal mass.

THE URINARY SYSTEM.

Everyone knows what kidneys look like—in fact, the term "kidney-shaped" is used to describe other objects. Within the kidneys the blood-vessels carrying waste materials subdivide and finally end up in little coils or glomeruli through which waste products are filtered into the other system, the system of tubes which, beginning as tiny cups around the glomeruli, become larger and larger until they join the ureter passing out at the foot of the kidney, the hilum, a point at which both the veins and tubes enter and leave. The kidneys, of course, lie one on each side in the loins, so that if one puts one's hands on the hips and then slides them farther back they will cover the area over the left and right kidney. The ureters pass down on each side to the bladder, which is the storage tank of the products excreted by the kidneys, and lies in the mid-line down low in the abdomen; it is somewhat pear-shaped, and at its base in men there lies the prostate gland—a gland which apparently has few functions but can be a nuisance. Its only known function is that it adds something to the semen from the testes without which the semen would be sterile. Then, from the base of the bladder a single tube, the urethra, passes to the outside. One can, in fact, visualise the urinary system as a capital Y, in which the two upper limbs are the ureters, the place where they meet is the bladder, and the single limb at the foot is the urethra. Clearly, then, there may be diseases of the kidneys, of the ureters, of the bladder, of the prostate gland, or of the urethra.

The amount of urine may be increased or diminished. It is *increased* in the following conditions: after drinking excess of fluids; after taking drugs (known as *diuretics*) which are given to increase the flow; in diabetes of both types—mellitus and insipidus; in some types of chronic kidney disease; and finally, in emotional states of excitement. It is *decreased* in the following conditions: acute nephritis; any disease in which fluid is being lost in other ways, such as diarrhoea or sweating in fevers; when the fluid intake is small; and when both ureters are blocked by stones. Passing a great deal of urine is known as *polyuria*, passing very little as *oliguria*, passing frequent small amounts is simply called *frequency*. Normally, the urine is acid, but in infections of the bladder it may become alkaline owing to decomposition by bacteria. Abnormal substances, or normal substances in abnormal quantities, may occur in the urine and give the doctor an indication of what is wrong. In fact, urine analysis is a very important part of medical diagnosis. Thus urea is a normal component of urine which is increased in fevers, wasting diseases, or diabetes; the amount of urea is to some extent a measure of the degree of tissue breakdown. Uric acid is found in small quantities in normal urine, but the amount is increased in fevers and after an attack of gout (uric acid is important in the causation of gout, but has nothing at all to do with rheumatism in general, so one may disregard the advertisements in the popular press showing unpleasant pictures of joints with sharp crystals of uric acid which are alleged to cause the pain of rheumatic disease). Oxalates are not ordinarily found in urine, but, since they occur in such foods as rhubarb and strawberries, and some people are unable to deal with them, such individuals may develop stones or have pain on passing urine after eating oxalate-containing fruits.

Two very important substances which ought not to be in normal urine are albumin and sugar. Albumin is a protein, and its presence in the urine indicates that the filters of the kidney are leaking —they are allowing protein to pass out which ought to remain in the body. Albumin is easily tested for, and its presence may indicate kidney disease or nephritis as it is usually called by doctors. On the other hand, small amounts of albumin occur in fevers and in nervous conditions —*functional albuminuria*. Sugar, too, should not be present, but its presence does not necessarily indicate diabetes; for small amounts may occur in nervous conditions or in some people after taking large quantities of carbohydrate.

Blood in the urine may give it an appearance which varies from bright red to a dark, smoky colour. It is found in many diseases: acute nephritis, stone, tumours, poisoning by certain drugs, infections such as bilharzia or malaria, papilloma (i.e., non-malignant tumour of the bladder), after injury, in high blood-pressure, scurvy, and blood diseases. Sometimes it occurs for no known reason at all.

It will be remembered that streptococcal infection of the throat may cause in some people disease of the valves in the heart or endocarditis. In such cases, although the germ is found in the throat, it is not found in the heart or indeed anywhere else in the body. *Acute nephritis* occurs in the same circumstances, with the sole difference that the kidneys instead of the heart are affected. The disease appears to be an allergic reaction to the toxins of the Streptococcus. The patient, often a child, has a sore throat (and even this may be absent or fail to be noticed) or sometimes the infection may arise in other sites: after scarlet fever, erysipelas, burns, and disease of the ear. A few days later there is headache, vomiting, pain in the loins, slight rise in temperature, and especially typical is *dropsy* or oedema. This begins in the face, first around the eyelids, and then affects the ankles; later it may become more general and affect the rest of the body. Blood and albumin are found in the urine, and the blood pressure is slightly raised. The outlook is usually good if the kidneys are rested by reducing the amount of protein taken in and also the amounts of salt and water. When this is done, the inflammation soon goes and no permanent harm results. In other cases, however, if treatment is inadequate or the condition severe, the symptoms may go, but the albumin found in the urine persists. This means that permanent damage has been done, and although there may be nothing else to show for many years, *chronic nephritis* develops. In this case, the blood pressure continues to rise, and since the filters of the kidneys no longer work efficiently, urea, the principal waste product of the body to be excreted in the urine, is retained in the blood and only small amounts escape from the system. Hence chronic nephritis sooner or later leads to heart failure or haemorrhage in the brain from the rising blood pressure, or to the form of poisoning known as *uraemia* which results from the retention of urea in the blood. Uraemia may come on suddenly or gradually, but ends in progressive coma, drowsiness, and unconsciousness. There may be convulsions similar to those of epilepsy, high fever, and difficulty in breathing to complicate the picture.

Another type of nephritis which seems to have nothing at all to do with streptococcal infections, and the cause of which is completely unknown, is *nephrosis*. Developing in early adult life, its onset is insidious, and the patient first shows signs of oedema in his white and puffy face and the swelling of his legs. (It should be said here that if you have swelling of the ankles or elsewhere, you would be foolish to jump to conclusions; for such swelling is common in many diseases—in heart disease, in allergic conditions, in neurotic illness, and even just from hot weather.) When the urine is examined in a case of nephrosis it is found to be full of albumin and, as in chronic nephritis, the blood urea starts to rise. The end results of nephrosis are the same as those of chronic nephritis and depend upon the damage originally done.

The modern diuretics of the thiazide group help to control the oedema and, provided enough healthy tissue remains, remove both the fluid and the waste-products.

In recent years there have been considerable advances in the development of the artificial kidney. Once only used within hospital, artificial kidneys or dialysers as they are known, can now be used in patients' own homes, thus obviating in some cases long journeys to hospital twice a week for treatment. Dialysis is a relatively temporary measure; renal transplants now offer real hope to many sufferers although there are far more suitable recipients than there are potential donors.

Pyelitis is an infection of the pelvis of the kidney, that is to say, of the part where the ureter leaves the kidney. It is usually caused by Escherichia coli, which is normally present in the body, or by the Streptococcus. These germs may reach the ureter through the blood-stream or may pass upwards from the bladder. Obstruction anywhere in the urinary tract which causes the urine to stagnate is liable to cause pyelitis. Symptoms come on suddenly, with high fever, pain in the loin (the infection is usually on one side only, and is commoner in women), and pain in the abdomen. When urine is passed there is a burning sensation, and it is passed frequently and in small amounts, On examination, the urine is found to be highly acid and full of Escherichia coli or whatever the causative germ may be. Pyelitis is fairly readily treated by the antibiotics or sulpha drugs. Plenty of fluids should be given and the urine made alkaline by administration of alkalis.

Cystitis means inflammation of the bladder, either acute or chronic, and its causes are much the same as in the case of pyelitis. There is pain over the lower abdomen, frequency, and sometimes slight fever. The treatment is as for pyelitis. *Urethritis* is an inflammation of the urethra, with burning pain on passing water and frequency. The most serious cause (although it can usually be easily dealt with now) is gonorrhoea. But non-specific urethritis is common, especially in the newly wed and in this case various germs or none may bring about pain and frequency; there is often a large neurotic element. Urethritis should be regarded as probably due to gonorrhoea, which has already been discussed elsewhere, when there is a thick, creamy discharge from the penis or discharge in women following sexual intercourse with an infected person.

Kidney stones or Renal calculi sometimes form, and, as in the case of gall-stones, what causes them is not certain. They may be caused by disorders of metabolism—that is, in the inability of the body to deal with calcium, proteins, uric acid, and other products; or by vitamin deficiency, obstruction in the urinary tract, and urinary infections. But when a stone or stones are formed various events may occur: thus it may remain in the kidney and cause no symptoms; or it may cause repeated attacks of pain, infection, and blood in the urine (haematuria); or it may completely block the passage of urine from the kidney to such a degree that it degenerates and becomes useless; or, lastly, it may pass into the ureter, and when this occurs very severe pain, known as *renal colic*, will occur. A stone passing down the ureter into the bladder may become stuck in the urethra, although this is uncommon, since a stone small enough to get down the ureters is likely to be capable of manoeuvring through the rest of the tract. In fact, about 80–90 per cent. of stones are passed spontaneously. Stones not passed spontaneously may have to be removed by operation, but whether this is undertaken or not depends on various factors, such as the general health of the patient, the amount of trouble caused by the stone, and the health of the other kidney —for it is dangerous to operate on one kidney unless one is sure that the other is functioning efficiently. Lithotripters are also used to fragment stones without needing invasive surgery.

If a stone blocks the passage of urine on one side for any length of time *hydronephrosis* may result, in which the part where the ureter enters the kidney swells with the retained urine. Ultimately much of the kidney may be destroyed by the back-pressure. The same effect may be produced by kinking of the ureter or anything else which causes obstruction. Sometimes children are born with hydronephrosis, and when the dilation is due to kinking of the tube the condition may be intermittent, with attacks of renal colic during which only small amounts of urine are passed; this is followed with relief and the passage of large quantities.

Tumours and Cysts. The kidney may also be the site of tumours and cysts which produce pain in the loins, sometimes a lump over the kidney which can be felt, and blood in the urine. Cancer of the bladder is a serious condition in which the bladder may have to be removed, so the urinary flow has then to be directed elsewhere. Either the ureters are brought out on to the skin surface, a procedure known as *cutaneous ureterostomy*, or they are implanted in the large bowel, so that the urine flows out with the faeces. This is described as *uretero-colostomy*.

There may also be benign tumours of the bladder or *papillomas*, which are soft and bleed easily; a great deal of blood is passed, but there is usually little or no pain. In this, and similar, diseases of the bladder examination of the inside of the organ is carried out by means of a cystoscope, a thin tube which is passed up the urethra with fibre-optic light guides which enable the surgeon to see what is going on. Instruments may also be passed through the tube, and simple papillomas can be cauterised. Similar instruments are used in the examination of the stomach (gastroscope) and the bronchial tubes (bronchoscope). When some obstruction in the outlet of the bladder or in the urethra occurs the bladder, of course, fills with urine, which cannot be passed, and very painful dilation occurs. In this case an attempt may be made to pass a catheter, a thin rubber tube, into the bladder to relieve the tension, or if this fails a *suprapubic cystotomy* is performed—an incision is made in the abdomen over the bladder and a tube inserted into it, through which the urine escapes. This is ordinarily a temporary expedient, and later when the patient's health has improved an attempt will be made to remove the cause of obstruction. The most common cause of such obstruction is *enlargement of the prostate gland* at the base of the bladder, which surrounds this area and the beginning of the ureter. About 40 per cent. of men over sixty have some degree of obstruction due to this cause, and about 20 per cent. of these require operation. The gland is about the size of a walnut, and, as we have seen, its function is to supply part of the fluid which makes up the semen, the male sex secretion. Enlargement of the prostate may be benign or malignant, and, although nobody knows just why, such benign enlargement tends to occur in most men in later life. There may be no symptoms, but characteristically there is frequency during the day and the need to get up at night to pass water. The flow of urine being impeded by constriction of the urethra, the passage is less forceful than normal, and there is a tendency for dribbling to occur. If the obstruction is severe and not relieved the back-pressure may be transmitted to the ureters and kidneys, resulting finally in kidney failure and uraemia. The prostate, except in cases of very mild enlargement, has to be removed either through the abdomen or through the perineum (the part of the body lying between the sex organs and the anus). Sometimes, in less serious cases, it is possible without an incision to cut away the obstructing part by an electrocautery inserted, as is a cystoscope, through the urethra. Prostatectomy was once a serious operation, all the more so because the patient was usually elderly and not in good condition, but new techniques and the use of antibiotics have greatly improved the outlook.

Cancer of the Prostate is a potentially serious disease, but if diagnosed early and is localised, can often be cured by radiotherapy. If the disease spreads, or has spread at the time of diagnosis, it can often be controlled by various hormone treatments or by drugs, or by other forms of radiation. Even when the disease has spread, its progress can sometimes be slow.

THE NERVOUS SYSTEM.

The nervous system consists of the central nervous system and the peripheral nervous system. The brain and spinal cord make up the former. The latter consists of the nerve fibres by which the central nervous system is connected to all parts of the body. Human beings have a more complicated brain than any other animal species, but it is only its complexity which makes it different from the brains of other mammals like rats and pigs and cows. We do not have the largest brains, since whales, for example, have much larger ones. Ours is not even the largest for the size of the body. Mice and dolphins and several other creatures have relatively larger brains when compared with body weight. Furthermore the cells and materials of which our brain is composed are virtually identical with those in other mammals, and its living properties are also the same.

Before describing some of the diseases of the nervous system it will be helpful to say a little about how it is made and how it works. Each human brain probably contains about ten thousand million (10,000,000,000) nerve cells and perhaps four or five times this number of supporting "glial" cells. Each nerve cell has many long thin branching projections, called dendrites, rather like the branches of a tree, leading to many thousands of "twigs" for each single nerve cell. At the end of each "twig" there is a special structure called a *synapse* by which contact is made with other nerve cells. It is through these connections that very large numbers of nerve cells give information (or send impulses) to each other so that they can be co-ordinated. As well as these dendritic branches, each nerve cell gives off one large trunk called the *axon*, down which final messages are sent as the result of all the information it receives from its dendrites. Some axons are many feet long. Some end in another synapse, by which the outgoing message is passed to yet another nerve cell. Some axons, those of the peripheral nerves, end directly on organs like muscles or glands, instructing them and making them work.

Messages are passed along dendrites and axons as electrical impulses. These are generated in the nerve cell "body." They are modified according to information received from other nerve cells and propagated down the axon. It is this superficial resemblance to a series of electrical cables which has given rise to comparisons of the brain with a telephone system or a computer, and as long as it is realised how infinitely more complicated each brain is than any known computer, the comparison is not a bad one. However, the brain generates its own electric power from the fuel brought in its own blood supply; and no spare parts or spare cables are available if the originals should get damaged, except in peripheral nerves. Furthermore the contact of one nerve cell with another through a synapse is not an electrical contact, and neither is the contact between a nerve and the muscle or other organ it is controlling. In both cases the connection is chemical. Thus when an electrical impulse arrives at the end of the nerve fibre, a chemical is released into the gap between it and the next nerve or organ, and it is this chemical which carries the stimulus forward. There is also an arrangement to neutralise the chemical transmitter when the impulse has been transmitted. So the resemblance to a telephone exchange or computer can sometimes be misleading.

Many of the nerve axons which transmit electrical impulses are clothed in fatty *myelin sheaths*, a little like the plastic insulation around an electric wire. Here again the resemblance is only partial, since the myelin sheaths are interrupted at regular intervals and these gaps in the insulation play an important role in transmitting the impulse. One of the important functions of the non-nervous *glial* cells of the brain is to manufacture and maintain the myelin sheaths.

Most of the functions of the brain are quite unknown, and even the ones we know about are very poorly understood. It is the organ of higher mental function, of the mind and intellect, but much remains to be done on linking the different functions of the brain with the structures found within it. The brain is known to control all bodily functions by means of *motor* and other nerves which carry impulses from the brain outwards to all parts of the body. Sometimes these are under our voluntary control; mostly they are involuntary, reflex or automatic. Reflex actions are the result of impulses passed inwards from the body towards the brain by means of sensory nerves. Information arriving in the brain about the various sensations like heat, pain, touch, position, the need for saliva or gastric juice or even the thought or smell of food, are acted on in the various "centres" in the brain. These send out instructions down the "motor" or "secretary" nerves which instruct the muscles or glands to take appropriate action. Thus a *reflex* has a "sensory ending" which appreciates some sort of sensation. This is converted into an electrical impulse which is sent towards the brain or spinal cord along a sensory or "afferent" nerve. The impulse arrives at a "centre" in the central nervous system which co-ordinates all the relevant information and issues instructions. These travel as impulses outwards, along "efferent" nerves towards "effector" organs like muscles or glands, and an appropriate action occurs automatically. The pathway from sensory ending to effector organ is called a *reflex arc*. Many reflex activities are partly under voluntary control, although mainly automatic. If you touch something hot

you will automatically withdraw your hand. But if it is a hot china cup which has cost you a lot of money, you are capable of overriding the tendency to drop it, at least for a time. Breathing is automatic, but it can also be controlled, again at least for a time.

Clearly the brain is a very delicately organised piece of machinery, and its cells are extremely specialised for their job. Achieving this kind of specialised perfection brings many difficulties, however, and the brain cells have become highly dependent on the proper functioning of the other body systems, especially the blood circulation, the respiratory system, and the systems regulating the detailed nutrient composition of the blood. Failure of these systems, even for a very short time, can damage the nerve cells. Nearly all death, from whatever original cause, is produced this way, by an ultimate interference with nerve cell function.

We have already mentioned that the brain and spinal cord are unable to repair or replace any components which get damaged. The vulnerability of the brain is even more obvious when it is realised how easily damage and destruction can occur. For example, unless a rich supply of oxygen and glucose is continuously arriving in the blood stream, brain cells will cease to function in a few seconds and will die in a few minutes, and they can never be replaced. This is in marked contrast to other tissues of the body. The leg, for example, may carry on for over half an hour without any blood at all because the muscle and other cells can find other ways of surviving. Thus the brain can be permanently damaged if the blood contains insufficient oxygen (through asphyxia), insufficient glucose, or if the blood supply is blocked or if the blood pressure falls. All these are likely to happen to any of us at any time, and so there are elaborate mechanisms trying to prevent them occurring. Much of the subject of physiology is concerned with the mechanisms designed to protect the brain, and most of us ultimately die because they eventually fail. One of the clever features of the body design is that all the mechanisms which protect the brain from a supply failure are controlled by the brain itself. Thus the brain has itself been made to control the heart beat and the breathing and the many other systems which are needed for its own survival.

In all that follows concerning disease of the nervous system it will be seen that the effects of neurological disease on the patient are the direct result of something going wrong with one of the structures or mechanisms we have described.

Diagnostic Techniques in Neurology. The doctor has many ways of testing the nervous system, most of which test its various functions as outlined in the introduction. Thus tests of sensation, muscular movement and reflexes of all kinds as well as the special functions of taste, smell, vision, hearing, speech and intellect play a part. A great deal can be learned about the brain by *arteriography*. In this test a radio-opaque substance is put into the arteries supplying the brain, and an X-ray picture taken immediately afterwards shows up all the blood vessels. *Ventriculography* is an X-ray examination after gas has been introduced into the brain cavities or ventricles which are normally filled with *cerebrospinal fluid*; *myelography* is an X-ray of the spinal cord after a radio-opaque substance has been injected into the space between the spinal cord and the bony vertebral canal which houses it.

The development of computed tomography, a relatively new concept in diagnostic radiology, has now made most of those "invasive" diagnostic techniques unnecessary. The equipment needed is expensive and is presently only available at a very few centres. Sometimes *radioactive isotopes* are put into the blood stream and carried into the brain where they can be detected from outside the skull by counters. *Electroencephalography* measures the electrical waves generated by the brain by placing electrodes on the scalp. *Electromyography* does the same for muscles.

Consciousness and Unconsciousness (Coma). Everyone knows what consciousness is until he tries to define it. Full consciousness is generally taken to imply not only wakefulness but the total complement of human mental faculties. In clinical medicine, however, something less than this is usually meant. For example a demented person, or one whose memory is lost (*amnesia*), or one whose powers of speech are lost (*aphasia*) may still be "conscious." There is really a continuous gradation between full consciousness and coma, passing through drowsiness and even "stupor" in which condition a patient can be aroused from coma but sinks back into it when left alone. Many different things can cause coma ranging from swelling of the brain, compressing it in its rigid box of bone, to disorders in other body systems resulting in a failure to provide for the brain's needs. Examples of the first are bleeding within the brain or *brain tumours*, both of which occupy space and can only do so by producing compression. In the second category are asphyxia preventing oxygen from reaching the brain, lack of glucose in the blood, circulatory failure in which there is insufficient blood, or insufficient blood pressure. Fainting is a comparatively minor example.

Sleep and Insomnia. Nobody knows what causes sleep, why it is necessary, and how it helps. It is quite different from coma or even stupor, since as much oxygen and glucose is necessary asleep as awake. Insomnia is experienced by everyone at some time, and for some reason is very distressing if it persists. There are three forms: failing to get to sleep, intermittent wakefulness, and awaking early. Nearly all insomniacs sleep more than they think. They should eat light evening meals and avoid stimulants like tea and coffee after mid-day. Elderly people should realise they need less sleep. Being cold or having a full bladder can be a cause. Or simply not being tired. Sedative drugs are a last resort, but they can be useful in "breaking the habit" of wakefulness. Obviously there may be psychological factors such as anxiety and excitement. *Narcolepsy*, or a true inability to keep awake is comparatively rare. Both narcolepsy and insomnia are really extreme examples of what all normal people suffer from occasionally.

Headache is man's most common pain. Here again we must distinguish between the very common varieties of comparatively trivial significance and the rare ones due to serious causes. Some headaches are due to continuous tightness in muscles of the scalp, and are often "nervous" or psychological in origin. Others result from nose blockage and congestion, sinus problems, eye strain, toothache, etc. Migraine is a special kind and will be described below. Very occasionally indeed headache is due to serious disease like brain tumour. Most headache results from "living it up" or being "run down," or both. The headache of alcoholic hangover is probably due to dehydration. It can often be avoided by consuming a great quantity of water (a half litre or so, before going to bed), but few people are prepared to do this in the circumstances. Be careful when using aspirin, which is a useful remedy for headache, since it is very dangerous for people with stomach complaints like gastritis or gastric or duodenal ulcer. Occasionally aspirin makes the stomach bleed, and this can be so severe as to kill. A safer pain killer is paracetamol. Be particularly careful in treating "hang-over" headaches by patent fizzy remedies. They are very effective, but often contain large quantities of aspirin described in small print by its proper name as acetyl salicylic acid.

Migraine. This is a very special variety of "sick headache" and requires special treatment under medical supervision. It has many different forms, but usually there is a definite sequence of events. An attack often starts with some alteration of vision. The patient has shimmering blind spots or other visual disorders. This is followed by a well localised severe headache which may end in nausea or vomiting. The whole thing is caused by a poorly understood disorder of the blood vessels. There are special drugs, mostly derivatives of ergot, which are effective, especially if used when the first signs of an attack appear. Although there is a direct physical cause for an attack, it is also certain that some of the trouble is psychological tenseness. People with migraine are often rather anxious, striving and perfectionist people. Also it has been noticed that attacks are much less frequent when the necessary pills are being carried available for use. However, as with all other conditions which are partly "psychological" in origin they are none the less distressing for the patient. It simply means that the treatment is also partly psychological in encouraging him to come to terms with his problems.

Menière's Disease is one of the conditions in which the organ of balance in the middle ear is affected, giving rise to *vertigo*, a form of giddiness. It usually begins in middle life in the same sort of person who sometimes has migraine. There is buzzing in the ears and some intermittent loss of hearing as well as vertigo. During an attack the patient may be unable to walk because of his loss of balance, and nausea and vomiting are common. Treatment is by special drugs, and occasionally an operation on the ear is necessary.

Epilepsy is a symptom, not a disease, which is common at all ages but especially children. It has been attributed to St. Paul, Julius Caesar, Napoleon, and (with more justice perhaps) to Dostoyevsky. Many varieties of attack occur often in the same patient, the commonest and best known being the *grand mal* or major seizure. In this the patient falls down unconscious and rigid and the jaw is clenched, so that there is danger of the tongue being bitten. This so-called tonic phase is followed, within a minute or so, by a clonic phase in which the limbs contract rhythmically. The attack ends with the patient going limp and gradually recovering consciousness, a process which may take up to an hour. Occasionally the patient has a brief warning, most often an indescribable feeling in the stomach. There are two common forms of minor seizure, one occurring mainly in children and the other more often in adults. The common minor attacks in children are often called *petit mal* or *absence*, which well describes the instantaneous and brief loss of consciousness often unaccompanied by any change in posture. Recovery is equally instantaneous. On the other hand, in the other forms of epilepsy which arise from various parts of the brain, but especially from the lobe under the temporal region, there is often a warning similar to that which may precede a major seizure. In these cases the patient shows only confusion, no definite loss of posture, but automatic activity such as fumbling with buttons, muttering, and grimacing. Following these attacks there may be a quite prolonged period of confusion in which the patient may wander away and occasionally may be violent. Criminal acts are very rarely carried out in this state.

A large number of people have had one or two fits in their lives, particularly at times of physical or psychological stress. "Fever" or "Febrile" convulsions (often called teething fits in the past) are extremely common in young children and are often thought of as something different from epilepsy since the attacks rarely continue in later years. This form of epilepsy and some cases of *petit mal* are the only forms in which hereditary factors are important in the causation, and these are the least serious forms of epilepsy. They are very rarely associated with serious physical or psychological disturbances. Most other forms of epilepsy are due to a scar or other area of brain damage. It is a proportion of these cases which develop the psychological disturbances that are occasionally very serious.

Not every patient who has had one or two fits need necessarily take regular anticonvulsant drugs; that is drugs which damp down the abnormal excessive activity of the brain that leads to the attacks. Many drugs are available of which the most important are phenobarbitone, phenytoin and clonazepam. The succinimides and troxidones are effective only against minor seizures. The choice is a matter of skilled medical judgment. Patients often find it difficult to get work because of the reluctance of employers to take on someone who may be more prone to accidents and whose fits may distress other workers. Obviously there are some jobs which epilepsy sufferers should not do because of the danger involved (from for example, moving machinery), and they should not drive a car. A few cases are so severe that work is almost impossible, but employers have a duty whenever possible to employ these people whose mental health may suffer greatly if they are made to feel outcasts and who ordinarily are as efficient, or even more so, as the next man. It is also hoped that employees will become less prejudiced about epilepsy as the general public become less ignorant about medical matters.

Congenital Malformations. The proper shape of the brain and spinal cord is achieved quite early in development by about the thirteenth week after conception. During this time very slight changes in the foetal environment can produce disastrous malformations. The drug thalidomide, for example, operated on other body systems while they were passing through this phase of construction. Some viruses can do the same thing. Most malformations are without known cause, but it is certain that something went wrong at this very early stage, and it only needs a very minor interference with the normal process to do the permanent damage. At about this time the bones of the spine are beginning to enclose, or form a roof over the developing spinal cord. Sometimes they fail to complete the process, resulting in *spina bifida*. If the coverings of the cord protrude through the defect, this is a *meningocoele*, and if the cord itself protrudes it is a *meningomyelocoele*. The whole protrusion may be covered with skin, but if it is not, the cord soon becomes infected. The effect on the patient is variable, according to the amount of damage to the nerve fibres in the cord, and there are varying degrees of paralysis and loss of sensation below the area involved together with loss of bowel and bladder control. Much help is often obtained from surgical repair, but many cases remain in a distressing condition always, and the only really useful attack on the problem is research to find the cause and prevent it happening. The same is true of the *malformations of the brain*. In one of these, hydrocephaly, the narrow channel is blocked which transmits the cerebrospinal fluid from the chambers within the brain where it is secreted to the outer coverings to be taken back into the blood stream. Blockage of the channel (or aqueduct) results in distension of the brain by fluid, enlargement of the head, and mental retardation. Sometimes a by-pass valve can be inserted to restore normal fluid circulation with very gratifying results.

Cerebral Palsy is a physically disabling condition of impaired muscle co-ordination caused before, during or shortly after birth by damage to or maldevelopment in the portion of the brain which controls movement. There are 3 main types: *spasticity, athetosis,* and *ataxia* depending on what area of the brain has been affected. Inherited defects do not play a large part in cerebral palsy. The general incidence of the disorder is thought to be 2.5 per 1,000 births. For further information and advice contact: the Spastics Society, 12 Park Crescent, London W1N 4EQ.

Motor Neurone Disease. This is a group of distressing diseases usually occurring in people over 40, in whom the parts of the brain and spinal cord which look after muscular movement degenerate. The group includes *amyotrophic lateral sclerosis, progressive muscular atrophy, progressive bulbar palsy,* and *primary lateral sclerosis.* The results are paralysis or weakness with wasting of the muscles of the body, including those concerned with arms, legs, breathing, speaking, etc. Nothing whatever is known of the cause. It is uncommon, but this is little comfort to the sufferer.

Parkinson's Disease, formerly known as the shaking palsy, derives its present name from the London physician James Parkinson (1755–1824) whose description established it as a clinical entity. It is one of the commonest illnesses to affect the human brain with more than one in 1,000 of the population as a whole (though one in 100 of those above 60 years of age) suffering from it. The average age of onset is about 55 though one in seven contract it in their thirties or forties. It has three classical features: shaking (or tremor), muscular rigidity and poverty of movement. A stooping, shuffling gait and a mask-like loss of facial expression are common. It is a progressive disease affecting patients in variable degrees of severity and different degrees of progression. A good deal can now be done to help these patients with drugs and since the condition results from a malfunctioning of brain cells which produce a chemical 'messenger' known as dopamine replacement of this substance by the drug levodopa (often accompanied by an additive in a combined preparation) is often the first line of treatment. Occasionally younger patients have benefited from surgical destruction of small areas of diseased brain. It is important to remember that many elderly people have some tremor of the head or hands called *senile tremor* and this is *not* parkinson's Disease. It is merely one of the features of achieving advanced seniority as a citizen. The Parkinson's Disease Society of 36 Portland Place, London W1N 3DG sponsors, from monies raised, medical research as well as promoting patient welfare.

Chorea. This is a group of diseases in which there is involuntary muscle movement, weakness, and emotional instability. There will be clumsiness, awkward gait, twitching of limbs, face, hands, trunk, or tongue. They include *acute chorea* or *St. Vitus' dance* occurring in children from 5 to 15, *hereditary* or *Huntington's chorea* occurring in a well-defined genetic pattern and beginning later, between 35 and 50. *Tics* or habit spasms are not part of these diseases but are often of psychological origin. They are usually eye blinking or head shaking.

Stroke Illness or Cerebrovascular Diseases. Strokes are due to diseases of the brain's blood vessels which either burst or get blocked. The same blood vessel disorders cause heart attacks by blocking the coronary arteries supplying the heart. Strokes and heart attacks together kill more people than any other single cause including cancer. They account for one death in every five. Perhaps less is known of the cause of this disease than is known about cancer, and much more research is needed to find out if it is to be prevented. The cause of the commonest cancer (of the lung) is now known and it can be prevented by stopping smoking. Perhaps the prevention of strokes and heart attacks will mean an equally difficult abstinence from all those foods which make us fat. At least it is known that being overweight leads to death from these causes, just as smoking may lead to death from lung cancer.

If any artery supplying blood to any part of the brain is blocked, the territory supplied will die; and the bodily functions for which that part of the brain is responsible will cease. The process is called *infarction* of the brain, the dead area being an *infarct.* The blockage is usually due to thrombosis (*see* **P30**) of the blood within a vessel, a *thrombus* being a rather complicated clot with a structure of its own. The underlying cause is the arterial disease, atheroma (*see* **P29**) together with stagnation of the circulation. About one blockage in ten is due to a small piece of a much larger thrombus in the heart chambers being flung into the blood stream and impacting in the distant vessel in the brain. This is *cerebral embolism* (*see* **P30**). If the area of dead or infarcted brain is not too large the patient will recover from his unconsciousness, but will be left with permanent loss of function (paralysis, etc.) related to that part of the brain.

When a blood vessel supplying the brain bursts, this causes *cerebral haemorrhage* or apoplexy. The vessel may be on the surface (*subarachnoid haemorrhage*) or in the depths of the tissue (*intracerebral haemorrhage*). Strokes tend to occur in older people, because the associated arterial disease is a product of age and high blood pressure. Occasionally a subarachnoid haemorrhage occurs in a younger person with an unsuspected malformation of the arteries of the base of the brain known as a *berry aneurysm.* This is a small berry-sized blown-out balloon due to a defect in the wall of the vessel. Berry aneurysms can often be treated surgically. Intracerebral haemorrhage carries a very poor outlook, however, since much brain tissue is often destroyed by the escaping blood, especially the deep tissues responsible for the vital functions. Haemorrhage within the brain cavity can also be caused by injury (*see concussion and compression,* **P21**).

Inflammatory Diseases of the Nervous System. The membranes covering the brain are called the meninges. Inflammation of these, nearly always by blood-borne infection or infection following injury, is called *meningitis.* Cerebrospinal or spotted fever which used to be common and very much feared was only one variety caused by a germ called "meningococcus." It is now rare. Almost any other germ may cause meningitis, and when the germ is susceptible to one of the antibiotics it is usually treatable. It will usually be necessary to identify the germ by taking a sample of cerebrospinal fluid from a convenient space around the spinal cord in the lower back. When the disease is caused by the tubercle bacillus (*tuberculous meningitis*) the problem is more difficult because the patient is often not so obviously ill until the later, less treatable stages. *Cerebral abscess,* or abscess of the brain is very serious because it occupies space in the closed box of the skull and compresses the brain, as well as being a destructive process. It may arise due to an infected piece of tissue or pus being carried to the brain in the blood stream from a distant site in the lungs or heart. When the brain or cord tissue is itself inflamed it is called *encephalitis* (brain) or *myelitis* (cord) or *encephalo-myelitis* (both).

Herpes zoster (Shingles) is a common viral infection of the nervous system which affects sensory nerve roots where they enter the spinal cord. The initial symptoms are of pain in the area supplied by the affected nerves—commonly one side of the trunk, the buttock or the face—followed by the appearance of blisters. Treatment is symptomatic, as there is no specific remedy. Soothing lotions may be applied to the blisters and analgesics given for the pain. The disease is fairly short-lived, but neuralgia may persist for weeks after the blisters have healed.

Shingles is interesting in that it is not a *primary* viral infection, but the result of reactivation of the varicella-zoster virus (so called because it causes *either* chicken pox or shingles) which has lain dormant in nerve root cells, probably since childhood. Primary infection with the virus at whatever age causes chicken pox, not shingles; if an adult who has never had chicken pox or shingles comes into contact with a child with chicken pox or an adult with shingles, he is likely to contract the former but not the latter.

Shingles is infectious from the time the blisters appear until they have crusted over and healed. However, it is not as infectious as chicken pox.

Multiple sclerosis is the most important of the *demyelinating diseases* in which the myelin or "fatty" sheaths which insulate nerve fibres appear to disintegrate. This occurs patchily and seemingly randomly throughout the central nervous system (*i.e.* the brain and spinal cord) and results in interference with the passage of impulses through the affected nerves. Changes in sensation, balance or muscular co-ordination occur at varying intervals of time and spaced out over months or years in such a way as to appear unconnected. There is at present no reliable, objective diagnostic test for multiple sclerosis and diagnosis has to be made from the history of such episodic symptoms. The cause is unknown, but from various pieces of evidence such as the odd distribution of the disease in the world one theory is that multiple sclerosis is the result of a recrudescence of a dormant viral infection which may be picked up during the teenage years. Others hold it to be an auto-immune disease. It is commonly held that once diagnosis of MS is made it means a sentence of years of increasingly severe disablement which will progress relentlessly and inexorably and reduce the patient to a helpless vegetable state in twenty or thirty years. That may be the case, but in fact such a gloomy picture is very uncommon. Much research has gone into the natural history of MS and it is clear that there are seven distinct patterns of the disease. These cover a wide range of symptom patterns from that characterised by a sudden onset of symptoms with relatively few relapses after the first year, to that manifested by sudden onset followed by unremitting relapses causing progressively greater degrees of physical impairment which may indeed lead to much distressing disability and relatively early

death. But between these two extremes, of which the first is far the commonest form for the disease to take and the latter relatively infrequent, there lies a whole range of disease patterns and prediction is difficult.

The Multiple Sclerosis Society exists to sponsor research, to care for patients and to give advice and support to friends and relatives. For more information write to them at their offices at 25 Effie Road Fulham, London SW6 1EE. The Scottish office is at 27 Castle Street, Edinburgh, EH2 3DN.

Brain Tumours. The brain is no exception to the rule that any cell in any tissue of the body can suddenly begin to disobey the body's rules regarding its growth and multiplication. A largely unknown mechanism governs how many cells of a certain type there ought to be and calls a halt to cell multiplication when this number is reached. Every now and then one of them turns a blind eye and goes on dividing, and the result is a tumour, or lump, of anarchic cells which obey no rules. Tumours are commonest in cells which normally go on dividing throughout life, in order to replace those lost by wear and tear. Examples are the cells lining the air passages in the lung, or the alimentary tract in the stomach or large bowel. Fortunately for the brain there is little cell division once it has grown. Nerve cells cannot divide at all in an adult life, and the supporting glial cells only do so in response to injury. Therefore primary brain tumours are much less common than those elsewhere. Also many brain tumours like many of those elsewhere, are benign or "innocent" tumours. They are not cancerous, and need only be removed for the patient to be completely cured. The brain, however, is at two major disadvantages compared with other tissues when it comes to tumours. One is that all tumours as they grow take up space, and space in the skull is already fully occupied. Thus even an innocent tumour can compress the brain within its rigid box of bone and become most dangerous until it is removed. The second disadvantage is due to the very large blood supply of the brain. Cancer in other parts of the body spreads partly by sending small pieces of itself to other tissues by way of the blood stream, and those tissues like liver, lung, kidney, and brain which have a big blood supply naturally receive more than their share of other tissues' tumour. These secondary deposits, or *metastases,* cause compression and other trouble in the brain much more frequently than the brain's own primary tumours. Indeed convulsions or other signs of brain disorder may be the first indication that there is a primary tumour in the lung or breast or elsewhere.

Diseases of Peripheral Nerves. Compared with the nerves of the central nervous system (brain and spinal cord), the peripheral nerves are comparatively rarely affected by disease. They have some similarities of structure with central nerve fibres in that their fibres are often covered with myelin sheaths and are arranged in bundles. A special feature, however, is that they are enclosed by connective tissue sheaths and it is probably these which allow a peripheral nerve to grow again, or regenerate, after it has been cut or damaged. Central nerve fibres are unable to do this. After *injury of a peripheral nerve* the part away from the centre is cut off from its parent cell body and it dies. All function, whether motor or sensory, is lost. But in the course of many months the central surviving part grows into the connective tissue sheaths which act like tubes to guide the new nerve to its destination. Provided the cut ends are close enough together and correctly aligned, and provided enough fibres reach their correct destination, good functional recovery is possible.

A disorder of a peripheral nerve is called a *neuropathy* and means nothing more than that. There are many kinds. One of the most distressing is *trigeminal neuralgia,* again fortunately rare. The trigeminal or fifth cranial nerve has a motor and sensory territory on the face. In this condition there are paroxysmal episodes of extremely severe pain which may resist all treatment except destruction of the nerve itself with consequent facial paralysis and loss of sensation. At the other more trivial extreme are the occasions when a leg "goes to sleep" or gets "pins and needles" after crossing it and pressing on a nerve for too long. *Bell's Palsy* is sudden loss of function of the seventh cranial nerve and there is again paralysis on one side of the face which usually recovers in time. Some bacterial diseases, especially leprosy, invade the nerves themselves. Chronic alcoholism may affect the nerves, as may diabetes, probably by interfering with the nutrition of the nerve cell. So may exposure to arsenic or lead or an unpleasant nerve poison which may contaminate cooking oil known as TOCP, or triorthocresylphosphate.

Muscular Dystrophies. These are a series of diseases of muscle in which there is progressive wasting and weakness of muscle, the causes of which are entirely unknown. They are divided up according to the age of onset and the muscles involved. *Duchenne's muscular dystrophy* occurs in the first decade of life. It affects most of the muscles eventually, including the heart muscle and those concerned with breathing, and so the outlook is not good. Other forms are inherited. The Muscular Dystrophy Group (Nattrass House, 35 Macaulay Rd. London SW4 0QP) gives great assistance to sufferers.

Myasthenia Gravis. This is a strange disorder of the mechanism which transmits instructions from nerve to muscle at the "neuromuscular junction," leading to extreme weakness.

MENTAL ILLNESS

Conventionally mental illness is divided into two categories, psychosis (madness), and neurosis (exaggerated symptoms of commonly experienced states). The dividing line is not a clear one though, since even the acts of a madman are understandable if you accept his view of the world. Psychoses are themselves divided into: *organic*, implying that we can identify a physical cause, and *functional*, where the brain structure appears to be intact but its performance is abnormal. This division is now seen to be very blurred since there are physical diseases and drugs which can lower the threshold for response, or alter a person's perceptions so that he appears to be mad, albeit temporarily. The more research is done, the more organic causes are found for abnormal behaviour, and the more hope is raised for successful medical intervention.

Organic Psychoses.

The organic psychoses result from actual damage to the brain. This damage can be caused by disease, as in syphilis; by tumours; by dietary deficiencies, as in inadequate vitamin B12 absorption; by poisons such as alcohol and lead; by drugs such as LSD or amphetamine; by problems of blood circulation such as heart failure or atheroma; and by genetic inheritance. The onset of illness can be either an acute confusional state or a chronic reaction known as *dementia*. The acute episode is characterised by an impairment of consciousness which may vary from difficulty in holding on to the point of a story, to actual coma. The chronic reaction, on the other hand, does not affect consciousness but intellect, memory and personality. Characteristically, memory for recent events is lost, while that for remote ones is preserved. About one in ten men and women over the age of 65 is likely to be affected. Since it is the most commonly and voluntarily ingested poison, it is worth giving a special mention to alcohol. It is hard to define what is meant by the term 'alcoholic', but anyone whose daily intake of alcohol exceeds 5 units is generally agreed to qualify. (A unit of alcohol is a half pint of beer, or a single measure of spirits, or a glass of wine). Alcohol-related disabilities can be classed as social, psychological and physical. Social problems are often noticed first, and include failure to perform an expected role as parent or spouse or at work, or breaking social rules as in driving offences. Psychological difficulties include increased depression and personality deterioration. *Delerium tremens,* (DTs), is an acute confusional state involving intense fear and restlessness with hallucinations. Most alcoholics experience blackouts ranging from momentary lapses to memory loss involving several hours. Intellectual impairment can occur and may be permanent, even after alcohol is abandoned.

Other physical problems associated with alcoholism include a doubled death rate, liver damage, gastritis, anaemia, increased rates of cancer, and infections such as TB. Sexual incompetence is common. The children of alcoholic mothers are at increased risk of deformity and growth retardation.

Functional Psychoses.

Functional psychoses broadly fall into two categories: *schizophrenia* and *manic depressive psychosis*. Schizophrenia was a term introduced by Eugene Bleuler in 1911 to describe a group of illnesses in which there was a splitting of the psychic functioning so that the association between two ideas was bizarre, and mood seemed inappropriate to the circumstances. Nowadays schizophrenia is diagnosed on the presence of certain accepted symptoms such as a lack of insight, auditory hallucinations especially of voices discussing the patient in derogatory terms, the idea that radio and TV programmes refer to him directly, unreasonable suspicions, or a flatness of response. However, the concept has been challenged by workers such as Thomas Szasz, who regards it as a medical fiction, and Scheff, who believed that many of the symptoms arose from being labelled 'mad'. It seems that schizophrenia occurs in all societies, but in less developed countries appears to be more acute yet to offer better prospects for recovery. About one person in a hundred will develop the condition, and there is an increased risk where close relations are affected. There are many theories of causation though an inheritance factor is clear, but there is argument about what this factor might be, and the extent to which its influence is affected by life events. Theories invoking abnormalities in the substances responsible for the transmission of signals within the brain itself are supported by the fact that some symptoms of schizophrenia can be induced experimentally. But as yet the physical theories are not wholly proven. The concept of the 'schizophrenogenic' mother who causes illness in her child, and the theory that abnormal dominance patterns in the family are the cause have proved equally hard to verify. The 'double bind' hypothesis of Bateson, that an emotionally disturbed parent, who says one thing to a child but at the same time suggests a deeper, contradictory, message will eventually cause the child to withdraw into a fantasy world, is another explanation. The personal construct theory of Bannister and Fransella says that we build up constructs and relationships between them in order to understand our world. In this theory if the construct of generous-mean is linked with those of honest–dishonest and gentle–violent, then we expect someone we know to be generous to be also honest and gentle. If these associations are weak or inconsistent, then the world is a chaotic and fearful place. Whatever the role of early experience in the causation of schizophrenia it is clear that current stress brings on an attack.

The treatment of schizophrenia was revolutionised by the introduction in the 1950s of phenothiazine drugs which not only tranquillise but also have specific anti-psychotic effects. The fact that schizophrenic patients are increasingly returned to their community, able to function, is due in large part to these pharmacological advances, and to the concept of 'milieu therapy' involving group activities, recreation and occupational therapies.

Manic depressive psychosis is characterised by swings of mood between depression and elation without apparent cause, and in this form is called the *bipolar* state. More frequently, the disease is *unipolar,* showing only periods of depression interspersed with periods of normality. The difficulty in defining depression as an illness is firstly to distinguish it from a symptom, and secondly to make a distinction between normal and morbid depression which is depression of greater severity and duration than would be expected in a given population from the apparent cause. This last is a very subjective rating and this makes depression a difficult subject for research. The expectancy that one will suffer a depressive illness in one's lifetime is about one to three per cent, with females more likely than males. Generally it is accepted as a phenomenon of later life, but can occur at any age. In depression the major symptom is of a persisting sad, despairing mood, especially severe on waking up. Agitation or marked slowing down may be present, and hallucinations are not uncommon.

Ideas of unworthiness, guilt and persecution are frequent, loss of appetite, loss of weight, loss of sexual drive and loss of menstruation are also common. The causation of depressive illness is another area where authorities are in dispute, and theories abound. Seligman points to learned helplessness as a cause. In his experiments animals exposed to repeated stresses beyond their control, exhibited apathy, difficulty in accepting that they could do anything to help themselves, loss of appetite, and reduced sociability. The idea that depression is the result of aggressive feelings which cannot be channelled out and so are turned in on oneself, is a simplified view of what Freud said. Some support is lent to this idea by the fact that depressive illness is less common in time of war. Certain biochemical changes have been found in the brains of depressed patients, and the anti-depressant drugs work in ways to correct these imbalances, but whether these intra-cellular changes are cause or effect, and how this comes about, is still not entirely clear. Treatment is by specific anti-depressant drugs of which there are now many, by psychotherapy of various kinds, and much more rarely now by electro-convulsive therapy (ECT) which can be life-saving in very severe cases. Treatment with lithium is often successful in reducing the severity of mood swings.

Mania is a state of elation, hurried speech, and physical overactivity. Irritability is common if the patient is frustrated. Grandiose plans are made and money can be lavishly spent. Gradually as the illness progresses the sufferer becomes confused, angry, hallucinated, incoherent and exhausted. Treatment is usually by tranquillising drugs.

Neurosis.

Neurosis as we now understand it is a concept we owe to Freud, and to him, too, we owe the distinction between the neurotic disorders of *hysteria*, *anxiety* and *obsessionality*, and the disorders of *personality*. Those in the latter category, while having no detectable disease, are treated by psychiatrists as if they had, and this is a decision of society as a whole since the alternative is to refer such people to the legal or social services. Because the category of neurosis is so vague, it is hard to put a figure on how many people may be affected, but researchers in general practice consultations estimate about one in ten women, and half that many men are at risk. The reason for this disparity is not clear, but may be due to factors such as the greater freedom for expression of frustration enjoyed by men in our society than women. The majority of neurotic illnesses clear up, and may do so spontaneously, although obsessional and hypochondriacal symptoms are more persistent than others.

Anxiety neurosis as a pathological state where anxiety is either unrelated to a recognisable threat, or the degree of anxiety is out of proportion to the threat. The mechanism of our response to a threat appears to depend on the level at which the threat is perceived, if at a conscious level, the response is fear, if at an unconscious level, the response is anxiety. Symptoms include weakness, dizziness, sweating and tiredness. The physical symptoms are themselves unpleasant and increase the feelings of being threatened. Treatment may be by reassurance and explanation, by psychotherapy aimed at bringing the threat into conscious appraisal, or by drugs which are now widely, and often inappropriately, prescribed. Phobic anxiety occurs when unreasonable fear is focused on a particular object or situation, and leads to avoidance, Agoraphobia, literally a fear of the market place, claustrophobia, fear of enclosed spaces, and animal phobias are well recognised. Social phobias, such as fear of eating in public or fear of vomiting are often harder for the sufferer to acknowledge. Phobic states are often associated with a traumatic event in the past, and avoidance through fear leads to a form of conditioning which reinforces the fear. Gradually the sufferer extends the range of feared and avoided stimuli. Behavioural therapy offers the chance to reverse this process.

Much is made of the manipulative nature of neurotics, and the idea of secondary gain, where the neurotic is perceived as getting the better of those around him by organising his, and other people's, lives to fit in with his symptoms. Certainly neurotic people can be very irritating in their demands and social failings, but their conscious experience is of personal suffering, their gains are at an unconscious level, and one cannot but be saddened by the waste their lives represent.

Suicide as a completed act is on the decline, but the rate of attempted suicide is rising. Most attempts are preceded by a warning of intention, often quite explicit. Men, especially alcoholic or physically ill men, are more likely to complete the attempt than are women for whom the attempt itself, rather than the ending of life, seems to be the important feature.

Mental Illness in Childhood.

Mental illness in childhood can refer to illness specific to children such as autism (*see below*), to emotional disorders, and to disorders of conduct. Because children are dependent on their families, much interest has centred on relationships within the family and on maternal deprivation as factors in the creation of childhood difficulties. The work of Bowlby highlighted problems consequent on the infant's need for attachment being denied, and he expressed the view that poor early experiences led to failures in later life to develop social relationships. Autism is a state where the child displays abnormalities of language, indifference to people, and ritual behaviour. Autistic children do not grow into schizophrenics, they grow up into autistic adults, and most remain severely handicapped. Phobias and obsessional behaviour are common in children and usually appear and disappear rapidly, especially with prompt intervention. Depressive illness is rare before puberty and where depressive features are seen it is usually in response to environment.

Conduct disorders include persistent lying, stealing, disobeying, truanting, fighting or setting fires. The distinction from delinquency is important since the latter implies breaking the law which is quite common in adolescence. There is a high correlation between these behaviours and difficulty in reading, though whether this is because of a shared impairment or the result of educational frustration is not clear. Treatment is by careful assessment of the family situation, and by social and educational intervention. The future is not rosy though, since about half the antisocial boys in one long-term study went on to be antisocial men in later life.

Anorexia nervosa is usually a disorder of adolescent girls in which food avoidance, weight loss, failure of menstruation and overactivity predominate. Anorexics often display a distorted view of their own bodies, being unable to see how thin they have become. The underlying difficulty may be a need to control something in their life at a time of actual dependence on parents, or an attempt to avoid the challenge of puberty and the demands, particularly of sexuality, that adulthood makes. Treatment is by behaviour modification, supervised weight gain, and psychotherapy. Bulimia nervosa is a variant in which meals, often very large meals, are eaten and then vomiting is induced to get rid of them.

Autism.

Autism is a profound life-long handicap which is now believed to be caused by brain malfunction; often occurring with other disorders, including mental retardation, which affects three times as many boys as girls. The spectrum of the autistic condition encompasses dramatically different degrees of severity, varying from profound handicap through to subtle problems of social understanding in people of apparently normal or even superior intelligence. With the right therapy at an early age, autistic people can become less indifferent to others and can develop social responsiveness at a simple level.

There is no present cure for autism; most children who are born autistic will die autistic and it is essential that people with autism are cared for in a special community by experienced and dedicated staff.

THE SKIN

The skin in the course of development before birth is particularly closely associated with the nervous system. It is therefore not surprising that so many skin diseases are influenced by emotional states. Other causes of skin disease are infectious, glandular disorders, vitamin deficiencies, and the numerous conditions for which no cause has been discovered, but which presumably are due to metabolic disorders.

One of the commonest skin symptoms is *itching* or *pruritus*. It may accompany many different general diseases, for example diabetes and jaundice. It may also be troublesome during the menopause (the change of life in women), in old age, or in nervous conditions. Sedatives and sex hormones sometimes help the itching during the menopause, and there are ointments which may be useful.

Itching in the region of the anus and genital organs is relatively common. It may be caused by worms, by irritating vaginal discharge, or by sugar in the urine, as in diabetes. The alteration in the normal bacteria of the bowel which follows treatment with various antibiotics also often causes anal pruritus and soreness. In many cases however the itching has some psychological cause. In treatment it is important to avoid ointments and creams which contain a local anaesthetic, because these substances can cause severe allergic reactions if used for longer than a few days, and may thus make the condition much worse. Treatment with a local corticosteroid application is more effective and safer.

Parasites, such as the *scabies* mite or *lice* can cause severe and persistent itching. The scabies mite is very small, and since it burrows under the skin surface, is unlikely to be seen; it is the cause of itching most commonly between the fingers and on the front of the wrists. The itching is worst when the body becomes heated, as in bed. Treatment consists of painting the body from head to foot with benzyl benzoate application, followed the next day by a hot bath. Since scabies is contracted through close personal contact with an infested person it is often desirable for several or all members of a family to be treated at the same time, even though only one of them may be affected. Lice are specialists, one type of which affects the scalp, another the body, and a third the genital area. Head lice are destroyed by washing with shampoos containing organophosphorus insecticides such as malathion, body lice by insecticides and genital (pubic) lice by shaving off hair and washing. Obviously, the clothes, especially in the case of body lice, should be disinfested, by using a hot iron particularly over the seams, which lice (for some inexplicable reason) seem to favour. Apart from the discomfort they cause, lice are dangerous as potential carriers of typhus fever.

Baldness, or Alopecia, is a very common and often distressing condition, as is manifested by the number of preparations advertised as curing it. When many preparations are offered for the treatment of one condition it is a fair judgment to assume that none of them is likely to be effective. There are, in fact, two types of baldness; one, which is much the commoner, is hereditary, and cannot be influenced in the slightest by any treatment, the other, *alopecia areata*, is caused by nervous stress, and would recover in most cases by itself, whether one used a solution of soot and water or the most expensive "hair food." There is no such thing as a hair food, any more than there is such a thing as a nerve food, and although it is probable that hair hygiene may delay baldness, it certainly cannot prevent it. All hair tonics and "foods" are useless, and their uselessness is only equalled by their costliness. Those who have lost their hair and find it growing again after using some alleged tonic are people who have had *alopecia areata* and whose hair would have grown back anyhow. In women the hair often thins out soon after a pregnancy, but a few months later it usually returns to normal. Alopecia is a common side effect of many modern drugs used in treating cancer, because these drugs affect rapidly-growing cells, including those in hair follicles.

Seborrhoea is a condition in which there is over-activity of the sebaceous glands. The most usual form it takes is *dandruff*. However, it takes other forms, and those who have dandruff may also have rashes on the face, shoulders, and chest. In these areas there is a patchy, greasy, and often itchy, rash which does not clear up until the primary condition in the scalp is dealt with. The scalp should be washed with one of the modern sulphur-containing shampoos at least twice a week, and the affected parts on the face and chest can be dealt with by the use of a sulphur lotion (*not* on any account by greasy ointments). Seborrhoea is not in itself difficult to treat, but since the condition depends on over-secretion of sebum, the skin lubricant, treatment may have to be persisted in during the years of early adulthood, when it is most active.

Erythema Intertrigo is, quite simply, the sort of irritation which occurs usually from excessive sweating under the armpits, between the legs, and under the breasts in women. All that need be done is to wash frequently and to dust the affected areas after washing with powder. This is the condition which, in the tropics, is known as "prickly heat" and elsewhere as a "sweat rash." In some people *hyperhidrosis* or *excessive sweating* is a problem, especially when the sweating is accompanied with body odour—the sort of thing that, according to the advertisements, "even your best friends won't tell you." There is little need for anyone in these days to suffer in this way: for the cosmetic firms have produced many highly efficient deodorants which not only control odour but also control the amount of sweating. Chlorophyll, which has been much advertised as removing odours, is effective when applied directly to surfaces which give off an unpleasant smell. It is however ineffective when taken by mouth, and does not prevent body odours. Stale sweat smells bad because it is decomposed by bacteria, and this type of body odour can be largely prevented by preparations containing harmless antiseptic and anti-perspirants.

Erysipelas is an infection of the skin caused by the haemolytic streptococcus. It begins as a red, raised area anywhere on the body where the germs have been able to enter through a small crack or cut in the skin. The red area advances and spreads over the body until the disease is got under control. Erysipelas is very infectious, and those who look after the patient should wash their hands thoroughly after contact. At one time the disease used to spread as an epidemic throughout the hospital wards, but this is very rare nowadays. Treatment is, of course, a matter for the doctor.

Chilblains used to be common in cold weather, especially in those with poor circulation. Ordinarily they occur in the toes and fingers, but may appear on the nose and ears. The part affected becomes swollen, dusky, and there is pain and itching, sometimes leading to ulceration. Protection of the body, especially the hands and feet, from cold is the best and the only really effective way of preventing chilblains. Warm lined gloves and footwear, and arm stockings or trousers should be worn outdoors. Adequate heating of rooms is essential: a temperature between 18° and 21°C is recommended. Most tablets, medicines, ointment, or creams for chilblains are useless. A skin affection caused by heat is rather grandiosely described as *erythema ab igne*, and used frequently to be seen on the legs of ladies addicted to roasting their legs before the fire. It takes the form of red patches on the front of the legs and can be removed only by avoiding the cause.

Dermatitis means "inflammation of the skin," and therefore the word could be, strictly speaking, applied to any skin disease. In fact the term is used almost interchangeably with the term *eczema*. There are three main types of dermatitis or eczema. The first, *primary irritant dermatitis* results from injury of the skin by some powerful chemical, such as strong alkali or turpentine. The second, *contact dermatitis* is due to sensitisation of the skin to some substance which is normally liable to cause this type of allergic sensitivity; examples are nickel (in jewellery and suspender buckles), epoxy resins, rubber additives, primulas and chrysanthemums, and even ingredients of cosmetics. Contact dermatitis may continue for a long time, even after the patient is no longer in contact with the offending material. The third type is often called *constitutional eczema*. Although the skin is apt to react adversely to various irritants and sensitisers the major part is played by the personality, and there is often a history of eczema, hay fever or asthma in the family. Treatment is more difficult, but local corticosteroids and tar, sedatives and psychological treatment can be of great help. Infantile eczema also belongs in this category, but in most patients it disappears as the child grows up.

Impetigo is an infectious skin disease caused primarily by the Streptococcus, but later often infected with staphylococci. It usually occurs on the face, and takes the form of blisters filled with pus on a red base; when the blisters burst their place is taken by yellow crusts. Impetigo is very infectious and easily spread by the fingers, dirty towels, or cloths; therefore, one of the first necessities is to prevent infection of others or reinfection of oneself by avoiding scratching and using a different towel each day, which must on no account be used by anyone else. Treatment is simple with an antibacterial ointment, so the main issue is prevention of contamination.

Urticaria or *Nettlerash* is a familiar skin disease in which itching weals appear on the skin, usually for no obvious reason. It is not infectious, and can be caused by nervous stress, certain drugs, allergy to some foods, or even exposure of the skin to cold. In some people it is possible to write on the skin with a fingernail: the "writing" appears in the form of weals. This is known as *dermographism*; it occurs in many normal persons as well as in many patients with urticaria. The antihistamine drugs are the most useful in the treatment of urticaria. Urticarial swelling of the tongue or throat requires urgent medical attention.

Acne, or "*Blackheads*," is a condition found on the face and shoulders; its appearance is so familiar that no description is necessary. Acne is one of those conditions which is the end result of many factors. There is, first, a greasy skin, the result of glandular upset (which is why the disease usually occurs in adolescence); secondly, there is infection of the skin; and thirdly, there is blockage of the sebaceous ducts, which ordinarily allow the grease from the skin to pass out on to the surface. Since the condition starts with excess secretion of grease, ointments should never be used, and probably the best applications are drying lotions containing some sulphur preparation which inhibits secretion of grease. The face should be frequently washed, and it is possible now to obtain detergent solutions which are both antiseptic and prevent grease formation. In severe cases ultraviolet ray treatment may be necessary. Advances are presently being made in the case of vitamin A in treating acne, but great care must be taken to avoid overdosage with this poisonous substance.

Rosacea. As has already been implied elsewhere, although the wages of sin may be extremely unpleasant, the wages of extreme virtue may be no less troublesome. Thus *rosacea*, in which the nose and cheeks become red and greasy and the skin coarsened, occurs alike to chronic alcoholics and elderly ladies with no vices other than a preference for strong tea. Both cases are associated with indigestion, since, regrettable as it may seem, strong tea and alcohol are about equally liable to cause the gastritis which may be at the root of this complaint. However, in many patients the chronic flushing is caused in other ways and psychological factors are important.

Lichen Planus is one of the numerous skin diseases which seem to be due to nervous states of tension. It may occur on any part of the body, but is most common on the front of the forearms and legs. The rash takes the form of nodules which are lilac in colour and have a dent on the top; when these disappear a stain is left behind. There is severe itching. Treatment is a matter for a doctor, as it also is in the case of *psoriasis*, a very common disease of largely unknown origin, which is extremely resistant to treatment. It tends to run in families. It takes the form of slightly raised papules, usually on the elbows and knees; typically the papules are covered with dry, silvery-looking scales. Apart from the rash, the patient is usually in perfectly good health and there is no itching. Many drugs have been used in psoriasis, notably chrysarobin, and while it is not difficult to cause the rash (which may occur anywhere on the body) to disappear in one area or even in all areas for a time it has a strong tendency to return.

Warts, or *Verrucae* are familiar enough. They are caused by a virus, and are, theoretically at least, contagious (although having removed many warts, the writer has never found them contagious). Most frequently they are found on the hands, but may occur elsewhere. Treatment is best carried out by a doctor, who will use a cautery, a caustic carbon dioxide frozen into "snow." A curious feature of the common wart is that it can sometimes be caused to disappear by suggestion, which is presumably why so many old wives charms are not necessarily without effect. Different altogether from the common wart is the *plantar wart*, which occurs on the soles of the feet and often causes a good deal of discomfort. It is best dealt with by a chiropodist or in bad cases by a skin specialist since it is highly infectious.

Ichthyosis is a disorder of skin formation with which some unfortunate people are born. The oil and sweat-producing glands do not function well and the skin is dry and scaly like the skin of a fish. It is, however, possible to help the condition, which does not affect the general health, by frequent alkaline baths to wash off the scales, and the subsequent use of lanolin to replace the lacking oil. Large doses of vitamin A seem to help in some cases, and there have been reports in the medical press of cases being helped by hypnosis; this, however, is very much a matter for speculation.

Cancer, Rodent Ulcer, and Cysts. Cancer of the skin occurs mostly in old people, and takes the form of what is described as an *epithelioma*. It is most common on the face or hands, and usually appears as a nodule which breaks down and produces an ulcer. The glands may later be affected, but such cancers can almost invariably be cured unless a considerable time has elapsed during which they have been neglected. Epitheliomas are much more common in persons over-exposed to the ultraviolet in sunlight, and there is great worry that their frequency will increase as the ozone layer of the atmosphere becomes more depleted. Great care should be taken in direct sunlight, especially when sunbathing. *Rodent ulcer* is a form of ulcer which appears on the inner corner of the eye or the side of the nose in old people. It does not spread over the body, but acts by eating into the tissues in the area where it has started. X-ray or operation is necessary, but the outlook is good. *Cysts* on the skin are due to blockage of the sebaceous glands. They may become very large, and are best removed, as they may become infected. They do not turn into cancer, and there is no such thing as "male" and "female" cysts. It does sometimes happen that *moles*, especially of the bluish-black type, may become malignant, forming a cancer called a malignant melanoma. This is a fast growing and extremely dangerous cancer, though cure rates after early treatment are good. Any change in size or shape of any mole must be shown to your doctor immediately.

Skin Grafts.

These are a very complex subject which can be only briefly discussed here. They are used basically for a number of conditions in which large areas of skin have been removed from the body, as in burns or serious accidents. In other cases, as in plastic surgery, grafts may be used to make a new nose, eyelids, and so on. The following are the main types:

Pinch Grafts are small, circular pieces of skin cut from some other part of the body. (The former method of using grafts from another person has been given up almost completely, since such grafts—except in the case of identical twins—never "take.") The small pieces are laid on the area without skin and gradually grow together. *Split-thickness grafts* are grafts removed from another part of the body by an instrument known as a dermatome, which cuts sections about 10 by 20 cm. containing part of the deep layers of the skin.

In *Full-thickness Grafts*, on the other hand, the whole thickness of the skin is removed from elsewhere and applied to an area which has to bear friction or heavy weights, such as the hand or the foot. Lastly, and this is largely used in plastic surgery, there is the *pedicle graft*, which, unfortunately although it is certainly the most exciting type, is rather difficult to describe. Briefly, if one, for example, wants to make a new nose, one cuts an area of skin and underlying fat about 5 cm wide and 12·5-15 cm long in the abdomen. One end, however, remains attached so that it gets adequate blood supply. The problem is how to get this tissue to the nose, and this is done by a complicated process of leap-frog. First, the free end of the graft is attached to the forearm, whilst its "root" remains in the original site, and when it begins to grow and get its blood supply from the arm, the original "root" is cut. So we now have a "sausage" of tissue attached to the arm. The arm is then lifted to the face and kept firmly in position there until the new free part becomes attached. It is then detached from the arm, modelled to the correct shape, and grows where the nose used to be!

THE JOINTS.

Rheumatism is a word most doctors wish did not exist. This is partly because they do not understand it, but mainly because it is a condition which strictly does not exist: which is small comfort to the many millions of people who are more or less totally incapacitated by it. The truth is it is used for a hotch-potch of very real diseases, in all of which there is pain and stiffness of what is called the musculo-skeletal system, i.e., the muscles and the joints. It may mainly involve the joints, in which case it should be called arthritis; or it may involve other structures near the joints like tendons, muscles and fibrous tissue. Joints may either suffer from inflammation or degeneration or both, and the trouble may be acute or chronic or both; so it is easy to see what a mix-up the subject becomes, especially when we must include the joints of the spine as well as the limbs, feet and hands.

A good deal of arthritis used to be due to various germs, but these types are much less common now that the infections causing them have become rarer or better treated. They used to include gonorrhoea, tuberculosis, septic joints, syphilis, brucellosis, typhoid fever, dysentery and so on. The importance of *rheumatic fever*, which is a reaction to an infection (streptococcal sore throat) rather than being actually caused by the Streptococcus, is not because it involves the joints. This arthritis quickly clears up, but there may also be disease of the heart which may be serious and has been described on **P27**.

Rheumatoid arthritis is a completely different condition in which there is non-infective inflammation of connective tissues throughout the body. In the joints, the normally smooth, lubricated synovial membrane lining the joint cavity becomes scarred, leading to distortion, especially of smaller joints like those of the hand. Another characteristic feature is its capacity to vary in severity from time to time, with a strong tendency to unexplainable periods when it gets better or worse. This makes it extremely difficult to know whether any form of treatment is being useful, since any response may have occurred in any case. As in all diseases which behave like this, especially those in which medical men are also baffled, there are almost as many theories and treatments as there are doctors. It has never been satisfactorily shown to be caused by infection, faulty nutrition, "glands," emotions or personality disturbance, nor is it convincingly inherited. The best current theory links it with an increased sensitivity reaction, perhaps to the body's own tissues, known as "autoimmunity." From the patient's point of view there is swelling and deformity of the joints with tenderness on pressure and pain on movement. Treatment involves a lengthy and complicated regime of rest, relief of pain with anti-inflammatory drugs such as aspirin, exercises and the application of heat, with attention to general physical and mental health. At some stage adrenal corticosteroids (cortisone and its derivatives) are often tried, but although these can give great relief they have to be very carefully used to avoid very unpleasant side-effects.

Osteoarthritis is another completely different condition closely related to the normal processes of ageing. Therefore it occurs in older people and tends to be in larger, weight-bearing joints of the spine, hips and knees rather than in the hand; although the end joint of the fingers is commonly affected. Hard wear and tear, especially that caused by overweight, or injury may be the beginning of it. It is *not* due to diet, and dieting has no part in treatment except in those who need to slim. Physiotherapy, including heat, is helpful. It is not such a relentless condition as rheumatoid arthritis and patients should be reassured about this.

Osteoporosis is a reduction in bone density without change in the chemical composition of bone, and has many causes including hormone imbalance, poor diet, age and long use of corticosteroid medicines. Hormone replacement therapy after the menopause is partly to prevent osteoporosis. Treatment is difficult, and it is better to avoid the condition by eating well and exercising regularly.

Fibrositis and other vague forms of "rheumatism" are very often manifestations of psychological problems. This does not make them any less real, but it directs treatment towards the mental state rather than to the joints and muscles.

EYES, EARS, NOSE AND THROAT.

Diseases of the *eyes* are very specialised and only very general information can be given here. The most common is inflammation of the conjunctiva causing redness and usually due to infection or some irritant substance or dust. If it persists and leads to hard crusts of yellow pus on waking in the morning, get it seen by a doctor for treatment probably with antibiotics. First-aiders are usually instructed how to remove small particles of grit from under the lids. It is important that these should not scratch the front of the eye—your window on the world—as this may lead to scarring and poor vision. So, above all, do not rub them in. Also, if you are fishing one out of someone else's eye, see it before removing it. Do not have a general sweep round in vague hopes of finding it. If in any doubts, obtain skilled help. Remember the eyes are part of the brain: the only visible part. Perhaps this is why people's eyes are so revealing.

Conditions such as glaucoma, cataract and disorders of vision are beyond the scope of this section.

Foreign bodies in the ears and nose are a constant minor problem with children. In these cases, whether they be peas, beads or peanuts, do *not* attempt to fish them out. They are doing no harm where they are, provided the child can be prevented from fiddling with them. Get him to a doctor who knows far better than you do about the delicate structures of the ear drum or the internal nose just behind the object, and has the proper gadget to get it out.

Sore throats are a nuisance we all have to put up with from time to time. If they last more than a few days they should be treated professionally. Persistent or recurrent sore throats are often due to over-eager treatment with antibiotics not allowing the body to learn how to fight the germs itself. Never prescribe antibiotics for yourself, especially in lozenge form, and only expect your doctor to give them when other measures have failed.

Tonsils and their inflammation may be a problem. It is comparatively rarely that they should be removed, yet every year hundreds of thousands of innocent children are subjected to this ritual cruelty to satisfy the misconceptions of their parents and the greed (or ignorance) of some surgeons. Of course there are many children who benefit so much from having tonsils out that the operation (which has real dangers) is worth doing. But please allow your doctor to decide if it is necessary, and do not pressurise him into recommending it. (The same is true of *circumcision*, for which there are no hygienic, and few medical indications. If your reasons for inflicting this cruel assault on your little boy are religious or emotional, then please admit it: but do not pretend it is "necessary" or even medically helpful.)

DISEASES OF WOMEN.

The *internal sexual organs* of a woman, like the urinary system, can best be described as shaped like a capital Y. At the tips of the arms of the Y are the female sex glands, the ovaries: the two arms running downwards are the Fallopian tubes: the point where the arms meet is the womb or uterus: the single leg of the Y is the vagina. These are the *primary sexual organs* of a woman and they undergo regular cyclical changes in response to the control exercised over them by the pituitary gland, situated in the base of the skull. This control is mediated by chemical messengers (hormones) secreted into the circulation. The ovaries also secrete hormones, oestrogen, and progesterone, and a delicate hormonal balance is maintained between the pituitary gland and the ovaries. Each month an egg cell (ovum) matures and is released from the ovary, usually midway between two menstrual periods: the ovum is wafted along the Fallopian tubes by waves of contraction and if fertilised embeds in the lining of the uterus which has been conditioned to nourish it by the ovarian hormones. If it is not fertilised the ovum escapes from the uterus, altered hormone levels then cause the lining of the uterus to be shed (this is menstruation), usually about 14 days after ovulation. After menstruation a new cycle begins; another ovum matures and a fresh lining grows in the uterus. These cyclical changes recur from puberty to the menopause. Menstruation does not occur during pregnancy, of which a missed period is often the first sign. However, women do miss periods even though they are not pregnant, and this usually means that some minor and temporary change has occurred in the hormone balance. If three consecutive periods are missed it is wise to consult a doctor.

The *breasts* are called *secondary sexual organs* and are also under the influence of the ovarian hormones. Two conditions which need treatment are *mastitis* and *cancer of the breast*, both of which are characterised by lumps within the breast tissue. Mastitis may be uncomfortable but is not dangerous and can be treated medically, whereas cancer is more serious. The distinction between mastitis and cancer can only be made by a doctor and any woman who discovers a lump in her breast must seek medical aid *at once*.

Abscesses also occur in the breast, nearly always when the mother is feeding her child. Here again, a lump appears, the breast becomes red and very tender, and the woman may be feverish. Treatment with antibiotics is sometimes successful, especially if the mother consults her doctor quickly, otherwise treatment is by a small operation.

The Ovaries. The two commonest diseases of the ovaries are cysts and disorders arising from hormonal imbalance. The symptoms of ovarian disease are usually abdominal or low back pains, and heavy and painful loss during the periods, which may become irregular. These signs should be taken as a warning to consult a doctor.

The Fallopian Tubes. Infection of the Fallopian tubes is called salpingitis. The membrane lining the tubes is continuous with the lining of the uterus, hence an infection is rarely confined to a circumscribed area in either the tubes or the uterus, and pelvic inflammatory disease is a better name for this condition. Pelvic inflammatory disease often follows an abortion, or childbirth where part of the afterbirth (placenta) has been retained, or can spread from an infection in a nearby organ, for example the appendix. Infection is sometimes conveyed by the blood from another septic source in the body. The gonococcus is another cause of infection. The disease is characterised by pain and tenderness in the lower part of the abdomen, accompanied by fever, general malaise and frequently (but not invariably) a vaginal discharge. The treatment of pelvic inflammatory disease is usually medical and is the same irrespective of the primary site of infection. Before the introduction of antibiotics the disease often became chronic and the Fallopian tubes were frequently blocked by a cicatrising scar, a cause of subsequent sterility.

The Uterus. This is a hollow muscular organ and both its musculature and its lining membrane can be the site of disease. *Fibroids* are non-malignant muscular tumours which develop in many women. The main symptom is a heavy menstrual loss and surgical removal of the uterus (hysterectomy) is often necessary. This can be a major operation, but trans-vaginal hysterectomy, which does not involve opening the abdomen, has made this operation much less daunting. Hysterectomy does not impair sexual pleasure, but no more babies can be conceived. Infection of the lining of the uterus is usually part of a generalised pelvic inflammatory disease (*see* Fallopian tubes).

Cancer of the Uterus and Cervical Smears. The uterus is pear-shaped and consists of a body and neck. The wide end is uppermost (the body) and the narrow neck (cervix) projects into the top of the vagina. Cancer of the cervix is commonest in middle-aged women who have married young and have had a large family; cancer of the body of the uterus usually occurs after the menopause and is more common in nulliparous women. The symptoms are variable and it is sufficient to emphasise that any woman who has unexpected bleeding, especially after intercourse, whether her periods have stopped or not, *must* see her doctor at once. The treatment depends on individual circumstances, but is usually by operation. It is now possible to detect cancer of the cervix long before symptoms develop and at a stage when the disease can be eradicated by a relatively small operation. This early detection has been made possible by the development of exfoliative cytology. Cells taken from the cervix (without discomfort to the woman) are examined under a microscope. This test is popularly known as the "cancer test" or "cervical smear." A cervical smear is often taken as part of the routine gynaecological examination by consultants, general practitioners, and family planning doctors, and a nationwide screening programme is now in force. It is a big step forward in preventive medicine and may ultimately solve the problem of cancer of the cervix. Every woman between the ages of 25 and 60 should have the test done at least once every 5 years.

Prolapse means a sagging down of the uterus into the vagina and the cervix may even appear at the outside. It is a result of frequent childbirth and laxness of the ligaments which support the uterus: weakness of the vaginal walls often occurs at the same time. The symptoms of uterine prolapse are low back pain and a heavy dragging feeling in the lower abdomen: these are often overshadowed by the distressingly embarrassing incontinence which results from lax vaginal walls. The stress of only a sneeze, a cough, or a giggle often causes the involuntary escape of urine. The cure is operative and very rewarding.

Dysmenorrhoea or pain with the periods, is very common and most women experience this symptom at some time or another. Very often a girl's first periods are troublesome, but dysmenorrhoea develops after a year or two: this suggests that a psychological element is involved. Dysmenorrhoea is a symptom which has many varying causes, and the sensible thing to do, if pain is troublesome, is to see a doctor.

Amenorrhoea means stopping of the periods in a young woman. It may signify pregnancy or glandular disease or it can be purely psychological and generally occurs in girls with anorexia.

Abortion means the death and expulsion of a foetus before the 28th week of pregnancy. Abortion may happen spontaneously (*i.e.* naturally) or be deliberately induced. If deliberate, it may be legal or illegal (although a woman who aborts herself commits no offence) and the Abortion Act 1967 defines those conditions in which abortion is legal. The two main symptoms of abortion are bleeding and abdominal pain. Any bleeding occurring during pregnancy ought to be reported at once. Pain starts in the back and lower abdomen and is usually spasmodic in character, and like colic it works up to a peak and then temporarily passes off. Any pregnant woman with pain and bleeding should go to bed at once and send for her doctor. When doctors are convinced that a pregnancy should be terminated then an abortion by surgical means may be performed in hospital.

FAMILY PLANNING

The Family Planning Service.

In Britain a service of *free* family planning advice and supplies is in operation, that is, *free* to the consumer. The service is the responsibility of the Department of Health and Social Security which delegates its running mainly to Area Health Authorities and Family Doctors. The service is available to men and women irrespective of age, marital status and nationality.

Sources of the Service.

1. *Area Health Authorities:* provide Family Planning Clinics in local Health Centres and sometimes in other buildings—*e.g.*, those taken over from the Family Planning Association. Some require an appointment but others provide a "walkin" service at certain specified times.
2. *Family Doctors:* 90% of doctors in the Health Service primary care sector (GPs) have contracted to supply family planning to women *either* (*a*) just for their own patients *or* (*b*) for any woman who wishes to consult them. This service may be either (i) methods excluding the intrauterine device ("IUCD" or "coil") or (ii) methods including the provison of IUCDs.
3. *Hospitals:* supply the service mainly
   (*a*) for the patients of that hospital referred from other departments and
   (*b*) for patients referred to their family planning clinics by the patients' own doctors (usually for IUCDs).
4. *Private Sector:*
   1. The Family Planning Association still provides clinics in some areas, including some special vasectomy clinics.
   2. Brook Advisory Centres operate in certain places and tend to specialise in advising the young.
   3. The Marie Stopes Clinic is in London (and advertises in the press).
   4. The British Pregnancy Advisory Service provides a pregnancy advisory service in some areas.
   5. Some Family Practitioners undertake vasectomies.
   6. Some hospital consultant surgeons do private vasectomies, female sterilisations and reversals of sterilisation operations.

How to find out about the Service.

Anyone wishing to use the service can obtain the

address of a clinic or a family doctor from any one of a number of sources.

1. *The Citizens Advice Bureau:* the address is in the telephone directory.
2. *The telephone directory:* Area Health Authority clinics are usually under the heading Health and subheading Clinic for each Health Authority. Private clinics will be under their own names.
3. *Area Health Authorities:* (H.Q. telephone number usually in Directory) Health Centres; Health Visitors; Nurses; Midwives; Family Doctors;* Any clinic (baby, dental etc.)
4. *Family doctors' surgeries.*
5. *School nurses, school teachers, school counsellors.*
6. *Social workers.*

N.B. If a person goes to a family doctor she may be required to sign a form to the effect that the doctor has undertaken to provide her with contraception for the following 12 months. This is not binding on her and if for any reason she is unable to return to that doctor, or does not wish to, she may still obtain help elsewhere, *e.g.*, at a clinic or from another doctor. The patient has the choice.
    At most, but not all, family planning clinics an appointment system operates.

* The list of Family Doctors issued by the Family Practitioners Committees is available in Public Libraries and Post Offices. Doctors in the list who offer Family Planning Services have "C" or "C +" after their names.

METHODS OF FAMILY PLANNING

Methods Used by the Woman.

"The pill" ("combined oral contraceptive pill").

This consists of two female type hormones, oestrogen (usually pronounced as if the first "o" were another "e", that is eestrogen), and progestogen.

Preparations:

Many different combinations of these two hormones are marketed. Nowadays most formulae contain 30–50 units (micrograms) of oestrogen, whereas twelve years ago most contained 100 units. Even the amount of progestogen has been reduced to the bare minimum which is effective. Most pills have the same amount of hormone throughout the course but some recently produced pills have differing amounts of progestogen during the course, giving the lowest total amount of hormone per month.

Mode of action:

The pill works by stopping the egg cell from being shed from the ovary, and if no egg cell is shed, no fertilisation can take place. They are thus virtually 100% effective as a contraceptive, the tiny proportion of failure which occurs being almost invariably due to human error, *e.g.*, forgetting to take the pill.

The menstrual cycle.

Some people may like to have a more detailed description of the way in which the pill affects the normal menstrual cycle.
    The menstrual cycle begins thus: A tiny part of the base of the brain (the *hypothalamus*) sends out a hormone called releasing factor (R.F.), which stimulates the pituitary gland to release a hormone called follicle stimulating hormone (F.S.H.). This in turn stimulates a group of folicles or egg sacs in the ovary. Each egg sac is a small fluid-filled bubble lined with special cells and containing an immature egg cell. The lining cells are stimulated to produce oestrogen and more and more of this accumulates in the blood stream. Eventually by "negative feedback" the oestrogen causes the pituitary gland to decrease the production of F.S.H. (*i.e.* high level of oestrogen → low level F.S.H.), and by "positive feedback" causes the pituitary gland to produce a sudden surge of another hormone called luteinising hormone, L.H. (*i.e.*, high level oestrogen → high level of L.H.). This L.H. causes the largest egg sac bubble to burst, releasing the egg cell, which is caught by the fringe at the free end of the uterine tube and wafted down the tube into the uterus,

during which time it can be fertilised. Meanwhile the burst bubble in the ovary turns yellow and is called the "yellow body" (or *corpus luteum*). This produces both oestrogen and another hormone progesterone which are both vital for the continuation and promotion of any pregnancy. If no pregnancy occurs the yellow body collapses after 14 days, the lining of the uterus is shed in menstruation, the level of oestrogen (and progesterone) in the blood drops, and this causes the pituitary gland to step up the output of F.S.H. again.

The combined pill consists of oestrogen and progestogen, similar to those hormones produced by the "yellow body". These act on the pituitary gland as they would in a pregnancy and prevent the release of F.S.H. and L.H., so that egg cells are neither prepared nor released. Thus, taking the pill is in some ways like being constantly pregnant, which until the present century was probably the most natural and likely way for a woman in the fertile age group to be.

Method of taking the pill.

A woman starts to take the pill initially on the 1st day of a normal period, or on the 5th day of a normal period, depending on the particular pill. If she starts on the first day, she is protected from risk of pregnancy immediately. If she starts on the fifth day she is not protected until she has taken 14 pills. The pill is taken for 21 days followed by a rest interval of 7 days and this pattern is repeated indefinitely. The pills are provided in packets of 21. (There is one pill which is supplied in packs of 22 and a rest interval of only 6 days is required.) During the seven days without the pill the "pill period" comes. This is not a true period, but is simply due to stopping the pill, when such lining of the womb as has been allowed to form, is shed.

Protection from pregnancy is maintained unless:

she is more than 4–12 hours late in taking a pill (depending on the pill dosage)
she misses a pill
she has diarrhoea or vomiting so that the pill is lost before it can be absorbed.

If protection is lost she should continue to take the pills in the ordinary way but use other contraceptives, *e.g.*, the sheath, as well until the end of that packet of pills.

A few pills are put up in packets with 7 inactive tablets as well as 21 active tablets, so that a pill is taken every day. These are useful for people who find the "on–off" regime difficult to remember.

Other drugs and the pill.

A few drugs hasten the breakdown of the pill in the body and so make it less effective. Such drugs include some of those used to treat epilepsy and some, but not by any means all, antibiotics, some drugs for treating rheumatism and one or two other drugs more rarely used. Conversely, the pill is suspected of making some other drugs less effective, for example some drugs for treating depression. It is always advisable for a woman to remind any doctor who is prescribing for her that she is taking the pill.

The pill is the commonest method of birth control being used in Britain. 28% of the 11 million women in the fertile age group 15–44 use it, according to the Family Planning Association estimate 1979. In the under-30 age group, recent estimates are that about 70% are using it. In spite of the fact that the pill affects in some degree, usually slight or moderate, much body chemistry and therefore many body systems, rather as pregnancy does, most people feel no different on the pill.

Pill problems and side-effects

Connected with "pill period".

Occasionally slight bleeding happens during the days when pills are being taken, particularly when a woman first starts to take the pill. If it is very slight it is called "spotting", if rather heavier, *i.e.*, necessitating the wearing of some sort of protection, it is referred to as "breakthrough bleeding". If this is in the first month or two of pill-taking it usually settles down spontaneously. If later on, a change of pill may be indicated. It can be due to erratic pill-taking, *i.e.*, being late taking a pill, or forgetting to take a pill, or it can be caused by having to take one of a very few other drugs which have the effect of hastening the breakdown of the pill in the body so that it does not have time to be effective. It is best to consult your doctor if bleeding happens, particularly if it happens when drug treatment is given. To be absolutely safe in those circumstances it is wise to use other contraceptives, *e.g.*, sheaths, as well until the end of that packet of pills.

Other side effects.

Occasionally, and usually in the early weeks of pill-taking, other side effects are experienced such as nausea, breast tenderness, headaches or weight gain. If these are troublesome and do not settle the pill may have to be changed or even, rarely, stopped. Some symptoms such as depression, general leg aches, and decreased interest in sex, are more doubtfully attributable to the pill and may have some quite other cause, but all these problems should be discussed with the doctor.

Headaches: Migraine headaches are usually one-sided, often associated with feeling sick or with actual vomiting and sometimes with disturbances of vision. Sometimes these headaches seem to improve when a woman takes the pill, but more often they seem to become more frequent. Sometimes they come only in the pill-free week. Often a change to a pill with a lower dose of oestrogen, or even to a progestogen-only pill, will eliminate such headaches.

It is advisable to stop taking the pill if

(a) *migraine occurs for the first time* when the pill is taken or
(b) migraine becomes "focal".

By "focal" is meant that other localised symptoms are experienced such as attacks of tingling or weakness on one side of the body, brief episodes of difficulty in speaking or visual disturbances such as transient loss of part of the field of vision. This might be a sign of a brief loss of blood supply to a part of the brain and a warning of the danger of stroke.

Headaches other than migraine: these are of course not uncommon in women who are not taking the pill. They are not uncommon in men. If they should increase when the pill is taken then changing the pill to one with a lower dose of oestrogen, or with a different progestogen (or even to one containing progestogen only) will help.

Blood pressure: In most women the blood pressure rises very slightly on the pill. In a few, it rises to above the normal level. Having a blood pressure higher than normal over a period of time renders a person more liable to diseases of the circulation. Fortunately the blood pressure is easy to monitor regularly.

Blood clotting: Blood clotting is a normal function of the body and is the body's way of sealing a cut or otherwise injured blood vessel. In women who take the pill various factors which influence blood clotting both in the blood itself and in the blood vessel wall, are altered, so that although the blood is slightly more liable to clot, the clot is more liable to be dissolved. The net result is still a slightly increased tendency to blood clotting (thrombosis).

Blood clotting or thrombosis can occur in a vein, or in an artery.

In a vein: It can extremely rarely occur in a normal vein in a person who is not taking the pill. It is only about four times more likely (or four times less unlikely) in a person taking the pill. If it occurs, it is usually in the deep veins of the leg, mainly because blood flow tends to be slowest there. It usually causes relatively little localised damage but very occasionally a piece of the blood clot can break off and be swept in the blood stream through the heart and into the lungs where it can block a blood vessel and even occasionally prove fatal.

N.B. Moderate varicose veins with no evidence of any past thrombosis are not reasons for not taking the pill.

In an artery (thrombosis) is due to the fact that "hardening of the arteries" (atherosclerosis) affects almost everyone and in the developed world has usually begun by the age of 20. Roughened patches on the artery wall allow blood clots to form on them and occasionally to block them. The pill slightly increases the risk of this happening, again by about 4–5 times. Other factors which more strongly increase the likelihood of this happening are smoking, which at less than 15 cigarettes/day increases the risk by 5 times and at more than 20 cigarettes/day increases the risk by 10 times,

increasing age, particularly the age of 35 years and older,

high blood pressure and

abnormal blood fats. A few people have these from birth, but this is a disorder which runs in families and can be detected by a blood test.

Clotting in an artery of the heart muscle is called coronary thrombosis. Clotting in an artery of the brain, and bleeding from an artery of the brain, which can result from a weak patch in a blood vessel and/or high blood pressure, are known as cerebral thrombosis or a stroke.

In October 1983 the results of one American and one British study of cancer among women using oral contraceptives were published in the medical press. The first of these appeared to suggest that long-term use of certain types of pill by younger women (under 25) may be associated with an increased risk of breast cancer; other previously published studies had shown no such connection. The British study showed that a group of women who had chosen to take a combined oral contraceptive had an increased incidence of cancer of the neck of the womb (cervical cancer) in comparison with a similar group of women who had elected to use intra-uterine contraceptive devices (*e.g.*, the coil). Both studies suggested that the progestogen content of mixed pills could be implicated. All the women in the pill group who had been found to have invasive cervical cancer were treated effectively.

The Committee on Safety of Medicines considered both these studies very carefully and concluded that women should be prescribed pills which had the lowest progestogen content but that there was no need for any woman to make an immediate change. Furthermore, the Committee endorsed the British study authors' recommendation that all long-term users of oral contraceptives should have regular cervical cytology examinations ("smears"). Of course, your family or clinic doctor will have all the Committee of Safety of Medicine's information and will know which pill to recommend.

Helpful side effects: the pill almost always prevents period pains. It also frequently reduces the unpleasant effects of "premenstrual tension" which some women experience, including feelings of depression, irritability and tenseness.

The Progestogen-only pill.

This pill, as its name implies, contains only one hormone, progestogen. It is sometimes called the mini-pill but as this name is also occasionally used for very low dose combined pills, it will be better to call it the progestogen-only pill, or P-O-P.

Until the past year or two this pill was used mainly by women who were breast feeding as it is 98 per cent effective as a contraceptive, but does not diminish the milk flow. A very small amount of the hormone does get into the milk; it is not known whether this can affect the baby but it is thought that it does not.

Recently the P-O-P is being more widely used, particularly by women over the age of 35, and also by younger women. It is probably the next most effective method of birth control to the combined pill, having a failure rate of rather less than 2 pregnancies among 100 women taking it for a year.

Mode of action: The P-O-P works mainly by making the secretion from the neck of the womb (the cervix) scanty and thick so that the sperms do not get through. The pill does not as a rule stop the egg cell from being shed, so that the periods which come are natural periods, though they may be lighter than usual because the pill does make the lining of the uterus thinner and less suitable for a fertilised egg cell to settle in. It also probably slows down the transporting of the egg cell in the uterine tubes by diminishing the waves of movement in them which normally help to get the egg cell into the uterus.

Side effects: There are two slight risks with the P-O-P. One is the slight risk of unwanted pregnancy. The other is the risk of the nuisance of irregular bleeding.

The irregular bleeding may take the form of more frequent, usually slight, bleeding or less frequent bleeding. Sometimes the periods cease altogether, or become extremely infrequent. This means that the very small amount of hormone in the pill is having a similar effect on the pituitary gland to that of the combined pill, so that it does not stimulate egg release in the ovaries. Provided it is ascertained that the pill-taker is not pregnant, the contraceptive effect is excellent in these people, and probably because the dose of hormone is so small the pituitary gland seems to recover its normal functions very rapidly when this pill is stopped. In general tests have shown that the P-O-P has far less effect on body chemistry than has the combined pill. Blood clotting and blood pressure seem to be little affected.

Method of taking the P-O-P.

The P-O-P is taken continuously and without breaks. Starting on the first day of a period it is taken every day. Because the effect on the secretion from the neck of the womb is greatest for the first six hours after taking it, it is advisable for it to be taken about six or seven o'clock in the evening, so that protection is high at bed time when intercourse is most likely. Because the effect rapidly declines after 24 hours it should be taken at the same time every day and not more than 2 hours late, otherwise the protection is broken. It takes about 2 weeks for the protection to build up initially, and the same after any break in protection due, for example, to being late taking a pill, missing a pill or pills or having a stomach upset.

The Coil or Intra Uterine Contraceptive Device (I.U.C.D.).

Coils are devices which are inserted into the uterus and remain there until a pregnancy is desired. All are made of plastic, some have very fine copper wire wound round them to increase their effectiveness. They are all highly effective, having a failure rate of about 2 pregnancies per 100 women using it for a year.

Various shapes of coils are used. The copper wire covered ones are the Copper 7, Gravgard, the Copper 1 and the Multiload. The plastic only ones are the Lippes loop and the Saf-T coil.

Each device has a thread attached to it which passes through the neck of the womb into the vagina. This can be pulled by the doctor when the coil is to be removed. A woman should never try to remove her coil herself.

The mode of action is not entirely clear, but the coil seems to prevent the fertilised egg cell from embedding in the uterus.

The method is generally considered to be more suitable for women who have had a baby than for those who have not, because in the latter the very slight risk of an infection ensuing is 7 times greater. An infection could occasionally, if untreated, proceed to involve the uterine tubes, even rarely sealing them. A woman fitted with a coil not infrequently has slightly longer and heavier and occasionally more painful periods than were usual for her.

The coil is used by about 5% of the 11 million women in the fertile age group 15–44.

The Cap or Diaphragm.

The cap or diaphragm is a circle of soft rubber with a firm rim which is inserted by the woman into the vagina so that it covers the neck of the womb (the cervix) and so physically prevents sperms from entering it. It is always used with a sperm-killing jelly or cream. There are a few different shapes of cap. Most are flat, but some are variations on a thimble shape and fit closely over the cervix. One of these is also made in plastic and can be used by a person who is allergic to rubber. The suitable cap size has to be estimated and the cap first fitted by a doctor (or nurse).

Method of use:

The cap can be put in anything up to 3 hours before intercourse, or longer if more sperm-killing preparation (spermicide) is inserted. The cap should be left in for 6–8 hours after intercourse, and if this happens again before 6 hours have elapsed, more spermicide is inserted and the cap is left in for a further 6 hours. It is then removed, washed with soft soap and water and stored in its box.

The cap has the advantage of being absolutely harmless to health. It does not affect the periods or the body systems or chemistry in any way.

It is slightly less effective than either pill or coil. The failure rate has been estimated variously as 2–8 per 100 women using it for a year, probably varying with the conscientiousness of the user.

It is used by about 3% of women in the fertile age group.

Method Used by the Man.

The sheath (or condom or French letter or "Durex"). The sheath is made of very fine rubber, nowadays almost always including a lubricant and usually including a spermicide. Most have a teat-shaped end to receive the semen.

Method of use: The air should be squeezed out of the teat end before the sheath is put on so that there is room for the semen and the sheath will not burst. The sheath should then be unrolled on to the erect penis before the penis makes any contact with the woman, as there can be a drop of fluid which contains sperms and is quite sufficient to make her pregnant. The man should hold the sheath in place when he withdraws. Unless the sheath contains spermicide the woman should always use a spermicidal pessary or foam in addition.

Advantages: Sheaths are completely harmless and in fact can give some protection against sexually transmitted diseases ("V.D.") They are readily available—*free* (when *prescribed* by the doctor) from all Area Health Authority Family Planning Clinics and on payment from chemists' shops and from slot machines which are found mainly in public houses, hotels, garages and service stations and sometimes in clubs, restaurants and holiday camps.

The failure rate is variously estimated at between 0·4 and 6 per 100 couples using it for a year and can be very low if the method is conscientiously used. The method is second only to the pill in the number of people using it—25 per cent of couples where the woman is in the fertile age-group.

Natural Methods of Birth Control.

These unfortunately are not very reliable. They are all based on the woman finding out when her egg cell is shed, *i.e.*, her "ovulation time", and avoiding intercourse around that time. Sperms can live in the vagina for up to 3 days and the egg cell lives for at least 48 hours after it is shed.

There are two methods of detecting ovulation time. The *calendar method* involves the woman in recording the length of her menstrual cycle for *at least* 6 months before it can any way be relied on. The woman must make a note of the first day of bleeding of each cycle. The last day of the cycle is the day before the next onset of bleeding. The calculation of the "safe period" is made by deducting 18 from the shortest cycle and 11 from the longest. For example, with a shortest cycle of 25 days and a longest of 31 the safe period would be *before* day 7 and *after* day 20 (25 − 18 = 7; 31 − 11 = 20). If only the safe period around day 20 is used the method is considererably more reliable.

The *temperature method* is based on the fact that immediately after ovulation there is a distinct rise in body temperature which persists until the next period starts. The method involves taking the temperature first thing every morning *before* eating, drinking or smoking and plotting it on a chart each day. The safe period begins about four days *after* ovulation (as detected by the rise in temperature) and continues until the next menstrual period begins.

Other more accurate home-methods of finding the moment of ovulation are being explored, including tests on the mucus from the cervix, which becomes thin, clear and "stringy" at ovulation times; tests on vaginal enzymes; and even urine tests, but no simple test requiring no expertise is yet available.

Coitus interruptus, withdrawal or "being careful".

This should be mentioned in this section on "natural methods" because it is probably used at some time by many couples. It means that the man withdraws his penis before climax or ejaculation. This requires great will-power at the height of sexual excitation. Even if withdrawal is achieved, it may be too late. There are enough sperms in the drop of fluid which emerges from the penis in the early stages of sexual stimulation to cause a pregnancy. The method is therefore highly fallible, frustrating and often futile—akin to "shutting the stable door . . ." Although it cannot be recommended, it is a method requiring no expert help or artificial equipment, and is better than nothing. The failure rate is at least 17%.

Sterilisation.

Sterilisation of the woman. Tubal tie or tubal ligation.

This means cutting the tubes which carry the egg cells from the ovary to the uterus. Although this is not a major operation it may involve a general anaesthetic and an abdominal operation. It can now sometimes be done through a very small cut under a local anaesthetic with an instrument called a laparoscope, which can shine a light into the abdomen through a quite narrow tube. At operation the uterine tubes are cut and a piece taken out before each end is sealed. In addition the cut end nearest the uterus may also be embedded in the uterine wall to make doubly sure that the two ends do not rejoin. Sometimes the tubes are not cut but gold clips are put on to close the lumens of the tubes.

The operation must be regarded as irreversible as it is extremely rarely possible to reverse it.

Sterilisation of the man. Vasectomy.

Vasectomy means cutting the tubes which carry the sperms into the semen or seminal fluid, which is the fluid produced during intercourse.

The testicles have two functions. One is to produce sperms. The other is to produce the hormone testosterone which gives a man his maleness, for example his deep voice and his beard, and his sex drive. The hormone is carried in the blood stream. The sperms are carried in special tubes called the *vas deferens* which run under the skin of the scrotum. Thus the tubes are easily accessible to the surgeon. At operation the tube on each side is cut and a small piece is removed. This is to leave a gap to prevent the cut ends from re-uniting. The cut ends are sealed and the skin cut closed. The operation takes 15–20 minutes, can be done under general or local anaesthetic, and causes minimal discomfort afterwards. The result of the operation is that the sperms formed in the testicle do not get through to the penis. They go on being formed, but are gradually broken down again and reabsorbed by the blood stream. The sperms which are already in the *vas* beyond the cut end will still go into the seminal fluid, and it may be 3 months before they have all been ejected. A sample of fluid is usually checked about 2 months after the operation, and another 2 weeks later. There is no visible change in the fluid, only under the microscope it can be seen that there are no sperms in it. Nor is there any change in a man's virility, potency or sex drive. A man should have the operation only if he is sure he will not wish for further children. Although in some cases it may be possible to reverse the operation and give him back his fertility this can never be certain. He should be prepared to accept that it is irreversible.

DRUG ABUSE AND DRUG DEPENDENCE.

This section of earlier editions of *Pears* was simply called "Addiction." This word is still much used, but is gradually being replaced by the terms in the present title, because ideas about the nature of the problem and methods of dealing with it are changing. Addiction is a word that conjures up rather 19th century ideas in the minds of readers: opium dens, inscrutable orientals, Sherlock Holmes injecting himself with cocaine—basically a phenomenon of foreign origin, rather frightening if its implications were not literary rather than factual, and not of great significance in Great Britain.

Drug Abuse.

It is now realised by doctors, research scientists, social workers, and the police—if still not by society as a whole—that the truth is quite different. The *abuse* of drugs in this country is at present of large proportions, increasing rapidly and showing no signs of diminishing. It is responsible each year for thousands of deaths by suicide and by accidental overdosage; for an enormous but virtually unmeasurable amount of private suffering; and for the loss to society, in terms of reduced working efficiency, of millions of man-hours every year. It has nothing to do with opium smoking which was never in any case more than the eccentricity of the few. Opium is virtually unused in medicine these days, though serious problems are caused by the illegal importation and distribution of drugs such as heroin and cocaine. Nonetheless, the problems today arise chiefly from the misuse of drugs given by doctors for their effects on the central nervous system—the painkillers, sleeping pills, "stimulants," and "tranquillisers."

Drugs and Medicines.

To the doctor, any substance is a drug that can be introduced into the body from outside, and that is capable of producing some detectable effect. Most such substances have a beneficial use. They are "medicines," and as such are given by doctors in suitable cases. Others, for example, nicotine (in cigarettes), alcohol (in beer, wine, or spirits), and carbon monoxide (in coal gas), are of doubtful benefit and of certain harm and are used by doctors, if at all, only under certain very special and usually experimental conditions.

Medicines may be classified under four main headings. First, there are those like quinine, or penicillin and other so-called antibiotics, that actually cure diseases by eradicating the organism (bacteria or other parasites) that cause disturbance of normal bodily function. Second, drugs such as insulin or the steroids overcome in the unhealthy the lack of some necessary substance a healthy body manufactures for itself: they must usually continue to be given for life. Third are the drugs which relieve the signs of disease—for example, there are many new drugs that lower the blood pressure or increase the output of urine—without being able to put right the disturbed basic situation which is the cause of the trouble. Fourth are drugs to relieve the patient's symptoms—which make him feel better, less breathless, take away his pain, help him to sleep, and so on—although we seldom know why they are able to do this. Indeed, in many cases we suspect that they are acting mainly as a token of help from doctor to patient, and so encouraging his body to fight a more successful battle on its own behalf.

There is no doubt that the genuine advances in beneficial drugs during the last forty years have been enormous; but the very successes of the penicillins, tetracyclines, antimalarials, hormones, and so on have bred in the public and in the medical profession itself an attitude of uncritical wonder. There have been relatively few drugs in the first and second categories mentioned above; and in the field of mental health, the importance of which is now so rightly emphasised, there are virtually none. Yet drugs which act upon the brain are often received as if they were curative although they may pose fresh problems rather than solve the old. Thus, although there are many drugs which act upon the mind, few do this in any fundamental sense; they relieve pain and anxiety, bring sleep and lessening of stress, and may allow the patient to recuperate himself during the relief they provide. But often this deeper change does not occur—sometimes because the doctor has not clearly seen his part in helping to bring it about—and then the symptomatic relief may come to be sought for its own sake.

Dangers of Long-term Medication with Drugs acting on the Brain.

1. *Toxic effects.* Drugs which act upon the nervous system, like any others, have characteristic toxic or unwanted effects of their own

(incidentally, these may become apparent rapidly; even, on rare occasions, after only a single dose). Such effects may have little or nothing to do with the desired effects for which they are being prescribed and taken. For example, it has only come to be realised quite recently that aspirin is liable to cause bleeding, which is occasionally serious, from the lining of the stomach in a large proportion of people who take aspirin regularly; or that phenacetin, another substance very frequently present in analgesics (*i.e.*, pain relievers) that can be bought from chemists without prescription, may lead (after prolonged use) to kidney damage. Some drugs may cause rashes and other allergic reactions in susceptible subjects; and jaundice, fainting, tremors, and motor disorders are known to occur in some patients taking a variety of other drugs.

2. *"Rebound."* The body works in such a way, over a variety of its activities, that it tends to return to a "neutral" position after it has departed from this for any reason. For example, over-eating tends to be followed by a lessening of appetite, at least for a time; the runner makes up for his air-deficit during the race by breathing more deeply thereafter; and if, at rest, you breathe for a time more rapidly and deeply than you need, this period will be followed by one in which you breathe *less* often than usual until the balance is restored. These illustrations—and there are others—have nothing to do with drugs; but in a similar way, it seems that if a continued pain, or an unpleasant emotional state such as anxiety or depression is changed into its opposite, or removed altogether by the use of a drug, the prior state may return with increased force when the drug is no longer taken. The "rebound" phenomenon, naturally, encourages the patient to take another dose, and so on.

3. *Habit formation.* This alternation of mood-changed-by-drug with the disturbed mood itself leads to the habit of taking the drug. The patient comes to rely upon it and to take it anyway, even before the unpleasant state has returned. At this stage he is said to be "habituated"; he has a psychological need for the drug, and later may become disturbed at the possibility that it will not be available when he needs it. This might not matter so greatly, if it were not that continued use of drugs in this way has physical consequences as well.

4. *Tolerance and habituation.* The body also tends to restore its own balance when drugs are given, too. It "learns" surprisingly quickly how to deal with substances with which it has never before been confronted, so that it eliminates subsequent doses more and more quickly and completely. Thus the effect of each successive dose is smaller and lasts for progressively shorter periods of time. To counter this, the patient tends to increase the dose: and the vicious circle continues. At this point he has become physically dependent upon the drug: and he may suffer physically—sometimes so severely that he dies—if supplies are not continued.

As he increases the dose in this way, so his tolerance of its effects increases, to such an extent that after prolonged use he may be taking doses of a drug that are five or ten times greater than those which will kill somebody not dependent upon them in this way. It sometimes happens that a patient develops a renewed craving at some point after a course of treatment, in which the dose of drug has been reduced without removing the underlying cause of his dependence. He may then obtain and use the dose he habitually took before treatment, not knowing that his body will have lost its tolerance of such doses. That dose is now as high for him as for any other person and so may be lethal. There has been a number of deaths for this reason.

Factors in the Causation of Dependence.

The risk of becoming dependent upon a drug is governed by three main factors; the drug itself, the personality of the individual who takes it, and the circumstances in which it is taken. Most adults have taken alcohol at one time or another, unless it is against their code to do so; yet *relatively* few are dependent upon it (relatively few, but many too many; more than half a million in the United Kingdom alone). Many of us have had morphine or some other strong analgesic for medical reasons, without becoming dependent upon it (whatever so-called addicts say, it is extremely rare for anyone to become dependent on an opiate because he was introduced to it in a medical setting). On the other hand, if we start to take such a drug "for kicks"—as more and more people, particularly teen-agers and young adults are doing—it is extremely probable that we shall become dependent upon it, and sooner rather than later at that. It is also probable that each one of us would become dependent, were he obliged to take it regularly, for long enough, and in sufficient dosage. Thus, although there are personalities—psychopathic, immature, or unstable—that are more prone than others to become dependent if they are exposed to the drug, there are also drugs that are more likely than others to cause such dependence no matter to whom they are given. The extent of the dependence will vary; with some, it is never physiological but remains psychological (but not the less real or disturbing for that). Also, the rate at which dependence develops may vary; and the picture presented by the dependent subject—the extent to which his normal life is impaired, or to which he becomes dangerous to himself or others—varies as well. In a very much oversimplified way, some of these relationships will now be summarised for certain substances.

Heroin, morphine and cocaine are usually injected. Barbiturates (sleeping pills) and amphetamines ("Benzedrine") are tablets or capsules, and marihuana ("reefer," hashish) is smoked in cigarettes. Heroin and cocaine are now usually taken together. Combinations of drugs often act differently from their individual constituents, and patients dependent upon them are even more difficult to treat. Barbiturate and amphetamine, also, are often mixed (as in "purple hearts"). There is considerable *psychological* dependence on heroin, morphine, cocaine, and amphetamine, but much less with marihuana. *Physiological* dependence is great with heroin and morphine, less with barbiturates, alcohol, and amphetamine in that order, and virtually nil

with cocaine and marihuana. Personality plays a greater part in initiating dependence on alcohol, marihuana, and barbiturates than with the others. Heroin, cocaine, and morphine are the cause of more antisocial tendencies in dependent people than alcohol, barbiturates, and amphetamine. The chief danger of marihuana (mere possession of which is illegal) seems to be that the search for it will lead the searcher into localities where his risk of exposure to even more dangerous influences is greatly increased. It is thus sometimes argued that if it were legal to consume marihuana, the number of young people who yearly become dependent upon the other more dangerous drugs would in fact decrease. There is as yet no evidence for or against this proposition. The number of drug dependent people in U.K. is rising fast for heroin and cocaine. This number is very large for alcohol, and is increasing in the case of barbiturates and marihuana. Very few people are dependent on morphine, and the number is not growing.

Treatment.

Exhortations, imprisonment, and other moralistic or legalistic approaches are useless. Treatment of any person dependent upon a drug is a matter for a qualified psychotherapist. It is liable to be time-consuming and frustrating for patient and doctor, and it is frequently unsuccessful. At present, there are too few specialists or centres where treatment can be obtained, although it is to be hoped that this situation will change as the problem is increasingly seen by our society to be of exceptional gravity.

When there is little or no chance of cure, prevention is certainly the best treatment. Drugs should only be taken on the prescription of a doctor: and the patient should remind him from time to time, if this be necessary, that he would like to dispense with his drugs as soon as the doctor thinks it possible. It should also be remembered that there is often no need to reach for the aspirin (or any other drug that anyone can buy from the chemist without prescription) at the first sign of a headache—or to reach for it at all to help one sleep or relax, for which purpose such drugs are in any case pharmacologically useless. A wait for ten minutes is good discipline, and will frequently resolve the problem to an extent that makes a drug unnecessary.

PART III. SPECIAL TOPICS

THE MENOPAUSE
(HORMONE REPLACEMENT THERAPY)

The word menopause properly refers only to the discontinuation of menstrual flow. It is one manifestation of the climacteric which is a transitional phase lasting between 1 and 5 years, in which the body adjusts to the cessation of ovarian hormonal activity. It usually occurs between the ages of 47 and 51 and is governed by familial and racial factors. Periods may cease suddenly but more usually decrease gradually with occasional missed cycles. Heavy or excessive loss is never a feature of the menopause and requires investigation. Post menopausal bleeding is defined as bleeding occurring 6 months after the last period. This should be regarded as pathological and similarly warrants investigation to exclude the possibility of a polyp or tumour, although most cases have no recognisable cause.

Continued regular bleeding beyond the age of 55 is unusual and should also be investigated. On the other hand, the menopause rarely occurs before the age of 40 years and the cessation of regular bleeding or amenorrhoea occurring at this time needs assessment to exclude pregnancy or hormone secreting tumours.

Effects of the Menopause

These result largely from the loss of the hormone oestrogen.

(1) Fertility is diminished but ovulation may occur for up to two years after the last menstrual bleed and, therefore, contraception should still be continued until this time. Up to 20/30 births per

year may occur in women around the age of 50 years.

(2) Lack of oestrogen leads to atrophy or degeneration of the reproductive organs. The uterus decreases in size, the vagina tends to lose its protective bacterial flora and becomes more susceptible to infection. Discomfort, irritation and painful intercourse may result. The ligaments which support the uterus and bladder neck weaken leading to prolapse and urinary problems such as frequency and dysuria.

(3) Abdominal symptoms such as bloating, indigestion and constipation can also be troublesome. Weight gain may also occur.

(4) The loss of the protective effect of oestrogen leads to an increase in atherosclerosis and it is at this time that the incidence of cardio-vascular disease in women increases to equal that of men.

(5) Osteoporosis, or loss of bone density, leads to back problems and increased susceptibility to serious fractures such as those of the hip.

Symptoms

75% of women have some problem but less than a quarter will consult their doctor.

Hot Flushes and Emotional Changes

Hot flushes can be very debilitating, they can be brought on by excitement, alcohol or a stuffy atmosphere and may last up to 15 minutes and can occur several times a day. They cause acute embarrassment and discomfort and are often associated with profuse sweating which leads to a disturbed sleep pattern. Hot flushes may also be accompanied by cold shivers, palpitations and chest pain.

Irritability, depression, insomnia and mood changes may occur. They are often associated with loss of concentration. Women worry about their loss of femininity and feel that they are less attractive to their partner. A dry vagina, painful intercourse and unpleasant urinary symptoms can lead to severe marital problems. This period in a woman's life often coincides with worries over difficult teenage children or elderly parents and can cause considerable stress.

HRT Treatment

This initially should be directed at reassurance that sexual life has not ended and that something can be done to help. HRT (hormone replacement therapy) is by far the most effective therapy and it is now far more widely used. It should be available to all but a few women. Some authorities recommend that treatment should take place regardless of symptoms but the British National Formulary is more conservative advising treatment only when required. The reason for the change of view is that it is now known that HRT is an extremely effective therapy against the damaging effects of osteoporosis. HRT successfully combats hot flushes, improves libido and urinary symptoms and leads to a general sense of well-being.

HRT is available as calendar packs of tablets, adhesive patches or implants. Oestrogen creams can be applied vaginally to give relief from local symptoms such as atrophy and soreness. For women who have had a hysterectomy continuous oestrogen therapy will suffice. For those who still have a womb, a progesterone tablet is added for 12 days of the monthly cycle. This combination leads to a regular monthly withdrawal bleed which simulates a period. Most women find this reassuring, although to a small number it is an inconvenience. The reason for the introduction of progesterone is that it leads to the regular shedding of the lining of the womb or endometrium, which occurs as the monthly bleed. We now know that this decreases the small but recognised incidence of endometrial cancer which can occur with unopposed oestrogen therapy.

The patches can be applied to any non-hairy areas of the waist and usually last for 4–5 days. Local irritation can occur and progesterone tablets will still need to be used if the patient has an intact uterus.

The implant is placed subcutaneously in the abdominal tissue. It requires a local anaesthetic but has the advantage of lasting for up to 6 months. It is very useful for those women who have had a hysterectomy and do not wish to take tablets. However, if side effects occur it cannot be removed.

The dose of hormone used is usually extremely small, much less than the dose of the oral contraceptive pill and therefore side effects are few. HRT is, however, contra-indicated with those who have a past medical history of malignant tumour of the breast or lining of the womb (endometrial carcinoma). Active hepatitis and liver problems will also tend to preclude its use. Hypertension is not necessarily a contra-indication as long as control is good and there is regular monitoring of blood pressure. Coronary heart disease is not itself a contra-indication and the incidence may actually be lower on those who are taking long term HRT. The incidence of serious stroke may also be reduced, although it is thought that to achieve these effects, women may have to take HRT for up to 10 years or more. Many doctors will feel reluctant about prescribing where there is a history of thrombo-embolism, i.e. deep vein thrombosis or pulmonary embolus.

The most lasting benefit from HRT is a reduction in effective bone loss and there is a 50% decrease in serious osteoporotic fracture in those who have been taking HRT for 10 years. Thin women who have a history of osteoporotic fracture, family history of osteoporosis, or who have had an early menopause have the most to gain from treatment. Side effects include breast tenderness and nausea. The possible long-term risk of a slight increase in breast cancer is debatable. However, it is important that women are fully assessed and examined before treatment is initiated and that cervical smears, breast and blood pressure checks should be carried out at regular intervals. For those whose medical history makes hormone replacement therapy inadvisable, other drugs are available to alleviate the distress of hot flushes.

TRANSPLANT SURGERY

Introduction

Transplantation is the area of surgery in which organs are transplanted from one part of a person to another, from one person to another, or from an animal to a person; the implantation of artificial organs and devices is a closely related field. Transplants are required when part of the body is damaged or diseased beyond recovery. For example, severe anaemia requires transplants of blood (transfusions), renal failure requires transplantation of kidneys, and irreversible cardiac disease requires blood vessel, valve or heart transplantation, or implantation of an artificial valve or a pacemaker.

Transplants coming from the patient's own body are called *autografts*, examples of which are skin grafts used in severe burns and hair transplantation, which is essentially a cosmetic procedure. Transplants coming from the same species are called *isografts*, and include blood transfusions, and transplants of kidneys, hearts and other organs from human donors. Transplants of organs taken from other animals are called *xenografts* – this is the area with the greatest potential for future development, because of advances in genetic engineering.

History

The history of transplantation is surprisingly long, some forms of autografting being traceable back to the sixth century B.C. Blood transfusion, which is the most common form of transplantation, was made possible by Harvey's discovery of blood circulation in 1628, and the first successful use was a transfusion of lamb's blood in 1667, though it was then almost ignored until the realisation that isografts were needed, in 1818, and only became routine after Landsteiner discovered blood groups as the basis of rejection in 1900.

Early studies on kidney transplantation were carried out around 1906 by Carrel, who developed the necessary surgical techniques in animals and showed that transplanted kidneys could function normally for a few days before failure, which he termed rejection, set in. It was a further 50 years before advances in the development of drugs for preventing rejection made transplantation a practicality. The first heart transplantation was carried out by Christian Barnard in 1967, though the technique had been essentially perfected in animals in the United States by the late 1950s. Recent developments have seen a number of cases of multiple organ transplants, such as combined heart-lung transplants and simultaneous grafting of liver, gall bladder, intestine, stomach and spleen.

Rejection

Although transplantation might at first seem an essentially surgical technique, it is the immunologists and pharmacologists who have made many of the advances in transplantation possible. This is because, apart from the complexity of the "plumbing" carried out by the surgeon, the main problems in transplantation result from rejection of the transplanted tissues and organs. Rejection is caused by the fact that all the cells of the body are marked by special antigens, called HLA or histocompatibility antigens, which are different in every individual. The purpose of having these differences is thought to be related to the body's systems for protecting itself against viral infections and cancer, both of which can lead to alterations in the antigens expressed on the cell surface. These changes stimulate the immune system to attack the cells bearing altered antigens, because the cells are no longer seen as "self" cells. Only the cornea, which lacks a blood supply and does not become infiltrated with lymphocytes and antibodies from the recipient, is exempt from rejection.

The immune system has two branches: cell-mediated immunity, in which the so-called T-cells recognise a cell as being "non-self," attach to it and destroy it, and humoral immunity, where antibodies in the blood bind to a cell, activating a number of destructive processes. The most important mechanism in graft rejection is cell-mediated immunity, which can affect any isograft or xenograft. Humoral immunity becomes important when the graft recipient has previously been exposed to antigens identical to or resembling those of the grafted organ or tissue, as occurs in pregnancy (the mother is exposed to the "self" antigens of the baby, which are different from her own), and in recipients who have had blood transfusions or previous transplants. Almost everyone has antibodies to, for example, pig tissue; although this may seem surprising, it is worth mentioning that the immune system is extremely sensitive to foreign materials, and that most of us are exposed to significant quantities of pig tissues in our food. Cell-mediated immunity is a slow process, and can be suppressed, while humoral responses are much faster and more aggressive, and are much harder to block.

Prevention of Rejection

Rejection can be overcome by three approaches. The first is to prevent it from occurring, which can be achieved by using autografts (in which there are no "non-self" antigens) and grafts from related donors – the closer the donor is related to the recipient, the more similar their "self" antigens, and the less of a problem rejection will be. Tissue matching is used to identify which HLA antigens are present in the recipient and in the donor tissue, in other words to determine how closely related the donor and recipient are, and transplants are ideally carried out only when good tissue matches are found. The idea of using xenografts from species closely related to humans, such as baboons, has generally proven unsuccessful.

The second approach is to interfere with the immunological systems causing rejection, which is done by using drugs that inhibit the development of immune cells or suppress their activity. An important problem with this method is that the immune system is also responsible for providing protection against infections, so that patients receiving this therapy have increased susceptibility, especially in the immediate post-grafting period when immunosuppressive therapy is more intense. Other methods that have been used include X-ray treatment to damage immune cells, and removal of the thymus and/or spleen, the sites at which immune cells acquire the ability to cause rejection.

The third approach consists of exploiting the phenomenon of desensitisation, where repeated exposure to foreign antigens reduces the recipient's immunological reactions to them. Thus, repeated small blood transfusions from the organ or tissue donor are now commonly carried out before a transplant.

Cytotoxic and Immunosuppressive Drugs

The drugs used against rejection include cytotoxic and immunosuppressive agents. Cytotoxic agents are also used in cancer, and work by damaging cells. An important example is azathioprine, which, in carefully adjusted doses, prevents the growth of the cells causing rejection without affecting the bone marrow – a side effect that has the serious consequences of increasing susceptibility to infection and bleeding. Immunosuppressive drugs include the corticosteroids cortisone, prednisone and prednisolone, which reduce immunity and inflammation, high doses also having a toxic action on lymph node cells. These agents do not damage blood-forming tissues, but long-term use, especially at high doses, results in dependence and can produce serious side effects such as weight gain, facial swelling, diabetes, osteoporosis ("brittle bones"), slowed wound healing, hypertension, and retardation of growth in children. Cyclosporine is another immunosuppressive drug which has powerful action against T-lymphocytes. Although very effective in preventing rejection, cyclosporine is toxic to the kidneys and increases the growth of facial and body hair.

Another treatment is to use anti-lymphocyte serum (ALS), usually prepared from horse blood, which contains antibodies specifically induced against the immune cells responsible for rejection. ALS is used as an addition to azathioprine and steroid treatment, and is particularly useful in cases resistant to steroids. Its disadvantage is that some people may be allergic to horse proteins. A recent modification of this method is to use monoclonal antibodies – these are antibodies produced in the laboratory by artificial hybrid cells, and have the advantage that they only contain the antibody that

is needed; future developments in genetic engineering should reduce the risk of allergy by using human genes to make the antibodies in bacteria. Immunosuppressive therapy must generally go on for long periods of time, because the immune system continues to react to the continual presence of the foreign tissues. However, dosages are generally reduced a short time after the transplant operation and in some cases can be stopped altogether, because the persistent presence of the foreign antigens tends to desensitise the immune system, as mentioned above.

The Future of Transplantation

Progress in transplantation will depend more on advances in immunosuppressive therapy, mechanical engineering and provision of donor tissues than on developments in surgical technique. In the first case, "ideal" immunosuppressive drugs are being sought that would specifically block the rejection reaction without affecting protection from infections and without producing side effects in other body systems. Engineering is important because non-biological implants do not cause immunological reactions; however, other reactions occur, and the challenge is to find inert materials with the physical strength to substitute for biological materials – which are extraordinarily strong and long-lasting because one of the most important properties of biological systems is that they continually adapt and repair their components.

The question of the provision of donor tissues and organs is at the threshold of a major step forward, because of genetic engineering techniques, and is the subject of intense study: the greatest problem in transplantation is the shortage of donor organs.

Xenografting is the obvious response to the shortage, but is associated with far more aggressive rejection reactions than isografting – without strong immunosuppression, a xenografted organ survives only for a matter of hours. This hyperacute rejection reaction is mostly due to a set of blood proteins called the complement cascade, which recognises foreign cells and destroys them by literally punching holes in them. This does not occur with the body's own cells because they have surface proteins that block the action of complement. Recent work has concentrated on transferring the genes for these proteins into pig embryos, so that the cells of adults also have the human protein on their surfaces, thus preventing attack by complement. Animal transplantation experiments with these organs first began in late 1994.

Although this approach would overcome the hyperacute phase of xenograft rejection, there remains the problem of histocompatibility at the MHC level. This is more difficult to solve because the genes concerned are extremely large and are more difficult to transfer into animal cells. In addition, making animals with MHC compatibility with humans would need a separate animal to be engineered for each human individual, because each human has his or her own unique set of MHC antigens. Nonetheless, the creation of animals whose tissues bear human MHC genes is now being contemplated. Other modifications may need to be made to the xenograft before transplantation, and modification may also have to be made to the recipient's immune system, for example by continued use of immunosuppressive agents, and by tolerisation to animal antigens, possibly by simultaneous transplantation of bone marrow from the donor animal.

Ethical Aspects

There are many ethical problems in transplantation, largely arising from the fact that removal of an organ from a live donor contravenes one of the most fundamental of ethics – that a doctor should do nothing that will harm the patient. Removal of organs from cadavers is also ethically difficult, in terms of defining when a person is truly dead, and in terms of conflicts between the donor's wishes for the fate of his or her body, and those of the family. Permission to remove organs for donation is almost always made at an emotionally stressful time, as only younger people's organs are suitable for transplants. There is currently much debate as to whether donor schemes should be opt-in, as in the UK, where a person opts in by carrying a donor card, or opt-out, as in Belgium, where opting out requires people to carry non-donor cards. A much more serious ethical problem is that of organ selling and stealing – in selling, money is offered to the living to give up, for example, a kidney or a cornea, and in stealing, organs are obtained from "organ to order" murder victims. In both selling and stealing, organs are generally obtained from victims in poor countries and used by patients in rich countries.

Although the use of genetically engineered animals might seem to overcome ethical questions, anti-vivisectionists show considerable opposition, while proponents of this approach ask what is the difference between killing an animal for its organs and killing it to consume its flesh. In both cases, the consequence for the animal is death and the consequence for the recipient/consumer is life. The only area free from ethical difficulties is the use of mechanical implants, but at the moment it appears that biological engineering is going to make far faster progress than mechanical engineering.

IMAGING IN MEDICAL DIAGNOSIS

Introductory Note

When you are admitted to hospital, the doctors have to identify exactly what is wrong with you before they start treatment. Diagnosis is based on a knowledge of what is normal and which diseases are associated with which abnormalities in which combinations.

The first thing the doctor will do is take a history and examine you. Descriptions of a pain, such as what type it is, where it is, when and how suddenly it started, to which other parts of the body it radiates, can often lead the doctor to a fairly precise diagnosis, as with the characteristic pain of angina. However, many symptoms are not this clear. For example, a vague abdominal pain may relate to problems with the stomach, intestines, liver, pancreas, kidneys, or other organs and tissues.

The doctor then uses his knowledge of the anatomy and physiology of normal organs and tissues to improve the diagnosis. Changes in organ and tissue function are investigated by looking for biochemical changes – mostly by a battery of blood tests, while anatomical changes are investigated by one or more of a number of imaging techniques.

Radiography

The most familiar imaging technique is based on the use of X-rays. These are electromagnetic waves with a wavelength between those of gamma rays and ultraviolet light, and can penetrate tissues to some extent. However, different tissues absorb and scatter different amounts of X-ray energy, so the amount reaching the photographic film used for detection depends on the "X-ray density" of the tissues through which the beam has passed. Bone has a high density, while fatty tissues have a low density, so the X-rays arriving at the film after passing through fatty tissue expose the film more than those passing through bone. This gives rise to the characteristic picture of white bones on a black background: the X-ray picture is actually a photographic negative, and is used in this format because more detail can be seen than would be possible with a positive print.

Contrast Radiography

The disadvantage of simple X-ray pictures is that the intensity of any given point of the image depends on the total absorption and scattering of X-ray energy by all the tissues through which the X-ray beam has passed: skin, fat, muscle, organs, ligaments, bone, *etc*. In addition, the differences in the amount of energy absorbed by different soft tissues (*e.g.* muscle and fat) are quite small. These factors reduce the resolution of the image, and reduce the utility of simple radiography for soft tissue diseases.

One approach to this problem is to inject radio-opaque substances (contrast media) into the body before taking the X-ray picture, which will then produce a clearer image of the structures containing them. For example, in angiography (X-rays of blood vessels), a series of X-rays is taken shortly after injection of a contrast medium into an artery, and the pictures show the flow of blood into all the vessels branching off from the one injected. In myelography, a contrast medium is injected into the space surrounding the spinal cord, and the

resulting X-ray shows abnormalities in spinal cord and backbone anatomy. Many other variations exist for other organs.

Computerised Tomography

Computerised tomography (CT scanning) is another method of increasing the resolution of radiography, and works by passing narrow X-ray beams through the body at a wide variety of angles. The patient is placed inside a large metal tube for body scans, or the head is placed in a smaller cavity for brain scans, and the X-ray beam generator and detector move rapidly around the body. X-rays passing through the body are detected by scintillation, and the intensity of the beam passing through each path is stored in a computer. Complex calculations are then carried out, using the path intensities from beams passing through a given point in the body from different directions, to determine the X-rays density of each point of the body. The computer can then plot the resulting X-ray densities on the screen, or print them out on photographic paper, to produce an image representing an X-ray of a cross-section through the part of the body that was scanned. Since the X-ray density of a tissue is measured independently of other tissues, and because the detectors are more sensitive than X-ray film, CT scans give better resolution of different soft tissues than do simple X-ray techniques. CT scanning was first used for examination of the brain, to detect tumors, enlargement of the ventricular system, *etc*, and was subsequently applied to the abdominal and thoracic regions for studies of the liver, pancreas, kidneys, lungs and other organs.

Ultrasound

Ultrasound is based on the same principles used in active sonar in submarines. Short pulses of very high frequency sound waves (2 MHz) are passed through the body from a piezoelectric transducer (which is called a "gong") and are reflected back to the transducer by surfaces at which the acoustic impedance (the resistance of a tissue to sound waves), which depends on the density and elasticity of the tissues, changes. A single pulse from the gong produces a series of echoes, one from each surface where the acoustic impedance changes, that is, from each surface between tissues with different properties. The distances of these surfaces from the transducer are measured from the time passing between sending the signal and receiving each echo. A gel is applied to the body surface before starting, because any air between the skin and the transducer blocks the entry of ultrasound into the body.

The more sophisticated type of ultrasound, called B-scanning, consists of sending pulses from a series of gongs mounted in a single holder, and arranged to send out pulses one after the other, so that the pulses from different gongs do not produce overlapping echoes. When the holder is moved over the body surface, a two-dimensional picture is built up, where one dimension represents the distance between gongs along the holder and the second represents the distance the holder is moved across the body; the brightness of the image is determined by the amount of ultrasound energy reflected to the transducer. This method is most familiar in pregnancy, where it can be used to determine the sex of a baby before it is born.

A further variation of the technique, called time-position scanning, is used for monitoring foetal heartbeats. An array of gongs is held stationary over the foetus, and signals are sent through the heart. For each transducer, a plot is made of the time taken for each echo to arrive against the times at which successive pulses were sent out. Plots from the gong whose pulse passes through the foetal heart show changes in the depth of the foetal heart surfaces from the gong, and monitoring these changes over a period of time reveals the foetal heart rate. Ultrasound methods are also very useful for a number of the other body systems, for example in the diagnosis of a variety of liver diseases.

Doppler Sonography

Doppler sonography is a variation of ultrasound scanning which is used for detecting motion. An ultrasound beam is directed towards a moving structure, and reflections are recorded. The frequency (pitch) of a sound is altered when the surface reflecting it is moving – just like a pitch of a car horn changes as it approaches and then recedes. Doppler sonography is used for measuring the rate of blood flow through vessels, where the frequency of sound reflected from moving blood cells is monitored. When Doppler measurements are combined with B-scanning, measurements of blood flow through a vessel can be combined with producing images of the vessels, which is much more informative for making precise diagnoses of vascular diseases such as atherosclerosis.

Magnetic Resonance Imaging (MRI)

This newer technique is based on nuclear magnetic resonance, and involves measuring the distribution of water in the body by detecting its hydrogen atoms. Hydrogen atoms in a strong stationary magnetic field absorb radio waves of a particular frequency, called the resonant frequency (other atoms do this as well, but are distinguished by having different resonant frequencies). When the radio frequency waves are switched off, the hydrogen atoms re-emit the energy they have absorbed, and these are detected and fed into a computer. As in CT scanning, the computer uses the distribution of signals to construct a two-dimensional cross-sectional image of the part of the body that was scanned. MRI scanning is useful in studies of the anatomy of most of the internal organs, and is thought to be safer than CT scanning, as exposure of the body to magnetic fields (albeit strong ones) and radio waves is not known to have any harmful consequences, which is not true of the X-rays used in CT scanning.

Scintigraphy

All the methods so far mentioned are based on the physical properties of organs and tissues, and give images purely of their anatomy. In many cases, it is useful to obtain images containing information about organ and tissue function: some abnormal tissues are anatomically indistinguishable by other imaging methods but have different physiological activity. The principle is that a radioactive substance is injected into the body, where it is taken up to different extents by different tissues. A scanner able to detect the emissions from the radioactive agent used is passed over the body and the intensity of the radiation detected is fed into a computer, which then constructs an image. This method is best known in the diagnosis of thyroid diseases: the thyroid gland makes a hormone called thyroxine, which contains iodine; iodine uptake by all other tissues is minimal. If radioactive iodine is injected into the body, it will be taken up by the thyroid gland, and produces a strong scintigraphic image, which outlines the shape and density of thyroid tissue. An underactive thyroid will produce a fainter than normal image, an enlarged thyroid (goitre) will produce a large image, a thyroid containing cysts will produce an image with patches of low density, and a thyroid containing tumours may produce an image with regions of high density. The method is also used in the diagnosis of a number of tumours which have abnormal metabolic activity. More recent advances involve labelling an antibody with a radioactive material, which produces an image of the tissues to which the antibody sticks. This is used in the detection of tumours, which sometimes have specific antigens which are recognised by the appropriately chosen antibodies.

Other Imaging Techniques

A number of other methods exist, but are generally of narrower application. Thermography consists of recording the infra-red (heat) waves given off, to measure the temperatures of different parts of the body surface. These temperatures depend on the physiological state of the organs and tissues; tumour tissues sometimes have greater metabolic activity, and hence higher temperatures, than surrounding normal tissues. However, the low resolution of thermography limits its applications, which include the detection of breast cancers and physiological studies of emotional responses.

Transillumination consists of examining part of the body illuminated from behind or within by a bright (but cool) light, often a small torch. Since most parts of the body do not transmit much light, the technique is limited; uses include examination of the breast for cysts and tumours, detection of infected sinuses, examination of meningomyeloceles in spina bifida to determine whether or not they contain the spinal cord or nerves, and diagnosis of testicular diseases.

PART IV. INDEX AND GLOSSARY

Abortus fever. *See* **Undulant fever,** 13 (2).

Abrasion. Any injury which rubs off the surface skin.

Acidity. *See* **Peptic ulcer,** 35 (2).

Acne, 53 (1).

Acromegaly, 43 (1).

Actinomycosis, 15 (1).

Acute chorea or St. Vitus' dance, 48 (2).

Acute nephritis, 44 (2).

Addison's disease, 43 (1).

Adrenal cortex, 43 (1).

Adrenocorticotrophic hormone (ACTH), 42 (2).

Agranulocytosis, 25 (2).

Aids, 11 (2)

Alcoholism, 50 (1).

Allergy. Abnormal sensitivity to any substance which does not affect normal people.

Alopecia, 52 (1).

Amenorrhœa, 56 (1).

Amnesia, 47 (1).

Amoebae, 8 (1).

Amoebic dysentery. 17 (2).

Amphetamine, 61 (1).

Amyotrophic lateral sclerosis, 48 (1).

Anaemias, 24–25.

Anaesthetic. Any drug used to abolish pain during an operation.

Anencephaly, 48 (1).

Aneurism, 30 (1).

Angina pectoris, 28 (1).

Ankylosis. Partial or complete fixation of a joint as after some types of arthritis. In other cases deliberately produced by surgery.

Ankylostomiasis, 18 (1).

Anorexia nervosa, 51 (2).

Anterior pituitary, 42 (2).

Anthrax, 14 (1).

Antibiotics, 9 (1)

Antibodies, 8 (2).

Antihistamine drugs, 4 (2), 5 (1).

Antiseptics, 8 (2).

Anxiety neurosis, 51 (2).

Aortic diseases, 30 (1).

Aphasia, 47 (1).

Aplastic anaemia, 24 (2).

Appendicitis, 36 (2).

Arteriography, 46 (2).

Arthritis, 54 (1).

Artificial respiration (kiss of life), 22 (1).

Ascites, 38 (2).

Aspirin, 60 (2), 36 (1); *see also* **Headache.**

Asthma, 31 (2).

Atheroma or Atherosclerosis, 29 (2).

Athlete's foot, 8 (1), 15 (1).

Autism, 51 (2).

Backache. A symptom which may be caused by many different diseases—sometimes disease of the vertebrae themselves, sometimes strain of the ligaments, and sometimes inflammation or spasm of the surrounding muscles. "Lumbago" is usually due to inflammation of the muscles in the small of the back. Backache from purely local causes may be treated temporarily by applying heat in the form of a kaolin poultice or a rubber hot-water bottle and taking two aspirin tablets a day. On the other hand, many cases of backache are due to disease elsewhere. The most important thing is to find out the cause, and therefore a doctor should be consulted.

Bacteria, 7 (1). **Bacterial diseases,** 12–14.

Bacteriophage, 7 (2).

Baldness, 52 (1).

Barbiturates, 61 (1).

Bell's palsy, 50 (1).

Beri-beri, 42 (1).

Berry aneurysm, 48 (2).

Bilharzia, 18 (1).

Birth control, 56–59.

Blackwater fever, 17 (1).

Bladder. *See under* **Urinary diseases,** 44–45.

Bleeding diseases, 26 (1).

Blood, function of the, 24 (1).

Blood, diseases of the, 24–26.

Blood Groups. Human blood plasma contains factors which clump, or agglutinate, the red cells of some other people's blood. The main blood groups are called A, B, AB, and O. The plasma of group A blood contains an anti-B factor and *vice versa*, so that people of groups A and B cannot accept each other's blood. Group AB contains neither anti-A nor anti-B factor and people with this group can therefore receive transfusions from both but can give to neither. Group O contains both anti-A and anti-B, and can therefore receive blood only from group O but can donate blood to all groups. It is important that transfused cells should not be agglutinated by the factors in the recipient's plasma. Apart from the so-called ABO system, there are several other blood groupings, one of which is mentioned under **Rhesus Factor.**

Blood poisoning (septicaemia), 13 (1).

Blood-pressure, 28 (2).

Blood-vessels, diseases of the, 29 (2)–30.

Botulism, 15 (1).

Brain. *See under* **Nervous system,** 45–50.

Brain tumour, 49 (2).

Breasts, 55 (1).

Bronchial asthma, 31 (2).

Bronchial carcinoma, *See* Lung cancer.

Bronchiectasis, 31 (2).

Bronchitis, 31 (1).

Bulimia nervosa, 51 (2).

Burns and Scalds, 19 (2).

Cachexia. Extreme wasting due to disease.

Caesarean operation. When the abdomen has to be opened to remove the child. (Named after Julius Caesar, who is said to have been born in this way.)

Caisson disease, 30 (1).

Cancer of the breast, 55 (1).

Cancer of the cervix, 55 (2).

Cancer of the colon, 37 (1).

Cancer of the liver, 39 (1).

Cancer of the lung, 33 (1), 33 (2).

Cancer of the oesophagus, 35 (2).

Cancer of the rectum, 37 (1).

Cancer of the stomach, 36 (2).

Cancer test (cervical smear), 55 (2).

Carbohydrates. The scientific name for sugars, starches and cellulose, 34 (1), 39–40.

Carbuncle. A large boil.

Cardiac neurosis, 27 (1).

Cataract, 54 (2).

Cerebral abscess, 49 (1).

Cerebral embolism, 48 (2).

Cerebral haemorrhage or apoplexy, 48 (2).

Cerebral palsy, 48 (1).

Cerebrovascular diseases, *see* **Stroke illness.**

Chadwick, Sir Edwin (1800–90). English social reformer, 6 (1).

Chancroid, 15 (2).

Change of life, 43 (2).

Chickenpox, 10 (1).

Chilblains, 52 (2).

Chill. This is not a proper medical word, but refers to the symptoms that occur when one first becomes infected with any germs which cause fever. When such germs enter the body, all the defending processes are mobilised and speeded up. The white cells in the blood increase in number, and the amount of energy used is greater than normal, causing the temperature to rise. This rise in temperature increases the ability of the body to fight back, and, in order to retain heat within the body, the blood-vessels in the skin contract so that less heat is lost by radiation. This makes the skin cold and pale. What is ordinarily called a chill is merely an infection by the germs causing cold and influenza. But a chill may be the preliminary to almost any infectious disease, such as measles, mumps, scarlet fever, pneumonia, and so on. The best treatment when the temperature is raised is to go to bed with as much warmth as possible. Hot drinks and hot-water bottles are helpful. See **Colds**, 10 (2).

Cholecystitis, 39 (1).

Cholera, 14 (1).

Cholesterol, 29 (2), 38 (1).

Chronic. A chronic disease is one which is prolonged and relatively mild, as opposed to an acute one which is short and severe.

Chronic nephritis, 44 (2).

Cilia, 31 (1).

Cirrhosis of the liver, 38 (2).

Claustrophobia. A physical symptom, which causes the individual to be afraid of enclosed spaces. See under **Obsessional neurosis**, 51 (1).

Cocaine, 61 (1).

Coccyx. The end of the spinal column.

Colds, 10 (2).

Colitis, 37 (1).

Coma, 46 (2).

Concussion, see **Head injuries**, 21 (1).

Congenital heart disease, 27 (2).

Conjunctivitis, 54 (2).

Consciousness and unconsciousness, 46 (2).

Constipation, 35 (1).

Contraception, See **Family Planning**, 56–59.

Coronary heart disease, 28 (1).

Coronary thrombosis, 28 (2).

Cortisone. A hormone produced by the suprarenal glands, 43 (1).

Cretin, 43 (1).

Cretinism, 43 (1).

C.S.F. (i.e, cerebrospinal fluid), 46 (2)

Cushing's disease, 43 (1).

Cutaneous ureterostomy, 45 (1).

Cystic fibrosis, 31 (2).

Cystitis, 45 (1).

Dandruff. See **Seborrhoea**, 52 (1).

Deficiency diseases, 41–2.

Dementia, 50 (1).

Demyelinating diseases, 49 (1).

Dengue, 11 (2).

Dermatitis, 52 (2).

Dhobie itch, 8 (1).

Diabetes insipidus, 43 (1).

Diabetes mellitus, 39 (1).

Diarrhoea, and vomiting, 14 (2).

Diet, 39–41.

Digestive tract, 34–38.

Diphtheria, 12 (1).

Diverticulitis, 37 (1).

Dropsy, 44 (2).

Drug abuse, 59–61

Duchenne's muscular dystrophy, 50 (1).

Ductless glands, 42 (2).

Duodenal ulcer, 35 (2).

Duodenum, 35 (2).

Dysentery, 14 (2).

Dysmenorrhoea, 55 (2).

E.C.T. The abbreviated form of the name for a modern type of treatment for certain psychiatric disorders—electro-convulsive-therapy. See under **Psychosis**, 50 (1).

Eczema, 52(2).

Ehrlich, Paul (1854–1915). German bacteriologist, 4 (1), 5 (2).

Electrocardiogram, (E.C.G.), 29 (2).

Electroencephalography, (E.E.G.), 46 (2).

Electromyography, (E.M.G.), 46 (2).

Elephantiasis, 18 (2).

Embolism, 30 (1), 32 (2).

Emphysema, 31 (1).

Empyema. A collection of pus in the lung (usually a complication of other diseases).

Encephalitis, 49 (1).

Encephalo-myelitis, 49 (1).

Endemic. Referring to a disease, means prevalent in a particular area.

Endocarditis. Disease of the valves of the heart, 29 (2).

Endocrine glands, 42–3.

Enzymes, 34 (1).

Epidemic jaundice. 16 (1).

Epilepsy, 47 (2).

Epithelioma (cancer of the skin), 54 (1).

Erysipelas, 52 (2).

Exocrine glands, 42 (2).

Eye, disease of the, 54 (2).

Fallopian tubes, 55 (1).

Family Planning, 56–59.

Farcy, 14 (1).

Fat embolism, 33 (1).

Fats. See **Diet**.

Fevers, general treatment of, 9.

Fibroids, 55 (2).

Fibrositis, 54 (2).

First Aid, 18–23

Fits. See **Epilepsy**.

Fleming, Sir Alexander (1881–1955). Scottish bacteriologist, discoverer of penicillin, 4 (1).

Food poisoning diseases, 14–15.

Fractures, 20 (2).

Frostbite, 30 (2).

Fungi, diseases caused by, 7 (2), 15 (1).

Gall-bladder, 38 (1).

Gallstones, 39 (1).

Ganglion. A small cystic swelling, usually on the wrist, dealt with by simple surgical treatment.

Gastric ulcer, 35 (2).

Geriatrics. The medical study of old age.

German Measles, 10 (1).

Gigantism, 43 (1).

Gingivitis. Inflammation of the gums due to infection and requiring treatment by a dentist.

Glanders, 14 (1).

Glandular diseases, 42–3.

Glandular fever, 11 (1).

Glaucoma, 54 (2).

Glial cells of the brain, 46 (1).

Goitre, 43 (1).

Gonadotrophic hormones, 42 (2).

Gonorrhoea, 15 (2).

Grand mal. See **Epilepsy**, 47 (2).

Graves' disease, 43 (1).

Growth hormone, 42 (2).

Gynaecology. The study of the diseases of women, 55–56.

Pellagra, 42 (1).

Penicillin, 9 (1), 60 (1).

Peptic ulcer, 35 (2).

Pericarditis, 29 (2).

Peripheral nerves, diseases of, 49 (2).

Peritonitis, 37 (2).

Pernicious anaemia, 25 (1).

Petit mal. *See* Epilepsy, 47 (2).

Physical injuries, 18–23.

Piles. *See* Haemorrhoids, 37 (2).

Pineal gland, 43 (2).

Pituitary gland, 42 (2).

Plague, 16 (2).

Plastic surgery, 53 (2).

Pleurisy, 33 (2).

Pneumoconiosis, 32 (2).

Pneumonia, 32 (1).

Poliomyelitis, 10 (2).

Polycythaemia, 25 (1).

Portal hypertension, 38 (1).

Posterior pituitary, 43 (1).

Prostate disease, 45 (2).

Protein, 34 (2), 39.

Protein-calorie deficiency, 41 (2).

Protozoal diseases, 16–17.

Pruritus, 52 (1).

Psittacosis, 12 (2).

Psychopathic personality, 51 (2).

Psychosis, 50 (1).

Psychosomatic diseases. Psychosomatic diseases are those physical ailments due to emotional causes. They include such complaints as high blood-pressure, gastric ulcer *etc*.

Pulmonary embolism, 32 (2).

Purpura, 26 (1).

Pyaemia, 13 (2).

Pyelitis, 44 (2).

Pyloric stenosis, 36 (1).

Pyorrhoea. An infection of the gums which causes the edges of the tooth sockets to bleed easily when the teeth are being brushed.

Rabies, 11 (1).

Raynaud's disease, 30 (2).

Rectum, cancer of the, 37 (1).

Reducing weight, 40–41.

Reed, Major Walter (1851–1902). American army surgeon, 11 (2).

Reflex actions, 46 (1).

Reflex arc, 46 (1).

Regional enteritis, 36 (2).

Relapsing fever, 16 (1).

Renal colic, 45 (1).

Respiratory system, diseases of the, 30–34.

Reticulosarcoma, 25 (2).

Rhesus Factor. Apart from the ABO blood group system (*see* **Blood Groups**) there is another blood group system (designated the Rh-system or Rhesus system). Everybody is either Rh-positive or Rh-negative. Three positive factors (denoted C, D, E) and three negative factors (denoted c, d, e) are involved. This system of blood factors is inherited separately from the ABO group, so that one may be A Rh+ or A Rh−, etc. Both the positive and the negative factors are antigenic, *i.e.*, if introduced into other blood they will stimulate the production of substances which act in some way against the cells introduced.

Rheumatic diseases. *See* Joints.

Rheumatic fever. *See* Rheumatic heart disease.

Rheumatic heart disease, 27 (2).

Rheumatoid arthritis, 54 (1).

Rickets, 42 (2).

Ringworm, 8 (1), 15 (1).

Rodent ulcer, 53 (2).

Rods and Cones are cells in the retina of the eye which convert light into nervous impulses which can be interpreted by the brain.

Rosacea, 53 (1).

Ross, Sir Ronald (1857–1932). English physician, 16 (1).

Roundworms, 18 (1).

Roux, Pierre Paul Emile (1853–1933). French physician and bacteriologist, 16 (1).

Rubella or German measles, 10 (1).

Rupture. *See* Hernia, 37 (1).

Salmonella infections, 14 (2).

Salvarsan, 15 (2).

Sandfly fever, 11 (2).

Scabies, 52 (1).

Scalds, 21 (2).

Scarlet fever, 12 (1).

Schizophrenia, 50 (2).

Scurvy, 42 (2).

Seborrhoea, 52 (1).

Senile tremor, 48 (2).

Septicaemia, 13 (1).

Sheehan's disease, 42 (2).

Shingles, 10 (1), 49 (1).

Shock, 19 (2).

Simmond's disease, 42 (2).

Simpson, Sir James Young (1811–70), Scottish physician, 5 (2).

Skin, 51–54.

Skin grafts, 53 (2).

Sleep and insomnia, 47 (1).

Sleeping sickness or Trypanosomiasis, 17 (1).

Smallpox, 11 (1).

Smoking. *See* Lung Cancer, Bronchitis, Bronchial Asthma.

Social medicine, new approaches in, 5–6.

Sore throat, 54 (2).

Spastic child, 48 (1).

Spina bifida, 48 (1).

Spirochaetes, 7 (2).

Staphylococcal food poisoning, 14-15.

Stomach, cancer of the, 36 (2).

Streptococcal infections, 12 (1).

Streptococcal sore throat, 12 (1), 27 (2), 54 (1).

Stroke, 29 (2), 48 (2).

Suprapubic cystotomy, 45 (2).

Sydenham, Thomas (1624–89), English physician, 5 (1).

Syphilis, 15 (2).

Tabes dorsalis, 15 (2).

Tachycardia, 29 (1).

Tapeworms, 17 (2).

Temperature. The body temperature is regulated by a small area at the base of the brain. Normally it should be about 37°C. *See* 9 (1).

Testis, 43 (2).

Tetanus, 13 (2).

Thalidomide, 4 (2).

Thermometer, use of. *See* **General treatment of fevers,** 9 (1).

Threadworms, 18 (1).

Thrombosis, 30 (2).

Thrush, 9 (1).

Thyroid gland, 43 (1).

Thyrotoxicosis, 43 (1).

Thyrotropic hormone, 42 (2).

Tics, 48 (2).

Tobacco-smoking, *See under* Lung Cancer, 33 (2).

Tonsils, 55 (1).

Toxaemia, 13 (2).

SPORTING COMPANION

This section provides a wide-ranging variety of tables giving numerous recent winners of popular sporting competitions. Included in this edition are post-war Olympic champions in such areas as athletics, ice-skating, skiing and swimming.

SPORTING COMPANION

AMERICAN FOOTBALL

WORLD CHAMPIONSHIP SUPERBOWL WINNERS

I (1967)	Green Bay Packers
II (1968)	Green Bay Packers
III (1969)	New York Jets
IV (1970)	Kansas City Chiefs
V (1971)	Baltimore Colts
VI (1972)	Dallas Cowboys
VII (1973)	Miami Dolphins
VIII (1974)	Miami Dolphins
IX (1975)	Pittsburgh Steelers
X (1976)	Pittsburgh Steelers
XI (1977)	Oakland Raiders
XII (1978)	Dallas Cowboys
XIII (1979)	Pittsburgh Steelers
XIV (1980)	Pittsburgh Steelers
XV (1981)	Oakland Raiders
XVI (1982)	San Francisco 49ers
XVII (1983)	Washington Redskins
XVIII ((1984)	Los Angeles Raiders
XIX (1985)	San Francisco 49ers
XX (1986)	Chicago Bears
XXI (1987)	New York Giants
XXII (1988)	Washington Redskins
XXIII (1989)	San Francisco 49ers
XXIV (1990)	San Francisco 49ers
XXV (1991)	New York Giants
XXVI (1992)	Washington Redskins
XXVII (1993)	Dallas Cowboys
XXVIII (1994)	Dallas Cowboys
XXIX (1995)	San Francisco 49ers

ASSOCIATION FOOTBALL

WORLD CUP WINNERS

1930	(In Uruguay)	Uruguay
1934	(In Italy)	Italy
1938	(In France)	Italy
1950	(In Brazil)	Uruguay
1954	(In Switzerland)	West Germany
1958	(In Sweden)	Brazil
1962	(In Chile)	Brazil
1966	(In England)	England
1970	(In Mexico)	Brazil
1974	(In West Germany)	West Germany
1978	(In Argentina)	Argentina
1982	(In Spain)	Italy
1986	(In Mexico)	Argentina
1990	(In Italy)	West Germany
1994	(In the USA)	Brazil

EUROPEAN CHAMPIONS

1960	(In France)	USSR
1964	(In Spain)	Spain
1968	(In Italy)	Italy
1972	(In Belgium)	West Germany
1976	(In Yugoslavia)	Czechoslovakia
1980	(In Italy)	West Germany
1984	(In France)	France
1988	(In West Germany)	Holland
1992	(In Sweden)	Denmark

EUROPEAN CHAMPIONS CUP WINNERS

1955–6	Real Madrid
1956–7	Real Madrid
1957–8	Real Madrid
1958–9	Real Madrid
1959–60	Real Madrid
1960–1	Benfica
1961–2	Benfica
1962–3	A C Milan
1963–4	Inter-Milan
1964–5	Inter-Milan
1965–6	Real Madrid
1966–7	Glasgow Celtic
1967–8	Manchester United
1968–9	A C Milan
1969–70	Feyenoord
1970–1	Ajax Amsterdam
1971–2	Ajax Amsterdam
1972–3	Ajax Amsterdam
1973–4	Bayern Munich
1974–5	Bayern Munich
1975–6	Bayern Munich
1976–7	Liverpool
1977–8	Liverpool
1978–9	Nottingham Forest
1979–80	Nottingham Forest
1980–1	Liverpool
1981–2	Aston Villa
1982–3	SV Hamburg
1983–4	Liverpool
1984–5	Juventus
1985–6	Steaua Bucharest
1986–7	FC Porto
1987–8	PSV Eindhoven
1988–9	A C Milan
1989–90	A C Milan
1990–1	Red Star Belgrade
1991–2	Barcelona
1992–3	Marseille
1993–4	A C Milan

EUROPEAN CUP–WINNERS' CUP WINNERS

1960–1	Fiorentina
1961–2	Atletico Madrid
1962–3	Tottenham Hotspur
1963–4	Sporting Lisbon
1964–5	West Ham United
1965–6	Borussia Dortmund
1966–7	Bayern Munich
1967–8	A C Milan
1968–9	Slovan Bratislava
1969–70	Manchester City
1970–1	Chelsea
1971–2	Glasgow Rangers
1972–3	A C Milan
1973–4	FC Magdeburg
1974–5	Dynamo Kiev
1975–6	Anderlecht
1976–7	Hamburg SV
1977–8	Anderlecht
1978–9	Barcelona
1979–80	Valencia
1980–1	Dynamo Tbilisi
1981–2	Barcelona
1982–3	Aberdeen
1983–4	Juventus
1984–5	Everton
1985–6	Dynamo Kiev
1986–7	Ajax Amsterdam
1987–8	Mechelen
1988–9	Barcelona
1989–90	Sampdoria
1990–1	Manchester United
1991–2	Werder Bremen
1992–3	Parma
1993–4	Arsenal
1994–5	Real Zaragoza

UEFA CUP WINNERS

1957–8	Barcelona	1971–2	Tottenham Hotspur	1982–3	Anderlecht
1959–60	Barcelona	1972–3	Liverpool	1983–4	Tottenham Hotspur
1960–1	A S Roma	1973–4	Feyenoord	1984–5	Real Madrid
1961–2	Valencia	1974–5	Borussia	1985–6	Real Madrid
1962–3	Valencia		Moenchengladbach	1986–7	IFK Gothenburg
1963–4	Real Zaragoza	1975–6	Liverpool	1987–8	Bayer Leverkusen
1964–5	Ferencvaros	1976–7	Juventus	1988–9	Napoli
1965–6	Barcelona	1977–8	PSV Eindhoven	1989–90	Juventus
1966–7	Dynamo Zagreb	1978–9	Juventus	1990–1	Inter-Milan
1967–8	Leeds United		Borussia	1991–2	Ajax Amsterdam
1968–9	Newcastle United		Moenchengladbach	1992–3	Juventus
1969–70	Arsenal	1979–80	Eintracht Frankfurt	1993–4	Inter-Milan
1970–1	Leeds United	1980–1	Ipswich Town	1994–5	Parma
		1981–2	IFK Gothenburg		

ENGLISH FOOTBALL LEAGUE CHAMPIONS (POST WAR)

1946–7	Liverpool	1971–2	Derby County
1947–8	Arsenal	1972–3	Liverpool
1948–9	Portsmouth	1973–4	Leeds United
1949–50	Portsmouth	1974–5	Derby County
1950–1	Tottenham Hotspur	1975–6	Liverpool
1951–2	Manchester United	1976–7	Liverpool
1952–3	Arsenal	1977–8	Nottingham Forest
1953–4	Wolverhampton Wanderers	1978–9	Liverpool
1954–5	Chelsea	1979–80	Liverpool
1955–6	Manchester United	1980–1	Aston Villa
1956–7	Manchester United	1981–2	Liverpool
1957–8	Wolverhampton Wanderers	1982–3	Liverpool
1958–9	Wolverhampton Wanderers	1983–4	Liverpool
1959–60	Burnley	1984–5	Everton
1960–1	Tottenham Hotspur	1985–6	Liverpool
1961–2	Ipswich Town	1986–7	Everton
1962–3	Everton	1987–8	Liverpool
1963–4	Liverpool	1988–9	Arsenal
1964–5	Manchester United	1989–90	Liverpool
1965–6	Liverpool	1990–1	Arsenal
1966–7	Manchester United	1991–2	Leeds United
1967–8	Manchester City	1992–3	Manchester United
1968–9	Leeds United	1993–4	Manchester United
1969–70	Everton	1994–5	Blackburn Rovers
1970–1	Arsenal		

Titles won since Football League began in 1888

18	Liverpool
10	Arsenal
9	Everton, Manchester United
7	Aston Villa
6	Sunderland
4	Newcastle United, Sheffield Wednesday
3	Blackburn Rovers, Huddersfield Town, Leeds United, Wolverhampton Wanderers
2	Burnley, Derby County, Manchester City, Tottenham Hotspur, Portsmouth, Preston North End
1	Chelsea, Ipswich Town, Nottingham Forest, Sheffield United, West Bromwich Albion

ENGLISH FOOTBALL ASSOCIATION CUP WINNERS (POST WAR)

1945–6	Derby County	1970–1	Arsenal
1946–7	Charlton Athletic	1971–2	Leeds United
1947–8	Manchester United	1972–3	Sunderland
1948–9	Wolverhampton Wanderers	1973–4	Liverpool
1949–50	Arsenal	1974–5	West Ham United
1950–1	Newcastle United	1975–6	Southampton
1951–2	Newcastle United	1976–7	Manchester United
1952–3	Blackpool	1977–8	Ipswich Town
1953–4	West Bromwich Albion	1978–9	Arsenal
1954–5	Newcastle United	1979–80	West Ham United
1955–6	Manchester City	1980–1	Tottenham Hotspur
1956–7	Aston Villa	1981–2	Tottenham Hotspur
1957–8	Bolton Wanderers	1982–3	Manchester United
1958–9	Nottingham Forest	1983–4	Everton
1959–60	Wolverhampton Wanderers	1984–5	Manchester United
1960–1	Tottenham Hotspur	1985–6	Liverpool
1961–2	Tottenham Hotspur	1986–7	Coventry City
1962–3	Manchester United	1987–8	Wimbledon
1963–4	West Ham United	1988–9	Liverpool
1964–5	Liverpool	1989–90	Manchester United
1965–6	Everton	1990–1	Tottenham Hotspur
1966–7	Tottenham Hotspur	1991–2	Liverpool
1967–8	West Bromwich Albion	1992–3	Arsenal
1968–9	Manchester City	1993–4	Manchester United
1969–70	Chelsea	1994–5	Everton

Wins since F.A. Cup began in 1872

8   Manchester United, Tottenham Hotspur
7   Aston Villa,
6   Arsenal, Blackburn Rovers, Newcastle United
5   Everton, Liverpool, The Wanderers, West Bromwich Albion
4   Bolton Wanderers, Manchester City, Sheffield United, Wolverhampton Wanderers
3   Sheffield Wednesday, West Ham United
2   Bury, Nottingham Forest, Old Etonians, Preston North End, Sunderland
1   Barnsley, Blackburn Olympic, Blackpool, Bradford City, Burnley, Cardiff City, Charlton Athletic,
    Chelsea, Clapham Rovers, Coventry City, Derby County, Huddersfield Town, Ipswich Town, Leeds
    United, Notts County, Old Carthusians, Oxford University, Portsmouth, Royal Engineers,
    Southampton, Wimbledon

FOOTBALL LEAGUE & F.A. CUP 'DOUBLE' WINNERS

1888–9	Preston North End	1970–1	Arsenal
1896–7	Aston Villa	1985–6	Liverpool
1960–1	Tottenham Hotspur	1993–4	Manchester United

ENGLISH FOOTBALL LEAGUE CUP WINNERS

1960–1	Aston Villa	1978–9	Nottingham Forest
1961–2	Norwich City	1979–80	Wolverhampton Wanderers
1962–3	Birmingham City	1980–1	Liverpool
1963–4	Leicester City	1981–2	Liverpool
1964–5	Chelsea	1982–3	Liverpool
1965–6	West Bromwich Albion	1983–4	Liverpool
1966–7	Queen's Park Rangers	1984–5	Norwich City
1967–8	Leeds United	1985–6	Oxford United
1968–9	Swindon Town	1986–7	Arsenal
1969–70	Manchester City	1987–8	Luton Town
1970–1	Tottenham Hotspur	1988–9	Nottingham Forest
1971–2	Stoke City	1989–90	Nottingham Forest
1972–3	Tottenham Hotspur	1990–1	Sheffield Wednesday
1973–4	Wolverhampton Wanderers	1991–2	Manchester United
1974–5	Aston Villa	1992–3	Arsenal
1975–6	Manchester City	1993–4	Aston Villa
1976–7	Aston Villa	1994–5	Liverpool
1977–8	Nottingham Forest		

SCOTTISH FOOTBALL LEAGUE CHAMPIONS (POST WAR)

1946–7	Rangers	1963–4	Rangers	1979–80	Aberdeen
1947–8	Hibernian	1964–5	Kilmarnock	1980–1	Celtic
1948–9	Rangers	1965–6	Celtic	1981–2	Celtic
1949–50	Rangers	1966–7	Celtic	1982–3	Dundee United
1950–1	Hibernian	1967–8	Celtic	1983–4	Aberdeen
1951–2	Hibernian	1968–9	Celtic	1984–5	Aberdeen
1952–3	Rangers	1969–70	Celtic	1985–6	Celtic
1953–4	Celtic	1970–1	Celtic	1986–7	Rangers
1954–5	Aberdeen	1971–2	Celtic	1987–8	Celtic
1955–6	Rangers	1972–3	Celtic	1988–9	Rangers
1956–7	Rangers	1973–4	Celtic	1989–90	Rangers
1957–8	Hearts	1974–5	Rangers	1990–1	Rangers
1958–9	Rangers	1975–6	Rangers	1991–2	Rangers
1959–60	Hearts	1976–7	Celtic	1992–3	Rangers
1960–1	Rangers	1977–8	Rangers	1993–4	Rangers
1961–2	Dundee	1978–9	Celtic	1994–5	Rangers
1962–3	Rangers				

Titles won since League began in 1890

45   Rangers
35   Celtic
4   Aberdeen, Hearts, Hibernian
2   Dumbarton
1   Dundee, Dundee United, Kilmarnock, Motherwell, Third Lanark

SCOTTISH CUP WINNERS (POST WAR)

1946–7	Aberdeen	1963–4	Rangers	1979–80	Celtic
1947–8	Rangers	1964–5	Celtic	1980–1	Rangers
1948–9	Rangers	1965–6	Rangers	1981–2	Aberdeen
1949–50	Rangers	1966–7	Celtic	1982–3	Aberdeen
1950–1	Celtic	1967–8	Dunfermline Athletic	1983–4	Aberdeen
1951–2	Motherwell	1968–9	Celtic	1984–5	Celtic
1952–3	Rangers	1969–70	Aberdeen	1985–6	Aberdeen
1953–4	Celtic	1970–1	Celtic	1986–7	St Mirren
1954–5	Clyde	1971–2	Celtic	1987–8	Celtic
1955–6	Hearts	1972–3	Rangers	1988–9	Celtic
1956–7	Falkirk	1973–4	Celtic	1989–90	Aberdeen
1957–8	Clyde	1974–5	Celtic	1990–1	Motherwell
1958–9	St Mirren	1975–6	Rangers	1991–2	Rangers
1959–60	Rangers	1976–7	Celtic	1992–3	Rangers
1960–1	Dunfermline Athletic	1977–8	Rangers	1993–4	Dundee United
1961–2	Rangers	1978–9	Rangers		
1962–3	Rangers				

Wins since Scottish Cup began in 1873

29	Celtic
26	Rangers
10	Queen's Park
7	Aberdeen
5	Hearts
3	Clyde, St Mirren, Vale of Leven
2	Dunfermline Athletic, Falkirk, Hibernian, Kilmarnock, Motherwell, Renton, Third Lanark
1	Airdrieonians, Dumbarton, Dundee, Dundee United, East Fife, Morton, Partick Thistle, St Bernard's

SCOTTISH LEAGUE CUP WINNERS

1946–7	Rangers	1963–4	Rangers	1979–80	Dundee United
1947–8	East Fife	1964–5	Rangers	1980–1	Dundee United
1948–9	Rangers	1965–6	Celtic	1981–2	Rangers
1949–50	East Fife	1966–7	Celtic	1982–3	Celtic
1950–1	Motherwell	1967–8	Celtic	1983–4	Rangers
1951–2	Dundee	1968–9	Celtic	1984–5	Rangers
1952–3	Dundee	1969–70	Celtic	1985–6	Aberdeen
1953–4	East Fife	1970–1	Rangers	1986–7	Rangers
1954–5	Hearts	1971–2	Partick Thistle	1987–8	Rangers
1955–6	Aberdeen	1972–3	Hibernian	1988–9	Rangers
1956–7	Celtic	1973–4	Dundee	1989–90	Aberdeen
1957–8	Celtic	1974–5	Celtic	1990–1	Rangers
1958–9	Hearts	1975–6	Rangers	1991–2	Hibernian
1959–60	Hearts	1976–7	Aberdeen	1992–3	Rangers
1960–1	Rangers	1977–8	Rangers	1993–4	Rangers
1961–2	Rangers	1978–9	Rangers	1994–5	Raith Rovers
1962–3	Hearts				

SCOTTISH LEAGUE, SCOTTISH CUP AND LEAGUE CUP 'TREBLE' WINNERS

1948–9	Rangers	1968–9	Celtic	1977–8	Rangers
1963–4	Rangers	1975–6	Rangers	1992–3	Rangers
1966–7	Celtic				

ATHLETICS

OLYMPIC CHAMPIONS (POST WAR)

Men's 100m
1948	Harrison Dillard (USA)
1952	Lindy Remigino (USA)
1956	Bobby Morrow (USA)
1960	Armin Hary (FRG)
1964	Robert Hayes (USA)
1968	James Hines (USA)
1972	Valeriy Borzov (USSR)
1976	Hasely Crawford (Tri)
1980	Allan Wells (UK)
1984	Carl Lewis (USA)
1988	Carl Lewis (USA)
1992	Linford Christie (UK)

Men's 200m
1948	Melvin Patton (USA)
1952	Andrew Stanfield (USA)
1956	Bobby Morrow (USA)
1960	Livio Berruti (Ita)
1964	Henry Carr (USA)
1968	Tommie Smith (USA)
1972	Valeriy Borzov (USSR)
1976	Donald Quarrie (Jam)
1980	Pietro Mennea (Ita)
1984	Carl Lewis (USA)
1988	Joe DeLoach (USA)
1992	Michael Marsh (USA)

Men's 400m
1948	Arthur Wint (Jam)
1952	George Rhoden (Jam)
1956	Charles Jenkins (USA)
1960	Otis Davis (USA)
1964	Michael Larrabee (USA)
1968	Lee Evans (USA)
1972	Vincent Matthews (USA)
1976	Alberto Juantorena (Cub)
1980	Viktor Markin (USSR)
1984	Alonzo Babers (USA)
1988	Steve Lewis (USA)
1992	Quincy Watts (USA)

Men's 800m
1948	Malvin Whitfield (USA)
1952	Malvin Whitfield (USA)
1956	Thomas Courtney (USA)
1960	Peter Snell (NZ)
1964	Peter Snell (NZ)
1968	Ralph Doubell (Aus)
1972	David Wottle (USA)
1976	Alberto Juantorena (Cub)
1980	Steve Ovett (UK)
1984	Joaquim Cruz (Bra)
1988	Paul Ereng (Ken)
1992	William Tanui (Ken)

Men's 1500m
1948	Henry Eriksson (Swe)
1952	Josef Barthel (Lux)
1956	Ron Delany (Ire)
1960	Herbert Elliott (Aus)
1964	Peter Snell (NZ)
1968	Kipchoge Keino (Ken)
1972	Pekka Vasala (Fin)
1976	John Walker (NZ)
1980	Sebastian Coe (UK)
1984	Sebastian Coe (UK)
1988	Peter Rono (Ken)
1992	Fermin Cacho (Spa)

Men's 5000m
1948	Gaston Reiff (Bel)
1952	Emil Zatopek (Cze)
1956	Vladimir Kuts (USSR)
1960	Murray Halberg (NZ)
1964	Robert Schul (USA)
1968	Mohamed Gammoudi (Tun)
1972	Lasse Viren (Fin)
1976	Lasse Viren (Fin)
1980	Miruts Yifter (Eth)
1984	Saïd Aouita (Mor)
1988	John Ngugi (Ken)
1992	Dieter Baumann (Ger)

Men's 10,000m
1948	Emil Zátopek (Cze)
1952	Emil Zátopek (Cze)
1956	Vladimir Kuts (USSR)
1960	Pyotr Bolontikov (USSR)
1964	William Mills (USA)
1968	Naftali Temu (Ken)
1972	Lasse Viren (Fin)
1976	Lasse Viren (Fin)
1980	Miruts Yifter (Eth)
1984	Alberto Cova (Ita)
1988	Brahim Boutayeb (Mor)
1992	Khalid Skah (Mor)

Men's Marathon
1948	Delfo Cabrera (Arg)
1952	Emil Zátopek (Cze)
1956	Alain Mimoun (Fra)
1960	Abebe Bikila (Eth)

1964	Abebe Bikila (Eth)
1968	Mamo Wolde (Eth)
1972	Frank Shorter (USA)
1976	Waldemar Cierpinski (GDR)
1980	Waldemar Cierpinski (GDR)
1984	Carlos Lopes (Por)
1988	Gelindo Bordin (Ita)
1992	Hwang Young-jo (SKo)

Men's Steeplechase
1948	Tore Sjöstrand (Swe)
1952	Horace Ashenfelter (USA)
1956	Christopher Brasher (UK)
1960	Zdzislaw Kryszkowiak (Pol)
1964	Gaston Roelants (Bel)
1968	Amos Biwott (Ken)
1972	Kipchoge Keino (Ken)
1976	Anders Gärderud (Swe)
1980	Bronislaw Malinowski (Pol)
1984	Julius Korir (Ken)
1988	Julius Kariuki (Ken)
1992	Matthew Birir (Ken)

Men's 110m Hurdles
1948	William Porter (USA)
1952	Harrison Dillard (USA)
1956	Lee Calhoun (USA)
1960	Lee Calhoun (USA)
1964	Hayes Jones (USA)
1968	Willie Davenport (USA)
1972	Rodney Milburn (USA)
1976	Guy Drut (Fra)
1980	Thomas Munkelt (GDR)
1984	Roger Kingdom (USA)
1988	Roger Kingdom (USA)
1992	Mark McKoy (Can)

Men's 400m Hurdles
1948	Roy Cochran (USA)
1952	Charles Moore (USA)
1956	Glenn Davis (USA)
1960	Glenn Davis (USA)
1964	Rex Cawley (USA)
1968	David Hemery (UK)
1972	John Akii-Bua (Uga)
1976	Edwin Moses (USA)
1980	Volker Beck (GDR)
1984	Edwin Moses (USA)
1988	Andre Phillips (USA)
1992	Kevin Young (USA)

Men's High Jump
1948	John Winter (Aus)
1952	Walter Davis (USA)
1956	Charles Dumas (USA)
1960	Robert Shavlakadze (USSR)
1964	Valeriy Brumel (USSR)
1968	Dick Fosbury (USA)
1972	Jüri Tarmak (USSR)
1976	Jacek Wszola (Pol)
1980	Gerd Wessig (GDR)
1984	Dietmar Mögenburg (FRG)
1988	Gennadiy Avdeyenko (USSR)
1992	Javier Sotomayor (Cub)

Men's Pole Vault
1948	Guinn Smith (USA)
1952	Robert Richards (USA)
1956	Robert Richards (USA)
1960	Donald Bragg (USA)
1964	Frederick Hansen (USA)
1968	Bob Seagren (USA)
1972	Wolfgang Nordwig (GDR)
1976	Tadeusz Slusarski (Pol)
1980	Wladyslaw Kozakiewicz (Pol)
1984	Pierre Quinon (Fra)
1988	Sergey Bubka (USSR)
1992	Maksim Tarasov (CIS/Rus)

Men's Triple Jump
1948	Arne Ahman (Swe)
1952	Adhemar Ferreira da Silva (Bra)
1956	Adhemar Ferreira da Silva (Bra)
1960	Jozef Schmidt (Pol)
1964	Jozef Schmidt (Pol)
1968	Viktor Saneyev (USSR)
1972	Viktor Saneyev (USSR)
1976	Viktor Saneyev (USSR)
1980	Jaak Uudmäe (USSR)
1984	Al Joyner (USA)
1988	Khristo Markov (Bul)
1992	Mike Conley (USA)

Men's Long Jump
1948	William Steele (USA)
1952	Jerome Biffle (USA)
1956	Gregory Bell (USA)
1960	Ralph Boston (USA)
1964	Lynn Davies (UK)
1968	Bob Beamon (USA)
1972	Randy Williams (USA)
1976	Arnie Robinson (USA)
1980	Lutz Dombrowski (GDR)
1984	Carl Lewis (USA)
1988	Carl Lewis (USA)
1992	Carl Lewis (USA)

Men's Shot
1948	Wilbur Thompson (USA)
1952	Parry O'Brien (USA)
1956	Parry O'Brien (USA)
1960	William Nieder (USA)
1964	Dallas Long (USA)
1968	Randy Matson (USA)
1972	Wladyslaw Komar (Pol)
1976	Udo Beyer (GDR)
1980	Vladimir Kiselyov (USSR)
1984	Alessandro Andrei (Ita)
1988	Ulf Timmermann (GDR)
1992	Mike Stulce (USA)

Men's Discus
1948	Adolfo Consolini (Ita)
1952	Sim Iness (USA)
1956	Al Oerter (USA)
1960	Al Oerter (USA)
1964	Al Oerter (USA)
1968	Al Oerter (USA)
1972	Ludvik Danek (Cze)
1976	Mac Wilkins (USA)
1980	Viktor Rashchupkin (USSR)
1984	Rolf Danneberg (FRG)
1988	Jürgen Schult (GDR)
1992	Romas Ubartas (Lit)

Men's Javelin
1948	Tapio Rautavaara (Fin)
1952	Cyrus Young (USA)
1956	Egil Danielsen (Nor)
1960	Viktor Tsibulenko (USSR)
1964	Pauli Nevala (Fin)
1968	Janis Lusis (USSR)
1972	Klaus Wolfermann (FRG)
1976	Miklós Németh (Hun)
1980	Dainis Kula (USSR)
1984	Arto Härkönen (Fin)
1988	Tapio Korjus (Fin)
1992	Jan Zelezny (Cze)

Men's Hammer
1948	Imre Németh (Hun)
1952	József Csermak (Hun)
1956	Harold Connolly (USA)
1960	Vasiliy Rudenkov (USSR)
1964	Romuald Klim (USSR)
1968	Gyula Zsivótzky (Hun)
1972	Anatoliy Bondarchuk (USSR)
1976	Yuriy Sedykh (USSR)
1980	Yuriy Sedykh (USSR)
1984	Juha Tiainen (Fin)
1988	Sergey Litvinov (USSR)
1992	Andrey Abduvaliyev (CIS/Tjk)

Men's Decathlon
1948	Robert Mathias (USA)
1952	Robert Mathias (USA)
1956	Milton Campbell (USA)
1960	Rafer Johnson (USA)
1964	Willi Holdorf (FRG)
1968	Bill Toomey (USA)
1972	Nikolay Avilov (USSR)
1976	Bruce Jenner (USA)
1980	Daley Thompson (UK)
1984	Daley Thompson (UK)
1988	Christian Schenk (GDR)
1992	Robert Zmelik (Cze)

Men's 20km Walk
1956	Leonid Spirin (USSR)
1960	Vladimir Golubnichiy (USSR)
1964	Kenneth Matthews (UK)
1968	Vladimir Golubnichiy (USSR)
1972	Peter Frenkel (GDR)
1976	Daniel Bautista (Mex)
1980	Maurizio Damilano (Ita)
1984	Ernesto Canto (Mex)

1988 Jozef Pribilinec (Cze)
1992 Daniel Plaza (Spa)

Men's 50km Walk
1948 John Ljunggren (Swe)
1952 Giuseppe Dordoni (Ita)
1956 Norman Read (NZ)
1960 Don Thompson (UK)
1964 Abdon Pamich (Ita)
1968 Christophe Höhne (GDR)
1972 Bernd Kannenberg (GDR)
1980 Hartwig Gauder (GDR)
1984 Raúl Gonzales (Mex)
1988 Vyacheslav Ivanenko (USSR)
1992 Andrey Perlov (CIS/Rus)

Men's 4 × 100m Relay
1948 USA
1952 USA
1956 USA
1960 West Germany
1964 USA
1968 USA
1972 USA
1976 USA
1980 USSR
1984 USA
1988 USSR
1992 USA

Men's 4 × 400m Relay
1948 USA
1952 Jamaica
1956 USA
1960 USA
1964 USA
1968 USA
1972 Kenya
1976 USA
1980 USSR
1984 USA
1988 USA
1992 USA

Women's 100m
1948 Fanny Blankers-Koen (Hol)
1952 Marjorie Jackson (Aus)
1956 Betty Cuthbert (Aus)
1960 Wilma Rudolph (USA)
1964 Wyomia Tyus (USA)
1968 Wyomia Tyus (USA)
1972 Renate Stecher (GDR)
1976 Annegret Richter (FRG)
1980 Lyudmila Kondratyeva (USSR)
1984 Evelyn Ashford (USA)
1988 Florence Griffith-Joyner (USA)
1992 Gail Devers (USA)

Women's 200m
1948 Fanny Blankers-Koen (Hol)
1952 Marjorie Jackson (Aus)
1956 Betty Cuthbert (Aus)
1960 Wilma Rudolph (USA)
1964 Edith Maguire (USA)
1968 Irena Szewinska (Pol)
1972 Renate Stecher (GDR)
1976 Bärbel Eckert (GDR)
1980 Bärbel Wöckel (née Eckert) (GDR)
1984 Valerie Brisco-Hooks (USA)
1988 Florence Griffith-Joyner (USA)
1992 Gwen Torrance (USA)

Women's 400m
1964 Betty Cuthbert (Aus)
1968 Colette Besson (Fra)
1972 Monika Zehrt (GDR)
1976 Irena Szewinska (Pol)
1980 Marita Koch (GDR)
1984 Valerie Brisco-Hooks (USA)
1988 Olga Bryzgina (USSR)
1992 Marie-José Pérec (Fra)

Women's 800m
1960 Lyudmila Shevtsova (USSR)
1964 Ann Packer (UK)
1968 Madeline Manning (USA)
1972 Hildegard Falck (FRG)
1976 Tatyana Kazankina (USSR)
1980 Nadezhda Olizarenko (USSR)
1984 Doina Melinte (Rom)
1988 Sigrun Wodars (GDR)
1992 Ellen van Langren (Hol)

Women's 1500m
1972 Lyudmila Bragina (USSR)
1976 Tatyana Kazankina (USSR)
1980 Tatyana Kazankina (USSR)
1984 Gabriella Doria (Ita)
1988 Paula Ivan (Rom)
1992 Hassiba Boulmerka (Alg)

Women's 3000m
1984 Maricica Puica (Rom)
1988 Tatyana Samolenko (USSR)
1992 Yelena Romanova (CIS/Rus)

Women's 10,000m
1988 Olga Bondarenko (USSR)
1992 Derartu Tulu (Eth)

Women's Marathon
1984 Joan Benoit (USA)
1988 Rosa Mota (Por)
1992 Valentina Yegorova (CIS/Rus)

Women's 80m Hurdles
1948 Fanny Blankers-Koen (Hol)
1952 Shirley Strickland (Aus)
1956 Shirley Strickland (Aus)
1960 Irina Press (USSR)
1964 Karin Balzer (GDR)
1968 Maureen Caird (Aus)

Women's 100m Hurdles
1972 Annelie Ehrhardt (GDR)
1976 Johanna Schaller (GDR)
1980 Vera Komisova (USSR)
1984 Benita Fitzgerald-Brown (USA)
1988 Yordanka Donkova (Bul)
1992 Paraskevi Patoulidou (Gre)

Women's 400m Hurdles
1984 Newal El Moutawakil (Mor)
1988 Debbie Flintoff-King (Aus)
1992 Sally Gunnell (UK)

Women's High Jump
1948 Alice Coachman (USA)
1952 Esther Brand (SAf)
1956 Mildred McDaniel (USA)
1960 Iolanda Balas (Rom)
1964 Iolanda Balas (Rom)
1968 Miloslava Rezková (Cze)
1972 Ulrike Meyfarth (FRG)
1976 Rosemarie Ackermann (GDR)
1980 Sara Simeoni (Ita)
1984 Ulrike Meyfarth (FRG)
1988 Louise Ritter (USA)
1992 Heike Henkel (Ger)

Women's Long Jump
1948 Olga Gyarmati (Hun)
1952 Yvette Williams (NZ)
1956 Elzbieta Krzesinska (Pol)
1960 Vyera Krepkina (USSR)
1964 Mary Rand (UK)
1968 Viorica Viscopoleanu (Rom)
1972 Heide Rosendahl (FRG)
1976 Angela Voigt (GDR)
1980 Tatyana Kolpakova (USSR)
1984 Anisoara Stanciu (Rom)
1988 Jackie Joyner-Kersee (USA)
1992 Heike Drechsler (Ger)

Women's Shot
1948 Micheline Ostermeyer (Fra)
1952 Galina Zybina (USSR)
1956 Tamara Tishkyevich (USSR)
1960 Tamara Press (USSR)
1964 Tamara Press (USSR)
1968 Margitta Gummel (GDR)
1972 Nadezhda Chizhova (USSR)
1976 Ivanka Khristova (Bul)
1980 Ilona Slupianek (GDR)
1984 Claudia Losch (FRG)
1988 Natalya Lisovskaya (USSR)
1992 Svetlana Krivelyova (CIS/Rus)

Women's Discus
1948 Micheline Ostermeyer (Fra)
1952 Nina Ponomaryeva (USSR)
1956 Olga Fikotová (Cze)
1960 Nina Ponomaryeva (USSR)
1964 Tamara Press (USSR)
1968 Lia Manoliu (Rom)

1972	Faina Melnik (USSR)
1976	Evelin Schlaak (GDR)
1980	Evelin Jahl (née Schlaak) (GDR)
1984	Ria Stalmach (Hol)
1988	Martina Hellmann (GDR)
1992	Maritza Marten (Cub)

Women's Javelin

1948	Herma Bauma (Aut)
1952	Dana Zátopková (Cze)
1956	Inese Jaunzeme (USSR)
1960	Elvira Ozolina (USSR)
1964	Mihaela Penes (Rom)
1968	Angéla Németh (Hun)
1972	Ruth Fuchs (GDR)
1976	Ruth Fuchs (GDR)
1980	Maria C. Colón (Cub)
1984	Tessa Sanderson (UK)
1988	Petra Felke (GDR)
1992	Silke Renk (Ger)

Women's Heptathlon

1984	Glynis Nunn (Aus)
1988	Jackie Joyner-Kersee (USA)
1992	Jackie Joyner-Kersee (USA)

Women's 10km Walk

1992	Chen Yueling (Chn)

Women's 4 × 100m Relay

1948	Holland
1952	USA
1956	Australia
1960	USA
1964	Poland
1968	USA
1972	West Germany
1976	East Germany
1980	East Germany
1984	USA
1988	USA
1992	USA

Women's 4 × 400m Relay

1972	East Germany
1976	East Germany
1980	USSR
1984	USA
1988	USSR
1992	CIS (united team)

BADMINTON

WORLD CHAMPIONS

	MEN	WOMEN
1977	Flemming Delfs (Denmark)	Lene Koppen (Denmark)
1980	Rudy Hartono (Indonesia)	Wiharjo Verawaty (Indonesia)
1983	Icuk Sugiarto (Indonesia)	Li Lingwei (China)
1985	Han Jian (China)	Han Aiping (China)
1987	Yang Yang (China)	Han Aiping (China)
1989	Yang Yang (China)	Li Lingwei (China)
1991	Zhao Jianhua (China)	Tang Jiuhong (China)
1993	Joko Suprianto (Indonesia)	Susi Susanti (Indonesia)
1994	Heryanto Arbi (Indonesia)	Susi Susanti (Indonesia)

ALL-ENGLAND CHAMPIONS (POST WAR)

	MEN	WOMEN
1947	Conny Jepsen (Sweden)	Marrie Ussing (Denmark)
1948	Jorn Skaarup (Denmark)	Kirsten Thorndahl (Denmark)
1949	Dave Freeman (USA)	Aase Jacobsen (Denmark)
1950	Wong Peng Soon (Malaya)	Tonny Olsen-Ahm (Denmark)
1951	Wong Peng Soon (Malaya)	Aase Jacobsen (Denmark)
1952	Wong Peng Soon (Malaya)	Tonny Olsen-Ahm (Denmark)
1953	Eddie Choong (Malaya)	Marie Ussing (Denmark)
1954	Eddie Choong (Malaya)	Judy Devlin (USA)
1955	Wong Peng Soon (Malaya)	Margaret Varner (USA)
1956	Eddie Choong (Malaya)	Margaret Varner (USA)
1957	Eddie Choong (Malaya)	Judy Devlin (USA)
1958	Erland Kops (Denmark)	Judy Devlin (USA)
1959	Tan Joe Hok (Indonesia)	Heather Ward (England)
1960	Erland Kops (Denmark)	Judy Devlin (USA)
1961	Erland Kops (Denmark)	Judy Hashman (née Devlin) (USA)
1962	Erland Kops (Denmark)	Judy Hashman (USA)
1963	Erland Kops (Denmark)	Judy Hashman (USA)
1964	Knud Nielsen (Denmark)	Judy Hashman (USA)
1965	Erland Kops (Denmark)	Ursula Smith (England)
1966	Tan Aik Huang (Malaya)	Judy Hashman (USA)
1967	Erland Kops (Denmark)	Judy Hashman (USA)
1968	Rudy Hartono (Indonesia)	Eva Twedberg (Sweden)
1969	Rudy Hartono (Indonesia)	Hiroe Yuki (Japan)
1970	Rudy Hartono (Indonesia)	Etsuko Takenaka (Japan)
1971	Rudy Hartono (Indonesia)	Eva Twedberg (Sweden)
1972	Rudy Hartono (Indonesia)	Noriko Nakayama (Japan)
1973	Rudy Hartono (Indonesia)	Margaret Beck (England)
1974	Rudy Hartono (Indonesia)	Hiroe Yuki (Japan)
1975	Sven Pri (Denmark)	Hiroe Yuki (Japan)
1976	Rudy Hartono (Indonesia)	Gillian Gilks (England)
1977	Flemming Delfs (Denmark)	Hiroe Yuki (Japan)
1978	Liem Swie King (Indonesia)	Gillian Gilks (England)
1979	Liem Swie King (Indonesia)	Lene Koppen (Denmark)
1980	Prakash Padukone (India)	Lene Koppen (Denmark)
1981	Liem Swie King (Indonesia)	Sun Ai Hwang (South Korea)
1982	Morten Frost (Denmark)	Zang Ailing (China)
1983	Luan Jin (China)	Zang Ailing (China)
1984	Morten Frost (Denmark)	Li Lingwei (China)
1985	Zhao Jianhua (China)	Han Aiping (China)
1986	Morten Frost (Denmark)	Kim Yun-Ja (South Korea)
1987	Morten Frost (Denmark)	Kirsten Larsen (Denmark)
1988	Ib Frederiksen (Denmark)	Gu Jiaming (China)
1989	Yang Yang (China)	Li Lingwei (China)
1990	Zhao Jianhua (China)	Susi Susanti (Indonesia)
1991	Ardy Wiranta (Indonesia)	Susi Susanti (Indonesia)
1992	Liu Jun (China)	Tang Jiuhong (China)
1993	Heryanto Arbi (Indonesia)	Susi Susanti (Indonesia)
1994	Heryanto Arbi (Indonesia)	Susi Susanti (Indonesia)

BASEBALL

WORLD SERIES WINNERS (POST WAR)

1946	St Louis Cardinals	1963	Los Angeles Dodgers	1979	Pittsburgh Pirates
1947	New York Yankees	1964	St Louis Cardinals	1980	Philadelphia Phillies
1948	Cleveland Indians	1965	Los Angeles Dodgers	1981	Los Angeles Dodgers
1949	New York Yankees	1966	Baltimore Orioles	1982	St Louis Cardinals
1950	New York Yankees	1967	St Louis Cardinals	1983	Baltimore Orioles
1951	New York Yankees	1968	Detroit Tigers	1984	Detroit Tigers
1952	New York Yankees	1969	New York Mets	1985	Kansas City Royals
1953	New York Yankees	1970	Baltimore Orioles	1986	New York Mets
1954	New York Yankees	1971	Pittsburgh Pirates	1987	Minnesota Twins
1955	Brooklyn Dodgers	1972	Oakland Athletics	1988	Los Angeles Dodgers
1956	New York Yankees	1973	Oakland Athletics	1989	Oakland Athletics
1957	Milwaukee Braves	1974	Oakland Athletics	1990	Cincinnati Reds
1958	New York Yankees	1975	Cincinnati Reds	1991	Minnesota Twins
1959	Los Angeles Dodgers	1976	Cincinnati Reds	1992	Toronto Blue Jays
1960	Pittsburgh Pirates	1977	New York Yankees	1993	Toronto Blue Jays
1961	New York Yankees	1978	New York Yankees	1994	No Competition
1962	New York Yankees				

Wins since World Series began in 1903

22 New York Yankees
9 St Louis Cardinals
5 Boston Red Sox, Cincinnati Reds, Los Angeles Dodgers, New York Giants, Philadelphia Athletics, Pittsburgh Pirates
4 Detroit Tigers, Oakland Athletics
3 Baltimore Orioles
2 Chicago Cubs, Chicago White Sox, Cleveland Indians, Minnesota Twins, New York Mets, Toronto Blue Jays
1 Boston Braves, Brooklyn Dodgers, Kansas City Royals, Milwaukee Braves, Philadelphia Phillies, Washington Senators

BASKETBALL

WORLD CHAMPIONS

MEN		WOMEN	
1950	Argentina	1953	USA
1954	USA	1957	USA
1959	Brazil	1959	USSR
1963	Brazil	1964	USSR
1967	USSR	1967	USSR
1970	Yugoslavia	1971	USSR
1974	USSR	1975	USSR
1978	Yugoslavia	1979	USA
1982	USSR	1983	USSR
1986	USA	1987	USA
1990	Yugoslavia	1990	USA
1994	USA	1994	Brazil

BOBSLEIGH

OLYMPIC CHAMPIONS (POST WAR)

Two-man Bob
1948 Felix Endrich and Friedrich Waller (Swi)
1952 Andreas Ostler and Lorenz Nieberl (FRG)
1956 Lamberto Dalla Costa and
       Giacomo Conti (Ita)
1964 Tony Nash and Robin Dixon (UK)
1968 Eugenio Monti and Luciano de Paolis (Ita)
1972 Wolfgang Zimmerer and
       Peter Utzschneider (FRG)
1976 Meinhard Nehmer and
       Bernhard Germeshausen (GDR)
1980 Erich Schärer and Josef Benz (Swi)
1984 Wolfang Hoppe and
       Dietmar Schauerhammer (GDR)
1988 Janis Kipurs and Vladimir Kozlov (USSR)
1992 Gustav Weder and Donald Acklin (Swi)
1994 Gustav Weder and Donald Acklin (Swi)

Four-man Bob
1948 USA
1952 West Germany
1956 Switzerland
1964 Canada
1968 Italy
1972 Switzerland
1976 East Germany
1980 East Germany
1984 East Germany
1988 Switzerland
1992 Austria
1994 Germany

Men's Luge Single-seater
1964 Thomas Köhler (GDR)

1968 Manfred Schmid (Aut)
1972 Wolfgang Scheidel (GDR)
1976 Detlef Günther (GDR)
1980 Bernhard Glass (GDR)
1984 Paul Hildgartner (Ita)
1988 Jens Müller (GDR)
1992 Georg Hackl (Ger)
1994 Georg Hackl (Ger)

Women's Luge Single-seater
1964 Ortrun Enderlein (GDR)
1968 Erica Lechner (Ita)
1972 Anna-Maria Müller (GDR)
1976 Margit Schumann (GDR)
1980 Vera Zozulya (USSR)
1984 Steffi Martin (GDR)
1988 Steffi Walter (née Martin) (GDR)
1992 Doris Neuner (Aut)
1994 Gerda Weissensteiner (Ita)

Luge Two-seater
1964 Josef Feistmantl and Manfred Stengl (Aut)
1968 Thomas Köhler and Klaus Bonsack (GDR)
1972 Paul Hildgartner and
          Walter Plaikner (Ita)
     Horst Hörnlein and
          Reinhard Bredow (GDR)
1976 Hans Rinn and Norbert Hahn (GDR)
1980 Hans Rinn and Norbert Hahn (GDR)
1984 Hans Stanggasinger and Franz Wembacher
     (FRG)
1988 Jörg Hoffman and Jochen Pietzsch (GDR)
1992 Stefan Krausse and Jan Behrendt (Ger)
1994 Kurt Brugger and Wilfred Huber (Ita)

CRICKET

TEST MATCHES *

England	Played	Won	Lost	Drawn
v. Australia (1876–1995)	284	90	111	83
v. India (1954–1993)	81	31	14	36
v. New Zealand (1929–1994)	75	34	4	37
v. Pakistan (1954–1991)	52	14	7	31
v. South Africa (1888–1994)	105	47	19	39
v. Sri Lanka (1982–1993)	5	3	1	1
v West Indies (1928–1994)	109	25	46	38
TOTAL	711	244	202	265

* Up to March 1995

WORLD CUP

1975	West Indies	1987	Australia
1979	West Indies	1992	Pakistan
1983	India		

COUNTY CHAMPIONSHIP (POST WAR)

1946	Yorkshire	1962	Yorkshire	1978	Kent
1947	Middlesex	1963	Yorkshire	1979	Essex
1948	Glamorgan	1964	Worcestershire	1980	Middlesex
1949	Middlesex	1965	Worcestershire	1981	Nottinghamshire
	Yorkshire	1966	Yorkshire	1982	Middlesex
1950	Lancashire	1967	Yorkshire	1983	Essex
	Surrey	1968	Yorkshire	1984	Essex
1951	Warwickshire	1969	Glamorgan	1985	Middlesex
1952	Surrey	1970	Kent	1986	Essex
1953	Surrey	1971	Surrey	1987	Nottinghamshire
1954	Surrey	1972	Warwickshire	1988	Worcestershire
1955	Surrey	1973	Hampshire	1989	Worcestershire
1956	Surrey	1974	Worcestershire	1990	Middlesex
1957	Surrey	1975	Leicestershire	1991	Essex
1958	Surrey	1976	Middlesex	1992	Essex
1959	Yorkshire	1977	Kent	1993	Middlesex
1961	Hampshire		Middlesex	1994	Warwickshire
1960	Yorkshire				

Wins and shared wins since Championship began in 1864

33	Yorkshire	6	Essex
20	Surrey	5	Worcestershire
19	Nottinghamshire	4	Gloucestershire, Warwickshire
13	Middlesex	2	Glamorgan, Hampshire
12	Lancashire	1	Derbyshire, Leicestershire
7	Kent		

NATWEST BANK TROPHY WINNERS

1963	Sussex	1974	Kent	1985	Essex
1964	Sussex	1975	Lancashire	1986	Sussex
1965	Yorkshire	1976	Northamptonshire	1987	Nottinghamshire
1966	Warwickshire	1977	Middlesex	1988	Middlesex
1967	Kent	1978	Sussex	1989	Warwickshire
1968	Warwickshire	1979	Somerset	1990	Lancashire
1969	Yorkshire	1980	Middlesex	1991	Hampshire
1970	Lancashire	1981	Derbyshire	1992	Northamptonshire
1971	Lancashire	1982	Surrey	1993	Warwickshire
1972	Lancashire	1983	Somerset	1994	Worcestershire
1973	Gloucestershire	1984	Middlesex		

SUNDAY LEAGUE WINNERS

1969	Lancashire	1978	Hampshire	1987	Worcestershire
1970	Lancashire	1979	Somerset	1988	Worcestershire
1971	Worcestershire	1980	Warwickshire	1989	Lancashire
1972	Kent	1981	Essex	1990	Derbyshire
1973	Kent	1982	Sussex	1991	Nottinghamshire
1974	Leicestershire	1983	Yorkshire	1992	Middlesex
1975	Hampshire	1984	Essex	1993	Glamorgan
1976	Kent	1985	Essex	1994	Warwickshire
1977	Leicestershire	1986	Hampshire		

BENSON & HEDGES CUP WINNERS

1972	Leicestershire	1980	Northamptonshire	1988	Hampshire
1973	Kent	1981	Somerset	1989	Nottinghamshire
1974	Surrey	1982	Somerset	1990	Lancashire
1975	Leicestershire	1983	Middlesex	1991	Worcestershire
1976	Kent	1984	Lancashire	1992	Hampshire
1977	Gloucestershire	1985	Leicestershire	1993	Derbyshire
1978	Kent	1986	Middlesex	1994	Warwickshire
1979	Essex	1987	Yorkshire		

GOLF

MAJOR TOURNAMENT WINNERS (POST WAR)

	UK Open	US Open	US Masters	PGA
1946	S Snead (USA)	L Mangrum (USA)	H Keiser (USA)	B Hogan (USA)
1947	F Daly (GBR)	L Worsham (USA)	J Demaret (USA)	J Ferrier (USA)
1948	H Cotton (GBR)	B Hogan (USA)	C Harmon (USA)	B Hogan (USA)
1949	B Locke (SAF)	C Middlecoff (USA)	S Snead (USA)	S Snead (USA)
1950	B Locke (SAF)	B Hogan (USA)	J Demaret (USA)	C Harper (USA)
1951	M Faulkner (GBR)	B Hogan (USA)	B Hogan (USA)	S Snead (USA)
1952	B Locke (SAF)	J Boros (USA)	S Snead (USA)	J Turnesa (USA)
1953	B Hogan (USA)	B Hogan (USA)	B Hogan (USA)	W Burkemo (USA)
1954	P Thomson (AUS)	E Furgol (USA)	S Snead (USA)	C Harbert (USA)
1955	P Thomson (AUS)	J Fleck (USA)	C Middlecoff (USA)	D Ford (USA)
1956	P Thomson (AUS)	C Middlecoff (USA)	J Burke (USA)	J Burke (USA)
1957	B Locke (SAF)	D Mayer (USA)	D Ford (USA)	L Herbert (USA)
1958	P Thomson (AUS)	T Bolt (USA)	A Palmer (USA)	D Finsterwald (USA)
1959	G Player (SAF)	B Caspar (USA)	A Wall (USA)	B Roseburg (USA)
1960	K Nagle (AUS)	A Palmer (USA)	A Palmer (USA)	J Hebert (USA)
1961	A Palmer (USA)	G Littler (USA)	G Player (SAF)	J Barber (USA)
1962	A Palmer (USA)	J Nicklaus (USA)	A Palmer (USA)	G Player (SAF)
1963	B Charles (NZL)	J Boros (USA)	J Nicklaus (USA)	J Nicklaus (USA)
1964	T Lema (USA)	K Venturi (USA)	A Palmer (USA)	B Nichols (USA)
1965	P Thomson (AUS)	G Player (SAF)	J Nicklaus (USA)	D Marr (USA)
1966	J Nicklaus (USA)	B Casper (USA)	J Nicklaus (USA)	A Geiberger (USA)
1967	R De Vicenzo (ARG)	J Nicklaus (USA)	G Brewer (USA)	D January (USA)
1968	G Player (SAF)	L Trevino (USA)	B Goalby (USA)	J Boros (USA)
1969	T Jacklin (GBR)	O Moody (USA)	G Archer (USA)	R Floyd (USA)
1970	J Nicklaus (USA)	T Jacklin (GBR)	B Casper (USA)	D Stockton (USA)
1971	L Trevino (USA)	L Trevino (USA)	C Coody (USA)	J Nicklaus (USA)
1972	L Trevino (USA)	J Nicklaus (USA)	J Nicklaus (USA)	G Player (SAF)
1973	T Weiskopf (USA)	J Miller (USA)	T Aaron (USA)	J Nicklaus (USA)
1974	G Player (SAF)	H Irwin (USA)	G Player (SAF)	L Trevino (USA)
1975	T Watson (USA)	L Graham (USA)	J Nicklaus (USA)	J Nicklaus (USA)
1976	J Miller (USA)	J Pate (USA)	R Floyd (USA)	D Stockton (USA)
1977	T Watson (USA)	H Green (USA)	T Watson (USA)	L Wadkins (USA)
1978	J Nicklaus (USA)	A North (USA)	G Player (SAF)	J Mahaffey (USA)
1979	S Ballesteros (SPA)	H Irwin (USA)	F Zoeller (USA)	D Graham (AUS)
1980	T Watson (USA)	J Nicklaus (USA)	S Ballesteros (SPA)	J Nicklaus (USA)
1981	B Rogers (USA)	D Graham (AUS)	T Watson (USA)	L Nelson (USA)
1982	T Watson (USA)	T Watson (USA)	C Stadler (USA)	R Floyd (USA)
1983	T Watson (USA)	L Nelson (USA)	S Ballesteros (SPA)	H Sutton (USA)
1984	S Ballesteros (SPA)	F Zoeller (USA)	B Crenshaw (USA)	L Trevino (USA)
1985	S Lyle (GBR)	A North (USA)	B Langer (WGR)	H Green (USA)
1986	G Norman (AUS)	R Floyd (USA)	J Nicklaus (USA)	B Tway (USA)
1987	N Faldo (GBR)	S Simpson (USA)	L Mize (USA)	L Nelson (USA)
1988	S Ballesteros (SPA)	C Strange (USA)	S Lyle (GBR)	J Sluman (USA)
1989	M Calcavecchia (USA)	C Strange (USA)	N Faldo (GBR)	P Stewart (USA)
1990	N Faldo (GBR)	H Irwin (USA)	N Faldo (GBR)	W Grady (AUS)
1991	I Baker-Finch (AUS)	P Stewart (USA)	I Woosnam (GBR)	J Daly (USA)
1992	N Faldo (GBR)	T Kite (USA)	F Couples (USA)	N Price (ZIM)
1993	G Norman (AUS)	L Janzen (USA)	B Langer (GER)	P Azinger (USA)
1994	N Price (ZIM)	E Els (SAF)	J M Olazabal (SPA)	N Price (ZIM)

RYDER CUP WINNERS (POST WAR)

USA v Great Britain

1947	Portland, Oregon	USA	1963	Atlanta, Georgia	USA
1949	Ganton, England	USA	1965	Southport, England	USA
1951	Pinehurst, North Carolina	USA	1967	Houston, Texas	USA
1953	Wentworth, England	USA	1969	Southport, England	Tied
1955	Thunderbird, California	USA	1971	St Louis, Missouri	USA
1957	Lindrick, England	Great Britain	1973	Muirfield, Scotland	USA
1959	Elorado, California	USA	1975	Laurel Valley, Pennsylvania	USA
1961	Royal Lytham, England	USA	1977	Royal Lytham, England	USA

USA v Europe

1979	Greenbrier, West Virginia	USA	1987	Columbus, Ohio	Europe
1981	Walton Heath, England	USA	1989	The Belfry, England	Tied
1983	PGA Course, Florida	USA	1991	Kiawah Island, South Carolina	USA
1985	The Belfry, England	Europe	1993	The Belfry, England	USA

Wins since competition began in 1927

USA	23
Great Britain/Europe	5
Tied	2

GREYHOUND RACING

THE DERBY WINNERS (POST WAR)

Year	Greyhound	Year	Greyhound
1945	Ballyhennessy Seal	1970	John Silver
1946	Monday's News	1971	Dolores Rocket
1947	Trev's Perfection	1972	Patricia's Hope
1948	Priceless Border	1973	Patricia's Hope
1949	Narrogar Ann	1974	Jimsun
1950	Ballymac Ball	1975	Tartan Khan
1951	Ballylanigan Tanist	1976	Mutts Silver
1952	Endless Gossip	1977	Balliniska Band
1953	Daws Dancer	1978	Lacca Champion
1954	Paul's Fun	1979	Sarah's Bunny
1955	Rushton Mack	1980	Indian Joe
1956	Dunmore King	1981	Parkdown Jet
1957	Ford Spartan	1982	Laurie's Panther
1958	Pigalle Wonder	1983	I'm Slippy
1959	Mile Bush Pride	1984	Whisper Wishes
1960	Duleek Dandy	1985	Pagan Swallow
1961	Palm's Printer	1986	Tico
1962	The Grand Canal	1987	Signal Spark
1963	Lucky Boy Boy	1988	Hit-the-Lid
1964	Hack Up Chieftain	1989	Lartigue Note
1965	Chittering Clapton	1990	Slippy Blue
1966	Faithful Hope	1991	Ballinderry Ash
1967	Tric-Trac	1992	Farloe Melody
1968	Camira Flash	1993	Ringa Hustle
1969	Sand Star	1994	Moral Standards

HOCKEY

MEN'S WORLD CUP CHAMPIONS		WOMEN'S WORLD CUP CHAMPIONS	
1971	Pakistan	1974	Holland
1973	Holland	1976	West Germany
1975	India	1978	Holland
1978	Pakistan	1981	West Germany
1982	Pakistan	1983	Holland
1986	Australia	1986	Holland
1990	Holland	1990	Holland
1994	Pakistan	1994	Australia

HORSE RACING

MAJOR RACE WINNERS (POST WAR)

GRAND NATIONAL WINNERS		DERBY WINNERS
1946	Lovely Cottage	Airborne
1947	Caughoo	Pearl Diver
1948	Sheila's Cottage	My Love
1949	Russian Hero	Nimbus
1950	Freebooter	Galcador
1951	Nickel Coin	Arctic Prince
1952	Teal	Tulyar
1953	Early Mist	Pinza
1954	Royal Tan	Never Say Die
1955	Quare Times	Phil Drake
1956	ESB	Lavandin
1957	Sundew	Crepello
1958	Mr What	Hard Ridden
1959	Oxo	Parthia
1960	Merryman II	St Paddy
1961	Nicolaus Silver	Psidium
1962	Kilmore	Larkspur
1963	Ayala	Relko
1964	Team Spirit	Santa Claus
1965	Jay Trump	Sea Bird II
1966	Anglo	Charlottown
1967	Foinavon	Royal Palace
1968	Red Alligator	Sir Ivor
1969	Highland Wedding	Blakeney
1970	Gay Trip	Nijinsky
1971	Specify	Mill Reef
1972	Well to Do	Roberto
1973	Red Rum	Morston
1974	Red Rum	Snow Knight
1975	L'Escargot	Grundy
1976	Rag Trade	Empery
1977	Red Rum	The Minstrel
1978	Lucius	Shirley Heights
1979	Rubstic	Troy
1980	Ben Nevis	Henbit
1981	Aldaniti	Shergar

GRAND NATIONAL WINNERS

1982	Grittar
1983	Corbiere
1984	Hallo Dandy
1985	Last Suspect
1986	West Tip
1987	Maori Venture
1988	Rhyme 'n' Reason
1989	Little Polvier
1990	Mr Frisk
1991	Seagram
1992	Party Politics
1993	–
1994	Miinnehoma
1995	Royal Athlete

DERBY WINNERS

1982	Golden Fleece
1983	Teenoso
1984	Secreto
1985	Slip Anchor
1986	Shahrastani
1987	Reference Point
1988	Kahyasi
1989	Nashwan
1990	Quest for Fame
1991	Generous
1992	Dr Devious
1993	Commander in Chief
1994	Ehrhaab

ICE HOCKEY

WORLD CHAMPIONS (POST WAR)

1947	Czechoslovakia	1964	USSR	1980	USA
1948	Canada	1965	USSR	1981	USSR
1949	Czechoslovakia	1966	USSR	1982	USSR
1950	Canada	1967	USSR	1983	USSR
1951	Canada	1968	USSR	1984	USSR
1952	Canada	1969	USSR	1985	Czechoslovakia
1953	Sweden	1970	USSR	1986	USSR
1954	USSR	1971	USSR	1987	Sweden
1955	Canada	1972	Czechoslovakia	1988	USSR
1956	USSR	1973	USSR	1989	USSR
1957	Sweden	1974	USSR	1990	USSR
1958	Canada	1975	USSR	1991	Sweden
1959	Canada	1976	Czechoslovakia	1992	Sweden
1960	USA	1977	Czechoslovakia	1993	Russia
1961	Canada	1978	USSR	1994	Canada
1962	Sweden	1979	USSR	1995	Finland
1963	USSR				

Wins since competition began in 1920

24	USSR	3	USA
11	Canada	1	Finland, Great Britain, Russia
6	Czechoslovakia, Sweden		

ICE SKATING

OLYMPIC CHAMPIONS (POST WAR)

Men's Figure Skating
1948	Richard Button (USA)
1952	Richard Button (USA)
1956	Hayes Alan Jenkins (USA)
1960	David Jenkins (USA)
1964	Manfred Schneldorfer (FRG)
1968	Wolfgang Schwarz (Aut)
1972	Ondrej Napela (Cze)
1976	John Curry (GB)
1980	Robin Cousins (GB)
1984	Scott Hamilton (USA)
1988	Brian Boitano (USA)
1992	Viktor Petrenko (CIS)
1994	Aleksi Urmanov (Rus)

Women's Figure Skating
1948	Barbara Ann Scott (Can)
1952	Jeanette Altwegg (GB)
1956	Tenley Albright (USA)
1960	Carol Heiss (USA)
1964	Sjoukje Dijkstra (Hol)
1968	Peggy Fleming (USA)
1972	Beatrix Schuba (Aut)
1976	Dorothy Hamill (USA)
1980	Anett Potzsch (GDR)
1984	Katarina Witt (GDR)
1988	Katarina Witt (GDR)
1992	Kristi Yamaguchi (USA)
1994	Oksana Baiul (Ukr)

Pairs
1948	Micheline Lannoy and Pierre Baugniet (Bel)
1952	Ria Falk and Paul Falk (Ger)
1956	Elisabeth Schwartz and Kurt Oppelt (Aut)
1960	Barbara Wagner and Robert Paul (Can)
1964	Lyudmila Belousova and Oleg Protopopov (USSR)
1968	Lyudmila Belousova and Oleg Protopopov (USSR)
1972	Irina Rodnina and Aleksey Ulanov (USSR)
1976	Irina Rodnina and Aleksandr Zaitsev (USSR)
1980	Irina Rodnina and Aleksandr Zaitsev (USSR)
1984	Yelena Valova and Oleg Vasiliev (USSR)
1988	Yekaterina Gordeyeva and Sergey Grinkov (USSR)
1992	Natalya Mishkutienok and Artur Dmitriyev (CIS)
1994	Ekaterina Gordeeva and Sergei Krinkov (Rus)

Ice Dancing
1976	Lyudmila Pakhomova and Aleksandr Gorshkov (USSR)
1980	Natalya Linitschuck and Gannadiy Karponosov (USSR)
1984	Jayne Torvill and Christopher Dean (GB)
1988	Natalya Bestemianova and Andre Bukin (USSR)
1992	Marina Klimova and Sergey Ponomarenko (CIS)
1994	Oksana Grichtuk and Yevgeny Platov (Rus)

Men's 500m Speed Skating
1948	Finn Helgesen (Nor)
1952	Kenneth Henry (USA)
1956	Yevgeny Grishin (USSR)
1960	Yevgeny Grishin (USSR)
1964	Richard McDermott (USA)
1968	Erhard Keller (Ger)
1972	Erhard Keller (Ger)
1976	Yevgeny Kulikov (USSR)
1980	Eric Heiden (USA)
1984	Sergei Fokichev (USSR)
1988	Uwe-Jens Mey (GDR)
1992	Uwe-Jens Mey (Ger)
1994	Aleksandr Golubev (Rus)

Men's 1000m Speed Skating
1976	Peter Mueller (USA)
1980	Eric Heiden (USA)
1984	Gaetan Boucher (Can)
1988	Nikolay Gulyayev (USSR)
1992	Olaf Zinke (Ger)
1994	Daniel Jansen (USA)

Men's 1500m Speed Skating
1948	Sverre Farstad (Nor)
1952	Hjalmar Andersen (Nor)
1956	Yevgeny Grishin (USSR)
1960	Roald Aas (Nor)
1964	Ants Antson (USSR)
1968	Cornelis Verkerk (Hol)
1972	Adrianus Schenk (Hol)
1976	Jan Egil Storholt (Nor)
1980	Eric Heiden (USA)
1984	Gaetan Boucher (Can)
1988	Andre Hoffman (GDR)
1992	Johann Olav Koss (Nor)
1994	Johann Olav Koss (Nor)

Men's 5000m Speed Skating
1948	Reider Liaklev (Nor)
1952	Hjalmar Andersen (Nor)
1956	Boris Shilkov (USSR)
1960	Viktor Kosichkin (USSR)
1964	Knut Johannesen (Nor)
1968	Fred Anton Maier (Nor)
1972	Adrianus Schenk (Hol)
1976	Sten Stensen (Nor)
1980	Eric Heiden (USA)
1984	Tomas Gustafsson (Swe)
1988	Tomas Gustafsson (Swe)
1992	Geir Karlsrad (Nor)
1994	Johann Olav Koss (Nor)

Men's 10,000m Speed Skating
1948	Ake Seyffarth (Swe)
1952	Hjalmar Andersen (Nor)
1956	Sigvard Ericsson (Swe)
1960	Knut Johannesen (Nor)
1964	Jonny Nilsson (Swe)
1968	Johnny Hoglin (Swe)
1972	Adrianus Schenk (Hol)
1976	Piet Kleine (Hol)
1980	Eric Heiden (USA)
1984	Igor Malkov (USSR)
1988	Tomas Gustafsson (Swe)
1992	Bart Veldkamp (Hol)
1994	Johann Olav Koss (Nor)

Women's 500m Speed Skating
1960	Helga Haase (GDR)
1964	Lydia Skoblikova (USSR)
1968	Lyudmila Titova (USSR)
1972	Anne Henning (USA)
1976	Sheila Young (USA)
1980	Karin Enke (GDR)
1984	Christa Rothenburger (GDR)
1988	Bonnie Blair (USA)
1992	Bonnie Blair (USA)
1994	Bonnie Blair (USA)

Women's 1000m Speed Skating
1960	Klara Guseva (USSR)
1964	Lydia Skoblikova (USSR)
1968	Carolina Geijssen (Hol)
1972	Monika Pflug (Ger)
1976	Tatiana Averina (USSR)
1980	Natalia Petruseva (USSR)
1984	Karin Enke (GDR)
1988	Christa Rothenburger (Hol)
1992	Bonnie Blair (USA)
1994	Bonnie Blair (USA)

Women's 1500m Speed Skating
1960	Lydia Skoblikova (USSR)
1964	Lydia Skoblikova (USSR)
1968	Kaija Mustonen (Fin)
1972	Dianne Holum (USA)
1976	Galina Stepanskaya (USSR)
1980	Annie Borchink (Hol)
1984	Karin Enke (GDR)
1988	Yvonne van Gennip (Hol)
1992	Jacqueline Berner (Ger)
1994	Emese Hunyadi (Aut)

Women's 3000m Speed Skating
1960	Lydia Skoblikova (USSR)
1964	Lydia Skoblikova (USSR)
1968	Johanna Schut (Hol)
1972	Christina Baas-Kaiser (Hol)
1976	Tatiana Averina (USSR)
1980	Bjorg Eva Jensen (Nor)
1984	Andrea Schone (GDR)
1988	Yvonne van Gennip (Hol)
1992	Gunda Niemann (Ger)
1994	Svetlana Bazhanova (Rus)

Women's 5000m Speed Skating
1988	Yvonne van Gennip (Hol)
1992	Gunda Niemann (Ger)
1994	Claudia Pechstein (Ger)

LAWN TENNIS

GRAND SLAM CHAMPIONSHIP WINNERS – MEN (POST WAR)

	Wimbledon	US Open	French Open	Australian Open
1946	Y Petra (FRA)	J Kramer (USA)	M Bernard (FRA)	J Bromwich (AUS)
1947	J Kramer (USA)	J Kramer (USA)	J Asboth (HUN)	D Pails (AUS)
1948	B Falkenberg (USA)	R Gonzales (USA)	F Parker (USA)	A Quist (AUS)
1949	T Schroeder (USA)	R Gonzales (USA)	F Parker (USA)	F Sedgman (AUS)
1950	B Patty (USA)	A Larsen (USA)	B Patty (USA)	F Sedgman (AUS)
1951	D Savitt (USA)	F Sedgman (AUS)	J Drobny (EGY)	D Savitt (USA)
1952	F Sedgman (AUS)	F Sedgman (AUS)	J Drobny (EGY)	K McGregor (AUS)
1953	V Seixas (USA)	T Trabert (USA)	K Rosewall (AUS)	K Rosewall (AUS)
1954	J Drobny (EGY)	V Seixas (USA)	T Trabert (USA)	M Rose (AUS)
1955	T Trabert (USA)	T Trabert (USA)	T Trabert (USA)	K Rosewall (AUS)
1956	L Hoad (AUS)	K Rosewall (AUS)	L Hoad (AUS)	L Hoad (AUS)
1957	L Hoad (AUS)	M Anderson (AUS)	S Davidson (SWE)	A Cooper (AUS)
1958	A Cooper (AUS)	A Cooper (AUS)	M Rose (AUS)	A Cooper (AUS)
1959	A Olmedo (USA)	N Fraser (AUS)	N Pietrangeli (ITA)	A Olmedo (USA)
1960	N Fraser (AUS)	N Fraser (AUS)	N Pietrangeli (ITA)	R Laver (AUS)
1961	R Laver (AUS)	R Emerson (AUS)	M Santana (SPA)	R Emerson (AUS)
1962	R Laver (AUS)	R Laver (AUS)	R Laver (AUS)	R Laver (AUS)
1963	C McKinley (USA)	R Osuna (MEX)	R Emerson (AUS)	R Emerson (AUS)
1964	R Emerson (AUS)	R Emerson (AUS)	M Santana (SPA)	R Emerson (AUS)
1965	R Emerson (AUS)	M Santana (SPA)	F Stolle (AUS)	R Emerson (AUS)
1966	M Santana (SPA)	F Stolle (AUS)	T Roche (AUS)	R Emerson (AUS)
1967	J Newcombe (AUS)	J Newcombe (AUS)	R Emerson (AUS)	R Emerson (AUS)
1968	R Laver (AUS)	A Ashe (USA)	K Rosewall (AUS)	B Bowrey (AUS)
1969	R Laver (AUS)	S Smith (USA)	R Laver (AUS)	R Laver (AUS)
1970	J Newcombe (AUS)	K Rosewall (AUS)	J Kodes (CZE)	A Ashe (USA)
1971	J Newcombe (AUS)	S Smith (USA)	J Kodes (CZE)	K Rosewall (AUS)
1972	S Smith (USA)	I Nastase (RUM)	A Gimeno (SPA)	K Rosewall (AUS)
1973	J Kodes (CZE)	J Newcombe (AUS)	I Nastase (RUM)	J Newcombe (AUS)
1974	J Connors (USA)	J Connors (USA)	B Borg (SWE)	J Connors (USA)
1975	A Ashe (USA)	M Orantes (SPA)	B Borg (SWE)	J Newcombe (USA)
1976	B Borg (SWE)	J Connors (USA)	A Panatta (ITA)	M Edmondson (AUS)
1977	B Borg (SWE)	G Vilas (ARG)	G Vilas (ARG)	R Tanner (USA)
1978	B Borg (SWE)	J Connors (USA)	B Borg (SWE)	G Vilas (ARG)
1979	B Borg (SWE)	J McEnroe (USA)	B Borg (SWE)	G Vilas (ARG)

	Wimbledon	US Open	French Open	Australian Open
1980	B Borg (SWE)	J McEnroe (USA)	B Borg (SWE)	B Teacher (USA)
1981	J McEnroe (USA)	J McEnroe (USA)	B Borg (SWE)	J Kriek (SAF)
1982	J Connors (USA)	J Connors (USA)	M Wilander (SWE)	J Kriek (SAF)
1983	J McEnroe (USA)	J Connors (USA)	Y Noah (FRA)	M Wilander (SWE)
1984	J McEnroe (USA)	J McEnroe (USA)	I Lendl (CZE)	M Wilander (SWE)
1985	B Becker (WGR)	I Lendl (CZE)	M Wilander (SWE)	S Edberg (SWE)
1986	B Becker (WGR)	I Lendl (CZE)	I Lendl (CZE)	—
1987	P Cash (AUS)	I Lendl (CZE)	I Lendl (CZE)	S Edberg (SWE)
1988	S Edberg (SWE)	M Wilander (SWE)	M Wilander (SWE)	M Wilander (SWE)
1989	B Becker (WGR)	B Becker (WGR)	M Chang (USA)	I Lendl (CZE)
1990	S Edberg (SWE)	P Sampras (USA)	A Gomez (ECU)	I Lendl (CZE)
1991	M Stich (GER)	S Edberg (SWE)	J Courier (USA)	B Becker (GER)
1992	A Agassi (USA)	S Edberg (SWE)	J Courier (USA)	J Courier (USA)
1993	P Sampras (USA)	P Sampras (USA)	S Brugera (SPA)	J Courier (USA)
1994	P Sampras (USA)	A Agassi (USA)	S Brugera (SPA)	P Sampras (USA)

GRAND SLAM CHAMPIONSHIP WINNERS – WOMEN (POST WAR)

	Wimbledon	US Open	French Open	Australian Open
1946	P Betz (USA)	P Betz (USA)	M Osborne (USA)	N Bolton (AUS)
1947	M Osborne (USA)	L Brough (USA)	P Todd (USA)	N Bolton (AUS)
1948	L Brough (USA)	M Du Pont (USA)	N Landry (FRA)	N Bolton (AUS)
1949	L Brough (USA)	M Du Pont (USA)	M Du Pont (USA)	D Hart (USA)
1950	L Brough (USA)	M Du Pont (USA)	D Hart (USA)	L Brough (USA)
1951	D Hart (USA)	M Connolly (USA)	S Fry (USA)	N Bolton (AUS)
1952	M Connolly (USA)	M Connolly (USA)	D Hart (USA)	T Long (USA)
1953	M Connolly (USA)	M Connolly (USA)	M Connolly (USA)	M Connolly (USA)
1954	M Connolly (USA)	D Hart (USA)	M Connolly (USA)	T Long (USA)
1955	L Brough (USA)	D Hart (USA)	A Mortimer (GBR)	B Penrose (AUS)
1956	S Fry (USA)	S Fry (USA)	A Gibson (USA)	M Carter (AUS)
1957	A Gibson (USA)	A Gibson (USA)	S Bloomer (GBR)	S Fry (USA)
1958	A Gibson (USA)	A Gibson (USA)	Z Kormoczy (HUN)	A Mortimer (GBR)
1959	M Bueno (BRA)	M Bueno (BRA)	C Truman (GBR)	M Reitano (AUS)
1960	M Bueno (BRA)	D Hard (USA)	D Hard (USA)	M Smith (AUS)
1961	A Mortimer (GBR)	D Hard (USA)	A Haydon (GBR)	M Smith (AUS)
1962	K Susman (USA)	M Smith (AUS)	M Smith (AUS)	M Smith (AUS)
1963	M Smith (AUS)	M Bueno (BRA)	L Turner (AUS)	M Smith (AUS)
1964	M Bueno (BRA)	M Bueno (BRA)	M Smith (AUS)	M Smith (AUS)
1965	M Smith (AUS)	M Smith (AUS)	L Turner (AUS)	M Smith (AUS)
1966	B-J King (USA)	M Bueno (BRA)	A Jones (GBR)*	M Smith (AUS)
1967	B-J King (USA)	B-J King (USA)	F Durr (FRA)	N Richey (USA)
1968	B-J King (USA)	M Court (AUS)*	N Richey (USA)	B-J King (USA)
1969	A Jones (GBR)*	M Court (AUS)*	M Court (AUS)*	M Court (AUS)*
1970	M Court (AUS)*	M Court (AUS)*	M Court (AUS)*	M Court (AUS)*
1971	E Goolagong (AUS)	B-J King (USA)	E Goolagong (AUS)	E Goolagong (AUS)
1972	B-J King (USA)	B-J King (USA)	M Court (AUS)*	V Wade (GBR)
1973	B-J King (USA)	M Court (AUS)*	B-J King (USA)	M Court (AUS)*
1974	C Evert (USA)	B-J King (USA)	M Court (AUS)*	E Goolagong (AUS)
1975	B-J King (USA)	C Evert (USA)	C Evert (USA)	E Goolagong (AUS)
1976	C Evert (USA)	C Evert (USA)	S Barker (GBR)	E Cawley (AUS)*
1977	V Wade (GBR)	C Evert (USA)	M Jauseovec (YUG)	K Reid (AUS)
1978	M Navratilova (CZE)	C Evert (USA)	V Ruzici (ROM)	C O'Neill (AUS)
1979	M Navratilova (CZE)	T Austin (USA)	C Evert (USA)	B Jordan (USA)
1980	E Cawley (AUS)*	C Evert (USA)	C Evert (USA)	H Mandlikova (CZE)
1981	C Evert (USA)	T Austin (USA)	H Mandlikova (CZE)	M Navratilova (USA)
1982	M Navratilova (USA)	C Evert (USA)	M Navratilova (USA)	C Evert (USA)
1983	M Navratilova (USA)	M Navratilova (USA)	C Evert (USA)	M Navratilova (USA)
1984	M Navratilova (USA)	M Navratilova (USA)	M Navratilova (USA)	C Evert (USA)
1985	M Navratilova (USA)	H Mandlikova (CZE)	C Evert (USA)	M Navratilova (USA)
1986	M Navratilova (USA)	M Navratilova (USA)	C Evert (USA)	—
1987	M Navratilova (USA)	M Navratilova (USA)	S Graf (WGR)	H Mandlikova (CZE)
1988	S Graf (WGR)	S Graf (WGR)	S Graf (WGR)	S Graf (WGR)
1989	S Graf (WGR)	S Graf (WGR)	A Sanchez (SPA)	S Graf (WGR)
1990	M Navratilova (USA)	G Sabatini (ARG)	M Seles (YUG)	S Graf (WGR)
1991	S Graf (GER)	M Seles (YUG)	M Seles (YUG)	M Seles (YUG)
1992	S Graf (GER)	M Seles (YUG)	M Seles (YUG)	M Seles (YUG)
1993	S Graf (GER)	S Graf (GER)	S Graf (GER)	M Seles (YUG)
1994	C Martinez (SPA)	A Sanchez (SPA)	A Sanchez (SPA)	S Graf (GER)

* Players who have won before under maiden names:
A Jones as A Hayden, M Court as M Smith, E Cawley as E Goolagong

DAVIS CUP WINNERS (POST WAR)

1946	USA	1963	USA	1979	USA
1947	USA	1964	Australia	1980	Czechoslovakia
1948	USA	1965	Australia	1981	USA
1949	USA	1966	Australia	1982	USA
1950	Australia	1967	Australia	1983	Australia
1951	Australia	1968	USA	1984	Sweden
1952	Australia	1969	USA	1985	Sweden
1953	Australia	1970	USA	1986	Australia
1954	USA	1971	USA	1987	Sweden
1955	Australia	1972	USA	1988	West Germany
1956	Australia	1973	Australia	1989	West Germany
1957	Australia	1974	South Africa	1990	USA
1958	USA	1975	Sweden	1991	France
1959	Australia	1976	Italy	1992	USA
1960	Australia	1977	Australia	1993	Germany
1961	Australia	1978	USA	1994	Sweden
1962	Australia				

Wins since competition began in 1900

30	USA	5	Sweden
26	Australia or Australasia	3	Germany or West Germany
9	Great Britain or British Isles	1	Czechoslovakia, Italy, South Africa
7	France		

MOTOR RACING

FORMULA ONE WORLD CAR CHAMPIONSHIP

	Driver		Car	Constructors Cup
1950	Giuseppe Farina	Italy	Alfa Romeo	
1951	Juan Manuel Fangio	Argentina	Alfa Romeo	
1952	Alberto Ascari	Italy	Ferrari	
1953	Alberto Ascari	Italy	Ferrari	
1954	Juan Manuel Fangio	Argentina	Maserati/Mercedes	
1955	Juan Manuel Fangio	Argentina	Mercedes-Benz	
1956	Juan Manuel Fangio	Argentina	Lancia-Ferrari	
1957	Juan Manuel Fangio	Argentina	Maserati	
1958	Mike Hawthorn	Great Britain	Ferrari	Vanwall
1959	Jack Brabham	Australia	Cooper-Climax	Cooper-Climax
1960	Jack Brabham	Australia	Cooper-Climax	Cooper-Climax
1961	Phil Hill	USA	Ferrari	Ferrari
1962	Graham Hill	Great Britain	BRM	BRM
1963	Jim Clark	Great Britain	Lotus-Climax	Lotus-Climax
1964	John Surtees	Great Britain	Ferrari	Ferrari
1965	Jim Clark	Great Britain	Lotus-Climax	Lotus-Climax
1966	Jack Brabham	Australia	Brabham-Repco	Brabham-Repco
1967	Denny Hulme	New Zealand	Brabham-Repco	Brabham-Repco
1968	Graham Hill	Great Britain	Lotus-Ford	Lotus-Ford
1969	Jackie Stewart	Great Britain	Matra-Ford	Matra-Ford
1970	Jochen Rindt	Austria	Lotus-Ford	Lotus-Ford
1971	Jackie Stewart	Great Britain	Tyrell-Ford	Tyrell-Ford
1972	Emerson Fittipaldi	Brazil	Lotus-Ford	Lotus-Ford
1973	Jackie Stewart	Great Britain	Tyrell-Ford	Lotus-Ford
1974	Emerson Fittipaldi	Brazil	McLaren-Ford	McLaren-Ford
1975	Niki Lauda	Austria	Ferrari	Ferrari
1976	James Hunt	Great Britain	McLaren-Ford	Ferrari
1977	Niki Lauda	Austria	Ferrari	Ferrari
1978	Mario Andretti	USA	Lotus-Ford	Lotus-Ford
1979	Jody Scheckter	South Africa	Ferrari	Ferrari
1980	Alan Jones	Australia	Williams-Ford	Williams-Ford
1981	Nelson Piquet	Brazil	Brabham-Ford	Williams-Ford
1982	Keke Rosberg	Finland	Williams-Ford	Ferrari
1983	Nelson Piquet	Brazil	Brabham-BMW	Ferrari
1984	Niki Lauda	Austria	McLaren-TAG	McLaren-Porsche
1985	Alain Prost	France	McLaren-TAG	McLaren-TAG
1986	Alain Prost	France	McLaren-TAG	Williams-Honda
1987	Nelson Piquet	Brazil	Williams-Honda	Williams-Honda
1988	Ayrton Senna	Brazil	McLaren-Honda	McLaren-Honda
1989	Alain Prost	France	McLaren-Honda	McLaren-Honda
1990	Ayrton Senna	Brazil	McLaren-Honda	McLaren-Honda
1991	Ayrton Senna	Brazil	McLaren-Honda	McLaren-Honda
1992	Nigel Mansell	Great Britain	Williams-Renault	Williams-Renault
1993	Alain Prost	France	Williams-Renault	Williams-Renault
1994	Michael Schumacher	Germany	Benneton-Ford	Williams-Renault

ROWING

THE UNIVERSITY BOAT RACE

1946	Oxford	1965–7	Oxford
1947–51	Cambridge	1968–73	Cambridge
1952	Oxford	1974	Oxford
1953	Cambridge	1975	Cambridge
1954	Oxford	1976–85	Oxford
1955–8	Cambridge	1986	Cambridge
1959–60	Oxford	1987–92	Oxford
1961–2	Cambridge	1993–95	Cambridge
1963	Oxford		
1964	Cambridge		

Overall results since race began in 1829

Cambridge 72   Oxford 68   Dead Heat 1

RUGBY LEAGUE

LEAGUE CHAMPIONS (POST WAR)

1945–6	Wigan	1970–1	St Helens
1946–7	Wigan	1971–2	Leeds
1947–8	Warrington	1972–3	Dewsbury
1948–9	Huddersfield	1973–4	Salford
1949–50	Wigan	1974–5	St Helens
1950–1	Workington Town	1975–6	Salford
1951–2	Wigan	1976–7	Featherstone Rovers
1952–3	St Helens	1977–8	Widnes
1953–4	Warrington	1978–9	Hull Kingston Rovers
1954–5	Warrington	1979–80	Bradford Northern
1955–6	Hull	1980–1	Bradford Northern
1956–7	Oldham	1981–2	Leigh
1957–8	Hull	1982–3	Hull
1958–9	St Helens	1983–4	Hull Kingston Rovers
1959–60	Wigan	1984–5	Hull Kingston Rovers
1960–1	Leeds	1985–6	Halifax
1961–2	Huddersfield	1986–7	Wigan
1962–3	Swinton/Hunslet	1987–8	Widnes
1963–4	Swinton/Oldham	1988–9	Widnes
1964–5	Halifax	1989–90	Wigan
1965–6	St Helens	1990–1	Wigan
1966–7	Wakefield Trinity	1991–2	Wigan
1967–8	Wakefield Trinity	1992–3	Wigan
1968–9	Leeds	1993–4	Wigan
1969–70	St Helens	1994–5	Wigan

Wins since competition began in 1906

16 Wigan
7   Huddersfield, St Helens
6   Hull, Salford
5   Hull Kingston Rovers
4   Swinton
3   Halifax, Leeds, Oldham, Warrington, Widnes
2   Bradford Northern, Hunslet, Leigh, Wakefield Trinity
1   Batley, Dewsbury, Featherstone Rovers, Workington Town

CHALLENGE CUP WINNERS (POST WAR)

1946	Wakefield Trinity	1971	Leigh
1947	Bradford Northern	1972	St Helens
1948	Wigan	1973	Featherstone Rovers
1949	Bradford Northern	1974	Warrington
1950	Warrington	1975	Widnes
1951	Wigan	1976	St Helens
1952	Workington Town	1977	Leeds
1953	Huddersfield	1978	Leeds
1954	Warrington	1979	Widnes
1955	Barrow	1980	Hull Kingston Rovers
1956	St Helens	1981	Widnes
1957	Leeds	1982	Hull
1958	Wigan	1983	Featherstone Rovers
1959	Wigan	1984	Widnes
1960	Wakefield Trinity	1985	Wigan
1961	St Helens	1986	Castleford
1962	Wakefield Trinity	1987	Halifax
1963	Wakefield Trinity	1988	Wigan
1964	Widnes	1989	Wigan
1965	Wigan	1990	Wigan
1966	St Helens	1991	Wigan
1967	Featherstone Rovers	1992	Wigan
1968	Leeds	1993	Wigan
1969	Castleford	1994	Wigan
1970	Castleford	1995	Wigan

Wins since competition began in 1897

16 Wigan
10 Leeds
7   Widnes
6   Huddersfield
5   Halifax, St Helens, Wakefield Trinity, Warrington
4   Bradford Northern, Castleford
3   Batley, Featherstone Rovers, Oldham, Swinton
2   Broughton Rangers, Dewsbury, Hull, Hunslet, Leigh
1   Barrow, Hull Kingston Rovers, Rochdale Hornets, Salford, Workington Town

RUGBY UNION

WORLD CUP WINNERS

1987 New Zealand   1991 Australia

FIVE NATIONS CHAMPIONSHIP WINNERS (POST WAR)

1947	England	1964	Scotland	1979	Wales
	Wales		Wales	1980	England
1948	Ireland	1965	Wales	1981	France
1949	Ireland	1966	Wales	1982	Ireland
1950	Wales	1967	France	1983	France
1951	Ireland	1968	France		Ireland
1952	Wales	1969	Wales	1984	Scotland
1953	England	1970	France	1985	Ireland
1954	England		Wales	1986	France
	France	1971	Wales		Scotland
	Wales	1972	No competition	1987	France
1955	France	1973	England	1988	France
	Wales		France		Wales
1956	Wales		Ireland	1989	France
1957	England		Scotland	1990	Scotland
1958	England		Wales	1991	England
1959	France	1974	Ireland	1992	England
1960	England	1975	Wales	1993	France
	France	1976	Wales	1994	Wales
1961	France	1977	France	1995	England
1962	France	1978	Wales		
1963	England				

Wins and shared wins since Championship began in 1883:

Wales	33
England	31
Scotland	21
Ireland	18
France	18

Grand Slam Winners:

England	11
Wales	8
France	4
Scotland	3
Ireland	1

Triple Crown Winners:

England	18
Wales	17
Scotland	10
Ireland	6

PILKINGTON CUP WINNERS

1972	Gloucester	1980	Leicester	1988	Harlequins
1973	Coventry	1981	Leicester	1989	Bath
1974	Coventry	1982	Gloucester & Moseley	1990	Bath
1975	Bedford		(shared)	1991	Harlequins
1976	Gosforth	1983	Bristol	1992	Bath
1977	Gosforth	1984	Bath	1993	Leicester
1978	Gloucester	1985	Bath	1994	Bath
1979	Leicester	1986	Bath	1995	Bath
		1987	Bath		

SWALEC CUP WINNERS

1972	Neath	1980	Bridgend	1988	Llanelli
1973	Llanelli	1981	Cardiff	1989	Neath
1974	Llanelli	1982	Cardiff	1990	Neath
1975	Llanelli	1983	Pontypool	1991	Llanelli
1976	Llanelli	1984	Cardiff	1992	Llanelli
1977	Newport	1985	Llanelli	1993	Llanelli
1978	Swansea	1986	Cardiff	1994	Cardiff
1979	Bridgend	1987	Cardiff	1995	Swansea

COURAGE ENGLISH LEAGUE CHAMPIONS

1987–8	Leicester	1991–2	Bath
1988–9	Bath	1992–3	Bath
1989–90	Wasps	1993–4	Bath
1990–1	Bath	1994–5	Leicester

HEINEKEN WELSH LEAGUE CHAMPIONS

1990–1	Neath	1993–4	Swansea
1991–2	Swansea	1994–5	Cardiff
1992–3	Llanelli		

SKIING

OLYMPIC CHAMPIONS (POST WAR)

**Men's Alpine Combination
(Downhill and Slalom)**
1948　Henri Oreiller (Fra)
1988　Hubert Stroiz (Aut)
1992　Josef Polig (Ita)
1994　Lasse Kjus (Nor)

Men's Downhill
1948　Henri Oreiller (Fra)
1952　Zeno Colò (Ita)
1956　Toni Sailer (Aut)
1960　Jean Vuarnet (Fra)
1964　Egon Zimmermann (Aut)
1968　Jean-Claud Killy (Fra)
1972　Bernhard Russi (Swi)
1976　Franz Klammer (Aut)
1980　Leonhard Stock (Aut)
1984　William Johnson (USA)
1988　Pirmin Zurbriggen (Swi)
1992　Patrick Ortlieb (Aut)
1994　Tommy Moe (USA)

Men's Slalom
1948　Edy Reinalter (Swi)
1952　Othmar Schneider (Aut)
1956　Toni Sailer (Aut)
1960　Ernst Hinterseer (Aut)
1964　Josef Stiegler (Aut)
1968　Jean-Claud Killy (Fra)
1972　Francisco Fernandez Ochoa (Spa)
1976　Piero Gros (Ita)
1980　Ingemar Stenmark (Swe)
1984　Phil Mahre (USA)
1988　Alberto Tomba (Ita)
1992　Finn-Christian Jagge (Nor)
1994　Thomas Stangassinger (Aut)

Men's Giant Slalom
1952　Stein Eriksen (Nor)
1956　Toni Sailer (Aut)
1960　Roger Staub (Swi)
1964　François Boulieu (Fra)
1968　Jean-Claud Killy (Fra)
1972　Gustavo Thoeni (Ita)
1976　Heini Hemmi (Swi)
1980　Ingemar Stenmark (Swe)
1984　Max Julen (Swi)
1988　Alberto Tomba (Ita)
1992　Alberto Tomba (Ita)
1994　Markus Wasmeier (Ger)

Men's Super Giant Slalom
1988　Franck Riccard (Fra)
1992　Kjetil Andre Aamodt (Nor)
1994　Markus Wasmeier (Ger)

**Women's Alpine Combination
(Downhill and Slalom)**
1948　Trude Beiser (Aut)
1988　Anita Wachter (Aut)
1992　Petra Kronberger (Aut)
1994　Pernilla Wiberg (Swe)

Women's Downhill
1948　Hedy Schlunegger (Swi)
1952　Trude Jochum (née Beiser) (Aut)
1956　Madeleine Berthod (Swi)
1960　Heidi Biebl (FRG)
1964　Christl Haas (Aut)
1968　Olga Pall (Aut)
1972　Marie-Thérèse Nadig (Swi)
1976　Rosi Mittermaier (FRG)
1980　Annemarie Moser-Pröll (Aut)
1984　Michela Figini (Swi)
1988　Marina Kiehl (FRG)
1992　Kerrin Lee-Gartner (Can)
1994　Katja Seizinger (Ger)

Women's Slalom
1948　Gretchen Fraser (USA)
1952　Andrea Mead-Lawrence (USA)
1956　Renée Colliard (Swi)
1960　Anne Heggtveit (Can)
1964　Christine Goitschel (Fra)
1968　Marielle Goitschel (Fra)
1972　Barbara Cochran (USA)

1976　Rosi Mittermaier (FRG)
1980　Hanni Wenzel (Lie)
1984　Paoletta Magoni (Ita)
1988　Vreni Schneider (Swi)
1992　Petra Kronberger (Aut)
1994　Vreni Schneider (Swi)

Women's Giant Slalom
1952　Andrea Mead-Lawrence (USA)
1956　Ossi Reichert (FRG)
1960　Yvonne Rüegg (Swi)
1964　Marielle Goitschel (Fra)
1968　Nancy Greene (Can)
1972　Marie-Thérèse Nadig (Swi)
1976　Kathy Kreiner (Can)
1980　Hanni Wenzel (Lie)
1984　Debbie Armstrong (USA)
1988　Vreni Schneider (Swi)
1992　Pernilla Wiberg (Swe)
1994　Deborah Compagnoni (Ita)

Women's Super Giant Slalom
1988　Sigrid Wolf (Aut)
1992　Deborah Compagnoni (Ita)
1994　Diann Roffe (USA)

**Men's 10km Cross-country
(Classical)**
1992　Vegard Ulvang (Nor)
1994　Bjørn Daelie (Nor)

Men's Pursuit Start
1994　Bjørn Daelie (Nor)

**Men's 30km Cross-country
(Classical)**
1956　Veikko Hakulinen (Fin)
1960　Sixten Jernberg (Swe)
1964　Eero Mäntyranta (Fin)
1968　Franco Nones (Ita)
1972　Vyacheslav Vedenin (USSR)
1976　Sergey Savelyev (USSR)
1980　Nikolay Zimyatov (USSR)
1984　Nikolay Zimyatov (USSR)
1988　Aleksey Prokurakov (USSR)
1992　Vegard Ulvang (Nor)
1994　Thomas Alsgaard (Nor)

Men's 50km Cross-country
1948　Nils Karlsson (Swe)
1952　Veikko Hakulinen (Fin)
1956　Sixten Jernberg (Swe)
1960　Kalevi Hämäläinen (Fin)
1964　Sixten Jernberg (Swe)
1968　Ole Ellefsaeter (Nor)
1972　Pal Tyldum (Nor)
1976　Ivar Formo (Nor)
1980　Nikolay Zimyatov (USSR)
1984　Thomas Wassberg (Swe)
1988　Gunde Svan (Swe)
1992　Bjørn Daelie (Nor)
1994　Vladimir Smirnov (Kaz)

**Men's 4 × 10km Cross-country
Relay**
1948　Sweden
1952　Finland
1956　USSR
1960　Finland
1964　Sweden
1968　Norway
1972　USSR
1976　Finland
1980　USSR
1984　Sweden
1988　Sweden
1992　Norway
1994　Italy

Men's Team Ski Jumping
1988　Finland
1992　Finland
1994　Germany

**Men's Nordic Combined – Skiing
and Jumping**
1948　Heikki Hasu (Fin)

1952	Simon Slåtvik (Nor)
1956	Sverre Stenersen (Nor)
1960	Georg Thoma (FRG)
1964	Tormod Knutsen (Nor)
1968	Franz Keller (FRG)
1972	Ulrich Wehling (GDR)
1976	Ulrich Wehling (GDR)
1980	Ulrich Wehling (GDR)
1984	Tom Sandberg (Nor)
1988	Hippolyt Kempf (Swi)
1992	Fabrice Guy (Fra)
1994	Fred Borre Lundberg (Nor)

Men's Team Nordic Combined

1988	West Germany
1992	Japan
1994	Japan

Men's Ski Jumping – Normal Hill

1948	Petter Hugstedt (Nor)
1952	Arnfinn Bergmann (Nor)
1956	Anti Hyvärinen (Fin)
1960	Helmut Recknagel (GDR)
1964	Viekko Kankkänen (Fin)
1968	Jiri Raska (Cze)
1972	Yukio Kasaya (Jap)
1976	Hans-Georg Aschenbach (GDR)
1980	Toni Innauer (Aut)
1984	Jens Weissflog (GDR)
1988	Matti Nykänen (Fin)
1992	Ernst Vettori (Aut)
1994	Espen Bredesen (Nor)

Men's Ski Jumping – Large Hill

1964	Toralf Engan (Nor)
1968	Vladimir Byeloussov (USSR)
1972	Wojciech Fortuna (Pol)
1976	Karl Schnabl (Aut)
1980	Jouko Törmänen (Fin)
1984	Matti Nykänen (Fin)
1988	Matti Nykänen (Fin)
1992	Toni Nieminen (Fin)
1994	Jens Weissflog (Ger)

Women's 5km Cross-country

1964	Klaudia Boyarskikh (USSR)
1968	Toini Gustafsson (Swe)
1972	Galina Kulakova (USSR)
1976	Helena Takalo (Fin)
1980	Raisa Smetanina (USSR)
1984	Marja-Liisa Hämäläinen (Fin)
1988	Marjo Matikainen (Fin)
1992	Marjet Lukkarinen (Fin)
1994	Ljubov Egorova (Rus)

Women's Pursuit Start

| 1994 | Ljubov Egorova (Rus) |

Women's 15km Cross-country
(Classical) (freestyle 1994)

| 1992 | Ljubov Egorova (CIS) |
| 1994 | Manuela Di Centa (Ita) |

Women's 20km Cross-country
(Freestyle)

| 1984 | Marja-Liisa Hämäläinen (Fin) |
| 1988 | Tamara Tikhonova (USSR) |

Women's 30km Cross-country

| 1992 | Stefania Belmondo (Ita) |
| 1994 | Manuela Di Centa (Ita) |

Women's 4 × 5km Cross-country
Relay

1956	Finland
1960	Sweden
1964	USSR
1968	Norway
1972	USSR
1976	USSR
1980	East Germany
1984	Norway
1988	USSR
1992	CIS
1994	Russia

SNOOKER

EMBASSY WORLD PROFESSIONAL CHAMPIONS

1976	Ray Reardon (Wales)
1977	John Spencer (England)
1978	Ray Reardon (Wales)
1979	Terry Griffiths (Wales)
1980	Cliff Thorburn (Canada)
1981	Steve Davis (England)
1982	Alex Higgins (Northern Ireland)
1983	Steve Davis (England)
1984	Steve Davis (England)
1985	Dennis Taylor (Northern Ireland)

1986	Joe Johnson (England)
1987	Steve Davis (England)
1988	Steve Davis (England)
1989	Steve Davis (England)
1990	Stephen Hendry (Scotland)
1991	John Parrott (England)
1992	Stephen Hendry (Scotland)
1993	Stephen Hendry (Scotland)
1994	Stephen Hendry (Scotland)
1995	Stephen Hendry (Scotland)

SPEEDWAY

WORLD CHAMPIONS (since 1970)

1970	Ivan Mauger (New Zealand)
1971	Ole Olsen (Denmark)
1972	Ivan Mauger (New Zealand)
1973	Jerry Szczakiel (Poland)
1974	Anders Michanek (Sweden)
1975	Ole Olsen (Denmark)
1976	Peter Collins (England)
1977	Ivan Mauger (New Zealand)
1978	Ole Olsen (Denmark)
1979	Ivan Mauger (New Zealand)
1980	Michael Lee (England)
1981	Bruce Penhall (USA)
1982	Bruce Penhall (USA)

1983	Egon Muller (West Germany)
1984	Erik Gundersen (Denmark)
1985	Erik Gundersen (Denmark)
1986	Hans Nielsen (Denmark)
1987	Hans Nielsen (Denmark)
1988	Erik Gundersen (Denmark)
1989	Hans Nielsen (Denmark)
1990	Per Jonsson (Sweden)
1991	Jan Pedersen (Denmark)
1992	Gary Havelock (England)
1993	Sam Ermolenko (USA)
1994	Tony Rickardson (Sweden)

SWIMMING

OLYMPIC CHAMPIONS (POST WAR)

Men's 50m Freestyle

| 1988 | Matt Biondi (USA) |
| 1992 | Aleksandr Popov (CIS) |

Men's 100m Freestyle

| 1948 | Walter Ris (USA) |
| 1952 | Clarke Scholes (USA) |

1956	Jon Henricks (Aus)
1960	John Devitt (Aus)
1964	Don Schollander (USA)
1968	Mike Wenden (Aus)
1972	Mark Spitz (USA)
1976	Jim Montgomery (USA)
1980	Jorg Woithe (GDR)

1984	Howdy Gaines (USA)
1988	Matt Biondi (USA)
1992	Aleksandr Popov (CIS)

Men's 200m Freestyle

1968	Mike Wenden (Aus)
1972	Mark Spitz (USA)
1976	Bruce Furniss (USA)
1980	Sergey Koplyakov (USSR)
1984	Michael Gross (FRG)
1988	Duncan Armstrong (Aus)

Men's 400m Freestyle

1948	William Smith (USA)
1952	Jean Boiteux (Fra)
1956	Murray Rose (Aus)
1960	Murray Rose (Aus)
1964	Don Schollander (USA)
1968	Mike Burton (USA)
1972	Brad Cooper (Aus)
1976	Brian Goodell (USA)
1980	Vladimir Salnikov (USSR)
1984	George DiCarlo (USA)
1988	Uwe Dassler (GDR)
1992	Yevgeniy Sadoviy (CIS)

Men's 1500m Freestyle

1948	James McLane (USA)
1952	Ford Konno (USA)
1956	Murray Rose (Aus)
1960	John Konrads (Aus)
1964	Bob Windle (Aus)
1968	Mike Burton (USA)
1972	Mike Burton (USA)
1976	Brian Goodell (USA)
1980	Vladimir Salnikov (USSR)
1984	Michael O'Brien (USA)
1988	Vladimir Salnikov (USSR)
1992	Kieren Perkins (Aus)

Men's 100m Backstroke

1948	Allen Stack (USA)
1952	Yoshinobu Oyakawa (USA)
1956	David Theile (Aus)
1960	David Theile (Aus)
1968	Roland Matthes (GDR)
1972	Roland Matthes (GDR)
1976	John Naber (USA)
1980	Bengt Baron (Swe)
1984	Rick Carey (USA)
1988	Daichi Suzuki (Jap)
1992	Mark Tewksbury (Can)

Men's 200m Backstroke

1964	Jed Graef (USA)
1968	Roland Matthes (GDR)
1972	Roland Matthes (GDR)
1976	John Naber (USA)
1980	Sándor Wladár (Hun)
1984	Rick Carey (USA)
1988	Igor Polyanskiy (USSR)
1992	Martin López-Zubero (Spa)

Men's 100m Breaststroke

1968	Don McKenzie (USA)
1972	Nobutaka Taguchi (Jap)
1976	John Hencken (USA)
1980	Duncan Goodhew (UK)
1984	Steve Lundquist (USA)
1988	Adrian Moorhouse (UK)
1992	Nelson Diebel (USA)

Men's 200m Breaststroke

1948	Joseph Verdeur (USA)
1952	John Davies (Aus)
1956	Masaru Furukawa (Jap)
1960	William Mulliken (USA)
1964	Ian O'Brien (Aus)
1968	Felipe Munoz (Mex)
1972	John Hencken (USA)
1976	David Wilkie (UK)
1980	Robertas Zhulpa (USSR)
1984	Victor Davis (Can)
1988	József Szabó (Hun)
1992	Mike Barrowman (USA)

Men's 100m Butterfly

1968	Doug Russell (USA)
1972	Mark Spitz (USA)
1976	Matt Vogel (USA)
1980	Pär Arvidsson (Swe)
1984	Michael Gross (FRG)
1988	Anthony Nesty (Sur)
1992	Pablo Morales (USA)

Men's 200m Butterfly

1956	William Yorzyk (USA)
1960	Mike Troy (USA)
1964	Kevin Berry (Aus)
1968	Carl Robie (USA)
1972	Mark Spitz (USA)
1976	Mike Bruner (USA)
1980	Sergey Fesenko (USSR)
1984	Jon Sieben (Aus)
1988	Michael Gross (FRG)
1992	Melvin Stewart (USA)

Men's 200m Individual Medley

1968	Charles Hickcox (USA)
1972	Gunnar Larsson (Swe)
1984	Alex Baumann (Can)
1988	Tamás Darnyi (Hun)
1992	Tamás Darnyi (Hun)

Men's 400m Individual Medley

1964	Richard Roth (USA)
1968	Charles Hickcox (USA)
1972	Gunnar Larsson (Swe)
1976	Rod Strachan (USA)
1980	Aleksandr Sidorenko (USSR)
1984	Alex Baumann (Can)
1988	Tamás Darnyi (Hun)
1992	Tamás Darnyi (Hun)

Men's 4 × 100m Freestyle Relay

1964	USA	1984	USA
1968	USA	1988	USA
1972	USA	1992	USA

Men's 4 × 200m Freestyle Relay

1948	USA	1972	USA
1952	USA	1976	USA
1956	Australia	1980	USSR
1960	USA	1984	USA
1964	USA	1988	USA
1968	USA	1992	CIS

Men's 4 × 100m Medley Relay

1960	USA	1980	Australia
1964	USA	1984	USA
1968	USA	1988	USA
1972	USA	1992	USA
1976	USA		

Men's Springboard Diving

1948	Bruce Harlan (USA)
1952	David Browning (USA)
1956	Robert Clotworthy (USA)
1960	Gary Tobian (USA)
1964	Kenneth Sitzberger (USA)
1968	Bernard Wrightson (USA)
1972	Vladimir Vasin (USSR)
1976	Philip Boggs (USA)
1980	Aleksandr Portnov (USSR)
1984	Greg Louganis (USA)
1988	Greg Louganis (USA)
1992	Mark Lenzi (USA)

Men's Highboard Platform Diving

1948	Samuel Lee (USA)
1952	Samuel Lee (USA)
1956	Joaquin Capilla (Mex)
1960	Robert Webster (USA)
1964	Robert Webster (USA)
1968	Klaus Dibiasi (Ita)
1972	Klaus Dibiasi (Ita)
1976	Klaus Dibiasi (Ita)
1980	Falk Hoffmann (GDR)
1984	Greg Louganis (USA)
1988	Greg Louganis (USA)
1992	Sun Shuwei (Chn)

Women's 50m Freestyle

1988	Kristin Otto (GDR)
1992	Yang Wenyi (Chn)

Women's 100m Freestyle

1948	Greta Andersen (Den)
1952	Katalin Szöke (Hun)
1956	Dawn Fraser (Aus)
1960	Dawn Fraser (Aus)
1964	Dawn Fraser (Aus)
1968	Jan Henne (USA)
1972	Sandra Neilson (USA)
1976	Kornelia Ender (GDR)
1980	Barbara Krause (GDR)
1984 {	Nancy Hogshead (USA)
	Carrie Steinseifer (USA)
1988	Kristin Otto (GDR)
1992	Zhuang Yong (Chn)

Women's 200m Freestyle
1968   Debbie Meyer (USA)
1972   Shane Gould (Aus)
1976   Kornelia Ender (GDR)
1980   Barbara Krause (GDR)
1984   Mary Wayte (USA)
1988   Heike Friedrich (GDR)
1992   Nicole Haislett (USA)

Women's 400m Freestyle
1948   Ann Curtis (USA)
1952   Valéria Gyenge (Hun)
1956   Lorraine Crapp (Aus)
1960   Chris Von Saltza (USA)
1964   Virginia Duenkel (USA)
1968   Debbie Meyer (USA)
1972   Shane Gould (Aus)
1976   Petra Thümer (GDR)
1980   Ines Diers (GDR)
1984   Tiffany Cohen (USA)
1988   Janet Evans (USA)
1992   Dagmar Hase (Ger)

Women's 800m Freestyle
1968   Debbie Meyer (USA)
1972   Keena Rothhammer (USA)
1976   Petra Thümer (GDR)
1980   Michelle Ford (Aus)
1984   Tiffany Cohen (USA)
1988   Janet Evans (USA)
1992   Janet Evans (USA)

Women's 100m Backstroke
1948   Karen Harup (Den)
1952   Joan Harrison (SAf)
1956   Judy Grinham (UK)
1960   Lynn Burke (USA)
1964   Cathy Ferguson (USA)
1968   Kaye Hall (USA)
1972   Melissa Belote (USA)
1976   Ulrike Richter (GDR)
1980   Rica Reinisch (GDR)
1984   Theresa Andrews (USA)
1988   Kristin Otto (GDR)
1992   Krisztina Egerszegi (Hun)

Women's 200m Backstroke
1968   Pokey Watson (USA)
1972   Melissa Belote (USA)
1976   Ulrike Richter (GDR)
1980   Rica Reinisch (GDR)
1984   Jolanda de Rover (Hol)
1988   Krisztina Egerszegi (Hun)
1992   Krisztina Egerszegi (Hun)

Women's 100m Breaststroke
1968   Djurdjica Bjedov (Yug)
1972   Catherine Carr (USA)
1976   Hannelore Anke (GDR)
1980   Ute Geweniger (GDR)
1984   Petra Van Staveren (Hol)
1988   Tania Dangalakova (Bul)
1992   Yelena Rudkovskaya (CIS/Bls)

Women's 200m Breaststroke
1948   Petronella van Vliet (Hol)
1952   Eva Székely (Hun)
1956   Ursula Happe (FRG)
1960   Anita Lonsbrough (UK)
1964   Galina Prozumenshchikova (USSR)
1968   Sharon Wichman (USA)
1972   Beverley Whitfield (Aus)
1976   Marina Koshevaya (USSR)
1980   Lina Kachushite (USSR)
1984   Anne Ottenbrite (Can)
1988   Silke Hörner (GDR)
1992   Kyoko Iwasaki (Jap)

Women's 100m Butterfly
1956   Shelley Mann (USA)
1960   Carolyn Schuler (USA)
1964   Sharon Stouder (USA)
1968   Lynette McClements (Aus)
1972   Mayumi Aoki (Jap)
1976   Kornelia Ender (GDR)
1980   Caren Metschuck (GDR)
1984   Mary T. Meagher (USA)
1988   Kristin Otto (GDR)
1992   Qian Hong (Chn)

Women's 200m Butterfly
1968   Ada Kok (Hol)

1972   Karen Moe (USA)
1976   Andrea Pollack (GDR)
1980   Ines Geissler (GDR)
1984   Mary T. Meagher (USA)
1988   Kathleen Nord (GDR)
1992   Summer Sanders (USA)

Women's 200m Individual Medley
1968   Claudia Kolb (USA)
1972   Sharon Gould (Aus)
1984   Tracy Caulkins (USA)
1988   Daniela Hunger (GDR)
1992   Lin Li (Chn)

Women's 400m Individual Medley
1964   Donna De Varona (USA)
1968   Claudia Kolb (USA)
1972   Gail Neall (Aus)
1976   Ulrike Tauber (GDR)
1980   Petra Schneider (GDR)
1984   Tracy Caulkins (USA)
1988   Janet Evans (USA)
1992   Krisztina Egerszegi (Hun)

Women's 4 × 100m Freestyle Medley
1948   USA
1952   Hungary
1956   Australia
1960   USA
1964   USA
1968   USA
1972   USA
1976   USA
1980   East Germany
1984   USA
1988   East Germany
1992   USA

Women's 4 × 100m Medley Relay
1960   USA
1964   USA
1968   USA
1972   USA
1976   East Germany
1980   East Germany
1984   USA
1988   East Germany
1992   USA

Women's Synchronized Swimming

Solo
1984   Tracie Ruiz (USA)
1988   Carolyn Waldo (Can)
1992   Kristen Babb-Sprague (USA)

Duet
1984   Candy Costie and Tracie Ruiz (USA)
1988   Michelle Cameron and Carolyn Waldo (Can)
1992   Karen and Sarah Josephson (USA)

Women's Springboard Diving
1948   Victoria Draves (USA)
1952   Pat McCormick (USA)
1956   Pat McCormick (USA)
1960   Ingrid Krämer (GDR)
1964   Ingrid Engel (née Krämer) (GDR)
1968   Sue Gossick (USA)
1972   Micki King (USA)
1976   Jennifer Chandler (USA)
1980   Irina Kalinina (USSR)
1984   Sylvie Bernier (Can)
1988   Gao Min (Chn)
1992   Gao Min (Chn)

Women's Highboard Platform Diving
1948   Victoria Draves (USA)
1952   Pat McCormick (USA)
1956   Pat McCormick (USA)
1960   Ingrid Krämer (GDR)
1964   Lesley Bush (USA)
1968   Milena Duchkova (Cze)
1972   Ulrika Knape (Swe)
1976   Elena Vaytsekhovskaya (USSR)
1980   Martina Jäschke (GDR)
1984   Zhou Jihong (Chn)
1988   Xu Yanmei (Chn)
1992   Fu Mingxia (Chn)

BIBLICAL GLOSSARY

This section provides an easy to use treasure-house of information about the biblical world. It presents a concise and valuable guide to the people, places and events which have had so much influence on the course of history.

THE LAND OF PALESTINE

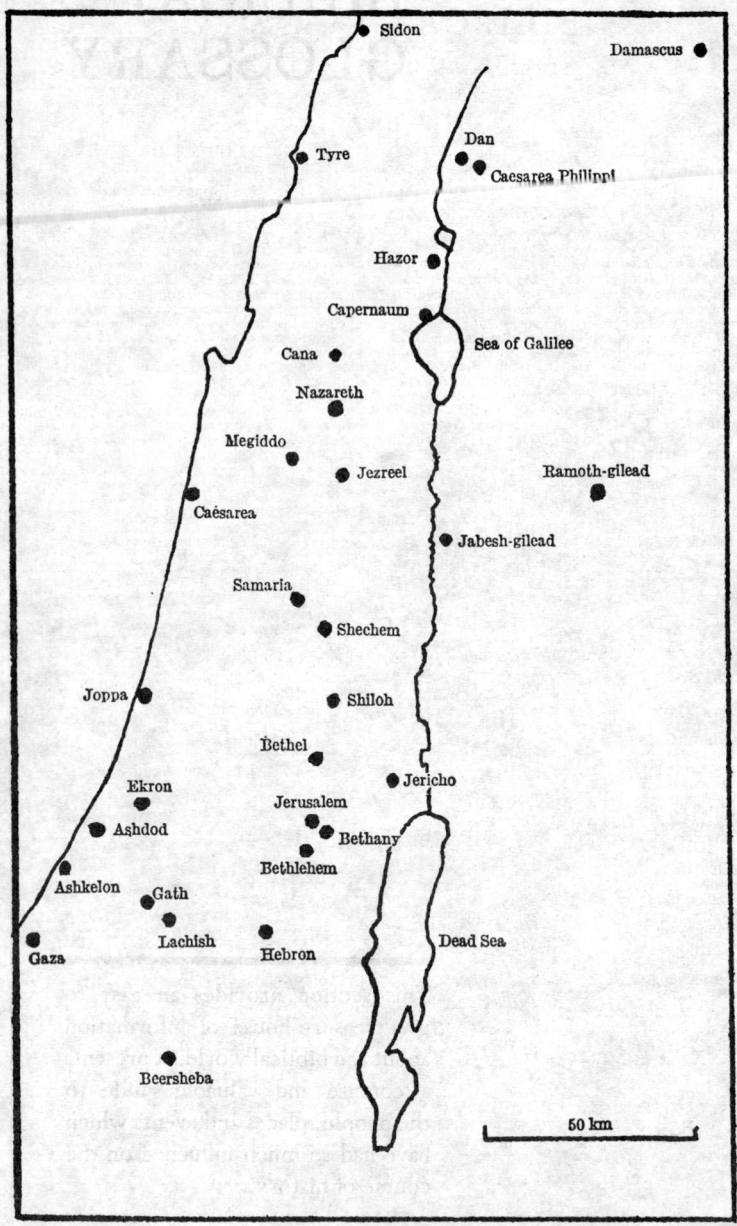

N.B. This map does not represent Palestine as it was at any one period of history. It shows most of the Palestinian locations mentioned in the text from whatever period.

BIBLICAL GLOSSARY

INTRODUCTION

There is a sense in which the Bible is part of every person's heritage. Though it is sometimes claimed that we are now living in a post-Christian era, the marks of a Christian culture are part of our everyday experience: the great cathedrals of our cities, the parish churches and village chapels of our countryside, the frequent allusions to biblical ideas or symbols in the works of many of our novelists, poets and playwrights, even the appearance of a Christian hymn, *Amazing Grace*, in the "pop" charts. At the root of this culture is the revelation of God offered by the Bible.

Even to those who do not accept the faith it proclaims, the Bible has much to commend it. It contains some fine poetry, vivid story-telling, deep insights into the human condition and moral guidance which has stood the test of time. It is also of enormous value simply as a historical resource. For Christians, of course, it is much more than this, a unique revelation of God.

It is not, however, an easy book. The modern British reader has to bridge a time-gap of at least 2,000 years (often much more) and enter into an alien culture if he is to become familiar with the biblical world. It is astonishing how many Christians have succeeded in making this transition with little or no help, and found that the Bible can still speak across the barriers of time and space. But today it should not be necessary for anyone to read the Bible unaided. Within the last century our understanding of the way the biblical writers worked, of the cultural background against which their lives were set, and of the wider historical and religious background of the surrounding nations have all increased enormously.

Much of this new knowledge is now available in large, definitive dictionaries of the Bible and in detailed commentaries on individual books. The reader who wishes seriously to improve his understanding of the Bible must consult such works. This section, however, is intended to offer assistance to those who do not possess more specialised works of reference, with information which is simply presented but does not gloss over the complexity of the issues, and which is based on the consensus of modern scholarly opinion.

ABBREVIATIONS USED IN GIVING BIBLICAL REFERENCES

Acts	Acts	Isaiah	Is	Nehemiah	Neh
Amos	Amos	James	Jas	Numbers	Num
Chronicles	Chr	Jeremiah	Jer	Obadiah	Obad
Colossians	Col	Job	Job	Peter	Pet
Corinthians	Cor	Joel	Joel	Philemon	Phlm
Daniel	Dan	John	Jn	Philippians	Phil
Deuteronomy	Deut	Jonah	Jon	Proverbs	Prov
Ecclesiastes	Ecc	Joshua	Josh	Psalms	Ps
Ephesians	Eph	Jude	Jude	Revelation	Rev
Esther	Esth	Judges	Judg	Romans	Rom
Exodus	Ex	Kings	Kgs	Ruth	Ruth
Ezekiel	Ezek	Lamentations	Lam	Samuel	Sam
Ezra	Ezra	Leviticus	Lev	Song of Songs	Song
Galatians	Gal	Luke	Lk	Thessalonians	Thes
Genesis	Gen	Malachi	Mal	Timothy	Tim
Habakkuk	Hab	Mark	Mk	Titus	Tit
Haggai	Hag	Matthew	Mt	Zechariah	Zech
Hebrews	Heb	Micah	Mic	Zephaniah	Zeph
Hosea	Hos	Nahum	Nah		

A

Aaron. The elder brother of Moses, he was appointed by God to be Moses' spokesman in the negotiations with the Egyptian Pharaoh for the release of the Jews (Ex 4:14). After the exodus, in Moses' absence, he made a golden calf for the people to worship (Ex 32:1–6). In spite of this lapse, tradition regards him as Israel's first High Priest (Ex 29:1–7).

Abednego. One of three young men who, according to the book of Daniel, survived being thrown into a blazing furnace for refusing to worship a gold statue set up by King Nebuchadnezzar (Dan 3:1–27).

Abel. The second son of Adam and Eve, he was killed by his elder brother Cain out of jealousy because God found Abel's offering of a lamb more acceptable than his offering of grain (Gen 4:1–8). The story probably reflects a feeling among traditionalists that the Jews had been corrupted by the agricultural civilisation of Canaan, and were less acceptable to God than when they had been shepherds.

Abiathar. When his father Ahimelech was killed by Saul for his unwitting involvement in David's escape, Abiathar fled to join David's outlaw band (1 Sam 22:16–23). He subsequently became David's High Priest, but was banished by Solomon because he supported Adonijah in the struggle for succession to the throne (1 Kgs 1:5–7, 26–27).

Abijah. King of Judah (915–913 B.C.).

Abner. Saul's commander-in-chief. After Saul's death he supported Ishbosheth, his only surviving son, as king of Israel, but soon became disenchanted with him. He was negotiating with David to transfer the allegiance of the northern tribes to him when he was murdered by David's commander, Joab, in pursuance of a family quarrel (2 Sam 3:6–27).

Abraham. Abraham, originally known as Abram, is regarded as the father of the Jewish people. While there are doubtless legendary elements in the stories told of him, there is no reason to question his historical existence, probably in the period 2000–1800 B.C. Through the stories of Abraham run two complementary themes: God's promises and Abraham's faith. God promises to Abraham that he will have numerous descendants, that they will occupy the land of Canaan and that they will be a source of blessing to all mankind (Gen 12:1–3). Abraham responds to these promises with faith, shown in his willingness to set out for the promised land not knowing where he is being led, and to sacrifice his son Isaac when he thinks that this is what God requires. Neighbouring peoples (e.g. the Moabites) still practised child sacrifice a thousand years later, and this story, as well as indicating Abraham's faith, reflects the early understanding of the Jews that God did not require human sacrifice.

Absalom. David's third son. After his sister Tamar had been raped by his elder half-brother Amnon, he plotted revenge and eventually had Amnon killed (2 Sam 13). As a result he had to flee to the small state of Geshur which his grandfather ruled. After three years he was permitted to return at the instigation of David's general, Joab, who probably felt that Amnon had only got his due punishment. He then proceeded to plot against his father, sowing seeds of discontent among the northern tribes especially (2 Sam 15:1–6) and finally raised an army to march on Jerusalem. David withdrew across the Jordan, gained time to organise loyal forces and crushed the rebels. In the decisive battle Absalom was killed by Joab, even though David had expressly instructed that he should not be harmed (2 Sam 18:6–15).

Acts of the Apostles. The book is clearly a sequel to Luke's gospel, being addressed to the same person, Theophilus, and referring to an earlier work which described "the things that Jesus did and taught from the time he began his work until the day when he was taken up to heaven." It is invaluable for the insight it gives into the first thirty years of the Christian church. Peter and Paul are the leading personalities in the book, yet the theme is not one of human heroes but of God at work among the community of believers through the gift of the Holy Spirit. The somewhat surprising ending, with Paul under house arrest in Rome, has led many to wonder whether the work was unfinished or a third volume planned, yet in some ways this is a most fitting conclusion—Paul in spite of everything proclaiming the good news at the very heart of the Roman empire.

Adam. The name is simply the Hebrew for "man". Adam is therefore to be thought of not as the first man in a historical sense but as the symbolic prototype of all mankind.

Adonijah. The fourth son of David. As the eldest surviving son by the time his father reached old age, he expected to succeed to the throne and had himself declared king by Abiathar and Joab before David's death. David, however, nominated Solomon to succeed him and Solomon soon found occasion to accuse Adonijah of treachery and have him put to death (1 Kgs 1:5–53, 2:13–25).

Agrippa, see **Herod Family.**

Ahab. King of Israel (869–850 B.C.). The son of Omri, who arranged his marriage to Jezebel, daughter of the king of Tyre, as part of his policy of friendly relations with Phoenicia. His chief fault was his failure to curb the excesses of his wife, who was determined to supplant the worship of Yahweh with the worship of her own god, Baal Melkart. He ignored the advice of the prophet Micaiah to go to battle against the Syrians at Ramoth-Gilead, where he was fatally wounded by an arrow.

Ahaz. King of Judah (735–715 B.C.). Ahaz came to the throne at a moment of crisis. King Pekah of Israel and King Rezin of Damascus had formed an allegiance against the powerful Assyrians, and were threatening to attack Judah if she did not join them. In desperation, and against the advice of Isaiah, he appealed to the Assyrians for help. This he received, but at the cost of becoming an Assyrian vassal. He is criticised by the biblical historians for taking part in idolatrous practices, and is even said to have sacrificed his own son (2 Kgs 16:1–4).

Ahaziah. (1) King of Israel (850–849 B.C.). The son of Ahab, within two years of coming to the throne he fell from a balcony and never recovered from his injuries (2 Kgs 1:2).

(2) King of Judah (842 B.C.). The son of Jehoram, he had the misfortune to be visiting his father's namesake, Jehoram king of Israel, at the time of Jehu's rebellion in which he was killed (2 Kgs 9:27–28).

Ahijah. A prophet from Shiloh who predicted the division of the kingdom after Solomon's death by tearing his robe into twelve pieces and giving ten of them (representing ten tribes) to Jeroboam, later to be the first king of the breakaway state of Israel (1 Kgs 11:29–40).

Ahimelech. The priest at Nob who unwittingly assisted David's escape from Saul by giving him food and a sword. He was subsequently killed by Saul together with all the other priests at Nob (1 Sam 21:1–9).

Alexandria. Though only mentioned four times in the Bible (all the references being in Acts), Alexandria had a large Jewish community almost from its foundation in 332 B.C. by Alexander the Great, and it was here that the Septuagint, the Greek translation of the Old Testament, was made during the third and second centuries B.C.

Amalekites. A nomadic people who lived in the desert regions to the south of Israel. They attacked the Israelites during their march from Egypt to the promised land, and were later attacked and defeated by both Saul and David (1 Sam 15:1–9, 30:1–20).

Amaziah. King of Judah (800–783 B.C.). After succeeding in regaining territory earlier lost to the Edomites, Amaziah got into an unnecessary and disastrous quarrel with King Jehoash of Israel from which he emerged the clear loser. He was eventually assassinated at Lachish, whence he had fled, having heard of a plot against his life (2 Kgs 14:1–19).

Ammonites. A trans-Jordanian tribe frequently at war with the Israelites. It was in action against the Ammonites that Saul proved his powers of leadership (1 Sam 11:1–15), and although David seems to have established good relations with King Nahash of Ammon, his son insulted David's envoys and bitter hostilities ensued. David ultimately took the Ammonite crown, but only after a long struggle (1 Sam 10:1–11:1, 13:26–31).

Amon. King of Judah (642–640 B.C.). The son of the hated Manasseh, he was soon assassinated because he continued in his father's idolatrous ways.

Amos. The first of the great reforming prophets of the eighth century B.C., we know relatively little about the man himself as opposed to what he taught. A herdsman and grower of figs from Tekoa in Judah, he prophesied in the cities of Israel to which he perhaps travelled to sell his produce. His prophetic career may have lasted as little as a few months sometime during the period 760–750 B.C.

Amos was appalled by a society in which an affluent minority exploited the poverty-stricken majority. Loans would be made to the poor, and when they were unable to repay them, their houses and land would be seized, or their children sold into slavery to pay off the debt. The use of false weights and measures by the merchants was commonplace, and bribery in the courts ensured that no case against them would ever succeed. Yet these same merchants made lavish sacrifices to God at the national shrines of Gilgal and Bethel.

Amos believed in a God of righteousness who demanded right living from his people. Furthermore, he was a God of limitless power who controlled the forces of the universe and directed the course of human history. If his people failed to see the evil of their ways he would use a foreign power as the instrument of his judgement upon them. The fact that they were a chosen people would not prevent this: indeed they, more than any other nation, should know what God required and their failure to meet his standards was all the more blameworthy.

The message of Amos is uncompromising, and needs to be balanced by the words of later prophets who saw the possibility of redemption as well as judgement. Nevertheless his importance is immense, as the man who proclaimed with a new clarity the incompatibility of worshipping God and exploiting one's fellow men.

Ananias. (1) A member of the early church who sold some property and gave part of the proceeds to the church, but claimed to have given all. Peter accused him of lying to God, and he fell down dead (Acts 5:1–6).

(2) A Christian in Damascus who, in response to a vision, went and baptised Saul following his conversion (Acts 9:10–19).

(3) The Jewish High Priest before whom Paul appeared after his arrest in the temple at Jerusalem (Acts 23:1–5).

Andrew. The brother of Simon Peter and one of the first disciples.

Annas. Though he had retired from the High Priesthood before the time of Jesus' trial, Annas continued to exercise influence through his son-in-law and successor, Caiaphas.

Antioch. (1) The capital of the Roman province of Syria and an important centre of early Christianity. It was here that disciples were first called Christians, and it was this church that sent Paul and Barnabas out on the first missionary journey (Acts 13:1–3).

(2) A city in Pisidia (part of Asia Minor) visited by Paul on his first missionary journey (Acts 13:13–52).

Apocalypse. Prophetic description of the end of the world from the Greek word meaning "revelation".

Apollos. A Jew from Alexandria who proclaimed the gospel in Ephesus but only knew about John's baptism as opposed to Christian baptism in the Holy Spirit. After Prisca and Aquila had explained Christianity more fully to him he went on to Corinth where, unfortunately, opposing factions developed according to whether they "followed" Apollos or other teachers (Acts 18:24–28, 1 Cor 1:12–13).

Aquila. A Jew who, with his wife Prisca, was expelled from Rome by an edict of Claudius and settled in Corinth. Here they welcomed Paul, and later worked with him in Ephesus (Acts 18:1–4, 24–26).

Aramaeans, *see* **Syrians.**

Areopagus. An open space in Athens, often used for public debates, and where Paul addressed the Athenians (Acts 17:16–34).

Ark of the Covenant. An ornate wooden chest believed to contain the stone tablets on which the ten commandments were written. It accompanied the Israelites throughout their nomadic wanderings and was then kept at Shiloh during the early years of the occupation of Palestine. Brought by the Israelites to encourage them in battle against the Philistines at Aphek, it was in fact captured, but the Philistines soon returned it, attributing a series of disasters to its presence. David brought it to Jerusalem, where Solomon eventually enshrined it in the temple. It is presumed to have remained there until the temple was destroyed by the Babylonians in 586 B.C.

Artemis. A Greek goddess identified with the Roman Diana. Her temple at Ephesus was famous, though the worship there seems to have been based on an earlier fertility cult.

Asa. King of Judah (913–873 B.C.).

Ascension. Although this is the word normally used to describe Jesus' departure from the earth, its significance is metaphorical rather than literal. It signifies the return of Jesus to God, and the taking up again of the power and authority he voluntarily laid down in order to share the human experience (Acts 1:6–11).

Ashdod. One of the five Philistine city-states.

Asher. (1) The eighth son of Jacob, his second by Zilpah, Leah's slave-girl.

(2) The tribe of Asher which occupied fertile land along the coastal plain north of Mount Carmel.

Ashkelon. One of the five Philistine city-states.

Assyria. A major power to the north-east of Israel for over two centuries. As early as 853 B.C. Ahab had to meet the threat of an Assyrian invasion, though it was not until the accession of Tiglath-pileser III to the Assyrian throne in 745 B.C. that Assyria took a dominating role in the affairs of Palestine. By 721 B.C. the northern kingdom of Israel had become an Assyrian province and the southern kingdom of Judah was paying heavy tribute. An attempt by Hezekiah to become independent from Assyria in 705 B.C. was punished by an invasion in which all the fortified cities of Judah except for Jerusalem itself were taken and destroyed. Judah remained subservient to Assyria until the Assyrian empire began to break up under pressure from the Medes and the Babylonians about 630 B.C.

Athaliah. Queen of Judah (842–837 B.C.). The wife of Jehoram, king of Judah and mother of Ahaziah, who succeeded him. When Ahaziah lost his life in Jehu's rebellion, Athaliah seized the throne and put to death all male members of the royal family except for Joash, one of Ahaziah's sons who was hidden by his aunt. After six years in hiding he was proclaimed king by members of the forces acting on the instructions of Jehoiada the priest, and Athaliah was killed.

Athens. Visited by Paul on his second missionary journey. The sermon he preached there (Acts 17:16–34) is notable for its attempt to speak to Greek thinkers in terms they would find familiar, but his success appears to have been slight and Athens was never an important centre of Christianity.

Atonement, Day of. The most solemn day of fasting in the Jewish calendar. The High Priest went into the most sacred part of the temple (the only day of the year on which this was permitted) to make a special offering in expiation of the sins of the people. These sins were symbolically transferred to a goat (the "scape-goat") which was then driven out into the wilderness (Lev 16:20–34).

B

Baal. The Hebrew word means simply "master", "owner" or "husband", and it was used as a general term for foreign gods, but especially for the Canaanite fertility god. Although the debased sexual practices associated with the worship of this god were fiercely condemned by Hebrew writers, it was probably through contact with Canaanite religion that the people of Israel came to view their own God as creator and lord of the world of nature.

Baasha. King of Israel (900–877 B.C.), and involved in a border dispute with Asa, king of Judah.

Babel, Tower of. The significance of the story is mythological rather than historical. Partly it is an attempt to explain the variety of human languages, but it also reflects a view long held in certain sectors of Israelite society that man's close relationship with God was broken once he began to build cities and become, in his own eyes, self-sufficient. Like the story of Adam's disobedience it regards human greed and arrogance as the root causes of his estrangement from God.

Babylonians. When the Babylonians and Medes destroyed Assyria they divided her empire between them, with the Babylonians taking the southern portion. They therefore took over from the Assyrians the dominating role in Palestinian affairs from 605 B.C. Rebellions against Babylonian overlordship in 598 B.C. and 589 B.C. were disastrously unsuccessful, the latter resulting in the destruction of Jerusalem and its temple and the exile of many of its people in 586 B.C.

Baptism. The origins of baptism are obscure. John the Baptist baptised as a sign of repentance (Mk 1:4–5), and the Jews are known to have used a form of baptism as a means of entry to the Jewish faith for non-Jews, though it is uncertain whether or not this custom was established before John started baptising. There is no record of Jesus baptising anyone, yet it seems to have been established as the mode of entry into the Christian church from earliest times (Acts 1:38). Baptism was first administered to adult believers, or sometimes to whole families on the conversion of the head of household (Acts 16:33), and from this seems to have sprung the practice of baptising infants of Christian parents.

Barabbas. According to an established custom of releasing a prisoner at Passover time, Pilate set free Barabbas in preference to Jesus on the insistence of the crowd (Jn 18:38–40).

Barnabas. A prominent member of the early church, invariably exerting an influence for good at crucial moments. He was the first to befriend Paul in Jerusalem after his conversion (Acts 9:26–27). Sent by the Jerusalem church to report on work among the Gentiles which had begun in Syrian Antioch, he made a favourable recommendation, remained himself to continue the work and brought Paul to join him (Acts 11:19–26). He was Paul's companion on the first missionary journey (Acts 13:1–3), but did not accompany him on the second journey for characteristic reasons. Paul did not want to take John Mark, who had failed them on the first journey, while Barnabas wanted to give him a second chance. Significantly Paul was later to become reconciled to John Mark, thus confirming Barnabas' judgement (2 Tim 4:11).

Bartholomew. One of the twelve disciples, *See* **Nathaniel.**

Baruch. Acted as scribe to Jeremiah and read out a message from Jeremiah in the temple precincts at a time when Jeremiah himself had been banned from speaking there (Jer 36:1–8).

Bathsheba. The wife of Uriah, an officer in King David's army. Because she was expecting a child by David, he gave orders that Uriah be left in an exposed position during the fighting against the Ammonites, and he was killed. Bathsheba's child died in infancy, but she subsequently bore Solomon (2 Sam 11:2–12:25).

Beersheba. A town on the southernmost border of Judah: hence the expression "from Dan to Beersheba" mean the whole of Israel.

Belshazzar. The last king of Babylon before its capture by the Persian monarch Cyrus in 539 B.C. Mentioned in the Bible only in the book of Daniel, particularly in the dramatic story of his downfall recorded in the fifth chapter.

Benjamin. (1) The twelfth son of Jacob, his second by Rachel, who died in giving birth to him (Gen 35:16–18).
(2) The tribe of Benjamin, occupying a relatively small area just north of Judah.

Bernice. The sister of Herod Agrippa II, she

heard with him Paul's defence of his conduct before the Roman governor Festus (Acts 25:13–26:31).

Bethany. A village just outside Jerusalem, the home of Lazarus, Martha and Mary. It was here that Jesus stayed on his final visit to Jerusalem.

Bethesda. A pool in Jerusalem believed to have healing properties, particularly when the waters were disturbed. The scene of one of Jesus' healing miracles in John 5:1–9.

Bethlehem. A town in Judaea some five miles south of Jerusalem and known from before King David's time. Chiefly famous as the birthplace of Jesus, although some scholars now believe it more likely he was born in or near Nazareth which was in Galilee.

Bildad. The second of Job's three "comforters" (Job 8).

Booths, *see* **Tabernacles.**

C

Caesarea. A city on the Palestinian coast built by Herod the Great and named after Caesar Augustus. The Roman governors of Palestine had their residence in Caesarea, and it was here that Paul was tried before Felix and Festus, spending the intervening two years under arrest (Acts 24:1–26:32).

Caiaphas. The High Priest during the time of Jesus' ministry, who presided at his examination before the Jewish Council.

Cain, *see* **Abel.**

Cana. A village in Galilee where Jesus attended a wedding celebration and, according to John 2:1–11, turned water into wine.

Canaanites. The people who occupied the territory subsequently taken over by the people of Israel. Their civilisation was materially more advanced than that of the people of Israel, but morally they lagged far behind and their cultic practices are frequently condemned by biblical writers.

Capernaum. A little frontier town by the Sea of Galilee which for a time was the centre of Jesus' ministry. It was here that he called Matthew (Mt 9:9) and performed a number of healings including that of the centurion's servant (Lk 7:1–9).

Carmel. The culmination of a spur branching westwards from the main north–south mountain range of Palestine and almost reaching the coast. It was the scene of Elijah's confrontation with the prophets of Baal (1 Kgs 18:19–40).

Chaldeans, *see* **Babylonians.**

Christ, *see* **Jesus** and **Messiah.**

Christian. A nickname, first used in Syrian Antioch (Acts 11:26), which gradually became the normal way of describing a follower of Christ. Elsewhere in the New Testament, Christians are referred to as followers of "the Way", Nazarenes or simply the saints.

Chronicles, Books of. These books give an account of the history of the Jews from the death of Saul to the return from the exile. They are therefore largely a retelling of events already recorded by earlier authors in the books of Samuel and Kings. The purpose of the chroniclers seems to have been to reassure their people of God's care for them in spite of the adversities recently suffered, and this leads them to present an unjustifiably rosy view of Israel's history (*e.g.* glorifying David's reign and glossing over his weaknesses). Consequently most scholars prefer to rely on the earlier and more sober accounts in Samuel and Kings, but, treated with caution, the information in Chronicles provides a useful supplement to the earlier records.

Colossians, Letter to the. As far as is known, Paul himself never visited Colossae, but the church there had been founded by Epaphras, a close associate of Paul (Col 1:7). Perhaps he felt some responsibility for the Colossian Christians because of this. The letter was probably written during Paul's imprisonment in Rome and appears to be a response to reports of false teachers in Colossae. These teachers suggest that there is a special kind of knowledge (over and above the knowledge of Christ) which is necessary for salvation, and they advocate an ascetic way of life. Paul's reply stresses that Christ alone is all-sufficient for the needs of his readers.

Commandments. There are, of course, many commandments in the Bible, but the ten commandments which God is said to have given to Moses on Mount Sinai have a special place. They are seen as the basis of God's agreement with the people of Israel and, significantly, combine religious and social obligations. In Israel's religion true worship and right living are not to be separated (Ex 20:1–17).

Corinth. Strategically situated at a major junction of trading routes, Corinth in New Testament times was a wealthy city which not even Athens could match in importance among the cities of Greece. It also had an evil reputation, however, because of its notoriously lax moral standards. Both its importance and its depravity may have commended it to Paul as a place to preach the Christian gospel. He spent 18 months there about A.D. 50 (Acts 18:1–18), and made at least one further visit, possibly two. His letters to the church at Corinth show that he was passionately concerned about its welfare.

Corinthians, Letters to the. Although Paul's correspondence with the Corinthians is collected into two letters in the New Testament, most scholars are agreed that they include parts of four separate communications summarised below:

(1) A letter of warning against pagan influences, a fragment of which appears in 2 Corinthians 6:14–7:1 and which is referred to in 1 Corinthians 5:9–13.

(2) The letter now known as 1 Corinthians.

(3) An extremely severe letter partly preserved in 2 Corinthians 10–13.

(4) A much more relaxed letter, perhaps showing relief that the severe letter had had the desired effect, and preserved in 2 Corinthians 1–9.

The letters afford valuable insights into the problems which faced a small Christian community set in a pagan environment, and into the relationship between Paul and a church which nearly drove him to distraction because of its waywardness and the depth of his concern for it.

Cornelius. A Roman centurion whose baptism by Peter represented an important step in the progress of the Christian church from a Jewish sect to a universal faith (Acts 10).

Covenant. The concept of the covenant—an agreement between God and man—is implicit throughout the Old Testament. The first explicit reference comes in the story of Noah where God makes a covenant to save Noah and his family from the impending flood, and subsequently agrees never again to send such a flood upon the earth. God then makes a covenant with Abraham to establish his descendants as a chosen people, though it should be noted that they are chosen to bring God's blessing to all nations (Gen 12:3). It is however, the covenant made at Sinai after the exodus that is regarded as the most important. In this covenant God offers the people of Israel a special place in his plans if they will serve him alone and obey his commandments (Ex 19:5–6). Again it is noteworthy that the people of Israel are to serve God as priests, *i.e.* as people who mediate the knowledge of God to others.

Covenant, Book of the. In 622 B.C. during the course of repairs on the temple, a scroll was discovered which is described as the Book of the Covenant. When this was brought to King Josiah he realised that his people had failed to live up to God's demands, and set in motion the most far-reaching religious reforms ever known in Judah. These included the suppression of all pagan cults, an edict that in future sacrifice could only take place in the temple in Jerusalem, and the re-institution of the Passover which had apparently not been celebrated for many years (2 Kgs 22:3–23:23). The close similarities between these measures and instructions contained in the book of Deuteronomy suggest that the Book of the Covenant was in fact the first edition of Deuteronomy. It is thought to have been written by pious Jews during the long and evil reign of Manasseh

(687–642 B.C.) as a re-statement and amplification of the covenant with Moses. Not daring to publish it openly at the time, they hid it in the temple, hoping that it would later be discovered and acted upon.

Creation. There are two creation stories in the Old Testament, a primitive version which nevertheless has considerable charm starting at Genesis 2:4, and the more familiar version with which Genesis begins, but which is actually later in origin. *See also* **Genesis**.

Cross. The supreme symbol of the Christian faith because it represents the depths of suffering Jesus was prepared to embrace in order to save mankind by inaugurating God's Kingdom upon earth. Crucifixion was the normal method of execution for those who did not possess Roman citizenship, and because the wounds inflicted were not in themselves very serious, a strong man could take days to die. According to Mark 15:44, Pilate was surprised that Jesus had died within hours.

Cyrus (*c.* 559–530 B.C.). The Persian king who overthrew the Babylonian empire and allowed the exiled Jews to return to their homeland.

D

Damascus. An ancient city, the capital of Syria. In the Old Testament, in fact, Damascus and Syria are synonymous. It was on his way to Damascus to persecute the Christian community there that Paul had his conversion experience.

Dan. (1) The fifth son of Jacob, his first by Bilhah, Rachel's slave-girl.

(2) The tribe of Dan, occupying a small area north of Judah and west of Benjamin.

(3) The city of Dan in the far north of Israel: hence the expression "from Dan to Beersheba" meaning the whole of Israel.

Daniel. Almost certainly written between 167 and 164 B.C., Daniel is one of the last of the books of the Old Testament chronologically. At this time the Greek ruler Antiochus Epiphanes was attempting systematically to destroy the Jewish religion. The book was written to encourage the resistance movement with stories of Daniel and his friends, who refused to compromise in religious matters during the Babylonian captivity some four hundred years earlier. The second half of the book contains obscure visions which appear to predict the ultimate downfall of pagan empires and the triumph of the people of God.

David. King of Israel from about 1000 to about 960 B.C. It is not clear whether David first came to Saul's attention as a skilled musician able to soothe him in his depressions (1 Sam 16:17–23) or as the shepherd boy who killed the Philistine champion Goliath (1 Sam 17:12–51). In either case he soon showed his military skill, and before long was receiving adulation greater than Saul himself (1 Sam 18:7). Saul's insane jealousy forced David to flee from his court and become an outlaw, eventually offering his services, and those of the 600 men who had joined him, to the Philistines as a way of keeping out of Saul's clutches (1 Sam 27:1–4).

Whilst nominally a Philistine vassal, David attacked traditional enemies of Israel such as the Amalekites, and distributed his booty among the tribe of Judah, thus indicating that his change of allegiance was a temporary expedient (1 Sam 30:1–31). When Saul was killed in battle David was immediately accepted as king of Judah (2 Sam 2:4), but the northern tribes were ruled by Saul's son, Ishbosheth, until he was assassinated by two of his officers (2 Sam 4:5–8).

As king of all Israel David rapidly subdued the Philistines (2 Sam 5:17–25), and soon turned his attention to the Ammonites, who had insulted his ambassadors (2 Sam 10:1–5). During the Ammonite war he successfully beat off a Syrian attack and subsequently annexed much Syrian territory. He also conquered the Moabites and the Edomites east of the Jordan. In the end he ruled an empire stretching some 725 kilometres from north to south and 185 kilometres from east to west.

David was not just a brilliant military tactician however. He was a statesman who understood the need for national unity and the crucial part to be played by his people's religion in achieving this. He established his capital in Jerusalem because it was close to the boundary between Judah and the northern tribes, and did not actually belong to any of the tribes, being still in the hands of the Jebusites. This was presumably to avoid inter-tribal jealousy. Although he did not build a temple, he brought the ark of the covenant to Jerusalem, thus establishing it as a religious centre and not just an administrative capital.

David's later years were marred by struggles among his sons to gain the throne, and he seems to have been uncharacteristically weak and indecisive in dealing with them.

Deborah, Song of. If this hymn of triumph over the enemy commander, Sisera, was composed at the time of the events, as seems likely, it dates from before 1100 B.C. and is therefore one of the oldest fragments of literature in the Old Testament (Judg 5:2–31).

Dedication, Feast of. A feast to commemorate the rededication of the temple following its desecration by the Greek ruler Antiochus Epiphanes in 168 B.C.

Demetrius. A silversmith of Ephesus who stirred up trouble for the Christian community because the success of Christianity was affecting the trade of those who made silver models of the temple of Artemis (or Diana), the local goddess (Acts 19:23–41).

Deuteronomy, see **Covenant, Book of the.**

Devil. Contrary to popular opinion, the devil has a very minor role in the biblical writings. In the book of Job, Satan is counsel for the prosecution at the court of God, and therefore not a figure of evil as such. At the beginning of Jesus' ministry the devil appears in the role of tempter (Lk 4:1–13) and elsewhere as the adversary of God (1 Jn 3:8). Strictly, Jewish and Christian monotheism seems to offer no place for a devil except as a subordinate of God, and perhaps he is best regarded as a valuable, but mythological expression of the reality of evil.

Diana, see **Artemis.**

Dispersion (Greek Diaspora). Over a period of centuries many Jews left Palestine for a variety of reasons. Some left in times of famine to seek food elsewhere, some fled from invading armies or were forcibly exiled, others went voluntarily to set up business in the major centres of commerce. By New Testament times these Jews of the Dispersion outnumbered those in Palestine, and there were few cities round the eastern Mediterranean without a sizeable Jewish colony. It is no accident that some of the most important figures in the early church—Stephen, Philip, Barnabas and Paul, for example—were Jews of the Dispersion, for their circumstances made them less fettered by tradition and more open to new thinking.

Dorcas. A Christian woman who lived in Joppa and was renowned for her good deeds among the poor. According to Acts 9:36–42 Peter restored her to life after she had died.

E

Ecclesiastes. A strange book to find in the Bible because of its apparently unrelenting pessimism. The burden of the author's message seems to be that there is no fulfilment to be found in human existence. Man's life on earth is governed by the endless cycle of the seasons, all too soon to be ended by death, beyond which there is no certainty of anything. Some commentators suggest that the author was simply exposing the limitations of a purely rational approach and thereby demonstrating the need for a wider view of human life based on trust in God, but if this was the author's intention he fails to make it at all explicit.

Edomites. Recognised as relations of the Jews because of their alleged descent from Esau, the Edomites were nevertheless often in conflict with the people of Israel. Their territory extended from the southern end of the Dead Sea to the Gulf of Aqaba, and was of importance because of its copper mines and because it afforded access to African trade routes via the Red Sea. David conquered the Edomites and Solomon made full use of the strategic advantages thus gained, but they gradually reasserted their independence and were never again completely subjugated by the people of Israel.

Egypt. Although the influence of Egypt on Palestinian affairs was less dramatic than that of the Mesopotamian empires of Assyria and Babylonia, it was far more persistent. From very early times the story of the Jews is linked with Egypt, and the great event of Jewish history is the escape from Egyptian captivity. During the period when Assyria and Babylon were at the height of their power, Egypt used the Palestinian states to foment trouble against them, promising assistance if they rebelled against their Mesopotamian overlords. The promised assistance did not always materialise, however, and when it did it was inadequate. After the destruction of the temple by the Babylonians in 586 B.C. a considerable number of Jews sought refuge in Egypt, and it was in Egypt during the third and second centuries B.C. that the Greek translation of the Old Testament was made. References to Egypt in the New Testament are far fewer, though Joseph and Mary are said to have fled there to protect their child from the wrath of Herod.

Ekron. One of the five Philistine city-states.

Elah. King of Israel (877–876 B.C.).

Eli. The priest who brought up Samuel (1 Sam 2:11).

Elihu. A young man who, after Job's three "comforters" had failed to persuade him of the error of his ways, made another attempt to do so (Job 32).

Elijah. A prophet from Tishbe in Gilead, Elijah is rightly considered one of the great figures of the Old Testament. He was the supreme champion of Israel's God at a time when Jezebel was trying to substitute the worship of her own god, Baal Melkart. This epic struggle is epitomised by the confrontation between Elijah and the prophets of Baal on Mount Carmel (1 Kgs 18:19–40). While many different interpretations of this story have been offered, ranging from the absolutely literal to the purely legendary, there can be no doubt whatever that the conflict it represents was real. Apart from this, however, the Elijah stories contain many pointers towards a more complete understanding of God. On Mount Horeb (Sinai) he realised that God was to be found in quiet reflection rather than in dramatic natural events, and the instructions he received there showed that God's power extended beyond Israel to the surrounding nations (1 Kgs 19:8–16). The encounter with King Ahab over Naboth's vineyard (1 Kgs 21:1–24), while not proclaiming anything new, is a forceful restatement of God's concern with social justice, and clearly anticipates the work of Amos.

Eliphaz. The first of Job's three "comforters" (Job 4).

Elisha. Though he is inevitably linked with his master and predecessor Elijah, Elisha is a very different character. More miraculous incidents are recorded about Elisha, yet many of them are trivial, e.g. recovering an axe-head from the river Jordan (2 Kgs 6:1–7), and the effect is to diminish rather than enhance his stature. Whereas Elijah was a largely solitary figure spending long periods in the wilderness, Elisha associated freely with the communities of prophets and lived in the capital city, Samaria, for at least part of his career. Though not always in sympathy with the kings of Israel, he advised them in military matters. He added little or nothing to the understanding of God achieved by Elijah, but some of the ways in which he exemplified that understanding are notable, e.g. the breadth of concern shown in the healing of Naaman, the commander of the Syrian army (2 Kgs 5:1–19).

Elizabeth. The mother of John the Baptist and a relative of Mary, mother of Jesus.

Emmanuel. The name, meaning "God with us", is in fact used in a prophecy of Isaiah to King Ahaz during a time of crisis. Isaiah says that a young woman will conceive and bring forth a son, whom she will name Emmanuel. He is saying, in effect, that in nine months' time the situation will have improved so much that parents will give their children a name expressive of God's care for his people. Though the immediate prophecy, therefore, refers to events in the immediate future, it is not surprising that Christians should have seen in these words the foreshadowing of God's presence with his people in Christ (Mt 1:22–23).

Epaphras. An associate of Paul who founded the church at Colossae (Col 1:7).

Epaphroditus. A Christian from Philippi who was sent by the Philippian church to render assistance to Paul during imprisonment, probably in Rome. While with Paul he had a serious illness and Paul thought it best to send him back home possibly taking the letter to the Philippians with him (Phil 2:25–30).

Ephesians, Letter to the. Although apparently written by Paul, there is considerable doubt as to the authorship of this letter. It was not uncommon in those times for a follower of a great teacher to write in the teacher's name and, far from being considered fraudulent, this was regarded as a mark of respect. The style of writing is not quite as in Paul's other letters, themes are introduced which appear nowhere else in his correspondence, and there is a remarkable absence of personal greetings considering that Paul had spent two years in Ephesus. If the author were not Paul, however, he was clearly well acquainted with Paul's writings, especially the letter to the Colossians, parts of which are quoted almost verbatim. The first part of the letter emphasises the unity of Christian believers, whose common life in Christ overrides all human distinctions, and the glory of the church which, whatever its human weaknesses, is Christ's body. The second part of the letter draws out the implications of this view of the church for practical living.

Ephesus (in Asia Minor). The capital of the Roman province of Asia and an important trading centre, Ephesus was famous for its temple of Artemis (Diana). It had a substantial Jewish population, and soon became an important centre of Christianity. Paul visited Ephesus as he returned from his second missionary journey (Acts 18:19–21) and subsequently spent two years there (Acts 19:1–10).

Ephraim. (1) Although he was Joseph's second son, he received from Jacob his grandfather the blessing normally due to the eldest, and established an important tribe (Gen 48:17–19).

(2) It appears that Joseph never had a tribe named after him, but he gave rise to two of the tribes of Israel, named after his sons Manasseh and Ephraim. The tribe of Ephraim occupied fertile land running down to the Mediterranean coast north of Dan and Benjamin and south of Manasseh. Its significance in the affairs of Israel was such that the northern kingdom was often referred to as Ephraim.

Epicureans. A school of Greek philosophers with whom Paul debated in Athens (Acts 17:18).

Esau. The first-born son of Isaac, he sold the birthright which was his by tradition to his younger brother, Jacob, for a bowl of soup (Gen 25:27–34). He is regarded as the ancestor of the Edomites.

Esther. Dated between 150 and 100 B.C., the book of Esther describes how a Jewish heroine of that name became queen to the Persian king, Xerxes, and was able to save her people from the evil plotting of one Haman. The book makes no mention of God at all, and it appears to have gained its place in the Old Testament purely as an expression of nationalist sentiments. The deliverance from Haman is still celebrated by Jews in the feast of Purim.

Eve. Adam's partner (Gen 2:21–24, 3:20). As Adam should be thought of as a symbolic prototype of mankind, so is Eve the typical woman rather than the first woman.

Exile. The term usually refers to the exile of the leading Jewish people in Babylon between 586 and 538 B.C., though there had been an earlier deportation in 597 B.C. This experience was of great importance to the Jews for a number of reasons. They had to learn how to worship God without the temple and without sacrifice, and so it was here that forms of worship developed which were based on the recollection of the

way God had led them throughout their history. This in turn stimulated interest in writing down their history, and it was during the exile that much of the editorial work on the historical books of the Old Testament was done. On the negative side, the Jews became more exclusive during the exile because of fears that intermarriage would result in the loss of their religious and national identity. The Jews, therefore, emerged from the exile purified but also hardened in a way that was not entirely to the good.

Exodus. The name given to the escape of the people of Israel from Egypt, an escape always seen as the supreme symbol of God's concern for them and an event still celebrated annually by Jews in the feast of the Passover. While some allowance has to be made for exaggeration of the incidents leading up to the escape, there is no reason to doubt the essential historical truth of the account. It appears that, originally having gone to Egypt because of famine in Palestine, the Jews had become slave-labourers working on Egyptian building projects. They were freed from this oppression about 1250 B.C. under the leadership of Moses with the assistance of a remarkable sequence of events known as the plagues of Egypt (Ex 7:14–12:36). The pursuing Egyptian army fell into a panic as their chariots sank in the waters of a shallow swamp, successfully crossed on foot by the Israelites, in the area of the Suez canal today. Whatever our interpretation of these events, the people of Israel had no hesitation in ascribing them to God.

Exodus, Book of. As its name implies the book of Exodus tells the story of the Jews' escape from Egypt, but it contains much else of importance besides. It includes the account of God's covenant with the people of Israel at Sinai based on the ten commandments, and goes on to give instructions about the construction of the ark and of the tent in which it is to be housed, as well as directions concerning worship.

Ezekiel. Ezekiel is probably the most difficult of the major prophets for the modern reader to come to grips with. Among the Jews deported to Babylon in the first exile of 597 B.C., his call to be a prophet came in Babylon and the whole of his prophetic ministry was carried out there, though his prophecies are directed to his people in Jerusalem as well as to the exiles. Many of the messages of Ezekiel are in the form of symbolic visions of great complexity; in fact, Ezekiel has been called "the father of apocalyptic", a kind of visionary writing represented elsewhere in the Bible by the books of Daniel and Revelation. The Old Testament book stresses the responsibility of the individual before God, rather than the people as a corporate body (Ezek 18:1–4), looks forward to the restoration of his people (Ezek 37:1–14) and presents a vision of the future temple and its worship (chapter 40 onwards). This interest in ritual, the result of his priestly status (Ezek 1:1) is in sharp contrast to earlier prophets who tend to condemn ritual, or at least the insincerity of ritual without righteousness.

Ezra. A lawyer who led a party of exiles to Jerusalem from Babylon about 460 B.C. (Ezra 7:1–9) and played a major role in the re-establishment of the worship of the temple. Unfortunately he shows the hard-line tendencies some of the Jews developed in exile, to the extent of insisting that Jews who had married foreign wives should get rid of them and their children. The book of Ezra relates events from the first return of exiles in 538 B.C. up to those in which Ezra himself was involved. It is not clear how much of the book is the work of Ezra and how much the work of later editors.

F

Felix. The Roman governor of Judaea from about A.D. 52 to 58, he had a Jewish wife and was apparently well informed about the Christian way (Acts 24:22–25). He kept Paul in custody for two years, having no cause to condemn him but unwilling to release him for fear of opposition from the Jewish leaders (Acts 24:27).

Festivals, see separate entries under **Dedication, Feast of; New Year; Passover; Tabernacles, Feast of; Weeks, Feast of.**

Festus. The Roman governor of Judaea who succeeded Felix about A.D. 58. He seems to have behaved with absolute correctness in his dealings with Paul, and would probably have set him free had not Paul taken the matter out of his hands by appealing to Caesar (Acts 25:1–12, 26:30–32).

G

Gabriel. The literal meaning of the name is simply "man of God". In Jewish tradition one of seven archangels, he is said to have announced the birth of John the Baptist to Zechariah (Lk 1:5–20) and of Jesus to Mary (Lk 1:26–38).

Gad. (1) Jacob's seventh son, his first by Zilpah, Leah's slave-girl.
(2) The tribe of Gad, holding territory east of the Jordan to the north of that occupied by Reuben.

Galatia. The ancient kingdon of Galatia was in central Asia Minor, but the Roman province of the same name included a much larger area reaching down to the Mediterranean coast. Paul visited several towns within the Roman province on his first missionary journey.

Galatians, Letter to. One of the earliest of Paul's letters, probably written in c. A.D. 54, though some scholars would date it to A.D. 49, making it the first of all his surviving letters. It was written, almost certainly, to the churches Paul founded in the Roman province of Galatia on his first missionary journey, and is unusual in being addressed to a group of churches rather than a single church. The purpose in writing is very clear: Paul has been told that there are people going round the churches claiming that circumcision and the acceptance of the Jewish law is a necessary part of Christianity. Paul writes with the utmost urgency and vigour to refute these claims. He himself had been a Pharisee and knew that the attempt to satisfy God by perfect obedience to the law was impossible. It was faith in Christ which had liberated him from that futile pursuit, and the last thing he wanted was to see anyone persuaded into taking up something he had only discovered by long and painful experience to be of no value. The letter gives some useful autobiographical information as Paul recounts the way in which he became an apostle, and lays the foundations for the more fully developed statement of his theology in the letter to the Romans some years later.

Galilee. The area west of the Sea of Galilee (actually an inland lake some 20 km long) where Jesus was brought up and spent the greater part of his ministry. In the time of Jesus it formed the northern part of the Roman province of Galilee and Peraea, governed by Herod Antipas.

Gallio. The proconsul of the Roman province of Achaia before whom Paul was accused during his eighteen-month stay at Corinth (Acts 18:12–17). An inscription from Delphi establishes that Gallio was in Corinth by A.D. 52, probably having been appointed the previous year. It is implied (though not definitely stated) in Acts that Paul's trial took place soon after Gallio's arrival, and if this is accepted it fixes Paul's ministry in Corinth within a year or so, providing a useful fixed point in the chronology of the early church.

Gamaliel. A well-known Jewish teacher who numbered Paul among his pupils (Acts 22:3), and who argued in the Jewish Council against trying to stamp out Christianity on the grounds that history would show whether it was a movement from God or a worthless novelty (Acts 5:34–40).

Gath. One of the five Philistine city-states.

Gaza. The southernmost of the five Philistine city-states.

Gedaliah. When Zedekiah, the last king of Judah, was taken in chains to Babylon in 586 B.C., the Babylonians appointed Gedaliah as governor. Though in his brief spell of office he seems to have acted with wisdom and humanity, he was soon assassinated by supporters of the royal house who regarded him as a traitor (2 Kgs 25:22–26).

Gehazi. Elisha's servant, condemned by Elisha for accepting gifts against his instructions from the healed Syrian commander, Naaman (2 Kgs 5:19–27).

Genesis. As the name implies, the first book of the Bible. Chapters 1–11 contain the acounts of the creation and the stories of Adam and Eve, Cain and Abel, Noah and the tower of Babel. These stories, though they may have some basis in historical fact, are important mainly for their mythological value. They are to be seen as parables, conveying in a vivid and often entertaining way, the convictions of their authors on immensely important matters—the nature of God, the nature of the universe and the nature of man. From chapter 12 onwards, with the entrance of Abraham into the story, the book is dealing with historical figures, however much allowance may have to be made for the inevitable legendary accretions acquired during centuries of handing down by word of mouth. Whatever their degree of historical accuracy, these stories of the early ancestors of the Jewish people are richly perceptive in their observations of human life and, above all, man's religious quest.

Gentiles. The word usually translated as Gentiles means literally "the peoples" or "the nations", i.e. the peoples other than the people of Israel. The Bible shows ambivalent attitudes among the Jews towards Gentiles. The covenants with Abraham and Moses both stress that the people of Israel are to be a blessing to "the nations", but during and following the exile the fear of religious and ethnic absorption made the Jews increasingly exclusive. Even in the early church there was a long and sometimes acrimonious debate before the mission to the Gentiles was accepted by all as an inevitable implication of Christian belief. It was this crucial decision which made Christianity a universal faith and no longer just a sect within Judaism.

Gethsemane. An olive grove on the western slopes of the Mount of Olives, facing Jerusalem across the Kidron valley, it was apparently Jesus' custom to go there with his disciples to avoid the crowds, and it was there that he was arrested (Mk 14:32–52).

Gibeah. A town some 7 km north of Jerusalem which was Saul's capital throughout his reign.

Gideon. Before the monarchy was established, the people of Israel relied on inspired leaders, known as judges, to raise armies and cope with enemy aggression as the need arose. Gideon was one such leader, renowned for his victory over the Midianites (Judg 7:1–22).

Gilgal. (1) A town on the west bank of the Jordan, just north of the Dead Sea, where the people of Israel first entered the "promised land" and Saul was later proclaimed king.
(2) A settlement north of Bethel where there was a community of prophets in the time of Elijah and Elisha (2 Kgs 2:1, 4:38).

God. The existence of God is never discussed in the Bible; it is simply assumed from start to finish. But if the biblical authors never question God's existence, they do question what sort of God he is and, as one would expect of a varied group of writers working over a period of many centuries, they do not all arrive at the same conclusion. Samuel believed that God demanded the total destruction of Israel's ancient enemy the Amalekites, severely criticised Saul because he had spared the life of Agag the Amalekite king, and himself cut him to pieces (1 Sam 15:1–33). The writer of 2 Kings 2:23–24 believed that God had punished some boys who had made fun of Elisha by causing them to be mauled by bears. Clearly these are primitive views of God which cannot be reconciled with the God revealed by Jesus.

In spite of these relics of primitive religion, however, the Bible as a whole presents a remarkably unified view of God, with most of the key concepts established at quite an early date in

Israel's history. The "otherness" of God is expressed in the idea that no man could look upon the face of God and live (Ex 33:20) or that anyone who touched the ark, representing God's presence, would be struck dead (2 Sam 6:6–8). Later on these primitive attempts to express belief in a God whose ways are unsearchable, whose powers are unlimited, whose holiness is literally aweful, and who is as far removed from man as the heavens are from the earth, find nobler expression in such passages as the call vision of Isaiah (Is 6:1–8) and many of the Psalms. But the God of the Bible, though far removed from man in his wisdom, power and purity, is never remote. From the very earliest stories in the Bible he is a God who involves himself in the life of men, both making demands on them and caring for them. What he demands from men is justice in their dealings with each other. The ten commandments (Ex 20:1–17) form the basis of the moral code by which men are to live, and it is significant that even the king is subject to these demands and open to criticism for failure (1 Kgs 21:17–19) unlike other monarchs of the day who were a law unto themselves. What he offers men is a constant concern for their welfare, seen at an early stage in the exodus and expressed most movingly among Old Testament writers by the prophet Hosea, who daringly compares God to a faithful husband whose love for his wife does not waver in spite of her infidelity. So the thinkers of the Old Testament prepared the way for one whose moral demands reached new and frightening heights in the commandment to "love your enemies and do good to those who hate you", but who offered men the means to reach these heights by their response to a God who "so loved the world that he sent his only begotten son".

Golgotha. The name of the place where Jesus was crucified, the word means "skull". Whether this is a reference to the shape of the hill or an indication that executions had long been carried out there is uncertain, as is the location.

Goliath. A Philistine warrior of enormous stature supposedly killed by David, though 2 Samuel 21:19 says that it was Elhaman who killed Goliath, and it seems possible that tradition transferred this exploit to the more famous David.

Gomorrah. One of five cities described in Genesis 14:3 as occupying the valley of Siddim. The location is not quite certain, but is thought to be covered now by the southern part of the Dead Sea. Notorious for its wickedness, the city was destroyed by burning sulphur according to Genesis 19:24–25.

Greeks. Apart from its literal meaning, the word is often used in the New Testament as a general word for non-Jews. Thus in Romans 1:16 Paul says that the gospel is the saving power of God for "the Jew first but the Greek also". Some modern versions use the translation "Gentile" when this is the sense intended.

H

Habakkuk. A prophet whose ministry coincided with the rise to power of the Babylonians in the closing years of the seventh century B.C. The Old Testament book views the ascendency of the Babylonians as an act of God, but nevertheless questions how God can countenance such ruthless people, and declares that they are doomed, whereas "the righteous shall live by faith" (Hab 2:4).

Hagar. The slave-girl of Abraham's wife Sarah. When it seemed that Sarah would never have a child, Hagar was given to him to bear his children, and gave birth to Ishmael (Gen 16:1–4, 15). After the birth of Sarah's own son, Isaac, she sent Hagar and Ishmael away, but God promised Abraham that Ishmael would become the father of a nation (Gen 21:9–20).

Haggai. A prophet who prophesied about 520 B.C. some twenty years after the first Jews had returned from the exile to Jerusalem. He said

that the reason for the poor harvests the people were getting was their failure to make a start on rebuilding the temple, and encouraged them to begin the rebuilding programme.

Haman. The villain of the book of Esther, an official at the Persian court who schemed to bring about the destruction of the Jews.

Hannah. The mother of Samuel, she was childless for many years and therefore considered to be out of favour with God. She made a promise that if God granted her a son she would dedicate him to the service of his sanctuary at Shiloh (1 Sam 1:1–28).

Hazael. An army officer who came to the Syrian throne shortly before 840 B.C. by suffocating the ruling monarch, Benhadad, in his bed. Elijah had been instructed to anoint Hazael king of Syria, but had not been able to do so before his death. Elisha is said to have told Hazael that he would become king, though he did not apparently anoint him (2 Kgs 8:7–15). Hazael was to be a scourge to Israel throughout his long reign, and it is significant that the people of Israel were prepared to see even an enemy who oppressed them as God's appointed agent.

Hazor. A large town in the far north of Israel, one of those which Solomon specially fortified and made into a garrison town for his chariot forces (1 Kgs 9:15–19).

Hebrew. The language in which the Old Testament was written. Over the last fifty years, archaeological work has brought to light a vast quantity of texts in Hebrew or closely related Semitic languages, and this has greatly increased our knowledge, making accurate translation possible where previously it was necessary to resort to conjecture.

Hebrews, Letter to the. Although traditionally ascribed to Paul, it has long been recognised that this is not one of Paul's letters, being quite unlike Paul's writing in both style and content. The main theme of the letter is an interpretation of the significance of Jesus' life and teaching based on the concept of priesthood—Jesus as the supreme mediator between God and man. It is most famous for its eleventh chapter on the nature of faith. The obviously Jewish outlook of the writer has led most commentators to assume that the letter was destined for a community of Jewish Christians, as the title implies, but even this has been questioned and it has to be said that authorship, destination and circumstances of writing remain conjectural.

Hebron. A city in the territory of Judah, it was David's capital for a time before the northern tribes accepted him as king and he established Jerusalem as the new religious and administrative centre. It had, however, been a city of importance for centuries before the Jews occupied Palestine.

Hermon. At over 2,800 m., Mt Hermon is the highest point in Palestine and also represents the far north-eastern frontier of Israel at the height of her power. It is considered by some to be the scene of the transfiguration because of its proximity to Caesarea Philippi.

Herod Family. Four Herods of four different generations are mentioned in the New Testament, in addition to Philip, who was also a member of the family. Herod the Great ruled the whole of the territory of the Jews (under Roman authority) from 40 to 4 B.C. He was the Herod ruling at the time of the birth of Jesus (which was incorrectly calculated when the Christian calendar was established: hence the anomaly of Jesus' birth taking place "before Christ"). Although suspicious and intolerant by nature, he kept his country free from conflict for 35 years, which was no mean achievement. On his death, his kingdom was divided between his three sons, Archelaus, Herod Antipas and Philip. Archelaus, however, was deposed in A.D. 6 and his territory came under the direct rule of a Roman governor. Herod Antipas, the Herod who had John the Baptist killed and before whom Jesus was tried, continued to rule Galilee and Peraea until his banishment in A.D. 39. Philip ruled Ituraea and Trachonitis until his death in A.D. 34. The territories of both Herod Antipas and Philip passed to Herod Agrippa I, who persecuted the Church and had James put to death (Acts 12:2). He himself died in A.D. 44 and was succeeded by

Herod Agrippa II, the king before whom Paul appeared in Acts 25.

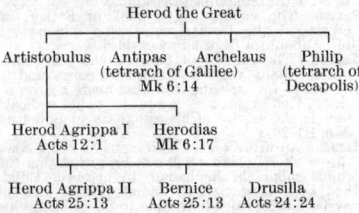

Herodias. Originally the wife of Philip (not the tetrarch), she was subsequently married to his half-brother Antipas. It was John the Baptist's objection to this marriage which brought about his imprisonment and eventual death (Mk 6:14–29).

Hezekiah. King of Judah (715–687 B.C.). Hezekiah came to the throne as a vassal of Assyria as his father, Ahaz, had been. The Assyrian ruler, Sargon II, was having difficulties elsewhere in his empire, however, and Hezekiah soon removed Assyrian religious objects from the temple, a step he might have hesitated to take but for the temporary Assyrian weakness. He also attacked the old Canaanite places of worship which were still used, and broke a bronze serpent allegedly made by Moses before which incense was burned. The exact extent of his religious reforms is uncertain, but it is clear that they were far-reaching. In spite of his removal of Assyrian cult objects from the temple, Hezekiah did not join other small Palestinian states, led by the Philistine city of Ashdod, in rebellion against the Assyrians in 713 B.C., perhaps because Isaiah opposed the enterprise. In 705 B.C., however, when Sargon II died, Hezekiah did refuse tribute to Assyria. Facing troubles elsewhere, it was 701 B.C. before the new king Sennacherib was able to move against Judah. When he did, he devastated 46 of Judah's fortresses and, in the words of his own inscription, shut up Hezekiah in Jerusalem "like a bird in a cage". What happened at this point is not clear. 2 Kings 18:14–16 says that Sennacherib demanded vastly increased tribute and Hezekiah meekly agreed. 2 Kings 18:17–19:37, however, relates how Hezekiah defied Sennacherib and the Assyrian had to return home after his army had been struck down by some mysterious agency. No attempt to reconcile these conflicting statements is entirely satisfactory, and this has led some scholars to suggest that the account of Hezekiah's successful defiance relates to a second invasion about 688 B.C. There is no corroborative evidence for this however.

Hinnom. A deep valley south-west of Jerusalem where child sacrifice was carried out according to Jeremiah 7:30–34. It is not clear from Jeremiah when this occurred (at no time was it a normal feature of Jewish religion), but it may have been during the long and evil reign of Manasseh (687–642 B.C.).

Hittites. A people referred to many times in the early period of Old Testament history from the time of the patriarchs to the establishment of the monarchy. It is now known that they ruled a considerable empire, centred on Asia Minor and achieving its maximum influence between 1400 and 1200 B.C.

Hosea. Hosea prophesied in the northern kingdom of Israel shortly after Amos (i.e. from about 750 B.C. onwards) during a period of political anarchy which was eventually to lead to the end of Israel as an independent kingdom in 721 B.C. His prophetic message is coloured throughout by his own experience of marriage, though the facts about his marriage are disputed, the evidence being ambiguous on many points. The most commonly accepted view is that his wife Gomer was unfaithful to him and eventually left him to become a prostitute. Falling upon hard times, she was sold into slavery, from which Hosea bought her back,

attempting to reform her by keeping her in seclusion for a period of time. Such a view certainly accords well with Hosea's daring portrayal of God as the faithful and persistent lover who will not abandon his faithless wife Israel. Although Hosea's message is therefore supremely hopeful, being based on the constant love of God for his people, it is not lacking in stern warnings of judgement, for the concept of God's love does not exclude the possibility of corrective punishment and Hosea is utterly appalled by the idolatry and unrighteousness of his people. Yet even God's judgement is seen as something positive, as a necessary step towards the re-establishment of a relationship between God and his people which is based on faithfulness on both sides.

Hoshea. King of Israel (732–724 B.C.). The last king of Israel, Hoshea came to the throne by the assassination of his predecessor Pekah. It was a period of Assyrian domination and for a while Hoshea wisely remained subservient to his Assyrian masters. When the capable Assyrian ruler Tiglath-pileser III died in 727 B.C., however, Hoshea made an alliance with Egypt and withheld tribute. The new Assyrian king Shalmaneser V, attacked and overran Israel, taking Hoshea captive in 724 B.C., though the capital city, Samaria, held out against the Assyrians until 721 B.C. Thereafter Israel was an Assyrian province.

I

Iconium. A city in the Roman province of Galatia visited by Paul and Barnabas on Paul's first missionary journey (Acts 13:51–14:6).

Immanuel, *see* **Emmanuel.**

Isaac. The son of Abraham and Sarah, he was nearly sacrificed to God until God showed Abraham that he did not require child sacrifice (Gen 22:1–14). His wife Rebecca bore him twin sons, Esau and Jacob, whose descendants became the Edomites and the people of Israel respectively.

Isaiah. It has long been recognised that the book of Isaiah is the work of three major prophets, often known for convenience as first, second and third Isaiah.

First Isaiah, also sometimes called Isaiah of Jerusalem, prophesied from "the year that King Uzziah died" (i.e. 742 B.C.) until at least the end of the eighth century B.C., and his work occupies chapters 1–39 of the book which bears his name. It has been said that Isaiah was more of a statesman than a prophet because of the close interest he took in Judah's affairs, and especially her foreign policy. Thus, when King Ahaz was threatened by Pekah of Israel and Rezin of Syria, Isaiah advised against taking panic measures because he believed the threat would be short-lived. Ahaz, however, ignored his advice, appealed to Assyria for help and became an Assyrian vassal for the remainder of his reign. Later Isaiah warned King Hezekiah against becoming involved in rebellion against Assyria led by the Philistine city-state of Ashdod, and this time his advice was heeded. He also constantly spoke out against reliance on Egyptian help against the Assyrians. But to call Isaiah a statesman rather than a prophet is to ignore the religious foundations of his political advice. He believed in a God whose control of history was absolute. He also believed that his people's difficulties were the result of their failure to put their trust in God and to meet his moral demands in their social life. For him, therefore, the way to solve their problems was to put these things right. Political intrigues and alliances with foreign nations were not only worthless but diverted attention from the real issues. For much of his career Isaiah regarded the Assyrians as instruments of God's judgement, and consequently argued that resistance to them was futile, but towards the end of his life he encouraged King Hezekiah in defying them, perhaps feeling that his people had now received sufficient punishment and certainly believing that the arrogance of the

Assyrians must in its own time come under God's judgement.

Second Isaiah, the author of chapters 40–55 of the prophetic book, was a prophet of the exile. Like the earlier Isaiah he had a profound belief in the utter sovereignty of God, and expresses this in some of the most beautiful and exalted language in the Old Testament. His most important contribution to religious thought, however, comes in the sections which speak of a suffering servant of the Lord. These passages are enigmatic, and it is not clear whether Isaiah was speaking of a past, present or future figure. What is important is the insight—quite astonishing in his time—that a man who set himself to serve God faithfully might be despised, reviled and rejected and that God might somehow bring healing to his people through such a person. Whatever Isaiah himself intended, it is hardly surprising that Christians equate the suffering servant with Christ.

Third Isaiah, responsible for chapters 56–66, mostly addresses people back in Jerusalem after the exile, offering them encouragement through his belief in a God who keeps his promises. It may seem strange to us that the work of three different prophets, living at different times, should have been combined in this way in one book under one name, yet the book does show a fundamental unity of outlook, especially in its proclamation of God's sovereignty. It seems possible that the first Isaiah left behind a group of disciples which continued in existence long after his death, a group which included the two later authors and which was responsible for the editing of the book of Isaiah as we know it.

Ishbosheth. The only one of Saul's four sons to survive his final tragic battle against the Philistines, Ishbosheth was accepted as king by the northern tribes while Judah proclaimed David as its king (2 Sam 2:8–11). David carefully avoided open confrontation with Ishbosheth while constantly weakening his position by diplomatic pressure. Abner, Saul's general, soon defected and Ishbosheth was eventually murdered in his bed by two of his officers (2 Sam 4:5–7).

Ishmael. The son Abraham had by Hagar, Sarah's slave-girl, when it seemed that Sarah herself would have no children (Gen 16:1–4, 15). After Sarah had Isaac, Hagar and Ishmael were driven out (Gen 21:9–20).

Israel. In the first instance this is the name given to Jacob by his mysterious opponent in the wrestling match at Peniel (Gen 32:22–28). His descendants therefore became the children of Israel, or simply Israel. When, after Solomon's reign, the northern tribes rebelled against his son Rehoboam, the term was reserved for the northern kingdom as opposed to the southern kingdom of Judah. Sometimes the term "all Israel" is used of the undivided kingdom to distinguish this usage from the later use for the northern kingdom only.

Issachar. (1) The ninth son of Jacob, his fifth by Leah.

(2) The tribe of Issachar which occupied a fairly small area west of the Jordan and south of the Sea of Galilee.

J

Jabesh-Gilead. A town just east of the Jordan which Saul delivered from the Ammonites (1 Sam 11:1–11). In gratitude the men of Jabesh-Gilead rescued the bodies of Saul and his sons from the Philistines and took them back to give them a decent burial (1 Sam 31:11–13).

Jacob. One of twin brothers, Jacob nevertheless had no claim on his father's property or the special blessing reserved for the eldest son because he was the second from his mother's womb. However, he first got his brother, Esau, to agree to sell his birthright (Gen 25:29–33) and then tricked his blind father Isaac into giving him the blessing (Gen 27:1–29). He fled from his father's wrath to his uncle Laban, in whom he met someone almost as crafty as himself. He served Laban for seven years for his younger daughter Rachel, only to find after his marriage that he had been given the elder daughter Leah (Gen 29:15–26). He then had to serve another seven years for Rachel. Nevertheless, Jacob prospered with Laban and returned a wealthy man to be reconciled with Esau (Gen 33:1–4). He ended his days in Egypt as the guest of his eleventh son, Joseph (Gen 47:11–12). The stories of Jacob which do not gloss over his failings, show a man who is often self-centred and careless about God in his early years, but who comes to see that God has plans for him and has in fact been caring for him throughout his life.

Jahweh, see Yahweh.

James. (1) One of the three disciples who were with Jesus on the mount of transfiguration (Mk 9:2–9). The brother of John and a son of Zebedee, he was later killed by Herod Agrippa I (Acts 12:1–2).

(2) Another disciple, the son of Alphaeus, of whom nothing more is known (Mk 4:18).

(3) The brother of Jesus who apparently became an apostle after a special resurrection appearance to him (1 Cor 15:7, Gal 1:19) and subsequently became leader of the Jerusalem church (Acts 15:13–21).

James, Letter of. Though some have identified the author as James the brother of Jesus, this can only be speculation, nor is there any clear indication to whom the letter was first addressed. It is a set of practical instructions on how to live the Christian life, and its emphasis on deeds (as opposed to Paul's emphasis on faith) led Luther to dismiss it as "a letter of straw". In reality, however, there is no conflict; for both James and Paul righteousness is a product of faith.

Jebusites. The original inhabitants of Jerusalem, they were not conquered by the people of Israel when they occupied Canaan but remained as an independent city-state. David took the city, however, by sending his men along a water tunnel, and established his capital there (2 Sam 5:6–10).

Jehoahaz. (1) King of Israel (815–801 B.C.). The son of Jehu, Jehoahaz was an ineffective ruler and spent the whole of his reign under Syrian domination.

(2) King of Judah (609 B.C.). The unfortunate Jehoahaz succeeded his father Josiah who had been killed in battle with the Egyptians. He was almost immediately deposed by the Egyptians in favour of his brother Eliakim, who took the throne-name Jehoiakim.

Jehoash. King of Israel (801–786 B.C.). A strong ruler who regained from Syria all the territory lost by his father Jehoahaz, and who also defeated King Amaziah of Judah after being provoked into a quarrel he did not seek.

Jehoiachin. King of Judah (598–597 B.C.). Jehoiachin came to the throne when a Babylonian army was already on the march against Jerusalem because of his father Jehoiakim's rebellion. Within three months he surrendered the city and was taken into exile where he spent the rest of his life.

Jehoiakim. King of Judah (609–598 B.C.). Placed on the throne by the Egyptians after they had killed his father Josiah in battle and deposed his elder brother Jehoahaz, Jehoiakim remained a vassal of Egypt until 605 B.C. when the Egyptians were routed by the Babylonians. He transferred his allegiance to Babylon, but in 601 B.C. another battle between the Egyptians and Babylonians on the Egyptian frontier resulted in the withdrawal of the Babylonian armies to reorganise. Interpreting this as weakness, Jehoiakim rebelled. In December 598 the Babylonians marched against him, and in the same month Jehoiakim died, possibly by assassination (this may be implied by Jeremiah 22:18, 36:30). Jeremiah, himself forced into hiding by Jehoiakim, is scathing in his criticism of the king as one who callously exploited his people and shed much innocent blood.

Jehoram. (1) King of Israel (849–842 B.C.). A son of Ahab, he actually succeeded his brother Ahaziah, who died after a short reign leaving no sons. During his reign the Moabites successfully rebelled against him, and the war against Syria, in which Ahab had lost his life, dragged on. It was while recovering from wounds received in the Syrian war that he was killed in Jehu's coup.

(2) King of Judah (849–842 B.C.). Like his contemporary and namesake in Israel, Jehoram of Judah lost territory to his enemies in Edom and also on the Philistine frontier. He was married to Ahab's sister (or possibly daughter) Athaliah, who was to seize the throne after the death of their son Ahaziah.

Jehoshaphat. King of Judah (873–849 B.C.). A capable ruler who allied himself with Omri and Ahab, his contemporaries in Israel, to subjugate enemies across the Jordan and, with rather less success, keep the Syrians at bay. In 2 Chronicles 19:4–11 we are told of a reform of the judicial system he carried out, and it seems from 2 Kings 3:14 that Elisha held him in considerable respect.

Jehu. Jehu was anointed king while serving as commander of Jehoram's army by one of the prophets acting on Elisha's instructions (2 Kgs 9:1–10). He promptly killed Jehoram, who was recovering from wounds in Jezreel, King Ahaziah of Judah who had the misfortune to be visiting him at the time, and the evil Jezebel who, as queen mother, still exercised considerable influence. He went on to exterminate every surviving member of the royal family and the worshippers of Baal. In so doing he broke the alliance with Judah, on which Israel's defence against her enemies largely depended, and deprived the nation of many of its leading figures. In spite of the ferocity of his coup, he was unable to withstand the aggression of Hazael, king of Syria, and lost all his territory across the Jordan.

Jephthah. One of the inspired leaders of Israel known as judges, before the days of the monarchy. He defeated the Ammonites, having made a vow to sacrifice the first living thing he met on his return if God gave him victory. In consequence he was compelled to sacrifice his own daughter (Judg 11:1–39).

Jeremiah. Jeremiah was called to be a prophet as a young man about 630 B.C. and prophesied until after the fall of Jerusalem to the Babylonians in 586 B.C. His long prophetic ministry therefore spanned the last years of Judah as an independent kingdom. His early prophecies paint a terrifying picture of impending disaster (Jer 5:23–31) which, in the short term at least, never materialised and made Jeremiah feel that God had made a laughing stock of him (Jer 20:7). Among the many fascinations of the book of Jeremiah are the frankness of the prophet's conversations with God and his reflections on how to distinguish true prophecy from false. When Josiah carried out his great religious reforms in 622 B.C. Jeremiah supported them and thus aroused the anger of his family, who were priests at Anathoth just outside Jerusalem and probably objected to the ban on sacrificial worship except in the temple (Jer 11:1–8,21). Although a supporter of the reforms initially, Jeremiah soon saw their limitations or even dangers: because the external forms of Judah's religion had been regularised people might become complacent, failing to realise that what God really required was a change of heart. It was this that led Jeremiah to speak of a new covenant written in men's hearts (Jer 31:31–34). From Jehoiakim's time onwards Jeremiah became increasingly unpopular because of his insistence that the presence of the temple would not save the Jews from the Babylonians, contrary to the accepted doctrine that God would never permit his city to be taken or his temple destroyed (Jer 26:1–11). During the siege of Jerusalem he was imprisoned and nearly killed as a traitor because he constantly advocated surrender and was suspected of deserting to the Babylonians (Jer 37:11–38:13). When Jerusalem finally fell, Jeremiah was permitted to remain rather than being taken into exile on the express instructions of King Nebuchadnezzar (Jer 39:11–14). After the murder of the newly appointed governor, Gedaliah, Jeremiah was taken against his will to Egypt by the remaining officials who fled there. Here he ended his days. In spite of the almost unrelieved tragedy of his life, Jeremiah was not without hope. At the height of the siege of Jerusalem he bought a plot of land from a kinsman as a symbol that people would one day have the confidence to engage in business again (Jer 32:1–15), and he wrote a letter to the first group of exiles, taken to Babylon in 597 B.C., declaring that the future of the nation was in their hands and that God had plans for their welfare (Jer 29:1–14).

Jericho. A very ancient city a few miles west of the Jordan, it was the first stronghold to be captured by Joshua after crossing the river. In Elijah's time it was the home of a company of prophets (2 Kgs 2:4–5), and in the gospels it is the setting for the healing of blind Bartimaeus and the rehabilitation of Zacchaeus (Lk 18:35–19:9).

Jeroboam I. King of Israel (922–901 B.C.). Jeroboam first appears as one of Solomon's officials in charge of forced labour. Told by the prophet Ahijah that he would receive ten of the twelve tribes of Israel, he became a marked man and had to flee to Egypt to escape Solomon's wrath (1 Kgs 11:26–40). After Solomon's death he returned to lead the northern tribes in their revolt against Rehoboam, and became the first king of the northern kingdom (1 Kgs 12:1–20). He established a capital at Shechem initially, but later moved to Tirzah, which remained the capital until the reign of Omri. Clearly he could not have his people going to the Jerusalem temple to worship, since the cult there celebrated amongst other things, God's eternal covenant with the house of David. He therefore established two rival centres at the ancient shrines of Dan and Bethel, and in each of them placed a golden calf. The significance of these animals is not in fact clear, but the biblical writers assume that they were idols and the name of Jeroboam is always associated by them with idolatry (1 Kgs 12:26–30).

Jeroboam II. King of Israel (786–746 B.C.). Long-lived and capable, in human terms Jeroboam II must be judged one of the most successful kings the northern kingdom ever had. The biblical record gives few details but states that he "restored the border of Israel from the entrance to Hamath as far as the Sea of Arabah" (2 Kgs 14:25). It appears from this that his north-eastern border stood where it had been in Solomon's time. The books of Amos and Hosea give a vivid picture of social conditions during Jeroboam's reign, a picture of great prosperity, but prosperity confined to a fortunate minority who cared little for the fate of the masses.

Jerusalem. An ancient city originally occupied by the Jebusites but captured from them by David. It made an ideal capital because of its military strength, because it was near the border between Judah and the northern tribes who were now being brought together again under David's rule, and because it did not actually belong to any of the tribes, having remained as an independent enclave until David took it. As time went on it acquired a mystical significance as the city of God, with the temple as his dwelling-place. This mystique was partly, though not entirely, destroyed by the experience of the exile, which showed that Israel's faith could survive without Jerusalem and its temple.

Jesse. The father of David (1 Sam 16:1).

Jesus. Without doubt more words have been written about Jesus than any other figure in history, and the debate still continues, not only about the historical facts but about their significance. It is impossible in a short article to do justice to the complexity of the issues arising from the life of this man, but the main facts of his public ministry may be stated with some certainty.

The existence of Jesus, as a religious leader put to death by the Romans at the instigation of the Jewish authorities, is attested by the contemporary Jewish historian Josephus. For the details of his life and teaching we have to rely mainly on the four gospels written some 35 to 65 years after his death. The earliest of these, Mark, does not record the birth of Jesus and the birth stories contained in Luke and Matthew are important more for their symbolic value than for their contribution to our historical knowledge. They do establish the date of Jesus' birth as about 4 B.C. (the obvious anomaly is due to the fact that when the

Christian calendar was established much later
the date of Jesus' birth was miscalculated).
Virtually nothing is known about his life until
he was nearly thirty when he received baptism
from John the Baptist and was confirmed in his
conviction that God had entrusted him with a
special mission and he retired to the wilderness
to reflect upon it (Lk 3:21–22, 4:1–13). When
he returned he declared his manifesto in the
synagogue at Nazareth using some words of
Isaiah, "to bring good news to the poor, to
proclaim liberty to the captive and recovery of
sight to the blind, to set free the oppressed, and
to announce that the time has come when God
will save his people". He proceeded to put
this manifesto into practice in both words and
actions. Jesus believed that the Kingdom of
God foreshadowed in the Old Testament was
about to be realised and his teaching was to
prepare people for that Kingdom which he
described in his parables. "Unless a man has
been born again he cannot see the Kingdom of
God" (Jn 3:3). Wherever he went he healed
the sick. Whether these were miracles in the
sense that normal physical laws were set aside
is, of course, open to question, but they are such
an integral part of the gospel records that they
cannot be ignored. It seems clear that Jesus
was able to heal people who could not otherwise
be healed in his day, and drove himself to
exhaustion in doing so, thus demonstrating in
practice the love of God he preached. Inevitably this made him popular, in the end embarrassingly so, for the people came to have expectations of him which he had no intention of fulfilling (Jn 6:14–15). As it became clear that he
was not going to lead his countrymen in throwing off the the yoke of Roman rule, disillusionment
set in. It had also become clear that alongside
the tremendous assurance of God's unwavering
love Jesus set demands far harder to meet than
those of the Old Testament. What other
teacher had ever required that they should love
their enemies and do good to those who hated
them (Mt 5:43–48)? The religious authorities
had never shared the popular enthusiasm for
Jesus, partly because of his disregard for sabbath rules (Mk 2:23–3:6) but even more so
because the note of authority in his teaching
put them to shame and seemed to imply a
special relationship with God (Mk 2:1–12).
Jesus, well aware that their net was closing
in around him, set out for Jerusalem for the
final confrontation (Lk 9:51). Here, having
failed to trap him by any legal method the
authorities arrested him by night with the con-
nivance of Judas (Mk 14:43–46), condemned
him in their own court on the charge of blasphemy (Mk 14:55–64) and rushed him before
the Roman governor on charges of political subversion (Mk 15:1–5). Within hours he was
dead, executed by crucifixion (Mk 15:24–37).
Yet not long afterwards his followers, who had
gone to ground after his arrest, were boldly
proclaiming his message regardless of the risks
and declaring that death had been unable to
hold him fast (Acts 2:22–24). In all the inevitable questioning over the resurrection of
Jesus one fact seems beyond dispute: that his
disciples were prepared to stake their lives on
its reality.

Jethro. A Midianite priest whose daughter
Zipporah was married to Moses (Ex 2:16–22).
He also advised Moses on the setting up of a
judicial system after the exodus (Ex 18:13–
26).

Jezebel. A Phoenician princess who was married
to Ahab, probably as part of his father Omri's
policy of friendly relations with the Phoenicians
for trade purposes. She was a fanatical devotee
of the Phoenician Baal Melkart and made strenuous efforts to introduce his worship to Israel,
equally strenuously opposed by Elijah (1 Kgs
18:19–40). Her involvement in Naboth's unjust execution (1 Kgs 21:1–15) shows a completely despotic view of the king's rights. She
outlived Ahab and continued to exercise an
evil influence as queen mother during the reigns
of his sons Ahaziah and Jehoram until killed in
Jehu's rebellion.

Jezreel. A city which seems to have been used as
a second capital by the kings of Israel about
the time of Ahab. It was here that Jehoram

went to recover from his wounds received in the
Syrian wars and where he was killed, together
with Jezebel, in Jehu's coup (2 Kgs 9:14–35).
Hosea named his first child Jezreel as a symbol
of judgement on the house of Jehu for its unnecessary brutality (Hos 1:3–4).

Joab. David's commander-in-chief and a considerable influence upon him. It was he who
persuaded David to accept Absalom back from
exile (2 Sam 14:1–24), though after Absalom's
death he took David to task for showing excessive grief over his rebellious son rather than
gratitude to those who had been loyal to him
(2 Sam 19:1–8). As David's life drew to a close
Joab backed Adonijah as his successor, but
David nominated Solomon, who subsequently
had Joab killed (1 Kgs 1:5–6, 2:28–34).

Joash. King of Judah (837–800 B.C.). The only
son of Ahaziah to escape Athaliah's slaughter,
he was kept in hiding for six years and then
proclaimed king at the age of seven on the
instructions of Jehoiada the priest (2 Kgs 11:1–
11). Under Jehoiada's influence he made repairs to the temple, but according to Chronicles
24:17–22 he showed a very different character
once Jehoiada was dead. Certainly he must
have aroused the hatred of his subjects, as he
was eventually assassinated.

Job. The book of Job is a protest against the
commonly accepted view that God rewards the
good with prosperity and punishes the wicked
with suffering. It postulates the case of a man
who had led a blameless life (Job's personal code
of conduct described in chapter 31 is astonishing
in its closeness to the ideals later proclaimed by
Jesus) who nevertheless suffers every conceivable disaster from the death of his children to
painful and disfiguring illness. The major part
of the book consists of dialogue between Job and
three of his friends (later joined by a fourth).
The friends try to convince Job that he must
have done something to deserve his misfortunes,
while Job continues to protest his innocence and
cannot accept this explanation of his suffering.
The book does not arrive at any specific answer
to the problem of innocent suffering but rejects
facile solutions, declaring in majestic poetry
that God is far greater than human understanding can encompass.

Joel. The book of Joel tells us nothing about the
author except his father's name, and there is no
clear indication when he lived, though a date in
the fifth or fourth century B.C. is likely. The
prophet regards a severe infestation of locusts
as a sign of God's judgement on his people, and
calls them to repent. He looks forward to a
time when God will pour out his spirit on everyone, men and women, young and old alike, a
passage quoted by Peter on the first Whit Sunday.

John. (1) John the Baptist. A kinsman of
Jesus, he was also his forerunner, preaching
repentance to all who would listen and baptising
them in the Jordan as a symbol of the new way
of life to which they committed themselves (Lk
3:3–14). Jesus accepted baptism from John
but then embarked on a very different kind of
ministry. It is clear, however, that the two
men regarded each other with the greatest respect (Lk 7:18–28). John was imprisoned by
Herod Antipas for criticising his marriage to his
half-brother's wife Herodias, and it was Herodias
who eventually engineered his execution (Mk
6:17–28).

(2) The brother of James, a son of Zebedee
and one of the inner group of disciples who were
with Jesus on the mount of transfiguration.
Though the identification between John and
"the disciple whom Jesus loved" in John's
gospel is not certain, it is widely assumed. In
the early days of the Christian church he was
a prominent leader with Peter (Acts 3:1–10,
4:1–21) but we hear relatively little of him
afterwards. His connection with the writing
of the fourth gospel is problematic (see next
entry).

John, Gospel of. The fourth gospel is clearly
different from the other three even to the casual
reader. To name only the most obvious difference, whereas the teaching of Jesus in the first
three gospels is in the form of short pithy sayings
or vivid parables, in John it appears as long
philosophical discourses. The gospel is not

therefore so much an account of the life of Jesus as an interpretation of its significance. But although the author has deliberately and freely recast the teaching of Jesus into a more explicitly theological form, this does not mean that he is not concerned with the historical truth; indeed, the leading British New Testament scholar of recent times has argued that in some respects the historical information in the fourth gospel is superior to that in the other three. The author then was a man of great intellectual stature who had long reflected on the significance of Jesus, and was capable of expressing his conclusions in a form more akin to Greek philosophical writing than traditional Jewish teaching, but who was also in contact with a good historical source independent of the other three gospels. John the disciple of Jesus, with his humble background as a Galilean fisherman, seems an unlikely author, but may well have been the source of the author's historical information.

John, Letters of. The three letters of John show many similarities with the fourth gospel in their vocabulary, style and thematic content, but there are some difficulties in ascribing them to the same author. If they were not by the author of the fourth gospel they were certainly written by someone thoroughly steeped in his way of thinking. The first letter is concerned with a form of false teaching which claims that there is a special way of knowing God open only to the initiated, that Jesus was not truly a physical person and that morality, having nothing to do with actions in the physical world has nothing to do with religion. In opposing this heresy John insists on the physical reality of Jesus and declares that knowing God is inseparable from loving others. Whereas the first letter appears to be a "circular" for general dissemination among the churches, the second is addressed to "the dear lady and her children"—probably a local church. It is much shorter but deals with the same false teaching. The third letter is addressed to an individual, Gaius, encouraging him and warning him against one Diotrephes.

Jonadab. The son of Rechab, he seems to have been the real founder of the Rechabites who tried to maintain the way of life of their forefathers, living in tents rather than houses and not planting crops or vineyards or drinking wine. Apart from this the only information we have on Jonadab is that he helped Jehu in his seizure of the throne (2 Kgs 10:15–17).

Jonah. The book of Jonah is in effect a short story, making a very important point in a humorous way. The essence of the story is Jonah's reluctance to preach to the people of Nineveh, the Assyrian capital, in case they listen to him and consequently enjoy the benefits of God's favour! His attempt to flee to a distant place out of God's reach is foiled by a storm and the great fish which conveniently deposits him on the Palestinian shore once more. Realising that he has no option but to do as God has told him, he goes and preaches to the people of Nineveh, who, as he had feared, repent of their evil and turn to God. Jonah consequently sulks over God's failure to punish them for their previous sins until God shows him how unreasonable his attitude is. The book is thus a witty but serious appeal to the Jews to broaden their conception of God and to rejoice in his concern for other nations. In spirit it comes close to several of the parables of Jesus, e.g. the parable of the prodigal son and his elder brother who refuses to rejoice over the return of the lost one.

Jonathan. One of the four sons of Saul whose reckless daring was largely responsible for a victory over the Philistines at the pass of Michmash (1 Sam 14:1–23). He is best known, however, for his unwavering friendship with David which survived his father's intense jealousy and David's ultimate exile (1 Sam 19:1–7, 20:1–42). He was killed, together with his father and two other brothers, in battle against the Philistines (1 Sam 31:1–4).

Joppa. A port on the Palestinian coast where Peter was staying when he had his vision showing him that there was no distinction between Jew and Gentile in God's sight (Acts 10:9–23).

Joram, see Jehoram.

Jordan. The river Jordan runs north–south from the foot of Mount Hermon to the Dead Sea through a rift valley which is below sea level for the greater part of its length. It forms a natural division between the central highlands of Palestine to the west and the plateau of the Transjordanian desert to the east. As well as being a natural barrier it is also a psychological one, the crossing of the Jordan having the same sort of significance for the people of Israel as the crossing of the Rubicon for Julius Caesar—a decisive step on the road to conquest.

Joseph. (1) The eleventh son of Jacob, his first by Rachel. A precocious child who provoked the enmity of his brothers, he was taken and sold as a slave in Egypt by Ishmaelite or Midianite traders. Not only is the story confused on this point but also as to whether he was sold to the traders by his brothers or rescued by the traders from a pit where his brothers had left him (Gen 37:12–35). After various vicissitudes in Egypt he gained high office by his power to interpret dreams, and in this position he was able both to help and test his brothers incognito when they came seeking corn in time of famine (Gen 41:1–45:14). Eventually he brought his father and brothers to live in Egypt (Gen 47:11–12). While there is no reason to doubt that the Joseph stories have a historical basis, they may well have been embellished in order to drive home the theological point made in Joseph's words to his brothers when he revealed his identity: "so it was not really you who sent me here but God" (Gen 45:8). Joseph gave rise to two of the tribes of Israel named after his sons Ephraim and Manasseh.

(2) The husband of Mary. Information on Joseph is sparse. He was a descendant of David (Mt 1:20), and worked as a village carpenter in Nazareth (Mt 13:55). He is not mentioned after the visit to Jerusalem when Jesus was twelve (Lk 2:41–51), and it seems a reasonable supposition that he had died before Jesus began his public ministry. This has led to the tradition, not necessarily true, that he was much older than Mary.

(3) Joseph of Arimathea. A rich Jew who was a member of the Jewish Council but who sympathised with Jesus and his cause. After Jesus' execution he requested the body from Pilate and had it buried in his own rock-hewn tomb (Mk 15:42–46).

Joshua. The book of Joshua takes its name from Moses' successor and records the invasion and settlement of Canaan by the people of Israel under his leadership. While it includes some very early material, the book has been extensively edited and did not reach its final form until centuries after the events it describes. It is generally considered that the picture it presents is a simplified one, representing the invasion of Canaan as a single co-ordinated campaign with Joshua as commander-in-chief. In fact, the likelihood is that the occupation was far more haphazard, with some of the tribes at least acting independently and Joshua commanding only the most successful part of the invasion forces. In particular there are indications in Joshua 15:13–14 and Judges 1:11–21 that the southern tribes of Judah, Simeon and Benjamin may have operated in isolation from the main body with a man called Caleb as their leader. The most famous incident in the conquest is undoubtedly the battle of Jericho, and controversy still rages on what actually happened on this occasion (Josh 6:1–20). In spite of the unresolved historical questions, the character of Joshua emerges clearly—a man of simple faith who believed that God had given the land of Canaan to the people of Israel and would continue to support them if they remained true to him.

Josiah. King of Judah (640–609 B.C.). Josiah is chiefly remembered for the great religious reform he carried out in 622 B.C. following the discovery in the temple of a Book of the Covenant which made him realise how far short his people had fallen from the standards God demanded. He closed down all pagan altars and, in order to prevent irregularities, decreed that sacrifice could only be offered in the temple in Jerusalem. These measures were extended even to parts of the old northern kingdom of

Israel, indicating the degree of freedom Josiah enjoyed due to the preoccupation of the Assyrians with survival against the Medes and Babylonians. He also reinstated the celebration of the Passover which had apparently lapsed (2 Kgs 23:1–23). In 609 B.C. the Egyptians marched through Judah on their way to render assistance to the beleaguered Assyrians, preferring to maintain a weakened Assyria in power than to face a strong Babylon. Josiah tried to stop them and was killed in battle at Megiddo.

Jotham. King of Judah (742–735 B.C.). The son of Uzziah, Jotham ruled as co-regent with his father for some years as his father had contracted "leprosy" (*i.e.* a disfiguring skin disease, not necessarily leprosy as it is known today), and could not carry out public duties. Little is said about Jotham except that he continued the good work of his father, building the upper gate of the temple. At the end of his reign he was under pressure from Pekah of Israel and Rezin of Syria to join an anti-Assyrian coalition, but this problem was left to his successor Ahaz.

Judaea. Like many names which denote an area, the term Judaea is used differently at different times. Its most common usage, however, is to denote the Roman province of Judaea, the area of southern Palestine which from A.D. 6 onwards came under the rule of a Roman governor rather than a member of the Herod family. It was this province which was governed by Pontius Pilate and later by Felix and Festus.

Judah. (1) The fourth son of both Jacob and Leah.

(2) The tribe of Judah which occupied a large area to the west of the Dead Sea and as far as the Egyptian frontier.

(3) The name of the southern kingdom after the northern tribes had broken away under Jeroboam I. While its boundaries coincided roughly with the old tribal area of Judah, it also included most of the territory of Benjamin.

Judas. (1) Judas, son of James, a disciple of Jesus about whom nothing else is known.

(2) Judas Iscariot, the disciple of Jesus who betrayed him. John 12:4–6 states that he was in charge of the common purse used by the disciples and stole from it, but apart from that there is little information on him prior to his act of betrayal. After betraying Jesus for 30 pieces of silver (Mt 26:14–16) he returned the money and committed suicide (Mt 27:3–5). His motives will always remain a matter of speculation. The most charitable view is that he was trying to force Jesus into a position where he would have to perform a dramatic miracle to save himself, thus convincing the sceptics, and he never anticipated that Jesus would let himself be killed.

Jude, Letter of. A short letter warning of the dangers of false teaching and the judgement which will befall those who distort the Christian message. Though it has been suggested on the basis of Mark 6:3 that the author was one of the brothers of Jesus, this is by no means certain, nor is there any clear indication to whom the letter was addressed.

Judge. The term is used in several senses in the Old Testament, including the modern sense of one who arbitrates in a legal dispute or enforces the law. There is, however, an important special use of the term to describe men like Gideon, Jephthah and Samson who exercised leadership among the tribes of Israel, especially in times of danger, during the period between the settlement of Canaan and the establishment of the monarchy. Their authority was regarded as God-given and was entirely personal, *i.e.* it did not extend to their sons. In many ways they acted as kings, but for a long time the establishment of a recognised monarchy was resisted on the grounds that it would be a denial of God's sovereignty (Judg 8:22–23).

Judges, Book of. This book deals with the history of the people of Israel during the period of the Judges, *i.e.* from the death of Joshua until shortly before the anointing of Saul as Israel's first king. It contains some material (*e.g.* the song of Deborah in chapter five) which is contemporaneous with the events described, and therefore of enormous historical value, though

like all the historical books of the Old Testament it was not edited into its final form until centuries later. Much of the book is concerned with the battles for survival against hostile tribes, but as in all the writings of the Old Testament the uniting theme is a theological one, tracing in Israel's history a recurring cycle of disobedience, oppression, repentance, deliverance leading after a time to forgetfulness, further disobedience and so on.

K

Kenites. A tribe which lived in southern Palestine and, unlike many of the surrounding tribes enjoyed friendly relations with the people of Israel, perhaps because they had religious affinities with them. Moses' father-in-law, Jethro, was a Kenite (Judg 1:16) and the Rechabites who long persisted as an ascetic group among the people of Israel appear to have been closely connected with the Kenites (1 Chr 2:55).

Kidron. A stream running through a deep valley to the east of Jerusalem and separating the city from the Mount of Olives.

Kings, Books of. The two books of Kings are the major source for nearly 400 years of the history of the people of Israel, from the accession of Solomon around 960 B.C., through the division of the kingdom on Solomon's death and the end of the northern kingdom after the fall of Samaria in 721 B.C., to the destruction of Jerusalem and the exile of the leading people by the Babylonians in 586 B.C. Like all the historical books of the Old Testament, it is a composite work containing material of different ages and not reaching its final form until centuries after some of the incidents described. Many of the major events recorded, however, can be confirmed by archaeological evidence from other sources, *e.g.* the Moabite stone, an inscription of Mesha, king of Moab, which describes relations between his people and the northern kingdom of Israel about the time of Jehoram and, except in minor details, agrees with the biblical record. The interest of the authors of Kings was not in history as an academic exercise, however, but history as it revealed the hand of God, and the kings of Israel and Judah are therefore judged by their loyalty to Yahweh, and the fortunes of their people are related to this. On this criterion all the kings of Israel are judged to have failed, but among the kings of Judah, Uzziah, Hezekiah and Josiah especially are regarded as good kings.

L

Laban. Jacob's uncle and the father of Leah and Rachel.

Lachish. An important city and stronghold about 50 km south-west of Jerusalem. Against both the Assyrians in 701 B.C. and the Babylonians in 587 B.C. it proved its defensive strength, in the latter campaign holding out longer than any other city except Jerusalem itself. Important archaeological finds have been made there, including the Lachish letters written in the heat of the Babylonian invasion.

Lamentations, Book of. Traditionally known as the Lamentations of Jeremiah, there is in fact no evidence to connect them with the prophet. The book is a collection of fine poems mourning the devastation of Jerusalem in 586 B.C. The third chapter expressed hope for the future, however, and the fifth is a prayer for mercy.

Laodicea. A city of Asia Minor near Colossae. The church there is referred to in Revelation 3:14–22 and criticised for its lukewarmness. There is particular irony in the author's claim that the church is blind, for Laodicea was famed for an eye ointment made there. It appears from Colossians 4:16 that Paul wrote a letter to Laodicea, though he never visited it as far as is known.

Last Supper, *see* **Lord's Supper.**

Lazarus. (1) The brother of Martha and Mary whom, according to John 11:17–44, Jesus raised to life again.

(2) The poor beggar in Jesus' parable of the rich man and Lazarus (Lk 16:19–31).

Leah. The elder daughter of Laban and first wife of Jacob. She bore six of Jacob's twelve sons (Gen 29:31–30:20).

Levi. (1) The third son of both Jacob and Leah.
(2) *See* **Matthew**.

Levites. It appears that the descendants of Levi never possessed any tribal territory of their own but were dispersed among the other tribes. At an early stage, by a process which is far from clear, they were associated with the priesthood, and it became the custom that only Levites could be priests, although not all Levites were. Later the term was used for an order of temple assistants with lower status than priests, as in the parable of the good Samaritan.

Leviticus. As the name of the book implies it is almost entirely concerned with Levitical or priestly duties (*see* above), the offering of worship and sacrifice, the maintenance of ritual purity and the proper response to God's holiness. To the modern reader who does not accept the need for physical sacrifice as part of worship, much of it may appear irrelevant or even repugnant, yet it represents a real desire to give to God the respect properly due to him, and it is not completely taken up with obscure ritual instructions, for it includes the words quoted with approval by Jesus, "love your neighbour as you love yourself" (Lev 19:18).

Lord's Prayer. This brief prayer, given by Jesus in response to a request from his disciples (Lk 11:1), is highly characteristic of his thought. It first places God at the centre of the worshipper's life and only then concerns itself with human needs, asking only for the basic physical requirements of food from day to day and the spiritual necessities of forgiveness and strength under testing.

Lord's Supper. The name given both to the last meal Jesus had with his disciples and to its re-enactment by the Christian community subsequently. The earliest account of the meal occurs in 1 Corinthians 11:23–26, and it is clear from the fact that Paul was instructing the Corinthian church in the proper celebration of the Lord's Supper that it was an established part of Christian worship by the mid-fifties A.D. Accounts are also given in the first three gospels. While John does not describe the meal itself, his treatment of the feeding of the five thousand is given strong sacramental overtones (Jn 6:25–58) which suggest a knowledge of the Lord's Supper. It is impossible to reconstruct with certainty the exact words of Jesus on this occasion, but it seems clear that he linked the breaking of bread and sharing of wine with his approaching sacrifice and ultimate triumph, and also with the new covenant (or new relationship) between God and man foreseen by Jeremiah (Mk 14:22–25).

Lot. A nephew of Abraham who journeyed with him to Canaan. Eventually they had to separate because their herds were too big to remain together, and Lot chose the plain of the Jordan near the Dead Sea as his territory. When escaping from the destruction of Sodom and Gomorrah his wife is said to have looked back and been turned into a pillar of salt (Gen 19:26).

Luke. Luke is referred to only three times in the New Testament, but is of special interest as being almost certainly the author of the third gospel and the book of Acts (*see* below). Only one of the references, that in Colossians 4:14, gives any information other than his name. Here he is spoken of as "our dear doctor", and since Paul has earlier named three people as the "only Jewish converts who work with me" it follows that Luke was a Gentile.

Luke, Gospel of. The question of the authorship of this gospel is closely linked to that of Acts, which is clearly a sequel to the gospel, being addressed to the same person Theophilus. The author of Acts sometimes uses the first person plural, showing that he was present himself for certain parts of the story, including Paul's crossing from Troas to Philippi on his second missionary journey and his voyage to Rome as a prisoner. It seems likely, therefore, that he would be among the people Paul names as his co-workers in his letters and, by a process of

elimination, Luke emerges as the strongest candidate. Since there is also a tradition going back to the second century that Luke was the author of the third gospel this seems a near certainty. About half the material in Luke's gospel comes from Mark (in those days copying another author's work, far from being considered unethical, was regarded a mark of respect), and some of the remainder comes from a collection of the sayings of Jesus which Matthew evidently used as well. Luke had other sources of his own, however, and it is to him that we owe the preservation of some of Jesus' best-loved parables including those of the good Samaritan and the prodigal son. He also gives us the delightful story of Zacchaeus and the account of the two disciples on the road to Emmaus. He lays special emphasis on Jesus' concern for Gentiles and outcasts, emphasises the role of women in his ministry and shows the importance of prayer in his life.

Lydia. A resident of Philippi and dealer in the purple-dyed cloth for which that area was famous, she was Paul's first convert there and opened her house to him and his companions (Acts 16:13–15).

Lystra. A city in the Roman province of Galatia visited by Paul during his first missionary journey (Acts 14:6–19).

M

Macedonia. A Roman province including parts of northern Greece, Albania and Yugoslavia with Philippi as its chief city. It was here that Paul first preached in Europe (as opposed to Asia Minor) in response to a vision of a man of Macedonia asking for his help (Acts 16:9–12).

Malachi. The book of Malachi clearly comes from some time after the reconstruction of the temple following the Babylonian exile. A probable date would be the first half of the fifth century B.C. The prophet takes his people to task for their laxity in the worship of God and their failure to obey the terms of God's covenant. He warns of God's judgement but also speaks of his saving power (Mal 4:2-3).

Malta. Paul was shipwrecked and spent the rest of the winter here on his journey to Rome (Acts 27:39–28:11).

Manasseh. (1) The elder of Joseph's two sons.
(2) The tribe of Manasseh, which occupied a large area on both banks of the Jordan to the north of Ephraim.
(3) King of Judah (687–642 B.C.). Regarded as the worst king in Judah's history, he actively promoted Assyrian and other pagan religious practices, sacrificed his own son and "killed so many innocent people that the streets of Jerusalem were flowing with blood" (2 Kgs 21:16).

Manna. The name of the food which God is said to have provided for the people of Israel during their wanderings in the wilderness (Ex 16:1–31). It is thought to have been a secretion formed by insects feeding on the scrublands of the desert.

Mark. The house of John Mark's mother, Mary, appears to have been the headquarters of the Jerusalem church (Acts 12:12). Paul and Barnabas took him to work with them in Antioch (Acts 12:25) and subsequently on the first missionary journey (Acts 13:5). He left them at Perga to return to Jerusalem, however, and this led to Paul refusing to take him on his second journey, with the consequence that Barnabas took him to Cyprus instead (Acts 15:36–40). It is clear from Colossians 4:10 and other references that Mark later became a close associate of Paul, and we are also told here that he was Barnabas' cousin. For his connection with the second gospel see below.

Mark, Gospel of. There is a tradition dating back to A.D. 135 that the second gospel was written by Mark on the basis of Peter's memories of the life and teaching of Jesus. It seems probable that Mark collected these reminiscences shortly before Peter's death in Nero's persecution of A.D. 64 and published his gospel in Rome soon afterwards. While the identification of this Mark with John Mark cannot be absolutely certain, it seems highly likely, since John Mark knew Peter from the early days in Jerusalem. The view that the gospel is based on the first-hand information of an eye-witness is borne out by the many vivid details it contains—details often omitted by Luke and Matthew when they later used Mark's work as a basis for their own. They had other material to include and economised on unnecessary detail. Mark's gospel is of special value, therefore, as the one with most direct links with the events described.

Martha. The sister of Mary and Lazarus, who gave Jesus hospitality at her home in Bethany just outside Jerusalem (Lk 10:38–41, Jn 11:1).

Mary. (1) The mother of Jesus. Our knowledge of Jesus' mother is very limited. The birth stories present her as a pious girl, open to God's bidding. Luke's account of the visit to Jerusalem when Jesus was twelve shows her anxious and somewhat uncomprehending of her unusual son (Lk 2:41–51), and it is later suggested (Mk 3:21) that she may have attempted to restrain Jesus in his public ministry. John records that she was present at the crucifixion, and that Jesus entrusted her to the "beloved disciple". By this time she must have been old by current standards and may well have died soon after.

(2) The sister of Martha and Lazarus, who was praised for her sense of priorities in listening to Jesus (Lk 10:38–41).

(3) Mary Magdalene. A woman whom Jesus cured of "seven demons" (Lk 8:2), and who became one of those who travelled with Jesus and his disciples ministering to their needs. She was present at the crucifixion, was among a group which discovered the empty tomb and was a witness of the resurrection (Mk 15:40, 16:1, Jn 20:11–18). The tradition which identifies her with the sinful woman of Luke 7:37 is wholly without foundation.

(4) The mother of James and Joseph. Another woman who followed Jesus to Jerusalem, witnessed his crucifixion and saw the empty tomb (Mk 15:40, 47, 16:1).

(5) The mother of John Mark (Acts 12:12).

Matthew. Also called Levi, Matthew was a tax collector before becoming one of the twelve disciples (Mt 9:9–13, cf. Mk 2:13–17).

Matthew, Gospel of. It is highly unlikely that the author of the gospel was the disciple Matthew, since he draws heavily on Mark for much of his material, and this would have been unnecessary for an eyewitness of the events. Like Luke, he also uses a collection of the sayings of Jesus in addition to some material of his own (*e.g.* the parable of the sheep and the goats). It is clear that the author was a Jewish Christian who was concerned among other things to stress the continuity between the Christian church and the old community of the people of Israel. Significantly, Matthew traces the ancestors of Jesus back to Abraham, whereas Luke traces them back to Adam, the symbolic father of the whole human race, and Matthew frequently states that events occurred in order to fulfil Old Testament prophecies. He arranges most of his material in five sections, possibly a conscious imitation of the Pentateuch (the five books of teaching which begin the Old Testament and have a special status among the Old Testament writings for Jews). Each section begins with a narrative and continues with the teaching of Jesus. It is the teaching of the first main sections in chapters 5–7 which constitutes the so-called Sermon on the Mount.

Megiddo. A city of strategic importance controlling the pass through the Carmel ridge from the coastal plain on the south to the Plain of Esdraelon on the north side. It was fortified by Solomon, and it was here that King Josiah lost his life in battle against the Egyptians. It is an important archaeological site.

Melchizedek. A king and priest who gave hospitality to Abraham (Gen 14:18–20) and who is referred to by the author of Hebrews as a forerunner of Christ, himself a priest-king (Heb 7:1–8:2).

Menahem. King of Israel (745–738 B.C.). Menahem secured the throne by the murder of his predecessor Shallum and a bloody struggle against his opponents. He gave tribute to the Assyrian ruler Tiglath-pileser III, hoping both to forestall any Assyrian designs on his territory and gain support to keep him in power. He raised the money by taxation, for which he was not popular.

Mephibosheth. A crippled son of Jonathan who was befriended by David (2 Sam 9:1–13), though he later entertained hopes of gaining the throne as the only remaining descendant of Saul (2 Sam 16:3). Perhaps because this was by now a totally unrealistic hope, David chose to overlook the matter (Sam 19:24–30).

Mesha. The king of Moab during Jehoram's reign, he succeeded in regaining much territory from Israel, according to an ancient inscribed stone known as the Moabite stone. This is consistent with 2 Kings 3:27, which implies that after a highly successful campaign against Mesha, the Israelite forces were unnerved by Mesha's sacrifice of his son and withdrew, having failed to bring the rebel into subjection.

Meshach. One of the three young men who, according to the book of Daniel, survived being thrown into a blazing furnace for refusing to worship a gold statue set up by King Nebuchadnezzar (Dan 3:1–27).

Mesopotamia. The fertile area between the rivers Tigris and Euphrates. It was from this land that Abraham came, and it was also the land of the Assyrians and Babylonians who had had such an influence on the history of the people of Israel.

Messiah. The Hebrew word means "anointed one" and therefore implies kingship. "Christ" is the Greek equivalent. The concept of a Messiah has a complex background, but essentially it was born out of Israel's calamitous history and a sense of disillusionment with her leaders. As a result of these factors the hope grew up of a future leader who would truly be God's representative and would consequently restore his people to the position of power and prosperity they enjoyed under David and Solomon. The balance between his spiritual and political functions seems to have been viewed differently by different groups, however, which may well explain why Jesus was apparently prepared to accept the title from his disciples (in a spiritual sense) while forbidding its general use for fear of misunderstanding (Mk 8:27–30).

Micah. A contemporary of Isaiah prophesying in the southern kingdom of Judah towards the end of the eighth century B.C., Micah pronounces God's judgement on his people for their failure to establish a just society and declares that not even the temple will be spared in the general destruction (Mic 3:12). His book is best known for its simple but searching statement of God's requirements: to do what is just, to show constant love and to walk in humble fellowship with God (Mic 6:8). Many scholars consider that the more hopeful elements in the book of Micah are later editorial insertions, and on this view Micah must be considered primarily as a prophet of judgement like Amos before him in the northern kingdom.

Micaiah. A prophet who, in contrast to the 400 court prophets, predicted disaster for King Ahab if he went to take Ramoth-Gilead from the Syrians (1 Kgs 22:1–35).

Miletus. A port near Ephesus. Paul called the leaders of the Ephesian church to meet him here on his last journey to Jerusalem, and warned them against false teachers (Acts 20:17–38).

Miriam. The elder sister of Moses, she is referred to as a prophetess when she leads the women of Israel in a song and dance of triumph after the crossing of the sea on the escape from Egypt (Ex 15:20–21).

Moabites. Occupying land east of the Dead Sea, the Moabites were generally hostile to the people of Israel. David conquered them, but they reasserted their independence in the period of weakness after the division of the kingdom, only to be subjugated again later by Omri. They were finally led to independence by Mesha while Jehoram was king of Israel.

Molech. A Canaanite god whose worship involved child-sacrifice. King Manasseh apparently worshipped him (2 Kgs 21:6), but Josiah desecrated the site of these sacrifices to prevent them happening again (2 Kgs 23:10).

Mordecai. The cousin and foster-father of Queen Esther (Esth 2:6–7).

Moses. If Abraham is the father of the Jewish race, Moses is the founder of Jewish religion. This does not mean, however, that the religion he established had no antecedents, but it was under Moses that it achieved its definitive form. While it is admittedly difficult to disentangle fact from legend in many of the stories of Moses, there is no reason to doubt their essential historical basis as recollections of the great leader who took the people of Israel from slavery in Egypt to the threshold of the promised land, and in the process firmly established their religious traditions. At the centre of Moses' religion is the concept of the covenant, an agreement between God and the people of Israel whereby God gives them a special position of responsibility in his plans and they pledge him their loyalty and obedience. This obedience is to be expressed not only in worship but also in behaviour towards others as laid down in the ten commandments. It is, in essence, a joyful religion because it springs from a sense of gratitude for what God has done, and in this respect as in many others, it is a precursor of Christianity.

N

Naaman. Commander of the Syrian army, cured of "leprosy" (*i.e.* a disfiguring skin disease) by Elisha (2 Kgs 5:1–19).

Naboth. Owner of a vineyard adjoining King Ahab's palace, he was put to death on false evidence at Jezebel's instigation so that Ahab could take the property in the absence of an heir (1 Kgs 21:1–16).

Nadab. King of Israel (901–900 B.C.). Assassinated within two years of his accession by Baasha whilst fighting the Philistines at Gibbethon (1 Kgs 15:27).

Nahum. The book is a poem exulting in the fall of the Assyrian capital Nineveh, which is seen as an example of God's judgement on a nation which had long taken for granted its dominant position and gave no thought to the suffering of its subject peoples. Nineveh fell in 612 B.C., and the poem appears to be contemporary with the event.

Naphtali. (1) The sixth son of Jacob, his second by Bilhah, Rachel's slave-girl.

(2) The tribe of Naphtali, occupying territory to the north and west of the Sea of Galilee.

Nathan. A prophet who advised David not to build a permanent temple in Jerusalem and rebuked him for his misconduct with Bathsheba. Nevertheless, he backed Bathsheba's son, Solomon, in the struggle for succession. It was largely through him that David was eventually persuaded to declare himself in Solomon's favour (1 Kgs 1:11–40).

Nathanael. Often identified with Bartholomew, since John omits all mention of Bartholomew but names Nathanael as one of the disciples. Brought to Jesus by Philip (who is linked with Bartholomew in the other gospels), Jesus referred to him as "a true Israelite in whom there is nothing false" (Jn 1:47).

Nazareth. The home of Joseph and Mary, and the place where Jesus lived until he began his itinerant ministry. Until then this small Galilean town was of no importance and is not even mentioned in the Old Testament.

Nazirite. A person dedicated to God's service and following an ascetic rule of life involving abstinence from alcohol and refusal to cut hair amongst other things. Samson was a Nazirite (Judg 13:2–24) and John the Baptist may have been (Lk 1:15).

Nebuchadnezzar. The Babylonian ruler (605–562 B.C.) under whose orders Jerusalem was taken and destroyed and the people exiled in 586 B.C. By the standards of his day he was not excessively ruthless, and it could be argued that only the intransigence of the Jews compelled him to treat them with severity.

Nehemiah. A Jewish exile who became cupbearer to the Persian king Artaxerxes and was allowed by him to go to Jerusalem as governor about 445 B.C. in order to accelerate reconstruction of the nation's life. The book of Nehemiah relates how he overcame opposition to get the walls of Jerusalem rebuilt. It also tells how Ezra read the law aloud to the people and got them to enter into an agreement to keep it. While it seems that the two men worked to-

gether on the re-establishment of the nation's religious and economic life, the relationship between them is not entirely clear.

New Year. Originally the Jewish New Year began in the autumn, but during the exile the Babylonian New Year starting in the spring was adopted. The autumn New Year was still maintained for cultic purposes, however, and there has been much speculation, based on strong but circumstantial evidence mainly from the Psalms, over the possibility that the autumn New Year was the occasion of a major religious festival celebrating and renewing the covenant.

Nicodemus. A member of the Jewish Council who sympathised with Jesus and came to see him by night—presumably fearful of associating with him openly (Jn 3:1–12). He objected to the Council condemning Jesus without giving him a chance to defend himself (Jn 7:50–51) and helped Joseph of Arimathea to give Jesus a decent burial (Jn 19:39–42).

Nineveh. The capital of Assyria until its destruction by the combined forces of the Medes and Babylonians in 612 B.C. Among the people of Israel it was legendary for its size and sinfulness (Jon 1:2).

Noah. While the story of Noah may have a historical basis, its primary value lies in what it says about God. It shows God as one who does not fully carry out the judgement which man's sinfulness deserves, but in his generosity makes a new start possible.

Numbers, Book of. The name of the book refers to two censuses of the people of Israel recorded in it, one just before they left Mount Sinai and the other about a generation later. The book covers the history of the people of Israel from the exodus until just before the crossing of the Jordan and lays down various rules for everyday life and worship.

O

Obadiah. (1) A high official under King Ahab who tried to protect loyal worshippers of Yahweh against the persecution of Queen Jezebel (1 Kgs 18:2–15).

(2) A prophet who wrote sometime after the fall of Jerusalem in 586 B.C., condemning the Edomites for taking advantage of Judah's plight to settle old scores, and predicting final victory for the people of Israel.

Omri. King of Israel (876–869 B.C.). Although Omri is only given six verses in the books of Kings (1 Kgs 16:23–28), and is condemned for leading his people into idolatry, he was a capable ruler who in a relatively short reign established good relations with both Judah and the Phoenician states, subjugated enemies east of the Jordan and built a new capital, Samaria.

Onesimus. A runaway slave who was converted by Paul and eventually sent back to his master Philemon, bearing with him the letter of that name.

P

Palestine. Derived from "Philistine", the name originally referred only to the southern part of the coastal plain around the Philistine cities, but it came to be used for the whole of the area bordering the eastern Mediterranean from the Lebanon southwards to the Egyptian frontier and across to the desert land of Transjordan.

Passover. A festival celebrated in spring by a special meal. Originally it probably derived from a custom of sacrificing the first lamb of the new season, but it became associated with the deliverance from slavery in Egypt, and it is as a way of remembering this that it has been celebrated ever since. It is followed by a week of eating unleavened bread, also in memory of the escape from Egypt.

Paul. We know more about Paul than about any other leader of the early church, our information coming both from Acts and his own letters. Born in Tarsus in Asia Minor, he was brought up in strictest Jewish tradition and studied under the renowned teacher, Gamaliel. He considered it his duty to persecute the Christian community, and was present at the stoning of Stephen, whose saintly behaviour towards his executioners almost certainly sowed the first seeds of doubt in his mind. These doubts culminated in a shattering conversion experience as he travelled to Damascus to continue his persecution of the Christians there. It was not until many years had elapsed, however, that Paul emerged as the leading figure in the mission to the Gentiles, and he did so at the instigation of Barnabas, who sent for him to help in the work at Antioch. Soon the church decided to send Paul and Barnabas on a missionary journey which took them first to Cyprus and then into the Roman province of Galatia. By this time some of the Jewish Christians were becoming alarmed at the large number of Gentile converts, and on their return they went to a gathering in Jerusalem to thrash out questions of policy with regard to the admission of Gentiles to the church. Here, Paul, more aware than anyone else of the futility of the Jewish law, strongly resisted the imposition of Jewish customs on Gentile converts, and appears to have won, though the argument was to rumble on for many years. Soon he undertook a second missionary journey with Silas, in the course of which he founded the first church in Europe at Philippi and stayed for eighteen months in Corinth. On a third journey he spent two years in Ephesus before revisiting the churches founded earlier during his second journey. On a visit to Jerusalem at the end of his third journey he was arrested by Roman guards during a disturbance in the temple courtyard when Jews alleged that he had taken Trophimus, a Gentile from Ephesus, into the temple. After two years' imprisonment during which he was neither condemned nor declared innocent, Paul appealed to Caesar and was duly sent to Rome. We are told in Acts 28:30 that he was there for two years, presumably waiting for his accusers to present a case against him, and this may imply that he was then released, since the rule was that a case must be presented within two years. However, this is not certain, and tradition has it that he died, together with Peter, in Nero's persecution of A.D. 64. From about A.D. 50 onwards Paul wrote numerous letters, mainly to churches he had founded, but occasionally to churches he had not visited himself, and some of these letters form a substantial part of the New Testament. Some have accused Paul of complicating the simple gospel preached by Jesus, yet the church today may owe its very existence to Paul's clear understanding that Christianity could not just remain an offshoot of Judaism, but must become a universal religion.

Pekah. King of Israel (737–732 B.C.). Seizing the throne by assassinating his predecessor, Pekah immediately entered an anti-Assyrian coalition with his Syrian neighbour Rezin. Together they made threats against Ahaz, king of Judah, who soon appealed to the Assyrians for help. In 733 B.C. Tiglath-pileser III attacked Israel, capturing many cities and deporting much of the population. It was possibly only Pekah's assassination by Hoshea, who promptly surrendered, which saved Israel from further destruction.

Pekahiah. King of Israel (738–737 B.C.). Assassinated after a short period by Pekah, probably because of discontent with his policy of submission to Assyria.

Pentateuch. The first five books of the Old Testament, having special significance for the Jews as the Torah, the basis of Jewish law.

Pentecost, *see* **Weeks, Feast of.**

Peter. The undisputed leader of the disciples, and of the Christian church during its earliest days. A Galilean fisherman, he was brought to Jesus by his brother Andrew and quickly became one of the inner group of disciples. He showed his leadership in his declaration of faith in Jesus as the Christ at Caesarea Philippi, and it was here that Jesus added the name Peter (the rock) to his original name Simon. After Jesus' arrest he denied all knowledge of him, but it could be argued that he was only exposed to this temptation because he had had the courage to follow Jesus to the High Priest's house. He was the first disciple to enter the empty tomb and preached the first Christian sermon on the day of Pente-

cost. He was also instrumental in paving the way for Gentiles to enter the church through the baptism of the Roman centurion Cornelius and his subsequent defence of this action (Acts 10:1–11:18). It is unfortunate, though understandable, that the emphasis in the second half of Acts on the work of Paul leave us in ignorance as to the subsequent development of Peter's ministry. Tradition has it that he founded the church in Rome, and died there in Nero's persecution of A.D. 64.

Peter, Letters of. There is considerable doubt whether either of these letters is by the disciple Peter, or indeed whether they are by the same author. The first letter is written to encourage Christians in Asia Minor who are suffering or are likely to suffer, for their Christian faith. If this were written during a specific period of persecution it would almost certainly have been that under the Roman emperor Domitian (A.D. 81–96), since Nero's persecution does not appear to have extended far beyond the capital, and this would rule out authorship by Peter if he had died in A.D. 64. The second letter, which shows a detailed knowledge of the letter of Jude, is a general warning against false teachers. Many scholars regard it as the latest document in the New Testament, with a date in the second century.

Pharaoh. The title of the kings of Egypt. The Pharaohs under whom the people of Israel served as forced labourers have not been identified with certainty, but the likelihood is that the Pharaoh at the time of the exodus was Rameses II (reigned 1304–1237 B.C.).

Pharisees. One of the chief sects within Judaism at the time of Jesus. The movement started as an attempt to bring everyday life more closely into conformity with the law of Judaism, so that religious observance became an integral part of daily living. Jesus would hardly have quarrelled with this aim, but the effect had been to emphasise trivial details and lose sight of basic principles. It was this, and the sense of self-righteousness so often engendered, that Jesus criticised in the Pharisees.

Philemon, Letter to. A short personal letter from Paul to a member of the church at Colossae. Onesimus, Philemon's slave, had run away to Rome, where he came into contact with Paul. Paul would have liked to keep him as he was proving so useful, but felt bound to return him to Philemon. begging Philemon to welcome him back not just as a slave but as a Christian brother.

Philip. (1) Ruler of Ituraea and Trachonitis (4 B.C.–A.D. 34), *see* **Herod family.**

(2) One of the twelve disciples about whom little is known, although John's gospel gives him slightly greater prominence than the other three (Jn 1:43–46, 12:20–22, 14:8–9).

(3) One of the seven deacons appointed to organise the distribution of resources in the system of sharing goods adopted by the early church in Jerusalem (Acts 6:1–6). In fact, he quickly became a notable evangelist, working among the Samaritans and also in southern Palestine, where he converted an Ethiopian official travelling home, before settling in Caesarea, where he still lived nearby thirty years later (Acts 8:4–40, 21:8).

Philippi. A city of Macedonia where Paul first preached in Europe (Acts 16:12).

Philippians, Letter to the. Unlike many of Paul's letters, the letter to the church at Philippi does not seem to have been written with any particular object in mind—to combat false teaching (Galatians) or pave the way for a possible future visit (Romans). It is simply keeping in touch with old friends, for the church at Philippi had apparently been the first to give Paul financial support so that he could be a full-time missionary without the necessity of plying a trade (Phil 4:15–16). Although he warns the Philippian Christians to be on their guard against any attempt to impose Jewish customs on them (Phil 3:2–7), he seems confident of their ability to maintain their Christian life against any opposition it encounters. The whole atmosphere of the letter is one of gratitude, joy and peace, all the more remarkable as Paul was in prison and possibly close to death as he wrote (Phil 1:20–24).

Philistines. A people who came from Crete or the Aegean islands to settle on the coastal plain of Palestine about the same time that the people of Israel were entering Canaan from the east. They were organised in five main city-states and were a serious threat to the Israelites because of their iron weapons (Israel being still in the Bronze Age), their use of chariots and their military form of government. After the period of acute antagonism which was brought to a close by David's unchallengeable superiority, they lived relatively peacefully apart from occasional incidents until, sometime after the exile, the Philistines disappeared as an independent entity.

Phoenicia. A term used to describe the coastal area north of Mount Carmel which is now the Lebanon. It was never a kingdom as such, but included a number of city-states, of which Tyre was the most important. The Phoenicians were seafarers and traders and times of prosperity in Israel often hinged upon good relations with Phoenicia, as in Solomon's reign.

Pilate, Pontius. The Roman governor of Judaea at the time of Jesus' execution, he does not seem to have handled the admittedly difficult task of governing the Jews particularly well. All the gospels represent him as resisting the death sentence on Jesus, however, and only passing it under Jewish pressure. John implies that the Jews had some kind of hold over Pilate: possibly because of previous blunders he could not afford to antagonise the Jews again. In fact, he was recalled to Rome c. A.D. 36, tried and imprisoned.

Priest. In the early period of Jewish religion there were no priests. The head of the family would perform any religious functions necessary. Samuel, however, is said to have condemned Saul for offering sacrifice, thereby usurping his proper function (1 Sam 13:8–14). This suggests that by now a specific priestly role was recognised. It was with the construction of the temple and the development of more elaborate rituals that a priesthood became essential, though it was the offering of sacrifice which remained the primary function.

Prisca, see Aquila.

Prophet. What marks a person out as a prophet has been much debated. The prophets of Baal on Mount Carmel present an extremely unedifying spectacle as they dance and cut themselves to invoke the power of their god (1 Kgs 18:26–29), yet there were prophets in Israel whose behaviour was not dissimilar (1 Sam: 10:10–13). There is clearly a vast gulf between such people and men of the calibre of Amos, Hosea or Jeremiah. The one thing they have in common is their enthusiasm for God. It is possible to trace the gradual transition from these primitive prophets who expressed themselves in emotional outbursts to the great religious thinkers of later times but to sum up the difference in terms of emotions against intellect (or any other pair of contrasting qualities) is an over-simplification. Possibly the best short definition of a prophet is "one who is convinced that God has something to say through him". Note that, although prophets were generally expected to have knowledge of future events, this is not an essential part of the Hebrew concept of prophecy.

Proselyte. One who was not a Jew by birth but who, by circumcision and a form of baptism, had become a Jew by faith. Acts 2:11 refers to the presence of proselytes in Jerusalem for the day of Pentecost.

Proverbs, Book of. This is basically a collection of short sayings offering advice on how to act in everyday situations, but, as with all the biblical writings, it emphasises an important theological belief—that all true wisdom comes from God and is based on respect for him. The sayings are traditionally ascribed to Solomon, who may indeed be responsible for some of them, but the compilation of the book certainly took place centuries after his death and incorporated much later material.

Psalms. It is a truism to say that the Psalms are the hymn book of the Old Testament, yet it is only recently that the implications of this obvious truth have been explored. If the Psalms were collected for use in corporate worship, we need to ask for each Psalm, "On what sort of occasion would these have been appropriate sentiments to express?" In recent years this approach has led to some interesting conclusions about the worship of the people of Israel, and greatly illuminated the Psalms themselves. For the ordinary reader, however, the attraction of these poems remains what it has always been—their expression of a very wide range of human emotions within an overall context of faith in God.

Publius. The chief official (his exact status is unclear) on Malta when Paul was shipwrecked there. Paul cured his father of a fever (Acts 28:7–10).

Q

Qirinius. Described by Luke as the governor of Syria at the time of Jesus' birth, though if this took place in the reign of Herod the Great, Luke is wrong on this point. He later had two terms of office as governor of Syria, but at this time commanded the Roman army there.

R

Rabbah. The Ammonite capital, captured by David. It was during the siege of Rabbah that David arranged for Uriah to be left exposed to the enemy, in order to marry his wife Bathsheba (2 Sam 11:14–17).

Rabbi. Sometimes translated "teacher", but implying rather more than this. It is a respectful title, suggesting that the one who uses it accepts the authority of the one to whom it is used. In John's gospel Jesus is addressed in this manner several times.

Rachel. Laban's younger daughter and Jacob's second wife, though she was his first choice (Gen 29:18–28). She bore him Joseph and Benjamin.

Rahab. A prostitute of Jericho who concealed two spies sent by Joshua, and was subsequently spared when the other inhabitants were slaughtered (Josh 1:1–21, 6:22–25).

Rameses. An Egyptian city where Israelite slave labour was used, and from which the people of Israel started out on the exodus. It was on the eastern edge of the Nile delta, and is generally identified with a city earlier known as Avaris and later as Tanis.

Ramoth-Gilead. A town on the border between Israel and Syria which was the scene of bitter fighting between these traditional enemies. It was here that Ahab died, and that Jehoram received the wounds from which he was recovering at the time of Jehu's coup.

Rebecca. The sister of Laban, wife of Isaac, and mother of the twins Esau and Jacob.

Rechabites. The descendants of Rechab, about whom we know nothing except that he was the father of Jonadab, who laid down the rules of the Rechabite community. He insisted that they lived in tents and refrained from alcohol, thus trying to protect them against the corrupting influences of Canaanite civilisation. Jeremiah commends the Rechabites for their faithfulness to these principles, in contrast to the lack of faithfulness found elsewhere among the people of Israel (Jer 35:1–17).

Red Sea. The name translated as "Red Sea" in older versions of the Bible is not always to be equated with the Red Sea as known today. References in the exodus story may be to a shallow inland lake in the region now cut through by the Suez Canal, and in 1 Kings 9:26 the reference is to the Gulf of Aqaba, the eastern limb of the Red Sea, rather than the Red Sea itself.

Rehoboam. King of Judah (922–915 B.C.). The son of Solomon, Rehoboam refused to listen to the grievances of his people at the beginning of his reign and as a consequence was faced with rebellion by the ten northern tribes under Jeroboam's leadership. Rehoboam was unable to prevent the division and soon gave up any attempt to reassert his authority over Israel. He lost nearly all his foreign territory, was invaded by the Egyptians and had to ransack his treasury to pay the tribute demanded (1 Kgs 12:1–24, 14:25–26).

Resurrection. It is quite clear from the book of Acts that the resurrection of Jesus was the central theme of early Christian preaching. It is equally clear that those who proclaimed the resurrection in this way stood a considerable risk of sharing the fate of their leader. It follows that they must have been absolutely certain in their own minds of the truth and importance of their claims. Because these claims are admittedly extraordinary, it is natural that people should have sought explanations in terms of natural causes, but no such explanation has proved entirely satisfactory. In any case, an extraordinary event is needed to explain the transformation in the behaviour of the disciples. Among those who believe in the resurrection it is, of course, possible to find a wide variety of interpretations as to what exactly took place.

Reuben. (1) The first-born son of both Jacob and Leah.

(2) The tribe of Reuben, which occupied an area on the eastern shore of the Dead Sea between Ammonite and Moabite territory.

Revelation, Book of. Without doubt the most difficult book in the New Testament for modern readers because its thought-forms and imagery are so remote from those to which we are accustomed. Written during a time of persecution, probably that of the emperor Domitian in the last decade of the first century, it declares in highly metaphorical language that the stage of human history is set in the context of an eternal scheme of things, in which God reigns supreme. Whatever their present sufferings, ultimate victory is assured to those who put their trust in Jesus. The writer describes himself as John, and some scholars have identified him with the disciple John, but there is no solid evidence for this. There is no question of the writer being the author of John's gospel or the letters of John.

Rezin. King of Syria (about 740–732 B.C.). An ally of Pekah, king of Israel, against the Assyrians. Together they threatened to attack Judah if King Ahaz would not join their coalition. Rezin was killed by the Assyrians when they finally took his capital, Damascus.

Romans. The Roman empire provides the context in which the events of the New Testament took place. Many Jews hated the Romans, and there were frequent misguided attempts at rebellion which culminated in the revolt of A.D. 66 and the eventual destruction of Jerusalem by the Romans in A.D. 70. In spite of occasional persecution, Roman rule was generally helpful to the spread of Christianity through its maintenance of political stability and good communications.

Romans, Letters to the. Paul's letter to the Romans was written to an already flourishing church which he did not know personally. Its purpose was apparently to pave the way for further missionary work in the western Mediterranean, using Rome as a base. Paul seems to feel it necessary to lay before the Roman church the gospel that he preaches, and this letter provides the most coherent statement of his theology that we possess. Its great emphasis is on faith in Jesus as the sole necessity for reconciliation with God, and the inadequacy of legalistic forms of religion where the follower's relationship with God depends on his having met God's demands in every detail.

Rome. The capital of the Roman empire, a church seems to have been established there at an early but unknown date. Tradition says it was founded by Peter, but there is no biblical evidence for this. Paul spent two years there under arrest and, again according to tradition, died there with Peter in Nero's persecution.

Ruth. The book of Ruth is one of the gems of the Old Testament. It tells how Ruth, the Moabite widow of an Israelite husband, decides to accompany her widowed mother-in-law, Naomi, back to her home town of Bethlehem. In so doing Ruth accepts Israel's God as her own. Boaz, a kinsman of Naomi, notices Ruth gleaning the remains of his barley field and ultimately marries her, and they give birth to Obed, David's grandfather. The story is a parable (as is suggested by the names of the chief characters, all

of them symbolic), but may rest on a historical fact, for much of the point of the story depends on Ruth being David's great-grandmother, and if this were made up the point would be lost. The book is essentially a plea for tolerance of mixed marriages, and as such it shows a liberality of outlook matched in the Old Testament only by the book of Jonah. Attempts to date the book have proved very difficult, but the most likely period is shortly after the exile, when the Jewish community was becoming more exclusive.

S

Sabbath. The observance of the sabbath as a day of rest and worship goes back at least to the time of Moses, yet it was only during the exile that it came to assume the importance it has had ever since for Jews. Deprived of temple worship, and living among aliens, strict sabbath observance became the identifying characteristic of a good Jew. By Jesus' time the number of rules about the sabbath was enormous, and while Jesus clearly supported the principle of the sabbath, he would not let his work be hindered by such petty rules. This became one of the major sources of friction between him and the Pharisees.

Sacrifice. Although the Jews came to realise at an early stage that God did not require human sacrifice (Gen 22:9–14), animal sacrifice continued to be part of their worship until the destruction of Herod's temple by the Romans. Many of the prophets questioned the value of the practice, however, declaring that what God really wanted was justice and compassion in all men's dealings with their fellows.

Sadducees. A major party within Judaism at the time of Jesus. They were mainly of priestly background and, because many of them occupied positions which depended on the good will of the Romans, they generally favoured a conciliatory approach. Unlike the Pharisees, many of whom commanded respect by their conscientiousness, the Sadducees were liked by no one.

Salome. One of the women who had followed Jesus from Galilee to Jerusalem, watched the crucifixion and saw the empty tomb.

Samaria. Originally the name referred to the new capital city built by Omri, king of Israel. It was increasingly used, however, as another term for the northern kingdom as a whole. After the kingdom had ceased to exist it denoted an area corresponding to the central part of the old kingdom.

Samaritan. An inhabitant of Samaria. The Jews considered Samaritans to be excluded from their ranks because, following the deportation of many Samaritan citizens by the Assyrians in 721 B.C. and the establishment of people from other parts of the Assyrian empire on their soil, many mixed marriages had taken place. Since the northern kingdom had always been considered idolatrous by southern Jews, this put them both religiously and socially beyond the pale.

Samson. A Nazirite, and one of the most famous of the judges. He seems to have had more valour than discretion, however, and provoked the Philistines needlessly (Judg 15:1–6). He paid for this unnecessary bravado with his life (Judg 16:4–30).

Samuel. Samuel was the last great leader of Israel before the establishment of the monarchy, and a unique figure combining the functions of prophet, priest, judge and even ruler. Undoubtedly the most significant part of his work was the creation of the monarchy, but unfortunately the role he played in this is far from clear. There are two conflicting accounts interwoven in 1 Samuel. One represents Samuel privately anointing Saul as king on God's instructions, and later arranging for a public acclamation of his kingship when he has proved himself in battle. The other suggests that the people demanded a king against Samuel's advice and that only under protest did he arrange a system for choosing a king by lots. Whatever his initial attitude, his support for Saul was soon withdrawn when Saul offered sacrifice instead of waiting for Samuel to do it (1 Sam 13:8–14) and failed to destroy totally the Amalekites according to Samuel's instructions (1 Sam 15:13–23). It seems clear that Samuel came to regard Saul as one who was usurping God's position, and his hostility did much to break the man who, willingly or otherwise, he had created king.

Samuel, Books of. The two books of Samuel cover an epoch-making period in Israel's history. They trace the development of a loose confederation of tribes, without any established form of government, into a considerable empire under a dynastic ruler. Like all the historical books, they contain material from a variety of sources, some much closer to the events than others. We are fortunate, however, to have in 2 Samuel 9–20 (and continuing in 1 Kings 1–2) a continuous source which is widely recognised as the finest piece of history writing of its time from anywhere in the world. The author deals with the reign of David in such a way that he can only have been a close associate of the king himself. Not only does he describe in detail David's conversations with his advisers, but he does it so vividly that the characters of the major participants are laid open to scrutiny. He is quite remarkable in his absence of bias. He paints a sympathetic portrait of David but does not gloss over his failings, and neither condemns nor attempts to justify his more questionable activities. About no other king in the history of the monarchy is our information so reliable.

Sanhedrin. A council meeting under the High Priest at Jerusalem which had ultimate authority in religious and legal matters except for the power to pass the death penalty. This was why the Jews had to take Jesus before Pilate. The stoning of Stephen appears to have been a flagrant violation of this restriction. How and when the Sanhedrin was established is uncertain, but it came to an end with the destruction of Jerusalem in A.D. 70.

Sarah. Wife of Abraham and mother of Isaac. One of a number of women in the Bible whose child was seen as a special mark of God's favour because it came late in life.

Saul. (1) As the first king of Israel shortly before 1000 B.C., Saul faced a near impossible task, and his undoubted courage in battle was not an adequate qualification. The people of Israel wanted a king to defend them from their enemies, especially the Philistines, but they were not yet ready to give up their tribal independence, or support a permanent army as opposed to a constantly changing collection of volunteers. So he occupied an uncomfortable position in which more was expected of him than of the judges of old, but without any constitutional means of exercising his authority. When Samuel, a powerful influence on public opinion, withdrew his support, Saul clearly felt exposed and vulnerable, and the popularity of the young hero David increased his sense of insecurity. When David fled from his jealousy, helped unwittingly by the priest Ahimelech, Saul's slaughter of Ahimelech and his household was widely regarded as unjust, and must have alienated the priesthood. Thereafter much of his time and energy was diverted into hunting down David when it could have been more usefully employed in other ways. His final battle was an act of desperation, meeting the Philistines on level ground at the foot of Mount Gilboa, where their chariots gave them a decisive advantage. In the early years of his reign he seems to have enjoyed success, however, ejecting the Philistines from the central mountain range and, temporarily at least, being sufficiently free from the Philistine threat to strike at other enemies across the Jordan and far to the south. When he died there seems to have been no move to dispense with a king, so in spite of his ultimate failure, he seems to have achieved the acceptance of the monarchy by his people and thus paved the way for his successors.

(2) The Hebrew name by which Paul was known before his conversion. He may have taken the Roman form of his name to signify that he was "a new man in Christ", or possibly in order to identify himself with the Gentiles.

Scapegoat. A goat on which the sins of all the people were symbolically laid before driving it out into the wilderness. This happened annually on the Day of Atonement (Lev 16:20–22).

Scribes. The scribes were the professional interpreters of the law from the exile onwards. Many of them were also Pharisees, and the two are often linked in the New Testament.

Scripture. The term can be applied to any body of writings, but in the New Testament (where it is sometimes used in the plural) it invariably refers to the Old Testament. The use of the term by Christians to signify the Bible as a whole naturally came later.

Scrolls, Dead Sea. A collection of about 500 documents, the first of them discovered in 1947, from caves near the Dead Sea. Written between 170 B.C. and A.D. 70, some of them relate to the life of the ascetic community to which they belonged and others are parts of the Old Testament. Surprisingly the most ancient manuscripts of the Old Testament previously known were mediaeval, yet the differences in the text are mostly insignificant.

Sennacherib. The king of Assyria who invaded Judah in 701 B.C., destroyed 46 of its fortified cities and shut up Hezekiah "like a bird in a cage" (to use the words of his own inscription). He did not take Jerusalem, but it is not clear whether this was because of a disaster in the Assyrian camp or because Hezekiah accepted his punitive terms of surrender.

Septuagint. The Greek translation of the Old Testament, so called because of a tradition that it was made by 72 scribes. The latin septuaginta actually means 70, and hence the use of LXX as an abbreviation.

Shadrach. One of three young men, who according to the book of Daniel, survived being thrown into a blazing furnace for refusing to worship a gold statue set up by King Nebuchadnezzar (Dan 3:1–27).

Shallum. King of Israel (745 B.C.). He came to the throne by assassinating his predecessor and died in the same manner a month later.

Shaphan. The high official of King Josiah who took the Book of the Covenant from the temple and read it to him (2 Kgs 22:3–10). His family later protected Jeremiah, particularly during Jehoiakim's reign.

Sheba, Queen of. Sheba, in the Arabian peninsula, was a trading nation. The visit of the Queen of Sheba to Solomon (1 Kgs 10:1–10, 13) was probably what would now be called a trade mission, with Solomon offering copper in exchange for spices.

Shechem. A town with ancient religious connections, since Jacob is said to have built an altar there (Gen 33:18–20). Centrally situated on the borders of Ephraim and Manasseh, it became the first capital of the northern kingdom.

Shiloh. A town where the tabernacle was taken after the occupation of Canaan and which became the site for a permanent temple, the central sanctuary for the confederation of Israelite tribes before the monarchy (1 Sam 1:3). Jeremiah refers to the destruction of this temple, most probably by the Philistines (Jer 7:12).

Sidon. Next to Tyre, the most important city of Phoenicia and a good port. Jesus passed through its territory on at least one occasion (Mk 7:31).

Silas. Sent with Paul and Barnabas to present the findings of the Council of Jerusalem to the church at Antioch, he subsequently became Paul's companion on the second missionary journey (Acts 16:22–41). Probably to be identified with the Silvanus mentioned in some of Paul's letters.

Siloam. The name of a pool within the city walls of Jerusalem, fed from a spring outside by a tunnel some 620 m long. The tunnel was cut by Hezekiah (2 Chr 32:30) and can still be seen today.

Simeon. (1) The second son of Jacob and Leah.
(2) The tribe of Simeon which originally possessed territory south of Judah but was then absorbed into its neighbour.

Simon. (1) see Peter.
(2) **Simon the Zealot**, one of the twelve disciples, whose name suggests that he started at

least with very different political ideals from Jesus (Mk 3:18).

(3) **Simon the Pharisee.** The man with whom Jesus was eating when a sinful woman anointed him (Lk 7:36–47).

(4) **Simon of Cyrene.** The man who was compelled to carry Jesus' cross (Mk 15:21).

(5) **Simon Magus.** A miracle-worker in Samaria who, when he saw the effects of the Holy Spirit on a group of converts Peter and John had laid hands on, tried to buy this power from them (Acts 8:9–24).

Sinai. The peninsula between the Gulf of Suez and the Gulf of Aqaba which was the first objective on the exodus from Egypt. Mount Sinai (also called Horeb) has not been identified with certainty. If the giving of the law was accompanied by volcanic activity, as certain elements of the account suggest, a site on the eastern side of the Gulf of Aqaba (and therefore not on the Sinai peninsula at all) would be preferable on geological grounds.

Smyrna. An important city on the Aegean coastline of Asia Minor. The book of Revelation (Rev 2:8–11) refers sympathetically to the church there and its steadfastness under persecution, but we know little else about it.

Sodom. A city of evil reputation, probably to be located in an area now covered by the southern part of the Dead Sea. The city was destroyed by burning sulphur (presumably a volcanic disturbance) according to Genesis 19:24–25.

Solomon. King of Israel (*c.* 960–922 B.C.). Solomon is traditionally regarded as a wise king, yet by the end of his reign his subjects were seething with discontent, and it would have taken a man of exceptional ability to win back their loyalty. Rehoboam, his son, was not such a man, and so the great empire of Solomon was reduced almost overnight to two insignificant states. For this Solomon must take much of the blame. His reputation for wisdom is not without foundation, however. Inheriting a large and relatively peaceful empire from his father, David, he was never in serious danger from enemies, though he strengthened his defences and added chariots to his army just in case. He was thus able to concentrate on economic policy and proved a genius at exploiting his position across a number of major trade routes as well as developing the copper mines south of the Dead Sea. The wealth generated by this economic development went into building his own palace and its ancillary buildings and the first temple. He allowed himself to get carried away by the splendour of his own designs, however, and got into such debts that not even heavy taxation could pay them and he had to give away territory to his neighbour Hiram, king of Tyre, in payment for the supply of cedar wood (1 Kgs 9:10–11). These measures, together with the system of forced labour introduced to man the copper mines and the building projects, were exceedingly unpopular. So was his marriage to foreign wives (often in pursuance of trade agreements) and his tolerance of their pagan religions. Less obviously the reign of Solomon saw the beginnings of an insidious trend towards the concentration of power in the hands of a small number of people, which led ultimately to the kind of social injustice so fiercely condemned by the prophets. That Solomon was clever is beyond dispute; whether he was wise may be debated.

Sosthenes. The leader of the synagogue at Corinth who was beaten by the Jews (Acts 18:17). The reason for this is not stated. Possibly he had shown sympathy towards Christianity, since a Sosthenes is associated with Paul in the writing of 1 Corinthians (1 Cor 1:1).

Stephen. Appointed originally as one of the seven administrators of the charitable work of the Jerusalem church (Acts 6:1–6), Stephen soon showed himself a powerful advocate of the Christian faith. He was brought before the Jewish Council on charges of denigrating the temple and denying the necessity for the law of Moses, and was illegally executed by stoning, the traditional Jewish method (Acts 6:8–60).

Stoics. Members of a Greek school of philosophers who believed in the suppression of the emotions so as to remain unaffected by life's adversities. Paul debated with the Stoics in Athens (Acts 17:18).

Stoning. The method of execution among the Jews, and the prescribed penalty for 18 crimes. The accusers were required to throw the first stone (Deu 17:5–7, *see* John 8:7 for Jesus' reaction to this rule).

Sychar. According to John 4:5–6 the site of Jacob's well. Usually identified with Shechem.

Synagogue. The development of synagogue worship was a response to three things: the law forbidding sacrifice except in the Jerusalem temple, the destruction of the temple in 586 B.C. and the dispersion of the Jews. As a result, the offering of sacrifice could no longer be a regular way of worship and a non-sacrificial form of worship had to be developed. This was based on the reading and exposition of the Law, interspersed with psalms and prayers, and it set the pattern for later Christian worship.

Syrians. Also known as Aramaeans, these people were Israel's immediate north-eastern neighbours. At one time forming several small kingdoms, they gradually coalesced into a single state which was frequently at war with Israel. Syria became a province of Assyria following the destruction of Damascus, the capital, in 732 B.C.

T

Tabernacle. The name given to the "tent of meeting", the place where Moses met with God and which represented God's presence among his people. An elaborate structure, it was in effect a travelling temple.

Tabernacles, Feast of. Known also as the Feast of Booths, the festival was both a celebration of the grape harvest and a recollection of the wilderness wanderings, symbolised by people living in temporary shelters (booths) throughout the week.

Tarsus. A city in Asia Minor which was the home of Paul. It had a large Jewish population, but was also noted for its Greek philosophers, and it was this dual background that equipped Paul especially to be a missionary to the Gentiles.

Temple. There were three successive temples in Jerusalem. Solomon's temple, the first, was destroyed by the Babylonians in 586 B.C. After the exile a second temple was built, but due to the circumstances of the time this seems to have been a relatively poor affair. Then in 19 B.C. Herod the Great began work on the third temple, a large and imposing structure in every way. Though substantially complete by Jesus' time the finishing touches were not added until about A.D. 60. Ten years later it was destroyed by the Romans.

Ten Commandments, *see* **Commandments.**

Tertullus. A Roman or Romano-Jewish lawyer whom the Jewish Council employed to present the case against Paul before Felix (Acts 24:1–9).

Tetrarch. Both Herod Antipas and Philip were known as tetrarchs because they each received roughly a quarter of Herod the Great's kingdom (the other half going to Archelaus).

Thaddeus. One of the twelve disciples (Mk 3:18), known in Luke as Judas, son of James (Lk 6:16).

Thessalonians, Letters to the. The two letters of Paul to the Thessalonians are the earliest writings in the New Testament unless, as some scholars think, Galatians came earlier. They were written from Corinth, within a short time of each other, about A.D. 52. Amongst other things they show that the church at that time still expected the second coming of Christ in a literal form quite shortly, and that this expectation had led to undesirable behaviour such as refusal to work any more. Although Paul's correspondence with the Corinthians two to three years later shows that he still thought in terms of a second coming then, it is not a theme which occurs in his later letters.

Thessalonica. The capital of Macedonia in northern Greece, the city was visited by Paul during his second missionary journey (Acts 17:1–9) and presumably on the short tour he made of the Greek churches following his ministry in Ephesus (Acts 20:1–6).

Thomas. One of the twelve disciples well characterised in John's gospel, where he appears as loyal but slow to learn. His confession of Jesus as "My Lord and my God" after the resurrection identifies Jesus with God more clearly than any other statement in the gospels, however (Jn 20:28).

Tiglath-pileser III. King of Assyria (745–727 B.C.). It was Tiglath-pileser who established the Assyrian dominance of Palestine which was to last well over a century. It was to him that Ahaz of Judah appealed for help against Israel and Syria, both of which were invaded and devastated.

Timothy. Born of a Jewish mother and Greek father, Timothy was a native of Lystra. When Paul revisited the city at the start of his second missionary journey he asked Timothy to join him. From this time onwards he was constantly with Paul or working elsewhere under Paul's oversight, and only three of the letters ascribed to Paul do not mention him.

Timothy, Letters to. There are difficulties in ascribing to Paul the two letters to Timothy. The style is not quite like Paul's, and the more formal organisation of the church suggests a later period. The most probable view is that they do contain fragments of personal notes written by Paul to Timothy, but that these have been used by a later author as the basis for general advice to church leaders. Similar considerations apply to the letter to Titus, which is often linked with the two letters to Timothy under the title of the Pastoral Letters.

Titus. A companion and co-worker of Paul, he seems to have been particularly involved in Paul's correspondence with Corinth, carrying his letters and acting as his representative (2 Cor 7:7, 8:16–17).

Titus, Letter to, see Timothy, Letters to.

Tongues, Speaking with. An outpouring of incomprehensible sounds which often accompanied a state of religious excitement in New Testament times, and still occurs in some churches today. The implication that the disciples actually spoke in foreign languages on the day of Pentecost is probably intended as a way of symbolising the universal relevance of the gospel. Paul warned against giving undue emphasis to this gift of the Spirit (1 Cor 14).

Tribes of Israel. Traditionally descended from the twelve sons of Jacob, the number remained twelve in spite of some changes. The descendants of Joseph in fact formed two tribes, named after his sons Ephraim and Manasseh, whereas Simeon fairly quickly became absorbed into Judah.

Tyre. The principal city of Phoenicia, and the centre of a city-state. The kings of Tyre were often on good terms with the kings of Israel, and the two nations traded to their mutual advantage (1 Kgs 5:1–11).

U

Unclean Foods. By long established tradition the Jews did not eat (and still do not eat) certain foods which were ritually unclean. This, and the fact that every meal was seen as a family religious occasion, meant that Jews rarely sat down at table with Gentiles. When Jewish and Gentile Christians began to associate with one another this was one of the difficulties they had to face (Rom 14:14–15).

Unleavened Bread, see Passover.

Ur. The home town of Abraham, sited in the southern part of the fertile flood-plain of the Tigris–Euphrates river system.

Urim and Thummim. Two objects used by a priest to determine God's will. It is not known how they were used, but the technique was probably to ask specific questions, to which the objects, on being thrown like dice, would then give a "yes" or "no" answer (1 Sam 14:41).

Uzziah. King of Judah (783–742 B.C.). Long-lived, capable and with the welfare of his people at heart, Uzziah was one of the better kings of Judah. He repaired and strengthened the defences of Jerusalem, re-equipped his army (with slings for hurling stones among other things), attacked the Philistine cities and recaptured from the Edomites the important port of Elath on the Gulf of Aqaba (2 Chr 26:1–15). Towards the end of his reign he was stricken by a skin disease and his public duties were taken over by his son Jotham.

W

Weeks, Feast of. Also known as Pentecost, the feast came at the end of the wheat harvest and later was associated with the giving of the Law on Sinai. It was during this feast that the apostles received the gift of the Holy Spirit (Acts 2:1–4).

Wisdom Literature. A name applied to books such as Proverbs, Job and Ecclesiastes which discuss philosophical issues or offer practical advice for living. There is a parallel literature from other middle-eastern civilisations, but the Hebrew literature is unique in its emphasis on the knowledge of God (and not merely academic knowledge but the knowing that comes from a relationship) as the basis of all wisdom.

Y

Yahweh. The proper name of the God of Israel was written as YHWH, there being no vowels in Hebrew. How it would have been pronounced (in fact it was considered too sacred ever to be spoken aloud) is a matter of speculation, but modern opinion favours Yahweh. Jehovah is an earlier and now outmoded attempt to render the same name.

Z

Zacchaeus. A tax collector of Jericho who became a follower of Jesus and generously compensated all those he had previously cheated (Lk 19:1–10).

Zadok. He appears to have been High Priest jointly with Abiathar during David's reign, but when Abiathar was banished by Solomon for supporting Adonijah in the struggle for succession, Zadok became the sole High Priest.

Zebulum. (1) The tenth son of Jacob, his sixth by Leah.
(2) The tribe of Zebulum which occupied a fairly small area of northern Israel surrounded by Manasseh, Issachar, Naphtali and Asher.

Zechariah. (1) King of Israel (746–745 B.C.). The son of Jeroboam II, he was assassinated by Shallum.
(2) A prophet who wrote chapters 1–8 of the book of Zechariah about 520 B.C. His prophecies look forward to the restoration of the temple and the new age about to dawn. Chapters 9–14 are from a later date.
(3) The father of John the Baptist.

Zedekiah. King of Judah (597–586 B.C.). The uncle of his predecessor Jehoiachin, he was placed on the throne by the Babylonians when Jehoiachin surrendered to them in 597 B.C. and was deported. In 589 B.C. Zedekiah himself rebelled and so precipitated the final crisis in the history of Judah. After Jerusalem fell in 586 B.C. he fled, but was captured, and after watching all his sons killed he was blinded and taken in chains to Babylon.

Zephaniah. A contemporary of Jeremiah, Zephaniah threatened a day of judgement against his people, primarily because of their unfaithfulness in worshipping other gods, but also he looked forward to repentance and restoration.

Zimri. King of Israel (876 B.C.). After assassinating his predecessor Elah, Zimri ruled for only seven days before committing suicide in order to avoid being murdered by Omri.

Zion. Originally just the name of one of the hills on which Jerusalem is built, it came to be a symbolic term indicating the dwelling-place of God and associated with the belief that he would always protect Jerusalem.

Zophar. The third of Job's "friends" (Job 11).

THE CLASSICAL WORLD

This new section in *Pears* provides a concise introduction to the world of ancient Greece and Rome. It introduces the reader to the history of an epic age which still exercises great fascination on the world. Readers may wish to refer to Section A for a chronology of events, Section B for prominent figures in the ancient world and Section I for the enduring mythology of classical Greece and Rome. A Special Topic in this edition provides an introduction to the civilisation of Ancient Egypt

THE CLASSICAL WORLD

A

Academy An open-air gymnasium in Athens containing the shrine of the local hero Academus, hence the name. Plato (**B48**) founded here his philosophical school, which was in a sense the world's first university. Philosophy, and particularly mathematics, were of fundamental importance to its studies. Plato taught at the school until his death in 347 B.C. It survived 900 years, until the Christian emperor Justinian suppressed all pagan philosophical schools in A.D. 529.

Achaeans Name given by the poet Homer to the Greek forces at Troy. These early Greek-speakers were probably among those sea-borne migrant raiders known to the ancient Egyptians and Hittites as "The Sea Peoples".

Achaean League A federation of 12 Greek city states of Achaea which first existed in the 4th century B.C., it was refounded in 281 B.C. by Aratus of Sicyon to defend the cities particularly against Sparta. It was frequently under Macedonian suzerainty, but effectively postponed for a century the eventual loss of Greek independence to Rome. The League had a federal constitution which allowed each city self-government but which provided for a common foreign policy and army.

Acropolis In general terms, a high citadel found in all Greek cities. Being the most easily defended area it was usually the oldest part of the town and it was here the patron gods of the city were believed to dwell and accordingly here their shrines and temples were built. The best known acropolis is that at Athens which was first inhabited around 2000 B.C. Its most famous structure on the acropolis is the Parthenon (*q.v.*), a temple to Athene built by Pericles between 447 and 432 B.C. and containing the famous statue of the goddess by Phidias, one of the Seven Wonders of the World.

Acta The public rulings of Roman magistrates, made within the competence of their own jurisdiction and with favourable auspices.

Aediles Roman municipal officials. Originally they were wardens of the temple of Ceres, Liber and Libera (gods of grain and wine) who held summary jurisdiction over trading disputes among the small community inhabiting the Aventine hill. In 367 B.C. two plebeian aediles (the equivalent of mayors) were given control of municipal affairs, control of the food supply and the police, and the provision of public games. The patricians formed a magistracy of curule aediles to supplement plebeian control of such affairs and in 366 B.C. the plebeian aediles were admitted to the new magistracy; henceforth the aediles were selected in alternate years from each order.

Aeolians Those Greeks settled on the north-west coast of Asia Minor and the islands of Tenedos and Lesbos. They originated from Boeotia and Thessaly in Greece and were forced to migrate *c* 1000 B.C. by the Dorian invasions.

Aerarii A class of Roman citizens not possessing full civil rights (*see* Citizenship) who were subject to a poll tax imposed by the censors and who could not hold office nor serve in the army. Full citizens might be reduced to this status by the censors for criminal convictions or for engaging in particular professions, *e.g.* acting, which were regarded as dishonourable.

Aerarium The Roman state treasury situated in the temple of Saturn. In the imperial period it was effectively superceded by the emperor's own treasury, the *fiscus*.

Aesymnetes In Greece, a governor possessing supreme power for a limited period. The aim of the institution was to suppress or otherwise end internal factional strife within Greek city states.

Aetolian League A confederacy of Greek states founded in late 4th century B.C. by Aetolia, which came to comprise most of northern Greece, Elis and parts of Arcadia. Its territory and influence continued to expand and its collaboration with

Rome helped her to defeat Macedonia in 197 B.C., but it quickly came under Roman suzerainty thereafter.

Agentes in Rebus Members of the imperial inspectorate instituted by the later Roman emperors to check abuses in provincial government.

Ager Publicus The land acquired by Rome during her conquest of Italy. Upon defeat of an enemy, she usually confiscated a third of that state's land which was used for founding colonies, distributed in allotments to individual Roman citizens, "loaned" back to the natives, or sold.

Agger The embankment around a Roman military camp, with a ditch on the outside.

Agora An open place and the centre of public affairs and commerce in the Greek *polis*. The *agora* itself was a sacred area usually containing the tombs of the city's founders and heroes and the temples of its patron deities; ritual worship and civic festivals would take place here. Political assemblies and tribunals were also held in the *agora*, around which the official buildings were situated.

Alae A Roman military term originally denoting those troops who were posted on the wings in battle. Under the Republic they were *socii* and invariably cavalry; during the imperial period Roman cavalry units were all termed *alae* and were auxiliary troops under the command of a *praefectus*.

Alimenta A system of public allowances for poor children in the Roman empire, by which state or municipal officials distributed the interest earned on investments in land. Originally the investments were granted by private benefactors to particular cities; later they were made by the emperors themselves. The writer Pliny suggests the aim was to raise the birthrate and hence (ultimately) recruitment to the army.

Amicitia The relationship of friendship between Rome and another state. It was not a formal treaty, but did imply diplomatic recognition. In the East particularly many individual rulers became "client kings" of the Roman people and later of the emperors.

Amphictyonies Associations of Greek states united partly by their proximity but more importantly by joint participation in religious worship and celebration of festivals. The foremost was that of the oracle at Delphi. Each member state had an equal vote in the administration of an amphictyony.

Amphitheatres Elliptically shaped buildings designed originally to house chariot races, gladiatorial contests, wild beast hunts and the like. They were pre-dated by the circus which remained the predominant home of the chariot race. Although regarded as a characteristic of Roman architecture, they were of Campanian origin. The largest was the Colosseum at Rome.

Annona In its most widely used sense, the term for the government controlled grain supply to Rome. Following a dramatic fall in Italian wheat production at the end of the Republic it became necessary to levy wheat as a tax on the provinces in order to feed the urban population. The largest supply came from Egypt. Augustus raised the number of recipients to 200,000; about one-fifth of Rome's population.

Antonines A dynasty of Roman emperors, whose name is derived from Antoninus Pius. Usually judged to have been sound administrators and just rulers, they were not blood-relations but adoptive sons of their predecessors. The dynasty consisted of Nerva (A.D. 96–98), Trajan (98–117), Hadrian (117–138), Antoninus (138–161), Marcus Aurelius (161–180) and Commodus (180–192). *See also* Section B for individual emperors.

Aqueducts The Greek technique for conducting water was to construct subterranean or ground-level channels designed to make maximum use of natural gradients. The Romans improved upon this by utilising concrete and vaulting to build superstructures capable of reducing the length of the water course and thereby keeping the water under pressure. Appius Claudius was responsible for building Rome's first aqueduct when he was censor in 312 B.C. Outside Rome aqueducts followed urbanisation on the Roman pattern; surviving examples include that at Segovia in Spain.

Aquila The "eagle" of each Roman legion and an object of special veneration, consisting of a pole surmounted by a silver (later gold) eagle which symbolised the *imperium* of Jupiter. It was carried by a veteran known as the *aquilifer* and stored in a special shrine when in camp. Its loss was traditionally cause for the disbandment of the legion. *See also* **Signa.**

Arches A characteristic feature of Roman architecture in which the one stone lintel gave way to semi-circular free stones, bricks or cement. Arches were used to support amphitheatres and aqueducts. The triumphal arch was exclusively Roman and was originally a sacred gate situated on a boundary crossing. Rome's principal arches were those of Constantine, Titus and Septimius Severus.

Archon A Greek term meaning "one who commands". It denoted the head state of a confederacy and also, in some cities, the supreme magistrate. In Athens the archons were magistrates who first appeared in the 9th century B.C. when a powerful aristocracy chose two officials to govern in conjunction with the king. The latter retained his important religious duties of consulting the gods and making sacrifices while one archon, the *polemarchos,* commanded the army and the other administered the state. Later the king came to be known as the *archon basileus* (literally King-Archon) and was subject to the same rules as his colleagues. By 686 B.C. the archonship was open to all nobles and renewed annually. As the economy developed and the lower classes faced slavery and famine in the mid 7th century B.C., the number of archons was increased to nine to meet the demands of government. On retiring the archons automatically became members of the council of the Areopagus. The office was now open only to the richest class, the *pentakosiomedimnoi,* and Solon (**B56**) left its character unchanged. Cleisthenes (**B15**) added a tenth archon in order that their number might correspond to his ten tribes; membership was extended to the second class, the *hippeis* (knights), and from 457 B.C. to nearly all citizens. However, the archonship had declined in importance from the early 5th century B.C. and government was effectively now in the hands of the *strategoi.* The word itself gives us monarchy (sole rule), oligarchy (rule of the few), and anarchy (no rulers).

Areopagus A rocky hill facing the Athenian acropolis, the site of the council of elders of the Athenian state. It originated during the Athenian monarchy, although it also had legendary forebears; the goddess Athene had established a court of the Areopagus to try Orestes for his mother's murder. The council survived the kings and came to include ex-archons; its powers were vague but far reaching, covering both domestic and foreign policy. Aristotle described it as the guardian of laws. Its sovereignty was left intact by Solon but under Cleisthenes its powers were reduced and transferred to new democratic bodies; however it remained a court and, as it could punish illegalities by state officials, it had a power of veto. However the democratic reformers Pericles and Ephialtes stripped it of this right, leaving it simply as a criminal court; by the 4th century B.C. the tribunal of the *Heliaea* had come to hold the most important trials and the Areopagus was left with jurisdiction over only arson, poisoning, premeditated murder and occasionally impiety.

Aries The Roman battering ram; a tree trunk tipped with a heavy iron ram's head and suspended by ropes from a mobile wooden framework with a protective roof. It was used to destroy city gates and walls during sieges.

Athens The leading Greek city state of the 5th century B.C. and the home of classical Greek democracy. At the dawn of Greek history the independent tribal communities of Ionian Attica were united in a monarchical state (named after her patron goddess Athene) in a process of centralisation known as synoecism. During the 7th century the monarchy was supplanted by a hereditary nobility, the *Eupatridai,* who alone had political rights. The bulk of the population

was gradually reduced to a state of serfdom and the political crisis this engendered induced the *Eupatridai* to appoint the noble Solon (**B56**) to revise the Athenian constitution in 594 B.C. Solon abolished serfdom and divided the people into three census classes (*pentakosiomedimnoi, hippeis* and *thetes*) with varying civic rights; but these reforms did not prevent a period of tyranny in the 6th century, and in 509 Cleisthenes (**B15**) took power to issue a new constitution that was to become the basis for the classical Athenian democracy. The 5th century was the height of Athens' power, based upon her maritime empire and commercial strength. Allied with Sparta she led the resistance to the Persian attempt to conquer Greece (480–479 B.C.) and thereafter turned the allied Ionian states of the Aegean into her own empire, a process arrested only by the disastrous Peloponnesian War against Sparta. Nonetheless this period of imperial expansion was also the zenith of political democracy at home, which was sealed by the judicial reforms of Pericles (**B47**); moreover, Athens was at this period the leading cultural centre of Greece, the home of Socrates (**B56**). Following her defeat by Sparta, Athens lost her hegemony but in the 4th century, encouraged by the orator Demosthenes, she nonetheless led the resistance of the Greek states to Philip of Macedon until Greek independence was extinguished in 336 B.C.

Atrium The central room in a Roman house (*see* **Domus**).

Auctoritas A Roman concept denoting the charismatic authority of a public figure or official which indicated he had the approval of the gods in his actions. It was an authority which those guiding Rome's affairs had to possess, as opposed to *potestas* (the legal authority conferred by the holding of a particular office) or *imperium* (the authority, frequently military, which was granted directly by the gods themselves). Hence the *auctoritas* of the Senate during the Republic confirmed the merits of any policy or measure it proposed.

Augur An "interpreter" of the will of the gods. The Romans believed that the gods issued warnings, or expressed approval, to man through natural signs and thus that their will could be gleaned by observations of natural phenomena. A *collegium* of ultimately 15 augurs existed; from 104 B.C. they were selected by co-option and from the time of Augustus were nominated by the emperor. As interpreters of divine will the augurs had great influence on when assemblies should meet, the validity of decisions, *etc.* Under the Empire the emperor himself was head of the *collegium.*

Auspices Signs sent by the gods to show their wishes and opinions on decisions and forthcoming enterprises. All Roman magistrates could take the auspices in relation to actions falling within their own sphere of duties (*e.g.* holding assemblies), but usually asked the assistance of augurs.

Auxilia Forces of non-Italian mercenaries fighting with the Roman army as auxiliary troops. They originated in the late Republic when the Roman deficiency in cavalry and light infantry made necessary recruitment outside Italy of specialist units. Their numbers grew rapidly in the Civil Wars of the late Republic. Gradually during the Empire the distinction between *auxilia* and the regular legions disappeared; auxiliary troops retiring after 25 years' service received Roman citizenship. Specialist *auxilia,* fighting under the overall command of a Roman *praefectus,* included Cretan archers, Balearic slingers, and Gallic cavalry.

B

Bacchae Female followers of the cult of Bacchus or Dionysus, the god of wine. Their male counterparts were the Bacchi. Worship of the god was characterised by wine-induced frenzies of a mystic nature (Bacchanalia). The cult originated in Thrace, spread to Greece in the 8th century B.C. and was introduced to Italy at the beginning of the 2nd. The practices of worship were so extreme (human sacrifice was rumoured) that the Senate forbade membership of Dionysiac associations on pain of death. Also known as *Bacchantes*, *Maenads* and *Thyiads*.

Ballista A Roman war engine, a form of large catapult throwing heavy weights.

Barbari The term applied by the Greeks to non-Greek speakers to signify their—to the Greeks—unintelligible babble. Often mistranslated as barbarians.

Barcids The family who led the Carthaginian forces in the Punic Wars against Rome. Hamilcar Barca conducted operations in Sicily (247 B.C.) in the First Punic War and led the peace negotiations with Rome. He died in 229 B.C., but his sons Hannibal (**B29**) and Hasdrubal succeeded him as Carthaginian generals in the Second Punic War.

Boeotian League The first significant movement towards federalism among the Greeks, the League was established in central Greece in the 6th century B.C. under the direction of the city-state of Thebes. It was both a military and religious unity with its own coinage and amphictyony. The League, of oligarchic states, was an ally of Sparta during the Peloponnesian War but later opposed Spartan hegemony after the fall of Athens. Thebes later rose to become the dominant state in Greece in the mid-4th century B.C.

Boule The council of elders which met to discuss affairs of state with early Greek kings. At Athens it came to be called the Council of the Areopagus to distinguish it from other councils. Under Solon (**B56**) a second *Boule* of 400 members was established to prepare business for the assembly or *Ecclesia*. Under Cleisthenes (**B15**) membership was increased to 500 and, under the overall control of the *Ecclesia*, this central council was the chief organ of state. Public finances, the construction of public works and the conduct of war were in its hands and it prepared every bill sent to the *Ecclesia* to become law.

C

Caelian One of the hills of Rome spanning an area from the plateau of the Esquiline to the Colosseum.

Caldarium *See* **Thermae**.

Campus Martius A marshy alluvial plain in a bend of the Tiber, situated north of the Capitol in Rome. It was outside the *pomerium*. From antiquity it was used for the taking of exercise, military gatherings (hence the name, the 'Field of Mars'), triumphs and census operations.

Capite Censi The lowest and poorest class of Roman citizen whose personal identity was the sole entry on the census records, as they possessed no property.

Capitol The most sacred of Rome's hills. It had two summits, the *Arx* or Citadel to the north and the Capitolium itself to the south. The temple of Jupiter was situated here. The name was also applied in other Roman cities to any group of buildings having the same characteristics as the Capitol in Rome.

Cataphracts Heavily mailed cavalrymen of the Parthian armies. The Romans gained first hand knowledge of their value when the expedition of Crassus into Parthia was destroyed in 53 B.C. By the 3rd century A.D. the Romans had adopted heavily mailed lancers of the Persian type into their own forces.

Censors The Roman magistrates who performed the census. Two were elected every five years (although custom ordained they resign after 18 months). Besides taking the census of persons and property, they drew up the lists of senators and equites. They possessed considerable moral jurisdiction and could brand with infamy anyone they wished on account of his private conduct.

Census Introduced by the sixth Roman king Servius Tullius (578–534 B.C.), it was originally a system of rating citizens according to their registered property. Every five years the citizens were assembled by the censors on the Campus Martius, counted and classified by age, means, and moral worth. They were drawn up by *centuriae* in military formation and the census was the basis of military organisation. Under the Empire the system was extended to the provinces

for fiscal purposes, but no longer had any bearing on military recruitment.

Centuriae Centuries, a classification originally introduced to Rome by the king Servius Tullius. By the 4th century B.C. the system had acquired a definite shape by which the citizenry was divided into five classes, and each (except the poorest class who were exempt from military service) was subdivided into varying numbers of *centuriae*, which theoretically consisted of 100 men. The division was also adopted for the purposes of the ballot. The *centuriae* were based on the census and survived to the end of the Republic. *See also* **Legion**.

Centurion A Roman military officer, originally in charge of a maniple consisting of 100 men. In the 4th century B.C. the maniple became two *centuriae*, each commanded by a centurion. He was of officer status and usually a veteran; exceptionally he might be elected by the legionaries themselves. *See also* **Primus Pilus**.

Choregoi Athenian citizens designated by the archons to pay for the training of lyric or dramatic choruses out of their own pockets. They thus subsidized state religious and dramatic festivals.

Circus A huge elliptical arena, particularly elongated. The circus was used mainly for chariot races whereas the amphitheatre which it predated was generally associated with gladiatorial contests. The best known was the Circus Maximus, the largest in Rome, which after Caesar's restorations could accommodate 50,000 spectators and 250,000 after Trajan's. The track was also used for triumphs.

Citizenship, Roman A highly prized possession giving the right to a variety of privileges, citizenship could be acquired by birth or in the case of slaves by emancipation. Full rights included the right to vote (*ius suffragii*); the right to hold a magistracy (*ius honorarium*); the right to serve in the army (*ius militae*); the right to contract a legal union (*ius conubii*); and the right to buy, own or sell property (*ius commercii*). All Italians were given citizenship after the Social War of the late Republic; it was later extended to individual provinces and in A.D. 212 to the whole Empire by emperor Caracalla.

Cleruchy An Athenian colony in which the settlers maintained their Athenian citizenship together with its rights and duties. Such emigration was led and directed by a chosen chief and the cleruchies were usually established in strategically important positions or in the territory of lukewarm allies. Cleisthenes started the system which spread widely in the 5th century B.C. making Athens highly unpopular among other states.

Clientela The Roman practice whereby men of no means attached themselves to a patron, usually the patrician head of a great family, receiving help and protection in return for the performance of clearly defined duties.

Cloaca Maxima Rome's largest sewer, a covered drain which crossed the Forum and opened via an arch into the Tiber. It was extensively restored in imperial times.

Cohort A Roman military unit introduced by the military reforms of Marius in the 2nd century B.C. It was brought in for tactical purposes, replacing the three lines of *hastati*, *principles* and *triarii* (*see* **Legion**) and consisting of six centuries. There were ten cohorts of nominally 600 men each to a legion. The commander of the cohort was the *tribunus cohortis*.

Collegium In the Roman world a legally-recognised association, *e.g.* of priests of the same cult or of magistrates of equal rank; or a private society of co-operating individuals, such as poets.

Colosseum The Flavian amphitheatre in Rome built by the emperor Vespasian but inaugurated in A.D. 80 during the reign of his son Titus. Elliptical in shape, the arena measured 80 metres by 54, with an outer wall 49 metres high and consisting of three storeys of open arches.

Column A characteristic Roman monument designed to commemorate triumphs. The first was the *Columna Maenia*, erected in 338 B.C. to celebrate Maenius' victory in the naval battle of Antium. Perhaps the most famous is the marble column of the emperor Trajan, build *c* A.D. 110 to celebrate his victory over the Dacians; the incidents of four campaigns are represented in a continuous spiral relief which shows 2500 figures.

Comitia A term applied to the various assemblies of the Roman people. The most ancient was the *Comitia Curiata*, established under the early kings (*see also* **Curiae**). After 509 B.C. the citizens assembled in the *Comitia Centuriata* and were grouped into classes according to wealth and property, each class being subdivided into *centuriae*. Under the Republic this assembly elected higher magistrates and voted on certain important laws. The *Comitia Tributa* appeared shortly afterwards based on the local tribes established by king Servius Tullius and developed from the *Concilium Plebis*; in 366 B.C. it was entrusted with the election of quaestors and aediles. Eventually the *Concilium Plebis* and *Comitia Tributa* became, with the Senate, the leading assemblies of the Republic.

Comitium The original meeting place of the *Comitia Curiata* and *Tributa* (*see* **Comitia**). It was an inaugurated *templum* of some 120 square metres to the north of the Forum (*q.v.*). Such a small area could only accommodate a fraction of Rome's population by the 2nd century B.C. so the assemblies were later moved to the Forum.

Concilium Plebis A plebeian assembly of Rome based on the four tribes of local character established by the early king Servius Tullius, to which a further 31 rural tribes were later added. It elected the plebeian tribunes. The *concilium* later became identified with the *Comitia Tributa* (*see* **Comitia**).

Concilium Principis Originally an advisory body established by the emperor Augustus. Under Claudius this "privy council" replaced the Senate as the court of trial for serious political crimes; and following the reigns of Hadrian (**B29**) and Commodus its political influence effectively supplanted that of the Senate. Under Hadrian the function of interpreting and revising Roman law devolved upon the *concilium*.

Consul, consulship The highest Roman magistracy established after 500 B.C. to replace the monarchy. There were two consuls with equal powers who together held supreme authority in the Republic. Originally called praetors ("headmen") their name was later changed to that of consul ("colleague"). The office was at first confined to the patrician class, but was extended to the plebeians after 367 B.C. Their tenure lasted one year and the consuls presided over the Senate and the *Comitia Centuriata* which originally elected them (although from the reign of the emperor Tiberius consuls were appointed by the Senate). Furthermore they had the right to introduce legislation. Following this year of office they became *consulares* (ex-consuls) and remained members of the Senate. The power of the office declined substantially upon the establishment of the Empire.

Curator A manager or guardian. In Roman private law it denoted a person holding a trusteeship, *e.g.* of a minor; in administrative law, someone given a special technical function beyond the usual sphere of a magistrate.

Curia The meeting place of the Roman Senate. Various buildings were used for the purpose from time to time and were thus given the name. The oldest was the *Curia Hostilia* in the Forum, attributed to the king Tullus Hostilius. It was replaced by the *Curia Julia* of Julius Caesar.

Curiae An administrative and political subdivision of the three early tribes of Rome. There were ten *curiae* to a tribe and the 30 *curiae* assembled together constituted the *Comitia Curiata* (*see also* **Comitia**), the assembly of the people called to ratify the laws and decisions of the kings.

Currency The Babylonians, Phoenicians and Egyptians had all used weighed silver and gold as a medium of exchange; but it was Lydia, in Asia Minor, which in the early 7th century B.C. first stamped coins whereby the state guaranteed weight and purity. Aegina and Euboea were the first Greek states to issue coinage and institute monetary systems, and eventually all Greek states developed mints. As gold was rare in Greece, coins were made of silver; the standard silver coin was the *stater*. Athens' currency, recognisable by the image of the owl of Athene which it carried, was used throughout her own empire. Rome's earliest currency was simple bronze bullion, *aes rude*. Stamped bronze (*aes signatum*) followed, each weight being one Roman pound in theory but less in practice. Rome did not

start minting its bronze coinage until *c.* 300 B.C. and her earliest silver coins appeared around 285 B.C. Silver coinage developed significantly in the 2nd century B.C. The most widely used coin was the silver *sestertius*, at one time worth 4·5 *asses* but in Caesar's day worth four; another silver coin, the *denarius*, was first minted in 269 B.C. and was initially worth 10 *asses* or 4 *sestertii*. The value of various coins fluctuated greatly throughout Rome's history: the authorities frequently devalued coins and in the early first century B.C. the Senate authorised an extensive debasement of silver and a reduction in the weight of copper coins. In 12 B.C. Augustus reserved to himself the right to mint gold and silver coins, leaving the Senate to issue the copper *asses* and brass *sestertii*. By the 4th century A.D. the monetary system had been brought near to collapse with "silver" coins becoming in fact copper pieces with a 4% wash of precious metal. Roman coins originally bore the images of gods, but later the heads of prominent magistrates and finally of the emperors became the usual designs.

Cursus Honorum The public career of a Roman statesman, the succession of magistracies which culminated in the consulship. It commenced with a decade of service in the army. This was followed by the various magistracies—quaestor, aedile, praetor and finally consul—two years having to elapse between the tenure of each office. The earliest age at which one could hold the consulship during the Republic was 41; under the Empire consuls might be elected or appointed from the age of 33.

D

Decemviri A Roman term applied to any extraordinary commission, *e.g.* that appointed in 451 B.C. which replaced the consuls and tribunes while it drew up the codification of Roman law known as the Twelve Tables.

Decimation The Roman military punishment for desertion or mutiny when whole units were involved. The guilty unit was assembled and the names of one in every ten men were drawn by lot. Those chosen were then executed.

Decuriones The members of the municipal council (*curia*) in the provincial cities of the Roman Empire. They would be ex-magistrates and were responsible for administering municipal affairs and, during the imperial period, for tax-collection. They were required to meet the expenses of many municipal functions themselves; in the 3rd century A.D. the office was made hereditary to prevent leading families avoiding this responsibility.

Delatores Informers who prosecuted in court and if successful, under Roman law, received a quarter of the possessions of the condemned. During the Empire it proved a very profitable profession.

Delian League A Greek confederation, headed by Athens and formed in 478-7 B.C. Its purpose was ostensibly to protect the Aegean cities which had been freed from Persian occupation after Xerxes (**B66**) failure to conquer Greece. The treasury of the League was kept on the island of Delos and its congresses met there. Athens eventually transformed the League into her own empire; in 454 B.C. the treasury was transferred to Athens. Only with her defeat in the Peloponnesian War did member states regain independence.

Demes The territorial and administrative divisions into which Athens and Attica were divided. They were introduced by Cleisthenes in the late 5th century B.C. as the basis of the Athenian state. At birth each Athenian was registered in the deme to which his father belonged and only thus did he obtain his civil rights. Each deme was a community with its patron deities, festivals, popular assemblies and mayor or *demarchos*.

Diadochi The "successors" of Alexander the Great, his generals who carved up his empire between themselves upon his death and sought to establish ruling dynasties in various parts of it. Three permanent kingdoms emerged: that of Antipater and his heirs in the Macedonian Empire, that of the Ptolemies in Egypt, and that of Seleucus and his successors in Syria and Mesopotamia.

Dictator An exceptional Roman magistrate, chosen by the Senate in times of national crisis. The office, the only one not held in a colleagueship, lasted six months. It seems to have been a vestige of primitive kingship and the dictator was not answerable to the veto of the tribunes nor had to take account of the right of appeal. The dictator chose a subordinate officer, the *magister equitum* or master of the horse. The last true dictator under the Republican constitution was Q. Fabius Maximus Cunctator who, unusually, was elected to the post during the 2nd Punic War. By the time Caesar (**B12**) had himself appointed dictator in 49 B.C. the office had lost its constitutional basis and become a legal nicety to disguise his tyranny.

Dioceses The administrative areas into which the Roman Empire was divided under the Tetrarchy (*q.v.*). The old provinces were broken up and 12 dioceses superimposed upon them according to racial or historical unities, *e.g.* the diocese of Spain. Italy was divided into two, centred on Milan in the north and Rome in the south.

Dokimasia The examination of their good citizenship and piety which Athenian magistrates, already chosen by ballot or lot, had to undergo before assuming office.

Domus A Roman house. Originally a rural dwelling adapted to urban needs, it consisted of a central living room with a kitchen garden at the back and an enclosed yard (later the *atrium*) at the front. The classical urban *domus* consisted of the *atrium*, a room open to the sky with a central sunken tank to collect rainwater (*impluvium*) and which housed the shrine to the gods of the house and hearth, the *Penates* and *Lares*. It was approached from the street along a narrow corridor, rooms to either side of which were frequently occupied as shops (*tabernae*) opening onto the street. Behind the atrium was the *tablinum*, originally the master's bedroom and later his study. On either side of the *tablinum* were the *alae*, two wings each consisting of a large room as living quarters. The kitchen (*culina*) was usually near the *tablinum* and the rear garden, and adjoined a lavatory. Variations upon this traditional design were numerous: the *atrium* often grew to a vast size in the houses of the rich, who had to receive large numbers of clients each day; at Pompeii the townhouses of the 1st century A.D. often had the principal living rooms at the rear, grouped around a garden or peristyle in the Greek fashion, and the *atrium* was reduced to a simple reception area.

Dorians The last wave of invaders of Greece in the classical world, who arrived from the north between 1200 and 1000 B.C. They were racially related to the existing settlers of Greece, whom Homer calls the Achaeans, both groups having originated in the Balkans. The Dorian invasion caused most Achaeans to migrate to the islands of the Aegean or to Asia Minor, where they became the ancestors of the classical Ionians; only Attica remained an Achaean bridgehead. In most places the Dorians fused with the local populace but in Sparta and Crete remained a distinct ruling class with the natives reduced to being serfs. The Peloponnesus was thus the centre of Dorian civilization.

E

Ecclesia The popular assembly at Athens, initially consisting of the nobility only but from the time of Solon open to all citizens. In the 5th century B.C. following the reforms of Cleisthenes, it was the embodiment of democracy to which all magistrates were answerable. It decided on bills prepared by the Council of Five Hundred or *Boule* and its decrees were supreme.

Edictum A public declaration made by a Roman magistrate on assuming office, announcing the manner in which he proposed to carry out his duties. The *edicta* helped the development of Roman law by defining primitive law more precisely or by modifying or replacing it.

Emperor The term *imperator*, from which emperor is derived, designated a Roman military commander who had been acclaimed by his soldiers as possessing *imperium*. He was recognised by the Senate and Roman people, and magistrates swore

allegiance to him. In 27 B.C. when Augustus founded the Principate he attempted to preserve the forms of the old constitution, regarding himself as *princeps*, that is first among equals, the leading senator. In fact his powers were much wider: he was eventually granted extensive proconsular *imperium* and tribunician powers (*see* **Consul** and **Tribune**) and was the supreme military leader who also convened the Senate and issued edicts. His successors Tiberius and Claudius sought radically to decrease the countervailing powers of the Senate and were largely successful; later emperors were granted divine status after death (a concept known as apotheosis) and by the 3rd century A.D. during their lifetimes.

Succession to the imperial throne came to depend on inheritance, adoption and occasionally force of arms. The successive dynasties of the first century A.D. were the Julio-Claudians, Flavians and Antonines; and in the second and third centuries non-Roman emperors—including African, Syrian and Illyrian dynasties—seized the throne largely on the basis of their military strength. Eventually all the sovereignty of the Roman people was transferred to the person of the emperor; by the time of Aurelian he was described as *dominus* or lord rather than *princeps* which had implied a legal parity of status. Imperial officials, directly appointed by the emperor, replaced the old magistracies in the provinces and in central administration. The system was modified by Diocletian (**B20**) in the 3rd century A.D. when he appointed a colleague, Maximian (*see* **Tetrarchy**). The empire was finally partitioned in A.D. 364 when the brothers Valentinian and Valens amicably divided it between them, Valens ruling the east from Constantinople and Valentinian the west from Rome.

Epheboi A Greek term denoting in general all adolescents, but in most states having an additional restricted usage referring to young men doing a term of military service. In Athens this was from age 18 and after two years' service they were granted full citizenship rights.

Ephetae An early Athenian jury consisting of 51 noble citizens aged 50 or over, which tried lesser cases of murder.

Ephors The ephors or "supervisors" were Dorian magistrates of particular importance. In Sparta there were five whose original function was to interpret divine will. By the 6th century B.C. they were annually elected and were the real authority in the state, supervising the rule of the two kings. After Sparta's victory in the Peloponnesian War the system became corrupt and in 227 B.C. King Cleomenes III terminated the office.

Equites The knights, or equestrians, of Rome. During the monarchy and Republic they were the class of citizens rich enough to be required to provide a horse for military service. In this early period there were ten *equites* to each *curia* and therefore 300 *equites* in total, divided into six *centuriae*. After the reforms of the Gracchi they became an "order" of society and formed a class of gentility based on wealth, alongside the Senate. Legal restrictions on senators' financial activities meant the *equites* formed a "capitalist" middle class running the banking system and carrying out public works contracts. Under the Empire the class provided most of the high administrators, *e.g.* the *praefectus* of Egypt.

Erechtheum The most venerated part of the Acropolis of Athens because of its historical and religious traditions. Rebuilt between 430 and 408 B.C., it was an enclosure housing nine different shrines.

Esquiline One of the seven hills of Rome, a plateau east of the original city, it later became one of the most aristocratic districts and home of the famous gardens of Maecenas, and eventually an imperial estate.

Etruscans *See* **L41**.

Eupatridai Greeks who were noble by birth, able to trace their descent from a known family of the heroic era. They were frequently rich landowners and at Athens in the early 6th century B.C. formed one of the four classes of citizens (the others being *zeugitai*, *demiourgoi* and *thetes*). Solon reduced their influence when he made wealth not birth the qualification for office-holding, but the *Eupatridai* continued to have considerable political influence, in part because they maintained the right to interpret religious law.

F

Fas A Roman legal concept denoting that which is lawful and not contrary to the will of the gods.

Fasces Bundles of elm or birch sticks tied by a red thong and carried by the lictors who attended the Roman consuls, to signify their authority. Outside the city of Rome an axe was added to the emblem to indicate the magistrate's power to execute as well as flog.

Fasti Originally those days in the Roman religious calendar when the praetor could fulfill his judicial functions. The term also applies to the running lists of their members kept by each board of magistrates (*fasti magistratuum*). Those of the consuls, the *fasti consulares*, provide a chronology of Roman history.

Fetiales A special college of Roman priests charged with performing the religious rites associated with foreign relations, particularly the declaration of war and the concluding of peace treaties. They originally existed not only in Rome but among the Sabines, Samnites and Latins as well.

Fides A Roman moral concept implying respect for undertakings or engagements and as such it was the basis of social order.

Flamines A very ancient priestly college of Rome appointed from amongst the patrician class by the early kings. There were 15 flamens or priests, the highest being of Jupiter. Various taboos attached to the latter, *e.g.* he could not touch a corpse (in order to preserve his ritual sanctity) nor could he leave Rome itself. After the expulsion of the kings the *flamines* were appointed by the *Pontifex Maximus*.

Flavians A dynasty of Roman emperors who succeeded the Julio-Claudians. Established by Vespasian (A.D. 69–79) (**B62**) after the civil war (commonly known as the Year of the Four Emperors) which followed Nero's (**B44**) reign, it was distinguished by the restoration of military security to the Empire and by the further encroachment of the powers of the Principate upon those of the Senate. Vespasian was succeeded by his sons Titus (A.D. 79–81) (**B60**) and Domitian (A.D. 81–96), whose reign ended in an anti-senatorial terror which led to the Flavians' overthrow and the accession of the Antonines.

Foedus A treaty between Rome and other states. The Roman theory of international relations rested on the concept of a contract; thus a declaration of war was really a claim for restoration to Rome of what she believed to be her rights. The only enemy recognised in law was the citizen of a country on whom war had been declared, a *hostis*, and only citizens on active duty could kill a *hostis*. From the 2nd century A.D. the term *foederati* was also given to barbarian allies who were allowed to settle on the frontiers of the Empire in order that they might defend their borders against invasion.

Forum The centre of life in Rome and in Roman cities, the site of public and private business. The Forum in Rome was an oblong shaped area on whose west side stood the Capitol, to the south the Palatine, and to the north the Quirinal, Viminal and Esquiline Hills. Originally it was a market place, as the name implies, but was also used for public meetings, festivals and games. The *Curia* of King Tullus Hostilius stood at the north-west corner; in front of this was the *comitium*—the meeting place of assemblies—and the *rostra*. The *Via Sacra* or Sacred Way, along which processions would advance, traversed the Forum. Public buildings and temples surrounded the open area. The original *Forum Romanum* was extensively restored through the centuries and later surrounded by other commemorative fora, notably those of Julius Caesar and the emperors Augustus, Vespasian, Nerva and Trajan.

Frigidarium *See* **Thermae**.

G

Genius To the Roman mind, a spirit inherent in a being or even a place. Thus a house possessed its own *genius* which embodied a greater divine power and which received offerings at the domestic altar; the *genius* of the *paterfamilias* (head of the family) also received worship. This concept of a personified spirit could also be applied to any body of men linked by a common interest through successive stages, *e.g.* a legion.

Gens, gentes Early Roman society consisted of patriarchal clans or *gentes*, members of which shared descent from a common ancestor. They possessed a gentile name, *e.g.* all members of the Julian clan were called Julius; and each clan had its own religious rites or *sacra*. Eventually the *gentes* split into individual families, *e.g.* the *gens Cornelia* clan was subdivided into the Cornelii Scipiones, Cornelii Sullae, Cornelii Lentuli, *etc*. The leading *gentes* were the Iulia (who produced Caesar), the Claudia (who produced the emperors Tiberius and Nero), the Aemilia, the Fabia, and the Sempronia.

Gerousia A council of Elders at Sparta. It consisted of the two kings and 28 members aged sixty or more. Its task was to prepare matters for hearing before the Assembly, to act as a court of justice in criminal cases, and to act as a general advisory body on political affairs.

Gladiators *See* **L51**.

Gymnasium A word derived from the Greek for naked, as the Greeks always stripped for exercise. Gymnasia were possibly originally intended for military training. All three of the known gymnasia of classical Athens were connected with shrines outside the city—the Academy with the shrine of Academus, the Lyceum with Apollo and the Cynosarges with Heracles. The establishment was an ideal place to sit around talking and the three gymnasia became respectively the philosophical schools of Plato, Aristotle and the Cynics.

H

Haruspices Originally Etruscan priests who practised an elaborate ritual of divination from the entrails of sacrificial animals. The Romans later adopted the practice.

Heliaea An Athenian judicial body, popularly constituted with the people sitting in sections as sworn judges. At first the archons retained judicial powers and the *Heliaea* was the court of appeal. But by degrees the archons' power was reduced to that of holding preliminary hearings and the *Heliaea* became the first and last court dealing with all cases save murder.

Hellenes, Hellenism The Greeks of the classical period termed themselves Hellenes and their country Hellas (in contrast to Homer's Achaeans). They traced their common descent from Hellen, an eponymous hero. In modern terms "Hellenism" refers to the culture flourishing in Greece, the Aegean isles, the coast of Asia Minor and Magna Graecia (the Greek settlements in Italy and Sicily) between 776 B.C. and the death of Alexander the Great in 323 B.C.

Helots When the Dorians invaded the Peloponnesus they dispossessed the original inhabitants and founded the state of Sparta on their land. These inhabitants were reduced to servitude and known as helots. Living as serfs they were forced to provide food for their Spartan masters, which left the latter free for military service. Helot revolts were common and the Spartans were always aware of their numerical inferiority to their subjects. The *Krypteia* (*q.v.*) was established to control them and once a year Sparta officially declared war on the helots, thus providing a formal excuse for the murder of potential troublemakers.

Hermae Square pillars ending in a human head with a protruding phallus in the middle. The hermae were of very ancient origin and stood at boundaries and crossroads as protective guardians.

Hetairai The Attic Greek term for women who were prostitutes. In the 5th to 3rd centuries B.C. many in the great cities were known for their sophistication as hostesses and entertainers and often became mistresses of the leading men of the state, *e.g.* Aspasia the companion of Pericles. Certain cults of leading female divinities, *e.g.* of Aphrodite at Corinth, moreover had sacred prostitutes residing at the cult centre. The term is not to be confused with *hetairiai*, the Greek word for brotherhoods which by extension later meant political factions.

Hetairoi The Companions, the royal bodyguard of the Macedonian kings and particularly of Alexander the Great.

Hippeis Greek cavalry. Secondary in function to the hoplites, they were first used regularly by Athens after the Persian Wars. As cavalrymen were required to provide their own horses, service was confined to rich men and the name was given to the second census classes of the Athenian citizenry after the Solonic reforms.

Hippodrome A Greek stadium for chariot and horse racing and a prototype of the Roman circus. No classical Greek hippodrome survives but they were probably similar to the Roman type.

Homoioi Those who were full citizens of Sparta, descended from the original Dorian founders of the state. They alone had political and legal rights and devoted themselves to military pursuits, supported by the labour of the helot serfs.

Homonoia An agreement between different Greek states or members of a community. It was revered as a religious ideal, due in part to the notable lack of unity among the Greeks.

Hoplite The heavily armoured Greek foot soldier who replaced the mounted warrior and chariot rider of the Homeric Iliad as the basis of Greek armies. Instead of hurling spears at long range, he carried a long thrusting spear and a shield held on the left arm. Hoplites were usually deployed in a formation called the phalanx. This type of troop appeared in the 8th century B.C. and survived until the Roman conquest; and was a consequence of advances in metalworking which made armour cheaper and available to the majority of citizens.

Hypocaust The Roman method of central heating in a building, domestic or public, it consisted originally of a raised floor heated from below by a furnace. In the first century A.D. the hypocaust was refined by the addition of hollow sections in walls and floors to conduct the heated air into other rooms. It was extensively used in Roman houses in cold climates, *e.g.* in Britain.

I

Imperator To the Romans one who was the direct interpreter of the will of the gods, whose actions confirmed the gods' approval; an invincible warrior and the supreme dispenser of justice. The title was conferred by the acclamation of troops in the field of battle, that is citizens on active service rather than the people at large. In a legal sense it denoted also the holder of *imperium. See also* **Emperor**.

Imperium The source of all political authority in the Roman world, it originated as a power exceptionally conferred upon the holder by the gods and an extension within the city of Rome of the omnipotence of Jupiter. During the monarchy the *imperium* was held by the kings as the interpreters of the will of the gods and later descended from them to the consuls, who in turn could relinquish it to the dictator. During an interregnum it was transmitted to and resided in the Senate. If the gods chose it could be directly conferred upon one individual, the *imperator*, whose military success was a sign of divine blessing; in this fashion it ultimately passed to the emperors. Plebeians, who did not have the right to communicate with the gods by taking auspices, originally could not exercise *imperium*.

Insulae Large tenements in Roman cities which were subdivided into flats. The ground floor was typically occupied by shops. Many were hastily constructed in lath-work; they collapsed with alarming frequency and Augustus limited their height to 70 feet. It is possible they developed from the traditional *domus*, as they resembled the front portion of a Roman house with the *atrium* removed.

Intercessio A Roman judicial action consisting of a veto which could nullify both public and private legal decisions. It was held by members of a *collegium* of magistracies: each could block another's decisions and the higher magistrates could overrule the lower. The tribunes of the plebeians could exercise the veto over all other officials.

Interrex The magistrate chosen by the Senate to govern during a vacancy in the Roman monarchy, which was an elective rather than hereditary office. The *interrex* governed the state whilst a king was being chosen and supervised the transition of authority to whoever was chosen. After the expulsion of the kings the office survived with the same name and function of presiding over any hiatus between elected magistrates.

Ionians Those Greeks settled along the central coastal region of Asia Minor around the Gulf of Smyrna, though the name was generally given to all Greeks in Asia Minor. They had originally invaded mainland Greece around 2000 B.C. but were forced to migrate across the Aegean by the Dorian invaders. They were ethnically related to the inhabitants of Attica, including the Athenians.

Ius For the Romans, law in general. The *Ius Civile* dealt with the rights of citizens (*see* **Citizenship**), the *Ius Gentium* was a composite code embodying the usage of surrounding states or nations and conceptions of equality; and the *Ius Naturae* was the "natural law" of Stoic doctrine from which various concepts were borrowed or applied to *Ius Civile*. The rights of a category of citizens or a community were defined in relation to the full rights of Roman citizenship, *e.g.* the *Ius Latii* or Latin rights embodied some but not all rights of the full citizen.

J

Janiculum A ridge of hills on the west bank of the Tiber near Rome, but never properly incorporated into the city.

Julian Calendar The Roman calendar was originally a lunar one based on months of 27 or 28 days each divided into phases, the *kalendae* (new moon), *nonae* (first quarter) and the *idus* (full moon). Originally there were ten months; later King Numa introduced a 12 month year. In order to allow synchronisation of the solar and lunar years an extra month of 22 or 23 days was added every second year. By the time of the late Republic the calendar had become chaotic and was replaced by one introduced by Julius Caesar in 46 B.C., which had 12 months of 30 and 31 days (except for February which had 28) and a leap year every fourth year. Modified by Pope Gregory XIII in 1582 it remains the basis of the modern calendar.

Julio-Claudians The dynasty of the first five Roman emperors, Augustus, Tiberius, Caligula, Claudius and Nero, so called because it was formed of two families, the Julian and the Claudian. Augustus was the natural grandnephew of Julius Caesar and became Caesar's adoptive son. His wife Livia had two sons, Tiberius and Drusus, by her first marriage to T. Claudius Nero. Tiberius was adopted by Augustus in A.D. 4, thus becoming a Julio-Claudian. His successor Caligula was the son of Germanicus, son of Tiberius' brother Drusus; Claudius was the younger brother of Germanicus; and Nero, who was adopted by his predecessor, was a nephew of Caligula and grandson of Germanicus. *See* **Section B** for individual emperors.

Jurisconsults Roman experts in law who gave opinions on legal matters in a private capacity. Originally Roman law, having a religious foundation, was known only to priests but was later codified in the Twelve Tables. In 304 B.C. the aedile Cn. Flavius published the complex rules pertaining to civil suits in a convenient form. It was now possible for all literate citizens to take an interest in civil law and a number of jurisconsults sprang up to publish compendia of laws and their own commentaries. Under the Empire they had great influence advising not only magistrates but also the emperor through the *concilium principis*.

K

Krypteia The Spartan "secret police" founded to deal with the dangers arising from the oppression of the helots. Spartan youths were encouraged to kill helots whom they suspected of plotting rebellion.

L

Lagides The dynasty which ruled Egypt from the death of Alexander the Great until the death of Cleopatra in 34 B.C. The name is derived from that of Lagus whose son Ptolemy I was the first *diadochus* (*see* Diadochi) to rule the country.

Latifundia Vast pastoral estates in Italy created from confiscated land and bankrupt smallholdings cheaply bought. They first appeared at the end of the 2nd Punic War and had the effect of driving the small proprietors from the land and into the cities, causing unemployment and social unrest and decreasing Italian wheat production. The brothers Gracchi attempted a notable reform of the system in the late 2nd century B.C. by breaking them up into individual properties again.

Laudatio The Roman funeral ovation. Originally confined to patricians, it became a public rite performed by the eldest son or even a magistrate, eulogizing the deceased.

Legati Military or civil representatives of the Senate or the Emperor; in a sense, ambassadors. The governor of a Roman province was usually accompanied by several *legati* whom he appointed to his staff with the approval of the Senate. Under the Empire *legati* were appointed to govern those provinces directly under imperial control.

Legion A Roman military unit, the number, recruitment and constitution of which varied at different times. Originally the whole army or levy of troops was called the *legio* and fought in a fashion similar to the Greek phalanx. Around the end of the 4th century B.C. a more flexible formation was adopted, by which the legion was arranged in three lines each of 10 maniples or 20 centuries. In the first line were the *hastati* who originally carried the *hasta*—a long spear for use at close quarters (later replaced by the *pilum*)—a short sword and full suit of armour; in the second line were the *principes* similarly armed; and in the third the *triarii* who continued to carry the *hasta*. In the late 2nd century B.C., following severe defeats at the hands of Germanic tribes, the army was completely reorganised by Marius. The property qualification for military service was abolished and henceforth soldiering became more of a "professional" career. The cohort also succeeded the maniple as a tactical formation. In theory the new legion consisted of 6,000 professional troops serving for 20 years, divided into 10 cohorts each of six centuries. In practice from the time of Marius until the imperial period the legion numbered only about 4,800 men, so the term *centuriae* was purely nominal as legions were never up to strength. Under the Empire the legion probably numbered 5,500; during Augustus' reign there was a standing army of 25 of them. Twenty years' service entitled provincials to Roman citizenship. The numbers given to legions originated during the Civil Wars of the late Republic but the names were of various origin and usually referred to the area of recruitment, *e.g. III Gallica*, or to patron gods, *e.g. VI Martia Victrix*.

Lex A Latin word which we translate as law but which denoted a juridicial action instigated by a magistrate and usually ratified by a citizen assembly. It implied a legal obligation on a body of citizens (*lex publica*) or only on certain of them (*lex privata*).

Libertas A Roman political concept denoting that freedom which guaranteed a minimum of personal rights. *Libertas* was not the right to question or challenge authority but rather permission to do what the law or ancient customs (*mos maiorum*) allowed.

Lictors Officials who originally attended the kings of Rome and later the consuls and praetors. Carrying the *fasces* to symbolise the *imperium* of the magistrates, they also put their decisions into effect and on occasion even acted as executioners.

Limes A Latin word originally meaning path; under the Empire it denoted a system of fortifications on certain strategic frontiers, *e.g.* the Rhine. In Britain the *limes* stretched 76 miles from modern Newcastle to the Solway Firth and between A.D. 122 and 127 was reconstructed in stone as Hadrian's Wall. *See* **Roman Walls, L106.**

Liturgy An Athenian institution by which rich citizens were compelled to finance certain public activities. The major ones were the trierarchy, by which a citizen had to equip and man a trireme or warship and the *choregia* or provision of a chorus for dramatic festivals.

Long Walls Originally two walls built in 458 B.C. by Cimon to link Athens to its port of Piraeus six miles away, thus securing access to the port and effectively making a twin town. The walls were destroyed by the Spartans after the Peloponnesian War but later rebuilt.

Ludi Roman games. Their origin is obscure but possibly rooted in ancient religious practice such as the rural cult of Ceres. The official *ludi*, financed by public funds, were initially the circus races and dramatic performances. These were later supplemented by gladiatorial contests and with wild beast hunts financed privately by young noble men and afterwards by the emperors. The number of days devoted to the games increased over the years; by A.D. 350 they occupied 176 days a year. The word *ludi* could also mean schools of instruction, *e.g.* of rhetoric, law or even gladiators.

Lupercalia A religious ceremony and fertility rite held annually on the Palatine hill at Rome, in honour of the god Faunus.

Lustration The performance of a purification ceremony conducted every five years at Rome by the censors. It usually took the form of a procession around whatever was to be purified.

Lyceum Aristotle's school at Athens so called because the gymnasium where he taught was near the grove of Lycian Apollo (a shrine). Because its members walked as they conversed it was also called the Peripatetic School from *peripatos* or covered walk.

M

Macellum A Roman provision market. Unlike the forum it was used only for the sale of food.

Maiestas For the Romans, a quality the possession of which elevated them above all other peoples. Derogation of the majesty of the Roman people (*maiestas populi Romani imminuta*) was a crime. Much political use of the law was made under the late Republic and particularly during the reign of the emperor Tiberius (**B60**), when trials were held before the Senate.

Maniple *See* **Legion.**

Metics Aliens, often from other Greek states, residing in Greek cities were known as *metoikoi*, *i.e.* those who dwell with. Usually craftsmen by profession they could not hold office, participate in assemblies, own land or marry native women. Occasionally they were granted *isoteleia*, the rights of full citizenship. They were very common at Athens but were excluded from Sparta.

Miliaria Roman milestones showing distances and often bearing other inscriptions.

Municipium A Latin term with various meanings used to denote the degrees to which individuals, and more commonly communities, shared the privileges and responsibilities of Roman citizenship. After Rome's victory over them in the Social War (*i.e.* the war of the *socii* or allies) of the 1st century B.C., all Italian cities became *municipia* and enjoyed full citizen rights. Under the Empire the difference between *municipia* and *coloniae* (colonies) lay in the latter's possession of full citizenship. Both had similar systems of administration analogous to that of Rome itself: two annually elected magistrates or *duoviri* (equivalent to consuls) assisted by two junior magistrates (equivalent to aediles), a council of *decuriones* (*q.v.*), the *curia* (equivalent to the Senate) and an assembly of townsfolk.

N

Naukrariai Each of Athens' four tribes, the Geleontes, Argadeis, Aigicoreis and Hopletes, was divided into twelve districts or *naukrariai*, each of which was obliged to provide a ship for the early Athenian navy. Following the reforms of Cleisthenes and the introduction of the new demes (*q.v.*) the system was abolished and replaced by liturgies.

Nomen The Latin word for name. In the classical

period all Roman males had three names, the *praenomen*, the gentile *nomen* (*see* **Gens**) and the *cognomen*. There were originally only 17 *praenomina* (what we could distinguish as the first or personal name, such as Marcus); but the gentile *nomen* was given to all members of a *gens*, male and female, and all free persons had one. The *cognomen* began as a purely personal appellation but later became hereditary within the *familiae* (*see* **Gens**). To mark any personal achievement *agnomina* might be adopted, *e.g.* the general P. Cornelius Scipio took the added name Africanus to commemorate his victory there over Hannibal. Freedmen (*liberti*) took the *praenomen* and *nomen* of the man who had freed them, retaining their slave name as a *cognomen*.

Nomoi In the Greek world, man-made laws. In the Athenian state they included the criminal and constitutional law; the *psephismata* or daily decrees of the Ecclesia; and the ancestral customs.

Nomothetae Lawmakers. In Athens the name was given to any commission appointed to draft or revise the laws.

Numen A supernatural power or powers (*numina*) which the Romans recognised and respected but did not envisage clearly: the *numen* was not a personified divinity with a definite sex *etc.* Rather *numina* could reside anywhere – in men, animals or even inanimate objects.

O

Officia Social duties of which a Roman of rank could not divest himself without being considered guilty of a serious dereliction of obligations, *e.g.* attendance at betrothals or marriages.

Onager A Roman war machine in the form of a portable catapult. The name means wild ass, because its rear end "kicked" upwards when it was fired.

Ostracism A system peculiar to Athens and rarely used whereby if the citizens considered any person to be a threat to democracy they might write his name on a piece of broken pottery (*ostrakon*) and if someone's name appeared on more than 6,000 shards he was banished from Athens for ten years. It was instituted by Cleisthenes in 507 B.C. as a means of peacefully removing potential tyrants. The ostracised person could however return after banishment and resume both his citizen rights and his property.

P

Paean A form of Greek lyric poetry; a poem with a dignified and solemn rhythm. Paeans were sung or recited, amongst other occasions, prior to battle.

Palaestra An open air Greek sports ground. The name is derived from *pale* or wrestling although other sports including running, boxing and jumping were held there. They were of a more "aristocratic" character than the gymnasia.

Palatine One of Rome's seven hills which lay between the Forum and the Tiber. From the time of Augustus it was the site of lavish homes and imperial palaces.

Panathenaea An Athenian summer festival held every four years in honour of the goddess Athene. Its date of origin is unknown, but it was remodelled in the early 6th century B.C. It involved athletic contests, poetry recitals, and at the climax a procession to the temple on the Acropolis. Here a new robe or *peplum* was offered to the goddess. The procession is depicted in the Elgin Marbles (the frieze of the Parthenon now in the British Museum).

Parthenon The magnificent temple of the goddess Athene built on the Athenian Acropolis between 447 and 432 B.C. Work was initially commenced on a temple after the battle of Marathon but it was destroyed during the Persian occupation of the city in 480 B.C. The statesman Pericles was responsible for its rebuilding, as a symbol of Athenian imperial democracy, and he commissioned Phidias' statue of Athene, one of the Seven Wonders of the World. The temple became a Christian church in the Byzantine period and

during the Ottoman period a mosque. It was largely destroyed in 1687 by Venetian bombardment, but its frieze was subsequently saved by the British antiquarian Lord Elgin and is now in the British Museum.

Paterfamilias The head of the Roman family and household. In early times he had very great power in what was a patriarchal society. He assumed *manus* or complete disciplinary control over his wife when he married; he had paternal authority (*patria potestas*) over his children; and *dominium* or mastership of the household slaves. Outside the house he alone was endowed with full legal responsibility (*e.g.* his wife and children had no legal personality and the *paterfamilias* took action at law on their behalf) and theoretically his authority included the power of life and death over the household.

Pater Patriae A Roman honorific title, "Father of His Country", first bestowed by the Senate on Cicero in 63 B.C. for suppressing the Catiline conspiracy; and upon Augustus in 2 B.C. and subsequent emperors.

Patricians The self-styled nobility of Rome, who formed a caste based on the leading families or *gentes* and for many years sought to exclude the plebeians from positions of power in the state. This social division does not seem to have arisen from any racial differences but from a progressive differentiation of wealth in the city. During the monarchy the patricians formed a powerful oligarchy and at the expulsion of the kings secured power in the new Republic, reserving to themselves the right to be consul and to sit in the Senate, *etc.* The political history of the Republic is therefore largely the attempt of the plebeians to wrest power from the patricians, although economic and social divisions long remained reinforced by the system of *clientela*.

Patronus In Roman public life, one who agreed to protect and assist another by making him his client. This social and economic institution was an important and permanent feature of Roman life extending beyond the ties of clients and great families to the sphere of foreign relations. A victorious general was responsible for organising conquered territory and could allocate it to his retinue, to friends or even to associate cities.

Pax Deorum A Roman religious concept (literally the "Peace of the Gods"), denoting a covenant between Rome and the gods. It preserved her security, being a guarantee of harmony between men and the divine powers.

Peloponnesian War (431–404 B.C.) The great war between Athens and Sparta. The two states had been allies in the 5th century against the Persian invasions of Greece, but the defeat of the Persian threat unleashed a struggle for supremacy between democratic Athens with her seaborne empire and oligarchic Sparta which dominated the Peloponnesus. Hostilities broke out when Sparta's ally, Thebes, seized the Athenian city of Plataea; but the main episode of the war was the annual expedition of the superior Spartan land forces into Attica which bottled up the Athenian army behind the Long Walls whilst the Spartans devastated Attica (431–425). Athenian troubles were deepened by a bubonic plague which ravaged the city between 430 and 427 and deprived her of the democratic leader Pericles. At the same time the Athenian fleet had undisputed control of all Greek waters. In this fashion two alliances faced each other: that of all the states of the Peloponnesus (except Argos and Achaea), Boeotia, Phocis, Locris and Ambracia against Athens and the Delian League. An interlude occurred between 421 and 414 (known as the Peace of Nicias) whilst the various states altered their alignment and Sparta tried to re-establish her hegemony over the Peloponnesus. In 415 however the Athenian democracy, incited by Alcibiades, launched a disastrous expedition against the city of Syracuse in Sicily; this ended in complete failure two years later with the loss of 40,000 men and 240 ships. Sparta seized the opportunity to reopen hostilities and Persian influence instigated revolts among Athens' allies; Persia even offered to finance the Spartan navy if the latter recognised her claims in Ionia. Dissent in Athens led an oligarchy to seize power (411) which attempted negotiation with Sparta but was soon deposed. The Spartan king Lysander had by now commenced a general reorganisation of the

Peloponnesian fleet; and in 406–405 he progressively wore down the Athenian navy, causing a general revolt to break out against Athens among the member states of the Delian League. The Spartan blockade of the city and starvation forced her surrender in 404 on extremely unfavourable terms: her navy was eliminated and the democracy overthrown. Thereafter Athens never regained her former power in Greece.

Peltasts Greek light infantry equipped with javelins as opposed to the thrusting spear of the hoplite. In democratic states the poorer classes who could not afford to provide themselves with heavy armour formed the peltasts.

Pentaskosiomedimnoi The highest census class of Athenian citizenry established by the constitutional reforms of Solon. The name denotes those who owned sufficient land to yield 500 bushels of agricultural produce (*e.g.* wheat and olive oil) a year.

Peregrini Foreigners dwelling in Roman territory who did not hold Roman citizenship but were given lesser "alien" rights. In 241 B.C. a special praetor was appointed to deal with their legal relations. They supplied the auxiliary troops for the legions and from the time of the emperor Claudius received full citizenship upon discharge.

Perioikoi Literally "those that dwell about", that is, in Greece neighbouring peoples who were the subjects of a state but had a certain degree of autonomous local government. *See also* **Sparta**.

Phalanx A Greek military tactical formation introduced in the 7th century B.C. The phalanx consisted of several ranks of heavily armoured hoplites who carried long thrusting spears, those of the rear rank being up to 24 feet long. A solid wall of horizontally held spears was thus presented to the enemy. The formation lacked manoeuvrability and under Philip of Macedon it became more loosely deployed: the aim was no longer to drive a wedge into the enemy but to engage and hold his forces whilst the cavalry broke through on the wings. As a military formation it survived until the more manoeuvrable Roman legions broke the Macedonian phalanx at the battle of Cynoscephalae in 197 B.C.

Phratry A group of several families amongst the primitive Greek tribes. The families formed themselves into a brotherhood, the phratry, which had a religious significance. The phratry stood between the clan and the family in the social order. As democracy asserted itself the aristocratic heads of the phratry lost their positions of authority and the phratry itself was divested of its economic and social importance.

Phylae "Tribes" in early and classical Greece. Originally an ethnic grouping formed around a common religious cult, it comprised the entire population of a kingdom who inhabited a deme but members made no claim to common descent. The Ionians were divided into four *phylae*, the Dorians into three. In 6th century Athens Cleisthenes decided to create new *phylae*, and redivided the population into ten, giving each its own hero and sanctuary (*see also* **Deme**). The tribes thus became political rather than religious or ethnic groups.

Pilum A Roman military javelin, consisting of a wooden shaft seven feet long with an iron head attached by rivets. It was thrown by the legionaries during their initial battle charge in order to break the enemy's formation before close combat with the sword. The *pilum* was so designed that on impact the iron head would bend, thus preventing it being returned by the enemy.

Piraeus The port near Athens, built on the urging of Themistocles to accommodate a growing fleet and replace the smaller port of Phalerum. It was linked to Athens by the Long Walls.

Pisistratids The dynasty of tyrants who ruled Athens between 560 and 510 B.C. It consisted of the benevolent tyrant Pisistratus who seized power in 560 and died in 527 and of his two sons Hipparchus and Hippias. The former was assassinated in 514, the latter expelled by the forces of democracy in 510.

Plebeians In the early history of Rome, those persons who were not members of the *gentes* which produced *patres* (fathers) of the state, *i.e.* the patrician class. The social division was probably of economic rather than racial origin. Admission to political office was denied them by the

patricians and the domestic history of the Republic is largely one of conflict between the two orders. The plebeians gradually extended their political rights (*see* **Tribune**) and occasionally would withdraw en masse from Rome, the last secession occurring in 286 B.C.

Polis The Greek city state. The Greek states generally consisted of a city with a surrounding district to support it. The ideal was one of moderate size, large enough for self-sufficiency but small enough for the citizens—who might live in the town or surrounding rural districts—to know one another. The *polis* was above all a political entity in which the citizens participated freely in government and thus fulfilled their civic duties.

Pomerium The boundary of the city of Rome which was ritually consecrated. The concept is of obscure origin but clearly signifies that the city territory was a religious entity. Army leaders could not enter the *pomerium* and legally retain their powers.

Pontifex Maximus The high priest of Rome. He assumed the religious duties of the early kings, which included charge of the calendar of religious festivals (*see* **Fasti**) and nomination of the *flamines* and Vestal Virgins. He had disciplinary powers over these bodies but his main role was an advisory one of ensuring that religious rites were correctly performed and suppressing foreign cults. Other priests (*pontifices*) were restricted to performing rituals. From the time of Augustus the emperor himself held the post.

Praefectura A district of Roman territory or a town, the control of which the *praetor urbanus* delegated to a *praefectus*.

Praefectus A Roman official appointed by the Senate, or later by the emperor, for a particular task. In the 3rd and 2nd centuries B.C. *praefecti* were often appointed to govern towns and colonies in Rome's Italian territories. Under the Empire they had charge of imperial provinces or the emperor's personal territories such as Egypt. Governors would be accompanied by a military *praefectus* and *praefecti* commanded the Roman fleet and the Praetorian Guard (*q.v.*). Others had responsibility for urban administration: the *praefectus annonae* had charge of provisioning Rome with food and the *praefectus vigilum* supervised the fire brigade.

Praetorian Guard An elite military unit stationed in Rome. During the Republic Roman generals had a personal bodyguard, the *cohors praetoria*, which gave its name to a permanent corps established by Augustus in 27 B.C. On a number of occasions the Guards intervened in politics, *e.g.* they assassinated the emperor Caligula and elected his successor Claudius. For a long time the troops were all of Italian origin but in A.D. 193 the Guards seized control of the city and auctioned off the imperial throne to the highest bidder. As a result Septimius Severus, on becoming emperor, disbanded them and replaced them with his own Illyrian troops.

Praetorium The general's tent in a Roman military camp, it lent its name to the permanent headquarters building of anywhere under Roman military administration, *e.g.* Pontius Pilate, procurator of Judaea, ruled from the *praetorium* in Jerusalem

Praetors "Headmen", a title given initially to the two Roman magistrates later known as consuls. In 366 B.C. the title was revived and given to new officials appointed to act as the consuls' delegates. They were expected to act in any capacity specified but their primary duty became that of supervising civil jurisdiction. The appointment was an annual one. Until 242 B.C. only one praetor existed, the *praetor urbanus*, responsible for the administration of justice in the city of Rome itself. In 242 the *praetor peregrinus* was also appointed to deal with lawsuits involving foreigners. As Roman territory expanded, more were added and, after their year of office, they would go abroad to govern provinces as propraetors. The propraetors were replaced by imperial *praefecti* during the Empire.

Primus Pilus The highest ranking "non-commissioned" officer and usually the longest serving in a Roman legion. The *primus pilus* was the leading centurion of the first cohort.

Princeps A concept developed under the late Roman Republic in which leading political figures came to be seen as premier citizens who could control the state by their authority. When Augustus established the Principate, it was nominally in his capacity as the senior senator (*princeps senatus*) and *princeps civium Romanorum*, the leading Roman citizen. The title implied however that he was merely the first among equals and not an absolute monarch; and in this way he wedded his position as emperor—actually achieved by his military leadership and control of the Caesarian party— onto the old republican constitution. However the possession of *imperium* by the emperors eventually made them monarchs in all but name, and by the time of Aurelian (A.D. 270–275) the term *dominus* or lord had come to replace that of *princeps*.

Principate The system of government established by Octavian in 27 B.C. and partially modified four years later. With the defeat of Mark Antony (*see* **Triumvirate**) in 31 B.C. Julius Caesar's grandnephew and heir Octavian became master of the Roman world, its military overlord and leader of the Caesarian party. But to avoid Caesar's fate of assassination, he contrived to disguise his dictatorship by adopting various republican constitutional forms. He had the Senate and People grant him both an extraordinary proconsular *imperium* over those provinces which were of strategic value, and the authority of the plebeian tribunes to be exercised at home. The name *Augustus*, "revered", was taken to emphasise his political primacy. In this way he effectively guided the politics of the state without the need to hold successive consulships. The term Principate is used to describe the early form of imperial rule before it assumed more monarchical characteristics in the 2nd century A.D. *See also* **Princeps**.

Procurator Roman officials appointed by the emperor to take sole charge of certain administrative departments. The imperial territories which were privately owned by the emperor were run by procurators and in the imperial provinces they assumed collection of direct taxes from the *publicani*.

Promagistrates Ex-magistrates who were sent to govern Roman provinces at the end of their magisterial term of office, *e.g.* proconsuls and propraetors. During the Empire imperial provinces were run by *legati pro praetore* (*see* **Legates**) aided in financial matters by a procurator. Quaestors, subordinate staff and friends were also available to help them.

Provincia Originally a term referring to the sphere of competency of a Roman magistrate, it came to mean also a military or administrative mission and eventually the territory itself on which the mission was performed. The western Mediterranean states conquered by Rome were at first incorporated into her own territory, but this system was not successful and firstly Sicily and then Sardinia and Corsica were designated *provinciae*. This pattern was subsequently followed throughout the Empire. The *provinciae* were given constitutions by the Roman Senate under a code known as the *Lex Provinciae* and during the Republic were designated either praetorian or proconsular, depending on the rank of the governor (*see* **Promagistrates**). Under the Empire provinces were either senatorial (*i.e.* ruled by ex-consuls or praetors with minimal military force) or imperial (*i.e.* governed by *legati* nominated by the emperor). Potentially rebellious areas were run by procurators directly in the emperor's name, *e.g.* Judaea. Egypt, which was a personal territory of the imperial throne, was governed by a *praefectus*. Under Diocletian the empire was divided into 12 dioceses and 96 provinces.

Proxenos A form of ambassador, roughly corresponding to the modern consul, in ancient Greece. However they did not belong to the city which they represented but to the state in which they represented it. Thus the *proxenos* of Sparta at Athens was an Athenian. The *proxenoi* managed permanent international relations as opposed to the *presbeis* who would carry out a specific and temporary mission.

Prytaneis A Greek term meaning "one who commands". As the state evolved the term came to be applied to the office of high magistrates. In 5th century Athens it was obvious that the governing Council of Five Hundred (*see* **Boule**) could not constantly meet to perform administrative functions; therefore 50 representatives of each of the ten tribes in turn acted as an administrative committee and were known as the *prytaneis* or presidents. Their power was administrative or executive and involved organising and presiding over assemblies, supervising religious worship, meeting ambassadors, *etc.*

Ptolemies *See also* **Lagides**. The Hellenistic dynasty which ruled Egypt from the time of its founder Ptolemy I to that of Cleopatra (**B15**). Its last representative was Ptolemy XV Philopator, also known as Caesarion. The son of Julius Caesar and Cleopatra, he was killed in 30 B.C. shortly after the death of his mother.

Publicanus A public contractor. The contract could be for public works or the like but was usually for tax gathering. The right of collection was auctioned to *publicani* whose profit lay in the excess collected over the amount bid at auction. The *publicani* formed large companies with headquarters in Rome and provincial agencies. Under the Empire the collection of direct taxes passed to the governing promagistrates but indirect taxes continued to be collected by them for a considerable time.

Q

Quaestiones Perpetuae Permanent criminal courts established at Rome in the 2nd century B.C. largely to abolish abuses of the system of trial before the tribal assembly. The first court appointed was *quaestio de rebus repetundis*, which could award damages in the case of misgovernment of a *provincia*. Sulla raised the number of courts to seven to cover the whole range of serious crime. The president of such a court was the praetor or a jury member called a *quaesitor*. Juries were chosen by lot from among the senatorial and equestrian ranks.

Quaestors Roman magistrates with criminal jurisdiction. Each operated within a certain sphere of crime. The earliest were the *quaestores parricidii* (trackers of murder) appointed by the king. In 421 B.C. two *quaestores consulis* were appointed as military paymasters while two *quaestores urbani* were given control of the State treasury. Under Sulla the number of quaestors was increased to 20. The magistracy declined in importance under the Empire and by the 4th century A.D. was an expensive but purely honorific office.

Quinquereme The standard warship in Greek states and the Roman Republic. It was a larger galley than the earlier trireme and was probably rowed by five oarsmen to each oar, hence the name.

Quirinal One of the Seven Hills of Rome, an oblong spur to the north of the city.

R

Renuntiatio A declaration of election by the people of Roman magistrates. It was an act of recognition of the embodiment of *imperium* in the magistrates or in a victorious general.

Repetundae Cases of alleged abuses of power by magistrates in Roman provinces, which from 149 B.C. were tried by a standing jury or *quaestio* under a praetor. Those guilty of the crime might be exiled. Much political use was made of the charge.

Rex King, of which the Romans traditionally had seven (Romulus, Numa Pompilius, Tullus Hostilius, Ancus Marcius, Tarquinius Priscus, Servius Tullius and Tarquinius Superbus). They are said to have ruled from Romulus' foundation of the city in 753 B.C. to the expulsion of Tarquinius Superbus in 509 B.C. and the foundation of the Republic. The Tarquins were of Etruscan origin. After the expulsion the office of *rex sacrorum* was established to continue their royal functions in religious rituals and sacrifices in order that the gods would continue to recognise and reside in the city.

Rhetoric The science of oratory and public debating. Practised in Greece it nonetheless reached its height at Rome where it was fundamental to the education required for public life and was taught in organised schools.

Roman Roads *See* L106.

Roman Towns *See* L106 and Z14.

Roman Walls *See* L106.

Rome The "Eternal City" sited on the banks of the Tiber. Traditionally founded in 753 B.C. by Romulus, it only really became a city in the 6th century under the Tarquins. During the Republic it had a population of 200–300,000; of 450,000 by the time of Augustus; and possibly one million under the Antonines. Administration was originally in the hands of the Senate. Under Augustus the city was reorganised and divided into 14 regions each subdivided into wards (*vici*). The city was ruled by kings until 509 B.C. when they were expelled and a republic came into existence; this lasted until 27 B.C. when Octavian Augustus established the Principate. Rome was henceforth ruled by emperors, although they themselves were not responsible for the creation of the Roman Empire. From the 6th century B.C. onwards Rome had been involved in wars with her Latin neighbours and from the 5th began an expansion in Italy (brought under Roman control by 282 B.C.) which eventually left her mistress of the Mediterranean world. The city itself was sacked in 390 B.C. by marauding Gauls but did not fall again until Alaric the Goth took it in A.D. 410. By this time Constantinople had been established, the Empire formally divided between East and West, and Ravenna had become the seat of the Western Empire.

Rostra The speaker's platform in the Roman Forum. It stood outside the *comitium* (*q.v.*) and took its name from the prows (*rostra*) of ships captured in the battle of Antium in 338 B.C. which were used to adorn it. Augustus replaced it with a new platform.

S

Sacramentum A Roman oath, the legal basis of military service and commercial contracts.

Sacred Band A body of elite Theban troops consisting of 300 young nobles, established by Epaminondas in the 4th century B.C. Their most distinguished hour was at the battle of Leuctra in 371 B.C. when Thebes and her allies defeated a Spartan force, an almost unheard of event in Greek history. The Sacred Band was annihilated by Philip of Macedon at the battle of Chaeronea (338 B.C.).

Satraps The provincial governors of the Persian empire. Their powers varied over time but some satraps enjoyed a high degree of independence from central government.

Saxon Shore The coastline of England from the Isle of Wight to the Wash. Along it the Romans built a string of forts around A.D. 300 in an attempt to ward off invasions by the Angles and Saxons. Later, when these pirates started coming from Frisia, it was extended along the coast of Yorkshire.

Secular Games Games (*see* **Ludi**) and sacrifices performed by the Roman state to commemorate the conclusion of a *saeculum*, an era fixed during the Republic as one century. Augustus held secular games in 17 B.C. to celebrate the establishment of his Principate and Claudius in A.D. 47 for the 800th birthday of Rome.

Seleucids *See also* **Diadochi**. The ruling dynasty in Syria founded by Seleucus I in 321 B.C. His successors reigned until Pompey made Syria a Roman province in 64 B.C.

Senate The Council of Elders under the Roman kings and the repository of power under the Republic. It was an assembly of nobles, recruitment to which depended on wealth, experience and fitness for office. The censors determined who was suitable. Originally membership was confined to the patrician class but became open to the plebeians in the 4th century B.C. and to provincials from the time of Caesar. There were about 300 senators at the foundation of the Republic, 600 under Sulla, and 900 under Caesar. Augustus established it as the highest judicial authority under the Empire. After its revolt against Nero the Senate was gradually excluded from political activity and its influence declined, partly as a result of deliberate attacks on its powers by the

emperors. The growing number of imperially appointed officials, the expansion of *concilium principis* and the tendency to promote the equestrian rather than the senatorial order undermined its political position. Having thus lost its executive functions, its provinces—and thus its income—were withdrawn from it. From A.D. 282 the Senate lost the right to validate the emperor's claim to the throne and from 300 its remaining judicial functions as well. However, it did retain a certain prestige based upon position: in the late Empire membership was extended to the higher echelons of the civil service. By this stage the great offices of state were held by large aristocratic landowners on semi-hereditary lines and these continued to assemble in the Senate. It was for reasons of its traditional prestige that Constantine saw fit to duplicate the body when he established Constantinople as the imperial capital.

Senatus Consultum The declaration of the advice of the Roman Senate to named magistrates of the state on a particular issue, which although not binding in law was so in practice. The most extreme form during the Republic was the *senatus consultum ultimum*, a declaration of public emergency, authorising the magistrates to use all means necessary to save the state.

Severi A dynasty of Roman emperors who ruled from A.D. 193 to 235. It was founded by Septimius Severus and continued by his sons Caracalla and Geta (who was murdered by his brother in A.D. 211). It ended with the reigns of Elagabalus and Alexander Severus. A Syrian military dynasty, the Severi introduced numerous eastern elements into Roman culture.

Signa *See also* **Aquila**. The other Roman legionary standards, apart from the *aquila*, such as the *imagines* or standards bearing medallions with the portrait of the emperor. They were carried by a *signifer*.

Social War *See* **Socii**.

Socii The 150 or so communities in Italy which were allied to Rome in a federation. They included Greeks, Latins, Etruscans, Illyrians *etc.* in those cities and regions which had signed a treaty (*foedus*) with Rome pledging friendship and military aid and relinquishing control of foreign affairs. In return Rome offered protection and did not collect taxes from them. Their troops were not incorporated into the legions but acted as separate units under Roman commanders. They were termed *socii* whilst troops of non-Italian allies were called *auxilia*. Their unsuccessful revolt against Rome in the period 91 to 87 B.C. is known as the Social War.

Sophists Not originally a pejorative term but one denoting a man skilled in a certain art, especially the teaching of rhetoric and philosophy. By the 5th century B.C. it had come to denote an itinerant professional teacher who usually charged high fees. The sophists were generally sceptical and their criticism of religion and the social order led to many of them facing charges of impiety.

Sparta A city built by the Dorians on the banks of the Eurotas in the Peloponnesus in the 9th century B.C. Spartan society was divided into three classes: the true citizen or *homoioi* with full rights to hold office; the *periokoi* who lived on the province's borders and who were pressed into military service; and helots, serfs tied to the soil with no legal rights at all. Alone in Greece the monarchy persisted at Sparta; in fact she had two kings whose families never intermarried and who were hereditary. Military and religious leaders, they led the warriors of the *homoioi* in the state council or *Gerousia* (*q.v.*), to which 28 warriors were elected by popular acclamation. This body of privileged men was supreme until the 8th century B.C. when the ephors forced the kings to share control of the state. The Spartan social order was strictly controlled. A male child belonged not to his parents but to the state (which determined whether he survived or was exposed at birth); his existence was entirely communal and even when married he did not live with his wife. Instead he lived with his fellow warriors and was supported by the *periokoi* and helots. The end result was an intensive social discipline and stress on martial values that made the Spartan army the most powerful in Greece. But the insularity of Sparta and her failure to develop politically led to her downfall. After the victory over her great rival Athens in the Peloponnesian War she nonetheless failed to dominate Greece by the imposition of oligarchies in other states and in the 4th century B.C. Spartan power was broken firstly by Thebes and then by Macedon.

S.P.Q.R. An abbreviation of the Latin phrase *Senatus Populusque Romanus* ("The Senate and Roman People"). It was the official "stamp" of the Roman Republic and Empire, appearing on public documents *etc.*, roughly equivalent to the British "H.M." for Her Majesty's.

Spolia Opima The spoils offered to the gods by a Roman general who had killed the enemy commander himself in single combat. The custom was reserved exclusively for the emperors during the Empire.

Stele A Greek word denoting a column, pillar or thin stone slab erected on tombs and in public places to commemorate the deceased, a public event, or a religious ceremony.

Stoa The philosophical school founded c. 300 B.C. by Zeno. Less well organised than the Academy or Lyceum it survived until at least A.D. 260; it was probably finally suppressed when the Christian emperor Justinian closed all pagan schools in A.D. 529. The Stoics believed virtue was based exclusively on knowledge and that only through knowledge of the truth could one live a virtuous, harmonious life. The name also refers to any type of building with a roof supported by columns.

Strategos An Athenian general. When Cleisthenes created the ten tribes of Athens, each supplied a military unit under the authority of members of the tribe, the first of whom was the *strategos*. Hence there were ten. By the 4th century B.C. they were elected annually but could hold office indefinitely in order to conduct campaigns. Hence Pericles' uninterrupted period of office between 443 and 429 B.C. They controlled operations, levied military tributes from the allies and conducted diplomatic missions. The near constant warfare of the period meant that politically they dominated the constitutional assemblies of the people and were the effective rulers of the state.

Sykophantai Those who brought private prosecutions before the Athenian courts, where no system of public prosecution existed. As a reward they received a share of any fines imposed and consequently abuses occurred with malicious accusations being made with a view to profit. To deter ill-founded prosecution an accuser winning less than one-fifth of the jury's votes was himself heavily fined.

Symposium A Greek drinking party, though the wine was heavily diluted and took second place to the entertainment. Music and song were prominent, but those in the literary genre provided for an open discussion and lively conversation.

T

Tabularium The state record office at Rome, chiefly serving the *Aerarium* (*q.v.*).

Templum The consecrated area in which the auspices were taken. It could be in the city, being the area in which omens were observed, or on the ground where the augur stood. The edifice (temple as we know it) on which sacrifices were made was built inside it so that the *templum* would include the altar and steps to it.

Tepidarium *See* **Thermae.**

Tessera In the Roman world an important item, being the token or tally entitling its holder to a tangible benefit or entertainment, *e.g.* free corn or a free seat at the games.

Tetrarchy The system of imperial government introduced by the Emperor Diocletian who appointed Maximian as a colleague, the two ruling as "Augusti". Military necessity also forced him to appoint two "Caesars", Constantius and Galerius in A.D. 293. Obviously the Caesars were successors to the Augusti and it was the "rule of the four" that gives us the term tetrarchy. However the system was held together only because of Diocletian's authority and did not long survive his death.

Thermae The Roman baths, and an important social institution. Bathing was a communal process and hence a social occasion. The long ritual began in the *apodyterium* or changing room

whence one progressed to the warm heat of the *tepidarium*; then came the intense dry heat of the *sudatorium* or sweating-room, which was intended to induce perspiration, after which one was rubbed with oil and scraped clean with a strigil. The process finished with a plunge in either the *caldarium* (hot bath) or the cold *frigidarium*. *Thermae* were generally provided with sports halls and libraries attached. Large baths were built by the emperors; surviving examples include those at Bath (Aquae Sulis) in England and the baths of Caracalla in Rome.

Thesmothetai A college of six judges instituted in 7th century Athens. Their task was to review defects in the Athenian judicial system and to keep a record of court decisions. They were elected annually.

Thetes Hired labourers and the humblest class of free men in a Greek *polis*. Solon admitted them to the Ecclesia and Heliaea but not to any magistracy. The *thetes* could not afford to undertake military service as hoplites, but at Athens did serve as rowers in the navy, the growth of which in the 5th century B.C. increased their influence in the Athenian democracy.

Thirty Tyrants In 404 B.C. as the Peloponnesian War ended, the Athenian oligarchs secured the aid of the Spartan king Lysander in forcing the democratic party to suspend the constitution. They then gave absolute power to the Thirty Tyrants whose reign of terror was long remembered with horror. Under them some 1,500 men were exiled or executed, but after little more than a year democracy was restored.

Tribunes A Roman term derived from *tribus* or tribe. The *tribuni* appear originally to have been some kind of tribal administrators. During the Republic, as the plebeians undertook a greater share of military service, they demanded more political power and looked to the tribunes to represent them to the Senate. When the plebeians seceded from the city in 449 B.C. in their struggle for political rights they elected two aediles and ten tribunes to act as their executive. The tribunes appeared for them before the Senate and sought to protect individuals against consular *imperium*; hence they soon outstripped the aediles in importance. In time they became personally inviolable and by 300 B.C. had brought the actions of all magistrates within their power of *intercessio* or veto, thus allowing them to suspend the business of government. Although they could not sit in the Senate, they could put motions before it and by 216 B.C. could summon and preside over it. When Augustus established the Principate in 27 B.C. one of the foremost powers which he was granted was the tribuncian power in perpetuity, so that he became the theoretical guardian of the Roman people. There also existed the office of military tribune, which during the late Republic was a junior rank occupied by young men of the senatorial class who were beginning a public career (*see* **Cursus Honorum**); under the Empire the tribunes were usually of equestrian rank.

Tribus A Roman tribe. The city was originally occupied by three tribes, the Ramnes, Tities and Luceres. They were later replaced by four urban and eventually 31 rustic ones which were political rather than racial divisions. *See also* **Comitia.**

Tributum A direct tax levied according to the property on Roman citizens and persons in the provinces *See also* **Publicanus.**

Trireme The principal type of Greek warship from the 6th century B.C. onwards. It was a long rowed galley of narrow beam which attacked by means of a ram and was probably crewed by three rowers to an oar, hence the name.

Triumph The ceremonial procession of a victorious Roman general to the temple of Jupiter on the Capitol, which during the Republic was awarded by the Senate for victory over a foreign enemy. Under the Empire the honour was confined to the imperial dynasty.

Triumvirate The First Triumvirate was a secret alliance made in 60 B.C. between the three most powerful Roman statesmen, Pompey, Caesar and Crassus. It was an unconstitutional agreement to further their individual ends by placing them in control of the Roman state. After Crassus' death it ended in civil war when the Senate tried unsuccessfully to support Pompey against Caesar. The Second Triumvirate was a publicly declared association between Octavian (later Augustus),

Mark Antony and Lepidus. They pledged to avenge the murder of Caesar and at the same time had an official commission to give Rome a new constitution. It was formed in 43 B.C. and renewed for a further five years in 37 B.C. It collapsed in the final civil war of the Republic, which led to Mark Antony's death (with Cleopatra) and Augustus' establishment of the Empire.

Tullianum The state prison in Rome's Forum. It had two floors, the lower being the underground dungeons where condemned prisoners were strangled or left to die of starvation.

Tyrants To the Greeks the tyrant was not a dictator in the modern sense, but rather an individual who had usurped authority and seized power and often acted as the champion of the people against an established aristocracy or plutocracy. Tyrannies flourished in the Hellenistic world in the 7th or 6th centuries B.C. It was only after democracy succeeded tyranny, *e.g.* in 5th century Athens, that the term came to be used pejoratively. Plato regarded tyranny as the worst form of government because the ruler was often susceptible to his own baser instincts. *See* **Pisistratids**.

V

Velites Roman light infantry. They were primarily used as slingers. Under the Marian reforms they were discarded and their place taken by *auxilia*.

Venationes Roman wild beast hunts introduced in the 2nd century B.C. *See* **Ludi** and **Gladiators**.

Vestal Virgins A Roman college of priestesses to the cult of Vesta, goddess of the hearth. They were selected by the Pontifex Maximus between the ages of six and ten and had to come from leading families. After a period of training they entered the college for a period of thirty years during which time they were required to remain virgins. The Pontifex Maximus supervised the college and the punishment for unchastity was burial alive. Their task was the perpetual one of keeping the sacred flame of Vesta and their residence was situated near her Temple in the Forum. The college existed until the 4th century A.D.

Via A Roman main street or high road. The most famous was the Via Appia built to link Rome and Capua in 312 B.C. Properly constructed roads were among the Romans' most important technological innovation and were vital for military security, allowing the rapid deployment of their small standing army all over the Empire. *See also* **Roman Roads, L106**.

Vigiles A force of 7,000 founded by Augustus as a fire brigade for Rome. It was composed of slaves and freedmen organised on paramilitary lines. Overall command was in the hands of the *praefectus vigilum*.

Vigintisexviri The name for the 26 minor magistrates who were responsible for the civic administration of Rome. Any prospective senator was required to have held one of these offices before entering the Senate itself, following a period of service as a military tribune. *See* **Cursus Honorum**.

Villa Originally a rural Italian residence, the centre of a farm or estate. The earliest villa comprised one room only (the later *tablinum* of the *domus*) and would have opened onto a farmyard of beaten earth. The term was subsequently applied to the rural retreats of the urban aristocracy, when the original villa was subjected to Greek influence and came to resemble the urban *domus*, with peristyle *etc.* Generally common to all rural villas throughout the Roman empire were features copied from Italy such as glass windows, mosaic floor and heating by hypocaust. Towards the fall of the Empire villas were frequently fortified sites.

Viminal One of Rome's hills between the Quirinal and the Esquiline.

Virtus The quality of masculinity which to the Romans implied the possession of self-discipline. Women did not possess *virtus* and were characterised by *impolentia sui*, an inability to control their own natures.

Votum A vow. It was a Greek and Roman practice to promise specified acts of devotion to the gods if they should grant certain favours. Magistrates might make vows on behalf of the state. During the Empire they were ritually made on behalf of the emperor's health by all classes.

Z

Zeugitai At Athens before the Solonic period, a name corresponding to 'farmers' and referring to those citizens of moderate income. Solon took it for the name of his third census class, applying it to those owning land sufficient to produce 200 bushels of agricultural produce a year. Most farmers and craftsmen were in this class and formed the hoplites of the Athenian army. From Cleisthenes' time they could be elected *strategoi* and, later on, archons.

SPECIAL TOPIC

ANCIENT EGYPT.

Introduction.

To the priests and guides of the XXVIIth Dynasty who supplied the ancient historian Herodotus (*c.* 480–425 B.C.) with much of the information about their country contained in the *Histories*, the IVth Dynasty Pharaohs who built the great pyramids were as remote as Julius Caesar is to us today. To the Greeks Egypt represented the ancient world, its priesthood reputedly possessed of closely-guarded knowledge drawing many to travel there. The following article outlines the long history of a civilisation whose technical accomplishments and antique grandeur still pose many questions.

Chronology of Dynastic Egypt *

Period	Dynasties	Approx Dates B.C.
Old Kingdom	I–II	3150–2700
Middle Kingdom	III–VI	2700–2200
New Kingdom	XII	1991–1785
Late Period	XVIII–XX	1552–1069
	XXV–XXX	747– 343

* Omitting three Intermediate Periods.

A Note on Chronology.

The division of the extensive period of Pharaonic rule in Egypt into dynasties originates with Manetho of Sebennytus, a Heliopolitan priest of the third century B.C. who wrote a history of his country in Greek, the *Egyptian Annals*. This work itself is not extant, but is known through the writings of Eusebius, Africanus and Josephus. Manetho's authorities were Egyptian temple records, and archaeology has indicated that his king-lists, if not his chronology, are fairly reliable. The further classification of the dynasties into periods such as the Old Kingdom and Intermediate Periods is comparatively recent and more arbitrary. Actual dates, in the earlier periods, are a matter of considerable uncertainty, constantly undergoing revision, and should by no means be regarded as precise.

Predynastic and Early Dynastic (Archaic) Egypt.

The world's longest river, the Nile, flows for over 4,000 miles to the Mediterranean Sea. Beyond the great cataracts its 750-mile course through Egypt discovers a land of contrasts. To the south Upper Egypt is closely girt by cliffs and desert, 600 miles long and just a few miles wide, while to the north Lower Egypt broadens into the fertile Delta as the river approaches the sea. Each year, swollen by rainfall in the mountains of Africa, the river flooded, depositing the rich black silt essential for agriculture. All life in Egypt from the earliest times was regulated by the annual rhythm of the Nile and Herodotus was entirely correct in describing Egypt itself as "the gift of the Nile". With a prevailing wind enabling travel under sail up-river (*i.e.*, southwards, against the current) the Nile also proved an efficient facilitator of communication and trade; furthermore, the papyrus reeds of the Delta were to provide an excellent writing material and a principal export commodity.

While climatic changes may have forced primitive attempts at farming as early as 12,000 B.C., it was not until *c.* 5000 B.C. that the 200,000-year-old Palaeolithic hunter-gatherer culture of the Nile Valley disappeared and its inhabitants adopted agricultural settlement and the domestication of animals. Neolithic Lower Egyptian settlements of the Early Predynastic Period such as Fayum 'A' and Merimde differed considerably from the contemporary Badarian culture of Upper Egypt, being less technologically and artistically developed. The Badarian culture of the south was succeeded by the first period of the important Naqada civilisation—a native development with links to its predecessor known as Naqada I (formerly termed Amratian; *c.* 4000–3600 B.C.). Development was gradual, until moves towards Dynastic civilisation were initiated by the advent of new arrivals to the south *c.* 3600 B.C., who imported new customs and new technology, resulting in stage II Naqada culture (formerly termed Gerzean). It is unlikely that the newcomers actually invaded Egypt, as has been suggested.

The Naqada Culture.

By the Unification period Naqada II cultural influence, and its later stage Naqada III, had dominated the south and also largely supplanted the more primitive Late Predynastic cultures of the north. Egyptian tradition has it that two rival kingdoms came into being, of Upper and Lower Egypt, their capitals at Hierakonpolis and Buto respectively, and that a powerful southern king Menes forcibly extended his control northwards, creating a unified state and founding the Ist Dynasty with a new capital at Memphis, near the old north–south border. It may be, however, that the Unification occurred more by natural evolution between 3300–3150 than by sudden force of arms at the latter date. The Ist Dynasty kings (*c.* 3150–2925 B.C.) were Narmer and Aha (both of whom have been identified with Menes) followed by Djer, Djet, Den, Adjib, Semerkhe and Qa'a. Interestingly, the Ist Dynasty may also have included a regnant queen, Merneith (Meryetnit). These rulers were buried at Abydos and much of our knowledge of the Early Dynastic Period is derived from these *mastaba* tombs. Excavation of non-funerary Archaic sites should soon increase. The Abydos tomb of Djer has furnished the Cairo Museum with the earliest royal jewellery of Egyptian antiquity. In the New Kingdom this already ancient tomb was declared to be the sepulchre of Osiris himself, Abydos being the pilgrimage-centre of the Osirian cult.

The ancient division of Egypt was never forgotten and the Pharaoh of much later times remained "king of the two lands". The Narmer Palette shows the king wearing both his own white (*Hedjet*) crown of the south and the red (*Deshert*) crown of the north. Eventually the double (*Pschent*) crown became the emblem of the Pharaohs of all Egypt. The symbolic institutions of Lower Egypt were not, therefore, simply replaced by those of the south.

The Expansion of Egyptian Power.

Aha evidently inherited a country sufficiently stable for him to have been able to apply himself to extending Egyptian control to the First Cataract, Djer pushing as far as the Second. Initially government continued in a dual form as before, but under the single divine authority of the Pharaoh as the incarnated god Horus of the royal solar cult. The administrative unit of Egypt prior even to Menes was the tribal *nome* (a Greek word = Egyptian *sepat*) of which there were finally 42. In addition, a sophisticated civil service existed in the Archaic Period to ensure equitable and efficient tax-collection. Each *nome* now had a governor assigned to it by the central administration, each of these *nomarchs* being required to supply soldiers for the national army, and a *nome*-based regimental structure probably existed. The *nomes* were not compelled to surrender their religious autonomy, each one possessing local deities particular to it. The Egyptian pantheon consequently retained many hundreds of ancient minor deities and underwent no simplification, as might have been expected as one result of a military unification of the country.

In trade, copper was imported from Sinai for use in tool-manufacture, although flint continued to be used for this purpose for some centuries. Timber for buildings was imported from Syria and Lebanon, while exporting to Byblos, Crete and Palestine is known by the IInd Dynasty.

The many early tombs at Abydos and Saqqara suggest continuous architectural and cultural development. The practice of mass sacrificial servant burials around the royal graves at Abydos appears to have lasted until the close of the 1st Dynasty. The conceived need to supply the deceased with worldly goods as well as food and drink (for his *ka*) in the next life was to result in tomb-plundering which led to increasingly elaborate and always unsuccessful methods of burial designed to foil the robbers.

Extant specimens of inscriptions from the period do not reveal a primitive written language, but one already developed. The earliest hieroglyphs show that phonetic characters were in use as well as a cursive form of the elaborate script. The concept of writing may have been brought in from Mesopotamia in the Late Predynastic Period. Much too of what is familiar in later Egyptian art and religious iconography was already fixed or part-developed by the period and many major cults well established.

Much of Egypt's future character was determined during the Late Predynastic (Naqada II and III) and Archaic Periods. Forms were established that were rigidly adhered to throughout later times, an Egyptian trait that has been criticised as a brake on invention and as creating a stagnant society and culture. Such a view, however, seems based on doubtful modern notions of "progress", and Egypt did indeed adapt when circumstances required it.

The Old Kingdom (Pyramid Age).

There is evidence during the IInd Dynasty (*c.* 2925–2700 B.C.) of civil disorder, apparently involving a conflict between the Horus cult and that of Set. One king changed his Horus name (one of three royal names then in use) Sekhemib to a Set name, Perabsen, but under the last king Khasekhemwy the troubles seem to have been settled on equal terms, for his name appears in a combined Horus-Set form, the *serekh* containing it being surmounted by the Typhonian animal in addition to the Horus falcon. His reign provided the domestic background necessary for the great leap forward of Dynasty III (*c.* 2700–2625 B.C.) which is generally taken as the first of the Old Kingdom as it marks the start of the Pyramid Age, a 500-year period of cultural development following the consolidation of political union. Netcherikhe-Djoser (-Zoser) was the Dynasty's second king, whose Step Pyramid at Saqqara with its great temple complex is Egypt's earliest known monument of stone construction, mud-brick and timber having been used in the main for earlier tombs. This was the innovation of Imhotep, Djoser's later-deified architect and a priest-astronomer of Annu (Heliopolis), with the title "Chief of the Observers". The pyramid-complex is testimony to the stability and increased resources of Memphite authority by the time of Dynasty III as well as a landmark in world architecture.

The sudden change from the step pyramids built by Djoser and his successors of the IIIrd Dynasty, which probably evolved from the stepped structures representing the primeval hillock of Atum found in Archaic tombs, to the true straight-sided pyramids is illustrated by the Meidum pyramid, built as a step pyramid either by Huni or Sneferu, but converted by Sneferu (first of the IVth Dynasty Pharaohs and father of Cheops) to a true pyramid at a later stage. Sneferu also built the Bent and Red pyramids at Dahshur. The reason for the change of form is unclear, but it was perhaps inspired by changed religious beliefs.

Just as absolute Pharaonic power reached a zenith during the Old Kingdom, so monumental stone architecture reached its acme under the great IVth Dynasty kings (*c.* 2625–2510 B.C.) who included the famed builders of the Gizeh pyramids Khufu (Cheops), Khafra (Chephren) and Menkaura (Mycerinos). The logistics involved in constructing these huge pyramids (the Great Pyramid contains over six million tons of rock and was originally 480 ft high) with just the simplest of tools continue to challenge explanation, but the technical superior-

ity of the IVth Dynasty builders can hardly be overstated. There are remains of some 90 pyramids in Egypt, yet those built during the Vth and VIth Dynasties were already greatly inferior to those of the IVth, although it is the pyramids of these later dynasties rather than the giants of the IVth Dynasty which contain the ancient Pyramid Texts, the oldest body of Egyptian religious writings. The pyramids at Saqqara of Unas (last of the Vth Dynasty kings), Teti, Pepi I, Merenra and Pepi II were among those found, chiefly by Gaston Maspero, to contain these carved and painted texts, thus uniquely preserved against the corruptions of copyists and later priestly recension.

Fresh debate currently surrounds these texts (believed to contain elements dating back to Predynastic times) which also involves the significance of the IVth Dynasty pyramids themselves. It has been long maintained that the texts (essentially magic spells to ensure the well-being of the king in the next life) and all pyramids were expressions of a predominantly solar religion. Some, however, recognising that the Pyramid Texts preserve a strong Osirian stellar element (gradually displaced by the solar) stress the importance of this element in connection with the IVth Dynasty, one ingenious theory even asserting that the IVth Dynasty Pharaohs were inspired by such astral beliefs to conceive at the outset a ground plan for their constructions at Gizeh, Dahshur and elsewhere, the three Gizeh pyramids designed to correspond to the stars Delta, Epsilon and Zeta Orionis (Orion's belt)—*i.e.*, a scheme to reproduce the celestial figure of Sahu-Orion, whom the Egyptians identified with Osiris, in the terrestrial Duat—the Memphite necropolis itself. Less controversially, fresh consideration is being given to the stellar alignments of the "ventilation-shafts" unique to the Great Pyramid, the southern two of which would indeed have aligned with Osiris-Orion and Isis-Sirius at the time the pyramid was constructed. Such intentional alignments allow the possibility of more accurate dating of monuments by taking into account the precessional effect. The matter of religion in the Pyramid Age is therefore one of great uncertainty, but growing debate. Astronomy will increasingly play a part in this field.

The cause of the fall of the IVth Dynasty is unknown, but it appears to have been attended by a progressive strengthening of the influence of the priesthood of Ra. At the end of the line Shepseskaf may have attempted to resist this growing Heliopolitan power-base. A religious-political upheaval evidently precipitated the rise of the Vth Dynasty kings who proceeded to erect sun temples, notably that of Niuserra near Abusir. Through some 260 years of the VIth Dynasty the Pharaohs' centralised power declined while that of the *nomarchs*, who had become independent, hereditary barons, increased, as did that of the priesthood. Pepi II was the Old Kingdom's last noteworthy Pharaoh, with a reputed reign of 90 years. Egypt then entered a dark age marked by invasion, famine, civil discord and the fragmentation of the country, an anarchic interval known as the First Intermediate Period. The lavish building of the past centuries and the upkeep of the royal mortuary temples must severely have drained Egypt's resources. In the ensuing disorder these tombs were plundered extensively.

The Middle Kingdom (Feudal Age).

Although Manetho documents Memphite kings of the VIIth and VIIIth Dynasties (*c.* 2200–2160 B.C.) during the early Intermediate Period, in truth their sphere of influence must have been relatively local. A (possibly considerable) measure of stability was maintained by the IXth and Xth Dynasties of Herakleopolis until a revolt led by the Theban *nomarch*, Intef I of Dynasty XI. Thus was government first exercised from Thebes in Upper Egypt, as yet an unremarkable provincial town, but destined to become Egypt's capital in the New Kingdom and one of the ancient world's great cities. Finally negating Herakleopolitan influence, Intef's third successor, the outstanding Mentuhotep II (Nebhepet-Ra), re-united Egypt *c.* 2040 B.C. and a cultural revival began, the XIth Dynasty closing with Mentuhotep IV (Nebtawi-Ra), whose Vizier founded the powerful XIIth Dynasty (*c.* 1991–1785 B.C.) as king Amenemhet (Ammenemes) I. Perhaps

T18

judging Thebes too distant from the fractious northern barons, Amenemhet established his capital city at Ithtawy, near Lisht, south of Memphis. Steps were taken to curb the *nomarchs* by appointing Thebans but because the Pharaoh, lacking the autocracy of the god-kings of Memphis, had now to rely on their co-operation to maintain order and had found it necessary to make grants of land to them, the Middle Kingdom—the classical period in Egyptian history—has been described as Egypt's Feudal Age. Its kings were the four Pharaohs Amenemhet and three called Sestrosis.

Sestrosis I built widely and extended the southern frontier to the Second Cataract where border fortresses were erected. Sestrosis III invaded Syria and largely restored royal control over the *nomarchs*. Gold was now available from the Nubian mines and work was undertaken, notably under Amenemhet III, a king of especial note who reigned for 45 years, on large scale irrigation and building projects. Amenemhet constructed the Labyrinth (his mortuary temple), seen and described by Strabo and Herodotus, at Hawara. Bronze was now widely used and foreign trade flourished.

During the years of anarchy the old assurances had vanished. A new literature born of the Intermediate Period shows awareness of the ever-present threat of disorder, of the overthrow of Maat. Some is deeply pessimistic, while some stresses the need for the kind treatment of the poor by their rulers, a significant departure from Old Kingdom attitudes.

This evolving sense of social justice was characteristic of the Middle Kingdom, while religion saw the popularisation of the cult of Osiris and the conception of the god as a judge of the dead, as well as the commencement of the rise of the minor Theban god Amon to a position of national pre-eminence as Amon-Ra. The idea of *post mortem* accountability for one's sins has obvious parallels in Christian beliefs, as, indeed, have the death and resurrection of Osiris. Any person, no longer just the Pharaoh and his favourites, who could afford the ritual apparatus could now secure the burial necessary to ensure after-life habitation in Osiris' kingdom, the Field of Reeds. Thus an expanded and revised religious literature (developed from the exclusively royal Pyramid Texts) was now inscribed in ordinary wooden coffins in the hieratic script, consequently being known today as the Coffin Texts. As this process of "democratization" continued into the New Kingdom, there evolved the best-known collection of these funerary texts, the 192 "Chapters of Coming Forth By Day", better known as the Book of the Dead, found on papyri in Theban and Saïte Recensions. The Middle Kingdom work *The Story of Sinuhe*, as well as exemplifying a flourishing classical literature in prose and verse, illustrates the great importance that Egyptians attached to proper burial in their own land by Egyptian priests. As to royal burial, while the XIth Dynasty rulers, remaining in Upper Egypt, constructed no pyramids but elaborate southern tombs, the XIIth Dynasty Pharaohs of Ithtawy did so—doubtless impressed by the awe-inspiring sight of the monuments of their Old Kingdom predecessors.

The New Kingdom (The Empire).

Egypt's Middle Kingdom, like the Old, ended with the gradual decay of central control and the fragmentation of the country under ineffectual rulers. Dynasties XIII–XVII (*c.* 1785–1553 B.C.) comprise the Second Intermediate Period (XI and XIII are sometimes included in the Middle Kingdom). This time, there was a new threat from the Hyksos, Semitic Asiatics from Palestine who overran the Delta and whose kings formed Dynasties XV and XVI. Possessed of superior weaponry, the Hyksos kings retained their Egyptian foothold for 150 years and extended their rule much further south. Only by adopting the foreigners' new weapons would the Egyptians be able to expel them. In particular, the Hyksos introduced the horse-drawn war-chariot which would later help the Egyptians to acquire an empire. While the Hyksos ruled from Avaris, distant Thebes retained some autonomy. The last king of the XVIIth (Theban) Dynasty Kamose repulsed the Hyksos to the Delta and they were finally pushed out into Palestine by Ahmose (Amasis) I, founder of the remarkable

XVIIIth Dynasty (*c.* 1552–1295 B.C.). This was the era of the Homeric warfare of the late Bronze Age, and in Egypt of the warrior-Pharaoh. From the XVIIth Dynasty the Blue or War Crown (*khepresh*) became a royal emblem.

The XVIIIth Dynasty.

The XVIIIth Dynasty comprises some of Egypt's most famous rulers, among them: Amenhotep (Amenophis) I, son of Ahmose; Tuthmosis (Thothmes) I, the first king to adopt a tomb hewn in the Valley of the Kings, burial-place of Dynasties XVIII–XX; Tuthmosis II and his queen Hatshepsut ("the first great woman in history"); Tuthmosis III, "the Napoleon of Ancient Egypt" who secured an empire that reached from the Sudan to the Euphrates; Amenhotep III, whose leisured reign saw Egypt at the height of her prosperity; his co-regent and son Amenhotep IV, better known as Akhenaten, with his beautiful queen, Nefertiti (Neferneferuaten); and Nebkheperure-Tutankhamen. Their Cyclopean buildings, including the terraced temple of Hatshepsut at Deir el-Bahri, the temple at Luxor and much of the temple of Amon at Karnak, are among Egypt's most celebrated monuments. There was close contact with the flourishing civilisation of Crete (Late Minoan I, II) at this period, the Minoans trading from Komo to the Delta area. Egypt was a centre of Mediterranean maritime commerce—much Mycenaean pottery has been found at Tell el-Amarna.

The empire was born of the necessity of protecting against further intrusions such as that of the Hyksos. The Nile Valley profited culturally by exposure to fresh influences as well as in terms of material wealth. Literature continued to thrive: from the Late New Kingdom the narrative *The Voyage of Wenamun* relates the adventures and misadventures of a rather pompous Egyptian traveller at a time when Egypt's prestige had waned.

Expansion underwent a 20-year setback when Hatshepsut as regent of the young Tuthmosis III usurped supreme power and avoided further military conquest. She is sometimes referred to as "the female king", for she adopted all the masculine trappings of the Pharaohs, even the symbolic false beard. Volumes have been written concerning the phenomenon of the "heretic" Amenhotep IV, inheritor and fanatical developer of the ephemeral monotheistic cult of the Aten at Tell el-Amarna. More interested, like his parent, in religious reform than in emulating the military conquests of his predecessors, Amenhotep IV continued his father's stance against the powerful priesthood of Amon. Abandoning Thebes after Amenhotep III's death, he transported his capital to a new city 200 miles away which he called Akhet-Aten ("The Horizon of the Aten") and changed his own name to Akhenaten (Ikhnaton). All other cults were zealously suppressed.

The Boy-King Tutankhamen.

The Amarna Period in art is notable for a striking (and inelegant) departure from long-established conventions, typically showing the king with his queen and daughters in a more humanised, domestic setting. However, after little over a decade in the new city Akhenaten died, succeeded by the boy-prince Tutankhaten. (The position of a possible co-regent Smenkhkare is unclear.) After Nefertiti's death government reverted to Thebes and the young king was renamed Tutankhamen, heralding the official restoration of the Theban deity. Akhet-Aten was abandoned, and the one ill-considered attempt in its history to reform Egyptian religion had failed. Tutankhamen's significance, therefore, lies in his role as a pawn in the Theban restoration. In other respects he was a minor king, probably crowned at the age of nine and dying at 18. His latter-day fame, of course, rests entirely on the sensation surrounding his tomb's discovery and opening by Howard Carter and Lord Carnarvon in 1922, some 3,300 years after being sealed by the Theban priests, and on the breathtaking funerary artefacts found to have escaped the ancient robbers. The discovery of a major subterranean tomb-complex at Saqqara in 1986—that of Maya, a senior official under Tutankhamen—showed that Egypt's sands still hold secrets.

With the end of the imperial line, Egypt's throne was occupied by General Horemheb, a violent reactionary who set about effacing all traces of the Aten cult. The empire had suffered since the reign of Amenhotep III, who had none of the fighting spirit of the Tuthmosids—particularly during the Amarna interlude. The Asiatic provinces fell away as a new menace, the Hittites, capitalised on Egyptian apathy; it fell to Seti (Sethos) I, of Dynasty XIX (c. 1295–1188 B.C.) to attempt the recovery of Syria. Seti I was one of the great warrior-kings. His superbly decorated tomb, with its famous ceiling of stars, is the most outstanding ever discovered in the Valley of the Kings, though like many it is now subject to an alarmingly accelerated level of decay.

Dynasties XIX and XX are those of the 11 kings named Ramesses; Ramesses II (Usimare), son of Seti, was a prolific builder (including the Rameseum and the temple-complex and four 67-foot-high statues at Abu-Simbel). Unlike the pyramid-building Pharaohs, Ramesses the Great used slave labour, now available in the form of prisoners of war. It may be that his labourers included the Hebrews, for Ramesses is the Pharaoh associated with the Biblical Exodus, and he is the poet Shelley's Ozymandias: "Look on my works, ye Mighty, and despair!"

The Hittite Wars.

Ramesses II's 67-year reign had opened with optimism, the ostentatious monuments attesting to no small confidence. Yet, by the death of Ramesses XI at the end of Dynasty XX (c. 1069 B.C.) Egypt's empire was lost, her decline now manifest. Ramesses II eventually signed a peace treaty—the first such recorded in history—with the Hittite Hattusilis III who was by then concerned with the Assyrian threat and took a daughter of Hattusilis as a royal wife further to establish good relations. Hostilities had reached their peak at the battle of Qadesh (c. 1275 B.C.) in which Ramesses narrowly averted the destruction of his forces. The Hittite Empire was broken c. 1200 B.C., according to the Egyptians by the same "Sea Peoples" who menaced them. In fact, it was probably by the Phrygians.

The Hittite Wars had drained Egypt and now she was compelled to look not to foreign conquest but to domestic security. Ramesses III's (Dynasty XX) much-vaunted repulsion of the attacks of the Sea Peoples, a century after Qadesh, is recorded in his mortuary temple at Medinet Habu, and highlights momentous developments outside Egypt, being a repercussive effect of a period of raiding and mass-migration during which Bronze Age Mycenaean culture was passing into legend and a Dark Age ensuing—the prologue to the drama of later Greek civilisation. The Near East was undergoing radical change. In short, the Iron Age was poised to overtake Egypt. Ramesses III's victory was a great one, but it was Egypt's last such triumph. His successors Ramesses IV–XI were kings of diminishing significance. Dynasties XXI–XXIV are sometimes designated the Third Intermediate Period (and XXV–XXX the Late Period; otherwise XXI–XXX comprise the Late Dynastic Period). Egypt was again divided and nevermore a major imperial power, yet her unique and stubbornly conservative culture remained intact during the foreign occupations that attended her thousand-year decline.

Late Dynastic and Graeco-Roman Egypt.

The threat of invasion to the Delta had necessitated the return of Egypt's capital to the north (to Piramesse, at Avaris) during Dynasty XIX and following the latest division of the country the priesthood of Amon governed Upper Egypt from Thebes, while Tanite Dynasty XXI (capital Tanis; 1069–945 B.C.) controlled Lower Egypt. This political situation was stabilised by intermarriage, but Egypt's influence abroad remained extremely limited. Tomb-robbery, rife since the time of the later Ramessides, continued in the Valley of the Kings.

Tutankhamen's tomb alone was overlooked, its entrance fortuitously concealed by debris excavated during the construction of the tomb of Ramesses VI directly above it. Priests, valley-guards and high officials connived in the plunder, but not all were corrupt and it was finally decided that the royal remains be collectively buried in secret locations. In 1881 a major cache of mummies was discovered at Deir el-Bahri, including those of the great Pharaohs Tuthmosis III, Seti I and Ramesses II.

Shoshenq I, founder of Dynasty XXII (945–715 B.C.), appears in 1 Kings 14.25 as "Shishak, king of Egypt" leading an invasion of Palestine after Rehoboam had succeeded Solomon—Egypt's first such expedition for three centuries. Shoshenq's family were Bubastite Libyan immigrants who had risen to prominence. His capital remained Tanis and for a century Egyptian prestige in the Near East recovered markedly but hopes for a new age of empire were not to be fulfilled. Shoshenq's successors gradually lost their grip on the country amid complex inter-dynastic feuding.

Egypt lay split into several factions and open to conquest. In a reversal of her former domination of Nubia, Egypt was now herself conquered by the lords of Napata below the Fourth Cataract who formed the Kushite XXVth Dynasty (747–656 B.C.), of which Piankhi (Py), Shabaka, Shabataka, Taharqa (2 Kings 19.9) and Tantamani were kings. Long influenced by Egyptian culture but insulated from Egypt's latest decline, Nubia's ascendency led not to an undermining of Egyptian tradition, but to a resurgence of Amonian conservatism. Particularly in sculpture, something of an artistic revival commenced, and these kings built small royal pyramid tombs—the first in 800 years. The past was keenly studied. From this period date the important Shabaka Texts, also known as the Memphite Theology—an engraved copy of crumbling Old Kingdom documents made at Shabaka's instigation to preserve the ancient texts for perpetuity, now in the British Museum.

The Rule of Psammetichus.

The Kushites were expelled with difficulty by Esarhaddon and Ashurbanipal during the expansion of Assyria. Memphis was taken in 671, again in 667 and Thebes was sacked in 664 (Nahum 3.8–10). The Assyrian overlords installed a Saïte prince, one Psammetichus, as Governor of Egypt who subsequently expelled their garrisons with the help of Greek, Lydian and Carian mercenaries, founding the Saïte XXVIth Dynasty (centres at Saïs and Memphis; 664–525 B.C.) as king Psammetichus (Psamtik) I. Nineveh fell to the Medes and Babylonians in 612. Psammetichus' commercial adroitness laid the foundations for a period of considerable prosperity with Egypt becoming a major producer of grain. While some dismiss the "Saïte Revival" as a decadent evocation of greater days, others detect a genuine cultural renaissance, albeit one fashioned on the past, during this 140-year "Pharaonic Indian summer".

Psammetichus was succeeded after 54 years by Necho II who commenced work on a canal to link the Nile and the Red Sea (completed by the Persians) and his Phoenician sailors successfully circumnavigated Africa. Psammetichus II reigned for just six years but set keenly about restoring Egypt's temples and again made use of Greek mercenaries. Ahmose (Amasis) II actively encouraged Greek settlement and links were strengthened by the granting of Naucratis as a trade-colony.

Saïte rule ended with the defeat of Psammetichus III at Pelusium by Cambyses' Persian forces in 525 B.C. and Egypt's addition to the conquests of Cyrus, but the open policy of Dynasty XXVI had anticipated Ptolemaic rule and allowed an important early Graeco-Egyptian interaction. The extent of Egypt's contribution to western civilisation via the Greeks is uncertain. Geometry and astronomy were both priestly disciplines and medicine is another area of likely influence—parallels between the Corpus Hippocraticum and Egyptian texts such as the Ebers and Edwin Smith Medical Papyri have been suggested, and Egyptian physicians were certainly admired by the Greeks for their skill. Abstract philosophy and empirical science, however, were provinces of Greek and not Egyptian thinking and caution is required in seeking Egyptian origins, for it became conventional for biographers to ascribe formative "studies in Egypt" to Greek *savants*, whether or not such studies had actually been undertaken.

Achaemenid Persian domination (Dynasty XXVII) persisted under Darius I, Xerxes I, Artaxerxes I and Darius II, but was successfully resisted by Dynasties XXVIII–XXX (404–343 B.C.). Dynasty XXX was Egypt's last taste of independent prosperity, during which extensive building works were carried out. The defeat of Egypt's last native Pharaoh Nectanebo II by the Persian Artaxerxes III (Ochus) in 343, some 2,800 years after the founding of the Ist Dynasty, might be said to mark the end of Ancient Egyptian history. Alexander's campaigns against Darius III and conquest of Egypt in 332 brought to an end the world of the Ancient Near East and mark the start of the Graeco-Roman Period in Egypt.

After Alexander's death in 323 Alexandria became the capital of the Ptolemies (Ptolemies I–XV; 304–30 B.C.). Alexander, Philip Arrhidaeus and Alexander IV are sometimes designated Dynasty XXXI, and the Ptolemies Dynasty XXXII. The Alexandrian Library established by Ptolemy I (Soter) grew into the greatest library of Antiquity; Ptolemy II (Philadelphus) founded the Museum (*Mouseion*) and Egyptian Alexandria became the foremost intellectual centre of the Hellenistic Age. The temples of Horus at Edfu, of Sebek and Haroeris at Kom Ombo and of Hathor at Dendera belong to the Ptolemaic period. Greek was now the administrative language of Egypt but elements of the Egyptian language, written in the Greek alphabet, were to survive in the form of Coptic.

The Coming of the Romans.

Roman involvement in Egypt deepened when Ptolemy XII (Auletes) sought recognition for his claim to the throne. His daughter Cleopatra VII (a Ptolemy, and therefore a Macedonian and not an Egyptian) famously involved herself with both Caesar and Mark Antony, having children by both men. Her aim was to revive the confused Ptolemaic succession and to secure the throne for herself and Caesarion, her son by Caesar, but her hopes were dashed by Octavian's victory over Antony at Actium in 31 B.C. after which both he and she committed suicide.

Octavian became Augustus and Egypt a Roman province, her great natural resources and the accumulated wealth of the Ptolemies making her a most valuable acquisition. As the "granary of Rome" her security was essential to the stability of the empire, but Egypt was to be ruined by Rome's increasing demands. Egyptian cults, particularly those of Isis and Osiris (the latter as Serapis) remained popular in the empire until their suppression by the Christians. Cynegius, Praetorian Prefect A.D. 384–8, sanctioned the destruction of Egyptian temples and in 392 paganism was officially proscribed by Theodosius.

All knowledge of the hieroglyphic language was lost by the fifth century and remained so until 1822, when, having recognised the significance of Coptic, the French philologist Jean François Champollion (1790–1832) published the *Lettre à M. Dacier relative à l'alphabet des hiéroglyphs phonétiques* that finally opened the way to the study of the Egyptian texts and of the civilisation of Ancient Egypt itself.

THE CINEMA

This section provides a brief but authoritative introduction to the world of the cinema. It includes sections on how the cinema has evolved, notes on the major directors, actors and actresses and a brief glossary of terms which anyone who enjoys the cinema will find of value. There are lists of the famous names who have won the coveted "Oscar" awards for Best Actor, Best Actress and Best Film.

TABLE OF CONTENTS

THE CINEMA

The cinema is the newest arrival among major art-forms—exactly one hundred years have elapsed since its invention by the Lumière brothers in 1895—and it is the last to gain widespread acceptance as such. Many still regard it as simply an escapist medium of mass entertainment. The purpose of this section is not only to provide basic information on major actors and directors, so that their work can be placed in some sort of overall context, but also to attempt to map out the developments—artistic, economic and technical—that have characterised the medium and influenced the course of its multiple and complex development.

I. THE EVOLUTION OF THE CINEMA

The Technical Background

The cinema brought to fruition a long-standing entertainment dream, the "moving picture"—suggestions of which go right back to the Bayeux Tapestry—which was popular with Victorian children in such forms as the Zoëtrope (Wheel of Life), featuring a cylinder with slats cut in and a piece of paper or tissue inside with drawings of, for example, a horse; as the inner layer was rotated, the horse would appear to gallop past the slats.

For the cinema as we know it today to develop, it was necessary for two fundamental principles to coincide: that of the persistence of vision (whereby an after-image of an object remains on the retina after the object itself has disappeared), and that whereby still images following one another in rapid succession give the impression of movement. Zoëtropes, What-the-Butler-Saw machines and other devices abounded towards the end of the nineteenth century, foreshadowing the first exhibition of "moving pictures" for admission money by the Lumière brothers from Lyon in 1895. The brothers owned a factory that manufactured cameras and photographic equipment, and envisaged the motion picture primarily as an extension and promotion of this. Their work, mostly documentary with a number of comic or light dramatic set-pieces, is seen as a major precursor of realism (q.v.) in the cinema. Roughly contemporary with them was the magician Georges Méliès, who made the first trick films, using a variety of special effects to tell ludicrous but entertaining science-fiction and pseudo-historical tales.

Despite many short-lived innovations (such as three-dimensional cinema, which necessitated the wearing of a special pair of spectacles), the technical battery of cinema has remained in many respects remarkably moderate. Special effects (as in Stanley Kubrick's *2001: A Space Odyssey* of 1968), the development of sophisticated animation techniques, quadrophonic sound in certain large city-centre cinemas, and an increasingly sophisticated range of colour techniques are all quantitative rather than qualitative modifications, and plans to enlarge the sensory battery of cinema through pumping appropriate scents in the cinema (and even providing spectators with suitable tactile stimuli) have remained in the realms of science-fiction. The major date in the history of the medium remains 1927, the year of the first sound film (*The Jazz Singer*, with Al Jolson). Sound was fiercely resisted for a long time (by Charlie Chaplin among others), but its possibilities were so rapidly recognised, not least by René Clair and Alfred Hitchcock who both made early innovatory use of it, that its survival was never long in jeopardy.

Introduction of Colour

Film-prints were tinted from the earliest days (a fact worth bearing in mind nowadays when we tend to think of all silent films as plain monochrome), but colour of a high technical standard did not become widely used until after the Second World War. Here the pattern is much more complex than with sound; many films still use black-and-white, not out of hostility to colour but because of its possibilities for producing a stylised, non-realistic

effect (as in Resnais's *Last Year in Marienbad* of 1961), or a sense of nostalgia (Woody Allen's *Manhattan* of 1979). Colour is also often used non-naturalistically, to evoke a mood or suggest a fantasy (as in Antonioni's *The Red Desert* of 1964 and—arguably—Hitchcock's *Marnie* of 1964), or to suggest a process of ironic distancing from a set of stylistic conventions (as with the deliberately lurid colours in Douglas Sirk's melodramas). Its use in most commercial films, alas, is often unimaginative and automatic, but it has shown that it can become a rich and important part of cinematic language, even when coexisting in the same film with black-and-white (Eisenstein's *Ivan the Terrible*, Part Two, 1945, Lelouch's *A Man and a Woman*, 1966, though in both films the reasons for the mixing of colour and monochrome were financial rather than aesthetic).

The Years of the "Big Screen"

The fifties and early sixties in Hollywood have come to be remembered as the years of the Big Screen—Cinerama, Cinemascope, and Todd-AO. All are variants of the expansion of the screen into a curved oblong. The initial tendency was for large-scale blockbusters (as exemplified by Cecil B. de Mille) to dominate, but these soon began to pall, and the big screen has shown itself capable of handling the cinema of analytical scrutiny (cf. Godard's *Pierrot le Fou* of 1965) as well as that of spectacular action. Colour, screen-size, and sound remain the three fundamental technical facets of the celluloid image.

MAJOR DATES AND THEIR SIGNIFICANCE

1895

On 28 December, the Lumière brothers gave the first paying show of films, at the Grand Café in Paris—a programme of documentary and comedy shorts which is still popular with film-society audiences today.

1896

2 February—the Lumière programme screened at the Regent Street Polytechnic in London, the first film-show in Britain.

1910

D. W. Griffith made a film in California, to escape the rigours of America's Eastern climate—the beginning of what was to become Hollywood.

1914

Charlie Chaplin signed a contract that gave him over $1000 per week—the highest-paid star in screen history up to this point.

1924

Formation of Metro-Goldwyn-Mayer by the amalgamation of three existing trusts. Eisenstein's first feature *Strike* crystallised the concern for film shown by the Bolshevik régime in Russia.

1925

First sign that the Scandinavian industries, second only to the USA at one point, would not be able to retain their supremacy; director Mauritz Stiller and actress Greta Garbo left Sweden for Hollywood. Eisenstein produced his first masterpiece, *The Battleship Potemkin* (see *montage*).

1927

Al Jolson's "You ain't heard nothing yet" in *The Jazz Singer*, the first words spoken on a film soundtrack.

1929

The Great Depression hit the American stock market. Because of the recent advent of sound and the tendency for people to spend more on entertainment in periods of recession, the cinema was one of the few sectors of the economy not to feel its worst effects. The German industry became the most commercially successful in Europe.

1933

Roosevelt elected President of the United States. His socially conscious "New Deal" had repercussions on the film industry, which turned increasingly away from escapist vehicles and towards films "with a social conscience".

1934

Foundation of the Legion of Decency in the USA to act as a self-appointed ethical police force for the cinema. Following on the Hays Code of twelve years earlier, which severely restricted controversial subject-matter, this inaugurated a period of extreme prudery and striving after respectability in Hollywood.

1939

The outbreak of the Second World War was marked by the banning of Renoir's *La Règle du Jeu* in France and the departure of many European directors for Hollywood. Fritz Lang had already left Germany in 1936; Renoir left France in 1940.

1940

The British Ministry of Information took over the GPO Film Unit and proceeded to sponsor a major series of wartime documentaries.

1941

Germany invaded Russia, and the entire Soviet industry turned itself over to the war effort. Orson Welles and John Huston meanwhile made their débuts in a relatively unaffected Hollywood with *Citizen Kane* and *The Maltese Falcon* respectively.

1942

Marcel Carné began work on *Les Enfants du Paradis* which took three years to make. One of the reasons for this was that it kept cast and production-team away from the fighting. First use of the term "neo-realism" (*q.v.*) by the Italian critic Umberto Barbaro.

1946

Hollywood began long-term decline.

1947

The decline was further accentuated by the campaign of persecution and harassment launched by Senator McCarthy to root "Communists" (*i.e.* liberals) out of the industry. The investigation begun on 18 October wreaked enormous personal, financial, and artistic havoc.

1948

French critic Alexandre Astruc predicted that the cinema would become "a means of writing just as flexible and subtle as written language", in an article that would have a tremendous effect on New Wave (*q.v.*) directors.

1949

Henry Cornelius's *Passport to Pimlico* inaugurated the immensely successful series of "Ealing comedies", whose humour and superb cast of character-actors ensured their enduring success.

1951

Kurosawa's *Rashomon* introduced the West to Japanese cinema.

1952

Invention of "three-D".

1959

Truffaut's *Les Quatre Cents Coups* and Godard's *Breathless* inaugurated what came to be known as the French "New Wave".

1960

Antonioni's *L'Avventura* was successful at the Cannes Film Festival despite noisy barracking. Hitchcock's *Psycho* was launched with publicity almost as harrowing as the film itself.

1961

Luis Buñuel was invited to return to Spain; he did so with *Viridiana*, which threw the Franco régime into a rage and survived only through a copy smuggled out.

1964

Dreyer's *Gertrud* was barbarically barracked at its première in Paris. This may well have contributed to its director's death four years later.

1968

The year of the Russian invasion of Czechoslovakia, the intensification of protest against the American war in Vietnam, the "May events" in Paris, and the worldwide upsurge of the libertarian "New Left" had important repercussions for the cinema in France (where film-makers took part in strikes and occupations, caused the closure of the Cannes Festival, and attempted an ambitious revision of their own industry), and in the United States, where the youth-rebellion movie of the fifties took on a new lease of life (see the success of *Easy Rider* the following year).

1975

Steven Spielberg shoots the biggest box-office success of all time with *Jaws*; it is beaten first by George Lucas's *Star Wars* in 1977, then by Spielberg's own *Close Encounters of the Third Kind* later the same year. Nagisa Oshima's *Ai No Corrida/Empire of the Senses*, a Franco-Japanese coproduction, is harassed in many countries (including Japan) for its erotic and political frankness, and at the same time hailed as a masterpiece.

1980

A new version of Abel Gance's *Napoleon*, reconstructed by the film-maker and historian, Kevin Brownlow, is shown to great acclaim in England, reviving an interest in silent film classics and their restoration for proper exhibition.

1982

Spielberg's *E.T. The Extra-Terrestrial* becomes the most commercially successful film ever made.

1987

Bernardo Bertolucci's *The Last Emperor* becomes the first Western film to be shot in Beijing (Peking). It coincides with a new Western interest in Chinese film, after recent festival successes by a new generation of film-makers emerging from the Beijing Film School.

Krzysztof Kieslowski's *A Short Film About Killing* (U.S. title: *Thou Shalt Not Kill*) is voted best film at the first European Film Awards.

1991

Britain's most honoured film-maker, Sir David Lean dies.

1993

Record-breaking box-office success of Steven Spielberg's film *Jurassic Park*.

1994

Steven Spielberg's *Schindler's List*, a harrowing account of the holocaust, receives great acclaim, winning numerous Oscars.

2. THE LEADING CINEMA DIRECTORS

Woody Allen (b. 1935)

Woody Allen first achieved star status as an actor in movies he himself directed, playing a walking worry-bead who wore his urban anxiety like a red badge of courage. Films like *Take the Money and Run* (1969), *Bananas* (1971) and *Love and Death* (1975) seemed to align him with prior film farceurs like his favourite, Bob Hope. Since then he has become more ambitious and intellectual, with films such as *Annie Hall* (1977) and *Stardust Memories* (1980) being anguished as well as amusing self-portraits, and *Interiors* (1978) being a study of family breakdown closer to Chekhov than Chaplin. Films such as *Zelig* (1983) and *The Purple Rose of Cairo* (1985) have shown him to be the technical equal of any contemporary American director, whilst *Hannah and her Sisters* (1986) and *Crimes and Misdemeanours* (1989) have the philosophical density of a Russian novel. He has become a rare phenomenon in modern cinema; prolific, unpredictable and artistically consistent, and someone whose films must be seen by anyone who cares for modern cinema and its development and modern civilisation and its discontents.

Robert Altman (b. 1925)

Innovative, iconoclastic director who shot to prominence with the military comedy *M:A:S:H* (1970), and then proceeded to subvert some of America's major film genres, notably in his western *McCabe and Mrs. Miller* (1971), which was more about the rise of capitalism than the growth of civilisation, and in his private-eye movie, *The Long Goodbye* (1973), where he debunked Raymond Chandler's knight-errant hero, Philip Marlowe. His epic and ironic fresco on the American Dream, *Nashville* (1975) was a highpoint of his career. Since then he has become ever more esoteric and experimental. Nevertheless, in films like his imaginative realisation of the play, *Come Back to the Five and Dime, Jimmy Dean, Jimmy Dean* (1982), and the made-for-TV biopic of Van Gogh, *Vincent and Theo* (1990), he has shown he can still spring some surprises. His Hollywood satire, *The Player* (1992) was his most acclaimed film for a decade.

Michelangelo Antonioni (b. 1912)

Antonioni was the director who made alienation fashionable in the early 1960s with his trilogy *L'Avventura* (1960), *La Notte* (1961) and *The Eclipse* (1962), which explored the gap between his characters' material affluence and their spiritual impoverishment. He also gave alienation a palpable visual form, each shot an eloquent comment on the tension between protagonist and environment. These films remain his greatest achievement, and in Monica Vitti he found a leading lady whose haunted performances greatly enhanced the emotional impact of his work. His other major films include *Le Amiche—The Girl Friends* (1955), *The Red Desert* (1964), *Blow-Up* (1966) and *The Passenger* (1975).

Ingmar Bergman (b. 1918)

The definitive example of the film artist, by virtue of the maturity and complexity of his themes and of the control he has had over all aspects of his films—writing, casting *etc.* Since he established his international reputation with a trio of masterly works in the 1950s—*Smiles of a Summer Night*

(1955), *The Seventh Seal* (1956) and *Wild Strawberries* (1957)—he has enjoyed almost complete creative freedom. Films like *The Seventh Seal*, *Through a Glass Darkly* (1960) and *Winter Light* (1962) test the validity of an individual's religious faith in a world of fearful cruelty, whilst a masterpiece like *Persona* (1966) is a revelatory study of character and creativity, superbly acted by Bibi Andersson and Liv Ullmann. There are those who criticise Bergman for the narrowness of his social range, his limited political vision, his spiritual masochism. But to Bergman the camera eye is the window of the soul and few have probed more deeply to the roots of human personality. And it is not all Scandinavian gloom. In *Fanny and Alexander* (1983), he created a wonderful reminder of his story-telling gifts, his rich visual sense, and his capacity to embrace life with all its pain, perils, and pleasures. His autobiography, *The Magic Lantern* was published in 1988; and his screenplay about the early life of his parents, *Best Intentions* (1992) was memorably filmed by Bille August.

Bernardo Bertolucci (b. 1940)

The Italian Communist Party evolved in the seventies the conception of the "historic compromise"—a tactical alliance on the part of a self-styled revolutionary party with progressive reformist forces. Bertolucci's aesthetic strategy can be seen as an (unconscious?) embodiment of this—a "message" of revolution often clothed in the glossy, star-studded forms of bourgeois Hollywood cinema (as in the two-part *1900* of 1976). Likewise, in *Last Tango in Paris* (1972), the brutal sexual frankness for which the film rapidly became notorious is cushioned by the reassuring Hollywood deep-orange glow in which the scenes are shot and the presence of attested Hollywood rebel Marlon Brando as the initiator. He won an Oscar for the opulent epic, *The Last Emperor* (1987), but his best films to date are his early works—*Before the Revolution* (1964), *The Spider's Stratagem* (1970), *The Conformist* (1970)—which combine an incisive political and psychological analysis with a poetic and lyrical style.

Robert Bresson (b. 1907)

The most reclusive and rigorous of French directors, expressing his religious themes through a style of pared-down purity. He rejects plot and for the most part uses non-professional actors, because acting is for the theatre, he believes, and what he is after is inner truth. His most famous film is *Diary of a Country Priest* (1950), but other works such as *A Man Escaped* (1956), *Pickpocket* (1959), *Balthazar* (1966) and *L'Argent* (1982) express his individuality equally strongly.

Luis Buñuel (1900–1983)

Buñuel began his career by collaborating with Salvador Dali on a surrealist short, *Un Chien Andalou* (1928) and then scandalised audiences with *L'Age d'Or* (1930), which attacked the Church ("Thank God I'm an atheist", Buñuel declared) and bourgeois morality (which Buñuel always found deeply immoral). A powerful, hallucinatory film about violence and poverty in the slums, *Los Olvidados* (1950) launched a second phase of his career, and his religious assaults were continued in *El* (1953), which equated religious orthodoxy with emotional repression, and *Nazarin* (1959) and *Viridiana* (1961), which showed the impossibility of a modern Christ surviving in today's society. In his final years, he took pleasure not so much in savaging the bourgeoisie as in, metaphorically speaking, poisoning their food, serving them a dainty cultural dish with a sinister undertaste. *Belle de Jour* (1967), *Tristana* (1970) and *The Discreet Charm of the Bourgeoisie* (1972) are all slyly subversive, surreal works, dealing with the split between appearance and reality, decorum and desire. He believed man was unconsciously a slave to custom and to social orthodoxy and, with his enthusiasm for symbols and the world of dreams, which reveal the hidden fears and desires of modern man, Buñuel did everything in his power to shock man out of his complacency. His impish spirit was also revealed in his appropriately liberating autobiography, *My Last Breath*, published in 1983.

Frank Capra (1897–1991)

The films of Sicilian-born Frank Capra embodied the American Dream. His major works were comedies with a strong moral lesson, and their message of optimism over adversity cheered up audiences during the Depression. His films were essentially variations on David and Goliath, with the common man victorious over seemingly insurmountable odds. His main characters, such as Gary Cooper's Mr. Deeds in *Mr. Deeds Goes To Town* (1936) or James Stewart's Mr. Smith in *Mr Smith Goes to Washington* (1939) were innocent idealists who vanquished the cynical, the crooked and the corrupt. After winning three directing Oscars in the 1930s, Capra never recovered his popularity after World War Two and retired after *A Pocketful of Miracles* in 1961. His testament is the aptly entitled *It's A Wonderful Life* (1946), a beautiful fantasy, with dark undertones, on the typical Capra theme that no man is born a failure.

Marcel Carné (b. 1909)

He occupied a role in the immediately pre-war cinema in many ways similar to that of Antonioni in the early sixties—the poet of an age's style of despair, whose fatalism receives tangible support and embodiment from the skilful use of decor and architecture. In Carné's case these were entirely studio-bound (his mature masterpieces eschewed location filming entirely), which may be one reason why his output has dated compared with, say, Renoir's. But *Quai des Brumes* (1938) and *Le Jour Se Leve* (1939) provide atmospheric frameworks for the acting of Jean Gabin, and *Les Enfants du Paradis* (1945), the three-and-a-half-hour tale of lost love and cynicism in the theatrical world of nineteenth-century Paris, remains exciting through its amalgam of "period" style and a tortured consciousness (particularly in the person of the poet and criminal Lacenaire) evocative of the time at which it was made. With Rene Clement (director of *Jeux Interdits*, 1952) and Henri-Georges Clouzot (maker of *Wages of Fear*, 1952 and *Les Diaboloques*, 1955) Carné fell out of fashion at the time of the less studio-and-script-bound films of the *Nouvelle Vague*, but in 1979, French critics voted *Les Enfants du Paradis* as the best French film ever made.

Claude Chabrol (b. 1930)

Like Godard and Truffaut, Chabrol first distinguished himself as an abrasive and articulate critic on the magazine *Cahiers du Cinema* before branching into direction. With Eric Rohmer (later also to become a director), he also wrote an influential book at this time on the films of Alfred Hitchcock. Hitchcock has been a strong influence on Chabrol's films, which are often cynical detective stories or psychological suspense thrillers set against carefully observed French provincial settings. He is a cool anatomist of the discreet charms and deadly passions of the bourgeoisie. His key films include *Les Cousins* (1958), *Les Bonnes Femmes* (1960), *Les Biches* (1968), *La Femme Infidele* (1969), *Killer!— Que la Bete meure* (1969), *Les Noces Rouges* (1973) and his best film, *Le Boucher* (1970).

Rene Clair (1898–1981)

The first and still the greatest European musical director. His early interest in asynchronous sound (*i.e.* that which does not always correspond to what we see going on on the screen) led him to attach equal importance to natural noise and music and to dialogue in his early sound films (such as *Sous les Toits de Paris* of 1930). A delight in dance—the choreographed quality of fights, chases and crowd scenes—permeates his two most successful works, *Le Million* and the simplistic but vivacious satire on industrialisation, *A Nous la Liberté* (both 1931).

Jean Cocteau (1889–1963)

A poet who expressed himself variously in fiction, drama, painting and drawing, and poetry as well as through the cinema. *Beauty and the Beast* (1946) was an imaginative telling of the familiar tale, with Jean Marais both frightening and poignant as the Beast. In *Orphée* of 1950 he produced one of the cinema's unquestioned fantastic masterpieces, using mirrors as links between the world of the living and that of the dead to great effect, and playing upon the connection between love and death in a way that must have influenced the makers of *Last Year in Marienbad* (Resnais and Robbe-Grillet) eleven years later.

Francis Ford Coppola (b. 1939)

The Godfather of modern American cinema, confidante and father-figure to the new generation of directors (such as George Lucas and Steven Spielberg) who emerged from film school to storm Hollywood in the early 1970s. Coppola's *The Godfather* (1972) and *The Godfather, Part II* (1974) combined the sweep of a dynastic family melodrama with a mature political analysis of corporate America. The former restored Marlon Brando to superstardom; the latter made stars of Al Pacino and Robert De Niro. Two other major films of the decade were *The Conversation* (1974), a tale of treacherous tapes and an atmosphere of paranoia that evoked Watergate; and *Apocalypse Now* (1979), in which America's incursion into Vietnam was interpreted as a mad, metaphysical journey into the heart of darkness. Since the trauma of *Apocalypse Now*, whose making was a nightmare that almost drove him mad, Coppola has seemed something of a lost soul in modern cinema, searching for inspiration, marking time and, with *Godfather III* (1990), revisiting old haunts. His version of *Dracula* (1992) has revived his career.

Constantin Costa Gavras (b. 1933)

The cinema's specialist director of the political thriller, throwing up large social issues of corruption and responsibility under the guise of suspense melodrama. He achieved international prominence with *Z* (1969), an indictment of the repressive regime in Greece, and he has had equal success in the mainstream commercial cinema, particularly with *Missing* (1982) and *Music Box* (1989).

George Cukor (1899–1983)

Cukor came to Hollywood from directing on the New York stage, and this theatrical background was an important clue to his work. His films were often adaptations of plays, like *Gaslight* (1944); he was always intrigued by theatrical people indulging a flair for the dramatic, either on stage, like Ronald Colman in *A Double Life* (1947), or in a courtroom, like Spencer Tracy and Katherine Hepburn in *Adam's Rib* (1949); and his films are particularly remembered for their performances, like Greta Garbo's in *Camille* (1937) or Judy Garland's in *A Star is Born* (1954). Cukor was one of the most civilised of Hollywood directors, versatile and visually stylish, but particularly revelling in the sex-war comedies of Tracy and Hepburn, like *Adam's Rib* and *Pat and Mike* (1952), which debated feminist issues ahead of their time.

Cecil B. De Mille (1881–1959)

The name synonymous above all others with bigness in the movies. His gigantic epics include *The Sign of the Cross* with Charles Laughton in 1932, and two spectacularly tasteless versions of *The Ten Commandments* (1923 and 1956). The films themselves matter less nowadays than the reputation for scale and the consistently successful box-office returns. Joseph L. Mankiewicz's observation on de Mille is worth quoting: "He had his finger up the pulse of America."

Vittorio De Sica (1902–1974)

Although he began his screen career as an actor, Vittorio De Sica is remembered principally for a remarkable group of films he made immediately after World War II, collaborating with writer Cesare Zavattini on works which are regarded as key examples of Italian neo-realism; *Shoeshine* (1946), *Bicycle Thieves* (1948) and *Umberto D* (1952). These sympathetic studies of the poor were heavily criticised in their own country (for political simplemindedness by the Left and for unflattering and unpatriotic portraiture of Italy by the Right) but were widely acclaimed abroad. With the decline of neo-realism in the early 1950s, De Sica was never to scale the same heights, though he did direct Sophia Loren to an Oscar winning performance in *Two Women* (1961), and experienced a later flourish of critical acclaim for two of his final films, *The Garden of the Finzi Continis* (1971) and *A Brief Vacation* (1973).

Carl Theodor Dreyer (1889–1968)

Still regarded as the greatest artist in the history of Danish cinema, though it was in France that he directed his first masterpiece, *The Passion of Joan of Arc* (1928), with its remarkable leading performance by Renee Falconetti in her only screen role. The austerity and apparent severe Protestant guilt that pervade his work compare interestingly with Robert Bresson's Catholic severity. Dreyer's last film, *Gertrud* (1964) was disgracefully derided at its premiere in Paris, but it is now regarded as one of his finest works, both for its steady satire of the bourgeoisie and its sympathy with women and hatred of their oppression. The slowness of his work still causes difficulty, but the fantastical quality of *Vampyr* (1932), and the undercutting of fanaticism in *Days of Wrath* (1943) and *Ordet/The Word* (1955) are nowadays better appreciated than they were at the time of release.

Sergei Eisenstein (1898–1948)

A prominent theorist as well as practitioner, whose Marxist awareness of society as founded upon conflict rather than harmony led him to develop a theory of montage, or meaning built up by collision and clash of images. This theory found illustration in what are at the same time highly effective Socialist propaganda films: *The Battleship Potemkin* of 1925, whose massacre-sequence on the steps of the port of Odessa is among the most famous in cinematic history, *October* of 1927 (in which the Menshevik or moderate leader Kerensky is denigrated when his image is followed by that of a peacock—an example of the montage technique), and the more dramatic and baroque *Ivan the Terrible* (Part one, 1942; Part two, 1945). This last caused Eisenstein to fall into disfavour with Stalin (who may have taken the portrait of the tyrant Ivan to be a reflection upon himself), and the financial difficulties and persecution because of his homosexuality led to his premature death of a heart attack. "Of all the arts", said Lenin, "for us the cinema is the most important". In Soviet Russia its most important voice was Eisenstein who, in finding filmic forms to express collectivism and brotherhood, gave substance to a national ideology.

Rainer Werner Fassbinder (1946–1982)

Phenomenally prolific hero of the new German cinema of the 1970s, Fassbinder's films at their best combined the political commitment of a Godard with the heady melodrama of a Hollywood director he much admired, Douglas Sirk. His best film is probably *The Marriage of Maria Braun* (1979), an extraordinary allegory of the history of post-war Germany with a magnetic leading performance from Hanna Schygulla. The best films in his melodramatic style are *The Merchant of Four Seasons* (1972), *The Bitter Tears of Petra von Kant* (1972), *Fear Eats the Soul* (1974) and *Veronika Voss* (1981).

Federico Fellini (1920–1993)

Fellini was an example of the director as star, delighting in treading a thin line between self-expression and self-indulgence. The films recall his early experience in the circus and as a cartoonist, being populated by grotesques and having a unique mixture of risk and spectacle, fantasy and fact. *I Vitelloni* (1953), a semi-autobiographical account of his wastrel adolescent days, established Fellini's reputation; it was enhanced by the international success of his next film, *La Strada* (1954), a parable of body and spirit, love and salvation. With *La Dolce Vita* (1960), a sensational view of contemporary Roman society, Fellini entered his decadent phase, which was to be continued in such films as *Fellini Satyricon* (1969) and Fellini's *Casanova* (1976). His most highly regarded films are his most autobiographical, *8½* (1963), in which a film director encounters a creative crisis and ransacks his past for inspiration, and *Amarcord* (1973) which is a remembrance of his childhood.

Robert Flaherty (1884–1951)

Often referred to as the "father of film documentary", Flaherty was actually as much a Romantic as a realist. He has been criticised for the imaginary absences in his movies but he was not a polemicist but a poet, making films that were either hymns to a vanishing way of life or recorded elemental struggles between Man and Nature. His best films were his first, and last: respectively, *Nanook of the North* (1922) and *Louisiana Story* (1948).

John Ford (1895–1973)

Generally acclaimed as the greatest director of Westerns. Particularly celebrated are those he made starring John Wayne: *Stagecoach* (1939), an odyssey of Western outcasts across hostile Indian territory: *The Searchers* (1956), in which Wayne's bitter racialism is eventually tamed; and *The Man Who Shot Liberty Valance* (1962) which pits Wayne against James Stewart. But he also excelled with Henry Fonda (*Drums Along the Mohawk* of 1939, and in non-Western films (*The Grapes of Wrath*, 1940). His greatest limitation is that he is pre-eminently a man's director, whose bourbon-soaked camaraderie and stress on tough, determined action in some of his less successful films palls rapidly. His greatest strengths are as the unsurpassed chronicler of pioneering America and as the sympathetic observer of the endurance of the common people; and his insights into prejudice, injustice and the tragedy of destroyed families. "This is the West, sir", says the newspaper editor of *Liberty Valance*. "When the legend becomes fact, print the legend". Ford printed the legend better than anyone. Other key films: *The Informer* (1935), *My Darling Clementine* (1946), *Fort Apache* (1948), *The Quiet Man* (1952).

Milos Forman (b. 1932)

Forman was one of a group of directors of the so-called Czech New Wave of the 1960s, whose comedies such as *A Blonde in Love* (1965) and *The Fireman's Ball* (1967) audaciously satirised authority, both parental and political. In Paris in 1968 when the Soviet tanks rolled into Prague and there was a clampdown on artistic expression, Forman eventually emigrated to America, where he has continued to score notable successes with offbeat films, most famously with *One Flew Over the Cuckoo's Nest* (1975) and *Amadeus* (1984).

Samuel Fuller (b. 1912)

A ferocious action director, castigated as neo-Fascist by his adversaries and lauded by his advocates for the tough, unsparing economy and desperate honesty of his work. He has worked across different genres: the spy-thriller (*Pickup on South Street*, 1953), the Western (*Run of the Arrow*, 1957) and, in *Shock Corridor* of 1963, his finest and most revelatory work, a remarkable amalgam of the investigative-journalist picture and the drama of psychological horror, perhaps, in its harrowing brutality, paralleling that of American society. His later films have been few and far between, though *White Dog* (1983) showed that, given the opportunity, Fuller had lost none of his bite.

Abel Gance (1889–1981)

"The day of the Image has arrived", proclaimed

Abel Gance at the triumphant premiere of his five-and-a-half-hour epic, *Napoleon* (1927), which deployed superimposition, slow-motion, split-screen, colour, and a triple-screen process, Polyvision, that anticipated Cinemascope by nearly thirty years. Alas, Gance was mistaken: sound was round the corner and the visual innovations of *Napoleon* were rendered virtually obsolete before they had begun. Not until the film's restoration in 1980 was Gance's achievement appreciated and his own reputation restored as one of the great innovators of the silent screen.

Jean-Luc Godard (b. 1930)

"We are the children of Marx and Coca-Cola", claimed Godard in the 1960s, when he seemed the most radical, innovative and controversial director in world cinema. Nowadays we are probably the children of McDonald's and market forces and his ideas and formal experiments seem correspondingly less urgent, more marginal. The turning-point was *Weekend* (1967), an apocalyptic black-comedy of chaos and cannibalism, of social and cultural breakdown. From his early films, which were often love letters to the Hollywood cinema, he had moved to an alternative political cinema that seemed to demand not audiences but disciples. Still, although his day is over, his influence on all spheres of alternative, independent, avant-garde film theory and practice has been immense. Other key films: *Breathless* (1959), *Vivre sa Vie* (1962), *Une Femme Mariee* (1964), *Pierrot le Fou* (1965), *Tout Va Bien* (1972).

D. W. Griffith (1875–1948)

Griffith more than any other individual was responsible for the cinema moving from short one and two-reelers to the grand epic scale. *The Birth of a Nation* (1915), despite overt racism, was the most exciting attempt the cinema had hitherto made to capture and reconstruct the course of historical events, and broke all box-office records as well as profoundly influencing Eisenstein. Its successor, *Intolerance* (1916), was even more grandiose and cost unimaginable sums by the standards of those days. Apart from *Broken Blossoms* (1919) and *Way Down East* (1920), Griffith's later films were undistinguished and his career ended in a prolonged, drink-sodden decline. Although sometimes criticised for his Victorian melodrama, Griffith is more properly remembered for his popularisation of feature-length narrative; his revelation of the creative possibilities of montage; and his encouragement of a new subtlety and realism in screen performance. He was the first figure in film history to give this new mass medium intellectual respectability.

Robert Hamer (1911–1963)

The problem child of Ealing studios, whose career was to decline due to alcoholism and what producer Michael Balcon was to call Hamer's "self-destructive streak", but who was responsible for at least three classics of British film: "The Haunted Mirror" episode from *Dead of Night* (1945); the neo-realist melodrama about the London underworld, *It Always Rains on Sunday* (1947); and, above all, the black comedy, *Kind Hearts and Coronets* (1949) in which Dennis Price purrs through some of the most suavely literate dialogue in British cinema as he attempts to kill off eight Alec Guinnesses on his way to a dukedom.

Howard Hawks (1896–1977)

The litmus-paper director for proponents of the auteur theory of criticism in the fifties and, even now that theory has been surpassed, probably the most versatile and consistent operator within the Hollywood studio system. It is certainly true that, whatever genre he worked in, it was worked on, transmuted and made more ambiguous; thus the Western *Rio Bravo* (1959) contains a minimum of big-scale outdoor action and a maximum of charged conversation. The private-eye classic *The Big Sleep* (1946) is concerned with Bogie's process of ironic self-discovery rather than with who-dunnit a question to which Hawks himself never worked out

the answer). The action in the civil-aviation drama *Only Angels Have Wings* (1939) takes place predominantly on the ground. His comedies, notably those with Cary Grant, hilariously subvert sex stereotypes, above all *Bringing Up Baby* (1938), whose plot vies in implausibility with W. C. Fields but whose thrusts at academic ossification, male chauvinism, and one-upmanship are masterfully worked into a framework of gag and slapstick.

Werner Herzog (b. 1942)

One of the most exciting of the young wave of German directors, his treatment of madness is particularly penetrating. This is normally undertaken within the context of a part-historical, part-fictional society, as with the paranoia of the sixteenth century Amazon conquistador in *Aguirre, Wrath of God* (1972), the scandalous insights of the supposed "savage" in *The Enigma of Kaspar Hauser* (1974), and the odd symbiosis between predator and victim in his Murnau remake *Nosferatu the Vampyre* (1978). "Dreams move mountains", says Herzog: it is his philosophy of film-making.

Sir Alfred Hitchcock (1899–1980)

For half a century the acknowledged master of mystery and suspense, whose coldly planned delight in playing on his audience's nerves has occasioned violent disagreement between those who see him as the medium's leading exponent of predestination and those for whom he is but a limited practical joker in bad taste. *Psycho* (1960) remains the most notorious film, less now perhaps for the murder of Janet Leigh in her shower than for the *coup de grace* when the murderer's "real identity" is revealed near the end. *North by North-West* of the previous year is among his least vicious and most accomplished works, a comic spy-thriller based (like so much that is funniest in Hollywood cinema) on a mistake involving the identity of Cary Grant. Sexually perverse or tabooed areas which the conventional narrative cinema perforce ignored or treated as marginal assume central (though often implicit) places in his work, which is perhaps his greatest source of interest to students of film: *cf.* the latent homosexuality in *Strangers on a Train* (1951), the Grand Guignol parody of an Oedipus complex in *Psycho* and of repression and the traumatic return of what has been "forgotten" (*i.e.* repressed) in *Marnie* (1964). In recent years his early British films have been revalued and upgraded, and the sexual politics of his films have been earnestly analysed. He has also been the subject of a scandalous biography by Donald Spoto, *The Dark Side of Genius*. But he continues to fascinate because of the multi-sided personality of his work, which reveals at once the mask of a joker of genius, a nihilist, a Catholic moralist, a Freudian sexual psychologist and, in perhaps his greatest work, *Vertigo* (1958) an anguished romantic. He was more than the "master of suspense": he made murder into an art form. Other key films include: *Blackmail* (1929), *The Thirty-Nine Steps* (1935), *Sabotage* (1937), *The Lady Vanishes* (1938), *Rebecca* (1940), *Shadow of a Doubt* (1943), *Notorious* (1946), *Rope* (1948), *Rear Window* (1954) and *The Birds* (1963).

John Huston (1906–1987)

1941 marked two of the most sensationally successful debuts in directorial history—Orson Welles with *Citizen Kane* and Huston's *The Maltese Falcon*, an elegantly perverse private-eye tale in which double-crosses occur at a bewildering rate, thereby setting the mould for the *film noir* that was so prominent later in the decade. Huston's career intermittently maintained this initial impetus, though public and critical reception of his works was not always judicious. *Freud: The Secret Passion* (1962), a remarkable drama ahead of its time, was ill received, whereas *The African Queen*, for which Bogart won an Oscar in 1952, is an overrated, though entertaining, film. Huston was intrigued by over-reachers, people who pursue their dreams to the point of obsession. Even when their obsessions blow up in their faces, as they do in two of his best films, *The Treasure of the Sierra Madre* (1948) and *The Man who would be King* (1975),

Huston is still impressed by the grandeur of human aspiration, by the ironies of courage and cowardice, by the stirring way humanity challenges its fate. His work was uneven but his career ended on a high note: a typically literate adaptation of a literary classic, *Under the Volcano* (1984); an impish Mafia black comedy, *Prizzi's Honor* (1985); and a serene rendering of James Joyce's elegiac short story, *The Dead* (1987). His direction also helped win Oscars for his family: for father Walter in *Sierra Madre*, and for daughter Anjelica in *Prizzi's Honor*. Other key films: *Key Largo* (1948), *Moby Dick* (1956), *The Misfits* (1961), *Reflections in a Golden Eye* (1967), *Fat City* (1972), *Wise Blood* (1979).

Elia Kazan (b. 1909)

Dynamic director who founded the Actor's Studio with Lee Strasberg and is responsible for bringing the Method style of acting into the American cinema. His association on three films with Marlon Brando—*A Streetcar named Desire* (1951), *Viva Zapata* (1952) and *On the Waterfront* (1954)—was particularly significant for its establishment of the prototype Kazan hero: a rebel, anguished and ambivalent about his personal situation and social responsibilities but with a tremendous drive to solve his problems. *On the Waterfront* was particularly controversial for its so-called "glorification of the informer" (an ex-Communist, Kazan had named names to the House UnAmerican Activities Committee in 1952). He also directed James Dean in *East of Eden* (1955), Montgomery Clift in *Wild River* (1960) and Robert De Niro in *The Last Tycoon* (1976), though in his later years he has occupied himself mainly in writing novels and a magnificent revelatory autobiography, *A Life*.

Krzysztof Kieslowski (b. 1941)

The greatest Polish directors, like Andrzej Wajda and Krzysztof Zanussi, see cinema as the nation's social conscience, the art-form that most courageously interrogates the country's moral and political values. Kieslowski is in that tradition and is best known abroad for his contemporary TV films on the theme of the Ten Commandments, two of which were expanded to feature-film length: *A Short Film About Killing* (1988) and *A Short Film About Love* (1989). Other key films include: *Camera Buff* (1979), *No End* (1984) and *The Double Life of Veronique* (1991).

Stanley Kubrick (b. 1928)

For Kubrick, the cinema is a laboratory for observation and experiment and his findings have revealed a mind of the highest intellect and provoked more critical debate than any American director since Orson Welles. Two films in the 1960s particularly confirmed his extraordinary gifts: the nuclear comedy, *Dr. Strangelove* (1964), which showed the tension between man and the machine; and his sci-fi epic, *2001: A Space Odyssey* (1968), a vast enigmatic meditation on evolution and the degree to which man has been mastered by the technology he has created. His following two films, *A Clockwork Orange* (1971) and *Barry Lyndon* (1975) were amongst the most controversial of the next decade, the former for its violence in depicting the issue of free-will, the latter for its sumptuousness in anatomising high society at the end of the eighteenth-century. Many were disappointed with his labyrinthine horror film, *The Shining* (1980) and his Vietnam movie *Full Metal Jacket* (1987), but he remains a key figure in modern film, analysing the tensions between the individual and history, man and science, language and social conditioning with a disturbingly clinical detachment. Other key films: *Paths of Glory* (1957), *Lolita* (1962).

Akira Kurosawa (b. 1910)

The first Japanese director to make a major impact on Western audiences, with *Rashomon*, the recounting of a rape and murder from four separate perspectives, which was the great success of the Venice Film Festival in 1951. Compared to such as Mizoguchi and Ozu his work looks Westernised, but this can be of positive benefit, as in the Samurai "Westerns" he made with the actor Toshiro Mifune, where classic Western plot-schemes are translated into stylised Japanese settings (*The Seven Samurai*, 1954; *Sanjuro*, 1962). He has also made highly praised adaptations of Shakespeare, *Throne of Blood* (1957), a version of *Macbeth*, and *Ran* (1985), an interpretation of *King Lear*. Psychological extremes have always excited Kurosawa, and his pulsating visual style can be understood in terms of finding a powerful visual pattern to reflect the feverish inner intensity of his characters. But one should not overlook the strong humanist vein in Kurosawa, expressed most movingly in *Living* (1952). Other key films: *Drunken Angel* (1948), *The Idiot* (1951), *I Live in Fear* (1955), *The Lower Depths* (1957) and *Kagemusha* (1980).

Fritz Lang (1890–1976)

Lang began as a leading exponent of German Expressionism, with the psychodrama *M* (1931), starring Peter Lorre as the self-hating child murderer, and *Metropolis* (1926), a science-fiction evocation of a nightmarish industrial city of the future. Goebbels was very taken with the latter film, and offered Lang the job of film-propaganda director to the Third Reich. Instead, he fled to America, and proceeded to provide auteurist critics with one of their juiciest test-cases by adapting his preoccupations with fate, revenge, and the social outcast to the turbulent American society of the pre-war and wartime years (*Fury*, 1936; *The Ministry of Fear*, 1944), and to genres such as the Western (*Rancho Notorious* in 1952) and the gangster film (*The Big Heat* in 1953). Two Edward G. Robinson performances—as a Professor implicated in murder in *The Woman in the Window* (1944) and as an artist infatuated with a prostitute in *Scarlet Street* (1945)—embody to perfection the typical Lang hero, trapped by personality, circumstance and environment. He is still arguably the most formidable pessimist in film history, but his presentation of fear and alienation in the modern metropolis has been profoundly influential on, among others, Godard, Hitchcock and Kubrick.

Sir David Lean (1908–1991)

The popular cinema's master story-teller. In *Brief Encounter* (1945), he made the British cinema's greatest love story; his Dickens' adaptations, *Great Expectations* (1946) and *Oliver Twist* (1948) have never been surpassed; and with *The Bridge on the River Kwai* (1957), *Lawrence of Arabia* (1962) and *Doctor Zhivago* (1965), he managed to align epic perspectives with intimate and intense characterisation. After the failure of *Ryan's Daughter* in 1970, his reputation slumped: "bourgeois impersonality" was the label given to his films. But the success of *A Passage to India* (1984) helped to force a re-evaluation of his work and recognise its individual qualities: the emotional repression of his heroines; the visionary madness of his heroes; the spirit of place that pulses in his films; and his sensitivity to the erratic, exotic emotions that lurk beneath the surface of English propriety. Other key films include: *The Sound Barrier* (1952), *Hobson's Choice* (1954) and *Summer Madness* (1955).

Joseph Losey (1909–1984)

There were several Joseph Loseys: the American Losey renowned for cogent moral fables such as *The Prowler* (1951) before the McCarthyist blacklist forced him out of America; the British Losey in which, with collaborators like actors Stanley Baker and Dirk Bogarde and writer Harold Pinter, he analysed the sexual mores and class corruption of English society, as in *The Servant* (1963), *Accident* (1967) and *The Go-Between* (1970); and the European Losey of the final phase of his career, when he adapted classics such as *A Doll's House* (1973) or Mozart's *Don Giovanni* (1980) or offered trenchant insights into recent political history, as in *The Assassination of Trotsky* (1972) and *Mr. Klein* (1976). With a style often verging on the baroque, Losey tackled a variety of subject matter, but the themes were consistent: the hypocrisy and deceit of dominant social and sexual attitudes. He was the most Brechtian of directors and had one of the most lucid intellects in movies. Other key films include: *The Boy with Green Hair* (1948), *Blind Date* (1959),

The Criminal (1960), *King and Country* (1964) and *Secret Ceremony* (1968).

Ernst Lubitsch (1892–1947)

The master of sophisticated sex comedy who, in Billy Wilder's phrase, "could do more with a closed door than most modern directors can do with an entire bedroom". Born in Berlin, Lubitsch brought a European flavour to Hollywood farce, satirising the pretension and insensitivity that sometimes go with wealth and position. His best remembered films are *Ninotchka* (1939), in which Garbo laughs, and *To Be or Not to Be* (1942), in which Jack Benny plays Hamlet. They are not only comedies: they are fervent anti-Nazi satires made at a time when Lubitsch must have known that the Europe of his youth, so wittily and lovingly evoked on screen, was being destroyed forever. Other key films, *Trouble in Paradise* (1932) and *The Shop Around the Corner* (1940).

Alexander Mackendrick (1912–1993)

The most consistently brilliant of the Ealing directors, making four of its most successful and enduring comedies: *Whisky Galore* (1949), *The Man in the White Suit* (1951), *The Maggie* (1954) and *The Lady-Killers* (1955). His American debut—an exposé of yellow journalism—*Sweet Smell of Success* (1957) was also remarkable, but after a series of abortive projects in the 1960s, Mackendrick retired from directing to become Dean of the film department of the California Institute of the Arts. He left behind a fascinating body of work, notable for its extraordinary insights into the world of children, its fascination with the dangers of innocence, and its mordant observation of the intricate yet inevitable ways in which humans fail to communicate. Other key films: *Mandy* (1952), *Sammy Going South* (1963) and *A High Wind in Jamaica* (1965).

Louis Malle (b 1932)

Formerly an assistant to Robert Bresson and Jacques Cousteau, Louis Malle has developed into one of the most esteemed of international directors. He has made films as dashing as *Zazie dans le Metro* (1960), as disturbing as *Lacombe Lucien* (1973), as atmospheric as *Atlantic City* (1980), and as moving as *Au Revoir les Enfants* (1987). Malle often challenges the norms of society and the boundaries of cinema, exploring such risky subjects as eroticism (in *Les Amants* in 1958), incest (in *Murmur of the Heart* in 1971) and child prostitution (in *Pretty Baby* in 1979) and yet still achieving popular success and critical acclaim. Isolation and social alienation are recurrent themes, fittingly so perhaps for one of the least predictable and most individualistic filmmakers of modern times. Other key films include: *Lift to the Scaffold* (1957), *Le Feu Follet* (1963), *My Dinner With Andre* (1982) and *Damage* (1992).

Joseph L. Mankiewicz (1909–1993)

To those who find Mankiewicz's films too wordy, he replied: "There can never be an excess of *good* talk". Mankiewicz was one of the most eloquent of Hollywood's writer directors, who began by writing dialogue for W. C. Fields and, he claims, Rin-Rin-Tin (an unused screen-play about a dog that hates its master, a familiar Mankiewicz theme). His greatest period was during the ten years after the War, in which he won the writing and directing Oscars for two consecutive years (for *A Letter to Three Wives* in 1949 and *All About Eve* in 1950) and also made Hollywood's best Shakespearian film (*Julius Caesar* in 1952). His career never really picked up momentum after his labours on the mammothly expensive *Cleopatra* (1963), though he was proud to claim that his last film *Sleuth* (1972) is the only film ever to have its entire cast—i.e. Laurence Olivier and Michael Caine—nominated for Oscars. There are a lot of interesting recurrent motifs in Mankiewicz—generation conflict, ghosts from the past that will not stay dead—and nobody has made more haunting use of the flashback. Other key films: *The Ghost and Mrs. Muir* (1947), *Five Fingers* (1952), *The Barefoot Contessa* (1954) and *Suddenly Last Summer* (1959).

Anthony Mann (1909–1967)

Anthony Mann is best remembered for a series of Westerns he made with actor James Stewart, which were striking for their dramatic use of landscape and the psychological instability of their heroes. In *Winchester 73* (1950), *Bend of the River* (1952), *The Naked Spur* (1953), and *The Far Country* (1955), Stewart plays an ostensibly noble but actually neurotic hero who, whilst undertaking a perilous journey across a treacherous landscape, must also root out the evil in himself. Mann also made fine thrillers, a classic epic (*El Cid* in 1961) and even a stylish musical (*The Glenn Miller Story* in 1954) but it was the Mann of the Western that really showed his quality as a director. Other key films: *The Man from Laramie* (1955), *Man of the West* (1958) and *The Fall of the Roman Empire* (1964).

Jean-Pierre Melville (1917–1973)

Something of a father figure of the *Nouvelle Vague* because of his economical and independent production methods. He made an exemplary adaptation of Jean Cocteau's novel *Les Enfants Terribles* (1950). However, he is most celebrated for a series of poetic, stylised existential gangster films. among them *Second Breath* (1966), *The Samurai* (1967), and *The Red Circle* (1970), which particularly took their inspiration from Melville's favourite director, John Huston. (Melville had chosen his pseudonym after his favourite author, Herman Melville: his actual surname was Grumbach). Perhaps his masterpiece, though, and certainly his most personal film, is *Army of the Shadows* (1969), a film about the French Resistance that drew on his own personal experience in the war.

Vincente Minnelli (1910–1986)

The name Vincente Minnelli is synonymous with the MGM musical—*Meet Me in St. Louis* (1944), *An American in Paris* (1951), *The Band Wagon* (1953), *Gigi* (1958) and others. Yet he was also adept at comedy, and did some remarkably intense melodramas, of which *Lust for Life* (1955), his bio-pic of Van Gogh, and *The Bad and the Beautiful* (1952), his glittering dissection of Hollywood ruthlessness, are particularly notable. He was interested in the plight of the artist in society, and the superiority of the world of imagination to that of reality. Hollywood's Dream Factory proved a most congenial environment for this most elegant of stylists. Other key films: *The Pirate* (1948), *Madame Bovary* (1949), *Father of the Bride* (1950). *Brigadoon* (1953), *The Cobweb* (1955) and *Some Came Running* (1958).

Kenji Mizoguchi (1898–1956)

For many, Mizoguchi is the greatest of all Japanese directors, but his films are still not that well known in the West. The most famous is *Ugetsu Monogatari* (1953), a ravishingly beautiful tale of two potters seduced by ghosts. Its articulation of history and fantasy, its lyrical style and its commitment to the treatment of women as equals are characteristic of the director. Other major films include: *The Story of the Last Chrysanthemums* (1939), *The Life of Oharu* (1952) and *Sansho the Bailiff* (1954).

F. W. Murnau (1889–1931)

Murnau is renowned for three classics of silent film: *Nosferatu* (1922), the cinema's first version of the *Dracula* story and still the most frightening; *The Last Laugh* (1924), credited as being one of the few silent films to dispense with titles and remarkable for its fluid camera movement; and *Sunrise* (1927), his first American film. Tragically he was killed in a car crash in 1931, his potential tantalisingly unfulfilled.

Max Ophuls (1902–1957)

For a long time regarded as a talented minor director of exquisite trifles, Ophuls has been reinstated by recent—notably feminist—criticism to his rightful place as one of the greatest of forties and fifties directors. *Lola Montes* (1955) was his last film, about the beautiful 'adventuress' who allows herself to be put on display in a circus ring at the end of her career. The swooping camera-movements and awareness of how feminine sexuality necessarily connotes being an object to be looked at are in evidence too in *Madame de . . .* (1953), as well as in the films he made in Austria, Germany and France before setting out to pursue his career in Hollywood. His best American film was the beautiful tragic romance, *Letter from an Unknown Woman* (1948); whilst both *Caught* (1949) and *The Reckless Moment* (1949) took conventional women's magazine material and, through intense visual style, transformed them into tense and subversive comments on romantic obsession and domestic imprisonment.

Nagisa Oshima (b. 1932)

An acute awareness of the theatrical in its widest sense–the need to treat urgent social questions as dialectical dramas rather than as ready-made events for the camera to record—and a sense of the inter-relationship of the erotic and the political unmatched by any other living director have coexisted fruitfully in Oshima's work since *Death by Hanging*—about an execution that isn't—in 1968. But his name became familiar to most filmgoers only with *Ai No Corrida* (otherwise *Empire of the Senses*) in 1975. An innkeeper and his ex-servant make untiring love until she, at his behest, strangles him in the moment of orgasm. The much-touted erotic frankness–certainly far less surrogate than that in *Last Tango in Paris*–assumes its importance only when seen in conjunction with the film's critique of the position of women in Japanese society. In his first international film, *Merry Christmas, Mr. Lawrence* (1983), he explored the strange bond which grows between a Japanese captain and a British prisoner of war: a variation of his typical themes of forbidden passion, and his preoccupation with society's "enemies" whose psychology he seeks to understand. More recently he has completed a documentary for the BBC, *Kyoto, My Mother's Place* (1991), which gives a fascinating account of his background. Other key films: *Diary of A Shinjuku Thief* (1968), *Boy* (1969), *The Ceremony* (1971) and *Empire of Passion* (1978).

Ermanno Olmi (b. 1931)

An Italian director whose work is characterised by a sympathy for the working man and by a concern for human dignity. In films such as *Il Posto* (1961) and *The Tree of Wooden Clogs* (1979), he has kept the spirit of neo-realism alive.

Yasujiro Ozu (1903–1963)

Like Mizoguchi, a director long known to the Western public through only one work—*Tokyo Story* of 1953, about a visit paid by an elderly couple to their children in the capital. Ozu's style is slow, his narrative-lines not exactly eventful, his photography from a low level (the seated position traditional for social intercourse in Japan) perhaps difficult for Westerners to adjust to. But now he is accepted as one of the most important innovators in film language, for the way in which his small-scale stories distil much that is important in Japanese life and history, and for the separating out of individual actions and gestures so that spectators have time fully to appreciate their implications. Key films include: *I Was Born But . . .* (1932), *Early Summer* (1951), *Good Morning* (1959) and *An Autumn Afternoon* (1962).

Pier Paolo Pasolini (1922–1976)

His notorious death—murdered by a homosexual pick-up—could almost have been engineered as a publicity stunt to launch his final film, *Salo or the 120 Days of Sodom* (1976), in which the combination of intense and complex visual lucidity with a recoiling from the tyrannies of the twentieth century already evident in *Pigsty* (1969) reaches its zenith. Ideological revulsion from the present and an interest in the possibilities of film language motivate Pasolini's curious "Marxist-Freudian-Catholic" rewritings of classics for the screen—*Medea* (1969) and *The Decameron* (1971). His complex artistry is seen at its best in his first film, *Accatone!* (1961) and *The Gospel According to St. Matthew* (1964), an austere rendering of the Biblical story far removed from the Hollywood epic, and movingly attempting to reconcile Pasolini's Marxist political outlook with his religious mysticism.

Sam Peckinpah (1925–1984)

A Hollywood maverick, associated with scenes of graphic violence photographed in loving slow motion. In fact, he had something of the visual lyricism and raucous male humour of John Ford, though whereas Ford disclosed the poetry behind America's pioneering past, Peckinpah explored its passions and perversions as well. He will always be remembered for *The Wild Bunch* (1969), his radical, revisionist Western that majestically dragged the genre, kicking and screaming, into the 20th century. Other key films: *Guns in the Afternoon* (1962), *Major Dundee* (1965), *Straw Dogs* (1971) and *Pat Garrett and Billy the Kid* (1973).

Arthur Penn (b. 1922)

An abrasive stylist, notable for his subversive way with popular film genres, his investigation of the reality behind legendary figures, and his insertion of counter-culture attitudes into mainstream movie-making. Key films: *The Left-Handed Gun* (1958), *The Miracle Worker* (1962), *Bonnie and Clyde* (1967), *Alice's Restaurant* (1969) and *Night Moves* (1975).

Roman Polanski (b. 1933)

From early Surrealist shorts, Polanski moved into feature-length dramas of sexual tension with *Knife in the Water* (1962) and *Repulsion* (shot in England in 1965). The reputation for kinkiness he thereby gained was tragically highlighted when his wife, the actress Sharon Tate, was butchered by crazed followers of Charles Manson in 1969. His major box-office success has been the private-eye drama *Chinatown* (1974), in which Polanski himself slits open the nose of the character played by Jack Nicholson. He also breathed flesh and blood into the horror film with *Rosemary's Baby* (1968) and fresh life into the filmed literary classic with *Tess* (1979). His traumatic life has been recounted in his autobiography, *Roman*. Other key films: *Cul-de-Sac* (1966), *Macbeth* (1971) and *The Tenant* (1976).

Michael Powell (1905–1990) and Emeric Pressburger (1902–1988)

British cinema's most full-blooded fantasists, who peaked in the 1940s with such passionate and visually imaginative films as *The Life and Death of Colonel Blimp* (1943), *I Know Where I'm Going* (1945), *A Matter of Life and Death* (1946), *Black Narcissus* (1947) and their greatest success, *The Red Shoes* (1948). From the late 1950s, Powell went solo and created an enormous furore with *Peeping Tom* (1960), which was critically reviled at the time but has since attained classic status and is deeply admired by cineastes and fellow directors such as Martin Scorsese.

Otto Preminger (1906–1986)

Talented tyrant who thrived on controversy, whether it involved the use of "naughty" words in *The Moon is Blue* (1953) or the depiction of the world of the drug addict in *The Man with the Golden Arm* (1955). His best films are the detective thriller, *Laura* (1945), one of a number of Preminger's features about mysterious, irresistible women who lure men to their doom; and the courtroom drama *Anatomy of a Murder* (1959), a masterpiece of objectivity and ambiguity. Other key films: *Angel Face* (1953), *Carmen Jones* (1954), *Bonjour Tristesse* (1957), *Advise and Consent* (1962) and *The Cardinal* (1963).

Nicholas Ray (1911–1978)

One of the most inventive and consistent of Hollywood action directors, whose rhetorical question summed up his philosophy of cinema: "If it were all in the script, why make the film?" *Rebel Without A Cause* (1955) blazed the trail for a host of movies about rebellious youth, but the dignity of James Dean's performance and the symbolic richness of Ray's *mise-en-scène* have caused it to survive longer than most of its imitators. He enjoyed success also with Bogart, *In a Lonely Place* (1950) and Robert Mitchum, *The Lusty Men* (1952). The critics of *Cahiers du Cinema* particularly championed Ray's more extreme stylistic exercises, such as the feminist Western, *Johnny Guitar* (1954) and the baroque gangster film, *Party Girl* (1958). Alienated youth, the rebel, the outsider: these were the figures with whom Ray identified, sometimes melodramatically, often poetically. Other key films: *They Live By Night* (1948), *Knock on Any Door* (1949), *On Dangerous Ground* (1952), *Bigger Than Life* (1956) and *Bitter Victory* (1957).

Satyajit Ray (1921–1992)

Pather Panchali of 1955 introduced Indian cinema to a wider audience, and launched a highly successful trilogy, completed by *Aparajito* of 1957 and *The World of Apu* of 1959. The withdrawn, analytical style of Ray's output expanded with some of his work in the seventies (see *Company Limited*, 1972) to a greater awareness of the problems of Westernised India. His films were rooted in the tradition of the humanist documentary, influenced by the social concern of Italian neo-realists, and inspired by the natural lyricism of a director like Jean Renoir. Other key films: *The Music Room* (1958), *Charulata* (1964), *Days and Nights in the Forest* (1970), *The Middle Man* (1976), *The Chess Players* (1977) and *The Home and the World* (1984).

Sir Carol Reed (1906–1976)

Reed's reputation as one of the key directors of post-war British cinema rests on a small number of films: the Expressionist, *Odd Man Out* (1947), the last day-in-the-life of an IRA man on the run, and two adaptations of Graham Greene stories, *The Fallen Idol* (1948) and *The Third Man* (1949). Overall his films are notable for a self-effacing craftsmanship, a sympathy with the world of children, and a fascination with confrontations between innocence and experience. He won an Oscar for *Oliver!* (1968). Other key films include *Outcast of the Islands* (1951), one of the cinema's best adaptations of Conrad; and *The Man Between* (1953), using its post-war Berlin setting less evocatively than post-war Vienna in *The Third Man* but a gripping human drama nonetheless.

Jean Renoir (1899–1979)

A career spanning nearly fifty years included one of the first great dramas to be shot entirely on location, *Toni*, made with a largely non-professional cast in the South of France in 1935; two magnificent performances from Michel Simon, in *La Chienne* (1931) and *Boudu Sauve Des Eaux* (1932); a period funded by the Left-wing Popular Front that produced the film about a workers' cooperative, *Le Crime de Monsieur Lange* (1935); and a forties and fifties output as an exile in Hollywood of considerable merit, including *The Southerner* of 1945. These would be enough to mark Renoir out as an all-time cinema great even were it not for his two pre-Second-World-War masterpieces, *La Grande Illusion* (1937), a drama set in a POW camp, and the matchless *La Regle du Jeu* of 1939. This savage and frequently hilarious drama of love, class-antagonism, mixed identity, and the ambiguous corruption of aristocratic style so quickly achieved recognition as a masterpiece that it requires an effort now to remind outselves that it was banned on first release, so clearly was its scathing criticism of French society recognised.

Alain Resnais (b. 1922)

Resnais began as a documentarist, and made his first feature film in 1959—*Hiroshima Mon Amour*, from a screenplay by the novelist Marguerite Duras. *Hiroshima*'s concern with the interaction of time, place and memory was taken up and amplified in *Last Year in Marienbad* (1961), where there is no reassuring continuity of character or coherence of time or space other than that imposed ambiguously, from moment to moment by the "eternal present" of the screen. Speculation about *Marienbad* reached quasi-metaphysical heights that have frequently tended to obscure the dazzling frozen eroticism of its *mise-en-scene*, its masterful exploitation of the dreamlike aspect of film-watching, and the performances of Georgio Albertazzi and Delphine Seyrig. Memory and imagination have continued to be important preoccupations in

his work, and he remains one of the great "modernist" innovators of contemporary cinema, continually exploring new areas of expression. Key films: *Night and Fog* (1956), *Muriel* (1963), *Providence* (1977) and *L'Amour a Mort* (1984).

Francesco Rosi (b. 1922)

Italian director who began as an assistant to Luchino Visconti and is perhaps best known as the maker of the Placido Domingo film of *Carmen* (1984). But Rosi's natural home is the world of political corruption and paranoia, and no modern film-maker can match him for his trenchant critique of the institutions of power. His most important films in this vein are *Salvatore Giuliano* (1961), *Hands Over the City* (1963), *The Mattei Affair* (1972), *Illustrious Corpses* (1976) *Christ Stopped at Eboli* (1979) and *Three Brothers* (1981).

Roberto Rosselini (1906–1977)

A key figure in the Italian neo-realist movement, whose early films were made on shoestring budgets and in often difficult conditions (see *Rome, Open City*, 1945, about the anti-Fascist Resistance, shot when Mussolini's troops were still occupying Rome). *Voyage in Italy* (1953), in its open-endedness and preoccupation with George Sanders' and Ingrid Bergman's fluctuating senses of cultural alienation, foreshadowed the hesitant psychological explorations of Antonioni. Other key films: *Germany Year Zero* (1948), *Stromboli* (1949) and *The Rise of Louis XIV* (1966).

Robert Rossen (1908–1966)

One of the most socially aware of Hollywood directors who made his mark in the later 1940s with a hard-hitting boxing saga *Body and Soul* (1947), which was actually an allegory of capitalist corruption, and the Oscar-winning *All the King's Men* (1949), an indictment of creeping political Fascism. But then, hounded by the House UnAmerican Activities Committee for his Communist affiliations, he finally recanted and named names. He was able to work again but became, according to friends, a haunted, withdrawn individual. But his last two films were remarkable returns to form: a study of character and courage around the pool table, *The Hustler* (1961), and a study of madness, *Lilith* (1964), which was condemned on its first release but has gained an underground reputation as one of the most lyrical films of the American cinema.

Martin Scorsese (b. 1942)

Arguably the most exciting of modern American film-makers. His movies are notable for their restless camera movement which reflects the inner tension of the characters. He has collaborated particularly closely with actor Robert De Niro, forging the most important actor-director partnership in American film since Brando and Kazan in the 1950s. Together they have made emotionally lacerating films about troubled masculinity and with a religious sense of redemption. Sometimes criticised for misogyny, Scorsese's films are nonetheless the most disturbing and challenging of contemporary mainstream cinema. Key films: *Mean Streets* (1973), *Taxi Driver* (1976), *Raging Bull* (1980), *The King of Comedy* (1983), *After Hours* (1985), *Goodfellas* (1990) *Cape Fear* (1991) and *The Age of Innocence* (1993).

Douglas Sirk (1900–1987)

Long regarded as a curiosity, a Danish expatriate whose melodramas, richly shot and distinguished by narrative flamboyance, were treated with mild patronisation. *Written on the Wind* (1956) was among the first to gain serious acceptance, with its dramatisation of the conflicts within a wealthy oil family whose problems (alcoholism, instability, sexual promiscuity) were sympathetically presented in a highly-coloured style that still managed to eschew portentousness or heavy realism. His other works, notably *All That Heaven Allows* (1955) and *Imitation of Life* (1959), also began to receive more serious and sympathetic treatment as ironic and subversive critiques of middle-class America: they had a profound influence on the work of Fassbinder.

Other key films: *There's Always Tomorrow* (1956), *Tarnished Angels* (1957) and *A Time to Love and A Time to Die* (1958).

Steven Spielberg (b. 1947)

The most successful director in the history of cinema, notably for four films: *Jaws* (1975), *Close Encounters of the Third Kind* (1977), *E.T.—the Extra-Terrestrial* (1982) and *Jurassic Park* (1993). The secret of his success is the blend of innocence and precociousness, the heart of a Peter Pan with the technique of an Alfred Hitchcock. His films are basically about ordinary people in extraordinary situations, and he directs these with a witty eye for the mores of American suburbia, a tremendous flair for suspense, and an unusually sympathetic presentation of the relationships between mothers and children. Recently a new maturity has come into his work with *The Color Purple* (1985), *Empire of the Sun* (1987) and *Schindler's List* (1993) but, like Peter Pan himself, he seems loth to leave the world of childhood: a recent film is a version of *Peter Pan* called *Hook* (1991). Other key films: *Duel* (1971), *The Sugarland Express* (1974) and *Raiders of the Lost Ark* (1981).

George Stevens (1904–1975)

Beginning his career as a cameraman on Laurel and Hardy shorts, Stevens' early reputation as a director was in comedy: *Woman of the Year* (1942) and *The More the Merrier* (1943). But his war experience, which included being part of the American force that liberated Dachau, changed his sensibility: comedy receded and his films became full of a feeling of tragic sacrifice. *The Diary of Anne Frank* (1959) is his memorial to the war dead. His own movie monument is probably a trio of films that encapsulates his sympathy for the outsider and constitutes his epic reassessment of the American Dream: *A Place in the Sun* (1951), *Shane* (1953), and *Giant* (1956). Other key films: *Alice Adams* (1935), *Gunga Din* (1939), *Talk of the Town* (1942), *I Remember Mama* (1948) and *The Greatest Story Ever Told* (1965).

Preston Sturges (1898–1959)

One of the first great writer-directors of the sound era in Hollywood, Sturges sold his screenplay *The Great McGinty* (1940) to Paramount for ten dollars on the condition he was allowed to direct. It was the first of eight comedies he wrote and directed within four years, each of which was interesting, some of which—*The Lady Eve* (1941), *Sullivan's Travels* (1942), *Palm Beach Story* (1942)—are classics. His comedies are distinguished by a frantic pace, tremendous ingenuity of dialogue and situation, and an air of shrill desperation. His characters comprise hapless millionaires, seductive gold-diggers and frustrated inventors, all whipped together in a sustained assault on what Sturges saw as all-American sacred cows—politics, motherhood, small-town life, the obsession with success. It is not surprising that his talent burnt out, but for a while his creative flame flared as brilliantly as anyone's.

Andrey Tarkovsky (1932–1986)

The greatest Soviet film-maker since Eisenstein—and the resemblance ends there. Tarkovsky found his inspiration not in the spirit of the Russian Revolution but in the spirituality of the classic Russian novel, and the questions his films posed were not about the nature of political power but about the possibilities of personal salvation. This inevitably brought him into conflict with the Soviet authorities, who disliked the unsocialist, surreal, avant-garde qualities in films such as *Andrei Rublev* (1966) and *Mirror* (1974). They also took exception to Tarkovsky's thinly concealed allegory of the struggles of the artist in a repressive society. His last films were made in exile, and his final film, *The Sacrifice* (1985), a typically hallucinatory drama about a dream of nuclear holocaust averted, was one of his most movingly accessible and affirmative. A dreamer, a poet, a prophet, Tarkovsky's provocative and challenging thoughts on cinema were published in his book, *Sculpting in Time* (1987). Other key films: *Ivan's Childhood* (1962), *Solaris* (1971), *Stalker* (1979) and *Nostalgia* (1982).

Francois Truffaut (1932–1984)

With Godard, one of the outstanding early names of the so-called French "New Wave". His early work reveals a delight in the possibilities of the cinematic medium (notably in evoking situations of emotional fluidity and ambiguity) that is often exhilarating, as in *Shoot the Pianist* (with Charles Aznavour, 1960) and his masterpiece, *Jules et Jim* (1961). This deals with a menage a trois in the France of the beginning of the century, portrayed with tragic irony and a light yet serious treatment of historical and cultural influences on the relationship between Catherine (Jeanne Moreau) and her two lovers, the German Jules and the Frenchman Jim. His first feature film, *The 400 Blows* (1959) drew on his own difficult childhood and delinquent adolescence, and later films like *L'Enfant Sauvage* (1970) also deal sensitively with the world of childhood. He then made films like *Fahrenheit 451* (1965) and *The Bride Wore Black* (1968) in homage to Hitchcock. In the 1970s he made two of his most haunting films on his favourite theme of romantic obsession, *The Story of Adele H* (1975) and *The Green Room* (1978), but he also made one of the most affectionate of all films about film-making, *Day for Night* (1973). Truffaut loved movies and his death left cineastes feeling that they had lost a member of the family.

Dziga Vertov (1896–1934)

The great documentary director, as Eisenstein was the great feature director, of the early Bolshevik Russian days. His principal work is *The Man with a Movie Camera* (1929), an exhilarating exploration of the relationship between the camera, the person holding it, and the subject-matter being filmed, and an illustration that documentary, propaganda, and artistic satisfaction are far from incompatible.

Jean Vigo (1905–1934)

A great Surrealist director, whose early death from tuberculosis meant that he produced only two feature films, both masterpieces: *Zero de Conduite* (1933), an account of a rebellion in a repressive boys' school whose fragmentary, night-marish quality (partly a result of the tight conditions under which it was shot) is exceptional, and *L'Atalante* (1934), about a honeymoon on a barge, a haunting blend of lyricism and realism.

Luchino Visconti (1906–1977)

The most emotive and extravagant of the Italian neo-realists. He came to attention with *La Terra Trema* (1948), about Sicilian fishermen; a mixture of tragic fatalism and concern for social change characteristic of Visconti pervades this, as it does the operatic *Rocco and his Brothers* of 1960 and his adaptation of the novel by Lampedusa, *The Leopard* (1963). Aristocrat yet communist, arthouse director who loved working with stars (like Dirk Bogarde and Burt Lancaster), Visconti was a strange mixture of extremes. His films dealt with forbidden passions; tormented heroes imprisoned by the standards of a society they despise; and superficially cultured ways of life in their death-throes. Nobody recreated the past more sumptuously on the screen than Visconti nor photographed doom more voluptuously. Other key films: *Ossessione* (1942), *Senso* (1954), *The Damned* (1969), *Death in Venice* (1971), *Ludwig* (1972) and *Conversation Piece* (1974).

Josef Von Sternberg (1894–1969)

The supreme exponent of cinema as icon, of the image whose lavish and elaborate composition is its most immediately apparent justification. Yet his work escapes the arid aestheticism this statement might suggest, through its awareness of the central importance of woman as pursuer/pursued and of the symbiosis between man's desire for humiliation and woman's desire to castrate. This makes *The Blue Angel* (1930) the most harrowing of the films Sternberg made with Marlene Dietrich; most exotic is probably *The Devil is a Woman* (1935). Other key films: *Morocco* (1930), *Shanghai Express* (1932) and *The Scarlet Empress* (1934).

Erich Von Stroheim (1885–1957)

"By God I told them the truth" said Stroheim of his classic film *Greed* (1923). Unfortunately for MGM, he told it at excessive length, and the film was cut from 42 to 10 reels in length. Stroheim's career as director never recovered from this. But John Grierson was to call him "the director of directors", for his unflinching realism and fanatical attention to detail. Billy Wilder thought he was ten years ahead of his time, though Stroheim contradicted him: "No—twenty". Key films: *Foolish Wives* (1922), *Merry-Go-Round* (1923) and *Queen Kelly* (1928).

Andrzej Wajda (b. 1926)

Perhaps the most important film-maker Poland has ever produced. He grew up in Poland during the Nazi occupation and his famous trilogy, *A Generation* (1955), *Kanal* (1956) and *Ashes and Diamonds* (1958)—records the wartime suffering and courage and the scramble for political power that followed the liberation. *Ashes and Diamonds*, in particular, with its charismatic performance by Zbigniew Cybulski, exemplifies Wajda's fascination with heroes who refuse to follow the tide of history and attempt to shape their own destinies through extreme action. For a time, history took second place to psychology and symbolism in his work. But in the mid 1970s, he returned head-on to contemporary issues, tackling the theme of censorship, political blackmail and the film-maker's responsibilities in *Man of Marble* (1976), and celebrating the rise of Solidarity in *Man of Iron* (1980) in a tone of prophetically precarious optimism. Wajda's films have often been set in transitional periods where one era has died and another is struggling to be born. His own career has also been subject to the turbulent tides of history, facing censorship, exile and rejection, but his achievements stand as an inspiring example of artistic talent surviving against difficult odds. Other key films: *Innocent Sorcerers* (1961), *Everything for Sale* (1968), *The Wedding* (1973), *The Conductor* (1980) and *Korczak* (1988).

Orson Welles (1915–1985)

Made his debut with *Citizen Kane* in 1941; fifty years later, it is still a popular choice as the best film ever made. Innovatory in film language in its bold and extensive use of "deep-focus"—the camera plunging into the imaginary "depth" of the screen), suggestive in its plot (about a tycoon, modelled on William Randolph Hearst, whose public success is seen as a remedy for private unhappiness), electric in the quality of its camerawork and ensemble acting, and with its finale (the "secret" of Kane's life—the name of his confiscated childhood sledge, Rosebud) the most ironically well-kept secret in cinema history, the film succeeded on so many levels that hind-sight almost suggests Welles's subsequent career had to be an anti-climax. He has filmed Shakespeare (*Chimes at Midnight*, 1966), Kafka (*The Trial*, 1963) and a "documentary" about forgeries (*F. for Fake*, 1975), none to the effect of *Kane*. Nevertheless the qualities of his other films should not be overlooked: the tenderness of *The Magnificent Ambersons* (1942), the *film noir* virtuosity of *Lady from Shanghai* (1948), the magisterial study of police corruption in *Touch of Evil* (1958). It is tempting to see *Kane* as a prophetic study of promise unfulfilled, and Welles's career certainly had more than its share of disappointments and frustrations. But he still remains a giant of the cinema, probing themes of power and corruption with that virtuoso camera style that he said "describes that sense of vertigo, uncertainty, lack of stability, that melange of movement and tension that is our universe".

Wim Wenders (b. 1945)

One of the major figures of the "New German Cinema" of the 1970s, cooler and less didactic than Fassbinder, more streetwise and less anti-American than Herzog. His ambivalent response to America's "Coca-colonisation" of Europe was explored in *The American Friend* (1977), which had guest roles for Nicholas Ray and Samuel Fuller; and films such as *The Goalkeeper's Fear of the Penalty* (1972) and *Kings of the Road* (1976) elaborated his interest in the alienation of the modern environment and the rootlessness of modern man. Wenders' films commonly start from place rather than plot and it is no surprise that his biggest international success to date is *Paris Texas* (1984), a film as remarkable for its disorienting landscape as its characters or story.

Billy Wilder (b. 1906)

"It's not important that a director knows how to write," said Billy Wilder, "but it is important that he knows how to read." Fleeing from Nazi Europe and becoming a Hollywood screenwriter for, among others, Ernst Lubitsch, Wilder became a director in order to protect his own scripts. *Double Indemnity* (1944), *The Lost Weekend* (1945) and *Sunset Boulevard* (1950) were wonderfully macabre demonstrations of his talents, and films like *Some Like it Hot* (1959) and *The Apartment* (1960) consolidated his reputation as the sharpest satirist in Hollywood, with an unusually mordant view of human nature that did not, however, preclude the possibility of redemption. *Sabrina* (1954) and *Avanti!* (1972) show the melting of American materialism by European romanticism. His care for structure, his unceasing verbal wit and the intelligence of his character development make Wilder's overall achievement the equal of any Hollywood director's of the sound era. Other key films: *Ace in the Hole* (1951), *Stalag 17* (1953), *Witness for the Prosecution* (1957), *One, Two, Three* (1961), *The Fortune Cookie* (1966), *The Private Life of Sherlock Holmes* (1970) and *Fedora* (1978).

William Wyler (1902–1981)

One of the master craftsmen of Hollywood film. As well as winning three Oscars for himself (for *Mrs. Miniver*, 1942; *The Best Years of Our Lives*, 1946; and *Ben-Hur*, 1959), he elicited more than a dozen Oscar-winning performances from his casts. Although he could handle the epic canvas as well as anyone, his forte was for drama in a confined setting and struggles for territorial advantage in a marriage or family. *The Little Foxes*, (1941), *The Heiress* (1949) and *Carrie* (1952) are all masterpieces of domestic claustrophobia. Whilst his heroes tended to be withdrawn figures, needing to be convinced of the necessity for action (like the pacifist hero of *The Big Country*, (1958)), his heroines are more often dynamic creatures, kicking against the constraints of a masculine world. No wonder he was Bette Davis's favourite director and directed her in some of her best films: *Jezebel* (1938), *The Letter* (1940) and *The Little Foxes*. Although recurrent patterns and themes are discernible in his films (unrequited love, class confrontations between the complacent and the envious), he tended, like Huston, to subordinate his personality to the requirements of the story. For this reason, he has often been underestimated by *auteurist* critics. But if a great director is simply someone who has made a number of great films, Wyler was a great director. Other key films: *Dodsworth* (1936), *Wuthering Heights* (1939), *Roman Holiday* (1952) and *The Children's Hour* (1961).

Fred Zinnemann (b. 1907)

Born in Vienna, Zinnemann came to America in 1929, but his career did not really take off until *The Search* in 1948, a story of European children orphaned by the war and which presaged a number of his films about the impact and aftermath of war. But it was the western *High Noon* (1952) that established both Zinnemann's reputation and his fundamental theme: that of individual conscience. At considerable personal risk but on a point of principle, a character takes a stand against a community or institution that wishes him to compromise and conform: it is the theme also of *From Here to Eternity* (1953), *The Nun's Story* (1959) and *A Man for All Seasons* (1966). Unusually for Hollywood, these were dramas of reaction, not action, and with melancholy rather than happy endings. Their critical and commercial success testified to Zinnemann's skill at popularising complex themes without compromising his vision. Other key films: *The Seventh Cross* (1944), *Act of Violence* (1949), *Member of the Wedding* (1952), *Day of the Jackal* (1973) and *Julia* (1977). He published his autobiography in 1991.

EXPLANATION OF SOME TERMS

auteurism a critical theory, popular in France in the fifties and sixties, that ascribed overall responsibility for the creation of a film to its director, and thereby provoked renewed critical analysis of much previously neglected Hollywood work. The "*politique des auteurs*" (auteur policy) was first stated by Francois Truffaut in the January 1954 issue of *Cahiers du Cinema*; the main exponent of the auteur "theory" in America was the critic Andrew Sarris.

cinema verité, literally "cinema truth"; it signified a kind of documentary cinema that used light-weight equipment, minimal crews (camera and sound) and interview techniques.

deep focus, a technique favoured by realists in which objects very near the camera as well as those far away are in focus at the same time: particularly associated with the cameraman Gregg Toland and the forties' films of Welles and Wyler.

film noir, films with a grim, urban setting that deal mainly with dark and violent passions in a downbeat way. Especially associated with American thrillers of the forties and early fifties.

genre, a type or class of film (*e.g.* the musical, the western).

German expressionism, a style of film common in Germany in the twenties, typified by dramatic lighting, distorted sets, symbolic action and characterisation as in, for example, *The Cabinet of Dr. Caligari* (Robert Wiene, 1920).

mise en scene, literally, "staging"—the way in which the elements and components in a film are arranged and encompassed by the camera, or the term usually used to denote that part of the cinematic process that takes place on the set, as opposed to montage, which takes place afterwards.

montage, the juxtaposition of material (successive shots, or items within a shot) to suggest meaning—as when Eisenstein in *Potemkin* evokes anger at the massacre by showing three successive shots of stone lions in various positions, shot to look as though they are one lion rising to its feet and roaring its fury.

movie brats, younger generation of Hollywood directors who exploded onto the scene in the early 1970s: *e.g.* Spielberg, George Lucas, Brian De Palma, Martin Scorsese.

neo-realism connected with movement out of the studio, shooting on real locations, sometimes the absence of a script and/or non-professional casts —all designed simultaneously to cut costs and increase the impression of spontaneity. In fact inaugurated by Renoir, but associated with Italian post-war directors (Rossellini, Visconti).

new wave, a loose, heterogeneous group of young French critics (Chabrol, Rivette, Truffaut, Godard), who went into direction in the late fifties and sixties. Much influenced by Hollywood action cinema, they relied heavily on hand-held cameras, a laconic and non-moralistic style, a general sense of existential amoralism.

screwball comedy, type of comedy popular in thirties' Hollywood characterised by frantic action, verbal wit, and a couple in a bizarre predicament, *e.g.* Capra's *It Happened One Night* (1934), Hawks's *Bringing Up Baby* (1938).

3. FAMOUS SCREEN ACTORS AND ACTRESSES

Julie Andrews (b. 1935)

The archetype of screen virtue who reached her peak of popularity in the mid-1960s with *Mary Poppins* (1964) and *The Sound of Music* (1965), in both of which her "English rose" image and pure singing voice enchanted audiences. She has since made a number of films for her second husband, director Blake Edwards, but without the same success.

"Fatty" Arbuckle (1887–1933)

Superb silent comedian whose career was ruined when accused of the rape and murder of a starlet Virginia Rappe at a wild Hollywood party in 1921. Although completely cleared of all charges, Arbuckle was never allowed to appear on the screen again (the whole story is told in David Yallop's book, *The Day the Laughter Stopped*). Buster Keaton, who owed his start in movies to Arbuckle, said he learnt everything about film from him.

Fred Astaire (1899–1987)

"Can't act, slightly bald, can dance a little", was the verdict of the screen test of Astaire, who, in partnership with Ginger Rogers, was to become the most stylish screen dancer in Hollywood history. He starred in such classic musicals as *Top Hat* (1935), *Swing Time* (1936), *Easter Parade* (1948) and *Funny Face* (1956). Turned to straight acting in his later career with such effect that Spencer Tracy felt threatened and sent the following wire to his friend: "You stop acting or I'll start dancing!"

Lauren Bacall (b. 1924)

One of the first examples of Hollywood's skill at playing on-and-off screen personas off against each other. Opposite Humphrey Bogart in *To Have and Have Not* (1944), she enchanted him on the screen as she did in real life while the film was being shot. Her performance there is a remarkably knowing and ironic one (particularly in the famous scene where she tells Bogart how to whistle for her if he wants anything), and she was to play similar roles opposite him in *The Big Sleep* (1946), *Dark Passage* (Delmer Daves, 1947) and *Key Largo* (John Huston, 1948). Although she was never really able to repeat her success with Bogart, her persona in these films is interesting as a contrast to the submissive view of women often purveyed by Hollywood.

Brigitte Bardot (b. 1934)

"Created" by her then-husband Roger Vadim in *And God Created Woman* (1956). She epitomised a certain popular view of French female sexuality—poutingly sensual, sporting a St. Tropez suntan and little else besides, as ardent and capricious in her off-screen romances as in those for the cameras. In Julien Duvivier's *La Femme et le Pantin* (1958) and Vadim's *Warrior's Rest* (1962) she exploited this role to perfection; but she did show that she had some acting ability in *Le Mepris*, made for Jean-Luc Godard in 1963, in *Viva Maria* (1965) for Louis Malle, and in *La Verité* (1960) for Henri-Georges Clouzot. Retired from the screen to devote herself to ecological issues.

Warren Beatty (b. 1937)

Many people think of Beatty's career as beginning with *Bonnie and Clyde* (Arthur Penn, 1967), in which his performance as the debonair yet sexually insecure bandit Clyde steals the show. But he sprang to prominence as early as 1961 (Elia Kazan's *Splendour in the Grass*), and has appeared infrequently, but always to great effect, ever since, his best post-Bonnie performance perhaps being the gambler McCabe in Altman's *McCabe and Mrs. Miller* (1971). Political and directorial ambitions have preoccupied him more than acting recently, and he won an Oscar for the direction of *Reds* (1981).

Jean-Paul Belmondo (b. 1933)

Sprang to fame with his performance as the confusedly amoral Michel Poiccard in Godard's *Breathless* (1959). This earned him recognition as one of the first "anti-heroes" of the European cinema, concerned with discovering himself through action and, in his second masterpiece for Godard, *Pierrot le Fou* (1965), contemplation as well. Both films featured Belmondo "betrayed", ostensibly by the women he chose (Jean Seberg and Anna Karina respectively), but as much by his own insecure openness. His later work (including *Borsalino* for Deray in 1970, and *Stavisky* for Resnais in 1974) tended to be glossier and more spectacular, to the detriment of the "anti-hero" persona.

Ingrid Bergman (1915–1982)

Enticed, like Greta Garbo, from Sweden to Hollywood at the end of the thirties, she became one of Hollywood's star actresses, particularly in exotic "European" roles like that of Humphrey Bogart's lost *grand amour* in Michael Curtiz's *Casablanca* (1943). She went on to freelance in Europe in the fifties, notably for Roberto Roselini (whom she married), in neo-realist classics such as *Stromboli* (1950) and *Voyage in Italy* (1953). Made a triumphant comeback to Hollywood in *Anastasia* (1956), and in her later years had great success in *The Murder on the Orient Express* (1974) for which she won her third Oscar and in Ingmar Bergman's *Autumn Sonata* (1978).

Sir Dirk Bogarde (b. 1921)

It takes an effort to remind ourselves that the Bogarde destroyed by his death-wish passion for a young boy in Visconti's *Death in Venice* (1971) began his acting career in British comedy features and acquired real prominence as the accident-prone medical student in the "Doctor" films of the late fifties. Joseph Losey first exploited his dramatic acting talent in *The Servant* (1963), which played off his British reserve against a highly-charged situation as Losey was also to do in *Accident* (1967). Semi-retired since his performance in Resnais's *Providence* (1977), he has since made an effective comeback in Bertrand Tavernier's *These Foolish Things* (1990).

Humphrey Bogart (1899–1957)

One of the all-time superstars. Bogart began as a stage actor and graduated to screen stardom with one of his theatre roles, the psychopathic gangster in Mayo's *The Petrified Forest* (1936). He became famous in the forties as an "outsider" figure, caught up in corrupt or devious situations from which he tried to stay aloof through a basic decency masquerading as hard-bitten cynicism. *Casablanca* (Michael Curtiz, 1943) revealed the persona to have a soft heart, in the scenes where he drinks to forget his love for Ingrid Bergman—or rather to remember it—and where he sacrifices it in the airport scene at the end with the immortal: "Here's looking at you, kid". For Howard Hawks he made *To Have and Have Not* in 1944 and *The Big Sleep* in 1946, both with Lauren Bacall and both exploiting the same persona. Small wonder that fifties anti-hero Belmondo elevated him to a god in *Breathless* (Godard, 1959), as did Woody Allen in a different way in *Play it Again, Sam* (1972). Closely associated with director John Huston, for whom he made six films, including *The Maltese Falcon* (1941), *The Treasure of the Sierra Madre* (1948) and the film for which he won his Oscar, *The African Queen* (1951).

Clara Bow (1905–1965)

Known as the "It" girl because of her enormously popular personal success in the film *It* (1927). Epitomised the "Roaring 20s" during the silent era but her career then foundered because of sound, scandals and mental illness. She was the Monroe of her time: a sad fate.

Marlon Brando (b. 1924)

Brando came to the cinema from the stage, a leading proponent of the "Method" school of acting which relied upon naturalistic empathy with the part rather than careful professional stylisation. Laconic violence, often tending to the inarticulate, was his early stock-in-trade, exemplified in *A Streetcar Named Desire* (1951) and *On The Waterfront* (1954), both directed by Elia Kazan. Other rebels vied with Brando in the late fifties and sixties, and his career went into an eclipse from which it was rescued by two very different, but remarkable, performances as men aware that they have passed their personal peak—the *Mafioso* Don

Corleone in Coppola's *The Godfather* (1972), and the self-loathing American in Bertolucci's *Last Tango in Paris* (1973). Has since tended to confine himself to expensive guest performances in movies like *Superman* (1980), though he gave a superb character performance as a Scottish liberal lawyer in the anti-apartheid drama, *A Dry White Season* (1989). Published a much publicised autobiography in 1994.

Louise Brooks (1906–1985)

Magnetic star whose film fame rests mainly on one charismatic performance: as Lulu in G. W. Pabst's *Pandora's Box* (1929). She retired from the screen in the early 1930s and had a reclusive life, though briefly surfaced to write a marvellous book of memoirs, *Lulu in Hollywood*,

Richard Burton (1925–1984)

Initially a leading stage Shakespearian, but better-known to the film-going public for his flamboyant romance with Elizabeth Taylor and his resonant performances in costume-dramas (*Cleopatra* for Joseph L. Mankiewicz in 1963) and macho action-dramas (Hathaway's *Raid on Rommel*, 1971). Despite much rubbish his performance as the verbally aggressive college professor in Mike Nichols's *Who's Afraid of Virginia Woolf?* (1966) marked him out as a great screen actor, as did his performance in *The Spy who came in from the Cold* (1966). He was nominated seven times for the coveted Oscar without winning: his last performance was as the sinister interrogator O'Brien in the 1984 screen adaptation of George Orwell's *1984*.

James Cagney (1899–1986)

Pugnacious leading man who started out as a dancer but whose energy and vitality made him ideal for the dynamic gangster movies of the 1930s, such as *Public Enemy* (1931), *Angels with Dirty Faces* (1938) and *The Roaring Twenties* (1939). Won an Oscar for *Yankee Doodle Dandy* (1942) but his most memorable characterisation was probably as the psychopathic, mother-fixated Cody Jarrett in Raoul Walsh's *White Heat* (1949).

Sir Charles Chaplin (1889–1977)

Still the most famous film star and director in the history of movies. His creation of the "little man"—the wistful tramp figure who fantasises his way out of the hardships of life—achieved success on an unprecedented scale and effectively made the transition from silent shorts to feature-length films, the most famous being *The Gold Rush* (1925). He fought hard against the coming of sound, refusing to use any apart from music and sound effects in *City Lights* (1931), where the blend of slapstick and suspense was particularly well achieved. His later films, like *Modern Times* (1936), *The Great Dictator* (1940) and *Monsieur Verdoux* (1947) were infused with his socialist political sympathies which set him at odds with the American authorities and led to his exile in 1952. His reputation has plummeted since his death, but he remains the most significant and creative film comic of the century. A recent bio-pic *Chaplin* (1992) has been made by Sir Richard Attenborough, starring Robert Downey Jnr.

Julie Christie (b. 1941)

Beautiful British actress who shot to international stardom with her performance in *Darling* (1965) and *Doctor Zhivago* (1965). Her best films include *Petulia* (1968), *The Go-Between* (1971), *McCabe and Mrs. Miller* (1971) and *Don't Look Now* (1973).

Montgomery Clift (1920–1966)

Now enjoys a vogue as one of the great Hollywood victims, destroyed by drink, pills and inability to come to terms with his homosexuality. This litany should not obscure the fact that he was a tremendously gifted screen actor, as a tormented priest in *I Confess* (Hitchcock, 1952), as a cowboy opposite John Wayne in Hawk's *Red River* (1948), or with Clark Gable and Marilyn Monroe in that most macabre of pictures (it marked the end of virtually all its stars' careers), John Huston's *The Misfits* of 1960. Other key performances include *A*

Place in the Sun (Stevens, 1951), *From Here to Eternity* (Zinnemann, 1953) and *Freud* (Huston, 1962). Speaking of his tormented personality, Marilyn Monroe once commented: "He's the only person I know who's in worse shape than I am."

Gary Cooper (1901–1961)

Cooper embodied quintessential American decency—not blustering like Wayne nor cynical like Bogart, the decent lad up from the country putting sophisticates to shame in *Mr. Deeds Goes to Town* (Frank Capra, 1936), the pacifist soldier in Hawks's *Sergeant York* (1941), or—his best-known role—the lone sheriff in Zinnemann's *High Noon* (1952).

Sean Connery (b. 1930)

Connery achieved fame as the first and best of the screen James Bonds, but has recently been recognised as one of the best character-actor stars of modern cinema. Won an overdue Oscar for *The Untouchables* (1987) and has also given fine character performances in such films as Hitchcock's *Marnie* (1964), *The Hill* (1965), *The Man Who Would be King* (1975), *Robin and Marian* (1976) and *The Name of the Rose* (1987).

Joan Crawford (1906–1977)

The leading unhappy-in-love female star of the thirties and early forties (as in Cukor's *The Women* of 1939), she won an Oscar for *Mildred Pierce* (Michael Curtiz, 1945). In later life a successful and immensely wealthy businesswoman, and better known perhaps as a star than for any individual performances, and as the subject of her daughter's sensational memoir, *Mommie Dearest*, filmed in 1981 with Faye Dunaway as Crawford. Played masochist to Bette Davis's sadist in the gleefully grotesque *Whatever Happened to Baby Jane?* (1962).

Bette Davis (1908–1989)

"Nobody's as good as Bette when she's bad" was the slogan coined for Bette Davis, who excelled at playing dynamic or queen-bitch heroines. Among her major screen performances were three for William Wyler, *Jezebel* (1938), *The Letter* (1940) and *The Little Foxes* (1941), and when her career seemed destined for oblivion in the late 1940s, she returned with one of the classic characterisations of the screen, as the dominating actress Margot Channing in *All About Eve* (1950). Her autobiography *The Lonely Life* (1962) is one of the frankest and most intelligent of any screen star.

Doris Day (b. 1924)

Pure, wholesome singing star who achieved her peak of popularity in the 1950s and early 1960s, particularly in a series of romantic comedies she made with Rock Hudson, including *Pillow Talk* (1959), *Lover Come Back* (1962) and *Send Me No Flowers* (1964). Recently appropriated by the feminists, who admire her screen persona for its career-woman independence and its healthy suspicion of male seductive strategies. Certainly someone who can upstage performers such as James Cagney (in *Love Me or Leave Me*, 1954), James Stewart (in *The Man Who Knew Too Much*, 1956) and Clark Gable (in *Teacher's Pet*, 1958) is no mean actress.

James Dean (1931–1955)

Made three starring feature roles before his death in a car crash in 1955. But those three, and particularly *Rebel Without a Cause* for Nicholas Ray in 1955, were enough to establish him as Hollywood's leading rebel (along with Brando—and how fascinating subsequent rivalry between their careers would have been). In *Rebel* Dean showed himself as a gentler, more idealistic figure than Brando, particularly in his "adoption" of the young runaway Sal Mineo. In *East of Eden* (Kazan, 1955), it is again his idealism that leads him to look out his mother, now running a whore-house, with disastrous results. In *Giant* (Stevens, 1956) he is an independent cowboy whose discovery of oil on his land will transform him into an isolated tycoon.

Robert De Niro (b. 1943)

The finest American screen actor since Brando, noted for the dedication with which he immerses himself in his roles (for example, his gaining sixty pounds in weight to play the role of Jake LaMotta in decline in *Raging Bull*). Has had a particularly important collaboration with director Martin Scorsese, for whom he has turned in some of his finest studies of violent yet tortured masculinity: *Mean Streets* (1973), *Taxi Driver* (1976), *Raging Bull* (1980), *Cape Fear* (1991). Other important films include: *The Godfather Part II* (1974), *The Deer Hunter* (1978).

Marlene Dietrich (1902–1992)

Overnight fame came her way when Joseph von Sternberg cast her as the sensuous and manipulative night-club singer Lola in *The Blue Angel* (1930). She manipulates Emil Jannings's school teacher there as Sternberg's camera manipulates her (and us the spectators), through a sequence of lushly masochistic masterpieces including *The Scarlet Empress* (1934). Her post-Sternberg career diversified into cabaret performance, and her subsequent movies, including *The Flame of New Orleans* for Rene Clair in 1941 and *Rancho Notorious* for Fritz Lang in 1952, did not attain the same heights as her work for Sternberg, though she gave striking performances in two Billy Wilder films, *A Foreign Affair* (1948) and *Witness for the Prosecution* (1957), and a memorable cameo in Welles's *Touch of Evil* (1958).

Kirk Douglas (b. 1916)

Dimpled-chin he-man of the American screen, who excelled in roles of unscrupulous, ambitious anti-heroes, such as those in *Champion* (1949), *Ace in the Hole* (1951) and *The Bad and the Beautiful* (1952), though a more sensitive and tormented side to his persona is also seen in such films as *Lust for Life* (1955), in which he plays Van Gogh and *Paths of Glory* (1957). The father of successful screen actor and producer, Michael Douglas.

Clint Eastwood (b. 1930)

In the great tradition of stars like John Wayne and Gary Cooper who projects pure Americanism and rectifies wrongs, though in a more ferocious manner than his predecessors. Became a star for his "Man With No Name" characterisation in Sergio Leone's violent, stylised "Dollars" westerns; and became a superstar after playing the tough cop in *Dirty Harry* (1971). Sometimes attacked for their Fascist overtones, Eastwood's films have also been praised for their strong female roles, Eastwood's willingness to examine his own screen persona, and their engagement with contemporary issues. Eastwood is also a talented director, sometimes starring in his own films (*e.g. The Outlaw Josey Wales*, 1976) and sometimes not (*Bird*, 1988). His revisionist Western *Unforgiven* (1992) was widely acclaimed as a classic and won him a directing 'Oscar'.

Douglas Fairbanks (1883–1939)

The supreme action man of silent cinema, excelling in such features as *The Three Musketeers* (1921), *Robin Hood* (1922) and *The Thief of Bagdad* (1924). Age and sound took their toll of his popularity as did his divorce from Mary Pickford in 1936, after a marriage of sixteen years. But during the silent era, nobody epitomised screen heroism more exuberantly.

W. C. Fields (1879–1946)

Fields is the polar opposite of Chaplin as a screen comedian, in that, while the "little man" courts audience affection, Fields does everything in his drunken, misogynistic, mean, cynical, ill-tempered power to repel it. Through such titles as *Mrs. Wiggs of the Cabbage Patch* (Norman Taurog, 1934) and *Never Give a Sucker an Even Break* (Edward Cline, 1941), he paraded preposterous situations (usually of his own invention), and a battery of dislikes that included wives, children, domestic animals and authority figures. His best films were *It's A Gift* (1935) and *The Bank Dick* (1940). When discovered on his death-bed reading the Bible, he explained that he was "looking for loopholes".

Peter Finch (1916–1977)

Rugged yet subtle screen performer, who won the British Academy Award four times for his performances in *A Town Like Alice* (1956), *The Trials of Oscar Wilde* (1960), *No Love for Johnnie* (1961) and *Sunday, Bloody Sunday* (1971). He won a posthumous Oscar for his performance in *Network* (1976).

Albert Finney (b. 1936)

Made a big impression with his first screen performances in such films as *Saturday Night and Sunday Morning* (1961) and *Tom Jones* (1963), and was hailed as "a second Olivier". But, unlike Richard Burton, he seemed to eschew screen stardom in favour of theatrical work. The most powerful of his recent film performances has been as the drunken Consul in Huston's adaptation of Malcolm Lowry's novel, *Under the Volcano* (1984).

Henry Fonda (1905–1982)

One of the major Hollywood leading men of the late thirties and forties, with distinguished starring roles for Fritz Lang (as the runaway in *You Only Love Once*, 1937) and John Ford (in *Young Mr. Lincoln* and *Drums Along the Mohawk*, both 1939). His honest and conscientious stance was just right for the immediate pre- and post-war years. After a lull in his screen career, he made a successful comeback in such films as *Mister Roberts* (1955), *Twelve Angry Men* (1957) and *The Best Man* (1964), and won a long-awaited Oscar for his last film, *On Golden Pond* (1981), in which he co-starred with his daughter Jane.

Jane Fonda (b. 1937)

Began her career in "sex-symbol" roles—in Hollywood and for her then husband Roger Vadim—that now appear incongruous in the light of her progressive political position (Edward Dmytryk's *Walk on the Wild Side*, 1962; Vadim's *Barbarella*, 1968). Her involvement with women's movement and anti-Vietnam campaigns took her into such films as *Klute* (Pakula, 1971), where she plays a prostitute who regards herself as "the only truly liberated woman". She won an Oscar for *Klute* and won again later in the decade for *Coming Home* (1978), confirming herself as one of the most accomplished of modern screen actresses.

Jean Gabin (1904–1976)

In many ways Gabin was for the French cinema of the thirties and forties what Gary Cooper or Henry Fonda were for Hollywood—the stoically decent man of the people whose malediction sprang from his very ordinariness. He excelled for two directors in particular: Marcel Carné for whom he played a deserter in *Quai des Brumes* and a workman in *Le Jour se Leve* (1938 and 1939 respectively), both of whom meet violent deaths as a result of falling in love, and Jean Renoir, in whose *La Bete Humaine* (1938) he was an engine-driver vainly struggling against homicidal urges. A less doom-laden performance, but one that revealed his particular strength as an ensemble player as well as a "star", was also for Renoir, as one of the soldiers who escape from a POW camp in *La Grande Illusion* (1937).

Clark Gable (1901–1960)

Hollywood's number one heartthrob in the years immediately preceding the war. His open-handed cheerfulness and easy-going Americanism now might appear dated and unconvincing, but they bowled over a long list of leading ladies, including Claudette Colbert (in Frank Capra's *It Happened One Night*, 1934) and Vivien Leigh (in the Fleming/Cukor/Wood success *Gone with the Wind*, 1939). He is proof that Hollywood male chauvinism did not need the bullying qualities of a John Wayne to make its mark. He gave perhaps his greatest performance in his last film, Huston's ill-fated *The Misfits* (1960).

Greta Garbo (1905–1990)

A career that lasted only seventeen years and a reclusive retirement combined to create the "Garbo myth", of world-weary, capricious and lonesome sensuality, which must be one of the most potent in cinema history. She moved from Sweden to Hollywood under the aegis of the director Mauritz Stiller in 1926, to become MGM's major star, whose every move was heralded by a barrage of studio publicity (thus, "Garbo talks!" before Clarence Brown's *Anna Christie* in 1930, and "Garbo laughs!" before *Ninotchka*, made for Ernst Lubitsch in 1939). Unlike her romantic co-star in the silent period, John Gilbert, Garbo triumphantly made the transition to talkies, her greatest successes being in *Queen Christina* (1934) and *Camille* (1937). But after the disaster of *Two-Faced Woman* (1941) she retired from the screen.

Judy Garland (1922–1969)

A prominent teenage star who became famous through her performance in *The Wizard of Oz* (Victor Fleming, 1939), where she first performed the song whose soaring yearning was to become her hallmark—"Over the Rainbow". She starred in musicals for her then-husband, Vincente Minnelli (including *Meet Me in St. Louis*, 1944), but the pattern of breakdown, emotional turmoil, and abuse of barbiturates had set in by the beginning of the fifties. Stage appearances and nervous breakdowns between them crowded out her mature film career, though her performance in *A Star is Born* (1954) was a tour-de-force and the greatest of her career.

Lillian Gish (1896–1993)

The longest career of movie actors—from D. W. Griffith's *An Unseen Enemy* (1912) through to Lindsay Anderson's *The Whales of August* (1987). She radiated innocence for Griffith in *The Birth of a Nation* (1915) and *Intolerance* (1916), before leaving his Biograph company to make more money, first for Inspiration and then for MGM. During the sound era, her screen appearances were intermittent, though she was particularly effective as the brave schoolma'am facing up to Robert Mitchum's demonic preacher in *The Night of the Hunter* (1955). Her performances in Griffith's *Broken Blossoms* (1919) and Victor Seastrom's *The Wind* (1928) are among the greatest of the silent film era.

Cary Grant (1904–1986)

His British origin shows in his debonair style and curious "mid-Atlantic" accent (imitated by Tony Curtis in Billy Wilder's *Some Like it Hot*, 1959). Beneath his gentlemanly urbanity, frenzy, even insanity, never seem far away, which accounts for the matchless ambiguity of his greatest performances—as the suspected wife-murderer in Hitchcock's *Suspicion* (1941), as baiting foil to Mae West in Wesley Ruggles's *I'm No Angel* (1933), as advertising man pursued across America by spies in *North by North-West* (Hitchcock, 1959), and above all the victim of the insecurity that stems from sex-stereotyping in the magnificent comedies he made opposite various leading ladies for Howard Hawks—*Bringing Up Baby* (with Katharine Hepburn, 1938), *His Girl Friday* (with Rosalind Russell, 1940), and *I Was a Male War Bride* (with Ann Sheridan, 1949). Small wonder that he won an Oscar in 1970 for "sheer brilliance".

Sir Alec Guinness (b. 1914)

Guinness came to prominence as a screen actor in the great Ealing comedies of the 1950s, notably *The Man in the White Suit* (1951), *The Lavender Hill Mob* (1952), and *The Ladykillers* (1955). He also developed a close working relationship with David Lean, and won an Oscar for his superb performance in Lean's *The Bridge on the River Kwai* (1957). An actor of unobtrusive subtlety and infinite resource, he achieved his biggest popular success in *Star Wars* (1977) but more representative of his skills are his masterly characterisations in such films as *Tunes of Glory* (1960) and *Little Dorritt* (1987).

Audrey Hepburn (1929–1993)

Enchanting elfin actress who won an Oscar in her first starring role, *Roman Holiday* (Wyler, 1953). She then proceeded to bewitch some of Hollywood's most eminent senior citizens—Humphrey Bogart in *Sabrina* (1954), Gary Cooper in *Love in the*

Afternoon (1957), Cary Grant in *Charade* (1963), Rex Harrison in *My Fair Lady* (1964). An adept comedienne, she also proved herself a formidable dramatic actress in *The Nun's Story* (1959), *The Children's Hour* (1961) and *Robin and Marian* (1976). She then virtually retired from the screen, though Spielberg cast her appropriately as an angel in *Always* (1989).

Katharine Hepburn (b. 1909)

The most intelligent and astringent of all screen comediennes—if not all screen actresses. She remained resolutely outside the mould of female stardom, regarded for years as box-office poison and relying on her mind rather than her body for impact. Her most celebrated films are those made with her long-time off-screen lover, Spencer Tracy—notably *Adam's Rib* and *Pat and Mike* for George Cukor (1949 and 1952 respectively), and *State of the Union* for Frank Capra in 1948. But her warm sharpness was equally in evidence with Cary Grant (*Bringing Up Baby* for Hawks in 1938) and Humphrey Bogart (*The African Queen* for John Huston in 1951). Winner of four best actress Oscars (more than any other recipient), she has recently published a set of autobiographical memoirs, *Me* (1991). Her greatest screen performances include *Alice Adams* (1935), *Summer Madness* (1955), *Suddenly Last Summer* (1959) and *Long Day's Journey into Night* (1962).

Charlton Heston (b. 1923)

Heston's first starring role was in C. B. DeMille's circus epic, *The Greatest Show on Earth* (1952). He has since specialised in epic roles, bringing dignity and integrity to the genre, particularly in his title performances in *Ben Hur* (1959) and *El Cid* (1961). His historical roles range from Cardinal Richelieu to General Gordon, from Moses to Michelangelo: his best modern film role has probably been in Welles's *Touch of Evil* (1958).

Dustin Hoffman (b. 1937)

Earnest, intense method actor whose perfectionism has sometimes driven co-stars to distraction (Olivier: "Dustin is very talented—but why doesn't he just act?") but has certainly produced the goods—Oscars for his performances in *Kramer vs. Kramer* (1979) and *The Rain Man* (1988). Other important roles: *The Graduate* (1967), *Lenny* (1974) and *All the President's Men* (1976).

William Holden (1918–1981)

Handsome leading man of the 1940s who was rescued from bland B-picture roles by Billy Wilder, who cast him as a screen writing gigolo in *Sunset Boulevard* (1950) and as a captive capitalist in *Stalag 17* (1953), for which Holden won an Oscar. After a lean spell in the 1960s, his career revived with his splendid leading performance in *The Wild Bunch* (1969), and before his death, he gave further thoughtful characterisations in *Network* (1976) and *Fedora* (1978). Other key roles: *Golden Boy* (1939), *Sabrina* (1954), *Picnic* (1955) and *The Bridge on the River Kwai* (1957).

Trevor Howard (1916–1987)

Leathery character actor of the British film, reputedly Graham Greene's favourite. Capable of acting just about anyone off the screen, which might be the reason that he only rarely got the parts (and therefore the recognition) that he deserved. Important films include: *Brief Encounter* (1945), *The Third Man* (1949), *Outcast of The Islands* (1951), *The Key* (1958), *Sons and Lovers* (1960), *Mutiny on the Bounty* (1962) and *Ludwig* (1972).

Rock Hudson (1925–1985)

Solid Hollywood leading man who sprang back into the public eye in the 1980s because of his death from AIDS. This rather contradicted his screen image as the all-American romantic hero. An effective screen actor in dramas such as *Giant* (1956) or comedies such as *Send Me No Flowers* (1964), he had, in retrospect, his most resonant role in John Frankenheimer's sci-fi horror film, *Seconds* (1966), where a dissatisfied middle-aged man fakes his own death and, through plastic surgery, starts a new life looking like Rock Hudson—and finds that soul-destroying also.

Emil Jannings (1884–1950)

A king of the German silent cinema, ruined by the coming of sound (which unkindly showed up his thick accent) and his collaboration with the Nazis. His massive self-sentimentalisation and Prussian obsession with lost status were triumphant in Murnau's *The Last Laugh* (1924), and even more so in his role as the puritanical schoolteacher Professor Rath, destroyed by his passion for Marlene Dietrich's Lola in Sternberg's *The Blue Angel* (1930). This performance remains the greatest monument of male sexual humiliation in cinema history. He epitomised silent film acting at its most Expressionist and expressive, though Luis Bunuel said he preferred Buster Keaton.

Boris Karloff (1887–1969)

Here again on- and off-screen personas interacted intriguingly. Mild mannered English cricket-loving gentleman William Henry Pratt became the best-known horror star in Hollywood history with his performance as the blundering yet tender-hearted monster in James Whale's *Frankenstein* in 1931. Thenceforth his legendary status was secure, and augmented by his work for Karl Freund (*The Mummy* of 1932) and Charles Vidor (*The Mask of Fu Manchu*, 1932). As moving as his performance in *Frankenstein* in many ways is his valedictory appearance in Peter Bogdanovich's *Targets* (shot in the year of his death) where he plays a retired Hollywood horror star whose essential kindness is appalled by the horror of contemporary American society.

Buster Keaton (1895–1966)

Arguably the greatest director and the greatest actor of the American silent era. As an actor, his deadpan appearance, often almost suicidal insistence on choreographing and carrying out all his own stunts, and awareness of the element of fantasy identification in cinema have ensured that his performances remain consistently exciting and do not date. As a director, he masterfully exploited the relationship between man and machine—driver/train and actor/camera—in *The General* of 1926, and that between cinema and dream in *Sherlock Junior* of 1924. His career was undermined as much by the classic Hollywood afflictions—marital problems and heavy drinking—as by the coming of sound. But his reputation has soared since his death, and works such as *Our Hospitality* (1923), *Seven Chances* (1925), *The Navigator* (1927) and *Steamboat Bill Jr.* (1928), along with his aforementioned films, are now regarded as movie classics. Appeared alongside Chaplin in an unforgettable routine in the latter's *Limelight* (1952).

Gene Kelly (b. 1912)

Arguably the most inventive and adventurous actor-choreographer of the American screen. Rival to Fred Astaire as Hollywood's dancing master, he was even more creative in furthering the boundaries of the film musical, particularly in a trio of magnificent musicals he co-directed with Stanley Donen: *On the Town* (1949), *Singin' in the Rain* (1952) and *It's Always Fair Weather* (1955).

Grace Kelly (1928–1982)

Aloof but elegant leading lady who made her first major impression as Gary Cooper's Quaker wife in *High Noon* (1952) and then as the archetypal Hitchcockian ice-cool blonde in *Dial M for Murder* (1954), *Rear Window* (1954) and *To Catch a Thief* (1955). Her dramatic prowess was revealed in her Oscar-winning role in *The Country Girl* (1954) but she gave up stardom for royalty when she married Prince Rainier of Monaco in 1956.

Deborah Kerr (b. 1921)

One of the most versatile and sensitive of British

screen actresses, whose persona of "English rose" was changed when she played the nymphomaniac wife of an Army Captain in *From Here to Eternity* (1953). She has seemed at her best either when playing nuns with a hint of neurosis—*Black Narcissus* (1947), *Heaven Knows, Mr. Allison* (1957)—or prim teachers or governesses wrestling privately with emotional repression—*The King and I* (1955), *Tea and Sympathy* (1956), *The Innocents* (1961).

Burt Lancaster (1913–1994)

Acrobat turned actor, who revealed a sensitive interior behind his action-man mask. He won an Oscar for his role as a religious charlatan in *Elmer Gantry* (1960), and a Venice Festival award for a more introvert performance in *Bird Man of Alcatraz* (1962). "A deeply mysterious man" was the verdict on him of Luchino Visconti, who directed him to great effect in *The Leopard* (1963) and *Conversation Piece* (1974), and he triumphed also under Louis Malle in *Atlantic City* (1980). He had a career of fascinating contrasts, between swashbuckling and sensitive roles. Other key films include: *The Killers* (1946), *The Crimson Pirate* (1952), *From Here to Eternity* (1953), *Sweet Smell of Success* (1957), *1900* (1976) and *Twilight's Last Gleaming* (1977).

Charles Laughton (1899–1962)

Bulky actor of phenomenal power and range, with the occasional tendency to ham but also capable of producing magical effects with a sympathetic director. It is sometimes thought that his heyday was in the thirties, when he excelled in *The Private Life of Henry VIII* (1933), *Ruggles of Red Gap* (1935), *Mutiny on the Bounty* (1935) and *The Hunchback of Notre Dame* (1939). But he was no less remarkable in later films such as *Hobson's Choice* (1954), *Witness for the Prosecution* (1957), *Spartacus* (1960) and *Advise and Consent* (1962). There is a sense of relish about his greatest acting, whether playing saint or sadist. One should not forget also his one and only film as director, an altogether remarkable, poetic thriller *The Night of the Hunter* (1955) that constitutes one of the most extraordinary directing debuts in the history of the cinema.

Laurel (1890–1965) and Hardy (1892–1957)

The first great comedy partnership in films, and never surpassed. Their films usually involve frantic attempts to gain social acceptance, as piano-movers or salesmen, that lead only to the disasters ruefully described by Hardy as "another fine mess". Their features, including *Pack Up Your Troubles* (Marshall and Raymond McCarey, 1932) and *A Chump at Oxford* (Alfred Goulding, 1940), retain the personas—sly and skinny Stan and overweight Ollie trying to cling on to his dignity—almost intact. The comedy of failure in its purest, most unpretentious form. Key films include: *Big Business* (1929), *The Music Box* (1932), *Sons of the Desert* (1934), *Way Out West* (1937).

Vivien Leigh (1913–1967)

Fragile and exquisite English actress who remarkably scored her greatest film triumphs in two quintessentially American roles: as Scarlett O'Hara in *Gone With the Wind* (1939) and as Blanche DuBois in *A Streetcar Named Desire* (1951). Married to Laurence Olivier in 1940, her later career was blighted by physical and mental illness. She was divorced from Olivier in 1960, and her last major film roles were in *The Roman Spring of Mrs. Stone* (1961) and *Ship of Fools* (1965).

Jack Lemmon (b. 1925)

Consummate film actor who is probably most associated in the public mind with a series of sublime comedy characterisations in films of Billy Wilder, such as *Some Like it Hot* (1959), *The Apartment* (1960) *The Fortune Cookie* (1966), and *Avanti!* (1972). But he is an equally forceful straight actor, as films such as *Days of Wine and Roses* (1962), *The China Syndrome* (1979), *Missing* (1982) and *Glengarry Glen Ross* (1992) demonstrate. The screen's best tragi-comedian since Chaplin.

Sophia Loren (b. 1934)

Epitomises the stereotype of Latin female sexuality for the moviegoer, much as Marcello Mastroianni does for the male. She began for Hollywood in ripely sensual roles (e.g. *Desire under the Elms* for Delbert Mann in 1958), before moving on to more demanding dramatic parts, such as Vittorio de Sica's *Two Women* for which she won an Oscar in 1961.

Peter Lorre (1904–1964)

Among his best-known films there is only one in which he actually starred: *M* for Fritz Lang in 1931, where he portrayed a demented child-murderer, contorting his features as much as Lang's direction contorted the screen images. But he became one of Hollywood's most memorable supporting actors, as the crazed hitman in Huston's *The Maltese Falcon* (1941), and for Michael Curtiz (in *Casablanca* of 1943 and *Passage to Marseilles* of 1944) and Frank Capra (*Arsenic and Old Lace*, 1944). Like Karloff but in a very different way, he excels at suggesting sensitivity beneath the contortions of horror and malice.

Shirley Maclaine (b. 1934)

Prodigiously talented dancer-cum-comedienne-cum dramatic actress. Won an Oscar for *Terms of Endearment* (1983), but her best films are the early ones: *The Trouble With Harry* (1955), *Some Came Running* (1958), *The Apartment* (1960), *The Children's Hour* (1961) and *Sweet Charity* (1969).

Fredric March (1897–1975)

One of Hollywood's finest character actors, particularly when portraying ostensibly decent men with darker sides to their personalities. This was shown to particular effect in *Dr. Jekyll and Mr. Hyde* (1932) but was also a feature of some other of his major roles: *Les Miserables* (1935), *The Best Years of our Lives* (1946), *Death of a Salesman* (1952), *Executive Suite* (1954) and *The Desperate Hours* (1955).

Marx Brothers: Chico (1887–1961), Harpo (1888–1964), Groucho (1890–1978)

Hollywood's undisputed great comic family. Their films rely on the way in which the three brothers' fortes complement one another, so that as soon as a threat from one quarter is averted another one will appear. Groucho's undammable flow of insult and wisecrack, Chico's illogicalities and prevarications (delivered in a heavy mock-Italian accent), and Harpo's mute mime form an unbeatable trio, whether in the early Paramount features (such as *Duck Soup* for Leo McCarey in 1933) or in their later work for MGM, where musical and romantic interludes irksomely break up the stream of comedy (as in *A Day at the Races*—Sam Wood, 1937). Their most popular film, and Groucho's favourite, was *A Night at the Opera* (1935).

James Mason (1909–1984)

Mason's style migrated successfully from the British industry (as in *Odd Man Out*—Carol Reed, 1947) to Hollywood and the international circuit. He was an urbane villain for Hitchcock in *North by North-West* (1959), and a suitable articulate and obsessed lover for *Lolita* (Stanley Kubrick, 1962), somewhat removed from the persona of the romantic sadist with which he had first shot to fame (in *The Man in Grey*, 1943 and *The Wicked Lady*, 1945). One of those screen actors like Trevor Howard or David Niven who seemed incapable of giving a bad performance, however bad the film was around him. When the film was good—like say, *Five Fingers* (1952), *A Star is Born* (1954), *The Verdict* (1982)—he could be quite exceptional.

Marcello Mastroianni (b. 1924)

The ultimate listless Latin lover, who seems wearied by the very thought of all the women to whom he is supposed to appeal. This quality in fact enables his screen persona to work quite subversively against the macho ideal of Hollywood, as in Fellini's *La Dolce Vita* (1959), where he plays a disillusioned journalist, or Antonioni's *La Notte* (1961), as the exhausted husband of Jeanne Moreau. His finest performance remains that in Fellini's *8¹/₂* (1963), as the film director (an obvious alter ego to Fellini), whose very prostration and inability to organise his neuroses into cinematic form at the end provide the mainspring that enables him to do so. The films with Fellini and Antonioni remain his best-known work. His most recent successes include *Macaroni* (1985), opposite Jack Lemmon; *Ginger and Fred* (1986), for Fellini; and a particularly intense performance in *The Beekeeper* (1986) for Greece's major contemporary director, Theo Angelopoulous.

Steve McQueen (1930–1980)

Supercool but smouldering anti-hero and loner, McQueen became a star after his POW antics on a motorbike in *The Great Escape* (1963), though the neurosis beneath the nonchalance had probably been better explored by director Don Siegel in *Hell is for Heroes* (1961). Best remembered for action roles like *The Magnificent Seven* (1960) or *Bullitt* (1968), McQueen was showing signs of greater artistic ambition towards the end of his life, producing as well as starring in an adaptation of Ibsen's *An Enemy of the People* (1979) and contributing a finely shaded, poignant performance in the elegiac Western, *Tom Horn* (1980).

Toshiro Mifune (b. 1920)

Japanese actor whose robust style, ironic as well as dramatic, is indelibly associated with the films he has made for Kurosawa, including *Seven Samurai* (1954), *Throne of Blood* (1957) and *Yojimbo* (1961). He has also appeared in the occasional Hollywood film, most notably opposite Lee Marvin in *Hell in the Pacific* (1969).

Robert Mitchum (b. 1917)

A deceptively outstanding film actor whose lazy style conceals enormous range and prodigious depth. Directors as exacting as John Huston (*Heaven Knows Mr. Allison*, 1957) and Fred Zinnemann (*The Sundowners*, 1960) have testified to Mitchum's exceptional abilities. Only once nominated for an Oscar (for *The Story of G.I. Joe*, 1945), his memorable performances are legion: *Pursued* (1947), *Build My Gallows High* (1947), *The Lusty Men* (1952), *The Night of the Hunter* (1955), *Cape Fear* (1962), *Ryan's Daughter* (1970), *The Friends of Eddie Coyle* (1973), *The Last Tycoon* (1976).

Marilyn Monroe (1926–1962)

Not the original cinematic sex symbol—that distinction belongs to Mary Pickford or Rudolph Valentino—but she is certainly the best-known. Nowhere else have the on-and-off screen persona interacted to such devastating, and finally destructive, effect. She began as a "dumb blonde" in the early fifties before producers and directors recognised in her vulnerability and ambivalent attitude towards her own sexuality—pride tempered by the desire to be appreciated for something more—outstanding qualities. Her best films remain comedies in which her ambivalence was played upon to enrich the texture of the movies: *Bus Stop* for Joshua Logan in 1956, and for Billy Wilder, *The Seven-Year Itch* of 1955, and *Some Like It Hot* in 1959. She was dismissed from her final project (Cukor's *Something's Got to Give*) for unreliability in 1960, and not long afterwards committed suicide. Revelations of her off-screen loneliness and the mysterious circumstances of her death went to fuel what is still Hollywood's most potent and macabre legend.

Jeanne Moreau (b. 1928)

Described as the "thinking man's actress", and whose name was synonymous with some of the greatest and most controversial European art movies of the late fifties and early sixties: Malle's *The Lovers* (1958), Truffaut's *Jules et Jim* (1961), Antonioni's *La Notte* (1962) and Buñuel's *Diary of a Chambermaid* (1964).

Paul Newman (b. 1925)

Blue-eyed boy of modern American film, exceptionally good looking and a considerable actor to boot. Early Oscar-nominated performances in *Cat on a Hot Tin Roof* (1958), *The Hustler* (1961), *Hud* (1963) and *Cool Hand Luke* (1967) testified to his great skill in revealing an attractive, adventurous side to roles which, in other hands, could have seemed unsympathetic and morbid. He finally won his Oscar for *The Color of Money* (1987), Scorsese's sequel to *The Hustler*. He has also proved himself a sympathetic director, particularly of his actress-wife Joanne Woodward, in films such as *Rachel, Rachel* (1968) and *The Glass Menagerie* (1987).

Jack Nicholson (b. 1937)

Nicholson broke into public prominence with his performance as the alcoholic ne'er-do-well in Hopper's *Easy Rider* (1969), and has remained at the top ever since with sardonic yet often tender performances. The versatility that often goes with understatement has enabled him to give outstanding performances as a drop-out classical musician (Bob Rafelson's *Five Easy Pieces* in 1970), a private eye (Polanski's *Chinatown* in 1974), and a rebel in a mental hospital (Milos Forman's *One Flew Over The Cuckoo's Nest*, 1975). Some recent performances have bordered on self-parody, notably *Batman* (1989), and others (for example, *The Shining*, 1980) have been distinctly controversial. At least he is never dull.

Sir Laurence Olivier (1907–1989)

Perhaps the most exciting and respected actor of his generation, Olivier will perhaps first be remembered and revered for his achievement as actor and director in bringing Shakespeare to vivid life on screen with *Henry V* (1944), *Hamlet* (1948) and *Richard III* (1955). But perhaps his most subtle screen acting was to be found in two films he made for Wyler, *Wuthering Heights* (1939) and *Carrie* (1952), and one for Hitchcock, *Rebecca* (1940). His later years were dogged by illness, and his last major film role was in Mankiewicz's *Sleuth* (1972).

Gregory Peck (b. 1916)

Archetypal screen symbol of liberal integrity, particularly embodied in his performance as the lawyer defending an unjustly accused Negro in *To Kill a Mockingbird* (1962), for which he justly won an Oscar. Other important films: *Gentleman's Agreement* (1947), *The Gunfighter* (1950), *Roman Holiday* (1953), *Moby Dick* (1956), *The Big Country* (1958), *The Stalking Moon* (1968) and *I Walk the Line* (1970).

Mary Pickford (1893–1979)

The sentimentality of her early performances for D. W. Griffith between 1909 and 1912, and her peak period as "America's Sweetheart" when married to Douglas Fairbanks (*Daddy Long Legs* for Marshall Neilan in 1919, *Pollyanna* for Paul Powell in 1920) are considerably less interesting today than her ideological role as what Basil Wright has dubbed the "hearth goddess" of domesticity and her early status as one of the first multi-millionaire film stars.

Sidney Poitier (b. 1924)

Ground-breaking black actor, who was one of the first Negroes to attain Hollywood star status. He won an Oscar for a now virtually forgotten movie, *Lilies of the Field* (1963), and is better remembered for such films as *The Defiant Ones* (1958), *In The Heat of the Night* (1967) and *Guess Who's Coming to Dinner* (1967). Also an accomplished director, though definitely in the commercial mainstream rather than in the radical alternative lane chosen by the new generation of black American directors such as Spike Lee and John Singleton.

Robert Redford (b. 1937)

Redford is distinguished from his "peer-group" stars such as Beatty and Nicholson by a resolute rejection of the trappings of stardom (he lives a reclusive countryside existence and claims never to have been unfaithful to his wife)—qualities which have been inexorably recuperated into the construction of his "star-image". Athletically handsome (like John Wayne he went to university on a sports scholarship), he struck gold with *Butch Cassidy and the Sundance Kid* (George Roy Hill, 1969), and created perhaps his most successful dramatic role in the Scott Fitzgerald adaptation, *The Great Gatsby* for Jack Clayton in 1974. His most important role in the 1980s was opposite Meryl Streep in *Out of Africa* (1985) but increasingly his interest seems to be turning to direction, understandably so since his directing debut, *Ordinary People* (1980) won him an Oscar.

Edward G. Robinson (1893–1973)

Made his name in gangster film roles such as *Little Ceasar* (1931) and as Johnny Rocco in Huston's *Key Largo* (1948). But he was actually a highly skilled actor in a variety of parts, at his best perhaps in two psychological dramas for Fritz Lang, *Woman in the Window* (1944) and *Scarlet Street* (1945); as the insurance investigator in Wilder's *Double Indemnity* (1944); and as a roguish diamond smuggler in Mackendrick's *Sammy Going South* (1963).

Simone Signoret (1921–1985)

Classy French actress who excelled at playing lovelorn women, most memorably in Jacques Becker's *Casque d'Or* (1952) and Jack Clayton's *Room at the Top* (1958). Among her other important films are *La Ronde* (1950), *Les Diaboliques* (1955), *The Army of the Shadows* (1969) and *Madame Rosa* (1977).

James Stewart (b. 1908)

Directors have found complex uses for the slow drawl and shy demeanour of this adroit screen actor: all-American integrity, in his films for Capra (*Mr. Smith goes to Washington*, 1939; *It's A Wonderful Life*, 1946); seething inner intensity in his Anthony Mann westerns; and romantic vulnerability in his Alfred Hitchcock movies, most disturbingly and tragically so in *Vertigo* (1958). A versatile performer, who combines exceptional dramatic power, seen at its best in Preminger's *Anatomy of a Murder* (1959), with a flair for comedy: his performance in the latter vein in Cukor's *Philadelphia Story* (1940) won him an Oscar.

Meryl Streep (b. 1951)

Currently the leading lady of the screen, who seems to snatch all the big parts, whether they be English, Danish, Polish, or Australian, let alone American. She might not always move the heart, but the acting intelligence and technique are formidable. Her key films include: *The Deer Hunter* (1978), *Kramer Vs. Kramer* (1979), *The French Lieutenant's Woman* (1981), *Sophie's Choice* (1982) and *Out of Africa* (1985).

Barbara Stanwyck (1907–1990)

Vibrant, strong actress, much appreciated by directors such as Capra, DeMille, Lang, Sirk for her utter professionalism. Her stock-in-trade was as a hard-as-nails heroine who knew her own mind and was sometimes not to be trusted. Nominated for an Oscar four times without winning for *Stella Dallas*, 1937; *Ball of Fire*, 1942; *Double Indemnity*, 1944; and *Sorry, Wrong Number*, 1948), she was finally given an honorary Oscar in 1982. Other key films: *The Bitter Tea of General Yen* (1933), *Annie Oakley* (1935), *The Lady Eve* (1941), *The Furies* (1950), *There's Always Tomorrow* (1956).

Gloria Swanson (1897–1983)

Perhaps the most glamorous of silent screen stars, particularly in her films for Cecil B. DeMille, like *Male and Female* (1919). She lost much of her wealth when producing *Queen Kelly* (1928), a film she stopped in mid-production owing to director Erich von Stroheim's extravagance: and talkies proved a problem. However, she made a triumphant return to the screen as Norma Desmond in Billy Wilder's *Sunset Boulevard* (1950), as the former

silent star dreaming of a comeback. When the brash screenwriter says she used to be big, she snaps back imperiously: "I *am* big. It's the pictures that got small."

Jacques Tati (1908–1982)

Like Keaton, Tati's claim to fame is based on his direction as much as on his acting. Indeed it could be said that the two have in a sense came into conflict in his later career, his directorial skill and concern with elaborate mechanised set-pieces causing his output to be irregular and often working against his lanky, absent-minded quality as a clown. *Mr. Hulot's Holiday* (1953) remains one of the greatest silent comedies in cinema history (sound was actually added after shooting, but its contribution to the comic impact is minimal), and Tati's greatest achievement in that film is perhaps the way in which he manages to render a specifically French social stereotype—the would-be sporting bourgeois on a seaside holiday—appealing to a much wider audience. Later films like *Mon Oncle* (1958), *Playtime* (1968) and *Traffic* (1971) have an almost mathematical precision in their comedy lay-out and a serious underlying theme: the decline of individuality in an age of mechanisation.

Elizabeth Taylor (b. 1932)

Started out as a child-star in Clarence Brown's *National Velvet* (1944) before graduating to become one of the major Hollywood sex symbols of the fifties, dark and sultry in Richard Brooks's *Cat on a Hot Tin Roof* (1958) and Mankiewicz's *Suddenly Last Summer* (1959). After her marriage to Richard Burton off-and-on screen persona were profitably played off against each other, these culminating in her Oscar-winning performance in Mike Nichols's *Who's Afraid of Virginia Woolf!* (1966). Directors like George Stevens and Joseph Losey have spoken glowingly of her skill as a screen actress, but it is as a star that she has excelled, and nobody has symbolised celluloid glamour more seductively. From being its loveliest child star, Elizabeth Taylor can now be fairly regarded as Hollywood's Queen Mother. Other important films: *Father of the Bride* (1950), *A Place in the Sun* (1951), *Butterfield 8* (1960), *Cleopatra* (1963), *Reflections in a Golden Eye* (1967) and *Secret Ceremony* (1968).

Shirley Temple (b. 1928)

The most famous of all child stars, so precociously talented at singing, dancing and emoting that Graham Greene opined in print that she was a midget, leading to a libel suit and the bankruptcy of the magazine he was writing for. The top box-office attraction of 1938, she was a has-been by 1940, and has spent her adult life engaged not in movies but in Republican politics. Main films include: *Little Miss Marker* (1934), *Wee Willie Winkie* (1937) and *Rebecca of Sunnybrook Farm* (1938).

Spencer Tracy (1900–1967)

Tracy successfully embodied in the thirties and forties certain "all-American" qualities—bluff decency, perceptive kind-heartedness, the "Honest Joe" syndrome—marked in such movies as Fritz Lang's *Fury* (1936) and Frank Borzage's *Big City* (1937). With Katharine Hepburn, he formed one of the archetypal American-movie couples. They strike sparks off each other in *Adam's Rib* and *Pat and Mike* for George Cukor (1949 and 1952 respectively), and in work for such directors as George Stevens and Frank Capra. An actor's actor, so natural that he seemed not to be acting at all, he was greatly admired by his peers, not least by Laurence Olivier, who commented: "I've learned more about acting from watching Tracy than in any other way. He has great truth in everything he does." His important films included: *San Francisco* (1936), *Captains Courageous* (1937), *Boys' Town* (1938), *Woman of the Year* (1942), *Father of the Bride* (1950), *The Actress* (1953), *Bad Day at Black Rock* (1955) and *Inherit the Wind* (1960).

Rudolph Valentino (1895–1926)

One of the first major Hollywood sex symbols whose funeral after a premature death from peritonitis was followed by thousands of sobbing fans. This now seems ironic due not only to changes in film fashions and sexual coding that make his savagely passionate oriental in *The Sheik* (George Melford, 1921) appear passé, but also to subsequent revelations about his unconsummated first marriage, homosexual tendencies and domination by his second wife, who took charge of his career and mismanaged it abominably. To women he symbolised exotic eroticism; to men, to quote an infamous *Chicago Tribune* editorial, a "painted pansy". His premature death (which is often a smart career move, as one cynical journalist remarked) only fanned the legend and the controversy. Other important films: *The Four Horsemen of the Apocalypse* (1921), *Blood and Sand* (1922) and *Son of the Sheik* (1926).

John Wayne (1907–1979)

Perhaps Hollywood's most loved and most hated star. Loved, by Western fans the world over for performances that set the mould for the horseback hero—big physically and spiritually, charismatically dominating with men, awkward and latently sentimental with women, always coming out on top in a crisis. Hated, for his uncompromising rightwing political stance which led him to endorse the McCarthyite persecutions of the fifties and to give active support to the American invasion of Vietnam, even making a film—*The Green Berets* (1968)—

in support of it. As an actor, he revealed in his best parts more sensitivity than he often cared to offscreen—as the outlaw Ringo in Ford's *Stagecoach* (1939) who ends up with the prostitute Dallas, as the tamed Comanche-hater Ethan Edwards in Ford's *The Searchers* (1956), who walks off into the barren landscape at the end, and as the sheriff in Hawk's *Rio Bravo* (1959), holding a motley posse together by force of personality. There are many who will forgive a film with Wayne in it anything, many who find his presence in itself almost unforgivable. He won an Oscar for *True Grit* (1969). Other important films: *Fort Apache* (1948), *Red River* (1949), *She Wore a Yellow Ribbon* (1949), *Sands of Iwo Jima* (1950), *The Quiet Man* (1952), *The Man Who Shot Liberty Valance* (1962) and *The Shootist* (1976).

Mae West (1892–1980)

"I was Snow White—but I drifted." So said Mae West, whose raunchy style was seen at its best on film in *She Done Him Wrong* (1933) and *I'm No Angel* (1933). This blousy buxom blonde appealed to men because of her sex-appeal, and to women because of the way she seized the sexual initiative from the male and sent up his desires. Unfortunately the production code of 1934, which laid down strict guidelines on the treatment of sex on film, inhibited Miss West's screen career. Other key films: *Belle of the Nineties* (1934), *My Little Chickadee* (1940).

4. THE OSCAR WINNERS

Introduction

The film industry's most glittering prize remains the Hollywood Academy Award, or 'Oscar'. The 'Oscar' came about as a result of the formation of the Academy of Motion Picture Arts and Sciences in 1927. The Academy thought it would gain additional prestige and publicity if it gave out annual awards for artistic and technical merit. The first awards ceremony was in May 1929 and was a modest affair. Nowadays the ceremony is a lavish spectacle watched by countless millions on television worldwide.

The Oscar itself is a gold-plated statuette of a knight holding a crusader's sword and standing on a reel of film whose five spokes symbolise the original branches of the Academy (actors, directors, producers, technicians and writers). Legend has it that the name comes from a secretary Margaret Herrick, later an executive director of the Academy, who commented one day that the statuette "reminds me of my uncle Oscar".

Ben Hur (1959) holds the record number of Oscars—11. *West Side Story* (1961) won 10; *Gone With the Wind* (1939), *Gigi* (1958) and *The Last Emperor* (1987) each won nine. Katharine Hepburn has won more major acting Oscars than any other star (4). Bette Davis, Louise Rainer, Olivia de Havilland, Ingrid Bergman, Glenda Jackson, Jane Fonda, Sally Field and Jodie Foster have won Best Actress twice; Spencer Tracy, Fredric March, Gary Cooper, Marlon Brando, Dustin Hoffman and Tom Hanks have done the same as Best Actor.

Whether the Oscars reflect merit or commercial pressures is still a debatable point. Raymond Chandler described the ceremony as the "motion picture industry's frantic desire to kiss itself on the back of the neck." Certainly there have been some glaring omissions: Alfred Hitchcock and Orson Welles never won a Best Director Oscar; and among the actors and actresses who failed to win Oscars for their performances were Charlie Chaplin, Greta Garbo, Cary Grant and Judy Garland. To repair such omissions, certain actors and directors have been given honorary Oscars for a lifetime's achievement.

There are many other prestigious awards connected with the film industry, particularly those donated by Film Festivals. It is also very evident that the Hollywood Academy's judgment of what constitutes the year's best film has not always stood the test of time.

Best Actor

1927–28	Emil Jannings, *The Way of All Flesh*
1928–29	Warner Baxter, *In Old Arizona*
1929–30	George Arliss, *Disraeli*
1930–31	Lionel Barrymore, *A Free Soul*
1931–32	Fredric March, *Dr Jekyll and Mr Hyde*; Wallace Beery, *The Champ* (tie)
1932–33	Charles Laughton, *Private Life of Henry VIII*
1934	Clark Gable, *It Happened One Night*
1935	Victor McLaglen, *The Informer*
1936	Paul Muni, *Story of Louis Pasteur*
1937	Spencer Tracy, *Captains Courageous*
1938	Spencer Tracy, *Boys Town*
1939	Robert Donat, *Goodbye Mr Chips*
1940	James Stewart, *The Philadelphia Story*
1941	Gary Cooper, *Sergeant York*
1942	James Cagney, *Yankee Doodle Dandy*
1943	Paul Lukas, *Watch on the Rhine*
1944	Bing Crosby, *Going My Way*
1945	Ray Milland, *The Lost Weekend*
1946	Fredric March, *The Best Years of Our Lives*
1947	Ronald Colman, *A Double Life*
1948	Laurence Olivier, *Hamlet*
1949	Broderick Crawford, *All the King's Men*
1950	José Ferrer, *Cyrano de Bergerac*
1951	Humphrey Bogart, *The African Queen*
1952	Gary Cooper, *High Noon*
1953	William Holden, *Stalag 17*
1954	Marlon Brando, *On the Waterfront*
1955	Ernest Borgnine, *Marty*
1956	Yul Brynner, *The King and I*
1957	Alec Guinness, *The Bridge on the River Kwai*
1958	David Niven, *Separate Tables*
1959	Charlton Heston, *Ben Hur*
1960	Burt Lancaster, *Elmer Gantry*
1961	Maximilian Schell, *Judgment at Nuremberg*
1962	Gregory Peck, *To Kill a Mockingbird*
1963	Sidney Poitier, *Lilies of the Field*
1964	Rex Harrison, *My Fair Lady*
1965	Lee Marvin, *Cat Ballou*
1966	Paul Scofield, *A Man for All Seasons*
1967	Rod Steiger, *In the Heat of the Night*
1968	Cliff Robertson, *Charly*
1969	John Wayne, *True Grit*
1970	George C. Scott, *Patton* (refused)
1971	Gene Hackman, *The French Connection*
1972	Marlon Brando, *The Godfather* (refused)
1973	Jack Lemmon, *Save the Tiger*

1974	Art Carney, *Harry and Tonto*	1985	Geraldine Page, *The Trip to Bountiful*
1975	Jack Nicholson, *One Flew Over the Cuckoo's Nest*	1986	Marlee Matlin, *Children of a Lesser God*
		1987	Cher, *Moonstruck*
1976	Peter Finch, *Network*	1988	Jodie Foster, *The Accused*
1977	Richard Dreyfuss, *The Goodbye Girl*	1989	Jessica Tandy, *Driving Miss Daisy*
1978	Jon Voigt, *Coming Home*	1990	Kathy Bates, *Misery*
1979	Dustin Hoffman, *Kramer vs. Kramer*	1991	Jodie Foster, *The Silence of the Lambs*
1980	Robert DeNiro, *Raging Bull*	1992	Emma Thompson, *Howards End*
1981	Henry Fonda, *On Golden Pond*	1993	Holly Hunter, *The Piano*
1982	Ben Kingsley, *Gandhi*	1994	Jessica Lange, *Blue Sky*
1983	Robert Duvall, *Tender Mercies*		
1984	F. Murray Abraham, *Amadeus*		**Best Film**
1985	William Hurt, *Kiss of the Spider Woman*		
1986	Paul Newman, *The Color of Money*	1927–28	*Wings*, Paramount
1987	Michael Douglas, *Wall Street*	1928–29	*Broadway Melody*, MGM
1988	Dustin Hoffman, *Rain Man*	1929–30	*All Quiet on the Western Front*, Universal
1989	Daniel Day-Lewis, *My Left Foot*	1930–31	*Cimarron*, RKO
1990	Jeremy Irons, *Reversal of Fortune*	1931–32	*Grand Hotel*, MGM
1991	Anthony Hopkins, *The Silence of the Lambs*		Special: *Mickey Mouse*, Walt Disney
1992	Al Pacino, *Scent of a Woman*	1932–33	*Cavalcade*, 20th Century-Fox
1993	Tom Hanks, *Philadelphia*	1934	*It Happened One Night*, Columbia
1994	Tom Hanks, *Forrest Gump*	1935	*Mutiny on the Bounty*, MGM
		1936	*The Great Ziegfeld*, MGM
		1937	*Life of Emile Zola*, Warner
	Best Actress	1938	*You Can't Take It With You*, Columbia
		1939	*Gone With the Wind*, Selznick International
1927–28	Janet Gaynor, *Seventh Heaven*	1940	*Rebecca*, Selznick International
1928–29	Mary Pickford, *Coquette*	1941	*How Green Was My Valley*, 20th Century-Fox
1929–30	Norma Shearer, *The Divorcee*		
1930–31	Marie Dressler, *Min and Bill*	1942	*Mrs Miniver*, MGM
1931–32	Helen Hayes, *Sin of Madelon Claudet*	1943	*Casablanca*, Warner
1932–33	Katharine Hepburn, *Morning Glory*	1944	*Going My Way*, Paramount
1934	Claudette Colbert, *It Happened One Night*	1945	*The Lost Weekend*, Paramount
1935	Bette Davis, *Dangerous*	1946	*The Best Years of Our Lives*, Goldwyn, RKO
1936	Luise Rainer, *The Great Ziegfeld*		
1937	Luise Rainer, *The Good Earth*	1947	*Gentleman's Agreement*, 20th Century-Fox
1938	Bette Davis, *Jezebel*	1948	*Hamlet*, Two Cities Film, Universal International
1939	Vivien Leigh, *Gone With the Wind*		
1940	Ginger Rogers, *Kitty Foyle*	1949	*All the King's Men*, Columbia
1941	Joan Fontaine, *Suspicion*	1950	*All About Eve*, 20th Century-Fox
1942	Greer Garson, *Mrs Miniver*	1951	*An American in Paris*, MGM
1943	Jennifer Jones, *The Song of Bernadette*	1952	*Greatest Show on Earth*, Cecil B. De Mille, Paramount
1944	Ingrid Bergman, *Gaslight*		
1945	Joan Crawford, *Mildred Pierce*	1953	*From Here to Eternity*, Columbia
1946	Olivia de Havilland, *To Each His Own*	1954	*On the Waterfront*, Horizon-American Corp. Columbia
1947	Loretta Young, *The Farmer's Daughter*		
1948	Jane Wyman, *Johnny Belinda*	1955	*Marty*, Hecht and Lancaster's Steven Productions UA
1949	Olivia de Havilland, *The Heiress*		
1950	Judy Holliday, *Born Yesterday*	1956	*Around the World in 80 Days*, Michael Todd Co. UA
1951	Vivien Leigh, *A Streetcar Named Desire*		
1952	Shirley Booth, *Come Back, Little Sheba*	1957	*The Bridge on the River Kwai*, Columbia
1953	Audrey Hepburn, *Roman Holiday*	1958	*Gigi*, Arthur Freed Production, MGM
1954	Grace Kelly, *Country Girl*	1959	*Ben-Hur*, MGM
1955	Anna Magnani, *The Rose Tattoo*	1960	*The Apartment*, Mirisch Co. UA
1956	Ingrid Bergman, *Anastasia*	1961	*West Side Story*, United Artists
1957	Joanne Woodward, *The Three Faces of Eve*	1962	*Lawrence of Arabia*, Columbia
		1963	*Tom Jones*, Woodfall Prod. UA-Lopert Pictures
1958	Susan Hayward, *I Want to Live*		
1959	Simone Signoret, *Room at the Top*	1964	*My Fair Lady*, Warner Bros.
1960	Elizabeth Taylor, *Butterfield 8*	1965	*The Sound of Music*, 20th Century-Fox
1961	Sophia Loren, *Two Women*	1966	*A Man for All Seasons*, Columbia
1962	Anne Bancroft, *The Miracle Worker*	1967	*In the Heat of the Night*, United Artists
1963	Patricia Neal, *Hud*	1968	*Oliver*, Columbia
1964	Julie Andrews, *Mary Poppins*	1969	*Midnight Cowboy*, United Artists
1965	Julie Christie, *Darling*	1970	*Patton*, 20th Century-Fox
1966	Elizabeth Taylor, *Who's Afraid of Virginia Woolf?*	1971	*The French Connection*, 20th Century-Fox
		1972	*The Godfather*, Paramount
1967	Katharine Hepburn, *Guess Who's Coming to Dinner*	1973	*The Sting*, Universal
		1974	*The Godfather, Part II*, Paramount
1968	Katharine Hepburn, *The Lion in Winter*; Barbra Streisand, *Funny Girl* (tie)	1975	*One Flew Over the Cuckoo's Nest*, United Artists
1969	Maggie Smith, *The Prime of Miss Jean Brodie*	1976	*Rocky*, United Artists
		1977	*Annie Hall*, United Artists
1970	Glenda Jackson, *Women in Love*	1978	*The Deer Hunter*, EMI
1971	Jane Fonda, *Klute*	1979	*Kramer vs. Kramer*, Columbia
1972	Liza Minelli, *Cabaret*	1980	*Ordinary People*, Paramount
1973	Glenda Jackson, *A Touch of Class*	1981	*Chariots of Fire*, Fox
1974	Ellen Burstyn, *Alice Doesn't Live Here Anymore*	1982	*Gandhi*, Columbia-Warner
		1983	*Terms of Endearment*, Paramount
1975	Louise Fletcher, *One Flew Over the Cuckoo's Nest*	1984	*Amadeus*, Columbia-Warner
		1985	*Out of Africa*, Universal
1976	Faye Dunaway, *Network*	1986	*Platoon*, Orion Pictures
1977	Diane Keaton, *Annie Hall*	1987	*The Last Emperor*, Columbia
1978	Jane Fonda, *Coming Home*	1988	*Rain Man*, United Artists
1979	Sally Field, *Norma Rae*	1989	*Driving Miss Daisy*, Warner Bros.
1980	Sissy Spacek, *Coal Miner's Daughter*	1990	*Dances with Wolves*, Guild
1981	Katharine Hepburn, *On Golden Pond*	1991	*The Silence of the Lambs*, Orion Pictures
1982	Meryl Streep, *Sophie's Choice*	1992	*Unforgiven*, Warner Bros.
1983	Shirley MacLaine, *Terms of Endearment*	1993	*Schindler's List*, Universal
1984	Sally Field, *Places in the Heart*	1994	*Forrest Gump*, Paramount

THE ENVIRONMENT

This section provides a brief introduction to the study of the environment in both the rich and poor countries of the world. It examines such topical subjects as energy problems, pollution, food resources, ecology and the outcome of the 1992 "Earth Summit". Special topics focus on the outcome of the UN Population Conference held in Cairo in 1994 and on the recommendations of the Royal Commission on Environmental Pollution.

TABLE OF CONTENTS

THE ENVIRONMENT

Editor's Note This section was specially written for *Pears* by Israel Berkovitch, a leading writer on environmental matters.

1. INTRODUCTION

"1 Human beings are at the centre of concerns for sustainable development. They are entitled to a healthy and productive life in harmony with nature.

4 In order to achieve sustainable development, environmental protection shall constitute an integral part of the development process and cannot be considered in isolation from it."

From the Rio Declaration, 1992.

"A fundamental change in life-style is vital if we are to protect our world for future generations" said the UK Environment Secretary John Gummer early in 1994 launching four government documents in response to the UN Earth Summit in Rio. Both these events are discussed in later parts of this Section. Meanwhile the public had indicated that air pollution from road traffic and factories was their main environmental concern at the end of 1993 according to an opinion survey by Survey Research Associates. Contrasting action with promises, the public were also generally disappointed with the government's performance in protecting the environment. It seemed that at long last, people were heeding the earlier caution by Mostafa Tolba, former Executive Director of the UN Environment Programme (UNEP); the notion that natural resources, such as clean air and fresh water are free goods, he warned "is a menace to life in the late 20th century". This section in *Pears* is devoted to examining what are current environmental trends, considered worldwide but with special attention to the European Union and Britain, and what needs to be done to ensure that mankind—now extensively plundering this planet—becomes a better guest. In recent years concern has grown among the informed public at the risks to the environment arising from man's activities and at the associated hazard of a major recoil that would damage mankind itself. An important stage in the development of world awareness was the holding of a UN Conference on the Human Environment in Stockholm in 1972. It called for an official organisation with a global commitment "to safeguard and enhance the environment for present and future generations of man".

A UN Environment Programme (UNEP) was quickly set up with Headquarters in Nairobi, Kenya. Responding to a decision of the UN General Assembly it has issued annual reports on the state of the environment. These widespread concerns were also reflected in environmental programmes forming part of the activities of several other UN agencies. Among them were those dealing with food and agriculture, health, education, atomic energy, meteorology, and maritime activities. Many of the developed nations set up relevant government ministries. In the UK a number of ministries were linked in 1970 into a Department of the Environment.

These changes signified greater understanding of the fact that human activities interact on each other and on our surroundings so that events in one place affect people and conditions in others and at other times. So the subject embraces such others as what we mean by quality of life, ecology, effects of population trends, food and energy supplies, reclaiming land and creating new environment, and the trends in pollution. We shall see these issues as interacting parts of a system that includes all living things, the air, water and soil, accessible parts of the earth's crust, and the exchange of radiation with the rest of the universe, the most important part being the receipt of vast amounts of energy from the sun. Whether we can meet the challenge and find ways of living in equilibrium with that environment depends on ourselves. Those of us living in the developed (or "industrialised") countries have the greater responsibility. We have greater wealth, more technology, better educated populations than the less-developed countries whose poverty limits the extent to which they can help themselves.

These issues are discussed in the relevant sections which follow. Readers may also wish to consult **Section G, Part III** on the **Less Developed Economies** and **Section F, Part V** on Development Anthropology.

2. QUALITY OF LIFE

The concept of quality of life is difficult to define since it depends on the criteria used to judge human welfare. Yet these must certainly include "recognition of the inherent dignity and of the equal and inalienable rights of all members of the human family" set out in the Universal Declaration of Human Rights adopted in 1948 by the UN. This states that all human beings are born free and equal in dignity and rights, naming among these the right to life, liberty and security of person, freedom from slavery, from torture or degrading treatment, from arbitrary arrest, and arbitrary interference. In the economic and social spheres it covers the right to social security, to work, to rest and leisure, to a standard of living adequate for health and well-being, including food, clothing and medical care, and to education. Policies directed at ensuring that man lives in equilibrium with his environment must be kept consistent with these humane requirements.

For example, it would not be acceptable to argue that the need to conserve resources demanded that consumption levels should be kept low in the countries that are at present poor; nor would it be consistent with the view that all human beings are equal to suggest that population should be more severely controlled in the poorer countries than in the richer ones. These are not "abstract" questions. They have arisen forcefully at several UN conferences. And the Stockholm Conference endorsed this wider view in its 26 Principles. The environment, it declared, should be "of a quality that permits a life of dignity and well-being". And so policies that promote apartheid, discrimination and foreign domination "stand condemned and must be eliminated". Representatives of the world's nations went on to agree that "environmental deficiencies generated by conditions of under-development and natural disasters pose grave problems and can best be remedied by accelerated development through the transfer of substantial quantities of financial and technological assistance as a supplement to the domestic effort of the developing countries". And the most terrible threat to the quality of life also received due mention: "Man and his environment must be spared the effects of nuclear weapons and all other means of mass destruction. States must strive to reach prompt agreement on ... complete destruction of such weapons."

A further UN World Conference on Human Rights in 1993 led to a stronger statement—the Vienna Declaration—and a Programme of Action for Human Rights.

Attempts have been made to devise an index of quality of life to replace the narrowly-based economic index known as the Gross Domestic Product (GDP). Among them have been the Genuine Progress Indicator (GPI) which adds in the value of housework, but subtracts costs due to pollution, accidents, loss of leisure time, and resource depletion. Applied to both the USA and to the UK by such bodies as the New Economics Foundation, these indices show a fall in sustainable welfare in recent years. In the UK, the United Nations Association with the Local Government Management Board is studying six local boroughs and consulting with local organisations to develop Sustainability Indicators including prevalence of asthma in children, the state of the trees, air pollution and the like.

The Quality of Working Life.

Several of the industrial countries now have projects to improve the *quality of working life*, particularly for workers in operations likely to induce stress. These are seen as production or clerical jobs with forced uniform pacing especially when the pace is rapid; repetitiveness and very short time cycles leading to monotony, triviality and meaninglessness in work; large impersonal organisations and also objectives that seem distant and unreal. To combat these undesirable features, Reg Sell in the UK Department of Employment recommended in 1983 that for a job to satisfy human needs it is likely to have these characteristics: some freedom on how it should be carried out * responsibility for work and equipment * some variety of task, pace or skills * some feedback from supervisors and "customers" * some understanding of how it fits into a total product or process * choice of whether to work as an individual or in a team * a reasonable goal giving a sense of achievement * some opportunity to learn * an understanding of their role and how it fits in with other roles * avoiding role conflict such as pressure for output and for safety * a reasonable physical environment * discussion with people affected of any changes including advances in technology.

The programme continues with a Work Research Unit (WRU) aiming "to encourage industry and commerce to adopt measures that can lead to better economic performance through improving the Quality of Working Life". Developing people as a resource, they add, means that we must look at ways of both increasing their contribution to the running of business and of satisfying their needs as human beings. (ACAS Advisory Booklet No.16, 1993).

As interest grew in the practice of Total Quality Management (TQM), the WRU pointed to the need to underpin it with a culture based on high quality of working life. This means creating more satisfying jobs at all levels, involving the workers, and viewing people as assets contributing knowledge, experience and skills. The strategy, summarised by Mr Graham James, calls for delegating responsibility, teamwork across boundaries, empowering people, integrating people with technology, and a shared sense of purpose. Included is a relation of trust between managers and unions. Results are high quality products (or services), reliable output and low absenteeism he reported in 1991.

There have also been big advances in attention to health and safety at work in the industrial countries, although this is less marked in the developing countries and companies of the industrial countries sometimes take advantage of this. The EC Social Action Programme (1973) includes the improvement of living and working conditions. It specifies that this must apply to disadvantaged groups including migrant workers, women workers, physically handicapped and young workers. Decisions since that date aim "to help ensure that wellbeing is spread fairly through all areas and all social groups so that conditions of competition are 'harmonised' through member states"—though progress has inevitably been hindered by heavy unemployment.

This programme is being continuously updated as part of what is called "The Social Dimension of the Internal Market". In respect of the health and safety activities, the EC Joint Research Centre has compiled several data bases on harmful chemical substances.

A major development by the EC—though alas opposed by the UK government—was the adoption in December 1989 of a Social Charter by its constituent governments by a vote of 11 to 1. This Charter sets out rights based on these fundamental principles: free movement of workers, fair remuneration, improvement of living and working conditions, social protection, freedom of association, vocational training, equal treatment of men and women, information, consultation and participation of workers, protecting health and safety, protecting children and adolescents, the elderly, and the disabled. Though it has been criticised for vagueness, it has an associated action programme.

At the Council Meeting in Maastricht (December 1991), the UK government maintained its opposition. The results were what some commentators called a "most bizarre addition to EC decision making". In the new Treaty, the 11 EC governments other than Britain agreed to implement this Social Charter (re-named Chapter). A further Commission statement in December 1993 emphasised that "the Community is fully committed to ensuring that economic and social progress go hand in hand".

Clean Water.

A UN Conference on Human Settlements (HABITAT) in 1976 became the first international forum to set out the need for a global approach to supplying safe water and proper sanitation. In 1980 the UN General Assembly launched the International Drinking Water Supply and Sanitation Decade, intended to promote these objectives during the period 1980–1990. This was also designated the UN Decade for Women and it was noted that lack of water particularly places burdens on women; there was correspondingly, a call for women to participate fully in planning and implementing water supply projects.

The great significance of this effort is that the World Health Organisation (WHO) estimates that 80 per cent of all sickness and disease is due to inadequate water or sanitation. This includes diarrhoea, trachoma, debilitation due to parasitic worms, and malaria. The action needed is seen as a combined operation involving a clean water supply, sanitation and related programmes of health education as an integral part of the total development process.

However in its 1991 report on the State of the World Environment, UNEP sadly had to report that the goals set—to provide all people with clean water supplies and adequate sanitation facilities by 1990—had not been achieved. Yet great progress had been made. About 1·4 billion people in developing countries had been provided with safe, clean water and about 1·5 billion with sanitation services.

Unhappily, this still leaves 1·2 billion people, 31% of the population in developing countries, without access to safe clean water; 1·8 billion (43%) do not have access to adequate sanitation. UNEP notes that the debt burden of developing countries has contributed to slowing down investment in projects for drinking water and sanitation. Charities and voluntary agencies such as Water Aid and Oxfam are active in helping people in poorer countries to provide themselves with safe water but their funds are limited.

Though generally industrial countries have cleaner water supplies, an ironic twist is that the EC, during 1989, was considering taking legal action against the UK for extensive infringements of EC law agreed by the UK, concerning water purity. During 1989, the UK water industry was privatised, and in October 1989 the Environment Secretary relaxed pollution standards for 835 sewage works to minimise risks of prosecution of the resulting water companies. In autumn 1991, the official National Rivers Authority reported that rivers, canals and estuaries were more heavily polluted than in 1985. This decline in purity reversed a gradual improvement that had occurred during earlier decades. But the Authority expected that current investment programmes would improve standards in the next five years.

In 1992 NRA reported that close working with industry and agriculture was bringing about changes needed to achieve sustained improvements in the water environment. There had been a steep decline in major pollution incidents. NRA also launched a Groundwater Protection Policy dealing with all risks to groundwater resources (which provide about 35% of public supply in England and Wales). But by 1994 its Chief Executive was warning that cuts in government grants (£70 million in 1993–94 down to £60m in 1995–96) meant that NRA was at the limit of its ability to deal with water pollution.

However, researchers in major industrial countries, including the USA, UK, and Denmark are also concerned about the effects of breakdown products of pesticides, detergents and other industrial chemicals which are finding their way into our water supplies. Current water purification treatments do not normally remove them. In particular some synthetic chemicals—notably nonyl phenol compounds, but also others—are suspected of acting on organisms in the same way as the natural sex hormones, the oestrogens. In rivers, experiments have confirmed that they disrupt the physiology of

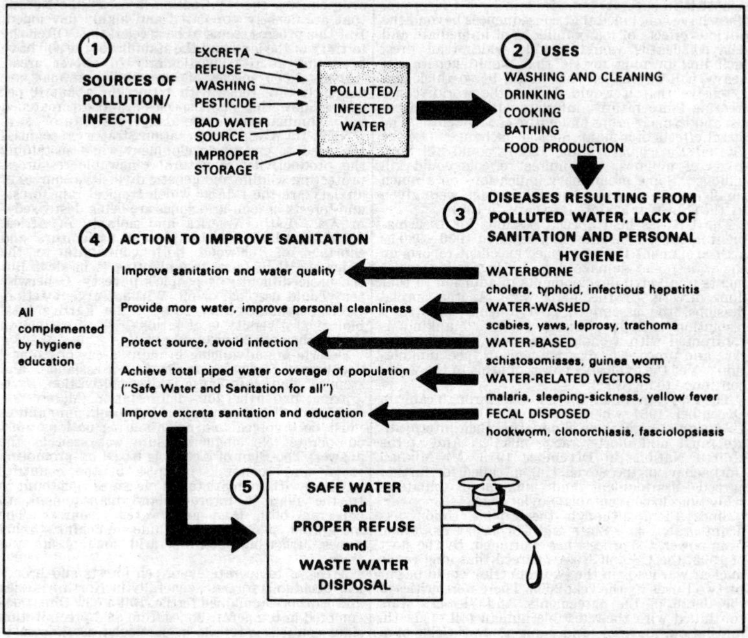

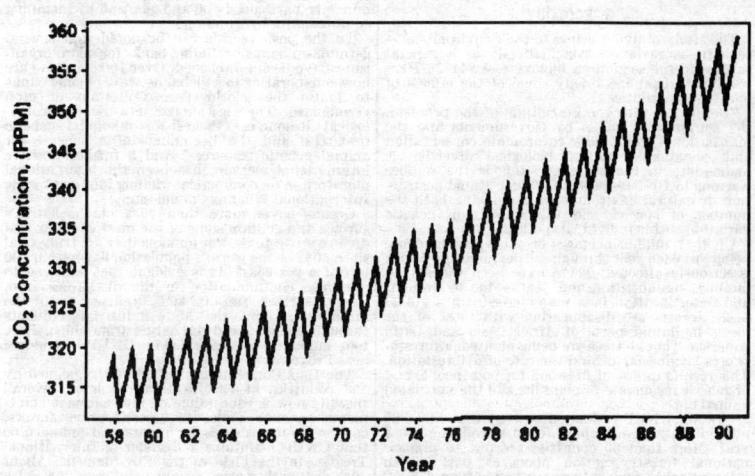

FIG. 1: PATHS TO SAFE WATER AND SANITATION

Source: "International Drinking Water Supply and Sanitation Decade 1981–90" (United Nations).

FIG. 2: ATMOSPHERIC CONCENTRATION OF CARBON DIOXIDE
(as measured at Mauna Loa Observatory, Hawaii)

Source: "The State of the Environment 1989"

male fish, in effect "feminising" them. The compounds that act on the body like oestrogen hormones are also suspected of being linked to doubling rates of human testicular cancer, and falling sperm counts in men; Medical Research Council workers think they may also be linked to increasing breast cancer rates in women.

Arms and Disarmament.

Environmental effects of a nuclear war have been the subject of detailed studies by distinguished scientists in several countries and by a UN group. They have concluded that consequences beyond the obvious effects of many millions of immediate and delayed deaths would include widespread fires, including burning forests that would generate a heavy pall of smoke. This would be so thick and extensive that it would darken the world, cause freezing temperatures, interfere with photosynthesis, and damage crops and entire eco-systems. "The direct effects of a major nuclear exchange" (see the journal *Environment* June 1988) "could kill hundreds of millions; the indirect effects could kill billions". Some preliminary indications on a much smaller scale of environmental damage were given by the Gulf War against Iraq early in 1991.

The UN has held Special Sessions for Disarmament in 1978, 1982 and 1988, declared 1970–1980 as a Disarmament Decade, issued excellent reports on the widespread damage done by increasing arma ments to all civil developments in addition to that done directly by the many wars. At the Special Sessions, the assembled governments adopted a resolution including these words: "Mankind is confronted with a choice—we must halt the arms race and proceed to disarmament or face annihilation". Yet the explosive power of arms in the world continued to increase.

The first signs of a material breakthrough came in December 1987 when the Soviet Union and the USA signed a treaty on eliminating their intermediate range and shorter range missiles. And at the United Nations in December 1988, Mr Mikhail Gorbachev, of the Soviet Union, called for further agreed disarmament and announced unilateral reductions in conventional Soviet arms.

Since then, although the Soviet Union has disintegrated as a State and Gorbachev has fallen from power, the process has continued. By the start of 1993, the US and Russia agreed that long range nuclear warheads in the two countries would be cut by two thirds by the year 2003. There were critics of the detail of the agreements, and "lesser" wars continued with their terrible human toll of death, mutilation, poverty and hunger. But risks of a world cataclysm from this source, with major world damage to the environment, seemed to recede.

3. ECOLOGY

The study of living beings in their environment—ecology—is reviewed systematically as a general subject in the section on biology (see **F44–7**). Here we aim to examine briefly some of the effects of man's own activities.

"Compared with the magnitude of the problem, the action being taken by Governments and the international community to promote conservation and sustainable use of biological diversity is inadequate in the extreme"; this is the sombre warning in UNEP's report for 1989. Rapid destruction of natural environments is reducing both the number of species and the amount of genetic variation within individual species.

Up to 7 million hectares of cultivated land are being lost each year through soil degradation. Africa is seriously affected. There have been widespread famines, malnutrition and deaths due to drought and desertification in a major crisis. On a global basis, forests are disappearing with most of the losses in humid parts of Africa, Asia and Latin America. Though trees are being planted, afforestation is lagging far behind the rate of deforestation. This results in loss of firewood for poor people and of genetic resources—of plant life and the associated animal life.

Overall, UNEP estimated in 1991 that 14 to 20 million hectares of tropical forest were being lost a year. More than 60 countries are due to prepare national forestry action plans as part of an international Tropical Forestry Action Plan. UNEP reports some moderate success. Investment in tropical forestry increased to US $ one billion in 1989. Also a Convention on International Trade in Endangered Species that came into force in 1975 is receiving increasing (nominal) support, with 95 countries subscribing to it in 1989, though countries do not necessarily enforce it vigorously. The UK "representative" for this Convention is the Nature Conservancy Council. It publishes a World Checklist of Threatened Amphibians and Reptiles.

There is nothing new in mankind modifying the "assemblage" of plants and animals (biomes) and even causing their extinction in areas like Europe that are densely populated and highly developed. But this process seems to be accelerating. Often the fertility of the land and the stability of the soil have been put at risk, particularly in poorer areas. "About 1,000 species of birds and mammals are currently threatened with extinction; about 10 per cent of flowering plant species are also threatened with elimination or are dangerously rare" says UNEP. Its World Conservation Strategy recognises the need to ensure development while sustaining the productivity of natural renewable resources, protecting wildlife and genetic diversity. Sources of anxiety are the rate at which tropical rain forests and forests in semi-arid zones are being destroyed—in Asia, Latin America and notably in Africa. "Slash-and-burn" techniques of agriculture and shortage of fuelwood both contribute to the damage. Much more tree-planting is needed. But the basic difficulty is people's poverty. Otherwise they could use coal or oil. Without urgent action, UNEP estimates that 25 % of the Earth's total biological diversity is at serious risk of extinction during the next 20 to 30 years.

Deserts are advancing in many areas of tropical deciduous forests, savannahs, grasslands and steppes. The main cause is over-cultivation, overgrazing, bad irrigation, deforestation. Massive resources need to be invested, but local communities must be involved and neighbouring nations must co-operate. No single measure was seen as the answer. The Plan of Action is based on promoting social and economic progress in the countries affected with many detailed measures then built in to the Plan to improve land management, to conserve both land and water resources. The integrated plans may include mulching, fixing dunes, irrigating, planting arid zone plants and trees.

Areas of temperate evergreen forests and broadleaf deciduous forests—generally in North America and Europe—remained fertile. But a new threat has emerged in temperate zones from acid precipitation since coniferous forests in particular are known to be sensitive. UNEP also found that parts of the Arctic tundra were threatened. This wilderness is an ecosystem that provides grazing ground for nomadic tribes, but there has been damage by the search for minerals, particularly oil and gas, and by installing equipment for hydropower.

On the positive side can be noted that several germplasm banks, including banks for micro-organisms, have been established. Over 100 countries are now collaborating in a global network of gene banks to house the World Base Collection of crop germoplasm. There is a similar network of Microbiological Resources Centres for microbial genetic resources, and the beginnings of a scheme for animal genetic resources. And a further positive international measure has been the international moratorium on commercial whaling imposed by the International Whaling Commission.

Oceans cover more than 70% of the Earth's surface and contain some of the most complex and diverse ecosystems. For humans they are truly vital since 60% of the world's population live within 100 km of a sea-coast. It is evident that we need to minimise contamination in the discharges from rivers, surface run-off and drainage from the hinterland, domestic and industrial effluents through outfalls, and discharges from ships. Here too, guidance is available—in UNEP's Regional Seas Programme.

The 1992 Convention on Biodiversity, signed by 153 countries at Rio, is discussed later. Overall there is now a wide range of international agreements on such topics as desertification, forests, conservation measures for plants and animals, so that UNEP maintains a Register of International Treaties in the Field of the Environment. About 40% deal with marine systems and over 25% with nature conservation and terrestrial living resources.

4. POPULATION

"Population growth increases the demand for goods and services and, if practices remain unchanged, implies increased environmental damage" warns the World Bank, in its 1992 major report on "Development and the Environment". In fact there has been some progress, but nowhere near enough.

Years of studies, forecasts, warnings and exhortations by population analysts of the manifold risks to mankind in the continuing growth of our numbers have at last, slowly, begun to have effect. Growth rates for population have declined overall and the Special Topic (*see* Y17) is devoted to this subject. Recent researches indicate that fertility rates in developing countries have fallen much more rapidly than they did in Europe during the period called the demographic transition. This is the change from high death rates and high birth rates through intermediate stages to low birth rates and low death rates. This recent faster rate of fall of fertility is attributed very largely to greater use of contraceptives.

Nevertheless the world's population was esti-mated to have reached about 5·5 billion (thousand million) in 1993, with about 93% of future growth due to be in developing countries. The world's Scientific Academies held an unprecedented joint conference in 1993 to prepare an appraisal of the dangers for the UN conference on Population and Development due in September 1994. But the UN Population Fund (UNFPA) has also pointed out that ". . . a country's people should be a resource not a liability. Problems arise when a population is out of balance with the resources required to sustain it, or when population is growing at such a rapid rate as to overtake the ability of governments . . . to provide proper services like health care and educa-tion, employment opportunities, and adequate housing." In many countries, large increases have been accompanied by rising living standards. But in developing countries, notably in Africa, rapid growth of population has occurred alongside decline in food, nutrition, drinking water and sanitation.

It is now widely realised that family size involves much more than successful contraception advice. For example, high death rates of children are a cause as well as an effect of high birth rates. Research has consistently shown that the education of women is of key importance. Educated women are more likely to use health services, they are less vulnerable to the risks of childbirth, they take more advantage of community services and have smaller families.

UNFPA had earlier adopted decisions that such programmes must be carried out in ways that respect the principle of voluntary decisions and are in keeping with cultural and religious values. It is also realised that if women marry young it not only has a major effect on family size but also damages the health of women and reduces their status in the family and the community. UNFPA proposes that child marriage is "recognised" as a violation of human rights.

Yet—in keeping with the points made above (Quality of Life)—the Declaration on Population and Development emphasises that all couples have the basic right to decide freely and responsibly the number of their children. But when they exercise this right they should take into account their responsibility to the community. Furthermore improving the status of women influences family life and size. These points endorse and develop those made at the first population conference. They logically lead to the final current recommendation that comprehensive population programmes are needed based on active co-operation between governments and communities.

Mortality and Health Policy.

When death rates go down, there is a delay before birth rates decline. It is as though people need time to adjust themselves. In assessing progress this must be allowed for.

It is comforting to be able to report that in the 1980s there was marked progress in improving health conditions throughout the world. Overall, infant mortality fell to 71 per 1,000 births per year in 1985–90 and life expectancy rose to 62 years at birth. Yet enormous gaps remain between rich and poor within and between countries. Des-pite the improvements, high infant mortality is a harrowing, but marked feature of the developing world. In 34 of these countries the rate remains at more than 100 per 1,000 births, compared with 9 per 1,000 in the industrial countries. Improvements in preventing child deaths are due to no single factor. They are attributed to better sanitation and public health, notably in controlling epidemic diseases. Further reductions in deaths depend on

better health services, living conditions and nutrition.

Urbanisation.

In search of a better life, people have moved in their millions from country to town, from poorer countries to richer, and—before the present wide-spread unemployment—from countries with abund-ant labour to those short of labour. The resulting problems have been aggravated by the further millions who have moved due to wars and political upheavals. In 1982 it was estimated that there were almost 10 million unsettled refugees. The poor people who have moved into towns have led to numbers in towns growing at 3 per cent per annum though world population as a whole was then growing at 1·7 per cent per annum. In the developing countries town populations are increas-ing at an estimated 4 per cent per annum. Nearly half the world population, it is reckoned, will be in towns in the year 2000.

As well as becoming a heavy burden on the re-sources of and organisation of the towns, this can be a severe drain on the countryside. For those who move are often the young or educated who could be most valuable to the countryside. It is therefore essential to invest in the country areas and to stimulate medium-sized cities to try and stem the flight to the large cities.

UNEP estimates that by the year 2000, the developing regions will have about 61 cities with populations over 4 million, compared to about 25 cities in the developed regions. All this strains the capacities of governments to provide basic services. Poor people live in shanty towns, with many social hazards—dirty water, no sanitation, liability to crime and drug addiction, liability to natural disasters and industrial accidents. Rich and poor often suffer from air pollution as discussed further below.

In the developed countries there tends to be an opposite movement, from big towns into the country. For the UK, the Council for the Preserva-tion of Rural England has warned that this is 'urbanising the countryside', undermining efforts to tackle dereliction in the cities and spoiling the countryside for city-dwellers themselves.

Population Density in the UK.

Though these discussions often tend to centre on the problems of crowded countries remote from our shores—and very much on the extra problems faced by the poorer ones—Britain is very directly in-volved. Statistics issued by the European Commu-nity show the UK with 233 inhabitants per square kilometre, well above the Community average. This puts us among the more densely populated coun-tries, though less than Belgium, Netherlands, or the pre-reunification Federal Republic of Germany.

For 1991 the population of the UK was estimated to be 57·8 million. It is projected to continue to grow slowly to over 62 million by 2031 mainly by excess of births over deaths before starting to decline. Little change in the proportions of those over pensionable age is expected between 1990 and 2001 but marked increases in the proportion over 75. In making these projections the Office of Population Censuses and Surveys (OPCS) expects an overall balance of immigrants and emigrants for the UK from 1991.

5. FOOD

During the 1980s a series of TV reports on starving people notably in sub-Saharan Africa provoked a great wave of public concern in West Europe, the Soviet Union and USA. Governments and voluntary organisations poured in a stream of both food and transport in a belated attempt to minimise the human toll. Yet ironically there had been bumper wheat crops in the developed countries and the EC had tens of millions of tonnes of corn in store.

Because of the continuing conditions of severe food shortage in many poor countries and their further deterioration, all too often, into actual famine, international bodies have taken decisions to try and minimise these risks—although the deeds have been far inferior to the grand words. Three

TABLE: CLASSIFICATION OF COUNTRIES (1990)

Developing Countries			
Low income			

Oil importers

Afghanistan	Chad	Madagascar	Sierra Leone
Bangladesh	Equatorial Guinea	Malawi	Somalia
Benin	Ethiopia	Mali	Sri Lanka
Bhutan	Fiji	Mozambique	Sudan
Burkina Faso	Ghana	Nepal	Surinam
Burma (Myanmar)	Guinea	Niger	Tanzania
Burundi	Guinea-Bissau	Pakistan	Togo
Cambodia	Haiti	Rwanda	Uganda
Cape Verde	India	Sao Tome and	Vietnam
Central African	Laos	Principe	Zaïre
Republic			

Oil exporters

China

Middle income			

Oil importers

Argentina	El Salvador	Korea, North	Paraguay
Barbados	Greece	Korea, South	Philippines
Bolivia	Guatemala	Lebanon	Portugal
Botswana	Guyana	Lesotho	Senegal
Brazil	Honduras	Liberia	Singapore
Cameroon	Hong Kong	Mauritania	Thailand
Chile	Israel	Mongolia	Turkey
Colombia	Ivory Coast	Morocco	Uruguay
Costa Rica	Jamaica	Nicaragua	Yemen
Cuba	Jordan	Panama	Zambia
Dominican Republic	Kenya	Papua New Guinea	Zimbabwe

Oil exporters

Algeria	Gabon	Malaysia	Syrian Arab Republic
Angola	Indonesia	Mexico	Trinidad and Tobago
Congo, PR	Iran	Nigeria	Tunisia
Ecuador	Iraq	Peru	Venezuela
Egypt			

Industrial Market Economies			
Australia	France	Japan	Spain
Austria	Germany	Luxembourg	Sweden
Belgium	Iceland	Netherlands	Switzerland
Canada	Ireland	New Zealand	United Kingdom
Denmark	Italy	Norway	United States
Finland			

High Income Oil Exporters			
Bahrain	Kuwait	Oman	Saudi Arabia
Brunei	Libya	Qatar	United Arab Emirates

Former Centrally Planned Economies under Communism			
Albania	Hungary	Romania	Slovakia
Bulgaria	Poland	Russia	Ukraine
Czech Republic			

Source: Based on the classification used in the *World Development Report 1983*. It does not include all countries with less than one million population and without production (or prospects of future production) of oil, gas, and coal. The classification has been amended to reflect the collapse of communism in Eastern Europe and the disintegration of the former Soviet Union in 1991.

major initiatives have been the establishment of the following:

International Emergency Food Reserve (IEFR)

Global Information and Early Warning System (GIEWS)

Food Security Assistance Scheme (FSAS).

Some success is being achieved by the GIEWS which has 98 participating governments. It receives and analyses a large amount of relevant information and alerted the world to impending severe food shortages in 1977 and 1980 in the Sahel and in sub-Saharan Africa; urgent action was taken and famines averted.

FSAS has also made progress. In over fifty countries it has helped improve food storage facilities, stock management, transport and port facilities, and helped set up national warning systems. But because there is still no international grain agreement, including arrangements for internationally held stocks, there is no assured buffer stock that would stabilise prices and help developing countries. It should be added, in reply to criticisms of food aid, that officers of the World Food Programme say they take care to use it in ways that avoid inducing dependence and they aim to build up capacities to produce food. For example, food may be given to poor landless labourers in exchange for work on land development or as interim supplies during land reform schemes. On these projects as a whole, FAO reports both progress and also unmet targets for aid. Another contentious area is the need to use fertilisers and pesticides. Against them are the arguments that they are expensive for poor farmers and that it should be possible to farm without using "chemicals" liable to add to environmental pollution. But the UN appraisals are that more food is needed to relieve malnourishment of the world's poorest people. 60 per cent of this increase must come from higher yields. Present cereal yields in tonnes per hectare are West Europe 3·5, USA 4·3, Asia 2·15, South America 1·95 and Africa 1·05. Much more fertiliser is needed to increase yields in developing countries and improved seeds. Then the crop must be protected by pesticides and good storage. Developing countries have severe losses due to rotting and pests. Strategies of governments must shift to helping the world's smallholders directly by aid, education, promoting co-operatives, providing seeds, equipment, storage, etc.—and credit to buy these urgent needs. And the crisis area for many years was Africa. But FAO notes that in all aid activities environment must be preserved; conservation is emphasised as a pre-condition of food security.

In respect of fish supplies, the world's nations have recognised in principle the risks of over-fishing and have adopted a UN Convention on the Law of the Sea. Yet UNEP has warned in 1993 that in practice some of the world's major fisheries are being fished at unsustainable rates.

Early in 1984, FAO issued the result of a further study with the International Institute for Applied Systems Analysis (IIASA) on Third World land resources. Carefully analysing country by country they concluded that these could feed more people living there than the number living now. But they had to upgrade their farming practices.

However there was little favourable to report at the FAO/WHO first global "Nutrition Summit" of over 160 nations at the end of 1992. "In a world that produces more than it consumes" stated its World Declaration "about 780 million people in developing countries—20% of their population—still do not have access to enough food to meet their daily needs ... 190 million children suffer from protein-energy malnutrition and more than 2,000 million people suffer from micronutrient deficiencies which can lead to blindness, mental retardation and death." The Conference called for action to eliminate hunger and malnutrition. This had several parts and included a call for increasing development assistance.

An entirely different problem has also been the subject of review by the UN as part of its Global Environment Monitoring System (GEMS). A report "Chemical Contaminants of Food" (1988) on levels of selected pesticides, industrial chemicals and natural toxins—with reservations—was generally reassuring. After checking for such pollutants as lead, mercury, polychlorinated biphenyls, DDT, aldrin and dieldrin, and for aflatoxins, the researchers decided that current levels, particularly in the industrialized countries, were well within established health criteria.

Two further dangers have been pinpointed by the World Health Organisation. Foodborne diseases have become a growing source of ill health; in the case of malnourished people, notably children, it often proves to be a cause of death. WHO stresses the importance of hygienic food handling practices.

In respect of the "hidden hunger" of deficiencies in supply of the micronutrients iodine, iron and vitamin A in diets, WHO notes that the treatment is exceptionally cost-effective. The capsules needed cost a few US cents year; WHO estimate that complete global control of these deficiencies would cost only US $2 million a year.

FAO also add their strong support to the campaign for trees. "Sound agroforestry practices can help to ensure the environmental stability that rural people need to sustain the production of food for their families".

6. ENERGY

There has been growing concern about the major environmental impacts of energy production, transport and use. For both this reason and the normal desire to improve economy there have been efforts to increase the efficiency of using energy particularly in the developed countries. These efforts have achieved some success as shown by steady decreases in industrial countries in total energy needed per unit growth of GNP for many years.

Nevertheless, commercial energy consumption has increased more than threefold over the last three decades. Most of this usage is in industrialised economies. However the poorer countries in general aim to raise their living standards by developing their own industries and using more energy. In turn this will demand growing supplies of sources of energy—likely to be mainly fossil fuels and generating more CO_2. The significance of this is discussed below, particularly in respect of the so-called "greenhouse effect".

The World Bank in a policy statement in 1993 stated it would give greater attention to transferring more energy-efficient and pollution-reducing technologies to the developing world. It planned that bank lending for electric power should focus on countries "with a clear commitment to improving the sector performance".

Total primary energy consumption worldwide (reported in the BP Statistical Review of World Energy 1993) was 7794·2 million tonnes of oil equivalent in 1992. This represented a mere 0·2% growth over the previous year, comprising a small rise in the industrial world, a larger one in the developing countries notably in Asia and a fall in the former Soviet and allied countries,

An important negative factor was that the steady improvement in energy economy noted above slowed worldwide in 1988. In the industrial nations forming the Organisation for Economic Co-operation and Development (OECD) for the first time for many years energy consumption grew in step with Gross Domestic Product.

Public pressure about pollution by sulphur dioxide led to the EC agreeing that by the end of this century sulphur dioxide emissions will be cut by two thirds and there will be corresponding cuts in other pollutants. But, in addition to the commercially traded fuels, large parts of the population in the developing world use firewood and they are suffering what is called the "firewood catastrophe". In several countries the time needed to collect a day's firewood is now a full day's work. Forest cover is diminishing as we noted earlier. The International Institute for Environment and Development has urged a combination of solutions for Africa that may be of wider application—village woodlots, increased tree growing on private land, better forest management, and rational use of crop residues. Even in the industrial countries, there is now growing attention to "energy forestry"—short rotation forestry for energy. There are programmes in Sweden, UK and in other European countries.

The World Bank estimates that the developing countries (see Table) account for one-fourth of the world's production and one-fifth of the world's consumption of commercial energy. (Incidentally, energy estimates have to differentiate between commercial energy and that based on collected sources such as firewood or cow-dung which do not enter into statistics.) But the shares of the developing countries in both consumption and production are rising rapidly. By 1995 the Bank expects them to account for one third of (commercial) production and one fourth of consumption. So, as a group, the developing countries are thought likely to continue to be net exporters of commercial energy to the rest of the world.

"Green Energy"

There is growing interest in using renewable forms of energy—sometimes called "Green Energy". However in practice only hydro-electricity contributes on a large enough scale to world commercial supplies to justify listing in statistical tables. Furthermore, these generally benign and non-polluting sources can introduce their own environmental problems. Major hydro-electric schemes may displace farmers from their land; using wood fuel in developing countries may aggravate the exploitation of women and children; in poor areas growing plants for energy may absorb resources better used for producing food. UNEP and the European Union (EU, formerly called the EC) have emphasised that projects have to be carefully assessed at an early stage to ensure that "green energy" is developed in an environmentally sound way.

In the EU, the Commission is trying to stimulate more use of renewables both by direct support and by proposing penalising carbon-based fuels by a carbon/energy tax. Its Alternative Energy programme includes these objectives for the year 2005;

* doubling all renewable sources from an estimated 4% of primary energy in 1991;
* trebling production of electricity from these sources;
* securing a market share of 5% of motor fuel usage for biofuels—mixing alcohols from plant sources with petrol, using vegetable oils in diesel engines.

There are high hopes for geothermal energy—Italy already produces 500 MW of electricity in this way—and there are several EU research projects including one in France to tap energy by injecting water into hot rocks at a depth of 4000 m. Further EU schemes in the UK include a wave power scheme off Dounreay generating 2 MW.

For the UK "Renewable sources can and should make a significant contribution to future energy supply" was the conclusion in 1992 of a government-appointed expert Renewable Energy Advisory Group. It recommended government intervention and favoured a partnership with industry to establish a self-sustaining market by the year 2005. By 2025 renewables should "plausibly" be contributing 20% of the 1991 electricity supply.

Both this group and earlier the Parliamentary Energy Select Committee wanted more attention to the "external costs" of all energy sources "because environmental costs are not currently reflected in energy prices". This referred to such issues as damage due to acid emissions when burning fossil fuels.

In 1994 the government stated that it was seeking to stimulate a commercial market in new and renewable energy with up to £3 billion of private sector investment; it was working towards 1500 MW Declared Net Capacity of new electricity generating capacity from renewable sources for the UK by 2000.

7. MAJOR THREATS TO THE BIOSPHERE

The Greenhouse Effect.

The atmosphere keeps us warm, like the glass in a greenhouse. Without the atmosphere, the Earth's surface temperature would average about minus 20°C instead of the current plus 15°C. UNEP summarises the effect in this way.

"Sunlight heats up the sea, land and vegetation. The warmed surface of the earth then radiates heat back towards space, but this outward flow of radiation is at much longer wavelengths than sunlight, in the infra-red part of the spectrum. On its way out some of this infra-red radiation is absorbed by trace gases. Nitrogen and oxygen ... play no part in the process. But relatively tiny parts of the trace gases—notably carbon dioxide and water vapour—trap the heat that keeps the planet inhabitable."

However human activities have been accentuating this heating. The concentration of carbon dioxide (CO_2) has increased largely due to burning of fossil fuels. And the effects are enhanced by other strongly heat-absorbing gases, notably methane, nitrous oxide, ozone and the chlorofluorocarbons (CFCs) used mainly as refrigerants, foaming agents and aerosol propellants.

Global warming in the range 1 to 3°C would lead to the seas rising due to ice melting and water expansion and would flood low-lying parts. These include many densely packed cities. It would cause climatic instability affecting ecosystems and agriculture.

Natural processes produce CO_2 from living organisms and decomposing vegetation. But these amounts were generally taken up by photosynthesis and by the oceans. Human activities release extra carbon dioxide by burning fuels and by destroying forests and other vegetation. "Halting destruction of rain forests would provide the best way of limiting the rise of carbon dioxide" states a study by the Royal Society (the UK academy of sciences).

In the UK a House of Commons Select Committee of all parties made a range of recommendations for energy policy to mitigate the green-house effect. At the core of their detailed proposals were that "no one other than governments can realistically be expected to fund or coordinate this basic R & D" and "market mechanisms alone will not produce an adequate response to global warming".

Yet ultimately the problem is global, particularly since the developing world will need greatly increased amounts of energy to raise their living standards and therefore technical and financial help in achieving this safely. So preventing the buildup of greenhouse gases, like the further problem of the ozone hole discussed below, will need urgent international measures and integrity in carrying them out.

This is part of the programme of UNCED (see below). The EC, as part of its own studies, has noted "the enormity of the challenge". Allowing for population increase, the present global average of emissions of CO_2 of about 1·45 tonnes of carbon per capita will have to be reduced to about 0·35 by the year 2030 to stabilise CO_2 concentration. The interim EC objective is to stabilize emissions in the EC at the 1990 level by the year 2000.

The UK draft response to UNCED in December 1992, a Discussion Document "Climate Change; our national programme for CO_2 emissions", was severely criticised by such bodies as the Association for the Conservation of Energy and the Royal Commission on Environmental Pollution. The latter urged the government to set targets for reducing CO_2 emissions from transport and adopting programmes to achieve them, since two thirds of the expected increase to the year 2020 will come from private cars. Car users impose costs on the environment. Yet the final response document "Sustainable Development" (discussed later) though stating that the government is "committed to taking measures aimed at returning CO_2 and other greenhouse gas emissions to their 1990 levels by 2000" set out only estimates and "scenarios" rather than a firm programme of action.

The Ozone Hole.

In the atmosphere, there is a layer of ozone (O_3) largely concentrated in the stratosphere especially between altitudes of 20 and 30 km. Though ozone in the troposphere is a harmful constituent, the ozone in the stratosphere protects the earth including ourselves from ultraviolet radiation (UV) coming from the sun. This UV would otherwise do immense damage to life. The Natural Environment Research Council (UK) claim to have been the first to have discovered that an "ozone hole" had developed over Antarctica. After much debate about its causes, scientific opinion eventually agreed that this was due to the greatly increased use of chlorofluorocarbons (CFCs). Though they were regarded as chemically inert materials, under conditions in the atmosphere with intense solar radiation, they have reacted with the ozone. Changes in the amount of chlorine oxide were inversely correlated with the ozone. As the chlorine oxide amounts increased the ozone amount fell.

A wide range of effects was expected. Among them were increases in skin cancers, damage to crops and animals, and changes in world weather patterns. In September 1987 a conference of the world's major producing and consuming nations, convened by the UN, agreed to reduce the release of CFCs by 50% by the end of the century (The "Montreal Protocol"). Later information suggested that this might be too little and too late. The requirements were "tightened up" at two following international meetings and further tightened for the EU by ministers in December 1993. The EU limits include the following:

CFCs—85% cut by 1994, phaseout by 1995.
Carbon tetrachloride—85% cut by 1994, phaseout by 1995.
Halons—Phaseout by 1994.
HCFCs—Freeze at 2·6% CFC use + total HCFC use 1989; cut in 4 stages to phaseout 2015.

(Note: Halons are a range of compounds containing bromine, used in fire extinguishers. They are very damaging to atmospheric ozone. HCFCs are hydrochlorofluorocarbons, used as refrigerants and foaming agents.)

The HCFCs do less damage than the CFCs but need to be controlled, then phased out. Yet, residues of all these substances will continue to damage the ozone layer for many years to come until they are eliminated. Late in 1992 appeared a harbinger of the new trend—the first CFC-free

refrigerator. Made by a German company called
DKK, it uses a mixture of propane and butane as
the coolant and pentane for the insulating foam.

Attention is now turning to the ozone damaging
effects of oxides of nitrogen (NOx) from jet
aircraft. New engines will be expected to generate
less NOx.

Representatives of developing countries have
pointed out that they will need assistance from
industrial countries in achieving improvements in
their living standards while avoiding using materials
liable to deplete the ozone layer. This also forms
part of the programme of the 1992 Earth Summit.

8. MAN-MADE LAND

In manufacturing new islands or recovering land
from the edge of the sea, new environment is
created. The new areas may be built up solidly from
the sea-bottom by filling up with sand or gravel, or
built up on supports, or floating and tethered. For a
crowded country, like Japan or the Netherlands,
this provides extra space.

Islands can also be useful for locating industrial or
other activities that many people find a nuisance—
like storing oil, running airports, manufacturing
products where the process creates noises or smells.
In these cases, they remove these activities from
intruding on other people's environments. In some
cases, work is set up at sea because there lies the
material that is to be worked, e.g. Britain's North
Sea oil and gas or Japan's coal. Islands may be
sternly functional, such as those in the North Sea;
but they may be elegantly dressed up like the so-
called THUMS islands near the Long Beach
Harbour of Los Angeles in California to avoid
changing the visual character of a holiday district.

The oldest man-made island is a Japanese one
built in 1640 to permit trading with Dutch traders
who were not allowed to set foot ashore within the
country. But the Dutch also have a long history of
both land reclamation and building islands. Both
countries are highly active today in such projects.

Near Osaka is Japan's latest airport built on an
island claimed to be the greatest civil engineering
project in the world. Three mountains were removed
to form its foundations and the terminal, opened in
1994, stands on 900 computer-monitored jacks to
keep the building level. Its area is 511 hectares and
the passenger terminal is a mile long.

9. POLLUTION

Though there has always been a certain amount
of concern about pollution since the start of the
Industrial Revolution, this was largely an interest
of relatively limited numbers of concerned people.
But during the 1960s there was a great upsurge of
anxiety which was reflected internationally by the
calling of the Stockholm UN Conference referred to
earlier.

In response to the rising public pressures, many
aspects of pollution are now being monitored and
action has been taken mainly in the industrial
countries, even though sometimes reluctantly and
with many warnings from industry and governments about the costs. In many areas there has
been a gratifying improvement. In the UK, for
example, urban concentration of smoke in 1989
was about one tenth of that in 1962–3 but the
improvement seems to have halted in the later
part of the 1980s. Sulphur dioxide emissions have
also fallen (by about 80% over the same period)
and also appear to show the same halt in improvement recently. Lead emissions have also shown a
marked reduction of pollution in response to
effective campaigns reflecting public concern. Emissions of oxides of nitrogen have increased in recent
years, mainly from increasing road transport. Both
these and the contribution from power stations are
being increasingly controlled by EC Directives.

Considering the world as a whole, a UNEP
report in 1988 was disturbingly headed "Are we
poisoning our peoples?" Global air monitoring
indicates that two thirds of the world's city dwellers
breathe air that contains "disturbingly high levels"
of sulphur dioxide and dust. Trends are for improvements in general in the most industrialised
countries while quality is getting worse in many
developing ones. The survey also covered nitrogen
dioxide, carbon monoxide and lead. It found that in
many developing countries emissions of all five

pollutants are increasing. These are serious tendencies in view of the harmful effects of the pollutants,
the often poor nutrition (and therefore resistance)
of the poor city-dwellers, the growing tendency to
industrialisation, and growth of city-dwelling in
developing countries.

There was alas no comfort from WHO and UNEP
in 1992 when further studies showed air pollution
"posing increasingly serious health problems in
some of the world's biggest cities". Of those
surveyed, Mexico City was the worst affected.
Motor vehicle traffic was indicted as a major source
of air pollution, often the single most important
source.

Volatile organic compounds (VOC), comprising
hundreds of compounds including unburnt petrol
and solvents, are now being monitored as threats to
health and environment. They include carcinogens
and compounds that form smog. Many originate in
natural emissions from plants, trees and animals;
others arise from plastics, finishes and coatings,
vehicle exhausts, and industrial processes. A new
learned society, Indoor Air International, has been
set up to study this group of atmospheric pollutants.

More generally, Elizabeth Dowdeswell, Executive
Director of UNEP, has warned "of the new and
burgeoning class of human ailments caused by
chemical contaminants in the environment" with
the poorer people at the greatest risk. UNEP "pulls
together" information into its International Register of Potentially Toxic Chemicals and acts with
WHO in a major programme on chemical safety.

Turning to rivers, those in Europe have shown
increases in nitrate concentrations due to changes
in agricultural practices including using more
fertilisers. This influences the quality of drinking
water. Pressure from the EU is leading to discussions of control on agricultural practices. There are
also EU pressures in respect of our often seriously
contaminated bathing beaches.

Opinion surveys for the UK National Rivers
Authority in 1993 showed that people were concerned about UK waters being dirtier than many
others in Europe and wanted more attention to
water cleanliness. People complained about high
profits of the water companies, but were also willing
to pay more for improved environmental standards.

The 1988 UNEP report quoted above gave even
more cause for concern in respect of river quality in
developing countries. Information was collected on
over 50 properties. They included bacteria, nitrates,
faecal coliforms, dissolved oxygen and heavy
metals. The study found very severe pollution
causing infant deaths in developing countries, in
many streams and rivers in South America, the
Indian sub-Continent and south-east Asia. Though
African rivers are poorly documented, they are
thought to present the same features.

The seas are becoming more polluted. By 1988
there were 820 marine and coastal protected areas
in the world. But a 1993 report (partly funded by
UNEP) of the US Centre for Marine Conservation
demands much more than this to protect future
food supplies and enable the oceans to act as a
treasure chest of medicines and raw materials.
Industrial pollution combined with hunting and
fishing are jointly blamed for putting the entire
marine realm at risk. The report proposes a
programme for sustainable harvesting of the oceans'
riches.

Disquiet over waste incineration at sea eventually
led eight North Sea countries to agree to reduce the
practice by 76% by the end of 1990 and to phase it
out by 1991. A further international agreement to
stop ships dumping plastics at sea took effect in
December 1988.

In 1994 a further research report confirmed the
devastating effect on health of the self-inflicted
pollution of smoking. Published in the British
Medical Journal, the results showed that the death
rate for smokers in the age range 35 to 69 was treble
the death rate of non-smokers. The most comforting
feature of the research was a finding that there were
survival benefits in quitting at any age.

Radioactivity.

There has been great public anxiety over risks due
to radioactivity and this insidious form of pollution
is monitored by public agencies in all the industrial
countries, with increased attention since the 1986
Chernobyl disaster (and public acknowledgement

of earlier UK disasters). There was a peak of strontium-90 in milk in 1964 and this has fallen steadily due to the virtual elimination of testing of nuclear weapons in the atmosphere. Radioactivity due to liquid effluents from processing factories (such as Sellafield), experimental stations (of UKAEA), and nuclear power stations has been the subject of extensive protests. However, they are all officially monitored and "exposure pathways" later examined in terms of the maximum exposure of the people most likely to suffer, called the "critical group". This is a calculation that takes account of both dose rates and the length of period of occupancy of the area emitting the radiation. It is then expressed as a percentage of the dose limit recommended by the International Commission on Radiological Protection. An international meeting in November 1993 agreed an indefinite ban on disposing of radioactive waste at sea. The UK and four other countries abstained, but the UK later accepted the decision in 1994.

The government has approved with strict safety requirements the start-up of the thermal oxide reprocessing plant (THORP) for treating spent nuclear fuel. Objectors claim this will increase ambient radioactivity and risk nuclear material falling into the hands of terrorists, but the operators (BNFL) deny both of these claims.

UK and EU objectives for radiological protection are officially based on the recommendations of the International Commission on Radiological Protection (ICRP). And, though eternal vigilance is of course necessary and local conditions may need attention, the overall problems of radiation exposure tend to be exaggerated. Our radiation exposure in the UK consists of some 87% from natural sources and 13% from man-made sources. Of the latter, medical irradiation provides almost the whole of the dose. Cosmic rays bombard the earth and produce radioactive material as they pass through the atmosphere; the ground contains naturally occurring uranium, radon and thoron. The food we eat and the air we breathe are slightly radioactive, so that our bodies are also slightly radioactive.

In line with ICRP recommendations, current official objectives in the UK are these:

"a all practices giving rise to radioactive wastes must be justified, *i.e.* the need for the practice must be established in terms of its overall benefit;

b radiation exposure of individuals and the collective dose to the population arising from radioactive wastes shall be reduced to levels which are as low as reasonably achievable, economic and social factors being taken into account;

c the effective dose equivalent from all sources, excluding background radiation and medical procedures, to representative members of a critical group should not exceed 1 mSv in any one year; however, effective dose equivalents of up to 5 mSv are permissible in some years provided that the total does not exceed 70 mSv over a lifetime".

Yet there remain important sources of concern. The EU is setting up what they call "a defence system" in the event of a further nuclear accident to provide information to governments and public on foodstuff standards. A further area (radon) is discussed below. Yet a third area of concern is the disposal of waste from military, nuclear power, industrial and medical use. In the UK a Nuclear Industry Waste Executive (NIREX) has been set up to dispose of all nuclear wastes "in such a way that future generations will be fully protected". The EU is reviving monitoring provisions of the Euratom Treaty to strengthen controls on movements of nuclear waste.

But the largest problem on earth is posed by the military nuclear waste of the USA where the safety aspects have been handled very secretively.

Electromagnetic Compatibility.

So much electrical and electronic equipment is now being introduced into homes, industry, commerce and transport that there is growing concern about "electromagnetic pollution". This means that this type of equipment may be disturbing or being disturbed by other such equipment. A European Directive on Electromagnetic Compatibility (EMC)

came into force at the start of 1992 with corresponding internal regulations in the UK. Electrical goods may not now emit electromagnetic radiation which will render other electrical equipment unreliable. Also, equipment must be immune to a certain level of emitted electromagnetic radiation (presumably from older equipment).

Genetically Modified Organisms.

Two sets of regulations issued in 1992, implementing EC Directives, now govern both the contained use and the deliberate release of genetically modified organisms. The government is advised by two independent expert committees with the aim of encouraging use of genetic resources without adverse effects on the environment.

Interior Environment.

Since most people in the industrialised countries spend most of their time indoors, the interior environment is also of great importance. In recent years there has been concern about the effects of radon-222, a naturally occuring radioactive gas. This is formed by radioactive decomposition of radium. It comes out of the ground, particularly in and around areas of igneous rock such as granite. In the open air it disperses, but in buildings it may accumulate. The gas itself decays into minute solid particles. If these are breathed in, they can be deposited in the lungs. In the UK the main areas with radon concentrations at a level that may cause concern are in some parts of Devon and Cornwall. The danger was first discovered in Sweden; research on limiting exposure is in progress particularly in Sweden, Britain, and the USA. For example in Britain there is now a Householders Guide to Radon.

More generally, there is liable to be some level of concentration of volatile organic pollutants in buildings, particularly in tightly sealed air-conditioned buildings. Plastics, varnishes, paints, organic filling for cavity walls, upholstery and its dyes are all suspected of possibly emitting slowly volatile pollutants. Some people tend to become ill in air-conditioned buildings and there is considerable—but inconclusive—discussion on the relative importance of psychological and chemical factors in causing these difficulties.

Bridging the issues of interior and exterior environments are new schemes by the Building Research Establishment for environmental assessments of new offices, superstores, supermarkets and homes. Buildings are rated by being given credits for global issues (CO_2 emissions, CFC, use of recycled materials), neighbourhood issues (such as the ecological value of the site) and indoor issues (such as air quality, hazardous materials and lighting). Capital investors and developers are said to find the resulting BREEAM certificates an asset in dealing with clients.

Noise.

One important area that does not show much progress is noise. Over the last twenty years the level of noise in urban areas has generally risen mainly because of traffic on land and in the air. This is a difficult area because of the trouble in measuring noise levels and interpreting their effects. Directives have been issued by the EC to bring this type of nuisance under control. In the UK, new Building Regulations tightened up standards for noise insulations in flat conversions. Further rules have been issued or planned to cover noise nuisance from new railway lines, noise in the street, loudspeakers, burglar alarms and aircraft noise; there is research into Noise Abatement Zones by local authorities and even a Working Group on dealing with noisy parties.

An EC Directive (86/188) requires workers to be protected from risks due to exposure to noise at work. The most effective way is to quieten machines at source. Methods of test are being internationally standardised. In the UK, noise data are required on all machines producing more than 85 dB(A). By 1992 a Directive extended this to machinery producing more than 70 dB(A). In addition approved designs of ear muffs have to be available for those cases where noise cannot be reduced to safe levels.

The Disposal of Wastes.

Worldwide, landfill sites used for dumping hazardous wastes have been found unsatisfactory. Corrosive materials, poisonous organics and metals have been left in unsafe condition. UNEP has been active in urging governments to research the issue and to take action. One of the actions has been the Global Convention to control transboundary movements of hazardous wastes, (Basle Convention), adopted in March 1989. It followed the revelations of dumping of such wastes by industrial countries in African states with no facilities for properly controlling the dumps. Industrial countries have also suffered from "cowboy" dumping practices, inadequate laws, and inadequate inspection arrangements, which have even led to homes being built on poisonous dumps. Reducing waste at its source, recycling it and reusing it are strongly recommended by UNEP. Both pressure groups and commercial interests urge separating metals from waste, burning the remainder safely and utilising the heat generated.

The inadequacies of UK laws on waste, including toxic waste, and of their enforcement has been severely criticised in recent years by such bodies as the House of Commons Environmental Committee, the Royal Commission on Environmental Pollution and the Royal Fine Arts Commission. Children had been found playing among drums of poison.

But most of the provisions of the Environmental Protection Act 1990 have now been brought into force. They include a Duty of Care. Anyone who has control of waste *at any stage* has to ensure that it is dealt with safely and legally. The Act includes new duties on people and authorities to keep areas, including railway tracksides, clear of litter. Surveys by the Tidy Britain Group suggest some improvements but a long way to go. Additional duties have been imposed on local authorities in respect of waste and recycling and some degree of financial assistance provided.

In Western Europe over 9 million cars are scrapped each year. Auxiliary industries are developing to maximise recovering useful materials and the car industry is working towards designs that will aid such recovery.

10. RESEARCH

The International Council of Scientific Unions has set up a major programme to study global change as part of the international geosphere-biosphere programme. They have set out to answer these specific questions:

* How is the chemistry of the global atmosphere regulated, and what is the role of terrestrial processes producing and consuming trace gases?
* How do ocean biogeochemical processes influence and respond to climate change?
* How does vegetation interact with physical processes in the hydrological cycle?
* How will climate change affect terrestrial ecosystems?

UK environmental research organisations are actively involved and coordinated through a Global Environmental Research Office. Its governing committee has set up a research framework on environmental processes, their impacts and the responses needed, identifying the highest priority areas. A surprising report in 1993 was that CO_2 concentration had increased at a rate slower than normal. This was attributed to a sequence of events following on the massive 1991 eruption of Mount Pinatubo in the Philippines that led to greater uptake of CO_2 by the oceans.

In considering action based on research, the Committee on Global Environmental Change has drawn attention to the Precautionary Principle. This rests on

* prudent action in advance of scientific certainty
* shifting the burden of proof to show no unreasonable harm
* ensuring that environmental well-being is given legitimate status
* developing best practice techniques.

A wide range of organisations in the UK and overseas are now including environmental impacts into their research programmes. Briefly, we can mention a group of projects of the Engineering and Physical Sciences Research Council entitled "Clean Technology". The intention is to develop processes, for services or producing goods, that are cleaner. or do not produce waste. Also, the Building Research Establishment has a programme on indoor air quality covering dampness, mould, bacteria, ventilation, radon, leakage of landfill gas into homes, and the "sick building syndrome". The Royal Commission on Environmental Pollution is studying pollution from incinerating of wastes. At the Open University an extensive programme looks at the interactions between energy systems organised by humans and the biosphere, viewed as a solar-powered system. Its aim is to "enable the energy needs of society to be met in an environmentally and socially appropriate manner".

Until 1993 the government's main environmental research centre was the Warren Spring Laboratory (WSL) monitoring air and marine pollution, studying methods of abating them, and preparing a National Atmospheric Emissions Inventory. It also researched minimising industrial waste and ways of recovering valuable materials from it. The laboratory was then merged with the commercial part of the Atomic Energy Authority, AEA Technology, becoming part of it, losing 150 of its original 250 WSL staff, and forming the National Environmental Technology Centre. This is a general consultancy and also continues the programmes transferred from WSL including the monitoring for the Department of the Environment.

Can the greenhouse gases be captured by technological means? A positive answer to this is the ambitious aim of a programme by the International Energy Association (IEA) operated by British Coal and supported by several other countries; they are aware that concern about the CO_2 generated may damage the market for coal.

The Director-General of the Agricultural and Food Research Council (AFRC) has stressed the need for sustainable agriculture, involving such themes as analysing the nitrogen cycle and fertiliser need, and integrated pest control. Fibres, fuels, pharmaceuticals, chemicals and construction materials can all be economically derived from crops, as they were before the industrial revolution.

The Royal Society, after carrying out its own investigation, has urged much more research on the project of using deep repositories for disposing of radioactive wastes, that are now stored on the surface. The aim is to ensure that this waste will not find its way to the surface in quantities that might harm people living nearby.

11. THE "EARTH SUMMIT"

"Working towards international agreements which respect the interests of all and protect the integrity of the global environmental and development system"; this was part of the Preamble to the Rio Declaration of the truly historic UN Conference on Environment and Development (UNCED), mercifully known briefly as the Earth Summit. Held in Rio de Janeiro, Brazil, and attended by 103 Heads of State or Government, it adopted this Declaration of 27 principles on sustainable development, intended to guide governments' actions. In order to achieve such development, it noted that the environment should be protected as an integral part of development. To help poorer developing nations in carrying out the necessary actions, several aspects of aid were urged covering trading patterns, scientific exchanges, and transfer of technologies, as well as transfer of resources.

Putting flesh on the bare bones of the Declaration, a voluminous document Agenda 21 formed a comprehensive programme of action "aimed at reshaping human activities in order to minimise environmental damage." Efforts should be made towards the greening of the world, the statement continued.

This was then further emphasised by the Convention on Biological Diversity (signed by 153 States). It was intended to ensure effective national action to curb the destruction of biological species, habitats and ecosystems.

A Convention on Climate Change (153 States) set an objective of stabilising the concentrations of greenhouse gases. "As a first step" developed countries would return to their 1990 levels of such emissions by the end of the decade. A Conference of

Parties will be established to decide on subsequent steps.

For forestry, only a statement of principles was adopted, not a legally binding Convention. It states that they provide resources for human needs and environmental values; they require sound management and conservation.

Maurice Strang, Secretary-General of UNCED, "celebrated" the decisions taken but warned that current levels of commitment did not yet match up to the level of the problems. Further action on desertification and forestry was urged. We needed a new mode of civic conduct involving "a political and ethical contract with nature ... seeing the earth as a vast interlocking whole ... a new pathway and a new economy, that is truly an *eco-nomic system*".

12. ACTION

The "Green" Movement.

"Throughout the last few years environment policy has steadily moved towards the top of the political agenda" said the retiring European Commissioner for the Environment, Mr. Stanley Clinton Davis in November 1988. The EC itself had passed some 60 items of relevant legislation in the previous four years. And the Community's basic treaties have been revised to include a separate chapter on environment for the first time. Reflecting the growing public concern a range of "Green" organisations has been set up. In the UK the Green Party startled the established political parties in the European Parliament elections (June 1989) by gaining 15% of the votes, though they failed to win a seat. Such bodies as Friends of the Earth, Greenpeace, Worldwide Fund for Nature and others continue to press through publications and demonstrations, for greater commitment to green issues by people and government. Some of the most spectacular of these have been "direct actions" by Greenpeace which has an International Board and offices in 20 countries. They have included placing themselves between whales and harpoonists, driving inflatables under barrels of toxic waste to prevent sea dumping, climbing of smoke stacks to draw attention to acid rain. With other organisations, they have exposed the many breaches of the agreement by the International Whaling Commission, noted earlier, to halt commercial whaling (these breaches are mainly through exploiting on false premises the exception allowed for "scientific research").

The combined effects of public opinion and similar green activities in many countries has led commercial companies, governments and the established political parties also to pay at least lip service to environmental issues.

Companies from 21 countries in 1993 set up a World Industry Council for the Environment (WICE) with the aim of supporting "environmental policies that favour economic growth and do not inhibit world trade".

In 1994, UNEP Industry and Environment Office (with the company SustainAbility) published a survey of what it called '100 pioneers in Environmental Reporting'. The companies—operating in Europe, North America and Japan—had reported on such issues as complying with regulations and pollution control, and on liability and product stewardship. Five levels of environmental disclosure were identified in the report and an 'embryonic grading system' was used to assess the reports.

"Towards Sustainability" (EU Programme).

Building on the objective included in the Maastricht Treaty of promoting sustainable growth respecting the environment, the EU Commission has produced a new Action Programme "Towards Sustainability" based on the concept of joint action by public authorities, private companies and the public. Initiatives have included Eco-labelling and Eco-management and -Audit. Eco-labelling is intended to promote design of products that have a reduced environmental impact during their entire life cycle and to provide customers with better information.

Tying together approaches in several member countries including the UK, the Commission proposed in 1993 integrated pollution prevention and control, preventing pollution being transferred from one place or medium into another, like extracting foul air from a workshop into the atmosphere.

EPA and White Paper 1990.

The UK Environmental Protection Act (EPA) 1990 was based on integrated pollution control and included
* new powers for local authorities
* public access to more information
* stricter controls over waste disposal, and encouragement of recycling.

An associated White Paper "This Common Inheritance" was announced as "The first really comprehensive statement of Government policy on the environment". The aims were;

to preserve and enhance the UK's natural and cultural heritage;
—to encourage the efficient use of energy and resources and meet the UK's commitments to reduce global warming, ozone depletion and acid rain;
—to keep the country's air and water clean and safe;
—to maintain effective controls over wastes and pollution and strengthen them where necessary;
—to keep up the UK's contribution to environmental research;
—to make everyone in Britain better informed and better able to play a part in enhancing the environment;
—to play a full part in international initiatives to deal with world environmental issues.

The government issued reports in 1991, 1992 and 1994 on the way it was meeting its commitments to the Earth Summit. It also emphasised, in domestic policy, a "change of direction". Economic means, as well as regulation, were to be used to deliver environmental goals. An example given was applying a lower tax rate on unleaded petrol to encourage its use.

UK Programme: "Sustainable Development"

"To meet the UK's commitments" under the Rio Convention on Climate Change, the government—after extensive consultation—published four documents early in 1994 setting out a programme and appointed both an expert panel on sustainability issues and a Round Table with representatives of the main sectors to discuss issues with ministers. The main document, *Sustainable Development: the UK Strategy*, is a wide-ranging factual survey of the current environmental situation with estimates of how it is likely to evolve over the next 20 years. It concludes with a section on "putting sustainability into practice" strong on exhortation, limited on action.

In at least one important area, the government is acting against the needs of the policies. For all the greenhouse gases, countries are committed to take measures aimed at returning emissions to 1990 levels by the year 2000. CO_2 is recognised as the most significant of these gases. The programme of expected reductions in emissions by 2000 is 10 million tonnes, a quarter of this being in transport. But the government is breaking up the currently unified rail network, and has a major roadbuilding programme which will increase road traffic; yet this traffic is noted as a major source of emissions and the programme states "better public transport will have an important role to play".

The expected reduction in emissions of CO_2 by 2000 in million tonnes of carbon is listed as:

Energy consumption in the home	4
Energy consumption by business	2·5
Energy consumption in the public sector	1
Transport	2·5
Total	10

Reductions are also "envisaged" in methane, nitrous oxide and other gases, equivalent to some 5% of total greenhouse gas emissions by the year 2000.

The Programme concludes by calling for government, local communities and invididuals to work together to protect the environment and achieve sustainable development.

However, commenting on the government's environment policy overall, Professor David Pearce, Professor of Environmental Economics at University College, London, argues that the authorities are paying lip service to green ideas; what is needed is binding integration of protection of the environment into the policy-making framework.

Draft legislation was published in 1994 for a new Environment Agency that would bring together the Inspectorate of Pollution, the National Rivers Authority and local waste regulation authorities. Though this was claimed to strengthen the effectiveness of integrated pollution control, environmentalists pointed to the wording describing its powers—namely "taking into account costs which are likely to be incurred and the benefits that are likely to accrue". This formulation is weaker than the existing powers and the text is due to be challenged in Parliament.

Transport Proposals.

With the exception of sulphur dioxide, transport is the most important source of the majority of air pollutants, stated a report by the Royal Commission on Environmental Pollution. Emissions from road vehicles, added the document "Transport and the Environment", are now the main influence on air quality over large areas of the country where there are no significant industrial emissions. The Commission proposed a basis for a sustainable transport policy needing co-ordinated action by government and industry. (*see* **Special Topic, Y18**). This included doubling the price of fuel, halving spending on motorways and trunk roads, and switching resources to boost the convenience of rail and other forms of public transport. First reactions by the government have been to set up an environmental policy unit to co-ordinate assessment of its roads programme. But there appeared to be no halt to the breakup of the rail network into separate privatised companies.

13. ENVIRONMENTAL ORGANISATIONS

Some organisations connected with care of the environment:

Ark, 498–500 Harrow Rd., London W9 3QA

British Society for Social Responsibility in Science, 9 Poland St., London W1V 3DG

Conservation Society Ltd., 12a Guildford St., Chertsey, Surrey KT16 9BQ

Conservation Trust, George Palmer School, Northumberland Ave., Reading, Berks.

Council for Environmental Conservation, Zoological Gardens, Regents Park, London NW1 4RY

Council for Environmental Education, University of Reading, London Rd., Reading RG1 5AO

Council for the Protection of Rural England, 4 Hobart Place, London SW1W 0HY

Countryside Commission, Crescent Place, Cheltenham, Glos GL50 3RA

Earthscan, 10 Percy St., London W1P 0DR

Ecoropa, 24 rue de l'Ermitage, 75020 Paris, France

Environment Council, 80 York Way, London N1 9AG

Environment, Department of, Marsham St., London SW1 3PY

Environmental Communicators Organisation, 8 Hooks Cross, Watton-at-Stone, Hertford SG14 3RY

Environmental Education Advisers Association (EEAA), Education Dept., Old County Hall, Truro, Cornwall

European Environment Agency, Copenhagen, Denmark

Field Studies Council, 62 Wilson St., London EC2A 2BU

Friends of the Earth, 26–28 Underwood St., London N1 7JQ

Global Environmental Research Office, Polaris House, North Star Ave., Swindon SN2 1EU

Green Alliance, 60 Chandos Place, London WC2N 4HG

Greenpeace Ltd., 30–31 Islington Green, London N1 8XE

Health and Safety Commission, 259 Old Marylebone Rd., London NW1 5RR

Health Education Council, 78 New Oxford St., London WC1A 1AH

Indoor Air International, Unit 179, 2 Old Brompton Rd., London SW7 3DQ

Industrial Air Pollution Inspectorate, Romney House, 43 Marsham St., London SW1P 3PY

Institute of Environmental and Offshore Medicine, The University, Aberdeen AB9 1FX

Institution of Environmental Health Officers, Chadwick House, Rushforth St., London SE1 0RB

Institution of Environmental Sciences Ltd., 14 Princes Gate, London SW7 1PU

Institution of Public Health Engineers, 13 Grosvenor Place, London SW1X 7EN

International Tropical Timber Organisation (ITTO), Yokohama, Japan

Living Earth, 10 Upper Grosvenor St., London W1X 9PA

National Association for Environmental Education (NAEE), West Midlands College of Higher Education, Gorway, Walsall WS1 3BD

National Environmental Technology Centre, Culham, Abingdon, Oxon, OX14 3DB

National Radiological Protection Board, Chilton, Didcot, Oxon OX11 0RQ

National Rivers Authority, 30 Albert Embankment, London SE1 7TL

National Society for Clean Air, 136 North St., Brighton, BN1 1RG

Natural Environment Research Council, North Star Avenue, Swindon SN2 1EU

Nature Conservancy Council, 20 Belgrave Square, London SW1X 8PY

New Economics Foundation, 112 Whitechapel Rd, London E1

Oxfam, Banbury Rd., Oxford, OX2 7DZ

Royal Commission on Environmental Pollution, Church House, Gt. Smith St., London SW1P 3BL

Royal Society for the Protection of Birds, The Lodge, Sandy, Beds, SG19 2DL

Royal Society of Health, 13 Grosvenor Place, London SW1X 7EN

Science and Engineering Research Council, North Star Ave, Swindon, Wilts, SN2 1ET.

Socialist Environment and Resources Association (SERA), 9 Poland St., London W1V 3DG

Tropical Forestry Action Programme, (TFAP) Via delle Terme di Caracalla, 00100 Rome, Italy

United Nations Information Centre, 20 Buckingham Gate, London SW1E 6LB

United Nations Educational, Scientific and Cultural Organisation, 7 Place de Fontenoy, 75700 Paris, France

United Nations Environment Programme, PO Box 30552, Nairobi, Kenya

Woodland Trust, Autumn Park, Dysart Rd, Grantham, Lincs, NG31 6LL

World Health Organisation, Division of Environmental Health, Avenue Appia, 1211 Geneva 27, Switzerland

Worldwatch Institute, 1776 Massachusetts Avenue NW, Washington DC, 20036 USA

WWF UK (World Wide Fund for Nature), Panda House, Weyside Park, Godalming, Surrey, GU17 1QU

11. CHRONOLOGY

Chronology of some of the events connected with care of the environment since 1970[1]:

1970 Department of the Environment established by combining several existing ministries
Royal Commission on Environmental Pollution established

1972 UN Conference on the Human Environabatement section on which legislation to the present day has been based

1974 Control of Pollution Act
Health and Safety at Work, etc., Act

1976 5th Report of Royal Commission on Environmental Pollution recommended an inspectorate for all forms of pollution

1979 Government decided to "axe" the Clean Air Council
1st International Agreement on transnational air pollution by governments of ECE (UN)

1980 First air quality standards in UK, by EC Directive

1981 Wildlife and Countryside Act

1982 White Paper on radioactive waste management
Special Session (10th anniversary) of UNEP

Convention on Conservation of Antarctic Marine Living Organisms came into effect protecting all marine organisms within its boundary
3rd UN Conference on Law of the Sea adopted a Convention including sections on exploitation of resources, conservation, preserving the marine environment. But US and UK (among others) refused to sign.

1983 9th Report of Royal Commission on Environmental Pollution recommending lead-free petrol was accepted by Government and will aim for this to apply throughout Europe
Royal Society agreed to investigate acidification of surface waters in Norway and Sweden with their Scientific Academies

1984 Government announced it is planning new powers for controlling pesticides.

1985 EC Directive on Environmental Impact Assessment

1986 New 'Central Unit on Environmental Issues' set up within Department of the Environment
Chemical explosion at Chernobyl Nuclear Power Station, Ukraine, USSR, spreads radioactive cloud over a large part of Europe
Unified Inspectorate of Pollution set up
Commission of the European Communities publishes proposed Fourth Environmental Action Programme

1987 European Year of the Environment until March 1988
Montreal Protocol on Substances that Deplete the Ozone Layer
Publication of "Our Common Future" (the Brundtland Report) by the UN

1988 Commission of the European Communities issues range of proposals including rules for protecting the ozone layer, for municipal waste incineration, for tighter control of hazardous waste, for protecting habitats of wild fauna and flora, measures against air pollution by vehicles, controlling production of gases relevant to "greenhouse effect"

1989 Massive pollution of Alaska coastline after oil spillage from *Exxon Valdez*
Basle Convention to control transboundary movements of hazardous wastes
Government published Environmental Protection Bill
EC Directive on controlling gases from car exhausts

1990 Environmental Protection Act
White Paper "This Common Inheritance"

1991 Massive pollution of Persian Gulf by wilful oil discharge by Iraqis from occupied Kuwait; wildlife ecological disaster feared after biggest oil slick in history
Sinking of supertanker *Haven* off Genoa threatens Mediterranean coastlines

1992 "Earth Summit". UN Conference on Environment and Development, Brazil

1993 Pollution of Shetlands from *Braer* oil tanker disaster

1994 Publication of UK Programme "Sustainable Development"
UN Cairo Conference on Population and Development
Report of Royal Commission on Environmental Pollution "Transport and the Environment"

1995 Growing protests at shipment of live animals overseas. Popular protests at Shoreham *etc.*

[1] This list draws heavily on *History of Pollution and its Control* kindly supplied by the National Society for Clean Air.

SPECIAL TOPICS

UN POPULATION CONFERENCE, CAIRO 1994

Introduction.

"An outstanding success" was the judgment of Mrs Nafis Sadik, head of the UN Population Fund, on the 1994 UN Conference in Cairo on Population and Development. It had survived major disputes on policy between its organisers and most delegations on the one hand and the Vatican delegation and some Muslim delegates on the other. Though the latter two groups had amended and tried to weaken parts of its conclusions, the Conference adopted a Programme of Action including expanded programmes on family planning and reproductive health care in developing countries. Overall, costs should rise to $17 billion in 2000, with the family planning component costing $10·2 billion in that year, both figures rising further to the year 2015. Overall, two thirds will be met by the countries themselves and the balance "from external sources". But low-income countries should receive a higher proportion of grants than this. The programme also covers child and maternal health, preventing sexually transmitted diseases (including preventing the spread of HIV/AIDS), and collecting population data. Great emphasis was placed on raising the status of women worldwide.

Problems of Population Growth.

Rapid growth of population, combined with poverty and lack of resources, noted the Conference, cause or exacerbate the degrading of the environment. So countries should adopt programmes integrating plans for population, environment and for eradicating poverty. Behind these concerns for the future lie disturbing facts.

World population is currently estimated at 5·6 thousand million (billion). Rate of growth is slowly declining. Yet the absolute numbers of the increments continue to increase and at present are over 86 million people a year. These annual increments of population are likely to stay above 86 million until the year 2015. In 1993 a unique "Science Summit" of the world's scientific academies had heard that growing population until recently was matched by similar increases in resources we could use. But now, warned the scientists, natural systems are being pushed ever closer to their limits. The indicators of severe stress to the environment included loss of biodiversity, increasing loss of forests, loss of topsoil and increasing concentration of greenhouse gases. Many developing countries are finding reduced supplies per head of water, food and fuelwood, with land, water and air more heavily polluted.

Yet there are promising features. The UN Conference noted "major shifts in attitude among the world's peoples and their leaders . . . resulting in the new comprehensive concept of reproductive health including family planning and sexual health". During the period 1985–1990 the numbers of people had grown at the rate of 1·7% per annum. But this rate is declining and expected to fall to 1·0% by the period 2020–2025.

However, aggregated data can mask important detail. For instance during the period 1985–90, fertility ranged from an estimated 8·5 children per woman in Rwanda to 1·3 children per woman in Italy. During that period nearly half the world's population lived in countries with growth rates of more than 2% per annum. These included nearly all the countries in Africa, two thirds of those in Asia and one third of those in Latin America. Other countries with nearly one quarter of the world's population (most of them in Europe) had growth rates of less than 1% per annum. Over the next 20 years, it is projected that population in the more developed regions will increase by about 120 million, while that of the less developed regions will grow by 1727 million. Against this great disparity in numbers must be set the fact that the developed countries make much more demand per head on world resources, so that controlling future numbers is a world problem not solely one for developing countries.

Varying Growth Rates.

There are big differences in trends in growth rates within the developing world. One group that have not yet started the decline in fertility (or are at an early stage) comprise most of the countries in sub-Saharan Africa and some in South Asia (excluding India). They may average up to 7 births per woman and a growth rate of up to 3% pa. But in Latin America, the fertility rates have fallen in the last 30 years from about 5·5 to 3·5 births per woman. In parts of Asia they fell even more quickly, dominated by the remarkable changes in China where fertility declined from 6·0 to 2·4 in the last 25 years.

The Conference Recommendations.

The UN Conference recommendations went far beyond helping poorer countries with contraceptive advice and supplies. They were based on the view that there were inter-relationships between population, sustained economic growth and sustainable development; and they demanded advances in the education, economic status and empowerment of women. Acknowledging the sovereign rights of each country to implement the recommendations with full respect for religious and ethical values, and the cultural backgrounds of its people, the Conference adopted a set of Principles that included these features:—

*Everyone is entitled to all the rights and freedoms of the UN Universal Declaration of Human Rights, without distinction of any kind such as race, colour, sex, language, religion, political or other opinion, national or social origin, property, birth or other status.

*People have the right to an adequate standard of living for themselves and their families, including adequate food, clothing, housing, water and sanitation.

*Human rights include the right to development, and the human person is the central subject of development.

*"Cornerstones of population programmes" are advancing gender equality and empowerment of women, and ensuring women's ability to control their own fertility.

*Development should improve the quality of life of people.

*To achieve sustainable development, States should eliminate unsustainable patterns of production and consumption.

*States should eradicate poverty. Needs of developing countries shall be given special priority and fully integrated into the world economy.

*Universal access to health-care services including those for reproductive health care should be without any form of coercion. Couples and individuals have the basic right to decide freely and responsibly the number and spacing of their children.

*The family is the basic unit of society, though various forms of family exist. Marriage must be entered into with the free consent of the intending spouses.

*Everyone has the right to education with particular attention to women and the girl-child.

*States and families should give the highest possible priority to children. The child has the right to be protected from all forms of violence including sale and trafficking.

*Countries should guarantee to all migrants all basic human rights as included in the Universal Declaration of Human Rights.

*Everyone has the right to enjoy in other countries asylum from persecution.

*Developed countries acknowledge their responsibility in the international pursuit of sustainable development and narrowing imbalances to benefit all countries, particularly the developing countries.

A detailed Programme of Action was adopted based on these Principles, calling on governments to commit themselves to achieving the objectives, following up the Conference with national and local action and publicity to promote public support.

An interesting consequence of the decline in fertility levels is that the proportion of older people will rise worldwide—a trend that is already noticeable in the developed countries. An important part of programmes for reducing the proportion of births must therefore be enhancing the self-reliance of elderly people and creating conditions for them to be able to continue working as long as they wish. This involves developing systems of health care and social support where these are needed.

And to those who commented on the cost of this programme, the Conference Report had this response. "None of the actions required—nor all of them combined—is expensive in the context of either current global development or military expenditures."

TRANSPORT AND THE ENVIRONMENT

In 1994, the Royal Commission on Environmental Pollution issued its report on Transport and the Environment. The objectives of the Royal Commission were to ensure that an effective transport policy at all levels of government is integrated with land use policy and gives priority to minimising the need for transport and increasing the proportions of trips made by environmentally less damaging modes. The recommendations of the Commission are set out below

1 To achieve standards of air quality, that will prevent damage to human health and the environment.

1: To achieve full compliance by 2005 with World Health Organization (WHO) health-based air quality guidelines for transport-related pollutants.

2: To establish in appropriate areas by 2005 local air quality standards based on the critical levels required to protect sensitive ecosystems.

2 To improve the quality of life, particularly in towns and cities, by reducing the dominance of cars and lorries and providing alternative means of access.

1: To reduce the proportion of urban journeys undertaken by car from 50% in the London area to 45% by 2000 and 35% by 2020, and from 65% in other urban areas to 60% by 2000 and 50% by 2020.

2: To increase cycle use to 10% of all urban journeys by 2005, compared to 2·5% now, and seek further increases thereafter on the basis of targets to be set by the government.

3: To reduce pedestrian deaths from 2·2 per 100,000 population to not more than 1·5 per 100,000 population by 2000, and cyclist deaths from 4·1 per 100 million kilometres cycled to not more than 2 per 100 million kilometres cycled by the same date.

3 To increase the proportions of personal travel and freight transport by environmentally less damaging modes and to make the best use of existing infrastructure.

1: To increase the proportion of passenger-kilometres carried by public transport from 12% in 1993 to 20% by 2005 and 30% by 2020.

2: To increase the proportion of tonne-kilometres carried by rail from 6·5% in 1993 to 10% by 2000 and 20% by 2010.

3: To increase the proportion of tonne-kilometres carried by water from 25% in 1993 to 30% by 2000, and at least maintain that share thereafter.

4 To halt any loss of land to transport infrastructure in areas of conservation, cultural, scenic or amenity value unless the use of the land for that purpose has been shown to be the best practicable environmental option.

5 To reduce carbon dioxide emissions from transport.

1: To reduce emissions of carbon dioxide from surface transport in 2020 to no more than 80% of the 1990 level.

2: To limit emissions of carbon dioxide from surface transport in 2000 to the 1990 level.

3: To increase the average fuel efficiency of new cars sold in the UK by 40% between 1990 and 2005, that of new light goods vehicles by 20%, and that of new heavy duty vehicles by 10%.

6 To reduce substantially the demands which transport infrastructure and the vehicle industry place on non-renewable materials.

1: To increase the proportion by weight of scrapped vehicles which is recycled, or used for energy generation, from 77% at present to 85% by 2002 and 95% by 2015.

2: To increase the proportion of vehicles tyres recycled, or used for energy generation, from less than a third at present to 90% by 2015.

3: To double the proportion of recycled material used in road construction and reconstruction by 2005, and double it again by 2015.

7 To reduce noise nuisance from transport.

1: To reduce daytime exposure to road and rail noise to not more than 65 dBL$_{Aeq}$. 16h at the external walls of housing.

2: To reduce night-time exposure to road and rail noise to not more than 59 dBL$_{Aeq}$. 8h at the external walls of housing.

Summary of Proposals.

The main points can be summarised as follows:—

Halve expenditure on motorways and trunk roads

Double the price of fuel

Increase investment in public transport over ten years

Tighten EC emission limits for all new vehicles

Vary duty on heavy vehicles according to emissions

Ban unleaded super-premium petrol

Encourage heavy-vehicle operators to use natural gas

Increase vehicle excise duty for less efficient cars

Abolish mileage thresholds for company cars

Increase enforcement of speed limits

Give grants for port facilities for coastal shipping

Invest to encourage Channel Tunnel freight to Scotland

Increase bus lanes and give buses priority at junctions

Encourage new light railway and tram systems in towns

Introduce more safe pedestrian routes and cycleways

Discourage air travel when rail is competitive

Restructure transport department to fit new approach.

GENERAL
COMPENDIUM

A collection of useful tables and data on a variety of unrelated subjects, including Archbishops of Canterbury, the British monarchy, Prime Ministers since 1721, rulers of the Roman world, United States Presidents, phases of the moon, sunrise and sunset, eclipses, Roman numerals, foreign phrases, national currencies and the Beaufort wind scale.

TABLE OF CONTENTS

GENERAL COMPENDIUM

ENGLISH MONARCHS
(A.D. 827–1603)

Monarch	Accession	Died	Age	Reigned

I.—BEFORE THE CONQUEST.

SAXONS AND DANES

Monarch	Accession	Died	Age	Reigned
Egbert	827	839	—	12
Ethelwulf	839	858	—	19
Ethelbald	858	860	—	2
Ethelbert	858	865	—	7
Ethelred	865	871	—	6
Alfred the Great	871	899	50	28
Edward the Elder	899	924	54	25
Athelstan	924	939	45	15
Edmund	939	946	25	7
Eadred	946	955	32	9
Eadwig	955	959	18	3
Edgar	959	975	32	17
Edward the Martyr	975	978	17	3
Ethelred II ("the Unready")	978	1016	48	37
Edmund Ironside	1016	1016	27	Apr.–Nov.
Canute the Dane	1017	1035	40	18
Harold I	1035	1040	—	5
Hardicanute	1040	1042	24	2
Edward the Confessor	1042	1066	62	24
Harold II	1066	1066	44	Jan.–Oct.

II.—FROM THE CONQUEST TO THE PRESENT DAY.

NORMANS

Monarch	Accession	Died	Age	Reigned
William I	1066	1087	60	21
William II	1087	1100	43	13
Henry I	1100	1135	67	35
Stephen, Count of Blois	1135	1154	50	19

PLANTAGENETS

Monarch	Accession	Died	Age	Reigned
Henry II	1154	1189	56	35
Richard I	1189	1199	42	10
John	1199	1216	50	17
Henry III	1216	1272	65	56
Edward I	1272	1307	68	35
Edward II	1307	dep. 1327	43	20
Edward III	1327	1377	65	50
Richard II	1377	dep. 1399	34	22
Henry IV ⎫	1399	1413	47	13
Henry V ⎬ Lancaster	1413	1422	34	9
Henry VI ⎭	1422	dep. 1461	49	39
Edward IV ⎫	1461	1483	41	22
Edward V ⎬ York	1483	1483	13	Apr.–June
Richard III ⎭	1483	1485	32	2

TUDORS

Monarch	Accession	Died	Age	Reigned
Henry VII	1485	1509	53	24
Henry VIII	1509	1547	56	38
Edward VI	1547	1553	16	6
Jane	1553	1554	17	9 days
Mary I	1553	1558	43	5
Elizabeth I	1558	1603	69	44

THE BRITISH MONARCHY
(1603 to the present day

Monarch	Accession	Died	Age	Reigned
STUARTS				
James I (VI of Scotland)	1603	1625	59	22
Charles I	1625	beh. 1649	48	24
COMMONWEALTH DECLARED, MAY 19, 1649				
Oliver Cromwell, Lord Protector . . .	1653–8	—	—	—
Richard Cromwell, Lord Protector .	1658–9			
STUARTS (RESTORATION)				
Charles II	1660	1685	55	25
James II (VII of Scotland) . .	1685	dep. 1688	68	3
Interregnum Dec. 11, 1688 to Feb. 13, 1689				
William III and Mary II	1689	1702	51	13
		1694	33	6
Anne	1702	1714	49	12
HOUSE OF HANOVER				
George I	1714	1727	67	13
George II	1727	1760	77	33
George III	1760	1820	81	59
George IV	1820	1830	67	10
William IV	1830	1837	71	7
Victoria	1837	1901	81	63
HOUSE OF SAXE-COBURG				
Edward VII	1901	1910	68	9
HOUSE OF WINDSOR				
George V	1910	1936	70	25
Edward VIII	1936	Abd. 1936	77	325 days
George VI	1936	1952	56	15
Elizabeth II	1952			

SCOTTISH MONARCHS
(1034–1603)

Monarch		Accession	Died
Duncan I	Son of Malcolm II	1034	1040
Macbeth	Slew Duncan in 1040	1040	1057
Malcolm III (Canmore)	Son of Duncan I	1058	1093
Donald Ban	Brother of Malcolm Canmore	1093	—
Duncan II	Son of Malcom Canmore, by first marriage	1094	1094
Donald Ban	Restored	1094	1097
Edgar	Son of Malcolm Canmore, by second marriage	1097	1107
Alexander I	Son of Malcolm Canmore	1107	1124
David I	Son of Malcolm Canmore	1124	1153
Malcolm IV (the Maiden)	Son of Henry, eldest son of David I	1153	1165
William I (the Lion)	Brother of Malcolm the Maiden	1165	1214
Alexander II	Son of William the Lion	1214	1249
Alexander III	Son of Alexander II, by second marriage	1249	1286
Margaret, Maid of Norway	Daughter of Eric II of Norway, granddaughter of Alexander III	1286	1290
John Baliol	Grandson of eldest daughter of David, Earl of Huntingdon, brother of William the Lion	1292	1296
Robert I (Bruce)	Great-grandson of 2nd daughter of David, Earl of Huntingdon, brother of William the Lion	1306	1329
David II	Son of Robert I, by second marriage	1329	1371
Robert II (Stewart)	Son of Marjorie, daughter of Robert I by first marriage, and Walter the Steward	1371	1390
Robert III	(John, Earl of Carrick) son of Robert II	1390	1406
James I	Son of Robert III	1406	1437
James II	Son of James I	1437	1460
James III	Eldest son of James II	1460	1488
James IV	Eldest son of James III	1488	1513
James V	Son of James IV	1513	1542
Mary	Daughter of James V, by second marriage	1542	1587
James VI (ascended the Throne of England 1603)	Son of Mary, by second marriage	1567	1625

BRITISH PRIME MINISTERS

	Party	Served
George II, 1727–60		
Sir Robert Walpole	Whig	1721–42
Earl of Wilmington	Whig	1742–3
Henry Pelham	Whig	1743–54
Duke of Newcastle	Whig	1754–6
Duke of Devonshire	Whig	1756–7
Duke of Newcastle	Whig	1757–60
George III, 1760–1820		
Duke of Newcastle	Whig	1760–2
Earl of Bute	Tory	1762–3
George Grenville	Whig	1763–5
Marquis of Rocking-ham	Whig	1766
Earl of Chatham	Tory	1766–8
Duke of Grafton	Whig	1766–9
Lord North	Tory	1770–82
Marquis of Rocking-ham	Whig	1782
Earl of Shelburne	Whig	1782–3
Duke of Portland	Coalition	1783
William Pitt	Tory	1783–1801
Viscount Sidmouth	Tory	1801–4
William Pitt	Tory	1804–6
Lord Grenville	Whig	1806–7
Duke of Portland	Tory	1807–9
Spencer Perceval (assassinated)	Tory	1809–12
George IV, 1820–30		
Earl of Liverpool	Tory	1812–27
George Canning	Tory	1827
Viscount Goderich	Tory	1827
Duke of Wellington	Tory	1827–30
William IV, 1830–7		
Earl Grey	Whig	1830–4
Viscount Melbourne	Whig	1834
Sir Robert Peel	Tory	1834–5
Viscount Melbourne	Whig	1835–7
Victoria, 1837–1901		
Viscount Melbourne	Whig	1837–41
Sir Robert Peel	Tory	1841–6
Lord John Russell	Whig	1846–52
Earl of Derby	Tory	1852
Earl of Aberdeen	Peelite	1852–5
Viscount Palmerston	Liberal	1855–8
Earl of Derby	Tory	1858–9
Viscount Palmerston	Liberal	1859–65
Earl Russell	Liberal	1865–66

	Party	Served
Earl of Derby	Conservative	1866–8
B. Disraeli	Conservative	1868
W. E. Gladstone	Liberal	1868–74
B. Disraeli	Conservative	1874–80
W. E. Gladstone	Liberal	1880–5
Marquis of Salisbury	Conservative	1885–6
W. E. Gladstone	Liberal	1886
Marquis of Salisbury	Conservative	1886–92
W. E. Gladstone	Liberal	1892–4
Earl of Rosebery	Liberal	1894–5
Marquis of Salisbury	Conservative	1895–1901
Edward VII, 1901–10		
Marquis of Salisbury	Conservative	1901–2
A. J. Balfour	Conservative	1902–5
Sir H. Campbell-Bannerman	Liberal	1905–8
H. H. Asquith	Liberal	1908–10
George V, 1910–36		
H. H. Asquith	Liberal	1910–15
H. H. Asquith	Coalition	1915–16
D. Lloyd George	Coalition	1916–22
A. Bonar Law	Conservative	1922–3
S. Baldwin	Conservative	1923–4
J. R. MacDonald	Labour	1924
S. Baldwin	Conservative	1924–9
J. R. MacDonald	Labour	1929–31
J. R. MacDonald	National	1931–5
S. Baldwin	National	1935–6
Edward VIII, 1936		
George VI, 1936–52		
S. Baldwin	National	1936–7
N. Chamberlain	National	1937–39
N. Chamberlain	War Cabinet	1939
W. S. Churchill	War Cabinet	1940–45
W. S. Churchill	Caretaker	1945
C. R. Attlee	Labour	1945–51
Sir W. S. Churchill	Conservative	1951–2
Elizabeth II, 1952–		
Sir W. S. Churchill	Conservative	1952–5
Sir A. Eden	Conservative	1955–7
H. Macmillan	Conservative	1957–63
Sir A. Douglas-Home	Conservative	1963–4
H. Wilson	Labour	1964–70
E. Heath	Conservative	1970–4
H. Wilson	Labour	1974–6
J. Callaghan	Labour	1976–9
Mrs. M. Thatcher	Conservative	1979–90
J. Major	Conservative	1990–

PRESIDENTS OF THE UNITED STATES

The terms are for four years; only President F. D. Roosevelt has served more than two terms.

	Party	Served
1. George Washington	Fed.	1789–97
2. John Adams	Fed.	1797–1801
3. Thomas Jefferson	Rep.	1801–9
4. James Madison	Rep.	1809–17
5. James Monroe	Rep.	1817–25
6. John Quincey Adams	Rep.	1825–9
7. Andrew Jackson	Dem.	1829–37
8. Martin Van Buren	Dem.	1837–41
9. William H. Harrison (died in office)	Whig	1841
10. John Tyler	Whig	1841–5
11. James K. Polk	Dem.	1845–9
12. Zachary Taylor (died in office)	Whig	1849–50
13. Millard Fillmore	Whig	1850–3
14. Franklin Pierce	Dem.	1853–7
15. James Buchanan	Dem.	1857–61
16. Abraham Lincoln (assassinated)	Rep.	1861–5
17. Andrew Johnson	Dem.	1865–9
18. Ulysses S. Grant	Rep.	1869–77
19. Rutherford B. Hayes	Rep.	1877–81
20. James A. Garfield (assassinated)	Rep.	1881
21. Chester A. Arthur	Rep.	1881–5
22. Grover Cleveland	Dem.	1885–9

	Party	Served
23. Benjamin Harrison	Rep.	1889–93
24. Grover Cleveland	Dem.	1893–7
25. William McKinley (assassinated)	Rep.	1897–1901
26. Theodore Roosevelt	Rep.	1901–9
27. William Howard Taft	Rep.	1909–13
28. Woodrow Wilson	Dem.	1913–21
29. Warren G. Harding (died in office)	Rep.	1921–3
30. Calvin Coolidge	Rep.	1923–9
31. Herbert C. Hoover	Rep.	1929–33
32. Franklin D. Roosevelt (died in office)	Dem.	1933–45
33. Harry S. Truman	Dem.	1945–53
34. Dwight D. Eisenhower	Rep.	1953–61
35. John F. Kennedy (assassinated)	Dem.	1961–3
36. Lyndon B. Johnson	Dem.	1963–9
37. Richard M. Nixon (resigned)	Rep.	1969–74
38. Gerald R. Ford	Rep.	1974–7
39. James Carter	Dem.	1977–81
40. Ronald Reagan	Rep.	1981–9
41. George Bush	Rep.	1989–93
42. Bill Clinton	Dem.	1993–

FOREIGN PHRASES

Fr., French. Gr., Greek. Ger., German. It., Italian. L., Latin. Sp., Spanish

à bas (Fr.), down, down with.
ab extra (L.), from without.
ab incunabilis (L.), from the cradle.
ab initio (L.), from the beginning.
ab intra (L.), from within.
à bon chat, bon rat (Fr.), to be a good cat, a good rat; well attacked and defended; tit for tat; a Rowland for an Oliver.
à bon marche (Fr.), cheap, a good bargain.
à bras ouverts (Fr.), with open arms.
absente reo (L.), the accused being absent.
absit invidia (L.), let there be no ill-will; envy apart.
ab uno disce omnes (L.), from one specimen judge of all the rest; from a single instance infer the whole.
ab urbe condità (L.), from the building of the city; *i.e.,* Rome.
a capite ad calcem (L.) from head to heel.
à chaque saint sa chandelle (Fr.), to each saint his candle; honour where honour is due.
à cheval (Fr.), on horseback.
à compte (Fr.) on account; in part payment.
à corps perdu (Fr.), with might and main.
à couvert (Fr.), under cover; protected; sheltered.
ad astra (L.), to the stars.
ad calendas Græcas (L.), at the Greek calends; *i.e.,* never, as the Greeks had no calends in their mode of reckoning.
à demi (Fr.), by halves; half-way.
a Deo et rege (L.), from God and the king.
ad hoc (L.), arranged for this purpose; special.
ad hominem (L.), to the man; to an individual's interests or passions; personal.
adhuc sub judice lis est (L.), the case has not yet been decided.
a die (L.), from that day.
ad infinitum (L.), to infinity.
ad interim (L.), in the meantime.
ad libitum (L.), at pleasure.
ad modum (L.), after the manner of.
ad nauseam (L.), to disgust or satiety.
ad referendum (L.), for further consideration.
ad rem (L.), to the purpose; to the point.
ad valorem (L.), according to the value.
affaire d'amour (Fr.), a love affair.
affaire d'honneur (Fr.), an affair of honour; a duel.
affaire de cœur (Fr.), an affair of the heart.
a fortiori (L.), with stronger reason.
à gauche (Fr.), to the left.
à genoux (Fr.), on the knees.
à haute voix (Fr.), aloud.
à huis clos (Fr.), with closed doors; secretly.
à belle étoile (Fr.), under the stars; in the open air.
à la bonne heure (Fr.), well timed; all right; very well; as you please.
à l'abri (Fr.), under shelter.
à la mode (Fr.), according to the custom or fashion.
à la Tartuffe (Fr.), like Tartuffe, the hero of a celebrated comedy by Molière; hypocritically.
al fresco (It.), in the open air; out-of-doors.
al più (It.), at most.
alter ego (L.), another self.
à merveille (Fr.), to a wonder; marvellously.
amor patriæ (L.), love of country.
amour-propre (Fr.), self-love, vanity.
ancien régime (Fr.), the ancient or former order of things.
anguis in herba (L.), a snake in the grass.
anno Christi (L.), in the year of Christ.
anno Domini (L.), in the year of our Lord.
anno mundi (L.), in the year of the world.
annus mirabilis (L.), year of wonders; wonderful year.
ante bellum (L.), before the war.
ante lucem (L.), before light.
ante meridiem (L.), before noon.
à outrance (Fr.), to the utmost; to extremities; without sparing.
à pied (Fr.), on foot.
à point (Fr.), to a point, just in time, exactly right.

a posse ad esse (L.), from possibility to reality.
ariston metron (Gr.), the middle course is the best; the golden mean.
arrière-pensé (Fr.), hidden thought; mental reservation.
au courant (Fr.), fully acquainted with
audi alterum partem (L.), hear the other side.
au fait (Fr.), well acquainted with; expert.
au fond (Fr.), at bottom.
auf Wiedersehen! (Ger.), till we meet again.
au pis aller (Fr.), at the worst.
au revoir (Fr.), adieu; till we meet again.
aut vincere aut mori (L.), either to conquer or to die; death or victory.
a verbis ad verbera (L.), from words to blows.
a vinculo matrimonii (L.), from the bond of matrimony.
à volonte (Fr.), at pleasure.
a vostra salute (It.) ⎫
à votre santé (Fr.)   ⎬ to your health.
a vuestra salud (Sp.) ⎭
bas bleu (Fr.), a blue-stocking; a literary woman.
beau monde (Fr.), the world of fashion.
beaux esprits (Fr.), men of wit, gay spirits.
beaux yeux (Fr.), fine eyes; good looks.
ben trovato (It.), well or cleverly invented.
bête noire (Fr.), a black beast; a bugbear.
bon gré mal gré (Fr.), with good or ill grace; willing or unwilling.
bonhomie (Fr.), good-nature; artlessness.
bonne bouche (Fr.), a delicate or tasty morsel.
bon vivant (Fr.), a good liver; a gourmand.
brutum fulmen (L.), a harmless thunderbolt.
canaille (Fr.), rabble.
candida Pax (L.), white-robed Peace.
casus belli (L.), that which causes or justifies war.
causa sine qua non (L.), an indispensable cause or condition.
caveat emptor (L.), let the buyer beware (or look after his own interest).
cela va sans dire (Fr.), that goes without saying; needless to say.
ceteris paribus (L.), other things being equal.
chacun à son goût (Fr.), every one to his taste.
cogito, ergo sum (L.), I think, therefore I exist.
comme il faut (Fr.), as it should be.
compos mentis (L.), sound of mind; quite sane.
compte rendu (Fr.), an account rendered; a report or statement drawn up.
conditio sine qua non (L.), a necessary condition.
conseil de famille (Fr.), a family consultation.
consensus facit legem (L.), consent makes the law.
consilio et animis (L.), by wisdom and courage.
consilio et prudentia (L.), by wisdom and prudence.
constantia et virtute (L.), by constancy and virtue.
contra bonos mores (L.), against good manners.
contretemps (Fr.), an unlucky accident; a hitch.
cordon bleu (Fr.), blue ribbon; a cook of the highest class.
cordon sanitaire (Fr.), a line of guards to prevent the spreading of contagion or pestilence.
corpus delicti (L.), the body or substance of a crime or offence.
corrigenda (L.), things to be corrected.
coup de grâce (Fr.), a sudden decisive blow in politics; a stroke of policy.
coup de soleil (Fr.), sunstroke.
credat Judæus Apella (L.), let Apella, the superstitious Jew, believe it (I won't); tell that to the marines.
cucullus non facit monachum (L.), the cowl does not make the friar.
cui bono? (L.), For whose advantage is it? to what end?
culpam pœna premit comes (L.), punishment follows hard upon crime.
cum grano salis (L.), with a grain of salt; with some allowance.
cum privilegio (L.), with privilege.
currente calamo (L.), with a fluent pen.
da locum melioribus (L.), give place to your betters.

damnant quod non intelligunt (L.), they condemn what they do not comprehend.

data et accepta (L.), expenditures and receipts.

de bon augure (Fr.), of good augury or omen.

de bonne grâce (Fr.), with good grace; willingly.

de die in diem (L.), from day to day.

de facto (L.), in point of fact; actual or actually.

dei gratia (L.), by God's grace.

de jure (L.), from the law; by right.

de mal en pis (Fr.), from bad to worse.

de novo (L.), anew.

deo volente (L.), God willing; by God's will.

de profundis (L.), out of the depths.

dernier ressort (Fr.), a last resource.

deus ex machina (L.), one who puts matters right at a critical moment; providential intervention.

dies non (L.), a day on which judges do not sit.

distingué (Fr.), distinguished; of genteel or elegant appearance.

dolce far niente (It.), a sweet doing-nothing; sweet idleness.

double entente (Fr.), a double meaning; a play on words.

dramatis personæ (L.), characters of the drama or play.

dum spiro, spero (L.), while I breathe, I hope.

ecce homo! (L.), behold the man!

eheu! fugaces labuntur anni (L.), alas! the fleeting years glide by.

einmal ist keinmal (Ger.), just once doesn't count.

en avant (Fr.), forward.

en badinant (Fr.), in sport; in jest.

en déshabillé (Fr.), in undress.

en famille (Fr.), with one's family; in a domestic state.

enfant terrible (Fr.), a terrible child, or one that makes disconcerting remarks.

enfin (Fr.), in short; at last; finally.

en passant (Fr.), in passing; by the way.

en plein jour (Fr.), in broad day.

en rapport (Fr.), in harmony; in agreement; in relation.

en règle (Fr.), according to rules; in order.

entente cordiale (Fr.), cordial understanding, especially between two states.

entre nous (Fr.), between ourselves.

en vérité (Fr.), in truth; verily.

e pluribus unum (L.), one out of many; one composed of many.

esprit de corps (Fr.), the animating spirit of a collective body, as a regiment, learned profession or the like.

et sequentes, et sequentia (L.), and those that follow.

et tu, Brute! (L.), and thou also, Brutus!

ex animo (L.), heartily; sincerely.

ex capite (L.), from the head; from memory.

ex cathedra (L.), from the chair or seat of authority, with high authority.

exceptio probat regulam (L.), the exception proves the rule.

ex curia (L.), out of court.

ex dono (L.), by the gift.

exeunt omnes (L.), all go out or retire.

exit (L.), he goes out.

ex mero motu (L.), from his own impulse, from his own free will.

ex nihilo nihil fit (L.), out of nothing, nothing comes; nothing produces nothing.

ex officio (L.), in virtue of his office.

ex post facto (L.), after the deed is done; retrospective.

face à face (Fr.), face to face.

façon de parler (Fr.), manner of speaking.

faire bonne mine (Fr.), to put a good face upon the matter.

fait accompli (Fr.), a thing already done.

fama clamosa (L.), a current scandal; a prevailing report.

faute de mieux (Fr.), for want of better.

faux pas (Fr.), a false step; a slip in behaviour.

festina lente (L.), hasten slowly.

fiat justitia, ruat cœlum (L.), let justice be done though the heavens should fall.

fiat lux (L.), let there be light.

fide et amore (L.), by faith and love.

fide et fiduciâ (L.), by fidelity and confidence.

fide et fortitudine (L.), with faith and fortitude.

fidei defensor (L.), defender of the faith.

fide non armis (L.), by faith, not by arms.

fide, sed cui vide (L.), trust, but see whom.

fides et justitia (L.), fidelity and justice.

fides Punica (L.), Punic faith; treachery.

filius nullius (L.), a son of nobody; a bastard.

finis coronat opus (L.), the end crowns the work.

flagrante bello (L.), during hostilities.

flagrante delicto (L.), in the commission of the crime.

floreat (L.), let it flourish.

fons et origo (L.), the source and origin.

force majeure (Fr.), irresistible compulsion; war, strike, Act of God, etc.

forensis strepitus (L.), the clamour of the forum.

fortuna favet fortibus (L.), fortune favours the bold.

functus officio (L.), having performed one's office or duty; hence, out of office.

gaudeamus igitur (L.), so let us be joyful!

genius loci (L.), the genius or guardian spirit of a place.

gradu diverso, via una (L.), the same road by different steps.

grande parure / *grande toilette* (Fr.), full dress.

guerra al cuchillo (Sp.), war to the knife.

Hannibal ante portas (L.), Hannibal before the gates; the enemy close at hand.

hiatus valde deflendus (L.), a chasm or deficiency much to be regretted.

hic et nunc (L.), here and now.

hic et ubique (L.), here and everywhere.

hic jacet (L.) here lies.

hic labor, hoc opus est (L.), this is a labour, this is a toil.

hic sepultus (L.), here buried.

hoc genus omne (L.), all of this sort or class.

hoi polloi (Gr.), the many; the vulgar; the rabble.

hominis est errare (L.), to err is human.

homme de robe (Fr.), a man in civil office.

homme d'affair (Fr.), a man of business.

homme d'esprit (Fr.), a man of wit or genius.

honi soit qui mal y pense (O. Fr.), evil to him who evil thinks.

honores mutant mores (L.), honours change men's manners or characters.

hors de combat (Fr.), out of condition to fight.

hors de propos (Fr.), not to the point or purpose.

hors d'œuvre (Fr.), out of course; out of order.

ich dien (Ger.), I serve.

idée fixe (Fr.), a fixed idea.

id est (L.), that is.

il a diable au corps (Fr.), the devil is in him.

Ilias malorum (L.), an Iliad of ills; a host of evils.

il penseroso (It.), the pensive man.

il sent le fagot (Fr.), he smells of the faggot; he is suspected of heresy.

imperium in imperio (L.), a state within a state; a government within another.

in actu (L.), in act or reality.

in articulo mortis (L.), at the point of death; in the last struggle.

in capite (L.), in chief.

in curia (L.), in court.

index expurgatorius / *index prohibitorius* (L.) a list of books prohibited to Roman Catholics.

in esse (L.), in being; in actuality.

in extenso (L.), at full length.

in extremis (L.), at the point of death.

in memoriam (L.), to the memory of; in memory.

in nubibus (L.), in the clouds.

in petto (It.), in (my) breast; to one's self.

in re (L.), in the matter of.

in sano sensu (L.), in a proper sense.

in situ (L.), in its original situation.

in vino veritas (L.), there is truth in wine; truth is told under the influence of intoxicants.

ipse dixit (L.), he himself said it; a dogmatic saying or assertion.

ipsissima verba (L.), the very words.

ipso facto (L.), in the fact itself.

ipso jure (L.), by the law itself.

jacta est alea (L.), the die is cast.

je ne sais quoi (Fr.), I know not what.

joci causa (L.), for the sake of a joke.

labor omnia vincit (L.), labour conquers everything.

l'allegro (It.), the merry man.

lapsus linguæ (L.), a slip of the tongue.

lares et penates (L.), household goods.

laus Deo (L.), praise to God.

le beau monde (Fr.), the fashionable world.

lector benevole (L.), kind or gentle reader.

le jeu n'en vaut pas la chandelle (Fr.), the game is not worth the candle; the object is not worth the trouble.

le mot de l'énigme (Fr.), the key to the mystery.

le point du jour (Fr.), daybreak.

lèse-majesté (Fr.), high-treason.

lettre de cachet (Fr.), a sealed letter containing private orders; a royal warrant.

lex loci (L.), the law or custom of the place.

lex non scripta (L.), unwritten law; common law.

lex scripta (L.), written law; statute law.

locum tenens (L.), a deputy.

lucri causa (L.), for the sake of gain.

magnum opus (L.), a great work.

mala fide (L.), with bad faith; treacherously.

mal à propos (Fr.), ill-timed; out of place.

malgré nous (Fr.), in spite of us.

malheur ne vient jamais seul (Fr.), misfortunes never come singly.

malum in se (L.), evil or an evil in itself.

mardi gras (L.), Shrove Tuesday.

mariage de convenance (Fr.), marriage from motives of interest rather than of love.

mauvais goût (Fr.), bad taste.

mauvaise honte (Fr.), false modesty.

mea culpa (L.), my fault; by my fault.

me judice (L.), I being judge; in my opinion.

mens agitat molem (L.), mind moves matter.

mens legis (L.), the spirit of the law.

mens sana in corpore sano (L.), a sound mind in a sound body.

meo periculo (L.), at my own risk.

meo voto (L.), according to my wish.

mise en scène (Fr.), the getting up for the stage, or the putting on the stage.

modus operandi (L.), manner of working.

more suo (L.), in his own way.

motu proprio (L.), of his own accord.

multum in parvo (L.), much in little.

mutatis mutandis (L.), with suitable or necessary alteration.

nervus probandi (L.), the sinews of the argument.

nihil ad rem (L.), irrelevant.

nil desperandum (L.), there is no reason to despair.

noblesse oblige (Fr.), rank imposes obligations; much is expected from one in good position.

nolens volens (L.), willing or unwilling.

nom de guerre (Fr.), a false or assumed name.

non compos mentis (L.), not of sound mind.

non sequitur (L.), it does not follow.

nosce te ipsum (L.), know thyself.

nota bene (L.), mark well.

nudis verbis (L.), in plain words.

obiter dictum (L.), a thing said by the way.

omnia vincit amor (L.), love conquers all things.

ora pro nobis (L.), pray for us.

O tempora! O mores! (L.), O the times! O the manners (or morals)!

ouï-dire (Fr.), hearsay.

padrone (It.), a master; a landlord.

par excellence (Fr.), by way of eminence.

pari passu (L.), at an equal pace or rate of progress.

particeps criminis (L.), an accomplice in a crime.

pas de quoi (Fr. abbrev. Il n'y a pas de quoi), don't mention it.

passim (L.), everywhere; in all parts of the book, chapter, etc.

pâté de foie gras (Fr.), goose-liver paté.

pater patriæ (L.), father of his country.

patres conscripti (L.), the conscript fathers; Roman senators.

pax vobiscum (L.), peace be with you.

per ardua ad astra (L.), through rough ways to the stars; through suffering to renown.

per capita (L.), by the head or poll.

per contra (It.), countrariwise.

per diem (L.), by the day; daily.

per se (L.), by itself; considered apart.

pied-à-terre (Fr.), a resting-place; a temporary lodging.

pis aller (Fr.), the worst or last shift.

plebs (L.), the common people.

poco a poco (It.), little by little.

poste restante (Fr.), to remain in the post-office till called for.

prima facie (L.), at first view or consideration.

primus inter pares (L.), first among equals.

pro forma (L.), for the sake of form.

pro patria (L.), for our country.

pro tanto (L.), for so much; for as far as it goes.

pro tempore (L.), for the time being.

quid pro quo (L.), one thing for another; tit for tat; an equivalent.

qui m'aime, aime mon chien (Fr.), love me, love my dog.

qui tacet consentit (L.), he who is silent gives consent.

quod erat demonstrandum (L.), which was to be proved or demonstrated.

quod erat faciendum (L.), which was to be done.

quod vide (L.), which see; refer to the word just mentioned.

quo jure? (L.), by what right?

raison d'être (Fr.), the reason for a thing's existence.

re (L.), in the matter or affair of.

reculer pour mieux sauter (Fr.), to draw back in order to make a better spring.

reductio ad adsurdum (L.), the reducing of a position to a logical absurdity.

requiescat in pace (L.), may he (or she) rest in peace.

respice finem (L.), look to the end.

respublica (L.), the commonwealth.

revenons à nos moutons (Fr.), let us return to our sheep; let us return to our subject.

re vera (L.), in truth.

sans peur et sans reproche (Fr.), without fear and without reproach.

sans rime ni raison (Fr.), without rhyme or reason.

sans souci (Fr.), without care.

sartor resartus (L.), the botcher repatched; the tailor patched or mended.

sauve qui peut (Fr.), let him save himself who can.

savoir-faire (Fr.), the knowing how to act; tact.

savoir-vivre (Fr.), good-breeding; refined manners.

semper idem (L.), always the same.

seriatim (L.), in a series; one by one.

sic passim (L.), so here and there throughout; so everywhere.

sicut ante (L.), as before.

sine die (L.), without a day being appointed.

sine mora (L.), without delay.

sine qua non (L.), without which, not; indispensable condition.

sotto voce (It.), in an undertone.

spirituel (Fr.), intellectual; witty.

stet (L.), let it stand; do not delete.

sub judice (L.), under consideration.

sub pæna (L.), under a penalty.

sub rosa (L.), under the rose; privately.

sub voce (L.), under such or such a word.

sui generis (L.), of its own or of a particular kind.

summum bonum (L.), the chief good.

tableau vivant (Fr.), a living picture; the representation of some scene by a group of persons.

tant mieux (Fr.), so much the better.

tant pis (Fr.), so much the worse.

tempora mutantur, nos et mutamur in illis (L.), the times are changing and we with them.

tempus fugit (L.), time flies.

tête-à-tête (Fr.), together in private.

tiers état (Fr.), the third estate; the commons.

to kalon (Gr.), the beautiful; the chief good.

to prepon (Gr.), the becoming or proper.

tour de force (Fr.), a feat of strength or skill.

tout à fait (Fr.), wholly; entirely.

tout à l'heure (Fr.), instantly.

toute de suite (Fr.), immediately.

tu quoque (L.), thou also.

ubique (L.), everywhere.

ubi supra (L.), where above mentioned.

ultra licitum (L.), beyond what is allowable.

ultra vires (L.), beyond powers or rights conferred by law.

urbi et orbi (L.), to the city (Rome), and the world.

utile dulci (L.), the useful with the pleasant.

ut infra (L.), as below.

ut supra (L.), as above stated.

vade in pace (L.), go in peace.

variæ lectiones (L.), various readings.

variorum notæ (L.), the notes of various commentators.

vede et crede (L.), see and believe.

veni, vidi, vici (L.), I came, I saw, I conquered.

verbatim et literatim (L.), word for word and letter for letter.

verbum sat sapienti (L.), a word is enough for a wise man.

ver non semper viret (L.), spring is not always green.

vexata quæstio (L.), a disputed question.

via media (L.), a middle course.

via trita, via tuta (L.), the beaten path is the safe path.

vice versa (L.), the terms of the case being reversed.

videlicet (L.), that is to say; namely.

vi et armis (L.), by force of arms; by main force; by violence.

vigilate et orate (L.), watch and pray.

vita brevis, ars longa (L.), life is short; art is long.

viva regina! (L.), long live the queen!

vivat rex! (L.), long live the king!

viva voce (L.), by the living voice; orally.

voilà (Fr.), behold; there is; there are.

voilà tout (Fr.), that's all.

volo, non valeo (L.), I am willing, but unable.

vox populi, vox Dei (L.), the voice of the people is the voice of God.

MAJOR NATIONAL CURRENCIES

Country	Currency
Albania	Lek
Argentina	Austral
Australia	Dollar
Austria	Schilling
Belgium/Lux.	Franc
Belize	Dollar
Bolivia	Peso Boliviano
Brazil	Real
Bulgaria	Lev
Burma (Myanmar)	Kyat
Canada	Dollar
Chile	Peso
China	Renminbi
Colombia	Peso
Costa Rica	Colón
Cuba	Peso
Czech Republic	Koruna
Denmark	Krone
Dominican Republic	Peso
Ecuador	Sucre
Egypt	Pound
El Salvador	Colón
Ethiopia	Dollar
Finland	Markka
France	Franc
Germany	D. Mark
Greece	Drachma
Guatemala	Quetzal
Guyana	Dollar
Haiti	Gourde
Hong Kong	Dollar
Hungary	Forint
Iceland	Króna
India	Rupee
Indonesia	Rupiah
Iran	Rial
Iraq	Dinar
Israel	Shekel
Italy	New Lira
Jamaica	Dollar
Japan	Yen
Jordan	Dinar
Kenya	K. Shilling
Lebanon	Pound
Malaysia	Ringgit
Mexico	Peso
Morocco	Dirham
Netherlands	Guilder
New Zealand	Dollar
Nicaragua	Córdoba
Nigeria	Naira
Norway	Krone
Pakistan	Rupee
Panama	Balboa
Paraguay	Guaraní
Peru	Inti
Philippines	Peso
Poland	Zloty
Portugal	Escudo
Romania	Leu
Russia	Rouble
Saudi Arabia	Rial
South Africa	Rand
Spain	Peseta
Sri Lanka	Rupee
Sweden	Krona
Switzerland	Franc
Syria	Pound
Tanzania	T. Shilling
Thailand	Baht
Trinidad and Tobago	T.T. Dollar
Tunisia	Dinar
Turkey	Lira
United Arab Emirates	Dirham
United Kingdom	Pound
U.S.A.	Dollar
Uruguay	Peso
Venezuela	Bolivar
Vietnam	Dong
Zaïre	Zaïre
Zambia	Kwacha
Zimbabwe	Dollar

ROMAN NUMERALS

I	1	LXX	70
II	2	LXXX	80
III	3	LXXXVIII	88
IV	4	XC	90
V	5	XCIX	99
VI	6	C	100
VII	7	CX	110
VIII	8	CXI	111
IX	9	CXX	120
X	10	CC	200
XI	11	CCXX	220
XII	12	CCC	300
XIII	13	CCCXX	320
XIV	14	CD	400
XV	15	D	500
XVI	16	DC	600
XVII	17	DCC	700
XVIII	18	DCCC	800
XIX	19	CM	900
XX	20	XM	990
XXX	30	M	1000
XL	40	MD	1500
L	50	MDCCC	1800
LV	55	MCMLXXX	1980
LX	60	MM	2000

INTERNATIONAL TIME-TABLE (GMT)

Place	Time h	Place	Time h
Adelaide	21 30	Melbourne	22 00
Amsterdam	13 00	Montreal	07 00
Ankara	14 00	Moscow	15 00
Athens	14 00	Nairobi	15 00
Auckland (N.Z.)	24 00	New York	07 00
		Oslo	13 00
Belgrade	13 00	Ottawa	07 00
Berlin	13 00	Panama	07 00
Bombay	17 30	Paris	13 00
Brisbane	22 00	Peking	20 00
Brussels	13 00	Perth (W.A.)	20 00
Budapest	13 00	Prague	13 00
Buenos Aires	09 00	Quebec	07 00
Cairo	14 00	Rangoon	18 30
Calcutta	17 30	Rio de Janeiro	09 00
Cape Town	14 00	Rome	13 00
Chicago	06 00	San Francisco	04 00
Copenhagen	13 00	St. John's (N.F.)	08 30
Gibraltar	13 00	Singapore	20 00
Helsinki	14 00	Stockholm	13 00
Hobart	22 00	Sydney	22 00
Hong Kong	20 00	Tehran	15 30
Istanbul	14 00	Tokyo	21 00
Jerusalem	14 00	Toronto	07 00
London	12 00	Vancouver	04 00
Madeira	12 00	Vienna	13 00
Madrid	13 00	Winnipeg	06 00
Malta	13 00	Yokohama	21 00
Mauritius	16 00		

GREEK ALPHABET

Α	α	Alpha	Ν	ν	nu	
Β	β	beta	Ξ	ξ	xi	
Γ	γ	gamma	Ο	ο	omicron	
Δ	δ	delta	Π	π	pi	
Ε	ε	epsilon	Ρ	ρ	rho	
Ζ	ζ	zeta	Σ	σ	sigma	
Η	η	eta	Τ	τ	tau	
Θ	θ	theta	Υ	υ	upsilon	
Ι	ι	iota	Φ	φ	phi	
Κ	κ	kappa	Χ	χ	chi	
Λ	λ	lambda	Ψ	ψ	psi	
Μ	μ	mu	Ω	ω	omega	

BANK AND PUBLIC HOLIDAYS

The number of public holidays in England and Wales comprise at present six bank holidays (New Year's Day, Easter Monday, May Day, Spring and Late Summer Holidays at the end of May and August respectively, and Boxing Day), with also two common law holidays (Good Friday and Christmas Day); in Scotland (beginning in 1996) seven bank holidays (New Year's Day, Good Friday, Easter Monday, May Day, Spring and Late Summer Holidays at the end of May and August respectively, and Christmas Day); and in Northern Ireland seven bank holidays (New Year's Day, St. Patrick's Day, Easter Monday, May Day, Spring Late Summer Holidays at the end of May and August respectively, and Boxing Day) plus two other public holidays (Easter Tuesday and the anniversary of the Battle of the Boyne).

1996   Bank Holidays in England and Wales—Jan 1, Apr 5, Apr 8, May 6, May 27, Aug 26, Dec 25, Dec 26.
         Northern Ireland—Jan 1, Mar 18, Apr 5, Apr 8, May 6, May 27, July 12, Aug 26, Dec 25, Dec 26.
         Scotland—Jan 1, Apr 5, Apr 8, May 6, May 27, Aug 26, Dec 25, Dec 26.

Note: There are holidays in lieu of those public holidays which fall at weekends. In Scotland and Northern Ireland a general holiday is not necessarily observed on the same day as a bank holiday.

THE SEASONS

	1995			1996		
	d	h	m	d	h	m
Vernal Equinox—Spring begins	Mar 21	02	14	Mar 20	08	03
Summer Solstice—Summer begins	June 21	20	34	June 21	02	24
Autumnal Equinox—Autumn begins	Sept 23	12	13	Sept 22	18	00
Winter Solstice—Winter begins	Dec 22	08	17	Dec 21	14	06

(All times are in GMT)

THE COUNTRY CODE

GUARD AGAINST THE RISK OF FIRE. Great damage is done every year to crops, plantations, woodlands, and heaths. A match or cigarette thrown away or a pipe carelessly knocked out, picnic fires not properly put out or lighted near dry crops, can quickly start a blaze.

FASTEN ALL GATES. If animals get out of a field they stray. As a result they may do serious damage to crops, suffer injury on the roads, or eat food that is harmful.

KEEP DOGS UNDER CONTROL. Animals are easily frightened, even by small, playful dogs. Stillbirths may be the result.

KEEP TO THE PATHS ACROSS FARM LAND. Crops are damaged by treading; flattened crops are difficult to harvest. Grass is a valuable crop.

AVOID DAMAGING FENCING, HEDGES, AND WALLS. If these are damaged, gaps will be caused. Where a man goes, an animal may follow.

LEAVE NO LITTER. Litter is not just unsightly, but often a danger as well. Broken glass and tins may injure animals and harm machinery.

SAFEGUARD WATER SUPPLIES. Countrymen often depend on wells and streams for water for themselves and for their animals.

PROTECT WILD LIFE, PLANTS, AND TREES. Wild animals should not be disturbed, plants uprooted, or trees treated roughly.

GO CAREFULLY ON COUNTRY ROADS. If there is no footpath, walkers are generally safer on the right, facing on-coming traffic. Care and patience are needed by motorists when passing farm animals.

RESPECT THE LIFE OF THE COUNTRYSIDE. Many of the machines and much of the business stock of which the farmer depends for his livelihood have to be kept in the open. Take care not to damage them.

THE BEAUFORT SCALE OF WIND FORCE

Beaufort number	Wind	Effect on land	Speed	
			mile/h	Knots
0	Calm	Smoke rises vertically	Less than 1	Less than 1
1	Light air	Direction shown by smoke but not by wind vanes	1–3	1–3
2	Light breeze	Wind felt on face; leaves rustle; wind vanes move	4–7	4–6
3	Gentle breeze	Leaves and twigs in motion; wind extends light flag	8–12	7–10
4	Moderate breeze	Raises dust, loose paper and moves small branches	13–18	11–16
5	Fresh breeze	Small trees in leaf begin to sway	19–24	17–21
6	Strong breeze	Large branches in motion; whistling in telegraph wires; difficulty with umbrellas	25–31	22–27
7	Moderate gale	Whole trees in motion; difficult to walk against wind	32–38	28–33
8	Fresh gale	Twigs break off trees; progress impeded	39–46	34–40
9	Strong gale	Slight structural damage occurs; chimney pots and slates blown off	47–54	41–47
10	Whole gale	Trees uprooted and considerable structural damage	55–63	48–56
11	Storm	Widespread damage, seldom experienced in England	64–75	57–65
12	Hurricane	Winds of this force rarely encountered outside tropical revolving storms[1]	Above 75	Above 65

[1] The most notable recent exception was the tremendous storm which devastated Southern England on the night of 15/16 October 1987. Storms of great severity also battered Britain in January and February 1990.

SUNRISE AND SUNSET FOR LONDON, 1996

		Rise	Set				Rise	Set				Rise	Set
		h m	h m				h m	h m				h m	h m
Jan	1	08 06	16 02	May	6	05 23	20 32	September	2	06 15	19 44
	8	08 05	16 10		13	05 12	20 43		9	06 26	19 28
	15	08 00	16 20		20	05 02	20 54		16	06 37	19 12
	22	07 53	16 31		27	04 54	21 03		23	06 49	18 56
	29	07 45	16 44						30	07 00	18 40
				June	3	04 48	21 11				
Feb	5	07 34	16 56		10	04 44	21 17	October	7	07 11	18 24
	12	07 22	17 09		17	04 43	21 21		14	07 23	18 09
	19	07 08	17 22		24	04 44	21 22		21	07 35	17 54
	26	06 54	17 34						28	06 47	16 41
				July	1	04 48	21 21				
March	4	06 39	17 47		8	04 54	21 17	November	4	07 00	16 28
	11	06 23	17 59		15	05 01	21 11		11	07 12	16 17
	18	06 08	18 11		22	05 10	21 03		18	07 24	16 07
	25	05 52	18 23		29	05 20	20 53		25	07 35	16 00
April	1	06 36	19 34					December	2	07 46	15 54
	8	06 20	19 46	August	5	05 31	20 41		9	07 54	15 52
	15	06 05	19 58		12	05 42	20 29		16	08 01	15 52
	22	05 50	20 09		19	05 53	20 15		23	08 05	15 55
	29	05 36	20 21		26	06 04	20 00		30	08 06	16 00

Note: These times are in GMT, except between 0100 on 31 Mar and 0100 on 27 Oct when the times are in BST (1 hour in advance of GMT).

PHASES OF THE MOON, 1996

	New Moon				First Quarter				Full Moon				Last Quarter		
	d	h	m		d	h	m		d	h	m		d	h	m
Jan	20	12	50	Jan	27	11	14	Jan	5	20	51	Jan	13	20	45
Feb	18	23	30	Feb	26	05	52	Feb	4	15	58	Feb	12	08	37
Mar	19	10	45	Mar	27	01	31	Mar	5	09	23	Mar	12	17	15
Apr	17	22	49	Apr	25	20	40	Apr	4	00	07	Apr	10	23	36
May	17	11	46	May	25	14	13	May	3	11	48	May	10	05	04
June	16	01	36	June	24	05	23	June	1	20	47	June	8	11	05
July	15	16	15	July	23	17	49	July	1	03	58	July	7	18	55
Aug	14	07	34	Aug	22	03	36	July	30	10	35	Aug	6	05	25
Sept	12	23	07	Sept	20	11	23	Aug	28	17	52	Sept	4	19	06
Oct	12	14	14	Oct	19	18	09	Sept	27	02	51	Oct	4	12	04
Nov	11	04	16	Nov	18	01	09	Oct	26	14	11	Nov	3	07	50
Dec	10	16	56	Dec	17	09	31	Nov	25	04	10	Dec	3	05	06
								Dec	24	20	41				

Note: All times are in GMT.

ECLIPSES, 1996

1. A total eclipse of the Moon on 3–4 April is visible from part of Antarctica, Indian Ocean, West Asia, Africa, Europe (including the British Isles), Iceland, Greenland, Atlantic Ocean, South America, West Indies and the eastern part of North America. The eclipse begins on 3 April at 22h 22m and ends on 4 April at 01h 58m. Totality lasts from 23h 27m on 3 April to 00h 53m on 4 April.

2. A partial eclipse of the Sun on 17–18 April is visible from New Zealand, part of Antarctica and the South Pacific Ocean. The eclipse begins on 17 April at 20h 31m and ends on 18 April at 00h 43m. The time of maximum eclipse is 22h 37m on 17 April, when 0.88 of the Sun's diameter is obscured.

3. A total eclipse of the Moon on 27 September is visible from part of Antarctica, extreme west Asia, Africa, Europe (including the British Isles), Iceland, Greenland, Atlantic Ocean and Arctic regions, the Americas except Alaska and the eastern part of Pacific Ocean. The eclipse begins at 01h 13m and ends at 04h 35m. Totality lasts from 02h 19m to 03h 29m.

4. A partial eclipse of the Sun on 12 October is visible from extreme north-east Canada, Greenland, Iceland, North Atlantic Ocean, Europe (including the British Isles) and North Africa. The eclipse begins at 12h 00m and ends at 16h 05m. The time of maximum eclipse is 14h 02m, when 0.76 of the Sun's diameter is obscured.

Source: H.M. Nautical Almanac Office. Reproduced with permission from data supplied to the Science and Engineering Council.

THE COMMONWEALTH

The Commonwealth of Nations is a free association of independent member nations and their dependencies. The political status of the member nations listed below is clarified and given legal substance in the *Statute of Westminster* drawn up in 1931, before the Commonwealth was founded, by the United Kingdom and the Dominions. The original Dominions were Australia, Canada, Irish Free State, Newfoundland, New Zealand and South Africa. On 1 June 1994, South Africa rejoined the Commonwealth, having left in 1961. There are currently (May 1995) 51 Members. The Secretary-General is Emeka Anyaoku (Nigeria).

Country	Capital	Status	Joined	Population
1. Antigua and Barbuda	St. John's	M	1981	65,900 (1991)
2. Australia	Canberra	M	1931	16,849,000 (1991)
3. The Bahamas	Nassau	M	1973	259,000 (1991)
4. Bangladesh	Dhaka	R	1972	108,000,000 (1991)
5. Barbados	Bridgetown	M	1966	258,600 (1991)
6. Belize	Belmopen	M	1981	193,000 (1990)
7. Botswana	Gaborone	R	1966	1,300,000 (1991)
8. Brunei	Bandar Seri Begawan	M*	1984	264,000 (1991)
9. Canada	Ottawa	M	1931	27,125,800 (1991)
10. Cyprus	Nicosia	R	1961	710,200 (1991)
11. Dominica	Roseau	R	1978	108,812 (1991)
12. The Gambia	Banjul	R	1965	880,000 (1991)
13. Ghana	Accra	R	1957	15,510,000 (1991)
14. Grenada	St. George's	M	1974	91,000 (1991)
15. Guyana	Georgetown	R	1966	990,000 (1989)
16. India	New Delhi	R	1947	846,300,000 (1991)
17. Jamaica	Kingston	M	1962	2,440,000 (1992)
18. Kenya	Nairobi	R	1963	25,910,000 (1991)
19. Kiribati	Tarawa	R	1979	71,000 (1991)
20. Lesotho	Maseru	M*	1966	1,825,000 (1991)
21. Malawi	Lilongwe	R	1964	8,560,000 (1991)
22. Malaysia	Kuala Lumpur	M*	1957	18,600,000 (1992)
23. Maldives	Male	R	1982(S)	213,200 (1990)
24. Malta	Valletta	R	1964	360,000 (1992)
25. Mauritius	Port Louis	R	1968	1,078,000 (1991)
26. Namibia	Windhoek	R	1990	1,402,000 (1991)
27. Nauru	Nauru	R	1968(S)	8,100 (1990)
28. New Zealand	Wellington	M	1931	3,435,000 (1991)
29. Nigeria	Abuja	R	1960	88,500,000 (1991)
30. Pakistan	Islamabad	R	1947*	114,000,000 (1991)
31. Papua New Guinea	Port Moresby	M	1975	3,530,000 (1990)
32. St. Kitts and Nevis	Basseterre	M	1983	41,900 (1990)
33. St. Lucia	Castries	M	1979	153,000 (1991)
34. St. Vincent and the Grenadines	Kingstown	M	1979(S)	108,000 (1991)
35. Seychelles	Victoria	R	1976	70,400 (1991)
36. Sierra Leone	Freetown	R	1961	4,260,000 (1991)
37. Singapore	Singapore	R	1965	2,760,000 (1991)
38. Solomon Islands	Honiara	M	1978	326,000 (1991)
39. South Africa	Pretoria	R	1931**	35,300,000 (1990)
40. Sri Lanka	Colombo	R	1948	17,250,000 (1991)
41. Swaziland	Mbabane	M*	1968	800,000 (1990)
42. Tanzania	Dar es Salaam	R	1961	25,090,000 (1991)
43. Tonga	Nuku'Alofa	M*	1970	103,000 (1991)
44. Trinidad and Tobago	Port of Spain	R	1962	1,250,000 (1991)
45. Tuvalu	Funafuti	M	1978(S)	9,317 (1991)
46. Uganda	Kampala	R	1962	16,600,000 (1991)
47. United Kingdom	London	M	1931	53,920,000 (1991)
48. Vanuatu	Port Vila	R	1980	154,000 (1992)
49. Western Samoa	Apia	M*	1970	168,000 (1988)
50. Zambia	Lusaka	R	1964	8,780,000 (1991)
51. Zimbabwe	Harare	R	1980	9,900,000 (1992)

M = Monarchy under Queen Elizabeth, represented by Governor-General in all countries except Britain.
M* = Country with its own monarchy. Brunei is a Sultanate.
R   = Republic.
(S) = Special Member.
*   = Pakistan left in 1972, rejoining in 1989.
** = South Africa left in 1961, rejoining in 1994.

Dependencies of Britain

Anguilla
Bermuda
British Antarctic Territory
British Indian Ocean Territory
British Virgin Isles
Cayman Islands
Falkland Islands and Dependencies
(South Georgia, South Sandwich Islands)

Gibraltar
Hong Kong (until 1997)
Montserrat
Pitcairn Islands Group
St. Helena and Dependencies (Ascension,
Tristan da Cunha)
Turks and Caicos Islands

Territories of Member Countries

Australia Norfolk Island, Heard Island, McDonald Island, Cocos (Keeling) Islands, Christmas Island, Asmore and Cartier Islands, Coral Sea Islands
New Zealand Cook Islands, Niue, Tokelau Islands

The Channel Islands and the Isle of Man are dependent territories of the crown and do not form part of the United Kingdom. They have their own legislative assemblies and legal and administrative systems.

POPES
(Since 1492)

Alexander VI	1492	Innocent XI	1676
Pius III	1503	Alexander VIII	1689
Julius II	1503	Innocent XII	1691
Leo X	1513	Clement XI	1700
Adrian VI	1522	Innocent XIII	1721
Clement VII	1523	Benedict XIII	1724
Paul III	1534	Clement XII	1730
Julius III	1550	Benedict XIV	1740
Marcellus II	1555	Clement XIII	1758
Paul IV	1555	Clement XIV	1769
Pius IV	1559	Pius VI	1775
St. Pius V	1566	Pius VII	1800
Gregory XIII	1572	Leo XII	1823
Sixtus V	1585	Pius VIII	1829
Urban VIII	1590	Gregory XVI	1831
Gregory XIV	1590	Pius IX	1846
Innocent IX	1591	Leo XIII	1878
Clement VIII	1592	St. Pius X	1903
Leo XI	1605	Benedict XV	1914
Paul V	1605	Pius XI	1922
Gregory XV	1621	Pius XII	1939
Urban VIII	1623	John XXIII	1958
Innocent X	1644	Paul VI	1963
Alexander VII	1655	John Paul I	1978
Clement IX	1667	John Paul II	1978
Clement X	1670		

ARCHBISHOPS OF CANTERBURY
(Since the Reformation)

1533	Thomas Cranmer	1768	Hon. Frederick Cornwallis
1556	Reginald Pole	1783	John Moore
1559	Matthew Parker	1805	Charles Manners Sutton
1576	Edmund Grindal	1828	William Howley
1583	John Whitgift	1848	John Bird Sumner
1604	Richard Bancroft	1862	Charles Thomas Longley
1611	George Abbot	1868	Archibald Campbell Tait
1633	William Laud	1883	Edward White Benson
1660	William Juxon	1896	Frederick Temple
1663	Gilbert Sheldon	1903	Randall Thomas Davidson
1678	William Sancroft	1928	Cosmo Gordon Lang
1691	John Tillotson	1942	William Temple
1695	Thomas Tenison	1945	Geoffrey Francis Fisher
1716	William Wake	1961	Arthur Michael Ramsey
1737	John Potter	1974	Frederick Donald Coggan
1747	Thomas Herring	1980	Robert Runcie
1757	Matthew Hutton	1991	George Carey
1758	Thomas Secker		

ARCHBISHOPS OF YORK
(Since 1900)

1891	William Maclagan	1961	Donald Coggan
1909	Cosmo Gordon Lang	1975	Stuart Blanch
1929	William Temple	1983	John Habgood
1942	Cyril Garbett	1995	David Hope
1956	Arthur Michael Ramsey		

RULERS OF THE ROMAN WORLD
(from 753 B.C. to 363 A.D.)

The Kingdom

753	Romulus (Quirinus)
716	Numa Pompilius
673	Tullus Hostilius
640	Ancus Marcius
616	L. Tarquinius Priscus
578	Servius Tullius
534	L. Tarquinius Superbus

The Republic

509	Consulate established
509	Quaestorship instituted
498	Dictatorship introduced
494	Plebeian Tribunate created
494	Plebeian Aedileship created
444	Consular Tribunate organized
435	Censorship instituted
366	Praetorship established
366	Curule Aedileship created
362	Military Tribunate elected
326	Proconsulate introduced
311	Naval Duumvirate elected
217	Dictatorship of Fabius Maximus
133	Tribunate of Tiberius Gracchus
123	Tribunate of Gaius Gracchus
82	Dictatorship of Sulla
60	First Triumvirate formed (Caesar, Pompeius, Crassus)
46	Dictatorship of Caesar
43	Second Triumvirate formed (Octavianus, Antonius, Lepidus)

The Empire

27	Augustus (Galus Julius Caesar Octavianus)
14	Tiberius I
37	Gaius Caesar (Caligula)
41	Claudius I
54	Nero
68	Galba
69	Galba; Otho, Vitellius
69	Vespasianus
79	Titus
81	Domitianus

96	Nerva
98	Trajanus
117	Hadrianus
138	Antoninus Pius
161	Marcus Aurelius and Lucius Verus
169	Marcus Aurelius (alone)
180	Commodus
193	Pertinax; Julianus I
193	Septimius Severus
211	Caracalla and Geta
212	Caracalla (alone)
217	Macrinus
218	Elagabalus (Heliogabalus)
222	Alexander Severus
235	Maximinus I (the Thracian)
238	Gordianus I and Gordianus II; Pupienus and Balbinus
238	Gordianus III
244	Philippus (the Arabian)
249	Decius
251	Gallus and Volusianus
253	Aemilianus
253	Valerianus and Gallienus
258	Gallienus (alone)
268	Claudius II (the Goth)
270	Quintillus
270	Aurelianus
275	Tacitus
276	Florianus
276	Probus
282	Carus
283	Carinus and Numerianus
284	Diocletianus
286	Diocletianus and Maximianus
305	Galerius and Constantius I
306	Galerius, Maximinus II, Severus I
307	Galerius, Maximinus II, Constantinus I, Licinius, Maxentius
311	Maximinus II, Constantinus I, Licinius, Maxentius
314	Maximinus II, Constantinus I, Licinius
314	Constantinus I and Licinius
324	Constantinus I (the Great)
337	Constantinus II, Constans I, Constantius II
340	Constantius II and Constans I
361	Julianus II (the Apostate)
363	Jovianus

Note: In 364 the Empire was divided between the brothers Valentinian (in the West) and Valens (East).

MAJOR TOWNS OF ROMAN BRITAIN

Andover	Levcomagus	Leicester	Ratae Coritanorum
Bath	Aquae Sulis	Lincoln	Lindum
Cambridge	Durolipons	London	Londinium
Caernarvon	Segontium	Manchester	Mamucium
Canterbury	Durovernum	Northwich	Condate
Carlisle	Luguvalium	Pevensey	Anderita
Carmarthen	Moridunum	Richborough	Rutupiae
Catterick	Cataractonium	Rochester	Durobrivae
Chelmsford	Caesaromagus	St. Albans	Verulamium
Chester	Deva	Severn R.	Sabrina
Chichester	Noviomagus Regnensium	Silchester	Calleva Atrebatum
Cirencester	Corinium Dobunnorum	South Shields	Arbeia
Colchester	Camulodunum	Thames R.	Tamesis
Doncaster	Danum	Towcester	Lactodorum
Dorchester	Durnovaria	Wash, The	Metarius Aestuarium
Dover	Portus Dubris	Wight. I. o.	Vectis
Dunstable	Durocobrivae	Winchester	Venta Belgarum
Exeter	Isca Dumnoniorum	Wroxeter	Viroconium Cornoviorum
Gloucester	Glevum	York	Eboracum
Ilchester	Lindinus		

INDEX

Each section has a letter and, where appropriate, the column is given in brackets after the page number, *e.g.*, F8(1), G25(2). Some of the sections are alphabetically arranged and index themselves. Their contents are not included here except where it is anticipated some special difficulty may arise. The sections "Medical Matters" and "The World of Music" have each a separate index and glossary.

U

V

W

X

Y

Z